R.E.D.
Compact Disc edition 16
CATALOGUE

Retail Entertainment Data Publishing Limited
Paulton House, 8 Shepherdess Walk, London N1 7LB, UK
Tel: +44 (0)171 566 8216   Fax: +44 (0)171 566 8259

MusicMaster Gramophone

Editor	Matthew Garbutt
Assistant Editor	Gary Ford
Editorial Assistants	Bruno MacDonald Howard Richardson Jane Scarratt
Product Manager	Chris Spalding
Sales & Marketing Manager	Brian Mulligan
Sales Manager	Marie-Clare Murray
Sales Executives	Adrian Pope Catherine Ayres
Production Manager	Keith Hawkins
Publishing Assistant	Becca Bailey
Publisher	Brenda Daly

All enquiries:
Retail Entertainment Data Publishing Ltd.
Paulton House, 8 Shepherdess Walk, London N1 7LB, UK
Tel: +44 (0)171 566 8216 Fax: +44 (0)171 566 8259

DPA
DIRECTORY PUBLISHERS
ASSOCIATION
ASSOCIATE MEMBER

Database typeset by BPC Whitefriars, Tunbridge Wells, Kent, UK

Cover design by Chris Spalding
Cover photograph by B. Roussel
Cover image supplied by The Image Bank, London, UK

Printed and bound in Great Britain by BPC Wheatons Ltd, Exeter, Devon, UK

ISBN 1 900105 02 0

Contents

Introduction

Welcome to the R.E.D. CD Catalogue, 16th Edition. Information on the 60,000 currently available albums on CD featured in this catalogue has been arranged into the following sections:

The **Distributors Index** lists all the major UK distributors and their contact details.

The **Main Section** of the book contains the majority of the recording data. The 'black strip' artist headings and subsequent recording titles are arranged alphabetically. Tracks are listed, where we have been advised, after the recording title. Catalogue numbers and format are displayed in bold, followed by issuing label, release date and distributors.

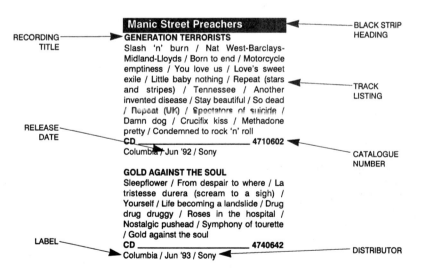

The **Compilations** section is arranged alphabetically by recording title and thereafter the layout is as the Main Section.

The **Soundtracks** section has been redesigned and is now arranged into three separate parts:

1 : Soundtracks – an alphabetical listing by title of film, show and TV soundtrack recordings.

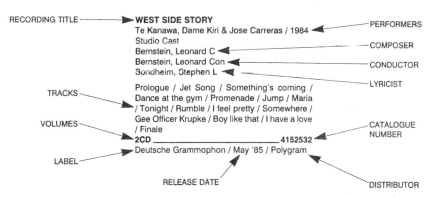

2 : Collections – soundtrack compilations listed by recording title.

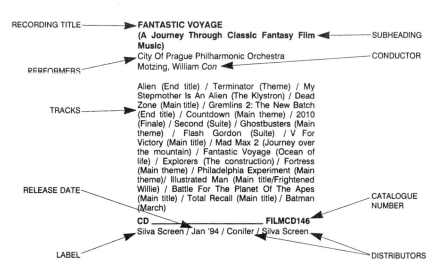

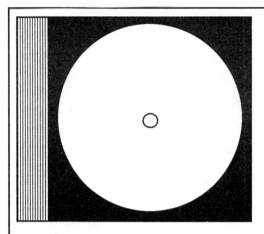

3 : Composer Collections – compilation recordings devoted to the work of specific composers. Listed alphabetically by composer.

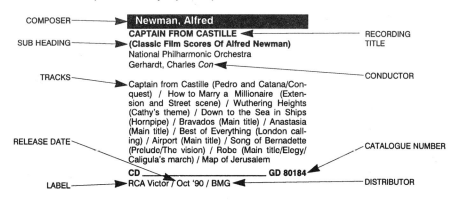

COMPOSER → **Newman, Alfred**

SUB HEADING → CAPTAIN FROM CASTILLE ← RECORDING TITLE
(Classic Film Scores Of Alfred Newman)
National Philharmonic Orchestra
Gerhardt, Charles Con ← CONDUCTOR

TRACKS → Captain from Castille (Pedro and Catana/Conquest) / How to Marry a Millionaire (Extension and Street scene) / Wuthering Heights (Cathy's theme) / Down to the Sea in Ships (Hornpipe) / Bravados (Main title) / Anastasia (Main title) / Best of Everything (London calling) / Airport (Main title) / Song of Bernadette (Prelude/The vision) / Robe (Main title/Elegy/Caligula's march) / Map of Jerusalem

RELEASE DATE → CATALOGUE NUMBER

CD _____ GD 80184 ← DISTRIBUTOR

LABEL → RCA Victor / Oct '90 / BMG ←

Where possible the Soundtracks Section features Performer, Composer, Lyricist and Conductor information. Subsequent recording details are arranged in a similar way to the Main Section.

OFFICIAL MUSICMASTER JAZZ & BLUES CATALOGUE 2ND EDITION

"The aim of this second Jazz & Blues Catalogue is to cater for the tastes of everyone remotely interested in jazz, blues and the many musical forms which make up the genre – so this book is a book for both the purist and the generalist"

– Graham Langley, Editor

This new and fully updated edition lists over 34,000 jazz and blues recordings, along with label information, catalogue numbers, track listings where advised, and an 8–page colour section of classic album covers. Also included are nearly 700 up-to-date biographies of all the major and most influential artists in these increasingly popular genres.

PRICE : £14.95 (PLUS POSTAGE & PACKING)

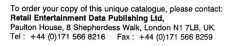

The Ultimate Source of Recorded Music Information

Imagine one product that gives virtually instant access to information on nearly 1,000,000 recordings and compositions by more than 100,000 classical and popular artists. A product that is both simple to use and regularly updated with all the latest information.

That product is the **R.E.D** CD-ROM.

Combining the entire **Gramophone** and **MusicMaster** databases, the **R.E.D** CD-ROM has been developed to give retailers, librarians, researchers and collectors access to the most comprehensive catalogues of classical and popular recorded music information currently available.

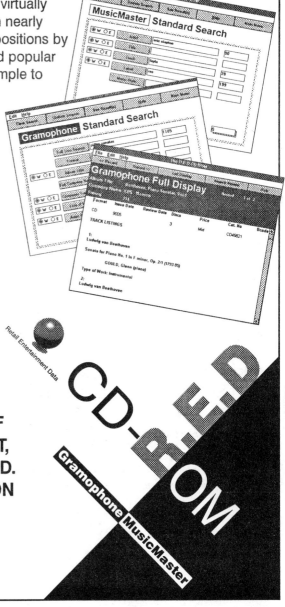

FOR MORE DETAILS OF THIS UNIQUE PRODUCT, PLEASE CALL THE R.E.D. SALES DEPARTMENT ON +44-(0)171 566 8216

Retail Entertainment Data Publishing Ltd
Paulton House, 8 Shepherdess Walk, London, N1 7LB, UK.
Tel: +44-(0)171 566 8215 Fax: +44-(0)171 566 8259

Distributors Index

3MV
Eastern Office
81-83 Weston Street
London
SE1 3RS
Tel 0171 378 8866
Fax...............0171 378 8855

ADA
Unit 8
Riverview Business
Centre
Riverview Road
Beverley
Humberside
HU17 0LD
Tel 01482 868024
Fax...............01482 868024

BMG
Lyng Lane
West Bromwich
West Midlands
B70 7ST
Tel 0121 500 5545
Fax...............0121 558 6880

CADILLAC
61-71 Collier Street
London
N1 9DF
Tel 0171 278 7391
Fax...............0171 278 7394

CARLTON HOME ENTERTAINMENT
The Waterfront
Elstree Road
Elstree
Hertfordshire
WD6 3BS
Tel 0181 207 6207
Fax...............0181 207 5789

CHARLY
156-166 Ilderton Road
London
SE15 1NT
Tel 0171 639 8603
Fax...............0171 639 2532

CM
Hookstone Park
Harrogate
North Yorkshire
HG2 7DB
Tel 01423 888979
Fax...............01423 885761

COMPLETE
12 Pepys Court
84 The Chase
Clapham Common
London
SW4 0NF
Tel 0171 498 9666
Fax...............0171 498 1828

CONIFER
Claremont House
Horton Road
West Drayton
Middlesex
UB7 8JL
Tel 01895 441808
Fax...............01895 420713

DIRECT
50 Stroud Green Road
London
N4 3EF
Tel 0171 263 1240
Fax...............0171 281 5671

DISC
36 Caxton Way
Watford
Hertfordshire
WD1 8UF
Tel 01923 255558
Fax...............01923 817968

DISCOVERY
Old Church Mission
Room
Kings Corner
Pewsey
Wiltshire
SN9 5BS
Tel 01672 563931
Fax...............01672 563934

DUNCANS
9 Market Place
Inverurie
Grampian
AB51 9PU
Tel 01467 621517
Fax...............01467 625536

EMI
Hermes Close
Tachbrook Park
Leamington Spa
Warwickshire
CV34 6RP
Tel 01926 888888
Fax...............0181 479 5992

GRAPEVINE
12 Oval Road
London
NW1 7DH
Tel 0171 284 0900
Fax...............0171 284 0522

GREENSLEEVES
Unit 14
Metro Centre
St John's Road
Isleworth
Middlesex
TW7 6NJ
Tel 0181 758 0564
Fax...............0181 758 0811

HARMONIA MUNDI
19-21 Nile Street
London
N1 7LR
Tel 0171 253 0863
Fax...............0171 253 3237

HOT SHOT
29a St Michael's Road
Headingley
Leeds
West Yorkshire
LS6 3BG
Tel 0113 274 2106
Fax...............0113 278 6291

JAZZ MUSIC
Glenview
Moylegrove
Cardigan
Dyfed
SA43 3BW
Tel 01239 881278
Fax...............01239 881296

JETSTAR
155 Acton Lane
Park Royal
London
NW10 7NG
Tel 0181 961 5818
Fax...............0181 965 7008

KOCH
24 Concord Road
London
W3 0TH
Tel 0181 992 7177
Fax...............0181 992 7124

MAGNUM MUSIC
Magnum House
High Street
Lane End
High Wycombe
Buckinghamshire
HP14 3JG
Tel 01494 882858
Fax...............01494 882631

NEW NOTE
Electron House
Cray Avenue
St Mary Cray
Orpington
Kent
BR5 3RJ
Tel 01689 877884
Fax...............01689 877891

PINNACLE
Electron House
Cray Avenue
St Mary Cray
Orpington
Kent
BR5 3PN
Tel 01689 870622
Fax...............01689 878269

PLASTIC HEAD
Units 15 & 15A
Bushell Business Estate
Hithercroft
Wallingford
Oxfordshire
OX10 9DD
Tel 01491 825029
Fax...............01491 826320

POLYGRAM
PO Box 36
Clyde Works
Grove Road
Romford
Essex
RM6 4QR
Tel 0181 910 1799
Fax...............0181 910 1675

ROLLERCOASTER
Rock House
London Road
St Marys Chalford
Gloucestershire
GL6 8PU
Tel 01453 886252
Fax...............01453 885361

ROOTS
250 Earlsdon Avenue
North
Coventry
West Midlands
CV5 6GX
Tel 01203 711935

SILVA SCREEN
Silva House
261 Royal College Street
London
NW1 9LU
Tel 0171 284 0525
Fax...............0171 482 2385

SONY
Rabans Lane
Aylesbury
Buckinghamshire
HP19 3BX
Tel 01296 395151
Fax...............01296 395551

SRD
70 Lawrence Road
London
N15 4EG
Tel 0181 802 3000
Fax...............0181 802 2222

SWIFT
3 Wilton Road
Bexhill-On-Sea
East Sussex
TN40 1HY
Tel 01424 220028
Fax...............01424 213440

THE R.E.D.
SOUNDTRACKS CATALOGUE
1ST EDITION

This is the first Soundtracks catalogue which combines the MusicMaster and Gramophone databases. This volume contains approximately 6,000 film, show and TV soundtracks released in the UK on all formats.

As well as an alphabetical listing by title, this book features an artist/composer index and a distributor index.

(326 pages)

PRICE : £14.95 (PLUS POSTAGE & PACKING)

From the film music of Sir William Walton to the TV music from "The Waltons"

Numerical

2 AM

LATE NIGHT SAX
Ain't no sunshine / Think twice / Saving all my love / I swear / Your love is king / Sexual healing / Careless whisper / Right here waiting / If you don't know me by now / Nothing compares 2 U / Let's get it on / Just the way you are / If you leave me now / I heard it through the grapevine / (Everything I do) I do it for you / Songbird / Three times a lady / When a man loves a woman
CD _____ CDEMTV 108
EMI / Jan '96 / EMI.

2 Bad

ANSWERMACHINE
CD _____ XM 039CD
X-Mist / Jul '93 / SRD.

2 Bad Card

HUSTLING ABILITY
CD _____ ONUCD 78
On-U Sound / Sep '95 / SRD / Jetstar.

2 Die 4

2 DIE 4
Walk right now / Now you got what it takes / Sorry I broke your smile / Living for the moment / Green with envy / Deliver me from evil / No bars at the zoo / Come inside / How can you believe in love / Warm your mind up (hey, hey) / Emotional earthquake
CD _____ 5139272
Polydor / Sep '92 / PolyGram.

2 Foot Flame

2 FOOT FLAME
Lindauer / To the sea / Already walking / MR II / Reinvention / Compass / Arbitrator / Cordoned off / Chisel
CD _____ OLE 1622
Matador / Oct '95 / Vital.

2 In A Room

VOLUME 1
CD _____ INACD 1
Big Life / Sep '89 / Pinnacle.

2 Nice Girls

LIKE A VERSION
I feel (like makin') love / Bang bang / Top of the world / Speed racer / Cotton crown / Scottish Air and Quickstep
CD _____ RTM 235 CD
Rough Trade / Feb '90 / Pinnacle.

2 Pac

ME AGAINST THE WORLD
Intro / If I die 2nite / Me against the world (feat. Dramacydal) / So many tears / Temptations / Young niggaz / Heavy in the game (feat. Richie Rich) / Lord knows / Dear Mama / It ain't easy / Can U get away / Old school / Fuck the world / Death around the corner / Outlaw (feat. Dramacydal)
CD _____ 8811000000
Interscope / Mar '95 / Warner Music.

STRICTLY 4 MY N.I.G.G.A.Z.
Holler if ya hear me / 2 Pac's theme / Point the finga / Something 2 die 4 / Last wordz / Souljah's revenge / Peep game / Strugglin' / Guess who's back / Representin' / Keep ya head up / Strictly 4 my N.I.G.G.A.Z. / Streetz R deathrow / I get around / Papa'z song / Five deadly venomz
CD _____ 756792209-2
Interscope / Feb '93 / Warner Music.

2 Rocks

WHEN SANITY IS ACTING KIND OF WILD
CD _____ WKFMXD 174
FM / Jul '91 / Sony.

2 Unlimited

GET READY
CD _____ HFCD 23
PWL / Feb '92 / Warner Music / 3MV.

NO LIMITS
CD _____ HFCD 32
PWL / May '93 / Warner Music / 3MV.

REAL THINGS
CD _____ HFCD 38
PWL / Jun '94 / Warner Music / 3MV.

2nd Communication

2ND COMMUNICATION
CD _____ KKUK 008CD
KK / '90 / Plastic Head.

MY CHROMOSOMAL FRIEND
CD _____ KK 044 CD
KK / Aug '90 / Plastic Head.

SECOND COMMUNICATION
CD _____ KK 038 CD
KK / '89 / Plastic Head.

2nd Heat

SHREDDERVISION
CD _____ RTN 41204
Rock The Nation / Nov '94 / Plastic Head.

2nd Orchestra

INTERACTION
CD _____ KKCD 066
KK / Feb '94 / Plastic Head.

2nd Power

DA SOUL MAN
People / Get busy / Livin' like a gangsta / Da soul man / Side / Fonkay drunk ghetto bass / People B trippin' / Make it fonkay / Private freak / Don't rush my beat (Only on MC and CD.) / S.O.S. (same ole story) (Only on MC and CD.)
CD _____ ICH 1102 CD
Ichiban / Apr '91 / Koch.

2nd Voice

CELEBRATE OUR DEATH
CD _____ HY 39100433CD
Hyperium / Aug '93 / Plastic Head.

3 Grand

3 BAD BROTHERS
CD _____ GRA 41572CD
Ichiban / May '94 / Koch.

3 Mustaphas 3

FRIENDS, FIENDS AND FRONDS
Si vous passez par la / Starehe Mustapha I, II and III / Maldita guajira / Linda Linda / Fiz'n / D.J. Trouble Fezz meets 3 Mustaphas 3 / Buke e kripe ne vater tone / Kalaxhoine / Anapse to Tsigaro / Shouffi rhirou / Niska banja / Kac kuzulu Ceylan / Selma
CD _____ CDORB 070
Globestyle / May '91 / Pinnacle.

HEART OF UNCLE
Awara hoon / Mama O / Anapse to tsigaro / Yeni yol / Kaba mustafa / Taxi driver / Aj zajdi zajdi jasno sonce / Sitna Lisa / Ovce-polsko oro / Kem kem / Trois fois trois (city version) / Vi bist du gevey zn far prohibish'n / Benga taxi / Trois fois trois (country version)
CD _____ CDORB 043
Globestyle / May '89 / Pinnacle.

SHOPPING
Ljubav kraj izvora/zvezdanova (skupovo) kolo / Shika shika / Xamenh evtexia/Fiz'n / Musafir / Szegerely farewell / Night off Beirut / Server / Shouffi rhirou / Valle e pogradecit / Darling don't say no (CD only) / Vou-lez vous danser
CD _____ CDORB 022
Fez-O-Phone / Aug '90 / Pinnacle.

SOUP OF THE CENTURY
Buke e kripe ne vater tone / Kalaxhojne / Zohar no.2 / Soba song / Golden clarinet / Ti citron / Sadilo mome / Tropnalo oro / This city is very exciting / Madre / Ya habibi, ya ghaybine / Mamo, snezhets navalyalo / Yo-gurt kovdum dolaba (Not on LP) / Televi-zyon (Not on LP) / Upovacko kolo (Not on LP)
CD _____ CDFEZ 004
Fez-O-Phone / Aug '90 / Pinnacle.

3 O'Clock

HAPPEN HAPPENED
CD _____ 346392
Frontier / Nov '93 / Vital.

3 Phase

SCHLANGEN FARM
CD Set _____ MONU 23CD
Mute / Nov '93 / Disc.

STRAIGHT ROAD
CD _____ EFA 017552
Tresor / Jul '94 / SRD.

3D's

VENUS TRAIL
CD _____ FNCD 281
Flying Nun / Apr '94 / Disc.

3LB Thrill

VULTURE
Born again / Diana / Baby comes clean / Stop inviting / Mary tells me / Jeff's fast one

---

/ Something will come / Bikini Island / Bad seed / Coffin nails / Collide / Embrace / Pinata
CD _____ 4817062
Epic / Dec '95 / Sony.

3rd And The Mortal

PAINTING ON GLASS
CD _____ VOW 051CD
Voices Of Wonder / Jan '96 / Plastic Head.

3rd Bass

DERELICTS OF DIALECT
Merchant of grooves / Derelicts of dialect / Ace in the hole / French toast / Portrait of the artist as a hand / Pop goes the weasel / Sea vessel soliloquy / Daddy rich in the land of 1210 / Word to the third / Herbalz in your mouth / Al's a b cee'z / No master plan no master race / Come in / No static at all / Eye jammie / Microphone techniques / Problem child / Three strikes 5000 / Kick 'em in the grill / Green eggs and swine / Check yourself (Only available on LP)
CD _____ 5235022
Def Jam / Jan '96 / PolyGram.

3rd Time Out

LETTER TO HOME
CD _____ ROUCD 0333
Rounder / Oct '95 / CM / Direct / ADA / Cadillac.

4 Deep

ANOTHER DAY IN THE JUNGLE
CD _____ POA 41642CD
Ichiban / May '94 / Koch.

4 Hero

PARALLEL UNIVERSE
CD _____ RIVCD 4
Reinforced / Jun '94 / SRD.

4 Non Blondes

BIGGER, BETTER, FASTER, MORE
Train / Superfly / What's up / Pleasantly blue / Morphine and chocolate / Spaceman / Old Mr.Heffer / Calling all the people / Dear Mr. President / Drifting / No place like home
CD _____ 756792112-2
WEA / Jun '93 / Warner Music.

4 Of Us

MAN ALIVE
Sensual thing / I miss you / Man alive / She hits me / Lift me up / Possessed / Baby Jesus / Love, hate and hope / Car crash at 80 mph / Boomtown / Stung, stuck and stranded / Hymn for her
CD _____ 4723262
Columbia / Oct '92 / Sony.

4 Skins

BEST OF THE 4-SKINS, THE
One law for them / Yesterday's heroes / Brave new world / Chaos / Wonderful world / Evil / Sorry / 1984 / A.C.A.B. / I don't wanna die / Plastic gangsters / Yesterday's heroes (single version) / Get out of my life / Justice / Jack the lad / Low life / Bread or blood / Seems to me / Norman / On the streets / Five more years / Betrayed / Saturday / Dambusters
CD _____ DOJOCD 140
Castle / Jun '93 / BMG.

FEW 4 SKINS MORE VOL. 1, A
Plastic gangsters / Jealousy / Yesterday's heroes / Justice / Jack the lad / Remembrance day / Manifesto / Wonderful world / Sorry / Evil / I don't wanna die / A.C.A.B. / Chaos / Five more years / Johnny go home / Gambler / I'll stick to my guns / On file / Forgotten hero / H.M.P / No excuse / Betrayed / City boy / New war
CD _____ LINK CD 015
Street Link / Oct '92 / BMG.

FISTFUL OF....FOUR SKINS, A
CD _____ AHOYCD 3
Captain Oi / Nov '93 / Plastic Head.

GOOD THE BAD AND THE 4 SKINS, THE
Plastic gangsters / Jealousy / Yesterday's heroes / Justice / Jack the lad / Remembrance day / Manifesto / Wonderful world / Sorry / Evil / I don't wanna die / A.C.A.B. / Chaos / One law for them
CD _____ AHOYCD 3
Captain Oi / Jul '93 / Plastic Head.

5-6-7-8's

CAN'T HELP IT
CD _____ ROCK 6096-2
Rockville / Mar '93 / CRD.

5ive Style

5IVE STYLE
CD _____ SP 309B
Sub Pop / Sep '95 / Disc.

5th Dimension

BEST OF THE FIFTH DIMENSION, THE
Last night I didn't get to sleep at all / One less bell to answer / Aquarius / Let the sunshine in / Wedding bell blues / Save the country / Love's lines, angles and rhymes / Puppet man / Up, up and away / Never my love / Together let's find love / Light sings / If I could reach you / Go where you wanna go / Sweet blindness / Working on a groovy thing / MacArthur park
CD _____ 74321 22545-2
Arista / Oct '94 / BMG.

7 Seconds

MUSIC, THE MESSAGE, THE
Ghost / Such and such / Music / Message / Kinda future / My gravity / See you tomorrow / Get a different life / Talkbox / My list / First ya told us / Born without a mind / Punk rock teeth / Girl song / I can remember / Even better plan / Kids are united (CD only.)
CD _____ 4814542
Epic / Dec '95 / Sony.

7 Year Bitch

SICK 'EM
CD _____ CZ 048CD
C/Z / Oct '92 / Plastic Head.

8 Bold Souls

ANT FARM
Half life / Little encouragement / Antfarm / Corner of walk and don't walk / Furthest from my mind / Big dig
CD _____ AJ 0114
Arabesque / Feb '95 / New Note.

SIDESHOW
CD _____ AJ 0103
Arabesque / Jul '94 / New Note.

8 From The Egg

8 FROM THE EGG
Underground hits / Black milk / So good / El cortez / Head funk / Fuzz / Gone / Liberation man
CD _____ OERCD002
Orange Egg / Aug '95 / Vital.

8 Storey Window

8 STOREY WINDOW.
CD _____ TOPPCD 006
Ultimate / Apr '94 / 3MV / Vital.

8 Up

LIE DOWN AND STAY CALM
Rubberneckin' / Ya don't quit / Not cometh of goest / Bottom end (buy the big issue) / Bup / Rip's rub / Keep it like that / Stan Gettes / Bright moments
CD _____ SJRCD 021
Soul Jazz / Oct '94 / New Note / Vital.

9.0

TOO FAR GONE
CD _____ RR 93442
Roadrunner / Dec '90 / Pinnacle.

9th Dream

RHYTHM AND IRRELEVANCE
Canfield / Play garden / Red of fire / Summer offering / Benediction / Letter in three parts / La lune de miel / Life a stormy point
CD _____ 450996257-2
Warner Bros. / May '94 / Warner Music.

10cc

10 CC IN CONCERT
Second sitting for the last supper / You've got a cold / Things we do for love / Art for art's sake / People in love / Wall Street shuffle / I'm Mandy fly me / Marriage bureau rendezvous / Good morning Judge / Honeymoon with B troop / Waterfall / I'm not in love
CD _____ PWKS 4050P
Carlton Home Entertainment / Apr '91 / Carlton Home Entertainment.

1

BLOODY TOURISTS
Dreadlock holiday / For you and I / Take these chains / Shock on the tube / Last night / Anonymous alcoholic / Reds in my bed / Life line / Tokyo / Old mister time / From Rochdale to Ocho Rios / Everything you've wanted to know about
CD _____ 8269212
Mercury / Jul '93 / PolyGram.

CHANGING FACES (The Very Best Of 10cc/Godley & Creme) (10cc & Godley & Creme)
Dreadlock holiday / Wall Street shuffle / Under your thumb / Life is a minestrone / Englishman in New York / Art for art's sake / Donna / Snack attack / Cry / Things we do for love / Wedding bells / I'm Mandy fly me / Good morning judge / Rubber bullets / Save a mountain for me / I'm not in love
CD _____ 816 355-2
Polydor / Mar '94 / PolyGram.

COLLECTION: 10CC
CD _____ CCSCD 214
Castle / Apr '89 / BMG.

DECEPTIVE BENDS
Good morning judge / Things we do for love / Marriage bureau / Rendezvous / People in love / Modern man blues / Honeymoon with B troop / I bought a flat guitar tutor / You've got a cold / Feel the benefit
CD _____ 8369482
Mercury / Jul '93 / PolyGram.

EARLY YEARS
CD _____ EARLD 12
Castle / Mar '93 / BMG.

FOOD FOR THOUGHT
Life is a minestrone / Don't hang up / Good morning judge / Last night / 1-2-5 / We've heard it all before / Twenty four hours / Dreadlock holiday / Rock 'n' roll lullaby / Take these chains / Power of love / Everyone / Feel the love / Food for thought
CD _____ 5500042
Spectrum/Karussell / May '93 / PolyGram / THE.

GREATEST HITS: 10 CC (1972-78)
Rubber bullets / Donna / Silly love / Dean and I / Life is a minestrone / Wall Street shuffle / Art for art's sake / I'm Mandy fly me / Good morning judge / Things we do for love / Dreadlock holiday / I'm not in love
CD _____ 800 056-2
Mercury / '83 / PolyGram.

HITS, THE
CD _____ 15193
Laserlight / Aug '91 / Target/BMG.

HOW DARE YOU
Art for art's sake / Don't hang up / Head room / How dare you / I wanna rule the world / Iceberg / I'm Mandy fly me / Lazy ways / Rock 'n' roll lullaby
CD _____ 836 949-4
Mercury / Feb '94 / PolyGram.

LIVE AND LET LIVE
Second sitting for the last supper / You've got a cold / Honeymoon with B troop / Art for art's sake / People in love / Wall Street shuffle / Ships don't disappear in the night / I'm Mandy fly me / Good morning judge / Feel the benefit / Things we do for love / Waterfall / I'm not in love (Seven-minute version.) / Modern man blues
CD _____ 838 861-2
Mercury / Feb '94 / PolyGram.

MEANWHILE
CD _____ 5132792
Polydor / Jan '92 / PolyGram.

MIRROR MIRROR
CD _____ AVEXCD 6
Avex / Aug '95 / 3MV.

ORIGINAL SOUNDTRACK, THE
Blackmail / Brand new day / Film of my love / Flying junk / I'm not in love / Life is a minestrone / Second sitting for the last supper / Une nuit a Paris / One night in Paris / Same night in Paris / Later the same night in Paris
CD _____ 830 776-2
Mercury / '88 / PolyGram.

SHEET MUSIC
Wall Street shuffle / Worst band in the world / Hotel / Old wild men / Clockwork creep / Just a wish / Battered and bruised / Jungleland / Tell me / No way out
CD _____ CLACD 186
Castle / Aug '90 / BMG.

VERY BEST OF THE EARLY YEARS, THE
CD _____ MCCD 107
MCI / May '93 / Disc / THE.

COME OUT AND ...
CD _____ NIGHTCD 008
Nightbreed / Nov '95 / Plastic Head.

THIRTEEN DAYS
Future blues / Shot down in flames / Morphine Bill / Angel / Crazy Bill / Kennedy said / Garden of Eden / Houseparty / Lonesome prairie / Melanie

---

BEST OF 13TH FLOOR ELEVATORS
CD _____ NTMCD 516
Nectar / Jan '96 / Pinnacle.

BEST OF THE 13TH FLOOR ELEVATORS
You're gonna miss me / I had to tell you / Never another / Thru the rhythm / Slip inside this house / Splash / Dr. Doom / Earthquake / May the circle remain unbroken / Levitation / She lives (in a time of her own) / I'm gonna love you too (live version) / Kingdom of heaven / Monkey island / Fire engine / You're gonna miss me (live version)
CD _____ 642370
EVA / Jun '94 / Direct / ADA.

I'VE SEEN YOUR FACE BEFORE
Fire engine / Tried to hide / Levitation / Don't fall down / Kingdom of heaven / You're gonna miss me / Reverberation (Doubt) / Monkey Island / Splash / She lives in a time of her own / Rollercoaster
CD _____ CDWIK 82
Big Beat / Jun '89 / Pinnacle.

LEVITATION - IN CONCERT
Levitation / Rollercoaster / Fire engine / Reverberation (Doubt) / Don't fall down / Tried to hide / Splash 1 / You're gonna miss me / Monkey island / Kingdom of heaven / She lives in a time of her own
CD _____ CDTB 147
Magnum Music / Mar '94 / Magnum Music Group.

OUT OF ORDER
Everybody needs somebody / To love / Before you accuse me / You don't know / I'm gonna love you too / You really got me / Splash / Fire engine / Roll over Beethoven / Word / Monkey Island / Rollercoaster
CD _____ CDTB 124
Magnum Music / Jun '93 / Magnum Music Group.

REUNION CONCERT, THE
Beast / Splash 1 / Don't slander me / You're gonna miss me / Clear night for love / Don't shake me lucifer / Bloody hammer / Two headed dog
CD _____ CDTB 153
Thunderbolt / Apr '95 / Magnum Music Group.

GYATSO
CD _____ PATH 12CD
Big Cat / Feb '94 / SRD / Pinnacle.

TWIN ACTION
Sweet tooth / Nature girl / Kum back / Golden candles / Revealer / Honey mink / Gram / Prock shake / Hotel 167 / Suncrush / Frosty hands / Life is strange / I won't let you down / Wet dream
CD _____ CRECD 164
Creation / Jul '94 / 3MV / Vital.

CRAYON
Aug. / Sixteen ink / Ray / Mystics 11 / Crank / Nuit N.
CD _____ OLE 1182
Matador / Dec '94 / Vital.

DONE
CD _____ CHE 12CD
Che / May '94 / SRD.

TRIBUTE TO A BUS
CD _____ CHE 26CD
Che / Mar '95 / SRD.

SALUTE
Knee deep / These eyes / Walkin' / Marching in time / Rain / Little sister / Pays off big / Just a wish / Battered and bruised / Jungleland / Tell me / No way out
CD _____ 07863610172
RCA / Jul '92 / BMG.

ENDLESS SEARCHING FOR SUBSTANCE, AN
CD _____ SR 9467
Silent / Oct '94 / Plastic Head.

GHETTO: MISFORTUNE'S WEALTH
Synopsis One: In the Ghetto/God save the world / Poverty's paradise / Brown-baggin' / Synopsis Two: Mother's Day / Mother's Day / Foodstamps / Ghetto: Misfortune's wealth / 24 Carat Black / God save the world
CD _____ CDSXE 090
Stax / Sep '93 / Pinnacle.

KEEPIN IT REAL
CD _____ W 1121372
We Bite / Jan '96 / Plastic Head.

UNDERGROUND
In case you missed it / What happened / Underground / Old devil moon / Hard times / After the rain / Manteca
CD _____ ANCD 8759
Antilles/New Directions / May '91 / PolyGram.

YOUR MOVE
CD _____ 5125242
Antilles/New Directions / Apr '92 / PolyGram.

MAXIN' WITH A FULL CLIP
Second without a pause / Code / Hole lotta nonsense / Tear the lid off / Rewind the future / Political frame-up / Measurement of the snucknose / Players rolling a stone / Both barrels / Dee / Watch my back / Push and shove (Not on LP) / Confusion on the inside (Not on LP)
CD _____ KEY 4104 CD
Gold Key / Apr '91 / Disc.

BANISH SILENCE
CD _____ WENCD 002
When / Jun '95 / BMG / Pinnacle.

DEBASEMENT TAPES
CD _____ CLEO 2143CD
Cleopatra / Jan '94 / Disc.

EMANATES
CD _____ MTB 018
TEQ / May '95 / Plastic Head.

EASTER, NOVEMBER A YEAR
CD _____ SA 54028
Semantic / Apr '94 / Plastic Head.

CAULDRON
And after / If not this time / Opus 777 / Things that concern you / Opus 11 / Red the sign post / For Paula / Rose / Fantasy / God bless the child / Cauldron / Fly free / Desire / Bad trip / Skins
CD _____ CDWIKD 158
Chiswick / Jan '96 / Pinnacle.

SMILIN' BUDDHA CABARET
Blame your parents / Radio luv song / Assoholic / Daisy / Once a killer / Punk grass / Lucy / Beyond the outsider / Don't listen to that / Ocean pearl / Higher / Friends end / What Buddy was / Save yourself / Nice to love you (CD only) / You don't get away (that easy) (CD only) / She la (CD only)
CD _____ REVXD 1001
Black / Nov '94 / Revolver Music.

BLIND ANGER AND HATE
CD _____ BHR 013
Burning Heart / Aug '95 / Plastic Head.

MORE OUT OF TODAY
CD _____ BHR 029CD
Burning Heart / May '95 / Plastic Head.

LANDING ON A RAT COLUMN
It's all overture / Agressive travelling / Fat chance / Ich bin heidi / Nib (Synthesizer party) / Tails in the sky / Ivory ball / Plonder on / Weird Granny / It's only a party / Dear Clare / Lens / Five miles / Julius Caesar (Live) / Do's and the dont's of path laying / Landing on a rat column (Live)
CD _____ FCR 001CD
Freshly Cut / Sep '94 / Vital.

SOUND OF MUSIC, THE
My machines / Microlour / Jam the box / Desire / Rushed / Sub seducer / Sound on sound / Poi et pas / Filter king / Highs / Finale / No
CD _____ RS 90578CD
R & S / Jul '95 / Vital.

PEEL SESSIONS
CD _____ SR 013
Snape / Apr '95 / Disc.

78th Fraser Highlander's.

LIVE IN SCOTLAND (78th Fraser Highlander's Pipe Band)
Slow airs / 4/4 Marches / Waulking songs medley / Solo pipe set / Reels-band, solo pipe, duet / Jigs / Slow air / Piobaireachd / Medley / Drum fanfare / Cape Breton medley / Journey to Skye
CD _____ LCOM 8016
Lismor / Jan '95 / Lismor / Direct / Duncans / ADA.

NOO THAT'S WHIT A CA'CEILIDH VOL.1 (78th Fraser Highlander's Pipe Band)
Dashing white sergeant / Dashing white sergeant (Encore) / Polka / Gay Gordons / Gay Gordons (encore) / St. Bernard's waltz / Eightsome reel / Strip the willow / Strip the willow (Encore) / Canadian barn dance / Canadian barn dance encore / Holley garel jig / Boston two step / Boston two step encore / Virginia reel / Military two step
CD _____ LISMOR 8016
Lismor / Jan '95 / Lismor / Direct / Duncans / ADA.

OFF GLIDE
CD _____ CDFRE 1
Parallel / Sep '93 / PolyGram.

QUAD CITY KNOCK
CD _____ WRA 8117CD
Wrap / Feb '94 / Koch.

QUAID CITY KNOCK
CD _____ WRA 8117C
Wrap / Jul '94 / Koch.

100 PROOF AGED IN SOUL
Somebody's been sleeping in my bed / Love is sweeter / One man's leftovers / I've come to save you / Ain't that lovin' you / Not enough love to satisfy / Age ain't nothing but a number / She's not just another woman / Too many cooks (spoil the soup) / I can't sit and wait / Backtrack / If I could see the light in the window / Driveway / Ninety day freeze (on her love) / Everything good is bad / I'd rather fight than switch / Don't scratch (where it don't itch) / Nothing sweeter than love / Since you been gone / Never my love
CD _____ HDHCD 504
HDH / Apr '92 / Pinnacle.

SELFTITLED
CD _____ HOO 392
Noise/Modern Music / Jul '95 / Pinnacle / Plastic Head.

ARE YOU LONESOME TONIGHT
CD _____ EMPRCD 009
Emporio / Feb '94 / THE / Disc / CM.

COUNTRY COLLECTION, THE
CD _____ EMPRCD 017
Emporio / Feb '94 / THE / Disc / CM.

GREAT AMERICAN COMPOSERS, THE
CD _____ EMPRCD 016
Emporio / Feb '94 / THE / Disc / CM.

GREAT LOVE SONGS, THE
CD _____ EMPRCD 008
Emporio / Feb '94 / THE / Disc / CM.

GREAT STRAUSS WALTZES, THE
CD _____ EMPRCD 015
Emporio / Feb '94 / THE / Disc / CM.

MAGIC OF HAWAII, THE
CD _____ EMPRCD 014
Emporio / Feb '94 / THE / Disc / CM.

MEMORIES ARE MADE OF THIS - THE 50'S
CD _____ EMPRCD 013
Emporio / Feb '94 / THE / Disc / CM.

MEMORIES ARE MADE OF THIS - THE 60'S
CD _____ EMPRCD 012
Emporio / Feb '94 / THE / Disc / CM.

MEMORIES ARE MADE OF THIS - THE 70'S
CD _____ EMPRCD 011
Emporio / Feb '94 / THE / Disc / CM.

MOONLIGHT SERENADES
CD _____ EMPRCD 002
Emporio / Feb '94 / THE / Disc / CM.

MUSIC FOR SWINGIN' LOVERS
CD _____ EMPRCD 020
Emporio / Feb '94 / THE / Disc / CM.

MUSIC FROM THE MOVIES
CD _____ EMPRCD 001
Emporio / Feb '94 / THE / Disc / CM.

MUSIC OF THE WORLD
CD _____ EMPRCD 006
Emporio / Feb '94 / THE / Disc / CM.

ON BROADWAY
CD _____ EMPRECD 018
Emporio / Feb '94 / THE / Disc / CM.

POWER & THE GLORY, THE
CD _____ EMPRCD 005
Emporio / Feb '94 / THE / Disc / CM.

RHAPSODY AND BLUES
CD _____ EMPRCD 003
Emporio / Feb '94 / THE / Disc / CM.

RODGERS, HAMMERSTEIN & HART
CD _____ EMPRCD 007
Emporio / Feb '94 / THE / Disc / CM.

THAT LATIN SOUND
CD _____ EMPRCD 004
Emporio / Feb '94 / THE / Disc / CM.

THEY WRITE THE SONGS
CD _____ EMPRECD 019
Emporio / Feb '94 / THE / Disc / CM.

108

SONGS OF SEPARATION
CD _____ LF 096CD
Lost & Found / Jun '94 / Plastic Head.

108 Grand

ALBUM, THE
CD _____ OMCD 002
OM / Nov '94 / SRD.

311

GRASS ROOTS
Lucky / Homebrew / Nutsympton / 8.16
a.m. / Omaha stylee / Apples science / Tai-
yed / Silver / Grass roots / Salsa / Lose /
Six / Offbeat / 1-2-3
CD _____ 4778942
Columbia / Jun '95 / Sony.

360's

ILLUMINATED
CD _____ LNKCD 1
Street Link / Oct '91 / BMG.

400 Blows

LOOK
CD _____ 9.00534
Trance / Nov '86 / SRD.

454 Big Block

YOUR JESUS
CD _____ CMCD 77084
Century Media / Sep '95 / Plastic Head.

500's

HUNGERS TEETH
CD _____ RER 5001
ReR Megacorp / May '94 / These / ReR
Megacorp.

808 State

EX.EL
San Francisco / Spanish heart / Leo Leo /
Qmart / Nephatiti / Lift / Ooops / Empire /
In yer face / Cubik / Lambrusco / Techno
bell / Olympic
CD _____ 9031737752
ZTT / Mar '91 / Warner Music.

Plan 9 / Moses / Contrique / Ten times ten
/ Timebomb / One in ten / Europa / Orbit /
Black morpheus / Southern cross / Nimbus
/ Colony
CD _____ 4509911002
ZTT / Feb '93 / Warner Music.

NINETY
Magical dream / Ancodia / Cobra bora / Pa-
cific 202 / Donkey doctor / 808080808 /
Sunrise / Fat shadow
CD _____ 2464612
ZTT / Nov '89 / Warner Music.

999

999
Me and my desire / Chicane destiny / Crazy
/ Your number is my number / Hit me / Ti-
tanic (My over) reaction / Pick it up / Emer
gency / No pity / Direct action / Briefing /
Nobody knows
CD _____ DOJOCD 149
Dojo / Sep '93 / BMG.

BIGGEST PRIZE IN SPORT, THE
Boys in the gang / Inside out / Trouble / So
long / Fun thing / Biggest prize in sport /
Hollywood / Stranger / Lie lie lie / Found out
too late / Made a fool of you / Boiler / Shake
/ English wipeout / Stop stop
CD _____ CDPUNK 67
Anagram / Nov '95 / Pinnacle.

FACE TO FACE
CD _____ OBSESSCD 003
Obsession / May '93 / Disc.

GREATEST HITS LIVE
Inside out / Hit me / Don't you know I need
you / White trash / Feelin' alright with the
crew / Obsessed / On the line / Let's face
it / Emergency / English wipe out / Nasty
nasty / Homicide / Lust, power and money
alive
CD _____ STR CD 026
Street Link / Oct '92 / BMG.

1000 Homo D.J's

SUPERNAUT
CD _____ CDDVN 5M
Devotion / Feb '92 / Pinnacle.

1910 Fruitgum Company

SIMON SAYS
CD _____ REP 4019-WX
Repertoire / Aug '91 / Pinnacle / Cadillac.

3080 Yen

HUMANOID HA HA
CD _____ EFA 123042
Vince Lombard / Dec '95 / SRD.

7669

EAST FROM A BAD BLOCK
Heree ah cumm / Session (interlude) / 69
ways to love a (black) man / Ma, I luv him
(interlude) / Joy / Shoot the M.F. in his
kneecap (interlude) / Changes / Conversation fo yo ass (interlude) / R.M.A. (Will you
remember me) / Crossover message (interlude) / Last song / Who dez bytches anyway (interlude) / So high / Tic away / By
your side / Cabaret (interlude) / Cloud 69 /
1-800 dial f... (interlude) / King size bed /
Shmoken' em up y'all (interlude) / Phillies,
40's and 69
CD _____ 532842-2
Motown / Mar '94 / PolyGram.

LIVE AND LOUD
Let's face it / Hit me / English wipe out /
Stranger / Feelin' alright with the crew /
Boys in the gang / Me and my desire /
Biggest prize in sport / Fun thing / Holly-
wood / Inside out / Homicide / Boiler
CD _____ LINKCD 107
Street Link / Jan '91 / BMG.

SEPARATES
Homicide / Tulse Hill night / Rael rean /
Let's face it / Crime (Pts. 1 & 2) / Feelin'
alright with the crew / Out of reach / Sub-
terfuge / Wolf / Brightest view / High energy
plan
CD _____ DOJOCD 150
Dojo / Sep '93 / BMG.

Black flowers for the bride / There is no
glory in Mary's story / Signed dangerous
from Hollywood / Bye bye bones / Everybody needs it / It's over now / Bye bye England / All of the days / Big fast car / Absolution / Deep in the shadow / Run for your
life / Don't tell me / Crazy crazy crazy /
White light
CD _____ CDGRAM 71
Cherry Red / Oct '93 / Pinnacle.

9353

MAKE YOUR LAST DAYS LOUD DAYS
CD _____ AS 6D
Adult Swim / May '93 / SRD.

**OVERDOSE AT YOUR MOTHER'S
HOUSE**
CD _____ AS 5D
Adult Swim / May '93 / SRD.

10,000 Maniacs

BLIND MAN'S ZOO
Eat for two / Please forgive us / Big parade
/ Trouble me / You happy puppet / Head-
strong / Poison in the well / Dust bowl /
Lion's share / Hateful hate / Jubilee
CD _____ K 9608152
Elektra / May '89 / Warner Music.

**HOPE CHEST (The Fredonia Recordings
1982-83)**
Planned obsolescence / Latin one / Katrina's fair / Pour de chirico / Grey victory /
National education week / Death of manolete / Orange / Tension / Anthem for
doomed youth / Daktari / Groove dub / Pit
viper / My mother the war
CD _____ 7559609622
Elektra / Oct '90 / Warner Music.

IN MY TRIBE
What's the matter here / Hey Jack Kerouac
/ Like the weather / Cherry tree / Painted
desert / Don't talk / Peace train / Gun shy
/ My sister Rose / Campfire song / City of
angels / Verdi cries
CD _____ K 9607382
Elektra / Nov '92 / Warner Music.

OUR TIME IN EDEN
Noah's dove / These are days / Eden / Few
and far between / Stockton gala days / Gold
rush brides / Jezebel / How you've grown /
Candy everybody wants / Tolerance / Circle
dream / If you intend / I'm not the man
CD _____ 7559613852
Elektra / Oct '92 / Warner Music.

UNPLUGGED
These are days / Eat for two / Candy every-
body wants / I'm not the man / Don't talk /
Hey Jack Kerouac / What's the matter here
/ Gold rush brides / Like the weather / Trou-
ble me / Jezebel / Because the night /
Stockton gala days / Noah's dove
CD _____ 755961569-2
WEA / Oct '93 / Warner Music.

WISHING CHAIR, THE
Can't ignore the train / Just as the tide was
flowing / Scorpio rising / Lilydale / Maddox
table / Everyone a puzzle lover / Arbor day
/ Back o' the moon / Tension makes a
tangle / Among the Americans / Grey victory / Cotton Alley / My mother the war
CD _____ 9604282
Elektra / '89 / Warner Music.

A

A Certain Ratio

FORCE
Only together / Bootsy / Fever 103 degrees / Naked and white / Mickey way / And then she smiled / Take me down / Anthem / Si fermi o gredo (Available on CD and cassette only)
CD _____ CREV 027CD
Rev-Ola / Oct '94 / 3MV / Vital.

GRAVEYARD AND THE BALLROOM, THE
CD _____ CREV 022CD
Rev-Ola / Oct '94 / 3MV / Vital.

I'D LIKE TO SEE YOU AGAIN
CD _____ CREV 025CD
Rev-Ola / Oct '94 / 3MV / Vital.

LOOKING FOR A CERTAIN RATIO - REMIX
CD _____ CRECD 159
Creation / Jun '94 / 3MV / Vital.

OLD AND THE NEW, THE
CD _____ CREV 026CD
Rev-Ola / Oct '94 / 3MV / Vital.

SEXTET
CD _____ CREV 024CD
Rev-Ola / Oct '94 / 3MV / Vital.

TO EACH
CD _____ CREV 023CD
Rev-Ola / Oct '94 / 3MV / Vital.

UP IN DOWNSVILLE
CD _____ CDROBERT 20
Rob's Records / Sep '92 / Pinnacle.

A One

FREE ASSOCIATION
CD _____ ZEN 004CD
China / Aug '95 / Pinnacle.

A Positive Life

SYNAESTHETIC
CD _____ RBADCD 10
Beyond / Oct '94 / Kudos / Pinnacle.

A Split Second

NEUROBEAT
CD _____ 842.424
Trance / '88 / SRD.

VENGEANCE C.O.D
CD _____ HY 210526
Hypertension / Feb '94 / Total/BMG / Direct / ADA.

A Subtle Plague

NO REPRISE
Young girl / I seperate / Same story / Microfaction / Weak and deprived / Growing upsidedown / Cheyenne's lullaby / I wanna kill the president / Planting minds / Ship song / Butcher's death parade / Dreaming you dead
CD _____ RTD 15730162
World Service / Jun '95 / Vital.

A Witness

PEEL SESSIONS: WITNESS (20.11.88 - 10.1.88)
I love you Mr Disposable Razors / Life - Final frontier / Helicopter tealeaf / Prince Microwave Bollard / Take me to the earth / McManus octaphone / Sunbed sentiment / Zip up
CD _____ SFPMACD 206
Strange Fruit / Dec '89 / Pinnacle.

A-Ha

EAST OF THE SUN, WEST OF THE MOON
Crying in the rain / I call your name / East of the sun and west of the moon / Waiting for her / Way we talk / Seemingly nonstop July / Early mornings / Slender frame / Sycamore leaves / Cold river / Rolling thunder
CD _____ 7599263142
WEA / Oct '90 / Warner Music.

HEADLINES AND DEADLINES
Take on me / Cry wolf / Touchy / You are the one / Manhattan skyline / Blood that moves the body / Early morning / Hunting high and low / Move to memphis / I've been losing you / Living daylights / Crying in the rain / I call your name / Stay on these roads / Train of thought / Sun always shines on TV
CD _____ 7599 267732
WEA / Nov '91 / Warner Music.

HUNTING HIGH AND LOW
Take on me / Train of thought / Hunting high and low / Blue sky / Living a boy's adventures tale / Sun always shines on TV / And

you tell me / Love is reason / Dream myself alive / Here I stand and face the rain
CD _____ 925300 2
WEA / Nov '85 / Warner Music.

MEMORIAL BEACH
Dark is the night / Move to Memphis / Cold as stone / Angel in the snow / Locust / Lie down in darkness / How sweet it was / Lamb to the slaughter / Between your mama and yourself / Memorial beach
CD _____ 936245229-2
WEA / Jun '93 / Warner Music.

SCOUNDREL DAYS
Scoundrel days / Swing of things / I've been losing you / October / Manhattan skyline / Cry wolf / Looking for the whales / Weight of the wind / Maybe maybe / Soft rains of April
CD _____ 9255012
WEA / Feb '95 / Warner Music.

STAY ON THESE ROADS
Blood that moves the body / Touchy / This alone is love / Hurry home / Living daylights / There's never a forever thing / Out of blue comes green / You are the one / You'll end up crying / Stay on these roads
CD _____ 9257332
WEA / Feb '95 / Warner Music.

A-La-Tex

ROUGH 'N' TUMBLE
Just sit back and laugh / Young dogs / Don't stop at the borderline / Signpost / Set me free / Girl from the west country / Gold of Eldorado / Loving chain / Don't leave me again / In the doghouse / I'll follow you / Parchman farm / I've got my foolhead on
CD _____ ZNCD 1008
Zane / Oct '95 / Pinnacle.

A.B. Skhy

A.B. SKHY
CD _____ OW 30011
One Way / Jul '94 / Direct / ADA.

A.C.

EVERYONE SHOULD BE KILLED
Some songs / Some more songs / Blur including new H.C. song / Even more songs / Tim / Judge / Spin cycle / Song 8 / Pavarotti / Unbelievable / Music sucks / Newest H.C. song #1 / Chiffon and chips / Guy Smiley / Seth / I'm not allowed to like A.C. anymore / EX.A Blur / G.M.O.T.R. / I'm wicked underground / Blur including G / Shut up Mike / Abomination of unnecessarily augmented... / Radio hit / Loser / When I think of the true punk rock bands / Eddy Grant / MTV is my source for new music / Song titles are fucking stupid / Having to make up song titles sucks / Well you know, mean Gene / Song 5 / Iron funeral / Chapel of gristle / Hellbent for leatherman / Alcoholic / Chump change / Slow song for split 7" / Des Bink's hairstyle / Newest H.C. song #2 / Greatful dead / Aging disgracefully / Brutally morbid axe of Satan / Surfer / You must be wicked underground if you own this / Choke edge / Otis Sistrunk / Russty knoife / Fred Bash / These are actual song titles / Our band is wicked sick (we have flu) / Guy le Fleur / Song 3 / Empire sandwich shop / Morrisey / Selling out by having song titles / Grindcore is very terrifying / Song 6 / Guy Lombardo
CD _____ MOSH 101CD
Earache / Nov '93 / Vital.

TOP 40 HITS
Some hits / Some more hits / Pepe, the gay waiter / Even more hits / M.J.C. / Flower shop guy / Living colour is my favourite black metal band / Lenny's in my neighbourhood / Stayin' alive (oi version) / Benchpressing the effects on Kevin Sharp's vocal's / Josue / Delicious face stuff / Nineteen to go / Stealing Seth's idea (The new book by John Chang) / Morbid dead guy / Believe in the King / Don't call Japanese hardcore Jap core / Shut up Mike / Hey, aren't you Gary Spivey / Breastfeeding JMJ. Bullocks' toenail collection / Fore play with a tree shredder / Two down five to go / I liked Earache better when Dig answered the phone / Brian dead / Newest H.C. Song #3 / Guy Ways of Steve Berger / Escape (Pina colada song) / Lives ruined by music / Still a freshman after all these years / I'm still standing / Art fag / John / Newest H.C. song / Song 9 / Cleft palate / A-Team / Old lady across the hall with no life / Shut up Paul / Lazy eye (once a hank, always a hank) / American woman
CD _____ MOSH 129CD
Earache / Apr '95 / Vital.

A.C. Acoustics

ABLE TREASURY
CD _____ ELM 21MCD
Elemental / Apr '94 / Disc.

A.C. Marias

ONE OF OUR GIRLS HAS GONE MISSING
Trilby's couch / Just talk / There's a scent of rain in the air / Our dust / So soon / Give me / To sleep / Looks like / Sometime / One of our girls has gone missing / Time was
CD _____ CDSTUMM 68
Mute / Aug '89 / Disc.

A.C. Temple

BLOWTORCH
CD _____ FU 6 CD
Furthur / Jul '88 / Pinnacle.

SOURPUSS
Sundown pet corner / Miss Sky / Stymied / Mother tongue / Crayola / Devil you know / Horsetrading / Mouthful / Faith is a windsock / Ringpiece / (Dirty) weekend
CD _____ BFFP 45CD
Blast First / Sep '89 / Disc.

A.D.

A.D.
CD _____ RGE 101-2
Enemy / Nov '94 / Grapevine.

DEAD WILL RISE
Joy for the world / If I could fly / Listen to the worlds / Pop song / Drop heavy / Bloodshed / Speak freely / Resting place / Dead will rise / Something special
CD _____ CDVEST 53
Bulletproof / Aug '95 / Pinnacle.

A.P.E.

STRIP LIGHT
CD _____ DOR 41CD
Dorado / Jun '95 / Disc.

A.R. Kane

69
CD _____ ROUGHCD 119
Rough Trade / Jun '88 / Pinnacle.

I
Hello / Crack up / What's all this then / Off into space / Yeti / Honeysuckle swallow / In a circle / Miles apart / Mars / Sugar wings / Down / Insect love / Catch my drift / Love from outer space / Timewind / Snow joke / And I say / Conundrum / Long body / Fast ka / Pop / Spook / Back home / Super vixons / Sorry / Challenge
CD _____ ROUGHCD 139
Rough Trade / Oct '89 / Pinnacle.

NEW CLEAR CHILD
Deep blue breath / Grace / Tiny little drop of perfumed time / Surf motel / Gather / Honey be (For Stella) / Cool as moons / Snow White's world / Pearl / Sea like a child / 3rd Stone / Sep '94 / Vital / Plastic Head.

REMIXES, THE
CD _____ RTCD 171
Rough Trade / May '90 / Pinnacle.

A.R.G.

ONE WORLD WITHOUT THE END
CD _____ BMCD 15
Black Mark / '92 / Plastic Head.

Aaberg, Philip

UPRIGHT
Upright / As if we didn't know / Every deep dream / Slow dance / Oh yes / Welcome to the Church of St. Anytime / New life, new View from Pony, Montana / Crying smile / Slow dance (piano reprise) / Thanks
CD _____ WD 1088
Windham Hill / Jun '91 / Pinnacle / BMG / ADA.

Aag

FIRE
CD _____ OZ 1002CD
Ozone / Jul '90 / SRD.

Aaliyah

AGE AIN'T NOTHING BUT A NUMBER
Throw your hands up / Back and forth / Age ain't nothing but a number / Down with the clique / At your best you are love / Me quite like you do / I'm so into you / Street thing / Young nation / Old scool / I'm down
CD _____ CHIP 149
Jive / Jul '94 / BMG.

Aardvarks

BARGAIN
Bargain day / Cheyenne woman / Office no.1 / Girl on a bike / Fly my plane / Mr. Inertia / Arthur C. Clarke / When the morning comes / Fifty hertz man / You're my loving way / Merry go round / Time to fly
CD _____ DELECCD 029
Delerium / Jun '95 / Vital.

Aaron, Lee

EMOTIONAL RAIN
CD _____ 341952
No Bull / Nov '95 / Koch.

Aatabou, Najat

VOICE OF THE ATLAS, THE
Baghi narjah / Finetriki / Shouffi rhirou / Lila ya shaba / Ouardatte Lajnane / Zourouni li-lah / Ditih
CD _____ CDORBD 069
Globestyle / Sep '91 / Pinnacle.

Abacush

LIFE
CD _____ ABACD 01
Abacush / May '94 / Jetstar.

Abana Ba Nasery

NURSERY BOYS GO AHEAD!
CD _____ CDORBD 076
Globestyle / Feb '92 / Pinnacle.

Abate, Greg

BOP CITY - LIVE AT BIRDLAND
CD _____ CCD 79513
Candid / Oct '93 / Cadillac / Jazz Music / Wellard / Koch.

DR. JEKYLL AND MR. HYDE (Abate, Greg Quintet with Richie Cole)
CD _____ CCD 79715
Candid / Nov '95 / Cadillac / Jazz Music / Wellard / Koch.

STRAIGHT AHEAD
CD _____ CCD 79530
Candid / Jul '93 / Cadillac / Jazz Music / Wellard / Koch.

Abba

ABBA
Mamma mia / Hey hey Helen / Tropical loveland / S.O.S. / Man in the middle / Bang a boomerang / I do I do I do I do / Rock me / Benny Andersson intermezzo N.1 / I've been waiting for you / So long / Waterloo / Hasta manana / Honey honey / Ring ring / Nina, pretty ballerina
CD _____ 831 596-2
Polydor / Mar '90 / PolyGram.

ABBA LIVE
Dancing queen / Take a chance on me / I have a dream / Does your Mother know / Chiquitita / Thank you for the music / Two for the price of one / Fernando / Gimme gimme gimme / Super trouper / Waterloo / Money money money / Name of the game / Eagle / On and on and on
CD _____ 829 951-2
Polydor / May '94 / PolyGram.

AGNETHA & FRIDA - THE SOUND OF ABBA
Heat is on / I know there's something going on / You're there / To turn the stone / Just one heart / That's tough / Turn the world around / I got something / We should be together / Shine / I won't let you go / Here we'll stay / Wrap your arms around me / Heart of the country
CD _____ 5502122
Spectrum/Karussell / Mar '94 / PolyGram / THE.

ALBUM, THE
Eagle / Take a chance on me / One man one woman / Name of the game / Move on / Hole in your soul / Girl with the golden hair / Three scenes from a mini musical
CD _____ 821 217-2
Polydor / Sep '92 / PolyGram.

ARRIVAL
My love my life / When I kissed the teacher / Dancing queen / Dum dum diddle / Knowing me, knowing you / Money, money, money / That's me / Why did it have to be me / Tiger / Arrival
CD _____ 821 319-2
Polydor / Sep '92 / PolyGram.

GOLD - GREATEST HITS
Dancing queen / Knowing me, knowing you / Take a chance on me / Mamma mia / Lay all your love on me / Super trouper / I have a dream / Winner takes it all / Money, money, money / S.O.S. / Chiquitita / Fer-

4

nando / Voulez vous / Gimme gimme
gimme / Does your mother know / One of
us / Name of the game / Thank you for the
music / Waterloo
CD _____ 5170072
Polydor / Sep '92 / PolyGram.

GREATEST HITS VOL.2
Take a chance on me / Gimme gimme
gimme / Money, money, money / Rock me
/ Eagle / Angel eyes / Dancing queen / Does
your mother know / Chiquitita / Summer
night city / Ronettes / Name of the game /
Thank you for the music / Knowing me,
knowing you
CD _____ 800 012-2
Polydor / Mar '90 / PolyGram.

HITS BOX, THE
CD Set _____ BOX D1
Carlton Home Entertainment / Nov '91 /
Carlton Home Entertainment.

HITS, THE (2)
Name of the game / Ring ring / Arrival /
Summer night city / Happy New Year / An-
gel eyes / Kisses of fire / Fernando / Day
before you came / Money, money, money /
Andante andante / Voulez vous / When I
kissed the teacher
CD _____ PWKS 500
Carlton Home Entertainment / Jan '88 /
Carlton Home Entertainment.

HITS, THE (3)
Winner takes it all / King has lost his crown
/ Dance (while the music still goes on) /
Gimme gimme gimme / Head over heels /
Rock me / I have a dream
CD _____ PWKS 507
Carlton Home Entertainment / Sep '88 /
Carlton Home Entertainment.

LOVE SONGS, THE
Under attack / Slippin' through my fingers /
Should I laugh or cry / Gonna sing you a
love song / Lovers (live a little longer) / Lov-
elight / I've been waiting for you / My love
my life / One man, one woman / Tropical
loveland / Another town another train /
When all is said and done / If it wasn't for
the night / So long
CD _____ PWKS 564
Carlton Home Entertainment / Dec '89 /
Carlton Home Entertainment.

MORE ABBA GOLD
CD _____ 519353-2
Polydor / May '93 / PolyGram.

RING RING
Ring ring / Another town another train / Disillusion / People need love / I saw it in the
mirror / Nine, pretty ballerina / Love isn't
easy (but it sure is hard enough) / Me and
Bobby and Bobby's brother / She's my kind
of girl / I am just a girl / Rock 'n' roll band
CD _____ 843 642-2
Polydor / May '91 / PolyGram.

SINGLES - THE FIRST 10 YEARS
Ring ring / Waterloo / So long / I do I do I
do I do I do / S.O.S. / Mamma mia / Fernando / Dancing queen / Money, money,
money / Knowing me, knowing you / Name
of the game / Take a chance on me / Summer night city / Chiquitita / Does your
mother know / Voulez vous / Gimme gimme
gimme / I have a dream / Winner takes it all
/ Super trouper / One of us / Day before
you came / Under attack
CD _____ 810 050-2
Polydor / Mar '90 / PolyGram.

SUPER TROUPER
Super trouper / Winner takes it all / On and
on and on / Andante Andante / Me and I /
Happy New Year / Our last summer / Piper
/ Lay all your love on me / Way old friends
do
CD _____ 800 023-2
Polydor / Sep '92 / PolyGram.

THANK YOU FOR THE MUSIC
CD Set _____ 523472-2
PolyGram / Nov '94 / PolyGram.

VISITORS, THE
Visitors / Head over heels / When all is said
and done / Soldiers / I let the music speak
/ One of us / Two for the price of one /
Slipping through my fingers / Like an angel
/ Passing through my room / Eagle
CD _____ 8000112
Polydor / Sep '92 / PolyGram.

VOULEZ VOUS
As good as new / Voulez vous / I have a
dream / Angel eyes / King has lost his
crown / Does your mother know / If it
wasn't for the night / Chiquitita / Lovers (like
a little longer) / Kisses of fire
CD _____ 821 320-2
Polydor / Mar '90 / PolyGram.

WATERLOO
Waterloo / Watch out / King Kong song /
Hasta manana / My mama said / Dance
(while the music still goes on) / Honey
honey / What about Livingstone / Gonna
sing you a love song / Suzy hang around
CD _____ 5500342
Spectrum/Karussell / Jun '93 / PolyGram /
THE.

Abbacadabra

ABBACADABRA
CD _____ ALMYCD 03
Almighty / Jan '93 / Total/BMG.

Abbasi, Rez

THIRD EAR
CD _____ EFA 015042
Ozone / Jul '95 / SRD.

Abbfinoosty

FUTURE
Owl / Future / Medusa / Workshop / Drink
with the Devil / Arabian sales / Wild ones /
Wish song / Wake up / Mama don't send /
Khatra dream / Wizard
CD _____ CYCL 005
Cyclops / May '94 / Pinnacle.

Abbott, Bobby

WELCOME TO GLENSHARRAGH
CD _____ LCOM 9046
Lismor / Jul '91 / Lismor / Direct /
Duncans / ADA.

Abbott, Gregory

SHAKE YOU DOWN
I got the feelin' / Say you will / Shake you
down / You're my angel / Magic / Wait until
tomorrow / Rhyme and reason / I'll find a
way
CD _____ 983310 2
Pickwick/Sony Collector's Choice / Oct '93
/ Carlton Home Entertainment / Pinnacle /
Sony.

Abbud, Malik Ahmel

JAZZ SAHARA
CD _____ OJCCD 18202
Original Jazz Classics / Jun '95 / Wellard /
Jazz Music / Cadillac / Complete/Pinnacle.

ABC

ABC 1
Look of love (parts 1 and 2) / Love's a dan-
gerous language / Man trap / Show me /
Date stamp / Valentine's day / Overture /
Beauty stab / When Smokey sings / 4 Ever
2 gether / If ever I thought you'd be lonely
/ Rage and then regret / Bite the hand /
Tears are not enough
CD _____ PWKS 4111P
Carlton Home Entertainment / Jul '92 / Carl-
ton Home Entertainment.

ABC 2
All of my heart / Where is the heaven / Real
thing / Greatest love of all / Look of love
(parts 3 and 4) / Between you and me / Vertigo / Poison arrow / Chicago (part 1 and 2)
/ Never more than now / Many happy returns / Jealous lover / Tower of London / A
to Z / Judy's jewels / That was then but this
is now
CD _____ PWKS 4132 P
Carlton Home Entertainment / Nov '92 /
Carlton Home Entertainment.

ABRACADABRA
Love conquers all / Unlock the secrets of
your heart / Answered prayer / Spellbound
/ Say it / Welcome to the real world / Satori
/ All that matters / This must be magic
CD _____ CDPCS 7355
Parlophone / Jun '91 / EMI.

ABSOLUTELY ABC (The Greatest Hits)
Poison arrow / Look of love / All of my heart
/ Tears are not enough / That was then but
this is now / S.O.S. / How to be a millionaire
/ Be near me / When Smokey sings / Night
you murdered love / Look of love, The (1990
remix) (Only on CD and cassette.) / When
Smokey sings (12" mix) (CD/MC only) / Be
near me (12" remix) (Only on CD and cas-
sette.) / One better world (12" remix) /
Ocean blue (Only on CD and cassette.)
CD _____ 64296722
Neutron / Apr '90 / PolyGram.

BEAUTY STAB
That was then but this is now / Love's a
dangerous language / If I ever thought
you'd be lonely / Power of persuasion /
Beauty stab / By default, by design / Hey
citizen / King money / Bite the hand / Unzip
/ S.O.S. / United Kingdom
CD _____ 8146612
Neutron / Nov '83 / PolyGram.

LEXICON OF LOVE, THE
Show me / Poison arrow / Many happy returns / Tears are not enough / Valentine's
day / Look of love / Date stamp / All of my
heart / 4 ever 2 gether / Look of
love
CD _____ 810 003 2
Neutron / Jun '82 / PolyGram.

**LEXICON OF LOVE, THE/BEAUTY STAB
(2CD Set)**
Show me / Poison arrow / Many happy returns / Tears are not enough / Valentine's
day / Look of love / Date stamp / All of my
heart / 4 ever 2 gether / Look of love (pt 4)
/ That was then but this is now / Love's a
dangerous language / If ever I thought

you'd be lonely / Power of persuasion /
Beauty stab / By default, by design / Hey
citizen / King money / Bite the hand / Unzip
/ S.O.S. / United Kingdom
CD Set _____ 5286002
Neutron / Aug '95 / PolyGram.

REMIX COLLECTION, THE
Tears are not enough / Alphabet soup / Poison arrow / Look of love / That was then
but this is now / How to be a millionaire /
Be near me / Ocean blue / Night you murdered love / King without a crown / One
better world / Real thing / Chicago (part 1
and 2) / Judy's jewels / Overture
CD _____ VSOP CD 182
Connoisseur / Mar '93 / Pinnacle.

TEARS ARE NOT ENOUGH
Poison arrow / Tears are not enough / Be
near me / Never more than now / Love's a
dangerous language / Bite the hand / Night
you murdered love / Greatest love of all /
Minneapolis / Vanity kills / Think again / I'm
in love with you / Real thing / Chicago
CD _____ 5500002
Spectrum/Karussell / May '93 / PolyGram /
THE.

UP
Never more than now / Real thing / One
better world / Where is the Heaven /
Greatest love of all / I'm in love with you /
Paper thin
CD _____ 8386462
Neutron / Oct '89 / PolyGram.

ABC Diablo

GIVE RISE TO DOUBTS
Common Cause / Sep '95 / Plastic Head /
SRD.

LAST INTOXICATION OF THE SENSES
CD _____ CC 001CD
Common Cause / Jun '93 / Plastic Head /
SRD.

Abcess

URINE JUNKIES
CD _____ RR 6923CD
Relapse / Nov '95 / Plastic Head.

Abdelli

NEW MOON
Adarghal introduction / Adarghal (The blind
in spirit) / Achaah (Resentment) / Lawan
(Time) / Walagh (I observe) / Ayafrouk (The
pigeon) / Imanza (Ancestors) / J.S.K. / Ig-
gantiw (There are no more stars in my sky)
/ Amegh asinigh (Bad news)
CD _____ CDRW 54
Realworld / Jun '95 / EMI / Sterns.

Abdul, Paula

FOREVER YOUR GIRL
Way that you love me / Knocked out / Op-
posites attract (Duet with the Wild Pair) /
State of attraction / I need you / Forever
your girl / Straight up / Next to you / Cold
hearted / One or the other
CD _____ CDSRN 19
Siren / Apr '92 / EMI.

HEAD OVER HEELS
Crazy cool / My love is for real / Ain't never
gonna give you up / Love don't come easy
/ If I were your girl / Sexy thoughts / Choice
is yours / Ho-down / Under the influence /
I never knew it / Get your groove on / Missing
you / It's all about feeling good / Cry for
me
CD _____ CDVUS 90
Virgin / Jun '95 / EMI.

**SHUT UP AND DANCE (THE DANCE
REMIXES)**
Cold hearted / Straight up / One or the other
/ Forever your girl / Knocked out / Way that
you love me / Opposites attract / Medley /
State of attraction
CD _____ CDVUS 28
Virgin / Apr '92 / EMI.

SPELLBOUND
Promise of a new day / Rock house / Rush
rush / Spellbound / Vibeology / Will you
marry me / U / My foolish heart / Blowing
kisses in the wind / To you / Alright tonight
/ Goodnight my love (pleasant dreams)
CD _____ CDVUS 33
Virgin / Jul '91 / EMI.

Abe, Kaoru

JAZZ BED
CD _____ PSFD 66
PSF / Dec '95 / Harmonia Mundi.

Abee, Steve

JERUSALEM DONUTS
CD _____ NAR 087 CD
New Alliance / May '93 / Pinnacle.

Abeng

UNCONQUEREBEL
CD _____ LRCD 001
Lush / Oct '94 / SRD.

Abercrombie, John

ANIMATO
Right now / Single moon / Agitato / First
light / Last light / For hope of hope / Bright
reign / Ollie Mention
CD _____ 841 779 2
ECM / Mar '90 / New Note.

CHARACTERS
Parable / Memoir / Telegram / Backward
glance / Ghost dance / Paramour / After-
thoughts / Evensong
CD _____ 8293722
ECM / '88 / New Note.

FAREWELL
CD _____ 500462
Musidisc / Nov '93 / Vital / Harmonia
Mundi / ADA / Cadillac / Discovery.

GATEWAY 2
Opening / Sing song / Blue / Reminiscence
/ Nexus
CD _____ 8473232
ECM / Dec '95 / New Note.

GETTING THERE
Sidekick / Upon a time / Getting there / Re-
member hymn / Thalia / Furs on ice /
Chance / Labour day
CD _____ 8334942
ECM / Feb '88 / New Note.

**JOHN ABERCROMBIE TRIO
(Abercrombie, John Trio)**
Furs on ice / Alice in Wonderland / Innerplay
/ Drum solo / Samurai hee-haw / Stella by
starlight / Beautiful love / Light beam / Four
on one / Haunted heart
CD _____ 8377562
ECM / Apr '89 / New Note.

NOVEMBER
Cat's back / J.S / Right brain patrol / Prel-
ude / November / Rise and fall / John's
walts / Ogeda / Tuesday afternoon / To be
/ Come rain or come shine / Big music
CD _____ 5190732
ECM / Oct '93 / New Note.

**SPEAK OF THE DEVIL (Abercrombie,
John Trio)**
Angel food / Now and again / Mahat / Cho-
rale / Farewell / BT-U / Early to bed /
Dreamland / Hell's gare
CD _____ 8496482
ECM / May '94 / New Note.

TIMELESS
Lungs / Love song / Ralph's piano waltz /
Red and orange / Remembering / Timeless
CD _____ 8291142
ECM / '87 / New Note.

WORKS: JOHN ABERCROMBIE
Red and orange / Night / Ralph's piano
waltz / Backward glance / Nightlake /
Dreamstalker / Isla / Sing song
CD _____ 8372752
ECM / Jun '89 / New Note.

Aberg, Lennart

GREEN PRINTS
CD _____ 1276-2
Caprice / Oct '87 / CM / Complete/
Pinnacle / Cadillac / ADA.

Abhisheki, Jitendra

**HYMNS FROM THE VEDAS AND
UPABNISHADS**
Salutations to the gurus / Peace chants /
Gayatri mantara / Bhhagavad selections /
Jayadeva's song to Krishna / Radha's
pangs for krishna / Hymn on the greatness
of shiva / Bhagavad gita verses chapter 2 /
O mind go to kasi (Sung in Hindu)
CD _____ RMSCD 105
Ravi Shankar Music Circle / May '94 /
Conifer.

Abigail

FEEL GOOD
CD _____ GAILCD 1
Rumour / Oct '94 / Pinnacle / 3MV / Sony.

Abigor

INVOKE THE DARK AGE
CD _____ SPV 08407962
Napalm / Apr '95 / Plastic Head.

ORKBLUT... THE RETALIATION
CD _____ SPV 08007992
SPV / May '95 / Plastic Head.

Abnegate

INSANE SOULS
CD _____ MOLTEN 002CD
Molten Head / Jul '95 / Plastic Head.

Abou-Khalil, Rabih

BETWEEN DUSK AND DAWN
CD _____ MMP 170886 CD
MMP / Mar '89 / New Note.

BLUE CAMEL
Sahara / Tsarka / Ziriab / Blue camel / On
time / Night in the mountains / Rabou Abou
Kabou / Beriut
CD _____ ENJ 70532
Enja / Oct '92 / New Note / Vital/SAM.

5

BUKRA
CD _____ MMP 170889 CD
MMP / Feb '89 / New Note.

NAFAS
CD _____ 8357812
ECM / Sep '88 / New Note.

ROOTS AND SPROUTS
Remembering Machghara / Walking on air /
Nida / Revelation / Wordless / Sweet tain /
Outlook / Caravan / Dreams of a dying city
CD _____ MMP 170890CD
MMP / Jul '90 / New Note.

SULTAN'S PICNIC, THE
Sunrise in Montreal / Solitude / Dog river /
Moments / Lamentation / Nocturne au vil-
laret / Happy sheik / Snake soup
CD _____ ENJ 80782
Enja / Oct '94 / New Note / Vital/SAM.

TARAB
Bushman in the desert / After dinner /
Awakening / Haneen wa hanaan / Lost cen-
turies / In search of the well / Orange fields
/ Tooth lost / Arabian waltz
CD _____ ENJ 70832
Enja / Oct '93 / New Note / Vital/SAM.

Aboud Abdel Al

**BEST OF MODERN BELLYDANCE
FROM ARABIA**
CD _____ EUCD 1244
ARC / Nov '93 / ARC Music / ADA.

Abrahams, Brian

**IMGOMA YABANTWANA (Abrahams,
Brian District Six)**
McGregorian chant / Home in a home / Ma-
ras dance / Django's jungle / Opskud (Let's
jump) / Imgoma yabantwana (Song for the
children) / Out of the question
CD _____ D 6002
District 6 / Jan '90 / Cadillac / Pinnacle.

Abrahams, Mick

ALL SAID AND DONE
Roadroller / Watch your step / Billy the kid
/ Black night / All tore down / Redway of
Milton Keynes / Long gone / Rock me right
/ So much trouble / Dear Jane / I wonder
who / All said and done / Cat's squirrel / Let
me love you baby
CD _____ ELITE 007 CD
Elite/Old Gold / May '91 / Carlton Home
Entertainment.

AT LAST
When I get back / Absent friends / Time
now to decide / Whole wide world / Up and
down (part 1) / Up and down (part 2) /
Maybe because / Good old days / You'll
never get it from me
CD _____ EDCD 335
Edsel / Sep '91 / Pinnacle / ADA.

LIVE - ALL TORE DOWN
CD _____ IGOCD 2011
Indigo / Nov '94 / Direct / ADA.

MICK ABRAHAMS
Greyhound Bus / Awake / Winds of change
/ Why do you do me this way / Big queen
/ Not to rearrange / Seasons
CD _____ BGOCD 95
Beat Goes On / Aug '94 / Pinnacle.

Abram, Vic

SERENISSIMA
CD _____ HY 2000104CD
Hypertension / Sep '93 / Total/BMG /
Direct / ADA.

Abrams, Muhal Richard

1-0 QA + 19
CD _____ 1200172
Black Saint / Oct '90 / Harmonia Mundi /
Cadillac.

BLU BLU BLU
CD _____ 1201172
Black Saint / Jan '92 / Harmonia Mundi /
Cadillac.

BLUES FOREVER
CD _____ BSR 0061
Black Saint / Jun '86 / Harmonia Mundi /
Cadillac.

DUET
CD _____ 120051-2
Black Saint / Jan '94 / Harmonia Mundi /
Cadillac.

FAMILYTALK
CD _____ 120132-2
Black Saint / Nov '93 / Harmonia Mundi /
Cadillac.

LEVELS & DEGREES OF LIGHT
CD _____ DELMARK 413
Delmark / Oct '89 / Hot Shot / ADA / CM /
Direct / Cadillac.

ONE LINE, TWO VIEWS
CD _____ 804692
New World / Dec '95 / Harmonia Mundi /
ADA / Cadillac.

**THINGS TO COME FROM THOSE NOW
GONE**
CD _____ DELMARK 430
Delmark / Sep '89 / Hot Shot / ADA / CM
/ Direct / Cadillac.

VIEW FROM WITHIN
CD _____ BSR 0081
Black Saint / Jun '86 / Harmonia Mundi /
Cadillac.

YOUNG AT HEART - WISE IN TIME
CD _____ DELMARK 423
Delmark / Oct '93 / Hot Shot / ADA / CM /
Direct / Cadillac.

Abrasive Wheels

VICIOUS CIRCLE
CD _____ AABT 807CD
Metalcore / May '92 / Plastic Head.

WHEN THE PUNKS GO MARCHING IN
CD _____ AHOY 25
Captain Oi / Nov '94 / Plastic Head.

Abraxas

SKIN THRILLS
CD _____ TF 136512
TFI / Jul '95 / Plastic Head.

Abruptum

IN UMBRA MALFTJAE
CD _____ ANTI-MOSH 009CD
Voices Of Wonder / Apr '94 / Plastic
Head.

Abscess

IN YOUR MIND
CD _____ EFA 111812
Glasnost / May '95 / SRD.

Abshire, Nathan

**FRENCH BLUES (Abshire, Nathan & The
Pinegrove Boys)**
CD _____ ARHCD 373
Arhoolie / Apr '95 / ADA / Direct /
Cadillac.

GREAT CAJUN ACCORDIONIST, THE
La valse de meche / La valse de bayou teche / La valse du kaplan / T'en as eu, t'en
n'auras plus / La calse de belezaire / Le
two-step de l'acadien / Cher ti-monde / Allons tuer la tortue / La valse des valses / Le
blues francais / La valse de grand basile /
Le two-step de choupique / Pauvre hobo /
J'aimerais connaitre / La valse de la porte
ouverte / Blues du tac tac / La valse du
reveur / Hip et taiau / Jolie blon / Pine grove
blues / La valse de choupique / Les flames
d'enfer / Le temps est apres finir
CD _____ CDCHD 401
Ace / Apr '93 / Pinnacle / Cadillac / Com-
plete/Pinnacle.

**PINE GROVE BLUES/THE GOOD TIMES
ARE KILLING ME**
Pine grove blues / La valse de Holly Beach
/ Games people play / Service blues / Musician's life / Fee-fee pon-cho / Lemonade
song / La valse de bayou teche / Sur la
courtableau / I don't hurt anymore / Phil's
waltz / Shamrock / Choupique two step /
Tracks of my buggy / Nathan's lafayette
two step / Dying in misery / Tramp sur la
rue / Partie a grand basile / J'ai etais au
balle / Valse de kaplan / If you don't love
me / Off shore blues / Let me hold your
hand / La noce a Rosalie
CD _____ CDCHD 329
Ace / Nov '93 / Pinnacle / Cadillac / Com-
plete/Pinnacle.

Abstinence

FRIGID
CD _____ SR 9468CD
Silent / Jan '95 / Plastic Head.

REVOLT OF CYBERCHRIST
CD _____ SR 9440
Furnace / Sep '94 / Plastic Head.

Absu

BARATHRUM V.I.T.R.I.O.L
CD _____ OPCD 020
Osmose / Apr '94 / Plastic Head.

SUN OF TIPERETH, THE
CD _____ OPCD 029
Osmose / May '95 / Plastic Head.

Abutilon

T.C.H.
CD _____ DOROBO 004CD
Dorobo / Oct '95 / Plastic Head.

Abysmal

PILLORAIN AGE
CD _____ CDAV 007
Avant Garde / Feb '95 / Plastic Head.

Abyss

OTHER SIDE, THE
CD _____ NB 1262
Nuclear Blast / Mar '95 / Plastic Head.

Abyssinians

ARISE
Oh Lord / Land is for everyone / Mightiest
of all / Meditation / Wicked men / Jah loves
/ Dem a come / South African enlistment /
Hey you / Let my days be long
CD _____ CDFL 9010
Frontline / Sep '90 / EMI / Jetstar.

BEST OF THE ABYSSINIANS, THE
Leggo beast / Let's my days be long / Satta
a masagana / Jason Whyte / Reason time /
Crashie sweeps / Jerusalem / Satta me
born ya / Love comes and goes / Tena
yistillin
CD _____ 111922
Musidisc / Mar '94 / Vital / Harmonia Mundi
/ ADA / Cadillac / Discovery.

SATTA MASSAGANA
CD _____ HBCD 120
Heartbeat / Mar '93 / Greensleeves /
Jetstar / Direct / ADA.

Ac Alun, John

OS NA DDAY YFORY
CD _____ SCD 2112
Sain / Dec '95 / Direct / ADA.

Ac Dhonncha, Sean

AN SPAILPIN FANACH
CD _____ CICD 006
Clo Iar-Chonnachta / Dec '94 / CM.

AC/DC

74 JAILBREAK
CD _____ 756792449-2
Atlantic / Sep '94 / Warner Music.

BACK IN BLACK
Back in black / Hell's bells / Shoot to thrill
/ Given the dog a bone / What do you do
for money honey / Rock 'n' roll ain't noise
pollution / Let me put my love into you / You
shook me all night long / Shake a leg / Have
a drink on me
CD _____ 756792418-2
Atlantic / Aug '94 / Warner Music.

BALLBREAKER
CD _____ 7559617802
Atlantic / Sep '95 / Warner Music.

BLOW UP YOUR VIDEO
Heatseeker / That's the way I wanna rock
'n' roll / Meanstreak / Go zone / Kissin' dy-
namite / Nick of time / Some sin for nuthin'
/ Ruff stuff / Two's up / This means war
CD _____ 781 828-2
Atlantic / Feb '88 / Warner Music.

DIRTY DEEDS DONE DIRT CHEAP
Dirty deeds done dirt cheap / Love at first
feel / Big balls / Rocker / Problem child /
There's gonna be some rockin' / Ain't no
fun waiting round to be a millionaire / Ride
on / Squealer
CD _____ 756792414-2
Atlantic / Jul '94 / Warner Music.

FLICK OF THE SWITCH
Rising power / Badlands / Brain shake /
Flick of the switch / Deep in the hole / Land-
slide / Guns for hire / Bedlam in Belgium
CD _____ 756792448-2
Atlantic / Jul '94 / Warner Music.

FLY ON THE WALL
Fly on the wall / Shake your foundations /
First blood / Danger / Sink the pink / Playing
with girls / Stand up / Hell or high water /
Back in business / Send for the man
CD _____ 781 263-2
Atlantic / Jul '85 / Warner Music.

**FOR THOSE ABOUT TO ROCK (WE
SALUTE YOU)**
For those about to rock (we salute you) /
Put the finger on you / Let's get it up / Inject
the venom / Snowballed / Evil walk / C.O.D.
/ Breaking the rules / Night of the long
knives / Spellbound
CD _____ 756792412-2
Atlantic / Jul '94 / Warner Music.

HIGH VOLTAGE
It's a long way to the top (if you wanna rock
'n' roll) / Rock 'n' roll singer / Jack / T.N.T.
/ Can I sit next to you girl / Little lover /
She's got balls / High voltage / Live wire
CD _____ 756792413-2
Atlantic / Jul '94 / Warner Music.

HIGHWAY TO HELL
Highway to Hell / Girl's got rhythm / Touch
too much / Beating around the bush / Shot
down in flames / Get it hot / If you want
blood (you've got it) / Love hungry / Night
prowler
CD _____ 756792419-2
Atlantic / Aug '94 / Warner Music.

IF YOU WANT BLOOD YOU'VE GOT IT
Riff raff / Hell ain't a bad place to be / Bad
boy boogie / Problem child / Whole
lotta Rosie / Rock 'n' roll damnation / High
voltage / Let there be rock / Rocker
CD _____ 756792447-2
Atlantic / Sep '94 / Warner Music.

LET THERE BE ROCK
Go down / Dog eat dog / Let there be rock
/ Bad boy boogie / Overdose / Crapsody in

blue / Hell ain't a bad place to be / Whole
lotta Rosie
CD _____ 756792445-2
Atlantic / Sep '94 / Warner Music.

LIVE
Thunderstruck / Shoot to thrill / Back in
black / Sin City / Who made who / Heat-
seeker / Fire your guns / Jailbreak / Jack /
Razor's edge / Dirty deeds done dirt cheap
/ Money talks / Hell's bells / Are you ready
/ That's the way I wanna rock 'n' roll / High
voltage / You shook me all night long /
Whole lotta Rosie / Let there be rock /
Bonny / Highway to hell / T.N.T. / For those
about to rock (we salute you)
CD _____ 7567922152
Atlantic / Nov '92 / Warner Music.

POWERAGE
Gimme a bullet / Down payment blues /
Gone shootin' / Riff raff / Sin City / Up to
my neck in you / What's next to the Moon
/ Cold hearted man / Kicked in the teeth
CD _____ 756792446-2
Atlantic / Sep '94 / Warner Music.

RAZOR'S EDGE, THE
Thunderstruck / Fire your guns / Money
talks / Razor's edge / Mistress for Christmas / Rock your heart out / Are you ready
/ Got you by the balls / Shot of love / Let's
make it / Goodbye and good riddance to
bad luck / If you dare
CD _____ 756 791 413 2
Atlantic / Sep '90 / Warner Music.

**WHO MADE WHO (Film Soundtrack for
Maximum Overdrive)**
Who made who / You shook me all night
long / D.T. / Sink the pink / Ride on / Hell's
bells / Shake your foundations / Chase the
ace / For those about to rock (we salute
you)
CD _____ 781 650-2
Atlantic / '88 / Warner Music.

Acanto

LABIRINTO
CD _____ BRAM 198902-2
Brambus / Nov '93 / ADA / Direct.

VERSO SERA
CD _____ BRAM 199123-2
Brambus / Nov '93 / ADA / Direct.

Acapella

WE HAVE SEEN HIS GLORY
Sing to the glory / We have seen his glory
/ Glory in his name / We will see Jesus /
How can I truly say / Good livin' / Talk to
Jah / Angels long to look / I understood /
To him who sits on the throne
CD _____ 7019299601
Nelson Word / Mar '92 / Nelson Word.

Acceleration

ACCELERATION
CD _____ 8334732
ECM / May '88 / New Note.

Accelerators

DREAM TRAIN
CD _____ FILERCD 404
Profile / Jun '91 / Pinnacle.

Accept

ACCEPT
Lady Lou / Tired of me / Seawinds / Take
him in my heart / Sounds of war / Free me
now / Glad to be alone / That's rock 'n' roll
/ Hell driver / Street fighter
CD _____ CLACD 404
Castle / Nov '95 / BMG.

BREAKER
Starlight / Breaker / Run if you can / Can't
stand the night / Son of a bitch / Burning /
Feelings / Midnight highway / Breaking up
again / Down and out
CD _____ CLACD 245
Castle / Apr '92 / BMG.

COLLECTION: ACCEPT
Lady Lou / I'm a rebel / Thunder and light-
ning / Breaker / Burning / Son of a bitch /
Fast as a shark / Restless and wild / Prin-
cess of the dawn / Ball to the wall / London
leather boys / Love child / Metal heart / Up
to the limit / Screaming for a love bite /
Monster man / TV War / King
CD _____ CCSCD 311
Castle / Oct '91 / BMG.

HUNGRY YEARS
Fast as a shark / Burning / Son of a bitch /
Princess of the dawn / I'm a rebel / Breaker
/ Restless and wild / King / Midnight
highway
CD _____ CLACD 405
Castle / Oct '95 / BMG.

I'M A REBEL
I'm a rebel / Save us / No time to lose /
Thunder and lightning / China lady / I wanna
be no hero / King / Do it
CD _____ CLACD 244
Castle / '92 / BMG.

OBJECTION OVERRULED
Bullet proof / I don't wanna be like you /
Slaves to metal / Objection overruled / This

one's for you / Sick, dirty and mean / Projectors of terror / All or nothing / Rich and famous / Anamos la vida / Instrumental
CD _____ 74321112466-2
RCA / Feb '93 / BMG.

STEEL GLOVE
CD _____ CCSCD 422
Castle / Oct '95 / BMG.

Accidents

KISS ME ON THE APOCALYPSE
CD _____ DRCD 004
Detour / Nov '95 / Swift / Jazz Music / Pinnacle.

Accused

GRINNING LIKE AN UNDERTAKER
CD _____ CDJUST 17
Music For Nations / Dec '90 / Pinnacle.

MARTHA SPLATTERHEAD'S MADDEST STORIES EVER TOLD
CD _____ WEBITE 43 CD
We Bite / Feb '89 / Plastic Head.

SPLATTER ROCK
CD _____ NMR 7103CD
Nasty Mix / Jun '92 / Pinnacle.

Accuser

CONFUSION ROMANCE
CD _____ CC 025052CD
Shark / May '95 / Plastic Head.

TAKEN BY THE THROAT
CD _____ 341682
No Bull / Oct '95 / Koch.

WHO DOMINATES WHO
CD _____ ATOMH 008CD
Atom / '89 / Cadillac.

Ace

BEST OF ACE, THE
How long / I'm a man / Ain't gonna stand for this no more / Rock 'n' roll runaway / Real feeling / Rock 'n' roll singer / You're all that I need / Twenty four hours / Crazy world / No future in your eyes / Tongue tied / Dream at long / Sail on my brother / I think it's gonna last
CD _____ SEECD 214
See For Miles/C5 / May '93 / Pinnacle.

VERY BEST OF ACE
CD _____ MCCD 123
Music Club / Aug '93 / Disc / THE / CM.

Ace Of Base

BRIDGE, THE
Beautiful life / Never gonna say I'm sorry / Lucky love / Edge of heaven / Strange ways / Ravine / Perfect world / Angels eyes / Whispers in blindness / My deja vu / Wave wet sand / Que sera / Just 'n' image / Experimental / Blooming
CD _____ 5296552
London / Nov '95 / PolyGram.

HAPPY NATION
CD _____ 517749-2
London / Jul '93 / PolyGram.

Acetone

CINDY
Come on / Pinch / Sundown / Chills / Endless summer / Intermission / Louise / Don't cry / No need swim / Barefoot on Sunday
CD _____ CDHUT 13
Hut / Oct '93 / EMI.

I GUESS I WOULD
Juanita / Late John Garfield blues / I guess I would / Sometimes you just can't win / All for the love of a girl / How sweet I roamed / Border lord
CD _____ HUTMCD 21
Hut / Jan '95 / EMI.

Acheron

RITES OF THE BLACK MASS
CD _____ TURBO 007CD
Turbo Music / Nov '92 / Plastic Head.

Achkar, Elie

MIDDLE EAST QANUN SONGS
CD _____ 925582
Buda / Jun '93 / Discovery / ADA.

Acid Bath

WHEN THE KITE STRING POPS
CD _____ RR 89782
Roadrunner / Oct '94 / Pinnacle.

Acid Drinkers

DIRTY MONEY - DIRTY TRICKS
CD _____ CDFLAG 59
Music For Nations / Jun '91 / Pinnacle.

STRIP TEASE
Strip tease / King kong bless you / Seek and destroy / Rock 'n' roll beast / Rats/ Feeling naity / Poplin twist / Masterhood of hearts devouring / You are lost my dear / Menel song/Always look on the bright side

of life / Blood is boiling / My caddish promise / Mentally deficient / Hell it is a place on earth / Ronnie and the brotherspider / I'm a rocker
CD _____ CDFLAG 76
Music For Nations / Nov '92 / Pinnacle.

Acid Jesus

ACID JESUS
CD _____ KLANGCD 1
Klang Elektronik / Aug '94 / Plastic Head.

Acid Reign

FEAR, THE
You never know / Insane ecstasy / Blind agression / Lost in solitude / Reflection of truths / Humanoia / Life in forms
CD _____ CDFLAG 31
Under One Flag / Mar '89 / Pinnacle.

OBNOXIOUS
CD _____ CDFLAG 39
Under One Flag / Jul '92 / Pinnacle.

WORST OF ACID REIGN, THE
CD _____ CDFLAG 60
Under One Flag / Sep '91 / Pinnacle.

Acid Scout

SAFARI
CD _____ EFA 122672
Disko B / Feb '95 / SRD.

Ackerman, Will

IMAGINARY ROAD
Moment / Region of clouds / If you look / Floyd's ghost / Wondering again what's behind the eyes / Dawn treader / Prospect of Darrow's barn / Brother A teaches 7 / Innocent moon / Moment, The (reprise) / If you look (version II) / Prospect of Darrow's barn (2)
CD _____ WD 1078
Windham Hill / Jul '91 / Pinnacle / BMG / ADA.

IT TAKES A YEAR
CD _____ 371003 2
Windham Hill / '85 / Pinnacle / BMG / ADA.

OPENING OF DOORS, THE
CD _____ 01934111142
Windham Hill / Sep '95 / Pinnacle / BMG / ADA.

PASSAGE
Remedios / Processional / Impending death of the virgin spirit / Pacific I / Bricklayer's beautiful daughter / Hawk circle / Annie's song / Passage
CD _____ 01934110142
Windham Hill / Jul '93 / Pinnacle / BMG / ADA.

PAST LIGHT
CD _____ CDW 1028
Windham Hill / Jan '86 / Pinnacle / BMG / ADA.

WINDHAM HILL RETROSPECTIVE, A
Bricklayer's beautiful daughter / Processional / Ventana / Santos and the well travelled bear / Slow motion roast beef restaurant seduction / Visiting / Anne's song / Impending death of the virgin spirit / Climbing in geometry / Opening of doors / Brother A teaches 7 / Seattle / Lago de montans (mountain lake) / Hawk circle / Region of clouds
CD _____ 01934111212
Windham Hill / Mar '93 / Pinnacle / BMG / ADA.

Ackles, David

AKA THE ROAD TO CAIRO
Road to Cairo / When love is gone / Sonny come home / Blue ribbons / What a happy day / Down river / Laissez-faire / Lotus man / His name is Andrew / Be my friend
CD _____ 755961595-2
Elektra / Oct '93 / Warner Music.

AMERICAN GOTHIC
American gothic / Love's enough / Ballad of the ship of state / One night stand / Oh California / Another Friday night / Family band / Midnight carousel / Waiting for the moving van / Blues for Billy Whitecloud / Montana song
CD _____ 755961597-2
Elektra / Oct '93 / Warner Music.

SUBWAY TO THE COUNTRY
Mainline saloon / That's no reason to cry / Candy man / Out on the road / Cabin on the mountain / Woman river / Inmates of the institution / Subway to the country
CD _____ 755961596-2
Elektra / Oct '93 / Warner Music.

Aconcha, Leandro

PIANO BAR (Aconcha, Leandro & Remi Chaudagne)
CD _____ CDSGP 0161
Prestige / Sep '95 / Total/BMG.

Acoustic Alchemy

AGAINST THE GRAIN
Against the grain / Lazeez / Different kind of freedom / Lady Laynda / Road dogs / Shot the loop / Papillion / Silent partner / Nouveau tango
CD _____ GRP 97832
GRP / Oct '94 / BMG / New Note.

BACK ON THE CASE
Alchemist / Jamaica heartbeat / Georgia Peach / Playing for time / When lights go out / Clear air for miles / Fire of the heart / Freeze frame / On the case / Break for the border
CD _____ GRP 96482
GRP / Aug '91 / BMG / New Note.

EARLY ALCHEMY
Santiago / Sarah Victoria / Last Summer song / Slap it down / Sira's song / Moonstone / Wind it up / Casino / Little bercheres / Amanecer / Waiting for you / Return flight / Daybreak / Dream of fair women
CD _____ GRP 96662
GRP / Feb '92 / BMG / New Note.

NEW EDGE
Oceans apart / Notting Hill two-step / Slow ride home / Cool as a rule / Santa cafe / Arc en ciel / London skyline / Liason / Until always / Rive gauche / Act of innocence
CD _____ GRP 97112
GRP / Mar '93 / BMG / New Note.

REFERENCE POINT
Reference point / Missing your touch / Take five / Same road, same reason / Make my day / Caravan of dreams / Homecoming / Cuban heels / Lullaby for the first born
CD _____ GRP 96142
GRP / Aug '90 / BMG / New Note.

Acoustic Art

INTERLUDE
CD _____ BEST 1024CD
Acoustic Music / Nov '93 / ADA.

Acoustick

OCTOBER
CD _____ ART 00052
Extreme / Nov '94 / Vital/SAM.

Acridity

FOR FREEDOM I CRY
CD _____ PROPH 2CD
Prophecy / Sep '91 / Plastic Head.

Acrimony

ACID ELEPHANT, THE
CD _____ GOD 019MCD
Godhead / Oct '95 / Plastic Head.

HYMNS TO THE STONE
CD _____ GOD 010
Godhead / May '95 / Plastic Head.

Acrophet

CORRUPT MINDS
Intro to corruption / Lifeless image / Crime for loving / Holy spirit / Ceremonial slaughter / Forgotten faith / Corrupt minds / Slaves of sin / From the depths / Living in today / Warped illusions / Victims of the holocaust
CD _____ RR 9523 2
Roadrunner / Nov '88 / Pinnacle.

Acrylic Tones

ACRYLIC TONES
CD _____ DRCD 002
Detour / Jan '95 / Detour.

Act Of Faith

ONE VISION
Whole thing / Lost on a breeze / Doing it with love / Love not love / Soul love / Perfect world / Dream about you / Summer in the city / What'cha gonna do for me / Lite up your life / All for love / Looking at the world
CD _____ BRCD 613
4th & Broadway / Mar '95 / PolyGram.

Action

ULTIMATE ACTION, THE
I'll keep holding on / Harlem shuffle / Never ever / Twenty fourth hour / Since I lost my baby / My lonely room / Hey Sha-lo-ney / Shadows and reflections / Something has hit me / Place / Cissy / Baby you got it / I love you (yeah) / Land of 1000 dances
CD _____ EDCD 101
Edsel / Jan '88 / Pinnacle / ADA.

Action Swingers

DECIMATION BOULEVARD
CD _____ TOAD 6CD
Newt / Jun '94 / Plastic Head.

QUIT WHILE YOUR AHEAD
CD _____ TOADCD 7
Newt / Oct '94 / Plastic Head.

Acuff, Roy

GREATEST HITS: ROY ACUFF
Lonesome old river blues / Were you there when they crucified my Lord / Tennessee waltz / Waiting for my call to glory / Mule light / Fireball mail / Night train to Memphis / Great speckled bird / If I could hear my mother pray again / Wreck of the highway / Freight train blues / Devil's train / It won't be long (Til I'm leaving) washbash cannonball
CD _____ 983256 2
Pickwick/Sony Collector's Choice / Aug '93 / Carlton Home Entertainment / Pinnacle / Sony.

KING OF COUNTRY MUSIC
Tied down / What will I do / Is it love or is it lies / Lonesome Joe / Sweep around your back door / Don't say goodbye / Swamp Lily / Sixteen chickens and a tamborine / Rushing around / Whoa mule / Sunshine special / I closed my heart's door / I mean planting a rose / River of crystal / Please daddy forgive / Streamline heartbreaker / Six more days / Thief upon thee tree / Don't judge your neighbor / Night spots (Of the town) / Great speckled bird / Lonely mound of clay / Pins and needles (In my heart) / Wabash cannonball / Great judgement morning / Wreck on the highway / Precious jewel / Night train to Memphis / That's what makes the jukebox play / Little Moses / What do you think about me / Oh those tombs / Come back little pal / Fireball mail / I'm building a home (in the sky) / Great Titanic / Goodbye Mr. Brown / Mother hold me tight / Crazy worried mind / Along the China coast / It's hard to love / Plant some flowers by my graveside / I wanta to be loved / I like mountain music / Jesus died for me / Thank god / Were you there when they crucified my Lord / How beautiful heaven must be / Unclouded day / Hold to God's unchanging hand / Lord build me a cabin / Where the soul never dies / Shake my mother's hand for me / Take my hand. Precious Lord / This world is not my home / Where could I go but to the Lord
CD Set _____ BCD 15652
Bear Family / Mar '93 / Rollercoaster / Direct / CM / Swift / ADA.

Acuna, Alex

**ALEX ACUNA & THE UNKNOWNS
(Acuna, Alex & The Unknowns)**
Te amo / Joe's red eye / Marionettes / Hoppin' it / Nice / Cocho San / Van nuys jam / Thinking of you / Psalms / Ten O'Clock groove
CD _____ MAXCD 1029
Maxus / Oct '92 / Harmonia Mundi.

Ad Vielle Que Pourra

AD VIELLE QUE POURRA
CD _____ GLCD 1099
Green Linnet / Mar '90 / Roots / CM / Direct / ADA.

COME WHAT MAY
CD _____ GLCD 1112
Green Linnet / Apr '92 / Roots / CM / Direct / ADA.

MUSAIQUE
CD _____ GLCD 4017
Green Linnet / Apr '94 / Roots / CM / Direct / ADA.

Adam Ant

ANTICS IN THE FORBIDDEN ZONE
Boruin / Whip in my sailas / Oar trouble / Kick / Kings of the wild frontier / Ant music / Dog eat dog / Los Rancheros / Killer in the home / Stand and deliver / Beat my guest / Prince Charming / Ant rap / Desperate but not serious / Place in the country / Friend or foe / Goody two shoes / Strip / Puss 'n' boots / Apollo 9 / Vive le rock
CD _____ 4687622
Columbia / Jun '91 / Sony.

**ANTMUSIC - THE BEST OF ADAM ANT
(Adam Ant/Adam & the Ants)**
CD _____ ARC 3100052
Arcade / Aug '93 / Sony / Grapevine.

B-SIDE BABIES
Beat my guest / Why do girls love horses / Yours yours yours / Kiss the drummer / Fall-in / Making history / Friends (version 2) / Red scab / Juanito the bandito / B side baby / Greta-X
CD _____ 4803622
Columbia / Apr '95 / Sony.

DIRK WEARS WHITE SOX (Adam & The Ants)
Car trouble / Nine plan failed / Catholic day / Idea / Never trust a man (with egg on his face) / Animals and men / Family of noise / Table talk / Day I met God
CD _____ 4805212
Columbia / Jul '95 / Sony.

KINGS OF THE WILD FRONTIER (Adam & The Ants)
Dog eat dog / Ant music / Feed me to the lions / Los rancheros / Ants invasion / Killer in the home / Kings of the wild frontier /

7

ADAM ANT (continued)

Magnificent five / Don't be square / Jolly
Roger / Making history / Human beings
CD _____ 477902 2
Columbia / Oct '94 / Sony.

**PEEL SESSIONS: ADAM & THE ANTS
(Adam & The Ants)**
Lov / It doesn't matter / Zerox / Friends /
You're so physical / Cleopatra / Ligotage /
Tabletalk / Animals and men / Never trust a
man (with egg on his face)
CD _____ SFRCD 115
Strange Fruit / Feb '91 / Pinnacle.

VIVE LE ROCK
Vive le rock / Miss thing / Razor keen / Rip
down / Scorpio rising / Apollo 9 / Hell's
eight acres / Mohair lockeroom pin-up boys
/ No zap / P.O.E. / Human bondage dem
(Available on cassette only)
CD _____ 4785042
Columbia / Feb '95 / Sony.

WONDERFUL
Won't take that talk / Beautiful dream /
Wonderful / 1969 again / Yin and yang /
Image of yourself / Alien / Gotta be a sin /
Vampires / Angel / Very long ride
CD _____ CDEMC 3687
EMI / Feb '95 / EMI.

Adams, Bruce

**LET'S FACE THE MUSIC (Adams,
Bruce/Alan Barnes Quintet)**
Let's face the music and dance / Blowing
with Bruce / Cool heights / Come back to
bed / Give a little whistle / When it's sleepy
time down South / Instep / Rosie B / Cu-
bicle / Thrill is gone / Raincheck / Hollywood
stampede
CD _____ ESSCD 269
Essential / Mar '95 / Total/BMG.

ONE FOOT IN THE GUTTER
CD _____ ESSCD 260
Essential / Feb '95 / Total/BMG.

**SIDE-STEPPIN' (Adams, Bruce/Alan
Barnes Quintet)**
CD _____ BEARCD 38
Big Bear / Mar '94 / BMG.
CD _____ ESSCD 249
Essential / Nov '94 / Total/BMG.

Adams, Bryan

BRYAN ADAMS
Hidin' from love / Win some lose some /
Wait and see / Give me your love / Wastin'
time / Don't ya say it / Remember / State
of mind / Try to see it my way
CD _____ CDMID 100
A&M / Oct '92 / PolyGram.

CUTS LIKE A KNIFE
Only one / Take me back / This time /
Straight from the heart / Cuts like a knife /
I'm ready / What's it gonna be / Don't leave
me lonely / Best was yet to come
CD _____ CDMID 102
A&M / Aug '91 / PolyGram.

INTO THE FIRE
Heat of the night / Into the fire / Victim of
love / Another day / Native son / Only the
strong survive / Rebel / Remembrance day
/ Hearts on fire / Home again
CD _____ CDMID 185
A&M / '92 / PolyGram.

LIVE LIVE LIVE
She's only happy when she's dancin' / It's
only love / Cuts like a knife / Kids wanna
rock / Hearts on fire / Take me back / Best
was yet to come / Heaven / Heat of the
night / Run to you / One night love affair /
Long gone / Summer of '69 / Somebody /
Walkin' after midnight / I fought the law /
Into the fire
CD _____ 3970942
A&M / Aug '94 / PolyGram.

RECKLESS
One night love affair / She's only happy
when she's dancin' / Run to you / Heaven
/ Somebody / Summer of '69 / Kids wanna
rock / It's only love / Long gone / Ain't
gonna cry
CD _____ CDA 5013
A&M / Feb '85 / PolyGram.

**SO FAR SO GOOD (Collection Of The
Best Of Bryan Adams)**
CD _____ 540157-2
A&M / Nov '93 / PolyGram.

WAKING UP THE NEIGHBOURS
Is your mama gonna miss ya / Hey honey
I'm packin' you in / Can't stop this thing we
started / Thought I'd died and gone to
heaven / Not guilty / Vanishing / House arrest / There's nothing I wouldn't do / There
will never be another tonight / All I want is
you / Depend on me / Everything I do (I do
it for you) / If you wanna leave me (can I
come too) / Touch the hand / Don't drop
that bomb on me
CD _____ 3971642
A&M / Oct '91 / PolyGram.

YOU WANT IT, YOU GOT IT
Lonely nights / One good reason / Don't
look now / Coming home / Fits ya good /
Tonight / Jealousy / You want it, you got it
/ Last chance / No one makes it right
CD _____ CDMID 101
A&M / Oct '92 / PolyGram.

Adams, Cliff

AT YOUR REQUEST
We'll gather lilacs / It had to be you / Barcarolle / Entertainer/Solace / Come rain or
come shine / That old black magic / Bewitched, bothered and bewildered / Air on
a G string / Dancing in the dark / Lonely
Man theme / Ole buttermilk sky / Intermezzo from Cavalleria Rusticana / La vie en
rose / Unforgettable/They didn't believe me
/ They can't take that away from me / Sophisticated lady / Adagio in G minor / Satin
doll / East of the sun and west of the moon
CD _____ CDMFP 6135
Music For Pleasure / Oct '94 / EMI.

**BEST OF SING SOMETHING SIMPLE,
THE (Adams, Cliff Singers)**
CD _____ PWKS 4187
Carlton Home Entertainment / Mar '94 /
Carlton Home Entertainment.

**SING SOMETHING SIMPLE (Adams,
Cliff Singers)**
I don't want to walk without you / Can't
smile without you / Mandy / If I had a hammer / Down by the riverside / He's got the
whole world in his hands / Marianne / I can
give you the starlight / Love is the reason /
Someday my heart will awake / We'll gather
lillacs / Singin' the blues / Truly fair / Feet
up / Chicka boom / My love is like a red red
rose / Liverpool Lou / Little children / How
do you do it / Ferry 'cross the Mersey / Little
bit of Heaven / Irish lullaby / If you're Irish
come into the parlour / It's a great day for
the Irish / I want a girl - just like the girl that
married dear old Dad / My mother's eyes /
Mother
CD _____ PWKS 660
Carlton Home Entertainment / Sep '90 /
Carlton Home Entertainment.

**SING SOMETHING SIMPLE - VERY
BEST OF CLIFF ADAMS SINGERS (3CD/
MC Set) (Adams, Cliff Singers)**
Sing something simple / Mame / One / Hello
Dolly / Give my regards to Broadway / To-
gether / Let me call you sweetheart / Daisy
bell / Three o'clock in the morning / After
the ball / September song / It don't mean a
ting if it ain't got that swing / Lookie, lookie,
lookie here come cookie / Chilli bom bom /
Let's all go to Mary's house / Five foot two
/ Your Mother should know / Penny lane / I
want to hold your hand / All my loving /
Green grow the rushes oh / Rainy days and
Mondays / We've only just begun / I won't
last a day without you / Top of the world /
Moonlight and roses / I'll see you in my
dreams / Down by the old mill stream /
Row, row, row / Paddlin' Madelin' home /
Bless this house / Broken doll / Shine on
harvest moon / Show me the way to go
home / California, here I come / By the
beautiful sea / You are the sunshine of my
life / By the rivers of Babylon / Green green
/ Tie a yellow ribbon round the old oak tree
/ Love me tender / Return to sender / Good
luck charm / Wooden heart / Upidee / Old
MacDonald had a farm / Little brown jug /
What shall we do with a drunken sailor /
There is a tavern in the town / Jesu, joy of
man's desiring / Cathy's clown / All I have
to do is dream / Walk right back / Singing
in the rain / Side by side / Way we were / I
don't want to walk without you / Can't smile
without you / Mandy / If I had a hammer /
Down by the riverside / He's got he whole
world in his hand / Marianne / I can give
you the starlight / Love is my reason /
Someday my heart will awake / We'll gather
lilacs / Singing the blues / My truley truly
fair / Feet up (pat him on the po po) / Chicka
boom / My love is like a red, red rose / Liverpool Lou / Little children / How do you do
it / Ferry across the Mersey / Little bit of
heaven, shure they call it Ireland / Too ra
loo ra loo ra, that's an Irish lullaby / Your
Irish come into the parlour / Great day for
the Irish / I want a girl (just like the girl that
married dear old dad) / My mothers eyes /
M.O.T.H.E.R. / Roses of Picardy / Darling,
je vous aime beaucoup / Pigalle / Under the
bridges of Paris / Michelle / Chanson
d'amour / Always / Let the rest of the world
go by / Til we meet again / In the good old
summertime / Little Annie Rooney / Beautiful dreamer / Old folks at home / Camptown
races / Oh Suzannah / Poor old Joe / Silver
threads among the gold / My old dutch /
One of the old ruins that Cromwell knocked
about a bit / Call round any old time / Down
at the old bull and bush / Any old iron /
Boiled beef and carrotts / In the evening by
the moonlight / Over the rainbow / You
made me love you / Meet me in St. Louis,
Louise / Couple of swells / Trolley song /
What have they done to my song, ma / I
believe in music / True love / Sweet Rosie
O'Grady / Band played on / You do something to me / It doesn't matter anymore / If
/ Go tell aunt Rhodie / Yello rose of Texas
/ Marching through Georgia / John Brown's
body / I'm gonna sit right down and write
myself a letter / When somebody think's
your wonderful / My very good friend the
milkman / There goes my everything / Am I
wasting my time / Java jive / Pennies from
heaven / I want some money / You're the
cream in my coffee / Let's call the whole
thing off / I'm alone because I love you /
Are you lonesome tonight / Ev'rthing's in
rhythm with my heart / Double dare you /
Michael, row the boat ashore / Bye bye love
/ Wake up little Susie / Bye bye blackbird /
Monday, Monday / Love grows where my
Rosemary goes / Where the blue of the
night / It's a sin to tell a lie / Home on the
range / I wonder where my baby is tonight
/ Old fashioned way
CD Set _____ BOXD 49T
Carlton Home Entertainment / Oct '95 /
Carlton Home Entertainment.

**SING SOMETHING SIMPLE AT
CHRISTMAS (Adams, Cliff Singers)**
Sing something seasonal / Christmas alphabet / Winter wonderland / Have yourself
a merry little Christmas / First Noel / Past
three o'clock / Mary's boy child / Little donkey / When a child is born / Twelve days of
Christmas / Little boy that Santa Claus forgot / I'm going home for Christmas / Jingle
bells / Little drummer boy / Ding dong merrily on high / Good Christian men rejoice /
Coventry carol / We wish you a Merry
Christmas / I saw Mommy kissing Santa
Claus / All I want for Christmas (is my two
front teeth) / Rudolph the red nosed reindeer / Do you hear what I hear / We three
kings / While shepherds watched their
flocks by night / Once in Royal David's city
/ Hark the herald angels sing / Good King
Wenceslas / Santa Claus is coming to town
/ Rockin' around the Christmas tree / Wonderful Christmas time / Silent night / Mistle-
toe and wine / Saviour's day / Holly and the
ivy / In the bleak midwinter / Away in a manger / O come all ye faithful (Adeste Fidelis)
/ Christmas song / White Christmas
CD _____ CDPR 104
Premier/MFP / Dec '94 / EMI.

**SING SOMETHING SIMPLE FOR
LOVERS (Adams, Cliff Singers)**
I don't know why / Glory of love / Love in
bloom / Melody of love / My wonderful one
/ Longing for you / Everywhere you go / Red
roses for a blue lady / Lover and his lass /
May you always / Matrimony / Forgotten
dreams / Lover's concerto / I just called to
say I love you / Let us be sweethearts / I'll
always be in love with you / I love my baby
/ Honeysuckle and the bee / I don't want
a tiny seed of love / Be my little baby bum-
bie bee / Love's last word / Pariez-moi
d'amour / That'a amore / You are my sunshine / Viva l'amour / These foolish things /
Peggy Sue / Every day / Moonlight sonata
/ Softly as I leave you / Stone in love with
you / All alone / Because I love you / Speak
to me pretty / Every thought of you / Touch
of your lips
CD _____ CDMFP 5997
Music For Pleasure / Oct '93 / EMI.

**SING SOMETHING SIMPLE THE
SINATRA WAY (Adams, Cliff Singers)**
I'm beginning to see the light / You make
me feel so young / I thought about you /
High hopes / London by night / Foggy day
/ Girl from Ipanema / All or nothing at all /
Fly me to the moon / It's nice to go trav'ling
/ Come fly with me / Three coins in the
fountain / Young at heart / All the way / New
York, New York / Chicago / My kind of town
(Chicago is) / Gender trap / Love and mar-
riage / Too marvellous for words / Swinging
down the lane / Somethin' stupid / Strang-
ers in the night / Lady is a tramp / It's all
right with me / Something's gotta give /
Nice 'n' easy / Witchcraft / At long last love
/ In the wee small hours of the morning / I
couldn't sleep a wink last night / Nancy with
the laughing face
CD _____ CDMFP 5930
Music For Pleasure / Nov '91 / EMI.

**SING SOMETHING SIMPLE VOL. 2
(Adams, Cliff Singers)**
CD _____ PWKS 4189
Carlton Home Entertainment / Mar '94 /
Carlton Home Entertainment.

**VERY BEST OF SING SOMETHING
SIMPLE VOL.3 (Adams, Cliff Singers)**
What have they done to my song Ma / I
believe in music / True love / Sweet Rosie
O'Grady / And the band played on / You do
something to me / It doesn't matter anymore / If / Go tell Aunt Rhodie / Yellow rose
of Texas / Marching through Georgia / John
Brown's body / I'm gonna sit right down
and write myself a letter / When somebody
thinks you're wonderful / My very good
friend the milkman / There goes my everything / Am I wasting my time / Java jive /
Pennies from heaven / I want some money
/ You're the cream in my coffee / Let's call
the whole thing off / I'm alone because I
love you / Are you lonesome tonight / Everything's in rhythm with my heart / I double
dare you / Michael, row the boat ashore /
Bye bye love / Wake up little Susie / Bye
bye blackbird / Monday, Monday / Love
grows (where my Rosemary goes) / Where
the blue of the night meets the gold of the
day / It's a sin to tell a lie / Home on the
range / I wonder where my baby is tonight
/ Old fashioned way / Sing something
simple
CD _____ PWKS 4166
Carlton Home Entertainment / Oct '93 /
Carlton Home Entertainment.

Adams, George

**CITY GATES (Adams, George & Don
Pullen Quartet)**
Wake up little Susie / Bye bye love /
Mingus metamorphosis / Samba for now /
Thank you very much Mr. Monk / Nobody
knows the trouble I've seen / City gates
CD _____ CDSJP 181
Timeless Jazz / Aug '91 / New Note.

**DECISIONS (Adams, George & Don
Pullen Quartet)**
Trees and grass and things / His eye is on
the sparrow / Message urgent / Decisions /
Triple over time / I could really for you
CD _____ CDSJP 205
Timeless Jazz / Feb '91 / New Note.

**DON'T LOSE CONTROL (Adams,
George & Don Pullen Quartet)**
CD _____ SNCD 1004
Soul Note / Jan '87 / Harmonia Mundi /
Wellard / Cadillac.

**EARTH BEAMS (Adams, George & Don
Pullen Quartet)**
Magnetic love / Dionysus / Saturday nite in
the cosmos / More flowers / Sophisticated
Alice
CD _____ CDSJP 147
Timeless Jazz / Mar '90 / New Note.

**HAND TO HAND (Adams, George &
Danny Richmond Quartet)**
CD _____ SNCD 1007
Soul Note / Jun '86 / Harmonia Mundi /
Wellard / Cadillac.

**LIVE AT MONTMARTRE (Adams,
George & Don Pullen Quartet)**
CD _____ CDSJP 219
Timeless Jazz / Jan '88 / New Note.

**LIVE AT VILLAGE VANGUARD (Adams,
George & Don Pullen Quartet)**
Necessary blues / Solitude / Intentions /
Diane
CD _____ SNCD 1094
Soul Note / May '85 / Harmonia Mundi /
Wellard / Cadillac.

SOUND SUGGESTIONS
CD _____ 5177552
ECM / Jul '94 / New Note.

Adams, John

CHAIRMAN DANCES, THE
Chairman dances / Christian zeal and
activity / Two fanfares for orchestra /
Tromba lontana / Short ride in a fast ma-
chine / Common tones in simple time
CD _____ 7559791442
Elektra Nonesuch / Jan '95 / Warner Music.

**CHAMBER SYMPHONY/GRAND
PIANOLA MUSIC**
CD _____ 7559792192
Elektra Nonesuch / Jan '95 / Warner
Music.

DEATH OF KLINGHOFFER, THE
CD _____ 7559792812
Elektra Nonesuch / Jan '95 / Warner
Music.

**FEARFUL SYMMETRIES/THE WOUND
DRESSER**
CD _____ 7559792182
Elektra Nonesuch / Jan '95 / Warner
Music.

HARMONIELEHRE
CD _____ 7559791152
Elektra Nonesuch / Dec '95 / Warner
Music.

HARMONIUM
Negative love (part one) / Because I could
not stop for death - Wild nights (part 2) /
Negative love (Poem by John Donne) / Be-
cause I could not stop for death (Poem by
Emily Dickinson) / Wild nights / Who do I /
Laughin' and clownin' / If I ever had a good
time / Scarred knees / Your love is so dog-
gone good / We don't see eye to eye /
Roadblock / Teach me to forget
CD _____ 8214652
ECM / Apr '87 / New Note.

HOODOO ZEPHYR
CD _____ 7559793112
Elektra Nonesuch / Jan '95 / Warner
Music.

NIXON IN CHINA (3CD Set)
CD Set _____ 7559791772
Elektra Nonesuch / Jan '95 / Warner
Music.

Adams, Johnny

AFTER DARK
CD _____ CD 2049
Rounder / '88 / CM / Direct / ADA /
Cadillac.

**BEST OF NEW ORLEANS RHYTHM &
BLUES VOL. 1**
CD _____ MG 9007
Mardi Gras / Feb '95 / Jazz Music.

FROM THE HEART
I feel like breaking up somebody's home /
Why do I / Laughin' and clownin' / If I ever
had a good thing / Scarred knees / From
the heart / Your love is so doggone good /
We don't see eye to eye / Roadblock /
Teach me to forget
CD _____ FIENDCD 26
Demon / Mar '92 / Pinnacle / ADA.

GOOD MORNING HEARTACHE
CD _____ ROU 2125CD
Rounder / Oct '93 / CM / Direct / ADA /
Cadillac.

ROOM WITH A VIEW OF THE BLUES
Room with a view / I don't want to do wrong
/ Not trustworthy / Neither one of us / Body
and fender man / I owe you / Wished I'd
never loved you at all / Hunt is on / Hunt is
never made
CD _____ FIENDCD 111
Demon / Sep '91 / Pinnacle / ADA.

VERDICT, THE
CD _____ ROUCD 2135
Rounder / Feb '95 / CM / Direct / ADA /
Cadillac.

Adams, Oleta

CIRCLE OF ONE
Rhythm of life / Get here / Circle of one /
You've got to give me room / I've got to
sing my song / I've got a right / Will we ever
learn / Everything must change
CD _____ 8487402
Fontana / Aug '91 / PolyGram.

EVOLUTION
CD _____ 5149652
Fontana / Jun '93 / PolyGram.

MOVIN' ON
Never knew love / Once in a lifetime / I knew
you when / You need to be loved / Slow
motion / We will meet again / This is real /
Life keeps moving on / Long distance love
/ Love begins at home / If this love should
ever end / New star / Between hello and
goodbye / Don't let the sun go down on me
CD _____ 5289002
Fontana / Feb '96 / PolyGram.

Adams, Pepper

**10 TO 4 AT THE 5-SPOT (Adams,
Pepper Quintet)**
CD _____ OJCCD 0312
Original Jazz Classics / Sep '93 / Wellard /
Jazz Music / Cadillac / Complete/Pinnacle.

**CONJURATION/FAT TUEDAY'S
SESSION**
CD _____ RSRCD 113
Reservoir Music / Nov '94 / Cadillac.

**COOL SOUND OF PEPPER ADAMS,
THE**
Bloos booze / Blues seein' red /
Like...what's this / Skippy
CD _____ SV 0198
Savoy Jazz / Nov '92 / Conifer / ADA.

MASTER, THE
Enchilada / Chelsea Bridge / Bossallegro /
Rue Serpente / Lovers of their time / My
shining hour
CD _____ MCD 5213
Muse / Sep '92 / New Note / CM.

OUT OF THIS WORLD
CD _____ FSRCD 137
Fresh Sound / Dec '90 / Jazz Music /
Discovery.

Adams, S.A.

REDEMPTION
CD _____ RTN 41209
Rock The Nation / Feb '95 / Plastic Head.

Adams, Terry

TERRIBLE
CD _____ 804732
New World / Aug '95 / Harmonia Mundi /
ADA / Cadillac.

Adams, Tom

RIGHT HAND MAN
Bluegrass breakdown / John Hardy / You
are my sunshine / Fiddle and the banjo / I
saw the light / Old rugged cross / Old Joe
Clark / Fireball mail / Polk country break-
down / Little Maggie / Cumberland gap
CD _____ CD 0282
Rounder / '90 / CM / Direct / ADA / Cadillac.

Adams, Yolanda

MORE THAN A MELODY
CD _____ 7901135921
Word / Sep '95 / Total/BMG.

Adamson, Barry

DELUSION
CD _____ CDIONIC 004
Mute / Aug '91 / Disc.

MOSS-SIDE STORY
Ring's the thing (On the wrong side of
relaxation/Under wraps/Central control/
Round up the usual suspects) / Real deep
cool (Sounds from the big house/Suck on
the honey of love/Everything happens to
me/The swinging detective) / Final Irony
(Autodestruction/Intensive care/ The most
beautiful girl in the world/Free at last) / For
your ears only (Alfred Hitchcock presents/
Chocolate milk shake/The man with the
golden arm)
CD _____ CDSTUMM 53
Mute / Feb '89 / Disc.

NEGRO INSIDE ME
CD _____ CDSTUMM 120
Mute / Jun '93 / Disc.

PRAYER MAT OF FLESH, A
CD _____ CDSTUMM 134
Mute / Oct '95 / Disc.

SOUL MURDER
CD _____ CDSTUMM 105
Mute / Apr '92 / Disc.

Add N To X

VERO ELECTRONICS
CD _____ BLOWUP 4CD
Blow Up / Jan '96 / SRD.

Adderley, Cannonball

AFRICAN WALTZ
African waltz / Barefoot Sunday blues /
Kelly blue
CD _____ OJCCD 258
Original Jazz Classics / Sep '93 / Wellard /
Jazz Music / Cadillac / Complete/Pinnacle.

**AUTUMN LEAVES (Adderley, Cannonball
& Miles Davis)**
CD _____ CD 53125
Giants Of Jazz / Jan '94 / Target/BMG /
Cadillac.

**CANNONBALL ADDERLEY
COLLECTION VOL. 3 (Jazz Workshop
Revisited)**
Pimitiva / Jessica's day / Unit 7 / Jive
samba / Marney / Mellow buno / Lillie
CD _____ LCD 13032
Landmark / Jul '88 / New Note.

**CANNONBALL ADDERLEY
COLLECTION VOL. 4 (The Poll Winners)**
Chant / Azule serape / Heart alone / Lolita
/ Au privave / Never will I marry
CD _____ LCD 13042
Landmark / Apr '91 / New Note.

**CANNONBALL ADDERLEY
COLLECTION VOL. 5 (At The
Lighthouse)**
Sack o' woe / Azule serape / Our delight /
Big P / Blue Daniel / Exodus / What is this
thing called love
CD _____ LCD 13052
Landmark / Apr '91 / New Note.

**CANNONBALL ADDERLEY
COLLECTION VOL. 6 (Cannonball Takes
Charge)**
If this isn't love / I guess I'll hang my tears
out to dry / Serenata / I've told every little
star / Barefoot Sunday blues / Poor butterfly
/ I remember you
CD _____ LCD 13062
Landmark / Apr '91 / New Note.

**CANNONBALL ADDERLEY
COLLECTION VOL. 7 (Cannonball In
Europe)**
P. Bouk / Gemini / Work song / Trouble in
mind / Dizzy's business
CD _____ LCD 13072
Landmark / Apr '91 / New Note.

CANNONBALL ADDERLEY IN CONCERT
CD _____ RTE 10042CD
RTE / Apr '95 / ADA / Koch.

COUNTRY PREACHER
Walk tall / Country preacher / Hummin' / Oh
babe / Afro Spanish omlette / Umbakwen /
Soli tomba / Oiga / Marabi / Scene
CD _____ CDP 8304522
Capitol Jazz / Oct '94 / EMI.

COUNTRY PREACHER
CD _____ CD 56053
Jazz Roots / Mar '95 / Target/BMG.

**DEEP GROOVE - BEST OF
CANNONBALL ADDERLEY**
Walk tall / Shake a lady / Why am I treated
so bad / Mercy mercy mercy / Do do do
(what now is next) / I'm on my way / Games
/ Happy people / Up and at it / Aries /
Taurus
CD _____ CDP 8307252
Blue Note / Sep '94 / EMI.

DISCOVERIES
With apologies to Oscar / Bohemia after
dark / Chasm / Late entry / Little taste /
Caribbean cutie / Spontaneous combustion
CD _____ SV 0251
Denon / Nov '94 / Conifer.

DIZZY'S BUSINESS
CD _____ MCD 47069
Milestone / Oct '93 / Jazz Music /
Pinnacle / Wellard / Cadillac.

**IN NEW YORK (Adderley, Cannonball
Quintet)**
CD _____ OJCCD 1422
Original Jazz Classics / Feb '92 / Wellard /
Jazz Music / Cadillac / Complete/Pinnacle.

**IN SAN FRANCISCO (Adderley,
Cannonball Quintet)**
CD _____ OJCCD 0352
Original Jazz Classics / Feb '92 / Wellard /
Jazz Music / Cadillac / Complete/Pinnacle.

**INSIDE STRAIGHT (Adderley,
Cannonball Quintet)**
Introduction / Inside straight / Saudade / Inner journey / Snakin' the grass / Five of a
kind / Second son / End

CD _____ OJCCD 750
Original Jazz Classics / Oct '93 / Wellard /
Jazz Music / Cadillac / Complete/Pinnacle.

JAZZ MASTERS
CD _____ 5226512
Verve / Apr '94 / PolyGram.

**JULIAN 'CANNONBALL' ADDERLEY
PRESENTING 'CANNONBALL'
(Adderley, Julian 'Cannonball')**
Spontaneous combustion / Still talkin' to ya
/ Little taste / Caribbean cutie / Flamingo
CD _____ SV 0108
Savoy Jazz / '93 / Conifer / ADA.

**JULIAN 'CANNONBALL' ADDERLEY
QUINTET (Adderley, Cannonball Quintet)**
CD _____ COD 020
Jazz View / Jun '92 / Harmonia Mundi.

KNOW WHAT I MEAN
Arriving soon / Well you needn't / New Delhi
/ Winetone star eyes / Lisa / Waltz for Deb-
bie / Goodbye / Who cares / Elsa / Toy /
Nancy / Venice / Know what I mean
CD _____ OJCCD 1052
Original Jazz Classics / Feb '92 / Wellard /
Jazz Music / Cadillac / Complete/Pinnacle.

**LIVE IN PARIS APRIL 1966 (Adderley,
Julian 'Cannonball')**
CD _____ 087172
Ulysse / Sep '95 / Discovery.

LUGANO 1963
Jessica's birthday / Jive samba / Bohemia
after dark / Dizzy's business / Trouble in
mind / Work song / Unit seven
CD _____ TCB 02032
TCB / Sep '95 / New Note.

MERCY, MERCY, MERCY
Fun / Games / Mercy mercy mercy / Sticks
/ Hippodelphia / Sack o' woe
CD _____ CDP 8299152
Capitol Jazz / Jul '95 / EMI.

NIPPON SOUL
CD _____ OJCCD 435
Original Jazz Classics / Feb '92 / Wellard /
Jazz Music / Cadillac / Complete/Pinnacle.

**PORTRAIT OF CANNONBALL (Adderley,
Julian 'Cannonball' Quintet)**
Minority / Minority (Take 2) / Minority (Take
3) / Straight life / Blue funk / Little taste /
People will say we're in love / Nardis (take
5) / Nardis (take 4)
CD _____ OJCCD 361
Original Jazz Classics / Apr '93 / Wellard /
Jazz Music / Cadillac / Complete/Pinnacle.

**PRESENTING CANNONBALL
ADDERLEY**
Spontaneous combustion / Still talkin' to ya
/ Little taste / Caribbean / Flamingo / With
apologies to Oscar / Late entry / Bohemia
after dark
CD _____ CY 78989
Savoy Jazz / Nov '95 / Conifer / ADA.

QUINTET PLUS
CD _____ OJCCD 306
Original Jazz Classics / Feb '92 / Wellard /
Jazz Music / Cadillac / Complete/Pinnacle.

RADIO NIGHTS
Little boy with the sad eyes / Midnight
mood / Star fell on Alabama / Fiddler on the
roof / Work song / Song my lady sings / Unit
seven / Cannonball monologues on / Oh
babe / Country preacher
CD _____ VNCD 2
Virgin / Feb '91 / EMI.

**SOMETHIN' ELSE (Adderley, Cannonball
& Miles Davis)**
Autumn leaves / Love for sale / Something
else / One for Daddy O / Dancing in the dark
/ Alison's uncle
CD _____ CDP 7463382
Blue Note / Mar '95 / EMI.

SPONTANEOUS COMBUSTION
Still talkin' to ya / Little taste / Caribbean
cutie / Bohemia after dark / Chasm / Willow
weep for me / Late entry / Spontaneous
combustion / Flamingo / Hear me talkin' to
ya / With apologies to Oscar / We'll be together again
CD _____ VGCD 650104
Vogue / Oct '93 / BMG.

**THINGS ARE GETTING BETTER
(Adderley, Cannonball & Milt Jackson)**
CD _____ OJCCD 0322
Original Jazz Classics / Feb '92 / Wellard /
Jazz Music / Cadillac / Complete/Pinnacle.

THIS HERE
CD _____ CD 53121
Giants Of Jazz / Nov '92 / Target/BMG /
Cadillac.

Adderley, Nat

BLUE AUTUMN (Adderley, Nat Quintet)
CD _____ ECD 220352
Evidence / Sep '92 / Harmonia Mundi /
ADA / Cadillac.

**GOOD COMPANY (Adderley, Nat
Quintet)**
CD _____ CHR 70009
Challenge / Jun '95 / Direct / Jazz Music /
Cadillac / ADA.

IN THE BAG (Adderley, Nat Sextet)
CD _____ OJCCD 648
Original Jazz Classics / Nov '95 / Wellard /
Jazz Music / Cadillac / Complete/Pinnacle.

MUCH BRASS (Adderley, Nat Sextet)
CD _____ OJCCD 848
Original Jazz Classics / Nov '95 / Wellard /
Jazz Music / Cadillac / Complete/Pinnacle.

ON THE MOVE (Adderley, Nat Quintet)
Malandro / Boy with the sad eyes / To wis-
dom, the prize / Naturally / Scene / Come
in out of the rain
CD _____ ECD 220642
Evidence / Nov '93 / Harmonia Mundi / ADA
/ Cadillac.

**TALKIN' ABOUT YOU (Adderley, Nat
Quintet)**
Talkin' about you, Cannon / I can't give you
anything but love / Arriving soon / Plum
street / Azule serape / Ill wind / Mo's theme
/ Big P
CD _____ LCD 15282
Landmark / May '91 / New Note.

THAT'S NAT
Porky / I married an angel / Big E / Kuzzin's
buzzin' / Ann springs / You better go now
CD _____ SV 0146
Savoy Jazz / '94 / Conifer / ADA.

WORKING (Adderley, Nat Quintet)
Work song / Chant / Plum street / Almost
always / Big J / Scene
CD _____ CDSJP 387
Timeless Jazz / Nov '93 / New Note.

Addy, Obo

TRADITIONAL MUSIC OF GHANA
CD _____ CDEB 2500
Earthbeat / May '93 / Direct / ADA.

Ade, King Sunny

LIVE JUJU
CD _____ RCD 10047
Rykodisc / Aug '91 / Vital / ADA.

Adeva

ALL THE HITS IN YA FACE
Respect / Musical freedom / Warning / I
thank you (mixes) / Beautiful love / Treat me
right / Ring my bell (mixes) / It should've
been me / Don't let it show on your face /
I'm the one for you / Until you come back
to me / Respect (Mix) (MC only)
CD _____ MOCD 3005
More Music / Feb '95 / Sound & Media.

HITS
Respect / I thank you / Warning / Beautiful
love / It should've been me / Independent
woman / Musical freedom (With Paul Simpson) / I'm the one for you / Don't let it show
on your face / Until you come back to me /
Ring my bell (With Monie Love)
CD _____ CTCD 30
Cooltempo / Oct '92 / EMI.

Adicts

27
Angel / Love sucks / Do it / That's happiness / Shangri la / Football fairy story / Rossini / Breakdown / Give me more / Fuck it
up / G.I.R.L. / What am I to do / Rockers in
rags / Let's dance / 7.27 / Bog / Come out
to play / Just wanna dance with you
CD _____ CDGRAM 68
Anagram / Sep '93 / Pinnacle.

**COMPLETE ADICTS SINGLES
COLLECTION, THE**
This week / Easy way out / Straight jacket
/ Organised confusion / Viva la revolution /
Steamroller / Numbers / Chinese takeaway
/ You'll never walk alone / Your song / Bad
boy / Joker in the pack / Shake rattle bang
your head / Tokyo / Old couple / A.D.X
Medley / Falling in love / It's a laugh / Sat-
urday night / Champ elysees / Sound of
music / Who split my beer / Cowboy
CD _____ CDPUNK 33
Anagram / Jun '94 / Pinnacle.

ROCKERS IN RAGS (Live in Alabama)
CD _____ FALLCD 046
Fallout / Jan '90 / Disc.

SHE'S A ROCKER
CD _____ 15394
Laserlight / Aug '91 / Target/BMG.

SONGS OF PRAISE
England / Hurt / Just like me / Tango / Telepathic people / Mary Whitehouse / Distortion / Get addicted / Viva la revolution / Calling calling / In the background / Dynasty /
Peculiar music numbers / Sensitive / Songs
of praise
CD _____ CLEO 2481CD
Cleopatra / Jan '94 / Disc.

SOUND OF MUSIC
CD _____ CLEO 3315CD
Cleopatra / Jan '94 / Disc.

THIS IS YOUR LIFE PLUS
CD _____ FALLCD 021
Fallout / Sep '92 / Disc.

ADICTS

TOTALLY ADICTED
Viva la revolution / Songs of praise / Get adicted / Sensitive / Just like me / Too young / Chinese takeway / Joker in the pack / Steamvoller / How sad / Let's go / Easy way out / Smart Alex / Troubadour / Tokyo / Crazy / Bad boy / Runaway / Come along / I wanna be sedated / Falling in love again / It's a laugh / Saturday night / Zimbabwe brothers are go
CD _____ DOJOCD 69
Dojo / Feb '94 / BMG.

Adiemus

SONGS OF SANCTUARY
Adiemus / Tintinnabulum / Cantus inaequalis / Cantus insolitus / In caelum fero / Cantus iteratus / Amate adea / Kayama / Hymn
CD _____ CDVE 925
Virgin / May '95 / EMI.

SONGS OF SANCTUARY (Limited Edition)
Adiemus / Tintinnabulum / Cantus inaequalis / Cantus insolitus / In caelum fero / Cantus iteratus / Kayama / Hymn / Tintinnabulum (edit) / Kayama (edit)
CD _____ CDVEX 925
Venture / Nov '95 / EMI.

Adler, Larry

BEST OF LARRY ADLER, THE
CD _____ SWNCD 004
Sound Waves / Oct '95 / Target/BMG.

GOLDEN ERA OF LARRY ADLER VOLUME 1
CD _____ CDSGP 0119
Prestige / Aug '94 / Total/BMG.

GOLDEN ERA OF LARRY ADLER VOLUME 2
CD _____ CDSGP 0120
Prestige / Oct '94 / Total/BMG.

MOUTH ORGAN VIRTUOSO, THE
I won't dance (introducing Lovely to look at) / Foggy day / Smoke gets in your eyes / Genevieve waltz / I got rhythm / Bolero / It ain't necessarily so / Continental / Londonderry air / Bach goes to town / Rififi / My melancholy baby / Someone to watch over me / Hora staccato / They all laughed / They can't take that away from me / Le gnsbi / Lover come back to me / La mer / Ritual fire dance / Bess, you is my woman now / Tiger rag / Rhapsody in blue / Gershwin - King of rhythm
CD _____ CDEMS 1543
EMI / Nov '94 / EMI.

PIANO ROLL RECORDINGS, THE
CD _____ CDSGP 0143
Prestige / Mar '95 / Total/BMG.

RHAPSODY IN BLUE
Continental / Smoke gets in your eyes / Sophisticated lady / Night and day / Tiger rag / Rhapsody in blue / Caravan / September in the rain / Moon at sea / Home town / Creole love call / Isn't this a lovely day (to be caught in the rain) / Rubenstein's melody in F / Love me forever / Solitude / They all laughed / I've got you under my skin / I know now / Whispers in the dark / it looks like rain in Cherry Blossom Lane / Hungarian dance / They can't take that away from me / With plenty of money and you / Why was I born / Stormy weather / I won't dance
CD _____ RAJCD 835
Empress / Oct '94 / THE.

Admiral Tibet

EXCITMENT
Call upon Jah Jah / Burn in flames / Set me free / Keep the fire burning / Not a fool for you / Want to talk / Never overcome / Excitment / Since you've been gone / Rude boys
CD _____ 117502
Musidisc / Aug '95 / Vital / Harmonia Mundi / ADA / Cadillac / Discovery.

REALITY TIME
CD _____ VYDCD 5
Vine Yard / Sep '95 / Grapevine.

TIME IS GOING TO COME, THE
CD _____ RNCD 2031
Rhino / Dec '93 / Jetstar / Magnum Music Group / THE.

Adolescents

BALBAO FUN ZONE
CD _____ RR 9494 2
Roadrunner / Nov '88 / Pinnacle.

Adorable

AGAINST PERFECTION
Glorious / Favourite fallen idol / A to fade in / I know you too well / Homeboy / Sistine chapel ceiling / Cut #2 / Crash sight / Still life / Breathless
CD _____ CRECD 138
Creation / Mar '93 / 3MV / Vital.

FAKE
Feed me / Vendetta / Man in a suitcase / Submarine / Lettergo / Kangaroo court /
Radio days / Go easy on her / Road movie / Have you seen the light
CD _____ CRECD 165
Creation / Sep '94 / 3MV / Vital.

Adulescents U.K.

SOCIETY OWES ME A LIVING
Society owes me a living / No no / Jelly machete / Witch of insanity / No war no more / Deathwish
CD _____ REPCD 001
Rage / Oct '94 / Nervous / Magnum Music Group.

Advent

ELEMENTS OF LIFE
There's no danger / Where in heaven / Audio illusion / Spaceism / Mad dog / It one jah / Overspray / Bad boy / Farencounters / domini / Call God / Lie / City limits
CD _____ TRUCD 8
Internal / Oct '95 / PolyGram / Pinnacle.

Adventures

SEA OF LOVE, THE
Drowning in the sea of love / Broken land / You don't have to cry / Trip to bountiful / Heaven knows which way / Hold me now / Sound of Summer / When your heart was young / One step from heaven
CD _____ 9607722
Elektra / Apr '88 / Warner Music.

Adverse, Anthony

SPIN
Paradise lost / Best friend / Wednesday's child / Cold winds / Centre of your world / Good girl / Night and day / No sweet surrender / Wastelands of your soul / Spin
CD _____ ACME 22 CD
El / Sep '89 / Pinnacle.

Adverts

CROSSING THE RED SEA
One chord wonders / Bored teenagers / New church / On the roof / Newsboys / Bombsite boys / No time to be 21 / Safety in numbers / Drowning men / On wheels / Great British mistake / Gary Gilmore's eyes / We who wait / New day dawning
CD _____ CLINK 001CD
Street Link / Aug '90 / BMG.

LIVE AND LOUD
Gary Gilmore's eyes / New boys / One chord wonders / On the roof / New day dawning / Quick step / Safety in numbers / Great British mistake / We who wait / New church / Bombsite boys / Bored teenagers / One chord wonders (encore)
CD _____ LINKCD 159
Street Link / Oct '92 / BMG.

Adzido

AKWAABA
CD _____ EUCD 1263
ARC / Mar '94 / ARC Music / ADA.

SIYE GOLI (Adzido Pan African Dance Ensemble)
CD _____ EUCD 1223
ARC / Sep '93 / ARC Music / ADA.

UNDER AFRICAN SKIES
CD _____ EUCD 1127
ARC / '91 / ARC Music / ADA.

Aero

MASQUELERO
CD _____ 8357672
ECM / Jul '88 / New Note.

Aerosmith

MASQUELERO
Make it / Somebody / Dream on / One way street / Mama Kin / Write me a letter / Movin' out / Walking the dog
CD _____ CK 64401
Columbia / Nov '94 / Sony.

AEROSMITH: INTERVIEW PICTURE DISC
CD P.Disc _____ CBAK 4032
Baktabak / Apr '91 / Baktabak.

BIG ONES
Walk on water / Love in an elevator / Rag doll / What it takes / Dude (looks like a lady) / Janie's got a gun / Cryin' / Amazing / Blind man / Deuces are wild / Other side / Crazy / Eat the rich / Angel / Livin' on the edge / Dude (looks like a lady) (live)
CD _____ GED 24546
Geffen / Oct '94 / BMG.

BOX OF FIRE (13 CDs)
CD Set _____ 477803-2
Columbia / Nov '94 / Sony.

CLASSICS LIVE
Train kept a rollin' / Kings and Queens / Sweet emotion / Dream on / Mama kin / Three mile smile (Reefer headed woman) / Lord of the thighs / Major Barbara
CD _____ 474971 2
Columbia / Nov '93 / Sony.

CLASSICS LIVE II
Back in the saddle / Walk this way / Movin' out / Draw the line / Same old song and dance / Last child / Let the music do the talking / Toys in the attic
CD _____ 474972 2
Columbia / Nov '93 / Sony.

DONE WITH MIRRORS
Let the music do the talking / My fist, your face / Shame on you / Reason a dog / She La / Gypsy boots / She's on fire / Hop / Darkness (MC only)
CD _____ GFLD 19052
Geffen / May '94 / BMG.

DRAW THE LINE
Draw the line / I wanna know why / Critical mass / Get it up / Bright light fright / Kings and queens / Hand that feeds / Sight for sore eyes / Milk cow blues
CD _____ 474966 2
Columbia / Nov '93 / Sony.

DRAW THE LINE/TOYS IN THE ATTIC/ ROCKS
CD Set _____ 4673852
CBS / Dec '90 / Sony.

GEMS
Rats in the cellar / Lick and a promise / Chip away the stone / No surprize / Mama kin / Adam's apple / Nobody's fault / Round and round / Critical mass / Lord of the Thighs / Jailbait / Train kept a rollin'
CD _____ 474973 2
Columbia / Nov '93 / Sony.

GET A GRIP
Intro / Eat the rich / Get a grip / Fever / Livin' on the edge / Flesh / Walk on down / Shut up and dance / Cryin' / Gotta love it / Crazy / Line up / Can't stop messin' / Amazing / Boogie man
CD _____ GED 24444
Geffen / Apr '93 / BMG.

GET YOUR WINGS
Same old song and dance / Lord of the thighs / Woman of the world / Train kept a rollin' / Spaced / SOS (too bad) / Seasons of wither / Pandora's box
CD _____ 474963 2
Columbia / Nov '93 / Sony.

GREATEST HITS: AEROSMITH
Dream on / Same old song and dance / Sweet emotion / Walk this way / Remember (walkin' in the sand) / Back in the saddle / Draw the line / Kings and queens / Come together / Last child
CD _____ 474969 2
Columbia / Nov '93 / Sony.

LIVE BOOTLEG
Back in the saddle / Sweet emotion / Lord of the thighs / Toys in the attic / Last child / Come together / Walk this way / Sick as a dog / Dream on / Mama kin / S.O.S. / Train kept a rollin' / Sight for sore eyes / Chip away the stone / I ain't got you / Mother popcorn
CD _____ 474967 2
Columbia / Nov '93 / Sony.

NIGHT IN THE RUTS
No surprize / Chiquita / Remember (walkin' in the sand) / Cheese cake / Three mile smile / Reefer head woman / Bone to bone (Coney Island white fish boy) / Mia / Think about it
CD _____ 474968 2
Columbia / Nov '93 / Sony.

PANDORA'S BOX
When I needed you / Make it / Movin' out / One way street / On the road again / Mama kin / Same old song and dance / Train kept a rollin' / Seasons of wither / Write me a letter / Dream on / Pandora's box / Rattlesnake shake / Walking the dog / Lord of the Thighs / Toys in the attic / Round and round / Krawhitham / You see me crying/Sweet emotion / No more no more / Walk this way / I wanna know why / Rats in the cellar / Last child / All your love / Soul saver / Nobody's fault / Lick and a promise / Adam's apple / Draw the line / Critical mass / Kings and Queens / Milkcow blues / I live in Connecticut / Three mile smile / Let it slide / Cheese cake / Bone to bone (Coney Island white fish boy) / No surprize / Come together / Downtown Charlie / Sharpshooter / Shithouse shuffle / South station blues / Riff and roll / Jailbait / Major Barbara / Chip away the stone / Helter skelter / Back in the saddle
CD Set _____ 4692932
Columbia / Dec '91 / Sony.

PANDORA'S TOYS
Sweet emotion / Draw the line / Walk this way / Dream on / Train kept a rollin' / Mama Kin / Seasons of wither / Big ten inch record / All your love / Helter skelter / Chip away the stone / Rattlesnake shake
CD _____ 476956 2
Columbia / Jun '94 / Sony.

PERMANENT VACATION
Hearts done time / Magic touch / Rag doll / Simoriah / Dude (looks like a lady) / St. John / Hangman jury / Girl keeps comin' apart / Angel / Permanent vacation / I'm down / Movie
CD _____ GFLD 19254
Geffen / May '94 / BMG.

PUMP
Young lust / F.I.N.E / Love in an elevator / Monkey on my back / Janie's got a gun / Other side / My girl / Don't get mad get even / Voodoo medicine man / What it takes
CD _____ GFLD 19255
Geffen / May '94 / BMG.

ROCK IN A HARD PLACE
Jailbait / Bitches brew / Cry me a river / Jig is up / Push comes to shove / Lightning strikes / Bolivian ragamuffin / Prelude to Joanie / Joanie's butterfly / Rock in a hard place
CD _____ 474970 2
Columbia / Nov '93 / Sony.

ROCKS
Back in the saddle / Last child / Rats in the cellar / Combination / Sick as a dog / Nobody's fault / Get the lead out / Lick and a promise / Home tonight
CD _____ 474965 2
Columbia / Nov '93 / Sony.

TOYS IN THE ATTIC
Toys in the attic / Uncle Salty / Adam's apple / Walk this way / Big ten inch record / Sweet emotion / No more no more / Round and round / You see me crying
CD _____ 4804142
Columbia / Jul '95 / Sony.

Affair

JUST CAN'T GET ENOUGH
If only you could be mine / Are you ready / Just can't get enough / Way we are / This man of mine / Something for nothing / Think it over / Take my love / I'm standing still / Wherever you are
CD _____ BRCD 596
4th & Broadway / Mar '95 / PolyGram.

Affected

FATE WORSE THAN A FATE WORSE THAN DEATH, A
Mind / Clawback / No one else / Wilt / Jenny 867/5309 / Blown / Never gonna see you again / Let it bleed / Sage / Misjudge me / Like you didn't know / Zilche / Empty promises
CD _____ 31060-2
Frontier / May '94 / Vital.

Afflicted

DAWN OF GLORY
CD _____ MASSCD 055
Massacre / Mar '95 / Plastic Head.

PRODIGAL SUN
CD _____ NB 063CD
Nuclear Blast / Nov '92 / Plastic Head.

Affolter, Heinz

ACOUSTIC ADVENTURE
Aftermath / Basia / Need you know / El patio / Man in a desert / Camino cielo / Triangle / Snow White / Crazy / Nadja's theme
CD _____ BW 034
B&W / Feb '95 / New Note.

ACOUSTIC REALITIES
Latin wind / Santa Lucia / You know / M Richard / Polish horses / Sparkling waters / Nadja / Nina's feeling blue / Tensions / Swallows
CD _____ BW 035
B&W / Jan '95 / New Note.

CHINA MOON
China moon / Life's miracle / Pay tomorrow / Tears in your eyes / Tell me why / Lithuania / Karma / Let's make it big / Omnipresent time / Waves
CD _____ BW 032
B&W / Sep '93 / New Note.

Afghan Whigs

GENTLEMEN
CD _____ BFFP 90CD
Blast First / Oct '93 / Disc.

African Children's Choir

WALKING IN THE LIGHT
Walking in the light / Man of the Lord / Be bold, be strong / Ndyahimbisa / Jubilant Africa / Awesome God / Generation song / Steal away / Seed to sow / Nimoljwe kana / Mpulia Ebiwobe (cries of the Lord) / From a distance / We are the world
CD _____ ALD 030
Alliance Music / Jun '95 / EMI.

African Headcharge

AKWAABA
Can't waste time / Yes I / Glory dawn / To fari hail / Heavy dance / Power from Zion / World peace / Cheer up / Walking thrill / All of the love / Ire day / Live good / Child's play
CD _____ JAZIDCD 129
Acid Jazz / Nov '95 / Pinnacle.

GREAT VINTAGE VOL. 1
CD _____ ONUCD 2
On-U Sound / Jul '89 / SRD / Jetstar.

10

GREAT VINTAGE VOL. 2
CD _____ ONUCD 3
On-U Sound / Sep '89 / SRD / Jetstar.

IN PURSUIT OF SHASAMANE LAND
CD _____ ONUCD 25
On-U Sound / Nov '93 / SRD / Jetstar.

OFF THE BEATEN TRACK
CD _____ ONULP 40CD
On-U Sound / Mar '88 / SRD / Jetstar.

SONGS OF PRAISE
CD _____ ONUCD 12
On-U Sound / '92 / SRD / Jetstar.

African Jazz Pioneers

AFRICAN JAZZ PIONEERS
Nonto sangoma / Yeka yeka / Hellfire / Hosh / Mzabalazo (hometown) / Ten ten special / Riverside special / Mbombela
CD _____ KAZCD 14
Kaz / Aug '90 / BMG.

MONTREUX
CD _____ KAZCD 2
Kaz / Jul '92 / BMG.

SIP 'N' FLY
CD _____ FLTRCD 511
Timbuktu / Jun '93 / Pinnacle.

Africjam

AFRICJAM DUB VOL. 1
CD _____ AJAMCD 002
Africjam / Oct '94 / Jetstar / SRD.

Afro-Cuba

ECLECTICISM
CD _____ JHCD 039
Ronnie Scott's Jazz House / Mar '95 / Jazz Music / Magnum Music Group / Cadillac.

After 7

AFTER 7
Don't cha think / In the heat of the moment / Can't stop / My only woman / Love's been so nice / One night / Ready or not / Sayonara
CD _____ CDVUS 7
Virgin / Sep '89 / EMI.

REFLECTIONS
Till you do me right / Cryin' for it / Save it up / Damn thing called love / How did he love you / What U R 2 me / How do you tell the one / Sprung on it / How could you leave / Givin' up this good thing / I like it like that / Honey (oh how I need you)
CD _____ CDVUS 88
Virgin / Jul '95 / EMI.

After Dinner

AFTER DINNER
After dinner / Sepia-ture / Accelerating etude. An / Soknya doll / Shovel and little lady / Cymbals at dawn / Glass tube / Dessert / Sepia-ture II / Walnut / Cymbals at dawn II / RE / Kitchen life / Glass tube II / Variation of Would you like some mushrooms / Ironclad mermaid / After dinner II / Room of hair-mobile
CD _____ RERSDCD 20
Recommended / Apr '91 / These / ReR Megacorp.

After Hours

UP TO HERE
CD _____ CMCD 069
Celtic Music / Mar '94 / CM / Roots.

After Tea

AFTER TEA
CD _____ REP 4236-WP
Repertoire / Aug '91 / Pinnacle / Cadillac.

After The Fire

DER KOMMISSAR
Der Kommissar / Who's gonna love you / Frozen rivers / Joy / Dancing in the shadows / Billy / 1980-F / Rich boys / Starlight / Laser love / Love will always make you cry / One rule for you / Sailing ship
CD _____ 4809732
Columbia / Aug '95 / Sony.

Afternoons

HOMAGE
CD _____ CBM 008CD
Cross Border Media / Jan '94 / Direct / ADA.

Age

ORION YEARS
CD _____ EFA 006532
Force Inc / Jul '94 / SRD.

Agent Orange

REAL LIVE SOUND
CD _____ 725292
Restless / Feb '95 / Vital.

This Is The Voice

THIS IS THE VOICE
CD _____ 725402
Restless / Feb '95 / Vital.

WHEN YOU LEAST EXPECT IT
CD _____ 722182
Restless / Feb '95 / Vital.

Agent Steel

UNSTOPPABLE FORCE
CD _____ CDMFN 66
Music For Nations / Aug '89 / Pinnacle.

Aghast

HEXERI IM ZWEILICHT
CD _____ CM 1033CD
Cold Meat Industry / Aug '95 / Plastic Head.

Agincourt

FLY AWAY
CD _____ HBG 123/6
Background / Apr '94 / Background.

Agnostic Front

CAUSE FOR ALARM
CD _____ CDJUST 3
Rough Justice / Aug '87 / Pinnacle.

LAST WARNING
CD _____ RR 90782
Roadrunner / Apr '95 / Pinnacle.

LIBERTY AND JUSTICE (FOR ALL)
CD _____ CDJUST 8
Rough Justice / Oct '87 / Pinnacle.

ONE VOICE
CD _____ RO 92222
Roadrunner / Apr '95 / Pinnacle.

RAW UNLEASHED
CD _____ GTA 002R051
Grand Theft Auto / Jul '95 / Plastic Head.

Agony

FIRST DEFIANCE, THE
Hey Suze / Falling rain / Discipline / Chasing dreams / Ah-ha / Sailors on the sea / Stalk the girls / Dream girl / Strung out on you / Country girl / Goodnight darling
CD _____ CDFLAG 19
Under One Flag / Apr '88 / Pinnacle.

Agony Column

BRAVE WORDS AND BLOODY KNUCKLES
CD _____ 341422
No Bull / Oct '95 / Koch.

Agothocles

BLACK CLOUDS DETERMINATE
CD _____ CYBER 10
Cyber / Aug '94 / Plastic Head.

THEATRICAL SYMBOLIZATION
CD _____ CYBERCD 2
Cyber / Jun '92 / Plastic Head.

Agressor

SATAN'S SODOMY
CD _____ BMCD 36
Black Mark / Jun '94 / Plastic Head.

SYMPOSIUM OF REBIRTH
CD _____ BMCD 55
Black Mark / Oct '91 / Plastic Head.

TOWARDS BEYOND
Intro / Forteress / Positronic showering / Antediluvian / Epileptic aura / Hyaloid / Crypt / Future past/Eldest things / Turkish march (CD only)
CD _____ BMCD 023
Black Mark / Sep '92 / Plastic Head.

Agudo, Luis

DONA FIA
CD _____ 12344-2
Red / Apr '93 / Harmonia Mundi / Jazz Horizons / Cadillac / ADA.

Agyeman, Eric

HIGH LIFE SAFARI
CD _____ STCD 3002
Sterns / Nov '92 / Sterns / CM.

Ahmad

AHMAD
Freak / Back in the day / Touch the ceiling / Jones / Can I party / You gotta be / We want the funk / Palladium / Homeboy's first / Ordinary people / Back in the day (Remix) (Available on CD & MC only.)
CD _____ 74321 19928-2
Arista / Jul '94 / BMG.

Ahmed, Abdullah Mussa

TAARAB MUSIC OF ZANZIBAR VOL.1
(Ahmed, Abdullah Mussa & Seif Salim)
Taksim in hijaz mode / Wawili Tunapedani / Taksim in nihawad mode / Nur el nujum / Taksim in sabah mode / Ulimwengu una visa / Taksim in sikka mode / Mpenzi wagu hawesi / Shada la maua / Safaa
CD _____ CDORB 032
Globestyle / Oct '88 / Pinnacle.

Ahsra

TROPICAL HEAT
Mosquito dance / Tropical heat / Pretty papaya / Nights in sweat / Don't stop the fan / Monsoon
CD _____ CDBT 138
Thunderbolt / Feb '91 / Magnum Music Group.

Ailana

MYSTERIOUS PLANET
CD _____ HNCD 1324
Hannibal / May '89 / Vital / ADA.

Ain Soph

KSHATRIYA
CD _____ EEE 21
Musica Maxima Magnetica / Aug '94 / Plastic Head.

Ainsworth, Alyn

MOTOWN PARTY (30 BLOCKBUSTER HITS)
Standing in the shadows of love / It's the same old song / Reach out, I'll be there / Walk away Renee / Supremes medley / Ain't no mountain high enough / I'm still waiting / Sir Duke / Superstition / Living for the city / I'm gonna make you love me / Signed, sealed, delivered (I'm yours) / With you I'm born again / Dancing in the street / What becomes of the broken hearted / I hear a symphony / My cherie amour / Stop in the name of love / Baby love / Where did our love go / You can't hurry love / Still water (love) / You are the sunshine of my life / Yester-me, yester-you, yesterday / I was made to love her / I just called to say I love you / Reach out and touch / Tears of a clown
CD _____ CDSIV 1127
Horatio Nelson / Jul '95 / THE / BMG / Avid/ BMG / Koch.

Aints

ASCENSION
CD _____ HOT 1035
Hot / Nov '93 / Vital.

AUTOCANNIBALISM
CD _____ HOT 1037CD
Hot / Aug '95 / Vital.

S.L.S.Q.
Intro / This perfect day / Erotic neurotic / Runaway / Know your product / River deep, mountain high / Audience rain chant / Messin' with the kid / Nights in venice
CD _____ AINTONECD
Hot / Aug '95 / Vital.

SHELF LIFE UNLIMITED - HOTTER THAN BLAZING PISTOLS
Like an oil spill / Ill wind / River deep, mountain high / It's still nowhere / Erotic neurotic / Aints go pop dancing / What's it like out there / Linda and Abilene
CD _____ HOT 1054CD
Hot / Aug '95 / Vital.

Air

AIR LORE
Ragtime dance / Buddy Bolden's blues / King Porter stomp / Paille Street / Weeping willow rag
CD _____ ND 86578
Bluebird / Apr '88 / BMG.

Air

AIR
CD _____ RSNCD 10
Rising High / Sep '93 / Disc.

Air Command Band...

SILENT SKY (Air Command Band Canadian Forces)
John Gay suite (Intrada/Romanza/Intermezzo/Finale) / Gordon Lightfoot medley (If you could read my mind/Early morning rain/ Pussy willows cats tails) / Far and Away (music from the film) / Copland portrait (music from Memphis Belle/Amazing Grace/ Steel lady/Flying home/The landing/Memphis Belle/Silent sky) / Wind beneath my wings / Music for a tattoo (Spitfire prelude/ Dambusters march/USAF march/Wish me luck as you wave me goodbye) / White cliffs of Dover / Airman's prayer / R.C.A.F. march past
CD _____ BNA 5100
Bandleader / Jul '95 / Conifer.

Air Liquide

AIR LIQUIDE LIVE
CD _____ RSNCD 37
Rising High / Jul '95 / Disc.

NEPHOLOGY
CD _____ RSNCD 15
Rising High / Apr '94 / Disc.

Air Supply

MAKING LOVE...THE BEST OF AIR SUPPLY
Lost in love / Even the nights are better / One that you love / Every woman in the world / Two less lonely people in the world / Chances / Making love out of nothing at all / All out of love / Here I am / Sweet dreams / Keeping the love alive / Now and forever
CD _____ 260757
Arista / May '90 / BMG.

Airdash

BOTH ENDS OF THE PATH
CD _____ BMCD 14
Black Mark / '92 / Plastic Head.

Airstream

RICKY TICK
Bright lights / Stay with me / I'll dream of you / Airstream / Follow through / Statue Queen / Fortuna / Jessica / My eyes / Brush your hair
CD _____ TPLP 36CD
One Little Indian / Mar '93 / Pinnacle.

Airto

SEEDS ON THE GROUND
CD _____ OW S2156841
Sequel / Sep '94 / BMG.

Airtribe

IGNITION
CD _____ EDM 41892
EDM / Oct '95 / EWM.

Aisha

DAUGHTERS OF ZION
CD _____ NG 538CD
Twinkle / May '93 / SRD / Jetstar / Kingdom.

TRUE ROOTS
CD _____ ARICD 084
Ariwa Sounds / Mar '94 / Jetstar / SRD.

Aitken, Laurel

EARLY DAYS OF BLUE BEAT, SKA AND REGGAE (Aitken, Laurel & Friends)
CD _____ BRMCD 025
Bold Reprive / Oct '88 / Pinnacle / Bold Reprive / Harmonia Mundi.

GODFATHER OF SKA
CD _____ CDGAZ 009
Gaz's Rockin' Records / Apr '95 / Pinnacle.

LONG HOT SUMMER (Aitken, Laurel & The Skatalites)
CD _____ PHZCD 59
Unicorn / Nov '93 / Plastic Head.

RINGO THE GRINGO
CD _____ PHZCD 50
Unicorn / Jun '93 / Plastic Head.

RISE AND FALL/IT'S TOO LATE
CD _____ PHZCD 71
Unicorn / Jun '94 / Plastic Head.

Akabu

WARRIOR QUEEN
CD _____ ONUCD 71
On-U Sound / Oct '88 / SRD / Jetstar.

Akademia

ANCIENT ECHOES
CD _____ 09026680552
RCA Victor / May '95 / BMG.

Akagi, Kei

MIRROR PUZZLE
CD _____ AQ 1028
Audioquest / Apr '95 / New Note.

Akers, Karen

JUST IMAGINE
Night, make my day / Nightingale sang in Berkeley Square / Remind me / Just imagine/You're nearer / Ain't misbehavin' / I'd rather be blue / More than you know / Angels, punks and raging queen / Twentieth century blues / I see the world through your eyes / My ship / I am your child / Two for the road
CD _____ DRGCD 5231
DRG / Sep '94 / New Note.

UNCHAINED MELODIES
If I sing / Sooner or later / Blame it on the summer night / I fall in love too easily / I never know when to say when / I waltz alone / How sad no one waltzes anymore / Picture in the hall / Life story / Unchained melody / Bewitched, bothered and bewildered / L'Annee ou Piccoli / Isn't it a pity / Every time we say goodbye / Here I'll stay / Falling in love again / What'll I do / Dream a little dream of me
CD _____ CDSL 5214
DRG / Mar '92 / New Note.

Akhenation

DIVINE SYMPHONIES
CD _____ CDAR 030
Adipocre / Jan '96 / Plastic Head.

Akiyoshi, Toshiko

AKIYOSHI/MARIANO QUARTET
(Akiyoshi, Toshiko/Charlie Mariano
Quartet)
CD _____ CCD 9012
Candid / Jun '88 / Cadillac / Jazz Music /
Wellard / Koch.

CARNEGIE HALL CONCERT
CD _____ 4778002
Sony Jazz / Jan '95 / Sony.

**DESERT LADY - FANTASY (Akiyoshi,
Toshiko Jazz Orchestra)**
Harlequin tears / Desert lady - fantasy /
Hangin' loose / Hiroko's delight / Broken
dreams / Be bop
CD _____ 477800-2
Columbia / Oct '94 / Sony.

INTERLUDE
Interlude / I know who loves you / Blue and
sentimental / I ain't gonna ask no more /
Pagliacci / Solitude / So in love / You
stepped out of a dream
CD _____ CCD 4324
Concord Jazz / Oct '87 / New Note.

**LIVE AT MAYBECK RECITAL HALL,
VOL. 36**
Village / Come Sunday / Con alma / Polka
dots and moonbeams / It was a very good
year / Things we did last summer / Old devil
moon / Sophisticated lady / Quadrille, anyone / Tempous fugit
CD _____ CCD 4635
Concord Jazz / Feb '95 / New Note.

REMEMBERING BUD
CD _____ ECD 220342
Evidence / Sep '92 / Harmonia Mundi /
ADA / Cadillac.

Akkerman, Jan

CAN'T STAND THE NOISE
Pietons / Everything must change / Back to
the factory / Journey (a real elegant gypsy)
/ Heavy treasure / Just because / Who
knows
CD _____ INAK 11001
In Akustik / Mar '95 / Magnum Music
Group.

COMPLETE GUITARIST, THE
Old tennis shoes / Come closer / Funkology
/ It could happen to you / Pietons / Journey
(a real elegant gypsy)
CD _____ CDCHARLY 17
Charly / Jun '86 / Charly / THE / Cadillac.

LIVE (Akkerman, Jan & Joachim Kuhn)
CD _____ INAK 868
In Akustik / Jun '95 / Magnum Music
Group.

PUCCINI'S CAFE
Burger's eyes / Your eyes in the whisky /
Spanish roads / Key to the highway / It
comes and goes / Albatross / Blue train /
Love is uneven / Puccini's cafe
CD _____ INAK 9027
In Akustik / May '95 / Magnum Music
Group.

Alaap

BEST OF ALAAP
CD _____ DMUT 001
Multitone / Mar '88 / BMG.

CHAM CHAM NACHDI PHIRAN
CD _____ DMUT 1121
Multitone / Mar '90 / BMG.

GOLD
CD _____ DMUT 1122
Multitone / Aug '90 / BMG.

IT'S BOOM
CD _____ DMUT 1291
Multitone / Jul '94 / BMG.

PATTAKA
You can't catch me / I didn't mean to be
mean / Crossing / Loretta
CD _____ BHANGRA 4CD
Multitone / Nov '88 / BMG.

SIMPLY ALAAP
CD _____ DMUT 1266
Multitone / Jan '94 / BMG.

Alabama Kids

EARTHMAN SUPERSMELL
CD _____ SCH 9117CD
Schemer / Oct '91 / Vital.

Alan, Josh

WORST, THE
CD _____ GORSE 6CD
Gorse / Jul '95 / Disc.

Alaniz, Joe

**TEJANO MEXICO (Alaniz, Joe & Chano
Cadena)**

CD _____ 90692-2
PMF / Jul '92 / Kingdom / Cadillac.

Alanski, Jay H.

HONEY ON A RAZOR BLADE
CD _____ 592204
FNAC / Oct '93 / Discovery.

Alarm

DECLARATION
Declaration / Marching on / Where were you
when the storm broke / Third light / Sixty
eight guns / We are the light / Shout to the
devil / Blaze of glory / Tell me / Deceiver /
Stand (prophecy) / Howling wind
CD _____ CDMID 103
A&M / Oct '92 / PolyGram.

STRENGTH
Knife edge / Strength / Dawn chorus / Spirit
of '76 / Day the ravens left the tower / Dee-
side / Father to son / Only the thunder /
Walk forever by my side
CD _____ IRLD 19006
IRS / Apr '92 / PolyGram / BMG / EMI.

Alaska

PACK, THE
CD _____ 845 089
Interchord / Oct '88 / CM.

Alastis

AND DEATH SMILED
CD _____ CDAR 029
Adipocre / May '95 / Plastic Head.

Albany, Joe

BIRD LIVES
CD _____ STCD 4164
Storyville / Feb '90 / Jazz Music / Wellard
/ CM / Cadillac.

Albatross

C'EST LA VIE LIVE IN FRANCE
CD _____ BSCD 4714
Blue Shadow / '92 / Swift.

Albert, Christine

UNDERNEATH THE LONE STAR SKY
CD _____ DOS 7014
Dos / Sep '95 / CM / Direct / ADA.

Albert, Morris

FEELINGS
CD _____ PRS 23009
Personality / Aug '93 / Target/BMG.

Alberto Y Los Trios...

**SNUFF ROCK: THE BEST OF THE
ALBERTOS (Alberto Y Los Trios
Paranoias)**
Old trust / Brrrr / I'll come if you let me /
Agnes / No change / Peon in the neck /
Happy to be on an island away from) Demis
Roussos / Teenager in schtuck / Italians
from outer space / Ballad of Colonel Callen
/ Fistful of spaghetti / Mandrax sunset var-
iations, part VI / Neville / Breakfast / Whole
food love / Holiday frog / Teenage promise
/ Willie Baxter's blues / It never rains in El
Paso / Whispering grass / Death of rock and
roll / Heads down no nonsense mindless
boogie / Jesus wept / Kill / Gobbing on life
/ Snuffin' like that / Snuffin' in a Babylon /
Twenty three / Dead meat / Juan Lopez /
Anadin / Pavlov / Anarchy in the UK
CD _____ MAUCD 604
Mau Mau / '91 / Pinnacle.

Alberto, Jose

DE PUERLO Y CON CLASE
Hacerte feliz / Eso parte del alma / juego de
amor / Hace falta tiempo / Pesando Todo
El Dia En Ti / Te repetiste / El temor me hizo
perderte / Baila que baila
CD _____ 66058057
RMM / Feb '95 / New Note.

ON TIME
Fotos y recuerdos / Quien como tu / Estas
a tiempo / Como ellas son / A la hora que
me llamen voy / Como fue / Con sandra en
la cama / Celia / Cuestion
CD _____ 66058093
RMM / Feb '96 / New Note.

Albino Slug

ALBINO SLUG
CD _____ MAD 001CD
Metal Art Disco / May '94 / Plastic Head.

BARRABBAS
CD _____ MAD 002
Mad / Mar '95 / Plastic Head.

Albion Band

1990
Yellow dress / Power and the glory / Fair-
ford breakdown / Fossie shuffle / Ramble
away / Flood / Nameless kind of hell / Adam
and Eve / Lock up your daughters / Party's
over

CD _____ TSCD 457
Topic / Aug '90 / Direct / ADA.

ACOUSTICITY
CD _____ HTD CD 13
HTD / Oct '93 / Pinnacle.

ALBION HEART
CD _____ HTDCD 30
HTD / Mar '95 / Pinnacle.

BBC LIVE IN CONCERT
CD _____ WINCD 041
Windsong / Aug '93 / Pinnacle.

**CAPTURED (The Albions Who Nearly
Got Away)**
Ball, anchor and chain / Yellow dress /
Horseshoe hornpipe/Chasing the jack / Par-
ty's over / Adam and Eve / Nameless kind
of hell / Fossie shuffle / Go north / Chapel
keithack/House in the county / Up the
crooked spire / Set their mouths to twisting
/ Hanging tree / Fireman's song
CD _____ HTDCD 19
HTD / Apr '94 / Pinnacle.

**LARK RISE TO CANDLEFORD (A
Country Tapestry)**
Girl I left behind me / Lemady/arise and pick
a posy / All of a row / Tommytoes / John
Dory / Witch Elder / Abroad for pleasure /
Day thou gavest Lord is ended / Battle of
the Somme / Grand circle dance / Speed
the plough / Snow falls / Cart music / Holly
and the ivy / Postman's knock / Hunt music
/ Scarlet and the blue / Dare to be a Daniel
/ Jacob's well
CD _____ CDSCD 4020
Charisma / Aug '92 / EMI.

**PROSPECT BEFORE US, THE (Albion
Dance Band)**
Uncle Bernard's/Jenny Lind / Hunt is up /
Varsoviana / Masque / Huntsman's chorus
/ Minuet / Wassail song / Picking of sticks/
The old mole / Merry Sherwood Rangers /
La texte estampie real / I wish I was single
again / Whim / Hopping down in Kent / Hor-
se's brawl / On Christmas night all chris-
tians sing
CD _____ CDEMS 1476
Harvest / Jul '93 / EMI.

RISE UP LIKE THE SUN
Ragged heroes / Poor old horse / Afro
blues/Danse Royale / Ampleforth/Lay me
low / Time to ring some changes / House
in the country / Primrose / Gresford disaster
/ Postman's knock / Pain and paradise /
Lay me low / Rainbow over the hill
CD _____ CDEMS 1460
EMI / Aug '92 / EMI.

SONGS FROM THE SHOWS - VOL. 1
CD _____ RGFCD 006
Road Goes On Forever / '92 / Direct.

SONGS FROM THE SHOWS - VOL. 2
CD _____ RGFCD 007
Road Goes On Forever / Feb '91 / Direct.

STELLA MARIS
CD _____ SPINCD 130
Making Waves / Oct '94 / CM.

Albion Jazz Band

ONE FOR THE GUV'NOR
CD _____ SOSCD 1206
Stomp Off / Oct '92 / Jazz Music /
Wellard.

THEY'RE ALL NICE TUNES
CD _____ SOSCD 1249
Stomp Off / May '93 / Jazz Music /
Wellard.

Albita

NO SE PARECE A NADA
Que manera de quererte / No se parece a
nada / Que culpa tengo yo / La esperanza
/ Bolero para nostalgiar / Solo porque vivo
/ Para que me beses tu / Quien le prohibe
/ Un solo beso / Mi guaguanco
CD _____ 4809432
Epic / Oct '95 / Sony.

Alboth

LIED
CD _____ PPP 118
PDCD / Apr '94 / Plastic Head.

Albright, Gerald

SMOOTH
Don't worry about it / I surrender / Sweet
baby / This is for the lover in you / G and
Lee / Just 2 b with u / Anniversary / Passion
/ Sedona / Say it with feeling
CD _____ 756782552-2
WEA / Mar '94 / Warner Music.

Albrigtsen, Steinar

BOUND TO WANDER
CD _____ RTMCD 52
Round Tower / Jan '94 / Pinnacle / ADA /
Direct / BMG / CM.

Alcapone, Dennis

FOREVER VERSION
Nanny version / Run run / Riddle I this /
Baby version / Sunday version / Version I

can feel / Forever version / Baby why ver-
sion / Dancing version / Midnight version /
Sweet talking version / Version you to the
ball
CD _____ CD 3505
Heartbeat / Nov '91 / Greensleeves / Jetstar
/ Direct / ADA.

GUNS DON'T ARGUE
CD _____ JMC 200115
Jamaica Gold / Jun '94 / THE / Magnum
Music Group / Jetstar.

PEACE AND LOVE
CD _____ RB 3014
Reggae Best / Apr '95 / Magnum Music
Group / THE.

UNIVERSAL ROCKERS
CD _____ RASCD 3221
Ras / Nov '92 / Jetstar / Greensleeves /
SRD / Direct.

WAKE UP JAMAICA
CD _____ RNCD 2118
Rhino / Sep '95 / Jetstar / Magnum Music
Group / THE.

Alcatrazz

LIVE SENTENCE
CD _____ CDMFN 134
Music For Nations / Jun '92 / Pinnacle.

NO PAROLE FROM ROCK'N'ROLL
CD _____ CDMFN 133
Music For Nations / Jul '92 / Pinnacle.

Alchemy

CELTIC PANPIPES
Ride on / Spinning wheel / Love thee dear-
est / Spancil Hill / She moved thru' the fair
/ Flight of the earls / My lagan love / Steal
away / Mountains of mourn / Sally gardens
/ Ag criost an siol / Carrickfergus / Derry air
/ Lonesome boatman / Mise Eire
CD _____ KCD 392
Irish / Jan '96 / Target/BMG.

Alcoholics Unanimous

DR. KEGGER MD
CD _____ TEAR 009CD
Tear It Up / Jan '96 / Plastic Head.

Alcorn, Alvin

GAY PARIS STOMPER
CD _____ AMCD 65
American Music / Aug '94 / Jazz Music.

Alden, Howard

**13 STRINGS (Alden, Howard & George
Van Eps)**
Just you, just me / My ideal / I hadn't any-
one till you / Beautiful friendship / Touch of
your lips / Ain't misbehavin' / Too marvel-
lous for words / Love walked in / Queerol-
ogy / How long has this been going on /
Mine / Embraceable you / Emaline
CD _____ CCD 4464
Concord Jazz / Jun '91 / New Note.

**CONCORD JAZZ GUITAR COLLECTIVE,
THE (Alden, Howard & Jimmy Bruno &
Frank Vignola)**
Bittersweet / Strictly confidential / String
thing / Mating call / Seven come eleven /
Body and soul / Donna Lee / Perdido /
Swing 39 / Four brothers / Song d'autumne
/ Ornithology
CD _____ CCD 4672
Concord Jazz / Dec '95 / New Note.

**ENCORE (Alden, Howard & Ken
Peplowski)**
It all depends on you / Palo alto / Since we
met / I hear a rhapsody / Dolphin / Wabash
/ Fading star / With every breath I take / You
CD _____ CCD 4654
Concord Jazz / Jul '95 / New Note.

**HAND CRAFTED SWING (Alden, Howard
& George Van Eps)**
CD _____ CCD 4513
Concord Jazz / Jul '92 / New Note.

MISTERIOSO (Alden, Howard Trio)
Song of the dove / Misterioso / Everything
but you / Waltz for Julie / This can't be love
/ Reflections in D
CD _____ CCD 4487
Concord Jazz / Nov '91 / New Note.

**SEVEN AND SEVEN (Alden, Howard &
George Van Eps)**
Surrender dear / I may be wrong, but I think
you're wonderful / Lullaby of Birdland /
Stella by starlight / Skylark / My romance /
Last night when we were young / Salute to
Basie / Night and day / Ja da / Just friends
CD _____ CCD 4584
Concord Jazz / Dec '93 / New Note.

**SNOWY MORNING BLUES (Alden,
Howard Trio)**
One morning in May / I'm through with love
/ Bye-ya / Melancholia / Sleepy time gal /
Le sucrier velours (Only on CD) / Dancers
in love (Only on CD) / Snowy morning blues
/ Ask me now / You leave me breathless /
Swing '39
CD _____ CCD 4424
Concord Jazz / Aug '90 / New Note.

YOUR STORY (The Music Of Bill Evans) (Alden, Howard & Frank Wess)
Tune for a lyric / Loose bloose / Displacement / Time remembered / Two lonely people / Funkallero / Only child / Laurie / Maxine / Five / Your story
CD _____ CCD 4621
Concord Jazz / Nov '94 / New Note.

Aldrich, Ronnie

HOUR OF RONNIE ALDRICH, AN (Aldrich, Ronnie & His Piano/Orchestra)
La mer / Hello / Bermuda triangle / Sound of the sea / Last farewell / Calypso / Stranger on the shore / Sailing / Trade winds / Begin the beguine / Arthur's theme / Memory (from 'Cats') / Hill Street Blues / Chariots of fire / Nights birds / Albareda / Stay / For Liza
CD _____ CC 220
Music For Pleasure / May '88 / EMI.

SEA DREAMS (Aldrich, Ronnie & His Two Pianos)
La mer / Hello / Sailing by / Bermuda triangle / Sound of the sea / Last farewell / Calypso / Stranger on the shore / Sailing / Trading winds / To all the girls I've loved before / How deep is the ocean
CD _____ SEWCD 1003
Seaward / May '92 / Target/BMG.

Ales, Brian

NAIVETE
Personal montuno / Low cloud / Mr. Dibala to me / Tango del suceso feliz / La casa ya en bongo / What mambo / Makye macca / This dream
CD _____ VBR 20542
Vera Bra / Mar '94 / Pinnacle / New Note.

Alesini, Nicola

MARCO POLO (Alesini, Nicola & Pier Luigi Andreoni)
Come morning / Quinsai / Yangchow / Golden way / Sumatra / M Polo / Il Libro dell'incessante accordo con il cielo / Maya / Buchara / Kubilay khan / Samarca / Valley of Pamir
CD _____ MASOCD 90069
Materiali Sonori / Dec '95 / New Note.

Alexander Brothers

ALEXANDER BROTHERS
CD _____ CDITV 568
Scotdisc / May '93 / Duncans / Ross / Conifer.

BEST OF THE ALEXANDER BROHERS
CD _____ MATCD 248
Castle / Nov '93 / BMG.

BEST OF THE ALEXANDER BROTHERS
Scotland, Scotland / Any dream will do / Mull of Kintyre / Oil rigger / Road to Dundee / Wild side of life / All along Loch Long / Nobody's child / Flying Scotsman / Caledonia / Northern lights of Aberdeen / Medley / Reels / Blackboard of my heart / He bought my soul at Calvary / Come by the hills / Jigs / Cornkisters / Farewell my love / Hiking song
CD _____ TRTCD 135
TrueTrax / Oct '94 / THE.

FLOWER OF SCOTLAND
Scotland the brave / Skye boat song / Campbeltown loch / Road and the miles to Dundee / Northern lights of old Aberdeen / My ain folk / Marie's wedding / Scottish soldier / Amazing grace / Heilan' lassie / Dawen tree / Wild roses / Cock o' the North / Tunes of glory / How are things in Glocca Morra / Flower of Scotland / These are my mountains (CD only.) / Two highlands lads (CD only.) / When you and I were young Maggie (CD only.) / Ballad of Glencoe (CD only.)
CD _____ CDMFP 5889
Music For Pleasure / Jun '90 / EMI.

GLORIOUS NORTH, THE
Glorious North / Caledonia / Hill o'Benachie / Lass of bon accord / Oil rigger / Northern lights of old Aberdeen / Dark island / Lonely scapa flow / Jigs medley / Farewell my love / McGinty's meal and ale
CD _____ CDITV 593
Scotdisc / Nov '94 / Duncans / Ross / Conifer.

NOW
Welcome medley / Nobody's child / Old button box / Pistonette / Gentle Annie / Inverary Inn / Daisy a day / Dark island / Doon in the wee room / When you and I were young Maggie / Sing along medley / Way old friends do / Home from the sea / On the rebound / Goodnight Bobby / Mary mack / Could I have this dance / Glencoe / Flying Scotsman / Bunch of thyme / Catch me if you can / Flower of Scotland
CD _____ LCDM 9023
Lismor / Aug '90 / Lismor / Direct / Duncans / ADA.

TOAST TO ABSENT FRIENDS, A
Opening medley / Any dream will do / Lass of bon accord / Oil rigger / Northern lights of old Aberdeen / Absent friends / Take me back / Working man / After all these years / Tartan / It is no secret / Jaqueline waltz / Helen of Inver-

garry / Marching through the heather / Bricklayer's song / Fisherman's son
CD _____ LCOM 6035
Lismor / Sep '92 / Lismor / Direct / Duncans / ADA.

Alexander, Arthur

ADIOS AMIGO (A Tribute To Arthur Alexander) (Various Artists)
CD _____ FIENDCD 754
Demon / Aug '94 / Pinnacle / ADA.

GREATEST, THE
Anna / Soldier of love / You don't care / Call me lonesome / Where have you been / Don't you know / All I need is you / Have her guessing / In the middle of it all / Without a song / Black night / You're the reason / I hang my head and cry / Dream girl / Are you / Shot of rhythm and blues / You better move on / Detroit city / Go home girl / Whole lot of trouble / I wonder where you are tonight
CD _____ CDCHD 922
Ace / Jun '89 / Pinnacle / Cadillac / Complete/Pinnacle.

LONELY JUST LIKE ME
If it's really got to be this way / Go home girl / Sally Sue Brown / Mr. John / Lonely just like me / Every day I have to cry / In the middle of it all / Genie in the jug / Johnny Heartbreak / All the time / There is a road / I believe in miracles
CD _____ 755961475-2
Elektra Nonesuch / Jul '93 / Warner Music.

YOU BETTER MOVE ON
CD _____ MCLD 19251
MCA / Oct '94 / BMG.

Alexander, Eric

NEW YORK CALLING (Alexander, Eric Quintet)
CD _____ CRISS 1077CD
Criss Cross / Nov '93 / Cadillac / Harmonia Mundi.

STRAIGHT UP
CD _____ DDCD 461
Delmark / Nov '93 / Hot Shot / ADA / CM / Direct / Cadillac.

Alexander, Monty

IVORY AND STEEL
CD _____ CCD 4124
Concord Jazz / Jul '88 / New Note.

JAMBOREE
CD _____ CCD 4359
Concord Picante / Oct '88 / New Note.

MAYBECK RECITAL HALL SERIES VOL. 40
When the saints go marching in / When I grow too old to dream / Close enough for love / Serpent / Where is love / Renewal / Island in the sun / Estate / (I love you) for sentimental reasons / Speak low / Smile
CD _____ CCD 4658
Concord Jazz / Aug '95 / New Note.

RIVER, THE
Stand up, stand up for Jesus / River / Serpent / Ave Maria / David danced before the Lord with all his might / Renewal / Ain't gonna study war no more (Only on CD) / Holy Holy Lord God Almighty / What a friend we have in Jesus / How great thou art
CD _____ CCD 4422
Concord Jazz / Aug '90 / New Note.

SATURDAY NIGHT (Alexander, Monty Quartet)
CD _____ MCD 024
Timeless Jazz / May '89 / New Note.

SO WHAT
CD _____ 591482
Black & Blue / Jun '91 / Wellard / Koch.

SOLO
CD _____ BLR 84 006
L&R / May '91 / New Note.

STEAMIN'
Pure imagination / Just a little bit / Dear Diz / 3000 Miles / Lively up yourself / Make believe / I'll never stop loving you / Maybe September / Tucker avenue stomp / Theme from Prawnbroker / Honest I do / When you go / Young at heart
CD _____ CCD 4636
Concord Jazz / Apr '95 / New Note.

TO NAT WITH LOVE
Unforgettable / What is this thing called love / Moonlight in Vermont / Honeysuckle rose / Three little words / Nature boy / Straighten up and fly right / Too marvellous for words / Yes sir that's my baby
CD _____ CHECD 12
Master Mix / Oct '91 / Wellard / Jazz Music / New Note.

TRIO (Alexander / Brown / Ellis)
CD _____ CCD 4136
Concord Jazz / Dec '90 / New Note.

TRIPLE TREAT II (Alexander, Monty & Ray Brown/Herb Ellis)
Lined with a groove / Straighten up and fly right / It might as well be Spring / Seven come eleven / Smile / I'll remember April /

Trip man (tracer and inst. mix) / Lester leaps in
CD _____ CCD 4338
Concord Jazz / May '88 / New Note.

TRIPLE TREAT III (Alexander, Monty & Ray Brown/Herb Ellis)
I told ya I love ya, now get out / In the wee small hours of the morning / Renewal / My one and only love / There will never be another you / Secret love / Hi-heel sneakers / I love you / Corcovado
CD _____ CCD 4394
Concord Jazz / '89 / New Note.

Alexander, Peter

DIE FRUHEN JAHRE
Das machen nur die Beine von Dolores / Bye bye mein Hawaii / Ich lade dich ein in die kleine Taverne / Erzahl mir keine Marchen / Im weissen weissen schnee / Sag es mit Musik Fahr auf dem Zigeunerwagen / Es ist ein abschied nur fur heut / Der alte Liebesbrief / Wenn ich dich seh' / Ich hab' nach dir soviel Heimweh Addio / Donna Grazia / Santa Fe / Wo am weg die apfel reifen ein musikus / Bumms / Weil du schon bist / Ich kusse ihre hand, Madame / Ich weiss es nicht / So ein kleines bisschen liebe / Isabella / Die sussesten fruchte (fressen nur die) / Braucht dein Herz keinen freund / Komm mit nach Palermo / Verliebte music / Ach, Herr Kuhn / Bolero (geheimnis der sudichen nachte) / Die panne panne mit Susanne / Gross kann sie sein, klein kann sie sein / Was versteht denn ein Cowboy von liebe / Margarita / Ich weiss was du dir denkst / Damais in Rom Angelina / Pony serenade / Tabak und Rum / Hannelore / Bella bella Donna / Optimisten boogie / Die alte kuckucksuhr / Es war das letzte mal / Alte lieder traute weisen / Das lied vom sonntag / Ein italiano / Nein nein ich will night bitte lass mich / Bella musica / Der alte stiefel / Ach hatt ich das gefuhl, doch mal / Keine angst vor grossen tieren / Immer wieder du / Jambalaya / Jonathan boogie / Kotettier nicht mit mir / Mein grosser bruder / Ich lieb dich so wie du bist / Die frau kommt direkt aus Spanien / Uno momento Maria / Plim plim, plum plum / Die sussesten fruchte (fressen nur die) (2) / Wir wir wir haben ein klavier / Was hat der Bobby mit der Lisa gemacht / Oh Mister Swoboda / Dann ist er furchtbar mude / In servent / Nicolo Nicolo Nicolo / Jede frau in bogota / Die freuen augen / Die schonen frauen haben immer recht / Es war in Napoli vor vielen Jahren / Continental / Es liegt was in der luft / Ich finde dich / Ich sing' heut vergnugt vor mich hin / Du bist die Richtige / Ich hap vor'm kussen immer lampenfieber / Der primas / Agustino / Der bunte traum / Schlager revue No. 8 / Weinlied/Sagbiem abschied leise verus
CD Set _____ BCD 15455
Bear Family / Jul '89 / Rollercoaster / Direct / CM / Swift / ADA.

STRASSE MEINER LEIDER
CD _____ BCD 15599
Bear Family / Feb '90 / Rollercoaster / Direct / CM / Swift / ADA.

Alexander, Ray

RAIN IN JUNE (Alexander, Ray Sextet)
Dizzy atmosphere / Nightingale sang in Berkeley Square / Lamp is low / Our love is here to stay / Let's fall in love / Rain in June / Angelique / Easy to love / Twinkletoes / Lady be good / Swinging on a star
CD _____ CDSGP 0139
Prestige / Jun '95 / Total/BMG.

Alexander, Texas

TEXAS ALEXANDER VOL 1 (1927-28)
Range in my kitchen blues / Long lonesome day blues / Cornbread blues / Section gang blues / Levee camp moan blues / Mama I heard you brought it right back home / Farm hand blues / Evil woman blues / Sabine River blues / Deep blue sea blues / No more woman blues / Don't you wish your baby was built up like mine / Bell cow blues
CD _____ MBCD 2001
Matchbox / Feb '93 / Roots / CM / Jazz Music / Cadillac.

TEXAS ALEXANDER VOL. 2 1928-30
CD _____ MBCD 2002
Matchbox / Jan '94 / Roots / CM / Jazz Music / Cadillac.

TEXAS ALEXANDER VOL. 3 1930-50
CD _____ MBCD 2003
Matchbox / Jan '94 / Roots / CM / Jazz Music / Cadillac.

Alexandria, Lorez

ALEXANDRIA THE GREAT
Show me / I've never been in love before / Satin doll / My one and only love / Over the rainbow / Get me to the church on time / Best is yet to come / I've grown accustomed to his face / Give me the simple life / I'm through with love / But beautiful / Little boat / Dancing on the ceiling / It might as well be Spring / Once / Wildest gal in town / Angel eyes / This could be the start of

something big / No more / That far away look
CD _____ MCAD 33116
Impulse Jazz / Jan '90 / BMG / New Note.

BAND SWINGS LOREZ
You're my thrill / Don't blame me / Ain't misbehavin' / What is this thing called love / Dancing on the ceiling / Love is just around the corner / I'm gonna sit right down and write myself a letter / Just you, just me / All the things you are / Thrill is gone / My baby just cares for me
CD _____ KCD 657
King/Paddle Wheel / Nov '92 / New Note.

I'LL NEVER STOP LOVING YOU
I should care / Love walked in / I'll never stop loving you / No moon at all / In the wee small hours of the morning / All my life / Like someone in love / For all we know / I could write a book
CD _____ MCD 5457
Muse / Feb '94 / New Note / CM.

LOREZ SINGS PRES (Late Session At An Intimate Club)
Fine and dandy / Fooling myself / D.B. blues / You're driving me crazy / Easy living / Polka dots and moonbeams / This year's kisses / There will never be another you / No eyes blues / Jumpin' with symphony Sid
CD _____ KCD 565
King/Paddle Wheel / Mar '90 / New Note.

MAY I COME IN
CD _____ MCD 5420
Muse / Nov '91 / New Note / CM.

SINGING SONGS EVERYONE KNOWS
CD _____ KCD 000676
King/Paddle Wheel / Sep '92 / New Note.

STANDARDS WITH A SLIGHT TOUCH OF JAZZ
Just one of those things / Then I'll be tired of you / Lush life / Sometimes I'm happy / Long ago and far away / But beautiful / I'm beginning to see the light / I can't believe that you're in love with me / Spring is here / Angel eyes / Better luck next time / I didn't know what time it was
CD _____ KCD 676
King/Paddle Wheel / Mar '90 / New Note.

STAR EYES
CD _____ MCD 5488
Muse / Feb '96 / New Note / CM.

TALK ABOUT COPY
CD _____ HCD 605
Hindsight / Oct '95 / Target/BMG / Jazz Music.

Alfred, Chuz

JAZZ YOUNG BLOOD
Message from home / Manta ray / I can't get started (with you) / Harlequin / Love comes to Mehitable Brown / Chuz duz
CD _____ SV 0211
Savoy Jazz / '94 / Conifer / ADA.

Algaion

OIMES ALGAION
CD _____ FMP 002CDM
Full Moon / Jun '95 / Plastic Head.

Alger, Pat

SEEDS
CD _____ SH 1041CD
Sugarhill / Jan '94 / Roots / CM / ADA / Direct.

TRUE LOVE AND OTHER STORIES
True love / Love star state of mind / Goin' gone / Like a hurricane / This town / Love can be a dangerous thing / I do / She came from Fort Worth / Forever lovin' you / Small town Saturday night / Once in a very blue moon / Blue highway 29
CD _____ SHCD 1029
Sugarhill / '91 / Roots / CM / ADA / Direct.

Alhambra

ART OF JUDEO-SPANISH SONG
CD _____ GV 127CD
Global Village / Nov '93 / ADA / Direct.

Ali, Salamat

NAZAKAT AND SALAMAT ALI (Ali, Salamat & Nazakat)
CD _____ HNCD 1332
Hannibal / Sep '91 / Vital / ADA.

Alias

METAL TO INFINITY
CD _____ RTN 41202
Rock The Nation / Nov '94 / Plastic Head.

Alias Ron Kavana

COMING DAYS
Galtee mor / Irish ways / Saddle the pony / Merrily kiss the quaker / Kinnegad slashers / Annie Mulligan's / Thoughts of Abilene / Psycho Mary's voodoo blues / Ain't that peculiar / Fox hunter's reel / Pennies for black babies / Cajun ceili / Freedom crazy / Walk don't walk / Hand me down (CD only) / Connemara (CD only) / Handcuffs (CD only)

/ Johnny (CD only) / If I had a rocket launcher
CD CDWIKD 94
Chiswick / Mar '91 / Pinnacle.

HOME FIRE
CD SPDCD 1043
Special Delivery / Jun '91 / ADA / CM / Direct.

ROLLIN' & COASTIN' (In Search Of America)
CD AP 042CD
Appaloosa / Apr '94 / ADA / Magnum Music Group.

THINK LIKE A HERO
Waxin' the gaza / Every man is a king (in the US of A) / Gone shopping / Soweto trembles (the Jo'burg jig) / Felice / This is the night (fair dues to "The Man") / Midnight on the water / Caoineadh roisin / Four horsemen / Rap 'n' reel / Tre ceather a hocht / Ochra at Killarney point to points (Available on CD and cassette only) / Reconciliation (Available on CD and cassette only)
CD CDWIK 88
Chiswick / Oct '89 / Pinnacle.

Alice Donut

BUCKETFULS OF SICKNESS AND HORROR (In An Otherwise Meaningless Life)
CD VIRUS 73CD
Alternative Tentacles / Jul '89 / Pinnacle.

DONUT COMES ALIVE
CD VIRUS 61CD
Alternative Tentacles / '92 / Pinnacle.

DRY HUMPING THE CASH COW
CD VIRUS 143CD
Alternative Tentacles / Apr '94 / Pinnacle.

MULE
CD VIRUS 82CD
Alternative Tentacles / Nov '90 / Pinnacle.

PURE ACID PARK
Millennium / Dreaming in Cuban / Freaks in love / Big cars and blow jobs / I walked with a zombie / Senator and the cabin boy / Mummenschantz pachinko / Insane / Shining path / Unspeakable pleasure of being me / Lost in space / Cain
CD VIRUS 163CD
Alternative Tentacles / Jul '95 / Pinnacle.

UNTIDY SUICIDES OF YOUR DEGENERATE CHILDREN
CD VIRUS 115CD
Alternative Tentacles / Sep '92 / Pinnacle.

Alice In Chains

ALICE IN CHAINS
Grind / Brush away / Sludge factory / Heaven beside you / Head creeps / Again / Shame in you / God am / So close / Nothin' song / Frogs / Over now
CD 4811142
CD 4811149
Columbia / Nov '95 / Sony.

DIRT
Them bones / Dam that river / Rain when I die / Down in a hole / Sick man / Rooster / Junkhead / Dirt / God smack / Hate to feel / Angry chair / Would
CD 472330-2
Columbia / Oct '92 / Sony.

FACELIFT
We die young / Man in the box / Sea of sorrow / Bleed the freak / I can't remember / Love hate love / It ain't like that / Sunshine / Put you down / Confusion / I know somethin' ('bout you) / Real thing
CD 4672002
Columbia / Oct '92 / Sony.

JAR OF FLIES/SAP
Rotten apple / Nutshell / I stay away / No excuses / Whale and wasp / Don't follow / Swing on this / Brother / Got me wrong / Right turn / Am I inside / Love story
CD Set 4757132
Columbia / Jan '94 / Sony.

Alien Boys

SEEDS OF DECAY
CD SR 330391CD
Semaphore / '91 / Plastic Head.

Alien Sex Fiend

ACID BATH
In God we trust / Dead and reburied / She's a killer / Hee-haw (here come the bone people) / Smoke my bones / Breakdown and cry (lay down and die goodbye) / E.S.T. (trip to the moon) / Attack + 2 / Boneshaker baby / I'm a product (CD only) / Thirty second coma (CD only)
CD CDMGRAM 18
Anagram / Mar '93 / Pinnacle.

ALL OUR YESTERDAYS (The Singles Collection 1983-87)
Ignore the machine / Lips can't go / R.I.P. / Dead and buried / E.S.T. (trip to the moon) / Drive my rocket (up Uranus) / I'm doing time in a maximum security twilight home / I walk the line / Smells like shit / Hurricane fighter plane
CD CDGRAM 34
Anagram / May '93 / Pinnacle.

ANOTHER PLANET
Bun ho / Everybody's dream / Radiant city / Spot your lucky warts / Sample my sausage / Outer limits / Instant Karma Sutra / So much to do, so little time / Alien / Wild green fiendy liquid / Nightmare zone / Another planet / Silver machine (On cassette only.)
CD CDGRAM 38
Anagram / Nov '88 / Pinnacle.

CURSE
Katch 22 / Now I'm feeling zombiefied / Stress / Blessings / Eat eat eat (an eye for an eye) / Ain't got no time to bleed / Bleeding reprise (Not on LP) / Dalisms / Burger bar baby / I think I / Mad daddy drives a UFO (Not on LP) / Wuthering wind (Not on LP) / Radio Jimi (Not on LP) / Hand of the silken (Not on LP) / Blessing in disguise (Not on LP)
CD CDGRAM 46
Anagram / Sep '90 / Pinnacle.

DRIVE MY ROCKET
CD CLEO 94122
Cleopatra / Aug '94 / Disc.

FIRST ALIEN SEX FIEND CD
I'm doing time in a maximum security twilight home / Mine's full of maggots / In and out of my mind / Spies / Fly in the ointment / Seconds to nowhere / Beaver destroys forests / Do you sleep / Depravity lane / E.S.T. (Trip to the moon) / Boneshaker baby / Ignore the machine / Attack
CD CDGRAM 25
Anagram / Apr '94 / Pinnacle.

HERE CUM GERMS
Here cum germs / Camel camel / Impossible mission / Isolation / My brain is in the cupboard above the kitchen sink / You are soul / Death / Boots on / They all call me crazee / Stuff the turkey
CD CDGRAM 31
Anagram / May '92 / Pinnacle.

I'M HER FRANKENSTEIN
CD CLEO 9508CD
Cleopatra / Jun '95 / Disc.

INFERNO
Inferno (mixes) / Human installation / Take off tune / Space 1 / Happy tune / Planet 1 / Human atmosphere / Happy finale / Alien installation / Dramatic tune / Moon tune / Planet 2 / Bad news / Space 2 / Alien atmopshere / Death tune / Sad finale / Moon tune (lunaphases mix) / Planet 2 (together dreamscape mix)
CD CDGRAM 80
Anagram / Oct '94 / Pinnacle.

IT/MAXIMUM SECURITY
Smells like shit / Manic depression / Believe it or not / April showers / Wop-bop / Get into it / Lesson one / Do it right / To be continued / I'm doing time in a maximum security twilight home / Mine's full of maggots / Do you sleep / In and out of my mind / Spies / Fly in the ointment / Seconds to nowhere / Beaver destroys forests / Do you sleep (version) / Depravity Lane
CD CDGRAM 26
Anagram / Nov '91 / Pinnacle.

LEGENDARY BATCAVE TAPES, THE
Wardance (of the Alien Sex Fiend) / In heaven / I walk alone / Outta control / I'm her Frankenstein / Boneshaker baby / R.I.P. / Wild women of Wongo / Funk in hell / Drive my rocket (up Uranus) / School's out
CD CDMGRAM 69
Anagram / Oct '93 / Pinnacle.

SINGLES 1983-1985, THE
Ignore the machine / Lips can't go / R.I.P. / New christian music / Dead and buried / E.S.T (trip to the moon) / Ignor the machine (electrode mix) / Doing time in a maximum twilight home / Walk the line / Smells like / Hurricane fighter plane / Impossible mission / Here cum germs / Stuff the turkey / Bun ho / Haunted house / Now I'm feeling zombiefied / Magic / Inferno
CD CDGRAM 99
Anagram / Oct '95 / Pinnacle.

TOO MUCH ACID
It lives again / I walk the line / Nightmare zone / Get into it / E.S.T. (trip to the moon) / So much to do, so little time / Haunted house / Smells like shit / Hurricane fighter plane / Sample my sausage / Boneshaker baby
CD CDGRAM 41
Anagram / May '93 / Pinnacle.

Alimatov, Turgen

TURGEN ALIMATOV
CD C 560086
Ocora / Jan '96 / Harmonia Mundi / ADA.

Alke, Bjorn

FOREVER LULU
CD DRCD 217
Dragon / Oct '89 / Roots / Cadillac / Wellard / CM / ADA.

JAZZ IN SWEDEN
CD 1072-2
Caprice / Oct '90 / CM / Complete/ Pinnacle / Cadillac / ADA.

All

ALLROY FOR PREZ
CD CRZ 004 CD
Cruz / Jan '90 / Pinnacle / Plastic Head.

ALLROY SEZ...
CD CRZ 001 CD
Cruz / Jan '90 / Pinnacle / Plastic Head.

ALLROY'S REVENGE
CD CRZ 006 CD
Cruz / Jan '90 / Pinnacle / Plastic Head.

BREAKING THINGS
CD CRZ 031CD
Cruz / Sep '93 / Pinnacle / Plastic Head.

DOT
CD CRZ 024 CD
Cruz / May '93 / Pinnacle / Plastic Head.

PERCOLATER
CD CRZ 022 CD
Cruz / May '93 / Pinnacle / Plastic Head.

All 4 One

ALL 4 ONE
So much in love / Oh girl / Better man / I swear / Down to the last drop / Without you (she's got) skillz / Breathless / Something about you / Bomb / Here if you're ready
CD 756782588-2
Atlantic / Apr '94 / Warner Music.

All About Eve

ALL ABOUT EVE
Flowers in our hair / Gypsy dance / In the clouds / Martha's harbour / Every angel / Shelter from the rain / She moved through the fair / Wild hearted woman / Never promise / What kind of fool
CD 8342602
Mercury / Aug '95 / PolyGram.

BBC LIVE IN CONCERT
CD WINCD 044
Windsong / Oct '93 / Pinnacle.

SCARLET AND OTHER STORIES
Road to your soul / Dream now / Gold and silver / Scarlet / December / Blind lemon Sam / More than the blues / Tuesday's child / Empty dancehall / Only one reason / Pearl fishermen
CD 8389652
Mercury / Aug '95 / PolyGram.

TOUCHED BY JESUS
Strange way / Farewell Mr. Sorrow / Wishing the hours away / Touched by Jesus / Dreamer / Rhythm of life / Mystery we are / Hide child / Ravens / Are you lonely / Share it with me (Only on MC and CD.)
CD 510 146 2
Mercury / Aug '91 / PolyGram.

WINTER WORDS, HITS AND RARITIES
CD 514 154-2
Mercury / Oct '92 / PolyGram.

All Souls' Orchestra

KENDRICK COLLECTION, THE (All Souls' Orchestra & Choir)
Lord is King / Servant King / Such love / Burn on / Fighter / May our worship be acceptable / May the fragrance of Jesus fill this place / Meekness and majesty
CD LANG D 003
Myrrh / '89 / Nelson Word.

PROM PRAISE AT THE ALBERT HALL (All Souls' Orchestra & Choir)
CD LANG D 001
Myrrh / '88 / Nelson Word.

PROM PRAISE FESTIVAL (Recorded Live At The Royal Albert Hall) (All Souls' Orchestra & Choir)
He's got the whole world in his hands / Give me joy / All people that on earth do dwell / Pomp and circumstance march No.4 / Let the bright seraphim / Hevenu Shalom Alechem / O happy day / Festival overture / At the river / Steal away / With loving hands / Death of Jesus / Fanfare for the common man / Easter prelude / He's alive / Come sing the praise of Jesus / Behold the man / Yours be the glory
CD LANGD 010
Alliance Music / May '95 / EMI.

All Star Big Band

BIG BAND SPECTACULAR
CD MATCD 239
Castle / Dec '92 / BMG.

All Stars

IN PHILADELPHIA 1948-49
CD 3801202
Jazz Archives / Oct '92 / Jazz Music / Discovery / Cadillac.

Allan, Johnnie

PROMISED LAND
Promised land / South to Louisiana / She's gone / Let's do it / Cry foolish heart / What'cha do / Your picture / Somebody else / Please accept my love / You got me whistling / I'll never love again / Secrets of love / Nights of misery / Cajun man / Graduation night (as you pass me by) / Please help me, I'm falling / Somewhere on Skid Row / Isle of Capri / Sweet dreams / I cried / Stranger to you / I can't wait / I'm missing you / Little fat man / Today I started loving you again / Homebound train / Let's go get drunk / Tennessee blues
CD CDCHD 380
Ace / Jun '92 / Pinnacle / Cadillac / Complete/Pinnacle.

Allan/Hallberg/Riedel

TRIO CONTROMBA
CD DRCD226
Dragon / May '88 / Roots / Cadillac / Wellard / CM / ADA.

Allaway/Antonia Quartet

SAMIZDAT
Crossing the rubicon / Next time round / Groovin' / Coopers calling / Blues for B.B. / Let this one go / Cogito ergo sum / Trick of the light / Leonard B / Peel me a grape / Samizdat / Seal it
CD CDAA 001
Mapa Music / Jan '95 / New Note.

Alldred, Bill

SWING THAT MUSIC (Alldred, Bill Goodtime Jazz Band)
CD BEARCD 31
Big Bear / Oct '90 / BMG.
CD ESSCD 246
Essential / Feb '95 / Total/BMG.

Allegro Milano

ALLEGRO MILANO PLAYS RONDO VENEZIANO
Magica melodia / La serenissima / Rondo Veneziano / Scaramucce / Visioni di venezia / Fantasia Venezia / Misteriosa Venezia / Rosso Veneziano / Musica...fantasia / Capriccio venziano / Odissea Veneziana / Carme veneziano / Venezia lunare / Andante Milano / Molto allegro / Alla turca
CD GRF 190
Tring / Jan '93 / Tring / Prism.

Allen, Carl

PICCADILLY SQUARE (Allen, Carl & Manhattan Projects)
Piccadilly Square / Autumn leaves / Round Midnight / Lullaby of birdland / Annie's mood / Biscuit man / New joy / What's new / In the still of the night / Afterthoughts
CD SJP 406
Timeless Jazz / Oct '93 / New Note.

Allen, Daevid

BANANA MOON
Time of your life / Memories / All I want is out of here / Fred the fish / White neck blooze / Stoned innocent Frankenstein / His adventures in the land of Flip / I am a bowl
CD CDLIK 63
Decal / May '90 / Charly / Swift.

DEATH OF ROCK AND OTHER ENTRANCES, THE
Death of rock / Poet for sale / Tally's birthday song / You never existed at all / Afraid / Radio gnome concert intro loop / Switch doctor / Gong ORFT invasion 1971
CD VP114 CD
Voice Print / Jan '93 / Voice Print.

LIVE 1963 (Allen, Daevid Trio)
Love is a careless sea / My head is a nightclub / Capacity travel (parts 1 - 4) / Song of the jazzman / Dear olde Benny Green is a-turning in his grave / Ya sunny WOT / Frederique la Poissonavec Frite sur le dos
CD VP 122CD
Voice Print / Mar '94 / Voice Print.

SHE
CD DMCD 1025
Demi-Monde / Feb '90 / Disc / Magnum Music Group.

TWELVE SELVES
Introdrone / Mystico Fanatico / Away away away / Colage/Bellyful of telephone / She/ Isis is calling / Collage patafisico/Divided alien manifesto / I love sex but / Wargasm / Children of the new world / O Wichitio / Sexual blueprint / Gaia / My heart's song
CD VP 111CD
Voice Print / Nov '93 / Voice Print.

VOICEPRINT RADIO SESSION
CD VPR 012CD
Voice Print / Oct '94 / Voice Print.

Allen, Eddie

ANOTHER'S POINT OF VIEW
Subject to change / Have you met Miss Jones / Ndutu / Modern times / Soul eyes / Perdido / Spur of the moment / Later

CD _____ ENJACD 80042
Enja / Oct '93 / New Note / Vital/SAM.

R 'N' B
Frick and frack / As quiet a it's kept / Clair-
voyant / Almost you / Schism / Seduction /
Quest
CD _____ ENJ 90332
Enja / Aug '95 / New Note / Vital/SAM.

Allen, Ernestine

LET IT ROLL
Let it roll / I want a little boy / Lullaby of
Broadway / Mean and evil / Love for sale /
Miss Allen's blues / Baubles, bangles and
beads / Man I love / Tea for two
CD _____ OBCCD 539
Original Blues Classics / Nov '92 / Com-
plete/Pinnacle / Wellard / Cadillac.

Allen, Geri

LIVE AT THE VILLAGE VANGUARD
(Allen, Geri & Charlie Haden/Paul
Motian)
CD _____ DIW 847
DIW / Jul '91 / Harmonia Mundi / Cadillac.

OPEN ON ALL SIDES IN THE MIDDLE
CD _____ MMCD 801013
Minor Music / Apr '90 / Vital/SAM.

PRINTMAKERS
CD _____ MMCD 8001
Minor Music / Apr '90 / Vital/SAM.

TWYLIGHT
CD _____ MMCD 801014
Minor Music / Apr '90 / Vital/SAM.

Allen, Harry

**CELEBRATION OF SAM FAIN (Allen,
Harry Trio)**
CD _____ ACD 261
Audiophile / Jan '93 / Jazz Music / Swift.

**CELEBRATION OF STRAYHORN (Allen,
Harry & Keith Ingham)**
CD _____ PCD 7101
Progressive / Apr '94 / Jazz Music.

CELEBRATION OF STRAYHORN NO.2
(Allen, Harry & Keith Ingham)
CD _____ PCD 7102
Progressive / Apr '94 / Jazz Music.

HOW LONG HAS THIS BEEN GOING ON
CD _____ PCD 7082
Progressive / '92 / Jazz Music.

**I KNOW THAT YOU KNOW (Allen, Harry
Trio)**
CD _____ CHECD 00104
Master Mix / Jul '92 / Wellard / Jazz
Music / New Note.

**I'LL NEVER BE THE SAME (Allen, Harry
& Howard Alden)**
All through the night / I won't dance / I'll
close my eyes
CD _____ CHECD 106
Master Mix / Jun '93 / Wellard / Jazz Music
/ New Note.

SOMEONE TO LIGHT UP YOUR LIFE
(Allen, Harry Quartet)
CD _____ CHECD 00100
Master Mix / Apr '92 / Wellard / Jazz
Music / New Note.

Allen, Henry 'Red'

1929-1933
CD _____ BLARGIOG 018
Classics / Dec '90 / Discovery / Jazz
Music.

1933-41
CD _____ TAXS 32
Tax / Aug '94 / Jazz Music / Wellard /
Cadillac.

COLLECTION VOL 1
CD _____ COCD 01
Collector's Classics / Dec '89 / Cadillac /
Complete/Pinnacle.

COLLECTION VOL 2
CD _____ COCD 02
Collector's Classics / Sep '92 / Cadillac /
Complete/Pinnacle.

COLLECTION VOL 3
CD _____ COCD 13
Collector's Classics / Oct '89 / Cadillac /
Complete/Pinnacle.

HENRY 'RED' ALLEN - 1936-37
CD _____ CD 590
Classic Jazz Masters / Sep '91 / Wellard /
Jazz Music / Jazz Music.

HENRY 'RED' ALLEN - 1937-41
CD _____ CLASSICS 628
Classics / '92 / Discovery / Jazz Music.

ORIGINAL 1933 TO 1941
River's takin' care of me / Believe it beloved
/ Rosetta / Body and soul / He ain't got
rhythm / K.K. boogie / Jack the bellboy /
When my dreamboat comes home
CD _____ TAXCD S-3
Tax / Apr '90 / Jazz Music / Wellard /
Cadillac.

SWING OUT
CD _____ TPZ 1037
Topaz Jazz / Jan '96 / Pinnacle / Cadillac.

Allen, Pete

BEAU SEJOUR
Seagull strut / Body and soul / I'm gonna
sit right down and write myself a letter / St.
Phillip's street breakdown / Elephant stomp
/ Roses of Picardy
CD _____ PAR 492 CD
PAR / Apr '01 / Charly / Wellard.

**JAZZ YOU LIKE IT (Allen, Pete & Clinton
Ford)**
Royal Garden blues / Melancholy baby /
Swanee River / Apple blossom time / Mood
indigo / Sailing down the Chesapeake Bay
/ Georgia / Wreck of ol' 97
CD _____ PAR 491 CD
PAR / Apr '91 / Charly / Wellard.

Allen, Rex

VOICE OF THE WEST
Tyin' knots in the Devil's tail / Moonshine
steer / Fireman cowboy / Today I started
loving you again / Windy Bill / Little Joe the
wrangler / When the work's all done this fall
/ Droop ears / Streets of Laredo / Braggin'
drunk from Wilcox / Gone girl / Catfish John
/ You never did give up on me / Just call
me lonesome / Reflex reaction
CD _____ BCD 15284
Bear Family / Aug '86 / Rollercoaster /
Direct / CM / Swift / ADA.

Allen, Ruth

RUTH ALLEN SONGBOOK
Who needs spring / You took the time / Last
time / At last I have someone / Leave me
to my dreams / All you have to do / Be a
little devil / This thing called love / Would I
still be me / Only just a phone call away /
Ah but that was a long time ago / Just
knock on any door / You're never too old /
January butterfly
CD _____ AST 1112
Astor / Dec '94 / Total/BMG.

Allen, Steve

STEVE ALLEN PLAYS JAZZ TONIGHT
Tangerine / One I love (belongs to somebody else) / Body and soul / After you've
gone / Don't cry little girl / Steve's blues /
Gone with the wind / Sinner kissed an angel
/ You go to my head / I can't get started
(with you) / Everyone can see how much I
love you / I should have told you so / Fine
and dandy
CD _____ CCD 4548
Concord Jazz / May '93 / New Note.

Allen, Terry

**PEDAL STEAL (Allen, Terry & The
Panhandle Mystery Band)**
CD _____ FATE 7655266
Fate / Apr '93 / Direct / ADA.

SILENT MAJORITY, THE
CD _____ FATE 7453266
Fate / May '93 / Direct / ADA.

SMOKIN' THE DUMMY
Heart of California / Cocaine cowboy /
Whatever happened to jesus / Helena Mon-
tana / Texas tears / Cajun roll / Feelin' easy
/ Night Cafe / Roll truck roll / Red bird /
Lubbock tornado (I don't know)
CD _____ FRCD 02
Fate / Apr / Direct / ADA.

Allen, Tex

LATE NIGHT
Wings of ceola / Things we'll never know /
You don't know what love is / Process
necessary / Mutti's buletten (Mama's ham-
burgers) / When you find a love / Estate
CD _____ MCD 5492
Muse / Feb '94 / New Note / CM.

Allen, Thomas

**IF I LOVED YOU (Allen, Thomas &
Valerie Masterson)**
CD _____ VIRCD 8317
Shanachie / Nov '93 / Koch / ADA /
Greensleeves.

**SONGS OF NORTHUMBRIA (Allen,
Thomas & Sheila Armstrong)**
CD _____ MWMCDSP 9
Mawson & Wareham / Jan '94 / BMG /
THE.

SONGS OF NORTHUMBRIA II
CD _____ MWMCDSP 12
Mawson & Wareham / Jan '94 / BMG /
THE.

Alleyne-Johnson, Ed

FLY BEFORE DAWN
CD _____ WINGCD 001
Backs / Jul '95 / Disc.

PURPLE ELECTRIC VIOLIN CONCERTO
Oxford suite / Inner city music / Improvisation / Concrete eden

CD _____ EQCD 001
Equation / Feb '93 / Disc.

ULTRAVIOLET
CD _____ EQCD 002
Equation / Jun '94 / Disc.

Allin, G.G.

HATED IN THE NATION
CD _____ RE 148CD
Reach Out International / Nov '94 /
Jetstar.

MURDER JUNKIES
CD _____ 422008
New Rose / May '94 / Direct / ADA.

TERROR IN AMERICA
CD _____ OVER 43CD
Overground / Nov '95 / SRD.

Allin, Ralph

TEA FOR THREE
Nightingale sang in Berkeley square / Hungarian dance no. 5 / Liebesleid / Cheek to
cheek / Misty / Ain't misbehavin' / Play
gypsy dance / Georgia on my mind / Tango
/ Czardas / Memory / Entertainer / Salut
d'amour / I can't give you anything but love
/ Way down yonder in New Orleans / Largo
from Winter, four seasons / Yesterday / Jo-
sika / I know him so well / Tea for two /
Summertime / Fiddler on the roof
CD _____ CDGRS 1246
Grosvenor / '91 / Target/BMG.

Allison

WAILING
CD _____ NGCD 544
Twinkle / Jul '94 / SRD / Jetstar /
Kingdom.

Allison, Bernard

NO MERCY
Rock me baby / Don't go to sleep on me /
Break 'in up / Change your way of living /
Driven wheel / Next generation / Boo boo's
boogie / Tin pan alley / Help
CD _____ INAK 9029CD
In Akustik / Dec '94 / Magnum Music
Group.

Allison, David

GUITAR GI-TAR
CD _____ LDL 1211CD
Lochshore / Mar '94 / ADA / Direct /
Duncans.

REPORTING
Birnam oak / Dreamdays / Excuse me /
Ceuta / Chinese whispers / Ishka / Spiral /
Journey / Something more comfortable /
Forgive, forget... / Border / Going home
CD _____ DUNCD 007
Dunkeld / Feb '92 / Direct / ADA / CM.

Allison, Luther

BAD LOVE
CD _____ RRCD 901295
Ruf / Aug '94 / Pinnacle / ADA.

BLUE STREAK
CD _____ TRIP 7712
Ruf / Nov '95 / Pinnacle / ADA.

HAND ME DOWN MY MOONSHINE
Good morning love / One more / Lightning
bolt / I need a friend / Castle / She's fine /
Stay with me / Farmer's child / Don't burn
my bread / You're the one / Hand me down
my moonshine / Meet me in my hometown
CD _____ INAK 9015CD
In Akustik / Jul '93 / Magnum Music Group.

LIVE '89
CD _____ RRCD 901309
Ruf / Apr '95 / Pinnacle / ADA.

LOVE ME PAPA
CD _____ ECD 260152
Evidence / Jan '92 / Harmonia Mundi /
ADA / Cadillac.

**SWEET HOME CHICAGO (Charly Blues -
Masterworks Vol. 37)**
Dust my broom / I got worries / You don't
love me / Goin' down / I'm gonna leave you
alone / Sweet home chicago
CD _____ CDBM 37
Charly / Jan '93 / Charly / THE / Cadillac.

Allison, Mose

BEST OF MOSE ALLISON, THE
CD _____ RSACD 814
Sequel / Oct '94 / BMG.

EARTH WANTS YOU, THE
Certified senior citizen / This ain't me / You
can't push people around / My ideal / Earth
wants you / Cabaret cards / Red wagon /
Variation on Dixie / What a shame / Nataral
born Malcolntent / Who's in, who's out /
Children of the future / I don't love you
CD _____ CDP 8276402
Blue Note / Dec '95 / EMI.

MY BACKYARD
Ever since I stole the blues / Big brother /
Stranger in my own hometown / Gettin'
paid waltz / That's your red waltz / Sleepy

lagoon / You call it joggin' / Sentimental fool
/ Was / Dr. Jekyll and Mr. Hyde / Long song
/ My backyard
CD _____ CDB1 93840
Blue Note / Apr '90 / EMI.

SINGS AND PLAYS
Seventh son / Eyesight to the blind / Yard-
bird suite / That's all right / Parchman farm
/ I hadn't anyone till you / Do nothin' 'til you
hear from me / Young man / Bye bye blues
CD _____ CDJZD 007
Fantasy / Sep '91 / Pinnacle / Jazz Music /
Wellard / Cadillac.

Allman Brothers

**ALLMAN BROTHERS BAND, THE
(Allman Brothers Band)**
Don't want you no more / It's not my cross
to bear / Black hearted woman / Trouble no
more / Every hungry woman / Dreams /
Whipping post
CD _____ 823 653-2
Polydor / '94 / PolyGram.

BROTHERS AND SISTERS
Wasted words / Ramblin' man / Come and
go blues / Jelly jelly / Southbound / Jessica
/ Pony boy
CD _____ 825 092-2
Polydor / Jan '89 / PolyGram.

**DECADE OF HITS 1969-1979, A (Allman
Brothers Band)**
Whipping post / Dreams / In memory of
Elizabeth Reed / One way out / Blue sky /
Wasted words / Revival / Crazy love / Little
Martha / Ain't wastin' time no more / Jes-
sica / Melissa / Southbound / Midnight rider
/ Ramblin' man / Statesboro blues
CD _____ 5111562
Polydor / Mar '92 / PolyGram.

EAT A PEACH
Ain't wastin' time no more / Le bers in A
minor / Melissa / Mountain jam / One way
out / Trouble no more / Stand back / Blue
sky / Little Martha
CD _____ 823 654-2
Polydor / Jul '88 / PolyGram.

**FILLMORE CONCERTS (Allman
Brothers Band)**
CD _____ 5172942
Polydor / Jan '93 / PolyGram.

**HELL & HIGH WATER (Best Of The
Arista Years)**
Hell and high water / Mystery woman /
From the madness of the west / I got a right
to be wrong / Angeline / Famous last words
/ Brothers of the road / Leavin' / Straight
from the heart / Judgement / Never knew
how much (I needed you)
CD _____ 07822187242
RCA / Sep '94 / BMG.

IDLE WIND SOUTH
CD _____ 833 334-2
Polydor / Mar '89 / PolyGram.

LIVE AT FILLMORE EAST (2CD Set)
Statesboro blues / (I) done somebody
wrong / They call it stormy Monday / You
don't love me / Hot lanta / In memory of
Elizabeth Reed / Whipping post
CD Set _____ 823 273-2
Polydor / Jul '88 / PolyGram.

**WHERE IT ALL BEGINS (Allman
Brothers Band)**
All night train / Sailin' cross the devil's sea
/ Back where it all begins / Soulshine / No
one to run with / Change my way of living /
Mean woman blues / Everybody's got a
mountain to climb / what's done is done /
Temptation is a gun
CD _____ 476884 2
Epic / Jul '94 / Sony.

Allman, Duane

ANTHOLOGY, AN
Hey Jude / Road of love / Goin' down slow
/ Weight / Games people play / Shake for
me / Rollin' stone / Mean old world / Layla
/ Stand back / Dreams / Little Martha
CD _____ 831 444-2
Polydor / Apr '89 / PolyGram.

Alloy

ALLOY
CD _____ VROOM 4
Engine / Aug '93 / Vital.

Allred, John

IN THE BEGINNING
CD _____ ARCD 19115
Arbors Jazz / Nov '94 / Cadillac.

Allyn, David

SOFT AS SPRING
CD _____ ACD 153
Audiophile / Jan '94 / Jazz Music / Swift.

Allyson, Karrin

AZURE-TE
How high the moon / Ornithology / Gee
baby / Bernie's tune / Night and day /
Blame it on my youth / Yardbird suite /
Good morning heartache / Stompin' at the

Savoy / Azure te / Some other time / Samba
'88
CD _____ CCD 4641
Concord Jazz / May '95 / New Note.

SWEET HOME COOKIN'
One note samba / I cover the waterfront /
Can't we be friends / Yeh yeh / Goodbye
pork pie hat / No moon at all / Sweet home
cookin' man / You are too beautiful / Social
call / Dindi / In a sentimental mood / I love
Paris
CD _____ CCD 4593
Concord Jazz / Apr '94 / New Note.

Almadraba

CANTOS DEL CAMPO Y DE LA MER
CD _____ CDH 008
Sonifolk / Dec '94 / ADA / CM.

Almanzor

TRIO DE VEUZE BRETAGNE
CD _____ AVPL 14CD
Diffusion Breizh / Apr '95 / ADA.

Almario, Justo

**JUSTO & ABRAHAM (Almario, Justo &
Abraham Laboriel)**
To him who sits on the throne / God is able
/ Medley: More love to thee/Jesus loves
me, this is know/We wo / He is exalted / I
will bless the Lord / Yahweeh / Medley:
Give thanks/Grateful heart / Amor, Algeria,
Paz / Righteousness, peace and joy / Times
of refreshing / Celebrate Jesus / Iamgo dei
(The image of God)
CD _____ 101S 8770732
101 South / May '95 / New Note.

Almeida, Laurindo

**ARTISTRY IN RHYTHM (Almeida,
Laurindo Trio)**
Chariots of fire / Astronauta / Andante / Te
amo / Artistry in rhythm / Always on my
mind / Slaughter on 10th Avenue / Up
where we belong / Almost a farewell / Liza
/ Puka shells in a whirl
CD _____ CCD 4238
Concord Jazz / Mar '94 / New Note.

**BAA-TOO-KEE (Almeida, Laurindo &
Bud Shank)**
CD _____ CD 53133
Giants Of Jazz / Nov '92 / Target/BMG /
Cadillac.

**BRAZILIAN SOUL (Almeida, Laurindo &
Charlie Byrd)**
CD _____ CCD 4150
Concord Picante / Jul '88 / New Note.

**BRAZILLIANCE VOLUME 1 (Almeida,
Laurindo & Bud Shank)**
CD _____ CDP 796 339 2
Blue Note / Jan '92 / EMI.

CHAMBER JAZZ
Dingue li bangue / Unaccustomed Bach /
Odeon / Bourree and double / Melissa / You
and I / Clair de Lune / Chopin a la breve /
Turuna
CD _____ CCD 4084
Concord Jazz / May '91 / New Note.

DANCE THE BOSSA NOVA
CD _____ CD 62055
Saludos Amigos / May '94 / Target/BMG.

**LATIN ODYSSEY (Almeida, Laurindo &
Charlie Byrd)**
Memory / Zum and ressurecion / El nino /
Gitanerias / Adios / El cavilan / Estrellita /
Turbilhao / Intermezzo malinconico
CD _____ CCD 4211
Concord Picante / Jan '90 / New Note.

**MUSIC OF THE BRAZILIAN MASTERS
(Almeida, Laurindo & Charlie Byrd)**
CD _____ CCD 4389
New Note / Oct '89 / New Note / Cadillac.

OUTRA VEZ (ONCE AGAIN)
Outra vez / Jolly crow / Danza five / Blue
skies / Goin' home / Samba de break / Bee-
thoven and Monk / Esacdo / Um a zero /
Carinhoso / Corcovado / Girl from Ipanema
/ Desafinado
CD _____ CCD 4497
Concord Jazz / Feb '92 / New Note.

**TANGO (Almeida, Laurindo & Charlie
Byrd)**
Orchids in the moonlight / Blue tango / Jal-
ousie / Los enamorados / La Rosita / Tango
alegre / La cumparsita / Moon was yellow /
Hernando's hideaway / Tanguero / Breakin
away
CD _____ CCD 4290
Concord Picante / Jul '88 / New Note.

Almighty

BLOOD, FIRE AND LIVE
Full force lovin' machine / Lay down the law
/ Destroyed / Resurrection mutha / You've
gone wild / Blood, fire and love / Wild and
wonderful / You are too seen nothin' yet
CD _____ 847 107-2
Polydor / Oct '89 / PolyGram.

BLOOD, FIRE AND LOVE
CD _____ 8413472
Polydor / Sep '89 / PolyGram.

CRANK
Ultraviolet / Wrench / Unreal thing / Jones-
town mind / Move right in / Crank and de-
ceit / United state of apathy / Welcome to
defiance / Way beyond belief / Crackdown
/ Sorry for nothing / Cheat / Shitzophrenic
CD _____ CDCHR 6086
Chrysalis / Sep '94 / EMI.

SOUL DESTRUCTION
Crucify / Free 'n' easy / Joy bang one time
/ Love religion / Bandaged knees / Praying
to the red light / Sin against the light / Little
lost sometimes / Devil's toy / What more do
you want / Hell to pay / Loaded
CD _____ 847 961-2
Polydor / Apr '91 / PolyGram.

Almond, Marc

FANTASTIC STAR
Caged / Out there / We need jealousy / Idol
(parts 1 & 2 All Gods fall) / Baby night eyes
/ Adored and explored (7" edit) / Child star
/ Looking for love (all in the wrong places) /
Addicted / Edge of heartbreak / Love to die
for / Betrayed / On the prowl / Come in
sweet assassin / Brilliant creatures / Shining
brightly
CD _____ 5286592
Some Bizarre/Mercury / Nov '95 /
PolyGram.

**MOTHER FIST AND HER FIVE
DAUGHTERS**
Mother fist / There is a bed / St. Judy /
Room below / Angel in her kiss / Mr. Sad /
Melancholy rose / Sea says / Champ / Ruby
red / Hustler
CD _____ CDFTH 2
Some Bizarre / Apr '87 / Pinnacle.

SINGLES '84-'87
Boy who came back / You have / Tender-
ness is a weakness / Stories of Johnny /
Love letters / House is haunted / Woman's
story / Ruby red / Melancholy rose / Mother
fist
CD _____ CDFTH 3
Some Bizarre / Nov '87 / Pinnacle.

STORIES OF JOHNNY
Traumas, traumas, traumas / Stories of
Johnny / House is haunted / Love letters /
Flesh is willing / Always / Contempt / I who
never / My candle burns / Love and little
white lies
CD _____ CDFTH 1
Some Bizarre / '87 / Pinnacle.

TENEMENT SYMPHONY
Meet me in my dream / Beautiful brutal
thing / I've never seen your face / Vaudeville
and burlesque / Champagne / Prelude /
Jackie / What is love / Trois chansons de
bilitis / Days of Pearly Spencer / My hand
over my heart
CD _____ 9031755182
Some Bizarre / Feb '95 / Pinnacle.

TREASURE BOX
City of nights / Waifs and strays (Grid mix)
/ King of the fools / Libertine's dream / Only
the moment (All the time in the world mix) /
Gambler / Tears run rings (La magia dance
mix) / Everything I wanted love to be / Something's gotten hold of my heart / Bittersweet (Big beat mix) / Frost comes tomorrow / She took my soul in Istanbul (Blue
mosque mix) / Stars we are (Full length mix)
/ Lover spurned (12" mix) / Real evil / Exotica rose / Desperate hours (Extended flamenco mix) / Old Jack's charm / These my
dreams are yours (Through the night mix) /
Sea still sings (Demo) / Madame de la luna
(Demo) / Death's diary (Demo) / Toreador in
the rain (Demo) / Orpheus in red velvet
(Demo) / Sensualist (Ultimate ecstacy mix)
CD Set _____ CDMATBOX 1
Parlophone / Aug '95 / EMI.

TWELVE YEARS OF TEARS
Tears run rings / Champagne / Bedsitter /
Mr. Sad / There is a bed / Youth / If you go
away / Jackie / Desperate hours / Waifs and
strays / Something's gotten hold of my
heart / What makes a man / Tainted love /
Say hello, wave goodbye
CD _____ 450992033-2
Some Bizarre / Apr '93 / Pinnacle.

VIRGIN'S TALE (VOL.1)
Stories of Johnny / Love letter / Blond boy
/ House is Haunted / Broken bracelets /
Cara a cara / Heel / Salty dog / Plague /
Little white cloud that cried / For one mo-
ment / Just good friends
CD _____ CDVM 9010
Virgin / Sep '92 / EMI.

VIRGIN'S TALE (VOL.2)
Gyp of the blood / World full of people /
Black lullabye / Pirate Jenny / Surabaya
Johnny / Two sailors on the beach / Anar-
coma / Jackal jackal / Broken hearted and
beautiful / I'm sick of you tasting of some-
body else
CD _____ CDVM 9011
Virgin / Sep '92 / EMI.

Alomar, Carlos

DREAM GENERATOR
Hallucination / Siamese dreams / Global al-
pha / Winkin' blinkin' and nod / Insomniac
/ Dream generator / R.E.M. / Feline lullaby
(Sam's song)

CD _____ 259.964
Private Music / Nov '89 / BMG.

Aloof

COVER THE CRIME
CD _____ 0630102322
East West / May '95 / Warner Music.

Aloof Proof

INSIDE THE QUIET
CD _____ CDCB 0103
Carbon Base / Jun '95 / Plastic Head.

Alpamayo

FOLKLORE DE PERU Y ECUADOR
CD _____ EUCD 1220
ARC / Sep '93 / ARC Music / ADA.

MUSIC FROM PERU & ECUADOR
CD _____ EUCD 1184
ARC / Apr '92 / ARC Music / ADA.

Alperin, Mikhail

**WAVE OF SORROW (Alperin, Mikhail &
Arkady Shilkloper)**
Song / Poem / Wave of sorrow / Toccata /
Unisons / Introduction and dance / Short
storey / Prelude in B minor / Miniature /
Epilogue
CD _____ 8396212
ECM / Jan '90 / New Note.

Alpert, Herb

MIDNIGHT SUN
Midnight sun / All the things you are /
Someone to watch over me / In the wee
small hours / Friends / Taste of honey /
Mona Lisa / I've grown accustomed to her
face / Silent tears and roses / Smile
CD _____ 3953912
A&M / Jun '92 / PolyGram.

VERY BEST OF HERB ALPERT
Lonely bull / Taste of honey / Tijuana taxi /
Spanish flea / Zorba the Greek / What now
my love / Casino Royale / This guy's in love
with you / Without her / Jerusalem / Rise /
Rotation / Keep your eye on me / Diamonds
/ Jump Street
CD _____ CDMID 170
A&M / Oct '92 / PolyGram.

Alpert, Pauline

PAULINE ALPERT
CD _____ GEMMCD 9201
Pearl / Dec '95 / Harmonia Mundi.

Alpha & Omega

**ALMIGHTY JAH (Alpha & Omega Meet
Dub Judah)**
CD _____ AOCD 077
Alpha & Omega / Oct '92 / Jetstar / SRD /
Greensleeves.

DANIEL/KING & QUEEN
CD _____ A&OCD 1
Alpha & Omega / Nov '93 / Jetstar / SRD /
Greensleeves.

DUB PLATE SELECTION VOLUME 1
CD _____ AOCD 95
Alpha & Omega / Apr '95 / Jetstar / SRD /
Greensleeves.

EVERYDAY LIFE
CD _____ AOCD 093
Alpha & Omega / Jun '93 / Jetstar / SRD /
Greensleeves.

FAITH IN THE DARK
CD _____ A&OCD 094
Alpha & Omega / Mar '94 / Jetstar / SRD /
Greensleeves.

OVERSTANDING/WATCH & PRAY
CD _____ AO27CD
Alpha & Omega / Sep '93 / Jetstar / SRD /
Greensleeves.

SIGNS, THE
CD _____ BTT 0292
Buback / Aug '94 / SRD.

SOUND SYSTEM DUB
CD _____ RUSCD 8216
Roir USA / Oct '95 / Plastic Head.

TREE OF LIFE
CD _____ A&OCD 96
Alpha & Omega / Nov '95 / Jetstar / SRD /
Greensleeves.

Alpha Band

**INTERVIEWS (Alpha Band & T-Bone
Burnett)**
Interviews / Cheap perfume / Ten figures /
Dogs / Last chance to dance / East of East
/ You angel you / Spark in the dark / Rich
man / Mighty man / Back in my baby's arms
again
CD _____ EDCD 272
Edsel / Jul '91 / Pinnacle / ADA.

Alpha Blondy

BEST OF ALPHA BLONDY
CD _____ SHANCD 43075

Shanachie / Oct '90 / Koch / ADA /
Greensleeves.

COCODY ROCK
Cocody rock / Tere / Super powers / Inter-
planetary revolution / Fangandan kameleba
/ Bory samory
CD _____ SH 64011
Shanachie / Dec '94 / Koch / ADA /
Greensleeves.

**JERUSALEM (Blondy, Alpha & The
Wailers)**
Jerusalem / Politique / Bloodshed in Africa
/ I love Paris / Kalachnikov love / Travailler
c'est trop dur / Mina / Poultevard de la mort
/ Dji
CD _____ STCD 1019
Sterns / Dec '87 / Sterns / CM.

Alphabet Soup

LAYIN' LOW IN THE CUT
Opression / Take a ride / First day, last night
/ What I am / Meditate / For your conscious
/ Walkin' roots / Zone / Year 2000 / Streets
/ Music in my head
CD _____ MR 0822
Mammoth / Feb '95 / Vital.

Alphaville

FOREVER YOUNG
Victory of love / Summer in Berlin / Big in
Japan / To Germany with love / Fallen angel
/ Forever young / In the mood / Sounds like
a melody / Jet set / Lies
CD _____ 2404812
WEA / Nov '84 / Warner Music.

Alston, Gerald

ALWAYS IN THE MOOD
CD _____ 5301342
Motown / Jan '93 / PolyGram.

Alt

ALTITUDE
We're all men / Penelope tree / When the
winter comes / Favourite girl / Swim / Ref-
uge tree / What you've done / Second swim
/ Girlfriend Guru / Mandala / I decided to fly
/ Day you were born / Halfway round the
world
CD _____ CDPCS 7377
Parlophone / Jun '95 / EMI.

Alta Moda

ALTA MODA
Train / Cool love / Julian / Wait / Push /
Back to back / Classique / No town (in
particular) / Draw a straight line / My million-
aire / Cool love (cooler re-mix) / Push (push
push in the mix)
CD _____ PCOM 1096
President / Aug '88 / Grapevine / Target/
BMG / Jazz Music / President.

Altan

FIRST TEN YEARS, THE (1986-1995)
CD _____ GLCD 1153
Green Linnet / May '95 / Roots / CM /
Direct / ADA.

HARVEST STORM
Pretty Peg/New ships a-sailing/Bird's nest/
Man from Bundoran / Donal Agus Morag /
King of the pipers / Seamus O'Shanahan's/
Walking in Liffey Street / Mo choill / Snowy
path / Drowsy Maggie/Rakish Paddy/Har-
vest storm / Si do Mhaimeo / Marley's/Mill
na maidi / Rosses highlands / Nobleman's
wedding / Bog an Lochain/Margaret reel/
Humours of Westport / Dobbin's flowery
vale
CD _____ GLCD 1117
Green Linnet / '92 / Roots / CM / Direct /
ADA.

HORSE WITH A HEART
Curlew/McDermott's reel/Three scones of
Boxty / Lass of Glenshee / Con Cassidy's
and Neil Gow's highlands/Moll and Tiarna /
McSweeney's reels / Road to Durham / An
t-Oilean Ur / An grianan/Horse with a heart
/ Bhean udai thall / Welcome home grainne/
Con McGinley's / Tuirse mo chroi / Come
ye bey atholl/Kitty O'Connor / An feochan /
Paddy's trip to Scotland/Dinky's/Shetland
fiddlers
CD _____ GLCD 1095
Green Linnet / Aug '89 / Roots / CM / Direct
/ ADA.

ISLAND ANGEL
Tommy Peoples/The windmill/Fintan Mc-
Manus / Brid og ni Mhaille / Fernanagh
highland/Donegal highland/John Doherty's
/ King George IV / An Mhaighdean Mhara /
Andy De Jarlis/Ingonish/Mrs. McGhee / Hu-
mours of Andytown/Kylebrack rambler/
Gladstone / Dulaman / Mazurka / Jug of
punch / Glory reel/Heathery cruach / An
cailin Gaelach / Drumnagarry/Pirrie wirrie/
Big John's / Island angel / Preety Peg/New
ships a-sailing/Birds nest/Man from
Bundoran
CD _____ GLCD 1137
Green Linnet / Oct '93 / Roots / CM / Direct
/ ADA.

RED CROW, THE
CD _____ GLCD 1109
Green Linnet / Mar '92 / Roots / CM / Direct / ADA.

Altar
YOUTH AGAINST CHRIST
CD _____ DOOO 33
Displeased / Oct '94 / Plastic Head.

Altar Of The King
ALTAR OF THE KING
CD _____ RTN 41203
Rock The Nation / Feb '95 / Plastic Head.

Altena, Maarten
CITIES AND STREETS
CD _____ ARTCD 6082
Hat Art / Aug '91 / Harmonia Mundi / ADA / Cadillac.

CODE (Altena, Maarten Ensemble)
CD _____ ARTCD 6094
Hat Art / Jan '92 / Harmonia Mundi / ADA / Cadillac.

RIF (Altena, Maarten Octet)
CD _____ ARTCD 6056
Hat Art / Nov '90 / Harmonia Mundi / ADA / Cadillac.

Alter Ego
ALTER EGO
CD _____ HHCD 6
Harthouse / Jun '94 / Disc / Warner Music.

DECODING THE HACKER MYTH
CD _____ HHCD 016
Harthouse / Feb '96 / Disc / Warner Music.

LYCRA
CD _____ HH 087CD
Harthouse / Feb '96 / Disc / Warner Music.

Alter Ego
MEMOIRES D'OUTREMER
CD _____ GL 4035CD
Green Linnet / Nov '95 / Roots / CM / Direct / ADA.

MEMORIES FROM OVERSEAS
CD _____ XENO 4035CD
Xenophile / Sep '95 / Direct / ADA.

Altered Images
HAPPY BIRTHDAY
Happy birthday / Love and kisses / Real toys / Idols / Legionaire / Faithless / Beckoning strings / Midnight / Day's wait / Leave me alone / Insects
CD _____ 932944-2
Pickwick/Sony Collector's Choice / Mar '94 / Carlton Home Entertainment / Pinnacle / Sony.
CD _____ 4805282
Columbia / May '95 / Sony.

PINKY BLUE
Pinky blue / See those eyes / Forgotten / Little brown head / See you later / Song sung blue / Funny funny me / Think that it might / I could be happy / Jump jump / Goodnight and I wish
CD _____ 983227 2
Pickwick/Sony Collector's Choice / Feb '94 / Carlton Home Entertainment / Pinnacle / Sony.

Altern 8
FULL ON MASK HYSTERIA
CD _____ TOPCD 1
Network / Jun '92 / Sony / 3MV.

Alternative Radio
WOOD, WIRE & SKIN
CD _____ PULCD 3
Pulse / Jul '95 / Grapevine.

Alternative TV
IMAGE HAS CRACKED - ATV COLLECTION
Alternatives / Action time vision / Why don't you do me right / Good times / Still life / Viva la rock 'n' roll / Nasty little lonely / Red / Splitting in two / Love lies limp / Life / How much longer / You bastard / Another coke / Life after life / Life after dub / Force is blind / Lost in a room / How much longer (different version) / You bastard (different version)
CD _____ CDPUNK 24
Anagram / Jan '94 / Pinnacle.

LIVE AT THE RAT CLUB 77
CD _____ OBSESSCD 005
Jungle / Sep '93 / Disc.

MY LIFE AS A CHILD STAR
CD _____ OVER 39CD
Overground / Oct '94 / SRD.

RADIO SESSIONS, THE
CD _____ OVER 44CD
Overground / Sep '95 / SRD.

Alternatives
BUZZ
Pudgy / Sex face / Black hole / Half cheek / sneek / Nubbing
CD _____ SST 245 CD
SST / Oct '89 / Plastic Head.

Altschul, Barry
VIRTUOSI (Altschul, Barry & Paul Bley/ Gary Peacock)
CD _____ 123844-2
IAI / May '92 / Harmonia Mundi / Cadillac.

Alvarez, Javier
PAPALOTL - TRANSFORMACIONES EXOTICAS
CD _____ CDSDL 390
Saydisc / Mar '94 / Harmonia Mundi / ADA / Direct.

Alvin & The Chipmunks
CHIPMUNK CHRISTMAS
It's beginning to look like Christmas / Chipmunk jingle bells / Chipmunk song / Spirit of Christmas / Have yourself a merry little Christmas / Crashup's Christmas / Here comes Santa Claus / Silent night / Sleigh ride / Deck the halls with boughs of holly / We wish you a Merry Christmas
CD _____ 4727402
Columbia / Nov '95 / Sony.

Alvin, Dave
BLUE BLVD
CD _____ DFGCD 8424
New Rose / Jun '94 / Direct / ADA.

EVERY NIGHT ABOUT THIS TIME
Every night about this time / 4th of July / Long white cadillac / Romeo's escape / Brother (on the line) / Jubilee train / Border radio / Fire away / New tattoo / You got me / I wish it were Saturday night
CD _____ FIENDCD 90
Demon / Apr '87 / Pinnacle / ADA.

KING OF CALIFORNIA
CD _____ HCD 8054
Hightone / Oct '94 / ADA / Koch.

MUSEUM OF HEART
CD _____ HCD 8049
Hightone / Jul '94 / ADA / Koch.

Alvin, Phil
COUNTRY FAIR 2000
CD _____ HCD 8056
Hightone / Nov '94 / ADA / Koch.

Always August
LARGENESS WITH (W)HOLES
CD _____ SST 135 CD
SST / Oct '87 / Plastic Head.

Alzir, Bud
BUD ALZIR
CD _____ HANCD 2
Hansome / Oct '95 / Pinnacle.

AM 4
AND SHE ANSWERED
CD _____ 8396202
ECM / Nov '89 / New Note.

Amaro Del
WORLD OF GYPSY MUSIC (Amaro Del & Big String Orchestra)
CD _____ 323055
Koch / Feb '94 / Koch.

Amarok
CANCIONES DE LOS MUNDOS PERDIDOS
CD _____ 21066CD
Sonifolk / Nov '95 / ADA / CM.

Amayon
PURULENCE SPLIT
CD _____ CDAR 016
Adipocre / Feb '94 / Plastic Head.

Amazing Blondel
AMAZING BLONDEL/A FEW FACES
CD _____ EDCD 421
Edsel / Mar '95 / Pinnacle / ADA.

Amazone
DEMONS
CD _____ NZ 019CD
Nova Zembla / Nov '94 / Plastic Head.

Ambassadors Of Funk
MONSTER JAM
CD _____ NOMIS 1 CD
Living Beat / Feb '89 / Grapevine.

Ambel, Eric
ROSCOE'S GANG
If you gotta go, go now / Total destruction to your mind / Girl that ain't got / Forever came today / Thirty days in the workhouse / Power lounger theme / Don't wanna be your friend / I waited for you / Next to the last waltz / Loose talk / You must have we confused / Vampire blues
CD _____ FIENDCD 157
Demon / Oct '89 / Pinnacle / ADA.

Ambient Warrior
DUB JOURNEYS
CD _____ CDLINC 007
Lion Inc. / Nov '95 / Jetstar / SRD.

Ambrose
AMBROSE (Ambrose & His Orchestra)
Don't let that moon get away / Says my heart / Love bug will bite you / Two sleepy people / Rhythm's OK in harlem / Blue skies are round the corner / Goodnight to you all / I've got a pocketful of dreams / Sailor, where art thou / While a cigarette was burning / Lord and Lady Whoozis / Moon or no moon / Lambeth Walk / Chestnut tree / I may be poor but I'm honest / Oh they're tough, mighty tough, in the West / In a little French casino / Fifty million robins can't be wrong / Smile when you say goodbye / Sympathy
CD _____ CDAJA 5066
Living Era / Feb '90 / Koch.

AT THE MAYFAIR HOTEL 1027 36 (Ambrose & His Orchestra)
Dance little lady / I'm more than satisfied / My heart stood still / My dream memory / Nicolette / Didn't I tell you / Little dream nest / Song of the sea / Somewhere / Then I'll be tired of you / Punch and Judy show / Ambrose's jubilee cavalcade / Humming to myself / For you / Lovable and sweet / 'S wonderful / Me and the man in the moon / Take your finger out of your mouth / Whispering pines of Nevada / Birth of the blues / Adoree' / Chirp chirp / Roll away clouds
CD _____ PASTCD 9713
Flapper / '90 / Pinnacle.

GLAMOUR OF THE THIRTIES (Ambrose & His Orchestra)
CD _____ PASTCD 7055
Flapper / Nov '94 / Pinnacle.

MIDNIGHT IN MAYFAIR (Ambrose & His Orchestra)
CD _____ CDSVL 207
Saville / Mar '90 / Conifer.

SUN HAS GOT HIS HAT ON, THE (Ambrose & His Orchestra)
I can't believe it's true / After tonight we say goodbye / Sun has got his hat on / Day by day / At eventide / Clouds will soon roll by / Streamline strut / Dames / Big Ben is saying goodnight / Memphis blues / I only have eyes for you / Who's been polishing the Sun / La cucarachn / Home James and don't spare the horses / Yip Neddy / I'm gonna wash my hands of you / Stay as sweet as you are / No, no, a thousand times no
CD _____ 2 BUR 002
Burlington / Sep '88 / CM.

Ambush
AMBUSH
CD _____ HHCD 5
Harthouse / Apr '94 / Disc / Warner Music.

LACH
CD _____ CC 008CD
Common Cause / May '95 / Plastic Head / SRD.

PIGS
CD _____ EFA 124062
Common Cause / Dec '95 / Plastic Head / SRD.

Amebix
ARISE
CD _____ VIRUS 46CD
Alternative Tentacles / Jul '94 / Pinnacle.

Amen Corner
BEST OF AMEN CORNER - HELLO SUSIE, THE
CD _____ CSL 6033
Immediate / Nov '93 / Charly / Target/ BMG.

NATIONAL WELSH COAST LIVE EXPLOSION COMPANY
MacArthur Park / Baby, do the Philly dog / You're my girl (I don't want to discuss it) / Shake a tail feather / So fine / (Our love) In the pocket / Penny Lane / High in the sky / Gin house / Bend me, shape me / (If paradise is) half as nice
CD _____ CDIMM 016
Charly / Feb '94 / Charly / THE / Cadillac.

VERY BEST OF AMEN CORNER
CD _____ 12360
Laserlight / Aug '94 / Target/BMG.

America
AMERICA
Riverside / Sandman / Three roses / Children / Here / I need you / Rainy day / Never found the time / Clarice / Donkey jaw / Pigeon song
CD _____ 7599272572
WEA / Jan '93 / Warner Music.

AMERICA LIVE
CD _____ 7599266902
WEA / Jan '96 / Warner Music.

HEARTS
Daisy Jane / Half a man / Midnight / Bell Tree / Old Virginia / People in the valley / Company / Woman tonight / Story of a teenager / Sister golden hair / Tomorrow / Seasons
CD _____ 9362459862
WEA / Jun '95 / Warner Music.

HISTORY - AMERICA'S GREATEST HITS
Horse with no name / I need you Sandman / Ventura highway / Don't cross the river / Only in your heart / Muskrat love / Tin man / Lonely people / Sister golden hair / Daisy Jane / Woman tonight
CD _____ 256169
WEA / Jan '87 / Warner Music.

HOURGLASS
Young moon / Hope / Sleeper train / Mirror to mirror / Garden of peace / Call of the world / Whole wide world / Close to the wind / Greenhouse / Ports-of-call / Everyone I meet is from California / You can do magic
CD _____ AGCD 494
American Gramophone / Jun '04 / New Note.

VIEW FROM THE GROUND
You can do magic / Never be lonely / You girl / Inspector Mills / Love on the vine / Desperate love / Right before your eyes / Jody / Sometimes lovers / Even the score
CD _____ NSPCD 509
Connoisseur / Mar '95 / Pinnacle.

American Boys' Choir
ON CHRISTMAS DAY
First Noel / Personent hodie / Sussex carol / Once in Royal David's City / Deck the halls with boughs of holly / Jesus Christ the apple tree / Twelve days of Christmas / O come all ye faithful (Adeste Fidelis) / God rest ye merry gentlemen / I sing of a maiden / Hark the herald angels sing / Salvator mundi
CD _____ RCD 30129
Rykodisc / Dec '92 / Vital / ADA.

American Breed
BEND ME SHAPE ME - BEST OF THE AMERICAN BREED
CD _____ VSD 5493
Varese Sarabande/Colosseum / Oct '94 / Pinnacle / Silva Screen.

American Jazz Orchestra
MUSIC OF JIMMY LUNCEFORD, THE
Lunceford special / What's your story / Morning glory / Belgium stomp / I'm alone with you / Yard dog Mazurka / Hi spook / For dancers only / Uptown blues / Annie Laurie / Margie / I wanna hear swing songs / Organ grinder swing
CD _____ 8208462
Limelight / May '92 / PolyGram.

PLAYS THE MUSIC OF JIMMIE LUNCEFORD
CD _____ MM 65072
Music Masters / Oct '94 / Nimbus.

American Jazz Quintet
FROM BAD TO BADDER
CD _____ 120114-2
Black Saint / Mar '92 / Harmonia Mundi / Cadillac.

American Music Club
CALIFORNIA
Firefly / Somewhere / Laughing stock / Lonely / Pale skinny girl / Blue and grey shirt / Bad liquor / Now you're defeated / Jenny / Western sky / Highway 5 / Last harbour
CD _____ FMCD 1
Demon / Apr '93 / Pinnacle / ADA.

EVERCLEAR
Why won't you stay / Rise / Miracle on 8th street / Ex-girlfriend / Crabwalk / Confidential agent / Sick of food / Dead part of you / Royal cafe / What the pillars of salt held up
CD _____ A 015D
Alias / Oct '91 / Vital.

KEEP ME AROUND
Keep me around / My role as the most hated singer in the local / Memo from aquatic park (CD) / Walking tune (CD) / Challenger (Home demo/MC) / Memo from Bernal Heights (MC)
CD _____ VSCDG 1464
Virgin / Jun '93 / EMI.

17

MERCURY
Gratitude walks / If I had a hammer / Challenger / I've been a mess / Hollywood 4-5-92 / What Godzilla said to God when his name wasn't... / Keep me around / Dallas, airports, bodybags / Apology for an accident / Over and done / Johnny Mathis' feet / Hopes and dreams of heaven's 10,000 whores / More hopes and dreams / Will you find me / Book of life
CD _____ CDV 2708
Virgin / Mar '93 / EMI.

SAN FRANCISCO
Fearless / It's your birthday / Can you help me / Love doesn't belong to anyone (not on LP) / Wish the world away / How many six packs does it take to screw in a light / Cape Canaveral (not on LP) / Hello Amsterdam / Revolving door / In the shadow of the valley (not on LP) / What holds the world together / I broke my promise / Thorn in my side is gone / I'll be gone / Fearless reprise (not on LP) / I just took my two sleeping pills and now I'm like a... (LP only)
CD _____ CDV 2752
Virgin / Sep '94 / EMI.

UNITED KINGDOM
Here they roll down / Dreamers of the dream / Never mind / United Kingdom / Dream is gone / Heaven of your hands / Kathleen / Hula maiden / Animal pen / California (Available on CD only)
CD _____ FMCD 2
Demon / Apr '93 / Pinnacle / ADA.

American Patrol Orchestra
SOUND OF THE BIG BANDS
Sounds of the big bands / Little brown jug / Frenesi / You made me love you / Listen to the mockingbird / Dark eyes / Why don't you do right / Bernie's tune / Cute / Patricia / Mr. Luck / Sing, sing, sing / Moonglow / Wild root / Blue eyes / I concentrate on you / When the saints go marching in / Crazy rhythm / Lonesome road / Swanee river / I've heard that song before / Clementine / Loch Lomond / Peter Gunn
CD _____ PWKM 4107
Carlton Home Entertainment / Jun '92 / Carlton Home Entertainment.

American Poijat
FINISH BRASS IN USA
CD _____ GVCD 810
Global Village / Mar '95 / ADA / Direct.

American Standard
WONDERLAND
CD _____ LF 177CD
Lost & Found / Jul '95 / Plastic Head.

Amhario
1990'S
CD _____ CDLINC 002
Lion Inc. / Jul '95 / Jetstar / SRD.

aMiniature
DEPTH FIVE RATE SIX
Physical climber / No bonds / Featurist / Weepo / Maestro / Ouisghian zodahs in panoply / Towner on the B side / Foreign room / Shadowned / Last night in Sakura's / Zero in trust / Hiker atlas
CD _____ 72740-2
Restless / Feb '94 / Vital.

MURK TIME CRUISER
He, the bad feeler / Peddler's talk / Bores spy / Maximun accident / Secret enemy / Prizefighters / Signer's strut / Murk time cruiser / Flux is flux / Long live soul miner
CD _____ 727882
Restless / Apr '95 / Vital.

Amisi, Reddy
PRUDENCE
CD _____ 503802
Declic / Apr '95 / Jetstar.

AMM
AMMUSIC 1966
CD _____ RERAMMCD
Recommended / '90 / These / ReR Megacorp.

NAMELESS UNCARVED BLOCK
CD _____ MR 20
Matchless / '90 / These / ReR Megacorp / Cadillac.

AMM III
IT HAD BEEN AN ORDINARY ENOUGH DAY IN PUEBLO, COLORADO.
Radioactivity / Convergence / Kline / Spitlefields' Slide / For A
CD _____ 8432062
ECM / May '91 / New Note.

Ammerians Octet
NOORDERZON
CD _____ BVHAASTCD 9306
Bvhaast / Oct '93 / Cadillac.

Ammons, Albert
ALBERT AMMONS 1936-39
CD _____ CLASSICS 715
Classics / Jul '93 / Discovery / Jazz Music.

Ammons, Gene
BOSS IS BACK, THE
CD _____ PCD 24129
Prestige / Dec '95 / Complete/Pinnacle / Cadillac.

BOSS TENOR
Hittin' the jug / Close your eyes / My romance / Canadian sunset / Blue Ammons / Confirmation / Savoy
CD _____ OJCCD 297
Original Jazz Classics / Feb '93 / Wellard / Jazz Music / Cadillac / Complete/Pinnacle.

GROOVE BLUES (Ammons, Gene All Stars)
CD _____ OJCCD 723
Original Jazz Classics / Nov '95 / Wellard / Jazz Music / Cadillac / Complete/Pinnacle.

JAMMIN' WITH GENE (Ammons, Gene All Stars)
CD _____ OJCCD 211
Original Jazz Classics / Nov '95 / Wellard / Jazz Music / Cadillac / Complete/Pinnacle.

PREACHIN'
CD _____ OJCCD 792
Original Jazz Classics / Nov '95 / Wellard / Jazz Music / Cadillac / Complete/Pinnacle.

RED TOP - THE SAVOY SESSIONS
El sino / Ineta / Wild Leo / Just chips / Street of dreams / Good time blues / Travellin' light / Red top / Fuzzy / Stairway to the stars / Jim Dawg / Big slam part 1 / Big slam part 2
CD _____ SV 0242
Savoy Jazz / Oct '94 / Conifer / ADA.

Amon Duul
AIRS ON A SHOESTRING
Hymn for the hardcore / Pioneer / One moment of anger is two pints of blood / Marcus Lied / Olaf
CD _____ CDTB 043
Thunderbolt / Aug '87 / Magnum Music Group.

DIE LOSUNG (Amon Duul & Bob Calvert)
Big wheel / Urban Indian / Adrenalin Rush / Visions of fire / Drawn to the flame / They call it home / Die Losung / Drawn to the flame (part 2)
CD _____ CDTB 115
Thunderbolt / '91 / Magnum Music Group.

FOOL MOON
Who who / Tribe / Tik tok song / Haupmotor / Hymn for the hardcore
CD _____ CDTL 011
The CD Label / Nov '89 / Jazz Music / THE.

FULL MOON
CD _____ CDTB 117
Thunderbolt / Mar '95 / Magnum Music Group.

HAWK MEETS PENGUIN,VOL.1
One moment of anger is two pints of blood / Meditative music from the third o before the p / Meditative music from the third o before the p #2
CD _____ CDTB 102
Thunderbolt / Jun '92 / Magnum Music Group.

MEETING OF THE MENMACHINES
Pioneer / Old one / Marcus Leid / Song / Thing's aren't always what they seem / Rundi drummer's nightmare
CD _____ CDTB 107
Magnum Music / Mar '93 / Magnum Music Group.

Amorphis
BLACK WINTER DAY
CD _____ NB 1172
Nuclear Blast / Mar '95 / Plastic Head.

KARELAIN ISTHMUS
CD _____ NB 072CD
Nuclear Blast / Oct '95 / Plastic Head.

TALES FROM 1000 LAKES
CD _____ NBCD 097
Nuclear Blast / Jun '94 / Plastic Head.

Amos, Tori
BOYS FOR PELE
Beauty queen / Horses / Blood roses / Father Lucifer / Professional widow / Mr. Zebra / Marianne / Caught a lite sneeze / Muhammad my friend / Hey Jupiter / Way down / Little Amsterdam / Talula / Not the Red Baron / Agent Orange / Doughnut song / In the springtime of his voodoo / Putting the damage on / Twinkle
CD _____ 7567828622
East West / Jan '96 / Warner Music.

LITTLE EARTHQUAKES
Crucify / Girl / Silent all these years / Precious things / Winter / Happy phantom /

China / Leather / Mother / Tear in your hand / Me and a gun / Little earthquakes
CD _____ 7567823582
East West / Jan '92 / Warner Music.

UNDER THE PINK
Pretty good year / God / Bells for her / Past the mission / Baker baker / Wrong band / Waitress / Cornflake girl / Icicle / Cloud on my tongue / Space dog / Yes, Anastasia
CD _____ 756782567-2
East West / Jan '94 / Warner Music.

Amps
PACER
Pacer / Tipp city / I am decided / Mom's drunk / Bragging party / Hoverin' / First revival / Full on idle / Breaking the split screen barrier / Empty glasses / She's a girl / Dedicated
CD _____ CAD 5016CD
4AD / Oct '95 / Disc.

Amsallem, Franck
REGARDS (Amsallem, Franck & Tim Ries Quartet)
CD _____ FRLCD 020
Freelance / Nov '93 / Harmonia Mundi / Cadillac / Koch.

Amuedo, Leonardo
DOLPHIN DANCE
CD _____ CHR 70008
Challenge / Aug '95 / Direct / Jazz Music / Cadillac / ADA.

Amundson, Monti
MEAN 18, THE
CD _____ TRACD 9914
Tramp / Jul '93 / Direct / ADA / CM.

An Emotional Fish
EMOTIONAL FISH, AN
Celebrate / Blue / Julian / Change / That demon jive / Grey matter / Lace Virginia / All I am / Colours / Brick it up
CD _____ 9031721492
WEA / Aug '90 / Warner Music.

JUNKPUPPETS
Rain / Harmony central / Sister change / If God was a girl / Careless child / Star / Hole in my heaven / Innocence / Half moon / Digging this hole / Yeah yeah yeah
CD _____ 450992357-2
WEA / May '93 / Warner Music.

An Teallach Ceilidh Band
SHIP IN FULL SAIL, A
Reels / Marches / Jigs / Song / Slip jig / Waltz / Slow air and reel / Polkas
CD _____ LCOM 5237
Lismor / Aug '94 / Lismor / Direct / Duncans / ADA.

Anacrusis
MANIC IMPRESSIONS
CD _____ CDZORRO 23
Metal Blade / Jul '91 / Pinnacle.

REASON
Stop me / Not forgotten / Silent crime / Afraid to feel / Vital / Terrified / Wrong / Misshapen intent / Child inside / Quick to doubt
CD _____ CDATV 9
Active / Feb '90 / Pinnacle.

SCREAMS & WHISPERS
Sound the alarm / Sense of will / Too many prophets / Release / Division / Tool of seperation / Grateful / Screaming breath / My soul's affliction / Driven / Brotherhood / Release (Remix)
CD _____ CDZORR 059
Metal Blade / May '93 / Pinnacle.

Anam
ANAM
CD _____ CACD 001CD
CACD / Apr '95 / ADA.

SAOIRSE
CD _____ CACD 002CD
CACD / Apr '95 / ADA.

Anao Atao
ESOTERIC STONES
Esoteric stones / Ros Keltek's favourite / Other side of Carna / Forest cry / International waters / Tinner's puzzle / An Gerrans / Quadrilles / Marrow / The Syntax's head / Yntra Deu Dyr
CD _____ KESCD 001
Kesson / Jul '94 / CM.

Anastasia Screamed
LAUGHING DOWN THE LIMEHOUSE
CD _____ NECK CD 2
Roughneck / Sep '90 / Disc.

MOONSHINE
CD _____ NECKCD 007
Roughneck / Oct '91 / Disc.

Anathema
PENTECOST 3
CD _____ CDMVILE 51
Peaceville / Mar '95 / Pinnacle.

SILENT ENIGMA, THE
Restless oblivion / Sunset of age / Silent enigma / Shroud of frost / Nocturnal emission / Dying wish / Alone / Cerulean twilight / Black orchid
CD _____ CDVILE 52
Peaceville / Oct '95 / Pinnacle.

Anche Passe
ENTRE TARENTELLE
CD _____ Y 225032CD
Silex / Dec '93 / ADA.

Ancient
SVARTALVHEIM
CD _____ POSH 006CD
Osmose / Jan '95 / Plastic Head.

Ancient Future
ASIAN FUSION
Prelude / Bookenka (the adventurer) / Trader / Mezgoof / Empress / Ja nam / Sunda straits / Morning sung / Sumbatico / Dusk song of the fisherman / Ladakh / Garuda
CD _____ ND 63023
Narada / Jun '93 / New Note / ADA.

NATURAL RHYTHMS
CD _____ PH 9006CD
Philo / Feb '94 / Direct / CM / ADA.

And Also The Trees
AND ALSO THE TREES
CD _____ NORMAL 85CD
Normal/Okra / Mar '94 / Direct / ADA.

EVENING OF THE 24TH
CD _____ NEW ROSE LEX 8CD
Normal/Okra / Mar '94 / Direct / ADA.

FAREWELL TO THE SHADE
Prince Rupert / Nobody Inn / Lady D'Arbanville / Pear tree / Horse fair / MacBeth's head / Belief in the rose / Misfortunes / Ill omen
CD _____ NORMAL 114CD
Normal/Okra / Mar '94 / Direct / ADA.

FROM HORIZON TO HORIZON
CD _____ NORMAL 154CD
Normal/Okra / Mar '94 / Direct / ADA.

GREEN IS THE SEA
CD _____ NORMAL 134CD
Normal/Okra / Mar '94 / Direct / ADA.

KLAXON, THE
CD _____ NORM 164CD
Normal/Okra / Mar '94 / Direct / ADA.

MILLPOND YEARS, THE
CD _____ NORMAL 100CD
Normal/Okra / Mar '94 / Direct / ADA.

RETROSPECTIVE 1983-1986, A
Shantell / Talk without words / Shrine / Midnight garden / Impulse of man / Twilights pool / Room lives in Lucy / Scarlet arch / Slow pulse boy / Maps in her wrists and arms / Dwelling place / Vincent Crane / Gone like the swallows / Virus meadow
CD _____ 422010
New Rose / May '94 / Direct / ADA.

VIRUS MEADOW
Slow pulse boy / Maps in her wrists and arms / Dwelling place / Vincent Crane / Jack / Headless clay woman / Gone like the swallows / Virus meadow
CD _____ NORMAL 90CD
Normal/Okra / Mar '94 / Direct / ADA.

And One
IST
CD _____ MA 612
Machinery / Nov '94 / Plastic Head.

SPOT
CD _____ MA34-2
Machinery / Nov '93 / Plastic Head.

Anders, Christian
SINGLE HITS (1968-1971)
CD _____ 16013
Laserlight / Aug '91 / Target/BMG.

Andersen, Arild
IF YOU LOOK FAR ENOUGH
If you look / Svev / For all we know / Backe / Voice / Woman / Place / Drink / Main man / Song I used to play / Far enough / Jonah
CD _____ 5139022
ECM / '90 / New Note.

SAGN
CD _____ 8496472
ECM / Oct '91 / New Note.

Anderson, Alistair
GRAND CHAIN, THE (With Steel Skies Band, Joe Hutton etc.)
CD _____ CROCD 216

Black Crow / Jun '88 / Roots / Jazz Music / CM.

Anderson, Angry

BEATS FROM A SINGLE DRUM
CD _____ CDGRUB 11
Food For Thought / Apr '89 / Pinnacle.

Anderson, Bill

MAGIC OF BILL ANDERSON, THE
CD _____ TKOCD 018
TKO / '92 / TKO.

Anderson, Bruford,...

ANDERSON, BRUFORD, WAKEMAN, HOWE (Anderson, Bruford, Wakeman, Howe)
Sound / Second attention / Soul warrior / Fist of fire / Brother of mine / Big dream / Nothing can come between us / Birthright / Meeting / I wanna learn / She gives me love / Who was the first / I'm alive / Teakbois / Order of the universe / Order theme / Rock gives courage / It's so hard to grow / Uni verse / Let's pretend
CD _____ 262155
Arista / Jan '92 / BMG.

EVENING OF YES, AN (Anderson, Bruford, Wakeman, Howe)
CD Set _____ CDRFL 002
Fragile / Nov '93 / Grapevine.

Anderson, Carl

HEAVY WEATHER SUNLIGHT AGAIN
I can't stop the rain / I'm all about you / I need your love / Love'll hold my baby to-night / Gather ye rosebuds / Heavy weather / God's gift to the world / Feel the night / Always come running / Black rain (Miles to go)
CD _____ GRP 97782
GRP / May '94 / BMG / New Note.

Anderson, Carleen

TRUE SPIRIT
True spirit / Morning loving / Mama said / Ain't givin' up on you / Only one for me / Nervous breakdown / Secrets / Let it last / Feet wet up / Welcome to changes / Ian Green's groove conclusion / Mama said (mixes) (Bonus track) / True spirit (mixes) (Bonus track) / Apparently nothin' (Bonus track) / Nervous breakdown (mix) (Bonus track) / Let it last (mix) (Bonus track)
CD _____ CIRCDX 30
Circa / Jun '94 / EMI.
CD Set _____ CIRCDD 30
Circa / Feb '95 / EMI.

Anderson, Cat

PLAYS W.C. HANDY
CD _____ BLE 591632
Black & Blue / Apr '91 / Wellard / Koch.

Anderson, Clive

BLUES ONE (Anderson, Clive Trio)
CD _____ DIW 607
DIW / Nov '91 / Harmonia Mundi / Cadillac.

Anderson, Eric

AVALANCHE
CD _____ 7559907780
WEA / Jan '96 / Warner Music.

ERIC ANDERSON
CD _____ 7599267782
WEA / Jan '96 / Warner Music.

Anderson, Ernestine

BE MINE TONIGHT
Sunday in New York / In a mellow tone / I'm comin' home again / Christopher Columbus / London by night / Little bird / Be mine tonight / Lend me your life / Sack full of dreams
CD _____ CCD 4319
Concord Jazz / Jul '87 / New Note.

ERNESTINE
CD _____ 5140762
Verve / May '93 / PolyGram.

GREAT MOMENTS WITH ERNESTINE ANDERSON
I love being here with you / Day by day / T'ain't nobody's business if I do / As long as I live / Don't get around much anymore / Please send me someone to love / Skylark / In a mellow tone / Someone else is step-pin' in / Time after time / Body and soul / Never make your move too soon
CD _____ CCD 4582
Concord Jazz / Nov '93 / New Note.

LIVE AT THE 1990 CONCORD JAZZ FESTIVAL (3RD SET)
Blues in the closet / I let a song go out of my heart / I should care / There is no greater love / Skylark / On my own / Never make your move too soon
CD _____ CCD 4454
Concord Jazz / May '91 / New Note.

SUNSHINE
Love / Summertime / Time after time / God bless the child / I've got the world on a string / I'm walkin' / I want a little boy / You are my sunshine / Satin doll / Sunny
CD _____ CCD 4109
Concord Jazz / Jan '92 / New Note.

WHEN THE SUN GOES DOWN
Someone else is steppin' in / In the evening / I love being here with you / Down home blues / I'm just a lucky so and so / Alone on my own / Mercy mercy mercy / Goin' to Chicago blues
CD _____ CCD 4263
Concord Jazz / '88 / New Note.

Anderson, Gladstone

BACK HOME
CD _____ RRCD 015
Roots Collective / Nov '95 / SRD / Jetstar / Roots Collective.

FOREVER DUB VOL.1
CD _____ RRCD 009
Roots Collective / Jun '94 / SRD / Jetstar / Roots Collective.

PEACE PIPE DUB
CD _____ RRCD 002
Roots Collective / Feb '93 / SRD / Jetstar / Roots Collective.

Anderson, Ian A.

UNRULY (English Country Blues Band)
CD _____ CDFMS 27
Hogue / Apr '93 / Sterns.

Anderson, Ivie

INTRODUCTION TO IVIE ANDERSON 1932-1942, AN
CD _____ 4020
Best Of Jazz / May '95 / Discovery.

IVIE ANDERSON (Anderson, Ivie & Duke Ellington)
CD _____ CD 14561
Jazz Portraits / May '95 / Jazz Music.

Anderson, John

PAN PIPES - ROMANCE OF IRELAND (Anderson, John Concert Orchestra)
Riverdance / Lark in the clear air / Meeting of the waters / O'Neills march / Rakes of Mallow / She moved through the fair / Brian Boru's march / Dublin's fair city / Cliffs of Dooneen / Lannigan's ball / Irish washer woman / Rose of the Tralee / Star of the county down / Endearing young charms / How can I keep from singing / Londonderry air / Sally gardens / Mo ghile mear
CD _____ MCD 60004
MCA / Nov '95 / BMG.

TOO TOUGH TO TAME
CD _____ UVLD 76008
New Sound Planet / Nov '89 / Pinnacle.

Anderson, John

I'M IN THE MOOD FOR SWING I
CD _____ LPCD 1021
Disky / Apr '94 / THE / BMG / Discovery / Pinnacle.

I'M IN THE MOOD FOR SWING II
CD _____ LPCD 1022
Disky / Apr '94 / THE / BMG / Discovery / Pinnacle.

Anderson, Jon

CHANGE WE MUST
State of independence / Shaker loops / Hearts / Alive and well / Kiss / Chagall duet / Run on, Jon / Candle song / View from the coppice / Hurry home / Under the sun / Majestic
CD _____ CDC 5550882
EMI / Oct '94 / EMI.

DESEO
Amor real / A-de-o / Bridges / Seasons / Floresta / Cafe / This child / Danca do ouro / Midnight dancing / Deseo / Latino / Bless this
CD _____ 01934111402
Windham Hill / May '94 / Pinnacle / BMG / ADA.

DESEO REMIXES, THE
Deep Floresta / Intercity 125 / Speed deep / Master Mute vs The Tone-E / FSOL Deseo reconstruction / Amor real / Master Mute / Bless this
CD _____ 72902103382
Windham Hill / Jul '95 / Pinnacle / BMG / ADA.

OLIAS OF SUNHILLOW
Ocean song / Meeting / Sound out the gal-leon / Dance of Ranyart Olias / Ooquaq en transic / Solid space / Moon ra chords song of search / To the runner / Naon / Transic to
CD _____ 7567802732
Atlantic / Jan '96 / Warner Music.

SONG OF SEVEN
For you for me / Some are born / Don't for-get / Heart of the matter / Hear it / Every-

---

body loves you / Take your time / Days / Song of seven
CD _____ 7567814752
Atlantic / Jan '96 / Warner Music.

Anderson, Laurie

BIG SCIENCE
From the air / Big science / Sweaters / Walking and falling / Born never asked / O superman / Example 22 / Let X = X / It tango
CD _____ K2 57002
WEA / Apr '82 / Warner Music.

BRIGHT RED
Speechless / Bright red / Puppet motel / Speak my language / World without end / Freefall / Muddy river / Beautiful pea green boat / Love among the sailors / Poison / In our sleep / Night in Baghdad / Tightrope / Same time tomorrow
CD _____ 936245534-2
WEA / Aug '94 / Warner Music.

MISTER HEARTBREAK
Sharkey's day / Langue d'armour / Gravity's angel / Blue lagoon / Excellent birds / Shar-key's night
CD _____ 925077 2
WEA / Jul '84 / Warner Music.

STRANGE ANGELS
Strange angels / Monkey's paw / Coolsville / Ramon / Baby doll / Beautiful red dress / Day the devil comes to getcha / Dream be-fore / My eyes / Hiawatha
CD _____ K 9259002
WEA / Mar '94 / Warner Music.

UGLY ONE WITH THE JEWELS
CD _____ 9362458472
WEA / Mar '95 / Warner Music.

Anderson, Leif

LEIF 'SMOKE RINGS' ANDERSON
Ancha / Aug '94 / Jazz Music / Wellard / Cadillac.
CD _____ ANC 9096-2

SWING SESSIONS VOL. 1 (Anderson, Leif 'Smokerings')
CD _____ ANC 9093
Ancha / Sep '94 / Jazz Music / Wellard / Cadillac.

Anderson, Lynn

COUNTRY GIRL
CD _____ PWK 005
Carlton Home Entertainment / '88 / Carlton Home Entertainment.

COWBOY'S SWEETHEART
CD _____ 12128
Laserlight / Jul '94 / Target/BMG.

LEGENDS IN MUSIC - LYNN ANDERSON
CD _____ LECD 056
Wisepack / Jul '94 / THE / Conifer.

ROSE GARDEN
CD _____ WMCD 5655
Woodford Music / Jun '92 / THE.

ROSE GARDEN
CD _____ CDCD 1191
Charly / Sep '94 / Charly / THE / Cadillac.

ROSE GARDEN
CD _____ ENTCD 242
Entertainers / Mar '92 / Target/BMG.

Anderson, Marian

SPIRITUALS (He's Got The Whole World In His Hands)
He's got the whole world in his hands / De-re's no hidin' place / I want Jesus to walk with me / Oh, didn't it rain / I am bound for de kingdom / Oh wasn't dat a wide ribber / My soul's been anchored in de lord / Lord I can't stay away / Sometimes I feel like a motherless child / Hold on / Scandalise my name / Great gittin' up mornin' / Done foun' my los' sheep / I stood on de ribber ob Jer-don / Behold that star / Heav'n Heav'n / Oh Peter, go ring dem bells / Trampin' / Hard trials / On heaven is one beautiful place / I know / Lord how come me here / Prayer is de key / He'll bring it to pass / You go / Jus' keep on singin' / Ain't got time to die / I been in de storm so long / I've been 'buked / Let's have a union / Jus' keep on singin'/ Ride on King Jesus
CD _____ 09026619602
RCA Victor / Jun '95 / BMG.

SPIRITUALS
CD _____ PASTCD 7073
Flapper / Aug '95 / Pinnacle.

Anderson, Moira

20 SCOTTISH FAVOURITES
Dark island / Farewell my love / Soft lowland tongue o' the borders / Loch Lomond / Al-ways Argyll / Jean annie / My love / Jo / Rowan tree / O Waly Waly / Isle of Mull / Sleeps the noon / O lovely land of Canada / Eriskay love lilt / Way old friends do / Ye banks and braes o' bonnie Doon / Duris-deer / Glencoe / Ae fond kiss / My ain folk / Calling me home / Amazing grace
CD _____ LCOM 9033

Lismor / Nov '90 / Lismor / Direct / Duncans / ADA.

MOIRA - IN LOVE
Time after time / Love is the sweetest thing / You light up my life / Shadow of your smile / More I see you / Until it's time for you to go / Nearness of you / I won't last a day without you / I just fall in love again / Some-times when we touch / If (CD only) / I'll walk alone (CD only) / You needed me (CD only) / Somewhere my love (CD only)
CD _____ DLCD 104
Dulcima / Oct '87 / Savoy / THE.

MOIRA ANDERSON
CD _____ PWK 101
Carlton Home Entertainment / '88 / Carlton Home Entertainment.

Anderson, Pink

BALLAD & FOLKSINGER
CD _____ OBCCD 577
Original Blues Classics / Jan '96 / Complete/Pinnacle / Wellard / Cadillac.

CAROLINA BLUES MAN
My baby left me this morning / Baby, please don't go / Mama where did you stay last night / Big house blues / Meet me in the bottom / Weeping willow blues / Baby I'm going away / I had my fun / Every day in the week / Thousand woman blues
CD _____ OBCCD 504
Original Blues Classics / Nov '92 / Com-plete/Pinnacle / Wellard / Cadillac.

Anderson, Ray

BIG BAND RECORD
Lips apart / Anabel at one / My wish / Raven-a-ning / Leo's place / Seven mon-sters / Waltz for Phoebe / Literary lizard / Don't mow your lawn
CD _____ GCD 79497
Gramavision / Sep '95 / Vital/SAM / ADA.

CHEER UP (Anderson, Ray & Hans Bennink/Christy Doran)
CD _____ ARTCD 6175
Hat Art / Dec '95 / Harmonia Mundi / ADA / Cadillac.

DON'T MOW YOUR LAWN
Don't mow your lawn / Diddleybop / Dam-aged but good / Alligatory peccadillo / What'cha gonna do with that / Airwaves / Blow your own horn / Disguise the limit
CD _____ ENJACD 80702
Enja / Aug '94 / New Note / Vital/SAM.

EVERYONE OF US
Funkalific / Brother can you spare a dime / Kind garnerish / Muddy and Willie / Snoo tune (for Anabel) / Lady day / Dear Lord
CD _____ GCD 79471
Gramavision / Sep '95 / Vital/SAM / ADA.

HEADS AND TALES
Hunting and gathering / Heads and tales / Matters of the heart / Unsung songs / Cheek to cheek / Tapajack / Tough guy / Road song / Drink and blather
CD _____ ENJ 90552
Enja / Nov '95 / New Note / Vital/SAM.

RIGHT DOWN YOUR ALLEY
CD _____ SNCD 1087
Soul Note / Dec '86 / Harmonia Mundi / Wellard / Cadillac.

WISHBONE
Gahtooze / Ah soca / Duke Ellington's sound of love / Gumbo here / Bupe Ham / Cheek to cheek / Wishbone suite
CD _____ GV 794542
Gramavision / Mar '91 / Vital/SAM / ADA.

Anderson, Roshell

ROLLING OVER
CD _____ ICH 1142CD
Ichiban / Feb '94 / Koch.

STEPPING OUT
Twilight state / Bodies talking / Peace / Vic-tim of a system / Better love / Passionate transition / Stepping out / Broken heart
CD _____ CDICH 1053
Ichiban / Mar '90 / Koch.

SWEET 'N' SOUR RHYTHM 'N' BLUES
Come on back / Leaving me / Chokin' kind / Grapevine will lie sometimes / Dearest darling / What do you expect from me / You wouldn't believe / Stop doggin' me
CD _____ CDICH 1035
Ichiban / Jun '89 / Koch.

Anderson, Stuart

ACTS NATURALLY
CD _____ CDITV 559
Scotdisc / Oct '92 / Duncans / Ross / Conifer.

STUART ANDERSON'S PARTY
Doon in the wee room / Bonnie Wee Jean-nie McCall / Donald, where's yer troosers / Stuart's song / Marriage / Coulter's candy / Ghostie / Catch me if you can / Wee Kirk-cudbright centipede / Come to the Ceilidh
CD _____ CDITV 502
Scotdisc / Nov '89 / Duncans / Ross / Conifer.

Anderson, Tom

SILVER BOW: SHETLAND FOLK FIDDLING (Anderson, Tom & Aly Bain)
Jack broke da prison door/Donald Blue/ Sleep soond / Lasses trust in Providence/ Bonnie Isle o'Whalsay / Da day dawn/Da cross reel / Shive her up/Ahint da deakes o'Voe / Da silver bow / Auld Foula reel/Wynadepla / Da slockit light/Smith o'Couster/ Da grocer / Da auld resting chair/Hamnavoe polka/Maggie's reel / Bridal march/Da bride's a bonnie ting / Jack is yet alive/Auld clettenroe / Da mill/Doon da Rooth / Pit hame da borrowed Claes/Wha'll dance wi' Wattie / Bush below da gairden / Soldier's joy / Shetland moods / Dean brig/Banks / Ferrie reel/Lay Dee at Dee/Spencie's reel / Up an'doon the harbour/Lucky can you link ony / Silvery voe/Pottinger's reel / If I get a bonnie lass/Jeannie shoke da bairn / Auld swaara / Faroe rum/Aandowin' at da Bow / Mrs. Jamieson's favourite/Lady Mary Ramsay / All da ships ir sailin'/Sheldor Geo/Mak a kishie needle dye / Fredtie's tune/Da blue yow / Full rigged ship/New rigged ship / Naanie an' Betty/A yow cam to wir door yarmin / Maggie O'Ham/Da Foula shaalds / Come agen ye're welcome/Da corbie an' da craw / Ian S. Robertson/Madam Vanoni
CD _____ TSCD 469
Topic / Sep '93 / Direct / ADA.

Anderson, Tony

STRICTLY DANCING: WALTZ (Anderson, Tony String Orchestra)
CD _____ 15341
Laserlight / May '94 / Target/BMG.

Anderson, Wayne

BACK TO THE GROOVE
CD _____ CPCD 8142
Charly / Nov '95 / Charly / THE / Cadillac.

Anderson, Willie

SWINGING THE BLUES (Anderson, Little Willie)
CD _____ CD 4930
Earwig / Feb '95 / CM.

Andes

LES GUARANIS
CD _____ 339353
Musidisc / Dec '86 / Vital / Harmonia Mundi / ADA / Cadillac / Discovery.

Andi Sex Gang

ARCO VALLEY
CD _____ FREUDCD 24
Jungle / Jul '89 / Disc.

Andress, Tuck

HYMNS CAROLS AND SONGS
Winter wonderland / Silent night / Coventry carol/What child is this / Jingle bells / Ave Maria / Little drummer boy / Santa Claus is coming to town / It came upon a midnight clear / Deck the halls with boughs of holly / O little town of bethlehem / Rudolph the red nosed reindeer / Angels we have heard on high
CD _____ 101352
Windham Hill / Oct '91 / Pinnacle / BMG / ADA.

RECKLESS PRECISION
Man in the mirror / Somewhere over the rainbow / If I only had a brain / Louie Louie / Body and soul / Sweet P / Stella by starlight / Manonash / Manha de Carnaval / Grooves of joy / Begin the beguine
CD _____ WD 0124
Windham Hill / Jun '91 / Pinnacle / BMG / ADA.

Andrews Sisters

ANDREWS SISTERS 1937-43
CD _____ 394672
Music Memoria / Mar '94 / Discovery / ADA.

ANDREWS SISTERS SHOW
CD _____ CDMR 1033
Derann Trax / Aug '91 / Pinnacle.

BEAT ME DADDY, EIGHT TO THE BAR (1937-1940)
Beat me Daddy, eight to the bar / Beer barrel polka / Bei mir bist du schon / Ciribiribin / Cock-eyed mayor of Kaunakakai / Ferryboat serenade / From the land of the sky blue water / Hold tight, hold tight / I love you too much / I want my mama / Let's have another one / Long time no see / Nice work if you can get it / 1-2-3 O'Leary / Oo-oo-oo-oh boom / Pagan love song / Pennsylvania 6-5000 / Rumboogie / Shortnin' bread / Well alright / Why talk about love / You don't know how much you can suffer
CD _____ CDAJA 5096
Living Era / Dec '95 / Koch.

BEST OF THE ANDREWS SISTERS, THE
CD _____ MATCD 318
Castle / Dec '94 / BMG.

BEST OF THE ANDREWS SISTERS, THE
CD _____ MCCD 199
Music Club / May '95 / Disc / THE / CM.

BOOGIE WOOGIE BUGLE BOY
Bei mir bist du schon / Joseph Joseph / Oh ma-ma / Sha-sha / When a Prince of a fella meets a Cinderella / Begin the beguine / Beer Barrel Polka / Jumpin' jive / Oh Johnny oh Johnny oh / South America Way / Let's have another one / Say si su / Rumboogie / Beat me Daddy, eight to the bar / Pennsylvania 6-5000 / Boogie woogie bugle boy
CD _____ HADCD 173
Javelin / May '94 / THE / Henry Hadaway Organisation.

CHRISTMAS WITH THE ANDREWS SISTERS
Winter wonderland / Jingle bells / Twelve days of Christmas / Sleigh bells / Christmas candles / Merry Christmas polka / Here comes Santa Claus / Jing-a-ling jing-a-ling / Christmas tree angel / (Toys gave a party for) Poppa Santa Claus / Merry Christmas at Grandmother's / Santa Claus is coming to town
CD _____ PWKM 4002
Carlton Home Entertainment / Oct '95 / Carlton Home Entertainment.

COLLECTION, THE
CD _____ COL 052
Collection / Jan '95 / Target/BMG.

CREAM OF THE ANDREWS SISTERS, THE
Beat me Daddy, eight to the bar / Joseph / Pennsylvania 6-5000 / Oh Johnny oh Johnny, oh / Bei mir bist du schon / Hold tight, hold tight / Rumboogie / Say "si, su" / South American way / Jumpin' jive / Where have we met before / Pagan love song / Oh, ma-ma / Sha-sha / Begin the beguine / Bugle boy / When a Prince of a fella meets a Cinderella / Just a simple melody / Love is where you find it / Why talk about love / Let's have another one
CD _____ PASTCD 9766
Flapper / Oct '91 / Pinnacle.

HOLD TIGHT IT'S THE ANDREWS SISTERS (20 Greatest Hits)
Don't sit under the apple tree / Sabre dance / Rum and coca cola / Put that ring on my finger / Twenty four hours of sunshine / I can dream, can't I / That lucky old sun / Coca roca / Pussy cat song / Lullaby of Broadway / Is you is or is you ain't my baby / Three caballeros / Accentuate the positive / Hold tight, hold tight / Beer barrel polka / Boogie woogie bugle boy / Pennsylvania polka / Victory polka
CD _____ DBCD 12
Dance Band Days / Dec '88 / Prism.

IN APPLE BLOSSOM TIME
Bei mir bist du schon / Oh ma-ma / Joseph Joseph / Jitterbug's lullaby / Ti-pi-tin / Hold tight, hold tight / Beer barrel polka / Long time no see / Well alright / Beat me Daddy / South American way / Oh Johnny / Beat me Daddy, eight to the bar / Eight to the bar / I'll be with you in apple blossom time / Rumboogie / Say si si / Hit the road / Sonny boy / Boogie woogie bugle boy / Yes my darling daughter / I love you too much
CD _____ CDCD 1060
Charly / Mar '93 / Charly / THE / Cadillac.

RUM AND COCA COLA
CD _____ RMB 75018
Remember / Nov '93 / Total/BMG.

SING, SING, SING
Beat me Daddy, eight to the bar / I'll be with you in apple blossom time / Oh johnny oh johnny oh / Bei mir bist du schon / Sing, sing, sing / Pennsylvania 6-5000 / Joseph Joseph / In the mood / Boogie woogie bugle boy / Don't sit under the apple tree / Hold tight, hold tight / I can dream, can't I / I got a gal in Kalamazoo / Coffee song / Lullaby of Broadway / Elmer's tune / Alexander's ragtime band (CD only.) / Don't be that way (CD only.) / Yes my darling daughter (CD only.) / Say si si (CD only.)
CD _____ CDMFP 6044
Music For Pleasure / Mar '89 / EMI.

SURE SCORE, A
Boogie woogie bugle boy / Buckle down Winsocki / It's the talk of the town / Baby, won't you please come home / Rum boogie / That's for me / Girl and a sailor / Waiting for the train to come in / Christmas candles / Begin the beguine / I wish I were in Michigan / Come to baby do / Patience and fortitude / Lily Belle / I'm gonna love that girl / Symphony / Put that ring on my finger / Tico-tico / Every time I fall in love / Pennsylvania polka
CD _____ DAWE 49
Magic / Feb '94 / Jazz Music / Swift / Wellard / Cadillac / Harmonia Mundi.

VERY BEST: ANDREWS SISTERS
CD _____ PWKM 4000
Carlton Home Entertainment / '90 / Carlton Home Entertainment.

Andrews, Chris

DIE SUPERHITS
CD _____ 15144
Laserlight / Aug '91 / Target/BMG.

GREATEST HITS

CD _____ PA 7162
Paradiso / Apr '94 / Target/BMG.

HIT SINGLE COLLECTABLES
CD _____ DISK 4508
Disky / Apr '94 / THE / BMG / Discovery / Pinnacle.

SIMPLY THE BEST
CD _____ WMCD 5707
Disky / Oct '94 / THE / BMG / Discovery / Pinnacle.

Andrews, Ernie

GREAT CITY, THE
Great city / Time after time / Jug and I got up this morning / Skylark / Fire and rain / If I loved you / Come back little girl / If I had your love
CD _____ MCD 5543
Muse / Dec '95 / New Note / CM.

NO REGRETS
When they ask about you / Don't you know I care (or don't you care to) / I'll never be free / You call it madness / Hunt is on / Until the real thing comes along / When did you leave Heaven / Sweet Lorraine / Sweet slumber
CD _____ MCD 5484
Muse / Nov '93 / New Note / CM.

Andrews, Harvey

25 YEARS ON THE ROAD
CD _____ HYCD 200 105
Hypertension / Feb '95 / Total/BMG / Direct / ADA.

SNAPS
CD _____ HYCD 295159
Hypertension / Dec '95 / Total/BMG / Direct / ADA.

SOMEDAY FANTASY
CD _____ LBEECD 006
Beeswing / Jan '95 / Roots / ADA / CM / Broadside.

SPRING AGAIN
CD _____ HYCD 200140
Hypertension / Mar '94 / Total/BMG / Direct / ADA.

WRITER OF SONGS
CD _____ LBEE 002CD
Beeswing / Jan '94 / Roots / ADA / CM / Broadside.

Andrews, Julie

JULIE ANDREWS - GREATEST HITS
CD _____ 983403-2
Pickwick/Sony Collector's Choice / Mar '94 / Carlton Home Entertainment / Pinnacle / Sony.

LOVE JULIE
Out of this world / Love / How deep is the ocean / Island / So in love / What are you doing / Come rain or come shine / Tea for two / My lucky day / Soundsketch / Where or when / Nobody does it better
CD _____ USACD 539
USA / Feb '89 / Charly / Jazz Music.

SOUND OF CHRISTMAS, THE
Hark the herald angels sing / In the bleak midwinter / See amid the winter's snow / It came upon a midnight clear / O little town of Bethlehem / What child is this / Silent night / Holy boy / Away in a manger / Rock-ing / I wonder as I wander / O come all ye faithful (Adeste Fidelis) / Patapan / Secret of Christmas
CD _____ PWKS 4035
Carlton Home Entertainment / Sep '93 / Carlton Home Entertainment.

Andrews, Maxene

MAXENE: AN ANDREWS SISTER
Bei mir bist du schoen / Don't sit under the apple tree / Remember / Fascinating rhythm / I'll be with you in apple blossom time
CD _____ CDSL 5218
DRG / May '92 / New Note.

Andrews, Ruby

KISS THIS
I want to rock with you baby (no. 2) / Since I met you / Que pasa / To the other woman (I'm the other woman) / Kiss this / Lovey dovey / Throw some more dirt on me (the shacking song) / Loving you no.44 / I got what I want at home / As in always...
CD _____ CDICH 1104
Ichiban / Oct '93 / Koch.

Andreyev Balalaika...

BALALAIKA (Andreyev Balalaika Ensemble)
CD _____ MCD 61713
Monitor / Jul '94 / CM.

Andromeda

RETURN TO SANITY
Background / Apr '94 / Background.
CD _____ HBG 122/5

SEE INTO THE STARS

CD _____ SARCD 003-4
Satellite / Mar '93 / Disc.

Andy, Bob

FIRE BURNING
CD _____ CDTRL 343
Trojan / Feb '95 / Jetstar / Total/BMG.

SONGS OF BOB ANDY, THE (Various Artists)
CD _____ JOVECD 1
Jove Music / Sep '93 / Jetstar / SRD.

YOUNG, GIFTED AND BLACK
CD _____ CDTRL 343
Trojan / Nov '94 / Jetstar / Total/BMG.

Andy, Horace

ELEMENTARY (Andy, Horace & The Rhythm Queen)
CD _____ RHCD 2016
Rhino / Jul '93 / Jetstar / Magnum Music Group / THE.

HITS FROM STUDIO ONE AND MORE
CD _____ RNCD 2116
Rhino / Sep '95 / Jetstar / Magnum Music Group / THE.

IN THE LIGHT
CD _____ BAFCD 6
Blood & Fire / May '95 / Grapevine / PolyGram.

LIFE IS FOR LIVING
CD _____ ARICD 106
Ariwa Sounds / Mar '95 / Jetstar / SRD.

SEEK AND YOU WILL FIND
CD _____ BLKCD 15
Blakamix / Nov '95 / Jetstar / SRD.

Andy, Kendrick

ANOTHER NIGHT IN THE GHETTO
CD _____ FBKCD 1
Fence Beater / Mar '95 / Jetstar.

Andyboy

ONE MAN, SIX STRINGS AND A WHOLE LOTTA MISERY
CD _____ WB 3117CD
We Bite / Jan '95 / Plastic Head.

Anekdoten

NUCLEUS
Nucleus / This far from the sky / Here / Harvest / Untitled / Rubankh / Pendylum swing / Book
CD _____ VIRTA 002
Cyclops / Jan '96 / Pinnacle.

Aneke, Aster

ASTER
CD _____ TERRACD 107
Sterns / Aug '89 / Sterns / CM.

Anesthesy

EXALTATION OF THE ECLIPSE
CD _____ BMCD 54
Black Mark / May '94 / Plastic Head.

Angel Cage

SOPHIE MAGIC
CD _____ ORGAN 016CD
Org / Jul '95 / Pinnacle.

Angel Corpus Christi

WHITE COURTESY PHONE
CD _____ ALMOCD 004
Almo Sounds / Nov '95 / Pinnacle.

Angel, Dave

TALES OF THE EXPECTED
Arabian nights / Big tight flares / Timeless / Scatman / Over here / Bump / It's too hot in here / Be bop / D.O.B. / Rudiments
CD _____ BVMCD 2
Blunted Vinyl / Oct '95 / Vital / PolyGram.

TRANCE LUNAR PARADISE
CD Set _____ SDIMCD 1
Sound Dimension / Dec '94 / Total/BMG.

Angel Voices

ANGEL VOICES
CD _____ QTVCD 018
Quality / Nov '92 / Pinnacle.

Angel Witch

ANGEL WITCH
Angel Witch / Gorgon / Atlantis / White witch / Confused / Sorceress / Sweet danger / Free man / Angel of death / Devil's tower
CD _____ CLACD 239
Castle / May '91 / BMG.

LIVE
Angel of death / Confused / Gorgon / Extermination day / Flight 19 / White witch / Sweet danger / Sorceress / Baphamet / Atlantis / Angel Witch

CD _____ CDZORRO 1
Music For Nations / May '90 / Pinnacle.

SCREAMIN' ASSAULT
She don't lie / Frontal assault / Something wrong / Straight from hell / Reawakening / Screamin' n' bleedin' / Waltz the night / Rendezvous with the blade / Goodbye / Take to the wing / Fatal kiss / Undergods / U.X.V.
CD _____ KILCD 1001
Killerwatt / Dec '88 / Kingdom.

Angelic Upstarts

ALTERNATIVE CHARTBUSTERS
CD _____ AOK 102
Street Link / Jan '92 / BMG.

ANGEL DUST (THE COLLECTED HIGHS)
Murder of Liddle Towers / Police oppression / I'm an upstart / Teenage warning / Never 'ad nothin' / Last night another soldier / Two million voices / Kids on the street / England / Hearts lament / Shotgun solution / Never say die / Woman in disguise / Solidarity / Lust for glory / Never give up / Waiting, hating / Reason why / Nobody was saved / Geordie's wife / Loneliness of the long distance runner / 42nd Street / Burglar / Five flew over the cuckoo's nest / As the passion / Young punk / Where we started
CD _____ CDMGRAM 7
Anagram / Aug '93 / Pinnacle.

BLOOD ON THE TERRACES/LOST AND FOUND
Pride of our passion / Everyday / I wanna knighthood / Heart attack in Paris / Four grey walls / I don't wanna fight the soviet / Our day will come / Blood on the terraces / Heroin is good for you / It's your life / I won't pay for liberty / Solidarity / Never return to hell / When will they learn / Tut shuffle / Box on / Living in exile / No nukes / Calypso / Never ad nothing (Live) / Leave me alone (live) / Teenage warning (live) / Last night another soldier (live) / Guns for the Afghan rebels (live)
CD _____ LOMACD 11
Loma / Feb '94 / BMG.

BOMBED OUT
CD _____ DOJOCD 198
Dojo / Aug '94 / BMG.

GREATEST HITS LIVE - ANGELIC UPSTARTS
Murder of liddle towers / Teenage warning / Police / Oppression / Young ones / We're gonna take the world / Last night / Another soldier / Guns for the Afghan rebels / Mr. Politician / Shotgun solution / I understand / Kids on the street / Enland / You're nicked / Two million voices / I'm an upstart / White riot / Leave me alone / Never 'ad nother
CD _____ DOJOCD 127
Dojo / Mar '93 / BMG.

INDEPENDENT SINGLES COLLECTION
Murder of the Liddle Towers / Police oppression / Woman in disguise / Lust for glory / Solidarity / 42nd Street / Five flew over the cuckoo's nest / Dollars and pounds / Don't stop / Not just a name / Leech / Leave me alone / White riot / Machine gun Kelly / Young ones / We're gonna take the world / England / Soldier / Thin red line / Brighton bomb / There's a drink in it
CD _____ CDPUNK 59
Anagram / May '95 / Pinnacle.

LIVE ANGELIC UPSTARTS
Teenage warning / Never had nothing / Four words / Last night another soldier / Guns for the Afghan rebels / Mr. Politician / Shotgun solution / Pride without prejudice / England / Police oppression / Kids on the street / I understand / You're nicked / Two million voices / I'm an upstart
CD _____ DOJOCD 169
Dojo / Feb '94 / BMG.

LIVE ON TOUR IN YUGOSLAVIA
CD _____ PUNXCD 2
Punx / Oct '95 / Total/BMG.

REASON WHY
Woman in disguise / Never give up / Waiting, hating / Reason why / Nobody was saved / Geordie's wife / Loneliness of the long distance runner / 42nd Street / Burglar / Solidarity / As the passion / Young punk / Where we started / Lust for glory / Five flew over the cuckoo's nest / Dollars and pounds / Don't stop / Not just a name / Leech / Leave me alone (live) / Murder of Liddle Towers / White riot
CD _____ CDGRAM 004
Anagram / Jun '92 / Pinnacle.

TWO MILLION VOICES
Two million voices / Ghost town / You're nicked / England / Heath's lament / Guns for the Afghan rebels / I understand / Men-si's marauders / Mr. Politician / Kids on the street / Jimmy / We're gonna take the world / Last night another soldier / I wish
CD _____ DOJOCD 81
Dojo / May '93 / BMG.

Angelo, Michael

NO BOUNDARIES
CD _____ THERM 419612
Thermometer / Sep '95 / Plastic Head.

Angelopoulos, Lycourgos

BYZANTINE MASS - AKATHISTOS HYMN (Angelopoulos, Lycourgos & The Greek Byzantine Choir)
CD _____ PS 65118/9
Playasound / Nov '93 / Harmonia Mundi / ADA.

Angels Ov Light

PSYCHICK YOUTH RALLY
CD _____ CSR 8CD
Cold Spring / Aug '95 / Plastic Head.

Angels With Dirty Faces

SOUNDS OF WORLD
CD _____ BFR 43101CD
Rock The Nation / Nov '94 / Plastic Head.

Anger

MIAMI, FLORIDA
CD _____ SPV 08436212
SPV / Nov '94 / Plastic Head.

Anger, Darol

CHIAROSCURO (Anger, Darol & Mike Marshall)
Dolphins / Saurian's farewell / Beneath the farewell / Beloved infidel / Placenza / Coming back / Dardanelles / Spring gesture
CD _____ CDW 1043
Windham Hill / '88 / Pinnacle / BMG / ADA.

LIVE AT MONTREUX: DAROL ANGER (Anger, Darol & Barbara Higbie Quintet)
CD _____ CDW 1036
Windham Hill / Jul '86 / Pinnacle / BMG / ADA.

Angina Pectoris

ANGUISH
CD _____ SPV 08445612
SPV / Oct '94 / Plastic Head.

Angkor Wat

CORPUS CHRISTI
CD _____ CDZORRO 5
Music For Nations / May '90 / Pinnacle.

Anglaspel

JAZZ IN SWEDEN 1982
CD _____ 1270
Caprice / Jan '89 / CM / Complete/ Pinnacle / Cadillac / ADA.

Angst

CRY FOR HAPPY
CD _____ SST 206 CD
SST / Nov '88 / Plastic Head.

Anhrefn

RASTA
CD _____ PLAY CD 7
Workers Playtime / Feb '89 / Pinnacle.

Anibaldi, Leo

VIRTUAL LANGUAGE, THE
CD _____ PWD 7448
Pow Wow / May '94 / Jetstar.

Animal New Ones

LAKE SIDE BASH
CD _____ FLIGHT 13013CD
Flight 13 / Nov '92 / Plastic Head.

Animals

ANIMALS WITH SONNY BOY WILLIAMSON (Newcastle, December 1963) (Animals & Sonny Boy Williamson)
Sonny's slow walk / Pontiac blues / My babe / I don't care no more / Baby don't you worry / Night time is the right time / I'm gonna put you down / Fattenin' frogs for snakes / Nobody but you / Bye bye Sonny bye bye / Coda
CD _____ CDCHARLY 215
Charly / Jul '90 / Charly / THE / Cadillac.

ANIMALS, THE
CD _____ 16137
Laserlight / Jul '95 / Target/BMG.

COMPLETE ANIMALS, THE (2CD Set)
Boom boom / Talking 'bout you / Blue feeling / Dimples / Baby let me take you home / Gonna send you back to Walker / Baby what's wrong / House of the rising sun / F-E-E-L / I'm mad again / Right time / Around and around / I'm in love again / Bury my body / She said yeah / I'm going to body easy / Story of Bo Diddley / Girl can't help it / I've been around / Memphis, Tennessee / Don't let me be misunderstood / Club a gogo / Roberta / Hallelujah, I love her so / Don't want much / I believe to my soul / Let the good times roll / Mess around / How you've changed / I ain't got you / Roberts / Bright lights big city / Worried life blues / Bring it on home to me / For Miss Caulker / I can't believe it / We gotta get out of this place / It's my life / I'm gonna change the world

Animals That Swim

WORKSHY
CD _____ ELM 24CD
Elemental / Sep '94 / Disc.

Anitas Livs

WILD WORLD WEB
CD _____ SLACD 014CD
Slask / Nov '95 / ADA.

Anka, Paul

GREATEST HITS COLLECTION
CD _____ [illegible]
Telstar / Nov '93 / BMG.

HAVING MY BABY
CD _____ 16122
Laserlight / May '95 / Target/BMG.

HIS GERMAN RECORDINGS
CD _____ BCD 15613
Bear Family / Feb '92 / Rollercoaster / Direct / CM / Swift / ADA.

PAUL ANKA
CD _____ 295036
Ariola / Oct '94 / BMG.

Ann Can Be

27 ON AND OFF
CD _____ TOODAMNHY 62
Too Damn Hype / Jan '95 / SRD.

Anna

101-1 SM
CD _____ CDFRE 3
Free / Oct '93 / Disc.

Annabouboula

GREEK FIRE
CD _____ SHCD 64027
Shanachie / Jul '91 / Koch / ADA / Greensleeves.

Annie Anxiety

JACKAMO (Bandez, Annie Anxiety)
As I lie in your arms / Bastinado / Chasing the dragon down Broadway / Jackamo / One mourning / Jak yo mama / Rise
CD _____ TPCD 4
One Little Indian / Jun '88 / Pinnacle.

CD Set _____ CDEM 1367
EMI / Jul '90 / EMI.

INSIDE LOOKING OUT (1965-1966 Decca Sessions)
Inside looking out / Outcast / Don't bring me down / Cheating / Help me girl / C.C. rider / One monkey don't stop now show / Maudie / Sweet little sixteen / You're on my mind / Clapping / Gin house blues / Squeeze her, tease her / What am I living for / I put a spell on you / That's all I am to you / She'll return it / Mama told me not to come / I just want to make love to you / Boom boom / Big boss man / Pretty thing
CD _____ NEXCD 153
Sequel / Feb '91 / BMG.

INSIDE OUT (Burdon, Eric & The Animals)
San Francisco nights / Ring of fire / I put a spell on you / Mama told me not to come / Good times / Help me girl / Sky pilot / Inside looking out / River deep, mountain high / When I was young / Monterrey / Sweet little sixteen / Gin house blues / Don't bring me down
CD _____ 5501192
Spectrum/Karussell / Oct '93 / PolyGram / THE.

LIVE AT THE CLUB A-GO-GO, NEWCASTLE
Let it rock / Gotta find my baby / Bo Diddley / Almost grown / Dimples / Boom boom (out go the lights) / C jam blues
CD _____ CDCD 1037
Charly / Mar '93 / Charly / THE / Cadillac.

LOVE IS
CD _____ OW 30338
One Way / Sep '94 / Direct / ADA.

MOST OF THE ANIMALS
CD _____ CDMFP 5218
Music For Pleasure / Feb '92 / EMI.

RARITIES
CD _____ PRCDSP 500
Prestige / Aug '92 / Total/BMG.

ROADRUNNERS (1966-1968 Live)
CD _____ RVCD 11
Raven / Oct '92 / Direct / ADA.

SINGLES PLUS
Baby let me take you home / Gonna send you back to Walker / House of the rising sun / Talkin' 'bout you / I'm crying / Take it easy / Don't let me be misunderstood / Club a gogo / Bring it on home to me / For Miss Caulker / We gotta get out of this place / I can't believe it / It's my life / I'm going to change the world / Bury my body / Dimples / She said yeah / Right time / Bright lights big city / Let the good times roll
CD _____ CZ 10
EMI / Aug '88 / EMI.

Ansill, Jay

ORIGAMI
CD _____ FF 530CD
Flying Fish / '92 / Roots / CM / Direct / ADA.

Antenna

HIDEOUT
Shine / Wallpaper / Stillife / Rust / Dreamy / Don't be late / Fade / Easy listening / Danger buggy / Second skin / Hallelujah / Grey St.
CD _____ MR 00462
Mammoth / Apr '93 / Vital.

Anthem

GYPSY WAYS
Gypsy ways (win, lose or draw) / Bad habits die hard / Cryin' heart / Midnight sun / Final risk / Love in vain / Legal killing / Silent child / Shout it out / Night stalker
CD _____ CDMFN 103
Music For Nations / Aug '90 / Pinnacle.

HUNTING TIME
Juggler / Evil touch / Sleepless night / Let your heart beat / Hunting time / Tears for the lovers / Jailbreak / Bottle bottom
CD _____ CDMFN 104
Music For Nations / Aug '90 / Pinnacle.

NO SMOKE WITHOUT FIRE
Shadow walk / Blinded pain / Love on the edge / Power and blood / Night we stand / Hungry soul / Do you understand / Voice of thunderstorm / Fever eyes
CD _____ CDMFN 101
Music For Nations / Aug '90 / Pinnacle.

Anthony, Doug

DEAD AND ALIVE (Anthony, Doug Allstars)
Chant / Sun / If you're happy/Waco / Gilbert and Sullivan 1 / Body science / Sailors arms / Necro-romancer / Skinhead sooty / Oprah / If you're happy 2 / Mommy dearest / Freak / Gilbert and Sullivan 2 / I fuck dogs / Moral dilemmas / World's best kisser / Joan of Arc / Breathers / Gilbert and Sullivan 3 / Wimmin / Throw your arms around me / Friends / There is nothing like a dame
CD _____ 4509941792
WEA / Oct '93 / Warner Music.

Anthony, Julie

I DREAMED A DREAM
CD _____ GNPD 2195
GNP Crescendo / '88 / Silva Screen.

Anthony, Marc

TODO A SU TIEMPO
Se me sigue olvidando / Te conozco bien / Hasta ayer / Nadie como ella / Te amare / Llegaste a mi / Y sigues siendo tu / Por amar se da tado / Vieja mesa

Annihilator

ALICE IN HELL
Crystal Ann / W.T.Y.D. / Burns like a buzzsaw blade / Schizos (are never alone) / Human insecticide / Alison Hell / Wicked mystic / Word salad / Ligeia
CD _____ RR 9488 2
Roadrunner / Apr '89 / Pinnacle.

BAG OF TRICKS
Alison Hell / Phantasmagoria / Back to the crypt / Gallery / Human insecticide / Fun Palace / W.T.Y.D. / Word salad / Live wire / Knight jumps Queen / Fantastic things / Bats in the belfry / Evil appetite / Gallery '86 / Alison Hell '86 / Phantasmagoria '86
CD _____ RR 8997-2
Roadrunner / Jul '94 / Pinnacle.

KING OF THE KILL
Box / King of the kill / Hell is a war / Bliss / Second to none / Annihilator / Twenty one / In the blood / Fiasco (slate) / Fiasco / Catch the wind / Speed / Bad child
CD _____ CDMFN 171
Music For Nations / Oct '94 / Pinnacle.

NEVER NEVER LAND
CD _____ RR 93742
Roadrunner / Jul '90 / Pinnacle.

SET THE WORLD ON FIRE
CD _____ RR 92002
Roadrunner / May '93 / Pinnacle.

Anonymous 4

LOVE'S ILLUSION
CD _____ HMU 907109
Harmonia Mundi / Oct '94 / Harmonia Mundi / Cadillac.

Another Fine Day

LIFE BEFORE LAND
CD _____ RBADCD 7
Beyond / Jun '94 / Kudos / Pinnacle.

Another Tale

NIGHTMARE VOICES
CD _____ HY 3910012
Hyperium / Nov '92 / Plastic Head.

21

CD _____ 66058072
RMM / Sep '95 / New Note.

Anthony, Mike

SHORT MORNING
CD _____ GPCD 005
Gussie P / Dec '92 / Jetstar.

Anthony, Ray

22 ORIGINAL BIG BAND RECORDINGS
CD _____ HCD 412
Hindsight / Sep '92 / Target/BMG / Jazz
Music.

SWEET AND SWINGIN' (1949-53)
CD _____ CCD 96
Circle / May '95 / Jazz Music / Swift /
Wellard.

Anthrax

AMONG THE LIVING
Among the living / Caught in a mosh / I am
the law / Efilnikufesin (N.F.L.) / Skeleton in
the closet / Indians / One world / A.D.I. Horror of it all / Imitation of life
CD _____ IMCD 186
Island / Mar '94 / PolyGram.

AMONG THE LIVING/ PERSISTENCE OF
TIME
CD Set _____ ITSCD 6
Island / Nov '92 / PolyGram.

ATTACK OF THE KILLER B'S
Milk (Ode to Billy) / Bring the noise / Keep
it in the family (live) / Startin' up a posse /
Protest and survive / Chromatic death / I'm
the man ('91) / Parasite / Pipeline / Sects /
Belly of the beast (live) / N.F.B.
CD _____ IMCD 180
Island / Mar '94 / PolyGram.

LIVE - THE ISLAND YEARS
Efilnikufesin (N.F.L.) / AIR / Parasite / Keep
it in the family / Caught in a mosh / Indians
/ Anti-social / Bring the noise / I am the law
/ Metal thrashing mad / In my world / Now
it's dark
CD _____ CID 8027
Island / Apr '94 / PolyGram.

PERSISTENCE OF TIME
Time / Blood / Keep it in the family / In my
world / Gridlock / Intro to reality / Belly of
the beast / Got the time / H8 red / One man
stands / Discharge
CD _____ IMCD 178
Island / Mar '94 / PolyGram.

SOUND OF WHITE NOISE, THE
Potter's field / Only / Room for one more /
Packaged rebellion / Hy pro glo / Invisible /
1000 points of hate / Black lodge / C11
H17... / Burst / This is not an exit
CD _____ 755961430-2
Elektra / May '93 / Warner Music.

SPREADING THE DISEASE
Gung ho / Armed and dangerous / Afters /
Enemy / S.S.C. / Stand or fall / Mad house
/ Lone justice / AIR
CD _____ IMCD 136
Island / Aug '91 / PolyGram.

STATE OF EUPHORIA
Be all, end all / Out of sight out of mind /
Make me laugh / Anti-social / Who cares
wins / Now it's dark / Schism / Misery loves
company / Thirteen / Finale
CD _____ IMCD 187
Island / Mar '94 / PolyGram.

Anti Cimex

MADE IN SWEDEN (LIVE)
CD _____ DISTC 53
Distortion / Sep '93 / Plastic Head.

RAPED ASS
CD _____ DISTCD 9
Distortion / Feb '95 / Plastic Head.

SCANDINAVIAN JAWBREAKER
CD _____ DISC 7
Discipline / Jul '93 / Pinnacle.

Anti Nowhere League

ANTI NOWHERE LEAGUE PUNK
SINGLES COLLECTION
Streets of London / So what / I hate people
(original) / Let's break the law (original) /
Woman / Rocker / World War III / For you /
Ballard of JJ Decay / Out on the wasteland
/ We will survive / Queen and country / So
what (live) / I hate people (live) / Snowman
(live) / Fuck around the clock (live)
CD _____ CDPUNK 44
Anagram / Jan '95 / Pinnacle.

BEST OF THE ANTI NOWHERE LEAGUE
Streets of London / I hate people / We are
the league / Let's break the law / Animal /
Woman / Rocker / For you / Ballad of JJ
Decay / Out on the wasteland / We will sur-
vive / Queen and country / On the water-
front / Let the country feed you (live) / Going
down (live) / Snowman (live) / So what (live)
CD _____ CLEO 07279CD
Cleopatra / Jan '94 / Disc.

LIVE AND LOUD
For you / Queen and country / Johannesburg / Wreck a nowhere / Streets of London

/ Crime / We will survive / Branded / Woman
/ Can't stand rock 'n' roll / We are the
league / Something else / Let the country
feed you / Let's break the law / I hate people / Snowman / On the waterfront / Going
down
CD _____ LINKCD 120
Street Link / Oct '90 / BMG.

PERFECT CRIME/ LIVE IN YUGOSLAVIA
Crime / Atomic harvest / On the waterfront
/ Branded / (I don't believe) This is my Eng-
land / Johannesburg / Shining / Working for
the company / System / Curtain / Let's
break the law / Streets of London / We will
survive / I hate people / For you / Woman /
Can't stand rock 'n' roll / Wreck a nowhere
/ Paint it black / We are the league
CD _____ LOMACD 9
Loma / Nov '92 / BMG.

WE ARE THE LEAGUE
We are the league / Animal / Woman / Can't
stand rock 'n' roll / (We will not) Rememeber
you / Snowman / Streets of London / I hate
people (remix) / Reck-a-nowhere / World
War III / Nowhere man / Let's break the law
(remix) / Rocker / So what
CD _____ DOJOCD 128
Dojo / Apr '93 / BMG.

Anti Pasti

CAUTION IN THE WIND
Caution in the wind / One Friday night / X
affair / Get out now / Mr. Mystery / East to
the West / See how they run / Hate circulation / Agent ABC / Best of us / Guinea
pigs / Beyond belief
CD _____ CDPUNK 53
Anagram / May '95 / Pinnacle.

LAST CALL, THE
No government / Brew your own / Another
dead soldier / Call the army (I'm alive) / City
below / Twenty four hours / Night of the war
cry / Freedom now / St. George (get's his
gun) / Last call / Ain't got me / Truth and
justice / Hell / I wanna be your dog
CD _____ CDPUNK 48
Anagram / Mar '95 / Pinnacle.

Anti System

ANTI-SYSTEM
CD _____ REB ICD
Rebellious Construction / Nov '92 / Plastic
Head.

Antidote

TRUTH, THE
CD _____ SHARK 026CD
Shark / Apr '92 / Plastic Head.

Antidote N.Y.C.

VIVA PENDEJOS
CD _____ CDATV 24
Active / Apr '92 / Pinnacle.

Antisect

IN DARKNESS THERE IS NO CHOICE
CD _____ 18524 2
Southern / Sep '94 / SRD.

Antiseen

HELL
CD _____ BSR 011CD
Tear It Up / Nov '95 / Plastic Head.

Antoine, Marc

CLASSICAL SOUL
Smart but casual / French dream / P C H
(Pacific coast highway) / Unity / Universal
language / Timeless line / Follow your bliss
/ New boundaries / Classical soul
CD _____ NYC 60102
NYC / Dec '94 / New Note.

URBAN GYPSY
Latin quarter / Quand le jazz hip-hop / Sand
castle / Steppin' / El matador / First rain /
Urban gypsy / Forget-me-not / Brazil 96 /
Paris jam / Hollywood insomnia / Storytime
CD _____ NYC 60202
NYC / Sep '95 / New Note.

Antolini, Charly

COOKIN' (Antolini, Charly Jazz Power)
After you've gone / My romance / Jumpin'
at the woodside / My ship / Yesterdays /
Dick blues / Soon / Tickle toe / Like some-
one in love / Perdido / Lady be good
CD _____ CDLR 45024
L&R / Feb '91 / New Note.

CRASH
CD _____ BLR 84 002
L&R / May '91 / New Note.

IN THE GROOVE
CD _____ INAK 806
In Akustik / Sep '95 / Magnum Music
Group.

Anton, Paul

PAUL ANTON
I know a man / Just don't matter / Forgive
me / What's a guy supposed to do / I know

a man (Smooth vibe) / We had it going on
/ Just say / Looking at you / In my life
CD _____ SIAMCD 108
Siam / Feb '95 / Siam / EWM.

Antones Women

BRINGING THE BEST IN BLUES
Something's got a hold on me / Hurtback /
Big town / Playboy / Neighour neighbour /
Down South in New Orleans / You'll lose a
good thing / I'm a good woman / Queen
Bee / But I forgive you / Cuban getaway /
Twelve bar blues / Richest one / Wrapping
up our love
CD _____ ANTCD 9902
Alligator / Jun '92 / Direct / ADA.

Antonov, Yuri

MIRROR
CD _____ MK 437052
Mezhdunarodnaya Kniga / Jul '92 /
Complete/Pinnacle.

Anuna

ANUNA
CD _____ 7567827332
Warner Bros. / Apr '95 / Warner Music.

INVOCATION
CD _____ DANU 002CD
Danu / Oct '94 / ADA.
CD _____ 7567828552
Atlantic / Jan '96 / Warner Music.

OMNIS
CD _____ DANU 005
Anuna Teo / Oct '95 / Direct.

Anvil

FORGED IN FIRE
CD _____ RR 349927
Roadrunner / '88 / Pinnacle.

METAL ON METAL
CD _____ RR 349917
Roadrunner / Jun '89 / Pinnacle.

Any Old Time

PHOENIX
CD _____ DARA 025CD
Dara / Jan '95 / Roots / CM / Direct / ADA
/ Koch.

Any Trouble

WRONG END OF THE RACE
Open fire / Old before your time / Lover's
moon / Lucky day / Coming of age / Baby,
now that I've found you / All the time in the
world / Wheels in motion / Turning up the
heat / Yesterday's love / Playing Bogart /
Eleventh hour / Cheating kind / Snapshot /
Between the black and the grey / Kid gloves
/ Like a man / Learning the game / Wrong
end of the race
CD _____ BGOCD 295
Beat Goes On / Nov '95 / Pinnacle.

Anyways

LOVE LIES
CD _____ PAXCD 011
Pax / Apr '92 / Pax Records.

AOS 3

DIVERSIONARY TACTICS
CD _____ ANOK 1CD
Inna State / Oct '95 / SRD.

GOD'S SECRET AGENT
CD _____ WOWCD 28
Words Of Warning / Sep '94 / SRD.

Apache Indian

MAKE WAY FOR THE INDIAN
Make way for the Indian / Armagideon time
/ Boba / Raggamuffin girl / I pray / Born for
a purpose / Back up / Right time / Who say
/ Boom shak-a-lak / Ansa dat
CD _____ CID 8016
Island / Mar '95 / PolyGram.

NO RESERVATIONS
Don raja (prelude) / Chok there / Fe real /
Fix up / AIDS warning / Guru / Wan' know
me / Come follow me / Don't touch / Ar-
ranged marriage / Drink problems / Movie
over India / Magic carpet / Badd Indian /
Don raja
CD _____ IMCD 215
Island / Mar '96 / PolyGram.

Aparis

DESPITE THE FIRE-FIGHTERS
EFFORTS
Sunrice / Waveterms / Welcome / Fire /
Green piece / Orange / Hannibal
CD _____ 5177172
ECM / May '93 / New Note.

Apartments

LIFE FULL OF FAREWELLS, A
Things you'll keep / Failure of love is a brick
wall / You became my big excuse / End of
some fear / Not every clown can be in the
circus / Thank you for making me beg / Pain

the days white / She sings to forget you /
All the time in the world
CD _____ HOT 1050CD
Hot / Mar '95 / Vital.

Apaza, L.

PERUVIAN HARP & MANDOLIN
CD _____ CDT 105CD
Music Of The World / Nov '95 / Target/
BMG / ADA.

Apazie, Don

DON APAZIE (Apazie, Don & His Havana
Casino Orchestra)
CD _____ HQCD 10
Harlequin / '91 / Swift / Jazz Music /
Wellard / Hot Shot / Cadillac.

Apes Pig & Spaceman

TRANSFUSION
Great place / Fragments / Do I need this /
Come round the world / Safety net / Twice
the man / Regurgitate / P.V.S / Take our
sorrow's swimming / Seep / Open season
CD _____ CDMFNX 192
CD _____ CDMFN 192
Music For Nations / Oct '95 / Pinnacle.

Apfelbaum, Peter

JODOJI BRIGHTNESS
CD _____ 5123202
Antilles/New Directions / Apr '92 /
PolyGram.

SIGNS OF LIFE
Candles and stones / Walk to the mountain
/ Grounding / Last door / Word is gifted /
Chant 2 / Forwarding / Samantha Smith /
Folksong No. 7 / Waiting
CD _____ ANCD 8764
Antilles/New Directions / May '91 /
PolyGram.

Aphex Twin

CLASSICS
Digeridoo / Flaphead / Phloam / Isopro-
phlex / Polynomial - C / Tamphex (head
fhug mix) / Phlange place / Dodeccaheed-
ron / Analogue bubblebath / En trange to
exit / Afx 2 / Metaphoristic / We have arrived
CD _____ RS 94035CD
R & S / Jan '95 / Vital.

I CARE BECAUSE YOU DO
CD _____ WARPCD 30
Warp / Apr '95 / Disc.

SELECTED AMBIENT WORKS 1985-
1992
Xtal / Tha / Pulsewidth / Ageispolis / Green-
calx / Heliospan / We are the music makers
/ Schotkey / Ptolemy / Hedphelym / Del-
phium / Actium
CD _____ AMB 3922 CD
Apollo / Dec '92 / Vital.

SELECTED AMBIENT WORKS VOL. 2
CD _____ WARPCD 21
Warp / Feb '94 / Disc.

Aphrodite's Child

666
Aegean sea / All the seats were occupied /
Altornont / Babylon / Battle of the beast /
Beast / Break / Capture of the beast / Do it
/ Four horsemen / Hic-et-nunc / Infinity /
Lamb / Lament / Loud loud / Marching
beast / Ofis / Seven trumpets / Seventh seal
/ System / Tribulation / Wakening beast /
Wedding of the lamb
CD _____ 838 430-2
Phonogram / '92 / PolyGram.

Apocalypse

APOCALYPSE
CD _____ CDFLAG 23
Under One Flag / Aug '89 / Pinnacle.

Apochrypha

AREA 54
Terrors holding on to you / Night in the fog
/ Instrubation #3 (instrumental) / Tian'an-
men Square / Refuse the offer that you
can't refuse / Catch 22 / Power elite / Area
54 / Detriment of man / Born to this world
CD _____ RR 93452
Roadrunner / Nov '90 / Pinnacle.

EYES OF TIME
CD _____ RR 9507 2
Roadrunner / Dec '88 / Pinnacle.

Apollo 440

MILLENNIUM FEVER
Rumble/Spirit of America / Liquid cool / Film
me and finish me off / I need something
stronger / Pain is a close up / Omega point
/ (Don't fear) the reaper / Astral America /
Millenium fever / Stealth requiem
CD _____ SSX 440 CD
Epic / Nov '94 / Sony.

22

Appellation Controllee

APPELLATION CONTROLLEE
CD _____ MW 1001CD
Music & Words / Jun '92 / ADA / Direct.

TIZ
CD _____ DIGIT 5679142
Dig It / Dec '95 / Direct.

Appleyard, Peter

BARBADOS COOL
Tangerine / Strrmpin' at the Savoy / Air mail special / Passion flower / Django / Prelude to a kiss / Memories of you / Fascinating rhythm / Broadway / Cherokee
CD _____ CCD 4475
Concord Jazz / Aug '91 / New Note.

BARBADOS HEAT
You stepped out of a dream / Body and soul / Take the 'A' Train / Satin doll / Caravan nuages / Here's that rainy day / Sing, sing, sing
CD _____ CCD 4436
Concord Jazz / Nov '90 / New Note.

April Wine

APRIL WINE
CD _____ REP 4212-WY
Repertoire / Aug '91 / Pinnacle / Cadillac.

ELECTRIC JEWELS
CD _____ RR 4212
Repertoire / Jul '93 / Pinnacle / Cadillac.

ON RECORD
CD _____ RR 4213
Repertoire / Jul '93 / Pinnacle / Cadillac.

Apu

SECRET OF THE ANDES
CD _____ ANT 1CD
Antara / May '94 / Direct / ADA.

Aquanettas

ROADHAUS
CD _____ ROCK 6131-2
Rockville / Jun '93 / SRD.

Aquaturbia

PSYCHEDELIC DRUGSTORE
CD _____ HBG 122/15
Background / Apr '93 / Background.

Aquila

AQUA DIVA
CD _____ PSY 013CD
PSY Harmonics / Oct '95 / Plastic Head.

Ar Braz, Dan

ACOUSTIC
CD _____ GLCD 3035
Green Linnet / Nov '93 / Roots / CM / Direct / ADA.

MUSIQUES POUR LES SILENCE A VENIR
CD _____ KMCD 02
Keltia Musique / Aug '89 / ADA / Direct / Discovery.

SONGS
CD _____ KMCD 14
Red Sky / '91 / CM / ADA / Direct.

Ar C'hoarezed Goadec

LED VEII LEDEII/DAñIED DL BRETAGNE
CD _____ KMCD 11
Keltia Musique / '91 / ADA / Direct / Discovery.

Ar Log

O AR-LOG IV/AR-LOG V
CD _____ SAIN 9068CD
Sain / Aug '94 / Direct / ADA.

Ar Menez, Dialouled

DIAOULED AR MENEZ
CD _____ CD 318
Diffusion Breizh / May '93 / ADA.

Ar Re Yaouank

BREIZH POSITIVE
CD _____ STSC 02CD
Diffusion Breizh / Apr '95 / ADA.

Arabesque

NIKRIZ (Arabesque & Hassan Erraji)
CD _____ TUGCD 001
Riverboat / Aug '89 / New Note / Sterns.

TRADITIONAL ARABIC MUSIC (Arabesque & Hassan Erraji)
Longa / Taksim hussayni / Ansam (Breezes) / Redile guelbi / Hiwar (dialogue) / Sama'l thaqil / Sidi blal / Cerga / Alway mizan / Bab arraja (The door of hope)
CD _____ CDSDL 387
Saydisc / Mar '94 / Harmonia Mundi / ADA / Direct.

Aranbee Symphony...

ARANBEE POP SYMPHONY ORCHESTRA, THE (Under the Direction of Keith Richard) (Aranbee Symphony Orchestra)
There's a place / Rag doll / I got you babe / We can work it out / Play with fire / Mother's little helper / In the midnight hour / Take it or leave it / Sittin' on a fence / I don't want to go on without you
CD _____ C5CD-522
See For Miles/C5 / Sep '90 / Pinnacle.

Arawi

DOCTRINE OF CYCLES, THE
CD _____ NA 029CD
New Albion / Oct '90 / Harmonia Mundi / Cadillac.

Arbete & Fritid

DEEP WOODS
CD _____ RESCD 501
Resource / Oct '93 / ADA.

Arbuckle, Les

BUSH CREW, THE
CD _____ AQ 1032
Audioquest / Apr '95 / New Note.

Arcadia

SO RED THE ROSE
Election day / Keep me in the dark / Goodbye is forever / Flame / Missing / Rose arcana / Promise / El diablo / Lady Ice
CD _____ CDPRG 1010
Parlophone / Aug '93 / EMI.

Arcady

AFTER THE BALL
Hennessey's / River / Barn dances / Field behind the plow / Heaven's gate / Lullybye / Jackie Daly's reels / Breton reels / Trios matelots du Port - De - Brest / I'd cross the wild Atlantic / Tripping down the stairs / After the ball / Spinsters waltz
CD _____ DARACD 037
Dara / Sep '93 / Roots / CM / Direct / ADA / Koch.

MANY HAPPY RETURNS
CD _____ SHCD 79095
Shanachie / Aug '95 / Koch / ADA / Greensleeves.

Arcane Device

FETISH
CD _____ SR 9009
Silent / Jul '94 / Plastic Head.

Arcansiel

STILL SEARCHING
CD _____ CONTECD 143
Contempo / Jun '90 / Plastic Head.

Arceneaux, Fernest

ZYDECO STOMP (Arceneaux, Fernest & Thunders)
CD _____ JSPCD 258
JSP / Jul '95 / ADA / Target/BMG / Direct / Cadillac / Complete/Pinnacle.

Arch Rival

IN THE FACE OF DANGER
In the face of danger / Time won't wait / Me against the world / Rock the night away / Fortune hunter / God bless America / Revolution / Shotgun at Midnight / Siren's song / Can you tell me why
CD _____ KILCD 1005
Killerwatt / Oct '93 / Kingdom.

Archer, Iain

PLAYING DEAD
CD _____ GUMCD 26
Sticky / May '95 / Total/BMG / SRD.

Archer, Tasmin

GREAT EXPECTATIONS
Sleeping satellite / Arienne / Lords of the new church / When it comes down to it / Somebody's daughter / Hero / Ripped inside / Halfway to heaven
CD _____ CDEMC 3624
EMI / Sep '92 / EMI.

Archers Of Loaf

ICKY METTLE
Web in front / Last word / Wrong / You and me / Might / Hate paste / Fat / Plumb line / Learo, you're a hole / Sick file / Toast / Backwash / Slow worm
CD _____ A 049D
Alias / Sep '93 / Vital.

VEE VEE
Step into the light / Harnessed in slums / Nevermind the enemy / Greatest of all time / Underdogs if Nipomo / Floating friends / 1985 / Fabroch nostalgia / Let the loser melt / Death in the park / Worst has yet to come / Underacheivers march and fight song
CD _____ A064 D
Alias / Mar '95 / Vital.

Archetype

ARCHETYPE
CD _____ CD 831
Diffusion Breizh / May '93 / ADA.

Archey, Jimmy

JIMMY ARCHEY
CD _____ BCD 310
GHB / Jun '94 / Jazz Music.

Archies

PEARLS FROM THE PAST
CD _____ KLMCD 017
Scratch / Apr '94 / BMG.

SUGAR SUGAR
CD _____ WMCD 5670
Woodford Music / Feb '93 / THE.

SUGAR SUGAR
Sugar sugar / Jingle jangle / Bang-shang-a-lang / Sugar and spice / Easy guy / Get on the line / Everything's alright / You little angel, you / Melody hill / Don't touch my guitar / Bicycles, roller skates and you / Seventeen ain't young / Rock 'n' roll music / Hot dog / Kissin' / Inside out - upside down / Feelin' so good (Skoo by-doo) / Who's your baby / Sunshine / Little green jacket / This love / This is the night / Don't need no bad girl
CD _____ 16221 CD
Success / Sep '94 / Carlton Home Entertainment.

Archon Satani

IN SHELTER
CD _____ DVLR 6CD
Dark Vinyl / Jan '95 / Plastic Head.

Arcwelder

PULL
CD _____ TG 108CD
Touch & Go / Feb '93 / SRD.

XERXES
CD _____ TG 126CD
Touch & Go / Apr '94 / SRD.

Arden, Jann

LIVING UNDER JUNE
Could I be your girl / Demolition love / Looking for it (finding heaven) / Insensitive / Gasoline / Wonderdrug / Living under June / Unloved / Good mother / It looks like rain / I would die for you
CD _____ 5403362
A&M / Mar '95 / PolyGram.

Arditti String Quartet

ARDITTI
Grosse fugue op. 133 / Quartet 1931 / Tetras / Quartet No. 3 / Coconino ... a shattered landscape
CD _____ GV 974402
Gramavision / Aug '90 / Vital/SAM / ADA.

Ardoin, Amade

I'M NEVER COMIN' BACK
CD _____ ARhB T007
Arhoolie / Jan '96 / ADA / Direct / Cadillac.

Area

AGATE LINES
CD _____ TMCD 59
Third Mind / Nov '90 / Pinnacle / Third Mind.

Arecibo

TRANS PLUTONIAN TRANSMISSIONS
CD _____ AT 002
Solielmoon Recordings / Mar '95 / Plastic Head.

Arena

SONGS FROM THE LIONS CAGE
Solomon / Crying for help IV / Midas vision / Jericho / Crying for help I / Out of the wilderness / Crying for help / Valley of the kings
CD _____ VGCD 001
Verglas Music / Feb '95 / Pinnacle.

Arena, Tina

DON'T ASK
Chains / Heaven help my heart / I remember (Sorento Moon) / Wasn't it good / Message / Love is the answer / Greatest gift / That's the way a woman feels / Baby be a man / Standing up / Show me heaven
CD _____ 4778869
Columbia / Dec '95 / Sony.

Argent

ALL TOGETHER NOW
Hold your head up / Keep on rolling / Tragedy / I am the dance of ages / Be my lover, be my friend / He's a dynamo / Pure love / Fantasia / Prelude / Finale
CD _____ 477377-2
Epic / Aug '94 / Sony.

ANTHOLOGY - ARGENT (Best of)
School girl / It's only money / Pleasure / Hold your head up / Thunder and lighting / Liar / God gave rock 'n' roll to you / Keep on rolling
CD _____ 9022932
Pickwick/Sony Collector's Choice / Mar '94 / Carlton Home Entertainment / Pinnacle / Sony.

ARGENT
Like honey / Liar / Be free / Schoolgirl / Dance in the smoke / Lonely hard road / Feelings inside / Freefall / Stepping stone / Bring you joy
CD _____ BGOCD 110
Beat Goes On / Aug '91 / Pinnacle.

ENCORE
Coming of Kohoutek / It's only money / God gave rock 'n' roll to you / Thunder and lightning / Music from the spheres / I don't believe in miracles / Dance of ages / Keep on rolling / Hold your head up / Time of the season
CD _____ BGOCD 206
Beat Goes On / Sep '93 / Pinnacle.

IN CONCERT
Be my lover, be my friend / Sweet Mary / Tragedy / Dance of ages / Fakir / Hold your head up / He's a dynamo
CD _____ WINCD 067
Windsong / Oct '94 / Pinnacle.

IN DEEP
CD _____ 4805292
Columbia / May '95 / Sony.

MUSIC FROM THE SPHERES
Music from the spheres / I don't believe in miracles / I am the dance of ages / Keep on rolling / Time of the season / Celebration / Tragedy / Man for all reasons / Like honey / Highwire / Dance in the smoke / It's only money / Sweet Mary / Chained / Rejoice / Pleasure
CD _____ ELITE 004 CD
Elite/Old Gold / Aug '93 / Carlton Home Entertainment.

Arguelles, Julian

HOME TRUTHS
CD _____ BDV 9503
Babel / Oct '95 / ADA / Harmonia Mundi / Cadillac / Diverse.

PHAEDRUS
Phaedrus / Invisible thread / Duet / Forests / Maxine / Red rag / Wild rice / Everything I love / Hi Steve
CD _____ AHUM 010
Ah-Um / Oct '91 / New Note / Cadillac.

Arguelles, Steve

ARGUELLES
Redman / Don't tell me now / Lucky star / Dis at ease / Cherry waltz / Blessed light / Elderberries / My heart belongs to Daddy / Guara / Hermana guapa / Tin tin / Trimmings
CD _____ AHUM 007
Ah-Um / Aug '90 / New Note / Cadillac.

Argyle Park

MISGUIDED
CD _____ REX 460132
Rex / Nov '95 / Cadillac.

Arizona Smoke Revue

BEST OF BLUEGRASS
Duelling banjos / Old Joe Clark / Earl's breakdown / Communications breakdown / Reuben's train / Foggy mountain breakdown / Old groundhog / Auld Lang Syne / Columbus George / Battle of New Orleans / Cannonball line / Black mountain rag / Teetotalers reel / Sailor's hornpipe / Orange blossom special
CD _____ 30363 00022
Country Skyline / Feb '96 / Carlton Home Entertainment.

Ark

SPIRITUAL PHYSICS
CD _____ MC 301CD
Mutilation Corps. / Jun '93 / Plastic Head.

Arkenstone, David

ANOTHER STAR IN THE SKY
Pool of radiance / Far far away / Light in the east / Under the canopy / Voices of the night / Another star in the sky / Taken by the wind / Canyon of the moon / Naked in the wind / Ride into midnight
CD _____ ND 62012
Narada / May '94 / New Note / ADA.

CHRONICLES
CD _____ ND 64007
Narada / Jun '93 / New Note / ADA.

IN THE WAKE OF THE WIND
Papillon (on the wings of the butterfly) / Dark dunes / Not too far to walk / Borderlands / Rug merchant / Firedance / Southern cross / Voyage of the stardancer / Overture / Stardancer / Morning sun on the sails / Lion's breath / Dances of the jankayla / Discovery
CD _____ CD 4003
Narada / Aug '92 / New Note / ADA.

QUEST OF THE DREAM WARRIOR
Prelude: Tallis the messenger / Rhythms of vision / Journey begins: Kyla's ride / Voice / Dance of the maidens / Magic forest / Road to the sea / Temple of vaal / Wings of the shadow / Homecoming
CD _____ ND 64008
Narada / Jun '95 / New Note / ADA.

SPIRIT OF OLYMPIA, THE (Arkenstone, David, Kostia & David Lanz)
Prelude: Let the games begin / Savannah runner / Memories of gold / Keeper of the flame / From the forge to the field / Heartfire / Celebration / Close without touching / Glory / Night in the village / Walk with the stars / Marathon man / Spirit of Olympia
CD _____ CD 4006
Narada / May '92 / New Note / ADA.

Armageddon

ARMAGEDDON
CD _____ REP 4235-WP
Repertoire / Aug '91 / Pinnacle / Cadillac.

INVISIBLE CIRCLE
CD _____ DEAF 013CD
Peaceville / '93 / Pinnacle.

Armagideon

EASE THE TENSION
CD _____ ASCD 001
Armagideon Sounds / Jun '95 / Jetstar / SRD.

STEPPIN' FORWARD
CD _____ ASCD 003
Armagideon Sounds / Mar '95 / Jetstar / SRD.

Armani, Robert

BLOW IT OUT
CD _____ ACVCD 013
ACV / Nov '95 / Plastic Head / SRD.

MADMAN STANDS
CD _____ ACVCD 007
ACV / Apr '95 / Plastic Head / SRD.

NEXT START
CD _____ ACVCD 4
ACV / Nov '93 / Plastic Head / SRD.

RIGHT TO SILENCE
CD _____ ACVCD 4
ACV / Jul '94 / Plastic Head / SRD.

Armatrading, Joan

CHRONICLES
CD Set _____ 5404052
A&M / Sep '95 / PolyGram.

JOAN ARMATRADING
Down to zero / Help yourself / Water with the wine / Love and affection / Save me / Join the boys / People / Somebody who loves you / Like fire / Tall in the saddle
CD _____ CDMID 104
A&M / Aug '91 / PolyGram.

ME, MYSELF, I
Me, myself and I / Ma me o beach / Friends / Is it tomorrow yet / Turn out the light / When you kissed me / All the way from America / Feeling in my heart (for you) / Simon / I need you
CD _____ 5500582
Spectrum/Karussell / Jun '93 / PolyGram / THE.

SHOW SOME EMOTION
Won'cha come on home / Show some emotion / Warm love / Never is too late / Peace in mind / Opportunity / Mama mercy / Get in the sun / Willow / Kissin' and a hugging
CD _____ CDMID 105
A&M / Oct '92 / PolyGram.

SQUARE THE CIRCLE
True love / Crazy / Wrapped around her / Sometimes I don't / Wanna go home / Square the circle / Weak woman / Can I get next to you / Can't get over you / (How I broke your heart) If women ruled the world / Cradled in your love
CD _____ 3958882
A&M / Jun '92 / PolyGram.

VERY BEST OF JOAN ARMATRADING
Love and affection / Down to zero / Drop the pilot / Show some emotion / Showdown stage / Willow / Rosie / I'm lucky / Me, myself and I / (I love it when you) call me names / Bottom to the top / More than one kind of love / Weakness in me / All the way from America
CD _____ 3971222
A&M / Apr '91 / PolyGram.

WHAT'S INSIDE
In your eyes / Everyday boy / Merchant of love / Shapes and sizes / Back on the road / Trouble / Shape of a pony / Can't stop loving you / Beyond the blue / Recommend my love / Would you like to dance / Songs / Lost the love
CD _____ 74321272692
RCA / May '95 / BMG.

WHATEVER'S FOR US
My family / City girl / Spend a little time / Whatever's for us / Child star / Visionary mountains / It could have been better / Head of the table / Mister, remember me / Conversation / Mean old man / All the king's gardens
CD _____ CLACD 143
Castle / Apr '89 / BMG.

Armed Forces

TAKE ON THE NATION
CD _____ CDMFN 136
Music For Nations / Jun '92 / Pinnacle.

Armored Saint

SAINTS WILL CONQUER
Raising fear / Nervous man / Book of blood / Can U deliver / Mad house / No reason to live
CD _____ CDZORRO 28
Metal Blade / Aug '91 / Pinnacle.

SYMBOL OF SALVATION
CD _____ CDZORRO 20
Metal Blade / Mar '91 / Pinnacle.

Armoured Angel

MYSTERIUM
CD _____ ID 000312CD
Modern Invasion / May '95 / Plastic Head.

STIGMARTYR
CD _____ NF 100012
Modern Invasion / Apr '95 / Plastic Head.

Armstrong Family

WHEEL OF THE YEAR, THE
CD _____ FF 594CD
Flying Fish / Feb '93 / Roots / CM / Direct / ADA.

Armstrong, James

SLEEPING WITH A STRANGER
CD _____ HCD 8068
Hightone / Dec '95 / ADA / Koch.

Armstrong, Louis

16 MOST REQUESTED SONGS
CD _____ 4767182
Sony Jazz / Jan '95 / Sony.

1924-1930 (6CD Set) (Armstrong, Louis & The Blues Singers)
See see rider blues / Jelly bean blues / Countin' the blues / Early in the morning / You've got the right key but the wrong key-hole / Of all the wrong you've done to me / Everybody loves my baby / Texas moaner blues / Papa, mama's all alone / Change-able daddy of mine / Baby, I can't use you no more / Trouble everywhere I roam / Poor house blues / Anybody here want to try my cabbage / Thunderstorm blues / If I lose, let me lose / Screamin' the blues / Good time flat blues / Mandy, make up your mind / I'm a little blackbird looking for a bluebird / Nobody knows the way I feel dis morning / Early every morn' / Cake walkin' babies from home / Broken busted blues / Pickin' on your baby / St. Louis blues / Reckless blues / Sobbin' hearted blues / Cold in hand blues / You've been a good ole wagon / You've got to beat me to keep me / Mining camp blues / Cast away / Papa de da da / World's jazz crazy (and so am I) / Railroad blues / My John blues / Nashville woman's blues / Careless lone blues / J.C. Holmes blues / I ain't gonna play no second fiddle / I miss my Swiss / You dirty mistreater / Come on coot do that thing / Have your chill, I'll be here when your fever rises / Find me at the greasy spoon / Just wait 'til you see my baby do the Charleston / Livin' high / Coal cart blues / Santa Claus blues / Squeeze me / You can't shush Katie (the grabbiest girl in town) / Lucy long / Low land blues / Kid man blues / Lazy woman blues / Lonesome lovesick blues / Gambler's dream / Sunshine baby / Adam and Eve had the blues / Furel in the morning / Washwoman blues / I've stopped my man / Lonesome all alone blues / Trouble in mind / G'man / You've got to go home on time / What kind o' man is that / Deep water blues / G'man, I told you / Listen to ma / Lonesome hours / Jealous woman like me / Special delivery blues / Jack O'diamonds / Mail train blues / I feel good / Man for every day in the week / Bridwell blues / St. Peter blues / He likes it slow / Pleadin' for the blues / Pratt city blues / Mess, Katie, mess / Lovesick blues / Lonesome weary blues / Dead drunk blues / Flood blues / You're a real sweetheart / Too busy / Was it a dream / Last night I dreamed you kissed me / I can't give you anything but love /

Baby / Sweetheart on parade / I must have that man / S'posin' / To be in love / Funny feathers / How do you do it that way / Ain't misbehavin' / Blue yodel no. 9 (Standing on the corner)
CD Set _____ CDAFS 1018-6
Affinity / Sep '91 / Charly / Cadillac / Jazz Music.

1925-26 (Armstrong, Louis & His Hot Five)
CD _____ CLASSICS 600
Classics / '91 / Discovery / Jazz Music.

1930-1931
CD _____ CLASSICS 547
Classics / Dec '90 / Discovery / Jazz Music.

1957
CD _____ CD 53153
Giants Of Jazz / Nov '95 / Target/BMG / Cadillac.

2 FACETS OF LOUIS
CD _____ 4737542
Sony Jazz / Jan '95 / Sony.

2ND ALLSTAR JAZZ FESTIVAL (Armstrong, Louis & His Allstars)
Krazy Kat / Jul '93 / Hot Shot / CM.

AIN'T MISBEHAVIN'
CD _____ AVC 504
Avid / Dec '92 / Avid/BMG / Koch.

ALL STARS COLLECTION 1950-56, THE
CD _____ CD 53091
Giants Of Jazz / Mar '92 / Target/BMG / Cadillac.

AMBASSADOR SATCH
CD _____ 4718712
Sony Jazz / Jan '95 / Sony.

BASIN STREET BLUES
CD _____ BLCD 760128
Black Lion / Jun '88 / Jazz Music / Cadillac / Wellard / Koch.

BEST OF LOUIS ARMSTRONG VOL.1
CD _____ DLCD 4001
Dixie Live / Mar '95 / Magnum Music Group.

BEST OF LOUIS ARMSTRONG VOL.2
CD _____ CDSGP 055
Prestige / Apr '93 / Total/BMG.

BEST OF LOUIS ARMSTRONG VOL.2
CD _____ DLCD 4014
Dixie Live / Mar '95 / Magnum Music Group.

BEST OF LOUIS ARMSTRONG, THE
CD _____ CDSGP 038
Prestige / Jan '93 / Total/BMG.

BIG BANDS VOL. 1 (1930-31)
CD _____ JSPCD 305
JSP / Oct '88 / ADA / Target/BMG / Direct / Cadillac / Complete/Pinnacle.

BLUES 'N' MORE
St. Louis blues / Ain't hater's blues / Yellow dog blues / Loveless dove / Black and blue / Ain't misbehavin' / Memphis blues / Squeeze me / Hesitating blues / Beale Street blues / Chante les bas / Atlanta blues / Blue turning grey over you / Long gone
CD _____ ELITE 013 CD
Elite/Old Gold / Aug '93 / Carlton Home Entertainment.

C'EST SI BON
Mame / When the saints go marching in / Ain't misbehavin' / Cabaret / Kiss to build a dream on / Please don't talk about me when I'm gone / Blueberry Hill / Hello Dolly / St. Louis blues / That's my desire / Mack the knife / Back o' town blues / Fly me to the moon / (Back home again in) Indiana / Tiger rag / Black and blue / C'est si bon / St. James infirmary / Someday you'll be sorry / Sweethearts on parade / Jelly roll blues
CD _____ CDGRF 036
Tring / '93 / Tring / Prism.

CHICAGO CONCERT 1956
Memphis blues / Frankie and Johnny / Tiger rag / Do you know what it means to miss New Orleans / Basin Street blues / Black and blue / West End blues / On the sunny side of the street / Struttin' with some barbecue / Manhattan / When it's sleepy time down South / (Back home again in) Indiana / Gypsy / Faithful hussar / Rockin' chair / Bucket's got a hole in it / Perdido / Clarinet marmalade / Mack the knife / Tenderly / You'll never walk alone / Stompin' at the Savoy / Margie / Mama's back in town / That's my desire / Kokomo / I love you so
CD _____ 471870 2
Columbia / Nov '93 / Sony.

COLLECTION - 25 TUNES
CD _____ COL 001
Collection / Jan '95 / Target/BMG.

COMPLETE TOWN HALL CONCERT, THE
Cornet chop suey / Our Monday date / Dear old Southland / Big butter and egg man / Tiger rag / Struttin' with some barbecue / Sweethearts on parade / St. Louis blues / Pennies from Heaven / On the sunny side of the street / I can't give you anything but

---

love / Back o' town blues / Ain't misbehavin' / Rockin' chair / Muskrat ramble / Save it pretty Mama / St. James Infirmary / Royal Garden blues / Do you know what it means to miss New Orleans / Jack Armstrong blues
CD _____ ND 897462
Jazz Tribune / Jun '94 / BMG.

ESSENCE OF ARMSTRONG
CD _____ PHONTCD 9308
Phontastic / Dec '94 / Wellard / Jazz Music / Cadillac.

ESSENTIAL HOT FIVE SIDES, THE
CD _____ JZ-CD324
Suisa / Feb '91 / Jazz Music / THE.

ESSENTIAL HOT SEVEN SIDES AND SOME RARITIES, THE
CD _____ JZ-CD325
Suisa / Feb '91 / Jazz Music / THE.

ESSENTIAL LOUIS ARMSTRONG, THE
CD _____ 4618702
Sony Jazz / Jan '95 / Sony.

ESSENTIAL LOUIS ARMSTRONG, THE #2
CD _____ 4716872
Sony Jazz / Jan '95 / Sony.

ESSENTIAL RECORDINGS 1925-1940 (4CD Set)
CD Set _____ CDDIG 17
Charly / Jun '95 / Charly / THE / Cadillac.

ESSENTIAL SATCHMO, THE
What a wonderful world / Blueberry Hill / Hello Dolly / La vie en rose / Cabaret / Lazy river / Whiffenpoof song / On the sunny side of the street / Georgia on my mind / When you're smiling / That lucky old sun / Home fire / Dream a little dream of me / Give me your kisses (I'll give you my heart) / Fantastic, that's you / Hellzapoppin' / Hello brother / Sunshine of love
CD _____ MCCD 088
Music Club / Dec '92 / Disc / THE / CM.

EVENING WITH LOUIS ARMSTRONG, AN
CD Set _____ GNPD 2-11001
GNP Crescendo / May '89 / Silva Screen.

FIRST SOLOS (Armstrong, Louis & King Oliver's Jazzband)
CD _____ JZ-CD323
Suisa / Feb '91 / Jazz Music / THE.

FLETCHER HENDERSON & LOUIS ARMSTRONG, 1924-1925 (Armstrong, Louis & Fletcher Henderson Orchestra)
Money blues / Why couldn't it be poor little me / I'll see you in my dreams / Tell me, dreamy eyes / My Rose Marie / Poplar Street blues / Shanghai shuffle / Mandy, make up your mind / Go 'long mule / Memphis bound / How come you do me like you do / Alabamy bound / Copenhagen / Meanest kind of blues / I miss my Swiss / Alone at last / Shanghai shuffle (2) / When you do what you do / Words / Carolina stomp / Bye and bye / Naughty man / Play me slow / T.N.T. / One of these days / Sugarfoot stomp
CD _____ CBC 1003
Timeless Historical / Jan '92 / New Note / Pinnacle.

FROM THE BIG BAND TO THE ALL STARS
Long long journey / Linger in my arms a little longer / Back o' town blues / Where the blues was born in New Orleans / I believe / You don't learn that in school / Rockin' chair / I never saw a better day / Hobo, you can't ride this train / Snafu / Whatta ya gonna do / No variety blues / Joseph and his brudders / Endie / Blues are brewin' / You're smiling / That it means to miss New Orleans / Mahogany Hall stomp / I wonder, I wonder, I wonder / Why doubt my love / It takes time / Jack Armstrong blues / Some day (You'll be sorry) / Fifty fifty blues / Song was born / Please, stop playing those blues / Before long / Lovely weather we're having / Rain rain
CD _____ ND 892792
Jazz Tribune / Jun '94 / BMG.

GEORGIA ON MY MIND
Old rockin' chair / (I'll be glad when you're dead) you rascal you / Wild man blues / Confessin' / Lazy river / Dinah / I ain't got nobody / Georgia bo bo / You're lucky to me / Monday date / St. James infirmary / Georgia on my mind / West End blues / Ain't misbehavin' / Knocking a jug / I can't believe that you're in love with me / St. Louis blues / Chinatown my Chinatown / Drop that sack / My sweet
CD _____ DBCD 17
Dance Band Days / Aug '90 / Prism.

GOLD COLLECTION, THE
CD _____ D2CD04
Recording Arts / Dec '92 / THE / Disc.

GREAT CONCERT, THE
CD _____ 401542CD
Musidisc / Jul '94 / Vital / Harmonia Mundi / ADA / Cadillac / Discovery.

GREAT LOUIS ARMSTRONG 1937 - 1941, THE
Yes suh / Wolverine blues / Cut off my legs and call me shorty / Cain and Abel / When it's sleepy time down South / Hep cats' ball

/ Do you call that a buddy / Down in honky tonk town / You run your mouth, I'll run my business / Save it pretty Mama / Perdido street blues / Me and brother blues / Struttin' with some barbecue / 2.19 Blues / (I'll be glad when you're dead) you rascal you / Lazy 'Sippi steamers / I'll get mine bye and bye / Harlem stomp / Hey lawdy mama / I double dare you / Public melody number one / Yours and mine
CD _____ PASTCD 7002
Flapper / Jan '93 / Pinnacle.

GREAT ORIGINAL PERFORMANCES
CD _____ RPCD 618
Robert Parker Jazz / Sep '93 / Conifer.

GUVNOR, THE
Mahogany hall stomp / St. Louis blues / I'm confessin' that I love you / Dinah / Chinatown, my Chinatown / Georgia on my mind / Lazy river / Rockin' chair / I hope Gabriel likes my music / Struttin' with some barbecue / I double dare you / Hear me talkin' to ya / Save it pretty Mama / Shoe shine boy / Red nose / West End blues / St. James infirmary / (I'll be glad when you're dead) you rascal you / You're luky to me / Wild man blues
CD _____ PAR 2015
Parade / Apr '95 / Koch / Cadillac.

HEAVENLY MUSIC 1949-57
CD _____ CLA 1916
Ambassador / Mar '94 / Wellard / Jazz Music / Cadillac.

HELLO DOLLY
CD _____ 3001002
Scratch / Jul '95 / BMG.

HIGHLIGHTS FROM HIS DECCA YEARS
Wild man blues / Weary blues / Georgia bo bo / Shanghai shuffle / I'm in the mood for love / Ol man hose / Skeleton in the closet / She's the daughter of a planter from Havana / Jubilee / Struttin' with some barbecue / Jeepers creepers / I'm confessin' that I love you / Wolverine blues / Perdido street blues / When it's sleepy time down South / I never knew / Ronettes / Muskrat ramble / Black and blue / Song is ended (but the melody lingers on) / You won't be satisfied (Until you break my heart) / You can't lose a broken heart / (I'll be glad when you're dead) you rascal you / Gone fishin' / That lucky old sun / My bucket's got a hole in it / La vie en rose / Someday / Baby, it's cold outside / Your cheatin' heart / Gypsy / Tin roof blues / Sometimes I feel like a motherless child / When you're smiling / Memories of you / King of the Zulus
CD _____ GRP 26382
GRP / Oct '94 / BMG / New Note.

HOT FIVE TO ALL-STARS (1925-56)
Alligator crawl / Wild man blues / Melancholy blues / Willie the weeper / Ory's creole trombone / Struttin' with some barbecue / Hotter than that / West End blues / Potato head blues / Keyhole blues / Gully low blues / Basin Street blues / S.O.L. blues / 12th Street rag / Savoy blues / Muskrat ramble / Cornet chop suey / Skid-dat-de-dat / Dance back sweet Papa / Yes, I'm in the barrel / Weary blues / Put 'em down / Monday date / Rockin' chair / Jack / Armstrong blues / Mahogany hall stomp / Do you know what it means to miss New Orleans / Where the blues was born in New Orleans / Blues for yesterday / Sugar / Long long journey / (I'll be glad when you're dead) you rascal you / Perdido street blues / 2.19 blues / Down in honky tonk town / Coal cart blues / Wolverine blues / Cut off my legs and call me shorty / Satchel mouth swing / Loved walked in / On the sunny side of the street / Swing that music / Dusky stevedore / That's my home / I surrender dear / Blue turning grey over you / That rhythm man / What did I do to be so black and blue / Struttin' with some barbecue #2 / All that meat and no potatoes / Ole Miss / Back o' town blues / (Back home again in) Indiana / That's my desire / Ain't misbehavin' / Aunt Hagar's blues / Tin roof blues / Panama / My bucket's got a hole in it / New Orleans function / Free as a bird / Didn't he ramble / When it's sleepy time down South
CD Set _____ CDB 1205
Giants Of Jazz / '92 / Target/BMG / Cadillac.

HOT FIVES AND HOT SEVENS
My heart / I'm in the barrel / Gut bucket blues / Come back sweet Papa / Georgia grind / Heebie jeebies / Cornet chop suey / Oriental strut / You're next / Muskrat ramble / Don't forget to mess around / I'm gonna gitcha / Droppin' shucks / Whosit / King of the Zulus / Big fat Ma and skinny Pa
CD _____ 4608012
CBS / May '90 / Sony.

HOT FIVES AND HOT SEVENS
CD _____ CD 56010
Jazz Roots / Aug '94 / Target/BMG.

HOT FIVES AND HOT SEVENS #2
CD _____ 4630522
Sony Jazz / Jan '95 / Sony.

HOT FIVES AND HOT SEVENS #3
CD _____ 4651892
CBS / Jul '88 / Sony.

HOT FIVES AND HOT SEVENS I (1926-27)
Lonesome blues / Sweet little papa / Jazz lips / Skid-dat-de-dat / I want a big butter and egg man / Sunset cafe stomp / You made me love you / Irish black bottom / Willie the weeper / Wild man blues / Chicago breakdown / Alligator crawl / Potato head blues / Melancholy blues / Weary blues / 12th Street rag
CD _____ JSPCD 312
JSP / Apr '90 / ADA / Target/BMG / Direct / Cadillac / Complete/Pinnacle.

HOT FIVES AND HOT SEVENS II
Willie the weeper / Wild man blues / Chicago breakdown / Alligator crawl / Potato head blues / 12th Street rag / Keyhole blues / S.O.L. blues / Gully low blues / That's when I'll come back to you / Put 'em down blues / Ory's creole trombone / Last time / Struttin' with some barbecue / Got no blues / Once in a while / I'm not rough / Hotter than that / Savoy blues
CD _____ JSPCD 313
JSP / Apr '90 / ADA / Target/BMG / Direct / Cadillac / Complete/Pinnacle.

HOT FIVES AND HOT SEVENS III
CD _____ JSPCD 314
JSP / Feb '92 / ADA / Target/BMG / Direct / Cadillac / Complete/Pinnacle.

HOT FIVES AND HOT SEVENS IV
CD _____ JSPCD 315
JSP / Jun '92 / ADA / Target/BMG / Direct / Cadillac / Complete/Pinnacle.

HOT FIVES AND HOT SEVENS VOL.1 1925-1926
CD _____ 781083-2
Jazztime / Aug '93 / Discovery / BMG.

HOT FIVES AND HOT SEVENS VOL.2 1926-1927
CD _____ 781084-2
Jazztime / Aug '93 / Discovery / BMG.

I GOT RHYTHM
I got rhythm / Honeysuckle rose / Jeepers creepers / Tiger rag / Muskrat ramble / Way down yonder in New Orleans / When the saints go marching in / Body and soul / Sweethearts on parade / You're driving me crazy / Just a gigolo / Ain't misbehavin' / Back o' town blues / C'est si bon / Stompin' at the Savoy / Shine / On the sunny side of the street / La vie en rose / Hucklebuck / Memories of you
CD _____ PWK 137
Carlton Home Entertainment / May '90 / Carlton Home Entertainment.

IMMORTAL CONCERTS (At the Symphony Hall-Boston, November 30, 1947) (Armstrong, Louis & His Allstars)
Mahogany Hall stomp / Black and blue / Royal Garden blues / That's my desire / C jam blues / Stars fell on Alabama / I cried for you / On the sunny side of the street / Tea for two / Baby, won't you please come home / Muskrat ramble / Lover / Body and soul / Steak face / High society / Boff boff
CD _____ ENTCD 235
Entertainers / Feb '88 / Target/BMG.

IN CONCERT AT WASHINGTON THEATRE
All That's Jazz / '92 / THE / Jazz Music.
CD _____ ATJCD 5957

INTRODUCTION TO LOUIS ARMSTRONG 1924-38
CD _____ 4004
Best Of Jazz / Dec '93 / Discovery.

JAZZ CLASSICS MASTERWORKS (Armstrong, Louis/Sidney Bechet)
Yes, I'm in the barrel / Struttin' with some barbecue / Cornet shop suey / Wild man blues / S.O.L. blues / Weary blues / Basin Street blues / Monday date / West End blues / Mahogany Hall stomp / On the sunny side of the street / Baby, won't you please come home / C-jam blues / Kansas City man blues / Jazz me blues / Honey suckle Rose
CD _____ 17051
Laserlight / Nov '95 / Target/BMG.

JAZZ MASTERS
CD _____ 519618-2
Verve / May '94 / PolyGram.

JAZZ PORTRAITS
Can anyone explain / My sweet hunk o'trash / You won't be satisfied (until you break my heart) / Fifty fifty blues / You can't lose a broken heart / Frim fram sauce / (I'll be glad when you're dead) you rascal you / Oops / Life is so peculiar / Dream a little dream of me / Struttin' with some barbecue / Necessary evil / Lazy bones / Long gone / Now you has jazz / Who walks in when I walk out / Boog it / Honeysuckle rose
CD _____ CD 14513
Jazz Portraits / May '94 / Jazz Music.

LEGENDARY, THE (Armstrong, Louis/Bessie Smith/ King Oliver)
CD _____ TKOCD 014
TKO / '92 / TKO.

LIVE 1938-1940 (Armstrong, Louis & Fats Waller)
CD _____ MM 31056
Music Memoria / Aug '93 / Discovery / ADA.

LIVE AT EXHIBITION GARDEN - VANCOUVER CANADA (Armstrong, Louis Allstars)
Rockin' chair / Where did you stay last night / Baby, it's cold outside / C Jam blues / Stompin' at the Savoy / I used to love you / La vie en rose / Lover / I love the guy / That's my desire / Royal garden blues / Ain't misbehavin'
CD _____ CDINS 5046
Charly / Dec '92 / Charly / THE / Cadillac.

LOUIS & LUIS (Original recordings 1929-1940) (Armstrong, Louis & Luis Russell)
Baby, won't you please come home / Bessie couldn't help it / Blue turning grey over you / 2.19 blues / Bye and bye / Confessin' / Dallas blues / Mahogany hall stomp / On the sunny side of the street / Our Monday date / Perdido blues / Public Melody Number One / Rockin' chair / St. Louis blues / Savoy blues / Struttin' with some barbecue / Sweethearts on parade / Swing that music / Thanks a million / West End blues / When it's sleepy time down South / When the saints go marching in / Wolverine blues / You run your mouth, I'll run my business / You're a lucky guy
CD _____ CD AJA 5094
Living Era / Sep '92 / Koch.

LOUIS ARMSTRONG
CD _____ LECD 050
Dynamite / May '94 / THE.

LOUIS ARMSTRONG
CD _____ 22701
Music / Nov '95 / Target/BMG.

LOUIS ARMSTRONG (2CD Set)
CD Set _____ R2CD 4004
Deja Vu / Jan '96 / THE.

LOUIS ARMSTRONG & EARL HINES (Armstrong, Louis & Earl Hines)
CD _____ 4663082
Sony Jazz / Jan '95 / Sony.

LOUIS ARMSTRONG & HIS ALL STARS (Armstrong, Louis & His Allstars)
CD _____ 15773
Laserlight / Jul '92 / Target/BMG.

LOUIS ARMSTRONG & HIS ALL STARS
CD _____ CD 14550
Jazz Portraits / Jul '94 / Jazz Music.

LOUIS ARMSTRONG & HIS ALL STARS (Armstrong, Louis & His Allstars)
When it's sleepy time down South / Hello Dolly / Blueberry Hill / Volare / St. James infirmary / Girl from Ipanema / (Back home again in) Indiana / Muskrat ramble / Mack the knife / I love Paris / Time after time / Cabaret / Tiger rag / When the saints go marching in / This could be the start of something big / Please don't talk about me when I'm gone / Stompin' at the Savoy / That's my desire / Closer walk with thee / Them there eyes / Avalon / Kiss to build a dream on / Ole miss
CD _____ STCD 4095
Storyville / Feb '89 / Jazz Music / Wellard / CM / Cadillac.

LOUIS ARMSTRONG & HIS ORCHESTRA 1940-1942 (Armstrong, Louis Orchestra)
CD _____ CLASSICS 685
Classics / Mar '93 / Discovery / Jazz Music.

LOUIS ARMSTRONG (1928-1931)
CD _____ HRM 6002
Hermes / Sep '88 / Nimbus.

LOUIS ARMSTRONG 1926-1927
CD _____ CLASSICS 585
Classics / Aug '91 / Discovery / Jazz Music.

LOUIS ARMSTRONG 1926-28 & BIG BANDS/ALTERNATIVES
CD _____ KJ 151FS
King Jazz / Oct '93 / Jazz Music / Cadillac / Discovery.

LOUIS ARMSTRONG 1931-47 (Armstrong, Louis Orchestra/Hot Seven/ Dixieland Seven)
CD _____ CD 14563
Jazz Portraits / May '95 / Jazz Music.

LOUIS ARMSTRONG 1959
CD _____ TAXCD 3712
Tax / '89 / Jazz Music / Wellard / Cadillac.

LOUIS ARMSTRONG AND EDMOND HALL'S ORCHESTRA (Live at Carnegie Hall, Feb 8 1947) (Armstrong, Louis & Edmond Hall's Orchestra)
New Orleans function / St. Louis blues / Muskrat ramble / Ain't misbehavin'
CD _____ 20802
Laserlight / Aug '94 / Target/BMG.

LOUIS ARMSTRONG AND HIS ALL STARS (1961-2)
CD _____ STCD 4012
Storyville / Feb '89 / Jazz Music / Wellard / CM / Cadillac.

LOUIS ARMSTRONG AND HIS ALL STARS (1947-50) (Armstrong, Louis & His Allstars)
CD _____ CD 53032
Giants Of Jazz / Sep '88 / Target/BMG / Cadillac.

LOUIS ARMSTRONG AND HIS ALL STARS (Armstrong, Louis & His Allstars)
CD _____ UCD 19002
Forlane / Jul '88 / Target/BMG.

LOUIS ARMSTRONG AND HIS BAND (1944-45) (Armstrong, Louis & his band)
CD _____ 90 509 2
Jazz Archives / Aug '91 / Jazz Music / Discovery / Cadillac.

LOUIS ARMSTRONG AND HIS GREAT BIG BAND
CD _____ JCD 19
Jass / Feb '91 / CM / Jazz Music / ADA / Cadillac / Direct.

LOUIS ARMSTRONG AND KING OLIVER
Just gone / Canal Street blues / Mandy Lee blues / I'm going to wear you off my mind / Chimes blues / Weatherbird rag / Dippermouth blues / Froggie Moore / Snake rag / Alligator hop / Zulu's ball / Workin' man blues / Krooked blues / Mabel's dream / Southern stomps (take 1) / Southern stomps (take 2) / Riverside blues / King Oliver / Jelly roll morton / Tom cat blues / Terrible blues / Santa Claus blues / Texas moaner blues / Of all the wrongs you've done to me / Nobody knows the way I feel this morning / Early every morn' / Cake walkin' babies from home
CD _____ MCD 47017 2
Milestone / Jun '93 / Jazz Music / Pinnacle / Wellard / Cadillac.

LOUIS ARMSTRONG COLLECTION, THE
Mame / Stompin' at the Savoy / I got rhythm / Honeysuckle rose / When the saints go marching in / Muskrat ramble / Way down yonder in New Orleans / Ain't misbehavin' / Royal garden blues / La vie en rose / Cabaret / Hucklebuck / I used to love you / Kis to build a dream on / Hello Dolly / Please don't talk about me when I'm gone / Just a gigolo / I'm your ding dong daddy from Dumas / Blueberry hill / I'm in the market for you / Peanut vendor / Mahogany hall stomp / St. Louis blues / You're lucky to me / That's my desire / I'm confessin' that I love you / Mack the knife / If I could be with you one hour tonight / Jeepers creepers / Basin Street blues / Body and soul / Back o' town blues / Memories of you / You're driving me crazy / I want a big butter and egg man / Shine / On the sunny side of the street / (Back home again in) Indiana / Dear old southland / Tiger rag / Bye and bye / Black and blue / Tea for two / Jelly Roll blues / Chimes blues / Dippermouth blues / C est si bon / Savoy stomp / I can't give you anything but love / St. James Infirmary / That rhythm man / Lover / Someday you'll be sorry / Snake rag / New Orleans stomp / Sweethearts on parade
CD Set _____ TFP 011
Tring / Nov '92 / Tring / Prism.

LOUIS ARMSTRONG COLLECTORS' EDITION
CD _____ DVX 812
Deja Vu / Apr '95 / THE.

LOUIS ARMSTRONG GOLD (2CD Set)
CD Set _____ D2CD 4004
Deja Vu / Jun '95 / THE.

LOUIS ARMSTRONG GREAT ALTERNATIVES - 1929-37
CD _____ KJ 153FS
King Jazz / Oct '93 / Jazz Music / Cadillac / Discovery.

LOUIS ARMSTRONG IN CONCERT
CD _____ RTE 10012CD
RTE / Apr '95 / ADA / Koch.

LOUIS ARMSTRONG LIVE IN PARIS
CD _____ ACDCH 553
Milan / Jun '90 / BMG / Silva Screen.

LOUIS ARMSTRONG PLAYS W.C. HANDY
St. Louis blues / Yellow dog blues / Loveless love / Aunt Hagar's blues / Louis Armstrong monologue / Long gone (from bowlin' green) / Memphis blues (or, Mister Crump) / Beale Street blues / Ole Miss / Chantez les bas (sing 'em low) / Hesitating blues / Atlanta blues (make me one pallet on your foot)
CD _____ 4509812
CBS / Mar '88 / Sony.

LOUIS ARMSTRONG VOL 1 - 1935 (Armstrong, Louis/Luis Russell/Victor Young)
Sunny side of the street / Ain't misbehavin' / I'm in the mood for love / You are my lucky star / I hope Gabriel likes my music / Solitude thanks a million / Shoe shine boy / Red sails in the sunset / On treasure island / Got a bran' new suit
CD _____ CLA 1901
Ambassador / Mar '94 / Wellard / Jazz Music / Cadillac.

LOUIS ARMSTRONG VOL 2 - 1936
Music goes round and around / Rhythm saved the world / I'm putting all my eggs in

one basket / Yes yes, my my / Somebody stole my break / I come from a musical family / If we never meet again / Lyin' to myself / Eventide / Swing that music / Dinah
CD _____ CLA 1902
Ambassador / Mar '94 / Wellard / Jazz Music / Cadillac.

LOUIS ARMSTRONG VOL 5 - 1938-39
Naturally / I've got a pocketful of dreams / I can't give you anything but love / Ain't misbehavin' / 12th street rag / Swing that music / Flat foot floogie / Elder Eatmore's sermon on throwing stones / Elder Eatmore's sermon on generosity / Tiger rag / Jeepers creepers / Let my people go / On the sunny side of the street / Blues / Honeysuckle rose / Shadrack / Nobody knows the trouble I've seen / Jeepers creepers (1) / What is this thing called swing / Rockin' chair / Bye bye bones
CD _____ CLA 1905
Ambassador / Jun '94 / Wellard / Jazz Music / Cadillac.

LOUIS ARMSTRONG VOL 6 - 1939-40
CD _____ CLA 1906
Ambassador / Mar '94 / Wellard / Jazz Music / Cadillac.

LOUIS ARMSTRONG VOL 7 (1940-41)
CD _____ CLA 1907
Ambassador / Jun '95 / Wellard / Jazz Music / Cadillac.

LOUIS ARMSTRONG VOL. 1 - 1925-27
CD _____ KJ 146FS
King Jazz / Oct '93 / Jazz Music Cadillac / Discovery.

LOUIS ARMSTRONG VOL. 2 - 1927-28
CD _____ KJ 147FS
King Jazz / Oct '93 / Jazz Music Cadillac / Discovery.

LOUIS ARMSTRONG VOL. 3 - 1928-29
CD _____ KJ 148FS
King Jazz / Oct '93 / Jazz Music Cadillac / Discovery.

LOUIS ARMSTRONG VOL. 4 - 1929-31
CD _____ KJ 149FS
King Jazz / Oct '93 / Jazz Music Cadillac / Discovery.

LOUIS ARMSTRONG VOL. 5 - 1931-32
CD _____ KJ 150FS
King Jazz / Oct '93 / Jazz Music Cadillac / Discovery.

LOUIS ARMSTRONG/COUNT BASIE ESSENTIALS (Armstrong, Louis & Count Basie)
CD _____ LECDD 640
Wisepack / Aug '95 / THE / Conifer.

LOUIS IN NEW YORK
CD _____ 4669652
Sony Jazz / Jan '95 / Sony.

LOUIS SINGS THE BLUES
CD _____ 07863662442
Novus / Jul '93 / BMG.

MACK THE KNIFE
When it's sleepy time down South / (Back home again) in Indiana / Now you has jazz / High society calypso / Mahogany hall stomp / Blue moon / Sweet Georgia Brown / Riff blues / Mack the knife / Lazy river / Stompin' at the Savoy
CD _____ CD 2310 941
Pablo / Jun '93 / Jazz Music / Cadillac / Complete/Pinnacle.

MAHOGANY HALL STOMP (Original Recordings 1927-36)
Mahogany Hall stomp / Rockin' chair / Savoy blues / Sweethearts on parade / Swing that music / Lyin' to myself / Thankful / I come from a musical family / Eventide / Red nose / If we never meet again / Peanut vendor / You're lucky to me / St. James infirmary / (I'll be glad when you're dead) you rascal you / Lazy river / I ain't got nobody / Ain't misbehavin'
CD _____ CDAJA 5049
Living Era / Nov '87 / Koch.

MAHOGANY HALL STOMP
Mahogany Hall stomp / I can't give you anything but love / Ain't misbehavin' / That rhythm man / Sweet Savannah Sue / Rockin' chair / Song of the Islands / Blue turning grey over you / I can't believe that you're in love with me / I'm in the market for you / Confessin' / Body and soul / You're driving me crazy / Them there eyes / Wrap your troubles in dreams (and dream your troubles away) / Star dust / I got rhythm / Between the Devil and the deep blue sea
CD _____ CDSVL 198
Saville / '88 / Conifer.

MAJESTIC YEARS, THE
CD _____ AVC 541
Avid / May '94 / Avid/BMG / Koch.

MASTERPIECES (Hot Five and Hot Seven 1925-28)
CD _____ CD 53001
Giants Of Jazz / Mar '92 / Target/BMG / Cadillac.

MASTERPIECES 1926-41
CD _____ 158132
Masterpieces / Mar '94 / BMG.

MASTERPIECES 1927-42
CD _____ 158142
Masterpieces / Mar '94 / BMG.

MOMENTS TO REMEMBER 1952-56
CD _____ CLA 1917
Ambassador / Aug '95 / Wellard / Jazz Music / Cadillac.

NEW ORLEANS FUNCTION
When it's sleepy time down South / (Back home again) in Indiana / Give me a kiss to build a dream on / My bucket's got a hole in it / Mack the knife / Ole Miss / C'est si bon / La vie en rose / New Orleans function / Free as a bird / Oh didn't he ramble
CD _____ ENTCD 206
Entertainers / Sep '87 / Target/BMG.

ON THE ROAD
CD _____ 15798
Laserlight / Jan '93 / Target/BMG.

ON THE SUNNY SIDE OF THE STREET
CD _____ JASSCD 19
Jass / Aug '90 / CM / Jazz Music / ADA / Cadillac / Direct.

PLAYS AND SINGS THE GREAT STANDARDS (1928-1932)
CD _____ BLE 592262
Black & Blue / Nov '92 / Wellard / Koch.

POCKET FULL OF DREAMS
Trumpet players lament / I double dare you / True confession / Let that be a lesson to you / Sweet as a song / So little time (so much to do) / Mexican swing / As long as you live, you'll be dead if you die / When the saints go marching in / On the sentimental side / It's wonderful / Something tells me / Love walked in / Naturally (natch-ra-ly) / I've got a pocket full of dreams / I can't give you anyth'n but love / Ain't misbehavin' / Got a bran new suit
CD _____ GRP 16492
GRP / Nov '95 / BMG / New Note.

POPS - THE HAPPY SOUND OF LOUIS ARMSTRONG (Armstrong, Louis Orchestra & All Stars)
CD _____ CDJJ 626
Jazz & Jazz / Jan '92 / Target/BMG.

PORGY AND BESS (Armstrong, Louis & Ella Fitzgerald)
Summertime / I got plenty o' nuttin' / My man's gone now / Bess, you is my woman now / It ain't necessarily so / There's a boat that's leaving shortly for New York / Bess, oh where's my Bess / I'm on my way / I loves you Porgy / Woman is a sometime thing
CD _____ 8274752
Verve / Feb '93 / PolyGram.

RADIO DAYS
CD _____ MCD 0562
Moon / Apr '94 / Harmonia Mundi / Cadillac.

SATCH PLAYS FATS
Honeysuckle rose / Blue turning grey over you / I'm crazy 'bout my baby / I've got a feeling I'm falling in love / Keepin' out of mischief now / All that meat and no potatoes / Squeeze me / Black and blue / Ain't misbehavin'
CD _____ 4509802
CBS / Feb '88 / Sony.

SATCHMO 1931-1947
CD _____ CD 56030
Jazz Roots / Nov '94 / Target/BMG.

SATCHMO AT SYMPHONY HALL
Mahogany hall stomp / Black and blue / Royal garden blues / Lover / Body and soul / Since I fell for you / Boff boff / Baby, won't you please come home / C-jam blues / Tea for two / Steak face / On the sunny side of the street / High society / Stars fell on Alabama / Muskrat ramble
CD _____ GRP 16612
American Decca / Feb '96 / BMG / New Note.

SATCHMO MEETS BIG T (1944-58) (Armstrong, Louis & Jack Teagarden)
CD _____ CD 53079
Giants Of Jazz / Mar '92 / Target/BMG / Cadillac.

SATCHMO'S CLASSIC VOCALS
When you're smiling / I'm a ding dong daddy from Dumas / If I could be with you one hour tonight / Body and soul / You're driving me crazy / Peanut vendor / When it's sleepy time down South / Shine / Just a gigolo / Walkin' my baby back home / I surrender dear / Hob / You can't ride this train / Public melody number one / Ex-ander's ragtime band / Once in a while / On the sunny side of the street / 's Wonderful / Love walked in / Jeepers creepers / Save it / Pretty Mama
CD _____ CDCD 1061
Charly / Mar '93 / Charly / THE / Cadillac.

SATCHMO'S GREATEST
Savoy blues / St. James infirmary / Ain't misbehavin' / Rockin' chair / Sweethearts on parade / (I'll be glad when you're dead) you rascal you / Lazy river / That's my home / I've got the world on a string / I gotta right to sing the blues / High society / Basin Street blues / Mahogany hall stomp / Sweet

Sue, just you / Just you / St. Louis blues / Swing that music
CD _____ CDCD 1008
Charly / Mar '93 / Charly / THE / Cadillac.

SATCHMO'S IMMORTAL PERFORMANCES (1929-47)
CD _____ CD 53088
Giants Of Jazz / Mar '90 / Target/BMG / Cadillac.

SATCHMO: A MUSICAL AUTOBIOGRAPHY VOL.1
CD _____ JUCD 2003
Jazz Unlimited / Jul '89 / Wellard / Cadillac.

SATCHMO: A MUSICAL AUTOBIOGRAPHY VOL.2
CD _____ JUCD 2004
Jazz Unlimited / Jun '89 / Wellard / Cadillac.

SATCHMO: A MUSICAL AUTOBIOGRAPHY VOL.3
CD _____ JUCD 2005
Jazz Unlimited / Dec '90 / Wellard / Cadillac.

SINGIN' N' PLAYIN'
Hello Dolly / Mack the knife / Muskrat ramble / Blueberry Hill / That's my desire / Ole Miss / When it's sleepy time down South / Kiss to build a dream on / St. James infirmary / (Back home again) in Indiana
CD _____ DC 8534
Denon / Apr '89 / Conifer.

SOMEDAY
CD _____ MCD 080
Moon / Dec '95 / Harmonia Mundi / Cadillac.

SPOTLIGHT ON LOUIS ARMSTRONG
Mack the knife / I got rhythm / Just a gigolo / When the saints go marching in / That's my desire / Heebie jeebies / Ain't misbehavin' / On the sunny side of the street / Cabaret / Blueberry hill / Hello Dolly / I can't give you anything but love / Sweethearts on parade / Jeepers creepers / You're driving me crazy / Way down yonder in New Orleans
CD _____ HADCD 140
Javelin / Feb '94 / THE / Henry Hadaway Organisation.

St. LOUIS BLUES
Mahogany hall stomp / St. Louis blues / I'm confessin' that I love you / Dinah / China-town, my chinatown / Georgia on my mind / Lazy river / Rockin' chair / Wild man blues / You're lucky to me / (I'll be glad when you're dead) you rascal you / St. James infirmary / West End blues / Red nose / Shoe shine boy / Save it pretty Mama / Hear me talkin' to ya / I double dare you / Struttin' with some barbecue / I hope Gabriel likes my music
CD _____ MUCD 9028
Start / Apr '95 / Koch.

St. LOUIS BLUES
CD _____ 4679192
Sony Jazz / Jan '95 / Sony.

STOCKHOLM 1959
CD _____ TAX 37122
Tax / Aug '94 / Jazz Music / Wellard / Cadillac.

SWING YOU CATS (Armstrong, Louis Orchestra)
Swing you cats / Honey don't you love me anymore / Some sweet day / Dusky Stevedore / You'll wish you'd never been born / I've got the world on a string / Mississippi basin / I gotta right to sing the blues / Sittin' in the dark / He's a son of the South / Sweet Sue
CD _____ SMS 51
Carlton Home Entertainment / Apr '92 / Carlton Home Entertainment.

TOGETHER AGAIN LIVE AT MONTREUX JAZZ FESTIVAL
CD _____ CD 20005
Pablo / May '86 / Jazz Music / Cadillac / Complete/Pinnacle.

TOWN HALL CONCERT PLUS
Rockin' chair / Ain't misbehavin' / Back o' town blues / Long long journey / I want a little girl / Mahogany hall stomp / Pennies from Heaven / St. James Infirmary / Save it pretty Mama / Someday you'll be sorry / Sugar / Snafu
CD _____ 74321 13036-2
RCA / Sep '93 / BMG.

TRIBUTE TO LOUIS ARMSTRONG (Various Artists)
CD _____ CDTTD 512
Timeless Traditional / Jul '94 / New Note.

ULTIMATE COLLECTION, THE
Blueberry hill / C'est si bon / Dream a little dream of me / Georgia on my mind / Hello Dolly / Jeepers creepers / Moon river / Only you / Up a lazy river / What a wonderful world / Basin Street blues / Rockin' chair / Someday you'll be sorry / Pennies from heaven / On the sunny side of the street / Tiger rag / Ain't misbehavin' / High society / wavoll (II) / Do you know what it means to miss New Orleans / Faithful hussar / Mack the knife

CD _____ 74321197062
Bluebird / May '94 / BMG.

WE HAVE ALL THE TIME IN THE WORLD (The Pure Genius Of Louis Armstrong)
What a wonderful world / C'est si bon / Blueberry hill / It don't mean a thing if it ain't got that swing / Mack the knife / Cabaret / Tiger rag / I'm just a lucky so and so / Hello Dolly / Georgia on my mind / Moon river / Nobody knows the trouble I've seen / Back o' town blues / Faithful hussar / Mood indigo / Jeepers creepers / Go down Moses / Only you (and you alone) / When the saints go marching in / We have all the time in the world
CD _____ CDEMTV 89
EMI / Nov '94 / EMI.

WEST END BLUES (Armstrong, Louis & His Hot Five)
CD _____ CD 14530
Jazz Portraits / Jan '94 / Jazz Music.

WEST END BLUES (1926-1933)
CD _____ IGOCD 2035
Indigo / Dec '95 / Direct / ADA.

WHAT A WONDERFUL WORLD
What a wonderful world / Cabaret / Home fire / Dream a little dream of me / Give me your kisses (I'll give you my heart) / Sunshine of love / Hello brother / There must be a way / Fantastic, that's you / I guess I'll get the papers and go home / Hellzapoppin'
CD _____ JHR 73507
Jazz Hour / Sep '93 / Target/BMG / Jazz Music / Cadillac.

WHAT A WONDERFUL WORLD
What a wonderful world / Everybody's / Georgia on my mind / On the sunny side of the street / Cabaret / Hello Dolly / Lazy river / When you're smiling / Whiffenpoof song / Blueberry Hill / La vie en rose / I can't give you anything but love / When it's sleepy time down South / Surrender dear / Some of these days / Exactly like you
CD _____ PLATCD 304
Platinum Music / Aug '88 / Prism / Ross.

WHEN YOU AND I WERE YOUNG, MAGGIE (Louis Armstrong 1946-1951)
CD _____ CLA 1915
Ambassador / Mar '94 / Wellard / Jazz Music / Cadillac.

YOU RASCAL YOU
When the saints go marching in / I'm confessin' that I love you / Our Monday date / You are my lucky star / As long as you'll be dead if you die / Red nose / Lyin' to myself / Solitude / Shoe shine boy / So little time / I double dare you / Love walked in / Public melody number one / True confession / I'm thankful / Red sails in the sunset / Eventide / Yours and mine / Hear me talkin' to ya / Save it pretty Mama / (I'll be glad when you're dead) you rascal you / When it's sleepy time down South
CD _____ RAJCD 821
Empress / Mar '94 / BMG.

YOU'RE DRIVING ME CRAZY
CD _____ 4729922
Sony Jazz / Jan '95 / Sony.

YOUNG LOUIS ARMSTRONG (1930-1933)
Blue yodel no. 9 (Standing on the corner) / That's my home (2 takes) / Hobo, you can't ride this train / I hate to leave you now (2 takes) / You'll wish you'd never been born / When you're smiling / St. James infirmary / Dinah / (I'll be glad when you're dead) you rascal you / When it's sleepy time down South / Nobody's sweetheart / I've got the world on a string / I gotta right to sing the blues / Hustlin' and bustlin' for baby / Sittin' in the dark / High Society / Basin Street blues / He's a son of the South / Some sweet day / Honey do / Swing you cats / Honey don't you love me anymore / Mississippi basin / Laughing Louis / Tomorrow night / Dusky stevedore / There's a cabin in the pines / Mighty river / Sweet Sue, just you / I wonder who / St. Louis blues / Don't play me cheap
CD _____ 74321 155172
Jazz Tribune / Jun '94 / BMG.

Armstrong, Vanessa

WONDERFUL ONE
CD _____ CHIP 78
Jive / Nov '89 / BMG.

Army Air Forces Overseas.

FAREWELL PERFORMANCES (Army Air Forces Overseas Orchestra)
CD _____ HCD 248
Hindsight / May '94 / Target/BMG / Jazz Music.

Army Of Lovers
GODS OF EARTH & HEAVEN
CD _____ 5191334
Polydor / Jul '93 / PolyGram.

Arnaz, Desi
BIG BANDS OF HOLLYWOOD (Arnaz, Desi Orchestra & Chico Marx Orchestra)
CD _____ 15767
Laserlight / Jul '92 / Target/BMG.

Arnaz, Lucie
JUST IN TIME
Lover / 'S Wonderful / Slow dancing / Sorry 'bout the whole darn thing / I love to dance/ I got lost in his arms / Things we did last summer / View from here / I'm beginning to see the light/Moonglow / My foolish heart / Just in time / Recipe for love / Another you / Witchcraft / Quiereme mucho / Make someone happy / Blue skies
CD _____ CCD 4573
Concord Jazz / Nov '93 / New Note.

Arnez, Chico
ESSENTIAL SALSA (Arnez, Chico & His Cubana Brass)
Rhythm is gonna get you / Mama you can't go / Do the salsa / Get on your feet / Girl from Brazil / Jezebel / 1-2-3 / Live for loving you / That's my desire / Oye mi canto (hear my voice) / Cheeky Chico / What goes around / 18th Century salsa / Specialization / Real wild house / Go away / Conga
CD _____ CDMFP 6174
Music For Pleasure / Sep '95 / EMI.

Arnold, Billy Boy
BACK WHERE I BELONG
CD _____ ALCD 4815
Alligator / Nov '93 / Direct / ADA.

ELDORADO CADILLAC
CD _____ ALCD 4836
Alligator / Nov '95 / Direct / ADA.

GOING TO CHICAGO
CD _____ TCD 5018
Testament / Jul '95 / Complete/Pinnacle / ADA / Koch.

I WISH YOU WOULD (Charly Blues - Masterworks Vol. 34)
Sweet on you baby / You got to love me / I wish you would / I was fooled / Don't stay out all night / I ain't got you / Here's my picture / You've got me wrong / My heart is crying / Kissing me at midnight / Prisoner's plea / No, no, no, no, no / Everyday, every night / Rockinitis
CD _____ CDBM 34
Charly / Jan '93 / Charly / THE / Cadillac.

Arnold, Eddy
CATTLE CALL/THEREBY HANGS A TALE
Streets of Laredo / Cool water / Cattle call / Leanin' on the old top rail / Ole faithful / Cowboy's dream / Wayward wind / Tumbling tumbleweeds / Cowpoke / Where the mountains meet the sky / Sierra Sue / Carry me back to the Lone Prairie / Jim I wore a tie today / Tom Dooley / Nellie sits a waitin' / Tennessee stud / Battle of Little Big Horn / Wreck of ol' 97 / Red headed stranger / Johnny Reb / Riders in the sky / Boot Hill / Ballad of Davy Crockett / Partners / Jesse James
CD _____ BCD 15441
Bear Family / Apr '90 / Rollercoaster / Direct / CM / Swift / ADA.

Arnold, Harry
HARRY ARNOLD
CD _____ ANC 9097-2
Ancha / Aug '94 / Jazz Music / Wellard / Cadillac.

PREMIARI - HARRY ARNOLD & HIS SWEDISH RADIO BAND
CD _____ ANC 9501
Ancha / Dec '94 / Jazz Music / Wellard / Cadillac.

Arnold, Kokomo
KING OF THE BOTTLENECK GUITAR 1934-1937
CD _____ BLE 592502
Black & Blue / Nov '92 / Wellard / Koch.

Arnold, P.P.
BEST OF P.P. ARNOLD (Kafunta/First Lady Of Immediate)
(If you think) you're groovy / Something beautiful happened / Born to be together / Am I still dreaming / First cut is the deepest / Everything's gonna be alright / Treat me like a lady / Would you believe / Speak to me / God only knows / Eleanor Rigby / Yesterday / Angel of the morning / It'll never happen again / As tears go by / To love somebody / Dreamin' / If you see what I mean / Though it hurts me badly (CD only) / Welcome home (CD only) / Life is but nothing (CD only) / Time has come (CD only)
CD _____ SEECD 235
See For Miles/C5 / Oct '88 / Pinnacle.

BEST OF P.P. ARNOLD - THE FIRST CUT IS THE DEEPEST, THE
CD _____ CSL 6035
Immediate / Nov '93 / Charly / Target/ BMG.

Arnold, Wayne
TOUGH LIFE
She makes me feel good / Keep giving your love / Ready when you are / Just take me back / Lucky tough life / You got what I need / Love is on your side / Everything reminds me / Love storm / You're the reason / All or nothing / Right back into love / Closer / How long does it take
CD _____ CD 013
About Time / Sep '92 / Target/BMG.

Arnoux, Viviane
CHEVAL ROUGE (Arnoux, Viviane & F. Michaud)
CD _____ 829062
Buda / Jul '95 / Discovery / ADA.

Arnstrom, Kenneth
SAXCESS
CD _____ NCD 8836
Phontastic / Dec '95 / Wellard / Jazz Music / Cadillac.

Arranmore
BY REQUEST
CD _____ FE 1418
Folk Era / Dec '94 / CM / ADA.

LIVE
CD _____ FE 1405
Folk Era / Nov '94 / CM / ADA.

Arrested Development
3 YEARS, 5 MONTHS AND 2 DAYS IN THE LIFE OF...
Man's final frontier / Mama's always on stage / People everyday / Blues happy / Mr. Wendal / Children play with earth / Raining revolution / Fishin' for religion / Give a man a fish / U / Eave of reality / Natural / Dawn of the dreads / Tennessee / Washed away
CD _____ CD25CR 25
Chrysalis / Mar '94 / EMI.

UNPLUGGED
Time / Give a man a fish / Gettin' / Natural / Searchin' for one soul / Raining revolution / Fishin' 4 religion (Mixes) / Mama's always on stage / U / Mr. Wendal (Mixes) / People everyday / Time (2) / Give a man a fish (Instrumental) / Gettin' (instrumental) / Searchin' for one soul (Instrumental) / Raining revolution (Instrumental) / U (Instrumental)
CD _____ CTCD 33
Cooltempo / Apr '93 / EMI.

ZINGALAMDUNI
WMFW (We must fight to win) / United minds / Ache'n for acres / United front / Africa's inside me / Pride / Shell / Mr. Landlord / Warm sentiments / Drum / In the sunshine / I Kneelin' at my altar / Fountain of youth / Ease my mind / Praisin' u
CD _____ CTCD 42
Cooltempo / Jun '94 / EMI.

Arriagada, Jorge
L'ENFANT DE L'HIVER
CD _____ TWI 8892
Les Disques Du Crepuscule / '90 / Discovery / ADA.

Arrow
BEST OF ARROW
Slouch hat / Memories of Norway / Memories of Jaren / Evening breakfast / Africa
CD _____ 100121 CD
Red Bullet / Sep '88 / Jetstar.

OUTRAGEOUS
CD _____ 040 CD
Arrow / Jan '94 / Jetstar.

PHAT
CD _____ ARROW 0043CD
Arrow / Dec '95 / Jetstar.

Arroyo, Joe
REBELLION
CD _____ WCD 012
World Circuit / Jul '89 / New Note / Direct / Cadillac / ADA.

Arson Garden
WISTERIA
CD _____ ASKD 66013
Vertebrae / Nov '92 / Vital.

Art Bears
HOPES AND FEARS
CD _____ ABCD 2
ReR Megacorp / Apr '92 / These / ReR Megacorp.

WINTER SONGS/THE WORLD AS IT IS TODAY
CD _____ RERABCD
ReR Megacorp / Jun '88 / These / ReR Megacorp.

Art Connection
STOLEN MOMENTS
CD _____ BEST 1035CD
Acoustic Music / Nov '93 / ADA.

Art Ensemble Of Chicago
ART ENSEMBLE OF CHICAGO (Art Ensemble Of Chicago & Fontella Bass)
CD _____ 500172
Musidisc / Nov '93 / Vital / Harmonia Mundi / ADA / Cadillac / Discovery.

DREAMING OF THE MASTERS SUITE
CD _____ DIW 854
DIW / Mar '92 / Harmonia Mundi / Cadillac.

EDA WOBU
CD _____ JMY 1008-2
JMY / Aug '91 / Harmonia Mundi.

FULL FORCE
CD _____ 8291972
ECM / Oct '86 / New Note.

LIVE IN BERLIN
CD _____ WWCD 2051
West Wind / Jan '91 / Swift / Charly / CM / ADA.

NICE GUYS
.la / Nice guys / Folkus / 597 50 / Cyp / Dreaming of the master
CD _____ 8278762
ECM / Jun '86 / New Note.

THIRD DECADE
CD _____ 8232132
ECM / Apr '85 / New Note.

TUTANKHAMUN
CD _____ BLCD 760199
Black Lion / Apr '95 / Jazz Music / Cadillac / Wellard / Koch.

Art Ensemble of Soweto
AMERICA-SOUTH AFRICA
CD _____ DIW 848
DIW / Aug '91 / Harmonia Mundi / Cadillac.

Art Lande
RUBISA PATROL
Celestial guests / Many chinas / Jaimi's birthday song / Romany / Corinthian melodies / For Nancy / Monk in his simple room
CD _____ 5198752
ECM / Mar '94 / New Note.

Art Of Noise
AMBIENT COLLECTION, THE
Opus 4 / Nothing was going to stop them / Island / Ode to Don Jose / Horndubaloud 727/Ransom in the sand / Robinson Crusoe / Art of love / Opus for 4 / Crusoe / Camilla / Counterpoint / Eye of a needle / Nation rejects
CD _____ WOLCD 1012
China / Apr '91 / Pinnacle.

BEST OF THE ART OF NOISE
Beat box / Moments in love / Close (to the edit) / Peter Gunn / Paranoimia / Legacy / Dragnet '88 / Kiss / Something always bad / pens / Opus 4
CD _____ WOLCD 1027
China / Aug '92 / Pinnacle.

DAFT
Love / Time for fear, A (who's afraid) / Beatbox (diversion 1) / Army now / Donna / Memento / How to kill / Realization / Who's afraid (on the Art of Noise) / Moments in love / Bright noise / Flesh in armour / Comes and goes / Snapshot / Close (to the edit) / (Three fingers of) Love
CD _____ 450994747-2
ZTT / Mar '94 / Warner Music.

FON MIXES
CD _____ WOLCD 1023
China / Nov '91 / Pinnacle.

IN NO SENSE I NONSENSE
Galleons of stone / Dragnet / Fin du temps / How rapid / Opus for four / Debut / E.F.L. / Ode to Don Jose / Day at the races / Counterpoint / Roundabout 727 / Ransom on the sand / Roller 1 / Nothing was going to stop them then, anyway / Crusoe / One earth
CD _____ WOLCD 1017
China / Jul '91 / Pinnacle.

INVISIBLE SILENCE
Opus for four / Paranoimia / Eye of a needle / Legs / Slip of the tongue / Backbeat / Instruments of darkness / Peter Gunn / Camilla / Chameleon's dish
CD _____ WOLCD 1016
China / Jul '91 / Pinnacle.

WHO'S AFRAID OF THE ART OF NOISE
Time for fear / Beat box / Snapshot / Close / Who's afraid (of the Art of Noise) / Moments in love / Memento / Hard to kill / Realization / Liquid sky
CD _____ 450994746-2
ZTT / Mar '94 / Warner Music.

Art Of Silence
ART OF SILENCE
CD _____ PERMCD 32
Permanent / Apr '95 / Total/BMG.

Artaek, Lagun
SONGS FROM THE BASQUE COUNTRY (Artaek, Lagun Groupe)
CD _____ ARN 64223
Arion / Jun '93 / Discovery / ADA.

Artango
DOUBLES JEUX
CD _____ ARN 62304
Arion / Jul '95 / Discovery / ADA.

PIANO - BANDONEON
CD _____ ARN 62245
Arion / Aug '93 / Discovery / ADA.

Artch
ANOTHER RETURN
CD _____ ACTCD 5
Active / Jul '91 / Pinnacle.

Artefakto
DES CONSTRUCTION
CD _____ CDZOT 113
Zoth Ommog / Oct '94 / Plastic Head.

Arthur
RIGHT OFF
CD _____ TGT 014CD
Target / Jul '94 / SRD.

Arthur, Davey
CELTIC SIDE SADDLE
Celtic side saddle / Hail Mary full of grace / Galway farmer / Fair city set / Emigrant / Over the ocean / Slip 'n' slides / Euston station / Mad lady and me / Walk / Sit you down / Ness pipers / Sister Marcella
CD _____ PRKCD 26
Park / Aug '94 / Pinnacle.

Arthur, Neil
SUITCASE
Breaking my heart / I love, I hate / Suitcase / Jumping like a kangaroo / I know these things about you / Heaven / That's what love is like / One day, one time / Jukebox theory / Beach
CD _____ CDCHR 6065
Chrysalis / Feb '94 / EMI.

Artificial Peace
DISCOGRAPH
CD _____ LF 038
Plastic Head / Jun '92 / Plastic Head.

Artillery
ARTILLERY 3
CD _____ NEATCD 1046
Neat / Aug '88 / Plastic Head.

BY INHERITANCE
7.00 from Tashkent / Beneath the clay / Bombard / Life in bondage / Razamanaz / Khomaniac / By inheritance / Don't believe / Equal at first / Back in the trash
CD _____ RO 93972
Roadrunner / May '90 / Pinnacle.

Artisan
BREATHING SPACE
CD _____ FESTIVAL 9CD
Festival / Oct '93 / CM / ADA / Roots.

ROCKING AT THE END OF TIME
CD _____ FESTIVAL 7CD
Festival / '92 / CM / ADA / Roots.

Arts & Decay
TRAIL OF TEARS
CD _____ HY 39100422CD
Hyperium / Nov '92 / Plastic Head.

Artwoods
C100 OXFORD STREET
Sweet Mary / If I ever get my hands on you / Goodbye sisters / Oh my love / I take what I want / Big city / She knows what to do / I'm looking for a saxophonist / Keep looking / I keep forgettin' / I feel good / One more heartache / Down in the valley / Be my lady / Stop and think it over / Don't cry no more
CD _____ ED CD 107
Edsel / Mar '83 / Pinnacle / ADA.

Arzachel
ARZACHEL
CD _____ DOCD 1983
Drop Out / Aug '94 / Pinnacle.

As One

CELESTIAL SOUL
CD _____ ELEC 26CD
New Electronica / Nov '95 / Pinnacle / Plastic Head.

REFLECTIONS
Mihara / Meridian / Orchila / Shamballa / Dance of the uighurs / Majik jar / Star gaze / Soleil levant / Lunate / Asa nisi masa / Moon over the moab
CD _____ ELEC 5CD
New Electronica / Apr '94 / Pinnacle / Plastic Head.

REFLECTIONS ON REFLECTIONS
CD _____ ELEC 23CD
New Electronica / '95 / Pinnacle / Plastic Head.

As Serenity Fades

EARTHBORN
CD _____ CDAR 018
Adipocre / May '94 / Plastic Head.

Asante

ASANTE MODE
Intro...Asante mode / Look what you've done / All about you / Don't push me away / Why / Don't say goodnight / People get ready / Prelude...what goes on / What's the plan / Dopest Ethiopian / Interlude...the phone call / Cathin' feelins
CD _____ 48113342
Columbia / Nov '95 / Sony.

Asgard

SONGS OF G
CD _____ BEST 1042CD
Acoustic Music / Nov '93 / ADA.

Ash

TRAILOR
CD _____ INFECT 14CD
Infectious / Oct '94 / Disc.

Ash, Daniel

COMING DOWN
Blue moon / Coming down fast / Walk this way / Closer to you / Day tripper / This love / Blue angel / Me and my shadow / Candy darling / Sweet little liar / Not so fast / Coming down
CD _____ BEGA 114CD
Beggars Banquet / Feb '91 / Warner Music / Disc.

FOOLISH THINGS DESIRED
CD _____ BBQCD 123
Beggars Banquet / May '93 / Warner Music / Disc.

Ashbrook, Karen

HILLS OF ERIN
CD _____ MMCD 207
Maggie's Music / Dec '94 / CM / ADA.

Ashby, Dorothy

JAZZ HARPIST
Thou swell / Stella by starlight / Dancing on the ceiling / Aeolian groove / Quietude / Spicy / Lamentation
CD _____ SV 0194
Savoy Jazz / Nov '92 / Conifer / ADA.

Ashby, Harold

I'M OLD FASHIONED
CD _____ STCD 545
Stash / '92 / Jazz Music / CM / Cadillac / Direct / ADA.

ON THE SUNNY SIDE OF THE STREET
Out of nowhere / There is no greater love / Honeysuckle rose / Pennies from heaven / It's the talk of the town / Satin doll / These foolish things / On the sunny side of the street / Scuffin' / In my solitude / Just squeeze me
CD _____ CDSJP 385
Timeless Jazz / Oct '92 / New Note.

VIKING, THE
CD _____ GEMCD 160
Gemini / '87 / Cadillac.

WHAT AM I HERE FOR (Ashby, Harold Quartet)
CD _____ CRISS 1054CD
Criss Cross / May '92 / Cadillac / Harmonia Mundi.

Asher D

RAGAMUFFIN HIP-HOP (Asher D & Daddy Freddy)
CD _____ MOLCD 999
Music Of Life / Jan '95 / Grapevine.

STILL KICKIN'
CD _____ ASHER 22CD
Music Of Life / Jul '91 / Grapevine.

Ashes & Diamonds

HEART OF AN ANGEL
CD _____ RHCD 4
River Head / Oct '93 / Pinnacle.

Ashford & Simpson

SOLID
Solid / Jungle / Honey I love you / Babies / Closest to love / Cherish forever more / To-night we escape (we make love) / Outta the world
CD _____ MUSCD 501
MCI / Sep '94 / Disc / THE.

Ashkaru

MOTHER TONGUE
Maray-Wollelaye / Tigel / Ring my faith / Bellema / Sigh like you do / Labour of love / Must give back / Énat / If I chose / Know joy
CD _____ 3202142
Triloka / Dec '95 / New Note.

Ashkhabad

CITY OF LOVE
Ayrylsa / Aglar men / Bayaty / Balam seni / Shalakho / Yaman ykbal / Bibining / Aisha / Kakan gyz / Ketshpelek / Garagum keshdeleri
CD _____ CDRW 34
Realworld / Apr '93 / EMI / Sterns.

Ashley, Steve

FAMILY ALBUM, THE
CD _____ RGFCD 002
Road Goes On Forever / Nov '91 / Direct.

Ashra

NEW AGE OF EARTH
Sunrain / Ocean of tenderness / Deep distance / Nightdust
CD _____ CDV 2080
Virgin / Jun '90 / EMI.

SUNRAIN
CD _____ CDOVD 463
Virgin / Jan '96 / EMI.

WALKIN' THE DESERT
First movement / Second movement / Third movement / Fourth movement / Desert
CD _____ CDTB 086
Thunderbolt / Apr '90 / Magnum Music Group.

Ashton, Susan

WAKENED BY THE WIND
Down on my knees / No one knows / My heart / Benediction / Ball and chain / I hear you / Land of nod / In my father's hands / In amazing grace land / Suffer in silence / Beyond justice to mercy
CD _____ SPD 1259
Alliance Music / Aug '95 / EMI.

WALK ON
Walk on / Here in my heart / Waiting for your love to come down / Song of reconciliation on my knees / Beyond justice to mercy / Land of Nod / Agree to disagree / Down on my knees / Beyond justice to mercy / Started as a whisper / There is a line / When are you coming back / Better angels of our nature / Benediction / Alice in Wonderland / Remember not (acoustic version)
CD _____ CDEMC 3689
EMI / Oct '94 / EMI.

Ashton, Tony

FIRST OF THE BIG BANDS/BBC LIVE IN CONCERT (Ashton, Tony & Jon Lord)
CD _____ 900117
Line / Oct '94 / CM / Grapevine / ADA / Conifer / Direct.

Ashtray Boy

HONEYMOON SUITE, THE
Ananda marga / Shirley MacLaine / Observatory Hill / There is a fountain / Time for a baby / How Charles destroyed the inland sea / Infidel / Little nature child / Hit / Love in a bakery / Honeymoon suite
CD _____ SR 1003
Scout / Jan '96 / Koch.

Asia

ALPHA
Don't cry / Smile has left your eyes / Never in a million years / My own time (I'll do what I want) / Heat goes on / Eye to eye / Last to know / True colours / Midnight sun / Open your eyes
CD _____ GFLD 19053
Geffen / Apr '92 / BMG.

AQUA
CD _____ WKFMXD 180
FM Coast To Coast / Feb '92 / Revolver Music.

ARIA
CD _____ CDVEST 8
Bulletproof / May '94 / Pinnacle.

ASIA
Go / Voice of America / Hard on me / Wishing / Rock 'n' roll dream / Countdown to zero / Love now till eternity / Too late / Suspicion / After the war / Heat of the moment / Only time will tell / Sole survivor / Time again / One step closer / Wildest dreams / Without you / Cutting it fine / Here comes the feeling
CD _____ GFLD 19054
Geffen / Nov '90 / BMG.

Asiabeat

ASIABEAT
CD _____ CDKUCK 11096
Kuckuck / Jun '92 / CM / ADA.

Asian Dub Foundation

FACTS AND FICTIONS
CD _____ NATCD 58
Nation / Oct '95 / Disc.

Askey, Arthur

BAND WAGGON (Askey, Arthur & Tommy Trinder & Richard Murdoch)
Adolf / (We're gonna hang out the) washing on the Siegfried Line / Big and stinkers moment musical / Worm / Big and stinkers parlour games / Chirrup / Seagull song / Proposal / Kiss me goodnight, Sergeant Major / How ashamed I was / Bee song
CD _____ PASTCD 9729
Flapper / Jan '91 / Pinnacle.

Asleep At The Wheel

PASTURE PRIME
Across the valley from the Alamo / Switchin' in the kitchen / Write your own song / Cotton eyed Joe / Baby / Shorty / That chick's too young to fry / Big beaver / This is the way we make a broken heart / Deep water / Natural thing to do / Liars moon / That's your red wagon
CD _____ FIENDCD 44
Demon / Mar '91 / Pinnacle / ADA.

TRIBUTE TO THE MUSIC OF BOB WILLIS & THE TEXAS PLAYBOYS
Red wing / Big ball in cowtown / Yearning (just for you) / Bring it on down to my house / Deep water / Blues for Dixie / Billy Dale / Across the Valley from the Alamo / Old fashioned love / Ida red / Misery / I wonder if you feel the way I do / Hubbin' it / Corine Corina / Still water runs the deepest / All night long / Got a letter from my kid today / Dusty skies
CD _____ CDP 7814702
Liberty / Nov '93 / EMI.

VERY BEST OF ASLEEP AT THE WHEEL
Cherokee boogie / I'll never get out of this world alive / Space buggy / Letter that Johnny Walker read / Let me go home whiskey / Trouble in mind / Runnin' after fools / Miles and miles of Texas / Route 66 / My baby thinks she's a train / Am I high / Ragtime Annie / Somebody stole his body / When love goes wrong / Louisiana 1927 / Ain't nobody here but us chickens / One o'clock jump
CD _____ SEECD 81
See For Miles/C5 / Nov '93 / Pinnacle.

Asmus Tietchens

ARCANE DEVICE
CD _____ SA 03
Stilleandacht / Nov '93 / Plastic Head.

Asmussen, Svend

MUSICAL MIRACLE VOL. 1 1935-40
CD _____ PHONTCD 9306
Phontastic / Dec '94 / Wellard / Jazz Music / Cadillac.

SLUKAFTER IN THE TIVOLI-COPENHAGEN (1984)
Believe it believed / Nadja / Exactly like you / Hot house / Body and soul / Coconut calypso / Someone to watch over me / Barney goin' / Out of nowhere / Pent-up house / Things ain't what they used to be
CD _____ PHONT CD 8804
Phontastic / Apr '90 / Wellard / Jazz Music / Cadillac.

SVEND AMUSSEN AT SLUK AFTER
CD _____ NCD 8804
Phontastic / '93 / Wellard / Jazz Music / Cadillac.

SVEND ASMUSSEN 1942 VOL.7
CD _____ THORANR 7
Hep / Oct '94 / Cadillac / Jazz Music / New Note / Wellard.

TWO OF A KIND (Asmussen, Svend & Stephane Grappelli)
CD _____ STCD 4088
Storyville / Feb '89 / Jazz Music / Wellard / CM / Cadillac.

Asphalt

257 KNOCK OUT
CD _____ DARK 0082
Dark Empire / Feb '95 / SRD.

Asphyx

ASPHYX
CD _____ CM 77063-2
Century Media / May '94 / Plastic Head.

CRUSH THE CENOTAPH
CD _____ CM 97232
Century Media / Sep '94 / Plastic Head.

LAST ONE ON EARTH
CD _____ 8497342
Century Media / Nov '92 / Plastic Head.

RACK, THE
CD _____ CM 97162
Century Media / Sep '94 / Plastic Head.

Assassin

DON'T WEAR SUITS
CD _____ JUCCD 01
Juce / May '95 / Grapevine.

INTERSTELLAR EXPERIENCE
CD _____ 087521
Steamhammer / '89 / Pinnacle / Plastic Head.

UPCOMING TERROR
CD _____ 087530
Steamhammer / '89 / Pinnacle / Plastic Head.

Asseccoires

VENDETTA
CD _____ EFA 063282
Ausfahrt / Nov '95 / SRD.

Assfort

EJACULATION
CD _____ DISCCD 012
Discipline / Sep '95 / Plastic Head.

Associates

POPERA
Party fears two / Club country / Eighteen Carat love affair / Love hangover / Those first impressions / Waiting for the loveboat / Breakfast / Take me to the girl / Heart of glass / Country boy / Rhythm divine / Tell me Easter's on Friday / Q Quarters / Kitchen person / Message oblique speech / White car in Germany
CD _____ 9031724142
WEA / Jan '91 / Warner Music.

SULK
It's better this way / Party fears two / Club country / Love hangover / Eighteen carat love affair / Arrogance gave him up / No / Skipping / White car in Germany / Gloomy Sunday / Associate
CD _____ K 2400052
WEA / Jul '88 / Warner Music.

Association

DON'T LOOK BACK
CD _____ 60562
Enja / Nov '90 / New Note / Vital/SAM.

Assuck

ANTICAPITAL
CD _____ CC 005CD
Common Cause / Jun '94 / Plastic Head / SRD.

Assumpaco, Itamar

INTERCONTINENTAL
CD _____ MES 159912
Messidor / Apr '93 / Koch / ADA.

SAMPA MIDNIGHT
CD _____ MES 158022
Messidor / Feb '93 / Koch / ADA.

Astaire, Fred

ASTAIRABLE FRED
CD _____ CDMRS 911
DRG / '88 / New Note.

ASTAIRE SINGS
CD _____ AVC 537
Avid / May '94 / Avid/BMG / Koch.

ASTAIRE STORY, THE
CD Set _____ 835 649-2
Polydor / Apr '89 / PolyGram.

CRAZY FEET
Night and day / My one and only / Fascinating rhythm / New sun in the sky / Louisiana / Swiss miss / I'd rather Charleston / High hat / Whichness of the whatness / I've got you on my mind / Puttin' on the Ritz / White heat / Dancing in the dark / Hang on to me / Oh gee, oh gosh / Not my girl / Half of it dearie blues / Babbitt and the bromide / I love Louisa / Funny face / Crazy feet
CD _____ CDAJA 5021
Living Era / Oct '88 / Koch.

CRAZY FEET
Crazy feet / I used to be colour blind / Fine romance / Yam / I'd better had / Let's call the whole thing off / Nice work if you can get it / Foggy day / We saw the sea / Let's face the music and dance / Let yourself go / Cheek to cheek / Yam step / They can't take that away from me / I'm

putting all my eggs in one basket / Way you look tonight / I'm building up to a awful let down / Pick yourself up / Night and day / Wedding in the spring / You were never lovelier / Shorty George / I'm old fashioned / Dearly beloved
CD _____ RAJCD 856
Empress / Oct '95 / THE.

CREAM OF FRED ASTAIRE, THE
We saw the sea / I'm putting all my eggs in one basket / Puttin' on the Ritz / Way you look tonight / Let's call the whole thing off / Hoops / Hang on to me / I'd rather charleston / Night and day / Crazy feet / Shall we dance / Fine romance / Top hat, white tie and tails / Wedding cake walk / Dig it / Just like taking candy from a baby / I've got you on my mind / Let's face the music and dance / So near and yet so far / Who cares / They all laughed / Isn't this a lovely day (to be caught in the rain) / Slap that bass / Cheek to cheek / I'd rather lead a band
CD _____ PASTCD 7013
Flapper / Aug '93 / Pinnacle.

FASCINATING RHYTHM
Shall we dance / Fascinating rhythm / Night and day / Crazy feet / Puttin' on the Ritz / My one and only / Babbitt and the bromide / I've got you on my mind / Foggy day / Let's call the whole thing off / New sun in the sky / High hat / Hang on to me / Funny face / They can't take that away from me / Nice work if you can get it
CD _____ HADCD 163
Javelin / May '94 / THE / Henry Hadaway Organisation.

FINE ROMANCE, A
CD _____ CDD 548
Progressive / May '91 / Jazz Music.

FRED ASTAIRE COLLECTOR'S EDITION
CD _____ DVGH 7022
Deja Vu / Apr '95 / THE.

GREAT MGM STARS: FRED ASTAIRE
Steppin' out with my baby / It only happens when I dance with you / Oops / Bachelor's dinner song / Baby doll / Seeing's believing / I wanna be a dancin' man / Every night at seven / I left my hat in Haiti / You're all the world to me / How could you believe me when I said I love you (when you know I've been a liar all my life) / Fated to be mated / Paris loves lovers / Ritz roll and rock / Nevertheless / Where did you get that girl / Three little words / Shine on your shoes / By myself / Triplets / I love Louisa / That's entertainment / All of you
CD _____ CDMGM 28
MGM/EMI / Feb '91 / EMI.

LET'S FACE THE MUSIC AND DANCE
Change partners / Cheek to cheek / I used to be colour blind / I'm putting all my eggs in one basket / Let's face the music and dance / No strings / Top hat, white tie and tails / Yam / Foggy day / I can't be bothered now / I've got beginner's luck / Let's call the whole thing off / Nice work if you can get it / Shall we dance / Slap that bass / They all laughed / They can't take that away from me / Things are looking up / Poor Mr Chisholm / Dearly Beloved / Fine romance / Pick yourself up / Way you look tonight / You were never lovelier / Since I kissed my baby goodbye
CD _____ CDAJA 5123
Living Era / Mar '94 / Koch.

LOVE OF MY LIFE
CD _____ DHDL 124
Halcyon / Sep '93 / Jazz Music / Wellard / Swift / Harmonia Mundi / Cadillac.

MR SONG AND DANCE
Fascinating rhythm / My one and only / No strings (I'm fancy free) / Isn't this a lovely day (to be caught in the rain) / Piccolino / Let's face the music and dance / I'm putting all my eggs in one basket / Let yourself go / Pick yourself up / Way you look tonight / They can't take that away from me / They all laughed / Let's call the whole thing off / Shall we dance / Nice work if you can get it / Foggy day / Things are looking up / I used to be colour blind / Yam / Poor Mr. Chisholm
CD _____ CDCD 1075
Charly / Mar '93 / Charly / THE / Cadillac.

NICE WORK (Fred Astaire Sings Gershwin)
Hang on to me / Fascinating rhythm / Half of it dearie blues / I'd rather Charleston / Funny face / Babbitt and the bromide / High hat / My one and only / They can't take that away from me / They all laughed / I've got beginner's luck / Let's call the whole thing off / Shall we dance / Slap that bass / Foggy day / Things are looking up / Nice work if you can get it / I can't be bothered now
CD _____ CDSVL 199
Saville / Apr '89 / Conifer.

PUTTIN' ON THE RITZ
CD _____ BSTCD 9108
Best Compact Discs / May '92 / Complete/Pinnacle.

PUTTIN' ON THE RITZ
CD _____ RMB 75010
Remember / Nov '93 / Total/BMG.

PUTTING ON THE RITZ
CD _____ MCCD 204
Music Club / May '95 / Disc / THE / CM.

SHALL WE DANCE
Shall we dance / Fascinating rhythm / Crazy feet / Puttin' on the ritz / Night and day / No strings / Top hat, white tie and tails / Cheek to cheek / Pick yourself up / Way you look tonight / Fine romance / Slap that bass / Beginner's luck / Let's call the whole thing off / They can't take that away from me / Shall we dance - finale
CD _____ RPCD 319
Robert Parker Jazz / Nov '94 / Conifer.

SONGS FROM THE MOVIES
No strings / Isn't this a lovely day (to be caught in the rain) / Top hat, white tie and tails / Cheek to cheek / Piccolino / We saw the sea / Let yourself go / I'd rather lead a band / I'm putting all my eggs in one basket / Let's face the music and dance / Pick yourself up / Way you look tonight / Fine romance / Bojangles of Harlem / Never gonna dance / Beginner's luck / Slap that bass / They all laughed / Let's call the whole thing off / They can't take that away from me / Shall we dance / I can't be bothered now / Things are looking up / Foggy day / Nice work if you can get it
CD _____ PPCD 78115
Past Perfect / Feb '95 / THE.

STARRING FRED ASTAIRE (SINGLE ALBUM)
CD _____ 4601272
CBS / Jan '90 / Sony.

STEPPIN' OUT - ASTAIRE SINGS
CD _____ 523006-2
Verve / Aug '94 / PolyGram.

STEPPIN' OUT WITH MY BABY
CD _____ 15189
Laserlight / Aug '91 / Target/BMG.

STEPPING IN PARADISE
CD _____ ENTCD 246
Entertainers / Jan '88 / Target/BMG.

Astle, Jeff

SINGS
Back home / Sugar sugar / Lovey dovey / Lily the pink / You're in my arms / Puppet on a string / Congratulations / Ob la di, ob la da / Glory O / Make me an island / Cinnamon stick / There'll always be an England / Sweet water / Summer sadness
CD _____ RETRO 805
RPM / Nov '95 / Pinnacle.

Astley, Rick

BODY AND SOUL
Ones you love / Waiting for the bell to ring / Hopelessly / Dream for us / Body and soul / Enough love / Natures gift / Remember the days / Everytime / When you love someone
CD _____ 74321 15633-2
RCA / Oct '93 / BMG.

HOLD ME IN YOUR ARMS
She wants to dance with me / Take me to your heart / I don't want to lose her / Giving up on love / Ain't too proud to beg / Put yourself in my place / Till then / Dial my number / I'll never let you down / I don't want to be your lover / Hold me in your arms
CD _____ PD 71932
RCA / Nov '88 / BMG.

WHENEVER YOU NEED SOMEBODY
Never gonna give you up / Whenever you need somebody / Together forever / It would take a strong, strong man / Love has gone / Don't say goodbye / Slippin' away / No more looking for love / You move me / When I fall in love
CD _____ ND 75150
RCA / Jan '92 / BMG.

Aston, Michael

WHY ME
CD _____ TX 51205CD
Triple X / Oct '95 / Plastic Head.

Astor, Peter

GOD AND OTHER STORIES
CD _____ DAN 9304CD
Danceteria / Feb '95 / Plastic Head / ADA.

SUBMARINE
CD _____ CRELPCD 065
Creation / May '94 / 3MV / Vital.

Astral Engineering

CHRONOGLIDE
CD _____ WI 01
Worm Interface / Feb '95 / Plastic Head.

Astral Navigations

HOLYGROUND
CD _____ HBG 122/1
Background / Jan '94 / Background.

Astral Pilot

ELECTRO ACUPUNCTURE
CD _____ HHCD 13

Harthouse / Aug '95 / Disc / Warner Music.

Astralasia

ASTROLOGY
CD _____ MEYCD 10
Magick Eye / Nov '95 / SRD.

AXIS MUNDI
CD _____ MEYCD 9
Magick Eye / May '95 / SRD.

PITCHED UP AT THE EDGE OF REALITY
CD _____ EYELPCD 8
Magick Eye / Oct '93 / SRD.

WHATEVER HAPPENED TO UTOPIA
CD _____ EYECDLP 5
Magick Eye / May '94 / SRD.

Astronauts

EVERYTHING'S A-OK/ASTRONAUTS ORBIT CAMPUS
Bo Diddley / If I had a hammer / It's so easy / Dream lover / Wine, wine, wine / Money / Big boss man / Stormy Monday blues / Shortnin' bread / I need you / What'd I say / Johnny B. Goode / Be bop a lula / Good golly Miss Molly / Let the good times roll / Linda Lou / Bony Moronie / Diddy wah diddy / Roll over Beethoven / Shop around / Greenback dollar / Summertime / Sticks and stones
CD _____ BCD 15443
Bear Family / Jul '89 / Rollercoaster / Direct / CM / Swift / ADA.

SURFIN' WITH THE ASTRONAUTS/ COMPETION COUPE
Baja / Surfin' USA / Miserlou / Surfer's stomp / Suzie Q / Pipeline / Kuk / Banzai pipeline / Movin' / Baby let's play house / Let's go trippin' / Batman / Little ford ragtop / Competition coupe / Hearse / Fifty five bird / Devil driver's theme / Happy ho Daddy / Our car club / Devil driver / Chevy scarfer / 4.56 Stingray / Aguila / 650 Scrambler
CD _____ BCD 15442
Bear Family / Jul '89 / Rollercoaster / Direct / CM / Swift / ADA.

Aswad

ANOTHER CHAPTER OF DUB VOLUME II
CD _____ BUBBCD 3
Gut / Jun '95 / Total/BMG.

ASWAD
Concrete slaves / Irie woman / Red up / Back to Africa / Natural progression / Ethiopian rhapsody / Can't stand the pressure / Rebel soul
CD _____ IMCD 58
Island / '89 / PolyGram.

BEST OF ASWAD, THE
CD _____ BUBBCD 4
Gut / Jul '95 / Total/BMG.

DISTANT THUNDER
Message / Don't turn around / Set them free / Smoky blues / I can't get over you / Give a little love / Tradition / Feelings / International melody / Bittersweet / Justice
CD _____ RRCD 27
Reggae Refreshers / Sep '91 / PolyGram / Vital.

DON'T TURN AROUND
Don't turn around / Woman / Justice / Give a little love / Message / Gave you my love / Babylon / Chasing for the breeze / Sons of criminals / 54-46 (was my number) / Hulet / Behold / Smoky blues / Bubbling
CD _____ 5500662
Spectrum/Karussell / Jun '93 / PolyGram / THE.

FIRESTICKS (12" mixes)
Warrior re-charge / Smoky blues / Fire / On and on / Smile / Next to you / Best of my love / Set them free / Warrior charge / Gotta find a way / Old firesticks / Chat to you / Hang on baby / Don't turn around / Help me crossover
CD _____ CIDM 1103
Mango / Jul '93 / Vital / PolyGram.

HULET
Behold / Sons of criminals / Judgement day / Not guilty / Can't walk the street / Corruption / Playing games / Hulet
CD _____ IMCD 56
Island / '89 / PolyGram.

LIVE AND DIRECT
Not guilty / Not satisfied / Your recipe / Roots rocking drum and bass line / African children / Soca rumba / Rockers medley / Love fire
CD _____ IMCD 54
Island / '89 / PolyGram.

NEW CHAPTER
African children / Natural progression / Ways of the Lord / I will keep on loving you / He gave the sun to shine / Tuff we tuff / Didn't know at the time / Zion / In a your rights / Candles / Love fire
CD _____ IMCD 55
Island / '89 / PolyGram.

NEW CHAPTER OF DUB/LIVE AND DIRECT/DISTANT THUNDER (3CD Set)
Dub fire / Mikaflame / Truth / Bammie blow / Tuffist / Shining dub / Zion I / Natural agression / Not guilty / Not satisfied / Your recipe / Roots rocking / Drums and bass line / African children / Soca rumba / Rocker's medley (Ease up/Your love's gotta hold on me/Revolution/Waterpumping) / Love fire / Message / Don't turn around / Set them free / Smokey blues / I can't get over you / Give a little love / Tradition / Feelings / International melody / Bittersweet / Justice
CD Set _____ 5241512
Island / Nov '95 / PolyGram.

RISE AND SHINE AGAIN
CD _____ BUBBCD 2
Gut / Mar '95 / Total/BMG.

SHOWCASE
Warrior charge / Babylon / Rainbow culture / It's not our wish / Three babylon / Back to Africa
CD _____ IMCD 57
Island / '89 / PolyGram.

TO THE TOP
Pull up / Wrapped up / Bubbling / Noh bada wid it / Gimme the dub / Nuclear soldier / Kool noh / Star of my show / Hooked on you
CD _____ IMCD 59
Island / Oct '89 / PolyGram.

TOO WICKED
Fire / Next to you / Best of my love / Confidential / Gotta find a way / Just can't take it / Dancing on my own / Smile / Love won't leave me / Got to get (to your loving) / Old fire stick / Hang on baby
CD _____ CIDM 1054
Mango / Sep '90 / Vital / PolyGram.

Async Sense

ASYNC SENSE
CD _____ EFA 127132
Imbalance / Apr '95 / SRD.

At The Gates

GARDEN OF GRIEF
CD _____ BS 04CD
Dolores / Aug '95 / Plastic Head.

RED IN THE SKY IS OURS/WITH FEAR I KISS THE BURNING DARKNESS
CD _____ CDVILE 59
Peaceville / May '91 / Pinnacle.

SLAUGHTER OF THE SOUL
Blinded by fear / Slaughter of the soul / Cold / Under the serpent sun / Into the dead sky / Suicide nation / World of lies / Unto others / Nausea / Need / Flames of the end
CD _____ MOSH 143CD
Earache / Oct '95 / Vital.

TERMINAL SPIRIT DISEASE
Swarm / Terminal spirit disease / World returned / Forever blind / Fevered circle / Beautiful wound / All life ends / Burning darkness (Live) / Kingdom gone (Live)
CD _____ CDVILE 47
Peaceville / May '95 / Pinnacle.

Ataraixa

MOON SANG, THE
CD _____ EFA 121622
Apollyon / Dec '95 / SRD.

Atori Teenage Riot

1995
Start the riot / Into the death / Raver bashing / Speed / Sex / Midi junkies / Delete yourself you got no chance to wine / Hel-zajagd auf nazis / Cyberpunks are dead / Atari teenage riot / Kids are united / Riot 1995
CD _____ DHRCD 001
Digital Hardcore / Apr '95 / Vital.

Atheist

ELEMENTS
Green / Water / Samba Briza / Air / Displacement / Animal / Mineral / Fire / Fractal point / Earth / See you again / Elements
CD _____ CDMFN 150
Music For Nations / Jul '93 / Pinnacle.

PIECE OF TIME
Piece of time / Unholy war / Room with a view / On they slay / Beyond / I deny / Why brother / Life / No truth
CD _____ CDATV 8
Active / Jan '90 / Pinnacle.

UNQUESTIONABLE PRESENCE
CD _____ CDATV 20
Music For Nations / Oct '91 / Pinnacle.

Athena

GREEK PARTY/SYRTAKI DANCE
CD _____ CDSGP 0117
Prestige / Apr '95 / Total/BMG.

Athenians

12 OF THE MOST POPULAR SYRTAKIS
CD _____ EUCD 1058
ARC / '89 / ARC Music / ADA.

ALEXIS SORBAS
CD _____ EUCD 1057
ARC / '89 / ARC Music / ADA.

ATHENIANS LIFE
CD _____ EUCD 1036
ARC / '89 / ARC Music / ADA.

BEST OF GREECE
CD _____ EUCD 1091
ARC / '89 / ARC Music / ADA.

GREEK POPULAR MUSIC
CD _____ EUCD 1024
ARC / '89 / ARC Music / ADA.

REMBETIKO
CD _____ EUCD 1063
ARC / '89 / ARC Music / ADA.

Atherton, Michael

AUSTRALIAN MADE, AUSTRALIAN PLAYED
CD _____ OZM 1008CD
Sounds Australian / Nov '95 / ADA.

Atkins, Chet

COLLECTION, THE
On the road again / Tenderly / Orange blossom special / Rodrigo's guitar concerto de Aranjuez / Take five / Caravan / Vincent / Mostly Mozart / Storms never last / Limehouse blues / Over the waves / It don't mean a thing if it ain't got that swing / Brandenburg / Struttin' / I'll see you in my dreams / Heart of glass / Black and white/ Ragtime Annie/Hot Toddy
CD _____ 74321140942
RCA / Jul '93 / BMG.

GALLOPIN' GUITAR
Guitar blues / Brown eyes cryin' in the rain / Ain'tcha tired of makin' me blue / I'm gonna get tight / Canned heat / Standing room only / Don't hand me that line / Bug dance / I know my baby loves me / Nashville jump / My guitar is my sweetheart / I'm pickin' the blues / Gone gone gone / Barnyard shuffle / Save your money / (I may be colour blind but) I know when... / I've been working on the guitar / Dizzy strings / Money, marbles and chalk / Wednesday night waltz / Guitar waltz / Telling my troubles to my old guitar / Dance of the goldenrod / Gallopin' guitar / Barber shop rag / Centipede boogie / Under the Hickory nut tree / I was bitten by the same bug twice / One more chance / Old buck dance / Boogie man boogie / Main street breakdown / Confusin' / Music in my heart / Indian love call / Birth of the blues / Mountain melody / You're always brand new / My crazy heart / Hybrid corn / Jitterbug waltz / One man boogie / Crazy rhythm (instrumental) / Crazy rhythm / Rustic dance / Rainbow / In the mood / Spanish fandango / Midnight / Goodbye blues / Your mean little heart / Sweet bunch of daisies / Blue gypsy / Third man theme / One man boogie (take D) / St. Louis blues / Listed knot / Lover come back to me / Stephen Foster medley / Hangover blues / Imagination / Black mountain rag / Guitar polka / Dream train / Meet Mr. Callaghan / Chinatown, my Chinatown / High rockin' swing / Pig leaf rag / Oh by jingo / Hello ma baby / Bells of St. Mary's / Country gentlemen / Memphis blues / Alice blue gown / 12th street rag / Peeping Tom / Three o'clock in the morning / Georgia camp meeting / City slicker / Dill pickle rag / Rubber doll rag / Beautiful Ohio (1) / Downhill drag / Avalon / Sunrise serenade / San Antonio rose / Set a spell / Mr. Misery / Get up and go (2) (Vocal: Red Kirk) / South / Alabama jubilee / Corine Corina / (Back home again in) Indiana / Red wing / Frankie and Johnny / Gay Ranchero / Ballin' the Jack / Honeysuckle rose / At the Darktown strutter's ball / Old spinning wheel / Silver bells / Under the double eagle / Have you ever been lonely / Caravan / Old man river / Mr. Sandman / New Spanish two-step
CD _____ BCD 15714
Bear Family / Oct '93 / Rollercoaster / Direct / CM / Swift / ADA.

NECK AND NECK (Atkins, Chet & Mark Knopfler)
Poor boy blues / Sweet dreams / There'll be some changes made / Just one time / So soft / Your goodbye / Yakety axe / Tears / Tahitian skys / I'll see you in my dreams / Next time I'm in town
CD _____ 4674352
CBS / Nov '90 / Sony.

READ MY LICKS
Young thing / Mountains of Illinois / After you're gone / Every now and then / Somebody loves me now / Norway (Norwegian mountain song) / Read my licks / Take a look at her now / Around the bend / Dream / Vincent
CD _____ 474628 2
Sony Music / Jul '94 / Sony.

Atlantic

POWER
It's only love / Power / War / Bad blood / Can't hold on / Hands of fate / Every beat of my heart / Dangerous games / Nothing to lose / Hard to believe
CD _____ CDMFN 168
Music For Nations / Oct '94 / Pinnacle.

Atlantic Ocean

WATERFALL
CD _____ HFCD 41
PWL / Sep '94 / Warner Music / 3MV.

Atlantic Starr

LOVE CRAZY
CD _____ 7599265452
WEA / Nov '91 / Warner Music.

VERY BEST OF ATLANTIC STARR, THE
CD _____ CDMID 152
A&M / Oct '92 / PolyGram.

Atlantis

ATLANTIS
CD _____ REP 4145
Repertoire / Jul '93 / Pinnacle / Cadillac.

IT'S GETTING BETTER
CD _____ REP 4232-WP
Repertoire / Aug '91 / Pinnacle / Cadillac.

Atlas, Natacha

DIASPORA
CD _____ NATCD 47
Nation / Jun '95 / Disc.

Atmosfear

DANCING IN OUTER SPACE
CD _____ CUTUPCD 009
Jump Cut / Jun '95 / Total/BMG / Vital/ SAM.

TRANCE PLANTS
CD _____ CUTUPCD 004
Jump Cut / Apr '94 / Total/BMG / Vital/ SAM.

Atmosphere

CRYSTAL EMOTION
CD _____ 710 113
Innovative Communication / Aug '90 / Magnum Music Group.

Atom Heart

BINARY AMPLIFIED SUPER STEREO
CD _____ RI 032CD
Fax / Nov '95 / Plastic Head.

MORPHOGENETIC FIELDS
CD _____ RTD 19519122
Our Choice / Nov '94 / Pinnacle.

Atom Heart Mother

SKIN 'EM UP, CHOP 'EM OUT RAWHIDE
CD _____ ABT 095 CD
Abstract / Oct '92 / Pinnacle / Total/BMG.

Atom Seed

GET IN LINE
CD _____ HMRXD 163
FM / Nov '92 / Sony.

Atomic 61

PURITY OF ESSENCE
CD _____ CSR 021CD
IFA / Oct '95 / Plastic Head.

TINNITUS IN EXTREMIS
CD _____ CSR 106CD
Cavity Search / Oct '95 / Plastic Head.

Atomic Rooster

ATOMIC ROOSTER
They took control of you / She's my woman / He did it again / Where's the show / In the shadows / Do you know who's looking for you / Don't lose your mind / Watch out / I can't stand it / Lost in space
CD _____ REP 4135-WZ
Repertoire / Aug '91 / Pinnacle / Cadillac.

BBC LIVE IN CONCERT
CD _____ WINCD 042
Windsong / Oct '93 / Pinnacle.

BEST OF ATOMIC ROOSTER
CD _____ DMCD 1020
Demi-Monde / Jun '89 / Disc / Magnum Music Group.

DEATH WALKS BEHIND YOU
Death walks behind you / Vug / Tomorrow night / Seven streets / Sleeping for years / I can't stand no more / Nobody else / Gershatzer
CD _____ REP 4069-WZ
Repertoire / Aug '91 / Pinnacle / Cadillac.

DEVIL HITS BACK, THE
CD _____ DMCD 1023
Demi-Monde / Nov '89 / Disc / Magnum Music Group.

DEVILS' ANSWER
CD _____ RRDCD 003
Receiver / Sep '89 / Grapevine.

HEADLINE NEWS
Hold your fire / Headline news / Taking a chance / Metal minds / Land of freedom / Machine / Dance of death / Carnival / Time
CD _____ VP 171CD
Voice Print / Nov '94 / Voice Print.

IN HEARING OF...
CD _____ REP 4068-WZ
Repertoire / Aug '91 / Pinnacle / Cadillac.

Atomic Spuds

GARBAGE SURFERS
CD _____ AS 007
Bananajuice / Jan '96 / Nervous.

Atomvinter

ATOMVINTER
CD _____ DISTCD 12LF
Distortion / Jun '95 / Plastic Head.

Atrocity

ART OF DEATH, THE
CD _____ CORE 10CD
Metalcore / Feb '92 / Plastic Head.

BLUT
CD _____ MASSCD 033
Massacre / Nov '94 / Plastic Head.

CALLING THE RAIN
CD _____ MASSCD 071
Massacre / Aug '95 / Plastic Head.

DIE LIEBE (Atrocity & Das Ich)
CD _____ MASSCD 069
Massacre / Nov '95 / Plastic Head.

HALLUCINATIONS
CD _____ NB 038CD
Nuclear Blast / Jan '91 / Plastic Head.

INFECTED
CD _____ CORE 3CD
Metalcore / Oct '90 / Plastic Head.

TODESSEHNSUCHT
CD _____ RR 91282
Roadrunner / Jan '94 / Pinnacle.

Atrophy

SOCIALIZED HATE
CD _____ RR 9518 2
Roadrunner / Oct '88 / Pinnacle.

Attack

ZOMBIES
CD _____ AHOY 22
Captain Oi / Nov '94 / Plastic Head.

Attaco Decente

BABY WITHIN US MARCHES ON
Will of one / Fear of freedom / Don't join their army / Bully / Natural anger / Dad was God / There comes a time / Middle ages / Rose grower / Baby within us marches on
CD _____ AONCD 002
All Or Nothing / Feb '88 / ADA / Direct.

CRYSTAL NIGHT
CD _____ AON 005
All Or Nothing / Oct '94 / ADA / Direct.

Attar, Bachir

IN NEW YORK (Attar, Bachir & Elliot Sharp)
CD _____ EMCD 114
Enemy / Mar '90 / Grapevine.

NEXT DREAM, THE
Ceremonies against the night of the devil / Under the shadow of liberty / 1001 nights / Here we stay / Mixed cultures / Full moon at the window / Next dream
CD _____ CMPCD 57
CMP / Jun '93 / Vital/SAM.

Attia, Adolphe

JEWISH LITURGICAL MUSIC
CD _____ CMT 274993
La Chant Du Monde / Oct '94 / Harmonia Mundi / ADA.

Attika

WHEN HEROES FALL
CD _____ MASSCD 023
Massacre / Feb '94 / Plastic Head.

Attractions

MAD ABOUT THE WRONG BOY
Arms race / Damage / Little Miss Understanding / Straight jacket / Mad about the wrong boy / Motorworld / On the third stroke / Slow patience / La la la la loved you / Single girl / Lonesome little room / Taste of poison / High rise housewife / Talk about me / Sad about girls / Camera camera
CD _____ FIENDCD 25
Demon / Jul '91 / Pinnacle / ADA.

Attrition

HIDDEN AGENDA, THE
CD _____ HY 39100812
Hyperium / Dec '93 / Plastic Head.

Atwell, Winifred

WINNIE'S PIANO PARTY
Make it a party (medley) / Cross hands boogie / Bumble boogie / Johnson rag / Serenata (Moszkowski) / Make it a party (medley part 2) / Plink plank plunk / Let's have a ball (medley) / At the woodchoppers' ball / Let's have a ball (medley part 2) / Let's rock 'n' roll (medley) / Black and white rag / Twelfth Street rag (Bowman) / Hamp's boogie woogie / Lazy train / Let's rock 'n' roll (medley part 2) / Brazillian rhapsody / I'll remember April / Britannia rag / Bewitched, bothered and bewildered
CD _____ PLCD 531
President / Oct '89 / Grapevine / Target/ BMG / Jazz Music / President.

Atwood, Eden

CAT ON A HOT TIN ROOF
For every man there's a woman / Twilight world / Silent movie / Cat on a hot tin roof / You've changed / My ship / Every time we say goodbye / Right as the rain / I'm glad there is you / Never let me go / Not while I'm around
CD _____ CCD 4599
Concord Jazz / Jun '94 / New Note.

NO ONE EVER TELLS YOU
I didn't know what time it was / I was the last one to know / Is you is or is you ain't my baby / Ballad of the sad young men / Old devil moon / Cow cow boogie / No one ever tells you / Too late now / Gentle rain / Nothing's changed / Them there eyes
CD _____ CCD 4560
Concord Jazz / Jul '93 / New Note.

THERE AGAIN
It never entered my mind / You're my thrill / Nearness of you / In love in vain / Music that makes me dance / I'm always drunk in San Francisco / Sonny boy / Everything I've got belongs to you / In the days of our love / Only you (and you alone) / You don't know what love is / Auld lang syne
CD _____ CCD 4645
Concord Jazz / Jun '95 / New Note.

Au Pairs

EQUAL BUT DIFFERENT
Pretty boys / Ideal woman / Come again / Monogamy / It's obvious / Love song / Repetition / Dear John / Set up / Headache / We're so cool / Armagh / Steppin' out / America / Sex without stress / Intact / Shakedown / Slider / Unfinished business
CD _____ RPM 139CD
RPM / Jun '94 / Pinnacle.

PLAYING WITH A DIFFERENT SEX
CD _____ RPM 107
RPM / Nov '92 / Pinnacle.

SENSE AND SENSUALITY
CD _____ RPM 111
RPM / Aug '93 / Pinnacle.

Audience

AUDIENCE
Banquet / Waverley stage coach / River boat Queen / Harlequin / Heaven was an island / Too late I'm gone / Maidens cry / Troubles / Going song / Paper round / House on the hill / Man on box / Leave it unsaid / Pleasant conversation
CD _____ RPM 148
RPM / Oct '95 / Pinnacle.

AUDIENCE UNCHAINED
Trombone gulch / Ain't the man you need / Indian summer / Raviole / I had a dream / Party games / In accord / I put a spell on you / Stand by the door / Nancy / It brings a tear / Thunder and lightnin' / Grief and disbelief / Hula girl / Belladonna / Moonshine / Barracuda Dan / Hard cruel world / Jackda W. / You're not smiling
CD _____ CDVM 9007
Virgin / Aug '92 / EMI.

FRIENDS, FRIENDS, FRIEND
CD _____ CASCD 1012
Charisma / Jun '92 / EMI.

HOUSE ON THE HILL, THE
Jackdaw / You're not smiling / I had a dream / Raviole / Eye to eye / I put a spell on you / House on the hill / Nancy
CD _____ CASCD 1032
Charisma / Oct '90 / EMI.

LUNCH
Stand by the door / Seven sore bruises / Hula girl / Ain't the man you need / In accord / Barracuda Dan / Thunder and lightning / Party games / Trombone gulch / Buy me an island
CD _____ CASCD 1054
Charisma / Feb '91 / EMI.

Audio Active

HAPPY HAPPER
CD _____ ONUCD 77
On-U Sound / Jun '95 / SRD / Jetstar.

HAPPY SHOPPING IN EUROPE
CD _____ EFA 186352
On-U Sound / Nov '95 / SRD / Jetstar.

WAY OUT IS THE WAY IN, THE (Audio Active & Laraaji)
New laughter mode (the way in) / Music and cosmic (feel yourself) / Think cosmically / How time flies / Laaraajingle / Space visitors for tea - tat lump on your head / Hither and zither / Blooper's dance floor / New laugher mode (the way out)
CD _____ ASCD 026
All Saints / Nov '95 / Vital / Discovery.

WE ARE AUDIO ACTIVE
CD _____ ONUCD 73
On-U Sound / Sep '94 / SRD / Jetstar.

Audio Assault Squad

COMIN' UP OUTTA THIS BITCH
CD _____ TED 41742CD
Ichiban / May '94 / Koch.

Auffret, Anne

ROUE GRALON NI HO SALUD (Auffret, Anne & Yann Fanch Kemener)
CD _____ KM 42CD
Keltia Musique / Feb '94 / ADA / Direct / Discovery.

Auger, Brian

AUGERNIZATION (The Best Of Brian Auger)
Freedom jazz dance / Second wind / Maiden voyage / I want to take you higher / Don't look away / Happiness is just around the bend / Dawn of another day / Listen here / Foolish girl / Whenever you're ready
CD _____ TNGCD 008
Tongue 'n' Groove / Jul '95 / Vital.

DEFINITELY WHAT (Auger, Brian & The Trinity)
CD _____ OW 30012
One Way / Sep '94 / Direct / ADA.

Augscholl, Charly

BUS STOP
CD _____ 322 424
Koch / Oct '91 / Koch.

August, Lynn

SAUCE PIQUANTE
CD _____ BT 1092CD
Black Top / Jul '93 / CM / Direct / ADA.

Auld, Georgie

CANYON PASSAGE (Auld, Georgie & His Orchestra)
CD _____ MVSCD 57
Musicraft / '88 / Warner Music.

Auld Reekie Dance Band

CAPITAL REELS
Dashing white sergeant / Dashing white sergeant (encore) / Eightsome reel / Foursome reel / Scottish waltz / Hamilton House (jig) / Hamilton House (encore) / Duke of Perth / Duke of Perth (encore) / Strip the willow (Jig) / Strip the willow / Duke and Duchess of Edinburgh / Duke and Duchess of Edinburgh (Encore) / Gay Gordons / Scottish reform (jig) / Scottish reform / Reel of the 51st division / Reel of the 51st division (encore)
CD _____ LCOM 5190
Lismor / May '95 / Lismor / Direct / Duncans / ADA.

Auldridge, Mike

EIGHT STRING SWING
Little rock getaway / Redskin rag / Bethesada / Swing scene / Caravan / Almost to Tulsa / Bluegrass boogie / Eight string swing / Brown's baggin' / Pete's place / Crazy red top / Stompin' at the Savoy (Features on CD only.)
CD _____ SHCD 3725
Sugarhill / '92 / Roots / CM / ADA / Direct.

HIGH TIME (Auldridge, Reid & Coleman)
CD _____ SH 3776CD
Sugarhill / '90 / Roots / CM / ADA / Direct.

Aura

BUTTERFLY CHRYSALIS CATERPILLAR
CD _____ INFECT 19CD
Infectious / May '95 / Disc.

Aural Expansion

REMIXED SHEEP
CD _____ SSR 159
Crammed Discs / Jan '96 / Grapevine / New Note.

SURREAL SHEEP
CD _____ SSR 143
SSR / Aug '95 / Grapevine.

Aurora

AURORA
Daddy Trane and cousin Wayne / Bluejerk / Music of my people / Ghosts / Two hats /

Like latin / Buell St. Blues / Round Midnight / I go / Pete's boogie
CD _____ CY 73148
Denon / May '89 / Conifer.

Aurora

LAND OF HARM AND APPLETREES
CD _____ CDSATE 03
Talitha / Jul '93 / Plastic Head.

Aurora Sutra

DIMENSION GATE, THE
CD _____ CDSATE 10
Music Research / Oct '93 / Plastic Head.

Austin, Claire

MEMORIES OF YOU (Austin, Claire & Don Ewell)
CD _____ ACD 143
Audiophile / Apr '93 / Jazz Music / Swift.

Austin Lounge Lizards

CREATURES FROM THE BLACK SALOON
Golden triangle / Hot tubs of tears / Pflugerville / Car Hank died in / Swingin' from your crystal chandeliers / Kool whip / We are in control / Didn't go to college / Saquaro / Keeping up with the Joneses / War between the States / Old fat and drunk / Chester Woolah / Anahuac
CD _____ WM 1000
Watermelon / Jun '93 / ADA / Direct.

HIGHWAY CAFE OF THE DAMNED
Highway Cafe of the Damned / Cornhusker refugee / Industrial strength tranquilizer / Wendell, the uncola man / Acid rain / I'll just have one beer / Dallas, Texas / Ballad of Ronald Reagan / When drunks go bad / Jalapeno Maria / Get a haircut Dad / Chester Ninitiz oriental garden waltz
CD _____ WM 1001
Watermelon / Jun '93 / ADA / Direct.

SMALL MINDS
CD _____ WM 1034
Watermelon / Nov '95 / ADA / Direct.

Austin, Lovie

CLASSICS 1924-26
CD _____ CLASSICS 756
Classics / Aug '94 / Discovery / Jazz Music.

Austin, Patti

CARRY ON
Carry on / Givin' in to love / I will remember you / How can I be sure / Why did she come in with you / I just can't let go / Monday, Monday / More I thing about it / Nobody to dance with / I'll be waiting for you / (Don't know) Whether to laugh or cry
CD _____ GRP 96602
GRP / Oct '91 / BMG / New Note.

THAT SECRET PLACE
That's enough for me / Ability to swing / Somebody make me laugh / Broken dreams / Rock steady / That secret place / Hurry home / Stars in your eyes
CD _____ GRM 40232
GRP / May '94 / BMG / New Note.

ULTIMATE COLLECTION, THE
Hold me / Ability to swing / Givin' in to love / We fell in love / Heat of heat / Reach / I'll keep your dream alive / Soldier boy / Love is gonna getcha / Girl who used to be me / You who brought me love / Through the test of time
CD _____ GRP 98212
GRP / May '94 / BMG / New Note.

Autechre

AMBER
CD _____ WARPCD 25
Warp / Nov '94 / Disc.

INCUNABULA
CD _____ WARPCD 17
Warp / Nov '93 / Disc.

TRI REPETAE
CD _____ WARPCD 38
Warp / Nov '95 / Disc.

Auteurs

AUTEURS VS. U-ZIQ
Lenny Valentino 3 / Daughter of a child / Chinese bakery / Lenny Valentino 1 / Lenny Valentino 2 / Underground movies
CD _____ DGHUTM 20
Hut / Oct '94 / EMI.

NEW WAVE
Show girl / Bailed out / American guitars / Junk shop clothes / Don't trust the stars / Just ask your heart / I'll wait for you / Don't throw away all those teardrops / Where are you / Togetherness / You are mine
CD _____ CDHUT 7
Hut / Mar '93 / EMI.

NOW I'M A COWBOY
Modern history (Accoustic version) / Features on HUTLPX 16 only.) / Lenny Valentino / Brain child / I'm a rich man's toy / New

french girlfriend / Upper classes / Chinese bakery / Sister like you / Underground movies / Life classes / Modern history / Daughter of a child
CD _____ CDHUT 16
Hut / May '94 / EMI.

Auto Creation

METTLE
CD _____ INTA 003CD
Intermodo / Aug '94 / Disc.

Automatic Head Detonator

WHAT THE FUCK DO YOU KNOW
CD _____ LF 001
Lo-Fi Recordings / Mar '95 / SRD.

Autonomex

EARLYMAN MEETS AUTONOMEX
CD _____ WOWCD 38
Words Of Warning / Oct '95 / SRD.

Autopsia

KRISTALLMACHT
CD _____ HY 85921076
Hyperium / Apr '94 / Plastic Head.

REQUIM POUR UN EMPIRE
CD _____ HY 185000CD
Hypertension / Nov '92 / Total/BMG / Direct / ADA.

Autopsy

SEVERED SURVIVAL/MENTAL FUNERAL AND...
CD _____ CDVILE 25
Peaceville / Aug '95 / Pinnacle.

SHITFUN
CD _____ CDVILE 49
Peaceville / Jul '95 / Pinnacle.

Autry, Gene

BACK IN THE SADDLE AGAIN (22 Cowboy Classics)
Back in the saddle again / I hang my head and cry / Tears on my pillow / Be honest with me / Goodbye little darling / Lonely river / Tweedle o'twill / Under fiesta stars / Le me cry on your shoulder / Blue canadian rockies / I was just walking out the door / Cowboy's trademark / Can't shake the sands of Texas from my shoes / Last mile home / Dixie cannonball / Cowboy blues / You're the only good thing / Voice in the choir / Angel song / New star is shining in heaven / Silver spurs / Keep rolling lazy longhorns
CD _____ CTS 55430
Country Stars / Aug '94 / Target/BMG.

Autumn Leaves

AUTUMN LEAVES
Building bridges / Light of your love / Right on / Keeping it cool / Vera cruz / Eye of the hurricane / Lies and alibis / Ten minutes romance / Rhythm of the road / Together we're strong / Swing across Texas / Steppin' out on me / Thank you for the time / Blue water / Don't it make ya wanna dance
CD _____ BCD 15734
Bear Family / May '93 / Rollercoaster / Direct / CM / Swift / ADA.

Ava & The Astronettes

PEOPLE FROM BAD HOMES
CD _____ GY 005
Trident / Mar '94 / Pinnacle.

Available Jelly

IN FULL FLAIL
CD _____ ECD 1013
Ear-Rational / Dec '90 / Impetus / Cadillac.

MONUMENT
CD _____ RAMBOY 07
Bvhaast / Oct '94 / Cadillac.

Avalon

HIGHER GROUND
Lion of the north / Sons of the sea / Into the mists / Soldier's dream / Palais de danse / Stretch the bowl / Wild cherry tree / Ellis isle
CD _____ IRCD 017
Lismor / Aug '92 / Lismor / Direct / Duncans / ADA.

Avalon, Frankie

FABULOUS FRANKIE AVALON, THE
Venus / Why / Dede Dinah / Gingerbread / Bobby Sox to stockings / Boy without a girl / Just ask your heart / I'll wait for you / Don't throw away all those teardrops / Where are you / Togetherness / You are mine
CD _____ CDFAB 007
Ace / Sep '91 / Pinnacle / Cadillac / Complete/Pinnacle.

FRANKIE AVALON
CD _____ REP 4158-WZ
Repertoire / Aug '91 / Pinnacle / Cadillac.

HIT SINGLE COLLECTABLES
CD _____ DISK 4501
Disky / Apr '94 / THE / BMG / Discovery / Pinnacle.

Ave Maria Avida

DISTANCE
CD _____ HY 39100652CD
Hyperium / Aug '93 / Plastic Head.

Average White Band

LET'S GO ROUND AGAIN - BEST OF THE AVERAGE WHITE BAND
CD _____ AHLCD 15
Hit / Mar '94 / PolyGram.

LIVE ON THE TEST
Put it where you want it / If I ever lose this heaven / Cloudy / Pick up the pieces / Person to person / I heard it through the grapevine / Star in the ghetto / When will you be mine / Please don't fall in love / Atlantic Avenue / Show your hand
CD _____ WHISCD 005
Windsong / Aug '94 / Pinnacle.

Aversion

FALL FROM GRACE
CD _____ CDVEST 41
Bulletproof / Feb '95 / Pinnacle.

Avery, Teodross

IN OTHER WORDS (Avery, Teodross Quartet)
High hopes / Our true love / One to love / Ancient civilisation / Edda / Possibilities are endless / What's new / Urban survival / Positive role models / In other words / Our struggle / Watching the sunrise
CD _____ GRP 97982
GRP / Mar '95 / BMG / New Note.

MY GENERATION
Addis abeba / Mode for my father / Theme for Malcolm / Lover man / To the east / Mr. Wonsey / Salome / Sphere / My generation / Anytime, anyplace / It's about that time
CD _____ IMP 11812
Impulse Jazz / Jan '96 / BMG / New Note.

Avia

AVIA
Wake up and sing out / Spring song of the masses / Russian lesson part 1 (goodbye) / Night watch / I don't love you / Russian lesson part 2 (home) / Celebration / Aviavial / Semaphore
CD _____ HNCD 1358
Hannibal / Jul '90 / Vital / ADA.

Avulsed

CARNIVORACITY
CD _____ RPS 007MCD
Repulse / Oct '95 / Plastic Head.

Awakening

INTO THY HANDS
CD _____ RRACD 0035
Reunion / '88 / Nelson Word.

Awankana

FLAMBOYAN
CD _____ SM 1804-2
Wergo / Nov '93 / Harmonia Mundi / ADA / Cadillac.

GENTLE RIVER
CD _____ SM 18022
Wergo / Feb '92 / Harmonia Mundi / ADA / Cadillac.

KINGDOM IS NOT AFAR, THE
CD _____ SM 1801-2
Wergo / Aug '92 / Harmonia Mundi / ADA / Cadillac.

RINGSEL
CD _____ SM 1805-2
Wergo / Nov '93 / Harmonia Mundi / ADA / Cadillac.

Awful Truth

AWFUL TRUTH
It takes so long / I should have known all along / Ghost of heaven / Drowning man / Circle of pain / Higher / No good reason / Mary
CD _____ CDZORRO 3
Metal Blade / Aug '90 / Pinnacle.

AWOL

WHAT IT BE LIKE
CD _____ BRY 4175CD
Ichiban / Apr '94 / Koch.

Axton, Hoyt

SNOWBLIND FRIEND
You're the hangnail in my life / Little white moon / Water for my horse / Funeral of the king / I light this candle / Never been to Spain / You taught me how to cry / Snowblind friend / Poncho and lefty / Seven come eleven / I don't know why I love you

CD _____ EDCD 426
Edsel / May '95 / Pinnacle / ADA.

Ayers, Kevin

BANANAMOUR
Don't let it get you down / Shouting in a
bucket blues / When your parents go to
sleep / Interview / International anthem /
Decadence / Oh wot a dream / Hymn /
Beware of the dog
CD _____ BGOCD 142
Beat Goes On / Jun '92 / Pinnacle.

CONFESSIONS OF DR DREAM
Day by day / See you later / Didn't feel
lonely till I thought of you / Everybody's
sometime and some people's all the time
blues / It begins with a blessing / Once I
awakened / But it ends with a curse / Ball-
bearing blues / Confessions of Dr. Dream /
Irreversible neural damage / Invitation / One
chance dance / Dr. Dream / Two goes into
four
CD _____ BGOCD 86
Beat Goes On / Oct '90 / Pinnacle.

DOCUMENT SERIES PRESENTS...
CD _____ CSAPCD 110
Connoisseur / Sep '92 / Pinnacle.

JOY OF A TOY
Joy of a toy continued / Clarietta rag / Song
for insane times / Eleanor's cake which ate
her / Oleh oleh bandu bandong / Town feel-
ing / Girl on a swing / Stop this train / Lady
Rachel / All this crazy gift of time
CD _____ BGOCD 78
Beat Goes On / '89 / Pinnacle.

KEVIN AYERS
CD _____ WINCD 018
Windsong / May '92 / Pinnacle.

KEVIN AYERS COLLECTION
Lady Rachel / May I / Puis-je / Stranger in
blue suede shoes / Caribbean moon /
Shouting in a bucket blues / After the show
/ Didn't feel lonely till I thought of you /
Once upon an ocean / City waltz / Blue star
/ Blaming it all on love / Strange song / Miss
Hanaga / Money, money, money
CD _____ SEECD 117
See For Miles/C5 / Jun '83 / Pinnacle.

RAINBOW TAKEAWAY
Blaming it all on love / Ballad of a salesman
who sold himself / View from the mountain
/ Rainbow takeaway / Waltz for you /
Beware of the dog / Strange song / Good-
night, goodnight / Hat song
CD _____ BGOCD 189
Beat Goes On / Apr '93 / Pinnacle.

**SHOOTING AT THE MOON (Ayers,
Kevin & The Whole World)**
May 1 / Colores para Dolores / Lunatics la-
ment / Underwater / Red, green and blue
you / Rheinhardt and Geraldine / Pisser
dans un violon / Oyster and the flying fish /
Clarence in Wonderland / Shooting at the
moon
CD _____ BGOCD 13
Beat Goes On / Apr '90 / Pinnacle.

**SOPORIFICS (June 1 1974) (Ayers,
Kevin & John Cale/Nico/Brian Eno)**
Driving me backwards / Baby's on fire /
Heartbreak hotel / End / May I / Shouting in
a bucket blues / Stranger in blue suede
shoes / Everybody's sometime and some
people's all the time blues / Two goes into
four
CD _____ IMCD 92
Island / Feb '90 / PolyGram.

SWEET DECEIVER
Observations / Guru banana / City waltz /
Toujours la voyage / Sweet deceiver /
Diminished but not finished / Circular letter
/ Once upon an ocean / Farewell again
CD _____ BGOCD 98
Beat Goes On / Aug '92 / Pinnacle.

THAT'S WHAT YOU GET BABE
That's what you get / Where do I go from
here / You never outrun your love / Given
and taken / Idiots / Super salesman /
Money, money, money / Miss Hanaga / I'm
so tired / Where do the stars end
CD _____ BGOCD 190
Beat Goes On / Jun '93 / Pinnacle.

WHATEVER SHE BRINGS WE SING
There is loving / Among us / Margaret oh
my / Song from the bottom of a well / What-
ever she brings we sing / Stranger in blue
suede shoes / Champagne cowboy blues /
Lullaby
CD _____ BGOCD 11
Beat Goes On / Jun '89 / Pinnacle.

YES WE HAVE NO MANANAS
Star / Mr. Cool / Owl / love's gonna turn
you round / Falling in love again / Help me
/ Ballad of Mr. Snake / Everyone knows the
song / Yes I do / Blue
CD _____ BGOCD 143
Beat Goes On / Apr '93 / Pinnacle.

Ayers, Roy

DRIVE
CD _____ CDICH 1028
Ichiban / Mar '94 / Koch.

ESSENTIAL GROOVE - LIVE
Everybody loves the sunshine / Hot / Red,
black and green / Searchin' / Love will bring
us back together / Don't wait for love / We
live in London baby / Long time ago / Poo
poo la la
CD _____ JHCD 035
Ronnie Scott's Jazz House / '88 / Jazz Music / Magnum Music Group / Cadillac.

EVERYBODY LOVES THE SUNSHINE
Hey u / Golden rod / Keep on walking / You
and me my love / Third eye / It ain't your
sign / People and the world / Everybody
loves the sunshine / Tongue power / Lonesome cowboy
CD _____ 833 844-2
Polydor / Sep '93 / PolyGram.

FAST MONEY (Live at Ronnie Scott's)
Spirit of doo doo / I wanna touch you /
Everybody loves the sunshine / Fast money
/ Battle of the vibes / Can't you see me /
Running away / Don't stop the feeling
CD _____ CLACD 335
Castle / '93 / BMG.

**GET ON UP, GET ON DOWN - BEST OF
ROY AYERS**
Turn me loose / Get on up, get on down /
Sweet tears / What you won't do for love /
Rhythm / You send me / This side of sun-
shine / Vibrations
CD _____ 519918-2
Polydor / Aug '93 / PolyGram.

GOOD VIBRATIONS
Everybody loves the sunshine / Easy to
move / Mission / Wrapped up in your love
/ X marks the spot / Poo poo la la / Ivory
tower
CD _____ JHCD 028
Ronnie Scott's Jazz House / Jan '94 / Jazz
Music / Magnum Music Group / Cadillac.

HOT
Can't you see me / Running away / Love
will bring us together / Lots of love / Every-
one loves the sunshine / Hot / Pete King /
Sweet tears / Philadelphia mambo / We live
in London baby
CD _____ JHCD 021
Ronnie Scott's Jazz House / Jan '94 / Jazz
Music / Magnum Music Group / Cadillac.

MYSTIC VOYAGE
CD _____ 5195672
Polydor / Aug '93 / PolyGram.

NASTE
Naste / Mama Daddy / Your love / Treasure
/ Swirl / Fantasy / Ole Jose / Baby, set me
free / No more trouble / Satisfaction / I like
it like that / Last XT / Nonsense
CD _____ 7863666132
Groovetown / Jun '95 / BMG.

SEARCHIN'
Searchin' / Yes / You send me / Mystic voy-
age (CD only) / Love will bring us together
(CD only) / Spirit of the Do Do / Long time
ago / Can you see me (CD only)
CD _____ JHCD 013
Ronnie Scott's Jazz House / Jan '94 / Jazz
Music / Magnum Music Group / Cadillac.

**SHINING SYMBOL - THE ULTIMATE
COLLECTION, A**
CD _____ 519378-2
Polydor / May '93 / PolyGram.

VIBESMAN (Live At Ronnie Scott's)
CD _____ MCCD 215
Music Club / Oct '95 / Disc / THE / CM.

VIBRANT
CD _____ VSOPCD 179
Connoisseur / Feb '93 / Pinnacle.

WAKE UP
Midnight after dark / Suave / Sweet talk /
Spirit of dodo '89 / Crack is in the mirror
(wake up) / You've got the power / Mystic
vibrations
CD _____ CDICH 1040
Ichiban / Oct '93 / Koch.

Ayibobo

FREESTYLE
CD _____ DIW 877
DIW / Jan '94 / Harmonia Mundi /
Cadillac.

Ayler, Albert

FONDATION MAEGHT NIGHTS
CD _____ COD 004
Jazz View / Mar '92 / Harmonia Mundi.

GOIN' HOME
CD _____ BLCD 760197
Koch / Nov '94 / Koch.

LIVE IN EUROPE
CD _____ LS 2902
Lagoon / Mar '93 / Magnum Music Group
/ THE.

LIVE IN GREENWICH VILLAGE
For John Coltrane / Change has come /
Truth is marching in / Our prayer
CD _____ MCAD 39123
Impulse Jazz / Jun '89 / BMG / New Note.

**TRUTH IS MARCHING IN (Ayler, Albert
Quintet)**
CD _____ 30003
Giants Of Jazz / Sep '92 / Target/BMG /
Cadillac.

**VIBRATIONS (Ayler, Albert & Don
Cherry)**
Ghosts / Children / Holy spirit / Vibrations /
Mothers
CD _____ FCD 41000
Freedom / Sep '87 / Jazz Music / Swift /
Wellard / Cadillac.

WITCHES AND DEVILS
CD _____ FCD 41018
Freedom / Jan '83 / Jazz Music / Swift /
Wellard / Cadillac.

AZ

DOE OR DIE
Uncut raw / Gimme your's / Ho happy
Jackie / Rather unique / I feel for you /
Sugar hill / Mo money / Mo murder (homi-
cide) / Doe or die / We can't win / Your
world don't stop / Sugar hill (remix)
CD _____ CTCD 51
Cooltempo / Nov '95 / EMI.

Azaad

DRUM 'N' DHOL
CD _____ DMUT 1078
Multitone / Jul '89 / BMG.

JUGNI
CD _____ DMUT 1152
Multitone / Nov '90 / BMG.

Azevedo, Geraldo

BEREKEKE
CD _____ 925632
Buda / Jun '93 / Discovery / ADA.

Aznavour, Charles

20 CHANSONS D'OR
Je m'voyais deja / Trousse - chemise / Les
plaisirs demodes / Qui / Les comediens /
La mamma / For me... formidable / Non, je
n'ai rien oublie / Le temps / Que c'est triste
venise / Tu t'laisses aller / Et pourtant / La
Boheme / Les deux guitares / Desormais /
Il faut savoir / Comme Ils Disent / Hier en-
core / L'amour c'est comme un jour / Em-
menez - moi
CD _____ CDEMC 3716
EMI / Jul '95 / EMI.

AZNAVOUR
Rapid 9547 / Aug '92 / Total/BMG.

COLLECTION VOL. 2, THE
CD _____ MUS 700006
Rapid 9547 / Aug '92 / Total/BMG.

LES COMEDIENS
CD _____ CD 352072
Duchesse / May '93 / Pinnacle.

**PARIS - PALAIS DES CONGRES
(Aznavour, Charles & Liza Minnelli)**
Prologue / Sound of your name / Mon
emouvant amour / Les Comedens / Sa jeunesse / Napoli chante / Vous et tu / La Marguerite / Tu t'laisses aller / Non je n'ai rien
oublie / Je bois / Comme ils disent / Les
plaisirs demodes / La Boheme / Je m'voyais deja / Pour faire une jam / Bonjour Paris
/ God bless the child / Old friend / Liza with
a Z / Sailor boys / Some people / J'ai deux
amours / Stepping out / Losing my mind / I
love a piano / Cabaret / New York, New
York / Our love is here to stay / Song is you
/ Old devil moon / How high in the sky /
Let's fall in love / I've got you under my skin
/ Dream / Unforgettable / I've grown accus-
tomed to her face / These foolish things /
Just a dream ago / How high the moon /
Just in time / Le temps
CD _____ CDEMD 1080
EMI / Jul '95 / EMI.

WE WERE HAPPY THEN
CD _____ CDSL 5189
DRG / '88 / New Note.

Azreal

THERE SHALL BE NO ANSWER
CD _____ NBAZ 001CD
Nuclear Blast / Nov '95 / Plastic Head.

Azrie, Abed

AROMATES
CD _____ 7559792412
Elektra Nonesuch / Jan '95 / Warner
Music.

Aztec Camera

DREAMLAND
Birds / Safe in sorrow / Black Lucia / Let
your love decide / Spanish horses / Dream
sweet dreams / Pianos and clocks / Sister
Anne / Vertigo / Valium summer / Belle of
the ball
CD _____ 450992492-2
WEA / May '93 / Warner Music.

FRESTONIA
CD _____ 0630119292
WEA / Oct '95 / Warner Music.

HIGH LAND, HARD RAIN
Oblivious / Boy wonders / Walk out to winter / Bugle sounds again / We could send
letters / Pillar to post / Release / Lost outside the tunnel / Back on board / Down the
dip / Haywire / Orchid girl / Queen's tattoos
CD _____ 4509928492
WEA / Sep '93 / Warner Music.

KNIFE
Just like the USA / Head is happy (heart's
insane) / Backdoor to heaven / All I need is
everything / Backwards and forwards / Birth
of the true / Knife / Still on fire
CD _____ K 2404832
WEA / Sep '93 / Warner Music.

LIVE ON THE TEST
Back door heaven / Boy wonders / Walk out
to winter / Orchid girl / Back on board / Bugle sounds again / Release / Oblivious / We
could send letters
CD _____ WHISCD 006
Windsong / Oct '94 / Pinnacle.

LOVE
Deep and wide and tall / How men are /
Everybody is a number one / More than a
law / Somewhere in my heart / Working in
a goldmine / One and one / Paradise / Kil-
lermont street
CD _____ K 2422022
WEA / Sep '93 / Warner Music.

STRAY
Stray / Crying scene / Get outta London /
Over my head / Good morning Britain / How
it is / Gentle kind / Notting Hill blues / Song
for a friend
CD _____ 9031716942
WEA / Sep '93 / Warner Music.

Azukx

EVERYTHING IS EVERYTHING
CD _____ MNTCD 1
Mantra / Oct '95 / Disc.

Azumah

LONG TIME AGO
Emigodini yasegoli / Nkombose / Woza
woza / Inkonjane mnyama / Saphelisizwe /
Zamadlozi / Intombenjant / Nyamsoro / Af-
rican unite
CD _____ KAZ CD 15
Kaz / Oct '91 / Disc.

Azymuth

AZIMUTH
CD Set _____ 5230102
ECM / Jul '94 / New Note.

AZYMUTH '85
Adios Iony / Dream - lost song / Who are
you / Breathtaking / Potion 1 / February
daze / Till bakeblikk / Potion 2
CD _____ 8275202
ECM / Dec '85 / New Note.

BEST OF AZYMUTH, THE
Club Morrocco / Cascades of the seven
waterfalls / Textile factory / Right on /
Somewhere in Brazil / Outubro / 500 miles
high / Dear Limmertz / Song of the jet / Ar-
eiras / All the carnaval / Maracana
CD _____ MCD 9160-2
Milestone / Apr '94 / Jazz Music / Pinnacle
/ Wellard / Cadillac.

CARIOCA
CD _____ MCD 9169
Milestone / Oct '93 / Jazz Music /
Pinnacle / Wellard / Cadillac.

CRAZY RHYTHM
CD _____ MCD 9156
Milestone / Oct '93 / Jazz Music /
Pinnacle / Wellard / Cadillac.

HOW IT WAS THEN...NEVER AGAIN
How it was then / Looking on / Whirlpool /
Full circle / How deep is the ocean / Stango
/ Mindiatyr / Wintersweet
CD _____ 4238202
ECM / Apr '95 / New Note.

JAZZ CARNIVAL - BEST OF AZYMUTH
Jazz carnival / Dear Limmertz / Estreito de
taruma / Cascade of the seven waterfalls /
Missing doto / Maracana / Samba da barra
/ Textile factory / Turma do samba / Papaia
/ Partido alto / Pantanal il swamp
CD _____ CDBGP 1007
BGP / Mar '88 / Pinnacle.

Azzola, Marcel

L'ACCORDEONISTE
CD _____ 521500-2
Verve / Jun '94 / PolyGram.

B

B Shops For The Poor

VISIONS AND BLUEPRINTS
CD _____ NWCD 2
Nu Wave / Oct '91 / Cadillac / ReR Megacorp.

B So Global

WORLD IS COVERED IN WINDOWS, THE
CD _____ CHILLUM 002
Chill Um / Jan '96 / Plastic Head.

B-12

ELECTRO-SOMA
CD _____ WARPCD 9
Warp / Apr '93 / Disc.

B-52's

B-52'S
Planet Claire / Fifty two Girls / Dance this mess around / Rock lobster / Lava / There's a Moon in the sky (called Moon) / Hero worship / 6060 842 / Downtown
CD _____ IMCD 1
Island / May '90 / PolyGram.

B-52'S/ WILD PLANET
CD Set _____ ITSCD 1
Island / Nov '92 / PolyGram.

BOUNCING OFF THE SATELLITES
Summer of love / Girl from Ipanema goes to Greenland / Housework / Detour thru your mind / Wig / Theme for a nude beach / Juicy jungle / Communicate / She brakes for rainbows
CD _____ IMCD 105
Island / May '90 / PolyGram.

COSMIC THING
Cosmic thing / Dead beat club / Junebug / Bush fire / Topaz / Dry county / Love shack / Roam / Channel Z / Follow your bliss
CD _____ K 9258542
WEA / Mar '90 / Warner Music.

DANCE THIS MESS AROUND (Best Of The B-52's)
Party out of bounds / Dirty back road / Wig / Rock lobster / Give me back my man / Planet Claire / Devil in my car / 6060 842 / Dance this mess around / Strobelight / Song for a future generation
CD _____ CID 9959
Island / Apr '90 / PolyGram.

GOOD STUFF
Tell it like it is / Hot pants explosion / Good stuff / Revolution earth / Dreamland / Is that you mo-dean / World's green laughter / Vision of a kiss / Breezin' / Bad influence
CD _____ 7599269432
WEA / Feb '95 / Warner Music.

MESOPOTAMIA
Loveland / Mesopotamia / Throw that beat in the garbage can / Deep sleep / Cake / Nip it in the bud
CD _____ IMCD 107
Island / May '90 / PolyGram.

PARTY MIX
Party out of bounds / Private Idaho / Give me back my man / Lava / Dance this mess around / Fifty two girls
CD _____ IMCD 106
Island / May '90 / PolyGram.

PLANET CLAIRE
Planet Claire / Rock lobster / Lava / Downtown / 6060-842 / 52 Girls / Give me back my man / Strobe light / Dirty back road / Loveland / Nip it in the bud / Song for a future generation / Wig / Girl from Ipanema goes to Greenland
CD _____ 5512102
Spectrum/Karussell / Aug '95 / PolyGram / THE.

WHAMMY!
Legal tender / Whammy kiss / Song for a future generation / Butterbean / Trism / Queen of Las Vegas / Don't worry / Big bird / Work that skirt
CD _____ IMCD 109
Island / May '90 / PolyGram.

WILD PLANET
Party out of bounds / Dirty back road / Running around / Give me back my man / Private Idaho / Quiche Lorraine / Strobelight / Fifty three miles West of Venus / Devils in my car
CD _____ IMCD 108
Island / May '90 / PolyGram.

B-Movie

DEAD GOOD TAPES
CD _____ WAXCD 1
Wax / Mar '88 / Disc.

B-Tribe

FIESTA FATALE
Intro (Sueno del cielo) / Fiesta fatal / Nadie entiende / Lo siento / Una vez mas / Love, tears, heartaches and devotion / Don't be emotional / You won't see me cry / Te quiero - interlude / Reprise - Fiesta fatal / Fiesta fatal
CD _____ 4509930622
East West / Sep '93 / Warner Music.

B. Bumble & The Stingers

NUT ROCKER AND ALL THE CLASSICS
Nut rocker / Bumble boogie / School day blues / Boogie woogie / Near you / Bee hive / Caravan / Nautilus / Nola / Rockin' on 'n' off / Mashed #5 / Apple knocker / Moon and the sea / All of me / Dawn cracker / Scales / 12th Street rag / Canadian sunset / Baby mash / Night time madness / In the mood / Chicken chow mein / Bumble bossa nova / Canadian sunset (Alt.)
CD _____ CDCHD 577
Ace / Jul '95 / Pinnacle / Cadillac / Complete/Pinnacle.

B.B. & The Blues Shacks

FEELIN' FINE TODAY
CD _____ CDST 01
Stumble / Nov '95 / Direct.

B.E.F.

MUSIC OF QUALITY AND DISTINCTION (VOL.1)
Ball of confusion / Secret Life of Arabia / There's a Ghost in my House / These Boots are made for Walking / Suspicious Minds / You keep me hangin' on / Wichita Lineman / Anyone who had a Heart / Perfect Day / It's Over
CD _____ CDBEF 1
Virgin / Aug '92 / EMI.

B.E.P.

RIPPER
CD _____ KI 57CD
Konkurrel / Jan '95 / SRD.

B.F.M.

CITY OF DOPE
City of dope / Go amazen' (do yo' thang) / Can't slow down / Am I black enough / Let yourself go / Why ya "p" ain't tight / Gimme a bottle / Larceny / Give it up / Pass the joint
CD _____ CDICH 1118
Ichiban / Oct '93 / Koch.

B.G.K.

NOTHING CAN GO WRONG
CD _____ VIRUS 52CD
Alternative Tentacles / '92 / Pinnacle.

B.L.O.W.

MAN AND GOAT ALIKE
CD _____ COTINDCD 1
Cottage Industry / Mar '95 / Total/BMG.

B.M.EX

APPOLONIA
CD _____ UCRCD 14
Union City / Jan '93 / EMI.

B.S.G.

WARM INSIDE
CD _____ XM 031CD
X-Mist / Apr '92 / SRD.

B.T.

IMA
CD _____ 0630123452
Perfecto/East West / Oct '95 / Warner Music.

B.W.F.

UNSENTIMENTAL
Unsentimental / Up-lifted / Unsentimental / Victim of riches / P.O.W. / Articles / Special one / Last days / Hole in my pocket / Said a prayer / Wish your life / Ain't no place like home
CD _____ 72715-2
Restless / May '94 / Vital.

B.Y.O.B.

B.Y.O.B.
Too good to let go / Ramifications of shaking one's ass / Change it / Distances / Go jazz go / Outerspacegethithang / Ramblifications of getting and saying high / Rackett / Day off in the life / Where ya going to

CD _____ RCD 10310
Rykodisc / Oct '94 / Vital / ADA.

B12

TIME TOURIST
CD _____ WARPCD 37
Warp / Feb '96 / Disc.

Baars, Ab

3900 CAROL COURT
CD _____ GEESTCD 12
Geest Gronden / Feb '89 / Cadillac.

KRANG
CD _____ GEESTCD 02
Geest Gronden / Sep '87 / Cadillac.

Baba Jam Band

KAYADA
CD _____ BEST 1036CD
Acoustic Music / Nov '93 / ADA.

Babble

STONE, THE
Downward pull of heaven's force / Tribe / You kill me / Spirit / Take me away / Stone / Beautiful / Space / Sunray dub / Drive
CD _____ 9362453872
WEA / Mar '94 / Warner Music.

Babe The Blue Ox

(BOX)
Home / Honey do / Chicken head bone sucker / Gymkhana / Spatula / Waiting for water to boil / Booty / Born again / National Geographic / Tongue tied / Snicker
CD _____ RTD 15715752
World Service / Jun '93 / Vital.

Babes In Toyland

FONTANELLE
CD _____ 185012
Southern / '92 / SRD.

NEMESISTER
CD _____ 9362458682
Warner Bros. / Apr '95 / Warner Music.

PAINKILLERS
CD _____ 185122
Southern / Jun '93 / SRD.

Babs, Alice

ALICE BABS & RED MITCHELL/ARNE DOMNERUS/NILS LINDBERG
CD _____ ABC 052
Bluebell / Mar '94 / Cadillac / Jazz Music.

FAR AWAY STAR (Babs, Alice & Duke Ellington/Nils Lindberg Orchestras)
Far away star / Serenade to Sweden / Spaceman / Jeep's blues / Daydream / Is God a three-letter word for love / Jump for joy / Warm valley / Blues for the maestro
CD _____ ABC 000005
Bluebell / Oct '94 / Cadillac / Jazz Music.

SWING IT 1939-1953
CD _____ PHONTCD 9302
Phontastic / Jun '94 / Wellard / Jazz Music / Cadillac.

Baby Bird

BAD SHAVE
KW Jesus TV roof appeal / Bad jazz / Too handsome / Steam train / Bad shave / O my God, you're a king / Restaurant is guilty / Valerie / Shop girl / W.B.T. / Hate song / 45 + Fat / Sha na na / Bug in a breeze / It's OK / Happy bus / Swinging from tree to tree
CD _____ BABYBIRDCD 002
Baby Bird / Oct '95 / Vital.

I WAS BORN A MAN
Blow it to the moon / Man's tight vest / Lemonade baby / CFC / Corner shop / Kiss your country / Kong blues / Dead bird sings / Baby bird / Farmer / Invisible tune / Alison / Love love love
CD _____ BABYBIRD
Baby Bird / Jul '95 / Vital.

Baby Chaos

SAFE SEX, DESIGNER DRUGS AND THE DEATH OF ROCK 'N' ROLL
CD _____ 450998052-2
Warner Bros. / Oct '94 / Warner Music.

Baby D

DELIVERANCE (1CD/MC/3LP/2CD Set)
Got to believe / So pure / Destiny / Come into my world / Casanova (Live Mix) / Winds of love / I need your loving / Daydreaming / Euphoria / Nature's warning / Take me to heaven / Let me be your fantasy / Have it all (CD Set Only) / Daydreaming - Acenhal-

lucination (CD Set Only) / So pure #2 (Mix/CD Set Only)
CD _____ 8286832
CD Set _____ 8287202
Systematic / Jan '96 / PolyGram.

Baby Doo & The Dentist

IN WORSHIP OF FALSE IDOLS
CD _____ TECLP 23CD
TEC / Jul '95 / SRD.

Baby Wayne

RAM D.J.
CD _____ HBCD 147
Heartbeat / Jan '94 / Greensleeves / Jetstar / Direct / ADA.

Babybird

FATHERHOOD
No children / Cooling towers / Cool and crazy thing to do / Bad blood / Neil Armstrong / May be / But love / Good weather / Not about a girl / Dustbin liner / Fatherhood / Failed old singer / Daisies / Godamn it, you're a kid / Aluminium beach / Iceberg / I didn't want to wake you up / Good night
CD _____ BABYBIRDCD 003
Baby Bird / Dec '95 / Vital.

Babyface

FOR THE COOL IN YOU
For the cool in you / Lady lady / Never keeping secrets / Rock bottom / And our feelings / Saturday / When can I see you / Illusions / Bit old fashioned / You are so beautiful / I'll always love you / Well alright
CD _____ 473949 2
Epic / Jan '94 / Sony.

Babylon Dance Band

BABYLON DANCE BAND
When I'm home / Bold beginnings / Reckoning / Shively spleen / Roger / Leave / Resources / See that girl / Jacob's chain / Shake
CD _____ OLE 033-2
Matador / May '94 / Vital.

Babylon Sad

KYRIE
CD _____ MASSCD 026
Massacre / Feb '94 / Plastic Head.

Bacharach, Burt

BEST OF BURT BACHARACH, THE
CD _____ 5404522
A&M / Jan '96 / PolyGram.

BURT BACHARACH/HAL DAVID SONGBOOK, THE (Various Artists)
I say a little prayer / What the world needs now is love / Alfie / Message to Michael / I just don't know what to do with myself / Do you know the way to San Jose / Trains four hours from Tulsa / Close to you / You'll never get to heaven (If you break my heart) / Anyone who had a heart / I'll never fall in love again / Walk on by / Story of my life / What's new pussycat / This guy's in love with you / Trains and boats and planes / Make it easy on yourself / House is not a home / Always something there to remind me / Look of love / Raindrops keep falling on my head / Wishin' and hopin' / Only love can break a heart / Promises, promises
CD _____ VSOPCD 128
Connoisseur / Jan '89 / Pinnacle.

GOLD SERIES
Raindrops keep falling on my head / Look of love / I'll never fall in love again / Do you know the way to San Jose / What the world needs now is love / Alfie / Reach out / Promises, promises / This guy's in love with you / Close to you / Make it easy on yourself / I say a little prayer / April fools / Bond street / Any day now / Pacific coast highway / House is not a home / One less bell to answer / Wives and lovers / Living together, growing together / Knowing when to leave
CD _____ CDMID 156
A&M / Oct '92 / PolyGram.

I'LL NEVER FALL IN LOVE AGAIN
Do you know the way to San Jose / I say a little prayer / I'll never fall in love again / No one remembers my name / This guy's in love with you / Time and tenderness / Wives and lovers / Raindrops keep falling on my head / Close to you / Look of love / Alfie / Where are you / Us / Another spring will make
CD _____ 5500572
Spectrum/Karussell / May '93 / PolyGram / THE.

33

MAGIC MUSIC OF BURT BACHARACH
(Various Artists)
CD _____ GRF 195
Tring / Jan '93 / Tring / Prism.

REACH OUT
Reach out for me / Alfie / Bond street / Are you there (with another girl) / What the world need now is love / Look of love / House is not a home / I say a little prayer / Windows of the world / Lisa / Message to Michael
CD _____ 3941312
A&M / Sep '95 / PolyGram.

Bachelors

CLASSIC ARTISTS
CD _____ JHD 049
Tring / Jun '92 / Tring / Prism.

COLLECTION: BACHELORS
Cecilia / Gonna build a mountain / Walk with faith in your heart / Marie / Well respected / Sound of silence / Elusive butterfly / Chapel in the moonlight / You'll never walk alone / Mame / Marta / My foolish heart
CD _____ PWK 067
Carlton Home Entertainment / Aug '88 / Carlton Home Entertainment.

GOLDEN HITS & PRECIOUS MEMORIES
CD _____ 8444862
Deram / Jan '96 / PolyGram.

Bachicha, Bianco

ORIGINAL TANGOS
CD _____ 995302
EPM / Jun '93 / Discovery / ADA.

Bachman

ANY ROAD
CD _____ 341082
Koch / Sep '93 / Koch.

Bachman-Turner Overdrive

ANTHOLOGY (2CD Set)
CD Set _____ 5149022
Phonogram / Jan '94 / PolyGram.

GREATEST HITS: BACHMAN TURNER OVERDRIVE
Lookin' out for no.1 / Hey you / Taking care of business / You ain't seen nothin' yet / Flat broke love / Rock 'n' roll nights / Roll on down the highway / Freeways / Down down / Let it ride / Can we all come together / Jamaica
CD _____ 8300392
Phonogram / Jan '86 / PolyGram.

NOT FRAGILE
Not fragile / Roll down the highway / You ain't seen nothin' yet / Free wheelin' / Sledgehammer / Blue moanin' / Second hand / Givin' it all away / Rock is my life, and this is my song
CD _____ 830 178-2
Phonogram / '92 / PolyGram.

ROLL ON DOWN THE HIGHWAY
You ain't seen nothin' yet / Roll on down the highway / Lookin' out for no.1 / Heartaches / Stayed awake all night / Just for you / Down and out man / Blue collar / Hey you / My wheel's won't turn / Takin' care of business / Stonegates / Not fragile / Away from home / Life ball goes on (I'm lonely) / Take it like a man / Shotgun rider / Sledgehammer
CD _____ 5504212
Spectrum/Karussell / Aug '94 / PolyGram / THE.

Back Bay Ramblers

BACK BAY RAMBLERS
CD _____ SOSCD 1262
Stomp Off / Dec '94 / Jazz Music / Wellard.

MY MAMA'S IN TOWN (Back Bay Ramblers & Jimmy Mazzy)
CD _____ SOSCD 1279
Stomp Off / Dec '94 / Jazz Music / Wellard.

Back To The Future

PROGRESSIVELY FUNKY
CD _____ HDHCD 502
HDH / Jul '91 / Pinnacle.

Back To The Planet

MESSAGES AFTER THE BLEEP
Tidal motion / Electro Ray's / Flexing muscles / Elemental bliss / Immanent deities / Never let them / Meditational thoughts / Colour sex / Criminal / Super powers / Under your skin
CD _____ BTTP 007CD
Arthur Mix / Mar '95 / Vital.

MIND & SOUL COLLABORATORS
CD _____ 828437-2
Parallel / Sep '93 / PolyGram.

Backhouse, Miriam

GYPSY WITHOUT A ROAD
Far away Tom / Widow / Farmers have gone East / Long lankin / Nasty spider / Dark side of the moon / John Riley / Keys of Canterbury / Gypsy without a road
CD _____ DORIS 1
Vinyl Tap / Mar '95 / Vinyl Tap.

Backstrom, Ola

OLA BACKSTROM
CD _____ GCD 21CD
Giga / Apr '95 / ADA.

Backtrack Blues Band

KILLIN' TIME
Killin' time / Heavy built woman / Cruesin' for a bluesin' / Like it or not / Work to do / Babe oh babe / Come on to me mama / Don't need nobody / I make my home in Florida / You'll come back someday
CD _____ ICH 9005CD
Ichiban / Jun '94 / Koch.

Backus, Gus

DIE SINGLES 1959-1961
CD _____ BCD 15482
Bear Family / '88 / Rollercoaster / Direct / CM / Swift / ADA.

HILLBILLY GASTHAUS
Saginaw Michigan / Terribly pretty / Tennessee waltz / Oh Susanna / Laughin' and singin' / House I call my home / Don't fence me in / Home on the range / San Antonio rose / Long is the road / Reach for me / Paint and glue / On top of Old Smokey / I'm coming home / Deshalb ich nach Alaska / Das gross stadt m'dchen / Tennesse waltz (German) / Oh Susanna (German) / Nur in Tennessee / Der letzte trapper / Oh Cathrin / Heim will ich gehn / San Antonio rose (German) / Lang, lang ist das her / He Alter John / Ese alles habo so schwer / Ein haus auf der Sierra / Es ist schon, Mutter
CD _____ BCD 15765
Bear Family / May '94 / Rollercoaster / Direct / CM / Swift / ADA.

MY CHICK IS FINE
My chick is fine / You can't got it alone / Big Willie broke jail tonight / Short on love / Linda / Little kiss / Whisper / Queen of the stars / Listen / Priscilla / Happy end in Switzerland / Vaya con dios / For stealing her away / Just say goodbye (and you can go) / I'm coming home / Lost and found / Something you've got / Guess you'll have to do without / It feels so good / Blind man in our town / Need you all the time / Autumn breeze / Turn around / for I smile 'cause I think of you / Touch on your heart / My scrapbook / Memories of Ofheidelberg / Wonderful rainbow
CD _____ BCDAH 15769
Bear Family / Nov '95 / Rollercoaster / Direct / CM / Swift / ADA.

Bacon, Max

HIGHER YOU CLIMB (Bacon, Max & His Orchestra)
CD _____ NTHEN 023CD
Now & Then / Jan '96 / Plastic Head.

Bad Boys Inc.

BAD BOYS INC.
Change your mind / Love here I come / I would give you forver / More to this world / Whenever you need someone / Falling for you girl / Take me away (I'll follow you) / Walking on air / You're my destiny / Honestly / Dream along with me tonight / Don't talk about love
CD _____ 540287-2
A&M / Oct '94 / PolyGram.

TAKE ME HOME
You're my destiny / Falling for you girl / Whenever you need someone / Walking on air / I would give you forever / I'm gonna miss you / Don't talk about love / Honestly / Take me home / Ain't nothing gonna keep me from you / Dream along with me tonight / Second chance / Heaven knows / Hearts of fire
CD _____ 540200-2
A&M / Jan '94 / PolyGram.

Bad Brains

GOD OF LOVE
CD _____ 9362458822
Warner Bros. / May '95 / Warner Music.

LIVE
CD _____ SST 160 CD
SST / May '93 / Plastic Head.

QUICKNESS
Soul craft / Voyage into infinity / Messengers / With the quickness / Gene machine / Don't bother me / Don't blow bubbles / Don't need me / No conditions / Silent tears / Prophet's eye / Endtro
CD _____ CARCD 4
Caroline / Jul '89 / EMI.

ROCK FOR LIGHT
Big takeover / Attitude / Right brigade / Joshua's song / I and I survive / Banned in DC / Supertouch / Destroy Babylon / FVK / Meek / / Coptic times / Sailin' on / Rock for light / Rally round jah throne / At the movies / Riot squad / How low can a punk get / We will not / Jam
CD _____ CARCD 12
Caroline / Feb '91 / EMI.

ROCK FOR LIGHT/I AGAINST I
Coptic times / Attitude / We will not / Sailin' on / Rally 'round jah throne / Right brigade / F V K / Riot squad / Meek shall inherit the earth / Joshua's song / Banned in DC / How low can a punk get / Big takeover / I and I survive / Destroy Babylon / Rock for light / At the movies / Intro / I against I / House of suffering / Re-ignition / Secret 77 / Let me help / She's calling you / Sacred love / Hired gun / Return to heaven
CD Set _____ LICD 921176
Line / May '92 / CM / Grapevine / ADA / Conifer / Direct.

Bad Company

10 FROM 6
Can't get enough / Feel like makin' love / Run with the pack / Shooting star / Movin' on / Bad company / Rock 'n' roll fantasy / Electric land / Ready for love / Live for the music
CD _____ 781 625-2
Atlantic / Jan '86 / Warner Music.

BAD COMPANY
Can't get enough / Rock steady / Ready for love / Don't let me down / Bad company / Way I choose / Movin' on / Seagull
CD _____ 756792441-2
Atlantic / Sep '94 / Warner Music.

BURNIN' SKY
CD _____ 756792450-2
Atlantic / Sep '94 / Warner Music.

COMPANY OF STRANGERS
CD _____ 7559618082
Atlantic / Aug '95 / Warner Music.

DANGEROUS AGE
One night / Shake it up / No smoke without fire / Bad man / Dangerous age / Dirty boy / Rock of America / Something about you / Way it goes / Love attack
CD _____ K 781 884 2
Atlantic / Aug '88 / Warner Music.

DESOLATION ANGELS
Rock 'n' roll fantasy / Crazy circles / Gone gone gone / Evil wind / Early in the morning / Lonely for your love / Oh, Atlanta / Take the time / Rhythm machine / She brings me love
CD _____ 756792451-2
Atlantic / Sep '94 / Warner Music.

FAME AND FORTUNE
Burning up / This love / Fame and fortune / Long walk / Valerie / Hold on my heart / That girl / When we made love / If I'm sleeping / Tell it like it is
CD _____ 7567816842
Atlantic / Jul '93 / Warner Music.

HERE COMES TROUBLE
How about that / Stranger than fiction / Here comes the trouble / This could be the one / Both feet in the water / Take this town / What about you / Little angel / Hold on to my heart / Broken hearted / My only one
CD _____ 7567917592
Atlantic / Oct '92 / Warner Music.

HOLY WATER
Holy water / Walk through fire / Stranger stranger / If you needed somebody / Fearless / Lay your love on me / Boys cry tough / With you in a heartbeat / I don't care / Never too late / Dead of the night / I can't live without you / Hundred miles
CD _____ 7567 91371 2
Atlantic / Jun '90 / Warner Music.

ROUGH DIAMONDS
Electric land / Untie the knot / Nuthin' on the TV / Painted face / Kickdown / Ballad of the band / Cross country boy / Old Mexico / Downhill ryder / Racetrack
CD _____ 756792452-2
Atlantic / Oct '94 / Warner Music.

RUN WITH THE PACK
Live for the music / Simple man / Honeychild / Love me somebody / Run with the pack / Silver blue and gold / Young blood / Do right by your woman / Sweet lil' sister / Fade away
CD _____ 756792435-2
Atlantic / Jul '94 / Warner Music.

STRAIGHT SHOOTER
Good lovin' gone bad / Feel like makin' love / Weep no more / Shooting star / Deal with the preacher / Wild fire women / Anna / Call on me
CD _____ 756782637-2
Atlantic / Jun '94 / Warner Music.

WHAT YOU HEAR IS WHAT YOU GET (The Best Of Bad Company - Live)
How about that / Holy water / Rock 'n' roll fantasy / If you needed somebody / Here comes trouble / Ready for love / Shooting star / No smoke without a fire / Feel like makin' love / Take this town / Movin' on / Good lovin' gone bad / Fist full of blisters / Can't get enough / Bad company

---

CD _____ 756792307-2
Atlantic / Dec '93 / Warner Music.

Bad Examples

SLOW MUSIC
CD _____ EFA 037652
Atatak / Nov '95 / SRD.

Bad Livers

DELUSIONS OF BANJER
CD _____ QS 14CD
Quarter Stick / Sep '92 / SRD.

HORSES IN THE MINES
CD _____ QS 20CD
Quarter Stick / May '94 / SRD.

Bad Manners

BEST OF BAD MANNERS
Lip up fatty / Special brew / Lorraine / Just a feeling / Can can / My girl lollipop / Walking in the sunshine / Skaville U.K. / This is ska / Midnight rider / You fat ... / Christmas time again / Gonna get along without you now
CD _____ BBSCD 010
Blue Beat / Sep '90 / Magnum Music Group / THE.

FATTY FATTY
CD _____ LG 21005
Lagoon / Jun '93 / Magnum Music Group / THE.

GREATEST HITS LIVE
Echo 4 + 2 / Just a feeling / Wooly bully / Only funkin / My girl lollipop / Undersea adventures of Ivor the engine / Lorraine / Samson and Delilah / Walking in the sunshine / Inner London violence / Special brew / Magnificent seven / Lip up fatty / Can can / El pussy cat / Ne-ne-na-na-na-na nu-nu
CD _____ DOJOCD 111
Dojo / Mar '93 / BMG.

INNER LONDON VIOLENCE
CD _____ LG 21094
Lagoon / Apr '94 / Magnum Music Group / THE.

SKINHEAD
CD _____ LG 21026
Lagoon / Jul '93 / Magnum Music Group / THE.

THIS IS SKA
CD _____ DOJOCD 245
Dojo / Jan '96 / BMG.

Bad Moon Rising

BAD MOON RISING
Hands on / If it ain't dirty / Without your love / Full moon / Lie down / Old flames / Built for speed / Dark side of babylon / Sunset after midnight / Wayward son
CD _____ CDFLAG 78
Under One Flag / Jan '93 / Pinnacle.

BLOOD
Dangerous game / Servants of the sun / Devil's son (Mother our children die) / Blood on the streets / Tears in the dark / Heart of darkness / Chains / Till the morning comes / Time will tell / Remember me
CD _____ CDFLAG 79
Under One Flag / Apr '93 / Pinnacle.

Bad News

CASH IN COMPILATION, THE
Hey hey bad news / Bad dreams / Warriors of Ghengis Khan / A.G.M. / Bohemian rhapsody / Pretty woman / O levels / Life with Brian / Bad news / Masturbike / Double entendre / Drink till I die / Cashing in on Christmas (Dub)
CD _____ DOJOCD 152
Dojo / Sep '93 / BMG.

Bad Religion

ALL AGES
CD _____ 864432
Epitaph / Nov '95 / Plastic Head / Pinnacle.

BAD RELIGION 1980-85
CD _____ E 864072 X
Epitaph / Nov '91 / Plastic Head / Pinnacle.

HOW COULD HE
CD _____ E 86407CD
Epitaph / Jul '93 / Plastic Head / Pinnacle.

RECIPE FOR HATE
CD _____ E 864202
Epitaph / Jun '93 / Plastic Head / Pinnacle.

STRANGER THAN FICTION
Incomplete / Leave me to me / Stranger than fiction / Tiny voices / Handshake / Better off dead / Infected / Television / Individual / Hooray for me / Slumber / Marked / Inner logic / What it is / 21st Century (digital boy)
CD _____ 477343-2
Columbia / Sep '94 / Sony.

Bad Sector

AMPOS
CD _____ STCD 009
Staalplaat / Sep '95 / Vital/SAM.

Bad Seed

BAD SEED
CD _____ CDMFN 179
Music For Nations / Mar '95 / Pinnacle.

Bad Yodellers

I WONDER
CD _____ SR 30190CD
Semaphore / Jan '92 / Plastic Head.

WINDOW
CD _____ SR 330591CD
Semaphore / '91 / Plastic Head.

Badarou, Wally

ECHOES
Keys / Hi life / Mambo / Voices / Canyons / Endless race / Chief inspector / Waltz / Jungle / Rain
CD _____ CID 104
Island / May '85 / PolyGram.

Badfinger

COME AND GET IT - BEST OF BADFINGER
Come and get it / Maybe tomorrow / Rock of all ages / Dear Angie / Carry on till tomorrow / No matter what / Believe me / Midnight caller / Better days / Without you / Take it all / Money / Flying / Name of the game / Suitcase / Day after day / Baby blue / When I say / Icicles / I can love you / Apple of my eye
CD _____ CDSAPCOR 28
Apple / Apr '95 / EMI.

Badgeman

KINGS OF THE DESERT
Secret diary of Jim Morrison's bastard / Sean's seen the light / Cupid's exploding harpoon / King of the desert / Montezuma's revenge / My flash on you / Crystals / Extraordinary girl / False yellow eyes / Make me feel / Going sane gain / P.A.F
CD _____ PAPCD 003
Paperhouse / Jul '90 / Disc.

Badloves

GET ON BOARD
CD _____ D 24025
Mushroom / Mar '94 / BMG / 3MV.

Baerwald, David

TRIAGE
Secret silken world / Got no shotgun hydrahead octopus blues / Nobody / Waiter / AIDS and armageddon / Postman / Bitter tree / China lake / Brand new morning / Born for love
CD _____ 395 392
A&M / Mar '93 / PolyGram.

Baez, Joan

BALLAD BOOK VOL 1, THE
CD _____ VFCD 7106
Start / May '89 / Koch.

BALLAD BOOK VOL 2, THE
CD _____ VFCD 7108
Start / Jun '89 / Koch.

DAY TIOM
CD _____ VFCD 7103
Start / Aug '89 / Koch.

BEST OF JOAN BAEZ
Diamonds and rust / Prison trilogy (Billy Rose) / Never dreamed you'd leave in summer / Please come to Boston / Sweeter for me / Gracias a la vida (Here's to life) / Forever young / Simple twist of fate / Love song to a stranger / Children and all that jazz / Imagine / Night they drove old Dixie down
CD _____ PWKS 544
Carlton Home Entertainment / Sep '89 / Carlton Home Entertainment.

BEST OF JOAN BAEZ
Diamonds and rust / Forever young / Prison trilogy / Simpel twist of fate / Never dreamed you'd leave in summer / Love song to a stranger / Please come to Boston / Children and all that jazz / Sweeter for me / Imagine / Gracias a la vida (heres to life) / Night they drove old Dixie down
CD _____ CDMID 108
A&M / Oct '92 / PolyGram.

COMPACT COLLECTION
CD _____ TPAK 30
Virgin / Nov '93 / EMI.

FAREWELL ANGELINA
Farewell Angelina / Daddy, you've been on my mind / It's all over now baby blue / Baby blue / Wild mountain thyme / Rangers command / Colours / Satisfied mind / River in the pines / Pauvre rutebeuf / Sagt mir wo die blumen sind / Hard rain's gonna fall
CD _____ VND 79200

Vanguard / Oct '95 / Complete/Pinnacle / Discovery.

GEMS
CD _____ 5501292
Spectrum/Karussell / Oct '93 / PolyGram / THE.

IMAGINE
Diamonds and rust / Night they drove old Dixie down / Simpel twist of fate / Imagine / In the quiet morning / Best of friends / Forever young / Prison trilogy / Jesse / Children and all that jazz / Please come to Boston / Never dreamed you'd leave in summer / Gracias a la vida (here's to life) / Sweeter for me / Love song to a stranger / Dida / Amazing grace
CD _____ CDMID 180
A&M / Mar '93 / PolyGram.

JOAN BAEZ #1
Silver dagger / East Virginia / Ten thousand miles / House of the rising sun / All my trials / Wildwood flower / Donna Donna / John Riley / Rake and the rambling boy / Little Moses / Mary Hamilton / Henry Martin / El preso numero nuevo
CD _____ VND 2077
Vanguard / Oct '95 / Complete/Pinnacle / Discovery.

JOAN BAEZ #2
CD _____ VND 2097
Vanguard / Oct '95 / Complete/Pinnacle / Discovery.

JOAN BAEZ IN CONCERT
CD _____ VMD 2122
Vanguard / Jan '96 / Complete/Pinnacle / Discovery.

JOAN BAEZ IN CONCERT VOL.2
Once I had a sweetheart / Jackaroe / Don't think twice, it's alright / We shall overcome / Portland Town / Queen of hearts / Manha de carnaval / Te ador / Long black veil / Fennario / Ne belle cardillo / With God on our side / Three fishers / Hush little baby / Battle hymn of the Republic
CD _____ VMD 2123
Vanguard / Jan '96 / Complete/Pinnacle / Discovery.

JOAN BAEZ VOL. 1
CD _____ VFCD 7101
Start / Oct '88 / Koch.

JOAN BAEZ VOL. 2
CD _____ VFCD 7102
Start / Oct '88 / Koch.

NIGHT THEY DROVE OLD DIXIE DOWN
Night they drove old dixie down / Brand new Tennessee waltz / Outside the Nashville City limits / Ghetto / My home's across the blue ridge mountains / Rock salt and nails / Help me make it through the night / Long black veil / I still miss someone / San Francisco Mabel Joy
CD _____ VFCD 7104
Start / Sep '88 / Koch.

NOEL
CD _____ VFCD 7107
Start / Oct '88 / Koch.

PLAY ME BACKWARDS
Play me backwards / Amsterdam / Isaac and Abraham / Stones in the road / Steal across the border / I'm with you / I'm with you (reprise) / Strange rivers / Through your hands / Dream song / Edge of glory
CD _____ CDV 2705
Virgin / Aug '92 / EMI.

RARE, LIVE & CLASSIC
CD Set _____ 662094
Vanguard / Mar '94 / Complete/Pinnacle / Discovery.

RING THEM BELLS
CD _____ GRACD 208
Grapevine / Sep '95 / Grapevine.

WHERE HAVE ALL THE FLOWERS GONE
Where have all the flowers gone / Riddle song / Last night I had the strangest dream / Johnny Cuckoo / She's a troublemaker / Railroad Bill / Lady gay (Child ballad no. 79) / Willie Moore / Tears in my eyes / Water is wide / Man of constant sorrow / Lonesome valley / Somebody got lost in a storm / Pilgrim of sorrow / Rambler gambler / On the banks of the Ohio / Birmingham Sunday
(CDST only) / Unquiet grave (CDST only) / When you hear them cuckoos hollerin' (CDST only) / Barbara Allen (CDST only) / El Preso Numero Nuevo (CDST only) / Let me babe (CDST only) / 33rd of August (CDST only) / Little Moses (CDST only) / Donna Donna (CDST only) / Rake and the rambling boy (CDST only) / Wildwood flower (CDST only) / I still miss someone (CDST only) / There but for fortune (CDST only) / Matty Groves (CDST only) / Death of Queen Jane (CDST only) / Stewball (CDST only) / Queen of hearts (CDST only) / Wagoner's lad (CDST only) / Black is the colour of my true love's hair (CDST only) / House of the rising sun (CDST only) / Henry Martin (CDST only) / All my trails (CDST only) / 10,000 miles (Fare thee well) (CDST only) / John Riley (CDST only) / Go 'way from my window (CDST only) / Mary Hamilton (CDST only) / Once I had a sweetheart (CDST only) / Silver dagger (CDST only) / Railroad boy

(CDST only) / Old Blue (CDST only) /. East Virginia (CDST only) / Lily of the West (CDST only)
CD Set _____ CD 333505
Duchesse / Nov '93 / Pinnacle.

Bagad Bleimor

SONEREZH GELTIEK
CD _____ KMCD 12
Keltia Musique / '91 / ADA / Direct / Discovery.

Bagad Brieg

DELC'H DA NOZ
CD _____ 433CD
Diffusion Breizh / Jul '95 / ADA.

Bagad De Lann Bihoue

BAGAD DE LANN BIHOUE
CD _____ KMCD 09
Keltia Musique / '91 / ADA / Direct / Discovery.

Bagad Kemper

BAGHAD KEMPER
CD _____ KMCD 05
Keltia Musique / Jul '90 / ADA / Direct / Discovery.

LIP AR MAOUT (Battering Rams)
CD _____ KMCD 50
Keltia Musique / Apr '95 / ADA / Direct / Discovery.

Bagad Ronsed-Mor

AG AN DOUAR D'AR MOR
CD _____ CD 426
Diffusion Breizh / Apr '94 / ADA.

Baha Men

KALIK
CD _____ 756792394-2
Warner Bros. / Sep '94 / Warner Music.

Bahia Black

BAHIA BLACK - RITUAL BEATING SYSTEM
Retrato calado / Capitao do asfalto / Seven powers / Uma viagem del baldes de Larry Wright / Olodum / Guia pro congal / Gwagwa o de / Follow me / Nina in the womb of the forest
CD _____ 5108562
Axiom / Mar '92 / PolyGram / Vital.

Bailey, Admiral

UNDISPUTED CHAMPION
CD _____ RNCD 2014
Rhino / Aug '93 / Jetstar / Magnum Music Group / THE.

Bailey, Benny

BENNY BAILY & THE CZECH-NORWEGIAN QUARTET (Bailey, Benny & The Norwegian Quartet)
CD _____ GEMCD 69
Gemini / Dec '87 / Cadillac.

BIG BRASS
CD _____ CCD 9011
Candid / Dec '87 / Cadillac / Jazz Music / Wellard / Koch.

FOR HEAVEN'S SAKE (Bailey, Benny Quintet)
Little jazz / Blues Last / Fortunan rights / Mood indigo / For heaven's sake / One for Wilton / No mo blues
CD _____ HHCD 1006
Hot House / May '95 / Cadillac / Wellard / Harmonia Mundi.

NO REFILL
Groovin high / Easy living / Gryce's grace / Serenade to a planet / Surinam / Early afternoon / No refil
CD _____ TCB 94202
TCB / Jul '94 / New Note.

Bailey, Chris

54 DAYS AT SEA
CD _____ DB 1145
Mushroom / Mar '94 / BMG / 3MV.

ENCORE
CD _____ 422009
Last Call / Oct '95 / Direct.

WHAT WE DID ON OUR HOLIDAYS
CD _____ ROSE 30 CD
New Rose / Aug '90 / Direct / ADA.

Bailey, Derek

CYRO
CD _____ INCUSCD 02
Incus / '90 / These / Cadillac.

FIGURING (Bailey, Derek & Barre Phillips)
CD _____ INCUSCD 05
Incus / '90 / These / Cadillac.

HAN (Bailey, Derek & Han Bennik)
CD _____ INCUSCD 02
Incus / '90 / These / Cadillac.

WIREFORKS (Bailey, Derek & Henry Kaiser)
CD _____ SH 5011
Shanachie / Apr '95 / Koch / ADA / Greensleeves.

Bailey, Mildred

BLUES SINGER 1929-37, THE
CD _____ JZCD 353
Suisa / Jan '93 / Jazz Music / THE.

BLUES SINGER 1937-39, THE
CD _____ JZCD 354
Suisa / Jun '93 / Jazz Music / THE.

HARLEM LULLABY
Georgia on my mind / Concentratin' / Harlem lullaby / Junk man / Ol' Pappy / Squeeze me / Downhearted blues / Porter's love song / Smoke dreams / Rockin' chair / Moon got in my eyes / It's the natural thing to do / Worried over you / Thanks for the memory / More than ever / Please be kind / I let a song go out of my heart / Rock it for me / My melancholy baby / Lonesome road
CD _____ CDAJA 5065
Living Era / Dec '89 / Koch.

LA SELECTION 1931-39
CD _____ 700092
Art Vocal / Nov '92 / Discovery.

ME AND THE BLUES
In love in vain / It's a womans perogative / I'll close my eyes / Me and the blues / At sundown / Lover come back to me / Born to be blue / You started something / Can't we be friends / All that glitters is not gold
CD _____ SV 0200
Savoy Jazz / Nov '92 / Conifer / ADA.

ROCKIN' CHAIR
CD _____ VJC 1006-2
Victorious Discs / Aug '90 / Jazz Music.

THAT ROCKIN' CHAIR LADY
CD _____ TPZ 1007
Topaz Jazz / Oct '94 / Pinnacle / Cadillac.

Bailey, Pearl

16 MOST REQUESTED SONGS
CD _____ CK 47082
Sony Jazz / Jan '95 / Sony.

BEST OF PEARL BAILEY
CD _____ ATJCD 8007
Disky / Jul '94 / THE / BMG / Discovery / Pinnacle.

Bailey, Philip

CHINESE WALL
Photogenic memory / I go crazy / Walking on the Chinese wall / For every heart that's been broken / Go / Easy lover / Show you the way to love / Time is a woman / Women children of the ghetto
CD _____ 474682
Columbia / Apr '95 / Sony.

CHINESE WALLS
Photogenic memory / I go crazy / Walking on the Chinese wall / For every heart that's been broken / Go / Easy lover / Show you the way to love / Time is a woman / Woman / Children of the ghetto
CD _____ 983282 2
Pickwick/Sony Collector's Choice / Mar '94 / Carlton Home Entertainment / Pinnacle / Sony.

Bailey, Richard

FIREDANCE
CD _____ CMML 89007CD
Music Maker / Jul '94 / Grapevine / ADA.

Bailey, Roy

BUSINESS AS USUAL
CD _____ CFCD 400
Fuse / Jul '94 / Direct / Roots / CM / ADA.

NEVER LEAVE A SONG UNSUNG
CD _____ CFCD 398
Fuse / Feb '88 / Direct / Roots / CM / ADA.

WHAT YOU DO WITH WHAT YOU'VE GOT
What you do with what you've got / Ugly ones / Let your hair hang down / Patience Kershaw / See it come down / Send me back to Georgia / Rose of York / Day before the war / If they come in the morning / Song of the exile / Hard times of old England / Burning times / New Year's Eve / Everything possible / Rollin' home
CD _____ CFCD 399
Fuse / Feb '89 / Direct / Roots / CM / ADA.

WHY DOES IT HAVE TO BE ME
CD _____ CFCD 396CD
Fuse / Jul '95 / Direct / Roots / CM / ADA.

Bailongo

TANGOLEANDA
CD _____ SYNCD 166
Syncoop / Jun '94 / ADA / Direct.

35

Bailter Space

VORTURU
CD _____ FNCD 295
Flying Nun / Apr '94 / Disc.

WAMMO
Untied / Splat / At five we drive / Zapped /
Colours / Retro / Glimmer / Voltage / D thing
/ Wammo
CD _____ OLE 1422
Matador / Jul '95 / Vital.

Bain, Aly

ALY BAIN
CD _____ WHIRLIE 001CD
Whirlie / Dec '93 / Roots / Duncans / CM /
ADA / Direct.

**ALY BAIN AND FRIENDS (Bain, Aly &
Various Artists)**
Waiting for the federals / Donald MacLean's
farewell to Oban / Sands of Burness / Miller's reel / Dean Cadalan Samhach / Kerryman's daughter / O'Keefe's plough / Sligo
maid / Humours of Ballinahinch / Gravel
walk / Out by East Da Vong / Maiden's
prayer / Jimmy Mann's reel / Aly's sound /
It's all just talk / Pearl / Floggin' / Chimes at
midnight / Humours of Tulla / Fox Hunter's
reel / St. Anne's reel / New road under my
wheels / Anne's tune / Love of the islands
/ Compliments to Dan R. MacDonald / Marie MacLennan's reel / Bonjour Tristesse
CD _____ CDTRAX 026
Greentrax / Mar '89 / Conifer / Duncans /
ADA / Direct.

ALY BAIN WITH YOUNG CHAMPIONS
Dr. Donaldson/The anvil / Ross Memorial
Hospital / Buain an Rainich/Brochan Lom/
Cockle gatherers / Balkan Hills/Duke of
Gordon/Deil and the dirk / Pear tree / Mr.
Michie/J.F. Dickie's delight/J.F. Dickie's reel
/ An Ataireachd Ard / Aspen bank / Ardg-
ualich/High road to Linton / Heaven's gate/
Le Grande Chaine/Waiting for the Federals
/ Conundrum/Mrs. Stewart of Grantully /
Morning dew/Blarney pilgrim/Langstrom's
pony / Helen Robertson / Humble tattie /
Ballachulish Glen / Leaving Lismor/Heights
of Dargai/Kilt is my delight / Wee burr stuck
tae ma apron / Midnight on the water/Bon-
aparte's retreat / Music of Spey / Sixereen/
Barrowburn reel/Fairy dance / Margaret's
waltz/Laird o'Drumblair/Deil among the
tailors
CD _____ SPRCD 1032
Springthyme / May '90 / Direct / Roots / CM
/ Duncans / ADA.

**ALY MEETS THE CAJUNS (Bain, Aly &
Various Artists)**
Midland two step / My friend / Mazuka /
Jongle a moi / Sassy on step / Jolie blon /
La contre danse a perepere / Water pump
/ J'ai ete au bal / Paper in my shoe / La vie
est pas donne / Back door / Chere toute
toute / Rosa majeur / Devant ta porte /
When I was poor
CD _____ LCOM 9009
Lismor / Oct '92 / Lismor / Direct / Duncans
/ ADA.

DOWN HOME
CD _____ LCOM 9027
Lismor / '90 / Lismor / Direct / Duncans /
ADA.

FOLLOW THE MOONSTONE
CD _____ WHIRLIECD 4
Whirlie / Oct '95 / Roots / Duncans / CM /
ADA / Direct.

LONELY BIRD
CD _____ WHIRLIE 2CD
Whirlie / Oct '88 / Roots / Duncans / CM /
ADA / Direct.

**PEARL, THE (Bain, Aly & Phil
Cunningham)**
CD _____ WHIRLIE 3CD
Whirlie / Oct '94 / Roots / Duncans / CM /
ADA / Direct.

Bainbridge, Harvey

INTERSTELLA CHAOS
CD _____ TASTE 40CD
Taste / Jan '95 / Plastic Head.

Baird, Dan

BUFFALO NICKEL
CD _____ 74321295172
De-Construction / Jan '96 / BMG.

**LOVE SONGS FOR THE HEARING
IMPAIRED**
One I am / Julie and lucky / I love you period
/ Look what you started / Look at what you
started / Seriously gone / Pick up the knife
/ Knocked up / Baby talk / Lost highway /
Dixie beauxderaunt
CD _____ 74321287582
American / Jun '95 / BMG.

Baiza, Joe

**PROSPEROUS AND QUALIFIED (Baiza,
Joe & The Universal Congress)**
CD _____ SST 180 CD
SST / May '93 / Plastic Head.

Bajourou

BIG STRING THEORY
Hakilma / Mansa / Mankan / Fanta barana
/ I ka di nye / Sora / Bastan toure / Nkani /
Jodoo
CD _____ CDORBD 078
Globestyle / Mar '93 / Pinnacle.

Baka Beyond

MEETING POOL, THE
Woosi / Ancestor's vice / Lupe / Ohureo /
Lost dance of Atlantis / Journey / Ndaweh's
dream / Booma lena
CD _____ HNCD 1388
Hannibal / Oct '95 / Vital / ADA.

**SPIRIT OF THE FOREST (Baka Beyond
& Martin Cradick)**
Spirit of the forest / Man who danced too
slowly / Canya jam / Ngombi / Baka play
baka / Nahwia / Elephant song / Bounaka
CD _____ HNCD 1377
Hannibal / Oct '93 / Vital / ADA.

Baka Pygmies

HEART OF THE FOREST
Yelli 1 / Yelli 2 / Yelli 3 / Water drums 1 /
Water drums 2 / Nursery rhyme / Veno-
louma / Ieta / Ngombi na peke 1 / Limbindi
and voices / Earth bow / Limbindi / Water
drums 3 / Welcome song / Banja's song /
Ngombi na peke 2 / Ngombi na peke 3 /
Acapella / Toji / Forest party / Distant yelli
CD _____ HNCD 1378
Hannibal / Oct '93 / Vital / ADA.

Bakardy, Vell

GENUINE LIQUA HITS
CD _____ 74321312652
RCA / Jan '96 / BMG.

Baked Beans

BAKED BEANS
Bake daga / Desert bean / Heintz 1 / Has
bean
CD _____ 450995346-2
Warner Bros. / Mar '94 / Warner Music.

Baker, Anita

COMPOSITIONS
Talk to me / Whatever it takes / Lonely /
More than you know / Fairy tales / Perfect
love affair / Soul inspiration / No one to
blame / Love you to the letter
CD _____ EKT 72CD
Elektra / Jul '90 / Warner Music.

GIVING YOU THE BEST THAT I GOT
Priceless / Lead me into love / Giving you
the best that I got / Good love / Rules /
Good enough / Just because I love you /
You belong to me
CD _____ 9608272
Elektra / Oct '88 / Warner Music.

RAPTURE
Sweet love / You bring me joy / Caught up
in the rapture / Been so long / Mystery / No
one in the world / Same ole love / Watch
your step
CD _____ 7559604445
Elektra / Nov '92 / Warner Music.

RHYTHM OF LOVE
Rhythm of love / Look of love / Body and
soul / Baby / I apologise / Plenty of room /
It's been you / You belong to me / Wrong
man / Only for a while / Sometimes I won-
der why / My funny valentine
CD _____ 755961555-2
Elektra / Sep '94 / Warner Music.

SONGSTRESS
Angel / You're the best thing yet / Feel the
need / Squeeze me / No more tears /
Sometimes / Will you be mine / Do you be-
lieve me
CD _____ 7559611162
Elektra / Nov '91 / Warner Music.

Baker Boys

FACING OUR TIME
CD _____ SITCD 9221
Sittel / Nov '95 / Cadillac / Jazz Music.

Baker, Chet

ALBERTS HOUSE
CD _____ REP 4167-WZ
Repertoire / Aug '91 / Pinnacle / Cadillac.

BALLADS FOR TWO
CD _____ INAK 856
In Akustik / Aug '95 / Magnum Music
Group.

BEST OF CHET BAKER
CD _____ DLCD 4020
Dixie Live / Mar '95 / Magnum Music
Group.

BEST OF CHET BAKER PLAYS, THE
Carson city stage / Imagination / All the
things you are / Bea's flat / Happy little sunbeam / Pro defunctus / Moonlight becomes
you / Stella by starlight / Darn the dream /
Sweet Lorraine / Worry river / A La / To
Mickey's memory / Jumpin' off a clef

CD _____ CZ 480
Blue Note / Sep '92 / EMI.

BRUSSELS 1964
CD _____ 449232
Landscape / Nov '92 / THE.

BUT NOT FOR ME
CD _____ STCD 584
Stash / Jun '94 / Jazz Music / CM /
Cadillac / Direct / ADA.

**CARNEGIE HALL CONCERT (Baker,
Chet & Gerry Mulligan)**
Lion for Lyons / For an unfinished woman /
My funny valentine / Song for strayhorn /
It's sandy at the beach / Bernies tune / K-
4 pacific / There will never be another you
CD _____ ZK 64769
Columbia / Nov '95 / Sony.

CHET
Alone together / How high the moon / It
never entered my mind / 'Tis Autumn / If
you could see me now / September song /
You my so nice to come home to / Time
on my hands / You, the night, and the
music
CD _____ OJCCD 087
Original Jazz Classics / Feb '92 / Wellard /
Jazz Music / Cadillac / Complete/Pinnacle.

CHET BAKER IN MILAN
CD _____ OJCCD 370
Original Jazz Classics / Feb '92 / Wellard /
Jazz Music / Cadillac / Complete/Pinnacle.

CHET BAKER IN TOKYO
CD _____ K 32Y6281
Concord Jazz / Jul '89 / New Note.

CHET BAKER SINGS AGAIN
CD _____ CDSJP 238
Timeless Jazz / '89 / New Note.

CHET IN PARIS (1955-6/Barclay Years)
CD Set _____ FSR CD 1/2
Fresh Sound / May '88 / Jazz Music /
Discovery.

COOL CAT
Swift shifting / Round Midnight / Caravelle
/ For all we know / Blue moon / My foolish
heart
CD _____ CDSJP 262
Timeless Jazz / Mar '90 / New Note.

COOLS OUT (Baker, Chet Quintet)
Extra mild / Halema / Jumpin' off a cliff /
Route / Lucius lou / Pawnee junction
CD _____ CDBOP 013
Boplicity / Feb '89 / Pinnacle / Cadillac.

DIANE (Baker, Chet & Paul Bley)
CD _____ SCCD 31207
Steeplechase / Jul '88 / Impetus.

EMBRACEABLE YOU
Night we called it a day / Little girl blue (instrumental) / Embraceable you / They all
laughed / There's a lull in my life / What is
there to say / While my lady sleeps / Forgetful / How long has this been going on /
Come rain or come shine / On Green Dolphin Street / Little girl blue (vocal) / You'lin'
light
CD _____ CDP 8316762
Pacific Jazz / Jun '95 / EMI.

**HAIG '53 - THE OTHER PIANO-LESS
QUARTET (Baker, Chet & Stan Getz)**
CD _____ CD 214W982
Philology / Mar '92 / Harmonia Mundi /
Cadillac.

**HEART OF THE BALLAD (Baker, Chet &
Enrico Pieranunzi)**
CD _____ W 20-2
Philology / Aug '92 / Harmonia Mundi /
Cadillac.

IN EUROPE - 1955
CD _____ 214 W42-2
Philology / Aug '91 / Harmonia Mundi /
Cadillac.

IN ITALY (Unissued 1975-1988)
CD _____ W 812
Philology / Apr '95 / Harmonia Mundi /
Cadillac.

IN NEW YORK
CD _____ OJCCD 2072
Original Jazz Classics / Feb '92 / Wellard /
Jazz Music / Cadillac / Complete/Pinnacle.

IN PARIS 1978 VOL. 2
CD _____ WW 2059
West Wind / Apr '91 / Swift / Charly / CM
/ ADA.

INTRODUCES JOHNNY
CD _____ OJCCD 433
Original Jazz Classics / Feb '92 / Wellard /
Jazz Music / Cadillac / Complete/Pinnacle.

IT COULD HAPPEN TO YOU
CD _____ OJCCD 303
Original Jazz Classics / Feb '92 / Wellard /
Jazz Music / Cadillac / Complete/Pinnacle.

ITALIAN MOVIES
CD _____ IRS 00631CD
Liuto / Oct '90 / Harmonia Mundi /
Cadillac.

ITALIAN SESSIONS, THE
Well you needn't / These foolish things /
Barbados / Star eyes / Somewhere over the

rainbow / Pent-up house / Ballata in forma
di blues / Blues in the closet
CD _____ ND 82001
Bluebird / May '90 / BMG.

JAZZ MASTERS
CD _____ 5169392
Verve / Apr '94 / PolyGram.

JAZZ PORTRAITS
Line for lyons / Cherry / Thrill is gone / But
not for me / My funny valentine / There will
never be another you / Time after time /
Daybreak / You don't know what love is /
Let's get lost / Love / I fall in love too easily
/ Just friends / I remember you / Long ago
and far away / That old feeling / My ideal /
Everything happens to me
CD _____ CD 14511
Jazz Portraits / May '94 / Jazz Music.

LAST CONCERT VOLS. 1 & 2
CD _____ ENJA 60742
Enja / Nov '91 / New Note / Vital/SAM.

LEGACY, THE
Here's that rainy day / How deep is the
ocean / Mr. B / In your own sweet way / All
of you / Dolphin dance / Look for the silver
lining / Django / All blues
CD _____ ENJ 90212
Enja / Jun '95 / New Note / Vital/SAM.

LET'S GET LOST
CD _____ CD 56024
Jazz Roots / Aug '94 / Target/BMG.

**LET'S GET LOST - THE BEST OF CHET
BAKER SINGS**
Thrill is gone / But not for me / Time after
time / I get along without you very well /
There will never be another you / Look for
the silver lining / My funny valentine / I fall
in love too easily / Daybreak / Just friends
/ I remember you / Let's get lost / Long ago
and far away / You don't know what love is
CD _____ CDP 7929322
Blue Note / Mar '95 / EMI.

LIVE AT FAT TUESDAY'S
CD _____ FSRCD 131
Fresh Sound / Sep '91 / Jazz Music /
Discovery.

LIVE AT NICK'S
CD _____ CRISSCD 1027
Criss Cross / Mar '90 / Cadillac /
Harmonia Mundi.

LIVE AT ROSENHEIMER
CD _____ CDSJP 233
Timeless Jazz / May '89 / New Note.

LIVE IN EUROPE 1956
CD _____ 556622
Accord / Apr '94 / Discovery / Harmonia
Mundi / Cadillac.

LIVE IN EUROPE 1956 VOL.2
CD _____ COD 034
Jazz View / Aug '92 / Harmonia Mundi.

LIVE IN SWEDEN
Lament / My ideal / Beatrice / You can't go
home again / But not for me / Ray's idea /
Milestones
CD _____ DRCD 178
Dragon / Sep '89 / Roots / Cadillac / Wel-
lard / CM / ADA.

MY FUNNY VALENTINE
My funny valentine / Someone to watch
over me / Moonlight becomes you / This is
always / I'm glad there is you / Time after
time / Sweet Lorraine / It's always you /
Let's get lost / Moon love / Like someone
in love / I've never been in love before / Isn't
it romantic / I fall in love too easily
CD _____ CDP 8282622
Pacific Jazz / Feb '94 / EMI.

NAIMA (Unusual Chet Volume 1)
CD _____ 214 W52-2
Philology / Aug '91 / Harmonia Mundi /
Cadillac.

NEWPORT YEARS, VOLUME 1, THE
CD _____ 214 W51-2
Philology / Aug '91 / Harmonia Mundi /
Cadillac.

NIGHT AT THE SHALIMAR CLUB, A
CD Set _____ 214 W59-2
Philology / Sep '91 / Harmonia Mundi /
Cadillac.

NIGHTBIRD (Live at Ronnie Scott's)
But not for me / Arboway / If I should lose
you / My ideal / Nightbird / Love for sale /
Shifting down / You can't go home again /
Send in the clowns
CD _____ CLACD 333
Castle / '93 / BMG.

NO PROBLEM (Baker, Chet Quartet)
CD _____ SCCD 31131
Steeplechase / '88 / Impetus.

ONCE UPON SUMMERTIME
CD _____ OJCCD 405
Original Jazz Classics / Feb '92 / Wellard /
Jazz Music / Cadillac / Complete/Pinnacle.

OUT OF NOWHERE
Fine and dandy / There will never be another you / Lady be good / Au privave / All
the things you are / Out of nowhere / There
is no greater love / Theme
CD _____ MCD 9191-2

Milestone / Apr '94 / Jazz Music / Pinnacle / Wellard / Cadillac.

PACIFIC JAZZ YEARS, THE
Freeway / My old flame / Five brothers / My funny valentine / Come out wherever you are / What's new / Half nelson / All the things you are / Bea's flat / Moon love / Happy little sunbeam / But not for me / I get along without you very well / I fall in love too easily / Let's get lost / You don't know what love is / Grey December / Rush job / Lullaby of the leaves / Dandy line / Carson city stage / Love nest / Lush life / Say when / Minor yours / Tynan time / Picture of health / C.T.A. / Mickey's memory / Lucious Lu / Jumpin' off a clef / Music to dance by / Festive minor / Song is you / Pro defunctus / Moonlight becomes you / Bockhanal / Stella by starlight / Half dozens / Foggy day / Mythe / Rebel at work / Let me be loved / Twenties late / Minor benign / Ponder / X
CD Set _____ CDS 7892922
Pacific Jazz / Mar '94 / EMI.

PLAYBOYS (Baker, Chet & Art Pepper)
For minors only / Original Pepper / Resonant emotions / Tynan time / Pictures of Heath / For miles and miles / C.T.A.
CD _____ CZ 345
Pacific Jazz / Aug '90 / EMI.

SHE WAS GOOD TO ME
CD _____ 4509542
Sony Jazz / Jan '95 / Sony.

SILENT NIGHTS
CD _____ DCCD 04
Scratch / Nov '94 / RMG.

SILENT NIGHTS/CHRISTMAS JAZZ ALBUM (Baker, Chet & Christopher Mason)
CD _____ CDVR 032
Varrick / '88 / Roots / CM / Direct / ADA.

SOMEWHERE OVER THE RAINBOW
Well you needn't / These foolish things / Star eyes / Somewhere over the rainbow / Pent-up house / Blues in the closet
CD _____ ND 90640
Bluebird / Apr '92 / BMG.

SPECIAL GUESTS (Baker, Chet & Larry Coryell)
CD _____ INAK 857
In Akustik / May '95 / Magnum Music Group.

STELLA BY STARLIGHT
CD _____ JHR 73551
Jazz Hour / Jun '92 / Target/BMG / Jazz Music / Cadillac.

TOGETHER - THE COMPLETE STUDIO RECORDINGS (Baker, Chet & Paul Desmond)
Tangerine / You can't go home again / How deep is the ocean / You'd be so nice to come home to / I'm getting sentimental over you/You've changed / Autumn leaves / Concierto de aranjuez
CD _____ 472984 2
Epic / Jan '93 / Sony.

WHEN SUNNY GETS BLUE
CD _____ SCCD 31221
Steeplechase / Jul '88 / Impetus.

WITCH DOCTOR (Baker, Chet & Lighthouse All Stars)
Loaded / I'll remember April / Winter wonderland / Pirouette / Witch doctor
CD _____ OJCCD 609-2
Original Jazz Classics / Feb '92 / Wellard / Jazz Music / Cadillac / Complete/Pinnacle.

WITH STRINGS
You don't know what love is / I'm through with love / Love walked in / You'd better go now / I married an angel / Love / I love you / What a difference a day makes / Why shouldn't I / Little duet / Wind / Trickleydidlier
CD _____ 4669682
Columbia / Apr '92 / Sony.

Baker, Duck

AMERICAN TRADITIONAL (Baker, Duck & Molly Andrews)
CD _____ DBMA 1CD
Dayjob / Jul '93 / ADA.

CLEAR BLUE SKY
CD _____ BEST 1065CD
Acoustic Music / Apr '95 / ADA.

MOVING BUSINESS, THE (Baker, Duck & Molly Andrews)
CD _____ DBMA 2CD
Dayjob / Oct '94 / ADA.

OPENING THE EYES OF LOVE
CD _____ SHAN 97025CD
Shanachie / May '93 / Koch / ADA / Greensleeves.

THOUSAND WORDS, A (Baker, Duck & John Renbourn)
CD _____ BEST 1021CD
Acoustic Music / Nov '93 / ADA.

Baker, Etta

ONE DIME BLUES
CD _____ CDROU 2112

Rounder / Sep '91 / CM / Direct / ADA / Cadillac.

Baker, George

STAR PORTRAIT: GEORGE BAKER SELECTION (Baker, George Selection)
CD _____ 16029
Laserlight / '93 / Target/BMG.

Baker, Ginger

AFRICAN FORCE
CD _____ ITM 1417
ITM / '89 / Tradelink / Koch.

GOING BACK HOME (Baker, Ginger Trio)
CD _____ 7567826522
Warner Bros. / Dec '94 / Warner Music.

PALANQUIN'S POLE (Baker, Ginger & African Force)
CD _____ ITM 1433
ITM / Apr '90 / Tradelink / Koch.

Baker, Josephine

EXOTIQUE
CD _____ PASTCD 7059
Flapper / Apr '95 / Pinnacle.

FABULOUS JOSEPHINE BAKER, THE
Paris ses amours / Le marchand de bonheur / Mo 'lo' / J'attendrai / Donnez moi la man / Je voudrais / La Seine / Sonny boy / Sous les toits de Paris / Mon p'tit bonhomme / En Avril a Paris / Saq beim Abschied leise 'Servus' / Don't touch my tomatoes
CD _____ 09026616682
RCA Victor / Jun '95 / BMG.

J'AI DEUX AMOURS
CD _____ CDCD 3007
Charly / Sep '94 / Charly / THE / Cadillac.

LEGEND IN HER LIFETIME, A
CD _____ WMCD 5674
Woodford Music / Feb '93 / THE.

MY GREATEST SONGS
La Seine / Sonny boy / Paris mes amours / Clopin clopant / Mon p'tit bonhomme / Mon 'lO / Avec / J'attendrai / La marchand de bonheur / Je voudrais / Don't touch my tomatoes / Medley: Paris je t'aime
CD _____ 74321 10732-2
RCA / Apr '93 / BMG.

Baker, Kenny

BOSS IS HOME, THE
CD _____ ESSCD 224
Essential / Oct '94 / Total/BMG.

TRIBUTE TO THE GREAT TRUMPETERS
I can't get started (with you) / And the angels sing / Tenderly / You made me love you / Satchmo / Morning glory / How long has this been going on / Georgia / Memories of you / Little jazz / Music goes round and round / Carnival time / Won't you come home, Bill Bailey / What's new / Sugar blues / Davenport blues / Echoes of Harlem / Our love is here to stay
CD _____ CDSIV 1124
Horatio Nelson / Jul '95 / THE / BMG / Avid/ BMG / Koch.

Baker, LaVern

SOUL ON FIRE
Soul on fire / Tomorrow night / Tweedlee Dee / That's all I need / Bop-ting-a-ling / Play it fair / Jim Dandy / My happiness forever / Get up, get up (you sleepy head) / Sill / I can't love you enough / Jim Dandy got married / I cried a tear / Whippersnapper / I waited to long / Shake a hand / How often / You said / Saved / See see rider
CD _____ 756782311-2
WEA / Mar '93 / Warner Music.

Baker, Marilyn

FACE TO FACE
Face to face / He is the rock / I know where you're coming from / Constantly amazed / Brand new heart / Lord I love you / He knows your sorrows / Don't deceive yourselves / When I think / Lord's my shepherd / O Lord you are so mighty / Open your ears / My God how great you are / I love to talk with Jesus
CD _____ WSTCD 9722
Nelson Word / Apr '92 / Nelson Word.

Baker, Mickey

ROCK WITH A SOCK
Guitar mambo / Riverboat / Love me baby / Oh happy day / Where is my honey / I'm tired / Stranger blues / I wish I knew / Down to the bottom / You better heed my warning / Midnight hours / Please tell me / Shake walkin' / Greasy spoon / Bandstand stomp / Rock with a sock / Old devil moon / Guitarambo / Spinnin' rock boogie / Ghost of a chance / Chloe / Man I love / Bobi, Mickey and Silvia / Hello stranger / My love / Woe woe is me / Can't get you on the phone / I'll always want you near
CD _____ BCD 15654
Bear Family / Aug '93 / Rollercoaster / Direct / CM / Swift / ADA.

Baker-Baldwin Radiogram..

OZARK BLUES (Baker-Baldwin Radiogram Washboards)
CD _____ SOSCD 1243
Stomp Off / Jul '93 / Jazz Music / Wellard.

Baker-Gurvitz Army

BAKER-GURVITZ ARMY
CD _____ REP 4163-WZ
Repertoire / Aug '91 / Pinnacle / Cadillac.

Bal Sagoth

BLACK MOON BROODS OVER LEMURIA, A
CD _____ NIHIL 4CD
Vinyl Solution / May '95 / Disc.

Balaam

PRIME TIME
Shame on you / Prime time / Next to me / What love is / Gathering dust / Eagle / She's not you / Mr. Business / Like a train / Burnin' / Just no good
CD _____ CDBLEED 1
Bleeding Hearts / Apr '93 / Pinnacle.

Balafon Marimba Ensemble

BALAFON MARIMBA ENSEMBLE, THE
CD _____ SHAN 670029CD
Shanachie / Feb '93 / Koch / ADA / Greensleeves.

HARARE TO KISINGANI
CD _____ SHCD 67004
Shanachie / Mar '94 / Koch / ADA / Greensleeves.

Balalaika Ensemble

KALAKOLTSCHIK
CD _____ EUCD 1064
ARC / '89 / ARC Music / ADA.

KALINKA
CD _____ EUCD 1054
ARC / '89 / ARC Music / ADA.

POPULAR FOLK SONGS FROM RUSSIA
Cossack's dance / Bandura / Oriental dance / Legend of the 12 brigands / Katjusche / Ej uchnjem / Wass duli / Bajuschki baju / White acacia / Uri balki / Tears fall out of clouds / Roaring volga
CD _____ EUCD 1126
ARC / '91 / ARC Music / ADA.

SONGS FROM THE TAIGA
CD _____ EUCD 1050
ARC / '89 / ARC Music / ADA.

WOLGA: BEST OF RUSSIAN FOLKSONGS
CD _____ EUCD 1146
ARC / Jan '92 / ARC Music / ADA.

Balanescu Quartet

ANGELS AND INSECTS
CD _____ CDSTUMM 147
Mute / Dec '95 / Disc.

Baldan, Bebo

EARTHBEAT (Baldan, Bebo & David Torn)
Desire / Earthbeat / Diving into the world / Niceday / Son leidas / Qhalili nu Birali / Asoka's / On Namah Shivaya / Santoor / Ralph
CD _____ MASOCD 90082
Materiali Sonori / Oct '95 / New Note.

Baldry, Long John

IT AIN'T EASY
Conditional discharge / Don't try to lay no Boogie-Woogie / Black girl / It ain't easy / Morning morning / I'm ready / Let's burn down the cornfield / Mr. Rubin / Rock me when he's gone / Flying
CD _____ LECD 901235
Line / Oct '94 / CM / Grapevine / ADA / Conifer / Direct.

IT STILL AIN'T EASY
Stony Plain / Oct '93 / ADA / CM / Direct.
CD _____ SP 1163CD

LET THE HEARTACHES BEGIN/WAIT FOR ME
Long and lonely nights / Stay with me baby / Every time we say goodbye / For all we know / Better by far / Let the heartaches begin / Wise to the ways of the world / Since I lost you baby / Smile / Annabella / We're together / I can't stop loving you / Sunshine of your love / Spanish Harlem / Henry Hannah's 42nd St. parking lot / Man without a dream / Cry like a baby / River deep, mountain high / How sweet it is (to be loved by you) / MacArthur Park / Bridadier McKenzie / Ligts of Cincinatti / Spinning wheel / Wait for me / Mexico / When the sun comes shining through
CD _____ BGOCD 272
Beat Goes On / May '95 / Pinnacle.

Balfa Toujours

LOOKING AT LONG JOHN
You've lost that lovin' feelin' / Only a fool breaks his own heart / Make it easy on yourself / Let him go / Drifter / Cry me a river / Stop her so night / Turn on your love light / I love Paris / Keep on runnin' / Ain't nothin' you can do / Bad luck soul / Got my mojo working / Gee baby ain't I good to you / Rool 'em Pete / You're breaking my heart / Hoochie coochie / Everyday (I got the blues) / Dimples / Five long years / My babe / Times are getting tougher / Goin' down slow / Rock the joint
CD _____ BGOCD 2
Beat Goes On / Dec '90 / Pinnacle.

MEXICO
Let the heartaches begin / Every time we say goodbye / Lights of Cincinatti / Since I lost you baby / Spinning wheel / Annabella (Who flies to me when she's lonely) / Stay with me baby / Sunshine of your love / It's too late now / When the sun comes shining through / For all we know / Spanish Harlem / Cry like a baby / How sweet it is (to be loved by you) / MacArthur Park / Smile / River deep, mountain high / Mexico (Underneath the sun in)
CD _____ 5507572
Spectrum/Karussell / Feb '95 / PolyGram / THE.

ON STAGE TONIGHT - BALDRY'S OUT
CD _____ HYCD 200135
Hypertension / Mar '95 / Total/BMG / Direct / ADA.

SILENT TREATMENT
CD _____ HYCD 200125
Hypertension / Mar '95 / Total/BMG / Direct / ADA.

Baldwin, James

LOVERS QUESTION, A
CD _____ TWI 9282
Les Disques Du Crepuscule / Oct '90 / Discovery / ADA.

Balfa Brothers

NEW YORK CONCERTS PLUS, THE
Jolie blon / Les flames d'enfer / Les bars de la prison / Two step de lacassine / I don't want you anymore / La valse de grand bois / J'ai passe devant ta porte / Hippy ti yo / Madame Sostan / La valse criminel / You had some but you won't have anymore / Tee yeaux noir / Chanson de les mardi gras / Dying in misery / In my old wagon / Cowboy waltz / Texas two step / Coeur criminel / Les traces de mon bogue / J'etais au balle / Valse de kaplan
CD _____ CDCHD 338
Ace / Oct '91 / Pinnacle / Cadillac / Complete/Pinnacle.

TRADITIONAL CAJUN MUSIC VOLS. 1 & 2
Drunkard's sorrow waltz / Lacassine special / My true love / La valse de Grand Bois / Family waltz / Newport waltz / Indian on a stomp / T'ai petite et t'ai meon / Two step a Hadley / Valse de Balfa / Parlez-nous a boire / Les blues de cajun / 'Tit galop pour mamou / Je suis Orphelin / T'en as eu mais t'en n'auras plus / Two step de l'anse a paille / La danse de Mardi Gras / Je me suis Marillie / Enterre moi pas / Chere joules roses / Chere bassette / J'ai passe devant ta porte / Les flames d'enfer / Madeleine
CD _____ CDCHD 955
Ace / Nov '90 / Pinnacle / Cadillac / Complete/Pinnacle.

Balfa, Dewey

SOUVENIRS & FAIT A LA MAIN (Balfa, Dewey & Friends)
Equand j'etais pauvre / La valse du Canada / La valse de deux familles / 1755 / Bienvenue au paradis / Fiddlesticks / J'ai pleure / Don't stop the music / La reel de joie / La mauvaise nouvelle / Watermelon reel / Grand mamou / Pauvre hobo / La jolie blonde / Back door / Valse de balfa / Blues a Leo Soileau / Two step a Nathan Abshire / Chere toute toute / J'ai passe devant ta porte / Les veuves de la coulee / Les flames d'enfer / T'ai petit et t'ai meon / Perrodin two step
CD _____ CDCHD 328
Ace / Jul '91 / Pinnacle / Cadillac / Complete/Pinnacle.

Balfa Toujours

A VIELLE TERRE HAUTRE
CD _____ SW 6121CD
Swallow / Jul '95 / ADA.

NEW CAJUN TRADITION
La vielle terre haute / True love waltz / Madam boso / Apres nous esperer / J'ai perdu mes lunettes / Reel de deshotels / Old fashioned two step / Les fleurs du Printemps / Rodair special / La maunatrice / La fille de la campagne / La valse de vieux vacher / Texas two step / Arrete pas la musique / Reel du melon d'eau / Pop, tu me parles toujours / L'anse aux pailles / La valse des Balfa / C'est tout perdu / Dans le coeur de basile / Two-step a tina / Toe truck blues
CD _____ CDCHD 613

37

Ace / Jun '95 / Pinnacle / Cadillac / Complete/Pinnacle.

Balkana

MUSIC OF BULGARIA, THE
CD _____ HNCD 1335
Hannibal / Oct '87 / Vital / ADA.

Balke, Jon

FURTHER (Balke, Jon & The Magnetic North Orchestra)
Departure / Step one / Horizontal song / Flying thing / Shaded place / Taraf / Moving carpet / Eastern forest / Changing forest / Wooden voices / Arrival
CD _____ 5217202
ECM / May '94 / New Note.

NONSENTRATION (Balke, Jon & Oslo 13)
Stealing space / Stealing space II / Stop / Blic / Constructing stop / Laws of freedom / Disappear here / Nord / Circling the square / Art of being
CD _____ 8496532
ECM / Feb '92 / New Note.

Ball

BALL 4 - HARDBALL
Hard ball / She's always driving / Timmy the toad man / Mary Jane / Road to Heaven / Ball four prelude / Ball one / Ball two / Ball three / Ball four / R.I.P.
CD _____ SDE 9018CD
Shimmy Disc / Mar '90 / Vital.

BIRD/PERIOD
It don't come easy / Bird / Charm / Long ago / Buick McKane / Spit shine / Wah wah / Dylan side / Eye / Scene's over / Ballad of Little Richard / Favourite day / French / Black Spring / St. Vitus dance / Theme B.A.L.L. / When is a man / If I break down / Love was the end / Burning wood / Another straight line / Just like the last time / Drink on it / Swim this way / Bangla Desh / All is sought in progress / King will never die / My TV is broken / I can never say / Treasure Island / In the woods / I could always be with you
CD _____ SDE 8907
Shimmy Disc / Nov '89 / Vital.

TROUBLE DOLL
Should brother kill / Never meant to say / Trouble world / This is war / Little Tex in trouble / Trash man / Trouble momma / I could always be with you / Cracked life of a cracked man / Flowers grow on the wall / French / When is a man / Bird / Charm / My T.V. is broken / King will never die / If I break down / It don't come easy / Love was the end / Just like the last time / Buick McKane / Little Tex's prelude (CD only.) / Reagans bush is on fire (CD only.) / Amazon (CD only.) / Trouble baby (CD only.) / TX-five (CD only.) / African sunset (CD only.) / Trouble finale (CD only.)
CD _____ SDE 8909CD
Shimmy Disc / Oct '89 / Vital.

Ball, Ed

IF A MAN EVER LOVED A WOMAN
CD _____ CRECD 195
Creation / Jul '95 / 3MV / Vital.

WONDERFUL WORLD OF ED BALL
CD Set _____ CRECD 183
Creation / Feb '95 / 3MV / Vital.

Ball, Kenny

BALL, BARBER & BILK (Ball, Kenny/ Chris Barber/Acker Bilk)
CD _____ MATCD 300
Castle / Sep '93 / BMG.

BEST OF KENNY BALL, THE (Hits & Requests) (Ball, Kenny & His Jazzmen)
March of the Siamese children / Muskrat ramble / I wanna be like you / Rondo / Su-kiyaki / T'ain't what you do / Kansas City stomps / Music goes round and round / Green leaves of summer / Acapulco 1922 / So do I / Midnight in Moscow / Samantha / Casablanca / Chimes blues / Hello Dolly / Original Dixieland one-step / Wild man blues / Basin Street blues / Ory's creole trombourne / When I'm sixty four / At the jazz band ball
CD _____ TRTCD 147
TrueTrax / Oct '94 / THE.

COLLECTION, THE
Midnight in Moscow / Alexander's ragtime band / Casablanca / Muskrat ramble / Samantha / Gavotte and rondo / Green leaves of summer / Wonderful world / Saturday night / From Russia with love / Someday / When the saints go marching in / March of the Siamese children / So do I / Cabaret / Pay off / Ace in the hole / Hello Dolly / Su-kiyaki / When I'm sixty four / Acapulco 1922 / I still love you all / Maple leaf rag / I shall not be moved
CD _____ CCSCD 258
Castle / Mar '90 / BMG.

DIXIE (Ball, Kenny & His Jazzmen)
Aura Lee / Sophie's rag / Sunshine time / Nicole / Lighting up the town / Stepping

along to the beat / Frankie and Johnny / My home town / Down Dixie way / Southland blue / Kibbutz girl / Honky stonkin'
CD _____ PWK 106
Carlton Home Entertainment / May '89 / Carlton Home Entertainment.

DIXIELAND CHRISTMAS, A
CD _____ PWKS 4219
Carlton Home Entertainment / Oct '95 / Carlton Home Entertainment.

GREENSLEEVES (Ball, Kenny & His Jazzmen)
Flow gently sweet Afton / Nobody knows you (when you're down and out) / I got rhythm / Ostrich walk / I shall not be moved / St. Louis blues / Greensleeves / My mother's eyes / I wanna be like you / Mood indigo / Them there eyes / Old folks / Sweet Georgia Brown
CD _____ CDTTD 505
Timeless Traditional / Jul '94 / New Note.

HAVE A DRINK ON ME (Ball, Kenny & His Jazzmen)
Samantha / At the jazz band ball / When I see an elephant fly / Basin Street blues / When somebody thinks you're wonderful / Midnight in Moscow / When I'm sixty four / Green leaves of summer / I shall not be moved / I wanna be like you / Tiger rag / Ten thousand years ago / So do I
CD _____ PWK 043
Carlton Home Entertainment / '88 / Carlton Home Entertainment.

HELLO DOLLY
Midnight in Moscow / March of the Siamese children / Sukiyaki / Maple Leaf rag / Swing low, sweet chariot / Down by the riverside / When I'm sixty four / Puttin' on the Ritz / At the jazz band ball / American patrol / Hello Dolly / Cabaret / Green leaves of summer / I got plenty o' nuttin' / Big noise from Winnetka / Acapulco 1922 / I love you / Samantha / Washington Square / Lazy river / Alexander's ragtime band
CD _____ 5507582
Spectrum/Karussell / Feb '95 / PolyGram / THE.

KENNY BALL PLAYS BRITISH
White cliffs of Dover / Eton boating song / Lincolnshire poacher / Men of Harlech / We'll keep a welcome in the hillside / British Grenadiers / Ilkley Moor / Lambeth walk / Danny boy / When Irish eyes are smiling / Scarborough Fair / Sweet Afton / Scotland the brave / Greensleeves / English country garden (CD only.)
CD _____ CDMFP 6072
Music For Pleasure / Mar '90 / EMI.

LIGHTING UP THE TOWN (Ball, Kenny & His Jazzmen)
CD _____ ISCD 113
Intersound / Jul '93 / Jazz Music.

ON STAGE
Midnight in Moscow / Rondo / Saturday night / Someday / I still love you all / Suki-yaki / Payoff / When I'm sixty four / Samantha / Green leaves of summer / So do I / Acapulco 1922 / 55 days at Peking / March of the Siamese children / Hello Dolly
CD _____ STOCD 102
Start / Mar '88 / Koch.

STEPPIN' OUT (Ball, Kenny & His Jazzmen)
CD _____ MATCD 209
Castle / Dec '92 / BMG.

STRICTLY JAZZ (Ball, Kenny & His Jazzmen)
CD _____ KAZCD 19
Kaz / Jul '92 / BMG.

VERY BEST OF KENNY BALL, THE (Ball, Kenny & His Jazzmen)
I got plenty o' nuttin' / Pennies from heaven / Teddy bear's picnic / Your feet's too big / Preacher / Stevedore stomp / Pay off / I still love you all / Royal garden blues / Ol' man river / I want a big butter and egg man / Flying high / You are the sunshine of my life / I can't get started / Midnight in Moscow / Samantha
CD _____ CDTTD 598
Timeless Jazz / Dec '95 / New Note.

Ball, Marcia

BLUE HOUSE
CD _____ ROUCD 3131
Rounder / Oct '94 / CM / Direct / ADA / Cadillac.

HOT TAMALE BABY
CD _____ CD 3095
Rounder / '88 / CM / Direct / ADA / Cadillac.

Ball, Michael

ALWAYS
Song for you / House is not a home / If I can dream / Cry me a river / You don't have to say you love me / Someone to watch over me / On Broadway / Tell me there's a heaven / Always on my mind / You'll never know / Stormy weather / You made me love you

COLLECTION, THE
Love changes everything / One step out of time / House is not a home / Cry me a river / You don't have to say you love me / Someone to watch over me / Stormy weather / As dreams go by / On Broadway / You made me love you / Secret of love / You'll never know (How much I love you) / Beautiful heartache / It's still you / Who needs to know / No one cries anymore / Holland Park / Simple affair of the heart / First man you remember
CD _____ 5517712
Spectrum/Karussell / Nov '95 / PolyGram / THE.

FIRST LOVE
Rose / Let the river run / Somewhere / If you could read my mind / (Something inside) So strong / How can I be sure / If you go away (Ne me quitte pas) / I'm gonna be strong / I'm so sorry / All by myself / Walk away / When you believe in love
CD _____ 4835992
Columbia / Jan '96 / Sony.

MICHAEL BALL
CD _____ 5113302
Polydor / May '92 / PolyGram.

ONE CAREFUL OWNER
Wherever you are / From here to eternity / Lovers we were / Take my breath away / Leave a light on / When we began / My arms are strong / I wouldn't know / All for nothing / In this life / Give me love / I'll be there
CD _____ 477280-2
Columbia / Aug '94 / Sony.

VERY BEST OF MICHAEL BALL, THE
Song for you / Sunset Boulevard / Holland Park / Love changes everything / No one cries anymore / One step out of time / We break our own hearts / Call on me / As dreams go by / Everyday everynight / No more steps to climb / House is not a home / Maria / Beautiful heartache / It's still you / If I can dream / Empty chairs at empty tables / Always on my mind / Simple affair of the heart / On Broadway
CD _____ 523891-2
PolyGram / Nov '94 / PolyGram.

Ball, Roger

STREET STRUTTIN'
CD _____ EFZ 1013
EFZ / May '95 / Vital/SAM.

Ball, Ronnie

ALL ABOUT RONNIE
Pennie Packer / Prez sez / I don't stand a ghost of a chance with you / Little quail / Citrus season / Sweet and lovely / Feather bed
CD _____ SV 0174
Savoy Jazz / '92 / Conifer / ADA.

Ball, Tom

BLOODSHOT EYES (Ball, Tom & Kenny Sultan)
CD _____ FF 386CD
Flying Fish / Feb '93 / Roots / CM / Direct / ADA.

TOO MUCH FUN (Ball, Tom & Kenny Sultan)
CD _____ FF 532CD
Flying Fish / '92 / Roots / CM / Direct / ADA.

Balla Et Ses Balladins

AFRICAN DANCE FLOOR CLASSICS
CD _____ ADC 302
PAM / Feb '94 / Direct / ADA.

Ballamy, Iain

ALL MEN AMEN
All men amen / Serendipity / Blennie / Haunted swing / Oaxaca / Meadow / This world / Further away
CD _____ BW 065
B&W / Mar '95 / New Note.

Ballantine, David

PAINT
CD _____ DTAB 16CD
Dtab / Nov '95 / ADA.

Ballard, Hank

DANCE ALONG (Ballard, Hank & The Midnighters)
CD _____ KCD 759
King/Paddle Wheel / Mar '90 / New Note.

HANK & THE MIDNIGHTERS (Vol. 2) (Ballard, Hank & The Midnighters)
Open up the back door / In the doorway crying / Oh so happy / Let 'em roll / E bosta cosi / Stay by my side / Daddy's little baby / Partners for life / Is your love for real / What made you change your mind / Let me hold your hand / Early one morning
CD _____ KCD 581
King/Paddle Wheel / May '93 / New Note.

MR RHYTHM & BLUES (Ballard, Hank & The Midnighters)
CD _____ KCD 000700
King/Paddle Wheel / Dec '92 / New Note.

NAKED IN THE RAIN (Ballard, Hank & The Midnighters)
CD _____ AFT 4137CD
Ichiban / Feb '94 / Koch.

ONE AND ONLY, THE
Sugaree / Rain down tears / Cute little ways / House without windows / Everybody dies wrong some time / So good to be home / Kansas City / I'll keep you happy / I'm crying mercy, mercy / She's got a whole lot of soul / I'll pray for you / Move, move, move
CD _____ KCD 674
King/Paddle Wheel / May '93 / New Note.

SING 24 SONGS (Ballard, Hank & The Midnighters)
CD _____ KCD 950
King/Paddle Wheel / Mar '90 / New Note.

SINGIN' AND SWINGIN' (Ballard, Hank & The Midnighters)
Teardrops on your letter / Ring-a-ling-a-ling / Let me hold your hand / Don't say your last goodbye / Whatsoever you do / Stingy little thing / Ashamed of myself / Twist / That house on the hill / Sweet mama do right / Ooh ooh baby / Tell them / Rock 'n' roll wedding / I'll be home someday
CD _____ KCD 618
King/Paddle Wheel / Dec '92 / New Note.

SPOTLIGHT ON BALLARD
CD _____ KCD 740
King/Paddle Wheel / Mar '90 / New Note.

THEIR GREATEST JUKE BOX HITS (Ballard, Hank & The Midnighters)
Work with me Annie / Moonrise / Sexy ways / Get it / Switchie witchie titchie / It's love baby / Annie had a baby / She's the one / Annie's Aunt Fanny / Crazy loving / Henry's got flat feet / Tore up over you
CD _____ KCD 541
King/Paddle Wheel / Mar '90 / New Note.

Ballard, Russ

SEER
CD _____ CDVEST 25
Bulletproof / Jul '94 / Pinnacle.

Ballas, Corky

PASSION 2 (Ballas, Corky & Shirley)
CD _____ DLD 1061
Dance & Listen / Dec '95 / Savoy.

Ballbusters

NO HANG UPS
CD _____ 0090674DDX
Deep Distraxion/Profile / Oct '95 / Pinnacle.

Ballero, Jimmy

JIMMY BALLERO AND THE RENEGADE BAND (Ballero, Jimmy & The Renegade Band)
CD _____ SCD 27
Southland / Feb '93 / Jazz Music.

Ballew, Michael

I LOVE TEXAS
Music is sweet / Greatest Texas song / Glenda Pearl / Ain't no future / I love Texas / Blue water / Country music / Rodeo cool / Hot spot / Lovin' me / Cheatin' / Take it slow / My family / Your daddy don't live in heaven / Pretending fool / Seminole County Jail / Crazy dreams / Dark side of the dancefloor / As precious as you are / Women love, love out there / Hazelwood Avenue
CD _____ BCD 15669
Bear Family / Jun '92 / Rollercoaster / Direct / CM / Swift / ADA.

YOU BETTER HOLD ON
Blue to the bone / Livin' in limbo / Nothin' on me / Tiny fingers, tiny toes / Texas gal / Blue water / Boot scootin' / Your memory is better than mine / You better hold on / Hill country wine / For the honey / Dig in, get tough / Today will never end
CD _____ BCDAH 15896
Bear Family / Jun '95 / Rollercoaster / Direct / CM / Swift / ADA.

Ballistic Brothers

LONDON HOOLIGAN SOUL
CD _____ JBOCD 3
Junior Boys Own / Sep '95 / Disc.

VOLUME 1 (Ballistic Brothers & Eccentric Afros)
NYX 2 / Gangstalane / Uschi's groove / It goes like this / M.C.F. 2870 / Blacker / Valley of the Afro temple / Grovers return
CD _____ DSTCD001
On Delancey Street / Jul '95 / Vital.

Ballochmyle

TOUCH OF COUNTRY, A
CD _____ CDSLP 622
Klub / Aug '94 / CM / Ross / Duncans / ADA / Direct.

Ballou Canta

BOLINGO SONIA (Ballou Canta & Soukous Stars)
CD _____ S 1829CD
Paris - Tropical / Nov '90 / Triple Earth.

Ballyclare Male Voice...

MARVELLOUS AND WONDERFUL (Ballyclare Male Voice Choir)
CD _____ CDPOL 906
Outlet / Jan '95 / ADA / Duncans / CM / Ross / Direct / Koch.

WALKING WITH GOD (Ballyclare Male Voice Choir)
CD _____ CDPOL 901
Outlet / Jan '95 / ADA / Duncans / CM / Ross / Direct / Koch.

Balogh, Kalman

GIPSY CIMBALOM, THE
CD _____ EUCD 1102
ARC / '91 / ARC Music / ADA.

ROMA VANDOR
CD _____ MW 4009CD
Music & Words / Apr '95 / ADA / Direct.

Balogh, Meta

GYPSY MUSIC FROM HUNGARY
CD _____ EUCD 1073
ARC / '89 / ARC Music / ADA.

Baltic Quartet

BALTIC QUARTET
CD _____ SITCD 9222
Sittel / Aug '95 / Cadillac / Jazz Music.

Baltimore

THOUGHT FOR FOOD
CD _____ SPV 08496112
SPV / Jul '94 / Plastic Head.

Bam Bam

BEST OF WESTBROOK CLASSICS
CD _____ EFAO 17822
Tresor / Mar '95 / SRD.

Bama Band

BAMA BAND, THE
Shop shop / Stand up / L.A. / I've changed my mind / Save that dress / What used to be crazy / Too voodoo / White cadillac / Stone cold and country / You can't get there from here
CD _____ 852176
Dixie Frog / Oct '93 / Magnum Music Group.

Bambaataa, Afrika

HIP HOP FUNK DANCE CLASSICS 1
CD _____ SPOCK 3CD
Music Of Life / Jul '91 / Grapevine.

HIP HOP FUNK DANCE CLASSICS 2
CD _____ SPOCK 4CD
Music Of Life / Aug '92 / Grapevine.

Bananarama

BUNCH OF HITS
Love in the first degree / Bad for me / I heard a rumour / Ain't no cure / I can't let you go / Hooked on love / Young at heart / Robert De Niro's waiting / Hotline to heaven / Dance with a stranger / Scarlett / Ghost / Rough justice / Cheers then
CD _____ 3000122
Spectrum/Karussell / May '93 / PolyGram / THE.

GREATEST HITS: BANANARAMA
Venus / I heard a rumour / Love in the first degree / I can't help it / I want you back / Love, truth and honesty / Nathan Jones / Really saying something / Shy boy / Robert De Niro's waiting / Cruel summer / It ain't what you do it's the way that you do it / Na na hey hey kiss him goodbye / Rough justice / Trick of the night (CD only) / Aie a mwana (CD only) / Venus (Mix) (CD only) / Love in the first degree (mix) (CD only)
CD _____ 828 106-2
London / Oct '88 / PolyGram.

PLEASE YOURSELF
CD _____ 8283572
London / Nov '92 / PolyGram.

Banchory Strathspey &...

GEOL NA FIDHLE (Banchory Strathspey & Reel Society)
CD _____ CDTIV 605
Scotdisc / Aug '95 / Duncans / Ross / Conifer.

Banco De Gaia

LAST TRAIN TO LHASA
CD _____ BARKCD 011
Planet Dog / May '95 / 3MV / Vital.

MAYA
CD _____ BARKCD 3
Ultimate / Feb '94 / 3MV / Vital.

Band

ACROSS THE GREAT DIVIDE (3 CDs)
Tears of rage / Weight / I shall be released / Chest fever / In a station / To kingdom come / Lonesome Suzie / Rag mama rag / Night they drove old dixie down / King Harvest (has surely come) / Rockin' chair / Whispering pines / Up on cripple creek / Across the great divide / Unfaithful servant / Shape I'm in / Daniel and the sacred harp / All la glory / Stage fright / When I paint my masterpiece / Moon struck one / Life is a carnival / River hymn / Don't do it / Calsonia mission / W.S. Walcott medicine show / Medicine show / Get up Jake / This wheel's on fire / Share your love with me / Mystery train / Acadian driftwood / Ophelia / It makes no difference / Living in a dream / Saga of Pepote Rouge / Right as rain / Who do you love / Do the honky tonk / He don't love you / katie's been gone / Bessie Smith / Orange juice blues / Ain't no cane on the brazos / Slippin' and slidin' / Twilight / Back to Memphis / Too wet to work / Loving you is sweeter than ever / Don't ya tell Henry / Endless highway / She knows / Evangeline / Out of the blue / Last waltz (refrain) / Last waltz (theme)
CD Set _____ CDBAND 1
Capitol / Nov '94 / EMI.

BAND, THE
Across the great divide / Rag mama rag / Night they drove old Dixie down / When you awake / Up on Cripple Creek / Whispering pines / Jemima surrender / Rockin' chair / Look out Cleveland / Jawbone / Unfaithful servant / King harvest (has surely come)
CD _____ CZ 70
EMI / Aug '88 / EMI.

JERICHO
CD _____ ESSCD 199
Essential / Jan '94 / Total/BMG.

LAST WALTZ, THE
Last waltz / Up on Cripple Creek / Who do you love / Helpless / Stage fright / Coyote / Dry your eyes / It makes no difference / Such a night / Night they drove old Dixie down / Mystery train / Mannish boy / Further on up the road / Shape I'm in / Down South in New Orleans / Ophelia / Tura lura larai (That's an Irish lullaby) / Caravan / Life is a carnival / Baby let me follow you down / I don't believe you (she acts like we never have met) / Forever young / I shall be released / Last waltz suite / Well / Evangeline / Out of the blue / Weight
CD _____ K 266076
WEA / Mar '88 / Warner Music.

LIVE AT WATKINS GLEN
Back to Memphis / Endless highway / I shall be released / Loving you is sweeter than ever / Too wet to work / Don't ya tell Henry / Rumour / Time to kill / Jam / Up on cripple creek
CD _____ CDP 8317422
Capitol / Apr '95 / EMI.

NORTHERN LIGHTS-SOUTHERN CROSS
Forbidden fruit / Hobo jungle / Ophelia / Acadian driftwood / Ring your bell / Rags and bones / It makes no difference / Jupiter hollow
CD _____ CZ 404
Capitol / Mar '91 / EMI.

TO KINGDOM COME
Back to Memphis / Tears of rage / To kingdom come / Long black veil / Chest fever / Weight / I shall be released / Up on Cripple Creek / Loving you is sweeter than ever / Rag mama rag / Night they drove old Dixie down / Jawn / Unfaithful servant / King harvest (has surely come) / Shape I'm in / W.S. Walcott medicine show / Daniel and the sacred harp / Stage fright / Don't do it (baby don't you do it) / Life is a carnival / When I paint my masterpiece / 4% pantomime / River hymn / Don't do it / Mystery train / Endless highway / Get up Jake / It makes no difference / Ophelia / Acadian driftwood / Christmas must be tonight / Saga of Pepote Rouge / Knockin' lost John
CD Set _____ CDS 792 169 2
Capitol / Sep '89 / EMI.

Band Of Hope

RHYTHMS AND REDS
CD _____ MFCD 512
Musikfolk / Aug '94 / Roots / Direct.

Band Of Outsiders

NO REFLECTION
CD _____ EFA 15658CD
Repulsion / Oct '92 / SRD.

Band Of Susans

BAND OF SUSANS-PEEL SESSIONS
I found that essence rare / Throne of blood / Child of the moon / Hope against hope / Which dream came true / Too late
CD _____ SFRCD 128
Strange Fruit / Feb '94 / Pinnacle.

HERE COMES SUCCESS
CD _____ BFFP 114CD
Blast First / Apr '95 / Disc.

HOPE AGAINST HOPE

Not even close / Learning to sin / Throne of blood / Elliott Abrams in hell / All the wrong reasons / I, the jury / No God / You were an optimist / Ready to bend / Hope against hope
CD _____ FU 005CD
Furthur / Apr '88 / Pinnacle.

LOVE AGENDA
CD _____ BFFP 43 CD
Blast First / Jan '89 / Disc.

NOW
Pearls of wisdom / Following my heart / Trash train / Paint it black / Now is now (Remix) / Paint it black (instrumental)
CD _____ RTD 15914912
World Service / Apr '93 / Vital.

VEIL
Mood swing / Not in this life / Red and the black / Following my heart / Stained glass / Last temptation of Susan / Truce / Trouble spot / Out of the question / Pearls of wisdom / Trollbinder's theme / Blind
CD _____ RTD 15715612
World Service / Jun '93 / Vital.

WIRED FOR SOUND
CD Set _____ BFFP 111CD
Blast First / Jan '95 / Disc.

Band Of The Life Guards

CROWN IMPERIAL
Emblazoned / Crown imperial / Wasps / Salute to the horse / Triumph of right / Rhapsody for trombone / Men of Harlech / Oboe concerto / Orb and sceptre
CD _____ MMCD 422
Music Masters / Nov '95 / Target/BMG.

Banda Olodum

O MOVIEMENTO
Alegria geral / Rosa / Amor de eva / Mul mulher / Literatura faraonica / Luz celeste / Requebra / Papa furado / O faio da dala / Suenos lejos / Jazz E blues / Te amo / Cara preta / Tropicum / Ideologia / Bahia viva
CD _____ 45099491222
East West / Feb '91 / Warner Music.

Bandit Queen

HORMONE HOTEL
Scorch / Back in the belljar / Miss Dandys / Nailbiter / Give it to the dog / Petals and razorblades / Overture for beginners / Big sugar emotional thing / Essence vanilla / Oestrogen / Frida Kahlo / Hormone hotel / Blue black (CD only)
CD _____ AMUSE 26CD
Playtime / Feb '95 / Pinnacle / Discovery.

Bandola

TIL TUESDAY
Till tuesday / Until the candle fades / Last song of summer / Defenceless
CD _____ BOTT 002 CD
Beechwood / Oct '92 / BMG / Pinnacle.

Bands Of The British Army

MARCHING TO GLORY
CD _____ MU 5009
Musketeer / Oct '92 / Koch.

Bandy, Moe

SINGS 20 GREAT SONGS OF THE AMERICAN COWBOY
Home on the range / I'm an old cowhand (from the Rio Grande) / Back in the saddle again / Streets of Laredo / Old faithful / Don't fence me in / San Antonio rose / Deep in the heart of Texas / Oklahoma hills / When it's springtime in the Rockies / Take me back to Tulsa / Red river valley / Cool water / Sioux City Sue / Tumbling tumbleweeds / Bury me not on the lone prairie / High noon / Good old paint / Strawberry roan / Old Chisholm trail
CD _____ PLATCD 3907
Platinum Music / '90 / Prism / Ross.

Bang Bang Machine

AMPHIBIAN
Breathless / Love and things / Tough Delilah / Fantasia / Slide / Show me your pain / Love it bleeds / When love comes down / Requiem of silence
CD _____ TOPPCD 036
Ultimate / Sep '95 / 3MV / Vital.

ETERNAL HAPPINESS
CD _____ TOPPCD 009
Ultimate / Jun '94 / 3MV / Vital.

Bang, Billy

LIVE AT CARLOS
CD _____ 121136-2
Soul Note / '88 / Harmonia Mundi / Wellard / Cadillac.

RAINBOW GLADIATOR (Bang, Billy Quartet)
CD _____ 121016-2
Soul Note / Nov '92 / Harmonia Mundi / Wellard / Cadillac.

TRIBUTE TO STUFF SMITH
CD _____ 121216-2
Soul Note / Nov '93 / Harmonia Mundi / Wellard / Cadillac.

VALVE NO. 10 (Bang, Billy Quartet)
CD _____ 1211862
Soul Note / Nov '91 / Harmonia Mundi / Wellard / Cadillac.

Bang Tango

LOVE AFTER DEATH
CD _____ CDMFN 174
Music For Nations / Feb '95 / Pinnacle.

Bang The Party

BACK TO PRISON
CD _____ WAFCD 4
Warriors Dance / Sep '90 / Pinnacle.

Bangalore Choir

ON TARGET
Angel in black / Loaded gun / If the good die young (we'll live forever) / Doin' the dance / Hold on to you / All or nothin' / Slippin' away / She can't stop / Freight train rollin' / Just one night
CD _____ 07599244332
Giant / Apr '92 / BMG.

Bangles

ALL OVER THE PLACE
Hero takes a fall / Live / James / All about you / Dover beach / Tell me / Restless / Going down to Liverpool / He's got a secret / Silent troatment / More than meets the eye
CD _____ 4500912
CBS / '84 / Sony.

DIFFERENT LIGHT
Manic Monday / In a different light / Walking down your street / Walk like an Egyptian / Standing in the hallway / Return post / If she knew what she wants / Let it go / September girls / Angels don't fall in love / Following / Not like you
CD _____ 465582
CBS / Mar '90 / Sony.

EVERYTHING
In your room / Complicated girl / Bell jar / Something to believe in / Eternal flame / Be with you / Glitter years / I'll set you free / Watching the sky / Some dreams come true / Make a play for her now / Waiting for you / Crash and burn
CD _____ 4629792
CBS / Jul '88 / Sony.

GREATEST HITS
Hero takes a fall / Going down to Liverpool / Manic monday / If she knew what she wants / Walk like an Egyptian / Walking down your street / Following / Hazy shade of winter / In your room / Eternal flame / Be with you / I'll set you free / Everything I wanted / Where were you when I needed you
CD _____ 4667692
CBS / Apr '95 / Sony.

TWELVE INCH MIXES
If she knew what she wants / Walking down your street / In your room / Manic Monday / Walk like an Egyptian
CD _____ 468988-2
Columbia / Nov '92 / Sony.

Banjo Express

OLD TIME COUNTRY MUSIC
CD _____ PV F18 T61
Disques Pierre Verany / '88 / Kingdom.

Bank Statement

BANK STATEMENT
Throwback / Queen of darkness / Raincloud / The big man / More I hide it / I'll be waiting / That night / Border / House needs a roof / Thursday the twelfth
CD _____ CDV 2600
Virgin / Apr '92 / EMI.

Banks, Peter

INSTINCT
CD _____ HTD CD 11
HTD / Feb '93 / Pinnacle.

TWO SIDES OF PETER BANKS
CD _____ OW S2118009
One Way / Sep '94 / Direct / ADA.

Banks, Tony

CURIOUS FEELING, A
From the undertow / Lucky me / Lie / After the lie / Curious feeling / Forever morning / You / Somebody else's dream / Waters of Lethe / For a while / In the dark
CD _____ CASCD 1148
Charisma / '88 / EMI.

DEAF FUGITIVE
This is love / Man of spells / And the wheels keep turning / Say you'll never leave me / Thirty three's / By you / At the edge of night / Charm / Moving under
CD _____ TBCD 1
Charisma / '88 / EMI.

SOUNDTRACKS
Shortcut to somewhere / Smilin' Jack Casey / Quicksilver suite / You call this victory / Lion of symmetry / Red wing suite
CD _____ CASCD 1173
Charisma / Jul '87 / EMI.

STILL
Red day on blue street / Angel face / Gift / Still it takes me by suprise / Hero for an hour / I wanna change the score / Water out of wine / Another murder of a day / Back to back / Final curtain
CD _____ CDV 2658
Virgin / Jun '91 / EMI.

Bannerjee, Nikhil

RAGA AHIR
CD _____ DSAV 1054
Multitone / Dec '95 / BMG.

Banton, Buju

BUJU BANTON MEETS GARNETT SILK AND TONY REBEL (Banton, Buju & Friends)
CD _____ RNCD 2033
Rhino / Oct '93 / Jetstar / Magnum Music Group / THE.

MR. MENTION
Batty rider / Love how the gal dem flex / Long black woman / Love how you sweet / Woman no fret / Have to get you tonight / Dickie / Love me brownin' / Buju movin' / Who say / How the world a run (CD only) / Bona fide love (Cd only)
CD _____ 522022-2
Mercury / Jan '94 / PolyGram.

TIL SHILOH
Shiloh / Till I'm glad to rest / Murderer / Champion / Untold stories / Not an easy road / Only man / Complaint / Chuck it so / How could you / Wanna be loved / It's all over / Hush baby love / What you're gonna do / Rampage
CD _____ 5241192
Loose Cannon / Jul '95 / Jetstar / PolyGram.

VOICE OF JAMAICA
CD _____ 5180132
Mercury / Aug '93 / PolyGram.

Banton, Mega

FIRST POSITION
CD _____ VPCD 1343
VP / Jan '94 / Jetstar.

NEW YEAR, NEW STYLE (Banton, Mega & Friends)
CD _____ SHCD 45020
Shanachie / Dec '94 / Koch / ADA / Greensleeves.

SHOWCASE (Mega Banton & Ricky General)
CD _____ BSCCD 17
Black Scorpio / Dec '93 / Jetstar.

Banton, Pato

COLLECTIONS
Baby come back / Bubbling hot / Don't sniff coke / Tudo de bom / Wize up / One world (not three) / Roots, rock, reggae / Gwarn / Go Pato / Bad man and woman / Never give in / Save your soul / All drugs out / Pato's opinion pt.2
CD _____ CDVX 2765
Virgin / May '95 / EMI.

MAD PROFESSOR RECAPTURES PATO BANTON (Banton, Pato & Mad Professor)
CD _____ ARICD 043
Ariwa Sounds / Feb '89 / Jetstar / SRD.

NEVER GIVE IN
Absolute perfection / My opinion / Don't Worry / Handsworth riot / Gwarn / Pato and Roger come again / Never give in / Don't sniff coke / Sattle Satan / King step / Hello Tosh
CD _____ GRELCD 108
Greensleeves / Feb '95 / Total/BMG / Jetstar / SRD.

Baphomet

TRUST
CD _____ MASSCD 027
Massacre / Apr '94 / Plastic Head.

Baptiste, David Jean

GROOVE ON A FOUR
CD _____ SAXCD 001
Saxology / Aug '95 / Harmonia Mundi / Cadillac.

Bar-Kays

GOTTA GROOVE BLACK ROCK
Don't stop dancing (to the music) / If this world was mine / In the hole / Funky thang / Jivin' round / Grab this thang / Dancing (to the music) Pt.2 / Street walker / Yesterday / Humpin' / Hey Jude / Baby I love you / I've been trying / You don't know like I know / Dance to the music / Piece of your peace / Six o'clock news report / How sweet it would be / Montego Bay

CD _____ CDSXD 962
Stax / Nov '90 / Pinnacle.

MONEY TALKS
Holy ghost / Feelin' alright / Monster / Money talks / Mean mistreater / Holy ghost (reborn)
CD _____ CDSXE 023
Stax / Jan '90 / Pinnacle.

SOUL FINGER
Knucklehead / Soul finger / With a child's heart / Bar-kays boogaloo / Hell's Angels / You can't sit down / House shoes / Pearl high / I want someone / Hole in the wall / Don't do that
CD _____ 8122702982
Atco / Jul '93 / Warner Music.

Baraban

IL VALZER DEI DISERTORI
CD _____ ACB 01
Robi Droli / Jan '94 / Direct / ADA.

Barazaz

ECHOUNDER
CD _____ CD 828
Diffusion Breizh / May '93 / ADA.

Barbarin, Paul

OXFORD SERIES VOL. 15
CD _____ AMCD 35
American Music / Jan '94 / Jazz Music.

STREETS OF THE CITY (Barbarin, Paul & His New Orleans Band 1950)
CD _____ 504 CD9
504 / Nov '95 / Wellard / Jazz Music / Target/BMG / Cadillac.

Barber, Chris

40 YEARS JUBILEE (Vol.1 1954-1955/ Vol.2 1955-1956 2CD Set)
Hiawatha rag / Jeep's blues / If I ever cease to love / Merrydown blues / Goin' to town / Lord, Lord, Lord / Someday sweetheart / When I move to the sky / On a Monday / Shout 'em Aunt Tillie / Spanish Mama / Please get him off my mind / See see rider / Black cat on the fence / In the evening / Midnight special / Papa de da da / Key-stone blues / Jailhouse blues / High society / Bye and bye / Magnolia's wedding day / Jelly bean blues / Everywhere you go / Goin' down the road feelin' bad / Long gone lost John / Tiger rag / Can't afford to do it / Original tuxedo rag / Bogalousa strut / How long blues / Railroad Bill / Whistling Rufus / Reckell blues / Panama / Back water blues / Big house blues / Royal telephone
CD Set _____ CDTTD 589
Timeless Traditional / Jul '95 / New Note.

40 YEARS JUBILEE AT THE OPERAHOUSE NURNBERG
Isle of capri / We sure do need him now / It's tight like that / Old rugged cross / Hush-a-bye / Worried man blues / Down by the riverside / Ice cream / Workin' man blues / Petite fleur / Sweet Georgia Brown / Brown / Slap 'n' slide / Tiger rag / Mile end stomp / Wild cat blues
CD _____ CDTTD 582
Timeless Jazz / Dec '94 / New Note.

ALL THAT JAZZ (Barber, Chris/Acker Bilk/Kenny Ball)
CD _____ KAZCD 18
Kaz / Jan '92 / BMG.

BARBER, BALL & BILK (Barber, Chris/ Acker Bilk/Kenny Ball)
Big noise from Winnetka / Sweet Sue, just you / Livery stable blues / Careless love / Willie the weeper / 1919 March / Sweet Georgia Brown / Bourbon street parade / Dinah / Burgundy St. Blues / Marching through Georgia / Petite fleur / Temptation rag / Chelsea cakewalk / Yama yama / South Rampart street parade / Bill Bailey, won't you please come home / Dardanella / Bugle boy march / Milenberg joys
CD _____ TRTCD 130
TrueTrax / Oct '94 / THE.

BARBER, BALL & BILK (Barber, Chris/ Acker Bilk/Kenny Ball)
CD _____ SSLCD 205
Savanna / Jun '95 / THE.

BEST SELLERS
CD _____ STCD 200
Storyville / Oct '87 / Jazz Music / Wellard / CM / Cadillac.

CHRIS BARBER (Barber, Chris & The Zenith Hot Stompers)
Ole Miss rag / Riverside blues / Just a little while to stay here / Bugle boy march / Saratoga swing / Precious Lord, take my hand / Sweet Georgia Brown / Goin' home / Panama rag / Sweet Sue, just you / Creole love call / Bye and bye
CD _____ CDTTD 582
Timeless Traditional / Feb '94 / New Note.

CHRIS BARBER & HIS NEW ORLEANS FRIENDS
Birth of the blues / Coquette / Ma, she's making eyes at me / Over in the glory land / Sentimental journey / Yes sir that's my baby / Eyes of Texas are upon you / Mood

indigo / My blue heaven / Let me call you sweetheart / Nobody's sweetheart / I ain't got nobody / Lord, lord, lord / Panama
CD _____ CDTTD 573
Timeless Jazz / Oct '93 / New Note.

CHRIS BARBER AND HIS JAZZ BAND IN CONCERT (Barber, Chris & His Jazz Band)
Bourbon Street Parade / New Blues / Willie the weeper / Mean mistreater / Yama yama man / Old man Mose / Mood indigo / Bear-cat crawl / Lowland blues / Panama / Savoy blues / Lonesome Road / Sheikh of Araby
CD _____ DM 23 CD
Dormouse / Aug '91 / Jazz Music / Target/ BMG.

CHRIS BARBER CONCERTS, THE (2CD Set)
Bourbon street parade / New blues / Willy the weeper / Mean mistreater / Yama yama man / Old man mose / Mood indigo / Bear-cat crawl / Lowland blues / Panama / Savoy blues / Lonesome road / Sheik or araby / Bill Bailey / You took advantage of me / Sweet Sue, just you / Moonshine / You rascal you / Bugle boy march / Pretty baby / Majorca / Indiana / Georgia grind / Rock in rhythm / My old kentucky home / Rent party blues / Careless love / Strange things happen everyday / Mama don't allow
CD Set _____ LACDD 55/56
Lake / Nov '95 / Target/BMG / Jazz Music / Direct / Cadillac / ADA.

CHRIS BARBER'S GREATEST HITS
CD _____ JW 77036
JWD / Jun '94 / Target/BMG.

CLASSICS CONCERT IN BERLIN (1959)
Climax rag / Gotta travel on / Chimes blues / Just a little while to stay here / 'S Wonderful / Lord, Lord, Lord / Revival
CD _____ CBJBCD 4002
Chris Barber Collection / Oct '88 / New Note / Cadillac.

COLLABORATION (Barber, Chris & Barry Martin)
CD _____ BCD 40
GHB / Mar '93 / Jazz Music.

COME FRIDAY (Barber, Chris Jazz & Blues Band)
Alligator hop / St. Louis blues / Wild cat blues / Come Friday / Sweet Sue, just you / Stevedore stomp
CD _____ BLR 84 011
L&R / May '91 / New Note.

CONCERT FOR THE BBC (Barber, Chris Jazz & Blues Band)
CD Set _____ CDTTD 509/10
Timeless Traditional / '86 / New Note.

ECHOES OF ELLINGTON VOL 1 (Barber, Chris Jazz & Blues Band)
Stevedore stomp / Jeep's blues / I'm slapping Seventh Avenue with the sole of my shoe / In a mellow tone / Prelude to a kiss / Second line / Perdido / Moon indigo / Shout 'em Aunt Tillie
CD _____ CDTTD 555
Timeless Traditional / Mar '91 / New Note.

ECHOES OF ELLINGTON VOL 2 (Barber, Chris Jazz & Blues Band)
Squatty roo / Blues for Duke / Take the 'A' train / Warm valley / Caravan / Sophisticated lady / It don't mean a thing if it ain't got that swing / Just squeeze me / Mooche / Jeep is jumpin'
CD _____ CDTTD 556
Timeless Traditional / Mar '91 / New Note.

ELITE SYNCOPATIONS (Great British Traditional Jazzbands Vol. 2)
Swipsey cakewalk / Bohemia rag / Elite syncopations / Cole's moan / Peach / St. George's rag / Favourite / Reindeer ragtime two step / Entertainer / Georgia cakewalk / Thriller rag / Whistling Rufus / Tuxedo rag / Bugle call rag
CD _____ LACD 43
Lake / Feb '95 / Target/BMG / Jazz Music / Direct / Cadillac / ADA.

ENTERTAINER, THE
CD _____ 8325932
Philips / Mar '94 / PolyGram.

ESSENTIAL CHRIS BARBER (Featuring Ottilie Patterson & Monty Sunshine)
Panama rag / Petite fleur / Savoy blues / I wish I could shimmy like my sister Kate / Sweet Georgia Brown / Thriller rag / Beale Street blues / Bill Bailey, won't you please come home / Bourbon Street parade / New blues / Trombone cholly / Texas moaner / Willie the weeper / Careless love / Everybody loves my baby / High society / Jailhouse blues / Make me a pallet on the floor / One sweet letter from you / Tishomingo blues / Trouble in mind / When you and I were young / Whistling Rufus / Wildcat blues
CD _____ KAZCD 13
Kaz / Oct '90 / BMG.

GREAT REUNION CONCERT, THE
Bourbon Street parade / Saturday night function / Martinique / Isle of Capri / Hush-a-bye / It's tight like that / Fairfield reunion / Bobby Shaftoe / On a Monday / Bury my body / Long gone lost John / Jenny's ball / Chimes blues / Whistling Rufus / Jazz me

blues / Just a sittin' and a rockin' / Steve-dore stomp
CD _____ CDTTD 553
Timeless Traditional / Jul '91 / New Note.

HOT GOSPEL 1963-1967 (Barber, Chris Jazzband)
CD _____ LACD 39
Lake / Sep '94 / Target/BMG / Jazz Music / Direct / Cadillac / ADA.

IN BUDAPEST
Lord, lord, lord / Mood indigo / Whistling Rufus / Some of these days / Mama he treats your daughter mean / Trad tavern
CD _____ STCD 408
Storyville / Jun '87 / Jazz Music / Wellard / CM / Cadillac.

IN CONCERT (Barber, Chris Jazz & Blues Band)
Take the 'A' train / Just a sittin' and a rockin' / Blues for yesterday / Summertime / Oh Lady be good / When you're smiling / Just a closer walk with thee / Lord, lord, you've sure been good to me / Shady green pastures / They kicked him out of heaven / Precious Lord, take my hand
CD _____ CDTTD 557
Timeless Traditional / Feb '91 / New Note.

IN CONCERT, VOL. 2
Bill Bailey, won't you please come home / You took advantage of me / Sweet Sue, just you / Moonshine man / (I'll be glad when you're dead) you rascal you / Bugle boy march / Pretty baby / Majorca / Georgia grind / Rockin' in rhythm / My old Kentucky home / Careless love / Strange things happen every day / Mama don't allow
CD _____ DM 24CD
Dormouse / '91 / Jazz Music / Target/BMG.

IN HIS ELEMENT
CD Set _____ CDTTD 572
Timeless Traditional / Jul '92 / New Note.

JAZZ BAND FAVOURITES (Barber, Chris Jazzband)
Petite fleur / Whistling Rufus / When the saints go marching in (part 1) / When the saints go marching in (part 2) / Sweet Georgia Brown / High society / Bugle call rag / Mack the knife / Hamp's blues / Bill Bailey, won't you please come home / I shall not be moved / O Sole Mio / Wini Wini (let's do the Tamoure) / Bonsoir Mes souvenirs / Good morning blues / Bad luck blues / Morning train / Frankie and Johnny / If I had a ticket / Great bear / Jeeps blues / Sweetest little baby
CD _____ CC 273
Music For Pleasure / Oct '91 / EMI.

JAZZ HOLIDAY (Meets Rod Mason's Hot Five) (Barber, Chris & Rod Mason's Hot Five)
CD _____ CDTTD 524
Timeless Traditional / Jul '94 / New Note.

JAZZ JAMBOREE (Barber, Chris/Acker Bilk/Kenny Ball)
CD _____ DCDCD 214
Castle / Nov '95 / BMG.

LIVE IN '85 (Barber, Chris Jazz & Blues Band)
CD _____ CDTTD 527
Timeless Traditional / Jul '94 / New Note.

LIVE IN EAST BERLIN
CD _____ BLCD 760502
Black Lion / Oct '90 / Jazz Music / Cadillac / Wellard / Koch.

MARDI GRAS AT THE MARQUEE (Barber, Chris & Dr. John)
CD _____ CDTTD 5546
Timeless Traditional / May '89 / New Note.

PANAMA (Barber, Chris & Wendell Brunious)
I wish I could shimmy like my sister Kate / Just a little while to stay here / Georgia on my mind / My blue heaven / Oh! lady be good / Careless love / Anytime / That's my desire / Panama
CD _____ CDTTD 568
Timeless Traditional / Oct '91 / New Note.

PETITE FLEUR
Petite fleur / When the saints go marching in / Wild cat blues / April showers / Sweet Georgia Brown / Majorca (Live) / High society / Whistling Rufus / Bourbon street parade (Live) / Trouble in mind / Everybody loves my baby / Jailhouse blues / When and I were young baby / Bill Bailey, won't you please come home / Beals Street blues / Mood indigo (Live) / (I'll be glad when you) you rascal you (Live) / Bye and bye / Savoy blues (Live)
CD _____ 5507442
Spectrum/Karussell / Feb '95 / PolyGram / THE.

SOUTH RAMPART STREET PARADE
CD _____ BLR 84 016
L&R / New Note.

STARDUST (Barber, Chris Jazz & Blues Band)
CD _____ CDTTD 537
Timeless Traditional / May '89 / New Note.

TAKE ME BACK TO NEW ORLEANS (Barber, Chris & Dr. John)
Take me back to New Orleans / Ti-pi-ti-na / Perdido street blues / New Orleans, Lou-

isiana / Decatur drive / New Orleans / Meet me on the Levee / Harlem rag / Ride on / Big bass drum (on a mardi gras day) / At the cemetery / Concert on Canal Street / Bourbon Street scene / Basin Street / Just a little while to stay here / Oration by Dr. John / What a friend we have in Jesus / When the saints go marching in / Concert in Canal Street / Buddy Bolden's blues / South Rampart street parade / Burgandy Street Blues / Canal Street Blues / Bourbon Street Parade / Do you know what it means to miss New Orleans / Professor Longhair's tip / Brass band blues / Basin Street blues
CD _____ BLC 760103
Black Lion / '92 / Jazz Music / Europe / Wellard / Koch.

ULTIMATE, THE (Barber, Chris/Acker Bilk/Kenny Ball)
I love you Samantha / Panama rag / Midnight in Moscow / Nobody knows you (when you're down and out) / Avalon / I wanna be like you / Christopher Columbus / Spanish harlem / That da da strain / Them there eyes / Stranger on the shore / That's my home / Good Queen Bess / Perdido street blues / Harlem rag / Mood indigo / Mary had a little lamb / When the saints go marching in / St. Louis blues / So do I / Muskrat ramble / Auf wiedersehen
CD Set _____ KAZ CD 4
Kaz / May '88 / BMG.

WHO'S BLUES
CD _____ BLR 84 009
L&R / May '91 / New Note.

Barbieri, Gato

CHAPTER ONE - LATIN AMERICA
Encuentros / La China I.eioncia arroo la / To be continued / India / Nunca mas
CD _____ MCAD 39124
Impulse Jazz / Jun '89 / BMG / New Note.

CHAPTER THREE: VIVA EMILIANO ZAPATA
Milongo triste / Lluvia azul / El sublime / La podrida / Cuando vuelva a tu lado / Viva Emiliano Zapata
CD _____ GRP 1112
GRP / Jan '92 / BMG / New Note.

GATO BARBIERI IN NEW YORK CITY
In search of the mystery / Michelle / Obsession no.2 / Cinematique
CD _____ 30019
Giants Of Jazz / Sep '92 / Target/BMG / Cadillac.

TWO PICTURES (1965-68)
CD _____ IRS 00632CD
Liuto / Oct '90 / Harmonia Mundi / Cadillac.

Barbieri, Richard

FLAME (Barbieri, Richard & Tim Bowness)
Night in heaven / Song of love and everything (parts 1 and 2) / Brightest blue / Flame / Trash talk / Time flown / Torch dance / Feel
CD _____ TPLP 58CD
One Little Indian / Sep '94 / Pinnacle.

Barbosa, Zelia

SERTAO E FAVELAS
CD _____ LDX 2741002
La Chant Du Monde / Aug '95 / Harmonia Mundi / ADA.

Barbosa-Lima, Carlos

BRAZIL, WITH LOVE (Barbosa-Lima, Carlos & Sharon Isbin)
Luiza / Felicidade / Chovendo na Rosiera / Garoto / Estrada do sol / Gabrielle / Passatempo / Vou vivendo / Pretencioso / Carinhoso / Brejeiro / Apandhi-Te, Cavaquinha / Bambino / Odeon
CD _____ CCD 4320
Concord Picante / Jul '87 / New Note.

CHANTS FOR THE CHIEF
A chamada dos ventos/Cancao naturna / Uirapuru do Amazonas / Cuhna-tan do Andira / Varando turos / Canto dos esquecidos/Yara levou o meu amor / Canto do missionario / Ventos do sertao / Canto da alvorada / Canto do verde-amado / Canoa furada/Cancao noturna/A chamada / Dos ventos - epilogo / Cajija de musica / Impressao de rua / Sonha yaya / Teotecacinte / Fantasy on an Hawaiian lullaby / Batucada / Entre olas / Panaderos / Cubanita / Corrion / De totana / Patio gitano / Alaiceria / Luna y clavel / Romance flamenco / Bailando
CD _____ CCD 4489
Concord Picante / Jan '92 / New Note.

MUSIC OF THE AMERICAS (Barbosa-Lima, Carlos & Sharon Isbin)
Sambo Chorado / Chants for the chief No. 3 / Chants for the chief No. 7 / Carioquinha / Mazurka No. 3 (Only on CD) / Caminho dos estados unidos / Brazil / Grande valsa / Lamento (Only on CD) / Cochichando / Um a zero / Lullaby for Janine / Playful equals (Only on CD) / Interlude dance (Only on CD) / Vera cruz / Always / I got rhythm / Kathy's waltz / In your own sweet way / Duke (Only on CD) / Timothy 'O'

CD _____ CCD 4461
Concord Jazz / May '91 / New Note.

PLAYS LUIZ BONFA AND COLE PORTER
Amor fascinante / Manha de carnaval / Xango / Sambolero / Na sombra da mangue - ira (in the shade of the / Passeio no Rio (a walk in Rio) / It's a lovely day today / Where or when / Begin the beguine / Let's do it / Still of the night / Night and day / Love for sale
CD _____ CCD 42008
Concord Concerto / Dec '90 / Pinnacle.

PLAYS MUSIC OF ANTONIO JOBIM AND GEORGE GERSHWIN
Cambinho de Pedra / Desafinado / Estrada branca / Stone flower / Corcovado / Amparo / One note samba (Only on CD) / Modinha (Only on CD) / Conta mais (Only on CD) / Prelude 1 / Prelude 2 / Promenade / Summertime / Swanee / 'S Wonderful / Merry Andrew / Man I love
CD _____ CCD 42005
Concord Concerto / Aug '90 / Pinnacle.

PLAYS THE ENTERTAINER AND OTHERS BY SCOTT JOPLIN
Entertainer / Heliotrope bouquet / Weeping willow / Solace / Maple leaf rag / Sugarcane / Chrysanthemum / Pleasant moments / Easy winners / Cascades
CD _____ CCD 42006
Concord Concerto / Aug '90 / Pinnacle.

TWILIGHT IN RIO
Twilight in Rio / Mi bossa blue (my blue bossa) / En la playa (at the beach) / Puerta de tierra / Etude on a theme by Mendelssohn / La alborada (dawn) / La mariposa (the butterfly) / Choro da saudade (choro of longing) / Danza paraguaya / Junto a tu corazon / Pais de abanico / El sueno de la munequita / Dinora / Um amor de valsa / Emerald / Sardius
CD _____ CCD 42017
Concord Concerto / Mar '95 / Pinnacle.

Barbour, Freeland

KILLIEKRANKIE
Glorious revolution / White rose / House of Stewart / Bluidy clavers / Cameronians march / Lands beyond forth / Tremble false Whigs / Band at distance, The / Dudhope / Green field of Dalcomera / Blair Castle / Braes of Glen Roy / Murray's siege / Mackay's advance / Men from Lochaber / Am feasgair samhraidh (the summer evening) / Allt Girnaig / Thickets of Raon Ruaraidh / Battle of Killiecrankie / MacBean's Chase / Flight and Pursuit / Urrard House / South to Dunkeld / Fiery cross / Battle of Dunkeld / Thanksgiving / There is no enemy in sight / Old Blair / Killiecrankie
CD _____ LAP CD 126
Lapwing / '89 / CM.

Barboza, Raul

MUSIC AFTER THE GUARANI INDIANS
CD _____ CDLLL 167
La Lichere / Aug '93 / Discovery / ADA.

MUSIC FROM THE BORDER
CD _____ 12453
Laserlight / Jul '95 / Target/BMG.

Barclay James Harvest

ALONE WE FLY
Crazy city / Mockingbird / Our kid's kid / Loving is easy / Rock 'n' roll lady / Fifties child / Blow me down / He said love / Rock 'n' roll star / On the wings of love / For no one / Hymn / Berlin (Love in the late / Shades of B hill / Waiting for the right time / Sideshow / Guitar blues / Poor boy blues / You need love
CD _____ VSOPCD 140
Connoisseur / Dec '90 / Pinnacle.

B.J.H. & OTHER SHORT STORIES
Medicine man / Someone there you know / Harry's song / Ursula (the Swansea song) / Little lapwing / Song with no meaning / Blue John blues / Poet / After the day / Crazy (over you) / Delph Town morn / Summer soldier / Thank you / Hundred thousand / Moonwater
CD _____ BGOCD 160
Beat Goes On / Nov '92 / Pinnacle.

BARCLAY JAMES HARVEST LIVE
Summer soldier / Medicine man / Crazy city / After the day / Great 1974 mining disaster / Galadriel / Negative earth / She said / Paper wings / For no one / Mockingbird
CD _____ VSOPCD 164
Connoisseur / Jun '91 / Pinnacle.

BEST OF BARCLAY JAMES HARVEST, THE
CD _____ 5119322
Polydor / Jan '89 / PolyGram.

CAUGHT IN THE LIGHT
CD _____ 5193032
Polydor / Jun '93 / PolyGram.

CONCERT FOR THE PEOPLE (BERLIN), A
Berlin / Loving is easy / Mockingbird / Sip of wine / Nova lepidopter / In memory of the martyrs / Life is for living / Child of the universe / Hymn

CD _____ 8000262
Polydor / Jan '89 / PolyGram.

EVERYONE IS EVERYBODY ELSE
CD _____ 833 448-2
Polydor / Feb '92 / PolyGram.

GONE TO EARTH
Hymn / Love is like a violin / Friend of mine / Poor man's moody blues / Hard hearted woman / Sea of Tranquility / Spirit on the water / Leper's song / Taking me higher
CD _____ 0000922
Polydor / Jan '89 / PolyGram.

HARVEST YEARS, THE
Early morning / Mr. Sunshine / Pools of blue / I can't go on without you / Eden unobtainable / Brother thrush / Poor wages / Taking some time on / When the world was woken / Good love child / Iron maiden / Dark now my sky / She said / Song for dying / Galadriel / Mocking bird / Vanessa Simmons / Happy old world (quad mix) / Ball and chain / Medicine man / Ursula (The Swansea song) / Someone there you know / Poet/After the day / I'm over you / Child of man / Breathless / When the city sleeps / Summer soldier / Hundred thousand smiles out / Moonwater / Joker / Good times
CD Set _____ CDEN 5014
Harvest / May '91 / EMI.

OCTOBERON
World goes on / May day / Ra / Rock 'n' roll / Star / Polk street rag / Believe in me / Suicide
CD _____ 8219302
Polydor / Oct '91 / PolyGram.

ONCE AGAIN
She said / Happy old world / Song for dying / Galadriel / Mockingbird / Vanessa Simmons / Ball and chain / Lady loves
CD _____ BGOCD 152
Beat Goes On / Nov '92 / Pinnacle.

RING OF CHANGES
Fifties child / Looking from the outside / Teenage heart / Highwire / Midnight drug / Waiting for the right time / Just a day away / Paraiso dos cavalos / Ring of changes
CD _____ 8116382
Polydor / Oct '88 / PolyGram.

SCORCERERS & KEEPERS
Just a day away / Titles / Sea of tranquility / Suicide / Love is like a violin / Song (they love to sing) / All right get down boogie (mu ala rusic) / Hold on / Alone in the night / On the wings of love / Poor boy blues / See me see you / Teenage heart / Love on the line
CD _____ 5500292
Spectrum/Karussell / Jun '93 / PolyGram / THE.

TURN OF THE TIDE
Waiting on the borderline / How do you feel now / Back to the wall / Highway for fools / Echoes and shadows / Death of a city / living / In memory of the martyrs
CD _____ 8000132
Polydor / Jul '88 / PolyGram.

Barde, Jerome

FELIZ
Marc / Dad's delight / No words / La Nina / Cecile / Citrons / Barde bleue / Ombrage / Feliz / Lefru / I'll be seeing you
CD _____ SSC 1042D
Sunnyside / Oct '91 / Pinnacle.

Bardens, Pete

BIG SKY
CD _____ HTDCD 22
HTD / Jun '94 / Pinnacle.

FURTHER THAN YOU KNOW
Sometime / Dream catcher / Sea of dreams / Real time / Coco loco / Bad boy (redemption song) / This could be like heaven / Rain talk
CD _____ MPCD 2601
Miramar / Oct '93 / New Note.

WATER COLORS
Journey / De profundis / Higher ground / Yellowstone blue / Is it any wonder / Water colors / Shape of the rain / Timepiece / Ghostwater
CD _____ MPCD 4001
Miramar / Jun '93 / New Note.

Bardo Pond

BUFO ALVARIUS
CD _____ CHE 33CD
Che / Sep '95 / SRD.

Bardots

EYE-BABY
Pretty O / Chained up / Cruelty blonde / Sister Richard / Slow asleep / Sunsetted / My cute thought / Obscenity thing / Gloriole / Caterina / A / Shallow
CD _____ CHEREE 031 CD
Cheree / Sep '95 / SRD.

Bare, Bobby

ALL AMERICAN BOY
CD _____ CTS 55428
Country Stars / Nov '94 / Target/BMG.

ALL AMERICAN BOY, THE (4 CDs)
Darlin' don't / Another love has ended / Down on the corner of love / Life of a fool / Beggar / Livin' end / Vampira / Tender years / When the one you love / All American boy / What you gonna do now / I'm hanging up my rifle / That's where I want to be / Lynching party / Sweet singin' Sam / More than a poor boy could give / No letter from my baby / Book of love / Can can ladies / Lorena / Zig zag twist / Island of love / Sailor man / These tender years / Lovesick / Great big car / Brooklyn bridge / That mean old clock / Day my rainbow fell / Above and beyond / Shame on me / To whom it may concern / Wallflower / I don't believe I'll fall in love today / Dear waste basket / Baby, don't believe him / I'm gettin' lonely / Heart of ice / Candy coated kisses / Gods were angry with me / I'd fight the world / Is it wrong (for loving you) / Dear waste backet / Detroit city / Lonely town / She called me baby / 500 miles away from home / It all depends on Linda / Worried man blues / Ho 'nstead on the farm / Abilene / Gotta travel on / Noah's ark / I wonder where you are tonight / Let me tell you about Mary / What kind of bird is that / Jeannie's last kiss / Miller's cave / Sittin' and thinkin' / Have I stayed away too long / Long way back to Tennessee / Long black limousine / Down in Mexico / I was coming home to you / Another bridge to burn / I've lived a lot in my time / He was a friend of mine / Take me home / When I'm gone / Sweeter than the flowers / Four strong winds / When the wind blows in Chicago / Just to satisfy you / Let it be me / In the misty moonlight / I love you / Too used to being with you / Together again / We'll sing in the sunshine / Out of our minds / I don't care / That's all I want from you / Invisible tears / Dear John letter / True love / Rosalie / Alle glauben dass ich glucklich bin / Times are gettin' hard / I'm a long way from home / Deepening snow / I'm a man of constant sorrow / She picked a perfect day / One day at a time / So soon / Countin' the hours - countin' the days / Don't think twice, it's alright / Blowin' in the wind / Della's gone / Lemon tree / It's all right / Salt Lake City / Changing my mind / Good old Tennessee / Das haus auf der sierra / Sixteen / Wilder wolfund brauner bar / Molly Brown / Little bit later on down the line / Got leavin' on her mind / Try to remember / All the good times are past and gone / Memories / Heaven help my soul / We helped each other out / In the same old way / Talk me some sense / You can't stop the wild wind from blowing / It ain't me babe / Long black veil / Passin' through / What color (is a man)
CD Set _____ BCD 15663
Bear Family / Jan '94 / Rollercoaster / Direct / CM / Swift / ADA.

BOBBY BARE SINGS LULLABYS, LEGENDS & LIES
Lullabys, legends and lies / Paul / Marie Lavaau / Daddy what if / Wonderful soup stones / Winner / In the hills of Shiloh / She's my ever lovin' machine / Mermaid / Rest awhile / Bottomless well / True story / Early in the morning / Rosalie's good eat's cafe
CD _____ BCD 15683
Bear Family / Apr '93 / Rollercoaster / Direct / CM / Swift / ADA.

GREATEST HITS
CD _____ WMCD 5681
Disky / Nov '93 / THE / BMG / Discovery / Pinnacle.

MERCURY YEARS 1970-72 (3 CDs)
That's how I got to Memphis / Come sundown / I took a memory to lunch / I'm her hoss if I never win a race / Woman you've been a friend to me / It's freezing in El Paso / Mrs. Jones your daughter cried all night / Don't it make you wanna go home / Mary Ann regrets / Leaving on a jet plane / Please / Waitress in the Main Street cafe / Please don't tell me how the story ends / How about you / Help me make it through the night / Rosalie / Dropping out of sight / Where have all the flowers gone / Travelling minstrel man / For the good times / Hello darlin' / Alabama rose / World is weighing heavy on my mind / Mama bake a pie (papa kill a chicken) / Coal river / Christian soldier / Don't you ever get tired of hurting me / West Virginia woman / New York City snow / Jesus is the only one that loves us / Loving her was easier (than anything I'll ever do again) / I need some good news bad / Me and Bobby McGee / Million miles to the city / Just the other side of nowhere / City boy / country born / Short and sweet / Puppet and the parakeet / Great society talking blues / Year that Clayton Delaney died / Roses are red / Lonely street / Crazy arms / Jesus Christ what a man / Fallen star / That's alright / Pamela Brown / When I want to love a lady / Love forever / Darby's castle / Lot of soul / Just in case / What am I gonna do / When love is gone / Lorena / Don't ask me, ask Marie / Laying here lying in bed / Take some and give some / Sylvia's mother / Footprints in the snow / Lord let a

41

lie come true / Under it all / Are you sincere / Even the bad times are good / High and dry / She gave her heart to Jethro / Music City U.S.A.
CD Set _____ BCD 15417
Bear Family / Dec '87 / Rollercoaster / Direct / CM / Swift / ADA.

Bare Necessities

TAKE A DANCE
CD _____ FF 564CD
Flying Fish / Apr '94 / Roots / CM / Direct / ADA.

Barefoot

BAREFOOT
Barefoot / Gobi wind / Roundabout / Street strut / Serengeti / Shooz off / Black Noah / Gitano de Paraguay / Africa / Breath of life
CD _____ 66052004
Global Pacific / Feb '91 / Pinnacle.

Barefoot Contessa

BAREFOOT CONTESSA
CD _____ LOLACD 1
Backs / Jun '95 / Disc.

Barely Works

BEST OF BARELY WORKS
Byker hill / As a thoiseach / This fire / Liberty / Blackberry blossom / Cuckoo's nest / Big river / Bread and water / Maybe I'm a fool / June / Back to the mountains / Moving cloud / Cliff / Treen beach / Pull me up / Old Joe Clarke / Riddle me wry / Stand together
CD _____ COOKCD 079
Cooking Vinyl / Feb '95 / Vital.

BIG BEAT, THE
White cockade / Bonaparte's retreat / Flop eared mule / Byker Hill / Big old road / Let's have a good time / Liberty / Blackberry blossom / Cuckoo's nest / It's not that bad anymore / Inventor / As a Thoiseach / Tropical hot dog night / Growing old man and woman
CD _____ COOKCD 024
Cooking Vinyl / Jul '90 / Vital.

DON'T MIND WALKING
Flowers of Edinburgh / Mr. McLeod's reel / Staten Island / My love is but a lassie yet / Petronella, Mississippi sawyer / Something'll have to change / Old Joe Clarke / Back to the mountains / Bread and water / This fire / Stand together
CD _____ COOKCD 045
Cooking Vinyl / Oct '91 / Vital.

Baren, Gasslin

OCCULT SONGS
CD _____ 1C 567 1999 48
Harmonia Mundi / '88 / Harmonia Mundi / Cadillac.

Barenaked Ladies

BORN ON A PIRATE SHIP
CD _____ 9362461282
Warner Bros. / Nov '95 / Warner Music.

GORDON
Hello city / Enid / Grade 9 / Brian Wilson / Be my Yoko Ono / Wrap your arms around me / What a good boy / King of bedside manor / Box set / I love you / New kid (on the block) / Blame it on me / Flag / If I had one hundred thousand dollars / Crazy
CD _____ 7599269562
East West / Aug '92 / Warner Music.

MAYBE YOU SHOULD DRIVE
CD _____ 936245709-2
Warner Bros. / Aug '94 / Warner Music.

Barenburg, Russ

HALLOWEEN REHEARSAL
CD _____ CD 11534
Rounder / '88 / CM / Direct / ADA / Cadillac.

MOVING PICTURES
CD _____ CD 0249
Rounder / Aug '88 / CM / Direct / ADA / Cadillac.

Bargad, Rob

BETTER TIMES (Bargad, Rob Sextet)
CD _____ CRISS 1086CD
Criss Cross / May '94 / Cadillac / Harmonia Mundi.

Bariu, Laver

SONGS FROM THE CITY
CD _____ CDORBD 091
Globestyle / Jan '96 / Pinnacle.

Bark Psychosis

HEX
Loom / Street scene / Absent friend / Big shot / Fingerspit / Eyes and smiles / Pendulum man
CD _____ CIRCD 29
Circa / Apr '94 / EMI.

Barker, Guy

INTO THE BLUE
Into the blue / J.J. swing / Oh Mr. Rex / Low down lullaby / Did it 'n' did it / Sphinx / Enigma / Ill wind / This is the life / Weatherbird rag
CD _____ 5276562
Verve / Jun '95 / PolyGram.

ISN'T IT
Sheldon the cat / Isn't it / In a mist / I get along without you very well / All or nothing / Amandanita / Good speed / Day and night / Lament for the black tower
CD _____ SPJCD 545
Spotlite / Jul '93 / Cadillac / Jazz Horizons / Swift.

Barker, Les

CARDI AND A BLOKE, A
CD _____ DOG 011
Mrs. Ackroyd / Dec '95 / Roots / Direct / ADA.

EARWIGO
CD _____ DOG 004CD
Mrs. Ackroyd / Apr '95 / Roots / Direct / ADA.

GNUS & ROSES (Mrs. Ackroyd Band)
CD _____ DOG 10CD
Mrs. Ackroyd / Jun '94 / Roots / Direct / ADA.

INFINITE NUMBER OF OCCASIONAL TABLES, AN
CD _____ DOG 008CD
Mrs. Ackroyd / Sep '94 / Roots / Direct / ADA.

ORANGES AND LEMMINGS (Mrs. Ackroyd Band)
CD _____ DOG 007CD
Mrs. Ackroyd / Sep '94 / Roots / Direct / ADA.

Barker, Sally

BEATING THE DRUM
CD _____ HY 200124CD
Hypertension / Mar '95 / Total/BMG / Direct / ADA.

IN THE SPOTLIGHT
CD _____ PUP 1 CD
Old Dog / Aug '89 / CM / Roots.

SALLY BARKER
CD _____ HY 200103CD
Hypertension / Feb '95 / Total/BMG / Direct / ADA.

TANGO/MONEY'S TALKING
CD _____ HYCD 200149
Hypertension / Mar '95 / Total/BMG / Direct / ADA.

THIS RHYTHM IS MINE
CD _____ HY 200106CD
Hypertension / Sep '93 / Total/BMG / Direct / ADA.

Barkin' Bill

GOTCHA
CD _____ DE 672
Delmark / Feb '95 / Hot Shot / ADA / CM / Direct / Cadillac.

Barking Tribe

SERPENT GO HOME
Pretty in print / Two important Pauls / White man's mind / Hide a prize / Breakaway / God knows what to do / Dammit to hell / Four fuses / Complain / With cretins as friends / Ain't as many girls as there used to be / Running down on my luck / City streets
CD _____ RCD 10200
Rykodisc / Sep '91 / Vital / ADA.

Barkmarket

EASY LISTENING CD, THE
CD _____ OUT 1012
Brake Out / Sep '92 / Vital.

Barley Bree

ANTHEM FOR THE CHILDREN
CD _____ SH 52020 CD
Shanachie / '90 / Koch / ADA / Greensleeves.

BEST OF BARLEY BREE, THE
CD _____ SHCD 52039
Shanachie / Mar '95 / Koch / ADA / Greensleeves.

Barleycorn

GREEN & GOLD
CD _____ DOCDK 108
Dolphin / May '94 / CM / Koch / Grapevine.

Barlow, Charles

DANSAN YEARS VOL. 10 (Barlow, Charles & Irven Tidswell)
CD _____ DACD 10
Dansan / Mar '95 / Savoy / President / Target/BMG.

DANSAN YEARS VOL. 9 (Barlow, Charles & Irven Tidswell)
CD _____ DACD 9
Dansan / Mar '95 / Savoy / President / Target/BMG.

Barlow, Lou

COLLECTION OF PREVIOUSLY RELEASED SONGS, A (Barlow, Lou & His Sentridoh)
CD _____ EFA 049402
City Slang / May '94 / Disc.

Barmy Army

ENGLISH DISEASE
CD _____ ONUCD 8
On-U Sound / Jun '94 / SRD / Jetstar.

Barnbrack

22 IRISH FOLK PUB SONGS
CD _____ CDHRL 199
Outlet / Feb '95 / ADA / Duncans / CM / Ross / Direct / Koch.

IRISH PUB FOLK SINGALONG
CD _____ CDPUB 024
Outlet / Oct '95 / ADA / Duncans / CM / Ross / Direct / Koch.

Barnes, Alan

LIKE MINDS (Barnes, Alan & David Newton)
Round Midnight / Blues in thirds / Batida differente / Poor butterfly / I'm just a lucky so and so / Lament for Javanette / Lull at dawn / Waltz for Sonny Criss / Walkin' shoes / Peacocks / Nobody else but me / Cotton tail
CD _____ FJCD 105
Fret / Nov '94 / New Note / Cadillac.

THIRSTY WORK
Ecaroh / Stars fell on Alabama / Groovy samba / Sweet and lovely / Stay as sweet as you are / Double take and fade away / Go home / Solitude / Autumn in New York / Thirsty work
CD _____ FJCD 106
Fret / Mar '95 / New Note / Cadillac.

Barnes, Emile

EMILE BARNES & LOUISIANA JOYMAKERS
CD _____ AMCD 13
American Music / Aug '95 / Jazz Music.

Barnes, George

2 GUITARS & A HORN (Barnes, George & Carl Kress)
CD _____ JCD 636
Jass / Jan '93 / CM / Jazz Music / ADA / Cadillac / Direct.

PLAYS SO GOOD
Night and day / I'm coming Virginia / Days of wine and roses / Don't get around much anymore / On a clear day / I've found a new baby / Honeysuckle rose / St. Louis blues / At sundown
CD _____ CCD 4067
Concord Jazz / Apr '94 / New Note.

Barnes, J.J.

KING OF NORTHERN SOUL
Whatever happend to our melody / On top of the world / Talk of the grapevine / Our love is in the pocket / Try it one more time / In and out of my life / Say it / Build a foundation / Sweet as a honey bee / Eternity / Happy road / That's just never enough / Please let me in / I've seen the light / Real humdinger / You can bet your love / Open the door to your heart / Sweet sherry
CD _____ 30359 90112
Motor City / Feb '96 / Carlton Home Entertainment.

Barnes, Jimmy

BARNESTORMING
CD _____ D 245212
Mushroom / May '94 / BMG / 3MV.

FLESH & WOOD
CD _____ TVD 93390
Mushroom / Dec '94 / BMG / 3MV.

HEAT
CD _____ TVD 93372
Mushroom / Jun '93 / BMG / 3MV.

Barker, Sally (INDEPENDENCY)

INDEPENDENCY
I know / Nothing feels / All different things / By-blow / Manman / Blood rush / Tooled up / Scum
CD _____ STONE 010CD
3rd Stone / Jul '94 / Vital / Plastic Head.

My Last Farewell

MY LAST FAREWELL
CD _____ DOCD 9010
Dolphin / Dec '88 / CM / Koch / Grapevine.

WALTZING FOR DREAMERS
CD _____ DOCDK 104
Dolphin / May '94 / CM / Koch / Grapevine.

Psyclone

PSYCLONE
CD _____ TVD 93433
Mushroom / Jun '95 / BMG / 3MV.

SOUL DEEP
CD _____ TVD 93344
Mushroom / Aug '94 / BMG / 3MV.

TWO FIRES
Lay down your guns / Let's make it last all night / Little darlin' / Love is enough / Hardline / One of a kind / Sister mercy / When your love is gone / Between two fires / Fade to black / Hold on
CD _____ TVD 93318
Mushroom / May '94 / BMG / 3MV.

Barnes, Johnny

SAMBA ROSSI
Samba rossi / Blue horizon / Boko's bounce / Hawk / Moonlight becomes you / Fascinating rhythm / Falling in love with you
CD _____ CLGCD 019
Calligraph / Feb '89 / Cadillac / Wellard / Jazz Music.

Barnes, Paul

PAUL BARNES & HIS POLO PLAYERS
CD _____ AMCD 55
American Music / Aug '95 / Jazz Music.

Barnes, Ricky

WELCOME TO HILLTOP USA (Barnes, Ricky & The Hootowls)
CD _____ OK 33025CD
Normal/Okra / Feb '95 / Direct / ADA.

Barnes, Roosevelt

HEARTBROKEN MAN, THE (Barnes, Roosevelt & The Playboys)
CD _____ R 2623
Rooster / Jul '95 / Direct.

Barnet, Charlie

CHARLIE BARNET & RHYTHM MAKERS 1938
CD _____ TAXCD 3715-2
Tax / Mar '94 / Jazz Music / Wellard / Cadillac.

CHEROKEE
Knockin' at the famous door / Cherokee / Count's idea / Right idea / Leapin' at the Lincoln / Afternoon of a moax (shake, rattle and roll) / Flying home / Rockin' in rhythm / Redskin rhumba / Lumby / Charleston Alley
CD _____ ND 90632
Bluebird / Apr '92 / BMG.

CHEROKEE
Cherokee/Redskin rhumba / Serenade to May / Side winds swing / Pompton turnpike / East side, west side / Charleston Alley / Skyliner / Blue juice / Wild mab of the fish pond / Southern fried / Smiles
CD _____ ECD 220652
Evidence / Nov '93 / Harmonia Mundi / ADA / Cadillac.

MORE (Barnet, Charlie & His Orchestra)
Evergreens / Stardust / Take the 'A' train / Goodbye / Early autumn / Flying home / I can't get started (with you) / Begin the beguine / Darn that dream / Midnight sun / One o'clock jump / Harlem nocturne
CD _____ ECD 22112
Evidence / Jan '95 / Harmonia Mundi / ADA / Cadillac.

Baron, Jean

BRITTANY
CD _____ ARN 64302
Arion / Jul '95 / Discovery / ADA.

DANSAL E BREIZ (Baron, Jean & Christian Anneix)
CD _____ KMCD 41
Keltia Musique / Aug '93 / ADA / Direct / Discovery.

DANSE DE BRETAGNE (Baron, Jean & Christian Anneix)
CD _____ KMCD 07
Keltia Musique / Jul '90 / ADA / Direct / Discovery.

Baron, Joey

RAISED PLEASURE DOT
CD _____ 804492
New World / Apr '94 / Harmonia Mundi / ADA / Cadillac.

Barone, Richard

BETWEEN HEAVEN AND CELLO
Certain harbours / Guinevere / Miss Jean / Before you were born / Forbidden / Beautiful human / Tangled in your web / Numbers with wings / To the pure / Barbarella / Ballrooms of mars / Standing in the line / Under someone's spell
CD _____ LICD 901289
Line / Sep '94 / CM / Grapevine / ADA / Conifer / Direct.

COOL BLUE HALO
Bullrushes / I belong to me / Visit / Tangled in your web / Silent symphony / Flew a falcon / Cry baby cry / Sweet blue cage / Man

who sold the world / Love is a wind that screams / Number with wings
CD _____ ROSE 171CD
New Rose / Sep '89 / Direct / ADA.

Baroudi, Hamid
CITY NO MAD
CD _____ EFA 042232
Vielklang / Aug '94 / SRD.

Barracudas
COMPLETE BARRACUDAS
Barracuda wavers / Surfers are back / Rendezvous / I can't pretend / We're living in violent times / Don't let go / This ain't my time / I saw my death in a dream last night / Somewhere outside / On the strip / Chevy baby / Summer fun / His last summer / (I wish it could be) 1965 Again / Somebody / KGB (Made a man out of me) / Campus tramp / California lament / Codeine / My little red book / Neighbourhood girls / Tokyo rose
CD _____ DOJOCD 99
Dojo / May '93 / BMG.

DROP OUT WITH THE BARRACUDAS
I can't pretend / We're living in violent times / Don't let go / Codine / This ain't my time / I saw my death in a dream last night / Somewhere outside / Summer fun / His last summer / Somebody / Campus tramp / On the strip / California lament / (I wish it could be) 1965 again
CD _____ VOXXCD 2009
Voxx / Jul '94 / Else / Disc.

ENDEAVOUR TO PERSEVERE
Dealing with today / Leaving home again / Song for Lorraine / World turned upside down / See her eyes again / Black snake / Way we've changed / She knows / Man with money / Pieces broken / Losin' streak / Corine / Barracuda / Stolen heart / Laughing at you
CD _____ MAUCD 642
Mau Mau / May '95 / Pinnacle.

MEANTIME
Grammar of misery / Bad news / I ain't no miracle worker / Be my friend again / Shades of today / Dead skin / Middle class blues / You've come a long way / Ballad of a liar / When I'm gone / Eleventh hour / Hear me calling
CD _____ MAUCD 641
Mau Mau / May '95 / Pinnacle.

SURF AND DESTROY
CD _____ 899027
New Rose / May '94 / Direct / ADA.

TWO SIDES OF A COIN
I want my woody back / Subway surfin' / Inside mind / Hour of degradation / Next time round / Take what he wants / Dead skin / Two sides of coin / Kingdom of pain / Twentieth Century myth / Very last day / Wastin time / Daggers of justice / There's a world out there / Seven and seven is / Codeine / Song for Lorraine / Fortunate son
CD _____ CDMGRAM 62
Anagram / May '95 / Pinnacle.

Barre, Martin
TRICK OF MEMORY, A
Bug / Way before your time / Bug bee / Empty cafe / Suspicion / I be thank you / Blues for all reasons / Trick of memory / Steal / Another view / Cold heart / Bug c / Morris minus / In the shade of the shadow
CD _____ TT 5009
XYZ / Apr '94 / XYZ.

Barrelhouse
STRAIGHT FROM THE SHOULDER
CD _____ MRM 005CD
Munich / Nov '93 / CM / ADA / Greensleeves / Direct.

Barrelhouse Jazz Band
DRIVING HOT JAZZ FROM THE 20'S
CD _____ BCD 49
GHB / Apr '94 / Jazz Music.

Barreto, Don
DON BARRETO ET SON ORCHESTRE CUBAIN, 1932-34 (Barreto, Don et Orchestre)
CD _____ HQCD 06
Harlequin / Oct '91 / Swift / Jazz Music / Wellard / Hot Shot / Cadillac.

Barrett, Dan
JUBILESTA
CD _____ ARCD 19107
Arbors Jazz / Nov '94 / Cadillac.

Barrett, Emma
LAST RECORDINGS 1974 & 1978 (Barrett, Sweet Emma)
CD _____ MG 9001
Mardi Gras / Feb '95 / Jazz Music.

Sweet Emma
CD _____ OJCCD 1832
Original Jazz Classics / Nov '95 / Wellard / Jazz Music / Cadillac / Complete/Pinnacle.

Barrett, Larry
BEYOND THE MISSISSIPPI
CD _____ GRCD 342
Glitterhouse / Oct '94 / Direct / ADA.

FLOWERS
CD _____ GRCD 298
Glitterhouse / Jan '94 / Direct / ADA.

Barrett, Syd
BARRETT
Baby lemonade / Love song / Dominoes / It is obvious / Rats / Maisie / Gigolo aunt / Waving my arms in the air / Wined and dined / Wolfpack / Effervescing elephant / I never lied to you
CD _____ CDGO 2054
Harvest / May '94 / EMI.

BEYOND THE WILDWOOD (A Tribute To Syd Barrett) (Various Artists)
No good trying / Octopus / Arnold Layne / Matilda mother / She took a long cold look / Long gone / If the sun don't shine / Baby lemonade / Wolfpack / Golden hair / No man's land / Apples and oranges / Two of a kind / Scream thy last scream / See Emily play (CD only) / Rats (CD only) / Gigolo aunt (CD only)
CD _____ ILLCD 100
Imaginary / May '90 / Vital.

CRAZY DIAMOND (THE COMPLETE SYD BARRETT)
Terrapin / No good trying / Love you / No man's land / Dark globe / Here I go / Octopus / Golden hair / Long gone / She took a long cold look / Feel / If it's in you / Late night / Octopus (Take 1 and 2) / It's no use / Waving / Love you (Take 1) / Love you (Take 2) / She took a long cold look (Take 4) / Golden hair (Take 5) / Baby lemonade / Love songs / Dominoes / It is obvious / Rats / Maisie / Gigolo aunt / Waving my arms in the air / I never lied to you (2) / Wined and dined / Wolfpack / Effervescing elephant / Terrapin (takes) / I never lied to you / Love song (Take 1) / Dominoes (take 1) / Dominoes (Take 2) / It is obvious (alt. takes) / Opel / Clowns and jugglers (Octopus) / Rats (2) / Golden hair (vocal) / Dolly rocker / Word song / Wined and dined (2) / Swan Lee (Silas Lang) / Birdie hop / Let's split / Lanky (Part 1) / Wouldn't you miss me (Dark globe) / Milky way / Golden hair (Inst.) / Gigolo aunt (Take 9) / Clowns and jugglers (Octopus) / Late night (Take 2) / Effervescing elephant (Take 2)
CD Set _____ SYDBOX 1
Harvest / Apr '93 / EMI.

MADCAP LAUGHS, THE
Terrapin / No good trying / Love you / No man's land / Here I go / Dark globe / Octopus / Golden hair / Long gone / She took a long cold look / Feel / If it's in you / Late night
CD _____ CDGO 2053
Harvest / May '94 / EMI.

OCTOPUS
Octopus / Swan Lee (Silas Lang) / Baby lemonade / Late night / Wined and dined / Golden hair / Gigolo aunt / Wolfpack / It is obvious / Lanky (part 1) / No good trying / Clowns and jugglers (Octopus) / Waving my arms in the air / Opel
CD _____ OLED OITIE
Cleopatra / Oct '94 / Disc.

OPEL
Opel / Clowns and jugglers (Octopus) / Rats / Golden hair / Dolly rocker / Word song / Wined and dined / Swan Lee (Silas Lang) / Birdie hop / Let's split / Lanky (part 1) / Wouldn't you miss me / Milky way / Golden hair (Inst.)
CD _____ CDGO 2055
Harvest / May '94 / EMI.

Barrett, Wild Willy
OPEN TOED AND FLAPPING
CD _____ PRKCD 29
Park / Apr '95 / Pinnacle.

Barretto, Ray
ANCESTRAL MESSAGES
New world spirit / Song for Chano / Freedom jazz dance / On a sunday afternoon / Beautiful love / Kikue / Aquablue / Gabriela / My Latin New York / Ancestral messages
CD _____ CCD 4549
Concord Picante / May '93 / New Note.

BEYOND THE BARRIO
Nadie se salva la rumba / Tu proprio dolor / Lucretia the cat / Aguadilla / Vive y vacila / Canto abacua / Cancion para el nino / Lo tuyo lo mio / Aguardiente d cana / Ya no puede ser / Tin tin deo / Prestame tu mujer / Eras
CD _____ CDHOT 518
Charly / Apr '95 / Charly / THE / Cadillac.

Carnaval
Manha de carnaval / Sugar's delight / Exodus / Descarga la moderna / Summertime / El negro y Ray / Mira que Linda / Coronando suave / Pachango oriental / Barretto en la tumbadora / Cumbamba / El Paso / Linda Mulata / Oye heck / Los Cueros / Pachanga suavecito / Ponte dura / Pachango para bailar
CD _____ FCD 24713
Fantasy / Oct '93 / Pinnacle / Jazz Music / Wellard / Cadillac.

INDESTRUCTIBLE
El hijo de obatalo / El Biablo / Yo tengo un amor / La familia / La orquestra / Llanto de coordrillo / Ay no / Indestructible / Adelante siempre voy / Algo nuevo
CD _____ CDHOT 502
Charly / Oct '93 / Charly / THE / Cadillac.

LIVE IN NEW YORK
Intro / Vaya / Ahora si que vamo a gozar / Bab ban quere / Guarare / Night Flowers (flores de noche) / Slo flo / Cocinando / Que viva la misica
CD _____ MES 159502
Messidor / Feb '93 / Koch / ADA.

PACHANGA
Exodus / Summertime / El paso / Manha de carnaval / Ponte dura / Pachanga para bailar / Sugar's delight / Descarga la moderna / Pachanga suavecito / El negro y ray / Cumbamba / Cocinando sauve / Linda mulata / Los cueros
CD _____ CD 62068
Saludos Amigos / Apr '95 / Target/BMG.

RAY BARRETTO 1939-43
CD _____ HQCD 36
Harlequin / Feb '94 / Swift / Jazz Music / Wellard / Hot Shot / Cadillac.

TABOO (Barretto, Ray & New World Spirit)
Taboo / Bomba-Riquen / Work song / Cancion del yunque (Song for the rain forest) / Guaji-Rita / 99 MacDougal St / Montuno blue / Brother Tom / Lazy afternoon / Effendi
CD _____ CCD 4601
Concord Picante / Jul '94 / New Note.

Barrister
FUJI GARBAGE
Refined Fuji garbage / Fuji worldwide
CD _____ CDORBD 067
Globestyle / Feb '91 / Pinnacle.

Barron, Bill
NEXT PLATEAU, THE
CD _____ MCD 5368
Muse / Sep '92 / New Note / CM.

TENOR STYLINGS, THE
Blast off / Ode to an Earth girl / Fox hunt / Oriental impressions / Back lash / Nebulae
CD _____ SV 0212
Savoy Jazz / '89 / Conifer / ADA.

Barron Knights
TWO SIDES OF YOU
CD _____ C5KCD 572
See For Miles/C5 / Aug '91 / Pinnacle.

Barron, Kenny
INVITATION
CD _____ CRISS 1044CD
Criss Cross / Apr '91 / Cadillac / Harmonia Mundi.

LIVE AT MAYBECK RECITAL HALL, VOL. 10
I'm getting sentimental over you / Witchcraft / Bud-like / Spring is here / Well you needn't / Skylark / And then again / Sunshower
CD _____ CCD 4466
Concord Jazz / Jun '91 / New Note.

MOMENT, THE
CD _____ RSRCD 112
Reservoir Music / Nov '94 / Cadillac.

ONLY ONE, THE
CD _____ RSRCD 115
Reservoir Music / Nov '94 / Cadillac.

RED BARRON DUO, THE (Barron, Kenny & Red Mitchell Trio)
CD _____ STCD 4137
Storyville / Feb '90 / Jazz Music / Wellard / CM / Cadillac.

RHYTHM-A-NING
CD _____ CCD 79044
Candid / Oct '91 / Cadillac / Jazz Music / Wellard / Koch.

SUNSET TO DAWN
Sunset / Flower / Swamp demon / Al-Kifha / Delores St. S.F. / Dawn
CD _____ MCD 6014
Muse / Sep '92 / New Note / CM.

WANTON SPIRIT
CD _____ 5223642
Verve / Dec '94 / PolyGram.

Barron, Ronnie
MY NEW ORLEANS SOUL
CD _____ AIM 1038
Aim / Apr '95 / Direct / ADA / Jazz Music.

Barros, Alberto
EL TITAN DE LA SALSA
Maldita duda / Vampiro / Confession / Perdi el control / Tu indiferencia / Fingiendo / Imagination / Sola quedaras / Reencarnado / Dosis pasional
CD _____ 00050004
RMM / May '95 / New Note.

Barrow, Arthur
EYEBROW RAZOR
CD _____ EFA 034192
Muffin / Aug '95 / SRD.

Barrow Side
WISH & THE WAY, THE
CD _____ RTMCD 66
Round Tower / Dec '94 / Pinnacle / ADA / Direct / BMG / CM.

Barry, John
BEAT GIRL/STRINGBEAT (Barry, John Seven & Orchestra)
City 2000 AD / Stripper / Cave / Made you / Car chase / Chicken / Blues for beatniks / It's legal / Immediate pleasure / Blondie's strip / End shot / Slaughter in Soho / It doesn't matter anymore / Sweet talk / Moody river / There's life in the old boy yet / Handful of songs / Like waltz / Rodeo / Donna's theme / Starfire / Baubles, bangles and beads / Zapata / Rum dee dum dee dah / Spanish harlem / Man from Madrid / Challenge
CD _____ PLAY 001
Play It Again / Aug '90 / Total/BMG.

EMBER YEARS VOLUME 1, THE
Elizabeth in London / Elizabeth walk / English garden / London theme / London waltz / Lovers / Fire of London / Elizabeth theme / Four in the morning / River walk / Lover's clasp / Norman's return / River ride / Lover's tension / First reconciliation / Norman leaves / Moment od decision / Judi come back
CD _____ PLAY 002
Play It Again / Mar '92 / Total/BMG.

EMBER YEARS VOLUME 2, THE
CD _____ PLAY 003
Play It Again / Mar '92 / Total/BMG.

EMI YEARS VOL.1, THE
Let's have a wonderful time / Rockabilly boogie / Zip zip / Three little fishes / Every which way / You've gotta way / Big guitar / Rodeo / Farrago / bee's knees / When the saints go marching in / Pancho / Long John / Snap 'n' whistle / Little John / For Pete's sake / Rebel rouser / Mab mab / 12th Street rag / Christella / Rockin' already / Walk don't run / Saturday's child / Wonderful / Good rockin' tonight / Hit and miss / I'm movin' on / Main title / Beat girl / Beat for beatniks / Big fella / Blueberry Hill / Never let go / Black stockings / Get lost Jack Frost / Bee's knees #2 / Pancho (2)
CD _____ CDEMS 1497
EMI / Jun '93 / EMI.

EMI YEARS VOL.2, THE
Magnificent seven / Skid row / Twist it / Watch your step / Dark rider / Matter of who / Iron horse / It doesn't matter anymore / Sweet talk / Moon river / There's life in the old boy yet / Handful of songs / Like waltz / Rodeo / Donna's theme / Starfire / Baubles, bangles and beads / Zapata / Rum-de-dum-de-da / Spanish Harlem / Man from Madrid / Challenge / Menace / Satin smooth / Agressor / Rocco's theme / Spinnerree
CD _____ CDEMS 1501
EMI / Jul '93 / EMI.

EMI YEARS VOL.3 ,THE (1962-1964)
James Bond theme / Blacksmith blues / Cutty Sark (Dateline TV theme) / Lost patrol / Roman Spring of Mrs Stone (theme from) / Tears / Blueberry Hill / Cherry pink and apple blossom white / Smokey Joe / Unchained melody / Party's over / Lolly theme / March of the Mandarins / Human jungle (alt. version) / Big safari / Mouse on the moon / Twangin' cheek / I'll be with you in apple blossom time / Volare / Human jungle. / Onward Christian spacemen / Seven faces / Twenty four hours ago / Jolly Bad Fellow (theme from) / Ouble cala / Seance on a Wet Afternoon / That fatal kiss
CD _____ CDEMS 1555
EMI / Sep '95 / EMI.

MUSIC OF JOHN BARRY
Born free / You only live twice / Goldfinger / Whisperers / From Russia with love / Wednesday's child / Quiller memorandum / Space march (capsule in space) / Girl with the sun in her hair / Thunderball / Wrong box / James Bond / 007 / Mr. kiss kiss bang bang / Chase / King rat / Seance on a wet afternoon / Ipcress file / Midnight cowboy / Romance for guitar and orchestra / On Her

Majesty's secret service / Appointment, Theme from / Lion in Winter
CD _____ 983379-2
Pickwick/Sony Collector's Choice / Apr '94 / Carlton Home Entertainment / Pinnacle / Sony.

Barry, Margaret

HER MANTLE SO GREEN (Barry, Margaret & Michael Gorman)
CD _____ TSCD 474
Topic / Aug '94 / Direct / ADA.

Barry, Stephen

BLUES UNDER A FULL MOON (Barry, Stephen Band)
CD _____ 1009-2
Blues Beacon / Apr '91 / New Note.

Barth, Bruce

IN FOCUS (Barth, Bruce Quintet)
I hear music / Escapade by night / Nefer bond / I got it bad / In search of... / Pinocchio / Louise / Persistence / Wildflower / Secret name
CD _____ ENJACD 80102
Enja / Oct '93 / New Note / Vital/SAM.

MORNING CALL
CD _____ ENJACD 80642
Enja / Sep '95 / New Note / Vital/SAM.

Barthelemy, Claude

SOLIDE (Barthelemy, Claude & Pierre Ledic/Charles Biddle)
CD _____ EVCD 316
Evidence / Feb '94 / Harmonia Mundi / ADA / Cadillac.

Bartholomew, Dave

BASIN STREET BREAKDOWN
Basin street breakdown / Golden rule / Bad habit / In the alley / Twins / Lawdy Lawdy Lord (part 1) / Lawdy Lawdy Lord (part 2) / Country boy / Pyramid / Messy bessy / I'll never be the same / Mr. Fool / Stormy weather / Nickel wine / Sweet home blues / Mother knows best / High flying woman / My ding a ling
CD _____ CDCHARLY 273
Charly / Jan '93 / Charly / THE / Cadillac.

Barton, Lou Ann

DREAMS COME TRUE (Barton, Lou Ann/Marcia Ball/Angela Strehli)
Fool in love / Good rockin' daddy / It hurts to be in love / Love sweet love / Gonna make it / You can if you think you can / I idolize you / Dreams come true / Bad thing / Turn the lock on love / Something's got a hold on me / Snake dance
CD _____ ANTCD 0014
Antones / Mar '91 / Hot Shot / Direct / ADA.

OLD ENOUGH
CD _____ ANTCD 0021
Antones / Oct '95 / Hot Shot / Direct / ADA.

Bartz, Gary

ALTO MEMORIES (Bartz, Gary & Sonny Fortune)
CD _____ 5232682
Verve / Dec '94 / PolyGram.

THERE GOES THE NEIGHBORHOOD
CD _____ CCD 79506
Candid / Oct '93 / Cadillac / Jazz Music / Wellard / Koch.

WEST 52ND STREET (Live at Birdland 1990)
West 52nd Street / Speak low / It's easy to remember / Counsins / Night has a thousand eyes
CD _____ CCD 79049
Candid / Jan '90 / Cadillac / Jazz Music / Wellard / Koch.

Barungwa

BARUNGWA (THE MESSENGERS)
Welcome / Siyahamba / Tutu / Ba naba Afrika / My Dali / Biko's dream / Abongcono / Vuyiso / Capitalismo / Na naba Afrika (Return)
CD _____ BW 070
B&W / Oct '95 / New Note.

Bascomb, Paul

BAD BASCOMB
CD _____ DD 431
Delmark / Aug '94 / Hot Shot / ADA / CM / Direct / Cadillac.

Base, Rob

BREAK OF DAWN (Base, Rob & D.J. E-Z Rock)
CD _____ 60802CLU
Edel / Jul '95 / Pinnacle.

INCREDIBLE BASE, THE
CD _____ FILERCD 285
Profile / Jan '90 / Pinnacle.

Basement 5

1965-1980/BASEMENT 5 IN DUB
CD _____ IMCD 145
Island / Jul '92 / PolyGram.

Bashful Brother Oswald

BROTHER OSWALD
CD _____ ROUCD 0013
Rounder / Jun '95 / CM / Direct / ADA / Cadillac.

Basia

LONDON, WARSAW, NEW YORK
Cruising for a bruising / Best friends / Brave new hope / Baby you're mine / Ordinary people / Reward / Until you come back to me / Copernicus / Not an angel / Take him back Rachel
CD _____ 4632822
Epic / Feb '90 / Sony.

SWEETEST ILLUSION, THE
Drunk on love / Third time lucky / Yearning / She deserves it/Rachel's wedding / Olive tree / Sweetest illusion / Perfect mother / More fire than flame / Simple pleasures / My cruel ways / Prayer of a happy housewife
CD _____ 476514 2
Epic / Oct '94 / Sony.

TIME AND TIDE
Promises / Run for cover / Time and tide / Freeze thaw / From now on / New day for you / Prime time TV / Astrud / How dare you / Miles away / Forgive and forget (CD/MC only)
CD _____ CK 53791
Epic / Feb '95 / Sony.

Basie, Count

1937-43 (Basie, Count Orchestra)
CD _____ CD 53072
Giants Of Jazz / Mar '92 / Target/BMG / Cadillac.

1944 (Basie, Count Orchestra)
CD _____ HCD 224
Hindsight / Jul '94 / Target/BMG / Jazz Music.

AIN'T MISBEHAVIN' (Basie, Count Orchestra)
CD _____ 15778
Laserlight / Jan '93 / Target/BMG.

AMERICANS IN SWEDEN VOL 1 (Basie, Count Orchestra)
CD _____ TAXCD 3701
Tax / Apr '88 / Jazz Music / Wellard / Cadillac.

AMERICANS IN SWEDEN VOL 2 (Basie, Count Orchestra)
CD _____ TAXCD 3702
Tax / Apr '88 / Jazz Music / Wellard / Cadillac.

ANTHOLOGY
CD _____ EN 517
Encyclopaedia / Sep '95 / Discovery.

APRIL IN PARIS (Basie, Count & Tony Bennett)
CD _____ MATCD 319
Castle / Dec '94 / BMG.

APRIL IN PARIS
Jumpin' at the woodside / I guess I'll have to change my plan / 9.20 special / Jeepers creepers / Swingin' the blues / With plenty of money and you / Shorty George / Chicago / Broadway / I've grown accustomed to her face / Out the window / Poor little rich girl / Lester leaps in / Anything goes / Are you having any fun / Dickie's dream / Growing pains / Jive at five / Life is a song / April in Paris
CD _____ TRTCD 171
TrueTrax / Dec '94 / THE.

ATOMIC MR. BASIE, THE (Basie, Count Orchestra)
Kid from Red Bank / Duet / After supper / Flight of the Foo birds / Double O / Teddy the toad / Whirly bird / Midnite blue / Splanky / Fantail / Li'l darlin'
CD _____ CD 53043
Giants Of Jazz / Jan '89 / Target/BMG / Cadillac.
CD _____ CDP 8286352
Blue Note / Mar '95 / EMI.

AUTUMN IN PARIS (Basie, Count Orchestra)
Whirly bird / Little pony / Corner pocket / Lovely baby / Blee blop blues / Nails / Kid from Red Bank / Spring is here / Why not / Well, alright, OK, you win / Roll 'em / Ol' man river / Duet / Gee baby ain't I good to you / One o'clock jump
CD _____ DAWE 13
Magic / Nov '93 / Jazz Music / Swift / Wellard / Cadillac / Harmonia Mundi.

AVENUE C (1944) (Basie, Count & Lester Young)
CD _____ CDJJ 604
Jazz & Jazz / Jul '89 / Target/BMG.

BASIE - ONE MORE TIME (Music from the Pen of Quincy Jones)
For Lena and Lennie / Rat race / Quince / Meet B B / Big walk / Square at the round table / I needs to be bee'd with / Jessica's day / Midnite sun never sets / Muttnik
CD _____ CDROU 1035
Roulette / Aug '91 / EMI.

BASIE AND FRIENDS
Easy does it / Zoot / Love me or leave me / N.H.O.P. / She's funny that way / Turna-round / Madame Fitz / Royal garden blues
CD _____ CD 2310925
Pablo / Apr '94 / Jazz Music / Cadillac / Complete/Pinnacle.

BASIE AND ZOOT (Basie, Count & Zoot Sims)
I never knew / It's only a paper moon / Blues for Nat Cole / Captain Bligh / Honeysuckle rose / Hardav / Mean to me / Surrender dear
CD _____ OJCCD 8222
Original Jazz Classics / Jun '95 / Wellard / Jazz Music / Cadillac / Complete/Pinnacle.

BASIE BOOGIE (Basie, Count Orchestra)
One o'clock jump / Basie boogie / Taps Miller / Red bank boogie / mead boogie / King / Hob nail boogie / Wild Bill's boogie / Little pony / Hozit / Beaver Junction / Nails / Squeeze me / Boone's blues / Jumpin' at the woodside
CD _____ JHR 73502
Jazz Hour / May '93 / Target/BMG / Jazz Music / Cadillac.

BASIE IN EUROPE
Hittin' twelve / Freckle face / Things ain't what they used to be / Whirly bird / More I see you / Orange sherbet / Way out Basie / Basie jumpin' at the Woodside
CD _____ DC 8533
Denon / Apr '89 / Conifer.

BASIE IN LONDON
CD _____ 8338052
Verve / Jan '94 / PolyGram.

BASIE IN SWEDEN
Little pony / Plymouth rock / Backwater blues / Who me / Corner pocket / Four, five, six / Splanky / In a mellow tone / April in Paris / Blues backstage / Good time blues / Peace pipe
CD _____ CDROU 1028
Roulette / Mar '91 / EMI.

BASIE JAM
Doubling blues / Hanging out / Red bank blues / One nighter / Freeport blues
CD _____ CD 2310 718
Pablo / May '94 / Jazz Music / Cadillac / Complete/Pinnacle.

BASIE JAM AT MONTREUX 1975
Billie's bounce / Festival blues / Lester leaps in
CD _____ CD 2310 750
Pablo / May '94 / Jazz Music / Cadillac / Complete/Pinnacle.

BASIE JAM NO.2
Mama don't wear no drawers / Doggin' around / Kansas City line / Jump
CD _____ OJCCD 631
Original Jazz Classics / Feb '92 / Wellard / Jazz Music / Cadillac / Complete/Pinnacle.

BASIE RHYTHM (Basie, Count & Harry James)
Shoe shine boy / Evening / Boogie woogie / Oh lady be good / Jubilee / When we're alone / I can dream, can't I / Life goes to a party / Texas chatter / Song of the wanderer / Dreamer in me / One o'clock jump / My heart belongs to daddy / Sing for your supper / You can depend on me / Cherokee (part I) / Cherokee (part II) / Blame it on my last affair / Jive at five / Thursday / Evil blues / Oh lady be good (2)
CD _____ HEPCD 1032
Hep / Jan '92 / Cadillac / Jazz Music / New Note / Wellard.

BASIE SWINGS - JOE WILLIAMS SINGS (Basie, Count & Joe Williams)
CD _____ 519852-2
Verve / Dec '93 / PolyGram.

BASIE'S BAG (Basie, Count Orchestra)
Firm roots / Three in one / Hampton strut / Basie's bag / Here's that rainy day / Count Basie remembrance suite
CD _____ CD 83358
Telarc / Jan '94 / Conifer / ADA.

BASIE'S BEST
Swinging at the daisy chain / Honeysuckle rose / Roseland shuffle / One O'Clock jump / John's idea / Time out / Topsy / Swingin' the blues / Blue and sentimental / Texas shuffle / Jumpin' at the woodside / Panna-sie stomp / Cherokee (Parts 1 and 2) / You can depend on me / Jive at five / Oh lady be good
CD _____ CDCD 1177
Charly / Apr '94 / Charly / THE / Cadillac.

BEST OF BOOGIE
CD _____ DLCD 4069
Dixie Live / Mar '95 / Magnum Music Group.

BEST OF COUNT BASIE
Tree frog / Sweet pea / Ticker / Flirt / Blues for Alfy / Billie's bounce / Festival blues / Jumpin' at the Woodside / Blue and sentimental / Red bank boogie / Shorty George / Rock-a-bye Basie / Every tub / Swingin'

the blues / Sent for you yesterday / Boogie woogie / Broadway / Texas shuffle / Tickle toe / Doggin' around / Dickie's dream / Topsy / Lester leaps in / Out the window
CD _____ CD 2405408
Pablo / Apr '94 / Jazz Music / Cadillac / Complete/Pinnacle.

BEST OF COUNT BASIE (The Roulette Years) (Basie, Count Orchestra)
Kid from red bank / Late late show / Flight of the Foo birds / Jive at five / Blue and sentimental / Lullaby of Birdland / Cute / Segue in C / Topsy / Jumpin' at the woodside / Broadway / Tickle toe / Scoot / For Lena and Lennie / Whirly bird / Down and double / Easy money / Turnabout / Taps miller / Old man river
CD _____ CDROU 1046
Roulette / Oct '91 / EMI.

BEST OF COUNT BASIE
Kid from Red Bank / Secret love / Cute / I cried for you (with Sarah Vaughan) / Blue and sentimental / Jumpin' at the woodside / Meet B.B. / Teach me tonight (With Sarah Vaughan & Joe Williams) / Moten swing (Live) / One o'clock jump (Live) / Whirly bird / Hallelujah, I love her so (With Joe Williams) / Makin' whoopee / Lullaby of Birdland / If I were a bell (With Sarah Vaughan & Joe Williams) / Jackson County Jubilee / Sunset glow / Tickle toe (With Lambert, Hendricks & Ross) / Old man river / Li'l darlin'
CD _____ CDMFP 6133
Music For Pleasure / Sep '94 / EMI.

BEST OF COUNT BASIE
CD _____ DLCD 4024
Dixie Live / Mar '95 / Magnum Music Group.

BEST OF COUNT BASIE BIG BAND (Basie, Count Orchestra)
CD _____ CDPBM 002
Pablo / '89 / Jazz Music / Cadillac / Complete/Pinnacle.

BEST OF COUNT BASIE ORCHESTRA
April in Paris / Misunderstood blues / Booze brothers / Do nothin' 'til you hear from me / Exactly like you / Autumn leaves / Hey I see you over there / Corner pocket / Count Basie remembrance suite / We be jammin' / Lady Carolyn / State of the art swing / One o'clock jump / Shiny stockings
CD _____ DC 8590
Denon / Jun '95 / Conifer.

BEST OF EARLY BASIE, THE
Honeysuckle rose / Roseland shuffle / Boogie woogie (I may be wrong) / One o'clock jump / John's idea / Good morning blues / Topsy / Oh, lady be good / Jive at five / Panassie stomp / Shorty George / Jumpin' at the woodside / Texas shuffle / Jumpin' around / Blues and sentimental / Swingin' the blues / Every tub / Sent for you yesterday / Blues in the dark / Don't you miss your baby / Out to the window
CD _____ GRP 16552
American Decca / Feb '96 / BMG / New Note.

BEST OF THE BASIE BIG BAND
Blues for Alfy / Heat's on / C.B. express / Sweet pea / Way out Basie / Featherweight / Katy / Prime time / Mr. Softie
CD _____ PACD 24054222
Pablo / Apr '94 / Jazz Music / Cadillac / Complete/Pinnacle.

BIG BAND MONTREUX '77
CD _____ OJCCD 377
Original Jazz Classics / Feb '92 / Wellard / Jazz Music / Cadillac / Complete/Pinnacle.

BLEE BLOP BLUES (Basie, Count Orchestra)
CD _____ CDJJ 619
Jazz & Jazz / Jan '92 / Target/BMG.

BLUES ALLEY
All heart / Blues alley / Cherokee / Night in Tunisia / Goin' to chicago blues / Kid from red bank / Shiny stockings / Shadow of your smile / Splanky / Basie's thought / Blues in Hoss's flat / Magic flea / One o'clock jump
CD _____ CDC 9060
LRC / Apr '95 / New Note / Harmonia Mundi.

BRAND NEW WAGON (Basie, Count Orchestra)
Bill's mill / Brand new wagon / One o'clock boogie / Swingin' the blues / St. Louis boogie / Basie's basement / Backstage at Stuff's / My buddy / Shine on harvest moon / Sugar / House rent boogie / South / Don't you want a man like me / Seventh Avenue express / Sophisticated swing / Your red wagon / Money is honey / Just a minute / Robbin's nest / Hey pretty baby / Bye bye baby
CD _____ ND 82292
Bluebird / Oct '90 / BMG.

BROADCAST TRANSCRIPTIONS 1944-45
CD _____ CD 884
Music & Arts / Sep '95 / Harmonia Mundi / Cadillac.

CHRONOLOGICAL 1936-1938, THE (Basie, Count Orchestra)
Shoe shine boy / Evening / Boogie woogie / Oh lady be good / Honeysuckle rose /

Pennies from Heaven / Swingin' at the daisy chain / Roseland shuffle / Exactly like you / Boo-hoo / Glory of love / Smarty / One o'clock jump / Listen my children / John's idea / Good morning blues / Our love was meant to be / Time out / Topsy / I keep remembering / Out the window / Don't you miss your baby / Let me dream / Georgianna
CD _____ CLASSIC 503
Classics / Apr '90 / Discovery / Jazz Music.

CHRONOLOGICAL 1938-1939, THE (Basie, Count Orchestra)
Blues in the dark / Sent for you yesterday / Every tub / Now will you be good / Swingin' the blues / Mama don't want no peas, no rice, no coconut oil / Blue and sentimental / Doggin' around / Stop beatin' around the mulberry bush / London Bridge is falling down / Texas shuffle / Jumpin' at the woodside / How long, how long blues / Dirty dozen / Hey lawdy mama / Fives / Boogie woogie / Dark rapture / Shorty George / Blues I like to hear / Do you wanna jump children / Pansie stomp / My heart belongs to daddy / Sing for your supper / Old red
CD _____ CLASSIC 504
Classics / Apr '90 / Discovery / Jazz Music.

CLASS OF '54
CD _____ BLC 760924
Black Lion / Oct '94 / Jazz Music / Cadillac / Wellard / Koch.

CLASSY PAIR, A (see under)

CORNER POCKET (Basie, Count Orchestra)
CD _____ CD 2312 132
Complete / May '94 / Complete/Pinnacle.

COUNT AT THE CHATTERBOX, THE (Basie, Count Orchestra)
CD _____ 3801162
Jazz Archives / Feb '93 / Jazz Music / Discovery / Cadillac.

COUNT BASIE
CD _____ PWK 032
Carlton Home Entertainment / '88 / Carlton Home Entertainment.

COUNT BASIE (2CD Set)
CD Set _____ R2CD 4012
Deja Vu / Jan '96 / THE.

COUNT BASIE & ANITA O'DAY 1945-1948 (Basie, Count & Anita O'Day)
CD _____ 157922
Jazz Archives / Jun '93 / Jazz Music / Discovery / Cadillac.

COUNT BASIE & HIS GREAT VOCALISTS
I can't believe that you're in love with me / Don't worry 'bout me / If I can't be here with you (one hour tonight) / Goin' to Chicago blues / I want a little girl / My old flame / If I didn't care / Moon nocturne / Somebody stole my gal / All of me / Angels sing / Between the devil and the deep blue sea / Blue shadows and white gardenias / That old feeling / Jivin' with Joe Jackson / Blue skies
CD _____ CK 66374
Sony Jazz / Jul '95 / Sony.

COUNT BASIE & HIS ORCHESTRA 1942
CD _____ CLASSICS 684
Classics / Mar '93 / Discovery / Jazz Music.

COUNT BASIE - 1940-41 (Basie, Count Orchestra)
CD _____ CLASSICS 623
Classics / '92 / Discovery / Jazz Music.

COUNT BASIE 1936-41 - CLASSICS BOX VI
CD Set _____ OJCCD 700642
Original Jazz Classics / Dec '93 / Wellard / Jazz Music / Cadillac / Complete/Pinnacle.

COUNT BASIE AND THE KANSAS CITY SEVEN (Basie, Count & The Kansas City Seven)
I'll always be in love with you / Snooky / Blues for Charlie Christian / Jaws / I'm confessin' that I love you / I want a little girl / Blues in C / Brio
CD _____ MCAD 5656
Impulse Jazz / '88 / BMG / New Note.

COUNT BASIE COLLECTION, THE
CD Set _____ 55514
Laserlight / Sep '93 / Target/BMG.

COUNT BASIE GOLD (2CD Set)
CD Set _____ D2CD 4012
Deja Vu / Jun '95 / THE.

COUNT BASIE ORCHESTRA 1943-44
CD _____ CLASSICS 801
Classics / Mar '95 / Discovery / Jazz Music.

COUNT BASIE, ARTIE SHAW & TOMMY DORSEY (3CD Set) (Basie, Count/Artie Shaw/Tommy Dorsey)
CD Set _____ MAK 102
Avid / Dec '93 / Avid/BMG / Koch.

COUNT ON THE COAST, VOL. 1 (Basie, Count & Joe Williams)
CD _____ PHONTCD 7555
Phontastic / '88 / Wellard / Jazz Music / Cadillac.

COUNT ON THE COAST, VOL. 2
CD _____ PHONTCD 7575
Phontastic / Oct '92 / Wellard / Jazz Music / Cadillac.

CREAM OF COUNT BASIE, THE VOL. 1
Lady be good / Panassie stomp / Blame it on my last affair / My heart belongs to daddy / Thursday / Jive at five / Sing for your supper / Smarty (you know it all) / Our love was meant to be / Let me dream / One o'clock jump / Honeysuckle rose / Dark rapture / Roseland shuffle / Fives / Boo-hoo / Boogie woogie / Glory of love / Cherokee / Dirty dozens / Stop beatin' around the Mulberry bush
CD _____ PASTCD 9774
Flapper / Feb '92 / Pinnacle.

CREAM OF COUNT BASIE, THE VOL. 2 (Basie, Count Orchestra)
Clap hands, here comes Charlie / Riff interlude / I left my baby / Don't worry 'bout me / What goes up must come down / Pound cake / Lester leaps in / Dickie's dream / How long blues / Red wagon / Exactly like you / Pennies from heaven / Swinging at the Daisy Chain / Listen my children / Our love was meant to be / Now will you be good / Swingin' the blues / You can depend on me / Georgianna / Blues I like to hear / Oh Red / Good morning blues
CD _____ PASTCD 9793
Flapper / Jun '92 / Pinnacle.

DO YOU WANNA JUMP
Georgianna / Sent for you yesterday / Panassie stomp / Blues I like to hear / Stop beatin' around the mulberry bush / Swingin' the blues / Texas shuffle / Shorty George / Blue in the dark / Every tub / Nor will you be good / Mama don't want no peas, no rice, no coconut oil / Blue and sentimental / Doggin' around / London Bridge is falling down / Jumpin' at the woodside / Dark rapture / Do you wanna jump children
CD _____ HEPCD 1027
Hep / Oct '89 / Cadillac / Jazz Music / New Note / Wellard.

ESSENTIAL COUNT BASIE #1
CD _____ 4600612
Sony Jazz / Jan '95 / Sony.

ESSENTIAL COUNT BASIE #2
CD _____ 4608282
Sony Jazz / Jan '95 / Sony.

ESSENTIAL COUNT BASIE #3
CD _____ 4610982
Sony Jazz / Jan '95 / Sony.

ESSENTIAL COUNT BASIE, THE
Clap hands, here comes Charlie / Tickle toe / Broadway / Jump the blues away / It's sand man / Ain't it the truth / For the good of your country / High tide / Queer street / Rambo / Stay cool / Stay on it / Golden bullet / Song of the Islands / One o'clock jump / Tootsie
CD _____ 467143 2
Columbia / Jul '93 / Sony.

ESSENTIAL V-DISCS, THE
CD _____ JZ-CD303
Suisa / Feb '91 / Jazz Music / THE.

FANCY PANTS (Basie, Count Orchestra)
Put it right there / By my side / Blue chip / Fancy pants / Hi five / Time stream / Samantha / Strike up the band
CD _____ CD 2310920
Pablo / Apr '94 / Jazz Music / Cadillac / Complete/Pinnacle.

FARMERS MARKET BARBEQUE
Way out Basie / St. Louis blues / Beaver junction / Lester leaps in / Blues for the barbeque / I don't know yet / Ain't that something / Jumpin' at the Woodside
CD _____ J33J 20056
Pablo / Apr '86 / Jazz Music / Cadillac / Complete/Pinnacle.

FOR THE SECOND TIME (Basie, Count & Kansas City 3)
Sandman / If I could be with you one hour tonight / Draw / On the sunny side of the street / One I love (belongs to somebody else) / Blues for Eric / I surrender dear / Race horse
CD _____ OJCCD 600
Original Jazz Classics / Feb '92 / Wellard / Jazz Music / Cadillac / Complete/Pinnacle.

FOUR TO A BAR (Basie, Count Orchestra)
Jive at five / Easy does it / Miss Thing / Love jumped out / If I could be with you one hour tonight / Between the devil and the deep blue sea / Don't worry 'bout me / You can depend on me / Clap hands, here comes Charlie / I left my baby / Swingin' the blues / Rock-a-bye Basie / Pound cake / Twelfth street rag / How long blues / Riff interlude / It's the same old south / One o'clock jump
CD _____ PAR 2030
Parade / Sep '94 / Koch / Cadillac.

FRANKLY SPEAKING
CD _____ 519849-2
Verve / Mar '94 / PolyGram.

FUN TIME (Basie, Count Orchestra)
Fun time / Why not / Li'l darlin' / In a mellow tone / Body and soul / Good time blues / I hate you baby / Lonesome blues / Whirly bird / One o'clock jump

CD _____ CD 2310945
Pablo / Apr '94 / Jazz Music / Cadillac / Complete/Pinnacle.

GET TOGETHER
Ode to pres / Basies bag / Like it used to be / Swinging on the cusp / My main men / I can't get started (with you) / What will i tell my heart / Talk of the town / I can't give you anything but love / I'm confessin' that I love you
CD _____ CD 2310924
Pablo / Apr '87 / Jazz Music / Cadillac / Complete/Pinnacle.

GOLD COLLECTION, THE
CD _____ D2CD12
Recording Arts / Dec '92 / THE / Disc.

GOLDEN YEARS VOL. 1 - 1937
CD _____ 158052
Jazz Archives / Dec '93 / Jazz Music / Discovery / Cadillac.

GOLDEN YEARS VOL. 2 - 1938
CD _____ 158062
Jazz Archives / Dec '93 / Jazz Music / Discovery / Cadillac.

GOLDEN YEARS VOL. 3 - 1940-44
CD _____ 158072
Jazz Archives / Dec '93 / Jazz Music / Discovery / Cadillac.

GOOD MORNING BLUES
Honeysuckle rose / Good morning blues / One o'clock jump / Listen my children / Sent for you yesterday / Topsy / Exactly like you / Georgina / Smarty / Now will you be good / Mama don't want no peas, no rice, no coconut oil / Swingin' the blues / Blame it on my last affair / Do you wanna jump children / Thursday / Doggin' around / Baby, don't tell on me / I can't believe that you're in love with me / Somebody stole my gal / Harvard blues
CD _____ CDHD 222
Happy Days / Sep '93 / Conifer.

I TOLD YOU SO
Tree frog / Flirt / Blues for Alfy / Something to live for / Plain brown wrapper / Sweet pea / Too close for comfort / Told you so / Git
CD _____ OJCCD 8242
Original Jazz Classics / Jun '95 / Wellard / Jazz Music / Cadillac / Complete/Pinnacle.

IN CONCERT
CD Set _____ RTE 15042
RTE / Aug '95 / ADA / Koch.

IN STOCKHOLM 1954 VOL.1
CD _____ TAX 37012
Tax / Aug '94 / Jazz Music / Wellard / Cadillac.

IN STOCKHOLM 1954 VOL.2
CD _____ TAX 37022
Tax / Aug '94 / Jazz Music / Wellard / Cadillac.

INDISPENSABLE COUNT BASIE
Bill's mill / Brand new wagon / One o'clock boogie / Futulie frustration / Swingin' the blues / St. Louis boogie / Basie's basement / Backstage at Stuff's / My buddy / Shine on harvest moon / Lopin' / I never knew / Sugar / Jungle king / I ain't mad at you / After you've gone / House rent boogie / South / Don't you want a man like me / Seventh Avenue express / Sophisticated swing / Guest in a nest / Your red wagon / Money is honey / Just a minute / Robbin's nest / Hey pretty baby / Bye bye baby / Just an old man's daydream / Let's jump / Teach me tonight
CD Set _____ ND 89758
RCA / Mar '94 / BMG.

INTRODUCTION TO COUNT BASIE 1936-44, AN
CD _____ 4026
Best Of Jazz / Nov '95 / Discovery.

JAZZ ARCHIVES
CD _____ 90 106 2
Jazz Archives / Jun '89 / Jazz Music / Discovery / Cadillac.

JAZZ MASTERS
CD _____ 5198192
Verve / Apr '93 / PolyGram.

JAZZ PORTRAITS (Basie, Count Orchestra)
Jumpin' at the woodside / One o'clock jump / Swingin' the blues / Tops / Every tub / Texas shuffle / Jive at five / Oh! Lady be good / Twelfth street rag / Clap hands, here comes Charlie / Dickie's dream / Lester leaps in / Tickle toe / I never knew / Jumped out / Super chief / Red bank boogie / Rhythm man
CD _____ CD 14506
Jazz Portraits / May '94 / Jazz Music.

JIVE AT FIVE
Blame it on my last affair / Blue and sentimental / Cherokee / Honeysuckle rose / How long blues / Jive at five / John's idea / Jumpin' at the woodside / Lady be good / Moten swing / One o'clock jump / Panassie stomp / Roseland shuffle / Shoe shine

boy / Swingin' at the daisy chain / Texas shuffle / Time out / You can depend on me
CD _____ CD AJA 5089
Living Era / '92 / Koch.

JUBILEE ALTERNATIVES (Basie, Count Orchestra)
Jumpin' at the woodside / I'm gonna move to the outskirts of town / I've found a new baby / Andy's blues / Avenue C / Basie's bag (Basie boogie) / More than you know / Let's jump / Harvard blues / One o'clock jump / Dinah / Baby, won't you please come home / Rock-a-bye Basie / Swing shift / Gee baby ain't I good to you / Beaver Junction / My what a fry
CD _____ HEPCD 38
Hep / Mar '90 / Cadillac / Jazz Music / New Note / Wellard.

JUMPIN' AT THE WOODSIDE (Basie, Count Orchestra)
Jumpin' at the woodside / One o'clock jump / Swingin' the blues / Topsy / Every tub / Texas shuffle / Jive at five / Oh lady be good / Twelfth street rag / Clap hands / Here comes Charley / Dickie's dream / Lester leaps in / Tickle toe / I never knew / Love jumped out / Super Chief / Red bank boogie / Rhythm man
CD _____ CD 56015
Jazz Roots / Aug '94 / Target/BMG.

JUMPIN' AT THE WOODSIDE
CD _____ JHR 73543
Jazz Hour / May '93 / Target/BMG / Jazz Music / Cadillac.

KANSAS CITY 6
Walking the blues / Blues for little jazz / Vegas drag / Wee baby / Scooter / St. Louis blues / Opus six
CD _____ OJCCD 449
Original Jazz Classics / Nov '95 / Wellard / Jazz Music / Cadillac / Complete/Pinnacle.

KANSAS CITY 7
Oh lady be good / Secrets / I want a little girl / Shoe shine boy / Count's place / Senator Whitehead / Tally ho Mr. Basie / What'cha talkin'
CD _____ CD 2310908
Pablo / Nov '95 / Jazz Music / Cadillac / Complete/Pinnacle.

KANSAS CITY SHOUT (Basie, Count/Joe Turner/Eddie Vinson)
My jug and I / Cherry red / Apollo daze / Standing on the corner / Stormy Monday / Signifying / Just a dream on my mind / Blues for Joe Turner / Blues for Joel / Everyday I have the blues / Blues au four
CD _____ CD 2310859
Pablo / May '94 / Jazz Music / Cadillac / Complete/Pinnacle.

KANSAS CITY SOUL (Basie, Count/Joe Turner/Eddie Vinson)
CD _____ 1311252
Pablo / '88 / Jazz Music / Cadillac / Complete/Pinnacle.

LEGEND - THE LEGACY, THE (Basie, Count Orchestra)
Booze brothers / Katherine The Great / Young and foolish / Do nothin' 'til you hear from me / Exactly like you / Papa Foss / Bring on the raindrops / Whirly bird / Count Basie remeberance suite / One O'Clock jump
CD _____ CY 73790
Denon / Jun '93 / Conifer.

LEGENDARY V-DISCS AND JUBILEE MASTERS (Basie, Count Orchestra)
CD _____ VJC 1018 2
Vintage Jazz Classics / Jun '91 / Direct / ADA / CM / Cadillac.

LESTER-AMADEUS (1936-38) (Basie, Count & Lester Young)
CD _____ PHONTCD 7639
Phontastic / Apr '94 / Wellard / Jazz Music / Cadillac.

LIVE 1938-39 (Basie, Count Orchestra & Lester Young)
CD _____ VJC 1033
Vintage Jazz Classics / '91 / Direct / ADA / CM / Cadillac.

LIVE 1954 AT THE SAVOY BALLROOM, NEW YORK (Basie, Count Orchestra)
CD _____ 11089
Laserlight / '88 / Target/BMG.

LIVE 1958-59 (Unissued Recordings)
Why not / In a mellow tone / So young so beautiful / Splanky / Back to the apple / Yogi / Bag a' bones / Moon is not green / Rat race / G'wan away / Plymouth rock / Chestnut Street rumble
CD _____ STATUSCD 110
Status / Oct '91 / Cadillac.

LIVE AT THE EL MOROCCO (Orchestra directed by Frank Foster) (Basie, Count Orchestra)
Gone an' git it y'all / Night at El Morocco / Kurtin on, right on / That's the kind of love I'm talking about / Corner pocket / Little Chicago fire / Shiny stockings / Angel eyes / Major Butts / Vignola express / Basie / One o'clock jump
CD _____ CD 83312
Scorpio / Jul '92 / Complete/Pinnacle.

45

LIVE IN ANTIBES 1968
Vine Street rumble / Pleasingly plump / Cherokee / Good times blues / Lonely Street / Night in Tunisia / Goin' to Chicago blues / I got rhythm / In a mellow tone / Basie's / Li'l darlin' / Blues in Hoss's flat / Everyday I have the blues / Wee baby blues / Stormy Monday blues / Magic flute / Jumpin' at the woodside
CD _______ FCD 112
France's Concert / Jun '88 / Jazz Music / BMG.

LIVE IN JAPAN '78
Heat's on / Freckle face / Ja da / Things ain't what they used to be / Bit of this and a bit of that / All of me / Shiny stockings / Left hand funk / John the III / Basie / Black velvet / Jumpin' at the Woodside
CD _______ CD 2308246
Pablo / May '94 / Jazz Music / Cadillac / Complete/Pinnacle.

LIVE IN SWITZERLAND
CD _______ LS 2907
Landscape / Nov '92 / THE.

LONG LIVE THE CHIEF (Basie, Count Orchestra)
You got it / April in Paris / Misunderstood blues / Autumn leaves / Foggy day / Hey, see you over there / Li'l darlin' / Bus dust / Corner pocket / Dr. Feelgood / Four five six / Shiny stockings
CD _______ CY 1018
Denon / Jan '87 / Conifer.

LOOSE WALK (Basie, Count & Roy Eldridge)
Loose walk / In a mellow tone / Makin' whoopee / If I had you / I surrender dear / 5400 North
CD _______ CD 2310928
Pablo / Aug '94 / Jazz Music / Cadillac / Complete/Pinnacle.

ME AND YOU
CD _______ CD 2310891
Pablo / May '86 / Jazz Music / Cadillac / Complete/Pinnacle.

MONTREUX '77 (Basie, Count Orchestra)
CD _______ CD 20019
Pablo / May '86 / Jazz Music / Cadillac / Complete/Pinnacle.

MOSTLY BLUES AND SOME OTHERS (Basie, Count & The Kansas City Seven)
I'll always be in love with you / Snooky / Blues for Charlie Christian / Jaws / I'm confessin' that I love you / I want a little girl / Blues in C / Brio
CD _______ CD 2310919
Pablo / Feb '87 / Jazz Music / Cadillac / Complete/Pinnacle.

ON THE ROAD (Basie, Count Orchestra)
Wind machine / Blues for Stephanie / John the III / There'll never be another you / Bootie's blues / Splanky / Basie / Watch what happens / Work song / In a mellow tone
CD _______ OJCCD 854
Original Jazz Classics / Nov '95 / Wellard / Jazz Music / Cadillac / Complete/Pinnacle.

ON THE ROAD '79
CD _______ CD 31121
Pablo / May '86 / Jazz Music / Cadillac / Complete/Pinnacle.

ONE O'CLOCK JUMP
Swingin' the blues / Lady be good / Topsy / One o'clock jump / Jumpin' at the woodside / Love jumped out / Dickie's dream / I never knew / Twelfth street rag / Lester leaps in / Super chief / Every tub / Tickle toe / Texas shuffle / Jive at five / Clap hands, here comes Charlie
CD _______ HADCD 175
Javelin / May '94 / THE / Henry Hadaway Organisation.

ONE O'CLOCK JUMP (LIVE) (Basie, Count Orchestra)
CD _______ 15797
Laserlight / Jan '93 / Target/BMG.

PLAYS THE MUSIC OF NEAL HEFTI AND BENNY CARTER (Basie, Count Orchestra)
CD _______ CD 53040
Giants Of Jazz / Mar '92 / Target/BMG / Cadillac.

PRIME TIME
Prime time / Bundle o'funk / Sweet Georgia Brown / Featherweight / Reaching out / Ja da / Great debate / Ya gotta try
CD _______ CD 2310797
Pablo / Oct '92 / Jazz Music / Cadillac / Complete/Pinnacle.

SHOUTIN' BLUES
Cheek to cheek / Just an old manuscript / Kayt / She's a wine-o / Shoutin' blues / Did you see Jackie Robinson hit that ball / St. Louis baby / After you've gone / Wonderful thing / Slider (take 1b) / Slider (take 1c) / Mine, too - Take 1C / Mine, too - Take 1d / Walking slow behind you / Normania (Bee bop blues) / Rocky mountain blues / Siler - take 2 / If you see my baby / Rat race / Sweets
CD _______ 7863 66158-2
Bluebird / Apr '93 / BMG.

SONNY LESTER COLLECTION
CD _______ CDC 9065
LRC / Nov '93 / New Note / Harmonia Mundi.

SOPHISTICATED SWING
Sophisticated swing / Cheek to cheek / Hey pretty baby / Your red wagon / One o'clock boogie / Money is honey / Don't you want a man like me / Shoutin' blues / After you've gone / Jungle King South / Swinging the blues / Walking slowly behind you / Bye bye baby
CD _______ 74321339492
Camden / Jan '96 / BMG.

SWING MACHINE, THE (1937-62) (Basie, Count Orchestra)
One o'clock jump / Swingin' the blues / Topsy / Every tub / Boogie woogie / Dickie's dream / 12th Street rag / Red wagon / Oh lady be good / Jive at five / Fives / Texas shuffle / Clap hands, here comes Charlie / Oh red / Tickle toe / I never knew / Sugar blues / Love jumped out / Super chief / Lester leaps in / Red bank boogie / Rhythm man / Fiesta in blue / Yeah man / What am I here for / April in Paris / There's a small hotel / Hob nail boogie / Blee blop blues / Basie talks / Paradise squat / Softly, with feeling / Beaver Junction / Nails / Did you see Jackie Robinson hit that ball / Seventh Avenue express / Mr. Roberts' roost / Mad boogie / King / Mutton leg / Patience and fortitude / Wild Bill's boogie / Stay cool / High tide / Jimmy's boogie woogie / Taps miller / Jumpin' at the woodside / Moten swing / Blue and sentimental / Sent for you yesterday / Blues in hoss's flat / Who me / Little pony / Legend / Goin' to Chicago blues / One o'clock junp / Shorty George / Duet / Double O / Splanky / Miss Missouri / Meetin' time / Stompin and jumpin'
CD Set _______ CDB 1210
Giants Of Jazz / '92 / Target/BMG / Cadillac.

SWINGIN' MACHINE LIVE, THE (Basie, Count Orchestra)
CD _______ LEJAZZCD 17
Le Jazz / Jun '93 / Charly / Cadillac.

SWINGTIME COLLECTION, VOL. 2, THE (Basie, Count Orchestra)
One o'clock jump / This could be the start of something big / Git / I can't stop loving you / April in Paris / Big brother / Jumpin' at the woodside / Shiny stockings / I needs to be bee'd with / Shake, rattle and roll / Blues for Eileen / Whirly bird / Pleasingly plump / All of me / Corner pocket
CD _______ CDAPS 1001
Charly / Sep '91 / Charly / THE / Cadillac.

TOPEKA, KANSAS '55
CD _______ JASSCD 17
Jass / '88 / CM / Jazz Music / ADA / Cadillac / Direct.

UNBEATABLE BASIE BEAT, THE
Honeysuckle rose / Blue and sentimental / Taxi war dance / John's idea / Topsy / Every tub / Swingin' the blues / Jumpin' at the woodside / Boogie woogie / How long blues / Panassie stomp / Jive at five / Lady be good / Doggin' around / Texas shuffle / Dickie's dream / Lester leaps in / Red bank boogie / Cherokee / One o'clock jump
CD _______ AVC 524
Avid / Apr '93 / Avid/BMG / Koch.

VOLUME 1 (1932/1937/1938)
CD _______ RPCD 602
Moidart / Aug '92 / Conifer / ADA.

VOLUME 2 (1938/1940)
CD _______ RPCD 603
Moidart / Aug '92 / Conifer / ADA.

WARM BREEZE
C.B. express / After the rain / Warm breeze / Cookie / Flight to Nassau / How sweet it is (to be loved by you) / Satin doll
CD _______ CD 311240
Pablo / May '86 / Jazz Music / Cadillac / Complete/Pinnacle.

YESSIR THAT'S MY BABY (Basie, Count & Oscar Peterson)
Blues for Roy / Teach me tonight / Joe Turner blues / Blues for cat / Yes sir that's my baby / After you've gone / Tea for two / Poor butterfly
CD _______ CD 2310923
Pablo / Apr '87 / Jazz Music / Cadillac / Complete/Pinnacle.

Basin Brothers

LET'S GET CAJUN
CD _______ FF 539CD
Flying Fish / Jul '92 / Roots / CM / Direct / ADA.

Basin Street Six

COMPLETE CIRCLE RECORDINGS, THE
CD _______ BCD 103
GHB / Aug '94 / Jazz Music.

Bass, Fontella

NO WAYS TIRED
CD _______ 7599793572
Elektra Nonesuch / Feb '95 / Warner Music.

RESCUED
CD _______ CHLD 19252
Chess/MCA / Oct '94 / BMG / New Note.

Bass-O-Matic

SET THE CONTROLS FOR THE HEART OF THE BASS
In the realm of the senses / Set the controls for the heart of the bass / Fascinating rhythm / Rat cut a bottle / Love catalogue / Zombie mantra / Freaky angel / Wicked love / Ease on by / My tears have gone
CD _______ CDV 2641
Virgin / Apr '92 / EMI.

Bassey, Shirley

ALL BY MYSELF
All by myself / This masquerade / If and when / He's out of my life / New York state of mind / Can you read my mind / Only when I laugh / Solitaire / New York medley / We don't cry out loud / That's what friends are for / Sorry seems to be the hardest word / Greatest love of all / Dio come ti amo
CD _______ MOCD 001
More Music / Feb '95 / Sound & Media.

BASSEY - THE EMI/UA YEARS
'S Wonderful / As long as he needs me / You'll never know / So in love / Reach for the stars / Who are we / I'll get by (as long as I have you) / Tonight / What now my love / Above all others / It could happen to you / It all depends on you / I who have nothing / Gone / How do you believe / Goldfinger / My child / Seesaw of dreams / It's yourself / Secrets / Stay on the island / Once in a lifetime / Liquidator / Mr. Kiss Kiss Bang Bang / Boy from Ipanema / More / House is not a home / Don't take the lovers from the world / Take away / I've got a song for you / Shirley / Give him your love / We were lovers / Who could love me / Do I look like a fool / Big spender / Dangerous game / La vita / I must know / This is my life / Without a word / If he walked into my life / To give / My love has two faces / Clown town / Does anybody miss me / I'll never fall in love again / (You are) My way of life / Bus that never comes / Fa fa fa (live for today) / Something / Spinning wheel / Yesterday I heard the rain / Sea and sand / What about today / You and I / Light my fire / Yesterday when I was young / Fool on the hill / Where do I begin / Till love touches your life / For the love of him / Vehicle / Diamonds are forever / Way a woman loves / For all we know / Greatest performance of my life / Lost and lonely / Way of love / Day by day / Ballad of the sad young men / If I should love again / Let me be the one / Never never never / Somehow / Going going gone / Make the world a little younger / Everything I own / All that went to waste / I'm not anyone / Jesse / Living / Natalie / If I never sing another song / Can't take my eyes off you / You take my heart away / Come in from the rain / Tomorrow morning / Razzle dazzle / You made me love you / My man / Nature boy / Greatest love of all / Moonraker / Just one of those things / Burn my candle (at both ends) / All the things you are / If I were a bell / Lovely way to spend the evening / Lot of livin' to do / No regrets / Typically English / Fly me to the moon / Please Mr. Brown / I'm a fool to want you / You / Johnny one note / I could have danced all night / Lovely way to spend an evening
CD Set _______ BASSEY 1
EMI / Nov '94 / EMI.

BORN TO SING
As I love you / Stormy weather / Love for sale / Birth of the blues / Hands across the sea / There's never been a night / Night and day / My funny valentine / Kiss me honey, honey kiss me / Gypsy in my soul / Crazy rhythm / How about you / Wayward wind / Born to sing the blues
CD _______ 5501852
Spectrum/Karussell / Mar '94 / PolyGram / THE.

CLASSIC TRACKS
CD _______ 5143472
Phonogram / Jan '94 / PolyGram.

COLLECTION: SHIRLEY BASSEY
Does anybody miss me / I'll never fall in love again / Never never no / Picture puzzle / I only miss him / As I love you / This is my life / Who am I / Funny girl / Sunny / I've been loved / Where is tomorrow / Think of me (You are) / My way of life / We / Give me you / It's always 4 a.m. / Hold me, thrill me, kiss me / Now you want to be loved / Medley: Goin' out of my head/You go to my head / Softly as I leave you / Time for us / Joker / I must know / You're gonna hear from me (CD only) / If you go away (Ne me quitte pas/CD only) / Burn my candle (at both ends) (CD only) / Shadow of your smile (CD only) / Kiss me honey, honey kiss me (CD only) / Impossible dream (CD only) / Johnny one note (CD only) / Summer wind (CD only) / Walking happy (CD only) / Strangers in the night (CD only) / Look for me tomorrow (I'll be gone) (CD only) / Let me sing and I'm happy (CD only) / On a clear day (you can see forever) (CD only) / It must be him (Seul sur son etoile/CD only) / All or nothing at all (CD only) / Dangerous games (CD only) / I'm glad there is you (CD only) / That's life (CD only) / (You are) My way of life (CD only) / You can have him (CD only) / Lady is a tramp (CD only) / You and I (CD only) / Big spender (CD only) / Sweet charity (CD only)
CD Set _______ CDDL 1239
EMI / Apr '93 / EMI.

DEFINITIVE COLLECTION, THE
What now my love / Something / As long as he needs me / As I love you / Big spender / Send in the clowns / I who have nothing / All by myself / This masquerade / If and when / He's out of my life / New York state of mind / Can you read my mind / Only when I laugh / Solitaire / New York, New York / We don't cry out loud / Natalie
CD _______ MDCD 3
MMG Video / Jan '94 / Magnum Music Group.

DIAMONDS (The Best Of Shirley Bassey)
Diamonds are forever / Something / Big spender / I who have nothing / For all we know / Where do I begin / Who can I turn to / Far away / Reach for the stars / Climb every mountain / Goldfinger / Never never never / If you go away / As long as he needs me / With these hands / What now my love / What kind of fool am I / I'll get by / You'll never know / This is my life
CD _______ CDP 790 469 2
EMI / May '88 / EMI.

DIAMONDS ARE FOREVER
CD _______ PRS 23011
Personality / Aug '93 / Target/BMG.

GOLDFINGER
CD _______ PRS 23010
Personality / Aug '93 / Target/BMG.

GREATEST HITS COLLECTION
CD _______ ST 5006
Star Collection / Nov '93 / BMG.

I'M IN THE MOOD FOR LOVE
What now my love / Moon river / Fools rush in / No regrets / I wish you love / Liquidator / Nearness of you / This love of mine / Where are you / If love were all / There will never be another you / Days of wine and roses / People / Second time around / Tonight / Strange how love can be / I'm in the mood for love / I get a kick out of you / Angel eyes / To be loved by a man / Hold me tight / I believe in you / Let's start all over again / I'm a fool to want you
CD _______ CC 241
Music For Pleasure / May '89 / EMI.

LIVE: SHIRLEY BASSEY
Goldfinger / Where am I going / I Capricorn / Let me sing and I'm happy / Johnny One Note / For all we know / I'd like to hate myself in the morning / I who have nothing / Day by day / And I love you so / Diamonds are forever / Narration / Big spender / Never, never, never / You and I / Something / This is my life / Lovely way to spend an evening / Party's over / Lovely way to spend an evening (2) / On a wonderful day like today / I get a kick out of you / Who can I turn to / You'd better love me / Other woman / He loves me / With these hands / Lot of livin' to do / I who have nothing (2) / La Bamba / You can have him / Second time around / Lady is a tramp / Somewhere / Lovely way to spend an evening (3)
CD Set _______ CDDL 1221
Music For Pleasure / Apr '92 / EMI.

LOVE ALBUM, THE
Something / What now my love / Where do I begin / Tonight / As long as he needs me / Time after time / As time goes by / With these hands / You'll never know / It must be him / Look of love / You made me love you / Softly as I leave you / I wish you love / Who can I turn to / Party's over / I'll never fall in love again (CD only.) / If you go away (Ne me quitte pas/CD only) / I get a kick out of you (CD only.) / Nearness of you (CD only.)
CD _______ CDMFP 5879
Music For Pleasure / Jan '92 / EMI.

NEW YORK, NEW YORK
CD _______ RMB 75002
Remember / Nov '93 / Total/BMG.

PLAYING SOLITAIRE
All by myself / This masquerade / If and when / He's out of my life / New York state of mind / Can you read my mind / Only when I laugh / Solitaire / New York, New York / Don't cry out loud
CD _______ PRCD 117
President / Mar '85 / Grapevine / Target/BMG / Jazz Music / President.

SHIRLEY BASSEY
CD _______ DINCD 21
Dino / May '91 / Pinnacle / 3MV.

SHIRLEY BASSEY - 40 GREAT SONGS
CD _______ DBP 102002
Double Platinum / Nov '93 / Target/BMG.

SHIRLEY BASSEY SINGS ANDREW LLOYD WEBBER
Memory / All I ask of you / Starlight Express / Last man in my life / Chanson d'enfance / I don't know how to love him / With one look / Macavity / Don't cry for me Argentina / Tell me on a Sunday / Wishing you were

somehow here again / As if we never said goodbye / Memory reprise
CD _____ CDDPR 114
Premier/MFP / Nov '93 / EMI.

SHIRLEY BASSEY: THE SINGLES
Something / Where do I begin / Diamonds are forever / Fool on the hill / Make the world a little younger / Big spender / Never never never / When you smile / If you go away / And I love you more / Somebody anybody miss me / For all we know / Goldfinger / No regrets / I who have nothing / What kind of fool am I
CD _____ CD MFP 6004
Music For Pleasure / Aug '88 / EMI.

SINGS THE MOVIES
CD _____ 5293992
PolyGram TV / Oct '95 / PolyGram.

SINGS THE MOVIES
Goldfinger / Where do I begin / Tonight / Big spender / Diamonds are forever / As long as he needs me / Lady is a tramp / As time goes by / You'll never walk alone / Climb every mountain / Moon river / Funny girl / Just one of those things / S'Wonderful / You'll never know / More / Liquidator / I don't know how to love him
CD _____ CDMFP 6205
Music For Pleasure / Nov '95 / EMI.

SOLID GOLD
CD Set _____ STACD 027/8
Telstar / Aug '92 / BMG.

SOMETHING
CD _____ RMB 75079
Remember / Apr '95 / Total/BMG.

SONGS FROM THE SHOWS
Moon river / People / Tonight / If love were all / Days of wine and roses / I believe in you / I've never been in love before / Far away / Lady is a tramp / Somewhere / It might as well be Spring / Don't rain on my parade / I get a kick out of you / Just one of those things / As long as he needs me / Where or when / 'S Wonderful / Every-thing's coming up roses / He loves me / Something wonderful / If ever I would leave you / You'll never walk alone
CD _____ CC 272
Music For Pleasure / Oct '91 / EMI.

SUPERSTAR
All by myself / Solitaire / Can you read my mind / He's out of my life / New York state of mind / If and when / Only when I laugh / This masquerade / New York, New York / Don't cry out loud
CD _____ PWK 016
Carlton Home Entertainment / '88 / Carlton Home Entertainment.

THIS IS
When you smile / Something / I get a kick out of you / Fly me to the moon / Sing / Lady is a tramp / Don't rain on my parade / Other side of me / I've got you under my skin / On a wonderful day like today / Somewhere / Lot of livin' to do / Once in a lifetime / Nobody does it like me / Goldfinger / As long as he needs me / Just one of those things / I who have nothing / Easy to love / Climb every mountain / Send in the clowns / Every time we say goodbye / Let there be love / What kind of fool am I / Everything's coming up roses / With these hands / Party's over / Tonight (CD set only) / Where do I begin (CD set only) / What now my love (CD set only) / No regrets (CD set only) / Big spender (CD set only) / Dia-monds are forever (CD set only)
CD Set _____ CDDL 1140
Music For Pleasure / May '91 / EMI.

Bassline Generation

JUNGLE EXPLORING
CD _____ EFA 127192
Mask / Apr '95 / Vital.

Bastards

WORLD BURNS TO DEATH
CD _____ LF 110CD
Lost & Found / Nov '94 / Plastic Head.

Bastro

BASTRO DIABLO GUAPO
CD _____ HMS 132 2
Homestead / Jul '89 / SRD.

Bates, Django

SUMMER FRUITS
CD _____ 514008-2
JMT / Jan '94 / PolyGram.

Bates, Martyn

LOVE SMASHED ON A ROCK
CD _____ IR 002CD
Integrity / Jan '90 / Vital.

STARS COME TREMBLING
CD _____ IR 011CD
Integrity / Oct '90 / Vital.

Bathers

LAGOON BLUES
CD _____ MAMCD 33962
Marina / Apr '94 / SRD.

SUNPOWDER
CD _____ MA 12
Marina / May '95 / SRD.

Bathory

BLOOD FIRE DEATH
Odens ride over Nordland / Golden wall of heaven / Pace 'til death / Dies irae / Fine day to die / Holocaust / For all those who died / Blood fire death
CD _____ BMCD 666-4
Black Mark / Oct '94 / Plastic Head.

HAMMERHEART
CD _____ BMCD 666-5
Black Mark / Oct '94 / Plastic Head.

JUBILEUM VOLUME 1
Rider at the gate of dawn / Crawl to your cross / Sacrifice / Dies irae / Through blood by thunder / You don't move me (I don't give a fuck) / Odens ride over Nordland / Fine day to die / War / Enter the eternal fire / Song to hall up high / Sadist / Under the runes / Equimanthorn / Blood fire death
CD _____ BMCD 666-7
Black Mark / Nov '92 / Plastic Head.

OCTAGON
CD _____ BMCD 66611
Black Mark / May '95 / Plastic Head.

REQUIEM
CD _____ BMCD 666
Black Mark / Nov '94 / Plastic Head.

RETURN.... THE
Revelation of doom / Total destruction / Born for burning / Wind of mayhem / Bestial lust / Possessed / Rite of darkness / Reap of evil / Son of the damned / Sadist / Return of the darkness and evil
CD _____ BMCD 666-2
Black Mark / May '92 / Plastic Head.

TWILIGHT OF THE GODS
CD _____ BMCD 666-6
Black Mark / '92 / Plastic Head.

Batimbos

MAITRES-TAMBOURS DU BURUNDI
Arrivee et salut a l'assistance / Offrande / Appel / Suite de danses rituelles / Suite de danses et d'appels rituels
CD _____ ARN 64016
Arion / '88 / Discovery / ADA.

Batiste, Milton

MILTON BATISTE
CD _____ BCD 324
GHB / Aug '94 / Jazz Music.

MILTON BATISTE & RUE CONTI JAZZ BAND
CD _____ LA 031CD
Lake / Nov '94 / Target/BMG / Jazz Music / Direct / Cadillac / ADA.

Batmobile

BAIL IS SET AT SIX MILLION DOLLARS
Kiss me now / Magic word called love / Can't find my way back home / Mystery Street / Calamity man / Shoot shoot / Gorilla rock / Gates of heaven / Girls, girls, girls / Hang on / 100 pounds of trouble / Ace of spades
CD _____ NERCD 035
Nervous / '90 / Nervous / Magnum Music Group.

Bators, Stiv

DEAD BOYS, THE
CD _____ 642002
New Rose / May '94 / Direct / ADA.

DISCONNECTED
CD _____ BCD 4043
Bomp / Feb '94 / Pinnacle.

Bats

COUCHMASTER
CD _____ FNCD 301
Flying Nun / Oct '95 / Disc.

DADDY'S HIGHWAY
CD _____ FNE 23CD
Flying Nun / Nov '88 / Disc.

FEAR OF GOD
CD _____ R 2832
Rough Trade / Mar '92 / Pinnacle.

SILVERBEET
CD _____ FNCD 260
Flying Nun / Sep '93 / Disc.

Battery

ONLY THE DIEHARD REMAIN
CD _____ LF 089CD
Lost & Found / May '94 / Plastic Head.

WE WON'T FALL
CD _____ LF 055
Lost & Found / Aug '93 / Plastic Head.

Battlefield Band

AFTER HOURS
CD _____ COMD 2001

Temple / Feb '94 / CM / Duncans / ADA / Direct.

ANTHEM FOR THE COMMON MAN
CD _____ COMD 2013
Temple / Feb '94 / CM / Duncans / ADA / Direct.

AT THE FRONT
Lady Carmichael / South of the Grampians / Mickie Ainsworth / Bachelor / Ge do theid mi do m'leabradh / Battle of Harlaw / Jenny Nettles / Grays of tongside / Tae the beg-gin' / Tamosher / Blackbird and the thrush / Moray club / Lang Johnnie More / Brown milkmaid / Dunnottar castle / Maid of Glen-garryedale / Disused railways / Lady Lerov / Stirling castle / Earl of Mansfield
CD _____ TP 56CD
Temple / Aug '94 / CM / Duncans / ADA / Direct.

BATTLEFIELD BAND
Silver spear / Humours of Tulla / Shipyard apprentice / Crossing the Minch / Minnie Hynd / Glasgow gaelic club / Brisk young lad / Birnie bouzie / Compliments of the band / A.A. Cameron's strathspey / Scott Skinner's compliments to Dr MacDonald / Bonnie Jean / Paddy Fahey's / Joseph's fancy / Hog's reel / It was a' for our rightful king / Inverness gathering / Marquis of Hunt-ly's strathspey / John MacNeil's reel / Miss Margaret Brown's favourite / Deserts of Tul-loch / Cruel brother
CD _____ TP 55CD
Temple / Aug '94 / CM / Duncans / ADA / Direct.

CELTIC HOTEL
Conway's farewell / Andy Renwick's Ferrett / Short coated Mary / Seacoalers / Return To Kashmagiro / Cuddly with the wooden leg / Jack the can / Ruvin' dies hard / Muinera sul sacrato delia chiesa / Hyoy Frwy-nen / E kostez an hebont / Celtic Hotel / Left handed fiddler / Floating crowbar / Ships are sailing / Lucy Campbell / June apple / We work the black seam / Tail o' the bank / Cran Tara / Madadh Ruadh
CD _____ COMD 2002
Temple / Feb '94 / CM / Duncans / ADA / Direct.

HOME GROUND
CD _____ COMD 034
Temple / Feb '94 / CM / Duncans / ADA / Direct.

HOME IS WHERE THE VAN IS
CD _____ COMD 2006
Temple / Feb '94 / CM / Duncans / ADA / Direct.

NEW SPRING
CD _____ COMD 2045
Temple / Feb '94 / CM / Duncans / ADA / Direct.

ON THE RISE
CD _____ COMD 2009
Temple / Feb '94 / CM / Duncans / ADA / Direct.

OPENING MOVES
Silver spear/Humours of Tulla / Shipyard apprentice / Cruel brother / Ge do theid mi do m'leabadh / Battle of Harlaw / Jenny Nettles/Grays of tongside / Tae the beggin / Tamosher / Blackbird and the thrush/ Moray club / Lang Johnnie More / Brown milkmaid/Dunnottar castle / Maid of Glen-garrydale / Disused railway / Lady Leroy / Miss Drummond of Perth/Fiddler's joy / Tra-ditional reel/Shetland fiddler / My last fare-well to stirling/Cuidich'n right / I hae laid a herrin' in salt/My wife's a wanton wee thing / Banks of the allan / Battler of Falkirk Muir / Jock MaGa's's fiddle/Centro's bonnet
CD _____ TSCD 468
Topic / Sep '93 / Direct / ADA.

QUIET DAYS
CD _____ COMD 2050
Temple / Feb '94 / CM / Duncans / ADA / Direct.

STAND EASY/PREVIEW
CD _____ COMD 2052
Temple / Feb '94 / CM / Duncans / ADA / Direct.

THERE'S A BUZZ
CD _____ COMD 2007
Temple / Feb '94 / CM / Duncans / ADA / Direct.

THREADS
CD _____ COMD 2062
Temple / Sep '95 / Duncans / ADA / Direct.

Bauer, Konrad

THREE WHEELS FOUR DIRECTIONS
(Bauer, Konrad Trio)
CD _____ VICTOCD 023
Victo / Nov '94 / These / ReR Megacorp / Cadillac.

TORONTO TÖNE
CD _____ VICTOCD 017
Victo / Nov '94 / These / ReR Megacorp / Cadillac.

Bauer, Uschi

YODEL HITS FROM USCHI BAUER
CD _____ 399382
Koch / Sep '92 / Koch.

Bauge, Andre

L'INOUBLIABLE
CD _____ CDP 7806582
Capitol / Apr '95 / EMI.

L'INOUBLIABLE
CD _____ UCD 19022
Forlane / Jun '95 / Target/BMG.

Bauhaus

BAUHAUS 1979-1983
Kick in the eye / Hollow hills / In fear of fear / Ziggy Stardust / Silent hedges / Lagartija Nick / Third uncle / Spirit / All we ever wanted was everything / She's in parties / Sanity assassin / Crowds / Double dare / In the flat field / Stigmata martyr / Bela Lu-gosi's dead / Telegram Sam / St. Vitus dance / Spy in the cab / Terror couple kill colonel / Passions of lovers / Mask
CD _____ BEGA 64CD
Beggars Banquet / Feb '88 / Warner Music / Disc.

BAUHAUS 1979-1983 VOL. 2
CD _____ BEGA 64 CD2
Beggars Banquet / Feb '88 / Warner Music / Disc.

BURNING FROM THE INSIDE
She's in parties / Antonin artaud / Wasp / King volcano / Who killed Mr. Moonlight / Slice of life / Honeymoon croon / Kingdom's coming / Burning from the inside / Hope / Lagartija Nick / Here's the dub / Departure / Sanity assassin
CD _____ BBL 45 CD
Lowdown/Beggars Banquet / Sep '88 / Warner Music / Disc.

IN THE FLAT FIELD
CD _____ CAD 13CD
4AD / Apr '88 / Disc.

MASK
Hair of the dog / Passion of lovers / Of lilies and remains / Hollow hills / Dancing / Kick in the eye / Muscle in plastic / In fear of fear / Man with the X-ray eyes / Mask
CD _____ BBL 29CD
Lowdown/Beggars Banquet / Oct '88 / Warner Music / Disc.

PRESS THE EJECT AND GIVE ME THE TAPE
In the flat field / Rosegarden funeral of sores / Dancing / Man with the X-ray eyes / Bela Lugosi's dead / Spy in the cab / Kick in the eye / In fear of fear / Hollow hills / Stigmata martyr / Dark entries
CD _____ BBL 38CD
Lowdown/Beggars Banquet / '89 / Warner Music / Disc.

SINGLES '81-'83
Passion of lovers / Kick in the eye / Spirit / Ziggy Stardust / Lagartija Nick / She's in parties
CD _____ BBP 4CD
Beggars Banquet / Dec '88 / Warner Music / Disc.

SKY'S GONE OUT, THE
Third uncle / Silent hedges / In the night / Swing the heartache / Spirit / Three shad-ows (part 1) / Three shadows (part 2) / Three shadows (part 3) / All we ever wanted was everything / Exquisite corpse
CD _____ BBL 42 CD
Lowdown/Beggars Banquet / '89 / Warner Music / Disc.

SWING THE HEARTACHE
Hair of the dog / Telegram Sam / Double dare / Terror couple kill colonel / Ziggy Star-dust / Third uncle / Silent hedges / Three shadows (pt. 2) / Party of the first part / Poison pen / Departure / Nightime / She's in parties / God in an alcove / In the flat field / In fear of fear / Swing the heartache / St. Vitus dance
CD _____ BEGA 103CD
Beggars Banquet / Jul '89 / Warner Music / Disc.

Baumann, Peter

PHASE BY PHASE
CD _____ CDOVD 464
Virgin / Jan '96 / EMI.

Bauza, Mario

944 COLUMBUS (Bauza, Mario & His Afro-Cuban Jazz Orchestra)
CD _____ MES 158282
Messidor / Apr '94 / Koch / ADA.

MY TIME IS NOW (Bauza, Mario & His Afro-Cuban Jazz Orchestra)
CD _____ MES 158252
Messidor / Jun '93 / Koch / ADA.

Baxter, Blake

VAULT, THE
CD _____ EFA 122762
Tresor / Oct '95 / SRD.

Baxter, Les

COLOURS OF BRAZIL/AFRICAN BLUE
Feliciade / Canta de ossanha / Balan samba / Day of the roses / Man and a woman / Who will buy / Somewhere in the hills / Goin' out of my head / Tristeza / Berimbau / Laia ladaia / Banda / Born free / Yellow sun / Flame tree / Zebra / Dark river / Topaz / Tree of life / Girl of Uganda / Magenta mountain / Johannesburg blues / Jalaba / Azure sands Kalahari
CD _____ GNPD 2036
GNP Crescendo / Oct '95 / Silva Screen.

Baxter, Shaun

JAZZ METAL
Strike up the band / Throw down / Chicken soup / G spot blues / Baxter's brew / Make it reel / Birdman / I'm not sure / Twelve bars from Mars / Gregory's girl / Open invitation
CD _____ ZCDSB 009
Zok / Jan '95 / Grapevine / PolyGram / Pinnacle / Koch.

Bay B Kane

GUARDIAN OF RUFF, THE
CD _____ WHSCD 1
Whitehouse / Jan '95 / Mo's Music Machine / Jetstar / Grapevine / Target/ BMG.

HAVE A BREAK
CD _____ WHSCD 5
Whitehouse / Nov '95 / Mo's Music Machine / Jetstar / Grapevine / Target/ BMG.

Bay City Rollers

ABSOLUTE ROLLERS
(Dancing on) A Saturday night / Shang-a-lang / Remember (sha la la) / Bye bye baby / I only want to be with you / All of me love all of you / Give a little love / Summer love sensation / Rebel rebel / Money honey / You made me believe in magic / Way I feel to-night / Another rainy day in New York City / It's a game / There goes my baby / Rock 'n' roll love letter / Bay City Rollers megamix
CD _____ 74321 265752
Arista / Aug '95 / BMG.

BAY CITY ROLLERS
CD _____ 295588
Ariola Express / Dec '92 / BMG.

Bay Laurel

UNDER A CLOUDED SKY
CD _____ NOX 003CD
Noxious / May '95 / Plastic Head.

Bayer Sager, Carole

...TOO
CD _____ 7559605302
Elektra / Jan '96 / Warner Music.

CAROLE BAYER SAGER
Come in from the rain / Until the next time / Don't wish too hard / Sweet alibis / Aces / I'd rather leave while I'm in love / Steal away again / You're moving out today / Shy as a violet / Home to myself
CD _____ 7559606172
Elektra / Jan '96 / Warner Music.

Bayete

MMALO-WE (Bayete & Jabu Khanyile)
Mmalo-we / Thabo / Retrenchment / Ten times love / Africa unite / Ubugwala / Emandulu / Ungayingeni / Culture disgrace / Celebrate life
CD _____ CIDM 1115
Mango / Dec '94 / Vital / PolyGram.

Baylor, Helen

LOOK A LITTLE
CD _____ DAYCD 4215
Nelson Word / May '93 / Nelson Word.

Bayne, Hamish

MAKING MUSIC (Bayne, Hamish & Martin Cole)
Rights of man / Off to California / Freedom come all ye / Newfoundland / Farewell rose of England / Lea rig / Dominic's mazurka / Helen of Kirkconnel / Halting march/The sloe / Gentle Annie / Connerys / Miss Rowan Davies / Fair and tender maidens / Off to Sheringham / Fond adieu
CD _____ FE 082CD
Fellside / '92 / Target/BMG / Direct / ADA.

Bayou Gumbo

BALD ON THE BAYOU
CD _____ BEANDOG 47CD
Beandog / May '93 / ADA.

Bazooka

BLOWHOLE
CD _____ SST 308CD
SST / Oct '94 / Plastic Head.

CIGARS, OYSTERS AND BOOZE
CD _____ SST 325CD
SST / Jan '96 / Plastic Head.

PERFECTLY SQUARE
CD _____ SST 296 CD
SST / May '93 / Plastic Head.

Bazz Mob

STRAIGHT 2 DA BAZZMENT
CD _____ FRE 42012
Fresh Entertainment / Mar '95 / Koch.

Bazzle, Germaine

NEW NEW ORLEANS MUSIC, VOL. 3
(Bazzle, Germaine & Friends)
CD _____ CD 2067
Rounder / '88 / CM / Direct / ADA / Cadillac.

BBC Big Band

AGE OF SWING
CD _____ EMPRBX 003
Empress / Sep '94 / THE.

BBC BIG BAND
Don't count / Song of the Volga boatmen / Street scene / King Porter stomp / Camptown races / Ol' man river / Herman's habit / Crescendo in blue / Alfresco / Say it isn't so / Opus in pastel / Magic time
CD _____ RBBCD 001
Radio Big Band / Feb '95 / New Note.

CITY LIFE
Strike up the band / I still care about us / I've got it bad, and that ain't good / But not for me / Singer / I let a song go out of my heart (with Don't get around much anymore) / Cotton tail / Declaration of love / Drop me off in Harlem / When my dream-boat comes home / I put a spell on you / City life / Blues and me / It don't mean a thing if it ain't got that swing
CD _____ RBBCD 003
Radio Big Band / Nov '93 / New Note.

BBC Concert Orchestra

BATTLE OF BRITAIN - 50TH ANNIVERSARY
Speedbird salutes the few / Mars / Winston Churchill speech / Fighter command / Hight-light / Spitfire prelude and fuge / Lie in the dark / Last enemy / O peaceful England / (We're gonna hang out the) washing on the Siegfried Line / We'll meet again / Armed forces medley / American hoedown / Speedbird salutes the few (theme)
CD _____ PZA 005 CD
Plaza / Sep '90 / Pinnacle.

BBC Philharmonic...

PORTRAIT OF GEORGE GERSHWIN
(BBC Philharmonic Orchestra)
CD _____ CDPC 5010
Prestige / Jan '94 / Total/BMG.

BBC Symphony Orchestra

MIDNIGHT
You stepped out of a dream / What are you doing the rest of your life / Smoke gets in your eyes / Midnight at the Mermaid / If I'll be seeing you / As time goes by / Easy to love / Misty morning / That lovely week-end / Where or when / Foots rush in / King Cole / Candlelight lovers / Laura / Nuages / These foolish things / Sunflower / Thanks for the memory
CD _____ PWKS 652
Carlton Home Entertainment / Jul '89 / Carlton Home Entertainment.

BBM

AROUND THE NEXT DREAM
Waiting in the wings / City of gold / Where in the world / Can't fool the blues / High cost of living / Glory days / Why does love (Have to go wrong) / Naked flame / I wonder (Why are you so mean to me) / Wrong side of town
CD _____ CDV 2745
Virgin / Jun '94 / EMI.

Be-Bop Deluxe

AXE VICTIM
Axe victim / Love is swift arrows / Jet silver and the dolls of venus / Third floor heaven / Night creature / Rocket cathedrals / Adventures in a Yorkshire landscape / Jets at dawn / No trains to heaven / Darkness (L'immoraliste) / Piece of mine (live) / Mill Street junction (Live) / Adventures in a Yorkshire landscape (live)
CD _____ CZ 327
EMI / Feb '91 / EMI.

LIVE - IN THE AIR-AGE
Life in the air age / Ships in the night / Piece of mind / Fair exchange / Mill Street junction / Adventures in a Yorkshire landscape / Blazing apostles / Shine / Sister seagull / Maid in heaven
CD _____ CZ 331
EMI / Feb '91 / EMI.

RADIOLAND
Life in the air age / Sister seagull / Third floor heaven / Blazing apostles / Maid in heaven / Kiss of light / Adventures in a Yorkshire landscape / Fair exchange / Ships in the night / Modern music / Dancing in the moonlight / Honeymoon on Mars / Lost in the neon world / New precision / Superenigmatix / Possession / Dangerous stranger / Islands of the dead / Panic in the world
CD _____ WINCD 065
Windsong / Aug '94 / Pinnacle.

RAIDING THE DIVINE ARCHIVES (Best of Be Bop Deluxe)
Jet Silver and the Dolls of Venus / Adventures in a Yorkshire landscape / Maid in Heaven / Ships in the night / Life in the air age / Kiss of light / Sister Seagull / Modern music / Japan / Panic in the world / Bring back the spark / Forbidden lovers / Electrical Language / Fair exchange (CD only.) / Sleep that burns (CD only.) / Between the worlds (CD only.) / Music in dreamland (CD only.)
CD _____ CZ 296
EMI / Apr '90 / EMI.

SINGLES A'S & B'S
Jet silver and the dolls of Venus / Between the worlds / Maid in heaven / Ships in the night / Kiss of light / Japan / Panic in the world / Electrical language / Third floor heaven / Lights / Crying to the sky / Shine / Futurist manifesto / Blue as a jewel / Surreal / Estate
CD _____ SEECD 336
See For Miles/C5 / Feb '92 / Pinnacle.

SUNBURST FINISH
Fair exchange / Heavenly homes / Ships in the night / Crying to the sky / Sleep that burns / Beauty secrets / Life in the air age / Like an old blues / Crystal gazing / Blazing apostles / Shine (CD only.) / Speed of the wind (CD only.) / Blue as a jewel (CD only.)
CD _____ CZ 329
EMI / Feb '91 / EMI.

Beacco, Marc

CROCODILE SMILE, THE
CD _____ 5134162
PolyGram Jazz / May '93 / PolyGram.

Beach Boys

15 GREATEST HITS, THE (Beach Boys/ Jan & Dean)
Surfin' safari / Surfer girl / Surfin' / Judy / Barbi / Luan / What is a young girl / Dead man's curve / City / Little old lady from Pasadena / Dead man's curve / Drag city / Little deuce coupe / Heart and soul / Ride the wild surf / Side-walk surfin'
CD _____ CD 34
Bescol / Jul '87 / CM / Target/BMG.

20 GOLDEN GREATS: BEACH BOYS
Surfin' USA / Fun, fun, fun / I get around / Don't worry baby / Little deuce coupe / When I grow up (to be a man) / Help me Rhonda / California girls / Barbara Ann / Sloop John B / You're so good to me / Good vibrations / Then I kissed her / Heroes and villains / Darlin' / Do it again / I can hear music / I break away
CD _____ CDEMTV 1
EMI / Nov '87 / EMI.

BEACH BOYS - GOOD VIBRATIONS, THE (Thirty Years Of The Beach Boys)
CD Set _____ CDS 7812942
Capitol / Oct '93 / EMI.

BEACH BOYS CONCERT & BEACH BOYS '69 (Beach Boys Live in London)
Fun, fun, fun / Little old lady from Pasadena / Little deuce coupe / Long tall Texan / In my room / Monster mash / Let's go trippin' / Papa oom mow mow / Wanderer / Hawaii / Graduation day / I get around / Johnny B. Goode / Darlin' / Wouldn't it be nice / Sloop John B / California girls / Do it again / Wake the world / Aren't you glad / Bluebirds over the world / Their hearts were full of spring / Good vibrations / God only knows / Barbara Ann / Don't worry baby / Heroes and villains
CD _____ CZ 325
Capitol / Jul '90 / EMI.

BEACH BOYS TODAY/SUMMER DAYS AND SUMMER NIGHTS
Do you wanna dance / Don't hurt my little sister / Help me Rhonda / Please let me wonder / Kiss me baby / In the back of my mind / Girl from New York City / Then I kissed her / Girl don't tell me / Let him run wild / Summer means new love / And your dreams come true / I'm so young (alt. take) / Graduation day (studio version) / Good to my baby / When I grow up (to be a man) / Dance, dance, dance / I'm so young / She knows me too well / Bull session with Big Daddy / Amusement Parks USA / Salt Lake City / California girls / You're so good to me / I'm bugged at my ole man / Little girl I once knew / Let me wild (alternate take) / Help me Rhonda (LP version) / Dance, dance, dance (alt. take)
CD _____ CZ 324
EMI / Jul '90 / EMI.

BEACH BOYS/JAN & DEAN (Beach Boys/Jan & Dean)
CD _____ CD 115
Timeless Treasures / Oct '94 / THE.

BEST OF THE BEACH BOYS, THE
California girls / Surfin' USA / Little deuce coupe / Fun, fun, fun / Surfer girl / I get around / Girls on the beach / Don't worry baby / When I grow up (to be a man) / All summer long / Wendy / Do you wanna dance / Dance, dance, dance / In my room / Help me Rhonda / Then I kissed her / Little girl I once knew / Barbara Ann / Sloop John B / You're so good to me / Caroline no / God only knows / Wouldn't it be nice / Heroes and villains / Good vibrations / Darlin' / Wild honey / Friends / Do it again / Blue birds over the mountain / I can hear music / Break away / Cotton fields / Forever / Tears in the morning / Disney girls / Surf's up / Sail on sailor / Rock 'n' roll music / Here comes the night / Lady Lynda / Sumahama / California dreamin' / Kokomo
CD _____ CDESTVD 3
Capitol / Jun '95 / EMI.

CHRISTMAS ALBUM
Little Saint Nick / Man with all the toys / Santa's beard / Merry Christmas baby / Christmas day / Frosty the snowman / We three kings of Orient are / Blue Christmas / Santa Claus is coming to town / White Christmas / I'll be home for Christmas / Auld Lang Syne
CD _____ CDMFP 6150
Music For Pleasure / Oct '94 / EMI.

CRUISIN'
Still cruisin' / Somewhere near Japan / Island girl / In my car / Kokomo / Wipeout / Make it big / I get around / Wouldn't it be nice / California girls
CD _____ CDFA 3294
Fame / May '93 / EMI.

ENDLESS SUMMER
Surfin' safari / Surfer girl / Catch a wave / Warmth of the sun / Surfin' USA / Be true to your school / Little deuce coupe / In my room / Shut down / Fun, fun, fun / I get around / Girls on the beach / Wendy / Let him wild / Don't worry baby / California girls / Girl don't tell me / Help me Rhonda / You're so good to me / All summer long / Good vibrations
CD _____ CDMFP 50528
Music For Pleasure / Jul '91 / EMI.

FRIENDS/20-20
Meant for you / Friends / Wake the world / Be here in the morning / When a man needs a woman / Passing by / Anna Lee, the healer / Little bird / Be still / Busy doing nothing / Diamond head / Transcendental meditation / Do it again / I can hear music / Bluebirds over the mountain / Be with me / All I want to do / Nearest faraway place / Cotton fields / I went to sleep / Time to get alone / Never learn not to love / Our prayer / Cabinessence / Breakaway / Celebrate the news / We're together again / Walk on by / Old folks at home/Ol' man river
CD _____ CZ 341
Capitol / Sep '90 / EMI.

FUN FUN FUN
CD _____ 15164
Laserlight / Aug '91 / Target/BMG.

I LOVE YOU
Good vibrations / Then I kissed her / God only knows / Darlin' / Help me Rhonda / All summer long / Wendy / Don't worry baby / You're so good to me / Why do fools fall in love / I can hear music / Wouldn't it be nice / Surfer girl / Devoted to you / I'm so young / There's no other (like my baby) / She means too well / Good to be my baby / Please let me wonder / I was made to love her
CD _____ CDMFP 5988
Music For Pleasure / Jun '93 / EMI.

L.A. (LIGHT ALBUM)
Good timin' / Lady Lynda / Full sail / Angel come home / Love surrounds me / Sumahama / Here comes the night / Baby blue / Going South / Shortnin' bread
CD _____ 9021272
Carlton Home Entertainment / Jul '89 / Carlton Home Entertainment.

PET SOUNDS
Caroline no / Wouldn't it be nice / You still believe in me / That's not me / Don't talk / I know there's an answer / Here today / I just wasn't made for these times / Pet sounds / Hang on to your ego (CD only.) / Unreleased background (CD only.) / Trombone dixie (CD only.)
CD _____ CDFA 3298
Fame / Nov '93 / EMI.

SHUTDOWN VOL 2 (Surfin' Girl)
Fun, fun, fun / Don't worry baby / In the parkin' lot / Cassius love vs Sonny Wilson / Warmth of the sun / This car of mine / Why do fools fall in love / Pom pom play girl / Keep an eye on summer / Shutdown / Louie Louie / Denny's drum
CD _____ CZ 311
Capitol / Jul '90 / EMI.

SMILEY SMILE/WILD HONEY
Heroes and villains / Vegetables / Fall breaks and back to winter / She's goin' bald / Little pad / Good vibrations / With me to-night / Wind chimes / Gettin' hungry / Wonderful / Whistle in / Wild honey / Aren't you glad / I gotta made to love her / Country air / Thing or two / Darlin' / I'd love just once to see you / Here comes the night / Let the wind blow / How she boogalooed it / Mama says / Heroes and villains (alt. take) / Good vibrations (various sessions) / Good vibrations (early take) / You're welcome / Their hearts were full of spring / Can't wait too long
CD _____ CZ 326
Capitol / Jul '90 / EMI.

STILL CRUISIN'
Still cruisin' / Somewhere near Japan / Island girl / In my car / Kokomo / Wipeout / Make it big / I get around / Wouldn't it be nice / California girls
CD _____ CDESTU 2107
Capitol / Sep '89 / EMI.

SUMMER DREAMS
I get around / Surfin' USA / In my room (Not on CD.) / Fun, fun, fun / Little deuce coupe / Warmth of the sun (Not on CD.) / Surfin' safari / Help me Rhonda / Good vibrations / Sloop John B / You're so good to me / God only knows / Then I kissed her / Wouldn't it be nice / Heroes and villains / Wild honey / California girls / Don't worry baby / All summer long (Not on CD.) / Wendy (Not on CD.) / When I grow up (to be a man) / Dance, dance, dance / Little girl I once knew / Barbara Ann / Do it again / Friends / Darlin' / Bluebirds over the mountain / I can hear music / Breakaway / Cotton fields / California dreamin'
CD _____ CDEMTVD 51
Capitol / Jun '90 / EMI.

SUMMER IN PARADISE
Hot fun in the summertime / Surfin' / Summer of love / Island fever / Still surfin' / Slow summer dance / (One summer night) / Strange things happen / Remember / Walking in the sand / Lahaina Aloha / Under the boardwalk / Summer in paradise / Forever
CD _____ CDFA 3321
Fame / Apr '95 / EMI.

SURFIN' SAFARI/SURFIN' USA
Surfin' safari / County fair / Ten little indians / Chug-a-lug / Little girl / 409 / Surfin' / Heads you win - tails I lose / Summertime blues / Cuckoo clock / Moon dawg / Shift / Surfin' USA / Farmer's daughter / Misirlou / Stoked / Lonely sea / Shut down / Noble surfer / Honky tonk / Lana / Surf jam / Let's go trippin' / Finders keepers / Cindy oh Cindy / Baker man / Land ahoy
CD _____ CZ 312
Capitol / May '90 / EMI.

Beaker, Norman

INTO THE BLUES (Beaker, Norman Band)
CD _____ JSPCD 230
JSP / Oct '89 / ADA / Target/BMG / Direct / Cadillac / Complete/Pinnacle.

Beal, Jeff

CONTEMPLATIONS
Contemplation / Improvisation - every moment / Being a tree / Improvisation - love / Improvisation - a deux / Maines / Dance / Improvisation - the call / Discovery / Unquiet city / First steps / Ascension
CD _____ 3202042
Triloka / May '94 / New Note.

THREE GRACES
Jazz habit / Three graces / I saw Isabella / Wrong number / Through a glass dimly / Watchers / Prayer of St. Francis / Dizzy spells / For miles / Waltz for Mary
CD _____ 3201972
Triloka / Jun '93 / New Note.

Beamer, Kapono

PARADISE FOUND
CD _____ ISCD 117
Intersound / Oct '91 / Jazz Music.

Bear

BEAR TRACKS
CD _____ BGR 010
BGR / Mar '95 / Plastic Head.

Bearcats

CAJUN TRACKS
CD _____ BCAT 04CD
Bearcat / Jun '94 / Direct / ADA.

Beard, Jim

LOST AT THE CARNIVAL
CD _____ LIP 890272
Lipstick / May '95 / Vital/SAM.

SONG OF THE SUN
Camieff / Parsley trees / Songs of the sun / Holodeck waltz / Diana / Baker's annex / Haydel Bay / Lucky charms / Long bashels / Sweet bumps / Crossing troll bridge
CD _____ ESJCD 231
Essential Jazz / Oct '94 / BMG.

Beasley, John

CAULDRON
Beehave yourself / Sierra / Cado baypi / Cauldron / Catalina / 11.11 / Run and hide / Zulu king / I'm outa' here
CD _____ 101342
Windham Hill Jazz / Jan '92 / New Note.

Beastialit

DEHYDRATED SPLIT
CD _____ METALAGE 1CD
Clay / Apr '94 / Cargo.

Beastie Boys

CHECK YOUR HEAD
Jimmy James / Funky boss / Pass the mic / Gratitude / Lighten up / Finger lickin' good / So what'cha want / Biz Vs. the nuge / Time for livin' / Something's got to give / Blue nun / Stand together / Pow / Groove Holmes / Live at P.J.'s / Mark on the bus / Professor Booty / In 3's / Mamaste
CD _____ CDEST 2171
Grand Royal / Apr '92 / EMI.

ILL COMMUNICATION
Sure shot / Tough guy / B boys makin' with the freak freak / Bobo on the corner / Root down / Sabotage / Get it together / Sabrosa / Update / Futterman's rule / Alright hear this / Eugene's lament / Flute loop / Do it / Ricky's theme / Heart attack man / Scoop / Shambala / Bodhisattva vow / Transitions
CD _____ CDEST 2229
Grand Royal / May '94 / EMI.

LICENSED TO ILL
Rhymin and stealin' / New style / She's crafty / Posse in effect / Slow ride / Girls / (You gotta) Fight for your right (to party) / No sleep till Brooklyn / Paul Revere / Hold it, now hit it / Brass monkey / Slow and low / Time to get ill
CD _____ 5273512
Def Jam / Jul '95 / PolyGram.

PAUL'S BOUTIQUE
To all the girls / Shake your rump / Johnny Ryall / Egg man / High plains drifter / Sounds of science / Three minute rule / Hey ladies / Five piece chicken dinner / Looking down the barrel of a gun / Car thief / What comes around / Shadrach / Ask for Janice / B boy bouillabaisse
CD _____ CDEST 2102
Capitol / May '92 / EMI.

ROOT DOWN
Root down (Free Zone Mix) / Root down (1) / Root down (2) (PP Balloon Mix) / Time to get ill / Heart attackman / Maestro / Sabrosa / Fluteloop / Time for livin' / Something's got to give
CD _____ CDEST 2262
Grand Royal / May '95 / EMI.

SOME OLD BULLSHIT
Egg raid on mojo (demo) / Beastie Boys / Transit cop / Jimi / Holy snappers / Riot fight / Ode to... / Michelle's farm / Egg raid on mojo / Transit cop (demo) / Cooky puss / Bonus batter / Beastie revolution / Cooky puss (censored version)
CD _____ CDEST 2225
Grand Royal / Mar '94 / EMI.

Beasts Of Bourbon

AXEMAN'S JAZZ
CD _____ REDCD 4
Normal/Okra / Mar '94 / Direct / ADA.

BLACK MILK
CD _____ RED 012CD
Normal/Okra / Mar '94 / Direct / ADA.

FROM THE BELLY OF THE BEASTS
CD _____ REDCD 30
Normal/Okra / Mar '94 / Direct / ADA.

JUST RIGHT
CD _____ REDCD 20
Normal/Okra / Mar '94 / Direct / ADA.

LOW ROAD, THE
CD _____ REDCD 26
Normal/Okra / Mar '94 / Direct / ADA.

SOUR MASH
CD _____ REDCD 5
Normal/Okra / Mar '94 / Direct / ADA.

Beat

BPM (The Very Best Of The Beat)
Mirror in the bathroom / Hands off...she's mine / Twist and crawl / Jackpot / Tears of a clown / Ranking fullstop / Rough rider / Best friend / Stand down Margaret / Too nice to talk to / All out to get you / Door of your heart / Drowning / Can't get used to losing you / I confess / Save it for later
CD _____ 74321231952
Arista / Jan '96 / BMG.

DANCE HALL ROCKERS (International Beat)
Blue Moon / Jan '96 / Magnum Music Group / Greensleeves / Hot Shot / ADA / Cadillac / Discovery.

Beat

LIVE (Special Beat)
Concrete jungle / Monkey man / Tears of a clown / Rough rider / Too much too young / Spar wid me / Rat race / Too nice to talk to / Get a job / Nite club / Gangsters / Ranking full stop / Mirror in the bathroom / Enjoy yourself
CD _____ RRCD 168
Receiver / Jul '93 / Grapevine.

LIVE IN JAPAN (Special Beat)
Concrete jungle / Monkey man / Tears of a clown / Rough rider / Too much too young / Get a job / Rat race / Spar wid me / Too nice to talk to / Too hot / Do nothing / Nite club / Noise in this world / Gangsters / Ranking full stop / Mirror in the bathroom / Doesn't make it alright / Enjoy yourself / Jackpot / Message to you Rudy / Save it for later / You're wondering now
CD _____ DOJOCD 146
Dojo / Jun '94 / BMG.

Beat Farmers

MANIFOLD
CD _____ SECT 10019
Sector 2 / Oct '95 / Direct / ADA.

TALES OF THE NEW WEST
Bigger stones / There she goes again / Reason to believe / Lost weekend / California kid / Never goin' back / Goldmine / Showbiz / Lonesome hound / Where do they go / Selfish heart
CD _____ FIENDCD 39
Demon / Sep '90 / Pinnacle / ADA.

VIKING LULLABYS
CD _____ SECTOR 210013
Sector 2 / Apr '95 / Direct / ADA.

Beat Happening

BLACK CANDY
CD _____ ROUGHCD 145
Rough Trade / Sep '89 / Pinnacle.

JAMBOREE
CD _____ SP 62B
Sub Pop / Mar '94 / Disc.

Beat In Time

DOG FIGHT
CD _____ WHOS 044 CD
Who's That Beat / Oct '90 / Vital.

Beat Poets

TOTALLY RADIO
CD _____ ILLCD 015
Imaginary / Aug '90 / Vital.

Beatlerape

BEATLERAPE, THE
CD _____ CI 9204
Staalplaat / Dec '95 / Vital/SAM.

Beatles

1962-1966
Love me do / Please please me / From me to you / She loves you / I want to hold your hand / All my loving / Can't buy me love / Hard day's night / And I love her / Eight days a week / I feel fine / Ticket to ride / Yesterday / Help / You've got to hide your love away / We can work it out / Day tripper / Drive my car / Norwegian wood / Nowhere man / Michelle / In my life / Girl / Paperback writer / Eleanor Rigby / Yellow submarine
CD _____ CDPCSP 717
Parlophone / Nov '93 / EMI.

1967-1970
Strawberry Fields forever / Penny Lane / Sergeant Pepper's lonely hearts club band / With a little help from my friends / Lucy in the sky with diamonds / Day in the life / All you need is love / I am the walrus / Hello goodbye / Fool on the hill / Magical mystery tour / Lady Madonna / Hey Jude / Revolution / Back in the U.S.S.R / While my guitar gently weeps / Ob la di ob la da / Get back / Don't let me down / Ballad of John and Yoko / Old brown shoe / Here comes the sun / Come together / Something / Octopus's garden / Let it be / Across the universe / Long and winding road
CD _____ CDPCSP 718
Parlophone / Nov '93 / EMI.

ABBEY ROAD
Come together / Something / Maxwell's silver hammer / Oh darling / Octopus's garden / I want you (she's so heavy) / Here comes the sun / Because / You never give me your money / Sun king / Mean Mr Mustard / Polythene Pam / She came in through the bathroom window / Golden slumbers / Carry that weight / End Her Majesty
CD _____ CDPCS 7088
Parlophone / Oct '87 / EMI.

ANTHOLOGY, THE (2 CD/MC/3 LP Set)
Free as a bird / That'll be the day / In spite of all the danger / Hallelujah / I love her so / You'll be mine / Cayenne / My bonnie / Ain't she sweet / Cry for a shadow / Searchin' / Three cool cats / Sheik of Araby / Like dreamers do / Hello little girl / Besame mucho / Love me do / How do you do it / Please please me / One after 909 (sequence) / One after 909 (complete) / Lend

me your comb / I'll get you / I saw her standing there / From me to you / Money (that's what I want) / You really got a hold on me / Roll over Beethoven / She loves you / Till there was you / Twist and shout / This boy / I want to hold your hand / Moonlight bay / Can't buy me love / All my loving / You can't do that / I love her / Hard's day night / I wanna be your man / Long tall Sally / Boys / Shout / I'll be back (take 2) / I'll be back (take 3) / You know what to do / No reply (demo) / Mr Moonlight / Leave my kitten alone / No reply / Eight days a week / Hey hey hey / Kansas City / Eight days a week (complete)
CD Set _____ CDPCSP 727
Parlophone / Nov '95 / EMI.

BEATLES BOX SET
CD Set _____ CDS 791 302 2
Parlophone / Oct '88 / EMI.

BEATLES EP COLLECTION (14 EP Set)
CD Set _____ CDBEP 14
Parlophone / Apr '92 / EMI.

BEATLES FOR SALE
No reply / I'm a loser / Baby's in black / Rock 'n' roll music / I'll follow the sun / Mr. Moonlight / Kansas City / Eight days a week / Words of love / Honey don't / Don't want to spoil the party / What you're doing / Everybody's tryin' to be my baby
CD _____ CDP 746 438 2
Parlophone / '88 / EMI.

BEATLES II
CD P.Disc _____ CBAK 4009
Baktabak / Apr '88 / Baktabak.

BEATLES TALK DOWN UNDER VOL. 1 (Australia 1964)
CD P.Disc _____ CBAK 4024
Baktabak / Jun '91 / Baktabak.

BEATLES TALK DOWN UNDER VOL. 2
CD P.Disc _____ CBAK 4034
Baktabak / Aug '90 / Baktabak.

BEATLES TAPES (David Wigg Interviews 1969-73)
Interview (part 1) June 1969 / Give peace a chance / Interview (Part 2) June 1969 / Come together / Interview October 1971 / Interview (Part 1) March 1970 / Because / Interview (Part 1) March 1970 / Hey Jude / Interview (Part 2) March 1969 / Here comes the sun / Interview (Part 2) March 1969 / Something / Interview December 1968 / Interview July 1970 / Interview (Part 1) December 1973 / Octopus's Garden / Interview (Part 2) December 1973 / Yellow submarine
CD Set _____ 847 185-2
Polydor / Oct '90 / PolyGram.

BEATLES, THE (The White Album)
Back in the U.S.S.R / Dear Prudence / Glass onion / Ob la di ob la da / Wild honey pie / Continuing story of bungalow Bill / Why don't we do it in the road / I will / Julia / Yer blues / Mother nature's son / Everybody's got something to hide except me and my monkey / Sexy Sadie / Helter skelter / Long long long / Revolution 1 / Honey pie / Savoy truffle / Cry baby cry / Revolution 9 / Goodnight
CD Set _____ CDS 746 443 8
Parlophone / Aug '87 / EMI.

CD SINGLES COLLECTION (22CD Singles Box Set)
Love me do / P.S. I love you / Please please me / Ask me why / From me to you / Thank you girl / She loves you / I'll get you / I want to hold your hand / This boy / Can't buy me love / You can't do that / Hard day's night / Things we said today / I feel fine / She's a woman / Ticket to ride / Yes it is / Help / I'm down / We can work it out / Day tripper / Paperback writer / Rain / Yellow submarine / Eleanor Rigby / Strawberry fields forever / Penny Lane / All you need is love / Baby, you're a rich man / Hello goodbye / I am the walrus / Lady Madonna / Inner light / Hey Jude / Revolution / Get back / Don't let me down / Ballad of John and Yoko / Old brown shoe / Something / Come together / Let it be / You know my name (look up the number)
CD Set _____ CDBSCP 1
Parlophone / Nov '92 / EMI.

COME TOGETHER (America Salutes The Beatles) (Various Artists)
I'll follow the sun / Something / One after 909 / Long and winding road / Come together / If I fell / Let it be / We can work it out / Yesterday / Can't buy me love / Nowhere man / Oh Darling / Help / Paperback writer / All my loving / Get back / In my life
CD _____ CDEST 2255
Liberty / Apr '95 / EMI.

COME TOGETHER VOL.2 (Various Artists)
Tomorrow never knows / Strawberry fields / Drive my car / I am the walrus / Not a second time / Yes it is / Because / Golden slumbers / If I needed someone
CD _____ NYC 60142
NYC / Apr '95 / New Note.

49

BEATLES

CONQUER AMERICA
CD P.Disc _____ CBAK 4001
Baktabak / Feb '88 / Baktabak.

DOWNTOWN DOES THE BEATLES
(Various Artists)
CD _____ KFWCD 113
Knitting Factory / Nov '94 / Grapevine.

EXOTIC BEATLES, THE (Various Artists)
Yellow submarine / Yellow submarine ondo
/ Lucy in the sky with diamonds / I should
have known better / I wanna be your man /
Penny Lane / She loves you / Come to-
gether / Step inside love / In my life / When
I'm sixty four / Please please me / There's
a place / Things we said today / Fool on the
hill / Paperback writer / I want to hold your
hand / Eleanor Rigby / We can work it out
/ I am the walrus / And I love her / I'll be
back / Her majesty / Goodnight
CD _____ PELE 003CD
Exotica / May '93 / Vital.

EXOTIC BEATLES, THE: PART 2
(Various Artists)
Let it be / I saw her standing there / Nowhere man / Sergeant Pepper's lonely
hearts club band / Yesterday / Rain / Can't
buy me love / Lady Madonna / Yellow submarine / Flying / Hard day's night / From
me to you / Desert island discs / It's for you
/ We love rock 'n' roll / Ob la di ob la da
(polka) / Hey Jude / Piggies / I am the walrus / Give peace a chance / All my loving /
Continuing story of Bungalow Bill / Day tripper / Nostalgia
CD _____ PELE 007CD
Exotica / Oct '94 / Vital.

HARD DAY'S NIGHT, A
I should have known better / If I fell / I'm
happy just to dance with you / And I love
her / Tell me why / Can't buy me love / Hard
day's night / Anytime at all / I'll cry instead
/ Things we said today / When I get home
/ You can't do that / I'll be back
CD _____ CDP 746 437 2
Parlophone / Feb '87 / EMI.

**HEAR THE BEATLES TELL ALL (A
Unique Collectors Item)**
CD _____ CDCD 1185
Charly / Sep '94 / Charly / THE / Cadillac.

HELP (Film Soundtrack)
Help / Night before / You've got to hide your
love away / I need you / Another girl / You're
going to lose that girl / Ticket to ride / Act
naturally / It's only love / You like me too
much / Tell me what you saw / I've just seen
a face / Yesterday / Dizzy Miss Lizzy
CD _____ CDP 746 439 2
Parlophone / Apr '87 / EMI.

HITS OF THE BEATLES (Various Artists)
CD _____ DCD 5276
Disky / Aug '92 / THE / BMG / Discovery /
Pinnacle.

**IN THEIR OWN WORDS - A
ROCKUMENTARY (5CD Set)**
CD Set _____ 15962
Laserlight / Dec '95 / Target/BMG.

INTROSPECTIVE: BEATLES
Twist and shout / I saw her standing there
/ Till there was you / Interview part one /
Roll over Beethoven / Hippy hippy shake /
Taste of honey / Interview part two
CD _____ CINT 5004
Baktabak / Jun '91 / Baktabak.

JOHN LENNON FOREVER
(Rockumentary #3)
CD _____ 12593
Laserlight / Dec '95 / Target/BMG.

**LENNON AND MCCARTNEY
SONGBOOK (Various Artists)**
Lucy in the sky with diamonds / Let it be /
Here, there and everywhere / Anytime at all
/ Day tripper / With a little help from my
friends / Hey Jude / In my life / I call your
name / Got to get you into my life / Tomorrow never knows / Get back / I saw her
standing there / Please please me / Things
we said today / Nowhere man / I've just
seen a face / From me to you / She came
in through the bathroom window / It's for
you / Step inside love / Bad to me / Yesterday / You've got to hide your love away
CD _____ VSOPCD 150
Connoisseur / Jun '90 / Pinnacle.

**LENNON AND MCCARTNEY
SONGBOOK II (Various Artists)**
It's only love / Misery / Blackbird / Lady Madonna / I want to hold your hand / I'll cry
instead / Love me do / Help / There's a
place / You won't see me / She's leaving
home / And I love him / For no one / With
a little help from my friends / This boy /
Drive my car / One and one is two / Like
dreamers do / Don't let me down / I am the
walrus / Rain / Nobody I know / Hello little
girl / Ticket to ride
CD _____ VSOPCD 162
Connoisseur / Nov '91 / Pinnacle.

LET IT BE
Two of us / Dig a pony / Across the universe
/ I me mine / Dig it / Let it be / Maggie Mae
/ I've got a feeling / One after 909 / Long
and winding road / Get back
CD _____ CDPCS 7096
Parlophone / Oct '87 / EMI.

LIVE AT THE BBC
Beatle greetings / From us to you / Riding
on a bus / I got a woman / Too much monkey business / Keep your hands off my
baby / I'll be on my way / Young blood /
Shot of rhythm and blues / Sure to fall /
Some other guy / Thank you girl / Sha la la
la / Baby, it's you / That's all right Mama /
Carol / Soldiers of love / Little rhyme / Clar-
abella / I'm gonna sit right down and cry
over you / Crying, waiting, hoping / Dear
wack / You really got a hold on me / To
know her is to love her / Taste of honey /
Long tall Sally / I saw her standing there /
Honeymoon song / Johnny B. Goode /
Memphis, Tennessee / Lucille / Can't buy
me love / From Fluff to you / Till there was
you / Crinsk dee night / Hard day's night /
Have a banana / I wanna be your man / Just
a rumour / Roll over Beethoven / All my loving / Things we said today / She's a woman
/ Sweet little sixteen / 1822 / Lonesome
tears in my eyes / Nothin' shakin' / Hippy
hippy shake / Glad all over / I just don't understand / So how come (no one loves me)
/ I feel fine / I'm a loser / Everybody's tryin'
to be my baby / Rock 'n' roll music / Ticket
to ride / Dizzy Miss Lizzy / Kansas City/Hey
hey hey hey / Set fire to that lot / Matchbox
/ I forgot to remember to forget / Love these
Goon shows / I got to find my baby / Ooh,
my soul / Ooh, my arms / Don't ever change
/ Slow down / Honey don't / Love me do
CD Set _____ CDPCSP 726
Apple / Dec '94 / EMI.

LIVE RECORDINGS (1962)
CD _____ CDTAB 5001
Baktabak / '88 / Baktabak.

LOST BEATLES INTERVIEWS, THE
(Rockummentary #1)
CD _____ 12591
Laserlight / Dec '95 / Target/BMG.

**LOVE 'EM DO (Hits That Inspired The
Beatles) (Various Artists)**
CD _____ CDINS 5063
Instant / Nov '92 / Charly.

**LOVE ME BLUE (The Music Of Lennon
& McCartney) (Various Artists)**
Can't buy me love / Eleanor Rigby / I want
to hold your hand / Yesterday / From me to
you / Hey Jude / In my life / Get back
CD _____ CDP 7948612
Blue Note / May '91 / EMI.

MAGICAL MYSTERY TOUR
Magical mystery tour / Fool on the hill / Fly-
ing / Blue jay way / Your mother should
know / I am the walrus / Hello goodbye /
Strawberry fields forever / Penny Lane /
Baby, you're a rich man / All you need is
love
CD _____ CDPCTC 255
Parlophone / Sep '87 / EMI.

PAST MASTERS VOL. 1
Love me do / From me to you / Thank you
girl / She loves you / I'll get you / I want to
hold your hand / This boy / Komm gib mir
deine hand / Sie liebt dich / Long tall Sally
/ I call your name / Slow down / Matchbox
/ I feel fine / She's a woman / Bad boy /
Yes it is / I'm down
CD _____ CDBPM 1
Parlophone / Aug '88 / EMI.

PAST MASTERS VOL. 2
Day tripper / We can work it out / Paper-
back writer / Rain / Lady Madonna / Inner
light / Hey Jude / Revolution / Get back /
Don't let me down / Ballad of John and
Yoko / Old brown shoe / Across the uni-
verse / Let it be / You know my name (look
up the number)
CD _____ CDBPM 2
Parlophone / Aug '88 / EMI.

**PAUL MCCARTNEY - BEYOND THE
MYTH (Rockumentary #4)**
CD _____ 12594
Laserlight / Dec '95 / Target/BMG.

PLEASE PLEASE ME
Taste of honey / I saw her standing there /
Misery / Anna / Chains / Boys / Ask me why
/ Please please me / Love me do / I love
you / Baby, it's you / Do you want to know
a secret / There's a place / Twist and shout
CD _____ CDP 746 435 2
Parlophone / Feb '87 / EMI.

REVOLVER
Taxman / Eleanor Rigby / I'm only sleeping
/ Love you to / Here, there and everywhere
/ Yellow submarine / She said she said /
Good day sunshine / And your bird can sing
/ For no one / Dr. Robert / I want to tell you
/ Got to get you into my life / Tomorrow
never knows
CD _____ CDP 746 441 2
Parlophone / Apr '87 / EMI.

RUBBER SOUL
Drive my car / Norwegian wood / You won't
see me / Nowhere man / Think for yourself
/ Word / Michelle / What goes on / Girl / I'm
looking through you / In my life / Wait / If I
needed someone / Run for your life
CD _____ CDP 746 440 2
Parlophone / Apr '87 / EMI.

**SECRET LIFE OF GEORGE HARRISON,
THE (Rockumentary #5)**
CD _____ 12595
Laserlight / Dec '95 / Target/BMG.

**SGT. PEPPER'S LONELY HEARTS
CLUB BAND**
Sergeant Pepper's lonely hearts club band
/ With a little help from my friends / Lucy in
the sky with diamonds / Getting better / Fix-
ing a hole / She's leaving home / Being for
the benefit of Mr. Kite / Within you without
you / When I'm sixty four / Lovely Rita /
Good morning good morning / Day in the
life
CD _____ CDPEPPER 1
Parlophone / Jun '87 / EMI.

**SHE LOVES YOU (Music Of The Beatles
- 16 Instrumental Hits) (Various Artists)**
CD _____ 5708574338073
Carlton Home Entertainment / Sep '94 /
Carlton Home Entertainment.

**SONGS OF LENNON & MCCARTNEY
(Various Artists)**
All my loving / Baby's in black / I don't want
to spoil the party / Paperback writer / With
a little help from my friends / We can work
it out / Little child / I'll follow the sun /
Eleanor Rigby / Fool on the hill / Long and
winding road / And I love her / Honey pie /
Continuing story of Bungalow Bill / This girl
CD _____ NEBCD 654
Sequel / Jun '93 / BMG.

**SONGS OF THE BEATLES (Various
Artists)**
Get back / And I love her / Eleanor Rigby /
Fool on the hill / You never give me your
money / Come together / I want you /
Blackbird / Something / Here, there and
everywhere / Long and winding road / Yes-
terday / Hey Jude
CD _____ 7567814832
East West / Feb '94 / Warner Music.

**SONGWRITING LEGENDS: LENNON &
MCCARTNEY (Nice 'n' easy series)
(Various Artists)**
CD _____ 8440822
Eclipse / Mar '92 / PolyGram.

**THINGS WE SAID TODAY - TALKING
WITH THE BEATLES (Rockumentary #2)**
CD _____ 12592
Laserlight / Dec '95 / Target/BMG.

WITH THE BEATLES
It won't be long / All I've got to do / All my
loving / Don't bother me / Little child / Till
there was you / Please Mr. Postman / Roll
over Beethoven / Hold me tight / You really
got a hold on me / I wanna be your man /
Devil in her heart / Not a second time /
Money
CD _____ CDP 746 436 2
Parlophone / Feb '87 / EMI.

YELLOW SUBMARINE
Yellow submarine / Only a northern song /
All you need is love / Hey bulldog / It's all
too much / All together now / Pepperland /
Sea of time / Sea of holes / Sea of monsters
/ March of the meanies / Pepperland laid to
waste / Yellow submarine in Pepperland
CD _____ CDPCS 7070
Parlophone / Aug '87 / EMI.

Beatnigs

BEATNIGS
CD _____ VIRUS 65CD
Alternative Tentacles / Jan '89 / Pinnacle.

Beatnik Filmstars

LAID BACK & ENGLISH
CD _____ LADIDA 027CD
La-Di-Da / Jul '94 / Vital.

Beaton, Alex

20 HITS OF SCOTLAND
Scots wha hae / Dumbarton's drums /
These are my mountains / Annie Laurie /
Wee castanettes / Man's a man for a' that
/ Ae fond kiss / Killiecrankie / Skye boat
song / Hey Johnny Cope / Amazing grace /
Stoutest man in the forty twa / Glencoe /
Scottish soldier / Flowers of the forest /
Loch Lomond / Big Nellie May / Rowan tree
/ Fower of Scotland / Bonnie Galloway /
Scotland the brave
CD _____ LCDM 9031
Lismor / Aug '90 / Lismor / Direct / Duncans
/ ADA.

Beats

UP UNTIL NOW
CD _____ CDCOT 102
Cottage / Oct '94 / THE / Koch.

Beats International

EXCURSION ON THE VERSION
Brand new beat / Change your mind / Love
is green / Echo chamber / Sun doesn't
shine / Herman / Three foot skank / No
more Mr. nice guy / Eyes on the prize / Ten
long years / In the ghetto / Come home
CD _____ 828 290 2
Go Beat / Feb '91 / PolyGram.

Beats The Hell Out Of Me

BEATS THE HELL OUT OF ME
Painfully / Buzz / Told / Behind my back /
Intro / Act like a man

Beau

BEAU/CREATION
Welcome / 1917 Revolution / Fising song /
Pillar of economy / Sundancer / Morning
sun / Ways of winter / Nine minutes / Spider
/ Is this your day / Blind faith / Release /
Silence returns / Imagination / Soldier of the
willow / Painted vase / Nations pride / Rain
/ Summer has gone / Welcome tag piece /
There was once a time / April meteor /
Creation / Ferris street / Reason to be
CD _____ SEECD 421
See For Miles/C5 / May '95 / Pinnacle.

Beau Brummels

AUTUMN IN SAN FRANCISCO
Laugh laugh / Just a little / You tell me why
/ Don't talk to strangers / In good time / Sad
little girl / Still in love with you baby / Stick
like glue / That's if you want me to / Can it
be / When it comes to your love / Gentle
wanderin' ways / I grow old / Lonely man /
She sends me
CD _____ EDCD 141
Edsel / Aug '90 / Pinnacle / ADA.

AUTUMN OF THEIR YEARS
She sends me / Tomorrow is another day /
She loves me / Woman / Dream on / Cry
some / I grow old / No lonelier man / This
is love / She's my girl / I'll tell you / Let me
in / Love is just a game / Till the day / I will
go / Stay with me awhile / I'm alone again
/ Down on me / Can't be so / Fine with me
/ Coming home / That's all that matter /
Laugh laugh / Still in love with you baby /
Just a little / When it comes to your love
CD _____ CDWIKD 127
Big Beat / Feb '94 / Pinnacle.

Bradley's Band

BRADLEY'S BAND
Turn around / Added attraction / Deep water / Long walking down to misery / Little
bird / Cherokee girl / I'm a sleeper / Loneliest man in town / Love can fall a long way
down / Jessica / Bless you California
CD _____ 7599268872
WEA / Jan '96 / Warner Music.

SIXTY SIX
CD _____ 7599268852
WEA / Jan '96 / Warner Music.

TRIANGLE
CD _____ 7599268862
WEA / Jan '96 / Warner Music.

Beaumont & Hannant

BASIC DATA MANIPULATION
CD _____ GPRCD 2
General Production Recordings / Nov '93 /
Pinnacle.

SCULPTURED
CD _____ GPRCD 9
General Production Recordings / Oct '94 /
Pinnacle.

TEXUROLOGY
CD _____ GPR 4CD
General Production Recordings / Apr '94 /
Pinnacle.

Beaumont, Howard

**AS TIME GOES BY, VOL. 3 (Together
Again) (Beaumont, Howard & John
Taylor)**
Together again / Say it isn't so / Love letters
in the sand / Smoke gets in your eyes / I'll
always be in love with you / Lollipops and
roses / Seems like old times / Nevertheless
/ Sun has got his hat on / Keep young and
beautiful / There's a small hotel / Room with
a view / Someone to watch over me /
Embraceable you / I wish you love / For all
we know / Steppin' out with my baby / Let's
face the music and dance / You'll never
know / Too late now / Room 504 / More
than you know / I'll never smile again /
Dream lover / Pal of my cradle days / I may
be wrong, but I think you're wonderful / I'm
beginning to see the light / Touch of your
lips / Time on my hands / As time goes by
/ We'll meet again
CD _____ CDGRS 1206
Grosvenor / '91 / Target/BMG.

HIGHLIGHTS
CD _____ CDGRS 1277
Grosvenor / May '95 / Target/BMG.

JUBILEE
Best of times / I am what I am / Nice and
easy / Where or when / Tender trap / These
foolish things / Mairi's wedding / Scotch on
the rocks / Scottish solider / Loch Lomond
/ Roaming' in the gloamin' / Scotland the
Brave / Manana / Enjoy yourself / Big brass
band from Brazil / Coffee song / Some
Moon river / Charade / It don't mean a thing
if it ain't got that swing / Happy feet / After
you've gone / Shine / When day is done /
On a slow boat to China / At last / I know
why / Losing my mind / When I fall in love
/ Fool on the hill / Watch what happens /

Blue velvet / Hey there / Norwegian wood / I've got a gal in Kalamazoo / Stompin' at the Savoy / Auntie Maggie's remedy / Fanlight fanny / With my little ukulele in my hand / When I'm cleaning windows / Leaning on a lamp-post / Thorn birds (Theme from) / My wild Irish rose / How can you buy Killarney / Come back Erin / Here's that rainy day / Love letters / My foolish heart / Stella by Starlight / World of our own / There's a kind of hush / It might as well rain until September / I only want to be with you / Raining in my heart
CD _____ CDGRS 1256
Grosvenor / Feb '95 / Target/BMG.

SHOWTIME VOL. 2
Me and my girl selection / Carousel selection / Oliver selection / Miss Saigon selection / Desert song medley / Seven brides for seven brothers selection (CD only)
CD _____ CDGRS 1262
Grosvenor / Feb '95 / Target/BMG.

YOU MUST REMEMBER THESE (As Time Goes By Vol.4) (Beaumont, Howard & John Taylor)
CD _____ CDGRS 1278
Grosvenor / May '95 / Target/BMG.

Beausoleil

ALLONS A LAFAYETTE & MORE
CD _____ ARHCD 308
Arhoolie / Apr '95 / ADA / Direct / Cadillac.

BAYOU BOOGIE
Zydeco gris gris / Fais pas ca / It's you I love / Dimanche apres-midi / Madame Bozo / Kolinda / Maman Rosin Boudreaux / Chez Seychelles / Jongle a moi / Flame will never die / La vaise de malchanceaux / Beausoleil boogie
CD _____ CD 6015
Rounder / '88 / CM / Direct / ADA / Cadillac.

CAJUN CONJA
CD _____ FIENDCD 704
Demon / Sep '91 / Pinnacle / ADA.

DANSE DE LA VIE
Danse de la vie / Dans le Grand Brouillard / L'ouragon / Dis-moi pas / Jeunes filles de la campagne / Quelle belle vie / R.D. special / Chanson pour Ezra / Menage a trois reels / Zydeco X / Je tombe aux Genoux / Attrape mes larmes / La fille de quatorze ans
CD _____ 812271221-2
Atlantic / Jun '93 / Warner Music.

HOT CHILI MAMA (Beausoleil & Michael Doucet)
CD _____ ARHCD 5040
Arhoolie / Apr '95 / ADA / Direct / Cadillac.

L'ECHO
CD _____ 812271808-2
Warner Bros. / Nov '94 / Warner Music.

PARLEZ-NOUS A BOIRE
CD _____ ARHCD 322
Arhoolie / Apr '95 / ADA / Direct / Cadillac.

THEIR SWALLOW RECORDINGS
J'ai vu le loup / Valse a Beausoleil / Twostep des freres Mathieu / Travailler ce'est trop dur / Potpourri cadjin / He, Mom / Valse des Balfa / Zydeco gris gris / Les barres de la prison / Hommage aux freres Balfa / Chanson / Love bridge waltz / Tu peux cognai / Contredanse de mamou / Reel de Dennis McGee / Blues a bebe / Talle du ronces / Blues de morse / Fi fi a Poncho / J'ai fait ta tour de grand bois / Je m'endors, je m'endors / La valse de grand bois / Tinnni.... trinnni?
CD _____ CDCHD 379
Ace / Sep '92 / Pinnacle / Cadillac / Complete/Pinnacle.

Beautiful South

0898 BEAUTIFUL SOUTH
CD _____ 8283102
Go Discs / Apr '92 / PolyGram.

CARRY ON UP THE CHARTS (Best Of The Beautiful South)
Song for whoever / You keep it all in / I'll sail this ship alone / Little time / My book / Let love speak up for itself / We are each other / Bell bottomed tear / 36D / Good as gold (stupid as mud) / Everybody's talkin' / Prettiest eyes / One last love song / Dream a little dream
CD _____ 8285722
Go Discs / Nov '94 / PolyGram.

CHOKE
Tonight I fancy myself / Let love speak up itself / I've come for my award / I think the answer's yes / Mother's pride / Rising of Grafton Street / My book / Should've kept my eyes shut / Lips / Little time / I hate you (but you're interesting)
CD _____ 8282342
Go Discs / Oct '90 / PolyGram.

MIAOW
CD _____ 828507-2
Go Discs / Mar '94 / PolyGram.

WELCOME TO THE BEAUTIFUL SOUTH
Song for whoever / Have you ever been away / From under the covers / I'll sail this

ship alone / Girlfriend / Straight in at 37 / You keep it all in / Woman in the wall / Oh Blackpool / Love is / I love you (but you're boring)
CD _____ AGOCD 16
Go Discs / Oct '89 / PolyGram.

Beautiful World

IN EXISTENCE
In the beginning / In existence / Evolution / Magicien du bonheur / I know / Silk road / Love song / Journey of the ancestors / Revolution of the heart / Coming of age / Spoken word / Wonderful world / Final emotion
CD _____ 450995120-2
WEA / Mar '94 / Warner Music.

Beauvoir, Jean

ROCKIN' IN THE STREET
CD _____ CDOVD 465
Virgin / Jan '96 / EMI.

Beaver & Krause

GANDHARVA
Soft / White / Saga of the blue beaver / Nine Moons In Alaska / Walkin' by the river / Short film for David / Bright shadows
CD _____ 9362454722
WEA / Feb '94 / Warner Music.

Becaud, Gilbert

ET MAINTENANT
CD _____ CD 352127
Duchesse / Jul '93 / Pinnacle.

Because

MAD SCARED DUMB AND GORGEOUS
CD _____ HAVENCD 1
Haven/Backs / May '92 / Disc / Pinnacle.

Bechet, Sidney

1937-1938
CD _____ CD 593
Classic Jazz Masters / Sep '91 / Wellard / Jazz Music / Jazz Music.

1938-40
CD _____ CLASSICS 608
Classics / Oct '92 / Discovery / Jazz Music.

AMERICAN FRIENDS
CD _____ VGCD 655623
Vogue / Jan '93 / BMG.

BECHET
Kansas City man blues / Old fashioned love / Texas moaner blues / Mandy, make up your mind / Papa de da da / Wild cat blues / Coal cart blues / Sweetie dear / I want you tonight / Ja da / Really the blues / I've found a new baby / When you and I were young Maggie / Shake it and break it / Old man blues / Wild man blues / Nobody knows the way I feel dis mornin' / Blues in thirds / Blues for you Johnny / Ain't misbehavin' / Save it pretty Mama / Stompy Jones
CD _____ PASTCD 9772
Flapper / Jan '92 / Pinnacle.

BECHET-MEZZROW QUINTET
CD _____ 401172CD
Musidisc / Jul '94 / Vital / Harmonia Mundi / ADA / Cadillac / Discovery.

BEST OF CHARLESTON (Bechet, Sidney & Claude Luter)
Dixie Live / Mar '95 / Magnum Classic
g. shipi
CD _____ DLCD 4070

BEST OF SIDNEY BECHET
CD _____ DLCD 4025
Dixie Live / Mar '95 / Magnum Music Group.

BLUES IN THIRDS
CD _____ LEJAZZCD 30
Le Jazz / Aug '94 / Charly / Cadillac.

BLUES IN THIRDS 1940-1941
CD _____ CD 53105
Giants Of Jazz / May '93 / Target/BMG / Cadillac.

COMPLETE SIDNEY BECHET 1 & 2 (1932 - 1941)
One o'clock jump / Preachin' blues / Old man blues / Blues in thirds / Ain't misbehavin' / Save it pretty Mama / Stompy Jones / Muskrat ramble / Coal black blues / Sweetie dear / Lay your racket / Maple leaf rag / Ja da / Really the blues / Weary blues / Indian Summer / I want you tonight / I've found a new baby / When you and I were young Maggie / Maggie / Sidney's blues / Shake it and break it / Wild man blues / Nobody knows the way I feel this morning / Make a pallet on the floor / St. Louis blues / Blues for you / Johnny / Eygptian fantasy
CD Set _____ ND 89760
Jazz Tribune / May '94 / BMG.

COMPLETE SIDNEY BECHET 3 & 4 (1941)
I'm coming Virginia (takes 1 & 2) / Limehouse blues / Georgia cabin (takes 1 & 2) / Texas moaner (takes 1 & 2) / Strange fruit / You're the limit (takes 1 & 2) / Rip up the

joint / Suey (takes 1 & 2) / Blues in the air (takes 1 & 2) / Mooche (takes 1 & 2) / Laughin' in rhythm / 12th Street rag (takes 1 & 2) / I know that you know (takes 1, 2 & 3) / Egyptian fantasy / Baby, won't you please come home / Slippin' and slidin' / Sheikh of Araby / Blues of Bechet / Swing parade (takes 1 & 2) / When it's sleepy time down South / I ain't gonna give nobody none o' this jelly roll (takes 1 & 2)
CD _____ ND 897592
Jazz Tribune / Jun '94 / BMG.

COMPLETE SIDNEY BECHET 5
Mood indigo (takes 1 & 2) / Lady be good (takes 1 & 2) / What's this thing called love (takes 1 & 2) / After you've gone / Bugle call rag/Ole Miss rag / St. Louis blues / Revolutionary blues / Comin' on with the come on (takes 1 & 2) / Careless love (takes 1 & 2) / Royal Garden blues (takes 1 & 2) / Everybody loves my baby (takes 1 & 2) / I ain't gonna give nobody none o' this Jelly Roll (takes 1 & 2) / If you see me comin' (takes 1 & 2) / Gettin' together (takes 1 & 2) / Rosetta / Minor jive / World is waiting for the sunrise / Who / Blues my baby gave to me / Rompin'
CD _____ 7432115519-2
Jazz Tribune / Jun '94 / BMG.

FREIGHT TRAIN BLUES
Sweetie dear / I want you tonight / I've found a new baby / Lay your racket / Maple leaf rag / Shag / Okey doke / Characteristic blues / Viper mad / Blackstick / When the sun sets down south (Southern sunset) / Sweet patootie / Freight train blues / Trixie blues / My Daddy rocks me (Part I) / My Daddy rocks me (Part II) / What a dream / Hold tight / Jungle drums / Chant in the night / Ja da / Really the blues / when you and I were young Maggie / Weary blues
CD _____ CDGRF 100
Tring / '93 / Tring / Prism.

GENIUS OF SIDNEY BECHET, THE
CD _____ JCD 35
Jazzology / Aug '95 / Swift / Jazz Music.

HOLD TIGHT 1938-46
CD _____ CDJJ 603
Jazz & Jazz / Jul '89 / Target/BMG.

IN CONCERT, OLYMPIA 1954
CD _____ VGCD 655625
Vogue / Jan '93 / BMG.

IN NEW YORK 1937-40
CD _____ JSPCD 338
JSP / Aug '92 / ADA / Target/BMG / Direct / Cadillac / Complete/Pinnacle.

INTRODUCTION TO JAZZ
CD _____ 4017
Best Of Jazz / Mar '95 / Discovery.

JAZZ AT STORYVILLE
CD _____ BLCD 760902
Black Lion / Jun '88 / Jazz Music / Cadillac / Wellard / Koch.

JAZZ CLASSICS VOL.1
Blue horizon / Weary blues / Summertime / Blame it on the blues / Milenberg joys / Days beyond recall / Salty dog / Dear old Southland / Weary wag blues
CD _____ CDP 7893842
Blue Note / Jan '94 / EMI.

JAZZ CLASSICS VOL.2
St. Louis blues / Up in Sidney's flat / Lord let me in the lifeboat / Pounding heart blues / Changes made / Magic hostess / Jackass blues / Jazz me blues / Blues for Tommy Ladnier / Old stack o'lee blues
CD _____ CDP 789385-2
Blue Note / Jan '94 / EMI.

JAZZ PORTRAITS
Shag / Maple leaf rag / Sweetie dear / I've found a new baby / Lay your racket / I want you tonight / Polka dot rag / T'aint a fit night out for a man or beast / When the sun sets down south (southern sunset) / Freight train blues / Chant in the night / Characteristic blues / Black stick blues / Jungle drums / Really the blues / Weary blues / When you and I were young Maggie / Ja da
CD _____ CD 14517
Jazz Portraits / May '94 / Jazz Music.

LA NUIT EST UNE SORCIERE
CD _____ 74321134142
Vogue / Jul '93 / BMG.

LIVE IN SWITZERLAND 1951 & 1954
CD _____ 44901-2
Landscape / Aug '93 / THE.

MASTERS OF JAZZ VOL.4
CD _____ STCD 4104
Storyville / May '93 / Jazz Music / Wellard / CM / Cadillac.

PARISIAN ENCOUNTER (Bechet, Sidney & Teddy Buckner)
Bravo / Aubergines / I can't get started (with you) / Souvenirs / Blue festival / Weary blues / Ain't misbehavin' / Sugar / Who's sorry now / All of me
CD _____ 655617
GNP Crescendo / May '91 / Silva Screen.

RARE SOPRANO SAX RECORDINGS (The Golden Age of Jazz)
CD _____ JZCD 364
Suisa / May '92 / Jazz Music / THE.

REALLY THE BLUES (Original recordings 1932-41)
Baby, won't you please come home / 2.19 blues / Blues in thirds / China boy / Egyptian fantasy / Four or five times / High society / I ain't gonna give nobody none o' this jelly roll / I thought I heard Buddy Bolden say / Indian summer / Lay your racket / Maple leaf rag / Mooche / Muskrat ramble / Nobody knows the way I feel dis mornin' / Perdido Street blues / Preachin' blues / Really the blues / Sheikh of araby / Strange time down South / Stompy Jones / Strange fruit / Texas moaner / When you and I were young Maggie / Wild man blues
CD _____ CDAJA 5107
Living Era / Jul '93 / Koch.

REVOLUTIONARY BLUES 1941-1951
Shimme-sha wabble / I wish I could shimmy like my sister Kate / Fidgety feet / Jelly roll blues / Mood indigo / Laura / St. Louis blues / Love for sale
CD _____ CD 53106
Giants Of Jazz / May '92 / Target/BMG / Cadillac.

SALLE PLAYEL, PARIS 1952
CD _____ CD 53177
Giants Of Jazz / Sep '94 / Target/BMG / Cadillac.

SERIE NOIRE
Pourtant / Un ange comme ca / South Rampart street parade / Blues dans le blues / Moi d'payer / Trottoir de Paris / Le hommes sont genereux / L'enchaines d'amour / Le blues de mes reves / Halle hallelujah / I had it but it's all gone now / Halle hallelujah (2) / Jumpin' Jack / Passport to paradise / Coquin de Boubou / Haco haco coucou / Chacun a sa chance / Shake 'em up / Un coup de cafard / Sans vous facher, respondezmoi / Le train du viewx noir / Le bidou
CD _____ 74321154652
Vogue / Oct '93 / BMG.

SIDNEY BECHET & MUGGSY SPANIER/DON EWELL/DOC EVANS VOL. 1
CD _____ DD 226
Delmark / Feb '95 / Hot Shot / ADA / CM / Direct / Cadillac.

SIDNEY BECHET & NEW ORLEANS FOOTWARMERS 1940-1941
CD _____ 882442
Music Memoria / Aug '93 / Discovery / ADA.

SIDNEY BECHET & NEW ORLEANS FOOTWARMERS 1941-1943
CD _____ 882452
Music Memoria / Aug '93 / Discovery / ADA.

SIDNEY BECHET - 1923-36
CD _____ CLASSICS 583
Classics / Oct '91 / Discovery / Jazz Music.

SIDNEY BECHET - 1940
CD _____ CLASSICS 619
Classics / '92 / Discovery / Jazz Music.

SIDNEY BECHET 1932 - 1951
CD Set _____ CDB 1214
Giants Of Jazz / Jul '92 / Target/BMG / Cadillac.

SIDNEY BECHET IN CONCERT
CD _____ 710440
RTE / Apr '95 / ADA / Koch.

SIDNEY DE PARIS 1943 & 1944
CD _____ 409392
Music Memoria / Nov '95 / Discovery / ADA.

Gr in l'3 OF NEW ORLEANS (Bechet, Sidney & Mezz Mezzrow)
American rhythm / Happy go lucky blues / Klook's blues / Out of nowhere / Mon homme / Orphan Annie's blues / Black and blue / Bugle call rag / Wolverine blues / High society / Blues for kicks / I found a new grove nobody none o' this jelly roll / My blue heaven / Careless love / Coquette / Reverend blues / Serenade to Paris
CD _____ 74321134082
Vogue / Jul '93 / BMG.

SUMMERTIME 1932-40
CD _____ CD 53104
Giants Of Jazz / Mar '92 / Target/BMG / Cadillac.

TOGETHER, TOWN HALL 1947 (Bechet, Sidney & Wingy Manone)
CD _____ 3801292
Jazz Archives / Jan '93 / Jazz Music / Discovery / Cadillac.

WEARY BLUES
CD _____ CD 56052
Jazz Roots / Mar '95 / Target/BMG.

WEARY BLUES
CD _____ JHR 73553
Jazz Hour / Jan '93 / Target/BMG / Jazz Music / Cadillac.

Beck

MELLOW GOLD
Loser / Pay no mind (snoozer) / Fuckin' with my head (Mountain dew rock) / Whiskeyclone / Hotel City 1997 / Soul suckin jerk /

Truckdrivin neighbors downstarirs / Sweet sunshine / Beercan / Steal my body home / Nightmare hippy girl / Motherfuker / Blackhole
CD _____ GED 24634
Geffen / Mar '94 / BMG.

ONE FOOT IN THE GRAVE
CD _____ KLP 28 CD
K / Nov '95 / SRD.

Beck, Elder Charles

ELDER BECK & ELDER CURRY 1930-39
CD _____ BDCD 6035
Blues Document / Apr '93 / Swift / Jazz Music / Hot Shot.

Beck, Gordon

ONE FOR THE ROAD
Good times, sometimes / Out of the shadows into the sun / Thoughts / Long, lean and lethal / What's this / Beautiful, but / One for the road / Shhhh / Pay now, live later
CD _____ JMS 186752
JMS / Nov '95 / BMG / New Note.

Beck, Jeff

BECKOLOGY
Trouble in mind / Nursery rhyme (Live) / Wandering man blues / Steeled blues / Heart full of soul / I'm not talking / I ain't done wrong / I'm a man / Shape of things ten years time ago / Hot house of Omagarashid / Lost women / Rack myh mind / Nazz are blue / Psycho daisies / Jeff's boogie / Too much monkey business (Live) / Sun is shining (Live) / You're a better man than I (Live) / Love me like I love you (Live) / Hi ho silver lining / Tallyman / Beck's bolero / I ain't superstitious / Rock my plimsoul / Jailhouse rock / Plynth (water down the drain) / I've been drinking / Definitely maybe / New ways/train train / Going down / I can't give back the love I feel for you / Superstition / Black cat moan (Live) / Blues deluxe BBA boogie / Jizz whizz / 'Cause we've ended as lovers / Goodbye pork pie hat / Love is green / Diamond dust / Freeway jam (Live) / Pump / People get ready / Escape / Gets us all in the end / Back on the street / Wild thing / Train kept a rollin' / Sleepwalk / Stumble / Big block / Where were you
CD Set _____ 4692622
Epic / May '94 / Sony.

BEST OF JEFF BECK, THE (featuring Rod Stewart)
Shapes of things / Morning dew / You shook me / I ain't superstitious / All shook up / Jailhouse rock / Plynth (water down the drain) / Hi ho silver lining / Tallyman / Love is blue / I've been drinking / Rock my plimsoul / Beck's bolero / Rice pudding / Greensleeves / Spanish boots
CD _____ CDMFP 6202
Music For Pleasure / Nov '95 / EMI.

BLOW BY BLOW
It doesn't really matter / She's a woman / Constipated duck / Air blower / Scatterbrain / 'Cause we've ended as lovers / Thelonious / Freeway jam / Diamond dust
CD _____ 4690122
Epic / Apr '94 / Sony.
CD _____ EK 64407
Epic / Nov '95 / Sony.

FLASH
Ambitious / Gets us all in the end / Escape / People get ready / Stop, look and listen / Get workin' / Ecstasy / Night after night / You know, we know / Get us all in the end / Ecstasy
CD _____ 982838 2
Pickwick/Sony Collector's Choice / Mar '94 / Carlton Home Entertainment / Pinnacle / Sony.

JEFF BECK/ERIC CLAPTON ESSENTIALS (Beck, Jeff & Eric Clapton)
CD _____ LECDD 039
Wisepack / Aug '95 / THE / Conifer.

LEGENDS IN MUSIC - JEFF BECK
CD _____ LECD 080
Wisepack / Jul '94 / THE / Conifer.

SHAPES OF THINGS
CD _____ CDCD 1186
Charly / Sep '94 / Charly / THE / Cadillac.

TRUTH/BECKOLA (Beck, Jeff Group)
Shapes of things / Let me love you / Morning dew / You shook me / Ol' man river / Greensleeves / Rock my plimsoul / Beck's bolero / Blues deluxe / I ain't superstitious / All shook up / Spanish boots / Girl from Mill Valley / Jailhouse rock / Plynth (water down the drain) / Hangman's knee / Rice pudding
CD _____ CZ 374
EMI / Feb '91 / EMI.

Beck, Joe

FINGER PAINTING
CD _____ EFA 034532
Wavetone / Nov '95 / SRD.

LIVE AT SALISHAN (Beck, Joe & Red Mitchell)
CD _____ 174033
Capri / Nov '93 / Wellard / Cadillac.

Becker, David

IN MOTION
Westward ho / Intro / In motion / Outta towner / Forgotten friends / Time has fun / Pepe / From the right side / Cobalt blue / Passion dance / Just because
CD _____ R27 91672
Bluemoon / Oct '92 / New Note.

Becker, Jason

PERPETUAL BURN
Altitudes / Perpetual blues / Mabel's fatal fable / Temple of the absurd / Eleven blue Egyptians / Dweller in the cellar / Opus pocus
CD _____ RR 9528 2
Roadrunner / Sep '88 / Pinnacle.

Becker, Walter

ELEVEN TRACKS OF WHACK
Down in the bottom / Junkie girl / Surf and or die / Book of liars / Lucky Henry / Hard up case / Cringemaker / Girlfriend / My Waterloo / This moody bastard / Hat too flat
CD _____ 74321226092
Giant / Nov '94 / BMG.

FOUNDERS OF STEELY DAN (Becker, Walter & Donald Fagen)
CD _____ RMB 75004
Remember / Nov '93 / Total/BMG.

PEARLS FROM THE PAST VOL. 2 - BECKER & FAGEN (Becker, Walter & Donald Fagen)
CD _____ KLMCD 22
Scratch / Jul '94 / BMG.

YOU GOTTA WALK IT LIKE YOU TALK IT (Becker, Walter & Donald Fagen)
You gotta walk it like you talk it / Flotsam and jetsam / War and peace / Roll back the meaning / You gotta walk it like you talk it (reprise) / Dog eat dog / Red giant/white dwarf / If it rains
CD _____ SEECD 357
See For Miles/C5 / Sep '92 / Pinnacle.

Beckett, Harry

ALL FOUR ONE
White sky / Time of day / One for all / Enchanted / Shadowy light / Happy 96 / Images of clarity / Better git it in your soul
CD _____ SPJCD 547
Spotlite / May '93 / Cadillac / Jazz Horizons / Swift.

BREMAN CONCERT (Beckett, Harry Quartet)
CD _____ WWCD 007
West Wind / Oct '88 / Swift / Charly / CM / ADA.

IMAGES OF CLARITY (Beckett, Harry & Didier Levallet/Tony Marsh)
CD _____ EVCD 315
Evidence / Feb '94 / Harmonia Mundi / ADA / Cadillac.

LIVE VOL 2. (Beckett, Harry & Courtney Pine)
CD _____ WWCD 2030
West Wind / Mar '93 / Swift / Charly / CM / ADA.

Becketts

MYTH
CD _____ BGRL 016 CD
Bad Girl / Sep '92 / Pinnacle.

Becton, William

BROKEN (Becton, William & Friends)
Broken / Still in love with you / Fall afresh / Sure won't forget / No turning back / In your arms of love / 'Til the end / Joy / Be encouraged / Closer to you / Courage to journey on / 'Til you take the pain away / Let the healing again / Since the Lord changed my life / 'Til the end (jazz version)
CD _____ CDK 9145
Alliance Music / Oct '95 / EMI.

Bedazzled

SUGARFREE
Stageshow day / Dumb / Summer song / Shut my mouth and start again / Haven't you heard / Teenage mother superior / What did you do / Railway children / Potstcards from here / Ouch
CD _____ 472020 2
Columbia / Sep '92 / Sony.

Bede, Arran

GOSSAMER MANSION
CD _____ CDLCDL 1221
Lochshore / Nov '94 / ADA / Direct / Duncans.

Bedford, David

GREAT EQUATORIAL
Great equatorial (Part 1 to part 6)
CD _____ VP 156CD
Voice Print / Oct '94 / Voice Print.

NURSES SONG WITH ELEPHANTS
It's easier than it looks / Nurses song with elephants / Some bright stars from queens college / Trona / Sad and lonely faces
CD _____ VP116 CD
Voice Print / Mar '93 / Voice Print.

ODYSSEY, THE
Penelope's shroud / King Aeolus / Penelope's shroud (2) / Phaeacian games / Penelope's shroud (3) / Sirens / Scylla and Charybdis / Penelope's shroud (4) / Circe's island / Penelope's shroud completed / Battle in the hall
CD _____ CDOVD 444
Virgin / Apr '94 / EMI.

SONG OF THE WHITE HORSE, THE
Prelude: Wayland's Smithy / White horse / Blowing stone / Song of the white horse / Postlude / Text / Choir 1 / Choir 2
CD _____ VP 110 CD
Voice Print / Feb '93 / Voice Print.

VARIATIONS ON A RHYTHM
CD _____ VP 180CD
Voice Print / Feb '95 / Voice Print.

VARIATIONS ON A RHYTHM OF MIKE OLDFIELD (Bedford, David Tom Newman & Mike Oldfield)
CD _____ VP 191CD
Voice Print / Mar '95 / Voice Print.

Bedhead

WHAT FUN LIFE WAS
CD _____ TRANCE 21CD
Trance / Apr '94 / SRD.

Bedlam Rovers

FROTHING GREEN
CD _____ NORM 171CD
Normal/Okra / Mar '94 / Direct / ADA.

LAND OF NO SURPRISE
CD _____ NORMAL 191CD
Normal/Okra / Aug '95 / Direct / ADA.

SQUEEZE YOUR INNER CHILD
CD _____ RTS 16
Return To Sender / Apr '95 / Direct / ADA.

WALLOW
CD _____ NORMAL 151CD
Normal/Okra / Mar '94 / Direct / ADA.

Bedouin Ascent

MUSIC FOR PARTICALS
CD _____ RSNCD 37
Rising High / Jul '95 / Disc.

SCIENCE, ART & RITUAL
CD _____ RSNCD 27
Rising High / Nov '94 / Disc.

Bee Gees

CHILDREN OF THE WORLD
CD _____ 8236582
Polydor / Nov '89 / PolyGram.

CUCUMBER CASTLE
If I only had my mind on something else / Then you left me / I was the child / Sweetheart / My thing / Turning tide / I.O.I.O. / Lord / I lay down and die / Bury me down by the river / Chance of love / Don't forget to remember
CD _____ 833 783 2
Polydor / Nov '89 / PolyGram.

E.S.P.
E.S.P. / You win again / Live or die / Giving up the ghost / Longest night / This is your life / Angela / Overnight / Crazy for your love / Backtafunk
CD _____ 9255412
WEA / Feb '95 / Warner Music.

EVER INCREASING CIRCLES
Three kisses of love / Batle of the blue and grey / Take hold of that star / Claustrophobia / could it be / Turn around and look at me / Theme from Jamie McPheeters / You wouldn't know / How many birds / Big chance / I don't think it's funny / How love was true / Glasshouse
CD _____ CDTB 132
Thunderbolt / '91 / Magnum Music Group.

HIGH CIVILISATION
High civilisation / Secret love / When he's gone / Happy ever after / Party with no name / Ghost train / Dimensions / Only love / Human sacrifice / Evolution / True confessions
CD (CD only) _____ 7599265302
WEA / Feb '95 / Warner Music.

HORIZONTAL
World / And the sun will shine / Lemons never forget / Really and sincerely / Birdie told me / With the sun in my eyes / Massachusetts / Harry Braff / Daytime girl / Earnest of being George / Change is made / Horizontal
CD _____ 833 659-2
Polydor / Mar '90 / PolyGram.

IDEA
Let there be love / In the Summer of his years / Down to earth / I've gotta get a message to you / When the swallows fly / I started a joke / Swansong / Kitty can / Indian gin and whisky dry / Such a shame / Idea / I have decided to join the airforce / Kilburn towers
CD _____ 833 660 2
Polydor / Nov '89 / PolyGram.

LIFE IN A TIN CAN
CD _____ 8337882
Polydor / Jul '92 / PolyGram.

ONE
Ordinary lives / Bodyguard / Tears / Flesh and blood / House of shame / One / It's my neighbourhood / Tokyo nights / Wish you were here / Will you ever let him
CD _____ 9258872
WEA / Feb '95 / Warner Music.

SIZE ISN'T EVERYTHING
Paying the price of love / Kiss of life / How to fall in love Pt 1 / Omega man / Haunted house / Heart like mine / Anything for you / Blue island / Above and beyond / For whom the bell tolls / Fallen angel / Decadance
CD _____ 519 945-2
Polydor / Sep '93 / PolyGram.

SPICKS AND SPECKS
CD _____ RMB 75068
Remember / Aug '93 / Total/BMG.

SPIRITS HAVING FLOWN
Tragedy / Too much heaven / Love you inside out / Reaching out / Spirits (having flown) / Living together / I'm satisfied / Until
CD _____ 827 335 2
Polydor / Nov '89 / PolyGram.

SPOTLIGHT ON BEE GEES
Wine and women / Turn around, look at me / How many birds / Claustrophobia / Three kisses of love / To be or not to be / I don't think it's funny / Spicks and specks / How love was true / Follow the wind / Take hold of that star / I was a lover, a leader of men / Second hand people / I am the world / Second hand people / Every day I have to cry / Monday's rain
CD _____ HADCD 105
Javelin / Feb '94 / THE / Henry Hadaway Organisation.

TALES FROM THE BROTHERS GIBB (A History in Song)
New York mining disaster 1941 / I can't see nobody / Holiday / Massachusetts / Barker of the U.F.O. / World / Sir Geoffrey saved the world / Sun will shine / Words / Sinking ships / Jumbo / Singer sang his song / I've got to get a message to you / I started a joke / First of May / Melody fair / Tomorrow / Sun in the morning / Saved by the bell / Don't forget to remember / If I only had my mind on something else / I.O.I.O. / Railroad / I'll kiss your memory / Lonely days / Morning of my life / How can you mend a broken heart / Country women / My world / On time / Run to me / Alive / Saw a new morning / Wouldn't it be someone / Elisa / King and country / Mr. Natural / Country woman / Don't want to live inside myself / It doesn't matter too much to me / Throw a penny / Charade / Jive talkin' / Nights on broadway / Fanny (Be tender with my love) / You should be dancing (Long version) / Love so right / Boogie child / Edge of the universe / How deep is your love / Stayin' alive / Night fever / More than a woman / If I can't have you / Don't throw it all away / Too much heaven / Tragedy / Love you inside out / He's a liar / Another lonely night in New York / Woman in you / Someone belonging to someone / Toys / My eternal love / Where tomorrow is / Letting go / ESP (Demo version) / You win again / Ordinary lives / One / Juliet / To love somebody
CD Set _____ 843 911-2
Polydor / Nov '90 / PolyGram.

TO BE OR NOT TO BE
Three kings of love / Battle of the blue and grey / Take hold of that star / Claustrophobia / Could it be / Turn around look at me / Theme from Jamie McPheeters / You wouldn't know / How many birds / Big chance / I don't think it's funny / How love was true / Glasshouse / Everyday I have to cry / Wine and women / Follow the wind / I was a lover / Children laughing / I want home / Spicks and specks / I am the world / Playdown / I don't know why I bother myself / Monday's rain / To be or not to be / Swcond hand people
CD _____ CDTB 170
Thunderbolt / Oct '95 / Magnum Music Group.

TOMORROW THE WORLD
Everyday I have to cry / Wine and women / Follow the wind / I was a lover / And the children laughing / I want home / Spicks and specks / I am the world / Playdown / I don't know why I bother myself / Monday's rain / To be or not to be / Second hand people
CD _____ CDTB 135
Magnum Music / Jan '92 / Magnum Music Group.

TRAFALGAR
How can you mend a broken heart / Israel / Greatest man in the world / It's just the way / Remembering / Somebody / Stop the music / Trafalgar / Don't wanna live inside myself / When do I / Dearest / Lion in winter / Walking back to Waterloo

CD _____ 833 786-2
Polydor / Mar '90 / PolyGram.

TWO YEARS ON
Two years on / Portrait of Louise / Man for all seasons / Sincere relation / Back home / First mistake I made / Lonely days / Alone again / Tell me why / Lay it on me / Every second, every minute / I'm weeping
CD _____ 833 785-2
Polydor / Mar '90 / PolyGram.

VERY BEST OF THE BEE GEES
You win again / How deep is your love / Night fever / Tragedy / Massachusetts / I've gotta get a message to you / You should be dancing / New York mining disaster 1941 / World / First of May / Don't forget to remember / Saved by the bell / Run to me / Jive talkin' / More than a woman / Stayin' alive / Too much heaven / Ordinary lives / To love somebody (Not on LP) / Nights on Broadway (Not on LP)
CD _____ 847 339-2
Polydor / Nov '90 / PolyGram.

Beechman, Laurie

TIME BETWEEN THE TIME
Another hundred people / It might be you / Look at that face / Very precious love / Long before I knew you / Look of love / House is not a home / I'll never stop loving you / Shining sea/Shadow of your smile / Soon it's gonna rain/Rain sometimes / Music that makes me dance / Time between the time / Never never land / Home
CD _____ DRGCD 5230
DRG / Nov '93 / New Note.

Beef Masters

SECRET PLACE
CD _____ VIRION 103
Sound Virus / Sep '94 / Plastic Head.

Beenie Man

BEENIE MAN GOLD
CD _____ CRCD 32
Charm / May '94 / Jetstar.

BEENIE MAN MEETS MAD COBRA
(Beenie Man & Mad Cobra)
CD _____ VPCD 1413
VP / Aug '95 / Jetstar.

BLESSED
Blessed / Slam / Freedom / Stop live in a de pass / Acid attack / Matie a come / Man moving / World dance / Tear off mi garment / New name / Weeping and mourning / Heaven vs hell / See a man face
CD _____ IJCD 3005
Island / Jul '95 / PolyGram.

DEFEND IT
CD _____ SVCD 3
Shocking Vibes / Feb '94 / Jetstar.

DIS UNU FI HEAR
CD _____ HCD 7010
Hightone / Nov '94 / ADA / Koch.

RUFF & RUGGED STRICTLY RAGGA
CD _____ RNCD 2041
Rhino / Jan '94 / Jetstar / Magnum Music Group / THE.

Beer, Phil

ALLANZA (Beer, Phil & Incantation)
CD _____ RGFCD 012
Road Goes On Forever / Nov '90 / Direct.

HARD HATS
Fireman's song (Mixes) / Chance / This far / Blinded by love / More / Blind fiddler / This year / Hard hats / She could laugh / Think it over
CD _____ HTDCD 24
HTD / Aug '94 / Pinnacle.

SHOW OF HANDS
CD _____ RGFCD 012
Road Goes On Forever / Nov '91 / Direct.

Bees, Andrew

MILITANT
CD _____ ML 818112
Music / Sep '95 / Jetstar.

Beesley, John

INSPIRATION
CD _____ CDGRS 1275
Grosvenor / Feb '95 / Target/BMG.

ORCHESTRALLY ORGANISED
Cabaret / All the things you are / Take five / Yellow submarine / Caravan / Gigue fugue / Whiter shade of pale / Waterloo march / Henry Mancini medley / I dreamed a dream / Bohemian rhapsody / Power of love / Olympic flame / Morning / Blue rondo a la turk / Summertime / Stars and stripes forever
CD _____ OS 204
Valentine / Mar '94 / Conifer.

PERFORMANCE
Trumpet blues and cantabile / Think twice / Songs of praise / I got rhythm / Bridge over troubled water / Jurassic park / Intermezzo from Cavalleria Rusticana / Night in Tunisia / Overture to the light Cavalry / Can you feel

the love tonight / Nutcracker suite - characteristic dances / Eleanor Rigby
CD _____ CDGRS 1282
Grosvenor / Nov '95 / Target/BMG.

Beeston Pipe Band

AMAZING GRACE
CD _____ EUCD 1189
ARC / Apr '92 / ARC Music / ADA.

Begley, Philomena

COUNTRY QUEEN FOR 30 YEARS
Every second / Look at us / Walkin', talkin', cryin', barely beatin' broken heart / Picture me (without you) / Bright lights and country music / Start living again / Bed you made for me / Home I'll be / Our wedding day / Just one time / If my heart had windows / Family tree / Last rose of summer / Life is not always a rainbow / Gold and silver days / Bing bang boom
CD _____ RITZRCD 522
Ritz / Nov '92 / Pinnacle.

IN HARMONY (Begley, Philomena & Mick Flavin)
No love left / Just between you and me / I'm wasting your time you're wasting mine / Till a tear becomes a rose / Always, always / We're strangers again / We'll get ahead someday / All you've got to do is dream / Daisy chain / Don't believe me I'm lying / You can't break the chains of love / Let's pretend we're not married tonight / How can I (help you forgive me) / Somewhere between
CD _____ RITZCD 0061
Ritz / Apr '91 / Pinnacle.

SILVER ANNIVERSARY ALBUM
Key is in the mailbox / Here today and gone tomorrow / Rose of my heart / Behind the footlights / Jeannie's afraid of the dark / Red is the rose / Dark island / Leavin' on your mind / Queen of the silver dollar / Blanket on the ground / Truck drivin' woman / One is one too many / Galway Bay / Old arboe
CD _____ RITZCD 505
Ritz / '90 / Pinnacle.

SIMPLY DIVINE (Begley, Philomena & Ray Lynam)
You don't know love / Simply divine / Together alone / Near you / Don't cross over an old love / Making plans / Sweetest of all / I'll never need another you / She sang the melody / As long as we're dreaming / Hold on / Fire of two old flames
CD _____ RITZSCD 425
Ritz / Apr '93 / Pinnacle.

Begley, Seamus

MELTEAL (Begley, Seamus & Stephen Cooney)
CD _____ HB 0004CD
Hummingbird / Oct '93 / ADA / Direct.

Begnagrad

BROKEN DANCE, A
CD _____ AAYACDT 1190
Ayaa Disques / Apr '91 / These / ReR Megacorp.

Beguiled

BLUE DIRGE
CD _____ EFA 11574-2
Crypt / Apr '94 / SRD.

Behan, Kathleen

WHEN ALL THE WORLD WAS YOUNG
CD _____ CLUNCD 046
Mulligan / Aug '86 / CM / ADA.

Beherit

H4180V21C
CD _____ SP 119CD
Spinefarm / Jun '94 / Plastic Head.

Beiderbecke, Bix

20 CLASSIC TRACKS
Jazz me blues / Somebody stole my gal / Ol man river / Wringin' and twistin' / Clarinet marmalade / Ostrich walk / Mississippi mud / Baby, won't you please come home / Goose pimples / Margie / Louisiana / Rhythm king / Three blind mice / Krazy cat / Good man is hard to find / Thou swell / Wa-da-da / Louise / Japanese sandman / Dusky stevedore
CD _____ CDMFP 6163
Music For Pleasure / May '95 / EMI.

AT THE JAZZ BAND BALL
CD _____ 4669672
Sony Jazz / Jan '95 / Sony.

AT THE JAZZ BAND BALL 1924-28
Fidgety feet / Tiger rag / Flock o'blues / I'm glad / Toddlin' blues / Davenport blues / In a mist / Riverboat shuffle / Ostrich walk / At the jazz band ball / Clementine / Deep down South / For no reason at all (in C) / From Monday on / I'm coming Virginia / Jazz me blues / Krazy kat / Mississippi mud / Sensation / My best gal turned me down / Singin' the blues / Way down yonder in New Orleans

CD _____ CDAJA 5080
Living Era / Apr '91 / Koch.

BEIDERBECKE AFFAIR, THE
Riverboat shuffle / Tiger rag / Davenport blues / I'm looking over a four leaf clover / Trumbology / Clarinet marmalade / Ostrich walk / Way down yonder in New Orleans / Three blind mice / Clementine / Royal garden blues / Coquette / When / Lovable / Is it gonna be long / Oh you have no idea / Felix the cat / T'aint so honey, taint so / I'd rather cry over you / Louisiana / Futuristic rhythm / Raisin' the roof / Rockin' chair / Strut Miss Lizzie / Georgia on my mind
CD _____ CDGRF 079
Tring / '93 / Tring / Prism.

BIX 'N' BING (Recordings From 1927-1929) (Beiderbecke, Bix/Bing Crosby/Paul Whiteman Orchestra)
Changes / Mary / There ain't no sweet man that's worth the salt of my tears / Sunshine / Mississippi mud / High water / From Monday on / Loveable / My pet / Louisiana / Do I hear you saying I love you / You took advantage of me / That's my weakness now / Because my baby don't mean maybe now / I'm in seventh heaven / Reaching for someone (and not finding anyone there) / Oh Miss Hannah / Your mother and mine / Waiting at the end of the road / T'ain't so honey, t'aint so
CD _____ CDAJA 5005
Living Era / Oct '88 / Koch.

BIX AND TRUMBAUER
CD _____ CDCD 1089
Charly / Apr '93 / Charly / THE / Cadillac.

BIX BEIDERBECKE
CD _____ DVX 08062
Deja Vu / May '95 / THE.

BIX BEIDERBECKE (2CD Set)
CD Set _____ R2CD 4023
Deja Vu / Jan '96 / THE.

BIX BEIDERBECKE & THE WOLVERINES
CD _____ CBC 10013
Timeless Jazz / Feb '94 / New Note.

BIX BEIDERBECKE 1924-27
CD _____ CLASSICS 778
Classics / Mar '95 / Discovery / Jazz Music.

BIX BEIDERBECKE 1924.
CD _____ CBC 1013
Bellaphon / Jun '93 / New Note.

BIX BEIDERBECKE AND THE CHICAGO CORNETS
Fidgety feet / Jazz me blues / Oh baby / Copenhagen / Riverboat shuffle / Susie / Royal garden blues / Tiger rag / I need some pettin' / Sensation / Lazy daddy / Tia Juana / Big boy / I'm glad / Flovk o' blues / Toddlin' blues / Davenport blues / Prince of Wails / When my sugar walks down the street / Steady roll blues / Mobile blues / Really a pain / Chicago blues / Hot mittens / Buddy's habit
CD _____ MCD 47019 2
Milestone / Jun '93 / Jazz Music / Pinnacle / Wellard / Cadillac.

BIX BEIDERBECKE GOLD (2CD Set)
CD Set _____ D2CD 4023
Deja Vu / Jun '95 / THE.

BIX.
Jazz Portraits / Jan '94 / Jazz Music.
CD _____ CD 14532

BIXOLOGY
Jazz me blues / At the jazz band ball / Royal garden blues / Carey / Clngin' the mines blues / Carey / Cingin' the mines / I'm coming Virginia / Way down yonder in New Orleans / For no reason at all in C / Goose pimples / Trumbology / Ostrich walk / Riverboat shuffle / Davenport blues / Copenhagen / Fidgety feet / Tiger rag / In a mist / Clementine / Thou swell / Ol' man river / Wa-da-da / Louisiana / Margie / I'll be a friend with pleasure / Bessie couldn't help it
CD _____ CD 53017
Giants Of Jazz / Jun '88 / Target/BMG / Cadillac.

CLASSIC YEARS, THE
CD _____ CDSGP 0178
Prestige / Nov '95 / Total/BMG.

CLASSICS 1927-30
CD _____ CLASSICS 788
Classics / Nov '94 / Discovery / Jazz Music.

COMPLETE BIX BEIDERBECKE, THE
CD Set _____ BIX BOX
IRD / Jul '91 / Harmonia Mundi / Cadillac.

FIDGETY FEET
Fidgety feet / Jazz me blues / Copenhagen / Riverboat shuffle / Oh baby / Susie / Sensation rag / Lazy daddy / Tiger rag / Big boy / Tia juana
CD _____ BIX 1
IRD / Jul '91 / Harmonia Mundi / Cadillac.

FROM MONDAY ON
CD _____ BIX 5
IRD / Jul '91 / Harmonia Mundi / Cadillac.

GENIUS OF BIX BEIDERBECKE
Jazz me blues / Thou swell / Royal garden blues / At the jazz band ball / Mississippi mud / Riverboat shuffle / T'ain't so, honey, t'ain't so / Clementine / Lonely melody / There ain't no sweet man that's worth the salt of my tears / Dardanella / Sugar / Since my best gal turned me down / Wa-da-da / Rhythm king / Clarinet marmalade / I'm coming Virginia / Crying all day / Deep down South / I'll be a friend with pleasure
CD _____ PASTCD 9765
Flapper / Oct '91 / Pinnacle.

GOLDEN AGE OF BIX BEIDERBECKE
Singin' the blues / Riverboat shuffle / I'm coming Virginia / There ain't no land like Dixieland to me / I'm wondering who / At the jazz band ball / Sorry / Crying all day / Since my best gal turned me down / Royal garden blues / Humpty Dumpty / In a mist / Trumbology
CD _____ CD-MFP 6046
Music For Pleasure / Nov '88 / EMI.

GOOSE PIMPLES
CD _____ BIX 4
IRD / Jul '91 / Harmonia Mundi / Cadillac.

GREAT ORIGINAL PERFORMANCES
CD _____ RPCD 620
Robert Parker Jazz / Sep '93 / Conifer.

I LIKE THAT
CD _____ BIX 8
IRD / Jul '91 / Harmonia Mundi / Cadillac.

I'M COMING VIRGINIA
CD _____ BIX 3
IRD / Jul '91 / Harmonia Mundi / Cadillac.

IN THE DARK
CD _____ BIX 9
IRD / Jul '91 / Harmonia Mundi / Cadillac.

INDISPENSABLE BIX BEIDERBECKE (1924-30)
I didn't know / Idolizing / Sunday / I'm proud of a baby like you / I'm looking over a four leaf clover / I'm gonna meet my sweetie now / Hoosier sweetheart / My pretty girl / Slow river / In my merry Oldsmobile / Clementine / Washboard blues / Changes / Mary / Lonely melody / San / Back in your own backyard / There ain't no sweet man that's worth the salt of my tears / Dardanella / From Monday on / Mississippi mud / Sugar / Coquette / Whenn / Lovable / My pet / Forget me not / Louisiana / You took advantage of me / Rockin' chair / Barnacle Bill the sailor / Deep down south / I don't mind walking in the rain / I'll be a friend with pleasure / Georgia on my mind / Bessie couldn't help it
CD Set _____ ND 89572
RCA / Mar '94 / BMG.

INTRODUCTION TO BIX BEIDERBECKE 1924-30, AN
CD _____ 4012
Best Of Jazz / Aug '94 / Discovery.

JAZZ ME BLUES
CD _____ JHR 73517
Jazz Hour / '91 / Target/BMG / Jazz Music / Cadillac.

JAZZ ME BLUES
CD _____ CDD 490
Progressive / Jul '91 / Jazz Music.

LEON BISMARCK 'BIX' BEIDERBECKE
Singin' the blues / Jazz me blues / All the jazz band ball / Royal garden blues / Sorry / I'm coming Virginia / Trumbology / Goose pimples / Riverboat shuffle / For no reason at all in C / Fidgety feet / Thou swell / Margie / Clementine / Ol' man river / Louisiana / In a mist / I'll be a friend with pleasure
CD _____ CD 56016
Jazz Roots / Aug '94 / Target/BMG.

MY MELANCHOLY BABY
CD _____ BIX 7
IRD / Jul '91 / Harmonia Mundi / Cadillac.

QUINTESSENCE, THE (2 CD)
CD Set _____ FA 215
Fremeaux / Nov '95 / Discovery / ADA.

RIVERBOAT SHUFFLE
CD _____ CDCD 1089
Charly / Jun '93 / Charly / THE / Cadillac.

SINGIN' THE BLUES
Trumbology / Clarinet marmalade / Singin' the blues / Ostrich walk / Riverboat shuffle / I'm going Virginia / Way down yonder in New Orleans / For no reason at all / Three blind mice / Blue river / There's a cradle in Caroline / In a mist / Wringin' and twistin' / Humpty and dumpty / Krazy kat / Baltimore / There ain't no land like Dixieland to me / I'm a fool for love / I'm wondering who
CD _____ 4663092
CBS / '91 / Sony.

SUNDAY
CD _____ BIX 2
IRD / Jul '91 / Harmonia Mundi / Cadillac.

THOU SWELL
CD _____ BIX 6
IRD / Jul '91 / Harmonia Mundi / Cadillac.

Being

SELECTED TRANSMISSIONS (2CD Set)
Mune / McLaren / Fotts / Mavebeep Pt.3 /
Flee / Ayemooth / Foamy / Ryam / Toobit /
Aquapan / Eeeshab / Toyled / Quickie
CD Set _____ SEE 006CD
Emissions / Feb '96 / Vital.

TIDES
CD _____ EFA 290092
Spacefrog / Nov '95 / SRD / Vital.

Beirach, Richie

ANTARCTICA
Ice shelf / Neptune's bellows / Penguins on
parade / Deception island / Mirage / Water
lilies (The cloud) / Empress
CD _____ ECD 220862
Evidence / Jun '94 / Harmonia Mundi / ADA
/ Cadillac.

CONVERGANCE (Beirach, Richie &
George Coleman)
Lamp is low / I wish I knew / Flamenco
sketches / Rectilinear / For B.C. / Riddles /
Zal / What is this thing called love / Infant
eyes
CD _____ 3201852
Triloka / May '92 / New Note.

DOUBLE EDGE (Beirach, Richie & David
Liebman)
CD _____ STCD 4091
Storyville / Feb '89 / Jazz Music / Wellard
/ CM / Cadillac.

ELEGY FOR BILL EVANS
CD _____ STCD 4151
Storyville / Feb '90 / Jazz Music / Wellard
/ CM / Cadillac.

EMERALD CITY (Beirach, Richie & John
Abercrombie)
Odin / Anse des flamands / Sleight of hand
/ Emerald city / On overgrown paths / Car-
nival supone
CD _____ 900522
Line / Jan '95 / CM / Grapevine / ADA /
Conifer / Direct.

LEAVING
CD _____ STCD 4149
Storyville / Feb '90 / Jazz Music / Wellard
/ CM / Cadillac.

LIVE AT MAYBECK RECITAL HALL
CD _____ CCD 4518
Concord Jazz / Aug '92 / New Note.

OMERTA
CD _____ STCD 4154
Storyville / Feb '90 / Jazz Music / Wellard
/ CM / Cadillac.

SELF PORTRAITS
CD _____ CMPCD 51
CMP / Jun '92 / Vital/SAM.

Bel Canto

BIRDS OF PASSAGE
CD _____ CRAMCD 065
Crammed Discs / '88 / Grapevine / New
Note.

SHIMMERING, WARM AND BRIGHT
CD _____ CRACD 077
Crammed Discs / Apr '92 / Grapevine /
New Note.

WHITE OUT CONDITION
CD _____ CRACD 57
Crammed Discs / Aug '93 / Grapevine /
New Note.

Bel, M'Bilia

BAMELI SOY
CD _____ SHCD 43025
Shanachie / Jul '91 / Koch / ADA /
Greensleeves.

Belafonte, Harry

BANANA BOAT SONG
CD _____ ENTCD 205
Entertainers / '88 / Target/BMG.

BEST OF HARRY BELAFONTE
CD _____ DLCD 4003
Dixie Live / Mar '95 / Magnum Music
Group.

CALYPSO FROM JAMAICA
Man smart, woman smarter / Kingston mar-
ket / Come back Liza / Calypso war / Island
in the sun / I do adore her / Belinda / Not
me / Hosanna / Jackass song / Kitch cav-
alcade / Mahalia, I want back my dollar /
Brown skin girl / Dolly dawn / Donkey city /
Coconut woman
CD _____ CD 62072
Saludos Amigos / Apr '95 / Target/BMG.

FOLK SONGS FROM THE WORLD
CD _____ CD 12518
Music Of The World / Feb '95 / Target/
BMG / ADA.

HARRY BELAFONTE RETURNS TO
CARNEGIE HALL
Jump down, spin around / Suzanne / Little
lyric of great importance / Chickens / Vai
chazkem / I do adore her / Ballad of Sigmund Freud / I've been driving on bald

mountain / Waterboy / Hole in the bucket /
Click song / One more dance / Ox drivers /
Red rosy bush / Didn't it rain / Hene ma tov
/ I know where / I'm going / Old King Cole
/ La bamba
CD _____ 09026626902
RCA Victor / Jun '95 / BMG.

ISLAND IN THE SUN
CD _____ WMCD 5643
Disky / May '94 / THE / BMG / Discovery /
Pinnacle.

SCARLET RIBBONS
Scarlet ribbons (for her hair) / Eden was just
like this / Man smart (woman smarter) / All
my trials / Cotton fields / Banana boat song
(Day-O) / Michael, row the boat ashore /
Hole in the bucket / Shenandoah / Cocoa-
nut woman / Island in the sun / Gotta travel
on / Jamaica farewell
CD _____ 74321339482
Camden / Jan '96 / BMG.

STATIONEN
CD _____ 16092
Laserlight / Jul '94 / Target/BMG.

VERY BEST OF HARRY BELAFONTE,
THE
CD _____ MCCD 059
Music Club / '92 / Disc / THE / CM.

Belden, Bob

WHEN DOVES CRY - THE MUSIC OF
PRINCE (Belden, Bob Ensemble)
Diamonds and pearls / Purple rain / Kiss /
When doves cry / Arms of Orion / Nothing
compares 2 U / 1999 / Little red corvette /
Question of U / When 2 R in love / Baby I'm
a star
CD _____ CDP 8295152
Blue Note / Oct '94 / EMI.

Belew, Adrian

ACOUSTIC ADRIAN BELEW
CD _____ DGM 95042
Discipline / May '95 / Pinnacle.

Belial

NEVER AGAIN
CD _____ LRC 666
Lethal / Feb '94 / Plastic Head.

Belile, Elspeth

YOUR ONLY OTHER OPTION
CD _____ NAR 111CD
SST / Sep '94 / Plastic Head.

Bell, Alan

WITH BREAD & FISHES
CD _____ DRGNCD 942
Dragon / Apr '94 / Roots / Cadillac /
Wellard / CM / ADA.

Bell Biv Devoe

POISON
Dope / B.B.D. (I thought it was me) / Let me
know something / Do me / Ronnie, Bobby,
Ricky, Mike / Ralph and Johnny (word to
the Mutha) / Poison / Ain't nut'in changed /
When will I see you smile / Again / I do need
you
CD _____ MCLD 19299
MCA / Oct '95 / BMG.

Bell, Carey

CAREY BELL'S BLUES HARP
CD _____ DE 622
Delmark / Dec '95 / Hot Shot / ADA / CM
/ Direct / Cadillac.

DEEP DOWN
CD _____ ALCD 4828
Alligator / Feb '95 / Direct / ADA.

DYNASTY (Bell, Carey & Lurrie)
CD _____ JSPCD 222
JSP / Feb '89 / ADA / Target/BMG / Direct
/ Cadillac / Complete/Pinnacle.

GOIN' ON MAIN STREET (Bell, Carey
Blues Harp Band)
Goin' on main street / I am worried / Hear-
aches and pain / Easy to love you / Train
ticket / When a woman get in trouble / Tribute to big Walter / I need you so bad / Man
and the blues
CD _____ CDLR 72006
L&R / Jul '94 / New Note.

HARPMASTER
CD _____ JSPCD 250
JSP / Jan '94 / ADA / Target/BMG / Direct
/ Cadillac / Complete/Pinnacle.

HARPSLINGER
What my Mama told me / Pretty baby /
Blues with a feeling / 85% / Sweet little
woman / It's so easy to love you / Strange
woman / Last night
CD _____ JSPCD 264
JSP / Nov '95 / ADA / Target/BMG / Direct
/ Cadillac / Complete/Pinnacle.

HEARTACHES AND PAIN
CD _____ DD 666
Delmark / May '94 / Hot Shot / ADA / CM
/ Direct / Cadillac.

Bell, Chris

I AM THE COSMOS
CD _____ RCD 10222
Rykodisc / Feb '92 / Vital / ADA.

Bell, Clive

SHAKUHACHI
CD _____ EUCD 1135
ARC / '91 / ARC Music / ADA.

Bell, Derek

ANCIENT MUSIC FOR THE IRISH HARP
Reminiscences of Sean O Riada / Colonel
O'Hara / Little Molly O / Love in secret / Soft
mild morning / Wexford bells / Lady Blaney
/ Within a mile of Edinburgh town / An buachaill Caol Dubh / Lady Iveagh/Black rose
bud / Dawning of the day/Green woods of
truagh/Captivating youth / Carolan's devotion / Churchyard of Creagan/Brown sloe
bush/Benevolent Father Dona / Lonesome/
An paistin fionn / Untitled air/Thomas a
Burca / Lulaby/Bardic hornpipe / Harp ser-
enade/Paraguayan dance in G / Dances
from the Quechua Indians
CD _____ CC 59CD
Claddagh / Feb '93 / ADA / Direct.

CAROLAN'S FAVOURITE (Music of
Carolan, Vol 2)
Carolan's favourite jig/Carolan's fancy /
Squire Wood's lamentation on ye refusal of
his halfpence / Sean Jones / Lady St. John
/ David Poer/Seamus Plunkett / Lament for
Terence O'Connor / Lady Dillon / Michael
O'Connor / Carolan's welcome/Madam
Keel / Right Reverend Lord bishop Mac-
Mahon of Clogher / Carolan's variations on
cock up your beaver
CD _____ CC 28CD
Claddagh / Jan '90 / ADA / Direct.

CAROLAN'S RECEIPT
Sidh Beag / Carolan's receipt for drinking /
Lady Athenry / Fanny Poer / Blind Mary /
Sir Festus Burke / Carolan's quarrel with the
landlady / Carolan's ramble to Cashel / Mrs.
Poer / John O'Connor / Ode to Whiskey /
George Brabazon / Mable Kelly / Madam
Maxwell/Carolan's nightcap/Lady Gethin /
Brighid Cruis / John O'Reilly / Carolan's
farewell to music
CD _____ CC 18CD
Claddagh / Nov '90 / ADA / Direct.

DEREK BELL'S MUSICAL IRELAND
She moved through the fair / Boys of Blue-
hill/Hillsborough Castle/Greencastle hornpipe / Carrickfergus / Little white cat / Gartan mothers lullaby / Im aonar seal / Down
by the Sally Gardens / Eileen my secret love
/ Piper through the meadow straying / Limerick's lamentation / Christ the seed / I wish
the shepherd's pet were mine
CD _____ CC 35CD
Claddagh / Nov '90 / ADA / Direct.

Bell, Ed

ED BELL 1927-30
CD _____ DOCD 5090
Blues Document / '92 / Swift / Jazz Music
/ Hot Shot.

Bell, Graeme

BEST OF DIXIELAND JAZZ, THE
South / Riverside blues / I'm crazy 'bout my
baby / Honey hush / Sugar / At a Georgia
camp meeting / Sentimental journey / Mel-
ancholy / T'aint watcha do / This one's for
Eric / Muskrat ramble
CD _____ 90778-2
PMF / Jul '94 / Kingdom / Cadillac.

Bell, Graham

ALL THE ROMANCES
CD _____ WCPCD 1010
President / Aug '94 / Grapevine / Target/
BMG / Jazz Music / President.

Bell, Lurrie

EVERYBODY WANTS TO WIN
CD _____ JSPCD 227
JSP / May '93 / ADA / Target/BMG /
Direct / Cadillac / Complete/Pinnacle.

MERCURIAL SON
CD _____ DE 679
Delmark / Dec '95 / Hot Shot / ADA / CM
/ Direct / Cadillac.

Bell, T.D.

IT'S ABOUT TIME (Bell, T.D. & Erbie
Bowser)
Black Magic / Apr '93 / Hot Shot / Swift /
CM / Direct / Cadillac / ADA.
CD _____ BMCD 9019

Bell Tower

POP DROPPER
CD _____ TOPPCD 002
Ultimate / Jul '94 / 3MV / Vital.

Bell, Vince

PHOENIX
CD _____ CD 1027
Watermelon / Sep '94 / ADA / Direct.

Bell, William

BEDTIME STORIES
CD _____ WIL 4128CD
Wilbe / Mar '94 / Koch.

BOUND TO HAPPEN/WOW
I forgot to be your lover / Hey Western union man / My whole world is falling down /
Everyday people / Johnny I love you / All
God's children got soul / Happy / By the
time I get to Phoenix / Bring the curtain
down / Smile can't hide a broken heart /
Born under a bad sign / I got a sure thing /
I can't make it (all by myself) / Till my back
ain't got no bone / All for the love of a
woman / My door is always open / Penny
for your thoughts / You'll want diamonds /
Winding winding road / Somebody's gonna
get hurt / I'll be home
CD _____ CDSXD 970
Stax / Apr '91 / Pinnacle.

LITTLE SOMETHING EXTRA, A
She won't be like you / All that I am / Let's
do something together / Forever wouldn't
be too long / You got me where you want
me / Quittin' time / That's my love / You
need a little something extra / There's a love
/ Never let me go / We got something good
/ Will you still love me tomorrow / Love will
find a way / What did I do wrong / Sacrifice
/ Love is after me / Life I live / Wait / You're
never too old
CD _____ CDSXD 037
Stax / Sep '91 / Pinnacle.

ON A ROLL
Getting out of your bed / If you don't use it
/ I need your love so bad / When you've got
the best / On a roll / I'm ready / I can do it
/ Short circuit / Holding on to love
CD _____ WIL 3007CD
Wilbe / Nov '89 / Koch.

PHASES OF REALITY
Save us / True love don't come easy / Fifty
dollar habit / What I don't know won't hurt
me / Phases of reality / If you really love him
/ Lonely for your love / Man in the street
CD _____ CDSXE 058
Stax / Jul '92 / Pinnacle.

SOUL OF A BELL, THE
Everybody loves a winner / You don't miss
your water / Do right woman, do right man
/ I've been loving you too long / Nothing
takes the place of you / Then you can tell
me goodbye / Eloise (hang on in there) / Any
other way / It's happening all over / Never
like this before / You're such a sweet thing
CD _____ 7567822522
Atlantic / Apr '95 / Warner Music.

Bellamy Brothers

BEST OF THE BEST
CD _____ SCD 22
Start / May '94 / Koch.

CRAZY FROM THE HEART/REBELS
WITHOUT A CLUE
Crazy from the heart / I'll give you all my
love tonight / Santa fe / It's rainin' girls /
Ying yang / Next down / Ramblin' again /
We don't wanna get for it / White trash /
White trash / Rebels without a clue / I'll help
you hurt him / Fountain of middle age /
Stayin' in love / Get your priorities in line /
Courthouse / Andy Griffith show / Little
naive
CD _____ SCD 24
Start / Nov '95 / Koch.

HEARTBREAK OVERLOAD
Rip off the knob / Not / Heartbreak overload
/ Blame it on the fire in my heart / On a
summer night / Sweet nostalgia / Bubba /
Stayin' in love / D-D-D-D-Divorce / Can I
come on home to you / Hemingway hide-
away / Andy Griffith Show / Hard on a heart
/ Nobody's perfect
CD _____ SCD 23
Start / May '95 / Koch.

LET YOUR LOVE FLOW
Let your love flow / If I said you had a
beautiful body would you hold it agains /
Sugar Daddy / Lovers live longer / Get into
reggae cowboy / Redneck girl / I need more
of you / Old hippie / Lie to you for your love
/ Feelin' the feelin' / Kids of the baby boom
/ Crazy from the heart / Rip off the knob /
No.1 / Miami moon / Life is a beach / Cow-
boy beat / Can I come home to you / Hard
way to make an easy living / She's gone
with the wind
CD _____ CTS 55432
Country Stars / Jan '96 / Target/BMG.

REALITY CHECK/ROLLIN' THUNDER
Too late / I could be persuaded / Have a
little compassion / May there be life before this
love / Makin' promises / What's this world
coming to / Forever ain't long enough / How
can you be everywhere at the same time /
I don't wanna lose you / Reality check / All
in the name of love / Down to you / She
don't know that she's perfect / Strength of
the weaker sex / Anyway I can / Rollin'

thunder / What's the dang deal / Our love / Lonely eyes / I make her laugh
CD _____ SCD 25
Start / Nov '95 / Koch.

SONS OF BEACHES
Shine them buckles / Big hair / Pit bulls and chain saws / Blue rodeo / Twang town / She's awesome / Old hippie (the sequel) / Native American / Feel free / Too much fun / We dared the lightening / Elvis, Marilyn and James Dean / Gotta get a little crazy / Jesus is coming
CD _____ SCD 27
Start / Oct '95 / Koch.

Bellamy, Peter

BOTH SIDES THEN
Barbaree / Trees they do grow high / Lord will provide / Gallant frigate Amphitrite / Roving on a winter's day / Derry gaol / Long time travelling / Shepherd of the downs / House carpenter / When I die / Edmund in the lowlands / Around Cape Horn / Turfman from Ardee / Amazing grace
CD _____ FLE 1002
Hokey Pokey / Oct '92 / ADA / Direct.

TRANSPORTS, THE
Overture / Ballad of Henry and Susannah / Us poor fellows / Robber's song / Ballad of Henry and Susannah (part 2) / I once lived in service / Norwich gaol / Sweet loving friendship / Black and bitter night / Humane turnkey / Plymouth mail / Green fields of England / Roll down / Still and silent ocean / Ballad of Henry and susannah (parts 3,4and5) / Convict's wedding dance
CD _____ TSCD 459
Topic / Aug '92 / Direct / ADA.

Belle, Regina

PASSION
Interlude / Passion / Quiet time / If I could / Do you wanna get serious / Dream in colour / My man (mon homme)
CD _____ 472301 2
Columbia / Mar '93 / Sony.

REACHIN' BACK
Reachin' back (intro) / Could it be I'm falling in love / Love TKO / You make me feel brand new / Hurry up this way again / Whole town's laughing / You are everything / Let me make love to you / I'll be around / Just don't want to be lonely / Didn't I blow your mind this time
CD _____ 4807622
Columbia / Sep '95 / Sony.

Belle Stars

HIT SINGLE COLLECTABLES
CD _____ DISK 4514
Disky / Apr '94 / THE / BMG / Discovery / Pinnacle.

SIGN OF THE TIMES
CD _____ 12365
Laserlight / May '94 / Target/BMG.

VERY BEST OF THE BELLE STARS, THE
CD _____ STIFFCD 5
Disky / Apr '94 / THE / BMG / Discovery / Pinnacle.

Bellson, Louie

1959 AT THE FLAMINGO HOTEL (Bellson, Louie & Big Band)
CD _____ JH 1026
Jazz Hour / Feb '93 / Target/BMG / Jazz Music / Cadillac.

DON'T STOP NOW
CD _____ 71000-2
Capri / Oct '94 / Wellard / Cadillac.

EAST SIDE SUITE (Bellson, Louie & His Jazz Orchestra)
Tenor time / What makes Moses run
CD _____ MM 5009
Music Masters / Oct '94 / Nimbus.

HOT
CD _____ MM 5008
Music Masters / Oct '94 / Nimbus.

LIVE AT JAZZ SHOWCASE (Bellson, Louie Four)
Sonny side / Duke's blues / 3 p.m. / I hear a rhapsody / Jam for your bread / Warm alley / Cherokee
CD _____ CCD 4350
Concord Jazz / Jul '88 / New Note.

LIVE AT THE CONCORD SUMMER FESTIVAL
Now and then / Here's that rainy day / My old flame / It might as well be spring / These foolish things remind me of you / Body and soul / True blue / Roto blues / Starship concord / Dig
CD _____ CCD 4025
Concord Jazz / May '95 / New Note.

LIVE FROM NEW YORK (Bellson, Louie & Big Band)
Soar like an eagle / Louie shuffle / Blow your horn / L.A. suite / Louie and Clark expedition / Francine / Santos
CD _____ CD 83334
Telarc / Jul '94 / Conifer / ADA.

LOUIS BELLSON AND HIS JAZZ ORCHESTRA (Bellson, Louie & His Jazz Orchestra)
It don't mean a thing if it ain't got that swing / Fascinating rhythm / Latin affair
CD _____ MMD 60120 Y
Music Masters / Jan '89 / Nimbus.

PEACEFUL THUNDER
CD _____ MM 65074
Music Masters / Oct '94 / Nimbus.

RAINCHECK
Raincheck / Alone together / I thought about you / Blue moon / Body and soul / Oleo / Song is you / Tristamente / Funky blues / More I see you
CD _____ CCD 4073
Concord Jazz / Nov '95 / New Note.

SALUTE (Bellson, Louie Quintet)
Chiara Scuro / Nov '95 / Jazz Music / Kudos.
CD _____ CRD 329

Belly

KING
Puberty / Seal my fate / Red / Silverfish / Super connected / Bees / King / Now they'll sleep / Untitled and unsung / Li'l Ennio / Judas my heart
CD _____ CAD 5004CD
CD _____ CADD 5004CD
4AD / Feb '95 / Disc.

STAR
CD _____ CAD 3002CD
4AD / Jan '93 / Disc.

Belmez

BESERKER
CD _____ SPV 08407952
Candlelight / Apr '95 / Plastic Head.

Belmondo Quintet

FOR ALL FRIENDS
CD _____ CHR 70016
Challenge / Aug '95 / Direct / Jazz Music / Cadillac / ADA.

Belmont, Martin

BIG GUITAR
CD _____ FMCD 3
Demon / Feb '91 / Pinnacle / ADA.

Beloved

BLISSED OUT
Up, up and away (happy sexy mix) / Wake up soon / Pablo (special K dub) / It's alright now (back to basics) / Hell (honky tonk) / Time after time (muffin mix) / Sun rising / Your love takes me higher
CD _____ 9031729072
East West / Nov '90 / Warner Music.

CONSCIENCE
Spirit / Sweet harmony / Outerspace girl / Lose yourself in me / Paradise found / You've got me thinking / Celebrate your life / Rock to the rhythm of love / Let the music take you / 1000 Years from today / Dream on
CD _____ 4509914832
East West / Nov '92 / Warner Music.

HAPPINESS
Hello / Your love takes me higher / Time after time / Don't you worry / Scarlet beautiful / Sun rising / I love you more / Wake up soon / Up, up and away / Found
CD _____ 2292450250 2
East West / Feb '95 / Warner Music.

Belton, Richard

MODERN SOUNDS IN CAJUN MUSIC
Cajun stripper / I have to forget you / Just a dream / Un autre soir d'ennui (Another sleepless night) / Cajun waltz / San Antonio rose / Madamme Sostan / Chrokee waltz / Who-diggie / Oh yea yi-yi / La jolie blonde / For the last time / Musician's paradise / Laisser les cajun danser / Give me another chance / J'ai pleurer pour toi / Oh lucille / I'm not a fool anymore / Cajun Fugitive / Won't be satisfied / Chere toute toute / Cette la j'aime / Roll on wagon wheel / She didn't know I was married / Heartbroken waltz / Cajun streak
CD _____ CDCHD 378
Ace / Jan '93 / Pinnacle / Cadillac / Complete/Pinnacle.

Beltram, Joey

PLACES
CD Set _____ 74321299132
RCA / Sep '95 / BMG.

Beltran, John

EARTH & NIGHTFALL
Blue world / Pluvial interlude / Synaptic transmission / Sub surface / Earth and nightfall / Mutualism / Dawn / Anticipation / Nitric / Fragile interlude / Aquatic / Vienna
CD _____ RS95072CD
R & S / Jun '95 / Vital.

Belvin, Jesse

BLUES BALLADEER, THE
Daddy loves baby / My love comes tumbling down / Dream girl / Confusin' blues / Baby don't go / Blues has got me / Hang your tears out to dry / Don't stop / Love me / Puddin' 'n' tane / Open up your heart / What's the matter / Ding dong baby / One little blessing / Gone / Love love of my life / Where's my girl / Let's try romance / Come back / Love of my life
CD _____ CDCHD 305
Ace / Nov '93 / Pinnacle / Cadillac / Complete/Pinnacle.

GOODNIGHT MY LOVE
Goodnight my love / (I love you) for sentimental reasons / I'll mess you up medley / Don't close the door / Senorita / Let me love you tonight / I need you so / My satellite / Just to say hello / Dream house / I'm not free / You send me / My baby / Let's make up / Summertime / I want you with me Christmas / Goodnight my love (alt take) / Sad and lonesome / Beware / What can I do without you / I'll make a bed
CD _____ CDCHD 336
Ace / Nov '93 / Pinnacle / Cadillac / Complete/Pinnacle.

Beme Seed

FUTURE IS ATTACKING
Future is attacking
CD _____ BFFP 50 CD
Blast First / Jul '89 / Disc.

Ben

BEN
CD _____ REP 4195-WP
Repertoire / Aug '91 / Pinnacle / Cadillac.

Ben, Jorge

GRANDS SUCES 78-85
CD _____ 824072
Buda / Nov '90 / Discovery / ADA.

Ben-Hur, Ronie

BACKYARD
Thrill is gone / Dance of the infidels / As me now / Backyard / Canal street / Never let me go / Audubon / Something to live for / Burgundy
CD _____ TCB 95902
TCB / Dec '95 / New Note.

Benatar, Pat

BEST SHOTS
Hit me with your best shot / Love is a battlefield / We belong / We live for love / Sex as a weapon / Invincible / Shadows of the night / Heartbreaker / Fire and ice / Treat me right / Heartbreaker / If you think you know how to love me / You better run
CD _____ CCD 1538
Chrysalis / Oct '87 / EMI.

CRIMES OF PASSION
Treat me right / You better run / Never wanna leave you / Hit me with your best shot / Hell is for children / Prisoner of love / Out a touch / Little paradise / I'm gonna follow you / Wuthering Heights / It's a lovely life / Eastern shadows / Joanna / Stretch / Poiliceman's ball / Stax / Taken in hand / Paradise lost / Box / Web of love / Dangerous woman
CD _____ ACCD 1275
Chrysalis / Jan '86 / EMI.

GRAVITY'S RAINBOW
Pictures of a gone world / Everybody lay down / Somebody's baby / Ties that bind / You and I / Disconnected / Crazy / Everytime I fall back / Sanctuary / Rise / Kingdom key / Tradin' down
CD _____ CDCHR 6054
Chrysalis / Oct '93 / EMI.

IN THE HEAT OF THE NIGHT
Heartbreaker / I need a lover / If you think you know how to love me / In the heat of the night / My clone sleeps alone / We live for love / Hated X / Don't let it show / No you don't / So sincere
CD _____ ACCD 1236
Chrysalis / Jul '94 / EMI.

TRUE LOVE
Bloodshot eyes / Payin' the cost to be the boss / So long / I've got papers on you / I feel lucky / True love / Good life / Evening / I get evil / Don't happen no more / Please come home for Christmas
CD _____ CCD 1805
Chrysalis / Feb '94 / EMI.

VERY BEST OF PAT BENATAR
Heartbreaker / We live for love / Promises in the dark / Fire and ice / Ooh ooh song / Hit me with your best shot / Shadows of the night / Anxiety (get nervous) / I want out / Lipstick lies / Love is a battlefield / We belong / All fired up / Hell is for children / Invincible / Somebody's baby / Everybody lay down / True love
CD _____ CDCHR 6070
Chrysalis / Apr '94 / EMI.

WIDE AWAKE IN DREAMLAND
All fired up / One love / Let's stay together / Don't walk away / Too long a soldier / Cool soldier / Cerebral man / Lift 'em on up / Suffer the little children / Wide awake in dreamland
CD _____ CD25CR 19
Chrysalis / Mar '94 / EMI.

Bender

LOST CITY OF DALSTON
CD _____ WOWCD 43
Words Of Warning / Jun '95 / SRD.

Benediction

DARK IS THE SEA
CD _____ NB 059CD
Nuclear Blast / Apr '92 / Plastic Head.

DREAMS YOU DREAD, THE
CD _____ NB 120CD
Nuclear Blast / Jun '95 / Plastic Head.

GRAND LEVELLER
CD _____ NB 048CD
Nuclear Blast / Sep '91 / Plastic Head.

GROTESQUE ASHEN EPITAPH, THE
CD _____ NB 088-2
Nuclear Blast / May '94 / Plastic Head.

SUBCONCIOUS TERROR
CD _____ 842971
Nuclear Blast / Aug '90 / Plastic Head.

TRANSCEND THE RUBICON
CD _____ NB 073CD
Nuclear Blast / Jan '93 / Plastic Head.

Beneke, Tex

JUKEBOX SATURDAY NIGHT (Beneke, Tex & The Glenn Miller Sound)
CD _____ VJC 1039
Vintage Jazz Classics / Nov '92 / Direct / ADA / CM / Cadillac.

Benito, Oscar

FOLKLORE DE PARAGUAY
CD _____ EUCD 1221
ARC / Sep '93 / ARC Music / ADA.

Bennett, Brian

CHANGE OF DIRECTION/ILLUSTRATED LONDON NOISE
Slippery Jim De Grize / Canvas / Whisper not / Memphis / Tricycle / Sunshine superman / On Broadway / Sunny afternoon / Little old lady / 98.6 / Con Alma / Change of direction / Love and occasional rain / I heard it through the grapevine / Chameleon / Just lookin' / Rocky raccoon / Ticket to ride
CD _____ SEECD 205
See For Miles/C5 / Aug '90 / Pinnacle.

MISTY
Wave / Laura / Misty / Close to you / Madrid / Love for sale / Who can I turn to / Shadow of your smile / What are you doing the rest of your life / Blue hankerchief
CD _____ C5CD 610
See For Miles/C5 / Sep '95 / Pinnacle.

Bennett, Don

CHICAGO CALLING (Bennett, Don Sextet)
CD _____ CCD 79713
Candid / Nov '95 / Cadillac / Jazz Music / Wellard / Koch.

SOLAR (Bennett, Don Trio)
CD _____ CCD 79723
Candid / Nov '95 / Cadillac / Jazz Music / Wellard / Koch.

Bennett, Duster

JUMPIN' AT SHADOWS
CD _____ IGOCD 2010
Indigo / Nov '94 / Direct / ADA.

OUT IN THE BLUE
CD _____ IGOCD 2018
Indigo / Apr '95 / Direct / ADA.

Bennett, Elinor

TELYNAU A CHAN/FOLK SONGS & HARPS
Clychau Aberdyfi / Ar lan y mor / Paid a deud / Merch y melinydd / Meillionen / Morfa Rhuddlan / Syr Harri Ddu / Codiad yr ehedydd / Ar hyd y nos / Gwyr Harlech / Dafydd y Garreg Wen / Y bore glas / Gwcw fach / Ei di'r deryn du / Y deryn pur / Cainc Dafydd broffwyd / Annhawdd ymadael / Pant corlan yr wyn / Hen benillion / Marwnad Sion Eos / Bugeilio'r gwenith gwyn / Huna blentyn / Y gwydd / Migildi magildi
CD _____ SCD 4041
Sain / Feb '95 / Direct / ADA.

Bennett, Gordon

ENGLISH PUBSONGS (Bennett, Gordon & The Good Times)
CD _____ CNCD 5980
Disky / Apr '94 / THE / BMG / Discovery / Pinnacle.

Bennett, Richard Rodney

HAROLD ARLEN'S SONGS
CD _____ ACD 168
Audiophile / Oct '93 / Jazz Music / Swift.

I NEVER WENT AWAY
CD _____ DE 5001
Delos / Aug '90 / Conifer.

SPECIAL OCCASIONS
Civil war ballet / Hero ballet / Within the quota / Ghost town
CD _____ DRGCD 6102
DRG / Apr '94 / New Note.

Bennett, Samm

BIG OFF, THE
CD _____ KFWCD 126
Knitting Factory / Nov '94 / Grapevine.

LIFE OF CRIME (Bennett, Samm & Chunk)
CD _____ KFWCD 110
Knitting Factory / Nov '94 / Grapevine.

Bennett, Tony

16 MOST REQUESTED SONGS
Because of you / Stranger in paradise / Rags to riches / Boulevard of broken dreams / Cold cold heart / Just in time / I left my heart in San Francisco / I wanna be around / Who can I turn to / For once in my life / This is all I ask / Smile / Tender is the night / Shadow of your smile / Love story
CD _____ 472418 2
Columbia / Nov '92 / Sony.

ALL TIME GREATEST HITS
Something / Love story / Maybe this time / Just in time / For once in my life / I left my heart in San Francisco / Because of you / Boulevard of broken dreams / Stranger in paradise / I wanna be around / Time for love / Who can I turn to / This is all I ask / Smile / Sing you sinners / Firefly / Put on a happy face / Love look away / Rags to riches / Where do I begin / Shadow of your smile
CD _____ 4688432
Columbia / Sep '91 / Sony.

BILL EVANS ALBUM
CD _____ OJCCD 439
Original Jazz Classics / Feb '92 / Wellard / Jazz Music / Cadillac / Complete/Pinnacle.

GREAT SONGS FROM THE SHOWS
Maybe this time / When can I turn to / Ol' man river / My funny valentine / Climb every mountain / On a clear day / I'll only miss her when I think of her / Love for sale / Ole devil moon / Taking a chance on love / Stranger in paradise / If I ruled the world / September song / Where or when / Have you met Miss Jones / They say it's wonderful
CD _____ PWKS 4171
Carlton Home Entertainment / Sep '93 / Carlton Home Entertainment.

HERE'S TO THE LADIES
People / I'm so in love again / Somewhere over the rainbow / My love went to London / Poor butterfly / Sentimental journey / Cloudy morning / Tenderly / Down in the depths / Moonlight in Vermont / Tangerine / God bless the child / Day break / You showed me the way / Honeysuckle Rose / Maybe this time / I got rhythm / My ideal
CD _____ 4812662
Columbia / Nov '95 / Sony.

HOLLYWOOD AND BROADWAY
CD _____ CDSIV 6145
Horatio Nelson / Jul '95 / THE / BMG / Avid/BMG / Koch.

I LEFT MY HEART IN SAN FRANCISCO
I left my heart in San Francisco / Once upon a time / Tender is the night / Smile / Love for sale / Taking a chance on love / Candy kisses / Have I told you lately that I love you / Rules of the road / Marry young / I'm always chasing rainbows / Best is yet to come
CD _____ 9022882
Pickwick/Sony Collector's Choice / Mar '90 / Carlton Home Entertainment / Pinnacle / Sony.

I LEFT MY HEART IN SAN FRANCISCO/I WANNA BE AROUND
I left my heart in San Francisco / Once upon a time / Tender is the night / Smile / Love for sale / Taking a chance on love / Candy kisses / Have I told you lately that I love you / Rules of the road / Marry young / I'm always chasing rainbows / Best is yet to come / Good life / If I ruled the world / I wanna be around / Love look away / Let's face the music and dance / Once upon a summertime / If you were mine / I will live my life for you / Someone to love it was me / Quiet nights
CD _____ 4775922
Columbia / Oct '94 / Sony.

IN PERSON (Bennett, Tony & Count Basie)
Just in time / When I fall in love / Taking a chance on love / Without a song / Fascinating rhythm / Solitude / Pennies from Heaven / Lost in the stars / Firefly / There will never be another you / Lullaby of Broadway / Ol' man river

CD
CK 64276
Legacy / Nov '94 / Sony.

LIFE IS A SONG
CD _____ 3001012
Scratch / Jul '95 / BMG.

MEL TORME & TONY BENNETT (Torme, Mel & Tony Bennett)
CD _____ CDCD 1076
Charly / Apr '93 / Charly / THE / Cadillac.

PERFECTLY FRANK
Time after time / I fall in love too easily / East of the sun and west of the moon / Nancy / I thought about you / Night and day / I've got the world on a string / I'm glad there is you / Nightingale sang in Berkeley Square / I wished on the moon / You go to my head / Lady is a tramp / I see your face before me / Day in, day out / Indian summer / Call me irresponsible / Here's that rainy day / Last night when we were young / I wanna be in love again / Foggy day / Don't worry 'bout me / One for my baby / Angel eyes / I'll be seeing you
CD _____ 472222-2
Columbia / Aug '94 / Sony.

PORTRAIT OF A SONG STYLIST
Shadow of your smile / Who can I turn to / When Joanna loved me / Don't worry 'bout me / It had to be you / Where or when / Ain't misbehavin' / Dancing in the dark / Second time around / Old devil moon / My funny valentine / Autumn leaves / Taste of honey / I left my heart in San Francisco / Toot toot tootsie / September song / Moment of truth / I'll be around
CD _____ HARCD 105
Masterpiece / Apr '89 / BMG.

RODGERS AND HART COLLECTION
Thou swell / Most beautiful / Small hotel / I've got five dollars / You took advantage of me / I wish I were in love again / This funny world / My heart stood still / My romance / Mountain greenery / This can't be love / Blue moon / Lady is a tramp / Lover / Manhattan / Spring is here / Have you met Miss Jones / Isn't it romantic / Wait till you see her / I could write a book
CD _____ CDSIV 1119
Horatio Nelson / Apr '93 / THE / BMG / Avid/BMG / Koch.

RODGERS AND HART SONGBOOK
This can't be love / Blue moon / Lady is a tramp / Lover / Manhattan / Spring is here / Have you met Miss Jones / Isn't it romantic / Wait till you see her / I could write a book / Thou swell / Most beautiful of all the world / There's a small hotel / I've got five dollars / You took advantage of me / I wish I were in love again / This funny world / My heart stood still / My romance / Mountain greenery
CD _____ CDXP 2102
DRG / Apr '88 / New Note.

SINGING AND SWINGING (Bennett, Tony & Count Basie)
CD _____ HADCD 184
Javelin / Nov '95 / THE / Henry Hadaway Organisation.

SINGS THE RODGERS AND HART SONGBOOK
This can't be love / Blue moon / Lady is a tramp / Lover / Manhattan / Spring is here / Have you met Miss Jones / Isn't it romantic / Wait till you see her / I could write a book / Thou swell / Most beautiful girl in the world / There's a small hotel / I've got five dollars / You took advantage of me / I wish I were in love again / This funny world / My heart stood still / My romance / Mountain greenery
CD _____ CDSIV 1138
Horatio Nelson / Jul '95 / THE / BMG / Avid/BMG / Koch.

SNOWFALL
Snowfall / My favourite things / Christmas song / Santa Claus is coming to town / We wish you a Merry Christmas / Silent night / O come all ye faithful (Adeste Fidelis) / Jingle bells / Where is love / Christmasland / I love the winter weather / I've got my love to keep me warm / White Christmas / Winter wonderland / Have yourself a merry little Christmas / I'll be home for Christmas (On reissues only)
CD _____ 4775972
Columbia / Nov '95 / Sony.

SPECIAL MAGIC OF TONY BENNETT
What is this thing called love / Love for sale / I'm in love again / You'd be so nice to come home to / Easy to love / It's all right with me / Night and day / Dream dancing / I've got you under my skin / Get out of town / Experiment / One / This funny world / Lost in the stars / As time goes by / I used to be colour blind / Mr. Magic
CD _____ JHD 053
Tring / Mar '93 / Tring / Prism.

STEPPIN' OUT
Steppin' out with my baby / Who cares / Top hat, white tie and tails / They can't take that away from me / Dancing in the dark / Shine on your shoes / He loves and she loves / They all laughed / I concentrate on you / You're all the world to me / All of you / Nice work if you can get it / It only happens when I dance with you / Shall we dance / You're easy to dance with / Change

partners / Cheek to cheek / I guess I'll have to change my plan / That's entertainment / By myself
CD _____ 474360 2
Columbia / Nov '93 / Sony.

TOGETHER AGAIN (Bennett, Tony & Bill Evans)
Child is born / Make someone happy / Bad and the beautiful / Lucky to be me / You're near me / Two lonely people / You don't know what love is / Maybe September / Lonely girl / You must believe in spring
CD _____ CDSIV 1122
Horatio Nelson / Jul '95 / THE / BMG / Avid/BMG / Koch.

UNPLUGGED
Old devil moon / Speak low / It had to be you / I love a piano / It amazes me / Girl I love (AKA the man I love) / Fly me to the moon / You're the world to me / Rags to riches / When Joanna loved me / Good life/I wanna be around / I left my heart in San Francisco / Steppin' out with my baby / Moonglow (With KD Lang) / They can't take that away from me (With Elvis Costello) / Foggy day / All of you / Body and soul / I don't mean a thing if it ain't got that swing / Autumn leaves
CD _____ 477170-2
Columbia / Aug '94 / Sony.

Benno, Marc

TAKE IT BACK TO TEXAS
Black cadillac / Easy travelin' gal / Mama's cookin' / Take it back to Texas / No problem child / Little Miss Rock 'n' roll / Mary played the pool hall / Greatest find
CD _____ SR 652303
Sky Ranch / Jun '92 / New Note.

Benoit, Blue Boy

PARLEZ-VOUS FRANCAIS
CD _____ CDLL 87
La Lichere / Aug '93 / Discovery / ADA.

PLUS TARD DANS LA SOIREE
CD _____ CDLL 187
La Lichere / Aug '93 / Discovery / ADA.

Benoit, David

BENOIT/FREEMAN PROJECT (Benoit, David & Russ Freeman)
Reunion / When she believed in me / Mediterranean nights / Swept away / End of our season / After the love has gone / Smarty-pants / It's the thought that counts / Mirage / That's all I could say
CD _____ GRP 97392
GRP / Feb '94 / BMG / New Note.

BEST OF DAVID BENOIT, THE
Drive time / Every step of the way / Cast your fate to the wind / Searching for June / M.W.A. / Linus and Lucy / Kei's song / Key to you / Freedom at midnight / Still standing / Wailea / Letter to Evan / Urban daydreams / Mediterranean nights
CD _____ GRP 98312
GRP / Oct '95 / BMG / New Note.

SHAKEN, NOT STIRRED
Wailea / I went to bat for you / Any other time / Carmel / Sparks flew / Shaken, not stirred / Chi Chi's eyes / Days of old / Jacqueline / Sarah's theme
CD _____ GRP 97872
GRP / Oct '94 / BMG / New Note.

THIS SIDE UP
Beach trails / Stingray / Land of the loving / Linus and Lucy / Sunset Island / Hymn for Aquino / Santa Barbara / Waltz for Debbie
CD _____ GRD 9541
GRP / Mar '87 / BMG / New Note.

Benoit, Tab

NICE AND WARM
CD _____ JR 012012
Justice / Apr '93 / Koch.

WHAT I LIVE FOR
CD _____ JR 12022
Justice / Oct '94 / Koch.

Benson, George

20/20
No one emotion / Please don't walk away / I just wanna hang around you / Nothing's gonna change my love for you / La march / New day / You are the love of my life / Hold me / Stand up / 20/20 / Shark bite
CD _____ 9251782
WEA / Feb '92 / Warner Music.

BAD BENSON
CD _____ 4508922
Sony Jazz / Jan '95 / Sony.

BEST OF GEORGE BENSON, THE
California dreamin' / Gentle rain / One rock don't make no boulder / Take five / Summertime / Theme from good king bad / Body talk / Summer of '42 / My latin brothers / Ode to a Kudu / I remember Wes / From now on
CD _____ 4654052
Columbia / Oct '92 / Sony.

BODY TALK
CD _____ 239206
Musidisc / Dec '86 / Vital / Harmonia Mundi / ADA / Cadillac / Discovery.

BREEZIN'
This masquerade / Six to four / Breezin' / So this is love / Lady / Affirmation
CD _____ K2 56199
WEA / Jun '89 / Warner Music.

COLLABORATION (Benson, George & Earl Klugh)
Mount Airey groove / Mimosa / Brazilian stomp / Dreamin' / Since you're gone / Collaboration / Jamaica / Romeo and Juliet
CD _____ 9255802
WEA / Feb '95 / Warner Music.

GEORGE BENSON COLLECTION, THE
Turn your love around / Love all the hurt away / Give me the night / Cast your fate to the wind / Love ballad / Nature boy / Last train to Clarksville / Livin' inside your love / Never give up on a good thing / On Broadway / White rabbit / This masquerade / Here comes the sun / Breezin' / Moody's mood / We got the love / Greatest love of all
CD _____ K2 66107
WEA / Jul '88 / Warner Music.

GEORGE BENSON COOKBOOK, THE
Cooker / Benny's back / Bossa rocka / All of me / Big fat lady / Benson's rider / Ready and able / Borgia stick / Return of the prodigal son / Jumpin' with symphony Sid
CD _____ 476903 2
Columbia / Sep '94 / Sony.

GIVE ME THE NIGHT
What's on your mind / Dinorah, Dinorah / Love dance / Star of the story / Midnight love affair / Turn out the lamplight / Love x love / Off Broadway / Moody's mood / Give me the night
CD _____ K 256823
WEA / Apr '84 / Warner Music.

GUITAR GIANTS
Love for sale / This masquerade / There will never be another you / All blues / Witchcraft / Blue bossa / Oleo / Li'l darlin'
CD _____ SMS 055
Carlton Home Entertainment / Oct '92 / Carlton Home Entertainment.

IN CONCERT - CARNEGIE HALL
Gone / Take 5 / Octane / Summertime
CD _____ 4608352
Sony Jazz / Jan '95 / Sony.

IN FLIGHT
Nature boy / Wind and I / World is a ghetto / Gonna love you more / Valdez in the country / Everything must change
CD _____ 256327
WEA / '86 / Warner Music.

IN YOUR EYES
Feel like makin' love / Inside love (so personal) / Lady love (one more time) / Love will come again / In your eyes / Never too far to fall / Being with you / Use me / Late at night / In search of a dream
CD _____ 923744 2
WEA / Jul '88 / Warner Music.

IT'S UPTOWN WITH THE GEORGE BENSON QUARTET (Benson, George Quartet)
Clockwise / Summertime / Ain't that peculiar / Jaguar / Willow weep for me / Foggy day / Hello birdie / Bullfight / Stormy weather / Eternally / Myna bird blues
CD _____ 476902 2
Columbia / Sep '94 / Sony.

JAZZ MASTERS
CD _____ 5218612
Verve / Feb '94 / PolyGram.

LEGENDS IN MUSIC - GEORGE BENSON
CD _____ LECD 068
Wisepack / Jul '94 / THE / Conifer.

LIL' DARLIN'
Witchcraft / Blue bossa / Oleo / Li'l darlin'
CD _____ CDTB 078
Thunderbolt / Sep '90 / Magnum Music Group.

LIVE AT CASA CARIBE (Benson, George Quartet)
CD _____ COD 011
Jazz View / Mar '92 / Harmonia Mundi.

LIVE AT CASA CARIBE VOL.2 (Benson, George Quartet)
CD _____ COD 035
Jazz View / Jun '92 / Harmonia Mundi.

LIVE AT CASA CARIBE VOL.3 (Benson, George Quartet)
CD _____ COD 036
Jazz View / Aug '92 / Harmonia Mundi.

LOVE REMEMBERS
I'll be good to you / Got to be there / My heart is dancing / Love of my life / Kiss and make up / Come into my world / Love remembers / Willing to fight / Somewhere Islands / Lovin' on borrowed time / Lost in love / Calling you
CD _____ 759926685-2
WEA / May '93 / Warner Music.

LOVE WALKED IN
All the things you are / Invitation / Love walked in / Dahlin's delight
CD _____ CDTB 088
Thunderbolt / Dec '90 / Magnum Music Group.

MASQUERADE
Love for sale / This masquerade / There will never be another you / All blues
CD _____ CDTB 072
Thunderbolt / Oct '89 / Magnum Music Group.

QUARTET ALL BLUES
CD _____ CDSGP 034
Prestige / Jul '92 / Total/BMG.

QUARTET BLUE BOSSA
CD _____ CDSGP 035
Prestige / Jul '92 / Total/BMG.

SILVER COLLECTION, THE
Billie's bounce / Low down and dirty / Thunder walk / Doobie doobie blues / What's new / I remember Wes / Windmills of your mind / Song for my father / Carnival joys / Giblet gravy / Walk on by / Sack o' woe / Groovin'
CD _____ 8234502
Verve / Sep '92 / PolyGram.

SPOTLIGHT ON GEORGE BENSON
Witchcraft / Love for sale / There will never be another you / All blues / Li'l darlin' / Oleo
CD _____ HADCD 102
Javelin / Feb '94 / THE / Henry Hadaway Organisation.

TENDERLY
You don't know what love is / Stella by starlight / Stardust / At the mambo inn / Here, There and Everywhere / This is all I ask / Tenderly / I could write a book
CD _____ 9259072
WEA / Jul '89 / Warner Music.

TWICE THE LOVE
Twice the love / Starting all over / Good habit / Everybody does it / Living on borrowed love / Let's do it again / Stephanie / Tender love / You're still my baby / Until you believe
CD _____ 925705 2
WEA / Aug '88 / Warner Music.

WHILE THE CITY SLEEPS
Shiver / Love is here tonight / Teaser / Secrets in the night / Too many times / Did you hear the thunder / While the city sleeps / Kisses in the moonlight
CD _____ 9254752
WEA / Feb '95 / Warner Music.

WHITE RABBIT
White rabbit / Summer of '42 / Little train / California dreamin' / El mar
CD _____ ZK 64768
Columbia / Nov '95 / Sony.

WITCHCRAFT
CD _____ JHR 73523
Jazz Hour / Sep '93 / Target/BMG / Jazz Music / Cadillac.

Bensusan, Pierre

BAMBOULE
CD _____ BEST 1040CD
Acoustic Music / Nov '93 / ADA.

SOLILAI
Nice feeling / Bamboule / Au jardin d'amour / Santa Monica / Suite flamande aux pommes / Milton / Salilai / Dea lua
CD _____ CMA 945CD
La Chant Du Monde / Jan '95 / Harmonia Mundi / ADA.

SPICES
Femme cambree / Mille vallees / Le bateau fiction / Shi big, shi mhor / Agadiramadan / La cour interieure / Last pint / Les voiles catalanes / Montsegur / Four am
CD _____ CMA 944CD
Danceteria / Jan '95 / Plastic Head / ADA.

WU WEI
CD _____ CMA 942
Danceteria / Oct '94 / Plastic Head / ADA.

Bent Back Tulips

LOOKING THROUGH
CD _____ ROSE 205 CD
New Rose / Aug '90 / Direct / ADA.

Bente's...

I GODLYNT LAG (Bente's Gammaldansorkester)
CD _____ B 1011CD
Musikk Distribujson / Dec '94 / ADA.

Bentley, Ed

BOLLA KEYBOARD BLUES
CD _____ CDSGP 003
Prestige / Jan '94 / Total/BMG.

METROPOLIS
CD _____ CDSGP 0137
Prestige / Sep '95 / Total/BMG.

Benton, Brook

20 GREATEST HITS
CD _____ RMB 75041
Remember / Nov '93 / Total/BMG.

ANTHOLOGY (2CD Set)
Rainy night in Georgia / Boll weevil song / It's just a matter of time / Hotel happines / So many ways / My true confession / I want to thank you / Lie to me / Shadrack / Kiddio / Fools rush in / Think twice / So close / For my hahy / Frankie and Johnny / Revenge / I got what I want / Ties that bind / It's just a house without you / I can't take my eyes off you / Mr. Bartender / Endlessly / Baby you've got what it takes) / Rocking good way / This time of year / It started all over again / Now is the time / ALI in love is fair / Wekend without feathers
CD Set _____ GP 20072
Gentle Price / Jan '96 / Target/BMG.

COLLECTION, THE
CD _____ COL 047
Collection / Jan '95 / Target/BMG.

ESSENTIAL COLLECTION
CD Set _____ LECD 622
Wisepack / Apr '95 / THE / Conifer.

GREAT LOVE SONGS
CD _____ 15102
Laserlight / Aug '91 / Target/BMG.

RAINY NIGHT IN GEORGIA
Rainy night in Georgia / It's just a matter of time / Boll weevil song / Baby, you got what it takes / Rockin' good way / Lie to me / So many ways / Hotel happiness / Kiddio / Endlessly / Revenge / Same one / Think twice
CD _____ CDCD 1047
Charly / Mar '93 / Charly / THE / Cadillac.

Benton, Buster

BLUES AT THE TOP
You're my lady / Blues and trouble / It's good in my neighbourhood / Lonesome for a dime / I wish't I knew / From Missouri / Dangerous woman / That's your thing / Can't wait to see my baby's face / In the ghetto / Honey bee / Hawk is coming / I must have a hole in my head / Cold man ain't no good / Money's the name of the game
CD _____ ECD 260302
Evidence / Feb '93 / Harmonia Mundi / ADA / Cadillac.

I LIKE TO HEAR MY GUITAR SING
I gotta find a big legged woman / My friends call me crazy / Little bluebird / How old Buster feels / Dust my broom / Woman can't live on love alone / Feels so bad / Sad on / I like to hear my guitar sing
CD _____ CDICH 1129
Ichiban / Oct '93 / Koch.

MONEY'S THE NAME OF THE GAME
Sweet 94 / You accuse me / Sit your fine self down / Money's the name of the game / As the years go passing by / Come and see about me / Sweet sixteen / Lean on me
CD _____ ICH 1046 CD
Ichiban / Oct '89 / Koch.

Benues

RISE UP AFRICA
CD _____ WWCD 07
World / Dec '88 / Grapevine.

Benzie, Ian F.

SO FAR
CD _____ CDLDL 1228
Lochshore / May '95 / ADA / Direct / Duncans.

Beowulf

2 CENTS
Throw your rock / Bullet hole / 140 Days / Two cents / Jumped in / Life ain't, life's only / Lack of knowledge / Superstar / No one knows no one / Only human / Badge abuse / Dope bag
CD _____ 727722
Restless / Apr '95 / Vital.

Berendsen, Ben

AMONG THE TREES (Berendsen, Ben & Marcel Van Der Heyden)
CD _____ 322801
Koch / Mar '93 / Koch.

Beresford, Steve

SIGNALS FOR TEA
CD _____ AVAN 013
Avant / Apr '95 / Harmonia Mundi / Cadillac.

Berezan, Jennifer

BORDERLINES
CD _____ FF 615CD
Flying Fish / Apr '94 / Roots / CM / Direct / ADA.

Berg, Bob

BACK ROADS
Back roads / Travellin' man / Silverado / When I fall in love / American gothic / Dreamer / Nighthawks
CD _____ CY 79042
Denon / Feb '93 / Conifer.

BEST OF BOB BERG, THE
Friday night at the Cadillac club / Kalimba / Pipes / Mayumi / In the shadows / Autumn leaves / Can't help lovin' dat man / Amazon / When I fall in love / Silverado
CD _____ DC 8593
Denon / Jun '95 / Conifer.

CYCLES (Berg, Bob/Mike Stern/Don Grolnick)
Bruze / Back home / Pipes / Diamond method / Company B / Mayumi / So far so / Someone to watch over me
CD _____ CY 72745
Denon / Feb '89 / Conifer.

ENTER THE SPIRIT
Second sight / Snapshot / Promise / Nature of the beast / Sometime ago / No moe / Night moves / Blues for Bella / I loves you / Porgy / Angles
CD _____ GRS 00052
GRP / May '93 / BMG / New Note.

IN THE SHADOWS
In the shadow / Crossing / I thought about you / Either or / Stay that way / Carry on / Games / Autumn leaves
CD _____ CY 76210
Denon / Jun '90 / Conifer.

RIDDLES
Morning star (A primeira estrela) / Something in the way she moves / Ramiro's dream / Children of the night / Riddle me this / Ebony eyes / Ahmed-6 / Coaster / For little Mia
CD _____ GRS 02112
GRP / Aug '94 / BMG / New Note.

SHORT STORIES
Friday night at the Cadillac Club / Words / Snakes / Kalimba / Search / Maya / That's the ticket / Junior
CD _____ CY 1768
Denon / Jun '92 / Conifer.

VIRTUAL REALITY
Can't help lovin' dat man / Water is wide / Loose bloose / Never will I marry / Tanka / Amazon / On second thought / Down snake hollow
CD _____ CY 75369
Denon / May '93 / Conifer.

Berg, Matraca

SPEED OF GRACE, THE
Slow poison / Tall drink of water / Let's face it, baby / I won't let go / Jolene / Guns in my head / Waiting for the sky to fall / Lying on the moon / Come on momma / River of no return
CD _____ 74321 19230-2
RCA / Mar '94 / BMG.

Berg, Rene

LEATHER, THE LONELINESS
CD _____ CMG 005CD
Communique / Nov '92 / Plastic Head.

Bergalli, Gustavo

ON THE WAY
CD _____ DRUD 212
Dragon / Oct '93 / Roots / Cadillac / Wellard / CM / ADA.

Bergamo, John

REPERCUSSION GROUP
CD _____ CMPCD 31
CMP / Jan '88 / Vital/SAM.

Bergcrantz, Anders

LIVE AT SWEET BASIL
CD _____ CRCD 225
Dragon / Oct '87 / Roots / Cadillac / Wellard / CM / ADA.

Bergens, Sodra

KAMARINSKAYA (Bergens, Sodra Balalaika Orchestra)
CD _____ XOUCD 103
Xource / Oct '93 / ADA / Cadillac.

Berger, Bengt

BITTER FUNERAL BEER BAND
In a Balinese bar / Two ewe songs / Upper region / Twisted pattern / Ammasu / Pre for Palme / Dar-Kpen: Gan da Yina / Praise drumming for ANC
CD _____ 8393082
ECM / '89 / New Note.

Berger, Karl

AROUND (Berger, Karl & Friends)
CD _____ 120112-2
Black Saint / May '91 / Harmonia Mundi / Cadillac.

Bergeron, Shirley

FRENCH ROCKING BOOGIE
French rocking boogie / J'ai fait mon idee / Old home waltz / Quel etoile / New country waltz / Perrodin two step / Chez Tanie / Mama and papa / Since that first time / True love waltz / J'ai passe devant ta porte / Poor hobo / La valse a August breaux / Eunice two step / La valse de cherokee / Bosco blues / Madam Sostan / La crepe a nazare / Chere Lasselle / Vermillion two step / La valse de grand bois / Chere toute toute
CD _____ CDCHD 353
Ace / Apr '92 / Pinnacle / Cadillac / Complete/Pinnacle.

Bergh, Totti

I HEAR A RHAPSODY
CD _____ GEMCD 148
Gemini / Nov '87 / Cadillac.

TENOR GLADNESS
CD _____ GEMCD 153
Gemini / Dec '89 / Cadillac.

Bergin, Johnny

COME DANCING
Everything's in rhythm with my heart / Please don't talk about me when I'm gone / Dream of me/Dreamy melody/Dream lover / Where the blue of the night/Sailing by / You brought a new kind of love to me/Undecided/A sky blue sh / Alexander's ragtime band / September in the rain/I'll string along with you / In a shady nook/Love letters in the sand / Deed I do / Goodbye blues / Blueberry hill/Goodnight sweetheart / We'll meet again/I don't want to walk without you / Breezin' along with the breeze / I saw stars/Auf weidersehn, sweetheart / Deep purple/Moonlight bay / Here's that rainy day / More I see you, The/Red sails in the sunset / Play to me gipsy / Ecstasy / When the red red robin/Glory of love / You're driving me crazy/Makin' whoopee/Roamin' in the Glomin
CD _____ SAV 173CD
Savoy / Jun '92 / THE / Savoy.

COME DANCING 2
Ma, he's making eyes at me/Moonstruck / You always hurt the one you love / Five foot two, eyes of blue / Some of these days/My blue heaven / If I had a talking picture of you / If I had my way/Pennies from heaven / Dancing with my shadow/Everything stops for tea / There's a land of begin again / Let us be sweethearts over again / I'll always be in love with you / Tennessee waltz/Far away places / Tell me I'm forgiven / Golden body/Come back to Sorrento / All I ask is dream of you/Ukelele lady/Soldiers of the Queen / Elmer's tune/Battle of New Orleans/Davy Crockett / You made me love you/A slow boat to China / Me and my shadow / Carolina in the morning / Maybe it's because I'm a Londoner/Lambeth walk / Japanese sandman/Old father Thames / Seven lonely days/Exactly like you/Glad rag doll / Lola rose/You are my everything/Spread a little happiness / Black hills of Dakota / Bye bye blues / 'S Wonderful
CD _____ SAV 192CD
Savoy / Jun '93 / THE / Savoy.

Bergin, Mary

FEADÓGA STÁIN
CD _____ CEFCD 071
Gael Linn / '89 / Roots / CM / Direct / ADA.

FEADÓGA STÁIN 2
CD _____ CEFCD 149
Gael Linn / Feb '93 / Roots / CM / Direct / ADA.

Bergin, Sean

LIVE AT THE BIMHUIS
CD _____ BVHAASTCD 9202
Bvhaast / Oct '93 / Cadillac.

Bergman, Borah

HUMAN FACTOR, THE (Bergman, Borah & Andrew Cyrille)
CD _____ 121212-2
Soul Note / Apr '93 / Harmonia Mundi / Wellard / Cadillac.

NEW FRONTIER, A
CD _____ 121030-2
Soul Note / May '94 / Harmonia Mundi / Wellard / Cadillac.

REFLECTIONS ON ORNETTE COLEMAN & THE STONE HOUSE (Bergman, Borah & Hamid Drake)
CD _____ 1212802
Soul Note / Jan '96 / Harmonia Mundi / Wellard / Cadillac.

Bergonzi, Jerry

LINEAGE
CD _____ 123237-2
Red / Mar '91 / Harmonia Mundi / Jazz Horizons / Cadillac / ADA.

SIGNED BY... (Bergonzi, Jerry & Joachim Kuhn)
CD ZZ 84104
Deux Z / Feb '94 / Harmonia Mundi / Cadillac.

TILT (Bergonzi, Jerry Quartet)
CD 1232452
Red / Mar '92 / Harmonia Mundi / Jazz Horizons / Cadillac / ADA.

Berigan, Bunny

1936
CD TAX 37102
Tax / Aug '94 / Jazz Music / Wellard / Cadillac.

1936-38 (Berigan, Bunny & His Rhythm Makers)
CD JASSCD 627
Jass / Oct '92 / CM / Jazz Music / ADA / Cadillac / Direct.

1938 BROADCASTS-PARADISE RESTAURANT
CD JH 1022
Jazz Hour / Feb '93 / Target/BMG / Jazz Music / Cadillac.

BUNNY & RED (Berigan, Bunny & Red McKenzie)
CD 3801032
Jazz Archives / Jun '92 / Jazz Music / Discovery / Cadillac.

BUNNY BERIGAN 1936-38
CD JCD 627
Jass / Feb '91 / CM / Jazz Music / ADA / Cadillac / Direct.

BUNNY BERIGAN AND HIS RHYTHM MAKERS - 1936 (Berigan, Bunny & His Rhythm Makers)
CD TAXCD 3710-2
Tax / Aug '94 / Jazz Music / Wellard / Cadillac.

BUNNY BERIGAN AND HIS RHYTHM MAKERS VOL. 2 1938 (Berigan, Bunny & His Rhythm Makers)
CD JASSCD 638
Jass / May '94 / CM / Jazz Music / ADA / Cadillac / Direct.

CLASSICS 1935-36
CD CLASSICS 734
Classics / Jan '94 / Discovery / Jazz Music.

CLASSICS 1936-1937
CD CLASSICS 749
Classics / Aug '94 / Discovery / Jazz Music.

CLASSICS 1937
CD CLASSICS 766
Classics / Aug '94 / Discovery / Jazz Music.

CLASSICS 1937-38
CD CLASSICS 785
Classics / Nov '94 / Discovery / Jazz Music.

CLASSICS 1938
CD CLASSICS 815
Classics / May '95 / Discovery / Jazz Music.

CLASSICS 1938-42
CD CLASSICS 844
Classics / Nov '95 / Discovery / Jazz Music.

DEVIL'S HOLIDAY
CD JCD 638
Jass / Jan '93 / CM / Jazz Music / ADA / Cadillac / Direct.

DOWN BY THE OLD MILL STREAM (Berigan, Bunny & His Orchestra)
CD 3801112
Jazz Archives / Feb '93 / Jazz Music / Discovery / Cadillac.

GANG BUSTERS (1938-1939)
When a prince / Livery stable blues / Let this be a warning / Why doesn't somebody / High society / Father dear father / Button, button / Rockin' rollers / Jubilee / Sobbin' blues / I cried for you / Deed I do / In a mist / Flashes / Davenport blues / Candlelights / In the dark / Walking the dog / Patty cake / Jazz me blues / You had it comin' to you / There'll be some changes made / Little gate's special / Gangbuster's holiday
CD HEPCD 1036
Hep / May '92 / Cadillac / Jazz Music / New Note / Wellard.

INTRODUCTION TO BUNNY BERIGAN 1935-39, AN
CD 4021
Best Of Jazz / May '95 / Discovery.

PIED PIPER 1935, THE
Nothin' but the blues / Troubled / Sometimes I'm happy / King Porter stomp / Jingle bells / Santa Claus came in spring / Honeysuckle rose / Blues / Song of India / Marie Liebestraum / Mendelssohn's spring song / Blue Lou / I can't get started (with you) / Prisoner's song / Trees / Russian lullaby / Wearing of the green / Pied piper / Jelly roll blues / Candlelights / I've found a new baby
CD 7863666152
Bluebird / Aug '95 / BMG.

PORTRAIT OF BUNNY BERIGAN
Me minus you / She reminds me of you / Troubled / Plantation moods / In a little Spanish town / Solo hop / Nothin' but the blues / Squareface / King Porter stomp / Buzzard / Tillie's downtown now / You took advantage of me / Chicken and waffles / I'm coming Virginia / Blues / Swing Mister Charlie / Blue Lou / Marie / Black bottom / Prisoner's song / I can't get started (with you)
CD CDAJA 5060
Living Era / Apr '89 / Koch.

SWINGIN' HIGH
CD TPZ 1013
Topaz Jazz / Feb '95 / Pinnacle / Cadillac.

THROUGH THE YEARS
CD 3801192
Jazz Archives / Feb '93 / Jazz Music / Discovery / Cadillac.

Berio, Luciano

ACOUSMATRIX 7, ELECTRONIC WORKS (Berio, Luciano & Bruno Maderna)
CD BVHAASTCD 9109
Bvhaast / Oct '94 / Cadillac.

Berk, Dick

EAST COAST STROLL
CD RSRCD 128
Reservoir Music / Nov '94 / Cadillac.

LET'S COOL ONE
CD RSRCD 122
Reservoir Music / Nov '94 / Cadillac.

Berlin

COUNT THREE AND PRAY
Will I ever understand you / You don't know / Like flames / Heartstrings / Take my breath away / Trash / When love goes to war / Hideaway / Sex me, talk me / Pink and velvet
CD 5509012
Spectrum/Karussell / Jan '95 / PolyGram / THE.

Berlin Contemporary Jazz.

BERLIN CONTEMPORARY JAZZ ORCHESTRA (Berlin Contemporary Jazz Orchestra)
CD 8417772
ECM / Oct '90 / New Note.

Berlin, Irving

IRVING BERLIN'S
CD VJC 1010-2
Victorious Discs / Feb '91 / Jazz Music.

Berline, Byron

DOUBLE TROUBLE (Berline, Byron & John Hickman)
CD SHCD 3750
Sugarhill / Aug '95 / Roots / CM / ADA / Direct.

FIDDLE AND A SONG
CD SHD 3838
Sugarhill / Oct '95 / Roots / CM / ADA / Direct.

NOW THERE ARE FOUR (Berline, Byron & Dan Crary & John Hickman)
Big dog / Train of memory / Weary blues from waiting / Moonlight motor inn / They don't play George Jones on MTV / Speak softly you're talking to my heart / Santa Anna / Leave me the way I am / Kodak 1955 / Hallelujah Harry
CD SH 3773 CD
Sugarhill / '90 / Roots / CM / ADA / Direct.

Berman, Sonny

WOODCHOPPER'S HOLIDAY (Berman, Sonny & Serge Chaloff)
CD C&BCD 111
Cool 'n' Blue / Oct '93 / Jazz Music / Discovery.

Bermejo, Mili

CASA CORAZON (Bermejo, Mili Quartet)
CD GLCD 4016
Green Linnet / May '94 / Roots / CM / Direct / ADA.

Bernard, James

ATMOSPHERICS
CD RSNCD 14
Rising High / Mar '94 / Disc.

Bernard, Rod

SWAMP ROCK 'N' ROLLER
Pardon Mr Gordon / Recorded in England / Memphis / Gimme back my cadillac / Who's gonna rock my baby / Forgive / My old mother in law / I might as well / Boss man's son / Fais do do / Loneliness / Colinda / I want somebody / Diggy liggy lo / Lawdy Miss Clawdy / Prisoner's song / Thirty days / That's alright mama / Lover's blues / Maybellene / Midnight special / My babe / Jambalaya / Big mamou / New Orleans / Give me love / Shake, rattle and roll / This should go on forever
CD CDCHD 488
Ace / May '94 / Pinnacle / Cadillac / Complete/Pinnacle.

Bernard-Smith, Simon

PRAISE HIM ON THE PANPIPES
CD SOPD 2050
Spirit Of Praise / May '92 / Nelson Word.

Berne, Tim

ANCESTORS, THE (Berne, Tim Sextet)
CD 121 061 2
Soul Note / Oct '90 / Harmonia Mundi / Wellard / Cadillac.

DIMINUTIVE MYSTERIES
CD 5140032
JMT / Jan '93 / PolyGram.

SANCTIFIED DREAMS
Velcho man / Hip doctor / Elastic lad / Blue alpha (for alpha) / Mag's groove / Terre haute
CD 4606762
CBS / Sep '88 / Sony.

Bernelle, Agnes

FATHER'S LYING DEAD ON THE IRONING BOARD
Homecoming / Chansonette / Bertha de Sade / Hafen-kneipe / Tootsies / Horse / Girl with brown mole / Night elegy / Ballad of the poor child / Hurdy gurdy / Nightingale
CD DIAB 815
Diabolo / Jul '95 / Pinnacle.

Bernhard, Sandra

EXCUSES FOR BAD BEHAVIOUR
CD 4773152
Sony Music / Jan '94 / Sony.

WITHOUT YOU I'M NOTHING
CD CDENV 528
Enigma / Jun '89 / EMI.

Bernie

I SAW THE LIGHT
I saw the light / This world is not my home / Me and Jesus / One day at a time / Morning has broken / Tramp on the streets / Precious memories / Fly away / Daddy sang bass / Why me Lord / Old rugged cross / Amazing grace / Rivers of Babylon / Swing low, sweet Chariot / He's got the whole world in his hands / Old country church / Safe in the arms of Jesus / Go tell it on the mountain / Will the circle be unbroken / When the saints go marching in / Count your blessings / Family bible / Rock of ages / How great thou art
CD PLATCD 339
Prism / Mar '93 / Prism.

Bernstein, Peter

SIGNS
CD CRISS 1095
Criss Cross / Apr '95 / Cadillac / Harmonia Mundi.

SOMETHIN'S BURNIN' (Bernstein, Peter Quartet)
CD CRISS 1079CD
Criss Cross / Nov '93 / Cadillac / Harmonia Mundi.

Bernstein, Steven Jesse

PRISON
CD SPCD 37195
Sub Pop / Jul '92 / Disc.

Beroard, Jocelyne

MILANS
CD COLCD 468723
Columbia / Dec '91 / Sony.

Berry, Benny

SOME THINGS NEVER CHANGE
CD HAWCD 171
Prism / Apr '91 / Prism.

Berry, Bill

HELLO REV (Berry, Bill LA Big Band)
Hello rev / Star crossed lovers / Bink / And how / Earl / Little song for Mex / Be your own best friend / Tulip or turnip / Boy meets horn / Cotton tail
CD CCD 4027
Concord Jazz / Aug '90 / New Note.

SHORTCAKE
Avalon / Betty / Bloose / I didn't know about you / Royal Garden blues / Moon song / I'm getting sentimental over you / I hadn't anyone till you
CD CCD 4075
Concord Jazz / Feb '95 / New Note.

Berry, Chu

BLOWING UP A BREEZE
CD TPZ 1024
Topaz Jazz / Jul '95 / Pinnacle / Cadillac.

CLASSICS 1937-41
CD CLASSICS 784
Classics / Nov '94 / Discovery / Jazz Music.

Berry, Chuck

20 GREAT TRACKS
Maybellene / Roll over Beethoven / Reelin' and rockin' / Rock 'n' roll music / Sweet little sixteen / Johnny B. Goode / No particular place to go / Memphis, Tennessee / Wee wee hours / You never can tell / Go go go / Downbound train / No money down / Havana moon / House of blue lights / Crying steel / I'm just a lucky so and so / Promised land / My Mustang Ford / Drifting heart
CD CDMFP 5936
Music For Pleasure / Apr '92 / EMI.

21 GREATEST HITS,THE
Maybellene / Sweet little sixteen / School days / Rock 'n' roll music / Johnny B. Goode / Carol / Reelin' and rockin' / Memphis, Tennessee / Bring another drink / Good lovin' woman / Roll over Beethoven / Back in the U.S.A / Sweet little rock 'n' roller / Oh baby doll / C.C. rider / Thirty days / Goodnight sweetheart / Back to Memphis / Check me out / My heart will always belong to you / I really do love you
CD CD 30
Bescol / May '87 / CM / Target/BMG.

AUDIO ARCHIVE
CD CDAA 049
Tring / Jun '92 / Tring / Prism.

BEST OF CHUCK BERRY, THE
Roll over Beethoven / No particular place to go / Memphis, Tennessee / Tulane / Havana moon / Wee wee hours / Nadine / Let it rock / Sweet little sixteen / Maybellene / Back in the U.S.A / Little queenie / Almost grown / Johnny B. Goode / School day / Oh baby doll / Sweet little rock 'n' roller / Reelin' and rockin' / Promised land / Rock 'n' roll music / Downbound train / Brown eyed handsome man / Merry Christmas baby / Bye bye Johnny / Around and around / No money down
CD MCCD 019
Music Club / May '91 / Disc / THE / CM.

CHESS MASTERS VOL. 1
Maybellene / Wee wee hours / Thirty days / You can't catch me / No money down / Brown eyed handsome man / Roll over Beethoven / Too much monkey business / School days / Rock 'n' roll music / Oh baby doll / Sweet little sixteen / Rockin' at the Philharmonic / Guitar boogie / Reelin' and rockin' / Johnny B. Goode
CD CDMF 076
Magnum Force / '91 / Magnum Music Group.

CHESS MASTERS VOL. 2
Around and around / Beautiful Delilah / Carol / Memphis, Tennessee / Sweet little rock 'n' roller / Little Queenie / Almost grown / Back in the U.S.A / Let it rock / Bye bye Johnny / Come on / Nadine / You never can tell / Promised land / No particular place to go / It wasn't me
CD CDMF 080
Magnum Force / Nov '91 / Magnum Music Group.

CHESS YEARS, THE (9CD Set)
CD Set CDREDBOX 2
Chess/Charly / Nov '92 / Charly.

CHUCK BERRY
CD CD 111
Timeless Treasures / Oct '94 / THE.

CHUCK BERRY COLLECTION
CD COL 002
Collection / Jun '95 / Target/BMG.

CHUCK BERRY IS ON TOP
CD CHLD 19250
Chess/MCA / Oct '94 / BMG / New Note.

CHUCK BERRY/GENE VINCENT ESSENTIALS (Berry, Chuck & Gene Vincent)
CD LECDD 625
Wisepack / Aug '95 / THE / Conifer.

DUCK WALK
CD ENTCD 263
Entertainers / Jul '88 / Target/BMG.

EP COLLECTION: CHUCK BERRY
CD SEECD 320
See For Miles/C5 / Jul '91 / Pinnacle.

FRUIT OF THE VINE
Downbound train / Wee wee hours / No money down / Drifting heart / Brown eyed handsome man / Havana moon / Oh baby doll / Anthony boy / Merry Christmas baby / Jo Jo Gunne / Childhood sweetheart / I got to find my baby / Worried life blues / Jaguar and the thunderbirds / Confessin' the blues / Thirteen question method / Things I used to do / You two / Little Marie / Dear Dad / It wasn't me / Ramona say yes / Tulane / Have mercy judge
CD CDRED 19
Charly / Jun '90 / Charly / THE / Cadillac.

GREAT 28 HITS, THE
CD CHLD 19116
Chess/MCA / Jan '94 / BMG / New Note.

HAIL, HAIL, ROCK & ROLL
Maybellene / Thirty days / No money down / Roll over Beethoven / Brown eyed handsome man / Too much monkey business / You can't catch me / School day / Rock 'n' roll music / Sweet little sixteen / Reelin' and rockin' / Johnny B. Goode / Around and around / Beautiful Delilah / Carol / Sweet little rock 'n' roller / Almost grown / Little Queenie / Back in the U.S.A / Memphis Tennesse / Too pooped to pop (Not on CD) / Let it rock / Bye bye johnny / I'm talking about you / Come on / Nadine / No particular place to go / You never can tell / Little Marie (Not on CD) / Promised land / Tulane (Not on CD) / My ding a ling (Not on CD)

CD _____ CPCD 8006
Charly / Oct '93 / Charly / THE / Cadillac.

LEGENDARY HITS
CD _____ 90156-2
Jazz Archives / Oct '92 / Jazz Music / Discovery / Cadillac.

LEGENDS IN MUSIC - CHUCK BERRY
CD _____ LECD 037
Wisepack / Nov '94 / THE / Conifer.

LET IT ROCK
CD _____ CDCD 1192
Charly / Sep '94 / Charly / THE / Cadillac.

LIVE ON STAGE
Schooldays / Sweet little sixteen / Roll over Beethoven / Everyday I have the blues / Bio / Maybellene/Mountain dew / Let it rock / Carol/Little Queenie / Keys to the highway / Got my mojo working / Reelin' and rockin' / Johnny B. Goode

CD _____ CDMF 092
Magnum Force / Mar '95 / Magnum Music Group.

LONDON SESSIONS, THE
Let's boogie / Mean old world / I will not let you go / London Berry blues / I love you / Reelin' and rockin' / My ding a ling / Johnny B. Goode

CD _____ CDRED 20
Charly / Jun '90 / Charly / THE / Cadillac.

ON THE BLUES SIDE
Confessin' the blues / runaround / Worried life blues / Things that I used to do / Blues for Hawaiians / Wee wee hours / I still got the blues / Down the road apiece / No money down / Stop and listen / Blue on blue / Sweet sixteen / I got to find my baby / I just want to make love to you / Merry Christmas baby / Deep feeling / Wee hour blues / Don't you lie to me / Ain't that just like a woman / Driftin' blues / Blue feeling

CD _____ CDCH 397
Ace / Sep '93 / Pinnacle / Cadillac / Complete/Pinnacle.

POET OF ROCK 'N' ROLL
CD Set _____ CDDIG 1
Charly / Feb '95 / Charly / THE / Cadillac.

ROCK 'N ROLL MUSIC
CD _____ CDCD 1018
Charly / Mar '93 / Charly / THE / Cadillac.

ROCKIT
Move it / Oh what a thrill / I need you baby / If I were / House lights / I never thought / Havana moon / Pass away

CD _____ CDMF 065
Magnum Force / Nov '88 / Magnum Music Group.

SWEET LITTLE EIGHTEEN
CD _____ 3001052
Scratch / Jul '95 / BMG.

TWO ON ONE: CHUCK BERRY & BO DIDDLEY (Berry, Chuck & Bo Diddley)
CD _____ CDTT 2
Charly / Apr '94 / Charly / THE / Cadillac.

Berry, Dave
BEST OF DAVE BERRY, THE
I love you babe / You're gonna need somebody / My baby left me / Hoochie coochie man / Diddley daddy / Same game / I'm gonna take your there / This strange effect / Crying game / Little things / Go on home / Don't gimme no lip child / Memphis, Tennessee / St. James infirmary / Alright baby / One heart between two / Mama / Forever / Baby, it's you / Picture me gone

CD _____ SEECD 384
See For Miles/C5 / Oct '93 / Pinnacle.

Berry, Heidi
BELOW THE WAVES
CD _____ CRECD 048
Creation / May '94 / 3MV / Vital.

HEIDI BERRY
CD _____ CAD 3009CD
4AD / Jun '93 / Disc.

LOVE
CD _____ CADCD 1012
4AD / Aug '91 / Disc.

Berry, Iris
LIFE ON THE EDGE IN STILETTOS
CD _____ NAR 108CD
SST / Jul '95 / Plastic Head.

Berry, John
STANDING ON THE EDGE
Every time my heart calls your name / Standing on the edge of goodbye / Prove me wrong / I think about it all the time / If I had any pride left at all / Desperate measures / What are we fighting for / There's no cross that love won't bear / Ninety miles an hour / I never lost you / You and only you

CD _____ CDEST 2265
Capitol / Jun '95 / EMI.

Berry, Leon Chu
PENGUIN SWING (Berry, Chu & Cab Calloway Orchestra)
CD _____ 3801082
Jazz Archives / Jun '92 / Jazz Music / Discovery / Cadillac.

Berry, Mike
ROCK 'N' ROLL BOOGIE... PLUS
I'm a rocker / Don't fight it / Love rocket / Don't ever change / Stay close to me / Hard times / Take me high / It's a hard hard rock / Tribute to Buddy Holly / Boogaloo dues / Midnight train / Hey Joe / One by one / Rebel without a cause / Take a heart / Dial my number / New Orleans / Wake up Suzy / Baby boy (CD only) / Low country woman (CD Only) / Hey baby (CD Only) / Think it over (CD Only) / Don't be cruel (CD Only)

CD _____ C5CD 541
See For Miles/C5 / Oct '92 / Pinnacle.

Berry, Richard
GET OUT OF THE CAR
Mad about you / Angel of my life / Yama yama pretty mama / Next time / Rockin' man / Oh oh, get out of the car / Crazy lover / I'm still in love with you / Jelly roll / Big John / One little prayer / Big break

CD _____ CDCH 355
Ace / Mar '92 / Pinnacle / Cadillac / Complete/Pinnacle.

Berry, Robert
PILGRIMAGE TO A POINT
No one else to blame / You've changed / Shelter / Another man / Love we share / Blame / Otherside / Freedom / Last ride into the sun

CD _____ CYCL 019
Cyclops / Apr '95 / Pinnacle.

Berryhill, Cyndi Lee
GARAGE ORCHESTRA
CD _____ UGCD 5502
Unique Gravity / Jul '95 / Pinnacle / ADA.

NAKED MOVIE STAR
CD _____ AWCD 1016
Awareness / Jul '89 / ADA.

Bert, Eddie
EDDIE BERT (Bert, Eddie & Hank Jones Trio)
Fragile / Stompin' at the Savoy / I should'a said / See you later / Three bass hit / What'd ya say / Billie's bounce

CD _____ SV 0183
Savoy Jazz / Oct '92 / Conifer / ADA.

ENCORE
Bert tram / One for Tubby / It's only sunshine / Opicana / Conversation / Crosstown / Manhattan suite

CD _____ SV 0229
Savoy Jazz / Oct '93 / Conifer / ADA.

HUMAN FACTOR, THE (Bert, Eddie Sextet)
CD _____ FSR 5005 CD
Fresh Sound / Nov '95 / Jazz Music / Discovery.

LIVE AT BIRDLAND (Bert, Eddie & J.R. Monterose)
CD _____ FSRCD 198
Fresh Sound / Dec '92 / Jazz Music / Discovery.

Bertoncini, Gene
ACOUSTIC ROMANCE
Edelweiss / Shadow of your smile / Girl talk / Two for the road / Gone with the wind / Round Midnight / Summer of '42 / What are you doing / Rest of your life / Stella by starlight / Emily / Invitation / Cavatina

CD _____ KICJ 155
King/Paddle Wheel / Feb '94 / New Note.

ART OF THE DUO, THE (Bertoncini, Gene & Michael Moore)
CD _____ STCD 6
Stash / '88 / Jazz Music / CM / Cadillac / Direct / ADA.

Bertone, Bruno
LA MUSICA FROM ITALY (Bertone, Bruno Mandoline Orchestra)
CD _____ 15209
Laserlight / '91 / Target/BMG.

STRICTLY DANCING: FOX-TROT (Bertone, Bruno Ballroom Orchestra)
CD _____ 15337
Laserlight / May '94 / Target/BMG.

Besses O' The Barn
HYMNS AND THINGS
Praise my soul the King of heaven / Eventide / Dem bones / Ave Maria / Simple gifts / Nun's chorus / Deep harmony / Jerusalem / Hymn tune medley (Jerusalem the golden; The old hundredth; Aberystwyth) / Aurelia / U, for the wings of a dove / God be in my head / Dear Lord and the father of mankind / Sandon / Thanks be to God

CD _____ CHAN 4529
Chandos / Aug '93 / Chandos.

SHOWCASE FOR BRASS
Three figures / In memoriam R.K. / Summer scherzo / Belmont variations / Northwest passage

CD _____ CHAN 4525
Chandos / May '93 / Chandos.

Best, Martin
CANTIGAS OF SANTA MARIA
CD _____ NI 5081
Nimbus / '88 / Nimbus.

DANTE TROUBADOURS, THE (Mediaeval music)
CD _____ NI 5002
Nimbus / '88 / Nimbus.

SONGS OF CHIVALRY (Mediaeval Music)
CD _____ NI 5006
Nimbus / '88 / Nimbus.

Best, Pete
BACK TO THE BEAT (Best, Pete Band)
My Bonnie / Roll over Beethoven / Dancing in the streets / Dizzie Miss Lizzie / Money / Love me do / Stand by me / Long tall Sally / I saw her standing there / Twist and shout / Hippy hippy shake / Johnny B. Goode / C'mon everybody

CD _____ PBSCD 2000
Graduate / Oct '95 / Graduate.

BEYOND THE BEATLES 1963-1968 (Best, Pete Combo)
All aboard / Why did you leave me baby / Shimmy like my sister Kate / I need your lovin' / I can't do without you now / I don't know why I do / I'll try anyway / I'm checking out now baby / Keys to my heart / She's alright / I'm blue / Castin' my spell / Off the hook / Pete's theme / Everybody / I wanna be there / Rock 'n' roll music / Don't play with me / Way I feel about you / I'll have everything too / How do you get to know her name / She's not the only girl in town / If you can't get her / More than I need myself

CD _____ CDMRED 124
Cherry Red / Jan '96 / Pinnacle.

Bestial Warlust
BLOOD AND VALOUR
CD _____ MIM 7321CD
Modern Invasion / Jan '96 / Plastic Head.

VENGEANCE WAR TIL DEATH
CD _____ MIN 7316-2
Modern Invasion / Feb '95 / Plastic Head.

Bethania, Maria
OLTIU D'AGUA
CD _____ 5120522
Philips / Jan '94 / PolyGram.

Bethlehem
DARK METAL
CD _____ CDAR 022
Adipocre / Jul '94 / Plastic Head.

Beto & The Fairlanes
SALSAFIED
CD _____ DOS 7009
Dos / Sep '94 / CM / Direct / ADA.

Betrayer
CALAMITY
CD _____ MNO 2CD
Nuclear Blast / Nov '94 / Plastic Head.

Betsy
ROUGH AROUND THE EDGES
All over my heart / If I don't stay the night / Love me like you mean it / Draggin' it back / Bits and pieces / Hard to believe / You can look (but you can't touch) / Southern wind / Passage / This house

CD _____ 7567 92428-2
Warner Bros. / Nov '94 / Warner Music.

Better Than Ezra
DELUXE
CD _____ 7559617842
Elektra / May '95 / Warner Music.

Bettie Serveert
LAMPREY
CD _____ BBQCD 169
Beggars Banquet / Jan '95 / Warner Music / Disc.

SOMETHING SO WILD
CD _____ BBQ 58CD
Beggars Banquet / Jun '95 / Warner Music / Disc.

Beuf, Sylvian Quartet
IMPRO PRIMO
CD _____ BBRC 9311
Big Blue / Jan '94 / Harmonia Mundi.

Bevan, Tony
ORIGINAL GRAVITY (Bevan, Tony & Greg Kingston & Matt Lewis)
CD _____ INCUSCD 03
Incus / '90 / These / Cadillac.

Beverly Sisters
SISTERS, SISTERS
CD _____ QPRM 601D
Polyphonic / Aug '93 / Conifer.

Bevis Frond
ANY GAS FASTER
Lord Plentiful reflects / Rejection day (am) / Ear song (olde world) / This corner of England / Legendary / When you wanted me / Lost rivers / Somewhere else / These dark days / Head on a pole / Your mind's gone grey / Old sea dog / Rejection day (pm) / Good old fashioned pain / Olde worlde

CD _____ CDRECK 18
Reckless / Jan '90 / Pinnacle.

AUNTIE WINNIE ALBUM, THE
CD _____ CDRECK 17
Reckless / Jul '89 / Pinnacle.

GATHERING OF FRONDS, A
CD _____ CDRECK 25
Reckless / Mar '92 / Pinnacle.

INNER MARSHLAND
CD _____ CDRECK 14
Reckless / Mar '89 / Pinnacle.

IT JUST IS
CD _____ WO 21CD
Woronzow / Oct '93 / Pinnacle.

MIASMA
CD _____ CDRECK 13
Reckless / Mar '89 / Pinnacle.

NEW RIVER HEAD
CD _____ WO 16CD
Woronzow / Sep '91 / Pinnacle.

SPRAWL
CD Set _____ WO 22CD
Woronzow / Oct '94 / Pinnacle.

SUPERSEEDER
CD _____ WO 26CD
Woronzow / Oct '95 / Pinnacle.

TRIPTYCH
CD _____ CDRECK 15
Reckless / Mar '89 / Pinnacle.

Bevoir, Paul
DUMB ANGEL
CD _____ TANGCD 8
Tangerine / May '94 / Disc.

HAPPIEST DAYS OF YOUR LIFE, THE
CD _____ TANGCD 2
Tangerine / Aug '92 / Disc.

Beyond
CHASM
CD _____ CDMFN 147
Music For Nations / Jul '93 / Pinnacle.

Beyond Belief
RAVE THE ABYSS
CD _____ SHARK 102CD
Shark / Jun '94 / Plastic Head.

Beyond Dawn
LONGING FOR SCARLET DAYS
CD _____ CDAR 019
Adipocre / May '94 / Plastic Head.

PITY LOVE
CD _____ CANDLE 012CD
Candlelight / Nov '95 / Plastic Head.

Bezet, Steve
ARCHAIC MODULATION
Man in the machine / Passion and hope / Maya and aliens / African marche / Harmonix / Closed eye view

CD _____ 450995347-2
Warner Bros. / Mar '94 / Warner Music.

Bhatt, Vishwa Mohan
BOURBON & ROSEWATER
CD _____ WLACS 47CD
Waterlilly Acoustics / Nov '95 / ADA.

GATHERING RAINCLOUDS
CD _____ WLAES 22CD
Waterlilly Acoustics / Nov '95 / ADA.

JUGALBANDI
CD _____ CDA 92059CD
Music Today / Jan '95 / ADA.

SASADAMANI
CD _____ WLAC 23CD
Waterlilly Acoustics / Oct '93 / ADA.

Bhattacharya, Pandit Amit

CLASSIC MUSIC FROM NORTH INDIA
CD _____ KMCD 54
Keltia Musique / Jul '95 / ADA / Direct / Discovery.

Bhundu Boys

FRIENDS ON THE ROAD
Radio Africa / Pombi / Ring of fire / Gonzo nachin'ai / Bitter to the south / Foolish harp/ Waerara / Anna / Church on fire / Don't forget Africa / Anyway / My best friend / Lizzie
CD _____ COOKCD 053
Cooking Vinyl / Feb '95 / Vital.

SHABINI
CD _____ AFRICD 02
Disc Afrique / Nov '87 / Roots / CM.

TRUE JIT
Jit jive / My foolish heart / Chemedzevana / Rugare / Vana / Wonderful world / Ndoi- tasei / Susan / African woman / Happy birthday / Jekesa / I don't think that man should sleep alone / Over you / Loving you / You shoulda kept a spare / Past / You make my nature dance / Perfect lovers / Af- ter midnite / I love your daughter / After dark
CD _____ 242203 2
WEA / Sep '87 / Warner Music.

TSVIMBO-DZE-MOTO (Sticks on Fire)
CD _____ AFRICD 03
Disc Afrique / Jun '87 / Roots / CM.

Biafra, Jello

I BLOW MINDS FOR A LIVING
CD Set _____ VIRUS 94CD
Alternative Tentacles / '92 / Pinnacle.

LAST SCREAM OF THE MISSING NEIGHBORS (Biafra, Jello & DOA)
CD _____ VIRUS 78CD
Alternative Tentacles / Feb '90 / Pinnacle.

PRAIRIE HOME INVASION
CD _____ VIRUS 137CD
Alternative Tentacles / Mar '94 / Pinnacle.

Bianchi, Maurico

AKTIVITAT
CD _____ DVLR 02
Dark Vinyl / Jan '94 / Plastic Head.

Bible

EUREKA
Skywriting / Honey be good / Skeleton crew / November brides / Cigarette girls / Crystal Palace / Wishing game / Red Hollywood / Tiny lights / Blue shoes stepping
CD _____ HAVENCD 5
Haven/Backs / Nov '95 / Disc / Pinnacle.

RANDOM ACTS OF KINDNESS
CD _____ HAVENCD 6
Haven/Backs / Nov '95 / Disc / Pinnacle.

WALKING THE GHOST BACK HOME
CD _____ HAVENCD 4
Haven/Backs / Nov '95 / Disc / Pinnacle.

Bickert, Ed

BORDER CROSSING
For all we know / Man I love / Goodnight my love / My funny valentine
CD _____ CCD 4216
Concord Jazz / '83 / New Note.

I WISHED ON THE MOON (Bickert, Ed Quartet)
C.T.A. / Easy street / Somewhere along the way / Blues for Tommy / Blues my naughty sweetie gives to me / Handful of stars / I wished on the moon / I'll never stop loving you
CD _____ CCD 4284
Concord Jazz / Nov '86 / New Note.

THIRD FLOOR RICHARD (Bickert, Ed Trio)
Band call / Together / Louisiana / I know why / One moment worth years / Tonite I shall sleep / I got a right to sing the blues / Circus / Third floor Richard / I surrender dear / This can't be love
CD _____ CCD 4380
Concord Jazz / Jul '89 / New Note.

Biddleville Quintette

BIDDLEVILLE QUINTETTE VOL. 1 (1926- 29)
CD _____ DOCD 5361
Blues Document / Jun '95 / Swift / Jazz Music / Hot Shot.

BIDDLEVILLE QUINTETTE VOL. 2 (1929)
CD _____ DOCD 5362
Blues Document / Jun '95 / Swift / Jazz Music / Hot Shot.

Biddulph, Rick

SECOND NATURE
CD _____ VP 178CD
Voice Print / Jan '95 / Voice Print.

Bif Naked

BIF NAKED
CD _____ CD 0086242
Edel / Nov '95 / Pinnacle.

Biff Bang Pow

ACID HOUSE ALBUM, THE
CD _____ CRECD 046
Creation / May '94 / 3MV / Vital.

GIRL WHO RUNS THE BEAT HOTEL
Someone stole my wheels / Love's going out of fashion / She never understood / He don't need that girl / She shivers inside / California here I come/ Are you from Dixie/ Ain't we got fun / Rose Rose I love you/ Buttons and bows/ In the middle of the / Leave the pretty girls alone/She wore a little taker's daughter/ Somebody loves (me/ For me and my gal) / Man on the flying trapeze/ In the twi-twi-twilight/ Mee / Is it true what they say about Dixie (medley inc. Mister Sandman) / Give me the moonlight give me the girl/ Ain't misbehavin'/ S / I've never seen a straight banana / You must have been a beautiful baby/ In a shanty in old Shan / Cheek to cheek/ Anything you can do/ You keep coming back k / Lady in red/ Fare thee well Annabelle/Oh! you beautiful
CD _____ CRECD 015
Creation / May '88 / 3MV / Vital.

L'AMOUR, DEMURE, STENHOUSEMUIR
CD _____ CRECD 099
Creation / May '94 / 3MV / Vital.

ME
CD _____ CRECD 071
Creation / May '94 / 3MV / Vital.

OBLIVION
CD _____ CRECD 020
Creation / Jun '88 / 3MV / Vital.

SONGS FOR THE SAD EYED GIRL
CD _____ CRECD 058
Creation / Jan '90 / 3MV / Vital.

Big Ass Truck

BIG ASS TRUCK
CD _____ UPSTART 024
Upstart / Nov '95 / Direct / ADA.

Big Audio Dynamite

F-PUNK
CD _____ RAD 11280
Radioactive / Jun '95 / Vital / BMG.

GLOBE, THE (B.A.D. II)
Rush / Can't wait (live) / I don't know / Globe / Innocent child / Green grass / Kool aid / In my dreams / When the time comes / Tea Party
CD _____ 4677062
Columbia / Jun '91 / Sony.

HIGHER POWER
Got to wake up / Harrow Road / Looking for a song / Some people / Slender Loris / Modern stoneage blues / Melancholy maybe / Over the rise / Why is it / Moon / Lucan / Light up my life / Hope
CD _____ 477239-2
Columbia / Nov '94 / Sony.

PLANET B.A.D.
Bottom line / E = MC2 / Medicine show / C'mon every beatbox / V / Thirteen / Sight- see MC1 / Just play music / Other 99 / Con- tact free / Rush / Globe / Looking for a song / Harrow road / Turned out a punk
CD _____ 4811332
Columbia / Sep '95 / Sony.

THIS IS BIG AUDIO DYNAMITE
Medicine show / Sony / E = MC2 / Bottom line / Sudden impact / Stone Thames / B.A.D. / Party
CD _____ 4629992
CBS / Nov '88 / Sony.

TIGHTEN UP VOL. 88
Rock non stop (all night long) / Other 99 / Funny names / Applecart / Esquerita / Champagne / Mr. Walker said / Battle of All Saints Road / Battle of New Orleans / Duel- in' banjos / Hip neck and thigh / Two thou- sand shoes / Tighten up vol. 88 / Just play music
CD _____ 4611992
CBS / Sep '94 / Sony.

Big Bad Smitty

MEAN DISPOSITION
CD _____ AIM 1037
Aim / Apr '95 / Direct / ADA / Jazz Music.

Big Band Charlie Mingus

LIVE AT THE T.T.B. PARIS VOL.1
CD _____ 121192-2
Soul Note / Nov '93 / Harmonia Mundi / Wellard / Cadillac.

LIVE AT THE T.T.B. PARIS VOL.2
CD _____ 121193-2
Soul Note / Nov '93 / Harmonia Mundi / Wellard / Cadillac.

Big Band Of Lausanne

ASTOR (Big Band Of Lausanne & Charles Papasoff)
Red kite / Exquise ésquisse / Selective in- finity / Signpost / Astor / Scorpio / I feel good / Welcome
CD _____ TCB 95502
TCB / Sep '95 / New Note.

Big Ben Banjo Band

BIG BEN BANJO PARTY
Rolling around the world/The best things in life are free / Who takes care of the care-
CD _____ CC 290
Music For Pleasure / Dec '92 / EMI.

BIG BEN BANJO PARTY
CD _____ MATCD 230
Castle / Dec '92 / BMG.

Big Big Train

GOODBYE TO THE AGE OF STEAM
CD _____ GEPCD 1007
Giant Electric Pea / May '94 / Pinnacle.

Big Black

BIG BLACK: LIVE
CD _____ BFFP 49CD
Blast First / Oct '89 / Disc.

HAMMER PARTY
CD _____ HMS 044 CD
Homestead / Jul '89 / SRD.

PIGPILE
CD _____ TG 81CD
Touch & Go / Nov '92 / SRD.

RICH MAN'S EIGHT TRACK
CD _____ BFFP 23CD
Blast First / Jun '88 / Disc.

SONGS ABOUT FUCKING
Power of independent trucking / Model / Bad penny / L dopa / Precious thing / Co- lumbian necktie / Kitty empire / Ergot ice- simir S Pulaski Day / Fish fry / Tiny, King of the Jews / Bombastic intro / He's a whore
CD _____ TG 24CD
Touch & Go / '94 / SRD.

Big Brother

CHEAPER THRILLS (Big Brother & The Holding Company)
Let the good times roll / I know you rider / Moanin' at midnight / Hey baby / Down on me / Whisperman / Women is losers / Blow my mind / Ball and chain / Coo coo / Gu- tra's garden / Harry
CD _____ EDCD 035
Edsel / Aug '90 / Pinnacle / ADA.

Big Car

NORMAL
Not the tunnel of love / Rosalita / Venus / Get started / Mad at the world / Amazing contradiction / Cats / Day by day / Shut up / Easy street
CD _____ 07599244432
Giant / May '92 / BMG.

Big Catholic Guilt

JUDGEMENT
CD _____ CHERRY 228902
Cherrydisc / Jun '94 / Plastic Head.

Big Chief

BIG CHIEF BRAND PRODUCT
CD _____ SPCD 89260
Sub Pop / Apr '93 / Disc.

MACK AVENUE SKULL GAME
CD _____ SP 109/285CD
Sub Pop / Sep '93 / Disc.

SHOUT OUT (Big Chief & Thornett)
CD _____ SPCD 135322
Sub Pop / Sep '94 / Disc.

Big Chill

HALFWAY TO HEAVEN
CD _____ CDMFN 142
Music For Nations / Sep '92 / Pinnacle.

Big Country

BUFFALO SKINNERS, THE
Alone / Seven waves / What are you work- ing for / One I love / Long way home / Sell- ing of America / We're not in Kansas / Ships / All go together / Winding wind / Pink marshmallow moon / Chester's farm
CD _____ CDNOIS 2
Chrysalis / Mar '93 / EMI.

COLLECTION 1982-1988, THE
Harvest home / In a big country / Close ac- tion / Storm / Wonderland / Belief in the small man / Girl with grey eyes / Tall ships go / Steeltown / Just a shadow / One great thing / Seer / Remembrance day / Sailor / King of emotion / Travellers / Thousand yard stare
CD _____ VSOPCD 178
Connoisseur / Jan '93 / Pinnacle.

CROSSING, THE
In a big country / Inwards / Chance / Thou- sand stars / Storm / Harvest home / Lost patrol / Close action / Fields of fire / Porroh man
CD _____ 812 870-2
Mercury / '83 / PolyGram.

IN A BIG COUNTRY
In a big country / Thousand stars / Tracks of my tears / Giant / One great thing / Hold the heart / Look away / Honky tonk woman / Restless natives / Longest day / Every- thing I need / Black skinned blue eyed boys / Fly like an eagle / Kiss the girl goodbye / Keep on dreaming / Freedom song
CD _____ 5508792
Spectrum/Karussell / Jul '95 / PolyGram / THE.

LEGENDS IN MUSIC - BIG COUNTRY
CD _____ LECD 043
Wisepack / Jul '94 / THE / Conifer.

LIVE IN CONCERT
Peace in our time / Wonderland / Seer / River of hope / Come back to me / Travell- ers / King of emotion / In a big country / I walk the hill / Fields of fire
CD _____ WINCD 075
Windsong / Oct '95 / Pinnacle.

NO PLACE LIKE HOME
We're not in Kansas / Republican party rep- tile / Dynamite lady / Keep on dreaming / Beautiful people / Hostage speaks / Beat the devil / Leap of faith / Ships / Into the fire
CD _____ 5102302
Phonogram / Jan '93 / PolyGram.

PEACE IN OUR TIME
King of emotion / Broken hearts / Thousand yard stare / From here to eternity / Every- thing I need / Peace in our time / Time for leaving / River of hope / In this place
CD _____ 836 325-2
Mercury / Sep '88 / PolyGram.

RADIO 1 SESSIONS
CD _____ CDNT 007
Strange Fruit / Jul '94 / Pinnacle.

SEER, THE/THE CROSSING (2CD Set)
Look away / Seer / Teacher / I walk the hill / Eiledon / One great thing / Hold the heart / Remembrance day / Red fox / Sailor / In a big country / Inwards / Chance / Thou- sand stars / Storm / Harvest home / Lost patrol / Close action / Fields of fire / Porroh man
CD Set _____ 5286072
Mercury / Aug '95 / PolyGram.

STEELTOWN
Flame of the west / East of Eden / Steel- town / Where the rose is sown / Come back to me / Tall ships go / Girl with grey eyes / Raindance / Great divide / Just a shadow
CD _____ 5500442
Spectrum/Karussell / Jun '93 / PolyGram / THE.

THROUGH A BIG COUNTRY (Greatest Hits)
In a big country / Fields of fire / Chance / Wonderland / Where the rose is sown / Just a shadow / Look away / King of emotion / East of Eden / One great thing / Teacher / Broken heart (thirteen valleys) / Peace in our time / Eiledon (Not on LP) / Seer (Not on LP) / Harvest home (Not on LP)
CD _____ 846 022-2
Mercury / May '90 / PolyGram.

WHY THE LONG FACE
CD _____ TRACD 109
Transatlantic / Jun '95 / BMG / Pinnacle / ADA.

WITHOUT THE AID OF A SAFETY NET
Harvest home / Just a shadow / Thirteen valleys / Storm / Chance / Look away / country / Peace in our time / What are you working for / Long way home / Lost patrol
CD _____ CDNOIS 5
Compulsion / Jun '94 / EMI.

Big Daddy

SERGEANT PEPPER'S LONELY HEARTS CLUB BAND
With a little help from my friends / Lucy in the sky with diamonds / Getting better / Fixing a hole / She's leaving home / Being for the benefit of Mr. Kite / Within you without you / When I'm sixty four / Lovely Rita / Good morning good morning / Sergeant Pepper's lonely hearts club band / Day in the life / Sergeant Pepper's lonely hearts club band (reprise)
CD _____ 8122703712
Rhino / Jul '93 / Warner Music.

Big Daddy Kane

LOOKS LIKE A JOB FOR...
Looks like a job for / How u get a record deal / Chocolate city / Prelude / Beef is on / Stop shammin' / Brother man, brother man / Rest in peace / Very special / Here comes Kane, scoob and scrap / Niggaz never learn / Give it to me / Nuff respect / Finale
CD _____ 936245128-2
Cold Chillin' / May '93 / Warner Music.

Big Dish

SATELLITES
Miss America / State of the union / Across the province / Give me some time / Twenty five years / Big town / Shipwrecked / Warning sign / Bona fide / Learn to love
CD _____ 9031733142
East West / Feb '91 / Warner Music.

Big Dogs

LIVE AT THE BIRCHMERE
CD _____ SCR 24
Strictly Country / Jul '95 / ADA / Direct.

Big Drill Car

ALBUM/TAPE/CD TYPE THING
CD _____ CRZ 008 CD
Cruz / Jan '90 / Pinnacle / Plastic Head.

SMALL BLOCK
CD _____ CRZ 014 CD
Cruz / May '93 / Pinnacle / Plastic Head.

Big Eighteen

LIVE ECHOES OF THE SWINGING BANDS
Tuxedo junction / Easy does it / Hors d'oeuvre / Blues on parade / Liza (all the clouds'll roll away) / Five o'clock drag / March of the toys / I'm prayin' humble / Campbells are swingin'
CD _____ 74321 13032-2
RCA / Sep '93 / BMG.

MORE LIVE ECHOES OF THE SWINGING BANDS
Summit ridge drive / Parade of the milk bottle caps / Swingtime in the rockies / Feet draggin' blues / Okay for baby / Quaker city jazz / Celery stalks at midnight / Skyliner / Organ grinder swing / Ton o'rock jump
CD _____ 74321 13033-2
RCA / Sep '93 / BMG.

Big Electric Cat

DREAMS OF A MAD KING
CD _____ CLEO 94952
Cleopatra / Jan '95 / Disc.

Big Eye

HIDDEN CORE, THE
CD _____ DUKE 027
Hydrogen Dukebox / Nov '95 / Vital / 3MV.

Big H

SPAGHETTI JUNCTION
CD _____ MGOUTCD 4
Outlaw / Aug '95 / BMG / Pinnacle.

Big Head Todd

SISTER SWEETLY
Broken hearted saviour / Sister sweetly / Turn the light out / Tomorrow never comes / It's alright / Groove thing / Soul for every cowboy / Ellis island / Bittersweet / Circle / Brother John
CD _____ 74321147992
Giant / Jun '94 / BMG.

STRATAGEM (Big Head Todd & The Monsters)
Kensington line / Stratagem / Wearing only flowers / Neckbreaker / Magdalena / Angel leads me on / In the morning / Candle / Ninety nine / Greyhound / Poor miss / Shadowlands
CD _____ 74321229042
Giant / Oct '94 / BMG.

Big Jig

BUG
CD _____ HYCD 295158
Hypertension / Nov '95 / Total/BMG / Direct / ADA.

Big Joe

COOL DYNAFLOW (Big Joe & The Dynaflows)
CD _____ TRCD 9915
Tramp / Apr '93 / Direct / ADA / CM.

LAYIN' IN THE ALLEY (Big Joe & The Dynaflows)
CD _____ BT 1098CD
Black Top / Feb '94 / CM / Direct / ADA.

Big Maceo

KING OF CHICAGO BLUES PIANO, THE
CD _____ FL 7009
Folklyric / Apr '95 / Direct / Cadillac.

Big Maybelle

BLUES, CANDY & BIG MAYBELLE
Candy / Ring dang dilly / Blues early, early / Little bird told me / So long / That's a good idea / Look now / Tell me who / Ramblin' blues / Rock house / I don't want to cry / Pitiful / Good man is hard to find / How it lies / Goin' home baby / Say it isn't so / If I could be with you one hour tonight / Goodnight wherever you are / White Christmas / Silent night / I ain't got nobody / I understand / I got it bad / Some of these days / Until the real thing comes along
CD _____ SV 0262
Savoy Jazz / Apr '95 / Conifer / ADA.

MAYBELLE SINGS THE BLUES
CD _____ CDRB 14
Charly / Nov '94 / Charly / THE / Cadillac.

Big Miller

LAST OF THE BLUES SHOUTERS, THE
CD _____ SCD 42
Southland / Feb '93 / Jazz Music.

Big Mountain

RESISTANCE
Hooligans / Resistance / Rise Rasta rise / Get together / Caribbean blue / Sweet and deadly / Troddin' / Know your culture / Soul teacher / Where do the children play / Retire / Inner city youth / Wante wante / Love is the only way / Bobbin' & weavin' / Hooligans dub (On CD)
CD _____ 74321299882
RCA / Oct '95 / BMG.

UNITY
Fruitful days / Revolution / Bordertown / Upful and right / Sweet sensual love / I would find a way / Tango ganas / Baby, I love your way / Young revolutionaries / Time has come / Big mountain / Baby I love your way (Spanish version) / Sweet sensual love (Spanish version)
CD _____ 74321219642
Giant / Aug '94 / BMG.

WAKE UP
Light'n up / Reggae inna summertime / Peaceful revolution / Rastaman / Back in the hill / Once again / Let you go / Touch my light / Beautiful day / Amor de lejos / Llena mi Vida / Reggae inna summertime (Spanglish) / Lick up tup
CD _____ 74321267482
Giant / Jun '95 / BMG.

Big Noise UK

GOOD MORNING BABY
Shame on you / Good morning baby / I want your love / Fade to grey / James Dean
CD _____ PCOM 1111
President / Apr '91 / Grapevine / Target/BMG / Jazz Music / President.

Big Rhythm Combo

TOO SMALL TO DANCE
CD _____ BM 9025CD
Black Magic / Aug '94 / Hot Shot / Swift / CM / Direct / Cadillac / ADA.

Big Sandy

ON THE GO (Big Sandy & The Flyrite Trio)
CD _____ NOHITCD 006
No Hit / Jan '94 / SRD.

SWINGIN' WEST (Big Sandy & The Flyrite Trio)
CD _____ HCD 8064
Hightone / Oct '93 / ADA / Koch.

Big Star

BIG STAR LIVE
CD _____ RCD 10221
Rykodisc / Feb '92 / Vital / ADA.

BIG STAR'S BIGGEST
Ballad of El Goodo / In the street / Don't lie to me / When my baby's beside me / Try again / Watch the sunrise / Life is white / What's goin' ahn / Back of a car / She's a mover / Way out west / September gurls / Jesus Christ / O'Dana / Holocaust / Kangaroo / Back car / Thank you friends
CD _____ LICD 900509
Line / Oct '94 / CM / Grapevine / ADA / Conifer / Direct.

NO.1 RECORD/RADIO CITY

Feel / Ballad of El Goodo / In the street / Thirteen / Don't lie to me / India song / When my baby's beside me / My life is right / Give me another chance / Try again / Watch the sunrise / O my soul / Life is white / Way out west / What's goin' ahn / You get what you deserve / Mod lang / Back of a car / Daisy glaze / She's a mover / September gurls / Morpha too / I'm in love with a girl
CD _____ CDWIK 910
Big Beat / Jan '90 / Pinnacle.

Big Stick

CRACK 'N' DRAG
CD _____ BFFP 25CD
Blast First / Nov '93 / Disc.

PRO-DRAG
CD _____ PWD 7456CD
IFA / Oct '95 / Plastic Head.

Big Three

BIG THREE FEATURING MAMA CASS, THE
I may be eight / Anna Fia / Tony and Delia / Grandfather's clock / Silkie / Ringo / Down in the valley / Wild women / All the pretty little horses / Glory glory / Come away Melinda / Young girl's lament / Banjo song / Winken blinken and nod / Ho honey ho / Young girl's lament / Banjo song / Sing hallelujah / Dark as a dungeon
CD _____ NEMCD 755
Sequel / Oct '95 / BMG.

Big Time Sarah

LAY IT ON 'EM GIRLS
CD _____ DD 659
Delmark / Jul '93 / Hot Shot / ADA / CM / Direct / Cadillac.

Big Tom

I'LL SETTLE FOR OLD IRELAND
CD _____ SWCD 1006
TC Records / Aug '92 / Pinnacle / Prism.

Big Twist

BIGGER THAN LIFE (Live from Chicago) (Big Twist & The Mellow Fellows)
CD _____ ALCD 4755
Alligator / May '93 / Direct / ADA.

PLAYING FOR KEEPS (Big Twist & The Mellow Fellows)
300 pounds of heavenly joy / Flip flop / I want your love / Pork salad Annie / Pouring water on a drowning man / I've got a problem / I brought the blues on myself / We're gonna make it / Just one woman
CD _____ ALCD 4732
Alligator / May '93 / Direct / ADA.

Big Vern

LULLABIES FOR LAGER LOUTS
CD _____ PRKCD 2
Park / Dec '89 / Pinnacle.

Big Wheel

SLOWTOWN
You shine, And / Down / Lied / Vicious cirle / Pete Rose / Birthday / Down the line / Daddy's at the wheel / Storm / Tuff skins / Bug bites / Lazy days
CD _____ MR 00472
Mammoth / Apr '93 / Vital.

Big Youth

A LUTA CONTINUA
CD _____ HBCD 28
Heartbeat / Sep '85 / Greensleeves / Jetstar / Direct / ADA.

DJ ORIGINATORS (Big Youth & Dillinger)
CD _____ RGCD 020
Rocky One / Dec '95 / Jetstar.

DREADLOCKS DREAD
Train to Rhodesia / House of dreadlocks / Lightning flash / Weak heart / Natty dread she want / Some like it dread / Marcus Garvey / Big Youth special / Dread organ / Blackman message / You don't care / Moving away
CD _____ CDFL 9006
Frontline / Sep '90 / EMI / Jetstar.

HIGHER GROUND
CD _____ VPCD 1440
VP / Oct '95 / Jetstar.

HIT THE ROAD JACK

What's going on / Hit the road Jack / Wake up everybody / Get up stand up / Jah man of Syreen / Ten against one / Hotter fire / Way of the light / Dread high ranking / Dread is the best
CD _____ CDTRL 137
Trojan / Sep '95 / Jetstar / Total/BMG.

JAMMING IN THE HOUSE OF DREAD
CD _____ DANCD 112
Danceteria / Nov '94 / Plastic Head / ADA.

MANIFESTATION
No nukes / Love fighting so / Turn me on / Mr. Right / Like it like that / Conqueror / Spiderman meet the Hulk / No way to treat a lady
CD _____ HBCD 46
Heartbeat / Apr '88 / Greensleeves / Jetstar / Direct / ADA.

REGGAE PHENOMENON
CD _____ CDTRD 411
Trojan / Mar '94 / Jetstar / Total/BMG.

SAVE THE WORLD
CD _____ 504002
Declic / Nov '95 / Jetstar.

SCREAMING TARGET
Screaming target / Pride and joy rock / Be careful / Tippertone rock / One of these fine days / Screaming target (2) / Killer / Solomon A Gunday / Honesty / I am alright / Lee a low / Concrete jungle
CD _____ CDTRL 61
Trojan / Mar '94 / Jetstar / Total/BMG.

SOME GREAT BIG YOUTH
World War III / Living / Roots foundation / Get on up / Dancing mood / Time alone will tell / Suffering / Love Jah with all of my heart / Green bay killing / We can work it out
CD _____ CDBM 015
Blue Moon / Jul '92 / Magnum Music Group / Greensleeves / Hot Shot / ADA / Cadillac / Discovery.

Bigard, Barney

BARNEY BIGARD & THE LEGENDS OF JAZZ
CD _____ BCD 338
GHB / Jun '95 / Jazz Music.

BARNEY BIGARD & THE PELICAN TRIO
CD _____ JCD 228
Jazzology / Oct '93 / Swift / Jazz Music.

Bigband Orchestra

LEGEND OF GLENN MILLER, THE
CD _____ 500582
Musidisc / Jan '94 / Vital / Harmonia Mundi / ADA / Cadillac / Discovery.

Bigeneric

MYRIADES
CD _____ EFA 698262
Spacefrog / Jul '95 / SRD / Vital.

Biggie Tembo

OUT OF AFRICA
CD _____ COOKCD 039
Cooking Vinyl / Feb '92 / Vital.

Biggs, Barry

SIDESHOW
CD _____ JMC 200117
Jamaica Gold / Jun '95 / THE / Magnum Music Group / Jetstar.

Biggun, Ivor

MORE FILTH DIRT CHEAP
Cockerel song / My shirt collar (it won't go stiff) / Southern breeze / Burglars holler / Gums and plums / John Thomas Allcock / I have a dog his name is Rover / My brothers magazine / Richard the third / Walking your blues away / Are mice electric / I can be the hot dog and you can be the bun / I wanna be a bear / I woke up dis moanin' / Terrific Teddy sings the blues / Ah feel so bad / Other educated monkey
CD _____ BBL 3 CD
Lowdown/Beggars Banquet / Sep '88 / Warner Music / Disc.

PARTNERS IN GRIME (Biggun, Ivor & Ivors Jivers)
Hide the sausage / Nobody does it like the ukelele man / Chantilly lace / Halfway up Virginia / Pussy song / Probing Andromeda / Majorca song / Sixty minute man / Toolbag Ted from Birkenhead / Where did the lead in my pencil go / Cue for a song / I've got a monster
CD _____ BBL 79 CD
Lowdown/Beggars Banquet / Jan '89 / Warner Music / Disc.

WINKERS ALBUM, THE
I've parted / Great grandad John / My brother's got files / Oh oh oh / Cucumber number / Underground music / Winker's paradise / Charabanc
CD _____ BBL 1 CD
Lowdown/Beggars Banquet / Jul '88 / Warner Music / Disc.

61

Bigjig

FEET TO THE FLOOR
CD _____ SMALLCD 9404
Smallworld / Apr '94 / Total/BMG / Direct /
ADA / Cadillac.

Bigod 20

SUPERCUTE
CD _____ CDZOT 122
Zoth Ommog / Nov '94 / Plastic Head.

Bijma, Greetje

BAREFOOT
Barefoot / Bosnia / Painter at work / As I
drive by / Glazed frost / Lonely walk / Kats-
jina / Sings with strings / Duck pond /
Guess where it's coming from / Vortex
CD _____ ENJ 80382
Enja / Oct '93 / New Note / Vital/SAM.

Bikaye, Zazou

GUILTY
CD _____ CRAM 062CD
Crammed Discs / Nov '88 / Grapevine /
New Note.

Bikini Kill

PUSSY WHIPPED
Blood one / Alien she / Magnet / Speed
heart / L'il red / Tell me so / Sugar / Star-
bellied boy / Hamster baby / Rebel girl /
Starfish / For Tammy Rae
CD _____ WIJ 028CD
Wiiija / Oct '93 / Vital.

YEAH YEAH YEAH YEAH
Double dare ya / Liar / Carnival / Suck my
left one / Feels blind / Thurston hearts the
who / White boy / This is not a test / Don't
need you / Jigsaw youth / Resist psychic
death / Rebel girl / Outta me
CD _____ KRS 204CD
Kill Rock Stars / Mar '94 / Vital.

Bilezikjian, John

**MUSIC FROM THE ARMENIAN
DIASPORA PLAYED ON THE OUD**
CD _____ GV 809CD
Global Village / May '94 / ADA / Direct.

Bilk, Acker

**ACKER BILK AND HIS PARAMOUNT
JAZZ BAND (Bilk, Acker & His
Paramount Jazz Band)**
CD _____ LACD 36
Lake / Oct '94 / Target/BMG / Jazz Music
/ Direct / Cadillac / ADA.

ACKER BILK IN HOLLAND
I can't believe that you're in love with me /
Clarinet marmalade / Mood indigo / Them
there eyes / Take the 'A' train / World is
waiting for the sunrise / Just a closer walk
with thee / Jeepers creepers / Lover man /
Watermelon man / I don't want to set the
world on fire / St. Thomas / Georgia / Senora Signora / Blues walk / Stranger on the
shore / Nobody's sweetheart / Once in a
while / Old music master
CD Set _____ CDTTD 506/7
Timeless Traditional / Nov '86 / New Note.

**ACKER BILK PLAYS LENNON &
MCCARTNEY**
CD _____ GNPD 2191
GNP Crescendo / '88 / Silva Screen.

ACKER BILK SONGBOOK
Just when I needed you most / I want to
know what love is / I just called to say I love
you / Longfellow serenade / Truly / Hundred
ways / Still / Always on my mind / Memory
/ Ships / Anytime / Do that to me one
more time / This masquerade / Stuck on
you / If ever you're in my arms again / Could
i have this dance / To all the girls I've loved
before / Three times a lady / Hello / Just
once
CD _____ CDGRF 056
Tring / '93 / Tring / Prism.

AFTER MIDNIGHT
Stranger on the shore / Right here waiting /
Room in your heart / Smack a Latin / An-
other day in paradise / Don't know much /
After midnight / Don't wanna lose you /
How am I supposed to live without you /
I'm not in love / Best of me / Anything for
you / Disney girls / If leaving is easy / When
summer comes / Traces of dreams
CD _____ PWKM 4019
Carlton Home Entertainment / Feb '96 /
Carlton Home Entertainment.

**AT SUNDOWN (Bilk, Acker & Humphrey
Lyttelton)**
At Sundown / When you and I were young
Maggie / You're exceptional to me / Lower
than low / Just a little while to stay here /
You're a lucky guy / Red beans and rice /
Wabash blues / Carry me back to old Vir-
ginny / Summertime / I used to love you /
Lonesome blues / Jazz me blues / Southern
sunset
CD _____ CLGCD 027
Calligraph / May '92 / Cadillac / Wellard /
Jazz Music.

BEST OF ACKER BILK, THE
CD _____ GNPD 2116
GNP Crescendo / Jul '94 / Silva Screen.

**BLAZE AWAY (Bilk, Acker & His
Paramount Jazz Band)**
Riverboat shuffle / I'm gonna sit right down
and write myself a letter / Black and tan fan-
tasy / Spain / Blaze away / Wabash blues /
Way down yonder in New Orleans / Aria /
Keepin' out of mischief now / Jazz me blues
/ Memphis blues / Exactly like you / Is you
is or is you ain't my baby / Singin' the blues
/ Please don't talk to me... / Stranger on the
shore
CD _____ CDTTD 543
Timeless Traditional / Mar '90 / New Note.

BRIDGE OVER TROUBLED WATER
Bridge over troubled water / Stranger on the
shore / Touch me in the morning / Evergreen / She / When I need you / You're my
best friend / Way we were / Raindrops keep
falling on my head / Amazing Grace / Raining in my heart / September song / Don't
cry for me Argentina / Aria / Talking in your
sleep / Misty / Without you / This guy's in
love with you / Forever autumn / Ebony and
ivory
CD _____ 5507322
Spectrum/Karussell / Mar '95 / PolyGram /
THE.

**CAN'T SMILE WITHOUT YOU (Bilk,
Acker, His Clarinet & Strings)**
CD _____ TRTCD 129
TrueTrax / Oct '94 / THE.

**CHALUMEAU (THAT'S MY HOME) (Bilk,
Acker & His Paramount Jazz Band)**
China boy / Nagasaki / Maryland march /
Creole jazz / Jazz me blues / Savoy blues /
New Orleans stomp / Buona sera / South /
Lazy river / Milenberg joys / Original Dixie-
land one-step / That's my home / Black
label blues
CD _____ APRCD 001
Apricot / Oct '95 / Target/BMG.

COLLECTION
CD _____ COL 070
Collection / Mar '95 / Target/BMG.

COLLECTION: ACKER BILK
CD _____ CCSCD 209
Castle / Jan '89 / BMG.

FEELINGS
CD Set _____ MBSCD 403
Castle / Nov '93 / BMG.

HEARTBEATS
Get here / Unchained melody / Somerset
skies / Crazy for you / Close to you / When
I'm back on my feet again / Rio nights / I've
got you under my skin / Sacrifice / Walk on
by / Cuts both ways / It's easy now / Here
we are / On Takapuna Beach / You've lost
that lovin' feelin' / Heartbeats
CD _____ PWKS 4084
Carlton Home Entertainment / Feb '96 /
Carlton Home Entertainment.

**HIS CLARINET & STRINGS LOVE
SONGS**
Evergreen / Miss you nights / Close to you
CD _____ PWKS 508
Carlton Home Entertainment / Sep '88 /
Carlton Home Entertainment.

**HITS, BLUES AND CLASSICS (Bilk,
Acker & His Paramount Jazz Band)**
Louisian-i-ay / Black and tan fantasy / My
baby just cares for me / Papa dip / That's
my home / Semper fidelis / Basin Street
blues / White cliffs of Dover / Blaze away /
Nairobi / Sleepy time down South / Savoy
blues / Just a closer walk with thee / South
/ Mood indigo / Buona sera / Ain't misbehavin' / Aria / Beale Street blues / Stranger
on the shore
CD _____ KAZ CD 10
Kaz / Aug '88 / BMG.

**I THINK THE BEST THING ABOUT THIS
RECORD IS THE MUSIC**
CD _____ BLR 84 04
L&R / New Note.

IMAGINE
Mull of Kintyre / Norwegian wood / Sailing
/ Send in the clowns / Stranger on the shore
/ Yesterday / Windmills of your mind / You
are the sunshine of my life / Aranjuez mon
amour / Aria / Ebony and ivory / Feelings /
Fool on the hill / Imagine / Michelle / Miss-
ing you
CD _____ PLS CD 511
Pulse / Jun '95 / BMG.

IN A MELLOW MOOD
CD _____ MATCD 213
Castle / Dec '92 / BMG.

JAZZ TODAY COLLECTION
CD _____ LACD 48
Lake / Jun '95 / Target/BMG / Jazz Music
/ Direct / Cadillac / ADA.

LOVE ALBUM, THE
When I fall in love / Groovy kind of love /
Silvery nights / Could've been / My love /
He ain't heavy, he's my brother / Good
times / One moment in time / Till I loved you
/ Candle in the wind / Tune for melody /
Take my breath away / Love changes
everything / Sweet crystal / Lady in red /
Every time we say goodbye

CD _____ PWKS 534
Carlton Home Entertainment / Feb '96 /
Carlton Home Entertainment.

MAGIC CLARINET OF ACKER BILK
CD _____ EMPRCD 513
Emporio / Jul '94 / THE / Disc / CM.

NEW ORLEANS DAYS
CD _____ LA 36CD
Lake / Jun '94 / Target/BMG / Jazz Music
/ Direct / Cadillac / ADA.

ON STAGE
Aria / Canio's tune / Pachelbel canon / You
are the sunshine of my life / Miss you nights
/ First of spring / Evergreen / Aranjuez mon
amour / Stranger on the shore / Chi mai /
Spanish harlem / Up in the world / Cavatina
/ Without you / Chariots of fire / Don't cry
for me Argentina
CD _____ STOCD 101
Start / Mar '88 / Koch.

OSCAR WINNERS
When you wish upon a star / For all we
know / Three coins in the fountain / Love
story / Last time I saw Paris / Swinging on
a star / Mona Lisa / Love is a many splendoured thing / Can you feel the love tonight
/ Up where we belong / All the way / You'll
never know / Days of wine and roses / It
might as well be spring / Hello Dolly / Over
the rainbow
CD _____ 3036000022
Carlton Home Entertainment / Oct '95 /
Carlton Home Entertainment.

REFLECTIONS
Stranger on the shore / Petit fleur / Georgia
on my mind / Ain't misbehavin' / I left my
heart in San Francisco / La paloma / Green-
sleeves / Sentimental journey / Moon river /
I'm in the mood for love / Creole love call /
Dinah / Shenandoah / Only you
CD _____ 5500462
Spectrum/Karussell / Jun '93 / PolyGram /
THE.

STRANGER ON THE SHORE
Stranger on the shore / Touch the wind /
Let it be me / First time I ever saw your face
/ Ramblin' rose / We've only just begun /
Morning has broken / I can't stop loving you
CD _____ CDCD 1056
Charly / Mar '93 / Charly / THE / Cadillac.

STRANGER ON THE SHORE
CD _____ 8307792
Philips / Mar '94 / PolyGram.

STRANGER ON THE SHORE
CD _____ MATCD 282
Castle / May '94 / BMG.

**TOGETHER AGAIN (Bilk, Acker & Ken
Colyers Jazzmen)**
CD _____ LACD 32
Lake / Oct '95 / Target/BMG / Jazz Music /
Direct / Cadillac / ADA.

VERY BEST OF ACKER BILK
Stranger on the shore / Way we were / Feelings / Send in the clowns / You are the sunshine of my life / What a wonderful world /
Aria / Windmills of your mind / This guy's in
love with you / Folks who live on the hill /
Wichita lineman / Bridge over troubled
water
CD _____ PWKM 4067
Carlton Home Entertainment / Jul '91 / Carlton Home Entertainment.

Billy Tipton's Memorial..

**SAXHOUSE (Billy Tipton's Memorial
Saxophone Quartet)**
CD _____ KFWCD 143
Knitting Factory / Feb '95 / Grapevine.

Bina, Sima

PERSIAN CLASSICAL MUSIC
CD _____ NI 5391
Nimbus / Apr '95 / Nimbus.

Bindu

SNAP TO IT
CD _____ DMUT 1274
Multitone / Jul '94 / BMG.

Bingham, Mark

I PASSED FOR HUMAN
CD _____ DOG 006CD
Ichiban / May '94 / Koch.

Binney, David

LUXURY OF GUESSING, THE
CD _____ AQ 1030
Audioquest / Apr '95 / New Note.

Biochip C

INSIDE (CHAPTER 2)
CD _____ EFA 008302
Anodyne / Jul '95 / SRD.

Biohazard

BIOHAZARD
CD _____ MCD 1067
MCA / Aug '94 / BMG.

State of the World Address

STATE OF THE WORLD ADDRESS
State of the world address / Down for life /
What makes us tick / Tales from the hard
side / How it is / Remember / Five blocks
to the subway / Each day / Failed territory
/ Lack there of / Pride / Human animal /
Cornered / Love denied
CD _____ 936245595-2
WEA / May '94 / Warner Music.

Biomuse

WRONG
4 Rubber feet / Race / Sine God / Very
approximately / Convolvotron / Medral / An-
aural / Ursonate / Ba-Umf (CD only.) /
Wrong (CD only.) / X (CD only.)
CD _____ WORDD 002
Language / Nov '95 / Grapevine.

Biosphere

MICROGRAVITY
Microgravity / Baby satellite / Tranquillizer /
Fairy tale / Cloudwalker 11 / Chromosphere
/ Cygnus-A / Baby interphase / Biosphere
CD _____ AMBCD 3921
Apollo / Jun '93 / Vital.

PATASHNIK
Phantasm / Startoucher / Decryption / Nov-
elty waves / Patashnik / Mir / Shield / Seti
project / Mestigoth / Botanical dimensions
/ Caboose / En-trance
CD _____ AMB 3927CD
Apollo / Feb '94 / Vital.

Biota

BELLOWING ROOM/TINCT
CD _____ RERB2CD
Recommended / '90 / These / ReR
Megacorp.

TINCT
CD _____ RERBCD 2
Recommended / Feb '88 / These / ReR
Megacorp.

TUMBLE
CD _____ RERBCD
Recommended / '90 / These / ReR
Megacorp.

Bird Nest Roy

BIRD NEST ROY
CD _____ FNECD 19
Flying Nun / '88 / Disc.

Bird, Ted

MADE IN AMERICA
Dirty little town / Land o' plenty / Drivin' in
Rhode Island / Still in your power / Hurri-
cane / Sadness in my eyes / Daddy's dia-
monds / Philadelphia kid / Southern Ohio /
Lady crystal / That far to fall / When she
gets drinkin' whiskey / On the radio / Dollar
bill / Allyson's waltz
CD _____ CDSL 5219
DRG / Aug '92 / New Note.

Bird, Tony

SORRY AFRICA
CD _____ CDPH 1135
Philo / Dec '90 / Direct / CM / ADA.

Bird, Tracy

TRACY BIRD
That's the thing about a memory / Back in
the swing of things / Someone to give my
love to / Holdin' heaven / Why / Out of control raging fire / Hat trick / Why don't that
telephone ring / Edge of a memory / Talk to
me Texas
CD _____ MCAD 10649
MCA / Mar '94 / BMG.

Birdland Stars

BIRDLAND STARS 1956
Bit of the blues / Two pairs of aces / Intro-
ductions by Condoli / Minorin' the blues /
Phil' er up / Roulette / Pee Wee speaks /
Hip boots / Ah funky new baby / Birdland
fantasy / Playboy / Conte's condolences
CD _____ 07863 66159-2
Bluebird / Apr '93 / BMG.

Birdsong Mesozoic

SONIC ECOLOGY
CD _____ RCD 20073
Rykodisc / Apr '92 / Vital / ADA.

Birke

JAZZ IN SWEDEN 1978
CD _____ 1145
Caprice / Nov '89 / CM / Complete/
Pinnacle / Cadillac / ADA.

Birmingham Jubilee...

**1926-1927 VOL.1 (Birmingham Jubilee
Singers)**
CD _____ DOCD 5345
Blues Document / May '95 / Swift / Jazz
Music / Hot Shot.

Birmingham Sunlights

FOR OLD TIME'S SAKE
CD _____ FF 588CD
Flying Fish / Nov '94 / Roots / CM / Direct / ADA.

Birthday Party

HITS
CD _____ DAD 2016CD
4AD / Oct '92 / Disc.

JUNKYARD
She's hit / Dead Joe / Dim locator / Hamlet pow pow pow / Several sins / Big Jesus trash can / Kiss me black / Six inch gold blade / Kewpie doll / Junkyard
CD _____ CAD 207 CD
4AD / Apr '88 / Disc.

MUTINY/BAD SEED
CD _____ CAD 301CD
4AD / Jul '89 / Disc.

PRAYERS ON FIRE
CD _____ CAD 104CD
4AD / Apr '88 / Disc.

Biscuit, Karl

AKTUALISMUS
CD _____ MTM 28CD
Made To Measure / Dec '92 / Grapevine.

Bishop, Elvin

ACE IN THE HOLE
CD _____ ALCD 4833
Alligator / Aug '95 / Direct / ADA.

BIG FUN
CD _____ ALCD 4767
Alligator / Apr '93 / Direct / ADA.

DON'T LET THE BOSSMAN GET YOU DOWN
Fannie Mae / Don't let the bossman get you down / Murder in the first degree / Kissing in the dark / My whiskey head buddies / Stepping up in class / You got to rock 'em / Come on in this house / Soul food / Rollin' with my blues / Devil's slide / Just your fool
CD _____ ALCD 4791
Alligator / May '93 / Direct / ADA.

TULSA SHUFFLE - BEST OF ELVIN BISHOP
Tulsa shuffle / How much more / Things (That) I used to do / Sweet potato / Honey bee / Prisoner of love / Party till the cows come home / Hogbottom / Be with me / So fine / Don't fight it (Feel it) / As the years go passing by / So good / Rock my soul / Rock bottom / Stomp / Stealin' watermelons / Last mile
CD _____ 4767222
Legacy / May '94 / Sony.

Bishop, Joni

EVERYDAY MIRACLES
CD _____ CDSGP 0134
Prestige / Nov '95 / Total/BMG.

Bishop, Walter Jr.

MILESTONES
CD _____ BLCD 760109
Black Lion / Feb '89 / Jazz Music / Cadillac / Wellard / Koch.

Bishops

BEST OF THE BISHOPS, THE
Train train / Baby you're wrong / Stay free / I want candy / I take what I want / Mr. Jones / I need you / Down in the bottom / You're in my way / Talk to you / Taste and try / Someone's got my number / Good times / Your Daddy won't mind / What's your number / Till the end of the day / These arms of mine / Rolling man / Paul's blues / No lies / Too much, too soon / Sometimes good guys don't wear white / Don't start me talkin' / Somebody's gonna get their head kicked in tonight / I don't like it / Route 66 / Train, train
CD _____ CDWIKD 150
Chiswick / Aug '95 / Pinnacle.

Bisi, Martin

ALL WILL BE WON
Camino de la India / Get it right / Brava / Hijos de Nadie / Rabbit dance / Broken hoop / For all our people / All will be won
CD _____ NAR 075 CD
New Alliance / Sep '93 / Pinnacle.

SEE YA IN TIAJUANA
CD _____ NAR 123CD
SST / Jul '95 / Plastic Head.

Bisiker, Mick

HOME AGAIN
Home again / Don't you go / Jigs / Katy Jane / Si beag si mor / Rose of Allendale / Maid from the shore / Mossy green banks of the lea / Jigs and reels / Downhills of life / Rainbows end
CD _____ FE 083CD
Fellside / Feb '88 / Target/BMG / Direct / ADA.

Bison, Fred

BEATROOTS
CD _____ WO 19CD
Woronzow / Apr '94 / Pinnacle.

Bisserov Sisters

PIRIN WEDDING AND RITUAL SONGS
CD _____ PAN 7005CD
Pan / Nov '95 / ADA / Direct / CM.

Bitch Funky Sex Machine

LOVE BOMB
CD _____ CDVEST 39
Bulletproof / Jan '95 / Pinnacle.

Bitchcraft

DON'T COUNT ON IT
CD _____ IT 0062
Iteration / Feb '95 / SRD.

Bitter End

HARSH REALITIES
CD _____ CDZORRO 10
Metal Blade / Jul '89 / Pinnacle.

Bivouac

FULL SIZE BOY
Not going back there again / Thinking / Trepanning / Gecko or skink / Monkey sanctuary / My only safe bet / Mattress / Mainbrake / Ding bong / Lounge lizard / Ray is related to the shark
CD _____ GED 24561
Geffen / Jul '95 / BMG.

TUBER
CD _____ ELM 11 CDX
Elemental / Jun '93 / Disc.

Bjork

BEST MIXES FROM THE ALBUM DEBUT (For All The People Who Don't Buy White Labels)
Human behaviour / One day (2 mixes) / Come to me (2 mixes) / Anchor song
CD _____ MUMCD 59
Mother / Oct '94 / PolyGram.

DEBUT
Human behaviour / Crying / Venus as a boy / There's more to life than this (Recorded live at the Milk Bar toilets) / Like someone in love / Big time sensuality / One day / Aeroplane / Come to me / Violently happy / Anchor song / Play dead
CD _____ TPLP 31CDX
One Little Indian / Nov '93 / Pinnacle.

POST
Army of me / Hyperballad / Modern things / It's oh so quiet / Enjoy / You've been flirting again / Isobel / Possibly maybe / I miss you / Cover me / Headphones
CD _____ TPLP 51CD
One Little Indian / Jun '95 / Pinnacle.

Bjornstad, Ketil

SEA, THE
CD _____ 5217182
ECM / Sep '95 / New Note.

WATER STORIES
Glacial reconstruction / Levels and degrees / Surface movements / View (part one) / Between memory and presentiment / Ten thousand years later / Waterfall / Flotation and surroundings / Riverscape / Approaching the sea / View (part two) / History
CD _____ 5190762
ECM / Sep '93 / New Note.

BKA

CLEVER
CD _____ FILERCD 405
Profile / Jun '91 / Pinnacle.

Black

ARE WE HAVING FUN YET
CD _____ NEROCD 9401
Nero Schwarz / Apr '94 / Total/BMG.

TURN LOOSE THE IDIOTS
CD _____ NORMAL 196CD
Normal/Okra / Jan '96 / Direct / ADA.

WONDERFUL LIFE
Ravel in the rain / Sixteens (CD only) / Leave yourself alone (CD only) / It's not you Lady Jane (CD only) / Hardly star crossed lovers / Wonderful life / Everything's coming up roses / Sometimes for the asking / Finder / Paradise / I'm not afraid / I just grew tired / Blue / Just making memories / Sweetest smile
CD _____ CDMID 166
A&M / Aug '91 / PolyGram.

Black & White Gospel...

LOOK TO GOD (Black & White Gospel Singers)
CD _____ FA 405
Fremeaux / Nov '95 / Discovery / ADA.

Black & White Minstrels

30 GOLDEN GREATS (Black & White Minstrels & The Joe Loss Orchestra)
Baby face / Ain't she sweet / Good ole mammy song / Nostalgia, Home town, Strollin', Underneath the arches / Y viva Espana / Happy feet/I want to be happy/Happy days are here again / Consider yourself / Mame / Tzena, tzena, tzena / Hava Nagila / Bring me sunshine / Paloma blanca / Old fashioned way / You are my sunshine / Laugh a happy laugh / Continental / Piccolino / When the red, red robin comes bob, bob, bobbin' along / Hopscotch / Mexican shuffle / Tijuana Taxi / La Bamba / (We're gonna) rock around the clock (the saint go marching in)
CD _____ CDMFP 5720
EMI / Mar '93 / EMI.

Black Ace

I'M THE BOSS CARD IN YOUR HAND
CD _____ ARHCD 374
Arhoolie / Apr '95 / ADA / Direct / Cadillac.

Black, Alastair

BALANDA DANCING (Black, Alastair & Stephen Richter)
CD _____ LARRCD 031
Larrikin / Jan '95 / Roots / Direct / ADA / CM.

Black, Andrea

ANDREA BLACK
CD _____ AKRCD 32
AKR / May '90 / Pinnacle.

JUMPING FROM THE WALL
CD _____ AKRCDA 38
AKR / Mar '95 / Pinnacle.

Black, Barry

BARRY BLACK
Train of pain / Mighty fields of tabacco / Broad majestic haw / Sandviken stomp / Fisherman thugs / Cockroaches / Vampire lounge / Staticus von carrborus / I can't breathe / Cowboys and thieves / Rabid dog / Blip / Animals are for eating / Golden throat
CD _____ A 085D
Alias / Oct '95 / Vital.

Black, Bill

GOES WEST & PLAYS (Black, Bill Combo)
CD _____ HIUKCD 124
Hi / Jun '93 / Pinnacle.

GREATEST HITS: BILL BLACK'S COMBO (Black, Bill Combo)
Do it rat / Josephine / Rollin' / Hearts of stone / Yogi / White silver sands / Blue tango / Willie / Ole buttermilk sky / Royal blue / Don't be cruel / Smoke part 2 / School days / Sweet little sixteen / Roll over Beethoven / Maybellene / Carol / Little queenie / Brown eyed handsome man / Nadine / Thirty days / Johnny B. Goode / Reelin' and rockin' / Memphis, Tennessee
CD _____ HIUKCD 115
Hi / '91 / Pinnacle.

LET'S TWIST HER/THE UNTOUCHABLE SOUND (Black, Bill Combo)
CD _____ HIUKCD 131
Hi / Jun '92 / Pinnacle.

MEMPHIS ROCK 'N' SOUL PARTY (Black, Bill & Willie Mitchell)
Don't be cruel / Honky tonk / Blueberry Hill / Hearts of stone / Movin' / Hey Bo Diddley / Work with me Annie / Twist-her / My girl Josephine / Night train / So what / Do it rat now / Monkey shine / School days / Memphis, Tennessee / Little queenie / Secret home / Buster Browne / At the woodchoppers' ball / That driving beat / Everything's gonna be alright / Champion / Bad eye / Sugar T / Mercy / Up-hard / 30-60-90 / Who's making love / Come see about me / My babe / I'm a midnight mover / Set free
CD _____ HIUKCD 102
Hi / Jul '89 / Pinnacle.

SOLID AND RAUNCHY AND MOVIN' (Black, Bill Combo)
Don't be cruel / Singin' the blues / Blueberry Hill / I almost lost my mind / Cherry pink / Mona Lisa / Honky Tonk / Tequila / Raunchy / You win again / Bo Diddley / Mack the knife / Movin' / What'd I say / Hey Bo Diddley / Witchcraft / Work with me Annie / Be bop a lula / My babe / Forty miles of bad road / Ain't that lovin' you baby / Honky train / Walk / Torquay
CD _____ HIUKCD 112
Hi / '91 / Pinnacle.

THAT WONDERFUL FEELING (Black, Bill Combo)
CD _____ HIUKCD 145
Hi / Aug '94 / Pinnacle.

Black Box

DREAMLAND
Everybody everybody / I don't know anybody else / Open your eyes / Fantasy /

Dreamland / Ride on time / Hold on / Ghost box / Strike it up
CD _____ 74321 15867-2
De-Construction / Sep '93 / BMG.

Black Cat Bones

BARBED WIRE SANDWICH
Chauffeur / Death Valley blues / Feelin' good / Please tell me baby / Coming back / Save my love / Four women / Sylvester's blues / Good lookin' woman
CD _____ SEECD 405
See For Miles/C5 / Jul '94 / Pinnacle.

Black, Christi

CHRISTI BLACK WITH STANDARD 3 (Black, Christi & Standard 3)
Bewitched, bothered and bewildered / I love you / I can't get started (with you) / Somebody loves me / Dindi / Black coffee / Speak low / More than you know / Thank you for the memory / It never entered my mind
CD _____ KICP 54
King/Paddle Wheel / Feb '91 / New Note.

Black, Cilla

BEST OF THE EMI YEARS: CILLA BLACK
You're my world (Il mio mondo) / Anyone who had a heart / Love of the loved / It's for you / You've lost that lovin' feelin' / I've been wrong before / Goin' out of my head / Love's just a broken heart / Alfie / Fool am I (Dimmelo parlami) / Sing a rainbow / Don't answer me / When I fall in love / Yesterday / Make it easy on yourself / What good am I / I only live to love you / Step inside love / Where is tomorrow / What the world needs now is love / Conversations / Surround yourself with sorrow / If I thought you'd ever change your mind / Something tells me (something's gonna happen tonight) / Liverpool lullaby / Baby we can't go wrong
CD _____ CDEMS 1410
EMI / Jun '91 / EMI.

CILLA'S WORLD
CD _____ SILVAD 3004
Silva Treasury / Nov '93 / Conifer / Silva Screen.

Black, Clint

NO TIME TO KILL
No time to kill / Thinking again / Good run of bad luck / State of mind / Bad goodbye (Duet with Wynonna Judd.) / Back to back / Half the man / I'll take Texas / Happiness alone / Tuckered out
CD _____ 7863662 392
RCA / Jul '93 / BMG.

ONE EMOTION
You walked by / Life gets away / One emotion / Summer's comin' / Untanglin' my mind / Hey hot rod / Change in the air / I can get by wherever you go / You made me feel / Good run of bad luck / Bad goodbye
CD _____ 74321 22957-2
RCA / Nov '94 / BMG.

PUT YOURSELF IN MY SHOES
Put yourself in my shoes / Gulf of Mexico / One more payment / Where are you now / Old man / This nightlife / Loving blind / Heart like mine / Good night loving
CD _____ PD 90544
RCA / Jan '90 / BMG.

Black Crowes

AMORICA
Gone / Conspiracy / High head blues / Cursed diamond / Non-fiction / She gave good / Sunflower / P.25 London / Ballad in urgency / Wiser time / Downtown money waster / Descending / Tied up and swallowed
CD _____ 74321236822
American / Oct '94 / BMG.

SHAKE YOUR MONEY MAKER
Twice as hard / Jealous again / Sister luck / Could I've been so blind / Seeing things / Hard to handle / Thick 'n' thin / She talks to angels / Struttin' blues / Stare it cold
CD _____ 74321248392
American / Dec '94 / BMG.

SOUTHERN HARMONY AND MUSICAL COMPANION, THE
Sting me / Remedy / Thorn in my pride / Bad luck blue eyes goodbye / Sometimes salvation / Hotel illness / Black moon creepin' / No speak, no slave / My morning song / Time will tell
CD _____ 74321248402
American / Dec '94 / BMG.

Black Crucifixion

PROMEATHEAN GIFT
CD _____ LMCD 222
Lethal / Nov '93 / Plastic Head.

Black, Dick

COME SEQUENCE DANCING
CD _____ CDKBP 510
Igus / Dec '89 / CM / Ross / Duncans.

63

DANCING TIME, MODERN SEQUENCE
(Black, Dick Scottish Dance Band)
CD _____ CDKBP 514
Igus / Dec '90 / CM / Ross / Duncans.

KEEP THE MUSIC GOING (Black, Dick
Scottish Dance Band)
CD _____ CDKBP 517
Klub / Mar '95 / CM / Ross / Duncans /
ADA / Direct.

Black Dog

BYTES
CD _____ WARPCD 8
Warp / Mar '93 / Disc.

SPANNERS
CD _____ PUPCD 1
Warp / Jan '95 / Disc.

TEMPLE OF TRANSPARENT BALLS
CD _____ GPRCD 1
General Production Recordings / Jul '93 /
Pinnacle.

Black, Donald

**WESTWIND (Scottish Mouth Organ
Music)**
Pipe jigs / J. Scott Skinner slow airs / Cape
Breton set / Slow airs / Welcome Christmas
morning / Shetland reels / Pipe slow air and
marches / Hebridean duet / Shores of Loch
Linnhe / Slow air and pipe marches / Touch
of the Irish / Lewis danns a rathad
CD _____ CDTRAX 091
Greentrax / Jul '95 / Conifer / Duncans /
ADA / Direct.

Black Dyke Mills Band

BLITZ
Blitz / Pageantry / Journey into freedom /
Tam O'Shanter's ride
CD _____ CHAN 8370
Chandos / Aug '85 / Chandos.

BROADWAY BRASS
There's no business like show business /
Oklahoma / Medley from West Side Story /
I have a love / Somewhere / I don't know
how to love him / Colours of my life / Where
is my love / Music of the night / Starlight
express / Bring him home / Wunderbar /
How to handle a woman / Summertime /
Medley from South Pacific / There is nothin'
like a dame / Wonderful guy / Some en-
chanted evening / That's entertainment
CD _____ CDMFP 5947
Music For Pleasure / Oct '92 / EMI.

COMPLETE CHAMPIONS
Contest march / Royal parks / Salute to
youth / Cloudcatcher fells
CD _____ CHAN 4509
Chandos / Apr '92 / Chandos.

ESSENTIAL DYKE
Queensbury / Le roi d'ts / Pandora / Deep
harmony / Galop / Macushla / Capriccio It-
alien / Knight templar / Cornet carillon / Rule
Britannia / Abide with me / Angels guard
thee / Hungarian rhapsody No. 1
CD _____ DOYCD 034
Doyen / Oct '94 / Conifer.

GREAT BRITISH MARCHES
Queensbury / Roll away Bet / Battle Abbey
/ O.R.B. / Senator / Invincible / Pompous
main / Cossack / Imperioso / Raby / Cap-
tain / Olympus / Knight templar
CD _____ DOYCD 039
Doyen / May '95 / Conifer.

GREAT BRITISH TRADITION, THE
Endeavour / West country fantasy / North
country fantasy / Sir Roger De Coverley /
Sally in our alley / On Ilkley Moor baht'at /
Fifth of August / Lincolnshire poacher / Car-
nival of the animals suite / Carmen fantasy
CD _____ CHAN 4524
Chandos / May '93 / Chandos.

GREGSON - BRASS MUSIC VOL.2
Prelude for an occasion / Plantagenets / Es-
say / Laudate dominum / Prelude and ca-
priccio / Concerto grosso / Partita
CD _____ DOYCD 044
Doyen / Nov '95 / Conifer.

LION AND THE EAGLE, THE
Yeoman of the guard / Phil the fluter's ball
/ Land of my fathers (Hen wlad fy nhadau)
/ Fantasia on the dargason / Scottish lament / Will ye no' come back again / Auld
lang syne / Pomp and circumstance march
No.4 / Stars and stripes forever / Rhapsody
on negro spirituals / Go down Moses / Pe-
ter, go ring dem bells / Every time I feel de
spirit / I'm a rollin' through an unfriendly
world / Stephen Foster fantasy / Camptown
races / My old Kentucky home / Beautiful
dreamer / Jeanie with the light brown hair /
Old folks at home / Oh Susanna / Old black
Joe / Strike up the band / Embraceable you
/ They can't take that away from me /
Someone to watch over me / Oh lady be
good / Rhapsody in blue / Man I love
CD _____ CHAN 4528
Chandos / Aug '93 / Chandos.

**MORE OF THE WORLD'S MOST
BEAUTIFUL MELODIES**
Your tiny hand is frozen / Celeste Aida /
Skye boat song / Bruch and Mendelssohn

violin concerto themes / Flower song / Holy
city / I hear you calling me / Ave Maria
CD _____ CHAN 8513
Chandos / '87 / Chandos.

Black Eagle Jazz Band

BLACK EAGLE JAZZ BAND, VOL. 7
CD _____ SOSCD 1224
Stomp Off / Oct '92 / Jazz Music /
Wellard.

DON'T MONKEY WITH IT
CD _____ SOSCD 1147
Stomp Off / Oct '92 / Jazz Music /
Wellard.

Black Earth

FEELING, THE
Never stop loving you / Too touch / You
made my night / Madelaine / Too late / Next
man / Marianne / How can I / Feeling / Para-
dise / Going kind of crazy
CD _____ PCOM 1103
President / '89 / Grapevine / Target/BMG /
Jazz Music / President.

Black Eg

BLACK EG
CD _____ CRECD 086
Creation / May '94 / 3MV / Vital.

Black Eyed Susans

ALL SOULS ALIVE
Curse on you / We could've been / Some-
one / Every gentle soul / Memories / Sheets
of rain / Reveal yourself / I can see now /
Apartment no. 9 / Dirty water / This one eats
souls
CD _____ 31061-2
Frontier / Jul '94 / Vital.

Black Family

BLACK FAMILY, THE
Broom o'the Cowdenknowes / Colannon /
Motorway song / Tomorrow is a long time /
Donkey riding / Will ye gang, love / Bramble
and the rose / Ploughboy lad / Warlike lads
of Russia / Dark and roving eye / James
Connolly / Wheel the perambulator
CD _____ DARACD 023
Dara / Jan '94 / Roots / CM / Direct / ADA
/ Koch.

TIME FOR TOUCHING HOME
Alabama John Cherokee / Rough ride / Old
bones / Farewell to the gold / Sweet liberty
/ Peat bog soldiers / Weave and mend /
Time alone / Song of the diggers / Since
Maggie went away / First Christmas / Eliza
Lee / This love will carry
CD _____ DARACD 035
Dara / Jan '94 / Roots / CM / Direct / ADA
/ Koch.

Black Flag

DAMAGED
CD _____ SST 007 CD
SST / May '93 / Plastic Head.

EVERYTHING WENT BLACK
CD _____ SST 015 CD
SST / May '93 / Plastic Head.

FAMILY MAN
CD _____ SST 026 CD
SST / May '93 / Plastic Head.

FIRST FOUR YEARS, THE
CD _____ SST 021 CD
SST / May '93 / Plastic Head.

IN MY HEAD
CD _____ SST 045 CD
SST / May '93 / Plastic Head.

LOOSE NUT
CD _____ SST 035 CD
SST / Feb '88 / Plastic Head.

MY WAR
CD _____ SST 023 CD
SST / May '93 / Plastic Head.

PROCESS OF WEEDING OUT
CD _____ SST 037 CD
SST / Sep '87 / Plastic Head.

SLIP IT IN
CD _____ SST 029 CD
SST / May '93 / Plastic Head.

WASTED...AGAIN
Wasted / T.V. party / Six pack / I don't care
/ I've had it / Jealous again / Slip it in / An-
nihilate this week / Loose nut / Gimmie gim-
mie / Louie Louie / Drinking and driving
CD _____ SST 166 CD
SST / Aug '87 / Plastic Head.

WHO'S GOT THE 10%
CD _____ SST 060 CD
SST / Aug '87 / Plastic Head.

Black, Frances

FRANCES BLACK & KIERAN GOSS
(Black, Frances & Kieran Goss)
CD _____ TRACD 112
Transatlantic / Oct '95 / BMG / Pinnacle /
ADA.

SKY ROAD, THE
CD _____ DARA 068CD
Dara / Jul '95 / Roots / CM / Direct / ADA
/ Koch.

TALK TO ME
All the lies that you have told me / Don't be
a stranger / On Grafton Street / Soldiers of
destiny / Talk to me while I'm listening / In-
tuition / Colder than Winter / Always wild /
Time of inconvenience / World of our own /
if love had wings
CD _____ 7567827362
Warner Bros. / Apr '95 / Warner Music.
CD _____ DARACD 056
Dara / Nov '95 / Roots / CM / Direct / ADA
/ Koch.

Black, Frank

CULT OF RAY, THE
Marsist / Men in black / Punk rock city / You
ain't me / Jesus was right / I don't want to
hurt you (every single time) / Mosh, don't
pass the guy / Kicked in the taco / Creature
crawling / Adventure and the resolution /
Dance war / Cult of Ray / Last stand of
Shazeb Andleeb
CD _____ 4816472
CD _____ 4816479
Dragnet / Jan '96 / Sony / SRD.

FRANK BLACK
CD _____ CAD 3004CD
4AD / Mar '93 / Disc.

TEENAGER OF THE YEAR
CD _____ DAD 4009CD
4AD / May '94 / Disc.

Black Girls

HAPPY
Happy / In the room / Cathedral / Car /
Charleston / Talk / Letter / Fat / Thunder /
I love you song / Tell you everything / Smart
man / Mother
CD _____ HNCD 1365
Hannibal / Sep '91 / Vital / ADA.

PROCEDURE
CD _____ HNCD 1348
Hannibal / Nov '89 / Vital / ADA.

Black Grape

**IT'S GREAT WHEN YOU'RE STRAIGHT...
YEAH**
Reverend Black Grape / In the name of the
father / Tramazi parti / Kelly's heroes / Yeah
yeah brother / Big day in the North / Shake
well before opening / Submarine / Shake
your money / Little Bob
CD _____ RAD 11224
Radioactive / Aug '95 / Vital / BMG.

Black, Ika

SPECIAL LOVE
CD _____ KMCD 004
Keyman / Oct '88 / SRD / Jetstar /
Greensleeves.

Black Lace

20 ALL TIME PARTY FAVOURITES
Agadoo / Hands up / Atmosphere /
D.I.S.C.O. / We danced we danced / Wig
wam bam / I just called to say I love you /
Viva Espana / I am the music man / Dancing
in the street / Superman / Simon says /
Birdie song / Brown girl in the ring / Soaking
up the sun / Let's twist again / Sailing /
Hokey cokey
CD _____ BLPFCD 1
Connoisseur / Nov '89 / Pinnacle.

ACTION PARTY
Agadoo / I am the music man / Wig wam
bam / Hi ho silver lining / Penny arcade /
Superman / Do the conga / Locomation /
Hippy hippy shake / Good golly Miss Molly
/ Twist and shout / Do you love me / Bump
/ Come on Eileen / Let's dance / Do wah
diddy diddy / Mandolin jiven' / Dancin' party
/ (We're gonna) Rock around the clock /
This ole house / Birdie song / Teardrops /
Knock three times / We danced we danced
/ Time warp (live)
CD _____ PLATCD 3915
Prism / Apr '93 / Prism.

SATURDAY NIGHT
CD _____ LACECD 2
Flair / Dec '94 / Total/BMG.

Black Lodge

COVET
CD _____ HNF 010CD
Head Not Found / Mar '95 / Plastic Head.

Black Lodge Singers

POW WOW WOW
CD _____ SPA 14286
Spalax / Nov '94 / Direct / ADA.

Black Lung

DEPOPULATION BOMB, THE
CD _____ NZ 036CD
Nova Zembla / May '95 / Plastic Head.

SILENT WEAPONS FOR QUIET WARS
CD _____ DOROBO 005CD
Dorobo / Oct '95 / Plastic Head.

Black, Marc

BIG DONG DHARMA
CD _____ ESP 3011-2
ESP / Jan '93 / Jazz Horizons / Jazz
Music.

Black, Mary

BABES IN THE WOOD
CD _____ GRACD 008
Grapevine / Jan '95 / Grapevine.

BY THE TIME IT GETS DARK
By the time it gets dark / Schoolday's over
/ Once in a very blue moon / Farewell fare-
well / Sparks might fly / Katy / Leaving the
land / There is a time / Jamie / Leaboy's
lassie / Trying to get the balance right
CD _____ GRACD 004
Grapevine / Jan '95 / Grapevine.

CIRCUS
CD _____ GRACD 014
Grapevine / Sep '95 / Grapevine.

COLLECTED
Mo Ghile Mear / Fare thee well my own /
True love / Men o' worth / She moved
through the fair / Love's endless war / Both
sides of the Tweed / My youngest son
came / Home today / Isle of St. Helena /
Don't explain / Everything that touches me
CD _____ GRACD 002
Grapevine / Jan '95 / Grapevine.

COLLECTION, THE
Moon and St. Christopher / No frontiers /
Babes in the wood / Carolina rua / Katie /
Columbus / Adam at the window / Ellis is-
land / Bright blue rose / Vanities / Only a
woman's heart / Song for Ireland / Tearing
up the town / There's a train that leaves
tonight
CD _____ GRACD 10
Grapevine / Jan '95 / Grapevine.

HOLY GROUND, THE
CD _____ GRACD 011
Grapevine / Jan '95 / Grapevine.

MARY BLACK
Rose of Allendale / Loving you / Loving
Hannah / My Donald / Crusader / Anachie
Gordon / Home / God bless the child / Ra-
re's hill
CD _____ GRACD 001
Grapevine / Jan '95 / Grapevine.

NO FRONTIERS
CD _____ GRACD 009
Grapevine / Jan '95 / Grapevine.

WITHOUT THE FANFARE
There's a train that leaves tonight / State of
heart / Night time / Crow on the cradle /
Greatest dream / Water is wild / Ellis island
/ Strange thing / Without the fanfare / As I
leave behind Neidin / Diamond days / Going
gone
CD _____ GRACD 003
Grapevine / Jan '95 / Grapevine.

Black Nasty

TALKING TO THE PEOPLE
Talking to the people / I must be in love /
Nasty soul / Getting funky round here /
Black nasty boogie / We're doin' our thing
/ I have no choice / It's not the world /
Rushin' sea / Booger the hooker
CD _____ CDSXE 091
Stax / Nov '93 / Pinnacle.

Black Note

JUNGLE MUSIC
No introduction / Dream of Elizabeth Brown
/ Introspection / Three wishes for Jackey /
Fifth Street Dick's / Call me in the morning
/ Maisha / Evil dancer / Unrequited / Jungle
music / Fourth grade (Remix)
CD _____ 476505 2
Columbia / Jul '94 / Sony.

Black Oak Arkansas

AIN'T LIFE GRAND
Taxman / Fancy Nancy / Keep on / Good
stuff / Rebel / Back door man / Love can
be found / Diggin' for gold / Crying shame
/ Let life be good to you
CD _____ RSACD 830
Sequel / Jun '95 / BMG.

EARLY TIMES
Someone something / When I'm gone / Let
us pray / Sly fox / Mean woman / No one
and the sun / Theatre / Collective thinking /
Older than grandpa
CD _____ CDSXE 067
Stax / Nov '92 / Pinnacle.

HIGH ON THE HOG
Swimmin' in deep water / Back to the band
/ Movin' / Happy hooker / Red hot lovin' /
Jim Dandy / Moonshine sonata / Why
shouldn't I smile / High 'n' dry / Madman
CD _____ RSACD 832
Sequel / Jun '95 / BMG.

HOT & NASTY

Mean woman (if you ever blues) / Uncle Lijah / Hot and nasty / Lord have mercy on my soul / When electricity came to Arkansas / Keep the faith / Fever in my mind / Hot rod / Gravel roads / Mutants of the monster / Jim Dandy / Happy hooker / Son of a gunn / Dixie / Everybody wants to see heaven / Diggin' for gold / Taxman / So you want to be a rock 'n' roll star
CD _____ 812271146-2
WEA / Mar '93 / Warner Music.

IF AN ANGEL CAME

Gravel roads / Fertile woman / Spring vacation / We help each other / Full moon ride / Our mind's eye / To make us what we are / Our eyes are on you / Mutants of the monster
CD _____ RSACD 831
Sequel / Jun '95 / BMG.

KEEP THE FAITH

Keep the faith / Revolutionary all American boys / Feet on earth, head in sky / Fever in my mind / Big ones still coming / White headed woman / We live on day to day / Short life line / Don't confuse what you don't know
CD _____ RSACD 828
Sequel / Jun '95 / BMG.

STREET PARTY

Dancing in the street / Sting me / Good good woman / Jailbait / Sure been working hard / Son of a gun / Brink of creation / I'm a man / Goin' home / Dixie / Everybody wants to see heaven / Hey y'all
CD _____ RSACD 829
Sequel / Jun '05 / BMG.

Black Ocean Drowning

BLACK OCEAN DROWNING
CD _____ EFA 08439CD
Dossier / Oct '92 / SRD.

Black Rock & Ron

HOT DANCE MUSIC
CD _____ 15355
Laserlight / Aug '91 / Target/BMG.

STOP THE WORLD
CD _____ CDSU 5
Supreme / Apr '89 / Pinnacle.

Black Rock Coalition

HISTORY OF OUR FUTURE
Son talkin' (intro) / H.O.P.E / Make it my world / Bluestime in America / Tough times / M.L.K...check / It will all / Think twice / Didn't live long / Hustler man / Son talkin' / Dadahdoodahda / Royal pain / Good guys / Michael Hill's Bluesband / Jupiter / Blue print / J.J. Jumpers / Blackasaurus mex / PBR Streetgang / Shock counsel
CD _____ RCD 20211
Rykodisc / Sep '91 / Vital / ADA.

Black Roots

BLACK ROOTS WITH FRIENDS
Juvenile delinquent / What them a do / Survival / Confusion / Move on / Release the flood (Not on LP) / Mash them dub (Not on LP) / Opportunity / Tribal war / Africa / Father / Chanting for freedom / Let it be me (Not on LP) / Jah Jah dub (Not on LP)
CD _____ NRCD 009
Nubian / Nov '93 / Jetstar / Vital.

DUB FACTOR 2 (The Dub Judah Mixes)
Tune hood / Not into war / Dust look back / People dub / Moving dub / Jah Jah dub / Mash them dub / Dub the youth / Warning from Jah / Now is the time / Chant it dub / Show them dub / Take heed 2 (Outro mix)
CD _____ NRCD 010
Nubian / Jul '94 / Jetstar / Vital.

DUB FACTOR: THE MAD PROFESSOR MIXES (Black Roots & Mad Professor)
CD _____ NRCD 007
Nubian / Nov '91 / Jetstar / Vital.

Black Rose

ROOM INSIDE
CD _____ CONTECD 168
Contempo / Oct '91 / Plastic Head.

Black Sabbath

BETWEEN HEAVEN AND HELL
CD _____ RAWCD 104
Raw Power / Oct '95 / BMG.

COLLECTION: BLACK SABBATH
Paranoid / Behind the wall of sleep / Sleeping village / Warning / War pigs / Hand of doom / Planet caravan / Electric funeral / Rat salad / Iron man / After forever / Supernaut / St. Vitus dance / Wheels of confusion / Snowblind / Killing yourself to live / Sabbra cadabra / Writ
CD _____ CCSCD 109
Castle / Jan '86 / BMG.

CROSS PURPOSES
I witness / Cross of thorns / Psychophobia / Virtual death / Immaculate deception / Dying for love / Back to Eden / Hand that rocks the cradle / Cardinal sin / Evil eye

CD _____ EIRSCD 1067
IRS/EMI / Jan '94 / EMI.

DEHUMANIZER
Computer god / After all / TV crimes / Letters from Earth / Master of insanity / Time machine / Sins of the father / Too late / I / Buried alive
CD _____ EIRSCD 1064
IRS/EMI / May '94 / EMI.

ETERNAL IDOL, THE
Shining / Ancient warrior / Hard life to love / Glory ride / Born to lose / Scarlet Pimpernel / Lost forever / Eternal idol
CD _____ 832 708-2
Vertigo / Nov '87 / PolyGram.

FORBIDDEN
Illusion of power / Get a grip / Can't get close enough / Shaking off the chains / I won't cry for you / Guilty as hell / Sick and tired / Rusty angels / Forbidden / Kiss of death
CD _____ EIRSCD 1072
IRS/EMI / Jun '95 / EMI.

HEADLESS CROSS
Gates of hell / Headless cross / Devil and daughter / When death calls / Kill in the spirit world / Call of the wild / Black moon / Nightwing
CD _____ EIRSACD 1002
IRS/EMI / May '94 / EMI.

HEADLESS CROSS/TYR/DEHUMANIZER (3CD Set)
Gates of hell / Headless cross / Devil & daughter / When death calls / Kill in the spirit world / Call of the world / Black moon / Nightwing / Anno mundi / Law maker / Jerusalem / Sabbath stones / Battle of Tyr / Odin's court / Valhalla / Feels good to me / Heaven in black / Computer God / After all / TV crimes / Letters from Earth / Master of insanity / Time machine / Sins of the father / Too late / I / Buried alive
CD Set _____ CDOMB 014
IRS/EMI / Oct '95 / EMI.

HEAVEN AND HELL
Neon knights / Children of the sea / Lady evil / Heaven and hell / Wishing well / Die young / Walk away / Lonely is the word
CD _____ ESMCD 330
Essential / Jan '96 / Total/BMG.

INTERVIEW, THE
CD P.Disc _____ CBAK 4071
Baktabak / Feb '94 / Baktabak.

IRON MAN
Sabbath bloody Sabbath / Wizard / Sweet leaf / Electric funeral / Into the void / Wheels of confusion / Paranoid / Iron man / Am I going insane (Radio) / Killing yourself to live / Snowblind / Hole in the sky / Laguna sunrise / War pigs
CD _____ 5507202
Spectrum/Karussell / Sep '94 / PolyGram THE.

LIVE AT LAST
Tomorrow's dream / Sweet leaf / Killing yourself to live / Cornucopia / War pigs / Laguna sunrise / Paranoid / Wicked world
CD _____ CLACD 203
Castle / Oct '90 / BMG.

LIVE EVIL
E 5150 / Neon knights / N.I.B. / Children of the sea / Voodoo / Black Sabbath / War pigs / Iron man / Mob rules / Heaven and hell / Sign of the Southern cross / Paranoid / Children of the grave / Fluff
CD _____ 8268812
Vertigo / Jul '88 / PolyGram.

MASTERS OF MISERY (A Black Sabbath Tribute) (Various Artists)
Shock wave / Snowblind / Zero the hero / Hole in the sky / Changes / Who are you / Lord of this world / N.I.B. / Wizard / Sweet leaf / Solitude
CD _____ TFCK 88607
Toys Factory / Jan '95 / Plastic Head.

MOB RULES
Turn up the night / Voodoo / Sign of the Southern Cross / E 5150 / Mob rules / Country girl / Slippin' away / Falling off the edge of the world / Over and over
CD _____ ESMCD 332
Essential / Jan '96 / Total/BMG.

NATIVITY IN BLACK (A Tribute To Black Sabbath) (Various Artists)
After forever / Children of the grave / Paranoid / Supernaut / Iron man / Lord of this world / Solitude / Symptom of the universe / Wizard / Sabbath bloody Sabbath / N.I.B. / War pigs / Black Sabbath
CD _____ 4776712
Sony Music / Oct '94 / Sony.

NEVER SAY DIE
Black Sabbath / Dirty women / Rock 'n' roll doctor / Electric funeral / Children of the grave / Paranoid / Snowblind / Never say die / Johnny Blade / Junior eyes / Hard road / Shock wave / Air dance / Over to you / Breakout / Swinging the chain
CD _____ 5501312
Spectrum/Karussell / Oct '93 / PolyGram THE.

OZZY OSBOURNE YEARS
Black Sabbath / Wizard / Behind the wall of sleep / N.I.B. / Evil woman / Sleeping

woman / Warning / War pigs / Paranoid / Planet Caravan / Iron man / Hand of doom / Fairies wear boots / Electric funeral / Sweet leaf / After forever / Embryo / Lord of this world / Solitude / Into the void / Wheels of confusion / Tomorrow's dream / Changes / Supernaut / Snowblind / Cornucopia / St. Vitus dance / Under the sun / Sabbath bloody Sabbath / National acrobat / Sabbra cadabra / Killing yourself to live / Who are you / Looking for today / Spiral architect / Hole in the sky / Symptom of the universe / Am I going insane (radio) / Thrill of it all / Megalomania / Writ
CD Set _____ ESBCD 142
Essential / Apr '91 / Total/BMG.

TECHNICAL ECSTASY
All moving parts / Backstreet kids / Dirty women / Gypsy / It's alright / Rock 'n' roll doctor / She's gone / You won't change me
CD _____ ESMCD 328
Essential / Jan '96 / Total/BMG.

TYR
CD _____ EIRSCD 1038
IRS/EMI / May '94 / EMI.

WE SOLD OUR SOULS FOR ROCK 'N' ROLL
Black Sabbath / Wizard / Warning / Paranoid / Wicked world / Tomorrow's dream / Fairies wear boots / Changes / Sweet leaf / Children of the grave / Sabbath bloody Sabbath / Am I going insane (radio) / Laguna sunrise / Snowblind
CD _____ CCSCD 249
Castle / Oct '90 / BMG.

Black Sheep

NON FICTION
Non fiction intro / Autobiographical / B.B.S. / City lights / Do your thing / E.F.F.E.C.T. / Freak y'all / Gotta get up / Let's get cozy / Me and my brother / North South East West / Peace to the niggas / Summa the time / We boys / Who's next / Without a doubt / Non fiction outro
CD _____ 5226852
Mercury / Jan '95 / PolyGram.

WOLF IN SHEEPS CLOTHING, A
Intro / U mean I'm not / Butt in the meantime / Have U.N.E. pull / Strobelite honey / Are U mad / Choice is yours / To whom it may concern / Similak child / Try counting sheep / Flavor of the month / La menage / L.A.S.M. / Gimme the finga / Hoes we knows / Go to hail / Black with N.V. / Pass the 40 / Blunted / For Doz that slept
CD _____ 8483682
Mercury / Oct '91 / PolyGram.

Black Slate

GET UP AND DANCE
CD _____ EXRCD 002
Elixir / Nov '95 / Jetstar.

Black Sorrows

BETTER TIMES
CD _____ TIMBCD 601
Timbuktu / Aug '93 / Pinnacle.

LUCKY CHARM
CD _____ TIMBCD 603
Timbuktu / Mar '95 / Pinnacle.

Black Star

NYOTA (Black Star & Lucky Star Musical Clubs)
Amana / Mpende anaekupenda / Nimekuja pasi haya / Chozi lanitoka / Hisani nakuusiya / Enyi wanadamu / Nazi / Duniani / Mnazi mkinda / Nini dawa ya mahaba / Bunduki / Rehema
CD _____ CDORB 044
Globestyle / Aug '89 / Pinnacle.

Black Star

TRIBUTE TO HAILE SELASSIE 1, A (King Of Kings)
CD Set _____ RASTA 3
Jungle / Jul '95 / Disc.

Black State Choir

PACHAKUTI
CD _____ PDCD PPP119
Head / May '95 / Total/BMG.

PERMACULTURE
CD _____ PPP 116
PDCD / Apr '94 / Plastic Head.

Black, Stanley

S'WONDERFUL
Memories are made of this / Holiday for strings / Blue tango / April in Portugal / 'S Wonderful / Poor people of Paris / Summer place / Limelight / Malaguena / Brazil / Hand in hand / Breeze and I / Girl from Ipanema / Granada / That old devil moon / Melodie d'amour / Soon / But not for me / On the street where you live / La cumparsita
CD _____ PLCD 527
President / Apr '90 / Grapevine / Target/ BMG / Jazz Music / President.

Black Survivors

NATION OF THE WORLD
CD _____ BSCD 001
Black Survivors / Aug '94 / Jetstar.

Black Tape For A Blue...

TEARDROP (Black Tape For A Blue Girl)
CD _____ HY 39100262
Hyperium / Nov '92 / Plastic Head.

Black Train Jack

NO REWARD
CD _____ CD RR 9070 2
Roadrunner / Jun '93 / Pinnacle.

YOU'RE NOT ALONE
Handouts / Not alone / Joker / What's the deal / Struggle / Alright then / Lottery / Regrets / Back up / Reason / Mr. Walsh blues / That reminds me
CD _____ RR 90172
Roadrunner / Apr '94 / Pinnacle.

Black Uhuru

ANTHEM
What is life / Party next door / Try it / Black Uhuru anthem / Botanical roots / Somebody's watching you / Bull in the pen / Elements
CD _____ RRCD 41
Reggae Refreshers / Jul '92 / PolyGram / Vital.

BLACK UHURU
Shine eye girl / Leaving to Zion / General penitentiary / Guess who's coming to dinner / Abortion / Natural reggae beat / Plastic smile
CD _____ CDVX 1004
Virgin / Jun '89 / EMI.

BRUTAL
Let us pray / Dread in the mountain / Brutal / City vibes / Great train robbery / Uptown girl / Vision / Reggae with you / Conviction or fine / Fit you haffe fit
CD _____ RASCD 3015
Ras / Jun '95 / Jetstar / Greensleeves / SRD / Direct.

BRUTAL DUB
Let us dub / Dub in the mountain / Brutalize me with dub / City dub / Dub you haffe dub / Robbery dub / Uptown dub / Visions of dub / Dub it with you / Conviction or a dub
CD _____ RASCD 3020
Ras / Nov '92 / Jetstar / Greensleeves / SRD / Direct.

CHILL OUT
CD _____ RRCD 43
Reggae Refreshers / Jun '88 / PolyGram / Vital.

DUB FACTOR, THE
Ion storm / Youth / Big spliff / Boof n baff b biff / Puffed out / Android rebellion / Apocalypse back breaker / Sodom / Slaughter
CD _____ RRCD 28
Reggae Refreshers / Sep '91 / PolyGram / Vital.

GUESS WHO'S COMING TO DINNER
CD _____ HBCD 18
Heartbeat / Apr '88 / Greensleeves / Jetstar / Direct / ADA.

IRON STORM
CD _____ R 279035
Mesa / Mar '94 / Total/BMG.

LIBERATION: THE ISLAND ANTHOLOGY
Chill out / Party next door / Black Uhuru anthem / Guess who's coming to dinner / Shine eye gal (live) / Sponji reggae / Wicked act / Botanical roots / Somebody's watching you / Utterance / Slaughter / I love King Selassie (live) / Darkness-dubness / Elements / What is life / Youth of Eglington / Youth right stuff / World is Africa / Happiness (live) / Mondays-killer / Tuesday / Solidarity / Ion storm / Try it / Bull in the pen / Sinsemilla / Puff she puff / Party in session
CD Set _____ CRNCD 1
Mango / Feb '94 / Vital / PolyGram.

LIVE
CD _____ SONCD 0080
Sonic Sounds / Nov '95 / Jetstar.

LIVE IN NEW YORK
CD _____ RBUCD 88000
Rohit / Aug '88 / Jetstar.

MYSTICAL TRUTH
Questions / Bassline / Slippin' into darkness / Give my love / Don't you worry / Dreadlock pall bearers / Payday / One love / Ozone layer / Living in the city / Young school girl / Mercy street / Tip of the iceberg
CD _____ 8122790442
WEA / Apr '93 / Warner Music.

POSITIVE DUB
Cowboy town / Firecity / Positive / My concept / Space within my heart / Dry weather house / Pain / Create
CD _____ RE 159CD
Reach Out International / Nov '94 / Jetstar.

RED
Youth of Eglington / Sponji reggae / Sistren / Journey / Utterance / Puff she puff / Rock stone / Carbine
CD _____ RRCD 18
Reggae Refreshers / Nov '90 / PolyGram / Vital.

REGGAE GREATS
Happiness / World in Africa / Sponji reggae / Youth of Eglington / Darkness / What is life / Bull in the pen / Elements / Push push / Right stuff
CD _____ IMCD 3
Island / Jul '89 / PolyGram.

SINSEMILLA
Happiness / World is Africa / Push push / There is fire / No loafing / Sinsemilla / Every dreadlocks / Vampire
CD _____ RRCD 12
Reggae Refreshers / Sep '90 / PolyGram / Vital.

Black Umfolosi

FESTIVAL - UMDLALO
Bazali bethu jazz song / Phetsheya kwezil-wandle over the seas / Ingoma yakwethu catch our song / Inobembela njiba / Em-thimbeni wedding / When shall wars / Saw-elu umfula ushangane / Salu 'randela / Gumboot dance / Helele mama Afrika / Side of the city / Take me home
CD _____ WCD 037
World Circuit / Sep '93 / New Note / Direct / Cadillac / ADA.

UNITY
CD _____ WCD 020
World Circuit / Oct '91 / New Note / Direct / Cadillac / ADA.

Black Voices

SPACE TO BREATHE
CD _____ T&M 005
Tradition & Moderne / Dec '95 / Direct / ADA.

WOMEN IN (E)MOTION FESTIVAL
CD _____ T&M 103
Tradition & Moderne / Nov '94 / Direct / ADA.

Black Watch Band

PIPES & DRUMS 1ST BATTALION (THE BLACK WATCH)
CD _____ CC 293
EMI / May '93 / EMI.

ROYAL HIGHLANDERS
Regimental call / Company marches / Pipes and drums set / Impressions on a Scottish air / Slow marches and quick marches / Royal highlanders
CD _____ BNA 5069
Bandleader / May '92 / Conifer.

Black Widow

BLACK WIDOW
CD _____ REP 4031-WZ
Repertoire / Aug '91 / Pinnacle / Cadillac.

SACRIFICE
In ancient days / Way to power / Come to the Sabbat / Conjuration / Seduction / At-tack of the demon / Sacrifice
CD _____ CLACD 262
Castle / '91 / BMG.
CD _____ REP 4067-WZ
Repertoire / Aug '91 / Pinnacle / Cadillac.

Black Byrds

ACTION/BETTER DAYS
Supernatural feeling / Lookin' ahead / Mys-terious vibes / Something special / Street games / Soft and easy / Dreaming about you / Dancin' dancin' / Loneliness for your love / Better days / Do it girl / Without your love / Do you wanna dance / Love don't strike twice / What's on your mind / Don't know what to say / What we have is right
CD _____ CDBGPD 090
BGP / Nov '94 / Pinnacle.

BEST OF THE BLACKBYRDS, THE
Blackbyrds' theme / Rock creek park / Time is movin' / Don't know what to say / Love don't strike twice / Supernatural feeling / Soft and easy / Do it fluid / Walking in rhythm / Happy music / Something special / Baby / Gut level / Dreaming about you / Mysterious vibes
CD _____ CDBGP 918
BGP / Jun '88 / Pinnacle.

BLACKBYRDS/FLYING START
Do it fluid / Gut level / Reggins / Runaway / Funkie junkie / Summer love / Life styles / Hot day today / I need you / Baby / Love is love / Blackbyrds' theme / Walking in rhythm / Future children / Happy endings / April showers / Spaced out
CD _____ CDBGPD 86
BGP / Jul '94 / Pinnacle.

CITY LIFE/UNFINISHED BUSINESS
Rock creek park / Thankful 'bout yourself / City life / All I ask / Happy music / Love so fine / Flying high / Hash and eggs / Time is movin' / In life / Enter in / You've got that

somthing / Party land / Lady / Unfinished business
CD _____ CDBGPD 089
BGP / Sep '94 / Pinnacle.

Blackeyed Biddy

HIGH SPIRITS
CD _____ DUNCD 014
Dunkeld / Jun '88 / Direct / ADA / CM.

PEACE, ENJOYMENT & PLEASURE
CD _____ CDTRAX 056
Greentrax / May '93 / Conifer / Duncans / ADA / Direct.

Blackfoot

AFTER THE REIGN
CD _____ CDVEST 15
Bulletproof / Jun '94 / Pinnacle.

MARAUDER
Good morning / Paying for it / Diary of a working man / Too hard to hand / Fly away / Dry county / Fire of the dragon / Rattle-snake rock 'n' roller / Searchin'
CD _____ 7567903852
WEA / Jan '93 / Warner Music.

MEDICINE MAN
Doin' my job / Stealer / Sleazy world / Not gonna cry any more / Runnin' runnin' / Chilled to d'bone / Guitar slingers song and dance
CD _____ CDMFN 106
Music For Nations / Oct '90 / Pinnacle.

Blackgirl

TREAT U RIGHT
Krazy / Treat U right / Can U feel it / Where did we go wrong / Chains / Ooh yeh (Smooth) / 90's Girl / Nubian prince / Things we used to do / Can't live without U / Let's do it again / Home
CD _____ 07863663592
Arista / Jul '94 / BMG.

Blackhawk

BLACKHAWK
CD _____ 07822187082
Arista / Sep '94 / BMG.

STRONG ENOUGH
Big guitar / Like there ain't no yesterday / Cast iron heart / I'm not strong enough to say no / Almost a memory now / King of the world / Bad love gone good / Any man with a heartbeat / Kiss is worth a thousand words / Hook, line and sinker
CD _____ 07822187922
Arista / Sep '95 / BMG.

Blackhouse

5 MINUTES AFTER I DIE
CD _____ BHCD 5
Nuclear Blast / Aug '93 / Plastic Head.

HOPE LIKE A CANDLE
CD _____ DV 12
Nuclear Blast / Aug '93 / Plastic Head.

PRO LIFE
CD _____ MHCD 006
Massacre / Nov '93 / Plastic Head.

Blackmadrid

ATLANTIC CROSSING: THE PEOPLE'S JOURNEY
CD _____ NAR 056 CD
New Alliance / May '93 / Pinnacle.

Blackman, Cindy

ARCANE
CD _____ MCD 5341
Muse / Sep '92 / New Note / CM.

CODE RED
Code red / Anxiety / Next time forever / Something for art (drum solo) / Round Mid-night / Circles / Face in the dark / Green
CD _____ MCD 5365
Muse / Nov '92 / New Note / CM.

ORACLE, THE
CD _____ MCD 5542
Muse / Feb '96 / New Note / CM.

TELEPATHY
Reves electriques du matin / Spank / Telep-athy / Well you needn't / Missing you / Club house / Reves electriques de l'apres midi / Jardin secret / Persuasion / Tune up / Re-ves electriques de minuit
CD _____ MCD 5437
Muse / Mar '94 / New Note / CM.

TRIO (Blackman, Cindy/Santi Debriano/Dave Fiuczynski)
CD _____ FRLCD 015
Freelance / Oct '92 / Harmonia Mundi / Cadillac / Koch.

Blackmore, Ritchie

ROCK PROFILE VOL 1
Return of the outlaws / Texan spiritual / If you gotta pick a baby / Big fat spider / Doo dah day / Thou shalt not steal / I'm not a bad guy / Ritchie Blackmore interview / Been invited to a party / Shake with me / Movin' in / Keep a knockin' / I shall be re-

leased / Playground / Wring that neck / Why didn't Rosemary / Living wreck / Guitar job / No, no, no / Highway star / A200 / Gypsy / Hold on / Show me the way to go home
CD _____ RPVSOPCD 143
Connoisseur / Oct '89 / Pinnacle.

ROCK PROFILE VOL 2
Getaway / Little brown jug / Honey hush / Train kept a rollin' / Gemini suite: guitar movement / Bullfrog / Good golly Miss Molly / Great balls of fire / Hurry to the city / Still I'm sad / Man on the silver mountain / Lady of the lake / Sixteenth century green-sleeves / I call, no answer / Son of Alerik
CD _____ RPVSOPCD 157
Connoisseur / Apr '91 / Pinnacle.

SESSION MAN
CD _____ RPM 120
RPM / Oct '93 / Pinnacle.

Blackout

BLACKOUT
CD _____ SHCD 6017
Sky High / Jul '95 / Jetstar.

Blackstones

OUTBURST
CD _____ CDSGP 0219
Prestige / Nov '95 / Total/BMG.

Blackstreet

BLACKSTREET
Intro (Blackstreet philosophy) / Baby be mine / U blow my mind / Hey love (keep it real) / I like the way you work / Good life / Physical thing / Make U wet / Booti call / Love's in need / Joy / Before I let you go / Confession (interlude) / Tonight's the night / Happy home / Wanna make love / Once in a lifetime / Givin' you all my lovin'
CD _____ 654492351-2
Warner Bros. / Jun '94 / Warner Music.

Blackthorne

AFTERLIFE
Cradle of the grave / Afterlife / We won't be forgotten / Breaking the chains / Over and over / Hard feelings / Baby you're the blood / Sex crime / Love from the ashes / All night long
CD _____ CDMFN 148
Music For Nations / May '93 / Pinnacle.

Blackwell

TRIBUTE TO BLACKWELL (Various Artists)
CD _____ 1201132
Black Saint / Nov '90 / Harmonia Mundi / Cadillac.

Blackwell, Ed

EL CORAZON (Blackwell, Ed & Don Cherry)
Mutron / Bemsha swing / Solidarity / Ara-bian nightingale / Roland Alphonso / Ma-kondi / Street dancin' / Short stuff / El cor-azon / Rhythm for runner / Near-in / Voice of the silence
CD _____ 8291992
ECM / Oct '86 / New Note.

OLD AND NEW DREAMS (Blackwell, Ed, Don Cherry & Redman)
CD _____ BSR 0013CD
Black Saint / Harmonia Mundi / Cadillac.

WHAT IT BE LIKE
Nebula / Grandma's shoes / Pentahouve / First love / Lito (Part 1,2,3,)
CD _____ ENJ 80542
Enja / Jul '94 / New Note / Vital/SAM.

Blackwell, Otis

BRACE YOURSELF (A Tribute To Otis Blackwell) (Various Artists)
CD _____ SHCD 5705
Shanachie / Apr '94 / Koch / ADA / Greensleeves.

OTIS BLACKWELL - 1953-55
CD _____ FLYCD 26
Flyright / Feb '91 / Hot Shot / Wellard / Jazz Music / CM.

Blackwell, Scrapper

VIRTUOSO GUITAR
CD _____ YAZCD 1019
Yazoo / Apr '91 / CM / ADA / Roots / Koch.

Blackwood Singers

GREATEST GOSPEL
I believe / Spirit of the living God / Glory glory clear the road / First day in heaven / House of God / This olde house / When the saints go marching in / Jonah / Amazing grace / I'll fly away / Yesterday / No further than your knees
CD _____ HADCD 171
Javelin / May '94 / THE / Henry Hadaway Organisation.

Blade

PLANNED AND EXECUTED
CD _____ BLADE 1208CD
Move/691 Influential / Jan '96 / Plastic Head.

Blade Fetish

ABSINTHE
CD _____ EFA 06480-2
Tess Europe / Mar '94 / SRD.

Blades, Ruben

AGUA DE LUNA
Isobel / No te Duermas / Blackaman / Ojos de Perro Azul / Claro Oscuro / Laura Farina / La cita / Agua de luna
CD _____ 15964
Messidor / Sep '89 / Koch / ADA.

ANTECEDENTE (Blades, Ruben Y Son Del Solar)
Juana mayo / 'Tas caliente / La marea / Contrabando / Patria / Noches del ayer / Nuestro adios / Nacer de ti / Plaza herrera
CD _____ 15993
Messidor / Aug '89 / Koch / ADA.

BUSCANDO AMERICA (SEARCHING FOR AMERICA)
Decisions / G D B D / Desapariciones / To-dos Vuelven / Caminos verdes / El Padre Antonio y el Monaguillo Andres / Buscando America
CD _____ 115926
Messidor / Jan '87 / Koch / ADA.

ESCENAS
Cuentas del alma / Tierra dura / La cancion del final del mundo / La sorpresa / Caina / Silencois / Muevete
CD _____ 1115939
Messidor / Jan '87 / Koch / ADA.

POETA LATINA
Mucho major / Anor pa'que / Ya no te Puedo Querer / Siembra / El Corrido / Del Caballa / Blanco / Usted / Noe / Cabeza de Hacha / Si yo pudier a andar / Tu me acos-tumbraste / Ganas / La pasado no perdona / Te odio y te Quiero / Para ser rumbero
CD _____ CDHOT 503
Charly / Oct '93 / Charly / THE / Cadillac.

POETRY
Tiburon / Ganas / Plastico / Solo / Paula / Buscando guyaba / Juan Gonzalez / Dime / Siembra / Manuela / Pablo Pueblo / Sin tu carino
CD _____ CDCHARLY 261
Charly / Jan '91 / Charly / THE / Cadillac.

Blades, Shaw

HALLUCINATION
CD _____ 9362458352
Warner Bros. / Mar '95 / Warner Music.

Blaggers ITA

BAD KARMA
Hits / 1994 / Man trap / Bad karma / Famine Queen / Stress / Abandon ship / Nation / Garden of love / Slam / Hate generator / Oxygen
CD _____ CDPCSD 156
Parlophone / Aug '94 / EMI.

UNITED COLOURS
CD _____ WOWCD 27
Words Of Warning / '94 / SRD.

Blair 1523

BEAUTIFUL DEBRIS
CD _____ VOXXCD 2060
Voxx / Mar '93 / Else / Disc.

Blake Babies

EARWIG
CD _____ MROO 1614
Mammoth / Nov '92 / Vital.

INNOCENCE AND EXPERIENCE
Wipe it up / Rain / Boiled potato / Lament / Cesspool / You don't give up / Star (Demo) / Sanctify / Out there / Girl in a box / I'm not your mother / Temptation eyes / Down-time / Over and over
CD _____ MR 058-2
Mammoth / Oct '93 / Vital.

NICELY, NICELY
Wipe it up / Her / Tom and Bob / Sweet burger LP / Bye / Let them eat chewy gra-nola bars / Julius fast body / Bitter n you / Swill and the cocaine sluts
CD _____ MR 086-2
Mammoth / Oct '94 / Vital.

SLOW LEARNER
CD _____ UTIL 006 CD
Utility / Jul '89 / Grapevine.

SUNBURN
CD _____ MROO 224
Mammoth / Nov '92 / Vital.

Blake, Eubie

MEMORIES OF YOU
Charleston rag / Chevy chase / Mirandy / Fizz water / Crazy blues / Memphis blues / Dangerous blues / Arkansas blues / Down

home blues / Good fellow blues / Don't tell your monkey man / Boll weevil blues / If you don't want me blues / I'm just wild about Harry / Memories of you

CD _____ BCD 112
Biograph / Jul '91 / Wellard / ADA / Hot Shot / Jazz Music / Cadillac / Direct.

Blake, John

QUEST
CD _____ 500582
Sunnyside / Nov '92 / Pinnacle.

Blake, Kenny

INTERIOR DESIGN
Hey mister / Take five / What can I say / Irene / Little stars / Harlem nocturne / Alladin / Babylon sisters / Soulmates / Oasis
CD _____ 101 S 7134 2
101 South / Jun '93 / New Note.

Blake, Norman

BACK HOME IN SULPHUR SPRINGS
CD _____ ROUCD 0012
Rounder / Nov '95 / CM / Direct / ADA / Cadillac.

BLAKE AND RICE (Blake, Norman & Tony Rice)
CD _____ CD 0233
Rounder / Aug '88 / CM / Direct / ADA / Cadillac.

BLIND DOG (Blake, Norman & Nancy)
CD _____ ROUNDERCD 0254
Rounder / '90 / CM / Direct / ADA / Cadillac.

FIELDS OF NOVEMBER/OLD & NEW
CD _____ FF 004CD
Flying Fish / May '93 / Roots / CM / Direct / ADA.

JUST GIMME SOMETHIN' I'M USED TO (Blake, Norman & Nancy)
CD _____ SHCD 6001
Shanachie / Apr '92 / Koch / ADA / Greensleeves.

NATASHA'S WALTZ (Blake, Norman & Nancy)
CD _____ CD 11530
Rounder / '88 / CM / Direct / ADA / Cadillac.

NORMAN & NANCY BLAKE COMPACT DISC
Hello stranger / New bicycle hornpipe / Marquis Huntley / Florida rag / Jordan am a hard road to travel / Belize / Elzic's farewell / Lighthouse on the shore / Grand junction / Butterfly weed / President Garfield's hornpipe / In Russia (we have parking lots too) / Wroxall / If I lose I don't care / Chrysanthemum / Lima road jig / Boston boy / Last night's joy / My love is like a red rose / Wildwood flower / Tennessee mountain fox chase
CD _____ CD 11505
Rounder / '88 / CM / Direct / ADA / Cadillac.

NORMAN BLAKE & TONY RICE 2 (Blake, Norman & Tony Rice)
It's raining here this morning / Lost Indian / Georgie / Father's hall / Two soldiers / Blackberry blossom / Eight more miles to Louisville / Lincoln's funeral train (The sad journey to Springfield) / Molly Bloom / D-18 Song (Thank you, Mr. Martin) / Back in yonder's world / Bright days / Salt creek
CD _____ CDROU 0266
Rounder / Jul '90 / CM / Direct / ADA / Cadillac.

BLOW TRAIN THROUGH GEORGIA
CD _____ CD 11526
Rounder / '88 / CM / Direct / ADA / Cadillac.

WHILE PASSING ALONG THIS WAY (Blake, Norman & Nancy)
CD _____ SHAN 6012CD
Shanachie / Apr '95 / Koch / ADA / Greensleeves.

WHISKEY BEFORE BREAKFAST
Hand me down my walking cane / Under the double eagle / Six white horses / Salt river / Old grey mare / Down at Mylow's house / Sleepy eyed Joe / Indian creek / Arkansas traveller / Girl I left in Sunny Tennessee / Mistrel boy to war has gone / Ash grove / Church Street blues / Macon rag / Fiddler's dream / Whiskey before breakfast / Slow train through Georgia
CD _____ ROUCD 063
Rounder / Aug '93 / CM / Direct / ADA / Cadillac.

Blake, Paul

DANCE
CD _____ LICD 900002
Line / Sep '92 / CM / Grapevine / ADA / Conifer / Direct.

Blake, Peter

PRIVATE DAWN
CD _____ WCL 110082
White Cloud / May '95 / Select.

Blake, Ran

DUKE DREAMS
CD _____ RN 121027-2
Soul Note / Oct '94 / Harmonia Mundi / Wellard / Cadillac.

EPISTROPHY
CD _____ 121177-2
Soul Note / Sep '92 / Harmonia Mundi / Wellard / Cadillac.

SOLO PIANO
CD _____ 1238422
IAI / Mar '92 / Harmonia Mundi / Cadillac.

THAT CERTAIN FEELING
CD _____ ARTCD 6077
Hat Art / Jul '91 / Harmonia Mundi / ADA / Cadillac.

Blake, Seamus

CALL, THE
CD _____ 1088CD
Criss Cross / Jan '95 / Cadillac / Harmonia Mundi.

Blakey, Art

1958: PARIS OLYMPIA
CD _____ 8326592
Fontana / Feb '92 / PolyGram.

APRIL JAMMING (Blakey, Art & The Jazz Messengers)
CD _____ CDJJ 627
Jazz & Jazz / Jan '92 / Target/BMG.

ART BLAKEY
CD _____ WWCD 2065
West Wind / Jan '91 / Swift / Charly / CM / ADA.

ART BLAKEY & THE JAZZ MESSENGERS (Blakey, Art & The Jazz Messengers)
CD _____ CDSJP 340
Timeless Jazz / Dec '90 / New Note.

ART BLAKEY & THE JAZZ MESSENGERS (Blakey, Art & The Jazz Messengers)
Alamode / Invitation / Circus / You don't know what love is / I hear a rhapsody / Gee baby, ain't I good to you
CD _____ IMP 11752
Impulse Jazz / Jan '96 / BMG / New Note.

ART BLAKEY IN CONCERT
CD Set _____ RTE 15022
RTE / Apr '95 / ADA / Koch.

ART COLLECTION (The best of)
Fuller love / Oh, by the way / Webb City / Second thoughts / In walked Bud / Dark side, light side / Jody
CD _____ CCD 4495
Concord Jazz / Jan '92 / New Note.

AT THE JAZZ CORNER OF THE WORLD, VOLS 1 & 2 (Blakey, Art & The Jazz Messengers)
Hipsippy blues / Justice / Theme / Close your eyes / Just coolin' / Chicken an' dumplins / M and M / Hi fly / Art's revelation
CD _____ CDP 8288882
Blue Note / May '94 / EMI.

BEST OF ART BLAKEY (Blakey, Art & The Jazz Messengers)
Moanin' / Blues march / Lester left town / Night in Tunisia / Dat dere / Mosaic (CD only.) / Free for all (CD only.)
CD _____ BNZ 32
Blue Note / Feb '90 / EMI.

BEST OF ART BLAKEY & THE JAZZ MESSENGERS, THE (Blakey, Art & The Jazz Messengers)
Moanin' / Blues march / Lester's left town / Night in Tunisia / Dat dere / Mosaic / Free for all
CD _____ CDP 7932052
Blue Note / Dec '95 / EMI.

BIG BEAT (Blakey, Art & The Jazz Messengers)
It's only a paper moon / Chess players / Sakeena's vision / Politely / Dat dere / Lester left town / It's only a paper moon (Alt.)
CD _____ MCD 47016
Milestone / Oct '93 / Jazz Music / Pinnacle / Wellard / Cadillac.

BIG BEAT, THE (Blakey, Art/Max Roach/Elvin Jones/Philly Joe Jones)
Caravan / High priest / Theme / Conversation / Mydrid's cha-cha / Larry-Larue / Lady luck / Buzz-at / Pretty Brown / Six and four / Stablemates / Carioca ("El Tambores") / Battery blues / Gone gone gone / Tribal message
CD _____ MCD 47014 2
Milestone / Apr '94 / Jazz Music / Pinnacle / Wellard / Cadillac.

BLUE NIGHT (Blakey, Art & The Jazz Messengers)
Two of a kind / Blue minor / Blue night / Body and soul / Mr. Combinated
CD _____ CDSJP 217
Timeless Jazz / Aug '90 / New Note.

BLUES MARCH (Blakey, Art & The Jazz Messengers)
CD _____ JHR 73539
Jazz Hour / May '93 / Target/BMG / Jazz Music / Cadillac.
CD _____ ATJCD 8009
All That's Jazz / Aug '94 / THE / Jazz Music.

COMPACT JAZZ BOX SET (Blakey, Art/Chet Baker/Anita O'Day/Memphis Slim)
CD Set _____ CD BOX 15
IMS / Jul '87 / PolyGram.

DAY WITH ART BLAKEY VOLUME 1, A
Summit / Breeze and I / Blues march / Moanin' / It's only a paper moon
CD _____ PRCDSP 201
Prestige / Aug '93 / Total/BMG.

FAREWELL (LIVE AT SWEET BASIL) (Blakey, Art & The Jazz Messengers)
Goma / Second thoughts / Uranus / Sudan blue / I thought about you / Blue 'n' boogie theme
CD Set _____ KICJ 41/2
King/Paddle Wheel / Jul '91 / New Note.

FEEL THE WIND (Blakey, Art & Freddie Hubbard)
CD _____ CDSJP 307
Timeless Jazz / Jun '89 / New Note.

FEELING GOOD (Blakey, Art & The Jazz Messengers)
CD _____ DCD 4007
Delos / '88 / Conifer.

HARD CHAMPION
CD _____ K32Y 6209
Electric Bird / Sep '88 / New Note.

HARD DRIVE, THE (Blakey, Art & The Jazz Messengers)
CD _____ CDCD 1095
Charly / Jun '93 / Charly / THE / Cadillac.

I GET A KICK OUT OF BU (Blakey, Art & The Jazz Messengers)
CD _____ 1211552
Soul Note / Nov '90 / Harmonia Mundi / Wellard / Cadillac.

IN SWEDEN (Blakey, Art & The Jazz Messengers)
Webb City / How deep is the ocean / Skylark / Gypsy folk tales
CD _____ ECD 22044
Evidence / Mar '93 / Harmonia Mundi / ADA / Cadillac.

JAZZ MESSENGER (Blakey, Art & Thelonious Monk)
Evidence / In walked Bud / Blue monk / I mean you / Rhythm a ning / Purple shades
CD _____ 756781332-2
Atlantic / Mar '93 / Warner Music.

JAZZ MESSENGERS (Blakey, Art & The Jazz Messengers)
Sacrifice / Cubano chant / Oscalypso / Nica's tempo / D's dilemma / Just for Marty
CD _____ 4809882
Sony Jazz / Dec '95 / Sony.

KEYSTONE 3 (Blakey, Art & The Jazz Messengers)
When it's sleepy time down South / When my sugar walks down the street / When I fall in love / As long as I live / America the beautiful / Louisiana / High society / I'll be with you in apple blossom time / I ain't got nobody / This is all I ask
CD _____ CCD 4196
Concord Jazz / Mar '90 / New Note.

KYOTO
CD _____ OJCCD 145
Original Jazz Classics / Feb '92 / Wellard / Jazz Music / Cadillac / Complete/Pinnacle.

LAUSANNE 1960, PART 1 (Blakey, Art & The Jazz Messengers)
Now's the time / Announcement / Lester left town / Noise in the attic / Dat dere / Kozo's waltz
CD _____ TCB 02022
TCB / Jul '95 / New Note.

LIVE AT BUBBA'S
Moanin' / My funny valentine / Soulful Mister Timmons / Au privave / Free for all
CD _____ CDGATE 7003
Kingdom Jazz / Oct '90 / Kingdom.

LIVE AT RONNIE SCOTT'S
On the ginza / Dr. Jekyll / Two of a kind / I want to talk about you
CD _____ CLACD 332
Castle / '93 / BMG.

LIVE IN EUROPE 1959 (Blakey, Art & The Jazz Messengers)
CD _____ LS 2916
Landscape / Nov '92 / THE.

LIVE IN STOCKHOLM 1959
CD _____ DRGCD 182
Dragon / Oct '88 / Roots / Cadillac / Wellard / CM / ADA.

MASTER OF DRUMS
CD _____ 722013
Scorpio / Sep '92 / Complete/Pinnacle.

MELLOW BLUES (Blakey, Art & The Jazz Messengers)
CD _____ MCD 0322
Moon / Jan '92 / Harmonia Mundi / Cadillac.

MIDNIGHT SESSION (Blakey, Art & The Jazz Messengers)
Casino / Biddle griddies / Potpourri / Ugh / Mirage / Reflections of Buhainia
CD _____ SV 0145
Savoy Jazz / Apr '93 / Conifer / ADA.

MIRAGE (Blakey, Art & The Jazz Messengers)
CD _____ VGCD 660130
Vogue / Jan '93 / BMG.

MOANIN' (Blakey, Art & The Jazz Messengers)
Moanin' / Moanin' (alt. take) / Are you real / Along came Betty / Drum thunder suite / Blues march / Come rain or come shine / Slide's delight / You don't know what love is / Blues for Eros / Moanin / Blue moon / Theme song
CD _____ CDP 7465162
Blue Note / Mar '95 / EMI.

NEW YEAR'S EVE AT SWEET BASIL (Blakey, Art & The Jazz Messengers)
Hide and seek / Little man / New York / I want to talk about you
CD _____ K32Y 6079
King/Paddle Wheel / Oct '87 / New Note.

NEW YORK SCENE
Oh by the way / It's easy to remember / Who cares / Controversy / Tenderly / Falafel
CD _____ CCD 4256
Concord Jazz / Sep '86 / New Note.

NIGHT IN TUNISIA, A (Blakey, Art & The Jazz Messengers)
Night in Tunisia / Sincerely Diana / So tired / Yama / Kozo's waltz
CD _____ BNZ 6
Blue Note / May '87 / EMI.

OH BY THE WAY (Blakey, Art & The Jazz Messengers)
Oh by the way / Duck soup / Tropical breeze / One by one / Sudan blue / My funny valentine / Alicia
CD _____ CDSJP 165
Timeless Jazz / Feb '92 / New Note.

ORIGINALLY (Blakey, Art & The Jazz Messengers)
CD _____ 4718722
Sony Jazz / Jan '95 / Sony.

PARIS 1958
CD _____ 74321101522
Bluebird / Jul '92 / BMG.

PARIS JAM SESSION (Blakey, Art & The Jazz Messengers)
Dance of the infidels / Bouncing with Bud / Midget / Night in Tunisia
CD _____ 8326922
Fontana / Mar '88 / PolyGram.

STANDARDS
CD _____ 292E6026
King/Paddle Wheel / Nov '89 / New Note.

STRAIGHT AHEAD
Falling in love with love / My romance / Webb City / How deep is the ocean / E.T.A. / Theme
CD _____ CCD 4168
Concord Jazz / Oct '90 / New Note.

UGETSU
One by one / Ugetsu / Time off / Ping pong / I didn't know what time it was / On the ginza
CD _____ OJCCD 090
Original Jazz Classics / Feb '92 / Wellard / Jazz Music / Cadillac / Complete/Pinnacle.

Blakey, Rev. Johnny

1927-1929 (Blakey, Rev. Johnny & Rev. M.L. Gipson)
CD _____ DOCD 5363
Document / Jul '95 / Jazz Music / Hot Shot / ADA.

Blameless

SIGNS WERE ALL THERE
CD _____ WOLCD 1059
China / Mar '95 / Pinnacle.

Blanca, Peres

STRICTLY DANCING: RHUMBA (Blanca, Peres Band)
CD _____ 15338
Laserlight / May '94 / Target/BMG.

Blanchard, Terence

BILLIE HOLIDAY SONGBOOK, THE
Detour ahead / Nice work if you can get it / Solitude / What a little moonlight can do / Good morning heartache / I cried for you / Don't explain / Fine and mellow / I cover the waterfront / Left alone / Strange fruit / Lady sings the blues
CD _____ 475926 2
Columbia / Apr '94 / Sony.

BLANCHARD, TERENCE

DISCERNMENT (Blanchard, Terence & Donald Harrison)
Worth the pain / When the saints go marching in / When I fall in love / Directions / Discernment / Are you sleeping / Akira / Dorchester House
CD _____ CCD 43008
Concord Jazz / Jan '86 / New Note.

MALCOLM X JAZZ SUITE
CD _____ 4736762
Sony Jazz / Jan '95 / Sony.

NEW YORK SECOND LINE (Blanchard, Terence & Donald Harrison)
New York second line / Oliver Twist / I can't get started (with you) / Duck steps / Dr. Drums / Isn't it so / Subterfuge
CD _____ CCD 43002
Concord Jazz / '88 / New Note.

ROMANTIC DEFIANCE
Premise / Unconditional / Betrayal of my soul / Divine order / Romantic defiance / Focus / Romantic processional / Morning after / Celebration
CD _____ 4804892
Sony Jazz / Jun '95 / Sony.

TERENCE BLANCHARD
Motherless child / Wandering wonder / Tomorrow's just a luxury / Goodbye / Au privave / Sing soweto / I'm getting sentimental over you / Azania / Amazing grace
CD _____ 468388 2
Columbia / Jan '95 / Sony.

Blancmange

HEAVEN KNOWS
Blind vision / Heaven knows where heaven is / I can see it / What's your problem / Feel me / Sad day / Living on the ceiling / Don't tell me / I've seen the word / Running thin / Waves / That's love / Blind vision / That's love / Why can't they leave things alone / Day before you came / God's kitchen
CD _____ ELITE 024CDP
Carlton Home Entertainment / Aug '93 / Carlton Home Entertainment.

SECOND HELPINGS (Best of Blancmange)
God's kitchen / I've seen the world / Feel me / Living on the ceiling / Waves / Game above my head / Blind vision / That's love that it is / Don't tell me / Day before you came / What's your problem
CD _____ 8280432
London / Jun '90 / PolyGram.

THIRD COURSE, THE
Feel me / I've seen the world / God's kitchen / I can't explain / Waves / Lose your love / No wonder they never made it back / Day before you came / All things are nice / Running thin / Game above my head / Wasted / Get out of that / Lorraine's my nurse
CD _____ 5501942
Spectrum/Karussell / Mar '94 / PolyGram / THE.

Bland, Bobby

BLUES IN THE NIGHT
Blue moon / If I hadn't called you back / Ask me 'bout nothin' (but the blues) / Jelly jelly / When you put me down / Blind man / Chains of love / Fever / Blues in the night / Loneliness hurts / Feeling is gone / I'm too far gone (to turn around) / Black night / Share your love with me
CD _____ CD 14531
Jazz Portraits / Jan '94 / Jazz Music.

CALIFORNIA ALBUM
This time I'm gone for good / Up and down world / It's not the spotlight / If loving you is wrong / I don't want to be right / Going down slow / Right place at the right time / Help me through the day / Where baby went / Friday the 13th child / I've got to use my imagination
CD _____ BGOCD 64
Beat Goes On / Jan '90 / Pinnacle.

DREAMER
Ain't no love in the heart of the city / I wouldn't treat a dog (the way you treated me) / Lovin' on borrowed time / End of the road / I ain't gonna be the first to cry / Dreamer / Yolanda / Twenty four hour blues / Cold day in hell / Who's foolin' who
CD _____ BGOCD 63
Beat Goes On / Oct '89 / Pinnacle.

LIVE AT LONG BEACH
CD _____ CDBL 750
Charly / Nov '94 / Charly / THE / Cadillac.

MASTER OF THE BLUES
CD _____ NTRCD 025
Nectar / Jun '94 / Pinnacle.

TOGETHER AGAIN - LIVE (Bland, Bobby & B.B. King)
Let the good times roll / Strange things happen / Feel so bad / Mother in law blues / Mean old world / Everyday I have the blues / Thrill is gone / I ain't gonna be the first to cry
CD _____ BGOCD 162
Beat Goes On / Feb '93 / Pinnacle.

TWO STEPS FROM THE BLUES
Cry cry cry / Two steps from the blues / I pity the fool / I'll take care of you / I'm not

ashamed / Don't cry no more / Lead me on / I've just got to forget you / Little boy blue / St. James infirmary
CD _____ BGOCD 163
Beat Goes On / Feb '93 / Pinnacle.

VOICE, THE
Who will the next fool be / I pity the fool / Don't cry no more / Ain't that lovin' you / I'm not ashamed / Cry cry cry / I'll take care of you / Call on me / Blue moon / Turn on your love light / Stormy Monday blues / Two steps from the blues / Ain't nothin' you can do / Ain't doing too bad Part 1 / Sometimes you gotta cry a little / Ain't no tellin' / Yield not to temptation / I'm too far gone (to turn around) / These hands (small but mighty) / Good time Charlie Part 1 / Ask me 'bout nothin' (but the blues) / Share your love with me / That did it / Shoes / Back in the same old bag again / Chains of love
CD _____ CHCD 323
Ace / Nov '93 / Pinnacle / Cadillac / Complete/Pinnacle.

Blanston, Gern

GERN BLANSTON
CD _____ CSR 014CD
Cavity Search / Oct '95 / Plastic Head.

Blasnost

BLASNOST
CD _____ BEST 1023CD
Acoustic Music / Nov '93 / ADA.

Blast

POWER OF EXPRESSION, THE
CD _____ SST 148 CD
SST / May '93 / Plastic Head.

TAKE THE MANIC RIDE
CD _____ SST 225 CD
SST / May '93 / Plastic Head.

Blast Off Country Style

C'MON AND ...
CD _____ TEENBEAT 131CD
Teenbeat / Mar '94 / SRD.

Blazers

EAST SIDE SOUL
CD _____ ROUCD 9053
Rounder / Jul '95 / CM / Direct / ADA / Cadillac.

SHORT FUSE
CD _____ ROU 9043CD
Rounder / Apr '94 / CM / Direct / ADA / Cadillac.

Blazing Redheads

BLAZING REDHEADS
Paradise drive / Cienega / Sea level / in search of... / Cha cha slippers / February song / Santa Fe / Get down (and stay down) / Final segment / Mozambo / Street dreamin' / My Picasso
CD _____ RR 26CD
Reference Recordings / Sep '91 / May Audio.

CRAZED WOMEN
CD _____ RR 41CD
Reference Recordings / Sep '91 / May Audio.

Bleachbath

BLEACHBATH
CD _____ VIRION 102
Sound Virus / Sep '94 / Plastic Head.

Bleed

GOOD TIMES ARE KILLING ME, THE
CD _____ BLEED 6CD
Bleed / Jul '95.

Bleedin' Hearts

SECONDS TO GO
CD _____ CSCCD 1003
CRS / Sep '95 / Direct / ADA.

Bleep & Booster

WORLD OF BLEEP & BOOSTER
Technotropolis / Sexy / Electro city / Genk / Find the light / Boosterdrome / Glock / Amber to atoms / Wonder of the world / Piano 1
CD _____ 828511-2
London / Sep '94 / PolyGram.

Blegvad, Peter

DOWNTIME
CD _____ RERPBCD 34
Recommended / Jul '88 / These / ReR Megacorp.

NAKED SHAKESPEARE, THE
How beautiful you are / Karen / Lonely too / First blow struck / Weird monkeys / Naked Shakespeare / Irma / Like a baby / Powers in the air / You can't miss it / Vermont / Blue eyed William
CD _____ CDV 2284
Virgin / Jun '91 / EMI.

Bleiming, Christian

JIVIN' TIME
CD _____ BEST 1010CD
Acoustic Music / Nov '93 / ADA.

Bleizi Ruz

MUSIQUES & DANSES DE BRETAGNE
CD _____ PL 3355/65CD
Diffusion Breizh / Jun '94 / ADA.

Blender, Everton

LIFT UP YOUR HEAD
CD _____ CDHB 169
Heartbeat / Jan '95 / Greensleeves / Jetstar / Direct / ADA.

Blenner, Serge

VISION ET POESIE
CD _____ SKYCD 8703053
Sky / Sep '95 / Koch.

Blessed Ethel

WELCOME TO THE RODEO
CD _____ 2DMCD 012
2 Damn Loud / Nov '95 / Pinnacle.

Blessed Rain

WHERE WILL YOU BE
CD _____ UGCD 5505
Unique Gravity / Oct '95 / Pinnacle / ADA.

Blessid Union Of Souls

HOME
I believe / Let me be the one / All along / Oh Virginia / Nora / Would you be there / Home / End of the world / Heaven / Forever for tonight / Lucky to be here
CD _____ CDEMC 3708
EMI / Jun '95 / EMI.

Bley, Carla

BIG BAND THEORY
On the stage in cages / Birds of paradise / Goodbye pork pie hat / Fresh impression
CD _____ 5199662
Watt / Oct '93 / New Note.

DUETS (Bley, Carla & Steve Swallow/ Andy Sheppard)
Baby baby / Walking batteriewoman / Utviklingssang / Ladies in Mercedes / Romantic notions / Remember / Ups and downs / Reactionary tango parts 1/2/3 / Soon I will be done with the troubles of this world (CD only)
CD _____ 8373452
ECM / Nov '88 / New Note.

ESCALATOR OVER THE HILL
CD Set _____ 8393102
ECM / Jan '90 / New Note.

EUROPEAN TOUR 1977
CD _____ 8318302
ECM / Jul '87 / New Note.

FLEUR CARNIVORE
CD _____ 8396622
Watt / Nov '89 / New Note.

GO TOGETHER (Bley, Carla & Steve Swallow/Andy Sheppard)
Sing me softly of the blues / Mother of the dead man / Masquerade / Ad infinitum / Copyright royalties / Peau douce / Doctor / Fleur carnivor
CD _____ 5176732
Watt / May '93 / New Note.

LIVE: CARLA BLEY
Blunt object / Lord is listenin' to ya, hallelujah / Time and us / Still in the room / Real life hits / Song sung long
CD _____ 8157302
ECM / Feb '86 / New Note.

MUSIQUE MECANIQUE
CD _____ 8393132
ECM / Sep '89 / New Note.

NIGHT-GLO
Pretend you're in love / Night-glo / Rut / Crazy with you / Wildlife (Horn-paws with out claws - sex with birds)
CD _____ 8276402
ECM / Dec '85 / New Note.

SEXTET
More Brahms / Houses and people / Girl who cried champagne / Brooklyn Bridge / Lawns / Healing power
CD _____ 8316972
ECM / Apr '87 / New Note.

SOCIAL STUDIES
CD _____ 8318312
ECM / Jul '87 / New Note.

SONGS WITH LEGS (Bley, Carla & Steve Swallow/Andy Sheppard)
Real life hits / Lord is listenin' to ya, hallelujah / Chicken / Misterioso / Wrong key donkey / Crazy with you
CD _____ 5270692
Watt / Feb '95 / New Note.

VERY BIG CARLA BLEY BAND, THE
United States / Strange arrangements / All fall down / Who will rescue you / Lo ultimo

CD _____ 8479422
Watt / Jul '92 / New Note.

Bley, Paul

ALONE AGAIN
CD _____ 1238402
IAI / May '94 / Harmonia Mundi / Cadillac.

ANNETTE (Bley, Paul/Various Artists)
CD _____ ARTCD 6118
Hat Art / Nov '92 / Harmonia Mundi / ADA / Cadillac.

AXIS
CD _____ 1238532
IAI / Jan '93 / Harmonia Mundi / Cadillac.

BLUES FOR RED
CD _____ 123238-2
Red / Mar '91 / Harmonia Mundi / Jazz Horizons / Cadillac / ADA.

CHANGING HANDS
CD _____ JUST 402
Justin Time / Jul '92 / Harmonia Mundi / Cadillac.

FABULOUS PAUL BLEY QUINTET, THE (Fabulous Paul Bley Quintet)
CD _____ 500542
Musidisc / Jan '94 / Vital / Harmonia Mundi / ADA / Cadillac / Discovery.

FOOTLOOSE
When will the blues leave / Floater / Turns / Around again / Syndrome / Cousins / King korn / Vashikar
CD _____ CY 78987
Savoy Jazz / Nov '95 / Conifer / ADA.

FRAGMENTS
CD _____ 8292802
ECM / Sep '86 / New Note.

IN A ROW
CD _____ ARTCD 6081
Hat Art / Aug '91 / Harmonia Mundi / ADA / Cadillac.

IN THE EVENINGS OUT THERE
Afterthoughts / Portrait of a silence / Soft touch / Speak easy / Interface / Allignment / Fair share / Article four / Married alive / Spe-cul-lay-ting / Tomorrow today / Note police
CD _____ 5174692
ECM / Sep '93 / New Note.

JAPAN SUITE
CD _____ 123849-2
IAI / Sep '92 / Harmonia Mundi / Cadillac.

LIVE AGAIN
CD _____ SCCD 31230
Steeplechase / Jul '88 / Impetus.

LIVE AT SWEET BASIL (Bley, Paul Group)
CD _____ 121235-2
Soul Note / Jun '91 / Harmonia Mundi / Wellard / Cadillac.

MEMOIRS (Bley, Paul, Charlie Haden & Paul Motian)
CD _____ 121240-2
Soul Note / May '92 / Harmonia Mundi / Wellard / Cadillac.

OPEN TO LOVE
Closer / Ida Lupino / Open to love / Started / Harlem / Seven / Nothing ever was anyway
CD _____ 8277512
ECM / May '87 / New Note.

OUTSIDE IN (Bley, Paul & Sonny Greenwich)
CD _____ JUST 692
Justin Time / Apr '95 / Harmonia Mundi / Cadillac.

PAUL BLEY QUARTET (Bley, Paul Quartet)
CD _____ 8352402
ECM / May '88 / New Note.

PAUL BLEY WITH GARY PEACOCK (Bley, Paul Trio)
Blues / Getting started / When will the blues leave / Long ago and far away / Moor / Gary / Big Foot / Albert's love theme
CD _____ 8431622
ECM / Oct '90 / New Note.

PAUL BLEY, NIELS HENNING, ORSTED PEDERSON (Bley, Paul, Niels Henning & Orsted Pederson)
CD _____ SCCD 31005
Steeplechase / Nov '90 / Impetus.

SWEET TIME
CD _____ JUST 56
Justin Time / Oct '94 / Harmonia Mundi / Cadillac.

TIME WILL TELL (Bley, Paul, Evan Parker & Barre Philips)
Poetic justice / Time will tell / Above the fenceline / You will, Oscar, you will / Sprung / No questions / Vine laces / Clawback / Testimony / Instance / Burlesque
CD _____ 5238192
ECM / Feb '95 / New Note.

TOUCHING
CD _____ BLCD 760195
Black Lion / Jun '94 / Jazz Music / Cadillac / Wellard / Koch.

Blige, Mary J.

MY LIFE
Intro / Mary Jane / You bring me joy / Marvin interlude / I'm the only woman / K. Murray interlude / My life / You gotta believe / I never wanna live without you / I'm going down / My life interlude / Be with you / Mary's joint / Don't go / I love you / No one else / Be happy / (You make me feel like a) Natural woman (MCD 11398 & MCC 11398 only.)
CD _____ MCD 11398
MCA / Jan '96 / BMG.

WHAT'S THE 411 - REMIX
Leave a message / You don't have to worry / My love / Real love / What's the 411 / Reminisce / Mary and Andre / Sweet thing / Love no limit / You remind me / Changes / I've been going through / I don't want to do anything
CD _____ MCD 10942
MCA / Dec '93 / BMG.

Blind Blake

BLIND BLAKE VOL.1
CD _____ DOCD 5024
Blues Document / Nov '93 / Swift / Jazz Music / Hot Shot.

Blind Guardian

BATTALIONS OF FEAR
CD _____ 859810
SPV / Sep '89 / Plastic Head.

Blind Idiot God

BLIND IDIOT GOD
CD _____ SST 104 CD
SST / May '93 / Plastic Head.

UNDERTOW
CD _____ EMY 1072
Enemy / Sep '92 / Grapevine.

Blind Illusion

SANE ASYLUM, THE
Sane asylum / Vengeance is mine / Kamikaze / Vicious vision / Bloodshower / Death noise / Smash the crystal / Metamorphosis of a monster
CD _____ CDFLAG 18
Under One Flag / Mar '88 / Pinnacle.

Blind Melon

BLIND MELON
Soak the sin / Tones of home / Ronettes / Paper scratcher / Dear ol' dad / Change / No rain / Deserted / Sleepyhouse / Holy man / Seed to a tree / Drive / Time
CD _____ CDEST 2188
Capitol / Mar '93 / EMI.

SOUP
Galaxie / Two times four / Vernie / Skinned / Toes across the floor / Walk / Dumptruck / Car seat (God's presents) / Wilt / Duke / St. Andrew's fall / New life / Mouthful of cavities / Lemonade
CD _____ CDEST 2261
Capitol / Aug '95 / EMI.

Blind Mr. Jones

STEREO MUSICALE
Sisters / Spooky Vibes / Regular Disease / Small caravan / Flying With Lux / Henna And Swayed / Lonesome Boatman / Unforgettable Waltz / Going on cold / Spook Easy / One Watt Above darkness / Dolores / Against The Glass
CD _____ CDBRED 100
Cherry Red / Oct '92 / Pinnacle.

TATOOINE
Hey / Disneyworld / Viva fisher / See you again / Big plane / Drop for days / Surfer baby / Please me / What's going on / Mesa
CD _____ CDBRED 113
Cherry Red / May '94 / Pinnacle.

Blink

MAP OF THE UNIVERSE, A
It's not my fault / Cello (Album mix) / Happy day / Everything comes, everything goes / Snow (Be precious) / Fundamentally lovable creature / Love me / Greatest trick / Going to Nepal / There's something wrong with Norman's mom / Christmas 22 / Is God really groovy / Separation
CD _____ CDPCS 7369
Parlophone / Aug '94 / EMI.

Blissed

RITE OF PASSAGE
CD _____ PODCD 029
Pod Communication / Aug '95 / Plastic Head.

Blitz

BEST OF BLITZ
Attack / Fight to live / Forty five revolutions / Never surrender / Razors in the night / Voice of a generation / Nation on fire / Youth / Warriors / Bleed / New age / Fatigue / Suf-

fragette city / Overdrive / Those days / Killing dream / Walkaway
CD _____ DOJOCD 123
Dojo / Mar '93 / BMG.

BLITZED ON ALL OUT ATTACK
Warriors (Alternative Version) / 4Q (demo) / Time bomb (Demo) / Criminal damage (Demo) / Razors in the night (Live) / Attack (Live) / Escape (Live) / Never surrender (Live) / Nation on fire (Live) / Warriors (Live) / Someone's gonna die (Live) / Forty five revolutions (Live) / Fight to live (Live) / Youth (Live) / I don't need you (Demo) / Propaganda (Demo) / Closedown (Demo) / Your revolution (Demo) / New age (Live) / Bleed (Live) / Caberet (Live) / Vicious (Live) / Escape (demo) / Youth (demo) / Bleed (demo) / Crimianl damage (Demo)
CD _____ DOJOCD 93
Dojo / Apr '93 / BMG.

COMPLETE BLITZ SINGLES COLLECTION
Someone's gonna die / Attack / Fight to live / Forty five revolutions / Never surrender / Razors in the night / Voice of a generation / Warriors / Youth (Alt. Take) / New age / Fatigue / Bleed (Remix) / Telecommunication / Teletron / Solar (Extended Mix) / Youth
CD _____ CDPUNK 25
Anagram / Dec '93 / Pinnacle.

VOICE OF A GENERATION
Warriors / Propaganda / Time bomb / Criminal damage / Fuck you / We are the boys / Bleed / I don't need you / Your revolution / Moscow / Voice of a generation / T.O. / Vicious / Nation on fire / Scream / 4Q / Escape / Closedown
CD _____ CDPUNK 1
No Future / Apr '92 / Pinnacle.

Blitz Babes

ON THE LINE
CD _____ SPENTUNIT 002CD
Spentunit / Aug '95 / Plastic Head.

Blitzkrieg

TIME OF CHANGES, A
Ragnarok / Inferno / Blitzkrieg / Pull the trigger / Armageddon / Hell to pay / Vikings / Time of changes / Saviour
CD _____ CLACD 268
Castle / '92 / BMG.

UNHOLY TRINITY
CD _____ NM 002CD
Neat / Nov '95 / Plastic Head.

Blizard, Ralph

SOUTHERN RAMBLE
CD _____ ROUCD 0352
Rounder / Aug '95 / CM / Direct / ADA / Cadillac.

Block

MEAN MACHINE
CD _____ CDZOT 101
Zoth Ommog / Nov '93 / Plastic Head.

Block, Rory

ANGEL OF MERCY
CD _____ NET 47CD
Munich / Apr '94 / CM / ADA / Greensleeves / Direct.

HOUSE OF HEARTS
CD _____ CD 3104
Rounder / '88 / CM / Direct / ADA / Cadillac.

I'VE GOT A ROCK IN MY SOCK
CD _____ CD 3097
Rounder / '88 / CM / Direct / ADA / Cadillac.

TURNING POINT
Turning point / Holdin' on / Far away / All of my life / Spiderboy / Gedachentrein / All as one / Heather's song / Old times are gone / Leavin' here / Down the highway / Tomorrow
CD _____ MRCD 145
Munich / Aug '94 / CM / ADA / Greensleeves / Direct.

WHEN A WOMAN GETS THE BLUES
CD _____ ROUCD 3139
Rounder / Apr '95 / CM / Direct / ADA / Cadillac.

WOMEN IN (E)MOTION FESTIVAL
CD _____ T&M 107
Tradition & Moderne / Jan '95 / Direct / ADA.

Blodwyn Pig

AHEAD RINGS OUT
It's only love / Sing me a song that I know / Up and coming / Change song / Dear Jill / Modern alchemist / Leave it with me / Ain't ya coming home, babe
CD _____ BGOCD 54
Beat Goes On / Aug '94 / Pinnacle.

GETTING TO THIS
Drive me / Variations on Nainos / See my way / Long lamb blues / Squirreling must go on / San Francisco sketches / Beach

scape / Fisherman's wharf / Telegraph hill / Close the door, I'm falling out of the room / Worry / Toys / To Rassman / Send your son to die
CD _____ BGOCD 81
Beat Goes On / Aug '94 / Pinnacle.

Bloedow, Oren

OREN BLOEDOW
CD _____ KFWCD 115
Knitting Factory / Nov '94 / Grapevine.

Blond, Leigh

BLUESNESS
CD _____ MRCD 162
Munich / Jun '92 / CM / ADA / Greensleeves / Direct.

Blonde On Blonde

CONTRASTS
Ride with Captain Max / Spinning wheel / No sleep blues / Goodbye / I need my friend / Mother Earth / All day and all night / Eleanor Rigby / Conversationally making the grade / Regency / Island on an island / Don't be too long / Jeanette Isabella / Country life
CD _____ SEECD 406
See For Miles/C5 / Jul '94 / Pinnacle.

Blondie

AUTOAMERICAN
Europa / Live it up / Here's looking at you / Tide is high / Angels on the balcony / Go through it / Do the dark / Rapture / Faces / T-Birds / Walk like me / Follow me
CD _____ CDCHR 6084
Chrysalis / Sep '94 / EMI.

BEAUTIFUL (The remix album)
Union city blue / Dreaming (mixes) / Rapture / Heart of glass / Sunday girl / Call me / Atomic (mixes) / Tide is high / Hanging on the telephone / Fade away and radiate
CD _____ CDCHR 6105
Chrysalis / Jul '95 / EMI.

BEST OF BLONDIE
Denis / Tide is high / In the flesh / Sunday girl / (I'm always touched by your) presence dear / Dreaming / Hanging on the telephone / Rapture / Picture this / Union city blue / Call me / Atomic / Rip her to shreds / Heart of glass
CD _____ CCD 1371
Chrysalis / Oct '81 / EMI.

BLONDIE
X offender / Rifle range / Look good in blue / In the sun / Shark in Jet's clothing / Man overboard / Rip her to shreds / Little girl lies / In the flesh / Kung fu girls / Attack of the giant ants
CD _____ CDCHR 6081
Chrysalis / Sep '94 / EMI.

BLONDIE AND BEYOND
Underground girl / English boys / Sunday girl (French version) / Susie and Jeffrey / Shayla / Denis / X offender / Poets problem / Scenery / Picture this / Angels on the balcony / Once I had a love / I'm gonna love you too / Island of lost souls / Call me (Spanish version) / Heart of glass (disco version) / Ring of fire (live) / Bang a gong (get it on) (live) / Heroes (live)
CD _____ CDCCHR 6063
Chrysalis / Jan '84 / EMI.

EAT TO THE BEAT
Dreaming / Hardest part / Union city blue / Shayla / Eat to the beat / Accidents never happen / Die young stay pretty / Slow motion / Atomic / Sound asleep / Victor / Living in the real world
CD _____ CPCD 1225
Chrysalis / Nov '92 / EMI.

HUNTER, THE
Orchid club / Island of lost souls / Dragonfly / For your eyes only / Beast / War child / Little Caesar / Danceway / Can I find the right words (to say) / English boys / Hunter gets captured by the game
CD _____ CDCHR 6083
Chrysalis / Sep '94 / EMI.

PARALLEL LINES
Fade away / Hanging on the telephone / One way or another / Picture this / Pretty baby / I know but I don't know / 11.59 / Will anything happen / Sunday girl / Heart of glass / I'm gonna love you too / Just go away
CD _____ CCD 1192
Chrysalis / Jul '94 / EMI.

PLASTIC LETTERS
Fan mail / Denis / Bermuda triangle / Youth nabbed as sniper / Contact in Red Square / (I'm always touched by your) presence dear / I'm on / I didn't have the nerve to say / No Love at the pier / No imagination / Kidnapper / Detroit 442 / Cautious lip
CD _____ CDCHR 6085
Chrysalis / Sep '94 / EMI.

PLATINUM COLLECTION, THE
X offender / In the flesh / Man overboard / Rip her to shreds / Denis / Contact in red square / Kung fu girls / I'm in E / (I'm always touched by your) presence dear / Poets problem / Detroit 442 / Picture this / Fade away and radiate / I'm gonna love you too / Just go away / Hanging on the telephone / Will anything happen / Heart of glass / Rifle range / 11.59 / Sunday girl / I know but I don't know / One way or another / Dreaming / Sound asleep / Living in the real world / Union city blue / Hardest part / Atomic / Die young stay pretty / Slow motion / Call me / Tide is high / Susie and Jeffrey / Rapture / Walk like me / Island of lost souls / Dragon fly / War child / Little Caesar / Out in the streets / Platinum blonde / Thin line / Puerto Rico / Once I had a love / Atomic (remix) / Rapture (remix)
CD Set _____ CDCHR 6089
Chrysalis / Oct '94 / EMI.

LIES
CD _____ CDVEST 12
Bulletproof / May '94 / Pinnacle.

Blondy, Alpha

RASTA POUE
CD _____ 387262
Syllart / Nov '92 / EMI / Sterns.

Blood

METAL CONFLICTS
CD _____ SPV 08412412
SPV / Apr '95 / Plastic Head.

Blood Farmers

SELF TITLED
CD _____ HOO 372
Noise/Modern Music / Apr '95 / Pinnacle / Plastic Head.

Blood Feast

CHOPPING BLOCK BLUES
CD _____ FLAME 1016CD
Flametrader / Nov '90 / Plastic Head.

KILL FOR PLEASURE
CD _____ SHARK 013 CD
Shark / Apr '90 / Plastic Head.

Blood From The Soul

TO SPRITE THE GLAND THAT BREEDS
Painted life / Image and the helpless / On fear and prayer / Guinea pig / Nature's hole / Vascular / To spite / Suspension of my disbelief / Yet to be savoured / Blood from the soul
CD _____ MOSH 089CD
Earache / Oct '93 / Vital.

Blood On The Saddle

FRESH BLOOD
CD _____ ROSE 126CD
New Rose / Sep '87 / Direct / ADA.

Blood, Sweat & Tears

BLOOD, SWEAT & TEARS
Variations on a theme by Satie / Smiling phases / Sometimes in winter / More and more / And when I die / God bless the child / Spinning wheel / You've made me so very happy / Blues
CD _____ BGOCD 28
Beat Goes On / Dec '88 / Pinnacle.

CHILD IS FATHER TO THE MAN
Overture / I love you more than you'll ever know / Morning glory / My days are numbered / Without her / Just one smile / I can't quit her / Meagan's gypsy eyes / Somethin' goin' on / House in the country / Modern adventures of Plato, Diogenes and Freud / So much love / Underture
CD _____ CK 64214
Columbia / Nov '95 / Sony.

COLLECTION
CD _____ CCSCD 379
Castle / Sep '93 / BMG.

SMILING PHASES
Smiling phases / More and more / Fire and rain / Lonesome Suzie / Somethin' comin' on / Cowboys and Indians / High on a mountain / Take me in your arms (rock me a little while) / Down in the flood / Touch me / Alone / Morning glory / Without her / Just one smile / Rollercoaster / Rosemary / Back up against the wall / Velvet
CD _____ ELITE 005CD
Elite/Old Gold / Aug '93 / Carlton Home Entertainment.

WHAT GOES UP (The Best Of Blood, Sweat & Tears/2CD Set)
Refugee from Yuhupitz / I can't quit her / House in the country / I love you more than you'll ever know / You've made me so very happy / More and more / Fire and rain / Sometimes in winter / Smiling phases / Spinning wheel / God bless the child / Children of the wind / Hi de ho / Lucretia / Mac evil / He's a runner / Something's coming on / 40,000 headmen / Go down gamblin' / Mama gets high / Lisa, listen to me / Valentine's day / John the baptist (Holy John) / So long Dixie / Snow queen / Maiden voyage / I can't move to the mountains / Time remembered / Roller coaster / Tell me that I'm wrong / Got to get you into my life / You're the one / Mean ole world (live)

CD Set _____ 4810192
Columbia / Jan '96 / Sony.

Bloodfire Posse

PRIMO
CD _____ RASCD 3108
Ras / Nov '92 / Jetstar / Greensleeves /
SRD / Direct.

Bloodgood

ALL STAND TOGETHER
S.O.S. / All stand together / Escape from
the fire / Say goodbye / Out of love / King-
dom come / Fear no evil / Help me /
Rounded are the rocks / Lies in the dark /
Streelight dance / I want to live in your heart
CD _____ CD 08793
Broken / Jan '92 / Broken.

Bloodlet

ELETIC
CD _____ VR 031CD
Victory Europe / Jan '96 / Plastic Head.

Bloodstar

ANYTIME ANYWHERE
CD _____ RR 90982
Roadrunner / Feb '93 / Pinnacle.

Bloom, Jane Ira

ART & AVIATION
Gateway to progress / Further into the night
/ Hawkin's parallel universe / Straight no
chaser/Miro / Oshumare / Art and aviation /
Most distant galaxy / I believe Anita / Lost
in the stars
CD _____ AJ 0107
Arabesque / Jun '93 / New Note.

Bloom, Luka

ACOUSTIC MOTORBIKE, THE
CD _____ 7599266702
Reprise / Jul '94 / Warner Music.

RIVERSIDE
Delerious / Dreams in America / Gone to
pablo / Man is alive / Irishman in Chinatown
/ Rescue mission / One / Hudson lady / This
is your life / You couldn't have come at a
better time / Hill of Allen
CD _____ 7599260922
Reprise / Feb '90 / Warner Music.

TURF
Cold comfort / True blue / Diamond mountain / Right here, right now / Sunny sailor
boy / Black is the colour of my true love's
hair / To begin to / Freedom song / Holding
back the river / Background noise / Fertile
rock / I did time / Sanctuary
CD _____ 936245608-2
Reprise / Jun '94 / Warner Music.

Bloomfield, Mike

AMERICAN HERO
Hully gully / Wings of an angel / Walking the
floor / Don't you lie to me / Junko partner /
Knockin' myself out / Women lovin' each
other / Cherry red / R.X. for the blues / You
must have Jesus
CD _____ CDBT 009
Thunderbolt / Feb '90 / Magnum Music
Group.

BETWEEN A HARD PLACE AND THE
GROUND
Eyesight to the blind / Linda Lou / Kansas
City blues / At the Darktown strutter's ball /
Mop mop / Call me a dog / I'm glad I'm
jewish / Great gifts from heaven / Lo though
I am with thee / Jockey blues / Between a
hard place and the ground / Uncle Bon's
barrelhouse blues / Wee wee hours / Vamp
in C / One of these days
CD _____ CDTB 076
Thunderbolt / Sep '90 / Magnum Music
Group.

BLUES, GOSPEL & RAGTIME
INSTRUMENTALS
CD _____ SHCD 99007
Shanachie / Mar '94 / Koch / ADA /
Greensleeves.

DON'T SAY THAT I AIN'T YOU MAN
(Essential Blues 1964-1969)
I've got you in the palm of my hand / Last
night / Feel so good / Goin' down slow / I
got my mojo working / Born in Chicago /
Work song / Killing floor / Albert's shuffle /
Stop / Mary Ann / Don't throw your love on
me so strong / Don't think about it baby /
It takes time / Carmelita skiffle
CD _____ 476721 2
Columbia / May '94 / Sony.

I'M WITH YOU ALWAYS
Eyesight to the blind / Frankie and Johnny
/ I'm with you always / Jockey blues / Some
of these days / Don't think about it baby /
Hymn tune / At the Darktown strutter's ball / Stag-
ger Lee / I'm glad I'm Jewish / A flat
boogaloo
CD _____ FIENDCD 92
Demon / Aug '90 / Pinnacle / ADA.

LIVE ADVENTURES OF MIKE
BLOOMFIELD AND AL COOPER
(Bloomfield, Mike & Al Cooper)
Opening speech / 59th Street bridge song
/ I wonder why / Her holy modal highness /
Weight / Mary Ann / Together / That's al-
right / Green onions
CD _____ ED CD 261
Edsel / Apr '88 / Pinnacle / ADA.

Bloss, Rainer

AMPSY
Oracle / From long ago / Energy / Adoring
multitudes / Psyche / I'm the heat / He's an
angel / Who the hell is she / Lights out baby
/ Love is a beginning
CD _____ CDTB 032
Thunderbolt / May '87 / Magnum Music
Group.

DRIVE INN PART 1
CD _____ 710 103
Innovative Communication / Apr '90 /
Magnum Music Group.

DRIVE INN PART 2
CD _____ 710 104
Innovative Communication / Apr '90 /
Magnum Music Group.

Blount, Chris

NEW ORLEANS JAZZ BAND
CD _____ PKCD 031
Arbors Jazz / Oct '94 / Cadillac.

OLD RUGGED CROSS, THE (Blount,
Chris New Orleans Jazz Band)
Mary wore a golden chain / Amazing grace
/ Lord, Lord, Lord / Only a look / Royal tel-
ephone / Old rugged cross / In the sweet
bye and bye / Hands of God / Lead me sav-
iour / It is no secret / Walking with the king
/ Evening prayer / Yes Lord I'm crippled /
His eye is on the sparrow / End of a perfect
day
CD _____ LACD 16
Lake / Nov '93 / Target/BMG / Jazz Music
/ Direct / Cadillac / ADA.

Blow

FLESHMACHINE
CD _____ PA 04CD
Soliellmoon Recordings / Mar '95 / Plastic
Head.

Blow Monkeys

BEST OF THE BLOW MONKEYS, THE
Man from Russia / He's shedding skin /
Atomic lullaby / Aeroplane city love song /
Forbidden fruit / Waiting for Mr Moonlight /
Wildflower / I nearly died laughing / It's not
unusual / Animal magic / Professor super
cool / Limping for a generation / Sweet mur-
der / Get it on
CD _____ 74321183262
Ariola Express / Feb '94 / BMG.

CHOICES (The Singles Connection)
Wait / Choice / Slaves no more / Celebrate
the day (after you) / Wicked ways / Diggin'
your scene / It doesn't have to be this way
/ Out with her / This is your life / It pays to
belong / Wait (2) (Not on LP) / Choice (2)
(Not on LP) / Man from Russia (CD only) /
Atomic lullaby (CD only) / Wildflower / For-
bidden fruit
CD _____ 7432113707-2
RCA / Apr '93 / BMG.

Blowzabella

BEST OF BLOWZABELLA
CD _____ OSMOCD 001
Osmosys / May '95 / Direct / ADA.

RICHER DUST, A
CD _____ PLCD 080
Plant Life / '88 / Soundalive / ADA /
Symposium.

VANILLA
CD _____ GLCD 3050
Green Linnet / Feb '95 / Roots / CM /
Direct / ADA.

WALL OF SOUND
CD _____ OSMOCD 005
Osmosys / Feb '96 / Direct / ADA.

Blue

RESISTANCE
Diamandra / Doctor / External / Black stone
/ Circle line / Division dub / Still moving /
Golden / Prisoner
CD _____ SOP 004CD
Sabres Of Paradise / Apr '95 / Vital.

Blue 101

FROZENLAND
CD _____ OOR 19CD
Out Of Romford / Jun '95 / Pinnacle /
SRD.

Blue Aeroplanes

FRIENDLOVERPLANE
CD _____ FIRE 33015
Fire / Oct '91 / Disc.

LIFE MODEL
CD _____ BBQCD 143
Beggars Banquet / Feb '94 / Warner
Music / Disc.

ROUGH MUSIC
CD _____ BBQCD 167
Beggars Banquet / Jan '95 / Warner
Music / Disc.

SPITTING OUT MIRACLES
CD _____ FIRE 33010
Fire / Oct '91 / Disc.

TOLERANCE
CD _____ FIRE 33003
Fire / Oct '91 / Disc.

Blue, Barry

VERY BEST OF BARRY BLUE, THE
CD _____ MCCD 103
MCI / May '93 / Disc / THE.

Blue Blood

BIG NOISE, THE
CD _____ CDMFN 93
Music For Nations / Oct '89 / Pinnacle.

UNIVERSAL LANGUAGE
CD _____ MFNCD 112
Music For Nations / Apr '91 / Pinnacle.

Blue Box

CAPTURED DANCE FLOOR
CD _____ 888 801
Tiptoe / Nov '89 / New Note.

Blue, Buddy

DIVE BAR CASANOVAS (Blue, Buddy
Band)
Right cross, left hook / I get a chill / Baby's
git the blues / Kill the dutchman / Boys from
syracuse / Check that chicken / It should
have been me / Nobody / Frim fram froo /
Bump Miss Suzie / Going down town
CD _____ FIENDCD 749
Demon / Feb '94 / Pinnacle / ADA.

Blue Caps

LEGENDARY BLUE CAPS, THE
Wrapped up in rockabilly / Baby blue / Yes
I love you baby / I got a baby / Blue cap
man / I lost an angel / Silly song / Lotta
lovin' / Say Mama / Down at the in den /
Dance to the bop / Johnny's boogie / Be
bop a Lula / Rap / Unchained melody / Jealous heart / September in the rain / Am I that
easy to forget / Jezebel / I dreamed of an
old love affair
CD _____ CDMF 089
Magnum Force / Jun '93 / Magnum Music
Group.

Blue Cats

TUNNEL, THE
CD _____ NERCD 069
Nervous / Sep '92 / Nervous / Magnum
Music Group.

Blue Cheer

BLITZKRIEG OVER NUREMBERG
Babylon / Girl next door / Ride with me /
Just a little bit / Summertime blues / Out of
focus / Doctor please / Hunter
CD _____ CDTB 091
Thunderbolt / Sep '90 / Magnum Music
Group.

HIGHLIGHTS AND LOWLIVES
Urban soldiers / Hunter of love / Girl from
London / Blues steel dues / Big trouble in
paradise / Flight of the enola gray / Hoochie
coochie man / Down and dirty
CD _____ CDTB 125
Thunderbolt / Jun '91 / Magnum Music
Group.

Blue, David

STORIES
CD _____ LECD 901059
Line / Mar '92 / CM / Grapevine / ADA /
Conifer / Direct.

Blue Dog

WHAT IS ANYTHING
CD _____ KFWCD 152
Knitting Factory / Feb '95 / Grapevine.

Blue Environment

ECHOSPACE
CD _____ AQDCD 002
Aquadar / Jul '95 / SRD.

SEA, SPACE, OCEAN
CD _____ AQUADAR 1CD
Aquadar / Sep '94 / SRD.

Blue For Two

SEARCH AND ENJOY
CD _____ RA 91392
Roadrunner / Sep '92 / Pinnacle.

Blue Hawaiians

CHRISTMAS ON BIG ISLAND
Christmas time is here / Jingle jangle /
White Christmas / Jungle bells / Blue
Christmas / Christmas on Big Island / Have
yourself a quiet little Christmas / Mele Ka-
likmaka / We four kings (little drummer boy)
/ Enchanted Xmas
CD _____ 7729212
Restless / Nov '95 / Vital.

Blue Hearts

HEART'S ABOUT TO BREAK
CD _____ 3 BC
Big Cactus / Nov '95 / Direct / ADA.

Blue Humans

CLEAR TO HIGHER TIME (Blue Humans
& Rudolph Grey)
CD _____ NAR 077 CD
New Alliance / May '93 / Pinnacle.

Blue Magic

BLUE MAGIC
Sideshow / Look me up / What's come over
me / Just don't want to be lonely / Stop to
start / Welcome to the club / Spell / Answer
to my prayer / Tear it down
CD _____ 7567804132
Atlantic / Jan '96 / Warner Music.

Blue Mink

VERY BEST OF BLUE MINK
CD _____ MCCD 117
Music Club / Aug '93 / Disc / THE / CM.

Blue Mountain Panpipe...

CHRISTMAS PANPIPE FAVOURITES
(Blue Mountain Panpipe Ensemble)
Little drummer boy / Christmas song / We
three kings / Stop the cavalry / I saw three
ships / Jingle bells / Mistletoe and wine /
Sleigh ride / Have yourself a merry little
Christmas / Good King Wenceslas / Silent
night / When a child is born / Deck the halls
/ Little donkey / Winter wonderland / Silver
bells / Jolly old St. Nicholas / Let it snow,
let it snow, let it snow / Happy holiday /
White Christmas
CD _____ CDMFP 6179
Music For Pleasure / Nov '95 / EMI.

PAN PIPE LOVE SONGS (Blue Mountain
Panpipe Ensemble)
Without you / To much love will kill you /
Sometimes when we touch / Lady in red /
When I fall in love / Whole new world / I'm
not in love / Get here / Love us all around /
You need me / Always on my mind / Wind
beneath my wings / Love lifted me / Power
of love / On the wings of love / I must have
been love / Greatest love of all / Everything
I do (I do it for you) / Secret love
CD _____ CDMFP 6169
Music For Pleasure / Jun '95 / EMI.

PANPIPE FAVOURITES (Blue Mountain
Panpipe Ensemble)
Whiter shade of pale / Live and let die / True
love ways / Spanish eyes / Wichita lineman
/ Wooden heart / When I'm sixty four / Unchained melody / Imagine / All time high /
Save the last dance for me / Help me make
it through the night / Que sera sera / Hey
Jude / Sailing / Silly love songs / Smoke
gets in your eyes / Michelle / Rhinestone
cowboy / Yesterday / And I love you so /
We've only just begun / Unforgettable / I
just called to say I love you / Fool on the
hill / Green green grass of home / Can't help
falling in love / I've never been to me / Let
it be / My guy / Nobody's child / And I love
her / Close to you / Something's gotten
hold of my heart / It's now or never / Mull
of Kintyre / Any dream will do / Wonder of
you / Tears on my pillow / When the girl in
your arms (is the girl in your heart) / Long
and winding road / My way
CD Set _____ CDTRBOX 196
Trio / Sep '95 / EMI.

Blue Nile

HATS
Downtown lights / Over the hillside / Let's
go out tonight / Headlights on the parade /
From a late night train / Seven am / Satur-
day night
CD _____ LKHCD 2
Linn / Apr '92 / PolyGram.

WALK ACROSS THE ROOFTOPS, A
Walk across the rooftops / Tinsel Town in
the rain / From rags to riches / Stay / Easter
parade / Heatwave / Automobile noise
CD _____ LKHCD 1
Linn / '88 / PolyGram.

Blue Note Six

FROM VIENNA WITH SWING
CD _____ JCD 243
Jazzology / Jun '95 / Swift / Jazz Music.

Blue Oyster Cult

AGENTS OF FORTUNE
This ain't the summer of love / True confessions / (Don't fear) the reaper / E.T.I. (Extra

Terrestrial Intelligence) / Revenge of Vera Gemini / Sinful love / Tattoo vampire / Morning final / Tenderloin / Debbie Denise
CD _____ 9827322
Pickwick/Sony Collector's Choice / Mar '94 / Carlton Home Entertainment / Pinnacle / Sony.
CD _____ 4680192
Columbia / Apr '95 / Sony.

CLUB NINJA
White flags / Dancin' in the ruins / Rock not war / Perfect water / Spy in the house of the night / Beat 'em up / When the war comes / Shadow warrior / Madness to the method
CD _____ 982841 2
Pickwick/Sony Collector's Choice / Mar '94 / Carlton Home Entertainment / Pinnacle / Sony.

CULT CLASSICS
(Don't fear) the reaper / E.T.I. (Extra Terresstial Intelligence) / M.E. 262 / This ain't the summer of love / Burning for you / O.D.D On life itself / Flaming telepaths / Godzilla, Astronomy / Cities on flame with rock 'n' roll / Harvester of eyes / Buck's boogie
CD _____ CDFRL 003
Fragile / Oct '94 / Grapevine.

LIVE 1976
Stairway to the stars / Harvester of eyes / Cities on flame / ME262 / Dominance and submission / Astronomy / E.T.I. (Extra Terrestrial Intelligence) / Buck's boogie / This ain't the summer of love / (Don't fear) the reaper
CD _____ CLACD 269
Castle / Oct '91 / BMG.

WORKSHOP OF THE TELESCOPES
(2CD Set)
Cities on flame with rock and roll / Transmaniacon MC / Before the kiss / Redcap / Stairway to the stars / Buck's boogie / Workshop of the telescopes / Red and the black / 7 screaming diz-busters / Career of evil / Flaming telepaths / Astronomy / Subhuman / Harvester of eyes / M.E. 262 / Born to be wild / Don't fear the reaper / This ain't the summer of love / E.T.I. (Extra Terrestrial Intelligence) / Godzilla / Goin' through the motions / Golden age of leather / Kick out the james / We gotta get out of this place / In thee / Marshall plan / Veteran of the psychic wars / Burnin' for you / Dominance and submission / Take me away / Shooting shark / Dancin' in the ruins / Perfect water
CD Set _____ 4809492
Columbia / Jan '96 / Sony.

Blue Pearl

NAKED
Naked in the rain / Down to you / Chemical thing / I never knew / Running up that hill / Chemical thing (ambient mix) (Not on LP) / Little brother / Alive / Rollover / Without love / Over you / Rollover (acapella) (Not on LP)
CD _____ BLRCD 4
Big Life / Dec '90 / Pinnacle.

Blue Pillar Organ

STREET ORGAN FAVOURITES
CD _____ SOW 90135
Sounds Of The World / Jan '95 / Target/BMG.

Blue Rhythm Boys

AT LAST
CD _____ CDWIK 108
Big Beat / Apr '92 / Pinnacle.

Blue Ridge Rangers

BLUE RIDGE RANGERS
Blue Ridge Mountain blues / Somewhere listening (on my name) / You're the reason / Jambalaya / She thinks I still care / California blues / Workin' on a building / Please help me, I'm falling / Have thine own way / I ain't never / Hearts of stone / Today I started loving you again
CD _____ CDFE 506
Fantasy / Oct '87 / Pinnacle / Jazz Music / Wellard / Cadillac.

Blue Rivers

FROM SKA TO REGGAE (Blue Rivers & The Maroons)
CD _____ LG 21078
Lagoon / May '93 / Magnum Music Group / THE.

Blue Sky Boys

IN CONCERT 1964
CD _____ CD 11536
Rounder / CM / Direct / ADA / Cadillac.

Bluebells

BEST OF THE BLUEBELLS
CD _____ 82840522
London / Apr '93 / PolyGram.

YOUNG AT HEART
CD _____ ST 5005
Star Collection / Nov '93 / BMG.

Blueberry Hill

D-DAY FAVOURITES 1944
CD _____ SOW 510
Sound Waves / May '94 / Target/BMG.

IT'S PARTY TIME
CD _____ SOW 520
Sound Waves / May '95 / Target/BMG.

Bluebird Society...

MUSIC OF HIGH SOCIETY (Bluebird Society Orchestra)
CD _____ ST 583
Stash / Jul '94 / Jazz Music / CM / Cadillac / Direct / ADA.

Bluebirds

SWAMP STOMP
CD _____ TX 1012CD
Taxim / Jul '95 / ADA.
CD _____ ICD 9407
Icehouse / Jul '95 / Hot Shot.

Blueboy

IF WISHES WERE HORSES
CD _____ SARAH 612CD
Sarah / Mar '95 / Vital.

UNISEX
So catch him / Cosmopolitan / Marble Arch / Joy of living / Fleetway / Also ran / Boys don't matter / Self portrait / Lazy thunderstorms / Finistere / Always there / Imipramine
CD _____ SARAH 620CD
Sarah / Apr '94 / Vital.

Bluerunners

CHATEAU CHUCK, THE
CD _____ MON 6118CD
Ichiban / Mar '94 / Koch.

Blues & Royals Band

BANDSTAND FAVOURITES
CD _____ MMCD 409
Music Masters / Mar '95 / Target/BMG.

Blues Band

BACK FOR MORE
Normal service / Victim of love / Not me / Blue collar / Can't get my ass in gear / Great crash / When I itches I scratch / Don't buy the potion / Bad boy / Down in the bottom / Leaving
CD _____ COBM 6
Cobalt / Sep '95 / Grapevine.

BRAND LOYALTY
Seemed like a good idea at the time / Rolling log / I want to be loved / Might as well be / What do you want / Big fine girl / Sure feels good / Little baby / Grits ain't groceries / Funny money / Take me home / Oo-oo-ee / So bad (Extra track on reissue.) / Ain't it tough (Extra track on reissue.)
CD _____ COBCM 5
Cobalt / Sep '95 / Grapevine.

FAT CITY
Fat city / Longing for you baby / Help me / I can't tell it all / Down to the river / Country blues / Cold emotions, frozen hearts / Killing me by degrees / Duisburg blues / So lonely / Too bad you're no good / Long time gone
CD _____ COBCM 1
Cobalt / Mar '95 / Grapevine.

ITCHY FEET
Talkin' woman blues / Who's right, who's wrong / Rock 'n' roll radio / Itchy feet / Ultimatum time / So lonely / Come on / Turn around / I can't be satisfied / Got to love you baby / Nothin' but the blues / Let your bucket down
CD _____ COBCM 4
Cobalt / Sep '95 / Grapevine.

OFFICIAL BLUES BAND BOOTLEG ALBUM
Talk to me baby / Flatfoot Sam / Two bones and a pick / Someday baby / Boom boom (out go the lights) / Come in / Death letter / Going home / I don't know / Diddy wah diddy
CD _____ COBCM 2
Cobalt / Mar '95 / Grapevine.

READY
Twenty nine ways / I'm ready / Hallelujah, I love her so / Sus blues / Noah Lewis blues / Treat her right / Lonely Avenue / Find yourself another fool / Hey hey little girl / Green stuff / Can't hold on / Cat / That's alright (CD/MC only) / Nadine (CD/MC only)
CD _____ COBCM 3
Cobalt / Mar '95 / Grapevine.

THESE KIND OF BLUES
Tobacco Road / Doin' alright / Time after time / Stealing / That's it, I quit / Bad penny blues / Let the four winds blow / Bad luck / Hard working man / These kind of blues / Smokestack lightnin'
CD _____ 900160
Line / Sep '94 / CM / Grapevine / ADA / Conifer / Direct.

Wire-less

CD _____ COBCD 1
Cobalt / Mar '95 / Grapevine.

Blues Boy Willie

BE WHO
Why are you cheatin' on me / Same ol' fishing hole / Crack up / Stealing your love tonight / Let me funk with you / Can we talk before we separate / Highway blues / Be who
CD _____ CDICH 1061
Ichiban / Oct '93 / Koch.

BE WHO, VOL. 2
Party all night / I still care / Break away / Rest of my life / Where is Leroy / Love darling love / Let's get closer / Be who, two
CD _____ ICH 1119CD
Ichiban / Jun '94 / Koch.

STRANGE THINGS HAPPENING
Leroy / Blues in this town / On more mile / Fly / Sweet home Chicago / Fishing trip / Let's go, let's go, let's go / Strange things happening
CD _____ CDICH 1038
Ichiban / Jun '89 / Koch.

Blues Brothers

BEST OF THE BLUES BROTHERS
Expressway / Everybody needs somebody to love / I don't know / She caught the Katy / Soul man / Rubber biscuit / Goin' back to Miami / Gimme some lovin' / B Movie / Boxcar blues / Flip flop fly
CD _____ 781 586-2
Atlantic / Jun '80 / Warner Music.

LIVE IN MONTREUX (Blues Brothers Band)
Hold on I'm comin' / In the midnight hour / She caught the katy / Thrill is gone / I can't turn you loose / Sweet home Chicago / Knock on wood / Rasie your hand / Peter Gunn / Soul finger / Hey bartender / Soul man / Everybody needs somebody to love / Green onions
CD _____ 9031716142
Atlantic / Feb '95 / Warner Music.

MADE IN AMERICA
Soul finger / Funky Broadway / Who's making love / Do you love me / Guilty / Perry Mason (theme from) / Riot in cell block 9 / Green onions / I ain't got you / From the bottom / Going to Miami
CD _____ 781 478-2
Atlantic / Jun '89 / Warner Music.

RED, WHITE AND BLUES (Blues Brothers Band)
You got the bucks / Red, white and blues / Can't play the blues (in an air conditioned room) / Early in the morning / One track train / Boogie thing / Never found a girl / Trick bag / Take you and show you / Big bird
CD _____ 9031772842
Atlantic / Jun '92 / Warner Music.

Blues Busters

IN MEMORY OF THE BLUES BUSTERS
CD _____ JMC 200114
Jamaica Gold / Sep '93 / THE / Magnum Music Group / Jetstar.

Blues Company

PUBLIC RELATIONS
Public relations / Red blood / Dance all night / Midnight train / Just can't keep from crying / Qui's gang / I've got the blues / Rhythm of Zydeco / Cry for me / Big bad wolf / Gambler / Blow Jay blow / Change / Crippled mind
CD _____ INAK 9018
In Akustik / Aug '95 / Magnum Music Group.

VINTAGE
CD _____ INAK 9036
In Akustik / Nov '95 / Magnum Music Group.

Blues Magoos

PSYCHEDELIC LOLLIPOP
CD _____ REP 4194-WZ
Repertoire / Aug '91 / Pinnacle / Cadillac.

Blues Mobile Band

NEW DAY YESTERDAY, A
CD _____ PRD 70772
Provogue / May '95 / Pinnacle.

OUT IN THE BLUE
What I do / She's gone / I'm going home / I can't stand it / To hard / Leave this town / I've got dreams to remember / Leave me alone / Tell me why / Helpless without you / Too late
CD _____ PRD 70852
Provogue / Nov '95 / Pinnacle.

Blues 'N' Trouble

BAG FULL OF BOOGIE
Bag full of boogie / Riding in my cadillac / Deep blue feeling / You got me spinnin' / Blues because of you / Breaking the ice / Good morning little school girl / Serenade

for a wealthy widow / Slim's chance / Drug store woman / Lookin' for my baby / Lowdown / Down in Dallas
CD _____ BAMCD 2
Barking Mad / Jul '94 / Conifer.

FIRST TROUBLE
Born in Chicago / Natural born lover / G.T. / Downtown Saturday night / Blues 'n' trouble / Sloppy drunk / Tearstains on my pillow / Mystery train / Wake up Mama / Deep blue feeling / Spank the plank
CD _____ 900326
Line / Oct '94 / CM / Grapevine / ADA / Conifer / Direct.

HAT TRICK
I got your number / Why / Cherry peaches / Travelling light / When the lights go down / Comin' home / What's the matter / Be mine tonight / Rockin' with you Jimmy / T.N.T / See my baby shake it / I don't need no doctor
CD _____ 900397
Line / Sep '94 / CM / Grapevine / ADA / Conifer / Direct.

NO MINOR KEYS/FIRST
CD _____ 921211
Line / Jun '94 / CM / Grapevine / ADA / Conifer / Direct.

POOR MOON
CD _____ BAMCD 1
Barking Mad / Feb '93 / Conifer.

Blues Project

LIVE AT TOWN HALL
CD _____ OW 30010
One Way / Jul '94 / Direct / ADA.

Blues Section

BLUES SECTION
CD _____ LRCD 3
Love / Dec '94 / Direct / ADA.

BLUES SECTION 2
CD _____ LXCD 604
Love / Aug '95 / Direct / ADA.

Blues Traveller

FOUR
Runaround / Stand / Look around / Fallible / Mountains win again / Freedom / Crash burn / Price to pay / Hook / Good, the bad and the ugly / Just wait / Brother John
CD _____ 5402652
Polydor / Nov '94 / PolyGram.

Bluesiana

BLUESIANA II
Fonkalishus / Dr. Blooze / Cowan woman / For art's sake / Skoshuss / Love's parody / Santa Rosalia / San Antone / Montana Banana / Tribute to Art
CD _____ 101332
Windham Hill Jazz / Aug '91 / New Note.

Bluesiana Triangle

BLUESIANA TRIANGLE
Heads up / Life's one way ticket / Shoo fly don't bother me / Need to be loved / Next time you see me / When the saints go marching in / For all we know
CD _____ WD 0125
Windham Hill / May '91 / Pinnacle / BMG / ADA.

Bluetones

EXPECTING TO FLY
Talking to clarry / Bluetonic / Cut some rug / Things change / Fountainhead / Carnt be trusted / Slight return / Putting out fires / Vampire
CD _____ BLUE 004CD
Superior Quality / Feb '96 / Vital.

Bluiett, Hamiet

EBU
CD _____ SNCD 1088
Soul Note / Jan '86 / Harmonia Mundi / Wellard / Cadillac.

SANKOFA/REAR GARDE
CD _____ 121238-2
Soul Note / Sep '93 / Harmonia Mundi / Wellard / Cadillac.

Blumfeld

LETAT AT MOI
CD _____ ABB 73CD
Big Cat / Feb '95 / SRD / Pinnacle.

Blunderbuss

CONSPIRACY
CD _____ HMS 2192
Homestead / Aug '95 / SRD.

Blunstone, Colin

ECHO BRIDGE
CD _____ PERMCD 38
Permanent / Sep '95 / Total/BMG.

LIVE AT THE BBC
Misty roses / Say you don't mind / Brother love / Something happens when you touch me / She's not there / Time of the season / Andorra / Caroline goodbye / I don't believe in miracles / Wonderful
CD _____ WINCD 079
Windsong / Dec '95 / Pinnacle.

MIRACLES
I don't believe in miracles / Loving and free / I'll never forget you / Misty roses / Keep the curtains closed today / You are the way for me / Who's that knocking / Caroline goodbye / Say you don't mind / Pondering / Beware / Care of cell 44 / Ain't it funny / How could we dare to be wrong / Wonderful / Beginning
CD _____ PWKS 4170
Carlton Home Entertainment / Sep '93 / Carlton Home Entertainment.

SINGS HIS GREATEST HITS
Say you don't mind / Old and wise / Caroline goodbye / Andorra / I don't believe in miracles / She's not there / Tell her no / Time of the season / What becomes of the broken hearted / Tracks of my tears / Still burning bright / Don't feel no pain
CD _____ CLACD 351
Castle / Aug '93 / BMG.

SOME YEARS IT'S THE TIME OF
She loves the way they love her / Misty roses / Caroline goodbye / Though you are far away / Mary won't you warm my bed / Let me come closer to you / Say you don't mind / I don't believe in miracles / How wrong can one man be / Andorra / How could we dare to be wrong / Wonderful / Beginning / Keep the curtains closed today / You who are lonely / It's magical / This is your captain calling
CD _____ EK 66449
Columbia / Jul '95 / Sony.

Blur

GREAT ESCAPE, THE
Stereotypes / Country house / Best days / Charmless man / Fade away / Top man / Universal / Mr. Robinson's quango / He thought of cars / It could be you / Ernold Same / Globe alone / Dan Abnormal / Entertain me / Yoko and Hiro
CD _____ FOODCD 14
Food / Sep '95 / EMI.

LEISURE
She's so high / Bang / Slow down / Repetition / Bad day / Sing / There's no other way / Fool / Come together / High cool / Birthday / War me down
CD _____ FOODCD 6
Food / Aug '91 / EMI.

MODERN LIFE IS RUBBISH
For tomorrow / Advert / Colin Zeal / Pressure on Julian / Star shaped / Blue jeans / Chemical world / Intermission / Sunday Sunday / Oily water / Miss America / Villa Rosie / Coping / Turn it up / Resigned / Commercial break
CD _____ FOODCD 9
Food / May '93 / EMI.

PARKLIFE
Girls and boys / Tracy Jacks / End of a century / Parklife / Bank holiday / Debt collector / Far out / To the end / London loves / Trouble in the message centre / Clover over Dover / Magic America / Jubilee / This is a low
CD _____ FOODCD 10
Food / Apr '94 / EMI.

Blurt

KENNY ROGERS GREATEST HITS: TAKE 2
CD _____ TBCD 666
Toeblock / Apr '89 / Vital.

Blyth Power

PARADISE RAZED
CD _____ DR 003CD
Downward Spiral / Feb '95 / Direct / ADA.

TEN YEARS INSIDE THE HORSE
Stand into danger / Hurling time / Probably going to rain / Hard summer long / He who would valiant be / Ne and Mr. Absolutley / Chilterns / Summer song / Song of the 3rd clause / Execution song / Right hand man / Inside the horse / Animal farm / Knight on Malta / Guns of castle cary / Van tempest / Pastor skull / Royal George
CD _____ CDMGRAM 83
Anagram / Aug '94 / Pinnacle.

'Blythe, Arthur

CALLING CARD
As of yet / Blue blues / Naima's love song / Hip dripper / Odessa / Elaborations / Jitterbug waltz / Break tune
CD _____ ENJ 90512
Enja / Feb '96 / New Note / Vital/SAM.

RETROFLECTION
Jana's delight / J.B. blues / Peacemaker / Light blue / Lenox avenue breakdown / Faceless woman / Break tune
CD _____ ENJ 80462
Enja / Mar '94 / New Note / Vital/SAM.

BMX Bandits

GETTING DIRTY
CD _____ CRECD 174
Creation / May '95 / 3MV / Vital.

LIFE GOES ON
CD _____ CRECD 133
Creation / Sep '93 / 3MV / Vital.

STAR WARS
CD _____ ASK 7CD
Vinyl Japan / '92 / Vital.

BNFL Band

COME FOLLOW THE BAND
Come follow the band / Arcadians / Summertime / Cheek to cheek / I got rhythm / I dreamed a dream / Pie Jesu / Slaughter on 10th Avenue / Another opening another show / Overture to Phantom of the Opera / Anything goes / Memory / West Side story / Till there was you / You'll never walk alone / Oklahoma
CD _____ DOYCD 018
Doyen / Oct '92 / Conifer.

PARTITE
CD _____ QPRL 062D
Polyphonic / Sep '93 / Conifer.

ROMANCE IN BRASS VOLUME 2
Kiss me again / Spread a little happiness / Just the way you are / Somewhere out there / Serenade for Toni / Annie Laurie / Girl with the flaxen hair / Meditation from thais / Li'l darlin' / Indian summer / Aubade / Love on the rocks / Romance de l'amour / Passing by / Myfanwy / Sweet shepherdess / Georgia on my mind / Folks that live on the hill / Memory
CD _____ QPRL 063D
Polyphonic / Apr '94 / Conifer.

UN VIE DE MATELOT
Un vie de matelot / Snowdon fantasy / Little suite for brass / Rococo variations / Land of the long white cloud
CD _____ QPRL 069D
Polyphonic / Oct '94 / Conifer.

Bo, Eddie

CHECK MR POPEYE
Check Mr. Popeye / Now let's Popeye / It must be love / Dinky doo / I'll do anything for you / Warm daddy / Roamin-itis / Hey there baby / I need someone / Tell it like it is / You got your mojo working / Ain't you ashamed / Baby I'm wise / Every dog has his day
CD _____ CD 2077
Rounder / '88 / CM / Direct / ADA / Cadillac.

Boat Band

BURNING THE WATER
CD _____ HAROCD 30
Harbour Town / Apr '95 / Roots / Direct / CM / ADA.

Bob & Earl

DANCETIME U.S.A. (Bob & Earl/The Olympics)
Baby, your time is my time / Big brother / Land of 1000 dances / I can't get away / My little girl / I'll keep running back / Dancin' everywhere / Send for me / Ooh honey babe / Harlem shuffle / Bounce Mine exclusively / Baby, do the philly dog / Duck / Same old thing / I'll do a little bit more / We go together / Secret agent
CD _____ GSCD054
Goldmine / Jul '95 / Vital.

Bob Delyn

GEDON
Gortoz pell zo gortoz gwell / Poeni dim / Llys Ifor Haul / Ffair y Bala / Corsydd Fyrjinia / Mil harddach wyt / Beaj iskis / Seance Watcyn Wynn / Y swn / Tren bach y sgwarnogod / Blodau haearn blodau glo / Y clewr olaf / Llewg zotrog oz Ilep zotrog (Kig ejen c'hoazh)
CD _____ CRAICD 021
Crai / Aug '94 / ADA / Direct.

Bobo, Willie

UNO DOS TRES
CD _____ 5216642
Verve / Feb '95 / PolyGram.

Bobs

COVER THE SONGS OF...
CD _____ ROUCD 9049
Rounder / Nov '94 / CM / Direct / ADA / Cadillac.

PLUGGED
CD _____ ROUCD 9059
Rounder / Oct '95 / CM / Direct / ADA / Cadillac.

SHUT UP AND SING
CD _____ ROU 9039CD
Rounder / Jan '94 / CM / Direct / ADA / Cadillac.

Bobs Your Uncle

CAGES
CD _____ ZULU 009CD
Zulu / Oct '95 / Plastic Head.

Bobvan

WATER DRAGON
Ay triste / Eyebrow and curved hair / Water dragon / Branle poitevin / Serendipity / Careful with that fax Eugene / Labbra Rosse / Shrinking of the gigantic / Perky Pat's lament / Memory
CD _____ SSR 127
SSR / Jan '94 / Grapevine.

Bocian, Michael

REVERENCE
CD _____ ENJACD 80962
Enja / Sep '95 / New Note / Vital/SAM.

Bock, Wolfgang

BISCAYA SUNSET
CD _____ SKYCD 8703054
Sky / Sep '95 / Koch.

Boddy, Ian

DEEP, THE
Standing at the edge / Dark descent / Deep / In the realm of poseidon / Leviathan / Flow current flow / Sirens call / Aquanaut / Re-emergence / Surface flight / Sub aquiem
CD _____ SER 006
Something Else / Sep '94 / Pinnacle.

DRIVE
Drive / Ice horizon / Alchemy / Crucifixus / Atlantis / Analogagogalog / Freeway / Southern comfort / Heaven's gate
CD _____ REAL 095
Surreal / Sep '91 / Surreal To Real / C & D Compact Disc Services.

JADE
CD _____ SER 003
Magnum Music / Sep '93 / Magnum Music Group.

ODYSSEY
Hyperion / Time remembered / Amazonia / Masquerade / Lammergeyer / Odyssey / Chameleon
CD _____ REAL 098
Surreal / Sep '89 / Surreal To Real / C & D Compact Disc Services.

UNCERTAINTY PRINCIPLE, THE
Times arrow / Virtual journey / Chromazone / Space cadet / Interstellar interlude No.1 / Cassiopeia's dream / Interstellar interlude No.2 / Sopernova / Uncertainty principle 1 / Uncertainty principle 2 / Uncertainty principle 3 / Beyond the event horizon / Times end
CD _____ SER 004
Something Else / Sep '94 / Pinnacle.

Bodner, Phil

FINE AND DANDY
CD _____ JHR 73511
Jazz Hour / May '93 / Target/BMG / Jazz Music / Cadillac.

NEW YORK JAM
CD _____ STB 2505
Stash / Sep '95 / Jazz Music / CM / Cadillac / Direct / ADA.

Body Count

BODYCOUNT
Smoked pork / Body Count's in the house / Now sports / Body Count / Statistic / Bowels of the devil / Real problem / KKK Bitch / Note / Voodoo / Winner loses / There goes the neighborhood / Oprah / Evil dick / Body Count anthem / Momma's gotta die tonight / Ice T/Freedom of speech
CD _____ 9362451392
WEA / Mar '94 / Warner Music.

BORN DEAD
Body m/f count / Masters of revenge / Killin' floor / Necessary evil / Drive-by / Last breath / Hey Joe / Shallow graves / Who are you / Street lobotomy / Born dead
CD _____ RSYND 2
Rhyme Syndicate / Sep '94 / EMI.

Bodychoke

MINDSHAFT
CD _____ FRR 003
Freek / Mar '94 / SRD.

Boe, Knut Ivar

FERDAMANN
CD _____ HCD 7100
Musikk Distribusjon / Dec '94 / ADA.

Boehmer, Conrad

ACOIUSMATRIX 5
CD _____ BVHAASTCD 9011
Bvhaast / Oct '93 / Cadillac.

IN ILO TEMPORE
CD _____ BVHAASTCD 9008
Bvhaast / Oct '93 / Cadillac.

WOUTERJE PIETERSE
CD _____ BVHAASTCD 9401/2
Bvhaast / Oct '94 / Cadillac.

Bofill, Angela

I WANNA LOVE SOMEBODY
CD _____ CHIP 134
Jive / Mar '93 / BMG.

Bogan, Lucille

LUCILLE BOGAN
CD _____ SOB 32352
Story Of The Blues / Dec '92 / Koch / ADA.

LUCILLE BOGAN VOL.1 1923-1930
CD _____ BDCD 6036
Blues Document / Apr '93 / Swift / Jazz Music / Hot Shot.

LUCILLE BOGAN VOL.3 1934-35
CD _____ BDCD 6038
Blues Document / Apr '93 / Swift / Jazz Music / Hot Shot.

Bogart, Deanna

CROSSING BORDERS
CD _____ FF 601CD
Flying Fish / Feb '93 / Roots / CM / Direct / ADA.

Bogguss, Suzy

ACES
Outbound plane / Aces / Someday soon / Let goodbye hurt like it should / Save yourself / Yellow river road / Part of me / Letting go / Music on the wind / Still hold on
CD _____ C2 95847
Capitol / Feb '92 / EMI.

SOMETHING UP MY SLEEVE
Diamonds and tears / Just like the weather / Just keep comin' back to you / You never will / You'd be the one / Take it to the limit / Hey Cinderella / Souvenirs / You wouldn't say that to a stranger / Take it like a man / No green eyes / Something up my sleeve
CD _____ 72438273982
Capitol / '93 / EMI.

VOICES IN THE WIND
Heartache / Drive south / Don't wanna / How come you go to her / Other side of the hill / In the day / Love goes without saying / Eat at Joe's / Lovin' a hurricane / Letting go / Cold day in July
CD _____ C2 98585
Liberty / Oct '92 / EMI.

Boghall & Bathgate...

INTERCONTINENTAL DRUMMERS FANFARE, THE (Boghall & Bathgate Caledonia)
CD _____ LCOM 9042
Lismor / Jul '91 / Lismor / Direct / Duncans / ADA.

Boghandle

STEP ON IT
Miserable and ugly / Get off / Hey mom / High toned son of a bitch / Hold back the tears / Don't give me that shit / Far from home / Loaded 'n' fucked / Only son / Fuck fun / Intoxicated
CD _____ BMCD 024
Black Mark / Jun '92 / Plastic Head.

Bogle, Eric

ERIC BOGLE SONGBOOK
Reason for it all / Nobody's moggy now / Hard hard times / Scraps of paper / If wishes were fishes / Front row cowboy / And the band played waltzing Matilda / Little Gomez / Aussie Bar-b-q / When the wind blows
CD _____ CDTRAX 028
Greentrax / Aug '89 / Conifer / Duncans / ADA / Direct.

ERIC BOGLE SONGBOOK VOLUME 2
Now I'm easy / Glasgow lullaby / No man's land / Do you know any Bob Dylan / My youngest son came home today / Belle of Broughton / Leaving Nancy / Singing the spirit home / Wee china pig / Leaving the land / Rosie / All the fine young men / Across the hills of home
CD _____ CDTRAX 051
Greentrax / Apr '92 / Conifer / Duncans / ADA / Direct.

HARD, HARD TIMES
CD _____ TUT 72162
Wundertute / Jan '94 / CM / Duncans / ADA.

I WROTE THIS WEE SONG (Live)
Sound of singing / Leaving the land / Silly slang song / Mirrors / Reason for it all / Flying finger filler / Vanya / Don't you worry about that / Somewhere in America / Them old song writing blues / Rosie / Feed the children / Singing the spirit home / Leaving Nancy / Now I'm easy / Plastic Paddy / No man's land / Never again- remember / Short white blues / Welcome home / Daniel smiling / Eric and the informers / Shelter / Gift of years

CD Set _____ CDTRAX 082D
Greentrax / Jan '95 / Conifer / Duncans / ADA / Direct.

MIRRORS
Refugee / One small life / Plastic Paddy / Welcome home / Flat story broke waltz / Vanya / Don't you worry about that / Mirrors / Song / Big (in a small way) / At risk / Never again - remember / Somewhere in America / Wouldn't be dead for quids / Wishing is free
CD _____ CDTRAX 068
Greentrax / Nov '93 / Conifer / Duncans / ADA / Direct.

NOW I'M EASY
CD _____ LRF 041CD
Larrikin / Mar '89 / Roots / Direct / ADA / CM.

SCRAPS OF PAPER
CD _____ LARRCD 104
Larrikin / Jun '94 / Roots / Direct / ADA / CM.

SINGING THE SPIRIT HOME
Old song / Lifeline / Singing the spirit home / Twenty years ago / All the fine young men / Leaving the land / Australian through and through / Lancelot and Guinevere / Silo / Shelter
CD _____ LRF 186CD
Larrikin / '88 / Roots / Direct / ADA / CM.

VOICES IN THE WILDERNESS
Peace has broken out / Lily and the poppy / Blues for Alex / What kind of man / Wilderness / Feed the children / Amazon / Silly slang song / Fences and walls / It's only Tuesday / Gift of years
CD _____ CDTRAX 040
Greentrax / Apr '91 / Conifer / Duncans / ADA / Direct.

WHEN THE WIND BLOWS
CD _____ LARRCD 144
Larrikin / Jun '94 / Roots / Direct / ADA / CM.

ESSENTIAL DANCEFLOOR ARTISTS VOL. 4
CD _____ DGPCD 699
Deep Beats / Jun '94 / BMG.

ANTLER DANCE
CD _____ OMM 2007CD
Omnium / Dec '94 / ADA.

OLD LEAD
CD _____ OMM 2001CD
Omnium / Dec '94 / ADA.

ORB
Kiepolka / Son, oh son / Tape decks all over hell / Snow on the hills / Army / Harout / Brave bombardier / Sota / Hard times / Glasena klingar / Town of Ballybay / Cunovo oro / Kaen lao gratop mai
CD _____ COOKCD 037
Cooking Vinyl / Sep '90 / Vital.

SONGS FROM THE GYPSY
CD _____ OMM 2013CD
Omnium / Jul '95 / ADA.

EAGLE BROTHER
CD _____ 521388-2
Verve / Jan '94 / PolyGram.

GULA GULA
Gula gula / Vilges soula / Balu badjel go nuoitan / Du laholja / It aat deahmme mu / Eadnan bakti / Oppskrift for Herrefolk / Dunne
CD _____ CDRW 13
Realworld / Jul '90 / EMI / Sterns.

LIEHKASTIN
CD _____ MB 94CD
Lean / Dec '94 / ADA.

SALMER PA VEIEN HJEM (Paus, Boine Persen, Bremmnes)
CD _____ FXC 105
Kirkelig Kultuverksted / Jul '93 / ADA.

BOINGO
Insanity / Hey / Mary / Can't see (useless) / Pedestrian wolves / Lost like this / Spider / War again / I am the walrus / Tender lumplings / Change / Helpless
CD _____ 74321189712
Giant / Oct '94 / BMG.

MAGIC MOMENT (Bois, Nordisle Orchestra)
Glory of love / I just called to say I love you / Say you, say me / Papa don't preach / Part time lover / Physical / Ai no corrida / Purple rain / Careless whisper / Just the way you are / Flashdance (what a feeling) / Chariots of fire / Stuck on you / Honesty / Hotel California / On my own / We are the world
CD _____ DC 8509
Denon / '88 / Conifer.

SAY YOU, SAY ME (Bois, Nordisle & Son Orchestre)
CD _____ CY 1002
Denon / '88 / Conifer.

SOUND STREAM TANGO (Bois, Nordisle Orchestra)
CD _____ CY 1012
Denon / Jan '89 / Conifer.

TWILIGHT SOUNDS (Bois, Nordisle Orchestra)
We've only just begun / Hey Jude / Michelle / Sound of silence / Whiter shade of pale / Yesterday / Hello Mr. Cunshine / I've the peace of all mankind / Bridge over troubled water / Impossible dream / Early in the morning / Scarborough Fair / Green fields / It never rains in Southern California / Long and winding road / Let it be / Sunrise sunset / Yesterday once more
CD _____ DC 8507
Denon / '88 / Conifer.

BOJAN Z QUARTET
No name value / Play ball / Zilbra / Mashala / Ginger pickles / Les instants / Grand od bora / Nishka bania / Spirito
CD _____ LBLC 6565
Label Bleu / Nov '95 / New Note.

BEARD OF STARS (T. Rex)
Prelude / Day laye / Woodland bop / First heart mighty dawn dart / Pavilions of sun / Organ blues / By the light of the magical moon / Wind cheetah / Beard of stars / Great horse / Dragon's ear / Lofty skies / Dove / Elemental child
CD _____ CLACD 317
Castle / '92 / BMG.

BEGINNING OF DOVES, THE
Jasper C. Debussy / Beyond the rising sun / Observations / You got the power / Sarah / Rings of fortune / Beginning of doves / Pictures of purple people / Jasmine '49 / Misty mist cat / Lunacy's back / Black and white incident / Eastern spell / Hippy gumbo / Crazy child / Hot rod Mama / Mustang Ford / One inch rock / Charlie / Black Sally was an angel
CD _____ RRCD 152
Receiver / Jul '93 / Grapevine.

BOLAN BOOGIE (T. Rex)
Get it on / Beltane walk / King of the mountain cometh / Jewel / She was born to be my unicorn / Dove / Woodland rock / Ride a white swan / Raw ramp / Jeepster / Fist heart mighty dawn dart / By the light of the magical moon / Summertime blues / Hot love
CD _____ CLACD 145
Castle / Apr '89 / BMG.

BOLAN'S ZIP GUN
Light of love / Solid baby / Precious star / Spaceboss / Token of my love / Think zinc / Till dawn / Girl in the thunderbolt suit / Golden belt / I really love you babe / Zip gun boogie
CD _____ EDCD 393
Edsel / May '94 / Pinnacle / ADA.

COLLECTION: T. REX (T. REX)
Hot rod mama / Strange orchestras / Chateau in Virginia Waters / Mustang Ford / Graceful fat Sheba / Deborah / Stacey Grove / Salamanda palaganda / Travelling tragition / Chariots of silk / Seal of seasons / Cat black (the wizard's hat) / She was born to be my unicorn / Woodland bop / Dove / Beard of stars / Elemental child / One inch rock / Seagull woman / Mambo Sun / Life's a gas / Ride a white swan / Jeepster
CD _____ CCSCD 136
Castle / '88 / BMG.

DANDY IN THE UNDERWORLD
Dandy in the underworld / Crimson moon / Universe / I'm a fool for you girl / I love to boogie / Visions of domino / Jason B Sad / Groove a little / Soul of my suit / Hang ups / Pain and love / Teen riot structure
CD _____ EDCD 395
Edsel / May '94 / Pinnacle / ADA.

DEFINITIVE TYRANNOSAURUS REX, THE (Tyrannosaurus Rex)
Deborah / Welder of words / Mustang Ford / One inch rock / Conseuala / Friends / Juniper suction / Warlord of the royal crocodiles / Chariots of silk / Iscariot / King of the rumbling spires / Once upon the seas of Abyssinia / By the light of the magical moon / Day laye / Great horse / Elemental child / Child star / Chateau in Virginia Waters / Salamanda paraganda / Stacey Grove / Eastern spell / Pewter suitor / Cat black (the wizards hat) / Seal of seasons / Misty coast of Albany / Do you remember / Blessed wild apple girl / Find a little wood / Pavilions of the sun / Lofty skies
CD _____ NEXCD 250
Sequel / Nov '93 / BMG.

EARLY RECORDINGS
CD _____ EMPRCD 545
Emporio / Nov '94 / THE / Disc / CM.

ELECTRIC WARRIOR (T. Rex)
Mambo sun / Cosmic dancer / Jeepster / Monolith / Lean woman blues / Get it on / Planet Queen / Girl / Motivator / Life's a gas / Rip off
CD _____ CLACD 180
Castle / Apr '90 / BMG.

ESSENTIAL COLLECTION, THE (Bolan, Marc & T.Rex)
CD _____ 5259612
PolyGram TV / Sep '95 / PolyGram.

FUTURISTIC DRAGON (T. Rex)
Futuristic dragon / Jupiter liar / Chrome sitar / All alone / New York City / My little baby / Calling all destroyers / Theme for a dragon / Sensation boulevard / Ride my wheels / Dreamy lady / Dawn storm / Casual agent
CD _____ EDCD 394
Edsel / May '94 / Pinnacle / ADA.

GREAT HITS 1972-77
CD _____ EDCD 401
Edsel / Oct '94 / Pinnacle / ADA.

GREAT HITS 1972-77: THE B-SIDES
CD _____ EDCD 402
Edsel / Oct '94 / Pinnacle / ADA.

INTROSPECTIVE: MARC BOLAN & T.REX (Bolan, Marc & T.Rex)
Baktabak / Nov '90 / Baktabak.

LEFT HAND LUKE (The Alternate Tanx) (T. Rex)
Tenement lady darling / Rapids / Mister mister / Broken hearted blues / Country honey / Mad Donna / Born to boogie / Life is strange / Street and the babe shadow / Highway knees / Left hand Luke / Children of the revolution / Solid gold easy action / Free angel / Mister mister #2 / Broken hearted blues #2 / Street and the babe shadow #2 / Tenement lady / Tenement lady #2 / Broken hearted blues #3 / Mad Donna #2 / Street and the babe shadow #3 / Left hand Luke (2)
CD _____ EDCD 410
Edsel / May '95 / Pinnacle / ADA.

LIGHT OF LOVE (T. Rex)
Light of love / Solid baby / Precious star / Token of my love / Space boss / Think zinc / Till dawn / Teenage dream / Girl in the thunderbolt suit / Explosive mouth / Venus moon
CD _____ EDCD 413
Edsel / May '95 / Pinnacle / ADA.

LOVE AND DEATH
You scare me to death / You've got the power / Eastern spell / Charlie / I'm weird / Hippy gumbo / Mustang Ford / Observations / Jasmine '49 / Cat black (the wizard's hat) / Black and white incident / Perfumed garden of Gulliver Smith / Wizard / Beyond the rising sun / Rings of fortune
CD _____ CDMRED 70
Cherry Red / Jan '91 / Pinnacle.

MESSING WITH THE MYSTIC: UNISSUED
CD _____ EDCD 404
Edsel / Oct '94 / Pinnacle / ADA.

PEEL SESSIONS: T REX (T. Rex)
CD _____ SFPSCD 031
Strange Fruit / Nov '94 / Pinnacle.

PREHISTORIC
CD _____ EMPRCD 589
Emporio / Oct '95 / THE / Disc / CM.

PROPHETS, SEERS AND SAGES (T. Rex)
Deborah / Stacey Grove / Wind quartets / Conesuala / Trelawny lawn / Aznageel the mage / Friends / Salamanda paligalliad / Our wonderful brownskin man / O Harley (the saltimbanques) / Eastern spell / Travelling tragition / Juniper suction / Scenes of dynasty
CD _____ CUCD 10
Disky / Oct '94 / THE / BMG / Discovery / Pinnacle.

RABBIT FIGHTER
CD _____ EDCD 403
Edsel / Oct '94 / Pinnacle / ADA.

SINGLES COLLECTION VOL 2 (T. Rex)
CD _____ MARCD 511
Marc On Wax / Nov '86 / Charly / Total / BMG.

SINGLES COLLECTION VOL 3 (T. Rex)
CD _____ MARCD 512
Marc On Wax / Nov '86 / Charly / Total / BMG.

SLIDER, THE
Metal guru / Mystic lady / Rock on / Slider / Baby boomerang / Spaceball ricochet / Buick McKane / Telegram Sam / Rabbit fighter / Baby strange / Ballrooms of Mars / Chariot choogle / Main man
CD _____ EDCD 390
Edsel / May '94 / Pinnacle / ADA.

STAND BY ME (Bolan, Marc & T.Rex)
Groover / Think zinc / Tenement lady / Rock on / Free angel / Telegram Sam / Stand by me / Country honey / Teen riot structure / Solid gold easy action / Truck on (Tyke) / Pain and love / Children of the revolution / Twentieth century boy / I really love you babe / Visions of Domino / Teenage dream

ELECTRIC WARRIOR / Metal guru / Casual agent / Tame my tiger / Precious star / Chariot choogle / Leopards featuring gardenia and the mighty slug
CD _____ VSOPCD 100
Connoisseur / Nov '88 / Pinnacle.

T. REX (T. Rex)
Get it on / Summertime blues / Beltane walk / Mustang Ford / Woodland rock / Life's a gas / Hot love / Jeepster / Motivator / Cosmic dancer / Hot rod mama / Is it love / Children of Rarn / Jewel / Visit / Childe / Time of love is now / Diamond meadows / Root of star / One inch rock / Summer deep / Seagull woman / Sun eye / Wizard
CD _____ CLACD 287
Castle / '92 / BMG.

T.REX: THE EARLY YEARS (T. Rex)
Ride a white swan / One inch rock / Wizard / Seagull woman / Beltane walk / Hot love / King of the mountain cometh / Get it on / There was a time / Raw ramp / Mambo sun / Rip off / Jeepster / Life's a gas
CD _____ EARLD 1
Dojo / Mar '92 / BMG.

TANX (Bolan, Marc & T.Rex)
Tenement lady / Rapids / Mister mister / Broken hearted blues / Shock rock / Country honey / Electric slim and the factory man
CD _____ EDCD 391
Edsel / May '94 / Pinnacle / ADA.

TILL DAWN (Bolan, Marc & T.Rex)
CD _____ MARCD 509
Marc On Wax / Nov '85 / Charly / Total / BMG.

UNCHAINED: UNRELEASED RECORDINGS VOL. 1 (1972 - Part 1) (Bolan, Marc & T.Rex)
Over the flats / Sugar baby / Children of the world / Did you ever / Alligator man / Shame on you / Guitar blues / Shadow blues / Cry baby (Acoustic/Electric) / Rollin' stone / What do I see / Shame on you (slide) / Always / Auto machine / Unicorn horn (A thousand Mark Field charms) / Jam / Sailors of the highway (wah wah)
CD _____ EDCD 411
Edsel / May '95 / Pinnacle / ADA.

UNCHAINED: UNRELEASED RECORDINGS VOL.2 (1972 - Part 2) (Bolan, Marc & T.Rex)
Wouldn't I be the one / Meadows of the sea / Mr. Motion (Versions 1 and 2) / City port / Just like me / Is it true / Zinc rider / Canyon / Fast blues - easy action / Bolan's blues / Shake it wind one / Work with me baby / Spaceball boot / Electric lips / Slider blues / Ellie May / My baby's new Porsche / Darklipped woman
CD _____ EDCD 412
Edsel / May '95 / Pinnacle / ADA.

UNICORN (T. Rex)
Unicorn / Chariots of silk / 'Pon a hill / Seal of seasons / Throat of winter / Cat black (the wizard's hat) / Stones for Avalon / She was born to be my unicorn / Like a white star, tangled and far / Tulip, that's what you are / Warlord of the royal crocodiles / Evenings of Damask / Sea beasts / Iscariot / Nijinsky hind / Pilgrim's tale / Misty coast of Albany / Romany soup
CD _____ CLACD 325
Castle / '92 / BMG.

CD _____ CUCD 11
Disky / Oct '93 / THE / BMG / Discovery / Pinnacle.

VERY BEST OF MARC BOLAN AND T-REX (T. Rex)
Telegram Sam / Metal guru / Children of the revolution / Solid gold easy action / Twentieth century boy / Truck on (tyke) / Teenage dream / Light of love / New York City / London boys / I love to boogie / Laser love / Lady / Born to boogie / Dandy in the underworld / Life's an elevator / All alone / Celebrate summer / Buick Mckane / Chariot choogle
CD _____ MCCD 030
Music Club / May '91 / Disc / THE / CM.

VERY BEST OF VOLUME 1, THE (Bolan, Marc & T.Rex)
Metal guru / Cadillac / New York City / To know you is to love you / London boys / Think zinc / Light of love / Midnight / Children of the revolution / Lady / Twentieth century boy / Sunken rags / Spaceball ricochet / Ride my wheels / Truck on (tyke) / Dandy in the underworld
CD _____ PWK 008
Carlton Home Entertainment / '89 / Carlton Home Entertainment.

ZINC ALLOY AND THE HIDDEN RIDERS OF TOMORROW (Bolan, Marc & T.Rex)
Venus loon / Sound pit / Explosive mouth / Galaxy / Change / Nameless wildness / Teenage dream / Liquid gang / Carsmile Smith and the old one / You got to live to stay alive / Interstellar soul / Painless persuasion v the meathawk imm / Avengers / Leopards featuring gardenia and the mighty slug
CD _____ EDCD 392
Edsel / May '94 / Pinnacle / ADA.

ZIP GUN BOOGIE (T. Rex)
Light of love / Solid baby / Precious star / Token of my love / Till dawn / Girl in the

thunderbolt suit / I really love you babe / Golden belt / Zip gun boogie
CD _____ RAPCD 506
Marc On Wax / Oct '87 / Charly / Total/ BMG.

Boland, Francy

TWO ORIGINALS (Boland, Francy & Kenny Clarke)
CD _____ 5235252
PolyGram Jazz / Jan '95 / PolyGram.

Bolek

MEMORIES OF POLAND
CD _____ MCD 71409
Monitor / Jun '93 / CM.

Bolin, Tommy

FROM THE ARCHIVES 1
CD _____ RPM 158
RPM / Jan '96 / Pinnacle.

PRIVATE EYES
Bustin' out of Rosey / Sweet burgundy / Post toastee / Shake the devil / Gypsy soul / Someday we'll bring our love home / Hello again / You told me that you loved me
CD _____ CCSCD 371
Castle / Aug '91 / BMG.

RETROSPECTIVE
CD _____ K 924248 2
Elektra / Sep '89 / Warner Music.

TEASER
Grind / Homeward / Strut / Dreamer savannah woman / Teaser / People, people / Marching powder / Wild dogs / Lotus
CD _____ 468016 2
Epic / May '94 / Sony.

Boll Weevils

HEAVYWEIGHT
CD _____ DSRCD 35
Dr. Strange / Sep '95 / Plastic Head.

Bolland, C.J.

4TH SIGN, THE
Mantra / Nightbread / Thrust / Aquadrive / Pendulum / Spring yard / Camargue / Inside out / Jungle man (Not on LP)
CD _____ RS 92024CD
R & S / Jul '93 / Vital.

D.J. KICKS
CD _____ K 7038CD
Studio K7 / Sep '95 / Disc.

ELECTRONIC HIGHWAY
Tower of Naphtali / Drum tower / Neural paradox / Spool / Con Spirito / Bones / Zenith / Nec plus ultra / Catharsis
CD _____ RS 95011CD
R & S / Oct '95 / Vital.

Bollin, Zuzu

TEXAS BLUES MAN
Big legs / Hey little girl / Blues in the dark / Kidney stew / Cold cold feeling / Why don't you eat where you slept last night / Headlight blues / How do you want your rollin' done / Leary blues / Rebecca / Zu's blues
CD _____ ANTCD 0018
Antones / Feb '92 / Hot Shot / Direct / ADA.

Bolling, Claude

VICTORY CONCERT, THE
CD _____ 887971
Milan / Aug '94 / BMG / Silva Screen.

WARM UP THE BAND
CD _____ 4684132
Sony Jazz / Jan '95 / Sony.

Bollock Brothers

BEST OF THE BOLLOCKS
CD _____ CDCRM 1011
Charly / Jul '93 / Charly / THE / Cadillac.

FOUR HORSEMEN OF THE APOCALYPSE, THE
Legend of the snake / Woke up this morning and found myself dead / Mistress of the macabre / Faith healer / King Rat / Four horsemen of the Apocalypse / Return to the garden of Eden / Loud, loud, loud / Seventh seal
CD _____ CDCHARLY 72
Charly / Mar '87 / Charly / THE / Cadillac.

LAST SUPPER, THE
Horror movies / Enchantment / Reincarnation of Bollock Brothers / Save our souls / Face in the mirror / Last supper / Act became real / Gift
CD _____ CDCHARLY 175
Charly / Feb '89 / Charly / THE / Cadillac.

LIVE - IN PUBLIC IN PRIVATE
Woke up this morning / Drac's back / Four horsemen of the Apocalypse / Count Dracula where's yer trousers / King Rat / Midnight Moses / Faith healer / Rock 'n' roll
CD _____ CDCHARLY 178
Charly / Nov '89 / Charly / THE / Cadillac.

LIVE PERFORMANCES (Official Bootleg)
Slow removal of Vincent Van Gogh's left ear / Loose / Horror movies / Bunker / Last sup-

per / Reincarnation of Bollock Brothers / New York / Holidays in the sun / Problems / Vincent / Pretty vacant / God save the queen
CD _____ CDCHARLY 174
Charly / Feb '89 / Charly / THE / Cadillac.

MYTHOLOGY
CD _____ 853544
SPV / '89 / Plastic Head.

NEVER MIND THE BOLLOCKS '83
Holidays in the sun / Problems / No feelings / God save the queen / Pretty vacant / Submission / New York / Seventeen / Anarchy in the U.K. / Liar / Bodies / EMI
CD _____ CDCHARLY 178
Charly / Dec '89 / Charly / THE / Cadillac.

Bolo, Yami

COOL AND EASY
CD _____ DSRCD 442
Tappa / Aug '93 / Jetstar.

FIGHTING FOR PEACE
CD _____ RAS 3141
Ras / Jun '94 / Jetstar / Greensleeves / SRD / Direct.

WAR MONGER
Johanna / Warmonger / Show me / Call me / African woman / Satr of love / Mind games / Maximum greedium / Spread jah love / Mr Big and in crime
CD _____ RFCD 002
Record Factory / Sep '95 / Jetstar.

Bolshoi

FRIENDS
Away / Modern man / Someone's daughter / Sunday morning / Looking for a life to lose / Romeo in clover / Books on the bonfire / Pardon me / Fat and jealous / Waspy
CD _____ BBL 76CD
Lowdown/Beggars Banquet / Jan '89 /
Warner Music / Disc.

LINDY'S PARTY
Auntie Jean / Please / Crack in smile / Swings And Roundabouts / She don't know / T.V. Man / Can you believe it / Rainy Day / Barrowlands / Lindy's Party
CD _____ BBL 86CD
Beggars Banquet / Feb '90 / Warner Music / Disc.

Bolthrower

4TH CRUSADE
CD _____ MOSH 070CD
Earache / Sep '94 / Vital.

FOR VICTORY
War / Remembrance / When glory beckons / For victory / Graven image / Lest we forget / Silent demise / Forever fallen / Tank (M.K.1) / Armageddon bound
CD _____ MOSH 120CD
Earache / Nov '94 / Vital.

IN BATTLE THERE IS NO LAW
CD _____ SOL 22 CD
Vinyl Solution / Feb '91 / Disc.

PEEL SESSIONS: BOLT THROUGH
Forgotten existence / Attack in the aftermath / Psychological warfare / In battle there is no law / Drowned in torment / Eternal war / Realm of chaos / Domination / Destructive infinity / Warmaster / After life / Lost souls domain / Forgotten existence
CD _____ SFRCD 116
Strange Fruit / Jun '91 / Pinnacle.

REALM OF CHAOS
Eternal war / Through the eye of terror / Dark millenium / All that remains / Lost souls domaine / Plague bearer / World eater / Drowned in torment / Realm of chaos
CD _____ MOSH 013CD
Earache / Sep '94 / Vital.

WAR MASTER
CD _____ MOSH 020CD
Earache / Sep '94 / Vital.

Bolton, Michael

EARLY YEARS, THE
Lost in the city / Everybody needs a reason / Your love / It's just a feelin' / Dream while you can / Take me as I am / These eyes / You mean more to me / If I had your love / Give me a reason / Tell me how you feel / Time is on my side
CD _____ ND 90593
RCA / Mar '92 / BMG.

EVERYBODY'S CRAZY
Everybody's crazy / Save our love / Can't turn it off / Call my name / Everytime / Desperate heart / Start breaking my heart / You don't want me bad enough / Don't tell me it's over
CD _____ 4666622
Columbia / May '91 / Sony.

GREATEST HITS 1985-1995
Soul provider / (Sittin' on) the dock of the bay / How am I supposed to live without you / How can we be lovers / When I'm back on my feet again / Georgia on my mind / Time, love and tenderness / When a man loves a woman / Missing you since / Steel bars / Said I loved you but I lied / Lean

on me / Can I touch you there / I promise you / I found someone / Love so beautiful / This river
CD _____ 4810022
Columbia / Sep '95 / Sony.

HUNGER, THE
Hot love / Wait on love / (Sittin' on) the dock of the bay / Gina / That's what love is all about / Hunger / You're all I need / Take a look at my face / Walk away
CD _____ 4601632
CBS / Aug '90 / Sony.

MICHAEL BOLTON
Fool's game / She did the same thing / Home town hero / Can't hold on, can't let go / Fighting for my life / Paradise / Back in my arms again / Carrie / I almost believed you
CD _____ 4667422
Columbia / Apr '92 / Sony.

MICHAEL BOLTON / EVERYBODY'S CRAZY / THE HUNGER
CD Set _____ 468327 2
Columbia / Jul '93 / Sony.

ONE THING, THE
Said I loved you but I lied / I'm not made of steel / One thing / Soul of my soul / Completely / Lean on me / Ain't got nothing if you ain't got love / Time for letting go / Never get enough of your love / In the arms of love / Voice of my heart
CD _____ 474355 2
Columbia / Nov '93 / Sony.

SOUL PROVIDER
Soul provider / Georgia on my mind / It's only my heart / How am I supposed to live without you / How can we be lovers / You wouldn't know love / When I'm back on my feet again / From now on / Love cuts deep / Stand up for love
CD _____ 4653432
Columbia / Aug '89 / Sony.

TIME, LOVE AND TENDERNESS
Love is a wonderful thing / Time, love and tenderness / Missing you now / Forever isn't long enough / Now that I found you / When a man loves a woman / We're not makin' love anymore / New love / Save me / Steel bars
CD _____ 4678122
Columbia / Apr '91 / Sony.

TIMELESS (THE CLASSICS)
Since I fell for you / To love somebody / Reach out, I'll be there / You send me / Yesterday / Hold on / I'm coming / Bring it on home to me / Knock on wood / Drift away / White Christmas
CD _____ 4723022
Columbia / Apr '91 / Sony.

Bolton, Polly

NO GOING BACK
CD _____ SPIN CD 134
Making Waves / May '90 / CM.

SONGS FROM A COLD OPEN FIELD
CD _____ PBBCD 02
PBB / May '93 / ADA.

Bomb Everything

ALL POWERFUL FLUID, THE
CD _____ CDDVN 10
Devotion / Jul '92 / Pinnacle.

Bomb Party

FISH
CD _____ NORMAL 103CD
Normal/Okra / May '89 / Direct / ADA.

Bomb The Bass

CLEAR
Bug powder dust / Sleepyhead / One to one religion / Dark heart / If you reach the border / Brain dead / 5ml Barrel / Somewhere / Sandcastles / Tidal wave / Empire
CD _____ BRCD 611
4th & Broadway / Mar '95 / PolyGram.

Bomber

FROM BURUNDI
You die / B.O.W. / Brain rape / Change of life / Fist fuck / Screams / Free beer / Urimodified / Dunk my head / Extreme astute / Hit 'em / Don't ask me / Butcher
CD _____ 847601
Steamhammer / '90 / Pinnacle / Plastic Head.

Bon

FULL CIRCLE COMING HOME
CD _____ EFA 130022
Ozone / Oct '94 / SRD.

Bon Jovi

7800 DEGREES FAHRENHEIT
In and out of love / Price of love / Only lonely / King of the mountain / Silent night / Tokyo road / Hardest part is the night / Always run to you / To the fire / Secret dreams
CD _____ 824 509-2
Vertigo / Jan '90 / PolyGram.

Bon Jovi

Runaway / She didn't know me / Shot through the heart / Love lies / Burning for love / Breakout / Come back / Get ready
CD _____ 814 982-2
Vertigo / Jul '84 / PolyGram.

BON JOVI: INTERVIEW PICTURE DISC
CD P.Disc _____ CBAK 4004
Baktabak / Apr '88 / Baktabak.

CROSS ROAD
CD _____ 522936-2
Vertigo / Oct '94 / PolyGram.

INTERVIEWS VOLUME 2, THE
CD P.Disc _____ CBAK 4070
Baktabak / Feb '94 / Baktabak.

KEEP THE FAITH
I believe / Keep the faith / I'll sleep when I'm dead / In these arms / Bed of roses / If I was your mother / Dry county / Woman in love / Fear / I want you / Blame it on the love of rock and roll / Little bit of soul / Save a prayer
CD _____ 5141972
Jambco / Nov '92 / PolyGram.

NEW JERSEY
Lay your hands on me / Bad medicine / Born to be my baby / Living in sin / Blood on blood / Stick to your guns / Homebound train / I'll be there for you / Ninety nine in the shade / Love for sale / Wild is the wind / Ride cowboy ride
CD _____ 836 345-2
Vertigo / Nov '88 / PolyGram.

SLIPPERY WHEN WET
Let it rock / You give love a bad name / Livin' on a prayer / Social disease / Wanted dead or alive / Raise your hands / Without love / I'd die for you / Never say goodbye / Wild in the streets
CD _____ 8302642
Vertigo / Sep '90 / PolyGram.

THESE DAYS
CD _____ 5282482
Jambco / Jun '95 / PolyGram.

Bon Jovi, Jon

BLAZE OF GLORY - YOUNG GUNS II
Billy get your guns / Blaze of glory / Santa Fe / Never say die / Bang a drum / Guano City / Miracle / Blood money / Justice in the barrel / You really got me now / Dyin' ain't much of a livin'
CD _____ 846 473 2
Vertigo / Aug '90 / PolyGram.

Bonano, Sharkey

SHARKEY BONANO 1928-1937
Panama / Dippermouth blues / Sizzling the blues / High society / Git wit it / Ideas / Everydoy loves my baby / Yes she do - no she don't / I'm satisfied with my gal / High society (2) / Mudhole blues / Swing in, swing out / Blowin' off steam / Mr. Brown goes to town / Wash it clean / When you're smiling / Swingin' on the Swanee shore / Old fashioned swing / Big boy blue / Swing like a rusty gate / Doodlebug / Magnolia blues / I never knew what a gal could do / Keep had a reason to believe in you
CD _____ CBC 1001
Timeless Historical / Jan '92 / New Note / Pinnacle.

Bond & Brown

TWO HEADS ARE BETTER THAN ONE...PLUS
Lost tribe / Ig the pig / Oobati / Amazing grass / Scunthorpe crabmeat train / Sideways boogie shuffle stomp / C.F.D.T. / Mass debate / Looking for time / Milk is turning sour in my shoes / Macumbe
CD _____ SEECD 345
See For Miles/C5 / Apr '92 / Pinnacle.

Bond, Eddie

ROCKIN' DADDY
Double duty lovin' / Talking off the wall / Love makes a fool (Everyday) / Your eyes / I got a woman / Rockin' Daddy / Slip, slip slippin in / Baby, baby , baby (What am I gonna rin) / Flip flop Mama / Boppin' Bonnie / You're part of me / King on your throne / They say we're too young / Backslidin / Love love love / Lovin' you, lovin' you / Hershey bar / One step close to you / Baby me (Without sax) / Broke my guitar / This old heart of mine / Show me (With sax) / One more memory / I can't quit / My backet's got a hole in it (Back home again in) Indiana (instrumental) / They'll never take her love from me / Day I found you / Standing in the window / Back street affair / Our secret rendezvous / I'd just be fool enough / You nearly lose your mind / I thought I heard you calling my name / Big boss man / In my solitude / Most of all I want to see Jesus / Where could I go / To the Lord / Satisfied / When they ring those golden bells / If we never meet again / Will I be lost or will I be saved / Just a closer walk with thee / Pass me not, o gentle saviour / I saw the light / Letter to God / Precious memories / Hallelujah way
CD Set _____ BCD 15708

Bear Family / May '93 / Rollercoaster / Direct / CM / Swift / ADA.

ROCKIN' DADDY
Rockin' daddy / Big boss man / Can't win for losing / When the jukebox plays / Hey Joe / Monkey and the baboon / Blues got me / Standing in your window / Look like a monkey / I'll step aside / Memphis, Tennessee / My bucket's got a hole in it / Winners circle / Juke joint Johnny / You'll never be a stranger to me / Boo bop da caa caa / Heart full of heartaches / Here comes the train / Someday I'll sober up / Double duty lovin' / Let's make the parting sweet / Tomorrow I'll be gone / One more memory / Country shindig / When the jukebox plays (2) / Raunchy / Cold dark waters / Your eyes / It's been so long darling / Your old standby / This old heart of mine
CD _____ STCD 1
Stomper Time / '92 / Magnum Music Group.

Bond, Graham

HOLY MAGIC
CD _____ REP 4106-WP
Repertoire / Aug '91 / Pinnacle / Cadillac.

WE PUT OUR MAGICK ON YOU
CD _____ REP 4107-WP
Repertoire / Aug '91 / Pinnacle / Cadillac.

Bond, Joyce

CALL ME
CD _____ OCD 33
Orbitone / Jan '90 / Jetstar.

NICE TO HAVE YOU BACK AGAIN
Nice to have you back again / Nothing ever comes easy / Love me and leave me / Lonesome Road / You've been gone too long / If I ever fall in love again / No other one is sweeter than you
CD _____ SPCD 06
Spindle / Dec '95 / Jetstar / Else.

YOU TOUCH MY HEART
CD _____ SPCD 04
Spindle / Dec '95 / Jetstar / Else.

Bondi Cigars

BAD WEATHER BLUES
CD _____ LRF 258
Larrikin / Oct '93 / Roots / Direct / ADA / CM.

Bonds, Gary U.S.

BEST OF GARY 'US' BONDS, THE
CD _____ MCCD 111
Music Club / Jun '93 / Disc / THE / CM.

GREATEST HITS: GARY U.S. BONDS (2)
CD _____ TRLGCD 100
Timeless Jazz / Sep '90 / New Note.

TAKE ME BACK TO NEW ORLEANS
Take me back to New Orleans / Send her to me / Shine on lover's moon / Please forgive me / Workin' for my baby / Give me one more chance / My little room / What a dream / Don't go to strangers / Food of love / Girl next door / What a crazy world / I'm that kind of guy / Call me for Christmas / Guida's Romeo and Juliet / Million tears / Time ol' story / My sweet Ruby Rose / I know why dreamers cry / I walk the line / Oh yeah oh yeah / Nearness of you / I love you so / I don't wanna wait (why wait 'til Saturday night)
CD _____ CDCHD 549
plete/Pinnacle.

Bone Machine

SEARCH AND DESTROY
CD _____ NTHEN 022CD
Now & Then / Jan '96 / Plastic Head.

Bone Structure

BONE STRUCTURE
On Green Dolphin Street / Vatican roulette / Modal T / Lush life / Doodlin' / Bone idle rich / Latin line / Shades of blue and green / Last minute waltz / Spanish white
CD _____ CLGCD 020
Calligraph / Jun '92 / Cadillac / Wellard / Jazz Music.

Bonesaw

ABANDONED
CD _____ LF 099CD
Lost & Found / Jun '94 / Plastic Head.

SHADOW OF DOUBT
CD _____ LF 189CD
Lost & Found / Jan '96 / Plastic Head.

WRITTEN IN STONE
CD _____ LF 140CD
Lost & Found / May '95 / Plastic Head.

Bonethugs N'Harmony

E1999 ETERNAL
Da introduction / East 1999 / Eternal / Crept and we came down '71 (the getaway) / Mr. Bill Collector / Budsmokers only / Crossroads / Me killa / Land of the heartless / No

shorts, no losses / First of the month / Budds lovaz / Die die die / Mr. Ouija 2 / Mo murda / Shots to the double glock
CD _____ 4810382
Epic / Jul '95 / Sony.

Bonewire

THROWN INTO MOTION
CD _____ NIHIL 3CD
Vinyl Solution / Mar '95 / Disc.

Boney M

10,000 LIGHTYEARS
CD _____ ACD 610 140
Ariola / Dec '88 / BMG.

ALL THE HITS
Rivers of Babylon / Daddy cool / Sunny / Brown girl in the ring / Rasputin / Ma Baker / hooray hooray it's a holi holiday / Painter man / Belfast / No woman, no cry / Mary's boy child / Gotta go home / Boney M megamix
CD _____ 74321128892
Arista / Jan '93 / BMG.

COLLECTION, THE
CD _____ 261670
Arista / Aug '92 / BMG.

DADDY COOL - GREATEST HITS
CD _____ 290 799
Ariola Express / Jun '92 / BMG.

GREATEST HITS
CD _____ TCD 2656
Telstar / Mar '93 / BMG.

GREATEST HITS OF ALL TIME - REMIX
Sunny / Daddy Cool / Rasputin / Ma Baker / Take the heat off me / Hooray hooray it's a holi holiday / Rivers of Babylon / No woman, no cry / Brown girl in the ring / Gotta go home / Painter man / Mary's boy child
CD _____ 259.476
Ariola / '90 / BMG.

NIGHT FLIGHT TO VENUS
Night flight to venus / Rasputin / Painter man / He was a steppenwolf / King of the road / Rivers of Babylon / Voodoo night / Brown girl in the ring / Never change lovers in the middle of the night / Heart of gold
CD _____ 74321212692
Arista / Jun '94 / BMG.

NIGHT FLIGHT TO VENUS/LOVE FOR SALE
Night light to venus / Rasputin / Painter man / He was a steppenwolf / King of the road / Rivers of Babylon / Voodoo night / Brown girl in the ring / Never change lovers in the middle of the night / Heart of gold / Ma baker / Love for sale / Belfast / Have you ever seen the rain / Gloria / Can you waddle / Plantation boy
CD Set _____ 74321260422
Arista / Mar '95 / BMG.

Bongos

DRUMS ALONG THE HUDSON
In the Congo / Bulrushes / Clay midgets / Video eyes / Glow in the dark / Telephoto lens / Certain harbours / Speaking sands / Burning bush / Automatic doors hunting / Zebra club / Three wise men / Mambo sun / Question ball
CD _____ 900770
Line / Oct '94 / CM / Grapevine / ADA / Conifer / Direct.

Bongchong

CRUDE
Le introducement / Things to come / Floggin set / If and when / Lee highway blues / Phosphene / Tamlinn / Hengmans reel / Dig a hole / Scotland / Frosty morning / A.K.A. Crude / Wedding row / Reprise
CD _____ DOOVFCD 1
Doovf / Oct '94 / CM / ADA.
CD _____ IRCD 032
Iona / Nov '95 / ADA / Direct / Duncans.

Bongwater

DOUBLE BUMMER
CD _____ SDE 8901CD
Shimmy Disc / Jan '91 / Vital.

TOO MUCH SLEEP
CD _____ SDE 9017CD
Shimmy Disc / Oct '90 / Vital.

Boni, Raymond

LE GOUT DU JOUR (Boni, Raymond Octet)
CD _____ CELP C18
CELP / Feb '92 / Harmonia Mundi / Cadillac.

Bonilla, Marc

EE TICKET
Entrance / White noise / Mannequin hotel / Commotion / Lycanthrope / Hit and run / Afterburner / Hurling blues skyward / Antonio's love jungle / Razor back / Slaughter on Memory Lane / Exit
CD _____ 7599267252
Reprise / Apr '92 / Warner Music.

Bonner, Joe

IMPRESSIONS OF COPENHAGEN
CD _____ ECD 220242
Evidence / Aug '92 / Harmonia Mundi / ADA / Cadillac.

MONKISMS
CD _____ 74030
Capri / Nov '93 / Wellard / Cadillac.

Bonner, Juke Boy

JUKE-BOY BONNER - 1960-67 (Bonner, Weldon 'Juke Boy')
Look out Lightning / Jumpin' with Juke Boy / Dust my broom / That a while ago / Three ring circus / Look out your window / True love darling / Jumpin' at the studio / I'm going up / Life is a dirty deal / Nine below zero
CD _____ FLYCD 38
Flyright / Oct '91 / Hot Shot / Wellard / Jazz Music / CM.

LIFE GAVE ME A DIRTY DEAL (Bonner, Weldon 'Juke Boy')
CD _____ ARHCD 375
Arhoolie / Apr '95 / ADA / Direct / Cadillac.

Bonnet, Graham

FORCEFIELD III (To Oz & Back) (Bonnet, Graham/Cozy Powell/Ray Fenwick/Jan Akkerman)
Hit and run / Always / Stay away / Desire / Tokyo / Who'll be the next in line / Wings on my feet / Firepower / Hold on / Rendezvous
CD _____ PCOM 1100
President / Oct '89 / Grapevine / Target/ BMG / Jazz Music / President.

HERE COMES THE NIGHT
CD _____ PCOM 1114
President / Jul '91 / Grapevine / Target/ BMG / Jazz Music / President.

Bonnet, Guy

CANTE (Bonnet Sings Trenet)
A la porte du garage / Mes jeunes annees / Y'a-d'la joie / La mer / Route N7 / Je chante / La java du Diable / Une noix / Le soleil et la lune / Que reste-t-il de nos amours / La jolie Sardane / Longtemps / Boum / Pour finir
CD _____ UCD 19112
Forlane / Nov '95 / Target/BMG.

Bonney, Graham

GRAHAM BONNEY
CD _____ 16008
Laserlight / Aug '91 / Target/BMG.

Bonney, Simon

EVERYMAN
CD _____ CDSTUMM 114
Mute / Jun '95 / Disc.

FOREVER
CD _____ CDSTUMM 99
Mute / May '92 / Disc.

Bonzo Dog Band

BESTIALITY OF BONZO DOG BAND
Intro and the outro / Canyons of your mind / Trouser press / Postcard / Mickey's son and daughter / Sport (the odd boy) / Tent / I'm the urban spaceman / Mr. Apollo / Shirt / Dad blead / Deadymades / Demostralia oaths / Can blue men sing the whites / Mr. Slater's parrot / Strain / We are normal / My pink half of the drainpipe / Jazz, delicious hot, disgusting cold / Big shot / Jollity farm / Humanoid boogie
CD _____ CZ 196
Liberty / Apr '90 / EMI.

CORNOLOGY
CD Set _____ CDDOG 1
EMI / Jun '92 / EMI.

DOG ENDS
My brother makes the noises for the talkies / I'm going to bring a watermelon to my girl tonight / Alley oop / Button up your overcoat / Mr. Apollo / Ready mades / Strain / Turkeys / King of Scurf / Waiting for the wardrobe / Straight from my heart / Rusty / Rawlinson end / Don't get me wrong / Fresh wound / Bad blood / Slush / Labio-dental fricative / Recycled vinyl blues / Trouser freak
CD _____ CZ 501
EMI / Jun '92 / EMI.

GORILLA
Cool Britannia / Equestrian statute / Jollity farm / I left my heart in San Francisco / Look out there's a monster coming / Jazz, delicious hot, disgusting cold / Death cab for a cutie / Narcissus / Intro and the outro / Mickey's son and daughter / Big shot / Music for the head ballet / Piggy bank love / I'm bored / Sound of music
CD _____ BGOCD 82
Beat Goes On / Jul '95 / Pinnacle.

INTRO, THE
Cool Britannia / Equestrian statute / Jollity farm / I left my heart in San Francisco / Look

out there's a monster coming / Jazz, delicious hot, disgusting cold / Death cab for cutie / Narcissus / Intro and the outro / Mickey's son and daughter / Big shot / Music for the head ballet / Piggy bank love / I'm bored / Sound of music / We are normal / Postcard / Beautiful Zelda / Can blue men sing the whites / Hello Mabel / Kama Sutra / Humanoid boogie / Trouser press / Pink half of the drainpipe / Rockaliser baby / Rhinocratic oaths / Mustachioed daughters
CD _____ CZ 499
EMI / Jun '92 / EMI.

OUTRO, THE
Hunting tigers out in Indiah / Shirt / Tubas in the moonlight / Dr. Jazz / Monster mash / I'm the urban spaceman / Ali Baba's camel / By a waterfall / Mr. Apollo / Canyons of your mind / You've done my brain in / Keynsham / Quiet talks and summer walks / Tent / We were wrong / Joke shop man / Bride stripped bare by 'bachelors' / Look at me I'm wonderful / What do you do / Mr. Slater's parrot / Sport (the odd boy) / I want to be with you / Noises for the leg / Busted
CD _____ CZ 500
EMI / Jun '92 / EMI.

UNPEELED
CD _____ SFRCD 134
Strange Fruit / May '95 / Pinnacle.

Boo, Betty

GRR, IT'S BETTY BOO
I'm on my way / Thing goin' on / Hangover / Curly and girly / Let me take you there / Gave you the Boo / Skin tight / Catch me / Close the door
CD _____ 4509909082
WEA / Nov '94 / Warner Music.

Boo Radleys

EVERYTHING'S ALRIGHT FOREVER
CD _____ CRECD 120
Creation / Mar '92 / 3MV / Vital.

GIANT STEPS
I hang suspended / Upon 9th and fairchild / Wish I was skinny / Leaves and sand / Butterfly McQueen / Rodney King / Thinking of ways / Barney (and me) / Spun around / If you want it, take it / Best lose the fear / Take the time around / Lazarus / One is for / Run my way runway / I've lost the reason
CD _____ CRECD 149
Creation / Aug '93 / 3MV / Vital.

LEARNING TO WALK
CD _____ R 3012
Rough Trade / Nov '93 / Pinnacle.

WAKE UP
CD _____ CRECD 179
Creation / Mar '95 / 3MV / Vital.

Boo-Yaa T.R.I.B.E.

DOOMSDAY
CD _____ CDVEST 20
Bulletproof / Jul '94 / Pinnacle.

NEW FUNKY NATION
Six bad brothers / Don't mess / Once upon a drive by / Psyko funk / R.A.I.D. / Riot pump / Rated R / New funky nation / Walk the line / Pickin' up metal / T.R.I.B.E.
CD _____ IMCD 120
4th & Broadway / Apr '91 / PolyGram.

Boogalusa

CARELESS ANGELS & CRAZY CAJUNS
CD _____ LDLCD 1208
Lochshore / Oct '93 / ADA / Direct / Duncans.

Boogie Monsters

RIDERS OF THE STORM: THE UNDERWATER ALBUM
Juggernauts / Recognised thresholds of negative stress / Boogie / Muzic appreciation (Sweet muzic) / Mark of the beast / Altered states of consciousness / Honeydrips in Gotham / Strange / Old man Jacob's well / Bronx bombas / Salt water Taffy (Slo jam) / Riders of the storm
CD _____ CDCHR 6079
Cooltempo / Aug '94 / EMI.

Book Of Wisdom

CATACOMBS
CD _____ NACD 201
Nature & Art / Oct '95 / Plastic Head.

Bookbinder, Roy

LIVE BOOK - DON'T START ME TALKIN'
CD _____ ROU 3130CD
Rounder / May '94 / CM / Direct / ADA / Cadillac.

ROY BOOKBINDER
CD _____ CD 3107
Rounder / '88 / CM / Direct / ADA / Cadillac.

Booker, Chuckii

NIICE N WIILD
Spinnin / Love is medicine / Out of the dark / You don't know / With all my heart / I git around / Games / Deep c diiver / Soul triilogy 1 / Soul triilogy 11 / Soul triilogy 111 / Niice n wiild / I should have loved you
CD _______ 7567824102
WEA / Nov '92 / Warner Music.

Booker, James

JUNCO PARTNER
Black minute waltz / Goodnight Irene / Pixie / On the sunny side of the street / Make a better world / Junco partner / Put out the light / Medley (Blues minute, Until the real thing comes along, Baby won't you please come home,) / Pop's dilemma / I'll be seeing you
CD _______ HANCD1359
Hannibal / Feb '93 / Vital / ADA.

KING OF THE NEW ORLEANS KEYBOARD
How do you feel / Going down slow / Classified / One hell of a nerve / Blues rhapsody / Rockin' pneumonia and the boogie woogie flu / Please send me someone to love / All by myself / Ain't nobody's business / Something you got / Harlem in Hamburg
CD _______ CDJP 1
JSP / Apr '92 / ADA / Target/BMG / Direct / Cadillac / Complete/Pinnacle.

RESSURECTION OF THE BAYOU MAHARAJAH
CD _______ ROU 2118CD
Rounder / Aug '93 / CM / Direct / ADA / Cadillac.

SPIDERS ON THE KEYS
CD _______ ROU 2119CD
Rounder / Oct '93 / CM / Direct / ADA / Cadillac.

Booker, Steve

DREAMWORLD
This side of heaven / Poet stone / Everytime you walk away / Running and hiding / Homeland / Shades of grey (CD only.) / Wedding day / I will be there / When the fire burns out / Songs from the river / Lay me down
CD _______ CDPCS 7347
Parlophone / Oct '90 / EMI.

Booker T & The MG's

AND NOW
My sweet potato / Jericho / No matter what shape / One mint julep / In the midnight hour / Summertime / Working in the coal mine / Don't mess up a good thing / Think / Taboo / Soul jam / Sentimental journey
CD _______ 8122702972
Atlantic / Jul '93 / Warner Music.

BEST OF BOOKER T AND THE MG'S
Green onions / Slim Jenkins place / Hip hug-her / Soul dressing / Summertime / Bootleg / Jelly bread / Tic-tac-toe / Can't be still / Groovin' / Mo' onions / Red beans and rice
CD _______ 756781218
Atlantic / Jan '93 / Warner Music.

BEST OF BOOKER T AND THE MG'S, THE
Time is tight / Soul limbo / Heads or tails / Over easy / Hip hug-her / Hang 'em high / Johnny I love you / Slum baby / Horse / Soul clap '69 / Sunday sermon / Born under a bad sign / Mrs. Robinson / Something / Light my fire / It's your thing / Fuquawi / Kinda easy like / Meditation / Melting pot
CD _______ CDSX 46
Stax / Apr '93 / Pinnacle.

BOOKER T SET, THE
Love child / Lady Madonna / Horse / Sing a simple song / Mrs. Robinson / This guy's in love with you / Light my fire / Michelle / You're all I need / I've never found a girl / It's your thing
CD _______ CDSXE 026
Stax / May '90 / Pinnacle.

DOIN' OUR THING
I can dig it / Expressway to your heart / Doin' our thing / You don't love me / Never my love / Exodus song / Beat goes on / Ode to Billie Joe / Blue on green / You keep me hangin' on / Let's go get stoned
CD _______ 8122710142
Atlantic / Jul '93 / Warner Music.

GREEN ONIONS
Green onions / Rinky dink / I got a woman / Mo' onions / Twist and shout / Behave yourself / Stranger on the shore / Lonely avenue / One who really loves you / You can't sit down / Woman, a lover, a friend / Comin' home baby
CD _______ 75678222552
Pickwick/Warner / Oct '94 / Pinnacle / Warner Music / Carlton Home Entertainment.

HIP HUG HER
Hip hug-her / Slim Jenkin's place / Soul sanction / Get ready / More / Double or nothing / Carnaby street / Slim Jenkins' joint / Pigmy / Groovin' / Booker's notion / Sunny
CD _______ 8122710132
Atlantic / Jul '93 / Warner Music.

IN THE CHRISTMAS SPIRIT
Jingle bells / Santa Claus is coming to town / Winter wonderland / White Christmas / Christmas song / Silver bells / Merry Christmas baby / Blue Christmas / Sweet little Jesus boy / Silent night / We three kings / We wish you a Merry Christmas
CD _______ 7567823382
Atlantic / Jul '93 / Warner Music.

MCLEMORE AVENUE
Golden slumbers / Here comes the sun / Come together / Because / Mean Mr Mustard / She came in through the bathroom window / Carry that weight / End / Something / You never give me your money / Polythene Pam / Sun king / I want you
CD _______ CDSXE 016
Stax / Nov '88 / Pinnacle.

MELTING POT
Melting pot / Back home / Chicken pox / Fuquawi / Kinda easy like / Hi ride / L.A. jazz song / Sunny Monday
CD _______ CDSXE 055
Stax / Sep '92 / Pinnacle.

PLAY THE HIP HITS
Baby scratch my back / Harlem shuffle / Hi-heel sneakers / Downtown / I was made to love her / Georgia on my mind / Wade in the water / Fannie Mae / Day tripper / You left the water running / Every beat of my heart / Ain't that peculiar / You can't do that / Wang dang doodle / On a Saturday night / Letter / Oo wee baby, I love you / Spoonful / I hear a symphony / You're so fine / Raunchy / You are my sunshine / Soul man / Gimme some lovin' / When something is wrong with my baby
CD _______ CDSXD 065
Stax / Apr '95 / Pinnacle.

SOUL DRESSING
Soul dressing / Tic-tac-toe / Big train / Jelly bread / Aw' mercy / Outrage / Night owl walk / Chinese checkers / Home grown / Mercy mercy / Plum Nellie / Can't be still
CD _______ 7567823372
Pickwick/Warner / Feb '95 / Pinnacle / Warner Music / Carlton Home Entertainment.

SOUL LIMBO
Be young, be foolish, be happy / Hang 'em high / Over easy / Eleanor Rigby / Sweet sweet baby / Foxy lady / La la means I love you / Willow weep for me / Soul limbo / Heads or tails / Born under a bad sign
CD _______ CDSXE 009
Stax / Apr '90 / Pinnacle.

THAT'S THE WAY IT SHOULD BE
Slip slidin' / Mo' greens / Gotta serve somebody / Let's wait awhile / That's the way it should be / Just my imagination / Camel ride / Have a heart / Cruisin' / I can't stand the rain / Sarasota sunset / I still haven't found what I'm looking for
CD _______ 474470 2
Columbia / Jun '94 / Sony.

Booker T Trio

GO TELL IT ON THE MOUNTAIN
CD _______ SHCD 114
Silkheart / Oct '92 / Jazz Music / Wellard / CM / Cadillac.

Boom, Barry

LIVING BOOM, THE
CD _______ FADCD 016
Fashion / Nov '90 / Jetstar / Grapevine.

TRUST ME
CD _______ MERCD 010
Merger / Jan '93 / Jetstar.

Boom Boyz

BOTTOM, THE
CD _______ BRY 4185CD
Ichiban / Mar '94 / Koch.

Boomers

ART OF LIVING
CD _______ 4509918542
WEA / Jan '96 / Warner Music.

WHAT WE DO
CD _______ 9031745152
WEA / Jan '96 / Warner Music.

Boomtown Rats

TONIC FOR THE TROOPS
Like clockwork / Blind date / I never loved Eva Braun / Living in an island / Don't believe what you read / She's so modern / Me and Howard Hughes / Can't stop / Watch out for the normal people / Rat trap
CD _______ 5140532
Mercury / Jul '93 / PolyGram.

Boon

TIN MAN
Tin man / Don't walk away / Kick or the kiss / Baby I know / Ever the way / Sleepy people / Every day / One from the heart / How deep (is your heart) / Growing wild in the desert / Tears me down / Knight
CD _______ RES 106CD
Resurgence / Sep '95 / Vital.

Boone, Daniel

BEAUTIFUL SUNDAY
CD _______ 12550
Laserlight / Jun '95 / Target/BMG.

Boone, Debbie

FRIENDS FOR LIFE
CD _______ CDO 3011
Nelson Word / '89 / Nelson Word.

SURRENDER
CD _______ LLD 3001
Nelson Word / Aug '85 / Nelson Word.

Boone, Pat

APRIL LOVE
Speedy Gonzales / Ain't that a shame / Love letters in the sand / Johnny Will / I'll be home / Moody River / Don't forbid me / Remember you're mine / Almost lost my mind / Why baby why / Wonderful time up there / April love
CD _______ CDCD 1046
Charly / Mar '93 / Charly / THE / Cadillac.

APRIL LOVE
Love letters in the sand / I love you more and more / I almost lost my head / Friendly persuasion / Mr. Blue / April love / Speedy Gonzales / Ain't that a shame / Tutti frutti / Don't forbid me / Wonderful time up there / I believe in music / I'll be home / Moody River / She fights that lovin' feelin' / Jambalaya / You lay so easy on my mind / Bernadine / Where there's a heartache / Poetry in motion
CD _______ HADCD 162
Javelin / May '94 / THE / Henry Hadaway Organisation.

APRIL LOVE
CD _______ RMB 75070
Remember / Apr '94 / Total/BMG.

BABY OH BABY
Baby, oh baby / Rose Marie / Baby sonnenschein / Wie eine lady / Ein goldener stern / Komm zu mir wenn du einsam bist / Oh lady / Nein nein valentina / Mary Lou / Wo find ich meine traume / Que pasa contigo / Y te quiero / Recuerdame siempre / Amor al reves / En cualquier lugar / Cartas en la arena / Tu che non hai amato mai / E fuori la pioggia cade / Se tu non fossi qui
CD _______ BCD 15645
Bear Family / Jun '92 / Rollercoaster / Direct / CM / Swift / ADA.

BEST OF PAT BOONE, THE
CD _______ MATCD 306
Castle / Oct '94 / BMG.

COLLECTION, THE
CD _______ COL 036
Collection / Jan '95 / Target/BMG.

FAMILY CHRISTMAS
CD _______ 12289
Laserlight / Nov '95 / Target/BMG.

GOLDEN GREATS
April love / Don't forbid me / I almost lost my mind / At my front door / Friendly persuassion (Thee I love) / Sugar moon / Moody river / I'll be home / Love letters in the sand / Gospel boogie / Remember your mine / Ain't that a shame / Main attraction / It's too soon to know / Why baby why / Speedy Gonzalez
CD _______ MCLD 19182
MCA / Mar '93 / BMG.

LOVE LETTERS IN THE SAND
CD _______ ENTCD 238
Entertainers / '88 / Target/BMG.

ULTIMATE HIT COLLECTION, THE
CD _______ 12387
Laserlight / Mar '95 / Target/BMG.

VERY BEST OF PAT BOONE
Love letters in the sand / Speedy Gonzalez / April love / I'll be home / Gospel boogie / Johnny will / Sugar moon / Ain't that a shame / Don't forbid me / Remember you're mine / I almost lost my mind / It's too soon to know / Moody river / Main attraction / There's a goldmine in the sky / Friendly persuasion
CD _______ PWK 074
Carlton Home Entertainment / Sep '88 / Carlton Home Entertainment.

Booth, Webster

MOONLIGHT AND YOU (Webster Booth Sings Songs of Romance)
World is mine tonight / Pale moon / Vienna / Stay with me forever / I love the moon / Always as I close my eyes / Moonlight and you / Brown bird singing / Princess Elizabeth / This year of theatreland / At dawning / Mifanwy / Song for you and me / Moon of romance / Serenade in the night / Way you look tonight / Serenata / In old Madrid / Elegie / Hindu song
CD _______ PASTCD 9709
Flapper / '90 / Pinnacle.

THREE GREAT TENORS (Booth, Webster & Josef Locke/Richard Tauber)
Lovely maid in the moonlight / My heart and I / Soldier's dream / English rose / Hear my song / Take a pair of sparkling eyes / Song of songs / When the stars are brightly shining / Serenade / March of the grenadiers / Wandering minstrel / Break of day / One alone / If I can help somebody / Faery song / You are my heart's delight / I'll walk beside you / Love is my reason / Goodbye / Lost chord
CD _______ CDSL 8248
EMI / Jul '95 / EMI.

Boothe, Ken

COLLECTION, THE
CD _______ RNCD 2124
Rhino / Nov '95 / Jetstar / Magnum Music Group / THE.

I AM JUST A MAN
CD _______ LG2 1101
Lagoon / Mar '95 / Magnum Music Group / THE.

KEN BOOTHE COLLECTION
CD _______ CDTRL 249
Trojan / Mar '94 / Jetstar / Total/BMG.

Boots & His Buddies

1935-1937
CD _______ JSPCD 327
JSP / Oct '91 / ADA / Target/BMG / Direct / Cadillac / Complete/Pinnacle.

BOOTS 1937-38
CD _______ CLASSICS 738
Classics / Feb '94 / Discovery / Jazz Music.

CLASSICS 1935-37
CD _______ OJCCD 732
Original Jazz Classics / Dec '93 / Wellard / Jazz Music / Cadillac / Complete/Pinnacle.

Bootstrappers

BOOTSTRAPPERS
CD _______ NAR 046 CD
New Alliance / May '93 / Pinnacle.

Booty, Charlie

AFTER HOURS
CD _______ SACD 108
Solo Art / Mar '95 / Jazz Music.

Booze & Blues

MOTORWAY LIGHTS
CD _______ BOO 003
B & B / Nov '94 / Jetstar / Else.

Booze Brothers

BREWERS DROOP
Where are you tonight / Rollercoaster / You make me feel so good / My old lady / Sugar baby / Rock steady woman / Louise / What's the time / Midnight special / Dreaming
CD _______ RATA 1
Ramble Tamble / May '94 / Target/BMG.

Bop Brothers

STRANGE NEWS
Thrill me / Cruisin' and coastin' / One mint julep / Big bad beautiful blues / Strange news / Money is getting cheaper / Long slow ride down / Little finger / Georgia on my mind / Chicken and the hawk
CD _______ ABACACD 1
Abacabe / Jul '95 / Hot Shot.

Bop Fathers

BOP FATHERS, VOL. 2
CD _______ COD 027
Jazz View / Jul '92 / Harmonia Mundi.

Bop Harvey

BREAD AND CIRCUSES
Bread and circuses / Vibe / Lazarus / Lazarus speaks / Dues due to dudu / Fun / Dub master / Can't blame the youth / Man in disguise / Poor Judge Bork
CD _______ 4676872
Epic / May '91 / Sony.

Boptails

HOT ROD WHEELS
CD _______ TBCD 2004
Nervous / Mar '93 / Nervous / Magnum Music Group.

Borderlands

FROM CONJUNTO TO CHICKEN SCRATCH
CD _______ SFWCD 40418
Smithsonian Folkways / Oct '94 / ADA / Direct / Koch / CM / Cadillac.

Bore, Sergio

TAMBORES URBANOS
Adivinhacao / Voices of percussion / Rumbata / Tambores urbanos / El cogollo /

|

Chama criolla / Stop killing the Amazon / El poliangito / Lamento Africano / Pingentes / Luz de lua / Marimba / Suite Brasila part 1
CD _____ ME 000342
Soulciety/Bassism / Oct '95 / EWM.

Boredoms

ONANIE BOMB MEETS THE SEX PISTOLS
Wipe out shock / Shoppers / Boredom Vs.SDI / We never sleep / Bite my bollocks / Young assouls / Call me God / No core punk / Lick'n cock boatpeople / Melt down boogie / Feedbackfuck / Anal eater / God from anal / Born to anal
CD _____ EN 001
Earthnoise / Sep '94 / Vital.

SOUL DISCHARGE '99
Your name is limitless / Bubblebop shot / Fifty two boredom (club mix) / Sun, gun / Z and U and T and A / TV Scorpion / Pow wow now / J.B. Dick and Tina Turner pussy / G.I.L. '77 / Jup-na-keeeeel / Catastro mix '99 / Milky way / Songs without electric guitars / Hamaiin disco bollocks / Hamaiin disco without bollocks
CD _____ EN 002
Earthnoise / Sep '94 / Vital.

WOW 2
CD _____ AVANT 026
Avant / Nov '93 / Harmonia Mundi / Cadillac.

Boris & His Bolshie...

PSYCHIC REVOLUTION (Boris & His Bolshie Balalaika)
Toadstool soup / Onward christian soldiers / Purple haze / Burnin' with the fire / Blacklisted blues / Voodoo chile / Moonsong / Goin' nowhere / Psychic revolution (sunsong)
CD _____ DELECCD 014
Delerium / Nov '94 / Vital.

Born Against

PATRIOTIC BATTLE HYMNS
CD _____ VMFM 612
Vermiform / Nov '94 / Plastic Head.

Born Jamericans

KIDS FROM FOREIGN
Instant death interlude / Warning sign / So ladies / Sweet honey / Informa fe dead / Cease and seckle / Ain't no stoppin' / Why do girls / Oh gosh / Nobody knows / Boom shak-a-tack
CD _____ 756792349-2
Warner Bros. / Jun '94 / Warner Music.

Bornkamp, Arno

REED MY MIND
CD _____ BVHAASTCD 9304
Bvhaast / Oct '94 / Cadillac.

Borrfors, Monica

SECOND TIME AROUND
CD _____ 1397
Caprice / Jun '85 / CM / Complete/Pinnacle / Cadillac / ADA.

YOUR TOUCH
CD _____ 1350
Caprice / Oct '90 / CM / Complete/Pinnacle / Cadillac / ADA.

Borstlap, Michiel

MICHIEL BORSTLAP LIVE
CD _____ CHR 70030
Challenge / Nov '95 / Direct / Jazz Music / Cadillac / ADA.

Bose, Miguel

SIGN OF CAIN, THE
One touch / Fire and forgiveness / They're only words / Home / Sign of cain / Hunter and the prey / Wako-shamen / I hold only you / mayo / Nada particular
CD _____ 450995053-2
East West / Feb '95 / Warner Music.

Boss

BORN GANGSTAZ
Call from mom / Deeper / Comin' to getcha / Mai sister is a bitch / Thelma and Louise / Drive-by / Progress of elimination / Livin' loc'd / Recipe of a hoe / Blind date with Boss / Catch a bad one / Born gansta / 1800 body bags / Diary of a mad bitch / 2 to da head / I don't give a fuck / Call from dad
CD _____ 474074 2
Columbia / Aug '93 / Sony.

Boss Hog

BOSS HOG
Winn coma / Sick / Beehive / Ski bunny / Green shirt / I dig you / Try one / What the fuck / I idolize you / Punkture / Strawberry / Walk in / Texas / Sam
CD _____ GED 24811
Geffen / Oct '95 / BMG.

Cold Hands

CD _____ EFA 08127CD
Amphetamine Reptile / Jan '91 / SRD.

Bostic, Earl

ALTO MAGIC IN HI-FI
Twilight time / Stairway to the stars / Rockin' with Richard / Be my love / Pinkie / Goodnight sweetheart / Over the waves rock / Geronimo / C jam blues / Wee-gee board / Wrecking rock / Home sweet home rock
CD _____ KCD 0597
King/Paddle Wheel / Mar '93 / New Note.

BEST OF BOSTIC
Flamingo / Always / Deep purple / Smoke rings / What, no pearls / Jungle drums / Serenade / I can't give you anything but love / Seven steps / I'm gettin' sentimental over you / Don't you do it / Steamwhistle jump
CD _____ KCD 500
King/Paddle Wheel / Mar '90 / New Note.

BLOWS A FUSE
Night train / 8.45 stomp / That's the groovy thing / Special delivery stomp / Moonglow / Mambostic / Earl blows a fuse / Harlem nocturne / Who snuck the wine in the gravy / Don't you do it / Disc jockey's nightmare / Flamingo / Steam whistle jump / What, no pearls / Tuxedo Junction
CD _____ CDCHARLY 241
Charly / Oct '90 / Charly / THE / Cadillac.

BOSTIC FOR YOU
Sleep / Moonglow / Velvet sunset / For you / Very thought of you / Linger awhile / Cherokee / smoke gets in your eyes / Memories / Embraceable you / Wrap your troubles in dreams (and dream your troubles away) / Night and day
CD _____ KCD 503
King/Paddle Wheel / Mar '90 / New Note.

DANCE MUSIC FROM THE BOSTIC WORKSHOP
Third man theme / Key / Does your heart beat for me / El choclo cha cha / Gondola / Sweet pea / Cuckoo / Sentimental journey / Barcarolle / Who cares / Rose Marie / Up there in orbit
CD _____ KCD 613
King/Paddle Wheel / Mar '90 / New Note.

DANCE TO THE BEST OF EARL BOSTIC
CD _____ KCD 000500
King/Paddle Wheel / Sep '92 / New Note.

FLAMINGO (Charly R&B Masters Vol. 16)
Flamingo / Sleep / Always / Moonglow / Ain't misbehavin' / You go to my head / Cherckee / Streamwhistle jump / What, no pearls / Deep purple / Mambostic / Sweet Lorraine / Where or when / Harlem nocturne / 720 in the books / Tuxedo junction / Night train / Special delivery stomp / Song of the Islands / Liebestraum / Liszt
CD _____ CDRB 16
Charly / Mar '95 / Charly / THE / Cadillac.

JAZZ TIME
CD _____ LEJAZZCD 52
Le Jazz / Jan '96 / Charly / Cadillac.

LET'S DANCE
Lover come back to me / Merry widow waltz / Cracked ice / Song of the Islands / Danube waves / Wrap it up / Blue skies / Ubangi stomp / Cherry bean / Earl's imagination / My heart at thy sweet voice / Liebestraum
CD _____ KBD E09
King/Paddle Wheel / Oct '88 / New Note.

Boston

BOSTON
More than a feeling / Peace of mind / Foreplay (long time) / Rock 'n' roll band / Smokin' / Hitch a ride / Something about you / Let me take you home tonight
CD _____ 4804132
Epic / Jul '95 / Sony.

DON'T LOOK BACK
Journey / It's easy / Man I'll never be / Feeling satisfied / Part / Used to bad news / Don't be afraid
CD _____ CD 86057
Epic / Mar '87 / Sony.

FOR REAL
CD _____ MCD 10973
MCA / May '94 / BMG.

THIRD STAGE
Amanda / We're ready / Launch / Cool the engines / My destination / New world / To be a man / I think I like it / Can'tcha say / Still in love / Hollyann
CD _____ MCLD 19066
MCA / Oct '92 / BMG.

Boston Pops Orchestra

CLASSIC ROCK
CD _____ 5501072
Spectrum/Karussell / Oct '93 / PolyGram / THE.

Bostonian Friends

PEACE FROM AFRICA
CD _____ 151472
EPM / Nov '92 / Discovery / ADA.

Boswell Sisters

ANTHOLOGY 1930-1940
CD _____ EN 518
Encyclopaedia / Sep '95 / Discovery.

BOSWELL SISTERS 1931-1935
CD _____ CD 56082
Jazz Hoots / Mar '95 / Target/BMG.

BOSWELL SISTERS COLLECTION VOL. 1 1931-32
CD _____ COCD 21
Collector's Classics / Mar '95 / Cadillac / Complete/Pinnacle.

IT'S THE GIRLS (Boswell Sisters & Connie Boswell)
It's the girls / That's what I like about you / Heebie jeebies / Concentratin' on you / Wha'd ja do to me / I'm all dressed up with a broken heart / When I take my sugar to tea / Don't tell him what happened to me / Roll on Mississippi roll on / I'm gonna cry (cryin' blues) / This is the missus / That's love / Life is just a bowl of cherries / My future just passed / What is it / Shine on harvest moon / Gee but'd like to make you happy / We're on the highway to Heaven / Time on my hands / Nights when I'm lonely / Shout, sister, shout / It's you
CD _____ CDAJA 5014
Living Era / Koch.

Bothy Band

AFTERHOURS (Recorded Live In Paris)
Kesh jig / Butterfly / Casadh an tsugain / Farewell to Erin / Heathery hills of Yarrow / Queen Jane / Pipe on the hob / Mary Willies / How can I live at the top of a mountain / Rosie Finn's favourite / Green groves of Erin
CD _____ GL 3016CD
Green Linnet / Jul '94 / Roots / CM / Direct / ADA.

BBC RADIO 1 IN CONCERT
CD _____ WINCD 060
Windsong / May '94 / Pinnacle.

BEST OF THE BOTHY BAND
Salamanca / Banshee / Sailor's bonnet / Petty peg / Craig's pipes / Blackbird / Maids of Mitchelstown / Casadh an tsupain / Music in the glen / Fionnghuala / Old hag you have killed me / Do you love an apple / Rip the calico / Death of Queen Jane / Green groves of Erin / Flowers of Red Hill
CD _____ GL 3001CD
Green Linnet / Jul '94 / Roots / CM / Direct / ADA.

BOTHY BAND
Kesh jig / Give us a drink of water / Flowers of the flock / Famous Ballymote / Green groves of Erin / Flowers of Red Hill / Do you love an apple / Julia Delaney / Patsy Geary's / Coleman's cross / Is trua nach bhfuil me in Eirinn / Navvy on the line / Rainy day / Tar road to Sligo / Paddy Clancy's jig / Martin Wynn's / Lonford tinker / Pretty peg / Craig's pipes / Hector the hero / Laird of Drumdair / Traveller / Humors of Lissade / Butterfly / Salamanca / Banshee / Sailor's bonnet
CD _____ GL 3011CD
Green Linnet / Jul '94 / Roots / CM / Direct / ADA.

OLD HAG YOU HAVE KILLED ME
Maids in the Glen / Fionnghuala / Old hag you have killed me / Farewell to Erin / Summer will come / Laurel tree / Sixteen come next Sunday / Old hag you have killed me / Calum Sgaire / Ballintore fancy / Maid of Coolmore / Michael Gorman's reel
CD _____ GL 3005CD
Green Linnet / Jul '94 / Roots / CM / Direct / ADA.

OUT OF THE WIND INTO THE SUN
Morning star / Maids of Mitchelstown / Rip the calico / Streets of Derry / Pipe on the hob / Sailor boy / Blackbird / Strayaway child / Factory girl / Slides
CD _____ GL 3013CD
Green Linnet / Jul '94 / Roots / CM / Direct / ADA.

Bottcher, Gerd

FUR GABI TU' ICH ALLES
Fur gabi tu ich alles / Du schaust mich an / Deine roten lippen / Adieu lebewohl goodbye (Tonight is so right for love) / Goodbye rock a hula baby / Wine nicht um mich / Geld wie heu / Man geht so leicht am gluck vorbei Tina Lou / Jambalaya / Ein dutzend and're manner / Oh Billy Billy Black / Sing / Sing denn mein zuhause das bist du / Susanna ich kenn' die / Strassen der welten / Ay ay ay ay oh / Signorina / Ich such' dich auf allen Wegen / Ich komme wieder / Du heut nacht / Carolin, Carolin / Meine braut, die kann das besser / Bing bang bungalow / Lady Lou / Ich finde nichts dabei
CD _____ BCD 15402
Bear Family / Dec '87 / Rollercoaster / Direct / CM / Swift / ADA.

Bottom 12

SONGS FOR THE DISGRUNTLED POSTMAN
CD _____ EFA 032502
Noise-O-Lution / Dec '95 / SRD.

Bouchard, Dominic

HEOL DOUR (Bouchard, Dominic & Cyrille Colas)
CD _____ KMCD 40
Keltia Musique / Aug '93 / ADA / Direct / Discovery.

VIBRATIONS
CD _____ KMCD 03
Keltia Musique / Jul '90 / ADA / Direct / Discovery.

Boucher, Judy

CAN'T BE WITH YOU TONIGHT
CD _____ OCD 024
Orbitone / Sep '86 / Jetstar.

DEVOTED TO YOU
CD _____ KU 106CD
Kufe / Apr '94 / Jetstar.

TEARS ON MY PILLOW
CD _____ KUCD 100
Kufe / Jul '92 / Jetstar.

Boudreaux, Helene

UNE DEUXIEME (Boudreaux, Helene & Pete Bergeron)
CD _____ SW 6120CD
Swallow / Jul '95 / ADA.

Bouffard, Patrick

MUSIC FOR HURDY GURDY FROM AUVERGNE
Ocora / Nov '90 / Harmonia Mundi / ADA. _____ C 560007

Boukan Ginen

JOU A RIVE
CD _____ XENO 4024
Xenophile / Feb '95 / Direct / ADA.

Boukman Experyans

KALFOU DANJERE
Bay bondye glwa / Tande m tande / Jou nou revolte / Kouman sa ta ye / Nanm nan boutey / Bade zile / Zanset nou yo / Nwel inosan / Eve / Fey / Vodou adjae / Kalfou danjere / Mayi a gaye
CD _____ CIDM 1113
Mango / Jun '94 / Vital / PolyGram.

LIBETE (PRAN POU PRAN'L)
Legba / Sa'm pedi / Libete (pran pou pran'l) / Ganga / Peye pou peye / Zan'j yo / Zili / Ki moun / Rar (ti celia) / Konbit zaka / Jou male
CD _____ CIDM 1117
Mango / Apr '95 / Vital / PolyGram.

VODOU ADJAE
Se kreyo'l nou ye / Nou l a / Plante / Ke'm pa sote / Pwazon rat / Malere / Mizak a manze' mizere're / Wet chen / Nou pap sa bliye
CD _____ CIDM 1072
Mango / Apr '91 / Vital / PolyGram.

Boulevard Of Broken...

IT'S THE TALK OF THE TOWN (Boulevard Of Broken Dreams)
CD _____ HNCD 1345
Hannibal / May '89 / Vital / ADA.

Boulton, Laura

NAVAJO SONGS
CD _____ SFWCD 40403
Smithsonian Folkways / Dec '94 / ADA / Direct / Koch / CM / Cadillac.

Bounty Killer

DOWN IN THE GHETTO
CD _____ GRELCD 210
Greensleeves / Nov '94 / Total/BMG / Jetstar / SRD.

GUNS OUT
CD _____ GRELCD 206
Greensleeves / Jul '94 / Total/BMG / Jetstar / SRD.

JAMAICA'S MOST WANTED
CD _____ GRELCD 195
Greensleeves / Jun '94 / Total/BMG / Jetstar / SRD.

NO ARGUMENT
CD _____ GRELCD 222
Greensleeves / Jul '94 / Total/BMG / Jetstar / SRD.

Bourbonese Qualk

BOURBONESE QUALK
CD _____ PRAXIS 5CD
Praxis / Feb '94 / Plastic Head.

FEEDING THE HUNGRY GHOST
CD _____ FUNFUNDVIERZIG 69
Funfundvierzig / Jun '94 / SRD.

MY GOVERNMENT
CD _____ CD 34
Funfundvierzig / Feb '90 / SRD.

UNPOP
CD _____ 2TF 13CD
TFI / Jul '95 / Plastic Head.

Bourelly, Jean-Paul

JUNGLE COWBOY
Love line / Tryin' to get over / Drifter / Hope
you find your way / Jungle cowboy / No
time to share / Can't get enough / Parade /
Mother Earth / Groove with me
CD _____ 8344092
JMT / May '91 / PolyGram.

TRIPPIN'
CD _____ EMY 1272
Enemy / Mar '92 / Grapevine.

Boutouk, Ian

**GIPSY CLASSICS (The Soul Of The
Gipsy Violin) (Boutouk, Ian & Batalonia
Gipsy Orchestra)**
CD _____ 995552
EPM / Jul '95 / Discovery / ADA.

Boutte, Lillian

I SING BECAUSE I'M HAPPY
CD _____ CDJC 11003
Timeless Jazz / Jan '88 / New Note.

JAZZ BOOK, THE
Now baby or never / Comes love / On
revival day / Don't worry 'bout me / Lover
come back to me / Muddy water / Tennessee waltz / That old feeling / Embraceable
you / Barefootin'
CD _____ BLU 10202
Blues Beacon / Dec '94 / New Note.

**LILLIAN BOUTTE WITH HUMPHREY
LYTTLETON AND BAND (Boutte, Lillian/
Humphrey Lyttelton & His Band)**
Back in your own backyard / Miss Otis re-
grets / Squiggles / I double dare you / Lillian
CD _____ CLGCD 018
Calligraph / Oct '88 / Cadillac / Wellard /
Jazz Music.

**LIVE IN TIVOLI (Boutte, Lillian & Her
American Band)**
CD _____ MECCACD 1030
Music Mecca / Jun '93 / Jazz Music /
Cadillac / Wellard.

Bouzouki Ensemble

SONGS OF GREECE
CD _____ SOW 90131
Sounds Of The World / Sep '94 / Target/
BMG.

Bovell, Dennis

AUDIO ACTIVE
CD _____ MTLP 008CD
Meteor / Oct '87 / Magnum Music Group.

DUB DEM SILLY
CD _____ ARKCD 107
Arawak / Oct '95 / Jetstar.

DUBMASTER
CD _____ JMC 200210
Jamaica Gold / Jan '94 / THE / Magnum
Music Group / Jetstar.

TACTICS
CD _____ LKJCD 010
LKJ / Mar '95 / Jetstar / Grapevine.

Bow Wow Wow

BEST OF BOW WOW WOW, THE
CD _____ RRCD 116
Receiver / Jul '93 / Grapevine.

**GO WILD - THE BEST OF BOW WOW
WOW**
I want Candy / Go wild in the country /
Prince of darkness / Cowboy / Baby, oh no
/ Do you wanna hold me / Golly golly go
buddy / Louis Quatorze / What's the time
(Hey buddy) / Joy of eating raw flesh / Elim-
ination dancing / Aphrodsiac / Mile high
club / T.V. savage / See jungle (See jungle
boy) / Chihuahua (12" version) / Go wild in
the country (12" Version) / Chihuahua
CD _____ 74321213362
Arista / Jun '94 / BMG.

I WANT CANDY
I want candy / Cowboy / Louis Quatorze /
Mile high club / W.O.R.K. (nah no no no my
daddy don't) / Fools rush in / I want my
baby on Mars / Gold he saw / Sexy Eiffel
towers / Radio G-string / C30 C60 C90 Go
/ Sun, sea and piracy / Uomo sea al parche
/ Giant sized baby thing
CD _____ PIPCD 021
Great Expectations / Nov '90 / BMG.

Bowdler, John

LET'S FACE THE MUSIC AND DANCE
CD _____ JB 001CD
Key / Oct '94 / CM.

Bowen, Ralph

MOVIN' ON (Bowen, Ralph Quintet)
CD _____ CRISS 1066CD
Criss Cross / Oct '92 / Cadillac /
Harmonia Mundi.

Bowen, Robin Huw

HARP MUSIC OF WALES
CD _____ CDSDL 412
Saydisc / Oct '95 / Harmonia Mundi / ADA
/ Direct.

HUNTING THE HEDGEHOG
CD _____ RHB 002CD
Teires / Jun '94 / ADA.

Bowers, Bryan

VIEW FROM HOME, THE
CD _____ FF 70037
Flying Fish / Oct '89 / Roots / CM / Direct
/ ADA.

Bowers, Graham

OF MARY'S BLOOD
CD _____ RWCD 001
Extreme / May '95 / Vital/SAM.

Bowie, David

1966
I'm not losing sleep / I dig everything / Can't
help thinking about me / Do anything you
say / Good morning girl / And I say to
myself
CD _____ CLACD 154
Castle / Dec '89 / BMG.

ALADDIN SANE
Watch that man / Aladdin Sane / Drive-in
Saturday / Panic in Detroit / Cracked actor
/ Time / Prettiest star / Let's spend the night
together / Jean genie / Lady grinning soul
CD _____ CDEMC 3579
EMI / Jul '90 / EMI.

CHANGESBOWIE
Space oddity / John I'm only dancing /
Changes / Ziggy Stardust / Suffragette City
/ Jean Genie / Diamond dogs / Rebel rebel
/ Young Americans / Fame '90 (remix) /
Golden years / Heroes / Ashes to ashes /
Fashion / Let's dance / China girl / Modern
love / Blue Jean / Starman (CD only) / Life
on Mars (CD only) / Sound and vision (CD
only)
CD _____ CDDBTV 1
EMI / Apr '90 / EMI.

DAVID BOWIE
Uncle Arthur / Sell me a coat / Rubber band
/ Love you till Tuesday / There is a happy
land / We are hungry men / When I live my
dream / Little bombardier / Silly boy blue /
Come and buy my toys / Join the gang /
She's got medals / Maid of Bond street /
Please Mr. Gravedigger
CD _____ 8000872
Deram / Jan '93 / PolyGram.

**DAVID LIVE (At Tower Theatre
Philadelphia)**
1984 / Rebel rebel / Moonage daydream /
Sweet thing / Changes / Suffragette city /
Aladdin Sane / All the young dudes /
Cracked actor / Rock 'n' roll with me /
Watch that man / Knock on wood / Dia-
mond dogs / Big brother / Width of a circle
/ Jean Genie / Rock 'n' roll suicide / Band
introduction (EMI issues only) / Here today,
gone tomorrow (EMI issues only) / Time
(EMI issues only)
CD Set _____ CDDBLD 1
EMI / Jun '95 / EMI.

DIAMOND DOGS
Future legend / Diamond dogs / Sweet
thing / Candidate / Rebel rebel / Rock 'n'
roll with me / We are the dead / 1984 / Big
brother / Chant of the ever circling skeletal
family / Dodo (EMI issues only) / Candidate
(demo) (EMI issues only)
CD _____ CDEMC 3584
EMI / Oct '90 / EMI.

**GOSPEL ACCORDING TO DAVID
BOWIE, THE**
Laughing gnome / Love you till Tuesday /
Did you ever have a dream / Rubber band
/ Little bombardier / Maid of Bond Street /
When I live my dream / London boys /
Karma man / Sell me a coat / There is a
happy land / She's got medals / Gospel ac-
cording to Tony Day / Let me sleep beside
you
CD _____ 5500212
Spectrum/Karussell / May '93 / PolyGram /
THE.

HEROES
Beauty and the beast / Joe the lion / Sons
of the silent age / Blackout / V2 Schneider
/ Sense of doubt / Moss garden / Neuköln
/ Secret life of Arabia / Heroes / Abdulmajid
(EMI issues only) / Joe the lion ('91 Mix)
(EMI issues only)
CD _____ CDEMD 1025
EMI / Aug '91 / EMI.

HUNKY DORY
Changes / Oh you pretty things / Eight line
poem / Life on Mars / Kooks / Quicksand /
Fill your heart / Andy Warhol / Song for Bob
Dylan / Queen bitch / Bewlay Brothers /

Bombers (EMI issues only) / Supermen (EMI
issues only) / Quicksand (demo version)
(EMI issues only) / Bewlay brothers (alter-
native mix) (EMI issues only)
CD _____ CDEMC 3572
EMI / Apr '90 / EMI.

**INTERVIEW COMPACT DISC: DAVID
BOWIE**
CD P.Disc _____ CBAK 4040
Baktabak / Sep '90 / Baktabak.

INTROSPECTIVE: DAVID BOWIE
I'm not losing sleep / I dig everything / Can't
help thinking about me / Interview part one
/ Do anything you say / Good morning girl
/ And I say to myself / Interview part two
CD _____ CINT 5001
Baktabak / Nov '90 / Baktabak.

LET'S DANCE
Modern love / China girl / Let's dance /
Without you / Ricochet / Criminal world /
Cat people (putting out fires) / Shake it /
Under pressure (CDVUS 96 only)
CD _____ CDVUS 96
Virgin / Nov '95 / EMI.

LODGER
Fantastic voyage / African night flight /
Move on / Yassassin / Red sails / D.J. /
Look back in anger / Boys keep swinging /
Repetition / Red money / I pray ole (EMI
issues only) / Look back in anger (1988 ver-
sion) (EMI issues only)
CD _____ CDEMD 1026
EMI / Aug '91 / EMI.

LOVE YOU TILL TUESDAY.
Space oddity / Love you till Tuesday / When
I'm five / Ching-a-ling / Laughing gnome /
Rubber band / Sell me a coat / Liza Jane /
When I live my dream / Let me sleep beside
you / London boys
CD _____ PWKS 4131P
Carlton Home Entertainment / Oct '92 /
Carlton Home Entertainment.

LOW
Speed of life / Breaking glass / What in the
world / Sound and vision / Always crashing
in the same car / Be my wife / New career
in a new town / Warszawa / Art decade /
Weeping wall / Subterraneans / Some are
(EMI issues only) / All saints (EMI issues
only) / Sound and vision (1991 remix) (EMI
issues only)
CD _____ CDEMD 1027
EMI / Aug '91 / EMI.

MAN WHO SOLD THE WORLD
Width of a circle / All the madmen / Black
country rock / After all / Running gun blues
/ Saviour machine / She shook me cold /
Man who sold the world / Supermen / Light-
ning frightening (EMI issues only) / Holy holy
(EMI issues only) / Moonage daydream (EMI
issues only) / Hang on to yourself (EMI is-
sues only)
CD _____ CDEMC 3573
EMI / Apr '90 / EMI.

NEVER LET ME DOWN
New York's in love / Too dizzy / Bang bang
/ Day in, day out / Time will crawl / Beat of
your drum / Never let me down / Zeroes /
Glass spider / Shining star (making my love)
/ '87 and cry / Julie (CDVUS 98 only) / Girls
(CDVUS 98 only) / When the wind blows
(CDVUS 98 only)
CD _____ CDVUS 98
Virgin / Nov '95 / EMI.

OUTSIDE
Leon take us outside / Outside / Heart's
filthy lesson / Small plot of land / Baby
Grace (a horrid cassette) / Hello spaceboy
/ Motel / I have not been to Oxford town /
No control / Algeria touchshriek / Voyeur of
utter destruction / Ramona A Stone/I am
with name / Wishful beginnings / We prick
you / Nathan Adler / I'm deranged / Thru'
these architects eyes / Strangers when we
meet
CD _____ 74321307022
RCA / Sep '95 / BMG.

PIN UPS
Rosalyn / Here comes the night / I wish you
would / See Emily play / Everything's alright
/ I can't explain / Friday on my mind / Sorrow / Don't bring me down / Shapes of
things / Anyway anyhow anywhere / Where
have all the good times gone / Growin' up
(EMI issues only) / Amsterdam (EMI issues
only)
CD _____ CDEMC 3580
EMI / Jul '90 / EMI.

RARESTONEBOWIE
All the young dudes / Queen bitch / Sound
and vision / Time / Be my wife / Footstom-
pin' / Ziggy Stardust / My death / I feel free
CD _____ GY 014
Trident / May '95 / Pinnacle.

**RISE AND FALL OF ZIGGY STARDUST
& THE SPIDERS FROM MARS**
Five years / Soul love / Moonage daydream
/ Starman / It ain't easy / Lady Stardust /
Star / Hang on to yourself / Ziggy Stardust
/ Suffragette city / Rock 'n' roll suicide /
John I'm only dancing (EMI issues only) /
Velvet goldmine (EMI issues only) / Sweet
head (EMI issues only) / Ziggy Stardust
(demo) (EMI issues only) / Lady Stardust
(demo) (EMI issues only)

CD _____ CDEMC 3577
EMI / Jun '90 / EMI.

SANTA MONICA '72
Ziggy Stardust / Changes / Superman / Life
on mars / Five years / Space oddity / Andy
Warhol / My death / Width of a circle /
Queen bitch / Moonage daydream / John
I'm only dancing / Waiting for the man /
Jean genie / Suffragette city / Rock 'n' roll
suicide
CD _____ GY 002
Trident / Mar '94 / Pinnacle.

SCARY MONSTERS
It's no game / Up the hill backwards / Scary
monsters (and super creeps) / Ashes to
ashes / Fashion / Teenage wildlife / Scream
like a baby / Kingdom come / Because
you're young / It's no game (part 2) / Space
oddity (EMI issues only) / Panic in Detroit
(EMI issues only) / Crystal Japan (EMI issues only) / Alabama song (EMI issues only)
CD _____ CDEMD 1029
EMI / May '92 / EMI.

**SINGLES COLLECTION, THE (2 CD/2
MC/3 LP)**
Space oddity / Changes / Starman / Ziggy
Stardust / Suffragette city / John I'm only
dancing / Jean genie / Drive-in Saturday /
Life on Mars / Sorrow / Rebel rebel / Rock
'n' roll suicide / Diamond dogs / Knock on
wood / Young Americans / Fame / Golden
years / TVC 15 / Sound and vision / Heroes
/ Beauty and the beast / Boys keep swing-
ing / D.J. / Alabama song / Ashes to ashes
/ Fashion / Scary monsters (and super
creeps) / Under pressure / Wild is the wind
/ Let's dance / China girl / Modern love /
Blue jean / This is not America / Dancing in
the street / Absolute beginners / Day in, day
out
CD Set _____ CDEM 1512
EMI / Nov '95 / EMI.

SPACE ODDITY
Space oddity / Unwashed and somewhat
slightly dazed / Letter to Hermione / Cygnet
committee / Janine / Wild eyed boy from
Freecloud / God knows I'm good / Memory
of a free festival / Occasional dream, An
CD _____ CDEMC 3571
EMI / Apr '90 / EMI.

STAGE
Hang on to yourself / Ziggy Stardust / Five
years / Soul love / Star / Station to station
/ Fame / TVC 15 / Warszawa / Speed of life
/ Art decade / Sense of doubt / Breaking
glass / Heroes / What in the world / Black-
out / Beauty and the beast / Alabama song
(EMI issues only)
CD Set _____ CDEMD 1030
EMI / Feb '92 / EMI.

STATION TO STATION
Station to station / Golden years / Word on
a wing / TVC 15 / Stay / Wild is the wind /
Word on a wing (live) (EMI issues only) /
Stay (live) (EMI issues only)
CD _____ CDEMD 1020
EMI / Apr '91 / EMI.

TONIGHT
Loving the alien / Don't look down / God
only knows / Tonight / Neighbourhood
threat / Blue Jean / Tumble and twirl / I keep
forgetting / Dancing with the big boys / This
is not America (CDVUS 97 only) / As the
world falls down (CDVUS 97 only) /
Absolute beginners (CDVUS 97 only)
CD _____ CDVUS 97
Virgin / Nov '95 / EMI.

YOUNG AMERICANS
Young Americans / Win / Fascination / Right
/ Somebody up there likes me / Across the
universe / Can you hear me / Fame / Who
can I be now (EMI issues only) / It's gonna
be me (EMI issues only) / John I'm only
dancing again (EMI issues only)
CD _____ CDP 7964362
EMI / Apr '91 / EMI.

Bowie, Lester

ALL THE MAGIC
For Louie / Spacehead / Ghosts / Trans tra-
ditional suite / Let the good times roll / Or-
ganic echo / Dunce dance / Charlie M (part
II) / Thirsty / Almost Christmas / Down home
/ Okra influence / Miles Davis meets Donald
Duck / Deb Deb's face / Monkey waltz /
Fraudulent fanfare / Organic echo (part II)
CD Set _____ 8106202
ECM / Nov '91 / New Note.

**AVANT POP (Bowie, Lester Brass
Fantasy)**
CD _____ 8295632
ECM / Sep '86 / New Note.

**FUNKY T. COOL T. (Bowie, Lester New
York Organ Ensemble)**
CD _____ DIW 853
DIW / Feb '92 / Harmonia Mundi /
Cadillac.

GREAT PRETENDER
Great pretender / It's howdy doody time /
When the doom (moon) comes over the
mountain / Rios negroes / Rose drop / Oh
how the ghost sings
CD _____ 8293692
ECM / '90 / New Note.

I ONLY HAVE EYES FOR YOU
I only have eyes for you / Think / Lament / Coming back Jamaica / Nonet / When the spirit returns
CD _____ 8259022
ECM / '90 / New Note.

ORGANIZER, THE (Bowie, Lester New York Organ Ensemble)
CD _____ DIW 821
DIW / Mar '91 / Harmonia Mundi / Cadillac.

TWILIGHT DREAMS (Bowie, Lester Brass Fantasy)
I am with you / Personality / Duke's fantasy / Thriller / Night time (is the right time) / Vibe waltz / Twilight dreams
CD _____ CDVE 2
Venture / Jun '88 / EMI.

WORKS: LESTER BOWIE
Charlie M / Rose drop / B funk / When the spirit returns / Let the good times roll
CD _____ 8372742
ECM / Jun '89 / New Note.

Bowles, Paul

BLACK STAR AT THE POINT OF DARKNESS
CD _____ SUBCD 01437
Sub Rosa / Jul '91 / Vital / These / Discovery.

Bowlfish

BISCUIT
CD _____ NECKCD 13
Roughneck / Oct '93 / Disc.

Bowlly, Al

GOODNIGHT SWEETHEART
Time on my hands / What are you thinkin' about baby / Guilty / Take it from me (I'm taking to you) / Oh Rosalita / Time alone will tell / Thank your father / Would you like to take a walk / I'll keep you in my heart / That's what I like about you / Bubbling over with love / Just one more chance / Dance hall doll / By the river Sainte Marie / You didn't have to tell me / By my side / Song of happiness / Lady play your mandolin / Smile, darn ya, smile / Goodnight sweetheart
CD _____ CDSVL 150
Saville / '88 / Conifer.

JUST A BOWL OF CHERRIES
Lady of Spain / Smile, darn ya, smile / Adeline / Save the last dance for me / Goodnight Vienna / All of me / My sweet Virginia / Auf wiedersehen my dear / Rain on the roof / Can't we talk it over / Just humming along / One more kiss / By the fireside / Weep no more my baby / Dinner at eight / This is romance / And so, goodbye / Wagon wheels / I idolize my baby's eyes / Falling in love / Life is just a bowl of cherries / You call it madness / Was that the human thing to do / Now that you're gone / You ought to see Sally on Sunday / Pied piper of Hamlin
CD _____ PASTCD 7003
Flapper / Feb '93 / Pinnacle.

LOVE IS THE SWEETEST THING
Love is the sweetest thing / When you wear your Sunday blue / You're a sweetheart / Dreaming / Bi mir bist du schoen / Man and his dream / Over the rainbow / Have you ever been lonely / Marie / It was a lover and his lass / What do you know about love / Something to sing about / Moon love / Little rain must fall / Bella bambina / Au revoir (but not goodbye) / I'll string along with you / In my little red book / Blow, blow thou winter wind / Goodnight sweetheart
CD _____ PAR 2024
Parade / Jul '94 / Koch / Cadillac.

PROUD OF YOU
Marie / Sweet someone / Colorado sunset / Is that the way to treat a sweetheart / When Mother Nature sings her lullaby / Two sleepy people / Sweet as a song / Goodnight angel / Any broken hearts to mend / Al Bowlly remembers (medley) (Lover come back to me/Dancing in the dark/I'm gonna sit right down and write myself a letter/Auf wiedersehen my dear) / Very thought of you / You're as pretty as a picture / Proud of you / True / Summer's end / There's rain in my eyes / Bei mir bist du schon / When the organ played 'O promise me' / While the cigarette was burning / Penny serenade
CD _____ CDAJA 5064
Living Era / Sep '89 / Koch.

SWEET SOMEONE
CD _____ CDMOIR 307
Memoir / Apr '94 / Target/BMG.

TWO SLEEPY PEOPLE
Two sleepy people / Goodnight angel / Any broken hearts to mend / Sweet as a song / When Mother Nature sings her lullaby / Is that the way to treat a sweetheart / Marie / Sweet someone / Colorado sunset / Al Bowlly remembers (Medley) / Very thought of you / You're as pretty as a picture / Proud of you / True / Penny serenade / While the cigarette was burning / When the organ played 'O promise me' / Bei mir bist du schon / There's rain in my eyes / Summer's end

CD _____ CDGRF 097
Tring / '93 / Tring / Prism.

VERY THOUGHT OF YOU, THE
Little white gardenia / Very thought of you / By the fireside / Close your eyes / Love is the sweetest thing / I'll do my best to make you happy / Rock your cares away / Don't say goodbye / Marching along together / Got a date with an angel / Good evening / Echo of a song / Bedtime story / I was true / Living in clover / Goodnight Vienna / Shout for happiness / Goodnight sweetheart
CD _____ 2 BUR 003
Burlington / Sep '88 / CM.

VERY THOUGHT OF YOU, THE
Whispering / Faded summer love / Tell me (you love me) / You didn't know the music / Dinah / Time alone will tell / Foolish facts / Eleven more months and ten more days / If I have to go on without you / My sweet Virginia / Out of nowhere / I'm so used to blanca / Amarillo / California here I come / Waiting for the Robert E. Lee / Baby face / Swanee / Come back to Sorrento / Edelweiss / Lara's theme / Quickstep / Breakaway blues / Pride of Erin / Twist and tweet / Gay Gordons / Old time waltz / Samba / Madison / Foxtrot / Tango / Barn dance / Siosh / Mississippi dip / Modern waltz
CD _____ RAJCD 837
Empress / Oct '94 / THE.

VERY THOUGHT OF YOU, THE
Time on my hands / Goodnight sweetheart / Sweet and lovely / Pied Piper of Hamlin / By the fireside / Love is the sweetest thing / How could we be strangers / Weep no more my baby / Love locked out / You ought to see Sally on Sunday / One morning in May / Very thought of you / Isle of Capri / Blue Hawaii / In my little red book / Penny serenade / They say / South of the border / Over the rainbow / Somewhere in France with you / When you wish upon a star / Who's taking you home tonight / Blow, blow thou winter wind / It was a lover and his lass
CD _____ CZ 306
EMI / May '90 / EMI.

Bowman, Gill

CITY LOVE
Your average woman / Very good year / Verses / Ballad of the four Mary's / Make it good / City love / Psychics in America / Story today / Lang-a-growing / Different game / If I didn't love you
CD _____ FECD 080
Fellside / Feb '91 / Target/BMG / Direct / ADA.

PERFECT LOVER
Take me home / Walking away / Rantin' dog / Dear friend / Comin' thro' the rye / This time / To be like you / Ae fond kiss / Dream Angus / Making friends / Somebody's baby
CD _____ CDTRAX 081
Greentrax / Sep '94 / Conifer / Duncans / ADA / Direct.

TOASTING THE LASSIES
Green grow the rashes / Now westlin' winds / Banks o'Doon / Sweet Tibbie Dunbar / Rantin' dog / Sweet afton / Auld lang syne / This in no my ain lassie / Rosebud by my early walk / Lea rig / De'il's awa' wi' tha exciseman / Ae fond kiss / Comin' thro' the rye
CD _____ CDTRAX 085
Greentrax / Feb '95 / Conifer / Duncans / ADA / Direct.

Bown, Alan

KICK ME OUT
My friend / Strange little friend / Flone / Perfect day / All I can do / Friends in St Louis / Still as stone / Prisoner / Kick me out / Children of the night / Gypsy girl / Wrong idea
CD _____ SEECD 393
See For Miles/C5 / Oct '93 / Pinnacle.

LISTEN/STRETCHING OUT
Wanted man / Crash landing / Loosen up / Pyramid / Forever / Curfew / Make us all believe / Make up your mind / Get myself straight / Messenger / Find a melody / Up above my hobby horse's head / Turning point / Build me a stage / Stretching out
CD _____ EDCD 362
Edsel / Jan '93 / Pinnacle / ADA.

Box & Banjo Band

DANCING PARTY
Hello Dolly / Margie / When you wore a tulip / Bye bye love / Heart of myself / I'm gonna sit right down and write myself a letter / Singin' the blues / Bless 'em all / After the ball was over / Oh dear what can the matter be / Locomotion / How do you do it / Roll out the barrel / Pack up your troubles / Who were you with last night / Happy wanderer / Yankee doodle boy / Dixie / She'll be coming round the mountains / Please help me, I'm falling / Crystal chandeliers / I can't stop loving you / Laughing samba / Wedding samba / Bluebell polka / You're free to go / Anna Marie / He'll have to go / Can Can / Nightingale sang in Berkeley Square / Birth of the blues / Once in a while / Peggy O'Neil / Garden where the praties grow / Teddy O'Neil / Wild rover / Loch Lomond / Bluebells of Scotland / Bonnie lass o'Fyvie / Mormond Braes / New York, New York

CD _____ LCOM 5209
Lismor / May '92 / Lismor / Direct / Duncans / ADA.

GO DANCING
Bye bye blackbird / At the Darktown strutter's ball / Alexander's ragtime band / You made me love you / Oh you beautiful doll / On the sunny side of the street / When Irish eyes are smiling / Lily McNally McNair / Too-ra-loo-ra-loo-ra / Let's twist again / Birdie dance / I love a lassie / Roamin' in the gloamin' / Stop your ticklin' Jock / Just a wee deoch an' Doris / Anniversary song / Bicycle built for two / I'll be your sweetheart / Alley cat / El Cumbanchero / Charleston / I wonder where my baby is tonight / Yes sir that's my baby / Side by side / Lily of Laguna / Carolina in the morning / Me and my gal / Isle of Capri / Jealousy / O sole mio / Camptown races / Steamboat Bill / Oh Susanna / Beautiful Sunday / Una paloma blanca / Amarillo / California here I come / Waiting for the Robert E. Lee / Baby face / Svanee / Come back to Sorrento / Edelweiss / Lara's theme / Quickstep / Breakaway blues / Pride of Erin / Twist and tweet / Gay Gordons / Old time waltz / Samba / Madison / Foxtrot / Tango / Barn dance / Slosh / Mississippi dip / Modern waltz
CD _____ LCOM 9020
Lismor / Sep '95 / Lismor / Direct / Duncans / ADA.

GO SEQUENCE DANCING (medleys)
Quickstep (1) (Strike up the band/Through the tulips/Two eyes of blue) / Quickstep (2) (The best things in life are free/I love my baby, my baby loves me/Button up your overcoat) / Cha cha (1) (There's a small hotel/Isn't this a lovely day/It had to be you) / Cha cha (2) (Tangerine/Always in my heart / Do re mi) / Foxtrot (1) (We'll gather lilacs/Red roses for a blue lady/Release me) / Foxtrot (2) (Rose Marie/Vila/Louise) / Tango (1) (The shadow of your smile/Come closer to me/Perfidia) / Tango (2) (In a little Spanish town/Blue tango/Mack the knife) / Rumba (Love is a many splendoured thing/Yesterday/September song) / Rumba #2 (Born free/Blue moon/Strangers in the night) / Old tyme waltz (1) (Oh in Antonio/Two lovely black eyes/It's my Mary Ellen, I'm shy/ You're a lassie from Lancashire) / Old tyme waltz (2) (After the ball was over/Down at the old bull and bush/In the good old summertime/Cruising down the river) / Waltz (1) (I wonder who's kissing her now/In the shade of the old apple tree/Little Sir Echo) / Waltz (2) (I'm forever blowing bubbles / Now is the hour/The last waltz) / Madison 1 (Ain't she sweet/When you wore a tulip/ S'wonderful/Where did you get that hat; only on CD) / Madison 2 (Pack up your troubles in your old kit bag/You are my sunshine/Don't dilly dally on the way/Sweet Georgia Brown; CD only) / Blues (1) (Show me the way to go home/On a slow boat to China/Red sails in the sunset; CD only) / Blues (2) (Look for the silver lining/If I had my way/The Londonderry air; CD only) / Quickstep (3) (Won't you come home Bill Bailey/Oh Johnny oh/Abie my boy) / Quickstep (4) (Dancing in the dark/You'd be so nice to come home to/Some of these days)
CD _____ LCDM 9021
Lismor / Jan '90 / Lismor / Direct / Duncans / ADA.

SINGALONGA SCOTLAND
Hundred thousand welcomes / Northern lights / Wee Cooper o' Fife / Skye boat song / Come in, come in / Strip the willow / Scottish soldier / Sailing up the Clyde / Annie Laurie / Star of Rabbie Burns / Dark island / Lassie come and dance with me / Auld hoose / Roses of Prince Charlie / Gay Gordons / Song of the Clyde / Wachlin' home / Bonnie Dundee / Auld lang syne
CD _____ LCOM 9017
Lismor / Sep '95 / Lismor / Direct / Duncans / ADA.

Box Tops

BOX TOPS, THE
CD _____ 295591
Ariola / Apr '93 / BMG.

Boxcar

VERTIGO
Gas stop (who do you think you are) / Insect / Vertigo / Freemason (you broke the promise) / Comet / Hit and run / 900 hours / Lelore / Cruel to you / This is the town / Index (Only on CD)
CD _____ VOLTCD 024
Volition / Mar '92 / Vital / Pinnacle.

Boxcar Willie

ACHY BREAKY HEART
Rockin' bones / Sally let your bangs hang down / Train of love / Maybellene / That's all right / Sixteen chickens and a tamborine / Mystery train / Pipeliner blues / No help wanted / Haunted house / Hank you're like your Daddy / Caribbean / Boney Maronie / Memphis / Achy breaky heart
CD _____ 5501342
Spectrum/Karussell / Oct '93 / PolyGram / THE.

CD _____ LCOM 5209 (duplicate?)

BOXCAR WILLIE & SPECIAL GUESTS
CD _____ MU 5061
Musketeer / Oct '92 / Koch.

HEART BREAKIN' HILLBILLY SONGS
Only in my mind / Lonesome old town / Long black veil around my heart / Forty nine nights / Why do you want me / Long black limousine / I don't feel like doing anything / Danny boy / Reflections of an old man / Cody, Wyoming / Nothing but memories / Long long train / If I didn't love you / Old King Cole
CD _____ RITZRCD 530
Ritz / Oct '93 / Pinnacle.

KING OF THE RAILROAD - 21 COUNTRY TRACKS
CD _____ CTS 55431
Country Stars / Sep '94 / Target/BMG.

KING OF THE ROAD
King of the road / Wabash cannonball / You are my sunshine / Boxcar blues / Don't let the stars get in your eyes / Your cheatin' heart / I saw the light / Wreck of ol' 97 / Hank and the hobo / Peace in the valley / Mule train / Hey good lookin' / Kaw-liga / Move it on over / London leaves / Rollin' in my sweet baby's arms / Divorce me C.O.D. / Red river valley / Heaven / San Antonio rose
CD _____ PLATCD 23
Platinum Music / Apr '88 / Prism / Ross.

LIVE AT WEMBLEY (Boxcar Willie & Friends)
Jambalaya / He'll have to go / You are my sunshine
CD _____ PWK 068
Carlton Home Entertainment / Aug '88 / Carlton Home Entertainment.

LIVE IN CONCERT
Wreck of ol' 97 / Mule train / Cold cold heart
CD _____ PWK 048
Carlton Home Entertainment / Jan '88 / Carlton Home Entertainment.

TWO SIDES OF BOXCAR
Freightline fever / Truck drivin' man / Phantom 309 / Truck drivin' son of a gun / Six days on the road / Teddy bear / Whiteline fever / Girl on a billboard / How fast them trucks will go / Truckers' prayer / Forty acres / Convoy / Spirit of America / Old Kentucky home / Dixie / Thank you old flag of mine / America / North to Alaska / Play the star spangled banner over me / Battle hymn of the Republic / Star spangled banner waving somewhere / Yankee doodle / America the beautiful / Battle of New Orleans
CD _____ CDGRF 151
Tring / Feb '93 / Tring / Prism.

Boy George

AT WORST... THE BEST OF BOY GEORGE AND CULTURE CLUB
Do you really want to hurt me / Time (clock of the heart) / Church of the poison mind / Karma chameleon / Victims / I'll tumble 4 ya / Miss me blind / Move away / Love is love / Love hurts / Everything I own / Don't cry / After the love / More than likely / Crying game / Generations of love (La la gone gaga mix) / Bow down mister (Small portion 2b polite mix) / Sweet toxic love (Deliverance mix)
CD _____ VTCD 19
Virgin / Oct '93 / EMI.

CHEAPNESS AND BEAUTY
Fun time / Blindman / Genocide peroxide / Sad / Satan's butterfly ball / Same thing in reverse / Cheapness and beauty / If I could fly / God don't hold a grudge / Evil is so civilised / Your love is what I am / Unfinished business / II adore
CD _____ CDV 2780
Virgin / May '95 / EMI.

SOLD
Sold / I asked for love / Keep me in mind / Everything I own / Freedom / Just ain't enough / Where are you now / Little ghost / Next time / We've got the right / To be reborn
CD _____ CDV 2430
Virgin / Jun '87 / EMI.

Boyack, Pat

BREAKIN' IN (Boyack, Pat & The Prowlers)
CD _____ BBCD 9557
Bullseye Blues / Dec '94 / Direct.

Boyce, Kim

TIME AND AGAIN
CD _____ MYRCD 6861
Myrrh / Jun '88 / Nelson Word.

Boyce, Max

LIVE AT TREORCHY
9-3 / Scottish trip / Ballad of Morgan the moon / Outside-half factory / Asso asso yakhozzi / Duw it's hard / Ten thousand instant Christians / Did you understand / Hymns and arias
CD _____ CDSL 8251
EMI / Jul '95 / EMI.

Boyd, Eddie

7936 SOUTH RHODES
You got to reap / Just the blues / She is real / I'll never stop (I can't stop loving you) / She's gone / Thank you baby / Third degree / You are my love / Blues is here to stay / Ten to one / Be careful / Blackslap
CD _____ BGOCD 195
Beat Goes On / May '95 / Pinnacle.

EDDIE BOYD & HIS BLUES BAND
(Boyd, Eddie Blues Band)
Too bad / Dust my broom / Unfair lovers / Key to the highway / Vacation from the blues / Steakhouse rock / Letter missin' blues / Ain't doing too bad / Blue coat man / Save her doctor / Rack 'em back / Too bad (part 2) / Big bell / Pinetop's boogie woogie / Night time is the right time / Train is coming
CD _____ 8440122
Deram / Jan '94 / PolyGram.

FIVE LONG YEARS
Five long years / Hello stranger / Where you belong / I'm comin' home / My idea / Big question / Come on home / Blue Monday blues / Eddie's blues / All the way / Twenty four hours of fear / Rock the rock / Rosa Lee / Hound dog
CD _____ ECD 260512
Evidence / Sep '94 / Harmonia Mundi / ADA / Cadillac.

LIVE IN SWITZERLAND
I'm coming home to you / Early in the morning / I ain't doing too bad at all / Mr. Highwayman / Little red rooster / I'm sitting here waiting / Third degree / Hard blues / I got a woman / Cool kind treatment / Five long years / She's the one / It's miserable to be alone / Save her doctor / Rattlin' and runnin' around / Reel good feeling / Her picture in the frame
CD _____ STCD 8022
Storyville / Mar '95 / Jazz Music / Wellard / CM / Cadillac.

THIRD DEGREE (Charly Blues - Masterworks Vol. 42)
CD _____ CDBM 42
Charly / Jun '93 / Charly / THE / Cadillac.

Boyer, Jean Pierre

GRILLER PISTACHE
CD _____ PS 65146CD
Playasound / Jul '95 / Harmonia Mundi / ADA.

Boyer, Lucienne

CHANSOPHONE 1926-31
CD _____ 701262
Chansophone / Jun '93 / Discovery.

Boyes, Jim

OUT OF THE BLUE
CD _____ NMV 1CD
No Master's Voice / Feb '93 / ADA.

Boyfriend

HAIRY BANJO
CD _____ RUST 003CD
Creation / Mar '93 / 3MV / Vital.

Boyle, Gary

TRIPLE ECHO
Peace green / Lost brothers / Angola / Let's hear it for Joe / Gilbreto / Bihar / 4 Wheel shuffle / Count city
CD _____ TJL 004CD
The Jazz Label / Oct '94 / New Note.

Boyle, Maggie

REACHING OUT
Proud man / Quiet land of Erin / Joe's in bed / Mountain streams where the moorcocks / October song / Lowlands of Holland / Has sorrow thy young blade / Busk busk bonnie lassie / Pancake Tuesday / Reaching out / Road to Ballinamuck
CD _____ RRACD 003
Run River / Feb '90 / Direct / ADA / CM.

Boyoyo Boys

BACK IN TOWN
Back in town / Maraba start 500 / Dayeyton special / Duba duba / Mapetla / Pulukwani centre / Brakpan no.2 / Dube station / Arcie special / Vezunyawo
CD _____ GRELCD 2003
Greensleeves / Jun '88 / Total/BMG / Jetstar / SRD.

TJ TODAY
Funny face / T.J. special / Gikeleza / Empty box / Tsou tsou / Boston special / Eloff street no.2 / Sofia / Nkosi / American jive
CD _____ GRELCD 2005
Greensleeves / Jan '89 / Total/BMG / Jetstar / SRD.

Boys

BEST OF THE BOYS, THE
CD _____ DOJOCD 137
Dojo / Mar '95 / BMG.

BOYS/ALTERNATIVE CHARTBUSTERS, THE
Sick on you / I call your name / Tumble with me / Tonight / I don't care / Soda pressing / No money / Turning grey / First time / Box number / Kiss like a nun / Cop cars / Keep running / Tenement kids / Living in the city / What'cha gonna do / Brickfield nights / U.S.I. / Taking on the world / Sway (Quien sera) / Do the contract / Heroine / Not ready / Teacher's pet / Classified Susie / T.C.P. / Neighbourhood brats / Stop stop stop / Talking / Backstage pass / Cast of thousands / School days
CD _____ LOMACD 12
Loma / Feb '94 / BMG.

LIVE AT THE ROXY
CD _____ RRCD 135
Receiver / Jul '93 / Grapevine.

TO HELL WITH THE BOYS
CD _____ LOMACD 20
Loma / Nov '94 / BMG.

Boys Next Door

DOOR, DOOR
CD _____ DOORCD 1
Grey Area / Mar '93 / Pinnacle.

Boys Of The Lough

DAY DAWN
CD _____ LOUGH 006CD
Lough / Dec '94 / Direct / Duncans / CM / ADA.

FAIR HILLS OF IRELAND
Bonnie labouring boy / Mickey Doherty's highland/Banks of the Allan/Maurice O'Keeff / Ban chnoic erin o / Wandering minstrel/Fasten the leg in her/Coleman's cross / Ook pick waltz / Midsummer's night/Tinker's daughter/Over the moor to Maggie / Father Brian MacDermott Roe / Joys of the lough/Lucky in love/Sleep sound in the morning / Pinch of snuff / Erin gra mo chroi / Ross memorial hospital / Lancers/Petronella/Ger the rigger / Wind that shakes the barley / Hunt
CD _____ LOUGHCD 005
Lough / Oct '89 / Direct / Duncans / CM / ADA.

FAREWELL AND REMEMBER ME
Sean Bui/Tommy Peoples/The lark in the morning / Leitrim queen / Lucky can du link ony/Pottinger's/Billy Nicholson / Farewell and remember me / Angus polka No.1/Angus polka No.2/Donegal barn dance / An spailpin fanach/The one-horned buck / Valencia harbour/The jug of punch/MacArthur Road / Lovely Ann / Holly bush/The new ships are sailing / Waterford waltz/The stronsay waltz
CD _____ LOUGHCD 002
Lismor / Oct '90 / Lismor / Direct / Duncans / ADA.

LIVE AT CARNEGIE HALL
Garrison Keillor / Maho snaps/Charlie Hunter/The mouse in the cupboard/The rose / I'll buy boots for Maggie/Brendan Begley's polka/O'Connor's / Leaving Glasgow/The Killarney boys of pleasure / Forest flower/James Byrne's reel/Jenny dang the weaver / Margaret's waltz/Captain Caswell/The jig of slurs / Flower of Magherally / Glencoe bridge march/Stirling castle/O'Keefe's polkas / On Raglan Road / Donegal jig / Donegal jig No.2 / Hanged man's reel / Kerryman's daughter/O'Keefe's plough/The sligo maid
CD _____ SA 001 CD
Sagem / Jul '90 / Duncans / Roots / CM.

WELCOMING PADDY HOME
When sick is it tea you want / Cape Breton wedding reel no 1 / Teelin march / Welcoming Paddy home / Miss Rowan Davies / Eugene Stratton / Antrim rose / Alexander's / Rose of Ardee / Tonbigbee waltz / Irish washerwoman
CD _____ LOUGHCD 001
Lough / Dec '94 / Direct / Duncans / CM / ADA.

Boystown Gang

CRUISIN' THE STREETS & DISC CHARGE
Remember me/Ain't no mountain high enough suite / Cruisin' the streets / Can't take my eyes off you / Come and get your love / Signed, sealed, delivered (I'm yours) / You're the one / Disco kicks / Can't take my eyes off you (reprise)
CD _____ MOCD 3004
More Music / Feb '95 / Sound & Media.

Boyz II Men

CHRISTMAS INTERPRETATIONS
CD _____ 5302572
Motown / Nov '93 / PolyGram.

COOLEYHIGHHARMONY
Please don't go / Lonely heart / This is my heart / Uhh ahh / It's so hard to say goodbye to yesterday / Motownphilly / Under pressure / Sympin' / Little things / Your love / End of the road
CD _____ 5300892
Motown / Oct '92 / PolyGram.

REMIX COLLECTION, THE
Under pressure / Vibin' / I remember / Water runs dry / U know / I'll make love to you / Uhh ahh / Motownphilly / On bended knee / Brokenhearted / Thank you / Sympin'
CD _____ 5305982
Motown / Oct '95 / PolyGram.

Boyzone

SAID AND DONE
CD _____ 5278012
Polydor / Aug '95 / PolyGram.

Braam, Bentje

BENTJE BRAAM (Braam, Bentje & Michiel)
CD _____ BVHAASTCD 9007
Bvhaast / Oct '93 / Cadillac.

Brackeen, Charles

ATTAINMENT (Brackeen, Charles Quartet)
CD _____ SHCD 110
Silkheart / May '89 / Jazz Music / Wellard / CM / Cadillac.

RHYTHM X
Rhythm X / Hourglass / Charles concept / C.B. Blues
CD _____ 66051019
Strata East / Sep '93 / New Note.

Brackeen, Jo Anne

FI-FI GOES TO HEAVEN
Estilo magnifico / Stardust / Fi Fi goes to heaven / Zingaro / I hear a rhapsody / Cosmonaut / Dr. Chang
CD _____ CCD 4316
Concord Jazz / Jul '87 / New Note.

HAVIN' FUN (Brackeen, Jo Anne Trio)
Thinking of you / I've got the world on a string / Emily / Just one of those things / This is always / Everything she wants / Manha de carnaval / Day by day
CD _____ CCD 4280
Concord Jazz / Jan '87 / New Note.

LIVE AT MAYBECK RECITAL HALL 1
Thou swelt / Dr. Chu Chow / Yesterdays / Curved space / My foolish heart / Calling Carl / I'm old fashioned / Strike up the band / Most beautiful girl in the world (CD only) / It could happen to you (CD only) / African Aztec (CD only)
CD _____ CCD 4409
Concord Jazz / Mar '90 / New Note.

NEW TRUE ILLUSION (Brackeen, Jo Anne & Clint Houston)
Steps what was / Search for peace / New true illusion / My romance / Freedent / Solar
CD _____ CDSJP 103
Timeless Jazz / Jun '91 / New Note.

TAKE A CHANCE
Recado bossa nova / Children's games / Estate / Cancao do sal / Frevo / Mountain flight / Island / Take a chance / Ponta de areia / Duduka / Mist on a rainbow
CD _____ CCD 4602
Concord Picante / Jul '94 / New Note.

WHERE LEGENDS DWELL
Where legends dwell / Oahu lizard / Picasso / Helen song / Consmic ties or mud pies / Doors and Anders / Edgar Irving Poe / For Stan / Can this Mcbee / Asian spell / Jump in Jack / How to think like a millionaire
CD _____ 66056021
Ken Music / Nov '92 / New Note.

Brackeen, Joanne

TURNAROUND
There is no greater love / Rubies and diamonds / Picasso / Bewitched, bothered and bewildered / Turnaround / Tricks of the trade
CD _____ ECD 221232
Evidence / Sep '95 / Harmonia Mundi / ADA / Cadillac.

Bracket

4 WHEEL VIBE
Circus act / Cool aid / Happy to be sad / John Wilkes Isolation booth / Tractor / Green apples / Closed caption / Trailer park / Fresh air / PC / G vibe / Warren's song part 4 / Two hotdogs for 99c / Metal one / Pessimist / Lazy / My stepson
CD _____ FLATCD 17
Hi Rise / May '95 / EMI / Pinnacle.

924 FORESTVILLE STREET
Get it nite / Dodge ball / Missing link / Sleep / Huge balloon / Stalking stuffer / Why should eye / Warren's song (pts 1 & 2) / Can't make me / Skanky love song / J. Weed / Rod's post
CD _____ FLATCD 15
Hi Rise / Mar '95 / EMI / Pinnacle.

Brad

SHAME
Buttercup / My fingers / Nadine / Screen / Twentieth century / Raise love / Bad for the soul / Down / Rock star / We
CD _____ 473596 2
Epic / Jul '95 / Sony.

Braden, Don

AFTER DARK (Braden, Don Septet)
CD _____ CRISS 1081CD
Criss Cross / May '94 / Cadillac / Harmonia Mundi.

LANDING ZONE
Landing zone / You are the sunshine of my life / Nightline / Body and soul / Break / Hillside / Come rain or come shine / Have you met Miss Jones / Blue spree / Amsterdam jam / Quadralog
CD _____ LCD 15392
Landmark / Mar '95 / New Note.

ORGANIC
Moonglow / Saving all my love / Walking / Brighter days / Cousin Esan / Twister / Belief / It might as well be spring / Plain ol'blues
CD _____ 4812582
Sony Jazz / Oct '95 / Sony.

TIME IS NOW, THE (Braden, Don Quintet)
CD _____ CRISS 1051CD
Criss Cross / Nov '91 / Cadillac / Harmonia Mundi.

Bradford

SHOUTING QUIETLY
CD _____ FOUND 001CD
Foundation 2000 / Feb '90 / Plastic Head.

Bradford, Alex

RAINBOW IN THE SKY
Packing up / Rainbow in the sky / Too close to heaven / I've found someone / Take the Lord along with you / Bells keep on ringing / I won't sell out / Oh my loving mother / Oh Lord, save me / Holy ghost / Let Jesus lead you / Captain Jesus / Life's candlelight / Feel like I'm running for the Lord / Dinner, Mr Rupe / It all belongs to him / Steal away / Over in Beulah land / I've got a job / Man is wonderful / Great consolation / What makes a man turn his back on God / Don't you want Jesus / See if I care
CD _____ CDCHD 413
Ace / Nov '93 / Pinnacle / Cadillac / Complete/Pinnacle.

TOO CLOSE
Too close to heaven / Lord, Lord, Lord / He lifted me / I don't care what the world may do / He leads me safely through / God is all / Just the name of Jesus / Right now / Don't let Satan turn you round / Life's candlelight / He'll wash you whiter than snow / Oh Lord, save me / Holy ghost / Crossing over Jordan / If mother knew / I dare you / I can't tarry / Without a God / Safe in Jesus' arms / Meeting ground / What did John do / There's only one way (to get to heaven) / What folks say about me / Truth will set you free / God searched the world / Lifeboat / Man is wonderful / Move upstairs / This may be the last time
CD _____ CDCHD 480
Ace / Jul '93 / Pinnacle / Cadillac / Complete/Pinnacle.

TOO CLOSE TO HEAVEN
One step / Walk through the streets / Just in time / Left my sins behind me / Let the Lord be seen in you / Climbing up the mountain / I wasn't gonna tell nobody / What about you / Lord looks out for me / Oh my Lord / Too close / Angel on vacation / When you pray / He always keeps his promises / They came out shouting / Let your conscience be your guide / Nothing but the holy ghost / Daniel is a prayin' man / Just to know / I made it in / I made God a promise
CD _____ CPCD 8114
Charly / Jul '95 / Charly / THE / Cadillac.

Bradford, Carmen

WITH RESPECT
Even Steven / Mr. Paganini / Look who's mine / High wire / Finally / Maybe now / Little Esther / Ain't no use / Was I in love alone / He comes to me in comfort / Nature boy
CD _____ ECD 22115
Evidence / Jun '95 / Harmonia Mundi / ADA / Cadillac.

Bradford, Geoff

RETURN OF A GUITAR LEGEND, THE
Going down slow / Broke and hungry / Dark side / Pontiac / Keys to the highway / Paris strut / Alimony / Red's piece / Hallelujah, I love her so / Blind Blake's rag / Blues jumped the devil / Auto-mechanics blues
CD _____ RNCD 001
Beat Goes On / Jun '95 / Pinnacle.

Bradford, Perry

PERRY BRADFORD & THE BLUES SINGERS (1923-27)
CD _____ DOCD 5353
Blues Document / Jun '95 / Swift / Jazz Music / Hot Shot.

Bradley, Tommie

TOMMIE BRADLEY & JAMES COLE
CD _____ DOCD 5189
Blues Document / Oct '93 / Swift / Jazz Music / Hot Shot.

Bradley, Will

FAMOUS DOOR BROADCASTS 1940
(Bradley, Will & Ray McKinley)
Fatal fascination / Flying home / All the things you are / When you wish upon a star / Old Doc Yak / In a little Spanish town / It's a blue world / Starlit hour
CD _____ TAXCD 3713
Tax / Oct '90 / Jazz Music / Wellard / Cadillac.

ORIGINAL 1940 RADIO TRANSCRIPTS
(Bradley, Will & His Orchestra)
CD _____ TAX 37132
Tax / Aug '94 / Jazz Music / Wellard / Cadillac.

Bradshaw, Tiny

GREAT COMPOSER, THE
CD _____ KCD 000653
King/Paddle Wheel / Dec '92 / New Note.

Brady, Paul

BACK TO THE CENTRE
CD _____ 8268092
Mercury / Apr '86 / PolyGram.

FULL MOON
Hard station / Not the only one / Take me away / Busted loose / Dance the romance / Crazy dreams / Helpless heart / Steel claw / Tootsies
CD _____ FIENDCD 34
Demon / Jan '93 / Pinnacle / ADA.

MOLLOY, BRADY, PEOPLES (Brady, Paul/Matt Molloy/Tommy Peoples)
Creel of turf / Tom Billys / Crosses of Annagh / McFadden's handsome daughter / Newport lass / Rambling pitchfork / Shamrock shore / Munster buttermilk / Connaught man's rambles / Speed the plough / Toss the feathers / Limerick lasses / Foxhunters / Mick Finns / Blackthorn / Fergal O'Gara / Cloon / Mulqueeney's / Out in the ocean / Rainy day / Grand canal / Scotsman over the border / Killavil / John Brennans / Drag her round the road / Graf spee
CD _____ GL 3018CD
Green Linnet / Jul '94 / Roots / CM / Direct / ADA.

PRIMITIVE DANCE
Steal your heart away / Soul commotion / Paradise is here / It's gonna work out fine / Awakening / Eat the peach / Don't start knocking / Just in case of accidents / Game of love
CD _____ 8321332
Mercury / Apr '87 / PolyGram.

SPIRITS COLLIDING
I want you to want me / Trust in you / World is what you make it / Marriage made in Hollywood / Help me to believe / You're the one / I will be there / After the party's over / Just in time / Love made a promise / Beautiful world
CD _____ 5268292
Mercury / May '95 / PolyGram.

TRICK OR TREAT
CD _____ 8484542
Mercury / Apr '91 / PolyGram.

TRUE FOR YOU
Great pretender / Let it happen / Helpless heart / Dance the romance / Steel claw / Take me away / Not the only one / Interlude / Trouble round the bend
CD _____ 8108932
Mercury / May '89 / PolyGram.

WELCOME HERE KIND STRANGER
CD _____ LUNCD 024
Mulligan / Aug '94 / CM / ADA.

Brady, Shane

LIVING ROOM, THE
CD _____ HY 200120CD
Hypertension / Feb '95 / Total/BMG / Direct / ADA.

Brady, Tim

IMAGINARY GUITARS
CD _____ JTR 8440-2
Justin Time / Nov '92 / Harmonia Mundi / Cadillac.

INVENTIONS
CD _____ JTR 8433-2
Justin Time / Apr '92 / Harmonia Mundi / Cadillac.

SCENARIO
CD _____ JTR 8445-2
Justin Time / Apr '94 / Harmonia Mundi / Cadillac.

Braff, Ruby

BRAVURA ELOQUENCE (Braff, Ruby Trio)

Ol' man river / Smile (who'll buy my violets) / Lonely moments (CD only) / Here's Cari / God bless the child / It's bad for me / I've grown accustomed to her face / Make sense (CD only) / I'm shooting high / Orange / Persian rug (CD only) / Trav'lin' light / Royal Garden blues / Judy medley
CD _____ CCD 4423
Concord Jazz / Aug '90 / New Note.

CORNET CHOP SUEY
Cornet chop suey / Nancy with the laughing face / Ooh, that kiss / On it again / Love me or leave me / It's the same old South / It had to be you / I must have that man / sweet and slow / Shoe shine boy / You're sensational/ love you Samantha/True love / Lover come back to me
CD _____ CCD 4606
Concord Jazz / Aug '94 / New Note.

EASY NOW
My walking stick / Willow weep for me / When my sugar walks down the street / Song is ended (but the melody lingers on) / Give my regards to broadway / This is my lucky day / Someday you'll be sorry / Yesterdays / For now / I just couldn't take it baby / Little man you've had a busy day / Swinging on a star / Old folks / Did you ever see a dream walking / Pocket full of dreams / Moonlight becomes you / Pennies from Heaven / Go fly a kite / Please / All alone / You're sensational / Too-ra-loo-ra-loo-ra / White Christmas
CD _____ 74321 18522-2
RCA / Jul '94 / BMG.

FIRST, A (Braff, Ruby & Scott Hamilton)
CD _____ CCD 4274
Concord Jazz / Jan '89 / New Note.

HEAR ME TALKIN'
You've changed / Hear me talkin' to ya / Don't blame me / No one else but you / Nobody knows you (when you're down and out) / Buddy Bolden's blues / Mean to me / Where's Freddy
CD _____ BLC 760161
Black Lion / Apr '92 / Jazz Music / Cadillac / Wellard / Koch.

HI-FI SALUTE TO BUNNY
Keep smiling at trouble / I can't get started (with you) / It's been so long / I'm coming Virginia / Marie / Downhearted blues / I got it bad and that ain't good / Somebody else is taking my place / Did I remember
CD _____ 74321185202
RCA / Jul '94 / BMG.

HUSTLIN' AND BUSTLIN'
Hustlin' and bustlin' / There's a small hotel / What's the reason / 'S wonderful / When it's sleepy time down South / Flaky / Fine and mellow / Ad lib blues
CD _____ BLCD 760908
Black Lion / Sep '88 / Jazz Music / Cadillac / Wellard / Koch.

LIVE AT THE NEW SCHOOL 174 (Braff, Ruby & George Barnes)
CD _____ CRD 126
Chiara Scuro / Aug '94 / Jazz Music / Kudos.

LIVE AT THE REGATTABAR
Persian rug / 'S wonderful / Louisiana / Sweet Sue, just you / Do it again / No one else but you / Crazy rhythm / Where are you / Between the devil and the deep blue sea / Orange / Give my regards to Broadway
CD _____ ARCD 19131
Arbors Jazz / Nov '94 / Cadillac.

MF MYSELF AND I (Braff, Ruby Trio)
Muskrat ramble / You've changed / Honey / Me, myself and I / When I fall in love / That's my home / Let me sing and I'm happy / You're a lucky guy / No one else but you / When you're smiling / Swan lake / Jubilee
CD _____ CCD 4381
Concord Jazz / Jul '89 / New Note.

MR. BRAFF TO YOU (Braff, Ruby Quintet)
CD _____ PHONT CD 7568
Phontastic / Apr '88 / Wellard / Jazz Music / Cadillac.

MUSIC FROM MY FAIR LADY (Braff, Ruby & Dick Hyman)
Wouldn't it be lovely / With a little bit of luck / I'm just an ordinary man / Rain in Spain / I could have danced all night / Ascot gavotte / On the street where you live / Show me / Get me to the church on time / Without you / I've grown accustomed to her face
CD _____ CCD 4393
Concord Jazz / '89 / New Note.

MUSIC FROM SOUTH PACIFIC (Braff, Ruby & Dick Hyman)
Bali Ha'i / Some enchanted evening / Cockeyed optimist / Wonderful guy / Happy talk / Dites moi / This nearly was mine / There is nothin' like a dame / Honeybun / Younger than Springtime / Bali Ha'i (final version)
CD _____ CCD 4445
Concord Jazz / Feb '91 / New Note.

PIPE ORGAN RECITAL PLUS ONE (Braff, Ruby & Dick Hyman)
When it's sleepy time down South / When I fall in love / When my sugar walks down the street / As long as I live / America the

beautiful / High society / I ain't got nobody / Louisiana / I'll be with you in apple blossom time / This is all I ask
CD _____ CCD 43003
Concord Jazz / Mar '90 / New Note.

PLAYS GERSHWIN (Braff, Ruby & George Barnes)
CD _____ CCD 6005
Concord Jazz / Jul '88 / New Note.

RODGERS AND HART (Braff, Ruby & George Barnes)
CD _____ CCD 6007
Concord Jazz / Jul '88 / New Note.

RUBY BRAFF & BUDDY TATE WITH NEWPORT ALLSTARS (Braff, Ruby & Buddy Tate & Newport Allstars)
Mean to me / Body and soul / I surrender dear / Lullaby of the leaves / Take the 'A' Train / Don't blame me
CD _____ BLC 760138
Black Lion / Oct '90 / Jazz Music / Cadillac / Wellard / Koch.

RUBY BRAFF & TEDDY WILSON/ NEWPORT ALL STARS JULY 1966 (Braff, Ruby & Teddy Wilson)
CD _____ EBCD 2120-2
Jazzband / Feb '95 / Jazz Music / Wellard.

RUBY BRAFF AND HIS NEW ENGLAND SONGHOUNDS VOL.2 (Braff, Ruby & His New England Songhounds)
Indian Summer / Thousand Islands / What's new / Heartaches / Cabin in the sky / You're a sweetheart / Please / All alone / Lullaby of birdland (Available on CD format only) / Nice work if you can get it (Available on CD format only) / As time goes by / Keepin' out of mischief now
CD _____ CCD 4504
Concord Jazz / May '92 / New Note.

RUBY BRAFF, VOLUME 1 (Braff, Ruby & His New England Songhounds)
CD _____ CCD 4478
Concord Jazz / Sep '91 / New Note.

SAILBOAT IN THE MOONLIGHT (Braff, Ruby & Scott Hamilton)
Lover come back to me / Where are you / Deed I do / When lights are low / Jeepers creepers / Milkman's matinee / Sweethearts on parade / Sailboat in the moonlight
CD _____ CCD 4296
Concord Jazz / Nov '86 / New Note.

Bragg, Billy

BACK TO BASICS
Milkman of human kindness / To have and have not / Richard / Lover's town revisited / New England / Man in the iron mask / Busy girl buys beauty / It says here / Love gets dangerous / From a Vauxhall Velox / Myth of trust / Saturday boy / Island of no return / This guitar says sorry / Lovers lie soldiers do / St. Swithins day / Strange things happen / Lover sings / Between the wars / World turned upside down / Which side are you on
CD _____ COOKCD 060
Cooking Vinyl / Nov '93 / Vital.

DON'T TRY THIS AT HOME
Accident waiting to happen / Moving the goalposts / Everywhere / Cindy of a thousand lives / You woke up my neighbourhood / Trust / God's footballer / Few / Mother of the bride / Tank park salute / Dolphins / North Sea bubble / Rumours of war / Wish you were her / Body of water
CD _____ COOKCD 062
Cooking Vinyl / Nov '93 / Vital.

INTERNATIONALE, THE
Internationale / I dreamt I saw Phil Ochs last night / March of the covert battalions / Red flag / My youngest son came home today
CD _____ UTILCD 011
Utility / May '92 / Grapevine.

PEEL SESSIONS: BILLY BRAGG
Lover's town / Between the wars / Which side are you on / Lover sings / Days like these / Marriage / Jeanne / Greetings to the new brunette / Chile your waters run red / She's got a new spell / Valentine's Day is over / Short answer / Rotting on remand / New England (CD only) / Strange things happen (CD only) / This guitar says sorry (CD only) / Love gets dangerous (CD only) / Fear is a man's best friend (CD only) / A13 trunk road to the sea (CD only)
CD _____ SFRCD 117
Strange Fruit / May '92 / Pinnacle.

VICTIM OF GEOGRAPHY
Greetings to the new brunette / Train train (Not on CD) / Marriage / Ideology / Levi Stubbs' tears / Honey I'm a big boy now / There is power in a union / Help save the youth of America / Wishing the days away / Passion / Warmest room / Home front / She's got a new spell / Must I paint you a picture / Tender Comrade / Price I pay / Little time bomb / Rotting on remand / Valentine's day is over / Life with the lions / Only one / Short answer / Waiting for the great leap forwards
CD _____ COOKCD 061
Cooking Vinyl / Nov '93 / Vital.

WORKERS PLAYTIME
She's got a new spell / Must I paint you a picture / Tender comrade / Price I pay / Lit-

tle time bomb / Rotting on remand / Valentine's day is over / Life with the lions / Only one / Short answer / Waiting for the great leap forwards
CD _____ AGOCD 15
Go Discs / Sep '88 / PolyGram.

Brahaspati, Sulochana

RAG BIULASKHANI TODI/RAGA MISHRA BHAIRAVI
CD _____ NI 5305
Nimbus / Sep '04 / Nimbus.

Brahem, Anouar

BARZAKH
Raf raf / Barzakh / Sadir / Ronda / Hou / Sarandib / Souga / Parfum de Gitane / Bou naouara / Kerkenah / La nuit des yeux / Le belvedera assiege / Oaf
CD _____ 8475402
ECM / May '91 / New Note.

CONTE DE L'INCROYABLE AMOUR
Etincelles / Le temps les genoux de la devineresse / L'oiseau de bois / Lumiere du silence / Conte de l'incroyable amour / Peshrev Hidjaz Homayoun / Diversion / Nayzak / Battements / En souvenir d'Iram retrouvee / Epilogue
CD _____ 5119592
ECM / Jun '92 / New Note.

KHOMSA
CD _____ 5270932
ECM / Feb '95 / New Note.

Brahms 'n' Liszt

CLASSICAL COCKNEY
Set sail / This is the 90's / Madame Belle Fruit / Music / Going nowhere / Miss Tu Tu / Flash the plastic / Daddy wouldn't buy me a pit bull / Henry VIII / China ship / Strollin' / Far too many love songs / Dagenham dustbins / Bill Bailey, Won't you please come home / Mabely Street / Pulling on a rope / Breezing along / All things bright and beautiful
CD _____ URCD 109
Upbeat / Jun '93 / Target/BMG / Cadillac.

Brain Pilot

BRAIN PILOT
CD _____ N 2007-2
Nova Zembla / Apr '94 / Plastic Head.

MIND FUEL
CD _____ NZ 037
Nova Zembla / Jul '95 / Plastic Head.

Brain Police

DRAIN
CD _____ BGR 004
BGR / Mar '95 / Plastic Head.

FUEL
CD _____ BGR 011CD
BGR / May '95 / Plastic Head.

Brainbox

PRIMORDIA
CD _____ W 230069
Nettwerk / Jun '95 / Vital / Pinnacle.

Braincell

LUCID DREAMING
CD _____ HHSP 007CD
Headhunter / May '95 / Disc / Warner Music.

Braindead Sound Machine

BRAINDEAD 2
CD _____ EFA 007602
Shockwave / Apr '95 / SRD.

Brainiac

BONSAI SUPERSTAR
CD _____ GROW 462
Grass / Jan '95 / SRD.

SMACK BUNNY BABY
I, fuzzbot / Ride / Smack bunny baby / Martian dance invasion / Cultural zero / Brat girl / Hurting me / I could own you / Anesthetize / Draag / Get away
CD _____ GROW 0042
Grass / Oct '93 / SRD.

Brainiac 5

WORLD INSIDE, THE
CD _____ CDRECK 1
Reckless / Jun '88 / Pinnacle.

Brainless

SUPERPUNKTUESDAY
CD _____ CDHOLE 005
Golf / Oct '95 / Plastic Head.

Brainpool

SODA
That's my charm / Every day / Girl lost / Come back / Wiping the stains / At school / In the countryside / Mr. Johnson cries / I feel good / (Let's get) Lucky in Kentucky /

Our own revolution / In your bedroom / Probably / We're sorry
CD _____ 476519 2
Epic / Nov '94 / Sony.

Bramhall, Doyle

BIRD NEST ON THE GROUND
CD _____ ANT 0027CD
Antones / Oct '95 / Hot Shot / Direct / ADA.

Branca, Glenn

SYMPHONY NO.1
CD _____ RE 125CD
Reach Out International / Nov '94 / Jetstar.

SYMPHONY NO.6 (Devil Choirs at the Gates of Heaven)
First movement / Second movement / Third movement / Fourth movement / Fifth movement
CD _____ BFFP 39CD
Blast First / Apr '89 / Disc.

WORLD UPSIDE DOWN
First movement (temple of the Venus, Part II) / Second movement / Third movement / Fourth movement / Fifth movement / Sixth movement (fluid density) / Seventh movement (polyhymnia)
CD _____ TWI 9602
Les Disques Du Crepuscule / Sep '92 / Discovery / ADA.

Branch, Billy

MISSISSIPPI FLASHBACK (Branch, Billy & The Sons Of Blues)
CD _____ GBWCD 005
GBW / Sep '92 / Harmonia Mundi.

WHERE'S MY MONEY (Branch, Billy & The Sons Of Blues)
Where's my money / You want it all / Third degree / Small town baby / Son of Juke / Sons of blues / Tell me what's on your mind / (Get up I feel like being a) sex machine / Eyesight to the blind / Take out the time
CD _____ ECD 26069
Evidence / Jul '95 / Harmonia Mundi / ADA / Cadillac.

Branco, Walter

MEU BALANEO
CD _____ MRBCD 002
Mr. Bongo / May '95 / New Note.

Brand New Heavies

BRAND NEW HEAVIES, THE
Dream come true / Stay this way / People get ready / Never stop / Put the funk back in it / Ride in the sky / Brand new heavies / Gimme one of those / Got to give / Sphynx / Dream come true (Mix)
CD _____ 8283002
Acid Jazz/FFRR / Mar '92 / PolyGram.
CD _____ JAZIDCD 023
Acid Jazz / Feb '95 / Pinnacle.

BROTHER SISTER
Back to love / Ten ton take / Mind trips / Spend some time / Keep together / Snake hips / Fake / People giving love / World keeps spinning / Forever / Daybreak / Midnight at the Oasis / Dream on dreamer / Have a good time / Brother sister
CD _____ 828557-2
Acid Jazz/FFRR / Apr '94 / PolyGram.

HEAVY RHYME EXPERIENCE VOL. 1
Bona fied funk (feat. Main Source) / It's getting hectic (feat. Gang Starr) / Who makes the loot (feat. Grand Puba) / Wake me when I'm dead (feat. Master Ace) / Jump 'n' move (feat. Jamalski) / Death threat (feat. Kool G Rap) / State of yo (feat. Black Sheep) / Do what I gotta do (feat. Ed O.G.) / Whatgabothat (feat. Tiger) / Soul Flower (feat. The Pharcyde)
CD _____ 828335-2
Acid Jazz/FFRR / Jul '92 / PolyGram.

Brand New Unit

UNDER THE BIG TOP
CD _____ EXC 0102
Excursion / May '94 / SRD.

Brand Nubian

EVERYTHING IS EVERYTHING
CD _____ 755961682-2
WEA / Oct '94 / Warner Music.

IN GOD WE TRUST
Allah u akbar / Ain't no mystery / Meaning of the 5% / Pass the gat / Black star line / Allah and justice / Godz / Travel jam / Brand Nubian rock the set / Love me or leave me alone / Steal ya ho / Steady bootleggin' / Black and blue / Punks get up to get beat down
CD _____ 7559613812
WEA / Feb '93 / Warner Music.

ONE FOR ONE
All for one / Concerto in X minor / Ragtime / To the right / Dance to my ministry / Drop the bomb / Wake up / Step to the rear / Slow down / Try to do me / Who can get busy like this man / Grand puba / Positive

and L.G dedication / Feels so good / Brand nubian (CD only)
CD _____ 7559609462
WEA / Feb '91 / Warner Music.

Brand X

DO THEY HURT
Noddy goes to Sweden / Voidarama / Act of will / Fragile / Cambodia / Triumphant limp / D.M.Z.
CD _____ CASCD 1151
Charisma / May '89 / EMI.

LIVESTOCK
Nightmare patrol / Ish / Euthanasia waltz / Isis mourning (Parts 1 & 2) / Malaga virgen
CD _____ CLACD 5
Virgin / May '89 / EMI.

MASQUES
Poke / Masques / Black moon / Deadly nightshade / Earth dance / Access to data / Ghost of Mayfield Lodge
CD _____ CASCD 1138
Charisma / May '89 / EMI.

MOROCCAN ROLL
Sun in the night / Why should I lend you mine / Maybe I'll lend you mine after all / Hate zone / Collapsar / Disco suicide / Orbits / Malaga virgen / Machocosm
CD _____ CASCD 1126
Charisma / May '89 / EMI.

PLOT THINS, THE (A History Of Brand X)
Nuclear burns / Born ugly / Why should I lend you mine / Disco suicide / Malaga virgen / Isis mourning (pt 1) / Poke / Ghost of Mayfield lodge / Dance of the illegal aliens / Algon / Cambodia / Triumphant limp
CD _____ CDVM 9005
Virgin / Oct '92 / EMI.

PRODUCT
Don't make waves / Dance of the illegal aliens / Soho / Not good enough - see me / Algon / Rhesus perplexus / Wal to wal / And so to F / April
CD _____ CASCD 1147
Charisma / May '89 / EMI.

UNORTHODOX BEHAVIOUR
Nuclear burn / Euthanasia waltz / Born ugly / Smacks of euphoric hysteria / Unorthodox behaviour / Running on three / Touch wood
CD _____ CASCD 1117
Charisma / May '89 / EMI.

Brandon, Bill

BEST OF BILL BRANDON
Can't we just sit down and talk about it / Just can't walk away / You don't have to say / Hands full of nothing / We fell in love while dancing / Baby, love is a two way street / You made my life so bright / No danger of heartbreak / Special occasion / Get it while it's hot
CD _____ NEMCD 746
Sequel / Aug '95 / BMG.

Brandon, Kirk

STONE IN THE RAIN
Stone in the rain / Communication / How long / Satellite / Children of the damned / Europa / Psycho woman / Revolver / Propaganda / Heroes (CD only) / Future world / Spirit tribe
CD _____ CDGRAM 92
Anagram / Mar '95 / Pinnacle.

Brandon, Mary-Ann

EVERYTHING I TOUCH
CD _____ AP 091CD
Appaloosa / Jun '92 / ADA / Magnum Music Group.

MARY-ANN BRANDON
CD _____ APP 6110CD
Appaloosa / Jun '94 / ADA / Magnum Music Group.

SELF APPOINTED HOMECOMING QUEEN
CD _____ APCD 070
Appaloosa / '92 / ADA / Magnum Music Group.

Brandy

BRANDY
CD _____ 7567826102
Warner Bros. / Nov '94 / Warner Music.

Brandywine Singers

WORLD CLASS FOLK
CD _____ FE 1402
Folk Era / Nov '94 / CM / ADA.

Branigan, Laura

LAURA BRANIGAN
Moonlight on water / Never in a million years / Let me in / Unison / Reverse psychology / Bad attitude / Smoke screen / Turn the beat around / No promise, no guarantee / Best was yet to come
CD _____ 7567820862
Atlantic / Apr '90 / Warner Music.

SELF CONTROL
Lucky one / Self control / Ti amo / Heart / Will you still love me tomorrow / Satisfaction / Silent partners / Breaking out / Take me / With every beat of my heart
CD _____ 780 147-2
Atlantic / '87 / Warner Music.

Brass Construction

BRASS CONSTRUCTION
CD _____ MUSCD 510
MCI / May '95 / Disc / THE.

MOVIN' & CHANGIN' (The Best Of Brass Construction)
Goodnews / Changing / What's on your mind (expression) / Love / Ha cha cha (funktion) / Movin' / Wake up / Message (inspiration) / L.O.V.E.U. / Help yourself / Perceptions (what's the right direction) / Got to get down / Can you see the light / Walkin' the line / Give and take
CD _____ CZ 525
EMI / Mar '94 / EMI.

Brass Monkey

COMPLETE BRASS MONKEY, THE
CD _____ TSCD 467
Topic / Sep '93 / Direct / ADA.

Brass Pennies

PRIDE OF ENGLAND
Rule Britannia / Rose of England / Oh I do like to be beside the seaside / All the nice girls love a sailor / Man who broke the bank at Monte Carlo / We'll meet again / White cliffs of Dover / Over the sticks / Sing as we go / Wish me luck as you wave me goodbye / Sally / Knees up Mother Brown / Bless em all / English country garden / John Peel / Robin Hood / Billy Boy / British grenadiers / There's a tavern in the town
CD _____ CDITV 581
Scotdisc / Aug '94 / Duncans / Ross / Conifer.

Bratland/Opheim

DAM (Bratland/Opheim & The Oslo Chamber Choir)
CD _____ FX 147CD
Musikk Distribusjon / Apr '95 / ADA.

Brave Boys

NEW ENGLAND TRADITIONS IN FOLK MUSIC
CD _____ 802392
New World / Sep '95 / Harmonia Mundi / ADA / Cadillac.

Brave Combo

BRAVE COMBO
CD _____ CD 9019
Rounder / '88 / CM / Direct / ADA / Cadillac.

MUSICAL VARIETIES
CD _____ CD 11546
Rounder / '88 / CM / Direct / ADA / Cadillac.

NO NO NO CHA CHA CHA
CD _____ CDROU 9035
Rounder / Apr '93 / CM / Direct / ADA / Cadillac.

POLKAS FOR A GLOOMY WORLD
CD _____ ROUCD 9045
Rounder / Jul '95 / CM / Direct / ADA / Cadillac.

POLKATHARSIS
Happy wanderer / Crazy Serbian butchers dance / Old country polka / Anniversary song / Who stole the kishka / La Rufalina / Lovesick / Accordions man / Mental polka / Jesuita en chihuahua / Westphalia waltz / Pretty dancing girl / Hey ba ba re bop
CD _____ CD 9009
Rounder / '88 / CM / Direct / ADA / Cadillac.

Brave Old World

BEYOND THE PALE
CD _____ ROU 3135CD
Rounder / Jul '94 / CM / Direct / ADA / Cadillac.

Bravo, Soledad

VOLANDO VOY
CD _____ MES 159662
Messidor / Apr '93 / Koch / ADA.

Braxton, Anthony

2 COMPOSITIONS (ENSEMBLE) 1989/ 1991
CD _____ ARTCD 606
Hat Art / Apr '92 / Harmonia Mundi / ADA / Cadillac.

4 COMPOSITIONS - 1992
CD _____ 120124-2
Black Saint / Nov '93 / Harmonia Mundi / Cadillac.

5 COMPOSITIONS 1986
CD _____ 1201062
Black Saint / Nov '92 / Harmonia Mundi / Cadillac.

8 DUETS, HAMBURG 1991
CD _____ CD 710
Music & Arts / Jun '92 / Harmonia Mundi / Cadillac.

ANTHONY BRAXTON: TOWN HALL 1972
CD _____ ARTCD 6119
Hat Art / Nov '92 / Harmonia Mundi / ADA / Cadillac.

COMPOSITION 96 FOR ORCHESTRA
CD _____ CDLR 169
Leo / Mar '94 / Wellard / Cadillac / Impetus.

COMPOSITION NO. 174
CD _____ LR 217
Leo / May '95 / Wellard / Cadillac / Impetus.

COMPOSITION NO.165
CD _____ NA 050 CD
New Albion / Nov '92 / Harmonia Mundi / Cadillac.

COVENTRY CONCERT, THE
CD _____ WWCD 001
West Wind / Jul '88 / Swift / Charly / CM / ADA.

CREATIVE ORCHESTRA (KOLN) 1978
CD _____ ARTCD 26171
Hat Art / Apr '95 / Harmonia Mundi / ADA / Cadillac.

CREATIVE ORCHESTRA 1987 (Pieces Nos. 1-6)
CD _____ ND 86579
Bluebird / Jun '88 / BMG.

DORTMUND 1976
CD _____ ARTCD 6075
Hat Art / Jul '91 / Harmonia Mundi / ADA / Cadillac.

DUETS (Braxton, Anthony & Mario Pavone)
CD _____ CD 786
Music & Arts / Nov '93 / Harmonia Mundi / Cadillac.

DUO (Braxton, Anthony & Evan Parker)
CD _____ CDLR 193
Leo / Mar '94 / Wellard / Cadillac / Impetus.

DUO 1976 (Braxton, Anthony & George Lewis)
CD _____ ART 6150CD
Hat Art / Jul '94 / Harmonia Mundi / ADA / Cadillac.

EIGHT (3): TRISTANO COMPOSITIONS 1989
CD _____ ARTCD 6052
Hat Art / Nov '90 / Harmonia Mundi / ADA / Cadillac.

ENSEMBLE (VICTORIAVILLE 1988)
CD _____ VICTOCD 07
Victo / Nov '94 / These / ReR Megacorp / Cadillac.

EUGENE (1989) (Braxton, Anthony & Northwest Creative Orchestra)
CD _____ 1201372
Black Saint / Jan '92 / Harmonia Mundi / Cadillac.

IF MY MEMORY SERVES ME RIGHT (Braxton, Anthony Quartet)
CD _____ WWCD 004
West Wind / Oct '88 / Swift / Charly / CM / ADA.

IN THE TRADITON VOL.2
CD _____ SCCD 31045
Steeplechase / Jul '88 / Impetus.

KNITTING FACTORY 1994 #1 (2CD Set)
CD Set _____ CDLR 222/3
Leo / Oct '95 / Wellard / Cadillac / Impetus.

MOMENT PRÉCLEUX (Braxton, Anthony & Derek Bailey)
CD _____ VICTOCD 02
Victo / Nov '94 / These / ReR Megacorp / Cadillac.

OPEN ASPECTS
CD _____ ARTCD 6106
Hat Art / Nov '93 / Harmonia Mundi / ADA / Cadillac.

QUARTET (LONDON) 1985 (Braxton, Anthony Quartet)
CD _____ CDLR 200/201
Leo / '90 / Wellard / Cadillac / Impetus.

SIX COMPOSITIONS (QUARTET) 1984
CD _____ BSR 0086
Black Saint / Jan '86 / Harmonia Mundi / Cadillac.

SIX MONK COMPOSITIONS
CD _____ 120116-2
Black Saint / Aug '88 / Harmonia Mundi / Cadillac.

TOGETHER ALONE (Braxton, Anthony & Joseph Jarman)
CD _____ DD 428
Delmark / Dec '94 / Hot Shot / ADA / CM / Direct / Cadillac.

TRIO (Braxton, Anthony & Evan Parker/ Paul Rutherford)
CD _____ CDLR 197
Leo / Nov '94 / Wellard / Cadillac / Impetus.

VICTORIAVII LE 1992 (Braxton, Anthony Quartet)
CD _____ VICTOCD 021
Victo / Nov '94 / These / ReR Megacorp / Cadillac.

WESLEYAN
CD _____ ARTCD 6128
Hat Art / Sep '93 / Harmonia Mundi / ADA / Cadillac.

WILLISAU 1991
CD _____ ARTCD 46100
Hat Art / Jul '92 / Harmonia Mundi / ADA / Cadillac.

Braxton, Toni

TONI BRAXTON
Another sad song / Breathe again / Seven whole days / Love affair / Candlelight / Spending my time with you / Love shoulda brought you home / I belong to you / How many ways / You mean the world to me / Best friend / Breathe again (Reprise)
CD _____ 74321 16268-2
Arista / Jan '94 / BMG.

Breach

FRICTION
CD _____ BHR 026CD
Burning Heart / Oct '95 / Plastic Head.

OUTLINES
CD _____ BHR 014
Burning Heart / Oct '94 / Plastic Head.

Breach, Joyce

CONFESSIONS
CD _____ ACD 269
Audiophile / Apr '93 / Jazz Music / Swift.

JOYCE BREACH & JERRY MELAGI TRIO (Breach, Joyce & Jerry Melagi)
CD _____ ACD 199
Audiophile / Aug '95 / Jazz Music / Swift.

LOVERS AFTER ALL
CD _____ ACD 282
Audiophile / Oct '93 / Jazz Music / Swift.

Bread

BREAD
CD _____ 0349735022
Elektra / Jan '96 / Warner Music.

LET YOUR LOVE GO
CD _____ RMB 75063
Remember / Aug '92 / Total/BMG.

MANNA
Let your love go / Take comfort / Too much love / If / Be kind to me / He's a good lad / She was my lady / Live in your love / What a change / I say again / Come again / Truckin'
CD _____ 0349735042
Elektra / Jan '96 / Warner Music.

ON THE WATERS
Why do you keep me waiting / Make it with you / Blue satin pillow / Look what you've done / I am that I am / Been too long on the road / I want you with me / Coming apart / Easy love / In the afterglow / Call on me / Other side of love
CD _____ 0349735032
Elektra / Jan '96 / Warner Music.

VERY BEST OF BREAD
Baby I'm a want you / Make it with you / Guitar man / Everything I own / If I don't matter to me / Didn't even know her name / Mother freedom / Took the last train / Lost without your love / Goodbye girl / Diary / If / Let your love go / Sweet surrender / Aubrey / Never let her go
CD _____ PWKS 518
Carlton Home Entertainment / Oct '89 / Carlton Home Entertainment.

Breakers

MILAN
CD _____ FWBR 1
Fast Western / May '95 / Grapevine.

Breaks

BEATDOWN VOL.1
CD _____ BSVCD 1
Bluntly Speaking Vol.1 / Jul '93 / SRD.

Breakstone, Joshua

REMEMBERING GRANT GREEN
Street of dreams / Idle moments / Grandstand / Falling in love / Moon river / Remember / Green's greenery
CD _____ KICJ 169
King/Paddle Wheel / Nov '93 / New Note.

SITTIN' ON THE THING WITH MING
CD _____ 74042-2
Capri / Oct '94 / Wellard / Cadillac.

WALK DON'T RUN (Breakstone, Joshua Quartet)
Lullaby of the leaves / Telstar / Ram-bunkshush / Perfidia / Walk don't run / Taste of honey / Apache / Caravan / Slaughter on 10th Avenue / Blue star
CD _____ ECD 22058
Evidence / Oct '93 / Harmonia Mundi / ADA / Cadillac.

Breath Of Life

LOST CHILDREN
CD _____ DW 076CD
Deathwish / Nov '95 / Plastic Head.

TASTE OF SORROW
CD _____ DW 1032
Deathwish / Jan '95 / Plastic Head.

Breathe

ALL THAT JAZZ
Jonah / All that jazz / Monday morning blues / Hands to heaven / All this I should have known / Any trick / Liberties of love / Won't you come back / For love or money / How can I fall / Don't tell me lies (extra track on Cassette)
CD _____ CDSRN 12
Siren / Aug '91 / EMI.

Breathin' Canyon Band

HARMONY OF A COUPLE, THE
CD _____ 042005MAN85
Mantra / Nov '94 / Direct / Discovery.

MOTHER AND CHILD
CD _____ 642086MAN86
Mantra / Nov '94 / Direct / Discovery.

Breathless

BETWEEN HAPPINESS AND HEARTACHE
CD _____ BREATHCD 10
Tenor Vosa / Oct '91 / Pinnacle.

CHASING PROMISES
CD _____ BREATHCD 7
Tenor Vosa / Apr '89 / Pinnacle.

HEARTBURST
CD _____ SAT 70012
Tenor Vosa / Feb '94 / Pinnacle.

Breathnach, Maire

ANGEL'S CANDLES
Mystic's slipjigs / Eist / Angel's candles / Carillion's/Moling / West ocean waltz / Swans at Coole / Beta/Carnival / Breatnaigh abu / Roundabout/Parallel / Goban/Halloween jig / Dreamer / Cuimhne / Aisling Samhna / Hop, skip, jump
CD _____ SCD 593
Starc / Jul '93 / ADA / Direct.

VOYAGE OF BRAN
CD _____ 7567827342
Warner Bros. / Apr '95 / Warner Music.

Breathnach, Siobhan

CELTIC HARP
CD _____ OSS 33CD
Ossian / Mar '94 / ADA / Direct / CM.

Breaux, Zachary

GROOVIN'
Coming home baby / Impressions / Picadillo / Alice / Where is the love / Red, black and green / Lagos / Thinking of Alexis
CD _____ JHCD 023
Ronnie Scott's Jazz House / Jan '94 / Jazz Music / Magnum Music Group / Cadillac.

LAIDBACK
Small town in Texas / Laid back / West side worry / Find a place / Going out of my head / Intro / Remember the sixties / Ten days before / Midnight cowboy / In the midst of it all / On 6th street
CD _____ NYC 60092
NYC / Oct '94 / New Note.

Brecker Brothers

COLLECTION: BRECKER BROTHERS
Skunk funk / Sponge / Squids / Funky sea, funky dew / Bathsheba / Dream theme / Straphangin' / East river
CD _____ ND 90442
RCA / Apr '90 / BMG.

OUT OF THE LOOP
Slang / Ecovation / Scrunch / Secret heart / African skies / When it was / Harpoon / Night crawler / Then she wept
CD _____ GRP 97842
GRP / Sep '94 / BMG / New Note.

RETURN OF THE BRECKER BROTHERS
Above and below / That's all there is to it / On the backside / Big idea / Bikutsi / Funk / Good gracious / New Guinea / Roppongi / Sozinho (alone) / Sperical
CD _____ GRP 96842
GRP / Aug '92 / BMG / New Note.

Brecker, Michael

NOTES
CD _____ INAK 8805
In Akustik / Jan '96 / Magnum Music Group.

Brecker, Randy

IN THE IDIOM
No scratch / Hit and miss / Forever young / Sang / You're in my heart / There's a Mingus a Monks us / Moontide / Little Miss P
CD _____ CY 1483
Denon / Oct '88 / Conifer.

LIVE AT SWEET BASIL
Sleaze factor / Thrifty man / Ting chang / Incidentally / Hurdy gurdy / Moontide / Mojoe
CD _____ GNPD 2210
GNP Crescendo / Jun '95 / Silva Screen.

Breeders

LAST SPLASH
CD _____ CAD 3014CD
4AD / Jun '93 / Disc.

POD
Glorious / Happiness is a warm gun / Hellbound / Fortunately gone / Opened / Limehouse / Doe / Oh / When I was a painter / Iris / Only in 3's / Metal man
CD _____ CAD 0006 CD
4AD / May '90 / Disc.

Breen, Ann

ANN BREEN IN CONCERT
CD _____ CDPLAY 1034
Play / Mar '93 / Avid/BMG.

DOWN MEMORY LANE
CD _____ PLAYCD 1036
Play / Apr '95 / Avid/BMG.

EVENING WITH ANN BREEN, AN
CD _____ PLACD 100
Prism / Oct '94 / Prism.

IT'S FOR MY DAD
It's for my dad
CD _____ DPLAY 1027
Play / Dec '92 / Avid/BMG.

SPECIALLY FOR YOU MOTHER
CD _____ PHCD 509
Outlet / Jan '95 / ADA / Duncans / CM / Ross / Direct / Koch.

WHEN I GROW TOO OLD TO DREAM
CD _____ CDPLAY 1023
Play / Dec '92 / Avid/BMG.

Breeze

INTIMATE MOMENTS
CD _____ TJCD 001
TJ / Nov '92 / Jetstar.

Brel, Jacques

GREATEST HITS
CD _____ CD 352111
Duchesse / Jul '93 / Pinnacle.

JACQUES BREL ALBUM, THE (Featuring Tom Mega/Phil Minton/Harry Beckett/Joachim Kuhn) (Various Artists)
CD _____ ITM 1455
ITM / Apr '92 / Tradelink / Koch.

NE ME QUITTE PAS
Ne me quitte pas / Marieke / On n'oublie rien / Les flamandes / Les p…p…p…ma de Paris / Quand on n'a l'amour / Les biches / Le prochain amour / Le moribond / La valise a mille temps / Je ne sais pas pourquoi
CD _____ 8130092
ECM / Jul '90 / New Note.

Bremnes, Kari

GATE VED GATE
CD _____ FXCD 143
Musikk Distribujson / Jan '95 / ADA.

Brennan, Dave

TAKE ME TO THE MARDI GRAS (Brennan, Dave Jubilee Jazzband)
Don't go 'way nobody / Dauphine Street blues / Bright star blues / Move the body over / Ride real ride / Roses of Picardy
CD _____ LACD 20
Lake / Nov '93 / Target/BMG / Jazz Music / Direct / Cadillac / ADA.

Brennan, Dennis

JACK IN THE PULPIT
CD _____ UPSTART 016
Upstart / May '95 / Direct / ADA.

Brennan, Maire

MAIRE
Ce leis / Against the wind / Oro / Voices of the land / Jealous heart / Land of youth / I believe (deep within) / Beating heart / No easy way / Atlantic shore
CD _____ 74321228212
RCA / Sep '94 / BMG.

MISTY EYED ADVENTURE
CD _____ 74321233552
RCA Victor / Nov '94 / BMG.

Brennan, Paul

FIRE IN THE SOUL (Brennan, Paul Band)
CD _____ CFE 090
Fellside / Apr '93 / Target/BMG / Direct / ADA.

Breschi, Antonio

AL KAMAR
CD _____ CHM 05
Flamencovision / Jun '94 / Pinnacle.

Breuer, Carolyn

FAMILY AFFAIR (Breuer, Carolyn & Hermann)
Prost / My ideal / Blue rock / Fidelidade / That silver hilversum / Lyrical excursion / Sunset one
CD _____ ENJACD 80022
Enja / Oct '93 / New Note / Vital/SAM.

SIMPLY BE (Breuer, Carolyn & Fee Claassen Quintet)
CD _____ CHR 70017
Challenge / Sep '95 / Direct / Jazz Music / Cadillac / ADA.

Breuker, Willem

BAAL/BRECHT/BREUKER
CD _____ BVHAASTCD 9006
Bvhaast / Oct '93 / Cadillac.

BOB'S GALLERY
CD _____ BVHAASTCD 8801
Bvhaast / Oct '93 / Cadillac.

DEZE KANT OP DAMES
CD _____ BVHAASTCD 9301
Bvhaast / Oct '93 / Cadillac.

HEIBEL
CD _____ BVHAASTCD 9102
Bvhaast / Oct '93 / Cadillac.

KOLLEKTIEF - TO REMAIN
CD _____ BVHAASTCD 8904
Bvhaast / Oct '93 / Cadillac.

METROPOLIS
CD _____ BVHAASTCD 8903
Bvhaast / Oct '93 / Cadillac.

MONDRIAAN STRINGS- PARADE
CD _____ BVHAASTCD 9101
Bvhaast / Oct '93 / Cadillac.

MUSIC FOR FILMS OF FREAK DE JONGE
CD _____ BVHAASTCD 9205
Bvhaast / Oct '93 / Cadillac.

OVERTIME/UBERSTUNDEN
CD _____ 92042
NM Classics / Feb '95 / Impetus.

VERA BETHS & MONDRIAAN STRINGS
CD _____ BVHAASTCD 8802
Bvhaast / Oct '93 / Cadillac.

Brewer, Jack

HARSH WORLD (Brewer, Jack Band)
CD _____ NAR 063 CD
New Alliance / May '93 / Pinnacle.

RHYTHM OR SUICIDE
CD _____ NAR 078CD
SST / Jun '95 / Plastic Head.

ROCKIN' ETHERLAL (Brewer, Jack Band)
CD _____ NAR 039 CD
New Alliance / Sep '90 / Pinnacle.

Brewer, Spencer

ROMANTIC INTERLUDE
Valley oaks / Celtic highlands / Blue northern / Tellurian rhapsody / Ghost mountain / Blue valentine / Ondine's dream / Caravanserai / Camelot
CD _____ ND 61035
Narada / Jun '93 / New Note / ADA.

SHADOW DANCER
CD _____ CD 144
Narada / Jul '92 / New Note / ADA.

Brewer, Teresa

GOLDEN HITS: TERESA BREWER
CD _____ PWK 074
Carlton Home Entertainment / Jan '89 / Carlton Home Entertainment.

MEMORIES OF LOUIS
CD _____ 4692832
Sony Jazz / Nov '92 / Sony.

TEENAGE DANCE PARTY
Hula hoop song / Ricky ticky song / Why baby why / Teardrops in my heart / Tweedle dee / After school / Rock love / Pledging my love / Lula rock a hula / On Treasure Island / If were a train / Gone / Empty arms / Since you went away / Dark moon / So shy / It's the same old jazz / Bobby / Jingle bell rock / Born to love
CD _____ BCD 15440

83

Bear Family / Apr '89 / Rollercoaster / Direct
/ CM / Swift / ADA.

VERY BEST OF TERESA BREWER
CD _____ SOW 710
Soundsrite / Jun '93 / THE / Target/BMG.

Brian Jonestown Massacre

METHODRONE
CD _____ BCD 4050
Bomp / Aug '95 / Pinnacle.

Briar, Celia

DARK ROSE
CD _____ WCL 11005
White Cloud / May '94 / Select.

Brick Layer Cake

TRAGEDY - TRAGEDY
CD _____ TG 127D
Touch & Go / Oct '94 / SRD.

Brickell, Edie

GHOST OF A DOG (Brickell, Edie & New Bohemians)
Mama help me / Black and blue / Carmelito / He said / Times like this / 10,000 angels / Ghost of a dog / Strings of love / Woyaho / Oak cliff bra / Stwisted / This eye / Forgiven / Me by the sea
CD _____ GFLD 19269
Geffen / Feb '95 / BMG.

PICTURE PERFECT MORNING
Tomorrow comes / Green / When the lights go down / Good times / Another woman's dream / Stay awhile / Hard times / Olivia / In the bath / Picture perfect morning / Lost in the moment
CD _____ GED 24715
Geffen / Aug '94 / BMG.

SHOOTING RUBBERBANDS AT THE STARS (Brickell, Edie & New Bohemians)
What I am / Little Miss S / Air of December / Wheel / Love like we do / Circle / Beat the time / She / Nothing / Now / Keep coming back
CD _____ GFLD 19268
Geffen / Feb '95 / BMG.

Brickman, Jim

BY HEART
Angel eyes / Lake Erie / Looking back / In a lover's eye / Nothing left to say / Little star / Sudden inspiration / Where are you now / If you believe / On the edge / All I ever wanted / By heart
CD _____ 01934111642
Windham Hill / Aug '95 / Pinnacle / BMG / ADA.

Bricktop's Jazz Babes

STOMPIN' AT THE JAZZ CAFE
CD _____ BCD 326
GHB / Jan '94 / Jazz Music.

Bride

SILENCE IS MADNESS
CD _____ CMGCD 002
Communique / Nov '90 / Plastic Head.

SNAKES IN THE PLAYGROUND
CD _____ CDMFN 156
Music For Nations / Nov '93 / Pinnacle.

Brides Of Funkenstein

BRIDES OF FUNKENSTEIN - LIVE
Introduction / War ship touchante / Birdie / Ride on / Bridesmaids / Vanish in our sleep / Together / Disco to go / James Wesley Jackson comedy spot
CD _____ NEMCD 719
Sequel / Nov '94 / BMG.

Bridewell Taxis

INVISIBLE TO YOU
CD _____ BLAG 007CD
Stolen / Jun '91 / Vital.

Bridewells

CAGE
CD _____ EXPALCD 14
Expression / Oct '92 / Pinnacle.

Bridget

BRIDGET OF CALIFORNIA
CD _____ GROW 0402
Grass / Feb '95 / SRD.

Bridgewater, Dee Dee

LIVE IN PARIS
All blues / Misty / On a clear day / Dr. Feelgood / There is no greater love / Here's that rainy day / Medley blues / Cherokee
CD _____ CDCHARLY 24
Charly / Jun '87 / Charly / THE / Cadillac.

PRECIOUS THINGS (Featuring Ray Charles)
CD _____ CDSGP 053
Prestige / Apr '93 / Total/BMG.

Brier

BEST OF IRISH FOLK, THE
CD _____ CHCD 1038
Chyme / Aug '94 / CM / ADA / Direct.

Brier, Tom

RISING STAR
CD _____ SDSCD 1274
Stomp Off / Jun '94 / Jazz Music / Wellard.

Brigades

TILL LIFE US DO PART
CD _____ DANCD 011
Danceteria / Apr '90 / Plastic Head / ADA.

Brigadier Jerry

HAIL HIM
CD _____ CDTZ 014
Tappa / Aug '93 / Jetstar.

ON THE ROAD
CD _____ RAS 3071CD
Ras / Feb '91 / Jetstar / Greensleeves / SRD / Direct.

Briggs, Anne

CLASSIC ANNE BRIGGS (Complete Topic Recordings)
Recruited collier / Doffin mistress / Lowlands away / My bonny boy / Polly Vaughan / Rosemary Lane / Gathering rushes in the month of May / Whirly whorl / Stonecutter boy / Martinmas time / Blackwater side / Snow it melts the soonest / Willie o' Winsbury / Go your way / Thorneymoor woods / Cuckoo / Reynardine / Young Tambling / Living by the water / My bonny lad
CD _____ FECD 78
Fellside / Nov '95 / Target/BMG / Direct / ADA.

Brighouse & Rastrick Band

COMPOSER'S CHOICE, THE
CD _____ HARCD 1122
Harlequin / Jul '95 / Magnum Music Group.

EVENING WITH BRIGHOUSE & RASTRICK BAND, AN
Floral dance / Overture to Mack and Mabel / Amazing grace / Great little army / Because / Le carnaval Romain (The Roman carnival) / Marching through Georgia / Nimrod / Army of the nile / Lento from Eurphoria concerto (1972) / Eriskay love lilt / Poet and peasant
CD _____ CDMFP 6151
EMI / Feb '95 / EMI.

FLORAL DANCE, THE
CD _____ 295941
Ariola / Oct '94 / BMG.

MARCHES & WALTZES
King cotton / Waltz of the flowers / Radetzky march / Westminster waltz / Espana / French military march / Waltz (Symphonie Fantastique) / Old comrades / West riding / Gold and silver / Cornish cavalier / Morning papers / B.B. and C.F. / Waltz from Sleeping Beauty / Colonel Bogey
CD _____ DOYCD 032
Doyen / Oct '94 / Conifer.

MUSIC OF ERIC BALL
CD _____ HARCD 1124
Harlequin / Jul '95 / Magnum Music Group.

ON THE BANDSTAND
British bandsman / Romance from 'the Gadfly' / Alpine samba / Napoli / Jubilee overture / Rhythm and blues / Carnival of Venice / March to the scaffold / Flower duet from Lakme / Overture-Waverley
CD _____ QPRL 031D
Polyphonic / Jun '88 / Conifer.

Bright, Ronnell

BRIGHT'S SPOT
Pennies from heaven / Gone with the wind / If I'm lucky / Blue Zepher / Struttin' in / I see your face before me / Bright's spot / Little girl blue
CD _____ SV 0220
Savoy / Jun '93 / Conifer / ADA.

Brightman, Sarah

AS I CAME OF AGE
River cried / As I came of age / Some girls / Love changes everything / Alone again or / Bowling green / Something to believe in / Take my life / Brown eyes / Good morning starshine / Yesterday / It must be tough to be that cool
CD _____ 843 563-2
Polydor / May '90 / PolyGram.

DIVE
Dive / Captain Nemo / Second element / Ship of fools / Once in a lifetime / Cape horn / Salty dog / Siren / Seven seas / Johnny wanna live / By now / Island / When it rains in America / La mer
CD _____ 540 083-2
A&M / Apr '95 / PolyGram.

SURRENDER (The Unexpected Songs)
Surrender / Unexpected song / Chanson d'enfance / Tell me on a Sunday / Nothing like you've ever known / Macavity: The mysterious cat / Gus: The theatre cat / Piano (memory the Italian version) / Everything's alright / Last man in my life / Pie Jesu / Amigos para siempre (friends for life) / No llores por mi Argentina (Don't cry for me Argentina) / Guardami (With one look Italian version) / There is more to love / Wishing you were somehow here again / Music of the night
CD _____ 5277022
Polydor / Oct '95 / PolyGram.

Brightside

FACE THE TRUTH
CD _____ LF 127
Lost & Found / Mar '95 / Plastic Head.

Brignola, Nick

IT'S TIME
CD _____ RSRCD 123
Reservoir Music / Nov '94 / Cadillac.

LIVE AT SWEET BASIL
CD _____ RSRCD 125
Reservoir Music / Nov '94 / Cadillac.

ON A DIFFERENT LEVEL
CD _____ RSRCD 112
Reservoir Music / Nov '94 / Cadillac.

RAINCHECK
Raincheck / Tenderly / Hurricane Connie / My ship / I wish I knew / Hesitation blues / Jo Spring / Jitterbug waltz / Darn that dream / North Star
CD _____ RSRCD 108
Reservoir Music / '89 / Cadillac.

TRIBUTE TO GERRY MULLIGAN (Brignola, Nick & Sal Salvador)
CD _____ STCD 574
Stash / Feb '94 / Jazz Music / CM / Cadillac / Direct / ADA.

WHAT IT TAKES
CD _____ RSRCD 117
Reservoir Music / Nov '94 / Cadillac.

Brilliant Corners

CREAMY STUFF
CD _____ MCQCD 006
McQueen / Sep '91 / Vital.

JOYRIDE
You don't know how lucky you are / This girl / Grow cold / I didn't see you / Emily / Nothing / Hemingway's back / Accused by the angels
CD _____ MCQCD 004
McQueen / May '89 / Vital.

Brim, John

ICE CREAM MAN, THE
CD _____ TONECOOLCD 1150
Tonecool / May '94 / Direct / ADA.

Brimble, Allister

SOUNDS DIGITAL
CD _____ AMBCD 1
AMB / Jun '94 / Plastic Head.

Brinsley Schwarz

BRINSLEY SCHWARZ
CD _____ REP 4421WY
Repertoire / Feb '94 / Pinnacle / Cadillac.

BRINSLEY SCHWARZ/DESPITE IT ALL
Hymn to me / Shining brightly / Rock 'n' roll women / Lady Constant / What do you suggest / Mayfly / Ballad of a has been Beauty Queen / Country girl / Slow one / Funk angel / Piece of home / Love song / Starship / Edbury Down / Old Jarrow
CD _____ BGOCD 239
Beat Goes On / Jun '94 / Pinnacle.

NERVOUS ON THE ROAD
Nervous on the road / It's been so long / Happy doing what we're doing / Surrender to the rhythm / Feel a little funky / I like it like that / Brand new you, brand new me / Home in my hand / Why why why
CD _____ BGOCD 289
Beat Goes On / Oct '95 / Pinnacle.

PLEASE DON'T EVER CHANGE
Hooked on love / I worry / Home in my hand / I won't make it without you / Speedoo / Why do we hurt the one we love / Don't ever change / Play that fast thing / Down in Mexico / Version
CD _____ EDCD 237
Edsel / Sep '90 / Pinnacle / ADA.

SILVER PISTOL
Dry land / Merry go round / One more day / Nightingales / Silver pistol / Last time I was fooled / Unknown number / Range war / Egypt / Niki Hoeke speedway / Ju ju man / Rockin' chair
CD _____ EDCD 190
Edsel / Sep '90 / Pinnacle / ADA.

Brise Glace

WHEN IN VANITAS
CD _____ GR 17CD
Skingraft / Sep '94 / SRD.

Brislin, Kate

OUR TOWN (Stecher, Jody & Kate Brislin)
Going to the west / Home / Old country stomp / In between dreams / Showerbread reel/The twisted arm / Too late, too late / Bramble and the rose / Our town / Twilight is stealing / Curtains of the night / Queen of the Earth and child of the stars / Roving on last winter's night / Henry the true mother / Won't you come and sing for me
CD _____ ROUCD 0304
Rounder / Jul '93 / CM / Direct / ADA / Cadillac.

Brissett, Annette

ANNETTE (Brissett, Annette & The Taxi Gang)
CD _____ RASCD 3088
Ras / Apr '92 / Jetstar / Greensleeves / SRD / Direct.

Bristol, Johnny

HANG ON IN THERE BABY
Hang on in there baby / Take good care of you for me / She came into my life / Do it to my mind / Love to have the chance to taste the wine / Love takes tears (you haven't learned to cry) / All goodbye's aren't gone / Memories don't leave like people do / It don't hurt no more / Love me for a reason / Leave my world / You and I / I sho like groovin' with ya / Feelin' the magic
CD _____ 5501812
Spectrum/Karussell / Sep '94 / PolyGram / THE.

Britannia Building...

BAND OF THE YEAR (Britannia Building Society Foden Band)
Spanish dance / Winter / You'll never walk alone / Tea for two / Solveig's song / Eighteenth variation from a rhapsody on a theme of Paganini / American in Paris / Postcard from Mexico / Pretty girl is like a melody / Puttin' on the ritz / Sweet and low / In the wood / Bolero
CD _____ GRCD 33
Grasmere / Apr '89 / Target/BMG / Savoy.

BEST OF BRASS AND VOICES, THE (Britannia Building Society Foden Band/ Halifax Choral Society)
Hallelujah chorus / Praise my soul / Swing low, sweet chariot / Oh God our help in ages past / Fantasy on North Country tunes / Onward, Christian soldiers / Chorus of the Hebrew slaves / Crimond / Grand march from Aida / Day thou gavest Lord is ended / Jerusalem / Pomp and circumstance #1
CD _____ DOYCD 041
Doyen / Aug '95 / Conifer.

BRASS WITH CLASS (Britannia Building Society Foden Band)
Britannia / Love's old sweet song / Dansa Brasiliera / To a wild rose / Bank holiday / On with the Motley / Cossack dance / Appalachian folk-song suite / Freedom / Dance sequence / Procession to the minster
CD _____ QPRL 037D
Polyphonic / Sep '88 / Conifer.

FESTIVAL OF BRASS 1992 (Britannia Building Society Foden Band)
CD _____ DOYCD 019
Doyen / Jan '93 / Conifer.

MUSIC OF JOHN MCCABE (Britannia Building Society Foden Band)
Salamander / Cloudcatcher fells / Desert 11 horizons / Images / Northern lights
CD _____ DOYCD 030
Doyen / May '95 / Conifer.

YEAR OF THE DRAGON (Britannia Building Society Foden Band)
CD _____ DOYCD 021
Doyen / May '93 / Conifer.

British Tuba Quartet

ELITE SYNCOPATIONS
CD _____ QPRZ 012D
Polyphonic / Apr '93 / Conifer.

EUPHONIC SOUNDS
Celestial suite / Il ritorno / They didn't believe me / Quartet for brass / Mon coeur se recommende a vous / John come kiss me now / Bocoxe / Favourite rag / Spiritual jazz suite / Greensleeves / Get me to the church on time / Air / Pink panther / Euphonis sounds / You made me love you / William Tell overture
CD _____ QPRL 009D
Polyphonic / Jun '92 / Conifer.

MARCH TO THE SCAFFOLD
Thunderer / Hava nagila / Dance of the sugar plum fairy / On the sunny side of the street / Glyder landscape / Sortie in E flat / Triplet for four tubas / Fugue / Battle royal / Dido's lament / Minitures for four valve instruments / Turkish march / In memoriam /

April is in my mistress' face / Sonatina for tuba quartet / March to the scaffold
CD _____ QPRZ 013D
Polyphonic / Jul '94 / Conifer.

Broadbent, Alan

CONCORD DUO SERIES (Broadbent, Alan & Gary Foster)
Ode to the road / Speak low / Wonder why / Lady in the lake / 317 East 32nd / What is this thing - hot house / If you could see me now / In your own sweet way / One morning in May / Relaxin' at Camarillo
CD _____ CCD 4562
Concord Jazz / Jul '93 / New Note.

LIVE AT MAYBECK RECITAL HALL, VOL. 14
I hear a rhapsody / Oleo / You've changed / Lennie's pennies / Nardis / Sweet and lovely / Don't ask why / Parisian thoroughfare
CD _____ CCD 4488
Concord Jazz / Dec '91 / New Note.

PACIFIC STANDARD TIME
Summer night / This one's for Bud / Easy living / Easy to love / I should care / Django / Beautiful love / In love in vain / Someday my prince will come / I've never been in love before / Reets and I
CD _____ CCD 4664
Concord Jazz / Sep '95 / New Note.

Broadside Band

ENGLISH COUNTRY DANCES
Cuckolds all in a row / Shepherd's Holyday or Labour in Vaine / Newcastle / Beggar boy / Picking of sticks / Faine I would if I could or Parthenia / Gathering peascods / Nightpeece or The shaking of the sheets / Chelsey Reach or Buckingham-House / Jameko / Epping Forest / Well-Hall / Fits come on me now or Bishop of Chester's jig / Mad robin / Red house / Mr. Beveridge's magot / Geud man of Ballangigh / To a new Scotch jigg / Childgrove / Wooly and Georgey / Portsmouth / Whitehall minuet / Bloomsberry market
CD _____ CDSDL 393
Saydisc / Mar '94 / Harmonia Mundi / ADA / Direct.

ENGLISH NATIONAL SONGS (Broadside Band & John Potter/Lucie Skeaping)
Greensleeves / Gather ye rosebuds while ye may / When the King enjoys his own again / Northern lass / Harvest home / Sally in our alley / Roast beef of old England / Vicar of Bray / Rule Britannia / God save the King / Nancy Dawson / Miller of the Dee / British Grenadiers / Hunting we will go / Drink to me only with thine eyes / Chapter of Kings / Lass of Richmond Hill / Begone dull care / Tom Bowling / Early one morning / Home sweet home
CD _____ CDSDL 400
Saydisc / Mar '94 / Harmonia Mundi / ADA / Direct.

JOHN PLAYFORD'S POPULAR TUNES
Greenwood / Heart's ease / Excuse me / Lady Catherine Ogle / Scotchman's dance / In the Northern lass / Never love thee more / Miller's jig / Granadees march / Saraband by Mr.Simon Ives / Lady Hatton's almaine / Prins Robbert Masco / Prince Rupert's march / Daphne / Lilliburlero / Parthenia / La volta / Jenny Pluck Pears / Daniel Cooper / Parson upon Dorothy / Nonesuch / Paul's steeple / Lady Nevils delight / Whisk / New rigaudon / Italian rant / Bouzar castle / Childgrove / Mr. Lane's minuet / Up with aily / Cheshire rounds / Hunt the squirrel
CD _____ CDSAR 28
Amon Ra / Jul '94 / Harmonia Mundi.

POPULAR 17TH CENTURY DANCE TUNES
CD _____ HMA 1901039CD
Musique D'Abord / Oct '94 / Harmonia Mundi.

SONGS & DANCES FROM SHAKESPEARE (Broadside Band & Deborah Roberts/John Potter)
Full fathom five thy Father lies / Where the bee sucks / O Mistress mine where are you roaming / Poor soul sat sighing / It was a lover and his lass / Sellengers round / Scottish jigge / Hoboken brawl / Staines morris / How should I your true love know / Tomorrow is St. Valentine's day / And will he not come again / In youth when I did love / Wooself cock, so black of hue / O sweet Oliver / When daffodils begin to peer / Jog on, jog on, the footpath way / Kemp's jig / Passamezzo pavan / Bargamasca / Queen Mary's dumpe / As you came from that holy land / I loathe that I did love / Bonny sweet robin / Come live with me / There dwelt a man / Farewell dear love / Fortune my foe / Earl of Essex measure / La volta / Sinkapace galliard / Coranto / Take, o take those lips away / Sigh no more ladies / Hark, hark, the lark / Lawn as white as driven snow / Get ye hence / When that I was and a little tiny boy
CD _____ CDSDL 409
Saydisc / Feb '95 / Harmonia Mundi / ADA / Direct.

Broberg, Basse

WEST OF THE MOON (Broberg, Basse & Red Mitchell)
CD _____ DRCD 235
Dragon / Oct '94 / Roots / Cadillac / Wellard / CM / ADA.

Brock, Dave

AGENT OF CHAOS (Brock, Dave & The Agent Of Chaos)
CD _____ SHARP 042CD
Flicknife / Apr '88 / Pinnacle.

STRANGE TRIPS & PIPE DREAMS
Hearing aid test / White zone / U.F.O. Line / Space / Pipe dream / Self / Something going on / Bosnia / Parasites are here on earth / Gateway / It's never too late / La forge / Encounter
CD _____ EBSSCD 116
Emergency Broadcast System / Jul '95 / Vital.

Brock, Herbie

BROCK'S TOPS (Brock, Herbie Trio)
If it's the last thing I do / Moon was yellow / Blues a Brock long / There'll never be another you / Four brothers / Sweet and lovely / Brock etude / Willow weep for me
CD _____ SV 0201
Savoy Jazz / Apr '93 / Conifer / ADA.

Brock, Jim

TROPIC AFFAIR
Pass-a-grill / Ladies of the calabash / Tropic affair / Anya / Quo qui's groove / Sidewalk / Palm-palm girls / O vazio
CD _____ RR 31CD
Reference Recordings / Sep '91 / Maze Audio.

Brock, Paul

MO CHAIRDIN
CD _____ CEFCD 155
Gael Linn / Jan '94 / Roots / CM / Direct / ADA.

Brodie, Mark

SHORES OF HELL, THE (Brodie, Mark & Beaver Patrol)
CD _____ SH 031CD
Shreder / Nov '95 / Plastic Head.

Broggs, Peter

CEASE THE WAR
Don't let the children cry / Cease the war / Mr. Sherriff man / My baby she's gone / Let's go party / Just can't stop praising Jah / Suzanne / Freedom for the people / I a field marshall / Ethiopia we're coming home
CD _____ RASCD 3022
Ras / '86 / Jetstar / Greensleeves / SRD / Direct.

RASTAFARI LIVETH
CD _____ RASCD 3001
Ras / Nov '92 / Jetstar / Greensleeves / SRD / Direct.

REASONING
CD _____ RASCD 3051
Ras / Jul '90 / Jetstar / Greensleeves / SRD / Direct.

RISE AND SHINE
You got to be wise / Rise and shine / I admire you / International farmer / Leggo mi hand / Bloodstain / Fuss and fight / I love to play reggae / Jah is the ruler / Rastaman chant Nyahbingi
CD _____ RASCD 3011
Greensleeves / Sep '93 / Total/BMG / Jetstar / SRD.

Broken Bones

BRAIN DEAD
CD _____ CDJUST 19
Rough Justice / Oct '92 / Disc.

DEATH IS IMMINENT
CD _____ CLEO 93092
Cleopatra / Dec '93 / Disc.

DEM BONES
CD _____ FALLCD 028
Fallout / Dec '90 / Disc.

F.O.A.D/BONECRUSHER
CD _____ FALLCD 041
Fallout / May '91 / Disc.

STITCHED UP
CD _____ CDJUST 18
Rough Justice / Oct '91 / Pinnacle.

Broken Hope

BOWELS OF REPUGNANCE
CD _____ CDZORRO 64
Metal Blade / Sep '93 / Pinnacle.

REPULSIVE CONCEPTION
CD _____ CDZORRO 85
Metal Blade / May '95 / Pinnacle.

SWAMPED IN GORE
CD _____ GC 189801
Recommended / Jul '92 / These / ReR Megacorp.
CD _____ 140962
Metal Blade / Nov '95 / Plastic Head.

Broken Pledge

MUSIQUE IRLANDAISE
CD _____ BCD 6801
Auvidis/Ethnic / Jan '95 / Harmonia Mundi.

Bromberg, Brian

BASSICALLY SPEAKING
CD _____ NOVA 9031
Nova / Jan '93 / New Note.

IT'S ABOUT TIME
CD _____ NOVA 9146
Nova / Jan '93 / New Note.

MAGIC RAIN
CD _____ CDENV 546
Enigma / Aug '89 / EMI.

Bronner, Till

MY SECRET LOVE
CD _____ MM 801051
Minor Music / Sep '95 / Vital/SAM.

Bronski Beat

HUNDREDS AND THOUSANDS
Heatwave / Why / Run from love / Hard rain / Smalltown boy / Junk / Mertley / Close to the edge / Cadillac car
CD _____ 5500432
Spectrum/Karussell / Jun '93 / PolyGram THE.

Brood

HITSVILLE
CD _____ IDI 2330CD
Dionysus / Sep '95 / Plastic Head.

Brook Brothers

BROOK BROTHERS, THE
CD _____ REP 4096-WZ
Repertoire / Aug '91 / Pinnacle / Cadillac.

Brook, Michael

COBALT BLUE
CD _____ CAD 2007CD
4AD / Jun '92 / Disc.

SHONA
CD _____ SINE 002
Sine / Sep '95 / Grapevine.

Brooker, Gary

ECHOES IN THE NIGHT
Count me out / Two fools in love / Echoes in the night / Ghost train / Mr. Blue Man / Saw the fire / Long goodbye / Hear what you're saying / Missing person / Trick of the night
CD _____ INCD 900076
Line / Sep '94 / CM / Grapevine / ADA / Conifer / Direct.

LEAD ME TO THE WATER/ECHOES IN THE NIGHT
CD _____ LICD 921195
Line / Sep '94 / CM / Grapevine / ADA / Conifer / Direct.

Brooklyn Funk Essentials

COOL, STEADY & EASY
Take the L train (to Brooklyn) / Creator has a master plan / Revolution was postponed because of rain / Brooklyn recycles / Madame Zazu / Headnaddas journey to the planet Addiskizm / Big apple boogaloo / Blow your brains out / Stickman crossing the Brooklyn bridge / Dilly dally / Take the L train (to 8 ave)
CD _____ DOR 022CD
Dorado / Jun '94 / Disc.

Brookmeyer, Bob

BOB BROOKMEYER & FRIENDS (Brookmeyer, Bob & Stan Getz)
Jive hoot / Misty / Wrinkle / Bracket / Skylark / Sometime ago / I've grown accustomed to her face / Who cares
CD _____ 468413 2
Columbia / Nov '93 / Sony.

BOB BROOKMEYER WITH STOCKHOLM JAZZ ORCHESTRA (Brookmeyer, Bob & Stockholm Jazz Orchestra)
Cats / Lies / Tick tock / Dreams / Missing work / Ceremony
CD _____ DRCD 169
Dragon / Sep '89 / Roots / Cadillac / Wellard / CM / ADA.

ELECTRICITY
Farewell, New York / Ugly music / White blues / Say ah / No song / Crystal Palace
CD _____ 892192
Act / Sep '94 / New Note.

Brookmeyer, Bob Quartet

OSLO (Brookmeyer, Bob Quartet)
With the wind and rain in your hair / Oslo / Later blues / Detour ahead / Tootsie sands / Alone together / Who could care / Caravan
CD _____ CCD 4312
Concord Jazz / Jul '87 / New Note.

Brookmeyer, Bob New Quartet

PARIS SUITE (Brookmeyer, Bob New Quartet)
CD _____ CHR 70026
Challenge / Sep '95 / Direct / Jazz Music / Cadillac / ADA.

STOCKHOLM JAZZ ORCH
CD _____ DRAGONCD 169
Dragon / Mar '87 / Roots / Cadillac / Wellard / CM / ADA.

Brooks & Dunn

BRAND NEW MAN
Brand new man / My next broken heart / Coll drink of water / Cheating on the blues / Neon moon / Lost and found / I've got a lot to learn / Boot scootin' boogie / I'm no good / Still in love with you
CD _____ 07822186582
Arista / Jul '91 / BMG.

WAITIN' ON SUNDOWN
CD _____ 782218765-2
RCA / Sep '94 / BMG.

Brooks, Bernard

CHEERS
CD _____ DLD 1017
Dance & Listen / Jul '93 / Savoy.

MOVING ON
CD _____ DLD 1060
Dance & Listen / Dec '95 / Savoy.

SWING AND SWAY NO. 1
CD _____ DLD 1005
Dance & Listen / Nov '93 / Savoy.

SWING AND SWAY NO. 3
Rose Marie / Only a rose / At the Balalaika / Blue tango / Don't get around much anymore / Makin' whoopee / Sunny side of the street / It's magic / Maybe / Sierra Sue / Marie Elena / I'm in the mood for love / Just one more chance / Carolina in the morning / You're driving me crazy / So what's new / 12th Street rag / Charleston / Are you lonesome tonight / Wonderful one / When you and I were seventeen / I wonder who's kissing her now / Carolina moon / Alice blue gown / You are my sunshine / Baby face / My blue heaven / Yes sir that's my baby / Sugartime / I'm looking over a four leaf clover / Oh what it seemed to be / Where are you / Please be kind / Music maestro please / Oh my papa / I wish you love / My special angel / Moving south
CD _____ DLD 1008
Dance & Listen / '92 / Savoy.

SWING AND SWAY NO. 5
CD _____ DLD 1012
Dance & Listen / Dec '92 / Savoy.

SWING AND SWAY NO. 7
CD _____ DLD 1018
Dance & Listen / Nov '93 / Savoy.

SWING AND SWAY NO. 8
CD _____ DLD 1021
Dance & Listen / '92 / Savoy.

SWING AND SWAY NO. 9
CD _____ DLD 1022
Dance & Listen / '92 / Savoy.

SWING AND SWAY, NO. 10
CD _____ DLD 1081
Dance & Listen / '92 / Savoy.

SWING AND SWAY, NO. 11
All of me / Some of these days / Beautiful dreamer / Ramona / Love letters in the sand / Deed I do
CD _____ DLD 1026
Dance & Listen / May '92 / Savoy.

SWING AND SWAY, NO. 12
That certain party/When you're smiling / If I had a talking picture of you/Clementine / King of the road/The man who comes around / On mother Kelly's doorstep/Underneath the arches / Babette/Charmaine / Dancing with tears in my eyes/I love you truly / Stars will remember / Hernando's hideaway / My melancholy baby/Taking a chance on love / Just walking in the rain/On a slow boat to China / There's a boy coming home on leave/Blue skies/Playmates / Rose Rose I love you/Nursie nursie / Always in my hair/There will never be another you / Stranger on the shore/More than ever / It's the tale of the town/Dance of the hours / Just walking in the rain/Singin' in the rain / Jingle jangle jingle/Who's been polishing the sun / I wonder where my baby is tonight / Silver wings/You always hurt the one you love / You, you, you/Too young / Snowbird/Don't sweetheart me / I'm thinking tonight of my blue eyes / Beautiful Ohio/ The shadow waltz / Just for a while/Santa Lucia
CD _____ DLCD 1029
Dance & Listen / Jul '92 / Savoy.

SWING AND SWAY, NO. 16
CD _____ DLD 1039
Dance & Listen / Jul '93 / Savoy.

Brooks, Big Leon

LET'S GO TO TOWN
CD _____ CD 4931
Earwig / Feb '95 / CM.

Brooks, Cecil III

NECK PECKIN' JAMMIE
Hill district / Yvette / Creepin' / One by one / Without a song / Blues citizens / Mood swings / In Jody's corner / Tenderly / Neck peckin' Jammie / Rhythms for mom's journey to heaven
CD _____ MCD 5504
Muse / Dec '94 / New Note / CM.

SMOKIN' JAZZ
CD _____ MCD 5521
Muse / Feb '96 / New Note / CM.

Brooks, Denice

YOU FILL MY DAYS
CD _____ 15375
Laserlight / Aug '91 / Target/BMG.

Brooks, Elkie

BEST OF ELKIE BROOKS, THE
Pearl's a singer / Sunshine after the rain / Don't cry out loud / Nights in white satin / Gasoline alley / I guess that's why they call it the blues / Growing tired / Ain't misbehavin' / Goin' back / Fool if you think it's over / Our love / Only love can break your heart / Runaway / Money / If you leave me now / Blue moon / Minutes / Lilac wine
CD _____ 5513292
THE.

BOOKBINDER'S KID
Sail on / Stairway to heaven / You ain't leavin' / Keep it a secret / When the hero walks alone / What's the matter baby / Can't wait all night / Kiss me for the last time / Love is love / Foolish games / Only love will set you free (Not on LP) / I can dream, can't I
CD _____ CLACD 327
Castle / '92 / BMG.

CIRCLES
CD _____ PERMCD 34
Permanent / Apr '95 / Total/BMG.

ELKIE BROOKS
CD _____ MATCD 258
Castle / Apr '93 / BMG.

FROM THE HEART
Last teardrop / Don't go changing your mind / We are all your children / One of a kind / Tell her / You and I (are you lonely) / Free to love / Suits my style / Got to get better / From the heart
CD _____ MSCD 1
Magnum Music / May '94 / Magnum Music Group.

INSPIRATIONS
CD _____ CDSR 008
Telstar / Jun '93 / BMG.

LIVE AND LEARN
Viva la money / On the horizon / He could have been an army / Rising cost of love / Dream dealer / Who's making love / If you can't beat me rocking / Heartache is on / Not enough lovin' yet / Falling star
CD _____ PWKS 552
Carlton Home Entertainment / Nov '89 / Carlton Home Entertainment.

NO MORE THE FOOL
No more the fool / Only women bleed / Blue jay / Break the chain / We've got tonight
CD _____ CLACD 326
Castle / May '93 / BMG.

NOTHIN' BUT THE BLUES
CD _____ CTVCD 1
Castle / Apr '94 / BMG.

ONE OF A KIND
CD _____ MSCD 1
Music De-Luxe / Apr '94 / Magnum Music Group.

PEARLS II
Goin' back / Our love / Gasoline alley / I just can't go on / Too much between us / Giving us hope / Money / Nights in white satin / Loving arms / Will you write me a song
CD _____ 5500602
Spectrum/Karussell / Jun '93 / PolyGram / THE.

PEARLS III
CD _____ MER 007
Tring / Mar '93 / Tring / Prism.

PRICELESS (Very best of Elkie Brooks)
Fool (if you think it's over) / Sunshine after the rain / If you leave me now / Going back / Lilac wine / Nights in white satin / Warm and tender love / Pearl's a singer / What'll I do / Love me or leave me / Don't cry out loud / Superstar / Blue moon / Only love can break your heart / Too busy thinking about my baby / Our love
CD _____ PWKS 4086
Carlton Home Entertainment / Jul '94 / Carlton Home Entertainment.

RICH MAN'S WOMAN
Where do we go from here / Take cover / Jigsaw baby / Roll me over / He's a rebel / One step on the ladder / Rock 'n' roll circus / Try a little love / Tomorrow
CD _____ PWKS 553
Carlton Home Entertainment / Oct '89 / Carlton Home Entertainment.

ROUND MIDNIGHT
Round Midnight / Cry me a river / Just for a thrill / Travelling light / Don't explain / Rainy day / All night long / What kind of man are you
CD _____ CLACD 403
Castle / '95 / BMG.

VERY BEST OF ELKIE BROOKS, THE
CD _____ CDLK 1986
A&M / Dec '88 / PolyGram.

WE'VE GOT TONIGHT
No more the fool / Break the chain / All or nothing / Hiding inside yourself / We've got tonight / Only women bleed / I can dream, can't I / You ain't leavin' / Love is love / Only love will set you free / Foolish games / Sail on / Hold the dream / No secrets (call of the wild) / Stairway to heaven / Kiss me for the last time
CD _____ 5507452
Spectrum/Karussell / Jan '95 / PolyGram / THE.

WE'VE GOT TONIGHT
CD _____ TRTCD 200
TrueTrax / Jun '95 / THE.

Brooks, Ernie

FALLING, THEY GET YOU
CD _____ 422501
New Rose / Nov '94 / Direct / ADA.

Brooks, Garth

BEYOND THE SEASON
Go tell it on the mountain / God rest ye merry gentlemen / Old man's back in town / Gift / Unto you this night / White Christmas / Friendly beasts / Santa looks a lot like Daddy / Silent night / Mary's dream / What child is this
CD _____ CDP 7987422
Liberty / Sep '92 / EMI.

CHASE, THE
That summer / Somewhere other than the night / Face to face / Every now and then / Mr. Right / Learning to live again / Walkin' after midnight / Dixie chicken / Night rider's lament
CD _____ CDESTU 2184
Liberty / Sep '92 / EMI.

FRESH HORSES
Old stuff / Cowboys and angels / Fever / That ol' wind / Rollin' / Change / Beaches of Cheyenne / It's midnight Cinderella / She's every woman / Ireland
CD _____ CDGB 1
Parlophone / Nov '95 / EMI.

HITS
Ain't going down (til the sun comes up) / Friends in low places / Burning bridges / Callin' Baton Rouge / River / Much too young (to feel this damn old) / Thunder rolls / American Honky-Tonk Bar Association / If tomorrow never comes / Unanswered prayers / Standing outside the fire / Rodeo / What she's doing now / We shall be free / Papa loved mama / Shameless / Two of a kind, workin' on a full house / That summer / Red strokes / Dance
CD _____ CDEST 2247
EMI / Dec '94 / EMI.

IN PIECES
Standing outside / Night I called the old man out / American honky-tonk bar association / One night a day / Kickin' and screamin' / Ain't going down (til the sun comes up) / Red strokes / Callin' baton rouge / Night will only know / Cowboy song / Fire
CD _____ CDEST 2212
Liberty / Aug '93 / EMI.

NO FENCES
If tomorrow never comes / Not counting you / Much too young (to feel this damn old) / Dance / Thunder rolls / New way to fly / Two of a kind, workin' on a full house / Victim of the game / Friends in low places / Wild horses / Unanswered prayers / Same old story / Mr. Blue / Wolves
CD _____ CDEST 2136
Capitol / Nov '90 / EMI.

ROPIN' THE WIND
Against the grain / Rodeo / What she's doing now / Burning bridges / Papa loved mama / Shameless / Cold shoulder / We bury the hatchet / In lonesome dove / River / Alabama clay / Everytime that it rains / Nobody gets off in this town / Cowboy Bill
CD _____ CDESTU 2162
Capitol / Jan '92 / EMI.

Brooks, Hadda

ANYTIME, ANYPLACE, ANYWHERE
Anytime anyplace anywhere / That's my desire / Don't go to strangers / Don't you think I ought to know / Man with the horn / But not for me / Rain sometime / heart of a

---

clown / Ol' man river / Dream / Foggy day / Trust in me / Please be kind/I'm blue / Stolen love / All of me
CD _____ DRGCD 91423
DRG / Sep '94 / New Note.

ROMANCE IN THE DARK
Variety bounce / That's my desire / Romance in the dark / Bully wully boogie / Out of the blue / Honey, honey, honey / Keep your hand on your heart / Bewildered / Jukebox boogie / Trust in me / Don't take your love from me / Schubert's serenade in boogie / Tough on my heart / When a woman cries / Say it with a kiss / I've got my love to keep me warm / I feel so good / It all depends on you / Don't call it love / Honky tonk boogie / Don't you think I ought to know / You won't let me go / Tootsie timesie
CD _____ CDCHD 453
Ace / Jun '93 / Pinnacle / Cadillac / Complete/Pinnacle.

Brooks III, Cecil

COLLECTIVE, THE
CD _____ MCD 5377
Muse / Sep '92 / New Note / CM.

Brooks, Lonnie

BAYOU LIGHTNING
Voodoo daddy / Figure head / Watchdog / Breakfast in bed / Worked up woman / Alimony / Watch what you got / I ain't superstitious / You know what my body needs / In the dark
CD _____ ALCD 4717
Alligator / May '93 / Direct / ADA.

HOT SHOT
Don't take advantage of me / Wrong number / Messed up again / Family rules / Back trail / I want all my money back / Mr. hot shot / One more shot
CD _____ ALCD 4731
Alligator / May '93 / Direct / ADA.

LET'S TALK IT OVER
CD _____ DD 660
Delmark / Jan '94 / Hot Shot / ADA / CM / Direct / Cadillac.

LIVE FROM CHICAGO
Two headed man / Trading post / In the dark / Got me by the tail / One more shot / Born with the blues / Eyeballin' / Cold lonely nights / Hideaway
CD _____ ALCD 4759
Alligator / May '93 / Direct / ADA.

SATISFACTION GUARANTEED
Temporary insanity / Man's gotta do / Feast or famine / Lyin' time / Little RR and CB / Wife for tonight / Family curse / Horoscope / Like Father, like son / Holding on to the memories / Accident / Price is right
CD _____ ALCD 4799
Alligator / May '93 / Direct / ADA.

SWEET HOME CHICAGO
CD _____ BLE 595542
Black & Blue / Apr '91 / Wellard / Koch.

TURN ON THE NIGHT
Eyeballin' / Inflation / Teenage boogie man / Heavy traffic / I'll take care of you / T.V. moan / Mother nature / Don't go to sleep on me / Something you got / Zydeco
CD _____ ALCD 4721
Alligator / May '93 / Direct / ADA.

WOUND UP TIGHT
Got lucky last night / Jealous man / Belly rubbin' music / Bewitched, bothered and bewildered / End of the rope / Wound up tight / Boomerang / Musta' been dreaming / Skid row / Hush mouth money
CD _____ ALCD 4751
Alligator / May '93 / Direct / ADA.

Brooks, Randy

1945-1947 (Brooks, Randy & His Orchestra)
CD _____ CCD 35
Circle / Mar '95 / Jazz Music / Swift / Wellard.

Broom, Bobby

NO HYPE BLUES
CD _____ CRISS 1109
Criss Cross / Dec '95 / Cadillac / Harmonia Mundi.

Broonzy, Big Bill

1955 LONDON SESSIONS, THE
When do I get to be called a man / Partnership woman / Southbound train / St. Louis blues / Mindind my own business / It feels so good / Saturday evening / Glory of love / Southern saga inc Joe Turner blues / In the evening / Going down this road feeling bad
CD _____ NEXCD 119
Sequel / Apr '90 / BMG.

BIG BILL BROONZY VOL. 10 (1940)
CD _____ DOCD 5132
Blues Document / Oct '92 / Swift / Jazz Music / Hot Shot.

BIG BILL BROONZY VOL. 12 1945-47
CD _____ BDCD 6047
Blues Document / Sep '94 / Swift / Jazz Music / Hot Shot.

BIG BILL BROONZY VOL. 4 (1935-36)
CD _____ DOCD 5126
Blues Document / Oct '92 / Swift / Jazz Music / Hot Shot.

BIG BILL BROONZY VOL. 5 (1936-37)
CD _____ DOCD 5127
Blues Document / Oct '92 / Swift / Jazz Music / Hot Shot.

BIG BILL BROONZY VOL. 6 (1937)
CD _____ DOCD 5128
Blues Document / Oct '92 / Swift / Jazz Music / Hot Shot.

BIG BILL BROONZY VOL. 7 (1937-38)
CD _____ DOCD 5129
Blues Document / Oct '92 / Swift / Jazz Music / Hot Shot.

BIG BILL BROONZY VOL. 8 (1938-39)
CD _____ DOCD 5130
Blues Document / Oct '92 / Swift / Jazz Music / Hot Shot.

BIG BILL BROONZY VOL. 9 (1939)
CD _____ DOCD 5131
Blues Document / Oct '92 / Swift / Jazz Music / Hot Shot.

BIG BILL BROONZY: 1935-1940
CD _____ BLE 592532
Black & Blue / Dec '92 / Wellard / Koch.

BLACK, BROWN AND WHITE
CD _____ 842743-2
Verve / Jan '93 / PolyGram.

GOOD TIME TONIGHT
I can't be satisfied / Long tall Mama / Worrying you off my mind - Part 1 / Too too train blues / Come home early / Hattie blues / I want my hands on it / Made a date with an angel (got no walking shoe / Horny frog / I believe I'll go back home / Good time tonight / Flat foot Susie with her flat yes yes / WPA rag / Going back to Arkansas / It's a low down dirty shame / Too many drivers / Woodie woodie / Whiskey and good time blues / Merry go round blues / You've got to hick the night trick
CD _____ 4672472
CBS / Oct '90 / Sony.

HISTORICAL RECORDINGS 1932-1937
CD _____ 157422
Blues Collection / Feb '93 / Discovery.

HOUSE RENT STOMP
Big Bill blues / Little city woman / Back water blues / Guitar shuffle / Romance without finance / Jacqueline / Lonesome / House rent stomp / Willie Mae blues / Saturday evening blues / Louise Louise blues / Key to the highway / Swing low, sweet chariot / Stump blues / Makin' my getaway / Boogie woogie / C.C. rider / Going down the road feelin' bad / Plowhand blues / I'm gonna move to the outskirts of town / How long blues
CD _____ CD 52007
Blues Encore / '92 / Target/BMG.

I FEEL SO GOOD
CD _____ IGOCD 2006
Indigo / Nov '94 / Direct / ADA.

REMEMBERING BIG BILL BROONZY
John Henry / Bill Bailey, won't you please come home / Blue tail fly / Leroy Carr / Trouble in mind blues / Stump blues / Get back / Willie Mae / Hey hey / Tomorrow / Walkin' down a lonesome road
CD _____ BGOCD 91
Beat Goes On / Dec '90 / Pinnacle.

SINGS FOLK SONGS
CD _____ SFWCD 40023
Smithsonian Folkways / Mar '95 / ADA / Direct / Koch / CM / Cadillac.

SOUTHERN BLUES (Charly blues - Masterworks Vol. 49)
CD _____ CDBM 49
Charly / Jun '93 / Charly / THE / Cadillac.

TREAT ME RIGHT
CD _____ TCD 1005
Rykodisc / Feb '96 / Vital / ADA.

YOUNG BIG BILL BROONZY 1928-35 (Broonzy, Bill)
CD _____ YAZCD 1011
Yazoo / Jun '91 / CM / ADA / Roots / Koch.

Bros

INTERVIEW COMPACT DISC: BROS
CD P.Disc _____ CBAK 4017
Baktabak / Nov '89 / Baktabak.

PUSH
When will I be famous / Drop the boy / Ten out of ten / Liar / Love to hate you / I owe you nothing / It's a jungle out there / Shocked / Cat among the pigeons
CD _____ 4606292
CBS / Mar '88 / Sony.

Brostrom, Hakan

CELESTIAL NIGHTS
CD _____ DRCD 257

Dragon / Oct '94 / Roots / Cadillac / Wellard / CM / ADA.

DARK LIGHT
CD _____ DRAGON 190
Dragon / May '89 / Roots / Cadillac / Wellard / CM / ADA.

Brother Beyond

GET EVEN
Chain gang smile / Somebody, somewhere / Restless / Shipwrecked / Sunset bars / I should have lied / How many times / Some-times good, sometimes bad, (sometimes better) / Think of you / King of blue / Act for love / Be my twin / Can you keep a secret / He ain't no competition / Harder I try
CD _____ CDPCS 7314
Parlophone / Nov '88 / EMI.

Brother Boys

BROTHERS BOYS
CD _____ NHD 1101
Zu Zazz / Aug '90 / Rollercoaster.

PLOW
Gonna row my boat / I got over the blues / Kiss the dream girl / Alone with you / Twist you up / Then and only then / Hoping that you're hoping / I see love / Blue guitar / Little box / Darkest day / Satellite shack / What will be in the fields tomorrow
CD _____ SH CD 3805
Sugarhill / '92 / Roots / CM / ADA / Direct.

PRESLEY'S GROCERY
CD _____ SHCD 3844
Sugarhill / Oct '95 / Roots / CM / ADA / Direct.

Brotherhood

XXIII
CD _____ CDBITE 7
Bite It / Aug '93 / EMI.

Brotherhood Of Breath

LIVE AT WILLISAU
CD _____ OGCD 001
Ogun / Sep '94 / Cadillac / Jazz Music / Charly.

Brotherhood Of Man

20 GREAT HITS
CD _____ CDPT 817
Prestige / Mar '92 / Total/BMG.

BEST OF BROTHERHOOD OF MAN (16 Super Hits)
CD _____ 12210
Laserlight / May '94 / Target/BMG.

GREATEST HITS
CD _____ CDSR 012
Telstar / Jun '93 / BMG.

SAVE YOUR KISSES FOR ME
CD _____ AVC 515
Avid / Dec '92 / Avid/BMG / Koch.

UNITED WE STAND
CD _____ 8206232
Deram / Jan '96 / PolyGram.

Brothers Brooks

BROTHERS BROOKS, THE
CD _____ DOS 7011
Dos / Dec '94 / CM / Direct / ADA.

Brothers Johnson

FUNKADELIA
Stompi / Dancin' free / Ain't we funkin' now / Real thing / You make me wanna wriggle / Come together / Thunder thumbs and lightnin' licks / Funk it (funkadelala) / Light up the night / I came here to party / Do it for love / It's you girl / Love is / You keep me coming back
CD _____ 5502242
Spectrum/Karussell / Aug '94 / PolyGram / THE.

Brothers Like Outlaw

MY AFRO'S ON FIRE (Outlaw Posse)
CD _____ GEECD 6
Gee Street / Jul '91 / PolyGram.

Brotzmann, Caspar

HOME
CD _____ BFFP 110CD
Blast First / Jan '95 / Disc.

KOKSOFEN
CD _____ ABBCD 052
Big Cat / Aug '95 / SRD / Pinnacle.

TRIBE, THE
CD _____ ZSCM 08
Special Delivery / Jul '92 / ADA / CM / Direct.

Brotzmann, Peter

DARE DEVIL
CD _____ DIW 857
DIW / May '92 / Harmonia Mundi / Cadillac.

DIE LIKE A DOG
CD _____ FMPCD 64
FMP / Oct '94 / Cadillac.

MACHINE GUN
CD _____ FMPCD 24
FMP / Mar '94 / Cadillac.

MARTZ COMBO - LIVE IN WUPPERETAL, THE
CD _____ FMPCD 47
FMP / May '89 / Cadillac.

RESERVE
CD _____ FMPCD 17
FMP / Apr '87 / Cadillac.

WIE DES LIEBEN SO SPIELD (Brotzmann, Peter & Werner Ludi)
CD _____ FMPCD 22
FMP / Jul '85 / Cadillac.

Broughton, Edgar

BANDAGES (Broughton, Edgar Band)
CD _____ CLACD 261
Castle / Jun '92 / BMG.

EDGAR BROUGHTON BAND (Broughton, Edgar Band)
CD _____ CSAPCD 109
Connoisseur / Oct '92 / Pinnacle.

EDGAR BROUGHTON BAND/IN SIDE OUT (Broughton, Edgar Band)
Evening over rooftops / Birth / Piece of my mind / Poppy / Don't even know what day it is / House of turnabout / Madhatter / Getting hard / What is a woman for / Thinking of you / For Dr Spock (part one) / For Dr Spock (Part two) / Get out of bed / There's nobody there / Side by side / Sister Angela / I got mad / They took it away / Homes fit for heroes / Gone blue / Chilly morning mamma / Rake / Totin this guitar / Double agent / It's not you / Rock 'n' roll
CD _____ BGOCD 179
Beat Goes On / Mar '93 / Pinnacle.

LIVE HITS HARDER (Broughton, Edgar Band)
CD _____ 0884948906
CTE / Dec '95 / Koch.

OORAH (Broughton, Edgar Band)
CD _____ BGOCD 114
Beat Goes On / Sep '91 / Pinnacle.

SING BROTHER SING (Broughton, Edgar Band)
CD _____ BGOCD 7
Beat Goes On / Feb '92 / Pinnacle.

WASA WASA (Broughton, Edgar Band)
CD _____ BGOCD 129
Beat Goes On / Feb '92 / Pinnacle.

Brown, Alison

SIMPLE PLEASURES
Mambo banjo / Leaving cottondale / Fan-tasy / Daytime TV / Wolf moon / From the coast / Weetabix / Bright and early / Waltz-ing with Tula / Reedy rooster / Sundaze / Simple pleasures
CD _____ VHD 74959CD
Vanguard / '91 / Complete/Pinnacle / Discovery.

Brown, Angela

ANGELA BROWN LIVE
CD _____ BEST 1038CD
Acoustic Music / Nov '93 / ADA.

BREATH TAKING BOOGIE SHAKING (Brown, Angela & Al Humphrey/C Christl)
CD _____ BEST 1004CD
Acoustic Music / Nov '93 / ADA.

WILD TURKEY (Brown, Angela & C. Christl)
CD _____ BEST 1017CD
Acoustic Music / Nov '93 / ADA.

Brown, Arthur

CHISHOLM IN MY BOSOM/DANCE
Need to know / Money wails / Let a little sunshine (into your life) / I put a spell on you / She's on my mind / Lord is my saviour / Chisholm in my bosom / We gotta get out of this place / Helen with the sun / Take a chance / Crazy / Hearts and minds / Dance / Out of time / Quietely with tact / Soul garden / Lord will find a way / Is there nothing beyond God
CD _____ SEECD 431
See For Miles/C5 / Aug '95 / Pinnacle.

GALACTIC ZOO DOSSIER (Arthur Brown's Kingdom Come)
Internal messenger / Space plucks / Galac-tic zoo / Metal monster / Simple man / Night of the pigs / Sunrise / Trouble / Brains / Galactic zoo (Cont) / Space plucks (Cont) / Galactic zoo (Cont.) / Creep / Creation / Gypsy escape / No time
CD _____ VP 135CD
Voice Print / Apr '93 / Voice Print.

JOURNEY (Arthur Brown's Kingdom Come)
Time captives / Triangles / Gypsy / Super-ficial roadblocks (a)Lost time (b)Superficial roadblocks (c)Corpora supercelstia) / Con-ception / Spirit of joy / Come alive

CD _____ VP 137CD
Voice Print / Apr '93 / Voice Print.

KINGDOM COME (Arthur Brown's Kingdom Come)
Teacher / Scientific experiment / Whirl pool / Hymn / Water / City melody / Traffic light song
CD _____ VP 136CD
Voice Print / Apr '93 / Voice Print.

ORDER FROM CHAOS - LIVE 1993
When you open the door / When you open the door (2) / King of England / Juices of love / Nightmare / Fire poem / Fire / Come and buy / Pick it up / Mandela / Time cap-tains / I put a spell on you
CD _____ VP 144CD
Voice Print / Mar '94 / Voice Print.

REQUIEM
Chant / Shades / Animal people / Spirits take flight / Gabriel / Requiem / Machanicla masseur / Busha-busha / Fire ant and the cockroaches / Tear down the wall / Santa put a spell on me / Pale stars / Chromatic alley / Falling up
CD _____ VP 125 CD
Voice Print / Feb '93 / Voice Print.

SPEAK NO TECH
King of England / Conversations / Strange romance / Not fade away / Morning was cold / Speak no tech / Names are names / Love lady / Big apple / Take a pic-ture / You don't know / Old friend my col-leage / Lost my soul in London / Joined for-ever / Mandala / Desert floor
CD _____ VPCD 124 CD
Voice Print / Feb '93 / Voice Print.

Brown, Barry

FAR EAST
CD _____ 78249700030
Channel One / Apr '95 / Jetstar.

SING ROOTS & CULTURE (Brown, Barry & Johnny Clarke)
CD _____ FMCD 002
Fatman / Nov '94 / SRD / Jetstar / THE.

Brown, Bobby

BOBBY
Humpin' around (Prelude) / Humpin' around / Two can play that game / Get away / Till the end of time / Good enough / Pretty little girl / Lovin' you down / One more night / Something in common / That's the way love is / College girl / Storm away / I'm your friend / Humpin' around (mix) (LP only) / Humpin' around (Epilogue)
CD _____ MCLD 19300
MCA / Oct '95 / BMG.

DON'T BE CRUEL
Don't be cruel / My prerogative / Roni / Rock wit'cha / Every little step / I'll be good to you / All day, all night / Take it slow
CD _____ MCLD 19212
MCA / Aug '93 / BMG.

TWO CAN PLAY THAT GAME
Two can play that game / Humpin' around / That's the way love is / Humpin' around / Something in common / Get away / On our own / My perogative / Every little step / Good enough / One more night / Rock wit'cha
CD _____ MCD 11334
MCA / Jul '95 / BMG.

Brown, Charles

CHARLES BROWN LIVE
Quicksand / Saving my love for you / Seven days long / Just the way you are / Black night / So long / Cottage for sale / Brown's boogie
CD _____ CDCBL 757
Charly / Oct '95 / Charly / THE / Cadillac.

COOL CHRISTMAS BLUES
CD _____ BBCD 9561
Bullseye Blues / Nov '94 / Direct.

DRIFTING AND DREAMING (Brown, Charles & Johnny Moore's Three Blazers)
Travelin' blues / I'll get along somehow / Copyright on your love / If you should ever leave / When your lover has gone / Blues because of you / Sail on blues / More than you know / You should show me the way / It had to be you / You are my first love / Seven saw concerto (part 1) / War-saw concerto (part 2) / You left me forsaken / How deep is the ocean / Nutmeg / It's the talk of the town / What do you know about love
CD _____ CDCHD 589
Ace / Jan '96 / Pinnacle / Cadillac / Com-plete/Pinnacle.

I'M GONNA PUSH ON (Live at Nosebacke) (Brown, Charles & Hjartslag)
Teardrops from my eyes / Black night / Please don't drive me away / Trouble blues / Please come home for Christmas / Just the way you are / Bad bad whiskey / I'm gonna push on / I wanna go back home to Gothenburg / I'll do my best
CD _____ RBD 200
Stockholm / Jan '91 / Swift / CM.

KINGDOM COME (Arthur Brown's Kingdom Come)
Teacher / Scientific experiment / Whirl pool / Hymn / Water / City melody / Traffic light song

JUST A LUCKY SO 'N' SO
CD _____ BB 9521CD
Bullseye Blues / Feb '94 / Direct.

ONE MORE FOR THE ROAD
I cried last night / Save your love for me / Who will the next fool be / Cottage for sale / Travellin' blues / I stepped in quicksand / Route 66 / One for my baby / My heart is mended / He's got you / I miss you so / Get yourself another fool
CD _____ ALCD 4771
Alligator / Aug '92 / Direct / ADA.

SINGS CHRISTMAS SONGS
CD _____ KCD 775
King/Paddle Wheel / Nov '92 / New Note.

THESE BLUES
CD _____ 523022-2
Verve / Oct '94 / PolyGram.

Brown, Clarence

GATE'S ON THE HEAT (Brown, Clarence 'Gatemouth')
CD _____ 5197302
Verve / Feb '94 / PolyGram.

MAN, THE (Brown, Clarence 'Gatemouth')
CD _____ 5237612
PolyGram Jazz / Feb '95 / PolyGram.

NO LOOKING BACK (Brown, Clarence 'Gatemouth')
Better off with the blues / Digging new ground / Dope / My own prison / Stop time / C jam blues / Straighten up and fly right / Peeper / Blue gummod catahoula (alligator eating boy) / I will be your friend / We're outta here
CD _____ ALCD 4804
Alligator / May '93 / Direct / ADA.

PRESSURE COOKER (Brown, Clarence 'Gatemouth')
CD _____ ALCD 4745
Alligator / May '93 / Direct / ADA.

REAL LIFE
Real Life / Okie Dokie stomp / Frankie and Johnny / Next time you see me / Take the 'A' train / Please send me someone to love / Catfish / St. Louis blues / What a shame what a shame
CD _____ CD 2054
Rounder / '88 / CM / Direct / ADA / Cadillac.

SAN ANTONIO BALLBUSTER (Charly Blues - Masterworks Volume 6) (Brown, Clarence 'Gatemouth')
May the bird of paradise fly up your nose (Alt.) / Cross my heart / Don't start me talkin' / Gate's salty blues / My time is ex-pensive / Goin' down slow / Long way home / Tippin' in / For now so long / May the bird of paradise fly up your nose
CD _____ CD BM 6
Charly / Apr '92 / Charly / THE / Cadillac.

STANDING MY GROUND
CD _____ ALCD 4779
Alligator / May '93 / Direct / ADA.

TEXAS SWING (Brown, Clarence 'Gatemouth')
CD _____ CD 11527
Rounder / '88 / CM / Direct / ADA / Cadillac.

Brown, Clifford

BEGINNING AND THE END, THE
I come from Jamaica / Ida red / Walkin' / Night in Tunisia / Donna Lee
CD _____ 477737-2
Columbia / Oct '94 / Sony.

BIRDLAND FEB. 1954 (Brown, Clifford & Art Blakey)
CD _____ CD 53033
Giants Of Jazz / Mar '90 / Target/BMG / Cadillac.

BLUE NOTE AND PACIFIC JAZZ RECORDINGS, THE (4CD Set)
Bellarosa / Carvin' the rock / Carvin' the rock (2) / Cookin' / Cookin' (2) / Brownie speaks / De-dah / You go to my head / Car-vin' the rock (3) / Wail bait / Wail bait (2) / Hymn of the Orient / Brownie eyes / Cher-okee / Cherokee (2) / Easy living / Minor mood / Hymn of the Orient (2) / Capri / Capri (2) / Lover man / Turnpike / Turnpike (2) / Sketch one / It could happen to you / Get happy / Get happy (2) / Daahound / Finders keepers / Joy spring / Gone with the wind / Bones for Jones / Blueberry hill / Tiny ca-pers / Tiny capers (2) / Split kick / Once in a while / Quicksilver / Wee dot / Blues / Night in Tunisia / Mayreh / Wee dot (2) / If I had you / Quicksilver (2) / Way you look tonight / Lou's blues / Now's the time / Confirmation
CD Set _____ CDP 8341952
Blue Note / Oct '95 / EMI.

CLIFF BROWN QUINTET & THE NEAL HEFTI ORCHESTRA (Brown, Clifford Quintet & Neal Hefti Orchestra)
CD _____ WWCD 2032
West Wind / Jan '91 / Swift / Charly / CM / ADA.

COMPLETE PARIS SESSIONS VOLUME 1, THE
Brown skins (2 Takes) / Deltitnu / Keeping up with Joneses / Conception (2 Takes) / All the things you are (2 Takes) / I cover the waterfront / Goofin' with me
CD _____ 74321154612
Vogue / Oct '93 / BMG.

COMPLETE PARIS SESSIONS VOLUME 2, THE
Minority (3 Takes) / Salute to the band box (2 Takes) / Strictly romantic / Baby (2 Takes) / Quick step (3 Takes) / Bum's rush (3 Takes) / No start, no end
CD _____ 74321154622
Vogue / Oct '93 / BMG.

COMPLETE PARIS SESSIONS VOLUME 3, THE
(Venez donc) Chez moi / All weird (3 takes) / Blue and brown / I can dream, can't I (3 takes) / Song is you (2 takes) / Come rain or come shine (2 takes) / It might as well be spring (2 takes) / You're a lucky guy (3 takes)
CD _____ 74321154632
Vogue / Oct '93 / BMG.

IN CONCERT (Brown, Clifford & Max Roach)
Jordu / I can't get started (with you) / I get a kick out of you / Parisian thoroughfare / All god's chillun got rhythm / Tenderly / Sunset eyes / Clifford's axe
CD _____ GNPD 18
GNP Crescendo / '88 / Silva Screen.

MEMORIAL ALBUM
Hymn of the Orient / Easy living / Minor mood / Cherokee / Wail bait / Brownie speaks / De-dah / Cookin' / Carvin' the rock / You go to my head
CD _____ BNZ 202
Blue Note / Aug '85 / EMI.

Brown, D.R.

LIVE IN THE MIND'S EYE
CD _____ BEARD 005 CD
Beard / Oct '92 / Pinnacle.

Brown, Deborah

JAZZ 4 JAZZ
Little Esther / Denise / Finally / It don't mean a thing if it ain't got that swing / Embraceable you / Since I fell for you / I thought about you / My romance / What is this thing called love / When we were one / Be bop / When I fall in love
CD _____ CDSJP 409
Timeless Jazz / Aug '93 / New Note.

Brown, Dennis

20 GOLDEN GREATS
CD _____ CDSGP 0104
Prestige / Oct '94 / Total/BMG.

20 MAGNIFICENT HITS
CD _____ DBP 1CD
Dennis Ting / Jul '93 / Jetstar / SRD.

ANOTHER DAY IN PARADISE
(Sittin' on) the dock of the bay / Last thing on my mind / Just a guy / My girl / Everybody needs love / Ain't that lovin' you / Another day in paradise / Queen Majesty / I'm still waiting / Conversation / Green green grass of home / Girl I got a date
CD _____ CDTRL 310
Trojan / Mar '94 / Jetstar / Total/BMG.

BEST OF DENNIS BROWN PT. 1
CD _____ JMGL 6048
Joe Gibbs / Jan '94 / Jetstar.

BEST OF DENNIS BROWN, THE
CD _____ CB 6004
Caribbean / Jan '96 / Magnum Music Group.

BEST OF VOL.1
CD _____ 60042
Declic / Nov '95 / Jetstar.

BEST OF VOL.2
CD _____ 60052
Declic / Nov '95 / Jetstar.

BROWN SUGAR
CD _____ RASCD 3207
Ras / '88 / Jetstar / Greensleeves / SRD / Direct.

CLASSIC HITS
CD _____ SONCD 0022
Sonic Sounds / Apr '92 / Jetstar.

COSMIC FORCE
CD _____ HBCD 135
Heartbeat / Apr '93 / Greensleeves / Jetstar / Direct / ADA.

DENNIS BROWN COLLECTION, THE
CD _____ DBP 1
Dennis Brown Productions / Jun '93 / Jetstar.

FACTS OF LIFE
CD _____ DIACD 0002
Diamond / Feb '95 / Discovery.

FOUL PLAY
CD _____ JGMLCD 4850
Joe Gibbs / Jan '94 / Jetstar.

FRIENDS FOR LIFE
CD _____ SHCD 45004
Shanachie / Jun '93 / Koch / ADA / Greensleeves.

GIVE PRAISES
CD _____ CDTZ 012
Tappa / Aug '93 / Jetstar.

GREATEST HITS: DENNIS BROWN
CD _____ RRTGCD 7709
Rohit / '88 / Jetstar.

HIT AFTER HIT
CD _____ RGCD 027
Rocky One / Feb '95 / Jetstar.

HOLD TIGHT
Hold tight / Indiscipline woman / Footstool / Let him go / When Spring is around / I've got your number / Worried man / Things in life
CD _____ LLCD 21
Live & Love / Sep '86 / Jetstar.

HOTTER FLAMES (Brown, Dennis & Frankie Paul)
CD _____ VPCD 1310
VP / Aug '93 / Jetstar.

I DON'T KNOW
CD _____ DGVCD 1600
Grapevine / Oct '95 / Grapevine.

IF I DIDN'T LOVE
CD _____ JMC 200202
Jamaica Gold / Dec '92 / THE / Magnum Music Group / Jetstar.

IT'S THE RIGHT TIME
CD _____ RNCD 2021
Rhino / Sep '93 / Jetstar / Magnum Music Group / THE.

JOSEPH'S COAT OF MANY COLOURS
Slave driver / Open your eyes / Creator / Cup of tea / Together brothers / Oh what a day / Well without water / Three meals a day / Home sweet home / Man next door
CD _____ CDBM 010
Blue Moon / Nov '88 / Magnum Music Group / Greensleeves / Hot Shot / ADA / Cadillac / Discovery.

JOY IN THE MORNING
CD _____ LG2 1106
Lagoon / Mar '95 / Magnum Music Group / THE.

LIGHT MY FIRE
CD _____ CDHB 154
Heartbeat / May '94 / Greensleeves / Jetstar / Direct / ADA.

LIVE AT MONTREUX: DENNIS BROWN
So jah say / Wolves and leopards / Ain't that lovin' you / Words of wisdom / Drifter / Milk and honey / Yabby you / Don't feel no way / Whip them Jah / Money in my pocket
CD _____ CDBM 016
Blue Moon / Apr '91 / Magnum Music Group / Greensleeves / Hot Shot / ADA / Cadillac / Discovery.

LIVE IN MONTEGO BAY
CD _____ SONCD 0039
Sonic Sounds / Jan '93 / Jetstar.

LOVE LIGHT
Little bit more / Tribulation / Rocking time / Caress me girl / Love light / Hold on to what you've got / Little village / Have you ever been in love
CD _____ CDBM 102
Blue Moon / Apr '95 / Magnum Music Group / Greensleeves / Hot Shot / ADA / Cadillac / Discovery.

LOVER'S PARADISE
CD _____ CDSGP 068
Prestige / Oct '93 / Total/BMG.

MONEY IN MY POCKET
Money in my pocket / Ah so we stay / Changing times / Silhouettes / Africa / Yagga yagga (you'll suffer) / I am the conqueror / Show us the way / Cassandra / No more will I roam
CD _____ CDTRL 311
Trojan / Mar '94 / Jetstar / Total/BMG.

MUSICAL HEATWAVE
Baby don't do it / What about the half / Don't you cry / Cheater / Let love in / Concentration / Silhouettes / He can't spell / Musical heatwave / I don't know / How could I let you get away / Lips of wine / Let me down easy / Changing times / Black magic woman / Money in my pocket / It's too late / Song my mother used to sing / Westbound train / Cassandra / I am the conqueror / No more will I roam / Why seek more / Moving away
CD _____ CDTRL 327
Trojan / Mar '94 / Jetstar / Total/BMG.

MY TIME
CD _____ RRTGCD 7713
Rohit / Jan '89 / Jetstar.

NO CONTEST (Brown, Dennis & Gregory Isaacs)
CD _____ GRELCD 133
Greensleeves / Jul '89 / Total/BMG / Jetstar / SRD.

ONE OF A KIND
CD _____ 111912
Musidisc / Mar '94 / Vital / Harmonia Mundi / ADA / Cadillac / Discovery.

OPEN THE GATE: GREATEST HITS VOL.2
CD _____ CDHB 177
Heartbeat / Apr '95 / Greensleeves / Jetstar / Direct / ADA.

OVERPROOF
CD _____ SHCD 43086
Shanachie / Jun '91 / Koch / ADA / Greensleeves.

PRIME OF DENNIS BROWN, THE
CD _____ MCCD 118
Music Club / Aug '93 / Disc / THE / CM.

SMILE LIKE AN ANGEL
Let me live / Pretend you're happy / Westbound train / Don't expect me to be your friend / Play girl / Smile like an angel / Poorer side of town / We will be free / Summertime / Silver words / My kind / Golden streets
CD _____ CDBM 034
Blue Moon / Jun '95 / Magnum Music Group / Greensleeves / Hot Shot / ADA / Cadillac / Discovery.

SO AMAZING (Brown, Dennis & Janet Kay)
CD _____ CDTRL 315
Trojan / Mar '94 / Jetstar / Total/BMG.

SOME LIKE IT HOT
CD _____ HBCD 107
Heartbeat / Nov '92 / Greensleeves / Jetstar / Direct / ADA.

TEMPERATURE RISING
CD _____ CDTRL 353
Trojan / Jun '95 / Jetstar / Total/BMG.

TRAVELLING MAN VOL.2, THE
CD _____ CB 6005
Caribbean / Jan '96 / Magnum Music Group.

UNCHALLENGED
CD _____ GRELCD 138
Greensleeves / Oct '89 / Total/BMG / Jetstar / SRD.

UNFORGETTABLE
CD _____ CRCD 24
Charm / Sep '93 / Jetstar.

VICTORY IS MINE
Victory is mine / Call me / We are in love / Don't give up / Everyday people / Sea of love / Just because / Should I / Jah can do it / Sad news
CD _____ CDBM 084
Blue Moon / Apr '91 / Magnum Music Group / Greensleeves / Hot Shot / ADA / Cadillac / Discovery.

VISION OF THE REGGAE KING
CD _____ GOLDCD 001
Goldmine / Jun '94 / Jetstar.

WOLVES AND LEOPARDS
Wolves and leopards / Emanuel / Here I come / Whip them Jah / Created by the Father / Party time / Rolling down / Boasting / Children of Israel / Lately girl
CD _____ CDBM 046
Blue Moon / Apr '87 / Magnum Music Group / Greensleeves / Hot Shot / ADA / Cadillac / Discovery.

YOU GOT THE BEST OF ME
CD _____ SAXCD 004
Saxon Studio / Oct '95 / Jetstar.

Brown, Donald

CAR TUNES
Car tunes / Theme for my father / Jay McShann / Blues for brother Jerome / Mr Felgeroulles / I didn't know what time it was / Being with you / There is a rose in Spanish harlem / Blues is my best friend / Car tunes (the end)
CD _____ MCD 5522
Muse / Dec '95 / New Note / CM.

SEND ONE YOUR LOVE
Whisper not / Sequel / Blues for Harold / Send one your love / Sweetest sounds / Second time around / Crazeology / Theme for Malcolm / Girl watching
CD _____ MCD 5479
Muse / Mar '94 / New Note / CM.

SOURCES OF INSPIRATION
CD _____ MCD 5385
Muse / Sep '92 / New Note / CM.

SWEETEST SOUNDS, THE
I used to think she was quiet / I should care / Gee baby ain't I good to you / Theme for Ernie / Sweetest sounds / Affaire d'amour / Natures folk song / Betcha by golly wow / Woody 'n' you / Night mist blues / Killing me softly
CD _____ 66053008
Jazz City / Feb '91 / New Note.

Brown, Earl

SYNERGY
CD _____ ARTCD 6177
Hat Art / Dec '95 / Harmonia Mundi / ADA / Cadillac.

Brown, Florie

IRISH FIDDLE TUNES
CD _____ EUCD 1308
ARC / Jul '95 / ARC Music / ADA.

Brown, Foxy

MY KINDA GIRL
CD _____ RASCD 3070
Ras / Feb '91 / Jetstar / Greensleeves / SRD / Direct.

Brown, Georgia

SINGS KURT WEILL / SINGS GEORGE GERSHWIN
September song / Jenny / Pirate Jenny / Alabama song / Speak low / It never was you / My ship / Mack the knife / Barbara song / Surabaya Johnny / Furchte dich nicht / Summertime / It ain't necessarily so / I loves you Porgy / I got plenty o' nuttin' / My man's gone now / Oh Lord, I'm on my way / Fascinating rhythm / But not for me / Blah blah blah / Slap that bass / How long has this been going on / Strike up the band
CD _____ SHE CD 9617
Pearl / '90 / Harmonia Mundi.

Brown, Glen

CHECK THE WINNER
CD _____ GRELCD 603
Greensleeves / May '90 / Total/BMG / Jetstar / SRD.

SENSI DUB VOLUME 6 (Brown, Glen & Roots Radics)
CD _____ OMCD 26
Original Music / Feb '93 / SRD / Jetstar.

WAY TO MOUNT ZION, THE
CD _____ RUSCD 8215
Roir USA / Oct '95 / Plastic Head.

Brown, Greg

IOWA WALTZ, THE
CD _____ RHRCD 01
Red House / Oct '95 / Koch / ADA.

LIVE ONE, THE
CD _____ RHRCD 78
Red House / Dec '95 / Koch / ADA.

POET GAME, THE
CD _____ RHRCD 68
Red House / May '95 / Koch / ADA.

Brown, Hylo

HYLO BROWN 1954 - 1960 (Brown, Hylo & The Timberliners)
Flower blooming in the wildwood / Put my little shoes away / Blue eyed darling / Will the angels play their harps for me / Old home town / Love and wealth / I'll be all smiles tonight / Gathering flowers from the hillside / Little Joe / Darling Nellie across the sea / When it's lamplighting time in the valley / Why do you weep dear willow / Test of love / Dark as a dungeon / Lost to a stranger / Sweethearts or strangers / In the graveyard beside the tomb / Wrong kind of life / I'll be broken hearted / Let's stop fooling our hearts / Lovesick and sorrow / Get lost, you wolf / One sided love affair / Only one / Prisoner's song / Nobody's darlin' but mine / One way train / Foolish pride / John Henry / There's more pretty girls than one / Stone wall (around my heart) / Shuffle of my feet / Your crazy heart / You can't relive the past / I've waited as long as I can / It's all over but the crying / Thunder clouds of love / Just any old love / Darlin' how can you forget so soon / Sweethearts and strangers
CD Set _____ BCD 15572
Bear Family / Mar '92 / Rollercoaster / Direct / CM / Swift / ADA.

Brown, James

COLD SWEAT
Give it up or turn it loose / Too funky in here / Little shoes away / Cold sweat / Try me / Get on the good foot / Get up offa that thing / Georgia on my mind / Hot pants / I got the feelin' / It's a man's man's man's world / Cold sweat / I can't stand it / Papa's got a brand new bag / I feel good / Please please please / Jam
CD _____ HADCD 164
Javelin / May '94 / THE / Henry Hadaway Organisation.

COLLECTION
CD _____ COL 003
Collection / Mar '95 / Target/BMG.

ESSENTIAL COLLECTION
CD Set _____ LECD 623
Wisepack / Apr '95 / THE / Conifer.

FUNKY PRESIDENT (Very Best Of James Brown)
CD _____ 5198542
Polydor / Jun '93 / PolyGram.

GODFATHER OF SOUL
It's a man's man's man's world / Papa's got a brand new bag / Nature boy / Think / Signed, sealed, delivered (I'm yours) / Please please please / How do you stop (live) / Call me super bad / Spinning wheel / Mona Lisa / This old heart / Good good

lovin' / Bewildered / (Get up I feel like being a) sex machine
CD _____ 5500402
Spectrum/Karussell / May '93 / PolyGram / THE.

GODFATHER OF SOUL, THE
CD _____ 100099
Scratch / Mar '95 / BMG.

GODFATHER OF SOUL, THE
It's a man's man's man's world / Super bad / Disco rap / Turn it loose (give it up) / It's too funky in here / Gonna have a funky good time / Try me / I got the feelin' / Get on the good foot / Prisoner of love / Get up offa that thing / Georgia on my mind
CD _____ MUCD 9009
Start / Apr '95 / Koch.

GODFATHER RETURNS, THE
Get up offa that thing / Hey America / Stormy Monday / Bodyheat / For once in my life / What the world needs now is love / Back stabbin' / Hot pants (She got to use what she got to get what she wants) / Stagger Lee / Need your love so bad / Woman / Never can say goodbye / Time after time / Georgia on my mind
CD _____ 5501992
Spectrum/Karussell / Sep '94 / PolyGram / THE.

GREATEST HITS
Get up offa that thing / Body heat / It's a man's man's man's world / I got the feelin' / (Get up I feel like being a) sex machine / Try me / Papa's got a brand new bag / Get on the good foot / Cold sweat / Please please please / Funky good time / It's too funky in here
CD _____ YDG 4613
Yesterday's Gold / Aug '93 / Target/BMG.

I'M REAL
Tribute / I'm real / Static / Time to get busy / She looks all types a good / Keep walkin' / Can't get enuff / It's your money / Godfather running the joint
CD _____ 834 755-2
Polydor / Jun '88 / PolyGram.

IN THE JUNGLE GROOVE
It's a new day / Funky drummer / Give it up or turn it loose(remix) / I got to move (Previously unreleased) / Talking loud and saying nothing(remix) / Get up, get into it and get involved / Soul power (re-edit) / Hot pants
CD _____ 829 624-2
Urban / May '88 / PolyGram.

JAMES BROWN LIVE
Give it up or turn it loose / It's a man's man's man's world / I got the feelin' / I can't stand it / Hot pants / Try me / I feel good today / Get up offa that thing / Please please please / Cold sweat / Georgia on my mind / It's too funky in here / Gonna have a funky good time / Get on the good foot / (Get up I feel like being a) sex machine
Laserlight / Jun '93 / Target/BMG.
_____ 15136

LIVE AT CHASTAIN PARK
Give it up or turn it loose / It's too funky in here / Try me / Get on the good foot / Get up offa that thing / Georgia on my mind / Hot pants / I got the feelin' / It's a man's man's man's world / I can't stand myself (when you touch me) / Papa's got a brand new bag / I got you (I feel good) / Please please please / Jam
CD _____ CDCD 1151
Charly / Apr '94 / Charly / THE / Cadillac.

LIVE AT THE APOLLO VOL.1
Opening fanfare / Try me / I don't mind / Lost someone (part 1) / Lost someone (part 2) / Night train / I'll go crazy / Think / Medley / Closing
CD _____ 843 479-2
Polydor / Jul '90 / PolyGram.

MESSIN' WITH THE BLUES
CD _____ 847 258-2
Polydor / Dec '90 / PolyGram.

PEARLS FROM THE PAST
CD _____ KLMCD 018
Scratch / Apr '94 / BMG.

PLEASE, PLEASE, PLEASE
Please please please / Try me / I feel that old feeling coming on / That's when I lost my heart / Chonnie on chon / Hold my baby's hand / Tell me what I did wrong / Baby cries over the ocean / Begging, begging / No, no, no, no / That dood it / I don't know / I walked alone / Love or a game / Let's make it / Just won't do right
CD _____ SING 8610
Sing / '88 / Charly.

SEX MACHINE - VERY BEST OF JAMES BROWN
Please please please / Think / Night train / Out of sight / Papa's got a brand new bag (part 1) / I got you (I feel good) / It's a man's man's man's world / Cold sweat / Say it loud, I'm black and I'm proud / Hey America / Make it funky / (Get up I feel like being a) sex machine / I'm a greedy man / Get on the good foot / Get up offa that thing / It's too funky in here / Livin' in America / Hot pants (Only on CD) / soul power (Only on CD)

_____ 845 828-2
Polydor / Nov '91 / PolyGram.

SOUL JUBILEE
Turn it loose / It's too funky in here / Gonna have a funky good time / Try me / Get on the good foot / Georgia / Hot pants / I got the feelin' / It's a man's man's man's world / Cold sweat / I can't stand it / Papa's got a brand new bag / I feel good / Please please please / Jam / Get up off that thing
CD _____ CDBM 081
Blue Moon / Apr '90 / Magnum Music Group / Greensleeves / Hot Shot / ADA / Cadillac / Discovery.

SOUL PRIDE
CD Set _____ 5178452
Polydor / May '93 / PolyGram.

STAR TIME
Please please please / Why do you do me / Try me / Tell me what I did wrong / Bewildered / Good good lovin' / I'll go crazy / I know it's true / Do the mashed potato (pt 1) / Think / Baby you're right / Lost someone / Night train / I've got money / I've got no money / I don't mind / Prisoner of love / Devil's den / Out of the blue / Out of sight / Grits / Maybe the last time / Papa's got a brand new bag (parts 1, 2 & 3) / Papa's got a brand new bag (part 1) / I got you (I feel good) / Ain't that a groove / It's a man's man's man's world / Money won't change you / Don't be a dropout / Bring it up (Hipster's avenue) / Let yourself go / Cold sweat / Get it together / I can't stand myself (when you touch me) (pt 1) / I got the feelin' / Lickin' stick / Say it loud, I'm black and I'm proud / There was a time (Live) / Give it up or turn it loose / I don't want nobody to give me nothing (Open up the door I'll get it myself) / Mother popcorn / Funky drummer / (Get up I feel like being a) sex machine / Super bad / Talkin' loud and sayin' nothing / Get up, get into it and get involved / Soul power, parts 1 and 2 / Brother rapp/Ain't it funky now (Live) / Hot pants (pt 1) / I'm a greedy man (pt 1) / Make it funky / It's a new day (Live) / I got ants in my pants (pt 1) / King Heroin / There it is, part 1 / Public enemy no.1 (pt 1) / Get on the good foot / I got a bag of my own / Doing it to death / Payback / Papa don't take no mess, part 1 / Stoned to the bone, part 1 / My thang / Funky president / Hot (I need to be loved, loved, loved) / Get up I feel like being a / Body heat (part 1) / It's too funky in here / Rapp payback / Unity, part 1
CD Set _____ 8491082
Polydor / May '91 / PolyGram.

TELL ME WHAT YOU'RE GONNA DO
(Brown, James & The Famous Flames)
Just you and me darling / I love you, yes I do / I don't mind / Come over here / bells / Love don't love nobody / Dancin' little thing / Lost someone / And I do just what I want / So long / You don't have to go / Tell me what you're gonna do
CD _____ CPCD 8053
Charly / Mar '95 / Charly / THE / Cadillac.

Brown, Jeri
UNFOLDING - THE PEACOCKS
CD _____ JUST 45-2
Justin Time / Apr '93 / Harmonia Mundi / Cadillac.

Brown, Jim
BACK TO THE COUNTRY (Brown, Jimmy & Willy Lee Harris)
CD _____ TCD 5013
Testament / Dec '94 / Complete/Pinnacle / ADA / Koch.

Brown, Jocelyn
ABSOLUTELY
CD _____ BR 1402
BR Music / Mar '95 / Target/BMG.

ESSENTIAL DANCEFLOOR ARTISTS VOL. 6
Somebody else's guy / I wish you would / Picking up promises / I'm caught up (in a never ending love affair) / I want to give you me / You don't have dancing on your mind / I hope it's the right time / Ain't no mountain high enough
CD _____ DGPCD 712
Deep Beats / Feb '95 / BMG.

JOCELYN BROWN COLLECTION
CD _____ CCSCD 386
Castle / Oct '93 / BMG.

Brown, Joe
JOE BROWN STORY, THE (Brown, Joe & The Bruvvers)
People gotta talk / Comes the day / Savage / At the Darktown struter's ball / Swagger / Jellied eels / Shine / Switch / Crazy mixed up kid / I'm Henery the Eighth (I am) / Good luck and goodbye / Popcorn / Picture of you / Lazybod's lament / Talking guitar / Lonely Island pearl / Your tender look / Other side of town / It only took a minute / All things bright and beautiful / That's what love will do / What's the name of the game / Casting my spell / What a crazy we're living in / Hava Nagila / You can't lie to a liar / Sweet little sixteen / Nature's time

for love / Spanish bit / Sally Ann / There's only one of you / Walkin' tall / Hercules unchained / You do things to me / Everybody calls me Joe / Don't / Just like that / Teardrops in the rain / Lonely Circus / Sicilian tarantella / Sea of heartbreak / Mrs. O's theme / Little ray of sunshine / Your loving touch / Satisfied mind / Th' wife / Rich man's son and the poor man's daughter / With a little help from my friends / Show me around
_____ NEDCD 235
Sequol / Oct '93 / BMG.

LIVE & IN THE STUDIO
See For Miles/C5 / Jun '94 / Pinnacle.
_____ C5MCD 612

PICTURE OF YOU, A
Picture of you / That's what love will do / It only took a minute / Sea of heartbreak / English country garden / S-H-I-N-E / With a little help from my friends / Alley oops (live) / Little ray of sunshine / What a crazy world we're livin' in (live) / Sweet little sixteen (live) / Hallelujah I love her so (live) / I'm Henry the eighth I am / Just like that / My favourite occupation / Hava nagila (the hora) / All things bright and beautiful / Nature's time
CD _____ 550 759-2
Spectrum/Karussell / Apr '95 / PolyGram / THE.

Brown, Kevin
ROAD DREAMS
CD _____ HNCD 1340
Hannibal / May '89 / Vital / ADA.

RUST
Don't quit / Hey Joe Louis / Write a bible of your own / Telephone tears / We'll be with you / If I had my way / You don't have to tell me / Southern Streets / Meltdown / Sunny side up
CD _____ HNCD 1344
Hannibal / May '89 / Vital / ADA.

Brown, Lee
1937-1940
CD _____ DOCD 5344
Blues Document / May '95 / Swift / Jazz Music / Hot Shot.

Brown, Les
22 ORIGINAL BIG BAND RECORDINGS
CD _____ HCD 408
Hindsight / Sep '92 / Target/BMG / Jazz Music.

BIG BAND CLASSICS (Brown, Les & Billy May)
CD _____ ISCD 129
Intersound / Jul '93 / Jazz Music.

DIGITAL SWING (Brown, Les & His Band Of Renown)
How high the moon / Let's get started (with you) / Blue skies / For all we know / What is this thing called love / I feel fine / Perky / One more blues / St. Louis blues / Come rain or come shine / Misty / You're nobody 'til somebody loves you / Yo Henry
CD _____ FCD 9650
Fantasy / Apr '94 / Pinnacle / Jazz Music / Wellard / Cadillac.

ELITCH GARDENS, DENVER 1959
CD _____ DSTS 1002
Status / Jazz Music / Wellard / Harmonia Mundi.

ELITCH GARDENS, DENVER 1959 VOL 2 (Brown, Les & His Band Of Renown)
CD _____ DSTS 1006
Status / Feb '95 / Jazz Music / Wellard / Harmonia Mundi.

GREAT LES BROWN, THE
CD _____ HCD 330
Hindsight / May '95 / Target/BMG / Jazz Music.

HEATWAVE (Brown, Les & His Band Of Renown)
CD _____ DAWE 54
Magic / Nov '93 / Jazz Music / Swift / Wellard / Cadillac / Harmonia Mundi.

LES BROWN & HIS GREAT VOCALISTS
Robin Hood / Lament to love / I guess I'll have to dream the rest / Good man is hard to find / I got it bad and that ain't good / 'Tis autumn / Sentimental journey / Sleigh ride in July / My dreams are getting better all the time / Day by day / I guess I'll get the papers and go home / OH how I miss you tonight / Comes the sandman (a lullaby) / Just a gigolo / Crosstown trolley / Rock me to sleep
CD _____ CK 66373
Columbia / Jul '95 / Sony.

LES BROWN AND HIS BAND
Leapfrog / Sentimental journey / You won't be satisfied / Floatin' / I've got the sun in the morning and the moon at night / Foggy day / Bizet has his day / All through the day / I've got my love to keep me warm / 'Tis Autumn / On the beach at Waikiki / 'S wonderful / My dreams are getting better all the time / Mexican hat dance / Just one of those things / Twilight time

CD Set _____ CK 45344
CBS / Apr '90 / Sony.

LES BROWN AND HIS BAND OF RENOWN (Brown, Les & His Band Of Renown)
CD _____ HCD 252
Hindsight / May '94 / Target/BMG / Jazz Music.

LES BROWN/JOHNNY MERCER/ MARGARET WHITING
CD _____ DAWE 68
Magic / Apr '01 / Jazz Music / Swift / Wellard / Cadillac / Harmonia Mundi.

SENTIMENTAL JOURNEY
CD _____ 825 493-2
PolyGram / '88 / PolyGram.

Brown, Marion
BACK TO PARIS
CD _____ FRLCD 002
Freelance / Oct '92 / Harmonia Mundi / Cadillac / Koch.

PORTO NOVO
Similar limits / Sound and structure / Improvisation / Qbic / Porto novo / And then they danced / Rhythmus #1
CD _____ BLCD 760200
Black Lion / Apr '95 / Jazz Music / Cadillac / Wellard / Koch.

WHY NOT (Brown, Marion Quartet)
CD _____ ESP 1040-2
ESP / Jan '93 / Jazz Horizons / Jazz Music.

Brown, Maxine
OH NO NOT MY BABY
Since I found you / Gotta find a way / I wonder what my baby's doing tonight / Let me give you my lovin' / It's torture / One in a million / Oh no not my baby / You're in love / Anything for a laugh / Coming back to you / Yesterday's kisses / Ask me / All in my mind / Little girl lost / I want a guarantee / Secret of livin' / Baby cakes / One step at a time / I've got a lot of love left in me / I don't need anything / Oh Lord what are you doing to me / I cry alone / Funny / Misty morning eyes / Love that man / Losing my touch / Put yourself in my place / It's gonna be alright
CD _____ CDKEND 949
Kent / Oct '90 / Pinnacle.

Brown, Nappy
APPLES AND LEMONS
Fishin' blues / Ain't no way / Get along / Lemon squeezin' daddy / Daddy / You showed me love / Lonely and blue / Don't be angry / Small red apples / Somebody's gonna jump outta the bushes
CD _____ ICH 1056 CD
Ichiban / Jun '90 / Koch.

AW, SHUCKS
You know it ain't right / Let love take care of the rest) / Aw shucks baby / Still holding on / It's not what you do / Mind your own business / True love / Chickadee / Night time (live jam version)
CD _____ ICH 9006CD
Ichiban / Jun '94 / Koch.

BLACK TOP BLUES-A-RAMA VOL.2 (Live At Tipitina's)
CD _____ CD 1045
Black Top / '88 / CM / Direct / ADA.

DON'T BE ANGRY
Is it true / That man / Honeties / T'm fed a woman / Just a little love / It's really you / Don't be angry / Land I love / I'm in the mood / Open up that door / I want to live / Skiddy woe / I'm getting lonesome / I cried like a baby / Little by little
CD _____ SV 0259
Savoy Jazz / Nov '94 / Conifer / ADA.

I DONE GONE OVER
CD _____ RBD 205
Mr. R&B / Apr '91 / Swift / CM / Wellard.

JUST FOR ME
CD _____ JSPCD 218
JSP / Jul '88 / ADA / Target/BMG / Direct / Cadillac / Complete/Pinnacle.

SOMETHING'S GONNA JUMP OUT THE BUSHES
CD _____ CD 1039
Black Top / '88 / CM / Direct / ADA.

TORE UP (Brown, Nappy & The Heartfixers)
CD _____ ALCD 4792
Alligator / May '93 / Direct / ADA.

Brown, Norman
JUST BETWEEN US
CD _____ 5300912
Motown / Feb '93 / PolyGram.

Brown, Pete
ARDOURS OF THE LOST RAKE (Brown, Pete & Phil Ryan)
CD _____ AUL 736
Aura / Apr '91 / Cadillac.

Brown, Phil

WHISTLING FOR THE MOON
Bowland air / Teddy O'Neill / Women of Ireland / Old man Quinn/Alexander's hornpipe / Lonesome boatman / Danny boy / Dark island / Copy nook / Endearing young charms / King of the fairies / Terminal love song / As I roved out / Leaboy's lassie / Down by the Sally Gardens / Whalley roundabout
CD _____ FSCD 34
Folksound / Oct '95 / Roots / CM.

Brown, Phil

DISCOVERY
At the sign of the swinging cymbal / Romance for violin and orchestra no.2 in F / Vienna is Vienna / Girl from Corsica / Up to the races / So eine liebe gibt es einmal nur / Carmen medley / Missing / London kid / At the woodchopper's ball / Eine kleine nachtmusik / Dizzy fingers / Mornings at seven / Taste of honey / Rare auld times / Abba medley / Discovery / Who cares
CD _____ CDRS 1284
Grosvenor / Nov '95 / Target/BMG.

Brown, Polly

BEWITCHED - THE POLLY BROWN STORY
That same old feeling / (It's like a) sad old kinda movie / All those days / Baby I won't let you down / To love somebody / Crazy love / Wild night / Amoreuse / Honey honey / Best of everything / That's the way love grows / Up in a puff of smoke / Special delivery / S.O.S. / You're my number one / One girl too late / Short down in flames / I need another song / Do you believe in love at first sight / Bewitched, bothered and bewildered / Believe in me / Angel / It's me you're leaving / Writing you a letter / Precious to me
CD _____ RPM 143
RPM / Apr '95 / Pinnacle.

Brown, Pud

PUD BROWN & NEW ORLEANS JAZZMEN
Jazzology / Apr '94 / Swift / Jazz Music.

PUD BROWN & THE SPIRIT OF NEW ORLEANS JAZZ BAND (Brown, Pud & The Spirit Of New Orleans Jazz Band)
CD _____ BCD 247
GHB / Aug '94 / Jazz Music.

PUD BROWN PLAYS CLARINET
CD _____ JCD 166
Jazzology / Apr '94 / Swift / Jazz Music.

Brown, Ray

AS GOOD AS IT GETS (Brown, Ray & Jimmy Rowles)
Sophisticated lady / That's all / Like someone in love / Looking back / Honey / Love / Alone together / Rosalie / Manha de carnaval / Who cares
CD _____ CCD 4066
Concord Jazz / Nov '92 / New Note.

BAM BAM BAM (Brown, Ray Trio)
CD _____ CCD 4375
Concord Jazz / May '89 / New Note.

BASS FACE (Brown, Ray Trio)
Milestones / Bass face / In the wee small hours of the morning / Tin Tin Deo CRS - CRAFT / Takin' a chance on love / Remember / Makin' whoopee / Phineas can be
CD _____ CD 83340
Telarc / Oct '93 / Conifer / ADA.

BLACK ORPHEUS
Days of wine and roses / I thought about you / Balck Orpheus / How insensitive / My foolish heart / Please send me someone to love / Ain't misbehavin' / When you wish upon a star / Things ain't what they used to be
CD _____ ECD 220762
Evidence / Feb '94 / Harmonia Mundi / ADA / Cadillac.

BROWN'S BAG
Blues for Eddie Lee / Keep on pumpin' / You are my sunshine / Time for love / Surrey with the fringe on top / Emily
CD _____ CCD 6019
Concord Jazz / Aug '91 / New Note.

DON'T FORGET THE BLUES (Brown, Ray All Stars)
Blues'd out / Jim / Night Train / If I could be with you one hour tonight / Rocks in my bed / You don't know me / Jumpin' the blues / Don't forget the blues
CD _____ CCD 4293
Concord Jazz / Jan '87 / New Note.

DON'T GET SASSY (Brown, Ray Trio)
Tanga / Con alma / Brown's new blues / Don't get sassy / Good life / Everything I love / Kelly's blues / When you go / Raincheck / In a sentimental mood / Squatty roo
CD _____ CD 83368
Telarc / Sep '94 / Conifer / ADA.

LIVE AT THE CONCORD JAZZ FESTIVAL - 1979 (Brown, Ray Trio)
Blue bossa / Bossa nova do marilla / Manha de carnaval / St. Louis blues / Fly me to the moon / Georgia on my mind / Here's that rainy day / Please send me someone to love / Honeysuckle rose
CD _____ CCD 4102
Concord Jazz / Mar '90 / New Note.

MOORE MAKES 4 (Brown, Ray Trio)
CD _____ CCD 4477
Concord Jazz / Oct '91 / New Note.

RED HOT RAY BROWN TRIO, THE
Have you met Miss Jones / Meditation / Street of dreams / Lady be good / That's all / Love me tender / How could you do a thing like this to me / Captain Bill
CD _____ CCD 4315
Concord Jazz / Oct '87 / New Note.

SOLAR ENERGY
Exactly like you / Cry me a river / Teach me tonight / Take the 'A' train / Mistreated but undefeated blues / That's all / Easy does it / Sweet Georgia Brown
CD _____ CCD 4268
Concord Jazz / New Note.

SOME OF MY BEST FRIENDS ARE....
Lover / Ray of light / Just a gigolo / St. Louis blues / Bag's groove / Love walked in / Nearness of you / Close your eyes / Giant steps / My romance / How come you do me like you do / If I love again / CD 83373
Telarc / Apr '95 / Conifer / ADA.

SOMETHING FOR LESTER
CD _____ OJCCD 412
Original Jazz Classics / Feb '93 / Wellard / Jazz Music / Cadillac / Complete/Pinnacle.

TASTY (Brown, Ray & Jimmy Rowles)
Sleepin' bee / I'm gonna sit right down and write myself a letter / Night is young and you're so beautiful / My ideal / Come Sunday / Close your eyes / Nancy with the laughing face / Smile
CD _____ CCD 4122
Concord Jazz / Jul '95 / New Note.

THREE DIMENSIONAL (Brown, Ray Trio)
Ja da / Paradise / You are my sunshine / Nancy / Gumbo hump / Classical in G / My romance / Take me out to the ball game / Ellington medley / Equinox / Time after time
CD _____ CCD 4520
Concord Jazz / Sep '92 / New Note.

TWO BASS HITS
CD _____ 74034
Capri / Nov '93 / Wellard / Cadillac.

Brown, Reverend Pearly

BARE IN CHANGE
CD _____ PRD 70742
Provogue / Mar '95 / Pinnacle.

PSYCHOMACHIA
There's a rumour going round / Nobody loves me / All I want / Happy face blues / Come 'ere babe / Big city ley bus / Voodoo chile (Slight return) / Sunset on time / Sad sad day / Dreamland / Hypnotised / Certified
CD _____ PRD 70872
Provogue / Jan '96 / Pinnacle.

Brown, Roy

BATTLE OF THE BLUES VOL.2 (Brown, Roy & Wynonie Harris)
R.B. / Hard luck blues / Dreaming blues / Along about sundown / Double crossin' woman / Sweet peach / Wrong woman / Brown angel / Wh / Man, have I got troubles / I'll never give up / Here comes the night / Luscious woman / Drinking blues / Nearer my love to thee / Tremblin'
CD _____ KCD 627
King/Paddle Wheel / Mar '90 / New Note.

BLUES DELUXE
Cadillac baby / Hard luck blues / New Rebecca / Sweet peach / Love don't love nobody / Dreaming blues / Good man blues / Too much lovin' ain't no good / Teenage jamboree / Train time blues / Bar room blues / Long about sundown / Beautician blues / Drum boogie / Double crossin' woman / Everybody / Mighty man / Wrong woman blues / Good rockin' man / I've got the last laugh now / Big town / Brown angel / Rock-a-bye baby / Lonesome lover / Answer to Big Town
CD _____ CDCHARLY 289
Charly / Nov '93 / Charly / THE / Cadillac.

COMPLETE IMPERIAL RECORDINGS, THE
Everybody / Tick of the clock / No greater thrill / Saturday night / Party doll / I'm stickin' with you / Let the four winds blow / I'm in love / Diddy-y-diddy-o / Crying over you / Slow down little Eva / Ain't gonna do it / Ivy league / Sail on little girl, sail on / I'm convinced of love / I'm ready to play / Hip shakin' baby / Be my love tonight / We're goin' rockin' tonight / I love you, I need you
CD _____ CZ 544
Capitol Jazz / Jul '95 / EMI.

MIGHTY, MIGHTY MAN
Mr. Hound Dog's in town / Bootleggin' baby / Trouble at midnight / Everything's alright /

This is my last goodbye / Don't let it rain / Up jumped the devil / No love at all / Ain't it a shame / Ain't no rockin' no more / Queen of diamonds / Gal from Kokomo / Fannie Brown got married / Worried life blues / Black diamond / Letter to baby / Shake 'em up baby / Rinky dinku doo / Adorable one / School bell rock / Ain't got no blues today / Good looking and foxy too
CD _____ CDCHD 459
Ace / Sep '93 / Pinnacle / Cadillac / Complete/Pinnacle.

Brown, Roy 'Chubby'

TAKE FAT AND PARTY
CD _____ 5298482
PolyGram TV / Nov '95 / PolyGram.

Brown, Rula

RULA
CD _____ BCR 1002
Bee Cat / Nov '95 / Jetstar.

Brown, Ruth

BLUES ON BROADWAY
Nobody knows you when you're down and out / Good morning heartache / If I can't sell it I'll keep sittin' on it / T'ain't nobody's business if I do / St. Louis blues / Blue / I'm just a lucky so and so / I don't break dance / Come Sunday
CD _____ FCD 9662
Fantasy / Mar '94 / Pinnacle / Jazz Music / Wellard / Cadillac.

HAVE A GOOD TIME
CD _____ FCD 9661
Fantasy / Nov '95 / Pinnacle / Jazz Music / Wellard / Cadillac.

LIVE IN LONDON
I've got the world on a string / I'm a lucky so and so / Have a good time / Fine and mellow / Loverman / Secret love / Fine Brown frame / It could happen to you / 5-10-15 Hours / Be anything (but be mine) / Since I fell for you / He's a real gone guy
CD _____ JHCD 042
Ronnie Scott's Jazz House / Sep '95 / Jazz Music / Magnum Music Group / Cadillac.

MISS RHYTHM
CD _____ 7567820612
Atlantic / Jul '93 / Warner Music.

MISS RHYTHM - GREATEST HITS
CD _____ RSDCD 816
Sequel / Oct '94 / BMG.

SONGS OF MY LIFE
CD _____ FCD 9665
Fantasy / Jun '94 / Pinnacle / Jazz Music / Wellard / Cadillac.

TAKIN' CARE OF BUSINESS
Takin' care of business / 5-10-15 hours / I can see everybody's baby / On my way / God holds the power / Oh what a dream / Teardrops from my eyes / So long / Seven days
CD _____ RBD 202
Mr. R&B / Dec '90 / Swift / CM / Wellard.

Brown, Sam

APRIL MOON
April moon / With a little love / Mindworks / Kissing gate / Where you are / Contradictions / Once in your life / Hypnotised / As one / Eye for an eye / Trouble soul / S'envolver / Henry (Not on LP) / Pride and joy (CD only) / Now and forever (CD only) / Way I love you (CD only)
CD _____ CDA 9014
A&M / Apr '90 / PolyGram.

KISSING GATE
Can I get a witness / Hypnotised / With a little love / Once in your life / April moon / Mind works / Contradictions / Kissing gate / S'envolver / Where are you / As one / Eye for an eye / Troubled soul / This feeling
CD _____ 5501132
Spectrum/Karussell / Oct '93 / PolyGram / THE.

STOP
Walking back to me / Your love is all / It makes me wonder / This feeling / Tea / Piece of my luck / Ball and chain / Wrap me up / I'll be in love / Merry go round / Sometimes / Can I get a witness / High as a kite / Nutbush City Limits (Available on CD only)
CD _____ CDMID 181
A&M / Jul '93 / PolyGram.

Brown, Sawyer

OUTSKIRTS OF TOWN
CD _____ CURCD 006
Curb / Mar '94 / PolyGram.

WANTIN' AND HAVIN' IT ALL
CD _____ CURCD 17
Curb / Sep '95 / PolyGram.

Brown, Shirley

DIVA OF SOUL
CD _____ DOMECD 7
Dome / Oct '95 / 3MV / Sony.

FOR THE REAL FEELING
When, where, what time / Crowding in on my mind / After a night like this / Dirty feelin' / Hang on Louie / Eyes can't see / Move me, move me / Love starved
CD _____ CDSXE 082
Stax / Nov '92 / Pinnacle.

WOMAN TO WOMAN
Woman to woman / Yes sir brother / It ain't no fun / As long as you love me / Stay with me baby / I've got to go on without you / It's worth a whipping / So glad to have you / Passion / I can't give you up / I need you tonight / Between you and me
CD _____ CDSXE 002
Stax / Nov '89 / Pinnacle.

Brown, Steven

1890-1990 LIVE IN PORTUGAL (Brown, Steven & Reininger, Blaine)
CD _____ TWI 9162
Les Disques Du Crepuscule / '88 / Discovery / ADA.

COMPOSES POUR LE THEATRE ET LE CINEMA
CD _____ TWI 8722
Les Disques Du Crepuscule / May '89 / Discovery / ADA.

DAY IS GONE, THE
CD _____ SUBCD 009 21
Sub Rosa / '89 / Vital / These / Discovery.

MUSIC FOR SOLO PIANO
Piano No 1 / Waltz / Ball / Hold me while I dream / Close little sixes / Fanfare / Egypt / Fall / Fantasie for clarinet and violin / R.W.F.
CD _____ TWI 102CD
Les Disques Du Crepuscule / Mar '90 / Discovery / ADA.

SEARCHING FOR CONTACT
CD _____ CDBIAS 055
Play It Again Sam / Jun '87 / Vital.

ZOO STORY
CD _____ MASO 90002
Materiali Sonori / '90 / New Note.

Brown, Tom

TOM BROWN & HIS NEW ORLEANS JAZZ BAND (Brown, Tom & His New Orleans Jazz Band)
CD _____ BCD 3
GHB / Aug '94 / Jazz Music.

Browne, Duncan

TRAVELLING MAN (Browne, Duncan & Sebastian Graham Jones)
CD _____ CDSGP 0114
Prestige / Sep '95 / Total/BMG.

Browne, Jackson

FOR EVERYMAN
Take it easy / Our Lady of the Well / Colours of the sun / I thought I was a child / These days / Redneck friend / Times you come / Ready or not / Sing my songs to me / For everyman
CD _____ 243 003
Asylum / Jan '87 / Warner Music.

HOLD OUT
Disco apocalypse / Hold on, hold out / Of missing persons / Call it a loan / That girl could sing / Hold out / Boulevard
CD _____ 252 226-2
Asylum / Jan '87 / Warner Music.

I'M ALIVE
I'm alive / My problem is you / Everywhere I go / I'll do anything / Miles away / Too many angels / Take this rain / Two of me, two of you / Sky blue and black / All good things
CD _____ 755961524-2
Asylum / Oct '93 / Warner Music.

JACKSON BROWNE
Jamaica say you will / Child in these hills / Song for Adam / Doctor my eyes / From silver lake / Something fine / Under the falling sky / Looking into you / Rock me on the water / My opening farewell
CD _____ 253022
Asylum / Dec '86 / Warner Music.

LATE FOR THE SKY
Late for the sky / Fountain of sorrow / Farther on / Late show / Road and the sky / For a dancer / Walking slow / Before the deluge
CD _____ 243 007
Asylum / Jan '87 / Warner Music.

LAWYERS IN LOVE
For a rocker / Lawyers in love / On the day / Cut it away / Downtown / Tender is the night / Knock on any door / Say it isn't true
CD _____ 960 268-2
Asylum / Jul '87 / Warner Music.

LIVES IN THE BALANCE
For America / Soldier of plenty / In the shape of a heart / Candy / Lawless Avenue / Lives in the balance / Till I go down / Black and white
CD _____ 9604572
Elektra / '86 / Warner Music.

PRETENDER, THE

Fuse / Your bright baby blues / Linda Paloma / Here come those tears again / Only child / Daddy's time / Sleep's dark and silent gate / Pretender

CD _____ 253 048

Asylum / Dec '86 / Warner Music.

RUNNING ON EMPTY

Running on empty / Road / Rosie / You love the thunder / Cocaine / Shaky town / Love needs a heart / Nothing but time / Load-out / Stay

CD _____ 253 070

Asylum / Jan '87 / Warner Music.

WORLD IN MOTION

World in motion / Enough of the night / Chasing you into the night / How long / Anything can happen / When the stone begins to turn / Word justice / My personal revenge / I am a patriot / Lights and virtues

CD _____ 9608322

Asylum / Feb '95 / Warner Music.

Browne, Kirk

CIVIL WAR GUITAR - CAMPFIRE MEMORIES

CD _____ SLCD 9002

Starline / Dec '94 / Jazz Music.

Browne, Ronan

SOUTH WEST WIND, THE (Browne, Ronan & Peter O'Loughlin)

Jenny picking cockles/Colliers' reel / Frieze breeches jig / Shaskeen/Five mile chase / Banks of Lough Gowna/Willie Clancy's Paidin O Raifeartaigh / Paidin O Raifeartaigh jig / Connaught heifers/Corney is coming / Bold trainer O / Dublin reel/Steampacket/ Hand me down the tackie / An ghaoth aniar aneas/Petticoat loose / Spike Island lassies/ Farewell to Connaught / Drunken gauger / Queen of the rushes/Chorus / Byrne's and Alfie's rambles / Bridie's joy/The spinner's delight / Thrush in the morning/Crooked road

CD _____ CC 47CD

Claddagh / Feb '93 / ADA / Direct.

Browne, Ronnie

SCOTTISH LOVE SONGS

Dumarton's drums / My love is like a red red rose / Come all ye fair and tender maidens / Touch and the go / Bonnie lass o'Fyvie / Loch Lomond / Bonnie Earl o'Moray / Canvas of my life / Kate Dalrymple / Massacre of Glencoe / Mary Hamilton / Queen's Maries / Leezie Lindsay / Sin I were a Baron's heir / Willie's gan tae Melville Castle / Parting glass

CD _____ CDITV 602

Scotdisc / Oct '95 / Duncans / Ross / Conifer.

Browne, Tom

MO'JAMAICA FUNK

Funkin' for Jamaica / Jam fo' reel / Everybody loves the sunshine / Milestones / That's what friends are for / Give me the night / Work song

CD _____ HIBD 8002

Hip Hop / Apr '95 / Conifer / Total/BMG / Silva Screen.

Browns

THREE BELLS, THE (8 CDs)

Rio de Janeiro / Looking back to see / Itsy bitsy teeny weeny yellow polka dot bikini (2) / Draggin' Main Street / You're love is as wild as the west wind / Cool green / Do memories haunt me / It's love I guess / I'm your man, I'm your gal / Set the dawgs on 'em / Jungle magic / You thought, I thought / Here today and gone tomorrow / Grass is green / Lookin' on / I take the chance / I can't see for lookin' / I'm in heaven / Goo goo dada / Just as long as you love me / Getting used to being lonely / Man with a plan / Sweet talk / Don't tell me your troubles / Last thing that I want / Preview of the blues / My Isle of golden dreams / I'm in heaven (2) / Guess I'm crazy / Sky princess / I'll hold you in my heart / How can it be imagination / I heard the bluebirds sing / It takes a long, long train with a red caboose / Don't use the word lightly / Waltz of the angels / Table next to me / Memory / You'll always be in my heart / Behave yourself, Jose / Just in time / Man in the moon / Ain't no way in this world / Crazy dreams / True love goes far beyond / Only one way to love you / Be my love / Land of golden dreams / Love is in season / Would you care / Trot / Beyond the shadow / This time I would know / Three bells / Wake up Jonah / Be my love (2) / Heaven fell last night / Your pretty blue eyes / Unchained melody / Indian love call / Blues stay away from me / Dream on / Where did the sunshine go / We should be together / Bye bye love / I still do / Only the lonely / I'm an ole lady's son tae me tender / Put on an old pair of shoes / Blue bells ring / Scarlet ribbons / Red sails in the sunset / That's my desire / That little boy of mine / Halfway to heaven / Teen-ex / Oh my Papa / Margo / Cool water / True love / Enchanted sea / Old lamplighter / Billy McCoy / Am I that easy to forget / Whiffenpoof song / Streamlined cannonball / My adobe hacienda / Pledge of love / Wabash blues / Who's gonna buy my ribbons / Margo (2) / Chandelier of stars / Eternally / Brighten the corner where you are / Blue skirt waltz / Have you ever been lonely / Lonely little robin / Wayward wind / Old village choir / High noon / Lavender blue / Blues in my heart / Chandelier of stars (2) / Whiffenpoof song (2) / Blue christmas / This land is your land / In the pines / Brighten the corner where you are (2) / Greenwillow christmas / Remember me / Twelfth of never / Nevada / Where I was (when we became strangers) / You're so much a part of me / Revenge / Bandit / Send me the pillow that you dream on / Down in the valley / Shenendoah / Columbus Stockade blues / Clementine / Poor wayfaring stranger / Ground hog / Poor wildwood flower / It's gonna shoe your pretty little feet / John B. Sails / My pretty quadroon / Down on the old plantation / My baby's gone / Alpha and omega / Foolish pride / Angel's dolly / Alpha and omega (2) / My baby's gone (2) / Whispering wine / Remember me (2) / Lord I'm coming home / How great thou art / Child of the King / Just as I am / Church in the wildwood / Evening prayer / In the garden / Whispering hope / When they ring those golden bells / Where no one stands alone / My latest sun is sinking fast / Faith unlocks the door / It's just a little heartache / No love at all / Buttons and bows / Old master painter / They call the wind Maria / Forty shades of green / Is it make believe / Everlasting / Twelfth rose / Watching my world fall apart / Oh no / Dear Teresa / Rumba boogie / Great speckled bird / Don't let the stars get in your eyes / Sugarfoot rag / Fair and tender ladies / Tragic romance / Four walls / You nearly lose your mind / Mansion on the hill / Wondering / Mommy please stay home with me / Anna / Prologue / Happy fool / Grass is red / Circuit ridin' preacher / Half breed / Young land / Gun, the gold, the girl / Mister and Mississippi / Blowin' in the wind / Tobacco road / Then I'll stop loving you / You're easy to remember / I know my place / My baby doesn't love me anymore / Love didn't pass me by / Outskirts of town / Tangled web / My destiny / Johnny I hardly knew you / Three hearts in a tangle / Everybody's darlin' plus mine / Meadow green / One take away one / No sad songs for me / I feel like crying / Big blizzard / Watch the roses grow / Little too much to dream / Little boy blue / Maybe tomorrow / I can stand it (as long as you can) / Gone / This heart of mine / I'm so lonesome I could cry / Yesterday's gone / You can't grow peaches on a cherry tree / Two of a kind / Spring time / When I stop dreaming / Too soon to know / Now I can live again / I will bring you water / June is as cold as December / I'd just be fool enough / Maker of raindrops and roses / Making plans / Born to be with you / Million miles from nowhere / Big daddy / Where does a little tear come from / Coming back to you / Do not ask for love / Gigawackers / Rhythm of the rain / Greener pastures / After losing you / Tip of my fingers / Four strong winds / Sorry I never knew you / Old country church / They tore the old country church down / Though your sins be as scarlet / He will set your fields on fire / Night watch / When I lift up my head / Taller than trees / Mocking bird / Jezebel / Rusty old halo / Weapon of prayer / I hear it now / Ride ride ride / Country boy's dream / All of me belongs to you / Where does the good times go / I'm a lonesome fugitive / Once / Walk through this world with me / Happy tracks / Misty blue / If the whole world stops lovin'

CD Set _____ BCD 15665

Bear Family / Dec '93 / Rollercoaster / Direct / CM / Swift / ADA.

Brownstone

FROM THE BOTTOM UP

Party wit me / Grapevyne / If you love me / Sometimes dancin' / I can't tell you why / Don't cry for me / Pass the lovin' / Fruit of life / True to me / Wipe it up / Deeper feelings / Half of you

CD _____ 4773622

MJJ Music / Jan '95 / Sony.

Brozman, Bob

DEVIL'S SLIDE

CD _____ CD 11557

Rounder / '88 / CM / Direct / ADA / Cadillac.

Brubeck, Darius

GATHERING FORCES 1 (Brubeck, Darius & Dan)

Earthrise / Three mile island / Kearsage strut / Just think about what happens / Tugela rail / Parrot / I say there's hope / Half of you

CD _____ BW 022

B&W / Sep '93 / New Note.

GATHERING FORCES 2

Kitu / Friendship ragga and boogie / Hariji / Mamazala / Amaselesele emvuleni (frogs) / October / Gathering forces

CD _____ BW 046

B&W / Feb '95 / New Note.

LIVE AT THE NEW ORLEANS & HERITAGE FESTIVAL 1990 (Afro Cool Concept) (Brubeck, Darius & Victor Ntoni)

Kwela mama / Lakutshon ilanga / Daveyton special / Mokotedi / Kilamanjaro

CD _____ BW 024

B&W / Oct '93 / New Note.

Brubeck, Dave

24 CLASSIC RECORDINGS (Brubeck, Dave Trio)

Fantasy / Jan '91 / Pinnacle / Jazz Music / Wellard / Cadillac.

CD _____ CDJZD 005

75TH BIRTHDAY CELEBRATION

CD _____ 83349CD

Telarc / Nov '95 / Conifer / ADA.

ALL THE THINGS WE ARE

Like someone in love / In your own sweet way / All the things you are / Deep in a dream / Here's that rainy day / Polka dots and moonbeams / It could happen to you / Don't get around much anymore

CD _____ 756781399-2

Atlantic / Mar '93 / Warner Music.

BACK HOME

Cassandra / (I'm afraid) the masquerade is over / Hometown blues / Two-part contention / Caravan

CD _____ CCD 4103

Concord Jazz / Jul '94 / New Note.

BLUE RONDO (Brubeck, Dave Quartet)

How does your garden grow / Festival hall / Easy as you go / Blue rondo a la turk / Dizzy's dream / I see, Satie / Swing bells / Strange meadowlark / Elana Joy

CD _____ CCD 4317

Concord Jazz / Aug '90 / New Note.

BRUBECK & DESMOND

CD _____ FCD 24727

Fantasy / Oct '93 / Pinnacle / Jazz Music / Wellard / Cadillac.

CONCORD ON A SUMMER NIGHT (Brubeck, Dave Quartet)

Benjamin / Koto Song / Black And Blue / Take five / Softly, William, softly

CD _____ CCD 4198

Concord Jazz / Nov '86 / New Note.

DAVE BRUBECK & PAUL DESMOND (Brubeck, Dave Octet & Paul Desmond)

Jeepers creepers / On a little street in Singapore / Trolley song / I may be wrong, but I think you're wonderful / Blue moon / My heart stood still / Let's fall in love / Over the rainbow / You go to my head / Crazy Chris / Give a little whistle / Oh lady be good / Tea for two / This can't be love

CD _____ OJCCD 101

Original Jazz Classics / Nov '95 / Wellard / Jazz Music / Cadillac / Complete/Pinnacle.

DAVE BRUBECK IN CONCERT (Brubeck, Dave Quartet)

Perdido / These foolish things / Stardust / Way you look tonight / I'll never smile again / I remember you / For all we know / All the things you are / Lullaby in rhythm

CD _____ FCD 60013

Fantasy / Mar '94 / Pinnacle / Jazz Music / Wellard / Cadillac.

DAVE BRUBECK QUARTET

CD _____ CDSH 2064

Derann Trax / Aug '91 / Pinnacle.

DAVE BRUBECK QUARTET (With Paul Desmond) (Brubeck, Dave Quartet)

Maria / I feel pretty / Somewhere / Tonight / Quiet girl / Dialogues for jazz combo and orchestra

CD _____ CD 53031

Giants Of Jazz / Aug '88 / Target/BMG / Cadillac.

DAVE DIGS DISNEY (Brubeck, Dave Quartet)

Alice in Wonderland / Give a little whistle / Heigh ho / When you wish upon a star / Someday my Prince will come / One song

CD _____ 4712502

Sony Jazz / Jan '95 / Sony.

ESSENTIAL DAVE BRUBECK QUARTET, THE (Brubeck, Dave Quartet)

CD _____ 4737342

Sony Jazz / Jan '95 / Sony.

FOR IOLA (Brubeck, Dave Quartet)

Polly / I hear a rhapsody / Thank you / Big bad blaze / For Iola / Summer song / Pange lingua march

CD _____ CCD 4259

Concord Jazz / Jul '88 / New Note.

GONE WITH THE WIND

Swanee river / Lonesome road / Georgia on my mind / Camptown races / Sort'nin' bread / Basin Street blues / Ol' man river / Gone with the wind

CD _____ 450984 2

Columbia / May '93 / Sony.

GREAT CONCERTS, THE

Pennies from Heaven / Blue rondo a la turk / Take the 'A' train / Wonderful Copenhagen / Tangerine / For all we know / Take five / Real ambassador / Like someone in love

CD _____ 4624032

CBS / May '90 / Sony.

GREATEST HITS: DAVE BRUBECK

Take five / I'm in a dancing mood / In your own sweet way / Camptown races / Duke / It's a raggy waltz / Bossa nova USA / Trolley song / Unsquare dance / Blue rondo a la turk / Mr. Broadway

CD _____ CD 32046

CBS / Jun '89 / Sony.

INTERCHANGES '54

Audrey / Jeepers creepers / Pennies from heaven / Why do I love you / Stompin' for Mili / Keepin' out of mischief now / Fine romance / Brother can you spare a dime / Sometimes I'm happy / Duke / (Back home again in) Indiana / Love walked in

CD _____ 4679172

Columbia / Apr '92 / Sony.

JAZZ AT COLLEGE OF THE PACIFIC (Brubeck, Dave Quartet)

CD _____ OJCCD 047

Original Jazz Classics / Feb '92 / Wellard / Jazz Music / Cadillac / Complete/Pinnacle.

JAZZ AT OBERLIN (Brubeck, Dave Quartet)

These foolish things / Perdido / Stardust / Way you look tonight / How high the moon

CD _____ OJCCD 046

Original Jazz Classics / Sep '93 / Wellard / Jazz Music / Cadillac / Complete/Pinnacle.

JAZZ COLLECTION (2CD Set)

Le souk / Stompin' for Mili / In your own sweet way / History of a boy scout (We crossed the Rhine) / Home at last / Someday my Prince will come / Tangerine / Golden horn / Georgia on my mind / Three to get ready / Blue rondo a la turk / Take five / Darktown strutter's ball / There'll be some changes made / Somewhere / Weep no more / Unsquare dance / Summer song / Non-sectarian blues / Bossa nova U.S.A. / It's a raggy waltz / World's fair / Fujiyama / Upstage rumba / My favourite things / La paloma azul / Recuerdo / St. Louis Blues

CD Set _____ 4804632

Columbia / Jul '95 / Sony.

JAZZ GOES TO COLLEGE

Balcony rock / Out of nowhere / Le souk / Take the 'A' train / Song is you / Don't worry 'bout me / I want to be happy

CD _____ 4656822

CBS / Feb '93 / Sony.

JAZZ IMPRESSIONS OF EURASIA

Nomad / Brandenburg Gate / Golden horn / Thank you / Marble arch / Calcutta blues

CD _____ 4712492

Columbia / Apr '92 / Sony.

JAZZ IMPRESSIONS OF NEW YORK

CD _____ 4669712

Sony Jazz / Jan '95 / Sony.

JUST YOU, JUST ME

Just you, just me / Strange meadowlark / It's the talk of the town / Brother can you spare a dime / Lullaby / Tribute / I married an angel / Music maestro please / Briar bush / Newport waltz / I understand / More than you know

CD _____ CD 83363

Telarc / Sep '94 / Conifer / ADA.

LAST SET AT NEWPORT

Introduction / Blues for Newport / Take five / Open the gates

CD _____ 756781382-2

Atlantic / Mar '93 / Warner Music.

LATE NIGHT BRUBECK (Live From Blue Note)

These foolish things / Here's that rainy day / Theme for June / Duke / This ain't what they used to be / C Jam blues / Don't get around much anymore / Who will take me home / Koto song / So wistfully sad / Mean to me

CD _____ CD 83345

Telarc / Mar '94 / Conifer / ADA.

LIVE AT THE BERLIN PHILHARMONIC (Brubeck, Dave & Gerry Mulligan)

Things ain't what they used to be / Blessed are the poor / Duke of New Orleans / Indian song / Limehouse blues / Lullaby de Mexico / St. Louis blues / Out of the way of the people / Basin street blues / Take five / Out of nowhere / Mexican jumpin' bean

CD _____ 4814152

Sony Jazz / Nov '95 / Sony.

LIVE IN 1956-57 (Brubeck, Dave Quartet)

CD _____ EBCD 21022

Jazzband / Aug '91 / Jazz Music / Wellard.

MOSCOW NIGHT

CD _____ CCD 4353

Concord Jazz / Jul '88 / New Note.

NEW QUARTET AT MONTREUX

CD _____ 269 613 2

Tomato / Mar '90 / Vital.

NIGHTSHIFT

Yesterdays / I can't give you anything but love / Travelin' blues / Thank you you go to my head / Blues for Newport / Ain't misbehavin' / Knives / River stay 'way from my door

CD _____ CD 83351

Telarc / May '95 / Conifer / ADA.

ONCE WHEN I WAS VERY YOUNG
Once when I was very young / What is this thing called love / Among my souvenirs / Dancin' in rhythm / Yesterdays / In a little Spanish town / Stardust / Shine on harvest moon / Gone with the wind / Please be kind / Once when I was very young (2)
CD _____ 844 298-2
Deram / Aug '92 / PolyGram.

PAPER MOON
Music maestro please / I hear a rhapsody / Symphony / I thought about you / It's only a paper moon / Long ago and far away / St. Louis blues / Music, Maestro, Please
CD _____ CCD 4178
Concord Jazz / Aug '92 / New Note.

PLAYS AND PLAYS AND PLAYS
Original Jazz Classics / Nov '95 / Wellard / Jazz Music / Cadillac / Complete/Pinnacle.

PLAYS MUSIC FROM WEST SIDE STORY (Brubeck, Dave Quartet)
CD _____ 4504102
Sony Jazz / Jan '95 / Sony.

QUARTET, THE
Castillian drums / Three to get ready / St. Louis Blues / Forty days / Summer song / Someday my Prince will come / Brandenburg Gate / In your own sweet way
CD _____ CDC 7681
LRC / Sep '93 / New Note / Harmonia Mundi.

QUIET AS THE MOON
Bicycle built for two / Linus and Lucy / Forty days / When I was a child / Quiet as the moon / Cast your fate to the wind / Benjamin / Looking at a rainbow / Desert and the parched land / Travelin' blues / Unisphere / When you wish upon a star
CD _____ 8208452
Limelight / Dec '91 / PolyGram.

REAL AMBASSADORS, THE (Brubeck, Dave & Louis Armstrong)
Everybody's comin' / Cultural exchange / Good reviews / Remember who you are / My one bad habit / Lonesome / Summer song / King for a day / Blow satchmo / Real ambassador / Nomad / In the lurch / One moment worth years / They say (The duke) / They say I look like God / I didn't know until you told me / Since love had it's way / Easy as you go / Swing bells/Blow satchmo / Finale
CD _____ 476897-2
Columbia / Aug '94 / Sony.

REFLECTIONS (Brubeck, Dave Quartet)
Reflections of you / Misty morning / I'd walk a country mile / My one bad habit / Blues for Newport / We will remember Paul / Michael, my second son / Blue Lake Tahoe
CD _____ CCD 4299
Concord Jazz / Jul '88 / New Note.

SOMEDAY MY PRINCE WILL COME (Brubeck, Dave Quartet)
CD _____ JHR 73572
Jazz Hour / Nov '93 / Target/BMG / Jazz Music / Cadillac.

STARDUST
Mam'selle / Stardust / Frenesi / Me and my shadow / At a perfect counter / Crazy Chris / Foggy day / Somebody loves me / Lyons busy / Look for the silver lining / Alice in wonderland / All the things you are / Lulu's back in town / My romance / Just one of those things
CD _____ FCD 24728
Fantasy / Jun '94 / Pinnacle / Jazz Music / Wellard / Cadillac.

TAKE ... THE GREATEST HITS
Take five / Camptown races / Trolley song / Unsquare dance / Blue rondo a la turk / Pennies from heaven / For all we know / Like someone in love / Strange meadowlark / Maria / Somewhere / What is this thing called love / Most beautiful girl in the world / Night and day
CD _____ ELITE 009CD
Elite/Old Gold / Aug '93 / Carlton Home Entertainment.

TAKE FIVE
Take five / Bossa nova USA / Unsquare dance / Someday my Prince will come / I'm in a dancing mood / It's a raggy waltz / Blue rondo a la turk / Kathy's waltz / My favourite things / Castillian drums / Duke / Trolley song
CD _____ VN 160
Viper's Nest / May '95 / Direct / Cadillac / ADA.

TAKE THE "FIVE" TRAIN
CD _____ MCD 0522
Moon / Apr '94 / Harmonia Mundi / Cadillac.

TIME IN
CD _____ 4746352
Sony Jazz / Jan '95 / Sony.

TIME OUT
Blue rondo a la turk / Strange meadowlark / Take five / Three to get ready / Kathy's waltz / Everybody's jumpin' / Pick up the sticks
CD _____ 4804122
Columbia / Jul '95 / Sony.

TIME SIGNATURES (4CD Set)
Curtain music / (Back home again in) Indiana / Body and soul / Undecided / Way you look tonight / Look for the silver lining / Over the rainbow / Perdido / Le souk / Stompin' for mili / Duke / Two part contention / In your own sweet way / History of a boy scout / Someday my Prince will come / Marble arch / Georgia on my mind / Three to get ready / Blue rondo a la turk / Strange meadowlark / Take five / At the Darktown strutter's ball / Offshoot / There'll be some changes made / Allegro blues / Somewhere / Weep no more / Charles Matthews Halleluja / Unsquare dance / Why Phillis / Kathy's waltz / Travellin' blues / Summer song / Real Ambassador / Non-sectarian blues / Bossa nova USA / It's a raggy waltz / World's fair / Fijiyama / Upstage rhumba / Little man with a candy cugar / My favourite things / Lost waltz / get a kick out of you / Koto song / La paloma azul / Estrellita / Forty days / Sapito / Recuerdo / St. Louis blues / Mr. Broadway / Caravan / Tritonis / Benjamin / Stardust
CD Set _____ 472776 2
Legacy / Jan '93 / Sony.

TRITONIS
Brother can you spare a dime / Like someone in love / Theme for June / Lord, Lord / Mr. Fats / Tritonis
CD _____ CCD 4129
Concord Jazz / Jul '95 / New Note.

WE'RE ALL TOGETHER AGAIN FOR THE FIRST TIME (Brubeck, Dave & Friends)
Truth / Unfinished woman / Koto song / Take five / Rotterdam blues / Sweet Georgia Brown
CD _____ 756781390-2
Atlantic / Mar '93 / Warner Music.

Brubeck, Matthew

GIRAFFES IN A HURRY (Brubeck, Matthew & David Widelock)
Bo's jazz / After the end / Dobrovnik / Hackensack / Black sand beach / Jolly blue giant / Almost April / Giraffes in a hurry / Other world music / Pannonica
CD _____ BW 042
B&W / Sep '94 / New Note.

REALLY (Brubeck, Matthew & David Widelock)
CD _____ CDJP 1030
Jazz Point / Nov '91 / Harmonia Mundi / Cadillac.

Bruce, Ed

PUZZLES
Puzzles / Blue denim eyes / By route of New Orleans / Shadows of her mind / Lonesome is me / Tiny golden locket / If I could just go home / Walker's woods / Give me Painted girls and wine / Price I pay to stay / Something else to mess your mind / I know better / Memphis morning / Blue bayou / Why can't I come home / Last train to Clarksville / Her sweet love and the baby / I'll take you away / Ninety seven more to go / I'd be best leaving you / Ballad of the drummer boy / Best be leaving you
CD _____ BCD 15830
Bear Family / Mar '95 / Rollercoaster / Direct / CM / Swift / ADA.

Bruce, Ian

BLODWEN'S DREAM
John / Factory life / Eldorado / Classical music / Ghost of the chair / Farewell deep blue / No noise / This peaceful evening / I can play you anything / Black fog / Blodwen's dream
CD _____ FECD 76
Fellside / Nov '95 / Target/BMG / Direct / ADA.

FREE AGENT
Scarborough settlers lament / Bizzie Lizzie / Hearts of Ohio / Find out who your friends are / Please be here / Out of sight (Rolling Stones) / Corners / No satisfaction / Bad bet / Anchor line / Dawn of a brand new day / Free agents / Ladies left behind / Find out who your friends are (reprise)
CD _____ IRCD 026
Iona / Jul '94 / ADA / Direct / Duncans.

OUT OF OFFICE
CD _____ FE 85CD
Fellside / Jul '92 / Target/BMG / Direct / ADA.

Bruce, Jack

CITIES OF THE HEART
Can you follow / Running thro' our hands / Over the cliff / Statues / First time I met the blues / Smiles and grins / Bird alone / Neighbor, neighbor / Born under a bad sign / Ships in the night / Never tell your Mother she's out of tune / Theme from an imaginary western / Golden days / Life on earth / NSU / Sittin' on top of the world / Politician / Spoonful / Sunshine of your love
CD _____ CMPCD 1004
CMP / Feb '94 / Vital/SAM.

JACK BRUCE IN CONCERT
You turned the tables on me / Folk song / Letter of thanks / Smiles and grins / We're going wrong / Clearout / Have you ever loved a woman / Powerhouse soul / You sure look good to me
CD _____ WINCD 076
Windsong / Aug '95 / Pinnacle.

MONKJACK
Third degree / Boy / Shouldn't we / David's harp / Know one blues / Time repairs / Laughing on music / Street / Folksong / Weird of Hermiston / Tightrope / Food / Immoral ninth
CD _____ CMPCD 1010
CMP / Sep '95 / Vital/SAM.

QUESTION OF TIME, A
Life on earth / Make love / No surrender / Flying / Hey now princess / Blues you can't lose / Obsession / Kwela / Let me be / Only playing games / Question of time
CD _____ 4656922
Epic / Jan '92 / Sony.

TRUCE (Bruce, Jack & Robin Trower)
Gonna shut you down / Gone too far / Thin ice / Last train to the stars / Take good care of yourself / Falling in love / Fat gut / Shadows touching / Little boy lost
CD _____ S21 17609
One Way / May '94 / Direct / ADA.

WILLPOWER
CD _____ 837 806-2
Polydor / May '89 / PolyGram.

Bruce-Harris, Kevin

AND THEY WALKED AMONGST THE PEOPLE
CD _____ 888 802
Tiptoe / Nov '89 / New Note.

Bruford, Bill

EARTHWORKS
Thud / Making a song and dance / Up North / Pressure / My heart declares a holiday / Emotional shirt / It needn't end in tears / Shepherd is eternal / Bridge Of Inhibition
CD _____ EEGCD 48
EG / '87 / EMI.

EARTHWORKS LIVE
Nerve / Up north / Stone's throw / Pilgrim's way / Emotional shirt / It needn't end in tears / All heaven broke loose / Psalm / Old song / Candles still flicker in Romania's dark / Brige of inhibition
CD _____ CDVE 922
Virgin / Apr '94 / EMI.

MASTER STROKES 1978-85
Hell's bells / Gothic 17 / Travels with myself / And someone else / Fainting in coils / Beelzebub / One of a kind (pts 1 & 2) / Drum also waltzes / Joe Frazier / Sahara of snow (pt 2) / Palewell park (Not on LP) / If you can't stand the heat (Not on LP) / Five G (Not on LP) / Living space (Not on LP) / Split seconds (Not on LP)
CD _____ EGCD 67
EG / '88 / EMI.

STAMPING GROUND
CD _____ 7243839476-2
Venture / Aug '94 / EMI.

Bruisers

CRUISIN' FOR A BRUISIN'
CD _____ LP 095
Lost & Found / Jul '94 / Plastic Head.

SOCIETY'S FOOLS
CD _____ LF 142CD
Lost & Found / May '95 / Plastic Head.

Brujeria

MATANDO GUEROS
Para de Venta / Leyes narcos / Sacrificio / Santa Lucia / Matando Gueros / Seis seis seis / Cruza la Frontera / Grenudos Locos / Chingo de Mecos / Narcos-Satanicos / Desperado / Culeros / Misas Negras (sacrificio III) / Chinga tu Madre / Verga del Brujo/Estan Chingados / Molestando Ninos Muertos / Machetazos / Castigo del Brujo / Christa de La Roca
CD _____ CD RR 9061 2
Roadrunner / Jun '93 / Pinnacle.

RAZA ODIADA
CD _____ RR 89232
Roadrunner / Oct '95 / Pinnacle.

Brundl's Basslab

BRUNDL'S BASSLAB (Brundl's Basslab & Barry Atischul)
CD _____ WW 2070
West Wind / Dec '92 / Swift / Charly / CM / ADA.

Brunel, Bunny

DEDICATION
CD _____ 500362
Musidisc / Nov '93 / Vital / Harmonia Mundi / ADA / Cadillac / Discovery.

Brunet, Alain

ROMINUS
CD _____ LBLC 6541
Label Bleu / Jan '92 / New Note.

Bruninghaus, Ranier

CONTINUUM
Strahlenspur / Stille / Continuum / Raga rag / Schattenfrei / Innerfern
CD _____ 8156792
ECM / '90 / New Note.

Brunning Sunflower Blues.

TRACKSIDE BLUES (Brunning Sunflower Blues Band)
CD _____ AP 031CD
Appaloosa / Jun '94 / ADA / Magnum Music Group.

Bruno, Francisco

EL LUGAR (THE PLACE) (Bruno, Francisco & Richie Havens)
CD _____ CDSGP 063
Prestige / Aug '93 / Total/BMG.

Bruno, Jimmy

BURNIN
Eternal triangle / Pastel / One for Amos / Love is here to stay / Burnin' / Moonlight in Vermont / Central Park West / Giant steps / Witchcraft / On the sunny side of the street / Rose for a peg / That's all
CD _____ CCD 4612
Concord Jazz / Sep '94 / New Note.

SLEIGHT OF HAND (Bruno, Jimmy Trio)
Egg plant pizza / Stompin' at the Savoy / Body and soul / Wheat thins / Night mist / Big shoes / Mandha de carnaval / Tenderly / Song for Jimmy and Susanna / All the things you are / Lionel's hat / Here's that rainy day
CD _____ CCD 4532
Concord Jazz / Nov '92 / New Note.

Bruno's Salon Band

LUCKY DAY
CD _____ SOSCD 1251
Stomp Off / May '93 / Jazz Music / Wellard.

Brunsden, Martin

OUT OF THE WOOD
CD _____ IS 01CD
Isis / Apr '94 / ADA / Direct.

Brus Trio

AIM
CD _____ DRCD 214
Dragon / Nov '87 / Roots / Cadillac / Wellard / CM / ADA.

Brutal Juice

I LOVE THE WAY THEY SCREAM WHEN THEY DIE
CD _____ VIRUS 157CD
Alternative Tentacles / Nov '94 / Pinnacle.

Brutal Obscenity

DREAM OUT LOUD
CD _____ PROPH 3-2CD
Prophecy / Jul '90 / Plastic Head.

IT'S BECAUSE OF THE BIRDS AND THE FLOWERS
Death is a damn good solution / Straight and stoned / Mom or dad / 1-2-3 / God is just a fairy tale / No more feelings left / Overtaking / It's because of the birds and the flowers / Emotion suicide / It's cruel (part 2) / Useless immortality / Defensor minor / Hangover D.D.D.
CD _____ CMFT 2CD
CMFT / Jun '89 / Plastic Head.

Brutal Truth

EXTREME CONDITIONS...
CD _____ MOSH 069CD
Earache / Sep '94 / Vital.

NEED TO CONTROL
Collapse / Black door mine / Turn face / God player / I see red / Iron lung / Bite the hand / Ordinary madness / Media blitz / Judgement / Brain trust / Choice of a new generation / Mainliner / Displacement / Crawlspace / B.T.I.T.B. (In Box Set only) / Bethroned (In Box Set only) / Painted clowns (In Box Set only) / Wish you were here (In Box Set only)
CD _____ MOSH 110CD
Earache / Nov '94 / Vital.

Brutality

SCREAMS OF ANGUISH
CD _____ NB 075CD
Nuclear Blast / Jul '93 / Plastic Head.

WHEN THE SKY TURNS BLACK
CD _____ NB 1152
Nuclear Blast / Jan '95 / Plastic Head.

Bruton, Stephen

RIGHT ON TIME
CD _____ DOS 7013
Dos / Jul '95 / CM / Direct / ADA.

WHAT IT IS
CD _____ DOSCD 7002
Dos / Sep '94 / CM / Direct / ADA.

Bruynel, Ton

LOOKING EARS
CD _____ BVHAASTCD 9214
Bvhaast / Oct '93 / Cadillac.

Bryan, Morgan

ASLEEP WHILE THE RAIN FALLS
CD _____ DCD 01
Dox Music / Oct '93 / Dox Music.

THORN
CD _____ DT 11
Dox Music / '94 / Dox Music.

UNDER EVERY SKY
CD _____ DCD 02
Dox Music / '94 / Dox Music.

Bryant, Don

COMIN' ON STRONG
CD _____ HIUKCD 133
Hi / Aug '92 / Pinnacle.

Bryant, Jimmy

SUNTIDE DESERT JAM (Bryant, Jimmy & Jody Reynolds & Les Paul)
Out of nowhere / Jammin' the blues / 9.20 special / Caravan / Back home again in) Indiana / Rose of desert view / Speedo / I can't get started (with you) / Yakety axe / Undecided / Market street blues / Rose room / How high the moon
CD _____ C5CD 611
See For Miles/C5 / Feb '94 / Pinnacle.

Bryant, Ray

MONTREUX '77
CD _____ OJCCD 371
Original Jazz Classics / Nov '95 / Wellard / Jazz Music / Cadillac / Complete/Pinnacle.

PLAYS BASIE & ELLINGTON
Jive at the Five / Swingin' the blues / 9.20 special / Teddy the toad / Blues for Basie / I let a song go out of my heart / It don't mean a thing if it ain't got that swing / Things ain't what they used to be
CD _____ 8322352
ECM / Mar '88 / New Note.

RAY BRYANT TRIO (Bryant, Ray Trio)
CD _____ OJCCD 793
Original Jazz Classics / Nov '95 / Wellard / Jazz Music / Cadillac / Complete/Pinnacle.

THROUGH THE YEARS VOLUME 1
CD _____ 5127642
Verve / May '92 / PolyGram.

THROUGH THE YEARS VOLUME 2
CD _____ 5129332
Verve / May '92 / PolyGram.

Bryant, Willie

CLASSICS 1935-36
CD _____ CLASSICS 768
Classics / Aug '94 / Discovery / Jazz Music.

Bryden, Beryl

BERYL BYRDEN 1975 & 1984
CD _____ ACD 113
Audiophile / Aug '94 / Jazz Music / Swift.

Bryson, Jeanie

I LOVE BEING HERE WITH YOU
CD _____ CD 83336
Telarc / May '93 / Conifer / ADA.

Bryson, Peabo

THROUGH THE FIRE
CD _____ 4742832
Sony Music / Jul '94 / Sony.

Brythoniaid Male Voice...

20 OF THE BEST (Brythoniaid Male Voice Choir)
CD _____ SCD 2018
Sain / Feb '93 / Direct / ADA.

Bubble Puppy

GATHERING OF PROMISES, A
Hot smoke and sasafrass / Todds tune / I've got to reach you / Lonely / Gathering of promises / Hurry sundown / Elizabeth / It's safe to say / Road to St Stephens / Beginning
CD _____ 642038
EVA / Jun '94 / Direct / ADA.

Bubonique

20 GOLDEN SHOWERS
Summer the first time / Think you're cool / Play that funky music / Cop lover / Cod-
sucker blues / My baby gave me rabies / Release the bats / Elvis '93 / Theme from chicken arse / Iron child / Yoda lady / Anytime anyplace it's O.K. / 2 J.G. / Stock Hausen and Waterman / East sheep station / Love me deadly kiss me headley / DLT 666 no idea / Bubonique American top 10 / Frank is frank / Jellypop porky jean / Dildo neighbour / Loce camp 7 / Nation of bubonique / Closedown
CD _____ KWCD 024
Kitchenware / Mar '93 / Sony / PolyGram / BMG.

TRANCE ARSE VOL.3
You can't fool the dead / Cod is love / Pianna / Truck turner / Sermon / Freestyle masterclass 1 - sawing / Talking' about talkin' about / Freebird / I've always liked hunting / Oi copper / Return of the nice age / What's E saying / Hey, handsome / Industrial woman / Rainbow buffalo cornwoman / Freestyle masterclass 2 - drilling / Q magazine / Kind of pure / George aid suite / Abbabortion / Sven of Newcastle
CD _____ KWCD 028
Kitchenware/Vital / Sep '95 / Vital.

Buccaneer

THERE GOES THE NEIGHBOURHOOD
CD _____ MAINCD 1
Main Street / Dec '94 / Jetstar.

Buchanan, Brian

AVENUES
CD _____ JFCD 002
Jazz Focus / Dec '94 / Cadillac.

Buchanan, Isobel

SONGS OF SCOTLAND
John Anderson, My Jo / I'm owre young tae marry yet / Ye banks and braes o' bonnie Doon / Aye waukin' o / Comin' thro' the rye / Queen's marries / My heart is sair / Deirdre's farewell to Scotland / Dursdeer / Rowan tree / Oor ain fireside / Mairi's wedding / Bonnie Earl O'Moray / Charlie is my darling / An plain folk
CD _____ LCOM 6038
Lismor / Sep '95 / Lismor / Duncans / ADA.

WHITE CLIFFS OF DOVER, THE (Songs and Music of the 40's) (Buchanan, Isobel & English Chamber Orchestra)
Calling all workers / Dambusters march / Knightsbridge march / Spitfire prelude and fugue / There'll always be an England / We'll meet again / White cliffs of Dover / Nightingale song in Berkeley square / When I grow too old to dream / Would you please oblige us with a Bren Gun / It's a lovely day tomorrow / I'll be seeing you / Love is the sweetest thing / All the things you are / Long ago and far away / So in love / Every time we say goodbye / I only have eyes for you / Always
CD _____ CD DCA 598
ASV / Nov '87 / Koch.

Buchanan, Jack

ELEGANCE
Night time / Living in clover / Fancy our meeting / Oceans of time / Like Monday follows Sunday / When we get our divorce / Not bad / Dancing honeymoon / And her mother came too / Who / Now that I've found you / You forgot your gloves / One I'm looking for / Sweet so an so / I think I can / Dapper Dan / Alone with my dreams / Two little bluebirds / Goodnight Vienna / It's not you / There's always tomorrow
CD _____ CDAJA 5033
Living Era / Koch.

JACK BUCHANAN
Fancy our meeting / You forgot your gloves / I've looked for trouble / This year, next year / Goodnight Vienna / Chirp chirp / Leave a little for me / Dapper Dan / One good tune deserves another / Let's say goodnight till the morning / Stand up and sing / Alone with my dreams / Weep no more baby / Who / Take a step / I think I can / Now that I've found you / Yes Mr. Brown / Don't love you / Living in clover / Jack Buchanan medley
CD _____ PASTCD 9763
Flapper / Oct '91 / Pinnacle.

THIS'LL MAKE YOU WHISTLE
CD _____ CMSCD 010
Movie Stars / Oct '91 / Conifer.

Buchanan, Roy

DANCING ON THE EDGE
Peter Gunn / Chokin' kind / Jungle gym / Drowning on dry land / Petal to the metal / You can't judge a book by the cover / Cream of the crop / Beer drinking woman / Whiplash / Baby, baby, baby / Matthew
CD _____ ALCD 4747
Alligator / May '93 / Direct / ADA.

EARLY ROY BUCHANAN
Mule train stomp / Pretty please / Mary Lou / Shuffle / Jam / Braggin' / Ruby baby / Am I the one
CD _____ KKCD 02
Krazy Kat / Oct '89 / Hot Shot / CM.

HOT WIRES
CD _____ ALCD 4756
Alligator / May '93 / Direct / ADA.

ROY BUCHANAN LIVE
Short fuse (instrumental) / Green onions (instrumental) / Strange kind of feeling / Pressure (instrumental) / Peter Gunn (instrumental) / Chicago smoke shop (instrumental) / Blues in E (instrumental) / Hey Joe / Foxy lady / Fantasia (instrumental)
CD _____ CDCBL 758
Charly / May '95 / Charly / THE / Cadillac.

SWEET DREAMS
CD _____ 5170862
Polydor / Jan '93 / PolyGram.

WHEN A GUITAR PLAYS THE BLUES
When a guitar plays the blues / Mrs. Pressure / Nickel and a nail / Short fuse / Why don't you want me / Country boy / Sneaking Godzilla through the alley / Hawaiian punch
CD _____ ALCD 4741
Alligator / May '93 / Direct / ADA.

Buchman, Rachel

JEWISH HOLIDAY SONGS FOR CHILDREN
CD _____ ROU 8028CD
Rounder / Jan '94 / CM / Direct / ADA / Cadillac.

Buck Pets

TO THE QUICK
Living is the biggest thing / Shave / Walk it to the payphone / To the quick / Nothing's ever gonna be alright again / Smiler with a knife / C'mon baby / Crutch / Rocket to you / Car chase / Worldwide smile / Manatee / Bargain (On CD only)
CD _____ 72726-2
Restless / Nov '93 / Vital.

Buck, Tuxedo

CUT RATE LIQUOR
CD _____ MRCD 159
Munich / Jun '92 / CM / ADA / Greensleeves / Direct.

Bucketheads

ALL IN THE MIND
Bomb (these sounds fall into my mind) / Sayin' dope / Sunset (new at) / Time and space (remix) / You're a runaway / Come and be gone / Got myself together (12" mix) / Jus' plain funny / I wanna know (Original raw mix) / Went / Little Louie Bonus / Bucketheads outro
CD _____ CDTIVA 1010
Positiva / Jan '96 / EMI.

Buckley, Jeff

GRACE
Mojo Pin / Grace / Last Goodbye / Lilac Wine / So real / Hallelujah / Lover / You should've come over / Corpus christi carol / Eternal life / Dream brother
CD _____ 475928-2
Columbia / Aug '94 / Sony.

LIVE AT SIN-E
CD _____ ABB 61CD
Big Cat / Mar '94 / SRD / Pinnacle.

Buckley, Tim

DREAM LETTER (Live In London 1968)
Introduction / Buzzin' fly / Phantasmagoria in two / Morning glory / Dolphins / I've been out walking / Earth is broken / Who do you love / Pleasant street / Love from room 109 - Strange feeling / Carnival song / Hallucinations / Troubadour / Dream letter / Happy time / Wayfaring stranger / You got me running / Once I was
CD Set _____ DFIENDCD 200
Demon / Jun '90 / Pinnacle / ADA.

GREETINGS FROM L.A.
Move with me / Get on top / Sweet surrender / Night hawkin' / Devil eyes / Hong Kong bar / Make it right
CD _____ 7599272612
Elektra / Jan '96 / Warner Music.

HAPPY SAD
Strange feeling / Buzzin' fly / Love from room 109 at the islander / Dream letter / Gypsy woman / Sing a song for you
CD _____ 7559740452
WEA / Feb '92 / Warner Music.

HONEY MAN
CD _____ ED 450CD
Edsel / Nov '95 / Pinnacle / ADA.

LIVE AT THE TROUBADOUR 1969
CD _____ EDCD 400
Edsel / Feb '94 / Pinnacle / ADA.

LOOK AT THE FOOL
Look at the fool / Bring it on up / Helpless / Freeway blues / Tijuana moon / Ain't it peculiar / Who could deny you / Mexicali voodoo / Down the street / Wanda Lu
CD _____ EDCD 294
Edsel / Oct '89 / Pinnacle / ADA.

MORNING GLORY
CD _____ BOJCD 009
Band of Joy / Jul '94 / ADA.

SEFRONIA
Dolphins / Honey man / Because of you / Peanut man / Martha / Quicksand / Stone in love / Sefron after Asklepiades after Kafka / Sefronia, the Kings chain / Sally go round the roses / I know I'd recognise your face
CD _____ EDCD 277
Edsel / Oct '80 / Pinnacle / ADA.

Buckner, Milt

GREEN ONIONS
CD _____ BLE 590872
Black & Blue / Oct '94 / Wellard / Koch.

MILT BUCKNER & ILLINOIS JACQUET (Buckner, Milt & Illinois Jacquet)
CD _____ PCD 7017
Progressive / Aug '94 / Jazz Music.

Buckner, Richard

BLOOMED
CD _____ GRCD 340
Glitterhouse / Oct '94 / Direct / ADA.

Bucks

DANCIN' TO THE CEILI BAND
Dancin' to the ceili band / Gra geal mo chroi / Rasher's and eggs / Ghost of winters gone / Auld time waltzes / Courtin' in the kitchen / What a time / ar puc ar buille / Hurray me boys hurray / Psycho ceili in Claremorris / Bucks set
CD _____ 450996653-2
Warner Bros. / Jul '94 / Warner Music.

Bucks Fizz

BEST AND THE REST, THE
CD _____ MER 010
Tring / Mar '93 / Tring / Prism.

BEST OF BUCKS FIZZ
Land of make believe / Making your mind up / Piece of the action / I hear tale / Run for your life / Talking in your sleep / Now those days are gone / My camera never lies / If you can't stand the heat / Heart of stone / Magical / London town / One of those nights / Golden days
CD _____ 74321 18327-2
Ariola Express / Feb '94 / BMG.

BEST OF BUCKS FIZZ
CD _____ 74321292792
RCA / Jul '95 / BMG.

GOLDEN DAYS
Golden days / Making your mind up / Piece if the action / Land of make believe / Camera never lies / If you can't stand the heat / When we were young / London town / I hear talk / Heart of stone / Magical / Rules of the game / You and your heart of blue / Now those days are gone / Where the ending starts / Oh Susanna
CD _____ PWKS 4125
Carlton Home Entertainment / Nov '92 / Carlton Home Entertainment.

Buckshot OD

OUTTA COURSE
CD _____ RR 89222
Roadrunner / Oct '95 / Pinnacle.

Buckwheat Zydeco

100% FORTIFIED ZYDECO
CD _____ CD 1024
Black Top / '88 / CM / Direct / ADA.

BUCKWHEAT ZYDECO & THE 11'S SONT PARTIS BAND (Buckwheat Zydeco & The 11's Sont Partis Band)
CD _____ CD 11528
Rounder / '88 / CM / Direct / ADA / Cadillac.

Budapest Gypsy Orchestra

BUDAPEST GYPSY ORCHESTRA
Ode / Feb '90 / CM / Discovery.
CD _____ CDODE 1310

Budapest Klezmer Band

FOLKLORE YIDDISH
CD _____ QUI 903070
Quintana / Apr '92 / Harmonia Mundi.

YIDDISH FOLKLORE
CD _____ HMA 1903070CD
Musique D'Abord / Aug '94 / Harmonia Mundi.

Budapest Ragtime Band

ELITE SYNCOPATIONS
CD _____ CDPAN 122
Pan / Apr '93 / ADA / Direct / CM.

Budd, Harold

AGUA
CD _____ SINE 003
Sine / Sep '95 / Grapevine.

BY DAWN'S EARLY NIGHT
Aztec hotel / Boy about 10 / Arcadia / Dead horse alive with flies / Photo of Santiago McKinn / Corpse at the shooting gallery / Albion farewell / Distant lights of Olancha recede / Down the slopes to the meadow / She dances by the light of the silvery moon / Blind bird / Saint's name spoken / Place of dead roads / Child in a sylvan field / Poems
CD _____ 7599266492
WEA / Aug '91 / Warner Music.

LOVELY THUNDER
Gunfighter / Sandtreader / Ice floes in Eden / Olancha farewell / Flowered knife shad-ows (for Simon Raymonde) / Gypsy violin
CD _____ EEGCD 46
EG / Oct '86 / EMI.

MOON AND THE MELODIES, THE
(Budd/Fraser/Guthrie/Raymonde)
Sea, swallow me / Memory gongs / Why do you love me / Eyes are mosaics / She will destroy you / Ghost has no home / Bloody and blunt / Ooze out and away, one how
CD _____ CAD 611CD
4AD / Nov '86 / Disc.

MUSIC FOR 3 PIANOS (Budd, Harold & Ruben Garcia & Daniel Lentz)
Pulse, pause, repeat / La muchacha de los suenos dorados / Iris / Somos tres / Mes-senger / La casa bruja
CD _____ ASCD 014
All Saints / Dec '92 / Vital / Discovery.

PEARL, THE (Budd, Harold & Brian Eno)
Late October / Stream with bright fish / Sil-ver ball / Against the sky / Lost in the hum-ming air / Dark eyed sister / Their memories / Pearl / Foreshadowed / Echo of night / Still return
CD _____ EEGCD 37
EG / Jan '87 / EMI.

SERPENT (IN QUICKSILVER)/ ABANDONED CITIES
Afar / Wanderer / Rub with ashes / Serpent on the Hill / Widows charm / Serpent (in quicksilver) / Dark star / Abandoned cities
CD _____ ASCD 08
All Saints / Oct '95 / Vital / Discovery.

WHITE ARCADES, THE
White arcades / Balthus bemused by colour / Child with a lion / Real dream of sails / Algebra of darkness / Totems of the red sleeved warrior / Room / Coyote / Kiss
CD _____ ASCD 03
All Saints / Feb '96 / Vital / Discovery.

Budd, Roy

HAVE A JAZZY CHRISTMAS (Budd, Roy Trio)
We three kings / Winter wonderland / When you wish upon a star / Ding dong merrily on high / Lieutenant Kije / Jingle bells
CD _____ CHECD 9
Master Mix / Nov '89 / Wellard / Jazz Music / New Note.

Buddy & Ghost Riders

FOR FOOLS ONLY
CD _____ BRAM 199232-2
Brambus / Nov '93 / ADA / Direct.

Budgie

BANDOLIER
CD _____ REP 4100-WZ
Repertoire / Aug '91 / Pinnacle / Cadillac.

BEST OF BUDGIE
Breadfan / I ain't no mountain / I can't see my feelings / Baby, please don't go / Zoom club / Breaking all the house rules / Parents / In for the kill / In the grip of a tyre-fitter's hand
CD _____ MCLD 19067
MCA / Oct '92 / BMG.

BUDGIE
CD _____ REP 4012-WZ
Repertoire / Aug '91 / Pinnacle / Cadillac.

IN FOR THE KILL
CD _____ REP 4027-WZ
Repertoire / Aug '91 / Pinnacle / Cadillac.

NEVER TURN YOUR BACK ON A FRIEND
CD _____ REP 4013-WZ
Repertoire / Aug '91 / Pinnacle / Cadillac.

SQUAWK
Whiskey river / Rocking man / Rolling home again / Make me happy / Hot as a docker's armpit / Drug store woman / Bottled / Young is a world / Stranded
CD _____ REP 4026-WZ
Repertoire / Aug '91 / Pinnacle / Cadillac.

Bue, Papa

EVERYBODY LOVES SATURDAY NIGHT (Bue, Papa Viking Jazz Band)
Everybody loves Saturday night / Yellow dog blues / Blueberry hill / Song was born / Weary blues / Tin roof blues / New Orleans / Mack the knife / Oh baby / I'm confessin' that I love you / Basin Street blues / Big butter and egg man / Maple leaf rag
CD _____ CDTTD 590
Timeless Traditional / Nov '93 / New Note.

ICE CREAM (Bue, Papa Viking Jazz Band)
CD _____ MECCAVCD 1000
Music Mecca / Jul '93 / Jazz Music / Cadillac / Wellard.

LIVE AT SLUKEFTER (Bue, Papa Viking Jazz Band)
CD _____ MECCACD 1028
Music Mecca / Jun '93 / Jazz Music / Cadillac / Wellard.

ON STAGE (Bue, Papa Viking Jazz Band)
CD _____ CDTTD 511
Timeless Traditional / Jan '86 / New Note.

SONG WAS BORN, A (Bue, Papa Viking Jazz Band)
CD _____ BLR 84 012
L&R / May '91 / New Note.

TIVOLI BLUES (Bue, Papa Viking Jazz Band)
CD _____ MECCACD 1001
Music Mecca / Aug '90 / Jazz Music / Cadillac / Wellard.

Buffalo

DEAD FOREVER
CD _____ REP 4141-WP
Repertoire / Aug '91 / Pinnacle / Cadillac.

Buffalo Road

HOTEL INCIDENT
CD _____ OLKCD 002
Backwater / Apr '95 / SRD.

Buffalo Springfield

AGAIN
Mr. Soul / Child's claim to fame / Everydays / Expecting to fly / Bluebird / Hung upside down / Sad memory / Good time boy / Rock 'n' roll woman / Broken arrow
CD _____ 790 391-2
Atlantic / '88 / Warner Music.

BUFFALO SPRINGFIELD
For what its worth / Sit down I think I love you / Nowadays Clancy can't even sing / Go and say goodbye / Pay the price / Burned / Out of my mind / Mr. Soul / Blue-bird / Broken arrow / Rock 'n' roll woman / Expecting to fly / Hung upside down / Child's claim to fame / Kind woman / On the way home / I am a child / Pretty girl why / Special care / Uno mundo / In the hour of not quite rain / Four days gone / Questions
CD _____ 756903892
Atlantic / Feb '92 / Warner Music.

LAST TIME AROUND
On the way home / It's so hard to wait / Pretty girl why / Four days gone / Carefree country day / Special care / Hour of not quite rain / Questions / I am a child / Merry go round / Uno mundo / Kind woman
CD _____ 756790393-2
Atlantic / Mar '94 / Warner Music.

RETROSPECTIVE (The Best Of Buffalo Springfield)
For what it's worth / Hello Mr. Soul / Sit down I think I love you / Kind woman / Blue-bird / On the way home / Nowadays Clancy can't even sing / Broken arrow / Rock 'n' roll woman / I am a child / Go and say goodbye / Expecting to fly
CD _____ K 7904172
Atlantic / Mar '88 / Warner Music.

Buffalo Tom

BIG RED LETTER DAY
Sodajerk / I'm allowed / Tree house / Would not be denied / Latest monkey / My responsibility / Dry land / Torch singer / Late at night / Suppose / Anything that / Dream
CD _____ BBQCD 142
Beggars Banquet / Sep '93 / Warner Music / Disc.

BIRD BRAIN
Bird brain / Caress / Enemy / Fortune teller / Directive / Skeleton key / Guy who is me / Crawl / Baby / Bleeding heart
CD _____ BBL 31CD
Beggars Banquet / Sep '95 / Warner Music / Disc.

BUFFALO TOM
Sunflower suit / Plank / Impossible / 500,000 warnings / Bus / Racine / In the attic / Flushing stars / Walk away / Reason why
CD _____ SST 250 CD
SST / Jul '89 / Plastic Head.

LET ME COME OVER
CD _____ SITU 36CD
Situation 2 / Mar '92 / Pinnacle.

SLEEPY EYED
CD _____ BBQCD 177
Beggars Banquet / Jul '95 / Warner Music / Disc.

Buffalo, Norton

LOVIN' IN THE VALLEY OF THE MOON/ DESERT HORIZON
Lovin' in the valley of the moon / One kiss to say goodbye / Ghetto hotel / Nobody wants me / Puerto de azul / Hangin' tree /

Another day / Rosalie / Jig is up / Eighteen wheels / Sea of key / Echoes of the last stampede / Desert horizon / Age old puppet / Wasn't it bad enough / Thinkin' 'bout you babe / Hopin' you'll come back / High tide in wingo / Walkin' down to Suzy's / Cold, cold city nights / Where has she gone / Sun comes in the morning / Anni in the morning
CD _____ EDCD 431
Edsel / Jul '95 / Pinnacle / ADA.

Buffett, Jimmy

ALL TIME GREAT HITS
Margaritaville / Fins / Come Monday / Vol-cano / Changes in latitudes / Cheeseburger in paradise / Son of a son of a sailor / Stars fell on Alabama / Miss you so badly / Why don't we get drunk / Pirate looks at forty / We went to Paris / Grapefruit - juicy fruit / Pencil thin mustache / Boat drinks / Chan-son pour les petits enfants / Banana repub-lic / Lat mango in Paris
CD _____ PLATCD 4903
Prism / Sep '94 / Prism.

Bufford, Mojo

STATE OF THE (BLUES) HARP.
CD _____ JSPCD 233
JSP / Mar '90 / ADA / Target/BMG / Direct / Cadillac / Complete/Pinnacle.

Bugbear

PLAN FOR THE ASSASINATION OF THE BUGBEAR
Theme from the bugbear / (I got a) New crush / Ride roughshod / Punkist / Mystic boy / Marlin / Damaged III / Dando moth-erfucker / Fucking through / Triple-brrr / Panik / I love the girl with the money shot face / Teen city intrigue / I like violence / 22 Boy whore / I hate my band
CD _____ MASKCD 049
Vinyl Japan / Jun '95 / Vital.

Buick 6

CYPRESS GROVE
CD _____ TX 1003CD
Taxim / Jan '94 / ADA.

Built To Spill

THERE'S NOTHING WRONG WITH LOVE
CD _____ EFAO 49632
City Slang / Oct '95 / Disc.

Buirski, Felicity

REPAIRS AND ALTERATIONS
Dream on / Heartless Hotel / Aha Song (I am the lord) / Executioner's song / Come to me darling / Marilyn / Travelling home / Rumpelstiltskin / Let there be light
CD _____ RRACD 004
Run River / Nov '90 / Direct / ADA / CM.

Bulba, Taras

SKETCHS OF BABEL
CD _____ HY 39100782
Hyperium / Nov '93 / Plastic Head.

Bulgarian National Folk..

PIRIN FOLK (Bulgarian National Folk Ensemble)
CD _____ CDPT 025
Prestige / Apr '95 / Total/BMG.

Bulgarian State..

RITUAL - LE MYSTERE DES VOIX BULGARES (Bulgarian State Television Female Choir)
CD _____ 7559793492
Elektra Nonesuch / Jan '95 / Warner Music.

Bulgarka Junior Quartet

LEGEND OF THE BULGARIAN VOICES
CD _____ EUCD 1331
ARC / Nov '95 / ARC Music / ADA.

Bull

GORDON ZONE
CD _____ HMS 197-2
Homestead / Jun '93 / SRD.

Bull City Red

COMPLETE RECORDINGS (1935-1939)
CD _____ SOB 035272
Story Of The Blues / Dec '92 / Koch / ADA.

Bull, Sandy

E PLURIBUS UNUM
CD _____ VND 6513
Vanguard / Mar '90 / Complete/Pinnacle / Discovery.

Bullet In The Head

JAWBONE OF AN ASS
CD _____ ORGAN 011-2
Lungcast / May '94 / SRD.

Bullet LaVolta

GIFT, THE
CD _____ TAANG 29CD
Taang / Nov '92 / Plastic Head.

Bunch, John

BEST THING FOR YOU, THE (Bunch, John Trio)
Best thing for you would be me / I loves you Porgy / Deed I do / Emily / Star eyes / Lucky to be me / Wave / Au privave / I can't get started (with you) / Jitterbug waltz
CD _____ CCD 4328
Concord Jazz / Oct '87 / New Note.

NEW YORK SWING (COLE PORTER COLLECTIVE) (Bunch, John & Bucky Pizzarelli)
Lady be good / Hi fly / Do nothin' 'til you hear from me / Dot's cheesecake / Stom-pin' at the Savoy / How am I to know / Slee-pin' bee / Polka dots and moonbeams / Jit-terbug waltz / Sunday / In a sentimental mood
CD _____ CDC 9055
LRC / Nov '92 / New Note / Harmonia Mundi.

Bundrick, John

RUN FOR COVER
CD _____ RMCCD 0198
Red Steel Music / Apr '95 / Grapevine.

Bunka, Roman

COLOUR ME CAIRO
CD _____ ENJACD 90832
Enja / Dec '95 / New Note / Vital/SAM.

Bunn, Teddy

SPIRITS OF RHYTHM
CD _____ JSPCD 307
JSP / Apr '89 / ADA / Target/BMG / Direct / Cadillac / Complete/Pinnacle.

Bunnett, Jane

RENDEZ VOUS/CUBA
CD _____ JUST 742
Justin Time / Sep '95 / Harmonia Mundi / Cadillac.

WATER IS WIDE, THE
Elements of freedom / Time again / Real truth / Serenade to a cuckoo / You must believe in spring / Influence peddling / Pan-nonica / Brakes' sake / Burning tear / Lucky strike / Water is wide / Rockin' in rhythm
CD _____ ECD 220912
Evidence / Jul '94 / Harmonia Mundi / ADA / Cadillac.

Bunny Rugs

TALKING TO YOU
CD _____ GRELCD 215
Greensleeves / May '95 / Total/BMG / Jetstar / SRD.

Burach

WEIRD SET, THE
All I ask / Boiling black kettle / Curve / Post-conscious modernisation of space / Candlelight reel / Jar o'lentils / Zombie song / Return to Milltown / Tarbolton lodge / Oni bucharesti / Green Loch / Vincent black lightening 1952 / Rest of your life / January the 8th / Overnice / Dick Gossips / Earl's chair / Halfway round / Walking the line / What shall we drink to tonight
CD _____ CDTRAX 093
Greentrax / Jul '95 / Conifer / Duncans / ADA / Direct.

Burbank, Albert

CREOLE CLARINETS (Burbank, Albert & Raymond Burke)
CD _____ MG 9005
Mardi Gras / Feb '95 / Jazz Music.

Burch, Elder J.E.

COMPLETE RECORDED WORKS 1927-29 (Burch, Elder J.E. & Rev. Beaumont)
CD _____ DOCD 5329
Blues Document / Mar '95 / Swift / Jazz Music / Hot Shot.

Burchell, Chas

UNSUNG HERO
Juicy Lucy / Bobbin' / Gone into it / Have you met Miss Jones / It's you or no one/ Shades / Marsh bars / Which way / Just squeeze me / Blue monk / Tickle toe / Come back / Sometimes / Sonnymoon for two / Solea
CD _____ IOR 70262
In & Out / Sep '95 / Vital/SAM.

Burdett, Phil

DIESEL POEMS (Burdett, Phil & The New World Troubadours)
Dreamworld's taking over / Rizla hoodlum - mythology Part 1 / Angel / Haunted fountain / Love light / My bluebird shirt / People only die in cartoons / Nihil (Nostalgia yo) /

Change the meaning / Closer to God like the moon / Impossible to love / They watered my whiskey down
CD _____ XXCD 24
F-Beat / Oct '93 / Pinnacle.

Burdon, Eric

COMEBACK SOUNDTRACK, THE
(Burdon, Eric & The Band)
CD _____ LICD 900058
Line / Sep '94 / CM / Grapevine / ADA / Conifer / Direct.

CRAWLING KING SNAKE
No more elmore / Crawling king snake / Take it easy / Dey won't / Wall of silence / Street walker / It hurts me too / Lights out / Bird on the beach
CD _____ CDTB 017
Magnum Music / Nov '92 / Magnum Music Group.

ERIC BURDON DECLARES WAR
Vision of Rassan / Dedication / Roll on Kirk / Tobacco Road / I have a dream / Blues for the Memphis Slim / Birth / Mother Earth / Mr. Charlie / Danish pastry / You're no stranger
CD _____ 74321305262
Avenue / Sep '95 / BMG.

GOOD TIMES (A Collection)
CD _____ 5117782
Polydor / Jul '93 / PolyGram.

LOST WITHIN THE HALLS OF FAME
CD _____ JETCD 1011
Jet / Apr '95 / Total/BMG.

MISUNDERSTOOD
CD _____ AIM 1054
Aim / Oct '95 / Direct / ADA / Jazz Music.

SINGS THE ANIMALS GREATEST HITS
House of the Rising Sun / Don't let me be misunderstood / We gotta get out of this place / It's my life / When I was young / Real me / Home dream / Stop / Paint it black / Nights in white satin / Tobacco road / Mother earth / City boy / Have mercy judge / Day in the life
CD _____ 74321305302
Avenue / Sep '95 / BMG.

THAT'S LIVE (Burdon, Eric & The Band)
CD _____ INAK 854 CD
In Akustik / '88 / Magnum Music Group.

WICKED MAN
CD _____ GNPD 2194
GNP Crescendo / '88 / Silva Screen.

Burgess, John

KING OF THE HIGHLAND PIPERS
CD _____ TSCD 466
Topic / May '93 / Direct / ADA.

Burgess, Mark

PARADYNING (Burgess, Mark & Yves Altana)
CD _____ GOODCD 8
Dead Dead Good / Oct '95 / Pinnacle.

Burgess, Sally

SALLY BURGESS SINGS JAZZ
CD _____ CDVIR 8308
TER / Dec '89 / Koch.

Burgess, Sonny

1956 - 1959
We wanna boogie / Red headed woman / Prisoner's song / All night long / Life's too short to live / Restless / Ain't got a thing / Daddy blues / Fannie Brown / Ain't gonna do it / You / Hand me down my walking cane / Please listen to me / Gone / My babe / My bucket's got a hole in it / Sweet misery / What'cha gonna do / Oh mama / Truckin' down the avenue / Feelin' good / So glad you're mine / One night / Always will / Little town baby / You're not mine / Mr. Blues / Find my baby for me / Tomorrow night / Tomorrow never comes / Skinny Ginny / So soon / Mama Loochie / Mama Loochie (2) / Itchy / Thunderbird / Kiss goodnight / Sadie's back in town / Smoochin' Jill / My baby loves me / One broken heart
CD Set _____ BCD 15525
Bear Family / Jul '91 / Rollercoaster / Direct / CM / Swift / ADA.

ARKANSAS WILD MAN, THE
We wanna boogie / Red headed woman / Prisoner's song / Restless / Ain't got a thing / Daddy blues / Hand me down my walking cane / Fannie Brown / One broken heart / Gone / Please listen to me / My babe / Sweet misery / Oh mama / Truckin' / Down tha avenue / What'cha gonna do / So glad you're mine / One night / My little town baby / Mr. Blues / Find my baby for me / Tomorrow night / Skinny Ginny / Mama Loochie / Sadie's back in town
CD _____ CPCD 8103
Charly / Jun '95 / Charly / THE / Cadillac.

TENNESSEE BORDER
Tennessee border / Enough of you / My heart is aching for you / Flattop joint / As far as I could go / Old old man / Automatic woman / There's talk in your sleep / Stuck up / I don't dig it

CD _____ FIENDCD 720
Edsel / Jun '92 / Pinnacle / ADA.

Burke, Joe

HAPPY TO MEET, SORRY TO PART
CD _____ GLCD 1069
Green Linnet / Feb '93 / Roots / CM / Direct / ADA.

PURE IRISH TRADITIONAL MUSIC ON THE ACCORDION
CD _____ PTCD 1015
Pure Traditional Irish / Jan '95 / ADA.

TAILOR'S CHOICE, THE
Dark woman of the Glen / Mills are grinding/ Paddy Doorhy's reel / Green blanket / Dean Brig of Edinburgh / Jack Coughlan's fancy / Coolin' / Sean Reid's fancy/Kerry reel / Mama's pet/Tailor's choice / Blind Mary / Humours of Quarry Cross/Jackson's bottle of brandy / Roisin Dubh / Fort of Kincora/ Caroline O'Neill's hornpipe / Were you at the Rock / Limestone rock/Banshee reel / O'Rahilly's grave
CD _____ GLCD 1045
Green Linnet / Aug '93 / Roots / CM / Direct / ADA.

TRADITIONAL MUSIC OF IRELAND
Bucks of Oranmore/Wind that shakes the barley / Dogs among the bushes/Gorman's / Trip to the cottage/Tatter Jack Walsh / Minny Foster/The banks / Sporting Nell/ Boyne hunt / Murray's reel/Smell of the bog / Patsy Tuohey's/Molly Ban / College groves/Rigging reel / Jackson's reel / Grey goose/Sixpenny money / Bonnie Kate/Jenny's chickens / Galway bay/Contradiction / Pat burke's jigs/Fraher's jigs / Longford spinster/Paddy Lynn's delight
CD _____ GLCD 1048
Green Linnet / Jun '93 / Roots / CM / Direct / ADA.

Burke, Kevin

CELTIC FIDDLE FEST (Burke, Kevin/ Johnny Cunningham/C. Lemaitre)
CD _____ GLCD 1133
Green Linnet / Oct '93 / Roots / CM / Direct / ADA.

EAVESDROPPER (Burke, Kevin & Jackie Daly)
CD _____ LUNCD 039
Mulligan / Aug '94 / CM / ADA.

IF THE CAP FITS
Kerry reel/Michael Coleman's reel/Wheels of the world / Dinney Delaney's/Yellow wattle / Mason's apron/Laington's reel / Paddy Fahy's jigs/Cliffs of Moher / Star of Munster / Biddy Martin's and Bill Sullivan's polkas/ Ger the Rigger / Bobby Casey's hornpipe / Toss the feathers / College groves/Pinch of snuff/Earl's chair / Woman of the house/Girl that broke my heart/Drunken tinker / Paddy Cronin/McFadden's handsome daughter / Hunter's purse/Toss the feathers
CD _____ GLCD 3009
Green Linnet / Aug '92 / Roots / CM / Direct / ADA.

OPEN HOUSE
CD _____ GLCD 1122
Green Linnet / Jun '92 / Roots / CM / Direct / ADA.

PORTLAND (Burke, Kevin & Michael O'Dohmnhaill)
Maudabawn chapel/Wild Irishman/Moher reel / Eirigh a shiuir / Breton Gavottes / Rolling waves/Market town/Scatter the mud / Aird ui chumhaing / Paddy's return/Willy Coleman's/Up in the air / Lucy's fling/ S'iomadh rud a chunnaic mi/Some say the Devil i i / Is fada Liom Uaim I / Tom Morrison's/Beare Island reel/George White's favourite / Dipping the sheep
CD _____ GLCD 1041
Green Linnet / Oct '88 / Roots / CM / Direct / ADA.

PROMENADE
CD _____ LUNCD 028
Mulligan / Aug '94 / CM / ADA.

SWEENEY'S DREAM
CD _____ OSS 18CD
Ossian / Mar '94 / ADA / Direct / CM.

UP CLOSE
Lord Gordon's reel / Finnish polka/Jessica's polka / Thrush in the straw/Health to the ladies/Boys of the town / Tuttle's reel/Bunch of green rushes/Maids of Mitchelstown / Shepherd's daughter/Jerusalem ridge / Michael Kennedy's reel / Bloom of youth/Molloy's favourite/Cabin hunter / Boys of Ballycastle/Stack of barley / Raheen medley / Rambler/Chapel bell / Peeler's jacket/Flax in bloom/Eileen curran / Orphan/Mist on the mountain/Stolen purse
CD _____ GLCD 1052
Green Linnet / Feb '90 / Roots / CM / Direct / ADA.

Burke, Malena

SALSEANDO
Para mi homenaje a matamoros / Longina / Chencha la gamba / Comprension / Me voy p'al pueblo / Bruca manigua / Capulito de aleli / De noche / Realidad y fantasia / Que bella

es Cuba / El madrugador / Seguire sin sonar
CD _____ PSCCD 1006
Pure Sounds From Cuba / Feb '95 / Henry Hadaway Organisation / THE.

Burke, Raymond

IN NEW ORLEANS (Burke, Raymond & Cie Frazier)
Gypsy love song / Hindustan / Dead bug blues / Wonderful one / I want somebody to love / At sundown / Oh daddy / All that I ask is love / I surrender dear / Sweet little you / Honky tonk town / Maybe you're mine / Blues in A flat / Dirty rag / All by myself
CD _____ 504CDS 27
504 / Sep '94 / Wellard / Jazz Music / Target/BMG / Cadillac.

RAYMOND BURKE & HIS SPEAKEASY BOYS
CD _____ AMCD 47
American Music / Jan '94 / Jazz Music.

Burke, Solomon

CHANGE IS GONNA COME, A
Love buys love / Got to get myself some money / Let it be you and me / Love is all that matters / Don't tell me what a man won't do for a woman / Change is gonna come / Here we go again / It don't get no better than this / When a man loves a woman
CD _____ FIENDCD 196
Demon / Oct '90 / Pinnacle / ADA.

HOME IN YOUR HEART (Best of Soloman Burke)
Home in your heart / Down in the valley / Looking for my baby / I'm hanging up my heart for you / Cry to me / Just out of reach / Goodbye baby (baby goodbye) / Words / Stupidity / Send me some lovin' / Go on back to him / Baby (I wanna be loved) / Can't nobody love you / Got to get you off my mind / Someone to love me / You're good for me / dance, dance, dance / Everybody needs somebody to love / Tonight's the night / Baby, come on home / If you need me / Price / Get out of my life woman / Save it / Take me (just as I am) / When she touches me / I wish I knew (how it would feel to be free) / Party people / Keep a light in the window / I feel a sin coming on / Meet me in the church / Someone is watching / Detroit city / Shame on me / I stayed away too long / It's just a matter of time / Since I met you baby / Time is a thief / Woman how do you make me love you like I do / It's been a change / What'd I say
CD _____ 8122702842
Atlantic / Jul '93 / Warner Music.

HOMELAND
CD _____ FIENDCD 737
Demon / Aug '93 / Pinnacle / ADA.

KING OF SOUL
Boo hoo hoo / Hold on I'm comin' / Sweeter than sweetness / Sidewalks, fences and walls / Let the love flow / More / Lucky / Please come back home to me
CD _____ CPCD 8014
Charly / Feb '94 / Charly / THE / Cadillac.

LIVE AT HOUSE OF BLUES
CD _____ BT 1108CD
Black Top / Dec '94 / CM / Direct / ADA.

LOVE TRAP
Love trap / Do you believe in the hereafter / Every breath you take / Daddy love bear / Isis / Nothing but the truth / Only God knows / Drive / Sweet spirit
CD _____ IVCD 21336
PolyGram TV / Jul '87 / PolyGram.

SOUL OF THE BLUES
CD _____ BT 1095CD
Black Top / Jan '94 / CM / Direct / ADA.

YOU CAN RUN BUT YOU CAN'T HIDE
To thee / Why do that to me / This is it / My heart is a chapel / Picture of you / You can run but you can't hide / Friendship ring / I'm not afraid / Don't cry / Christmas presents / I'm in love / Leave my kitten alone / No man walks alone / I'm all alone / I need you tonight / Walking in a dream / You are my one love / For you and you alone
CD _____ RBD 108
Mr. R&B / Apr '91 / Swift / CM / Wellard.

Burland, Dave

BENCHMARK
CD _____ FC 004CD
Fat Cat / Jul '94 / Direct / ADA / CM.

HIS MASTERS CHOICE
CD _____ RGFCD 009
Road Goes On Forever / '92 / Direct.

SINGS RICHARD BURLAND
CD _____ RGFCD 005
Road Goes On Forever / '92 / Direct.

Burma Jam

EMERGENCY BROADCAST SYSTEM
CD _____ NAUGH 1012
Naugh / Jan '93 / Vital.

Burmer, Richard

BHAKTI POINT
CD _____ CDFOR 17047-2
Miles Music / Mar '88 / Wellard / New Note / Cadillac.

Burn

SO FAR, SO BAD
CD _____ FONECD 001
Formula One / Aug '95 / Plastic Head.

SPARK TO A FLAME
CD _____ FONECD 003
Formula One / Jan '96 / Plastic Head.

Burn, Chris

HENRY COWELL CONCERT, A
CD _____ ACTA 7
Acta / Oct '94 / Cadillac / Acta / Impetus.

Burnell, Kenny

MOON AND SAND
Moon and sand / My ship / For once in my life / U.M.M.G. / Blue bossa / Stolen moments / Love for sale / Lost in the stars
CD _____ CCD 4121
Concord Jazz / Jun '92 / New Note.

Burnett, T-Bone

B52 BAND & THE FABULOUS SKYLARKS
One Way / Sep '94 / Direct / ADA.
CD _____ MCAD 22140

BEHIND THE TRAP DOOR
Strange combination / Amnesia and jealousy (oh Lana) / Having a wonderful time wish you were here / Law of average / My life and the women who lived it / Welcome home, Mr.Lewis
CD _____ VEXCD 3
Demon / Aug '92 / Pinnacle / ADA.

Burnette, Dorsey

GREAT SHAKIN' FEVER
Great shakin' fever / Don't let go / Dying ember / raining in my heart / Sad boy / He gave me my hands / Good good lovin' / Full house / Feminine touch / It's no sin / Creator / Biggest lover in town / Buckeye road / That's me without you / No one but him / Cry for your love / Rains came down / Country boy in the army / Somebody nobody wants / It could've been different / Little child / With all your heart / Look what you've missed / Gypsy magic / I would do anything
CD _____ BCD 15545
Bear Family / '93 / Rollercoaster / Direct / CM / Swift / ADA.

Burnette, Johnny

BURNETTE BROTHERS, THE (Burnette, Johnny & Dorsey)
CD _____ RSRCD 005
Rockstar / Dec '94 / Rollercoaster / Direct / Magnum Music Group / Nervous.

COMPLETE RECORDINGS (Burnette, Johnny Rock 'N' Roll Trio)
Rockabilly boogie / Please don't leave me / Rock memory / Lonesome train (on a lonesome track) / Sweet love on my mind / My love, you're a stranger / Your baby blue eyes / I love you so / Train kept a rollin' / All by myself / Drinkin' wine spo-dee-o-dee / Blind stay away from me / Honey hush / Lonesome tears in my eyes / I just found out / Chains of love / Lonesome train (on a lonesome track) (alt) / I love you so (master) / If you want it enough / Butterfingers / Eager beaver baby / Touch me / Tear it up / Oh baby babe / You're undecided / Midnight train / Shattered dreams
CD _____ BCD 15474
Bear Family / '88 / Rollercoaster / Direct / CM / Swift / ADA.

R 'N' R TRIO / TEAR IT UP (Burnette, Johnny Rock 'N' Roll Trio)
Beat Goes On / Jun '93 / Pinnacle.
CD _____ BGOCD 177

THAT'S THE WAY I FEEL
CD _____ RSRCD 006
Rockstar / Dec '94 / Rollercoaster / Direct / Magnum Music Group / Nervous.

Burnin' Chicago Blues...

BOOGIE BLUES (Burnin' Chicago Blues Machine)
CD _____ GBW 003
GBW / Mar '92 / Harmonia Mundi.

Burning Flames

DIG
If you get what you want / Chook and dig / Island girl I'm on fire / Workey workey / Forbidden fruit / Nice time / Tout moun dance
CD _____ CIDM 1088
Mango / Aug '91 / Vital / PolyGram.

WORKEY WORKEY
CD _____ CPCD 8134
Charly / Jan '96 / Charly / THE / Cadillac.

Burning Red Ivanhoe

BURNING RED IVANHOE
CD _____ REP 4209-WP
Repertoire / Aug '91 / Pinnacle / Cadillac.

Burning Spear

DRY AND HEAVY
Any river / Sun / It's a long way around / I.W.I.N. / Throw down your arms / Dry and heavy / Wailing / Disciples / Shout it out
CD _____ RRCD 40
Reggae Refreshers / Jul '93 / PolyGram / Vital.

FAR OVER
Heartbeat / '88 / Greensleeves / Jetstar / Direct / ADA.

FITTEST OF THE FITTEST, THE
Fittest of the fittest / Fireman / Bad to worst / Repatriation / Old Boy Garvey / 2000 years / For you / In Africa / Vision
CD _____ HBCD 22
Heartbeat / '88 / Greensleeves / Jetstar / Direct / ADA.

HAIL H.I.M
African teacher / African postman / Cry blood Africa / Hail H.I.M. / Jah a go raid / Columbus / Road foggy / Follow Marcus Garvey / Jah see and know
CD _____ HBCD 145
Heartbeat / Jun '94 / Greensleeves / Jetstar / Direct / ADA.

JAH KINGDOM
Mango / Aug '91 / Vital / PolyGram.

KEEP THE SPEAR BURNING
CD _____ CIDD 9377
Island / '89 / PolyGram.

LIVE 1993
CD _____ 503582
Declic / Sep '94 / Jetstar.

LIVING DUB VOL. 1
CD _____ HBCD 131
Heartbeat / Jun '93 / Greensleeves / Jetstar / Direct / ADA.

LIVING DUB VOL. 2
CD _____ HBCD 132
Greensleeves / Jan '94 / Total/BMG / Jetstar / SRD.

LOVE AND PEACE (Live)
CD _____ CDHB 175
Heartbeat / Jan '95 / Greensleeves / Jetstar / Direct / ADA.

MEK WI DWEET
Mek wi dweet / Garvey / Civilization / Elephants / My roots / Great man / African woman / Take a look / One people / Mek we dweet in dub
CD _____ CIDM 1045
Mango / Jun '90 / Vital / PolyGram.

ORIGINAL BURNING SPEAR, THE
CD _____ SONCD 0023
Sonic Sounds / Apr '92 / Jetstar.

RASTA BUSINESS
CD _____ 406042
Declic / Nov '95 / Jetstar.

REGGAE GREATS
Door peep / Slavery days / Lion / Black disciples / Man in the hills / Tradition / Throw down your arms / Social living / Marcus Garvey / Dry and heavy / Black wa-da-da (Invasion) / Sun
CD _____ IMCD 5
Island / Jul '89 / PolyGram.

RESISTANCE
CD _____ HBCD 33
Heartbeat / '88 / Greensleeves / Jetstar / Direct / ADA.

SOCIAL LIVING
Marcus children suffer / Social living / Nayah Keith / Institution / Marcus senior / Civilised reggae / Mr. Garvey / Come / Marcus say Jah no dead
CD _____ BAFCD 004
Blood & Fire / Oct '94 / Grapevine / PolyGram.

WORLD SHOULD KNOW, THE
CD _____ HBCD 119
Greensleeves / Feb '93 / Total/BMG / Jetstar / SRD.

Burns, Eddie

DETROIT (Burns, Eddie Band)
Orange driver / When I get drunk / Kidman / Bottle up and go / Inflation blues / Detroit / Butterfly / Boom boom / Time out / New highway 61 / Blue jay
CD _____ ECD 260242
Evidence / Feb '92 / Harmonia Mundi / ADA / Cadillac.

Burns, Hugh

DEDICATION
CD _____ BRGCD 15
Bridge / Nov '95 / Grapevine.

Burns, Jerry

JERRY BURNS
Pale red / Casually unkind / Hardly me / Fall for lovers / Sometimes I'm wild / Crossing over / Simple heart / Completely my dear / Safe in the rain / Stepping out slowly
CD _____ 4716452
Columbia / Jun '92 / Sony.

Burns Sisters

CLOSE TO HOME
CD _____ CDPH 1178
Philo / Aug '95 / Direct / CM / ADA.

Burnside, R.L.

BAD LUCK CITY
CD _____ FIENDCD 741
Demon / Nov '93 / Pinnacle / ADA.

Burrage, Ronnie

SHUTTLE
CD _____ SSCD 8052
Sound Hills / Apr '94 / Harmonia Mundi / Cadillac.

Burrell, Dave

DAVE BURRELL PLAYS ELLINGTON AND MONK
In a sentimental mood / Lush life / Come Sunday / Straight no chaser / Sophisticated lady / Flower is a lovesome thing
CD _____ DC 8550
Denon / Jun '89 / Conifer.

HIGH WON - HIGH TWO
CD _____ BLCD 760206
Black Lion / Nov '95 / Jazz Music / Cadillac / Wellard / Koch.

IN CONCERT (Burrell, Dave & David Murray)
CD _____ VICTOCD 016
Victo / Nov '94 / These / ReR Megacorp / Cadillac.

WINDWARD PASSAGES
CD _____ ARTCD 6138
Hat Art / Feb '94 / Harmonia Mundi / ADA / Cadillac.

Burrell, Kenny

BEST OF KENNY BURRELL, THE
Now see how you are / Cheetah / D.B. Blues / Phinupi / Chitlins con carne / Midnight blue / Love your spell is everywhere / Loie / Daydream / Togethering / Summertime / Jumpin' blues / Jeannine
CD _____ CDP 8304932
Blue Note / Apr '95 / EMI.

BLUE LIGHTS, VOL.1
Phinupi / Yes baby / Scotch blues / Man I love / I never knew
CD _____ BNZ 223
Blue Note / Aug '89 / EMI.

BLUESIN' AROUND
CD _____ 4722392
Sony Jazz / Jan '95 / Sony.

ELLINGTON A LA CARTE
take the 'a' train / Sultry serenade / Flamingo / In a mellow tone / Don't worry 'bout me / Azure / I ain't got nothin' but the blues / Do nothin' 'til you hear from me / Mood indigo
CD _____ MCD 5435
Muse / Jul '95 / New Note / CM.

FROM VANGUARD WITH LOVE
Opening introduction / I mean you / Maya's dance / Yardbird suite / Manteca / Black and tan fantasy / Lament / Along came you / Fungi Mama / Good news blues
CD _____ KICJ 212
King/Paddle Wheel / Dec '94 / New Note.

JAZZMEN DETROIT
Afternoon in Paris / You turned the tables on me / Apothegh / Your host / Cotton tail / Tom's thumb
CD _____ SV 0176
Savoy Jazz / Jul '93 / Conifer / ADA.

LIVE AT THE VILLAGE VANGUARD (Burrell, Kenny Trio)
Night long / Will you still be in my mind / I'm a fool to want you / Trio / Broadway / Soft winds / Just a sittin' and a rockin' / Well you needn't / Second balcony jump / Willow weep for me / Work song / Woody 'n' you / In the still of the night / Don't you know I care (or don't you care to) / Love you madly / It's getting dark
CD _____ LEJAZZCD 22
Le Jazz / Feb '94 / Charly / Cadillac.

LOTUS BLOSSOM
Warm valley / I don't stand a ghost of a chance / If you could see me now / Lotus blossom / Once upon a summertime / For once in my life / Minha saudade / Young and foolish / Old folks / They can't take that away from me / There will never be another / Night has a thousand eyes / I'm falling for you / Satin doll
CD _____ CCD 4668
Concord Jazz / Oct '95 / New Note.

Burrell, Roland

BEST OF ROLAND BURRELL
CD _____ CDSGP 054
Prestige / Jun '93 / Total/BMG.

Burrito Brothers

DOUBLE BARREL
She's single again / New shade of blue / Price of love / Ain't love just like the rain / One more time / Sailor / No easy way out / Tonight / Hearts in my eyes / Ain't worth the powder / Late in the night / I'm confessing / Let your heart do the talking
CD _____ CDSD 079
Sundown / Nov '95 / Magnum Music Group.

Burroughs, Chris

WEST OF TEXAS
CD _____ ROSE 203 CD
New Rose / Jul '90 / Direct / ADA.

Burroughs, William S.

ELVIS OF LETTERS (Burroughs, William S. & Gus Van Sant)
Burroughs break / Word is virus / Millions of images / Hipster be-bop junkie
CD _____ TK91CD 001
T/K / Jun '94 / Pinnacle.

SPARE ASS ANNIE AND OTHER TALES (Burroughs, William S. & Disposable Heroes Of Hiphoprisy)
CD _____ BRCD 600
4th & Broadway / Oct '93 / PolyGram.

Burrowes, Roy

LIVE AT THE DREHER - PARIS 1980 (Burrowes, Roy Sextet)
CD _____ 151992
Marge / Jun '93 / Discovery.

Burrows, Stuart

FAVOURITE SONGS OF WALES
CD _____ SCD 2032
Sain / Dec '94 / Direct / ADA.

Burrus, Terry

FREE SPIRIT
Finally in love / Period of time / Nite and day / Don't cry / This one's for you / Love ties / Free spirit / Hold on to me / Tell me how you feel / I'm on your side
CD _____ ICHCD 1124
Ichiban / Oct '91 / Koch.

Burton, Abraham

CLOSEST TO THE SUN
Minor march / Laura / E = MC2 / Romancing you / So gracefully / Corrida de Toros / Left alone / Closest to the sun / So gracefully (version)
CD _____ ENJACD 80742
Enja / Aug '94 / New Note / Vital/SAM.

MAGICIAN, THE
I can't get started / Little Melonae / Addition to the family / It's to you / Mari's soul / Gnossienne # 1 / Magician
CD _____ ENJ 90372
Enja / Nov '95 / New Note / Vital/SAM.

Burton, Aron

PAST, PRESENT AND FUTURE
CD _____ EARWIGCD 4927
Earwig / Oct '93 / CM.

Burton, Gary

3 IN JAZZ (Burton, Gary/Sonny Rollins/ Clark Terry)
Hello, young lovers / Gentle wind and falling tear / You are my lucky star / I could write a book / Sounds of the night / Clelito lindo / Stella by starlight / Blue comedy / There will never be another you / Blues tonight / When my dreamboat comes home
CD _____ 74321218252
RCA Victor / Nov '94 / BMG.

APPLES AND ORANGES
Kato's revenge / Monk's dream / For heaven's sake / Bento box / Blue monk / O grand amor / Laura's dream / Opus half / My romance / Times like these / Eiderdown
CD _____ GRP 98052
GRP / Mar '95 / BMG / New Note.

CRYSTAL SILENCE (Burton, Gary & Chick Corea)
Senor Mouse / Arise, her eyes / I'm your pal / Desert air / Crystal silence / Falling grace / Feelings and things / Children's song / What game shall we play today
CD _____ 8313312
ECM / Mar '88 / New Note.

DREAMS SO REAL (Music of Carla Bley)
CD _____ 8333292
ECM / Jul '88 / New Note.

DUET: GARY BURTON & CHICK COREA (Burton, Gary & Chick Corea)
CD _____ 8299412
ECM / Oct '88 / New Note.

GARY BURTON & THE BERKLEE ALL STARS (Burton, Gary & The Berklee All Stars)
CD _____ JD 3301
JVC / Jul '88 / New Note.

HOTEL HELLO (Burton, Gary & Steve Swallow)
CD _____ 8355862
ECM / '90 / New Note.

LIVE IN CANNES
My foolish heart / One / No more blues / Night has a 1000 eyes / Autumn leaves / African flower / Bogota
CD _____ JWD 102214
JWD / Apr '95 / Target/BMG.

NEW QUARTET, THE
Open your eyes you can fly / Coral / Tying up loose ends / Brownout / Olhos de gato / Mallet man / Four or less / Nonsequence
CD _____ 8350022
ECM / Sep '88 / New Note.

NEW VIBE MAN IN TOWN
Joy spring / Over the rainbow / Like someone in love / Minor blues / Our waltz / So many things / Sir John / You stepped out of a dream
CD _____ 74321218282
RCA / Jan '95 / BMG.

PASSENGERS (Burton, Gary & Eberhard Weber)
CD _____ 8350162
ECM / Oct '88 / New Note.

REAL LIFE HITS
Syndrome / Beatle / Fleurette Africaine (the African flower) / Ladies in Mercedes / Real life hits / I need you here / Ivanushka Durachok
CD _____ 8252352
ECM / '88 / New Note.

RING (Burton, Gary Quintet)
Mevlevia / Unfinished sympathy / Tunnel of love / Intrude / Silent spring / Colours of chloe
CD _____ 8291912
ECM / Oct '86 / New Note.

THROB (Burton, Gary & Keith Jarrett)
Grow your own / Moonchild / In your quiet place / Como en Vietnam / Fortune smiles / Raven speaks
CD _____ 8122715942
Atlantic / Mar '94 / Warner Music.

TIMES SQUARE
CD _____ 5219822
ECM / Jul '94 / New Note.

WHIZ KIDS (Burton, Gary Quartet)
Last clown / Yellow fever / Soulful Bill / La divetta / Cool train / Loop
CD _____ 8311102
ECM / Mar '87 / New Note.

WORKS: GARY BURTON
Olhos de gato / Desert air / Tunnel of love / Vox humana / Three / Brotherhood / Chelsea bells / Coral / Domino biscuit
CD _____ 8232672
ECM / Oct '88 / New Note.

Burton, Gary

TENNESSEE FIREBIRD (Burton, Gary & Friends)
Gone / Tennessee firebird / Just like a woman / Black is the colour of my true love's hair / Faded love / Panhandle rag / I

Midnight at the Village Vanguard

MIDNIGHT AT THE VILLAGE VANGUARD
Bemsha swing / Little sunflower / Cup bearers / Ruby my dear / Cotton tail / My one and only love / Come Sunday/David danced / Parker's mood / Do what you gotta do / Kenny's theme
CD _____ KICJ 178
King/Paddle Wheel / Jun '94 / New Note.

MIDNIGHT BLUE
Chitlins con carne / Mule / Soul lament / Midnight blue / Wavy gravy / Gee baby ain't I good to you / Saturday night blues
CD _____ CDP 7463992
Blue Note / Sep '92 / EMI.

MONDAY STROLL (Burrell, Kenny & Frank Wess)
Monday stroll / East wind / Wess side / Southern exposure / Wolafunt's lament / Over the rainbow / Kansas city side
CD _____ SV 0246
Savoy Jazz / Oct '94 / Conifer / ADA.

SOULERO
Hot bossa / Mother in law / People / Sabella / Girl talk / Suzy / Tender gender / La petite mambo / If someone had told me / I'm confessin' that I love you / My favourite things / I want my baby back / Con alma / Soulero / Wild is the wind / Blues fuse
CD _____ GRP 18082
GRP / Oct '95 / BMG / New Note.

TIN TIN DEO
Tin Tin Deo / Old folks / Have you met Miss Jones / I remember you / Common ground / If you could see me now / I hadn't anyone till you / La petite mambo
CD _____ CCD 4045
Concord Jazz / Jul '94 / New Note.

can't help it / I want you / Alone and for-
saken / Walter L. / Born to lose / Beauty
contest / Epilogue
CD _____ BCD 15458
Bear Family / Jun '89 / Rollercoaster / Direct
/ CM / Swift / ADA.

Burton, James

CORN PICKIN' AND SLICK SLIDIN'
(Burton, James & Ralph Mooney)
Columbus Stockade blues / Texas waltz /
It's such a pretty world today / Moonshine
/ Laura / There goes my everything / I'm a
lonesome fugitive / My elusive dreams /
Corn pickin' / Your cheatin' heart / Spanish
eyes / Sneaky strings
CD _____ SEECD 377
See For Miles/C5 / Aug '93 / Pinnacle.

Burton, Joe

St. LOUIS BLUES
CD _____ PS 012CD
P&S / Sep '95 / Discovery.

SUBTLE SOUND
CD _____ PS 006CD
P&S / Sep '95 / Discovery.

TASTY TOUCH OF JOE BURTON, THE
CD _____ PS 013CD
P&S / Sep '95 / Discovery.

Burton, Larry

HUSTLER'S PARADISE
CD _____ BRAM 199233-2
Brambus / Nov '93 / ADA / Direct.

Burton, Rahn

POEM, THE (Burton, Rahn Trio)
CD _____ DIW 610
DIW / Nov '92 / Harmonia Mundi /
Cadillac.

Burton, W.E. 'Buddy'

BUDDY BURTON & ED 'FATS' HUDSON
1928-36 (Burton, W.E. 'Buddy' & Ed
'Fats' Hudson)
CD _____ JPCD 1511
Jazz Perspectives / Dec '94 / Jazz Music /
Hot Shot.

Burzum

BURZUM/ASKE
CD _____ AMAZON 003CD
Misanthropy / May '95 / Plastic Head.

DET SOMEGAG VAR
CD _____ AMAZON 002CD
Misanthropy / Oct '94 / Plastic Head.

FILOSOFEM
CD _____ AMAZON 009BK
Misanthropy / Jan '96 / Plastic Head.

HVIS LYSET TAR OSS
CD _____ AMAZON 001
Misanthropy / Aug '94 / Plastic Head.

Busaras, David

SMEGMA 'STRUCTIONS DON'T RHYME
CD _____ SR 1008
Scout / Jan '96 / Koch.

Busby, Colin

BIG SWING BAND FAVOURITE (Busby,
Colin Big Swing Band)
At the woodchoppers' ball / Sing, sing, sing
/ April in Paris / Take the 'A' train / String
of pearls / Begin the beguine / One o'clock
jump / Skyliner / In the mood / St. Louis
blues march / Satin doll / Little brown jug
CD _____ CDSIV 1117
Horatio Nelson / Jul '95 / THE / BMG / Avid/
BMG / Koch.

Busby, Sid

PORTRAITS (Busby, Sid & The Berkeley
Orchestra)
Portrait of my love / With a song in my heart
/ Days of wine and roses / I can't get started
(with you) / My son, my son / Serenade in
blue / Java / Stardust / As time goes by /
Serenata / And this is my beloved / Love
changes everything / Violino tzigano / When
a love affair has ended
CD _____ PCOM 1105
President / Aug '90 / Grapevine / Target/
BMG / Jazz Music / President.

SO MANY STARS (Busby, Sid & The
Berkeley Orchestra)
Nessun dorma / Cuban Pete / Memories of
you / Tango desiree / Estrellita / Deep purple / Just the way you are / Dindi / Cool
cool Luke / Wave / Easy does it / Bess, you
is my woman now / Someday my prince will
come / Inter city 125 / Going home / So
many stars
CD _____ PCOM 1138
President / Dec '94 / Grapevine / Target/
BMG / Jazz Music / President.

TRIBUTES (Busby, Sid Big Band)
Strike up the band / I'll be around / Carnival
/ Song for Jilly / Ruby / C jam blues / I've
heard that song before / I don't want to

walk without you / It's been a long, long
time / String of pearls / Blues for two / Moment of truth / Lush life / Moonlight serenade / Trees in Grosvenor Square / You
made me love you
CD _____ PCOM 1118
President / Nov '91 / Grapevine / Target/
BMG / Jazz Music / President.

Bush

16 STONE
CD _____ 6544925312
Warner Bros. / May '95 / Warner Music.

Bush Chemists

DUBS FROM ZION VALLEY (Bush
Chemists Meet Jonah Dan)
CD _____ JKPD 001CD
JKP / Jul '95 / SRD.

LIGHT UP YOUR SPLIFF
CD _____ DNCD 005
Conscious Sounds / Jan '96 / SRD.

STRICTLY DUBWISE
CD _____ WWCD 6
Wibbly Wobbly / Jul '94 / SRD.

Bush, Kate

DREAMING, THE
Sat in your tap / There goes a tenner / Pull
out the pin / Suspended in Gaffa / Leave it
open / Dreaming / Night of the swallow / All
the love / Houdini / Get out of my house
CD _____ CZ 396
EMI / Mar '91 / EMI.

HOUNDS OF LOVE
Running up that hill / Hounds of love / Big
sky / Jig of life / Mother stands for comfort
/ Cloudbusting / And dream of sheep / Un-
der ice / Waking the witch / Watching you
without me / Hello Earth / Morning fog
CD _____ CZ 361
EMI / Oct '90 / EMI.

KATE BUSH: INTERVIEW DISC
CD P.Disc _____ CBAK 4011
Baktabak / Apr '88 / Baktabak.

KICK INSIDE, THE
Moving / Saxophone song / Strange phenomena / Kite / Man with the child in his
eyes / Wuthering Heights / James and the
cold gun / Feel it / Oh to be in love /
L'amour looks something like you / Them
heavy people / Room for the life / Kick
inside
CD _____ CDEMS 1522
EMI / Sep '94 / EMI.

LIONHEART
Symphony in blue / In search of Peter Pan
/ Wow / Don't push your foot on the heart-
brake / Oh England my lionheart / Full
house / In the warm room / Kashka from
Baghdad / Coffee homeground / Hammer
horror
CD _____ CDEMS 1523
EMI / Sep '94 / EMI.

NEVER FOR EVER
Babooshka / Delius / Blow away / All we
ever look for / Egypt / Wedding list / Violin
/ Infant kiss / Night scented stock / Army
dreamers / Breathing
CD _____ CZ 360
EMI / Oct '90 / EMI.

NEVER FOREVER
CD Set _____ KB 2
UFO / Oct '92 / Pinnacle.

RED SHOES, THE
Rubber band girl / And so is love / Eat the
music / Moments of pleasure / Song of Sol-
omon / Lily / Red shoes / Top of the city /
Constellation of the heart / Big stripey lie /
Why should I love you / You're the one
CD _____ CDEMD 1047
EMI / Nov '93 / EMI.

SENSUAL WORLD, THE
Sensual world / Love and anger / Fog /
Reaching out / Heads we're dancing /
Deeper understanding / Between a man
and a woman / Never be mine / Rocket's
tail / This woman's work / Walk straight
down the middle (CD only)
CD _____ CDEMD 1010
EMI / Oct '89 / EMI.

THIS WOMAN'S WORK (Anthology
1979-1990 - 8CD Set)
Empty bullring / Ran tan waltz / Passing
through air / December will be magic again
/ Warm and soothing / Lord of the reedy
river / Ne t'en fui pas / Un baiser d'enfant /
Under the ivy / Burning bridge / My lagan
love / Handsome cabin boy / Not this time
/ Walk straight down the middle / Be kind
to my mistakes / I'm still waiting / Ken / One
last look around the house before we go... /
Experiment IV / Them heavy people / Don't push
your foot on the heartbrake (live) / James
and the cold gun (live) / L'amour looks
something like you (live) / Running up that
hill (Mix) / Cloudbusting (Organon mix) /
Hounds of love (alternative) / Big sky (Mix)
/ Experiment IV (12" mix) / Moving / Saxophone song / Strange phenomena / Kite /
Man with the child in his eyes / Wuthering
Heights / James and the cold gun / Feel it

/ Oh to be in love / L'amour looks something like you / Room for the life / Kick inside / Symphony in blue / In search of Peter
Pan / Wow / Don't push your foot on the
heartbrake / Oh England my lionheart / Full
house / In the warm room / Kashka from
Baghdad / Coffee homeground / Hammer
horror / Babooshka / Delius / Blow away /
All we ever look for / Egypt / Wedding list /
Violin / Infant kiss / Night scented stock /
Army dreamers / Breathing / Running up
that hill / Hounds of love / Big sky / Mother
stands for comfort / Cloudbusting / And
dream of sheep / Under ice / Waking the
witch / Jig of life / Watching you without me
/ Hello Earth / Morning fog / Sat in your lap
/ There goes a tenner / Pull out the pin /
Suspended in gaffa / Leave it open /
Dreaming / Night of the swallow / All the
love / Houdini / Get out of my house / Sensual world / Love and anger / Fog / Reaching out / Heads we're dancing / Deeper understanding / Between a man and a woman
/ Never be mine / Rocket's tail / This woman's work
CD Set _____ CDKBBX 1
EMI / Oct '90 / EMI.

WHOLE STORY, THE
Wuthering Heights / Cloudbusting / Man
with the child in his eyes / Breathing / Wow
/ Hounds of love / Running up that hill /
Experiment IV / Dreaming / Babooshka / Big sky
(VHS only)
CD _____ CDKBTV 1
EMI / Nov '86 / EMI.

Bush, Sam

LATE AS USUAL
CD _____ CD 0195
Rounder / '88 / CM / Direct / ADA /
Cadillac.

Bush, Stan

DIAL 818 888 8638
I got it bad for you / One kiss away / Total
surrender / Come to me / Hold your head
up high / Are you over me / Come on / In
the name of love / Hero of the heart / Take
this heart / Take my love
CD _____ CDVEST 7
Bulletproof / Mar '94 / Pinnacle.

Bushfire

DIDGERIDOO MUSIC OF THE
AUSTRALIAN ABORIGINEES
CD _____ EUCD 1224
ARC / Sep '93 / ARC Music / ADA.

Bushkin, Joe

ROAD TO OSLO/PLAY IT AGAIN, JOE
Now you has jazz / Hallelujah / Bess you is
my woman / How long has this been going
on / Man I love / Yesterday / Ain't been the
same since the Beatles / There'll be a hot
time in the town of Berlin / Oh look at me
now / I love a piano / Phone call to the past
/ I've grown accustomed to her face /
Someday I'll be sorry / Sunday of the Shepherdess / Sail away from Norway / I can't
get started (with you) / Someday you'll be
sorry / Man that got away / One for my baby
/ It had to be you / Learnin' the blues / There's always the blues / Our love is here to
stay / What's new
CD _____ DRGCD 8490
DRG / Feb '95 / New Note.

Bushwick Bill

PHANTOM OF THE RAPPA
Phantom's theme / Wha cha gonna do /
Times is hard / Who's the biggest / Ex-girl-
fiend / Only God knows / Already dead /
Bushwicken / Subliminal criminal / Inhale
exhale / Mr. President / Phantom's reprise
CD _____ CDVUS 91
Virgin / Jun '95 / EMI.

Business

BEST OF THE BUSINESS
Out in the cold / Streets where you live /
Harry May / N.J. Blacklist / Suburban rebels
/ Product / Smash the disco / Disco girls /
H-Bomb / Blind justice / Get out while you
can / Guttersnipe / Real enemy / Loud,
proud and punk / Get out of my house /
Outlaw / Saturday's heroes / Front line /
Spanish jails / Freedom / Coventry / No
emotions / Do a runner / Welcome to the
real world / Fear in your heart / Never say
never / Look at him now / Drinking and
driving
CD _____ DOJOCD 124
Dojo / Apr '93 / BMG.

COMPLETE SINGLES COLLECTION
Harry May / National insurance blacklist /
Step into Christmas / Dayo / Disco girls /
Smash the discos / Loud, proud and punk
/ H-bomb / Last train to Clapham Junction
/ Law and order / Do they owe us a living /
Tell us the truth / Foreign girl / Out law / Drinking
and driving / Hurry up Harry / H-bomb (live)
/ Do a runner / Coventry / Welcome to the
real world / No emotions / Anywhere but
here / All out / (You're) Going down in
history

CD _____ CDPUNK 57
Anagram / Jun '95 / Pinnacle.

KEEP THE FAITH
CD _____ CM 77083-2
Century Media / Oct '94 / Plastic Head.

SINGALONG A BUSINESS (The Best of
the Business)
Suburban rebels / Blind justice / Loud,
proud and punk / Real enemy / Spanish jails
/ Product / National insurance blacklist (employers blacklist) / Get out of my house /
Saturday's heroes / Out in the cold / Smash
the discos / Harry May / Drinking and driving / Hurry up Harry
CD _____ AHOY 19
Captain Oi / Nov '94 / Plastic Head.

SUBURBAN REBELS
CD _____ LOMACD 32
Loma / Aug '94 / BMG.

WELCOME TO THE REAL WORLD
CD _____ AHOYCD 2
Captain Oi / May '93 / Plastic Head.

Buskirk, Paul

NACOGDOCHES WALTZ
CD _____ JR 17012
Justice / Apr '94 / Koch.

Busters

94 ER HITS
CD _____ WL 2478CD
Weser / Jul '95 / Plastic Head.

CHEAP THRILLS LIVE
CD _____ WL 2461CD
Weser / Jul '95 / Plastic Head.

COUCH POTATOES
CD _____ WL 2449CD
Weser / Jul '95 / Plastic Head.

DEAD OR ALIVE
CD _____ WL 2457CD
Weser / Jul '95 / Plastic Head.

LIVE IN MONTREUX
CD _____ WL 24902CD
Weser / Nov '95 / Plastic Head.

RUDER THAN RUDE
CD _____ WL 2453CD
Weser / Jul '95 / Plastic Head.

RUDER THAN YOU
CD _____ PHZCD 27
Unicorn / Sep '93 / Plastic Head.

SEXY MONEY
CD _____ WL 2477CD
Weser / Jul '95 / Plastic Head.

Butera, Sam

BY REQUEST (Butera, Sam & The
Wildest)
When you're smiling / Just a gigolo/I ain't
got nobody / For once in my life / Up a lazy
river / Ol' man mose / Night train / Lover is
a 5 letter word / Alexander's ragtime band
/ Margie / Come to the cabaret / Mari-
yootch / St. Louis blues / Your rascall you
/ French poodle / My first, my last / Closer
to the bone / Greenback dollar bill
CD _____ JASCD 314
Jasmine / Aug '95 / Wellard / Swift / Conifer
/ Cadillac / Magnum Music Group.

HOT NIGHTS IN NEW ORLEANS
Shine the buckle / Chicken scratch / Sam's
clan / Easy rocking / Wailin' walk / Screw
driver / Things I love / Do you care / I don't
want to set the world on fire / Tout / Long
ago / Giddyap baby / Sweep up / Sam's
reverie / Who's got the key / Ooh / Linda /
Tout, The (version) / Ooh (version)
CD _____ BCD 15449
Bear Family / Apr '89 / Rollercoaster / Direct
/ CM / Swift / ADA.

SHEER ENERGY (Butera, Sam & The
Wildest)
Let the good times roll / For you / I can't
get started (with you) / Jump, jive and wail
/ Glow worm / Closer to the bone / Hard
hearted Hannah / Body and soul / Night
train / Rosetta / You ain't to ordinary
woman / Pennies from heaven / Kansas
City / Why not / Ol' man river
CD _____ JASCD 313
Jasmine / Jul '95 / Wellard / Swift / Conifer
/ Cadillac / Magnum Music Group.

TRIBUTE TO LOUIS PRIMA
Josephine / Please no lean on the bell /
That old black magic / Please no squeeza
da banana / Medley: Robin Hood / Buona
sera / White cliffs of Dover / I got you under
my skin / Angelina / Oh Marie / Felicia / No
capicia / Medley / Tiger rag / Just the way
you are / Romance without finance / Exodus / Che-la-luna
CD _____ JASCD 319
Jasmine / Mar '95 / Wellard / Swift / Conifer
/ Cadillac / Magnum Music Group.

TRIBUTE TO LOUIS PRIMA #2
CD _____ JASCD 320
Jasmine / Apr '95 / Wellard / Swift /
Conifer / Cadillac / Magnum Music Group.

Buthelezi, Mzikayifani

FASHION MASWEDI
Amadyisi / Usizi / Umkhwewami / Mkami / Isighaza / Uze ungikholise / Inkunzi emmyama / Come back / Inyanga / Kuyesinda / Bangifuna ngandlela / Kungeneni laye khaya
CD _____ GRELCD 2007
Greensleeves / Feb '89 / Total/BMG / Jetstar / SRD.

Butler, Carl

CRYING MY HEART OUT OVER YOU
(Butler, Carl & Pearl)
Crying my heart out over you / Fools like me / Garden of shame / Dog eat dog / If teardrops were pennies / Holding on with open arms / Take me back to Jackson / Don't let me cross over / Blue eyes and waltzes / My joy / Precious memories / I hope we walk the last mile together
CD _____ BCD 15739
Bear Family / Jul '93 / Rollercoaster / Direct / CM / Swift / ADA.

Butler, George

KEEP ON DOING WHAT YOU'RE DOING
(Butler, George 'Wild Child')
CD _____ BMCD 9015
Black Magic / Nov '93 / Hot Shot / Swift / CM / Direct / Cadillac / ADA.

STRANGER
CD _____ BB 9539CD
Bullseye Blues / Aug '94 / Direct.

Butler, Henry

ORLEANS EXPERIMENT
CD _____ WD 0122
Windham Hill Jazz / Mar '92 / New Note.

Butler, Jerry

ICE MAN
CD _____ CDRB 30
Charly / Nov '95 / Charly / THE / Cadillac.

TIME & FAITH
CD _____ ICH 1151CD
Ichiban / Feb '94 / Koch.

WHATEVER YOU WANT
Rainbow Valley / Lonely soldier / Thanks to you / When trouble calls / Aware of love / Isle of sirens / It's too late / Moon River / Woman with soul / Let it be whatever it is / I almost lost my mind / Good times / Give it up / Believe in me / Just for you / For your precious love
CD _____ CDSGP 083
Prestige / Sep '93 / Total/BMG.

Butler, Jonathan

BEST OF JONATHAN BUTLER, THE
CD _____ CHIP 133
Jive / Mar '93 / BMG.

Butler, Margie

CELTIC LULLABY
CD _____ EUCD 1191
ARC / Apr '92 / ARC Music / ADA.

MAGIC OF THE CELTIC HARP, THE
CD _____ EUCD 1316
ARC / Jul '95 / ARC Music / ADA.

Butler Twins

NOT GONNA WORRY ABOUT TOMORROW
Finally found me a girl / My Baby's coming home / Not gonna worry about tomorrow / I know you don't love me baby / 1-900 / You don't need me / Going down a long country road / Crackhouse baby / That old devil (crossroads) / Bring it on back to me / Travellin' down south
CD _____ JSPCD 257
JSP / Apr '95 / ADA / Target/BMG / Direct / Cadillac / Complete/Pinnacle.

Butt, Clara

HEART OF THE EMPIRE
Enchantress / O lovely night / Abide with me / Land of Hope and Glory / Softly and gently / Sweetest flower / Kashmiri song / O rest the Lord / Lost chord / Annie Laurie / Rosary / Home sweet home / Barbara Allen / Trees / Shenandoah / Minstrel boy / Swanee river / Love's old sweet song / Handel's Largo / Keys of Heaven / Softly awakes my heart / Rule Britannia
CD _____ PASTCD 7012
Flapper / Aug '93 / Pinnacle.

Butterbeans

ELEVATOR PAPA, SWITCHBOARD MAN
(Butterbeans & Susie)
You're a no count triflin' man / Watch your step / Get away from my window / Radio papa / What it takes to bring you back / Better stop knockin' me around / Papa ain't no Santa Claus
CD _____ JSPCD 329
JSP / Oct '91 / ADA / Target/BMG / Direct / Cadillac / Complete/Pinnacle.

Butterfield, Paul

BETTER DAYS
CD _____ 812270877-2
WEA / Mar '93 / Warner Music.

IT ALL COMES BACK
CD _____ 812270878-2
WEA / Mar '93 / Warner Music.

NORTH SOUTH
CD _____ 812270880-2
WEA / Mar '93 / Warner Music.

PAUL BUTTERFIELD BLUES BAND
(Butterfield Blues Band)
Born in Chicago / Shake your moneymaker / Blues with a feeling / Thank you Mr. Poobah / Last of my mojo working / Mellow down easy / Screamin' / Our love is drifting / Mystery train / Last night / Look over yonder's wall
CD _____ 7559 60647-2
Pickwick/Warner / Nov '94 / Pinnacle / Warner Music / Carlton Home Entertainment.

Butterfly Child

HONEYMOON SUITE, THE
Mother have mercy / Passion is the only fruit / Ghost on your shoulder / Flaming burlesque / Unwashed, uncool / Carolina and the be bop review / Deep south / Louis as Anna / Six urchins / Botany bay / Towns come tumblin' / I shall hear in heaven
CD _____ DEDCD 019
Dedicated / Jan '96 / Vital.

ONOMATOPOEIA
CD _____ R 3082
Rough Trade / Aug '93 / Pinnacle.

Butthole Surfers

HAIRWAY TO STEVEN
CD _____ BFFP 29CD
Blast First / Feb '88 / Disc.

HOLE TRUTH AND NOTHING BUTT, THE
CD _____ TR 35CD
Trance / Mar '95 / SRD.

INDEPENDENT WORM SALOON
Who was in my room last night / Wooden song / Tongue / Chewin' George Lucas' chocolate / Goofy's concern / Alcohol / Dog inside your body / Strawberry / Some dispute over T-shirt sales / Dancing fool / You don't know me / Annoying song / Dust devil / Leave me alone / Edgar / Ballad of naked men / Clean it up
CD _____ CDEST 2192
Capitol / Mar '93 / EMI.

LOCUST ABORTION TECHNICIAN
Sweat loaf / Graveyard (1) / Graveyard (2) / Pittsburgh to Lebanon / Weber / Hay / Human cannonball / U.S.S.A. / O-men / Kuntz / Twenty two going on twenty three
CD _____ BFFP 15CD
Blast First / Jun '87 / Disc.

PIOUHGD
CD _____ DAN 069CD
Danceteria / Dec '94 / Plastic Head / ADA.

Buttons & Bows

FIRST MONTH OF SUMMER, THE
John D McGurk's / I les de la Madeleine / First month of summer / Fitmaurice's polka / Sir Sidney Smith / Man from Bundoran / Humours of Kinvara / Green garters / Inisheer / Gypsy hornpipe / Margaret's waltz / Four courts / Joyous waltz / Piper's despair
CD _____ GLCD 1079
Green Linnet / Feb '92 / Roots / CM / Direct / ADA.

GRACE NOTES
CD _____ CEFCD 151
Gael Linn / Jan '94 / Roots / CM / Direct / ADA.

Buzzcocks

ANOTHER MUSIC IN A DIFFERENT KITCHEN
Fast cars / No reply / You tear me up / Get on our own / Love battery / Sixteen / I don't mind / Fiction romance / Autonomy / I need / Moving away from the pulsebeat
CD _____ CDFA 3199
Fame / May '88 / EMI.

ANOTHER MUSIC IN A DIFFERENT KITCHEN/LOVE BITES
Fast cars / No reply / You tear me up / Get on our own / Love battery / Sixteen / I don't mind / Fiction romance / Autonomy / I need / Moving away from the pulsebeat / Real world / Ever fallen in love / Operator's manual / Nostalgia / Just lust / Sixteen again / Walking distance / Love is lies / Nothing left / E.S.P. / Late for the train
CD _____ CDPRDT 12
EMI / Apr '94 / EMI.

DIFFERENT KIND OF TENSION, A
Paradise / Sitting 'round at home / You say you don't love me / You know you can't help it / Mad mad Judy / Raison d'etre / I don't know what to do with my life / Money / Hollow inside / Different kind of tension / I believe / Radio nine

---

CD _____ CZ 93
EMI / Jun '88 / EMI.

FRENCH
CD _____ DOJOCD 237
Dojo / Sep '95 / BMG.

LEST WE FORGET
CD _____ RE 158CD
Reach Out International / Nov '94 / Jetstar.

LIVE AT THE ROXY 2ND APRIL 1977
Orgasm addict / Get on your own / What do I get / Sixteen / Oh shit / No reply / Fast cars / Friends of mine / Time's up / Boredom
CD _____ RRCD 131
Receiver / Jul '93 / Grapevine.

LOVE BITES
Real world / Ever fallen in love / Operator's manual / Nostalgia / Just lust / Sixteen again / Walking distance / Love is lies / Nothing left / E.S.P. / Late for the train
CD _____ CDFA 3174
Fame / May '88 / EMI.

OPERATORS MANUAL (Buzzcocks Best)
Orgasm addict / What do I get / I don't mind / Autonomy / Fast cars / Get on our own / Sixteen / Fiction romance / Love you more / Noise annoys / Ever fallen in love / Operators manual / Nostalgia / Walking distance / Nothing left / ESP / Promises / Lipstick / Everybody's happy nowadays / Harmony in my head / You say you don't love me / I don't know what to do with my life / I believe / Are everything / Radio nine
CD _____ CDEM 1421
EMI / Oct '91 / EMI.

PEEL SESSIONS: BUZZCOCKS (2)
Fast cars / Pulse beat / What do I get / Noise annoys / Walking distance / Last for the train / Promises / Lipstick / Everybody's happy nowadays / Sixteen again / I don't know what to do with my life / Mad mad Judy / Hollow inside / E.S.P.
CD _____ SFRCD 104
Strange Fruit / May '94 / Pinnacle.

PRODUCT (3CD Set)
Fast cars / No reply / You tear me up / Get on your own / Love battery / Sixteen / I don't mind / Fiction romance / Autonomy / I need / Moving away from the pulsebeat / Real world / Ever fallen in love / Operator's manual / Nostalgia / Just lust / Walking distance / Love is lies / Nothing left / E.S.P. / Late for the train / Paradise / Sitting 'round at home / You say you don't love me / You know you can't help it / Mad mad Judy / Raison D'etre / I don't know what to do with my life / Money / Hollow inside / Different kind of tension / I believe / Radio nine / Orgasm addict / Love you more / Promises / Everybody's happy nowadays / Harmony in my head / Whatever happened to / Oh shit / Noise annoys / Lipstick / Why can't I touch it / Something's gone wrong again / Breakdown / What do I get / Times up / Are everything / Strange thing / What do you know / Why she's a girl from the chainstore / Airwaves dream / Running free / I look alone
CD Set _____ PRODUCT 1
EMI / May '95 / EMI.

SINGLES GOING STEADY
Orgasm addict / What do I get / I don't mind / Love you more / Ever fallen in love / Promises / Everybody's happy nowadays / Harmony in my head / Whatever happened to / Oh shit / Autonomy / Noise annoys / Just lust / Lipstick / Why can't I touch it / Something's gone wrong again
CD _____ CDFA 3241
Fame / Oct '90 / EMI.

TRADE TEST TRANSMISSION
CD _____ ESSCD 195
Castle / May '93 / BMG.

By All Means

BY ALL MEANS
I surrender to your love / I'm the one who loves you / You decided to go / I believe in you / I want to thank you / Let's get started now / Slow jam (can I have this dance with you) / Somebody save me / Does it feel good to you / We're into this groove
CD _____ BRCD 520
4th & Broadway / May '88 / PolyGram.

IT'S REAL
CD _____ 530077-2
Motown / Feb '93 / PolyGram.

Byard, Jaki

BLUES FOR SMOKE
CD _____ CCD 9018
Candid / May '89 / Cadillac / Jazz Music / Wellard / Koch.

EMPIRICAL
CD _____ MCD 6010
Muse / Sep '92 / New Note / CM.

PHANTASIES (Byard, Jaki & The Apollo Stompers)
CD _____ SNCD 1075
Soul Note / Dec '86 / Harmonia Mundi / Wellard / Cadillac.

PHANTASIES II (Byard, Jaki & The Apollo Stompers)
CD _____ 121175-2
Soul Note / Jun '91 / Harmonia Mundi / Wellard / Cadillac.

Byas, Don

ALL THE THINGS YOU ARE
CD _____ JHR 73541
Jazz Hour / Sep '93 / Target/BMG / Jazz Music / Cadillac.

DON BYAS ON BLUE STAR
Please don't talk about me when I'm gone / Mad monk / Billie's bounce / I surrender dear / Red cross / Cynamo A / Summertime / Stardust / Ol' man river / Night and day / Man I love / Georgia on my mind / Easy to love / Over the rainbow / Where or when / En la casa / Somebody loves me / Riviera blues (blues a la Don) / Laura / Smoke gets in your eyes / Old folks at home / Don't blame me / I cover the waterfront
CD _____ 8334052
ECM / Mar '88 / New Note.

LIVING MY LIFE
CD _____ VGCD 650122
Vogue / Jan '93 / BMG.

LOVER MAN
If I had you / Lover man / I can't give you anything but love / Remember my forgotten man / GDB / Time on my hands / Blues for Don Carlos / Sweet Lorraine / April in Paris / Don't blame me / Unknown original / No one but you / Darling je vous aime beaucoup / Le musicien / Lover come back to me / I can't get started (with you) / Athena / Sincerely / Minor encamp / Cerisier rose et pommier blanc / Hold my hand / Un jour tu verras / Just one of those things / Anatole
CD _____ 74321154702
Vogue / Oct '93 / BMG.

NIGHT IN TUNISIA, A
CD _____ BLCD 760136
Black Lion / Oct '90 / Jazz Music / Cadillac / Wellard / Koch.

SAVOY JAM PACK
Riffin' and jivin' / Free and easy / Worried and blue / Don's idea / Savoy jam party / 1944 stomp / What do you want with my heart / Sweet and lovely / White rose kick / My deep blue dream / Byas'd opinion / Candy / How high the moon / Donby / Byas a drink / I don't know why / Old folks / Cherokee / September in the rain / Living my life / To each his own / They say it's wonderful / Cynthia's in love / September song / St. Louis blues
CD _____ SV 0268
Savoy Jazz / Sep '95 / Conifer / ADA.

WALKIN'
CD _____ BLCD 760167
Black Lion / Oct '93 / Jazz Music / Cadillac / Wellard / Koch.

Bygraves, Max

CHEERS
CD _____ CDSIV 1143
Horatio Nelson / Jul '95 / THE / BMG / Avid/BMG / Koch.

COLLECTION: MAX BYGRAVES
Wish me luck as you wave me goodbye / We'll all go riding on / Rainbow / Sunny side up / When the guards on parade / Good morning / Jingle jangle / I've got sixpence / Bless 'em all / Mairzy doats and dozy doats / Far away places / You don't have to tell me / Let bygones be bygones / Boogie woogie bugle boy / You always hurt the one you love / Tangerine / That old black magic / There, I've said it again / That lovely weekend / I don't know why
CD _____ CCSCD 232
Castle / Nov '89 / BMG.

EMI YEARS: MAX BYGRAVES
You're a pink toothbrush / Friends and neighbours / Little Sir Echo / Gang that sang heart of my heart / Mr. Sandman / Big head / Ballad of Davy Crockett / Good idea son / Chip chopper Charlie / I wish I could sing like Jolson / Cowpuncher's cantata / Out of town / Nothin' to do / Dummy song / Gilly gilly ossenfeffer Katzenellenbogen by the sea / Meet me on the corner / Little I a-plander / Pendulum song / Seventeen tons / True loves and false lovers
CD _____ CDEMS 1396
EMI / Apr '91 / EMI.

EVENING WITH MAX, AN
CD _____ DSHCD 7002
D-Sharp / Dec '92 / Pinnacle.

GOLDEN MEDLEYS
I don't know why I love you (I just do) / You made me love you / Me and my shadow / Moonlight and roses / You were meant for me / You are my sunshine / Let the rest of the world go by / Let me call you sweetheart / Girl of my dreams / Where the blue of the night meets the gold of the day / Everybody loves somebody / Just one more chance / What a wonderful world / Nightingale sang in Berkeley Square / I left my heart in San Francisco / One of those songs / Baby face / Toot toot tootsie goodbye / Swanee / Happy days are here again / Powder your face with sunshine / I'm looking

over a four leaf clover / When you're smiling / Put your arms around me honey / Wyoming Lullaby / What'll I do / When your hair has turned to silver / Till we meet again / It had to be you / I'll get by / I'll string along with you / I'll be seeing you / You'd be so nice to come home to / I love you because / True love / Charmaine / I'll be your sweetheart / When I grow too old to dream / Who's taking you home tonight / Good night sweetheart / Au revoir / Auf wiedersehen sweetheart / Arrivederci Roma / Goodbye blues
CD _____ 5507602
Spectrum/Karussell / Mar '95 / PolyGram / THE.

MAX BYGRAVES
Cowpuncher's cantana / Cry of the wild goose / Riders in the sky / Mule train / Jezebel / True love and false lovers / Little Sir Echo / Big head (Big 'ead) / You're a pink toothbrush / I wish I could sing like Jolson / (The gang that sang) heart of my heart / Out of town / Ballad of Davy Crockett / Try another cherry tree / By the light of the silvery moon / Peggy O'Neil / When you wore a tulip / If you were the only girl in the world / For me and my girl / Friends and neighbours / Gilly gilly ossenfeffer katzenellenbogen by the sea / Mr. Sandman / Pendulum song / Gretna Green / Meet me on the corner / Little Laplander / Good idea son / Seventeen sons / Tomorrow / Say si si / She's a lassie from Lancashire / When Irish eyes are smiling / I Belong to Glasgow / Any old iron
CD _____ CC 271
Music For Pleasure / Aug '91 / EMI.

SINGA LONGA CHRISTMAS
CD _____ TOTCD 5
Telegram / Dec '95 / Pinnacle.

SINGALONG WITH MAX
CD _____ MATCD 289
Castle / Mar '94 / BMG.

SINGALONG WITH MAX BYGRAVES
CD _____ PWK 042
Carlton Home Entertainment / '88 / Carlton Home Entertainment.

SINGALONG YEARS, THE
Don't bring Lulu / Ma, he's making eyes at me / Yes sir that's my baby / I wonder where my baby is tonight / Who's sorry now / Amy, wonderful Amy / Underneath the arches / Home town / South of the border / Is it true what they say about Dixie / Baby face / California here I come / I've got a lovely bunch of coconuts / You're a pink toothbrush / Who wants to be a millionaire / Beatles medley / What a wonderful world / Tie a yellow ribbon round the ole oak tree / Dance in the old-fashioned way / Neighbours / It's bad / Repeats
CD _____ 74321183232
Ariola Express / Feb '94 / BMG.

SINGALONGAWARYEARS
CD _____ MCCD 102
MCI / May '93 / Disc / THE.

SINGALONGAWARYEARS VOL. 2
This is the army Mr. Jones / Fleet's in port again / Army, Navy and Airforce / Roll out the barrel / I'm gonna get lit up (when the lights go on in London) / Chattanooga choo choo / Jeepers creepers / I've got a gal in Kalamazoo / Three little fishes / You'd be so nice to come home to / If I should fall in love again / You don't have to tell me / One day when we were young / I remember you / Don't sit under the apple tree / Yes my darling daughter / Woodpecker song / Put your arms around me honey / That lovely weekend / It's been a long, long time / You must have been a beautiful baby / Blueberry hill / Sentimental journey / Pennies from heaven / Hokey cokey / Horsey horsey / Under the spreading chestnut tree / Lambeth walk / White Christmas
CD _____ MCCD 159
Music Club / May '94 / Disc / THE / CM.

SONGS LIKE THEY USED T'BE
Fing's ain't what they used to be / You need hands / Who made the morning / When you come to the end of a lollipop (Live) / Little train / Every streets a coronation street / (In) a shanty in old Shanty Town / Lazybones / Bells of Avignon / Ain't that a grand and glorious feeling / Over the rainbow / I'd do anything / They're changing guards at Buckingham Palace / You're a pink toothbrush / O main Papa (Oh my Papa) / Little white lies / Gotta have rain
CD _____ 5500952
Spectrum/Karussell / Oct '93 / PolyGram / THE.

TIE A YELLOW RIBBON
CD _____ MATCD 226
Castle / Dec '92 / BMG.

BYLES
CD _____ CDHB 45
Heartbeat / Oct '95 / Greensleeves / Jetstar / Direct / ADA.

AQUARELLE
Concerto grosso / Canta mais / In a mist / 'S wonderful / Man I love / I got rhythm /

Quintet (Mozart K 581) / Los Angeles aquarelle suite / In the dark / Modinha / Candlelights
CD _____ CCD 42016
Concord Concerto / Apr '94 / Pinnacle.

BLUEBYRD
It don't mean a thing if it ain't got that swing / Vou vivendo / Nice work if you can get it / Jitterbug waltz / Soft light and sweet music / Ain't got nothing but the blues / This can't be love / Carinhoso / Mama I'll be home someday / Isn't it a lovely day / Saturday night fish fry
CD _____ CCD 4082
Concord Jazz / Oct '91 / New Note.

BOSSA NOVA - GUITAR JUBILEE (Byrd, Charlie & Joao Gilberto)
CD _____ CD 62006
Jasmine / Oct '93 / Wellard / Swift / Conifer / Cadillac / Magnum Music Group.

BOSSA NOVA YEARS, THE (Byrd, Charlie Trio)
Meditation / One note samba / Corcovado / Triste / Dindi / O pato / Girl from Ipanema / Samba d'Orpheus / How insensitive / Wave / P'ra dizer adeus / O nosso amor
CD _____ CCD 4468
Concord Jazz / Jul '91 / New Note.

BRAZILVILLE (Byrd, Charlie & Bud Shank)
Zingaro / Brazilville / Saquarema / Speak low / Yesterdays / Charlotte's fancy / What are you doing the rest of your life
CD _____ CCD 4173
Concord Picante / Jul '88 / New Note.

CHARLIE BYRD CHRISTMAS ALBUM
O come all ye faithful (Adeste Fidelis) / Deck the halls with boughs of holly / Mistletoe and holly / Lullay lullay (thou tiny little child) / What child is this / Hark the herald angels sing / Christmas song / Silent night / Good King Wenceslas / First Noel / In the bleak midwinter / God rest ye merry gentlemen / Oh Christmas tree (O Tannenbaum) / White Christmas / Angels we have heard on high / Holly and the ivy / Have yourself a merry little Christmas
CD _____ CCD 42004
Concord Jazz / Nov '90 / New Note.

DU HOT CLUB DE CONCORD
Swing '59 / Golden earrings / Lamentos / Carinhoso / Till the clouds roll by / Jubilee / Frenesi / At the seaside (na praia) / Gypsy boots (sapatos novos) / Old New Orleans Blues / Cottontail / Perfidia / Moon river / Besame mucho / They didn't believe me
CD _____ CCD 4674
Concord Jazz / Nov '95 / New Note.

GREAT GUITARS II (Byrd, Charlie & Barney Kessel)
Lover / Makin' whoopee / Body and soul / Outer drive / On green dolphin street / Nuages: Going out of my head
CD _____ CCD 4023
Concord Jazz / Mar '95 / New Note.

HITS
CD _____ 15298
Laserlight / May '94 / Target/BMG.

I'VE GOT THE WORLD ON A STRING
I'm gonna sit right down and write myself a letter / Blue skies / How deep is the ocean / Gee baby ain't I good to you / I've got the world on a string / Goody goody / They can't take that away from me / Avalon / Just you, just me / One to nothing / Don't get around much anymore / Satin doll / Travallin' as / Someone to light up my life / So dance samba / Imagination / Straight no chaser
CD _____ CDSJP 427
Timeless Jazz / May '95 / New Note.

ISN'T IT ROMANTIC (Byrd, Charlie Trio)
Isn't it romantic / I could write a book / Cheek to cheek / Very thought of you / Thou swell / One morning in May / I didn't know what time it was / There's a small hotel / Someone to watch over me / Thought about me / Last night when we were young
CD _____ CCD 4252
Concord Jazz / Aug '92 / New Note.

IT'S A WONDERFUL WORLD (Featuring Scott Hamilton) (Byrd, Charlie Trio)
CD _____ CCD 4374
Concord Jazz / May '89 / New Note.

JAZZ 'N' SAMBA
CD _____ HCD 606
Hindsight / Aug '95 / Target/BMG / Jazz Music.

JAZZ RECITAL
Prelude / My funny valentine / Little girl blue / My heart stood still / Blue interlude / Spring is here / Foggy day / Spanish guitar blues / Chuck a tuck / Homage to Charlie Christian
CD _____ SV 0192
Savoy Jazz / Nov '92 / Conifer / ADA.

MIDNIGHT GUITAR
Blues from night people / First show / 2 a.m. / Four o'clock funk / Blues my naughty sweetie gives to me / Blue prelude / This can't be love / Jive at five
CD _____ SV 0247
Savoy Jazz / Oct '94 / Conifer / ADA.

MOMENTS LIKE THIS
Little girls at play / Si tu vois ma mere / My ideal / Rose of the Rio Grande / Too late now / Rosetta / Russian lullaby / As long as I live / Wang wang blues / Prelude to a kiss / Soon / Polka dots and moonbeams / Moments like this / Don't explain
CD _____ CD 4627
Concord Jazz / Jan '95 / New Note.

SUGARLOAF SUITE
CD _____ CCD 4114
Concord Jazz / Jul '88 / New Note.

TAMBU (Byrd, Charlie & Cal Tjader)
CD _____ FCD 6169453
Fantasy / Jun '87 / Pinnacle / Jazz Music / Wellard / Cadillac.

125TH STREET NYC
Pretty baby / Gold the moon, white the sun / Giving it up / Marilyn / People suppose to be free / Veronica / Morning / I love you
CD _____ 1046710192
Discovery / May '95 / Warner Music.

BEST OF DONALD BYRD
Change (makes you want to hustle) / You and music / Black Byrd / Think twice / Onward 'til morning / Lanasana's priestess / Street lady / Flight time / Places and spaces / Wind parade / Dominoes (Live) / Steppin' into tomorrow / Just my imagination / Love's so far away / Dominoes (Live)
CD _____ BNZ 285
Blue Note / Feb '92 / EMI.

BLACKBYRD
Flight time / Black Byrd / Love's so far away / Mr. Thomas / Sky high / Slop jar blues / Where are we going
CD _____ BNZ 294
Blue Note / Aug '92 / EMI.

BYRD'S WORD
Winterset / Gotcha goin' n' comin' / Long green / Stareyes / Someone to watch over me
CD _____ SV 0132
Savoy Jazz / '92 / Conifer / ADA.

CITY CALLED HEAVEN, A
King Arthur / I'll always remember / City called heaven / Back down in Lu Easy Anna / Byrd song / Del Valle / Remember me / Not necessarily the blues
CD _____ LCD 15302
Landmark / Aug '93 / New Note.

EARLY BYRD - THE BEST OF THE JAZZ SOUL YEARS
Slow drag / West of Pecos / Books Bossa / Jelly roll / Mustang / Blackjack / Weasil / Dude / Emperor / Little rasti (On LP only)
CD _____ BNZ 316
Blue Note / Jun '93 / EMI.

FIRST FLIGHT
CD _____ DELMARK 407
Delmark / Feb '87 / Hot Shot / ADA / CM / Direct / Cadillac.

GETTING DOWN TO BUSINESS (Byrd, Donald Sextet)
Theme for Malcolm / That's all there is to love / Pomponio / I got it bad and that ain't good (Available on CD only) / Certain attitude / Loneliest / Around the corner
CD _____ LCD 15232
Landmark / Mar '90 / New Note.

GROOVIN' FOR NAT
Hush / Child's play / Angel eyes / Smoothie / Suede / Friday's child / Out of this world / Groovin' for Nat
CD _____ BLCD 760134
Black Lion / '88 / Jazz Music / Cadillac / Wellard / Koch.

HARLEM BLUES
Harlem blues / Fly, little Byrd / Voyage a deux / Blue monk / Alter ego / Sir Master Kool Guy
CD _____ LCD 15162
Landmark / Jul '88 / New Note.

KOFI
Kofi / Fufu / Perpetual love / Elmina / Loud minority
CD _____ CDP 8318752
Blue Note / Apr '95 / EMI.

NEW PERSPECTIVE , A
Elijah / Beast of burden / Cristo redentor / Black discipline / Chant
CD _____ BNZ 157
Blue Note / Oct '90 / EMI.

COMPLETE RECORDINGS (1929-1931) (Byrd, John & Walter Taylor)
CD _____ SOB 035172
Story Of The Blues / Dec '92 / Koch / ADA.

LOVE LESSONS
Walking to Jerusalem / Love lessons / 4 to 1 in Atlanta / Heaven in my woman's eyes / Honky-tonk dancing machine / You lied to me / Down on the bottom / Don't need that heartache / Have a good one / Walkin' in
CD _____ MCAD 11242
MCA / Nov '95 / BMG.

20 ESSENTIAL TRACKS FROM THE BOXED SET
Mr. Tambourine Man / I'll feel a whole lot better / All I really want to do / Turn turn turn / 5-D / Eight miles high / Mr. Spaceman / So you want to be a rock 'n' roll star / Have you seen her face / Lady friend / My back pages / Goin' back / Ballad of Easy Rider / Jesus is just alright / Chestnut mare / I wanna grow up to be a politician / He was a friend of mine / Paths of victory / From a distance / Love that never dies
CD _____ 4716652
Columbia / Jul '91 / Sony.

5D/NOTORIOUS BYRD BROTHERS/ SWEETHEART OF THE RODEO (3CD Set)
5-D (Fifth dimension) / Wild mountain thyme / Mr. Spaceman / I see you / What's happening / I come and stand at every door / Eight miles high / Hey Joe (where you gonna go) / Captain soul / John Riley / 2-4-2 Foxtrot (the lear jet song) / Artificial energy / Goin' back / Natural harmony / Draft morning wasn't / Born to follow / Get to you / Change is now / Old John Robertson / Tribal gathering / Dolphin's smile / Space odyssey / You ain't goin' nowhere / I am a pilgrim / Christian life / You don't miss your water / You're still on my mind / Pretty boy Floyd / Hickory wind / Hundred years from now / Blue Canadian rockies / Life in prison / Nothing was delivered
CD Set _____ 477520 2
Columbia / Oct '94 / Sony.

BYRDMANIAX
CD _____ CLCD 900930
Line / Sep '94 / CM / Grapevine / ADA / Conifer / Direct.

BYRDS PLAY DYLAN, THE
Mr. Tambourine man / All I really want to do / Chimes of freedom / Spanish Harlem incident / Time they are a changin' / Lay down your weary tune / My back pages / You ain't goin' nowhere / Nothing was delivered / This wheel's on fire / It's all over now baby blue / Baby blue / Lay lady lay / Positively 4th street
CD _____ 983399-2
Pickwick/Sony Collector's Choice / Apr '94 / Carlton Home Entertainment / Pinnacle / Sony.

BYRDS, THE
Full circle / Sweet Mary / Changing heart / For free / Born to rock 'n' roll / Things will be better / Cowgirl in the sand / Long live the King / Borrowing time / Laughing / See the sky about to rain
CD _____ 7559609552
WEA / Jan '93 / Warner Music.

DR BYRDS & MR HYDE
This wheel's on fire / Old blue / Your gentle way of loving me / Child of the universe / Nashville West / Drug store truck drivin' man / King Apathy III / Candy / Bad night at the whiskey / Medley: My back pages / B.J. blues / Baby, what you want me to do
CD _____ BGOCD 107
Beat Goes On / Aug '91 / Pinnacle.

FIFTH DIMENSION
5-D (fifth dimension) / Wild mountain thyme / Mr. Spaceman / I see you / What's happening / I come and stand at every door / Eight miles high / Hey Joe (where you gonna go) / Captain soul / John Riley / 2-4-2 foxtrot (the lear jet song)
CD _____ BGOCD 106
Beat Goes On / Aug '91 / Pinnacle.

GREATEST HITS: BYRDS
Mr. Tambourine man / I'll feel a whole lot better / Bells of Rhymney / Turn turn turn / All I really want to do / Chimes of freedom / Eight miles high / Mr. Spaceman / 5-D (fifth dimension) / So you want to be a rock 'n' roll star / My back pages
CD _____ 4678432
Columbia / Feb '91 / Sony.

MR. TAMBOURINE MAN/TURN TURN TURN/YOUNGER THAN YESTERDAY (3CD Set)
CD Set _____ 4683382
Columbia / '92 / Sony.

SWEETHEART OF THE RODEO
You ain't goin' nowhere / I am a pilgrim / Christian life / You don't miss your water / You're still on my mind / Pretty boy Floyd / Hickory wind / Hundred years from now / Blue Canadian Rockies / Life in prison / Nothing was delivered
CD _____ 4681782
Columbia / Aug '93 / Sony.

TIME BETWEEN (A Tribute To The Byrds) (Various Artists)
CD _____ ILLCD 004
Imaginary / Jun '89 / Vital.

ULTIMATE BYRDS, THE (4CD/MC Set)
Mr. Tambourine man / I'll feel a whole lot better / Chimes of freedom / She has a way / All I really want to do / Spanish harlem incident / Bells of Rhymney / It's all over now baby blue / She don't care about time / Turn, turn, turn / It won't be wrong / Lay down your weary tune / He was a friend of mind / World turns all around her / Day walk (never before) / Times are a-changing / 5-

D (Fifth dimension) / I know my rider / Eight miles high / Why / Psychodrama City / I see you / Hey Joe (where you gonna go) / Mr. Spaceman / John Riley / Roll over Beethoven / So you want to be a rock 'n' roll star / Have you seen her face / My back pages / Time between / It happens each day / Renaissance Fair / Everybody's been burned / Girl with no name / Triad / Lady friend / Old John Robertson / Goin' back / Draft morning / Wasn't born to follow / Dolphin's smile / Reputation / You ain't goin' nowhere / Christian life / I am a pilgrim / Pretty boy Floyd / You don't miss your water / Hickory wind / Nothing was delivered / Hundred years from now / Pretty Polly / Lazy days / This wheel's on fire / Nashville West / Old blue / Drug store truck drivin' man / Bad night at the whiskey / Lay lady lay / Mae Jean goes to Hollywood / Easy rider theme / Oil in my lamp / Jesus is just alright / Way beyond the sun / Tulsa county / Deportee / Lover of the Bayou / Willin' / Black mountain rag / Positively 4th Street / Chestnut mare / Just a season / Kathleen's song / Truck stop girl / Just like a woman / Stanley's song / Glory glory / I trust / I wanna grow up to be a politician / Green apple quick step / Tiffany Queen / Bugler / Lazy waters / Farther along / White's lightning / He was a friend of mine / Paths of victory / From a distance / Love that never dies
CD Set _____ 4676112
Columbia / Dec '90 / Sony.

YOUNGER THAN YESTERDAY
So you want to be a rock 'n' roll star / Have you seen her face / C.T.A. / Renaissance fair / Time between / Everybody's been burned / Thoughts and words / Mind gardens / My back pages / Girl with no name / Why
CD _____ 467045-2
Columbia / Sep '94 / Sony.

Byrne, David

DAVID BYRNE
Long time ago / Angels / Crash / Self made man / Back in the box / Sad song / Nothing at all / My love is you / Lillies of the valley / You and eye / Strange ritual / Buck naked
CD _____ 936245558-2
Sire / May '94 / Warner Music.

FOREST, THE
Ur / Kish / Dura europus / Nineveh / Ava / Machu picchu / Teotihuacan / Asuka / Samara (Mc and Cd only) / Tula (Mc and Cd only)
CD _____ 7599265842
Sire / Jun '91 / Warner Music.

FORRO
O fole roncou / Festa do interior / Tum tum tum / Dando de bom / Querubim / O sucesso da zefinha / E de dae agua na boca / Vou com voce / Asa branca / Recordacao de vaquerio / Bom demais / Tarde nordestina / Feira de caruaru / O aniversario do seu vava / Chiclete com banana / Rejeicao / Estrela miudo / Sanforninha choradeira

CD _____ 7599263232
Sire / Jan '91 / Warner Music.

REI MOMO
Independence day / Make believe mambo / Call of the wild / Dirty old town / Rose tattoo / Dream police / Don't want to be part of your world / Marching through the wilderness / Lie to me / Women vs. men / Carnival eyes / I know sometimes a man is a wrong / Loco de amor (Not on LP) / Good and evil (Not on LP) / Office cowboy (Not on LP)
CD _____ 9259902
Sire / Feb '95 / Warner Music.

UH-OH
Now I'm your mom / Girls on my mind / Something ain't right / She's mad / Hanging upside down / Twistin' in the wind / Walk in the dark / Cowboy's mambo / Tiny town / Somebody
CD _____ 7599267992
Sire / Feb '95 / Warner Music.

Byrne, Donna

LET'S FACE THE MUSIC AND DANCE
CD _____ ST 579
Stash / Jun '94 / Jazz Music / CM / Cadillac / Direct / ADA.

Byrne, James

ROAD TO GLENLOUGH, THE
CD _____ CC 52CD
Claddagh / Nov '95 / ADA / Direct.

Byron

BYRON
CD _____ WKFMXD 173
FM Coast To Coast / Mar '92 / Revolver Music.

Byron, Don

MUSIC FOR SIX MUSICIANS
CD _____ 7559793542
Elektra Nonesuch / '95 / Warner Music.

PLAYS THE MUSIC OF MICKEY KATZ
CD _____ 7559793132
Elektra Nonesuch / May '93 / Warner Music.

TUSKEGEE EXPERIMENT
CD _____ 7559792802
Elektra Nonesuch / May '92 / Warner Music.

Bystanders

BIRTH OF MAN
That's the end / (You're gonna) hurt yourself / My love - come home / 98.6 / Royal blue summer sunshine day / Make up your mind / Green grass / Cave of clear light / Painting the time / This time / Have I offended the girl / If you walk away / Stubborn kind of fellow / Pattern people / When jezamine goes / This world is my world
CD _____ SEECD 301
See For Miles/C5 / '90 / Pinnacle.

C

C & C Music Factory

GONNA MAKE YOU SWEAT
Gonna make you sweat / Here we go / Things that make you go hmmmm / Just a touch of love (everyday) / Groove of love (what's this world called love) / Live happy / Ooh baby / Let's get funkee / Givin' it to you / Bang that beat
CD _____ 4678142
Columbia / Apr '94 / Sony.

ULTIMATE
Gonna make you sweat (everybody dance now) / Here we go let's rock and roll / Love of love / Robi-robs boriqua anthem / Deeper love / Keep it comin' / Do you wanna get funky / Take a toke / I found love
CD _____ 4811172
Columbia / Oct '95 / Sony.

C.A. Quintet

TRIP THRU HELL
CD _____ 852126
EVA / May '94 / Direct / ADA.

C.I.A.

ATTITUDE
CD _____ CDFLAG 68
Under One Flag / Jul '91 / Pinnacle.

IN THE RED
Extinction / In the red / N.A.S.A. / Flight 103 / Turn to stone / Natas / Buried alive / Mind over matter / Moby Dick (part 2) / Samantha
CD _____ CD FLAG 40
Music For Nations / May '90 / Pinnacle.

C.W.S. Band

LAND OF THE MOUNTAIN AND THE FLOOD
CD _____ HARCD 1123
Harlequin / Jul '95 / Magnum Music Group.

Caballero, Don

FOR RESPECT
CD _____ EFA 049292
City Slang / Oct '93 / Disc.

Cabaret Voltaire

1974-1976
CD _____ CABS 15CD
Mute / Mar '92 / Disc.

2 X 45
CD _____ CABS 9 CD
Mute / Oct '90 / Disc.

8 CREPUSCULE TRACKS
Sluggin for Jesus (part 1) / Sluggin for Jesus (part 2) / Fools game-sluggin for Jesus (part 3) / Yashar / Your agent man / Gut level / Invocation / Shaft
CD _____ NORMAL 59CD
Normal/Okra / Mar '94 / Direct / ADA.

CONVERSATION, THE
Exterminating angel / Brutal but clean / Message / Let's start / Night rider / I think / Heat / Harmonic parallel / Project 80 (Pts 1-4) / Exterminating angel (Outro)
CD Set _____ AMB 4934CD
Apollo / Jul '94 / Vital.

COVENANT, THE SWORD AND THE ARM OF THE LORD, THE
L 21st / I want you / Hell's home / Kick back / Arm of the Lord / Warm / Golden halos / Motion rotation / Whip blow / Web
CD _____ CVCD 3
Virgin / Sep '91 / EMI.

CRACKDOWN, THE
24-24 / In the shadows / Talking time / Animation / Over and over / Just fascination / Why kill time (when you can kill yourself) / Haiti / Crackdown / Diskono (MC only) / Double vision (MC only) / Badge of evil (MC only) / Moscow (MC only)
CD _____ CVCD 1
Virgin / Apr '86 / EMI.

DRAIN TRAIN, THE
CD _____ CABS 12 CD
Mute / '88 / Disc.

GOLDEN MOMENTS OF CABARET VOLTAIRE, THE
CD _____ RUF CD 6001
Rough Trade / Oct '87 / Pinnacle.

HAI
CD _____ CABS 11 CD
Rough Trade / Nov '82 / Pinnacle.

JOHNNY YES NO
CD _____ CABSCD 10
Mute / Oct '90 / Disc.

LISTEN UP WITH CABARET VOLTAIRE
CD _____ CABS 5 CD
Mute / Jun '90 / Disc.

LIVE AT THE LYCEUM
CD _____ CABS 13 CD
Mute / '88 / Disc.

LIVE AT THE YMCA
CD _____ CABS 4 CD
Mute / Jun '90 / Disc.

LIVING LEGENDS
CD _____ CABS 6 CD
Mute / Jun '90 / Disc.

MICROPHONIES
Do right / Operative / Digital rasta / Spies in the wires / Earthshaker (Theme) / James Brown / Slammer / Blue heat / Sensoria
CD _____ CVCD 2
Virgin / Sep '91 / EMI.

MIX UP
CD _____ CABS 8 CD
Mute / Oct '90 / Disc.

PLASTICITY
CD _____ EXCD 003
Plastex / Jul '92 / Vital.

RED MECCA
CD _____ CABS 3 CD
Mute / Jun '90 / Disc.

THREE MANTRAS
CD _____ CABS 7 CD
Mute / Jun '90 / Disc.

VOICE OF AMERICA
CD _____ CABS 2 CD
Mute / Jun '90 / Disc.

Cabazz

FAR AWAY
CD _____ DRCD 194
Dragon / Jan '89 / Roots / Cadillac / Wellard / CM / ADA.

KAOTIKA
CD _____ DRCD 241
Dragon / Oct '94 / Roots / Cadillac / Wellard / CM / ADA.

Cable Regime

ASSIMILATE AND DESTROY
CD _____ PPP 110
PDCD / Sep '93 / Plastic Head.

KILL LIES ALL
CD _____ STC 17CD
Sentrax Corporation / Aug '94 / Plastic Head.

LIFE IN THE HOUSE OF THE ENEMY
CD _____ CDPPP 108
PDCD / Nov '92 / Plastic Head.

Cables, George

BY GEORGE
Bess, you is my woman now / My man's gone now / I got rhythm / Embraceable you / Someone to watch over me / Foggy day / Summertime
CD _____ CCD 14030
Contemporary / Apr '91 / Jazz Music / Cadillac / Pinnacle / Wellard.

INTRODUCING JEFF JEROLAMON
CD _____ CCD 79522
Candid / Nov '92 / Cadillac / Jazz Music / Wellard / Koch.

LIVE AT MAYBECK RECITAL HALL, VOL. 35
Over the rainbow / Helen's song / Bess, you is my woman now / Someone to watch over me / You don't know what love is / Lullaby / Everything happens to me / Goin' home / Little B's poem
CD _____ CCD 4630
Concord Jazz / Jan '95 / New Note.

NIGHT AND DAY (Cables, George Trio)
CD _____ DIW 606
DIW / Sep '91 / Harmonia Mundi / Cadillac.

Cabrette

CORNEMUSE D'AUVERGNEL 1895-1976
CD _____ Y 225104
Silex / Aug '93 / ADA.

Cacavas, Chris

CHRIS CACAVAS AND JUNKYARD LOVE (Cacavas, Chris & Junkyard Love)
Driving misery / Wrecking yard / Angel on a mattress spring / Blue river / Jukebox lullabye / Truth / I didn't mean that / Load off me / Honeymoon
CD _____ SERV 006CD
World Service / Nov '89 / Vital.

DWARF STAR
CD _____ RTS 14
Return To Sender / Dec '94 / Direct / ADA.

GOOD TIMES
CD _____ NORMAL 140CD
Normal/Okra / Sep '93 / Direct / ADA.

NEW IMPROVED PAIN (Cacavas, Chris & Junkyard Love)
CD _____ NORMAL 200CD
Normal/Okra / Oct '95 / Direct / ADA.

PALE BLONDE HELL
CD _____ NORM 170CD
Normal/Okra / Mar '94 / Direct / ADA.

SIX STRING SOAPBOX
CD _____ RTS 1CD
Normal/Okra / Mar '94 / Direct / ADA.

Cachao

MASTER SESSIONS VOLUME 1
Al fin te vi / Isora club / Mambo / El son no ha muerto / Lindo yambu / Mi guajira / Lluvia, viento y cana / Marianao social club / A gozar con mi combo / Cachao's guiro / El alcalde / Descarga Cachao
CD _____ 477282 2
Epic / Nov '94 / Sony.

Cacophony

SPEED METAL SYMPHONY
CD _____ RR 349577
Roadrunner / Feb '91 / Pinnacle.

Cactus

CACTUS
CD _____ 7567802902
Atlantic / Jan '96 / Warner Music.

Cactus Rain

IN OUR OWN TIME
We the people / Till comes the morning / Hopes and fears / Self / Walker / Look of love / Mystery train / Sun a blazing / Danny's ocean / Each day / Counting to ten / Senses
CD _____ CDIX 96
Virgin / Jun '91 / EMI.

Cadaver

HALLUCINATING ANXIETY
CD _____ NECRO 4 CD
Necrosis / Dec '90 / Vital.

IN PAINS
CD _____ MOSH 071CD
Earache / Oct '92 / Vital.

Cadaverous Condition

IN MELANCHOLY
CD _____ LRC 008
Lethal / Feb '94 / Plastic Head.

Caddick, Bill

WINTER WITH FLOWERS
CD _____ FLED 3004
Fledg'ling / Jul '95 / CM / ADA / Direct.

Cadell, Meryn

ANGEL FOOD FOR THOUGHT
Secret / Bumble bee / Flight attendant / Being in love / Inventory / Deep sixin' / Knitting / I say / Wait / I been redeemed / Spelling bee / Sweater / Joe application / Pope / Sharkhead / Martina / Maidenform / Confide / Clothes / Barbie
CD _____ 7599268772
WEA / Aug '92 / Warner Music.

Cadets

STRANDED IN THE JUNGLE (The Legendaray Modern Recordings)
Let's rock 'n' roll / Fools rush in / My clumsy heart / Annie met Henry / Rollin' stone / Don't be angry / Hands across the table / Smack dab in the middle / Pretty Evey / Love can do most anything / Baby ya know / Love bandit / Why did I fall in love / Church bells may ring / Car crash / Ring chimes / Heartbreak hotel / Dancin' Dan / Rum Jamaica rum / Don't / I got loaded / I'll be spinning / Sugar baby / Stranded in the jungle
CD _____ CDCHD 534
Ace / Sep '94 / Pinnacle / Cadillac / Complete/Pinnacle.

Cadillac Tramps

IT'S ALRIGHT
CD _____ CDVEST 28
Bulletproof / Aug '94 / Pinnacle.

Cadillacs

BEST OF THE CADILLACS
Gloria / No chance / Down the road / Window lady / Speedoo / Zoom / You are / Woe is me / Betty my love / Girl I love / Sugar sugar / My girl friend / Speedo ic back / Peek-a-boo / Zoom boom zing / Please Mr. Johnson / Romeo / Tell me today
CD _____ NEMCD 604
Sequel / Aug '90 / BMG.

COMPLETE JOSIE SESSIONS, THE
Gloria / I wonder why / Wishing well / Carelessly / I want to know about love / No chance / No chance (alt) / Sympathy sympathy / Party for two / Party for two (alt) / Corn whiskey / Down the road / Window lady / Speedoo (alt) / Speddoo / Zoom boom zing / Let me explain (alt) / Let me explain / You are (version 1) / Zoon (version 3) / Oh wahtcha do / Shock-a-doo / You are / Why / (That's) All I need / Baby's coming home to me baby / Girl I love / Betty my love / Woe is me / Rudolph the red nosed reindeer / Don't take your love from me / If you want to be a woman of mine / About that girl named Lou / Sugar sugar / Broken heart / C'mon home baby / Hurry home / Lucy / From this day on / My girlfriend / Don't be mad with my heart / Buzz buzz buzz / Yeah yeah baby / Holy smoke baby / I want to know / Ain't you gonna / It's spring / Speedoo is back / Look a hore / Great googly moo / Copy cat / Oh oh Lolita / Peek-a-boo / Jelly bean / Please Mr. Johnson / Your heart is so blind / Cool it fool / Jay Walker / Who ya gonna kiss / Vow / Naggity nag / You're not in love with me / Bad Dan McGoon / Romeo Romeo / Always my darling / Dumbell / Still you left me baby / Dum dee dum dum / Frankenstein / I want to be loved / I'm in love / Tell me today / Let me down easy / It's love / That's why / Louise / Rock 'n' roll is here to stay / Boogie man / I'll never let you go / Wayward wanderer
CD Set _____ BCD 15648
Bear Family / Mar '95 / Rollercoaster / Direct / CM / Swift / ADA.

Cadogan, Susan

HURT SO GOOD
CD _____ CDTRL 122
Trojan / Jun '95 / Jetstar / Total/BMG.

Caducity

WEILIAON WIELDER
CD _____ SHR 012CD
Shiva / Nov '95 / Plastic Head.

Caesar

LIVE AT CAESAR'S PALACE
CD _____ E 12251CD
Disko B / Sep '93 / SRD.

Cage, John

SIXTY EIGHT/QUARTETS I-VIII
CD _____ ARTCD 6168
Hat Art / Dec '95 / Harmonia Mundi / ADA / Cadillac.

SIXTY-TWO MESOSTICS RE MERCE CUNNINGHAM
CD Set _____ AHTCD 28093
Hat Art / Jan '92 / Harmonia Mundi / ADA / Cadillac.

Cain, Chris

SOMEWHERE ALONG THE WAY
CD _____ BPCD 5024
Blind Pig / Dec '95 / Hot Shot / Swift / CM / Roots / Direct / ADA.

Cain, Jackie

JACKIE & ROY FOREVER (Cain, Jackie & Roy Kral)
CD _____ 01612651282
Music Masters / Dec '95 / Nimbus.

Cain, Mike

STRANGE OMEN
CD _____ CCD 790505
Candid / Apr '91 / Cadillac / Jazz Music / Wellard / Koch.

WHAT MEANS THIS
CD _____ CCD 79529
Candid / Mar '93 / Cadillac / Jazz Music / Wellard / Koch.

Caine, Jackie

ALEC WILDER COLLECTION (Caine, Jackie & Roy Kral)
CD _____ ACD 257
Audiophile / Oct '92 / Jazz Music / Swift.

TRIBUTE TO ALAN J. LERNER (Caine, Jackie & Roy Kral)
CD _____ ACD 230
Audiophile / Oct '92 / Jazz Music / Swift.

Caine, Uri

SPHERE MUSIC
CD _____ 514007-2
JMT / May '94 / PolyGram.

Caiola, Al

DEEP IN A DREAM
Love letters / There'll never be another you / I got it bad / Everything happens to me / Deep in a dream / You are too beautiful / I got a crush on you / Thunderbird
CD _____ SV 0205
Savoy Jazz / Apr '93 / Conifer / ADA.

SERENADE IN BLUE
Serenade in blue / Don't worry 'bout me / Moments like this / Early Autumn / Black and blue / Indian summer / Blue the night / Dram-buie
CD _____ SV 0232
Savoy Jazz / Nov '93 / Conifer / ADA.

Cajun Aces

ACES HIGH
CD _____ PGR 001CD
Pine Grove / Jul '94 / Direct / ADA.

Cake Kitchen

FAR FROM THE SUN
CD _____ HMS 198-2
Homestead / Jul '93 / SRD.

Calderazzo, Joey

IN THE DOOR
In the door / Mikell's / Spring is here / Missed / Domes mode / Loud-zee / Chub-by's lament / Pest
CD _____ CDP 795 138 2
Blue Note / Mar '91 / EMI.

SECRETS
Secrets / No one knows I'm here / Aurora / Scriabin / Echoes / Filles de Kilimanjaro / Last visit home / ATM
CD _____ AQCD 1036
Audioquest / Aug '95 / New Note.

Cale, J.J.

CLOSER TO YOU
Long way home / Sho-biz blues / Slower baby / Devil's nurse / Like you used to / Borrowed time / Rose in the garden / Brown dirt / Hard love / Ain't love funny / Closer to you / Steve's song
CD _____ CDV 2746
Virgin / Jun '94 / EMI.

EIGHT
Money talks / Losers / Hard times / Reality / Takin' care of business / People lie / Un-employment / Trouble in the city / Tear-drops in my tequila / Livin' here too
CD _____ 8111522
Mercury / Sep '89 / PolyGram.

FIVE
Thirteen days / Boilin' pot / I'll make love to you anytime / Don't cry sister / Too much for me / Sensitive kind / Friday / Lou easy Ann / Let's go to Tahiti / Katy Kool lady / Fate of a fool / Mona
CD _____ 8103132
Mercury / Jul '93 / PolyGram.

GRASSHOPPER
City girls / Devil in disguise / One step ahead of the blues / You keep me hangin' on / Downtown L.A. / Can't live here / Grasshopper / Drifter's wife / Thing going on / Nobody but you / Mississippi river / Does your mama like to reggae / Dr. Jive
CD _____ 800 038-2
Mercury / '83 / PolyGram.

NATURALLY
Call me the breeze / Call the doctor / Don't go to strangers / Woman I love / Magnolia / Clyde / Crazy mama / Nowhere to run / After midnight / River runs deep / Bringing it back / Crying eyes
CD _____ 830 042-2
Mercury / Jan '87 / PolyGram.

OKIE
Crying / I'll be there (if you ever want me) / Starbound / Rock 'n' roll records / Old man and me / Ever lovin' woman / Cajun moon / I'd like to love you baby / Anyway the wind blows / Precious memories / Okie / I got the same old blues
CD _____ 8421022
Mercury / May '90 / PolyGram.

REALLY
Lies / Everything will be alright / I'll kiss the world goodbye / Changes / Right down here / If you're ever in Oklahoma / Riding home / Going down / Soulin' / Playin' in the streets / Mo Jo / Louisiana woman
CD _____ 8103142
Mercury / Aug '89 / PolyGram.

SHADES
Carry on / Deep dark dungeon / Wish I had not said that / Pack my jack / If you leave

---

her / Mama don't / What do you expect / Cloudy day / Love has been and gone
CD _____ 8001052
Mercury / Aug '89 / PolyGram.

SPECIAL EDITION
Cocaine / Don't wait / Magnolia / Devil in disguise / Sensitive kind / Carry on after midnight / Money talks / Call me the breeze / Lies / City girls / Cajun moon / Don't cry sister / Crazy mama
CD _____ 818 633 2
Mercury / Jun '84 / PolyGram.

TEN
CD _____ ORECD 523
Silvertone / Sep '92 / Pinnacle.

TRAVELOG
Lean on me / Who's talking / Humdinger / End of the line / Tijuana / shanghai'd / New Orleans
CD _____ ORECD 507
Silvertone / Mar '94 / Pinnacle.

TROUBADOUR
Hey baby / I'm a gypsy man / You got me on so bad / Trackin' light / Woman that got away / Cherry / You got something / Hold on / Let me do it to you / Ride me high / Cocaine / Super blue
CD _____ 800 001-2
Mercury / '83 / PolyGram.

Cale, John

23 SOLO PIECES
CD _____ YMCD 007
Yellow Moon / Nov '95 / Vital.

ACADEMY IN PERIL
Philosopher / Brahms / Legs Larry at tele-vision centre / Academy in peril / Intro (Days of steam) / Faust / Balance / Captain Mor-gan's lament / King Harry John Milton
CD _____ 7599269302
WEA / Oct '93 / Warner Music.

ARTIFICIAL INTELLIGENCE
Every time the dogs bark / Dying on the vine / Sleeper / Vigilante lover / Chinese takea-way / Song of the valley / Fade away to-morrow / Black rose / Satellite walk
CD _____ BBL 68CD
Lowdown/Beggars Banquet / Jan '89 / Warner Music / Disc.

FEAR
Fear is a man's best friend / Buffalo ballet / Barracuda Emily / Ship of fools / Gun / Man who couln't afford to orgy / You know we more than I know / Momma scuba
CD _____ IMCD 140
Island / Aug '91 / PolyGram.

FRAGMENTS OF A RAINY SEASON
CD _____ HNCD 1372
Hannibal / Oct '92 / Vital / ADA.

GUTS
Guts / Mary Lou / Helen of Troy / Pablo Picasso / Leaving it up to you / Fear is a man's best friend / Gun / Dirty-ass rock and roll / Rock 'n' roll / Heartbreak hotel
CD _____ IMCD 203
Island / Jul '94 / PolyGram.

HELEN OF TROY
My Maria / Helen of Troy / China Sea / En-gine / Save us / Cable hogue / I keep a close watch / Pablo Picasso / Coral moon / Baby, what you want me to do / Sudden death / Leaving it up to you / Sylvia said
CD _____ IMCD 177
Island / Mar '94 / PolyGram.

HONI SOIT
Honi soit / Dead or alive / Strange times in Casablanca / Fighter pilot / Wilson Joliet / Streets of Laredo / River bank / Russian roulette / Magic and lies
CD _____ CDMID 1936
A&M / Jul '94 / PolyGram.

PARIS 1919
Child's Christmas in Wales / Hanky panky no how / Endless plain of furtune / Andal-ucia / MacBeth / Paris 1919 / Graham Greene / Half past France / Antarctica starts here
CD _____ 759925926-2
WEA / Oct '93 / Warner Music.

PARIS S'EVEILLE - SUIVI D'AUTRES COMPOSITIONS
CD _____ YMCD 006
Yellow Moon / Nov '95 / Vital.

SLOW DAZZLE
Mr. Wilson / Taking it all away / Dirty-ass rock and roll / Darling I need you / Rollaroll / Heartbreak hotel / Ski patrol / I'm not the loving kind / Guts / Jeweller
CD _____ IMCD 202
Island / Jul '94 / PolyGram.

SONGS FOR DRELLA (Cale, John & Lou Reed)
Smalltown / Open house / Style it takes / Work / Trouble with classicists / Starlight / Faces and names / Images / Slip away / It wasn't me / I believe / Nobody but you / Dream / Forever changed / Hello it's me
CD _____ 7599261402
WEA / Apr '90 / Warner Music.

VINTAGE VIOLENCE
Hello there / Gideon's bible / Adelaide / Big white cloud / Cleo / Please / Charlemagne

---

/ Bring it on up / Amsterdam / Ghost story / Fairweather friends
CD _____ 477356-2
Columbia / Aug '94 / Sony.

WORDS FOR THE DYING
Introduction / There was a saviour / On a wedding anniversary / Interlude II / Lie still, sleep becalmed / Do not go gentle into that good night / Songs without words I / Songs without words II / Soul of Carmen Miranda
CD _____ ASCD 009
All Saints / Oct '95 / Vital / Discovery.

ZONE
CD _____ TWI 952CD
Les Disques Du Crepuscule / Jan '92 / Discovery / ADA.

Caledonian Fiddle...

IN CONCERT (Caledonian Fiddle Orchestra)
CD _____ CDLOC 1057
Lochshore / Dec '90 / ADA / Direct / Duncans.

Caledonian Heritage Pipes

AMAZING GRACE
CD _____ CDITV 515
Scotdisc / Jul '90 / Duncans / Ross / Conifer.

Calennig

DWR GLAN
Ynys Skye / Nantgwenith/Pibddawns Ffren-gig / Ar lan y mor/Meillionen o Feirionnydd / Pwt ar y bys/Cambro Br / Blwyddyn hen-ydd dda / Calennig pentywyn/A droau/An dro pen ar bed/Y gwcw fach / Dwr glan/Y lili/Nyth y gwcw/Ty coch Caerdydd / Blooming rose of South Wales / Llantrisant/ Y bregeth/Young fellow from Llyn/Beth yw'r haf i / Lanthenac
CD _____ SCD 4025
Sain / Feb '95 / Direct / ADA.

TRADE WINDS
CD _____ SCD 2091
Sain / Jun '95 / Direct / ADA.

Calgary Highlander Band

80 YEARS OF GLORY
CD _____ BNA 5051
Bandleader / Apr '91 / Conifer.

Calglia

MUSIC OF THE BALKANS & ANATOLIA VOL.2
CD _____ PANCD 2007
Pan / May '93 / ADA / Direct / CM.

Caliche

MUSIC OF THE ANDES
Festival of the flowers / Andean dawn / Memories of the lake / Flight of the Condor / Bell bird / Returning to a new time / Winds from the South / Silver paper / She left my crying
CD _____ CDSDL 388
Saydisc / Mar '94 / Harmonia Mundi / ADA / Direct.

California

TRAVELER
Rocker arm reel / Walk in the Irish rain / Scissors, paper and stone / My sweet blue eyed darling / Spurs / Farmers son / Cali-fornia traveler / I'll dry every tear that falls / Whiplash / Sasquatch / Uncle Pen / Band of angels
CD _____ SHCD 3803
Sugarhill / '92 / Roots / CM / ADA / Direct.

California Cajun...

NONC ADAM TWO-STEP (California Cajun Orchestra)
CD _____ ARHCD 436
Arhoolie / Sep '95 / ADA / Direct / Cadillac.

NOT LONESOME ANYMORE (California Cajun Orchestra)
CD _____ ARHCD 416
Arhoolie / Apr '95 / ADA / Direct / Cadillac.

California Guitar Trio

INVITATION
Train to lamy suite / Punta patri / Toccata and fugue in d minor / Fratres / Train to Lamy / Apache / Above the clouds / Prelude circulation / Good, the bad and the ugly
CD _____ DGM 9501
Discipline / Apr '95 / Pinnacle.

YAMANASHI BLUES
Yamanashi blues / Melrose Avenue / Cor-rente / Walk don't run / Ricercar / Pipeline / Beeline / Chromatic fugue in D minor / Tenor madness / Sleepwalk / Carnival / Prelude in C minor / Ciaccona / Blockhead / Kan-non power
CD _____ DGM 9301
Discipline / Aug '94 / Pinnacle.

California Jam

LIVE RECORDING 1952
CD _____ CDJJ 629
Jazz & Jazz / Jan '92 / Target/BMG.

California, Randy

EURO-AMERICA/SHATTERED DREAMS
Toy guns / This is the end / Mon ami / Rude reaction / Calling you / Wild thing / Easy love / Fearless leader / Five in the morning / Skull and crossbones / Breakout / Hey Joe / Shattered dreams / All along the watch-tower / Don't bother me / Downer / Second child / Man at war / Killer weed / Hand gun / Radio man / Run to your lover
CD Set _____ LICD 921173
Line / Mar '92 / CM / Grapevine / ADA / Conifer / Direct.

KAPTAIN KOPTER AND HIS TWIRLY BIRDS
Downer / Devil I don't want nobody / Day tripper / Mother and child reunion / Things yet to come / Rain / Rainbow
CD _____ EDCD 164
Edsel / Aug '93 / Pinnacle / ADA.

Callier, Terry

NEW FOLK SOUND OF TERRY CALLIER, THE
900 Miles / Oh dear, what can the matter be / Johnny be gay if you can / Cotton eyed joe / Spin spin spin / I'm a drifter
CD _____ CDBGPM 101
BGP / Nov '95 / Pinnacle.

VERY BEST OF TERRY CALLIER
CD _____ CDARC 514
Charly / Apr '94 / Charly / THE / Cadillac.

Calloway, Blanche

CLASSICS 1925-35
CD _____ CLASSICS 783
Classics / Nov '94 / Discovery / Jazz Music.

Calloway, Cab

1932-1934
CD _____ CLASSICS 544
Classics / Dec '90 / Discovery / Jazz Music.

BEST OF THE BIG BANDS
Minnie the moocher / Beale Street Mama / Angeline / Bye bye blues / Minnie the Moocher's weddin' day / Dinah / Wake up and live / Pickin' up the cabbage / You gotta ho-di-ho / Reefer man / Jumpin' jive / Manhattan jam / I gotta go places and do things baby to forget you / Eddie was a lady / Take the 'A' train / F.D.R. Jones
CD _____ 4666182
CBS / '91 / Sony.

BEST OF THE BIG BANDS (Calloway, Cab & Chu Berry)
Yours is my heart alone / Mr. Meadowland / Dreaming out loud / Nobody / Man I love / I'm always chasing rainbows / I hear a rhapsody / Corn silk you're dangerous / This is new / Perfidia / Lazy river / Yours / Oh! Look at me now / Amapola / Smoke gets in your eyes
CD _____ 4716572
Columbia / Aug '93 / Sony.

CAB AND CO.
Evening / Harlem hospitality / Lady with the fan / Harlem camp meeting / Zaz zuh zaz / Father's got his glasses on / Minnie the moocher (takes 1 and 2) / Scat song (takes 1 and 2o) / Kicking the gong around / The-re's a cabin in the cotton / I learned about love from her (takes 3 & 4) / Little town gal / Long about midnight / Moon glow / Jitter-bug / Hotcha razz ma tazz / Margie / Ema-line / Ol' Joe Louis / Your voice / Roomin' house boogie / I beeped when I shoulda bopped / I need lovin' / Just a crazy song / It looks like Susie / Growlin' Dan / Con-centratin' on you / Last dollar / Oh you sweet thing
CD Set _____ ND 89560
Jazz Tribune / May '94 / BMG.

CAB CALLOWAY & HIS ORCHESTRA (1939-42) (Calloway, Cab & His Orchestra)
CD _____ CD 14567
Jazz Portraits / May '95 / Jazz Music.

CAB CALLOWAY & HIS ORCHESTRA 1940-1942
CD _____ CLASSICS 682
Classics / Mar '93 / Discovery / Jazz Music.

CAB CALLOWAY - 1940-41 (Calloway, Cab & His Orchestra)
CD _____ CLASSICS 629
Classics / '92 / Discovery / Jazz Music.

CAB CALLOWAY AND HIS ORCHESTRA (Calloway, Cab & His Orchestra)
CD _____ SMS 47
Carlton Home Entertainment / Apr '92 / Carlton Home Entertainment.

CAB CALLOWAY AND HIS ORCHESTRA - 1939-40
CD _____ CD 595
Classic Jazz Masters / Sep '91 / Wellard / Jazz Music / Jazz Music.

CAB CALLOWAY AND HIS ORCHESTRA 1940 (Calloway, Cab & His Orchestra)
CD _____ CLASSICS 614
Classics / Feb '92 / Discovery / Jazz Music.

CAB CALLOWAY ON FILM 1934-1950
CD _____ FLYCD 944
Flyright / Feb '95 / Hot Shot / Wellard / Jazz Music / CM.

CONJURE
Author reflects on his 35th birthday / Sputin / General science / My brothers / St. Louis women / Beware - don't listen to this song / Loup garrou means change into / Nobody was there / Running for the office of love / Petit Kid Everett / Bitter chocolate / Minnie the moocher
CD _____ AMCL 1015
American Clave / May '90 / New Note / ADA / Direct.

CRUISIN' WITH CAB (Calloway, Cab & His Orchestra)
Get with it / That old black magic / Airmail stomp / Jealous / I've got a girl named Netty / Basically blue / You got it / Blue Serge suit / One o'clock jump / This is always / All by myself in the moonlight / Jumpin' jive / Everybody eats when they come to my house / I don't want to love you / Yesterdays / Cruisin' with Cab / Stormy weather / Duck trot
CD _____ TPZ 1010
Topaz Jazz / Oct '94 / Pinnacle / Cadillac.

FRANTIC IN THE ATLANTIC
I got a girl named Netty / This is always / Jealous / Blue serge suit / One o'clock jump / Frantic in the Atlantic / Jumpin' jive / Airmail stomp / Cruisin' with cab / You got it / That old black magic / Everybody eats when they come to my house / Duck trot
CD _____ DBCD 10
Dance Band Days / Dec '88 / Prism.

HI DE HO MAN
CD _____ 4716892
Sony Jazz / Jan '95 / Sony.

HI-DE-HI-DE-HO
Hi de ho man (that's me) / I'll be around / Summertime / It ain't necessarily so / Kicking the gong around / (I'll be glad when you're dead) You rascal you / Minnie the Moocher / I see a million people (but all I can see is you) / St. James Infirmary / Stormy weather / Jumpin' jive
CD _____ 74321185242
RCA Victor / Oct '94 / BMG.

HI-DE-HO (Calloway, Cab & His Orchestra)
Minnie the moocher / Long about midnight / Moonglow / Margie / Scar song / (I'll be glad when you're dead) you rascal you / Harlem camp meeting / There's a cabin in the cotton / Father's got his glasses on / Nobody's sweetheart / Between the devil and the deep blue sea / Kicking the gong around / Hotcha razz ma tazz / Jitterbug / Harlem hospitality / Lady with the fan / Zaz zuh zaz
CD _____ PAR 2008
Parade / Apr '95 / Koch / Cadillac.

HI-DE-HO MAN, THE
St. Louis blues / Minnie the moocher / St. James infirmary / Nobody's sweetheart / Six or seven times / (I'll be glad when you're dead) you rascal you / Kicking the gong around / Between the devil and the deep blue sea / Minnie the moocher's wedding day / Seat song / Bugle call rag / Blues in my heart / Sweet Georgia Brown / Mood Indigo / Dinah / Aw you dawg
CD _____ HADCD 174
Javelin / May '94 / THE / Henry Hadaway Organisation.

INTRODUCTION TO CAB CALLOWAY 1930-42, AN
CD _____ 4011
Best Of Jazz / Aug '94 / Discovery.

JUMPIN' JIVE
Minnie the moocher / St. James infirmary / Six or seven times / Bugle call rag / Corine Corina / Scat song / Minnie the moocher's wedding day / Keep that hi-de-hi in your soul / Nagasaki / Wedding of Mr and Mr Swing / Jive the jumpin' jive / Calling all bars / Jonah joins the cab / Hey doc
CD _____ CDCD 1072
Charly / Mar '93 / Charly / THE / Cadillac.

KICKING THE GONG AROUND
Minnie the moocher / Without rhythm / Aw you dog / Bugle call rag / Downhearted blues / Nightmare / Black rhythm / Yaller / Between the Devil and the deep blue sea / Nobody's sweetheart / Trickeration / St. Louis blues / Mood indigo / Farewell blues / (I'll be glad when you're dead) you rascal you / My honey's lovin' arms / Some of these days / Six or seven times / Somebody stole my gal / Kicking the gong around

---

CD _____ CDAJA 5013
Living Era / Sep '90 / Koch.

KING OF HI-DE-HO (Calloway, Cab & His Orchestra)
Minnie the moocher / Man from Harlem / Chinese rhythm / Jumpin' jive / Scat song / Trickeration / Kicking the gong around / Lonesome nights / Run little rabbit / Bye bye blues / Ad-de-day
CD _____ CDHD 260
Happy Days / Mar '95 / Conifer.

KING OF HI-DE-HO 1934-47, THE
CD _____ CD 53096
Giants Of Jazz / Mar '92 / Target/BMG / Cadillac.

KINGS OF THE COTTON CLUB (Calloway, Cab & Scatman Crothers)
CD _____ 15378
Laserlight / Jan '93 / Target/BMG.

LIVE IN 1944
CD _____ MRCD 123
Magnetic / Sep '91 / Magnum Music Group.

MINNIE THE MOOCHER
Nagaski / Hoy hoy / Jumpin' jive / Give baby give / I want to rock / Minnie the moocher / Honey dripper / Hi de ho man / Jungle king / Calloway boogie / Two blocks down town to the left / Chicken ain't nothin' but a bird / I can't give you anything but love / Stormy weather / You got it / Everybody eats when they come to my house / Afternoon moon / This is always / Duck trot / That old black magic / How big can you get / Hey now hey now / Birth of the blues / We the cats shall help you / Foo a little ballyhoo
CD _____ CD 56073
Jazz Roots / Mar '95 / Target/BMG.

MINNIE THE MOOCHER
Tring / '93 / Tring / Prism. _____ CDGRF 077

SOUNDTRACKS AND BROADCASTINGS - 1943/1944 (Calloway, Cab & His Orchestra)
Bojangles steps in / Easy Joe / Ain't that something / Everybody dance / Honeydripper / Let's go Joe / Jumpin' jive / Angels sing / Birth of the blues / Fiesta in brass / I've got you under my skin / Lady whistle bait / Russian lullaby / Foo a little bally-hoo / 9.20 Special
CD _____ 550232
Jazz Anthology / Feb '94 / Harmonia Mundi / Cadillac.

Calvert, Eddie

EMI YEARS: EDDIE CALVERT
Oh mein papa / Poor people of Paris / Stranger in paradise / April in Portugal / On a slow boat to China / Love is a many splendoured thing / I'm getting sentimental over you / Sucu sucu / My son, my son / malaguena / Cherry pink and apple blossom white / Mandy (the pansy) / Around the world / Forgotten dreams / My Yiddishe Momme / Summertime / John and Julie / Little serenade (Piccolissima serenata) / I love Paris / Zambesi
CD _____ CDEMS 1461
EMI / Aug '92 / EMI.

Calvert, Robert

BLUEPRINTS FROM THE CELLAR
CD _____ BGOCD 135
Beat Goes On / Oct '92 / Pinnacle.

CAPTAIN LOCKHEED AND THE STARFIGHTERS
CD _____ BGOCD 5
Beat Goes On / Oct '88 / Pinnacle.

FREQ REVISITED
Ned ludd / Talk one / Acid rain / Talk two / All the machines are quiet / Talk three / Picket line / Talk four / Cool courage of the bomb / Squad / Talk five / Work song / Lord of the Hornets / Greenfly and the rose
CD _____ CDMGRAM 55
Anagram / Jun '92 / Pinnacle.

HYPE
Over my head / Ambitious / It's the same / Hanging out on the seafront / Sensitive / Evil rock / We like to be frightened / Teen ballad of Deano / Flight 105 / Luminous green glow of the dashboard / Greenfly and the rose / Lord of the hornets
CD _____ SEECD 278
See For Miles/C5 / '89 / Pinnacle.

LIVE AT THE QUEEN ELIZABETH HALL
Evil rock / Catch a falling starfighter / Gremlins / Aerospace age inferno / Test tube conceived / Working down a diamond mine / All the machines are quiet / Work song / Telekinesis / Acid rain / Lord of the hornets
CD _____ BGOCD 187
Beat Goes On / Apr '93 / Pinnacle.

TEST TUBE CONCEIVED
Telekinesis / I hear voices / Fanfare for the perfect race / On line / Save them from the scientists / Fly on the wall / Thanks to the scientists / Test tube conceived / In vitro breed / Rah rah man
CD _____ CDTB 113
Thunderbolt / '91 / Magnum Music Group.

Calvin Party

LIFE AND OTHER SEX TRAGEDIE, THE
All messed up / Monster / Song from England / Messalina / Gun / Alphabet song / Look back in angst ah / Taxi man / None the less / Less is more / Mass
CD _____ PROBE 038CD
Probe Plus / Mar '95 / Vital.

Camacho, Wichy

LA ROMANCE
Desilucionado / Todo por amor / Dime carino / Me das libertad / Me pides que te ame / Amor de fantasia / Dosis del amor / Solicito un amor
CD _____ 66058079
RMM / Nov '95 / New Note.

Camaleon, Entra

JAZZ IN SWEDEN 1981
CD _____ 1260
Caprice / Nov '89 / CM / Complete/ Pinnacle / Cadillac / ADA.

Camara, Ladsi

AFRICA, NEW YORK (Master Drummer)
CD _____ LYRCD 7345
Lyrichord / Jul '94 / Roots / ADA / CM.

Camel

CAMEL
Slow yourself down / Mystic queen / Six ate / Separation / Never let go / Curiosity / Arubaluba
CD _____ CP 002CD
Camel Productions / Jul '93 / Pinnacle.

DUST & DREAMS
CD _____ CP 001CD
Camel Productions / Jul '93 / Pinnacle.

HARBOUR OF TEARS
CD _____ CP 006CD
Camel Productions / Jan '96 / Pinnacle.

LANDSCAPES
City lights / Landscapes / Reflections / Freefall / Echoes / Refugee / Missing / Spirit of the water / Air born / First light / Skylines / Raindances / Sanctuary/ Fritha / Last farewell / Beached / Stationary traveller / Dead and dagger / Your love is stranger than mine
CD _____ ELITE 003 PCD
Elite/Old Gold / May '91 / Carlton Home Entertainment.

NEVER LET GO (LIVE '92)
CD Set _____ CP 004CD
Camel Productions / Oct '93 / Pinnacle.

ON THE ROAD 1972
CD _____ CP 003CD
Camel Productions / Jul '93 / Pinnacle.

ON THE ROAD 1982
Sasquatch / Highways of the sun / Hymn of her / Neon magic / You are the one / Drafted / Lies / Captured / Heart's desire / Heroes / Who we are / Manic / Wait and never let go
CD _____ CP 005CD
Camel Productions / Jan '95 / Pinnacle.

RAIN DANCES
First light / Metronome / Tell me / Highways of the sun / Unevensong / One of these days I'll get an early night / Skylines / Elke / Rain dances
CD _____ 8207252
Deram / Jan '93 / PolyGram.

SNOW GOOSE
Great marsh / Rhayader / Rhayader goes to town / Sanctuary / Fritha / Snow goose / Friendship / Rhayader alone / Flight of the snow goose / Preparation / Dunkirk / Epitaph / Fritha alone / La princesse perdue / Pressure points / Refugee / Stationary traveller
CD _____ 8000802
Deram / Jul '93 / PolyGram.

Camelia Jazz Band

THAT'S MY HOME
CD _____ JCD 249
Jazzology / Aug '95 / Swift / Jazz Music.

Cameo

EMOTIONAL VIOLENCE
Emotional violence / Money / Raw but tasty / Front street / Kid don't believe it / Another love / Don't crash / Love yourself / Nothing less than love / That kind of guy
CD _____ 7599267342
Reprise / Mar '92 / Warner Music.

Cameron Highlanders Of...

ADVANCE (Cameron Highlanders Of Ottawa)
CD _____ BNA 5108
Bandleader / Jan '95 / Conifer.

Cameron, Doug

MIL AMORES
CD _____ CD 3010
Narada / Aug '92 / New Note / ADA.

Cameron, Steve

TITANIC SUITE, THE
CD _____ VTRCD 1
Titanic / Mar '88 / EMI.

Camilla's Little Secret

STEPS, THE
CD _____ SNRCD 944
S&R / May '95 / Pinnacle.

Camilo, Michel

MICHEL CAMILO
Suite sandrine part 1 / Nostalgia / Dreamlight / Crossroads / Sunset (Interlude/Suite sandrine) / Yarey / Pra voce / Blue brossa / Caribe
CD _____ 4633302
Sony Jazz / Dec '90 / Sony.

ON FIRE
CD _____ 4658802
Sony Jazz / Jan '95 / Sony.

ON THE OTHER HAND
On the other hand / City of angels / Journey / Impressions / Silent talk 1 / Forbidden fruit / Suite sandrine part 3 / Birk's works / Silent talk 2
CD _____ 4669372
Epic / Aug '90 / Sony.

ONE MORE ONCE
One more once / Why not / Resolution / Suite sandrine #3 / Dreamlight / Just kidding / Caribe / Suntan / On the other hand / Not yet
CD _____ 477753-2
Columbia / Oct '94 / Sony.

RENDEZVOUS
CD _____ 4737722
Sony Jazz / Jan '95 / Sony.

WHY NOT?
Just kidding / Hello and goodbye / Thinking of you / Why not / Not yet / Suite Sandrine #5
CD _____ K32Y 6031
King/Paddle Wheel / Sep '89 / New Note.

Campbell Family

SINGING CAMPBELLS, THE
Fur does bonnie lorna lie / Sleep till yer mammy / Nicky tams / Road and the miles to Dundee / Drumdelgie / I ken faur I'm gaun / My wee man's a miner / Fa, fa, fa wid be a bobby / Foul Friday / Me an' mi mither / We these kings of Orient are / Bogie's bonnie belle / Cruel mother / Lang-a-growing / Lady Eliza / Will ye gang love / I wish i wish / McGinty's meal and ale
CD _____ OSS 97CD
Ossian / Aug '94 / ADA / Direct / CM.

Campbell, Al

BOUNCE BACK
CD _____ ALCD 002
Al Campbell / Jun '94 / Jetstar.

IT'S MAGIC
CD _____ ALCD 001
Al Campbell / Jun '94 / Jetstar.

RASTA TIME
CD _____ LG 21056
Lagoon / Feb '93 / Magnum Music Group / THE.

SOULFUL, THE
CD _____ RNCD 2067
Rhino / Jul '94 / Jetstar / Magnum Music Group / THE.

Campbell, Ali

BIG LOVE
Big love (intro) / Happiness / That look in your eyes / Let your yeah be yeah / You can cry on my shoulder / Somethin' stupid / Big love / You could meet somebody / Talking blackbird / Pay the rent / Drive it home / Stop the guns
CD _____ CDV 2783
Kuff / Jun '95 / EMI.

Campbell, Anthony

YOUR SPECIAL GIFT
CD _____ CAMCD 3
Stringbean / Oct '95 / Jetstar.

Campbell, Blind James

BLIND JAMES CAMPBELL
CD _____ ARHCD 438
Arhoolie / Jun '95 / ADA / Direct / Cadillac.

Campbell, Chris

MEETINGS WITH REMARKABLE ALLOYS
CD _____ JHR 2021
Larrikin / Feb '95 / Roots / Direct / ADA / CM.

RINGS OF FIRE
CD _____ JHR 2022
Larrikin / Nov '94 / Roots / Direct / ADA / CM.

Campbell, Cornell

NATTY DREAD IN A GREENWICH FARM
CD _____ TSL 104CD
Striker Lee / Jul '95 / Jetstar / THE.

TELL THE PEOPLE
CD _____ CDSGP 072
Prestige / May '94 / Total/BMG.

Campbell, Don

ALBUM, THE
CD _____ JGLGCD 01
Juggling / May '94 / Jetstar.

Campbell, Eddie C.

BADDEST CAT ON THE BLOCK, THE
Hye baby / Nineteen years old / I'm in love
with you baby / Tears are for losers / Early
in the morning / Same thing / Cha cha blues
/ Cheaper to keep her
CD _____ JSPCD 216
JSP / Jul '88 / ADA / Target/BMG / Direct /
Cadillac / Complete/Pinnacle.

LET'S PICK IT
Messin' with my pride / Don't throw your
love on me so strong / All my whole life /
All of my life / Double dutch / Red light /
Cold and hungry / Love me with a feeling /
Dream / Let's pick it / Big leg mama / That
will never do
CD _____ ECD 260372
Evidence / Sep '93 / Harmonia Mundi / ADA
/ Cadillac.

MIND TROUBLE
CD _____ DTCD 3014
Double Trouble / Aug '88 / CM / Hot Shot.

THAT'S WHEN I KNOW
CD _____ BPCD 5014
Blind Pig / Dec '94 / Hot Shot / Swift /
CM / Roots / Direct / ADA.

Campbell, Gene

**GENE CAMPBELL & WILLIE REED
1928-1935 (Campbell, Gene & Willie
Reed)**
CD _____ BDCD 6043
Blues Document / May '93 / Swift / Jazz
Music / Hot Shot.

Campbell, Glen

BEST OF GLEN CAMPBELL, THE
CD _____ MATCD 303
Castle / Oct '94 / BMG.

BOY IN ME, THE
Boy in me / Living the legacy / Where time
stands still / Call it even / Come harvest
time / Best is yet to come / Something to
die for / Mercy's eyes / All I need is you /
Amazing grace
CD _____ 8441875372
Alliance Music / May '95 / EMI.

COUNTRY BOY
Country boy / Back in the race / This land
is your land / Galveston / Your cheatin'
heart / Tennessee home / Twelve string
special / California / Rhinestone cowboy /
Country girl / 500 miles away from home /
Gentle on my mind / Arkansas / I'm so lone-
some I could cry / True grit / Oklahoma
Sunday morning
CD _____ CD MFP 6034
Music For Pleasure / Oct '88 / EMI.

GLEN CAMPBELL IN CONCERT
Rhinestone cowboy / Gentle on my mind /
Medley / By the time I get to Phoenix /
Dreams of an everyday housewife / Heart-
ache number three / Please come to Boston
/ It's only make believe / Crying / Blue grass
medley / Milk cow blues / Rollin' in my
sweet baby's arms / I'm so lonesome I
could cry / Southern nights / Amazing grace
/ Try a little kindness / Mull of Kintyre
CD _____ TRTCD 163
TrueTrax / Dec '94 / THE.

GLEN CAMPBELL IN CONCERT
CD _____ 15346
Laserlight / Aug '91 / Target/BMG.

GLEN CAMPBELL LIVE
CD _____ EMPRCD 523
Empress / Sep '94 / THE.

GREATEST HITS - LIVE
Rhinestone cowboy / Gentle on my mind /
Medley (Wichita Lineman, Galveston &
Country Boy) / By the time I get to Phoenix
/ Dreams of an everyday housewife / Heart-
ache number two / Please come to Boston
/ It's only make believe / Crying / Blue grass
medley / Milk cow blues / Rollin' in my
sweet baby's arms / I'm so lonesome I
could cry / Southern nights / Amazing grace
/ Try a little kindness / Mull of Kintyre / In
your loving arms again / It's your world girls
and boys / Trials and tribulations
CD _____ CDGRF 182
Tring / Feb '93 / Tring / Prism.

IN CONCERT: GLEN CAMPBELL
Rhinestone cowboy / Gentle on my mind /
Wichita lineman / Galveston / Country boy
/ By the time I get to Phoenix / Dreams of
an everyday housewife / Heartache number
three / Please come to Boston / Trials and
tribulations / Crying/Blue grass medley /

Milk cow blues / Rollin' in my sweet baby's
arms / I'm so lonesome I could cry / Southern nights / Amazing grace / Try a little kindness / In your loving arms again / It's your
world girls and boys / Mull of Kintyre
CD _____ CPCD 8003
Charly / Oct '93 / Charly / THE / Cadillac.

LIVE 1994
CD _____ 12437
Laserlight / Mar '95 / Target/BMG.

LOVE SONGS: GLEN CAMPBELL
Gentle on my mind / Reason to believe / By
the time I get to Phoenix / It's only make
believe / Honey come back / Country girl /
One last time / I'm getting used to the crying / Last thing on my mind / Everything a
man could ever need / Dream baby / Hey
little one / Your cheatin' heart / This is Sarah's song / Let go / God only knows / How
high did we go (CD only.) / If this is love (CD
only.) / Love is not a game (CD only.) / For
my woman's love (CD only.)
CD _____ CDMFP 5881
Music For Pleasure / Apr '90 / EMI.

MAGIC OF GLEN CAMPBELL, THE
CD _____ TKOCD 001
TKO / '92 / TKO.

RHINESTONE COWBOY
CD _____ WMCD 5666
Disky / Oct '94 / THE / BMG / Discovery /
Pinnacle.

RHINESTONE COWBOY
CD _____ MU 5027
Musketeer / Oct '92 / Koch.

TWENTY GOLDEN GREATS
Rhinestone cowboy / Both sides now / By
the time I get to Phoenix / Too many morn-
ings / Wichita lineman / One last time /
Don't pull your love, then tell me goodbye /
Reason to believe / It's only make believe /
Honey come back / Give me back that old
familiar feeling / Galveston / Dreams of an
everyday housewife / Last thing on my mind
/ Where's the playground / Try a little kind-
ness / Country boy / All I have to do is
dream / Amazing grace
CD _____ CZ 363
EMI / Oct '90 / EMI.

UNCONDITIONAL LOVE
Unconditional love / We will / Right down to
the memories / Livin' in a house full of love
/ Healing hands of time / Next to you / So-
mebody's doin' me right / I'm gone this time
/ Once a day / Light of a clear blue morning
CD _____ CDP 790992 2
Capitol / Jun '91 / EMI.

VERY BEST OF GLEN CAMPBELL
Rhinestone cowboy / Wichita lineman / Galveston / By the time I get to Phoenix / Try
a little kindness / My little one / Where's the
playground / Gentle on my mind / Dreams
of an everyday housewife / All I have to do
is dream / Dream baby / It's only make believe / Sunflower / Southern nights / Country boy
CD _____ CDMFP 6023
Music For Pleasure / Apr '88 / EMI.

WICHITA LINEMAN
Wichita lineman / True grit / Hound dog
man / By the time I get to Phoenix / Country
girl / God only knows / Galveston / Let it be
me / Your cheatin' heart / Kentucky means
paradise / Early morning song / If you could
read my mind / Rhinestone cowboy / Gentle
on my mind / Until it's time for you to go /
Heart to heart / Highwayman / Words /
Southern nights / Take these chains from
my heart / Part time love / Any which way
you can / Too late to worry, too blue to cry
CD _____ VSOPCD 120
Connoisseur / Apr '90 / Pinnacle.

Campbell, Ian

**THIS IS ACROSS (Campbell, Ian Folk
Group)**
CD _____ ESMCD 357
Essential / Jan '96 / Total/BMG.

Campbell, John

HOWLIN' MERCY
Ain't afraid of midnight / When the levee
breaks / Down in the hole / Look what love
can do / Saddle up my pony / Firin' line /
Love's name / Written in stone / Wiseblood
/ Wolf among the lambs
CD _____ 7559614402
Elektra / Feb '93 / Warner Music.

**LIVE AT MAYBECK RECITAL HALL,
VOL. 29**
Just friends / You and the night and the mu-
sic / Invitation / Easy to love / Emily / I wish
I knew / Darn that dream / Touch of your
lips
CD _____ CCD 4581
Concord Jazz / Nov '93 / New Note.

MAN AND HIS BLUES, A
CD _____ CCD 11019
Crosscut / '92 / ADA / CM / Direct.

ONE BELIEVER
Devil in my closet / Angel of sorrow / Wild
streak / Couldn't do nothin' / Tiny coffin /
World of trouble / Voodoo edge / Person to
person / Take me down / One believer

CD _____ 7559610864
Elektra / Oct '91 / Warner Music.

Campbell, Mike

LOVING FRIENDS
CD _____ ACD 279
Audiophile / May '95 / Jazz Music / Swift.

ONE ON ONE
CD _____ ACD 259
Audiophile / Jun '93 / Jazz Music / Swift.

Campbell, Naomi

BABYWOMAN
Love and tears / I want to live / Ride a white
swan / Life of leisure / Babywoman / Looks
swank (spooky) / Picnic in the rain / When
I think about love / All through the night /
Sunshine on a rainy day / I want to live
(reprise)
CD _____ 476887 2
Epic / Oct '94 / Sony.

Campbell, Rocky

VALLEY OF TEARS
CD _____ ANGELLA 001CD
Angella / May '95 / Jetstar.

Campbell, Roy

NEW KINGDOM
CD _____ DD 456
Delmark / Jan '93 / Hot Shot / ADA / CM /
Direct / Cadillac.

Campbell, Royce

6 X 6
Happy blues / Love for sale / Milestones /
Naima / Agular blues / Day into night / In-
terplay / Softly as in a morning sunrise /
Darn that dream / Dancing on the ceiling
CD _____ KICJ 220
King/Paddle Wheel / Feb '95 / New Note.

Campbell, Sarah Elizabeth

LITTLE TENDERNESS, A
Mexico / I never meant to fall / Part of a
story / Waltz with you / Geraldine and
Ruthie Mae / Heartache / Tell me baby / To
remember / My heart can't seem to forget
/ I could use a little tenderness
CD _____ DJD 3220
Dejadisc / Nov '95 / Direct / ADA.

RUNNING WITH YOU
CD _____ DJD 3210
Dejadisc / May '94 / Direct / ADA.

Campbell, Tevin

I'M READY
Can we talk / Don't say goodbye girl / In-
terlude / Halls of desire / I'm ready / What
do I say / Uncle sam / Paris 1798430 / Al-
ways in my heart / Shhh / Brown eyed girl
/ Infant child
CD _____ 936245388-2
Qwest / Oct '93 / Warner Music.

T.E.V.I.N.
Interlude/over the rainbow and on to the
sun / Tell me what you want me to do / Li'l
brother / Strawberry letter 23 / One song /
Round and round / Just asking me to / Perfect world / Look what we'd have (if you
were mine) / She's all that
CD _____ 7599262912
Qwest / Apr '92 / Warner Music.

Campbells

POWER & HONESTY
CD _____ IRVCD 562
Scotdisc / Apr '93 / Duncans / Ross /
Conifer.

Campi, Ray

EAGER BEAVER BOY
Hot dog / All the time / Boogie boogie boo
/ Rock it / Thought of losing / Waffle stom-
pin' mama / Blue ranger / Ballin' keen / Let
'er roll / Dobro daddio from Del Rio / Born
to be wild / How low can you feel / Where
my sweet baby goes / Tribute to 'You know
who' / Eager beaver boy / Pretty mama /
One part stops where the other begins /
Pinball millionaire / When two ends meet /
Good time woman / It ain't me (piano ver-
sion) / Chug-a-lug / Parts unknown /
Wicked wicked woman / Shelby county pe-
nal farm / Don't give your heart to a rambler
/ Play anything / Major label blues
CD _____ BCD 15501
Bear Family / Sep '90 / Rollercoaster /
Direct / CM / Swift / ADA.

ORIGINAL ROCKABILLY ALBUM, THE
Caterpillar / It ain't me / Let go of Louise /
Livin' on love / My screamin' screamin'
Mimi / Long tall Sally / Johnny's jive / Play
it cool / Give that love to me / You can't
catch me / I didn't mean to be mean /
Crossing / Loretta
CD _____ CDMF 063
Magnum Force / Jul '90 / Magnum Music
Group.

ROCKABILLY ROCKET
Second story man / Don't get pushy / Cravin' / Separate ways / Gonna bid my blues
goodbye / How can I get on top / Little
young girl / Chew tobacco rag / You don't
rock and roll at all / Ruby Ann / I don't know
why you still come around / Runnin' after
fools / Jimmie skins the blues
CD _____ CDMF 046
Magnum Force / May '94 / Magnum Music
Group.

TAYLOR, TEXAS 1988
Curtain of tears / Haunted hungry heart /
Woods are full of them now / Dessau waltz
/ When they operated on papa / Butterball
bounce / Wild side of live / That's that / Mil-
lion tears / Honk your horn / Love for sale /
Honky tonk women / Bermuda grass waltz
CD _____ BCD 15486
Bear Family / Nov '89 / Rollercoaster /
Direct / CM / Swift / ADA.

Campoli, Alfredo

**ALDREDO CAMPOLI AND HIS SALON
ORCHESTRA (Campoli, Alfredo & his
Salon Orchestra)**
Mosquitoes' parade / Shadow waltz / El-
gar's serenade / Little valley in the mountains / Snowman / Czardas / Liszt, Chopin
and Mendelssohn / Mouse in the clock / Si-
monetta / Musical box / Wild violets / Parade of the pirates / Cavatina / Moths
around the candle flame / Waltzing to Archibald Joyce / Serenade / Love in idleness
/ Knave of diamonds / Fairy tale / In old
Vienna / La petite tonkinoise / Garden of
roses
CD _____ PASTCD 9707
Flapper / '90 / Pinnacle.

CAMPOLI'S CHOICE
CD _____ PASTCD 7744
Flapper / Jun '91 / Pinnacle.

SALON MUSIC OF THE THIRTIES
Ah sweet mystery of life / Butterfly / Canary
/ Czardas / Daddy long legs / Goodnight
waltz / Grasshoppers dance / Gypsy love
song / Her first dance / Hiawatha / Moths
around the candle flame / Old Spanish
tango / Old spinning wheel / Old violin /
Only my song / Pale Volga moon / La petite
tonkinoise / Popular Viennese waltzes (selection) / Softly awakes my heart / Song of
paradise / Tell me tonight / Waltzing to Irving Berlin
CD _____ CDAJA 5135
Living Era / Jul '94 / Koch.

Can

ANTHOLOGY
CD Set _____ SPOONCD 3031
Grey Area / Oct '94 / Pinnacle.

CAN DELAY 1968
Butterfly / Pnoom / Nineteen century man /
Thief / Man named Joe / Uphill / Little star
of Bethlehem
CD _____ SPOONCD 012
Mute / Jul '89 / Disc.

CANNIBALISM III
CD _____ SPOONCD 22
Mute / Jan '95 / Disc.

EGE BAMYASI
Pinch / Sing swan song / One more night /
Vitamin C / Soup / I'm so green / Spoon
CD _____ SPOONCD 008
Mute / Jul '89 / Disc.

FUTURE DAYS
Future days / Spray / Moonshake / Bel-air
CD _____ SPOONCD 009
Mute / Jul '89 / Disc.

INNER SPACE
All gates open / Safe / Sunday jam / Sodom
/ Spectacle / Can can / Ping pong / Can be
CD _____ CDTB 020
Thunderbolt / '88 / Magnum Music Group.

LANDED
Full moon on the highway / Half past one /
Hunters and collectors / Vernal equinox /
Red hot Indians / Unfinished
CD _____ CDV 2041
Virgin / Jun '88 / EMI.

LIVE AT THE BBC
Up the Bakerloo line / Return to BBC city /
Tape kebab / Tony wanna go / Geheim /
Mighty girl
CD _____ SFRCD 135
Strange Fruit / Aug '95 / Pinnacle.

MONSTER MOVIE
Father cannot yell / Mary Mary so contrary
/ Outside my door / Yoo doo right
CD _____ SPOONCD 004
Mute / Jul '89 / Disc.

OUT OF REACH
Serpentine / Pauper's daughter and I / No-
vember / Seven days awake / Give me no
'roses' / Like inobe God / One more day
CD _____ CDTB 025
Thunderbolt / Nov '88 / Magnum Music
Group.

RITE TIME
CD _____ SPOONCD 29
Grey Area / Oct '94 / Pinnacle.

SOON OVER BABALUMA
Dizzy dizzy / Come sta, la luna / Splash / Chain reaction / Quantum physics
CD _____ SPOONCD 010
Mute / Jul '89 / Disc.

SOUNDTRACKS
Deadlock / Tango whiskeyman / Don't turn the light on, leave me alone / Soul desert / Mother sky / She brings the rain
CD _____ SPOONCD 005
Mute / Jul '89 / Disc.

Canadian All Stars

EUROPEAN CONCERT
CD _____ SKCD 2-3055
Sackville / Oct '94 / Swift / Jazz Music / Jazz Horizons / Cadillac / CM.

Canadian Brass

RENAISSANCE MEN
CD _____ 09026681082
RCA Victor / Nov '95 / BMG.

SWINGTIME
Artistry in rhythm / Blue rondo a la Turk / Back home in Indiana / 'Round about midnight / AT the Woodchopper's ball / Lady is a tramp / Sugar blues / Man I love / Whatever happened to the dream / Concierto de Aranjuez / I found love / Ellington medley (Mood Indigo, Don't get around much anymore, Take the A train) / One o'clock jump
CD _____ 09026683152
RCA Victor / Oct '95 / BMG.

Canadian Forces School...

CANADA SUPREME (Canadian Forces School Of Music Band)
CD _____ BNA 5066
Bandleader / Nov '92 / Conifer.

Canambu

SON CUBANO: THE RHYTHM STICKS
CD _____ CORA 123
Corason / Apr '95 / CM / Direct / ADA.

Canavan, Josie

O AIRD GO HAIRD (Canavan, Josie & Tommy)
CD _____ CICD 044
Clo Iar-Chonnachta / Dec '94 / CM.

Cancer

BLACK FAITH
CD _____ 0630107522
East West / Jul '95 / Warner Music.

Candi

CANDI
Under your spell / Missing you / Shine on / Independent / Love makes no promises / Dancing under a Latin moon / Dance with me / Lucky night / Pleasure island / Closer than ever
CD _____ EIRSACD 1007
IRS / Mar '89 / PolyGram / BMG / EMI.

Candido

DANCIN' AND PRANCIN'
Dancin' and prancin' / Jingo / Thousand finger man / Rock and shuffle
CD _____ CPCD 8074
Charly / Mar '95 / Charly / THE / Cadillac.

Candlebox

CANDLEBOX
Don't you / Change / You / No sense / Far behind / Blossom / Arrow / Rain / Mothers dream / Cover me / He calls home
CD _____ 9362453132
Maverick / Jul '93 / Warner Music.

WIDELUX
CD _____ 9362459622
Maverick / Aug '95 / Warner Music.

Candlemass

AS IT IS, AS IT WAS (The Best Of Candlemass)
Solitude / Bewitched / Dying illusion / Demon's gate / Mirror mirror (Live) / Samaritan / Into the unfathomed tower / Bearer of pain / Where the runes still speak / At the gallows end / Mourner's lament / Tale of creation / Ebony throne / Under the oak / Well of souls / Dark are the veils of death / Darkness in paradise / End of pain / Sorcerer's pledge / Solitude '87 / Crystal ball '87 / Bullfest '93
CD _____ CDMFN 166
Music For Nations / Oct '94 / Pinnacle.

CANDLEMASS LIVE IN STOCKHOLM 9TH JUNE 1990
Well of souls / Bewitched / Dark reflections / Demon's gate / Through the infinitive halls of death / Mirror mirror / Sorceror's pledge / Dark are the veils / Solitude / Under the oak / Bells of Acheron / Samaritan / Gallows end
CD _____ CDMFN 109
Music For Nations / Nov '90 / Pinnacle.

Chapter Six

CHAPTER SIX
CD _____ CDMFN 128
Music For Nations / May '92 / Pinnacle.

EPICUS DOOMICUS METALLICA
CD _____ BD 013
Black Dragon / Apr '95 / Else.

TALES OF CREATION
CD _____ MFNCD 95
Music For Nations / Sep '89 / Pinnacle.

Candler, Norman

MAGIC DREAMS (Candler, Norman Strings)
CD _____ ISCD 116
Intersound / Oct '91 / Jazz Music.

MAGIC STRINGS VOL. 1
CD _____ ISCD 001
Intersound / Jul '93 / Jazz Music.

MAGIC STRINGS VOL. 2
CD _____ ISCD 002
Intersound / Jul '93 / Jazz Music.

SOFT MAGIC, THE (Candler, Norman & The Magic Strings)
CD _____ ISCD 101
Intersound / Oct '89 / Jazz Music.

Cannata

WATCHING THE WORLD
CD _____ NTHEN 3
Now & Then / Sep '95 / Plastic Head.

Canned Heat

BIG HEAT, THE (3CD Set)
Rollin' and tumblin' / Bullfrog blues / Evil is going on / Help me / Story of my life / Road song / On the road again / World in a jug / Amphetamine Annie / Owl song / Marie Laveau / Fried hockey boogie / Pony blues / My mistake / Going up the country / Walking by myself / Boogie music / One kind favour / Chipmunk song / Parthenogenesis / Same all over / Change my ways / Canned heat / Sic 'em pigs / Poor moon / Time was / Do not enter / Big fat / Get off my back / Down in the gutter but free / Sugar bee / Shake it and break it / That's all right / My time ain't long / Skat / Let's work together / Future blues / So sad (the world's in a tangle) / London blues / Sneakin' around / Hill's stomp / Rockin' with the King / Utah / Keep it clean / Harley Davidson blues / Don't deceive me / You can run but you sure can't hide / Lookin' for my rainbow / Rock 'n' roll music / Framed / Election blues / So long wrong
CD Set _____ CANNED 7802752
Liberty / Sep '92 / EMI.

BURNIN' LIVE
CD _____ AIM 1033CD
Aim / Oct '93 / Direct / ADA / Jazz Music.

CANNED HEAT
Rollin' and tumblin' / Bullfrog blues / Evil is going on / Going down slow / Catfish blues / Dust my broom / Help me / Big road blues / Story of my life / Road song / Rich woman
CD _____ SEECD 268
See For Miles/C5 / Aug '90 / Pinnacle.

FUTURE BLUES
CD _____ BGOCD 49
Beat Goes On / Sep '89 / Pinnacle.

HISTORICAL FIGURES AND ANCIENT HEADS
Sneakin' around / Rockin' with the king / Long way from L.A. / That's all right / Hill's stomp / I don't care what you tell me / Cherokee dance / Utah
CD _____ BGOCD 83
Beat Goes On / Aug '90 / Pinnacle.

INTERNAL COMBUSTION
CD _____ AIM 1044
Aim / Apr '95 / Direct / ADA / Jazz Music.

LET'S WORK TOGETHER (Best Of Canned Heat)
On the road again / Bullfrog blues / Rollin' and tumblin' / Amphetamine Annie / Fried hockey boogie / Sic 'em pigs / Poor moon / Let's work together / Going up the country / Boogie music / Same all over / Time was / Sugar bee / Rockin' with the king / That's alright mama / My time ain't long / Future blues (CD only.) / Pony blues (CD only.) / So sad (the world's in a tangle) (CD only.) / Chipmunk song (CD only.)
CD _____ CZ 226
Liberty / Sep '89 / EMI.

LIVE
CD _____ CDCD 1104
Charly / Jul '93 / Charly / THE / Cadillac.

LIVE AT THE TURKU ROCK FESTIVAL, 1971
She don't want me no more / Let's work together / On the road again / That's all right / Hill stomp / Long way from L.A. / Watch yourself / Canned Heat boogie / Late night blues
CD _____ BTCD 979409
Beartracks / Mar '90 / Rollercoaster.

LIVE IN AUSTRALIA
CD _____ AIM 1003CD
Aim / Oct '93 / Direct / ADA / Jazz Music.

LIVE IN EUROPE-'70
CD _____ BGOCD 12
Beat Goes On / Sep '89 / Pinnacle.

NEW AGE
CD _____ BGOCD 85
Beat Goes On / Dec '90 / Pinnacle.

ON THE ROAD AGAIN
On the road again / Amphetamine Annie / My crime / Time was / Going up the country / Sugar bee / Whiskey headed woman / Bullfrog blues / Let's work together / World in a jug / Fried hockey boogie / Rollin' and tumblin' / I'm her man / Dust by broom / Parthenogenesis (CD only.)
CD _____ CDFA 3222
Fame / Oct '89 / EMI.

PEARLS FROM THE PAST VOL. 2 - CANNED HEAT
CD _____ KLMCD 015
Scratch / May '94 / BMG.

ROCK LEGENDS VOL.1
CD _____ SMS 053
Carlton Home Entertainment / Sep '92 / Carlton Home Entertainment.

STRAIGHT AHEAD
Big road blues / I've got my mojo working / Pretty thing / Louise / Dimples / Talk to me baby / Straight ahead / Rollin' and tumblin' / I'd rather be a devil / It hurts me too / Bullfrog blues / Sweet sixteen / Dust my broom
CD _____ CDTB 130
Thunderbolt / Dec '91 / Magnum Music Group.

UNCANNED (The Best Of Canned Heat)
On the road again (Alternate take) / Nine below zero / TV Mama / Rollin' and tumblin' / Bullfrog blues / Evil is going on / Goin' down slow / Dust my broom / Help me / Story of my life / Hunter / Whiskey and wimmen / Shake, rattle and roll / Mean old world / Fannie Mae / Gotta boogie (The world boogie) / My crime / On the road again / Evil woman / Amphetamine Annie / Old owl song / Christmas blues / Going up the country / Time was / Low down (and high up) / Same all over / Big fat (The fat man) / It's all right / Poor moon / Sugar bee / Shake it and break it / Future blues / Let's work together / Wooly bully / Human condition / Long way from L.A. / Hill's stomp / Rockin' with the king / Harley Davidson blues / Rock 'n' roll music
CD _____ CDEM 1543
Liberty / Aug '94 / EMI.

Cannibal Corpse

BLEEDING
Staring through the eyes of the dead / Fucked with a knife / Stripped, raped and strangled / Pulverized / Return to flesh / Pick-axe murders / She was asking for it / Bleeding / Force fed broken glass / Experiment in homicide
CD _____ CDZORRO 67
Metal Blade / Mar '94 / Pinnacle.

BUTCHERED AT BIRTH
CD _____ CDZORRO 26
Metal Blade / Aug '94 / Pinnacle.

EATEN BACK TO LIFE
Shredded humans / Put them to death / Scattered remains, splattered brains / Rotting head / Bloody chunks / Buried in the backyard / Edible autopsy / Mangled / Born in a casket / Undead will feast / Skull full of maggots
CD _____ CDZORRO 12
Metal Blade / Sep '90 / Pinnacle.

HAMMER SMASHED FACE
Hammer smashed face / Exorcist / Zero the hero / Meat hook sodomy / Shredded humans
CD _____ CDMZORRO 57
Metal Blade / Apr '93 / Pinnacle.

TOMB OF THE MUTILATED
CD _____ CDZORRO 49
Metal Blade / Sep '92 / Pinnacle.

Cannibals

BREAST OF THE CANNIBALS
CD _____ CDHIT 2
Hit / Feb '95 / Disc.

Canning, Francis

MY DREAMS OF LONG AGO
After all these years / Let the rest of the world go by / Village where I went to school / Old rugged cross / If those lips could only speak / If I had my life to live over / Fool such as I / True love / Mother's love's a blessing / I will love you all my life / When I grow too old to dream / Old rustic bridge by the mill / My dreams of long ago / Maggie / Sunshine of your smile / Pal of my cradle days / Silver threads among the gold / I'll be your sweetheart
CD _____ LCOM 3006
Lismor / Sep '95 / Lismor / Direct / Duncans / ADA.

Cannon, Ace

ACES HI/PLAYS THE GREAT SHOW TUNES

CD _____ HIUKCD 125
Hi / Jun '93 / Pinnacle.

ROCKIN' ROBIN
CD _____ HADCD 198
Javelin / Nov '95 / THE / Henry Hadaway Organisation.

TUFF SAX/MOANING SAX
Tuff sax / Trouble in mind / St. Louis blues / Wabash blues / Basin Street blues / Cannonball / Blues in my heart / Blues stay away from me / Lonesome Road / Careless love / Kansas City / I've got a woman / Moanin' the blues / Trouble in mind (version 2) / Prisoner's song / I love you because / Last date / Singin' the blues / It's all in the game / No letter today / I left my heart in San Francisco / I can't get started (with you) / Prisoner of love / Moanin'
CD _____ HIUKCD 121
Hi / Sep '91 / Pinnacle.

Cannon, Gus

GUS CANNON, VOL. 1 (1927 - 28)
Blues Document / Feb '92 / Swift / Jazz Music / Hot Shot.
CD _____ DOCD 5032

GUS CANNON, VOL. 2 (1929 - 30) (Cannon, Gus & Noah Lewis)
CD _____ DOCD 5033
Blues Document / Feb '92 / Swift / Jazz Music / Hot Shot.

LEGENDARY 1928-30 RECORDINGS, THE (Cannon, Gus & his Jug Stompers)
Minglewood blues / Big railroad blues / Madison street rag / Springdale blues / Ripley blues / Pig ankle strut / Noah's blues / Hollywood rag / Heartbreakin' blues / Feather bed / Cairo rag / Bugle call rag / Viola Lee blues / Rileys wagon / Last chance blues / Tired chicken blues / Going to Germany / Walk right in / Mule get up in the alley / Roosters crowing blues / Jonestown blues / Pretty Mama blues / Bring it with you when you come / Wolf river blues / Money never runs out / Prison wall blues
CD _____ JSPCD 610
JSP / Jun '94 / ADA / Target/BMG / Direct / Cadillac / Complete/Pinnacle.

Cannon's Jug Stompers

COMPLETE
CD _____ YAZCD 1082
Yazoo / Apr '91 / CM / ADA / Roots / Koch.

Canter, Robin

OBOE COLLECTION
CD _____ CDSAR 22
Amon Ra / '88 / Harmonia Mundi.

Canterbury Cathedral...

CANTERBURY CAROLS (Canterbury Cathedral Choir)
O come, all ye faithful / Sussex carol / Stille nacht (Silent night) / Once in royal David's city / Ding dong merrily on high / Candlelight carol / God rest ye merry Gentlemen / Three kings / O little town of Bethlehem / Gaudete, Chrestus natus est / In the bleak midwinter / While shepherds watched their flocks by night / Away in a manger / Hark the herald angels sing / Toccata for organ (Dubois)
CD _____ YORKCD 109
York Ambisonic / Oct '95 / Target/BMG.

Canticum Puellius

ENDLESS
CD _____ CDSATE 14
Music Research / Jan '95 / Plastic Head.

Cantor, Eddie

MAKIN' WHOOPEE
That's the kind of a baby for me / Mandy / My wife is on a diet / Girlfriend of a boyfriend of mine / Okay toots / When my ship comes in / There's nothing too good for my baby / Over somebody else's shoulder / Hello, sunshine, hello / Makin' whoopee / Earful of music / Put a tax on love / Making the best of each day / What a perfect combination / Man on the flying trapeze / Yes yes (my baby says yes) / If I give up the saxophone / Look what you've done / Hungry women / Build a little home
CD _____ CMSCD 006
Movie Stars / '89 / Conifer.

Cantovivo

ANTOLOGIA
CD _____ BRAM 199120-2
Brambus / Nov '93 / ADA / Direct.

Canvey Island Allstars

ESCAPE FROM OIL CITY
CD _____ FOAMCD 4
On The Beach / Apr '91 / Pinnacle / Direct.

Canyon Dreams

TANGERINE DREAMS
Shadow flyer / Canyon carver / Water's gift / Canyon voices / Sudden revelation / Matter of time / Purple nighfall / Colorado dawn
CD _____ MPCD 2801
Miramar / Jun '93 / New Note.

Cao, Emilio

CARTAS MARINAS
CD _____ F 1021CD
Sonifolk / Jun '94 / ADA / CM.

Capart, Louis

MARIE-JEANNE GABRIELLE
CD _____ KMCD 06
Keltia Musique / '91 / ADA / Direct / Discovery.

PATIENCE
CD _____ KMCD 13
Keltia Musique / '91 / ADA / Direct / Discovery.

Capelino

LA COPINE
CD _____ BMCD 281
Munich / May '94 / CM / ADA / Greensleeves / Direct.

Capella Cordina

MISSA L'HOMME ARME
CD _____ LEMS 8009
Lyrichord / Aug '94 / Roots / ADA / CM.

TWO THREE VOICE MASSES, THE
CD _____ LEMS 8010
Lyrichord / Aug '94 / Roots / ADA / CM.

Capercaillie

BLOOD IS STRONG, THE
Aignish / Arrival / Iona / Calum's road / Fear / Dean Cadalan samhach / Grandfather mountain / An atairreachd ard / 'S fhada learn an oidhche gheamhraidh / Hebrides / Lordship of the isles / Arrival reprise / Columcille / Downtown Toronto
CD _____ SURCD 014
Survival / Jun '95 / Pinnacle.

CAPERCAILLIE
Miracle of being / When you return / Grace and pride / Tobermory / Take the floor / Stinging rain / Aladsair / Crime and passion / Bonaparte / When you return (2)
CD _____ SURCD 018
Survival / May '95 / Pinnacle.

CROSSWINDS
Puirt-a-beul / Soraidh bhuam gu barraidh / Glenorchy / Am buachaille ban / Haggis / Brenda Stubbart's set / Ma theid mise tuilleagh / David Glen's / Urnaigh a 'bhan-thigreach / My laggan love/Fox on the town / An ribhinn donn
CD _____ GLCD 1077
Green Linnet / May '92 / Roots / CM / Direct / ADA.

DELIRIUM
Rann na mona / Waiting for the wheel to turn / Aodann Strathbain / Cape Breton song / You will rise again / Kenny MacDonald's jigs (Not available on LP) / Dean saor an spiorad (Not available on LP) / Cois ich a ruin (walk my beloved) / Dr. MacPhail's reel / Heart of the highland / Brelsleach / Islay Ranter's reels (Not available on LP) / Servant to the slave
CD _____ SURCD 015
Survival / May '95 / Pinnacle.

GET OUT
Waiting for the wheel to turn / Pige ruadh ((i) Dean cadalan sambach (ii) Servant to the slave) / Silver spear reels / Outlaws / Cois ich a ruin (walk my beloved) / Fear a'bhata / Dr. MacPhail's trance
CD _____ SURCD 016
Survival / May '95 / Pinnacle.

SECRET PEOPLE
Bonaparte / Grace and pride / Tobar Mhoire (Tobermory) / Miracle of being / Crime of passion / Whinney hills jigs / An eala bhan (the white swan) / Seice Ruairidh (Roddy's drum) / Stinging rain / Hi rim bo / Four stone walls / Harley ashtray / Oran / Black fields
CD _____ SURCD 017
Survival / May '95 / Pinnacle.

SIDEWAULK
Alasdair Mhic Cholla Ghasda / Balindore / Fisherman's dream / Sidewaulk reels / Iain Ghlinn'Cuaich / Fosgail an Dorus / Turnpike / Both sides of the tweed / Weasel / Oh mo Dhuthaich
CD _____ CDGL 1094
Green Linnet / Feb '89 / Roots / CM / Direct / ADA.

TO THE MOON
To the moon / Claire in heaven / Wanderer / Price of fire / Rob Roy reels / Ailein Duinn / Nil si / Crooked mountain / Quady's alabi / Collector's daughter / Only you
CD _____ SURCD 019
Survival / Oct '95 / Pinnacle.

Capers, Valerie

COME ON HOME
Night in Tunisia / Out of all (he's chosen me) / Odyssey / I've never been in love before / One note samba / Come and show a mellow tone / Tell him thanks / It's all right with me
CD _____ 4781792
Sony Music / Apr '95 / Sony.

Capitol Punishment

FIRST LINE-UP, THE
CD _____ WB 1078166-2
We Bite / Sep '93 / Plastic Head.

LIVIN' ON THE EDGE OF A RAZOR
Livin' on the edge of a razor / This is how it should be done / Murder / B-insane bass / Caliber 380 / Death sentence / Them hoes / Non-believers / Penbound / Aggravated MC / Stunt bitch / Find you some business / Livin' on the edge of a razor (instrumental)
CD _____ WRA 8102 CD
Wrap / Nov '91 / Koch.

MESSIAH COMPLEX
CD _____ WB 210-2
We Bite / Apr '94 / Plastic Head.

Capleton

PROPHECY
Tour / Big time / Obstacle / Leave Babylon / Heathen reign / Don't dis the trinity / No competetion / Wings of the morning / See from afar
CD _____ 5292642
RAL / Oct '95 / PolyGram.

Capp, Frank

FRANK CAPP TRIO PRESENTS RICKEY WOODWARD (Capp, Frank Trio)
Oleo / Au privave / If I should lose you / Speak low / Sweet Lorraine / Polka dots and moonbeams / Doxy / Three bears / You tell me
CD _____ CCD 4469
Concord Jazz / Jul '9 / New Note.

IN A HEFTI BAG (Capp, Frank Juggernaut)
I'm shoutin' again / Cherry point / Flight of the Foo birds / Kid from Red Bank / Splanky / Fantail / Li'l darlin' / Duet / Whirly bird / Cute / Awful nice to be with you / Bag a' bones / Midnight blue / Dinner with my friends / Teddy the toad / Scoot / Late date
CD _____ CCD 4655
Concord Jazz / Jul '95 / New Note.

QUALITY TIME
Dip stick / Back to Brea / I've never been in love before / Daahoud / There you have it / Tadd's delight / 9:20 Special / Sophisticated lady / Things ain't what they used to be
CD _____ CCD 4677
Concord Jazz / Dec '95 / New Note.

Capp-Pierce Juggernaut

CAPP-PIERCE JUGGERNAUT
Avenue C / All heart / Moten swing / Basie / Mr. Softie / It's sand man / Dickie's dream / Take the 'A' train / Wee baby blues / Roll 'em Pete
CD _____ CCD 4040
Concord Jazz / Jun '91 / New Note.

JUGGERNAUT STRIKES AGAIN
One for Marshall / I remember Clifford / New York shuffle / Chops, fingers and sticks / You are so beautiful / Parker's mood / Word from Bird / Charade / Things ain't what they used to be / Little Pony
CD _____ CCD 4183
Concord Jazz / Aug '90 / New Note.

Cappella

U GOT 2 KNOW
U got 2 know / U got 2 let the music / Don't be proud / U and me / Everybody / Move on baby / What I gotta do / Shake your body / Big beat / Move it up / U got 2 know (Mix)
CD _____ CAPCD 1
Internal / Mar '94 / PolyGram / Pinnacle.

Cappelletti, Arrigo

TRANSFORMATION (W.OLIVIER MANOURI) (Cappelletti, Arrigo Quartet)
CD _____ Y225024
Silex / Jun '93 / ADA.

Capris

CAPRIS 1954-1958
CD _____ FLYCD 8
Flyright / Oct '93 / Hot Shot / Wellard / Jazz Music / CM.

Captain & Tennille

SCRAPBOOK
Do that to me one more time / Love on a shoestring / You've never done it like that before / Lonely night (Angel face) / No love in the morning / Baby I still got it / Keeping our love warm / Love will keep us together / Can't stop dancing / Until you come back to me / Shop around / You need a woman

tonight / Happy together (A fantasy) / Way I want to touch you
CD _____ 5501212
Spectrum/Karussell / Oct '93 / PolyGram / THE.

Captain Beefheart

BLUE JEANS AND MOONBEAMS
Captain's holiday / Pompadour swamp / Party of special things to do / Blue jeans and moonbeans / Twist ah luck / Further than we've gone / Rock 'n' roll's evil doll / Observatory quest / Same old blues
CD _____ CDV 2023
Virgin / Jun '88 / EMI.

CARROT IS AS CLOSE AS A RABBIT GETS TO A DIAMOND
Sugar bowl / Past sure is tense / Happy love song / Floppy boot stomp / Blue jeans and moonbeans / Run paint run run / This is the day / Tropical hot dog night / Observatory crest / Host the ghost the most holy O / Harry Irene / I got love on my mind / Pompadour swamp / Love lies / Sheriff of Hong Kong / Further than we've gone / Candle mambo / Light reflected off the oceans of the moon / Carrot is as close as a rabbit gets to a diamond
CD _____ CDVM 9028
Virgin / Jul '93 / EMI.

DOC AT THE RADAR STATION
Hothead / Ashtray heart / Carrot is as close as a rabbit gets to a diamond / Run paint run run / Sue Egypt / Brickbats / Dirty blue gene / Best batch yet / Telephone / Flavour bud living / Sheriff of Hong Kong / Making love to a vampire with a monkey on my knee
CD _____ CDV 2172
Virgin / Jun '88 / EMI.

I MAY BE HUNGRY BUT I SURE AIN'T WEIRD (The Alternate Captain Beefheart)
Trust us (take 6) / Beatle bones n' smokin' stones (part 1) / Moody Liz (take 8) / Safe as milk (take 12) / Gimme dat harp boy / On tomorrow (instrumental) / Trust us (take 9) / Safe as milk (take 5) / Big black baby shoes (instrumental) / Flower pot (Mixes) / Dirty blue gene (Instrumental)
CD _____ NEXCD 215
Sequel / Jun '92 / BMG.

ICE CREAM FOR CROW
Ice cream for crow / Host the ghost the most holy O / Semi-multicoloured caucasian / Hey Garland, I dig your tweed coat / Evening bells / Cardboard cut-out sundown / Past sure is tense / Ink mathematics / Witch doctor love / 81 poop hatch / Thousanth and tenth day of the human totem pole / Skeleton makes good
CD _____ CDV 2237
Virgin / Apr '88 / EMI.

LEGENDARY A & M SESSIONS
Diddy wah diddy / Who do you think you're fooling / Moonchild / Frying pan / Here I am I always am
CD _____ BLIMPCD 902
Edsel / Mar '92 / Pinnacle / ADA.

LONDON 1974
CD _____ MPG 74025
Movieplay Gold / Nov '93 / Target/BMG.

MIRROR MAN (Captain Beefheart & His Magic Band)
Tarotplane / Kandy korn / 25th century quaker / Mirror man
CD _____ CLACD 235
Castle / May '91 / BMG.

SAFE AS MILK (Captain Beefheart & His Magic Band)
Sure nuff 'n' yes I do / Zig zag wanderer / Call on me / Dropout boogie / I'm glad / Electricity / Yellow brick road / Abba zaba / Plastic factory / Where there's a woman / Grown so ugly / Autumn's child
CD _____ CLACD 234
Castle / May '91 / BMG.

SHINY BEAST (BAT CHAIN PULLER)
Floppy boot stomp / Tropical hot dog night / Ice rose / Harry Irene / You know you're a man / Bat chain puller / When I see mummy I feel like a mummy / Owed t Alex / Candle mambo / Love lies / Suction prints / Apes-ma
CD _____ CDV 2149
Virgin / Jul '87 / EMI.

SPOTLIGHT KID/CLEAR SPOT (Captain Beefheart & His Magic Band)
I'm gonna booglarize you baby / White jam / Blabber 'n smoke / When it blows it's stacks / Alic in blunderland / Spotlight kid / Click clack / Grow fins / There ain't no Santa Claus / Glider / Low yo yo stuff / Nowadays a woman's gotta hit a man / Too much time / Circumstances / My head is my only house unless it rains / Sum zoom spark / Clear spot / Crazy little thing / Long neck bottles / Her eyes are a blue million miles / Big eyes beans from Venus / Goldne birdies
CD _____ 9259262492
Warner Bros. / Aug '90 / Warner Music.

STRICTLY PERSONAL
Ah feel like acid / Safe as milk / Trust us / Son of mirror man-mere man / On tomorrow / Beatle bones n' smokin' stones / Gimme dat harp boy / Kandy korn

CD _____ CZ 529
EMI / Jul '94 / EMI.

TROUT MASK REPLICA
Hair pie: Bake II / Pena / Well / When Big Joan sets up / Fallin' ditch / Sugar 'n' spikes / Ant man bee / Orange claw hammer / Wild life / She's too much for my mirror / Hobo chang ba / Blimp (mousetrapreplica) / Steal softly thru snow / Old fart at play / Veteran's day poppy
CD _____ 759927196-2
Warner Bros. / Sep '94 / Warner Music.

UNCONDITIONALLY GUARANTEED
Upon the my-o-my / Sugar bowl / New electric ride / Magic be / Happy love song / Full moon hot sun / I got love on my mind / This is the day / Lazy music / Peaches
CD _____ CDV 2015
Virgin / Jun '88 / EMI.

Captain Gumbo

BACK A LA MAISON
CD _____ CDMW 2006
Music & Words / Apr '93 / ADA / Direct.

CHANK-A-CHANK
CD _____ MW 2012CD
Music & Words / Aug '94 / ADA / Direct.

ONE MORE TWO STEP
CD _____ MW 2001CD
Music & Words / Jun '92 / ADA / Direct.

Captain Hollywood

ANIMALS & HUMANS
CD _____ PULSE 20CD
Pulse 8 / Apr '95 / Pinnacle / 3MV.

LOVE IS NOT SEX
CD _____ INT 179
Pulse 8 / Apr '95 / Pinnacle / 3MV.

Captain Rizz

MANIFESTO
Vodoo Rizz / Rizz's radio song / Rizz's anthem / City of angels / St. Cecelia / Rizz's radio song (instrumental) / Voodoo Rizz (instrumental)
CD _____ EBSCD 112
Emergency Broadcast System / Feb '95 / Vital.

Captain Sensible

LIVE AT THE MILKY WAY
Interstella overcoat / Jet boy jet girl / Smash it up / Back to school / Come on Geoffrey Brown / Happy talk / Kamikaze millionaire / Exploding heads and teapots / Love song / Neat neat neat / New rose / Wot / Looking at you / Hey Joe / Glad it's all over
CD _____ BAH 12
Humbug / Aug '94 / Pinnacle.

MEATHEAD
CD Set _____ BAH 14
Humbug / Aug '94 / Pinnacle.

REVOLUTION NOW
CD _____ BAH 3
Humbug / Feb '93 / Pinnacle.

UNIVERSE OF GEOFFREY BROWN, THE
CD _____ BAH 4
Humbug / Mar '93 / Pinnacle.

Caravan

BATTLE OF HASTINGS
CD _____ HTDCD 41
HTD / Oct '95 / Pinnacle.

BEST OF CARAVAN
And I wish I were stoned again / Don't worry / Francoise-for-Richard-Musical / Can't be long now (Medley) / Warlock / No backstage pass / Dog, the dog, he's at it again / Love in your eye / To catch me a brother / In the land of grey and pink / Memory Iain Hugh
CD _____ C5CD-505X
See For Miles/C5 / Apr '93 / Pinnacle.

CANTERBURY COLLECTION
It's never too late / What'cha gonna tell me / All aboard / Piano player / Sally don't change it / Bright shiny day / Clear blue sky / Bet you wanna take it all / Hold on hold on / Corner of me eye / Taken my breath away
CD _____ CD KVL 9028
Kingdom / Jan '87 / Kingdom.

CARAVAN IN CONCERT
CD _____ WINCD 003
Windsong / Sep '91 / Pinnacle.

COOL WATER
CD _____ HTDCD 18
HTD / Feb '94 / Pinnacle.

CUNNING STUNTS
CD _____ HTDCD 52
HTD / Jan '96 / Pinnacle.

EVENING OF MAGIC, AN (Sinclair, Richard)
In the land of grey and pink / Only the brave/plan it earth / Share it / Videos / Heather / Going for a song / O Caroline / Nine feet underground / Felafel shuffle / Cruising / Emily / Halfway between heaven

and earth / It didn't matter anyway / Golf girl
CD _____ HTDCD 17
HTD / Jan '94 / Pinnacle.

LIVE 1990
CD _____ NINETY 2
Demon / Mar '93 / Pinnacle / ADA.

SONGS AND SIGNS
Songs and signs / Love in your eye / World is yours / Mirror the day / Show of our lives / Welcome the day / Surprise surprise / Hello hello / Winter wine / For Richard
CD _____ ELITE 002 PCD
Elite/Old Gold / May '91 / Carlton Home Entertainment.

WITH AN EAR TO THE GROUND
With an ear to the ground / Be alright / Place of my own / Can't be long now / Lover / Magic man / Wraiks and ladders / Nothing at all / L'auberge du sanglier
CD _____ ELITE 017CDP
Elite/Old Gold / Aug '91 / Carlton Home Entertainment.

Caravans

AMAZING GRACE
Amazing grace / Just like him / Nobody knows like the Lord / Sacred Lord / Lord stay with me / To whom shall I turn / I'm ready to serve the Lord / No coward soldier / Till I meet the Lord / Jesus will save / Till you come / Lord don't leave us now / Jesus and me / One of these old days / Everything you need / What will tomorrow bring / I don't mind / It must not suffer loss / I'm going thru' / Place like that
CD _____ CPCD 8088
Charly / Apr '95 / Charly / THE / Cadillac.

Caravanserai

SHOCK HORO
CD _____ SAMIZDAT 03CD
Samizdat / Apr '95 / ADA.

Caravensari

PIG
CD _____ SZDATCD 02
Samizdat / Jul '93 / ADA.

Carawan Family

HOMEBREW
CD _____ FF 609CD
Flying Fish / Apr '94 / Roots / CM / Direct / ADA.

Carawan, Guy

TREE OF LIFE
CD _____ FF 525CD
Flying Fish / '92 / Roots / CM / Direct / ADA.

Carbo, Gladys

STREET CRIES
CD _____ 121 197 2
Soul Note / Oct '90 / Harmonia Mundi / Wellard / Cadillac.

Carbon

LARYNX
CD _____ SST 194 CD
SST / May '93 / Plastic Head.

TRUTHTABLE
CD _____ HMS 202-2
Homestead / Jul '93 / SHD.

Carbon, Lisa

POLYESTER
CD _____ CAT 026CD
Rephlex / Jan '96 / Disc.

Carbonell, Augustin

AUGUSTIN 'BOLA' CARBONELL
CD _____ MES 158142
Messidor / Apr '93 / Koch / ADA.

CARMEN
Alegrias de cascorro / Travesia la comadre / Minerico / Gina / Esencia jonda / Galicia / Coral / Alchacon / Carmen / Improvisation
CD _____ 158142
Messidor / Aug '92 / Koch / ADA.

Carbonized

DISHARMONIZATION
CD _____ FDN 2006
Foundation 2000 / Sep '93 / Plastic Head.

Carcamo, Pablo

20 BEST OF CARIBBEAN TROPICAL MUSIC (Carcamo, Pablo & Jaime Mella)
CD _____ EUCD 1112
ARC / '91 / ARC Music / ADA.

BEST OF CARIBBEAN TROPICAL MUSIC
CD Set _____ EUCD 1322
ARC / Nov '95 / ARC Music / ADA.

CARIBBEAN TROPICAL MUSIC, VOL. 2
CD _____ EUCD 1162
ARC / '91 / ARC Music / ADA.

CARIBBEAN TROPICAL MUSIC, VOL. 3
CD _____ EUCD 1201
ARC / Sep '93 / ARC Music / ADA.

CUMBIA DANCE PARTY (Carcamo, Pablo & Enrique Ugarte)
CD _____ EUCD 1234
ARC / Nov '93 / ARC Music / ADA.

FLY AWAY HOME
CD _____ EUCD 1128
ARC / '91 / ARC Music / ADA.

IT'S TIME FOR MAMBO (Carcamo, Pablo & Vanessa Lawicki/Miguel Castro)
CD _____ EUCD 1225
ARC / Sep '93 / ARC Music / ADA.

MAGIC OF THE PARAGUAYAN AND THE INDIAN FLUTES (Carcamo, Pablo & Oscar Benito)
CD _____ EUCD 1245
ARC / Nov '93 / ARC Music / ADA.

MI CHILOE
CD _____ EUCD 1095
ARC / '91 / ARC Music / ADA.

MOST POPULAR SONGS FROM CHILE, THE
CD _____ EUCD 1217
ARC / Sep '93 / ARC Music / ADA.

MY INSPIRATION
CD _____ EUCD 1181
ARC / Apr '92 / ARC Music / ADA.

SAMBA BOSSA (Carcamo, Pablo, Hossam Ramzy & Ulrick Stiegler)
CD _____ EUCD 1142
ARC / '91 / ARC Music / ADA.

Carcass

HEARTWORK
Buried dreams / Carnal fudge / No love lost / Heartwork / Embodiment / This mortal coil / Albeit macht fleisch / Blind bleeding the blind / Doctrinal expletives / Death certificate
CD _____ MOSH 097CD
Earache / Sep '94 / Vital.

NECROTICISM - DESCANTING THE INSALUBRIOUS
Inpropgation / Corporeal jigsore quandary / Symposium of sickness / Pedigree butchery / Incarnated solvent abuse / Carneous coffin / Lavaging expectorate of Lysergide composition / Forensic clinicism - The Sanguine article
CD _____ MOSH 042CD
Earache / Sep '94 / Vital.

REEK OF PUTRIFICATION
Genital grinder / Regurgitation of giblets / Pyosisified (still rotten to the gore) / Carbonized eye-sockets / Frenzied detruncation / Vomited anal tract / Festerday / Fermenting innards / Excreted alive / Suppuration / Foeticide / Microwaved utergestation / Splattered cavities / Psychopathologist / Burnt to a crisp / Pungent excruciation / Manifestation of verrucose urethra / Oxidised razor masticator / Malignant defecation
CD _____ MOSH 006CD
Earache / Sep '94 / Vital.

SYMPHONIES OF SICKNESS
CD _____ MOSH 018CD
Earache / Sep '94 / Vital.

Carcrash International

FRAGMENTS OF A JOURNEY IN HELL
CD _____ CLEO 94612
City Slang / Apr '94 / Disc.

Cardiacs

ALL THAT GLITTERS IS A MARE'S NEST
CD _____ ALPHCD 018
Alphabet Business Concern / May '95 / Plastic Head.

ARCHIVE CARDIACS
CD _____ ALPHCD 000
Alphabet Business Concern / May '95 / Plastic Head.

BELLEYE
CD _____ ORGAN 011CD
Org / Apr '95 / Pinnacle.

CARDIACS LIVE
Icing on the world / In a city lining / Tarred and feathered / Loosefish scapegrace / Is this the life / To go off and things / Gina Lollibrigida / Goosegash / Cameras / Big ship
CD _____ ALPHCD 010
Alphabet Business Concern / May '95 / Plastic Head.

LITTLE MAN AND A HOUSE AND THE WHOLE WORLD WINDOW, A
Back to the cave / Little man and a house / In a city lining / Is this the life / Interlude / Dive / Icing on the world / Breakfast line / Victory / R.E.S. / Whole world window / I'm eating in bed (reissue only)
CD _____ ALPHCD 007

Alphabet Business Concern / May '95 / Plastic Head.

ON LAND AND IN THE SEA
CD _____ ALPHCD 012
Alphabet Business Concern / May '95 / Plastic Head.

RUDE BOOTLEG
CD _____ ALPHCD 005
Alphabet Business Concern / May '95 / Plastic Head.

SAMPLER
CD _____ ALPHCD 019
Alphabet Business Concern / May '95 / Plastic Head.

SEASIDE
CD _____ ALPHCD 013
Alphabet Business Concern / May '95 / Plastic Head.

SONGS FOR SHIPS AND IRONS
CD _____ ALPHCD 014
Alphabet Business Concern / May '95 / Plastic Head.

Cardigans

LIFE
Carnival / Gordon's garden party / Daddy's car / Sick and tired / Tomorrow / Rise and shine / Beautiful one / Travelling with Charley / Fine / Celia inside / Hey, get out of my way / After all / Sabbath bloody Sabbath
CD _____ 5235562
Stockholm / Jun '95 / PolyGram.

Cardona, Milton

BEMBE
CD _____ AMCLCD 1004
American Clave / Jul '94 / New Note / ADA / Direct.

Caretaker Race

HANGOVER SQUARE
CD _____ FOUND CD 2
Foundation 2000 / Jul '90 / Plastic Head.

Carey, Mariah

DAYDREAM
Fantasy / Underneath the stars / One sweet day / Open arms / Always be my baby / I am free / When I saw you / Long ago / Melt away / Forever / Daydream interlude / Looking in
CD _____ 4813672
Columbia / Sep '95 / Sony.

EMOTIONS
Emotions / And you don't remember / Can't let go / Make it happen / If it's over / You're so cold / So blessed / To be around you / Till the end of time / Wind / Vanishing
CD _____ 4688512
Columbia / Oct '91 / Sony.

MARIAH CAREY
Vision of love / There's got to be a way / I don't wanna cry / Someday / Vanishing / All in your mind / Alone in love / You need me / Sent from up above / Prisoner / Love takes time
CD _____ 4668152
CBS / Aug '90 / Sony.

MARIAH CAREY UNPLUGGED
Emotions / If it's over / Someday / Vision of love / Make it happen / I'll be there / Can't let go
CD _____ 4710862
Columbia / Jul '92 / Sony.

MERRY CHRISTMAS
Silent night / All I want for Christmas is you / O holy night / Christmas (Baby please come home) / Miss you most (at Christmas time) / Joy to the world / Jesus born on this day / Santa Claus is coming to town / Hark the herald angels sing/Gloria (In Excelsis Deo) / Jesus oh what a wonderful child / God rest ye merry gentlemen
CD _____ 477342 2
Columbia / Nov '94 / Sony.

MUSIC BOX
Dream lover / Hero / Anytime you need a friend / Music box / Now that I know / Never forget you / Without you / Just to hold you once again / I've been thinking about you / All I've ever wanted / Everything fades away
CD _____ 474270 2
Columbia / Sep '93 / Sony.

Carey, Mutt

MUTT CAREY & LEE COLLINS (Carey, Mutt & Lee Collins)
CD _____ AMCD 72
American Music / Jan '94 / Jazz Music.

Caribbean Clan

ULTIMATE IN REGGAE
CD _____ HADCD 176
Javelin / Nov '95 / THE / Henry Hadaway Organisation.

Caribbean Orchestra

CARIBBEAN SUNSET
CD _____ 15482
Laserlight / Aug '92 / Target/BMG.

Carioca

CARIOCA
Revoada / Pitanga / Alvorada / Briza / Branca / Despertar / Brilho / Caminho do sol / Bemtev / Revoada final
CD _____ 517709-2
Carmo / Jul '93 / Pinnacle / New Note.

Carle, Frankie

1946 BROADCASTS (Carle, Frankie & His Orchestra)
CD _____ JH 1008
Jazz Hour / '91 / Target/BMG / Jazz Music / Cadillac.

FRANKIE CARLE 1944-1946 (Carle, Frankie & His Orchestra)
CD _____ CCD 43
Circle / Jul '93 / Jazz Music / Swift / Wellard.

FRANKIE CARLE 1944-1949 (Carle, Frankie & His Orchestra)
CD _____ CCD 146
Circle / Jul '93 / Jazz Music / Swift / Wellard.

Carless, Dorothy

THAT LOVELY WEEKEND
Daddy / It can't be wrong / My sister and I / Room 504 / That lovely weekend / You too can have a lovely romance / Love stay in my heart / We three / Until you fall in love / Where's my love / I want to be in Dixie / This is no laughing matter / When the sun comes out / Our love affair / I can't love you anymore / I'll always love you / I'd know you anywhere / I guess I'll have to dream the rest / I'm sending my blessing / Ragtime cowboy Joe / Never a day goes by / Walkin' by the river
CD _____ RAJCD 849
Empress / May '95 / THE.

Carlin, Bob

FUN OF OPEN DISCUSSION (Carlin, Bob & John Hartford)
CD _____ ROU 0320CD
Rounder / Apr '95 / CM / Direct / ADA / Cadillac.

Carlisle, Belinda

BELINDA
Mad about you / I need a disguise / Since you're a rich man / I feel the magic / I never wanted a rich man / Band of gold / Gotta get to you / From the heart / Shot in the dark / Stuff and nonsense
CD _____ IRLD 19002
MCA / Apr '92 / BMG.

BEST OF BELINDA - VOLUME 1
Heaven is a place on Earth / Same thing / Circle in the sand / Leave a light on for me / Little black book / Summer rain / Vision of you / I get weak / La luna / I plead insanity / World without you / Do you feel like I feel / Half the world / Runaway horses
CD _____ BELCD 1
Offside / Sep '92 / EMI.

HEAVEN ON EARTH
Heaven is a place on Earth / Circle in the sand / I feel free / Should I let you in / World without you / I get weak / We can change / Fool for love / Nobody owns me / Love never dies
CD _____ CDV 2496
Virgin / Nov '88 / EMI.

LIVE YOUR LIFE BE FREE
CD _____ CDV 2680
Virgin / Oct '91 / EMI.

REAL
Goodbye day / It's too real (big scary animal) / Too much water / Lay down your arms / Where love hides / One with you / Wrap my arms / Tell me / Windows of the world / Here comes my baby
CD _____ CDV 2725
Offside / Oct '93 / EMI.

Carlisle, Una Mae

COMPLETE
Now I lay me down to dream / Papa's in bed with his britches on / If I had you / You made me love you / Walkin' by the river / I met you then / Blitzkrieg baby / Beautiful eyes / There'll be some changes made / It's sad but true / I see a million people / Oh I'm evil / You mean so much to me / Boogie wooglie piggy / Can't help lovin' dat man / It ain't like that / I'm the one who loves you / Anything / City called heaven / My wish / Coffee and cakes / Moonlight masquerade / Don't tetch it / So long Shorty / I'm tryin' / Sweet talk / Close shave / Bugler's dilemma / It's only a paper moon / Fifi's rapsody / Night whispers / Tweed me / Move over / Wondering where / Keep smilin' / Comin' back / No blues at all / St. Louis blues

CD _____ ND 89484
Jazz Tribune / Jun '94 / BMG.

UNA MAE CARLISLE (Carlisle, Una Mae & Savannah Churchill 1944)
T'aint yours / Without you baby / I'm a good good woman / Ain't nothin' much / I like it 'cause I love it / You gotta take your time / He's the best little Yankee to me / I speak so much about you / Teasin' me / You and your heart of stone / You're gonna change your mind / Rest of my life / He's commander in chief of my heart / Two faced man / Tell me your blues / Fat meat is good meat / That glory day (CD only) / Crying need for you (CD only) / I carry the torch for you (CD only) / Behavin' myself for you (CD only)
CD _____ HQCD 19
Harlequin / Jun '94 / Swift / Jazz Music / Wellard / Hot Shot / Cadillac.

Carlo & The Belmonts

CARLO AND THE BELMONTS
We belong together / Such a long way / Santa Margherita / My foolish heart / Teenage Clementine / Little orphan girl / Five minutes more / Write me a letter / Brenda the great pretender / Ring-a-ling / Baby doll / Mairzy doats and dozy doats / Story of love / Kansas City
CD _____ CHCHD 251
Ace / Jun '91 / Pinnacle / Cadillac / Complete/Pinnacle.

Carlos, Don

DAY TO DAY LIVING
Hog and goat / I like it / Dice cups / Roots man party / Hey Mr. Babylon / Street life / English woman / I'm not crazy / At the bus stop
CD _____ GRELCD 45
Greensleeves / Sep '89 / Total/BMG / Jetstar / SRD.

DEEPLY CONCERNED
Deeply concerned / Cool Johnny cool / Ruff we ruff / Jah people unite / Black station white station / Satan control them / Money lover / Night rider / Crazy girl
CD _____ RASCD 3029
Ras / Aug '88 / Jetstar / Greensleeves / SRD / Direct.

EASE UP (Carlos, Don & Gold)
CD _____ RASCD 3150
Ras / Jun '94 / Jetstar / Greensleeves / SRD / Direct.

HARVEST TIME
Fuss fuss / I Love Jah / Harvest time / In pieces / White squall / Magic man / Young girl / Music crave / Hail the roots
CD _____ CDBM 066
Blue Moon / Jul '93 / Magnum Music Group / Greensleeves / Hot Shot / ADA / Cadillac / Discovery.

PLANTATION (Carlos, Don & Gold)
Plantation / Promise to be true / Tear drops / Declaration of rights / Aint too proud to beg / Pretty baby
CD _____ TWCD 1062
Tamoki Wambesi / Nov '95 / Jetstar / SRD / Roots Collective / Greensleeves.

PROPHECY
Gimme gimme your love / Crucial situation / Version / Working everyday / Live in harmony / Prophecy / Jah hear my plea
CD _____ CDBM 054
Blue Moon / Nov '88 / Magnum Music Group / Greensleeves / Hot Shot / ADA / Cadillac / Discovery.

RAVING TONIGHT (Carlos, Don & Gold)
CD _____ RASCD 3005
Ras / Nov '92 / Jetstar / Greensleeves / SRD / Direct.

TIME IS THE MASTER
CD _____ RASCD 3217
Ras / Nov '92 / Jetstar / Greensleeves / SRD / Direct.

Carlotti, J.M.

PACHIQUELI VEN DE NEUCH (PROVENCE)
CD _____ Y225034
Silex / Jun '93 / ADA.

Carlton, Larry

KID GLOVES
Kid gloves / Preacher / Michele's whistle / Oui oui si / Heart to heart / Just my imagination / Where be Mosada / Farm jazz / Terry T. / If I could I would
CD _____ GRP 96832
GRP / Aug '92 / BMG / New Note.

RENEGADE GENTLEMAN
Crazy Mama / R.C.M / Sleep medicine / Cold day in hell / Anthem / Amen A.C. / Never say naw / Farm jazz / Nothin' comes / Bogner / Red hot poker / I gotta right
CD _____ GRP 97442
GRP / Aug '93 / BMG / New Note.

SINGING/PLAYING
CD _____ EDCD 439
Edsel / Oct '95 / Pinnacle / ADA.

Carman, Jenks Tex

HILLBILLY HULA
Hillbilly hula / Another good dream gone wrong / Hilo march / Gosh I miss you all the time / Locust hill rag / Calssons go rolling along / Samoa stomp / Dixie cannonball / Sweet luwanna / My lonely heart and I / Indian polka / I'm a poor lonesome fellow / Don't feel sorry for me / My trusting heart / Gonna stay right here / (I've recieved) A penny postcard / Ten thousand miles (Away from home) / I could love you darling / You tell her, I s-t-u-t-t-e-r / Blue memories
CD _____ BCD 15574
Bear Family / Mar '92 / Rollercoaster / Direct / CM / Swift / ADA.

Carmel

COLLECTED (A Collection of Work 1983-1990)
And I take it for granted / Sally / It's all in the game / I'm not afraid of you / Every little bit / I have fallen in love (Je suis tombee amoureuse) / More, more, more / You can have him / Bad day / J'oublierai ton nom / I'm over you
CD _____ 828 219 2
London / May '92 / PolyGram.

DRUM IS EVERYTHING, THE
More, more, more / Stormy weather / Drum is everything / I thought I was going mad / Prayer / Rockin' on suicide / Rue St. Denis / Willow weep for me / Tracks of my tears / Bad day
CD _____ 8202212
London / Jun '85 / PolyGram.

GOOD NEWS
Java / You're all I need / Heaven / Angel / Letter to Margaret / You're on my mind / Circle line / Good news / Chasin' rainbows
CD _____ 4509900442
East West / Aug '92 / Warner Music.

WORLD GONE CRAZY
CD _____ 4509991552
Warner Bros. / Feb '95 / Warner Music.

Carmello, Janusz

PORTRAIT
When the saints go marching in / Some time ago / Fun run / Song for Babyshka / Tiny capers / Li'l darlin' / Joy spring / Daydream / Lover man
CD _____ HEPCD 2044
Hep / Sep '90 / Cadillac / Jazz Music / New Note / Wellard.

Carmen

FANDANGOES IN SPACE/DANCING ON A COLD WIND
Bulerias / Bullfight / Stepping stone / Sailor song / Lonely house / Por tarantos / Looking outside / Tales of Spain / Retirando / Fandangos in space / Reprise finale / Viva mi Sevilla / I've been crying / Drifting along / She flew / Purple flowers / Remembrances
CD Set _____ LICD 921150
Line / Jun '92 / CM / Grapevine / ADA / Conifer / Direct.

Carmen, Phil

BACK FROM L.A. LIVE
CD _____ HYCD 200148
Hypertension / Mar '95 / Total/BMG / Direct / ADA.

Carmichael's Ceilidh

CARMICHAEL'S CEILIDH
CD _____ CDLOC 1081
Klub / Jul '94 / CM / Ross / Duncans / ADA / Direct.

Carmichael, Anita

COME WITH ME
CD _____ SAXCD 004
Saxology / May '94 / Harmonia Mundi / Cadillac.

PLAYS DINNER JAZZ
CD _____ SAXCD 009
Saxology / Aug '95 / Harmonia Mundi / Cadillac.

UNADULTERATED, THE
CD _____ SAXCD 003
Saxology / Aug '95 / Harmonia Mundi / Cadillac.

Carmichael, Hoagy

HOAGY CARMICHAEL 1927-1944
Washboard blues / Stardust / Rockin' chair / Georgia / Lazy river / Lazybones / Moon country / Two sleepy people / Little old lady
CD _____ CBC 1011
Timeless Jazz / Jun '93 / New Note.

HOAGY CARMICHAEL 1951
CD _____ FLYCD 912
Flyright / Oct '92 / Hot Shot / Wellard / Jazz Music / CM.

HOAGY CARMICHAEL VOL.1
CD _____ HOAGY 1
JSP / Jul '94 / ADA / Target/BMG / Direct / Cadillac / Complete/Pinnacle.

HOAGY CARMICHAEL VOL.2
CD _____ HOAGY 2
JSP / Mar '95 / ADA / Target/BMG / Direct / Cadillac / Complete/Pinnacle.

JAZZ PORTRAIT
CD _____ CD 14585
Complete / Nov '95 / THE.

MR MUSIC MASTER
Mr. Music Master / Stardust / Rockin' chair / Moon country / Riverboat shuffle / Two sleepy people / Hong Kong blues / One morning in May / Lazy river / I get along without you very well / Blue orchids / Little old lady / Georgia on my mind / Sing me a swing song / Lazy bones / Washboard blues / Snowball / Small fry / Sing it way down low
CD _____ PASTCD 7004
Flapper / Mar '93 / Pinnacle.

STARDUST (1927-60)
Giants Of Jazz / May '95 / Target/BMG / Cadillac.
CD _____ CD 53192

Carmichael, John

DANCE AWAY (Carmichael, John & His Band)
CD _____ CDLOC 1055
Lochshore / Jul '90 / ADA / Direct / Duncans.

Carnage

DARK RECOLLECTIONS
CD _____ NECRO 3 CD
Necrosis / Dec '90 / Vital.

Carnahan, Danny

CUT & RUN (Carnahan, Danny & Robin Petrie)
CD _____ FLE 1006CD
Fledg'ling / Jun '94 / CM / ADA / Direct.

Carne, Jean

LOVE LESSONS
Don't stop doin' whatcha doin' / Make love / Good thing goin' on / So I can love you / Have I told you that I love you / No one does it better / Fallin' for you / It's not for me to say / Misty / Someone to watch over me
CD _____ XECD 6
Expansion / Dec '95 / Pinnacle / Sony / 3MV.

Carneiro, Nando

VIOLAO
Violao / Charada / Poromim / Juliana / As gralhas / G.R.E.S. luxo artezanal / O compones / Liza
CD _____ 8492122
Carmo / May '91 / Pinnacle / New Note.

Carnes, Kim

MISTAKEN IDENTITY
Bette Davis eyes / Hit and run / Mistaken identity / When I'm away from you / Draw of the cards / Break the rules tonite / Still hold on / Don't call it love / Miss you tonite / My old pals
CD _____ MUSCD 507
MCI / Nov '94 / Disc / THE.

SWEET LOVE SONG OF MY SOUL
Sweet love song of my soul / Everything has got to be free / Do you want to dance / I won't call you back / To love / To love somebody / Fell in love with a poet / One more river to cross / You can do it to me anytime / Rest on me
CD _____ CDTB 084
Thunderbolt / '89 / Magnum Music Group.

Carnivore

RETALIATION
CD _____ RR 9597-2
Roadrunner / Apr '89 / Pinnacle.

Caron, Alain

RHYTHM 'N' JAZZ
Bump / Fat cat / District 6 / Slam the clown / Little Miss March / I C U / Cherokee drive / Flight of the bebop bee / Donna Lee / Intuitions
CD _____ JMS 186782
JMS / Nov '95 / BMG / New Note.

Carousel

ABCDEFGHIJKLMNOPQRSTUVWXYZ
CD _____ MASKCD 050
Vinyl Japan / Feb '95 / Vital.

Carpathian Forest

THROUGH CHASMS, CAVES
CD _____ CDAV 011
Avant Garde / Jul '95 / Plastic Head.

Carpathian Full Moon

SERENADES IN BLOOD
CD _____ CDAV 006
Avant Garde / Sep '94 / Plastic Head.

Carpendale, Howard

SINGLE HITS - 1966-68
CD _____ 16006
Laserlight / Aug '91 / Target/BMG.

Carpenter, Mary-Chapin

COME ON, COME ON
Hard way / He thinks he'll keep her / Rhythm of the blues / I feel lucky / Bug / Not too much to ask / Passionate kisses / Only a dream / I am a town / Walking through fire / I take my chances / Come on come on
CD _____ 4718982
Columbia / Apr '95 / Sony.

HOMETOWN GIRL
Lot like me / Other streets and other towns / Hometown girl / Downtown train / Family hands / Road is just a road / Come on home / Waltz / Just because / Heroes and heroines
CD _____ 473915-2
Columbia / Jun '93 / Sony.

SHOOTING STRAIGHT IN THE DARK
Going out tonight / Right now / More things change / When she's gone / Middle ground / Can't take love for granted / Down at the twist and shout / When Halley came to Jackson / What you didn't say / You win again / Moon and St Christopher
CD _____ 4674682
Columbia / Oct '91 / Sony.

STATE OF THE HEART
How do / Something of a dreamer / Never had it so good / Read my lips / This shirt / Quittin' time / Down in Mary's land / Goodbye again / Too tired / Slow country dance / It don't bring you
CD _____ 4666912
Sony Music / Aug '94 / Sony.

STONES IN THE ROAD
Why walk when you can fly / House of cards / Stones in the road / Keeper for every flame / Tender when I want to be / Shut up and kiss me / Last word / End of my private days / John Doe No.24 / Jubilee / Outside looking in / Where time stands still / This is love
CD _____ 477679-2
Columbia / Apr '95 / Sony.

Carpenters

CARPENTERS
Rainy days and Mondays / Saturday / Let me be the one / (A place to) hideaway / For all we know / Superstar / Druscilla penny / One love / Bacharach and David medley / Sometimes
CD _____ 5500632
Spectrum/Karussell / May '93 / PolyGram / THE.

CHRISTMAS PORTRAIT
O come, o come Emmanuel / Overture / Christmas waltz / Sleigh ride / It's Christmas time / Sleep well little children / Have yourself a merry little Christmas / Santa Claus is coming to town / Christmas song / Silent night / Jingle bells / First snowfall / Merry Christmas darling / I'll be home for Christmas
CD _____ CDMID 147
A&M / Oct '92 / PolyGram.

CLOSE TO YOU
We've only just begun / Love is surrender / Maybe it's you / Reason to believe / Help / Close to you / Baby, it's you / I'll never fall in love again / Crescent moon / Mr. Guder / I kept on loving you / Another song
CD _____ CDMID 138
A&M / Oct '92 / PolyGram.

FROM THE TOP (4CD Set)
CD Set _____ 3968752
A&M / Oct '91 / PolyGram.

HORIZON
Aurora / Only yesterday / Desperado / Please Mr. Postman / I can dream, can't I / Solitaire / Happy / Goodbye and I love you (I'm caught between) / Love me for what I am / Eventide
CD _____ CDMID 141
A&M / Oct '92 / PolyGram.

IF I WERE A CARPENTER (A Tribute To The Carpenters) (Various Artists)
Goodbye to love / Top of the world / Superstar / Close to you / For all we know / It's going to take some time / Solitaire / Hurting each other / Yesterday once more / Calling occupants of interplanetary craft / Rainy days and Mondays / Let me be the one / Bless the beasts and children / We've only just begun
CD _____ 5402582
A&M / Sep '94 / PolyGram.

Carmel (continued)

SLEEPWALK
Last nite / Blues bird / Song for Katie / Frenchman's flat / Upper kern / 10 p.m. / You gotta get it while you can / Sleepwalk
CD _____ GRP 01262
GRP / Aug '92 / BMG / New Note.

INTERPRETATIONS (A 25th Anniversary Celebration)
Without a song / Sing / Bless the beasts and children / When I fall in love / From this moment on / Tryin' to get the feeling again / When it's gone / Where do I go from here / Desperado / Superstar / Rainy days and Mondays / Ticket to ride / If I had you / Please Mr. Postman / We've only just begun / Calling occupants of interplanetary craft / Little girl blue / You're the one / Close to you
CD _____ 540 251-2
A&M / Oct '94 / PolyGram.

KIND OF HUSH, A
There's a kind of hush / You / Sandy / Goofus / Can't smile without you / I need to be in love / One more time / Boat to sail / I have you / Breaking up is hard to do
CD _____ CDMID 142
A&M / Oct '92 / PolyGram.

LIVE AT THE PALLADIUM
Flat baroque / There's a kind of hush / Jambalaya / Piano picker / Strike up the band / 'S wonderful / Fascinating rhythm / Warsaw concerto / From this moment on / Carpenters medley / We've only just begun
CD _____ PWKS 572
Carlton Home Entertainment / Mar '90 / Carlton Home Entertainment.

LOVELINES
Lovelines / Where do I go from here / Uninvited guest / If we try / When I fall in love / Kiss me the way you did last night / Remember when lovin' took all night / You're the one / Honolulu City lights / Slow dance / If I had you / Little girl blue
CD _____ CDMID 148
A&M / Oct '92 / PolyGram.

MADE IN AMERICA
Those good old dreams / Strength of a woman / Back in my life again / When you've got what it takes / Somebody's been lyin' / I believe you / Touch me when we're dancing / When it's gone / Beechwood 4-5789 / Because we are in love
CD _____ CDMID 146
A&M / Oct '92 / PolyGram.

NOW AND THEN
Sing / This masquerade / Heather / Jambalaya / I can't make music / Yesterday once more / Fun, fun, fun / End of the world / Da doo ron ron / Dead man's curve / Johnny angel / Night has a thousand eyes / Our day will come / One fine day
CD _____ CDMID 140
A&M / Oct '92 / PolyGram.

ONLY YESTERDAY (Richard & Karen Carpenter's Greatest Hits)
Yesterday once more / Superstar (remix) / Rainy days and mondays / Top of the world / Ticket to ride / Goodbye to love (remix) / This masquerade / Hurting each other / Solitaire / We've only just begun / Those good old dreams / Please Mr. Postman / I won't last a day without you / Touch me when we're dancing / Jambalaya / For all we know / All you get from love is a love song / Close to you / Only yesterday / Calling occupants of interplanetary craft
CD _____ CDA 1990
A&M / Mar '90 / PolyGram.

PASSAGE
B'wana she no home / All you get from love is a love song / I just fell in love again / On the balcony of the Casa Rosada / Don't cry for me Argentina / Sweet sweet smile / Two sides / Man smart, woman smarter / Calling occupants of interplanetary craft
CD _____ CDMID 143
A&M / Oct '92 / PolyGram.

REFLECTIONS
I need to be in love / I just fall in love again / Baby it's you / Can't smile without you / Beechwood 45789 / Eve / All of my life / Reason to believe / Your baby doesn't love you anymore / Maybe it's you / Ticket to ride / Sweet sweet smile / Song for you / Because we are in love (The wedding song)
CD _____ 5515932
Spectrum/Karussell / Nov '95 / PolyGram / THE.

SINGLES 1969-73, THE
We've only just begun / Top of the world / Ticket to ride / Superstar / Rainy days and Mondays / Goodbye to love / Yesterday once more / It's going to take some time / Sing / For all we know / Hurting each other / Close to you
CD _____ CDA 63601
A&M / Jun '84 / PolyGram.

SINGLES 1974-1978, THE
Sweet sweet smile / Jambalaya / Can't smile without you / I need to be in love with out you / All you get from love is a love song / Only yesterday / Solitaire / Please Mr. Postman / I need to be in love / Happy / There's a kind of hush / Calling occupants of interplanetary craft
CD _____ CDA 19748
A&M / '88 / PolyGram.

SONG FOR YOU, A
Song for you / Top of the world / Hurting each other / It's going to take some time / Goodbye to love / Intermission / Bless the beasts and children / Flat baroque / Piano

---

picker / I won't last a day without you / Crystal lullaby / Road ode
CD _____ CDMID 139
A&M / Oct '92 / PolyGram.

TICKET TO RIDE
CD _____ CDMID 137
A&M / Oct '92 / PolyGram.

TREASURES
Close to you / Let me be the one / Bless the beasts and children / Desperado / Don't cry for me Argentina / Make believe it's your first time / Help / Baby, it's you / Road ode / Look to your dreams / Now / Reason to believe / I just fall in love again / I need to be in love / Because we are in love / Eve
CD _____ PWKS 4089
Carlton Home Entertainment / Sep '94 / Carlton Home Entertainment.

VOICE OF THE HEART
Now / Sailing on the tide / Make believe it's your first time / Two lives / At the end of a song / Ordinary fool / Your baby doesn't love you anymore / Look to your dreams
CD _____ CDMID 144
A&M / Oct '92 / PolyGram.

Carr, Vikki

UNFORGETTABLE, THE
He's a rebel / Mirror / Only love can break a heart / Bye bye blackbird / How does the wine taste / Unforgettable / It must be him / With pen in hand / Alfie / Can't take my eyes off you / By the time I get to Phoenix / Never my love / All my love / Singing my song / Sunday morning coming down / Yesterday when I was young / Walk away / If you love me (I won't care) / Poor butterfly / Everything I touch turns to tears
CD _____ CDSL 8255
Music For Pleasure / Sep '95 / EMI.

Carrack, Paul

21 GOOD REASONS
How long / Real feeling / No future in your eyes / You're all that I need / Tempted / Do me lover / Oh how happy / Rumour / I need you / Always better with love / Little unkind / One good reason / Don't shed a tear / Button off my shirt / When you walk in the room / I live by the groove / Only my heart can tell / Battlefield / Loveless / Silent running / Living years
CD _____ CDCHR 6067
Chrysalis / Feb '94 / EMI.

BLUE VIEWS
Eyes of blue / For once in our lives / No easy way out / Oh oh oh my my my / Only a breath away / Nothing more than a memory / Somewhere in your heart / Love will keep us alive / Always have always will / Don't walk over me / How long
CD _____ EIRSCD 1075
IRS/EMI / Jan '96 / EMI.

Carrasco, Joe 'King'

BANDIDO ROCK (Carrasco, Joe 'King' Y Las Coronas)
CD _____ CD 9012
Rounder / '88 / CM / Direct / ADA / Cadillac.

BORDER TOWN (Carrasco, Joe 'King' & The Crowns)
Escondido / Hola coca cola / Who bought the guns / Are you Amigo / Put me in jail / Mr. Bogota / Walk it like you talk it / Current events (are making me tense) / Cucaraca taco / Baby let's go to Mexico / Vamos a bailar / Tamale baby
CD _____ ROSE 40CD
New Rose / '88 / Direct / ADA.

Carreg Lafar

YSBRYD Y WERIN
CD _____ SCD 2102
Sain / Jan '96 / Direct / ADA.

Carreras, Jose

BOLEROS & LOVE SONGS OF SPAIN
CD _____ CD 396
Bescol / Aug '94 / CM / Target/BMG.

BRILLIANT VOICE, THE
CD _____ MU 5042
Musketeer / Oct '92 / Koch.

FRIENDS FOR LIFE (Romantic Songs Of The World)
CD _____ 4509902302
WEA / Jul '93 / Warner Music.

JOSE CARRERAS SINGS ANDREW LLOYD WEBBER
Memory / Phantom of the opera / Music of the night / You / Pie Jesu / Tell me on a Sunday / Half a moment / There's me / Starlight express / Unexpected song / Love changes everything
CD _____ 256924 2
WEA / Nov '89 / Warner Music.

WHITE CHRISTMAS
White Christmas / O come all ye faithful (Adeste fidelis) / Agnus dei / Caro mio ben / Maria / Pieta, Signore / What child is this / Mille cherubini / Pregaria / Panis angelicus / El romanc / Andantino / Silent night
CD _____ DSHCD 7010
D-Sharp / Nov '95 / Pinnacle.

Carrere, Tia

DREAM
State of grace / I wanna come home with you tonight / Innocent side / I never even told you / Gift of perfect love / Surrender / Love is a cannibal / We need to belong / Our love / Dream a perfect dream
CD _____ 936245300-2
WEA / Oct '93 / Warner Music.

Carrier, Chubby

DANCE ALL NIGHT (Carrier, Chubby & Bayou Swamp Band)
CD _____ BP 5007CD

---

somewhere, somehow / Act right / What do you know about love / Now that I'm free / Heartbreak melody / Please Mr. Jailer / Weatherman / If these walls could speak / Touch and go / If I pray / Finders keepers / Things you do to me / How many times
CD _____ CDCHD 513
Ace / Jan '94 / Pinnacle / Cadillac / Complete/Pinnacle.

Carr, James

SOUL SURVIVOR
Soul survivor / Man worth knowing / Put love first / I can't leave your love alone / Things a woman need / Daydreaming / All because of your love / I'm into something / Memphis after midnight / That's how strong a woman's love is
CD _____ CDCH 487
Ace / Oct '93 / Pinnacle / Cadillac / Complete/Pinnacle.

TAKE ME TO THE LIMIT
Take me to the limit / Sugar shock / Love attack / You gotta love your woman / High on your love / She's already gone / Our garden of Eden / I can't leave your love alone / What's a little love between friends / Lack of attention
CD _____ CDCH 310
Ace / Jan '91 / Pinnacle / Cadillac / Complete/Pinnacle.

Carr, Leroy

1929-35
CD _____ PYCD 17
Magpie / Nov '92 / Hot Shot.

DON'T CRY WHEN I'M GONE
Barrelhouse woman / Alabama women blues / You left me crying / 11.29 blues / How long has that evening train been gone / Suicide blues / Sloppy drunk blues / 'Fore day rider / Rocks in my bed
CD _____ PYCD 07
Magpie / Apr '90 / Hot Shot.

HURRY DOWN SUNSHINE
CD _____ IGOCD 2016
Indigo / Mar '95 / Direct / ADA.

NAPTOWN BLUES
CD _____ ALB 1011CD
Aldabra / Mar '94 / CM / Disc.

REMAINING TITLES, THE (Carr, Leroy & Scrapper Blackwell)
CD _____ SOB 035382
Story Of The Blues / Oct '92 / Koch / ADA.

Carr, Romey

WOMAN KNOWS, A
Bonny banks of Loch Lomond / Nae luck about the house / Ae fond kiss / Wee willie winkie / My love is like a red red rose / Ertahay ha ta Eili / Whistle and I'll come to you my lad / Queen's Marines / Charlie is my darling / Amazing grace (the lord is my shepherd) / Ca' the yowes / Ye banks and brae's o'bonnie doon / In praise of Islay / Cockle gatherer / Hush-a-bye-baby / Bonnie wee thing / Wee Cooper o' Fife / I left my dearie lying here / Peat-fire flame / Auld lang syne
CD _____ ALBACD 01
Alba / Sep '95 / Pinnacle.

Carr, Sister Wynona

DRAGNET FOR JESUS
Each day / Lord Jesus / I want to go to heaven and rest / I'm a pilgrim traveller / I heard the news (Jesus is coming again) / Our father / He said he would / I see Jesus / Don't miss that train / I heard mother pray one day / Good old way / See his blessed face / Did he die in vain / I know someday God's gonna call me / Conversation with Jesus / Ball game / Letter to heaven / In a little while / Untitled instrumental / Operator, operator / Dragnet for Jesus / Fifteen rounds for Jesus / Nobody but Jesus / Just a few more days
CD _____ CDCHD 411
Ace / Nov '93 / Pinnacle / Cadillac / Complete/Pinnacle.

JUMP JACK JUMP
Jump jack jump / Till the well runs dry / Boppity bop (boogity boog) / Should I ever love again / I'm mad at you / Old fashioned love / Hurt me / It's raining outside / Nancy rhyme rock / Ding dong daddy / Someday,

---

Blind Pig / Mar '94 / Hot Shot / Swift / CM / Roots / Direct / ADA.

Carrier, Roy

AT HIS BEST
CD _____ ZNCD 1010
Zane / Nov '95 / Pinnacle.

SOULFUL SIDE OF ZYDECO (Carrier, Roy & Joe Walker)
CD _____ ZNCD 1003
Zane / Oct '95 / Pinnacle.

Carroll, Baikida

DOOR OF THE CAGE
CD _____ 1211232
Soul Note / Apr '95 / Harmonia Mundi / Wellard / Cadillac.

Carroll, Barbara

EVERYTHING I LOVE
You'd be so nice to come home to / Ace in the hole / I wish I could forget you / As long as I live / Song for Griffin / Hundred years from today / Now's the time / Everything I love / Heavenly / That face / Chelsea bridge
CD _____ DRGCD 91438
DRG / Dec '95 / New Note.

OLD FRIENDS
CD _____ ACD 254
Audiophile / Feb '91 / Jazz Music / Swift.

THIS HEART OF MINE
Way you look tonight / I wanna be yours / Sweet lilacs / On second thought/Why can't I / Lester leaps in / Some other time / Rain sometimes / Whenever a soft rain falls / It's like reaching for the moon / Never let me go / In some other world / This heart of mine
CD _____ 91416
DRG / Jul '94 / New Note.

Carroll, Cath

TRUE CRIME MODEL
Easter bunny song / Into day / I know / True crime model / Mississippi factory town / Jimmy's candy / Just once / L'amour c'est ca / Lullaby for a steeplejack / Breathe for me
CD _____ TB 1672
Matador / Aug '95 / Vital.

Carroll, Diahann

TRIBUTE TO ETHEL WATERS
CD _____ WW 2405
West Wind / Nov '92 / Swift / Charly / CM / ADA.

Carroll, Dina

SO CLOSE
Special kind of love / Hold on / This time / Falling / So close / Ain't no man / Express / Heaven sent / You'll never know / Don't be a stranger / Why did I let you go (On CD only) / If I knew you then (On CD only)
CD _____ 540034-2
A&M / Jan '93 / PolyGram.

Carroll, Jeanne

TRIBUTE TO WILLIE DIXON (Carroll, Jeanne & C. Christi/Willie Dixon)
CD _____ BEST 1014CD
Acoustic Music / Nov '93 / ADA.

Carroll, Karen

GOSPEL
Glory glory since I laid my burdens down / I want to be a christian / He's got the whole world in his hands / Peace, be still / Amazing grace / Oh happy day / Walk with me / Jesus is on the mainline / Doxology / When the saints go marching in
CD _____ HFCD 002
Hot Fox / Jun '93 / New Note.

HAD MY FUN
CD _____ DE 680
Delmark / Dec '95 / Hot Shot / ADA / CM / Direct / Cadillac.

Carroll, Liane

CLEARLY
CD _____ BRGCD 19
Bridge / Oct '95 / Grapevine.

Carroll, Liz

FRIEND INDEED, A
CD _____ SHCD 34013
Shanachie / Aug '95 / Koch / ADA / Greensleeves.

KISS ME KATE (Carroll, Liz & Tommy McGuire)
CD _____ SHCD 34012
Shanachie / Oct '95 / Koch / ADA / Greensleeves.

LIZ CARROLL
Reel Beatrice/Abbey reel / Out on the road/ Princess Nancy / For Eugene/Gravity hill / Clarke's favourite/Pigeon on the gate / Tune for Mairead and Anna Ni Mhaonaigh / Sock in the hole/Hole in the sock / Mrs. Carroll's Strathspey/Chapter 16 / Helicopters-

Crossing the Delaware / Sister's reel/Wynding the hay / Lacey's jig/Tune for Charles/ Geese in the bog / Par cark/Baiting the hook/Jumping the white nut eater / Greenleaf Strathspey/Setting sun / Wee dollop/ Houseboat / G reel/Merle's tune / Western reel/Road to recovery

CD _____ **GLCD 1092**
Green Linnet / Feb '91 / Roots / CM / Direct / ADA.

TRION
CD _____ **FF 70586**
Flying Fish / Jul '92 / Roots / CM / Direct / ADA.

Cars

CARS, THE
Good times roll / My best friend's girl / Just what I needed / I'm in touch with your world / Don't cha stop / You're all I've got tonight / Bye bye love / Moving in stereo / All mixed up
CD _____ **K 252088**
Elektra / Jan '84 / Warner Music.

GREATEST HITS: CARS
Just what I needed / Since you're gone / You might think / Good time roll / Touch and go / Drive / Tonight she comes / My best friend's girl / Heartbeat city / Let's go / Magic / Shake it up
CD _____ **9604642**
Elektra / Nov '85 / Warner Music.

HEARTBEAT CITY
Looking for love / Jackie / Not the night / Drive / Shooting for you / Why can't I / Magic / You might think / I do refuse / Stranger eyes / Hello again
CD _____ **9602962**
Elektra / Jul '84 / Warner Music.

JUST WHAT I NEEDED - ANTHOLOGY (2CD Set)
CD Set _____ **0349735062**
Elektra / Jan '96 / Warner Music.

Carson, Ernie

ERNIE CARSON & GOOSE HOLLOW GANG
CD _____ **BCD 297**
GHB / Apr '94 / Jazz Music.

OLD BONES (Carson, Ernie & Castle Jazz Band)
CD _____ **SOSCD 1283**
Stomp Off / Mar '95 / Jazz Music / Wellard.

WHER'M I GONNA LIVE (Carson, Ernie & Castle Jazz Band)
CD _____ **SOSCD 1277**
Stomp Off / Dec '94 / Jazz Music / Wellard.

Carson, Lori

WHERE IT GOES
Down here / Waking to the dream of you / You won't fall / Petal / Twisting my words / Where it goes / Through the cracks / Fell into the loneliness / Anyday / Christmas
CD _____ **727872**
Restless / Apr '95 / Vital.

Carsten, Mannie

JUST A KISS (Mannie Carsten's Hot Jazz Syndicate)
CD _____ **CD 1201**
Hep / Oct '94 / Cadillac / Jazz Music / New Note / Wellard.

Carter, Anita

RING OF FIRE
Ring of fire / Fair and tender ladies / Satan's child / Fly pretty swallow / As the sparrow goes / All my trials / Voice of the bayou / Sour grapes / Johnny I hardly knew you / My love / Kentuckian song / Five short years ago / No my love, no farewell / Running back / Take me home / John John John / John Hardy / I never will marry / In the highways / Bury me beneath the willow / Beautiful isle o'er the sea / Wildwood flower
CD _____ **BCD 15434**
Bear Family / '88 / Rollercoaster / Direct / CM / Swift / ADA.

Carter, Benny

1936
CD _____ **CLASSICS 541**
Classics / Dec '90 / Discovery / Jazz Music.

BENNY CARTER 1940-41
CD _____ **CLASSICS 631**
Classics / '92 / Discovery / Jazz Music.

BENNY CARTER IN EUROPE 1936-7
Black bottom / Mighty like the blues / Pardon me pretty baby / Just a mood / Royal garden blues / Rambler's rhythm / Lazy afternoon / I scott nobody / Waltzin' the blues / When day is done / Bugle call rag / There'll be some changes made / If only I could read your mind / Gin and jive / New street swing / I'll never give in / Stay in / Somebody loves me / Blues in my heart / My buddy / Nightfall / I've got two lips

CD _____ **PASTCD 7023**
Flapper / Sep '93 / Pinnacle.

BENNY CARTER, 1928-1952
Charleston is the best dance, after all / Old fashioned love / Apologies / Sendin' the vipers / Thirty fifth and Calumet / I'm in the mood for swing / Very thought of you / Cocktails for two / Takin' my time / Cuddle up, huddle up / Babalu / There, I've said it again / Midnight / My favourite blues / Lullaby to a dream / What a difference a day makes / Sunday / Ill wind / Back bay boogie / Tree of hope / Lullaby in blue / Cruisin' / I wanna go home / You belong to me / Love is cynthia / Sunday afternoon / Georgia on my mind
CD Set _____ **ND 89761**
Jazz Tribune / May '94 / BMG.

CENTRAL CITY SKETCHES (Carter, Benny & The American Jazz Orchestra)
Lonesome nights / Easy money / Doozy / When lights are low / Kiss from you / Sleep / Central City blues / Hello / People / Promenade / Remember / Sky dance / Doozy #2 / Symphony in riffs / Souvenir / Blues in my heart
CD _____ **CIJD 60126 X**
Music Masters / Jan '89 / Nimbus.

COMPLETE RECORDINGS VOL. 1 (3CD Set)
Goodbye blues / Cloudy skies / Got another sweetie now / Bugle call rag / Dee blues / Do you believe in love at first sight / Wrap your troubles in dreams (and dream your troubles away) / Tell all your daydreams to me / Swing it / Synthetic love / Six bells stampede / Love you're not the one for me / Blue interlude / I never knew / Once upon a time / Krazy kapers / Devil's holiday / Lonesome nights / Symphony in riffs / Blue Lou / Shoot the works / Dream lullaby / Everybody shuffle / Swingin' at Maida vale / Night fall / Big Ben blues / These foolish things / When day is done / I've got two lips / Just a mood / Swingin' the blues / Scandal in flat / Accent on swing / When I could only read your mind / I gotta go / When lights are low / Waltzing the blues / Tiger rag / Blue / Some of these days / Gloaming / Poor butterfly / Drop in next time your passing / Man I love / That's how the first song was born / There'll be some changes made / Jingle bells / Royal garden blues / Carry me back to old Virginny / Gin and jive / Nagasaki / There's a small hotel / I'm in the mood for swing / Rambling in C / Black bottom / Rambler's rhythm / New street swing / I'll never give in
CD _____ **CDAFS 1022-3**
Affinity / Oct '92 / Charly / Cadillac / Jazz Music.

COOKIN' AT CARLOS 1
You'd be so nice to come home to / All the things you are / Key Largo / Just friends / My romance / 'S Wonderful / Time for the blues
CD _____ **MM 5033**
Music Masters / Oct '94 / Nimbus.

COSMOPOLITE: THE OSCAR PETERSON VERVE SESSIONS
CD _____ **521673-2**
Verve / Oct '94 / PolyGram.

DEVIL'S HOLIDAY (1933-1934)
Swing it / Synthetic love / Six bells stampede / Love you're not the one for me / Blue interlude / I never knew / Once upon a time / Krazy kapers / Devil's holiday / Lonesome nights / Symphony in riffs / Blue Lou / Free love / Dissonance / Swingin' with Mezz / Old fashioned love / Apologies / Sendin' the vipers / 35th and calumet / Shoot the works / Dream lullaby / Everybody shuffle
CD _____ **JSPCD 331**
JSP / Apr '91 / ADA / Target/BMG / Direct / Cadillac / Complete/Pinnacle.

GENTLEMAN AND HIS MUSIC, A
Sometimes I'm happy / Blues for George / Things ain't what they used to be / Lover man / Idaho / Kiss from you
CD _____ **CCD 4285**
Concord Jazz / Jan '87 / New Note.

GROOVIN' IN LA 1946
CD _____ **HECPD 15**
Hep / Nov '92 / Cadillac / Jazz Music / New Note / Wellard.

IN RIFFS, 1930-37
Bugle call rag / Everybody shuffle / Shoot the works / Dee blues / Swing it / Nightfall / Bream lullaby / Pardon me pretty baby / Lazy afternoon
CD _____ **CDAJA 5704**
Living Era / Jan '91 / Koch.

IN THE MOOD FOR SWING
I'm in the mood for swing / Another time another place / Courtship / Rock me to sleep / Janel / Romp / Summer serenade / Not so blue, You, only you / Blue moonlight / South side samba
CD _____ **CIJD 60144 T**
Music Masters / Jan '89 / Nimbus.

INTRODUCTION TO BENNY CARTER 1929-40
CD _____ **4001**
Best Of Jazz / Dec '93 / Discovery.

JAZZ GIANT
Old fashioned love / I'm coming Virginia / Walkin' thing / Blue Lou / Ain't she sweet / How can you lose / Blues my naughty sweetie gives to me
CD _____ **OJCCD 167**
Original Jazz Classics / Oct '92 / Wellard / Jazz Music / Cadillac / Complete/Pinnacle.

JAZZ PORTRAIT
CD _____ **CD 14583**
Complete / Nov '95 / THE.

LIVE BROADCASTS 1939-48 (Carter, Benny & His Orchestra)
CD _____ **JH 1005**
Jazz Hour / Oct '91 / Target/BMG / Jazz Music / Cadillac.

MEETS OSCAR PETERSON
Pablo / Apr '92 / Jazz Music / Cadillac / Complete/Pinnacle.
CD _____ **CD 2310926**

MONTREUX '77 (Carter, Benny Quartet)
CD _____ **OJCCD 374**
Original Jazz Classics / Nov '95 / Wellard / Jazz Music / Cadillac / Complete/Pinnacle.

OVER THE RAINBOW (Carter, Benny All Star Sax Ensemble)
Blues for lucky lovers / Straight talk / Over the rainbow / Out of nowhere / Gal from Atlanta / Pawnbroker / Easy money / Ain't misbehavin'
CD _____ **CIJD 60196Y**
Music Masters / '89 / Nimbus.

SKYLAND DRIVE & TOWARDS
CD _____ **PHONTCD 9305**
Phontastic / Apr '94 / Wellard / Jazz Music.

SYMPHONY IN RIFFS
Blue interlude / Blues in my heart / Bugle call rag / Dee blues / Devil's holiday / Dream lullaby / Everybody shuffle / Just a mood / Lazy afternoon / Lonesome nights / Nightfall / Once upon a time / Pardon me pretty baby / Pastoral / Shoot the works / Skip it / Swing it / Swingin' with Mezz / Symphony in riffs / Waltzing the blues / When lights are low / You understand
CD _____ **CDAJA 5075**
Living Era / '91 / Koch.

THESE FOOLISH THINGS
Blue interlude / How come you like me like you do / Once upon a time / Devil's holiday / Lonesome nights / Shoot the works / Dream lullaby / Blue Lou / Krazy kapers / Symphony in riffs / I never knew / Music at sunrise / Firebird / Everybody shuffle / Synthetic love / Swingin' at Maida Vale / These foolish things / When day is done / Just a mood / Big Ben blues / Nightfall
CD _____ **CDGRF 087**
Tring / '93 / Tring / Prism.

Carter, Betty

AT THE VILLAGE VANGUARD
CD _____ **519581-2**
Verve / Dec '93 / PolyGram.

DROPPIN' THINGS
CD _____ **843 991-2**
Verve / Mar '91 / PolyGram.

FEED THE FIRE
CD _____ **5236002**
Verve / Oct '94 / PolyGram.

NOT ABOUT THE MELODY
CD _____ **5138702**
Verve / Apr '92 / PolyGram.

ROUND MIDNIGHT
CD Set _____ **ATJCD 8008**
All That's Jazz / Aug '94 / THE / Jazz Music.

ROUND MIDNIGHT
Do something / Every time we say goodbye / My shining hour / Something wonderful / What's new / By the bend on the river / I'm pulling through / Round Midnight / Sunny with the fringe on top
CD _____ **CDROU 1031**
Roulette / Mar '91 / EMI.

Carter, Bo

BANANA IN YOUR FRUIT BASKET
CD _____ **YAZCD 1064**
Yazoo / Apr '91 / CM / ADA / Roots / Koch.

BO CARTER, VOL. 1 (1928-31)
CD _____ **DOCD 5078**
Blues Document / Mar '95 / Swift / Jazz Music / Hot Shot.

BO CARTER, VOL. 2 (1931-34)
CD _____ **DOCD 5079**
Blues Document / Mar '95 / Swift / Jazz Music / Hot Shot.

BO CARTER, VOL. 3 (1934-36)
CD _____ **DOCD 5080**
Blues Document / Mar '95 / Swift / Jazz Music / Hot Shot.

BO CARTER, VOL. 4 (1936-38)
CD _____ **DOCD 5081**
Blues Document / Mar '95 / Swift / Jazz Music / Hot Shot.

BO CARTER, VOL. 5 (1938-40)
CD _____ **DOCD 5082**
Blues Document / Mar '95 / Swift / Jazz Music / Hot Shot.

Carter, Carlene

ACTS OF TREASON
Love like this / Lucky ones / Little acts of treason / He will be mine / Come here you / Change / Hurricane / Go wild / You'll be the one / All night long / Come here you (reprise)
CD _____ **74321294872**
Giant / Aug '95 / BMG.

I FELL IN LOVE
I fell in love / Come on back / Sweetest thing / My Dixie darling / Goodnight Dallas / One love / Leaving side / Guardian angel / Me and the wildwood rose / You are the one / Easy from now on
CD _____ **7599261392**
Reprise / Jan '96 / Warner Music.

LITTLE ACTS OF TREASON
CD _____ **74321259892**
Giant / Aug '95 / BMG.

MUSICAL SHAPES/BLUE NUN
CD _____ **FIENDCD 703**
Demon / Sep '91 / Pinnacle / ADA.

Carter, Chris

SPACE BETWEEN
CD _____ **ICC 1CD**
Mute / Jan '92 / Disc.

Carter, Clarence

BEST OF CLARENCE CARTER, THE
CD _____ **RSACD 801**
Sequel / Oct '94 / BMG.

BETWEEN A ROCK AND A HARD PLACE
Things ain't like they used to be / Straw that broke the camel's back / I ain't leaving, girl / Too weak to fight / Pickin' 'em down layin' 'em down / I'm between a rock and a hard place / I've got a thing for you baby / If you see my lady / Love building
CD _____ **CDICH 1068**
Ichiban / Oct '93 / Koch.

DOCTOR CC
Dr. CC / I stayed away too long / If you let me take you home / Leftover love / You been cheatin' on me / Try me / Let's funk / Strokin'
CD _____ **ICH 1003CD**
Ichiban / Oct '93 / Koch.

DOCTOR'S GREATEST PRESCRIPTIONS, THE (The Best Of Clarence Carter)
Strokin' / Trying to sleep tonight / Messin' with my mind / I was in the neighbourhood / Dr. C.C. / Love me with a feeling / I'm not good, I'm the best / I'm the best / Slip away / Grandpa can't fly his kite / Kiss you all over / I've got a thing for you baby / I'm between a rock and a hard place
CD _____ **ICH 1116CD**
Ichiban / Feb '94 / Koch.

DYNAMIC CLARENCE CARTER, THE
I'd rather go blind / Think about it / Road of love / You've been a long time comin' / Light my fire / That old time feeling / Steal away / Let me comfort you / Look what I got / Too weak to fight / Harper Valley PTA / Weekend love
CD _____ **7567803772**
Atlantic / Jan '96 / Warner Music.

HOOKED ON LOVE
CD _____ **CDICH 1016**
Ichiban / Mar '94 / Koch.

MESSIN' WITH MY MIND
CD _____ **ICH 1001**
Ichiban / Oct '93 / Koch.

PATCHES - THE BEST OF CLARENCE CARTER
CD _____ **CDSGP 0131**
Prestige / Dec '94 / Total/BMG.

SNATCHING IT BACK (The Best of Clarence Carter)
Tell Daddy / Slipped, tripped and fell in love / I can't see myself / Too weak to fight / Looking for a love / Step by step / Patches / Soul deep / Kind woman / Making love / Back door Santa
CD _____ **8122702862**
WEA / Jul '93 / Warner Music.

TOUCH OF THE BLUES
I'm not just good, I'm the best / Rock me baby / Why do I stay here / It's a man down there / All night, all day / Kiss you all over / Stormy Monday blues / Dance to the blues
CD _____ **CDICH 1032**
Ichiban / Oct '93 / Koch.

Carter, Dean

PERSISTENCE OF VISION
CD _____ **THEBES 002CD**
Oedipus / Nov '92 / Plastic Head.

Carter, Deana

DID I SHAVE MY LEGS FOR THIS
Angel without a prayer / Rita Valentine / I've loved enough to know / I can't shake you / Are you coming home today / Did I shave my legs for this / Turn those wheels around / Graffiti Bridge / Before we ever heard goodbye / We share a wall / Don't let go / Just what you need
CD _____ CDEST 2249
Capitol / Mar '95 / EMI.

Carter Family

ANCHORED IN LOVE
CD _____ ROU 1064CD
Rounder / Jan '94 / CM / Direct / ADA / Cadillac.

MY CLINCH FAMILY HOME
CD _____ ROU 1065CD
Rounder / Jan '94 / CM / Direct / ADA / Cadillac.

ON BORDER RADIO VOL.1
CD _____ ARHCD 411
Arhoolie / Jan '96 / ADA / Direct / Cadillac.

WHEN THE ROSES BLOOM IN DIXIELAND
CD _____ ROUCD 1066
Rounder / Nov '95 / CM / Direct / ADA / Cadillac.

WORRIED MAN BLUES
CD _____ ROUCD 1067
Rounder / Nov '95 / CM / Direct / ADA / Cadillac.

Carter, James

JURASSIC CLASSICS
Take the 'A' train / Out of nowhere / Epistrophy / Ask me now / Equinox / Sansu / Oleo
CD _____ 4786122
Sony Jazz / Jun '95 / Sony.

ON THE SET
CD _____ DIW 875
DIW / Nov '93 / Harmonia Mundi / Cadillac.

Carter, Joe

DUETS
CD _____ ST 578
Stash / Jul '94 / Jazz Music / CM / Cadillac / Direct / ADA.

Carter, John

FIELDS
CD _____ 188809 2
Gramavision / Feb '89 / Vital/SAM / ADA.

SEEKING (Carter, John & Bobby Bradford)
CD _____ ARTCD 6085
Hat Art / Aug '91 / Harmonia Mundi / ADA / Cadillac.

SHADOWS ON THE WALL
'Sippi strut / Spats / City streets / And I saw them / 52nd Street stomp / Hymn to freedom
CD _____ 794 222
Gramavision / Mar '90 / Vital/SAM / ADA.

Carter, Lisa

COUNTRY ROADS
CD _____ SOV 017CD
Sovereign / Jan '93 / Target/BMG.

Carter, Ron

ATUDES
CD _____ 1046710122
Discovery / May '95 / Warner Music.

PASTELS
Woolaphant / Ballad / One bass rag / Pastels / Twelve plus twelve
CD _____ OJCCD 665
Original Jazz Classics / Sep '93 / Wellard / Jazz Music / Cadillac / Complete/Pinnacle.

RON CARTER PLAYS BACH
CD _____ 8308902
ECM / Mar '88 / New Note.

TELEPHONE (Carter, Ron & Jim Hall)
Telephone / Indian Summer / Candlelight / Chorale and dance / Alone together / Stardust / Two's blues
CD _____ CCD 4270
Concord Jazz / Sep '86 / New Note.

THIRD PLANE (Carter, Ron, Tony Williams & Herbie Hancock)
Third plane / Quiet times / Lawra / Stella by starlight / United blues / Dolphin dance
CD _____ OJCCD 754
Original Jazz Classics / Apr '94 / Wellard / Jazz Music / Cadillac / Complete/Pinnacle.

UPTOWN CONVERSATION
CD _____ 7567819552
Atlantic / Apr '95 / Warner Music.

WHERE (Carter, Ron & Eric Dolphy/Mal Waldron)
Rally / Bass duet / Softly as in a morning sunrise / Where / Yes indeed / Saucer eyes

CD _____ OJCCD 432-2
Original Jazz Classics / May '93 / Wellard / Jazz Music / Cadillac / Complete/Pinnacle.

Carter, Sara

SARA & MAYBELLE (Carter, Sara & Maybelle)
Lonesome pine special / Hand that rocked the cradle / Spanish / Home / Ship that never returned / Three little strangers / Sun of the soul / Weary prodigal son / While the band is playing Dixie / Farther on / No more goodbyes / Happiest day of all / Charlie Brooks / I told them what you're fighting for / We all miss you Joe / San Antonio rose / Mama's Irish jig / Black mountain rag / Let's be lover's again / Give me your love and I'll give mine / Letter from home / There's a mother always waiting / Tom cat's kitten / Kitty Puss
CD _____ BCD 15471
Bear Family / Jul '93 / Rollercoaster / Direct / CM / Swift / ADA.

Carter U.S.M.

101 DAMNATIONS
Road to domestos / Every time a church bell rings / Twenty four minutes from Tulse Hill / All American national sport, An / Sheriff Fatman / Taking of Peckham 123 / Cheese-toppers A-go-go / Good grief Charlie Brown / Midnight on the murder mile / Perfect day to drop the bomb / G.I. blues
CD _____ ABBCD 101
Big Cat / Aug '95 / SRD / Pinnacle.

1992 - THE LOVE ALBUM
1993 / Is wrestling fixed / Only living boy in New Cross / Suppose you gave a funeral and nobody came / England / Do re me, so far so good / Look mum, no hands / While you were out / Skywest and crooked / Impossible dream
CD _____ CD25CR 24
Chrysalis / Mar '94 / EMI.

30 SOMETHING
My second to last will and testament / Anytime anyplace anywhere / Prince in a pauper's grave / Shoppers' paradise / Billy's smart circus / Bloodsport for all / Sealed with a Glasgow kiss / Say it with flowers / Falling on a bruise / Final comedown
CD _____ CCD 1897
Chrysalis / Feb '92 / EMI.

POST HISTORIC MONSTERS
Two million years BC / Music that nobody likes / Midday crisis / Cheer up, it might never happen / Stuff the jubilee / Bachelor for Baden Powell / Spoilsports personality of the year / Suicide isn't painless / Being here / Evil / Sing fat lady sing / Travis / Lean on me I won't fall over / Lenny and Terence / Under the thumb and over the moon
CD _____ CDCHR 7090
Chrysalis / Sep '93 / EMI.

STARRY EYED AND BOLLOCK NAKED
Is this the only way to get through to you / Granny farming in the UK / R.S.P.C.E. / Twin tub with guitar / Alternative Alf Garnett / Re-educating Rita / 2001 / Clockwork orange / 90's revival / Nation of shoplifters / Watching the big apple turn over / Turn on, tune in and switch off / When Thesauruses ruled the earth / Bring on the girls / Always the bridesmaid, never the bride / Her song / Commercial fucking suicide (Part 1) / Stuff the jubilee / Glam rock cops
CD _____ CDCHR 6069
Chrysalis / Mar '94 / EMI.

STRAW DONKEY - THE SINGLES
Sheltered life / Sherrif Fatman / Rubbish / Anytime, anyplace, anywhere / The impossible dream / Lean on me I won't fall over / Lenny and Terence / Glam rock cops / Let's get tattoos / Young offender's mum / Born on the 5th of November
CD _____ CDCHR 6110
Chrysalis / Oct '95 / EMI.

WORRY BOMB
Cheap 'n' cheesy / Airplane food/Airplane fast food / Young offender's mum / Gas (man) / Life and soul of party dies / My defeatist attitude / When thistledom is delinquent / Me and Mr. Jones / Let's get tattoos / Going straight / God, Saint Peter and the Guardian Angel / Only looney left in town / Ceasefire / Alternative Alf Garnet / Do re me, so far so good / Bachelor for Baden Powell (live) / Re-educating Rita (live) / Only living boy in New Cross (live) / Lean on me I won't fall over (live) / Granny farming in the UK (live) / Travis (live) / Sing fat lady sing (live) / Lenny and Terence (live) / Commercial fucking suicide (part 1)
CD _____ CDCHR 6096
Chrysalis / Feb '95 / EMI.

Carter, Wilf

DYNAMITE TRAIL - THE DECCA YEARS, 1954-58
One golden curl / My mountain high yodel song / I'm gonna tear down the mailbox / Maple leaf waltz / There's a tree on a rocky mountain road / I bought a rock for a rocky mountain gal / Shoo shoo sh'lala / Sunshine bird / Kissing on the sly / Alpine milkman / Dy-

namite trail / Strawberry road / Ragged but right / There's a padlock on your heart / Yodelin' song / On a little two acre farm / Strawberry road (2) / My little lady / Silver bell yudel / Away out on the mountain / Blind boy's prayer / X's from down in Texas / Let a little sunshine in your heart / There's a bluebird on your windowsill / My French Canadian girl / Sick, sober and sorry / Sinner's prayer / My prairie rose / Yodeling my babies to sleep / Born to lose
CD Set _____ BCD 15507
Bear Family / Jul '90 / Rollercoaster / Direct / CM / Swift / ADA.

PRAIRIE LEGEND, A (Carter, Wilf & Montana Slim)
Farewell, sweetheart, farewell / Old Shep / I've hung up my chaps and saddle / You'll get used to it / I ain't gonna hobo no more / Don't be mean, I wasn't mean to you / Sinner's prayer / Plant some flowers by my graveside / There's a goldstar in her window / My blue skies / Put me in your pocket / Smilin' through tears / Born to lose / No letter today / Our Canadian flag / So hard to start all over again / I'll never die of a broken heart / Dreaming of my blue eyes / Memories bring heartaches to me / My Queen of the prairies / Rye whiskey / One golden curl / Hang the key on the bunkhouse door / I'm a fool for foolin' around / There's a loveknot in my lariat / It's later than you think / Too many blues / Singing on borrowed time / Just an old forgotten letter / She lost her cowboy pal / Ol' lonely / If we can't be sweethearts, why can't we be... / Don't cry over me / Sharing your love with somebody new / Don't wait till Judgement Day / Cowboy days ain't ramblin' days no more / 'Neath a blanket of stars / I never knew that I could be so blue / It's just a wild rose I'm sending / Where the sleepy Rio's flowing / You'll be sorry you turned me down / Dream lullaby yodel / It's hard to forget you / Tramp's mother / Take away those blues around my heart / Midnight train / I'm gonna tear down the mailbox / It can't be done / All I need is some more lovin' / (There's a) Bluebird on your windowsill / When the iceworms nest again / Shackles and chains / No, no, don't ring those bells / Give a little, take a little / Unfaithful one / Little shirt my mother made for me / Guilty conscience / Take it easy blues / My heart's closed for repairs / My wife is on a date / Let's go back to the bible / She'll be there / I wish there were only three days in the year / When that love bug bites you / Just a woman's smile / Rudolph the red nosed reindeer / Apple, cherry, mince and choc'late cream / Jolly old St. Nicholas / KP blues / Blue Canadian Rockies / Dear Evalina / My Oklahoma rose / What cigarette is best / Sick, sober and sorry / Teardrops don't always mean a broken heart / Wha hoppen / Punkinhead (The little bear) / Night before Christmas in Texas that is / Goodbye Maris (I'm off to Korea) / Driftwood on the river / Manhunt / (All you gave me) Mockingbird love / Square dance boogie / Sweet little lover / Huggin', squeezin', kissin', teasin' / Sleep one little sleep / Alabama Saturday night / Hot foot boogie / I remember the rodeo / Pete Knight, the King of the cowboys / When the iceworms nest again (2) / My little grey haired Mother in the west / He rode the strawberry roan / Rattlin' cannonball / Calgary roundup / That silver haired daddy of mine / Smoke went up the chimney just the same / Capture of Albert Johnson / Beautiful girl of the prairie / Singing in my last roundup
CD Set _____ BCD 15754
Bear Family / Nov '93 / Rollercoaster / Direct / CM / Swift / ADA.

Carter-Lewis

CARTER-LEWIS STORY (Carter-Lewis & The Southerners)
Back on the scene / So much in love / Here's hopin' / Poor Joe / Two-timing baby / Will it happen to me / Tell me / My broken heart / Your Momma's out of town / Somebody told my girl / Skinny Minnie / Easy to cry / sweet and tender romance / Who told you / My world fell down / Lonely room / Willow tree / Let's go to San Francisco / Let's go back to San Francisco / Walk in the sky / Blow away / White dove / Tahiti farewell / Night to be remembered / Rise Sally rise / I want to be where you are
CD _____ NEXCD 234
Sequel / Jun '93 / BMG.

Carthy, Eliza

ELIZA CARTHY & NANCY KERR (Carthy, Eliza & Nancy Kerr)
CD _____ MCR 3991CD
Mrs. Casey / Nov '93 / Direct / ADA.

SHAPE OF SCRAPE (Carthy, Eliza & Nancy Kerr)
CD _____ MCR 5992CD
Mrs. Casey / Jul '95 / Direct / ADA.

Carthy, Martin

BECAUSE IT'S THERE
Nothing rhymed / May song / Swaggering Boney / Lord Randal / Long John, old John and Jackie North / Jolly tinker / Lovely Joan

/ Three cripples / Siege of Delhi / Death of young Andrew
CD _____ TSCD 389
Topic / May '95 / Direct / ADA.

BUT TWO CAME BY (Carthy, Martin & Dave Swarbrick)
Ship in distress / Banks of the sweet primroses / Long lankin / Brass band music
CD _____ TSCD 343
Topic / May '94 / Direct / ADA.

COLLECTION, THE
CD _____ GLCD 1136
Green Linnet / Jan '94 / Hoots / CM / Direct / ADA.

CROWN OF HORN
Bedmaking / Locks and bolts / King Knapperty / Geordie / Willie's lady / Virginny / Worcestershire wedding / Bonnie lass o'Anglesey / William Taylor the poacher / Old Tom of Oxford / Palaces of gold
CD _____ TSCD 300
Topic / Oct '95 / Direct / ADA.

KERSHAW SESSIONS
CD _____ ROOTCD 002
Strange Fruit / Jun '94 / Pinnacle.

MARTIN CARTHY
High Germany / Trees they do grow high / Sovay / Ye mariners all / Queen of hearts / Broomfield hill / Springhill mine disaster / Scarborough Fair / Lovely Joan / Barley and the rye / Wind that shakes the barley / Two magicians / Handsome cabin boy / And a begging I will go
CD _____ TSCD 340
Topic / May '93 / Direct / ADA.

OUT OF THE CUT
Devil and the feathery wife / Reynard the fox / Song of the lower classes / Rufford Park poachers / Molly Oxford / Rigs of the time / I sowed some seeds / Frair in the well / Jack Rowland / Old horse
CD _____ TSCD 426
Topic / Aug '94 / Direct / ADA.

PRINCE HEATHEN (Carthy, Martin & Dave Swarbrick)
Arthur McBride / Salisbury Plain / Polly on the shore / Rainbow / Died for love / Staines Morris / Reynardine / Seven yellow gypsies / Little Musgrave / Wren
CD _____ TSCD 344
Topic / Jun '94 / Direct / ADA.

RIGHT OF PASSAGE
Ant and the grasshopper / Eggs in her basket / Stitch in time / McVeagh / Hommage a roche proulx / All in green / Company policy / Banks of the Nile / La carde use / Bill Norrie / Sleepwalker / Cornish young man / Dominion of the sword
CD _____ TSCD 452
Topic / Dec '88 / Direct / ADA.

RIGS OF THE TIMES (The Best Of Martin Carthy)
Skewball / Ant and the grasshopper / Foxhunt / Devil and the feathery wife / Sheepstealer / Begging song / Geordie / Billy boy / Lovely Joan / Sovay / Bill Norrie / Question of sport / Old horse / All of a row / Work life out to keep life in / Rigs of the time / Such a war has never been / Dominion of the sword / Byker hill
CD _____ MCCD 145
Music Club / Dec '93 / Disc / THE / CM.

SECOND ALBUM
Two butchers / Ball o'yarn / Farewell Nancy / Lord Franklin / Rambling sailor / Lowlands of Holland / Fair maid on the shore / Brufton town / Box on her head / Newlyn town / Brave Wolfe / Peggy and the soldier / Sailor's life
CD _____ TSCD 341
Topic / Sep '93 / Direct / ADA.

Cartland, Barbara

GREAT ROMANTIC SONGS
CD _____ CDSIV 6132
Horatio Nelson / Jul '95 / THE / BMG / Avid/BMG / Koch.

Cartwright, Deirdre

DEBUT (Cartwright, Deirdre Group)
Spartia / Slipper 15s 8d / I thought of you / Trap / When pushing comes to shoving / Grand loup / Pisces moon / One more / Walk with me
CD _____ BTF 9401
Blow The Fuse / Oct '94 / New Note.

Carty, John

CAT THAT ATE THE CRADLE (Carty, John & Brian McGrath)
CD _____ CICD 099
Clo Iar-Chonnachta / Aug '94 / CM.

Carvenius, Rolf

ROLF CARVENIUS & HIS SINGING CLARINET
CD _____ CCCD 2
Cloetta / Feb '95 / Jazz Music / Cadillac.

Carvin, Michael

BETWEEN ME & YOU
CD _____ MCD 5370
Muse / Sep '92 / New Note / CM.

EACH ONE TEACH ONE
Surrey with the fringe on top/Eternal triangle / Waltz for Gina / Nails (to Michael Carvin) / Smoke gets in your eyes / Recife's blues / I don't stand a ghost of a chance with you / One by one
CD _____ MCD 5485
Muse / Feb '95 / New Note / CM.

Cary, Marc

CARY ON
Vibe / Afterthought / When I think of you / So gracefully / We learn as we go / Trial / Melody in C / He who hops around
CD _____ ENJ 90232
Enja / May '95 / New Note / Vital/SAM.

Cascade

LET IT BE ME
CD _____ CDOK 3007
OK / Nov '88 / Ross.

Case, Harry

IN A MOOD
Ride 'em off / Native drums / Chasing the goon / Quick wire / Jam / Carry me home / Midnight samba / In a mood / Air dancer / Mother-son
CD _____ CDICH 1037
Ichiban / Jul '89 / Koch.

Case, Peter

SINGS LIKE HELL
CD _____ GRCD 351
Glitterhouse / Dec '94 / Direct / ADA.

Casey, Al

BEST OF FRIENDS (Casey, Al & Jay McShann)
Deed I do / One o'clock jump / Going to Kansas City / One sweet blues / How deep is the ocean / Anything hallo / Little girl / Honky tonk train blues
CD _____ JSPCD 224
JSP / Apr '89 / ADA / Target/BMG / Direct / Cadillac / Complete/Pinnacle.

JIVIN' AROUND
Surfin' hootenanny / El aguila / Thunder beach / Baja / Surfin' blues / Lonely surfer / Guitars, guitars, guitars / Hearse / Ramrod / Caravan / Surfin' blues part II / Surfs you right / Cookin' / Hot food / Indian love call / Jivin' around / Doin' the shotish / Doin' it / Huckleback / Full house / Laughin' / Monte carlo / Huckleberry hound / Chicken feathers / Easy pickin' / What are we gonna do in '64
CD _____ CDCHD 612
Ace / Aug '95 / Pinnacle / Cadillac / Complete/Pinnacle.

SIDEWINDER
Undecided / You come a long way from St. Louis / Sidewinder / Ashokan farewell / Endless sleep / Limeshouse blues / Saguaro sunrise / Route 1 / Plectrum banjo medley / Fool
CD _____ BCDAH 1585
Bear Family / Aug '95 / Rollercoaster / Direct / CM / Swift / ADA.

TRIBUTE TO FATS, A
CD _____ 1044
Jazz Point / Jan '95 / Harmonia Mundi / Cadillac.

Casey, Nollaig

CAUSEWAY (Casey, Nollaig & Arty McGlynn)
Causeway / Cabbage and cale / Sel Le Thoil / Jack Palance's reel / Tra an phearla / Rainy summer / Stor mo chiroi / Comanche moon / Trip to Tokyo / Dun na sead / Murals / Lois na banrfona
CD _____ TARA 3035
Tara / Aug '95 / CM / ADA / Direct / Conifer.

Cash, Johnny

1958–1986 THE CBS YEARS
Oh what a dream / I still miss someone / Pickin' time / Don't take your guns to town / Five feet high and rising / Seasons of my heart / Legend of John Henry's hammer / Ring of fire / Ballad of Ira Hayes / Orange Blossom special / Folsom Prison blues / San Quentin / Boy named Sue / Sunday morning coming down / Man in black / One piece at a time / Riders in the sky / Without love / Baron / Highway patrolman
CD _____ 4504662
CBS / May '87 / Sony.

AMERICAN RECORDINGS
Delia's gone / Let the rain blow the whistle / Beast in me / Drive on / Why me Lord / Thirteen / Oh bury me not / Bird on the wire / Tennessee stud / Down there by the train / Redemption / Like a soldier / Man who couldn't cry
CD _____ 74321236852
American / Oct '94 / BMG.

BEST OF JOHNNY CASH
CD _____ MATCD 331
Castle / Jun '95 / BMG.

BEST OF THE SUN YEARS 1955–1961
CD _____ MCCD 082
Music Club / Sep '92 / Disc / THE / CM.

BIGGEST HITS
Don't take your guns to town / Ring of fire / Understand your man / One on the right is on the left / Rosanna's going wild / Folsom Prison blues / Baddy sand bass / Boy named Sue / Sunday morning coming down / Flesh and blood / Thing called love / One piece at a time / There ain't no good chain gang / Riders in the sky / Baron
CD _____ CD 32304
Columbia / Jun '91 / Sony.

BITTER TEARS (Ballads Of The American Indian)
Big foot / As long as the grass shall grow / Apache tears / Custer / Talking leaves / Ballad of Ira Hayes / Drums / White girl / Old Apache squaw / Vanishing race / Intro
CD _____ CK 66507
Columbia / Feb '95 / Sony.

BLOOD, SWEAT AND TEARS
Legend of John Henry's hammer / Tell him I'm gone / Another man done gone / Busted / Casey Jones / Nine pound hammer / Chain gang / Waiting for a train / Roughneck
CD _____ CK 66508
Columbia / Feb '95 / Sony.

BOOM CHICKA BOOM
Backstage pass / Farmer's almanac / Family bible / I love you, I love you / Monteagle Mountain / Cats in the cradle / Don't go near the water / Harley / Hidden shame / That's one you owe me
CD _____ 8421552
Mercury / Feb '90 / PolyGram.

BORN TO LOSE
I walk the line / Ballad of a teenage queen / Big river / Wreck of ol' 97 / Folsom prison blues / Rock Island line / Luther played the boogie / Straight A's in love / Get rhythm / Next in line / You're the nearest thing to heaven
CD _____ CDINS 5007
Instant / Jul '89 / Charly.

CLASSIC CASH
Get rhythm / Long black veil / I still miss someone / Blue train / Five feet high and rising / Don't take your guns to town / Guess things happen that way / I walk the line / Ballad of Ira Hayes / Folsom Prison blues / Tennessee flat top box / Thing called love / Cry cry cry / Sunday morning coming down / Peace in the valley / Home of the blues / I got stripes / Ring of fire / Ways of a woman in love / Suppertime
CD _____ 834 526-2
Mercury / Mar '89 / PolyGram.

COLLECTION, THE
CD _____ COL 004
Collection / Jan '95 / Target/BMG.

COLLECTION: JOHNNY CASH
Wide open road / Cry cry cry / Folsom Prison blues / So doggone lonesome / Mean eyed cat / New Mexico / I walk the line / I love you because / Straight A's in love / Home of the blues / Rock Island line / Country boy / Doin' my time / Big river / Ballad of a teenage queen / Oh lonesome me / You're the nearest thing to heaven / Always alone / You win again / Hey good lookin' / Blue train / Katy too / Fools hall of fame / Ways of a woman in love / Down the street to 301
CD _____ CCSCD 146
Castle / Feb '93 / BMG.

COME ALONG AND RIDE THIS TRAIN
Come along and ride this train / Loading coal / Slow rider / Lumberjack / Dorraine of ponchartrain / Going to Memphis / When papa played the dobro / Boss Jack / Old Doc Brown / Legend of John Henry's hammer / Tell him I'm gone / Another man done gone / Casey Jones / Nine pound hammer / Chain gang / Busted / Waiting for a train / Roughneck / Pick a bale of cotton / Cotton pickin' hands / Hiawatha's vision / Hammer and nails / Shifting whispering sands / Ballad of Boot Hill / I ride an old paint / Hardin wouldn't run / Mr. Garfield / Streets of Laredo / Johnny Reb / Letter from home / Bury me not on the lone prairie / Mean as hell / Sam Hall / Twenty five minutes to go / Blizzard / Sweet Betsy from Pike / Green grow the lilacs / Rodeo hand / Stampede / Remember the Alamo / Reflections / Big foot / As long as the grass shall grow / Apache tears / Custer / Talking leaves / Ballad of Ira Hayes / Drums / White girl / Old apache squaw / Vanishing race / Paul Revere / Road to Kaintuck / Battle of New Orleans / Lorena / Gettysburg address / Big battle / Come and take a trip in my airship / These are my people / From the sea to shining sea / Whirl and the suck / Call daddy from the mine / Frozen four hundred pound to middin' cotton picker / Walls of a prison / Masterpiece / You and Tennessee / She came from the mountains / Another song to sing / Flint arrowhead / Cisco Clifton's fillin' station / Shrimpin' sailin' / From sea to shining sea / Hit the road and go / If

it wasn't for the Wabash river / Lady / After the ball / No earthly good / Wednesday car / My cowboy's last ride
CD Set _____ BCD 15563
Bear Family / May '91 / Rollercoaster / Direct / CM / Swift / ADA.

COUNTRY BLUES
Wreck of ol' 97 / Get rhythm / Luther played the boogie / Two timin' woman / Next in line / Belshazar / Hey porter / I heard that lonesome whistle / Train of love / Sugartime / Don't make me go / There you go / Boy named Sue / Jackson / Daughter of the railroad man / Go on blues / Mama's baby / So do I / Folsom prison blues (Live) / In a young girl's mind / One piece at a time / How did you get away from me / Rodeo hand / Walking the blues
CD _____ VSOPCD 121
Connoisseur / Apr '90 / Pinnacle.

COUNTRY CHRISTMAS
CD _____ 15417
Laserlight / Nov '95 / Target/BMG.

FOLSOM PRISON BLUES
Cry cry cry / Folsom prison blues / So doggone lonesome / I walk the line / Get rhythm / There you go / Train of love / Next in line / Don't make me go / Home of the blues / Give my love to Rose / Ballad of a teenage queen / Big river / Guess things happen that way / Come in stranger / Ways of a woman in love / You're the nearest thing to heaven / It's just about time / Luther played the boogie / Thanks a lot / Katy too / Goodbye little darling / Straight A's in love / I love you because / Mean eyed cat / Oh lonesome me / Rock island line / Down the street to 301
CD _____ CPCD 8101
Charly / Jun '95 / Charly / THE / Cadillac.

GET RHYTHM (Cash, Johnny & The Tennessee Two)
Get rhythm / Mean eyed cat / You win again / Country boy / Two timin' woman / Oh lonesome me / Luther's boogie / Doin' my time / New Mexico / Belshazar / Sugartime
CD _____ CDCD 1054
Charly / Mar '93 / Charly / THE / Cadillac.

GREAT COUNTRY LOVE SONGS
CD _____ PWK 014
Carlton Home Entertainment / '88 / Carlton Home Entertainment.

GREATEST HITS: JOHNNY CASH
CD _____ WMCD 5661
Woodford Music / Aug '92 / THE.

GREATEST HITS: JOHNNY CASH VOL. 1
Jackson / I walk the line / Ballad of Ira Hayes / Orange blossom special / One on the right is on the left / Ring of fire / It ain't me babe / Understand your man / Rebel - Johnny Yuma / Five feet high and rising / Don't take your guns to town
CD _____ 983318 2
Pickwick/Sony Collector's Choice / Nov '93 / Carlton Home Entertainment / Pinnacle / Sony.

GUESS THINGS HAPPEN THAT WAY
CD _____ CDCD 1154
Charly / Jul '94 / Charly / THE / Cadillac.

HEROES (Cash, Johnny & Waylon Jennings)
Folks out on the road / I'm never gonna roam again / American by birth / Field of diamonds / Heroes / Even cowgirls get the blues / Love is the way / Ballad of forty dollars / I'll always love you - in my own crazy way / One too many mornings
CD _____ 983305 2
Pickwick/Sony Collector's Choice / Oct '93 / Carlton Home Entertainment / Pinnacle / Sony.

I WALK THE LINE
CD _____ CTS 55406
Country Stars / Jan '92 / Target/BMG.

ITCHY FEET - 20 FOOT-TAPPIN' GREATS
Folsom prison blues / I walk the line / Ring of fire / Forty shades of green / I still miss someone / There ain't no good chain gang / Busted / Twenty five minutes to go / Orange blossom special / It ain't me babe / Boy named Sue / San Quentin / Don't take your guns to town / One on the right is on the left / Jackson / Hey porter / Daddy sang bass / I got stripes / Thing called love / One piece at a time
CD _____ 4681162
Columbia / Apr '95 / Sony.

JOHNNY CASH
Wanted man / Wreck of ol' 97 / I walk the line / Darling companion / Starkville City jail / San Quentin / Boy named Sue / Peace in the valley / Folsom Prison blues
CD _____ 9825862
Pickwick/Sony Collector's Choice / Jul '91 / Carlton Home Entertainment / Pinnacle / Sony.

JOHNNY CASH
CD _____ 12373
Laserlight / Oct '95 / Target/BMG.

JOHNNY CASH IN CONCERT
CD _____ TRTCD 188
TrueTrax / Jun '95 / THE.

MAN IN BLACK

Ring of fire / I walk the line / Get rhythm (Live) / It Ain't Me Babe / I still miss someone / Ghost riders in the sky / Daddy sang bass / Jackson / One piece at a time / Orange blossom special / Folsom prison blues (Live) / San Quentin (Live) / Boy named Sue (Live) / Thing called love / Don't take your guns to town / Wanted man / Big river / Without love / No expectations / Highway patrolman / Singin' in
CD _____ MOODCD35
Columbia / Aug '94 / Sony.

MAN IN BLACK 1963-69 PLUS, THE (6 CDST)
Ring of fire / Matador / I'd still be there / Still in town / El matador (spanish) / Fuego d'amour (spanish) / My old faded rose / It ain't me babe / Don't think twice it's alright / One too many mornings / Mama, you've been on my mind / I walk the line / Folsom prison blues / Wreck of the old '97 / Hey porter / Big river / All God's children ain't free / Amen / When it's springtime in Alaska / You wild Colorado / Danny Boy / I still miss someone / Give my love to Rose / Goodbye little darlin' goodbye / Dark as a dungeon / Bottom of the mountain / Understand your man / Time and time again / Hardin wouln't run / Certain kinda hurtin / How did you get away from me / Bad news / Cup of coffee / Dirty old egg sucking hound / One on the right is one on the left / Concerning your new song / Bug that tried to crawl around the world / Flushed from the bathroom of your heart / Dirty old egg sucking dog / Take me home / Song of the coward / Please don't play red river valley / Foolish questions / Singing stars queen / Austin prison / Boa constrictor / Everybody loves a nut / Sound of laughter / Joe Bean / Frozen lagger / Baby is mine / Happy to with with you / You love me / You'll be alright / Fast boat to Sidney / Long legged guitar pickin' man / Pack up your sorrows / Jackson / Is this my destiny / Wound time can't erase / You comb her hair / Ancient history / Happiness is you / Guess things happen that way / I got a woman / What I'd say / Oh, what a good thing we had / No, no, no / Shanty town / What'd I say / Matador (spanish) / Wer kennt den weg / In Virginia / Kleine Rosmarie / Besser so, Jenny Jo / Thunderball / Sons of Katie Elder / Put the sugar to bed / Red velvet / Rosanna's going wild / Wind changes / On the line / Roll call / You beat all I ever saw / I tremble for you / Cattle call / Bill's theme / Spanish Harlem / Folk singer / Southwind / Devil to pay / Cause I love you / See Ruby fall / Rout # 1 / Box 144 / Sing a travelling song / If I were a carpenter / To beat the devil / Blisterd / Wrinkled, crinkled, wadded dollar bill / I've got a thing about trains / Six white horses / Jesus was a carpenter / Man in black / Christmas spirit / I heard the bells on Christmas day / Blue Christmas / Gifts they gave / Here was a man / Christmas as I knew it / Silent night / Little drummer boy / It came upon a midnight clear / Ringing the bells for jim / We are the shepherds / Who kept the sheep / Ballad of the harpweavers / Wildwood flowers / Engine 143 / Keep on the sunnyside / Single girl, married girl / Banks of the Ohio / My clinch mountain home / Lonesome valley / Worried man blues / Brown hearted lover / Brown eyes / I'm working on a building / Gathering flowers from the hillside / When the roses bloom again / I taught the weeping willow / Rock island line / Ballad of Ira Hayes
CD Set _____ BCD 15588
Bear Family / Nov '95 / Rollercoaster / Direct / CM / Swift / ADA.

MAN IN BLACK VOL. 1 (5 CDs)
Wide open road (2 versions) / You're my baby / My treasure (2 versions) / Hey porter (2 versions) / Folsom Prison blues (2 versions) / My two tone / Cry cry cry / Port of lonely hearts / I couldn't keep from crying / New Mexico / So doggone lonesome / Mean eyed cat / Luther played the boogie / Rock 'n' roll Ruby / I walk the line (2 versions) / Brakeman's blues / Get rhythm (2 versions) / Train of love (2 versions) / There you go / One more ride / I love you because (2 versions) / Goodbye little darling / Straight A's in love / Don't make me go (2 versions) / Next in line / Home of the blues (2 versions) / Give my love to Rose (2 versions) / Rock Island line / Wreck of ol' 97 / Belshazar / Country boy / Leave that junk alone / Doin' my time / If the good Lord's willing / (I heard that) lonesome whistle / I was there when it happened / Remember me / Big river / Ballad of a teenage queen (2 versions) / Goodnight Irene / Come in stranger (2 versions) / Guess things happen that way / Sugartime (2 versions) / Born to lose / You're the nearest thing to heaven / Story of a broken heart / Always alone (2 versions) / Story of a broken heart (false starts) / You tell me / Life goes on / You win again / I could never be ashamed of you / Hey good lookin' / I can't help it / Cold cold heart / Blue train / Katy too / Ways of a woman in love (2 versions) / Fools hall of fame (2 versions) / Thanks a lot / It's just about time (2 versions) / I forgot to remember to forget / I just thought you'd like to know / Down the street to 301 / Oh

what a dream (2 versions) / I'll remember you (2 versions) / Drink to me / What do I care / Suppertime / It was Jesus / Mama's baby / Troubador / Run softly blue river / All over again / That's all over / Frankie's man / Johnnie / Walking the blues / Lead me father / That's enough / I still miss someone / Pickin' time / Don't take your guns to town / I'd rather die young / Shepherd of my heart / Cold shoulder
CD Set _____ BCD 15147
Bear Family / Sep '90 / Rollercoaster Direct / CM / Swift / ADA.

MAN IN BLACK VOL.2, THE (1959-1962)
Snow in his hair / I saw a man / Lead me gently home / Are all the children in / Swing low, sweet chariot / I call him / Old account / He'll be a friend / These things shall pass / It could be you / God will / Great speckled bird / Were you there / He'll understand and say well done / God has my fortune laid away / When I've learned / I got shoes / Let the lower lights be burning / If we never meet again / When I take my vacation in heaven / When he reached down his hand for me / Taller than trees / I won't have to cross Jordan alone / My god is real / These hands / Peace in the valley / Day in the Grand Canyon / I'll remember you / I got stripes / You dreamer you / Five feet high and rising / Rebel Johnny Yuma / Lorena / Second honeymoon / Fable of Willie Brown / Smiling Bill McCall / Johnny Yuma / Man on the hill / Hank and Joe and me / Caretaker / Clementine / I want to go home / Old Apache squaw / Don't step on mother's roses / My grandfather's clock / I couldn't keep from crying / My shoes keep walking back to you / I will miss you when you go / I feel better all over / Bandana / Wabash blues / Viel zu spat / Woistzuhause, mama / I heartbeat / Hello again / Tall man / Girl in Saskatoon / Locomotive man / Losing kind / Five minutes to live / Forty shades of green / Big battle / Blues for two / Jeri and Nina's melody / Why do you punish me / Just one more / Seasons of my heart / Honky tonk girl / I'm so lonesome I could cry / Time changes everything / I'd just be fool enough / Transfusion blues / Lovin' locomotive man / Mr. Lonesome / Folsom Prison blues / I walk the line (Take 6-slow, take 9-fast.) / Hey pardner / I forgot more than you'll ever know / There's a mother always waiting / Tennessee flat top box / Sing it pretty Sue / Little at a time / So do I / Bonanza / Shamrock doesn't grow in California / I'm free from the chain gang now / Delia's gone / Lost on the desert / Accidentally on purpose / You remember me / In the jailhouse now / Let me down easy / In them cottonfields back home / You won't have to go far / No one will ever know / Danger zone / I'll be all smiles tonight / Send a picture of Mother / Hardin wouldn't run / Blue bandana / So doggone lonesome / Johnny Reb
CD Set _____ BCD 15562
Bear Family / Aug '91 / Rollercoaster Direct / CM / Swift / ADA.

NOW, THERE WAS A SONG
Seasons of my heart / I feel better all over / I couldn't keep from crying / Time changes everything / My shoes keep walking back to you / I'd just be fool enough (to fall) / Transfusion blues / Why do you punish me (for loving you) / I will miss you when you go / I'm so lonesome I could cry / Just one more / Honky tonk girl
CD _____ CK 66506
Columbia / Feb '95 / Sony.

PERSONAL CHRISTMAS COLLECTION
Christmas spirit / I heard the bells on Christmas day / Blue Christmas / Christmas as I knew it / Little drummer boy / Christmas with you / Silent night / Joy to the world / Away in a manger / O little town of Bethlehem / Hark the herald angels sing / O come all ye faithful (Adeste Fidelis)
CD _____ CK 64154
Columbia / Nov '95 / Sony.

RING OF FIRE
Ring of fire / Thing called love / I walk the line / Long black veil / Cats in the cradle / Goin' by the book / As long as I live / Ways of a woman in love / Night Hank Williams came to town / Folsom Prison blues / Five feet high and rising / Mystery of life / That's one you owe me / Suppertime / Family bible / Big light / Sixteen tons / Peace in the valley
CD _____ 5509322
Spectrum/Karussell / Mar '95 / PolyGram THE.

RING OF FIRE (His Greatest Hits Live)
CD _____ CDCD 1253
Charly / Jun '95 / Charly / THE / Cadillac.

SUN YEARS, THE (3CD Set)
Wide open road / You my baby / Folsom Prison blues / Two timin' woman / Goodnight Irene / Port of lonely hearts / My treasure / Cry cry cry / Hey porter / Luther played the boogie / So doggone lonesome / Mean eyed cat / I couldn't keep from crying / New Mexico / Rock 'n' roll Ruby / Get rhythm / I walk the line / Train of love / There you go / One more ride / Goodbye little darling / I love you because / Straight A's in love / Don't make me go / Next in line / Give my love to Rose / Home of the blues / Wreck

of ol' 97 / Rock Island line / Belshazar / Leave that junk alone / Country boy / Doin' my time / If the good Lord's willing / (I heard that) lonesome whistle / Remember me / I was there when it happened / Come in stranger / Big river / Ballad of a teenage queen / Oh lonesome me / Guess things happen that way / You're the nearest thing to Heaven / Sugartime / Born to lose / Always alone / Story of a broken heart / You tell me / Life goes on / You win again / I could never be ashamed of you / Cold cold heart / Hey good lookin' / I can't help it / Blue train / Katy too / Ways of a woman in love / Thanks a lot / It's just about time / I just thought you'd like to know / I forgot to remember to forget / Down the street to 301
CD Set _____ CDSUNBOX 5
Sun / Oct '95 / Charly.

TENNESSEE TOPCAT
CD _____ CTJCD 1
Stomper Time / Apr '95 / Magnum Music Group.

UP THROUGH THE YEARS '1955 - 1957'
Cry cry cry / Hey Porter / Folsom Prison blues / Luther played the boogie / So doggone lonesome / I walk the line / Get rhythm / Train of love / There you go / Goodbye little darling / I love you because / Straight A's in love / Next in line / Don't make me go / Home of the blues / Give my love to Rose / Rock Island line / Wreck of ol' 97 / Ballad of a teenage queen / Big river / Guess things happen that way / Come in stranger / You're the nearest thing to heaven / Blue train
CD _____ BCD 15247
Bear Family / Nov '86 / Rollercoaster Direct / CM / Swift / ADA.

Cash, Rosanne

RETROSPECTIVE
Our little angel / On the surface / All come true / Wheel / Sleeping in Paris / 707 / Runaway train / I'm only sleeping / It hasn't happened yet / On the inside / What we really want / I count the tears / Pink bedroom / Seventh Avenue / Lover is forever
CD _____ 4816132
Columbia / Nov '95 / Sony.

RIGHT OR WRONG
Right or wrong / Take me, take me / Man smart, woman smarter / This has happened before / Anybody's darlin' (anything but me) / No memories hangin' around / Couldn't do nothin' right / Seeing's believing / Big river / Not a second time
CD _____ 983254 2
Pickwick/Sony Collector's Choice / Feb '94 / Carlton Home Entertainment / Pinnacle / Sony.

WHEEL, THE
Wheel / Seventh avenue / Change partners / Sleeping in Paris / You won't let me in / From the ashes / Truth about you / Tears falling down / Roses in the fire / Fire of the newly alive / If there's a God on my side
CD _____ 472977 2
Columbia / May '93 / Sony.

Casino Steel

CASINO STEEL & HOLLYWOOD BRATS, ETC (Various Artists)
Little ole wine drinker me / You can't hurt a memory / Ruby / Cajun invitation / Strange brew / Ballad of the sad cafe / Dust of the angels wings / Waiting for the lady / Candy / Suckin' on Suzie / Independent girl / Ghost riders in the sky / Honky tonk night / Chez Maximes / This ain't America / Little rebel / Gotta serve somebody
CD _____ MISSCD 1993
Mission Discs / Aug '93 / Pinnacle.

Cassandra Complex

GRENADE
CD _____ CXM 1001
Play It Again Sam / Nov '87 / Vital.

SEX AND DEATH
Kneel to the (Boss) / Mouth of heaven / War against sleep / Come out / Satisfy me / Give me what I need / Devil's advocate / You make me sick / Voices / Realm of the senseless / Frankie teardrop / In memoriam JC / You still make me sick
CD _____ BIAS 255CD
Play It Again Sam / Nov '93 / Vital.

Cassell, Debbie

ANGEL IN LABOUR
CD _____ MAUVED 003
Mauve / Feb '95 / Pinnacle.

Cassiber

FACE WE ALL KNOW, A
This was the way it was / Remember / Old Gods / Two o'clock in the morning / Philosophy / Gut / Start the show / Screaming comes across the sky / They go in under archways / They have begun to move / Time gets faster / It's never quiet / Screaming holds / Philosophy (2) / Philosophy (3) / I was old / Way it was / To move
CD _____ RERCCD

Recommended / Apr '91 / These / ReR Megacorp.

Cassidy, David

DAYDREAMER
CD _____ ST 5004
Star Collection / Nov '93 / BMG.

HIS GREATEST HITS LIVE
Tenderly / Darlin' / Thin ice / Someone / Daydreamer / Romance / Cherish / Rock me baby / Last kiss / Please please me / I'm a clown / I think I love you / How can I be sure
CD _____ CDTRACK 3
Starblend / Jan '86 / Prism.

Cassidy, Jane

MARY ANN MCCRACKEN (Cassidy, Jane & Maurice Leyden)
CD _____ ASH 004CD
Ash / Apr '95 / Ash / ADA.

Cassidy, Patrick

CHILDREN OF LIR, THE
CD _____ 7567827442
Warner Bros. / Apr '95 / Warner Music.

CRUIT
CD _____ CEFCD 130
Gael Linn / Jan '94 / Roots / CM / Direct / ADA.

Cast

WINNOWING
CD _____ CUL 104CD
Culburnie / Oct '95 / Ross / ADA.

Cast

ALL CHANGE
Alright / Promised land / Sandstorm / Mankind / Tell it like it is / Four walls / Fine time / Back of my mind / Walkaway / Reflections / History / Two of a kind
CD _____ 5293122
Polydor / Sep '95 / PolyGram.

Cast Of Thousands

PASSION
This is love / Passion / September / Tear me down / Girl / Immaculate deception / Colour fields / This experience / Thin line / Nothing is forever
CD _____ CDAFTER 6
Fun After All / Jun '88 / Pinnacle.

Castle, Ben

BIG CELEBRATION (Castle, Ben & Roy)
CD _____ KMCD 735
Kingsway / Jun '94 / Total/BMG / Complete/Pinnacle.

Castle, Joey

ROCK AND ROLL DADDY-O
CD Set _____ BCD 15560
Bear Family / Apr '92 / Rollercoaster Direct / CM / Swift / ADA.

Castle, Pete

FALSE WATERS
CD _____ MATS 012CD
Steel Carpet / Nov '95 / ADA.

Castro, Miquel

EXOTIC RHYTHMS OF LATIN AMERICA
CD _____ EUCD 1214
ARC / Sep '93 / ARC Music / ADA.

Castro-Neves, Oscar

BRAZILIAN SCANDALS
CD _____ JD 3302
JVC / Jul '88 / New Note.

TROPICAL HEART
Holding with an open hand / You are my romance / New hope / If the dance is over / Envelope / I still do / My heart surrenders / Maya's gift / I have seen tomorrow / Jasmina's perfume / Souvenirs / Tropical heart / Lullaby for a magical child
CD _____ JVC 20262
JVC / Dec '93 / New Note.

Casual

FEAR ITSELF
CD _____ CHIP 148
Jive / Feb '94 / BMG.

Casus Belli

TAILGUNNRANGELES
CD _____ ARRCD 64007
Amphetamine Reptile / Aug '95 / SRD.

Cat Rapes Dog

FUNDAMENTAL
CD _____ KK 045
KK / '88 / Plastic Head.

GOD, GUNS AND GASOLINE
CD _____ KK 034 CD
KK / Sep '90 / Plastic Head.

MAXIMUM OVERDRIVE
CD _____ KK 031
KK / Nov '89 / Plastic Head.

RARITIES (Best Of Cat Rapes Dog - 2CD Set)
CD Set _____ KK 134DCD
KK / Jul '95 / Plastic Head.

Cat Sun Flower

CHILDISH
CD _____ EFA 127752
Freak Scene / Oct '95 / SRD.

Catatonia

CATATONIA
CD _____ CRAI 039CDS
Crai / Dec '93 / ADA / Direct.

Catchers

MUTE
Beauty No.3 / Cotton dress / Apathy / Country freaks / Worm out / Jesus spaceman / Song for Autumn / Hollowed / Shifting / Sleepy head / La luna / Epitaph
CD _____ SETCD 018
Setanta / Oct '94 / Vital.

Caterpillar

THOUSAND MILLION MICRONAUGHTS
CD _____ CPS 021CD
Compulsive / Jun '94 / SRD.

Catfish Keith

CHERRY BALL
Mr. Catfish's advice / Cool can of beer / Your head's too big / By and by I'm going see the King / Cherry ball / Rabbits in your drawers / Swim deep, pretty mama / Hawaiian cowboy / Deep sea moan / Goin' up north to get my hambone boiled / Ramblin' blues / Leave my wife alone / Mama don't you sell it, papa don't you give it away / That ain't no way for me to get along
CD _____ FTRCD 003
Fish Tail / Sep '93 / Hot Shot.

JITTERBUG SWING
Jitterbug swing / Slap a suit on you / Come back old devil / Blues at midnight / 12th street rag / Move to Louisiana / Gonna give that life / Preachin' the blues / Goin' down to Memphis / Texas tea party / Oh, captain / Fistful of riffs / Police and a sergeant / Tell everybody / Takin' my time
CD _____ FTRCD 002
Fish Tail / Nov '93 / Hot Shot.

PEPPER IN MY SHOE
Jealous hearted see / Knockin' myself out / Saturday night stroll / Oh Mr Catfish / Daddy, where you been / Pepper in my shoe / You got to move / Tell me, baby / Nineteen bird dogs / Howling tom cat
CD _____ FTRCD 001
Fish Tail / Nov '93 / Hot Shot.

Catharsis

ET S'AIMER...ET MOURIR
CD _____ SPA 14280
Spalax / Nov '94 / Direct / ADA.

Cathedral

CARNIVAL BIZARRE, THE
Vampire sun / Hopkins (witchfinder general) / Utopian blaster / Night of the seagulls / Carnival bizarre / Electric grave / Palace of the fallen majesty / Blue light / Fangalactic supergoria / Interias cave
CD _____ MOSH 130CD
Earache / Sep '95 / Vital.

ETHEREAL MIRROR, THE
Violet vortex / Ride / Enter the worms / Midnight mountain / Fountain of innocence / Grim luxuria / Jaded entity / Ashes you leave / Phantasmagoria / Imprisoned in flesh
CD _____ MOSH 077CD
Earache / Sep '94 / Vital.

FOREST OF EQUILIBRIUM
CD _____ MOSH 043CD
Earache / Sep '94 / Vital.

IN MEMORIAM
Mourning of a new day / All your sins / Ebony tears / March
CD _____ RISE 008MCD
Rise Above / Jan '96 / Vital / Plastic Head.

Catherine Wheel

CHROME
CD _____ 518039-2
Fontana / Jul '93 / PolyGram.

FERMENT
Texture / I wanna touch you / Black metallic / Indigo is blue / She's my friend / Shallow / Ferment / Flower to hide / Tumble down / Bill and Ben / Salt
CD _____ 5109032
Fontana / Feb '92 / PolyGram.

HAPPY DAYS
God inside my head / Way down / Little muscle / Heal / Empty head / Receive / My exhibition / Eat my dust you insensitive fuck / Shocking / Love tips up / Judy staring at the sun / Hole / Fizzy love / Kill my soul / Glitter
CD _____ 5147172
Fontana / Nov '95 / PolyGram.

Catherine's Cathedral

EQUILIBRIUM
CD _____ NOX 004CD
Noxious / Sep '95 / Plastic Head.

INTOXICATION
CD _____ NOX 001CD
Noxious / Oct '94 / Plastic Head.

Catherine, Philip

I REMEMBER YOU (Catherine, Philip Trio)
CD _____ CRISS 1048CD
Criss Cross / Nov '91 / Cadillac / Harmonia Mundi.

MOODS VOL.1 (Catherine, Philip Trio)
CD _____ CRISS 1060CD
Criss Cross / Oct '92 / Cadillac / Harmonia Mundi.

MOODS VOL.2
CD _____ CRISS 1061CD
Criss Cross / Nov '93 / Cadillac / Harmonia Mundi.

SLEEP MY LOVE (Catherine, Philip & Charlie Mariano)
CD _____ CMP CD 05
CMP / '91 / Vital/SAM.

TRANSPERANCE
CD _____ INAK 8701CD
In Akustik / '88 / Magnum Music Group.

TWIN HOUSE (Catherine, Philip & Larry Coryell)
Ms. Julie / Homecoming / Airpower / Twin house / Mortgage on your soul / Gloryell / Nuages / Twice a week
CD _____ 92022
Act / Apr '94 / New Note.

Catingub, Matt

HI TECH BIG BAND
CD _____ CDSB 2025
Sea Breeze / Nov '88 / Jazz Music.

Catley, Marc

FINE DIFFERENCE (Catley, Marc & Geoff Mann)
We are one / One of the green things / Keep on / Calling / Love is the only way / This time / Freedom / Closer to you / True riches / War is won / Growth / All along the way / Weep for the city / Theospeak / Somewhere here / Hosea / Hello
CD _____ PCDN 133
Plankton / Apr '92 / Plankton.

MAKE THE TEA
Make the tea / Jesus stops traffic / Ethnic praise / All glory to the wealthy / Newpraise / This is the day after yesterday / Times seven / P-r-r-raise the-e-e Lord / Jesus was so nice / Jesus you really are just God / Come to the quiet / Come and fill me with your power holy spirit / Lying in the spirit / Shepherding song / Lord I still just want to praise you / Now Lord in the outgoing faith situation / Lord / Hard livin' guy / If I had a rhyming dictionary / Gonna rock you tonite / Legend of ham 'n' egg / Hundred miraculous things before breakfast
CD _____ PCDN 135
Plankton / May '92 / Plankton.

OFF THE END OF THE PIER SHOW, THE (Catley, Marc & Geoff Mann)
Over the edge / River - blue water / River - white water / River - delta / Twittering machine / Terence the termite stares down his underpants in growing am / In the wilderness / Europe after the rain
CD _____ PCDN 130
Plankton / Aug '91 / Plankton.

Catmen

CUTTING THROUGH THE RED TAPE
CD _____ NERDCD 60
Nervous / Feb '91 / Nervous / Magnum Music Group.

Catney, Dave

FIRST FLIGHT
CD _____ JR 004012
Justice / Sep '92 / Koch.

JADE VISIONS
CD _____ JR 004022
Justice / Nov '92 / Koch.

REALITY RD
CD _____ JR 04032
Justice / Jun '94 / Koch.

Cato, Pauline

CHANGING TIDES (Cato, Pauline & Tom McConville)
Go to Berwick Johnny/High road to Linton / Omnibus/Beeswing / Gypsy's lullaby/Billy Pigg's hornpipe / Gardebylaten/Rejnlaender/Trettondagsmarschen / Keel row / South shore/De'il amang the tailors / Hector the hero/Iron man / Willafjord/Miss Mc-Leods/Sleep soond in da mornin' / Ned of the hill / I'll get wedded in my auld claes/ Coffee bridge / Golden eagle/Alexander's hornpipe / Roslin Castle/Jump at the sun / Forth bridge/Easy club reel / Peacock follows the hen/(Another) peacock follows the hen / Peacock's revenge
CD _____ PC 002CD
Cato / Oct '94 / Direct / ADA.

WANSBECK PIPER, THE
Calliope house/Tripping upstairs / Captain Ross/Cuckold come out of the amrey (Variations) / Piper's weird / Carrick hornpipe/ Happy hours / Lament for Ian Dickson / Acrobat / Wild hills o' Wannies / Town green polka/Bluebell polka / Exhibition/The hawk / Neil Gow's lament for the death of his second wife / Rowley burn/Remember me / Lady's well/Random (Variations) / Wallington Hall/Locomotive / Moving cloud/New high level (Whinham)/Mason's apron
CD _____ PCC 01CD
Cato / Aug '92 / Direct / ADA.

Cattle Company

HERO
CD _____ JHS 003
Bunny / Dec '94 / Bunny.

Caudel, Stephen

BOW OF BURNING GOLD
CD _____ NAGE 17CD
Art Of Landscape / May '88 / Sony.

IMPROMPTU ROMANCE
CD _____ CDSGP 9023
Prestige / Apr '95 / Total/BMG.

Caught In The Act

RELAPSE OF REASON
CD _____ NTHEN 025CD
Now & Then / Jan '96 / Plastic Head.

Caught On The Hop

NATION OF HOPKEEPERS
CD _____ HARCD 024
Harbour Town / Oct '93 / Roots / Direct / CM / ADA.

Cauld Blast Orchestra

DURGA'S FEAST
CD _____ ECLCD 9410
Eclectic / Jan '96 / Pinnacle.

SAVAGE DANCE
Reels within wheels / Tower of babel stomp / Cauld blast / Savage dance / Oyster wives' rant / Tarbolton lodge / Railyard band / Rantin' reel / Green shutters / Bottle hymn of the republic / Quaich
CD _____ ECLCD 9002
Eclectic / Jan '96 / Pinnacle.

Cause For Alarm

CAUSE FOR ALARM
CD _____ VE 19CD
Victory / Mar '95 / Plastic Head.

SPLIT CD (Cause For Alarm & Warzone)
CD _____ VR 0126
Victory / Jan '96 / Plastic Head.

Causing Much Pain

SOUTHERN POINT OF VIEW, A
CD _____ THT 4211
Ichiban / Aug '95 / Koch.

Cavallaro, Carmen

UNCOLLECTED 1946, THE (Cavallaro, Carmen & His Orchestra)
CD _____ HCD 112
Hindsight / Nov '94 / Target/BMG / Jazz Music.

Cavanagh, Page

DIGITAL PAGE VOL.2, THE
CD _____ SLCD 9006
Starline / Jun '94 / Jazz Music.

Cavatina

MUSIC OF ROMANCE, THE
Misty / Greensleeves / Send in the clowns / Allegretto / En bateau (petite suite) / Summer of '42 / Gymnopedie No.1 / She moved through the fair / Fantasy on themes of Japanese folk songs / Moon river / Sonatina no.4 for harp / Cavatina
CD _____ PWK 086
Carlton Home Entertainment / Feb '89 / Carlton Home Entertainment.

SOUND OF CHRISTMAS, THE
Sleigh ride / Ding dong merrily on high / Good King Wenceslas / First Noel / Ave Maria / What child is this / God rest ye merry gentlemen / Little drummer boy / Holly and the ivy / Golden bells / Past three o'clock / O Little town of Bethlehem / Christmas

song / Walking in the air / Little shepherd boy / In the bleak midwinter / Trio from l'enfance du Christ, Opus 25 / Coventry carol / We three kings of Orient are / Holy boys / Interlude from Ceremony Of Carols, Opus 28 / Amid the roses Mary sits / Rudolph the red nosed reindeer / White Christmas / Silent night
CD _____ PWK 123
Carlton Home Entertainment / Oct '95 / Carlton Home Entertainment.

Cave, Nick

FIRST BORN IS DEAD, THE (Cave, Nick & The Bad Seeds)
CD _____ CDSTUMM 21
Mute / Apr '88 / Disc.

FROM HER TO ETERNITY (Cave, Nick & The Bad Seeds)
Avalanche / Cabin fever / Well of misery / From here to eternity / In the ghetto / Moon in the ghetto / St. Huck / Wings off flies / Box for black Paul / From here to eternity (1987)
CD _____ CDSTUMM 17
Mute / '87 / Disc.

GOOD SON, THE (Cave, Nick & The Bad Seeds)
Foi na cruz / Good son / Sorrow's child / Weeping song / Ship song / Hammer song / Lament / Witness song / Lucy
CD _____ CDSTUMM 76
Mute / Apr '90 / Disc.

HENRY'S DREAM (Cave, Nick & The Bad Seeds)
Papa won't leave you, Henry / I had a dream, Joe / Straight to you / Brother my cup is empty / Christina the astonishing / When I first came to town / John Finns' wife / Loom of the land / Jack the ripper
CD _____ CDSTUMM 92
Mute / Apr '92 / Disc.

KICKING AGAINST THE PRICKS (Cave, Nick & The Bad Seeds)
CD _____ CDSTUMM 28
Mute / Aug '86 / Disc.

LET LOVE IN (Cave, Nick & The Bad Seeds)
Do you love me / Nobody's baby now / Lover man / Jangling Jack / Red right hand / I let love in / Thirsty dog / Ain't gonna rain anymore / Lay me low / Do you love me part 2
CD _____ CDSTUMM 123
Mute / Apr '94 / Disc.

LIVE SEEDS (Cave, Nick & The Bad Seeds)
CD _____ CDSTUMM 122
Mute / Sep '93 / Disc.

MURDER BALLADS (Cave, Nick & The Bad Seeds)
CD _____ LCDSTUMM 138
Mute / Jan '96 / Disc.

TENDER PREY (Cave, Nick & The Bad Seeds)
CD _____ CDSTUMM 52
Mute / Nov '88 / Disc.

YOUR FUNERAL, MY TRIAL (Cave, Nick & The Bad Seeds)
CD _____ CDSTUMM 34
Mute / Feb '87 / Disc.

Caveman

POSITIVE REACTION
CD _____ FILERCD 406
Profile / Apr '91 / Pinnacle.

WHOLE 5 YARDS
CD _____ FILERCD 429
Profile / May '92 / Pinnacle.

Caveman Shoestore

FLUX
Knife edge / Pond at night / Actualize / Four year old / Ticket to obscurity / Kurtain / All this air / Lightning / Henzyme / Underneath the water / Underneath the city / Cold
CD _____ TK 93CD056
T/K / Jun '94 / Pinnacle.

Cavendish Dance Band

St. ANDREW'S BALL
CD _____ SAB 200
Target / May '94 / Target/BMG.

Cazazza, Monte

WORST OF MONTE
CD _____ MONTE 1CD
Grey Area / Jun '92 / Pinnacle.

CBQ

CIRCLES AND TRIPLETS
CD _____ DRCD 203
Dragon / May '87 / Roots / Cadillac / Wellard / CM / ADA.

Cecilio & Kapono

CECILIO AND KAPONO
CD _____ CK 32928

Pickwick/Sony Collector's Choice / Jun '88 / Carlton Home Entertainment / Pinnacle / Sony.

ELUA
CD _____ CK 33689
Pickwick/Sony Collector's Choice / Jun '88 / Carlton Home Entertainment / Pinnacle / Sony.

NIGHT MUSIC
CD _____ CK 34300
Pickwick/Sony Collector's Choice / Jun '88 / Carlton Home Entertainment / Pinnacle / Sony.

Ceddo

UNCHAINED
CD _____ ITMP 970052
ITM / Jan '91 / Tradelink / Koch.

Cee Cee Beaumont

PRE-STRESSED
CD _____ DAMGOOD 66CD
Damaged Goods / Jul '95 / SRD.

Ceiver, Jiri

HEADPHONE
CD _____ HHCD 14
Harthouse / Oct '95 / Disc / Warner Music.

Celebrity Skin

GOOD CLEAN
CD _____ TX 93112
Roadrunner / Aug '91 / Pinnacle.

Celestial Season

FOREVER SCARLET
CD _____ CDAR 015
Adipocre / Feb '94 / Plastic Head.

SOLAR LOVERS
CD _____ DOOO 38CD
Displeased / Apr '95 / Plastic Head.

Celestin, Papa

NEW ORLEANS CLASSICS (Celestin, Papa & Sam Morgan)
Original tuxedo rag / Careless love / Black rag / I'm satisfied you love me / My Josephine / Station calls / Give me some more / Dear Almanzoer / Papa's got the jim-jams / As you like it / Just for you dear, I'm crying / When I'm with you / It's jam up / Sweetheart of T.K.O. / Ta ta daddy / Steppin' on the gas / Everybody's talking about Sammy / Mobile song / Sing on / Short dress gal / Bogalousa strut / Down by the riverside / Over in the glory land
CD _____ AZCD 12
Azure / Nov '92 / Jazz Music / Swift / Wellard / Azure / Cadillac.

Celibate Rifles

BLIND EAR
Johnny / Worlds keep turning / Electravision mantra / Dial om / Wonderful life / Sean O'Farell / Belfast / Cycle / They're killing us all (to make the world safe) / O salvation / El Salvador / Fish and trees
CD _____ HOT 1046CD
Hot / Oct '94 / Vital.

CELIBATAE RIFLES, THE
CD _____ HOT 1007CD
Hot / Nov '92 / Vital.

HEAVEN ON A STICK
CD _____ HOT 1038CD
Hot / Jun '95 / Vital.

KISS KISS BANG BANG
Back in the red / Temper, temper / J.N.S. / Pretty colours / Nether world / Some kinda feeling / New mistakes / Carmine vattelly (N.Y.N.Y.C.) / City of fun / Conflict of instinct / Sometimes / Burn my eye / S.O.S.
CD _____ HOT 1029CD
Hot / Nov '92 / Vital.

PLATTERS DU JOUR
Kent's theme / Let's get married / Twenty four hours (SOS) / Tubular greens / Pretty pictures / Out in the west again / Summer holiday blues / Merry Christmas blues / Wild desire / I'm waiting for the man / Sometimes / E = MC2 / Six days on the road / Zorquie girl / Eddie (Acoustic version) / Ice blue / Thank you America / Back in the red / Rainforest / Dancing barefoot / Jesus on TV / More things change / Junk
CD _____ HOT 1033-34CD
Hot / Oct '94 / Vital.

ROMAN BEACH PARTY
CD _____ HOT 1030CD
Hot / Nov '92 / Vital.

SIDEROXYLON
CD _____ HOT 1001CD
Hot / Mar '93 / Vital.

SOFA
Killing time / Wild desire / Sometimes / Bill Bonney regrets / Jesus on TV / Johnny / Electravision mantra / Wonderful life / More things change / Oceanshore / New mistakes / Back in the red / Ice blue / This week

/ Nether world / Glasshouse / Frank Hyde
(slight return) / Darlinghurst confidential /
Pretty pictures / Gonna cry
CD _____ HOT 1043CD
Hot / Jul '95 / Vital.

TURGID MIASMA OF EXISTENCE, THE
CD _____ HOT 1024CD
Hot / Nov '92 / Vital.

YIZGARNNOFF
Brickin' around / Word about Jones / Cycle
/ Downtown / Johnny / Happy house /
Dream of night / Groovin' in the land of love
/ E and M.T.V. / Electravision mantra / 2000
light years from home / More things change
/ Tubular greens / Invisible man / Glass-
house / O salvation / Oceanshore / Baby,
please don't go
CD _____ HOT 1041CD
Hot / Jul '95 / Vital.

Cell

LIVING ROOM
CD _____ EFA 049332
City Slang / Feb '94 / Disc.

SLO-BLO
CD _____ EO 4909CD
City Slang / Nov '92 / Disc.

Cello

ALVA
CD _____ BIOCD 04
Messerschmitt / Mar '94 / Plastic Head.

Cellophane

HANG UPS
CD _____ MINTCD 10
Mint Tea / Oct '94 / Disc.

Celtic Frost

EMPEROR'S RETURN
CD _____ NCD 003
Noise/Modern Music / '88 / Pinnacle /
Plastic Head.

MORBID TALES/EMPERORS RETURN
CD _____ NCD 3
Noise/Modern Music / '88 / Pinnacle /
Plastic Head.

**PARCHED WITH THIRST AM I, AND
DYING (1984-1992)**
Idols of Chagrin / A... descent to Babylon /
Return to the Eve / Juices like wine / Inevit-
able factor / Heart beneath / Cherry
orchards / Tristesses de la lune / Wings of
solitude / Usurper / Journey into fear /
Downtown Hanoi / Circle of the tyrants / In
the chapel in the moonlight / I won't dance
/ Name of my bride / Mexican radio / Under
Appolyon's sun
CD _____ N0191-2
Noise/Modern Music / Mar '92 / Pinnacle /
Plastic Head.

TO MEGA THERION
CD _____ NO 0313
Noise/Modern Music / Jul '92 / Pinnacle /
Plastic Head.

VANITY/NEMESIS
Heart beneath / Wine in my hand (third from
the sun) / Wings of solitude / Name of my
bride / This island earth / Restless seas /
Phallic tantrum / Kiss or a whisper / Vanity
/ Nemesis / Heroes (CD only.)
CD _____ NO 1992
Noise/Modern Music / Jul '92 / Pinnacle /
Plastic Head.

Celtic Thunder

CELTIC THUNDER
Mark Quinn's polkas / Deadly wars / Six-
penny money/Blackthorn stick / Bold thady
quill / All the way to Birmingham/Roaring
Mary / Best years of our lives / Phillippine
soldier / Woman of the house/Paddy Lynn's
delight / Gem of the Roe / Doug Lang's/My
brother Seamus/P.J. Conway's slide /
Johnny Doyle / Wise maid/Cup of tea/Shee-
han's reel
CD _____ GLCD 1029
Green Linnet / Feb '88 / Roots / CM / Direct
/ ADA.

LIGHT OF OTHER DAYS, THE
CD _____ GLCD 1086
Green Linnet / Jan '90 / Roots / CM /
Direct / ADA.

Cement

CEMENT
Living sound delay / Shout / I feel / Four /
Prison love / Six / Blue / Too beat / Take it
easy / Old days / Reputation shot / Chip
away / KCMT
CD _____ RTD 15715732
World Service / Jun '93 / Vital.

MAN WITH THE ACTION HAIR, THE
Man with the action hair / Killing an angel /
Pile driver / Crying / Dancing from the
depths of the fire / Life on the sun / Sleep
/ Train / King Arthur / Hotel Aiablo / Bonnie
Brae / Magic number / Power and the
magic
CD _____ RTD 15717452
World Service / Aug '94 / Vital.

Cemetary

BLACK VANITY
CD _____ BMCD 59
Black Mark / Oct '94 / Plastic Head.

EVIL SHADE OF GREY, AN
Dead red / Where the rivers of madness
stream / Dark illusions / Evil shade of grey /
Sidereal passing / Scars / Nightmare lake
/ Souldrain
CD _____ BMCD 020
Black Mark / Jun '92 / Plastic Head.

Cenotaph

RIDING OUR BLACK OCEANS
CD _____ CYBERCD 13
Cyber / Feb '95 / Plastic Head.

THIRTEEN THRENODIES
CD _____ KK 001CD
Planet K / May '95 / Plastic Head.

Central Band Of The...

**CANADA REMEMBERS (Central Band
Of The Canadian Forces)**
Air force overture / Vera Lynn medley /
March: je me souviens / Bless 'em all' /
Never again / Normandy landing / Salute to
the big bands / March: Canada overseas /
Nightfall in camp / March: Athene / Seven
seas overture / Lili Marlene / God save the
Queen
CD _____ BNA 5105
Bandleader / Jul '94 / Conifer.

Central Hall Choir

**TWENTY ONE HYMNS METHODISTS
LOVE TO SING**
Angel voices ever singing / All the name of
Jesus / Come let us sing of a wonderful love
/ Crown him with many crowns / Fill thou
my life / Great is Thy faithfulness / Hark my
soul / Holy Father, in thy mercy / How great
thou art / I will sing the wondrous story / I'll
praise my maker / In heavenly love abiding
/ Jesus shall reign / Man of sorrows / My
heart and voice I raise / O breath of God /
Saviour, Thy dying love / Sun of my soul /
This, this is the God we adore / We have a
gospel to proclaim / When morning gilds
the skies
CD _____ CDCA 921
Alpha / '91 / Abbey Recording.

Central Nervous System

REALITY CHECK
CD _____ WB 1122CD
We Bite / Jul '95 / Plastic Head.

Centry In Dub

THUNDER MOUNTAIN
CD _____ WWCD 03
Wibbly Wobbly / Mar '95 / SRD.

Century

RELEASE THE CHAINS
CD _____ DNCCD 4
Conscious Sounds / May '95 / SRD.

Century, Penny

CLOUDS
CD _____ 5113982
Polydor / Jan '93 / PolyGram.

Ceolbeg

SEEDS TO THE WIND
Mazurka set / Senorita Ana Rocio / Seeds
to the wind / Coupit yowe set / Glenlivet /
A the airts / Here's a health tae the sauters
/ Cajun two-step / Johnny Cope / See the
people run / Lord Galloway's lamentation
CD _____ CDTRAX 048
Greentrax / Dec '91 / Conifer / Duncans /
ADA / Direct.

UNFAIR DANCE, AN
Zito the bubbleman / Galicia revisited / Jolly
beggar / Gale warning / Culler's way /
Stand together / Wild west waltz / Ceol
beag / Seton's lassie / Train journey north /
My love is like a red red rose / Sleeping tune
CD _____ CDTRAX 058
Greentrax / Jul '93 / Conifer / Duncans /
ADA / Direct.

Ceoltoiri

CELTIC LACE
CD _____ MMCD 201
Maggie's Music / Dec '94 / CM / ADA.

SILVER APPLES OF MOON
CD _____ MMCD 202
Maggie's Music / Dec '94 / CM / ADA.

Cephas, John

DOG DAYS OF AUGUST
CD _____ FF 394CD
Flying Fish / May '93 / Roots / CM / Direct
/ ADA.

**FLIP, FLOP AND FLY (Cephas, John &
Phil Wiggins)**
CD _____ FF 58CD
Flying Fish / May '93 / Roots / CM / Direct
/ ADA.

**SWEET BITTER BLUES (Cephas,
Bowling Green John & Phil Hea
Wiggins)**
Bittersweet blues / St. James infirmary / I
saw the light / Sickbed blues / Piedmont rag
/ Dog days of August / Roberta-a-thousand
miles from home / Highway 301 / Hoodoo
woman / Louisiana chase / Bowling green
rag / Bye bye baby / Last fair deal gone
down / Big boss man / Burn your bridges /
Running and hiding
CD _____ ECD 260502
Evidence / Sep '94 / Harmonia Mundi / ADA
/ Cadillac.

Cerbone, Lisa

CLOSE YOUR EYES
CD _____ UGCD 5503
Unique Gravity / Oct '95 / Pinnacle / ADA.

Cerebral Fix

DEATH EROTICA
Death erotica / World machine / Clarissa /
Haunted eyes / Mind within mine / Spin-
tered wings / Creator of outcasts / Angel's
kiss / Still in mind / Raft of Medusa / Never
again / Too drunk to funk / Burning / Living
after midnight
CD _____ CDFLAG 75
Under One Flag / Nov '92 / Pinnacle.

Ceremonial Oath

CARPET
CD _____ BS 02CD
Black Sun / Apr '95 / Plastic Head.

Cerletti, Marco

RANDOM AND PROVIDENCE
Setting the sales / Glasshouse in the desert
/ La ville blanche / Sundown / Random and
providence / Light over darkness / Encore
toi / Web / Birds of paradise / Art of weath-
ering November
CD _____ VBR 20392
Vera Bra / Nov '90 / Pinnacle / New Note.

Cetera, Peter

ONE MORE STORY
Best of times / One good woman / Peace
of mind / Heaven help this lonely man /
Save me / Holding out / Body language
(there in the dark) / You never listen to me
/ Scheherazade / One more story
CD _____ 925704 2
WEA / Aug '88 / Warner Music.

SOLITUDE/SOLITAIRE
Big mistake / They don't make 'em like they
used to / Glory of love / Queen of the mas-
querade ball / Daddy's girl / Next time I fall
/ Wake up love / Solitude/Solitaire / Only
love knows why
CD _____ 92547422
WEA / Aug '90 / Warner Music.

WORLD FALLING DOWN
Restless heart / Even a fool can see / Feels
like heaven / Wild ways / World falling down
/ Man in me / Where there's no tomorrow /
Last place God made / Dip your wings /
Have you ever been in love
CD _____ 7599268942
WEA / Jun '93 / Warner Music.

Ceyleib People

TANYET
Aton 1: Leyshem / Zendan / Ceyladd beyta
/ Becal / Ddom / Toadda BB / Aton 11: Dyl
/ Ralin / Tygstyl / Pendyl / Jacayl / Menyatt
dyl com
CD _____ DOCD 1991
Drop Out / Jan '92 / Pinnacle.

Chabenat, Giles

**DE L'EAU ET DES AMANDES
(Chabenat, Giles & Frederic paris)**
CD _____ Y 225060CD
Silex / Nov '95 / ADA.

Chacksfield, Frank

MILLION SELLERS
CD _____ 8441882
Eclipse / Jul '93 / PolyGram.

Chadbourne, Eugene

**TERROR HAS SOME STRANGE
KINFOLK (Chadbourne, Eugene & Evan
Johns)**
CD _____ VIRUS 119CD
Alternative Tentacles / Jun '93 / Pinnacle.

Chahine, Khalil

HEKMA
Les paradis artifociels / La street / Doud /
Hekma / Adieu, donc / Jinns / Et tout autour
/ La mort du roi / Les amants / La 10 base
CD _____ ND 000082
Mountain/EWM / Oct '95 / EWM.

Chain Gang

PERFUMED
Dead at the Meadowlands / Metallands / Kill
for you / Beijing / Cut of the drug Czar's
head / Satanic rockers / Pal / Kill the bounc-
ers at the Ritz / Nam / Brother and sister /
That's how strong my love is / Rockland /
Born in Brazil / Prostitute / Guts boss / My
fly / Cannibal him / Piss your pants / Son
of Sam / Murder for the millions / Wrestler
/ OTB / Label this
CD _____ OLE 019-2
Matador / Mar '94 / Vital.

Chainsaw Kittens

ANGEL ON A WIRE
Kick kid / Angel on the range / John Wayne
dream / Mary's belated wedding present /
Lazy little dove / Sgt whore / Little fishies
CD _____ MR 0059-2
Mammoth / Oct '93 / Vital.

POP HEIRESS
CD _____ 7567923182
WEA / Feb '95 / Warner Music.

Chainsaw Sisters

HOT SAUCE
CD _____ NM 7CD
No Master's Voice / Apr '95 / ADA.

Chairmen Of The Board

SOUL AGENDA
Chairman Of The Board / Working on a
building of love / Bravo, hooray / (You've
got me) dangling on a string / Everything's
Tuesday / I'll come crawling / Elmo James
/ Give me just a little more time / All we
need is understanding / Men are getting
scarce / Let me down easy / Pay to the
piper / Patches / Tricked and trapped (by a
tricky trapper) / Bless you (Available on CD
only) / When will she tell me she needs me
(Available on CD only) / Try on my love for
size (Available on CD only) / Bittersweet
(Available on CD only) / Everybody's got a
song to sing (Available on CD only) / Finders
keepers (Available on CD only)
CD _____ HDHCD 007
HDH / Oct '89 / Pinnacle.

Chaix, Henri

JIVE AT FIVE
CD _____ SKCD 2-2035
Sackville / Jun '94 / Swift / Jazz Music /
Jazz Horizons / Cadillac / CM.

JUMPIN' PUMPKINS (Chaix, Henri Trio)
CD _____ SKCD 2-2020
Sackville / Jun '93 / Swift / Jazz Music /
Jazz Horizons / Cadillac / CM.

Chakraborty, A.

STRING OF ELEGANCE
CD _____ DSAV 1009
Multitone / Jan '95 / BMG.

Chalfont, Chubby

**RUGBY SONGS SING-A-LONG
(Chalfont, Chubby & The Chafers)**
CD _____ NBNCD 01
Disky / May '94 / THE / BMG / Discovery /
Pinnacle.

Chalice

UP TILL NOW
CD _____ RASCD 3026
Ras / Nov '87 / Jetstar / Greensleeves /
SRD / Direct.

Chalice Dub

CHALICE DUB
CD _____ ROTCD 006
Reggae On Top / Feb '95 / Jetstar / SRD.

Challengers

MAN FROM UNCLE
More / Cast your fate to the wind / Taste of
honey / Walk don't run / Only the young /
Work song / Born free / Telstar / Stranger
on the shore / Memphis / Lonely bull /
Penetration / Summer place / In crowd
rebel rouser / Somewhere my love / Mr.
Mojo / Alley cat / Tequila / Man from
U.N.C.L.E. / Pipeline / Strangers in the night
/ Out of limits / Raunchy / Wipeout
CD _____ EDCD 350
Edsel / Jul '92 / Pinnacle / ADA.

Challis, Bill

**BILL CHALLIS AND HIS ORCHESTRA
1936 (Challis, Bill & Orchestra)**
CD _____ CCD 71
Circle / Jun '95 / Jazz Music / Swift /
Wellard.

GOLDKETTLE PROJECT, THE
CD _____ CCD 118
Circle / '89 / Jazz Music / Swift / Wellard.

Chaloff, Serge

FABLE OF MABEL, THE
You brought a new kind of love to me / Fable of Mabel / Let's jump / Zdot / On baby / Salute to tiny / Sherry / Easy Street / All I do is dream of you
CD _____ BLCD 760923
Black Lion / Oct '90 / Jazz Music / Cadillac / Wellard / Koch.

Chamber Jazz Sextet

PLAYS PAL JOEY
I could write a book / My funny valentine / I didn't know what time it was / Zip / Lady is a tramp
CD _____ CCD 9030
Candid / Jun '88 / Cadillac / Jazz Music / Wellard / Koch.

Chambers, Dennis

GETTING EVEN
Fortune dance / Opener / Keep walking / Red eyes / Getting even / Widow's peak / Boo / Until we return
CD _____ 101 S877079
101 South / Jan '96 / New Note.

Chambers, Joe

PHANTOM OF THE CITY
CD _____ CCD 79517
Candid / Mar '92 / Cadillac / Jazz Music / Wellard / Koch.

Chambers, Ken

ABOVE YOU
CD _____ TAANG 83
Taang / Aug '94 / Plastic Head.

Chambers, Paul

JUST FRIENDS (Chambers, Paul & Cannonball Adderley)
Ease it / Just friends / I got rhythm / Julie Ann / Awful mean / There is no greater love
CD _____ LEJAZZCD 24
Le Jazz / Feb '94 / Charly / Cadillac.

Chameleon

CHAMELEON
CD _____ FLYCD 100
Fly / Nov '89 / Bucks Music.

Chameleons

FAN AND THE BELLOWS, THE
CD _____ GOODCD 9
Dead Dead Good / Feb '96 / Pinnacle.

LIVE IN TORONTO
Swamp thing / Person isn't safe anywhere these days / Monkeyland / Pleasure and pain / Singing rule Britannia (while the walls close in) / In shreds / Less than human / Paradiso / Home is where the heart is / Soul in isolation (CD only) / Second skin (CD only) / Caution / Splitting in two (CD only)
CD _____ ILLCD 036
Imaginary / Jun '92 / Vital.

PEEL SESSIONS: THE CHAMELEONS
Fan, the bellows / Here today / Looking inwardly / Things I wish I'd said / Don't fall / Nostalgia / Second skin / Perfumed garden / Dust to dust / Return of the roughnecks / One flesh / Intrigue in Tangiers / P.S. goodbye
CD _____ SFRCD 114
Strange Fruit / Dec '90 / Pinnacle.

RADIO 1 EVENING SHOW SESSIONS
CD _____ CDNT 1
Night Tracks / Jan '93 / Grapevine / Pinnacle.

SCRIPT OF THE BRIDGE
Don't fall / Here today / Monkeyland / Seal skin / Up the down escalator / Less than human / Pleasure and pain / Thursday's child / As high as you can go / Person isn't safe anywhere these days / Paper tiger / View from a hill / Nostalgia / In shreds
CD _____ GOODCD 6
Dead Dead Good / Jul '95 / Pinnacle.

STRANGE TIMES
Mad Jack / Caution / Soul in isolation / Swamp thing / Time / End of time / Seriocity / In answer / Childhood / I'll remember / Tears / Paradiso / Inside out / Ever after / John I'm only dancing / Tomorrow never knows
CD Set _____ GFLDD 19207
Geffen / Jun '93 / BMG.

WHAT DOES ANYTHING MEAN BASICALLY
CD _____ GOODCD 7
Dead Dead Good / Jul '95 / Pinnacle.

Champaign

HOW 'BOUT US
Can you find the time / Party people / Whiplash / I'm on fire / How 'bout us / Spinnin' / Dancin' together again / Lighten up / If one more morning
CD _____ 982990 2

Pickwick/Sony Collector's Choice / Aug '93 / Carlton Home Entertainment / Pinnacle / Sony.

Champion, Simon

CAMPFIRES AND DREAMTIME
Campfires / Echoes / Turu-etya / Storyteller / Valley of the kings / Set sail / Far away
CD _____ EUCD 1218
ARC / Sep '93 / ARC Music / ADA.

Champlin, Bill

RUNAWAY
CD _____ 7559609712
Elektra / Jan '96 / Warner Music.

Champs

GO CHAMPS GO/EVERYBODY'S ROCKIN'
Go champs go / El rancho rock / I'll be there / Sky high / What's up buttercup / Lollipop / Tequila / Train to nowhere / Midnighter / Robot walk / Just walking in the rain / Night beat / Everybody's rockin' / Chariot rock / Caterpillar / Turnpike / Lavenia / Mau mau stomp / Rockin' Mary / Subway / Toast / Bandido / Ali baba / Foggy river
CD _____ CDCHD 451
Ace / Jun '93 / Pinnacle / Cadillac / Complete/Pinnacle.

TEQUILA
Tequila / Train to nowhere / Sombrero / Experiment in terror / La cucaracha / Too much tequila / Turn pike / Beatnik / El rancho rock / Midnighter / Chariot rock / Subway / Limbo rock / Red eye / Gone train / Caramba
CD _____ CDCH 227
Ace / Jan '94 / Pinnacle / Cadillac / Complete/Pinnacle.

TEQUILA
CD _____ WMCD 5659
Woodford Music / Jul '92 / THE.

WING DING
Wing ding / TNT / Percolator / Swanee river blues / Baja / Roughneck / Istanbul / Stampede / Shiverin' and shakin' / Lowdown / Siesta / Volkswagen / Suicide / Cherokee stomp / Shiver / Rockin' crickets / Fireball / Hot line / You are my sunshine / Wildwood flower / Clubhouse / Eternal love / Rattler / 20,000 leagues / Double eagle rock / Jumping bean / Man from Durango / Roots
CD _____ CDCHD 460
Ace / Oct '93 / Pinnacle / Cadillac / Complete/Pinnacle.

Chance, James

LIVE IN NEW YORK (Chance, James & the Contortions)
CD _____ DANCD 082
Danceteria / Nov '94 / Plastic Head / ADA.

LOST CHANCE
CD _____ RUSCD 8214
Roir USA / Oct '95 / Plastic Head.

SOUL EXORCISM
CD _____ RE 191CD
Reach Out International / Nov '94 / Jetstar.

Chancey, Vincent

WELCOME MR. CHANCEY
Man say something / Spell / Night to remember / Day in ocho rios / Barefoot Bahian girl / Chazz
CD _____ IOR 70202
In & Out / Sep '95 / Vital/SAM.

Chandeen

SHOCKED BY LEAVES
CD _____ HY 39100942
Hyperium / Apr '94 / Plastic Head.

Chandell, Tim

LOVE LETTERS
CD _____ PILPCD 115
Pioneer / May '93 / Jetstar.

Chandler, Gene

NOTHING CAN STOP ME - GREATEST HITS
CD _____ VSD 5515
Varese Sarabande/Colosseum / Apr '95 / Pinnacle / Silva Screen.

Chandler, Kerri

SHAKE YOUR ASS
CD _____ BB 04142CD
Broken Beat / Jan '96 / Plastic Head.

Chandra, Ram

MUSIC FROM INDIA
CD _____ 15439
Laserlight / Jun '92 / Target/BMG.

Chandra, Sheila

WEAVING MY ANCESTORS' VOICES
Speaking in tongues I / Dhyana and donalogue / Ever so lonely/Eyes/Ocean / En-

chantment / Call / Bhajan / Speaking in tongues II / Sacred stones / Om namaha shiva
CD _____ CDRW 24
Realworld / May '92 / EMI / Sterns.

ZEN KISS, THE
La sagesse (Women, I'm calling you) / Speaking in tongues III / Waiting / Shehnai song / Love it is a killing thing / Speaking in tongues IV / Woman and child / En mireal del penal / Sailor's life / Abbess Hildegard / Kafi noir
CD _____ CDRW 45
Realworld / May '94 / EMI / Sterns.

Change

GLOW OF LOVE, THE
Lover's holiday / It's a girl's affair / Angel in my pocket / Glow of love / Searching / End
CD _____ 7599234382
WEA / Jan '96 / Warner Music.

Change Of Season

COLD SWEAT
CD _____ RTN 41205
Rock The Nation / Feb '95 / Plastic Head.

Changing Faces

CHANGING FACES
Stroke you up / Foolin' around / Lovin' ya boy / One of those things / Keep it right there / Am I wasting my time / Feeling all this love / Thoughts of you / Come closer / Baby your love / Movin' on / Good thing / All is not gone
CD _____ 756792369-2
Warner Bros. / Oct '94 / Warner Music.

Changui

AHORA SI - HERE COMES CHANGUI
CD _____ CORACD 121
Corason / Feb '95 / CM / Direct / ADA.

Channel

STATION IDENTIFICATION
Station identification / Channel 1 / Lock it up / Channel 2 / What / Mad izm / Who u represent / Homicide ride / Alpha and omega / Build and destroy / Down goes the devil / Channel 4 / Sex for the sport / Channel 3 / Reprogram
CD _____ CDEST 2252
Capitol / Apr '95 / EMI.

Channel 3

HOW DO YOU OPEN THE DAMN THING
CD _____ LP 098
Lost & Found / Jul '94 / Plastic Head.

I'VE GOT A GUN/AFTER THE LIGHTS GO OUT
Fear of life / Out of control / I've got a gun / Wetspots / Accident / You make me feel cheap / You lie / Catholic boy / Waiting in the wings / Strength in numbers / Double standard boys / Life goes on / What about me / Separate peace / No love / After the lights go out / Truth and trust / I'll take my chances / All my dreams / Can't afford it / I didn't know / Manzanar / Mannequin
CD _____ CDPUNK 2
Anagram / Jun '94 / Pinnacle.

Channel Light Vessel

AUTOMATIC
Testify / Train travelling north / Dog day afternoon / Ballyhoods / Place we pray for / Bubbling blue / Duende / Flaming creatures / Bill's last waltz / Thunderous accordions / Fish owl moon / Little luminaries
CD _____ ASCD 019
All Saints / Apr '94 / Vital / Discovery.

Channel Zero

CHANNEL ZERO
No light at the end of their tunnel / Tales of worship / Pioneer / Succeed or bleed / Never alone / Inspiration to violence / Painful jokes / Save me / Animation / Run with the torch
CD _____ BIAS 268CD
Play It Again Sam / Jun '94 / Vital.

STIGMATIZED FOR LIFE
Chrome dome / Repetition / Stigmatized for life / America / Play a little / Gold / Testimony / Unleash the dog / Big now / Last gasp
CD _____ BIAS 259CD
Play It Again Sam / Jun '94 / Vital.

UNSAFE
Suck my energy / Heroin / Bad to the bone / Help / Lonely / Run W.T.T. / Why / No more / Unsafe / Dashboard devils / As a boy / Man on the edge
CD _____ BIAS 290CD
Play It Again Sam / Feb '95 / Vital.

Channing, Carol

JAZZ BABY
Jazz baby / Thoroughly modern Millie / Join us in a cup of tea / Doin' the old yahoo step / Little game of tennis / Teeny weeny weeny nest of two / Ain't misbehavin' / You've got

to see Mama ev'ry night / Ma, he's making eyes at me / You're the cream in my coffee / Baby, won't you please come home / Good man is hard to find / Button up your overcoat / Wouldn't you like to lay your head upon my pillow / Little girl from Little Rock / Bye bye baby / Homesick blues / Diamonds are a girl's best friend
CD _____ DRGCD 13112
DRG / Apr '94 / New Note.

Chantays

PIPELINE
CD _____ VSD 5491
Varese Sarabande/Colosseum / Oct '94 / Pinnacle / Silva Screen.

TWO SIDES OF.../PIPELINE
CD _____ REP 4114-WZ
Repertoire / Aug '91 / Pinnacle / Cadillac.

Chantel

CLUB GUERILLA
CD _____ IC 008CD
Ladomat / May '95 / Plastic Head.

Chantels

BEST OF THE CHANTELS
He's gone / Plea / Maybe / I've lied / So real / Every night (I pray) / Whoever you are / I love you so / How could you call it off / Prayee / Sure of love / Memories / If you try / I can't take it (there's our song again) / Goodbye to love / Look in my eyes / Well I told you
CD _____ NEMCD 605
Sequel / Oct '90 / BMG.

Chantre, Teofilo

TERRA & CRETCHEU
CD _____ 086722
Melodie / Jul '95 / Triple Earth / Discovery / ADA / Jetstar.

Chaos UK

ENOUGH TO MAKE YOU SICK/THE CHIPPING SODBURY TAPES
Head on a pole / Vicious cabaret / Kettlehead / Midas touch / Loser / Drink thudd / 2010 (The day they made contact) / Urban nightmare / Cider I up landlord / Down on the farm / C-rap / Intro / World stock market / Indecision / Kill / Uniform choice / No taxi / Think / Rises from the rubble / Brain bomb / Too cool for school, too stupid for the real world (Let's form a band) / Courier / Farmyard (Cider house mix)
CD _____ CDPUNK 12
Anagram / May '93 / Pinnacle.

FLOGGIN THE CORPSE
Intro / Maggie / Hate / Police protection / No security / Kill your baby / Selfish few / False prophets / End is nigh / Parental love / Victimised / Four minute warning / Farmyard / Victimised part 2
CD _____ CDPUNK 65
Anagram / Oct '95 / Pinnacle.

LIVE IN JAPAN
Kill your baby / Indecision / Four minute warning / Too cool for school, too stupid for the real world / Head on a pole / Farmyard boogie / Vicious / Lawless Britain / Detention centre / Mid touch / 2010 (The day they made contact) / Crap song / Cider I up landlord / Down on the farm / Police story / Speed (Encore)
CD _____ DOJOCD 114
Dojo / Feb '94 / BMG.

RADIOACTIVE (Chaos UK & Extreme Noise Terror)
CD _____ RRCD 201
Receiver / Jun '95 / Grapevine.

RAW NOISE
CD _____ DISCCD 6
Vinyl Japan / Jul '92 / Vital.

SHORT SHARP SHOCK (Lawless Britain)
Lawless Britain / Living in fear / Detention centre / Suport / Control / People at the top / Global domination / No one seems to really care / Farmyard stomp (again)
CD _____ CDPUNK 71
Anagram / Feb '96 / Pinnacle.

TOTAL CHAOS
Selfish few / Fashion change / You'll never own me / End is nigh / Victimised / Parental love / Leech / Chaos / Mentally insane / Urban guerilla / Farmyard boogie / Four minute warning / Kill your baby / Army / No security / What about a future / Hypocrite / Senseless conflict
CD _____ CDPUNK 26
Anagram / Feb '94 / Pinnacle.

TWO FINGERS IN THE AIR PUNK ROCK
CD _____ CM 77053-2
Century Media / Jan '94 / Plastic Head.

Chaotic Dischord

FUCK RELIGION, FUCK POLITICS.../ DON'T THROW IT ALL AWAY
Rock 'n' roll swindle / Don't throw it all away / Stab your back / Sausage, beans and chips / Who killed E.T. (I killed the fucker) /

22 Hole Doc Martens / Anarthy in Wool-
worths / Batcave benders meet / Alien
durex machine / City claustraphobia / Boy
Bill / Wild mohicans (for wattie) / S.O.A.H.C.
/ Sound of music / Cider 'n' dogs / Destroy
peace 'n' freedom / Boring bastards /
Shadow / Anti christ / 77 in 82 (What's it
got to do with you) / There woz cows / Al-
ternative culture / Loud, tuneless 'n thick
(Ugly's too good for you)
CD _____ CDPUNK 72
Anagram / Feb '96 / Pinnacle.

THEIR GREATEST FUCKIN' HITS
Fuck religion, fuck polities, fuck the lot of
you / Fuck the world / Fuck off and die /
Loud, tuneless and thick / Are students safe
/ Anarchy in woolworths / You bastards
can't fuck us around / Psycho hippy skateboard punx / Destroy peace and freedom /
Sausage beans and chips / Anti-christ / Life
of Brian / Never trust a friend / City claustrophobia / Who killed E.T. (I killed the fucker)
/ I am the sturgeon / There was cows / Get
off my fuckin' allotment / Me and my girl
(seal clubbing) / Goat fuckin' unity killerz
from hell / Sound of music / Pop stars /
Twenty two hole Doc Martens / Boy Bill /
Sold out to the GPO / S.oach / Glue accident / Great rock 'n' roll swindle / Don't
throw it all away / Stab your back
CD _____ CDPUNK 27
Anagram / Mar '94 / Pinnacle.

Chaperals

ANOTHER SHOW
Hello everybody / Lucky guy / Falling leaves
/ Lover's question / Sh-boom / White cliffs
of Dover / Motorbiene / Angels listened /
Jitterbug Mary / Sitting in my room / Zoom,
zoom, zoom / So allein / In gee-home is
where the heart is
CD _____ BCD 15573
Bear Family / Jul '91 / Rollercoaster / Direct
/ CM / Swift / ADA.

Chapin, Harry

GREATEST STORIES-LIVE
Dreams go by / W.O.L.D / Saturday morn-
ing / I wanna learn a love song / Mr. Tanner
/ Better place to be / Let time go lightly /
Cats in the cradle / Taxi / Circle / 30,000
pounds of bananas / She is always seven-
teen / Love is just another world / Shortest
story
CD _____ 9606302
Elektra / '89 / Warner Music.

Chapin, Thomas

ANIMA (Chapin, Thomas Trio)
CD _____ KFWCD 121
Knitting Factory / Nov '94 / Grapevine.

I'VE GOT YOUR NUMBER
I've got your number / Drinkin' / Time waits
/ Moon ray / Don't look now / Present /
Walking wounded / Rhino
CD _____ AJ 0110
Arabesque / Nov '93 / New Note.

INSOMNIA (Chapin, Thomas Trio)
CD _____ KFWCD 132
Knitting Factory / Feb '95 / Grapevine.

THIRD FORCE (Chapin, Thomas Trio)
CD _____ KFWCD 103
Knitting Factory / Nov '92 / Grapevine.

YOU DON'T KNOW ME
Izzit / Kaokoland / Kunene / Opuwo / Na-
mibian sunset / Kura kura / Goodbye / You
don't know me
CD _____ AJ 0115
Arabesque / Jun '95 / New Note.

Chaplin, Charlie

20 SUPER HITS
CD _____ SONCD 0003
Sonic Sounds / Oct '90 / Jetstar.

**CHARLIE CHAPLIN MEETS PAPA SAN
(Charlie Chaplin & Papa San)**
CD _____ RNCD 2068
Rhino / Aug '94 / Jetstar / Magnum Music
Group / THE.

LIVE AT CLARENDON
CD _____ DHV 1CD
Tamoki Wambesi / Nov '95 / Jetstar / SRD
/ Roots Collective / Greensleeves.

OLD AND NEW TESTAMENT
CD _____ RASCD 3090
Ras / Apr '92 / Jetstar / Greensleeves /
SRD / Direct.

QUENCHIE
CD _____ TWCD 1028
Tamoki Wambesi / Dec '95 / Jetstar / SRD
/ Roots Collective / Greensleeves.

RED POND/CHAPLIN CHANT
CD _____ TWCD 1014
Tamoki Wambesi / Apr '94 / Jetstar / SRD
/ Roots Collective / Greensleeves.

TAKE TWO
CD _____ RASCD 3060
Ras / Jul '90 / Jetstar / Greensleeves /
SRD / Direct.

Chapman, Colin

FOLK SONGS
CD _____ CCLP 1001
Total / Oct '92 / Total/BMG.

Chapman, Michael

**BEST OF MICHAEL CHAPMAN, THE
(1969-1971)**
Naked ladies and electric ragtime / Rainmaker / You say / In the valley / Kodak
ghosts / Postcards of Scarborough / It
didn't work out / Last lady song / Wrecked
again / First leaf of autumn / Soulful lady /
Polar bear fandango (CD only) / All in all (CD
only) / Fennario (CD only) / Shuffle boat river
farewell (CD only) / Small stones (CD only)
CD _____ SEECD 230
See For Miles/C5 / Sep '88 / Pinnacle.

FULLY FLEDGED SURVIVOR
Fishbeard sunset / Soulful lady / Rabbit hills
/ March rain / Kodak ghosts / Andru's easy
rider / Trinkets and rings / Aviator / Naked
ladies and electric ragtime / Stranger in the
room / Postcards of Scarborough
CD _____ C5CD-527X
See For Miles/C5 / Apr '93 / Pinnacle.

HEARTBEAT
Heartbeat / All is forgiven / Chuckie / Africa
/ Minute you leave / Tristesse / Redskin
bridge / Tendresse / Heartbeat reprise
CD _____ NAGE 12CD
Art Of Landscape / Jun '87 / Sony.

NAVIGATION
CD _____ PLAN 007CD
Planet / Jul '95 / Grapevine / ADA / CM.

Chapman, Roger

CHAPPO
Midnite child / Hang on to a dream / Face
of stone / Pills / Always gotta pay in the end
/ Moth to a flame / Shapes of things / Keep
forgettin' / Let's spend the night together /
Who pulled the night down
CD _____ CLACD 299
Castle / Apr '92 / BMG.

HE WAS SHE WAS YOU WAS WE WAS
Higher round / Ducking down / Making the
same mistake / Blood and sand / King bee
/ That same thing / Face of stone / Hyenas
only laugh for fun
CD _____ CLACD 373
Castle / Apr '94 / BMG.

HYENAS ONLY LAUGH FOR FUN
Prisoner / Hyenas only laugh for fun / Killing
time / Wants nothing chained / Long good-
bye / Blood and sand / Common touch /
Goodbye (reprise) / Hearts on the floor /
Step up / Take a bow / Jukebox mama
CD _____ CLACD 305
Castle / Jun '92 / BMG.

LIVE IN BERLIN
Shadow on the wall / How how how / Let
me down / Mango crazy
CD _____ CLACD 313
Castle / Jun '92 / BMG.

LIVE IN HAMBURG
Moth to a flame / Keep forgettin' / Midnite
child / Who pulled the nite down / Talking
about you / Going down / Short list / Can't
get in / Keep a knockin' / Hoochie coochie
man / Let's spend the night together
CD _____ CLACD 320
Castle / Nov '92 / BMG.

MAIL ORDER MAGIC
Unknown soldier (can't get to heaven) / He
was, she was / Barman / Right to go /
Dusting down / Making the same mistake
/ Another little hurt / Mail order magic /
Higher ground / Ground floor
CD _____ CLACD 301
Castle / Apr '92 / BMG.

MANGO CRAZY
Mango crazy / Toys: do you / I read your
file / Los los Bailadores / Blues breaker /
Turn it up loud / Let me down / Hunt the
man / Rivers run dry / I really can't go
straight / Room service /
Hegoshegoyougoamigo
CD _____ CLACD 304
Castle / Jun '92 / BMG.

SHADOW KNOWS, THE
Busted loose / Leader of man / Ready to
roll / I think of you now / Sitting up pretty /
How how how / Only love is in the red /
Sweet vanilla / I'm a good boy now
CD _____ CLACD 370
Castle / Mar '94 / BMG.

TECHNO PRISONERS
Drum / Wild again / Techno prisoners /
Black forest / We will touch again / Run for
your love / Slap bang in the middle / Who's
been sleeping in my bed / Ball of confusion
CD _____ CLACD 371
Castle / Mar '94 / BMG.

WALKING THE CAT
Kick it back / Son of Red Moon / Stranger
than strange / Just a step away (let's go) /
Fool / Walking the cat / J and D / Come the
dark night / Hands off / Jivin' / Saturday
night kick back
CD _____ CLACD 372
Castle / '94 / BMG.

ZIPPER

Zipper / Running with the flame / On do die
day / Never love a rolling stone / Let the
beat get heavy / It's never too late to do-
ron-ron / Woman of destiny / Hoodoo me
up
CD _____ CLACD 314
Castle / '92 / BMG.

Chapman, Steven Curtis

HEAVEN IN THE REAL WORLD
Heaven in the real world / King of the jungle
/ Dancing with the dinosaur / Mountain /
Treasure of you / Love and learn / Burn the
ships / Remember your chains / Heartbeat
of heaven / Still listening / Facts and facts /
Miracle of mercy
CD _____ SPD 1408
Alliance Music / Jul '95 / EMI.

Chapman, Topsy

**TOPSY CHAPMAN & MAGNOLIA
JAZZBAND**
CD _____ BCD 320
GHB / Apr '94 / Jazz Music.

Chapman, Tracy

CROSSROADS
Crossroads / Freedom now / Be careful of
my heart / Born to fight / This time / Bridges
/ Material world / Sub city / Hundred years
/ All that you have is your soul
CD _____ K 960 8882
Elektra / Sep '89 / Warner Music.

MATTERS OF THE HEART
Bang bang bang / So / I used to be a sailor
/ Love that you had / Woman's work / If
these are the things / Short supply
CD _____ 75596125-2
Elektra / Nov '93 / Warner Music.

NEW BEGINNINGS
CD _____ 7559618502
Elektra / Nov '95 / Warner Music.

TRACY CHAPMAN
Talkin' bout a revolution / Fast car / Across
the lines / Behind the wall / Baby can I hold
you / Mountains O' things / She's got her
ticket / Why / For my lover / If not now... /
For you
CD _____ 9607742
Elektra / Apr '88 / Warner Music.

Chapman-Whitney...

**BBC RADIO 1 LIVE IN CONCERT
(Chapman-Whitney Streetwalkers)**
CD _____ WINCD 061
Windsong / Jun '94 / Pinnacle.

Charity, Pernell

VIRGINIAN, THE
Woke up on the hill / War blues / I'm climbing on top of the hill / Black rat swing / Pig
meat Mama / Flying the kite / Mammy / Evil
hearted woman / Richmond blues / Blind
man / Find me home / Come back, baby,
come / I don't see why / Blind lemon's
blues / Dig myself a hole
CD _____ TRIX 3309
Trix / Nov '95 / New Note.

Charlap, Bill

**PIANO & BASS (Charlap, Bill & Sean
Smith)**
CD _____ PCD 7092
Progressive / Jan '94 / Jazz Music.

SOUVENIR (Charlap, Bill Trio)
CD _____ CRISS 1108
Criss Cross / Dec '95 / Cadillac /
Harmonia Mundi.

Charlatans

BETWEEN 10TH AND 11TH
CD _____ SITU 37CD
Situation 2 / Mar '92 / Pinnacle.

CHARLATANS, THE
CD _____ BBQCD 174
Beggars Banquet / Aug '95 / Warner
Music / Disc.

SOME FRIENDLY
You're not very well / White shirt / Only one
I know / Opportunity / Then / 109 (pt 2) /
Polar bear / Believe you me / Flower / Sonic
/ Sproston green
CD _____ BBL 30CD
Beggars Banquet / Sep '95 / Warner Music
/ Disc.

UP TO OUR HIPS
Come in number 21 / I never want an easy
life if me and he were ever to get ther / Can't
get out of bed / Feel flows / Autograph /
Jesus Hairdo / Up to our hips / Patrol / An-
other rider up in flames / Inside looking out
CD _____ BBQCD 147
Beggars Banquet / Mar '94 / Warner Music
/ Disc.

Charlatans

FIRST ALBUM/ALABAMA BOUND
CD _____ 842020
EVA / Jun '94 / Direct / ADA.

Charles & Eddie

CHOCOLATE MIX
Keep on smilin' / Jealousy / 24-7-365 /
Wounded bird / Peace of mind / Sunshine
and happiness / Smile my way / She's so
shy / I can't find the words / Little piece of
heaven / Dear God / To someone else /
Zarah / Your love / Best place in the world
/ Goodbye song
CD _____ CDEST 2256
Capitol / May '95 / EMI.

DUOPHONIC
House is not a home / N.Y.C. / Would I lie
to you / Hurt no more / I understand / Un-
conditional / Love is a beautiful thing /
Where do we go from here / Father to son
/ December 2nd / Be a little easy on me /
Vowel song / Shine / Bonus cut
CD _____ CDESTU 2186
Capitol / May '95 / EMI.

Charles River Valley Boys

BEATLE COUNTRY
CD _____ ROUCDSS 41
Rounder / Apr '95 / CM / Direct / ADA /
Cadillac.

Charles, Bobby

LOUISIANA RHYTHM & BLUES MAN
CD _____ CDRB 31
Charly / Nov '95 / Charly / THE / Cadillac.

SMALL TOWN TALK
Street people / Long face / I must be in a
good place now / Save me Jesus / He's got
all the whisky / Let yourself go / Grow too
old / I'm that way / Tennessee blues
CD _____ SEECD 218
See For Miles/C5 / Mar '88 / Pinnacle.

WISH YOU WERE HERE RIGHT NOW
CD _____ SPCD 1203
Stony Plain / May '95 / ADA / CM / Direct.

Charles, Ray

ALONE IN THE CITY
CD _____ RMB 75009
Remember / Nov '93 / Total/BMG.

AUDIO ARCHIVE
I wonder who's kissing her now / Let's have
a ball / Goin' down slow / Sittin' on top of
the world / Alone in the city / Blues is my
middle name / This love of mine / Now she's
gone / Can anyone ask for more / C.C. rider
/ Rockin' chair blues / Hey now / Sentimental blues / Can't you see darling / Tell me
baby / Baby, let me hold your hand / I won't
let you go / I'm gonna drown myself / Snow
is fallin' / If I give you my love
CD _____ CDAA 003
Tring / Jan '92 / Tring / Prism.

BACK HOME
CD _____ CDCD 1128
Charly / Mar '93 / Charly / THE / Cadillac.

BEST OF RAY CHARLES
CD _____ DLCD 4008
Dixie Live / Mar '95 / Magnum Music
Group.

**BEST OF RAY CHARLES - THE
ATLANTIC YEARS**
It should've been me / Don't you know /
Blackjack / I've got a woman / What would
I do without you / Greenbacks / Come back
/ Fool for you / This little girl of mine / Hal-
lelujah, I love her so / Lonely avenue / It's
alright / Ain't that love / Swanee river rock
/ That's enough / What I'd say / (Night time)
is the right time / Drown in my own tears /
Tell the truth (Live) / Just for a thrill
CD _____ 812271722-2
Atlantic / Aug '94 / Warner Music.

BEST OF RAY CHARLES, THE
Hard times / Rock house / Sweet sixteen
bars / Doodlin' / How long blues / Blues
waltz
CD _____ 756781368-2
Atlantic / Mar '93 / Warner Music.

BLUES
What have I done / Goin' down slow / Now
she's gone / Rockin' chair blues / Sentimental blues / Can anyone ask for more /
Honey honey / Baby, won't you please
come home / You always miss the water
(when the well runs dry) / How long / Alone
in the city / Let's have a ball / This love of
mine / Can't you see darling / If I give you
my love / Some day (Blues is my middle
name) / Don't put all your dreams in one
basket / I found my baby there / She's on
the ball
CD _____ 16223CD
Success / Oct '94 / Carlton Home
Entertainment.

BLUES & JAZZ ANTHOLOGY, THE
Someday / Sun's gonna shine again / Midnight hour / Worried life blues / Low society
/ Losing hand / Sinner's prayer / Funny (but
I still love you) / Feelin' sad / I wonder who /
Nobody cares / Ray's blues / Mr. Charles
blues / Black jack / Come back / Fool for
you / hard times (no one knows better than
I) / Drown in my own tears / What would I
without you / I want a little girl / Early in the
morning / Night time is the right time / Two
years of torchure / I believe to my soul /

Man I love / Music music music / I surrender dear / Hornful soul / Ain't misbehavin' / Doodlin' / Sweet sixteen bars / Undecided / Rock house / X-ray blues / Love on my mind / Fathead / Bill for Bennie / Hard times / Willow weep for me / Spirit feel
CD _____ 8122716072
Atlantic / Mar '94 / Warner Music.

BLUES IS MY MIDDLE NAME
Goin' down slow / Alone in the city / Now she's gone / Rockin' chair blues / Sentimental blues / Can anyone ask for more / Let's have a ball / This love of mine / Can't you see darling / If I give you my love / Sittin' on top of the world / Kiss me baby / I'm gonna drown myself / Snow is fallin' / Blues is my middle name / I wonder who's kissing her now / C.C. rider / Hey now / Tell me baby / All to myself alone / Baby, let me hold your hand / I won't let you go / I'm glad for your sake / Walkin' and talkin' / I'm wonderin' and wonderin' / I found my baby there
CD _____ CDGRF 033
Tring / '93 / Tring / Prism.

CLASSIC YEARS, THE
Sticks and stones / Georgia on my mind / Ruby / Hard hearted Hannah / Theme that got / One mint julep / I've got news for you / Hit the road Jack / Unchain my heart / Hide nor hair / At the club / I can't stop loving you / Born to lose / You don't know me / You are my sunshine / Your cheatin' heart / Don't set me free / Take these chains from my heart / No one / Without love (there is nothing) / Busted / That lucky old sun / Baby don't you cry / My heart cries for you / My baby don't dig me / No one to cry to / Smack dab in the middle / Makin' whoopee / Cry / Crying time / Together again / Let's go get stoned / Please say you're fooling / I don't need no doctor / In the heat of the night / Yesterday / Eleanor Rigby / Understanding and nine more
CD _____ CDSGP 0121
Prestige / Jun '94 / Total/BMG.

COLLECTION VOL.1
Your cheatin' heart / Hit the road Jack / Georgia on my mind / Unchain my heart / One mint julep / Take these chains from my heart / I can't stop loving you / Busted / You are my sunshine / Your cheatin' heart / Let's go get stoned / My heart cries for you / Feel so bad / Lucky old sun / Smack dab in the middle / Crying time / If it wasn't for bad luck / In the heat of the night / Eleanor Rigby / Born to lose / No one / Hard hearted Hannah / Yesterday
CD _____ CCSCD 241
Castle / Mar '90 / BMG.

COLLECTION VOL.2
CD _____ CCSCD 328
Castle / Apr '92 / BMG.

COLLECTION: RAY CHARLES
Yesterday / Your cheatin' heart / Georgia on my mind / I can't stop loving you / Busted / Together again / Take these chains from my heart / Crying time / Half as much / Here we go again / Born to lose / Eleanor Rigby / You don't know me / Hit the road Jack / I gotta woman (live) / What'd I say
CD _____ RCLD 101
Arcade / Mar '90 / Sony / Grapevine.

ESSENTIAL COLLECTION
CD Set _____ LECD 607
Wisepack / Apr '95 / THE / Conifer.

FRIENDSHIP
Two old cats like us / This old heart of mine / We didn't see a thing / Who cares / Rock 'n' roll shoes / Friendship / It ain't gonna worry my mind / Little hotel room / Crazy old soldier / Seven Spanish angels
CD _____ 9825942
Pickwick/Sony Collector's Choice / Oct '93 / Carlton Home Entertainment / Pinnacle / Sony.

GENIUS + SOUL = JAZZ
From the heart / I've got news for you / Moanin' / Let's go / One mint julep / I'm gonna move to the outskirts of town / Stompin' room only / Mr. C / Strike up the band / Birth of the blues / Alabamy bound / Basin Street blues / New York's my home
CD _____ CLACD 339
Castle / Aug '93 / BMG.

GENIUS OF RAY CHARLES, THE
CD _____ 756781338-2
Atlantic / Jun '93 / Warner Music.

GEORGIA TIME
I had it all / Do I ever cross your mind / Workin' man's woman / I was on Georgia time / Two old cats like us / This ole heart / Friendship / This page on my mind / Slip away / Love is worth the pain / Rock 'n' roll shoes / Stranger in my own hometown / Let's call the whole thing off / Save the bones for Henry Jones / Nothing like a hundred miles / I wish I'd never loved you at all
CD _____ PWKS 4169
Carlton Home Entertainment / Sep '93 / Pinnacle.

GOLD COLLECTION, THE
CD _____ D2CD05
Recording Arts / Dec '92 / THE / Disc.

GREAT RAY CHARLES, THE
Ray / Melancholy baby / Black coffee / There's no you / Doodlin' / Sweet sixteen bars / I surrender dear / Undecided
CD _____ 756781731-2
Atlantic / Jun '93 / Warner Music.

GREATEST COUNTRY & WESTERN HITS
CD _____ PRS 23002
Personality / Jun '95 / Target/BMG.

GREATEST COUNTRY AND WESTERN HITS
Your cheatin' heart / Hey good lookin' / Take these chains from my heart / Don't tell me your troubles / I can't stop loving you / Just a little lovin' / It makes no difference now / You don't know me / You are my sunshine / Someday (you'll want me to want you) / I love you so much it hurts / Careless love / Oh, lonesome me / Midnight / No letter today / Crying time / Together again / Don't let her know / I'll never stand in your way (Only on CD.) / Hang your head in shame (Only on CD.)
CD _____ NEXCD 100
Sequel / Dec '89 / BMG.

HEY NOW
Confession blues / Can anyone ask for more / This love of mine / How long blues / Blues before sunrise / I've had my fun / C.C. rider / Late in the evening blues / Th'ego song / I wonder who's kissing her now / Lonely boy / Baby, won't you please come home / I'm glad for your sake / Kiss me baby / Hey now / Snow is fallin' / Misery in my heart / Let me hear you call my name / Why did you go / Walkin' and talkin'
CD _____ CDCD 1069
Charly / Mar '93 / Charly / THE / Cadillac.

HIS GREATEST HITS
CD _____ PRS 23005
Personality / '93 / Target/BMG.

I WISH YOU WERE HERE TONIGHT
3/4 time / I wish you were here tonight / Ain't your memory got no pride at all / Born to love me / I don't want no stranger sleepin' in my bed / I love your flow / You feel good all over / String bean / You've got the longest leaving act in town / Shakin' your head
CD _____ 9022892
Pickwick/Sony Collector's Choice / Apr '90 / Carlton Home Entertainment / Pinnacle / Sony.

IF I GIVE YOU MY LOVE
Alone in the city / Can anyone ask for more / Rockin' chair blues / Let's have a ball / If I give you my love / Can't see you darling / This love of mine / Sentimental blues / Now she's gone / Going down slow
CD _____ PD 50014
IMS / May '88 / PolyGram.

LIVE
Hot rod / Blues waltz / In a little Spanish town / Sherry / Right time / Fool for you / I got a woman / Talkin' 'bout you / Swanee river rock / Yes indeed / Frenesi / Spirit feel / Tell the truth / Drown in my own tears / What'd I say
CD _____ 756781732-2
Atlantic / Jun '93 / Warner Music.

LIVING LEGEND
CD _____ ARC 94642
Arcade / Mar '93 / Sony / Grapevine.

MY WORLD
My world / Song for you / None of us are free / So help me God / Let me take over / One drop of love / If I could / Love has a mind of its own / I'll be there / Still crazy after all these years
CD _____ 759926735-2
WEA / Mar '93 / Warner Music.

RAY CHARLES
CD _____ LECD 049
Dynamite / May '94 / THE.

RAY CHARLES (2CD Set)
CD Set _____ R2CD 4005
Deja Vu / Jan '96 / THE.

RAY CHARLES AND BETTY CARTER (Charles, Ray & Betty Carter)
Every time we say goodbye / You and I / Goodbye we'll be together again / People will say we're in love / Cocktails for two / Side by side / Baby, it's cold outside / Together / For all we know / It takes two to tango / Alone together / Just you and me / But on the other hand baby / I never see Maggie alone / I like to hear it sometimes
CD _____ CLACD 340
Castle / '93 / BMG.

RAY CHARLES AND BETTY CARTER (Charles, Ray & Betty Carter)
CD _____ PRS 23003
Personality / '93 / Target/BMG.

RAY CHARLES COLLECTION
Yesterday / Your cheatin' heart / I can't stop loving you / Eleanor Rigby / Hit the road Jack
CD _____ RCLD 101
Westmoor / Aug '92 / Target/BMG.

RAY CHARLES GOLD (2CD Set)
CD Set _____ D2CD 4005
Deja Vu / Jun '95 / THE.

ROCK + SOUL = GENIUS
CD _____ JMY 1009-2
JMY / Aug '91 / Harmonia Mundi.

SEE SEE RIDER
See see rider / Sentimental blues / She's on the ball / This love of mine / How long blues / You never miss the water / Someday / Baby, let me hold your hand / Baby, won't you please come home (2) / Ain't that fine / Don't put all your dreams in one basket / Why did you go / Let me hear you call my name / Sittin' on top of the world / Going down slow (I've had my fun) / Can't you see darling / What have I done / Money honey / Blues before sunrise / Snow is fallin' / Baby, won't you please come home
CD _____ MUCD 9011
Start / Apr '95 / Koch.

SOUL MEETING (Charles, Ray & Milt Jackson)
Hallelujah, I love her so / Blue genius / X-ray blues / Soul meeting / Love on my mind / Bags of blues
CD _____ 756781951-2
Atlantic / Mar '93 / Warner Music.

TWO IN ONE (Charles, Ray & Nat King Cole)
CD _____ CDTT 8
Charly / Apr '94 / Charly / THE / Cadillac.

Charles, Teddy

ON CAMPUS (Charles, Teddy & Zoot Sims)
CD _____ FSCD 43
Fresh Sound / Oct '90 / Jazz Music / Discovery.

Charles, Tina

I LOVE TO LOVE
I love to love (but my baby loves to dance) / You set my heart on fire (part 1) / Hey boy / Take all of me / Love me like a lover / Why / Hold me / Disco fever / Disco love
CD _____ 983277 2
Pickwick/Sony Collector's Choice / Sep '93 / Carlton Home Entertainment / Pinnacle / Sony.

Charleston Chasers

PLEASURE MAD
Stomp Off / Aug '95 / Jazz Music / Wellard.
CD _____ SOSCD 1287

THOSE CHARLESTON DAYS
CD _____ SOV 024CD
Sovereign / Aug '94 / Target/BMG.

Charlesworth, Bob

MUSIC FOR THE 3RD EAR
CD _____ WWCD 12
Wibbly Wobbly / Sep '95 / SRD.

Charlesworth, Dick

DICK CHARLESWORTH & HIS CITY GENTS
CD _____ BCD 272
GHB / Aug '95 / Jazz Music.

Charley's War

1000 YEARS OF CIVILISATION
CD _____ SRC 10CD
Snoop / Nov '92 / Plastic Head.

Charlie & His Orchestra

1941-42
Harlequin / Oct '91 / Swift / Jazz Music / Wellard / Hot Shot / Cadillac.
CD _____ HQCD 03

1941-44 VOL.2
Harlequin / '91 / Swift / Jazz Music / Wellard / Hot Shot / Cadillac.
CD _____ HQCD 09

Charlie Parker Memorial..

CHARLIE PARKER MEMORIAL BAND, THE (Charlie Parker Memorial Band)
Marduke / Out of nowhere / Don't blame me / Sweet Rosa / Little Willie leaps / Max the invincible reach / Star eyes / Lazit beat / Bird of paradise / Visa
CD _____ CDSJP 373
Timeless Jazz / Nov '93 / New Note.

Charlottes

THINGS COME APART
Liar / Prayer song / See me, feel me / By my side / Mad girls love song / Beautify / Love in the emptiness / We're going wrong / Blue / Venus
CD _____ CDBRED 92
Cherry Red / Jan '91 / Pinnacle.

Chas & Dave

AIN'T NO PLEASING YOU
Ain't no pleasing you / That's what I like / My melancholy baby / Sunday / One o' them days / Poor old Mr. Woogie / Bored stiff / Turn that noise down / Rabbit / Wish I could write a love song / That old piano / Nobody / Miss you all the

time / Flying / Stop dreaming / London girls / There in your eyes / I miss ya gel / Mustn't grumble
CD _____ TRTCD 149
TrueTrax / Oct '94 / THE.

ALL TIME JAMBOREE BAG
CD _____ CTMCD 208
Castle / Oct '91 / BMG.
CD Set _____ DCDCD 218
Castle / Nov '95 / BMG.

BEST OF CHAS & DAVE
Poor old Mr. Woogie / Bored stiff / Don't anyone speak English / Turn that noise down / Beer belly / Behave yourself / Ain't no pleasing you / I miss ya gel / Lonnie D / Wallop / Rabbit / That old piano / That's what I like / London girls / Give it some stick, Nick / Nobody / Flying / Margate / Musn't grumble / Word from Anne / Stop dreaming / Give it gavotte / Wish I could write a love song
CD _____ MATCD 207
Castle / Dec '92 / BMG.

CHAS & DAVE'S ROCK 'N' ROLL PARTY
CD _____ TCD 2794
Telstar / Nov '95 / BMG.

ONE FING 'N' ANUVVER
Ponders End allotments club / Better get your shoes on / Dry party / Ballad of the rich / Deceived / One fing 'n' anuvver / It's so very hard / Woortcha / I'm a rocker / Old time song / Old dog and me
CD _____ RTCD 901144
Line / Sep '92 / CM / Grapevine / ADA / Conifer / Direct.
CD _____ 901144
Line / May '95 / CM / Grapevine / ADA / Conifer / Direct.

STREET PARTY
CD _____ TCD 2765
Telstar / Apr '95 / BMG.

Chassagnite, Francois

SAMYA CYNTHIA
CD _____ CDLLL 97
La Lichere / Aug '93 / Discovery / ADA.

Chastain

SICK SOCIETY
CD _____ MASSCD 076
Massacre / Nov '95 / Plastic Head.

VOICE OF THE CULT, THE
Voice of the cult / Live hard / Chains of love / Share yourself with me / Child of evermore / Soldiers of the flame / Evil for evil / Take me home / Fortune teller
CD _____ RR 9548 2
Roadrunner / Jul '88 / Pinnacle.

WITHIN THE HEAT
Excursions into reality / Visionary / Nightmares / Zfunknc / In your face / Desert nights / Danger zone F107 / Return of the 6 / Within the heat / It's still in your eyes / Pantheon
CD _____ RR 9484 2
Roadrunner / Jan '89 / Pinnacle.

Chastain, David T.

7TH OF NEVER, THE
CD _____ MASSCD 077
Massacre / Oct '95 / Plastic Head.

MOVEMENTS THROUGH TIME
Thunder and lightning / 827 / Fortunate and happenstance / Citizen of hell / Blitzkrieg / Oracle within / New York rush / We must carry on / Capriccio / In E minor / No man's land / Seven Hills groove / Now or never / Trapped in the wind / Zoned in danger / Bargin
CD _____ KCLCD 1002
Killerwatt / Oct '93 / Kingdom.

NEXT PLANET PLEASE
CD _____ CDVEST 9
Bulletproof / May '94 / Pinnacle.

Chateau Neuf...

SPELL (Chateau Neuf Spelemannslag)
CD _____ HCD 7104CD
Helio / Apr '95 / ADA.

Chatham, Rhys

DIE DONNERGOTTER
CD _____ HMS 120 2
Homestead / Apr '89 / SRD.

DO IT TWICE
CD _____ DCD 9002
Dossier / Apr '88 / SRD.

Chattaway, Jay

SPACE AGE
CD _____ ND 66003
Narada / Nov '92 / New Note / ADA.

Chatuye

HEARTBEAT IN THE MUSIC
CD _____ ARHCD 383
Arhoolie / Apr '95 / ADA / Direct / Cadillac.

Chaurand, Anne

CELTIA
CD _____ ECLCD 9613
Eclectic / Feb '96 / Pinnacle.

Chaurasia, Hariprasad

RAG AHIR BHAIRAV
CD _____ NI 5111
Nimbus / Sep '94 / Nimbus.

RAG BHIMPALASI
CD _____ NI 5298
Nimbus / Sep '94 / Nimbus.

RAG KAUNSI KANHRA
CD _____ NI 5182
Nimbus / Sep '94 / Nimbus.

RAG LALIT
CD _____ NI 5152
Nimbus / Sep '94 / Nimbus.

RAGA DARBARI KANADA/DHUN IN RAGA
CD _____ NI 5638
Nimbus / Sep '94 / Nimbus.

Chaves, Guillermo

EL SUSPIRO DEL MORO (FLAMENCO)
(Chaves, Guillermo/ Marc Loopuyt/ Adel Shamseddin)
CD _____ AUB 006777
Auvidis/Ethnic / Apr '93 / Harmonia Mundi.

Chavez

GONE GLIMMERING
Nailed to the blank / Spot / Break up your band / Ghost by the sea / Relaxed fit / Wakeman's air / Flaming gong / In our pools / Pentagram ring / Laugh track
CD _____ OLE 1332
Matador / Jul '95 / Vital.

Chavis, Boozoo

BOOZOO CHAVIS
Boozoo's theme song / I'm ready me / Dog hill / Keep your dress tail down / Johnnie billy goat / Goin' to la maison / Forty one days / Oh yae yae / Tee black / Zydeco hee haw / Don't worry about Boozoo / Berandette
CD _____ 7559611462
Elektra Nonesuch / Jul '91 / Warner Music.

BOOZOO, THAT'S WHO
CD _____ ROU 2126CD
Rounder / Jan '94 / CM / Direct / ADA / Cadillac.

LEGENDS OF ZYDECO: SWAMP MUSIC VOL.7
CD _____ US 0203
Trikont / Apr '95 / ADA / Direct.

LIVE AT RICHARD'S ZYDECO DANCE HALL VOL.1 (Chavis, Boozoo & The Magic Sounds)
CD _____ CD 2069
Rounder / '88 / CM / Direct / ADA / Cadillac.

LIVE AT THE HABIBI TEMPLE
CD _____ ROUCD 2130
Rounder / Sep '94 / CM / Direct / ADA / Cadillac.

Chawner, Suzanna

ON PRIMROSE HILL
CD _____ RTMCD 67
Round Tower / Nov '94 / Pinnacle / ADA / Direct / BMG / CM.

Che

GUERRILLA WARFARE AND SOAPOWDER
CD _____ EXPALCD 9
Expression / May '91 / Pinnacle.

Cheap 'n' Nasty

BEAUTIFUL DISASTER
CD _____ WOLCD 1002
China / May '91 / Pinnacle.

Cheap Trick

ALL SHOOK UP
Stop this game / Just got back / Baby loves to rock / Can't stop it but I'm gonna try / World's greatest lover / High priest of rhythmic noise / Love comes a-tumblin' down / I love you honey but I hate your friends / Go for the throat / Who'd king
CD _____ EK 36498
Pickwick/Sony Collector's Choice / Jun '88 / Carlton Home Entertainment / Pinnacle / Sony.

CHEAP TRICK
Hot love / Speak now or forever hold your peace / He's a whore / Mandocello / Ballad of T.V. violence / Ello kiddies / Daddy should have stayed in High School / Taxman / Mr. Thief / Cry cry / Oh Candy
CD _____ EK 34400
Pickwick/Sony Collector's Choice / Jun '88 / Carlton Home Entertainment / Pinnacle / Sony.

COLLECTION: CHEAP TRICK

CD _____ CCSCD 309
Castle / Oct '91 / BMG.

GREATEST HITS, THE
Magical mystery tour / Dream police / Don't be cruel / Tonight it's you / She's tight / I want you to want me (live) / If you want my love / Ain't that a shame (live) / Surrender / Flame / I can't take it / Can't stop fallin' into love / Voices
CD _____ 4690862
Epic / Apr '94 / Sony.

IN COLOR
Hollo there / Dig eyes / Drowned / I want you to want me / You're all talk / Oh Caroline / Clock strikes ten / Southern girls / Come on come on / So good to see you
CD _____ 982833 2
Carlton Home Entertainment / Nov '92 / Carlton Home Entertainment.

LAP OF LUXURY
Let go / No mercy / Flame / Space / Never had a lot to lose / Don't be cruel / Wrong side of love / All we need is a dream / Ghost town / All wound up
CD _____ 982839 2
Carlton Home Entertainment / Oct '92 / Carlton Home Entertainment.

NEXT POSITION PLEASE
I can't take it / Borderline / I don't love her anymore / Next position please / Younger girls / Dancing the night away / 3-D / You say jump / Y.O.Y.O.Y / Won't take no for an answer / Heaven's falling / Invaders of the heart
CD _____ EK 38794
Pickwick/Sony Collector's Choice / Jun '88 / Carlton Home Entertainment / Pinnacle / Sony.

WOKE UP WITH A MONSTER
My gang / Woke up with a monster / You're all I wanna do / Never runout of love / Didn't know I had it / Ride the pony / Girlfriends / Let her go / Tell me everything / Cry baby / Love me for a minute
CD _____ 9362454252
WEA / Mar '94 / Warner Music.

Cheatham, Doc

AT BERN JAZZ FESTIVAL (Cheatham, Doc & Jim Galloway)
CD _____ SKCD 2-3045
Sackville / Jun '93 / Swift / Jazz Music / Jazz Horizons / Cadillac / CM.

DOC CHEATHAM LIVE
CD _____ NI 4023
Natasha / Feb '94 / Jazz Music / ADA / CM / Direct / Cadillac.

EIGHTY-SEVEN YEARS OF DOC CHEATHAM
That's my home / Okay baby / Love you madly / Blues in my heart / Sleep / New Orleans / Muskrat ramble / Was it a dream / Wolverine blues / Round Midnight / Miss Brown to you / Have you met Miss Jones / My buddy / I guess I'll get the papers and go home
CD _____ 474047 2
Columbia / Apr '94 / Sony.

HEY DOC
CD _____ BLE 590902
Black & Blue / Apr '91 / Wellard / Koch.

SWINGING DOWN IN NEW ORLEANS
CD _____ JCD 233
Jazzology / Dec '95 / Swift / Jazz Music.

Cheatham, Jeannie

BACK TO THE NEIGHBORHOOD
CD _____ CCD 4373
Concord Jazz / Apr '89 / New Note.

BASKET FULL OF BLUES
Blues like Jay McShann / Heaven or hell blues / Buddy Bolden's blues / Song of the wanderer / Basket full of blues / All the time / Baby, where have you been / Band rat blues / Little girl blue/Am I blue / Bye 'n' bye blues / Ballad of the wannabes / Don't cha boogie with your black drawers off
CD _____ CCD 4501
Concord Jazz / Mar '92 / New Note.

BLUES AND THE BOOGIE MASTERS
What we do for fun / Lead dog blues / Little bitty bluebird blues / Don't let me wake up / Blues and the boogie masters / Lonesome road / Line in the sand / Too many goodbyes / Up in Rickey's room / Leave that woman blues / Please send me someone to love
CD _____ CCD 4579
Concord Jazz / Nov '93 / New Note.

HOMEWARD BOUND
Permanent solution / Going down slow / Daddy-O / Trouble in mind / You don't have to go / Hello little boy / Detour ahead / Sometimes it be that way
CD _____ CCD 4321
Concord Jazz / Jul '87 / New Note.

SWEET BABY BLUES
Brand new blues / Roll 'em Pete / Sweet baby blues / I got a mind to ramble / Ain't nobody's business / Muddy water blues / Cherry red / Meet me with your black drawers on

CD _____ CCD 4258
Concord Jazz / Nov '89 / New Note.

Checker, Chubby

LEGENDS IN MUSIC - CHUBBY CHECKER
CD _____ LECD 062
Wisepack / Jul '94 / THE / Conifer.

LET'S TWIST AGAIN
Remember / Nov '93 / Total/BMG. RMB 75058

MR. TWISTER
CD _____ CDCD 1043
Charly / Mar '93 / Charly / THE / Cadillac.

PEARLS FROM THE PAST VOL. 2 - CHUBBY CHECKER
Scratch / Apr '94 / BMG. KLMCD 014

ULTIMATE COLLECTION, THE (16 All Time Classics)
Twist / Limbo rock / Dancin' party / Hey babba needle / Loddy lo / Slow twistin' / Fly / Party time / Let's twist again / Let's limbo some more / Birdland / Dance the mess around / Popeye (The hitchiker) / Twenty miles / Twist it up / Hucklebuck
CD _____ ECD 3045
K-Tel / Jan '95 / K-Tel.

Cheech & Chong

GREATEST HITS
Earache my eye / Dave / Let's make a dope deal / Basketball Jones / Blin melon chitlin' / Sister Mary elephant / Sergeant Stadanko / Dave (2) / Cruisin' / Continuing adventures of Pedro De Pacas / Pedrn and man at the drivein / Trippin' in court
CD _____ 7599236142
WEA / Jan '93 / Warner Music.

Cheeks, Judy

RESPECT
Reach (Radio Edit) / So in love (The real deal) / Could it be (Falling in love) / This time / Forgive and forget / You're the story of my life / Respect / Joy to the world / As long as you're good to me / Different love / I'm only here / Wishing on the same star (MC/ CD only) / Single tear (MC/CD only)
CD _____ CDTIVA 1005
Positiva / Jun '91 / EMI.

Cheer Accident

DUMB ASK
CD _____ NM 001CD
Neat / Nov '95 / Plastic Head.

Cheito

CHEITO
Tu y yo / El baile de la vela / Piñuela la bella / Promesa / La montadera / Tu territorio / Mal de amores / Baila sonero / Te juro / Que decir / Contrapunto musical
CD _____ 476938 2
Epic / Nov '94 / Sony.

Chelsea

ALTERNATIVE, THE
Alternative / Weirdos in wonderland / More than a giro / Wasting time / Ever wonder / Where is everything / You can be there too / What's wrong with you / Oh no / Too late / Dreams of dreams / Ode to the travellers
CD _____ WLO 24662
Weser / Oct '94 / Plastic Head.

LIVE AND WELL
CD _____ PUNXCD 1
Punx / Oct '95 / Total/BMG.

LIVE AT THE MUSIC MACHINE 1978
CD _____ REM 016 CD
Released Emotions / Mar '92 / Pinnacle.

TRAITORS GATE
CD _____ WL 2480-2
Weser / Aug '94 / Plastic Head.

UNRELEASED STUFF
I'm on fire / Come on / No flowers / Urban kids / Twelve men / Trouble is the day / Young toy / Decide / Curfew / Look at the outside / Don't get me wrong / Fools and soldiers / Comeon
CD _____ CLAYCD 101
Clay / Jul '94 / Cargo.

Chelsea F.C.

BLUE IS THE COLOUR
Blue is the colour / Chirpy chirpy cheep cheep / Football is / Give me back my soccer boots / Maybe it's because I'm a Londoner / Let's all go down the Strand / On mother Kelly's doorstep / Strollin' / Let's all sing together / Song sung blue / Stop and take a look / Son of my father / Alouette
CD _____ MONDE 19CD
Cherry Red / Oct '94 / Pinnacle.

Chemical Brothers

EXIT PLANET DUST
Leave home / In dust we trust / Song to the siren / Three little birdies down beats / Fuck up beats / Chemical beats / Life is sweet /

Playground for a wedgeless firm / Chico's groove / One too many mornings / Alive: alone
CD _____ XDUSTCD 1
Virgin / Jun '95 / EMI.

Chemical People

ANGELS 'N' DEVILS
CD _____ CRZ 019 CD
Cruz / May '93 / Pinnacle / Plastic Head.

CHEMICAL PEOPLE
CD _____ CRZ 023 CD
Cruz / May '93 / Pinnacle / Plastic Head.

LET IT GO
CD _____ CRZ 025 CD
Cruz / May '93 / Pinnacle / Plastic Head.

RIGHT THING, THE
CD _____ CRZ 013 CD
Cruz / Aug '90 / Pinnacle / Plastic Head.

SO SEXIST
CD _____ CRZ 002 CD
Cruz / Jan '90 / Pinnacle / Plastic Head.

SOUNDTRACKS
CD _____ CRZ 020 CD
Cruz / May '93 / Pinnacle / Plastic Head.

TEN-FOLD HATE
CD _____ CRZ 007 CD
Cruz / Jan '90 / Pinnacle / Plastic Head.

Chemirani, Djamchid

TRADITION CLASSIQUE DE L'IRAN - VOL. 1 (Le Zarb)
CD _____ HMA 190368
Musique D'Abord / Nov '93 / Harmonia Mundi.

Chemlab

BURN OUT AT THE HYDROGEN BAR
Codeine, glue and you / Suicide jag / Chemical halo / Neurozone / Elephant man / Rivethead / Derailer / Summer of hate
CD _____ CDDVN 21
Devotion / Jun '93 / Pinnacle.

Cheneour, Paul

TIME HAS COME, THE
Med mig sjalv / Time has come / First find an angel / Glass bead game / Who will cry / Rain / Moontide / Village / Snaewa / Shroud / Fantasie I / Fantasie II / Fantasie III / Knots / Rain #2 / Nasrudin
CD _____ RGM 294CD
Red Gold Music / Feb '95 / Red Gold Music.

Chenier, Clifton

60 MINUTES WITH THE KING OF ZYDECO
CD _____ ARCD 301
Arhoolie / Apr '95 / ADA / Direct / Cadillac.

BOGALUSA BOOGIE
CD _____ ARHCD 347
Arhoolie / Apr '95 / ADA / Direct / Cadillac.

BON TON ROULET
CD _____ ARHCD 345
Arhoolie / Apr '95 / ADA / Direct / Cadillac.

CAJUN SWAMP
CD _____ 260606D
Tomato / May '88 / Vital.

CAJUN SWAMP MUSIC LIVE
CD _____ 269 621 2
Tomato / Nov '94 / Vital.

CLIFTON CHENIER IN NEW ORLEANS
Boogie Louisiana / Cotton picker blues / J'aime pain de mais / Pousse cafe waltz / Hello Rosa-Lee / Jusque parce que je t'aime / Boogie in Orleans / Rumblin' on the bayou / I'm gonna take you home tonite / Mon vieux buggy / Crying my heart out to you / Tous les jours / Mardi gras boogie
CD _____ GNPD 2119
GNP Crescendo / Sep '95 / Silva Screen.

CLIFTON CHENIER SINGS THE BLUES (Home Cookin' & Prophesy Sides From 1969)
CD _____ ARHCD 351
Arhoolie / Apr '95 / ADA / Direct / Cadillac.

FRENCHIN' THE BOOGIE
Caldonia / Laissez le bon temps roulez / Tu peux cogner mais tu peux pas rentrer (Keep-a-knockin'...) (Full Translation: Keep-a-knockin' but you can't come in.) / Blues de la vache a lait (Milkcow blues) / Moi, j'ai une petite femme (I got a woman) / Tous les jours mon coeur est blue (Everytime I see you) / Choo choo ch' boogie / La valse de Paris / Shake, rattle and roll / Going down slow (in Paris) / Aye, aye mama / Don't you lie to me
CD _____ 5197242
Verve / Apr '93 / PolyGram.

KING OF THE BAYOUS
CD _____ ARHCD 339
Arhoolie / Apr '95 / ADA / Direct / Cadillac.

KING OF ZYDECO LIVE AT MONTREUX
CD _____ ARHCD 355
Arhoolie / Apr '95 / ADA / Direct / Cadillac.

LIVE AT LONG BEACH & SAN FRANCISCO BLUES FESTIVAL
CD _____ ARHCD 404
Arhoolie / Apr '95 / ADA / Direct / Cadillac.

LIVE AT St. MARK'S
CD _____ ARHCD 313
Arhoolie / Apr '95 / ADA / Direct / Cadillac.

LOUISIANA BLUES AND ZYDECO
CD _____ ARHCD 329
Arhoolie / Apr '95 / ADA / Direct / Cadillac.

MY BABY DON'T WEAR NO SHOES
CD _____ ARHCD 1098
Arhoolie / Apr '95 / ADA / Direct / Cadillac.

ON TOUR
CD _____ 157722
Blues Collection / Feb '93 / Discovery.

OUT WEST
CD _____ ARHCD 350
Arhoolie / Apr '95 / ADA / Direct / Cadillac.

TOO MUCH FUN (Chenier, Clifton & His Red Hot Louisiana Band)
CD _____ ALCD 4830
Alligator / Apr '95 / Direct / ADA.

ZODICO BLUES & BOOGIE
Boppin' the rock / Ay tet fee / Cat's dreamin' / Squeeze box boogie / Things I did for you / Think it over / Zodico stomp / Yesterday (I lost my best friend) / Chenier's boogie / I'm on my way (back home to you) / All night long / Opelousas hop / Wherever you go I'll go / Clifton's dreamin'
CD _____ CDCHD 389
Ace / May '92 / Pinnacle / Cadillac / Complete/Pinnacle.

Chenille Sisters

HAUTE CHENILLE (A Retrospective)
CD _____ RHRCD 81
Red House / Jan '96 / Koch / ADA.

TRUE TO LIFE
CD _____ RHRCD 67
Red House / May '95 / Koch / ADA.

Cher

ALL I REALLY WANT TO DO/SONNY SIDE OF CHER/CHER (3CD Set)
All I really want to do / I go to sleep / Needles and pins / Don't think twice / She thinks I still care / Dream baby / Bells of Rhymney / Girl don't come / See see rider / Come and stay with me / Cry myself to sleep / Blowin' in the wind / Bang bang (my baby shot me down) / Young girl (une entante) / Where do you go / Our day will come / Elusive butterfly / Like a rolling stone / Ol' man river / Come to your garden / Girl from Ipanema / It's not unusual / Time / Milord / Twelfth of never / You don't have to say you love me / I feel something in the air / Will you love me tomorrow / Until it's time for you to go / Cruel war / Catch the wind / Pied piper / Homeward bound / I want you / Alfie
CD Set _____ CDOMB 005
EMI / Oct '95 / EMI.

CHER
I found someone / We all sleep alone / Bang bang (my baby shot me down) / Main man / Give our love a chance / Perfection / Dangerous times / Skin deep / Working girl / Hard enough getting over you
CD _____ GFLD 19192
Geffen / Mar '93 / BMG.

CHER'S GREATEST HITS 1965-1992
Oh no not my baby / Whenever you're near / Many rivers to cross / Love and understanding / Save up all your tears / Shoop shoop song (It's in his kiss) / If I could turn back time / Just like Jesse James / Heart of stone / I found someone / We all sleep alone / Bang bang (my baby shot me down) / dead ringer for love / Dark lady / Gypsies, tramps and thieves / I got you babe
CD _____ GED 24439
Geffen / Nov '92 / BMG.

CHER/FOXY LADY
Way of love / Gypsies, tramps and thieves / He'll never know / Fire and rain / When you find out where you're goin' let me know / He ain't heavy, he's my brother / I hate to sleep alone / I'm in the middle / Touch and go / One honest man / Living in a house divided / It might as well stay Monday (from now on) / Song for you / Down down down / Don't try to close a rose / First time / Let me down easy / If I knew then / Don't hide your love / Never been to Spain
CD _____ MCLD 19208
MCA / Jul '93 / BMG.

GYPSYS, TRAMPS & THIEVES
CD _____ MPG 74017
Movieplay Gold / May '93 / Target/BMG.

HALF BREED/DARK LADY
My love / Two people clinging to a thread / Half breed / Greatest song I ever heard / How can you mend a broken heart / Carousel man / David's song / Melody / Long and winding road / God-forsaken day / Chastity's sun / Train of thought / I saw a man and he danced with his wife / Make the man love me / Just what I've been lookin' for / Dark lady / Miss subway of 1952 / Dixie girl / Rescue me / What'll I do / Apples don't fall far from the tree
CD _____ MCLD 19209
MCA / Oct '95 / BMG.

HEART OF STONE
If I could turn back time / Just like Jesse James / You wouldn't know love / Heart of stone / Still in love with you / Love on a rooftop / Emotional fire / All because of you / Does anybody really fall in love anymore / Starting over / Kiss to kiss / After all
CD _____ GEFD 24239
Geffen / Jan '91 / BMG.

IT'S A MAN'S WORLD
CD _____ 0630126702
WEA / Nov '95 / Warner Music.

LOVE HURTS
Save up all your tears / Love hurts / Love and understanding / Fires of Eden / I'll never stop loving you / One small step / World without heroes / Could've been love / When love calls your name / When lovers become strangers / Who you gonna believe / Shoop shoop song (it's in his kiss)
CD _____ GFLD 19266
Geffen / Feb '95 / BMG.

OUTRAGEOUS
Prisoner / Holdin' out for love / Shoppin' / Boys and girls / Mirror image / Hell on wheels / Holy smoke / Outrageous
CD _____ CDTB 131
Thunderbolt / Jun '91 / Magnum Music Group.

TAKE ME HOME/PRISONER
Take me home / Wasn't it good / Say the word / Happy was the day we met / Git down / Love and pain / Let this be a lesson to you / It's too late to love me now / My song (too far gone) / Prisoner / Holdin' out for love / Shoppin' / Boys and girls / Mirror image / Hell on wheels / Holy smoke / Outrageous
CD _____ 5500382
Spectrum/Karussell / May '93 / PolyGram / THE.

Cherish The Ladies

BACK DOOR, THE
Character's Polka/The Warlock/The Volunteer/The Donegal Trav / Back door / Redican's/Sean Ryan's/Take the bull by the horns / Galway Hornpipe/Dessie O'Connor/Mother reel / Coal Quay market/Happy days/Rabbit in the field / Maire Mhor / If ever you were mine / Paddy O'Brien's/Toss the feathers/Jenny Dang the weaver / My own native land / Pepin Arsenault/The Shepherd's daughter/A bunch in the dark / Three weeks we were wed / Jessica's polka / Tear the Calico/I have no money / Carrigdhoun / Redican's mother / Humours of Westport/The morning dew/The glass of beer/Yougha
CD _____ GLCD 1119
Green Linnet / Nov '92 / Roots / CM / Direct / ADA.

IRISH WOMEN MUSICIANS IN AMERICA
CD _____ SHCD 79053
Shanachie / Mar '95 / Koch / ADA / Greensleeves.

OUT & ABOUT
Old favourite/Flogging reel/Leave my way/ The Kerryman / Spoon river / Ladies of Carrick/Kinnegad slashers/Old man Dillon / Declan's waltz/Waltz Duhamel / Cameronian set (M'Inntinn Raoir/Duke of gordon/The Cameronian/Lady of the house) / Inisheer / O'Keefe's/Shepherd's   lamb/Johnny O'Leary / Roisin dubh / Le voyage de Cacmouret/House of Hamill / Cat rambles to the child's saucepan/Maire O'Keefe/Harry Brad / Missing piece / Out and about set (Wandering minstrel/Fred Rice's polkas/Cabin hunter/Out and about)
CD _____ GLCD 1134
Green Linnet / Oct '93 / Roots / CM / Direct / ADA.

Cherry Blades

IN-DEPENDANCE
CD _____ ILLUSION 028CD
Imaginary / Apr '91 / Vital.

Cherry, Don

DONA NOSTRA
In memoriam / Fort cherry / Arrows / M'bizo / Race face / Prayer / What reason could O give / Vienna / Ahaye-da
CD _____ 5217272
ECM / Apr '94 / New Note.

MU (THE COMPLETE SESSION)
Brilliant action / Amejelo / Total vibrations / Sun of the east / Terrestrial beings / Mystics of my sound / Dollar brand / Spontaneous composing / Exert / Man on the moon / Bamboo night / Teo-teo can / Smiling faces / Going places / Psycho drama / Theme albert heath / Theme dollar brand / Babyrest / Time for
CD _____ CDAFF 774
Affinity / Jun '93 / Charly / Cadillac / Jazz Music.

SYMPHONY FOR IMPROVISERS
CD _____ CDP 8289762
Blue Note / Sep '94 / EMI.

Cherry, Ed

FIRST TAKE
CD _____ 519942-2
Groovin' High / Jun '94 / PolyGram.

Cherry, Neneh

HOMEBREW
Sassy / Money love / Move with me / I ain't gone under yet / Twisted / Buddy X / Somedays / Trout / Peace in mind / Red paint
CD _____ CIRCD 25
Circa / Oct '92 / EMI.

RAW LIKE SUSHI
Buffalo stance / Manchild / Kisses on the wind / Inna city mamma / Next generation / Love ghetto / Heart / Phoney ladies / Outre risque locomotive / So here I come / My bitch (CD only) / Heart (it's a demo) (CD only) / Buffalo stance (sukka mix) (CD only) / Manchild (Mix) (CD only)
CD _____ CIRCD 8
Circa / Apr '92 / EMI.

Cherry People

CHERRY PEOPLE, THE
And suddenly / Girl on the subway / On to something new / Imagination / Mr. Hyde / Do something to me / Ask the children / I'm the one who loves you / Don't hang me up girl / Light of love
CD _____ NEMCD 723
Sequel / May '95 / BMG.

Cherub

SARC ART
CD _____ MASSCD 045
Massacre / Jan '95 / Plastic Head.

Cherubs

HEROIN MAN
CD _____ TR 24CD
Trance / Jun '94 / SRD.

Chesapeake

FULL SAIL
CD _____ SHCD 3941
Sugarhill / Dec '95 / Roots / CM / ADA / Direct.

RISING TIDE
CD _____ SH 3827CD
Sugarhill / May '95 / Roots / CM / ADA / Direct.

Chesapeake Minstrels

CREOLE BELLES
Plantation medley / Jeanie with the light brown hair / Some folks / Creole medley / Pasquinade / Gentle Annie / Dixie's land / Hiawatha / Bethena / Creole belles / Maple leaf rag / My old Kentucky home / Waiting for the Robert E. Lee
CD _____ CDH 88009
Helios / May '88 / Select.

Chescoe, Laurie

LAURIE CHESCOE'S GOOD TIME JAZZ
I wanna girl / Dans les rues D'Antibes / Is you is or is you ain't my baby / My blue heaven / Limehouse blues / I want a little girl / Bloodshot eyes
CD _____ JCD 002
Jazzology / Oct '90 / Swift / Jazz Music.

Cheshire Regiment

ROAD TO VITEZ, THE
Royal salute / Star Trek / Raging Bull / Xylophobia / High on a hill / Assembly march / Cheshire Regiment troop / Regimental march sequence / Gershwin / Post horn galop / Who's sorry now / Road to Vitez / West Side Story / Best years of our lives / Highland Cathedral / Ode to joy and last post
CD _____ MMCD 432
Music Masters / Nov '95 / Target/BMG.

Chesky, David

TANGOS AND DANCES
CD _____ JD 72
Chesky / Aug '92 / Complete/Pinnacle.

Chesnutt, Vic

DRUNK
Sleeping man / Bourgeois and biblical / One of many / When I ran off and left her /

Dodge / Gluefoot / Drunk / Naughty fatalist / Super Tuesday / Kick my ass
CD _____ TXH 022-2
Texas Hotel / Mar '94 / Pinnacle.

IS THE ACTOR HAPPY
CD _____ TXH 0232
Texas Hotel / Mar '95 / Pinnacle.

LITTLE
Isadora Duncan / Danny Carlisle / Giupetto / Bakersfield / Mr. Riely / Rabbit box / Speed racer / Soft Picasso / Independence Day / Stevie Smith
CD _____ TXH 0202
Texas Hotel / Jan '95 / Pinnacle.

SAMPLER
CD _____ TXHO 213
Texas Hotel / Jul '94 / Pinnacle.

WEST OF ROME
Latent blatant / Withering away / Sponge / Where were you / Lucinda Williams / Florida / Stupid pre-occupation / Panic / Miss Mary / Steve Willougby / West of Rome / Big huge valley / Soggy tongues / Fuge
CD _____ TXH 0212
Texas Hotel / Mar '94 / Pinnacle.

Chester, Bob

BOB CHESTER & HIS ORCHESTRA 1940-41
CD _____ CCD 44
Circle / Jan '94 / Jazz Music / Swift / Wellard.

Chesterfields

KETTLE
Nose out of joint / Ask Johnny Dee / Two girls and a treehouse / Shame about the rain / Everything a boy could ever need / Kiss me stupid / Thumb / Storm Nelson / Holiday hymn / Oh Mr. Wilson / Boy who sold his suitcase / Completely and utterly
CD _____ ASKCD 030
Vinyl Japan / Sep '93 / Vital.

Chestnut, Mark

ALMOST GOODBYE
It sure is Monday / Woman, sensuous woman / Almost goodbye / I just wanted you to know / April's fools / Texas is bigger than it used to be / My heart's too broke (To pay attention) / Vickie Vance gotta dance / Till a better memory comes along / Will
CD _____ MCAD 10851
MCA / Mar '94 / BMG.

Chevalier, Maurice

CHARMER, THE
Paris sera toujours Paris / You took the words right out of my mouth / Appelez ca comme vous voulez / Hello beautiful / Ma pomme / Walkin' my baby back home / No-tre espoir / Oh, come on, be sociable / Mimi / On top of the world alone / Toi et moi / Mama Inez / Nouveau bonheur / Sweepin' the clouds away / La chanson du macon / March de menilmontant
CD _____ HADCD 158
Javelin / May '94 / THE / Henry Hadaway Organisation.

ENCORE MAURICE
Hello beautiful / Up on top of a rainbow (sweepin' the clouds away) / Ca m'est egal / On top of the world alone / Mais ou est ma Zou-Zou / It's a great life / Mama Inez / Toi et moi / Savez-vous / Bon soir / Goodnight Cherie / Paris je t'aime d'amour / Walkin' my baby back home / Mon coeur / Nobody's using it now / Vous etes mon nouveau bonheur / Right now / Les ananas / O come on be sociable / Lovin' in the moonlight / Paris stay the same / You brought a new kind of love to me / Mon cocktail d'amour / Dites moi ma mere
CD _____ CD AJA 5016
Living Era / Feb '87 / Koch.

IMMORTAL MAURICE CHEVALIER, THE
CD _____ CD 118
Timeless Treasures / May '95 / THE.

ON TOP OF THE WORLD
Valentine / It's a habit of mine / Wait till you see Ma cherie / On top of the world, alone / Sweepin' the clouds away / All I want is just one girl / mama Inez / Toi et moi / You brought a new kind of love / Living in the sunlight / Paris stay the same / My love parade / Dites moi ma mere / Quand on est tout seul / Walkin' my baby back home / Oh, come on, be sociable / You took the words right out of my mouth / Hello beautiful / Mimi / Ma pomme / Ah Si vous connaissiez ma poule / Singing a happy song / Rhythm of the rain
CD _____ PASTCD 9711
Flapper / '90 / Pinnacle.

PARIS JE T'AIME
CD _____ RMB 75023
Remember / Nov '93 / Total/BMG.

Chi-Lites

BEST OF THE CHI-LITES
Give it away / Let me be the man my daddy was / Twenty four hours of sadness / I like

your lovin' (Do you like mine) / Are you my woman (tell me so) / For god's sake give more power to the people / Have you seen her / Oh girl / Coldest day of my life / We need order / Letter to myself / Stoned out of my mind / I found sunshine / Homely girl / Too good to be forgotten / There will never be any peace (until God is seated at the... / Toby / It's time for love / You don't have to go

CD _____ CDKEN 911
Kent / Jun '87 / Pinnacle.

BEST OF THE HITS, THE
Homely girl / Toby / For god's sake give more power to the people / I want to pay you back (For loving me) / Too good to be forgotten / Twenty four hours of sadness / Lonely man / Coldest day of my life / You don't have to go / There will never be any peace (Until God is seated at the co / I found sunshine / It's time for love / Give it away / Oh girl / Stoned out of my mind / Have you seen her / Letter to myself / Let me be the man my Daddy was / We are neighbours
CD _____ CPCD 8051
Charly / Mar '95 / Charly / THE / Cadillac.

GREATEST HITS
CD _____ KWEST 5402
Disky / Mar '93 / THE / BMG / Discovery / Pinnacle.

HAVE YOU SEEN HER
CD _____ PWKS 4240
Carlton Home Entertainment / Feb '95 / Carlton Home Entertainment.

JUST SAY YOU LOVE ME
Happy music / Solid love affair / Just you and I tonite / Just say you love me / Inner city blues / There's a change / Eternity / Only you
CD _____ CDICH 1057
Ichiban / Mar '94 / Koch.

SWEET SOUL MUSIC
Have you seen her / Heavenly body / Strung out / Round and round / Give me a dream / Super mad / All I wanna do is make love to you / Love shock / Me and you / Tell me where it hurts / Oh girl / Get down with me / Hot on a thing (called love) / Never speak to a stranger / Whole lot of good loving / Try my side of love
CD _____ CPCD 8019
Charly / Feb '94 / Charly / THE / Cadillac.

VERY BEST OF THE CHI-LITES, THE
Have you seen her / For god's sake give more power to the people / Oh girl / Coldest day of my life / Homely girl / Are you my woman (tell me so) / Let me be the man my daddy was / There will never be any peace (until god is se / I found sunshine / Too good to be forgotten / It's time for love / You don't have to go / I like your lovin' / Stoned out of my mind / Give it away / Letter to myself
CD _____ MCCD 029
Music Club / May '91 / Disc / THE / CM.

Chiarelli, Rita

JUST GETTING STARTED
CD _____ HYCD 200151
Hypertension / Jul '95 / Total/BMG / Direct / ADA.

ROAD ROCKET
CD _____ HYCD 200137
Hypertension / Mar '95 / Total/BMG / Direct / ADA.

Chiasson, Warren

GOOD VIBES FOR KURT WEILL
CD _____ ACD 236
Audiophile / Jun '93 / Jazz Music / Swift.

Chic

BELIEVER
Believer / You are beautiful / Party everybody / Give me the lovin' / In love with music / You got some love for me / Take a closer look / Show me your light
CD _____ 7567801072
Atlantic / Jan '96 / Warner Music.

BEST OF CHIC VOL.2, THE
Rebels are we / What about me / Twenty six / Will you cry (when you hear this song) / Stage fright / Real people / Hangin' / Give me the lovin' / At last I am free / Just out of reach / When you love someone / Your love is cancelled / Flash back / You can't do it alone / Tavern on the green
CD _____ 812271086-2
Atlantic / Mar '93 / Warner Music.

C'EST CHIC
Le freak / Chic cheer / I want your love / Happy man / Dance, dance, dance / Savoir faire / At last I am free / Sometimes you win / Funny bone / Everybody dance
CD _____ 7567815522
Atlantic / Feb '93 / Warner Music.

CHIC
Dance, dance, dance / Sao Paulo / You can get by / Everybody dance / Est-ce que c'est chic / Falling in love with you / Strike up the band

CD _____ 7567804072
Atlantic / Feb '92 / Warner Music.

CHIC-ISM
Chic mystique / Your love / Jus' a groove / Something you can feel / One and only one / Doin' that thing to me / Chicism / In it to win it / My love's for real / Take my love / High / M.M.F.T.C.F. / Chic mystique (reprise)
CD _____ 7599263942
Atlantic / Feb '95 / Warner Music.

MEGACHIC (The Best Of Chic Vol. 1)
Megachic (medley) / Chic cheer / My feet keep dancing / Good times / I want your love / Everybody dance / Le freak / Dance, dance, dance
CD _____ 2292417502
Atlantic / Aug '90 / Warner Music.

REAL PEOPLE
Real people / Rebels are we / You can't do it alone / Chip off the old block / I got protection / Open up / I loved you more / Twenty six
CD _____ 7567804202
Atlantic / Jan '96 / Warner Music.

RISQUE
Good times / Warm summer night / My feet keep dancing / My forbidden lover / Can't stand to love you / Will you cry (when you hear this song) / What about me
CD _____ 7567804062
Atlantic / Feb '91 / Warner Music.

TAKE IT OFF
Flashback / Take it off / Just out of reach / Telling lies / Stage fright / So fine / Baby doll / Your love is cancelled / Play Ray / Would you be my baby
CD _____ 7567804212
Atlantic / Jan '96 / Warner Music.

TONGUE IN CHIC
Hangin' / I feel your love comin' on / When you love someone / Chic / Hey fool / Sharing love / City lights
CD _____ 7567800312
Atlantic / Jun '96 / Warner Music.

Chicago

25 OR 6 TO 4
CD _____ CDSGP 0126
Prestige / Oct '94 / Total/BMG.

BEGINNINGS
25 or 6 to 4 / Beginnings / Does anybody really know what time it is / Purple song / Questions / I'm a man / Liberation
CD _____ CDCD 1034
Charly / Mar '93 / Charly / THE / Cadillac.

CHICAGO 14
Manipulation / Upon arrival / Song for you / Where did the lovin' go / Birthday boy / Overnight cafe / I'd rather be rich / American dream
CD _____ 982834 2
Carlton Home Entertainment / Oct '92 / Carlton Home Entertainment.

CHICAGO 17
Stay the night / We can stop the hurtin' / Hard habit to break / Only you / Remember the feeling / Along comes a woman / You're the inspiration / Please hold on / Prima donna / Once in a lifetime
CD _____ 925060 2
WEA / Jul '84 / Warner Music.

CHICAGO 18
Niagra falls / Forever / If she would have been faithful / 25 or 6 to 4 / Will you still love me / Over and over / It's alright / Nothin's gonna stop us now / I believe / One more day
CD _____ 9255092
WEA / Oct '86 / Warner Music.

CHICAGO 5
Prelude to Aire / Aire / Devil's sweet / Italian from New York / Hanky panky / Lifesaver / Happy man / (I've been) searchin' so long / Mongonucleosis / Song of the evergreens / Byblos / Wishing you were here / Call on me / Woman don't want to love me / Skinny boy
CD _____ 983301 2
Pickwick/Sony Collector's Choice / Apr '92 / Carlton Home Entertainment / Pinnacle / Sony.

CHICAGO TRANSIT AUTHORITY, THE (Chicago Transit Authority)
Does anybody really know what time it is / Beginnings / Questions 67 and 68 / Listen / Poem 58 / Free form guitar / South California purples / I'm a man / Prologue, August 29 / Someday / Liberation / Introduction
CD _____ 474788 2
Columbia / Nov '94 / Sony.

GREATEST HITS: CHICAGO
25 or 6 to 4 / Does anybody really know what time it is / Colour my world / Just you 'n' me / Saturday in the park / Never been in love before / Feeling stronger every day / I'm a man / Make me smile / Wishing you were here / Call on me / I've been searchin' so long / Beginnings
CD _____ CD 32535
Columbia / Mar '91 / Sony.

GROUP PORTRAIT
CD Set _____ 4692092
Legacy / May '94 / Sony.

HEART OF CHICAGO, THE
If you leave me now / Baby what a big surprise / Take me back to Chicago / Hard to say I'm sorry / Love me tomorrow / Hard habit to break / You're the inspiration / Along comes a woman / Remember the feeling / If she would have been faithful / What kind of man would I be / Look away / Where did the loving go / Only you / Will you still love me
CD _____ WX 328CD
WEA / Feb '94 / Warner Music.

HOT STREETS
CD _____ 982942-2
Pickwick/Sony Collector's Choice / Mar '94 / Carlton Home Entertainment / Pinnacle / Sony.

IN CONCERT
Beginnings / Purples / I'm a man / Questions 67 and 68 / Does anybody really know what time it is / 25 or 6 to 4 / Liberation
CD _____ HADCD 172
Javelin / May '94 / THE / Henry Hadaway Organisation.

LEGENDS IN MUSIC - CHICAGO
CD _____ LECD 075
Wisepack / Jul '94 / THE / Conifer.

LIVE IN TORONTO
Beginnings / Purples / 25 or 6 to 4 / Does anybody really know what time it is / I'm a man / Questions 67 and 68 / Liberation
CD _____ CDTB 103
Thunderbolt / Jul '95 / Magnum Music Group.

NIGHT AND DAY
Moonlight serenade / Night and day / Chicago / Blues in the night / In the mood / Caravan / Take the 'A' train / String of pearls / Don't get around much anymore / Sophisticated lady / Goody goody / Dream a little dream
CD _____ 74321267672
Giant / Jun '95 / BMG.

Chicago All Stars

WHEN I LOST MY BABY
CD _____ CM 10003
Magnum Music / Oct '92 / Magnum Music Group.

Chicago Beau

CHICAGO BEAU & FRIENDS
CD _____ GBW 009
GBW / Feb '94 / Harmonia Mundi.

MY ANCESTORS
CD _____ GBW 004
GBW / Mar '92 / Harmonia Mundi.

Chicago String Band

CHICAGO STRING BAND
CD _____ TCD 5006
Testament / Oct '94 / Complete/Pinnacle / ADA / Koch.

Chichester Cathedral...

CELEBRATION OF CHRISTMAS (Chichester Cathedral Choir)
Joy to the world / Virgin Mary / Gift carol / How far is it to Bethlehem / Sleigh ride / Child is born / Make we mery on this fent / Yuletide souffle / Whistle while you work / Deck the halls with boughs of holly / Good King Wenceslas / White Christmas / Ding dong merrily on high / Our joyfulst feast / Love came down at christmas / I come for the highest heaven / Troika from 'Lieutenant Kije' / Joseph dearest / Rise up shepherd and follow
CD _____ BNA 5027
Bandleader / '88 / Conifer.

Chicken Chest

ACTION PACKED
CD _____ RE 174CD
Reach Out International / Nov '94 / Jetstar.

Chickenpox

DINNER DANCE AND LATE NIGHT MUSIC
CD _____ BHR 025CD
Burning Heart / Jul '95 / Plastic Head.

Chicory Tip

CHICORY TIP
CD _____ 12377
Laserlight / May '95 / Target/BMG.

Chief Groovy Loo

GOT 'EM RUNNING SCARED
CD _____ WRA 8116CD
Wrap / Jan '94 / Koch.

Chiefs Of Relief

CHIEFS OF RELIEF
CD _____ RRCD 122
Receiver / Jan '90 / Grapevine.

Chieftains

ANOTHER COUNTRY
Wabash cannonball / Morning dew/Father Kelly's reels / I can't stop loving you / Heartbreak hotel / Heartbreak hotel/Cliffs of Moher (jig) / Cotton eyed Joe / Nobody's darlin' but mine / Goodnight Irene
CD _____ 09026609392
RCA / Nov '92 / BMG.

BEST OF THE CHIEFTAINS
Up against the Buachalawns / Boil the breakfast early / Friel's kitchen / No.6 the Coombe / O'Sullivan's march / Sea image / Speic seoigheach / Dogs among the bushes / Job of journeywork / Oh the breeches full of stitches / Chase around the windmill / Toss the feathers / Ballinasloe Fair / Cailleach an airgid / Cuil addha slide / Pretty girl / Wind that shakes the barley / Reel with the Beryle
CD _____ 4716662
Columbia / May '92 / Sony.

BOIL THE BREAKFAST EARLY
Boil the breakfast early / Mrs. Judge / March: Oscar and Malvina / When a man's in love / Bealach an doirin / Ag taisteal na blarnan / Carolan's welcome / Up against the buachalawns / Gol na mban san ar / Chase around the windmill toss the feathers / Bailinasloe Fair / Cailleach an Airgid / Cuil addha slide / Pretty girl
CD _____ 4803662
Columbia / Apr '95 / Sony.

CHIEFTAINS LIVE
Morning dew / George Brabazon / Kerry slides / Carolcfergus / Carolan's concerto / Foxhunt / Round the house and mind the dresser / Caitlin trial / For the sakes of old decency / Carolan's farewell to music / Banish misfortune / Tarbolton/The pinch of snuff / Star of munster/Flogging reel / Limerick's lamentation / O'Neill's march / Ril mhor
CD _____ CC 21CD
Claddagh / Apr '89 / ADA / Direct.

CHIEFTAINS, VOL 1
Se fath mo Bhuartha / Lark on the Strand / An fhallaingin mhuimhneagh / Trim the velvet / An combra Donn/Murphy's hornpipe / Cailin na Gruaige Doinne / Comb your hair or curl it/Boys of Ballisodare / Musical priest/Queen of May / Walls of Liscarroll jig / Dhruimfhionn donn dilis / Connemara stocking/Limestone rock/Dan Breen's reel / Casadh an tSugain / Boy in the Gap / St. Mary's / Church Street polka / Garrett Barry/The battering ram / Kitty goes milking/Rakish Paddy
CD _____ CC 2CD
Claddagh / Nov '90 / ADA / Direct.

CHIEFTAINS, VOL 10
Christmas eve / Salut a la Compagnie / My love is in America / Manx music / Master Crowley's reels / Pride of Pimlico / An Faire / Turtle dove / Sir Arthur Shaen/Madam Cole / Garech's wedding / Cotton eyed Joe
CD _____ CC 33CD
Claddagh / Nov '90 / ADA / Direct.

CHIEFTAINS, VOL 2
Banish misfortune/Gillian's apples / Planxty George Brabazon / Bean an fhir rua / O'Farrell's welcome to Limerick / An p018 Fionn/Mountain top / Foxhunt / An mhaighdean mhara / Tie the bonnet/O'Deurila's / Pigtown/Tie the ribbons/Bag of potatoes / Humours of whiskey/Hardiman the fiddler / Donald Og / Brian Boru's march / Sweeney's polka/Denis Murphy's polka / Scartagien polka
CD _____ CC 7CD
Claddagh / Aug '92 / ADA / Direct.

CHIEFTAINS, VOL 3
Strike the gay harp / Lord Mayo / Lady on the island / Sailor on the rock / Sonny's mazurka / Tommy Hunt's jig / Eibi gheal chiuin ni chearbhaill / Defahunty's hornpipe / Hunter's purse / March of the King of Laois / Carolan's concerto / Tom Billy's / Road to Lisdoonvarna / Merry sisters / An ghaoth aneas / Lord Inchiquin / Trip to Sligo / An raibh tu ag an Gcarraig / John Kelly's / Merrily kiss the Quaker / Dennis Murphy's
CD _____ CC 10CD
Claddagh / Jan '93 / ADA / Direct.

CHIEFTAINS, VOL 4
Drowsy Maggie / Morgan Magan / Tip of the whistle / Bucks of Oranmore / Battle of Aughrium / Morning dew / Carrickfergus / Hewlett / Cherish the ladies / Lord Mayo / Mna ban / Star above the garter / Weavers
CD _____ CC 14CD
Claddagh / Oct '88 / ADA / Direct.

CHIEFTAINS, VOL 5
Timpan reel / Tabhair dom do lamh / Three Kerry polkas / Ceol Bhriotanach / Churchles knock on the door / Robber's glen / An ghe agus an gra geal / Humours of Carolan / Sambradh Sambradh (Summertime Summertime) / Kerry slides

CHIEFTAINS

CD _____ CC 16 CD
Claddagh / '88 / ADA / Direct.

CHIEFTAINS, VOL 6
Chattering magpie / First Tuesday of Autumn/Green grow the rushes O / Bonaparte's retreat / Away with ye / Caledonia / Princess Royal/Blind Mary/John Drury / Rights of man / Round the house and mind the dresser
CD _____ CC 20CD
Claddagh / Nov '90 / ADA / Direct.

CHIEFTAINS, VOL 7
Away we go again / Dochas / Hedigan's fancy / John O'Connor / Friel's kitchen / No. 6 The Coombe / O'Sullivan's march / Ace and deuce of pipering / Fairies / Lamentation and dance / Oh the breeches full of stitches
CD _____ 9826572
Pickwick/Sony Collector's Choice / Nov '91 / Carlton Home Entertainment / Pinnacle / Sony.

CHIEFTAINS, VOL 8
Session / Dr. John Hart / Sean sa cheo / Fairies' hornpipe / Sea image / If I had Maggie in the wood / An speic seogheach / Dogs among the bushes / Miss Hamilton the job of journeywork / Wind that shakes the barley / Reel with the Beryle
CD _____ CC 29CD
Claddagh / Dec '93 / ADA / Direct.

CHIEFTAINS, VOL 9
Boil the breakfast early / Mrs. Judge / March: Oscar and Malvina / When a man's in love / Path through the wood / Travelling through Blarney / Carolan's welcome / Up against the Buachalawns / Gol na mBan san Ar / Chase around the windmill
CD _____ CC 30CD
Claddagh / '88 / ADA / Direct.

GREATEST HITS
Millenium celtic suite / Wexford carol / Iron man / Stray away child / Here's a health to the company / Coolin' medley / Boffyflow and Spike / O'Mahoney's frolics / Dan tros fisel / Heulliadenn tonniou breizh-izel
CD _____ 74321339452
Camden / Jan '96 / BMG.

IRISH EVENING, AN
CD _____ RD 60916
RCA / Jun '92 / BMG.

LIVE IN CHINA
Full of joy / In a suzhow garden / If I had Maggie in the wood / Reason for my sorrow / Chieftains in China / Planxty irwin / Off the great wall / Tribute to O'Carolan / Wind from the south / China to Hong kong
CD _____ CC 42CD
Claddagh / Aug '85 / ADA / Direct.

LONG BLACK VEIL, THE
Mo ghile mear / Long black veil / Foggy dew / Have I told you lately that I love you / Changing your demeanor / Lily of the west / Coast of Malabar / Dunmore lassies / Ferny Hill / Tennessee waltz / Tennessee mazurka / Rocky road to Dublin
CD _____ 74321251672
RCA / Jan '95 / BMG.

MAGIC OF THE CHIEFTAINS
O'Mahoney's frolics / Coolin' medley / Wexford carol / Marches / Boffyflow and Spike / Celtic wedding / Here's a health to the company / Strayaway child / Iron man / Millennium celtic suite / Dans tro fisel / Heuliadenn tonniou breizh-izel
CD _____ MCCD 048
Music Club / Jan '92 / Disc / THE / CM.

Chiffons

ONE FINE DAY
CD _____ RMB 75071
Remember / Apr '94 / Total/BMG.

Child, Jane

HERE NOT THERE
Mona Lisa smiles / Do whatcha do / Monument / All I do / Sshhh / Perfect love / I do not feel as good as you / Heavy smile / Calling / Step out of time / Sarasvati / Here not there
CD _____ 9362452962
Warner Bros. / Sep '93 / Warner Music.

Childish, Billy

AT THE BRIDGE (Childish, Billy & The Singing Loins)
CD _____ DAM 22CD
Damaged Goods / Apr '94 / SRD.

CAPTAIN CALYPSO'S HOODOO PARTY/LIVE IN THE NETHERLANDS (Childish, Billy & The Black Hands)
CD _____ SCRAG 3UP
Hangman's Daughter / Sep '94 / SRD.

Children

EVERY SINGLE DAY
CD _____ SKY 72015
Sky / Sep '94 / Koch.

Children Of Dub

SILENT POOL
CD _____ BACCYCD 002
Diversity / Oct '95 / 3MV / Vital.

Children Of Judah

WAITING BY THE GATES OF EDEN
CD _____ TRIBE 001CD
Wall Of Sound / Jun '95 / Disc / Soul Trader.

Children Of Selma

WHO WILL SPEAK FOR THE CHILDREN?
CD _____ CD 8008
Rounder / '88 / CM / Direct / ADA / Cadillac.

Children Of The Bong

SIRIUS SOUNDS
Polyphase / Ionosperic state / Interface reality / Veil / Underwater (Dub) / Life of plant earth / Squigglasonica / Visitor
CD _____ BARKCD 012
Planet Dog / Jul '95 / 3MV / Vital.

Children On Stun

TORNIQUETS OF LOVE DESIRE
CD _____ CLEO 72082
Cleopatra / Aug '94 / Disc.

Childs Brothers

WELSH WIZARDS (Childs Brothers & The Tredegar Town Band)
CD _____ DOYCD 022
Doyen / May '93 / Conifer.

Childs, Billy

HIS APRIL TOUCH
Where it's at / His April touch / Four by five / Miles to go before I sleep / New world disorder / Memory and desire / Rapid transit / Hand picked rose of a fading dream
CD _____ WD 0131
Windham Hill / May '91 / Pinnacle / BMG / ADA.

I'VE KNOWN RIVERS
I've known rivers / I've known rivers (part 2) / Starry night / Lament / Way of the new world / This moment / Realism / Somewhere I have never travelled / Siren serenade
CD _____ GRP 00142
GRP / Feb '95 / BMG / New Note.

PORTRAIT OF A PLAYER
It's you or no one / End of innocence / Flanagan / Never let me go / Satellite / Island / Bolivia / Easy living / 34 Skidoo / Darn that dream
CD _____ 0193 10144-23
Windham Hill Jazz / Mar '93 / New Note.

TAKE FOR EXAMPLE THIS
CD _____ WD 0113
Windham Hill Jazz / Mar '92 / New Note.

TWILIGHT IS UPON US
CD _____ WD 0118
Windham Hill Jazz / Mar '92 / New Note.

Childs, Toni

HOUSE OF HOPE
CD _____ 3971492
A&M / Aug '91 / PolyGram.

UNION
Don't walk away / Walk and talk like angels / Stop you're fussin' / Dreamer / Let the rain come down / Zimbabwe / Hush / Tin drum / Where's the ocean
CD _____ 3951752
A&M / Apr '95 / PolyGram.

Chilli Willi

BONGOS OVER BALHAM (Chilli Willi & Red Hot Peppers)
CD _____ CRESTCD 007
Mooncrest / Apr '91 / Direct / ADA.

Chills

KALEIDOSCOPE WORLD
Kaleidoscope world / Satin doll / Frantic drift / Rolling moon / Bite / Flame thrower / Pink frost / Purple girl / This is the way / Never never go / Don't even know her name / Bee bah bee bah bee boe / Whole weird world / Dream by dream / Doledrums (CD only) / Hidden bay (CD only) / I love my leather jacket / Great escape
CD _____ FNE 013CD
Normal/Okra / Mar '94 / Direct / ADA.

SOFT BOMB
CD _____ 8283222
Slash / Nov '92 / PolyGram.

SUBMARINE BELLS
Heavenly pop hit / Tied up in chain / Oncoming day / Part past part fiction / Singing in my sleep / I soar / Dead wee / Familiarity breeds contempt / Don't be a memory / Efforece and deliquesce / Sweet times / Submarine bells

CD _____ 828 191 2
London / Mar '90 / PolyGram.

Chilton, Alex

ALEX CHILTON
CD _____ 422051
New Rose / May '94 / Direct / ADA.

CLICHES
CD _____ NR 422481
New Rose / Jan '94 / Direct / ADA.

FEUDALIST TARTS
CD _____ ROSE 68CD
New Rose / Jul '85 / Direct / ADA.

HIGH PRIEST
CD _____ 422053
New Rose / May '94 / Direct / ADA.

LIKE FLIES ON SHERBERT
Boogie shoes / My rival / Hey little child / Hook or crook / I've had it / Rock hard / Girl after girl / Waltz across Texas / Alligator man / Like flies on sherbert
CD _____ 900486
Line / Oct '94 / CM / Grapevine / ADA / Conifer / Direct.
CD _____ COOKCD 095
Cooking Vinyl / Jan '96 / Vital.

LIVE IN LONDON
CD _____ CREV 015CD
Rev-Ola / Jun '93 / 3MV / Vital.

MAN CALLED DESTRUCTION, A
CD _____ RRCD 901312
Ruf / May '95 / Pinnacle / ADA.

Chimera

LUGHNASA
CD _____ FLUTE 4CD
Beechwood / May '93 / BMG / Pinnacle.

Chimes

CHIMES
Love so tender / Heaven / True love / 1-2-3 / Underestimate / Love comes to mind / I still haven't found what I'm looking for (street mix) / Don't make me wait / Stronger together / Stay / I still haven't found what I'm looking for
CD _____ 4664812
CBS / Jun '90 / Sony.

China Beach

SIX BULLET RUSSIAN ROULETTE
CD _____ RTN 41213
Rock The Nation / Aug '95 / Plastic Head.

China Black

BORN
Searching / Stars / Almost see you (somewhere) / Born / Go your own way / Where / No surprise / Sunrise / I love life / Child o'nature
CD _____ 5237552
Wild Card / Feb '95 / PolyGram.

China Crisis

AUTOMATICALLY YOURS
CD _____ TLGCD 005
Telegraph / Sep '95 / BMG.

CHINA CRISIS COLLECTION
African and white / No more blue horizons / Christian / Tragedy and mystery / Working with fire and steel / Wishful thinking / Hanna Hanna / Black man ray / King in a catholic style / You did cut me / Arizona sky / Best kept secret / It's everything / St. Saviour square / Scream down at me (Limited edition CD set only) / Cucumber garden (CD set only) / Golden handshake for every daughter (CD set only) / Some people I know (CD set only) / Instigator (Italian Fuzzbox Version (CD set only)) / Little Italy (CD set only) / Greenacre Bay (CD set only) / No ordinary sorrow (CD set only) / Dockland (CD set only) / Forever I and I (CD set only) / Performing seals (CD set only) / Occupation (CD set only) / Watching over burning fields (CD set only) / Animalistic (Day At The Zoo Mix (CD set only))
CD _____ CDV 2613
Virgin / Sep '90 / EMI.

DIARY (A Collection)
Black man Ray / Animalistic (A Day At The Zoo Mix) / Hampton beach / Red letter day / Diary of a hollow horse / Strength of character / When the piper calls / Christian / Golden handshake for every daughter / Hanna Hanna / African and white / Here comes a raincloud / King in a catholic style / Blue sea / Tragedy and mystery / Wishful thinking
CD _____ CDVIP 109
Virgin VIP / Nov '93 / Carlton Home Entertainment / THE / EMI.

DIFFICULT SHAPES AND PASSIVE RHYTHMS (Some People Think It's Fun To Entertain)
Seven sports for all / No more blues horizons / Feel to be driven away / Some people I know to lead fantastic lives / Christian / African and white / Are we a worker / Red sails / You never see it / Temptations big blue eyes / Jean walks in fresh fields

CD _____ CDV 2243
Virgin / Jul '87 / EMI.

WARPED BY SUCCESS
CD _____ STACD 001
Stardumb / Aug '94 / BMG.

WHAT PRICE PARADISE
It's everything / Arizona sky / Safe as houses / World's apart / Hampton beach / Understudy / Best kept secret / We do the same / June bride / Days work for the days done / Trading in gold (CD only)
CD _____ CDV 2410
Virgin / Nov '86 / EMI.

WORKING WITH FIRE AND STEEL-POSSIBLE POP SONGS VOL.2
Working with fire and steel / When the piper calls / Hanna Hanna / Animals in the jungle / Here comes a raincloud / Wishful thinking / Tragedy and mystery / Papua / Gates of door to door / Soulful awakening
CD _____ CDV 2286
Virgin / Sep '84 / EMI.

China White

ADDICTION
CD _____ AGO 712
Noise/Modern Music / May '95 / Pinnacle / Plastic Head.

Chinafrica

CREATION
CD _____ CACD 01
Graylan / Jul '95 / Jetstar / Grapevine / THE.

Chippendales

CHIPPENDALES
CD _____ CDSR 035
Telstar / Nov '93 / BMG.

Chirag Penchan

BHANGRA PARTY
CD _____ DMUT 003
Multitone / Apr '88 / BMG.

DEKHO DEKHO
CD _____ DMUT 1073
Multitone / Jul '89 / BMG.

Chisholm, George

WITH MAXINE DANIELS & JOHN PETTERS BAND (Chisholm, George/ Maxine Daniels & John Petters)
Swinging down memory lane / Riverboat shuffle / Happiness is a thing called Joe / Do nothin' 'til you hear from me / I've got my love to keep me warm / Zing went the strings of my heart
CD _____ CMJCD 011
CMJ / Mar '90 / Jazz Music / Wellard.

Chittison, Herman

HERMAN CHITTISON 1933-41
CD _____ CLASSICS 690
Classic Jazz Masters / May '93 / Wellard / Jazz Music / Jazz Music.

P.S. WITH LOVE
CD _____ IAJRCCD 1006
IAJRC / Jun '94 / Jazz Music.

Chiweshe, Stella

AMBUYA/NDIZVOZVO (Chiweshe, Stella & The Earthquake)
Chachimurenga / Nehondo / Njuzu / Mugomba / Chamakuwende / Kasahwa / Chipindura / Ndinogarochema / Sarura Wako
CD _____ CDORB 029
Globestyle / May '89 / Pinnacle.

Choates, Harry

FIDDLE KING OF CAJUN SWING
CD _____ ARHCD 380
Arhoolie / Apr '95 / ADA / Direct / Cadillac.

Chocolate

SUBSTITUTE FOR SEX
CD _____ DPROMCD 15
Dirter Promotions / Aug '93 / Pinnacle.

Chocolate

HUNG, GIFTED & SLACK
CD _____ CDWOOS 8
Out Of Step / Oct '95 / Pinnacle.

Chocolate Dandies

CHOCOLATE DANDIES 1928-1940
CD _____ 157982
Jazz Archives / Jun '93 / Jazz Music / Discovery / Cadillac.

Chocolate Watch Band

44
Don't need your lovin' / No way out / It's all over now baby blue / I'm not like everybody else / Misty lane / Loose lip sync ship / Are you gonna be there (at the love in) / Gone and passes by / Sitting there standing / She

weaves a tender trap / Sweet young thing / I ain't no miracle worker / Blues theme
CD _____ CDWIK 25
Big Beat / May '90 / Pinnacle.

INNER MYSTIQUE/ONE STEP BEYOND
Voyage of the triste / In the past / Inner mystique / I'm not like everybody else / Medication / Let's go, let's go (Aka Thrill on the hill) / It's all over now baby blue / I ain't no miracle worker / Uncle Morris / How ya been / Devil's motorcycle / I ain't been no doctor / Flowers / Fireface / And she's lonely
CD _____ CDWIK 111
Big Beat / Apr '90 / Pinnacle.

NO WAY OUT...PLUS
Let's talk about girls / In the midnight hour / Come on / Dark side of the mushroom / Hot dusty road / Are you gonna be there (at the love in) / Gone and passes by / No way out / Expo 2000 / Gossamer wings / Sweet young thing / Baby blue / Misty lane / She weaves a tender trap / Milk cow blues / Don't let the sun catch you crying / Since you broke my heart / Misty lane (Remix)
CD _____ CDWIK 118
Big Beat / Jun '93 / Pinnacle.

Chodack, Walter

RAGTIME (The Best Of Scott Joplin)
CD _____ MAN 4638
Mandala / Oct '94 / Mandala / Harmonia Mundi.

Choice

GREAT SUBCONSCIOUS CLUB, THE
Me maybe / Breakfast / I smoke a lot / Walk away / Elegia / My heart / I wanna meet the man / What the hell is love / I will return to you / Ballad of Lea and Paul / Winter / Laughing as I pray
CD _____ 474949 2
Epic / Jun '94 / Sony.

Choir

CHOIR PRACTICE
I'd rather you leave me / It's cold outside / When you were with me / Don't change your mind (rehersal version) / Dream of one's life / In love's shadow (mod's demo) / I'm slippin' (Mod's demo) / Leave me be (mod's demo) / I'd rather you leave me (rehearsal version) / Treeberry / Smile / A to F / I only did it 'cause I felt so lonely / Don't change your mind / Anyway I can / Boris' lament / David Watts / These are men
CD _____ CDSC 11018
Sundazed / Apr '94 / Rollercoaster.

Choir Of York Minster

CHRISTMAS AT YORK MINSTER
CD _____ YORKCD 846
York Ambisonic / Oct '95 / Target/BMG.

Chokebore

ANYTHING NEAR WATER
CD _____ ARRCD 61004
Amphetamine Reptile / May '95 / SRD.

MOTIONLESS
CD _____ ARRCD 43/289
Amphetamine Reptile / Aug '93 / SRD.

Chop Shop

RECOVERED PIECES
Intro / Fili brustaita / Danny days / Carnival ride / Kick the ballistics / Stoop / Drop da new flavor / X-break / Dab'l do ya / Shaolin shoot out
CD _____ ME 000362
Soulciety/Bassism / Sep '95 / EWM.

Chordettes

FABULOUS CHORDETTES, THE
Lollipop / Born to be with you / Eddie my love / Wedding / Mr. Sandman / Teenage goodnight / Just between you and me / Soft sands / Zorro / No other arms, no other lips / Lay down your arms / Never on Sunday
CD _____ CDFAB 005
Ace / Sep '91 / Pinnacle / Cadillac / Complete/Pinnacle.

MAINLY ROCK'N'ROLL
True love goes on and on / Mr. Sandman / Lonely lips / Hummingbird / Wedding / Eddie my love / Born to be with you / Lay down your arms / Teenage goodbye / Echo of love / Just between you and me / Soft sands / Photograph / Baby come-a-back-a / Zorro / Love is a two way street / No other arms, no other lips / Girl's work is never done / No wheels / Lonely boy / Charlie Brown / I cried a tear / Pink shoelaces / Tall Paul / To know him is to love him / My heart stood still / For me and my gal / Broken vow / Never on Sunday / Faraway star / In the deep blue sea
CD _____ CDCHD 934
Ace / Jul '90 / Pinnacle / Cadillac / Complete/Pinnacle.

Chords

LIVE AT THE RAINBOW
Something's missing / Happy families / It's no use / Now it's gone / I'm not sure / British way of life / So far away / I'll keep on holding on / Tumbling down / Maybe tomorrow / Breaks my heart/This is what they want
CD _____ DOJOCD 178
Dojo / Jun '94 / BMG.

Chosen Gospel Singers

LIFEBOAT, THE
Before this time another year / Ananais / Don't you know the man / Come by here / Family prayer / Leaning on the Lord / 1-2-3 / Lord will make a way somewhere / It's getting late in the evening / No room at the hotel / Watch ye therefore / I'm going back with him / I've tried / Lifeboat is coming / What a wonderful sight / Don't worry 'bout me / When I get home / On the main line / Stay with Jesus / Prayer for the doomed
CD _____ CDCHD 414
Ace / Nov '93 / Pinnacle / Cadillac / Complete/Pinnacle.

Chowdhury, Subroto Roy

BAGESHREE
Raga brageshree parts 1 to 4 / Raga sindhi bhairavi part 1 to 2
CD _____ 8888212
Tiptoe / Dec '95 / New Note.

MORNING
CD _____ CDJP 1033
Jazz Point / Feb '93 / Harmonia Mundi / Cadillac.

Chris & Carla

LIFE FULL OF HOLES
CD _____ GRCD 360
Glitterhouse / Feb '95 / Direct / ADA.

SHELTER FOR AN EVENING
CD _____ SPCD 92/264
Sub Pop / Jul '93 / Disc.

Chris & Cosey

EXOTICA
CD _____ CDBIAS 069
Play It Again Sam / Oct '87 / Vital.

MUZIK FANTASTIQUE
CD _____ BIAS 221CD
Play It Again Sam / Sep '92 / Vital.

TRUST
CD _____ CDBIAS 124
Play It Again Sam / Jan '88 / Vital.

Chrissos, Theo

WHITE ROSE OF ATHENS, THE
CD _____ CNCD 5952
Disky / Jul '93 / THE / BMG / Discovery / Pinnacle.

Christ Agony

DAEMOONSETH ACT II
CD _____ CDAR 024
Fringe / Mar '95 / Plastic Head.

Christian Death

ALIVE
CD _____ FREUDCD 29
Jungle / Jul '89 / Disc.

AMEN (2CD Set)
CD Set _____ CM 77107
Century Media / Nov '96 / Plastic Head.

ANTHOLOGY OF BOOTLEGS
CD _____ NOS 1006 CD
Nostradamus / May '88 / Disc.

ASHES
CD _____ NORMAL 15CD
Normal/Okra / May '94 / Direct / ADA.

ATROCITIES
CD _____ NORMAL 18CD
Normal/Okra / May '94 / Direct / ADA.

CATASTROPHE BALLET
CD _____ CONTECD 105
Contempo / Nov '87 / Plastic Head.
CD _____ N 181CD
Normal/Okra / Jan '96 / Direct / ADA.

DEATHWISH
CD _____ NORMAL 84CD
Normal/Okra / May '94 / Direct / ADA.

DOLL'S THEATRE
CD _____ CLEO 62082
Cleopatra / Jun '94 / Disc.

INSANUS, ULTIO, MISERICORDIAQUE
CD _____ FREUDCD 48
Jungle / Jan '95 / Disc.

JESUS POINTS THE BONE
CD _____ FREUDCD 39
Jungle / Mar '92 / Disc.

ONLY THEATRE OF PAIN
Cavity - First Communion / Figurative theatre / Burnt offerings / Mysterious Iniquitatis / Dream for mother / Deathwish / Romeo's distress / Dogs / Stairs uncertain

journey / Spiritual cramp / Resurrection - Sixth Communion / Prayer / Desperate Hell / Cavity
CD _____ FCD 1007
Frontier / Aug '93 / Vital.

PART 1: ALL THE LOVE (All the Love, All the Hate)
CD _____ FREUDCD 33
Jungle / Dec '89 / Disc.

PATH OF SORROW, THE
CD _____ CLEO 39932
Cleopatra / Mar '94 / Disc.

RAGE OF ANGELS, THE
CD _____ CLEO 81252
Cleopatra / May '94 / Disc.

SCRIPTURES
CD _____ NORMAL 65
Normal/Okra / May '94 / Direct / ADA.

SEX AND DRUGS AND JESUS CHRIST
CD _____ FREUDCD 050
Jungle / Aug '92 / Disc.

SEXY DEATH GOD
CD _____ CDVEST 26
Bulletproof / Aug '94 / Pinnacle.

TALES OF INNOCENCE
CD _____ CLEO 9109-2
Cleopatra / Dec '93 / Disc.

WIND KISSED PICTURES
CD _____ NORMAL 76CD
Normal/Okra / Jan '96 / Direct / ADA.

Christian, Charlie

1939-1941 (Christian, Charlie & Benny Goodman)
CD _____ CD 56059
Jazz Roots / Mar '95 / Target/BMG.

AIRCHECKS AND PRIVATE RECORDINGS
CD _____ JZCD 379
Recording Arts / Jun '93 / THE / Disc.

CHARLIE CHRISTIAN WITH BENNY GOODMAN (Christian, Charlie & Benny Goodman)
CD _____ CD 14545
Jazz Portraits / Jan '94 / Jazz Music.

GENIUS OF THE ELECTRIC GUITAR
Rose room / Seven come eleven / Till Tom special / Gone with "what" wind / Grand slam / Six appeal / Wholly cats / Royal Garden blues / As long as I live / Benny's bugle / Breakfast feud / I found a new baby / Solo flight / Blue in B / Waiting for Benny / Airmail special
CD _____ 4606122
Sony Jazz / Jan '95 / Sony.

GENIUS OF THE ELECTRIC GUITAR
CD _____ CD 53049
Giants Of Jazz / May '90 / Target/BMG / Cadillac.

GUITAR WIZARD
CD _____ LEJAZZCD 11
Le Jazz / Jun '93 / Charly / Cadillac.

IMMORTAL, THE
CD _____ 17032
Laserlight / Jul '94 / Target/BMG.

JAZZ GUITAR VOL.2, THE
CD _____ CD 56027
Jazz Roots / Nov '94 / Target/BMG.

LIVE 1939-41 (Christian, Charlie/Benny Goodman Sextet & Orchestra)
CD _____ 3804999
Jazz Archives / Oct '92 / Jazz Music / Discovery / Cadillac.

SOLO FLIGHT (Christian, Charlie/Benny Goodman Sextet & Orchestra)
CD _____ TPZ 1017
Topaz Jazz / Feb '95 / Pinnacle / Cadillac.

SWING TO THE BOP
CD _____ NI 4020
Natasha / Feb '94 / Jazz Music / ADA / CM / Direct / Cadillac.

TOGETHER (Christian, Charlie & Lester Young)
CD _____ 3801062
Jazz Archives / Jun '92 / Jazz Music / Discovery / Cadillac.

Christian, Emma

BENEATH THE TWILIGHT
CD _____ EM 001CD
Manx Productions / Oct '94 / ADA / Direct.

Christian, Frank

FROM MY HANDS
CD _____ PM 2011
Palmetto / Nov '95 / Direct.

Christian, James

RUDE AWAKENING
CD _____ NTHEN 12
Now & Then / Sep '95 / Plastic Head.

Christian, Judie

EZPERIENCE
CD _____ DD 454
Delmark / Nov '92 / Hot Shot / ADA / CM / Direct / Cadillac.

Christian, Neil

NEIL CHRISTIAN & THE CRUSADERS 1962-1973 (Christian, Neil & The Crusaders)
Road to love / Little bit of something else / Honey hush / She's got the action / Wanna lover / She said yeah / Count down / You're all things bright and beautiful / My baby left me / I remember / Feel in the mood / What would your mamma say / I like it / All last night / One for the money / Get a load of this / Give the game away / Two at a time / Oops / Bit by bit / Bad girl / Gonna love you baby / Yakety yak / Crusading / That's nice / Dedicated follower of fashion / Let me in / Big beat in
CD _____ SEECD 342
See For Miles/C5 / Mar '92 / Pinnacle.

Christians

BEST OF THE CHRISTIANS, THE
CD _____ CIDTV 6
Island / Nov '93 / PolyGram.

CHRISTIANS, THE
Forgotten town (Theme for BBC TV series / Hooverville / Born again / Ideal world / Save a soul in every town / And that's why / Hooverville / One in a million / Sad songs
CD _____ IMCD 162
Island / Mar '93 / PolyGram.

COLOUR
Man don't cry / I found out / Greenbank Drive / All talk / Words / Community of spirit / There you go again / One more baby in black / In my hour of need
CD _____ IMCD 181
Island / Mar '94 / PolyGram.

HAPPY IN HELL
CD _____ IMCD 182
Island / Mar '94 / PolyGram.

Christianson, Denny

SUITE MINGUS (Christianson, Denny Big Band)
CD _____ JUST 15-2
Justin Time / Jun '92 / Harmonia Mundi / Cadillac.

Christie Brothers

CHRISTIE BROTHERS STOMPERS (Christie Brothers Stompers)
CD _____ SGC/MELCD 20/1
Cadillac / Jan '94 / Cadillac / Wellard.

Christie, Lou

GLORY RIVERS (Buddah Years)
Genesis and the third verse / Rake up the leaves / Johnstown kite / Canterbury road / I'm gonna make you mine / I'm gonna get married / Are you getting any sunshine / She sold me magic / Life is what you make it / I just love / Boys lazed on the veranda / Tell her / Indian lady / Glory river / Wood child / Paper song / Chuckie wagon / Campus rest / Lighthouse / Look out the window / Paint America love / Shuffle on down of Pittsburgh
CD _____ NEX CD 187
Sequel / Jul '92 / BMG.

LIGHTNING STRIKES
CD _____ RMB 75048
Remember / Nov '93 / Total/BMG.

Christie, Tony

BEST OF TONY CHRISTIE
CD _____ MCCD 185
Music Club / Nov '94 / Disc / THE / CM.

BEST OF TONY CHRISTIE, THE
CD _____ MCLD 19204
MCA / May '93 / BMG.

Christie-Tyler Cory Band

BRASS FROM THE VALLEYS
Mephistopheles / Bohemian rhapsody / Don't it make my brown eyes blue / Portrait of a city / Trittico / Triple gold / Rule Britannia / Adagio from Spartacus / Celtic suite / Miller magic
CD _____ QPRL 044D
Polyphonic / Jun '90 / Conifer.

Christlieb, Pete

CONVERSATIONS WITH WARNE (Christlieb, Pete & Warne Marsh)
CD _____ CRISS 1103
Criss Cross / Oct '95 / Cadillac / Harmonia Mundi.

CONVERSATIONS WITH WARNE, VOL. 1
CD _____ CRISS 1043CD
Criss Cross / Apr '91 / Cadillac / Harmonia Mundi.

Christ's Hospital Choir

CHRISTMAS CAROLS
Break forth, o beautious heavenly light / O come all ye faithful / Tommow shall be my dancing day / Nativity carol / Hymn to the virgin / Of the fathers heart begotten / Von himmel hoch / Maiden most gentle / Noel nouvelet / Eastern monarchs / Puer nayus in Bethlehem / God rest ye merry gentlemen / In dulci jubilo / O little town of Bethlehem / Ding dong merrily on high / Once in Royal David's city / No small wonder / Out of your sleep / Lo he comes with clouds / Descending / Hark the herlad angels sing
CD _____ 3037600012
Carlton Home Entertainment / Oct '95 / Carlton Home Entertainment.

Christy, June

DAY DREAMS
I let a song go out of my heart / If I should lose you / Day dream / Little grass skirt / Skip rope / I'll bet you do / Way you look tonight / Everything happens to me / I'll remember April / Get happy / Somewhere (if not in heaven) / Mile down the highway (there's a toll bridge) / Do it again / He can come back anytime he wants to / Body and soul / You're blase
CD _____ CDP 8320832
Capitol Jazz / Aug '95 / EMI.

IMPROMPTU (Christy, June & Lou Levy Sextet)
My shining hour / Once upon a summertime / Show me / Everything must change / Willow weep for me / I'll remember April / Trouble with hello is goodbye / Autumn serenade / Sometime ago / Angel eyes
CD _____ DSCD 836
Discovery / Jun '93 / Warner Music.

JUNE CHRISTY 1977
CD _____ STCD 4168
Storyville / Feb '90 / Jazz Music / Wellard / CM / Cadillac.

JUNE CHRISTY VOLUME 2 - THE UNCOLLECTED 1957
CD _____ HCD 235
Hindsight / Sep '94 / Target/BMG / Jazz Music.

LOVELY WAY TO SPEND AN EVENING, A
Lovely way to spend an evening / From this moment on / Let there be love / I'll take romance / Midnight sun / How high the moon / Rock me to sleep / It's a most unusual day / Willow weep for me / It don't mean a thing if it ain't got that swing / Lullaby in rhythm / That's all
CD _____ JASMCD 2528
Jasmine / May '92 / Wellard / Swift / Conifer / Cadillac / Magnum Music Group.

SPOTLIGHT ON JUNE CHRISTY
How high the moon / I remember you / Give me the simple life / Midnight sun / They can't take that away from me / Bewitched / Until the real thing comes along / Imagination / He's funny that way / Song is for you / I'll take romance / When the sun coms out / Don't get around much anymore / How long has this been going on / As long as I live / When you wish upon a star / For all we know / Goodbye
CD _____ CDP 8285352
Capitol / Jul '95 / EMI.

THROUGH THE YEARS
CD _____ HCD 260
Hindsight / Aug '95 / Target/BMG / Jazz Music.

UNCOLLECTED 1946, THE
CD _____ HCD 219
Hindsight / Jun '94 / Target/BMG / Jazz Music.

Chroma

MUSIC ON THE EDGE
Prelude to music on the edge / Fanfare for the common man / Overture / Lesson / True confessions / Twotege nou / Squids / Concierto de Aranjuez / Afterwords / Glazed / Upside downside
CD _____ R2 79475
CTI / May '92 / Sony.

Chrome

3RD FROM THE SUN
Third from the Sun / Firebomb / Future ghosts / Armageddon / Heartbeat / Off the line / Shadows of 1,000 years
CD _____ CLEO 95332
Cleopatra / Aug '95 / Disc.

BLOOD ON THE MOON/ETERNITY
CD _____ EFA 7490 CD
Dossier / Jun '89 / SRD.

CHROME SAMPLER VOLUME 1
CD _____ EFA 084612
Dossier / Jun '89 / SRD.

CHRONICLES I & II
CD _____ EFA 7499
Dossier / Jun '89 / SRD.

CLAIRAUDIENT SYNDROME, THE
CD _____ EFA 08456-2
Dossier / Jul '94 / SRD.

HALF MACHINE LIP MOVES
T.V. as eyes / Zombie warfare (can't let you down) / March of the chrome police (a cold clamey bombing) / You've been duplicated / Mondo anthem / Half machine lip moves / Abstract nympho / Turned around / Zero time / Creature eternal / Critical mass
CD _____ DCD 9009
Dossier / '85 / SRD.

HAVING A WONDERFUL TIME IN THE JUICE DOME
CD _____ EFA 084622
Dossier / Mar '95 / SRD.

INTO THE EYES OF THE ZOMBIE KINGS (Chrome & Damon Edge)
CD _____ DCD 9004
Dossier / Aug '88 / SRD.

LYON CONCERT, THE/ANOTHER WORLD
If you come around / I found out today / Our good dreams / Stranger from another world / Moon glow / Sky said / Loving lovely lover / We are connected / Saniby / As we stand here in time / March of the rubber people / Ghosts of the long forgotten future / Version two (raining milk) / Source improves / Frankenstein's party
CD _____ EFA 7709CD
Dossier / Jun '89 / SRD.

THIRD FROM THE SUN
CD _____ DCD 9012
Dossier / Mar '89 / SRD.

Chrome Cranks

CHROME CRANKS, THE
Dark room / Subway man / Driving bad / Eight track mind / No. 1 girl / Doll in a dress / Backdoor maniac / Stuck in a cave / Lo-end buzz / Outta my heart
CD _____ PCP 0162
PCP / Jan '95 / Vital.

DEAD COOL
CD _____ EFA 115902
Crypt / May '95 / SRD.

Chrome Molly

SLAP HEAD
Out of our minds / Gimme that line again / Red hot red rock / Shotgun / Loosen up / Caught with the bottle again / Sitter the children / Assinine nation / Pray with me / Now / Little voodoo magic
CD _____ CDMFN 98
Music For Nations / May '90 / Pinnacle.

Chron Gen

BEST OF CHRON GEN
CD _____ AHOY 18
Captain Oi / Nov '94 / Plastic Head.

LIVE AT THE WARDORF IN SAN FRANCISCO
CD _____ PUNXCD 3
Punx / Oct '95 / Total/BMG.

Chrysanthemums

IS THAT A FISH ON YOUR SHOULDER OR ARE YOU JUST PLEASED...
CD _____ 2/3 EGGSCD
Egg Plant / Feb '92 / Pinnacle.

LITTLE FLECKS OF FOAM AROUND BARKING EGG PLANT
CD _____ FOUR EGGS CD
Egg Plant / Jul '90 / Pinnacle.

ODYSSEY AND ORACLE
CD _____ SIX EGGS CD
Egg Plant / May '89 / Pinnacle.

Chuchuk, Raymond

LET'S DANCE
CD _____ SAV 190CD
Savoy / Jun '93 / THE / Savoy.

Chuckle Brothers

TO YOU TO ME
CD _____ DMCD 10130
ICC / Oct '95 / Total/BMG.

Chug

SASSAFRAS
CD _____ FNCD 300
Flying Nun / Nov '94 / Disc.

Chumbawamba

ANARCHY
Give the anarchist a cigarette / Timebomb / Homophobia / On being pushed / Heaven/Hell / Love me / Georgina / Doh / Blackpool rock / This years thing / Mouthful of shit / Never do what you are told / Bad dog / Enough is enough / Rage
CD _____ TPLP 46CD
One Little Indian / Apr '94 / Pinnacle.

ENGLISH REBEL SONGS 1381-1914
Cutty wren / Digger's song / Collier's march / Triumph of General Ludd / Chartist anthem / Song on the times / Smashing of the van / World turned upside down / Poverty knock / Idris strike song / Hanging on the old barbed wire

CD _____ TPLP 64CD
One Little Indian / Feb '95 / Pinnacle.

LOVE/HATE
CD _____ TPLP 66CD
One Little Indian / Oct '95 / Pinnacle.

PICTURES OF STARVING CHILDREN SELL RECORDS (& Never Mind The Ballots)
How to get your band on the television / British colonialism and the BBC / Commercial break / Unilever / More whitewashing / Interlude: Beginning to take it back / Dutiful servants and political masters / Coca-colonisation / In a nutshell invasion / Always tell the voter what the voter wants to hear / Come on baby (let's do the revolution) / Wasteland / Today's sermon / Ah-men / Mr. Heseltine meets his public / Candidates find common ground
CD _____ TPLP 63CD
One Little Indian / Feb '95 / Pinnacle.

SHHH
CD _____ 185152
Southern / Oct '94 / SRD.

SHOWBUSINESS
Never do what you are told / Rappoport / Give the anarchist a cigarette / Heaven/Hell / Hungary / Homophobia / Morality / Bad dog / Stitch that / Mouthful of shit / Nazi / Jimbomb / Slad aid
CD _____ TPLP 56CD
One Little Indian / Oct '95 / Pinnacle.

SLAP
Ulrike / Tiananmen square / Cartrouble / Chase PC'd flee attack by own dog / Ruben's has been shot / Rappoport's testament: I never gave up / Slap / That's how grateful we are / Meinhof
CD _____ TPLP 65CD
One Little Indian / Feb '95 / Pinnacle.

Church

ALMOST YESTERDAY 1981-1990
CD _____ RVCD 43
Raven / Dec '94 / Direct / ADA.

SOMETIME ANYWHERE
Day of the dead / Lost my touch / Loveblind / My little problem / Maven / Angelica / Lullaby / Eastern / Places at once / Business woman / Authority / Fly home / Dead man's dream
CD _____ 07822187272
Arista / Jun '94 / BMG.

Church Bells

CHURCH BELLS OF ENGLAND
CD _____ CDSDL 378
Saydisc / Sep '89 / Harmonia Mundi / ADA / Direct.

Church, J.

NOSTALGA FOR NOTHING
CD _____ SKIP 037CD
Broken Rekids / Nov '95 / Plastic Head.

Church Of God

IN HIM I LIVE (Church Of God & Saints Of Christ)
CD _____ LYRCD 7423
Lyrichord / Dec '94 / Roots / ADA / CM.

Church Of Raism

CHURCH OF RAISM
CD _____ CRECD 057
Creation / Dec '89 / 3MV / Vital.

Ciani, Suzanne

NEVERLAND
Neverland / Tuscany / Mosaic / Aegean wave / Summer's day / Life in the moonlight / When love dies / Adagio / Mother's song / Lumiere
CD _____ 259758
Arista / Aug '89 / BMG.

SEVEN WAVES
First wave / Birth of Venus / Second wave / Sirens / Third wave / Love in the waves / Fourth wave / Wind in the sea / Fifth wave / Water lullaby / Sixth wave / Deep in the sea / Seventh wave / Sailing away
CD _____ 259.968
Private Music / Nov '89 / BMG.

Cianide

DYING TRUTH, THE
CD _____ GC 189806
Recommended / Jul '92 / These / ReR Megacorp.

Ciccu, Bianca

GUSCH, THE (Ciccu, Bianca & Randy Brecker)
CD _____ ITM 1440 CD
ITM / Apr '90 / Tradelink / Koch.

Cicion Tropical...

CYCLONE TROPICAL (Cicion Tropical Orchestra La Colegiala)
CD _____ UCD 19108
Forlane / Jul '95 / Target/BMG.

Ciletti, Miles

LONG DAYS & MONSTER NIGHTS
CD _____ NAR 091CD
SST / Sep '94 / Plastic Head.

Cimarons

BEST OF CIMARONS
CD _____ CC2 703
Crocodisc / Nov '92 / THE / Magnum Music Group.

MAKA
CD _____ CC 2704
Crocodisc / Jun '93 / THE / Magnum Music Group.

PEOPLE SAY
CD _____ LG 21006
Lagoon / Jun '93 / Magnum Music Group / THE.

Cinderella

LONG COLD WINTER
Falling apart at the seams / Gypsy road / Last mile / Long cold winter / If you don't like it / Coming home / Fire and ice / Take me back / Bad seamstress blues / Don't know what you got (til it's gone) / Second wind
CD _____ 834 612-2
Vertigo / Jul '88 / PolyGram.

STILL CLIMBING
CD _____ 522947-2
Vertigo / Nov '94 / PolyGram.

Cinorama

GARDEN, THE GARDEN
CD _____ D 63
PSF / Aug '95 / Harmonia Mundi.

Ciotti, Roberto

ROAD 'N' RAIL
CD _____ CDSGP 039
Prestige / Jan '93 / Total/BMG.

Circle

PARIS CONCERT
Nefertitti / Song for the newborn / Duet / Lookout farm / Kalvin 73, variation - 3 / Toy room / No greater love
CD _____ 8434632
ECM / Oct '90 / New Note.

Circle Jerks

GROUP SEX
CD _____ 46002 L
Frontier / May '92 / Vital.

GROUP SEX/WILD IN THE STREET
CD _____ FCD 1002
Frontier / Aug '92 / Vital.

Circle Of Dust

CIRCLE OF DUST
CD _____ REX 460112
Rex / Nov '95 / Cadillac.

Circle X

CELESTIAL
Kyoko / Pulley / Crow's ghost / Gothic fragment / Some things don't grow back / Tell my horse / Big picture / Cabin 9 / Waxed fruit / Celestial / They come prancing
CD _____ OLE 091-2
Matador / Jul '94 / Vital.

Circus

BRISTOL STREET
Godwhat / My daughter / In limbo / Bristol Street / Cold Alice / Weekdays (1) / Weekdays (2) / Things you left (1) / Island / What can I say / Wave in the night / Bristol Street (instrumental) / Things you left (2)
CD _____ PCOM 1143
President / Oct '95 / Grapevine / Target/BMG / Jazz Music / President.

SURFACE TENSION
Relove / Sanctuary / Interview / Falling / Sometimes / Walk in the country / Swallow's tale / Interlude / Light of the morning / Reunion / I need a drink / Awake / Stationary traveller / Dream / Child's play
CD _____ PCOM 1127
President / Aug '93 / Grapevine / Target/BMG / Jazz Music / President.

Circus In Town

D'ARCY LOVES LIQUORICE, LACE & LEATHER
Lace (slippy) / Vanquished / Waiting for dawn / Oxford dreams / Please Mr. President / Pick-up man / Nothing / D'Arcy / Wild prairie / Toreador / Outclause / Hollywood lies / Resurrection / Lace / Circus in town / Liquorice laughs
CD _____ CIT 005
Darius Doll / Feb '95 / Darius Doll.

Circus Lupus

SOLID BRASS
CD _____ DIS 79D
Dischord / Jul '93 / SRD.

Cirque Du Soleil

SALTIMBANCO
CD _____ 74321257072
RCA / Dec '95 / BMG.

Citania

CITANIA
CD _____ H 002CD
Sonifolk / Jun '94 / ADA / CM.

O ASUBIO DO PADRINO
CD _____ J 101CD
Sonifolk / Jun '94 / ADA / CM.

Citizen Fish

FREE SOULS IN A TRAPPED
CD _____ FISH 24CD
Bluurg / Apr '94 / SRD.

LIVE FISH
CD _____ FISH 29CD
Bluurg / Nov '93 / SRD.

MILLENNIA MADNESS
CD _____ FISH 34CD
Bluurg / Sep '95 / SRD.

Citizen Z

FLUXUS AND THE FIST EP (Citizen Z Vs The Continuum)
CD _____ BLAZE 92CD
Fire / Oct '95 / Disc.

Citizen's Arrest

CITIZEN ARREST
CD _____ LF 086CD
Lost & Found / Jun '94 / Plastic Head.

COMPLETE DISCOGRAPHY
CD _____ LF 086
Lost & Found / Mar '94 / Plastic Head.

Citreon, Soesja

SINGS THELONIOUS MONK
In walked bud / In twilight / Come with me / Round Midnight / Well you needn't / Underneath this cover / Blue monk / Sure it can be done
CD _____ CDJC 11021
Timeless Jazz / Feb '95 / New Note.

City Waites

PILLS TO PURGE MELANCHOLY (City Waites & Richard Wistreich)
Blowzabella, my bouncing dxie / As oyster nan stood by her tub / There was a lass of Islington / Would ye have a young virgin / With my strings of small wire / Like a ring without a finger / When for air I take my mare / Young Colin cleaving of a beam / Do not rumple my top knot / Come jug my honey let's to bed
CD _____ CDSDL 382
Saydisc / Mar '94 / Harmonia Mundi / ADA / Direct.

City West Quartet

CHATTERBOX
CD _____ BRAM 199230-2
Brambus / Nov '93 / ADA / Direct.

CIV

SET YOUR GOALS
CD _____ 7567926032
Atlantic / Nov '95 / Warner Music.

Ciyo

URBAN ATMOSPHERE
Groove / Don't diss me / Don't let him get to you / If love's a gift of life / Home deh yah / We know we are / Get out the way...beep beep / Love is around...love is found / Days of feelings / Just give me a break / Give me the night / Urban atmosphere
CD _____ DIVCD 01
Diverse / May '94 / Grapevine.

Clail, Gary

DREAMSTEALERS
Speak no evil / These things are worth fighting for / Dreamstealers / Decadance / No comfort / Peacemaker / Trouble / Who pays the piper / Isolation / Free / Behind every fortune
CD _____ 74321119202
RCA / May '93 / BMG.

EMOTIONAL HOOLIGAN, THE (Clail, Gary & On-U Sound System)
Food, clothes and shelter / Monk track / Escape / Emotional hooligan / Magic penny / Human nature / Crocodile eyes / Dreams / Beef / Temptation / False leader (Not on LP)
CD _____ 74321158662
RCA / Sep '93 / BMG.

Clair Obscur

COLLECTION OF ISOLATED TRACKS 1982-88, A
CD _____ EFA 015602
Apocalyptic Vision / Oct '95 / Plastic Head / SRD.

IN OUT
CD _____ AV 001CD
Apocalyptic Vision / Oct '93 / Plastic Head / SRD.

ROCK
CD _____ EFA 015502
Apocalyptic Vision / Oct '95 / Plastic Head / SRD.

Clan Sutherland Pipe Band

CLAN SUTHERLAND PIPE BAND
CD _____ EUCD 1311
ARC / Jul '95 / ARC Music / ADA.

Clancy, Aoipe

IT'S ABOUT TIME
CD _____ BM 559CD
Beaumex / Jul '95 / ADA.

Clancy Brothers

28 SONGS OF IRELAND (Clancy Brothers & Tommy Makem)
O'Donnell aboo / Croppy box / Rising of the moon / Foggy dew / Ministrel boy / Wind that shakes the barley / Tipperary far away / Kelly, the boy from Killane / Kevin Barry / Whack for the diddle / Men of the West / Eamonn an chnuic (Ned of the hills) / Nell Flaherty's Drake / Boulavogue / Whisky you're the devil / Maid of the sweet brown knowe / Moonshiner / Bold thady quill / Rosin the beau / Finnegan's wake / Real old mountain dew / Courtin' in the kitchen / Mick McGuire / Jug of punch / Johnny McEldoo / Cruiscin lan / Partlairge / Parting glass
CD _____ IHCD 10
Irish Music Heritage / Jul '89 / Prism.

BOYS WON'T LEAVE THE GIRLS ALONE, THE (Clancy Brothers & Tommy Makem)
Bold O'Donaghue / I'll tell me ma / Wild mountain thyme / Rothsay o / Marie's wedding / Singing bird / Holy ground / South Australia / As I roved out / MacPherson's lament / Wild colonial boy / Shoals of herring / I know who is sick / Old woman from Wexford
CD _____ SH 52015 CD
Shanachie / Dec '87 / Koch / ADA / Greensleeves.

CHRISTMAS WITH THE CLANCY BROTHERS
CD _____ SHAN 52017 CD
Shanachie / Apr '88 / Koch / ADA / Greensleeves.

CLANCY BROTHERS IN CONCERT (Clancy Brothers & Tommy Makem)
Isn't it grand / Bold boys / Mountain dew / Whistling gypsy rover / Finnegan's wake / Carrickfergus / Haul away Joe / Wild rover / Red haired Mary / Jug of punch / Leaving of Liverpool / Wild colonial boy / Holy ground / Wild mountain thyme
CD _____ PLATCD 335
Platinum Music / Jul '92 / Prism / Ross.

REUNION (Clancy Brothers & Tommy Makem)
Isn't it grand / Mountain dew / Whistling gypsy rover / Finnegan's wake / Carrickfergus / Haul away Joe / Wild rover / Red haired Mary / Jug of punch / Leaving of Liverpool / Wild colonial boy / Holy ground / Wild mountain thyme
Ogham / Apr '88 / Roots / Duncans / CM.

TUNES & TALES OF IRELAND LIVE
CD _____ FE 2061
Folk Era / Dec '94 / CM / ADA.

Clancy, Willie

MINSTREL FROM CLARE, THE
Langstern pony uilleann pipes / Templehouse / Over the moor to Maggie whistle / Bruachna carraige baine pipes / Erin's lovely lea / Killavil fancy / Dogs among the bushes / Family ointment vocal / Dear Irish boy / Caoineadh an spailpin whistle / Pipe on the hob / Gander vocal / Legacy jig whistle / Flogging reel pipes / Going to the riddles vocal / Spailpin a ruin pipes
CD _____ GL 3091CD
Green Linnet / Sep '94 / Roots / CM / Direct / ADA.

PIPERING OF WILLIE CLANCY, VOL 1
West wind/Sean Reid's fancy / Rocks of Bawn / Old bush / Will you come down to Limerick / Bold trainer O / Rolling wave / An Ghaoth Aniar-Aneas / Garrett Barry's Mazurka / Jenny picking cockles/My love is in America / Bright lady / Lady's pantaletts/ Ravelled Hank of Yarn / Fairly Molly Brannigan/Green fields of America / Kitty got a clinking coming from the fair / Bonny bunch of roses / Down the back lane / Paidin O Raifeartaigh / Clancy's jig / Jenny tie the bonnet/Corney is coming

PIPERING OF WILLIE CLANCY, VOL 2
Sean O Duibhir a Ghleanna / Caislean dhun guaire / McKenna's / Casadh an tSugain / Harvest home / I buried my wife and danced on her grave / Chaillgh, do mhairis me / Fowler on the moor / Bimis as ol s ag pogadh na mban / Milliner's daughter / Trip o'er the mountain / Connaught heifers / Steampacket / Gold ring / Kitty goes milking / Banish misfortune / An buachaill caol dubh / As phis fhliuch / Rakish paddy / Father's jig / Garrett Barry's / Dark is the colour of my true love's hair / Chief O'Neill's favourite / Jenny's welcome to Charlie
CD _____ CC 39CD
Claddagh / Jul '93 / ADA / Direct.

Clannad

BACK2BACK
CD Set _____ 74321206932
RCA / Sep '95 / BMG.

BANBA
Na leatha bhi / Banba oir / There for you / Mystery game / Struggle / I will find you / Soul searcher / Ca de sin don te sin / Other side / Sunset dreams / Gentle place
CD _____ 74321139612
RCA / May '93 / BMG.

CLANNAD 2
An gabhar ban / Eleanor Plunkett / Coinleach glas an fhomhair / Rince Philib a Cheoil / By chance it was / Rince Briotunach / Dheanainn sugradh / Gaoth barra na d'tonn / Teidhm abhaile riu / Fairly shot of her / Chuaigh me 'na rosann
CD _____ CEFCD 041
Gael Linn / Jan '94 / Roots / CM / Direct / ADA.

CLANNAD IN CONCERT
CD _____ TFCB 5001
Third Floor / Oct '94 / Total/BMG / ADA / Direct.

CRANN ULL
Ar a ghabhail 'n a 'chuain damh / Last rose of Summer / Cruscin Ian / Bacach Shile Andai / La coimhthioch fan dtuath / Crann ull / Gathering mushrooms / Bunan bui / Planxty Browne
CD _____ TARACD 3007
Tara / Nov '90 / CM / ADA / Direct / Conifer.

DÚLAMÁN
Gael Linn / Jan '94 / Roots / CM / Direct / ADA.
CD _____ CEFCD 058

FUAIM
Na Buachailli Alainn / Mheall Si Lena Glorthai Me / Bruachna carraige baine pipes / La Brea Fan Dtuath / An tull / Strayed away / Ni La Na Gaoithe La Na Scoib / Lish young buy a boron / Mhorag's Na Horo Ghealaidh / Green fields of Gaothdobhair / Buaireadh / An Phosta
CD _____ COOKCD 035
Cooking Vinyl / Apr '90 / Vital.

LEGEND
Robin (the hooded man) / Now is here / Herne / Together we / Darkmere / Strange Island / Scarlet inside / Lady Marian / Battles / Ancient forest
CD _____ ND 71703
RCA / Aug '88 / BMG.

MACALLA
Caislean oir / Wild cry / Closer to your heart / Almost seems (too late to turn) / In a lifetime / Buachaill an Eirne / Blackstairs / Journey's end / Northern skyline
CD _____ 74321 16035-2
RCA / Sep '93 / BMG.

PAST PRESENT
Harry's Game / Closer to your heart / Almost seems (too late to turn) / Hunter / Lady Marian / Sirius / Coinleach glas an fhomair / Second nature / World of difference / In a lifetime / Robin (the hooded man) / Something to believe in / Newgrange / Buachaill an eirne / White fool / Stepping stone
CD _____ 74321289612
RCA / Aug '95 / BMG.

SIRIUS
In search of a heart / Second nature / Turning tide / Skellig / Stepping stone / White fool / Something to believe in / Live and learn / Many roads / Sirius
CD _____ ND 75149
RCA / Jan '92 / BMG.

Clapton, Eric

24 NIGHTS (Eric Clapton live)
Badge / Running on faith / White room / Sunshine of your love / Watch yourself / Have you ever loved a woman / Worried life blues / Hoodoo man / Pretending / Bad love / Old love / Wonderful tonight / Bell bottom blues / Hard times / Edge of darkness
CD _____ 7599260402
Reprise / Nov '90 / Warner Music.

461 OCEAN BOULEVARD
Get ready / Give me strength / I can't hold out much longer / I shot the sheriff / Let it grow / Mainline Florida / Motherless children / Please be with me / Steady rollin' man / Willie and the hand jive
CD _____ 839 874-2
Polydor / Nov '89 / PolyGram.

ANOTHER TICKET
Something special / Black rose / Another ticket / I can't stand it / Hold me cord / Floating bridge / Catch me if you can / Rita Mae / Blow wind blow
CD _____ 827 579-2
Polydor / Feb '87 / PolyGram.

AUGUST
It's in the way that you use it / Run / Tearing us apart / Bad influence / Hung up on your love / I take a chance / Hold on / Miss you / Holy Mother / Behind the mask
CD _____ 9254762
Duck / Feb '95 / Warner Music.

BACKLESS
Early in the morning / Golden ring / If I don't be there by morning / I'll make love to you anytime / Promises / Roll it / Tell me that you love me / Tulsa time / Walk out in the rain / Watch out for Lucy
CD _____ 813 581-2
Polydor / Jan '89 / PolyGram.

BACKTRACKIN'
Cocaine / Strange brew / Spoonful / Let it rain / Have you ever loved a woman / Presence of the Lord / Crossroads / Roll it over / Can't find my way home / Blues power / Further on up the road / I shot the Sheriff / Knockin' on Heaven's door / Lay down Sally / Promises / Swing low, sweet chariot / Wonderful tonight / Sunshine of your love / Tales of brave Ulysses / Badge / Little wing / Layla
CD _____ 8219372
Polydor / Feb '85 / PolyGram.

BEGINNINGS
CD _____ CDCD 1174
Charly / Jul '94 / Charly / THE / Cadillac.

BEHIND THE SUN
She's waiting / See what love can do / Same old blues / Knock on wood / Something's happening / Forever man / It all depends / Tangles in love / Never make you cry / Just like a prisoner / Behind the sun
CD _____ 925166 2
Duck / Apr '85 / Warner Music.

BLUESBREAKERS (Clapton, Eric & John Mayall)
All your love / Hideaway / Little girl / Another man / Double crossin' time / What'd I say / Key to love / Parchman farm / Have you heard / Ramblin' on my mind / Steppin' out / It ain't right
CD _____ 8000862
Deram / Nov '88 / PolyGram.

CREAM OF ERIC CLAPTON
Layla / Bad / feel free / Sunshine of your love / Strange brew / White room / Cocaine / I shot the sheriff / Behind the mask / Forever man / Lay down Sally / Knockin' on Heaven's door / Wonderful tonight / Let it grow / Promises / I've got a rock 'n' roll heart / Heart / Crossroads
CD _____ 5110722
Polydor / Nov '91 / PolyGram.

CROSSROADS (4CD Set)
CD Set _____ 835 261-2
Polydor / Apr '88 / PolyGram.

ERIC CLAPTON & THE YARDBIRDS
CD _____ 100100
Scratch / Oct '94 / BMG.

ERIC CLAPTON WITH THE YARDBIRDS
CD _____ CD 12337
BR Music / Apr '94 / Target/BMG.

FROM THE CRADLE
Blues before sunrise / Third degree / Reconsider baby / Hoochie coochie man / Five long years / I'm tore down / How long blues / Goin' away baby / Blues leave me alone / Sinner's prayer / Motherless child / It hurts me too / Someday after a while / Standing around crying / Driftin' / Groaning the blues
CD _____ 936245735-2
Reprise / Sep '94 / Warner Music.

JOURNEYMAN
Pretending / Anything for your love / Bad love / Running on faith / Hard times / Hound dog / No alibis / Run so far / Old love / Breaking point / Lead me on / Before you accuse me
CD _____ 92620742
Reprise / Oct '89 / Warner Music.

MISTER SLOWHAND
CD Set _____ PULS 201
Pulsar / Oct '95 / BMG.

MONEY AND CIGARETTES
Everybody oughta make a change / Shape you're in / Ain't going down / I've got a rock 'n' roll heart / Man overboard / Pretty girl / Man in love / Crosscut saw / Slow down Linda / Crazy country hop
CD _____ 9237732
Reprise / Feb '95 / Warner Music.

NO REASON TO CRY
Beautiful things / County jail / Carnival / Sign language / County jail blues / All our past times / Hello old friend / Double trouble / Innocent times / Hungry / Black summer rain
CD _____ 8135822
Polydor / Jul '93 / PolyGram.

RAINBOW CONCERT
Badge / Roll it over / Presence of the Lord / Pearly queen / After midnight / Little wing
CD _____ 5274722
Polydor / May '95 / PolyGram.

STAGES OF CLAPTON (Various Artists)
Stepping out / Ramblin' on my mind / Hideaway / Have you heard / Outside woman blues / Crossroads / They call it stormy Monday / Well alright / Bell bottom blues / Blues power (Live) / Driftin' blues / Mean ol' Frisco
CD _____ 5500282
Spectrum/Karussell / May '93 / PolyGram / THE.

STRICTLY THE BLUES
CD _____ KAZCD 30
Kaz / Oct '94 / BMG.

SURVIVOR
I wish you would / For your love / Certain girl / Got to hurry / Too much monkey business / I don't care no more / Bye bye bird / Twenty three hours too long / Baby don't worry / Take it easy baby
CD _____ CDTB 013
Thunderbolt / Mar '95 / Magnum Music Group.

THERE'S ONE IN EVERY CROWD
We've been told (Jesus coming soon) / Swing low, sweet chariot / Little Rachel / Don't blame me / Sky is crying / Singin' the blues / Better make it through the day / Pretty blue eyes / High / Opposite
CD _____ 8296492
Polydor / Jul '88 / PolyGram.

UNPLUGGED
Signe / Before you accuse me / Hey hey / Tears in heaven / Lonely stranger / Nobody knows you (when you're down and out) / Layla / Running on faith / Walkin' blues / Alberta / San Francisco Bay blues / Malted milk / Old love
CD _____ 9362450242
WEA / Aug '92 / Warner Music.

Clare, Allen
ALLEN CLARE & LENNY BUSH (Clare, Allen & Lenny Bush)
CD _____ CHECD 00108
Master Mix / Nov '93 / Wellard / Jazz Music / New Note.

Clarinette Quintet
BAZH DU
CD _____ Y 225031CD
Silex / Dec '93 / ADA.

Clarion
FROM THE OAK
CD _____ BAK 002CD
Bakkus / Jul '95 / ADA.

Clarion Fracture Zone
BLUE SHIFT
CD _____ VBR 27052
Vera Bra / Sep '91 / Pinnacle / New Note.

Clark, Dave Five
GLAD ALL OVER AGAIN
Glad all over / Do you love me / Bits and pieces / Can't you see that she's mine / Don't let me down / Anyway you want it / Catch us if you can / Having a wild weekend / Because / I like it like that / Over and over / Reelin' and rockin' / Come home / You got what it takes / Everybody knows / Try too hard / I'll be yours my love / Good old Rock 'N' Roll Medley (Good old Rock 'N' Roll, Sweet little sixteen, Long tall Sally, Chantilly lace, Whole lotta shakin' goin' on, Blue suede shoes, Good old Rock 'N' Roll) / Here comes summer / Live in the sky / Red Balloon / Sha-na-na hey hey kiss him goodbye / More good old Rock 'N' Roll Medley (Rock 'N' Roll music, Blueberry hill, Good golly Miss Molly, The blues have, Keep-a-knockin', Rock 'N' Roll music) / Put a little love in your heart / Everybody get together
CD _____ CDEMTV 75
EMI / Apr '93 / EMI.

Clark, David Anthony
AUSTRALIA BEYOND THE DREAMTIME
CD _____ WCL 110132
White Cloud / May '95 / Select.

TERRA INHABITATA
CD _____ WCL 11007
White Cloud / May '94 / Select.

Clark, Dee
HEY LITTLE GIRL
I just can't help myself / When I call on you / Just like a fool / Seven nights / Oh little girl / Wondering / Nobody but you / Just keep it up / Hey little girl / How about that / Blues get off my shoulder / At my front door / You're looking good / Your friends / Because I love you / Raindrops / (Don't) walk away from me / I'm going back to school / Shook up over you / I'm a soldier boy

CD _____ CDRB 19
Charly / Apr '95 / Charly / THE / Cadillac.

Clark, Gary
TEN SHORT SONGS ABOUT LOVE
This is why, J / We sail on stormy waters / St. Jude / Short song about love / Make a family / Freefloating / Baby blue No.2 / Nancy / Any Sunday morning / Making people cry / Sail on / Jackson in your kitchen
CD _____ CIRCD 23
Circa / Apr '93 / EMI.

Clark, Gene
AMERICAN DREAMER 1964-1974
CD _____ RVCD 21
Raven / Feb '93 / Direct / ADA.

GENE CLARK & THE GOSDIN BROTHERS (Clark, Gene & The Gosdin Brothers)
Echoes / Think I'm gonna feel better / Tried so hard / Is yours is mine / Keep on pushing / I found you / So you say you lost your baby / Elevator operator / Same one / Couldn't believe her / Needing someone
CD _____ ED CD 263
Edsel / Apr '88 / Pinnacle / ADA.

NO OTHER
Life's greatest fool / Silver raven / No other / Strength of strings / From a silver phial / Some misunderstanding / True one / Lady of the North
CD _____ LECD 900889
Line / Sep '94 / CM / Grapevine / ADA / Conifer / Direct.

ROADMASTER
She's the kind of girl / One in a hundred / Here tonight / Full circle song / In a misty morning / Rough and rocky / Roadmaster / I really don't want to know / I remember the railroad / She don't care about time / Shooting star
CD _____ ED CD 198
Edsel / Jun '90 / Pinnacle / ADA.

SILHOUETTED IN LIGHT (Clark, Gene & Carla Olsen)
Your fire burning / Number one is to survive / Love wins again / Fair and tender ladies / Photograph / Set you free this time / Last thing on my mind / Gypsy rider / Train leaves here this morning / Almost Saturday night / Del Gato / I'll feel a whole lot better / She don't care about time / Speed of the sound of loneliness / Will the circle be unbroken
CD _____ FIENDCD 710
Demon / Feb '92 / Pinnacle / ADA.

SO REBELLIOUS A LOVER (Clark, Gene & Carla Olsen)
Drifter / Gypsy rider / Every angel in heaven / Del gato / Deportees / Fair and tender ladies / Almost Saturday night / I'm your toy / Why did you leave me / Don't it make you wanna go home / Are we still making love
CD _____ FIENDCD 89
Demon / Aug '87 / Pinnacle / ADA.

THIS BYRD HAS FLOWN
Tambourine man / Vanessa / Rainsong / C'est la bonne rue / If you could read my mind / Dixie flyer / Feel a whole lot better / Rodeo rider / All I want / Something about you / Made for love / Blue raven
CD _____ EDCD 436
Edsel / Jul '95 / Pinnacle / ADA.

Clark, Glen
LOOKING FOR A CONNECTION
CD _____ DOSCD 7006
Dos / Sep '95 / CM / Direct / ADA.

Clark, Guy
BOATS TO BUILD
Baton Rouge / Picasso's mandolin / How'd you get this number / Boats to build / Too much / Ramblin' Jack and Mahan / I don't love you much do I / Jack of all trades / Madonna w/Child ca. 1969 / Must be my baby
CD _____ 7559614422
Elektra Nonesuch / Jul '93 / Warner Music.

CRAFTSMAN
CD _____ CDPH 118485
Philo / Jun '95 / Direct / CM / ADA.

OLD FRIENDS
CD _____ SHCD 1026
Sugarhill / Aug '95 / Roots / CM / ADA / Direct.

OLD NUMBER ONE
Rita Ballou / L.A. freeway / She ain't goin' nowhere / Nickel for the fiddler / That old time feeling / Texas - 1947 / Desperados waiting for the train / Like a coat from the cold / Instant coffee blues / Let him roll
CD _____ EDCD 285
Edsel / Jul '90 / Pinnacle / ADA.

TEXAS COOKIN'
Texas cookin' / Anyhow I love you / Virginia's real / It's about time / Good to love you lady / Broken hearted people / Black haired boy / Me I'm feelin' the same / Ballad of Laverne and Captain Flint / Last gunfighter ballad

CD _____ EDCD 287
Edsel / Jul '90 / Pinnacle / ADA.

Clark, Ian
IAN CLARK PLAYS THE MELODIES OF SCOTLAND
CD _____ CDSLP 615
Igus / Dec '89 / CM / Ross / Duncans.

Clark, John
Il SUONO
Mustang Sally / Buster's move / Groove from the Louvre / Hot fired fish / Miradita / Il suono delle ragazze che ridono / Pretty loose
CD _____ CMPCD 59
CMP / Oct '93 / Vital/SAM.

Clark, Louis
BEST OF HOOKED ON CLASSICS (Clark, Louis & Royal Philharmonic Orchestra)
Hooked on classics (pts 1 & 2) / Can't stop the classics / Night at the opera / Hooked on America / Symphonies of the seas / Hooked on a can can / Also sprach Zarathustra / Journey through the classics / Hooked on Tchaikovsky / Hooked on romance (opus 3) / Tales of the Vienna waltz / If you knew Sousa / If you knew Sousa (and friends) / Scotland the brave
CD _____ 74321101112
RCA / Aug '92 / BMG.

CLASSICS FOR THE MILLIONS (Clark, Louis & Royal Philharmonic Orchestra)
CD _____ SYCD 6320
Disky / May '94 / THE / BMG / Discovery / Pinnacle.

HOOKED ON CLASSICS - THE ULTIMATE PERFORMANCE (Clark, Louis & Royal Philharmonic Orchestra)
Hooked on romance / Hooked on classics (pt 3) / Journey through the classics #2 / Can't stop the classics / Hooked on Mozart / Hooked on Baroque / Hooked on Bach / Hooked on Rodgers and Hammerstein / Journey through America / Hooked on a song
CD _____ 74321 15558-2
Ariola Express / Sep '93 / BMG.

PLAY THE QUEEN COLLECTION
Flash / Play the game / We are the champions / Don't stop me now / Love of my life / Killer Queen / You're my best friend / Teo torriatte / Under pressure / Crazy little thing called love / Bohemian rhapsody
CD _____ CDMFP 5945
Music For Pleasure / Oct '92 / EMI.

Clark, Mike
FUNK STOPS HERE, THE (Clark, Mike, Paul Jackson, Kenny Garrett & Jeff Pittson)
CD _____ TIP 8888112
Enja / Jul '92 / New Note / Vital/SAM.

GIVE THE DRUMMER SOME (Clark, Mike Sextet)
CD _____ STCD 19
Stash / Aug '90 / Jazz Music / CM / Cadillac / Direct / ADA.

MIKE CLARK SEXTET (Clark, Mike Sextet / Ricky Ford & Jack Walrath)
CD _____ STCD 22
Stash / Oct '91 / Jazz Music / CM / Cadillac / Direct / ADA.

Clark, Petula
BEST OF PETULA CLARK
CD _____ MATCD 206
Castle / Dec '92 / BMG.

DOWNTOWN
Downtown / Sign of the times / This is my song / I couldn't live without your love / You're the one / I know a place / Kiss me goodbye / Colour my world / Mad about you / Don't sleep in the subway / Good life / Other man's grass / My love / Give it a try / Strangers in the night / Call me
CD _____ 15103
Laserlight / Jan '93 / Target/BMG.

DOWNTOWN
True love never runs smooth / Baby / It's mine / Now that you've gone / Tell me (that it's love) / Crying through a sleepless night / In love / Music / Be good to me / This is goodbye / Let me tell you / You belong to me / Downtown / I will follow him / Darling Cheri / You'd better love me
CD _____ NEBCD 661
Sequel / Oct '93 / BMG.

DOWNTOWN
Downtown / Don't sleep in the subway / Romeo / I don't know how to love him / If for all we know / I couldn't live without your love / Where do I go from here / Welcome home / Thank you / This is my song / Sailor / Colour my world / Fly me to the moon / Memories are made of this / I get along without you very well / Night has a thousand eyes / Chariot / Happy heart / My love
CD _____ 5507332

Spectrum/Karussell / Mar '95 / PolyGram / THE.

EP COLLECTION: PETULA CLARK
Cinderella Jones / With your love / Who needs you / While the children play / Slumming on Park Avenue / I've grown accustomed to his face / Love me again / Here, there and everywhere / Welcome home / My favourtie things / Have I the right / Downtown / Gotta tell the world / Everything in the garden / Hold on to what you've got / Life and soul of the party / I couldn't live without your love / Long before I knew you (CD only) / In a little moment (CD only) / Baby it's me (CD only) / True love never runs smooth (CD only) / Strangers and lovers (Cd only) / We can watch (CD only) / Wasn't it you (Cd only) / Come rain or come shine (CD only) / What would I be (CD only)
CD _____ SEECD 306
See For Miles/C5 / Dec '90 / Pinnacle.

EP COLLECTION: PETULA CLARK VOL. 2
I know a place / Tell me / In love / Let me tell you / You'd better love me / Every little bit hurts / Time for love / This is my song / Monday, Monday / I'm begging you / On the path of glory / Resist / Winchester Cathedral / Homeward bound / Jack and John / Music / Forgetting you / Be good to me / My love / Where am I going / 31st of June / Show is over / Colour my world / Here comes the morning / Fancy dancin' man / Bang bang / Groovy kind of love
CD _____ SEECD 381
See For Miles/C5 / Oct '93 / Pinnacle.

GOLD
CD _____ GOLD 207
Disky / Apr '94 / THE / BMG / Discovery / Pinnacle.

GREATEST HITS: PETULA CLARK
CD _____ GNPD 2170
GNP Crescendo / '88 / Silva Screen.

I KNOW A PLACE
Dancing in the street / Strangers and lovers / Everything in the garden / In crowd / Heart / You're the one / Foggy day / Gotta tell the world / Every little bit hurts / Call me / Goin' out of my head / I know a place / Jack and John / You'd better come home / Sound of love / Round every corner
CD _____ NEBCD 660
Sequel / Jan '95 / BMG.

I LOVE TO SING
Madamoiselle de paris / On the atchison, topeka and the Santa Fe / I get along without you very well (except sometimes) / Fly me to the moon / Gotta have me go with you / George / There's nothing more to say / Nighty-night / Valentino / Imagination / Thankyou / Saturday sunshine / You'd better love me / Forgetting you / Round about / Never will I / Sound of love / Look at me / Nothing much matters / Make way for love / At the crossroads / What a song / Only when to love me / Big love sale / Make a time for loving / What I did for love / Downtown / Sailor / Romeo / My friend the sea / I love to sing / I will follow him / I know a place / Things go better with coca-cola / You'd better come home / Round every corner / You're the one / My love / Just say goodbye / Sign of the times / I couldn't live without your love / Who am I / Colour my world / This is my song / Don't sleep in the subway / High / Other man's grass / Kiss me goodnight / Don't give up / Look at mine / You and I / I don't know how to love him / Superstar / Take good care of your heart / Love will find a way / Gotta be better than this / After you / Gotta be home / There from a dream / Goodbye Mr. Chips / Things to do / Conversations in the wind / Support your nearest love / Cranes flying south / Melody man / Beautiful sounds / Song is love / I've got to know / I think of you / Lifetime of love / Coming back to you again / On the road / Goin' out of my head / Maybe
CD Set _____ NXTCD 265
Sequel / Jul '95 / BMG.

JUMBLE SALE
CD Set _____ NEDCD 198
Sequel / Feb '92 / BMG.

LIVE AT THE COPACABANA
Put on a happy face / I've seen that face before / My love / I couldn't live without your love / Come rain or come shine / I know a place / Typically English / I couldn't live without your love / Santa Lucia / Hello Dolly / Call me / M'sieure m'sieure / My name is Petula (in) a shanty in old Shanty Town / So nice top come home to / Dear hearts
CD _____ NEBCD 653
Sequel / Jun '93 / BMG.

LOVE SONGS: PETULA CLARK
Don't sleep in the subway / This is my song / My love
CD _____ PWK 080
Carlton Home Entertainment / Jan '89 / Carlton Home Entertainment.

MY GREATEST
Downtown / If you ever go away / I couldn't live without your love / My love / Song of my life / Send away the clowns / We'll still be friends /

Don't sleep in the subway / My love / All my life / Other man's grass / Colours of love / Kiss me goodbye / Show is over
CD _____ CDMFP 6053
Music For Pleasure / Jan '89 / EMI.

MY LOVE
My love / Hold on to what you've got / We can work it out / Time for love / Just say goodbye / Life and soul of the party / Sign of the times / 31st of June / Where did we go wrong / I can't remember (ever loving you) / Dance with me / If I were a bell / Rain / Love is a long journey / Your way of life
CD _____ NEBCD 658
Sequel / Jun '94 / BMG.

NIXA YEARS VOL.1, THE
Suddenly there's a valley / Band of gold / Memories are made of this / Forever faithful / To you, my love / Another door opens / Million stars above / With all my heart / 'Allo mon coeur / Papayer / Tout ce que veut Lola / Histoire D'un amour / Guitare et tambourin / Java pour Petula / Mon couer danse avec la chance / Tango au L'esquimau / Prends mon couer / Lune de miel / Che sbadato / Ne joue pas / Que voulez vous de plus / Je t'aime / Liebe in St. Tropez / Du bist mein anfang und mein schluss / Hark the herald angels sing / List our merry carol / Once in Royal David's City / Little Jesus / Holly and the ivy / Away in a manger
CD _____ RPM 138
RPM / Aug '94 / Pinnacle.

NIXA YEARS VOLUME TWO, THE
Gonna find me a bluebird / Alone / Baby lover / Little blue man / Devotion / St. Tropez / Fibbin' / Where do I go from here / Dear Daddy / Through the looking glass / Let's get lost / I love to sing / All through the day / You're a sweetheart / Don't blame me / More I see you / Moi j'prefere l'amour a tout ca / Dis-moi / Tra ma pluie et mon beau temps / Grand-mere / Non et non / Garde ta derniere danse pour moi / Sur un tapis volant / Calcutta (ma fete a moi) / Marin / Les gens diront / Calender girl / Ya ya twist / Si c'est oui, c'est oui / Bye bye mon amour
CD _____ RPM 144
RPM / Nov '94 / Pinnacle.

OTHER MAN'S GRASS IS ALWAYS GREENER, THE/PETULA-KISS ME GOOD
Smile / Black coffee / Answer me my love / Other man's grass is always greener / Today, tomorrow / I could have danced all night / At the crossroads / Ville de france / Cat in the window (bird in the sky) / For love / Ballad of a sad young man / Don't give up / Have another dream on me / Your love is everywhere / One in a million / Beautiful in the rain / This girl's in love with you / Kiss me goodbye / Sun shines out of your shoes / We're falling in love again / Days / Why can't I cry / Good life
CD _____ SEECD 435
See For Miles/C5 / Oct '95 / Pinnacle.

POLYGON YEARS VOL.1
You go to my head / Out of a clear blue sky / Music music music / Blossoms on the bough / Silver dollar / Talky talky talky / Who spilt coffee on the carpet / You are my true love / You're the sweetest in the land / Beloved be faithful / Fly away Peter, fly away Paul / Tennessee waltz / Sleepy eyes / Teasin' / Black note serenade / May kway / Clickety clack / Manandi / Broken heart / That's how a love song is born / Cold cold heart / Tell me truly / Song of the mermaid / It had to be you / Card I buy in love / Where did my snowman go / Teasin' #2
CD _____ RPM 130
RPM / Jun '94 / Pinnacle.

POLYGON YEARS VOL.2
Anytime is teatime now / Made in heaven / Temptation rag / My love is a wanderer / Take care of yourself / Christopher Robin at Buckingham Palace / Three little kittens / Poppa Piccolino / Who-is-it song / Little shoemaker / Helpless / Meet me in Battersea Park / Long way to go / Smile / Somebody / Christmas carols / Little Johnny Rainbow / Majorca / Fascinating ryhthm / Get well soon / Romance in Rome / Chee Chee oo chee / Crazy Otto rag / Pendulum song / How are things with you / Tuna puna Trinidad / Chee chee oo chee #2
CD _____ RPM 131
RPM / Jun '94 / Pinnacle.

PORTRAIT OF PETULA
Happy heart / If ever you're lonely (Lontago dagli occhi) / Games people play / Love is the only thing / When I was a child / Ad / My funny valentine / Lovin' things / When I give my heart / Let it be me / Some / Windmills of your mind / When you return / Have another dream on me / One in a million / Your love is everywhere
CD _____ NEBCD 659
Sequel / Jun '95 / BMG.

PYE YEARS #1 (Don't Sleep In The Subway)
Never on a Sunday / You can't keep me from loving you / What now my love / Why don't they understand / Have I the right / Volare / One more sunrise / I want to hold your hand / Love me with all your heart / Boy from Ipanema / I who have nothing /

Hello Dolly / This is my song / Groovin' / Lover man / San Francisco / Eternally / Resist / Don't sleep in the subway / Imagine / Love is here / How insensitive / I will wait for you / On the path of glory / High / Here comes the morning / Show is over
CD _____ RPM 146
RPM / Jun '95 / Pinnacle.

PYE YEARS #2
CD _____ RPM 159
RPM / Jan '96 / Pinnacle.

SPECIAL COLLECTION
Sailor / I know a place / After the hill / Spring in September / City lights / Today / Don't give up / Downtown / Beautiful in the rain / Sun shines out of your shoes / Why can't I cry / We're falling in love again / Don't sleep in the subway / I couldn't live without your love / He made me a woman / For all we know / One step behind / Man in a million / Other man's grass / My funny valentine / That's what life is all about / Neon rainbow / It don't matter to me / If
CD _____ CCSCD 236
Castle / Mar '90 / BMG.

YOU ARE MY LUCKY STAR
It's foolish but it's fun / Sonny boy / Zing went the strings of my heart / Alone / I, yi, yi, yi / Goodnight my love / I wish I knew / Slumming on Park Avenue / As time goes by / It's the natural thing to do / Afraid to dream / You are my lucky star / I yi yi yi yi (I like you very much)
CD _____ C5CD-551
See For Miles/C5 / Jan '90 / Pinnacle.

Clark, Roy

MAKIN' MUSIC (Clark, Roy & Clarence 'Gatemouth' Brown)
CD _____ MCAD 22125
One Way / Jul '94 / Direct / ADA.

Clark, Sanford

FOOL, THE
Fool / Man who made an angel cry / Love charms / Cheat / Lonesome for a letter / Ooh baby / Darling dear / Modern romance / Travellin' man / Swanee river rock / Lou / Usta to be my baby / Nine pound hammer / Glory of love / Don't care / Usta be my baby (2)
CD _____ BCD 15549
Bear Family / Jun '92 / Rollercoaster / Direct / CM / Swift / ADA.

SHADES
Better go home (throw that blade away) / Pledging my love / Girl on Death Row / Step aside / (They call me) Country / Shades / Fool / Climbin' the walls / Once upon a time / It's nothing to me / Where's the door / Big lie / Calling all hearts / Black Jack county chain / Big big day tomorrow / Bad case of you / Wind will blow (demo) / Streets of San Francisco / Oh Julie / Kung Fu U / Mother Texas (you been a mother to me) / Taste of you / Movin' on / Wind will blow / Feathers / Now I know I'm not in Kansas / Nine pound hammer
CD _____ BCD 15731
Bear Family / Jul '93 / Rollercoaster / Direct / CM / Swift / ADA.

Clark Sisters

MIRACLE
It's gonna be alright / Miracle / Simply yes / Call me / I don't know why / He's a real friend / Amazing grace / Jesus is the best thing / No doubt about it / Work to do
CD _____ SPD 1368
Alliance Music / Aug '95 / EMI.

Clark, Sonny

COOL STRUTTIN'
Cool struttin' / Blue minor / Sippin' at bells / Deep night / Royal flush / Lover
CD _____ CDP 7465132
Blue Note / Mar '95 / EMI.

SONNY CLARK, MAX ROACH, GEORGE DUVIVIER (Clark, Sonny/Max Roach/George Duvivier)
CD _____ COD 009
Jazz View / Mar '92 / Harmonia Mundi.

Clark, Terry

COLOR CHANGES
CD _____ CCD 79009
Candid / Jan '89 / Cadillac / Jazz Music / Wellard / Koch.

WHAT A WONDERFUL WORLD (For Louis & Duke)
CD _____ 473714 2
Sony Jazz / May '94 / Sony.

Clark, W.C.

HEART OF GOLD
CD _____ BT 1103CD
Black Top / May '94 / CM / Direct / ADA.

Clarke, Ann

UNSTILL LIFE
CD _____ 0888362
SPV / May '91 / Plastic Head.

Clarke, Anthony J.

I GET LOST
CD _____ JP 00102
Splash / May '94.

Clarke, Buddy

ONCE AND FOR ALWAYS
CD _____ JCD 631
Jass / '92 / CM / Jazz Music / ADA / Cadillac / Direct.

Clarke, Dave

ARCHIVE ONE
Rhapsody in red / Protective custody / No one's driving / Woki / Southside / Wisdom to the wise / Tales of two cities / Storm / Miles away / Thunder / Splendour
CD _____ 74321320672
De-Construction / Jan '96 / BMG.

Clarke, Gilby

PAWNSHOP GUITARS
Cure me... or kill me / Black / Tijuana jail / Black and blues / Johanna's chopper / Let's get lost / Pawnshop guitar / Dead flowers / Jail guitar doors / Hunting dogs / Shut up
CD _____ CDVUS 76
Virgin / Jul '94 / EMI.

Clarke, Johnny

AUTHORISED ROCKERS
Rockers time now / It's green and cold / African roots / Be holy my brothers and sisters / Satta a masagana / Stop the tribal war / Declaration of rights / Let's give jah jah praises / Wish it would go on forever / Natty dreadlocks stand up right / Prophesy a fulfilled / Marcus Garvey / Roots, natty roots, natty congo / Wrath of jah / Legalize it / I'm still waiting / Let go violence / Academy award version / Cry tough / Crazy baldheads / Simmer down / Jah jah see them come / Freedom blues
CD _____ CDFL 9014
Frontline / Jun '91 / EMI / Jetstar.

GOLDEN HITS
CD _____ SONCD 0081
Sonic Sounds / Nov '95 / Jetstar.

Clarke, Kenny

BOHEMIA AFTER DARK
Bohemia after dark / Chasm / Willow weep for me / Hear me talkin' to ya / With apologies to Oscar / We'll be together again / Late entry
CD _____ SV 0107
Savoy Jazz / Apr '92 / Conifer / ADA.

KENNY CLARKE & ERNIE WILKINS (Clarke, Kenny & Ernie Wilkins)
Pru's bloose / I dig you the most / Cute tomato / Summer evening / Oz the wizard / Now's the time / Plenty for Kenny
CD _____ SV 0222
Savoy Jazz / Oct '93 / Conifer / ADA.

KENNY CLARKE MEETS THE DETROIT JAZZ MEN
You turned the tables on me / Your host / Cotton tail / Apothegh / Tricrotism / Afternoon in Paris / Tom's thumb
CD _____ SV 0243
Savoy Jazz / Oct '94 / Conifer / ADA.

TELEFUNKEN BLUES
Strollin' / Sonor / Blue's mood / Skoot / Telefunken blues / Klook's nook / Baggin' the blues / Inhibitions
CD _____ SV 0106
Savoy Jazz / Apr '92 / Conifer / ADA.

Clarke, Mick

ALL THESE BLUES (Clarke, Mick Band)
CD _____ APCD 034
Appaloosa / '92 / ADA / Magnum Music Group.

LOOKING FOR TROUBLE (Clarke, Mick Band)
CD _____ APCD 038
Appaloosa / '92 / ADA / Magnum Music Group.

NO COMPROMISE (Clarke, Mick Band)
CD _____ TX 1006CD
Taxim / Dec '93 / ADA.

TELL THE TRUTH (Clarke, Mick Band)
CD _____ TX 1001CD
Taxim / Dec '93 / ADA.

WEST COAST CONNECTION
CD _____ BRAM 198801-2
Brambus / Aug '95 / ADA / Direct.

Clarke, Stanley

CLARKE/DUKE PROJECT #1 (Clarke, Stanley & George Duke)
CD _____ 4682232
Sony Jazz / Jan '95 / Sony.

CLARKE/DUKE PROJECT #2 (Clarke, Stanley & George Duke)
Put it on the line / Atlanta / Trip you in love / You're gonna love it / Good times / Great danes / Every reason to smile / Try me baby / Heroes

CD _____ EK 38934
Sony Jazz / Jul '95 / Sony.

CLARKE/DUKE PROJECT #3 (Clarke, Stanley & George Duke)
Pit bulls (An endangered species) / Oh Oh / No place to hide / Somebody else / Mothership connection / Right by my side / From the deepest corner of my heart / Lady / Find out who you are / Quiet time / Fingerprints / Always
CD _____ 4670112
Sony Jazz / Jan '95 / Sony.

COLLECTION: STANLEY CLARKE
CD _____ CCSCD 242
Castle / Jun '90 / BMG.

EAST RIVER DRIVE
CD _____ 4737972
Sony Jazz / Jan '95 / Sony.

I WANNA PLAY FOR YOU
Rock 'n' roll jelly / All about / Jamaican boy / Christopher Ivanhoe / My greatest hits / Strange weather / I wanna play for you / Just a feeling / Streets of Philadelphia / School days / Quiet afternoon / Together again / Blues for Mingus / Off the planet / Hot fun
CD _____ 4773132
Sony Jazz / Jan '95 / Sony.

IF THIS BASS COULD ONLY TALK
If this bass could talk / I wanna play for you / Funny how time flies / Bassically taps / Working man / Come take my hand / Stories to tell / Tradition
CD _____ 4608832
Epic / Jan '93 / Sony.

JOURNEY TO LOVE
Silly putty / Journey to love / Hello, Jeff / Song to John / Concerto for jazz-rock orchestra
CD _____ 4682212
Sony Jazz / Jan '95 / Sony.

LIVE 1976-1977
CD _____ 4689592
Sony Jazz / Jan '95 / Sony.

LIVE AT THE GREEK
CD _____ 4766022
Sony Jazz / Jan '95 / Sony.

RITE OF SPRING, THE (Clarke, Stanley & Al Di Meola/Jean-Luc Ponty)
CD _____ 8341672
Gai Saber / Dec '95 / Vital.

ROCKS, PEBBLES AND SAND
Danger street / All hell broke loose / Rocks, pebbles and sand / You / Me together / Underestimation / We supply / Story of a man and a woman / She thought I was Stanley Clarke / Fool again / I nearly went crazy (until I realised what had occurred)
CD _____ 4682222
Sony Jazz / Jan '95 / Sony.

SCHOOLDAYS
CD _____ 4682182
Sony Jazz / Jan '95 / Sony.

STANLEY CLARKE
Vulcan princess / Yesterday Princess / Lopsy lu / Power / Spanish phases for strings and bass / Life suite (part 1) / Life suite (part 2) / Life suite (part 3) / Life suite (part 4)
CD _____ 4682182
Sony Jazz / Jan '95 / Sony.

Clarke, William

BLOWIN' LIKE HELL
CD _____ ALCD 4788
Alligator / Mar '93 / Direct / ADA.

GROOVE TIME
CD _____ ALCD 4827
Alligator / Dec '94 / Direct / ADA.

SERIOUS INTENTIONS
Pawnshop bound / Trying to stretch my money / Educated fool / Going down this highway / I know you're fine / Driving my life away / Chasin' the gator / With a tear in my eye / It's been a long time / Work song / I feel like jumping / Soon forgotten
CD _____ ALCD 4806
Alligator / May '93 / Direct / ADA.

Clash

BLACK MARKET CLASH
Capital Radio / Prisoner / Pressure drop / Cheat / City of the dead / Time is tight / Bankrobber (dub) / Armagideon time / Justice tonight / Kick it over
CD _____ 4687632
Columbia / Jan '91 / Sony.

CLASH, THE
Janie Jones / Remote control / I'm so bored with the USA / White riot / Hate and war / What's my name / Deny / London's burning / Career opportunities / Cheat / Protex blue / Police and thieves / 48 hours / Garage land
CD _____ 4687832
Columbia / Jun '91 / Sony.

CLASH, THE (American Version)
CD _____ CD 32232
Columbia / Jan '95 / Sony.

CLASH

**CLASH, THE/GIVE 'EM ENOUGH ROPE/
COMBAT ROCK (3CD Set)**
CD Set _____ 4673832
Columbia / Dec '90 / Sony.

COMBAT ROCK
Inoculated city / Know your rights / Car jamming / Should I stay or should I go / Rock
the Casbah / Red angel dragnet / Straight
to hell / Overpowered by funk / Atom tan /
Sean Flynn / Ghetto defendant / Death is a
star
CD _____ CD 32787
Columbia / Jul '92 / Sony.

CUT THE CRAP
Dictator / Dirty punk / We are The Clash /
Are you ready / Cool under heat / Movers
and shakers / This is England / Three card
trick / Play to win / Finger poppin' / North
and South / Life is wild
CD _____ 4651102
CBS / '91 / Sony.

GIVE 'EM ENOUGH ROPE
Safe European home / English civil war /
Tommy gun / Julie's been working for the
drug squad / Last gang in town / Guns on
the roof / Drug stabbing time / Stay free /
Cheapskates / All the young punks (new
boots and contracts)
CD _____ CD 32444
CBS / '91 / Sony.

LONDON CALLING
London calling / Brand new Cadillac /
Jimmy Jazz / Hateful / Rudie can't fail /
Spanish bombs / Right profile / Lost in the
supermarket / Clampdown / Guns of Brix-
ton / Wrong 'em / Boyo / Death or glory /
Koka cola / Card cheat / Lover's rock / I'm
not down / Revolution rock / Four horsemen
CD _____ 4601142
CBS / '91 / Sony.

ON BROADWAY (3CD/MC Set)
CD Set _____ 4693082
Legacy / May '94 / Sony.

SANDINISTA
Hitsville UK / Junco partner / Leader / Rebel
waltz / Look here / One more time / Corner
soul / Equaliser / Call up / Broadway /
Junkie slip / Version city / Crooked beat /
Up in heaven / Midnight log / Lose this skin
/ Kingston advice / Let's go crazy
CD Set _____ 4633642
Columbia / Apr '89 / Sony.

SINGLES, THE
White riot / Remote control / Complete con-
trol / Clash city rockers / White man in Ham-
mersmith Palais / Tommy gun / English Civil
War / I fought the law / International love /
Train in vain / Bankrobber / Call up / Hitsville
UK / Magnificent seven / This is radio clash
/ Know your rights / Rock the casbah /
Should I stay or should I go
CD _____ 4689462
Columbia / Nov '91 / Sony.

**STORY OF THE CLASH VOL.1, THE (2
CD/MCs)**
Magnificent seven / This is Radio Clash /
Straight to hell / Train in vain / I fought the
law / Somebody got murdered / Bankrob-
ber / Rock the Casbah / Should I stay or
should I go / Armageddon time / Guns of
Brixton / Clampdown / Lost in the super-
market / White man in Hammersmith Palais
/ London's burning / Janie Jones / Tommy
gun / Complete control / Capital radio /
White riot / Career opportunities / Clash city
rockers / Safe European home / Stay free /
London calling / Spanish bombs / English
civil war / Police and thieves
CD Set _____ 4602442
Columbia / Oct '95 / Sony.

SUPER BLACK MARKET CLASH
1977 / Protex blue (LP only) / Deny (LP only)
/ Cheat (LP only) / 48 Hours (LP only) / Listen / Jail guitar doors / City of the dead /
Prisoner / Pressure drop / One-two crush
on you / Groovy times / Gates of the west
/ Capital radio two / Time is tight / Kick it
over / Bankrobber (dub) / Stop the world /
Cool out / First night back in London / Long
time jerk / Cool confusion / Magnificent
dance / This is radio clash / Mustapha
dance
CD _____ 474546 2
Columbia / Jan '94 / Sony.

TWELVE INCH MIXES
London calling / Magnificent dance / This is
radio clash / Rock the casbah / This is
England
CD _____ 450123-2
Columbia / Nov '92 / Sony.

Classen, Martin

**STOP AND GO (Classen, Martin
Quartet)**
CD _____ BEST 1033CD
Acoustic Music / Nov '93 / ADA.

Classic Jazz Quartet

COMPLETE RECORDINGS
CD _____ JCD 138
Jazzology / Jun '95 / Swift / Jazz Music.

COMPLETE RECORDINGS #2
CD _____ JCD 139
Jazzology / Jun '95 / Swift / Jazz Music.

Classical Brass

MUSIC FROM THE CIVIL WAR
CD _____ MM 67075
Music Masters / Oct '94 / Target/BMG.

Clastrier, Valentin

**PALUDE (Clastrier, Valentin & Michael
Riessler/Carlo Rizzo)**
CD _____ WER 8009
Wergo / Dec '95 / Harmonia Mundi / ADA
/ Cadillac.

Clau De Lluna

CERCLE DE GAL-LA
CD _____ H 039CD
Sonifolk / Jun '94 / ADA / CM.

FICA-LI, NOIA
CD _____ 20049CD
Sonifolk / Jun '94 / ADA / CM.

Clawfinger

DEAF, DUMB, BLIND
Nigger / Truth / Rosegrove / Don't get me
wrong / I need you / Catch me / Warfair /
Wonderful world / Sad to see your sorrow /
I don't care
CD _____ 450993321-2
WEA / Aug '93 / Warner Music.

USE YOUR BRAIN
CD _____ 4509996312
Warner Bros. / Apr '95 / Warner Music.

Clawhammer

PABLUM
CD _____ E 864252
Epitaph / Nov '92 / Plastic Head /
Pinnacle.

Clawson, Cynthia

HYMN SINGER
CD _____ DAYCD 4162
Dayspring / '88 / Nelson Word.

Clay, Joe

DUCKTAIL
Duck tail / Did you mean jelly bean (what
you said cabbage head) / Crackerjack /
Goodbye goodbye / Sixteen chicks / Slip-
ping out and sneaking in / Doggone it / Get
on the right track baby / You look good to
me
CD _____ BCD 15516
Bear Family / Jul '90 / Rollercoaster / Direct
/ CM / Swift / ADA.

Clay, Judy

**BILLY VERA AND JUDY CLAY (Clay,
Judy & Billy Vera)**
CD _____ SCL 2101
Ichiban Soul Classics / May '95 / Koch.

Clay, Otis

CALL ME
CD _____ WAY 269510-2
Waylo / Apr '90 / Charly.

GOSPEL TRUTH, THE
CD _____ BP 5005CD
Blind Pig / May '94 / Hot Shot / Swift /
CM / Roots / Direct / ADA.

ON MY WAY HOME
CD _____ BBCD 9536
Bullseye Blues / Jun '93 / Direct.

ONLY WAY IS UP, THE
CD _____ WAY 269504-2
Waylo / Apr '90 / Charly.

OTIS CLAY 45'S
CD _____ HILOCD 1
Hi / Dec '93 / Pinnacle.

THAT'S HOW IT IS
CD _____ HIUKCD 110
Hi / Jul '91 / Pinnacle.

Clayderman, Richard

BALLERINA
CD _____ MSCD 15
Music De-Luxe / Mar '95 / Magnum Music
Group.

CARPENTERS COLLECTION, THE
Yesterday once more / There's a kind of
hush (all over the world) / We've only just
begun / Superstar / Top of the world / Rainy
days and Mondays / (They long to be) close
to you / Only yesterday / For all we know /
Please Mr. Postman / I won't last a day
without you / Solitaire / Meldley: For all we
know, We've only just begun / Sing
CD _____ 8286882
Delphine / Oct '95 / PolyGram.

CHRISTMAS (RICHARD CLAYDERMAN)
White Christmas / Handel's Largo / Jesu joy
of man's desiring / Silver bells / Christmas
concerto / He was born the holy child /
Moonlight sonata / Leise rieselt der schnee
/ Romance / Candles twinkle / On the
Christmas tree
CD _____ 5506442

Spectrum/Karussell / Nov '94 / PolyGram /
THE.

CHRISTMAS ALBUM, THE
White Christmas / On Christmas tree /
Christian midnight / He was born the holy
child / Silent night / Ave Maria / Christmas
concerto / Rudolph the red nosed reindeer
/ Little drummer boy / Moonlight sonata /
Jingle bells / Softly falls the snow / Largo /
Romance / Jesu joy of man's desiring /
Santa Claus is coming to town / Silver bells
CD _____ PWKS 4085P
Carlton Home Entertainment / Oct '91 /
Carlton Home Entertainment.

CLASSIC PIANO GALA
CD _____ 280724
BR Music / Jun '95 / Target/BMG.

CLASSIC TOUCH
Dream of Olwen / Variation of a theme of
Paganini / Pathetique (Beethoven) / Liebes-
traum (Liszt) / Warsaw concerto / Piano
concerto in A minor (Grieg) / Cornish rhap-
sody / Piano concerto no.2 (Rachmaninov)
/ Rhapsody in blue / Concerto No. 1/ B flat
minor Op. 23 / Piano concerto No.21 in C major
CD _____ 8202992
Delphine / Oct '90 / PolyGram.

FROM THE HEART
Clouds / Tender love / Your eyes in my eyes
/ Remember me / Moonlighting / Italian girl
/ Loneliness / Living without you / Such a
beautiful waltz / Broken heart / First love /
Lady said / Girl from Asia
CD _____ PWKS 536
Carlton Home Entertainment / '89 / Carlton
Home Entertainment.

HOLLYWOOD AND BROADWAY
Night and day / Bewitched, bothered and
bewildered / Embraceable you / Long ago
and far away / Way you look tonight /
Smoke gets in your eyes / People / All the
things you are / I've grown accustomed to
her face / On the street where you live / If I
loved you / You'll never walk alone
CD _____ 828 028-2
Delphine / Oct '90 / PolyGram.

**IN HARMONY (Clayderman, Richard &
James Last)**
I will always love you / Streets of Philadelphia / Pastorale / Savev the best for last /
Capriccio romantico / Have I told you lately
that I love you / Everytime you go away /
Strangers in paradise / Goodnight girl / Legend of Greensleeves / When a man loves a
woman / True love / Nocturno / Another day
in paradise / Andantino semplice / When
you tell me that you love me / Love is all
around
CD _____ 523824-2
Polydor / Oct '94 / PolyGram.

**LITTLE NIGHT MUSIC, A (12 Classic
Love Songs)**
I just called to say I love you / I'm not in
love / Sailing / For all we know / We've only
just begun without you / Nights in white
satin / Careless whisper / Power of love /
Whiter shade of pale / Nothing's gonna
change my love for you / Just the way you
are / Princess of the night
CD _____ 5501332
Spectrum/Karussell / Oct '93 / PolyGram /
THE.

LOVESONGS
CD _____ 270799
BR Music / Jun '95 / Target/BMG.

MUSIQUES DE L'AMOUR
Man and a woman / My way / Lara's theme
/ Parlez-moi d'amour / When a man loves a
woman / Strangers in the night / Voyage a
Venise / Ave Maria / Aline / La vraie mu-
sique de l'amour / Feelings / Tristesse / Un
homme et une femme / Love me tender /
Plaisir d'amour / Michelle / Jardin Street
CD _____ 822 440-2
Delphine / Nov '84 / PolyGram.

MY CLASSIC COLLECTION
Four seasons: spring / Swan / Italian sym-
phony no.1 - A sharp/opus 90 / Aria / Waltz
in A flat / Cavalleria rusticana / Barcarolle /
Nocturne - D flat major/ opus 27 / Forever
green / Hill Street Blues / Mahogany /
Sleepy shores / Evergreen / Tara's theme /
Over the rainbow / Medley: Four Seasons
CD _____ 828 228 2
Delphine / Jun '92 / PolyGram.

REVERIES
Dolannes melodie / Yesterday / Liebes-
traum / Don't cry for me Argentina / La vie
en rose / Hymne a la joie / Pour elise / Ex-
odus / Ballade pour Adeline / Romeo and
Juliet / Elizabethan serenade / Bridge over
troubled water / Love story / Moon river /
Sonate au Clair de Lune (Debussy) / La mer
/ Barcarolle
CD _____ 818 629 2
Delphine / '86 / PolyGram.

RICHARD CLAYDERMAN
L for love (A comme armour) / La mer / My
way / Lyphard melody / Tristesse / Fur Elise
/ Ballade pour Adeline / Romeo and Juliet /
Bach gammon / Sentimental melody / Liebestraum / Moonlight sonata / Romeo and
Juliet / Murmers / I have a dream / Woman
in love / Thorn birds / Feelings / Up where
we belong / Bright eyes / Ebony and ivory

/ Bridge over troubled water / Chariots of
fire / Memory / Only you / How deep is your
love / Don't cry for me Argentina
CD _____ 828 003-2
Delphine / Oct '90 / PolyGram.

ROMANTIC
Broken hearts / Heartbeat / Love in vain /
Because / Dancing alone / Moonlit shores /
Listen on my love / Longing / Piano solo /
Lonely sea
CD _____ PWKS 532
Carlton Home Entertainment / Jul '89 / Carl-
ton Home Entertainment.

SONGS OF LOVE
Bretts (Theme) / Howard's Way / Easten-
ders / Nikita / Do you know where you're
going to / Lady in red / Take my breath
away / You are my world / We are the world
/ I know him so well / Eleana / Colin Maillard
/ Eroica / La sorellina / All By myself / I
dreamed a dream / All I ask of you
CD _____ 8209952
Delphine / Oct '90 / PolyGram.

SOUVENIRS
Love at first sight / Letter to my mother /
Ocean / Wedding of love / Sagittarius / Diva
/ So sad / Secret garden / Journey to Ven-
ice / Dream story / Pastoral / Rondo for a
little child / Doves from the Tenere / Regrets
/ Childhood memories / Time passing
CD _____ PWKS 4030P
Carlton Home Entertainment / Oct '90 /
Carlton Home Entertainment.

SPECIAL COLLECTION, A
Love at first sight / Ocean / Sagittarius / So
sad / Journey to Venice / Pasoral / Doves
from the Tenere / Childhood memories /
Letter to my mother / Wedding of love /
Diva / Secret garden / Dream story / Rondo
for a little child / Regrets / Time passing /
Remember me / Clouds / Loneliness /
Tender love / Such a beautiful waltz / First
love / Girl from Asia / Moonlighting / Italian
girl / Living without you / Your eyes in my
eyes / Broken heart / Lady said / Broken
hearts / Love in vain / Dancing alone / Lis-
ten oh my love / Piano solo / Heartbeat /
Berceuse / Moonlight shores / Longing /
Lonely sea
CD Set _____ BOXD 15
Carlton Home Entertainment / Nov '91 /
Carlton Home Entertainment.

SUN AND THE FLOWER, THE
CD _____ MSCD 10
Magnum Music / Oct '94 / Magnum Music
Group.

**TOGETHER AT LAST (Clayderman,
Richard & James Last)**
From a distance / Everything I do (I do it for
you) / Sacrifice / Moonfire / Careless whis-
per / Pretty ballerina / Chancer (theme) /
Wind beneath my wings / Any dream will do
/ Unchained melody / Indigo bay / Promise
me / Reflections / Candle in the wind
CD _____ 5115252
Polydor / Oct '91 / PolyGram.

Claypool, Philip

CIRCUS LEAVING TOWN, A
CD _____ CURCD 18
Curb / Nov '95 / PolyGram.

Clayton Brothers

MUSIC, THE
CD _____ 74037
Capri / Nov '93 / Wellard / Cadillac.

Clayton, Buck

BADEN-SWITZERLAND
CD _____ SKCD 2-2028
Sackville / Jul '93 / Swift / Jazz Music /
Jazz Horizons / Cadillac / CM.

**BLOW THE BLUES (Clayton, Buck &
Buddy Tate)**
CD _____ OJCCD 850
Original Jazz Classics / Nov '95 / Wellard /
Jazz Music / Cadillac / Complete/Pinnacle.

**BUCK CLAYTON & BUDDY TATE
(Clayton, Buck & Buddy Tate)**
CD _____ OJCCD 7572
Original Jazz Classics / Jun '95 / Wellard /
Jazz Music / Cadillac / Complete/Pinnacle.

**COPENHAGEN CONCERT (Clayton,
Buck All Stars)**
CD _____ SCCD 36006/7
Steeplechase / Nov '90 / Impetus.

JAM SESSION 1975
CD _____ CRD 143
Chiara Scuro / Nov '95 / Jazz Music /
Kudos.

**SWINGIN' DREAM, A (Clayton, Buck &
Swing Band)**
CD _____ STCD 16
Stash / Oct '92 / Jazz Music / CM /
Cadillac / Direct / ADA.

Clayton, Jay

**JAZZ ALLEY TAPES, THE (Clayton, Jay
& Don Lamphere)**
You're a weaver of dreams / Serenade to
you / Softly as in a morning sunrise / I remember Clifford / New stores / Love for sale

/ I've grown accustomed to her face / My silent love / Mr. P.C. / A.C.
CD _____ HEPCD 2046
Hep / Sep '92 / Cadillac / Jazz Music / New Note / Wellard.

Clayton, John

GROOVE SHOP (Featuring Hamilton Jazz Orchestra) (Clayton, John & Jeff)
CD _____ 740212
Capri / '90 / Wellard / Cadillac.

HEART AND SOUL (Clayton-Hamilton Orchestra)
CD _____ 74028
Capri / Nov '93 / Wellard / Cadillac.

SUPER BASS (Clayton, John & Ray Brown)
CD _____ 740182
Capri / '90 / Wellard / Cadillac.

Clayton, Lee

ANOTHER NIGHT
CD _____ PRLD 700812
Provogue / Nov '89 / Pinnacle.

BORDER AFFAIR/NAKED CHILD
CD _____ EDCD 434
Edsel / Oct '95 / Pinnacle / ADA.

SPIRIT OF TWILIGHT
CD _____ PRD 70652
Provogue / Sep '94 / Pinnacle.

Clayton, Peter

DOCTOR PETER CLAYTON - 1935-1942 (Clayton, Doctor Peter)
CD _____ DOCD 5179
Blues Document / Oct '93 / Swift / Jazz Music / Hot Shot.

Clayton, Steve

LOVE IS SAID IN MANY WAYS
CD _____ STCD 559
Stash / Oct '93 / Jazz Music / CM / Cadillac / Direct / ADA.

Clayton, Vikki

IN FLIGHT
CD _____ RGF 013CD
Road Goes On Forever / Aug '93 / Direct.

IT SUITS ME WELL
CD _____ TRUCKCD 021
Terrapin Truckin' / Sep '94 / Total/BMG / Direct / ADA.

MIDSUMMER CUSHION
CD _____ CDSGP 008
Prestige / Jun '94 / Total/BMG.

Clayton, Willie

AT HIS BEST
CD _____ ICH 1503
Ichiban / Dec '93 / Koch.

CHICAGO SOUL GREATS (Clayton, Willie & Otis Clay)
It's time you made up your mind / I must be losing you / Baby you're ready / Too much of nothing / Gotta have money / Hello, how have you been / Say yes to love / Abracadabra / When I'm gone / That wall / If I could reach out / Let me be the one / I didn't know the meaning of pain / Woman don't live here no more / You can't escape the hands of love / You did something to me / It was jealousy
CD _____ HILOCD 16
Hi / Jul '95 / Pinnacle.

FEELS LIKE LOVE
CD _____ ICH 1155CD
Ichiban / Feb '94 / Koch.

NO GETTING OVER ME
CD _____ ICH 1182
Ichiban / Aug '94 / Koch.

Clea & McLeod

BEYOND OUR MEANS
CD _____ UTIL 009 CD
Utility / Feb '90 / Grapevine.

Clean

CLEAN COMPILATION
Billy two / At the bottom / Tally ho / Anything could happen / Point that thing somewhere else / Flowers / Fish / Beatnik / Getting older / Slug song / Oddity / Whatever I do (wherever I go)
CD _____ FNE 3CD
Flying Nun / Nov '88 / Disc.

COMPILATION
CD _____ FNCD 154
Flying Nun / Jun '95 / Disc.

GREAT UNWASHED
CD _____ FNCD 208
Flying Nun / Jun '95 / Disc.

MODERN ROCK
CD _____ FNCD 292
Flying Nun / Feb '95 / Disc.

ODDITIES
CD _____ FNCD 223
Flying Nun / Jun '95 / Disc.

VEHICLE
CD _____ FNCD 147
Flying Nun / Jun '95 / Disc.

Cleaners From Venus

BACK FROM THE CLEANERS
CD _____ TANGCD 014
Tangerine / Oct '95 / Disc.

GOLDEN CLEANERS
CD _____ TANGCD 3
Tangerine / Oct '95 / Disc.

Clear Blue Sky

CLEAR BLUE SKY
CD _____ REP 4110-WP
Repertoire / Aug '91 / Pinnacle / Cadillac.

Clearwater, Eddy

BLUES HANGOUT
CD _____ ECD 260082
Evidence / Jan '92 / Harmonia Mundi / ADA / Cadillac.

BOOGIE MY BLUES AWAY
CD _____ DD 678
Big Mo / Aug '95 / Direct / ADA.

CHIEF, THE
CD _____ R 2615
Rooster / Dec '94 / Direct.

Cleary, Jon

ALLIGATOR LIPS & DIRTY RICE
Go ahead baby / Long distance lover / C'mon second line / Groove me / In the mood / Big chief / Let them talk / Pick up the pieces / Burnt mouth boogie
CD _____ CDCH 377
Ace / Mar '93 / Pinnacle / Cadillac / Complete/Pinnacle.

Cleftones

BEST OF THE CLEFTONES
CD _____ NEMCD 603
Sequel / Aug '90 / BMG.

Clegg, Johnny

IN MY AFRICAN DREAM
CD _____ SHAKACD 3
Safari / Aug '94 / Pinnacle.

Clement, Giles

WES SIDE STORIES (Clement, Giles Quartet)
CD _____ 500492
Musidisc / Nov '93 / Vital / Harmonia Mundi / ADA / Cadillac / Discovery.

Clements, Vassar

GRASS ROUTES
Beats me / Westport Drive / Come on home / Florida blues / Other end / Rain rain rain / Rambling / Rounder's blues / Fiddlin' will / Non-stop / Flame of love / Turkey in the straw
CD _____ CDROU 0287
Rounder / Feb '92 / CM / Direct / ADA / Cadillac.

HILLBILLY JAZZ
CD _____ FF 101CD
Flying Fish / Jul '92 / Roots / CM / Direct / ADA.

HILLBILLY JAZZ RIDES AGAIN
Hillbilly jazz / Don't hop don't skip / Airmail special / Say goodbye to the blues / Swing street / Woodsheddin' / Be a little discreet / Hillbilly jazz on vacation / Caravan / How can I go on without you / Triple stop boogie / Take a break
CD _____ FF 385CD
Flying Fish / May '93 / Roots / CM / Direct / ADA.

Clemons, Clarence

PEACEMAKER
Peace prayer / Into the blue forest / Abraxas / Miracle / Serenity / Spirit dance
CD _____ 72445110322
Zoo Entertainment / Jun '95 / BMG.

Click Click

BENT MASSIVE
CD _____ BIAS 144 CD
Play It Again Sam / '89 / Vital.

RORSCHACH TESTING
Awake and watching / Perfect stranger / Fifteen minutes / Playground / Head fuck / Whirlpool / Vacuum shop / What a word
CD _____ CDBIAS 090
Play It Again Sam / '88 / Vital.

YAKUTSKA
Yakutska
CD _____ CDBIAS 126
Play It Again Sam / '89 / Vital.

Cliff, Dave

SIPPIN' AT BELLS (Cliff, Dave & Geoff Simkins)
Back to back / Sal's line / How deep is the ocean / Easy to love / Nobody knows the trouble I've caused / I guess I'll hang my tears out to dry / Nightingale sang in Berkeley Square / Lester's blues / Sippin' at bells / Conception / Once I loved / Touch of your lips / That old feeling / Indian summer
CD _____ SPJCD 553
Spotlite / Jul '95 / Cadillac / Jazz Horizons / Swift.

Cliff, Jimmy

BEST OF JIMMY CLIFF
Hard road to travel / Sooner or later / Sufferin' in the land / Keep your eye on the sparrow / Struggling man / Wild world / Vietnam / Another cycle / Wonderful world, beautiful people / Harder they come / Let your yeah be yeah / Synthetic world / I'm no immigrant / Give and take / Many rivers to cross / Going back west / Sitting in limbo / Come into my life / You can get it if you really want / Goodbye yesterday
CD _____ RRCD 50
Reggae Refreshers / Mar '96 / PolyGram / Vital.

COOL RUNNER LIVE IN LONDON, THE
Intro (Jimmy Jimmy) / Africa / Yeah ho / Rub-a-dub / Peace / Rock steady / Save the planet / Many rivers to cross / Limbo / Third world people / Many rivers to cross / Samba reggae (live & studio versions) / Rebel in me / Wonderful world, beautiful people / Justice / Higher and deeper love / Baby let me feel it (MC only) / True story (MC only) / Shout for freedom (MC only)
CD _____ MOCD 3010
More Music / Feb '95 / Sound & Media.

FOLLOW MY MIND
Look at the mountains / Jimmy I'm gonna live, I'm gonna love / Going mad / Dear mother / Who feels it, knows it / Remake the world / No woman, no cry / Wahjahka man / Hypocrite / If I follow my mind / You're the only one
CD _____ 7599263112
WEA / Jan '96 / Warner Music.

FUNDAMENTAL REGGAY
Fundamental reggae / Under the sun, moon and stars / Rip off / On my life / Commercialization / Oh Jamaica / No. 1 rip off man / Brother / House of exile / Long time no see / My love is as solid as rock / My people / Actions speak louder than words / Brave warrior / Fundamental reggay / Under the sun moon and stars
CD _____ SEECD 83
See For Miles/C5 / Apr '93 / Pinnacle.

GIVE THE PEOPLE WHAT THEY WANT
Son of man / Give the people what they want / Experience / Shelter of your love / Majority rule / Let's turn the tables / Material world / World in trap / What are you doing with your life / My philosophy
CD _____ 9031748252
WEA / Jan '96 / Warner Music.

I AM THE LIVING
I am the living / All the strength we got / It's the beginning of the end / Gone clear / Love again / Morning train / Satan's kingdom / Another summer
CD _____ 0630129912
WEA / Jan '96 / Warner Music.

IN CONCERT (The Best Of Jimmy Cliff)
You can get it if you really want / Vietnam / Fountain of life / Many rivers of cross / Wonderful world, beautiful people / Under the sun, moon and stars / Wild world / Harder they come / Struggling man / Sitting in limbo
CD _____ 7599272322
WEA / Feb '92 / Warner Music.

JIMMY CLIFF
Many rivers to cross / Vietnam / My ancestors / Hard road to travel / Wonderful world, beautiful people / Sufferin' in the land / Hello sunshine / Use what I got / That's the way life goes / Come into my life
CD _____ CDTRL 16
Trojan / Mar '94 / Jetstar / Total/BMG.

JIMMY CLIFF LIVE
Intro / Jimmy Jimmy / Africa / Yeah ho / Rub a dub / Peace / Rock steady / Save our planet Earth / Many rivers to cross / Sitting in limbo / Third world people / Harder they come / Samba reggae / Rebel in me / Wonderful world, beautiful people / No justice / Higher and deeper love
CD _____ 16224CD
Success / Oct '94 / Carlton Home Entertainment.

MANY RIVERS TO CROSS
CD Set _____ CDTRL 342
Trojan / Jan '94 / Jetstar / Total/BMG.

REGGAE GREATS
Vietnam / Sitting in limbo / Struggling man / Let your yeah be yeah / Bongo man / Harder they come / Sufferin' in the land / Many rivers to cross / Hard road to travel / You can get it if you really want / Sooner or later

Climax Blues Band

CD _____ RRCD 22
Reggae Refreshers / Nov '90 / PolyGram / Vital.

SAVE OUR PLANET EARTH
CD _____ 106 552
Musidisc / Feb '94 / Vital / Harmonia Mundi / ADA / Cadillac / Discovery.

UNLIMITED
CD _____ CDTRJ 100
Trojan / Nov '90 / Jetstar / Total/BMG.

Clifford, Billy

BILLY CLIFFORD
CD _____ OSS 11CD
Ossian / Mar '88 / ADA / Direct / CM.

Clifford, Linda

IF MY FRIENDS COULD SEE ME NOW
If my friends could see me now / You are, you are / Runaway love / Broadway gypsy lady / I feel like falling in love / Please darling, don't say goodbye / Gypsy lady
CD _____ CPCD 8158
Charly / Jan '96 / Charly / THE / Cadillac.

RIGHT COMBINATION (Clifford, Linda & Curtis Mayfield)
Right combination / I'm so proud / Ain't no love lost / It's lovin' time / Love's sweet sensation / Between you baby and me
CD _____ CPCD 8072
Charly / Jun '94 / Charly / THE / Cadillac.

Clifton, Bill

EARLY YEARS 1957-1958, THE
Girl I left in Tennessee / Dixie darlin' / You don't know / Blue darlin' / I'll be there Mary dear / Paddy on the turnpike / I'll wander back someday / Darling Corey / When you kneel at my mother's grave / Blue ridge mountain blues / Are you alone / Springhill disaster / I'm living the right life now / Lonely heart blues / Cedar Grove / You go to your church / Walking in my sleep / Pal of yesterday / Just another broken heart / Little white washed chimney
CD _____ CD 1021
Rounder / '92 / CM / Direct / ADA / Cadillac.

Clifton, Ian

MUSIC FOR LIFE
CD _____ DLD 1033
Dance & Listen / Mar '93 / Savoy.

MUSIC FOR LIFE NO 2
Blackpool belle / I've told every little star / Aria / Yellow bird / Friends and neighbours / Put on a happy face
CD _____ DLD 1041
Dance & Listen / Nov '93 / Savoy.

Climax Blues Band

BLUES FROM THE ATTIC
CD _____ HTDCD 15
HTD / Oct '93 / Pinnacle.

CLIMAX CHICAGO BLUES BAND
Mean old world / Insurance / Going down this road / You've been drinking / Don't start me talkin' / Wee baby blues / Twenty past one / Stranger in your town / How many more years / Looking for my baby / Lonely, And / Entertainer
CD _____ C5CD 555
See For Miles/C5 / Oct '92 / Pinnacle.

COULDN'T GET IT RIGHT - PLUS
Couldn't get it right / Berlin blues / Chasing change / Losin' the humbles / Shopping bag people / Sense of direction / Before you reach the grave / Reaching out / Right now / Cobra / Rollin' home / Sav'ry gravy / Sky high / Loosen up / Running out of time / Mr. Goodtime / I am constant / Mighty fire
CD _____ SEECD 222
See For Miles/C5 / Jul '88 / Pinnacle.

DRASTIC STEPS
California sunshine / Lonely avenue / Deceiver / Ordinary people / Winner / Couldn't get it right / Fool for the bright times / Good times / Trouble / American dream / Couldn't get it right (Mix) (MC only)
CD _____ C5CD 573
See For Miles/C5 / Sep '91 / Pinnacle.

F.M./LIVE...PLUS
All the time in the world / Flight / Seventh son / Let's work together / Standing by a river / So many roads, so many trains / You make me sick / Shake your love / Going to New York / I am constant / Mesopotamania / Country hat
CD _____ SEECD 279
See For Miles/C5 / Sep '89 / Pinnacle.

HARVEST YEARS, THE ('69-'72)
Please don't help me / Hey baby everything's gonna be alright / Yeh yeh yeh / Everyday / Towards the sun / You make me sick / Reap what I've sowed / Shake your love / Looking for my baby / Flight / Mole on the dole / That's all / Insurance / Wee baby blues / Crazy about my baby / All right blue / Cut you loose
CD _____ SEECD 316
See For Miles/C5 / Jun '91 / Pinnacle.

LOT OF BOTTLE, A

Country hat / Everyday / Reap what I've sowed / Brief case / Alright blue / Seventh son / Please don't help me / Morning, noon and night / Long lovin' man / Louisiana blues / Cut you loose
CD _____ C5CD-548
See For Miles/C5 / Jan '90 / Pinnacle.

PLAYS ON

Flight / Hey baby's everything gonna be alright yeah yeah yeah / Cubano chant / Little girl / Mum's the word / Twenty past two / Temptation rag / So many roads / City ways / Crazy about my baby
CD _____ C5CD 556
See For Miles/C5 / Oct '92 / Pinnacle.

RICH MAN

Rich man / Mole on the dole / You make me sick / Standing by a river / Shake your love / All the time in the world / If you wanna know / Don't you mind people grinning in your face
CD _____ C5CD-553
See For Miles/C5 / '90 / Pinnacle.

TIGHTLY KNIT

Hey man / Shoot her if she runs / Towards the sun / Come on in my kitchen / Who killed McSwiggen / Little link / St. Michael's blues / Bide my time / That's all
CD _____ C5CD-557
See For Miles/C5 / Jun '90 / Pinnacle.

Climie, Simon

SOUL INSPIRATION

Soul inspiration / Does your heart still break / Love in the right hands / Dream with me / Oh how the years go by / Don't give up so easy / Spell / Don't waste time (Make your move) / Losing you / Life goes on
CD _____ 472220 2
Epic / Jan '93 / Sony.

Cline, Patsy

ALWAYS

Always / Love letters in the sand / Crazy arms / Bill Bailey, won't you please come home / Have you ever been lonely / You made me love you / I can see an angel / That's my desire / Your cheatin' heart / That's how a heartache begins / I love you so much it hurts / Half as much / You belong to me
CD _____ PWKS 502
Carlton Home Entertainment / Sep '93 / Carlton Home Entertainment.

BEST OF PATSY CLINE

Walkin' after midnight / I fall to pieces / Crazy / Who can I count on / She's got you / Strange / When I get thru with you / Imagine that / Someone / Heartaches / Sweet dreams / Faded love / When you need a laugh / He called me baby / Anytime
CD _____ PWKS 524
Carlton Home Entertainment / Sep '93 / Carlton Home Entertainment.

BEST OF PATSY CLINE

CD _____ DCD 5323
Disky / Dec '93 / THE / BMG / Discovery / Pinnacle.

BEST OF PATSY CLINE

CD _____ WMCD 5656
Woodford Music / Jun '92 / THE.

COLLECTION

CD _____ COL 007
Collection / Oct '95 / Target/BMG.

CRAZY DREAMS

Hidin' out / Turn the cards slowly / Church, a courtroom and then goodbye / Honky tonk merry go round / I love you honey / Come on in (and make yourself at home) / I cried all the way to the altar / Stop, look and listen / I've loved and lost again / Dear God / He will do for you (what he's done for me) / Walkin' after midnight / Heart you break may be your own / Pick me up on your way down / Poor man's roses / Today, tomorrow and forever / Fingertips / Stranger in my arms / Don't ever leave me again / Try again / Too many secrets / Then you'll know / Three cigarettes in an ashtray / That wonderful someone / In care of the blues / Hungry for love / I can't forget / I don't wanta / Ain't no wheels on this ship / Stop the world (and let me off) / Walking dream / Cry not for me / If I could see the world / Just out of reach / I can see an angel / Let the teardrops fall / Never no more / If I could only stay asleep / I'm moving along / I'm blue again / Love love love me honey do / Yes I understand / Gotta lot of rhythm in my soul / Life's railway to heaven / Just a closer walk with thee / Lovesick blues / How can I face tomorrow / There he goes / Crazy dreams
CD Set _____ CDSD 3.001
Sundown / Jul '90 / Magnum Music Group.

CRAZY DREAMS

CD _____ TRTCD 177
TrueTrax / Jun '95 / THE.

DEFINITIVE PATSY CLINE, THE

CD _____ ARC 94992
ARC / Sep '92 / ARC Music / ADA.

DISCOVERY

I don't wanta / Then you'll know / Don't ever leave me again / Two cigarettes in an ashtray / In care of the blues / Your cheatin' heart / Man upstairs / Stop the world (and let me off) / Try again / Walkin' dream / Too many secrets / Down by the riverside / Come on in / Ain't no wheels on this ship / Hungry for love / Walkin' after midnight
CD _____ PLATCD 5902
Prism / Sep '94 / Prism.

DREAMING

Sweet dreams / I fall to pieces / Crazy / Heartaches / Tra le la le la triangle / Have you ever been lonely / Faded love / Your cheatin' heart / She's got you / Walkin' after midnight / San Antonio rose / Three cigarettes in an ashtray / When I need a laugh / Always
CD _____ PLATCD 303
Platinum Music / Dec '88 / Prism / Ross.

ESSENTIAL COLLECTION

CD Set _____ LECD 608
Wisepack / Apr '95 / THE / Conifer.

ESSENTIAL COLLECTION, THE

CD Set _____ MCAD 410421
MCA / Nov '91 / BMG.

JUST OUT OF REACH

CD _____ MU 5072
Musketeer / Oct '92 / Koch.

LEGENDS IN MUSIC - PATSY CLINE

CD _____ LECD 052
Wisepack / Aug '94 / THE / Conifer.

LOVE COUNTRY

True love / Heartaches / Your cheatin' heart / Half as much / I love you so much it hurts / Love letters in the sand / Seven lonely days / Why can't he be you / Your kinda love / Sweet dreams / That's how a heartache begins / There he goes again / Have you ever been lonely / He called me baby / I'll sail my ship alone / You belong to me / Someday (you'll want me to want you) / Lovin' in vain / I fall to pieces / Leavin' on your mind
CD _____ MCLD 19240
MCA / May '94 / BMG.

LOVE SONGS

CD _____ CDMFP 5957
Music For Pleasure / Jan '92 / EMI.

MAGIC OF PATSY CLINE, THE

CD _____ TKOCD 003
TKO / '92 / TKO.

ONE AND ONLY PATSY CLINE, THE

Stop the world / Walkin' after midnight / Just a closer walk with thee / Just out of reach / I've loved and lost again / Fingerprints / Stranger in my arms / Poor man's roses / I can see an angel / If I could only stay asleep / I'm blue again / Today, tomorrow and forever / I love you honey / Never no more / Love love love me honey / Let the teardrops fall / I'm moving alone / Stop, look and listen
CD _____ ECD 3086
K-Tel / Jan '95 / K-Tel.

PATSY CLINE

Just a closer walk with thee / Never no more / Ain't no wheels on this ship / He'll do for you / Honky tonk merry go round / Poor man's roses / Pick me up / Turn the cards slowly / Dear God / I love you honey / I can't forget you / Crazy dreams
CD _____ CD 102
Timeless Treasures / Oct '94 / THE.

PATSY CLINE

Deja Vu / May '95 / THE.
CD _____ DVAD 6072

PATSY CLINE/BRENDA LEE ESSENTIALS (Cline, Patsy & Brenda Lee)

CD _____ LECDD 628
Wisepack / Aug '95 / THE / Conifer.

PREMIER COLLECTION

Gotta lot of rhythm in my soul / In care of the blues / Hungry for love / Lovesick blues / Stranger in my arms / Crazy dreams / Honky tonk merry go round / I cried all the way to the altar / A church, a courtroom, then goodbye / I've loved and lost again / Three cigarettes in an ashtray / I can't forget / Just out of reach / I love you honey / Poor man's roses / Pick me up / Heart you break may be your own / Turn the cards slowly / That wonderful someone / Don't ever leave me / Dear God / He'll do for you / Never no more / Always / Half as much / Have you ever been lonely / That's how a heartache begins / Bill Bailey, Won't you please come home / Love letters in the sand / Wayward wind / You belong to me / I love you so much it hurts / That's my desire / I can see an angel / You made me love you / Crazy midnight / I fall to pieces / Crazy / Who can I count on / She's got you / Strange / When I get thru with you / Imagine that / So lonely / Heartaches / Leavin' on your mind / Sweet dreams / Faded love / When you need a laugh / He called me baby / Anytime
CD Set _____ BOXD 40T
Carlton Home Entertainment / Oct '94 / Carlton Home Entertainment.

SPOTLIGHT ON PATSY CLINE

Walkin' after midnight / I cried all the way to the altar / In care of the blues / I can't forget you / I love you honey / Just out of reach / Walking dream / Today, tomorrow and forever / Let the teardrops fall / Hungry for love / Too many secrets / Never no more / Stop the world / I don't wanna / Turn the cards slowly / I've loved and lost again
CD _____ HADCD 130
Javelin / Feb '94 / THE / Henry Hadaway Organisation.

STOP THE WORLD

In care of the blues / Stop the world / Too many secrets / Ain't no wheels on this ship / If I could only stay asleep / Never no more / Love me honey do / Three cigarettes in an ashtray / Honky tonk merry go round / Life's railway to heaven / Try again / Fingerprints / Turn the cards slowly / I cried all the way to the altar / Cry not for me / I love you honey / I'm blue again / Let the teardrops fall / Hidin' out
CD _____ MUCD 9029
Start / Apr '95 / Koch.

SWEET DREAMS WITH...

CD _____ ENTCD 267
Entertainers / Oct '87 / Target/BMG.

TODAY, TOMORROW AND FOREVER

Walkin' after midnight / Stop, look and listen / Yes I understand / I can see an angel / Just out of reach / Walking dream / Then you'll know / Don't ever leave me again / I can't forget you / I'm hungry, hungry for your love / I don't wanna / I'm moving along / Gotta lot of rhythm in my soul / Just a closer walk with thee / I've loved and lost again / Todya, tomorrow and forever / If I could see the world / Come on in / Pick me up on your way down / Heart you break may be your own / In care of the blues / Stop the world / Too many secrets / Ain't no wheels on this ship / If only I could stay asleep / Never no more / Love me honey do / Three cigarettes in an ashtray / Honky tonk merry go round / Life's railway to heaven / Try again / Fingerprints / Turn the cards slowly / I cried all the way to the altar / Cry not for me / I love you honey / I'm blue again / Let the teardrops fall / Hidin' out
CD Set _____ PAR 2305
Start / Mar '95 / Koch.

UNFORGETTABLE

Gotta lot of rhythm in my soul / In care of the blues / Hungry for love / Lovesick blues / Stranger in my arms / Crazy dreams / Honky tonk merry go round / I cried all the way to the altar / Church, a courtroom and then goodbye / I've loved and lost again / Three cigarettes in an ashtray / I can't forget you / Just out of reach / I love you honey / Poor man's roses / Pick me up on your way down / Heart you break may be your own / Turn the cards slowly / That wonderful someone / Don't ever leave me again / Just a closer walk with thee / Dear God / He'll do for you / Never no more
CD _____ PWK 017
Carlton Home Entertainment / Feb '96 / Carlton Home Entertainment.

VERY BEST OF PATSY CLINE, THE

CD Set _____ DCDCD 207
Castle / Jun '95 / BMG.

WALKIN' AFTER MIDNIGHT (28 Country Classics)

Walkin' after midnight / I've loved and lost again / Poor man's roses / Turn the cards slowly / I cried all the way to the altar / Pick me up on your way down / Stranger in my arms / Honky tonk merry go round / Church a courtroom and then goodbye / Three cigarettes in an ashtray / Never no more / Dear God / Lovesick blues / If I could stay asleep / Just out of reach / Then you'll know / I love honey / Fingerprints / There he goes he'll do for you (what he's done for me) / I can't forget you / Today, tomorrow and forever / Crazy dreams / I can see an angel / If I could see the world
CD _____ PLATCD 27
Platinum Music / Jul '89 / Prism / Ross.

WALKIN' AFTER MIDNIGHT

Walkin' after midnight / Gotta lot of rhythm in my soul / Just out of reach / Church, a courtroom and then goodbye / I don't wanna / Stop, look and listen / Three cigarettes in an ashtray / I can see an angel / Poor man's roses / I'm blue again / Cry not for me / Honky tonk merry go round / Life's railway to heaven / Just a closer walk with thee
CD _____ 5500542
Spectrum/Karussell / May '93 / PolyGram / THE.

WALKIN' AFTER MIDNIGHT (2)

CD _____ CTS 55404
Country Stars / Jan '92 / Target/BMG.

WALKING AFTER MIDNIGHT

Walkin' after midnight / I've loved and lost again / I can't forget / Just out of reach / I'm hungry, hungry for your love / I can see an angel / Walking dream / If I could see the world / Hidin' out / Too many secrets
CD _____ CDCD 1066
Charly / Mar '93 / Charly / THE / Cadillac.

Clinton, Bill

BILL CLINTON JAM SESSION

CD _____ PRES 001CD
Pres / Nov '94 / Direct.

Clinton, George

COMPUTER GAMES

CD _____ MUSCD 511
MCI / May '95 / Disc / THE.

FIFTH OF FUNK

CD _____ ESSCD 280
Essential / Feb '95 / Total/BMG.

GEORGE CLINTON FAMILY SERIES PART 1 (Various Artists)

Go for yer funk / Funk it up / Funkin' for my momma's rent / Send a gram / Who in the funk do you think you are / Better days / Chong song / Michelle / Sunshine of your love / Interview
CD _____ ESSCD 185
Castle / Oct '92 / BMG.

GEORGE CLINTON FAMILY SERIES PART 2 (Various Artists)

May Day (S.O.S.) / These feet are made for dancin' (footstranger) / Booty body ray for the plush funk / I really envy the sunshine / Lickety split / Common law wife / Superspirit / Love don't come easy / I can't stand it / Monster dance / We're just funkers / Interview
CD _____ ESSCD 189
Castle / Jan '93 / BMG.

GEORGE CLINTON FAMILY SERIES PART 3 ("P" Is The Funk) (Various Artists)

Clone communicado / Does disc with dat / Shove on / Rock jam / Love is something / Every booty (get on down) / Personal problems / Bubblegum gangster / She's crazy / Think right / In the cabin of my Uncle Jam (P is the funk) / My love / Interview / Commercials
CD Set _____ ESSCD 190
Castle / May '93 / BMG.

GEORGE CLINTON FAMILY SERIES PART 4 (Testing Positive For The Funk) (Various Artists)

Live up (to what she thinks of me) / Secrets / She never do's things / Take my love / Just for play / Off the wall / Get it on / Triune / Superstar madness / One angle / Twenty bucks / To care / Comin' down from your love / Interview
CD _____ ESSCD 198
Castle / Sep '93 / BMG.

HEY MAN, SMELL MY FINGER

Martial law / Paint the white house black / Way up / Dis beat disrupts / Get satisfied / Hollywood / Rhythm and rhyme / Big pump / If true love / Right in my hello / Maximumisness / Kick back / Flag was still there / Martial law (Hey man, smell my finger)
CD _____ NPG 60532
New Power Generation / Mar '95 / Grapevine / THE.

HYDRAULIC FUNK (P-Funk All Stars)

Pump up and down / Pumpin' it up / Copy cat / Hydraulic pump / Throw your hands up in the air / Generator pap / Acupuncture / One of those summers / Catch a keeper / Pumpin' you is so easy / Generator pop (mix)
CD _____ CDSEWD 097
Westbound / Jun '95 / Pinnacle.

P. FUNK ALL-STARS LIVE (P-Funk All Stars)

Audience chant: P funk / Do that stuff (Introducting the band) / Cosmic slop / Let's take it to the stage / Mothership connection / I call my baby pussycat / Give up the funk / (Not just) knee deep / Maggot brain / Atomic dog / Flashlight / One nation under a groove (On CD only)
CD Set _____ CDSEW2 031
Westbound / Oct '90 / Pinnacle.

SAMPLE SOME OF DISC, SAMPLE SOME OF DAT

CD _____ MOLCD 36
Music Of Life / Nov '94 / Grapevine.

SAMPLE SOME OF DISC, SAMPLE SOME OF DAT VOL. 2

CD _____ MOLCD 33
Music Of Life / Sep '93 / Grapevine.

Clinton, Larry

FEELING LIKE A DREAM

Feeling like a dream / Jump Joe / I want to rock / Because of you / Nobody knows the trouble I've seen / Taboo / Sahara / Dance of the reed flutes / Arab dance / I may be wrong / Do you call that a buddy / Rockin' chair / Camptown races
CD _____ HEPCD 1047
Hep / Nov '95 / Cadillac / Jazz Music / New Note / Wellard.

LARRY CLINTON - 1941-49 (Clinton, Larry & His Orchestra)
CD _____ CCD 58
Circle / '92 / Jazz Music / Swift / Wellard.

SHADES OF HADES (Clinton, Larry & Bea Wain)
Big dipper / Snake charmer / Midnight in the madhouse / I double dare you / I cash clo'es / Two dreams got together / Swing lightly / Military madcaps / I've got my heart set on you / Mr. Jinx stay away from me / True confession / Shades of Hades / Abba dabba / Dr. Rhythm / Campbells are swingin' / Always and always / Jubilee / I was doing all right / One rose (that's left in my heart) / Our love is here to stay / Wolverine blues / Oh Lady be good / Scrapin' the toast
CD _____ HEPCD 1037
Hep / Oct '93 / Cadillac / Jazz Music / New Note / Wellard.

Clinton, Michelle T.

BLACK ANGELES (Clinton, Michelle T. & Wanda Coleman)
CD _____ NAR 031 CD
New Alliance / May '93 / Pinnacle.

Clique

SELF PRESERVATION SOCIETY
CD _____ DRCD 003
Detour / Jul '95 / Detour.

Clock

IT'S TIME
Axel f / Whoomph (there it is) / Everybody / Holding on in the house (Live version) / Keep the fires burning / Rythm holding on / Keep pushin' / Clock carnival / Secret (Instrumental) / Clock ten to two megamix
CD _____ MCD 11355
MCA / Sep '95 / BMG.

Clock DVA

BLACK WORDS ON WHITE PAPER
CD _____ DD 172
Contempo / Oct '93 / Plastic Head.

COLLECTIVE
CD Set _____ HY 39100
Hyperium / Aug '94 / Plastic Head.

DIGITAL SOUNDTRACKS
Sensual engine / Cycom / Presence / Sound sweep / Chemicals / Delta machines / Stills in emotion / Inversion / Operator / E-Wave / Diminishing point / Stations of the mind
CD _____ CONTECD 217
Contempo / Jan '93 / Plastic Head.

MAN AMPLIFIED
CD _____ CONTECD 182
Contempo / Mar '92 / Plastic Head.

SIGN
CD _____ CONTECD 225
Contempo / Sep '93 / Plastic Head.

THIRST
CD _____ CONTEDISC 192
Contempo / May '92 / Plastic Head.

WHITE SOULS IN BLACK SUITS
CD _____ CONTECD 157
Contempo / May '92 / Plastic Head.

Clooney, Rosemary

16 MOST REQUESTED SONGS
Come on-a my house / Botch-a-me (ba-ba baciani piccina) / Hey there / Be my life's companion / Tenderly / Mixed emotion / Mambo italiano / You'll never know / When you wish upon a star / Half as much / This ole house / I could have danced all night / It might as well be spring / In the cool, cool, cool of the evening / Blues in the night / Too young
CD _____ CK 4403
Columbia / May '95 / Sony.

BLUE ROSE (Clooney, Rosemary & Duke Ellington)
CD _____ 4720852
Sony Jazz / Jan '95 / Sony.

BOTCH-A-ME
CD _____ WW 88020
World Music / May '93 / Pinnacle.

DEMI-CENTENNIAL
Danny boy / Coffee song / I'm confessin' that I love you / I left my heart in San Francisco / Old friends / White Christmas / There will never be another you / Falling in love again / Sophisticated lady / How will I remember you / Mambo italiano / Promise I'll never say goodbye) / Heart's desire / We'll meet again / Time flies / Dear departed past
CD _____ CCD 4633
Concord Jazz / Mar '95 / New Note.

EVERYTHING'S COMING UP ROSIE (Clooney, Rosemary & Nat Pierce Quintet)
I cried for you / I can't get started (with you) / Do you know what it means to miss New Orleans / I've got such a crush on you / As time goes by / More than you know / Foggy day / Hey there

CD _____ CCD 4047
Concord Jazz / Jun '89 / New Note.

EVERYTHING'S ROSIE
CD _____ HCD 255
Hindsight / Nov '94 / Target/BMG / Jazz Music.

FOR THE DURATION
No love, no nothin' / Don't fence me in / I don't want to walk without you / Every time we say goodbye (CD only.) / You'd be so nice to come home to / Sentimental journey / For all we know / September song / These foolish things / They're either too young or too old / More I see you / White cliffs of Dover / Saturday night is the loneliest night of the week (CD only.) / I'll be seeing you
CD _____ CCD 4444
Concord Jazz / Feb '91 / New Note.

GIRL SINGER
Nice 'n' easy / Sweet Kentucky ham / Autumn in New York / Miss Otis regrets / Let there be love / Lovers after all / From this moment on / More than you know / Wave / We fell in love anyway / It don't mean a thing if it ain't got that swing / I'm checkin' out (goodbye) / Of course it's crazy / Straighten up and fly right / Best is yet to come
CD _____ CCD 4496
Concord Jazz / Feb '92 / New Note.

ROSEMARY CLOONEY SING BALLADS
CD _____ CCD 4282
Concord Jazz / '85 / New Note.

ROSEMARY CLOONEY SINGS COLE PORTER
CD _____ CCD 185
Concord Jazz / '89 / New Note.

ROSEMARY CLOONEY SINGS HAROLD ARLEN
Hooray for love / Happiness is a thing called love / One for my baby / Get happy / Ding dong the witch is dead / Out of this world / My shining hour / Let's take the long way home / Stormy weather
CD _____ CCD 4210
Concord Jazz / '83 / New Note.

SHOW TUNES
I wish I were in love again / I stayed too long at the fair / How are things in Glocca Morra / When do you start / I'll see you again / Guys and dolls / Manhattan / Everything I've got / Come back to me / Taking a chance on love / All the things you are
CD _____ CCD 346
Concord Jazz / Jan '89 / New Note.

SINGS RODGERS, HART & HAMMERSTEIN
OH what a beautiful morning / People will say we're in love / Love look away / Gentleman is a dope / It might as well be Spring / Sweetest sounds / I could write a book / You took advantage of me / Lady is a tramp / Little girl blue / My romance / Yours sincerely (CD only.)
CD _____ CCD 4405
Concord Jazz / '91 / New Note.

SINGS SHOW TUNES
CD _____ CCD 4364
Concord Jazz / '91 / New Note.

SINGS THE LYRICS OF IRA GERSHWIN
But not for me / Nice work if you can get it / How long has this been going on / Fascinating rhythm / Love is here to stay / Strike up the band / Long ago and far away / They all laughed / Man that got away / They can't take that away from me
CD _____ CCD 4112
Concord Jazz / Mar '90 / New Note.

SINGS THE LYRICS OF JOHNNY MERCER
CD _____ CCD 4333
Concord Jazz / Dec '87 / New Note.

SINGS THE MUSIC OF IRVING BERLIN
It's a lovely day today / Be careful it's my heart / Cheek to cheek / How about me / Best thing for you would be me / I got lost in his arms / There's no business like show business / Better luck next time / What'll I do / Let's face the music and dance
CD _____ CCD 4255
Concord Jazz / '85 / New Note.

SINGS THE MUSIC OF JIMMY VAN HEUSEN
Love won't let you get away / I thought about you / My heart is a hobo / Second time around / It could happen to you / Imagination / Like someone in love / Call me irresponsible / Walking happy / Last dance
CD _____ CCD 4308
Concord Jazz / Mar '87 / New Note.

STILL ON THE ROAD
Take me back to manhattan / Rules of the road / On the road again / Let's get away from it all / Road to Morocco / Let's eat home / Till we meet again / Still crazy after all these years / Ol' man river / Moonlight Mississippi / (Back home again in) Indiana / Corcovado (Quiet nights) / How deep is the ocean / How are things in Glocca Morra / Still on the road
CD _____ CCD 4590
Concord Jazz / Mar '94 / New Note.

TRIBUTE TO BILLIE HOLIDAY - "HERE'S TO MY LADY"
CD _____ CCD 4081
Concord Jazz / Jul '92 / New Note.

WITH LOVE
Just the way you are / Way we were / Alone at last / Come in from the rain / Meditation / Hello, young lovers / Just in time / Tenderly / Will you still be mine
CD _____ CCD 4144
Concord Jazz / '89 / New Note.

Close Lobsters

HEADACHE RHETORIC
CD _____ FIRE 33017
Fire / Oct '91 / Disc.

Closedown

NEARFIELD
CD _____ SR 9469CD
Silent / Jan '95 / Plastic Head.

Clout

CLOUT
CD _____ 12366
Laserlight / May '94 / Target/BMG.

Cloven Hoof

DOMINATOR
Rising up / Nova battlestar / Reach for the sky / Warrior of the wasteland / Invaders / Fugitive / Dominator / Road of eagles
CD _____ HMRXD 113
FM / Aug '88 / Sony.

Cloverleaf

BORN A RIDER
CD _____ HY 200129CD
Hypertension / Mar '95 / Total/BMG / Direct / ADA.

Clovers

DOWN IN THE ALLEY
One mint julip / Good lovin' / Don't you know I love you / Wonder where my baby's gone / Ting a ling / Crawlin' / Hey Miss Fanny / Lovey dovey / Middle of the night / Fool fool fool / I've got my eyes on you / I confess / Your cash ain't nothin' but trash / Little Mama / Down in the alley / Nip slip / Devil or angel / Blue velvet / In the morning time / Love bug / If I could be loved by you
CD _____ 756782312-2
Atlantic / Mar '93 / Warner Music.

Club 69

ADULTS ONLY
Diva / Let me be your underwear / Sugar pie guy / Pleasure / Take a ride / Fantasy / Unique / My secret wish / Riding into battle with her high heels on / Love is the message / Warm leatherette / Diva (remix) / Theme
CD _____ TRIUK 008CD
Tribal UK / Oct '95 / Vital.

Clusone

CLUSONE 3
CD _____ RAMBOY 05
Bvhaast / Oct '94 / Cadillac.

I AM AN INDIAN
CD _____ GCD 79505
Gramavision / Oct '95 / Vital/3MV / ADA.

SOFT LIGHTS AND SWEET MUSIC
CD _____ ART 6153CD
Hat Art / Jul '94 / Harmonia Mundi / ADA / Cadillac.

Cluster

CLUSTER & BRIAN ENO (Cluster & Brian Eno)
CD _____ SKYCD 3010
Sky / Nov '94 / Koch.

CURIOSUM
CD _____ SKYCD 3063
Sky / May '95 / Koch.

GROSSES WASSER
CD _____ SKYCD 3027
Sky / Nov '94 / Koch.

SOWIESOSO
CD _____ SKYCD 3005
Sky / Nov '94 / Koch.

Clutch

CLUTCH
CD _____ 7559617552
Warner Bros. / Jun '95 / Warner Music.

TRANS NATIONAL SPEEDWAY LEAGUE
Shogun named Marcus / El jefe speaks / Binge and purge / Twelve Ounce epilogue / Bacchanal / Milk of human kindness / Rats / Earthworm / Heirloom 13 / Walking in the great shining path of monster trucks / Effigy
CD _____ 7567922812
Warner Bros. / Oct '93 / Warner Music.

CMU

SPACE CABARET/OPEN SPACES
Space cabaret / Song from the 4th era / Doctor am I normal / Light shine / Voodoo man / Japan / Mystical sounds / Archway 272 / Distand thought, a point of light / Dream / Henry / Slow and lonesome blues / Clown / Open spaces
CD _____ SEECD 373
See For Miles/C5 / Jun '93 / Pinnacle.

Coal Porters

LAND OF HOPE & CROSBY
CD _____ SID 002
Prima / Sep '94 / Direct.

REBELS WITHOUT APPLAUSE
CD _____ RUB 17
Rubber / Jul '95 / Roots / Jazz Music / CM / Direct / ADA.

Coasters

GREATEST HITS
CD _____ 7567903862
Atlantic / Jul '93 / Warner Music.

JUST COASTIN'
I got to boogie / If I had a hammer / Poison ivy / Young blood / Along came Jones / Searchin' / Charlie Brown / Yakety yak / Benjamin and Loretta / Chick is guilty
CD _____ C5CD 579
See For Miles/C5 / Feb '92 / Pinnacle.

LEGENDS IN MUSIC - THE COASTERS
CD _____ LECD 076
Wisepack / Jul '94 / THE / Conifer.

VERY BEST OF THE COASTERS, THE
Riot in cell block 9 / Smoky Joe's cafe / Down in mexico / Searchin' / Idol with the golden head / Young blood / yakety yak / Charlie Brown / Along comes Jones / That is rock and roll / I'm a hog for you / Poison ivy / What about us / Run red run / Little Eygpt / Shoppin' for clothes / Sorry but I'm gonna have to pass
CD _____ 954832656-2
Atlantic / Mar '94 / Warner Music.

WHAT IS THE SECRET TO YOUR SUCCESS, 1957-64
My baby comes to me / Gee Golly / Sorry but I'm gonna have to pass / Teach me how to shimmy / The P.T.A.
CD _____ RBD 102
Mr. R&B / Jan '91 / Swift / CM / Wellard.

YAKETY YAK
CD _____ 8122714282
Carlton Home Entertainment / Oct '94 / Carlton Home Entertainment.

Coates, Eric

ERIC COATES
CD _____ GEMM CD 9973
Gemm / Sep '92 / Pinnacle.

Coates, Johnny

PORTRAIT
Let's get lost / Ding dong the witch is dead / If I love again / Love is the sweetest thing / Little girl blue / Sha-ga-da-ga-da / Coates oats / Between the devil and the deep blue sea / Skylark / My lucky day / If there is someone lovelier than you
CD _____ SV 0234
Savoy Jazz / Nov '93 / Conifer / ADA.

Cobb, Arnett

AGAIN WITH MILT BUCKNER (Cobb, Arnett & Milt Buckner)
CD _____ BLE 590522
Black & Blue / Apr '91 / Wellard / Koch.

ARNETT BLOWS FOR 1300
CD _____ DD 472
Delmark / Dec '94 / Hot Shot / ADA / CM / Direct / Cadillac.

BLUE AND SENTIMENTAL (Cobb, Arnett & Red Garland Trio)
CD _____ PCD 24122
Prestige / Nov '95 / Complete/Pinnacle / Cadillac.

IT'S BACK
CD _____ PCD 7037
Progressive / '91 / Jazz Music.

LIVE IN PARIS, 1974 (Cobb, Arnett & Tiny Grimes)
CD _____ FCD 133
France's Concert / '89 / Jazz Music / BMG.

SMOOTH SAILING
CD _____ OJCCD 323
Original Jazz Classics / Dec '95 / Wellard / Jazz Music / Cadillac / Complete/Pinnacle.

TENOR TRIBUTE (Cobb, Arnett, Jimmy Heath & Joe Henderson)
CD _____ 121 184 2
Soul Note / Oct '90 / Harmonia Mundi / Wellard / Cadillac.

Cobb, Jimmy

ENCOUNTER
CD _____ PHIL 66-2

Philology / Oct '94 / Harmonia Mundi / Cadillac.

Cobb, Junie C.

COLLECTION 1926-29
CD _____ COCD 14
Collector's Classics / Oct '91 / Cadillac / Complete/Pinnacle.

Cobbs, Willie

DOWN TO EARTH
CD _____ R 2628
Rooster / Nov '94 / Direct.

Cobham, Billy

BEST OF BILLY COBHAM, THE
Quadrant 4 / Snoopy's search / Red baron / Spanish moss / Moon germs / Stratus / Pleasant pheasant / Solo panhandler / Do whatcha wanna
CD _____ 7567815582
Atlantic / Jan '93 / Warner Music.

FLIGHT TIME
CD _____ INAK 8616CD
In Akustik / '88 / Magnum Music Group.

SPECTRUM
Quadrant 4 / Searching for the right door / Spectrum / Anxiety / Taurian matador / Stratus / To the women in my life / Le lis / Snoopy's search / Red Baron
CD _____ 7567814282
East West / Jan '93 / Warner Music.

STRATUS
CD _____ INAK 813 CD
In Akustik / '88 / Magnum Music Group.

TRAVELLER, THE
Alfa waves / All that your soul provides / Balancing act / What if / Dipping the biscuits in the soup / Fragolino / Just one step away / Nautus Creole blues / On the inside track / Soul provider
CD _____ ECD 220982
Evidence / Jul '94 / Harmonia Mundi / ADA / Cadillac.

Cobra Verde

VIVA LA MUERTE
Was it good / Gimme your heart / Montenegro / Despair / Debt / Already dead / Until the killing time / I thought you knew (what pleasure was) / Cease to exist
CD _____ SCT 036-2
Matador / Oct '94 / Vital.

Coburn, Pamela

MUCH LOVED MUSIC
CD _____ CDCFP 9009
Classics For Pleasure / Jul '87 / EMI.

Cochabamba

GREATEST HITS: COCHABAMBA
CD _____ PV 758 11
Disques Pierre Verany / '88 / Kingdom.

Cochise

BEST OF COCHISE
Past loves / Trafalgar day / Moment and the end / Watch this space / China / That's why I sing the blues / Strange image / Down country girls / Home again / Another day / Love's made a fool of you / Cajun girl / Diamonds / Blind love / Thunder in the city / Midnight moonshine
CD _____ EDCD 254
Edsel / Sep '92 / Pinnacle / ADA.

Cochran, Charles

HAUNTED HEART
CD _____ ACD 177
Audiophile / May '95 / Jazz Music / Swift.

Cochran, Eddie

C'MON EVERYBODY
C'mon everybody / Sweetie pie / I almost lost my mind / Proud of you / Guybo / I remember / Stockin's 'n' shoes / Rock 'n' roll blues / Undying love / My love to remember / Never / Little angel / Nervous breakdown / Teenage heaven / Weekend / Sittin' in the balcony / Twenty flight rock / Milk cow blues / Blue suede shoes / Hallelujah, I love her so / Something else / Summertime blues / Jeannie Jeannie Jeannie / My way / Cherished memories / Teenage cutie / Long tall Sally / Eddie's blues / Cut across shorty / Pretty girl / Three steps to heaven
CD _____ CDECR 1
Liberty / Mar '88 / EMI.

CRUISIN THE DRIVE IN
CD _____ RSRCD 009
Rockstar / Jan '96 / Rollercoaster / Direct / Magnum Music Group / Nervous.

EARLY YEARS, THE
Skinny Jim / Half loved / Tired and sleepy / That's what it takes to make a man / Pink pegged slacks / Open the door / Country jam / Don't bye bye baby me / My love to remember / Guybo / Dark lonely street / If I were dying / Jelly bean / Latch on / Slow

down / Fool's paradise / Bad baby doll (Not on LP) / Itty bitty Betty (Not on LP) / Heart of a fool (Not on LP) / Instrumental blues (Not on LP)
CD _____ CDCH 237
Ace / Nov '93 / Pinnacle / Cadillac / Complete/Pinnacle.

EDDIE COCHRAN
Summertime blues / My way / I remember / Three steps to heaven / Skinny Jim / Completely sweet / Lonely / Long tall Sally / C'mon everybody / Teenage heaven / Boll weevil song / Pretty girl / Cherished memories / I'm ready / Sweetie pie / Eddie's blues
CD _____ CDMFP 5748
Music For Pleasure / May '92 / EMI.

EDDIE COCHRAN BOX SET, THE
Tired and sleepy / Fool's paradise / Open the door / Slow down / Pink peg slacks / Latch on / My love to remember / Yesterday's heartbreak / I'm ready / Blue suede shoes / Long tall Sally / Half loved / Skinny Jim / I almost lost my mind / Twenty flight rock / That's my desire / Completely sweet / Cotton picker / Sittin' in the balcony / Dark lonely street / One kiss / Mean when I'm mad / Drive-in show / Cradle baby / Undying love / Am I blue / Tell me why / Sweetie pie / I'm alone because I love you / Stockings 'n' shoes / Proud of you / Lovin' time / Teenage cutie / Never / Jeannie Jeannie Jeannie / Pocket full of hearts / Little Lou / Pretty girl / Teresa / Nervous breakdown / Summertime blues / Love again / Let's get together / Lonely / C'mon everybody / Don't ever let me go / Teenage heaven / I've waited so long / My way / I remember / Three stars / Rock 'n' roll blues / Weekend / Think of me / Boll weevil song / Three steps to heaven / Cut across shorty / Cherished memories / Guybo / Strollin' guitar / Eddie's blues / Jam sandwich / Hammy blues / Fourth man theme / Country jam / Hallelujah, I love her so / Something else / Money honey / Have I told you lately that I love you / Milk cow blues / I don't like you no more / Sweet little sixteen / White lightning / Jelly bean / Little angel / Don't bye bye baby me / You oughta see grandma rock / Heart-breakin' mama / Slowly but surely / Keeper of the key / Let's coast awhile / I want Elvis for Christmas / How'd ja do / Don't wake up the kids / Willa Mae / It happened to me / Chicken shot blues
CD Set _____ CDECB 1
Liberty / Mar '91 / EMI.

EP COLLECTION: EDDIE COCHRAN
Skinny Jim / Twenty flight rock / Sittin' in the balcony / Blue suede shoes / Pink peg slacks / Mean when I'm mad / Stockin's 'n' shoes / Jeannie Jeannie Jeannie / Pretty girl / Teresa / Sweetie pie / C'mon everybody / Summertime blues / I remember / Rock 'n' roll blues / Milk cow blues / Little angel / Cherished memories / Three steps to heaven
CD _____ SEECD 271
See For Miles/C5 / Jan '91 / Pinnacle.

L.A. SESSIONS
CD _____ RSRCD 003
Rockstar / Apr '94 / Rollercoaster / Direct / Magnum Music Group / Nervous.

MIGHTY MEAN
CD _____ RSRCD 008
Rockstar / May '95 / Rollercoaster / Direct / Magnum Music Group / Nervous.

ORIGINALS - EDDIE COCHRAN/FATS ROCK AND ROLLIN'/BLUE JEAN BO
(3CD Set) (Cochran, Eddie/Fats Domino/Gene Vincent)
Singin' to my baby / Sittin' in the balcony / Completely sweet / Undying love / I'm alone / Because I love you / Lovin' time / Proud of you / Am I blue / Twenty flight rockers / Drive in show / Mean when I'm mad / Stockins'n'shoes / Tell me why / Have I told you lately that I love you / Cradle baby / One kiss / My blue heaven / Swanee river hop / Second line jump / Goodbye / Careless love / I love her / I'm in love again / When my dreamboat comes home / Are you going my way / If you need me / My heart is in your hands / Fats frenzy / Blue jean bop / Jezebel / Who slapped John / Ain't she sweet / I flipped / Waltz of the wind / Jump back / Wedding bells / Jumps, giggles and shouts / Lazy river / Bop street / Pet o' my heart
CD _____ CDOMB 006
EMI / Oct '95 / EMI.

ROCK 'N' ROLL LEGEND
Pink peg slacks / Latch on (version 1) / My love to remember / Heart of a fool / Yesterday's heartbreak / Latch on (version 2) / Tired and sleepy / Fool's paradise / Slow down / Open the door / Skinny Jim / Half loved / Drownin' all my sorrows / Let's coast awhile / Dark lonely street / Guybo / Take my hand / Jelly bean / Don't bye bye baby me / Chicken shot blues
CD _____ RSRCD 001
Rockstar / Apr '94 / Rollercoaster / Direct / Magnum Music Group / Nervous.

SUMMERTIME BLUES
CD _____ RMB 75054
Remember / Nov '93 / Total/BMG.

VERY BEST OF EDDIE COCHRAN (10th/15th Anniversary Album)
C'mon everybody / Three steps to heaven / Weekend / Skinny Jim / Completely sweet / Milk cow blues / Cut across shorty / Hallelujah, I love her so / Something else / Blue suede shoes / Eddie's blues (Instr.) / Sittin' in the balcony / Summertime blues / Twenty flight rock / Three stars / Cherished memories
CD _____ CDFA 3019
Fame / Mar '90 / EMI.

Cochrane, Brenda

VOICE, THE
You're the voice / Pearl's a singer / Right here waiting for you / New York, New York / You've lost that lovin' feelin' / You make me turn / I want to know what love is / Wind beneath my wings / Easy to love / Put the weight on my shoulders / All night long
CD _____ 843 141-2
Polydor / Mar '90 / PolyGram.

Cochrane, Michael

SONG OF CHANGE (Cochrane, Michael Trio)
CD _____ 121251-2
Soul Note / Nov '93 / Harmonia Mundi / Wellard / Cadillac.

Cochrane, Tom

RAGGED ASS ROAD
I wish you well / Wildest dreams / Just scream / Paper tiger / Crawl / Ragged Ass Road / Flowers in the concrete / Dreamer's dream / Message / Best waste of time / Will of the gun / Song before I leave
CD _____ CDEST 2268
Capitol / Oct '95 / EMI.

Cock 'N' Bull Band

BELOW THE BELT
CD _____ C & B 104CD
Cock & Bull / Dec '93 / ADA.

Cock Sparrer

SHOCK TROOPS
UN Recordings / Aug '93 / Plastic Head.
CD _____ AHOYCD 4

SHOCK TROOPS/RUNNIN RIOT IN 84
CD _____ SLOG CD 4
Slogan / Aug '92 / BMG.

Cockburn, Bruce

CHRISTMAS
O come all ye faithful (Adeste fidelis) / Early on one Christmas morn / O little town of Bethlehem / Riu Riu Chiu / I saw three ships / Down in yon forest / Les Angesdans nos campagnes / Go tell it on the mountain / Shepherds / Silent night / Iesus ahatonnia (the huron carol) / God rest ye merry gentlemen / It came upon a midnight clear / Mary had a baby / Joy to the world
CD _____ 4747122
Columbia / Dec '94 / Sony.

DANCING IN THE DRAGON'S JAWS
Creation dream / Hills of the morning / Badlands flashback / Northern lights / After the rain / Wondering where the lions are / Incandescent blue / No footprints
CD _____ 4803642
Columbia / Apr '95 / Sony.

DART TO THE HEART
Listen for the laugh / All the ways I want you / Bone in my ear / Burden of the angel/beast / Scanning these crowds / Southland of the heart / Train in the rain / Someone I used to love / Love loves you too / Sunrise on the Mississippi / Closer to the light / Tie me at the crossroads
CD _____ 475649 2
Columbia / Jun '94 / Sony.

LIVE
Silver wheels / World of wonders / Rumours of glory / See how I miss you / After the rain / Call it democracy / Wondering where the lions are / Nicaragua / Broken wheel / Stolen land / Always look on the bright side of life / Tibetan side of town (Not on LP) / To raise the morning star (Not on LP) / Maybe the poet (Not on LP)
CD _____ COOKCD 024
Cooking Vinyl / Apr '90 / Vital.

STEALING FIRE
CD _____ 4803632
Columbia / Apr '95 / Sony.

Cocker, Joe

BEST OF JOE COCKER, THE
Unchain my heart (90's version) / You can leave your hat on / When the night comes / Up where we belong (Duet with Jennifer Warnes) / Now that the magic has gone / Don't you love me anymore / I can hear the river / Sorry seems to be the hardest word / Shelter me / Feels like forever / Night calls / Don't let the sun go down on me / Now that you're gone / Civilised man / When a woman cries / With a little help from my friends
CD _____ CDESTU 2187
Capitol / Oct '92 / EMI.

CIVILIZED MAN
Civilized man / There goes my baby / Come on in / Tempted / Long drag off a cigarette / I love the night / Crazy in love / Girl like you / Hold on (I feel our love is changing) / Even a fool would let go
CD _____ EJ 2401392
Capitol / Apr '92 / EMI.

COCKER
You can leave your hat on / Heart of the matter / Inner city blues / Love is on a fade / Heaven / Shelter me / A to Z / Don't you love me anymore / Livin' without your love / Don't drink the water
CD _____ CDEST 2009
Capitol / Jul '94 / EMI.

COCKER HAPPY
Hitchcock railway / She came in through the bathroom window / Marjorine / She's so good to me / Hello little friend / With a little help from my friends / Delta lady / Darling be home soon / Do I still figure in your life
CD _____ CLACD 238
Castle / May '91 / BMG.
CD _____ CUCD 01
Disky / Oct '94 / THE / BMG / Discovery / Pinnacle.

COLLECTION: JOE COCKER
I can stand a little rain / It's a sin when you love somebody / Jamaica say you will / High time we went / Just like a woman / Do I still figure in your life / With a little help from my friends / Lawdy Miss Clawdy / Darling be home soon / Hello little friend / Pardon me sir / Marjorine / Midnight rider (Live in L.A.) / Love the one you're with (live in L.A.) / Bird on the wire / Feeling alright / Let's get stoned / Girl from the North Country / Give peace a chance / She came in through the bathroom window / Space captain / Letter / Delta lady / Honky tonk women / Cry me a river
CD _____ CCSCD 126
Castle / '86 / BMG.

COLLECTION: JOE COCKER VOL.2
CD _____ CCSCD 304
Castle / Oct '91 / BMG.

ESSENTIAL, THE
Up where we belong / Sweet lil' woman / Easy rider / Threw it away / Ruby Lee / Many rivers to cross / Taking back the night / Honky tonk woman / Sticks and stones / Cry me a river / Please give peace a chance / She came in thru the bathroom window / Letter / Delta lady
CD _____ 5514082
Spectrum/Karussell / Aug '95 / PolyGram / THE.

FAVOURITE RARITIES
CD _____ RA 95022
BR Music / Sep '94 / Target/BMG.

FIRST TIME
CD _____ 5501262
Spectrum/Karussell / Oct '93 / PolyGram / THE.

HAVE A LITTLE FAITH
Let the healing begin / Have a little faith in me / Simple things / Summer in the city / Great divide / Highway highway / Too cool / Soul time / Out of the blue / Angeline / Hell and high water / Standing knee deep in a river / Take me home
CD _____ CDEST 2233
Capitol / Sep '94 / EMI.

I CAN STAND A LITTLE RAIN
Put out the light / I can stand a little rain / I get mad / Sing me a song / Moon is a harsh mistress / Don't forget me / You are so beautiful / It's a sin when you love somebody / Performance / Guilty
CD _____ CLACD 144
Castle / Apr '89 / BMG.

JAMAICA SAY YOU WILL
(That's what I like) in my woman / Where am I now / I think it's going to rain today / Forgive me now / Oh mama / Lucinda / If I love you / Jamaica say you will / It's all over but the shouting / Jack O'Diamonds
CD _____ CLACD 237
Castle / May '91 / BMG.

JOE COCKER
Dear Landlord / Bird on the wire / Lawdy Miss Clawdy / She came through the bathroom window / Hitchcock Railway / That's your business / Something / Delta lady / Hello little friend / Darling be home soon
CD _____ CLACD 236
Castle / May '91 / BMG.

JOE COCKER LIVE
Feeling alright / Shelter me / Hitchcock railway / Up where we belong / Guilty / You can leave your hat on / When the night comes / Unchain my heart / With a little help from my friends / Your as so beautiful / Letter / She came in through the bathroom window / High time we went / What are you doing with a fool like me / Living in the promised land
CD _____ CDESTSP 25
Capitol / May '90 / EMI.

LEGEND, THE ESSENTIAL COLLECTION
Up where we belong / With a little help from my friends / Delta lady / Letter / She came in through the bathroom window / Whiter shade of pale / Love the one you're with /

You are so beautiful / Let it be / Just like a woman / Many rivers to cross / Talking back to the night / Fun time / I heard it through the grapevine / Please give peace a chance (live) / Don't let me be misunderstood / Honky tonk women (live) / Cry me a river (live)
CD _____ 5154112
Polydor / Jun '92 / PolyGram.

LIVE IN L.A.
Dear landlord / Early in the morning / Didn't you know (you'd have to cry sometime) / St. James infirmary / What kind of man are you / Hitchcock railway / Midnight rider / High times we went / Love the one you're with
CD _____ CLACD 189
Castle / Aug '90 / BMG.

LONG VOYAGE HOME, THE (4CD Set)
With a little help from my friends / I'll cry instead / Those precious words / Marjorine / Bye bye blackbird / Just like a woman / Don't let me be misunderstood / Do I still figure in your life / Feelin' alright / I shall be released / I don't need no doctor / Let it be / Delta lady / She came in through the bathroom window / Hitchcock railway / Dear landlord / Darling be home soon / Something / Wake up little Susie / Letter / Space Captain / Cry me a river / Let's go get stoned / Please give peace a chance / Blue medley / Midnight rider / High time we went / Black-eyed blues / Midnight rider / Woman to woman / Something to say / She don't mind / Pardon me Sir / Put out the light / I can stand a little rain / Moon is a harsh Mistress / You are so beautiful / Guilty / I think it's going to rain today / Jamaica say you will / Jealous kind / Catfish / Song for you / Fun time / I'm so glad I'm standing here today / Ruby Lee / Many rivers to cross / So good so right / Up where we belong / I love the night / Civilized man / Edge of a dream / You can leave your hat on / Unchain my heart / I've got to use my imagination / I'm your man / When the night comes / Can't find my way home / Don't let the sun go down on me / You've got to hide your love away / Love is alive / With a little help from my friends #2
CD Set _____ 5402362
A&M / Dec '95 / PolyGram.

LUXURY YOU CAN AFFORD
Fun time / Watching the river flow / Boogie baby / Whiter shade of pale / I can't say no / Southern lady / I know (you don't want me no more) / What you did to me last night / Lady put the light out / Wasted years / I heard it through the grapevine
CD _____ 7559608212
Elektra / Jan '96 / Warner Music.

MAD DOGS AND ENGLISHMEN
Honky tonk women / Sticks and stones / Cry me a river / Bird on the wire / Feeling alright / Superstar / Let's go get stoned / I'll drown in my own tears / When something is wrong with my baby / I've been loving you too long / Girl from the North Country / Give peace a chance / She came in through the bathroom window / Space captain / Letter / Delta lady
CD Set _____ CDA 6002
A&M / '88 / PolyGram.

MIDNIGHT RIDER
CD _____ WMCD 5701
Disky / Oct '94 / THE / BMG / Discovery / Pinnacle.

NIGHT CALLS
Feels like forever / I can hear the river / Now that the magic has gone / Unchain my heart (90's version) / Night calls / There's a storm coming / Can't find my way home / Don't let the sun go down on me / When the night comes / Five women / Love is alive / Please no more / Out of the rain / When a woman cries
CD _____ CDESTU 2167
Capitol / Feb '92 / EMI.

ONE NIGHT OF SIN
When the night comes / I will live for you / I've got to use my imagination / Letting go / Just to keep from drowning / Unforgiven / Another mind gone / Fever / You know it's gonna hurt / Bad bad sign / I'm your man / One night
CD _____ CDEST 2098
Capitol / Feb '91 / EMI.

SHEFFIELD STEEL
Look what you've done / Shocked / Seven days / Marie / Ruby Lee / Many rivers to cross / Talking back to the night / Just like always / Sweet little woman / So good, so right
CD _____ IMCD 149
Island / Jul '92 / PolyGram.

SIMPLY THE BEST
CD _____ WMCD 5705
Disky / Oct '94 / THE / BMG / Discovery / Pinnacle.

SOMETHING TO SAY
Pardon me sir / High time we went / She don't mind / Black eyed blues / Something to say / Midnight rider / Do right woman, do right man / Woman to woman / St. James infirmary
CD _____ CLACD 207
Castle / Dec '90 / BMG.

SPACE CAPTAIN
Honky tonk women / Love the one you're with / Letter / She came in through the bathroom window / Cry me a river / Delta lady
CD _____ CD 853 010
Cube / '88 / Bucks Music.

UNCHAIN MY HEART
Unchain my heart / One / Two wrongs don't make a right / I stand in wonder / River's rising / Isolation / All our tomorrows / Woman loves a man / Trust in me / Satisfied / You can leave your hat on
CD _____ CDEST 2045
Capitol / Aug '92 / EMI.

VERY BEST OF JOE COCKER, THE (The Voice)
With a little help from my friends / Honky tonk women / Delta lady / Marjorine / Don't let me be misunderstood / Something / Pardon me sir / Talking back to the night / Up where we belong (With Jennifer Warnes.) / She came in through the bathroom window / Letter / Just like a woman / Jamaica say you will / Cry me a river / Midnight rider / Let it be
CD _____ BRCD 104
BR Music / Jun '94 / Target/BMG.

WITH A LITTLE HELP FROM MY FRIENDS
Feeling alright / Bye bye blackbird / Change in Louise / Marjorie / Just like a woman / Do I still figure in your life / Sandpaper Cadillac / Don't let me be misunderstood / With a little help from my friends / I shall be released
CD _____ CLACD 172
Castle / Feb '90 / BMG.

WITH A LITTLE HELP FROM MY FRIENDS
With a little help from my friends / Marjorie / Letter / Dear landlord / Bird on the wire / Lawdy miss clawdy / She came in through the bedroom window / Hitchcock railway / That's your business now / Something / Delta lady / Hello little friend / Darling be home soon / Feeling alright / Bye bye blackbird / Change in Louise / Just like a woman
CD _____ 846 316
Cube / '88 / Bucks Music.

Cockersdale

BEEN AROUND FOR YEARS
CD _____ FE 101CD
Fellside / Jul '94 / Target/BMG / Direct / ADA.

Cockney Rebel

LIVE AT THE BBC
CD _____ WINCD 073
Windsong / Jun '95 / Pinnacle.

Cockney Rejects

BEST OF THE COCKNEY REJECTS, THE
Flares in slippers / Police car / I'm not a fool / East end / Bad man / Headbanger / Join the rejects / Where the hell is Babylon / War on the terraces / Oi oi oi / Hate of the city / Rocker / Greatest cockney rip off / We can do anything / We are the firm / I'm forever blowing bubbles / Here we go again / Motorhead (Live) / Easy life (Live) / On the streets again / Power and the glory / Teenage fantasy
CD _____ DOJOCD 82
Dojo / May '93 / BMG.

GREATEST HITS VOL.1
I'm not a fool / Headbanger / Bad man / Fighting in the streets / Shitter / Here they come again / Join the rejects / East End / New song / Police car / Someone like you / They're gonna put me away / Are you ready to ruck / Where the hell is Babylon / I'm forever blowing bubbles / West side boys
CD _____ DOJOCD 136
Dojo / Feb '94 / BMG.

GREATEST HITS VOL.2
War on the terraces / In the underworld / Oi oi oi / Hate of the city / With the boys / Urban guerilla / Rocker / Greatest cockney rip off / Sitting in a cell / On the waterfront / We can do anything / It's alright / Sub-culture / Blockbuster / Fifteen nights / We are the firm
CD _____ DOJOCD 138
Dojo / Feb '94 / BMG.

GREATEST HITS VOL.3
CD _____ DOJOCD 168
Dojo / Nov '93 / BMG.

LETHAL
CD _____ NEATCD 1049
Neat / Jan '96 / Plastic Head.

POWER AND THE GLORY
Power and the glory / Because I'm in love / On the run / Lemon / Friends / Van Bollocks / Teenage fantasy / It's over / On the streets again / BYC / Greatest story ever told
CD _____ DOJOCD 174
Dojo / Nov '93 / BMG.

WILD ONES/LETHAL
CD _____ LOMACD 38
Loma / Nov '94 / BMG.

Coco Steel & Lovebomb

IT
CD _____ WARPCD 24
Warp / Aug '94 / Disc.

Cocoa T

CAN'T LIVE SO
CD _____ SHCD 45016
Shanachie / May '94 / Koch / ADA / Greensleeves.

COME LOVE ME
CD _____ VPCD 1395
VP / Feb '95 / Jetstar.

LOVE ME
CD _____ DBTXCD 1
Digital B / Mar '95 / Jetstar.

RIKERS ISLAND
CD _____ GRELCD 156
Greensleeves / Dec '90 / Total/BMG / Jetstar / SRD.

SWEET LOVE
CD _____ RASCD 3161
Ras / Mar '95 / Jetstar / Greensleeves / SRD / Direct.

TUNE IN
CD _____ GRELCD 200
Greensleeves / May '94 / Total/BMG / Jetstar / SRD.

Coctails

PEEL
CD _____ EFA 121142
Moll / Aug '95 / SRD.

Cocteau Twins

BLUE BELL KNOLL
Blue bell knoll / Athol brose / Carolyn's fingers / For Phoebe still a baby / Itchy Glowbo / Cico buff / Suckling The Mender / Spooning good singing gum / Kissed out red floatboat / Ella megalast burls forever
CD _____ CAD 807CD
4AD / Sep '88 / Disc.

FOUR CALENDAR CAFE
CD _____ 5182592
Fontana / Oct '93 / PolyGram.

GARLANDS
Blood bitch / Wax and wane / But I'm not / Blind dumb deaf / Gail overfloweth / Shallow than hallow / Hollow men / Garlands
CD _____ CAD 211 CD
4AD / '86 / Disc.

HEAD OVER HEELS
When mama was moth / Sugar hiccup / In our angelhood / Glass candle grenades / Multifoiled / In the gold dust rush / Tinderbox, The (of a heart) / My love paramour / Musette and drums / Five ten fiffyfold
CD _____ CAD 313 CD
4AD / '86 / Disc.

HEAVEN OR LAS VEGAS
Cherry coloured funk / Pitch the baby / Iceblink luck / Fifty fifty clown / Heaven or Las Vegas / I wear your ring / Fotzepolitic / Wolf in the breast / River, road and rail / Frou-frou foxes in the midsummer fires
CD _____ CAD 0012 CD
4AD / Sep '90 / Disc.

MILK AND KISSES
Violaine / Serpentskirt / Tishbite / Half gifts / Calfskin smack / Rilkean heart / Ups / Eperdu / Treasure hiding / Seekers who are lovers
CD _____ 5145012
Fontana / Feb '96 / PolyGram.

PINK OPAQUE
CD _____ CAD 513 CD
4AD / Jan '86 / Disc.

TINY DYNAMITE/ECHOES IN A SHALLOW BAY
CD Set _____ BAD 510/511 CD
4AD / Oct '86 / Disc.

TREASURE
Ivo / Lorelei / Beatrix / Persephone / Pandora - for Cindy / Amelia / Aloysius / Cicely / Otterley / Donimo
CD _____ CAD 412 CD
4AD / '86 / Disc.

VICTORIA LAND
Lazy calm / Fluffy tufts / Throughout the dark months of April and May / Whales tales / Oomingmac / Little spacey / Feet-like fins / How to bring a blush to the snow / Thinner the air
CD _____ CAD 602 CD
4AD / '86 / Disc.

Code

ARCHITECT, THE
Blind in the darkness / Criminals / No resistance / Cities apart III / Cities apart IV / Workers / Gentle science / Atlantic / Blind in the sun / Grand architect / Bleak moments

CD _____ TM 89452
Third Mind / Mar '95 / Pinnacle / Third Mind.

Codeine

WHITE BIRCH, THE
CD _____ SPCD 118299
Sub Pop / May '94 / Disc.

Codona

CODONA
Like that of sky / Codona / Colemanwonder: race face, sortie, Sir Duke / Mumakata / New light
CD _____ 8293712
ECM / '90 / New Note.

CODONA 2
Que faser / Godumaduma / Malinye / Drip dry / Walking on eggs / Again and again, again
CD _____ 8333322
ECM / Jul '88 / New Note.

CODONA 3
Goshakabuch / Hey da ba doom / Travel by night (Lullaby.) / Trayra boia / Clicky clacky / Inner organs
CD _____ 8274202
ECM / Feb '86 / New Note.

Coe, David Allan

COMPASS POINT/I'VE GOT SOMETHING TO SAY
Heads or tails / Three times loser / Gone (like) / Honey don't / Lost Merle and me / Loving her (will make you lose your mind) / Fish aren't bitin' today / X's and O's (kisses and hugs) / I've got something to say / Back to Atlanta / I could never give you up (for someone else) / Take it easy rider / Great Nashville railroad disaster / Hank Williams Junior Junior / Get a little dirt on my hands / If you hold the ladder (I'll climb to) / This bottle (in my hand) / Take this job and shove it too / Lovin' you comes so natural
CD _____ BCD 15841
Bear Family / Mar '95 / Rollercoaster / Direct / CM / Swift / ADA.

HUMAN EMOTIONS/SPECTRUM VII
Would you lay with me (in a field of stone) / If this is just a game / You can count on me / Mississippi river queen / Tomrrow is another day / Human emotions / Love's cheatin' line / Whiskey and women / Jack Daniels if you please / Suicide / Rollin' with the punches / On my feet again / Fall in love with you / What can I do / Sudden death / Fairytale morning / Seven mile bridge / Now's the time / Love is just a porpoise / Please come back to Boston
CD _____ BCD 15840
Bear Family / Mar '95 / Rollercoaster / Direct / CM / Swift / ADA.

INVICTUS (MEANS) UNCONQUERED/ TENNESSE WHISKEY
Rose knows / Ain't it funny / Way love can do ya / If you ever think of me / Purple heart / London homesick blues / Stand by your man / As far as this feeling will take us / Someplace to come when it rains / Best game in town / I love robbing banks / Tennessee whiskey / I knew I've given bout all I can take / Pledging my love / I'll always be a fool for you / (Sittin' on) the dock of the bay / Juanita / We've got a bad thing goin' / D-R-U-N-K / Little orphan Annie / Bright morning light
CD _____ BCD 15842
Bear Family / Mar '95 / Rollercoaster / Direct / CM / Swift / ADA.

LONGHAIRED REDNECK/ RIDES AGAIN
Long haired redneck / Whon she's got me (Where she wants me) / Revenge / Texas lullaby / living on the run / Family reunion / Rock 'n' roll holiday / Free born rambling man / Spotlight / Dakota the dancing bear, Part 2 / Willie, Waylon and me / House we've been calling home / Young Dallas cowboy / Sense of humour / Pumkin certer barn dance / Willie, Waylon and Me (Reprise) / Lately I've been thinking too much lately / Laid back and wasted / Under Rachel's wings / Greener than the grass we laid on / If that ain't country
CD _____ BCD 15707
Bear Family / Mar '93 / Rollercoaster / Direct / CM / Swift / ADA.

MYSTERIOUS RHINESTONE COWBOY, THE/ ONCE UPON A RHYME
Sad country song / Crazy Mary / River / 33rd of august / Bossier city / Atlanta song / Old men tell me / Desperados waiting for the train / I still sing the old songs / Old grey goose is dead / Would you lay with me (in a field of stone) / Jody like a melody / Loneliness in Ruby's eyes / Would you be my lady / Sweet vibrations / Another pretty country song / Piece of wood and steel / Fraulein / Shine it on / You never even called me by my name
CD _____ BCD 15706
Bear Family / Mar '93 / Rollercoaster / Direct / CM / Swift / ADA.

TATTOO/FAMILY ALBUM
Just to prove my love for you / Face to face / You'll always live inside of me / Play me a sad song / Daddy was a god fearin' man / Canteen of water / Maria is a mystery / Just

in time / San Francisco Mabel Joy / Hey gypsy / Family album / Million dollar memories / Divers do it deeper / Guilty footsteps / Take this job and shove it / Houston, Dallas, San Antone / I've got to have you / Whole lot of lonesome / Bad impressions / Heavenly Father, Holy Mother
CD _____ BCD 15839
Bear Family / Mar '95 / Rollercoaster / Direct / CM / Swift / ADA.

Coe, Tony

CANTERBURY SONG
Canterbury song / How beautiful is the night / Light blue / Sometime ago / Re: person I knew / I guess I'll hang my tears out to dry / Lagos / Blue in green
CD _____ HHCD 1005
Hot House / Jun '89 / Cadillac / Wellard / Harmonia Mundi.

SOME OTHER AUTUMN
Aristotle blues / Some other autumn / Line up blues / Body and soul / Reka / Together / Regrets / Perdido / When your lover has gone / In a mellow tone / U.M.M.G.
CD _____ HEPCD 2037
Hep / Jan '96 / Cadillac / Jazz Music / New Note / Wellard.

Coen, Jack

BRANCH LINE, THE (Irish Traditional Music From Galway to New York) (Coen, Jack & Charlie)
Scatter the mud / Larry Redigan's jig / Sailor's cravat / Repeal of the union / John Conroy's jig / Peach blossom / Fidler's consort / Jim Conroy's reel / Pullet / Redican's mother / Humours of Kilkenny / Mike Coen's polka / Branch line / Have a drink with me / Blarney pilgrim / Two woodford flings / Waddling gander / O'Connell's jig on top of Mount Everest / Lads of Laois / Green groves of Erin / Tongs by the fire / Spinning wheel / Whelan's reel / Jenny dang the weaver / Jack Coen's jig / Paddy O'Brien's jig
CD _____ GLCD 3067
Green Linnet / Oct '93 / Roots / CM / Direct / ADA.

WARMING UP (Coen, Jack/Martin Mulhaire/Seamus Connolly)
CD _____ GL 1135CD
Green Linnet / Mar '94 / Roots / CM / Direct / ADA.

Coffee Sergeants

MOONLIGHT TOWERS
CD _____ DJD 3204
Dejadisc / May '94 / Direct / ADA.

Coffin Break

NO SLEEP TILL STARDUST MOTEL
CD _____ CZ 038
C/Z / Sep '94 / Plastic Head.

Cogan, Alma

A-Z OF ALMA, THE
Red silken stockings / To be worthy of you / Would you / To be loved by you / Homing waltz / Meet me on the corner / Waltz of Paree / Pretty bride / Blue tango / I went to your wedding / IFN / Take me in your arms and hold me / Somebody loves me / Happy Valley sweetheart / If I had a penny / On the first warm day / Hug me a hug / Sittin' in the sun / If I had a golden umbrella / Mystery Street / My love my love / Wasted tears / Isn't life wonderful / Over and over again / Love me again / Bell bottom blues / Make love to me / Do do do do it again / What am I gonna do Ma / Skinny Minnie / Christmas cards / Mrs. Santa Claus / Blue again / Naughty lady of Shady Lane / More than ever now / Dreamboat / Tika tika tok / Irish mambo / Keep me in mind / Where will the dimple be / Give a fool a chance / Banjo's back in town / Go on by / Herando's hideaway / Twenty tiny fingers / Love and marriage / Sycamore tree / Don't ringa da bell / Funny funny funny / Summer love / That's happiness / What you've done to me / Love is / Wouldn't it be lovely / With a little bit of luck / Stairway of love / Volare / This little girl's gone rockin' / Once in a while / Must be Santa / Just couldn't resist her with her pocket transistor / Ja da / Cowboy Jimmy Joe / Keep me in your heart / All alone / Let's face the music and dance / She's funny that way / Man I love / You were meant for me / Oom pah pah / I want to whisper something / I love you much too much / My one and only love / Baubles, bangles and beads / Goodbye Joe / Let me love you / If love were all / Tell him / Just once more / Hava nagila / Tenessee waltz / I knew right away / Birds and the bees / Now that I found you / Snakes and snails / How many nights, how many days / Eight days a week / Yesterday / There's a time and place / Hello baby
CD Set _____ CDALMA 1
EMI / Oct '94 / EMI.

EMI YEARS: ALMA COGAN (Best Of)
You, me and us / Bell bottom blues / Mambo Italiano / Got an idea / Last night on the back porch / It's all been done before / Lucky lips / Fly away lovers / Little shoe-

maker / Chiqu chaqui / I can't tell a waltz from a tango / Ricochet / I love you bit / Never do a tango with an eskimo / Little things mean a lot / Gettin' ready for Freddy / Mama says / Dreamboat / Said the little moment / In the middle of the house
CD _____ CDEMS 1378
EMI / Jan '91 / EMI.

HOUR OF ALMA COGAN, AN
To be worthy of you / Till I waltz again with you / Till they've all gone home / Bell bottom blues / Jilted / Canoodlin / Rag / This ole house / I can't tell a waltz from a tango / (Don't let the) Kiddygeddin / Softly, softly / Dreamboat / Willie can / Lizzie Borden / Birds and the bees / Why do fools fall in love / Whatever Lola wants (Lola gets) / Cahntez, chantez / Fabulous / Party time / Please Mr. Brown / Sugartime / Sorry, sorry, sorry / Pink shoelaces / We got you / Train of love / Just couldn't resist her with her pocket transistor
CD _____ CC 8240
EMI / Nov '94 / EMI.

WITH LOVE IN MIND
Somebody loves me / Can't help falling in love / Hello, young lovers / Our love affair / Love me as though there were no tomorrow / Love is just around the corner / Let me love you / If love were all / With you in mind / I dream of you (more than you dream I do) / Let's fall in love / In other words / My heart stood still / But beautiful / You'll never know / All I do is dream of you / What is there to say / Don't blame me / Falling in love with love / More I see you / I can't give you anything but love / It's April in love be-fore / Lady's in love with you / I'm in the mood for love
CD _____ CDB 906582
Music For Pleasure / Sep '88 / EMI.

Cohen, Leonard

COHEN LIVE
Dance me to the end of love / Bird on the wire / Everybody knows / Loan of arc / There is a war / Sisters of mercy / Hallelujah / I'm your man / Who by fire / One of us cannot be wrong / If it be your will / Heart with no companion / Suzanne
CD _____ 477171-2
Columbia / Aug '94 / Sony.

DEATH OF A LADIES MAN
True love leaves no traces / Iodine / Paper thin hotel / Memories / I left a woman waiting / Don't go home with your hard-on / Fingerprints / Death of a ladies man
CD _____ 4086042
Columbia / Apr '95 / Sony.

FUTURE, THE
Future / Waiting for the miracle / Be for real / Closing time / Anthem / Democracy / Light as the breeze / Always / Tacoma trailer
CD _____ 472498 2
Columbia / Nov '92 / Sony.

FUTURE, THE/SONGS OF LEONARD COHEN
CD Set _____ 4724982 D
Columbia / Feb '93 / Sony.

GREATEST HITS: LEONARD COHEN
Suzanne / Sisters of mercy / So long, Marianne / Bird on the wire / Lady Midnight / Partisan / Hey, that's no way to say goodbye / Famous blue raincoat / Last year's man / Chelsea Hotel no.2 / Who by fire / Take this longing
CD _____ CD 32644
Columbia / Jun '89 / Sony.

I'M YOUR FAN (The Songs Of Leonard Cohen) (Various Artists)
Who by fire / Hey, that's no way to say goodbye / I can't forget / Stories of the street / Bird on the wire / Suzanne / So long, Marianne / Avalanche N.2 / Don't go home with your hard-on / First we take Manhattan / Chelsea hotel / Tower of song / Take this longing / True love leaves no traces / I'm your man / Singer must die / Hallelujah / Tower of song (2)
CD _____ 9031755982
East West / Sep '91 / Warner Music.

I'M YOUR MAN
First we take Manhattan / Ain't no cure for love / Everybody knows / I'm your man / Take this waltz / Jazz police / I can't forget / Tower of song
CD _____ 4606422
Columbia / Feb '88 / Sony.

NEW SKIN FOR OLD CEREMONY/ SONGS FROM A ROOM (2CD Set)
Is this what you want / Chelsea hotel no.2 / Lover lover lover / Field Commander Cohen / Why don't you try / There is a war / Singer must die / I tried to leave you / Who by fire / Take this longing / Leaving green sleeves / Like a bird on the wire / Story of Isaac / Bunch of lonesome heroes / Partisan / Seems so long ago / Old revolution / Butcher / You know who I am / Lady midnight / Tonight will be fine
CD Set _____ 4610122
Columbia / Jul '92 / Sony.

RECENT SONGS
Guests / Humbled in love / Window / Came so far for beauty / Lost Canadian (Un Canadien errant) / Traitor / Our lady of solitude

/ Gypsy's wife / Smoky life / Ballad of the absent mare
CD _____ 4747502
Columbia / Apr '94 / Sony.

SO LONG, MARIANNE
Who by fire / So long, Marianne / Chelsea Hotel no.2 / Lady midnight / Sisters of mercy / Bird on the wire / Suzanne / Lover lover lover / Winter lady / Tonight will be fine / Partisan / Diamonds in the mine
CD _____ 4605002
Columbia / Oct '95 / Sony.

SONGS FROM A ROOM
Bird on the wire / Story of Isaac / Bunch of lonesome heroes / Seems so long ago / Nancy / Old revolution / Butcher / You know who I am / Lady Midnight / Tonight will be fine
CD _____ 32072
Columbia / May '90 / Sony.

SONGS FROM A ROOM/SONGS OF LOVE AND HATE (2CD Set)
Bird on the wire / Story of Isaac / Bunch of lonesome heroes / Seems so long ago / Nancy / Old revolution / Butcher / You know who I am / Lady Midnight / Tonight will be fine / Avalanche / Last year's man / Dress rehearsal rag / Diamonds in the mine / Love calls you by your name / Famous blue raincoat / Sing another song / Boys / Joan of Arc
CD Set _____ 4784802
Columbia / Mar '95 / Sony.

SONGS FROM A ROOM/VARIOUS POSITIONS/I'M YOUR MAN (3CD Set)
CD Set _____ 4722682
Columbia / Oct '92 / Sony.

SONGS OF LEONARD COHEN, THE
Suzanne / Master song / Winter lady / Stranger song / Sisters of mercy / So long, Marianne / Hey, that's no way to say goodbye / Stories of the street teachers / One of us cannot be wrong
CD _____ 4686002
Columbia / Oct '91 / Sony.

SONGS OF LEONARD COHEN, THE/ SONGS OF LOVE AND HATE/LIVE SONG (3CD Set)
CD _____ 4741462
Columbia / Jan '95 / Sony.

SONGS OF LOVE AND HATE
Avalanche / Last year's man / Dress rehearsal rag / Diamonds in the mine field / Love calls you by your name / Famous blue raincoat / Sing another song / Joan of Arc
CD _____ 476799 2
Columbia / May '95 / Sony.

TOWER OF SONG (A Tribute To Leonard Cohen) (Various Artists)
Everybody knows / Coming back to you / Sisters of mercy / Hallelujah / Famous blue raincoat / Ain't no cure for love / I'm your man / Bird on a wire / Suzanne / Light as the breeze / If it be your will / Story of Isaac
CD _____ 5402592
A&M / Sep '95 / PolyGram.

VARIOUS POSITIONS
Dance me to the end of love / Coming back to you / Law / Night comes on / Hallelujah / Captain / Hunter's lullaby / Heart with no companion / If it be your will
CD _____ 4655692
Columbia / Nov '89 / Sony.

Cohen, Marc

MY FOOLISH HEART
Snow fall / My foolish heart / Walkin' / So long ago / I fall in love too easily / How will the blues leave / At night / Mash / Just in time / In blue
CD _____ 66053014
Jazz City / Feb '91 / New Note.

Cohn, Al

BODY & SOUL (Cohn, Al & Zoot Sims)
CD _____ MCD 5356
Muse / Sep '92 / New Note / CM.

COHN'S TONES
Groovin' with Gus / Infinity / How long has this been going on / Let's get away from it all / Ah Moore / Jane Street / I'm tellin' ya / That's what you think
CD _____ SV 0187
Savoy Jazz / Oct '92 / Conifer / ADA.

KEEPER OF THE FLAME (Cohn, Al & The Jazz Seven)
Bilbo baggins / Mood indigo / Casa 50 / Keeper of the flame / High on you / Feel more like I do now
CD _____ JHCD 022
Ronnie Scott's Jazz House / Jan '94 / Jazz Music / Magnum Music Group / Cadillac.

MEETS AL PORCINO
CD _____ 474981 2
Sony Jazz / May '94 / Sony.

NONPAREIL
Take four / Unless it's you / El Cajon / Raincheck / Mr. George / Girl from Ipanema / This is new / Blue hodge / Expense account
CD _____ CCD 4155
Concord Jazz / Nov '92 / New Note.

PROGRESSIVE AL COHN, THE
Infinity / Groovin' with Gus / How long has this been going on / Let's get away from it all / That's what you think / I'm tellin' ya / Jane Street / Ah-moore / That's what you think (master)
CD _____ SV 0249
Savoy Jazz / Oct '94 / Conifer / ADA.

TOUR DE FORCE (Cohn, Al/Scott Hamilton/Buddy Tate)
Blues up and down / Tickle toe / Let's get away from it all / Soft winds / Stella by starlight / Broadway / Do nothin' 'til you hear from me / Jumpin' at the woodside / Bernie's tune / Rifftide / If
CD _____ CCD 4172
Concord Jazz / Aug '90 / New Note.

Cohn, Marc

MARC COHN
Walking in Memphis / Ghost train / Silver Thunderbird / Dig down deep / Walk on water / Miles away / Saving the best for last / Strangers in a car / Twenty nine ways / Perfect love / True companion
CD _____ 7567821782
Atlantic / Apr '91 / Warner Music.

RAINY SEASON, THE
Blues up and down / Rainy season / Mama's in the moon / Don't talk to her at night / Paper walls / From the station / Medicine man / Baby king / She's becoming gold / Things we've handed down
CD _____ 7567824912
Atlantic / Feb '95 / Warner Music.

Cohn, Steve

ITTEKIMASU
CD _____ ITM 970059
ITM / Apr '91 / Tradelink / Koch.

Coil

GOLD IS THE METAL
CD _____ NORMAL 77
Normal/Okra / May '94 / Direct / ADA.

HELLRAISER
CD _____ COILCD 001
Solar Lodge / Feb '89 / SRD.

UNNATURAL HISTORY
CD _____ LOCICD 2
Threshold House / '89 / SRD.

Cojazz

COJAZZ VOL.1
Invitation / Have you / Mascarade is over / Cheek to cheek / Mr. T / It might as well be spring / Soul eyes / Missile blues
CD _____ TCB 89102
TCB / Feb '95 / New Note.

Colaiuta, Vinnie

VINNIE COLAIUTA
I'm tweeked / Attack of the 20lb pizza / Private earthquake: Error 7 / Chauncey / John's blues / Slink / Darlene's song / Momoska (dub mix) / Bruce Lee / If one was one
CD _____ GRS 00132
GRP / Nov '94 / BMG / New Note.

Colclough, Phil

PLAYERS FROM A DRAMA (Colclough, Phil & June)
CD _____ CMCD 060
Celtic Music / '91 / CM / Roots.

Cold Blood

LYDIA
CD _____ 7599263382
Atlantic / Jan '96 / Warner Music.

THRILLER
CD _____ 7599263372
Atlantic / Jan '96 / Warner Music.

Cold Chisel

CIRCUS ANIMALS
You got nothing I want / Bow river / Forever now / Taipan / Hound dog / Wild colonial boy / No good for you / Numbers fall / When the war is over / Letter to Allan
CD _____ 2292549312
East West / Jan '96 / Warner Music.

EAST
Standing on the outside / Never before / Choir girl / Rising sun / My baby / Tomorrow / Cheap wine / Best kept lies / ITA / Star hotel / Four walls / My turn to cry
CD _____ 2292549302
East West / Jan '96 / Warner Music.

RAZOR SANGS
CD _____ 2292568272
East West / Jan '96 / Warner Music.

TWENTIETH CENTURY
CD _____ 2292503902
East West / Jan '96 / Warner Music.

Cold Steel

BRACING THE FALL
CD _____ TURBO 008CD
Turbo Music / Nov '92 / Plastic Head.

FREAKBOY
CD _____ TURBO 005CD
Turbo Music / Nov '92 / Plastic Head.

Cold Sweat

4 PLAY
Foreplay one / You are everything / Round Midnight / Spinning around / Foreplay two / If this world were mine / Secret gardens / Foreplay three / Going in circles / In the rain / Whip appeal / Nefertiti / La la (means I love you) / Foreplay four
CD _____ 8344442
JMT / May '91 / PolyGram.

Coldcut

JOURNEYS BY DJ VOL.8
CD _____ JDJCD 8
Music Unites / Oct '95 / Sony / 3MV / SRD.

PHILOSOPHY
Philosophy / Chocolate box / Pearls before swine / What are we living for / Leaving home / Dreamer / Peace and love / Kinda natural / Angel heart / Autumn leaves / Sign / Fat bloke / Rare leaves
CD _____ 74321 16426-2
Arista / Feb '94 / BMG.

SOME LIKE IT COLD
Find a way / Ride the pressure / R U ready / Mi sueno / Bass 4 luv / Original box / Chaos thing / Screw loose
CD _____ 74321251402
Arista / Mar '95 / BMG.

WHAT'S THAT NOISE
People hold on / Fat (Party and bullshit) / (I'm) in deep / My telephone / Reportage (theme) / Which doctor / Stop this crazy thing (Mixes) / No connection / Smoke 1 / Doctorin' the house (mix) / What's that noise / Beat's and pieces
CD _____ 74321251412
Arista / Mar '95 / BMG.

Coldstream Guards

LONDON SALUTE
London salute / State procession / Cockney lover / Bank holiday / Westminster waltz / Birdcage walk / Clarinet on the town / Royal windsor / Covent garden / Knightsbridge march / Nightingale sang in Berkley Square / Cockney cocktail / Foggy day in Camden town / Overture 'Cockaigne (in London town) / March finale / Boys in the old brigade / When the guards are on parade / Coldstream march 'Milanollo
CD _____ BNA 5119
Bandleader / Oct '95 / Conifer.

MARCHE MILITARE (Coldstream Guards Band)
CD _____ MATCD 260
Castle / Apr '93 / BMG.

MARCHES I - BRITISH (Coldstream Guards Regimental Band)
CD _____ CO 73806
Denon / Dec '89 / Conifer.

MARCHES II - AMERICAN & EUROPEAN GUARDS (Coldstream Guards Regimental Band)
Washington Post / Stars and stripes forever / Radeztzky march
CD _____ CO 73807
Denon / Dec '89 / Conifer.

MASTERPIECES FOR BAND (Coldstream Guards Regimental Band)
Two Irish tone sketches / Folk song suite / Toccata marziale / Gaelic fantasy / Suites for military band / Three humouresques / Theme and variations
CD _____ BNA 5002
Bandleader / Nov '86 / Conifer.

MUSIC OF ANDREW LLOYD WEBBER (Coldstream Guards Band)
Phantom of the opera / Think of me / All I ask of you / Music of the night / Pie Jesu / Hosanna / Cats overture / Skimbleshanks / the railway cat / Old gumbie cat / Macavity / Memory / I am the starlight / Engine of love / Only you / Race is on / Make up my heart / Light at the end of the tunnel / Starlight express / I'm only you / You're very me / Capped teeth and Caesar salad / Tell me on a Sunday / Take that look off your face / Variations 1-4 / Andrew Lloyd Webber - Symphonic Study
CD _____ BNA 5025
Bandleader / '88 / Conifer.

NATIONAL ANTHEMS VOL. 1 (Coldstream Guards Regimental Band)
CD _____ CO 74500
Denon / May '92 / Conifer.

NATIONAL ANTHEMS VOL. 2 (Coldstream Guards Regimental Band)
CD _____ CO 74501
Denon / May '92 / Conifer.

NULLI SECUNDUS (Coldstream Guards Band)
CD _____ MMCD 430
Music Masters / Aug '93 / Target/BMG.

OUT THE ESCORT (Coldstream Guards Band)
CD _____ BNA 5052
Bandleader / Feb '92 / Conifer.

Cole, B.J.

HEART OF THE MOMENT
In at the deep end / Icarus enigma / Eastern cool / Indian willow / Three piece suite / Sands of time / Promenade and arabesque / Kraken wakes / Forever amber / Adagio in blue
CD _____ RES 107CD
Resurgence / May '95 / Vital.

TRANSPARENT MUSIC
CD _____ HNCD 1325
Hannibal / May '89 / Vital / ADA.

Cole, Bobby

DANCE-DANCE-DANCE
Diana / Thorn birds / Look for the silver lining / Music maestro please / Whispering / On Mother Kelly's doorstep / Rock-a-bye your baby with a Dixie melody / Don't bring Lulu / Put your arms around me honey / My blue Heaven / Bring me sunshine / Sheikh of Araby / Powder your face with sunshine / Memories / For ever and ever / I'm always chasing rainbows / Something tells me / All my loving / Hey Jude / I love Paris / Serenata / Melancholy baby / Sleepy time gal
CD _____ SAV 107CD
Savoy / May '93 / THE / Savoy.

Cole, Cozy

CLASSICS 1944
CD _____ CLASSICS 819
Classics / May '95 / Discovery / Jazz Music.

Cole, Freddy

I'M NOT MY BROTHER, I'M ME
CD _____ SSC 1054D
Sunnyside / Jan '92 / Pinnacle.

LIVE AT BIRDLAND WEST
My hat's the size of my head / I almost lost my mind / Am I blue / Pretend / Walkin' my baby back home / This heart of mine / Send for me / Somewhere along the way / Ballerina / I'm not my brother, I'm me / He was the king / Copacabana ripple
CD _____ 17015
Laserlight / Dec '95 / Target/BMG.

THIS IS THE LIFE
Easy to love / Somewhere down the line / This is the life / Don't change your mind about me / When love is looking your way / I loved you for a minute / Sweet beginning / Sunday king of love / Place in the sun (Movin' on)
CD _____ MCD 5503
Muse / Apr '95 / New Note / CM.

Cole, Holly

TEMPTATION
Take me home / Train song / Jersey girl / Temptation / Falling down / Invitation to the blues / Cinny's waltz / Frank's theme / Little boy blue / I don't wanna grow up / Tango 'til they're sore / Looking for the heart of Saturday night / Soldier's things / I want you / I'll be your mirror / Bring on the rose / Shiver me timbers
CD _____ CDP 8343482
Capitol Jazz / Sep '95 / EMI.

Cole, Jude

START THE CAR
Start the car / World's apart / Open road / Just another night / Tell the truth / Intro / Right there now / First your money (then your clothes) / It comes around / Blame it on fate / Place in the line
CD _____ 7599268982
WEA / Aug '92 / Warner Music.

VIEW FROM 3RD STREET
Hallowed ground / House full of reasons / Time for letting go / This time it's us / Compared to nothing / Baby, it's tonight / Get me through the night / Stranger to myself / Heart of blues / Prove me wrong
CD _____ 7599261642
WEA / Aug '90 / Warner Music.

Cole, Lloyd

1984 - 1989 (Cole, Lloyd & The Commotions)
CD _____ 837 736-2
Polydor / Mar '89 / PolyGram.

BAD VIBES
Morning is broken / So you'd like to save the world / Holier than thou / Love you so what / Wild mushrooms / My way to you / Too much of a good thing / Fall together / Mr. Wrong / Seen the future / Can't get arrested
CD _____ 518318-2
Fontana / Oct '93 / PolyGram.

EASY PIECES (Cole, Lloyd & The Commotions)
Rich / Why I love country music / Pretty gone / Grace / Cut me down / Brand new friend / Lost weekend / James / Minor character / Perfect blue / Her last fling / Big world / Nevers end
CD _____ 5500352
Spectrum/Karussell / May '93 / PolyGram / THE.

LOVE STORY
Trigger happy / Sentimental fool / I didn't know that you cared / Love ruins everything / Baby / Be there / June bride / Like lovers do / Happy for you / Traffic / Let's get lost / For crying out loud
CD _____ 5285292
Fontana / Sep '95 / PolyGram.

MAINSTREAM (Cole, Lloyd & The Commotions)
My bag / Twenty nine / Mainstream / Jennifer / Mr. Malcontent / Sean Penn blues / Big snake / Hey rusty / These days
CD _____ 833 691-2
Polydor / Oct '87 / PolyGram.

RATTLESNAKES (Cole, Lloyd & The Commotions)
Perfect skin / Speedboat / Rattlesnakes / Down on Mission Street / Forest fire / Charlotte Street / 2 CV / Four flights up / Patience / Are you ready to be heartbroken
CD _____ 823 683-2
Polydor / PolyGram.

Cole, Nat King

18 SONGS
CD _____ CD 62052
Saludos Amigos / May '94 / Target/BMG.

1943-49 VOCAL SIDES, THE (Cole, Nat King Trio)
CD _____ 11044
Laserlight / Jun '86 / Target/BMG.

1949-1951
CD _____ CD 53160
Giants Of Jazz / Aug '95 / Target/BMG / Cadillac.

1949-1960
CD _____ CD 53166
Giants Of Jazz / Nov '95 / Target/BMG / Cadillac.

20 GOLDEN GREATS: NAT KING COLE
Sweet Lorraine / Straighten up and fly right / Nature boy / Dance, ballerina, dance / Mona Lisa / Too young / Love letters / Smile / Around the world / For all we know / When I fall in love / Very thought of you / On the street where you live / Unforgettable / It's all in the game / Ramblin' rose / Portrait of Jennie / Let there be love / Somewhere along the way / Those lazy, hazy, crazy days of summer
CD _____ CDEMTV 9
Capitol / Dec '87 / EMI.

20 GREATEST LOVE SONGS
Stardust / Answer me / Autumn leaves / Walkin' my baby back home / These foolish things / There goes my heart / Nightingale sang in Berkeley Square / You made me love you / Blossom fell / Move / Love letters / OH how I miss you tonight / Brazilian love song / You're my everything / Love is a many splendoured thing / You'll never know / He'll have to go / Stay as sweet as you are / More I see you / Party's over
CD _____ CDEMTV 35
EMI / Dec '87 / EMI.

ANATOMY OF A JAM SESSION
Black market stuff / Laguna leap / I'll never be the same / Swingin' on central / Kicks
CD _____ BLC 760137
Black Lion / Oct '94 / Jazz Music / Cadillac / Wellard / Koch.

ANY OLD TIME (Cole, Nat King Trio)
Little joy from Chicago / Sunny side of the street / Candy / Any old time / (Back home again in) Indiana / Man I love / Trio grooves in Brooklyn / That'll just about knock me out / Too marvellous for words / Besame mucho / Wouldn't you like to know more
CD _____ GOJCD 1031
Giants Of Jazz / Mar '95 / Target/BMG / Cadillac.

AUDIO ARCHIVE
You're the cream in my coffee / Bugle call rag / Sweet Georgia Brown / Too marvellous for words / Sweet Lorraine / Yes sir that's my baby / Frim fram sauce / it's only a paper moon / If you can't smile and say yes / Cole's bop blues / Trouble with me is you / Miss thing / Man on the keys (live) / Satchel mouth baby / On the sunny side of the street (Live) / Last but not least (live) / Tea for two (Live) / Nat meets June (live) / Don't cry crybaby
CD _____ CDAA 002
Tring / Jan '93 / Tring / Prism.

BEST OF NAT KING COLE, THE
CD _____ DLCD 4004
Dixie Live / Mar '95 / Magnum Music Group.

BEST OF THE NAT KING COLE ORCHESTRA, THE
CD _____ CDP 7982882
Capitol Jazz / Jan '93 / EMI.

BEST OF THE NAT KING COLE TRIO, THE (The vocal classics 1942-46) (Cole, Nat King Trio)
All for you / Straighten up and fly right / Gee baby, ain't I good to you / If you can't smile and say yes / Sweet Lorraine / Embraceable you / It's only a paper moon / I realize now / I'm a shy guy / You're nobody 'til somebody loves you / What can I say after I say I'm sorry / I'm thru with love / Come to baby / Do / Frim fram sauce / How does it feel / (Get your kicks on) Route 66 / Baby, baby all the time / But she's my buddy's chick / You call it madness (but I call it love) / Best man / (I love you) for sentimental reasons / You're the cream in my coffee
CD _____ CDP 8335712
Capitol Jazz / Nov '95 / EMI.

BILLY MAY SESSIONS, THE
Walkin' my baby back home / What does it take / Walkin' / I'm hurting / Angel eyes / Lover come back to me / Can't I / Papa loves mambo / Teach me tonight / Blue moon / With you on my mind / Don't try / Send for me / Let's make love / Don't get around much anymore / Song is ended (but the melody lingers on) / You'll never know / Just for the fun of it (alternate take) / Who's sorry now / These foolish things / Once in a while / Just one of those things / I should care / Party's over / Just for the fun of it / Cottage for sale / I understand / When your lover has gone / Ebony rhapsody / Day in, day out / Too little, too late / When my sugar walks down the street / Cold cold heart / Let's face the music and dance / Something makes me want to dance with you / I'm gonna sit right down and write myself a letter / Rules of the road / Warm and willing / Bidin' my time / Moon love
CD Set _____ CDS 7895452
Capitol Jazz / Sep '93 / EMI.

BODY AND SOUL
CD _____ CDCD 1087
Charly / Apr '93 / Charly / THE / Cadillac.

CAPITOL COLLECTORS SERIES: NAT KING COLE
Straighten up and fly right / Route 66 / (I love you) for sentimental reasons / Christmas song / Nature boy / Too young / Walkin' my baby back home / Pretend / Answer me / Darling je vous aime beaucoup / Blossom fell / Send for me / Non dimenticar (Don't forget) / Ramblin' rose / Dear lonely hearts / All over the world / Those lazy-hazy-crazy days of summer / L.O.V.E. / Mona Lisa / Unforgettable
CD _____ CZ 303
Capitol / Apr '90 / EMI.

CHRISTMAS WITH NAT & DEAN (Cole, Nat King & Dean Martin)
Christmas song / Let it snow, let it snow, let it snow / White Christmas / Frosty the snowman / Winter wonderland / Happiest Christmas tree / Deck the halls with boughs of holly / O tannenbaum / Silent night / Brahms lullaby / Buon natale / O come all ye faithful (Adeste fidelis) / Rudolph the red nosed reindeer / Little boy that Santa Claus forgot / Cradle in Bethlehem / Christmas blues / Mrs. Santa Claus / Caroling, caroling / O little town of Bethlehem / O holy night / Joy to the world (CD only.) / God rest ye merry gentlemen
CD _____ CDMFP 5902
Music For Pleasure / Dec '94 / EMI.

CLASSICS 1936-40
CD _____ CLASSICS 757
Classics / Aug '94 / Discovery / Jazz Music.

CLASSICS 1939-41
CD _____ CLASSICS 773
Classics / Aug '94 / Discovery / Jazz Music.

CLASSICS 1941-43
CD _____ CLASSICS 786
Classics / Nov '94 / Discovery / Jazz Music.

COLLECTION
CD _____ COL 008
Collection / Apr '95 / Target/BMG.

COLLECTION, THE
Sweet Lorraine / Love is here to stay / Autumn leaves / Dance, ballerina, dance / September song / Beautiful friendship / Fly me to the moon / Let there be love / Mona Lisa / Pick yourself up / More I see you / Just one of those things / Let's fall in love / Love is the thing / Stay as sweet as you are / Love letters / When I fall in love / Stardust / Around the world / Too young / Very thought of you / On the street where you live / Ramblin' rose / Almost like being in love / Don't get around much anymore / Once in a while / These foolish things / I'm gonna sit right down and write myself a letter / This can't be love / For all we know / Lush life / Jet / Somewhere along the way / Because you're mine / Pretend / Mother Nature and Father Time / Can't I / Tenderly / Smile / Blossom fell / Dreams can tell a lie / Too young to go steady / Love me as though there were no tomorrow / To the ends of the earth / Time and the river / That's you / That Sunday that summer / Look no further / People / Song is ended (but the melody lingers on) (CD only) / Azure te (CD only) / Serenata (CD only) / Party's

135

over (CD only) / Cottage for sale (CD only) / There goes my heart (CD only) / Ain't misbehavin' (CD only)
CD Set _____ CDMFPBOX 5
Music For Pleasure / Dec '92 / EMI.

COMPLETE AFTER MIDNIGHT SESSIONS
CD _____ CDP 748 328 2
Capitol / Feb '88 / EMI.

COMPLETE EARLY TRANSCRIPTIONS
CD _____ VJC 1026/7/8/9
Vintage Jazz Classics / Oct '92 / Direct / ADA / CM / Cadillac.

EARLY FORTIES
CD _____ FSRCD 139
Fresh Sound / Dec '90 / Jazz Music / Discovery.

ESSENTIAL V-DISCS, THE
CD _____ JZCD 342
Suisa / Jan '93 / Jazz Music / THE.

GOLD COLLECTION, THE
CD _____ D2CD10
Recording Arts / Dec '92 / THE / Disc.

GOT A PENNY
I'm lost / Let's spring one / Beautiful moons / Got a penny / All for you / Fine sweet and tasty / My lips remember your kisses / Vom vim veedle / Bugle call rag / Let's pretend / Melancholy Madeline / Pitchin' up the boogie / Honky tonk tavern
CD _____ CDSGP 047
Prestige / May '93 / Total/BMG.

GREAT GENTLEMEN OF SONG - SPOTLIGHT ON NAT KING COLE
She's funny that way / Sunday, Monday or always / Crazy she calls me / Spring is here / You'll never know / Funny (not much) / I want a little girl / Am I blue / Until the real thing comes along / Embraceable you / Should I / Say it isn't so / Too marvellous for words / Mood indigo / For you / I remember you / That's all / Lights out
CD _____ CDP 8293932
Capitol / Aug '95 / EMI.

GREAT NAT KING COLE 1940 - 1956
CD _____ 11086
Laserlight / '88 / Target/BMG.

IT'S ALMOST LIKE BEING IN LOVE (Cole, Nat King Trio)
It's almost like being in love / It's only a paper moon / Jumpy jitters / Nothing ever happens / Let's do things / Sentimental blue / What'cha doing to my heart / Love me sooner / I'm through with love / Flo and Joe / Go bongo / Yes sir that's my baby / Tiny's excercise / Gee baby ain't I good to you / Baby I need you / Bop kick
CD _____ DBCD 15
Dance Band Days / Jul '89 / Prism.

JAZZMAN, THE
CD _____ TPZ 1012
Topaz Jazz / Feb '95 / Pinnacle / Cadillac.

LEGENDS IN MUSIC - NAT KING COLE
CD _____ LECD 070
Wisepack / Jul '94 / THE / Conifer.

LET'S FACE THE MUSIC AND DANCE
Let's face the music and dance / Let there be love / Route 66 / Something makes me want to dance with you / More I see you / Answer me / These foolish things / Dance, ballerina, dance / Midnight flyer / Sweet Lorraine / Straighten up and fly right / Fly me to the moon / Just one of those things / I'm gonna sit right down and write myself a letter / Ain't misbehavin' / Girl from Ipanema / Papa loves mambo / Baby, won't you please come home / Blue moon / Party's over
CD _____ CDEST 2228
Capitol / Apr '94 / EMI.

LET'S FALL IN LOVE
When I fall in love / Stardust / Around the world / Too young / Very thought of you / On the street where you live / Ramblin' rose / Just one of those things / Let's fall in love / Almost like being in love / Don't get around much anymore / I'm gonna sit right down and write myself a letter / This can't be love / For all we know / Somewhere along the way (CD only) / Cottage for sale (CD only) / There goes my heart (CD only) / Ain't misbehavin' (CD only)
CD _____ CDMFP 5895
Music For Pleasure / Oct '90 / EMI.

LIVE AT THE SANDS
Ballerina / Funny (not much) / Continental / I wish you love / You leave me breathless / Thou swell / My kind of love / Surrey with the fringe on top / Where or when / Miss Otis regrets (she's unable to lunch today / Joe Turner blues
CD _____ CDEMS 1110
Capitol / Mar '91 / EMI.

LOVE IS A MANY SPLENDOURED THING
CD _____ CDSGP 097
Prestige / Mar '94 / Total/BMG.

LOVE IS THE THING
When I fall in love / End of a love affair / Stardust / Stay as sweet as you are / When can I go without you / Maybe it's because I love you too much / Love letters / Ain't

misbehavin' / I thought about Marie / At last / It's all in the game / When Sunny gets blue / Love is the thing
CD _____ BU 11
Capitol / Mar '88 / EMI.

NAT 'KING' COLE 1943-44
CD _____ CLASSICS 804
Classics / Mar '95 / Discovery / Jazz Music.

NAT KING COLE
Sweet Lorraine / It's only a paper moon / Gone with the draft / Route 66 / You're the cream in my coffee / Too marvelous for words / Honeysuckle rose / Sweet Georgia Brown / Easy listening blues / What is this thing called love / This autumn / Baby Early morning blues / Jumpin' at capitol / Stompin' down broadway / Somebody loves me / Tea for two
CD _____ 22713
Music / Dec '95 / Target/BMG.

NAT KING COLE
Sweet Lorraine / It's only a paper moon / Gone with the draft / Route 66 / You're the cream in my coffee / Too marvelous for words / Honeysuckle rose / Sweet Georgia Brown / Easy listening blues / What is this thing called love / This autumn / Baby Early morning blues / Jumpin' at capitol / Stompin' down Broadway / Somebody loves me / Tea for two
CD _____ DVX 08092
Deja Vu / May '95 / THE.

NAT KING COLE (2CD Set)
CD Set _____ R2CD 4010
Deja Vu / Jan '96 / THE.

NAT KING COLE (CD BOXSET)
Straighten up and fly right / Jumpin' at capitol / Sweet Lorraine / Embraceable you / It's only a paper moon / What is this thing called love / You can depend on me / I'm through with love / Sweet georgia brown / Frim fram sauce / Route 66 / Baby, baby, all the time (Alternate version) / You call it madness / Christmas song / (I love you) for sentimental reasons / When I take my sugar to tea / Too marvellous for words / Blues in my shower / Kee-mo Ky-mo (The magic song) / Save the bones for Henry Jones / Nature boy / Lost April / Portrait of Jennie / Bop-kick / For all we know / Lush life / My baby just cares for me / Can I come in for a second / I'll never say Never Again again / Mona Lisa / Ev'ry day (I fall in love) / Orange coloured sky / Jet / Too young / Red sails in the sunset / Unforgettable / Walkin' my baby back home / Ruby and the pearl / Somewhere along the way / You stepped out of a dream / Funny (Not much) / Pretend / Angel eyes / Lover come back to me / That's all / If love is good to me / Blue gardenia / Our love is here to stay / This can't be love / Darling Je vous aime beaucoup / Answer me my love / Smile / My one isin (In life) / Open up the doghouse (Two cats are comin' out) / If I give my heart to you / Blossom fell / If I may / It could happen to you / Autumn leaves / There will never be another you / Let's fall in love / Night lights / To the ends of the earth / Candy / Ballerina / Caravan / Stardust / When I fall in love / When Sunny gets blue / Send for me / Don't get around much anymore / I should care / Party's over / St. Louis blues / Looking back / Very thought of you / But beautiful / Avalon / Late late show / To whom it may concern / Non dimentica (Don't forget) / Standin' in the need of prayer / Best thing for you / Perfidia / Wild is love / Thou swell / Where or when / Mr. Cole won't rock and roll / I remember you / Nightingale sang in Berkeley Square / Touch of your lips / Poinciana (Song of the tree) / Day in, day out / Azure te / Ramblin' rose / Say it isn't so / That Sunday that summer / On the street where you live / I don't want to see tomorrow / L.O.V.E.
CD Set _____ CDS 7997772
Capitol / Nov '92 / EMI.

NAT KING COLE CHRISTMAS ALBUM, THE
Christmas song / Deck the halls with boughs of holly / Frosty the snowman / I saw three ships / Buon Natale (Merry Christmas to you) / O come all ye faithful (Adeste fidelis) / O little town of Bethlehem / Little boy that Santa Claus forgot / O'Tannenbaum / First Noel / Little Christmas / Joy to the world / O holy night / Caroling, caroling / Cradle in Bethlehem / Away in a manger / God rest ye merry gentlemen / Silent night
CD _____ CDMFP 5976
EMI / Dec '94 / EMI.

NAT KING COLE GOLD (2CD Set)
CD Set _____ D2CD 4010
Deja Vu / Jun '95 / THE.

NAT KING COLE LIVE (Cole, Nat King & Nelson Riddle Orchestra)
Two different worlds / Thou swell / Mona Lisa / Night lights / Too young / That's my girl / But not for me / Repeat after me / True love / Little girl / Love letters / Just in time / Unforgettable / Love me tender / My foolish heart / Sweet Sue, just you / Somewhere along the way / This can't be love / I'm sitting on top of the world / You are my first love / It's just a little street / Toyland
CD _____ DATOM 1

A Touch Of Magic / Apr '94 / Harmonia Mundi.

NAT KING COLE STORY
Straighten up and fly right / Sweet Lorraine / It's only a paper moon / Route 66 / (I love you) for sentimental reasons / Christmas song / Nature boy / Lush life / Calypso blues / Mona Lisa / Orange coloured sky / Too young / Unforgettable / Somewhere along the way / Walkin' my baby back home / Pretend / Blue gardenia / I am in love / Answer me / Smile / Darling je vous aime beaucoup / Sand and the sea / If I may / Blossom fell / To the ends of the earth / Night lights / Ballerina / Stardust / Send for me / St. Louis blues / Looking back / Non dimenticar / Paradise / Oh, Mary, don't you weep
CD Set _____ CDS 7951292
Capitol / May '91 / EMI.

NAT KING COLE TRIO (Cole, Nat King Trio)
CD _____ CD 53005
Giants Of Jazz / Mar '92 / Target/BMG / Cadillac.

NAT KING COLE TRIO (1943-47) (Cole, Nat King/Oscar Moore/Johnny Miller)
CD _____ CD 14566
Jazz Portraits / May '95 / Jazz Music.

NAT KING COLE TRIOS 1947-48 (Cole, Nat King & Duke/Woody/Pearl Bailey)
CD _____ VJC 1011 2
Vintage Jazz Classics / Oct '91 / Direct / ADA / CM / Cadillac.

NATURE BOY
CD _____ CDCD 1087
Charly / Jun '93 / Charly / THE / Cadillac.

ONE AND ONLY NAT KING COLE, THE
Sweet Lorraine / Love is here to stay / Autumn leaves / Dance, ballerina, dance / September song / Beautiful friendship / Fly me to the moon / Let there be love / Mona Lisa / Pick yourself up / More I see you / Just one of those things / Let's fall in love / Love is the thing / Stay as sweet as you are / Love letters / Azure te (CD only.) / Serenata (CD only.) / Party's over (CD only.)
CD _____ CDMFP 6082
Music For Pleasure / Mar '90 / EMI.

RARE RADIO RECORDINGS
CD _____ JZCD 343
Suisa / Oct '93 / Jazz Music / THE.

ROUTE 66
CD _____ 90107-2
Jazz Archives / Oct '92 / Jazz Music / Discovery / Cadillac.

SHOWS VOLUME 1
CD _____ OTA 101902
On The Air / Mar '95 / Target/BMG.

SHOWS VOLUME 2
CD _____ OTA 101903
On The Air / Mar '95 / Target/BMG.

SHOWS VOLUME 3
CD _____ OTA 101904
On The Air / Mar '95 / Target/BMG.

SINGLES
Lush life / Jet / Somewhere along the way / Because you're mine / Faith can move mountains / Pretend / Mother Nature and Father Time / Can't I / Tenderly / Smile / Blossom fell / Dreams can tell a lie / Too young to go steady / Love me as though there were no tomorrow / To the ends of the earth / Time and the river / That's you / That Sunday that summer / Look no further / People
CD _____ CDMFP 5939
Music For Pleasure / Dec '92 / EMI.

STRAIGHTEN UP AND FLY RIGHT (Cole, Nat King Trio)
CD _____ CDCD 1234
Charly / Jun '95 / Charly / THE / Cadillac.

SWEET GEORGIA BROWN
CD _____ CDGRF 038
Tring / Jun '92 / Tring / Prism.

SWEET LORRAINE
Sweet Lorraine / Honeysuckle rose / Gone with the draft / This side up / Babs / Scotchin' with soda / Slow down / Early morning blues / This will make you laugh / Stop the red light's on / Hit the ramp / I like to riff / Call the police / Are you fer it / That ain't right / Hit that jive Jack
CD _____ CDCD 1012
Charly / Mar '93 / Charly / THE / Cadillac.

THIS IS NAT KING COLE (2CD Set)
When I fall in love / On the street where you live / Ramblin' Rose / Gee baby, ain't I good to you / I'm an errand boy for rhythm / Honeysuckle rose / End of a love affair / When the world was young / Where can I go without you / Nightingale sang in Berkeley Square / Let's fall in love / Arriverderci Roma / Best thing for you / Tangerine / Late late show / I got it bad and that ain't good / Open up the doghouse / For you my love / Autumn leaves / More I see you / Dance ballerina dance / Fly me to the moon / Get out and get under the moon / Miss Otis regrets / Continental / Surrey with the fringe on top / Girl from Ipanema / My kind of girl / Pretend / Smile / Breezin' along with the breeze / Les feuilles mortes / Aqui

se hable en Amore / Make believe land / Day isn't long enough / Happy new year / Miss me / Blossom fell / Too young to go steady
CD Set _____ CDDL 1305
Music For Pleasure / Nov '95 / EMI.

TO WHOM IT MAY CONCERN
Thousand thoughts of you / You're bringing out the dreamer in me / My heart's treasure / If you said no / Can't help it / Lovesville / Unfair / This morning it was summer / To whom it may concern / Love-wise / Too much / In the heart of Jane Doe
CD _____ CDP 8317732
Capitol / Mar '95 / EMI.

TOO MARVELLOUS FOR WORDS (Cole, Nat King Trio)
CD _____ CDCD 1130
Charly / Mar '93 / Charly / THE / Cadillac.

TRIO RECORDINGS VOL.1, THE
CD _____ 15746
Laserlight / Aug '92 / Target/BMG.

TRIO RECORDINGS VOL.2, THE
CD _____ 15747
Laserlight / Aug '92 / Target/BMG.

TRIO RECORDINGS VOL.3, THE
CD _____ 15748
Laserlight / Aug '92 / Target/BMG.

TRIO RECORDINGS VOL.4, THE
CD _____ 15749
Laserlight / Aug '92 / Target/BMG.

TRIO RECORDINGS VOL.5, THE
CD _____ 15750
Laserlight / Aug '92 / Target/BMG.

TRIO RECORDINGS VOLS 1-5, THE
CD Set _____ 15915
Laserlight / Aug '92 / Target/BMG.

UNFORGETTABLE
Unforgettable / Too young / Mona Lisa / (I love you) for sentimental reasons / Pretend / Answer me / Portrait of Jennie / What'll I do / Lost April / Red sails in the sunset / Make her mine / Hajji baba
CD _____ CDEMS 1100
Capitol / Mar '91 / EMI.

UNFORGETTABLE
CD _____ CDCD 1255
Charly / Jun '95 / Charly / THE / Cadillac.

UNFORGETTABLE NAT KING COLE, THE
Unforgettable / Dance, ballerina, dance / It's all in the game / Let there be love / St. Louis blues / Beautiful friendship / Let's fall in love / Nature boy / Ramblin' rose / Smile / Serenata / Tenderly / Love is a many splendoured thing / Stay as sweet as you are / Love letters / Christmas song
CD _____ CDEMTV 61
EMI / Nov '91 / EMI.

UNFORGETTABLE NAT KING COLE, THE
Somewhere along the way / Love me tender / But not for me / Mona Lisa / Too young / Unforgettable / True love / Love letters / You are my first love / Take me back to Toyland / This can't be love / Two different worlds / Just in time / It's only a paper moon / To the ends of the earth / Tea for two / Somebody loves me / Sweet Lorraine
CD _____ BSTCD 9113
Best Compact Discs / Apr '94 / Complete/Pinnacle.

VOCAL SIDES, THE
CD _____ 15718
Laserlight / Sep '92 / Target/BMG.

WILD IS LOVE
Introduction / Hundreds and thousands of girls / It's a beautiful evening / Tell her in the morning / Are you disenchanted / Pick-up / Beggar for the blues / World of no return / In love again / Stay with it / Wouldn't you know / He who hesitates / Wild is love - finale
CD _____ CDP 8285112
Capitol / Mar '95 / EMI.

Cole, Natalie

EVERLASTING
Everlasting / Jump start / Urge to merge / Split decision / When I fall in love / Pink cadillac / I live for your love / In my reality / I'm the one / More than the stars / What I must do (Track on cassette only.)
CD _____ 7559611142
Elektra / Jul '91 / Warner Music.

GOOD TO BE BACK
Safe / As a matter of fact / Rest of the night / Miss you like crazy / I do / Good to be back / Gonna make you mine / Starting over again / Don't mention my heartache / I can't cry / Someone's rocking my dreamboat / Wild women do (Reissue only.)
CD _____ 7559611152
Elektra / Jul '91 / Warner Music.

HOLLY & IVY
CD _____ 755961704-2
Elektra / Nov '94 / Warner Music.

SOPHISTICATED LADY
This will be / Good morning heartache / Touch me / Unpredictable you / Sophisticated lady / Joey / I've got love on my mind / Needing you / Your face stays in my mind / Can we get together again / Heaven is with you / Our love / I love you so / Keep smiling / Not like mine / Be thankful / Who will carry on / You / Oh daddy / Stand by
CD _____ CDMFP 5984
Music For Pleasure / Jun '93 / EMI.

SOUL OF NATALIE COLE, THE (1975-1980)
This will be / Lovers / Mr. Melody / Annie Mae / I can't break away / La costa / Peaceful living / (I've seen) Paradise / Stairway to the stars / Inseparable / I love him so much / Be mine tonight / What you won't do for love / Still i love / Love will find you / Party lights / This will be (remix)
CD _____ CDEST 2157
Capitol / Oct '91 / EMI.

TAKE A LOOK
I wish you love / I'm beginning to see the light / Swingin' shepherd blues / Crazy he calls me / Cry me a river / Undecided / Fiesta in blue / I'm gonna laugh you right out of my life / Let there be love / It's sand man / Don't explain / As time goes by / Too close for comfort / Calypso blues / This will make you laugh / Lovers / All about love / Take a look
CD _____ 755961496-2
Elektra / Jun '93 / Warner Music.

UNFORGETTABLE
Very thought of you / It's only a paper moon / Route 66 / Mona lisa / I .O.V.E. / This can't be love / Smile / Lush life / That Sunday / That summer / Orange coloured sky / (I love you) for sentimental reasons / Straighten up and fly right / Avalon / Don't get around much anymore / Too young / Nature boy / Darling / Je vous aime beaucoup / Almost like being in love / Thou swell / Non dimenticar / Our love is here to stay
CD _____ 755961049-2
Elektra / Jun '91 / Warner Music.

Cole, Paula

HARBINGER
CD _____ 9362460412
Warner Bros. / Nov '95 / Warner Music.

Cole, Richie

ALTO MADNESS
Price is right / Common touch / Last tango in Paris / Island breeze / Big Bo's paradise / Remember your day off... / Moody's mood
CD _____ MCD 5155
Muse / Sep '92 / New Note / CM.

BOSSA INTERNATIONAL
CD _____ MCD 9180
Milestone / Oct '93 / Jazz Music / Pinnacle / Wellard / Cadillac.

HOLLYWOOD MADNESS
Hooray for Hollywood / Hi fly / Tokyo rose sing the Hollywood blues / Relaxin' at Camarillo / Malibu breeze / I love Lucy / Waiting for Waits / Hooray for Hollywood (reprise)
CD _____ MCD 5207
Muse / Feb '86 / New Note / CM.

NEW YORK AFTERNOON
Dorothy's den / Waltz for a rainy be-bop evening / Alto madness / New York afternoon / It's the same thing everywhere / Stormy weather (Trenton style.) / You'll always be my friend
CD _____ MOB 8118
Muse / Sep '92 / New Note / CM.

POPBOP
Overjoyed / Eddie Jefferson / On a misty night / L.Dorado kaddy / La bamba / When you wish upon a star / Spanish harlem / Star trek 1 / Sonomascope / Saxophobia / Straight no chaser
CD _____ MCD 9152-2
Milestone / Jan '94 / Jazz Music / Pinnacle / Wellard / Cadillac.

SIDE BY SIDE
Save your love for me / Naughayde reality (Live spiral.) / Scrapple from the apple / Donna Lee / Polka dots and moonbeams (Richie Cole alto sax solo.) / Eddie's mood / Side by side
CD _____ MCD 6016
Muse / Sep '92 / New Note / CM.

SIGNATURE
Sunday in New York / Trade winds / Doing the jungle walk / Occasional man / Rainbow lady / Take the cole train / If ever I would leave you / Peggy's blue skylight / America the beautiful
CD _____ MCD 9162-2
Milestone / Jan '94 / Jazz Music / Wellard / Cadillac.

YAKETY MADNESS! (Cole, Richie & Boots Randolph)
CD _____ 15473
Laserlight / Jan '94 / Target/BMG.

Coleman, Anthony

DISCO BY NIGHT
CD _____ AVAN 011

Avant / Nov '92 / Harmonia Mundi / Cadillac.

Coleman, Bill

BILL COLEMAN
CD _____ JCD 196
Jazzology / Apr '94 / Swift / Jazz Music.

BILL COLEMAN IN PARIS 1936/38
After you've gone / I'm in the mood for love / Joe Louis stomp / Coquette / Exactly like you / Hangover blues / Rose room / (Back home again in) Indiana / Bill street blues / Merry go round broke down / I ain't got nobody / Baby, won't you please come home / Big boy blues / Swing guitars / Bill Coleman blues / In a little Spanish town / I double dare you / Way down yonder in New Orleans / I wish I could shimmy like my sister Kate
CD _____ DRGCD 8402
DRG / Sep '93 / New Note.

CLASSICS 1936-38
CD _____ CLASSICS 764
Classics / Jun '94 / Discovery / Jazz Music.

FONSEQUE/ FLEUR
CD _____ 873121
Milan / Aug '92 / BMG / Silva Screen.

IN PARIS 1936-1938
CD _____ 8402
DRG / Feb '94 / New Note.

MEETS GUY LAFITTE
CD _____ BLCD 760182
Black Lion / Apr '93 / Jazz Music / Cadillac / Wellard / Koch.

Coleman, Bob

CINCINNATI BLUES (1928-1936) (Coleman, Bob Cincinnati Jug Band)
CD _____ SOB 035192
Story Of The Blues / Dec '92 / Koch / ADA.

Coleman, Cy

WHY TRY TO CHANGE ME NOW
CD _____ PS 003CD
P&S / Sep '95 / Discovery.

Coleman, Gary B.B.

BEST OF GARY B.B. COLEMAN
One eyed woman / Baby scratch my back / Cloud 9 / Word of warning / I fell in love on a one night stand / Merry Christmas baby / Watch where you stroke / Think before you act / If you can beat me rockin' / St. James infirmary / I won't be your fool / Christmas blues (Instr.)
CD _____ ICH 1065CD
Ichiban / Jun '94 / Koch.

DANCIN' MY BLUES AWAY
Word of warning / Think before you act / What's the name of that thing / I gotta play the blues for you / Dancin' my blues away / Maybe love wasn't meant for me / Can't spend my money / Blues at sunrise
CD _____ CDICH 1049
Ichiban / Dec '89 / Koch.

IF YOU CAN'T BEAT ME ROCKIN'
Watch where you stroke / Cloud 9 / Please don't dog me / If the washing don't get you / If you can beat me rockin' / It just ain't right / Rub my back / St. James Infirmary / Hideaway / Tell me what to do / Los con-quintadores_ chocolates_ / Lost_ on_ 23rd street / Fantasy / Shifting gears / Can't we smile
CD _____ CDICH 1018
Ichiban / Mar '88 / Koch.

ONE NIGHT STAND
Baby scratch my back / Sitting and waiting / I just can't lose this blues / I'll take care of you / I wrote this song for you / As the years go passing by / I fell in love on a one night stand / Going down
CD _____ CDICH 1034
Ichiban / Oct '93 / Koch.

ROMANCE WITHOUT FINANCE IS A NUISANCE
She ain't ugly / Don't give away that recipe / If you see my one eyed woman / Dealin' from the bottom of the deck / Romance without finance / Food stamp Annie / Mr. Chicken Stew / Mr. B's frosting
CD _____ CDICH 1107
Ichiban / Oct '93 / Koch.

Coleman, George

AMSTERDAM AFTER DARK
Amsterdam after dark / New arrival / Lo-Joe / Autumn in New York / Apache dance / Blondie's waltz
CD _____ CDSJP 129
Timeless Jazz / Mar '91 / New Note.

AT YOSHI'S
They say it's wonderful / Good morning heartache / Laig gobblin' blues / Ten / Up jumped Spring / Father / Soul eyes
CD _____ ECD 220212
Evidence / Aug '92 / Harmonia Mundi / ADA / Cadillac.

BONGO JOE
CD _____ ARHCD 1040
Arhoolie / Apr '95 / ADA / Direct / Cadillac.

MANHATTAN PANORAMA
CD _____ ECD 220192
Evidence / Jun '92 / Harmonia Mundi / ADA / Cadillac.

MY HORNS OF PLENTY (Coleman, George Quartet)
Lush life / Conrad / My romance / Sheikh of Araby / You mean so much to me / Old folks
CD _____ 8372782
Birdology / Jan '92 / PolyGram.

PLAYING CHANGES
Laura / Siorra / Moment's notice
CD _____ JHCD 002
Ronnie Scott's Jazz House / Jan '94 / Jazz Music / Magnum Music Group / Cadillac.

Coleman, Michael

1891-1945
CD _____ CEFCD 161
Gael Linn / Jan '94 / Roots / CM / Direct / ADA.

Coleman, Ornette

ART OF THE IMPROVISERS
CD _____ 7567909782
Atlantic / Apr '95 / Warner Music.

AT THE GOLDEN CIRCLE VOL 2
Snowflakes and sunshine / Morning song / Riddle / Antiques
CD _____ BNZ 101
Blue Note / Aug '89 / EMI.

BEAUTY IS A RARE THING (Complete Atlantic Recordings - 6CD Set)
Focus on sanity / Chrology / Peace / Congeniality / Lonely woman / Monk and the nun / Just for you / Eventually / Una muy bonita / Bird food / Change of the century / Music always / Face of the bass / Forerunner / Free / Circle with a hole in the middle / Ramblin' / Little symphony / Tribes of New York / Kaleidoscope / Rise and shine / Mr. and Mrs. People / Blues connotation / I heard it over the radio / P.S Unless one has (Blues connotation No.2) / Revolving doors / Brings goodness / Joy of a toy / To us / Humpty dumpty / Fifth of Beethoven / Motive for its use / Moon inhabitants / Legend of bebop / Some other / Embraceable you / All / Folk tale / Poise / Beauty is a rare thing / First take / Free jazz / Proof readers / Wru / Check up / Alchemy of Scott La Faro / Ecs / Enfant / Ecars / Cross breeding / Harlem's Manhattan / Mapa / Abstraction / Variants on a theme of thelonious monk (criss-cross)
CD Set _____ 812271410-2
Atlantic / Feb '94 / Warner Music.

CHANGE OF THE CENTURY
Ramblin' / Free / Face of the bass / Forerunner / Bird food / Una muy bonita / Change of the century
CD _____ 756781341-2
Atlantic / Jun '93 / Warner Music.

CHAPPAQUA SUITE (2CD Set)
Part one / Part two / Part three / Part four
CD _____ 4805842
Sony Jazz / Dec '95 / Sony.

DEDICATION TO POETS AND WRITERS
CD _____ 30010
Giants Of Jazz / Sep '92 / Target/BMG / Cadillac.

FREE JAZZ
Little symphony / Rise and shine / Kaleidoscope / Revolving doors / Legend of bebop / Embraceable you / Folk tale / Free jazz
CD _____ CD 53214
Giants Of Jazz / Jan '96 / Target/BMG / Cadillac.

FREE JAZZ - THAT'S JAZZ
Free jazz (part 1) / Free jazz (part 2)
CD _____ 756781347-2
Atlantic / Mar '93 / Warner Music.

SHAPE OF JAZZ TO COME, THE
Lonely woman / Eventually / Peace / Focus on sanity / Congeniality / Chronology
CD _____ 756781339-2
Atlantic / Jun '93 / Warner Music.

SOMETHING ELSE
CD _____ OJCCD 163
Original Jazz Classics / Feb '93 / Wellard / Jazz Music / Cadillac / Complete/Pinnacle.

SONG X (Coleman, Ornette & Pat Metheny)
Song X / Mob job / Endangered species / Video games / Kathelin Gray / Trigonometry / Song X (2) / Long time no see
CD _____ GFLD 19195
Geffen / Mar '93 / BMG.

TOMORROW IS THE QUESTION
Tomorrow is the question / Tears inside / Mind and time / Compassion / Giggin' / Rejoicing / Lorraine / Turnaround / Endless
CD _____ OJCCD 3422
Original Jazz Classics / Apr '89 / Wellard / Jazz Music / Cadillac / Complete/Pinnacle.

Coleman, Steve

BLACK SCIENCE (Coleman, Steve & Five Elements)
X format (standard deviation) / Twister / Turbulence / Beyond all we know / Vial of calm / Black phonemics / Ghost town / Magneto / Cross fade / Black phonemics (reprise)
CD _____ PD 83119
Novus / Jul '91 / BMG.

DEF TRANCE BEAT (Modalities Of Rhythm) (Coleman, Steve & Five Elements)
Flint / Verifiable / pedagogy / Dogon / Multiplicity of approachs (Afrikan way of knowing.) / Khu (Divine will) / Pad thai / Jeannine's sizzling patterns of force / Mantra (Intonation of power) / Salt peanuts
CD _____ 01241631812
Novus / Apr '95 / BMG.

DROP KICK (Coleman, Steve & Five Elements)
Ramses / Drop kick / Terra nova / Journeyman / Sinbius web / Tschanz / Contemplation / Shit on the fly / Bates motel / Z Train
CD _____ 01241631442
Novus / Oct '92 / BMG.

PHASE = SPACE (Coleman, Steve & Dave Holland)
CD _____ DIW 865
DIW / Jan '93 / Harmonia Mundi / Cadillac.

RHYTHM IN MIND
Slipped again / Left of center / Sweet dawn / Pass it on / Vet blues / Zic / Afterthoughts
CD _____ PD 90654
Novus / May '92 / BMG.

RHYTHM PEOPLE
Rhythm people / Blues shifting / No conscience / Neutral zone / Ain't goin' out like that / Step'n / Dangerous / Ice moves / Posse / Armageddon (Cold blooded)
CD _____ PD 83092
Novus / Nov '90 / BMG.

TALE OF THREE CITIES EP (Coleman, Steve & Metrics)
Be bop / I am who I am / Science / Get open / Slow burn / Left to right
CD _____ 74321247472
Novus / Jul '95 / BMG.

TAO OF MAD PHAT, THE (Coleman, Steve & Five Elements)
Tao of Mad Phat / Alt-shift-return / Collected meditations / Changing of the guard / Guards on the train / Relax your guard / All the guards enter / Enter the rhythm (people) / Incantation / Laid back schematics / Polymad nomads / Little girl on fire
CD _____ 01241631602
Novus / Nov '93 / BMG.

Coleman, Wanda

BERSERK ON HOLLYWOOD BOULEVARD
CD _____ NAR 059 CD
New Alliance / May '93 / Pinnacle.

HIGH PRIESTESS OF WORD
CD _____ NAR 048 CD
New Alliance / May '93 / Pinnacle.

Coles, Johnny

NEW MORNING (Coles, Johnny Quartet)
CD _____ CRISS 1005CD
Criss Cross / Oct '92 / Cadillac / Harmonia Mundi.

WARM SOUND, THE
CD _____ 3/8042
Koch / Jan '96 / Koch.

Colianni, John

MAYBECK RECITAL HALL SERIES VOL.37
Blue and sentimental / Stardust / What's your story Morning Glory / It never entered my mind / Londonderry air / Don't stop the carnival / When your lover loves you / Ja da / Basin Street blues / I never knew / Baby, won't you please come home / Tea for two / Goodbye / Heart shaped box
CD _____ CCD 4643
Concord Jazz / May '95 / New Note.

Colin, Daniel

PRESTIGE DE L'ACCORDEON VOL. 1
CD _____ 242052
Wotre Music / Nov '92 / New Note.

Colina, Michael

SHADOW OF URBANO
Joy dancing / Shades / Shadow of Urbano / Hong Kong flu / Doctor of desire / Fast break / Lady and the tramp / Drifter
CD _____ 259.967
Private Music / Nov '89 / BMG.

Coll, Brian

AT HOME IN IRELAND
CD _____ CDBC 505
Outlet / Jan '95 / ADA / Duncans / CM / Ross / Direct / Koch.

Collapsed Lung

JACKPOT GOALIE
Maclife intro / Maclife / Down with the plaid fad / Eat my goal / Interactive / I may not know the score but / Something ordinary / Burn rubber soul / Filthy's fix / Dis MX / Begrudgit / Slack agenda
CD _____ BLUFF 015CD
Deceptive / Apr '95 / Vital.

Collective Soul

HINTS, ALLEGATIONS & THINGS LEFT UNSOLVED
CD _____ 756782596-2
Warner Bros. / Aug '94 / Warner Music.

Collectors

COLLECTORS, THE
What is love / She / Howard Christman's older / Lydia purple / One act play
CD _____ 901009
Line / Oct '94 / CM / Grapevine / ADA / Conifer / Direct.

GRASS AND THE WILD STRAWBERRIES
Grass and wild strawberries / Things to remember / Don't turn away / Teletype click / Seventeenth summer / Long rain / My love delights me / Dream of desolation / Rainbow of fire / Early morning / Sheep on the hillside
CD _____ 901013
Line / Oct '94 / CM / Grapevine / ADA / Conifer / Direct.

Collectors

ASTRONAUT GIRL
CD _____ CITREC 02
Citizen / Oct '93 / Plastic Head.

DESOLATION ANGELS
CD _____ CITRE 03
Citizen / Oct '94 / Plastic Head.

Collet, Danny

LOUISIANA SWAMP CATS
CD _____ FF 628CD
Flying Fish / Dec '93 / Roots / CM / Direct / ADA.

Collette

ATTITUDE
CD _____ REVXD 135
FM / Mar '93 / Sony.

Collie, Mark

UNLEASHED
Hard lovin' woman / It is no secret / All I want is you / Waiting / Ring of fire / Rainy day woman / When you belonged to me / God didn't make me that strong / Lonely streak / Unleashed
CD _____ MCAD 11055
MCA / Aug '94 / BMG.

Collie, Max

FRONTLINE BACKLINE (Collie, Max & his Rhythm Aces)
Royal Garden blues / Kinklets / Down by the river / Gate mouth / Muskrat ramble / St. Louis blues / Isle of Capri / Ory's Creole trombone / Mahogany hall stomp / Lazy river / (I'll be glad when you're dead) you rascal you / Sing on / Oh you beautiful doll / You always hurt the one you love / Sweet Sue, just you
CD _____ CDTTD 504
Timeless Jazz / Feb '95 / New Note.

HIGH SOCIETY SHOW, THE (Collie, Max & his Rhythm Aces)
CD _____ RCD 108
Reality / Oct '92 / New Note / Jazz Music / Wellard / Cadillac.

LATEST & GREATEST (Collie, Max & his Rhythm Aces)
Dippermouth blues / Fidgety feet / My man / Martinique / Travelling blues / Nobody knows you're down and out / When you and I were young Maggie / Buddy's bolero / Tell me your dreams / Mabel's dream / Down in Honky Tonk town / Young woman blues / Froggy moor rag / Shimmee sha wabble / Savoy blues
CD _____ RCD 113
Reality / Nov '95 / New Note / Jazz Music / Wellard / Cadillac.

MAX COLLIE & FRIENDS PART 1
CD _____ RCD 113
Reality / Aug '94 / New Note / Jazz Music / Wellard / Cadillac.

MAX COLLIE & FRIENDS PART 2
CD _____ R 113C
Reality / Aug '94 / New Note / Jazz Music / Wellard / Cadillac.

SENSATION
CD _____ CDTTD 503
Timeless Traditional / Jan '88 / New Note.

THRILL OF JAZZ, THE (Collie, Max & his Rhythm Aces)
CD _____ RCD 111
Reality / Mar '90 / New Note / Jazz Music / Wellard / Cadillac.

WORLD CHAMPIONS OF JAZZ (Collie, Max & his Rhythm Aces)
Too bad / Sweet like this / Salutation march / 'S wonderful / I'm crazy 'bout my baby / Didn't he ramble / Ragtime dance / Dans les rues D'Antibes / Fidgety fingers
CD _____ BLCD 760512
Black Lion / Nov '95 / Jazz Music / Cadillac / Wellard / Koch.

Collins Kids

HOP, SKIP AND JUMP
Go away don't bother me / Rock 'n' roll polka / Move a little closer / My first love / Hush money / I wish / Cuckoo rock / Beetle bug bop / I'm in my teens / Rockaway rock / They're still in love / Make him behave / Hop, skip and jump / Shortnin' bread rock / Just because / Hoy hoy / Hot rod / Heartbeat / Mama worries / Party / Walking the floor over you / Missouri waltz / You are my sunshine / Soda poppin' around / Young heart / Ain't you ever / What'cha gonna do now / Waitin' and watchin' / Home of the blues / Lonesome road / Early American / Rockin' gypsy / Bye bye / Hurricane / Mercy / Rock boppin' baby / Whistle bait / Sweet talk / Spur of the moment / Rebel / Johnny Yuma / There'll be some changes made / Fireball mail / T-bone / What about tomorrow / Get along home Cindy / You've been gone too long / One step down / There stands the one / Wild and wicked love / Hey mama boom a lacka / More than a friend / Pied piper poodle / Blues in the night / Another man done gone / Sugar plum / Kinda like love / Are you certain / That's your affair
CD Set _____ BCD 15537
Bear Family / Aug '91 / Rollercoaster / Direct / CM / Swift / ADA.

ROCKIN' ON TV 1957-1961
CD _____ KKCD 14
Krazy Kat / Oct '94 / Hot Shot / CM.

Collins, Albert

ALBERT COLLINS LIVE
You're so high / You accuse me / I get the feeling / Angel mercy / Icy blue / Trouble was money / Playing with my mind / Too many dirty dishes / Things I used to do / Black cat bone
CD _____ CDCBL 756
Charly / Oct '95 / Charly / THE / Cadillac.

COLD SNAP
Cash talkin' / Bending like a willow tree / Good fool is hard to find / Lights are on but nobody's home / I ain't drunk / Hooked on you / Too many dirty dishes / Snatchin' it back / Fake ID
CD _____ ALCD 4752
Alligator / May '93 / Direct / ADA.

COLLINS MIX
There's gotta be a change / Honey hush / Master charge / If trouble was money / Don't lose your cool / If you love me like you say / Frosty / Tired man / Moon is full / Collin's mix / Same old thing
CD _____ VPBCD 17
Virgin / Nov '93 / EMI.

DON'T LOSE YOUR COOL
Got togettin' / My mind is trying to leave me / I'm broke / Don't lose your cool / When a guitar plays the blues / But I was cool / Melt down / Ego trip / Quicksand
CD _____ ALCD 4730
Alligator / May '93 / Direct / ADA.

FROSTBITE
If you love me like you say / Blue Monday hangover / I got a problem / Highway is like a woman / Brick / Don't go reaching across my plate / Give me my blues / Snowed in
CD _____ ALCD 4719
Alligator / May '93 / Direct / ADA.

FROZEN ALIVE
Frosty / Angel of mercy / I got that feeling / Caledonia / Things I used to do / Got a mind to travel / Cold cuts
CD _____ ALCD 4725
Alligator / May '93 / Direct / ADA.

ICE PICKIN'
Talking woman blues / When the welfare turns its back on you / Ice pick / Cold cold feeling / Too tired / Master charge / Conversation with Collins / Avalanche
CD _____ ALCD 4713
Alligator / May '93 / Direct / ADA.

ICEMAN
Mr. Collins, Mr. Collins / Iceman / Don't mistake kindness for weakness / Travellin' South / Put the shoe on the other foot / I'm beginning to wonder / Head rag / Hawk / Blues for Gabe / Mr. Collins, Mr. Collins (reprise)
CD _____ VPBCD 3
Virgin / Feb '91 / EMI.

LIVE '92/'93 (Collins, Albert & The Icebreakers)
Iceman / Lights are on but nobody's home / If you love me (like you say) / Put the shoe on the other foot / Frosty / Travellin' South

/ Talkin' woman / My woman has a black cat bone / I ain't drunk / T-bone shuffle
CD _____ VPBCD 27
Pointblank / Oct '95 / EMI.

LIVE IN JAPAN (Collins, Albert & The Icebreakers)
Listen here / Tired man / If trouble was money / Jealous man / Stormy Monday / Skatin' / All about my girl
CD _____ ALCD 4733
Alligator / May '93 / Direct / ADA.

SHOWDOWN (Collins, Albert/Johnny Copeland/Robert Cray)
T-bone shuffle / Moon is full / Lion's den / She's into something / Bring your fine self home / Black cat bone / Dream / Albert's alley / Black Jack
CD _____ ALCD 4743
Alligator / May '93 / Direct / ADA.

Collins, Bootsy

BACK IN THE DAY - THE BEST OF BOOTSY COLLINS
Ahh...the name is Bootsy baby / Stretchin' out (in a rubber band) / Pinocchio theory / Hollywood squares / I'd rather be with you / What so never the dance / Can't stay away / Jam fan (hot) / Mug push / Body slam / Scenery / Vanish in our sleep / Psychoticbumpschool (live)
CD _____ 7599226581-2
Warner Bros. / Aug '94 / Warner Music.

BLASTERS OF THE UNIVERSE (Bootsy's New Rubber Band)
Blasters of the universe / A / Funk express card / Bad girls / Back n the day / Where r the children / Female troubles (The national anthem) / Wide track / Funk me dirty / Blasters of the universe 2 (The sequel) / Goodnight Eddie / Sacred place / Half pass midnight / It's a silly serious world
CD Set _____ RCD 90307-08
Rykodisc / Aug '94 / Vital / ADA.

BOOTSY PLAYER OF THE YEAR
CD _____ 7599263352
WEA / Jan '96 / Warner Music.

JUNGLE BASS (Bootsy's Rubber Band)
Jungle bass / Disciples of funk / Interzone / Jungle bass (Mix)
CD _____ BRECD 550
4th & Broadway / Jul '90 / PolyGram.

KEEPIN' DAH FUNK ALIVE 4 (1995) (Bootsy's New Rubber Band)
Intro / Ahh the name is Bootsy, baby / Bootsy (What's the name of this town) / Psychoticbumpschool / Pinocchio theory / Hollywood squares / Bernie solo / One nation under a groove / P Funk (wants to get funked up) / Cosmic slop / Flash light / Bootzilla / Roto-rooter / I'd rather be with you / Sacred place / Stretchin' out (In a rubber band) / Touch somebody / Night of the thumpasaurus peoples / Keepin' da funk alive 1994-5
CD Set _____ RCD 9032324
Rykodisc / Aug '96 / Vital / ADA.

LORD OF THE HARVEST (Zillatron)
Bugg light / Fuzz face / Exterminate / Smell the secrets / Count zero / Bootsy and the beast / No fly zone the devils playground / Passion continues
CD _____ RCD 10301
Black Arc / Jun '94 / Vital.

NAME IS BOOTSY BABY, THE
CD _____ 7599229722
WEA / Jan '96 / Warner Music.

ONE GIVETH, THE COUNT TAKETH AWAY, THE
Shine o'Myte (rap popping) / Landshark / Count Dracula / Funkateer, I / Lexicon (of love) / So nice you name him twice / What's wrong radio / Music to smile by / Play on playboy / Take a lickin' and keep on kickin' / Funky funkateer
CD _____ 7599236672
WEA / Jan '96 / Warner Music.

STRETCHIN' OUT (Bootsy's Rubber Band)
Stretchin' out (In a rubber band) / Psychotic bum school / Another point of view / I'd rather be with you / Love vibes / Physical love / Vanish in our sleep
CD _____ 7599263342
WEA / Jan '96 / Warner Music.

THIS BOOT IS MADE FOR FONK-N (Bootsy's Rubber Band)
Under the influence of a groove / Bootsy get live / Do good / Jam fan / Chug-a-lug / Shejam / Reprise
CD _____ 7599232952
WEA / Jan '96 / Warner Music.

ULTRA WAVE
CD _____ 7599263362
WEA / Jan '96 / Warner Music.

Collins, Cal

OHIO STYLE (Collins, Cal Quartet)
Falling in love with love / East of the sun and west of the moon / Be anything / Bag's groove / Affair to remember / Skylark / I've got the world on a string / I don't stand a ghost of a chance with you / Tumbling tumbleweeds / Ill wind / Sweet Sue, just you / Until the real thing comes along

CD _____ CCD 4447
Concord Jazz / Feb '91 / New Note.

Collins, Dave & Ansil

DOUBLE BARREL
CD _____ RASCD 3225
Ras / Jan '96 / Jetstar / Greensleeves / SRD / Direct.

Collins, Edwyn

GORGEOUS GEORGE
Campaign for real rock / Girl like you / Low expectations / Out of this world / If you could love me / North of heaven / Gorgeous George / It's right in front of you / Make me feel again / You got it all / Subsidence / Occupy your mind (On MC & LP only.)
CD _____ SETCD 014
Setanta / Jul '95 / Vital.

HELLBENT ON COMPROMISE
Means to an end / You poor deluded fool / It might as well be you / Take care of yourself / Graciously / Someone else besides / My girl has gone / Now that it's love (Not on LP) / Everything and more / What's the big idea / Time of the preacher - long time gone
CD _____ FIENDCD 195
Demon / Oct '90 / Pinnacle / ADA.

HOPE AND DESPAIR
Coffee table song / Fifty shades of blue / You're better than you know / Pushing it to the back of my mind / Darling they want it all / Wheels of love / Beginning of the end / Measure of the man / Testing time / Let me put your arms around you / Wide eyes child in me / Ghost of a chance
CD _____ FIENDCD 144
Demon / Aug '95 / Pinnacle / ADA.

Collins, Glenda

BEEN INVITED TO A PARTY (1963-1966)
I lost my heart at the fairground / I feel so good / If you gotta pick a baby / Baby it hurts / Nice wasn't it / Lollipop / Everybody got to fall in love / Johnny loves me / Paradise for two / Thou shalt not steal / Been invited to a party / Something I got to tell you / My heart didn't lie / It's hard to believe it / Don't let it rain on Sunday / in the first place
CD _____ CSAPCD 108
Connoisseur / Aug '90 / Pinnacle.

Collins, Joyce

SWEET MADNESS
CD _____ ACD 262
Audiophile / Sep '91 / Jazz Music / Swift.

Collins, Judy

AMAZING GRACE
Somebody soon / Since you asked / Both sides now / Sons of / Suzanne / Farewell to Tarwathie / Father / Albatross / In my life / Amazing grace
CD _____ 9548 316162
Carlton Home Entertainment / Jan '93 / Carlton Home Entertainment.

AMAZING GRACE
CD _____ TCD 2265
Telstar / Jul '87 / BMG.

COLORS OF THE DAY - THE BEST OF JUDY COLLINS
Someday soon / Since you asked / Both sides now / Sons of / Suzanne / Farewell to Tarwathie / Who knows where the time goes / Sunny Goodge Street / My father (always promised) / Albatross / In my life / Amazing grace
CD _____ 9606812
Elektra / Sep '82 / Warner Music.

HARD TIMES FOR LOVERS
Hard times for lovers / Marie / Happy end / Desperado / I remember sky / Starmaker / Dorothy / I'll never say goodbye / Through the eyes of love / Where or when
CD _____ 7559605362
Carlton Home Entertainment / Oct '94 / Carlton Home Entertainment.

LIVE AT NEWPORT 1959
CD _____ VCD 77013
Vanguard / Oct '95 / Complete/Pinnacle / Discovery.

WIND BENEATH MY WINGS
CD _____ 15451
Laserlight / May '94 / Target/BMG.

Collins, Kathleen

TRADITIONAL MUSIC OF IRELAND
CD _____ SHAN 34010CD
Shanachie / Apr '95 / Koch / ADA / Greensleeves.

Collins, Lui

BAPTISM OF FIRE
CD _____ GLCD 1060
Green Linnet / '92 / Roots / CM / Direct / ADA.

MADE IN NEW ENGLAND
CD _____ GLCD 1056
Green Linnet / Feb '89 / Roots / CM /
Direct / ADA.

THERE'S A LIGHT
CD _____ GLCD 1061
Green Linnet / Feb '92 / Roots / CM /
Direct / ADA.

Collins, Phil

...BUT SERIOUSLY
Hang in long enough / That's just the way
it is / Do you remember / Something happened on the way to heaven / Colours / I
wish it would rain down / Another day in
paradise / Heat on the street / All of my life
/ Saturday night and Sunday morning / Father to son / Find a way to my heart
CD _____ CDV 2620
Virgin / Nov '89 / EMI.

BOTH SIDES
Both sides of the story / Can't turn back the
years / Everyday / I've forgotten everythin'
/ We're sons of our fathers / Can't find my
way / Survivors / We fly so close / There's
a place for us / We want and we wonder /
Please come out tonight
CD _____ CDV 2800
Virgin / Oct '93 / EMI.

FACE VALUE
In the air tonight / This must be love / Behind the lines / Roof is leaking / Droned /
Hand in hand / I missed again / You know
what I mean / I'm not moving / If leaving me
is easy / Tomorrow never knows / Thunder
and lightning
CD _____ CDV 2185
Virgin / EMI.

HELLO I MUST BE GOING
I don't care anymore / I cannot believe it's
true / Like China / Do you know, do you
care / You can't hurry love / It don't matter
to me / Thru these walls / Don't let him steal
your heart away / West side / Why can't I
wait till morning
CD _____ CDV 2252
Virgin / Jun '88 / EMI.

HITS OF PHIL COLLINS (Various Artists)
CD _____ DCD 5260
Disky / Aug '92 / THE / BMG / Discovery /
Pinnacle.

NO JACKET REQUIRED
Sussudio / Only you know and I know /
Long long way to go / Don't want to know
/ One more night / Don't lose my number /
Who said I would / Doesn't anybody stay
together anymore / Inside out / Take me
home / We said hello goodbye (CD only)
CD _____ CDV 2345
Virgin / Feb '85 / EMI.

SERIOUS HITS LIVE
Something happened on the way to heaven
/ Against all odds / Who said I would / One
more night / Don't lose my number / Do you
remember / Another day in paradise / Separate lives / In the air tonight / You can't
hurry love / Two hearts / Sussudio / Groovy
kind of love / Easy lover / Take me home
CD _____ PCVCD 1
Virgin / Nov '90 / EMI.

SERIOUSLY ORCHESTRAL (The Hits Of Phil Collins) (Royal Philharmonic Orchestra)
In the air tonight / Groovy kind of love / Easy
lover / Do you remember / I wish it would
rain down / Against all odds / Another day
in paradise / Two hearts / One more night /
Take me home
CD _____ CDVIP 122
Virgin VIP / Sep '93 / Carlton Home Entertainment / THE / EMI.

YOU CAN'T HURRY LOVE (Music of Phil Collins - 16 Instrumental Hits) (Various Artists)
CD _____ 5708574-338141
Carlton Home Entertainment / Sep '94 /
Carlton Home Entertainment.

Collins, Sam

JAILHOUSE BLUES
CD _____ YAZCD 1070
Yazoo / Apr '91 / CM / ADA / Roots /
Koch.

Collins, Shirley

ANTHEMS IN EDEN SUITE (Collins, Shirley & Dolly)
Meeting - searching for lambs / Courtship,
A - the wedding song / Denying / Foresak-
ing - our captain cried / Dream - lowlands /
Leavetaking (pleasant and delightful) /
Awakening / New beginning, A - the staines
morris / Rembleaway / Ca' the ewes / God
dog / Bonnie cuckoo / Nellie / Gathering
rushes in the month of May / Gower wassail
/ Beginning
CD _____ CDEMS 1477
Harvest / Jul '93 / EMI.

FOR AS MANY AS WILL (Collins, Shirley & Dolly)
Lancashire lass / Never again / Lord Allen-
water / Beggar's opera medley / O Polly you
might have toy'd and kist / Oh what pain it
is to part / Miser thus a shilling sees /

Youth's the season made for joys / Hither
dear husband, turn your eyes / Lumps of
plum pudding / Gilderoy / Rockley firs /
Sweet Jenny Jones / German tune / Moon
shines bright / Harvest home medley (Peas,
beans, oats and the barley) / Mistress's
health / Poor Tom
CD _____ FLED 1003CD
Fledg'ling / Jan '94 / CM / ADA / Direct.

LOVE, DEATH AND THE LADY (Collins, Shirley & Dolly)
Death of the lady / Glenlogie / Oxford girl /
Are you going to leave me / Outlandish
knight / Go from my window / Young girl
cut down in her prime / Geordie / Salisbury
/ Fair maid of Islington / Six dukes / Polly
on the shore / Plains of Waterloo
CD _____ CZ 534
EMI / Jul '94 / EMI.

SWEET PRIMROSES
All things are quite silent / Cambridgeshire
May Carol / Spencer the rover / Rigs of time
/ Cruel Mother / Bird in the bush / Streets
of Derry/False bride / Locks and bolts ram-
bleaway / Brigg fair / Higher Germaine /
George Collins / Babes in the wood / Down
in yon forest / Magpie's nest / False true
love / Sweet primroses
CD _____ TSCD 476
Topic / Aug '95 / Direct / ADA.

Collins, Tommy

LEONARD (5CD Set)
Campus boogie / Too beautiful to cry /
Smooth sailin' / Fool's gold / You gotta
have a license / Let me love you / There'll
be no other / I love you more and more
each day / Boob-i-lak / You better not do
that / I always get a souvenir / High on a
hilltop / Untied / What'cha gonna do now /
Love-a-me, s'il vous plait / You're for me /
I'll be gone / Wait a little longer / Let down
/ It tickles / It's nobody's fault but yours / I
guess I'm crazy / You oughta see pickles
now / Those old love letters from you / I
wish I had died in my cradle / I'll never,
never let you go / I'll always speak well of
you / What kind of sweetheart are you / No
love have I / All of the monkeys ain't in the
zoo / That's the way love is / How do I say
goodbye / Man we all ought to know / Are
you ready to go / Think it over boys / I think
of you yet / Upon this rock / Feet of the
traveler / Don't you love me anymore /
Retirement in heaven / What have you done
/ Love is born / I'm nobody's fool but yours
/ O Mary don't you weep / Did you let your
light shine / In the shadow of the cross /
When I survey the wondrous cross / Who
at my door is standing / My saviour's love
/ Where could I go but to the Lord / What
a friend we have in Jesus / Each step of the
way / Softly and tenderly / That's why I love
him / Jesus keep me near the cross / Amazing grace / Old rugged cross / Hearts don't
break / You belong in my arms / Hundred
years from now / Little June / My last
chance with you / Sidewalks of New York /
Last letter / Oklahoma hills / Great speckled
bird / Broken engagement / Wreck of ol' 97
/ I'm just here to get my baby out of jail /
Have I told you lately that I love you / It
makes no difference now / Let's live a little
/ I'll keep on loving you / I overlooked an
orchard / I wonder if you feel the way I do
/ Juicy fruit / Black cat / We kissed again
with tears / Keep dreaming / Don't let me
stand in his footsteps / Summer's almost
gone / Take me back to the good old days
/ Oh what a dream / Let her go / When did
right become wrong / If I could just go back
/ I got mine / You'd better be nice / I can
do that / I got mine (live) / Shindig in the
barn / Million miles / Good goody gumdrop
/ Clock on the wall / Bee that gets the honey
/ It's a big jump / It's a pretty good ol' world
after all / Take me back to the good old
days (With chorus) / What a dream
(Without chorus) / Klipps kloppa / If you
can't bite, don't growl / Man gotta do what
a man gotta do / Man machine / Girl on
sugar pie lane / Poor, broke, mixed up mess
of a heart / Be serious Ann / Fool's castle /
Little time for a little love / I'm not getting
anywhere with you / Two sides of life /
You're everything to me / Big dummy / There's no girl in my life anymore / Sherry / I'm
not looking for an angel / Don't wipe the
tears that you cry / Birmingham / Put me
irons, lock me up (Throw away the key) /
Sam Hill / It's to much like lonesome / Wine
take me away / General delivery U.S.A /
Roll truck roll / If that's the fashion / Piedras
negras / Laura / Branded man / Cincinnati,
Ohio / Break my mind / I made a prison
band / Best thing I've done in my life /
Woman you have been told / Sunny side of
life / He's gonna have to catch me first
CD Set _____ BCD 15577
Bear Family / Jan '93 / Rollercoaster / Direct
/ CM / Swift / ADA.

Collinson, Dean

LIFE AND TIMES
Hello hello / Words to that effect / Life and
times / This time / Louise / Russian roulette
/ Game for losers (she is out there) / Run-
aways / Measure upon measure / Welcome
to the club
CD _____ 74321134682
Arista / Sep '93 / BMG.

Collinson, Lee

SLIP THE DRIVER A FIVER
Fledg'ling / May '95 / CM / ADA / Direct.
CD _____ FLED 3003

Collister, Christine

LIVE
CD _____ FLECD 1004
Fledg'ling / Sep '94 / CM / ADA / Direct.

Colm

SERUM
CD _____ NR 422480
New Rose / Jan '94 / Direct / ADA.

Cologne

EARLY ELECTRONIC MUSIC
CD _____ BVHAASTCD 9106
Bvhaast / Oct '93 / Cadillac.

Colombo

COMPOSITIONS 1924-42
CD _____ FA 009CD
Fremeaux / Nov '95 / Discovery / ADA.

Colombo, Lou

I REMEMBER BOBBY
It all depends on you / I don't stand a ghost
of a chance with you / Octopus rag / Mem-
ories of you / (I'm afraid) the masquerade is
over / My romance / I remember Bobby /
Three little words / Emily / Gypsy / Avalon
/ Easy living / I let a song go out of my heart
CD _____ CCD 4435
Concord Jazz / Nov '90 / New Note.

Colon, Willie

CONTRABANDO
Bailando asi / Manana amor / Contrabando
/ Che che cole / Barrunto / Te conozco /
Calle luna calle sol / Lo que es de juan /
Pregunta por ahi / Especial no.5 / Soltera /
Quien eres
CD _____ MES 159592
Messidor / Apr '93 / Koch / ADA.

TIEMPO PA'MATAR
El diablo / Tiempo pa'matar / Noche de lose
enmascarados / Callejon sin salido / Volo /
Falta de consideracion / Gitana / Serenata
CD _____ MES 159272
Messidor / Feb '93 / Koch / ADA.

TOP SECRETS (Colon, Willie & Legal Alien)
CD _____ MES 159802
Messidor / Jun '93 / Koch / ADA.

Color Me Badd

TIME & CHANCE
Intro / Time and chance / Groovy now / Let
me have it all / Roseanna's little sister / How
deep / La tremenda (Intro) / In thee / Sunshine choose / Bells / Wildflower / Living
without her / Close to heaven / Trust me /
Let's start with forever / God is love / God
is love (Outro) / Let's la vie / I remember
CD _____ 74321166742
RCA / Nov '93 / BMG.

Colorblind James...

SOLID BEHIND THE TIMES (Colorblind James Experience)
CD _____ RHRCD 52
Red House / Oct '95 / Koch / ADA.

STRANGE SOUNDS FROM THE BASEMENT (Colorblind James Experience)
Ribbon cutting time / Don't be so hard on
yourself / Acorn girl / I think I know what
you mean / Colorblind's night out / Oh,
come on / Sidewalk sale / Strange sounds
(from the basement) / Jesus at the still / O
Sylvia / Two headed girl / Not for sale / Call
me sometime
CD _____ COOKCD 042
Cooking Vinyl / Nov '90 / Vital.

Colosseum

COLLECTION: COLOSSEUM
CD _____ CCSCD 287
Castle / May '91 / BMG.

COLLECTORS COLOSSEUM, THE
Jumping off the sun / Those about to die /
I can't live without you / Beware the Ides of
March / Walking in the park / Bolero / Rope
ladder to the moon / Grass is greener
CD _____ NEXCD 255
Sequel / Sep '93 / BMG.

COLOSSEUM (LIVE)
Rope ladder to the moon / Walking in the
park / Skelington / Tanglewood '63 / Encore... Stormy Monday blues / Lost angeles / I can't live without you
CD _____ NEXCD 201
Sequel / Feb '92 / BMG.

DAUGHTER OF TIME
Three score and ten, Amen / Time lament /
Take me back to doomsday / Daughter of
time / Theme for an imaginary western /
Bring out your dead / Downhill and shad-
ows / Time machine

CD _____ NEXCD 256
Sequel / Sep '93 / BMG.

EPITAPH
Walking in the park / Bring out your dead /
Those about to die / Beware the Ides of
March / Daughter of time / Valentine suite
CD _____ RAWCD 014
Raw Power / Apr '86 / BMG.

IDES OF MARCH, THE
Those about to die / Beware the ides of
March / Machine demands a sacrifice / El-
egy / Walking in the park / Backwater blues
/ Time machine (live) / Bring out your dead
/ Theme for an imaginary Western / Daugh-
ter of time / Rope ladder to the moon / Bo-
lero / Encore... Stormy Monday blues (live)
CD _____ 5507342
Spectrum/Karussell / May '95 / PolyGram /
THE.

REUNION CONCERT 1994
Those about to die / Elegy / Valentine suite
/ January's search / February's valentyne /
Grass is always greener / Theme for an
imaginary western / Machine demands a
sacrifice / Solo colinia / Lost Angeles /
Stormy Monday blues
CD _____ INT 31602
Intuition / May '95 / New Note.

STRANGE NEW FLESH (Colosseum II)
Dark side of the Moog / Down to you /
Gemini and Leo / Secret places / On sec-
ond thoughts / Winds
CD _____ CLACD 104
Castle / '86 / BMG.

THOSE WHO ARE ABOUT TO DIE .../ VALENTYNE SUITE
Walking in the park / Plenty hard luck / Ma-
darin / Debut / Beware the ides of march /
Road she walk / Before / Backwater blues
/ Those about to die / Kettle / Elegy / Butty's
blues / Machine demands a sacrifice / Sac-
rifice / Valentyne suite
CD _____ NEXCD 161
Sequel / Dec '90 / BMG.

Colour Club

COLOUR CLUB
Welcome to the Colour Club / Scene / Free-
dom words / Great issue: Freedom / Trust
in me / Consumption / Scene II / On and on
/ Scene III / Chicago / Cultures of jazz /
Scene IV / Howbtsuntinkikdis / Scene V /
State of mind / Don't wait too long
CD _____ JVC 20342
JVC / Aug '94 / New Note.

Colour Of Memory

OLD MAN & THE SEA, THE
Grace / Rigmarole / Rain parade / Emotional
fish / Changed days / Into my own / Always
with me / Days on end / Sun fire majestic /
Old man and the sea
CD _____ IRCD 028
Iona / Jan '95 / ADA / Direct / Duncans.

Colour Trip

COLOURTRIP
CD _____ MASSCD 014
Massacre / Feb '94 / Plastic Head.

FULL TIME FUNCTION
CD _____ 08436272
SPV / Dec '95 / Plastic Head.

GROUND LEVEL SEX TYPE THING
CD _____ SPV 08436222
SPV / Dec '94 / Plastic Head.

Colourbox

COLOURBOX
Suspicion / Arena / Say you / Just give 'em
whiskey / You keep me hangin' on / Moon
is blue / Manic / Sleepwalker / Inside informer / Punch
CD _____ CAD 508 CD
4AD / '86 / Disc.

COLOURBOX MINI LP
CD _____ MAD 315 CD
4AD / Nov '86 / Disc.

Colourhaus

WATER TO THE SOUL
Moving mountains / We talk to the angels /
Stone roses / Innocent child / Missing the
beat / Ghost train / I would walk the earth /
Colour me you / Waves / Feather in the fire
/ All the way to Marakesh / Oxygen (Nos-
feratu-the seduction)
CD _____ 7567921232
East West / Aug '92 / Warner Music.

Coltrane, John

AFRICA BRASS SESSIONS 1 & 2
Africa / Blues minor / Greensleeves (version)
/ Greensleeves / Song of the underground
railroad / Africa (version)
CD _____ MCAD 42001
Impulse Jazz / Jun '89 / BMG / New Note.

AFRO BLUE IMPRESSIONS
Lonnie's lament / Naima / Chasin' the trane
/ My favourite things / Afro blue / Cousin
Mary / I want to talk about you / Spiritual /
Impressions
CD Set _____ 2620101

Pablo / '94 / Jazz Music / Cadillac / Complete/Pinnacle.

AVANT GARDE, THE (Coltrane, John & Don Cherry)
CD _____ 7567900412
Atlantic / Jul '93 / Warner Music.

BAGS AND TRANE (Coltrane, John & Milt Jackson)
Bags and trane / Three little words / Night we called it a day / Be bop / Late late blues
CD _____ 756781348-2
Atlantic / Jun '93 / Warner Music.

BAHIA
CD _____ OJCCD 415
Original Jazz Classics / Feb '92 / Wellard / Jazz Music / Cadillac / Complete/Pinnacle.

BEST OF JOHN COLTRANE (LIVE)
Afro blue / Promise / Every time we say goodbye / Bye bye blackbird / Chasin' the trane
CD _____ CD 2310886
Pablo / Apr '94 / Jazz Music / Cadillac / Complete/Pinnacle.

BEST OF JOHN COLTRANE, THE
My favourite things / Naima / Giant steps / Equinox / Cousin Mary / Central Park West
CD _____ 756781366-2
Atlantic / Jun '93 / Warner Music.

BLACK PEARLS
Black pearls / Lover come back to me / Sweet sapphire blues / Believer / Nakatini serenade / Do I love you because you're beautiful
CD _____ OJCCD 352
Original Jazz Classics / Feb '92 / Wellard / Jazz Music / Cadillac / Complete/Pinnacle.

BLUE TRAIN
Blue train / Moments notice / Locomotion / I'm old fashioned / Lazy bird
CD _____ CDP 7460952
Blue Note / Mar '95 / EMI.

BYE BYE BLACKBIRD
Bye bye blackbird / Traneing in
CD _____ OJCCD 681
Original Jazz Classics / Feb '92 / Wellard / Jazz Music / Cadillac / Complete/Pinnacle.

CATTIN' WITH C & Q (Coltrane, John & Paul Quinichette)
CD _____ OJCCD 460-2
Original Jazz Classics / Apr '92 / Wellard / Jazz Music / Cadillac / Complete/Pinnacle.

CHIM CHIM CHEREE AND OTHER RARITIES
CD _____ JZ-CD318
Suisa / Feb '91 / Jazz Music / THE.

COAST TO COAST (Coltrane, John Quartet)
CD _____ MCD 0352
Moon / Jan '92 / Harmonia Mundi / Cadillac.

COLLECTION
CD _____ CCSCD 418
Castle / May '95 / BMG.

COLLECTION VOL. 2
CD _____ CCSCD 435
Castle / May '95 / BMG.

COLTRANE
Bakai / Violets for your furs / Time was / Straight street / While my lady sleeps / Chronic blues
CD _____ OJCCD 020
Original Jazz Classics / Oct '92 / Wellard / Jazz Music / Cadillac / Complete/Pinnacle.

COLTRANE AND LUSH LIFE
Lush life / I love you / Trane's slow blues / I hear a rhapsody / Violets for your furs / Time was / Straight street / While my lady sleeps / Chronic blues
CD _____ CDJZD 001
Prestige / Jan '91 / Complete/Pinnacle / Cadillac.

COLTRANE JAZZ
Little old lady / Village blues / My shining hour / Fifth house / Harmonique / Like Sonny / I'll wait and pray / Some other blues / Like Sonny (2) / I'll wait and pray (2)
CD _____ 7567813442
Atlantic / Feb '92 / Warner Music.

COLTRANE PLAYS THE BLUES
Blues to Elvin / Blues to Bechet / Blues to you / Mr. Day / Mr. Syms / Mr. Knight / Untitled original
CD _____ 756781351-2
Atlantic / Jun '93 / Warner Music.

COLTRANE TIME
CD _____ CDP 7844612
Blue Note / Feb '92 / EMI.

COLTRANE'S SOUND
Night has a thousand eyes / Central Park West / Liberia / Body and soul / Equinox / Satellite / 26-2 / Body and soul (2)
CD _____ 756781358-2
Atlantic / Mar '93 / Warner Music.

COMPLETE AFRICA BRASS VOLS. 1 & 2 (2CD Set)
Greensleeves / Song of the underground railroad / Greensleeves (alternate take) / Damned don't cry / Africa (first version) / Blues minor / Africa (alternate take) / Africa

CD Set _____ IMP 21682
Impulse Jazz / Oct '95 / BMG / New Note.

COUNTDOWN (Coltrane, John & Wilbur Harden)
Wells Fargo - take 1 / Wells Fargo - take 2 / E.F.F.P.H. / Countdown (Take 1) / Rhodomagnetics 1 / Rhodomagnetics 2 / Snuffy / West 42nd street
CD _____ VGCD 650102
Vogue / Oct '93 / BMG.

DAKAR
Dakar / Mary's blues / Route 4 / Velvet scene / Witches' pet / Cat walk / C.T.A. / Interplay / Anatomy / Light blue / Soul eyes
CD _____ OJCCD 393
Original Jazz Classics / Feb '92 / Wellard / Jazz Music / Cadillac / Complete/Pinnacle.

DIG IT (Coltrane, John & Red Garland Quintet)
Billie's bounce / Crazy rhythm / C.T.A. / Lazy Mae
CD _____ OJCCD 392
Original Jazz Classics / Apr '93 / Wellard / Jazz Music / Cadillac / Complete/Pinnacle.

EUROPEAN TOUR, THE
Promise / I want to talk about you / Naima / Mr. P.C.
CD _____ PACD 23082222
Pablo / Jul '94 / Jazz Music / Cadillac / Complete/Pinnacle.

EVERYTIME WE SAY GOODBYE (Coltrane, John Quartet)
CD _____ NI 4003
Natasha / Jun '93 / Jazz Music / ADA / CM / Direct / Cadillac.

GIANT STEPS
Giant steps / Cousin Mary / Countdown / Spiral / Syeeda's song flute / Naima / Mr. P.C.
CD _____ 781 337-2
Atlantic / '87 / Warner Music.

IMPRESSIONS
India / Up against the wall / Impressions / After the rain
CD _____ CDCD 1009
Charly / Mar '93 / Charly / THE / Cadillac.

IN A SOULFUL MOOD
In a sentimental mood / Tunji / Soul eyes / Inchworm / Nancy / Blues minor / After the rain / You don't know what love is / I want to talk about you / Alabama / Naima / Afro blue
CD _____ MCCD 170
MCI / Sep '94 / Disc / THE.

JAZZ PORTRAITS
Trane's blues / Sweet Sue, just you / Soultrane / Mating call / Mook / Chronic blues / While my lady sleeps / Straight street / Bakay
CD _____ CD 14507
Jazz Portraits / May '94 / Jazz Music.

JOHN COLTRANE & KENNY BURRELL (Coltrane, John & Kenny Burrell)
CD _____ OJCCD 300
Original Jazz Classics / Oct '92 / Wellard / Jazz Music / Cadillac / Complete/Pinnacle.

JOHN COLTRANE AND THE JAZZ GIANTS
CD _____ FCD 60014
Fantasy / Oct '93 / Pinnacle / Jazz Music / Wellard / Cadillac.

JUAN LES PINS JAZZ FESTIVAL (Antibes July 1965)
CD _____ CD 53068
Giants Of Jazz / May '92 / Target/BMG / Cadillac.

LAST TRANE
CD _____ OJCCD 394
Original Jazz Classics / Feb '92 / Wellard / Jazz Music / Cadillac / Complete/Pinnacle.

LEGENDARY MASTERS, THE (Unissued or rare 1951-65)
CD Set _____ RARECD 11/15
Recording Arts / Apr '88 / THE / Disc.

LEGENDARY MASTERS, THE (1951-58) (Unissued or rare)
Good bait / Birk's works / Thru for the night / Castle rock / Don't blame me / I've got a mind to ramble blues / Don't cry baby blues / In a mellow tone / Globetrotter / Tune up / Walkin' / Four
CD _____ RARECD 11
Recording Arts / '88 / THE / Disc.

LEGENDARY MASTERS, THE (1961-62) (Unissued or rare)
Chim chim cheree / Naima / Bye bye blackbird / I want to talk about you
CD _____ RARECD 13
Recording Arts / '88 / THE / Disc.

LEGENDARY MASTERS, THE (1961-65) (Unissued or rare)
Love supreme (Acknowledge/Resolution/Pursuance/Psalm) / Good bait / Thru for the night / Don't blame me / Don't cry baby blues / Globetrotter / Walkin' / Chim chim cheree / Bye bye blackbird / Roy / Impressions / Mr. P.C. / Cousin Mary / Lonnie's lament / Birk's works / Castle rock / I've got a mind to ramble blues / In a mellow tone / Tune up / Four / Acknowledgement (part 1) / Spiritual / Naima / I want to talk about you / Chasin' the trane / Afro blue /

My favourite things / Miles mode / Body and soul
CD _____ RARECD 12
Recording Arts / '88 / THE / Disc.

LEGENDARY MASTERS, THE (1962-63) (Unissued or rare)
My favourite things / Cousin Mary / Miles mode / Lonnie's lament / Body and soul
CD _____ RARECD 15
Recording Arts / '88 / THE / Disc.

LEGENDARY MASTERS, THE (1963-64) (Unissued or rare)
Roy / Chasin' the trane / Impressions / Afro blue / Mr. P.C.
CD _____ RARECD 14
Recording Arts / '88 / THE / Disc.

LIVE AT BIRDLAND (2)
Mr. P.C. / Miles mode / My favourite things / Body and soul
CD _____ CDCHARLY 68
Charly / Jun '87 / Charly / THE / Cadillac.

LIVE IN COMBLAIN-LA-TOUR 1965
Landscape / Feb '93 / THE.

LIVE IN EUROPE 1960 (Coltrane, John & Miles Davis)
CD _____ LS 2910
Landscape / Nov '92 / THE.

LIVE IN JAPAN (4CD Set)
Afro blue / Peace on Earth / Crescent / Peace on Earth (2) / Leo / My favourite things
CD Set _____ GRP 41022
GRP / Jul '91 / BMG / New Note.

LIVE IN PARIS
Naima / Impressions / Blue valse / Afro blue / Impressions (2nd version)
CD _____ LEJAZZCD 31
Le Jazz / Sep '94 / Charly / Cadillac.

LIVE IN SEATTLE
Cosmos / Out of this world / Body and soul / Tapestry in sound / Evolution / Afro blue
CD Set _____ GRP 21462
GRP / Nov '94 / BMG / New Note.

LIVE IN STOCKHOLM - 1961
My favourite things / Blue train / Naima / Impressions
CD _____ CDCHARLY 117
Charly / May '88 / Charly / THE / Cadillac.

LIVE IN STOCKHOLM - 1963
Mr. P.C. / Traneing in / Spiritual / I want to talk about you
CD _____ CDCHARLY 33
Charly / Dec '86 / Charly / THE / Cadillac.

LOVE SUPREME, A - IN CONCERT
CD _____ JZCD 317
Suisa / Oct '92 / Jazz Music / THE.

MAJOR WORKS OF JOHN COLTRANE, THE (2CD Set)
Ascension I / Ascension II / Om / Kula se mama / Selflessness
CD Set _____ GRP 21132
Impulse Jazz / Jan '92 / BMG / New Note.

MEDITATIONS
Love / Consequences / Serenity / Father, Son and Holy Ghost
CD _____ MCAD 39139
Impulse Jazz / Oct '90 / BMG / New Note.

MEETS ERIC DOLPHY
CD _____ MCD 0692
Moon / Aug '95 / Harmonia Mundi / Cadillac.

MY FAVOURITE THINGS
My favourite things / Every time we say goodbye / Summertime / But not for me
CD _____ 756781346-2
Atlantic / Mar '93 / Warner Music.

MY FAVOURITE THINGS (A Jazz House With John Coltrane)
CD _____ JHR 73538
Jazz Hour / May '93 / Target/BMG / Jazz Music / Cadillac.

MY FAVOURITE THINGS IN CONCERT AND OTHER RARITIES
CD _____ JZ-CD320
Suisa / Feb '91 / Jazz Music / THE.

NEW WAVE IN JAZZ (Coltrane, John & Archie Shepp)
Nature boy / Ham bone / Brilliant corners / Plight / Blue free / Intellect
CD _____ GRP 11372
GRP / Mar '94 / BMG / New Note.

OLE COLTRANE
Ole / Dahomey dance / Aisha / To her ladyship
CD _____ 781349-2
Atlantic / Feb '94 / Warner Music.

OM
CD _____ MCAD 39118
Impulse Jazz / Jun '89 / BMG / New Note.

ON STAGE 1962
CD _____ 556 632
Accord / Apr '94 / Discovery / Harmonia Mundi / Cadillac.

PARIS CONCERT, THE
Mr. P.C. / Inchworm / Every time we say goodbye
CD _____ OJCCD 781

Original Jazz Classics / Jun '94 / Wellard / Jazz Music / Cadillac / Complete/Pinnacle.

PRESTIGE RECORDINGS, THE (16CD Set)
CD Set _____ 16PCD 44052
Prestige / Jan '92 / Complete/Pinnacle / Cadillac.

PRIVATE RECORDINGS - 1951-58
CD _____ JZ-CD316
Suisa / Feb '91 / Jazz Music / THE.

ROY AND OTHER RARITIES
CD _____ JZ-CD319
Suisa / Feb '91 / Jazz Music / THE.

SETTIN' THE PACE
I see your face before me / If there's someone lovelier than you / Little Melonae / Rise and shine
CD _____ OJCCD 078
Original Jazz Classics / Feb '92 / Wellard / Jazz Music / Cadillac / Complete/Pinnacle.

STANDARD COLTRANE
CD _____ OJCCD 246
Original Jazz Classics / Feb '92 / Wellard / Jazz Music / Cadillac / Complete/Pinnacle.

STARDUST SESSION, THE
Spring is here / Invitation / I'm a dreamer (aren't we all) / Love thy neighbour / Don't take your love from me / My ideal / Stardust / I'll get by
CD _____ PRCD 24056
Prestige / Jul '94 / Complete/Pinnacle / Cadillac.

STELLAR REGIONS
Creation / Sun star / Stellar regions / Iris / Offering / Configuration / Jimmy's mode / Tranesonic / Stellar regions (alternate take) / Sun star (alternate take) / Tranesonic (alternate take)
CD _____ IMP 11692
Impulse Jazz / Oct '95 / BMG / New Note.

SUNSHIP
Sun ship / Dearly beloved / Amen / Attending / Ascent
CD _____ IMP 11672
Impulse Jazz / Nov '95 / BMG / New Note.

TENOR CONCLAVE (Coltrane, John & Hank Mobley/Al Cohn/Zoot Sims)
CD _____ OJCCD 127
Original Jazz Classics / Jul '94 / Wellard / Jazz Music / Cadillac / Complete/Pinnacle.

TRANE'S BLUES - 1955-57
CD _____ CD 53058
Giants Of Jazz / Mar '90 / Target/BMG / Cadillac.

TRANEING IN - WITH THE RED GARLAND TRIO
Traneing in / Slow dance / Bass blues / You leave me breathless / Soft lights and sweet music
CD _____ OJCCD 189
Original Jazz Classics / Mar '92 / Wellard / Jazz Music / Cadillac / Complete/Pinnacle.

WHEELIN' & DEALIN'
CD _____ OJCCD 672
Original Jazz Classics / May '93 / Wellard / Jazz Music / Cadillac / Complete/Pinnacle.

Columbia Orchestra

DANCING THROUGH SILVER SCREEN (Columbia Ballroom Orchestra)
New York, New York / Mrs. Robinson / I just called to say I love you / As time goes by / Sentimental journey / Stranger in the night / Way we were / Gonna fly now (Rocky theme) / Mona Lisa / When you wish upon a star / Tammy / Jealousy / Around the world / Scarborough Fair / Sound of silence / Chariots of fire / To love again / Over the rainbow
CD _____ DC 8504
Denon / '88 / Conifer.

LET'S DANCE - COMPETITION DANCE 1 (Like a Virgin) (Columbia Ballroom Orchestra)
What a feeling / Summer place / Copacabana / Aquarius / I like Chopin / Superstar / Granada / Raindrops keep falling on my head / Magical / Fascination / Pearl fishers / Mona Lisa / Annapola / Cabaret / New York, New York / Like a virgin / Love is blue / Dancing queen / Casablanca / Jungle drums / Just the way you are
CD _____ DC 8526
Denon / Jul '88 / Conifer.

LET'S DANCE - COMPETITION DANCE 2 (We Are The World) (Columbia Ballroom Orchestra)
When you wish upon a star / Try to remember / Nathalie / Rosita / Adios pampa mia / Killing me softly / Red roses for a blue lady / We are the world / Carnavalito / La reine de saba / Jambalaya / Tammy / Scarborough Fair / Tango delle rose / Beat it / Days of wine and roses / From Russia with love / Mrs. Robinson / Cherry blossom time
CD _____ DC 8527
Denon / Jul '88 / Conifer.

LET'S DANCE - INVITATION TO DANCE PARTY 1 (I Could Have Danced All Night) (Columbia Ballroom Orchestra)
Tennessee waltz / Danny boy / La Malaguena / Quien sera / Sunrise sunset / Sing, sing, sing / Sans toi mamie / La cumparsita / Tea for two / Time for us / Thriller / Stardust / Tonight / Jalousie / In the mood / Changing partners / I could have danced all night / Strangers in the night / Over the rainbow / Two guitars / Strangers
CD _____ DC 8521
Denon / Jul '88 / Conifer.

LET'S DANCE - INVITATION TO DANCE PARTY 2 (I Kiss Your Little Hand Madame) (Columbia Ballroom Orchestra)
Besame mucho / In einer kleinen konditorei / When the saints go marching in / Thirteen jours en France / Passion flower / Les parapluies de Cherbourg / Shadow of your smile / Blauer himmel / Begin the beguine / Edelweiss / Cerezo roza / Sentimental journey / Love is a many splendoured thing / Il pleut sur la route / Moon river
CD _____ DC 8522
Denon / Jul '88 / Conifer.

LET'S DANCE - LATIN COLLECTION (Chariots of Fire) (Columbia Ballroom Orchestra)
To love again / Where do I begin / Chariots of fire / Melody fair / Lover's concerto / Ballroom jive / Tico-tico / Mr. Lonely / Say you, say me / Babalu / Quizas quizas quizas / Stuck with you / Place in the sun / Someday you'll be old / Boogie woogie jive / Hello Dolly / When you're smiling / South of the border / Viva paso doble
CD _____ DC 8524
Denon / Jul '88 / Conifer.

LET'S DANCE - MODERN COLLECTION (Michelle) (Columbia Ballroom Orchestra)
Around the world / Fly me to the moon / Charade / La Rosita / El amenecer / Michelle / Autumn leaves / Summertime / Moonlight serenade / (I'm afraid) the masquerade is over / Nocturne / Top of the world / Sing / Liebestraum / Le professionel / Amazing grace / Tango notturno / Blue tango / Felicia / Wonderland by night / Smoke gets in your eyes / St. Louis blues
CD _____ DC 8525
Denon / Jul '88 / Conifer.

LET'S DANCE VOL.10
CD _____ CK 1012
Denon / '88 / Conifer.

LET'S DANCE VOL.3 (Love Me Tender) (Columbia Ballroom Orchestra)
Mauvais garcon / Petite fleur / Bei mir bist du schon / El choclo / Breeze and I / Greensleeves / Carioca / As time goes by / Estrellita / Romance de amor / Mambo No.5 / Love me tender / Little brown jug / Way we were / Siboney / I really don't want to know / Venus / I left my heart in San Francisco / String of pearls / Taboo / Farewell waltz
CD _____ DC 8523
Denon / Jul '88 / Conifer.

LET'S DANCE VOL.8
CD _____ C 327897
Denon / '88 / Conifer.

Colvin, Shawn

COVER GIRL
CD _____ 4772402
Columbia / Aug '94 / Sony.

FAT CITY
Polaroids / Tennessee / Tenderness on the block / Round of blues / Monopoly / Orion in the sky / Climb on (a back that's strong) / Set the prairie on fire / Object of my affection / Kill the messenger / I don't know why
CD _____ 467961 2
Columbia / Apr '93 / Sony.

STEADY ON
Steady on / Diamonds in the rough / Shotgun down the avalanche / Stranded another long one / Cry like an angel / Something to believe in / Story / Ricochet in time / Dead of the night
CD _____ 4661422
Columbia / Aug '95 / Sony.

Colyer, Ken

AT THE THAMES HOTEL
Milneberg joys / Lowland blues / Trombonium / Short dress gal / Blue skies / Glory of love / Hindustan / Hiawatha rag
CD _____ JOY CD 4
Joy / Aug '91 / President / Jazz Music / Wellard.

COLYER'S PLEASURE (Colyer, Ken Jazzmen)
Teasing rag / After you've gone / Highway blues / Dardanella / I can't escape from you / You always hurt the one you love / Creole bo bo / Honeysuckle rose / Barefoot boy / Mahogany Hall stomp / Gettysburg march / La Harpe St. blues / Thriller rag / I'm travelling / Virginia strut
CD _____ LACD 34
Lake / Nov '94 / Target/BMG / Jazz Music / Direct / Cadillac / ADA.

DECCA SKIFFLE SESSION 1954-57
Midnight special / Casey Jones / K.C. Moan / Take this hammer / Down by the riverside / Go down, old Hannah / Streamline train / Old Riley / Downbound train / Stack o lee blues / Mule skinner blues / Grey goose / Sporting life / House rent stomp / I can't sleep / This train / Midnight hour blues / Go down sunshine / Ella Speed
CD _____ LACD 7
Lake / Mar '94 / Target/BMG / Jazz Music / Direct / Cadillac / ADA.

DECCA YEARS 1953-1954, THE (Colyer, Ken Jazzmen)
CD _____ LACD 14
Lake / Sep '94 / Target/BMG / Jazz Music / Direct / Cadillac / ADA.

DECCA YEARS 1955-59, THE (Colyer, Ken Jazzmen)
CD _____ LA 001CD
Lake / Jan '94 / Target/BMG / Jazz Music / Direct / Cadillac / ADA.

IN HOLLAND (Colyer, Ken & Butch Thompson)
CD _____ MECCACD 1032
Music Mecca / Nov '94 / Jazz Music / Cadillac / Wellard.

JUST A LITTLE WHILE TO STAY HERE
Just a little while to stay here / Saturday night function / Lead me on / Lily of the valley / Sometimes my burden is so hard to bear / Lord, Lord, Lord / Just a closer walk with thee / Nobody's fault but mine
CD _____ CMJCD 012
CMJ / Oct '90 / Jazz Music / Wellard.

KEN COLYER & CHRIS BLOUNT
CD _____ KCT 5CD
Ken Colyer / Oct '92 / Jazz Music / Wellard.

KEN COLYER & RAYMOND BURKE 1952-53 (Colyer, Ken & Raymond Burke)
CD _____ 504CD 23
504 / Oct '93 / Wellard / Jazz Music / Target/BMG / Cadillac.

KEN COLYER TRUST BAND PLAY NEW ORLEANS JAZZ (Colyer, Ken Trust Band)
Yes Lord I'm crippled / Alexander's ragtime band / Over the waves / Breeze / Salutation march / Panama rag / Lights out / Bogalousa strut / Amazing Grace / Darktown strutter's ball / San Jacinto blues / Precious Lord / Silver bell / Sing on / Washington and Lee swing / My life will be sweeter some day
CD _____ URCD 112
Upbeat / Aug '94 / Target/BMG / Cadillac.

LIVE AT THE PIZZA EXPRESS, LONDON, FEBRUARY 1985 (Colyer, Ken Jazz Quartet)
Blame it on the blues / How long blues / Willie the weeper / Dinah / Dallas blues / (Back home again in) Indiana / Scatterbrain, Liza / Sweet Lorraine / Weary blues
CD _____ AZCD 33
Azure / Jan '95 / Jazz Music / Swift / Wellard / Azure / Cadillac.

MORE OF KEN COLYER & HIS JAZZMEN 25/1/72 (Colyer, Ken & His Hand Picked Jazzmen)
Pretty baby / Sing on / Snag it / Wabash blues / Louisian-I-Ay / Tishomingo blues / Black cat on the fence / High society
CD _____ KCT 3CD
Ken Colyer / Apr '91 / Jazz Music / Wellard.

ONE FOR MY BABY (Colyer, Ken Jazzmen)
Royal Garden blues / High society / Drop me off in Harlem / Bogalousa strut / One for my baby / Stardust / Tiger rag
CD _____ JOYCD 1
Joy / Aug '91 / President / Jazz Music / Wellard.

PAINTING THE CLOUDS WITH SUNSHINE
CD _____ BLCD 760501
Black Lion / Oct '90 / Jazz Music / Cadillac / Wellard / Koch.

RAGTIME REVISITED (Colyer, Ken Jazzmen)
Cataract rag / Grace and beauty / Minstrel man / Pineapple rag / Chrysanthemum / Tuxedo rag / Joplin's sensation / Harlem rag / Heliotrope bouquet / Ragtime oriole / Fig leaf rag / Kinklets / Thriller rag
CD _____ JOY CD 2
Joy / Aug '91 / President / Jazz Music / Wellard.

SENSATION (Colyer, Ken Jazzmen)
Dippermouth blues / Heliotrope bouquet / Beale Street blues / Fig leaf rag / Gravier Street blues / Canal street blues / World is waiting for the sunrise / Girls go crazy / Entertainer / If ever I cease to love / Sensation / Perdido street blues / Kinklets / Maryland my Maryland
CD _____ LACD 1
Lake / Nov '93 / Target/BMG / Jazz Music / Direct / Cadillac / ADA.

SERENADING AUNTIE (Ken Colyer - BBC Recordings 1955-60)
Carolina moon / In the evening / Papa dip / Tell me your dreams / My blue heaven /

Perdido street blues / Clarinet marmalade / When I leave the world behind / Eccentric rag / Riverside blues / Thriller rag / Hilarity rag / Yancey stomp / Heliotrope bouquet / Creole song / Chrysanthemum rag / You've got to see mama ev'ry night / Ice cream / Dinah / Going home / World is waiting for the sunrise
CD _____ URCD 111
Upbeat / Apr '94 / Target/BMG / Cadillac.

SPIRITUALS VOL.1 (Colyer, Ken Jazzmen)
We shall walk through the streets of the city / Darkness on the Delta / It's nobody's fault but mine / My life will be sweeter someday / Were you there when they satisfied my soul / Sometimes my burden is so hard to bear / Old rugged cross
CD _____ JOY CD 5
Joy / Aug '91 / President / Jazz Music / Wellard.

SPIRITUALS VOL.2 (Colyer, Ken Jazzmen)
Ghost soldier / Precious Lord / In the sweet bye and bye / Ain't you glad / Sing on / Just a closer walk with thee / Lead me saviour
CD _____ JOY CD 6
Joy / Aug '91 / President / Jazz Music / Wellard.

STUDIO 51 REVISITED (Colyer, Ken Jazzmen)
Lady be good / Dusty rag / Fidgety feet / Perdido street blues / Ace in the hole / Muskrat ramble / Yes Lord I'm crippled / Riverside blues / In the sweet bye and bye / Wolverine blues
CD _____ LACD 25
Lake / Jan '95 / Target/BMG / Jazz Music / Direct / Cadillac / ADA.

SUNNY SIDE OF KEN COLYER, THE (Colyer, Ken All Stars)
Sunny side of the street / Yaaka hula hickey dula / Canal Street blues (Slow) / Canal street blues (Fast) / Royal garden blues / Bill Bailey, Won't you please come home / Chloe / You always hurt the one you love / Everywhere you go the sunshine follows you
CD _____ URCD 113
Upbeat / Jul '94 / Target/BMG / Cadillac.

TOO BUSY (1985 at Harlow)
Tunes too busy / My old Kentucky home / Tishomingo blues / Down home rag / Old rugged cross / One sweet letter from you / Bogalousa strut / Snag it / Nobody's fault but mine / Home sweet home
CD _____ CMJCD 008
CMJ / Jul '89 / Jazz Music / Wellard.

UP JUMPED THE DEVIL
Sensation rag / Milnburg joys / When you wore a tulip / Mazie (Martha) / Up jumped the devil / Moose march / Breeze / Bourbon street parade / Red sails in the sunset / Dr. Jazz / Tiger rag
CD _____ URCD 114
Upbeat / Apr '95 / Target/BMG / Cadillac.

WATCH THAT DIRTY TONE OF YOURS (There are ladies present) (Colyer, Ken Jazzmen)
Till then / One sweet letter from you / Arkansas blues / Poor butterfly / Bugle boy march / If you're a viper / Running wild / My gal Sal / Black and blue / Swipsey cakewalk
CD _____ JOY CD 3
Joy / Aug '91 / President / Jazz Music / Wellard.

WHEN I LEAVE THE WORLD BEHIND (Colyer, Ken & Sam Rimington)
When I leave the world behind / Mabel's dream / Dr. Jazz / Wabash blues / Down home rag / Darkness on the delta / Old spinning wheel / Old black Joe / Careless love / After you've gone
CD _____ LACD 19
Lake / Feb '95 / Target/BMG / Jazz Music / Direct / Cadillac / ADA.

Combelle, Alix

ALIX COMBELLE 1935-40
CD _____ CLASSICS 714
Classics / Jul '93 / Discovery / Jazz Music.

CLASSICS 1940-41
CD _____ CLASSICS 751
Classics / May '94 / Discovery / Jazz Music.

CLASSICS 1942-43
CD _____ CLASSICS 782
Classics / Nov '94 / Discovery / Jazz Music.

Combustible Edison

I, SWINGER
Cadillac / Millionaire's holiday / Breakfast at Denny's / Intermission / Cry me a river / Impact / Guadaloupe / Carnival of souls / Veldt / Surabaya Johnny / Spy Vs. spy / Theme from The Tiki Wonder Hour
CD _____ EFAO 49342
City Slang / Mar '94 / Disc.

SCHIZOPHONIC
CD _____ RTD 34600022
City Slang / Feb '96 / Disc.

Come

DON'T ASK, DON'T TELL
CD _____ BBQCD 160
Beggars Banquet / Sep '94 / Warner Music / Disc.

Comecon

CONVERGING CONSPIRACIES
CD _____ CM 77075-2
Century Media / Jan '94 / Plastic Head.

FABLE FROLIC
CD _____ CM 77094CD
Century Media / Sep '95 / Plastic Head.

Comedian Harmonists

COMEDIAN HARMONISTS
Barber of Seville / Must I, then / When Sonia danced in Russian style / Sleep my little Prince / Good moon, you go so gently / Minuet / Creole love call / Little lightness / Blue Danube waltz / Court serenade / Marie Marie / Auf wiedersehen my dear / Liebesleid / Boy saw a rosebush / Woodcutter's song / Village music / Old ship piano / Let's have another beer / In the hayloft / Perpetuum mobile
CD _____ PASTCD 7000
Flapper / Jan '93 / Pinnacle.

Comet Gain

CASINO CLASSICS
Footstompers / Million and nine / Turnpike county blue / Last night / Original arrogance / Another girl / Music upstairs / Villain / Stay with me / Charlie / Just seventeen / Ghost of the roman empire / Intergalactic starbed / Chevron action flash
CD _____ WIJ 042CD
Wiija / Apr '95 / Vital.

Coming Up Roses

I SAID BALLROOM
CD _____ UTIL 005 CD
Utility / Jul '89 / Grapevine.

Commander Cody

BAR ROOM CLASSICS
CD _____ AIM 1024CD
Aim / Sep '93 / Direct / ADA / Jazz Music.

LET'S ROCK
Let's rock / Rockin' over China / Midnight on the strand / To jump mind / Angel got married / Truckstop at the end of the world / One more ride / Your cash ain't nothin' but trash / Rockabilly funeral / Transfusion / Home of rock 'n' roll
CD _____ BPCD 72086
Blind Pig / Dec '94 / Hot Shot / Swift / CM / Roots / Direct / ADA.

VERY BEST OF COMMANDER CODY AND HIS LOST PLANET (Commander Cody & His Lost Planet Airmen)
Back to Tennessee / Wine do yer stuff / Seeds and stems (again) / Daddy's gonna treat you right / Family Bible / Lost in the ozone / Hot rod Lincoln / Beat me daddy, eight to the bar / Truckstop rock / Truck drivin' man / It should've been me / Watch my .38 / Everybody's doin' it now / Rock that boogie / Smoke, smoke, smoke / Honeysuckle honey / Sunset on the sage (live) / Cryin' time (live)
CD _____ SEECD 64
See For Miles/C5 / Aug '91 / Pinnacle.

WORST CASE SCENARIO (Commander Cody & His Lost Planet Airmen)
CD _____ AIM 1043
Aim / Apr '95 / Direct / ADA / Jazz Music.

Commando

BATTLE OF THIS WEEK
CD _____ MNWCD 190
MNW / Mar '90 / Vital / ADA.

Commodores

ALL THE GREAT LOVE SONGS
Sweet love / Just to be close to you / Easy / Three times a lady / Say when / Still / Loving you / Sail on / Old fashioned love / Jesus is love / Lady (you bring me up) / Oh no / This love / Lucy
CD _____ 530151-2
Motown / Jan '93 / PolyGram.

COMMODORES, THE
CD _____ 12465
Laserlight / Oct '95 / Target/BMG.

COMPACT COMMAND PERFORMANCES (14 Greatest Hits)
Machine gun / Slippery when wet / Sweet love / Fancy dancer / Easy / Brick house / Too hot to trot / Three times a lady / X-rated movie / Sail on / Still / Wonderland / Old-fashioned love / Lady (you bring me up)
CD _____ 530096-2
Motown / Jan '93 / PolyGram.

HITS VOL. 1 & 2
CD _____ AR 9902121
Arcade / Feb '94 / Sony / Grapevine.

141

RISE UP
Cowboys to girls / Rise up / Losing you / Who's making love / Sing a simple song / Baby this is forever / Love canoe / Come by here / Keep on dancing
CD _____ CDBM 035
Blue Moon / Apr '87 / Magnum Music Group / Greensleeves / Hot Shot / ADA / Cadillac / Discovery.

VERY BEST OF THE COMMODORES, THE
Easy / Three times a lady / Nightshift / Brick house / Machine gun / Zoom / Old fashion love / Sail on / Lady (you bring me up) / Oh no / Too hot ta trot / Zoo (the human zoo) / Still / Sweet love / Janet / Flying high / Only you / Animal instinct / Just to be close to you / Wonderland
CD _____ 5305472
Motown / Jul '95 / PolyGram.

XX NO TRICKS
CD _____ FG 2-809
Freestyle / Mar '94 / Freestyle.

Common Language

FLESH IMPACT
CD _____ BFFP 84CD
Blast First / Sep '93 / Disc.

Communards

HEAVEN
You are my world / Czardas / So cold the night / Tomorrow / Annie / Hold on tight / If I could tell you / There's more to love (than boy meets girl) / Zing went the strings of my heart / I do it all for love / Sanctified / Judgement day / Heaven's above / Victims (Live)
CD _____ 5500932
Spectrum/Karussell / Oct '93 / PolyGram / THE.

Como, Perry

20 GREATEST HITS: PERRY COMO (VOL.1)
Magic moments / Caterina / Catch a falling star / I know / When you were sweet sixteen / I believe / Try to remember / Love makes the world go round / Prisoner of love / Don't let the stars get in your eyes / Hot diggity (dog ziggity boom) / Round and round / If I loved you / Hello, young lovers / Delaware / Moonglow / Killing me softly / More / Dear hearts and gentle people / I love you and don't you forget it
CD _____ ND 89019
RCA / Apr '90 / BMG.

20 GREATEST HITS: PERRY COMO (VOL.2)
And I love you so / For the good times / Close to you / Seattle / Tie a yellow ribbon / Walk right back / What kind of fool am I / Days of wine and roses / Where do I begin / Without a song / It's impossible / I think of you / If / We've only just begun / I want to give / Raindrops keep falling on my head / You make me feel so young / Temptation / Way we were / Sing
CD _____ ND 89020
RCA / Apr '92 / BMG.

GREATEST VOCALIST, THE
CD _____ CDSR 067
Telstar / May '95 / BMG.

LIVING LEGEND
CD _____ ARC 94632
Arcade / Nov '92 / Sony / Grapevine.

LOVE SONGS, THE
CD _____ MCCD 125
Music Club / Sep '93 / Disc / THE / CM.

MAGIC MOMENTS
Magic moments / Round and round / More / Don't let the stars get in your eyes / In the still of the night / Papa loves mambo / Me and my shadow / I've got a feeling I'm falling in love / Catch a falling star / Hot diggity (dog ziggity boom) / Wanted / It happened in Monterey / You do something to me / For me and my gal / One for my baby / It's a good day / Mandolins in the moonlight / And I love you so / Killing me softly / Caterina / I left my heart in San Francisco / Days of wine and roses / It's impossible / Raindrops keep falling on my head / Hello, young lovers / We've only just begun / Yesterday / Way we were
CD _____ PWKS 4124
Carlton Home Entertainment / Nov '92 / Carlton Home Entertainment.

PERRY COMO CHRISTMAS ALBUM, THE
Christmas Eve / Do you hear what I hear / Christ is born / Little drummer boy / There is no Christmas like a home Christmas / O Holy night / Caroling, caroling / First Noel / Hark the herald angels sing / Silent night / Silver bells / Toyland / Have yourself a merry little Christmas / Ave Maria
CD _____ ND 81929
Arista / Oct '94 / BMG.

TAKE IT EASY
Bridge over troubled water / El condor pasa / Way we were / When I need you / Feelings / Wind beneath my wings / Michelle / Yesterday / For the good times (Only on CD) / You are so beautiful / Killing me softly /

Most beautiful girl / You are the sunshine of my life / Sunrise sunset / Sing / Close to you / We've only just begun / And I love you so (Only on CD)
CD _____ ND 90490
RCA / Nov '90 / BMG.

TILL THE END OF TIME
CD _____ CDCD 1256
Charly / Jun '95 / Charly / THE / Cadillac.

WORLD OF DREAMS
World of dreams / Jason / Long life, lots of happiness / Wonderful baby / Someone who cares / What's one more time / Love looks so good on you / Meditation / There'll never be another night like this / That's you / Beats there a heart so true / I thought about you / Unchained melody / When she smiles / So it goes / Where you're concerned / You're following me / Stand beside me / How insensitive / Hawaiian wedding song / Dancin' / Everybody is looking for an answer / You are my world / Bless the beasts and the children
CD _____ 74321 278492
RCA / Aug '95 / BMG.

Compagnia Sonadur Di...

PAS EN AMUR (Compagnia Sonadur Di Ponte Caffaro)
CD _____ ACB 05
Robi Droli / Jan '94 / Direct / ADA.

Company

COMPANY 91 - VOL.1
CD _____ INCUSCD 16
Incus / Oct '94 / These / Cadillac.

COMPANY 91 - VOL.2
CD _____ INCUSCD 17
Incus / Oct '94 / These / Cadillac.

COMPANY 91 - VOL.3
CD _____ INCUSCD 15
Incus / Oct '94 / These / Cadillac.

ONCE
CD _____ INCUSCD 04
Incus / '90 / These / Cadillac.

Compton, Mike

CLIMBING THE WALLS (Compton, Mike & David Grier)
Climbin' the walls / Honky tonk swing / Waters street waltz / Black mountain rag / Bye bye blue / Going up Caney / Huffy / Over the waterfall / Flop eared mule / New five cents / Paul's blues / Fun's all over
CD _____ CDROU 0280
Rounder / '91 / CM / Direct / ADA / Cadillac.

Compulsion

COMFORTER
Rapejacket / Basketcase / Mall monarchy / Ariadne / Late again / Air raid for the neighbours / Yancy Dangerfield delusions / Lovers / I am John's brain / Bad cooking / Dick, Dale, Rick and Ricky / Oh my foul life / Jean could be wrong
CD Set _____ TPLP 59CDL
One Little Indian / Mar '94 / Pinnacle.

Comsat Angels

FICTION
After the rain / Zinger / Now I know / Not a word / Ju ju money / More / Pictures / Birdman / Don't look now / What else / It's history / After the rain (2) / Private party / Mass
CD _____ RPM 157
RPM / Jan '96 / Pinnacle.

GLAMOUR
CD _____ CSA 103LE
CD _____ CSA 103
RPM / Jun '95 / Pinnacle.

SLEEP NO MORE
Eye dance / Sleep no more / Be brave / Gone / Dark parade / Diagram / Restless / Goat of the West / Light years / Our secret / Eye of the lens / Another world / At sea / (Do the) Empty house / Red planet revisited
CD _____ RPM 156
RPM / Jan '96 / Pinnacle.

TIME CONSIDERED (BBC SESSIONS)
CD _____ RPM 106
RPM / Nov '92 / Pinnacle.

UNRAVELLED (Dutch Radio Sessions #1)
After the rain / Always near / Beautiful monster / Cutting edge / Field of tall flowers / SS 100X / Our secret / Storm of change / Citadel / Driving / My mind's eye / Shiva descending
CD _____ RPM 123
RPM / Jul '94 / Pinnacle.

WAITING FOR A MIRACLE
Missing in action / Baby / Independence day / Waiting for a miracle / Total war / On the beach / Monkey pilot / Real story / Map of the world / Postcard / Home is the range / We were
CD _____ RPM 155
RPM / Jan '96 / Pinnacle.

Comus

FIRST UTTERANCE
Diana / Herald / Drip drip / Song to Comus / Bite / Bitten / Prisoner
CD _____ BGOCD 275
Beat Goes On / Aug '95 / Pinnacle.

Concept In Dance

DIGITAL ALCHEMY
CD _____ DICD 123
Beggars Banquet / Oct '94 / Warner Music / Disc.

TRIBAL SCIENCE
CD _____ DICCD 124
Beggars Banquet / Aug '95 / Warner Music / Disc.

Conception

LAST SUNSET
Prevision / Building a force / War of hate / Bowed down with sorrow / Fairy's dance / Another world / Elegy / Last sunset / Live to survive / Among the Gods
CD _____ N 0232-2
Noise/Modern Music / Jan '94 / Pinnacle / Plastic Head.

PARALLEL MINDS
CD _____ NO 2182
Noise/Modern Music / Oct '93 / Pinnacle / Plastic Head.

Concord Jazz All Stars

AT THE NORTHSEA FESTIVAL VOL. 2
Vignette / Emily / That's your red wagon / Sweet Lorraine / Can't we be friends / Out of nowhere / Once in a while / In a mellow tone
CD _____ CCD 4205
Concord Jazz / '83 / New Note.

ON CAPE COD
Man I love / This is always / Recado bossa nova / It never entered my mind / Cherokee / All my tomorrows / Bewitched, bothered and bewildered / As long as I live / Time after time
CD _____ CCD 4530
Concord Jazz / Feb '93 / New Note.

OW!
Ow / Fungi mama / My shining hour / I'll close my eyes / Why did I choose you / Blue hodge / I love being here with you / All blues / Down home blues
CD _____ CCD 4348
Concord Jazz / Jul '88 / New Note.

TAKE EIGHT
CD _____ CCD 4347
Concord Jazz / Jul '88 / New Note.

Concrete Minds

LOST OUR MINDS
CD _____ CUS 41802CD
Ichiban / May '94 / Koch.

Concrete Sox

NO WORLD ORDER
CD _____ LF 048
Lost & Found / Aug '93 / Plastic Head.

Condell, Sonny

SOMEONE TO DANCE WITH
CD _____ SCD 295CD
Starc / Jan '95 / ADA / Direct.

Condon, Eddie

1930-1944
CD _____ CD 53183
Giants Of Jazz / Nov '95 / Target/BMG / Cadillac.

1933-1940
CD _____ CD 56078
Jazz Roots / Jul '95 / Target/BMG.

CLASSICS 1938-40
CD _____ CLASSICS 759
Classics / Aug '94 / Discovery / Jazz Music.

CLASSICS 1942-43
CD _____ CLASSICS 772
Classics / Aug '94 / Discovery / Jazz Music.

DIXIE LAND AT THE JAZZ BAND BALL (Condon, Eddie & George Wettling)
CD _____ CD 53175
Giants Of Jazz / Jan '95 / Target/BMG / Cadillac.

EDDIE CONDON 1927-38
CD _____ CLASSICS 742
Classics / Feb '94 / Discovery / Jazz Music.

HIS JAZZ CONCERT
CD _____ STCD 530
Stash / Feb '91 / Jazz Music / CM / Cadillac / Direct / ADA.

IN JAPAN
CD _____ CRD 154
Chiara Scuro / Dec '95 / Jazz Music / Kudos.

JAZZ ON THE AIR - EDDIE CONDON FLOOR SHOW
Them there eyes / Blues in my heart / Riverboat shuffle
CD _____ 20803
Laserlight / Mar '88 / Target/BMG.

LIVE IN 1944, VOL. 3 (Condon, Eddie & His All Stars)
CD _____ JCD 634
Jass / '92 / CM / Jazz Music / ADA / Cadillac / Direct.

RINGSIDE AT CONDON'S
Dixieland one step / Keepin' out of mischief now / Squeeze me / Memphis blues / Dippermouth blues / Sweet Georgia Brown / Wrap your troubles in dreams (and dream your troubles away) / One I love / Just the blues / Makin' whoopee/You made me love you / I can't give you anything but love / Beale Street blues / Mandy make your mind up / Blues my naughty sweetie gives to me
CD _____ SV 0231
Savoy Jazz / Oct '93 / Conifer / ADA.

TOWN HALL CONCERTS VOL.8
CD Set _____ JCD 1015/16
Jazzology / Jul '93 / Swift / Jazz Music.

TOWN HALL CONCERTS, VOL. 1 (Condon, Eddie & His All Stars)
Jazz me blues / Cherry / I'm coming Virginia / Love nest / Big butter and egg man / Oh Katharina / Impromptu ensemble / Sugar / It's been so long / Mandy, make up your mind / September in the rain / Song of the wanderer / Walking the dog
CD _____ JCECD 1001/2
Jazzology / Oct '92 / Swift / Jazz Music.

TOWN HALL CONCERTS, VOL. 2
CD Set _____ JCECD 1003/4
Jazzology / Swift / Jazz Music.

TOWN HALL CONCERTS, VOL. 3
CD _____ JCECD 1005/6
Jazzology / Oct '92 / Swift / Jazz Music.

TOWN HALL CONCERTS, VOL. 4
CD Set _____ JCECD 1007/8
Jazzology / Oct '92 / Swift / Jazz Music.

TOWN HALL CONCERTS, VOL. 5
CD Set _____ JCECD 1009/10
Jazzology / Oct '91 / Swift / Jazz Music.

TOWN HALL CONCERTS, VOL. 6
CD Set _____ JCECD 1011/12
Jazzology / Oct '92 / Swift / Jazz Music.

TOWN HALL CONCERTS, VOL. 9
CD _____ JCD 1017/18
Jazzology / Jan '94 / Swift / Jazz Music.

WE DIG DIXIELAND JAZZ
Tiger rag / Village blues / Black and blue / Who's sorry now / When it's sleepy time down South / Clarinet marmalade / Joe's blues / Some of these days / I told you once / Georgia on my mind
CD _____ SV 0197
Savoy Jazz / Jun '93 / Conifer / ADA.

WINDY CITY JAZZ
CD _____ TPZ 1026
Topaz Jazz / Aug '95 / Pinnacle / Cadillac.

Conemelt

CONFUSE AND DESTROY
Misty traincrash / Flashermac / Cuckoo clock rock / Joys of surface noises / Big up hte conemelt / Overbite nightmare / Espionage / Big and clever track / Pushbutton twist / Motorskating
CD _____ SOP 007CD
Emissions / Jan '96 / Vital.

Confessor

CONDEMNED
CD _____ MOSH 044CD
Earache / Oct '91 / Vital.

Confetti

RETROSPECTIVEl E.P.
Who's big and clever now / It's kinda funny / Yes please / Tomorrow who knows / Warm / Jenny / Bridge 61 / Diet / Whatever became of Alice and Jane / Here again / River island / Nothing II / Corduroy / Anyone can make a mistake / Once more
CD _____ ASKCD 039
Vinyl Japan / Sep '94 / Vital.

Conflict

CONCLUSION
CD _____ MORTCD
Mortarhate / Dec '93 / Disc.

EMPLOYING ALL MEANS NECESSARY
CD _____ CLEO 1023CD
Cleopatra / Jan '94 / Disc.

IT'S TIME TO SEE WHO'S WHO NOW
CD _____ MORTCD 110
Mortarhate / May '94 / Disc.

ONLY STUPID BASTARDS USE EMI
CD _____ MORTCD 130
Mortarhate / Jan '95 / Disc.

STANDARD ISSUE 2
CD _____ MORTCD 170
Mortarhate / Jan '96 / Disc.

THESE COLOURS DON'T RUN
CD _____ MORTCD 080
Mortarhate / Oct '93 / Disc.

WE WON'T TAKE NO MORE
CD _____ MORTCD 150
Mortarhate / Aug '95 / Disc.

Confront

ONE LIFE - DRUG FREE
CD _____ LF 097CD
Lost & Found / Aug '94 / Plastic Head.

Confront, James

TEST ONE REALITY
CD _____ SST 305CD
SST / Mar '95 / Plastic Head.

Confrontation

CONFRONTATION
CD _____ LF 139CD
Lost & Found / Mar '95 / Plastic Head.

Conglomerate

**PRECISELY THE OPPOSITE OF WHAT
WE NOW KNOW TO BE TRUE**
CD _____ DIS 004
FMR/Dissenter / Oct '95 / Harmonia
Mundi / Cadillac.

Congo, Roy

**BIG CITY (Congo, Roy & Jah Power
Band)**
CD _____ SPVCD 0845529
Red Arrow / Dec '94 / SRD / Jetstar.

Congolomerate

BIBLE SAYS, THE
CD _____ IMPCD 18921
Impetus / '90 / CM / Wellard / Impetus /
Cadillac.

Congos

HEART OF THE CONGOS
CD Set _____ BAFCD 9
Blood & Fire / Jan '96 / Grapevine /
PolyGram.

Congregation

EGHAM
CD _____ FIREMCD 55
Fire / Oct '95 / Disc.

Conjunto Alma De...

**ARRIBA TIERRA CALIENTE (Conjunto
Alma De Apatzingan)**
CD _____ ARHCD 426
Arhoolie / Apr '95 / ADA / Direct /
Cadillac.

Conjunto Bernal

MI UNICO CAMINO
CD _____ ARHCD 344
Arhoolie / Apr '95 / ADA / Direct /
Cadillac.

Conjunto Casino

MOLIENDA CAFE
CD _____ CCD 507
Caney / Nov '95 / ADA / Discovery.

Conjunto Cespedes

UNA SOLA CASA
CD _____ GLCD 4007
Green Linnet / Jul '93 / Roots / CM /
Direct / ADA.

VIVITO Y COLEANDO
CD _____ XENO 4033CD
Xenophile / Jun '95 / Direct / ADA.

Conjunto Clasico

CLASICO DE NUEVO
Tu mi estrella / Hipocresia / Gracias amor /
Se que volvera / Una dia de abril / No te
quiero como amiga / Contigo me voy / Me
enamore
CD _____ 66058092
RMM / Feb '96 / New Note.

Conjunto Explosao Do...

**BEST OF CARNIVAL IN RIO VOL.3
(Conjunto Explosao Do Samba)**
CD _____ EUCD 1137
ARC / '91 / ARC Music / ADA.

Conklin, Larry

POET'S ORCHESTRA
CD _____ INAK 9020CD
In Akustik / Jun '93 / Magnum Music
Group.

SNOW TIGER, THE
CD _____ INAK 8901
In Akustik / Jul '95 / Magnum Music
Group.

Conley, Arthur

SOUL DIRECTIONS
Funky Street / Burning fire / Otis sleep on /
Hearsay / This love of mine / Love comes
and goes / People sure act funny / How to
hurt a guy / Get another fool / Put our love
together
CD _____ 7567803862
Atlantic / Jan '96 / Warner Music.

SWEET SOUL MUSIC
CD _____ 7567802842
Atlantic / Jan '96 / Warner Music.

**SWEET SOUL MUSIC - THE BEST OF
ARTHUR CONLEY**
CD _____ SCL 2105
Ichiban Soul Classics / Nov '93 / Koch.

Conlon, Eddie

1933-40
CD _____ CD 14557
Jazz Portraits / Jul '94 / Jazz Music.

Connacht Ramblers

CONNACHT RAMBLERS
CD _____ RR 001CD
RR / Jan '95 / ADA.

Connection

MUSIC FOREVER
CD _____ CDBOP 019
Boplicity / Jul '95 / Pinnacle / Cadillac.

Conneff, Kevin

WEEK BEFORE EASTER, THE
Ellen Brown / Hornpipes / I'm here because
I'm here / John Barber / McAuliffe's polkas
/ Flower of Magherally / Salt / Dark eyed
gipsies / Fair maid won't you call me your
Darling / Cape breton reel / Green fields of
America / Gathering mushrooms / Estonian
waltz / Week before Easter
CD _____ CCF 23CD
Claddagh / Feb '93 / ADA / Direct.

Connells

RING
Slackjawed / Carry my picture / Doin' you /
Find out / Eyes on the ground / Spiral / Hey
you / New boy / Disappointed / Burden /
Any day now / Running Mary / Logan street
/ Wonder why / Living in the past
CD _____ 8286602
London / May '95 / PolyGram.

Connelly, Chris

PHENOBARB BAM-BA-LAM
CD _____ CDDVN 13
Devotion / Jul '92 / Pinnacle.

WHIPLASH BOYCHILD
CD _____ CDDVN 14
Devotion / Oct '92 / Pinnacle.

Connick, Harry Jr.

20
Avalon / Blue skies / Imagination / Do you
know what it means to miss New Orleans /
Basin Street blues / Lazy river / Please don't
talk about me when I'm gone / Stars fell on
Alabama / 'S wonderful / If I only had a dream
/ Do nothin' 'til you hear from me
CD _____ 4629962
Columbia / Mar '89 / Sony.

25
Stardust / Music, maestro, please / On the
street where you live / After you've gone /
I'm an old cowhand (From the Rio Grande)
/ Moments notice / Tangerine / Didn't he
ramble / Caravan / Lazy bones / Muskrat
ramble / This time the dream is on me / On
the Atchison, Topeka and the Santa Fe
CD _____ 472809 2
Columbia / Jan '93 / Sony.

BLUE LIGHT, RED LIGHT
Blue light, red light / Blessing and a curse /
You didn't know me when / Jill / He is they
are / With imagination (I'll get there) / If I
could give you more / Last payday / It's
time / She belongs to me / Sonny cried /
Just kiss me
CD _____ 4690872
Columbia / Apr '95 / Sony.

ELEVEN
Sweet Georgia Brown / Tin roof blues / Wol-
verine blues / Jazz me blues / Dr. Jazz /
Muskrat ramble / Lazy river / Joe Avery's
place / Way down yonder in New Orleans
CD _____ 472808 2
Columbia / Mar '93 / Sony.

FOREVER FOR NOW
It had to be you / Love is here to stay /
Forever for now / Stardust / Do you know
what it means to miss New Orleans / Rec-
ipe for love / Last pitch / Heavenly /
Blue light, red light / But not for me / Little
clown / Where or when / Don't get around
much anymore / You don't know me when
/ It's all right with me / We are in love
CD _____ 4738732
Columbia / Jun '93 / Sony.

Harry Connick Jr

Love is here to stay / Little clown / Zealousy
/ Sunny side of the street / I mean you /
Vocation / On Green Dolphin Street / Little
waltz / E
CD _____ 4604904
Columbia / Aug '94 / Sony.

SHE
She / Between us / Here comes the big parade / Trouble / (I could only) whisper your
name / Follow the music further / Joe slam
/ Honestly now (safety's just danger out of
place) / She blessed be the one / Funky
dunky / That party / Booker
CD _____ 476816-2
Columbia / Aug '94 / Sony.

WE ARE IN LOVE
We are in love / Only 'cause I don't have
you / Recipe for love / Drifting / Forever for
now / nightingale sang in berkeley square /
Heavenly / Just a boy / I've got a great idea
/ I'll dream of you again / It's all right with
me / Buried in blue
CD _____ 4667362
Columbia / Apr '94 / Sony.

WHEN MY HEART FINDS CHRISTMAS
Sleigh ride / When my heart finds Christmas
/ (It must have been ol') Santa Claus /
Blessed dawn of Christmas day / Let it
snow, let it snow, let it snow / Little drummer boy / Ave Maria / Parade of the wooden
soldiers / What child is this / Christmas
dreaming / I pray on Christmas / Rudolph
the red nosed reindeer / O holy night / What
are you doing New Year's Eve
CD _____ 474551 2
Columbia / Nov '93 / Sony.

Connie & Babe

**DOWN THE ROAD TO HOME (Connie &
Babe & The Backwoods Boys)**
CD _____ ROUCD 0298
Rounder / Nov '95 / CM / Direct / ADA /
Cadillac.

Conniff, Ray

16 MOST REQUESTED SONGS
'S wonderful / Sometimes I'm happy / You
do something to me / They can't take that
away from me / I'd like to teach the world
to sing / A time for us (Theme from Romeo
and Juliet) / Lara's (Theme from Dr. Zhivago) / Ravel's Bolero / Where do I begin?
(Theme from Love Story) / Way we were /
Speak softly love (Theme from The Godfather) / We've only just begun / I write the
songs / Just the way you are / Emotion /
How deep is your love / You light up my life
CD _____ 4720462
Columbia / Jan '94 / Sony.

BROADWAY RHYTHM
CD _____ CK 08064
Pickwick/Sony Collector's Choice / Jun
'88 / Carlton Home Entertainment /
Pinnacle / Sony.

CONCERT IN RHYTHM, VOL 1
CD _____ CK 08022
Pickwick/Sony Collector's Choice / Jun
'88 / Carlton Home Entertainment /
Pinnacle / Sony.

**ENCORE - 16 MOST REQUESTED
SONGS**
Begin the beguine / Besame mucho /
Thanks for the memory / Love is a many
splendoured thing / It's been a long, long
time / Memories are made of this / Midnight
lace, part 1 / Hi Lili hi Lo / Invisible tears /
Try to remember / This is my song / Red
roses for a blue lady / It's impossible / First
time I ever saw her face / Seasons in the
sun / Memory
CD _____ 4805142
Columbia / May '95 / Sony.

FRIENDLY PERSUASION
CD _____ CT 9010
Columbia / Jan '94 / Sony.

**HELLO YOUNG LOVERS (Conniff, Ray &
His Orchestra & Chorus)**
Hello, young lovers / As time goes by / You
do something to me / People will say we're
in love / Moonlight serenade / It might as
well be Spring / I'll see you again / Where
or when / Cheek to cheek / Easy to love /
Laura / Way you look tonight / I could have
danced all night / Smoke gets in your eyes
/ They can't take that away from me
CD _____ PWKS 579
Carlton Home Entertainment / Jun '90 /
Carlton Home Entertainment.

HOLLYWOOD RHYTHM
CD _____ CK 08117
Pickwick/Sony Collector's Choice / Jun
'88 / Carlton Home Entertainment /
Pinnacle / Sony.

I WILL SURVIVE (Conniff, Ray & Singers)
I will survive / Reunited / I want your love /
She believes in me / Practice makes perfect
/ If not for you / Hallelujah / Twenty third
psalm / Little music box dancer / Love you
inside out
CD _____ 983404-2

**Pickwick/Sony Collector's Choice / Mar '94
/ Carlton Home Entertainment / Pinnacle /
Sony.**

INVISIBLE TEARS
CD _____ CT 9064
Columbia / Jan '94 / Sony.

RAY CONNIFF
CD _____ CD 326
Entertainers / Apr '94 / Target/BMG.

**RAY CONNIFF PLAYS THE
CARPENTERS**
Yesterday once more / I won't last a day
without you / Top of the world / Rainy days
and Mondays / For all we know / Sing / Su-
perstar/There was a boy / We've only just
begun / Hurting each other / Bless the
beasts and children / Song for you / Close
to you
CD _____ 983401-2
Pickwick/Sony Collector's Choice / Apr '94
/ Carlton Home Entertainment / Pinnacle /
Sony.

SPEAK TO ME OF LOVE
CD _____ CT 8950
Columbia / Jan '94 / Sony.

**WE WISH YOU A MERRY CHRISTMAS
(Conniff, Ray & Singers)**
Jolly old St. Nicholas / Little drummer boy /
Holy night / We three kings of Orient are /
Deck the halls with boughs of holly / Ring
Christmas bells / Let it snow, let it snow, let
it snow / Count your blessings (instead of
sheep) / We wish you a Merry Christmas /
Twelve days of Christmas / First Noel / Hark
the herald angels sing / O come all ye faith-
ful (Adeste Fidelis)
CD _____ 4814372
Columbia / Nov '95 / Sony.

Connolly, Brian

LET'S GO
CD _____ KLMCD 054
Scratch / Jul '95 / BMG.

Connolly, John

AN TOILEAN AERACH
CD _____ CICD 063
Clo Iar-Chonnachta / Jan '94 / CM.

Connolly, Kevin

MY MY MY
CD _____ EFR 103
Eastern Front / Feb '94 / Direct / ADA.

Connolly, Rita

RITA CONNOLLY
Venezuela / Miracles / Factory girl/Same old
man / Alice in Jericho / Fanny Hawke / It's
really pouring / Two of us / Amiems / Red
dust / Dreams in the morning / Close your
eyes
CD _____ TARACD 3029
Tara / Jul '92 / CM / ADA / Direct / Conifer.

VALPARAISO
Ocean floor / Valparaiso / Lizzie Finn / Ripples in the rockpools / Piccadilly / His name
is Elvis / Two white horses / Shakin' the
blues away / Sun song / Rio / Great guns
roar / Quiet land of Erin
CD _____ TARACD 3033
Tara / Nov '95 / CM / ADA / Direct / Conifer.

Connolly, Seamus

HERE AND THERE
Reel le blanc / Pat the budgie / Le reel /
Reel of the birdmen / Larry's delight /
Dominick McCarthy's Irish barndance/
Saunder's fort / I'll always remember you /
Dr. Gilbert/Flax in bloom / Sheila Coyle's
reel / Bells of congress/Dance for the milk-
maker/Kitty O'Brien / Marian McCarthy/
Jockey to the fair / Thirteen arches/
Thoughts of Carignan / Man in the bog/
O'Brien from Newtown / Carraigin Ruadh /
Earl gray/Mrs. Macinroy of Lude/Spey in
spate
CD _____ GLCD 1098
Green Linnet / Feb '92 / Roots / CM / Direct
/ ADA.

NOTES FROM MY MIND
CD _____ GLCD 1087
Green Linnet / Jan '88 / Roots / CM /
Direct / ADA.

Connor, Chris

AS TIME GOES BY
Falling in love with love / As time goes by /
September in the rain / Gone with the wind
/ Strike up the band / Lovely way to spend
an evening / Foggy day / Goodbye
CD _____ ENJ 70612
Enja / Nov '92 / New Note / Vital/SAM.

LONDON CONNECTION
CD _____ ACD 246
Audiophile / Jun '93 / Jazz Music / Swift.

OUT OF THIS WORLD
I hear music / All about Ronnie / Why
shouldn't I / Come back to Sorrento / Out
of this world / Cottage for sale / How long
has this been going on / Goodbye / Lush
life / He's coming home / Riding high / All

dressed up with a broken heart / Trouble is a man / All this and heaven too / Someone to watch over me / Fly me to the moon / From this moment on
CD _____ CDCD 1081
Charly / Apr '93 / Charly / THE / Cadillac.

SWEET & SWINGING
CD _____ ACD 208
Audiophile / Aug '94 / Jazz Music / Swift.

Connor, Joanna

BELIEVE IT
CD _____ 900772
Line / Oct '94 / CM / Grapevine / ADA / Conifer / Direct.

LIVING ON THE ROAD
CD _____ INAK 9022
In Akustik / Jul '95 / Magnum Music Group.

ROCK AND ROLL GYPSY
CD _____ RRCD 901315
Ruf / May '95 / Pinnacle / ADA.

Connors, Bill

ASSEMBLER
Crunchy / Sea coy / Get it to go / Assembler / Add eleven / Tell it to the boss / It be FM
CD _____ 900519
Line / Jan '95 / CM / Grapevine / ADA / Conifer / Direct.

DOUBLE UP
Subtracks / Tud / Floor to floor / Crunchy cuts up / Long distance / Out by twelve
CD _____ 900826
Line / Jan '95 / CM / Grapevine / ADA / Conifer / Direct.

OF MIST & MELTING
Melting / Not forgetting / Face in the water / Aubade / Cafe vue / Unending
CD _____ 847324 2
ECM / Jun '93 / New Note.

STEP IT
Lydia / Pedal / Step it / Cookies / Brody / Twinkle / Titan / Flickering lights
CD _____ ECD 220802
Evidence / Mar '94 / Harmonia Mundi / ADA / Cadillac.

SWIMMING WITH A HOLE IN MY BODY
Feet first / Wade / Sing and swim / Frog stroke / Surrender to the water / Survive / With strings attached / Breath
CD _____ 8490782
ECM / Mar '92 / New Note.

Connors, Norman

BEST OF NORMAN CONNORS (The Buddah Collection)
Once I've been there / You are my starship / Mother of the future / Captain Connors / Be there in the morning / Kwasi / This is your life / Betcha by golly wow / Valentine love / Stella / Butterfly / Kingston / We both need each other / Romantic journey
CD _____ NEXCD 118
Sequel / Aug '90 / BMG.

DANCE OF MAGIC/DARK OF LIGHT
Dance of magic / Morning change / Blue / Give the drummer some / Dark of light / Butterfly dreams / Laughter / Black lightning / Twilight zone / Song for Rosa
CD _____ NEMCD 683
Sequel / Jun '95 / BMG.

SATURDAY NIGHT SPECIAL/YOU ARE MY STARSHIP (2 albums on one CD)
Saturday night special / Dindi / Maiden voyage / Valentine love / Akia / Skin diver / Kwasi / We both need each other / Betcha by golly wow / Bubbles / You are my starship / Just imagination / So much love / Creator has a master plan
CD _____ NEXCD 186
Sequel / May '92 / BMG.

THIS IS YOUR LIFE
Stella / This is your life / Wouldn't you like to see / Listen / Say you love me / Captain Connors / You make me feel brand new / Butterfly / Creator / Captain Connors (Mix)
CD _____ NEMCD 637
Sequel / Mar '93 / BMG.

Consolidated

BUSINESS OF PUNISHMENT
Cutting / Business of punishment / Born of a woman / Das habe ich nicht gewusst / No answer for a dancer / Meat, meat, meat and meat / Dog and pony show / Today is my birthday / Butyric acid / Woman shoots John / Consolidated buries the mammoth / Worthy victim / Recuperation / Empowerless / Emancipate yourself
CD _____ 828514-2
London / Jun '94 / PolyGram.

FRIENDLY FASCISM
CD _____ NET 033CD
Nettwerk / May '91 / Vital / Pinnacle.

PLAY MORE MUSIC
Industrial music is fascism / Tool and die / CNN / Praxis 'Bold as love' / We came here for music, play it / Accept me for what I am / Veggie beat manifesto / Why I'm in the klan / Hello are you there / Infomodities 92

/ Animal rights/Abortion rights / Wendy O Matic / One more song / He / I reckon you should shut the fuck up and play some music / You suck / Men's movement / Gone fishing / Labor vs. Leisure / Day on the green / More music/Hip-O crats / Industry corporate / This isn't a fuckin' press conference / Crackhouse / More music please
CD _____ NET 040CD
Nettwerk / Sep '92 / Vital / Pinnacle.

Consort Of Musicke

MADRIGALS AND WEDDING SONGS FOR DIANA
All creatures now are merry minded / Hence stars too dim of light / Songs from a wedding maske / 1607 / Now hath Flora robb'd her bowers / Move now with measur'd sound / Shows and nightly revels / Triumph now with joy / Time that leads the fatal round / Lady Oriana / Welcome back night / Hark all ye lovely saints / Come gentle swains / As Vesta was from Latmos hill descending / 1614 / Bring away this sacred tree / Go happy man / While dancing rests / Come ashore merry mates / Woo her and win her / You meaner beauties of the night / Mark how the blushful morn / Long live fair Oriana
CD _____ CDA 66019
Hyperion / Feb '89 / Select.

Conspiracy Of Silence

FACELESS
CD _____ SHR 013MCD
Shiva / Nov '95 / Plastic Head.

Conte, Luis

BLACK FOREST
Do the shrimp / Working in a coalmine / I can take you there / Black forest / Susarasa / Polo / Mere wotimbo / Krimson and khaos / Yoruban paradise / El solar
CD _____ CY 74100
Denon / Dec '89 / Conifer.

LA COCINA CALIENTE
Tu sabes / Ahora si / Mujaka / Para para / Tingo talango / Even he paid / Chevereando / Killer Joe / No place to hide this heart / Luisongo / Spankin'
CD _____ CY 30001
Denon / Jun '88 / Conifer.

Conte, Paolo

900
Novecento / Il treno va / Una di queste notti / Pesce veoce dal baltico / La Donna della tua vita / Per quel che vale / Inno in de bemolle / Gong oh / I giardini pensil hanno fatto li loro tempo / Schiava del politeama / Chiamami adesso / Brillantina / Do do
CD _____ 450991033-2
East West / Jun '93 / Warner Music.

Contemporary Piano...

KEY PLAYERS, THE (Contemporary Piano Ensemble)
CD _____ DIW 616
DIW / Feb '94 / Harmonia Mundi / Cadillac.
CD _____ 4756462
Sony Jazz / Jan '95 / Sony.

Conti, Ivan

BATIDA DIFERENTE
CD _____ ITM 94004
ITM / Nov '92 / Tradelink / Koch.

Continental Drifters

CONTINENTAL DRIFTERS
CD _____ MON 6123
Monkey Hill / Sep '94 / Direct.

Continentals

REASON WE SING, THE
CD _____ WSTCD 9696
Nelson Word / '88 / Nelson Word.

Contours

VERY BEST OF THE CONTOURS, THE
Storm warning / Revenge / I'm coming home to you / Running in circles / When it rains it pours / Face up to the fact / Magic lady / Head over heels / Blinded by the light / One day too late / Look out for the stop sign / Under loves control / Flashback / Rise above it / Gonna win you back / Spread the news around / Ready or not here I come / Heaven sent
CD _____ 3035990052
Carlton Home Entertainment / Oct '95 / Carlton Home Entertainment.

Contraband

DE RUYTER SUYTE
CD _____ BVHAASTCD 9104
Bvhaast / Jun '87 / Cadillac.

LIVE AT THE BIMHUIS
CD _____ BVHAASTCD 8906
Bvhaast / Jun '88 / Cadillac.

Control Freak

LOW ANIMAL CUNNING
CD _____ CSR 021CD
Cavity Search / Oct '95 / Plastic Head.

Controlled Bleeding

BODY SAMPLES
CD _____ EFA 5321 D
Dossier / Mar '93 / SRD.

CONTROLLED BLEEDING
CD _____ CLEO 1022CD
Cleopatra / Jan '94 / Disc.

CURD
CD _____ EFA 7726 D
Dossier / Mar '93 / SRD.

MUSIC FROM THE VAULTS
CD _____ DV 21
Dark Vinyl / Mar '94 / Plastic Head.

PETS FOR MEAT (Controlled Bleeding & Doc Wor Mirran)
CD _____ EFA 12205-2
Crypt / Apr '94 / SRD.

SONGS FROM THE DRAIN
CD _____ EFA 08547-2
Dossier / Jun '94 / SRD.

Conundrum

TOMORROW TRADITION
CD _____ CDLOC 1085
Klub / Apr '95 / CM / Ross / Duncans / ADA / Direct.

Convicted Felons

YEAR OF THE NO NIGGAS IS OVER, THE
CD _____ ROC 41692CD
Ichiban / May '94 / Koch.

Convulse

REFLECTIONS
CD _____ NB 114CD
Nuclear Blast / Jan '95 / Plastic Head.

Conway, Francie

WAKE UP
Wake up (introduction) / New York skyline / It's a bedsit / Sweet Carronlaoe / Not even the president / Wake up / Striking it rich / Your drug is Hollywood / Somebody stole my gal / Walking on seashells / Spanish nights / She haunts me / Somewhere in heaven / To the edge of time / One night in Amsterdam
CD _____ RTMCD 22
Round Tower / Jan '91 / Pinnacle / ADA / Direct / BMG / CM.

Conway, Russ

BEST OF RUSS CONWAY
CD _____ MATCD 212
Castle / Dec '92 / BMG.

EP COLLECTION, THE
Call of the sea / Side saddle / It's my mother's birthday today / That's a plenty / Soho fair / Darktown strutter's ball / Falling tears / Wedgewood blue / Rocking horse cowboy / Empty saddles / Ragtime cowboy Joe / Pixillated penguin / Let the big wheel keep turning / Pal Joey pops (medley) / Musical chairs / Musical chairs (Medley more party pops) / Part 2 Even more party pops part 1 (Medley) / More and more party pops - part 2 (Medley) / Scots pops (Medley) / I'll be seeing you / Twelth street rag (CD only) / Temptation rag (CD only)
CD _____ SEECD 310
See For Miles/C5 / Feb '91 / Pinnacle.

GREATEST HITS: RUSS CONWAY
Side saddle / Mack the knife / Westminster waltz / Pixillated penguin / Snow coach / Sam's song / Always / Wedding of the painted doll / World outside / China tea / Lesson one / When you're smiling / I'm looking over a four leaf clover / When you wore a tulip / Row row row / For me and my gal / Shine on harvest moon / By the light of the silvery moon / Side by side / Roulette / Toy balloons / Pepe / Royal event / Lucky five / Passing breeze / Got a match / Always you and me / Pablo / Fings ain't wot they used t be / Polka dots / Where do little birds go / Forgotten dreams / Music music music / If you were the only girl in the world / I'm nobody's sweetheart now / Yes sir that's my baby / Some of these days / Honeysuckle and the bee / Hello hello, who's your lady friend / (In) a shanty in old Shanty Town
CD _____ CC 203
Music For Pleasure / May '88 / EMI.

MAGIC PIANO OF RUSS CONWAY
Walk in the Black Forest / Ain't misbehavin' / Cast your fate to the wind / When somebody thinks you're wonderful / Poor people of Paris / Misty / Trudie / I'm always chasing rainbows / Bewitched, bothered and bewildered / Nightingale sang in Berkeley Square / Old pi'anna rag / Sleepy shores / My very good friend the milkman / Alligator crawl / Satin doll / Oh babe what would you say / Alley cat / China tea / I'm gonna sit

right down and write myself a letter / Chopsticks / Tiger rag / It's not goodbye
CD _____ PWK 052
Carlton Home Entertainment / Jan '89 / Carlton Home Entertainment.

PURE IVORY - A DOUBLE CELEBRATION (4 CD/MCs)
Time to celebrate (with Norman Newell & Rita Williams) / Roll the carpet up / Westminster waltz / Spotlight waltz / Red cat (Le chat rouge) / Piano pops no. 1 (pt 1) / Around the world/Tammy/We will make love / Lantern slide / Harry Lime theme / Jumping for joy / Whistling cat / Toby's walk / Love like ours / Side saddle / Piano pops no. 8 (pt 2) / Kiss me honey honey (kiss me) / Does your chewing gum lose its flavour on the bedpost over n / Tomboy / Russian rag / Gigi medley / Night they invented champagne / Parisians / Thank heaven for little girls / Trampolina / Wee boy of Brussels / Rule Britannia / Key to love / Rustling / Music Man selection (Medley: Seventy six trombones/Till there was you/Lida Rose) / Tin Pan Alley / Parade of the Poppets / Lulu / Bingo / Singing bells / Primera / Blitz medley (Far away/The day after tomorrow/Down the lane) / Angelo / What will they do without us (with Billy Cotton) / Late extra / Celebration day / Matador from Trinidad (with John Barry & his Orchestra) / Primera (2) (with Michael Collins & his Orchestra) / Mr. Happy / Happy Jose / Alone again / Gigolo / Raggity tune / For Pete's sake / Tell me in September (Dimelo en Septiembre) / Portugese washerwoman / Nicola / Cuban romance / Gold rush / Bedouin in Baghdad / Spartans with Norrie Paramour & his Orchestra) / Casino / Calcutta / Little leprechaun / Concerto for lovers / Beggars of Rome / I'm shy Mary Ellen I'm shy / Urchins of Paris / Crunch (with Les Reed & his Orchestra) / Patient heart / Stay awhile (with Les Reed & his Orchestra) / Felicity Grey / Love is a many splendoured thing (with The Band of HM The Royal Marines) / Life is good (with The Band of HM The Royal Marines) / Startime / My concerto for you / Dream of Olwen / Dusk / Autumn concerto / Jeannie / Exodus / Legend of the Glass Mountain / Limelight / Londonderry air / Our love / Skye boat song / Story of a starry night / Something for Mum / Try a little tenderness / April showers / I love the moon / In a shanty in old shantytown / It's my mother's birthday today / Little street / Folks who live on the hill / If you were the only girl in the world / Look for the silver lining / Tara's theme / Three coins in the fountain / Secret love / Laura / It might as well be Spring / Picnic, Theme from / April in Portugal / Song of Delilah / Love is the sweetest thing / More wonderful than you / My funny valentine / Concerto for Memories theme / I'm old fashioned / More / Among my souvenirs / Some enchanted evening / This is my lovely day / Hello young lovers / Almost like being in love / So in love / On the street where you live / We'll gather lilacs / If I loved you / You've done something to my heart / Tonight / Party's over
CD Set _____ CDRUSS 1
EMI / Sep '95 / EMI.

Cooder, Ry

BOOMER'S STORY
Boomer's story / Cherry ball blues / Crow black chicken / Axe sweet Mama / Maria Elena / Dark end of the street / Rally round the flag / Coming in on a wing and a prayer / President Kennedy / Good morning Mr. Railway man
CD _____ 7599263982
WEA / Jan '93 / Warner Music.

BOP TILL YOU DROP
Little sister / Go home girl / Very thing that makes you rich makes me poor / I think it's gonna work out fine / Down in Hollywood / Look at granny run run / Trouble / Don't mess up a good thing / I can't win
CD _____ 256691
WEA / '83 / Warner Music.

BORDERLINE
634 5789 / Speedo is back / Why don't you try me / Down in the boondocks / Johnny Porter / Way we make a broken heart / Crazy about an automobile / Girls from Texas / Borderline / Never make a move too soon
CD _____ 256864
WEA / '88 / Warner Music.

CHICKEN SKIN MUSIC
Bourgeois blues / I got mine / Always lift him up / He'll have to go / Smack dab in the middle / Stand by me / Yellow roses / Chloe / Goodnight Irene
CD _____ 254083
WEA / '88 / Warner Music.

GET RHYTHM
Get rhythm / Low commotion / Going back to Okinawa / Thirteen question method / Women will rule the world / All shook up / I can tell by the way you smell / Across the borderline / Let's have a ball
CD _____ 925639 2
WEA / Dec '87 / Warner Music.

INTO THE PURPLE VALLEY
How can you keep on moving / Billy the kid / Money honey / F.D.R. in Trinidad / Tear-

drops will fall / Denomination blues / On a Monday / Hey porter / Great dreams of heaven / Taxes on the farmer feeds us all / Vigilante man
CD _____ 244142
WEA / '88 / Warner Music.

JAZZ
Big bad Bill is sweet William now / Face to face that I shall meet him / Pearls / Tia Juana / Dream / Happy meeting in glory / In a mist / Flashes / Davenport blues / Shine / Nobody / We shall be happy
CD _____ 256488
WEA / '88 / Warner Music.

MEETING BY THE RIVER, A (Cooder, Ry & V.M. Bhatt)
CD _____ WLACS 029
Topic / Apr '93 / Direct / ADA.

MUSIC BY RY COODER (2CD Set)
CD Set _____ 9362459872
WEA / Jun '95 / Warner Music.

PARADISE AND LUNCH
Tamp 'em up solid / Tattler / Married man's a fool / Jesus on the mainline / It's all over now / Fool about a cigarette / Feeling good / If walls could talk / Mexican divorce / Ditty wa ditty
CD _____ 244260
WEA / Oct '87 / Warner Music.

RY COODER
Alimony / France chance / One meat ball / Do re mi / Old Kentucky home / How can a poor man stand such times and live / And live / Available space / Pig meat / Police dog blues / Goin' to Brownsville / Dark is the night
CD _____ 7599275102
WEA / May '95 / Warner Music.

SHOW TIME
School is out / Alimony / Jesus on the mainline / Dark end of the street / Viva sequin / Do re mi / Volver, volver / How can a poor man stand such times and live / Smack dab in the middle
CD _____ 7599273192
WEA / Aug '92 / Warner Music.

SLIDE AREA,THE
U.F.O. has landed in the ghetto / I need a woman / Gypsy woman / Blue suede shoes / Mama don't treat your daughter mean / I'm drinking again / Which came first / That's the way love turned out for me
CD _____ K2 56976
WEA / Jul '88 / Warner Music.

TRESPASS
Video drive-by / Trespass / East St. Louis / Orgill Bros. / Goose and lucky / You think it's on now / Solid gold / Heroin / Totally boxed in / Give 'em cops / Lucy in the trunk / We're rich / King of the street / Party lights
CD _____ 9362452202
WEA / Feb '93 / Warner Music.

WHY DON'T YOU TRY ME TONIGHT
How can a poor man stand such times and live / Available space / Money honey / Tattler / He'll have to go / Smack dab in the middle / Dark end of the street / Down in Hollywood / Little sister / I think it's gonna work out fine / Crazy about an automobile / 634 5789 / Why don't you try me
CD _____ K 2408642
WEA / '86 / Warner Music.

BARBARA COOK SINGS THE WALT DISNEY SONG BOOK
When you wish upon a star / Give a little whistle / Pink elephants on parade / When I see an elephant fly / With a smile and a song / Lavender blue / Zip a dee doo dah / Dream is a wish your heart makes / Second star to the right / Baby mine / Someone's waiting for you / Sooner or later / I'm late / Someday my Prince will come
CD _____ PWK 090
Carlton Home Entertainment / Feb '89 / Carlton Home Entertainment.

CLOSE AS PAGES IN A BOOK
It's not where you start / Close as pages in a book / I can't give you anything but love / Make the man love me / Exactly like you / April snow / Don't blame me / I'm in the mood for love / On the sunny side of the street / Way you look tonight / Bojangles of Harlem / I must have that man / April fooled me/I'm way ahead
CD _____ DRGCD 91412
DRG / Nov '93 / New Note.

LIVE FROM LONDON
Sing a song with me / Let me sing and I'm happy / Beauty and the beast / Never never land / Can you read my mind / Come rain or come shine / Ship in a bottle / Sweet dreams / I see your face before me / Change partners / I'm beginning to see the light / I had myself a true love / Sweet Georgia Brown / Errol Flynn / Love don't need a reason / He was too good to me / Losing my mind / Accentuate the positive / Why did I choose you / In between goodbyes
CD _____ DRGCD 91430
DRG / Oct '94 / New Note.

TILL THERE WAS YOU (Broadway Years)
CD _____ 379052
Koch / Aug '95 / Koch.

TEMPEST
Tempest / Cascada / Breeze from Saintes Maries / Baghdad / Parasol / Dance of spring / Soledad / Orbit / Fate (parasol reprise) / Jumpstart
CD _____ ND 63035
Narada / Dec '95 / New Note / ADA.

SOMETHIN'S COOKIN'
Detour ahead / Illusion of grandeur / Heavy blue / Hindsight / Chi chi / Fiesta Espanol (Mixes) / Detour ahead (alt.) / Hindsight (alt.) / Chi-chi (alt.)
CD _____ MCD 5470
Muse / Jun '93 / New Note / CM.

NIGHT WORK
CD _____ ENJACD 50332
Enja / May '95 / New Note / Vital/SAM.

HEAVEN IS MY HOME (Cooke, Sam & The Soul Stirrers)
That's heaven to me / Deep river / I thank God / Heaven is my home / God is standing by / Pass me not / Steal away / Must Jesus bear his cross alone / Lead me / Jesus / Trouble in mind / Sometimes / Somebody
See For Miles/C5 / Jul '88 / Pinnacle.

HITS OF THE 50'S
Hey there / Mona Lisa / Too young / Great pretender / You, you, you / Unchained melody / Wayward wind / Secret love / Song from Moulin Rouge / I'm walking behind you / Cry / Venus / All the way / Since I met you baby / I wish you love / Cry me a river
CD _____ 74321260562
RCA / Jun '95 / BMG.

IN THE BEGINNING (Cooke, Sam & The Soul Stirrers)
He's my friend (until the end) / I'm gonna build on that shore / Jesus wash away my troubles / Must Jesus bear the cross alone / Jesus I'll never forget / Nearer to thee / Any day now / Touch the hem of his garment / I don't want to cry / Lovable / For-ever (alternative take) (CD only) / I'll come running back to you / Happy in love / I need you now / That's all I need to know / One more river (CD only) / He's so wonderful (CD only) / Jesus gave me water (CD only) / That's all I need to know (alternative take) (CD only) / I don't want to cry (alternative take) (CD only) / Forever / Lovable (alternative take) (CD only)
CD _____ CDCHD 281
Ace / Nov '89 / Pinnacle / Cadillac / Complete/Pinnacle.

MAGIC OF SAM COOKE, THE
You send me / Only sixteen / Stealing kisses / Talk of the town / I love you most of all / Comes love / Lover come back to me / Everybody loves to cha cha / Little things you do / Good morning heartache / Win your love for me / Moonlight in Vermont / There, I've said it again / Stealaway / All of my life / That lucky old sun / God bless this child / When I fall in love
CD _____ MMB 881
Music Club / May '91 / Disc / THE / CM.

MAN AND HIS MUSIC, THE
Meet me at Mary's place / Good times / Shake / Sad mood / Bring it on home to me / That's where it's at / That's heaven to me / Touch the hem of his garment / You send me / I'll come running back to you / Win your love for me / Wonderful world / Cupid / Just for you / Chain gang / Only sixteen / When a boy falls in love / Rome wasn't built in a day / Everybody loves to cha cha / Nothing can change this love / Love will find a way / Another Saturday night / Having a party / Twistin' the night away / Somebody have mercy / Ain't that good news / Soothe me / Change is gonna come
CD Set _____ PD 87127
RCA / Apr '86 / BMG.

SAM COOKE
CD _____ 295039
Ariola / Oct '94 / BMG.

SAM COOKE WITH THE SOUL STIRRERS (Cooke, Sam & The Soul Stirrers)
Peace in the valley / It won't be very long / How far am I from Canaan / Just another day / Come and go to that land / Any day now / He'll make a way / Nearer to thee / Be with me, Jesus / One more river / I'm so glad (trouble don't last always) / Wonderful / Farther along / Touch the hem of his garment / Jesus wash away my troubles / Must Jesus bear the cross alone / That's heaven to me / Were you there / Mean old world / Lord remember me / Lovable / Forever / I'll come running back to you / That's all I need to know / I don't want to cry
CD _____ CDCHD 359

Ace / Nov '91 / Pinnacle / Cadillac / Complete/Pinnacle.

SAM COOKE'S NIGHT BEAT
CD _____ 5285672
London / Sep '95 / PolyGram.

TWO ON ONE (Cooke, Sam & Jackie Wilson)
CD _____ CDTT 1
Charly / Apr '94 / Charly / THE / Cadillac.

WONDERFUL WORLD
There, I've said it again / Let's go steady again / When I fall in love / Little things you do / You send me / Ol' man river / Moonlight in Vermont / Around the world / Danny boy / Ain't misbehavin' / Summertime / Wonderful world / Everybody loves to cha cha / Along the Navajo trail / Someday you'll want me to want you / I cover the waterfront / Mary Mary Lou / Love you most of all / Only sixteen / Win your love for me
CD _____ CDFA 3195
Fame / May '88 / EMI.

YOU SEND ME
CD _____ CDCD 1093
Charly / Apr '93 / Charly / THE / Cadillac.

COMPLETE COOKIES
Chains / Don't say nothin' bad about my baby / Girls grow up faster than boys / Will power / Old crowd / Stranger in my arms / Softly in the night / Foolish little girl / I want a boy for my birthday / On Broadway / Only to other people / I never dreamed / I'm into something good / We love and learn / Randy / They're jealous of me
CD _____ NEMCD 649
Sequel / Jun '94 / BMG.

ASSIMILATION
CD _____ DOR 38CD
Dorado / Apr '95 / Disc.

COOLEY
CD _____ CEFCD 044
Gael Linn / Jan '94 / Roots / CM / Direct / ADA.

ALL TIME HIGH
We're all alone / I don't want to talk about it / Loving arms / Closer you get / You're so fine / (Your love has lifted me) Higher and higher / Way you do the things you do / All time high / We've got tonight / Wishin' and hopin' / You / One fine day / I'd rather leave while I'm in love / Words
CD _____ 5500792
Spectrum/Karussell / May '93 / PolyGram / THE.

CHEROKEE
CD _____ PERMCD 31
Permanent / May '95 / Total/BMG.

COLLECTION, THE
We're all alone / I'd rather leave while I'm in love / (Your love has lifted me) higher and higher / Crazy love / Seven bridges road / I believe in you / Bird on the wire / I'll be your baby tonight / I don't want to talk about it / Words / One fine day / Fool that I am / Tempted / All time high / Walk on in / Wishin' and hopin' / Slow dancer / You / Quat at inspiration / You're on fire
CD _____ 5518162
Spectrum/Karussell / Nov '95 / PolyGram / THE.

GREATEST HITS
CD _____ CDMID 109
A&M / Oct '92 / PolyGram.

LOVE LESSONS
Heart don't fail me now / Just a kiss away / Nobody but you / If you find it / love lessons / Ain't no reason / You've got the best of me / Girlfriend / One heartbeat / I want to know what love is / Cherokee
CD _____ AA 093162
Start / Nov '94 / Koch.

IT TAKES A THIEF
Fantastic voyage / County line / Mama I'm in love with a gangsta / Hand on my nutsac / Ghetto cartoon / Smokin' / Can-o-corn / U know hoo / It takes a thief / Ghetto squad / Fo da hood / N da closet / On my way to Harlem / Sticky fingers / Thought you knew / Ugly woman / I remember
CD _____ TBCD 1099
Tommy Boy / Oct '94 / Disc.

BACK IN HIS OWN BACKYARD
CD _____ ARCD 19109
Arbors Jazz / Nov '94 / Cadillac.

MEITEAL (Cooney, Chris & Philomena Begley)

CD _____ HBCD 0004
Hummingbird / Jul '93 / ADA / Direct.

FUNNY OLD WORLD
CD _____ NMV 3CD
No Master's Voice / Mar '94 / ADA.

DO YOU NOT KNOW
CD _____ KIE 6CD
Konkurrel / Jan '95 / SRD.

CLASSICS 1938-41 (Cooper, Al & His Savoy Sultans)
CD _____ OJCCD 728
Original Jazz Classics / Dec '93 / Wellard / Jazz Music / Cadillac / Complete/Pinnacle.

ALICE COOPER LIVE 1968
CD _____ EDCD 320
Edsel / Feb '92 / Pinnacle / ADA.

BEAST OF ALICE COOPER, THE
School's out / Under my wheels / Billion dollar babies / Be my lover / Desperado / Is it my body / Only women bleed / Elected / Eighteen / Hello hooray / No more Mr. Nice Guy / Teenage lament '74 / Muscle of love / Department of youth
CD _____ 2417812
WEA / Nov '89 / Warner Music.

BILLION DOLLAR BABIES
Hello hooray / Raped and freezin' / Elected / Unfinished sweet / No more Mr. Nice Guy / Generation landslide / Sick things / Mary Ann / I love the dead / Billion dollar babies
CD _____ 7599 27269-2
WEA / Jan '93 / Warner Music.

CLASSICKS
Poison / Hey stoopid / Feed my Frankenstein / Love's a loaded gun / Stolen prayer / House of fire / Lost in America / It's me / Under my wheels (live) / Billion dollar babies (live) / Eighteen (live) / No more Mr. Nice Guy (live) / Only women bleed (live) / School's out (live) / Fire
CD _____ 4808452
Epic / Oct '95 / Sony.

CONSTRICTOR
CD _____ MCLD 19068
MCA / Jan '94 / BMG.

HEY STOOPID
Hey stoopid / Love's a loaded gun / Snakebite / Burning our bed / Dangerous tonight / Might as well be on Mars / Feed my Frankenstein / Hurricane years / Little by little / Die for you / Dirty dreams / Wind up toys
CD _____ 4684162
Epic / Jun '92 / Sony.

KILLER
Under my wheels / Be my lover / Halo of flies / Desperado / You drive me nervous / Yeah yeah yeah / Dead babies / Killer
CD _____ K 9272552
WEA / Sep '89 / Warner Music.

LADIES MAN
Freak out / Painting a picture / I've written home to mother / Science fiction / For Alice / Nobody likes me / Going to the river / Ain't that just like a woman
CD _____ CDTB 090
Thunderbolt / Feb '91 / Magnum Music Group.

LAST TEMPTATION, THE
Sideshow / Nothing's free / Lost in America / Bad place anytime / You're my temptation / Stolen prayer / Unholy war / Lullaby / It's me / Cleansed by fire
CD _____ 476594 2
Epic / Jun '94 / Sony.

LEGENDS IN MUSIC - ALICE COOPER
CD _____ LECD 085
Wisepack / Sep '94 / THE / Conifer.

LIVE AT THE WHISKEY A GO GO, 1969
No longer umpire / Today Mueller / Ten minutes before the worm / Levity ball / Nobody likes me / B.B. on Mars / Sing slow, sweet cheerio / Changing arranging
CD _____ NESTCD 903
Edsel / Mar '92 / Pinnacle / ADA.

RAISE YOUR FIST AND YELL
Lock me up / Give the radio back / Freedom / Step on you / Not that kind of love / Prince of Darkness / Time to kill / Chop chop chop / Gail / Roses on white lace
CD _____ MCLD 19137
MCA / Nov '91 / BMG.

ROCK LEGENDS VOL.2
Ain't that just like a woman / Painting a picture / Instrumental / I've written home to mother / Freak out song / Goin' to the river / Nobody likes me / Science fiction
CD _____ SMS 054
Carlton Home Entertainment / Oct '92 / Carlton Home Entertainment.

SCHOOL'S OUT
Luney tune / Gutter Cats vs The Jets / Blue turk / My stars / Public animal no. 9 / Alma master / Grand finale / School's out

---

CD _____ 9272602
WEA / Jun '89 / Warner Music.

3NAKES AND DEAD BABIES
CD P.Disc _____ CBAK 4037
Baktabak / Apr '90 / Baktabak.

TRASH
Poison / Spark in the dark / House of fire /
Why trust you / Only my heart talkin' / Bed
of nails / This maniac's in love with you /
Trash / Hell is living without you / I'm your
gun
CD _____ 4651302
Epic / Aug '89 / Sony.

Cooper, Bob

MOSAIC
CD _____ 74026
Capri / Nov '93 / Wellard / Cadillac.

Cooper Clarke, John

DISGUISE IN LOVE
I don't want to be nice / Psyche sluts 1 and
2 / (I've got a brand new) tracksuit / Teenage werewolf / Readers' wives / Post-war
glamour girl / (I married) a monster from outerspace / Salome Maloney health fanatic /
Strange bedfellows / Valley of the lost
women
CD _____ 4805302
Columbia / May '95 / Sony.

SNAP CRACKLE AND BOP
Evidently chickentown / Conditional dis-
charge / Sleepwalk / 23rd / Beasley Street
/ Thirty six hours / Belladonna / The it man
/ Limbo / Distant relation
CD _____ 477380-2
Epic / Aug '94 / Sony.

Cooper, Jim

NUTVILLE
CD _____ DD 457
Delmark / Jan '93 / Hot Shot / ADA / CM /
Direct / Cadillac.

Cooper, Lindsay

OH MOSCOW
CD _____ VICTOCD 015
Victo / Nov '94 / These / ReR Megacorp /
Cadillac.

RAGS
CD _____ RER LCD
Recommended / Apr '91 / These / ReR
Megacorp.

Cooper, Mike

**AVANT ROOTS (Cooper, Mike &
Vivienne Dogan Corringham)**
CD _____ MASHCD 002-2
Mash / Dec '93 / Cadillac.

DO I KNOW YOU/TROUT STEEL
Link / Journey to the East / First song /
Theme in C / Thinking back / Think she
knows me now / Too late now / Wish she
was with me / Do I know you / Start of a
journey / Looking back / That's how / Sitting
here watching / Goodtimes / I've got mine
/ Don't talk too fast / Trout steel / In the
mourning / Hope you see / Pharoah's
march / Weeping rose
CD _____ BGOCD 276
Beat Goes On / Nov '95 / Pinnacle.

Cooper, Pete

WOUNDED HUSSAR, THE
CD _____ FFS 002CD
Fiddling From Scratch / Oct '93 / ADA /
Direct.

Cop Shoot Cop

ASK QUESTIONS LATER
CD _____ ABBCD 045
Big Cat / Apr '93 / SRD / Pinnacle.

CONSUMER REVOLT
CD _____ ABB 033CD
Big Cat / Apr '92 / SRD / Pinnacle.

RELEASE
CD _____ ABB 69CD
Big Cat / Aug '95 / SRD / Pinnacle.

WHITE NOISE
CD _____ ABB 029CD
Big Cat / Oct '91 / SRD / Pinnacle.

Copas, Cowboy

TRAGIC TALES OF LOVE & LIFE
CD _____ KCD 00714
King/Paddle Wheel / Feb '93 / New Note.

Cope, Julian

20 MOTHERS
CD _____ ECHCD 5
Echo / Sep '95 / Pinnacle / EMI.

AUTOGEDDON
CD _____ ECHCD 1
Echo / Jul '94 / Pinnacle / EMI.

**FLOORED GENIUS (The Best Of Julian
Cope)**
CD _____ CID 8000
Island / Aug '92 / PolyGram.

FLOORED GENIUS 2
CD _____ CDNT 003
Night Tracks / Nov '93 / Grapevine /
Pinnacle.

FRIED
Reynard the fox / Bill Drummond said /
Laughing boy / Me singing / Sunspots /
Bloody assizes / Search party / O king of
chaos / Holy love / Torpedo
CD _____ 822 832-2
Mercury / Mar '96 / PolyGram.

JEHOVAHKILL
Soul desert / No hard shoulder to cry on /
Akhenaten / Mystery trend / Upwards at 45
/ Cut my friends down / Necropolis / Slow
rider / Gimme back my flag / Poet is priest
/ Julian H. Cope / Subtle energies commis-
sion / Fa-fa-fa-fine / Fear loves this place /
Tower / Peggy Suicide is missing
CD _____ IMCD 189
Island / Mar '94 / PolyGram.

MY NATION UNDERGROUND
Five o'clock world / Charlotte Anne / China
doll / I'm not losing sleep / Vegetation / My
nation underground / Someone like me /
Great white hoax
CD _____ IMCD 138
Island / Aug '91 / PolyGram.

PEGGY SUICIDE
Pristeen / Double vegetation / East easy
rider / Promised land / Hanging out and
hung up on the line / Safesurfer / If you
loved me at all / Drive she said / Soldier blue
/ You... / Not raving but drowning / Head /
Leperskin / Beautiful love / Western front
1992 C.E. / Hung up and hanging out to dry
/ American lite / Las Vegas basement
CD _____ IMCD 188
Island / Mar '94 / PolyGram.

**SAINT JULIAN/ MY NATION
UNDERGROUND**
CD Set _____ ITSCD 11
Island / Nov '92 / PolyGram.

St. JULIAN
Crack in the clouds / Trampoline / Shot
down / Eve's volcano (Levitation on) /
Space hopper / Planet ride / World shut
your mouth / St. Julian / Pulsar / Screaming
secrets
CD _____ IMCD 137
Island / Aug '91 / PolyGram.

WORLD SHUT YOUR MOUTH
Umpteenth unnatural blues (Included in box
set only.) / World shut your mouth / Bandy's
first jump / Greatness and perfection of love
/ Elegant chaos / Kolly Kibber's birthday /
Head hang low / Metranil vavin / Sunshine
playroom / Lunatic and fire pistol
CD _____ 818 365 2
Mercury / Mar '96 / PolyGram.

Copeland, Johnny

**AIN'T NOTHIN' BUT A PARTY (Live in
Houston, Texas)**
CD _____ CD 2055
Rounder / '88 / CM / Direct / ADA /
Cadillac.

FURTHER ON UP THE ROAD
CD _____ AIM 1032CD
Aim / Oct '93 / Direct / ADA / Jazz Music.

TEXAS TWISTER
Midnight fantasy / North Caroline / Don't
stop by the creek son / Excuses / Jessanne
/ Houston / When the rain starts fallin' / I de
go now / Early in the morning / Twister /
Idiom / Easy to love / Media / Morning cof-
fee / Jelly roll / Where or when
CD _____ CD 11504
Rounder / '88 / CM / Direct / ADA /
Cadillac.

WHEN THE RAIN STARTS FALLIN'
CD _____ CD 11515
Rounder / '88 / CM / Direct / ADA /
Cadillac.

Copernicus

NO BORDERLINE
CD _____ MCD 2089
Humbug / Jun '94 / Pinnacle.

Copland, Marc

AT NIGHT
CD _____ 500592
Sunnyside / Nov '92 / Pinnacle.

**STOMPIN' WITH SAVOY (Copland, Marc
Quintet)**
Equinox / I got rhythm / I loves you Porgy /
Footprints / Easy to love / Lover man /
Woody'n you / Blue in green / One finger
snap / All blue
CD _____ CY 75853
Savoy Jazz / Nov '95 / Conifer / ADA.

Copley, Al

**GOOD UNDERSTANDING (Copley, Al &
The Fabulous Thunderbirds)**
CD _____ SECD 754
Suffering Egos / Apr '94 / Direct.

LIVE AT MONTREUX
CD _____ OMCD 1201
One Mind / Nov '94 / Direct.

ROYAL BLUE (Copley, Al & Hal Singer)
CD _____ BT 1054CD
Black Top / '92 / CM / Direct / ADA.

Copper Family

COPPERSONGS VOL.2
CD _____ COPP 002CD
Coppersongs / Nov '95 / ADA.

Copper, Monique

BABAR & DOOS MEL SPEELGOOD
CD _____ BVHAASTCD 8907
Bvhaast / Apr '89 / Cadillac.

Copperpot, Chester

SHORTCUTS
CD _____ DOLCD 019
Dolores / Apr '95 / Plastic Head.

Coppin, Johnny

COUNTRY CHRISTMAS, A
CD _____ RSKCD 114
Red Sky / Jan '96 / CM / ADA / Direct.

**EDGE OF DAY (Music & Poetry)
(Coppin, Johnny & Laurie Lee)**
CD _____ RSKCD 108
Red Sky / May '89 / CM / ADA / Direct.

FORCE OF THE RIVER
River song / Reach out for you / Just for
you / Shining stars / Full force of the river /
All depends on you / May not be far away
/ Rise with the dawn / Border county road
/ On a hill in Shropshire / LOng lost love
CD _____ RSKCD 112
Red Sky / Oct '93 / CM / ADA / Direct.

**GLOUCESTERSHIRE COLLECTION, THE
(Forest & Vale & High Blue Hill/English
Morning)**
In Flanders / Song of Gloucestershire / Pi-
per's wood / Fisherman of Newnham /
Cotswold love / Briar roses / Legacy /
Warning / High road / Field of Autumn /
Have wondered / Cotswold farmers / This
night the stars / English morning / Everlast-
ing mercy / Dover's hill / Hill / Torn Long's
post / High hill / Holy brook / East wind /
Winter / Cotswold tiles / Roads go down
CD _____ RSKCD 015/107
Red Sky / Feb '95 / CM / ADA / Direct.

**SONGS & CAROLS FOR A WEST
COUNTRY CHRISTMAS**
Intro: Lord of all this Revelling / Glouces-
tershire Wassail / Song for loders / My
dancing day / Sans Day carol / Come all
you worth Christian friends / Sailor's carol /
Glastonbury thorn (theme) / Oxen / Inno-
cent's song / O little town of Bethlehem /
Wiltshire carol / Virgin most pure / Birth /
Campden carol / Flowering of the thorn
CD _____ RSKCD 111
Red Sky / Nov '90 / CM / ADA / Direct.

Coptic Rain

11/11
CD _____ DY 142
Dynamica / Jul '95 / Pinnacle.

DIES IREA
CD _____ DY 22
Dynamica / Oct '93 / Pinnacle.

Cordelia's Dad

COMET
CD _____ 179CD
Normal/Okra / Apr '95 / Direct / ADA.

CORDELIA'S DAD
CD _____ OK 011CD
Normal/Okra / Mar '94 / Direct / ADA.

HOW CAN I SLEEP
CD _____ OKRACD 33019
Normal/Okra / Mar '94 / Direct / ADA.

JOY FUN GARDEN, THE
CD _____ RTS 3CD
Normal/Okra / Mar '94 / Direct / ADA.

Cordle, Larry

**LARRY CORDLE, LARRY DUNCAN &
LONESOME STANDARD TIME (Cordle,
Larry & Larry Duncan)**
Lonesome standard time / Delta queen /
You can't do wrong and get by / Fields of
home / Lower on the hog / Castellion
springs / Down the road to gloryland / Ken-
tucky king / Little Cecil / Old river rock /
Highway 40 blues / Lonesome dove / You
can't take it with you when you go
CD _____ SH CD 3802
Sugarhill / '92 / Roots / CM / ADA / Direct.

Cordola, Lanny

ELECTRIC WARRIOR, ACOUSTIC SAINT
Intro (a new beginning) / Behold this
dreamer cometh / Angry candy / Looney
tunes / Ish kabibble / When shiloh comes /
Birenbau / Farbage valves / Marriage of figaro (sort of) / Slappy white / Zulu jam /
Shadows over my heart / Neesh taps / Ja-

Iapeno man / Django / Hungry hallow /
Plymouth rock / Sadako / Jabberwocky /
Vindaloo / Fripp / Summertime / Echo boy
/ Groom Lake / All the things you are /
Amazing grace
CD _____ FLD 9274
Frontline / Apr '92 / EMI / Jetstar.

Corea, Chick

**A.R.C. (Corea, Chick & Holland &
Altschul)**
Nefertiti / Ballad for Tillie / A.R.C. / Vedana
/ Thanatos / Games
CD _____ 8336782
ECM / Mar '88 / New Note.

AKOUSTIC BAND, THE
Autumn leaves / So in love / Morning sprite
/ Circles / Spain
CD _____ GRP 95822
GRP / Feb '89 / BMG / New Note.

ALIVE (Corea, Chick Akoustic Band)
On Green Dolphin Street / Round Midnight
/ Hackensack / Sophisticated lady /
U.M.M.G. / Humpty dumpty / How deep is
the ocean / Morning sprite
CD _____ GRP 96272
GRP / Dec '90 / BMG / New Note.

**BENEATH THE MASK (Corea, Chick
Elektric Band)**
Beneath the mask / Little things that count
/ One of us is over 40 / Wave goodbye /
Lifescape / Jammin' E. Cricket / Charged
particles / Free step / Ninety nine flavours /
Illusions
CD _____ GRP 96492
GRP / Aug '91 / BMG / New Note.

**BEST OF RETURN TO FOREVER
(Return To Forever)**
Musician / Romantic warrior / So long
Mickey Mouse / Majestic dance / Music
magic / Hello again / Sorceress
CD _____ 4682062
Sony Jazz / Jan '95 / Sony.

**CHICK COREA IN CONCERT (Corea,
Chick & Gary Burton)**
Senor Mouse / Bud Powell / Crystal silence
/ Tweak / Falling grace / Mirror mirror / Song
to Gayle / Endless trouble, endless pleasure
CD _____ 8214152
ECM / '84 / New Note.

CHILDREN'S SONGS
CD _____ 8156802
ECM / Apr '84 / New Note.

COME RAIN OR COME SHINE
Seabreeze / I ain't mad at you / Moments
notice / Blues for Oliver / It don't mean a
thing if it ain't got that swing / Come rain or
come shine / Fiesta piano solo
CD _____ AAOHP 93332
Start / Dec '94 / Koch.

EARLY DAYS
Brain / Converge / Waltz for Bill Evans /
Sundance / Dave / Vamp / Jamala
CD _____ DC 8541
Denon / Apr '89 / Conifer.

EXPRESSIONS
Lush life / This nearly was mine / It could
happen to you / My ship / I didn't know
what time it was / Monk's mood / Oblivion
/ Panonica / Someone to watch over me /
Armando's rhumba / Blues for art / Stella
by starlight / Anna / I want to be happy /
Smile
CD _____ GRP 97732
GRP / May '94 / BMG / New Note.

JAZZ MASTERS
CD _____ 519820-2
Verve / May '94 / PolyGram.

LEPRECHAUN, THE
CD _____ 519798-2
Verve / Dec '93 / PolyGram.

LIGHT AS A FEATHER
You're everything / Light as a feather / Cap-
tain Marvel / 500 miles high / Children's
song / Spain
CD _____ 8271482
PolyGram Jazz / Mar '93 / PolyGram.

**MASTERS OF PIANO (Corea, Chick &
Teddy Wilson)**
Sea breeze / Moments notice / Come rain
or come shine / Fiesta piano solo / I ain't
mad at you / Man in love / Prelude to a kiss
CD _____ 722015
Scorpio / Sep '92 / Complete/Pinnacle.

MY SPANISH HEART
Love castle / Gardens / Day danse / My
Spanish heart / Night streets / Hilltop / Sky,
The - parts 1 and 2 / Wind dance / Arman-
do's rhumba / Prelude to El Bozo - parts 1-
3 / Spanish fantasy (parts 1-4)
CD _____ 825 657-2
Verve / Jan '93 / PolyGram.

**PAINT THE WORLD (Corea, Chick
Elektric Band)**
Paint the world / Blue miles / Tone poem /
C.T.A. / Silhouette / Space / Ant and the
elephant / Tumba island / Ritual / Ished /
Spanish sketch / Final frontier / Reprise
CD _____ GRP 97412
GRP / Feb '94 / BMG / New Note.

PIANO IMPROVISATIONS
Noon Song / Song for Sally / Ballad for Anna / Song of the wind / Sometime ago / Where are you now
CD _____ 8119792
ECM / '88 / New Note.

PIANO IMPROVISATIONS VOL 2
CD _____ 8291902
ECM / New Note.

RETURN TO FOREVER
Return to forever / Crystal silence / What game shall we play today / Sometime ago - la fiesta
CD _____ 8119782
ECM / Mar '88 / New Note.

RETURN TO FOREVER LIVE (2CD Set) (Return To Forever)
CD Set _____ 4689232
Sony Jazz / Jan '95 / Sony.

ROMANTIC WARRIOR (Return To Forever)
Medieval overture / Sorceress / Romantic warrior / Majestic dance / Magician / Duel of the jester and the tyrant (Part 1 and 2)
CD _____ 4682052
Columbia / Nov '93 / Sony.

SEPTET
First movement / Second movement / Third movement / Fourth movement / Fifth Movement / Temple of Isafahan
CD _____ 8272582
ECM / New Note.

SEVENTH GALAXY (Return To Forever)
CD _____ 8253362
Polydor / Apr '92 / PolyGram.

TIME WARP (Corea, Chick Quartet)
New life / Wish / Terrain / Day danse / That old feeling / New waltz / Round midnight
CD _____ GRS 00152
GRP / Aug '95 / BMG / New Note.

TRIO MUSIC
Trio improvisations 1,2,3 / Duet improvisation 1,2,3,4,5 / Slippery when wet / Rhythm-a-ning / Round Midnight / Eronel / Think of one / Little rootie tootie / Reflections / Hackensack / Music of Thelonious Monk
CD Set _____ 8277022
ECM / May '87 / New Note.

TRIO MUSIC LIVE IN EUROPE
Loop / I hear a rhapsody / Night and day / Summer night / Prelude no.2 / Mock up / Hittin' / Microvisions
CD _____ 8277692
ECM / Dec '86 / New Note.

VOYAGE
Mallorca / Diversions / Star Island / Free fall / Hong Kong
CD _____ 8234682
ECM / New Note.

WHERE HAVE I KNOWN YOU BEFORE
Beyond the seventh galaxy / Earth juice / Shadow of Lo / Song to the Pharoah Kings / Vulcan worlds / Where have I danced with you before / Where have I known you before / Where have I loved you before
CD _____ 825 206-2
Verve / Feb '92 / PolyGram.

WORKS: CHICK COREA
Where are you now / Noon song / Children's song / Brasilia / Slippery when wet / Duet improvisation / New place / La Fiesta / Return to forever / Song of the wind / Round Midnight / Rhythm-a-ning / Senor Mouse / Sometime ago / Addendum
CD _____ 8254262
ECM / Jun '89 / New Note.

Cormack, Arthur

NUAIR BHA MI OG
CD _____ COMD 2016
Temple / Feb '94 / CM / Duncans / ADA / Direct.

RUITH NA GAOITH (CHASING THE WIND)
CD _____ COMD 2032
Temple / Feb '94 / CM / Duncans / ADA / Direct.

Cormann, Enzo

MINGUS CUERNAVACA (Cormann, Enzo & Jean-Marc Padovani)
CD _____ LBLC 6549
Label Bleu / Apr '92 / New Note.

Corn Dollies

EVERYTHING BAG
CD _____ MC 015 CD
Medium Cool / Jul '88 / Vital.

Cornell

SILVER JUBILEE
CD _____ RNCD 2024
Rhino / Sep '93 / Jetstar / Magnum Music Group / THE.

Cornershop

WOMAN'S GOTTA HAVE IT
6 a.m. Jullander shere / Honk Kong book of Kung Fu / My dancing days are gone / Call all destroyer / Camp orange / Never leave

yourself (vocal overload mix) / Jamsimran King / Wog / Looking for a way in / 7.20 a.m. Jullander shere
CD _____ WIJ 045CD
Wiiija / Apr '95 / Vital.

Cornerstone

OUT OF THE VALLEY
CD _____ FE 1411
Folk Era / Dec '94 / CM / ADA.

Cornerstone

BEATING THE MASSES
CD _____ LF 159CD
Lost & Found / Jul '95 / Plastic Head.

Cornfield, Klaus

LITTLE TIGERS (Cornfield, Klaus & Lotzi Lapislazuli)
CD _____ EFA 11312CD
Musical Tragedies / Aug '93 / SRD.

Cornwell, Hugh

CORNWELL, COOK AND WEST (Cornwell, Cook & West)
CD _____ UFO 009CD
UFO / Jun '92 / Pinnacle.

WIRED
CD _____ TRANSCD 1
Transmission / Jun '93 / Total/BMG.

Coroner

CORONER
CD _____ NO 2122
Noise/Modern Music / Apr '95 / Pinnacle / Plastic Head.

GRIN
Dream path / Lethargic age / Internal conflicts / Cavaet (To the coming) / Serpent moves / Status: Still thinking / Theme for silence / Paralized, mesmerized / Grin (Nails hurt) / Host
CD _____ N 0210-2
Noise/Modern Music / May '93 / Pinnacle / Plastic Head.

MENTAL VORTEX
CD _____ NO 1772
Noise/Modern Music / Aug '91 / Pinnacle / Plastic Head.

Corporal Punishment

INTO THE NERVE OF PAIN
CD _____ SPI 018CD
Spinefarm / Jun '95 / Plastic Head.

Corrette, Michel

LE NOUVEAU QUATUOR
CD _____ CSAR 57
Saydisc / Nov '92 / Harmonia Mundi / ADA / Direct.

Corridos

TRAGEDIAS DE LA FRONTERA (2CD/Book Set)
CD Set _____ FL 7019/7020
Folklyric / Apr '95 / Direct / Cadillac.

Corries

BEST OF THE CORRIES
Flower of Scotland / Road to Dundee / Skye boat song / Wild mountain thyme / Annie Laurie / Parcel o' rogues / Lord of the dance / Ae fond kiss / Wild rover / October song / Highland lament / Tiree love song / Blow ye winds / Kismuil's galley / Lowlands of Holland / I'm a rover
CD _____ PWKS 4054P
Carlton Home Entertainment / Apr '91 / Carlton Home Entertainment.

BONNET, BELT AND SWORD
Hot asphalt / Cam ye o'er frae France / Joy of my heart / Jolly beggar / Bring back my granny to me / Glenlyon lament / Johnny Cope / Gabentunzie king / Haughs o' Cromdale / Banks of Newfoundland / Parcel o' rogues / North sea holes / Katie Bairdie / Oor wee school / I once loved a lass / Blow ye winds in the morning / My brother Bill's a fireman
CD _____ BGOCD 271
Beat Goes On / Mar '95 / Pinnacle.

COMPACT COLLECTION, THE
Flower of Scotland / Dumbarton's drums / Portree kid / Glencoe / Bricklayer's song / Come o'er the stream / MacPherson's rant / Roses of Prince / Lammas tide / Massacre of Glencoe / Ettrick lady / Turn ye tae me / Sherramuir fight / Dark Lochnagar / King fa-reweel / Man's a man for a' that
CD _____ LCOM 9006
Lismor / Mar '88 / Lismor / Direct / Duncans / ADA.

FLOWER OF SCOTLAND
Stirling Brig / Kelvingrove / Vicar and the frog / Bona line / Loch song / Black Douglas / Bonnie ship the Diamond / Mothers, daughters, wives / Tibbie dunbar / Shen-andoah / Castle of Dromore / Food blues / Flower of Scotland

CD _____ MOICD 002
Moidart / Jun '94 / Conifer / ADA.

IN CONCERT/SCOTTISH LOVE SONGS
Johnny lad / Lord of the dance / Flower of Scotland / Wild mountain thyme / Ca' the yowes / Bonnie lass o'Fyvie / Skye boat song / Wild rover / Kid songs / Hills of Ard-morn / Tiree love song / Annie Laurie / Ae fond kiss / Nut brown maiden / Sally free and easy / Liverpool Judies / Granny's in the cellar / Road to Dundee / Hunting tower / Lowlands of Holland
CD _____ BGOCD 267
Beat Goes On / Feb '95 / Pinnacle.

SCOTS WHA'HAE
Stirling Brig / Black Douglas / Scots wha hae / Lammas tide / Battle of Harlaw / Lock the door Lariston / Haughs o' Cromdale / Bonnie Dundee / Braes o'Killiecrankie / Sherramuir fight / News from Moidart / Johnny Cope / King Fareweel
CD _____ MOICD 009
Moidart / Apr '94 / Conifer / ADA.

SILVER COLLECTION
Killiecrankie / Rise rise / News from Moidart / Johnny Cope / Lock the door Lariston / Scots wha hae / I will go / Loch Lomond / Skye boat song / Welcome Royal Charlie / Parcel o' rogues / Barrett's privateers / Queen's Maries / Jock O'Braidslee / Bonnie lass o'Fyvie / Haughs o' Cromdale / Rose of Allendale / Westering home / Twa recruiting sergeants / Wild mountain thyme
CD _____ MOICD 005
Moidart / Jun '93 / Conifer / ADA.

VERY BEST OF THE CORRIES
Black Douglas / Wha wadna fecht for Charlie / Isle of Skye / I will go / Sound the pi-broch / Derwentwater's farewell / Flood Garry / Bonnie Dundee / Peggy Gordon / Boys of Barehill and Derry hornpipe / Abigail / Tartan mother's lullaby / Maids, when you're young never wed an old man / Rose of Allendale / Kiss the children for me Mary / Westering home
CD _____ CC 246
Music For Pleasure / May '90 / EMI.

Corringham, Vivienne...

POPULAR TURKISH FOLK SONGS (Corringham, Vivienne Dogan & George Hadjineophytou)
CD _____ EUCD 1166
ARC / '91 / ARC Music / ADA.

Corrosion Of Conformity

ANIMOSITY
Loss for words / Mad world / Consumed / Holier / Positive outlook / Prayer / Intervention / Kill death / Hungry child / Animosity
CD _____ CDZORRO 44
Metal Blade / Apr '93 / Pinnacle.

BLIND
CD _____ RO 92362
Roadrunner / Apr '95 / Pinnacle.

DELIVERANCE
Heaven's not overflowing / Albatross / Clean my wounds / Without wings / Broken man / Senor Limpio / Man de mono / Seven days / 2121313 / My grain / Deliverance / Shake like you / Shelter / Pearls before swine
CD _____ 4776832
Columbia / Oct '94 / Sony.

EYE FOR AN EYE
Tell me / Indifferent / Habid dogs / Hed-neckkk / Minds are controlled / Broken will / L.S. / Co-exist / Dark thoughts / What / Positive outlook / College town / Eye for an eye / Poison planet / Negative outlook / No drunk / Not safe / Nothing's gonna change
CD _____ INCDD 002/3
Product Inc. / Jun '94 / Vital.

TECHNOCRACY
Technocracy / Hungry child / Happily ever after / Crawling / Ahh blugh / Intervention / Technocracy (2) / Crawling (2) / Happily ever after (2)
CD _____ CDZORRO 53
Metal Blade / Apr '93 / Pinnacle.

Corrs

FORGIVEN NOT FORGOTTEN
CD _____ 7567926122
Atlantic / Feb '96 / Warner Music.

Cortez, Dave 'Baby'

DAVE 'BABY' CORTEZ
Shake / Watermelon man / Boy from New York City / Can't buy me love / How sweet it is (to be loved by you) / Twine time / Stagger Lee / Yeh, yeh / Searchin' / Come see about me / Where did our love go / Paper tiger / Tweetie pie / Things ain't what they used to be / Count down part 1 / Count down part 2 / Belly rub part 1 / Belly rub part 2 / Do any dance / Peg leg / Sticks and stones / My sweet baby parts 1 and 2 / In orbit / Summertime / You talk too much / Hula hoop / Come back
CD _____ NEMCD 751
Sequel / Aug '95 / BMG.

HAPPY ORGANS, WILD GUITARS AND PIANO SHUFFLES
Happy organ / Piano shuffle / Cat nip / Hey hey hey / Mardi gras / Fiesta / Love me as I love you / Whistling organ / Hurricane / Deep in the heart of Texas / Do the slop / You're just right / Red sails in the sunset / Calypso love song / Dave's / I'm happy / Summertime / Tootsie / It's a sin to tell a lie / Boogie piano / Boogie organ / Shift / Organ bounce / Swinging piano / Riffin'
CD _____ CDOIHD 006
Ace / Jun '93 / Pinnacle / Cadillac / Complete/Pinnacle.

Cortez, Jayne

WOMEN IN (E)MOTION FESTIVAL (Cortez, Jayne & The Firespitters)
CD _____ T&M 106
Tradition & Moderne / Nov '94 / Direct / ADA.

Coryell, Larry

BOLERO (Coryell, Larry & Brian Keane)
Improvisation on Bolero / Nothing is forever / Something for Wolfgang Amadeus / Tombeau de couperin (Prelude from) / Elegancia del sol / Fancy frogs / 6 Watch hill road / Blues in Madrid / Motel time / At the airport / Brazilia / Piece for Larry / La pluie / Patty's song
CD _____ ECD 22046
Evidence / Mar '93 / Harmonia Mundi / ADA / Cadillac.

BOLERO AND SCHEHERAZADE
CD _____ 810 024-2
Philips / May '93 / PolyGram.

COMING HOME
Good citizen swallow / Glorielle / Twelve and twelve / Confirmation / It never entered my mind
CD _____ MCD 5303
Muse / Jan '86 / New Note / CM.

ELEVENTH HOUSE
CD _____ VND 79342
Vanguard / Oct '95 / Complete/Pinnacle / Discovery.

EQUIPOISE
Unemployed Floyd / Tender tears / Equipoise / Christina / Joy Spring / First things first
CD _____ MCD 5319
Muse / Feb '87 / New Note / CM.

FALLEN ANGEL
Inner city blues / Pieta / Fallen / Thus spoke z / Never never / Stella by starlight / Angel in sunset / Monk's corner / Stardust / Westerly winds / Misty / Moors / I remember bill
CD _____ ESJCD 237
Essential Jazz / Oct '94 / BMG.

QUIET DAY IN SPRING, A (Coryell, Larry & Urbaniak, Michal)
CD _____ SCCD 311 87
Steeplechase / '88 / Impetus.

SHINING HOUR
CD _____ MCD 5360
Muse / Sep '92 / New Note / CM.

SPACES
Spaces / Rene's theme / Gloria's step / Wrong is right / Chris / New year's day in Los Angeles-1968
CD _____ VND 79345
Vanguard / Oct '95 / Complete/Pinnacle / Discovery.

TOGETHER (Coryell, Larry & Emily Remler)
Arabian nights / Joy Spring / Ill wind / How my heart sings / Six beats, six strings / Gerri's blues / First things first
CD _____ CCD 4289
Concord Jazz / Nov '86 / New Note.

TOKUDO
CD _____ MCD 5350
Muse / Sep '92 / New Note / CM.

Coryell, Murall

EYES WIDE OPEN
CD _____ BIGMO 30232
Big Mo / Aug '95 / Direct / ADA.

Cosmetic

SO TRANQUILIZIN
All things must change / Be my girl / Take it to the top / All my love / N-er-gize me / About the money / So tranquilizin / Jet set
CD _____ 1883102
Gramavision / '85 / Vital/SAM / ADA.

Cosmic Baby

THINKING ABOUT MYSELF
Thinking about myself / Treptow / Tag 20000 / Another day in another city / Brooklyn / Au dessous des nuages / Comic greets Florida.... in Berlin / Fantasia / Loops of infinity (contemplative) / Movements in love
CD _____ 7432119605-2
RCA / Apr '94 / BMG.

Cosmic Jokers

SCI FI PARTY
CD _____ SPA 14884
Spalax / Nov '94 / Direct / ADA.

Cosmic Psychos

PALOMINO PIZZA
CD _____ EFA 0492409
City Slang / May '93 / Disc.

SELF TOTALLED
CD _____ ARRCD 63006
Amphetamine Reptile / May '95 / SRD.

Cosmic Trigger

SOLAR ECLIPSE
CD _____ SR 9345
Silent / Jan '94 / Plastic Head.

Cosmic Twins

COSMIC TWINS
CD _____ GRCD 312
Glitterhouse / Sep '94 / Direct / ADA.

Cosmoalpha

MUSIC FOR A SUMMER'S DAY
Elvis Presley medley / Only you / Sunny / I can't stop loving you / Neil Sedaka medley / Proud Mary / Rock 'n' roll music / Paul Anka Medley / Daydream believer / Unchained melody / What'd I say / Soul train / Joy to the world / Spinning wheel / California dreamin' / Aquarius / My girl / Place in the sun
CD _____ DC 8508
Denon / '88 / Conifer.

SOUND STREAM
CD _____ CY 1001
Denon / '88 / Conifer.

Cosmotheka

KEEP SMILING THROUGH (Hit Songs Of World War II)
Smiling through / Wish me luck as you wave me goodbye / I love to sit with Sophie in the shelter / I did what I could with my gas mask / Whitehall warriors / Lili Marlene / D-day dodgers / Roll me over / We'll meet again / Follow the white line / I get along without you very well / Hey little hen / Dig dig dig to victory / They're all under the counter / I'm gonna get lit up (when the lights go on in London) / Knees up Mother Brown / Medley
CD _____ EMPRCD 509
Emporio / Apr '94 / THE / Disc / CM.

Cossu, Scott

ISLANDS
Ohana / Gypsy dance / St. Croix / Islands / Harlequin messenger / Vashon poem / Oristano sojourn / Fawn
CD _____ CDWQ 1033
Windham Hill / '86 / Pinnacle / BMG / ADA.

WINDHAM HILL RETROSPECTIVE, A
Oristano sojourn / Gwenlaise / Desert lightning / Manhattan underground / Fawn / Country faire / Ode to Shiva / Sweet rose / Ohana / Switchback / Sanibel / Purple mountain / Islands / Bajun carnival / Angel steps
CD _____ 111122
Windham Hill / Mar '92 / Pinnacle / BMG / ADA.

Costanzo, Sonny

PROMISES TO KEEP (Costanzo, Sonny & Czech Radio Big Band)
CD _____ CR 0002-2
Czech Radio / Nov '95 / Czech Music Enterprises.

Costello, Elvis

ALMOST BLUE (Costello, Elvis & The Attractions)
Why don't you love me / Sweet dreams / I'm your toy / Tonight the bottle let me down / Brown to blue / Good year for the roses / Sittin' and thinkin' / Colour of the blues / Too far gone / Honey hush / How much I've lied
CD _____ DPAM 7
Demon / Oct '94 / Pinnacle / ADA.

ARMED FORCES
Senior service / Oliver's army / Big boys / Green shirt / Party girl / Goon squad / Busy bodies / Sunday's best / Chemistry class / Two little Hitlers / Accidents will happen
CD _____ DPAM 3
Demon / Oct '94 / Pinnacle / ADA.

BEST OF ELVIS COSTELLO - THE MAN
Watching the detectives / Oliver's army / Alison / Accidents will happen / Pump it up / High fidelity / Pills and soap / (I don't want to go to) Chelsea / New lace sleeves / Good year for the roses / I can't stand up for falling down / Clubland / Beyond belief / New Amsterdam / Green shirt / Everyday I write the book / I wanna be loved / Shipbuilding
CD _____ FIENDCD52X
Demon / Mar '93 / Pinnacle / ADA.

BLOOD AND CHOCOLATE
Uncomplicated / I hope you're happy now / Tokyo storm warning / Home is anywhere you hang your head / I want you / Home are you straight or are you blind / Blue chair / Battered old bird / Crimes of Paris / Poor Napoleon / Next time round
CD _____ FIENDCD 80X
Demon / Mar '93 / Pinnacle / ADA.

BRUTAL YOUTH
Pony St. / Kinder murder / Thirteen steps lead down / This is hell / Clown strike / You tripped at every step / Still too soon to know / 20% amnesia / Sulky girl / London's brilliant parade / My science fiction twin / Rocking horse road / Just about glad / All the rage / Favourite hour
CD _____ 936245535-2
Warner Bros. / Mar '94 / Warner Music.

GET HAPPY (Costello, Elvis & The Attractions)
Love for tender / Opportunity / Imposter / Secondary modern / King horse / Possession / Man called uncle / Clowntime is over / New Amsterdam / High fidelity / I can't stand up for falling down / Black and white world / Five gears in reverse / B Movie / Motel matches / Human touch / Beaten to the punch / Temptation / I stand accused / Riot act
CD _____ DPAM 5
Demon / Apr '94 / Pinnacle / ADA.

GIRLS, GIRLS, GIRLS
Watching the detectives / (I don't want to go to) Chelsea / Alison / Shipbuilding / I want you / American without tears / Oliver's army / This year's girl / Lover's walk / Pump it up / Strict time / Temptation / High fidelity / Lovable / Mystery dance / Big tears / Uncomplicated / Lipstick vogue / Man out of time / Brilliant mistake / New lace sleeves / Accidents will happen / Beyond belief / Black and white world / Green shirt / Loved ones / New Amsterdam / Red shoes / King horse / Big sister's clothes / Man called Uncle / Party girl / Shabby doll / Motel matches / Tiny steps / Almost blue / Riot act / Love field / Possession / Poisoned rose / Indoor fireworks / Pills and soap / Sunday's best / Watch your step / Less than zero / Clubland / Tokyo storm warning
CD _____ FIENDCD 160
Demon / Oct '89 / Pinnacle / ADA.

GOODBYE CRUEL WORLD (Costello, Elvis & The Attractions)
Only flame in town / Home truth / Room with no number / Inch by inch / Worthless thing / Love field / I wanna be loved / Comedians / Joe Porterhouse / Sour milk cow blues / Great unknown / Deportees club / Peace in our time
CD _____ DPAM 10
Demon / Feb '95 / Pinnacle / ADA.

IMPERIAL BEDROOM
Beyond belief / Tears before bedtime / Shabby doll / Long honeymoon / Man out of time / Almost blue / And in every home / Loved ones / Human hands / Kid about it / Little savage / Boy with a problem / Pidgin English / You little fool / Town crier / Only flame in town / Room with no number / Inch by inch / Worthless thing / Love field / I wanna be loved / Comedians / Joe Porterhouse / Sour milk cow blues / Great unknown / Deportees club / Peace in our time
CD _____ DPAM 8
Demon / Oct '94 / Pinnacle / ADA.

JULIET LETTERS (Costello, Elvis & Brodsky Quartet)
Jacksons, Monk and Rowe / This sad burlesque / Romeo's seance / I thought I'd write to Juliet / Last post / First to leave / Damnation's cellar / Birds will still be singing / Deliver us / For other eyes / Swine / Expert rites / Dead letter / I almost had a weakness / Why / Who do you think you are / Taking my life in your hands / This offer is unrepeatable / Dear sweet filthy world / Letter home
CD _____ 9362451802
WEA / Jan '93 / Warner Music.

KOJAK VARIETY
Strange / Hidden charms / Remove this doubt / I threw it all away / Leave my kitten alone / I've been young before / Must you throw dirt in my face / Everybody's cryin' mercy / Bama lama bama loo / Pouring water on a drowning man / Payday / Very thought of you / Please stay / Runnin' out of fools / Days
CD _____ 9362459032
Warner Bros. / May '95 / Warner Music.

MIGHTY LIKE A ROSE
Other side of summer / Hurry down doomesday / How to be dumb / All grown up / Invasion hit parade / Harpies bizzare / After the fall / Georgie and her mirror / So like Candy / Couldn't call it unexpected No. 2 / Playboy to a man / Sweet pear / Broken / Couldn't call it unexpected No. 4
CD _____ 7599265752
Demon / Feb '95 / Warner Music.

MY AIM IS TRUE
Welcome to the working week / Miracle man / No dancing / Blame it on Cain / Alison / Sneaky feelings / Red shoes / Less than zero / Mystery dance / Pay it back / I'm not angry / Waiting for the end of the world

CD _____ DPAM 1
Demon / Oct '93 / Pinnacle / ADA.

OUT OF OUR IDIOT
Blue chair / Seven day weekend / Turning the town red / Heathrow Town / People's limousine / So young / American without tears (No. 2 Twilight version) / Get yourself another fool / Walking on thin ice / Baby, it's you / From head to toe / Shoes without heels / Baby's got a brand new hairdo / Flirting kind / Black sails in the sunset / Imperial bedroom / Stampling grams
CD _____ FIENDCD 67X
Demon / Mar '93 / Pinnacle / ADA.

PUNCH THE CLOCK
Everyday I write the book / Pills and soap / Shipbuilding / Let them all talk / Boxing day / Love went mad / Greatest thing / Element within / Charm school / Invisible man / Mouth almighty / King of thieves / World and his wife
CD _____ DPAM 9
Demon / Feb '95 / Pinnacle / ADA.

SPIKE
This town / Let him dangle / Deep dark truthful mirror / Veronica / God's comic / Chewing gum / Tramp the dirt down / Stalin Malone / Satellite / Pads, paws and claws / Baby plays around / Miss Macbeth / Any king's shilling / Coal train robberies / Last boat leaving
CD _____ 925848-2
Warner Bros. / Jan '89 / Warner Music.

TEN BLOODY MARYS AND TEN HOW'S YOUR FATHERS (Costello, Elvis & The Attractions)
Clean money / Girls talk / Talking in the dark / Radio sweetheart / Big tears / Crawling to the USA / Just a memory / Watching the detectives / Stranger in the house / Clowntime is over (no.2) / Getting mighty crowded / Hoover factory / Tiny steps / Peace, love and understanding / Dr. Luther's assistant / Radio radio / Black and white world / Wednesday week / My funny valentine / Ghost train
CD _____ FIENDCD 27X
Demon / Mar '93 / Pinnacle / ADA.

THIS YEAR'S MODEL
Beyond belief / Tears before bedtime / Shabby doll / Long honeymoon / Man out of time / Almost blue / And in every home / Loved ones / Human hands / Kid about it / Little savage / Beat / Pump it up / Hand in hand / Lip service / Living in Paradise / Lipstick vogue / Night rally / No action / This years girl / Little triggers / You belong to me / (I don't want to go to) Chelsea
CD _____ DPAM 2
Demon / Oct '93 / Pinnacle / ADA.

TRUST
Clubland / Lover's walk / You'll never be a man / Pretty words / Strict time / Luxembourg / Watch your step / New lace sleeves / From a whisper to a scream / Different finger / White knuckles / Shot with his own gun / Fish'n'chip paper / Big sisters clothes
CD _____ DPAM 6
Demon / Oct '94 / Pinnacle / ADA.

TWO & HALF YEARS - THE ELVIS COSTELLO BOXSET (My Aim Is True/ This Years Model/Armed Forces/Live CD)
CD Set _____ DPAMBOX1
Demon / Oct '93 / Pinnacle / ADA.

VERY BEST OF ELVIS COSTELLO & THE ATTRACTIONS (Costello, Elvis & The Attractions)
CD _____ DPAM 13
Demon / Oct '94 / Pinnacle / ADA.

Coster, Tom

FORBIDDEN ZONE, THE
In the beginning / Jazz lament / Shall me / Father-daughter / Lover man / Voyage to nowhere / Waste land/Jam / Blue and cool / Group / Blues for D.C. / Fix / Closing thought
CD _____ JVC 20402
JVC / Nov '94 / New Note.

LET'S SET THE RECORD STRAIGHT
To be or not to be / Slick / Dance of the spirits / Then and now / Thinking of you / Mr. MD / Best of friends / Turkish delight / Blue blues / Welcome to my chambers / Caribbean sunset / For the folks back home
CD _____ JVC 20252
JVC / Nov '93 / New Note.

Cotten, Elizabeth

FREIGHT TRAIN (North Carolina Folk Songs & Tunes)
CD _____ SFWCD 40009
Smithsonian Folkways / May '95 / ADA / Direct / Koch / CM / Cadillac.

Cottle, Laurence

LIVE
Every offence / DR 10 / Underhill pavillion / Bouncing with Bud / Quite firm
CD _____ JITCD 9504
Jazzband / Jan '96 / Jazz Music / Wellard.

Cotton, Billy

THAT RHYTHM MAN 1928-31 (Cotton, Billy & His Band)
Sing a new song / We just couldn't say goodbye / Leave the pretty girls alone / Look what I've got / Margie / Georgia on my mind / Somebody loves you / (I'll be glad when you're dead) you rascal you / Day by day / Bessie couldn't help it / Nut sut song / Man with the mandolin / Lights out / Bon voyage cherie / Aurora / Fifty million robins can't be wrong / Man who comes around / Never took a lesson in my life / Woe is me / Shoe shine boy / Mammy bong
CD _____ 2 BUR 007
Burlington / Sep '88 / CM.

THINGS I LOVE ABOUT THE 40'S, THE (Cotton, Billy & His Band)
Bottle party / I'm gonna get it up (when the lights go on in London) / Yeah man / That lovely weekend / You'll be happy little sweetheart in the spring / Shine / Hold tight, hold tight / Toy trumpet / Things I love / Dere's jazz in dem here horns / Margie / Nut sut song / Man with the mandolin / Lights out / Bon voyage cherie / Aurora / Fifty million robins can't be wrong / Man who comes around / Never took a lesson in my life / Woe is me / Shoe shine boy / Mammy bong
CD _____ RAJCD 814
Empress / Feb '94 / THE.

WAKEE WAKEE! (Cotton, Billy & His Band)
Somebody stole my gal / Bugle call rag / I'm just wild about Harry / Third tiger / Mood indigo / Fancy our meeting / So green / Ooo-la-la / It's only a paper moon / Rhapsody in blue / Skirts / Best wishes / Sweep / Mrs. Bartholomew / You don't understand / Why has a cow got four legs / St. Louis blues / She was only somebody's daughter / Night owl / Young and healthy / You're getting to be a habit with me / Shuffle off to Buffalo / Forty second steet / Smile, darn ya, smile
CD _____ C5CD-513
See For Miles/C5 / Aug '90 / Pinnacle.

Cotton, James

100% COTTON (Cotton, James Band)
Boogie thing / One more mile / All walks of life / Creeper creeps again / Rocket 88 / How long can a fool go wrong / I don't know / Burner / Infatuation / Fever
CD _____ OW 27670
One Way / May '94 / Direct / ADA.

HARP ATTACK (Cotton, James/Junior Wells/Carey Bell/Billy Branch)
Down home blues / Who / Four hand out of my pocket / Little car blues / My eyes keep me in trouble / Broke and hungry / Hit man / Black night / Somebody changed the lock / Second hand man / New kid on the block
CD _____ ALCD 4790
Alligator / May '93 / Direct / ADA.

HIGH COMPRESSION
Diggin' my potatoes / Ying yang / Twenty three hours too long / No more doggin' / No cuttin' loose / Ain't doing too bad / Sunny road / Superharp / Easy loving / High compression
CD _____ ALCD 4737
Alligator / Oct '93 / Direct / ADA.

HIGH ENERGY (Cotton, James Band)
Hot and cold / Chicken heads / Hard time / Got a feeling / Weather report (the weather man said) / Rock 'n' roll music (ain't nothing new) / Fannie Mae / Caldonia / James theme / Keep cooking mama
CD _____ OW 27671
One Way / May '94 / Direct / ADA.

LIVE AND ON THE MOVE VOL. 1 (Cotton, James Band)
CD _____ OW 24835
One Way / May '94 / Direct / ADA.

LIVE AT ANTONES
CD _____ ANTCD 0007
Antones / Jan '93 / Hot Shot / Direct / ADA.

LIVE AT ELECTRIC LADY (Cotton, James Band)
Back at the chicken shack / Off the wall / Rocket 88 / Don't start me talkin' / Georgia swing / One more mile / I got my mojo working / How long can a fool go wrong / Blow wind blow / Mean old world / I don't know / Boogie thing / Stormy Monday / Fever
CD _____ NEXCD 224
Sequel / Nov '92 / BMG.

LIVE FROM CHICAGO (Mr Superharp himself)
Here I am / Part time love / Just to be with you / Hard headed / When it rains it really pours / Cross your heart / Come back baby / Born in Chicago / Creeper
CD _____ ALCD 4746
Alligator / May '93 / Direct / ADA.

LIVE: ON THE MOVE
Cotton boogie / One more mile / All walks of life / Born in Missouri / Flip flop and fly / Mojo / Rocket 88 / Goodbye my lady / I don't know / Caldonia / Boogie thing / Good

morning little school girl / Oh baby you don't have to go / Help me / Fannie Mae / Hot and cold / Teeny weeny bit / Blow wind blow / How long can a fool go wrong
CD _____ NEXCD 123
Sequel / Jun '90 / BMG.

MIGHTY LONG TIME
Straighten up baby / Everything gonna be alright / Black nights / Blow wind blow / Sugar sweet / Moanin' at midnight / Baby please / Hold me in your arms / Call it stormy Monday / 300 pounds of joy / Northside cadillac / Mighty long time
CD _____ ANTCD 0015
Antones / Mar '91 / Hot Shot / Direct / ADA.

TAKE ME BACK
CD _____ CD 72587
Blind Pig / '88 / Hot Shot / Swift / CM / Roots / Direct / ADA.

Coughlan, Mary

LOVE FOR SALE
CD _____ FIENDCD 730
Demon / May '93 / Pinnacle / ADA.

LOVE ME OR LEAVE ME
Ancient rain / Double cross / I'd rather go blind / Invisible to you / Ride on / Leaf from a tree / Delaney's gone back on the wine / Sunday mornings / Red ribbon / Ice cream man / There is a bed / Francis of Assisi / Beach / Man of the world / Seduced / T'ain't nobody's business if I do / I get along without you very well / Handbags and gladrags / Whiskey didn't kill the pain
CD _____ 450994400G-2
WEA / Feb '94 / Warner Music.

SENTIMENTAL KILLER
There is a bed / Hearts / Magdalen laundry / Francis of Assisi / Love in a shadow / Ain't no cure for love / Handbags and gladrags / Just a friend of mine / Ballad of a sad young man / Not up to scratch / Sentimental killer
CD _____ 9032772752
WEA / Jun '92 / Warner Music.

TIRED AND EMOTIONAL
Double cross / Beach / Meet me where they play the blues / Delaney's gone back on the wind / Sense of silence (S.O.S) / Nobody's business - the tango / Mama just wants to barrelhouse all night long / Country fair dance (The cowboy song) / Lady in green / Seduced
CD _____ 242094 2
WEA / Mar '87 / Warner Music.

UNCERTAIN PLEASURES
Man of the world / I can dream, can't I / Whiskey didn't kill the pain / Leaf from a tree / Little death / Invisible to you / I get along without you very well / Heartbreak hotel / Red ribbon / Mother's little helper
CD _____ WX 333CD
WEA / Mar '90 / Warner Music.

UNDER THE INFLUENCE
Laziest girl / Ice cream van / Parade of clowns / My land is too green / Ride on / Good morning heartache / Fisheen only / A.W.O.L. / Dice / Don't smoke in bed / Blue surrender / Sunday morning / Copa
CD _____ 2421852
WEA / Feb '95 / Warner Music.

Coulibaly Brothers

ANKA DIA : SONGS & DANCES FROM BURKINA FASO
CD _____ AUB 006775
Auvidis/Ethnic / Apr '93 / Harmonia Mundi.

Coulter, Phil

AMERICAN TRANQUILITY
CD _____ KCD 376
Irish / Jul '95 / Target/BMG.

CLASSIC TRANQUILITY
CD _____ FSCD 001
Four Seasons / Jan '93 / Direct / ADA.

COLLECTION
CD _____ DINCD 2
Telstar / May '92 / BMG.

ESSENTIAL COLLECTION, THE
CD _____ KCD 367
Irish / Jul '95 / Target/BMG.

LIVE EXPERIENCE, THE
Steal away / Play away / Derry air / Old man / Mancini magic / Thiarna Dean Trocaire / Ballad of the William Bloat / I'll tell me Ma / Cal / Local hero / Hoedown / Bonny boy / Mid term break / Scorn not his simplicity / Ballad and blarney / Mo ghile mear / Miss eire / Town I loved so well
CD _____ KCD 379
Irish / Jan '96 / Target/BMG.

LOCAL HEROES
CD _____ RTECD 165
Four Seasons / Jan '95 / Direct / ADA.

PEACE AND TRANQUILITY
CD _____ FSCD 003
Four Seasons / Jan '93 / Direct / ADA.

PHIL COULTER'S CHRISTMAS
CD _____ FSCD 005
Four Seasons / Sep '94 / Direct / ADA.

SCOTTISH TRANQUILITY
Flower of Scotland / Skye boat song / Will ye no' come back again / Loch Lomond / Dark Island / I belong to Glasgow / Ye banks and braes o' bonnie Doon / Wild mountain thyme / Annie Laurie / Rowan tree / Lochnagar / Amazing grace / Eriskay love lilt/Westering home / Red red rose/Bonnie Mary of Argyll / No awa' tae bid awa'/Scotland the brave / Auld lang syne
CD _____ MCCD 071
Music Club / Jun '92 / Disc / THE / CM.

SEA OF TRANQUILITY
CD _____ FSCD 002
Four Seasons / Jan '93 / Direct / ADA.

SERENITY
CD _____ FSCD 004
Four Seasons / Jan '93 / Direct / ADA.

WORDS & MUSIC
CD _____ FSCD 007
Four Seasons / Sep '94 / Direct / ADA.

Count Basic

LIFE THINK IT OVER
Prelude / Is it real / All time high / Healer / M.L in the sunshine / Joy, peace and happiness / Animal print / Strange life / Hide and seek / Jazz in the house / So close / Walk tall
CD _____ SPR 30202
Spray / Oct '95 / EWM.

Count Bass-D

PRE-LIFE CRISIS
Dozens / Sandwiches (I got a feeling) / T-boz (part 1/2) / Shake / T-boz tried to talk to me / Carmex / I got needs / Broke Thursday / Agriculture / Brown / Hate game / Pink tornado / Sunday school / Baker's dozen
CD _____ 4783732
Columbia / Oct '95 / Sony.

Count Bishops

SPEEDBALL + 11
Route 66 / I ain't got you / Beautiful Delilah / Teenage letter / Cry to me / Buzz me babe / Sweet little sixteen / Honey I need / Carol / Don't start crying now / Mercy mercy / Reelin' and rockin' / Down the road again / I'm a man / I want candy
CD _____ CDWIKM 161
Chiswick / Nov '95 / Pinnacle.

Count Five

PSYCHOTIC REACTION
Double decker bus / Pretty big mouth / World / Psychotic reaction / Peace of mind / They're gonna get you / Morning after / Can't get your lovin' / You must believe me / Teeny bopper, teeny bopper / Merry go round / Contrast / Revelation in slow motion / Declaration of independence
CD _____ EDCD 225
Edsel / Oct '87 / Pinnacle / ADA.

Count Raven

DESTRUCTION OF THE VOID
Until death do us part / Hippies triumph / Destruction of the void / Let the dead bury the dead / Northern lights / Leaving the warzone / Angel of death / Final journey / On ones hero / Europa
CD _____ HELL019CD
Hellhound / Apr '94 / Plastic Head.

HIGH ON INFINITY
Jim / Children's holocaust / In honour / Madman from waco / Masters of all evil / Ode to Rebecca / High on infinity / Ordinary loser / Traitor / Dance / Coming / Lost world / Cosmos
CD _____ HELL 026
Hellhound / Apr '94 / Plastic Head.

STORM WARNING
Intro (Count Raven) / Inam naudemina / True revelation / In the name of rock 'n' roll / Sometimes a great nation / Within the garden of mirrors / Devastating age / How can it be / Social warfare
CD _____ HELL 009CD
Hellhound / Apr '94 / Plastic Head.

Counting Crows

AUGUST AND EVERYTHING AFTER
Round here / Omaha / Mr. Jones / Perfect blue buildings / Anna begins / Time and time again / Rain King / Sullivan Street / Ghost train / Raining in Baltimore / Murder of one
CD _____ GED 24528
Geffen / Feb '94 / BMG.

Country All Stars

JAZZ FROM THE HILLS
Stompin' at the Savoy / Tennessee rag / Do something / Indiana march / Sweet Georgia Brown / Midnight train / In a little Spanish town / My little girl / Lady in red / Mania / It goes like this / What's the reason I'm not pleasin' you / When it's darkness on the delta / Vacation train / Fiddle patch / Fiddle sticks
CD _____ BCD 15728
Bear Family / Oct '93 / Rollercoaster / Direct / CM / Swift / ADA.

Country Dance Kings

COUNTRY DANCE CLUB USA VOL.1
CD _____ 33012
Irish / Jun '95 / Target/BMG.

COUNTRY DANCE CLUB: DENIM DANCIN'
CD _____ 33112
Irish / Jun '95 / Target/BMG.

COUNTRY LINE DANCE
CD _____ 31422
Irish / Jun '95 / Target/BMG.

Country Gazette

HELLO OPERATOR
CD _____ FF 112CD
Flying Fish / Jul '92 / Roots / CM / Direct / ADA.

TRAITOR IN OUR MIDST/DON'T GIVE UP YOUR DAY JOB
Lost indian / Keep on pushin' / I wish you knew / Hot burrito breakdown / I might take you back again / Forget me not / Tried so hard / Anna / If you're ever gonna love me / Aggravation / Sound of goodbye / Swing low sweet chariot / Huckleberry hornpipe / Fallen eagle / I don't believe you met my baby / Deputy Dalton / Teach your children / My Oklahoma / Down the road / Winterwood / Honky cat / Snowball / Lonesome blues / Singin' all day and dinner on the ground
CD _____ BGOCD 298
Beat Goes On / Nov '95 / Pinnacle.

Country Gentlemen

COUNTRY GENTLEMEN FEAT. RICKY SKAGGS ON FIDDLE
Travelling kind / Souvenirs / Leaves that are green / Irish Spring / Home in Louisiana / City of New Orleans / House of the rising sun / Catfish John / Heartaches / One morning in May / Bringing Mary home / Welcome to New York
CD _____ VND 73123
Vanguard / Jun '90 / Complete/Pinnacle / Discovery.

COUNTRY SONGS OLD AND NEW
CD _____ SFCD 40004
Smithsonian Folkways / Dec '94 / ADA / Direct / Koch / CM / Cadillac.

SUGARHILL COLLECTION
CD _____ SHCD 2207
Sugarhill / Aug '95 / Roots / CM / ADA / Direct.

Country Teasers

COUNTRY TEASERS
CD _____ EFA 115942
Crypt / Apr '95 / SRD.

Counts

WHAT'S UP THE FRONT THAT - COUNTS
What's up front that counts / Rhythm changes / Thinking single / Why not start all over again / Pack of lies / Bills / Motor city / What's it all about
CD _____ CDSEWM 063
Southbound / Nov '94 / Pinnacle.

County, Jayne

DEVIATION
CD _____ CSA 105
RPM / Jul '95 / Pinnacle.

LET YOUR BACKBONE SLIP
Max's / Are you a boy or are you a boy / '28 Noel T Berlin / Lady Dye twist / Time machine (I wish I had) / Mr. Normal / Fun in Amerika / Where Queens collide (part 1) / No one woman can satisfy no one man all the time / Tomorrow is another day / Plain of nazca / I fell in love with a Russian soldier / Love lives in lies / Black black window / Midnight pal / Waiting for the marines / Bad in bed
CD _____ RPM 145
RPM / Jul '95 / Pinnacle.

PUNK COLLECTION, THE (From Sneakers To Stilettos) (County, Wayne & The Electric Chairs)
Eddie and Sheena / Rock 'n' roll Cleopatra / (If you don't want to fuck me) fuck off / Toilet love / Mean mutha fuckin' man / Night time / Trying to get on the radio / Evil minded momma / I had too much to dream last night / Crest / Waiting for the marines / Midnight pal / Berlin / Storm the gates of heaven / Cry of angels / Speed demon / Mr. Norman / Man enough to be a woman / To-morrow is another day / Wonder woman / Wall city girl / Boy with the stolen face / C3 / Think straight / Something new / Two years too late / Let them free / Hell (version) / Six guns / Now's the time
CD _____ RPM 119
RPM / Oct '93 / Pinnacle.

WAYNE COUNTY - ROCK 'N' ROLL CLEOPATRA (County, Wayne)
CD _____ RPM 119
RPM / Oct '93 / Pinnacle.

Courage Of Lassie

SING OR DIE
CD _____ TMCD 055
Third Mind / Oct '90 / Pinnacle / Third Mind.

THIS SIDE OF HEAVEN
CD _____ BBQCD 146
Beggars Banquet / Apr '94 / Warner Music / Disc.

Course Of Empire

INITIATION
Hiss / White vision blowout / Gear / Breed / Apparition / Infested / Invertebrate / Sacrifice / Minions / Initiation / Chiluahphile
CD _____ 72445110542
Zoo Entertainment / Aug '94 / BMG.

Cousin Joe

BAD LUCK BLUES
Boxcar shorty / Life is a one way ticket / Take a lesson from your teacher / Bad luck blues / I'm living on borrowed time / That's enough / Goin' down slow / Chicken and the hawk / Levee blues / Railroad porter blues / I don't want no second hand love / Tore down
CD _____ ECD 260462
Evidence / Mar '94 / Harmonia Mundi / ADA / Cadillac.

COMPLETE VOL.1 1945-47
CD _____ BMCD 6001
Blue Moon / Sep '95 / Magnum Music Group / Greensleeves / Hot Shot / ADA / Cadillac / Discovery.

COMPLETE VOL.2 1946-47, THE
CD _____ BMCD 6002
Blue Moon / Sep '95 / Magnum Music Group / Greensleeves / Hot Shot / ADA / Cadillac / Discovery.

Cousins, Dave

BRIDGE, THE (Cousins, Dave & Brian Willoughby)
CD _____ RGFCD 020
Road Goes On Forever / Aug '94 / Direct.

OLD SCHOOL SONGS (Cousins, Dave & Brian Willoughby)
CD _____ RGFCD 004
Road Goes On Forever / '92 / Direct.

Cousins, Roy

10 YEARS AFTER (Cousins, Roy & The Royals)
CD _____ TWCD 1005
Tamoki Wambesi / Aug '95 / Jetstar / SRD / Roots Collective / Greensleeves.

PICK UP THE PIECES (Cousins, Roy & The Royals)
CD _____ TWCD 1004
Tamoki Wambesi / Mar '94 / Jetstar / SRD / Roots Collective / Greensleeves.

Couturier, Francois

PASSAGIO
CD _____ LBLC 6543
Label Bleu / Jun '92 / New Note.

Couza, Jim

APPALACHIAN BEACH PARTY (Couza, Jim & Durberville)
CD _____ DRGNCD 922
Dragon / Jan '93 / Roots / Cadillac / Wellard / CM / ADA.

JUBILEE
Mississippi jubilee (year of jubilo) / You've joined our hearts / My old man / Invention No. 13 / Gallo del cielo / Cranes over Hiroshima / Puncheon floor (Oklahoma rooster) / St. Paul's song / Poor wayfaring stranger / There were roses / If you don't love your neighbour / Jubilee
CD _____ FSCD 6
Folksound / Aug '89 / Roots / CM.

MUSIC FOR THE HAMMERED DULCIMER
Jenny leid polka / Johnny get your hair cut / Intrada and Minuet / Londonderry Air / Maid at the spinning / Nola / High cauled cap / As I roved out / Miss Hamilton / Christine's Waltz / Bells of St. Mary's / Devil's dream / Enchanted valley / La belle Katherine / Harper's hornpipe / Swinging on a gate / Norwegian wood / Flower of England / Snowflake / Los ejes de mi carreta / Perfect cure me / Tripping round the marines / Peel the carrot / Take five
CD _____ CDSDL 335
Saydisc / Mar '94 / Harmonia Mundi / ADA / Direct.

OUT OF THE SHADOWLAND
Canon in D / Song of the whale / Falls of Richmond / Hard love / Kitchen girl / I'll tickle Nancy / Christmas factory / Forever / Green Willis / Out of the Shadowland / Concerto no. 1 / Jonah and the whale / Wish I could fall in love / William Tell overture / St. Francis prayer / Seek ye first
CD _____ FSCD 14
Folksound / Aug '94 / Roots / CM.

Covenant

SPECTRES AT THE FEAST
CD _____ COVCD 0002
Covenant / Nov '94 / Else.

Coverdale, David

WHITESNAKE/NORTHWINDS
Lady / Time on my side / Blindman / Goldies place / Whitesnake / Peace lovin' man / Sunny days / Hole in the sky / Celebration / Keep on giving me love / Northwinds / Give me kindness / Time and time again / Queen of hearts / Only my soul / Say you love me / Breakdown
CD _____ VSOPCD 118
Connoisseur / Nov '88 / Pinnacle.

Coverdale-Page

COVERDALE PAGE (Coverdale, David & Jimmy Page)
Shake my tree / Waiting on you / Take me for a little while / Pride and joy / Over now / Feeling hot / Easy does it / Take a look at yourself / Don't leave me this way / Absolution blues / Whisper a prayer for the dying
CD _____ CDEMD 1041
EMI / Jul '94 / EMI.

Covington, Robert

BLUES IN THE NIGHT
Trust in me / I just want to make love to you / Better watch your step / I Don't care / Playing on me / Blues in the night / I want to know / Mean mistreater / I want to thank ya
CD _____ ECD 260742
Evidence / Oct '95 / Harmonia Mundi / ADA / Cadillac.

Covington, Trisha

CALL ME
Why you wanna play me out / Same old thang / Slow down all in love is fair / So tight / Call me / Let's get it on / Bedtime / Don't leave me lonely / Givin' it up / Anything anytime / Why you wanna play me out (K's reprise)
CD _____ 4744732
Columbia / Jan '95 / Sony.

Coward, Sir·Noel

1928-38 CLASSIC RECORDINGS
CD _____ CDCHD 168
Happy Days / Jul '90 / Conifer.

I'LL SEE YOU AGAIN (His Greatest Recordings)
Could you please oblige me with a Bren Gun / Dearest love / Dream is over / I travel alone / I'll see you again / Imagine the duchess's feelings / Let's say goodbye / London pride / Lorelei / Lover of my dreams / Mad dogs and Englishmen / Mary Make-Believe / Most of ev'ry day / Mrs. Worthington / Medley (Parisian pierrot/Poor little rich girl/A room with a view/Dance, little lady) / Private lives (2 scenes) / Shadow play (scene) / Stately homes of England / We were dancing / Where are the songs we sung / World weary
CD _____ CDAJA 5126
Living Era / Mar '94 / Koch.

LIVE IN LAS VEGAS AND NEW YORK
CD _____ CD 47253
Sony Classical / Nov '91 / Sony.

LONDON PRIDE
Lorelei / Dream is over / Zigeuner / World weary / Let's say goodbye / We were dancing / Parisian Pierrot / Poor little rich girl / Room with a view / Dance little lady / Someday I'll find you / Any little fish / If you could only come with me / I'll see you again / London pride / Last time I saw Paris / Could you please oblige us with a bren gun / Imagine the Duchess's feelings / Private Lives / Shadowplay / Red peppers / Family album
CD _____ CDHD 216
Happy Days / Sep '93 / Conifer.

MASTER'S VOICE, THE (His HMV Recordings 1928-1953)
Room with a view / Dance little lady / Mary make-believe / Try to learn to love / Lorelei / Dream is over / Zigeuner / World weary / Private lives / Half caste woman / Any little fish / Cavalcade prologue / Cavalcade - vocal selection / Lover of my dreams / Cavalcade vocal selection part 2 / Cavalcade epilogue / Noel Coward medley part 1 / Noel Coward medley part 2 / Let's say goodbye / Party's over now / Something to do with Spring / Mad dogs and Englishmen / Medley / I'll follow my secret heart (pts 1 & 2) / Melanie's aria part 1 / Melanie's aria part 2 / I travel alone / Most of ev'ry day / Love in bloom / Fare thee well / Mrs. Worthington / We were so young / Then play, orchestra, play / You were there / Has anybody seen our ship / Man about town / Family album / Parisian Pierrot / We were dancing / Dearest love / Where are the songs we sung / Stately homes of England / Gypsy melody / Dearest love (Operetta) / I'll see you again / Just let me look at you / Poor little rich girl / London pride / Last time I saw Paris / Could you please oblige us with a bren gun / There have been songs

in England / Imagine the Duchess's feelings / It's only you / Don't let's be beastly to the Germans / Welcoming land / I'm old fashioned / You'd be so nice to come home to / Sigh no more ladies / I wonder what happened to him / Matelot / Nina / Never again / Wait a bit Joe / Bright was the day / This is a changing world / His excellency regrets / 1-2-3 / Uncle Harry / I never knew / I saw no shadow / Josephine / Don't make fun of the fair / Sail away / Why does love get in the way / I like America / Time and again / There are bad times just around the corner
CD Set _____ COWARD 1
EMI / Sep '92 / EMI.

MORE COMPACT COWARD
Room with a view / Shadow play / We were dancing / Something to do with Spring / I'll see you again / Poor little rich girl / Zigeuner / Stately homes of England / Dearest love / World weary / Uncle Harry / Half caste woman / Family album / Dance little lady / Don't let's be beastly to the Germans / Nina / Matelot / Don't make fun of the festival / Wait a bit Joe / Sail away
CD _____ CDEMS 1417
EMI / Aug '91 / EMI.

TOGETHER WITH MUSIC (Coward, Sir Noel & Mary Martin)
CD _____ CDXP 1103
DRG / '88 / New Note.

Cowboy Junkies

BLACKED EYED MAN
Southern rain / Oregon hill / This street, than man, this life / Horse in the country / If you were the woman, and I was the man / Murder, tonight, in the trailer park / Black eyed man / Winter's song / Last spike / Cowboy Junkies lament / Townes' blues / To live is to fly
CD _____ PD 90620
RCA / Feb '92 / BMG.

CAUTION HORSES, THE
Sun comes up, it's Tuesday morning / Cause cheap is how I feel / Thirty summers / Mariner's song / Powder finger / Where are you tonight / Witches / Rock and bird / Escape is so easy / You will be found again
CD _____ 74321 18357-2
RCA / Feb '94 / BMG.

TRINITY SESSION, THE
Mining for gold / I don't get it / To love is to bury / Dreaming my dreams with you / Postcard blues / Misguided angel / I'm so lonesome I could cry / 200 more miles / Sweet Jane / Walkin' after midnight / Blue moon revisited (song for Elvis) (CD only.) / Working on a building (CD only.)
CD _____ 74321 18356-2
RCA / Feb '94 / BMG.

Cowboy Killers

DAI LAUGHING
CD _____ DISC 9
Discipline / Jan '94 / Pinnacle.

Cowboy Mouth

LIFE AS A DOG
CD _____ MA 8
Marina / Jan '95 / SRD.

Cowdrey, Lewis

IT'S LEWIS
CD _____ ANT 0029CD
Antones / Jul '94 / Hot Shot / Direct / ADA.

Cowell, Henry

PIANO MUSIC
CD _____ SFCD 40801
Smithsonian Folkways / Jul '93 / ADA / Direct / Koch / CM / Cadillac.

Cowell, Stanley

BACK TO THE BEAUTIFUL
Theme for Ernie / Wall / It don't mean a thing if it ain't got that swing / But beautiful / Sylvia's place / Come Sunday (on CD only) / Carnegie six / St. Croix / Prayer for peach (on CD only) / Nightingale sang in Berkeley Square
CD _____ CCD 4396
Concord Jazz / Nov '89 / New Note.

SUCH GREAT FRIENDS (Cowell, Stanley, Billy Harper, Reggie Workman & Billy Hart)
Sweet song / Destiny is yours / Layla joy / East harlem nostalgia
CD _____ 66051008
Strata East / May '91 / New Note.

TRAVELLIN' MAN
CD _____ BLCD 760178
Black Lion / Mar '93 / Jazz Music / Cadillac / Wellard / Koch.

Cowie, Charlie

UNSQUARE DANCE
Le reel de grandmere / Centennial jig / Joys of Quebec / Paris waltz / American rag / Maitland River / Ned Kendall / Snowshoer / Spin and glow / McDowall's breakdown / Mamou two step / Coryn Street / Rocky

mountain / Kinloss clog / Cowal gathering / Duncan Johnstone / Silver spear / Salley Gardens / Jackie Coleman's / Knotted chord / Last cheater's waltz / Turnpike reek / Schottische / Lilting fisherman / Rose wood / Syracuse / Snug in the blanket / Spanish two step / Mouth of the tobique / Janet's piano lesson / Mrs. Forbes Leith / Little house on the hill / Paddy Carey's / Pet of the pipers / House in the garden / Rowe's division / Baker's breakdown
CD _____ LCM 5207
Lismor / '91 / Lismor / Direct / Duncans / ADA.

Cowlan, Paul F.

PAPER DEVILS & SPIRITS OF FIRE
CD _____ BRAM 199236-2
Brambus / Nov '93 / ADA / Direct.

SECOND CLASS HOTEL
CD _____ BRAM 198904-2
Brambus / Nov '93 / ADA / Direct.

Cows

OLD GOLD 1989-1991
CD _____ ARRCD 68011
Amphetamine Reptile / Jan '96 / SRD.

ORPHAN'S TRAGEDY
CD _____ ARRCD 55/335
Amphetamine Reptile / Sep '94 / SRD.

COWWS Quintet

GROOVES 'N' LOOPS
CD _____ FMPCD 59
FMP / Oct '94 / Cadillac.

Cox, Carl

CARL COX F.A.C.T. (2CD/2MC/3LP) (Various Artists)
Hot the heels of love / Late night / Secrets of meditation / Cactus / Ego acid / Hope / Orange theme / Amphetamine / Psycho trip / Elektra / Phat man / Like that / Drum / Singularity / Kosmos / Raz / Pulsar cycle / Fuzz (Not on LP) / Sacred circles (Not on LP) / First question (Not on LP) / Deep in you (Not on LP) / Phosphene (Not on LP) / Tonight (Not on LP) / No more worry (Not on LP) / Coda back again (Not on LP) / Torway (Not on LP) / Meet my modern (Not on LP)
CD Set _____ REACTCD 056
React / Feb '95 / Vital.

FANTAZIA III (Made In Heaven - The Carl Cox Remix) (Various Artists)
Montana (Let yourself go) / Natural high / Mayorca / Move on / Space / Musika / We gonna funk / Space child / Too high / Power of love / Time to let go / You got me / Free the feeling / In the machines / Let me see ya move / Big band / War path / Moon / Aah yeah
CD _____ FANTA 005CDR
Fantazia Music / Aug '94 / 3MV / Sony.

Cox, Deborah

DEBORAH COX
Sentimental / Who do U love / I'm your natural woman / Sound of my tears / Call me / My radio / Never gonna break my heart again / It could've been you / My first night with you / Just be good to me / Where do we go from here
CD _____ 74321325752
Arista / Nov '95 / BMG.

Cox, Derek

20 PIANO FAVOURITES (Cox, Derek & His Music)
As time goes by / One day I'll fly away / Canadian sunset / With one more look at you / Impossible dreams / Can't smile without you / Three times a lady / Eleanor Rigby / Michelle / With a little help from my friends / Memory / I know him so well / Serenata / Hello / Moonlight serenade / She's out of my life / Greensleeves / How deep is your love / I just called to say I love you / My way / Scarborough fair
CD _____ CDSIV 1126
Horatio Nelson / Jul '95 / THE / BMG / Avid / BMG / Koch.

MAGIC OF ANDREW LLOYD WEBBER
Phantom of the opera / All I ask of you / Music of the night / Memory / King Herod's song / Any dream will do / Jesus Christ superstar / I don't know how to love him / Don't cry for me Argentina / Mr. Mistoffelees / Starlight express / Close every door / I expected song
CD _____ CDSIV 1113
Horatio Nelson / Jul '95 / THE / BMG / Avid / BMG / Koch.

VIVA BRAZIL (Cox, Derek & his Bossa Nova Rhythm)
One Note Samba / Desafinado / Quiet nights and quiet stars / Once I Loved / So many stars / Wave / Someone to light up my life / Girl From Ipanema / How Insensitive / Dindi / Tristeza / Manha de carnival / Surfboard / Abanda / Meditation / Sheila's Theme / Just a little bossa nova / Samba d'Orpheus / Adieu Tristeza / Brazil
CD _____ CDSIV 1136

Horatio Nelson / Jul '95 / THE / BMG / Avid / BMG / Koch.

Cox Family

BEYOND THE CITY
CD _____ ROUCD 0327
Rounder / May '95 / CM / Direct / ADA / Cadillac.

EVERYBODY'S REACHING OUT FOR SOMEONE
Standing by the bedside of a neighbour / Look me up by the ocean door / Everybody's reaching out for someone / Little white washed chimney / Cry baby cry / I've got that old feeling / But I do / Why not confess / Pardon me / My favorite memory / When God dips his pen of love in my heart / Backroads
CD _____ CDROU 0297
Rounder / May '93 / CM / Direct / ADA / Cadillac.

Cox, Ida

I CAN'T QUIT MY MAN
CD _____ CDAFS 1015
Affinity / Sep '91 / Charly / Cadillac / Jazz Music.

IDA COX VOL. 1 1923
CD _____ DOCD 5322
Blues Document / Mar '95 / Swift / Jazz Music / Hot Shot.

IDA COX VOL. 2 1924-25
CD _____ DOCD 5323
Blues Document / Mar '95 / Swift / Jazz Music / Hot Shot.

IDA COX VOL. 3 1927-38
CD _____ DOCD 5324
Blues Document / Mar '95 / Swift / Jazz Music / Hot Shot.

IDA COX VOL. 4 1927-38
CD _____ DOCD 5325
Blues Document / Mar '95 / Swift / Jazz Music / Hot Shot.

Cox, Michael

JOE MEEK STORY VOL.4 - THE BEST OF MICHAEL COX
Angela Jones / Along came Caroline / Lonely road / Teenage love / Linda / Sweet little sixteen / Cover girl / Young only once / Honey 'cause I love you / Stand up / In April / Don't you break my heart / Hark is that a cannon I hear / I've been thinking / Say what a party / Say that again / Rave on / Just say hello / Gypsy / It ain't right
CD _____ NEXCD 243
Sequel / Nov '93 / BMG.

Coxhill, Lol

EAR OF BEHOLDER
Introduction / Hungerford / Deviation dance / Two little pigeons / Don Alfonso / Open Piccadilly / Feedback / How insensitive / Conversation / Mango walk / Piccadilly with hoofs / Rasa moods / Collective improvisation / I am the walrus / Rhythmic hooter / Lover man / Zoological fun / Little trip one shoot / Dat's why darkies were born / Series of superbly played mellotron codas
CD _____ SEECD 414
See For Miles/C5 / Oct '94 / Pinnacle.

HOLYWELL CONCERT, THE (Coxhill, Lol/Haslam/Rutherford/Riley)
CD _____ SLAMCD 302
Slam / '90 / Cadillac.

THREE BLOKES (Coxhill, Lol & Evan Parker/Steve Lacy)
CD _____ FMPCD 63
FMP / Oct '94 / Cadillac.

Coyne, Kevin

ADVENTURES OF CRAZY FRANK, THE
Born crazy / Drunk again / Moon madness / You're so wonderful / Crazy dream / Devil calling / Married / Deep the darkness / I stood up / Playing the fool / Heart of hearts / Perversion / Frankies dream No.1 / Frankies dream No.2 / Time for tears / Blast of glory / Never ending
CD _____ CD 388701742
Rockport / Oct '95 / Pinnacle.

BURSTING BUBBLES
Only one / Children's crusade / No melody / Learn to swim - learn to drown / Mad boy No. 2 / Dark dance hall / I don't know what to do / Little piece of heaven / Day to day / Golden days / Old fashioned love song
CD _____ CDV 2152
Virgin / Jun '91 / EMI.

CASE HISTORY ...PLUS
God bless the bride / White horse / Uggy's song / Need somebody / Evil island home / Araby / My message to the people / Mad boy / Sand all yellow / I'm all aching / Leopard never changes it's spots
CD _____ SEECD 410
See For Miles/C5 / Sep '94 / Pinnacle.

COMPLETE PEEL SESSIONS: KEVIN COYNE
Marlene / Cheat me / Evil island home / Miner's song / Ey up me duck / Do not shout

at me father / Need somebody / Poor swine / Rivers of blood / That's rock'n'roll / Leopard never changes it's spots / I couldn't love you
CD _____ SFRCD 112
Strange Fruit / Jul '90 / Pinnacle.

DYNAMITE DAZE
Dynamite daze / Brothers of mine / Lunatic / Are we dreaming / Take me back to Dear old Blighty / I really live round here (false friends) / I am / Amsterdam / I only want to see you smile / Juliet and Mark / Woman, woman, woman / Cry / Dance of Bourgeoise
CD _____ CDV 2096
Virgin / Jun '91 / EMI.

ELVIRA: SONGS FROM THE ARCHIVES 1979-83
Stand up for England / I'm a girl / Debutante / Leopard never changes it's spots / Golden days / Bad boys / Long arm of the law / Think of sunshine / Elvira / Better than you / North / Born in 1944 / Blood in the night / Rambling Germany blues / Bimbo / Up
CD _____ GH 70122
Golden Hind / Mar '95 / Voice Print.

EVERYBODY'S NAKED
Millionaires song / I couldn't love you / Not the way / We don't talk too much / Here comes the morning / City crazy / Take me back in your arms / Last time blues / Slave / Old hippie / Radio / Everybody's naked (in their way)
CD _____ IMC 57218023CK
Zabo / Nov '94 / Vital.

LEGLESS IN MANILA
Big money man / Gina's song / Money machine / Raindrop on the river / Nigel in Napoli / Zoo wars / Black cloud / Legless in Manila / Don't raise an argument / Cycling
CD _____ GH 70062
Golden Hind / Nov '94 / Voice Print.

MARJORY RAZORBLADE
Marjory Razorblade / Marlene / Talking to no one / Eastbourne ladies / Old soldier / I want my crown / Nasty, lonesome valley / House on the hill / Cheat me / Jack and Edna / Everybody says / Mummy / Heaven in my view / Karate king / Dog Latin / This is Spain / Chairman's ball / Good boy / Chicken wing
CD _____ CDVM 2501
Virgin / Sep '90 / EMI.

MATCHING HEAD AND FEET
Saviour / Lucy / Lonely lovers / Sunday morning sunrise / Rock 'n' roll hymn / Mrs. Hooley go home / It's not me / Turpentine / Tulip / One fine day
CD _____ CDV 2033
Virgin / Jun '91 / EMI.

POINTING THE FINGER
There she goes / As I recall / Children of the deaf / One little moment / Let love reside / Sleeping, waking / Pointing the finger / You can't do that / Song of the womb / Old lady
CD _____ MAUCD 640
Mau Mau / Aug '94 / Pinnacle.

RABBITS (Coyne, Kevin & Siren)
Stride / Mandy Lee / Marilyn / Why why why / Cheat me / Whole lotta shakin' goin' on / Flowering cherry / Trouble in mind / God bless the bride / Bottle up and go / Blues before sunrise / I need you / John the baptist / Lunatic laughs / Big pistol Mama / Hot potato / Start walking / Let's dance / Forked lightening / Wait until dark
CD _____ DJC 001
Voice Point / Oct '94 / Voice Print.

ROMANCE ROMANCE (Coyne, Kevin & The Paradise Band)
Ready for love / Happy, happy / Chances / It's all over / Seventeenth Floor / Theresa / No kindness, no pity / Heaven song / Lovers and friends / Wild eyes / Best friend / Impossible child / Neighbourhood girl
CD _____ SPV 8492602
Voice Point / Dec '94 / Voice Print.

SIGN OF THE TIMES
CD _____ CDVM 9029
Virgin / Aug '92 / EMI.

STUMBLING ONTO PARADISE
I'm still here / Pack of lies / How is your luck / Sunshine home / Tear me up / No revolution / Victoria smiles / Charming / Winter into summer / Love for five minutes / Back home boogie
CD _____ GH 70102
Golden Hind / Nov '94 / Voice Print.

TOUGH AND SWEET
Little Miss Dynamite / Precious love / Burning head II / Really in love / Ponytail song / Elvis is dead / Totally naked II / Walls have ears / Baby blue / Talking money / Slow burner / All the loving / No lullabies / It's amazing II / Tell me Tony / Now's the time / Getting old / Some day / Love and money / Let's get romantic / Creeper
CD _____ GH 70092
Golden Hind / Jun '94 / Voice Print.

WILD TIGER LOVE (Coyne, Kevin & The Paradise Band)
Bungalow / Sensual / Cafe crazy / Looking in your eyes / Open up the gates / Go Sally go / American girls / Fish brain / Fooled

again / Don't you look (that way) / Raindrops on the window / Passions pleasure
CD _____ CD 3887001240
Golden Hind / Oct '94 / Voice Print.

Cozens, Chris

SYNTHESIZER GREATEST HITS
Eve of the war / Chariots of fire / Oxygene / Axel F / Crockett's theme / Magic fly / Autobahn / Telstar / Toccata / Chung kuo / Tokyo rendezvous / Miami Vice / Pulstar / Love theme from Bladerunner / Equinoxe / Birdland / Sweet lullaby (CD only) / Moments in love (OD only) / Friends of Mr. Cairo (CD only)
CD _____ CDMFP 6134
Music For Pleasure / Sep '94 / EMI.

Crack

SO 92
Happy birthday / For he's a jolly good fellow / For she's a jolly good lady / Auld lang syne / Congratulations / Happy anniversary / Christmas megamix / Irish national anthem / Number one (jingle)
CD _____ SUNCD 5
Sound / Sep '94 / Direct / ADA.

Cracker

CRACKER
Teen angst (what the world needs now) / Happy birthday to me / This is cracker soul / I see the light / St. Cajetan / Mr. Wrong / Someday / Can I take my gun to heaven / Satisfy you / Another song about the rain / Don't fuck me up (with peace and love) / Dr. Bernice
CD _____ CDVUS 48
Virgin / Apr '92 / EMI.

KEROSENE HAT
Low / Movie star / Get off this / Kerosene hat / Take me down to the infirmary / Nostalgia / Sweet potato / Sick of goodbyes / I want everything / Lonesome Johnny blues / Let's go for a ride / Loser / Hi-desert biker meth lab / Euro-trash girl / I ride my bike / Kerosene hat (Accoustic)
CD _____ CDVU 67
Virgin / Jun '94 / EMI.

Crackerbash

TIN TOY
CD _____ EFA 11397CD
Musical Tragedies / Aug '93 / SRD.

Craddock, Billy Crash

WELL DON'T YOU KNOW
Sweet pie / School day dreams / Lulu Lee / Ah poor little baby / I miss you so much / Blabbermouth / Am I to be the one / Sweetie Pie / Well don't you know / Boom boom baby / Don't destroy me (What makes you) / Treat me like you do / I want it / Since she turned seventeen / All I want is you / Letter of love / One last kiss / Is it true or is it false / Report card of love / Heavenly love / Goodtime Billy
CD _____ BCD 15610
Bear Family / Jun '92 / Rollercoaster / Direct / CM / Swift / ADA.

Cradle Of Filth

PRINCIPLE OF EVIL MADE FLESH
CD _____ NIHIL 1CD
Vinyl Solution / Mar '94 / Disc.

Cradle Of Spoil

SOLAR ECLIPSE
CD _____ EFA 125192
Celtic Circle / Apr '95 / SRD.

Craig, Carl

LANDCRUISING
CD _____ 4509998652
Blanco Y Negro / Apr '95 / Warner Music.

Craig, Cathryn

PORCH SONGS
CD _____ GOLDCD 001
Goldrush / Jul '95 / Direct.

Craig, Sara

SWEET EXHAUST
CD _____ 0072112ATT
Edel / Jul '95 / Pinnacle.

Crain

HEATER
Foot sanding / Save me your head / Valium and alcohol / Waste kings / Blistering / Knock your daylights out / Hey cops / Bricks / One who hangs / Broken heart of a neutron star
CD _____ 72751-2
Restless / Apr '94 / Vital.

Cramer, Floyd

JUST ME AND MY PIANO
Root beer rag / Time in a bottle / For the good times / Last date / Always on my mind / Blue eyes cryin' in the rain / It was almost

like a song / Homecoming / Hank Williams tribute / Your cheatin' heart / You win again / I'm so lonesome I could cry / Why don't you love me / Jambalaya / I saw the light / T.D.'s boogie woogie / Georgia on my mind
CD _____ SORCD 0032
D-Sharp / Oct '94 / Pinnacle.

KING OF COUNTRY PIANO
CD _____ PWKS 4222
Carlton Home Entertainment / Nov '94 / Carlton Home Entertainment.

Cramps

DATE WITH ELVIS, A
How far can too far go / Hot pearl snatch / People ain't no good / What's inside a girl / Kizmiaz / Cornfed dames / Chicken / Womanneed / Aloha from hell / It's just that song
CD _____ CDWIK 46
Big Beat / Apr '86 / Pinnacle.

FLAMEJOB
Mean machine / Ultra twist / Let's get fucked up / Nest of cuckoo birds / I'm customized / Sado county auto show / Naked girl falling down the stairs / How come you do me / Upside down and upside down / Trapped love / Swing the big eyed rabbit / Strange love / Blues blues blues / Sinners / Route 66
CD _____ CRECD 170
Creation / Oct '94 / 3MV / Vital.

OFF THE BONE
Human fly / Way I walk / Domino / Surfin' bird / Lonesome town / Garbage man / Fever / Drug train / Love me / I can't hardly stand it / Goo goo muck / She said / Crusher / Save it / New kind of kick
CD _____ ILPCD 12
IRS / Jan '87 / PolyGram / BMG / EMI.

ROCKINN-REELININAUCKLANDNEWZEALANDXXX
Hot pearl snatch / People ain't no good / What's inside a girl / Cornfed Dames / Sunglasses after dark / Heartbreak Hotel / Chicken / Do the clam / Aloha from Hell / Can your pussy do the dog / Blue moon baby / Georgia Lee Brown / Lonesome town
CD _____ CDWIKD 132
Big Beat / Aug '94 / Pinnacle.

SMELL OF FEMALE
Most exalted potentate of love / You got good taste / Call of the wig hat / Faster pussycat / I ain't nothin' but a gorehound / Psychotic reaction
CD _____ CDWIKM 95
Big Beat / Feb '91 / Pinnacle.

STAY SICK
Bop pills / God damn rock 'n' roll / Bikini girls with machine guns / All women are bad / Creature from the black leather lagoon / Shortnin' bread / Daisys up your butterfly / Everything goes / Journey to the center of a girl / Mama oo pow pow / Saddle up a buzz buzz / Mule skinner blues / Her love rubbed off (CD only)
CD _____ CDWIKD 126
Big Beat / Jan '94 / Pinnacle.

Cran

CROOKED STAIR
CD _____ CBM 002CD
Cross Border Media / Oct '93 / Direct / ADA.

Cranberries

EVERYBODY ELSE IS DOING IT, SO WHY CAN'T WE
CD _____ CID 8003
Island / Feb '94 / PolyGram.

EVERYBODY ELSE IS DOING IT, SO WHY CAN'T WE/NO NEED TO ARGUE (2CD Set)
I still do / Dreams / Sunday / Pretty / Waltzing back / Not sorry / Linger / Wanted / Still can't... / I will always / How / Put me down / Ode to my family / I can't be with you / Twenty one / Zombie / Empty / Everything I said / Icicle melts / Disappointment / Ridiculous thoughts / Dreaming my dreams / Yeats' grave / Daffodil lament / No need to argue
CD Set _____ ISDCD 1
Island / Nov '95 / PolyGram.

NO NEED TO ARGUE
Ode to my family / I can't be with you / Twenty one / Zombie / Empty / Everything I said / Icicle melts / Disappointment / Ridiculous thoughts / Dreaming my dreams / Yeats grave / Daffodils lament / No need to argue
CD _____ CID 8029
Island / Aug '94 / PolyGram.

Crane

345S
CD _____ ELM 7CD
Elemental / Jan '93 / Disc.

Crane River Jazz Band

GREAT BRITISH TRADITIONAL JAZZBANDS VOL.5

Balling the Jack / Maryland my Maryland / After dark / Moose march / Canal street blues / Down by the riverside / Winnin' boy blues / You tell me your dream / Tishomingo blues / When I leave the world behind / Saturday night function / Ain't gonna give nobody none of my jellyroll / I'm travelling / Washington and Lee swing / South
CD _____ LACD 57
Lake / Dec '95 / Target/BMG / Jazz Music / Direct / Cadillac / ADA.

Crane, Tony

FEEL LIKE DANCING
CD _____ DLD 1020
Dance & Listen / '92 / Savoy.

GEE BUT IT'S GOOD
CD _____ DLD 1036
Dance & Listen / May '93 / Savoy.

Cranes

FOREVER
Forever / Cloudless / Jewel / Far away / Adrift / Clear / Sun and sky / And ever / Golden / Rainbows
CD _____ DEDCD 009
Dedicated / Apr '93 / Vital.

LOVED
CD _____ DEDCD 016
Dedicated / Sep '94 / Vital.

SELF NON SELF
CD _____ DEDCD 006
Dedicated / Jun '92 / Vital.

Cranioclast

ICONCLASTER
CD _____ EEE 09CD
Musica Maxima Magnetica / Sep '93 / Plastic Head.

Cranitch, Matt

ANY OLD TIME
CD _____ CLUNCD 047
Mulligan / Oct '83 / CM / ADA.

IRISH FIDDLE BOOK, THE
CD _____ OSS 4CD
Ossian / Jan '87 / ADA / Direct / CM.

SMALL ISLAND, A (Cranitch, Milne & Sullivan)
CD _____ OSS 70CD
Ossian / Dec '94 / ADA / Direct / CM.

TAKE A BOW
CD _____ CDOSS 05
Ossian / Apr '93 / ADA / Direct / CM.

Craobh Rua

MORE THAT'S SAID THE LESS THE BETTER
CD _____ CDLDL 1215
Klub / Jul '94 / CM / Ross / Duncans / ADA.

Crary, Dan

JAMMED IF I DO
CD _____ SH 3824CD
Sugarhill / Oct '94 / Roots / CM / ADA / Direct.

LADY'S FANCY
Huckleberry hornpipe / Lime rock / If the devil dreamed about playing flamenco / With a flatpick / Jenny's waltz / Sally Goodin / Julie's reel / Dill pickle rag / Pretty little liddian / Grey eagle / Lady's fancy
CD _____ ROUCD 0099
Rounder / Dec '94 / Direct / ADA / Cadillac.

TAKE A STEP OVER
Bugle call rag / Take a step over / Great tunes/Dumb names medley / Raleigh and special / Come hither / Willow, the wandering gypsy / Hot canary / Traditional suite in "E" medley / Lord build me a cabin
CD _____ SHCD 3770
Sugarhill / Jan '89 / Roots / CM / ADA / Direct.

THUNDERATION
Banderilla / Depoe Bay / West O' the moon / Amsterdance / Songs of Makoraka-o / Thunderation / Lady's fantasy / Lime rock / Andante in steel / Denouement
CD _____ SHCD 1135
Sugarhill / '91 / Roots / CM / ADA / Direct.

Crash Test Dummies

GHOST THAT HAUNTS ME, THE
Winter song / Comin' back song (The bereft man's song) / Superman's song / Country life / Here on earth (I'll have my cake) / Ghost that haunts me / Thick necked man / Androgynous / Voyage / At my funeral
CD _____ 74321283342
RCA / Aug '95 / BMG.

GOD SHUFFLED HIS FEET
God shuffled his feet / Afternoons and coffeespoons / Mmm mmm mmm mmm / In the days of the cinema / Swimming in your ocean / Here I stand before me / I think I've disappeared / How does a duck know /

When I go out with artists / Psychic / Two knights and maidens / Untitled
CD _____ 74321 20152-2
RCA / May '94 / BMG.

Crash Worship

ASESINOS
CD _____ RUSCD 8212
Roir USA / Jul '95 / Plastic Head.

Crass

BEST BEFORE 1984
CD _____ CRASS 5CD
Crass / Oct '90 / SRD.

CHRIST THE ALBUM
CD _____ BOLLOX2U2 CD
Crass / Oct '90 / SRD.

FEEDING OF THE 5,000
CD _____ 621984 CD
Crass / Oct '90 / SRD.

PENIS ENVY
CD _____ 321984 CD
Crass / Oct '90 / SRD.

STATIONS OF THE CRASS
Stations of the crass / Mother Earth / White punks on hope / You've got big hands / Darling / System / Bigman / Hurry up Gary / Gas man cometh / Democrats / Contaminational power / Time out / I ain't thick, it's just a trick / Fun going on / Crutch of society / Heard too much about / Chairman of the board / Tired / Walls / Upright citizen / System (2) / Big man / Banned from the Roxy / Hurry up Gary (2) / Middle class, working class / Fight war, not wars / Shaved women / Fun going on (2) / Unknown songs / Do they owe us a living / Punk is dead
CD _____ 521984 CD
Crass / Oct '90 / SRD.

YES SIR I WILL
CD _____ 121984/2 CD
Crass / Oct '90 / SRD.

Craven, Beverley

BEVERLEY CRAVEN
Promise me / Holding on / Woman to woman / Memory / Castle in the clouds / You're not the first / Joey / Two of a kind / I listen to the rain / Missing you
CD _____ 4670532
Epic / Jul '90 / Sony.

LOVE SCENES
Love scenes / Love is the light / Look no further / Mollie's song / In those days / Feels like the first time / Blind faith / Lost without you / Winner takes it all
CD _____ 474517-2
Epic / Sep '93 / Sony.

Craw

CRAW
CD _____ CHK 002
Choke Inc. / Feb '94 / SRD.

Crawdaddys

CRAWDADDY EXPRESS
I'm a lover not a fighter / You can't judge a book by the cover / Down the road apiece / Let's make it / Raining in my heart / I'm movin' on / Mystic eyes / Oh baby doll / Bald headed woman / Come see me / Got you in my soul / Times are getting tougher than tough / Down in the bottom / Crawdaddy Express / I wanna put a tiger in your tank
CD _____ VOXXCD 2001
Voxx / Oct '94 / Else / Disc.

HERE TIS
CD _____ VOXXCD 2046
Voxx / Oct '94 / Else / Disc.

Crawford, Hank

SOUTH CENTRAL
Falling in love with love / I should care / South Central / I want to talk about you / In a mellow tone / Conjunction Mars / Fool that I am / Splanky / O holy night
CD _____ MCD 9201
Milestone / Oct '93 / Jazz Music / Pinnacle / Wellard / Cadillac.

Crawford, Hugh

READY OR NOT
CD _____ DIVCD 04
Diverse / Nov '94 / Grapevine.

Crawford, Johnny

BEST OF JOHNNY CRAWFORD
Cindy's birthday / Rumours / Your nose is gonna grow / Proud / Patti Ann / Daydreams / Cindy's gonna cry / Just woke me / Janie please believe me / What happened to Janie / Lonesome town / Lucky star / Devil or angel / Sandy / Debbie / Your love is growing old / That's all I want from you / Cry on my shoulder / I don't need you / Mr. Blue / Girl next door (Once upon a time) / We belong together / No one really loves a clown / Sittin' and watchin'
CD _____ CDCHD 429

Crawford, Kevin

'D' FLUTE ALBUM
CD _____ KBSCD 77
Kerbstone / Oct '94 / Direct / ADA.

Crawford, Michael

EFX
CD _____ TCD 2810
Telstar / Dec '95 / BMG.

LOVE SONGS
CD _____ TCD 2748
Telstar / Nov '94 / BMG.

MICHAEL CRAWFORD - STAGE AND SCREEN
West Side story / What'll I do / Unexpected song / If loved you / Before the parade passes by / When you wish upon a star / In the still of the night / Memory / Not a day goes by / Bring him home / You'll never walk alone
CD _____ CDSR 060
Telstar / Aug '94 / BMG.

PERFORMS ANDREW LLOYD WEBBER
CD _____ TCD 2544
Telstar / Nov '91 / BMG.

TOUCH OF MUSIC IN THE NIGHT, A
CD _____ TCD 2676
Telstar / Oct '93 / BMG.

WITH LOVE
CD _____ CDSR 061
Telstar / Aug '94 / BMG.

Crawford, Randy

ABSTRACT EMOTIONS
Can't stand the pain / Actual emotional love / World of fools / Betcha / Higher than anyone can count / Desire / Getting away with murder / Overnight / Almaz / Don't wanna be normal
CD _____ 925423 2
WEA / Jul '86 / Warner Music.

DON'T SAY IT'S OVER
I'm glad there is you / Love's mystery / Can we bring it back / Keep me loving you / In my life / Elusive boogie / Mad over you / Why can't we take a chance / Year after year / Don't say it's over
CD _____ 936245381-2
WEA / Nov '93 / Warner Music.

EVERYTHING MUST CHANGE
Everything must change / I let you walk away / I'm easy / I had to see you one more time / I've never been to me / Don't let me down / Something so right / Soon as I touched him / Only your love lasts / Gonna give lovin a try
CD _____ 7599273072
WEA / Feb '92 / Warner Music.

MISS RANDY CRAWFORD
Hallelujah glory hallelujah / I can't get you off my mind / I'm under the influence of you / Over my head / Desperado / Take it away from her (put it on me) / Single woman, married man / Half steppin' / This man / At last
CD _____ 7599265672
WEA / Feb '93 / Warner Music.

NAKED AND TRUE
Cajun moon / Give me the night / Glow of love / Purple rain / Forget me nots / I'll be around / Joy inside my tears / Come into my life / What a difference a day makes / Holding back the years / All the king's horses
CD _____ 0630109612
WEA / Jul '95 / Warner Music.

NIGHTLINE
Happy feet / This old heart of mine / Lift me up / Ain't no foolin' / Go on and live it up / Nightline / Living on the outside / Why / Bottom line / In real life
CD _____ 923976 2
WEA / May '87 / Warner Music.

NOW WE MAY BEGIN
Now we may begin / Blue flame / When your life was low / Last night at danceland / Tender falls the rain / One day I'll fly away / Same old story (same old song)
CD _____ 759923412
WEA / Feb '92 / Warner Music.

RAW SILK
I stand accused / Declaration of love / Someone to believe in / Endlessly / Love is like a newborn child / Where there was darkness / Nobody / I hope you'll be very unhappy without me / I got myself a happy song / Just to keep you satisfied / Blue mood
CD _____ 7599273862
WEA / Feb '93 / Warner Music.

RICH AND POOR
Knockin' on heaven's door / Every kinda people / Wrap U up / This is love / Seperate lives / Believe that love can change the world / Rich and poor / Cigarette in the rain / Love is / I don't feel much like crying / All it takes is love
CD _____ 9260022
WEA / Oct '89 / Warner Music.

Crawford, Ray

SMOOTH GROOVE
CD _____ CCD 9028
Candid / May '89 / Cadillac / Jazz Music / Wellard / Koch.

Crawford, Stephanie

TIME FOR LOVE, A (Crawford, Stephanie & Michel Graillier)
CD _____ BBRC 9103
Big Blue / Nov '92 / Harmonia Mundi.

Crawley

SUPERSONIC
CD _____ SPV 08436202
SPV / Oct '94 / Plastic Head.

Crawlpappy

DELUXE
CD _____ WB2-094CD
We Bite / Nov '92 / Plastic Head.

Cray, Robert

BAD INFLUENCE (Cray, Robert Band)
Phone booth / Grinder / Got to make a comeback / So many women, so little time / Where do I go from here / Waiting for a train / March on / Don't touch me / No big deal / Bad influence
CD _____ 8302452
Mercury / Jul '93 / PolyGram.

DON'T BE AFRAID OF THE DARK (Cray, Robert Band)
Don't be afraid of the dark / Your secret's safe with me / Acting this way / Don't you even come / I can't go home / Across the line
CD _____ 8349232
Mercury / Aug '88 / PolyGram.

FALSE ACCUSATIONS (Cray, Robert Band)
Porch light / Change of heart, change of mind / She's gone / Playin' in the dirt / I've slipped her mind / False accusations / Last time / Payin' for it now / Sonny
CD _____ 8302462
Mercury / Jul '93 / PolyGram.

I WAS WARNED
CD _____ 512 721 2
Mercury / Jan '93 / PolyGram.

MIDNIGHT STROLL (Cray, Robert Band & Memphis Horns)
CD _____ 8466522
Mercury / Sep '90 / PolyGram.

SCORE, THE (Charly Blues - Masterworks Vol. 16)
Too many cooks / Score / Welfare / That's what I'll do / I'd rather be a wino / Who's been talkin' / Sleeping in the ground / I'm gonna forget about you / Nice as a fool can be / If I'm thinkin' what I'm thinkin'
CD _____ CDBM 16
Charly / Apr '92 / Charly / THE / Cadillac.

SHAME & SIN
CD _____ 518517-2
Mercury / Oct '93 / PolyGram.

STRONG PERSUADER (Cray, Robert Band)
Smoking gun / I guessed I showed her / Right next door (because of me) / Nothin' but a woman / Still around / More than I can stand / Foul play / Ronettes / Fantasized / New blood
CD _____ 830 568-2
Mercury / Nov '86 / PolyGram.

TOO MANY COOKS
Too many cooks / Score / When the welfare turns it back on you / That's what I'll do / I'd rather be a wino / Who's been talkin' / Sleeping in the ground / I'm gonna forget

about you / Nice as a fool can be / If you're thinkin' what I'm thinkin'
CD _____ 2696532
Tomato / Oct '91 / Vital.

Crayton, Pee Wee

THINGS I USED TO DO
CD _____ VND 6566
Vanguard / Oct '95 / Complete/Pinnacle / Discovery.

Crazy

CRAZIAH THAN EVER
CD _____ JW 056CD
Soca / Feb '94 / Jetstar.

CRAZY FOR YOU
CD _____ JW 067CD
JW / Feb '95 / Jetstar.

Crazy Alice

WHEEL
CD _____ EVRCD 14
Eve / Nov '92 / Grapevine.

Crazy Backward Alphabet

CRAZY BACKWARD ALPHABET
Blood and the ink / Det Enda Raka / Get it you / Welfare elite / Ghosts / Lobster on the rocks / Sarayushka (La Grange) / Dropped D / Book of Joel / Bottoms up / We are in control / Maran II
CD _____ SST 110 CD
SST / May '93 / Plastic Head.

Crazy Cavan

COOL AND CRAZY
CD _____ 107352
Musidisc / Mar '94 / Vital / Harmonia Mundi / ADA / Cadillac / Discovery.

HEY, TEENAGER
CD _____ 107332
Musidisc / Mar '94 / Vital / Harmonia Mundi / ADA / Cadillac / Discovery.

ROLLIN' THROUGH THE NIGHT
CD _____ 107342
Musidisc / Mar '94 / Vital / Harmonia Mundi / ADA / Cadillac / Discovery.

ROUGH, TOUGH & READY
CD _____ 107072
Musidisc / Mar '94 / Vital / Harmonia Mundi / ADA / Cadillac / Discovery.

Crazy Horse

CRAZY HORSE
Gone dead train / Dance, dance, dance / Look at all the things / beggar's day / I don't want to talk about it / Carolay / Dirty, dirty / Nobody / I'll get by / Crow Lady Jane
CD _____ 759926808-2
Reprise / Apr '94 / Warner Music.

LEFT FOR DEAD
CD _____ SERV 009CD
World Service / Nov '89 / Vital.

Creach, Papa John

I'M THE FIDDLE MAN
CD _____ OW 30004
One Way / Jul '94 / Direct / ADA.

ROCK FATHER
CD _____ OW 30005
One Way / Jul '94 / Direct / ADA.

Cream

ALTERNATIVE ALBUM, THE
CD _____ ITM 960002
ITM / Oct '92 / Tradelink / Koch.

CREAM BOX SET
CD Set _____ CR 1
UFO / Oct '92 / Pinnacle.

CREAM LIVE VOL. 2
Deserted cities of the heart / White room / Politician / Tales of brave Ulysses / Sunshine of your love / Steppin' out
CD _____ 8236612
Polydor / May '88 / PolyGram.

DESERTED CITIES (THE CREAM COLLECTION)
Wrapping paper / Sittin' on top of the world / Passing on the time / NSU / Swlabr / Deserted cities of the heart / Anyone for tennis / Born under a bad sign / Dreaming / Take it back / Dance the night away / Toad / Tales of brave Ulysses (Live) / I feel free
CD _____ PWKS 4127P
Carlton Home Entertainment / Oct '92 / Carlton Home Entertainment.

DISRAELI GEARS
Strange brew / Sunshine of your love / World of pain / Dance the night away / Blue condition / Tales of brave Ulysses / We're going wrong / Outside woman blues / Take it back / Mother's lament
CD _____ 8236362
Polydor / Nov '90 / PolyGram.

FRESH CREAM
CD _____ 8275762
Polydor / Nov '90 / PolyGram.

VERY BEST OF CREAM, THE
White room / I feel free / Tales of brave Ulysses / I'm so glad / Toad / Sunshine of your love / Strange brew / NSU / Born under a bad sign / Badge / Crossroads
CD _____ 523752-2
PolyGram / Jan '95 / PolyGram.

WHEELS OF FIRE (In The Studio - Live At The Fillmore)
CD Set _____ 8275782
Polydor / Nov '90 / PolyGram.

Cream 8

EMERALD TOUCH, THE
CD _____ SPV 08423622
SPV / May '95 / Plastic Head.

Creaming Jesus

TOO FAT TO RUN, TO STUPID TO HIDE
CD _____ FREUDCD 36
Jungle / Dec '90 / Disc.

Creation

HOW DOES IT FEEL TO FEEL
How does it feel to feel / Life is just beginning / Through my eyes / Ostrich man / I am the walker / Tom / Tom / Girls are naked / Painter man / Try and stop me / Biff bang pow / Making time / Cool jerk / For all that I am / Nightmares / Midway down / Can I join your band
CD _____ EDCD 106
Edsel / Aug '90 / Pinnacle / ADA.

LAY THE GHOST
CD _____ COCRD 001
Cohesion / Oct '93 / Grapevine.

MARK 4/THE CREATION (Mark Four/Creation)
CD _____ 842058
EVA / May '94 / Direct / ADA.

PAINTER MAN
CD _____ NESTCD 904
Demon / Apr '93 / Pinnacle / ADA.

Creation Of Death

PURIFY YOUR SOUL
CD _____ CDFLAG 62
Music For Nations / Sep '91 / Pinnacle.

Creation Rebel

HISTORIC MOMENTS VOL II
CD _____ ONUCD 74
On-U Sound / Mar '95 / SRD / Jetstar.

HISTORIC MOMENTS VOLUME 1 (Dub From Creation/Rebel Vibrations)
CD _____ ONUCD 72
On-U Sound / Jul '94 / SRD / Jetstar.

LOWS AND HIGHS
Independent man / Rebel party / Reasoning / No peace / Love I can feel / Rubber skirt / Creation rebel / Creative involvements
CD _____ CDBRED 33
Cherry Red / Jul '91 / Pinnacle.

THREAT TO CREATION (Creation Rebel & New Age Steppers)
Chemical specialists / Threat to creation / Eugenic device / Last sane dream / Pain staker / Earthwire line / Ethos / Design / Final frontier
CD _____ CDBRED 21
Cherry Red / Jul '91 / Pinnacle.

Creator, Carlos

PURE GUITAR
Radio guitar / Snake dance / Wet blues / Mad kisses / Making satanic train / Grand Prix / Bound for Istanbul / European guitars / Elixir of life / E.T. calling / 711Q / Nightmare continutes
CD _____ PCOM 1113
President / Jul '91 / Grapevine / Target/ BMG / Jazz Music / President.

Creators

HAVE A MASTERPLAN
CD _____ BS 002CD
Blindside / Feb '96 / Disc.

Credit To The Nation

DADDY ALWAYS WANTED ME TO GROW A...
CD _____ TPLP 54CD
One Little Indian / Feb '96 / Pinnacle.

TAKE DIS
CD _____ TPLP 44CDH
One Little Indian / Apr '94 / Pinnacle.

Credo

FIELD OF VISION
Rules of engagement / Goodboy / Don't look back / Alicia / Power to the Nth degree / Phantom / Sweet scarlet whisper / Party / Kindness
CD _____ CYCL 012
Cyclops / Sep '94 / Pinnacle.

Creedence Clearwater...

10 CD COLLECTION (Creedence Clearwater Revival)
I put a spell on you / Working man / Suzie Q / Ninety nine and a half (won't do) / Get down woman / Porterville / Gloomy / Walk on the water / Born on the bayou / Bootleg / Graveyard train / Good golly miss molly / Penthouse pauper / Proud Mary / Keep on chooglin' / Green river / Commotion / Tombstone shadow / Wrote a song for everyone / Bad moon rising / Lodi / Sinister purpose / Night time is the right time / Down on the corner / It came out of the sky / Cotton fields / Poorboy shuffle / Feelin' blue / Don't look now / Midnight special / Side of the road / Effigy / Ramble tamble / Before you accuse me / Ooby dooby / Lookin' out my back door / Run through the jungle / Up around the bend / My baby left me / Who'll stop the rain / I heard it through the grapevine / Long as I can see the light / Pagan baby / Sailor's lament / Chameleon / Have you ever seen the rain / I wish I could hide away / Born to move / Hey tonight / It's just a thought / Molina / Rude awakening / Lookin' for a reason / Hello Mary Lou / Cross tie walker / Take it like a friend / Need someone to hold / Tearin' up the country / Someday never comes / What are you gonna do / Sail away / Door to door / Sweet Hitch-Hiker / Door to door (live) / Green river (live) / Suzie Q (Live) / It came out of the sky (live) / Travellin' Band (Live) / Fortunate son (Live) / Commotion (live) / Lodi (live) / Bad moon rising (live) / Proud Mary (live) / Up around the bend (live) / Hey tonight (live) / Keep on chooglin' (live)
CD Set _____ FCDCCR 10
Fantasy / Oct '92 / Pinnacle / Jazz Music / Wellard / Cadillac.

BAYOU COUNTRY (Creedence Clearwater Revival)
Born on the bayou / Bootleg / Graveyard train / Good golly Miss Molly / Penthouse pauper / Proud Mary / Keep on chooglin'
CD _____ CDFE 502
Fantasy / Aug '87 / Pinnacle / Jazz Music / Wellard / Cadillac.

CHOOGLIN' (Creedence Clearwater Revival)
I heard it through the grapevine / Keep on chooglin' / Suzie Q / Pagan baby / Born on the bayou
CD _____ CDFE 517
Fantasy / Jun '93 / Pinnacle / Jazz Music / Wellard / Cadillac.

CHRONICLE (20 Greatest hits) (Creedence Clearwater Revival)
Suzie Q / I put a spell on you / Proud Mary / Bad moon rising / Lodi / Green river / Commotion / Down on the corner / Fortunate son / Travellin' band / Who'll stop the rain / Up around the bend / Run through the jungle / Lookin' out my back door / Long as I can see the light / I heard it through the grapevine / Have you ever seen the rain / Hey tonight / Sweet hitch hiker / Some day never comes
CD _____ CDCCR 2
Fantasy / Jun '87 / Pinnacle / Jazz Music / Wellard / Cadillac.

CHRONICLE VOL.2 (Creedence Clearwater Revival)
Walk on the water / Suzie Q (Part 2) / Born on the Bayou / Good golly Miss Molly / Tombstone shadow / Wrote a song for everyone / Night time is the right time / Cotton fields / It came out of the sky / Don't look now / Midnight special / Before you accuse me / My baby left me / Pagan baby / I wish I could hide away / It's just a thought / Molina / Born to move / Lookin' for a reason / Hello Mary Lou
CD _____ CDCCR 3
Fantasy / Jun '87 / Pinnacle / Jazz Music / Wellard / Cadillac.

COSMO'S FACTORY (Creedence Clearwater Revival)
Ramble tamble / Before you accuse me / Lookin' out my back door / Run through the jungle / Up around the bend / My baby left me / Who'll stop the rain / I heard it through the grapevine / Long as I can see the light / Travellin' band / Ooby dooby
CD _____ CDFE 505
Fantasy / Aug '87 / Pinnacle / Jazz Music / Wellard / Cadillac.

CREEDENCE CLEARWATER REVIVAL (Creedence Clearwater Revival)
I put a spell on you / Working man / Suzie Q / Ninety nine and a half (won't do) / Get down, woman / Porterville / Gloomy / Walk on the water
CD _____ CDFE 501

CREEDENCE COUNTRY (Creedence Clearwater Revival)
Lookin' for a reason / Don't look now / Lodi / My baby left me / Hello Mary Lou / Ramble tamble / Cotton fields / Before you accuse me / Wrote a song for everyone / Ooby dooby / Cross tie walker / Lookin' out my back door
CD _____ CDFE 518
Fantasy / Sep '92 / Pinnacle / Jazz Music / Wellard / Cadillac.

CREEDENCE GOLD (Creedence Clearwater Revival)
Proud Mary / Down on the corner / Bad moon rising / I heard it through the grapevine / Midnight special / Have you ever seen the rain / Born on the Bayou / Suzie Q
CD _____ CDFE 515
Fantasy / Aug '91 / Pinnacle / Jazz Music / Wellard / Cadillac.

GREEN RIVER (Creedence Clearwater Revival)
Bad moon rising / Cross tie walker / Sinister purpose / Night time is the right time / Green River / Commotion / Tombstone Shadow / Wrote a song for everyone / Lodi
CD _____ CDFE 503
Fantasy / '88 / Pinnacle / Jazz Music / Wellard / Cadillac.

HEY TONIGHT (Creedence Clearwater Revival)
CD _____ 825 174-2
Fantasy / '88 / Pinnacle / Jazz Music / Wellard / Cadillac.

LIVE IN EUROPE (Creedence Clearwater Revival)
Born on the bayou / It came out of the sky / Fortunate son / Lodi / Proud Mary / Hey tonight / Green River / Suzie Q / Travelin' band / Commotion / Bad moon rising / Up around the bend / Keep on chooglin'
CD _____ CDFE 514
Fantasy / Feb '90 / Pinnacle / Jazz Music / Wellard / Cadillac.

MARDI GRAS (Creedence Clearwater Revival)
Lookin' for a reason / Take it like a friend / Need someone to hold / Tearin' up the country / Some day never comes / What are you gonna do / Sail away / Hello Mary Lou / Door to door / Sweet hitch hiker
CD _____ CDFE 513
Fantasy / Aug '89 / Pinnacle / Jazz Music / Wellard / Cadillac.

MORE CREEDENCE GOLD (Creedence Clearwater Revival)
Hey tonight / Run through the jungle / Fortunate son / Bootleg / Lookin' out my back door / Molina / Who'll stop the rain / Sweet hitch-hiker / Good golly Miss Molly / I put a spell on you / Don't look now / Lodi / Porterville / Up around the bend
CD _____ CDFE 516
Fantasy / Aug '91 / Pinnacle / Jazz Music / Wellard / Cadillac.

PENDULUM (Creedence Clearwater Revival)
Pagan baby / I wish I could hide away / It's just a thought / Rude awakening number two / Sailor's lament / Chameleon / Born to move / Hey tonight / Molina / Have you ever seen the rain
CD _____ CDFE 512
Fantasy / Aug '89 / Pinnacle / Jazz Music / Wellard / Cadillac.

WILLY AND THE POORBOYS (Creedence Clearwater Revival)
Down on the corner / It came out of the sky / Cotton fields / Poor boy shuffle / Feelin' blue / Fortunate son / Don't look now / Midnight special / Side of the road / Effigy
CD _____ CDFE 504
Fantasy / Aug '87 / Pinnacle / Jazz Music / Wellard / Cadillac.

Creek

STORM THE GATE
Storm the gate / Foxy / I love / Passion / Fountain of youth / On my way / Rock me tonight / Girl is crying / Hanky panky / Climb / Bad light
CD _____ CDMFN 102
Music For Nations / Jul '90 / Pinnacle.

Creep

NO PAIN
CD _____ SPCD 90262
Sub Pop / May '93 / Disc.

Creepmine

CHIAROSCURO
CD _____ M 7015CD
Mascot / Oct '95 / Vital.

Creeps

BLUE TOMATO
CD _____ 2292462462
East West / May '90 / Warner Music.

Crematory

ILLUSIONS
CD _____ MASSCD 080
Massacre / Oct '95 / Plastic Head.

JUST DREAMING
CD _____ MASSCD 031
Massacre / Jun '94 / Plastic Head.

TRANSMIGRATION
CD _____ MASSCD 016
Massacre / Nov '93 / Plastic Head.

Crepillon, Pierre

DREUZ KRIEZ BREIZ (Crepillon, Pierre & L. Bigot)
CD _____ KMCD 56
Keltia Musique / Jul '95 / ADA / Direct / Discovery.

Cresent

NOW
CD _____ PUNK 011CD
Planet / Dec '95 / SRD.

Cressida

ASYLUM
CD _____ REP 4105-WP
Repertoire / Aug '91 / Pinnacle / Cadillac.

Crests

BEST OF THE CRESTS, THE (Crests & Johnny Maestro)
Sixteen candles / Step by step / Trouble in Paradise / Angels listened in / Pretty little angel / Model girl / Six nights a week / I thank the moon / Journey of love / It must be love / Mr. Happiness / What a surprise / Gee (but I'd give the world) / Flower of love / Isn't it amazing / Year ago tonight / Young love / I'll remember in the still of the night
CD _____ CHCHD 322
Ace / Apr '91 / Pinnacle / Cadillac / Complete/Pinnacle.

BEST OF THE REST, THE
Learning 'bout love / Molly Mae / I.O.U. / I do / Keep away from Carol / Paper crown / Way you look tonight / Earth angel / Let me be the one / Beside you / Always you / Test of love / Six nights a week / Let true love begin / My special angel / Step by step / Say it isn't so / Isn't it amazing / Out in the cold again / Besame baby / Strangelove / Rose and a baby Ruth / If my heart could write a letter / We've got to tell them / Silhouettes / Angels listened in / You took the joy out of Spring / Dream maker / Warning voice
CD _____ CDCHD 322
Ace / Apr '91 / Pinnacle / Cadillac / Complete/Pinnacle.

Crickets

COLLECTION/CALIFORNIA SUN - SHE LOVES YOU
La Bamba / All over you / Everybody's got a little problem / I think I've caught the blues / We gotta get together / Playboy / Lonely avenue / My little girl / Teardrops fall like rain / Right or wrong / You can't be in between / Don't try to change me / Lost and alone / I'm not a bad guy / I want to hold your hand / California sun / She loves you / Fool never learns / Slippin' and slidin' / I saw her standing there / Lonely avenue (2) / Please please me / Money / From me to you / You can't be in between (2) / Come **
CD _____ BGOCD 251
Beat Goes On / Mar '95 / Pinnacle.

DOUBLE EXPOSURE
My little girl / I fought the law / Oh boy / That'll be the day / When you ask about love / Tell me how / It doesn't matter anymore / Baby my heart / Rave on / Maybe baby / Brown eyed handsome man / Teardrops fall like rain / Everyday / Think it over / More than I can say / Don't ever change / Peggy Sue / Well alright / True love ways / (They call her) La bamba / It's so easy / Love's made a fool of you
CD _____ RCCD 3006
Rollercoaster / Nov '93 / CM / Swift.

IN STEP WITH THE CRICKETS
More than I can say / Rockin' pneumonia and the boogie woogie flu / Great balls of fire / Ting-a-ling / Just this once / Deborah / Baby my heart / When you ask about love / Time will tell / Sweet love / I fought the law / Love's made a fool of you / Someone, someone / Don't cha know / Why did you leave / Smooth guy / So you're in love / Peggy Sue got married
CD _____ MCLD 19243
MCA / May '94 / BMG.

RAVIN' ON - FROM CALIFORNIA TO CLOVIS
CD _____ RSRCD 002
Rockstar / Apr '94 / Rollercoaster / Direct / Magnum Music Group / Nervous.

ROCK 'N' ROLL MASTERS (Best of The Crickets)
My little girl / Teardrops fall like rain / Lost and alone / Little Hollywood girl / What'd I say / Right or wrong / Blue Monday / La

Bamba / Lonely Avenue / Don't ever change / Willie and the hand jive / I think I've caught the blues / Summertime blues / Love is strange / I'm not a bad guy / Now hear this / Thoughtless (CD only.) / Slippin' and slidin' (CD only.) / Someday (CD only.) / I believe in you (CD only.)
CD _____ CZ 155
Liberty / Aug '89 / EMI.

SINGLES COLLECTION 1957-1960, THE (Holly, Buddy & The Crickets)
That'll be the day / I'm looking for someone to love / Oh boy / Not fade away / Maybe baby / Tell me how / Think it over / Fool's paradise / It's so easy / Lonesome tears / Love's made a fool of you / Someone someone / When you ask about love / Deborah / Baby my heart / More than I can say / Don't cha know / Peggy Sue got married / Sweet love / I fought the law
CD _____ PWKS 4205
Carlton Home Entertainment / May '94 / Carlton Home Entertainment.

SOMETHING OLD, SOMETHING NEW
Willie and the hand jive / Don't ever change / Summertime blues / Searchin' / Little Hollywood girl / Pretty blue eyes / What I'd say / Parisienne girl / Blue blue day / Love is strange / He's old enough to know better / Blue Monday / La bamba / Lonely adventure / Teardrops fall like rain / Thoughtless / My little girl / Playboy
CD _____ BGOCD 242
Beat Goes On / Sep '94 / Pinnacle.

Crime & The City Solution

ADVERSARY - LIVE
CD _____ CDSTUMM 110
Mute / Sep '93 / Disc.

BRIDE SHIP, THE
Shadow of no man / Stone / Keepsake / Free world / Greater head / Dangling man / Bride ship / New world
CD _____ CDSTUMM 65
Mute / Apr '89 / Disc.

PARADISE DISCOTHEQUE
CD _____ CDSTUMM 78
Mute / Aug '90 / Disc.

ROOM OF LIGHTS
CD _____ CDSTUMM 36
Mute / '88 / Disc.

SHINE
All must be love / Fray so slow / Angel / On every train (grain will bear grain) / Hunter / Steal to the sea / Home is far from here / On every train (grain will bear grain)(12") / All must be love (early version)
CD _____ CDSTUMM 59
Mute / Apr '88 / Disc.

Crimson Glory

CRIMSON GLORY
CD _____ RR 349655
Roadrunner / Dec '88 / Pinnacle.

TRANSCENDENCE
CD _____ RR 9508 2
Roadrunner / Nov '88 / Pinnacle.

Criner, Clyde

BEHIND THE SUN
Song to tell a tale to sing / Just might be that way / Arco iris / Spider / Black Manhattan / Morning until night / Kinesis / Behind the sun
CD _____ PD 83029
RCA / Mar '89 / BMG.

COLOUR OF DARK, THE
Celebration / Divine providence / Colours / Man from two planets / Anima de novo / Tarot / Llaquic llaguic (sad sad) / Blue rose / Zenith cycle / Coincidence / Llaquic llaquic (sad sad) part 2 / Colour of dark
CD _____ PD 83066
RCA / Dec '89 / BMG.

Criptanite

TALEZ FROM THE CRYPT
CD _____ WRA 8130CD
Wrap / May '94 / Koch.

Crisis

8 CONVULSIONS
CD _____ TOODAMNHY 72
Too Damn Hype / Jan '95 / SRD.

Crisis Children

I'D LIKE TO PAINT AN AEROPLANE
CD _____ NEATCD 63
Neat / Oct '92 / Plastic Head.

Crisis Of Faith

LAND OF THE FREE
CD _____ LF 059CD
Lost & Found / Aug '93 / Plastic Head.

Crispell, Marilyn

CASCADES (Crispell, Marilyn & Barry Guy/Gerry Hemingway)
CD _____ CD 853

Music & Arts / Jan '96 / Harmonia Mundi / Cadillac.

CIRCLES
CD _____ VICTOCD 012
Victo / Nov '94 / These / ReR Megacorp / Cadillac.

CRISPELL & HEMINGWAY (Crispell, Marilyn & Hemingway)
CD _____ KFWCD 117
Knitting Factory / Oct '92 / Grapevine.

GAIA (Crispell, Marilyn/Reggie Workman/Doug James)
CD _____ CDLR 152
Leo / Feb '88 / Wellard / Cadillac / Impetus.

HIGHLIGHTS FROM THE 1992 AMERICAN TOUR (Crispell, Marilyn Trio)
CD _____ CD 758
Music & Arts / Apr '93 / Harmonia Mundi / Cadillac.

HYPERION (Crispell, Marilyn & Peter Brotzmann/Hamid Drake)
CD _____ CD 852
Music & Arts / Dec '95 / Harmonia Mundi / Cadillac.

INTERFERENCE (Crispell, Marilyn & Tim Berne)
CD _____ CD 851
Music & Arts / Dec '95 / Harmonia Mundi / Cadillac.

LABYRINTHS
CD _____ VICTOCD 06
Victo / Nov '94 / These / ReR Megacorp / Cadillac.

LIVE IN BERLIN
CD _____ 120069-2
Black Saint / Nov '93 / Harmonia Mundi / Cadillac.

LIVE IN ZURICH (Crispell, Marilyn Trio)
CD _____ CDLR 122
Leo / '90 / Wellard / Cadillac / Impetus.

OVERLAPPING HANDS (Crispell, Marilyn & Irene Schweizer)
CD _____ FMPCD 2
FMP / Aug '87 / Cadillac.

SANTUERIO
CD _____ CDLR 191
Leo / Feb '94 / Wellard / Cadillac / Impetus.

Criss, Sonny

CRISSCRAFT
Isle of Celia / Blues in my heart / This is for Ben / All night long / Crisscraft
CD _____ MCD 6015
Muse / Sep '92 / New Note / CM.

OUT OF NOWHERE
All the things you are / Dreamer / El tiante / My ideal / Out of nowhere / Brother can you spare a dime / First one
CD _____ MCD 5089
Muse / Sep '92 / New Note / CM.

THIS IS CRISS
CD _____ OJCCD 430
Original Jazz Classics / Nov '95 / Wellard / Jazz Music / Cadillac / Complete/Pinnacle.

Critters Buggin'

GUEST
Shag / Kickstand hog / Critter's theme / Jski / S/4 F.T.D. / Fretless nostril / Double pot roast backpac / Naked truth / Los lobos
CD _____ 4783762
Epic / Jul '95 / Sony.

Crivits

DRIVE
Drive
CD _____ LF 068
Lost & Found / Jan '94 / Plastic Head.

STARE
CD _____ LF 148CD
Lost & Found / May '95 / Plastic Head.

Cro-Mags

ALPHA OMEGA
CD _____ CM 9730CD
Century Media / Jun '92 / Plastic Head.

HARD TIMES IN AN AGE OF QUARREL
CD _____ CM 77072-2
Century Media / Jun '94 / Plastic Head.

NEAR DEATH EXPERIENCE
CD _____ CM 77050-2
Century Media / Sep '93 / Plastic Head.

Croce, A.J.

THAT'S ME IN THE BAR
That's me in the bar / Pass me by / Checkin' in / Music box / Some people call it love / I mean what I said / Night out on the town / Callin' home / I confess / Sign on the line / Maybe I'm to blame / Digin' a hole / She's waiting for me / I meant what I said
CD _____ 1005821272
Private Music / Jul '95 / BMG.

Croce, Jim

50TH ANNIVERSARY
CD Set _____ ESDCD 188
Essential / Dec '92 / Total/BMG.

COLLECTION: JIM CROCE
Time in a bottle / Operator (that's not the way it feels) / Salon Saloon / Alabama rain / Dreamin' again / It doesn't have to be that way / I'll have to say I love you in a song / Lover's cross / Thursday / These dreams / Long time ago / Photographs and memories
CD _____ CCSCD 154
Castle / Jan '86 / BMG.

DOWN THE HIGHWAY
I got a name / Mississippi lady / New York's not my home / Chain gang medley / Chain gang / He don't love you / Searchin' / You don't mess around with Jim / Ol' man river / Which way are you going / Bad, Bad Leroy Brown / Walkin' back to Georgia / Box no.10 / Speedball Tucker / Alabama rain
CD _____ CLACD 118
Castle / '88 / BMG.

FINAL TOUR, THE
Operator (that's not the way it feels) / Roller derby queen dialogue / Roller derby queen / Next time,this time / Trucker dialogue / Speedball trucker / New York's not my home / Hard time losin' man / Ball of Kerrymuir dialogue / Ball of Kerrymuir dialogue / Careful man dialogue / Careful man / Shopping for clothes / These dreams
CD _____ CLACD 341
Castle / Jun '94 / BMG.

LEGEND OF JIM CROCE, THE
CD _____ RR 34 9841
Roadrunner / Jan '92 / Pinnacle.

PHOTOGRAPHS AND MEMORIES (His greatest hits)
Bad, Bad Leroy Brown / Operator (that's not the way it feels) / Photographs and memories / Rapid Roy (The stock car boy) / Time in a bottle / New York's not my home / Workin' at the car wash blues / I got a name / I'll have to say I love you in a song / You don't mess around with Jim / Lover's cross / One less set of footsteps / These dreams / Roller Derby Queen
CD _____ CLACD 119
Castle / Jun '88 / BMG.

SIMPLY THE BEST
CD _____ WMCD 5703
Disky / Oct '94 / THE / BMG / Discovery / Pinnacle.

TIME IN A BOTTLE
Time in a bottle / Operator (that's not the way it feels) / Salon and saloon / Alabama rain / Dreamin' again / It doesn't have to be that way / I'll have to say I love you in a song / Lover's cross / Thursday / These dreams / Long time ago / Photographs and memories
CD _____ CLACD 117
Castle / Nov '86 / BMG.

Crocker, Barry

EMOTIONS
CD _____ HADCD 192
Javelin / Nov '95 / THE / Henry Hadaway Organisation.

Crocker, John

ALL OF ME
Smiles / Don't blame me / My gal Sal / I love you / All of me / Between the devil and the deep blue sea / Tangerine / Poor butterfly / She's funny that way / Exactly like you / Stealin' apples
CD _____ CDTTD 585
Timeless Traditional / May '94 / New Note.

EASY LIVING (Crocker, John Quartet)
Avalon / I can't get started (with you) / Lady be good / Shine / Fine time / I hadn't any-one till you / Have you met Miss Jones / Easy living / Rose room / After you've gone
CD _____ CDTTD 561
Timeless Traditional / Aug '91 / New Note.

Croker, Brendan

BOAT TRIPS IN THE BAY (Croker, Brendan & The 5 O'Clock Shadows)
CD _____ ORECD 510
Silvertone / Apr '90 / Pinnacle.

CLOSE SHAVE, A (Croker, Brendan & The 5 O'Clock Shadows)
CD _____ MRCD 129
Munich / Mar '87 / CM / ADA / Greensleeves / Direct.

GREAT INDOORS
CD _____ ORECD 517
Silvertone / Aug '91 / Pinnacle.

REDNECK STATE OF THE ART
CD _____ WFRCD 004
L&J / Oct '91 / Grapevine.

Crombie, Tony

ATMOSPHERE (Crombie, Tony & His Rockets)

Beryl's bounce / Ninth man / St. James Infirmary / Invitation / Stompin' at the Savoy / Duke's joke / Panic stations / I'll close my eyes / Small talk / Perpetual lover / Shapes / Copy cats
CD _____ CDREN 002
Renaissance / Jul '89 / Wellard / Jazz Music.

SWEET, WILD AND BLUE
Cocktails for two / Wrap your troubles in dreams (and dream your troubles away) / So near, so far / I've got the world on a string / Embraceable you / Tulip or turnip / To each his own / Tender trap / Hold my hand / All the way / It's magic / High and mighty / So rare / Percussion staccato / I should care / For you alone / Summertime / You are my lucky star
CD _____ CDREN 003
Renaissance / '89 / Wellard / Jazz Music.

TONY CROMBIE AND FRIENDS
Tango '89 / Sophisticated lady / Moonglow / Twelve note samba / Raising the temperature / Fallen bird / I don't stand a ghost of a chance with you / Serenade in blue / Allison Adamant / Autumn rustle / Prelude to a kiss / So near, so far / Rabbit pie / Child of fancy / Viva Rodriguez
CD _____ CDREN 001
Renaissance / Jul '89 / Wellard / Jazz Music.

Cromwell, Rodney

LET THE PICTURE PAINT ITSELF
Let the picture paint itself / Give my heart a rest / Stuff that works / Big heart / Loving you makes me strong / Best years of our lives / I don't fall in love so easy / That ol'door / Rose of Memphis / Once in a while
CD _____ MCD 11042
MCA / Aug '94 / BMG.

Cronos

ROCK 'N' ROLL DISEASE
Message of war / Rock 'n' roll disease / Midnight eye / Lost and found / Love is infectious / Sexploitation / Super power / Aphrodisiac / Sweet savage sex / Bared to the bone / Dirty tricks dept.
CD _____ NEATCD 1051
Neat / Jan '96 / Plastic Head.

VENOM
CD _____ NM 003CD
Neat / Nov '95 / Plastic Head.

Cronos Train

BRIDES OF CHRIST
CD _____ TATCD 23
Tatra / Aug '95 / Plastic Head.

Cronshaw, Andrew

ANDREW CRONSHAW CD, THE
Voice of silence / Wexford carol / Andro and his cutty gun / Galician processional / Harry Bloodgood's famous jig/American Boot dance / Blacksmith / Fingal's cave / Yowe came to our door / Ships in distress/St Kilda rowing song/Go to sea no more / Pandeirada de entrimo/Gentle dark eyed Mary / Empty places / Dark haired youth/Taladh ar slanair / Freumh as craobh taigh challadair / Wasps in the woodpile / Turning the tide / Seana Mheallan / Giullan nam bo / Ho ho nighean donn/First of May/Prince of Wale's jig / Saratoga hornpipe / Old highland air
CD _____ TSCD 447
Topic / Sep '89 / Direct / ADA.

LANGUAGE OF SNAKES, THE
CD _____ SPDCD 1050
Special Delivery / Sep '93 / ADA / CM / Direct.

Crooked Jack

TOMORROW MUST WAIT
Rambling rover / Hermless / Magie cockabendie / Jigs and reels / Belfast mill / Working man / Auchtertool / Loch tay boat song / New teacher / March, strathspey and reel / Come by the hills / In search of you
CD _____ LCOM 5224CD
Lismor / Jan '94 / Lismor / Direct / Duncans / ADA.

Crooks

LIVE IN NOVOSIBIRSK
CD _____ PAN 151CD
Pan / Mar '95 / ADA / Direct / CM.

Crooks, Richard

ALL OF MY HEART
All of my heart / My song goes round the world / Ah! fuyez / Douce image / Mother o' mine / Thora / E Lucevan le stelle / Ah / Moon of my delight / Neapolitan love song (t'amo) / Il mio tesoro / Until una furtive lagrima / Little love / Little kiss (Un peu d'amour) / Preislied / Songs my mother taught me / Nirvana / O song divine
CD _____ CDHD 167
Happy Days / Oct '89 / Conifer.

FOR YOU ALONE
CD _____ CDMOIR 431
Memoir / Oct '95 / Target/BMG.

SMILIN' THROUGH
Ah sweet mystery of life / One alone / Song of songs / Rio Rita / Love everlasting / Serenade / Because / Beautiful Isle of somewhere / If I am dreaming / I love thee / Parted / Bird songs at eventide / Open your window / Vienna / Holy city / Lost chord / Smilin' through / Too late tomorrow / Yours is my heart alone / Just to linger in your arms / Gypsy moon / Only a rose
CD _____ CDHD 215
Happy Days / Jan '90 / Conifer.

Cropdusters

IF THE SOBER GO TO HEAVEN
CD _____ DOJOCD 202
Dojo / Nov '94 / BMG.

Cropper, Steve

JAMMED TOGETHER (Cropper, Steve/ Pop Staples / Albert King)
What'd I say / Opus de soul / Big bird / Trashy dog / Water / Tupelo / Baby, what you want me to do / Homer's theme / Don't turn your healer down / Knock on wood
CD _____ CDSXE 028
Stax / Jul '90 / Pinnacle.

WITH A LITTLE HELP FROM MY FRIENDS
Crop dustin' / Land of 1000 dances / ninety nine and a half (won't do) / Boogaloo down Broadway / Funky Broadway / With a little help from my friends / Oh pretty woman / I'd rather drink muddy water / Way I feel tonight / In the midnight hour / Rattlesnake
CD _____ CD3XE 000
Stax / Aug '92 / Pinnacle.

Crosby, Bing

20 GOLDEN GREATS: BING CROSBY
Swinging on a star / Gone fishin' / White Christmas / You are my sunshine / Moonlight bay / Pennies from Heaven / Mac-Namara's band
CD _____ MCLD 19218
MCA / Jan '95 / BMG.

ALL THE CLOUDS WILL ROLL AWAY (Crosby, Bing/Judy Garland/Andrews Sisters)
CD _____ JSPCD 702
JSP / May '93 / ADA / Target/BMG / Direct / Cadillac / Complete/Pinnacle.

BEST OF BING CROSBY (2)
CD _____ ENTCD 248
Entertainers / Mar '92 / Target/BMG.

BING CROSBY
CD _____ MATCD 253
Castle / Apr '93 / BMG.

BING CROSBY
Beautiful dreamer / Darling Nellie Gray / Ah sweet mystery of life / Deep purple / Sweethearts / Where the blue of the night meets the gold of the day / Pennies from heaven / Out of nowhere / How deep is the ocean / Street of dreams / Brother can you spare a dime / Ghost of chance / Please / Dancing in the dark / Stardust / I found a million dollar baby / Goodnight sweetheart / White Christmas
CD _____ BSTCD 9114
Best Compact Discs / Apr '94 / Complete/ Pinnacle.

BING CROSBY & FRIENDS
Gone fishin' / Couple of song and dance men / Swinging on a star / Pennies from heaven / Zing a little zong / You are my sunshine / Moonlight bay / In the cool, cool, cool of the evening / Where the blue of the night meets the gold of the day / Anything you can do / White christmas / Road to Bali / Spaniard that blighted my life / Whiffenpoof song / Life is so peculiar / Mac-Namara's band / Too ra loo ra loo ra / Noon came up with a great idea / Mr. Gallagher and Mr. Shean / Connecticut
CD _____ MCCD 089
Music Club / Nov '92 / Disc / THE / CM.

BING CROSBY 1926-1932
Pretty lips / Muddy water / I'm coming Virginia / Mississippi mud/I left my sugar standing in the rain / Changes / Mary / Ol' man river / Make believe / From Monday on / Lovable / Louisiana / You took advantage of me / T'aint so, honey t'aint so / Susianna / Spell of the blues / Let's do it (let's fall in love) / My kinda love / So the bluebirds and the blackbirds got together / Had a talking picture of you / Happy feet / Three little words / One more time / Dinah / St. Louis blues
CD _____ CBC 1004
Timeless Historical / Jan '92 / New Note / Pinnacle.

BING CROSBY SINGS MORE GREAT SONGS
There's no business like show business / Secret love / Stranger in paradise / Accentuate the positive / I'll be seeing you / I love Paris / People will say we're in love / They can't take that away from me / You must have been a beautiful baby / Nightingale sang in Berkeley Square / You made me love you / Red sails in the sunset / Wrap your troubles in dreams (and dream your troubles away) / Georgia on my mind / Autumn leaves

---

CD _____ PWK 088
Carlton Home Entertainment / Feb '89 / Carlton Home Entertainment.

BING CROSBY/NAT KING COLE ESSENTIALS (Crosby, Bing & Nat King Cole)
CD _____ LECDD 641
Wisepack / Aug '95 / THE / Conifer.

BING SINGS BERLIN, RODGERS & HART
Soft lights and sweet music / On a roof in Manhattan / How deep is the ocean / I'm playing with fire / Soon / Down by the river / It's easy to remember / Alexander's ragtime band / Now it can be told / When I lost you / God bless America / Bombardier song / Angels of mercy / I'll capture your heart / Lazy / Happy holiday / Let's start the New Year right / Abraham / Be careful it's my heart / Easter Parade / Song of freedom / I've got plenty to be thankful for / White Christmas
CD _____ CDHD 232
Happy Days / Sep '93 / Conifer.

BING SINGS THE GREAT SONGS
Begin the beguine / Fine romance / Ol' man river
CD _____ PWK 065
Carlton Home Entertainment / '88 / Carlton Home Entertainment.

BING SWINGS WITH JOHN SCOTT TROTTER ORCHESTRA (Crosby, Bing & John Scott Trotter Orchestra)
Painting the clouds with sunshine / Shanghai / Lady be good / Everywhere you go / So tired / Easter parade / Bali Ha'i / Lazy bones
CD _____ DAWE 48
Magic / Nov '93 / Jazz Music / Swift / Wellard / Cadillac / Harmonia Mundi.

BING'S BEST
Where the blue of the night meets the gold of the day / Sweet and lovely / Dinah / Shine / Sweet Georgia brown / Cabin in the cotton / Some of these days / Here lies love / You're beautiful tonight my dear / You're getting to be a habit with me / You've got me crying again / Temptation / May I / June in January / With every breath I take / I'm an old cowhand (from the Rio Grande) / Pennies from heaven / Sweet Leilani / Mr. gallagher and Mr. Shean / You must have been a beautiful baby
CD _____ CDCD 1071
Charly / Mar '93 / Charly / THE / Cadillac.

BING'S BUDDIES (1951 Crosby And Guests)
Bright eyes / Painting the clouds with sunshine / Sweet violets / Wang wang blues / Domino / I only have eyes for you / Buttermilk sky
CD _____ DAWE 41
Magic / Sep '93 / Jazz Music / Swift / Wellard / Cadillac / Harmonia Mundi.

BLUE OF THE NIGHT, THE
Where the blue of the night meets the gold of the day / Sweet and lovely / Dinah / Shine / Sweet georgia Brown / Cabin in the cotton / Some of these days / You're beautiful to-night my dear / You're getting to be a habit with me / You've got me crying again / Temptation / May I / June in January / With every breath I take / I'm an old cowhand (from the Rio Grande) / Mr. Gallagher and Mr. Shean / You must have been a beautiful baby
CD _____ MSCD 12
Music De-Luxe / '90 / Magnum Music Group.

BLUE SKIES
Waiting for the evening mail / I wish you love / Chances are / Where or when / What is there to say / Sunday / They didn't believe me / This can't be love / I can't get started (with you) / I guess I'll have to change my plan / Try a little tenderness / What is this thing called love / Pardon my ideal / Don't take your love from me / Tender trap / Love is just around the corner / Crazy rhythm / I've grown accustomed to her face / Come rain or come shine / She's funny that way / We're in the money / Little man you've had a busy day / At sundown
CD _____ TRTCD 151
TrueTrax / Dec '94 / THE.

CHRISTMAS SONGS (Wartime Christmas Broadcasts)
CD _____ VJC 1017 2
Vintage Jazz Classics / Oct '91 / Direct / ADA / CM / Cadillac.

CHRISTMAS WITH BING CROSBY
Christmas is a comin' / Rudolph the red nosed reindeer / Sleigh ride / Deck the halls with boughs of holly / That Christmas feeling / Looks like a cold cold winter / I heard the bells on Christmas day / Silent night / First snowfall / Marshmallow world / Snow / Sleigh bell serenade / Is Christmas only a tree / Little Jack Frost get lost / Snowman / Happy holiday
CD _____ PWKS 4219
Carlton Home Entertainment / Oct '95 / Carlton Home Entertainment.

CHRISTMAS WITH BING CROSBY
CD _____ MCCDX 022
Music Club / Nov '93 / Disc / THE / CM.

CHRISTMAS WITH BING CROSBY (1)
CD _____ TCD 2468
Telstar / Dec '91 / BMG.

COLLECTION VOL.1
I'm crazy over you / Rose of Mandalay / Happy go lucky you and broken hearted me / Waiting at the end of the road / I found you / Starlight (help find the one I love) / Love you funny thing / Shadows on the window / You're still in my heart / Southern medley / Lazy day / With summer coming on / Love me tonight / We're a couple of soldiers
CD _____ 982581 2
Pickwick/Sony Collector's Choice / Aug '91 / Carlton Home Entertainment / Pinnacle / Sony.

COLLECTION, THE
CD _____ COL 009
Collection / Jan '95 / Target/BMG.

COLLECTION: BING CROSBY
CD _____ CCSCD 275
Castle / Oct '90 / BMG.

EP COLLECTION: BING CROSBY
Road to Morocco / That's a plenty / Moments to remember / Suddenly there's a valley / Oh loneliness of evening / Sailing down the Chesapeake Bay / Sing soft, sing sweet, sing gentle / Me and the moon / Got the moon in my pocket / Young at heart / Mademoiselle de Paris / Morgen / Domenica / It had to be you / Something in common / Look at your heart / Possibility's there / Longest walk / Seventeenth summer / Moon was yellow / Pale moon / Chicago style / Oh baby mine I get so lonely / La mer / Under Paris skies / White Christmas
CD _____ SEECD 360
See For Miles/C5 / Sep '92 / Pinnacle.

ESSENTIAL COLLECTION
CD Set _____ LECD 612
Wisepack / Apr '95 / THE / Conifer.

EVERYTHING I HAVE IS YOURS
Blacksmith blues / Come what may / I dreamt I dwelt in Marble Hall / Glow worm / Feet up / Pittsburgh, Pennsylvania / Please Mr. Sun / Cockeyed optimist / When the red roses grow / Girl in the bonnet of blue / Everything I have is yours / Thousand violins / Dark moon / Now that I need you / Maybe it's because / When the midnight choo choo leaves for Alabam' / If I had my way / Blues my naughty sweetie gives to me / Down yonder / Lady of Spain / Zip a dee doo dah / P.S. I love you / If this isn't love / Ole buttermilk sky / Great day / I git the sun in the morning / It's a grand day you go to my head / Old lamp lighter
CD _____ CDGRF 016
Tring / '93 / Tring / Prism.

GREAT YEARS, THE
Deep in the heart of Texas / White Christmas / Wait till the sun shines Nellie / Moonlight becomes you / Road to Morocco / You are my sunshine / Walking the floor over you / Yes indeed / Mr. Meadowlark / Where the blue of the night meets the gold of the day / Let's all meet at my house / Do you ever think of me / Between a kiss and a sigh / When day is done / Be honest with me / Sing me a song of the islands / Tea for two / Tumbling tumbleweeds / Miss you / Along the Santa Fe trail / Start the day right / I want my Mama
CD _____ PASTCD 7027
Flapper / Nov '93 / Pinnacle.

HERE LIES LOVE (A Selection of Love Songs)
Very thought of you / Love thy neighbour / June in January / You've got me crying again / May I / With every breath I take / Temptation / Let me call you sweetheart / Sweet and lovely / Love in bloom / You're getting to be a habit with me / I love you truly / Someday, sweetheart / You're beautiful tonight my dear / Love is just around the corner / Just a wearyin' for you / It must be true / Here lies love
CD _____ CD AJA 5043
Living Era / Sep '90 / Koch.

HEY, LOOK US OVER (Crosby, Bing & Rosemary Clooney)
Introduction / Isn't it a lovely day / Anything you can do / They say it's wonderful / Ain't we got fun / Let's take a walk around the block / Summertime / Let's call the whole thing off / People will say we're in love / Lover / Hey look me over / Let's put out the lights / They can't take that away from me / Everytime I see you I'm in love again / Paris medley
CD _____ JASCD 318
Jasmine / Nov '93 / Wellard / Swift / Conifer / Cadillac / Magnum Music Group.

HOLIDAY INN (By Irvin Berlin) (Crosby, Bing & Fred Astaire)
CD _____ VJC 1012 2
Vintage Jazz Classics / Oct '91 / Direct / ADA / CM / Cadillac.

HOLLYWOOD GUYS AND DOLLS VOL 1
CD _____ PARCD 005
Parrot / Dec '94 / THE / Wellard / Jazz Music.

HOLLYWOOD GUYS AND DOLLS VOL 2
CD _____ PARCD 006
Parrot / Dec '94 / THE / Wellard / Jazz Music.

I'M AN OLD COWHAND
Don't fence me in / Home on the range / I'm an old cowhand (from the Rio Grande) / Take me back to my boots and saddle / Silver on the sage / When the bloom is on the sage / Tumbling tumbleweeds / After sundown / El rancho grande / Singing hills / Along the Santa Fe trail / Clementine / San Antonio rose / Deep in the heart of Texas / Who calls / Pistol packin' Mama / Ridin' down the canyon / San Fernando valley / Empty saddles (In the old corral) / Round up lullaby / Old oaken bucket / We'll rest at the end of the trail / Twilight on the trail / Goodbye little darlin' goodbye / Last round-up
CD _____ CDAJA 5160
ASV / May '95 / Koch.

IMMORTAL BING CROSBY
CD _____ AVC 535
Avid / May '94 / Avid/BMG / Koch.

JAZZIN' BING CROSBY 1927-1940, THE (2CD Set)
I'm coming Virginia / Side by side / Mississippi mud / I left my sugar standing in the rain (and she melted away) / Mary / There ain't no sweet man that's worth the salt of my tears / From Monday on / High water / Louisiana / T'aint so honey, tain't so / Because my baby don't mean maybe now / Rhythm king / I'm crazy over you / Susianna / If I had you / Spell of the blues / Let's do it (let's fall in love) / My kinda love / So the bluebirds and the blackbirds got together / Oh Miss Hannah / Waiting at the end of the road / After you've gone / One more time / I'm sorry dear / Dinah / St. Louis blues / Shine / Shadows on the window / Cabin in the cotton e / How deep is the ocean / Sweet Sue, just you / My honey's lovin' arms / Somebody stole Gabriel's horn / Stay on the right side of the road / Blue prelude / I'm hummin', I'm whistlin', I'm singin' / Someday sweetheart / Moonburn / Pennies from heaven / Don't be that way / Mr. Gallagher and Mr. Shean / You must have been a beautiful baby / Yodelin' jive / Rhythm on the river / Yes indeed
CD Set _____ CDAFS 1021-2
Affinity / Jun '93 / Charly / Cadillac / Jazz Music.

JUST BREEZIN' ALONG
Breezin' along with the breeze / How are things in Glocca Morra / Heatwave / Best things in life are free / My heart stood still / I got rhythm / Good old times / Cabaret / Send in the clowns / Only way to go / Have a nice day / Some sunny day / At my time of life / With a song in my heart / Razzle dazzle / That's what life is all about
CD _____ CZ 5
EMI / Oct '87 / EMI.

MOONLIGHT BECOMES YOU
CD _____ CDCD 1200
Charly / Sep '94 / Charly / THE / Cadillac.

OLD LAMPLIGHTER, THE
CD _____ CDSGP 0127
Prestige / Dec '94 / Total/BMG.

ON THE SENTIMENTAL SIDE (20 Classic Tracks of the 30's)
Black moonlight / How deep is the ocean / Stardust / Dancing in the dark / I'm through with love / Sweet is the word for you / Between a kiss and a sigh / Funny old hills / I found a million dollar baby / I have eyes / If you should ever need me / I'm building a sailboat of dreams / Joobalai / My heart is taking lessons / On the sentimental side / Our big love scene / Sing a song of sixpence / beams / That sly old gentleman / Thine alone / You're a sweet little headache
CD _____ CDAJA 5072
Living Era / Aug '90 / Koch.

ON THE SENTIMENTAL SIDE, THE
My heart is taking lessons / Funny old hills / Joobalai / East side of heaven / Hang your heart on a hickory limb / On the sentimental side / This is my night to dream / I have eyes / You're a sweet little headache / That sly old gentleman / Apple for the teacher / Man and his dream / Still the bluebird sings / April played the fiddle / I haven't time to be a millionaire / In my merry oldsmobile / Medley of Gus Edwards / Go fly a kite / Meet the sun halfway / Moon and the willow tree
CD _____ MUCD 9030
Start / Apr '95 / Koch.

ON TREASURE ISLAND
CD _____ JSPCD 703
JSP / May '93 / ADA / Target/BMG / Direct / Cadillac / Complete/Pinnacle.

ONLY FOREVER
Only forever / Rhythm on the river / That's for me / When the moon comes over Madison Square / You're dangerous / Birds of a feather / Apple for the teacher / Still the bluebird sings / Go fly a kite / If I had my way / Too romantic / Sweet potato piper / April played the fiddle / I haven't time to be a millionaire / Meet the sun halfway / Man and his dream / I have eyes / You're a sweet little headache / It's always you /

155

Birth of the blues / My melancholy baby / Waiter and the porter and the upstairs maid
CD _____ RAJCD 802
Empress / Oct '93 / THE.

POCKETFUL OF DREAMS
CD _____ CDD 457
Conifer / Jan '92 / Conifer.

QUINTESSENTIAL, THE
CD _____ CTVCD 211
Castle / Nov '92 / BMG.

RADIO YEARS, THE
CD _____ GNPD 9051
GNP Crescendo / '88 / Silva Screen.

RADIO YEARS, VOL 2
CD _____ GNPD 9052
GNP Crescendo / '88 / Silva Screen.

REMEMBERING
Please / Did you ever see a dream walking / I've got the world on a string / Sweet Georgia Brown / I don't stand a ghost of a chance with you / My honey's loving arms / Down the old ox road / How deep is the ocean / Temptation / St. Louis blues / Dinah / Somebody stole Gabriel's horn / Stay on the right side of the road / Someday, sweetheart / Some of these days / Shine / I'm coming Virginia / There's a cabin in the pines
CD _____ CDHD 123
Happy Days / May '93 / Conifer.

SPOTLIGHT ON BING CROSBY & ROSEMARY CLOONEY (Crosby, Bing & Rosemary Clooney)
White Christmas / Have yourself a merry little Christmas / Silent night / It came upon a midnight clear / Away in a manger / Christmas song / O'litte town of Bethlehem / Little drummer boy / Rudolph the red nosed reindeer / Jingle bells / O come all ye faithful (Adeste fidelis)
CD _____ HADCD 110
Javelin / Feb '94 / THE / Henry Hadaway Organisation.

START OFF EACH DAY WITH A SONG (Crosby, Bing & Jimmy Durante)
CD _____ JSPCD 701
JSP / May '93 / ADA / Target/BMG / Direct / Cadillac / Complete/Pinnacle.

SWINGING ON A STAR
CD _____ PASTCD 7065
Flapper / Jun '95 / Pinnacle.

SWINGING ON A STAR
CD _____ CDCD 1235
Charly / Jun '95 / Charly / THE / Cadillac.

THAT'S JAZZ
St. Louis blues / Please / Temptation / Did you ever see a dream walking / I don't stand a ghost of a chance with you / Down the old ox road / Black moonlight / Where the blue of the night meets the gold of the day / Last round-up / Someday sweetheart / How deep is the ocean / Our big love scene / Song of the Islands / Dinah / I'm an old cowhand (from the Rio Grande) / Wrap your troubles in dreams (and dream your troubles away) / Blue Hawaii / Sailor beware / Sweet Leilani / Pennies from heaven / Happy go lucky you and broken hearted me / Thanks
CD _____ PASTCD 9739
Flapper / Mar '91 / Pinnacle.

THOSE GREAT WORLD WAR II SONGS
CD _____ DBG 53042
Double Gold / Apr '95 / Target/BMG.

TOO MARVELLOUS FOR WORDS
CD _____ CPCD 8149
Charly / Nov '95 / Charly / THE / Cadillac.

TOO MARVELOUS FOR WORDS
CD _____ CDGR 105
Charly / Jan '96 / Charly / THE / Cadillac.

TWO ON ONE: BING CROSBY & FRANK SINATRA (Crosby, Bing & Frank Sinatra)
CD _____ CDT 6
Charly / Apr '94 / Charly / THE / Cadillac.

VISIT TO THE MOVIES, A
CD _____ 15411
Laserlight / Jan '93 / Target/BMG.

WHITE CHRISTMAS
CD _____ CD 50001
Lotus / Dec '88 / Jazz Horizons / Impetus.

WHITE CHRISTMAS
CD _____ 15444
Laserlight / Nov '95 / Target/BMG.

Crosby, Bob

1937 - 1938 (Crosby, Bob & His Bobcats)
CD _____ SWAGGIECD 501
Swaggie / Jun '93 / Jazz Music.

1939 (Crosby, Bob & His Bobcats)
CD _____ SWAGGIECD 502
Swaggie / Jan '94 / Jazz Music.

1940 (Crosby, Bob & His Bobcats)
CD _____ SWAGGIECD 503
Swaggie / Jun '93 / Jazz Music.

22 ORIGINAL BIG BAND RECORDINGS
CD _____ HCD 409
Hindsight / Sep '92 / Target/BMG / Jazz Music.

BIG NOISE STATUS, THE
CD _____ DHDL 126
Halcyon / Dec '94 / Jazz Music / Wellard / Swift / Harmonia Mundi / Cadillac.

BOB CROSBY & HIS BOB CATS VOL. 4
CD _____ SWAGGIECD 504
Swaggie / Dec '94 / Jazz Music.

BOB CROSBY & HIS DIXIELAND BOBCATS 1939-42 (Crosby, Bob & His Bobcats)
CD _____ JH 1043
Jazz Hour / Jun '95 / Target/BMG / Jazz Music / Cadillac.

BOB CROSBY & HIS ORCHESTRA (Crosby, Bob & His Orchestra)
CD _____ HCD 245
Hindsight / Sep '94 / Target/BMG / Jazz Music.

BOB CROSBY'S BOB CATS VOL.1
Stumbling / Who's sorry now / Coquette / Fidgety feet / You're driving me crazy / Can't we be friends / Lookin' the loop / Mama's gone goodbye / March of the bob cats / Palesteena / Slow mood / Big foot jump / Big crash from China / Five point blues / Way down yonder in New Orleans / Do you ever think of me
CD _____ CD 501
Swaggie / Oct '91 / Jazz Music.

HOW CAN YOU FORGET (Crosby, Bob & His Orchestra)
CD _____ DHDL 125
Halcyon / Nov '93 / Jazz Music / Wellard / Swift / Harmonia Mundi / Cadillac.

I REMEMBER YOU - THE BOB CROSBY MEMORIAL ALBUM
CD _____ VJC 1046
Vintage Jazz Classics / Aug '93 / Direct / ADA / CM / Cadillac.

MARCH OF THE BOBCATS (Crosby, Bob & The Bop Cats)
CD _____ JHR 73534
Jazz Hour / May '93 / Target/BMG / Jazz Music / Cadillac.

SOUTH RAMPART STREET PARADE
South Rampart street parade / Long time no see / Slow mood / Boogie woogie Maxie / Angry / Skater's waltz in swingtime / Big noise from Winnetka / It was a lover and his lass / Blow, blow thou winter wind / Oh, mistress mine / Sigh no more ladies / My inspiration / World is waiting for the sunrise / When my dreamboat comes home / Ja da / What's new (I'm free) / Rose of Washington square / Fidgety feet / Eye opener / Begin the beguine / Hundustan / Wahington and Lee Swing / Walking the floor over you / I'm prayin' humble / Peruna
CD _____ CDHD 219
Happy Days / May '93 / Conifer.

STOMP OFF, LET'S GO
Big noise from Winnetka / Call me a taxi / Diga diga doo / Dixieland shuffle / Dogtown blues / Gin mill blues / Gypsy love song / Grand terrace rhythm / I'm free / March of the bob cats / Milk cow blues / Muskrat ramble / Ooh looka there, ain't she pretty / Panama / Savoy blues / Smoky Mary / South Rampart Street parade / Spain / Stomp off, let's go / Stumbling / Swing Mister Charlie / Till we meet again / Wolverine blues / Yancey special
CD _____ CDAJA 5097
Living Era / Nov '92 / Koch.

STRANGE ENCHANTMENT (Vol. 8/1938-39) (Crosby, Bob & His Orchestra)
My inspiration / Your lovely, Madame / Deep in a dream / Summertime / Loopin' the loop / Skater's waltz / Stomp off and let's go / Smoky Mary / South Rampart Street parade / Song of the wanderer / Cherry / Eye opener / Begin the beguine / Hindustan / Long time no see / Mournin' blues / Don't worry 'bout me / I never knew heaven could speak / If I were sure of you / Strange enchantment
CD _____ DHDL 127
Halcyon / May '95 / Jazz Music / Wellard / Swift / Harmonia Mundi / Cadillac.

STRANGE NEW RHYTHM IN MY HEART - VOL. 4 (Crosby, Bob Orchestra)
CD _____ DHDL 122
Halcyon / Nov '93 / Jazz Music / Wellard / Swift / Harmonia Mundi / Cadillac.

YOU CAN CALL IT SWING (Crosby, Bob & His Orchestra)
CD _____ DHDL 121
Halcyon / Sep '93 / Jazz Music / Wellard / Swift / Harmonia Mundi / Cadillac.

YOU'RE DRIVING ME CRAZY (Crosby, Bob & His Orchestra)
CD _____ DHDL 123
Halcyon / Mar '93 / Jazz Music / Wellard / Swift / Harmonia Mundi / Cadillac.

Crosby, David

IT'S ALL COMING BACK TO ME NOW
CD _____ 7567826202
Atlantic / Mar '95 / Warner Music.

THOUSAND ROADS
Hero / Too young to die / Old soldier / Through your hands / Yvette in english /

Thousand roads / Columbus / Helpless heart / Coverage / Natalie
CD _____ 756782484-2
Atlantic / May '93 / Warner Music.

WIND ON THE WATER (Crosby, David & Graham Nash)
Carry me / Mama lion / Bittersweet / Take the money and run / Naked in the rain / Love work out / Low down payment / Cowboy of dreams / Homeward through the haze / Fieldworker / To the last whale / Wind on the water
CD _____ CDTB 128
Thunderbolt / Nov '91 / Magnum Music Group.

Crosby, Stills & Nash

4 WAY STREET (2CD Set) (Crosby, Stills, Nash & Young)
On the way home / Cowgirl in the sand / Southern man / Teach your children / Don't let it bring you down / Ohio / Triad / Forty nine bye byes / Carry on / Lee shore / Love the one you're with / Find the cost of freedom / Chicago / Pre-road downs / Right between the eyes / Long time gone / Suite: Judy blue eyes
CD _____ K2 60003
Atlantic / Mar '87 / Warner Music.

AMERICAN DREAM (Crosby, Stills, Nash & Young)
American dream / Got it made / Name of love / Don't say goodbye / This ole house / Nighttime for the generals / Shadowland / Drivin' thunder / Clear blue skies / That girl / Compass / Soldiers of peace / Feel your love / Night song
CD _____ 781 886-2
Atlantic / Nov '88 / Warner Music.

BEST OF CROSBY, STILLS & NASH (4CD Set)
Suite: Judy blue eyes / Helplessly hoping / You don't have to cry / Wooden ships / Guinevere / Marrakesh express / Long time gone / Blackbird / Lady of the island / Song with no words (tree with no leaves) / Almost cut my hair / Teach your children / Horses through a rainstorm / Deja vu / Helpless / Four plus twenty / Laughing / Carry on/ questions / Woodstock / Ohio / Love the one you're with / Our house / Old times good times / Lee shore / Music is love / I'd swear there was somebody here / Man in the mirror / Black queen / Military madness / Urge for going / I used to be a king / Simple man / Southbound train / Change dirt / My love is a gentle thing / Word game / Johnny's garden / So begins the task / Turn back the pages / See the changes / It doesn't matter / Immigration man / Chicago/We can change the world / Homeward through the haze / Where will I be / Page 43 / Carry me / Cowboy of dreams / Bittersweet / To the last whale...a critical mass/Wind on water / Prison song / Another sleep song / Taken at all / In my dreams / Just a song before I go / Shadow captain / Dark star / Cathedral / Wasted on the way / Barrel of pain (half life) / Southern cross / Daylight again/Find the cost of freedom / Thoroughfare gap / Wild tales / Cold rain / Got it more / Tracks in the dust / As I come of age / 50/50 / Drive my car / Delta / Soldiers of peace / Yours and mine / Haven't we lost enough / After the dolphin / Find the cost of freedom
CD _____ 7567823192
Atlantic / Dec '91 / Warner Music.

CARRY ON
Woodstock / Marrakesh express / You don't have to cry / Teach your children / Love the one you're with / Almost cut my hair / Wooden ships / Dark star / Helpless / Chicago/We can change the world / Our house / A.Mass/B.Wind on the water / Change partners / Just a song before I go / Ohio / Wasted on the way / Southern cross / Suite: Judy blue eyes / Carry on/questions / Horses through a rainstorm / Johnny's garden / Helplessly hoping / Lee shore / Taken at all / Shadow captain / As I come of age / Drive my car / Dear Mr. Fantasy / In my dreams / Yours and mine / Haven't we lost enough / After the dolphin / Find the cost of freedom
CD _____ 7567804872
Atlantic / Dec '91 / Warner Music.

CROSBY, STILLS AND NASH
Suite: Judy blue eyes / Marrakesh express / Guinevere / You don't have to cry / Pre-road downs / Wooden ships / Lady of the island / Helplessly hoping / Long time gone / Forty nine bye byes
CD _____ 756782651-2
Atlantic / Aug '94 / Warner Music.

DAYLIGHT AGAIN
Turn your back on love / Wasted on the way / Southern cross / Into the darkness / Delta / Since I met you / Too much love to hide / Song for Susan / You are alive / Might as well have a good time / Daylight again
CD _____ 756782672-2
Atlantic / Oct '94 / Warner Music.

DEJA VU (Crosby, Stills, Nash & Young)
Carry on / Teach your children / Almost cut my hair / Helpless / Woodstock / Deja vu / Our house / Four plus twenty / Country girl / Everybody I love you

CD _____ 756782649-2
Atlantic / Aug '94 / Warner Music.

LIVE IT UP
Live it up / If anybody had a heart / Tomboy / Haven't we lost enough / Yours and mine / (Got to keep) open / Straight line / House of broken dreams / Arrows / After the dolphin
CD _____ 7567 82101-2
Atlantic / Jun '90 / Warner Music.

REPLAY
Carry on / Marrakesh express / Just a song before I go / First things first / Shadow captain / To the last whale / Love the one you're with / Pre-road downs / Change partners / I give you give blind / Cathedral
CD _____ 756782679-2
Atlantic / Dec '94 / Warner Music.

SO FAR (Crosby, Stills, Nash & Young)
Deja vu / Helplessly hoping / Wooden ships / Teach your children / Ohio / Find the cost of freedom / Woodstock / Our house / Helpless / Guenevere / Suite: Judy Blue eyes
CD _____ 756782648-2
Atlantic / Sep '94 / Warner Music.

Crosland, Ben

NORTHERN RUN, THE
Blues for Lex / Sunshower / Away too long / Don't you dare / Northern run / Break a leg / Pause for thought / Blue / Take the coltrane / Confluence
CD _____ JCCD 101
Jazz Cat / Sep '95 / New Note.

Cross

SHOVE IT
Shove it / Heaven for everyone / Love on a tightrope (like an animal) / Cowboys and indians / Stand up for love / Love lies bleeding / Rough justice / Second shelf mix (CD only) / Conceal
CD _____ CDV 2477
Virgin / '88 / EMI.

Cross, Christopher

CHRISTOPHER CROSS
Say you'll be mine / I really don't know anymore / Spinning / Never be the same / Poor Shirley / Ride like the wind / Light is on / Sailing / Minstrel gigolo
CD _____ 256 789
WEA / Jul '89 / Warner Music.

RENDEZVOUS
Rendezvous / Deputy Dan / Night across the world / Angry young men / In the blink of an eye / Is there something / Isn't it love / Nothing will change / Driftin' away / Fisherman's tale
CD _____ 74321 10291-2
Arista / Oct '92 / BMG.

WINDOW
Been there, done that / Wild wild West / Wishing well / Thinkin' bout you / Jan's tune / Open up my window / Nature's way / Uncharted hearts / Before I go / Love is calling
CD _____ 74321246542
Arista / Jun '95 / BMG.

Cross, David

BIG PICTURE, THE
CD _____ CDR 104
Red Hot / Mar '94 / THE.

MEMOS FROM PURGATORY
Poppies / Meantime / First policeman / Animal / New dawn / Postscript / Bizarre bazaar / Basking in the blue
CD _____ CDR 103
Red Hot / Mar '94 / THE.

TESTING TO DESTRUCTION (Cross, David Band)
CD _____ CDR 107
Red Hot / Nov '94 / THE.

Cross, Mike

BEST OF THE FUNNY STUFF
CD _____ SH 1010CD
Sugarhill / Mar '94 / Roots / CM / ADA / Direct.

HIGH POWERED, LOW FLYING
CD _____ SHCD 1011
Sugarhill / Mar '94 / Roots / CM / ADA / Direct.

Cross, Sandra

100% LOVERS ROCK
CD _____ ARCD 096
Ariwa Sounds / Jun '94 / Jetstar / SRD.

COMET IN THE SKY
Who's finally won / Comet in the sky / Blinded by love / Whole world / I need a man / My only desire / Styler boy / Why oh why / Free South Africa / I want you so badly
CD _____ ARICD 034
Ariwa Sounds / Oct '88 / Jetstar / SRD.

COUNTRY LIFE
CD _____ ARICD 026
Ariwa Sounds / Feb '89 / Jetstar / SRD.

FOUNDATION OF LOVE
CD _____ ARICD 047
Ariwa Sounds / Jun '92 / Jetstar / SRD.

Cross, Tim

CLASSIC LANDSCAPE
CD _____ NAGE 3CD
Art Of Landscape / Jan '86 / Sony.

Crouch, Andraé

MERCY
Say so / Give it all back to me / Love in my light / Love somebody like me / Nobody else like you / Mercy / This is the Lord's doing / We love it here / He's the light / Mercy interlude / God still loves me
CD _____ 9362454322
Warner Bros. / Jul '95 / Warner Music.

Crow, Dan

OOPS
CD _____ CD 8007
Rounder / '88 / CM / Direct / ADA / Cadillac.

Crow, Sheryl

TUESDAY NIGHT MUSIC CLUB
Run baby run / Leaving Las Vegas / Strong enough / Can't cry anymore / Solidity / Na na song / No one said it'd be easy / What can I do for you / All I wanna do / We do what we can / Reach around jerk (CDST only) / Can't cry anymore (livo) (CDST only) / What can I do for you (live) (CDST only) / Leaving Las Vegas (live) (CDST only) / No-one said it would be easy (live) (CDST only) / Volvo cowgirl (CDST only)
CD _____ 540126-2
A&M / Oct '93 / PolyGram.
CD Set _____ 5403682
A&M / May '95 / PolyGram.

Crowbar

CROWBAR/LIVE + 1
High rate extinction / All I had (I gave) / Will that never dies / No quarter / Self inflicted / Negative pollution / Existance is punishment / Holding nothing / I have failed / Self inflicted (Live) / Fixation (Mixes) / I have failed (Live) / All I had (Live) / Numb sensitive (Live)
CD _____ CDVEST 5
Bulletproof / Apr '94 / Pinnacle.

OBEDIENCE THRU SUFFERING
CD _____ CDVEST 42
Bulletproof / Feb '95 / Pinnacle.

TIME HEALS NOTHING
CD _____ CDVEST 51
Bulletproof / May '95 / Pinnacle.

Crowbar

DAY THE FURNITURE ARGUED, THE
Day the furniture argued / Deep down / Tower of Babel / Manufactured eye / Talking windmill / Electric infa / Chemistry of dub / Millenium lights
CD _____ MASS 023CD
Infinite Mass / Mar '95 / Pinnacle.

Crowd Of Isolated

MEMORIES & SCARS
CD _____ XM 025CD
X-Mist / Apr '92 / SRD.

Crowded House

CROWDED HOUSE
World where you live / Now we're getting somewhere / Don't dream it's over / Mean to me / Love you till the day I die / Something so strong / Hole in the river / I walk away / Tombstone / That's what I call love
CD _____ CDEST 2016
Capitol / Feb '94 / EMI.

CROWDED HOUSE/TEMPLE OF LOW MEN/WOODFACE (3CD Set)
World where you live / Now we're getting somewhere / Don't dream it's over / Mean to me / Love you 'til the day I die / Something so strong / Hole in the river / I walk away / Tombstone / That's what I call love / I feel possessed / Kill eye / Into temptation / Mansion in the slums / When you come / Never be the same / Love this life / Sister madly / In the lowlands / Better be home soon / Chocolate cake / It's only natural / Fall at your feet / Tall trees / Weather with you / Whispers and moans / Four seasons in one day / There goes God / Fame is / All I ask / As sure as I am / Italian plastic / She goes on / How will you go
CD Set _____ CDOMB 001
Capitol / Oct '95 / EMI.

TEMPLE OF LOW MEN
I feel possessed / Kill eye / Into temptation / Mansion in the slums / When you come / Never be the same / Love this life / Sister madly / In the lowlands / Better be home soon
CD _____ CDEST 2064
Capitol / Jul '88 / EMI.

TOGETHER ALONE
Kare kare / In my command / Nails in my feet / Black and white boy / Fingers of love / Pineapple head / Locked out / Private Universe / Walking on the spot / Distant sun / Catherine wheels / Skin feeling / Together alone
CD _____ CDESTU 2215
Capitol / Nov '93 / EMI.

WOODFACE
Chocolate cake / It's only natural / Fall at your feet / Tall trees / Weather with you / Whispers and moans / Four seasons in one day / There goes God / Fame is / All I ask / As sure as I am / Italian plastic / She goes on / How will you go
CD _____ CDEST 2144
Capitol / Jun '91 / EMI.

Crowe, Bobby

SHORES OF LOCH ALVIE, THE (Crowe, Bobby & His S.C. Band)
CD _____ GRCD 48
Grasmere / '92 / Target/BMG / Savoy.

Crowe, J.D.

FLASHBACK (Crowe, J.D. & The New South)
CD _____ ROUCD 0322
Rounder / Nov '94 / CM / Direct / ADA / Cadillac.

GOING BACK (Crowe & McLaughlin)
CD _____ ROU 314CD
Rounder / Jan '94 / CM / Direct / ADA / Cadillac.

J.D. CROWE AND THE NEW SOUTH (Crowe, J.D. & The New South)
Old home place / Some old day / Rock salt and nails / Sally Goodin / Ten degrees / Nashville blues / You are what I am / Summer wages / I'm walkin' / Home sweet home revisited / Cryin' Holly
CD _____ CD 0044
Rounder / '88 / CM / Direct / ADA / Cadillac.

STRAIGHT AHEAD
CD _____ CD 0202
Rounder / Jun '87 / CM / Direct / ADA / Cadillac.

Crowell, Rodney

DIAMONDS AND DIRT
Crazy baby / I couldn't leave you if I tried / She's crazy for leaving / After all this time / I know you're married / Above and beyond / It's such a small world / I didn't know I could lose you / Brand new rag / Last waltz
CD _____ 4608732
CBS / Apr '89 / Sony.

JEWEL OF THE SOUTH
Say you love me / Candy man / Please remember me / Ballad of Possum Potez / Thinking about leaving / Ladder of love / Just say yes / Storm of love / Love to burn / Jewel of the South / Que' es amor (what is love)
CD _____ MCD 11223
MCA / Jun '95 / BMG.

KEYS TO THE HIGHWAY, THE
My past is present / If looks could kill / Soul searchin' / Many a long and lonesome highway / We gotta go on meeting like this / Faith is mine / Tell me the truth / Don't let your feet slow you down / That we're alone / Things I wish I'd said / I guess we've been together for too long / You've been on my mind
CD _____ 4660022
CBS / Sep '94 / Sony.

Crowforce

CROWFORCE
CD _____ CDDVN 1
Devotion / Jul '92 / Pinnacle.

Crowley, Jimmy

CAMP HOUSE BALLADS (Crowley, Jimmy & Stoker's Lodge)
CD _____ CLUNCD 031
Mulligan / Jan '92 / CM / ADA.

Crown Heights Affair

ESSENTIAL DANCEFLOOR ARTISTS VOL. 1
Dreaming a dream / Foxy lady / Dancin' / Far out / I'm gonna love you forever / Galaxy of love / You gave me love / Use your body and soul / Say a prayer for two
CD _____ DGPCD 665
Deep Beats / Mar '94 / BMG.

Crown Of Thorns

BURNING, THE
CD _____ BS 005CD
Black Sun / Jan '96 / Plastic Head.

CROWN OF THORNS
CD _____ NTHEN 8
Now & Then / Jun '95 / Plastic Head.

RAW THORNS
CD _____ NTHEN 13
Now & Then / Jun '95 / Plastic Head.

Crown Of Thornz

TRAIN YARD BLUES
CD _____ LF 151CD
Lost & Found / May '95 / Plastic Head.

Crowsdell

DREAMETTE
CD _____ ABB 83CD
Big Cat / Apr '95 / SRD / Pinnacle.

Crucial Robbie

CRUCIAL VIEW
CD _____ ARICD 056
Ariwa Sounds / Oct '90 / Jetstar / SRD.

Crucial Vibes

CONTROL YOURSELF
CD _____ CDSGP 061
Prestige / Jun '93 / Total/BMG.

Crucial, Lloydie

JUNGLE IN THE SUBURBS
CD _____ LCCD 002
Lloydie Crucial / Feb '95 / Jetstar.

JUNGLEMANIA VOL. 1 (Crucial, Lloydie & The Concrete Junglist Crew)
CD _____ LCCDLP 001
Lloydie Crucial / Oct '94 / Jetstar.

Crucifix

DEHUMANIZATION
CD _____ 18523 2
Southern / Sep '94 / SRD.

Crucifixion

DESERT OF SHATTERED HOPES
CD _____ 9040172
Mausoleum / Apr '95 / Grapevine.

Crucifucks

OUR WILL BE DONE
CD _____ VIRUS 111
Alternative Tentacles / '92 / Pinnacle.

Crudup, Arthur

ARTHUR 'BIG BOY' CRUDUP MEETS THE MASTER BLUES BASSISTS (Crudup, Arthur 'Big Boy')
CD _____ DD 621
Delmark / Mar '95 / Hot Shot / Jazz Music / Direct / Cadillac.

ARTHUR 'BIG BOY' CRUDUP VOL.1 (Crudup, Arthur 'Big Boy')
CD _____ DOCD 5201
Blues Document / Oct '93 / Swift / Jazz Music / Hot Shot.

ARTHUR 'BIG BOY' CRUDUP VOL.2 (Crudup, Arthur 'Big Boy')
CD _____ DOCD 5202
Blues Document / Oct '93 / Swift / Jazz Music / Hot Shot.

ARTHUR 'BIG BOY' CRUDUP VOL.3 (Crudup, Arthur 'Big Boy')
CD _____ DOCD 5203
Blues Document / Oct '93 / Swift / Jazz Music / Hot Shot.

ARTHUR 'BIG BOY' CRUDUP VOL.4 (Crudup, Arthur 'Big Boy')
CD _____ DOCD 5204
Blues Document / Oct '93 / Swift / Jazz Music / Hot Shot.

FATHER OF ROCK 'N' ROLL, THE
I'm in the mood / Ethel Mae / My mama don't allow me / Look no yonder wall / Too much competition / My baby left me
CD _____ CD 52025
Blues Encore / Feb '93 / Target/BMG.

MEAN OL' FRISCO (Charly Blues - Masterworks Vol. 50)
CD _____ CDBM 50
Charly / Jun '93 / Charly / THE / Cadillac.

THAT'S ALL RIGHT MAMA
If I get lucky / Gonna follow my baby / Mean ol' frisco / Cool disposition / Rock me mama / Keep your arms around me / That's your red wagon / She's gone / So glad you're mine / Chicago blues / Crudup's after hours / That's all right / Shout, sister, shout / She ain't nothing but trouble / My baby left me / Too much competition / Second man blues / I'm gonna dig myself a hole / Mr. So and so / My wife and woman / I love you / She's got no hair
CD _____ ND 90653
Bluebird / May '92 / BMG.

Cruel Frederick

BIRTH OF THE CRUEL
CD _____ SST 127 CD
SST / May '93 / Plastic Head.

WE ARE THE MUSIC WE PLAY
CD _____ SST 290 CD
SST / May '93 / Plastic Head.

Cruel Sea

THIS IS NOT THE WAY HOME
CD _____ REDCD 25
Red Eye / Aug '94 / Direct.

THREE-LEGGED DOG
CD _____ 5275372
PolyGram / Jun '95 / PolyGram.

Cruise, Julee

FLOATING INTO THE NIGHT
Floating / Falling / I remember / Mysteries of love / Into the night / I float alone / Nightingale / Swan / World spins
CD _____ 7599258592
WEA / Feb '90 / Warner Music.

VOICE OF LOVE, THE
This is our night / Space for love / Movin' / You on / Friends for life / Up in flames / Kool kat walk / Until the end of the world / She would die for love / In my other world / Questions in a world of blues / Voice of love
CD _____ 9362453902
WEA / Oct '93 / Warner Music.

Crumbsuckers

LIFE OF DREAMS
CD _____ CDJUST 4
Rough Justice / Aug '91 / Pinnacle.

Crumit, Frank

EVERYBODY'S BEST FRIEND
Riding down from Bangor / There's no one with endurance like a man who sells insurance / Wrap me up in my tarpaulin jacket / Pig got up and slowly walked away / Frankie and Johnny / My girl ran away / Prune song / Antonio Pasquale Ramonio / Donald the dub / I'm in love with Susan / Nagasaki / Three trees / King of Zulu / Who, Josephine / I don't work for a living / Tale of a ticker / What kind of noise annoys an oyster / High silk hat and a gold top walking cane / Grandson of Abdul Abulbul Amir / Dashing marine
CD _____ CDHD 139
Happy Days / Nov '88 / Conifer.

MOUNTAIN GREENERY
Bride's lament / Mountain greenery / Abdul Abulbul Amir / Thanks for the buggy ride / Carib-blue / Kingdom coming and the year of Jubilo / Ukelele lady / Jack is every inch a sailor / Oh by jingo, oh by gee / Prune song / Girlfriend / Billy boy / King of Borneo / Get away old man get away / Down in the cane break / Crazy words crazy tune / Gay caballero / Insurance man (CD only)
CD _____ CD AJA 5001
Living Era / Oct '93 / Koch.

RETURN OF THE GAY CABELLERO
I'm bettin' the roll on roamer / Donald the dub / Lady of my dreams taught me how to play second fiddle / I learned about women from her (around the corner) / Pretty little Italian bimbo down on the bamboo isle / Granny's old armchair / I'm a specialist / Would you like to take a walk / And then he took up golf / Wake Nicodemus / Oh, baby (don't say no say maybe) / Dolan's poker party / I married the Bootlegger's daughter / Little brown jug / Return of Abdul Abulbul Amir
CD _____ CD AJA 5012
Living Era / Oct '93 / Koch.

Crumly, Pat

BEHIND THE MASK (Crumly, Pat Quartet)
Behind the mask / Voyage / I'll remember April / You don't know what love is / Island / Carib-blue / This heart of mine / Transside / Little off beat / Polka dots and moonbeams / Contemplation / It should lose you / Behind the mask (Second version)
CD _____ SPJCD 549
Spotlite / May '93 / Cadillac / Jazz Horizons / Swift.

FLAMINGO
Nightwalk / Beautiful love / Bewitched, bothered and bewildered / Slow burn / Flamingo / Here's that rainy day / Eucalypso / Days of wine and roses / Three little words / My old flame / Flamebirds / Two degrees East - three degrees West / It might as well be spring / Way you look tonight
CD _____ SPJCD 550
Spotlite / Jun '94 / Cadillac / Jazz Horizons / Swift.

Crunt

CRUNT
CD _____ TRCD 19
Trance / Feb '94 / SRD.

Crusaders

COLLECTION, THE
CD _____ CCSCD 420
Castle / Mar '95 / BMG.

CRUSADERS AND BEYOND, THE
Street life / Inherit the wind / Stomp and buck dance / Burnin' up the carnival / No matter how high I get) I'll still be looking up

CRUSADERS

to you / Keep that same old feeling / Snow-flakes / Brazos river / Breakdown / Soul shadows / Let's dance together / Time bomb / Voices in the rain
CD _____ MCCD 163
MCI / Jul '94 / Disc / THE.

CRUSADERS BEST, THE
Street life / Way back home / Feeling funky / Tough talk / Do you remember when / Message from the inner city / Eleanor Rigby / Carnival of the night / My Mama told me / I'm so glad I'm standing here today / Put it where you want it
CD _____ PWKS 4231
Carlton Home Entertainment / Nov '94 / Carlton Home Entertainment.

GREATEST CRUSADE, THE
Street life / Hustler / Rodeo drive (High steppin') / Marcella's dream / Rainbow seeker / Burning up the carnival / Snowflake / Spiral / Nite crawler / Rainbow visions / Hold on (I feel our love is changing) / Chain reaction (MC only) / Carnival of the night / Ballad for Joe (Louis) / Inherit the wind / Some people just never learn / (No matter how high I get) I'll still be looking up to you / Oasis / It happens every day / Fly with the wings of love / Soul caravan / Fairy tales / I'm so glad I'm standing here today / Put it where you want it / Elegant evening / Free as the wind (MC only) / Search for soul / Survivor
CD _____ CLBCD 5501
Calibre / Feb '95 / Sound & Media.

HAPPY AGAIN (Jazz Crusaders)
Lock it down / When your so far away / Midnite moods / Top of the world / Fool's rush in / Are you a part of me / Slyzappit / Rockslide / La luz el dia / Jamaica / Travelin' inside your love / Young rabbits / Uh huh oh yea
CD _____ 9950322
Sin-Drome / Jul '95 / New Note.

HEALING THE WOUNDS
Pessimisticism / Mercy mercy mercy / Little things mean a lot / 'Cause we've ended as lovers / Shake dance / Maputo / Running man / Healing the wounds
CD _____ GRD 9638
GRP / May '91 / BMG / New Note.

HOLLYWOOD
CD _____ 5303062
Verve / Apr '94 / PolyGram.

LIVE IN JAPAN
Rainbow seeker / Hustler / Sweet gentle love / Spiral / Melodies of love / Carmel / So far away / Brazos river breakdown / In all my wildest dreams / Put it where you want it
CD _____ GRP 97462
GRP / Nov '93 / BMG / New Note.

OLD SOCKS, NEW SHOES
CD _____ 5303072
Verve / Apr '94 / PolyGram.

PASS THE PLATE
CD _____ 530308-2
PolyGram Jazz / Nov '94 / PolyGram.

SAMPLE A DECADE
So far away / Bayou bottoms / Soul shadows / Don't let it get you down / My mama told me so / I'm so glad I'm standing here today / Soul caravan / Nite crawler / Fairytales / Honky tonk struttin' / Chain reaction / And then there was the blues / Street life / Hold on / Snow flake / Rhapsody and blues / Sweet 'n' sour / Night ladies / Rodeo drive (high steppin') / Free as the wind
CD _____ VSOPCD 131
Connoisseur / Jan '89 / Pinnacle.

SOUL SHADOWS
Night theme / Stomp and buck dance / Spiral / Street life / Feel it / 'Cause we've ended as lovers / Ballad for Joe (Louis) / Destiny / I felt the love / Soul shadows / Way it goes / Night ladies
CD _____ VSOPCD 212
Connoisseur / Feb '95 / Pinnacle.

STREET LIFE
Street life / My lady / Rodeo drive (high steppin') / Carnival of the night / Hustler / Night faces / Inherit the wind
CD _____ MCLD 19004
MCA / Apr '92 / BMG.

ULTIMATE COLLECTION
CD _____ NTRCD 035
Nectar / Mar '95 / Pinnacle.

Crusaders For Real Hip...

DEJA VU/ IT'S '82 (Crusaders For Real Hip Hop)
CD _____ PCD 1428
Profile / Jul '92 / Pinnacle.

Crush, Bobby

DOUBLE DECKER PARTY
CD _____ PLATCD 5920
Platinum Music / Jul '92 / Prism / Ross.

HOLLYWOOD AND BROADWAY
Why God / Bohemian rhapsody / I dreamed a dream / Tears in heaven / Love moves in mysterious ways / Everything I do (I do it for you) / Beauty and the beast / Love can't happen / Places that belong to you / Any

dream will do / Music of the night / Some-one to watch over me
CD _____ PLATCD 3919
Prism / Apr '93 / Prism.

Crusher

ACT 2-UNDERMINE
CD _____ NO 2312
Noise/Modern Music / Nov '93 / Pinnacle / Plastic Head.

Crust

CRUSTY LOVE
CD _____ TRCD 23
Trance / May '94 / SRD.

Cruz, Celia

AZUCAR NEGRA
CD _____ 66058025
RMM / Jun '93 / New Note.

EL MERENGUE
CD _____ CD 62002
Saludos Amigos / Apr '94 / Target/BMG.

IRREPETIBLE
Que le den candela / Bembelequa / Limon Y menta / Marion ague / Drume negrita / Caballero y dama / Enamorada de ti / La guagua / Cuando cuba se acabe de liberar
CD _____ 66058054
RMM / Feb '95 / New Note.

MADRE RUMBA
CD _____ CD 62016
Saludos Amigos / Apr '94 / Target/BMG.

MADRE RUMBA (Cruz, Celia & Sonora Matancera)
CD _____ CD 3557
Cameo / Jul '95 / Target/BMG.

MAMBO DEL AMOR
CD _____ CD 62007
Saludos Amigos / Apr '94 / Target/BMG.

RITMOY Y CALOR DE CUBA CON
CD _____ BMB 504CD
Blue Moon / Nov '95 / Magnum Music Group / Greensleeves / Hot Shot / ADA / Cadillac / Discovery.

SALSA Y MERENGUUE
CD _____ CD 62054
Saludos Amigos / May '94 / Target/BMG.

Crybabys

CRYBABYS, THE
CD _____ RRCD 142
Receiver / Apr '91 / Grapevine.

Cryner, Bobbie

GIRL OF YOUR DREAMS
CD _____ MCD 11324
MCA / Jan '96 / BMG.

Crypt Of Kereberos

WORLD OF MYTHS
CD _____ CDAR 013
Adipocre / Feb '94 / Plastic Head.

Cryptic Slaughter

SPEAK YOUR PEACE
Born too soon / Insanity by the numbers / Death styles of the poor and lonely / Divided minds / Killing time / Still born, again / Co-exist / One thing or another / Speak your piece
CD _____ CDZORRO 6
Metal Blade / Jul '90 / Pinnacle.

STREAM OF CONSCIOUSNESS
Circus of fools / Aggravated / Last laugh / Overcome / Deteriorate / See through you / Just went back / Drift / Altered visions / One last thought / Whisker biscuit / Addicted
CD _____ RR9 521 2
Roadrunner / Nov '88 / Pinnacle.

Cryptopsy

BLASPHEMY MADE FLESH
CD _____ IR 011CD
Invasion / Apr '95 / Plastic Head.

Crystal Trip

CRYSTAL TRIP
CD _____ GULL 2CD
Seagull / Sep '93 / SRD.

Crystals

BEST OF THE CRYSTALS
There's no other (like my baby) / Oh yeah, maybe baby / Uptown / What a nice way to turn 17 / He hit me (and it felt like a kiss) / No one ever tells you / He's a rebel / I love you, Eddie / Another country, another world / Please hurt me / He's sure the boy I love / Look in my eyes / Da doo ron ron / Heart-breaker / Then he kissed me / Ronettes / Little boy / Girls can tell / All grown up
CD _____ PSCD 1007
Phil Spector Int. / Sep '92 / EMI.

CTC

CLOSER THAN CLOSE AND FRIENDS
CD _____ CUTUPCD 003
Jump Cut / Mar '94 / Total/BMG / Vital/SAM.

Cuarto Patria

UNA COQUETA, A
Corason / Jan '94 / CM / Direct / ADA. _____ CO 106

Cuban All Stars

PASSPORTE
Presentation / Rumberos de ayer / Descarga pa' gozar / Donde va mulata / Anga / Blem blem blem / Tata se ha vuelto loco / La clave de los primros
CD _____ ENJ 90192
Enja / Apr '95 / New Note / Vital/SAM.

Cubanate

ANTIMATTER
Blackout / Bodyburn / Revolution time / Autonomy / Junky / Exert / Disorder / Sucker / Switch / Forceful / Bodyburn (remix) / Kill or cure
CD _____ DYCD 12
Dynamica / Sep '93 / Pinnacle.

CYBERIA
CD _____ DY 82E
Dynamica / Nov '95 / Pinnacle.

Cuber, Ronnie

BARITONE MADNESS LIVE AT NICK'S (Cuber, Ronnie & Nick BRignola)
Softly as in a morning sunrise / Caravan / In a sentimental mood / What's new / Night in Tunisia / Blue train / Crack down
CD _____ CDSJP 341
Timeless Jazz / Dec '95 / New Note.

SCENE IS CLEAN, THE
Scene is clean / Adoracion / Song for Pharoah / Arroz con pollo / Mazambo / Fajardo / Tee's bag / Flamingo
CD _____ MCD 9218-2
Milestone / Jul '94 / Jazz Music / Pinnacle / Wellard / Cadillac.

Cucchi, Flavio

FLAVIO CUCCHI PLAYS BARRIOS & VILLA-LOBOS
CD _____ EUCD 1096
ARC / Jan '92 / ARC Music / ADA.

FROM YESTERDAY TO PENNY LANE
CD _____ EUCD 1247
ARC / Mar '94 / ARC Music / ADA.

GUITAR - CROSSING OVER
CD _____ EUCD 1326
ARC / Nov '95 / ARC Music / ADA.

PLAYS BROUWER
CD _____ EUCD 1192
ARC / Apr '92 / ARC Music / ADA.

Cuckooland

POP SENSIBILITY
CD _____ DAMGOOD 67CD
Damaged Goods / Jun '95 / SRD.

Cud

ASQUARIUS
CD _____ 3953902
A&M / Apr '95 / PolyGram.

ELVIS BELT
Slack time / Make no bones / Treat me bad / Punishment-reward relationships / Under my hat / Lola / Urban spaceman / Art / You're the boss / Only (a prawn in Whitby) / Hey wire / I've had it with blondes
CD _____ ILL CD 013
Imaginary / Apr '92 / Vital.

LEGGY MAMBO
CD _____ ILLCD 021
Imaginary / Oct '90 / Vital.

SHOWBIZ
Somebody snatched my action / ESP / Waving and drowning / Sticks and stones / Mystery deepens / Slip away / One giant love / I reek of choc / Not necessarily evil / You lead me / Tourniquet / Neurotica
CD _____ 540211-2
A&M / Apr '95 / PolyGram.

WHEN IN ROME, KILL ME
When in Rome, kill me / Only (a prawn in Whitby) / Bibi couldn't see / Strange kind of love / Push and shove / Day crime paid / When in Rome, kill me again / I've had it with blondes / Van van van / Vocally speaking / Wobbly jelly / Alison Springs / Epicurean's answer / Bomba boy
CD _____ ILLCD 500
Imaginary / Apr '92 / Vital.

Cudgels

GOD'S CHILDREN
CD _____ BULL 90CD
Bring On Bull / Jul '92 / Vital / SRD.

Cues

WHY
Yes sir / Why / Crackerjack / Burn that candle / Poppa loves momma / Charlie Brown / Crazy crazy party / You're on my mind / Ladder / Destination 2100 and 65 / Prince or pauper / Rock 'n' roll Mr. Oriole / Warm spot / Girl I love / Oh my darlin' / Killer diller / I pretend / Be my wife / Don't make believe / Only you / Fell for your loving, I / Hot rotten soda pop / So near and yet so far / Forty leven dozen ways / Schoochie schoochie / Yes sir (2) / Ol' man river
CD _____ BCD 15510
Bear Family / May '91 / Rollercoaster / Direct / CM / Swift / ADA.

Cuesta, Ivan

A TI, COLOMBIA (Cuesta, Ivan Y Sus Baltimore Vallent)
CD _____ ARHCD 388
Arhoolie / Apr '95 / ADA / Direct / Cadillac.

Cuevas, Sergio

LA HARPE INDIENNE DU PARAGUAY
Camino de San Juan / Maquinita / Feliz Navidad / Harpa serenata / Pajaro campana / A mi dos amores / Nuevo baile / Poncho cuatro colores / Golpe llanero / Danza indiana / Barrio rincon / Magnolia / Balada de mi sueno / Pa i Zacaria
CD _____ ARN 64040
Arion / '88 / Discovery / ADA.

Cuffe, Tony

WHEN FIRST I WENT TO CALEDONIA
When first I went to Caledonia / Miss Wharton Duff/The mare / Iron horse / Caledonia / Dr. MacInnes' fancy / Buchan turnpike / Lass o' paties mill / Weary pund o' tow / Paddy Kelly's brew / Otterburn / Scalloway lasses / Humours of Tulla / Miss Forester
CD _____ IRCD 011
Iona / Feb '94 / ADA / Direct / Duncans.

Cugat, Xavier

CUBAN MAMBO
CD _____ CD 62003
Saludos Amigos / Apr '94 / Target/BMG.

EL AMERICANO
El Americano / Yo quiero un mambo / Strangers in the dark / Que rico el mambo / Uuuh / Anything can happen - mambo / Mambo ay ay ay / Riviera mambo / Jamay / Maracaibo / Humpty dumpty / Mambo mania / Flute nightmares / Mambo gitano / Mambo OK / El Manjuano / Mondongo / Mambo at the Waldorf
CD _____ CD 62078
Saludos Amigos / Jan '93 / Target/BMG.

ME GUSTA LA CONGA (Cugat, Xavier & His Orchestra)
CD _____ CD 62009
Saludos Amigos / Jan '93 / Target/BMG.

PARA VIGO ME VAY (Cugat, Xavier & His Orchestra)
CD _____ CD 62044
Saludos Amigos / Nov '93 / Target/BMG.

TO ALL MY FRIENDS
New Cucaracha / Golden sunset / La Bamba / Que lindas in Mexicanas / Despedida / Cielito lindo / Banana boat song (Day O) / Cuban holiday / Adius marquita Linda / Barbados baila / Diamante negro / Braziliana
CD _____ ISCD 146
Intersound / Jun '95 / Jazz Music.

XAVIER CUGAT (Cugat, Xavier & His Band)
CD _____ HQCD 14
Harlequin / '92 / Swift / Jazz Music / Wellard / Hot Shot / Cadillac.

XAVIER CUGAT & DINAH SHORE 1939-1945 (Cugat, Xavier & Dinah Shore)
CD _____ HQCD 29
Harlequin / Oct '93 / Swift / Jazz Music / Wellard / Hot Shot / Cadillac.

XAVIER CUGAT 1944 & 1945 (Cugat, Xavier & His Orchestra)
CD _____ CCD 59
Circle / Aug '94 / Jazz Music / Swift / Wellard.

Cul De Sac

I DON'T WANT TO GO TO BED
CD _____ FNCD 330
Flying Nun / Jun '95 / Disc.

Cullum, Jim

HOORAY FOR HOAGY (Cullum, Jim & His Jazz Band)
CD _____ ACD 251
Audiophile / '91 / Jazz Music / Swift.

MUSIC OF JELLY ROLL MORTON (Cullum, Jim & His Jazz Band)
CD _____ SOSCD 1254
Stomp Off / Jul '93 / Jazz Music / Wellard.

SUPER SATCH (Cullum, Jim Big Band)
CD _____ SOSCD 1148
Stomp Off / Jan '88 / Jazz Music / Wellard.

Cult

CEREMONY
CD _____ BEGA 122CD
Beggars Banquet / Oct '91 / Warner Music / Disc.

COMPLETE RECORDINGS (Death Cult)
God's zoo / Brothers grimm / Ghost dance / Horse nation / Christians / God's zoo (these times)
CD _____ SIT 2329CD
Situation 2 / '91 / Pinnacle.

CULT
CD _____ BBQCD 164
Beggars Banquet / Sep '94 / Warner Music / Disc.

DREAMTIME
Horse nation / Butterflies / Flower in the desert / Bad medicine waltz / Spiritwalker / 83rd dream / Go West / Gimmick / Dreamtime / Rider in the snow
CD _____ BBL 57 CD
Lowdown/Beggars Banquet / Oct '88 / Warner Music / Disc.

ELECTRIC
Wild flower / Peace dog / Li'l devil / Aphrodisiac jacket / Electric ocean / Bad fun / King country man / Born to be wild / Love removal machine / Outlaw / Memphis hip shake
CD _____ BEGA 80CD
Beggars Banquet / Jan '88 / Warner Music / Disc.

INTERVIEW DISC
CD P.Disc _____ CBAK 4027
Baktabak / Sep '90 / Baktabak.

LOVE
Nirvana / Big neon glitter / Love / Brother wolf, sister moon / Rain / Phoenix / Hollow man / Revolution / She sells sanctuary / Black angel
CD _____ BEGA 65 CD
Beggars Banquet / Oct '85 / Warner Music / Disc.

PURE CULT (The Best Of The Cult)
CD _____ BEGA 130CD
Beggars Banquet / Jan '93 / Warner Music / Disc.

SONIC TEMPLE
Fire woman / Sun king / Sweet soul sister / Soul asylum / Soldier blue / Edie (ciao baby) / American horse / Automatic blues / Wake up time for freedom / New York City
CD _____ BEGA 98 CD
Beggars Banquet / Mar '89 / Warner Music / Disc.

SOUTHERN DEATH CULT (Southern Death Cult)
All glory / Fat man / Today / False faces / Crypt / Crow / Faith / Vivisection / Apache / Moya
CD _____ BBL 46CD
Lowdown/Beggars Banquet / Jul '88 / Warner Music / Disc.

Cultural Roots

PRETTY WOMAN
CD _____ LG2 1073
Lagoon / Mar '93 / Magnum Music Group / THE.

Culture

BALDHEAD BRIDGE
Them a payaka / How can I leave jah / Baldhead bridge / Behold I come / Love shine bright / Jah love / Zion gate / So long babylon / Fool I (and I)
CD _____ SHCD 44017
Shanachie / Mar '94 / Koch / ADA / Greensleeves.

CULTURE AT WORK
CD _____ SHANCD 43047
Shanachie / '89 / Koch / ADA /
Greensleeves.

CULTURE IN DUB - 15 DUB SHOTS
CD _____ HBCD 173
Heartbeat / Aug '94 / Greensleeves / Jetstar / Direct / ADA.

CUMBOLO
They never love in this time / Innocent blood / Cumbolo / Poor Jah people / Natty never get weary / Natty dread naw run / Down in Jamaica / This train / Payday / Mind who you beg for help
CD _____ SHANCD 44005
Shanachie / '88 / Koch / ADA / Greensleeves.

IN CULTURE
CD _____ JMC 200201
Jamaica Gold / Sep '94 / THE / Magnum Music Group / Jetstar.

LION ROCK
CD _____ NETCD 1005
Munich / Apr '95 / CM / ADA / Greensleeves / Direct.

PEACE AND LOVE
CD _____ CPCD 8024
Charly / Feb '94 / Charly / THE / Cadillac.

STRICTLY CULTURE
CD _____ MCCD 158
Music Club / May '94 / Disc / THE / CM.

TOO LONG IN SLAVERY
Behold / Poor jah people / Stop the fussing and fighting / Cumbolo / Work on Natty / Tell me where you get it / Iron sharpening iron / International rebel / Too long in slavery / Shepherd / Holy mount zion / Never get weary / Citizen as a peaceful dub
CD _____ CDFL 9011
Frontline / Sep '90 / EMI / Jetstar.

TROD ON
CD _____ HBCD 137
Heartbeat / Jun '93 / Greensleeves / Jetstar / Direct / ADA.

TWO SEVENS CLASH
Callin' rasta for I / I'm alone in the wilderness / Pirate days / Two sevens clash / I'm not ashamed / Get ready to ride the lion to Zion / Black starliner / Jah pretty face / See them a comin' / Natty dread taking over
CD _____ SHANCD 44001
Shanachie / '88 / Koch / ADA / Greensleeves.

WINGS OF A DOVE
Marcus / Why worry about them / Marriage in canaan / Wings of a dove / Freedom time / Rub-a-dub style / Pass on / Campyard / Too much pressure / England fireplace
CD _____ SHCD 43097
Shanachie / Jul '92 / Koch / ADA / Greensleeves.

Culture Beat

REMIX ALBUM
Der erdbeermund (Get Into Magic Mix) / No deeper meaning (Technology Mix) / I like you (Zulu Mix) / Mr. Vain (Mr. House Mix) / Got to get it (Hypnotic Mix) / Anything (Trance Mix) / World in your hands / Adelante / DMC Megamix (Vorsprung Durch Culture Beat)
CD _____ 4776692
Epic / Jan '95 / Sony.

SERENITY
Serenity (prolog) / Mr. Vain / Got to get it / World in your hands / Adelante / Rocket to the moon / Anything / Key to your heart / Other side of me / Hurt / Mother Earth / Serenity (epilog) / ID Tania / ID Jay
CD _____ 474101 2
Epic / Sep '93 / Sony.

Culture Ceilidh Band

AFTER THE CEILIDH
CD _____ CDITV 543
Scotdisc / May '93 / Duncans / Ross / Conifer.

Culture Club

BEST OF CULTURE CLUB, THE
Do you really want to hurt me / White boy / Church of the poison mind / Changing everyday / War song / I'm afraid of me / It's a miracle / Dream / Time (Clock of the heart) / Dive / Victims / I'll tumble 4 ya / Miss me blind / Mistake no. 3 / Medal song / Karma chameleon
CD _____ CDVIP 102
Virgin / Sep '94 / EMI.

COLLECT 12" MIXES PLUS
Move away / Miss me blind/It's a miracle / God thank you woman / I'll tumble 4 ya / Love is cold / Do you really want to hurt me / Everything I own / Colour by numbers / From luxury to heartache / Time / Black money / Love is love / Man shake / War song
CD _____ CDVIP 116
Virgin VIP / Mar '94 / Carlton Home Entertainment / THE / EMI.

COLOUR BY NUMBERS
Karma chameleon / It's a miracle / Black money / Changing everyday / That's the way / Church of the poison mind / Miss me blind / Mr. Man / Storm keeper (CD and cassette only) / Victims
CD _____ CDV 2285
Virgin / Feb '92 / EMI.

KISSING TO BE CLEVER
White boy / You know I'm not crazy / I'll tumble 4 ya / Take control / Love twist / Boy boy (I'm the boy) / I'm afraid of me (remix) / White boys can't control it / Do you really want to hurt me
CD _____ CDV 2232
Virgin / Jul '87 / EMI.

THIS TIME
Do you really want to hurt me / Move away / I'll tumble 4 ya / Love is love / Victims / Karma chameleon / Church of the poison mind / Miss me blind / Time (Clock of the heart) / It's a miracle / War song / I'll tumble 4 ya (US 12" remix) (CD only) / Miss me blind (US 12" remix) (CD only)
CD _____ CDVTV 1
Virgin / Apr '92 / EMI.

WAKING UP WITH THE HOUSE ON FIRE
Dangerous man / War song / Unfortunate thing / Crime time / Mistake no.3 / Dive / Medal song / Don't talk about it / Mannequin / Hello goodbye
CD _____ CDV 2330
Virgin / Oct '84 / EMI.

Culture Musical Club

TAARAB MUSIC OF ZANZIBAR VOL.4
Sibadili / Mwiko / Bingwa amekwenda kapa / Subalkhen mpenzi / Kupendana kwetu sisi / Sasa sinaye / Jipeleleze / Nimtakaye hataki / Mbuzi / Nieye / Umenita azizi (Available on CD format only.)
CD _____ CDORBD 041
Globestyle / May '89 / Pinnacle.

Culturemix

CULTUREMIX (Culturemix & Bill Nelson)
Luna park / Radio head / Housewives on drugs / Dancematic / Four postcards home / Zebra / Exile / Tangram / Cave paintings
CD _____ RES 113CD
Resurgence / Nov '95 / Vital.

Cultus Sanguine

CULTUS SANGUINE
CD _____ WLR 006CD
Wounded Love / Jul '95 / Plastic Head.

Cunliffe, Bill

PAUL SIMON SONG BOOK, A
You can call me Al / I do it for your love / Oh, Marion / One trick pony / Scarborough Fair / Jonah / Still crazy after all these years / Mrs. Robinson / America / Boxer / 59th Street bridge song (Feelin' groovy) / Bridge over troubled water
CD _____ 77005
Discovery / Nov '93 / Warner Music.

RARE CONNECTION, A
Stella by starlight / Chick it out / Jamaican lounge lizards / Cityscape / Rare connection / Big slide / Joyous dance / Minnesota / Miyako / Nobody else but me
CD _____ 77007
Discovery / Apr '94 / Warner Music.

Cunningham, John

FAIR WARNING
Celtic society's quickstep/42nd Highlander's farewell / Archibald MacDonald of Keppoch / Planxty Drew/Planxty Wilkinson / Sad is my fate / Lord Drummond/Lady Margaret Stewart/Crarae / Logan water / Drovers lads/Hug of brown ale / Waulkin o' the fauld / Fair warning
CD _____ GLCD 1047
Green Linnet / Oct '88 / Roots / CM / Direct / ADA.

Cunningham, John

SHANKLY GATES
CD _____ LADIDA 020
La-Di-Da / Jul '94 / Vital.

Cunningham, Phil

AIRS AND GRACES
CD _____ GLCD 3032
Green Linnet / Nov '93 / Roots / CM / Direct / ADA.

PALOMINO WALTZ, THE
Bombardier beetle/Webbs wonderful / Rosa Memorial Hospital / Palomino waltz/Donna's waltz / Four stroke reel/Martin O'Connor's flying clog / Leaving Glen Affric / Ceilidh funk / Wedding / Violet Tulloch's welcome to the Crask of Aigas / Laird of Drumblair / Ciara McCarthy's lullaby
CD _____ GLCD 1102
Green Linnet / Nov '92 / Roots / CM / Direct / ADA.

REBOX
CD Set _____ GLCD 200
Green Linnet / May '94 / Roots / CM / Direct / ADA.

RELATIVITY (Cunningham, Phil & Johnny/O Domhnaill,M./Ni Dhomhnail, T.)
Hut on Staffin Island / Sandy MacLeod of Garafad / Soft horse reel / There was a lady / Gile Mear / Gracelands / When Barney flew / Big slide / Leaving Brittany / Pernod waltz / An seanduine doite / John Cunningham's return to Edinburgh / Heather fields/Bell reel / Limerick lasses / Ur-Chill an Chreagain
CD _____ GLCD 1059
Green Linnet / Feb '88 / Roots / CM / Direct / ADA.

Cuozzo, Mike

MIGHTY MIKE
There'll never be another you / What is this thing called love / Nancy / Walk up / Evening at Papa Joe's / Undersided
CD _____ SV 0207
Savoy Jazz / Apr '93 / Conifer / ADA.

Cure

BOYS DON'T CRY
Boys don't cry / Plastic passion / 10.15 Saturday night / Accuracy / Object / Jumping someone else's train / Subway song / Killing an arab / Fire in Cairo / Another day / Grinding halt / World War / Three imaginary boys
CD _____ 815 011-2
Fiction / Jun '92 / PolyGram.

CONCERT - THE CURE LIVE
Shake dog shake / Primary / Charlotte sometimes / Hanging gardens / Give me it / Walk / Hundred years / Forest / 10.15 Saturday night / Killing an arab / Heroin face / Boys don't cry / Subway song / At night / In your house / Drowning man / Other voices / Funeral party / All mine / Forever
CD _____ 823 682-2
Fiction / Jun '92 / PolyGram.

CURE 16CD BOX SET
CD Set _____ 5135992
Fiction / Jun '92 / PolyGram.

CURE: INTERVIEW PICTURE DISC
CD P.Disc _____ CBAK 4003
Baktabak / Apr '88 / Baktabak.

DISINTEGRATION
Plainsong / Closedown / Last dance / Fascination Street / Same deep water as you / Homesick / Pictures of you / Love song / Lullaby / Prayers for rain / Disintegration / Untitled
CD _____ 8393532
Fiction / Jun '92 / PolyGram.

ENTREAT
Pictures of you / Closedown / Last dance / Fascination Street / Prayers for rain / Disintegration / Homesick / Untitled
CD _____ 8433592
Fiction / Jun '92 / PolyGram.

FAITH
All cats are grey / Carnage visors / Doubt / Drowning man / Faith / Funeral party / Holy hour / Other voices / Primary
CD _____ 827 687-2
Fiction / Jun '92 / PolyGram.

HEAD ON THE DOOR, THE
In between days / Kyoto song / Blood / Six different ways / Push / Baby screams / Close to me / Night like this / Screw / Sinking
CD _____ 827 231-2
Fiction / Jun '92 / PolyGram.

JAPANESE WHISPERS
Let's go to bed / Walk / Love cats / Dream / Just one kiss / Upstairs room / Lament / Speak my language
CD _____ 8174702
Fiction / Jun '92 / PolyGram.

KISS ME, KISS ME, KISS ME
Kiss / Catch / Torture / If only tonight we could sleep / Why can't I be you / How beautiful you are... / Snakepit / Just like heaven / Hot hot hot / All I want / One more time / Like cockatoos / Icing sugar smooth / Perfect girl / Thousand hours / Shiver and shake / Fight
CD _____ 832 130-2
Fiction / Jun '92 / PolyGram.

MIXED UP
Lullaby (extended) / Close to me (Paul Oakenfold mix) / Fascination Street (USA mix) / Walk (1990 version) / Love song (remix) / Forest (1990 remix) / Pictures of you (Chuck New mix) / Hot hot hot (extended) / Why can't I be you (extended) / Caterpillar (Chuck New mix) / In between days (William Orbit mix) / Never enough (big mix)
CD _____ 847 099-2
Fiction / Jun '92 / PolyGram.

PARIS
CD _____ 5199942
Fiction / Oct '93 / PolyGram.

PORNOGRAPHY
Pornography / Hanging gardens / Hundred years / Siamese twins / Figurehead / Strange day / Cold / Short term effect
CD _____ 827 688-2
Fiction / Jun '92 / PolyGram.

SEVENTEEN SECONDS
At night / Final sound / Forest / In your house / M / Play for today / Reflection / Secrets / Seventeen seconds / Three
CD _____ 825 354-2
Fiction / Jun '92 / PolyGram.

SHOW
Tape / Open / High / Pictures of you / Lullaby / Just like heaven / Fascination Street / Night like this / Trust / Doing the unstuck / Walk / Let's go to bed / Friday I'm in love / In between days / From the edge of the deep green sea / Never enough / Cut / End
CD _____ 519 951-2
Fiction / Sep '93 / PolyGram.

STARING AT THE SEA
Killing an Arab / 10.15 Saturday night / Boys don't cry / Jumping someone else's train / Forest / Play for today / Primary / Other voices / Charlotte sometimes / Hanging gardens / Let's go to bed / Walk / Love cats / Caterpillar / I'm cold / Another journey by train / In between days / Close to me / Descent (CD only) / Splin-

tered in her head (MC only) / Mr. Pink eyes (MC only) / Happy the man (MC only) / Throw your foot (MC only) / Exploding boy (MC only) / Few hours after this (MC only) / Man inside my mouth (MC only) / Stop dead (MC only) / New day (MC only)
CD _____ 8292392
Fiction / May '86 / PolyGram.

THREE IMAGINARY BOYS
Accuracy / Another day / Fire in Cairo / Foxy lady / Grinding halt / It's not you / Meat hook / Object / So what / Subway / 10.15 Saturday night / Three imaginary boys
CD _____ 827 686 2
Fiction / Jun '92 / PolyGram.

TOP, THE
Caterpillar / Piggy in the mirror / Empty world / Bananafishbones / Top / Shake dog shake / Bird mad girl / Wailing wall / Give me it / Dressing up
CD _____ 8211362
Fiction / Jun '92 / PolyGram.

WISH
Open / High / Apart / From the edge of the deep green sea / Wendy time / Doing the unstuck / Friday I'm in love / Trust / Letter to Elise / Cut / To wish impossible things / End
CD _____ FISCD 20
Fiction / May '92 / PolyGram.

Curiosity

BACK TO FRONT
Work it out / Hang on in there baby / Gimme the sunshine (Original) / Vibezin' / Addict / Killing me softly / Call on me / Gimme the sunshine (Ron's mystery) / Music's a mystery / Spice it up / Fall in again / Work it out (2)
CD _____ 74321 16657-2
RCA / Oct '93 / BMG.

VERY BEST OF CURIOSITY KILLED THE CAT, THE (Curiosity Killed The Cat)
Down to Earth / Relax / Go go ahead / Red lights / Shallow memory / First place / Cascade / Free / Name and number / Ball and chain / Keep on trying / Mile high / Know what you know / Ordinary day / Bullet / Misfit
CD _____ PWKS 4100P
Carlton Home Entertainment / Mar '92 / Carlton Home Entertainment.

Curless, Dick

TRAVELLING THROUGH
CD _____ ROUCD 3137
Rounder / Aug '95 / CM / Direct / ADA / Cadillac.

WELCOME TO MY WORLD
CD _____ RRCD 007
Rocade / Aug '93 / Direct / ADA.

Curlew

BEAUTIFUL WESTERN SADDLE, A
CD _____ RUNE 50
Cuneiform / Nov '87 / ReR Megacorp.

Currie, Billy

STAND UP AND WALK
Change of heart / French viola / Liberation / Ritual bliss / Stand up and walk / Ultravox / Requiem / Jam-boree / Crisis / Hatchback mania / Santa Claus / Irish widdershins
CD _____ HFMCD 001
Hot Food Music / Aug '95 / Pinnacle.

Curry, Clifford

CLIFFORD'S BLUES
CD _____ AP 122
Appaloosa / Oct '95 / ADA / Magnum Music Group.

PROVIDER, THE
CD _____ APP 6115CD
Appaloosa / Jun '94 / ADA / Magnum Music Group.

Cursed

RHAPSODY
CD _____ DW 20629CD
Deathwish / Jan '92 / Plastic Head.

Curson, Ted

PLENTY OF HORN
Caravan / Nosruc / Things we did last summer / Dem's blues / Ahma (see ya) / Flatted fifth / Bali Ha'i / Antibes / Mr. Teddy
CD _____ CDBOP 018
Boplicity / Mar '94 / Pinnacle / Cadillac.

TEARS FOR DOLPHY
CD _____ BLCD 760190
Black Lion / Jun '94 / Jazz Music / Cadillac / Wellard / Koch.

TED CURSON GROUP FEATURING ERIC DOLPHY
CD _____ COD 016
Jazz View / Jun '92 / Harmonia Mundi.

Curtin, Dan

SILICON DAWN
CD _____ PF 18CD
Peacefrog / Sep '94 / Disc.

WEB OF LIFE
Matter of sound / Quantum / Biotic / Intersellar perception / Out of sight and mind / Path / Subconscious / Awareness / 3rd from the sun / Envision
CD _____ PF 038CD
Peacefrog / Sep '95 / Disc.

Curtis, Amy

PEACE FOR LOVE
CD _____ FSR 5004CD
Fresh Sound / Mar '95 / Jazz Music / Discovery.

Curtis, Mac

BLUE JEAN HEART
Grandaddy's rockin' / Just so you call me / Half hearted love / If I had me a woman / Low road / That ain't nothing but right / Don't you love me / You ain't treatin' me right / I'll be gentle / Say so / Blue jean heart / Goosebumps / You are my very special baby / What you want / Little Miss Linda / Missy Ann
CD _____ CDCHARLY 164
Charly / Feb '91 / Charly / THE / Cadillac.

Curtis, Sonny

NO STRANGER TO THE RAIN
I'm no stranger to the rain / Hello Mary Lou / You are the lesson I never learned / When Amarillo blows / Back when has been lover / I saved my last name for you / Bad case of love / Think it over / That'll be the day / More than I can say / Well alright / Rock around with Ollie Vee / Midnight shift
CD _____ RITZCD 509
Ritz / '91 / Pinnacle.

Curved Air

AIR CONDITIONING
It happened today / Stretch / Screw / Blind man / Vivaldi / Hide and seek / Propositions / Rob one / Situation
CD _____ 9010230
Line / Jun '94 / CM / Grapevine / ADA / Conifer / Direct.
CD _____ 7599264332
WEA / Jan '96 / Warner Music.

LIVE: CURVED AIR
CD _____ HTDCD 49
HTD / Dec '95 / Pinnacle.

LOVECHILD
Exsultate Jubilate / Lovechild / Seasons / Flasher / Joan / Dancer / Widow / Paris by night
CD _____ CLACD 342
Castle / Jun '94 / BMG.

MIDNIGHT WIRE
Woman on a one night stand / Day breaks my heart / Pipe of dreams / Orange Street blues / Dance of love / Midnight wire / It happened today
CD _____ HTDCD 50
HTD / Dec '95 / Pinnacle.

SECOND ALBUM
Young mother / Backstreet luv / Jumbo / You know / Puppets / Everdance / Bright summer's day / Piece of mind
CD _____ 7599264342
WEA / Jan '96 / Warner Music.

Cusack, Michael

PIPERS OF DISTINCTION
CD _____ CDMON 807
Monarch / Jul '90 / CM / ADA / Duncans / Direct.

Cusan Tan

RIDGE, THE
CD _____ SCD 2116
Sain / Jan '96 / Direct / ADA.

Cusp

SPACE AND TIME LIQUIDS AND METAL
CD _____ WM 8
Swim / Nov '95 / SRD / Disc.

Cussick, Ian

TREASURE ISLAND
Catch you later / We are the refugees / Who dares wins / Treasure island / Restless heart / Ye Jacobites by name / Enemy / Wild West / Fire and ice / Lowlands / Love the one you're with / Proud Mary / Tobacco Road
CD _____ 900684
Line / Jan '95 / CM / Grapevine / ADA / Conifer / Direct.

Custy, Tola

SETTING FREE (Custy, Tola & Cyril O'Donoghue)
CD _____ CICD 098
Clo Iar-Chonnachta / Aug '94 / CM.

Cutler, Chris

DOMESTIC STORIES (Cutler, Chris & Lutz Glandien)
CD _____ LSMCD 1
ReR Macecorp / Mar '93 / These / ReR Megacorp.

MOSCOW, PRAGUE AND WASHINGTON (Cutler, Chris & Fred Frith)
CD _____ RERCCFFCD
Recommended / '90 / These / ReR Megacorp.

Cutler, Ivor

LIFE IN A SCOTCH SITTING ROOM
CD _____ CREV 035CD
Rev-Ola / May '95 / 3MV / Vital.

Cutting Crew

BEST OF CUTTING CREW, THE
(I just) died in your arms / Any colour / Fear of falling / Everything but my pride / Contact high / Tip of your tongue / One for the mockingbird / I've been in love before / Life in a dangerous time / Don't look back / Scattering / Christians / (I just) died in your arms (mix) / Reach for the sky / (Between a) rock and a hard place / If that's the way you want it
CD _____ CDVIP 121
Virgin VIP / Dec '93 / Carlton Home Entertainment / THE / EMI.

Cutting Edge

TURNING THE TIDE
Turning the tide / Seagate salsa / Beechgrove / Jig of slurs / When she sleeps / Sniffer's delight / Ass in the graveyard / Silver spire / O'Keefe's no.7 / Ceilidh Dave / Miss Rowan Davies / Shandon bells / Gorgon's Ola / Rudy's reggae / Lilly
CD _____ NGCD 1007
Ninegates Music / Jan '95 / ADA.

Cutty Ranks

FROM MI HEART
CD _____ SHCD 45001
Shanachie / Jun '93 / Koch / ADA / Greensleeves.

Cutty Wren

PARSON'S HAT
CD _____ CICD 101
Clo Iar-Chonnachta / Dec '94 / CM.

Cyan Kills E Boli

DO NOT OPEN
CD _____ EFA 155862
Gymnastic / Nov '95 / SRD.

Cyber-Tec

LET YOUR BODY DIE
CD _____ SPV 07661112
SPV / Jan '96 / Plastic Head.

Cybertech

PHAROS
CD _____ CUTUPCD 010
Jump Cut / Jun '95 / ºotal/BMG / Vital/SAM.

Cybertron

INTERFACE (The Roots Of Techno)
Clear / Eden / Enter / Techno city / Cosmic cars / Alleys of your mind / Megiddo / R 9 / Cosmic raindance / El Salvador / Vision
CD _____ CDSEWD 069
Southbound / Jan '94 / Pinnacle.

Cyco Mike

LOST MY BRAIN... (ONCE AGAIN)
I love destruction / All I ever get / F.U.B.A.R. / All kinda crazy / Gonna be alright / Save a peace for me / Nothing to lose / Ain't gonna get me / Lost my brain once again / It's always something / Cyco Mike wants you / Ain't mess'n around
CD _____ 4811362
Epic / Oct '95 / Sony.

Cygnus X

HYPERMETRICAL
CD _____ EYEUKCD 006
Eye Q / Nov '94 / Disc / Warner Music.

Cymande

CYMANDE
Message / Brothers on the slide / Dove / Bra / Fug / For baby woh / Rickshaw / Equitorial forest / Listen / Getting it back / Anthracite / Willy's headache / Genevieve / 'Pon de jungle / Rastafarian folk song / One more / Zion I
CD _____ NEX CD 202
Sequel / Jul '92 / BMG.

Cynic

FOCUS
CD _____ RR 91692
Roadrunner / Sep '93 / Pinnacle.

Cyphyrs

GURUS & GANGSTERS
More I know / I know you so well / Winter heart / Wednesday in the rain / Parting shots / Miracle / Busy town / Heartless woman / Tonight / Dive / Catherine Walters / Gurus and gangsters
CD _____ MAJ 001CD
Majja / Jul '95 / Majja.

Cypress Hill

BLACK SUNDAY
I wanna get high / I ain't goin' out like that / Insane in the brain / When the ship goes down / Lick a shot / Cock the hammer / Interlude / Li'l Putos / Legalize it / Hits from the bong / What go around come around, kid / A to the K / Hand on the glock / Break 'em off some
CD _____ 474075 2
Ruff House / Jul '93 / Sony.

CYPRESS HILL
Pigs / How I could just kill a man / Hand on the pump / Hole in the head / Ultraviolet dreams / Light another / Phuncky feel one / Break it up / Real estate / Stoned is the way of the walk / Psycobetabuckdown / Something for the blunted / Latin lingo / Funky Cypress Hill shit / Tres eqyis / Born to get busy
CD _____ 4688932
Ruff House / May '94 / Sony.

TEMPLE OF BOOM
Spark another owl / Throw your set in the air / Stoned raiders / Illusions / Killa hill niggas / Boom biddy bye bye / No rest for the wicked / Make a move / Killafornia / Funk freakers / Locotes / Red light visions / Strictly hip hop / Let it rain / Everybody must get stoned / D.J. Muggs Buddha mix
CD _____ 4781272
CD Set _____ 4781279
Ruff House / Oct '95 / Sony.

Cyrille, Andrew

METAMUSICIANS' STOMP (Cyrille, Andrew & Maono)
CD _____ 120025-2
Black Saint / Nov '93 / Harmonia Mundi / Cadillac.

MY FRIEND LOUIS (Cyrille, Andrew Quintet)
CD _____ DIW 858
DIW / Jun '92 / Harmonia Mundi / Cadillac.

NAVIGATOR, THE
CD _____ 1210622
Soul Note / May '94 / Harmonia Mundi / Wellard / Cadillac.

NUBA
CD _____ 120030-2
Black Saint / May '94 / Harmonia Mundi / Cadillac.

X MAN
CD _____ RN 121098-2
Soul Note / Oct '94 / Harmonia Mundi / Wellard / Cadillac.

Cyrka, Jan

BEYOND THE COMMON GROUND
CD _____ CDGRUB 22
Food For Thought / Mar '92 / Pinnacle.

SPIRIT
CD _____ CDGRUB 29
Food For Thought / Oct '93 / Pinnacle.

Cyrus, Billy Ray

IT WON'T BE THE LAST
CD _____ 51475824-2
Mercury / Jul '93 / PolyGram.

SOME GAVE ALL
Could've been me / Achy breaky heart / She's not cryin' anymore / Wher'm I gonna live / These boots are made for walkin' / Someday, somewhere, somehow / Never thought I'd fall in love with you / Ain't no good goodbye / I'm so miserable / Some gave all
CD _____ 510635-2
Mercury / Mar '92 / PolyGram.

STORM IN THE HEARTLAND
CD _____ 5260812
Mercury / Mar '95 / PolyGram.

Czukay, Holger

CANAXIS
CD _____ SPOONCD 15
Mute / Jan '95 / Disc.

FULL CIRCLE (Czukay, Holger/Jah Wobble/Jaki Liebezeit)
How much are they / Where's the money / Full circle R.P.S. (No. 7) / Mystery R.P.S. (No. 8) / Trench warfare / Twilight world
CD _____ CDOVD 437
Virgin / May '92 / EMI.

MOVING PICTURES
CD _____ CDSTUMM 125
Mute / May '93 / Disc.

ROME REMAINS ROME
Hey ba ba re bop / Blessed Easter / Sudetenland / Hit hit flop flop / Perfect world / Music in the air / Der osten ist rot (the east is red) (CD only) / Das massenmedium (CD only) / Photo song (CD only) / Ronrad (CD only) / Michy (CD only) / Esperanto socialiste (CD only) / Traum mal wieder (CD only)

CD _____ **CDV 2408**

Virgin / '88 / EMI.

D

D Ream

D:REAM ON VOL.1
Take me away / U R the best thing / Un-
forgiven / I like it / Glorious / So long movin'
on / Picture my world / Blame it on me /
Things can only get better / Star
CD _____ 450993371-2
Magnet / Apr '94 / Warner Music.

WORLD
CD _____ 0630117962
Magnet / Sep '95 / Warner Music.

D-Generation

D GENERATION
No way out / Sins of America / Guitar mafia
/ Feel like suicide / Waiting for the nect big
parade / Falling / Wasted years / Stealing
time / Ghosts / Frankie / Working on the
avenue / Vampire nation / Degeneration
CD _____ CDCHR 6092
Chrysalis / Oct '94 / EMI.

D-Influence

GOOD 4 WE
Good lover / I'm the one / Funny (how
things change) / Good 4 we / No illusions /
Journey / Changes / For you I sing this song
/ Sweetest things
CD _____ 7567951882
East West / Aug '92 / Warner Music.

PRAYER 4 UNITY
CD _____ 7559617512
East West / Jul '95 / Warner Music.

D-Note

BABEL
Judgement / Babel / Now's the time / Aria
/ Bronx bull / Rain / Pharoah / River sea /
Message / Lychia / Scheme of things / D
votion
CD _____ DOR 012CD
Dorado / Apr '93 / Disc.

CRIMINAL JUSTICE
CD _____ DOR 32CD
Dorado / Jan '95 / Disc.

D-Roc

ENGLEWOOD 4 LIFE
CD _____ WRA 8152
Wrap / Jan '96 / Koch.

D-Train

D-TRAIN - THE COLLECTION
CD _____ CCSCD 387
Castle / Oct '93 / BMG.

**ESSENTIAL DANCEFLOOR ARTISTS
VOL. 2**
You're the one for me / Keep on / Don't you
wanna ride (the D-Train) / Walk on by / Keep
giving me love / Something's on your mind
/ Music / Thank you / You're the reason
CD _____ DGPCD 666
Deep Beats / Mar '94 / BMG.

GO FOR IT BABY
CD _____ TRCD 9916
Tramp / Nov '93 / Direct / ADA / CM.

D. Maximillian

MY STORY
CD _____ BLKMCD 10
Blakamix / Oct '94 / Jetstar / SRD.

D.A.D.

HELPYOURSELFISH
Reconstrucdead flat / Written in water / Helpyourselfish / Soulbender unowned / Blood
in/Out candid / Prayin' to a God / Naked
(but still stripping) / Are we alive here / It's
when it's wrong it's right
CD _____ CDCHR 6101
Chrysalis / Apr '95 / EMI.

RISKIN' IT ALL
Bad craziness / D. Law / Day of the wrong
moves / Rock 'n' rock radar / I won't cut
my hair / Down that dusty 3rd world road /
Makin' fun of money / Smart bot can't tell
ya / Riskin' it all / Laugh 'n' a 1/2
CD _____ 7599267722
WEA / Oct '91 / Warner Music.

D.A.F.

**DIE KLEINEN UN DIE BOSEN (Deutsch
Amerikanische Freundschaft)**
CD _____ CDSTUMM 1
Mute / Apr '92 / Disc.

D.B.F.

NOT BOUND BY THE RULES
You deceive yourself / Election's just a farce
/ Suicide Billy / Make it a lie / Too wide apart

/ Narrow-minded / Not bound to rules /
Nothing to prove / Rape your mind / Too
much wasn't said / Am I too weak / Religion
/ Blank minds / No personality
CD _____ 853881
SPV / Jul '89 / Plastic Head.

D.B.'s

DB'S/REPERCUSSION
Black and white / Dynamite / She's not worried / Fight / Espionage / Tearjerkin' / Baby
talk / Cycles per second / Bad reputation /
Big brown eyes / I'm in love / Moving in your
sleep / Judy/Happenstance / We were
happy there / Living a lie / From a window
to a screen / Ask for Jill / Amplifier / Soul
kiss / Neverland / Storm warning / Ups and
downs / Nothing is wrong / In Spain / I feel
good today
CD Set _____ LICD 921191
Line / Mar '92 / CM / Grapevine / ADA /
Direct.

PARIS AVENUE
CD _____ MON 6122
Monkey Hill / Jan '95 / Direct.

RIDE THE WILD TOM TOM
We should be in bed / Everytime anytime /
Let's live for today / Little hands / You got
it wrong / Tell me two times / Nothing is
wrong / Purple hose / Ash / I read New York
Rocker / Walking the ceiling (it's good to be
alive) / Baby talk / Dynamite (original demo)
/ Soul kiss (part one) / Bad reputation /
Modern boys and girls / What about that car
/ What's the matter with me / Fight / She's
green, I'm blue / If and when / Soul kiss
(part two) / Death of rock / Purple hose
(slight return) / Hardcore Judy / Spy in the
house of love
CD _____ RSACD 805
Sequel / Dec '94 / BMG.

D.C. Talk

FREE AT LAST
Luv is a verb / That kinda girl / Jesus is just
alright / Say the words / Socially acceptable
/ Free at last / Time is... / Hard way / Lean
on me / I don't want it / Word 2 the Father
CD _____ FFD 3002
Alliance Music / Jul '95 / EMI.

D.C.3

VIDA
CD _____ SST 156 CD
SST / Jul '89 / Plastic Head.

D.C.S.

BHANGRA'S GONNA GET YOU
CD _____ DMUT 1086
Multitone / Jul '89 / BMG.

D.I.

STATE OF SHOCK
Hated / Clownhouse / What is life / Run-
around / Colors and blood / It's not right /
Paranoid's demise / Dream / Better than ex-
pected / Martyr man / Lexicon devil
CD _____ CDVEST 14
Bulletproof / May '94 / Pinnacle.

TRAGEDY AGAIN
Tragedy again / Chiva / Nick the whip /
Manhole / Sasha / Diablo I / Blue velvet /
Backseat driver / Love to me is a sin / On
our way / Diablo II
CD _____ EM 94262
Roadrunner / Dec '89 / Pinnacle.

D.I.Y.

STRICTLY FOR GROOVERS
CD _____ WARPCD 18
Warp / Dec '93 / Disc.

D.J. Dimitri

JOURNEYS BY DJ VOL.3
CD _____ JDJ 13CD
Music Unites / Mar '95 / Sony / 3MV /
SRD.

D.J. Duke

JOURNEYS BY DJ VOL.2
CD _____ JDJ 12CD
Music Unites / Jan '95 / Sony / 3MV /
SRD.

D.J. Food

RECIPE FOR DISASTER, A
Dark river / Inosan / Scratch yer head /
Brass neck / Fungle junk / Half step / Dusk
/ Bass city roller / Spiral / Scratch yer butt
/ Akaire / Little samba / Scientific youth /
SE 1 / Hipslop
CD _____ ZENCD 020
Ninja Tune / Oct '95 / Vital / Kudos.

REFRIED FOOD
Strange taste / Spiral dub / Freedom / Sexy
bits / Scratch yer head / Mella / Half step /
Turtle soup / Spiral / Dark lady / Dark river
/ Dark blood / Consciousness
CD _____ ZENCD 021
Ninja Tune / Feb '96 / Vital / Kudos.

D.J. Hurricane

HURRA, THE
Now you do / Elbow room / Four fly guys /
Can we all get along / Stick em up / Pat
your foot / Get blind / Comin' off / What's
really going on / Where's my niggas at /
Hurra / Pass me the gun / Feel the blast
CD _____ WIJ 043CD
Wiiija / Feb '95 / Vital.

D.J. Jazzy Jeff

**CODE RED (D.J. Jazzy Jeff & The Fresh
Prince)**
CD _____ CHIP 140
Jive / Nov '93 / BMG.

**HOME BASE (D.J. Jazzy Jeff & The
Fresh Prince)**
CD _____ CHIP 116
Jive / Sep '91 / BMG.

D.J. Keoki

MIXING IT UP WITH
CD _____ MM 800352
Moonshine / Jul '95 / Disc.

WE ARE ONE
CD _____ SUB 4D
Subversive / Oct '95 / 3MV / SRD.

D.J. Krush

MEISO
Only the strong survive / Anticipation /
What's behind the darkness / Meiso / By
path 1 / Blank / Ground / By path 2 / Most
wanted man / By path 3 / 3rd eye / Oce
9504 / Duality / By path - would you take it
CD _____ MW 039CD
Mo Wax / Sep '95 / Vital.

STRICTLY TURNTABILIZED
Intro / Lunation / Fucked up pendulum / Ke-
muri / Loop / Silent ungah / Interlude / Dig
this vibe / Yeah / To the infinity / Nightmare
of ungah (sandro in effect)
CD _____ MW 025CD
Mo Wax / Nov '94 / Vital.

D.J. Loops

BEATS TO SAMPLE
Evil / Bone / Slip / Light up / Stuffed /
Moved / Pumped / Middle / Fatso / Tooty /
Tooty 11 / So bad / Mash up / Holey / Buzz
/ Baz / Batty / Slam
CD _____ BRCD 608
4th & Broadway / Feb '94 / PolyGram.

D.J. Nemesis

JAMM ATTACK RAVE BEATS
CD _____ STARMIX 3CD
Music Of Life / Feb '92 / Grapevine.

D.J. Quik

QUIK IS THE NAME
CD _____ FILERCD 402
Profile / Apr '91 / Pinnacle.

SAFE & SOUND
CD _____ FILECD 462
Profile / Feb '95 / Pinnacle.

D.J. Rap

INTELLIGENCE (D.J. Rap & Voyager)
Mad up / Abyss / Losing control / Burning
love / Spiritual aura / Two loves / Drum /
Roughest gunark / See the future / Baby
don't keep me waiting
CD _____ PTCD 001
Proper Talent / Sep '95 / Vital.

JOURNEY INTO DRUM BASS
CD _____ JDJDB 1CD
Music Unites / Mar '95 / Sony / 3MV /
SRD.

D.J. Red Alert

**SLAMMIN' VINYL (D.J. Red Alert & Mike
Slammer)**
CD _____ GUMH 011
Gumh / Nov '94 / SRD.

D.J. Smurf

VERSASTYLES
CD _____ WRA 81452
Wrap / Mar '95 / Koch.

D.J. Spike

TASTELESS CUTS
Baby bye / Gaps in space / Mr. President /
Spike part one / M.P.B. 105 / German / De-
signer drugs / Stick out
CD _____ BL 001 CD
Blanc / Apr '92 / Pinnacle.

D.J. SS

ROLLERS CONVENTION
CD _____ FORM 4CD
Formation / Nov '94 / SRD.

D.J. Supreme

**STOLEN BEATS & RIPPED OFF
SCRATCHES**
Superstition Revisited / Incorporated Beat /
Hammonds drummer / Big soul / Kool's re-
turn / Radio break / Impeach - the sequel /
Buddy's solo / Hard 'n' horny / Love break
/ Dead ringer / Jungle vibes / Forty Scratch
vibes
CD _____ STARMIX 4CD
Music Of Life / Oct '92 / Grapevine.

D.J. Toolz

BREAKBEATS 'N' GROOVES VOL.1
Takin 1 back / Slots / Funky donkey / To
the beat y'all / Eight ins for Rita / Drummer
/ Thirteenth break / Flute of the groove /
Col' favour / Smoove B / Bus stop / Gimmi
gimmi / Twenty dollars / Biz beat / Congo
soul / Texas B boy
CD _____ TOOLCD 001
Ninja Tune / Jul '93 / Vital / Kudos.

BREAKBEATS 'N' GROOVES VOL.4
KC (On CD only) / Hey girl / Out at lunch /
Drum and bass / Drum and er / Uncle Bob
/ Tap it, unwrap it / Offside trap / Doobie
doobie doobie (On CD only) / Soul break /
Number 1 Ventire fan / We meet again Mr
Bond / Route 1 / Orgasmic / Yeah / Egg 'n'
bacon / Going green (On CD only) / Bony
arse beats (On CD only)
CD _____ TOOLCD 004
Ninja Tune / Jul '95 / Vital / Kudos.

D.J. Triple

**JUNGLE BREAKS & BEATS (D.J. Triple
& Bassman)**
CD _____ MOLCD 38
Music Of Life / Mar '95 / Grapevine.

D.N.S

BOMBS AND CLOUDS
CD _____ MA35-2
Machinery / Dec '93 / Plastic Head.

D.O.A.

DAWNING OF A NEW ERROR
CD _____ VIRUS 106CD
Alternative Tentacles / Feb '92 / Pinnacle.

GREATEST SHITS
CD _____ QQP 019CD
QQP / Nov '92 / Plastic Head.

LOGGERHEADS
CD _____ VIRUS 130CD
Alternative Tentacles / Sep '93 / Pinnacle.

MURDER
CD _____ 723762
Restless / Feb '95 / Vital.

TALK - ACTION = 0
CD _____ 725062
Restless / Feb '95 / Vital.

THIRTEEN FLAVOURS OF DOOM
CD _____ VIRUS 117CD
Alternative Tentacles / Oct '92 / Pinnacle.

D.O.C.

HELTER SKELTER
CD _____ 74321288282
RCA / Jan '96 / BMG.

D.O.P.

MUSICIANS OF THE MIND
D.O.P. (Don' Oh yeah / Take me / Groovy
beat (part 1) / Dance spirit / Future le funk
/ Let's party / Get out on this dancefloor /
Dancefloor / Oh no / Don't stop the music
/ Ric / Groovy beat
CD _____ GRCD 003
Guerilla / Jul '94 / Pinnacle.

MUSICIANS OF THE MIND VOL.2
Come to me / Together / String vest / On
/ Party rockin' / Satisfy / Here I go / Ooh la
la / Electronic funk / Lust / Catwalk
CD _____ GRCD 010
Guerilla / Jul '94 / Pinnacle.

D.R.I.

CROSSOVER
CD _____ ROTCD 2092
Rotten / Nov '95 / Plastic Head.

DEALING WITH IT
Snap / Marriage / Counter attack / Nursing home blues / Give my taxes back / Equal people / Bail out / Evil minds / I'd rather be sleeping / Yes ma'am / God is broke / I don't need society / Explorer / On my way home / Argument the war / Slit my wrists
CD _____ ROT 2091CD
Rotten / Nov '95 / Plastic Head.

DEFINITION
CD _____ ROTCD 2093
Rotten / Nov '95 / Plastic Head.

DIRTY ROTTEN
CD _____ ROTCD 001
Rotten / Nov '95 / Plastic Head.

FOUR OF A KIND
All for nothing / Manifest destiny / Gone too long / Do the dream / Shut up / Modern world / Think for yourself / Slumlord / Dead in a ditch / Suit and the guy / Man unkind
CD _____ COMZORRO 46
Metal Blade / Aug '92 / Pinnacle.

FULL SPEED AHEAD
CD _____ ROT 2099CD
Rotten / Nov '95 / Plastic Head.

THRASH ZONE
CD _____ 398147002CD
Metal Blade / Oct '95 / Plastic Head.

D.Y.S.

FIRE AND ICE
CD _____ TG 2981CD
Taang / Jul '91 / Plastic Head.

D3

SPONTANEOUS COMBUSTION
Spontaneous combustion / Dormar / Politics / Dreamtime / Fourth up / Antico invierno / Fragments
CD _____ TUTUCD 888126
Tutu / Mar '92 / Vital/SAM.

Da Brat

FUNKDAFIED
Da shit you can't fuc wit / Ya all y'll / Fire it up / Celebration time / Deeper / Funkdafied / May da funk bw wit'cha / Ain't no thang / Come and get some / Mind blowin' / Give it to you
CD _____ 4769980 2
Columbia / Oct '94 / Sony.

Da Costa, Paulino

SUNRISE
Taj Mahal / I'm going to Rio / African sunrise / Walkman / O mar e meu chao / You came into my life / My love / You've got a special kind of love / Carioca / Groove
CD _____ CD 2312143
Pablo / Apr '94 / Jazz Music / Cadillac / Complete/Pinnacle.

Da Costa, Tico

BRAZIL ENCANTO
CD _____ CDC 211
Music Of The World / Jun '93 / Target/BMG / ADA.

Da Lench Mob

GUERILLAS IN THE MIST
Capital punishment in America / Buck the devil / Lost in the system / You and your heroes / All on my nut sac / Guerillas in tha mist / Lenchmob also in the group / Ain't got no class / Freedom got an A.K. / Ankle blues / Who ya gonna shoot wit that / Lord have mercy / Inside tha head of a black man
CD _____ 7567922062
Street Knowledge / Nov '92 / Warner Music.

PLANET OF DA APES
Scared lil' nigga / Chocolate city / Cut throats / King of the jungle / Who is it / Planet of da apes / Goin' bangin / Mellow madness / Enviromental terrorist / Set the shit straight / Trapped / Final call
CD _____ CDPTY 110
Priority/Virgin / Dec '94 / EMI.

Da Silva, Jorginho

EL BOSSA NOVA
CD _____ 12385
Strictly Dancing / Feb '95 / Target/BMG.

Da Willys

SATUHDAY NITE PALSY
CD _____ OUTCD 105
Brake Out / Aug '91 / Vital.

Da Youngstas

NO MERCY
CD _____ 7567923702
WEA / Nov '94 / Warner Music.

Dabany, Patience

CENTRAL AFRICAN REPUBLIC
Levekisha / Pitie / Sango ya mawa / Opoungou andimba / Abagui alobi / Jalousie / Ayangal kelio / Ne t'inquietes pas / Patience II / Fly girl
CD _____ CDEMC 3677
EMI / May '94 / EMI.

Dada

AMERICAN HIGHWAY FLOWER
Ask the dust / Feet to the sun / All I am / Scum / Pretty girls make graves / Gogo / Feel me don't you / Real soon / Green Henry / Eight track mind / S.F. bar '63 / I / Heaven and nowhere
CD _____ EIRSCD 1068
IRS / Sep '94 / PolyGram / BMG / EMI.

PUZZLE
Dorina / Mary sunshine rain / Dog dizz knee land / Surround / Here today, gone tomorrow / Posters / Timothy / Dim / Who you are / Puzzle / Moon
CD _____ EIRSCD 1066
IRS / Apr '93 / PolyGram / BMG / EMI.

Daddies Sing Goodnight

COLLECTION OF SLEEPYTIME STORIES
CD _____ SH 3821CD
Sugarhill / Mar '94 / Roots / CM / ADA / Direct.

Daddy Freddie

BIG ONE, THE
CD _____ MDLCD 35
Music Of Life / Aug '95 / Grapevine.

NOW OR NEVER
Haul and pull / Now or never / Respect due (Feat : Frankie Paul & Heavy D) / Vibe up (break 1) / Jah Jah gives me vibes / Give me a little lovin' (Feat : Heavy D) / Don number 1 / Rappin' music (Feat : Supercat)
CD _____ FREDDY 2CD
Music Of Life / Oct '92 / Grapevine.

STRESS
CD _____ FREDDYCD 1
Music Of Life / Feb '91 / Grapevine.

Dadi, Marcel

COUNTRY GUITAR FLAVOURS
CD _____ 982532
EPM / Nov '92 / Discovery / ADA.

Daemion

DARK OPERA OF THE ANCIENT WAR SPIRIT
CD _____ CDAR 020
Adipocre / May '94 / Plastic Head.

Dag

RIGHTEOUS
Intro / Sweet little lass / Righteous (City pain) / Your mama's eyes / Home / Lovely Jane / You can lick it (if you try) / Even so / Plow / Candy / Sat morning / As / Do me good
CD _____ 4765152
Columbia / Sep '95 / Sony.

Dag Nasty

1985 - 1986
CD _____ SPLS 042
Selfless / Nov '92 / SRD.

FIELD DAY
CD _____ WB 3040-2
We Bite / Sep '93 / Plastic Head.

Dagar Brothers

RAG KAMBHOJI
CD _____ CDT 114
Topic / Apr '93 / Direct / ADA.

Dagar, Zia Mohiuddin

RUNDRA VINA
CD _____ NI 5402CD
Nimbus / Jul '94 / Nimbus.

Dagir, Abdu

MALIK AT-TAQASIM
Longa nahawand / Layali zaman / Samai kurd / Longa agam / Quartertone bycicle / Nidaa / Nil
CD _____ ENJACD 80122
Enja / Oct '93 / New Note / Vital/SAM.

D'Agostino, Peppino

CLOSE TO THE HEART
CD _____ BEST 1039CD
Acoustic Music / Nov '93 / ADA.

Dagradi, Tony

DREAMS OF LOVE
CD _____ CD 2071
Rounder / '88 / CM / Direct / ADA / Cadillac.

Dahl, Jeff

ULTRA UNDER
CD _____ TX 93172
Roadrunner / Apr '91 / Pinnacle.

Dahlander, Nils-Bertil

FROM SWEDEN WITH LOVE
CD _____ ECD 102
Everyday / Jun '95 / Jazz Music / Cadillac.

Daigrepont, Bruce

PETIT CADEAU
CD _____ ROU 6060CD
Rounder / May '94 / CM / Direct / ADA / Cadillac.

STIR UP THE ROUX
Laissez-faire / La valse de la riviere rouge / Disco et fais do-do / Les traces de mon bogue / Le two-step de marksville / Les filles cajines / Un autre soir ennuyant / Frisco zydeco / Stir up the roux
CD _____ CD 6016
Rounder / '88 / CM / Direct / ADA / Cadillac.

Dairo, I.K.

ASHIKO
CD _____ GL 4018CD
Green Linnet / Aug '94 / Roots / CM / Direct / ADA.

I REMEMBER (Dairo, I.K & His Blue Spots)
CD _____ CDC 212
Topic / Apr '93 / Direct / ADA.

JUJU MASTER
CD _____ OMCD 009
Original Music / Nov '90 / SRD / Jetstar.

Daisy Chainsaw

ELEVENTEEN
CD _____ TPLP 100CD
One Little Indian / Sep '92 / Pinnacle.

FOR THEY KNOW NOT WHAT THEY DO
Future free / Belittled and beaten down / Sleeping with heaven / Love me forever / Candyfloss / Life tomorrow / Zebra head / Unit shifter / Diamond of the desert / Mosquito / Greatest God's divine / Voice of a generation / Looking for an angel
CD _____ TPLP 111CD
One Little Indian / Jun '94 / Pinnacle.

Daisy Cutter

SHITHAMMER DELUXE
CD _____ ROCK 60802
Rockville / Mar '93 / SRD.

TRUCK FIST
CD _____ ROCK 6134-2
Rockville / Apr '94 / SRD.

Dako, Del

BALANCING ACT
CD _____ SKCD 2-2021
Sackville / Jun '93 / Swift / Jazz Music / Jazz Horizons / Cadillac / CM.

Dalakopa

EVI ALLE IHOPA
CD _____ HCD 7109
Helin / Nov '95 / ADA.

Dalby, Graham

LET'S DANCE FOXTROT (Dalby, Graham & Grahamophones)
CD _____ LTD 102702
Let's Dance / Apr '95 / Target/BMG.

LET'S DANCE LATIN AMERICAN
CD _____ LTD 102705
Let's Dance / May '95 / Target/BMG.

LET'S DANCE THE SLOW FOXTROT (Dalby, Graham & Grahamophones)
CD _____ LTD 102704
Let's Dance / Apr '95 / Target/BMG.

LET'S DANCE THE TANGO (Dalby, Graham & Grahamophones)
CD _____ LTD 102703
Let's Dance / Apr '95 / Target/BMG.

LET'S DANCE THE WALTZ (Dalby, Graham & Grahamophones)
CD _____ LTD 102701
Let's Dance / Jun '95 / Target/BMG.

LET'S DANCE VOL.1 (Dalby, Graham & Grahamophones)
CD _____ LTD 102706
Let's Dance / Jun '95 / Target/BMG.

LET'S DANCE VOL.2 (Dalby, Graham & Grahamophones)
CD _____ LTD 102707
Let's Dance / Jun '95 / Target/BMG.

LET'S DANCE VOL.3 (Dalby, Graham & Grahamophones)
CD _____ LTD 102708
Let's Dance / Jun '95 / Target/BMG.

LET'S DANCE VOL.4 (Dalby, Graham & Grahamophones)
CD _____ LTD 102709
Let's Dance / Jun '95 / Target/BMG.

LET'S DANCE VOL.5 (Dalby, Graham & Grahamophones)
CD _____ LTD 102710
Let's Dance / Jun '95 / Target/BMG.

Dalcan, Dominique

ENTRE L'ETOILE & LE CARRE
Typical blues / Entre l'etoilr and le carre / Promesse celeste / Un jour sur deux / Une epee dans le dos / Comment faut-il faire / Up and down / Les annees bleues / Naked and so shy / Une direction contraire
CD _____ CRAM 074CD
Crammed Discs / Nov '93 / Grapevine / New Note.

Dale, Colin

OUTER LIMITS VOL.1 (Various Artists)
CD _____ KICKCD 10
Kickin' / Jun '94 / SRD.

OUTER LIMITS VOL.2 (Various Artists)
CD _____ KICKCD 21
Kickin' / May '95 / SRD.

Dale, Dick

TRIBAL THUNDER
CD _____ HCD 8046
Hightone / Mar '95 / ADA / Koch.

UNKNOWN TERRITORY
CD _____ HCD 8055
Hightone / Mar '95 / ADA / Koch.

Daley & Lorien

DREAMS OF THE YES MEN
CD _____ EUCD 1193
ARC / Apr '92 / ARC Music / ADA.

Daley, Lloyd

IT'S SHUFFLE 'N' SKA TIME
CD _____ JMC 200221
Jamaica Gold / Jun '95 / THE / Magnum Music Group / Jetstar.

Daley, Martin

ARCHITECTS OF TIME (Daley, Martin & Duncan Lorien)
Structure / Bermuda / Architects of time / Into the oasis / Eleven days / Thank you / Waiting for Karl / Spirit warrior
CD _____ EUCD 1154
ARC / Jun '91 / ARC Music / ADA.

Dali's Car

WAKING HOUR
Dali's car / His box / Cornwall stone / Artemis / Create and melt / Moonlife / Judgement is the mirror
CD _____ BBL 52 CD
Lowdown/Beggars Banquet / Jan '89 / Warner Music / Disc.

Dallas Jazz Orchestra

THANK YOU, LEON
Back in town / Anand / Miami beach / Willow weep for me / Latin dream / Alison's tune / Basin Street blues / Reggae blues / Tickle toe / Yesterdays / Bikini beach / Thank you! Leon
CD _____ CDSB 2041
Sea Breeze / Oct '91 / Jazz Music.

Dalli, Toni

BEST OF TONI DALLI, THE
See For Miles/C5 / Jul '91 / Pinnacle.
CD _____ C5CD 570

Dallwitz, Dave

HOOKED ON RAGTIME - VOL. 1 (Dallwitz, Dave Euphonic Ragtime Ensemble)
CD _____ BCD 321
GHB / Jan '94 / Jazz Music.

HOOKED ON RAGTIME - VOL. 2 (Dallwitz, Dave Euphonic Ragtime Ensemble)
CD _____ BCD 322
GHB / Jan '94 / Jazz Music.

Dalriada

ALL IS FAIR
Haughs o' Cromdale / Scots wha hae / Green grow the rashes / Jock o'Hazeldean / Ye Jacobites by name / Will ye no' come back again / Johnny Cope / Loch Lomond / Macphersons' farewell / Ae fond kiss / Caledonia / Grey man
CD _____ IR 015 CD
Iona / Nov '91 / ADA / Direct / Duncans.

Dalseth, Laila

TIME FOR LOVE, A
CD _____ GEMCD 151
Gemini / Oct '90 / Cadillac.

TRAVELLIN LIGHT
CD _____ GEMCD 154
Gemini / Apr '89 / Cadillac.

Daltrey, Roger

BEST OF ROGER DALTREY
Martyrs and madmen / Say it isn't so Joe / Oceans away / Treasury / Free me / Without your love / It's a hard life / Giving it all away / Avenging Annie / Proud / You put something better inside me
CD _____ 847 855-2
Polydor / May '91 / PolyGram.

DALTREY
One man band / Way of the world / You are yourself / Thinking / You and me / It's a hard life / Giving it all away / Story so far / When the music stops / Reasons / Reprise - One man band
CD _____ 5272592
Polydor / Apr '95 / PolyGram.

Daltry, Peter

DREAM ON
Dust / Going back to bohemia / Fitzgerald / Tender is the night / Ravenswing / Richard and I / Nothing more than this / Felt like the moon / Unicorn / Eighteen summers / Dream on / Roundway Hill
CD _____ VP 196CD
Voice Print / Mar '95 / Voice Print.

Daly, Glen

HEART OF SCOTLAND, THE
CD _____ SSLCD 105
Savanna / Aug '92 / THE.

Daly, Jackie

BUTTONS AND BOWS (Daly, Jackie/ Seamus & Manus McGuire)
Blue Angel / Esther's reel/Trip to Kinvara / Old resting chair / Crowley's reels / Norwegian waltz/Liza Lynn / Dionne reel / Waltz from Orsa / Barn dances / My love is an Arbutus / Waltz clog / La Bastringue / Bog carrot
CD _____ GLCD 1051
Green Linnet / Jun '93 / Roots / CM / Direct / ADA.

JACKIE DALY
CD _____ OSS 30CD
Ossian / Mar '94 / ADA / Direct / CM.

JACKIE DALY & SÉAMUS CREAGH (Daly, Jackie & Séamus Creagh)
CD _____ CEFCD 057
Gael Linn / Jan '94 / Roots / CM / Direct / ADA.

MANY'S A WILD NIGHT
CD _____ CEFCD 176
Gael Linn / Dec '95 / Roots / CM / Direct / ADA.

MUSIC FROM SLIABH LUACHRA (Vol.6)
Tom Sullivan's / Johnny Leary's / Jim Keefe's / Keefe's / Clog / Tir na nog / Callaghan's hornpipe / Rising sun / Pope's toe / Glin cottage polkas / Paddy scully's / Gallant tipperay / Walsh's / Ballyvourine polka / Johnny Mickey's / Trip to the Jacks / Where is the cat / Banks of Sullane / Braidy Martin's / Ger the rigger / Glenside cottage / Tdim gan airgead / Willie Reilly / Murphy's / Going to the well for water
CD _____ GLCD 3065
Green Linnet / Jun '92 / Roots / CM / Direct / ADA.

Daly, Vic

SO AM I
CD _____ ADITZ 1
Album Zutique / Dec '95 / Else.

Dama & D'Gary

LONG WAY HOME
CD _____ SH 64052CD
Shanachie / Oct '94 / Koch / ADA / Greensleeves.

D'Ambrosio, Meredith

IT'S YOUR DANCE
Giant steps / Once upon a tempo / Listen little girl / Devil may care / August moon / Nobody else but me / Humpty dumpty heart / It's your dance / Underdog / It isn't so good it couldn't be better / Off again on again / No one remembers but me / Miss Harper goes bizarre / Strange meadowlark
CD _____ SSC 1011 D
Sunnyside / Feb '86 / Pinnacle.

LOVE IS NOT A GAME
Daybreak / In April / Autumn serenade / Young and foolish / I love you / You, I love / Quiet now / Get used to it baby / That old sweet song / Heaven sent / All or nothing at all / This lament / Indian summer / Peace / Oh look at me now / But now look at me / Love is not a game
CD _____ SSC 1051D
Sunnyside / Jun '91 / Pinnacle.

MEREDITH....ANOTHER TIME
All of us in it together / Aren't you glad / I love you / It's so peaceful in the country / Rain rain (don't go away) / Dear Bix / Lazy

afternoon / Where's the child I used to hold / Love is a simple thing / You are there / While we're young / Small day tomorrow / Child is born / Piano player / Someday my Prince will come / Such a lonely girl am I / Wheelers and dealers / I was doing all right / Skylark
CD _____ SSC 1017D
Sunnyside / Nov '90 / Pinnacle.

SHADOWLAND
CD _____ 500602
Sunnyside / Nov '92 / Pinnacle.

Dameron, Tadd

MATING CALL
CD _____ OJCCD 212
Original Jazz Classics / Oct '92 / Wellard / Jazz Music / Cadillac / Complete/Pinnacle.

Damia

1928-35
CD _____ 123
Chansophone / Nov '92 / Discovery.

LA TRAGEDIENNE DE LA CHANSON
CD _____ UCD 19075
Forlane / Jun '95 / Target/BMG.

Damianio, Peter

MERRY CHRISTMAS & A HAPPY NEW YEAR (Damianio, Peter & His Orchestra)
CD _____ CDSGP 116
Prestige / Jan '94 / Total/BMG.

Damn Yankees

DAMN YANKEES
Coming of age / Bad reputation / Runaway / High enough / Damn yankees / Come again / Mysified / Rock city / Tell me how you want it / Pile driver
CD _____ 7599261592
WEA / Mar '94 / Warner Music.

DON'T TREAD
Don't tread on me / Fifteen minutes of fame / Where you goin' now / Dirty dog / Mr. Please / Silence is broken / Firefly / Someone to believe / This side of hell / Double coyote / Uprising
CD _____ 9362450252
WEA / Aug '92 / Warner Music.

Damnation

NO MORE DREAMS OF HAPPY ENDINGS
CD _____ JT 1020CD
Jade Tree / Sep '95 / Plastic Head.

Damned

ALTERNATIVE CHARTBUSTERS
Thanks for the night / I think I'm wonderful / Lovely money / Ignite / Dozen girls / Bad time for Bonzo / Neat neat neat (Live) / Fan club (Live) / I feel alright (live) / Love song (Live) / I smash it up / Disco man
CD _____ AOK 101
Street Link / Jan '92 / BMG.

BEST OF THE DAMNED
New rose / Neat neat neat / I just can't be happy today / Jet boy jet girl / Hit and miss / There ain't no sanity clause / Smash it up (parts 1 and 2) / Plan 9 channel 7 / Ra bid (over you) / Wait for the world / History of the world (part 1)
CD _____ CDDAM 1
Big Beat / Oct '87 / Pinnacle.

BLACK ALBUM, THE
Wait for the blackout / Lively arts / Silly kids games / Drinking about my baby / Hit and miss / Dr. Jekyll and Mr. Hyde / Thirteenth floor vendetta / Curtain call (Available on CD only) / Twisted nerve / Sick of this and that / History of the world (part 1) / Therapy
CD _____ CDWIK 906
Big Beat / '87 / Pinnacle.

COLLECTION: THE DAMNED
Ignite / Generals / Dozen girls / Bad time for Bonzo / Gun fury / Thanks for the night / History of the world (part 1) / Lively arts / There ain't no sanity clause / White rabbit / Melody Lee / Lovely money / Disco man / I think I'm wonderful / Help (live) / I just can't be happy today (live) / Love song (live) / Neat neat neat (Live) / New rose (Live) / Noise noise noise (Live) / Smash it up / Wait for the blackout
CD _____ CCSCD 278
Castle / Dec '90 / BMG.

DAMNED BUSTERS
Disco man / Thanks for the night / I think I'm wonderful / Lovely money / Ignite / Dozen girls / Bad time for Bonzo / Neat neat neat (Live) / Fan club (live) / I feel alright (live) / Love song (live) / Smash it up
CD _____ STR CD 034
Street Link / Oct '92 / BMG.

DAMNED BUT NOT FORGOTTEN
Dozen girls / Lovely money / I think I'm wonderful / Disguise / Take that / Torture me / Disco man / Thanks for the night / Take me away / Some girls are ugly / Nice cup of tea / Billy bad breaks
CD _____ DOJOCD 21
Dojo / '86 / BMG.

DAMNED, DAMNED, DAMNED
Neat neat neat / Fan club / I fall / Born to kill / Stab your back / Feel the pain / New rose / Fish / See her tonite / One of the two / So messed up / I feel alright
CD _____ FIENDCD 91
Demon / Apr '87 / Pinnacle / ADA.

ETERNALLY DAMNED (The Very Best Of The Damned)
Neat neat neat / New rose / Problem child / Don't cry wolf / Stretcher case baby / Sick of being sick / Love song / Smash it up / I just can't be happy today / History of the world (Part 1) / White rabbit / Disco man / Nasty / There ain't no sanity clause / Shadow of love / Grimly fiendish / Eloise / Is it a dream / Alone again or / Gigolo
CD _____ MUSCD 017
MCI / May '94 / Disc / THE.

FINAL DAMNATION
See her tonite / Neat neat neat / Born to kill / I fall / Fan club / Fish / Help / New rose / I feel alright / I just can't be happy today / Wait for the blackout / Melody Lee / Noise noise noise / Love song / Smash it up / Looking at you / Last time
CD _____ CLACD 338
Castle / '94 / BMG.

FROM THE BEGINNING
Thanks for the night / Lovely money / Dozen girls / I think I'm wonderful / Take that / Last time (live) / I just can't be happy today (live) / Noise noise noise (live) / Love song (live) / Smash it up (live) / Help (live) / Generals / Stranger on the town / Take me away / Under the floor again / Pleasure and the pain
CD _____ 550 747-2
Spectrum/Karussell / Apr '95 / PolyGram / THE.

LIGHT AT THE END OF THE TUNNEL (2CD/MC Set)
CD Set _____ MCLDD 19007
MCA / Apr '92 / BMG.

LIVE AT NEWCASTLE CITY HALL
CD _____ RRCD 181
Receiver / May '93 / Grapevine.

LIVE AT SHEPPERTON
Love song / Second time around / I just can't be happy today / Melody Lee / Help / Neat neat neat / Looking at you M.C. / Smash it up (parts 1 and 2) / New rose / Plan 9 channel 7
CD _____ CDWIKM 27
Big Beat / Jun '88 / Pinnacle.

M.C.A SINGLES A'S AND B'S
CD _____ VSOPCD 174
Connoisseur / Jul '92 / Pinnacle.

MACHINE GUN ETIQUETTE
Love song / Machine gun etiquette / I can't be happy today / New rose / Anti-pope / These hands / Plan 9 channel 7 / Noise noise noise / Looking at you / Liar / Smash it up (Part 1) / Smash it up (Part 2) / Ballroom blitz (Available on CD only) / Suicide (Available on CD only) / Rabid (over you) (Available on CD only) / White rabbit (Available on CD only)
CD _____ CDWIK 905
Big Beat / '86 / Pinnacle.

MUSIC FOR PLEASURE
Problem child / Don't cry wolf / One way love / Politics / Stretcher case baby / Idiot box / You take my money / Alone / Your eyes / Creep (you can't fool me) / You know
CD _____ FIENDCD 108
Demon / Apr '88 / Pinnacle / ADA.

NOISE (The Best Of The Damned Live)
CD _____ EMPRCD 592
Emporio / Oct '95 / THE / Disc / CM.

NOT THE CAPTAIN'S BIRTHDAY PARTY
You take my money / Creep (you can't fool me) / Fan club / Problem child / I fall / So messed up / New rose / Feel alright / Born to kill
CD _____ VEXCD 7
Demon / Oct '91 / Pinnacle / ADA.

PEEL SESSIONS
CD _____ SFRCD 121
Strange Fruit / Oct '93 / Pinnacle.

PHANTASMAGORIA
Street of dreams / Shadow of love / There'll come a day / Sanctum sanctorum / Is it a dream / Grimly fiendish / Edward the bear / Eighth day / Trojans / I just can't be happy today
CD _____ MCLD 19069
MCA / Oct '91 / BMG.

SCHOOL BULLIES, THE
CD _____ RRCD 179
Receiver / Jul '93 / Grapevine.

SKIP OFF TO SCHOOL TO SEE THE DAMNED
New rose / Help / Neat neat neat / Stab your back / Singalongascabies / Stretcher case baby / Sick of being sick / Problem child / You take my money / Don't cry wolf / One way love
CD _____ VEXCD 12
Demon / Sep '92 / Pinnacle / ADA.

STRAWBERRIES
Ignite / Generals / Stranger on the town / Dozen girls / Dog / Gun fury / Pleasure and

pain / Life goes on / Bad time for Bonzo / Under the floor again / Don't bother me
CD _____ CLEO 1029-2
Cleopatra / Dec '93 / Disc.

TALES FROM THE DAMNED
CD _____ CLEO 71392
Cleopatra / Dec '93 / Disc.

TOTALLY DAMNED
Fun factory / Generals / Stranger / On the town / Gun fury / Born to kill (Live) / I fall / Fish (Live) / Help (Live) / New rose (Live) / I just can't be happy today (Live) / Wait for the blackout (Live) / Noise noise noise (Live) / Looking at you (Live) / Disguise / Take that / Torture me / Take me away / Some girls are ugly / Billy bad breaks
CD _____ DOJOCD 65
Dojo / Feb '94 / BMG.

Damon & Naomi

WONDEROUS WORLD OF....
CD _____ SP 322B
Sub Pop / Nov '95 / Disc.

Damone, Vic

16 MOST REQUESTED SONGS
On the street where you live / War and peace / Almost like being in love / Smoke gets in your eyes / Do I love you because you're beautiful / Affair to remember / You're breaking my heart / Angela mia / Maria / Gigi / Separate tables / But beautiful / Pleasure of her company / Serenade in blue / In the blue of evening
CD _____ 472197 2
Columbia / Nov '92 / Sony.

BEST OF VIC DAMONE LIVE, THE
CD _____ RCD 8204
Ranwood / May '89 / Jazz Music.

FEELINGS
Feelings / Lazy afternoon / Ghost riders in the sky / Softly / Windmills of your mind / People / Top of the world / Farewell to paradise / Over the rainbow
CD _____ MU 3004
Musketeer / Oct '92 / Koch.

ON THE STREET WHERE YOU LIVE
CD _____ MU 5074
Musketeer / Oct '92 / Koch.

ON THE STREET WHERE YOU LIVE
When lights are low / Close your eyes / Tender is the night / No strings / Once upon a time / Little girl / Alright OK you win / What kind of fool am I / Ooh looka there, ain't she pretty / Affair to remember / Call me irresponsible / Wives and lovers / Again / I'm gonna miss you / Cathy / Vieni vieni / Dearly beloved / Maria / Lost in the stars / On the street where you live
CD Set _____ CDSL 8277
Music For Pleasure / Nov '95 / EMI.

SINGS THE GREAT SONGS
By the time I get to Phoenix / Softly as I leave you / Didn't we / Look of love / Come back to me / For once in my life / Top of the world / Feelings / If I / Windmills of your mind / You / Little green apples / Can't take my eyes off you / MacArthur Park / Here's that rainy day / Almost close to you / We have all the time in the world / Lazy afternoon
CD _____ PWK 134
Carlton Home Entertainment / May '90 / Carlton Home Entertainment.

SONG IS YOU, THE
CD _____ CDCD 1077
Charly / Apr '93 / Charly / THE / Cadillac.

SPOTLIGHT ON VIC DAMONE
In the still of the night / Laura / Shangri la / Close your eyes / Let's sit this one out / Diane / After the lights go down / Ebb tide / Is you is or is you ain't my baby / There, I've said it again / Little girl / Poincian song (Ke kali nei au) / Change partners / I could write a book / Ruby / Hawaiian wedding song (Ke kali nei au) / Let's face the music and dance / Make this a slow goodbye
CD _____ CDP 8285132
Capitol / Jul '95 / EMI.

THAT TOWERING FEELING/YOUNG AND LIVELY
You stepped out of a dream / War till you see her / So in love / Spring is here / Let's fall in love / Smoke gets in your eyes / Time on your hands / I'm glad there is you / Touch of your lips / All the things you are / Cheek to cheek / Last night when we were young / We could make such beautiful music / It had to be you / In the blue of evening / I got it bad / Serenade in blue / Very thought of you / Spring will be a little late this year / Imagination / Solitude / What is there to say / Everytime we say goodbye
CD _____ 4810142
Columbia / Aug '95 / Sony.

VIC DAMONE COLLECTOR'S EDITION
CD _____ DVAD 6022
Deja Vu / Apr '95 / THE.

Dan Air Scottish Pipe...

BEST OF SCOTTISH PIPES AND DRUMS (Dan Air Scottish Pipe Band)

CD _____ EUCD 1150
ARC / '91 / ARC Music / ADA.

Dan Ar Bras
SEPTEMBER BLEU
CD _____ KMCD 38
Keltia Musique / May '94 / ADA / Direct /
Discovery.

THEME FOR THE GREEN LANDS
0D _____ KMCD 48
Keltia Musique / May '94 / ADA / Direct /
Discovery.

Dan, Jonah
INTERGALACTIC DUB ROCK
CD _____ ACTCD 002
Abba Christos Tafari / Jan '96 / SRD /
Jetstar.

Dan, Teddy
UNITED STATES OF AFRICA
CD _____ RMCD 013
Roots Man / Nov '94 / Jetstar.

Dance 2 Trance
REVIVAL
Surrealistic pillow / Purple onions / Neil's
aurora / Land of Oz / Enuf Eko / Christopher
/ Mrs. Canabis / Morning star / Fly, fly
dragonfly / Warrior
CD _____ 74321260282
Logic / Feb '95 / BMG.

Dance, Heather
HIGHLAND WELCOME
CD _____ CDLOC 1083
Klub / Oct '94 / CM / Ross / Duncans /
ADA / Direct.

Danceable Weird Shit
HERE'S THE RECORD
CD _____ WD 6662CD
World Domination / Sep '90 / Pinnacle.

Dancefloor Virus
BALLROOM, THE
Message in a bottle / De do do do de da
da da / Bed's too big without you / When
the world is running down / Walking on the
moon / Synchronicity / Every breath you
take / Spirits in a material world / Don't
stand so close to me
CD _____ 4804872
Epic / Nov '95 / Sony.

Dancetime Orchestra
OLD TIME CHAMPIONSHIP DANCES
CD _____ SAV 183CD
Savoy / May '93 / THE / Savoy.

Dancing Fantasy
MIDNIGHT BOULEVARD
CD _____ 710 105
Innovative Communication / Aug '90 /
Magnum Music Group.

Dancing Feet
IN THAT LAND ACROSS THE SEA
CD _____ DFO 2CD
Diffusion Breizh / Apr '94 / ADA.

Dancing French Liberals
POWERLINE
CD _____ SKIP 342
Broken Rekids / May '95 / Plastic Head.

Dancing Strings
ENCORE
CD _____ LCOM 5225
Lismor / Oct '93 / Lismor / Direct /
Duncans / ADA.

Dando Shaft
REAPING THE HARVEST
Coming home to me / Railway / Magnetic
beggar / Pass it on / Kalyope driver / Prayer
/ Sometimes / Waves upon the ether /
Dewet / Riverboat / Harp lady I bombed /
Black prince of paradise / When I'm weary
/ Till the morning comes / Whispering Ned
/ Road song / Is it me / It was good / Rain
(Available on CD only) / Cold wind (Available
on CD only) / In the country (Available on
CD only) / End of the game (Available on
CD only)
CD _____ SEECD 291
See For Miles/C5 / Jan '90 / Pinnacle.

SHADOWS ACROSS THE MOON
CD _____ HT 001CD
Happy Trail / Oct '94 / ADA.

D'Andrea, Franco
**ENROSADIRA (D'Andrea, Franco & Luis
Agudo)**
CD _____ 1232432
Red / Nov '91 / Harmonia Mundi / Jazz
Horizons / Cadillac / ADA.

Dandridge, Putney
1935-36
Mr. Bluebird / Ol' man river / It's a sin to tell
a lie
CD _____ CBC 1023
Timeless Jazz / Sep '95 / New Note.

CLASSICS 1935-36
CD _____ CLASSICS 846
Classics / Nov '95 / Discovery / Jazz
Music.

Danemo, Peter
BARABAN
CD _____ DRAGON 206
Dragon / Sep '89 / Roots / Cadillac /
Wellard / CM / ADA.

D'Angelo
BROWN SUGAR
Brown sugar / Alright / Jonz in my bonz /
Me and those dreaming eyes of mine / Shit,
damn Motherfucker / Smooth / Cruisin' /
When we get by / Lady / Higher
CD _____ CTCD 46
Cooltempo / Jun '95 / EMI.

Danger Gens
LIFE BETWEEN CIGARETTES
CD _____ CMR 1022
Crunch Melody / Jul '95 / 3MV / Vital.

Dangerous Toys
PISSED
CD _____ CDVEST 30
Bulletproof / Sep '94 / Pinnacle.

Daniel, Jack
ON TOUR ACROSS AMERICA
CD _____ SB 5
GNP Crescendo / May '93 / Silva Screen.

Daniels, Bebe
STOP, IT'S WONDERFUL
Deep purple / Stop it's wonderful / As round
and round we go / Start the day right / Your
company's requested / It's a small world /
Give a little whistle / I'm singing to a million
/ There I go / Rio Rita / Little swiss whistling
/ Imagination / Nursie Nursie / Somewhere
in France with you / Mother's prayer at twi-
light / Our love / Three little fishes / With the
wind and rain in your hair / Little Sir Echo /
Little boy who never told a lie / Ling'ring on
your doorstep / (I'm afraid) the masquerade
is over
CD _____ RAJCD 850
Empress / May '95 / THE.

Daniels, Chris
IS MY LOVE ENOUGH
CD _____ FIENDCD 744
Demon / Nov '93 / Pinnacle / ADA.

Daniels, Dee
CLOSE ENCOUNTER
Blues in the night / Laverne walk / Georgia
/ On green dolphin street / Never make your
move too soon / Nigerian market place /
Lover man / J.C. Blues / Centerpiece / April
in Paris / Things ain't what they used to be
CD _____ CDSJP 312
Timeless Jazz / Jun '94 / New Note.

LET'S TALK BUSINESS
CD _____ 740272
Capri / '90 / Wellard / Cadillac.

Daniels, Eddie
**BENNY RIDES AGAIN (Daniels, Eddie &
Gary Burton)**
Sing, sing, sing / Stompin' at the Savoy /
Moonglow / Airmail special / Let's dance /
Slipped disc / Memories of you / Avalon /
In a mist / Grand slam / After you've gone
/ Goodbye / Knockin' on wood
CD _____ GRP 96652
GRP / May '92 / BMG / New Note.

BRIEF ENCOUNTER
Brief encounter / Child is born / Path / Sway
/ There is no greater love / Ligia
CD _____ MCD 5154
Muse / Sep '92 / New Note / CM.

FIVE SEASONS, THE
CD _____ SHCD 5017
Shanachie / Jan '96 / Koch / ADA /
Greensleeves.

MEMO'S FROM PARADISE
Spectralight / Dreaming / Heartline / Love
of my life / Homecoming / Memo's from
Paradise / Seventh heaven / Capriccio twi-
light / Impressions from ancient dreamers /
Flight of the dove / Eight-pointed star (Bo-
nus track on CD only.)
CD _____ GRPD 9651
GRP / May '88 / BMG / New Note.

Daniels, Joe
SWING IS THE THING
Avalon / Basin Street blues / It don't mean
a thing if it ain't got that swing / Power

house / Who / Crashing through / Somebody stole my gal / No name jive / Swing is
the thing / Steepin' out to swing / Darktown
strutter's ball / Red light / Whirlwind /
Downbeat / Lady be good / Red robin rag
/ When you're smiling / Swing fan / Honeysuckle rose / Time on my hands / Drum
boogie / Jammin' sessions / Beat me
Daddy, eight to the bar / Fats' in the fire
CD _____ RAJCD 853
Empress / May '95 / THE.

Daniels, Luke
**LUKE DANIELS & FRANK KILKELLY
(Daniels, Luke & Frank Kilkenny)**
CD _____ ACS 019CD
Acoustics / Aug '94 / Conifer / Direct /
ADA.

TARANTELLA
CD _____ ACS 023CD
Acoustics / Aug '95 / Conifer / Direct /
ADA.

Daniels, Maxine
POCKETFUL OF DREAMS, A
I've got a pocketful of dreams / With you in
mind / Deep purple / Seems like old times
/ Change partners / Sunshine of love /
Something 'bout you baby I like / When you
wish upon a star / Leaning on a lamp-post
/ Into each life some must fall / Broken
doll / For all we know / Over the rainbow /
Talk to the animals
CD _____ CLGCD 016
Calligraph / Oct '93 / Cadillac / Wellard /
Jazz Music.

Danielsson, Lars
CONTINUATION
Hit man / Continuation / Long ago and far
away / Flykt / Falin' down / Hymn / It never
entered my mind / Namtih / Fatima / Solar
/ Postludium
CD _____ CDLR 45085
L&R / Aug '94 / New Note.

NEW HANDS
CD _____ DRAGON 125
Dragon / Jan '89 / Roots / Cadillac /
Wellard / CM / ADA.

POEMS
CD _____ DRAGON 209
Dragon / May '87 / Roots / Cadillac /
Wellard / CM / ADA.

Danish Radio Big Band
CRACKDOWN (1st UK tour (1987))
Mr. CT / Vismanden / Ballad for Benny /
Crackdown / From one to another / Say it /
Malus scorpio ritus / Cherry juice / Big
dipper
CD _____ HEPCD 2041
Hep / Apr '90 / Cadillac / Jazz Music / New
Note / Wellard.

SUITE FOR JAZZ BAND
Nervous Charlie / November / Daydream /
Suite for jazz band / This is all I ask / On
Green Dolphin Street / Groove merchant /
Well you needn't
CD _____ HEPCD 2051
Hep / May '92 / Cadillac / Jazz Music / New
Note / Wellard.

Danko, Harold
AFTER THE RAIN
0D _____ 0000 01050
Steeplechase / Sep '95 / Impetus.

FIRST LOVE SONG, THE
First love song / Devil may care / Spring can
really hang you up the most / European
passion / Cliches / Eleanor Rigby / Swift
shifting / To start again / Why did I choose
you / Young ali heart
CD _____ 66053011
Jazz City / Feb '91 / New Note.

Danko, Rick
**DANKO/FJELD/ANDERSEN (Danko,
Rick & Jonas Fjeld/Eric Andersen)**
Driftin' away / Blue hotel / One more shot /
Mary I'm comin' back home / River /
Judgement day / When morning comes to
America / Wrong side of town / Sick and
tired / Angels in the snow / Blaze of glory /
Last thing on my mind
CD _____ RCD 10270
Rykodisc / Oct '93 / Vital / ADA.

RICK DANKO
What a town / Brainwash / New Mexico /
Tired of waiting / Sip the wine / Java blues
/ Sweet romance / Small town talk / Shake
it / Once upon a time
CD _____ ED CD 317
Edsel / Apr '90 / Pinnacle / ADA.

**RIDIN' ON THE BLINDS (Danko, Rick &
Jonas Fjeld/Eric Andersen)**
CD _____ GR 4080CD
Grappa / Apr '95 / ADA.

Dankworth, Jackie
**FIRST CRY (Dankworth, Jackie &
Anthony Kerr)**

CD _____ EFZ 1010
EFZ / Jan '95 / Vital/SAM.

Dankworth, John
**INNOVATIONS (Dankworth, John & The
London Symphony Orchestra)**
Take five / We've only just begun / Here,
there and everywhere
CD _____ PWK 059
Carlton Home Entertainment / Apr '88 /
Carlton Home Entertainment.

**NEBUCHADNEZZAR (Dankworth
Generation Big Band)**
Maggot / It ain't necessarily so / Early June
/ Song for my lad / Day I met Kenny G /
Every time we say goodbye / Black narcis-
sus / Ida Lupino / Down to earth / Up for
an oscar / Emily / Song for my lady
CD _____ JHCD 029
Ronnie Scott's Jazz House / Mar '94 / Jazz
Music / Magnum Music Group / Cadillac.

**RHYTHM CHANGES (Dankworth
Generation Big Band)**
I got rheumatics / Just once more / Around
the track / Jelly mould blues / Going back,
going on / Thoughts / Pigs head copanitza
/ All things
CD _____ JHCD 043
Ronnie Scott's Jazz House / Nov '95 / Jazz
Music / Magnum Music Group / Cadillac.

Danleers
ONE SUMMERNIGHT
One summer night / My flaming heart / Per-
lude to love / Wheelin' and dealin' / Picture
of you / Really love you, I / You're everything / Whole mess of trouble / Just look
around / Can't sleep, I / Your love / (I live)
half a block from an angel / If you don't care
/ Little lover / I'll always believe in you /
Light of love / I'll be forever yours / I'm looking around / Foolish / Angels sent you /
Were you there / If / Where is love / Think
it over baby / Love you better leave me
alone
CD _____ BCD 15503
Bear Family / May '91 / Rollercoaster /
Direct / CM / Swift / ADA.

Danny & The Juniors
**BACK TO THE HOP (Original Swan
Recordings 1960-1962)**
CD _____ RCCD 3005
Rollercoaster / Sep '92 / CM / Swift.

Danny Wilson
BEBOP MOPTOP
Imaginary girl / Second summer of love / I
can't wait / If you really love me (let me go)
/ If everything you said was true / Loneli-
ness / I was wrong / Charlie boy / Never
gonna be the same / Desert hearts / NYC
Shanty / Goodbye Shanty Town / Ballad of
me and Shirley MacLaine
CD _____ CDV 2594
Virgin / Aug '91 / EMI.

BEST OF DANNY WILSON, THE
Davy / Mary's prayer / Girl I used to know
/ I won't forget / Second summer of love /
Get happy / Never gonna be the same / I'll
be waiting / Living to learn / Nothing ever
goes to plan / Broken china (live)
CD _____ CDVIP 139
Virgin VIP / Sep '95 / Carlton Home Enter-
tainment / THE / EMI.

MEET DANNY WILSON
Davy / Mary's prayer / Lorraine parade / Aberdeen / Nothing ever goes to plan / Broken
china / Steamtrains to the milkyway / Spencer Tracey / You remain an angel / Ruby's
golden wedding / Girl I used to know / Five
friendly aliens / I won't be here when you
get home
CD _____ CDV 2419
Virgin / '87 / EMI.

SWEET DANNY WILSON
Never gonna be the same / Ballad of me
and Shirley MacLaine / If you really love me
(Let me go) / Mary's prayer / Girl I used to
know / Pleaser to pleasure / Davy / Ruby's
golden wedding / I can't wait / I won't be
here when you get home / Second Summer
of love / From a boy to a man
CD _____ CDV 2669
Virgin / Aug '92 / EMI.

Danzig
DANZIG
Twist of Cain / Not of this world / She rides
/ Soul on fire / Am I demon / Mother / Pos-
session / End of time / Hunter / Evil thing
CD _____ 74321248412
American / Apr '95 / BMG.

DANZIG 4
Brand new God / Little whip / Cantspeak /
Going down to die / Until you call on the
dark / Dominion / Bringer of death / Sadis-
tikal / Son of the morning star / I don't mind
the pain / Stalker song / Let it be captured
CD _____ 74321236812
American / Oct '94 / BMG.

HOW THE GODS KILL
CD _____ 74321248432
American / Apr '95 / BMG.

LUCIFUGE
Long way back from hell / Killer wolf / I'm the one / Devil's plaything / Blood and tears / Pain in the world / Snakes of Christ / Tired of being alone / Her black wings / 777 / Girl
CD _____ 74321248422
American / Apr '95 / BMG.

THRALL/DEMONSWEATLIVE
It's coming down / Violet fire / Trouble / Snakes of Christ (live) / Am I demon (live) / Sistinas (live) / Mother (live)
CD _____ 74321248442
American / Apr '95 / BMG.

Daou, Vanessa

ZIPLESS
Long tunnell of wanting you / Dear Anne Sexton / Alcestis of the poetry circuit / Sunday afternoon / Autumn perspective / Near the black forest / My love is too much / Becoming a nun / Smoke / Autumn reprise
CD _____ MCD 11278
MCA / Nov '95 / BMG.

Dapogny, Jim

JAMES DAPOGNY & HIS CHICAGOANS
CD _____ SOSCD 1263
Stomp Off / Oct '93 / Jazz Music / Wellard.

Darby, Blind Teddy

BLIND TEDDY DARBY 1929-1937
CD _____ BDCD 6042
Blues Document / May '93 / Swift / Jazz Music / Hot Shot.

D'Arby, Terence Trent

INTRODUCING THE HARDLINE ACCORDING TO TERENCE TRENT D'ARBY
If you all get to Heaven / If you let me stay / Wishing well / I'll never turn my back on you (fathers words) / Dance little sister / Seven more days / Let's go forward / Rain / Sign your name / As yet untitled / Who's loving you
CD _____ 4509112
CBS / Apr '95 / Sony.

TERENCE TRENT D'ARBY'S SYMPHONY OR DAMN (Exploring The Tension Inside The Sweetness)
Welcome to the Monasteryo / She kissed me / Do you love me like you say / Baby let me share my love / Delicate / Neon messiah / Penelope please / Wet your lips / Turn the page / Castilian blues / T.I.T.S./FandJ / Are you happy / Succumb to me / I still love you (Extra track included with LP version.) / Seasons (Extra track included in LP version.) / Let her down easy (Extra track included in LP version.)
CD _____ 473561 2
Columbia / May '93 / Sony.

TERENCE TRENT D'ARBY'S VIBRATOR
Vibrator / Supermodel sandwich / Holding onto you / Read my lips (I dig your scene) / Supermodel sandwich with cheese / Resurrection / It's been said
CD _____ 4785052
Columbia / May '95 / Sony.

TOUCH WITH TERENCE TRENT D'ARBY, THE
CD _____ 839 308-2
Polydor / Aug '89 / PolyGram.

Darby, Tom

COMPLETE RECORDINGS (Darby, Tom & Jimmie Tarlton)
Down in Florida on a hog / Birmingham town / Birmingham jail / Columbus Stockade blues / Gamblin' Jim / Lonesome in the pines / After the ball / I can't tell you why / I love you / Irish police / Hobo tramp / Alto waltz / Mexican rag / Birmingham jail # 2 / Rainbow division / Country girl valley / Lonesome railroad / If you ever learn to love me / If I had listened to my Mother / Traveling yodel blues / Heavy hearted blues / New York hobo / All bound down in Texas / Touring yodel blues / Slow wicked blues / Black Jack moonshine / Ain't gonna marry no more / Down in the old cherry orchid / When the bluebirds nest again / Beggar Joe / When you're far away from home / Birmingham rag / Sweet Sarah blues / Little Bessie / I left her heart at the river / Jack and May / Captain won't you let me go home / Going back to my Texas home / Whistling songbird / Freight train ramble / Lonesome Frisco line / Down among the sugar cane / Black sheep / Little ola / Once I had a sweetheart / Maple on the hill / My father died a drunkyard / Franke Dean / Pork chops / On the banks of a lonely river / Faithless husband / Hard time blues / Rising sun blues / My little blue heaven / Carrie love / By the old oaken bucket / Louise / Lowe Bonnie / After the sinking of the Titanic / New Birmingham jail / Roy Dixon / Moonshine blues / She's waiting for me / That lonesome Frisco line / Thirteen years in Kilbie prison / Once I had a fortune / Dixie

mail / Weaver's blues / Sweetheart of my dreams / Ooze up to me / Let's be friends again / By the oaken bucket
CD Set _____ BCDCI 15764
Bear Family / Jun '95 / Rollercoaster / Direct / CM / Swift / ADA.

Darc, Daniel

PARCE QUE (Darc, Daniel & Bill Pritchard)
CD _____ BIAS 100CD
Play It Again Sam / '90 / Vital.

Dardanelle

COLORS OF MY LIFE, THE
CD _____ STCD 544
Stash / '91 / Jazz Music / CM / Cadillac / Direct / ADA.

DARDANELLE & DAG WALTON'S BIG BAND (Dardanelle & Dag Walton)
CD _____ ACD 227
Audiophile / Oct '92 / Jazz Music / Swift.

DOWN HOME
CD _____ ACD 214
Audiophile / Oct '92 / Jazz Music / Swift.

ECHOES SINGING LADIES
CD _____ ACD 145
Audiophile / Mar '95 / Jazz Music / Swift.

NEW YORK NEW YORK
CD _____ STCD 547
Stash / '92 / Jazz Music / CM / Cadillac / Direct / ADA.

SWINGIN' IN LONDON
CD _____ ACD 278
Audiophile / Jan '94 / Jazz Music / Swift.

Darensbourg, Joe

N'ORLEANS STATESMEN
CD _____ BCD 313
GHB / Aug '94 / Jazz Music.

Darin, Bobby

AS LONG AS I'M SINGIN'
CD _____ JASSCD 4
Jass / Oct '91 / CM / Jazz Music / ADA / Cadillac / Direct.

GREATEST HITS
Mack the knife / Dream lover / Splish splash / If I were a carpenter / Queen of the hop / Early in the morning / Plain Jane / Girl who stood beside me / Funny what love can do / Quarter to nine / Once upon a time / I wish I were in love again
CD _____ HADCD 152
Javelin / May '94 / THE / Henry Hadaway Organisation.

SPOTLIGHT ON BOBBY DARIN
Alabamy bound / Blue skies / You'll never know / Standing on the corner / I'm beginning to see the light / Good life / Oh look at me now / Just in time / You made me love you / All of you / There's a rainbow 'round my shoulder / Fly me to the moon / I got rhythm / All by myself / I wanna be around / Nightingale sang in Berkley Square / Call me irresponsible / My buddy / Always / I'm sitting on top of the world
CD _____ CDP 8285122
Capitol / Apr '95 / EMI.

Dark

ZYEZN GAMBALLE & MENTALWORLD
CD _____ MABCD 008
MAB / Sep '94 / Plastic Head.

Dark Angel

DARKNESS DESCENDS
Darkness descends / Burning of Sodom / Hunger of the undead / Merciless death / Death is certain (life is not) / Black prophesies / Perish in flames
CD _____ CDFLAG 6
Under One Flag / '89 / Pinnacle.

DECADE OF CHAOS (The Best Of Dark Angel)
CD _____ CDMFLAG 70
Under One Flag / Jul '92 / Pinnacle.

LEAVE SCARS
CD _____ CDFLAG 30
Under One Flag / Jan '89 / Pinnacle.

LIVE SCARS
CD _____ CDFLAG 42
Under One Flag / Jul '89 / Pinnacle.

TIME DOES NOT HEAL
CD _____ CDFLAG 54
Under One Flag / Feb '91 / Pinnacle.

Dark Heresy

ABSTRACT PRINCIPLES
CD _____ USR 020CD
Unisound / Nov '95 / Plastic Head.

Dark Lantern

DARK LANTERN
CD _____ SP 002CD
Silent Pocket / Nov '95 / ADA.

Dark Tranquility

GALLERY
CD _____ OPCD 033
Osmose / Jan '96 / Plastic Head.

OF CHAOS AND ETERNAL LIGHT
CD _____ SPI 023CD
Spinefarm / May '95 / Plastic Head.

SKYDANCER
CD _____ SPI 16-2
Spinefarm / Nov '93 / Plastic Head.

Darkfield

DANCE ON THE GRAVE, A
CD _____ RPS 005CD
Repulse / Jun '95 / Plastic Head.

Darkman

WORLDWIDE
CD _____ 5294162
Wild Card / Oct '95 / PolyGram.

Darkness

BROKEN HARD
CD _____ 15389
Laserlight / Aug '91 / Target/BMG.

Darkness & Light

CRESCENT
CD _____ CRCD 201
Scratch / Jan '95 / BMG.

Darkseed

ROMANTIC TALES
CD _____ IR 010CD
Invasion / Apr '95 / Plastic Head.

Darkthrone

PANZERFAUST
CD _____ FOG 005CD
Moonfog / May '95 / Plastic Head.

Darling

FAMOUS
CD _____ COD 1
Codfunk / Jan '96 / Total/BMG.

Darling, David

CELLO
Darkwood / No place nowhere / Fables / Darkwood II / Lament / Two or three things / Indiana Indian / Totem / Psalm / Choral / Bell / In November / Darkwood III
CD _____ 5119822
ECM / Sep '92 / New Note.

CYCLES
Cycle song / Cycle #1: Namaste / Fly / Ode / Cycle #2: Trio / Cycle #3: Quintet and coda / Jessica's sunwheel
CD _____ 8431722
ECM / Nov '91 / New Note.

DARKWOOD
Dawn / In motion / Journey / Light / Earth / New morning / Returning / Picture / Medivial dance / Searching / Up side down / Beginning / Passage
CD _____ 5237502
ECM / Feb '95 / New Note.

Darling, Erik

BORDER TOWN AT MIDNIGHT
CD _____ FE 1417
Folk Era / Dec '94 / CM / ADA.

Darlingheart

WISH YOU WERE HERE
CD _____ DHCD 3
Fontana / Jul '93 / PolyGram.

D'Arnell, Andrea

VILLERS-AUX-VENTS
CD _____ 422498
New Rose / May '94 / Direct / ADA.

Darren, James

BEST OF JAMES DARREN, THE
Angel face / I ain't sharin' Sharon / Because they're young / Goodbye cruel world / Her royal majesty / Conscience / Gotta have love / Mary's little lamb / Life of the party / Hail to the conquering hero / Pin a medal on Joey / They should have given you the oscar / Put on a happy face / Just think of tonight / Punch and Judy
CD _____ NEMCD 694
Sequel / Aug '94 / BMG.

Darrow, Chris

FRETLESS
CD _____ TX 2012CD
Taxim / Jan '94 / ADA.

SOUTHERN CALIFORNIA DRIVE, A
CD _____ LICD 900236
Line / Mar '92 / CM / Grapevine / ADA / Conifer / Direct.

Daryll-Ann

COME AROUND
Come around / Doll / Shamrock / Good thing / Mirror mind / Ocean girl
CD _____ HUTDM 44
Hut / May '94 / EMI.

SEABORNE WEST
Stay / Low light / Doctor and I / Sheila / Allright / Holida why / You're so vain / Birthmark / Boy you were / Liquid / H.P. confirm / Soft and fat
CD _____ CDHUT 26
Hut / Apr '95 / EMI.

Das Damen

DAS DAMEN
CD _____ SST 040 CD
SST / May '93 / Plastic Head.

JUPITER EYE
CD _____ SST 095 CD
SST / May '93 / Plastic Head.

MARSHMELLOW CONSPIRACY
CD _____ SST 218 CD
SST / '88 / Plastic Head.

TRISKAIDEKAPHOBE
CD _____ SST 190 CD
SST / May '93 / Plastic Head.

Das EFX

DEAD SERIOUS
Mic checka / Jussummen / They want efx / Looseys / Dum dums / East coast / If only / Brooklyn to T-neck / Klap ya handz / Straight out the sewer
CD _____ 7567918272
Atlantic / May '92 / Warner Music.

HOLD IT DOWN
CD _____ 7559618292
Atlantic / Sep '95 / Warner Music.

STRAIGHT UP SEWASIDE
Intro / Undaground rappa / Gimme dat micraphone / Check it out / Interlude / Freak it / Rappaz / Interview / Baknaffek / Kaught in da ak / Wontu / Krazy wit da books / It'z lik dat / Host wit da most
CD _____ 756792265-2
Atlantic / Dec '93 / Warner Music.

Das Ich

DIE PROPHETEN
CD _____ EFA 11201
Danse Macabre / Apr '93 / SRD.

SATANISCHE VERSE
CD _____ EFA 11232-2
Danse Macabre / Jul '94 / SRD.

STAUB
CD _____ EFA 11236-2
Danse Macabre / Nov '94 / SRD.

STIGMA
CD _____ EFACD 11233-2
Danse Macabre / Jun '94 / SRD.

Das Klown

LAUGHIN' STACK
CD _____ EFA 122152
Poshboy / Oct '94 / Disc.

Das Pferd

KISSES (Das Pferd & Randy Becker)
CD _____ ITM 1430
ITM / Jan '91 / Tradelink / Koch.

Dash Rip Rock

GET YOU SOME OF ME
CD _____ SECT 10021
Sector 2 / Jan '96 / Direct / ADA.

Dat Blygu

LIBERTINO
CD _____ ANKST 037CD
Ankst / Jun '93 / SRD.

Datblygu

WYAU/PYST
CD _____ ANKST 60CD
Ankst / Sep '95 / SRD.

Dauerlutscher

DAUERLUTSCHER
CD _____ LF 067
Lost & Found / Mar '94 / Plastic Head.

Daughters Of Zion

AISHA
CD _____ NGCD 538
Twinkle / May '93 / SRD / Jetstar / Kingdom.

Daun, Tom

ALL IN A GARDEN GREEN (Harp Music)
CD _____ TUT 167
Wundertute / Oct '94 / CM / Duncans / ADA.

Dave & Deke Combo

MOONSHINE MELODIES
CD _____ NOHITCD 009
No Hit / Jan '94 / SRD.

Dave Dee, Dozy, Beaky,...

BEST OF DAVE DEE, DOZY, BEAKY, MICK & TICH (Dave Dee, Dozy, Beaky, Mick & Tich)
Legend of Xanadu / Bend it / Save me / Hold tight / Touch me, touch me / Wreck of the Antoinette / Snake in the grass / No time / My woman's man / Zabadak / Okay / You make it move / Mr. President / Don Juan / Sun goes down / Is it love / Last night in Soho
CD _____ 5518232
Spectrum/Karussell / Nov '95 / PolyGram THE.

HITS (Dave Dee, Dozy, Beaky, Mick & Tich)
CD _____ 12274
Laserlight / Apr '94 / Target/BMG.

ZABADAK (Dave Dee, Dozy, Beaky, Mick & Tich)
Legend of Xanadu / Bend it / Save me / Mr. President / My woman's man / All I want to do / Master Llewellyn / I'm on the up / If I were a gardener / Zabadak / Okay / Don Juan / She's so good / Hands off / Help me / Hard to love you / Nose for trouble / We've got a good thing goin'
CD _____ 5509392
Spectrum/Karussell / Jan '95 / PolyGram THE.

Davenport, Cow Cow

ACCOMPANIST, THE
CD _____ BDCD 6040
Blues Document / May '93 / Swift / Jazz Music / Hot Shot.

Davern, Kenny

I'LL SEE YOU IN MY DREAMS
CD _____ MM 5020
Music Masters / Oct '94 / Nimbus.

KENNY DAVERN
CD _____ CRD 324
Chiara Scuro / Feb '95 / Jazz Music / Kudos.

LIVE AND SWINGING (Davern, Kenny & John Peters)
That's a plenty / Man I love / Poor butterfly / Royal Garden blues / Blue monk / Love me or leave me
CD _____ CMJCD 001
CMJ / '88 / Jazz Music / Wellard.

NEVER IN A MILLION YEARS (Davern, Kenny & Dick Wellstood)
CD _____ CHR 70019
Challenge / Jun '95 / Direct / Jazz Music / Cadillac / ADA.

ONE HOUR TONIGHT (Davern, Kenny & Dick Wellstood)
Elsa's dream / Pretty baby / Love is the thing / If I could be with you one hour tonight
CD _____ MM 5003
Music Masters / Oct '94 / Nimbus.

Davey, Shaun

GRANUAILE
Dubhdarra / Ripples in the rockpools / Defence of Hens Castle / Free and easy / Rescue of Hugh de Lacy / Dismissal / Hen's march / Death of Richard-an-iarainn / Sir Richard Bingham / Spanish Armada / New age
CD _____ TARACD 3017
Tara / Feb '86 / CM / ADA / Direct / Conifer.

PILGRIM, THE
CD _____ TARA 3032CD
Tara / Oct '94 / CM / ADA / Direct / Conifer.

RELIEF OF DERRY SYMPHONY
CD _____ TARACD 3024
Tara / Jul '92 / CM / ADA / Direct / Conifer.

David & David

BOOMTOWN
Boomtown / Rock for the forgotten / Welcome to the boomtown / Swallowed by the cracks / Ain't so easy / Being alone together / River's gonna rise / Swimming in the ocean / All alone in the big city / Heroes
CD _____ CDA 5134
A&M / '89 / PolyGram.

David & Jonathan

VERY BEST OF DAVID & JONATHAN
Michelle / Softly whispering your name / You ought to meet my baby / This golden ring / Bye bye brown eyes / I know / Speak her name / Ten storeys high / I've got that girl on my mind / You've got your troubles / Lovers of the world unite / Laughing fit to cry / Be sure / Scarlet ribbons / Gilly gilly ossenfeffer katzenellenbogen by the sea / How bitter the taste of love / Every now and

then / One born every minute / See me cry / She's leaving home
CD _____ C5CD-507
See For Miles/C5 / Jul '90 / Pinnacle.

David, Ian

I MUST JUST LEAVE A KISS
I must just leave a kiss / Sail with you only / Our room / Let me at least stay in your heart / Power behind the throne / Latin calipso / Babe / My airline hostess (coffee or tea) / Chivalry and song / Now I find
CD _____ DVDCD 1
Zonespec / Sep '89 / EMI.

David, Jean

CHIR HACHIRIM - THE SONG OF SONGS
CD _____ 926282
Buda / Jul '95 / Discovery / ADA.

David, Kal

DOUBLE TUFF
CD _____ SC 880042
Lipstick / May '95 / Vital/SAM.

Davidson, Matthew

SPACE SHUFFLE & OTHER FUTURISTIC RAGS
CD _____ SOSCD 1252
Stomp Off / May '93 / Jazz Music / Wellard.

Davies, Craig

GROOVIN' ON A SHAFT CYCLE
CD _____ ROUGHCD 132
Rough Trade / Apr '90 / Pinnacle.

LIKE NARCISSUS
CD _____ ROUGHCD 122
Rough Trade / Jun '88 / Pinnacle.

Davies, Dave

DAVE DAVIES AND GLAMOUR
CD _____ MAUCD 617
Mau Mau / Sep '92 / Pinnacle.

Davies, Debbie

LOOSE TONIGHT
CD _____ BPCD 5015
Blind Pig / Dec '94 / Hot Shot / Swift / CM / Roots / Direct / ADA.

PICTURE THIS
Picture this / Don't take advantage of me / Twenty four hour fool / I wonder why (you're so mean to me) / Livin' on lies / Better off with the blues / Sidetracked / Lovin' cup / Buzz me / San-Ho-Zay / How long / Still I win your love / Going back to luka
CD _____ FIENDCD 732
Demon / Jun '93 / Pinnacle / ADA.

Davies, Ray

DANSAN YEARS VOL. 11 (Davies, Ray & Irven Tidswell)
CD _____ DACD 11
Dansan / Mar '95 / Savoy / President / Target/BMG.

DANSAN YEARS VOL. 12 (Davies, Ray & Irven Tidswell)
CD _____ DACD 12
Dansan / Mar '95 / Savoy / President / Target/BMG.

Davies, Steve Gwyn

AN UBHAL AS AIRDE
CD _____ VITAL 02CD
Vital Spark / Nov '95 / ADA.

Davis, Alvin

LET IT BLOW
CD _____ FMJXD 186
Ripe / Nov '94 / Jetstar.

LET THE VIBES DECIDE
CD _____ RIPEXD 213
Ripe / Feb '95 / Total/BMG.

Davis, Anthony

GHOST FACTORY, THE
CD _____ GCD 79429
Gramavision / Sep '95 / Vital/SAM / ADA.

MIDDLE PASSAGE
Behind the rock / Middle passage / Particle W / Proposition for life
CD _____ GRCD 8401
Gramavision / Feb '85 / Vital/SAM / ADA.

TRIO 2 (Davis, Anthony, James Newton & Abdul Wadud)
Who's life / Thursday's child / Eclipse / Kiano / Invisible island / First movement / Second movement / Third movement / Simultaneity / Flat out
CD _____ 794 412
Gramavision / Mar '90 / Vital/SAM / ADA.

Davis, Art

LIFE
CD _____ SN 1143CD

Soul Note / Sep '95 / Harmonia Mundi / Wellard / Cadillac.

Davis, Betty

BETTY DAVIS
CD _____ UFOXY 1CD
UFO / Oct '93 / Pinnacle.

Davis, Blind John

BLIND JOHN DAVIS 1938
I had a dream / I know the baby loves me / Hey hey Mama / Woman I love / I heard an echo / Trick's done turned on you / Don't lie to me / Harlem blues / When the blues came out to sing / Pretty blues for listening / When I've been drinking / Bartender's bounce / Penny pinching blues
CD _____ ECD 260562
Evidence / Sep '94 / Harmonia Mundi / ADA / Cadillac.

BLIND JOHN DAVIS WITH JEANNE CARROLL (Davis, Blind John & Jeanne Carroll)
CD _____ CDLR 72002
L&R / Jul '94 / New Note.

FIRST RECORDING SESSIONS
CD _____ SOB 35202
Story Of The Blues / Dec '92 / Koch / ADA.

Davis, Carlene

REGGAE SONGBIRD
CD _____ RRTGCD 7703
Rohit / '88 / Jetstar.

SONGS OF FREEDOM
CD _____ LG 21076
Lagoon / Mar '93 / Magnum Music Group / THE.

Davis, Cedell

FEEL LIKE DOIN' SOMETHING WRONG
CD _____ FIENDCD 745
Demon / Nov '93 / Pinnacle / ADA.

Davis, Charles

REFLECTIONS (Davis, Charles & Barry Harris)
CD _____ 123247-2
Red / Nov '92 / Harmonia Mundi / Jazz Horizons / Cadillac / ADA.

Davis, Eb

GOOD TIME BLUES (Davis, Eb Bluesband)
CD _____ BEST 1016CD
Acoustic Music / Nov '93 / ADA.

Davis, Eddie 'Lockjaw'

EDDIE 'LOCKJAW' DAVIS & MICHAEL STARCH TRIO/KARL RATZER (Davis, Eddie 'Lockjaw' & Michael Starch Trio/ Karl Ratzer)
CD _____ WOLF 120588
Wolf / Mar '95 / Jazz Music / Swift / Hot Shot.

EDDIE 'LOCKJAW' DAVIS/ MICHEL ATTENOUX & HIS ORCHESTRA (Davis, Eddie 'Lockjaw' / Michel Attenoux & his Orchestra)
CD _____ STCD 5009
Storyville / May '93 / Jazz Music / Wellard / CM / Cadillac.

JAW'S BLUES
CD _____ ENJACD 30972
Enja / Jan '95 / New Note / Vital/SAM.

JAWS
CD _____ OJCCD 218
Original Jazz Classics / Nov '95 / Wellard / Cadillac / Complete/Pinnacle.

LOCKJAW COOKBOOK, VOL. 1
CD _____ OJCCD 652
Original Jazz Classics / Feb '92 / Wellard / Jazz Music / Cadillac / Complete/Pinnacle.

LOCKJAW COOKBOOK, VOL. 2
CD _____ OJCCD 653
Original Jazz Classics / Feb '92 / Wellard / Jazz Music / Cadillac / Complete/Pinnacle.

MODERN JAZZ
Dizzy atmosphere / It's the talk of the town / Leapin' on Lenox / This is always / Bean-o / I'll remember April / Moonlight in Vermont / Johnny come lately / You go to my head / Foggy day / Tenderly / Way you look tonight
CD _____ KCD 506
King/Paddle Wheel / Mar '90 / New Note.

SWINGIN' 'TIL GIRLS
CD _____ SCCD 31058
Steeplechase / Jul '88 / Impetus.

TOUGH TENORS (Davis, Eddie 'Lockjaw' & Johnny Griffin)
Again 'n' again / Tin tin deo / If I had you / Jim dawg / When we were one / Gigi
CD _____ 8212932
Milestone / Jun '86 / CM / Jazz Music / Pinnacle / Wellard / Cadillac.

WITH MILT (Davis, Eddie 'Lockjaw' & Sonny Stitt)
CD _____ CDC 9028
LRC / Mar '91 / New Note / Harmonia Mundi.

Davis, Guy

STOMP DOWN RIDER
CD _____ RHRCD 80
Red House / Dec '95 / Koch / ADA.

Davis, James

CHECK-OUT TIME (Davis, James 'Thunderbird')
I'm ready now / You did me wrong / Hello sundown / Check our time / What else is there to do / If I had my life to live over / Your turn to cry / Come by here / I should've known better / Case of love / Bloodshot eyes / Dark end of the street
CD _____ FIENDCD 149
Demon / Mar '92 / Pinnacle / ADA.

Davis, Janet-Lee

MISSING YOU
CD _____ FADCD 30
Fashion / Apr '95 / Jetstar / Grapevine.

Davis, Jesse

HIGH STANDARDS
Rush hour / I hear a rhapsody / Isms / Peace / Jubilation / Hues / Big push / On a misty night / Strike up the band / Just a little blues
CD _____ CCD 4624
Concord Jazz / Nov '04 / New Note.

YOUNG AT ART
East of the sun and west of the moon / Brother Roj / I love Paris / Ask me now / Georgiana / Waltz for Andre / Little flowers / One for cannon / Tipsy / Fine and dandy
CD _____ CCD 4565
Concord Jazz / Aug '93 / New Note.

Davis, Jesse Ed

JESSE ED DAVIS
CD _____ 7567803032
Atlantic / Jan '94 / Warner Music.

Davis, Larry

BLUES KNIGHTS (Davis, Larry & Byther Smith)
Giving up on love / I tried / Teardrops / That's all right / I don't have a mother / I'm a honey bee / What is this / Don't make me talk to much / Addressing the nation with the blues / I'm broke
CD _____ ECD 260422
Evidence / Mar '94 / Harmonia Mundi / ADA / Cadillac.

I AIN'T BEGGIN' NOBODY
CD _____ ECD 26016
Evidence / Feb '93 / Harmonia Mundi / ADA / Cadillac.

SOONER OR LATER
How could you do it to me / I'm working on it / Penitentiary blues / You'll need another favour / Help the poor / Letter from my darling / Goin' out west (part 1 and 2) / 102 St. blues / How long / Bluebird / Littlerock
CD _____ CDBB 9511
Bullseye Blues / Sep '92 / Direct.

Davis, Linda

SOME THINGS ARE MEAN
CD _____ 7822188042
Arista / Jan '96 / BMG.

Davis, Link

1948-1963
CD _____ KKCD 06
Krazy Kat / Jul '93 / Hot Shot / CM.

BIG MAMOU
Big mamou / Pretty little dedon / Mamou waltz / Hey garcon / Lonely heart / Time will tell / Gumbo ya-ya (everybody talks at once) / Falling for you / Crawfish crawl / You're little but you're cute / Mama say no / Every time I pass your door / You show up missing / Cajun love / Kajalena / Va t'cacher
CD _____ EDCD 279
Edsel / Mar '92 / Pinnacle / ADA.

Davis, Little Sammy

I AIN'T LYIN'
CD _____ DE 682
Delmark / Dec '95 / Hot Shot / ADA / CM / Direct / Cadillac.

Davis, Meg

CLADDAGH WALK, THE
For Ireland I'd not tell her name / Castle of Dromore / Burning West Indies / She moved through the fair / Broom o the Cowdenknowes / Claddagh walk / Lake of Ponchartrain / If I were a blackbird / P stands for Paddy / Eileen Aroon / My Lagan love / Loch Tay boat song / Queen of May / Last Leviathan
CD _____ LCDM 9030

Lismor / Nov '90 / Lismor / Direct / Duncans / ADA.

Davis, Michael

MIDNIGHT CROSSING
CD _____ LIP 890352
Lipstick / Dec '95 / Vital/SAM.

Davis, Miles

'58 SESSIONS
On Green Dolphin Street / Fran dance / Stella by starlight / Love for sale / Straight no chaser / My funny valentine / Oleo
CD _____ 4679182
Columbia / Apr '92 / Sony.

AGHARTA
Prelude / Maiysha / Interlude / Theme from Jack Johnson
CD _____ 467897 2
Columbia / Sep '93 / Sony.

AMANDLA
Catembe / Big time / Jo Jo / Jilli / Cobra / Hannibal / Amandla / Mr. Pastorius
CD _____ K 925873-2
WEA / May '89 / Warner Music.

AND MODERN JAZZ GIANTS
CD _____ OJCCD 347
Original Jazz Classics / Feb '92 / Wellard / Jazz Music / Cadillac / Complete/Pinnacle.

AT FILLMORE (2CD Set)
CD _____ 476909 2
Columbia / Oct '94 / Sony.

AT LAST (Davis, Miles & The Lighthouse All Stars)
Infinity promenade / Round Midnight / Night in Tunisia / Drum conversation / At last
CD _____ OJCCD 480
Original Jazz Classics / Feb '92 / Wellard / Jazz Music / Cadillac / Complete/Pinnacle.

AT THE ROYAL ROOST 1948 & BIRDLAND 1950-53
52nd street (theme) / Half Nelson / You go to my head / Chasin' the Bird / Hot house / Wee / Tempus fugit / Kaeree (out of the blue) / Move / Tenderly / Night in Tunisia / Dig
CD _____ LEJAZZCD 45
Le Jazz / Jun '95 / Charly / Cadillac.

AURA
Intro / White / Yellow / Orange / Red / Green / Blue / Electric red / Indigo / Violet
CD _____ 4633512
Columbia / Oct '89 / Sony.

BALLADS
Baby, won't you please come home / I fall in love too easily / Bye bye blackbird / Basin Street blues / Once upon a summertime / Song no.2 / Wait till you see her / Corcovado
CD _____ 4610992
Columbia / Apr '89 / Sony.

BEST OF MILES DAVIS
CD _____ DLCD 4023
Dixie Live / Mar '95 / Magnum Music Group.

BEST OF MILES DAVIS, THE
Move / Godchild / Budo / Dear old Stockholm / Donna / Yesterdays / Tempus fugit / Enigma / C.T.A. / Well you needn't / It never entered my mind / Weirdo / Something else / Autumn leaves
CD _____ BNZ 286
Blue Note / Feb '92 / EMI.

BIRDLAND DAYS
CD _____ FSCD 124
Fresh Sound / Jan '91 / Jazz Music / Discovery.

BIRDLAND SESSIONS
CD _____ LEJAZZCD 23
Le Jazz / Feb '94 / Charly / Cadillac.

BIRTH OF THE COOL
Move / Jeru / Moon dreams / Venus De Milo / Budo / Deception / Darn that dream (CD only.) / Godchild / Boplicity / Rocker / Israel / Rouge
CD _____ CDP 7928622
Capitol / Sep '92 / EMI.

BIRTH OF THE COOL/MILES DAVIS VOL.1/MILES DAVIS VOL.3 (3CD Set)
Move / Jeru / Moon dreams / Venus de Milo / Budo / Deception / Godchild / Boplicity / Rocker / Israel / Rouge / Tempus fugit / Kelo / Enigma / Ray's idea / How deep is the ocean / C.T.A. / Dear old Stockholm / Chance it / Yesterdays / Donna / C.T.A. (2) / Would'n you / Take off / Weirdo / Would'n you (2) / I waited for you / Ray's idea (2) / Donna (2) / Well you needn't / Leap / Lazy Susan / Tempus fugit (2) / It never entered my mind
CD Set _____ CDOMB 007
Blue Note / Oct '95 / EMI.

BITCHES BREW
Pharaoh's dance / Bitches brew / Spanish key / John McLaughlin / Miles runs the voodoo down / Sanctuary
CD Set _____ 4606022
Columbia / Oct '91 / Sony.

BITCHES BREW LIVE
CD _____ JZCD 373
Recording Arts / Nov '92 / THE / Disc.

BLUE HAZE
CD _____ CDSGP 042
Prestige / Mar '93 / Total/BMG.

BLUE MOODS
CD _____ OJCCD 043-2
Original Jazz Classics / Oct '93 / Wellard / Jazz Music / Cadillac / Complete/Pinnacle.

BOPPING THE BLUES
Don't sing me the blues (Takes 1/2) / I've always got the blues (Takes 1-3) / Don't explain to me baby (Takes 1 - 4) / Baby, won't you make up your mind (Take 1)
CD _____ BLCD 760102
Black Lion / Jun '88 / Jazz Music / Cadillac / Wellard / Koch.

CBS YEARS 1955-85 (4CD Set)
Generique / All blues / Eighty one / Blues for Pablo / Summertime / Straight no chaser / Footprints / Florence sur les Champs Elysees / I thought about you / Someday my Prince will come / Bye bye blackbird / My funny valentine / Love for sale / Budo / Miles / Files de Kilimanjaro / Fran dance / Seven steps to heaven / Flamenco sketches / So what / Water babies / Saeta / Masqualero / Pinocchio / Summer night / Fall / It's about that time / Sivad / What it is / Ms. Morrisine / Shout / Honky Tonk / Star on Cicely / Thinkin' one thing and doin' another / Miles runs the voodoo down
CD _____ 4632462
Columbia / Jan '95 / Sony.

CHRONICLE: THE COMPLETE PRESTIGE RECORDINGS (8CD/12LP)
Ahmad's blues / Airegin / Bag's groove / Bemsha swing / Bitty ditty / Blue haze / Blue 'n' boogie / Blue room / Blues by five / Bluing / But not for me / Changes / Compulsion / Conception / Denial / Diane / Dig / Dr. Jackie / Down / Doxy / Ezz-thetic / Floppy / For adults only / Four / Gal in Calico / Green haze / Half nelson / Hibeck / How am I to know / I could write a book / I know / I didn't / I see your face before me / I'll remember April / If I were a bell / In your own sweet way / It could happen to you / It's only a paper moon / Just squeeze me / Love me or leave me / Man I love / Miles ahead / Minor march / Morpheus / My funny valentine / My old flame / Night in Tunisia / No line / Odjenar / Old devil moon / Oleo / Out of the blue / Round Midnight / Salt peanuts / Serpent's tooth / Smooch / Solar / Something I dreamed last night / S'posin' / Stablemates / Surrey with the fringe on top / Swing spring / Tasty pudding / Theme / There is no greater love / Trane's blues / Tune up / Vierd blues / Walkin' / Well you needn't / When I fall in love / When lights are low / Whispering / Will you still be mine / Willie the wailer / Wouldn't you / Yesterdays / You don't know what love is / You're my everything
CD Set _____ 8 PCD 012
Prestige / Apr '92 / Complete/Pinnacle / Cadillac.

CIRCLE IN THE ROUND
Circle in the round / Two bass hit / Love for sale / Blues No. 2 / Teo's bag / Side car / Splash sanctuary / Guinevere
CD Set _____ 467989 2
Columbia / Sep '93 / Sony.

COLLECTION: MILES DAVIS
Milestones / Gone / So what / I thought about you / Walkin' / Frelon brun / Miles runs the voodoo down / Medley gemini / Double image / Fat time / What it is / Human nature
CD _____ CCSCD 243
Castle / Jun '90 / BMG.

COLLECTORS ITEM
Compulsion / Serpent's tooth / Round Midnight / In your own sweet way / Vierd blues / No line / My old flame / Nature boy / There's no you / Easy living / Alone together
CD _____ OJCCD 071
Original Jazz Classics / Feb '92 / Wellard / Jazz Music / Cadillac / Complete/Pinnacle.

COMPLETE CONCERT 1964, THE (My Funny Valentine & Four More)
Introduction by Mort Fega / My funny valentine / All of you / Go go (Theme and re-introduction) / Stella by starlight / All blues / I thought about you / So what / Walkin' / Joshua / Go go (Theme and announcement) / Four / Seven steps to heaven / There is no greater love / Do go
CD Set _____ 471246 2
Columbia / May '93 / Sony.

CONCERTO DE ARANJUEZ (Davis, Miles & Gil Evans)
CD _____ GOJCD 53023
Giants Of Jazz / Aug '88 / Target/BMG / Cadillac.

CONCERTO DE ARANJUEZ 1958-1960
CD _____ CD 56045
Jazz Roots / Nov '94 / Target/BMG.

CONCIERTO DE ARANJUEZ
CD _____ CD 14543
Jazz Portraits / Jan '94 / Jazz Music.

COOKIN' AND RELAXIN' (Davis, Miles Quintet)
Cookin' - My funny valentine / Blues by five / Airegin / Tune up / When the lights are low / Relaxin' / You're my everything / I could write a book / Oleo / It could happen to you / Woody 'n' you
CD _____ CDJZD 003
Prestige / Jan '91 / Complete/Pinnacle / Cadillac.

COOL
If I were a bell / You're my everything / I could write a book / Oleo / It could happen to you / Woody 'n' you
CD _____ MSCD 19
Music De-Luxe / Nov '95 / Magnum Music Group.

COTE BLUES
CD _____ JMY 1010-2
JMY / Aug '93 / Harmonia Mundi.

DAVISIANA (Davis, Miles Quintet)
CD _____ MCD 0332
Moon / Jan '92 / Harmonia Mundi / Cadillac.

DECOY
Decoy / Robot 415 / Code MD / Freaky deaky / What is it / That's right / That's what happened
CD _____ CD 25951
Columbia / Sep '93 / Sony.

DIG (Davis, Miles & Sonny Rollins)
CD _____ OJCCD 005
Original Jazz Classics / Feb '92 / Wellard / Jazz Music / Cadillac / Complete/Pinnacle.

DOO BOP
Mystery / Doo bop song / Chocolate chip / High speed chase / Blow / Sonya / Fantasy / Duke booty / Mystery (reprise)
CD _____ 7599269382
WEA / Mar '94 / Warner Music.

DOWN
CD _____ CDJJ 620
Jazz & Jazz / Jan '92 / Target/BMG.

E.S.P.
E.S.P. / Eighty one / Little one / R.J. / Agitation / Iris / Mood
CD _____ 4678992
Columbia / Oct '91 / Sony.

ESSENTIAL MILES DAVIS, THE
Round Midnight / My funny valentine / Concierto De aranjuez / Summertime / All blues / Milestones / Walkin
CD _____ 4671442
Columbia / Aug '92 / Sony.

EVOLUTION OF A GENIUS 1945-1954
Now's the time / Donna Lee / Milestones / Jeru / Boplicity / Rocker / Ezz-thetic / Yesterdays / Compulsion / Tempus fugit / Tune up / It never entered my mind / Old devil moon / I'll remember April / Walkin' / But not for me
CD _____ CD 53009
Giants Of Jazz / Mar '92 / Target/BMG / Cadillac.

EVOLUTION OF A GENIUS 1954-1958 (Davis, Miles & Friends)
CD _____ GOJCD 53063
Giants Of Jazz / Mar '92 / Target/BMG / Cadillac.

EVOLUTION OF A GENIUS 1957-1958
CD _____ CD 53071
Giants Of Jazz / May '93 / Target/BMG / Cadillac.

FILLES DE KILIMANJARO
Frelon brun (brown hornet) / Tout de suit / Petits machins (little stuff) / Filles de Kilimanjaro (girls of Kilimanjaro) / Mademoiselle Mabry
CD _____ 4670882
Columbia / Oct '91 / Sony.

FIRST MILES
Mile stone / Little Willie leaps / Half nelson / Sippin' at bells / That's the stuff you gotta watch / Pointless Mama blues / deep sea blues / Bring it on home
CD _____ CY 78995
Savoy Jazz / Nov '95 / Conifer / ADA.

FRIDAY NIGHT AT THE BLACK HAWK, SAN FRANCISCO VOL. 1
CD _____ 4633342
Columbia / Jan '95 / Sony.

GET UP WITH IT
He loved him madly / Maiysha / Honky tonk / Rated X / Calypso frelimo / Red China blues / Mtume / Billy Preston
CD _____ 9211552
Line / Jun '94 / CM / Grapevine / ADA / Conifer / Direct.

GREEN DOLPHIN STREET (Davis, Miles Quintet)
CD _____ NI 4002
Natasha / Jun '93 / Jazz Music / ADA / CM / Direct / Cadillac.

HIGHLIGHTS FROM THE PLUGGED NICKEL
Milestones / Yesterdays / So what / Stella by starlight / Walkin' / 'Round about midnight
CD _____ 4814032
Sony Jazz / Nov '95 / Sony.

IN A SILENT WAY
Ssh peaceful / In a silent way / It's about that time
CD _____ 4509822
Columbia / Oct '93 / Sony.

IN CONCERT
CD _____ 476910 2
Columbia / Oct '94 / Sony.

JATP STOCKHOLM 1960
CD _____ TAXCD 3716
Tax / Aug '95 / Jazz Music / Wellard / Cadillac.

JAZZ AT THE PLAZA VOL. 1
CD _____ 4715102
Columbia / Jan '95 / Sony.

JAZZ PORTRAITS
Now's the time / Night in Tunisia / Donna Lee / Cheryl / Milestones / Half nelson / Marmaduke / Jeru / Boplicity / Rocker / Ezz-thetic / Yesterdays / Constellation / Tempus fugit / Tune up / It never entered my mind / Old devil moon / I'll remember April
CD _____ CD 14503
Jazz Portraits / May '94 / Jazz Music.

JEAN PIERRE
CD _____ 4745582
Columbia / Jan '95 / Sony.

KIND OF BLUE
So what / Freddie Freeloader / Blue in green / Al blues / Flamenco sketches
CD _____ 4606032
Columbia / Sep '93 / Sony.
CD _____ CK 64403
Columbia / Nov '94 / Sony.
CD _____ 4804102
Columbia / Jul '95 / Sony.

KIND OF BLUE/MILESTONES/STELLA BY STARLIGHT
CD Set _____ 4722742
Columbia / Oct '92 / Sony.

LEGENDARY MASTERS, THE (1948-1952)
Godchild / Moon dreams / Hallucinations / Darn that dream / Move (mood) / Conceptions / Opmet (out of the blue) / Chase / Why do I love you / S'il vous plait / Move / Max making wax / Tune up / Bye bye blackbird / Rollin' blowin' walkin' / But not for me / Night in Tunisia / Fran dance / Walkin' / It never entered my mind / Round Midnight / What's new / Blues for pablo / On Green Dolphin Street
CD _____ RARECD 08
Recording Arts / '88 / THE / Disc.

LEGENDARY MASTERS, THE (1956-1959)
Tune up / Walkin' / Bye bye blackbird / It never entered my mind / Rollin' blowin' walkin' / Round Midnight / But not for me / What's new / Night in Tunisia / Blues for Pablo
CD _____ RARECD 09
Recording Arts / '88 / THE / Disc.

LEGENDARY MASTERS, THE (1960)
Walkin' / Fran dance / On Green Dolphin Street / So what
CD _____ RARECD 10
Recording Arts / '88 / THE / Disc.

LEGENDARY MASTERS, THE (BOX SET) (Unissued or rare 1948-60)
CD Set _____ RARECD 08/10
Recording Arts / Apr '88 / THE / Disc.

LEGENDARY STOCKHOLM CONCERT (Davis, Miles & John Coltrane)
CD _____ NI 4011
Natasha / Jun '93 / Jazz Music / ADA / CM / Direct / Cadillac.

LIVE AT MONTREUX (Davis, Miles & Quincy Jones)
Introduction by Claude Nobs and Quincy Jones / Boplicity / Introduction to Miles ahead medley / Springsville / Maids of cadiz / Duke / My ship / Miles ahead / Blues for pablo / Introduction to Porgy and Bess medley / Orgone / Gone gone gone / Summertime / Here come de honey man / Pan piper / Solea
CD _____ 9362452214-2
Warner Bros. / Sep '93 / Warner Music.

LIVE AT NEWPORT 1958 & 1963 (2CD Set) (Davis, Miles & Thelonious Monk)
Introduction (1) / Ah-leu-cha / Straight no chaser / Fran dance / Two bass hit / Bye bye blackbird / Theme / Introduction (2) / Criss cross / Light blue / Nutty / Blue monk / Epistrophy
CD Set _____ C2K 53585
Columbia / Oct '94 / Sony.

LIVE AT THE PLUGGED NICKEL 1965 (8CD Set)
If I were a bell / Stella by starlight / Walkin' / I fall in love too easily / Theme / My funny valentine / Four / When I fall in love / Agitation / Round Midnight / Milestones / All of you / Oleo / No blues / I thought about you / On green dolphin street / So what / Autumn leaves / All blues / Yesterdays
CD Set _____ CXK 66955
Sony Jazz / Jul '95 / Sony.

LIVE IN 1958-59 (Davis, Miles All Stars)
CD _____ EBCD 21012
Flyright / Dec '90 / Hot Shot / Wellard /
Jazz Music / CM.

**LIVE IN SINDELFINGEN 1964 (Davis,
Miles Quintet)**
CD _____ JZCD 372
Recording Arts / Nov '92 / THE / Disc.

**LIVE IN St LOUIS & PARIS 1963 (Davis,
Miles Quintet)**
CD _____ JZCD 371
Recording Arts / Nov '92 / THE / Disc.

**LIVE IN STOCKHOLM (1960) (Davis,
Miles & John Coltrane)**
CD _____ CD 53014
Giants Of Jazz / Mar '92 / Target/BMG /
Cadillac.

**LIVE IN STOCKHOLM 1960 COMPLETE
(Davis, Miles & John Coltrane/Sonny
Stitt)**
CD _____ DRCD 228
Dragon / Sep '89 / Roots / Cadillac /
Wellard / CM / ADA.

**LIVE MILES (More Music From The
Legendary Carnegie Hall Concert)**
CD _____ 4600642
Columbia / Jan '95 / Sony.

LIVE TUTU (Davis, Miles Band)
CD _____ JZCD 375
Recording Arts / Nov '92 / THE / Disc.

**MAN WITH THE HORN (Davis, Miles &
John Coltrane)**
Fat time / Backseat Betty / Shout Aida /
Man with the horn / Ursula
CD _____ 4007012
Columbia / Sep '93 / Sony.

MELLOW MILES
Miles / Summertime / So what / Time after
time / Miles ahead / Freddie freeloader /
Bye bye blackbird / Pfrancing / Round Mid-
night / It ain't necessarily so / Human nature
CD _____ 4694402
Columbia / Dec '91 / Sony.

MILES AHEAD
Springville / Maids of Cadiz / Duke / My
ship / Miles ahead / Blues for Pablo / New
rhumba / Meaning of the blues / Lament / I
don't wanna be kissed
CD _____ CD 14540
Jazz Portraits / Jan '94 / Jazz Music.

MILES AHEAD 1956-58
CD _____ CD 56038
Jazz Roots / Jul '95 / Target/BMG.

**MILES AND COLTRANE (Davis, Miles &
John Coltrane)**
CD _____ 4608242
Columbia / Oct '93 / Sony.

MILES AND HORNS
CD _____ OJCCD 053
Original Jazz Classics / Feb '92 / Wellard /
Jazz Music / Cadillac / Complete/Pinnacle.

**MILES DAVIS & KEITH JARRETT LIVE
(Davis, Miles Band)**
CD _____ JZCD 374
Recording Arts / Nov '92 / THE / Disc.

**MILES DAVIS & LENNIE TRISTANO
(Davis, Miles & Lennie Tristano)**
CD _____ NI 4015
Natasha / Aug '93 / Jazz Music / ADA /
CM / Direct / Cadillac.

**MILES DAVIS & MILT JACKSON (Davis,
Miles & Milt Jackson)**
CD _____ OJCCD 012
Original Jazz Classics / Feb '92 / Wellard /
Jazz Music / Cadillac / Complete/Pinnacle.

MILES DAVIS & THE JAZZ GIANTS
CD _____ FCD 60015
Fantasy / Oct '93 / Pinnacle / Jazz Music /
Wellard / Cadillac.

MILES DAVIS - LIVE IN EUROPE 1988
CD _____ OMDCD 101
OMD / Mar '93 / Koch.

MILES DAVIS COLLECTION
CD _____ COL 035
Collection / Jun '95 / Target/BMG.

MILES DAVIS GOLD (2CD Set)
CD Set _____ D2CD 4022
Deja Vu / Jun '95 / THE.

MILES DAVIS IN CONCERT
CD Set _____ 710455
RTE / Apr '95 / ADA / Koch.

**MILES DAVIS QUINTET (Lincoln Centre
1964) (Davis, Miles Quintet)**
CD _____ CD 53047
Giants Of Jazz / Mar '92 / Target/BMG /
Cadillac.

MILES IN ANTIBES
CD _____ 4629602
Columbia / Jan '95 / Sony.

MILES IN BERLIN
CD _____ CD 62976
Columbia / Jan '95 / Sony.

MILES IN THE SKY
Stuff / Paraphernalia / Black comedy /
Country son

CD _____ 477209 2
Columbia / Sep '93 / Sony.

MILES SMILES
Orbits / Circle / Footprints / Dolores / Free-
dom jazz dance / Gingerbread boy
CD _____ 4710042
Columbia / Apr '92 / Sony.

MILESTONES
CD _____ 4608272
Columbia / Oct '93 / Sony.

MILESTONES 1945-54
CD _____ CD 56009
Jazz Roots / Aug '94 / Target/BMG.

MISCELLANEOUS DAVIS
Hackensack / Round Midnight / Now's the
time / Four / Walkin' / Lady be good / All of
you / Four (1)
CD _____ JUCD 2050
Jazz Unlimited / Nov '94 / Wellard /
Cadillac.

MUSINGS OF MILES, THE
I didn't / Will you still be mine / Green haze
/ I see your face before me / Night in Tunisia
/ Gal in Calico
CD _____ OJCCD 004
Original Jazz Classics / Feb '92 / Wellard /
Jazz Music / Cadillac / Complete/Pinnacle.

NEFERTITI
Nefertiti / Fall / Hand jive / Madness / Riot
/ Pinocchio
CD _____ 4670892
Columbia / Oct '91 / Sony.

NEW MILES DAVIS QUINTET
CD _____ OJCCD 006
Original Jazz Classics / Feb '92 / Wellard /
Jazz Music / Cadillac / Complete/Pinnacle.

ON THE CORNER
On the corner / New York girl / Thinkin' one
thing and doin' another / Vote for Miles /
Black satin / One and one / Helen Butte /
Mr. Freedom X
CD _____ 4743712
Columbia / Feb '94 / Sony.

PANGAEA (2CD Set)
Zimbabwe / Gondwana
CD _____ 467087 2
Columbia / Sep '93 / Sony.

PARAPHERNALIA
CD _____ JMY 1013-2
JMY / Aug '92 / Harmonia Mundi.

PARIS CONCERT
CD _____ JZCD 341
Suisa / Jan '93 / Jazz Music / THE.

**PORGY AND BESS (Davis, Miles & Gil
Evans Orchestra)**
Buzzard song / Bess, you is my woman
now / Gone gone gone / Summertime /
Bess, oh where's my Bess / Prayer / O Doctor Jesus / Fisherman / Strawberry and devil
crab / My man's gone now / It ain't necessarily so / Here come de honey man / I
loves you Porgy / There's a boat that's leaving shortly for New York
CD _____ 4509852
Columbia / Oct '93 / Sony.

QUIET NIGHTS
CD _____ CD 85556
Columbia / Jan '95 / Sony.

**RARITIES AND PRIVATE COLLECTIONS
1956-59**
CD _____ JZ-CD314
Suisa / Feb '91 / Jazz Music / THE.

**REAL BIRTH OF THE COOL - RARE
AND LIVE**
CD _____ JZ-CD313
Suisa / Feb '91 / Jazz Music / THE.

ROUND ABOUT MIDNIGHT
Round Midnight / Ah leu cha / All of you /
Bye bye blackbird / Tadd's delight' / Dear
old Stockholm
CD _____ 4606052
Columbia / Oct '91 / Sony.

ROUND MIDNIGHT
CD _____ GOJCD 53045
Giants Of Jazz / Mar '92 / Target/BMG /
Cadillac.

**SATURDAY NIGHT AT THE BLACK
HAWK, SAN FRANCISCO VOL. 2**
CD _____ 4651912
Columbia / '88 / Sony.

SEVEN STEPS TO HEAVEN
Basin Street blues / Seven steps to heaven
/ I fall in love too easily / So near, so far /
Baby, won't you please come home /
Joshua
CD _____ 4669702
Columbia / Apr '92 / Sony.

SKETCHES OF SPAIN
Concierto de Aranjuez / Amor brujo / Pan
piper / Saeta / Solea
CD _____ 4606042
Columbia / Jan '95 / Sony.

SOME DAY MY PRINCE WILL COME
Someday my Prince will come / Old folks /
Drad-dog / Teo / I thought about you /
Pfancing
CD _____ 4663122
Columbia / Jan '95 / Sony.

SORCERER
Prince of Darkness / Vonetta / Limbo / Mas-
qualero / Pee Wee / Sorcerer
CD _____ 4743692
Columbia / Sep '93 / Sony.

STAR PEOPLE
Come get it / It gets better / Speak / Star
people / U'un I / Star on Cicely
CD _____ CD 25395
Columbia / Sep '93 / Sony.

**STEAMIN' WITH THE MILES DAVIS
QUINTET**
CD _____ OJCCD 391
Original Jazz Classics / Feb '92 / Wellard /
Jazz Music / Cadillac / Complete/Pinnacle.

**THEIR GREATEST CONCERT (Davis,
Miles & John Coltrane)**
CD _____ JZ-CD315
Suisa / Feb '91 / Jazz Music / THE.

TRANSITION
CD _____ MRCD 125
Magnetic / Sep '91 / Magnum Music
Group.

TRIBUTE TO JACK JOHNSON
Right off / Yesternow
CD _____ 471003 2
Columbia / Sep '93 / Sony.

**TRIBUTE TO MILES DAVIS, A (With H.
Hancock/W. Shorter/R. Carter/W.
Roney/T. Williams) (Various Artists)**
So what / R.J. / Little one / Pinocchio / El-
egy / Eighty one / All blues
CD _____ 936245059-2
WEA / Mar '94 / Warner Music.

TUNE UP (Davis, Miles & Stan Getz)
CD _____ NI 4008
Natasha / Jun '93 / Jazz Music / ADA /
CM / Direct / Cadillac.

TUTU
Tutu / Tomaas / Portia / Splatch / Backyard
ritual / Perfect way / Don't lose your mind /
Full nelson
CD _____ 925490 2
WEA / Oct '86 / Warner Music.

WALKIN'
Walkin' / Blue 'n' boogie / Solar / You don't
know what love is / Love me or leave me
CD _____ OJCCD 213
Original Jazz Classics / Feb '92 / Wellard /
Jazz Music / Cadillac / Complete/Pinnacle.

WALKIN'
CD _____ CD 14537
Jazz Portraits / Jan '94 / Jazz Music.

WE WANT MILES
Jean Pierre / Backseat Betty / Fast track /
My man's gone now / Kix
CD _____ 469902 2
Columbia / Sep '93 / Sony.

WHAT I SAY VOL.1
CD _____ JMY 1015-2
JMY / Apr '94 / Harmonia Mundi.

WHAT I SAY VOL.2
CD _____ JMY 1016-2
JMY / Apr '94 / Harmonia Mundi.

WORKIN' (Davis, Miles Quintet)
CD _____ OJCCD 296
Original Jazz Classics / Feb '92 / Wellard /
Jazz Music / Cadillac / Complete/Pinnacle.

WORKIN' AND STEAMIN'
It never entered my mind / Four / In your
own sweet way / Theme, The (take 1) / Trane's blues / Ahmad's blues / Half Nelson /
Theme, The (take 2) / Surrey with the fringe
on top / Salt peanuts / Something I
dreamed last night / Diane / Well you
needn't / When I fall in love
CD Set _____ 4PRCD 8805
Prestige / Oct '93 / Complete/Pinnacle /
Cadillac.

YOU'RE UNDER ARREST
One phone call / Street scenes / Human nature / Ms. Morrisine / Katia (prelude) / Time
after time / You're under arrest / Then there
were none / Something's on your mind
CD _____ 468703 2
Columbia / Sep '93 / Sony.

Davis, Morgan

MORGAN DAVIS
CD _____ SP 1148CD
Stony Plain / Oct '93 / ADA / CM / Direct.

Davis, Rev. Gary

COMPLETE EARLY RECORDINGS, THE
CD _____ YAZCD 2011
Yazoo / Oct '94 / CM / ADA / Roots /
Koch.

FROM BLUES TO GOSPEL
CD _____ BCD 124
Biograph / '92 / Wellard / ADA / Hot Shot
/ Jazz Music / Cadillac / Direct.

**GOSPEL BLUES & STREET SONGS
(Davis, Rev. Gary & Pink Anderson)**
John Henry / Everyday in the week / Ship /
Titanic / Greasy greens / Wreck of ol' 97 /
I've got mine / He's in the jailhouse now /
Blow Gabriel / Twelve gates to the city /
Samson and Delilah / Oh Lord / Search my
heart / Get right church / You got to go

down / Keep your lamp trimmed and burning / There was a time that I was blind
CD _____ OBCCD 524
Original Blues Classics / Nov '92 / Com-
plete/Pinnacle / Wellard / Cadillac.

HARLEM STREET SINGER
Samson and Delilah / Let us get together
right down here / I belong to the band /
Pure religion / Great change since I been
born / Death don't have no mercy / Twelve
gates to the city / Goin' to sit down on the
banks of the river / Tryin' to get home / Lo
I be with you always / I am the light of this
world / Lord I feel just like goin' on
CD _____ OBCCD 547
Original Blues Classics / Nov '92 / Com-
plete/Pinnacle / Wellard / Cadillac.

I AM A TRUE VINE (1962-63)
I am a true vine / Lord stand by me / Won't
you hush / Mean old world / Moon is goin'
down / Sportin' life blues / Get right church
/ Blow Gabriel / Slippin' til my gal comes in
partner / Wall hollow blues / Blues in E /
Piece without words / Whoopin' blues / I
want to be saved
CD _____ HTCD 07
Heritage. / '91 / Swift / Roots / Wellard /
Direct / Hot Shot / Jazz Music / ADA.

PURE RELIGION AND BAD COMPANY
CD _____ SFWCD 40035
Smithsonian Folkways / Oct '94 / ADA /
Direct / Koch / CM / Cadillac.

REVEREND BLIND GARY DAVIS
I'm going to sit down on the banks of the
river / Twelve gates to the city / I heard the
angels singing / Twelve sticks / Make be-
lieve stunt / Waltz time candyman / C rag /
Walking dog blues
CD _____ HTCD 03
Heritage / Oct '89 / Swift / Roots / Wellard
/ Direct / Hot Shot / Jazz Music / ADA.

SAY NO TO THE DEVIL
Say no to the devil / Time is drawing near /
Hold to God's unchanging hand / Bad com-
pany brought me here / I decided to go
down / Lord I looked down the road / Little
Bitty baby / No one can do me like Jesus /
Boy in the wilderness / Trying to get to
heaven in due time
CD _____ OBCCD 519
Original Blues Classics / Nov '92 / Com-
plete/Pinnacle / Wellard / Cadillac.

SIGN OF THE SUN
Sun is going down / When the train comes
along / If I had my way / Twelve gates /
God's gonna separate / Get right Church /
Saints / God don't work like a natural man
/ There's destruction in this land
CD _____ HTCD 03
Heritage / Oct '90 / Swift / Roots / Wellard
/ Direct / Hot Shot / Jazz Music / ADA.

Davis, Richard

NOW'S THE TIME
CD _____ MCD 6005
Muse / Sep '92 / New Note / CM.

Davis, Rue

YOU ARE MY HONEY POO
CD _____ KON 4213
Kon-Kord / Aug '95 / Koch.

Davis, Sammy Jnr.

COLLECTION: SAMMY DAVIS JR
After today / Candy man / Fabulous places
/ Where are the words / All that jazz / I'm
always chasing rainbows / Lonely is the
name / We'll be together again / Every time
we say goodbye / Going's great / If my
friends could see me now / I'm a brass
band / All the good things in life / People
tree / Good life / Please don't take your time
/ Come back to me / I've gotta be me / She
believes in me / At the crossroads
CD _____ CCSCD 225
Castle / May '89 / BMG.

GREAT, THE
That old black magic / Hey there / Something's gotta give / Stan' up an' fight (until
you hear de bell) / Someone to watch over
me / I'll know / Frankie and Johnny / Sit
down you're rockin' the boat / because of
you (CD only) / Back track (CD only) / Glad
to be unhappy (CD only) / Lonesome road
(CD only) / Lady is a tramp / Song and
dance man / Circus / Adelaide / New York's
my home / Love me or leave me / Easy to
love / All of you
CD _____ CDMFP 6055
Music For Pleasure / Mar '89 / EMI.

I GOT PLENTY OF NUTTIN'
CD _____ 15190
Laserlight / Aug '91 / Target/BMG.

WHAM OF SAM, THE
Lot of livin' to do / Begin the beguine / My
romance / Too close for comfort / Soon /
Falling in love with love / Thou swell / Can't
we be friends / Guys and dolls / Blame it
on my youth / Let there be love / Bye bye
blackbird
CD _____ 9362456372
Reprise / Feb '94 / Warner Music.

WHAT I'VE GOT IN MIND
CD _____ CDCD 1228
Charly / Jun '95 / Charly / THE / Cadillac.

Davis, Sara

TUNDRA
CD _____ CAKECD 14
Soundcakes / Jun '94 / 3MV / Sony.

Davis Sisters

MEMORIES
I forgot more than you'll ever know / Sorrow and pain / Rock-a-bye boogie (master) / You're gone / Sorrow and pain (fast version) / You're gone (swinging version) / Heartbreak ahead (overdub) / Jealous love / Kaw-Liga / Rag mop / Your cheatin' heart / Crying steel guitar waltz / Just when I needed you / Tomorrow's just another day to cry / Tomorrow I'll cry / Jambalaya / Takin' time out for tears / Rock-a-bye boogie (alt.) / Gotta git a goin' / You weren't ashamed to kiss me last night / Foggy mountain top / Just like me / Don't take him for granted / I've closed the door / Medley (Rock-a-bye boogie; I forgot more than you'll ever know; Gotta git a-goin) / She loves him and he loves me / Single girl / Show me / Christmas boogie / Fiddle diddle boogie / Everlovin' / Come back to me / Tomorrow I'll cry over you / When I stop lovin' you / I'll get him back / It's the girl who gets the blame / Toodle-ooh (to you) / Baby be mine / Blues for company / Lonely and blue / Let's go steady / Lying brown eyes / Everywhere he went / Take my hand, precious Lord / Dig a little deeper in God's love
CD _____ BCD 15722
Bear Family / Jul '93 / Rollercoaster / Direct / CM / Swift / ADA.

Davis, Skeeter

END OF THE WORLD, THE
End of the world / Silver threads and golden needles / Mine is a lonely life / Once upon a time / Why I'm walkin' / Don't let me cross over / My colouring book / Where nobody knows me / Keep your hands off my baby / Something precious / Longing to hold you again / He called me baby
CD _____ TC 017
That's Country / Mar '94 / BMG.

SHE SINGS THEY PLAY (Davis, Skeeter & NRBQ)
Things to you / Everybody wants a cowboy / I can't stop loving you now / Heart to heart / Ain't nice to talk like that / Everybody's clown / Someday my Prince will come / How many tears / You don't know what you got till you lose it / Roses on my shoulder / Temporarily out of order / May you never be alone
CD _____ CD 3092
Rounder / '88 / CM / Direct / ADA / Cadillac.

Davis, Spencer

24 HOURS - LIVE IN GERMANY (Davis, Spencer Band)
CD _____ INAK 859
In Akustik / Mar '95 / Magnum Music Group.

8 GIGS A WEEK (2CD Set) (Davis, Spencer Group)
Dimples / I can't stand it / Jump back / Here right now / Searchin' / Midnight train / It's gonna work out fine / My babe / Kansas City / Every little bit hurts / Sittin' and thinkin' / I'm blue / She put the hurt on me / I'll drown in my own tears / I'm getting better / Goodbye Stevie / Strong love / Georgia on my mind / It hurts me so / Oh pretty woman / Look away / This hammer / Please do something / Let me down easy / Somebody help me / Watch your step / Nobody knows you when you're down and out / Midnight special / When I come home / High time baby / Hey darling / I washed my hands in muddy water / You must believe me / Trampoline / Since I met you baby / Mean woman blues / Dust my broom / When a man loves a woman / Neighbour neighbour / On the green light / Stevie's blues / Take this hurt off me / Stevie's groove / I can't get enough of it / Waltz for Lumumba / Together till the end of time / Gimme some lovin' / Back into my life again / I'm a man / Blues in F
CD Set _____ CRNCD 5
Island / Dec '95 / PolyGram.

CATCH YOU ON THE REBOP (Live '73) (Davis, Spencer Group)
Let's have a party / Catch you on the rebop / I'm a man / Man jam / Gimme some lovin' / Living in a back street / Trago, gluggo, tomorrow the world / Lega eagle shuffle / Fastest thing on / One night / Trouble in mind / Tumble down tenament row / Hanging around / Mr. Operator
CD _____ RPM 150
RPM / Jun '95 / Pinnacle.

KEEP ON KEEPING ON
Keep on running / Somebody help me / I'm a man / Gimme some loving / Blood runs hot / Don't want you no more / Love is on a roll / Crossfire / Private number / No other baby / Mistakes / It must be love / Such a good woman

CD _____ MSCD 4
Music De-Luxe / Apr '94 / Magnum Music Group.

KEEP ON RUNNING (Davis, Spencer Group)
CD _____ RC 82149
Royal Classics / Mar '93 / Complete/ Pinnacle.

KEEP ON RUNNING
CD _____ CDCD 1193
Charly / Sep '94 / Charly / THE / Cadillac.

LIVE TOGETHER
CD _____ INAK 8410
In Akustik / Sep '95 / Magnum Music Group.

SPOTLIGHT ON SPENCER DAVIS
Love is on a roll / Keep on running / It must be love / Somebody help me / Don't want you no more / Crossfire / I'm a man / Private number / Such a good woman / Gimme some lovin' / No other baby / Blood runs hot / Mistakes
CD _____ HADCD 123
Javelin / Feb '94 / THE / Henry Hadaway Organisation.

TAKING OUT TIME 1967-69 (Davis, Spencer Group)
CD _____ RPMCD 127
RPM / May '94 / Pinnacle.

Davis, Tyrone

BEST OF THE FUTURE YEARS, THE
CD _____ ICH 1153CD
Ichiban / Feb '94 / Koch.

I'LL ALWAYS LOVE YOU
I'll always love you / Prove my love / Talk to you / Let me love you / Do U still love me / Can I change my mind / Woman needs to be loved / Mom's apple pie
CD _____ CDICH 1103
Ichiban / Oct '93 / Koch.

SOMETHING'S MIGHTY WRONG
CD _____ ICH 1135CD
Ichiban / Apr '94 / Koch.

YOU STAY ON MY MIND
You stay on my mind / Let me be your pacifier / I found myself when I lost you / All because of your love / You can win if you want / I won't let go / Something good about a woman / You're my heart / You're my soul
CD _____ ICH 1170CD
Ichiban / May '94 / Koch.

Davis, Walter

DAVIS CUP
Snake it / Loodle lot / Sweetness / Rumba rhumba / Minor mind / Millie's delight
CD _____ CDP 8320982
Blue Note / Aug '95 / EMI.

ENGINEER'S BLUES
CD _____ ALB 1012CD
Aldabra / Aug '92 / CM / Disc.

FIRST RECORDINGS 1930-1932
CD _____ JSPCD 605
JSP / Aug '92 / ADA / Target/BMG / Direct / Cadillac / Complete/Pinnacle.

ILLUMINATION
Scorpio rising / Illumination / Ronnie's a dynamite lady / Backgammon / Abide with me / Crowded elevator / La strada / Biribinya nos states / Just one of those things / Pranayama / I'll keep loving you
CD _____ DC 8553
Denon / Jun '89 / Conifer.

Davison, Wild Bill

AFTER HOURS
CD _____ JCD 22
Jazzology / '92 / Swift / Jazz Music.

AM I BLUE
Blue room / I surrender dear / Monday date / If I had you / I never knew / Am I blue / Running wild
CD _____ JSPCD 236
JSP / Apr '90 / ADA / Target/BMG / Direct / Cadillac / Complete/Pinnacle.

AT BIRDLAND
CD _____ 4714272
Sony Jazz / Jan '95 / Sony.

JAZZ ON A SATURDAY AFTERNOON, VOL. 1
CD _____ JCD 37
Jazzology / '92 / Swift / Jazz Music.

JAZZ ON A SATURDAY AFTERNOON, VOL. 2
CD _____ JCD 38
Jazzology / '92 / Swift / Jazz Music.

JUST A GIG
CD _____ JCD 191
Jazzology / '91 / Swift / Jazz Music.

LADY OF THE EVENING
CD _____ JCD 143
Jazzology / '92 / Swift / Jazz Music.

RUNNING WILD
Blue room / I surrender dear / Monday date / Am I blue / You took advantage of me / If I had you / I never knew / (Back home again

in) Indiana / Sleepy time down South / I want to be happy / Sunny side of the street / Running wild
CD _____ JSPCD 1044
JSP / Oct '90 / ADA / Target/BMG / Direct / Cadillac / Complete/Pinnacle.

S'WONDERFUL (Davison, Wild Bill & His New Yorkers)
CD _____ JCD 181
Jazzology / '92 / Swift / Jazz Music.

SHOWCASE
CD _____ JCD 83
Jazzology / '92 / Swift / Jazz Music.

SOLO FLIGHT
CD _____ JCD 114
Jazzology / '92 / Swift / Jazz Music.

STARS OF JAZZ (Davison, Wild Bill/ Freddy Randall & His Band)
CD _____ JCD 62
Jazzology / Oct '91 / Swift / Jazz Music.

STARS OF JAZZ, VOL. 2 (Davison, Wild Bill/Freddy Randall & His Band)
CD _____ JCD 63
Jazzology / Oct '91 / Swift / Jazz Music.

SWEET AND LOVELY (Davison, Wild Bill & Strings)
CD _____ STCD 4060
Storyville / Feb '90 / Jazz Music / Wellard / CM / Cadillac.

THIS IS JAZZ (Volume 1)
CD _____ JCD 42
Jazzology / '92 / Swift / Jazz Music.

TOGETHER AGAIN (Davison, Wild Bill & Ralph Sutton)
Limehouse blues / Am I blue / Grandpa's spells / Three little words / Reunion blues / Back in your own backyard / I've got the world on a string / Rockin' chair
CD _____ CMJCD 003
CMJ / Apr '89 / Jazz Music / Wellard.
CD _____ STCD 8216
Storyville / Dec '95 / Jazz Music / Wellard / CM / Cadillac.

WILD BILL DAVISON & HIS FAMOUS JAZZ BAND (Davison, Wild Bill & His Famous Jazz Band)
CD _____ JCD 103
Jazzology / '92 / Swift / Jazz Music.

Dawkins, Jimmy

ALL FOR BUSINESS
CD _____ DELMARK 634
Delmark / Dec '87 / Hot Shot / ADA / CM / Direct / Cadillac.

B PHUR REAL
CD _____ DOG 9110
Wild Dog / Aug '95 / Koch.

BLUES AND PAIN
CD _____ DOG 9108CD
Wild Dog / Jun '94 / Koch.

BLUES FROM ICELAND (Dawkins, Jimmy/Chicago Beau/Blue Ice Bragason)
Welfare line / That's alright / You don't love me / Feel so bad / Too much alcohol / Sometimes I have a heartache / Nightlife / One room country shack / Help me / Tin pan alley
CD _____ ECD 26064
Evidence / Mar '95 / Harmonia Mundi / ADA / Cadillac.

FEEL THE BLUES (1985 Chicago studio recording)
Feel the blues / Highway man blues / Last days / Love somebody / Christmas time blues / Have a little mercy
CD _____ JSPCD 206
JSP / Jan '88 / ADA / Target/BMG / Direct / Cadillac / Complete/Pinnacle.

HOT WIRE 81
You just a baby child / Ruff times / Welfare line / Kold actions / Roc-kin-sole / Peeper's music / My way
CD _____ ECD 260432
Evidence / Mar '94 / Harmonia Mundi / ADA / Cadillac.

TRIBUTE TO ORANGE (Dawkins, Jimmy & Gatemouth Brown/Otis Rush)
All for business / You've got to keep on trying / Ain't never had nothing / Born in poverty / Marcelle Morgantini's Cassoulet / Your love / Tribute to orange / Mississippi bound / Life is a mean mistreater / Mean Atlantic ocean / Serves you right to suffer / Marcelle, Jacques et Luc / Ode to Billy Joe
CD _____ ECD 260312
Evidence / Feb '93 / Harmonia Mundi / ADA / Cadillac.

Dawn

TIE A YELLOW RIBBON
CD _____ BR 1452
BR Music / Jun '94 / Target/BMG.

Dawn

NIER SOLEN GAR NIFER FUR EVUGHER
CD _____ NR 006CD
Necropolis / Apr '95 / Plastic Head.

Dawn, Dolly

MEMORIES OF YOU
CD _____ ACD 201
Audiophile / Feb '91 / Jazz Music / Swift.

Dawson

CHEESE MARKET
CD _____ GRUFF 11CD
Gruff Wit / Nov '95 / SRD.

Dawson, Julian

LIVE ON THE RADIO
CD _____ WM 1003
Watermelon / Jun '93 / ADA / Direct.

Dawson, Peter

OLD FATHER THAMES
Drum major / Mountains of Mourne / Smuggler's song / Friend of mine / Gay highway / Yeomen of England / Jovial monk am I / Shipmates o'mine / Bandolero / Volunteer organist / Boots / Bachelor gay / Give me the rolling sea / Love could I only tell thee / When the Sergeant Major's on parade / Invictus / Old father Thames / Sons of the sea / Floral dance / On the road to Mandalay / Phil the fluter's ball / Waiata poi / Sylvia / Waltzing Matilda
CD _____ CDHD 224
Happy Days / Aug '93 / Conifer.

PETER DAWSON
Floral dance / Drake goes west / Glorious Devon / Up from Somerset / When the Sergeant Major's on parade / Vulcan's song / Non piu'andrai / Largo al factotum / Toreador's song (Bizet 'Carmen') / Bachelor gay / Smuggler's song / Yeomen of England / Old father Thames / Phil the fluter's ball / Waltzing Matilda / Ol' man river / Waiata poi / Drum major / I am a roamer
CD _____ GEMM CD 9336
Pearl / '90 / Harmonia Mundi.

SCOTTISH AND IRISH SONGS
Auld sangs o'home / Auld hoose / O sing to me an Irish song / Mountains of Mourne / Star o' Rabbie Burns / Jug of punch / Border ballad / Off to Philadelphia / There far far awa' / Away in Athlone / Paddy's wedding / Father O'Flynn / Molly of Donegal / Pride of Tipperary / Turn ye tae me / She is far from the land / With my shilelagh under me arm / Fiddler of Dooney / Kerry dance / Phil the fluter's ball
CD _____ MIDCD 008
Moidart / Jul '95 / Conifer / ADA.

SINGS THE YEOMAN OF ENGLAND
CD _____ PASTCD 7007
Flapper / Jun '93 / Pinnacle.

SOMEWHERE A VOICE IS CALLING
El Abanico / Banjo song / Boots / Cobbler's song / Down among the dead men / Drum major / Fishermen of England / Fleet's not in port very long / Floral dance / Friend o' mine / Give me the rolling sea / Glorious Devon / If those lips could only speak / In a monastery garden / Jerusalem / Love and wine / Man who brings the sunshine / Mountains o' Mourne / Snowbird / Somewhere a voice is calling / Tomorrow is another day / Waiata poi / Waltzing Matilda / We saw the sea / Winding road
CD _____ CD AJA 5114
Living Era / Sep '93 / Koch.

SONGS OF THE SEA
Drake's drum / Outward bound / Old superb / Devon, O Devon / Homeward bound / Sons of the sea / Shipmates o'mine / Admiral Benbow / At Santa Barbara / Cargoes / Rocked in the cradle of the deep / Tune the bosun played / Jolly Roger / Anchored / Rolling down to Rio / Little Admiral
CD _____ GEMM CD 9381
Pearl / '90 / Harmonia Mundi.

Dawson, Ronnie

MONKEY BEAT
CD _____ NOHITCD 008
No Hit / Jan '94 / SRD.

ROCKIN' BONES
Rockin' bones / Congratulations to me / Do do do / Who's been here / Action packed / Tied down / I make the love / Riders in the sky / Jump and run / Tired of waitin' / I'm on your wagon / Who put the cat out / Reelin' and rockin' / Straight skirts / Searchin' for my baby / Everybody clap your hands
CD _____ NOHITCD 001
No Hit / Jan '94 / SRD.

Day, Bobby

ROCKIN' ROBIN
Rockin' Robin / Bluebird, the buzzard and the oriole / Over and over / Come seven / Honeysuckle baby / My blue Heaven / I don't want to / When the swallows come back to Capistrano / Beep beep beep / Ain't gonna cry no more / Little bitty pretty one / Life can be beautiful / That's all I want / Mr. and Mrs. rock 'n' roll / Sweet little thing / Three young rebs from Georgia
CD _____ CDCH 200
Ace / May '91 / Pinnacle / Cadillac / Complete/Pinnacle.

Day, Dennis

AMERICA'S FAVOURITE IRISH TENOR
CD ______ CDSG 402
Starline / Aug '89 / Jazz Music.

Day, Doris

'S WONDERFUL
CD ______ HCD 226
Hindsight / Mar '95 / Target/BMG / Jazz Music.

10 MOST REQUESTED SONGS
Sentimental journey / My dreams are getting bigger all the time / It's magic / Love somebody / Again / Bewitched, bothered and bewildered / Would I love you (love you, love you) / Why did I tell you I was going to Shanghai / Starbust / Guy is a guy / When I fall in love / Secret love / If I give my heart to you / I'll never stop loving you / Whatever will be will be (Que sera sera) / Everybody loves a lover
CD ______ 4721952
Columbia / May '95 / Sony.

BEST OF DORIS DAY, THE
CD ______ MATCD 315
Castle / Dec '94 / BMG.

BEST OF THE BANDS (Day, Doris & Les Brown)
While the music plays on / Aren't you glad you're you / I'll always be with you / T'aint me / Beau night in hotchkiss corner / Last time I saw you / Come to me baby / Do / We'll be together again / Easy as pie / There's good blues tonight / Booglie wooglie piggy / Let's be buddies / Barbara Allen / Sooner or later / Dig it / It could happen to you
CD ______ 4669582
Columbia / '91 / Sony.

BIG BAND'S GREATEST VOCALIST
CD ______ CDSH 2078
Derann Trax / Aug '91 / Pinnacle.

COLLECTION
CD ______ COL 071
Collection / Mar '95 / Target/BMG.

CUTTIN' CAPERS & BRIGHT AND SHINY
Cuttin' capers / Steppin' out with my baby / Makin' whoopee / Lady's in love with you / Why don't we do this more often / Let's take a walk around the block / I'm sitting on top of the world / Get out and get under the moon / Fit as a fiddle / Me too / I feel like a feather in the breeze / Let's fly away / Bright and shiny / I want to be happy / Keep smilin', keep laughin', be happy / Singin' in the rain / Gotta feelin' / Happy talk / Make someone happy / Riding high / On the sunny side of the street / Clap yo' hands / Stay with the happy people
CD ______ 477593 2
Columbia / Oct '94 / Sony.

DAY BY DAY/DAY BY NIGHT (2CD Set)
Song is you / Hello my lover, goodbye / Goodbye / But not for me / I remember you / I hadn't anyone till you / But beautiful / Autumn leaves / Don't take your love from me / There will never be another you / Gone with the wind / Gypsy in my soul / Day by day / I see your face before me / Close your eyes / Night we called it a day / Dream a little dream of me / Under a blanket of blue / You do something to me / Stars fell on Alabama / Moon song / Wrap your troubles in dreams (and dream your troubles away) / Soft as the starlight / Moonglow / Lamp is low
CD ______ 473749 2
Columbia / Feb '94 / Sony.

DORIS DAY AND ANDRE PREVIN (Day, Doris & Andre Previn)
Falling in love again / Give me time / My one and only love / Remind me / Wait 'til I see him / Close your eyes / Fools rush in / Control yourself / Who are we to say (obey your heart) / Yes / Nobody's heart / Daydreaming
CD ______ PWKS 583
Carlton Home Entertainment / May '90 / Carlton Home Entertainment.

DORIS DAY CHRISTMAS ALBUM
Silver bells / I'll be home for Christmas / Snowfall / Toyland / Let it snow, let it snow, let it snow / Be a child at Christmas time / Winter wonderland / Christmas song / Christmas present / Have yourself a merry little Christmas / Christmas waltz / White Christmas
CD ______ PWKS 4034
Carlton Home Entertainment / Sep '93 / Carlton Home Entertainment.

DORIS DAY COLLECTOR'S EDITION
CD ______ DVGH 7032
Deja Vu / Apr '95 / THE.

DORIS DAY SINGS SONGS FROM CALAMITY JANE/PAJAMA GAME
CD ______ 4676102
Columbia / Jul '93 / Sony.

DORIS DAY/PEGGY LEE ESSENTIALS (Day, Doris & Peggy Lee)
CD ______ LECDD 633
Wisepack / Aug '95 / THE / Conifer.

GIRL NEXT DOOR, THE
CD ______ ENTCD 223
Entertainers / Nov '87 / Target/BMG.

GREAT VOCALIST, THE
CD ______ CDSR 050
Telstar / Nov '94 / BMG.

IT'S MAGIC
It takes time / Pete / My young and foolish heart / Tell me, dream face (What am I to you) / I'm still sitting under the apple tree / Just an old love of mine / That's the way he does it / Why should we both be lonely / Papa, won't you dance with me / Say something nice about me baby / It's magic / Just imagine / Pretty baby / Confess / Love somebody / Tacos, Enchilados and Beans / No moon at all / Put 'em in a box (deep blue sea)) / Imagination / It's the sentimental thing to do / I've only myself to blame / Thoughtless / It's a quiet town (In Crossbone county) / Someone like you / My dream is yours / I'm in love / It's you or no one / My darling, My darling (With orchestra) / That certain party / His fraternity pin / If you will marry me / You was / I'll string along with you / Powder your face with sunshine / Don't gamble with romance / I'm beginning to miss you / That old feeling / When your lover has gone / You go to my head / How it lies, how it lies, how it lies / If I could be with you one hour tonight / Everywhere you go / Again (Where are you) Now that I need you / Blame my absent minded heart / Let's take an old fashioned walk / You're my thrill / Bewitched, bothered and bewildered / At the cafe rendezvous / It's a great feeling / It's better to conceal than reveal / You can have him / Sometimes, I'm happy / Land of love (come my love and live with me) / I didn't know what time it was / I'm confessin' that I love you / Last mile home / Canadian capers (Cuttin' capers) / Here comes Santa Claus / Ol' St Nicholas / It's on the tip of my tongue / River Seine (La Seine) / (It happened at the) festival of roses / Three rivers, The (The Allegheny, Susquehanna and the Old Mo / (There's a) Bluebird on your windowsill / Crocodile tears / Game of broken hearts / Quicksilver / I'll never slip around again / I don't wanna be kissed by anyone but you / With you anywhere you are / Save a little sunbeam (For a rainy, rainy day) / Mama what'll I do / I said my pyjamas (and put on my prayers) / Enjoy yourself / I may be wrong, but I think you're wonderful / Very thought of you / Too marvellous for words / With a song in my heart / Spesh'lly you / Marriage ties / Before I loved you / I went a wooing / I didn't slip, I wasn't pushed, I fell / Hoop dee doo / I can't get over a boy like you (Loving a girl like me) / I've forgotten you / I'll be around / Darn that dream / Here in my arms / Tea for two / I only have eyes for you / Do do do / Crazy rhythm / I know that you know / Oh me, oh my / I want to be happy / He's such a gentleman / Load of hay / I love the way you say goodnight / Orange coloured sky / Comb and paper polka / Pumpernickel / You are my sunshine / Everlasting arms / David's Psalm / Christmas story / I've never been in love before / Bushel and a peck / You love me / Best thing for you / If I were a bell / Silver bells / It's a lovely day today / From this moment on / I am loved / Nobody's chasing me / Ten thousand four hundred thirty-two sheep / You're getting to be a habit with me / Somebody loves me / Please don't talk about me when I'm gone / Just one of those things / Lullaby of Broadway / I love the way you say good night / (In) a shanty in old Shanty Town / Fine and dandy / Would I love you (Love you, love you) / Say something nice about me baby (2) / It's magic #2 / Pretty baby, / Thoughtless, / It's you or no one #2 / My darling, my darling (With piano) / His fraternity pin (2) / Let's take an old fashioned walk, / You're my thrill (2) / Do do do (2)
CD Set ______ BCD 15609
Bear Family / Mar '93 / Rollercoaster / Direct / CM / Swift / ADA.

LATIN FOR LOVERS/LOVE HIM
Quiet nights of quiet stars / Fly me to the moon / Meditation / Dansero / Summer has gone / How insensitive / Slightly out of tune / Our day will come / Be true to me / Latin for lovers / Perhaps perhaps perhaps / Be mine tonight / Can't help falling in love / Since I fell for you / Losing you / Fool such as I / As long as he needs me / Whisper away / Moonlight lover / Love him / Lollipops and roses / Softly as I leave you / Funny / Night life
CD ______ 4810182
Columbia / Aug '95 / Sony.

LEGENDS IN MUSIC - DORIS DAY
CD ______ LECD 091
Wisepack / Sep '94 / THE / Conifer.

LES BROWN & HIS ORCHESTRA WITH DORIS DAY
CD ______ HCD 103
Hindsight / Nov '94 / Target/BMG / Jazz Music.

LOVE ALBUM, THE
CD ______ VISCD 2
Vision / Nov '94 / Pinnacle.

PERSONAL CHRISTMAS COLLECTION
Christmas song / Silver bells / Here comes Santa Claus / Ol' Saint Nicholas / Christmas story / Have yourself a merry little Christmas / Be a child at Christmas time / Toyland / Christmas present / Christmas waltz / Winter wonderland / Snowfall / White Christmas / Let it snow, let it snow, let it snow
CD ______ CK 64153
Columbia / Nov '95 / Sony.

PORTRAIT OF A SONG STYLIST
More / Fly me to the moon / Some day I'll find you / Slightly out of tune / Autumn leaves / People will say we're in love / In the still of the night / You stepped out of a dream / Little girl blue / On the street where you live / Stepping out with my baby / Softly as I leave you / Oh but I do / Quiet nights of quiet stars / Hello my lover, goodbye / Night and day / Stars fell on Alabama / My ship
CD ______ HARCD 101
Masterpiece / Apr '89 / BMG.

SECRET LOVE
It's so laughable / Something wonderful / We kiss in a shadow / Very good advice / Tell me (why nights are lonely) / Till we meet again / Moonlight baby / My life's desire / I'm forever blowing bubbles / Every little moment / Love ya / Cuddle up a little closer / Why did I tell you I was going to Shanghai / Lonesome and sorry / Ask me (because I'm so in love) / Kiss me goodbye love / Got him off my hands / Baby doll / Oops / If that doesn't do it / Domino / Makin' whoopee / It had to be you / My buddy / One I love / Moonlight bay / I'll see you in my dreams / I wish I had a girl / Ain't we got fun / Nobody's sweetheart / How lovely cooks the meat / Sugarbush / Guy is a guy / Little kiss goodnight / Gently Johnny / Who who who / Take me in your arms / Make it soon / My love and devotion / It's magic / When I fall in love / Cherries / April in Paris / No two people / You can't lose me / I know a place / That's what makes Paris Paree / I'm gonna ring the bell tonight / Second star to the right / Your Mother and mine / Mr. Tip toe / Ma says, Pa says / Full time job / Beautiful music to love you by / You have my sympathy / Let's walk that way / Candy lips / Be my little baby / King Chanticleer / If you were the only girl in the world / Your eyes have told me so / Just one girl / By the light of the silvery moon / When the red, red robin comes bob, bob, bobbin' along / Purple cow / Kiss me again stranger / Black hills of Dakota / 'Tis Harry I'm planning to marry / Just blew in from the windy city / This too shall pass away / Woman's touch / Choo choo train / Secret love / I can do without you / Deadwood stage / Love you Dearly / Lost in loveliness / I speak to the stars / What every girl should know / Blue bells of broadway / Kay Muleta / Anyone can fall in love / Jimmy unknown someone / Else's roses / If I give my heart to you / There's a rising moon for every falling star / You, my love / Hold me in your arms / Till my love comes to me / Ready, willing and able / Two hearts, two kisses (make one love) / Foolishly yours / I'll never stop loving you / Love's little island (1) / Ooh bang jiggly jang let it ring / I've gotta sing away these blues / Live it up / I'm a big girl now / When I'm happy / Love's little island / It all depends on you / You made me love you / Stay on the right side / Mean to me / Everybody loves my baby / Sam the old accordion man / Shaking the blues away / Ten cents a dance / Never look back / At sundown / Love me or leave me / Overture / You made me love you (I didn't want to do it)
CD Set ______ BCD 15746
Bear Family / Mar '95 / Rollercoaster / Direct / CM / Swift / ADA.

SENTIMENTAL JOURNEY
More I see you / At last / Come to baby do / I had the craziest dream / I don't want to walk without you / I'll never smile again / I remember you / Serenade in blue / I'm beginning to see the light / It could happen to you / It's been a long, long time / Sentimental journey
CD ______ 9825832
Pickwick/Sony Collector's Choice / Jun '91 / Carlton Home Entertainment / Pinnacle / Sony.

SENTIMENTAL JOURNEY
Blue skies / Sentimental journey / I can't give you anything but love / Everything I have is yours / I got it bad and that ain't good / Day by day / In the moon mist / Kiss to remember / There's good blues tonight / Moon on my pillow / I'm making believe / While the music plays on / Beau night in hotchkiss corner / Easy as pie / Booglie wooglie piggy / Let's be buddies / Barbara Allen / Dig it
CD ______ BSTCD 9115
Best Compact Discs / Apr '94 / Complete/ Pinnacle.

SENTIMENTAL JOURNEY
CD ______ HCD 200
Hindsight / Nov '94 / Target/BMG / Jazz Music.

SENTIMENTAL JOURNEY
My blue heaven / September in the rain / 'S wonderful / You brought a new kind of love to me / Stardust / Blue skies / I've gotta sing away these blues / I can't give you anything but love / Sentimental journey / I could write a book / Singin' in the rain / I'm a big girl now / S'posin' / You ought to be in pictures / I'm in the mood for love / Be anything, but be mine / I got it bad and that ain't good / Light your lamp / Hundred years from today / Just you, just me / Don't worry 'bout me / Crying my heart out for you
CD ______ TRTCD 164
TrueTrax / Dec '94 / THE.

SENTIMENTAL JOURNEY
Singin' in the rain / I've got it bad, and that ain't good / Blue skies / Crying my heart out for you / I'm in the mood for love / s'posin' / My blue heaven / Star dust / I gotta sing away these blues / I'm a big girl now / September in the rain / You brought a new kind of love to me / Hundred years from today / Be anything, but be mine / Light up your lamp / Don't worry 'bout me / Sentimental journey
CD ______ MUCD 9015
Start / Apr '95 / Koch.

SENTIMENTAL JOURNEY, A
CD ______ CDCD 1254
Charly / Jun '95 / Charly / THE / Cadillac.

SHOW TIME/DAY IN HOLLYWOOD (2CD Set)
Showtime (part one) / I got the sun in the morning / Ohio / I love Paris / When I'm not near the boy I love / People will say we're in love / I've grown accustomed to his face / Surrey with the fringe on top / They say it's wonderful / Wonderful guy / On the street where you live / Showtime (part two) / Tea for two / Lullaby of Broadway / Cuddle up a little closer / I may be wrong, but I think you're wonderful / Makin' whoopee / Be my little baby bumble bee / Secret love / Till we meet again / Ain't we got fun / Just one of those things / It had to be you / Love me or leave me
CD ______ 475750 2
Columbia / Feb '94 / Sony.

WHAT EVERY GIRL SHOULD KNOW
What every girl should know / Mood indigo / When you're smiling / Fellow needs a girl / My kinda love / What's the use of wonderin' / Something wonderful / Hundred years from today / You can't have everything / Not only should you love him / What does a woman do / Everlasting arms / I enjoy being a girl
CD ______ PWKS 4042
Carlton Home Entertainment / Feb '91 / Carlton Home Entertainment.

Day, Jimmy

STEEL & STRINGS (Golden Steel Guitar Hits)
Panhandle rag / Roadside rag / Texas playboy rag / Remington ride / Coconut grove / Boot hill drag / Bud's bounce / B. Bowman's hop / Georgia steel guitar / Steelin' the blues / Indian love call / Please help me, I'm falling / I love you because / Am I that easy to forget / Fallen star / She thinks I still care / Making believe / I love you so much it hurts / Wild side of life / Release me / Funny how time slips away / I can't stop loving you / I fall to pieces
CD ______ BCD 15583
Bear Family / Apr '92 / Rollercoaster / Direct / CM / Swift / ADA.

Dayne, Taylor

CAN'T FIGHT FATE
With every beat of my heart / I know the feeling / Heart of stone / Up all night / Wait for me / I'll be your shelter / You can't fight fate / Love will lead you back / You meant the world to me / Ain't no good
CD ______ 260321
Arista / Mar '94 / BMG.

GREATEST HITS
Say a prayer (Mixes) / Tell it to my heart (Mixes) / I'll always love you / Can't get enough of your love (Mixes) / With every beat of my heart / Love will lead you back / Don't rush me / Prove your love / I'll be your shelter / Heart of stone / Send me a lover / I'll wait (Mixes)
CD ______ 7822187742
Arista / Jan '96 / BMG.

TELL IT TO MY HEART
Tell it to my heart / In the darkness / Don't rush me / I'll always love you / Prove your love / Do you want it right now / Carry your heart / Want ads / Where does that boy hang out / Upon the journey's end
CD ______ 258898
Arista / Jan '93 / BMG.

Daytona

CHICANE
CD ______ ZULU 010CD
Zulu / Oct '95 / Plastic Head.

Dazzling Killmen

FACE OF COLLAPSE
CD ______ GR 12CD
Skingraft / Apr '94 / SRD.

D'Cruze

CONTROL
CD _____ SUBBASECD 1
Suburban Base / Oct '95 / SRD.

De Alvear, Maria

EN AMOR DURO
CD _____ ARTCD 6112
Hat Art / Jan '93 / Harmonia Mundi / ADA / Cadillac.

De Bora, Naomi

PRIVATE EYES
CD _____ BRAM 199128-2
Brambus / Nov '93 / ADA / Direct.

De Buddelschipper

SHANTIES AND SEEMANNSLIEDER
CD _____ EUCD 1178
ARC / '91 / ARC Music / ADA.

De Burgh, Chris

AT THE END OF A PERFECT DAY
Broken wings / Round and round / I will / Summer rain / Discovery / Brazil / In a country churchyard / Rainy night in Paris / If you really love her let her go / Perfect day
CD _____ CDMID 112
A&M / Oct '92 / PolyGram.

BEAUTIFUL DREAMS
Missing you / Carry me (Like a fire in your heart) / Discovery / Snows of New York / In love forever / Shine on / Lady in red / In dreams / I'm not crying over you / Always on my mind / Say goodbye to it all / One more mile to go
CD _____ 5404322
A&M / Oct '95 / PolyGram.

BEST MOVES
Every drop of rain / In a country churchyard / Patricia the stripper / Satin green shutters / Spanish train / Waiting for the hurricane / Broken wings (Live) / Lonely sky / Spaceman came travelling / Crusader / Traveller
CD _____ 3950832
A&M / Apr '95 / PolyGram.

CRUSADER
Carry on / I had the love in my eyes / Something else again / Girl with April in her eyes / Just in time / Devil's eyes / It's such a long way home / Old fashioned people / Quiet moments / Crusader / You and me
CD _____ CDMID 113
A&M / Oct '92 / PolyGram.

EASTERN WIND
Traveller / Record company bash / Tonight / Wall of silence / Flying home / Shadows and light / Some things never change / Tourist attraction / Eastern wind
CD _____ CDMID 167
A&M / Aug '91 / PolyGram.

FAR BEYOND THESE CASTLE WALLS
Hold on / Key / Windy night / Sin City / New moon / Watching the world / Lonesome cowboy / Satin green shutters / Turning around / Goodnight
CD _____ CDMID 110
A&M / Oct '92 / PolyGram.

FLYING COLOURS
Sailing away / Carry me (like a fire in your heart) / Tender hands / Night on the river / Leather on my shoes / Suddenly love / Missing you / I'm not scared anymore / Don't look back / Just a word away / Risen Lord / Last time I cried / Simple truth (a child is born) (On CD only.)
CD _____ 3952242
A&M / Apr '95 / PolyGram.

GETAWAY, THE
Don't pay the ferryman / Living on the island / Crying and laughing / I'm counting on you / Getaway / Ship to shore / Borderline / Where peaceful waters flow / Revolution / Light a fire / Liberty
CD _____ 3949292
A&M / Apr '95 / PolyGram.

HIGH ON EMOTION- LIVE FROM DUBLIN
CD _____ 3970862
A&M / Apr '95 / PolyGram.

INTO THE LIGHT
One word straight to the heart / For Rosanna / Leader / Vision / What about me / Last night / Fire on the water / Fatal charm of romance / Lady in red / Say goodbye to it all / Spirit of man / Fatal hesitation
CD _____ 3951212
A&M / Apr '95 / PolyGram.

INTO THE LIGHT/ FLYING COLOURS
(2CD Set)
Last night / Ballroom of romance / Say goodbye to it all / Fata hesitation / For Rosanna / What about me / Carry me / Night on the river / Suddenly love / Fire on the water / Lady in red / Spirit of man / One word / Leader / Sailing away / Tender hands / Leather on my shoes
CD _____ CDA 24116
A&M / Jul '92 / PolyGram.

MAN ON THE LINE

Ecstasy of flight (I love the night) / Sight and touch / Taking it to the top / Head and the heart / Sound of a gun / High on emotion / Much more than this / Man on the line / Moonlight and vodka / Transmission ends
CD _____ CDMID 188
A&M / Jul '93 / PolyGram.

POWER OF TEN
Where will we be going / By my side / Heart of darkness / In your eyes / Separate tables / Talk to me / Brother John / Connemara coast / Shine on / Celebration / She means everything to me / Making the perfect man
CD _____ 3971882
A&M / Apr '95 / PolyGram.

SPANISH TRAIN AND OTHER STORIES
Spanish train / Lonely sky / This song for you / Patricia the stripper / Spaceman came travelling / I'm going home / Painter / Old friend / Tower / Just another poor boy
CD _____ CDMID 111
A&M / Oct '92 / PolyGram.

SPARK TO A FLAME
This waiting heart / Don't pay the ferryman / Much more than this / Sailing away / Lady in red / Borderline / Say goodbye to it all / Ship to shore / Missing you / Diamond in the dark / Tender hands / Spaceman came travelling / Where peaceful waters flow / High on emotion / Spanish train / Fatal hesitation
CD _____ CDBCD 100
A&M / Oct '89 / PolyGram.

THIS WAY UP
This silent world / This is love / This weight on me / Here is your paradise / Oh my brave hearts / Blonde hair, blue jeans / Son and the father / Up here in heaven / You are the reason / Love's got a hold on me / Snows of New York
CD _____ 540 233-2
A&M / May '94 / PolyGram.

De Cadiz, Beni

GREAT FIGURES OF FLAMENCO VOL. 17
CD _____ LDX 274992
La Chant Du Monde / Jun '94 / Harmonia Mundi / ADA.

De Cana, Flor

MUEVETE (MOVE IT)
CD _____ FF 70463
Flying Fish / Jul '89 / Roots / CM / Direct / ADA.

De Chiaro, Giovanni

GUITAR ON BROADWAY, THE
CD _____ CRC 2172
Centaur / Jan '94 / Complete/Pinnacle.

De Dakar, Etoile

VOLUME 2: PHIAPATHIOLY
Thiapathioly / Dokhama say ne ne / Diandioli / Dounyan / Defal gnou guiss / Dagotte
CD _____ STCD 3006
Sterns / Mar '94 / Sterns / CM.

De Dannan

ANTHEM
Wren's nest / Let it be / Johnstone hornpipe / Connie from Constantinople / Johnny I hardly knew you / Ril and Spideal / Anthem for Ireland / Jimmy Byrnes and Dinkies / Diglake fields / Duo in G / Paddy's lamentation
CD _____ DARCD 013
Dara / Sep '93 / Roots / CM / Direct / ADA / Koch.

BALLROOM
CD _____ GLCD 3040
Green Linnet / Feb '95 / Roots / CM / Direct / ADA.

JACKET OF BATTERIES, A
CD _____ CMCD 066
Celtic Music / Oct '94 / CM / Roots.

MIST COVERED MOUNTAINS, THE
Mac's fancy/Mist covered mountain / Cameronian reel/Doon reel / Seamaisin / Mulvihill's reel/Dawn / Banks of the Nile / Johnny Leary's polka/O'Keefe's polka/Johnny do I miss you / Mr. O'Connor / Henry Joy / Cottage in the grove/Sean Ryan's reel / Maire Mhor / Langstrom's pony/Tap room/Lord Ramsey's reel
CD _____ CEFCD 087
Gael Linn / Jan '94 / Roots / CM / Direct / ADA.

STAR SPANGLED MOLLY, THE
CD _____ TFCB 5006CD
Third Floor / Oct '94 / Total/BMG / ADA / Direct.

De Fabriek

PWZ
CD _____ EFA 015622
Apocalyptic Vision / Sep '95 / Plastic Head / SRD.

De Falla Trio

MUSIC FOR THREE GUITARS
CD _____ CCD 42011
Concord Concerto / Dec '87 / Pinnacle.

De Forest, Carmaig

DEATHGROOVELOVEPARTY
CD _____ KFWCD 145
Knitting Factory / Feb '95 / Grapevine.

De France, Jean Michel

FEELINGS (The music of the pan flute)
Woman in love / Man and a woman / La mer / My heart in my hands / About the clouds / Love serenade / Dolannes melodie / Guernica / We are the world / Feelings / Autumn leaves / Adagio / Song for Anna / Liebestraum / El love Maria / Summer love affair / El condor pasa
CD _____ PWK 130
Carlton Home Entertainment / May '90 / Carlton Home Entertainment.

MEMORIES (Music Of The Pan Flute)
CD _____ PWK 085
Carlton Home Entertainment / '91 / Carlton Home Entertainment.

De Franco, Buddy

BORN TO SWING
CD _____ HCD 701
Hindsight / Nov '94 / Target/BMG / Jazz Music.

BUENOS AIRES CONCERTS, THE
Billie's bounce / Triste / Ja da / Yesterdays / Mood indigo / Scrapple from the apple / Street of dreams / Song is you
CD _____ HEPCD 2014
Hep / Nov '95 / Cadillac / Jazz Music / New Note / Wellard.

FIVE NOTES OF BLUES
CD _____ 500302
Musidisc / Nov '93 / Vital / Harmonia Mundi / ADA / Cadillac / Discovery.

HARK (De Franco, Buddy & Oscar Peterson Quartet)
All too soon / Summer me, Winter me / Llovisna (Light rain) / By myself / Joy spring / This is all I ask / Hark / Why am I
CD _____ OJCCD 867
Original Jazz Classics / Nov '95 / Wellard / Jazz Music / Cadillac / Complete/Pinnacle.

De Goal, Charles

DOUBLE FACE
CD _____ ROSE 96CD
New Rose / Dec '86 / Direct / ADA.

De Graaf, Dick

SAILING
CD _____ CHR 70024
Challenge / Sep '95 / Direct / Jazz Music / Cadillac / ADA.

De Graaff, Rein

NOSTALGIA
How high the moon / Alone together / Afternoon in Paris / I cover the waterfront / Cherokee / Au privave / Nostalgia / Ablution / Lennie's pennies / Dreamstepper / Subconscious - Lee
CD _____ CDSJP 429
Timeless Jazz / Jul '95 / New Note.

De Grassi, Alex

DEEP AT NIGHT
Mirage / Deep at night / Charlotte / Short order / Indian Summer / Blue trout / Waltz / Arcos / Mirror / Hidden voices
CD _____ WD 1100
Windham Hill / May '91 / Pinnacle / BMG / ADA.

WINDHAM HILL RETROSPECTIVE, A
Overland / Causeway / Western / Window / Clockwork / Blue trout / White rain / Cumulus / Momentary change of heart / Luther's lullaby / Charlotte / Turning, turning back / Children's dance / Mirage / Slow circle II / Blood and jasmine
CD _____ 111132
Windham Hill / Mar '92 / Pinnacle / BMG / ADA.

WORLD'S GETTING..., THE
CD _____ 01934111312
Windham Hill / May '95 / Pinnacle / BMG / ADA.

De Johnette, Jack

ALBUM ALBUM (Special edition)
Festival / New Orleans strut / Zoot suite / Ahmad the terrible / Monk's mood / Third world anthem
CD _____ 8234672
ECM / Jan '89 / New Note.

NEW DIRECTIONS
CD _____ 8293742
ECM / Jan '89 / New Note.

NEW DIRECTIONS IN EUROPE

Salsa for Eddie / Bayou fever / Where or Wayne / Multo spillagio
CD _____ 8291582
ECM / '88 / New Note.

PIANO ALBUM, THE
CD _____ LCD 15042
Landmark / Aug '88 / New Note.

PICTURES
Picture 1 / Picture 2 / Picture 3 / Picture 4 / Picture 5 / Picture 6
CD _____ 519284-2
ECM / Jun '93 / New Note.

SPECIAL EDITION (De Johnette, Jack Special Edition)
One for Eric / Zoot suite / Central Park West / India / Journey to the twin planet
CD _____ 8276942
ECM / Jan '89 / New Note.

TIN CAN ALLEY (De Johnette, Jack Special Edition)
Tin can alley / Pastel rhapsody / Riff raff / Gri gri man / I know
CD _____ 5177542-2
ECM / Nov '93 / New Note.

WORKS: JACK DEJOHNETTE
Bayou fever / Gri gri man / To be continued / One for Eric / Unshielded desire / Blue
CD _____ 8254272
ECM / Jun '89 / New Note.

De Jong, Tracie

LONGEST DAY, THE
CD _____ CDMANU 1440
Manu / Dec '93 / Discovery / ADA.

De Jonge, Henk

JUMPING SHARK
CD _____ BVHAASTCD 9103
Bvhaast / Nov '90 / Cadillac.

De La Isla, Camaron

GRAND FIGURES OF FLAMENCO VOL. 15
CD _____ LDX 274957
La Chant Du Monde / May '94 / Harmonia Mundi / ADA.

De La Matrona, Pepe

GREAT SINGERS OF FLAMENCO VOL.2
CD _____ LDC 274 829
La Chant Du Monde / '88 / Harmonia Mundi / ADA.

De La Rosa, Tony

ATOTONILCO
CD _____ ARHCD 362
Arhoolie / Apr '95 / ADA / Direct / Cadillac.

ES MI DERECHO
CD _____ ROUCD 6066
Rounder / Jun '95 / CM / Direct / ADA / Cadillac.

De La Soul

3 FEET HIGH AND RISING
Intro / Magic number / Change in speak / Cool breeze on the rocks / Can U keep a secret / Jenifa (taught me) / Ghetto thang / Transmitting live from Mars / Eye know / Take it off / Little bit of soap / Tread water / Say no go / Do as De La does / Plug tunin' / De La orgee / Buddy / Description / Me, myself and I / This is a recording 4 living in a fulltime era / I can do anything / D.A.I.S.Y. age / Plug tunin' (12" mix) / Potholes in my lawn
CD _____ DLSCD 1
Big Life / Jul '95 / Pinnacle.

DE LA SOUL IS DEAD
Intro / Oodles of O's / Talkin' 'bout Hey Love / Pease porridge / Skit 1 / Johnny's dead aka Vincent Mason (live from the BK lounge) / Roller skating jam named 'Saturdays' / WRMS' dedication to the bitty / Bitties in the BK lounge / Skit 2 / My brother's a basehead / Let, let me in / Afro connections at a hi 5 (in the eyes of the hoodlum) / Rap de rap show / Millie pulled a pistol on Santa / Who do U worship / Skit 3 / Kicked out the house / Pass the plugs / Not over till the fat lady plays the demo / Ring ring ring (ha ha hey) / WRMS: cat's in control / Skit 4 / Shwingalokate / Fanatic of the B word / Keepin' the faith / Skit 5
CD _____ BLRCD 8
Big Life / Jul '95 / Pinnacle.

De Lone, Austin

DE LONE AT LAST
Blithe'd ale boogie / Deeper well / Little little record / Big big fun / Visions of Johanna / No money / Done doin' good / Beaver strut / Louise / My baby, my baby / Put your wig back on / For Lesley
CD _____ FIENDCD 706
Demon / Oct '91 / Pinnacle / ADA.

De Marez, Cas

CATHEDRALE DE CHANT
CD _____ BAR 011
Staalplaat / Sep '95 / Vital/SAM.

De Mbanga, Labiro

NDINGA MAN CONTRE-ATTAQUE : NA WOU GO PAY (Protest Songs From Cameroon)
CD _____ LBLC 2506
Indigo / Jan '93 / Direct / ADA.

De Melo, Armenio

SPIRIT OF FADO, A (De Melo, Armenio & Jose Maria Nobrega)
CD _____ PS 65705
Playasound / Feb '93 / Harmonia Mundi / ADA.

De Norte A Sur

FOLKSONGS FROM VENEZUELA
CD _____ EUCD 1149
ARC / '91 / ARC Music / ADA.

INSPIRATION MEXICANA - SONGS & DANCES FROM MEXICO (De Norte A Sur & Friends)
CD _____ EUCD 1196
ARC / Sep '93 / ARC Music / ADA.

De Palma, Victor

COME DANCING (De Palma, Victor & His Orchestra)
CD _____ CDSGP 060
Prestige / Oct '93 / Total/BMG.

De Paul, Lynsey

JUST A LITTLE TIME
Sugar me / Getting a drag / Words don't mean a thing / We got love / Storm in a teacup / Dancing on a Sunday night / Just a little time / Instant love / Now and then / Won't somebody dance with me / Sugar me (club mix) / Getting a drag (club mix)
CD _____ MSCD 9
Magnum Music / Oct '94 / Magnum Music Group.

De Ridder, Willem

SNUFF (De Ridder, Willem & Hafler Trio)
CD _____ SPL 2
Touch / Oct '95 / These / Kudos.

De Shannon, Jackie

WHAT THE WORLD NEEDS NOW
Buddy / Heaven is being with you / You won't forget me / Needles and pins / Hello and goodbyes / When you walk in the room / Till you walk in / Breakaway / Should I cry / I remember the boy / Dream boy / Don't turn your back on me / Dream / the world needs now is love / Lifetime of lonliness / Come and get me / Splendor in the grass / Forgranted / Windows and doors / I can make it with you / 500 miles from yesterday / Where does the sun go / It shines on you too / Reason to believe / Weight / Came and stay with me / Put a little love in your heart / Love will find a way / Brighton Hill
CD _____ CZ 539
EMI / Aug '94 / EMI.

YOU'RE THE ONLY DANCER/QUICK TOUCHES
CD _____ EDCD 420
Edsel / May '95 / Pinnacle / ADA.

De Tecalitlan, Vargas

MEXICO'S PIONEER MARIACHIS VOL.3 (Their First Recordings 1937-1947)
CD _____ FL 7015
Folklyric / Apr '95 / Direct / Cadillac.

De Utrera, Pitine

GUITARRA FLAMENCA
CD _____ ARN 64237
Arion / Jun '93 / Discovery / ADA.

De Ville, Willy

BIG EASY FANTASY
CD _____ 122151
Wotre Music / Jun '96 / New Note.

LOUP GAROU
CD _____ 0630124562
Warner Bros. / Jan '96 / Warner Music.

MIRACLE
Due to gun control / Could you would you / Heart and soul / Assassin of love / Spanish Jack / Storybook love / Southern politician / Angel eyes / Miracle
CD _____ RVCD 41
Raven / Nov '94 / Direct / ADA.

VICTORY MIXTURE
Hello my lover / It do me good / Key to my heart / Beating like a tom tom / Every dog has its day / Big blue diamonds / Teasin' you / Ruler of my heart / Who shot the La / Junkers blues
CD _____ 652304
New Rose / Mar '95 / Direct / ADA.

De Zes, Winden

SAX SEXTET - MAN MET MUTS
CD _____ DVHAA&TCD 0004
Bvhaast / Dec '87 / Cadillac.

Deacon Blue

FELLOW HOODLUMS
James Joyce soles / Fellow hoodlums / Your swaying arms / Cover from the sky / Day that slackie bumped the jail / Wildness / Brighter star than you will shine / Twist and shout / Closing time / Goodnight Jamsie / I will see you tomorrow / One day I'll go walking
CD _____ 4685502
Columbia / Jun '91 / Sony.

OUR TOWN (Deacon Blue Greatest Hits)
Dignity / Wages day / Real gone kid / Your swaying arms / Fergus sings the blues / I was right and you were wrong / Chocolate girl / I'll never fall in love again / When will you (make my telephone ring) / Twist and shout / Your town / Queen of the new year / Only tender love / Cover from the sky / Love and regret / Beautiful stranger (Available on LP only) / Will we be lovers / Loaded / Bound to love / Still in the mood
CD _____ 4666422
Columbia / Apr '94 / Sony.

RAINTOWN
Born in a storm / Raintown / Ragman / He looks like Spencer Tracy now / Loaded / When will you (make my telephone ring) / Chocolate girl / Dignity / Very thing (Theme from BBC TV series'Take Me Home') / Love's great fears / Town to be blamed / Riches / Kings of the Western world / Shifting sands / Suffering / Ribbons and bows / Angeliou / Just like boys
CD _____ 4505492
CBS / Feb '88 / Sony.

RAINTOWN/WHEN THE WORLD KNOWS YOUR NAME (2CD Set)
Born in a storm / Raintown / Ragman / He looks like Spencer Tracy now / Loaded / When will you (make my telephone ring) / Chocolate girl / Dignity / Very thing / Love's great fears / Town to be blamed / Riches / Kings of the Western world / Queen of the New Year / Wages day / Real gone kid / Love and regret / Circus lights / This changing light / Sad love girl / Fergus sings the blues / World is lit by lightning / Silhouette / Hundred things / Your constant heart / Orphans
CD Set _____ 466532
CBS / Feb '90 / Sony.

WHATEVER YOU SAY, SAY NOTHING
Your town / Only tender love / Peace and jobs and freedom / Hang your head / Bethlehem's gate / Will we be lovers / Fall so freely down / Cut lip / Last night I dreamed of Henry Thomas / All over the world
CD _____ 473527 2
Columbia / Mar '93 / Sony.

WHEN THE WORLD KNOWS YOUR NAME
Queen of the New Year / Real gone kid / Circus lights / Sad loved girl / Hundred things / Silhouette / Wages day / Love and regret / This changing light / Fergus sings the blues / Orphans / World is lit by lightning
CD _____ 4633212
CBS / Oct '95 / Sony.

Dead Beat

FILE UNDER FUCK
CD _____ LF 134MCD
Lost & Found / May '95 / Plastic Head.

Dead Boys

NIGHT OF THE LIVING DEAD BOYS
CD _____ BCD 4017
Bomp / Mar '94 / Pinnacle.

Dead Brain Cells

UNIVERSE
CD _____ CDJUST 14
Rough Justice / Jul '90 / Pinnacle.

Dead C

TRAPDOOR FUCKING EXIT
Heaven / Hell is now love / Mighty / Power / Bury / Bury (refutation, omnium, haeresium) / Sky / Bone / Krassed / Calling slowly / Helen said this / Acoustico
CD _____ SB 0212
Matador / Aug '95 / Vital.

WHITE HOUSE, THE
Voodoo spell / New snow / Your hand / (PROCHAM) / Bitcher / Outside
CD _____ SB0402
Matador / Aug '95 / Vital.

Dead Can Dance

AION
Arrival and the reunion / Mephisto / Fortune presents gifts not according / End of words / Wilderness / Garden of Zephirus / Saltarello / Song of Sibyl / As the bell rings the Maypole sign / Black sun / Promised womb / Radharc

CD _____ CAD 0007CD
4AD / Apr '90 / Disc.

DEAD CAN DANCE
Fatal impact / Trial / Frontier / Fortune / Ocean / East of Eden / Threshold / Passage in time / Wild in the woods / Musica eternal
CD _____ CAD 404 CD
4AD / Feb '87 / Disc.

INTO THE LABRYNTH
CD _____ CAD 3013CD
4AD / Jun '93 / Disc.

PASSAGE IN TIME, A
CD _____ CAD 1010CD
4AD / Oct '91 / Disc.

SERPENTS EGG, THE
Host of Seraphim / Orbis de ignis / Severance / Writing on my father's hand / In the kingdom of the blind / Chant of the paladin / Song of Sophia / Echolalia / Mother tongue / Ulysses
CD _____ CAD 808CD
4AD / Oct '94 / Disc.

SPLEEN AND IDEAL
This tide / De profundis / Ascension / Circumradiant dawn / Cardinal sin / Mesmerism / Enigma of the absolute / Advent / Abatar / Indoctrination / Out of the depth of sorrow / Design for living
CD _____ CAD 512CD
4AD / Jan '86 / Disc.

TOWARD THE WITHIN
CD _____ DAD 4015CD
4AD / Oct '94 / Disc.

WITHIN THE REALM OF A DYING SUN
Anywhere out of the world / Windfall / In the wake of adversity / Xavier / Dawn of the iconoclast / Cantara / Summoning up the muse / Persphone (the gathering of flowers)
CD _____ CAD 705CD
4AD / Jul '87 / Disc.

Dead Famous People

ALL HAIL THE DAFFODIL
CD _____ LADIDA 016CD
La-Di-Da / Jul '94 / Vital.

ARRIVING LATE IN TORN AND FILTHY JEANS
CD _____ UTIL 007 CD
Utility / Jul '89 / Grapevine.

Dead Flowers

ALTERED STATE CIRCUS
Elephant's eye was eerie / Altered state circus / Warm within - chemical binolculas / Slough factor 9 / Full fist / Free the weed / Vodaphone in Oz (On CD only.)
CD _____ DELECCD 022
Delerium / Oct '94 / Vital.

DEAD FLOWERS
CD _____ RUNECD 002
Mystic Stones / Aug '92 / Vital.

SMELL THE FRAGRANCE
Absolution / Drowning / Jesus toy / Piece of sky / So far gone / Can't understand / Swimming around / Manic depression / Third eye shades / Crack down / Cut shapes
CD _____ CDRUNE 002
Mystic Stones / Oct '93 / Vital.

Dead Fly Boy

DEAD FLY BOY
CD _____ SECTOR2 1001
Sector 2 / Jul '95 / Direct / ADA.

Dead Fucking Last

PROUD TO BE
CD _____ 864532
Epitaph / Aug '95 / Plastic Head / Pinnacle.

Dead Kennedys

BEDTIME FOR DEMOCRACY
CD _____ VIRUS 50CD
Alternative Tentacles / Jan '92 / Pinnacle.

FRANKENCHRIST
CD _____ VIRUS 45CD
Alternative Tentacles / Feb '92 / Pinnacle.

FRESH FRUIT FOR ROTTING VEGETABLES
Kill the poor / Forward to death / When ya get drafted / Let's lynch the landlord / Drug me / Your emotions / Chemical warfare / California uber alles / I kill children / Stealing people's mail / Funland at the beach / Ill in the head / Holiday in Cambodia / Viva Las Vegas
CD _____ VIRUS 1CD
Alternative Tentacles / '88 / Pinnacle.
CD _____ CDBRED 10
Cherry Red / Mar '95 / Pinnacle.

GIVE ME CONVENIENCE OR GIVE ME DEATH
CD _____ VIRUS 57CD
Alternative Tentacles / Sep '87 / Pinnacle.

PLASTIC SURGERY DISASTERS
Government flu / Terminal preppie / Trust your mechanic / Well paid scientist / Buzzbomb / Forest fire / Halloween / Winnebago warrior / Riot / Bleed for me / I am the owl

Dead On

ALL FOR YOU
CD _____ 367 0005.3
Mausoleum / Oct '91 / Grapevine.

Dead Or Alive

YOUTHQUAKE
You spin me round (like a record) / I wanna be a toy / D.J. hit that button / In too deep / Big daddy of the rhythm / Cake and eat it / Lover come back to me / My heart goes bang / It's been a long time / Lover come back to me (extended mix)
CD _____ 477853 2
Epic / Oct '94 / Sony.

Dead Orchestra

SOUNDS LIKE TIME TASTES
CD _____ MASSCD 064
Massacre / Aug '95 / Plastic Head.

Dead Ringer Band

RED DESERT SKY
CD _____ LARRCD 302
Larrikin / Nov '94 / Roots / Direct / ADA / CM.

Dead World

MACHINE, THE
CD _____ NB 089-2
Nuclear Blast / Jan '94 / Plastic Head.

Dead Youth

INTENSE BRUTALITY
CD _____ GCI 9800
Plastic Head / Jun '92 / Plastic Head.

Deadeye Dick

DIFFERENT STORY, A
New age girl (Many Moon) / Perfect family / Your love is killing me / Marguerite / Oath / Anyone / Sentimental crap / Like a shadow / Molly / Different story / Lucky one
CD _____ CDCHR 6099
Chrysalis / Mar '95 / EMI.

Deadguy

FIXATION ON A CO WORKER
CD _____ VR 030
Victory Europe / Jan '96 / Plastic Head.

Deadly Nighshades

DEADLY NIGHTSHADES, THE
Totally female / Monster / Love blackmailer / James / That song / Vampire / Train / Who's that living next door / Nocturnal / Stray cats / Red turns to brown / Twilight
CD _____ HOT 1051
Hot / Feb '96 / Vital.

Deadspot

ADIOS DUDE
Addiction / Right through you / Inside / Backspot / Friday night in hell / This means war / Power tool / Another day / My death / Jesus is my best friend
CD _____ HMRXD 149
Heavy Metal / May '90 / Sony.

BUILT IN PAIN
CD _____ CZ 032CD
C/Z / Oct '91 / Plastic Head.

Deaf School

SECOND COMING
What a way to end it all / Shake some action / Hi Jo hi / Nearly moonlight night motel / Taxi / Ronnie Zamora / Thunder and lightning / Blue velvet / Princess princess / I wanna be your boy / Lines / Capaldis cafe / Second honeymoon / Final act
CD _____ FIEND CD 135
Demon / Oct '88 / Pinnacle / ADA.

Deal, Bill

BEST OF BILL DEAL AND THE RHONDELLS (Deal, Bill & The Rhondells)
I've been hurt / What kind of fool do you think I am / May I / Are you ready for this / Can I change my mind / Words / Touch me / I've gotta be me / Soulful strut / It's too late / Everybody's got something to hide / Nothing succeeds like success / Swinging tight / I'm gonna make you love me / I've got my needs / Harlem shuffle / River deep, mountain high / Hooked on a feeling / Hey bulldog / Tuck's theme / So what if it rains / I live in the night

CD _____ NEMCD 644
Sequel / Apr '94 / BMG.

Dean Close School Chapel

MICHAELMAS TO WHITSUNTIDE (Dean Close School Chapel Choir)
Sing lullaby / And there were shepherds / Break forth / Lo now we count them blessed / Miserere mei / Three kings / When to the temple Mary went / Spirit of the Lord / Little road to Bethlehem / Crucifixus / I waited for the Lord / Ascendit Deus / Tibi Christe / Beata nobis gaudia / Haec dies / Caelos ascendit hodie / Wash me throughly / Alleluia, a new work / Strife is o'er
CD _____ CDPS 405
Alpha / '91 / Abbey Recording.

Dean, Elton

ALL THE TRADITION (Dean, Elton & Howard Riley Quartet)
Darn that dream / Longest day / Crescent / Convivial convocation / I remember Clifford
CD _____ SLAMCD 201
Slam / Apr '91 / Cadillac.

ELTON DEAN & HIS UNLIMITED SAXOPHONE COMPANY
CD _____ OGCD 002
Ogun / Oct '92 / Cadillac / Jazz Music / Charly.

TWO'S AND THREE'S
He who dares / P.R. Department / Uprising / Reconciliation / K.T. / Riolity / Duke
CD _____ VP 167CD
Voice Print / Aug '94 / Voice Print.

Dean, Graham

GRAHAM DEAN QUARTET, THE
CD _____ GFD 001
Scorpio / Jun '94 / Complete/Pinnacle.

Dean, Jimmy

BIG BAD JOHN
Big bad John / I won't go huntin' with you Jake / Smoke, smoke, smoke / Dear Ivan / To a sleeping beauty / Cajun Queen / P.T. 109 / Walk on boy / Little bitty big John / Steel man / Little black book / Please pass the biscuits / Gonna raise a ruckus tonight / Day that changed the world / Gotta travel on / Sixteen tons / Oklahoma Bill / Night train to Memphis / Make the waterwheel roll / Lonesome road / Grasshopper MacCleod / Old Pappy's new banjo / You're nobody 'til somebody loves you / Cajun Joe / Nobody / Kentucky means paradise
CD _____ BCD 15723
Bear Family / Jul '93 / Rollercoaster / Direct / CM / Swift / ADA.

GREATEST HITS: JIMMY DEAN
Big bad John / Cajun Queen / Harvest of sunshine / Little black book / Steel men / First thing every morning (and the last thing at night) / Sam Hill / P.T. 109 / To a sleeping beauty / Farmer and the Lord / I won't go huntin' with you Jake / With you Jake (But I'll go chasin' wimmin)
CD _____ 983000 2
Pickwick/Sony Collector's Choice / Aug '93 / Carlton Home Entertainment / Pinnacle / Sony.

Deanta

DEANTA
CD _____ GLCD 1126
Green Linnet / May '93 / Roots / CM / Direct / ADA.

READY FOR THE STORM
CD _____ GL 1147CD
Green Linnet / Oct '94 / Roots / CM / Direct / ADA.

Dear Janes I

SOMETIMES I
Girl of your dreams / Niagara tears / Brides of the cross / Dear Jane / Air traffic / Sometimes I / Outside my window / My guilty hand / Some small corner / Jesus put me down / I'm heading home / PMP
CD _____ TRACD 104
Transatlantic / Feb '95 / BMG / Pinnacle / ADA.

Dear Mr. President

DEAR MR. PRESIDENT
Hey daddy have you / Fate / What's the world coming to / Love and violence / Queen of my parade / Fatal desire / Get It Together / Who killed Santa Claus
CD _____ 925637 2
Atlantic / Sep '88 / Warner Music.

Dearie, Blossom

CHRISTMAS SPICE, IT'S SO NICE
CD _____ CHECD 00103
Master Mix / '91 / Wellard / Jazz Music / New Note.

ET TU BRUCE
Bruce / Hey John / Someone's been sending me flowers / You have lived in autumn / Alice in Wonderland / Satin doll / Riviera / Inside a silent tear

CD _____ CDCHE 5
Master Mix / Aug '89 / Wellard / Jazz Music / New Note.

NEEDLEPOINT MAGIC
Ballad of the shape of things / Lush life / When the world was young / I'm hip / Baby, it's cold outside / I like you, you're nice / Sweet surprise / I'm shadowing you / Sweet Georgie fame / Peel me a grape / Two sleepy people
CD _____ CDCHE 3
Master Mix / Oct '91 / Wellard / Jazz Music / New Note.

SINGS AND PLAYS SONGS OF CHEALSEA', VOL. 10
My attorney Bernie / Everything I've got / C'est Le Printemps / When in Rome / Let the flower grow / My new celebrity is you / What time is it now / You fascinate me so / There ought to be moonlight saving time / Chelsea Aire
CD _____ CDCHE 2
Master Mix / Jan '90 / Wellard / Jazz Music / New Note.

TWEEDLE DUM AND TWEEDLE DEE (Dearie, Blossom & Mike Renzi)
CD _____ CHECD 00101
Master Mix / '91 / Wellard / Jazz Music / New Note.

UPON A SUMMERTIME
CD _____ 5172232
Verve / Feb '93 / PolyGram.

VOCAL CLASSICS
CD _____ 8379342
Verve / Feb '93 / PolyGram.

WINCHESTER IN APPLE BLOSSOM TIME
Spring can really hang you up the most / Sunday afternoon / Wonderful guy / To touch the hand of love / Wheelers and dealers / Jazz musician / Surrey with the fringe on top / Love is an elusive celebration / Lucky to be me / You're for loving / Summer is gone / Sammy / It amazes me / If I were a bell
CD _____ CHECD 8
Master Mix / '89 / Wellard / Jazz Music / New Note.

Death

BEST OF DEATH
CD _____ CDMFLAG 71
Under One Flag / Aug '92 / Pinnacle.

HUMAN
CD _____ RC 92382
Roadrunner / Apr '95 / Pinnacle.

INDIVIDUAL THOUGHT PATTERNS
Overactive imagination / Jealousy / Trapped in a corner / Nothing is everything / Mentally blind / Individual thought patterns / Destiny / Out of touch / Philosopher / In human form
CD _____ RR 90792
Roadrunner / Apr '95 / Pinnacle.

SCREAM BLOODY GORE
Infernal death / Zombie ritual / Denial of life / Sacrificial / Mutilation / Regurgitated guts / Baptized in blood / Torn to pieces / Evil dead / Scream bloody gore
CD _____ CDFLAG 12
Under One Flag / Jun '87 / Pinnacle.

SYMBOLIC
CD _____ RR 89572
Roadrunner / Mar '95 / Pinnacle.

Death Angel

FROLIC THROUGH THE PARK
Third floor / Road mutants / Why you do this / Bored / Confused / Guilty of innocence / Open up / Shores of sin / Cold gin / Mind rape
CD _____ 772549-2
Restless / Jul '94 / Vital.

ULTRA-VIOLENCE
Thrashers / Evil priest / Voracious souls / Kill as one / Ultra violence / Mistress of pain / Final death / IPFS
CD _____ 772548-2
Restless / Jul '94 / Vital.

Death Of Samantha

WHERE THE WOMEN WEAR THE GLORY
CD _____ HMS 121CD
Homestead / Nov '88 / SRD.

Death SS

HEAVY DEMONS
CD _____ BABEDISCCD 002
Plastic Head / Jul '92 / Plastic Head.

Deathcore

SPONTANEOUS
CD _____ 842976
Nuclear Blast / Sep '90 / Plastic Head.

SPONTANEOUS UNDERGROUND
CD _____ NB 034CD
Nuclear Blast / Oct '92 / Plastic Head.

Deathfolk

DEATHFOLK
CD _____ NAR 047 CD
New Alliance / May '93 / Pinnacle.

DEATHFOLK 2
CD _____ NAR 076 CD
New Alliance / May '93 / Pinnacle.

Deathless

ANHEDONIA
CD _____ EL 104
Electrip / Nov '92 / Plastic Head.

NONDEATHLESS
CD _____ EL 105CD
Electrip / Sep '93 / Plastic Head.

Deathprod

TREETOP DRIVE
CD _____ MAD 004
Mad / Mar '95 / Plastic Head.

Deaville, Gillman

WAYS TO FLY
CD _____ FF 70636
Flying Fish / Nov '94 / Roots / CM / Direct / ADA.

DeBarge, El

HEART, MIND & SOUL
Where you are / Can't get enough / Where is my love / You got the love I want / It's got to be real / Slide / I'll be there / Special song / Starlight, moonlight, candlight / You are my dream / Heart, mind and soul
CD _____ 936245375-2
Warner Bros. / Jun '94 / Warner Music.

Debriano, Santi

OBEAH
CD _____ FRLCD 008
Freelance / Oct '92 / Harmonia Mundi / Cadillac / Koch.

PANAMANIACS (Debriano, Santi Group)
CD _____ FRLCD 019
Freelance / Nov '93 / Harmonia Mundi / Cadillac / Koch.

SOLDIERS OF FORTUNE
CD _____ FRLCD 012
Freelance / Oct '92 / Harmonia Mundi / Cadillac / Koch.

Debris

EPIC SOUNDTRACKS
CD _____ RTS 20
Return To Sender / Jan '96 / Direct / ADA.

Debustrol

NEUROPATOLOG
CD _____ MONITOR 2
Monitor / Jan '92 / CM.

Decameron

MAMMOTH SPECIAL
Rock 'n' roll woman / Mammoth special / Just enough like home / Glimpse of me / Late on Lady Day / Breakdown of the song / Cheetah / Jan / Stonehouse / Parade / Empty space
CD _____ CRESTCD 013
Mooncrest / Oct '90 / Direct / ADA.

Decan, Chen

CHINESE FOLK MUSIC (Decan, Chen Chinese Ensemble)
CD _____ EUCD 1167
ARC / '91 / ARC Music / ADA.

Decimator

CARNAGE CITY STATE MOSH PATROL
Raider / Mutoids / F H Blood Island / C.C.S.M.P. / Devil's bridge / Rogue decimator / Dustbowl / Stealer of souls
CD _____ NEAT 1047D
Neat / '89 / Plastic Head.

DIRTY, HOT & HUNGRY
CD _____ NEATCD 1052
Neat / Nov '92 / Plastic Head.

Decollation

CURSED LANDS
CD _____ POSH 0004
Listenable / Oct '93 / Plastic Head.

Decomposed

FUNERAL OBSESSION
CD _____ CYBERCD 2
Cybersound / May '92 / Vital.

HOPE FINALLY DIED
CD _____ CANDLE 003CD
Candlelight / Jan '94 / Plastic Head.

Deconstruction

DECONSTRUCTION
LA Song / Single / Get at 'em / Iris / Dirge / Fire in the hole / Son / Big sur / Hope /

One / America / Sleepyhead / Wait for history / That is all / Kilo
CD _____ 74321 248522
American / Aug '95 / BMG.

Dedale

CHRONIQUES URBAINES
CD _____ DP 93009CD
Mustradem / Apr '94 / ADA.

LE MAITRE DHU
CD _____ DP 91007CD
Mustradem / Apr '94 / ADA.

NO PAST
CD _____ DP 9501CD
Mustradem / Aug '95 / ADA.

OBSESSION
CD _____ DP 92008CD
Mustradem / Apr '94 / ADA.

Dedication Orchestra

IXESHA
CD Set _____ OGCD 102103
Ogun / Dec '94 / Cadillac / Jazz Music / Charly.

Dee, Brian

CLIMB EVERY MOUNTAIN
I have dreamed / I should care / Your song / Pete Kelly's blues / Nuages / Koo / Instep / Day by day / You are the sunshine of my life / Uncle's friend / Triple play / I surrender Dear / How insensitive / Dream / To the shores of Tripoli / Unforgettable / Homebase / Climb every mountain
CD _____ SPJCD 552
Spotlite / May '95 / Cadillac / Jazz Horizons / Swift.

SECOND SIGHT (Dee, Brian Trio)
Bruised blues / Certain smile / Dream dancing / Elba mel delba / Second sight / Seven steps to heaven / In your own sweet way / Hermitage / Promised land / More bruised blues
CD _____ SPJCD 543
Spotlite / May '93 / Cadillac / Jazz Horizons / Swift.

Dee, David

GOIN' FISHIN'
Heatin' me up / Rainy night in Georgia / If I knew then / Special way of making love / Part time love / Goin' fishin' / Workin' this dream overtime / Lead me on / Thought my lovin' was over
CD _____ CDICH 1114
Ichiban / Oct '93 / Koch.

Dee Dee Brave

DEE DEE BRAVE
CD _____ CHAMCD 1025
Champion / Sep '91 / BMG.

Dee, Joey

HEY, LET'S TWIST (Best of Joey Dee & The Starliters) (Dee, Joey & The Starlighters)
Peppermint twist (part 1) / Peppermint twist (part 2) / Hey, let's twist / Roly poly / Joey's blues (Featuring Dave Brigati. CD only.) / Shout / Irresistible you (CD only.) / Crazy love (CD only.) / Everytime (I think about you) - part I / What kind of love is this / I lost my baby / Keep your mind on what you're doing (CD only.) / Help me pick up the pieces / Baby, you're driving me crazy / Hot pastrami / Dance, dance, dance / Ya ya / Fannie Mae
CD _____ CDROU 5010
Roulette / Aug '90 / EMI.

LIVE AT THE PEPPERMINT LOUNGE/ BACK AT THE PEPPERMINT LOUNGE (Dee, Joey & The Starlighters)
Peppermint twist / Ram-bunk-shush / Ya Ya / Sticks and stones / Shout / Peppermint twist (2) / Hold it / Fanny Mae / Honky tonk / Hot pastrami (with mashed potatoes) / C.C. rider / Talkin' 'bout you / Long tall Sally / Raindrops / Hello Josephine / Money (that's what I want) / Kansas City / You must have been a beautiful baby / Will you still love me tomorrow / Have you ever had the blues
CD _____ NEMCD 648
Sequel / Feb '94 / BMG.

Dee, Johnny

LOVE COMPILATION
Theme for Johnny Dee / When my heart goes wild / Goodbye flip flap guitar / Why I like Max Eider (Part 1) / Blue girl from north town / Day in Waterloo / Hey gentle girl / Bachelor kisses / So what / Why I like Max Eider (Part 3)
CD _____ MASKCD 038
Vinyl Japan / Mar '94 / Vital.

Dee, Kiki

ALMOST NAKED
CD _____ TB 01
Tickety Boo / Oct '95 / Grapevine.

PERFECT TIMING
Star / Loving you is sweeter than ever / Wild eyes / Twenty four hours / Perfect timing / Midnight flyer / There's a need / Another break / Love is just a moment away / You are my hope in this world
CD _____ 74321 19317-2
RCA / Apr '94 / BMG.

Dee, Sonny

CHICAGO - THAT'S JAZZ VOL.2 (Dee, Sonny Allstars)
Who's sorry now / My cutie's due at two to two / You're in kentucky sure as you're born / Trouble in mind / Mandy, make up your mind / Is it true what they say about Dixie / When / Mama's gone goodbye / Goodbye / Do you know what it means to miss New Orleans / Moonglow / Who cares / It's been so long / Lady's in love with you / Blue and broken hearted / Miss Annabelle Lee / Since my best gal turned me down
CD _____ LACD 28
Lake / Mar '93 / Target/BMG / Jazz Music / Direct / Cadillac / ADA.

Deebank, Maurice

INNER THOUGHT ZONE
Watery song / Four corners of the earth / Study No.1 / Golden hills / Silver fountain of Paradise Square / So Serene / Dance Of Deliverance / Pavanne / Tale from Scriabins lonely trail / Maestoso Con Anima
CD _____ CDMRED 61
Cherry Red / Nov '92 / Pinnacle.

Deee-Lite

DEW DROPS IN THE GARDEN
CD _____ 755961526-2
Elektra / Jul '94 / Warner Music.

INFINITY WITHIN
Runaway / Electric shock / Heart be still / Come on in, the dreams are fine / Two clouds above nine / Rubber lover / I had a dream... / Fuddy duddy judge / Pussy cat meow / I.F.O. / Thank you everyday / I won't give up
CD _____ 7559613132
Elektra / Jun '92 / Warner Music.

WORLD CLIQUE
Good beat / Power of love / Try me on...I'm very you / Smile on / What is love / World clique / E.S.P. / Groove is in the heart / Who was that / Deep ending w/plogo / Deee-lite theme (Mc,Cd only) / Build the bridge
CD _____ 7559609572
Elektra / Sep '90 / Warner Music.

Deems, Barrett

HOW D'YOU LIKE IT SO FAR
CD _____ DE 472
Delmark / Dec '95 / Hot Shot / ADA / CM / Direct / Cadillac.

Deep Forest

BOHEME
Anathasia / Marta's song / Gathering / Lament / Bulgarian melody / Deep folk song / Freedom cry / Twosome / Cafe europa / Katharina / Boheme
CD _____ 4786232
Columbia / May '95 / Sony.

DEEP FOREST
Deep forest / Sweet lullaby / Hunting / Night bird / First twilight / Savannah dance / Desert walk / White whisper / Second twilight / Sweet lullaby (mix) / Forest hymn
CD _____ 474178 2
Columbia / Feb '94 / Sony.

Deep Freeze Production

SLOWBONE
Cruise of the spacebird / Sleeper / Get this / Zombie warning / Somehow someway / Under your spell / Sometimes / Theme to a prelude / Showdown at Voodoo Creek / Free / Lost soul of arch stanton / Feelin' good
CD _____ SSRCD 1
Sureshot / Mar '95 / Vital.

Deep Purple

24 CARAT PURPLE
Woman from Tokyo / Fireball / Strange kind of woman / Never before / Black night / Speed king / Smoke on the water / Child in time
CD _____ CDFA 3132
Fame / Oct '87 / EMI.

ANTHOLOGY, THE (2CD/MC Set)
Hush / Mandrake root / Shield / Wring that neck / Bird has flown / Bloodsucker / Speed king / Black night / Child in time / Fireball / Strange kind of woman (live) / Highway star / Smoke on the water / Pictures of home / Woman from Tokyo / Smooth dancer / Sail away / Lay down stay down / Burn (live) / Stormbringer / Hold on / Gypsy / Mistreated (live) / Gettin' tighter / Love child / You keep on moving / No one came
CD Set _____ CDEM 1374
EMI / Mar '91 / EMI.

BATTLE RAGES ON, THE
Battle rages on / Lick it up / Anya / Talk about love / Time to kill / Ramshackle man / Twist in the tale / Nasty piece of work / Solitaire / One man's meat
CD _____ 74321154202
RCA / Aug '95 / BMG.

BOOK OF TALIESYN/SHADES OF DEEP PURPLE/DEEP PURPLE (3CD Set)
Listen, learn, read on / Wring that neck / Kentucky woman / Exposition / We can work it out / Shield / Anthem / River deep, mountain high / And the address / Hush / One more rainy day / Prelude / Happiness / I'm so glad / Mandrake / Root / Help / Love help me / Hey Joe / Chasing shadows / Blind / Lalena / Fault line / Painter / Why didn't Rosemary / Bird has flown / April
CD Set _____ CDOMB 002
Harvest / Oct '95 / EMI.

BURN
Burn / Might just take your life / Lay down stay down / Sail away / You fool no one / What's goin' on here / Mistreated / A-Zoo
CD _____ CZ 203
EMI / Jul '89 / EMI.

CHILD IN TIME
Nobody's home / Mean streak / Wasted sunsets / Hungry daze / Unwritten law / Mad dog / Spanish archer / Mitzi dupree / Woman from Tokyo (live) / Child in time (live) / Strange kind of woman (live) / Highway star (live)
CD _____ 5513392
Spectrum/Karussell / Aug '95 / PolyGram / THE.

COME HELL OR HIGH WATER
Highway star / Black night / Twist in the tale / Perfect strangers / Anyone's daughter / Child in time / Anya / Speed king / Smoke on the water
CD _____ 74321234162
RCA / Oct '94 / BMG.

COME TASTE THE BAND
Comin' home / Lady Luck / Gettin' tighter / Dealer / I need love / Drifter / Love child / This time around / Owed to 'G' / You keep on moving
CD _____ CDFA 3318
Fame / Jul '95 / EMI.

CONCERTO FOR GROUP AND ORCHESTRA
Wring that neck / Child in time / Moderato - allegro: First movement / Andante: Second movement / Vivace - presto: Third movement
CD _____ CZ 342
EMI / Jul '90 / EMI.

DEEP PURPLE
Chasing shadows / Blind / Lalena / Fault line / Painter / Why didn't Rosemary / Bird has flown / April part 1
CD _____ CDFA 3317
Fame / Apr '95 / EMI.

DEEP PURPLE FAMILY ALBUM (Various Artists)
If you've gotta pick a baby / You'll never stop me loving you / I take what I want / I can see through you / Hush / Sun's a risin' / Black night / Into the fire (live) / Burn / Love is all / You keep on moving / Kill the king (Live) / Arabella (Live) / Northwinds / L.A. cut off / Stallion / Nervous / Clouds and rain / Perfect strangers (live)
CD _____ VSOPCD 187
Connoisseur / May '93 / Pinnacle.

DEEP PURPLE IN CONCERT
Speed king / Wring that neck / Child in time / Mandrake root / Highway star / Strange kind of woman / Lazy / Never before / Space truckin' / Lucille / Smoke on the water
CD Set _____ CDEM 1434
EMI / Feb '92 / EMI.

DEEPEST PURPLE
Black night / Speed king / Fireball / Strange kind of woman / Child in time / Woman from Tokyo / Highway star / Space truckin' / Burn / Demon's eye / Stormbringer / Smoke on the water
CD _____ CDFA 3239
Fame / Jul '90 / EMI.

FIREBALL
Fireball / No, no, no / Demon's eye / Mule / Fools / No one came / Anyone's daughter
CD _____ CZ 30
EMI / Jan '88 / EMI.

GEMINI SUITE-LIVE
Guitar/Voice / Organ/Bass / Drums/Finale
CD _____ RPM 114
RPM / Jul '93 / Pinnacle.

HOUSE OF BLUE LIGHT
Bad attitude / Unwritten law / Call of the wild / Mad dog / Black and white / Hard lovin' woman / Spanish archer / Strangeways / Mitzi dupree / Dead or alive
CD _____ 831 318-2
Polydor / Jan '87 / PolyGram.

IN ROCK (25th Anniversary Edition)
Speed king / Blood sucker / Child in time / Flight of the rat / Into the fire / Living wreck / Hard lovin' man / Black night / Studio chat 1 / Speed king (1) (piano version) / Studio chat 2 / Cry free (Roger Glover Mix) / Studio chat 3 / Jam stew (Unreleased Instrumental)

/ Studio chat 4 / Flight of the rat (90's Vocal Mix Bass Up) / Studio chat 5 / Woffle and speed king (Roger Glover Remix) / Studio chat 6 / Black night #1 (unedited Roger Glover mix)
CD _____ CDDEEPP 1
Harvest / Jun '95 / EMI.

INTERVIEW PICTURE DISC
CD P.Disc _____ CBAK 4054
Baktabak / Apr '92 / Baktabak.

KNEBWORTH LIVE 1985
Highway star / Nobody's home / Strange kind of woman / Gypsy's kiss / Perfect strangers / Lazy / Knocking at your back door / Space truckin' / Difficult to cure / Speed king / Black night / Smoke on the water
CD _____ DPVSOPCD 163
Connoisseur / Jun '91 / Pinnacle.

KNOCKING AT YOUR BACK DOOR
CD _____ 511438-2
Polydor / Mar '92 / PolyGram.

LIVE IN JAPAN
Highway star / Child in time / Mule (drum solo) / Strange kind of woman / Lazy / Space truckin' / Black night / Speed king
CD _____ CDEM 1510
EMI / Nov '93 / EMI.

MACHINE HEAD
Highway star / Maybe I'm a Leo / Pictures of home / Never before / Smoke on the water / Lazy / Space truckin'
CD _____ CDFA 3158
Fame / May '89 / EMI.

MADE IN EUROPE (LIVE)
Burn / Mistreated / Lady double dealer / You fool no one / Stormbringer
CD _____ CZ 344
EMI / Jul '90 / EMI.

MADE IN JAPAN
Highway star / Child in time / Smoke on the water / Mule / Strange kind of woman / Lazy / Space truckin'
CD _____ CDFA 3268
Fame / Oct '92 / EMI.

NOBODY'S PERFECT - LIVE
Highway star / Strange kind of woman / Perfect strangers / Hard lovin' woman / Bad attitude / Knocking at your back door / Child in time / Lazy / Black night / Woman from Tokyo / Smoke on the water / Space truckin'
CD _____ 835 897-2
Polydor / Jun '88 / PolyGram.

ON THE WINGS OF A RUSSIAN FOXBAT
Burn / Lady Luck / Getting tighter / Lovechild / Smoke on the water / Space truckin' / You fool no one / Stormbringer / Highway star / Going down / Highway star / Smoke on the water/Georgia on my mind
CD _____ DPVSOPCD 217
Connoisseur / May '95 / Pinnacle.

PERFECT STRANGERS
Knocking at your back door / Under the gun / Nobody's home / Mean streak / Perfect strangers / Gypsy's kiss / Wasted sunsets / Hungry daze / Not responsible (MC only)
CD _____ 823 777-2
Polydor / Mar '91 / PolyGram.

PROGRESSION
Perfect strangers / Under the gun / Knocking at your back door / Gypsy's kiss / Not responsible / Black night (live) / Smoke on the water (live) / Hush / Bad attitude / Dead or alive / Hard lovin' woman / Call of the wilff
CD _____ 5500272
Spectrum/Karussell / May '93 / PolyGram / THE.

PURPENDICULAR
CD _____ 74321338022
RCA / Jan '96 / BMG.

PURPLE RAINBOWS
Black night / Speed king / Child in time (Not on LP) / Strange kind of woman / Fireball / Smoke on the water / Woman from Tokyo (Not on LP) / Perfect strangers / Hush ('88) / Since you been gone / I surrender / Fool for your loving (original) / Here I go again (US remix) / Night games / Rock 'n' roll children
CD _____ 845534-2
PolyGram TV / Apr '94 / PolyGram.

SCANDINAVIAN NIGHTS
Wring that neck / Speed king / Into the fire / Paint it black / Mandrake root / Child in time / Black night
CD Set _____ DPVSOPCD 125
Connoisseur / Oct '88 / Pinnacle.

SHADES OF DEEP PURPLE
And the address / Hush / One more rainy day / Prelude: happiness / I'm so glad / Mandrake root / Help / Love help me / Hey Joe
CD _____ CDFA 3314
Fame / Feb '95 / EMI.

SINGLES - A'S & B'S
Hush / One more rainy day / Emmaretta / Wring that neck / Hallelujah / April, part 1 / Black night / Speed king / Strange kind of woman / I'm alone / Demon's eye / Fireball

/ Kentucky woman / Bird has flown / Never before / When a blind man cries / Smoke on the water / Black night (live) / Might just take your life / Coronarias rediq / You keep on moving / Lovechild
CD _____ CDP 781 009 2
EMI / Jan '93 / EMI.

SLAVES AND MASTERS
King of dreams / Cut runs deep / Fire in the basement / Truth hurts / Breakfast in bed / Love conquers all / Fortune teller / Too much is not enough / Wicked ways
CD _____ 7432118719-2
RCA / Apr '94 / BMG.

STORMBRINGER
Stormbringer / Love don't mean a thing / Holy man / Hold on / Lady double dealer / You can't do it right / High ball shooter / Gypsy / Soldier of fortune
CD _____ CZ 142
EMI / Oct '88 / EMI.

THIRD ALBUM
Chasing shadows / Blind / Lalena / Painter / Why didn't Rosemary / Bird has flown / April
CD _____ CZ 172
Harvest / Mar '89 / EMI.

WHO DO WE THINK WE ARE
Woman from Tokyo / Mary Long / Super trouper / Smooth dancer / Rat bat blue / Place in line / Our lady
CD _____ CDFA 3311
Fame / Dec '94 / EMI.

Deep Throat

VERSION 3.0
CD _____ CDDVN 20
Devotion / Jun '93 / Pinnacle.

Deepika

I ALT SLAGS LYS
CD _____ FXCD 118
Kirkelig Kulturverksted / Jul '93 / ADA.

Dees, Sam

SECOND TO NONE
We always come back strong / Tag / Your love is like a boomerang / Number one, second to none / Home wreckers / Your fool or your man / World don't owe you nothing / I like to party / I'm gonna give you just enough rope (To hang yourself) / Cry to me / Who are you gonna love (Your woman or your wife) / Good guys don't always win / Vanishing love / Nothing comes to a sleeper but a dream / I wish that I could be him / False alarm / You've been doing wrong for so long / Win or lose / Run to me / Help me / World / Touch me with your love / Just my alibi / Worn out broken heart
CD _____ CDKEND 125
Kent / Jun '95 / Pinnacle.

Def Leppard

ADRENALIZE
Let's get rocked / Heaven is / Make love like a man / Tonight / White lightning / Stand up (kick love into motion) / Personal property / Have you ever / I wanna touch you / Tear it down
CD _____ 5109782
Bludgeon Riffola / Mar '92 / PolyGram.

CONVERSATIONALIZE
CD P.Disc _____ CBAK 4029
Baktabak / Feb '94 / Baktabak.

HIGH 'N' DRY
High 'n' dry (Saturday night) / You got me runnin' / Let it go / Another hit and run / Lady strange / On through the night / Mirror mirror (look into my eyes) / No, no, no / Bringin' on the heartbreak / Switch 625
CD _____ 818 836 2
Bludgeon Riffola / Jan '89 / PolyGram.

HYSTERIA
Women / Rocket / Animal / Love bites / Pour some sugar on me / Armageddon it / Gods of war / Don't shoot shotgun / Run riot / Hysteria / Excitable / Love and affection
CD _____ 830 675-2
Bludgeon Riffola / '87 / PolyGram.

ON THROUGH THE NIGHT
Answer to the master / Hello America / It could be you / It don't matter / Overture / Rock brigade / Rocks off / Satellite / Sorrow is a woman / When the walls came tumblin' down
CD _____ 8225 332
Bludgeon Riffola / Jan '89 / PolyGram.

PYROMANIA
Rock rock (til you drop) / Photograph / Stagefright / Too late for love / Die hard the hunter / Foolin' / Rock of ages / Comin' under fire / Action not words / Billy's got a gun
CD _____ 810308-2
Bludgeon Riffola / '88 / PolyGram.

RETRO ACTIVE
CD _____ 5183052
Bludgeon Riffola / '88 / PolyGram.

VAULT
Pour some sugar on me / Photograph / Love bites / Let's get shocked / Two steps behind / Animal / Heaven is / Rocket / When

love and hate collide / Action / Make love like a man / Armageddon it / Have you ever needed someone so bad / Rock of ages / Hysteria / Bringin' on the heartbreak
CD _____ 5286562
CD Set _____ 5286572
Bludgeon Riffola / Oct '95 / PolyGram.

Defecation

PURITY DILUTION
CD _____ NB 018CD
Nuclear Blast / Nov '92 / Plastic Head.

Defects

DEFECTIVE BREAKDOWN
CD _____ AHOY 29
Captain Oi / Dec '94 / Plastic Head.

Definition Of Sound

EXPERIENCE
Boom boom / Pass the vibes / Lucy / Will you love me / Experience / Here comes the sun / Feels like heaven / Child / Take me on / Mama's not coming home / Wishes in the wind
CD _____ 5287402
Fontana / Oct '95 / PolyGram.

LICK, THE
Looking good / Can I get over / What are you under / Together / Move your body / She hangs out / Sunshine and rain / Too young to know / Travelling man / Cry
CD _____ CIRCD 24
Circa / Sep '92 / EMI.

LOVE AND LIFE
When a lion awakens / Now is tomorrow / Passion and pain / Wear you love like heaven / Reality / Rise like the sun / What's goin' on / Dream girl / Change / Blues / Moira Jane's cafe / Won / City lights / Time is running out
CD _____ CIRCD 14
Circa / Jun '91 / EMI.

Defleshed

MA BELLE SCALPELLE
CD _____ IR 009CD
Invasion / Apr '95 / Plastic Head.

DeFrancesco, Joey

ALL ABOUT MY GIRL
Grilled cheese and bacon / Polka dots and moonbeams / Donna Lee / Alone together / Save your love for me / Blues for Joe F. / When Sunny gets blue / All about my girl
CD _____ MCD 5528
Muse / Sep '94 / New Note / CM.

LIVE AT THE 5 SPOT
Eternal one / Embraceable you / I'll remember April / Work song / Moonlight in Vermont / Impressions / All of me / Spectator
CD _____ 474045 2
Columbia / Apr '94 / Sony.

STREET OF DREAMS, THE
CD _____ BIGMO 20252E
Big Mo / Nov '95 / Direct / ADA.

DeFrancesco, John

COMIN' HOME
Comin' home baby / Bye bye blackbird / Satin doll / Watermelon man / Summertime / Organ blues / Soft winds / I've got a woman
CD _____ MCD 5531
Muse / Jul '95 / New Note / CM.

DOODLIN'
Doodlin' / All blues / Sonnymoon for two / Do you want to dance / Don't get around much anymore / Here's that rainy day / Blues for L.D.
CD _____ MCD 5501
Muse / Aug '93 / New Note / CM.

Defranco, Ani

NOT A PRETTY GIRL
CD _____ RBR 007CD
Righteous Babe / Nov '95 / ADA.

Defunkt

AVOID THE FUNK (Defunkt Anthology)
CD _____ HNCD 1320
Hannibal / May '89 / Vital / ADA.

CRISIS
CD _____ EMY 1352
Enemy / Mar '92 / Grapevine.

CUM FUNKY
CD _____ EMY 140-2
CD Set _____ EMY 144-2
Enemy / Nov '94 / Grapevine.

DEFUNKT SPECIAL EDITION (Live Tribute To Muddy Waters & Jimi Hendrix)
CD _____ EMY 148-2
Enemy / Nov '94 / Grapevine.

LIVE AND REUNIFIED
CD _____ EMY 145-2
Enemy / Nov '94 / Grapevine.

LIVE AT THE KNITTING FACTORY
CD _____ KFWCD 104
Knitting Factory / Nov '94 / Grapevine.

LIVE AT THE KNITTING FACTORY, NYC
CD Set _____ EMY 122
Enemy / Sep '91 / Grapevine.

DeGruy, Phil

INNUENDO OUT THE OTHER
Innuendo out the other / My girl / If I only had a brain / Naima / They can't take that away from me / Dear Sur / Wave / When the saints go marchin' in / When you wish upon a star / Woolly bully / Lazy bird / Blackbird / My bells / Blues for Rod Sterling / Freight train / See you in my dreams / Claire de lune / Out of the (music) box and inot the (John) Cage
CD _____ NYC 60132
NYC / Oct '95 / New Note.

Degville, Martin

WORLD WAR FOUR
CD _____ RRCD 138
Receiver / Apr '91 / Grapevine.

Deicide

AMON : FEASTING THE BEAST
Lunatic of God's creation / Sacrificial suicide / Crucifixation / Carnage in the temple of the damned / Dead by dawn / Blaspherererion / Feasting the beast / Day of darkness / Oblivious to nothing
CD _____ RR 91112
Roadrunner / Feb '93 / Pinnacle.

LEGION
CD _____ RC 91922
Roadrunner / Jun '92 / Pinnacle.

ONCE UPON THE CROSS
CD _____ RR 89492
Roadrunner / May '95 / Pinnacle.

Deighton Family

ACOUSTIC MUSIC TO SUIT MOST OCCASIONS
Travelling light / Matchbox / Two little boys / Muddy roads / Boll weevil song / Keep that candle burning / All shook up / Tennessee wig walk / Money / Handsome molly / Tin whistle / Blue suede shoes / Going down the road / Give the fiddler a dram
CD _____ FMSD 5010
Rogue / '89 / Sterns.

ROLLING HOME
I love you because / I can see clearly now / Save the last dance for me / Road to Newcastle / Green rolling hills of West Virginia / Reuben's train / Under the Boardwalk / I forgot to remember to forget / When I get home / Leather britches / Rollin' home / Has he got a friend / Gilbert Clancy's reel
CD _____ GLCD 1116
Green Linnet / '92 / Roots / CM / Direct / ADA.

Deighton, Matt

VILLAGER
CD _____ FOCUSCD 1
Focus / Jun '95 / Pinnacle.

Deine Lakaien

ACOUSTIC
CD _____ EFA 155882
Gymnastic / Sep '95 / SRD.

DARK STAR TOUR '92
CD _____ EFA 15567
Gymnastic / Apr '93 / SRD.

Deiseal

LONG LONG NOTE, THE
Shores of loch Ghamhna / Si beag si mor / Raindrops/The first of May / My love I miss her so / Long (long) note / Soporific/The rights of man / Mna na hEireann / Stranger at the gate/Boston blues / Lord inchiquin / Lakeside
CD _____ SCD 193
Starc / Jan '94 / ADA / Direct.

Deity Guns

100M
CD _____ RIK 001CD
Semantic / Feb '94 / Plastic Head.

TRANS LINES APPOINTMENT
CD _____ ABBCD 047
Big Cat / May '93 / SRD / Pinnacle.

Dekker, Desmond

ACTION (Dekker, Desmond & The Aces)
CD _____ LG 21106
Lagoon / Nov '94 / Magnum Music Group / THE.

BLACK & DEKKER
Israelites / Lickin' stick / It mek / Please don't bend / Many rivers to cross / Hippo / 007 / Workout / Problems / Rude boy train / Pickney gal / Why fight
CD _____ STIFFCD 11
Disky / Jan '94 / THE / BMG / Discovery / Pinnacle.

BLACK & DEKKER/COMPASS POINT
Israelites / Lickin' stick / It mek / Please don't bend / Many rivers to cross / Hippo /

007 / Workout / Problems / Rude boy train / Pickney gal / Why fight / I'll get by / Moving on / We can and shall / Hurt so bad / Isabella / Come back to me / Build a believe/My destiny / Big headed / That's my woman / Allamanna
CD _____ DOJOCD 77
Dojo / Feb '94 / BMG.

COMPASS POINT
I'll get by / Moving on / We can and shall / Hurt so bad / Isabella / Come back to me / Cindy / I do believe / My destiny / Big headed / That's my woman / Allamanna
CD _____ REP 4223-WY
Repertoire / Aug '91 / Pinnacle / Cadillac.

CRUCIAL CUTS - BEST OF DESMOND DEKKER
CD _____ MCCD 115
Music Club / Jun '93 / Disc / THE / CM.

ISRAELITES
Israelites / Beware / Everybody join hands / It mek / Sing a little song / Busted lad / My world is blue / Mother nature / Money and friends / No place like home
CD _____ CDTRO 9104
Trojan / Aug '92 / Jetstar / Total/BMG.

ISRAELITES
CD _____ CDCD 1078
Charly / Apr '93 / Charly / THE / Cadillac.

ISRAELITES
CD _____ 12361
Laserlight / May '94 / Target/BMG.

KING OF KINGS (Dekker, Desmond & The Specials)
CD _____ CDTRL 324
Trojan / Mar '94 / Jetstar / Total/BMG.

KING OF SKA
CD _____ CDTRL 292
Trojan / Mar '94 / Jetstar / Total/BMG.

MUSIC LIKE DIRT
King of SKA / It's a shame / Rudie got soul / Rude boy train / Mother's young gal / Sweet music / You've got your troubles / Keep a cool head / Mother long tongue / Personal possession / Bongo gal / Don't blame me / Hey Grandma / Music like dirt / Nincompoop / It mek / Problems / Coconut water
CD _____ CDTRL 301
Trojan / Mar '94 / Jetstar / Total/BMG.

OFFICIAL LIVE AND RARE (Dekker, Desmond & The Aces)
CD Set _____ CDTRD 404
Trojan / Nov '89 / Jetstar / Total/BMG.

ORIGINAL REGGAE HITSOUND, THE (Dekker, Desmond & The Aces)
007 / Get up, Edina / Beautiful and dangerous / Shing a ling / Pretty Africa / Wise man / Sabotage / Unity / It pays / Israelites / It mek / Warlock / Archie wah wah / Pickney girl / Reggae recipe / You can get it if you really want / Hippopotamus song / Lickin' stick / More you live
CD _____ CDTRL 226
Trojan / Mar '94 / Jetstar / Total/BMG.

VOICE OF SKA (Dekker, Desmond & The Aces)
CD _____ EMPRCD 594
Emporio / Oct '95 / THE / Disc / CM.

Del Amitri

CHANGE EVERYTHING
CD _____ 3953852
A&M / Jun '92 / PolyGram.

DEL AMITRI
Heard through a wall / Hammering heart / Former owner / Sticks and stones girl / Deceive yourself (in ignorant heaven) / I was here / Crows in a wheatfield / Keepers / Ceasefire / Breaking bread
CD _____ CCD 1499
Chrysalis / Dec '90 / EMI.

TWISTED
Food for songs / Start with me / Here and now / One thing left to do / Tell her this / Being somebody else / Roll to me / Crashing down / It might as well be you / Never enough / It's never too late to be alone / Driving with the brakes on
CD _____ 5403962
A&M / Aug '95 / PolyGram.

WAKING HOURS
Kiss this thing goodbye / Opposite view / Move away Jimmy Blue / Stone cold sober / You're gone / When I want you / This side of the morning / Empty / Hatful of rain / Nothing ever happens
CD _____ 3970102
A&M / Apr '95 / PolyGram.

Del Gastor, Paco

FLAMENCO DE LA FRONTERA
CD _____ NI 5352
Nimbus / Oct '94 / Nimbus.

Del Rey, Teisco

MANY MOODS OF TEISCO DEL REY
CD _____ UPSTART 007
Upstart / Jul '94 / Direct / ADA.

Del Tha Funky Homosapien

I WISH MY BROTHER GEORGE WAS HERE
What is a booty / Mistadobalina / Wacky world of rapid transit / Pissin' on your steps / Dark skin girls / Money for sex / Ahonetwo, ahonetwo / Prelude / Dr. Bombay / Sunny meadowz / Sleepin' on my couch / Hoodz come in dozens / Same old thing / Ya lil crumbsnatchers
CD _____ 755961133-2
Elektra / Dec '91 / Warner Music.

NO NEED FOR ALARM
You're in shambles / Catch a bad one / Wack M.C.'s / No need for alarm / Boo boo heads / Treats for the kiddies / Worldwide / No more worries / Wrongplace / In and out / Don't forget / Miles to go / Check it ooout / Thank youse
CD _____ 755961529-2
Elektra / Dec '93 / Warner Music.

Del-Vikings

COME GO WITH ME
Come go with me / Don't be a fool / In the still of the night / Yours / I'm spinning / Over the rainbow / White cliffs of Dover
CD _____ FLYCD 34
Flyright / Apr '91 / Hot Shot / Wellard / Jazz Music / CM.

DEL-VIKINGS VOL.2
CD _____ FLYCD 53
Flyright / Nov '92 / Hot Shot / Wellard / Jazz Music / CM.

Delafose, Geno

FRENCH ROCKIN' BOOGIE
CD _____ ROUCD 2131
Rounder / Aug '94 / CM / Direct / ADA / Cadillac.

Delafose, John

BLUES STAY AWAY FROM ME (Delafose, John & The Eunice Playboys)
CD _____ ROU 2121CD
Rounder / Jan '94 / CM / Direct / ADA / Cadillac.

JOE PETE GOT TWO WOMEN
CD _____ ARHCD 335
Arhoolie / Apr '95 / ADA / Direct / Cadillac.

LIVE AT RICHARD'S ZYDECO DANCE HALL (Vol. 2) (Delafose, John & The Eunice Playboys)
CD _____ CD 2070
Rounder / '88 / CM / Direct / ADA / Cadillac.

Delagado, Luis

AL ANDALUS
CD _____ 21042CD
Sonifolk / Jun '94 / ADA / CM.

Delakian, Michel

BIARRITZ
CD _____ BBRC 9107
Big Blue / Dec '91 / Harmonia Mundi.

Delaney & Bonnie

ACCEPT NO SUBSTITUTE
Get ourselves together / Someday / Ghetto / When the battle is over / Dirty old man / Love me a little bit longer / I can't take it much longer / Do right woman, do right man / Soldiers of the cross / Gift of love
CD _____ CDTB 050
Thunderbolt / Feb '88 / Magnum Music Group.

HOME
It's been a long time coming / We can love / Everybody loves a winner / Just plain beautiful / Pour your love on me / Right now love / My baby specializes / Things get better / Hard to say goodbye / Piece of my heart
CD _____ CDSXE 029
Stax / May '90 / Pinnacle.

ON TOUR WITH ERIC CLAPTON (Delaney & Bonnie/Friends)
Things get better / Poor Elijah / Only you know and I know / I don't want to discuss it / That's what my man is for / Where there's a will / Comin' home / Little Richard medley
CD _____ 7567903972
Atlantic / Feb '92 / Warner Music.

Delaney's Rhythm Section

NO JOKIN'...WE'RE SMOKIN'
CD _____ BIZ 10012
Three / Sep '95 / EWM.

Delano, Peter

PETER DELANO
CD _____ 519602-2
Verve / Mar '94 / PolyGram.

Delavier, Katrien

IRISH HARP, THE
CD _____ PS 65095
Playasound / Sep '92 / Harmonia Mundi / ADA.

Delerium

FACES FORMS AND ILLUSIONS
CD _____ DCD 9008
Dossier / May '89 / SRD.

MORPHEUS
CD _____ DCD 9010
Dossier / '89 / SRD.

SEMANTIC SPACES
CD _____ W 230092
Nettwerk / Apr '95 / Vital / Pinnacle.

SPHERE
CD _____ EFA 08453-2
Dossier / Feb '94 / SRD.

SPHERES II
CD _____ EFA 08460 2
Dossier / Sep '94 / SRD.

SYROPHENIKAN
CD _____ DCD 9015
Dossier / '89 / SRD.

ZZOOOUHH
CD _____ PROPH 1CD
Prophecy / Jan '91 / Plastic Head.

Delevantes

LONG ADOUT THAT TIME
CD _____ ROUCD 9041
Rounder / May '95 / CM / Direct / ADA / Cadillac.

Delgado, Isaac

EL ANO QUE VIENE
El ano que viene / No me mires a los ojos / Ayudeme senora / Por que paro / La rompecorazones / La vida sin esperanza / Ella todo y nada / Yo tengo un corazon / Sopresa de amor / Potpurri para el sonero
CD _____ 66058089
RMM / Feb '96 / New Note.

Delgado, Junior

MR. FIXIT
CD _____ RNCD 2055
Rhino / May '94 / Jetstar / Magnum Music Group / THE.

TREASURE FOUND
CD _____ IMCD 001
Incredible Music / Mar '95 / Jetstar.

Delicatessen

SKIN TOUCHING WATER
I'm just alive / C.F. Kane / Zebra/Monkey/ Liar / Red, blue and green / Watercress / Classic adventure / Appeased / Chomsky / You cut my throat, I'll cut yours / Sick of flying saucers / Smiling you're stupid / Inviting both sisters out to dinner / Advice / Love's liquid / Froth / If she was anybody else
CD _____ STFCD 001X
CD _____ STFCD 001
Starfish / May '95 / Pinnacle.

Delicious Monster

JOIE DE VIVRE
CD _____ FLUTE 7CD
Flute / Oct '93 / Pinnacle.

Delico, Stephane

AQUARELLES
CD _____ ED 13024CD
L'Empreinte Digitale / Jul '95 / Harmonia Mundi / ADA.

Dello, Pete

INTO YOUR EARS...PLUS (Dello, Pete & Friends)
It's what you've got / There's nothing that I can do for you / I'm a gambler / Harry the earwig / Do I still figure in your life / Uptight Basil / Taking the heart out of love / Here me only / On a time said Sylvie / Good song / It's the way / Go away / Arise Sir Henry / Madam Chairman (of the committee)
CD _____ SEECD 257
See For Miles/C5 / Sep '89 / Pinnacle.

Dells

PASSIONATE BREEZES (Best Of The Dells 1975-1991)
CD _____ 5280922
Mercury / Sep '95 / PolyGram.

SECOND TIME
Can we skip that part / You can depend on me / My lady, so perfect for me / No win situation / Hott / That's how heartaches are made / Thought of you just a little too much / Sweetness
CD _____ URG 4108CD
Urgent / Sep '91 / Koch.

Delmar, Elaine

S'WONDERFUL
Some of my best friends / Touch of your lips / In a sentimental mood / 'S Wonderful / Stardust / I did it all for you / Little girl blue / Carioca / They can't take that away from me / We could be flying / They say it's wonderful / Ol' man river / There's a small hotel for sale
CD _____ JHRCD 027
Ronnie Scott's Jazz House / Sep '91 / Jazz Music / Magnum Music Group / Cadillac.

Delmirani, Ugo

BRAZILIAN SONG BOOK
Felicidade / Uptown samba / Cancao do sal / Mixing / Arrastao / Barquinho diferente / Partido novo / Lullaby / San Salavador
CD _____ JM 005
JM / Oct '95 / New Note.

Delmonas

DELMONAS/ DELMONAS 5
Dr. Goldfoot / Heard about him / Why don't you smile now / Black elk speaks / Hound dog / Delmona / I feel like giving in / Keep your big mouth shut / When I want you / Black Ludella / Your love / Don't fall in love (every single time) / Jealousy / Jealousy (French version) / That boy of mine / Can't sit down / Kiss me honey / I've got everything I need / Uncle Willy / Farmer John / You did him wrong / Dangerous charms / Long drop / I feel alright
CD _____ ASKCD 032
Vinyl Japan / Oct '93 / Vital.

Delmore Brothers

FREIGHT TRAIN BOOGIE
Blues stay away from me / Freight train boogie / Trouble ain't nothin' but the blues / Boogie woogie baby / Rounder's blues / Mobile boogie / Used car blues / Pan American blues / Pan American boogie / Field hand man / Brown's ferry blues / Peach tree street boogie / Blues you never lose / Steamboat boogie / Muddy water / Sand mountain blues / Hillbilly boogie / You can't do wrong and get by / Kentucky Mountain / Weary day / Take it to the Captain
CD _____ CDCHD 455
Ace / Aug '93 / Pinnacle / Cadillac / Complete/Pinnacle.

Delray, Leon

I'M STILL WAITIN'
All the lonely girls / Please don't ask me why / Macho man / I'm not in love / My love for you / Day by day / Good mornin' / I wanna be free (Creepin') / Unfree / I'm still waiting (for your call) / I wonder will we ever learn / I wanna be free (reprise)
CD _____ 101S 8770572
101 South / Nov '93 / New Note.

Delta 9

NO BLUFF
CD _____ 503632
Declic / Apr '95 / Jetstar.

Delta Angel

SILHOUETTE
CD _____ FILERCD 413
Profile / Jun '91 / Pinnacle.

Delta Of Venus

NEUTRAL, A
CD _____ SR 1006
Scout / Jan '96 / Koch.

Deltas

BOOGIE DISEASE
CD _____ NERDCD 002
Nervous / Jun '95 / Nervous / Magnum Music Group.

LIVE
Raging sea / You can't judge a book by the cover / As you like it / Tuffer than tuff / Boogie disease / Gimme the drugs / Cigarette / Cool off baby / Teenage ball / Long black train / Honky tonk women / Nine below zero / I got you / How come you do me / Kokomo
CD _____ JE 256
Visionary/Jettisoundz / Mar '93 / THE / Pinnacle.

TUFFER THAN TUFF LIVE
CD _____ LOMACD 34
Loma / Nov '94 / BMG.

Deltones

NANA CHOC CHOC IN PARIS
CD _____ PHZCD 31
Unicorn / Jan '89 / Plastic Head.

Deluigi, Silvana

TANGOS
CD _____ SM 16132
Wergo / Jan '96 / Harmonia Mundi / ADA / Cadillac.

TANGUERA - WOMAN IN TANGO
CD _____ SM 1503-2
Wergo / Nov '92 / Harmonia Mundi / ADA / Cadillac.

Demasse, Seleshe

SONGS FROM ETHIOPIA
CD _____ SM 1516-2
Wergo / Nov '93 / Harmonia Mundi / ADA / Cadillac.

Dembo, Konte

BAATOTO
CD _____ WWCD 05
World / Dec '88 / Grapevine.

DeMent, Iris

INFAMOUS ANGEL
Let the mystery be / These hills / Hotter than mojave in my heart / When love was young / Our town / Fifty miles of elbow room / Infamous angel / Sweet forgiveness / After you've gone / Mama's opry / Higher ground
CD _____ 936245238-2
Warner Bros. / May '93 / Warner Music.

MY LIFE
Sweet is the melody / You've done nothing wrong / Calling for you / Childhood memories / No time to cry / Troublesome waters / Mom and Dad's waltz / Easy's getting harder every day / Shores of Jordan / My life
CD _____ 936245493-2
Warner Bros. / Mar '94 / Warner Music.

Demented Are Go

BEST OF DEMENTED ARE GO, THE
Pervy in the park / Busty hymen / Holy hack jack / Pickled and preserved / Transvestite blues / PVC chair / Nuke mutants / Satan's rejects / Cripple in the woods / Call of the wired / Surf ride to oblivion / Shadow crypt / Human slug / Sick spasmoid / Country woman / One shrp knife / Brain damaged chile / Flight 103
CD _____ DOJOCD 125
Dojo / May '93 / BMG.

IN SICKNESS AND IN HEALTH/KICKED OUT OF HELL
Be bop a lula / Pervy in the park / (I was born on a) Busted hymen / Holy hack jack / Frenzied beat / Pickled and preserved / Crazy horses / Transvestite blues / Rubber buccaneer / Vibrate / Rubber love / Nuke mutants / PVC chair / Don't go into the woods / Satan's rejects / Human slug / Cripple in the woods / Decomposition / Cast iron arm / Call of the wired / Rubber plimsoles / Shadow crypt / Surf ride to oblivion / Old black Joe / Sick spasmoid / Vietnam / Jet tune boogie
CD _____ LOMACD 15
Loma / Feb '94 / BMG.

LIVE AT THE KLUB FOOT APRIL '87
CD _____ DOJOCD 23
Dojo / Jun '94 / BMG.

TANGENITAL MADNESS
CD _____ DAGCD 1
Fury / Apr '95 / Magnum Music Group / Nervous.

Demented Ted

PROMISE IMPURE
Existance lies beneath / Despair / Psychopathology / Incisions / Liquid remains / Gehillcide / Between two eternities / Forgotten
CD _____ CDVEST 2
Bulletproof / Mar '94 / Pinnacle.

Dementia

RECUPERATE FROM REALITY
CD _____ CORPSE 003CD
Tombstone / Oct '91 / Nervous.

Demolition 23

DEMOLITION 23
CD _____ CDMFN 176
Music For Nations / Oct '94 / Pinnacle.

Demolition Hammer

EPIDEMIC OF VIOLENCE
CD _____ CM 97282
Century Media / Sep '94 / Plastic Head.

TIMEBOMB
CD _____ CM 77071-2
Century Media / Aug '94 / Plastic Head.

TORTURED EXISTENCE
CD _____ 0897132
Century Media / Sep '90 / Plastic Head.

Demon

BLOW OUT
CD _____ SONICCD 11
Sonic / May '92 / Total/BMG.

BRITISH STANDARD APPROVED
CD _____ SONICCD 6
Sonic / Sep '90 / Total/BMG.

ONE HELLUVA NIGHT (Live in West Germany)
CD Set _____ DEMONCD 1
Sonic / Aug '90 / Total/BMG.

PLAGUE, THE
Plague / Nowhere to run / Fever in the city / Blackheath / Writings on the wall / Only sane man / Step to far
CD _____ HTDCD 36
HTD / Jul '95 / Pinnacle.

TAKING THE WORLD BY STORM
Commercial dynamite / Taking the world by storm / Life brigade / Remembrance day / What do you think about hell / Blue skies in Red Square / Time has come
CD _____ HTDCD 32
HTD / Mar '95 / Pinnacle.

Demone, Gitane

LOVE FOR SALE
CD _____ CD 004
Dark Vinyl / Jan '91 / Plastic Head.

Demoniac

PREPARE FOR WAR
CD _____ EOR 003CD
Osmose / Apr '95 / Plastic Head.

Dempsey, Little Jimmy

GUITAR MUSIC
CD _____ CNCD 5937
Disky / Jun '92 / THE / BMG / Discovery / Pinnacle.

Demus, Chaka

BAD BAD CHAKA
CD _____ 792112
Jammy's / Jan '94 / Jetstar.

CHAKA DEMUS & PLIERS GOLD (Demus, Chaka & Pliers)
Bogle dance / Thief / Nuh me / World a girls / Winning machine / You send come call me / Blood in a eyes / Sweet Jamaica / Love up de gal / Terror girl wine / Pretty face
CD _____ CRCD 11
Charm / Apr '92 / Jetstar.

CHAKA DEMUS MEETS SHABBA RANKS
CD _____ RNCD 2101
Rhino / Apr '95 / Jetstar / Magnum Music Group / THE.

GAL WINE (Demus, Chaka & Pliers)
CD _____ VYDCD 7
Vine Yard / Sep '95 / Grapevine.

GAL WINE WINE (Demus, Chaka & Pliers)
CD _____ GRELCD 173
Greensleeves / Jul '92 / Total/BMG / Jetstar / SRD.

RUFF THIS YEAR (Demus, Chaka & Pliers)
CD _____ RASCD 3112
Greensleeves / Apr '93 / Total/BMG / Jetstar / SRD.

TEASE ME (Demus, Chaka & Pliers)
Tease me / She don't let nobody / Nuh betta nuh deh / Bam bam / Friday evening / Let's make it tonight / One nation under a groove / Tracy / Sunshine day / Murder she wrote / Roadrunner / I wanna be your man / Twist and shout / Gal wine and shout
CD _____ CIDMX 1102
Mango / Jan '91 / Vital / PolyGram.

WORLD ENTERPRISE (Demus, Chaka & Pliers)
CD _____ RNCD 2028
Rhino / Nov '93 / Jetstar / Magnum Music Group / THE.

Den Fule

LUGUMLEIK
CD _____ XOUCD 104
Xource / Oct '94 / ADA / Cadillac.

SKALV
CD _____ XOU 109CD
Xource / Apr '95 / ADA / Cadillac.

Denayer, Oscar

ACCORDION FAVOURITES
CD _____ HRCD 8056
Disky / Sep '94 / THE / BMG / Discovery / Pinnacle.

Denim

DENIM ON ICE
Great pub rock revival / If fell off the back of the lorry / Romeo Jones is in love / Bumburger / Supermodels / Shut up Sidney / Mrs. Mills / Best song in the world / Synthesizers in the rain / Job centre / Council house / Glue and smack / Jane Suck died in 77 / Grandad's false teeth / Silly rabbit / Don't bite too much out of the apple / Myriad of hoops / Denim on ice
CD _____ ECHCD 008
Echo / Feb '96 / Vital.

Denio, Amy

BIRTHING CHAIR BLUES
CD _____ KFWCD 111
Knitting Factory / Nov '94 / Grapevine.

Denison/Kimball Trio

SOUL MACHINE
CD _____ GR 22CD
Skingraft / May '95 / SRD.

WALLS IN THE CITY
CD _____ GR 16CD
Skingraft / Oct '94 / SRD.

Dennehy, Tim

WINTER'S TEAR, A (Traditional & Original Songs Of Love, Loss & Longing)
CD _____ CICD 002
Clo Iar-Chonnachta / Dec '93 / CM.

Dennerlein, Barbara

BARBARA DENNERLEIN
CD _____ CD 250964
Bebab / Nov '91 / Harmonia Mundi / Cadillac.

LIVE ON TOUR (Dennerlein, Barbara, Oscar Klein & Charly Antolini)
CD _____ CD 250965
Bebab / Nov '91 / Harmonia Mundi / Cadillac.

Dennis, Denny

I SING YOU A THOUSAND LOVE SONGS
May I have the next romance with you / I stumbled over love / Time on my hands / Hurry home / Rosita / Sweet is the word for you / I have eyes / If I should fall in love again / Will you remember / Goodnight my love / Sweet someone / Pretty little quaker girl / Thru the courtesy of love / Deep purple / I let a song go out of my heart / Blue Hawaii / South of the border / Always and always / Dearest love / Where are the songs we sung
CD _____ PAR 2026
Parade / Jul '94 / Koch / Cadillac.

TRIBUTE, A
Angels never leave heaven / Bird on the wing / Blue skies are just around the corner / Did you ever see a dream walking / Glory of love / Goodbye to summer / Hear my song Violetta / I fall in love with you every day / I was lucky / I wished on the moon / I'll string along with you / If you please / In the middle of a kiss / In the mission by the sea / Just one more chance / Let's call the whole thing off / Let's face the music and dance / Louise / Mexicali Rose / South of the border / Stardust / Two sleepy people / Way you look tonight / Whispers in the dark / Would you
CD _____ CDAJA 5127
Living Era / '94 / Koch.

Denny & Dunipace Pipe...

PLAY SCOTLANDS BEST (Denny & Dunipace Pipe Band)
Scotland the brave (Traditional.4/4 March.) / Rowan tree (Traditional.4/4 March.) / Bonnie Galloway (Traditional.4/4 March.) / Old rustic bridge (Traditional.4/4 March.) / Black Watch polka (Polka & Jias) / Mull of Kintyre (Polka & Jias) / Green hills (3/4 March) / When the battle is over / Lynn Shannon's wedding / Dunipace (Traditional) / Danish knife grinder's spring song (Traditional) / Crossing the Minch (Traditional) / A.A. Cameron's strathspey (Traditional) / Miller of Drone (Traditional) / Donald's wedding (Traditional) / McFarlane's reel (Traditional) / John Wilson / Muckin' o' Geordie's byre / Glendaurel highlanders / Bonnie Dundee / Amazing grace / Day thou gavest Lord is ended / Flower of Scotland (Slow Air & 2/4 March) / MacKay's farewell to the 71st / Rose among the heather / Fiddlers' joy / De'il among the tailors / Pigeon on the gate / Kate Dalrymple / Going home / Mist covered mountains of home / Morag of Dunvegan / Skye boat song / Dark island / Highland wedding / Susan Macleod / Kate Robertson / Barren rocks of Aden / Highland laddie / Mhairi's wedding / Black bear / Flowers of the forest / Drum salute
CD _____ CD ITV 385
Scotdisc / May '87 / Duncans / Ross / Conifer.

Denny, Martin

EXOTIC SOUNDS OF MARTIN DENNY, THE
CD _____ CREV 039CD
Rev-Ola / Jul '95 / 3MV / Vital.

Denny, Sandy

ATTIC ATTACKS 1972-1984, THE
CD _____ SPDCD 1052
Special Delivery / Jun '95 / ADA / CM / Direct.

BEST OF SANDY DENNY
Listen listen / Lady / One way donkey ride / It'll take a long time / Farewell, farewell /

Tam Lin / Pond in the stream / Late November / Solo / Sea / Banks of the Nile / Next time around / For shame of doing wrong / Stranger to himself / I'm a dreamer / Who knows where the time goes
CD _____ IMCD 217
Island / Mar '96 / PolyGram.

NORTH STAR GRASSMAN AND THE RAVENS
Late November / Blackwater side / Sea Captain / Down in the flood / John the gun / Next time around / Optimist / Let's jump the broomstick / Wretched Wilbur / North star grassman and the ravens / Crazy lady blues
CD _____ IMCD 133
Island / Jun '91 / PolyGram.

RENDEZVOUS
I wish I was a fool for you / Gold dust / Candle in the wind / Take me away / One way donkey ride / I'm a dreamer / All our days / Silver threads and golden needles / No more sad refrains
CD _____ HNCD 4423
Hannibal / Jan '87 / Vital / ADA.

SANDY
CD _____ IMCD 132
Island / Jun '91 / PolyGram.

SANDY AND THE STRAWBS (Denny, Sandy & The Strawbs)
Nothing else will do / Who knows where the time goes / How everyone but Sam was a hypocrite / Sail away to the sea / And you need me / Poor Jimmy Wilson / All I need is you / Tell me what you see in me / I've been my own worst friend / Two weeks last summer / Always on my mind / Stay a while with me / On my way
CD _____ HNCD 1361
Hannibal / Jul '91 / Vital / ADA.

WHO KNOWS WHERE THE TIME GOES
Lady / Nothing more / Memphis Tennessee. / Solo / John the gun / Knockin' on Heaven's door / Who knows where the time goes / Music weaver / Take away the load / Sweet Rosemary / Now and then / By the time it gets dark / What is true / Sail away to the sea / Farewell, farewell / Quiet joys of brotherhood / Tamlin / You never wanted me / Autopsy / One more chance / Stranger to himself / Pond and the stream / Banks of the Nile / Two weeks last summer / Late November / Gypsy Davey / Winter winds / Sea / When will I be loved (Solo.) / Listen / Next time around / Tomorrow is a long time / One way donkey ride / Burton Town / Blackwater side / It'll take a long time / Walking the floor over you / Friends / For shame of doing wrong / I'm a dreamer / Full moon
CD Set _____ HNCD 5301
Hannibal / Feb '92 / Vital / ADA.

Denson, Karl

BABY FOOD
CD _____ MM 801048
Minor Music / May '95 / Vital/SAM.

CHUNKY PECAN PIE
Waltz for Leslie / Is it a bell / Fried bananas / Heart of the wanderer / Blue eyed peas / Banana boy / In order to form a more perfect union
CD _____ MM 801041
Minor Music / Jun '94 / Vital/SAM.

Dentists

BEHIND THE DOOR I KEEP THE UNIVERSE
This is not my flag / Space man / Sorry is not enough / In orbit / Faces on stone / Smile like oil on water / Tremendous Many / Gas / Brittle sin and flowers / Apple beast / Water for a man on fire / Waiter
CD _____ 756792288-2
WEA / Mar '94 / Warner Music.

DRESSED
CD _____ ME 2001
Metwo / Aug '92 / Pinnacle.

POWDERED LOBSTER FIASCO
Pocket of silver / Charms and the girls / Outside your inside / Box of Sun / Beautiful day / I can see your house from up here / We thought we'd gone to Heaven / Leave me alive / All coming down / Snapdragon
CD _____ SHED 002 CD
Creation / Jun '93 / 3MV / Vital.

Denver, John

BACK HOME AGAIN
Back home again / On the road / Grandma's feather bed / Matthew / Thank God I'm a country boy / Music is you / Annie's song / It's up to you / Cool and green and shady eclipse / Sweet surrender / This old guitar
CD _____ ND 85193
RCA / Oct '87 / BMG.

EARTH SONGS
Windsong / Rocky mountain suite / Rocky mountain high / Sunshine on my shoulders / Eagle and the hawk / Eclipse / Children of the universe / To the wild country / American child / Calypso / Islands / Earth day every day (celebrate)

FAREWELL ANDROMEDA
I'd rather be a cowboy / Berkeley woman / Please daddy / Angel from Montgomery / River of love / Rocky mountain suite / Whisky basin blues / Sweet misery / Zachary and Jennifer / We don't live here no more / Farewell Andromeda
CD _____ ND 85195
RCA / Feb '89 / BMG.

FLOWER THAT SHATTERED THE STONE, THE
Thanks to you / Postcard from Paris / High, wide and handsome / Eagles and horses / Little further north / Raven's child / Ancient rhymes / Gift you are / I watch you sleeping / Stonehaven sunset / Flower that shattered the stone (Mixes)
CD _____ MCCD 154
Music Club / Feb '94 / Disc / THE / CM.

GREATEST HITS
Take me home country roads / Follow me / Starwood in Aspen / For baby (for Bobbie) / Rhymes and reasons / Leaving on a jet plane / Eagle and the hawk / Sunshine on my shoulders / Goodbye again / Poems, prayers and promises / Rocky mountain high
CD _____ ND 90523
RCA / Nov '90 / BMG.

GREATEST HITS VOL.2
Annie's song / Perhaps love (With Placido Domingo.) / Fly away (With Olivia Newton John.) / Like a sad song / Looking for space / Thank God I'm a country boy / Grandma's feather bed / Back home again / I'm sorry / My sweet lady / Calypso / This old guitar
CD _____ 74321154802
RCA / Oct '93 / BMG.

HIGHER GROUND
Alaska and me / Higher ground / Whispering Jesse / Never a doubt / Deal with the ladies / Sing Australia / Country girl in Paris / For you / All this joy / Falling leaves / Bread and roses / Homegrown tomatoes
CD _____ PD 90240
RCA / Oct '88 / BMG.

HIGHER GROUND
CD _____ MCCD 197
Music Club / Mar '95 / Disc / THE / CM.

IN CONCERT
Music is you / Farewell Andromeda / Mother nature / Summer / Toledo / Matthew / Rocky mountain suite / Sweet surrender / Grandma's feather bed / Annie's song / Eagle and the hawk / My sweet lady / Annie's other song / Rhymes and reasons / Forest lawn / Blue grass / Thank God I'm a country boy / Take me home, country roads / Poems, prayers and promises / Rocky mountain high / This old guitar
CD _____ HP 93482
Happy Price / Jan '96 / Target/BMG.

TWO DIFFERENT DIRECTIONS
CD _____ DBP 102008
Double Platinum / Oct '95 / Target/BMG.

WILDLIFE CONSERVATION SOCIETY CONCERT
Rocky mountain high / Rhymes and reasons / Country roads / Back home again / I guess he'd rather be in Colorado / Matthew / Sunshine on my shoulders / You say the battle is over / Eagles and horses / Darcy Farrow / Whispering Jesse / Me and my uncle / Wild mountain skies / Leaving on a jet plane/Goodbye again / Bet on the blues / Harder they fall / Shanghai breeze / Fly away / Song for all lovers / Dreamland express / For you / Is it love / Falling out of love / Annie's song / Poems prayers and promises / Calypso / Amazon / This old guitar
CD _____ 4806942
Columbia / Aug '95 / Sony.

Denver, Karl

JUST LOVING YOU
From a Jack to a King / Garden party / I can't stop loving you / San Fernando / King of the road / Just loving you / Song for Maria / Walk on by / Won't give up / Runaway / Voices of the Highlands / Little bitty tear / Travelling light / Answer to everything / Story of my life
CD _____ PZA 004CD
Plaza / Oct '93 / Pinnacle.

Denzil

PUB
Fat loose and fancies me / Running this family / Rake around the grave / Useless / Sunday service Hengistbury Head / Too scared to be true / Bastard son of Elvis / Funny moon / Shame / Who made you so cynical about me / Autistic / If only Alan won the pools / Seven years in these boots / Your sister song / Cutie / Goodnight darling
CD _____ 74321189662
RCA / Jan '95 / BMG.

Deodato, Eumir

PRELUDE/DEODATO 2
CD _____ 4505582
CBS / Jan '94 / Sony.

Department S

IS VIC THERE
CD _____ MAUCD 633
Mau Mau / Mar '93 / Pinnacle.

Depeche Mode

101
Pimpf / Behind the wheel / Strangelove / Sacred (Not on LP) / Something to do / Blasphemous rumours / Stripped / Somebody / Things you said / Black celebration / Shake the disease / Nothing (Not on LP) / Pleasure little treasure / People are people / Question of time / Never let me down again / Question of lust / Master and servant / Just can't get enough / Everything counts
CD _____ CDSTUMM 101
Mute / Jan '89 / Disc.

BLACK CELEBRATION
Black celebration / Fly on the windscreen (Final) / Question of lust / Sometimes / It doesn't matter / Question of time / Stripped / Here is the house / World full of nothing / Dressed in black / New dress / But not tonight (CD only) / Breathing in fumes (CD only) / Black day (CD only)
CD _____ CDSTUMM 26
Mute / Jan '86 / Disc.

BROKEN FRAME, A
CD _____ CDSTUMM 9
Mute / Disc.

CONSTRUCTION TIME AGAIN
CD _____ CDSTUMM 13
Mute / Jan '86 / Disc.

MUSIC FOR THE MASSES
Things you said / Strangelove / Sacred / Little 15 / Behind the wheel / I want you now / To have and to hold / Nothing / Pimpf / Agent Orange / Never let me down again (Mixes) / To have and to hold (Spanish taster) / Pleasure little treasure (Glitter mix)
CD _____ CDSTUMM 47
Mute / Sep '87 / Disc.

SINGLES '81-'85
People are people / Master and servant / It's called a heart / Just can't get enough / See you / Shake the disease / Everything counts / New life / Blasphemous rumours / Leave in silence / Get the balance right / Love in itself / Dreaming of me
CD _____ CDMUTEL 1
Mute / '85 / Disc.

SOME GREAT REWARD
If you want to / Master and servant / Lie to me / Something to do / Blasphemous rumours / Somebody / People are people / It don't matter / Stories of old / Pipeline / Everything counts / Two minute warning
CD _____ CDSTUMM 19
Mute / '84 / Disc.

SONGS OF FAITH AND DEVOTION
I feel you / Walking in my shoes / Condemnation / Mercy in you / In your room / Get right with me / Rush / One caress / Higher love / Judas
CD _____ CDSTUMM 106
Mute / Apr '93 / Disc.

SONGS OF FAITH AND DEVOTION - LIVE
CD _____ LCDSTUMM 106
Mute / Dec '93 / Disc.

SPEAK AND SPELL
New life / Just can't get enough / I sometimes wish I was dead / Puppets / Boys say go / No disco / What's your name / Photographic / Tora tora tora / Big muff / Any second now
CD _____ CDSTUMM 5
Mute / Jun '88 / Disc.

VIOLATOR
World in my eyes / Sweetest perfection / Personal Jesus / Halo / Waiting for the night / Enjoy the silence / Policy of truth / Blue dress / Clean
CD _____ CDSTUMM 64
Mute / Mar '90 / Disc.

Depravity

SILENCE OF THE CENTURIES
CD _____ CDAR 017
Adipocre / May '94 / Plastic Head.

Depth Charge

NINE DEADLY VENOMS
CD _____ STEAM 100CD
Vinyl Solution / Nov '94 / Disc.

Der 3 Raum

DER DRITTE RAUM
CD _____ HHCD 8
Harthouse / Nov '94 / Disc / Warner Music.

Deranged

ARCHITECTS OF PERVERSIONS
CD _____ RPS 002MCD
Repulse / Apr '95 / Plastic Head.

Derek & The Dominoes

DEREK AND THE DOMINOES IN CONCERT (2CD Set)
Why does love got to be so sad / Got to get better in a little while / Let it rain / Presence of the Lord / Tell the truth / Bottle of red wine / Roll it over / Blues power / Have you ever loved a woman
CD Set _____ 8314162
Polydor / Jan '94 / PolyGram.

LAYLA REMASTERED - 20TH ANNIVERSARY EDITION (2CD/MC Set)
CD Set _____ 8470832
Polydor / Oct '90 / PolyGram.

LIVE AT FILLMORE
CD Set _____ 521682-2
Polydor / Feb '94 / PolyGram.

Derise, Joe

HOUSE OF FLOWERS
CD _____ ACD 153
Audiophile / Apr '93 / Jazz Music / Swift.

SINGS & PLAYS THE JIMMY VAN HEUSEN ANTHOLOGY
CD _____ ACD 234
Audiophile / Oct '92 / Jazz Music / Swift.

Derome, Jean

CONFITURES DE GAGAKU
CD _____ VICTOCD 05
Victo / Oct '94 / These / ReR Megacorp / Cadillac.

Derrane, Joe

GIVE US ANOTHER
CD _____ GLCD 1149
Green Linnet / Jun '95 / Roots / CM / Direct / ADA.

IRISH ACCORDION, THE
CD _____ COP 5008CD
Cop / Mar '94 / ADA.

Derriere Le Mirroir

ALIBI
CD _____ EFA 11902-2
Apollyon / Jan '94 / SRD.

PREGNANT
CD _____ EFA 11931-2
Derriere / Mar '94 / SRD.

Derringer, Rick

BACK TO THE BLUES
Trouble in paradise / Blue suede blues / Mean town blues / Sorry for your heartache / Sink or swim / Diamond / Cry baby / Unsolved mystery / Blue velvet
CD _____ RR 90482
Roadrunner / Jun '93 / Pinnacle.

ELECTRA BLUES
CD _____ RR 89682
Roadrunner / Sep '94 / Pinnacle.

Dervish

BOYS OF SLIGO, THE
Donegal set / Dolphin / Clapton jigs / Thos Byrnes / Man of Arran / Jackson's / Cliffs of Glencolumbkille / Sligo set / Martin Wynne's / Lad O'Beirne's / McDermotts / Raphoe reel / Chestnut tree / Boys of sligo / Montaghan twig / World's end set / Eddie Hully's jigs / Datum from Camden Town / Key of the Convent / Tommie people's reel / Dancing bear / Oreaga / Walsh's fancy / Congress / Spoil the dance
CD _____ SUNCD 1
Sound / Sep '94 / Direct / ADA.

HARMONY HILL
CD _____ WHRL 001CD
Whirling Discs / Aug '93 / ADA / Direct.

PLAYING WITH FIRE
CD _____ WHRL 002
Whirling Discs / Apr '95 / ADA / Direct.

Des, Henri

DES NO.5
CD _____ MCD 237 684
Accord / '88 / Discovery / Harmonia Mundi / Cadillac.

Des Plantes, Ted

TED DES PLANTES
CD _____ JCD 225
Jazzology / Oct '93 / Swift / Jazz Music.

Descendents

ALL
CD _____ SST 112 CD
SST / May '93 / Plastic Head.

BONUS FAT
Bonus fat
CD _____ SST 144 CD
SST / May '93 / Plastic Head.

ENJOY
CD _____ SST 242 CD
SST / Sep '90 / Plastic Head.

HALLRAKER
CD _____ SST 205 CD
SST / May '93 / Plastic Head.

I DON'T WANT TO GROW UP
CD _____ SST 143 CD
SST / Feb '88 / Plastic Head.

LIVEAGE
All / I'm not a loser / Silly girl / I wanna be a bear / Coolidge / Weinerschnitel / I don't want to grow up / Kids / Wendy / Get the time / Descendents / All-o-gistics / Myage / My dad sucks / Van / Surburban home / Hope / Clean sheets
CD _____ SST 163 CD
SST / Jan '88 / Plastic Head.

MILO GOES TO COLLEGE
CD _____ SST 142 CD
SST / May '93 / Plastic Head.

SOMERY
CD _____ SST 259 CD
SST / May '93 / Plastic Head.

TWO THINGS AT ONCE
CD _____ SST 145 CD
SST / May '93 / Plastic Head.

Desert Rose Band

LIFE GOES ON
CD _____ 4748692
Curb / Dec '93 / PolyGram.

Desford Colliery Band

ANDREW LLOYD WEBBER IN BRASS (Desford Colliery Caterpillar Band)
CD _____ 340472
Koch / Dec '94 / Koch.

GREGSON (Desford Colliery Caterpillar Band)
Dances and arias / Concerto for french horn and brass band / Connotations / Of men and mountains
CD _____ DOYCD 017
Doyen / Nov '92 / Conifer.

Designer

GOIN' DE DISTANCE
CD _____ JW 057CD
Soca / Feb '94 / Jetstar.

Desmond, Johnny

ONCE UPON A TIME/BLUE SMOKE
All the things you are / My heart stood still / Night and day / Where or when / Symphony / Together / I'll be seeing you / I'll walk alone / I'll remember April / Sweet Lorraine / Amor / Time on my hands / I'm through with love / No-one ever tells you / Party's over / I gotta right to sing the blues / It's a lonesome old town / Blue smoke / Last night when we were young / Why shouldn't I / Imagination / That old feeling / You go to my heart / I'm glad there is you / Bluesmoke
CD _____ 4810162
Columbia / Aug '95 / Sony.

Desmond, Paul

LIKE SOMEONE IN LOVE
Just squeeze me / Tangerine / Meditation / Nuages / Like someone in love / Things ain't what they used to be
CD _____ CD 83319
Telarc / Nov '92 / Conifer / ADA.

PAUL DESMOND & THE MJQ (Desmond, Paul & The MJQ)
CD _____ 474984 2
Sony Jazz / May '94 / Sony.

PAUL DESMOND QUARTET AND JIM HALL (Desmond, Paul & Jim Hall)
CD _____ CD 53224
Giants Of Jazz / Nov '95 / Target/BMG / Cadillac.

POLKA DOTS AND MOON BEAMS
When Joanna loved me / Polka dots and moonbeams / Here's that rainy day / Easy living / I've grown accustomed to your face / Bewitched, bothered and bewildered
CD _____ ND 90637
Bluebird / Apr '92 / BMG.

PURE DESMOND
Squeeze me / I'm old fashioned / Nuages / Why shouldn't I / Everything I love / Warm valley / Till the clouds roll by / Mean to me / Song from M.A.S.H. / Wave
CD _____ ZK 64767
Epic / Nov '95 / Sony.

TAKE TEN
Take ten / El prince / Alone together / Embarcadero / Black orpheus / Nancy / Samba d'Orpheus / One I love
CD _____ 07863 66146-2
Bluebird / Apr '93 / BMG.

TWO OF A MIND (Desmond, Paul & Gerry Mulligan)
All the things you are / Stardust / Two of a mind / Blight of the fumble bee / Way you look tonight / Out of nowhere
CD _____ ND 90364
Bluebird / Aug '89 / BMG.

Desmond, Trudy

R.S.V.P
I've got the world on a string / That's all / How long has this been going on / If I were a bell / I concentrate on you / Blame it on my youth / Just for a thrill / All or nothing at all / In the wee small hours of the morning / I'm a fool to want you / How did he look / Just one of those things / It's all right with me
CD _____ TJA 10024
Jazz Alliance / Jun '94 / New Note.

TAILOR MADE
Day by day / Goody goody / I see your face before me / Lucky to be me / I'm shadowing you / By myself / Anyone can whistle / I thought about you / Make someone happy / Guess I'll hang my tears out to dry / People will say we're in love / I'll never be the same
CD _____ TJA 10015
Jazz Alliance / Oct '92 / New Note.

Desotos

CRUISIN' WITH THE DESOTOS
CD _____ WCD 9026
Wilson Audiophile / Sep '91 / Quantum Audio.

Despair

DECAY OF HUMANITY
Decay of humanity / Delusion / Distant territory / Radiated / Cry for liberty / Victims of vanity / Silent screaming / Satantic verses
CD _____ 8497122
Century Media / Aug '90 / Plastic Head.

Desperadoes Steel...

JAMMER, THE (Desperadoes Steel Orchestra)
Jammer / No pan / Ah goin an party tonight / Moliendo cafe / Africa / Rebecca / Symphony in G / Musical volcano
CD _____ DE 4023
Delos / Jan '94 / Conifer.

Des'ree

I AIN'T MOVIN'
Herald the day / Crazy maze / You gotta be / Little child / Strong enough / Trip on love / I ain't movin' / Living in the city / In my dreams / Love is here / I ain't movin' (Percussion reprise)
CD _____ 475843 2
Sony Soho2 / May '94 / Sony.

MIND ADVENTURES
Average man / Feel so high / Sun of '79 / Why should I love you / Stand on my own ground / Competitive world / Mind adventures / Laughter / Save me / Momma, please don't cry
CD _____ 4712632
Sony Soho2 / Feb '92 / Sony.

Destiny

NOTHING LEFT TO FEAR
CD _____ CDATV 18
Music For Nations / May '91 / Pinnacle.

Destroy All Monsters

BORED
You're gonna die / November 22nd 1963 / Meet the creeper / Nobody knows / What do I get / Goin' to town
CD _____ CDMRED 94
Cherry Red / Oct '91 / Pinnacle.

DESTROY ALL MONSTERS (LIVE)
CD _____ FC 050CD
Fan Club / '90 / Direct.

NOVEMBER 22ND 1963
CD _____ 892011MIG 11
Revenge / Nov '94 / Pinnacle.

Destroyer 666

VIOLENCE IS THE PRINCE OF THIS WORLD
CD _____ MIM 7320CD
Modern Invasion / Jan '96 / Plastic Head.

Destruction

DESTRUCTION
CD _____ UAM 0447
UAM / Oct '95 / Plastic Head.

INFERNAL OVERKILL/SENTENCE OF DEATH
CD _____ 857529
Steamhammer / '89 / Pinnacle / Plastic Head.

LIVE WITHOUT SENSE
CD _____ CDNUK 125
Noise/Modern Music / Feb '89 / Pinnacle / Plastic Head.

MAD BUTCHER/ETERNAL DEVASTATION
CD _____ 851860
SPV / '89 / Plastic Head.

Desultory

BITTERNESS
CD _____ CDZORR 077
Metal Blade / Jun '94 / Pinnacle.

Det-Ri-Mental

XENOPHOBIA
Bhangra attack / Informer / Total revolution / Richmans world (suffering pt 2) / Children of a rat race (aye man) / Sista India / Bank robber / Babylon / Living on the edge / Unknown identity (Inn-a-England)
CD _____ DEBTCD 003
Debt / Oct '95 / Vital.

Detective

DETECTIVE
Recognition / Got enough love / Grim reaper / Nightingale / Detective man / Ain't none of your business / Deep down / Wild hot summer / One more heartache
CD _____ 7567914152
Atlantic / Jan '96 / Warner Music.

IT TAKES ONE TO KNOW ONE
Help me up / Competition / Are you talkin' to me / Dynamite / Something beautiful / Warm love / Betcha won't dance / Fever / Tear jerker
CD _____ 7567804032
Atlantic / Jan '96 / Warner Music.

Detest

DORVAL
CD _____ NB 104
Nuclear Blast / Mar '94 / Plastic Head.

Dethmuffen, Miles

CLUTTER
CD _____ QTZ 01-2
Quartz / Apr '94 / SRD.

Dethrone

LET THE DAY BEGIN
CD _____ CDFLAG 41
Under One Flag / Sep '90 / Pinnacle.

Detour

HONKY TONKIN' TIL IT HURTS
CD _____ 15377
Laserlight / Aug '91 / Target/BMG.

Detroit Emeralds

DO ME RIGHT/YOU WANT IT YOU GOT IT
Do me right / Wear this ring (With love) / Long live the king / What you gonna do about me / You can't take this love for you, from me / Just now and then / Lee / If I love your love / And I love her / I can't see myself (Doing without you) / Holding on / Afraid our love is gone / You want it, you got it / There's love for me somewhere / I'll never sail the sea again / Take my love / Feel the need / I've got to move / Baby let me take you (In my arms) / I bet you get the one you love / Till you decide to come home / Radio promo medley: (You want it you got it, Do me right, Wear this ring, Feel the need in me, Baby let me take you in my arms)
CD _____ CDSEWD 067
Westbound / Apr '93 / Pinnacle.

I'M IN LOVE WITH YOU
Shake your head / You're getting a little too smart / What'cha gonna wear tomorrow / My dreams have got the best of me / So long / I think of you (You control me) / Heaven couldn't be like this/Without you baby
CD _____ CDSEW 006
Westbound / Jun '89 / Pinnacle.

I'M IN LOVE WITH YOU/FEEL THE NEED IN ME
Shake your head / So long / You're getting too smart / I think of you (You control me) / What'cha gonna wear tomorrow / Heaven couldn't be like this/without you baby / My dreams have got the best of you / Set it out / Take it or leave it / Feel the need in me / Wednesday / Love for you / Look what has happened to our love / Sexy ways / Love has come to me
CD _____ CDSEWD 068
Westbound / Nov '93 / Pinnacle.

Detroit Spinners

DANCIN' AND LOVIN'
Disco ride / Body language / Let's boogie, let's dance / Medley: Working my way back to you / Forgive me girl / With my eyes / One one two two boogie woogie avenue (home of the boogie...
CD _____ 8122711152
Atlantic / Jan '96 / Warner Music.

LOVE TRIPPIN'
Love trippin' / Heavy on the sunshine / Medley: Cupid / I've loved you for a long time / I just want to be with you / Street wise / Working my way back to you / I just want to fall in love / Now that you're mine again / Split decision / I'm takin' you back / Pipe dream / Body language

179

CD _____ 7567803782
Atlantic / Jan '96 / Warner Music.

SWEET SOUL MUSIC
It's a shame / Together we can make such sweet music / At sundown / I've got to hold myself a brand new baby / Pay them no mind / My whole world ended (the moment you left me) / Souly ghost / Message from a black man / It hurts to be in love / Can sing a rainbow/Love is blue / That's what girls are made for / We'll have it made / Bad bad weather (till you come home) / O-o-h child / My lady love
CD _____ 550 4082
Spectrum/Karussell / Aug '94 / PolyGram / THE.

Detroit, Marcella

JEWEL
Jewel / I believe / Perfect world / Art of melancholy / James Brown / Detroit / Ain't nothing like the real thing / I'm no angel / I want to take you higher / You don't tell me everything / Cool people / Out of my mind / Prima Donna
CD _____ 828491-2
London / Mar '94 / PolyGram.

Detroiters

OLD TIME RELIGION (Detroiters & Golden Echoes)
He walks with me / Mother on the train take 2 / Mother on the train take 3 / Angels watching over me / I trust in Jesus / Ride on king Jesus / Mother, don't cry about your child / Let Jesus lead you / Mother, I need your prayer / Old time religion / Sometimes / Body and soul / Shady green pastures / Where shall I be / Down on my knees / My life is in his hands / When the saints go marching in (take 2) / When the saints go marching in / When I lay my burden down / I'm so happy in the service of the lord / Waiting and watching / Yield not to temptation take 1 / Yield not to temptation take 2 / Yield not to temptation take 3
CD _____ CDCHD 467
Ace / Mar '93 / Pinnacle / Cadillac / Complete/Pinnacle.

Deuce

ON THE LOOSE
Call it love / Talk to me / What you wanna be / Rumours / Let's call it a day / I need you / Boyfriend girlfriend / I'll be there for you / I was wrong / Kiss it
CD _____ 8286642
London / Aug '95 / PolyGram.

Deus

MY SISTER IS MY CLOCK
Middlewave / Almost white / Health insurance / Little ghost / How to row a cat / Only a colour to her / Sick sugar / Sweetness / Horror party jokes / Void / Sans titre pour sira / Glovesong / Lorre in the forest
CD _____ IMCD 8031
Island / Jan '95 / PolyGram.

WORST CASE SCENARIO
Intro / Suds and soda / W.C.S. (1st draft) / Jigsaw you / Morticiachair / Via / Right as rain / Mute / Let's get lost / Hotellounge (be the death of me) / Share your hip / Great American nude / Secret hell / Divebomb djingle
CD _____ CID 8028
Island / Aug '94 / PolyGram.

Deuter-D

CALL OF THE UNKNOWN-SELECTED PIECES 1972-1986
Starchild / Peru le Peru / Call of the unknown / Sky beyond clouds / Cathedral / From here to here / High road / Alchemy / Pacifica / Silence is the answer / Haleakala mystery / Album / Solitary bird / Echo of the beast / Back to a planet / La llaha il allah
CD Set _____ CDKUCK 076/077
Kuckuck / Feb '87 / CM / ADA.

CICADA
From here to here / Light / Cicada / Sun on my face / From here to here (reprise) / Sky beyond clouds / Haiku / Alchemy / Between two breaths
CD _____ CDKUCK 056
Kuckuck / Feb '87 / CM / ADA.

HENON
Nada / Sha / Ebony / Basho / Ari / Gentle darkness / Terra Linda / Indian girl / Fjaril / Rainmoon / Chicken itza
CD _____ CDKUCK 11099
Kuckuck / Jul '92 / CM / ADA.

LAND OF ENCHANTMENT
Pierrot / Maui morning / Silver air / Waves and dolphins / Santa Fe / Celestial harmony / Peru le Peru / Petite fleur / Wind of dawn
CD _____ CDKUCK 081
Kuckuck / Jan '88 / CM / ADA.

NIRVANA ROAD
CD _____ CDKUCK 068
Kuckuck / Jul '84 / CM / ADA.

SANDS OF TIME
CD _____ CDKUCK 120902
Kuckuck / Feb '91 / CM / ADA.

Deutsch, Alex

PINK INC. (Deutsch, Alex, George Garzone & Jammaladeen Tacuma)
CD _____ DIW 852
DIW / Nov '91 / Harmonia Mundi / Cadillac.

Deutscher, Drafi

DIE DECCA JAHRE 1963-68
Teeny / Shu-bi-do the slop / Grun, grun ist Tennessee / Kleine Peggy Lou / Shake hands / Come on let's go / Cinderella baby / Es ist besser, wenn du gebst / Keep smiling / Es war einmal / Hast du alles vergessen / Heute male ich dein Bild, Cindy Lou / Mr. Tambourine man / Keiner weiss, wie es morgen sein wird / Nimm mich so wie ich bin / Ich geh' durch's Feuer fur dich / Marmor, Stein und Eisen bricht / Das sind die einsamen jahre / Honey bee / Hello little girl / Ich hab' den mond in meiner tasche / An deiner seite / Old old Germany / Mit schirm, Frack und Melone / Mit schirm, charme und melone / Die goldene zeit / Take it easy / Was sind sie ohne Regen / Sweet dreams for you my love / Darlin' / Der hauptmann von Kopenick / Zwei fremde augen / Rock 'n' roll lady / Alice im Wunderland / Marble breaks, iron bends / Wanna take you home / Summertime / Bachelor boy / Trouble / Amanda / Wake up / Crying in the morning / Bleib, oh bleib / Junge leute brauchen liebe / Shake your hands / Good golly Miss Molly / Memphis, Tennessee / Roll over Beethoven / What'd I say / What's the matter baby / Mit siebzehn fangt das Leben erst an / Komm zu mir / Zip a dee doo dah / Lion sleeps tonight / Hippy hippy shake / Shakin' all over / Ready Teddy / Marnor, stein und eisen bricht / Wunder / I don't need that kind of lovin' / Language of love / Tranen der liebe / Ich will frei sein / Welche farbe had die welt / He's got the whole world in his hands / Noah's arche / Waterloo / Denn da waren wir beide noch kinder / Liebe, gluck und treue / Bring grusse zu Mary
CD Set _____ BCD 15416
Bear Family / Dec '87 / Rollercoaster / Direct / CM / Swift / ADA.

HITS, PSEUDONYMC AND RARITATEN
CD _____ REP 4113-WZ
Repertoire / Aug '91 / Pinnacle / Cadillac.

Deux Filles

SILENCE AND WISDOM
CD _____ BAH 1
Humbug / Feb '93 / Pinnacle.

Devas

EMBODIED
CD _____ MSECD 016
Mouse / Oct '95 / Grapevine.

Devastation

SIGNS OF LIFE
Eye for an eye / Manic depressive / Retribution / Contaminated / Escape to violence / Desolation / Signs of life / Tomorrow we die / Fear of the unknown
CD _____ CDFLAG 44
Under One Flag / Jul '90 / Pinnacle.

DeVaughan, William

BE THANKFUL FOR WHAT YOU GOT/ FIGURES CAN'T CALCULATE
Give the little man a great big hand / Something's being done / Blood is thicker than water / Kiss and make up / You gave me a brand new start / Be thankful for what you got / Sing a love song / You can do it / We are his children / Be thankful for what you've got (1980) / Hold on to love / Boogie Dan / Figures can't calculate (the love I have for you) / Love comes so easy with you / You send me / I've never found a girl
CD _____ NEMCD 700
Sequel / Nov '94 / BMG.

BE THANKFUL FOR WHAT YOU'VE GOT
CD _____ CHELD 1002
Start / Jun '89 / Koch.

Devi, Girija

GIRIJA DEVI IN CONCERT
CD _____ C 560056
Ocora / Oct '95 / Harmonia Mundi / ADA.

Deviants

PARTIAL RECALL
Billy the monster / Trouble coming every day / Broken statue / Whole things starts / But Charlie it's still moving / Observe the ravens / Society of the horseman / Summertime blues / Don't talk to me Mary / You can't move me / In my window box / Epitaph can point the way / Mona the whole trip / People call me crazy / Half price drinks / Death of a dream machine
CD _____ DOCD 1989
Drop Out / Sep '92 / Pinnacle.

PTOOFF
CD _____ DOCD 1988
Drop Out / Nov '92 / Pinnacle.

Deviate

CRISIS OF CONFIDENCE
CD _____ MASSCD 042
Massacre / Oct '94 / Plastic Head.

Deviated Instinct

RE-OPENING OLD WOUNDS
CD _____ DAR 011CD
Desperate Attempt / Nov '94 / SRD.

Devil Dogs

30 SIZZLING SLABS
CD _____ EFA 11561 CD
Crypt / Jun '93 / SRD.

CHAOS BLAST
CD _____ MT 218CD
Empty / Sep '95 / Plastic Head / SRD.

CHOAD BLAST
CD _____ EFA 12357-2
Empty / Mar '94 / Plastic Head / SRD.

Devilhead

YOUR ICE CREAM'S DIRTY
Too mcuh protection / Your mistake / Don't make me / There Polly / Troubled moon / Devilhead / Down on the cow / Birthday / We like you / Cup of tea / Funeral march
CD _____ 4783772
Epic / Jul '95 / Sony.

Devine, Sydney

50 COUNTRY WINNERS
Country roads / Early morning rain / Gentle on my mind / Hello Mary Lou / Oh lonesome me / Sea of heartbreak / Lonesome number one / Blue blue day / Four walls / He'll have to go / You're free to go / Sweet dreams / Send me the pillow that you dream on / Satin sheets / Wild side of life / This song is just for you / Blackboard of my heart / Married by the bible, divorced by the law / Crying time / Together again / I can't stop loving you / I Take these chains from my heart / Dear God / Where could I go but to the Lord / House of gold / You'll never walk alone / Blanket on the ground / Old flames / Blowin' in the wind / Sing me / Tiny bubbles / Early shells / Stand beside me / Gypsy woman / You're my best friend / Till the rivers all run dry / Please help me, I'm falling / Fraulein / I fall to pieces / It keeps right on a-hurtin' / Eighteen yellow roses / Ramblin' rose / Red roses for a blue lady / Irene / Lucille / Amanda / Lovesick blues / Singin' the blues / Knee deep in the blues / Long gone lonesome blues
CD Set _____ PLATCD 18
Platinum Music / Oct '87 / Prism / Ross.

CRYING TIME
Crying time / Broken engagement / My son calls another man daddy / Long black limousine / Two little orphans / Eighteen yellow roses / Old Shep / Letter edged in black / Nobody's child / I ain't crying, mister / Gentle mother / Come home rolling stone
CD _____ EMPRCD 505
Emporio / Apr '94 / THE / Disc / CM.

GREEN GRASS OF HOME, THE
CD _____ CDITV 530
Scotdisc / Dec '90 / Duncans / Ross / Conifer.

NORFOLK COUNTRY
CD _____ CDITV 598
Scotdisc / Nov '94 / Duncans / Ross / Conifer.

Devlins

DRIFT
I knew that / Everytime you go / Turn you around / Drift / Almost made you smile / Alone in the dark / Someone to talk to / Necessary evil / As far as you can go / I don't want to be like this / Until the light shines through
CD _____ CDEST 2260
Capitol / Jun '95 / EMI.

Devo

COMPACT COLLECTION
CD Set _____ TPAK 38
Virgin / Oct '94 / EMI.

DEVO LIVE
Gates of steel / Be stiff / Planet Earth / Freedom of choice (Theme song.) / Whip it / Girl U want
CD _____ CDV 2106
Virgin / May '93 / EMI.

DUTY NOW FOR THE FUTURE
Devo corporate anthem / Clockout / Timing x / Wiggly world / Block head / Strange pursuits / S.I.B. (swelling itching brain) / Triumph of the will / Day my baby gave me a surprise / Pink pussycat / Secret agent man / Smart patrol / Redeye express / Mr. DNA
CD _____ CDV 2125
Virgin / May '93 / EMI.

FREEDOM OF CHOICE
Girl u want / It's not right / Snowball / Don' to' lov / Freedom of choice / Gates of steel / Cold war / Don't you know / That's pep / Mr. B's ballroom / Planet Earth

CD _____ CDV 2241
Virgin / May '93 / EMI.

HARD CORE DEVO
CD _____ 422105
New Rose / May '94 / Direct / ADA.

HARDCORE VOLUME 2
CD _____ RCD 20208
Rykodisc / Sep '91 / Vital / ADA.

HOT POTATOES: THE BEST OF DEVO
Jocko Homo / Mogoloid / Satisfaction / Whip it / Girl u want / Freedom of choice / That's good / Working in a coalmine / Deco corporate anthem / Be stiff / Gates of steel / Come back Jonee / Secret agent man / Day my baby gave me a surprise / Beautiful world / Big mess / Whip it (remix)
CD _____ CDVM 9016
Virgin / Aug '93 / EMI.

LIVE MONGALOID YEARS
CD _____ RCD 20209
Rykodisc / Oct '92 / Vital / ADA.

NEW TRADITIONALISTS
Through being cool / Jerkin' back 'n' forth / Pity you / Soft things / Race of doom / Going under / Love without anger / Super thing / Beautiful world / Enough said
CD _____ CDV 2125
Virgin / May '93 / EMI.

NOW IT CAN BE TOLD
CD _____ 727552
Restless / Feb '95 / Vital.

OH NO IT'S DEVO
Time out for fun / Peek-a-boo / Out of sync / Explosions / That's good / Patterns / Big mess / Speed racer / What I must / I desire / Deep sleep
CD _____ CDV 2241
Virgin / May '93 / EMI.

Q:ARE WE NOT MEN.A:WE ARE DEVO
Uncontrollable urge / Satisfaction / Praying hands / Space junk / Monogoloid / Jocko homo / Too much paranoias / Gut feeling / Slap your mammy / Sloppy (I saw my baby gettin') / Shrivel up / Come back Jonee
CD _____ CDV 2106
Virgin / May '93 / EMI.

SMOOTH NOODLE MAPS
Stuck in a loop / Post post-modern man / When we do it / Spin the wheel / Morning dew / Chance is gonna cum / Big picture / Pink jazz trancers / Jimmy / Devo has feelings too / Dawghaus
CD _____ 727572
Restless / Feb '95 / Vital.

TOTAL DEVO
Baby doll / Disco dancer / Some things never change / Plain truth / Happy guy / Shadow / I'd cry if you died / Agitated / Man turned inside out / Blow up
CD _____ 727562
Restless / Feb '95 / Vital.

Dexy's Midnight Runners

BBC LIVE IN CONCERT
T.S.O.P. / Burn it down / Precious / Jackie Wilson said (I'm in heaven when you smile) / Come on Eileen / Respect / Soon / Plan B / Geno / Old / Celtic soul brothers / There there my dear / Show me
CD _____ WINCD 047
Windsong / Sep '93 / Pinnacle.

BECAUSE OF YOU
Celtic soul brothers / Show me / Liars A to E / This is what she's like / Let's make this precious / Soon / Reminisce (Part 1) / Because of you / Let's get this straight / Old / All in all / One of those things / Dubious / Occasional flicker
CD _____ 5500032
Spectrum/Karussell / May '93 / PolyGram / THE.

RADIO 1 SESSIONS
CD _____ CDNT 009
Night Tracks / Jun '95 / Grapevine / Pinnacle.

SEARCHING FOR THE YOUNG SOUL REBELS
Burn it down / Tell me when my light turns to green / Teams that meet in the caffs / I'm just looking / Geno / Seven days too long / I couldn't help it if I tried / Thankfully not living in Yorkshire it doesn't apply / Keep it / Love part one / There there my dear
CD _____ CZ 31
EMI / Jan '88 / EMI.

TOO RYE AYE
Celtic soul brothers / Let's make this precious / All in all / Old / Plan B / Jackie Wilson said (I'm in heaven when you smile) / I'll show you / Liars to be / Until / Come on Eileen
CD _____ 810 054-2
Mercury / Jan '83 / PolyGram.

TOO RYE AYE/DON'T STAND ME DOWN (2CD Set)
Celtic soul brothers / Let's make this precious / All in all (this one last wild waltz) / Jackie Wilson said (I'm in heaven when you smile) / Old / Plan B / I'll show you / Liars A to E / Until I believe in my soul / Come on Eileen / Occasional flicker / This is what she's like / Knowledge of beauty / One of

those things / Reminisce part 2 / Listen to this / Waltz
CD Set _____ 5286082
Mercury / Aug '95 / PolyGram.

VERY BEST OF DEXY'S MIDNIGHT RUNNERS, THE
Come on Eileen / Jackie Wilson said (I'm in heaven when you smile) / Let's get this straight / Because of you / Show me / Celtic soul brothers / Liars A to E / One way love / Old / Geno / There there my dear / Breakin' down the walls of heartache / Dance stance / Plan B / Keep it / I'm just looking / Soon / This is what she's like / Soul finger
CD _____ 846 460-2
Mercury / May '91 / PolyGram.

Deyess

LITTLE GODDESS
CD _____ STCD 1040
Sterns / Oct '92 / Sterns / CM.

Dezi, Dao

DAO DEZI WORLD MIX ALBUM
Hebrides / La jument de mishao / Kokerkero / Ti eliz iza / Tri martold / King of the fairies / Gaspesie / An tri breur / Digor / Till eliz iza
CD _____ CDPCS 7371
Parlophone / Feb '95 / EMI.

D'Gary

MALAGASY GUITAR
CD _____ SHCD 65009
Shanachie / May '93 / Koch / ADA / Greensleeves.

Dhar, Sheila

VOYAGE INTERIEUR
CD _____ C 560017/18
Ocora / Jan '93 / Harmonia Mundi / ADA.

Dhomont, Francis

ACOUSMATRIX 8/9
CD _____ BVHAASTCD 9107/8
Bvhaast / Oct '93 / Cadillac.

Di Franco, Ani

ANI DI FRANCO
CD _____ RBR 001CD
Righteous Babe / Jul '95 / ADA.

IMPERFECTLY
CD _____ RBR 003CD
Righteous Babe / Jul '95 / ADA.

LIKE I SAID - SONGS 1990-91
CD _____ RBR 005CD
Righteous Babe / Jul '95 / ADA.

NOT SO SOFT
CD _____ RBR 002CD
Righteous Babe / Jul '95 / ADA.

OUT OF RANGE
CD _____ HAVENCD 3
Haven/Backs / Jan '95 / Disc / Pinnacle.

PUDDLE DIVE
CD _____ HAVENCD 2
Haven/Backs / Jan '95 / Disc / Pinnacle.

WOMEN IN (E)MOTION FESTIVAL
CD _____ T&M 105
Tradition & Moderne / Nov '94 / Direct / ADA.

Di Gojim

NOCH À SJOH
CD _____ SYNCD 161
Syncoop / Jun '94 / ADA / Direct.

Di Leva

NAKED NUMBER ONE
Naked number one / Mr. Thomas / Hell is made of love / Adam and Eve / Keep on dying / Never (the beggar song) / To the fairytale / Spaceflower (Part 1) / Time is a crime / Spaceflower (Part 2) / I'm not alone / Hiding behind water / Goddess of earth
CD _____ AUMCD 001
Spaceflower / May '95 / Plastic Head.

Di Meola, Al

BEST OF AL DI MEOLA
July / Traces of a tear / Maraba / Song to the Pharoah Kings / Etude / Rhapsody of fire / Coral / Beijing demons / Ballad
CD _____ BNZ 305
Blue Note / Feb '93 / EMI.

CASINO
Egyptian danza / Chasin' the voodoo / Dark eye tango / Senor mouse / Fantasia suite for two guitars / Viva la danzarina / Guitars of the exotic isle / Rhapsody Italia / Bravoto fantasia / Casino
CD _____ 4682152
Sony Jazz / Jan '95 / Sony.

COLLECTION: AL DI MEOLA
CD _____ CCSD 310
Castle / Sep '91 / BMG.

ELECTRIC RENDEZVOUS
God bird / Change / Electric rendezvous / Passion, grace and fire / Cruisin' / Black cat

shuffle / Ritmo de la noche / Somalia / Jewel inside a dream
CD _____ 4682162
Columbia / Nov '93 / Sony.

ELEGANT GYPSY
Flight over Rio / Midnight tango / Mediterranean suntrance / Race with devil on Spanish highway / Lady of Rome / Sister of Brazil / Elegant gypsy suite
CD _____ 4682132
Sony Jazz / Jan '95 / Sony.

HEART OF THE IMMIGRANTS
Nightclub 1960 / Vistaero / Carousel requiem / Tango II / Under a dark moon / Bordel 1900 / Indigo / Heru mertar/Don't go so far away / Parranda / Someday my Prince will come / Cafe 1930 / They love me from fifteen feet away / Milonga del angel
CD _____ RZ 79052
Tomato / May '93 / Vital.

KISS MY AXE
South bound traveller / Embrace / Kiss my axe / Morocco / Gigi's playtime rhyme (interlude No. 1) / One night last June / Phantom / Erotic interlude (interlude No. 2) / Global safari / Interlude 3 / Purple orchids / Prophet (interlude No.4) / Oriana (September 24, 1988)
CD _____ 700782
Tomato / Jul '92 / Vital.

LAND OF THE MIDNIGHT SUN
Wizard / Sarabande from violin sonata in B minor / Pictures of the sea (love theme) / Land of the midnight sun / Golden dawn suite (morning fire) / Calmer of the tempests / From ocean to the clouds / Short tales of the Black Forest
CD _____ 4682142
Sony Jazz / Jan '95 / Sony.

ORANGE & BLUE
CD _____ 5237242
PolyGram Jazz / Oct '94 / PolyGram.

SPLENDIDO HOTEL
CD _____ 4670902
Sony Jazz / Jan '95 / Sony.

TOUR DE FORCE
CD _____ 4682172
Sony Jazz / Jan '95 / Sony.

Di Novi, Gene

RENAISSANCE OF A JAZZ MASTER
CD _____ CCD 79708
Candid / Oct '95 / Cadillac / Jazz Music / Wellard / Koch.

Diabate, Mama

N'NA NIWALE
CD _____ PAMOA 205
PAM / Feb '94 / Direct / ADA.

Diabate, Sekouba

LE DESTIN
CD _____ OA 202
PAM / Feb '94 / Direct / ADA.

Diabate, Sona

KANKELE TI
CD _____ PAM 401
PAM / Feb '94 / Direct / ADA.

Diabate, Toumani

DJELIKA
Djelika / Mankoman djan / Cheik oumar bah / Marielle / Kandjoura / Aminata santoro / Tony Vanuel / Sankoun djubl
CD _____ HNCD 1380
Hannibal / Sep '95 / Vital / ADA.

KAIRA
CD _____ HNCD 1338
Hannibal / May '89 / Vital / ADA.

Diablos Rising

666
CD _____ CD 023
Osmose / Oct '94 / Plastic Head.

BLOOD, VAMPIRISM AND SADISM
CD _____ KROHN 02CD
Osmose / Nov '95 / Plastic Head.

Diamond Accordion Band

PLAY COUNTRY GREATS
CD _____ EMPRCD 510
Emporio / Apr '94 / THE / Disc / CM.

SING-A-LONG PARTY
CD _____ EMPRCD 591
Emporio / Oct '94 / THE / Disc / CM.

Diamond Head

AM I EVIL?
Am I evil / Heat'of the night / Don't you ever leave me / Borrowed time / To Heaven from Hell / Dead reckoning / Lightning to the nations / Sucking my love
CD _____ WKFMXD 92
FM / Sep '94 / Sony.

BEHOLD THE BEGINNING
It's electric / Prince / Sweet and innocent / Sucking my love / Streets of gold / Play it

loud / Shoot out the lights / Waited too long / Helpless
CD _____ HMRXD 165
Heavy Metal / May '91 / Sony.

DEATH & PROGRESS
CD _____ ESSCD 192
Essential / Jun '93 / Total/BMG.

DIAMOND HEAD
CD _____ HMRXD 92
Heavy Metal / May '87 / Sony.

DIAMOND HEAD - FRIDAY ROCK SHOW SESSIONS
Sweet and innocent / Lightning to the nations / Am I evil / In the heat of the night / Borrowed time / Don't you ever leave me / Sucking my love / Play it loud
CD _____ FRSCD 006
Raw Fruit / Mar '92 / Pinnacle.

DIAMOND HEAD - IN THE BEGINNING
CD _____ WKFMCD 165
FM / Feb '91 / Sony.

EVIL LIVE
CD Set _____ ESDCD 219
Essential / Sep '94 / Total/BMG.

Diamond Rio

CLOSE TO THE EDGE
Oh me, oh my, sweet baby / In a week or two / It does get better than this / Sawmill road / Calling all hearts (Come back home) / This Romeo ain't got Julie yet / I was meant to be with you / Old weakness (Coming on strong) / Demons and angels / Nothing in this world / Close to the edge
CD _____ 07822186562
Arista / Oct '93 / BMG.

LITTLE STRONGER, A
CD _____ 07822187452
Arista / Aug '94 / BMG.

Diamond, Jim

JIM DIAMOND
I won't let you down / I should have known better / Hi ho silver (theme from Boon) / Not man enough / Our love / I still love you / We dance the night away / It's true what they say / If you're gonna break my heart / Devil in my eyes / Child's heart / Goodnight tonight
CD _____ 843 847-2
PolyGram TV / May '93 / PolyGram.

SUGAR ROLLEY DAYS
CD _____ JDACD 1
Righteous / Sep '94 / Total/BMG.

Diamond, Neil

12 GREATEST HITS VOLUME 2
Beautiful noise / Hello again / Forever in blue jeans / September morn / Desiree / You don't bring me flowers / America / Be / Longfellow serenade / If you know what I mean / Yesterday's songs / Love on the rocks
CD _____ CD 85844
CBS / May '87 / Sony.

20 GOLDEN GREATS: NEIL DIAMOND
CD _____ DMCTV 2
MCA / Feb '91 / BMG.

BEAUTIFUL NOISE
Beautiful noise / Stargazer / Lady oh / Don't think / Feel / Surviving the life / If you know what I mean / Street life / Home is a wonderful heart / Jungletime / Signs / Dry your eyes
CD _____ 4504522
CBS / Mar '91 / Sony.

BEST YEARS OF OUR LIVES
Best years of our lives / Hard times for young lovers / This time / Everything's gonna be fine / Hooked on the memory of you / Take care of me / Baby can I hold you / Carmelita's eyes / Courtin' disaster / If I couldn't see you again / Long hard climb
CD _____ 4632012
CBS / Nov '89 / Sony.

CHRISTMAS ALBUM, THE
O come o come Emmanuel/We three kings of Orient are / Silent night / Little drummer boy / Santa Claus is coming to town / Christmas song / Morning has broken / Happy Christmas (war is over) / White Christmas / God rest ye merry gentlemen / Jingle bell rock / Hark the herald angels sing / Silver bells / You make it feel like Christmas / Holy night
CD _____ 472410-2
Columbia / Nov '92 / Sony.

CHRISTMAS ALBUM, THE Vol.2
Joy to the world / Mary's boy child / Deck the halls/We wish you a merry Christmas / Winter wonderland / Have yourself a merry little Christmas / I'll be home for Christmas / Rudolph the red nosed reindeer / Sleigh ride / Candlelight carol / Away in a manger / O come all ye faithful (Adeste Fidelis) / O little town of Bethlehem / Angels we have heard on high / First Noel / Hallelujah chorus
CD _____ 477598 2
Columbia / Nov '94 / Sony.

CLASSICS - THE EARLY YEARS
Kentucky woman / Cherry, Cherry / Solitary man / You got to me / I got the feelin' (oh no no) / Thank the Lord for the night time / I'm a believer / Girl, you'll be a woman soon / Shilo / Do it / Red red wine / Boat that I row
CD _____ CD 32349
CBS / Apr '89 / Sony.

GREATEST HITS, THE (1966-1992)
Solitary man / Cherry, Cherry / I got the feelin' (oh no no) / Thank the Lord for the night time / Girl, you'll be a woman soon / Kentucky woman / Shilo / You got to me / Brooklyn roads / Red red wine / I'm a believer / Sweet caroline / Soolaimon / Cracklin' rosie / Song sung blue / Play me / Holly holy / Morning side / Crunchy granola suite / Brother love's travelling salvation show / I am... I said / Longfellow serenade / Beautiful noise / If you know what I mean / Desiree / September morn / You don't bring me flowers (With Barbra Streisand) / Forever in blue jeans / Hello again / America / Love on the rocks / Yesterday's songs / Heartlight / Headed for the future / Heartbreak hotel (With Kim Carnes) / All I really need is you
CD Set _____ 4715022
Columbia / Jun '92 / Sony.

HEARTLIGHT
Heartlight / I'm alive / I'm guilty / Hurricane / Lost among the stars / In Ensenada / Fool for you / Star flight / Front page story / Comin' home / First you have to say you love me
CD _____ 982835 2
Pickwick/Sony Collector's Choice / Mar '94 / Carlton Home Entertainment / Pinnacle / Sony.

HOT AUGUST NIGHT
Prologue / Crunchy granola suite / Done too soon / Dialogue / Solitary man / Cherry, Cherry / Sweet Caroline / Porcupine pie / You're so sweet / Red red wine / Soggy pretzels / And the grass won't pay no mind / Shilo / Girl, you'll be a woman soon / Play me / Canta libre / Morningside / Song sung blue / Cracklin' Rosie / Holly holy / I am... I said / Walk off / Soolaimon / Brother Love's travelling salvation show / Encore
CD Set _____ MCLDD 19042
MCA / Apr '92 / BMG.

HOT AUGUST NIGHTS II
Song of the whales / Headed for the future / September morn / Thank the Lord for the night time / Cherry, Cherry / Sweet Caroline / Hello again / Love on the rocks / America / Forever in blue jeans / You don't bring me flowers / I dreamed a dream / Back in L.A. / Song sung blue / Cracklin' Rosie / I am... I said / Holly holy / Soolaimon / Brother Love's travelling salvation show / Heartlight
CD _____ 4604082
CBS / Nov '87 / Sony.

LIVE IN AMERICA (2MC/CD Set)
America / Hello again / Kentucky woman / You got me / Cherry, Cherry / I'm a believer / Sweet Caroline / Love on the rocks / Hooked on the memory of you / Lady oh / Beautiful noise / Play me / Up on the roof / You've lost that lovin' feelin' / River deep, mountain high / I who have nothing / Missa / Soolaimon / Holly holy / Grass won't pay no mind / You don't bring me flowers / September morn / Hava nagila / Solitary man / Red red wine / Song sung blue / Forever in blue jeans / Crunchy granola suite / Brother Love's travelling salvation show
CD Set _____ 477211 2
CBS / Jun '94 / Sony.

LOVE AT THE GREEK
Kentucky woman / Sweet Caroline / Last Picasso / Longfellow serenade / Beautiful noise / Lady oh / Stargazer / If you know what I mean / Surviving the life / Glory road / Song sung blue / Holly Holy / Brother Love's travelling salvation show / Jonathan Livingstone Seagull / I've been this way before / Be / Dear father / Lonely looking sky / Sanctus / Skybird / Be (encore)
CD _____ CD 95001
CBS / Mar '87 / Sony.

LOVESCAPE
If there were no dreams / Mountains of love / Someone who believes in you / When you miss your love / Fortunes of the night / One hand, one heart / Hooked on the memory of you / Wish everything was alright / Way / Sweet L.A. days / All I really need is you / Lonely lady no.17 / I feel you / Common ground
CD _____ 4688902
Columbia / Oct '91 / Sony.

MOODS
Song sung blue / Porcupine pie / High rolling man / Canta Libre / Captain sunshine / Play me / Gitchy goomy / Walk on water / Theme / Prelude in E Major / Morningside
CD _____ MCLD 19043
MCA / Apr '92 / BMG.

NEIL DIAMOND SONGBOOK (Various Artists)
CD _____ VSOPCD 173
Connoisseur / Jun '92 / Pinnacle.

PRIMITIVE
Turn around / Primitive / Fire on the tracks / Brooklyn on a Saturday night / Sleep with me tonight / Crazy / My time with you / Love's own song / It's a trip / You make it feel like Christmas / One by one
CD _____ 982636 2
Pickwick/Sony Collector's Choice / Aug '91 / Carlton Home Entertainment / Pinnacle / Sony.

SERENADE
I've been this way before / Rosemary's wine / Lady Magdelene / Last Picasso / Longfellow serenade / Yes I will / Reggae strut / Gift of song
CD _____ 982195 2
Carlton Home Entertainment / Sep '93 / Carlton Home Entertainment.
CD _____ 4650122
Columbia / Dec '95 / Sony.

STONES
I am... I said / Last thing on my mind / Husbands and wives / Chelsea morning / Crunchy Granola Suite / Stones / If you go away / Suzanne / I think it's going to rain today
CD _____ MCLD 19118
MCA / Apr '92 / BMG.

TAP ROOT MANUSCRIPT
Cracklin' Rosie / Free life / Coldwater morning / Done too soon / He ain't heavy, he's my brother / African trilogy / I am the lion / Madrigal / Soolaimon / Missa / African suite / Child's song
CD _____ MCLD 19119
MCA / Aug '92 / BMG.

UP ON THE ROOF - SONGS FROM THE BRILL BUILDING
You've lost that lovin' feelin' / Up on the roof / Love potion no.9 / Will you still love me tomorrow / Don't be cruel / Do wah diddy diddy / I who have nothing / Do you know the way to San Jose / River deep, mountain high / Groovy kind of love / Spanish Harlem / Sweets for my sweet / Happy birthday sweet sixteen / Ten lonely guys / Save the last dance for me
CD _____ 474356 2
Columbia / Oct '93 / Sony.

VELVET GLOVES AND SPIT (2CD Set)
Two bit manchild / Modern day version of love / Honeydrippin' times / Pot smoker's song / Brooklyn roads / Shilo / Sunday sun / Holiday inn blues / Practically newborn / Knackelflerg / Merry go round
CD _____ MCLD 19044
MCA / Apr '92 / BMG.

VERY BEST OF NEIL DIAMOND
Sweet Caroline / Cracklin' rosie / Song sung blue / I am... I said
CD _____ PWKS 510
Carlton Home Entertainment / Feb '96 / Carlton Home Entertainment.

YOU DON'T BRING ME FLOWERS
American popular song / Forever in blue jeans / Remember me / You've got your troubles / You don't bring me flowers / Dancing bumble bee bumble boogie / Mothers and daughters, fathers and sons / Memphis flyer / Say maybe / Diamond girl
CD _____ 4687822
Columbia / Aug '91 / Sony.

Di'Anno, Paul

IRON MEN, THE
CD _____ ASBCD 004
Scratch / Jul '95 / BMG.

SOUTH AMERICAN ASSAULT
CD _____ SPV 084-38952
SPV / Aug '94 / Plastic Head.

Dias, Jose Barrense

ESCULTOR DE IMAGEM
CD _____ KAR 973
Kardum / Sep '93 / Discovery.

Dias, Sergio

MIND OVER MATTER
CD _____ EXPALCD 8
Expression / Aug '91 / Pinnacle.

Diatta, Pascal

SIMNADE (Diatta, Pascal & Sona Mane)
CD _____ FMSD 2017
Rogue / Aug '89 / Sterns.

Diaz, Alirio

ART OF SPANISH GUITAR, THE
CD _____ 14129
Laserlight / Jun '94 / Target/BMG.

Diaz, Diomedes

CANTANDO (Diaz, Diomedes & Nicholas Colacho Mendoza)
Esperanza / Cantando / Te necesito / Myriam / Cardon guarjiro / El medallon / Por amor a dios / Paisana mia / Siempre contigo / Las cosas del amor
CD _____ CDORB 055
Globestyle / Mar '90 / Pinnacle.

Diaz, Hugo

20 BEST OF CLASSICAL "TANGO ARGENTINO" (Diaz, Hugo Trio)
CD _____ EUCD 1094
ARC / '91 / ARC Music / ADA.

TANGO ARGENTINO (Diaz, Hugo Trio)
CD _____ EUCD 1327
ARC / Nov '95 / ARC Music / ADA.

Diaz, Joaquin

AFFINITES
CD _____ CD 001CD
Caskabel / Nov '95 / ADA.

Dibango, Manu

AFRIJAZZY
Masa lemba / Bushman promenade / Gombo sauce / Soir au village / Makossa / Kango / Doula serenade / Abelley sphere
CD _____ EMY 1372
Enemy / Oct '92 / Grapevine.

BAO BAO
CD _____ MAUCD 632
Mau Mau / Nov '92 / Pinnacle.

ELECTRIC AFRICA
CD _____ CPCD 8152
Celluloid / Nov '95 / Charly.

NEGROPOLITAINES
CD _____ 859052
Melodie / Nov '92 / Triple Earth / Discovery / ADA / Jetstar.

POLYSONIK
CD _____ EXPALCD 7
Expression / May '91 / Pinnacle.

SOUL MAKOSSA
Soul makossa / Rencontre / Taoumba / Moni / New bell 'hard pulsation' / O Boso / Kata kata / Soukouss / Pepe soup / Essimo / Nights in Zeralda
CD _____ 139 215
Musidisc / Aug '90 / Vital / Harmonia Mundi / ADA / Cadillac / Discovery.

WAKAFRIKA
Soul Makossa / Biko / Wakafrika / Emma / Homeless / Lady / Hi-life / Wimoweh / Am oh / Jingo / Pata pata / Diarabi / Ca va chouia
CD _____ BLM 001CD
Blue Music / Jun '94 / Pinnacle / CM / ADA.

Diblo

MONDO RY
CD _____ 41008-2
Melodie / Jul '91 / Triple Earth / Discovery / ADA / Jetstar.

Dicabor

DICABOR
Space Teddy / Feb '95 / SRD.
CD _____ EFA 004102

Dick Nixons

PAINT THE WHITE HOUSE BLACK
CD _____ 422106
New Rose / Jun '94 / Direct / ADA.

Dick, Robert

THIRD STONE FROM THE SUN
CD _____ 804352
New World / Sep '93 / Harmonia Mundi / ADA / Cadillac.

Dickens, Hazel

FEW OLD MEMORIES, A
CD _____ CD 11529
Rounder / '88 / CM / Direct / ADA / Cadillac.

HAZEL & ALICE (Dickens, Hazel & Alice Gerrard)
Mining camp blues / Hello stranger / Green rolling hills of West Virginia / Few more years shall roll / Two soldiers / Sweetest gift, a mother's smile / Tomorrow I'll be gone / My better years / Custom made woman blues / Don't put her down, you helped put her there / You gave me a song / Pretty bird / Gallop to Kansas
CD _____ ROUCD 0027
Rounder / May '95 / CM / Direct / ADA / Cadillac.

Dickenson, Vic

VIC DICKENSON SEPTET
CD Set _____ 662221
Vanguard / Jan '94 / Complete/Pinnacle / Discovery.

Dickerson, Stefan

ROMANZA
Pescadero pointe / Brazilian sunrise / Old dreams, new wings / Morning view / When love cries / Sarabande / Spanish love / Alone in oblivion / Romanza / Sahara montage
CD _____ 101S8770512
101 South / Jul '94 / New Note.

Dickies

IDJIT SAVANT
CD _____ CDHOLE 002
Golf / May '95 / Plastic Head.

WE AREN'T THE WORLD
CD _____ RE 140CD
Reach Out International / Nov '94 / Jetstar.

Dickinson, Bruce

BALLS TO PICASSO
Cyclops / Hell no / Gods of war / 1000 Points of light / Laughing in the hiding bush / Change of heart / Shoot all the clowns / Fire / Sacred cowboy / Tears of the dragon
CD _____ CDEMDX 1057
EMI / Jun '94 / EMI.

TATTOOED MILLIONAIRE
Son of a gun / Tattooed millionaire / Born in '58 / Hell on wheels / Gypsy road (Dive dive dive) / Dive dive dive / All the young dudes / Lickin' the gun / Zulu Lulu / No lies
CD _____ CDEMS 1542
EMI / Jul '94 / EMI.

Dickinson, Jimmy

SPRING POEMS
CD _____ FC 064CD
Fan Club / Aug '90 / Direct.

Dickson, Barbara

AFTER DARK
Right moment / Same sky / Only a dream in Rio / Lush life / I don't believe in you / Caravan / Fortress around your heart / I think it's going to rain today / It's money that I love / Pride (in the name of love) / No milk today / I know him so well
CD _____ CLACD 302
Castle / Aug '92 / BMG.

BARBARA DICKSON ALBUM
January February / In the night / It's really you / Day and night / Can't get by without you / Anytime you're down and out / I'll say it all again / Hello stranger / Goodbye my heart / Plane song / Now i don't know
CD _____ 9827272
Pickwick/Sony Collector's Choice / Mar '94 / Carlton Home Entertainment / Pinnacle / Sony.

DARK END OF THE STREET
CD _____ TRACD 117
Transatlantic / Nov '95 / BMG / Pinnacle / ADA.

DON'T THINK TWICE IT'S ALL RIGHT
Don't think twice, it's alright / With God on our side / When the ship comes in / Maggie's farm / Tears of rage / Oxford town / You ain't goin' nowhere / When I paint my masterpiece / Times they are a changin' / Ring them bells / Hard rain's gonna fall / Blowin' in the wind
CD _____ MOODCD 25
Columbia / Aug '92 / Sony.

GOLD
I know him so well / Missing you / Another good day for goodbye / Touch touch / Anyone who had a heart / Day in the life / You send me / What is love
CD _____ CLACD 297
Castle / '92 / BMG.

NOW AND THEN
Follow you follow me / Fine partly cloudy / I think it's going to rain today / Friend in need / It might be you / Fortress around your heart / If you go away / Same sky / September song / If you're right / How long / Peter / West coast of Clare / Tenderly / I don't believe in you / Angie baby / Who are you anyway / Caravans / No milk today / Day in the life / Thousands are sailing / Dream of you / It's raining again today / Every now and then
CD _____ VSOPCD 166
Connoisseur / Jul '91 / Pinnacle.

PARCEL OF ROGUES, A
Van diemen's land / My lagan love / My Johnny was a shoemaker / Fine flowers in the valley / I once loved a lad / Jock O'Hazeldean / Sule skerry / Farewell to whisky / Lovely Joan / Donald Og / Geordie / Dark end one / Parcel o' rogues
CD _____ CTVCD 126
Castle / Feb '94 / BMG.

RIGHT MOMENT, THE
Right moment / Tenderly / She moved through the fair / Time after time / Follow you, follow me / It's raining again today / Wouldn't it be good / Boulder to Birmingham / Who are you anyway / Vanishing days of love / Angie baby / Making history / Fine partly cloudy / If you go away
CD _____ CLACD 310
Castle / Sep '92 / BMG.

YOU KNOW IT'S ME
Think it over / Little by little in love / You know it's me / Hold on / We'll believe in lovin' / Only seventeen / You got me / I know you, you know me / I believe in you / My heart lies
CD _____ 9829822

Dickies
CD _____ CDHOLE 002
Golf / May '95 / Plastic Head.

Dictators

FUCK 'EM IF THEY CAN'T TAKE A JOKE
CD _____ DANCD 052
Danceteria / Nov '94 / Plastic Head / ADA.

Diddley, Bo

20TH ANNIVERSARY OF ROCK 'N' ROLL, THE
Ride the water (part 1) / Not fade away / Kill my body / Drag on / Ride on the water (part 2) / Bo Diddley jam - I'm a man / Hey Bo Diddley / Who do you love / Bo Diddley's a gun slinger / I'm a man
CD _____ EDCD 318
Edsel / '91 / Pinnacle / ADA.

AIN'T IT GOOD TO BE FREE
Ain't it good to be free / Bo Diddley put the rock in rock 'n' roll / Gotta be a change / I don't want your welfare / Mona, where's your sister / Stabilize yourself / I don't know where I've been / I ain't gonna force it on you / Evil woman / Let the fox talk
CD _____ 422107
New Rose / May '94 / Direct / ADA.

BEFORE YOU ACCUSE ME
CD _____ CDCD 1208
Charly / Jan '95 / Charly / THE / Cadillac.

BO DIDDLEY - THE CHESS YEARS (12CD Box Set)
I'm a man / Little girl / Bo Diddley / You don't love me (You don't care) / Diddley daddy / She's fine, she's mine / Pretty thing / Heart o-matic love / Bring it to Jerome / Spanish guitar / Dancing girl / Diddy wah diddy / I'm looking for a woman / I'm bad / Who do you love / Cops and robbers / Down home special / Hey Bo Diddley / Mona (I need you baby) / Say boss man / Before you accuse me / Say man / Hush your mouth / Bo's guitar / Clock strikes twelve / Dearest Darling / Willie and Lillie / Bo meets the monster / Crackin' up / Don't let it go / I'm sorry / Oh yeah / Blues blues / Great Grandfather / Mamma mia / Bucket / What do you know about love / Lazy woman / Come on baby / Nursery rhyme (Puttentang) / Mumblin' guitar / I love you so / Story of Bo Diddley / She's alright / Limber / Say man back again / Run Diddley Daddy / Roadrunner / Spend my life with you / Love you baby / Diddlin' / Cadillac / Limbo / Look at my baby / You know I love you / Let me in / Signifying blues / Live my life / Scuttle bug / Love me / Deed and deed / Walkin' and talkin' / Travelin' west / Crawdad / Ride on Josephine / No more lovin' / Do what I say / Doing the crawdaddy / Whoa / Mule (shine) / Cheyenne / Sixteen tons / Working man / Gunslinger / Somewhere / Sick and tired / Huckleberry bush / All together / Mess around / Shank / Twister / Bo Diddley is a lover / Love is a secret / Bo diddley is loose / Congo / Aztec / Jeanne / Bo's vacation / Hong Kong / Mississippi / Quick draw / You're looking good / Back home / Not guilty / Moon baby / Untitled instrumental / My babe / Detour / Stay sharp / Pills (love's labours lost) / Bo's bounce / I want my baby / Two flies / Background / Please Mr. Engineer / Doin' the jaguar / I know, I'm alright / For the love of Mike / Mr. Khrushchev / You all green / Bo's twist / I can tell / You can't judge a book by the cover / Sad sack / Rock 'n' roll / Mama don't allow no twistin' / Give me a break / Babes in the woods / Who may your lover be / Here 'tis / Bo's a lumberjack / (Extra read all about) Ben / Help out / Gimme gimme / Same old thing / Diana / Met you on a Saturday / Put the shoes on willie / Pretty girl / Old man river / Surfer's love call / Cookie headed Diddley / Greatest lover in the world / Surf sink or swim / Low tide / Africa speaks / Memphis / Old smokey / Bo Diddley's dog / I'm alright / Mr. Custer / Bo's waltz / What's buggin' you / Monkey Diddle / Hey good lookin' / Mama keep your big mouth shut / Jo-Ann / When the saints go marching in / Mush mouth Millie / London stomp / Rooster stew / Mummy walk / La la la / Yeah yeah yeah / Rain man / I wonder why (people don't like me) / Brother bear / Bo Diddley's hoot'nanny / Let's walk awhile / You ain't bad / Somebody beat me / Greasy spoon / Let me pass / Tonight is ours / Soul food / Let the kids dance / Hey red riding hood / He's so mad / Stop my monkey / Root hoot / Stinkey / Cornbread / Fireball / 500% more man / We're gonna get married / Easy / Do the frog / Yakky doodle / Ooh baby / Back to school / Juke / Long distance call / I just want to make love to you / Sad hours / Wrecking my love life / Boo-ga-loo before you go / Little red rooster / Sweet little angel / Goin' down slow / Spoonful / I'm high again / Another sugar Daddy / Bo Diddley 1969 / Soul train / Elephant man / I've got a feeling / If the bible's right / Power house / Funky sly / Shut up woman / Back soul / You Bo Diddley / I don't like you / Hot buttered blues / Bo's beat / Chuck's beat / I love you more than anything / Shape I'm in / Pollution / Bad moon rising / Down on the corner / I said shutup woman / Bad side of the

moon / Lodi / Go for broke / Look at granma / Woman / Hey Jerome / Take it all off / I've had it hard / Bad trip / Good thing / Infatuation / Bo Diddley-itis / I hear you knocking / Make a hit record / Do the robot / Get out of my life / Don't want no lyin' woman / Bo-jam / Husband in law / Sneakers on a rooster / Going down / I've been workin' / Hit or miss / He's got all the whisky / Bite you / Evelee / Stop the pusher / You've got a lot of nerve / I'm sweet on you baby / You got to love me baby / Rollercoaster / I got to go / Billy's blues / Billy's blues #2 / She's alright (unedited) / Signifying blues (extended version) / Pretty baby / You can shimmy / I'm hungry / Oh yes / Watusi bounce / Soup maker / Hey, go go
CD Set _____ CDREDBOX 8
Charly / Feb '94 / Charly / THE / Cadillac.

BO DIDDLEY IS A LOVER
Not guilty / Hong Kong, Mississippi / You're looking good / Bo's vacation / Congo / Bo Diddley is a lover / Aztec / Back home / Bo Diddley is loose / Love is a secret / Quick draw / Two flies / Help out / Diana / Mamma mia / What do you know about love / My babe
CD _____ SEECD 391
See For Miles/C5 / Dec '93 / Pinnacle.

BO'S BLUES
Down home special / You don't love me (you don't care) / Blues blues / 500% more man / Live my life / She's fine, she's mine / Heart-o-matic love / Bring it to Jerome / Pretty thing / You can't judge a book by the cover / Clock strikes twelve / Cops and robbers / Run diddley daddy / Before you accuse me / Diddy wah diddy / Bo's blues / Little girl / I'm a man / I'm bad / Who do you love / I'm looking for a woman / Two flies
CD _____ CDCHD 396
Ace / Aug '93 / Pinnacle / Cadillac / Complete/Pinnacle.

CHESS MASTERS, THE
I'm a man / Diddley daddy / Pretty thing / Bring it to Jerome / Diddy wah diddy / Who do you love / Hey Bo Diddley / Mona / Say boss man / Before you accuse me / Say man / Hush your mouth / Dearest darling / Crackin' up / I'm sorry / Mumblin' guitar / Roadrunner / Sixteen tons / Ride on Josephine / You can't judge a book by the cover
CD _____ CDMF 077
Magnum Force / '90 / Magnum Music Group.

EP COLLECTION: BO DIDDLEY
Little girl / Put the shoes on Willie / Run Diddley daddy / Bo Diddley / I'm a man / Bring it to Jerome / Pretty thing / Greatest lover in the world / She's fine, she's mine / Hey good lookin' / Deed and deed I do / I'm sorry / Dearest darling / Bo meets the monster / Rooster stew / Bo's a lumberjack / Let me in / Hong Kong, Mississippi / Hey Bo Diddley / Before you accuse me / Story of Bo Diddley / You're looking good / I'm looking for a woman (Available on CD only) / Hush your mouth (Available on CD only)
CD _____ SEECD 321
See For Miles/C5 / Jul '91 / Pinnacle.

HEY BO DIDDLEY
Bo Diddley / Hey Bo Diddley / I'm a man / Bring it to Jerome / Diddley daddy / Before you accuse me / Pretty thing / Who do you love / Dearest darling / You can't judge a book by the cover / Say, mam / I'm looking for a woman / Roadrunner / Mona / Cops and robbers / Story of Bo Diddley / Say horeman / Hush your mouth / Nursery rhyme / I'm sorry / Live my life
CD _____ CDRB 1
Charly / Apr '94 / Charly / THE / Cadillac.

HEY BO DIDDLEY/BO DIDDLEY
Hey Bo Diddley / I'm a man / Detour / Before you accuse me / Bo Diddley / Hush your mouth / My babe / Roadrunner / Shank / I know / Here 'tis / I'm looking for a woman / I can tell / Mr. Khrushchev / Diddlin' / Give me a break / Who may your lover be / Bo's bounce / You can't judge a book by the cover / Babes in the woods / Sad sack / Mama don't allow no twistin' / You all gone / Bo's twist
CD _____ BGOCD 287
Beat Goes On / Jul '95 / Pinnacle.

I'M A MAN
Bo Diddley / I'm a man / Pretty thing / Who do you love / Mona / Say man / Hush your mouth / Roadrunner / You can't judge a book by the cover / Cops and robbers / Hey Bo Diddley / Crackin' up / Little fool / Dancing girl / Diddy wah diddy / Bring it to Jerome
CD _____ CDCD 1019
Charly / Mar '93 / Charly / THE / Cadillac.

IN CONCERT WITH MAINSQUEEZE
CD _____ AIM 1023CD
Aim / Oct '93 / Direct / ADA / Jazz Music.

LEGENDARY HITS
CD _____ 90158-2
Jazz Archives / Oct '92 / Jazz Music / Discovery / Cadillac.

LET ME PASS...PLUS
Let me pass / Stop my monkey / Greasy spoon / Tonight is ours / Root toot / Slinkey / Hey red riding hood / Let the kids dance

---

/ He's so mad / Soul food / Cornbread / Somebody beat me / 500% more man / Mama keep your big mouth shut / We're gonna get married / Easy
CD _____ SEECD 392
See For Miles/C5 / Jan '94 / Pinnacle.

LIVING LEGEND
CD _____ ROSE 188CD
New Rose / Sep '89 / Direct / ADA.

MIGHTY BO DIDDLEY, THE
CD _____ TX 51161CD
Triple X / Sep '95 / Plastic Head.

SIGNIFYING BLUES (Charly Blues - Masterworks Vol. 42)
CD _____ CDBM 43
Charly / Jun '93 / Charly / THE / Cadillac.

STORY OF BO DIDDLEY
CD _____ 3001062
Scratch / Jul '95 / BMG.

Die Art

BUT
CD _____ RTD 19519042
Our Choice / Nov '94 / Pinnacle.

Die Cheerleader

FILTH BY ASSOCIATION
CD _____ ABT 097CD
Abstract / Oct '93 / Pinnacle / Total/BMG.

Die Kreuzen

CENTURY DAYS
CD _____ TGLP 30CD
Touch & Go / Aug '88 / SRD.

Die Krupps

FINAL REMIXES, THE
To the hilt / Paradise of sin / Language of reality / Fatherland / Worst case scenario / Shellshocked / Crossfire / Bloodsuckers / Iron man / Inside out / New temptation / Dawning of doom / Ministry of fear / Hi tech low life / Metal machine music / Rings of steel
CD _____ ATLASCDD 006
Equator / Sep '94 / Pinnacle.

METALLE MASCHINEN MUSIK
CD _____ KRUPPS 1CD
Grey Area / Aug '91 / Pinnacle.

ODYSSEY OF THE MIND
Last flood / Scent / Metalmorphasis / Isolation / Final option / Alive / Odyssey / LCD / Eggshell / Jekyll or Hyde
CD _____ CDXMFN 187
CD _____ CDXMFN 187
Music For Nations / Jul '95 / Pinnacle.

Die Lustigen Junggesellen

EDELWEISS
CD _____ CNCD 5996
Disky / Jul '94 / THE / BMG / Discovery / Pinnacle.

Die Monster Die

CHROME MOLLY
CD _____ JBM 1 CD
Johnson Brothers Music / Mar '93 / SRD.

Die Toten Hosen

LEARNING ENGLISH, LESSON 1
CD _____ CDVIR 11
Virgin / Mar '92 / EMI.

LOVE, PEACE AND MONEY
Return of Alex / Year 2000 / All for the sake of love / Love song / Sexual / Diary of a lover / Put your money where your mouth is (Buy me) / Love is here / More and more / My land / Wunsch dir was / Wasted years / Perfect criminal / Love machine / Chaos bros.
CD _____ CDVIR 27
Virgin / Dec '94 / EMI.

Died Pretty

DOUGHBOY HOLLOW
Doused / D.C. / Sweetheart / Godbless / Satisfied / Stop myself / Battle of Stanmore / Love song / Disaster / Out in the rain / Turn your head
CD _____ BEGA 121CD
Beggars Banquet / '92 / Warner Music / Disc.

EVERY BRILLIANT EYE
Sight unseen / Underbelly / Herr godiva / Face toward the sun / Prayer / Ture fools fall / Whitlam Square / Rue for the day / From the dark
CD _____ BEGA 108CD
Beggars Banquet / Apr '90 / Warner Music / Disc.

LOST
Lost / As must have / Winterland / Crawls away / Towers of strength / Out of my hands / Springenfall / Caesar's cold / One day / Free dirt
CD _____ BEGA 101CD
Beggars Banquet / Apr '89 / Warner Music / Disc.

Dieform

ARCHIVES AND DOCUMENTS
CD _____ NORMAL 95 CD
Normal/Okra / '89 / Direct / ADA.

ARCHIVES AND DOCUMENTS (RE-RELEASE)
Face against ground / Bondage / New York / Serenade / Serial clones / Deadline 2 / North valley / Necrox x / Third generation / Shaved girls / Was / Nostalgia / Tomorrow / Crash in the sky / Eternal language / Reflex 3 / Criminal passion / Sing song / Dance music / Maldoror / Es lebe the tod 3 / Murder /projection / Tote kinder aus deutschland / Ataxia / Uns kill / Psychotrope / Dog handler / Purple rain / Newel/ light / Crypt / Song of parlysis / Oltre / Fleshwounds / Post mortem / Sad memory
CD Set _____ TUECD 9202
Tuesday / Mar '95 / Vital.

DIE PUPPE
CD _____ NORMAL 81 CD
Normal/Okra / '89 / Direct / ADA.

PHOTOGRAMMES
CD _____ NORMAL 106 CD
Normal/Okra / '89 / Direct / ADA.

POUPEE MECHANIQUE
CD _____ NORMAL 83 CD
Normal/Okra / '89 / Direct / ADA.

SOME EXPERIENCES WITH SHOCK
CD _____ NORMAL 82 CD
Normal/Okra / '89 / Direct / ADA.

TEARS OF EROS
CD _____ HY 39100032
Hyperium / Jul '93 / Plastic Head.

Dieheim, Susan

DESERT EQUATIONS (Dieheim, Susan & Richard Horowitz)
Ishtar / Got away / I'm a man / Tear / Azax attra / Jum jum / Armour / Desert equations
CD _____ MTM 8CD
Made To Measure / Sep '88 / Grapevine.

Diesel Park West

FREAKGENE
CD _____ PERMCD 29
Permanent / Apr '95 / Total/BMG.

VERSUS THE CORPORATE WALTZ
CD _____ FIENDCD 747
Demon / May '93 / Pinnacle / ADA.

Dietrich, Marlene

COLLECTION
CD _____ COL 054
Collection / Mar '95 / Target/BMG.

COME UP AND SEE ME
CD _____ 213352
Milan / Jul '94 / BMG / Silva Screen.

DAS LIED IST AUS
CD _____ RMB 75052
Remember / Nov '93 / Total/BMG.

ESSENTIAL MARLENE DIETRICH, THE
Ich bin von kopf bis fuss auf liebe eingestellt (Falling in love again) / Quand l'amour meurt / Give me the man / Leben ohne liebe kannst du nicht / Mein blondes baby / Allein in einer grossen stadt / Peter / Lola / Wer wird den weinen / Johnny wenn du geburtstag hast / Lili Marlene / Dejeuner du matin / Ou vont les fleurs / Wenn die soldaten / In den kasernen / Und wenn er wiederkommt / Wenn der sommer müde / Illusion (J'étais on the lonely side) / Blowin' in the wind / Der welt war jung (When the world was young) / Where have all the flowers gone / Ich werde dich lieben (Theme for young lovers) / Der trommelmann (The little drummerboy) / Auf der mundharmonika
CD _____ CDEMS 1399
EMI / May '91 / EMI.

FOR THE BOYS IN THE BACKROOM
Lili Marlene / Black market / Johnny / Boys in the backroom / You've got that look / This world of ours / You do something to me
CD _____ BSTCD 9109
Best Compact Discs / May '92 / Complete/ Pinnacle.

I COULDN'T BE SO ANNOYED
CD _____ RMB 75053
Remember / Nov '93 / Total/BMG.

MARLENE
Kinder, heute'abend / Leben ohne liebe kannst du nicht / Falling in love again / Ich bin die fesche Lola / Quand l'amour meurt / Johnny / Mein blondes baby / Wenn die beste freundin / Wenn ich mir'was wunschen durfte / Allein in einer grossen stadt / Ich bin von kopf bis fuss auf liebe eingestellt (Falling in love again (original German version)) / Es liegt in der luft/potpourri / Nimm dich in acht vor blonden frauen / Give me the man
CD _____ CD AJA 5039
Living Era / Oct '88 / Koch.

MARLENE DIETRICH
CD _____ LCD 6006/7
Fresh Sound / Jan '93 / Jazz Music / Discovery.

MARLENE DIETRICH
CD _____ 16058
Laserlight / May '94 / Target/BMG.

MARLENE DIETRICH COLLECTOR'S EDITION
Deja Vu / Apr '95 / THE.

MARLENE DIETRICH IN LONDON
I can't give you anything but love / Laziest girl in town / Shir Hatan / La vie en rose / Jonny / Go away from my window / Allein in einer grossen stadt / Lili Marlene / Das lied ist aus / Lola / I wish you love
CD _____ CDSBL 13110
DRG / Nov '92 / New Note.

MARLENE DIETRICH LIVE AT THE CAFE DE PARIS
CD _____ CD 47254
Sony Classical / Nov '91 / Sony.

SEI LIEB ZU MIR
CD _____ RMB 75056
Remember / Aug '93 / Total/BMG.

Diez Brothers

CLOSE UP
CD _____ ISCD 114
Intersound / Oct '91 / Jazz Music.

Dif Juz

EXTRACTIONS
Crosswinds / Starting point / Love insane / Twin and earth
CD _____ CAD 505 CD
4AD / Feb '87 / Disc.

Difference Engine

BREADMAKER
Five listens / Simon's day / Never pull / Tsunami / Flat / Bugpowder / Epiphany
CD _____ LADIDA 034
La-Di-Da / Jul '94 / Vital.

Different Trains

ON THE RIGHT TRACK
Birth / This is life / Bits of dust / Dust in the wind / Market place / In my house / Sweet children / Class / To be continued / Workmen / Work / Rain / Tired tide / Swim against the tide / Cruel trick
CD _____ GEPCD 1008
Giant Electric Pea / Apr '94 / Pinnacle.

Diga Rhythm Band

DIGA
Sweet sixteen / Magnificent sevens / Happiness is drumming / Razooli / Tal mala
CD _____ RCD 10101
Rykodisc / Sep '91 / Vital / ADA.

Digable Planets

BLOWOUT COMB
May 4th movement / Black ego / Dog it / Jettin' / Borough check / Highing fly / Dial 7 (Axiomos of creamy spices) / Art of easing / K.B.'s Alley (mood dudes groove) / Graffiti / Blowing down / Ninth Wonder (Blackitolism) / For corners
CD _____ CDCHR 6087
Cooltempo / Oct '94 / EMI.

REACHIN' (A NEW REFUTATION OF TIME AND SPACE)
It's good to be here / Pacifics / Where I'm from / What cool breezes do / Time and space / Rebirth of slick / Last of the spiddyunda / Jimmi diggin' cats / La femme fetel / Escapism / Appointment at the fat clinic / Nickel bags / Swoon units / Examination of what
CD _____ CDCHR 6064
Cooltempo / Jan '94 / EMI.

Digance, Richard

LIVE AT THE QEH/COMMERCIAL ROAD
Dear Diana / Summertime day in Stratford / Down petticoat lane / Drinking with Rosie / Journey of the salmon / Up on the seventh floor / Drag queen blues (nearly) / Right back where I started / Taken my lifetime away / I want to be there when you made it / Suicide Sam / Jungle cup final / East end ding dong / Think of me / Jumping Jack frog / Nightingale sang in Berkeley Square / Beauty Queen / Goodbye my friend, goodbye / Heavyweight Albert / Back Street international / Jimmy Greaves
CD _____ BGOCD 304
Beat Goes On / Nov '95 / Pinnacle.

Digital Orgasm

COME DANCIN'
Another world / Startouchers / Time to believe / Switch the mood / Magick / Running out of time (remix) / Moog eruption / Keep on flying / This generation / Reality / Running out of time / Moog eruption (remix)
CD _____ 4509905022
Dead Dead Good / Aug '92 / Pinnacle.

Digital Poodle

DIVISION
Division / Forward march / Totalitarian / Head of Lenin / Left/right / Binary / Elek-

tronic espionage / Reform / Crack / Red star / Rifle
CD _____ LUDDITECD 222
Death Of Vinyl / Mar '94 / Vital.

Digital Underground

SONS OF THE P
DFLO shuffle / Heartbeat props / No nose job / Sons of the P / Flowin' on the D-line / Kiss you back / Tales of the funky / Higher heights of spirituality / Family of the underground / D-flowstrumental / Good thing we-'re rappin'
CD _____ BLRCD 12
Big Life / Oct '91 / Pinnacle.

Digits

LITTLE MISCARRIAGE
CD _____ TG 103CD
Touch & Go / Oct '92 / SRD.

Digweed, John

JOURNEYS BY DJ VOL.4
CD _____ JDJCD 4
Music Unites / Feb '94 / Sony / 3MV / SRD.

Dillard & Clark

FANTASTIC EXPEDITION OF DILLARD & CLARK (Dillard, Doug & Gene Clark)
Out on the side / She darked the sun / Don't come rollin' / Train leaves here this morning / Radio song / Git it on brother (git in line brother) / In the plan / Something's wrong / Why not your baby / Lyin' down the middle / Don't be cruel
CD _____ EDCD 192
Edsel / Jun '90 / Pinnacle / ADA.

THROUGH THE MORNING, THROUGH THE NIGHT (Dillard, Doug & Gene Clark)
No longer a sweetheart of mine / Through the morning, through the night / Rocky top / So sad / Corner street bar / I bowed my head and cried holy / Kansas City Southern / Four walls / Polly / Rollin' in my sweet baby's arms / Don't let me down
CD _____ EDCD 195
Edsel / Feb '91 / Pinnacle / ADA.

Dillard, Rodney

LET THE ROUGH SIDE DRAG
CD _____ FF 537CD
Flying Fish / Jul '92 / Roots / CM / Direct / ADA.

Dillard, Varetta

GOT YOU ON MY MIND
Square dance rock / If (you want to be my baby) / Got you on my mind / Mama don't want (what papa don't want) / One more time / I'm gonna tell my Daddy on you / Skinny Jimmy / Darling listen to the words of this song / Leave a happy fool alone / See see rider blues / That's why I cry / I got a lot of love / Undecided / Pray for me mother / I miss you Jimmy (Tribute to James Dean) / Star of fortune / Rules of love / Falling / Old fashioned / Honey / What'll I do / Just nightly / Give me the night / Time was / I can't help myself / That old feeling / Cherry blossom / Pennies from Heaven / Night is never long enough
CD _____ BCD 15431
Bear Family / Jul '89 / Rollercoaster / Direct / CM / Swift / ADA.

LOVIN' BIRD, THE
(Twee twee twee) the lovin' bird / Teaser / Good to me / Mercy Mr. Percy / Whole lot of lip / What can I say / I don't know what it is but I like it / Hey sweet love / You don't know what you're missing / Little bitty tear / Positive love / You ain't foolin' nobody / You better come home / You know I'm too good for you / Wondering where you are / Scorched / Good gravy baby / One more time / Star of fortune / Rules of love / Old fashioned
CD _____ BCD 15432
Bear Family / Jul '89 / Rollercoaster / Direct / CM / Swift / ADA.

Dillard-Hartford-Dillard

GLITTER GRASS/PERMANENT WAVE
CD _____ FF 036CD
Flying Fish / Feb '93 / Roots / CM / Direct / ADA.

Dillards

LET IT FLY
Darlin' boys / Close the door lightly / Old train / Big ship / Missing you / Out on a limb / Ozark nights / Tears won't dry in the rain / Livin' in the house / One too many mornings / Let it fly / Wizard of song
CD _____ VHD 79460
Vanguard / Jul '91 / Complete/Pinnacle / Discovery.

MOUNTAIN ROCK
Caney Creek / Don't you cry / Reason to believe / Big bayou / Walkin' in Jerusalem / I've just seen a face / High sierra / Never see my home again / Somebody touched

me / Fields have turned brown / Orange blossom special (13 minutes)
CD _____ 15295
Laserlight / Aug '91 / Target/BMG.

TRIBUTE TO THE AMERICAN DUCK/ROOTS & BRANCHES
CD _____ BGOCD 306
Beat Goes On / Feb '96 / Pinnacle.

Dillinger

CB 200
CD _____ RRCD 30
Reggae Refreshers / Sep '91 / PolyGram / Vital.

COCAINE
Cocaine in my brain / Jah love / Funkey punk / Mickey Mouse crab louse / I thurst / Loving pauper / Flat foot hustlin' / Crabs in my pants / Marijuana in my brain / Cocaine (remix)
CD _____ CPCD 8020
Charly / Feb '94 / Charly / THE / Cadillac.

FUNKY PUNK
CD _____ LG 21061
Lagoon / Nov '92 / Magnum Music Group / THE.

I NEED A WOMAN
CD _____ RB 3004
Reggae Best / May '94 / Magnum Music Group / THE.

SAY NO TO DRUGS
CD _____ LG 21003
Lagoon / Jun '93 / Magnum Music Group / THE.

THREE PIECE SUIT
CD _____ LG 21081
Lagoon / Aug '93 / Magnum Music Group / THE.

TOP RANKING
CD _____ RNCD 2129
Rhino / Nov '95 / Jetstar / Magnum Music Group / THE.

Dillingham, Todd

ART INTO DUST
Little visions / Girl of the scene / You don't mind / Art into dust / Celebration bonfire / It really matters / Never want to see / Fading (just for you) / Fine time no time / African device / Fly / Crabs adventury / Luminous glow / Green pears / Am I alone / Interstellar overdrive (24 minute bonus)
CD _____ VP 121CD
Voice Print / Jan '93 / Voice Print.

SGT. KIPPER
CD _____ WO 25CD
Woronzow / Jul '95 / Pinnacle.

VAST EMPTY SPACES
Vast empty spaces / Shiny girl / Myriad girl-paintings / Rely on me / Dollis broof / Millero / Wonderland / Mullardo / Tranquil water / Nine you dont' want to / Up the ass of a swan / Animal bizarre / Where is the brave
CD _____ VP 153CD
Voice Print / Aug '94 / Voice Print.

VOICEPRINT RADIO SESSION
CD _____ VPR 002CD
Voice Print / Oct '94 / Voice Print.

Dillon, Cheralee

CITRON
CD _____ GRCD 380
Glitterhouse / Dec '95 / Direct / ADA.

POOL
CD _____ GRCD 310
Glitterhouse / Feb '94 / Direct / ADA.

Dillon Fence

OUTSIDE IN
CD _____ MR 0492
Mammoth / Jun '93 / Vital.

ROSEMARY
CD _____ MR 00332
Mammoth / Nov '92 / Vital.

Dillon, Leonard

ONE STEP FORWARD
CD _____ PRCDSP 400
Prestige / Jun '92 / Total/BMG.

Dillon, Phyllis

LOVE WAS ALL I HAD (Dillon, Phillis)
CD _____ RNCD 2088
Rhino / Dec '94 / Jetstar / Magnum Music Group / THE.

ONE LIFE TO LIVE
CD _____ TICD 15004
Studio One / Mar '95 / Jetstar.

Dillon, Sandy

DANCING ON THE FREEWAY
CD _____ GY 004
Trident / Mar '94 / Pinnacle.

Dils

I HATE THE RICH
CD _____ DAMGOOD 008
Damaged Goods / Jul '92 / SRD.

Dim Stars

DIM STARS
CD _____ PAPCD 014
Paperhouse / Apr '92 / Disc.

Dime Bag

DIME BAG
CD _____ HB 10
Heatblast / Mar '93 / SRD.

Dimensional Holofonic...

LSD 3D (Dimensional Holofonic Sound)
Acid / Evil acid / Compound-25 version / This is acid / 3-D Dub version / Psych-o-delics / Flashbacks / Bad acid
CD _____ BIAS 246CD
Play It Again Sam / Apr '93 / Vital.

Dimple Minds

LIVE IN ALZHEIM
CD _____ SPV 08476932
SPV / May '95 / Plastic Head.

Din

FANTASTIC PLANET
CD _____ HY 39100162CD
Hyperium / Nov '92 / Plastic Head.

Dingle

RED DOG
Hot dingle wood / Haemorrhage / Birdy num num / Xylocheese / Fred Lane / Fleas / Ouise / Vodka tonic / Sailing / Journey on a davenport / Ba da da da / Without hot water / Still going / Still going (instrumental) / Soliloquy / Drinking song / 2-Note / Nuevo imperial / Celine / Mambo samba / Java
CD _____ NAR 110CD
New Alliance / May '94 / Pinnacle.

Dink

DINK
Three big bags / Running red / Green mind / Water / Urban suicide (Hippie Killer Mix) / Angels / Heroin song / Get on it / In her head / Rocks / Dirt
CD _____ CDEST 2248
Capitol / Jun '95 / EMI.

Dinosaur Jnr

BUG
CD _____ BFFP 31 CD
Blast First / Oct '88 / Disc.

FOSSILS
CD _____ SST 275 CD
SST / May '93 / Plastic Head.

GREEN MIND
Wagon / Puke and cry / Flying cloud / How'd you pin that one on me / Water / Muck / Thumb / Green mind / Blowing it / I live for that look
CD _____ 9031734482
Blanco Y Negro / Feb '91 / Warner Music.

WHERE HAVE YOU BEEN
Out there / Start choppin' / What else is new / On the way / Not the same / Get me / Drawerings / Hide / Goin' home / I ain't sayin'
CD _____ 4509916272
Blanco Y Negro / Feb '93 / Warner Music.

WITHOUT A SOUND
Feel the pain / I don't think so / Yeah right / Outta hand / Grab it / Even you / Mind glow / Get out of this / On the brink / Seemed like the thing to do / Over your shoulder
CD _____ 450996933-2
Warner Bros. / Aug '94 / Warner Music.

YOU'RE LIVING ALL OVER ME
CD _____ SST 1330 CD
SST / May '93 / Plastic Head.

Dio

DIAMONDS (The Best Of Dio)
Holy diver / Rainbow in the dark / Don't talk to strangers / We rock / Last in line / Evil eyes / Rock 'n' roll children / Sacred heart / Hungry for heaven / Hide in the rainbow / Dream evil / Wild one / Lock up the wolves
CD _____ 512206-2
Vertigo / Jun '92 / PolyGram.

HOLY DIVER
Stand up and shout / Holy diver / Gypsy / Caught in the middle / Don't talk to strangers / Straight through the heart / Invisible / Rainbow in the dark / Shame on the night
CD _____ 811 021-2
Vertigo / Mar '88 / PolyGram.

Dion

DREAM ON FIRE
CD _____ VR 3327
Vision / Oct '92 / Pinnacle.

I wonder why / Teen angel / Where or when / You better not do that / Just you / I got the blues / Don't pity me / Teenager in love / Wonderful girl / Funny feeling / I've cried before / That's my desire / No one knows / I can't go on
CD _____ CDCHM 107
Ace / Jul '89 / Pinnacle / Cadillac / Complete/Pinnacle.

RETURN OF THE WANDERER/FIRE IN THE NIGHT
Looking for the heart of Saturday night / You've awakened something in me / Pattern of my lifeline / Street heart theme / Spanish Harlem incident / Fire in the night / Hollywood / Street mama / You are my star / Midtown American main street gang / Guitar queen / (I used to be a) Brooklyn dodger / Power of love within / Do you believe in magic / We don't talk anymore / Midnight lover / All quiet on 34th Street / Poor boy
CD _____ CDCHD 936
Ace / Jun '90 / Pinnacle / Cadillac / Complete/Pinnacle.

RUNAROUND SUE
Runaround Sue / Somebody nobody wants / Dream lover / Life is but a dream / Wanderer / Runaway girl / I'm gonna make it somehow / Majestic / Could somebody take my place tonight / Little star / Lonely world / In the still of the night / Kansas City / Take good care of my baby
CD _____ CDCHM 148
Ace / Aug '89 / Pinnacle / Cadillac / Complete/Pinnacle.

LAURIE, SABINA & UNITED ARTISTS SIDES VOLUME 1, THE (Belmonts)
Come on little angel / Tell me why / Smoke from your cigarette / That background music / Know about me / My love is real / Searching for a new love / I don't know how to cry / I need someone / Hombre / Don't get around much anymore / Why / You're like a mystery / Today my love has gone away / I got a feeling / I don't know why / We belong together / Such a long way / Come take a walk with me / Ann-Marie / Diddle-dee-dum / I confess / Summertime / I Walk on boy / Now it's all over / Not responsible / Time to dream / Dancin' girl / Have you heard / (I've got) More important things to do / Tell my why
CD _____ CDCHD 58C
Ace / Aug '95 / Pinnacle / Cadillac / Complete/Pinnacle.

Dion, Celine

CELINE DION
Introduction / Love can move mountains / Show your emotion / If you asked me to / If you could see me now / Halfway to heaven / Beauty and the beast / With this tear / Did you give enough love / If I were you / I love you, goodbye / Little bit of love / Water from the moon / Nothing broken but my heart / Where does my heart beat now (On 4715080/8/9 only)
CD _____ 471508-9
Epic / Nov '92 / Sony.

CELINE DION/UNISON
Love can move mountains / Show some emotions / If you asked me to / If you could see me now / Halfway to heaven / Did you give enough love / If I were you / Beauty and the beast / I love you, goodbye / Little bit of love / Water from the moon / With this tear / Nothing broken but my heart / (If there was) Any other way / If love is out of the question / Where does my heart beat now / Last to know / I'm loving every moment with you / Love by another name / Unison / I feel too much / If we could start over / Have a heart
CD Set _____ DIONCD 2
Epic / May '95 / Sony.

COLOUR OF MY LOVE, THE
Power of love / Misled / Think twice / Only one road / Everybody's talkin' my baby down / Next plane out / Real emotion / When I fall in love / Love doesn't ask why / Refuse to dance / I remember L.A. / No living without loving you / Lovin' proof / Just walk away / Colour of my love
CD _____ 474743 2
Epic / Feb '94 / Sony.

D'EUX
Pour que tu maimes encore / Le ballet / Regarde moi / Je seia pas / La moire d'abra-ham destin / Les derniers seront les premiers / Mrai ou tu iras / J'attendais / Priere paienne / Vole
CD _____ 4802862
Epic / Sep '95 / Sony.

FOR YOU
CD _____ DSHLCD 7021
D-Sharp / Jan '96 / Pinnacle.

UNISON
(If there was) any other way / If love is out of the question / Where does my heart beat now / Last to know / I'm loving every moment with you / Love by another name / Unison / I feel too much / If we could start over / Have a heart

Diop, Wasis

NO SANT
CD _____ 5265652
Mercury / Jan '96 / PolyGram.

Diorio, Joe

DOUBLE TAKE
CD _____ RMCD 4502
Ram / Sep '93 / Harmonia Mundi /
Cadillac.

MORE THAN FRIENDS
CD _____ RMCD 4514
Ram / Apr '94 / Harmonia Mundi /
Cadillac.

WE WILL MEET AGAIN
CD _____ RMCD 4501
Ram / Sep '93 / Harmonia Mundi /
Cadillac.

Dioubate, Oumou

LANCEY
CD _____ STCD 1046
Sterns / Oct '93 / Sterns / CM.

Dioulasso, Bob

BALAFONS, PERCUSSIONS, ETC
CD _____ 824812
Buda / Nov '90 / Discovery / ADA.

Diplomats

DIPLOMATS
CD _____ RIPEXD 197
Ripe / Nov '95 / Total/BMG.

Dire Straits

ALCHEMY -- LIVE
Once upon a time in the west / Expresso
love / Private investigations / Sultans of
swing / Two young lovers / Telegraph Road
/ Solid rock / Going home (theme from Lo-
cal Hero) / Romeo and Juliet
CD _____ 818 243-2
Vertigo / '87 / PolyGram.

BROTHERS IN ARMS
So far away / Money for nothing / Walk of
life / Your latest trick / Why worry / Ride
across the river / Man's too strong / One
world / Brothers in arms
CD _____ 824 499-2
Vertigo / May '85 / PolyGram.

COMMUNIQUE
Angel of mercy / Follow me home / Lady
writer / News / Once upon a time in the
West / Communique / Portobello belle / Single headed sailor / Where do you think
you're going / So far away / Money for nothing / Walk of life / Your latest trick / Why
worry / Ride across the river / Man's too
strong / One world / Brothers in arms
CD _____ 800 052-2
Vertigo / '87 / PolyGram.

DIRE STRAITS
Down to the waterline / Water of love / Set-
ting me up / Six blade knife / Southbound
again / Sultans of swing / In the gallery
CD _____ 800 051-2
Vertigo / '87 / PolyGram.

LIVE AT THE BBC
Down to the waterline / Six blade knife /
Water of love / Wild West End / Sultans of
swing / Lions / What's the matter baby /
Tunnel of love
CD _____ WINCD 072
CD _____ WINCD 072X
Windsong / Jun '95 / Pinnacle.

LOVE OVER GOLD
Telegraph Road / Private investigations / In-
dustrial disease / It never rains / Love over
gold
CD _____ 8000882
Vertigo / '84 / PolyGram.

MAKING MOVIES
Tunnel of love / Romeo and Juliet / Skatea-
way / Expresso love / Les boys / Hand in
hand / Solid rock / Down to the waterline /
Water of love / Setting me up / Six blade
knife / Southbound again / Sultans of swing
/ In the gallery / Wild West End / Lions
CD _____ 8000502
Vertigo / '87 / PolyGram.

MONEY FOR NOTHING
Sultans of swing / Down to the waterline /
Portobello belle (live) / Twisting by the pool
/ Romeo and Juliet / Where do you think
you're going / Walk of life / Private investi-
gations / Money for nothing / Tunnel of love
/ Brothers in arms / Telegraph Road
CD _____ 836 419-2
Vertigo / Oct '88 / PolyGram.

ON EVERY STREET
Calling Elvis / On every street / When it
comes to you / Fade to black / Bug / You
and your friend / Heavy fuel / Iron hand /
Ticket to heaven / My parties / Planet of
New Orleans / How long
CD _____ 5101602
Vertigo / Sep '91 / PolyGram.

ON THE NIGHT
Calling Elvis / Walk of life / Heavy fuel / Ro-
meo and Juliet / Private investigations /
Your latest trick / On every street / You and
your friend / Money for nothing / Brothers
in arms
CD _____ 514766-2
Vertigo / Apr '94 / PolyGram.

Direct Hits

MAGIC ATTIC
CD _____ TANGCD 9
Tangerine / Oct '94 / Disc.

Directions In Groove

DIRECTIONS IN GROOVE
CD _____ 518436-2
Mercury / Dec '93 / PolyGram.

Dirtcoldfight

HYMNAL
CD _____ CSR 017CD
Cavity Search / Oct '95 / Plastic Head.

Dirty 3

DIRTY 3
CD _____ ABB 93CD
Big Cat / Aug '95 / SRD / Pinnacle.

Dirty Dozen Brass Band

JELLY
Jelly jazz / Georgia swing / Freakish / Side-
walk blues / Red light district / Milenberg
joys / Medley: Mr. Ray J/Dead man blues /
Jungle blues / Shoe shiner's drag / Wolver-
ine blues / Jelly roll's misgiving / Pearls /
New Orleans blues / Kansas City stomp /
Medley: The one and only/Georgia swing
reprise
CD _____ 473059 2
Columbia / Jul '93 / Sony.

LIVE: MARDI GRAS IN MONTREUX
CD _____ CD 2052
Rounder / '88 / CM / Direct / ADA /
Cadillac.

MY FEET CAN'T FAIL ME NOW
Blackbird special / Do it fluid / I ate up the
apple tree / Bongo beep / Blue monk /
Caravan / St. James infirmary / Li'l Liza
Jane / Mary Mary / My feet can't fail me
now
CD _____ CCD 43005
George Wein Collection / Oct '84 / New
Note.

**OPEN UP (WHATCHA GONNA DO FOR
THE REST OF YOUR LIFE)**
Use your brain / Open up (whatcha gonna
do for the rest of your life) / Lost souls (of
Southern Louisiana) / Deore sceadu (dark
shadow) / Dominique / Charlie Dozen /
Song for Lady M / Remember when /
Darker shadows / Eyomzi
CD _____ 4683652
Columbia / Oct '91 / Sony.

Dirty Hands

LETTERS FOR KINGS
CD _____ BNVCD 10
Black & Noir / Jan '92 / Plastic Head.

Dirty Looks

ONE BAD LEG
CD _____ CDMFN 178
Music For Nations / Jan '95 / Pinnacle.

Dis Bonjour A La Dame

DIS BONJOUR A LA DAME
CD _____ 0630104362
East West / Jul '95 / Warner Music.

Disappear Fear

DEEP SOUL DIVER
CD _____ CDPH 1173
Philo / May '95 / Direct / CM / ADA.

DISAPPEAR FEAR
CD _____ CDPH 1171
Philo / Aug '95 / Direct / CM / ADA.

LIVE AT THE BOTTOM LINE
CD _____ CDPH 1172
Philo / Jun '95 / Direct / CM / ADA.

Discard

FOUR MINUTES PAST MIDNIGHT
CD _____ RIP 001
Ripping / Sep '94 / Plastic Head.

Discharge

**DISCHARGED (A Tribute To Discharge)
(Various Artists)**
CD _____ PREACH 001CD
Rhythm Vicar / Jun '92 / Plastic Head.

SEEING, FEELING, BLEEDING
CD _____ NB 085
Nuclear Blast / Dec '93 / Plastic Head.

WHY
Vision of war / Look at tomorrow / Maimed
and slaughtered / Ain't no feeble bastard /
Massacre of innocence / Doomsday / Does

this system work / Why / Mania for conquest / Is this to be / State violence / State
control
CD _____ PLATE 002CD
Clay / Apr '93 / Cargo.

Disciples

FOR THOSE WHO UNDERSTAND
CD _____ BSL 101CD
Boomshakalacka / Nov '95 / SRD /
Jetstar.

HAIL HIM IN DUB
CD _____ RRCD 014
Roots Collective / Oct '95 / SRD / Jetstar
/ Roots Collective.

RESONATIONS
Eastern fire / Wild fire / From Genesis to
revelation / Root of creation / Mabrak /
Thunder and lightning / Fire burn / Faithful
man / Inner spirit / Iyaman say / After the
battle (Features on CD.) / Tribute to Don
(Features on CD.) / Salute to the brave (Fea-
tures on CD.)
CD _____ NLX 5004CD
Cloak & Dagger / May '95 / Vital.

STORM CLOUDS
CD _____ TEMCD 001
Third Eye / Mar '95 / SRD.

Disco Inferno

D.I. GO POP
In sharky water / New clothes for the new
world / Starbound : All burnt out and nowhere to go / Crash at every speed / Even
the sea sides against us / Next year / Whole
wide world ahead / Footprints in snow
CD _____ R 3072
Rough Trade / Feb '94 / Pinnacle.

IN DEBT
Entertainment / Arc in round / Broken / Emi-
gre / Interference / Leisure time / Set sail /
Hope to God / Freethought / Bleed clean /
Next in line / Incentives / Waking up /
Glancing away / Fallen down the wire / No
edge no end
CD _____ CHE 004 CD
Che / Sep '95 / SRD.

Disco Tex

**GET DANCING (Disco Tex & The
Sexolettes)**
CD _____ CHELD 1003
Start / Aug '89 / Koch.

Dismember

LIKE AN EVER FLOWING
CD _____ NB 047CD
Nuclear Blast / Aug '91 / Plastic Head.

Disembowelment

**TRANSCENDENCE INTO THE
PERIPHERAL**
CD _____ NB 096-2
Nuclear Blast / Jan '94 / Plastic Head.

Disfear

BRUTAL SIGHT OF WAR, A
CD _____ LF 060CD
Lost & Found / Aug '93 / Plastic Head.

Disgust

BRUTALITY OF WAR
Intro / Mother earth / Millions suffer and die
/ Horrific end / Thrown into oblivion / Civil-
isation decoys / Relentless slaughter / And
still... / Light of death / What kind of mind /
You have no right / Sea of tears / Anarchist
cry / Heaps of flesh / Outro
CD _____ MOSH 104CD
Earache / Nov '93 / Vital.

Disgusting

SHAPESHIFTERBIRTHBLUES
CD _____ HNF 011CD
Head Not Found / Nov '95 / Plastic Head.

Disharmonic Orchestra

EXPOSITIONSPROPHYLAXE
CD _____ 8429812
Nuclear Blast / Dec '90 / Plastic Head.

PLEASURE DOME
CD _____ SPV 084-76772
SPV / Jun '94 / Plastic Head.

Disley, Diz

**DIZ DISLEY & HIS STRING QUARTET
AT THE WHITE BEAR**
CD _____ JCD 212
Jazzology / Mar '95 / Swift / Jazz Music.

Dismember

CASKET GARDEN
CD _____ NB 1302
Nuclear Blast / Mar '95 / Plastic Head.

INDECENT AND OBSCENE
CD _____ NB 077CD
Nuclear Blast / Jul '93 / Plastic Head.

Massive Killing Capacity

MASSIVE KILLING CAPACITY
CD _____ NBCD 123
Nuclear Blast / Sep '95 / Plastic Head.

PIECES
CD _____ NB 060CD
Nuclear Blast / Apr '92 / Plastic Head.

Disorder

COMPLETE DISORDER
Today's war / Violent crime / Complete dis-
order / Insane youth / You've got to be
someone / More than fights / Daily life /
Rampton song / Provocated war / Bullshit
everyone / Three blind mice / Buy I gurt pint
/ Stagnation / Life / Out of order / Con-
demned / Media / Suicide children /
Preachers / Remembrance day
CD _____ CDPUNK 46
Anagram / Feb '95 / Pinnacle.

LIVE IN OSLO/VIOLENT WORLD
Complete disorder / Daily life / More than
fights / Remembrance day / Maternal ob-
session / Bent edge / Provocated wars /
God nose / Education / Driller killer / Pris-
oner of conscience / Stagnation / Life /
Rampton / After 16 / Fuck your nationality /
Out of order / Rhino song / Intro 21 / Ate
seconds 22 / Another fight another day /
Gods are born in the USA / I don't like war
/ Joleen 26 / Fur else / Health hazard / To-
days world / Violent world / Dope not Pope
/ Distortion til U vomit / Take what you need
CD _____ CDPUNK 39
Anagram / Oct '94 / Pinnacle.

**MASTERS OF THE GLUENIVERSE
(Disorder/Mushroom Attack)**
CD _____ DAR 010CD
Desperate Attempt / Nov '94 / SRD.

UNDER THE SCALPEL BLADE
Driller killer / Education / Security guard /
Go-song / Transparency / Victim of the NHS
/ Bent edge / Rhino song / God nose /
Overproduction / Other side of the fence /
Fuck your nationality / Men make frontiers
/ Prisoner of conscience / After / Double
standards / Be bad be glad / Marriage story
/ Love and flowers / Togetherness and more
CD _____ CDPUNK 19
Anagram / Oct '93 / Pinnacle.

Disposable Heroes Of...

**HYPOCRISY IS THE GREATEST
LUXURY (Disposable Heroes Of
Hiphoprisy)**
Satanic reverses / Famous and dandy (like
Amos 'n' Andy) / Television (the drug of a
nation) / Language of violence / Winter of
the long hot summer / Hypocrisy is the
greatest luxury / Everyday life has become
a health risk / INS Greencard A-19 191 500
/ Socio-genetic experiment / Music and politics / Financial leprosy / California uber alles / Water pistol man
CD _____ BRCD 584
4th & Broadway / Apr '92 / PolyGram.

Disrupt

UNREST
CD _____ RR 69062
Nuclear Blast / Dec '94 / Plastic Head.

Dissect

SWALLOW SWOUMING MASS
CD _____ CYBERCD 5
Cyber / Sep '93 / Plastic Head.

Dissecting Table

ULTIMATE PSYCHOLOGICAL
CD _____ DVLR 3
Dark Vinyl / Aug '94 / Plastic Head.

ZIGOKU
CD _____ DVO 16CD
Dark Vinyl / Sep '93 / Plastic Head.

Dissection

SOMBERLAIN
CD _____ NFR 006
No Fashion / Jan '05 / Plastic Head.

STORM OF THE LIGHTS BANE
CD _____ NB 129CD
Nuclear Blast / Jan '96 / Plastic Head.

Dissober

SOBER LIFE
CD _____ DISTCD 0
Distortion / Jun '94 / Plastic Head.

Distant Cousins

DISTANT COUSINS
CD _____ GHETTCD 002
Ghetto / Mar '89 / Sony.

DISTANT COUSINS (REMIX)
CD _____ GHETTD 2X
Ghetto / Apr '90 / Sony.

Distorted Pony

INSTANT WINNER
CD _____ TRANCE 22CD
Trance / Apr '94 / SRD.

185

District Six

IMGOMA YABANTWANA
CD _____ D6 002
D6 / Mar '90 / New Note.

Ditch Witch

EVERYWHERE, NOWHERE
CD _____ GROW 12-2
Grass / Apr '94 / SRD.

Dive

CONCRETE JUNGLE
CD _____ MHCD 018
Minus Habens / May '94 / Plastic Head.

Diverse Interpreten

CLASSIC REFERENCE
CD _____ BLR 84 008
L&R / May '91 / New Note.

REFERENCE
CD _____ BLR 84 001
L&R / May '91 / New Note.

REFERENCE, II
CD _____ BLR 84 020
L&R / May '91 / New Note.

REHEARSAL
CD _____ BLR 84 010
L&R / May '91 / New Note.

Diversion

JAM TOMORROW
CD _____ TOAD 3CD
Newt / May '94 / Plastic Head.

Divine

BORN TO BE CHEAP
Gang bang / Alphabet rap / Native love / Shake it up / Shoot your shot / Love reaction
CD _____ CDMGRAM 84
Anagram / Aug '94 / Pinnacle.

CREAM OF DIVINE
CD _____ PWKS 4228
Carlton Home Entertainment / Nov '94 / Carlton Home Entertainment.

Divine Comedy

FANFARE FOR THE COMIC MUSE
CD _____ SETCDM 002
Setanta / Aug '90 / Vital.

LIBERATION
Festive Road / Death of a supernaturalist / Bernice bobs her hair / I was born yesterday / Your Daddy's car / Europop / Timewatching / Popsinger's fear of the pollen count / Queen of the South / Victoria falls / Three sisters / Europe by train / Lucy
CD _____ SETCD 013
Setanta / Aug '93 / Vital.

PROMENADE
Bath / Going downhill fast / Booklovers / Seafood song / Geronimo / When the lights go out all over Europe / Summerhouse / Neptune's daughter / Drinking song / Ten seconds to midnight / Tonight we fly
CD _____ SETCD 013
Setanta / Mar '94 / Vital.

Divine Horsemen

DEVIL'S RIVER
CD _____ ROSE 102CD
New Rose / Dec '86 / Direct / ADA.

SNAKE HANDLER
CD _____ SST 140 CD
SST / May '93 / Plastic Head.

Divine Soma Experience

WELCOME TO THE LAND OF DRAGONS
Ravi Shankar's bizarre sitar (dub) / Somae / Music is magic / Impossible possibilities / Chillout and chill'um / Icaro (Magical curing song)
CD _____ DIVINE 001CD
Divine / Sep '94 / Vital.

Dixie Cups

HIT SINGLE COLLECTABLES
CD _____ DISK 4511
Disky / Apr '94 / THE / BMG / Discovery / Pinnacle.

Dixie Stompers

AIN'T GONNA TELL NOBODY
CD _____ DD 224
Delmark / Aug '94 / Hot Shot / ADA / CM / Direct / Cadillac.

Dixie Waste

START THE MADNESS
CD _____ VIRION 104
Sound Virus / Sep '94 / Plastic Head.

Dixon, Bill

VADE MECUM
CD _____ SN 121208-2

Soul Note / Oct '94 / Harmonia Mundi / Wellard / Cadillac.

Dixon, Don

IF I'M A HAM WELL YOU'RE A SAUSAGE
Don Dixon (aged 8) and his sister Anne / Praying mantis / Southside girl / Just rites / Girls L.T.D. / Borrowed time / Your sister told me / Heart in a box / Renaissance eyes / Teenage suicide / Million angels sigh / Oh cheap chatter / I can hear the river / Gimme little sign / Calling out for love / Bad reputation / Sweet surrender / Don Dixon (age 8) and his sister Susan
CD _____ MAUCD 616
Mau Mau / Feb '92 / Pinnacle.

MOST OF THE GIRLS LIVE IN TOWN
Praying Mantis / (You're a) big girl now / Swallowing pride / Wake up / Talk to me / Pocket / Skin deep / Eyes on fire / Girls L.T.D. / Just rites / Ice on the river / Renaissance eyes / Fighting for my life / Southside girl
CD _____ FIENDCD 60
Demon / Jan '86 / Pinnacle / ADA.

ROMANTIC DEPRESSIVE
CD _____ SHCD 5501
Sugarhill / Apr '95 / Roots / CM / ADA / Direct.

Dixon, Floyd

MARSHALL TEXAS IS MY HOME
Hard living alone / Please don't go / Old memories / Hole in the wall / Time brings about a change / Me quieras / Call operator 210 / Ooh eee ooh eee / Chicken growing / Carlos / Nose trouble / Reap what you sow / Judgement day / Instrumental shuffle / Hey bartender / Never can tell when a woman changes her mind / Oh baby / What is life without a home / Rita / I'll always love you / Oooh little girl
CD _____ CDCHD 361
Ace / Nov '93 / Pinnacle / Cadillac / Complete/Pinnacle.

MR MAGNIFICENT HITS AGAIN
CD _____ IMP 706
IMP / Sep '95 / Discovery / ADA.

Dixon, Reginald

AT THE BLACKPOOL TOWER WURLITZER
Blackpool song mixture medleys 7 and 8 / Canadian capers / Dixon hits medleys 3 and 7 / Dixonland medley 2 / Dixontime medleys 1, 2, 3, 9 and 10 / Dixon request medley / Fifty years of song medley / Goodnight / In a Persian market / It's time to sing Sweet Adeline again / Parade of the tin soldiers / Sanctuary of the heart / Sunrise serenade / Tauber memories medley / Waltz memories medley / Was love a dream
CD _____ CDAJA 5134
Living Era / Jul '94 / Koch.

MAGIC OF REGINALD DIXON, THE
Over the waves / Whatever will be will be (Que sera sera) / My resistance is low / At sundown / Dancing with tears in my eyes / Pasadena / Bewitched, bothered and bewildered / Pretty girl is like a melody / Is it true what they say about Dixie / Sweet and lovely / Broadway medley / I can't give you anything but love / Peg o' my heart / Red roses for a blue lady / Sunshine of your smile / Second hand rose / There, I've said it again / Yes sir that's my baby / This is my lovely day / Shine / You can't stop me from dreaming / When you wore a tulip / Guilty / If you knew Susie like I know Susie / Happy days and lonely nights / On a slow boat to China / Nobody's sweetheart / Shepherd of the hills / Alice blue gown / Bill Bailey, won't you please come home / Am I wasting my time on you / My sweetie went away / Oh johnny oh johnny oh / Glad rag doll / Time on my hands / Jeepers creepers / Amazing grace / Old rugged cross / I do like to be beside the seaside / Pigalle / Lullaby of Broadway / Carolina moon / Toot toot tootsie / Dream of Olwen / South of the border / Stein song / Wistful waltz / Storm at sea / Life on the ocean wave / Jack's the lad / Drunken sailor / Anchors aweigh / Skye boat song / Fingal's cave / Imperial echoes / Whispering / Beer barrel polka / Charmaine / Harry Lime theme / Minuet / At the Darktown strutter's ball / Anniversary waltz / MacNamara's band / I kiss your hand, Madame / Happy days are here again / When the saints go marching in
CD Set _____ CDDL 1060
EMI / Apr '93 / EMI.

MUSIC MAESTRO PLEASE (The early years)
You can't stop me dreaming / Little old lady / Whispers in the dark / Horsey horsey / Afraid to dream / Goodnight to you all / Music goes around and around / Lights out / Take me back to my boots and saddle / When the poppies bloom again / I dream of San Marino / I'm in a dancing mood / In the chapel in the moonlight / Way you look tonight / When a lady meets a gentleman down South / When I'm with you / Fine romance / Sing baby sing / Did your mother come from Ireland / When did you leave Heaven / Oh my goodness / It looks like rain

in Cherry Blossom lane / Greatest mistake of my life / Wake up and live / Is it true what they say about Dixie / Sweetheart let's grow old together / Touch of your lips / Bells across the meadow / Music maestro please / Little lady make believe / Lost / Lovely lady / Glory of love / Sally / Love is everywhere / Looking on the bright side / Smile when you say goodbye / When I grow too old to dream / Sing as we go / Desert song / Deep in my heart dear / Dream lover / Laughing Irish eyes / It's a sin to tell a lie / On the beach at Bali-bali / At the cafe continental / Empty saddles / Pretty girl is like a melody / You're here, you're there / Ten pretty girls / Love is good for anything that ails you / Martial moments / Martial moments (2)
CD _____ GRCD 44
Grasmere / '91 / Target/BMG / Savoy.

REGINALD DIXON AT THE BLACKPOOL TOWER
Medley / St. Louis blues/Limehouse blues/Jealousy / My blue heaven/Star dust/Goodnight sweetheart / Bolero / I hate myself/Isle of Capri/My song for you / I won't dance/Lovely to look at/Smoke gets in your eyes / Hustle of spring / With my eyes open I'm dreaming/If/I never had a chance / Harlemania/Ain't misbehavin'/My sweetie went away / Ma, he's making eyes at me/Alexander's ragtime band / Medley #2 / I'll walk beside you (medley with One Day When We Were Young) / Dream lover/Nobody's using it now/March of the Grenadiers/Lo / Skater's waltz / Why do I love you/You are my love/Oi' man river / Somebody stole my gal / Love makes the world go round/Change partners / Sweet music/Ev'ryday/Fare thee well Annabelle / Sunrise serenade / When Mother Nature sings her lullaby / Bugle call rag / Medley #3
CD _____ PASTCD 7039
Flapper / May '94 / Pinnacle.

TOWER BALLROOM FAVOURITES
Tiger rag / Autumn leaves / Moonlight serenade / These foolish things / Dardanella / Elizabethan serenade / La paloma / Russian rag / Peanut vendor / Wedding of the painted doll / Temptation rag / Czardas / Sabre dance / Sweet and lovely / Canadian capers / Continental / Jealousy / 12th Street rag / Deep purple / Cherokee / Toy trumpet / Stardust
CD _____ CC 255
Music For Pleasure / May '90 / EMI.

Dixon, Willie

BLUES DICTIONARY VOL.2
CD _____ RTS 33046
Roots / Jun '93 / Pinnacle.

BLUES DICTIONARY VOL.3
CD _____ RTS 33047
Roots / Jun '93 / Pinnacle.

BLUES DICTIONARY VOL.5
CD _____ RTS 33049
Roots / Jun '93 / Pinnacle.

CRYIN' THE BLUES (Live At Liberty Hall) (Dixon, Willie & Johnny Winter)
Sittin' and cryin' the blues / Spoonful / I just want to make love to you / Chicago here I come / Tore down / You know it ain't right / Mean mistreater/Baby what you want me to do / Roach stew / Killing floor
CD _____ CDTB 166
Thunderbolt / Mar '95 / Magnum Music Group.

HIDDEN CHARMS
CD _____ ORECD 515
Silvertone / Mar '94 / Pinnacle.

I'M THE BLUES
Pain in my heart / My babe / Walking the blues / (Back home again in) Indiana / Hoochie coochie man / Little red rooster / Spoonful
CD _____ CD 52026
Blues Encore / Mar '93 / Target/BMG.

WILLIE DIXON BOX SET
CD Set _____ CHD 216500
MCA / Sep '90 / BMG.

WILLIE'S BLUES (Dixon, Willie & Memphis Slim)
Nervous / Good understanding / That's my baby / Slim's thing / That's all I want baby / Don't you tell nobody / Youth to you / Sittin' and cryin' the blues / Bluit for comfort / I got a razor / Go easy / Move me
CD _____ OBCCD 501
Original Blues Classics / Nov '92 / Complete/Pinnacle / Wellard / Cadillac.

WILLIE'S BLUES (Dixon, Willie & Memphis Slim)
CD _____ CDCHD 349
Ace / Jun '92 / Pinnacle / Cadillac / Complete/Pinnacle.

Diyici, Senem

TAKALAR (Diyici, Senem Sextet)
CD _____ CDLLL 17
La Lichere / Aug '93 / Discovery / ADA.

Djole, Africa

LIVE - THE CONCERT IN BERLIN 1978
CD _____ FMPCD 01
FMP / Feb '86 / Cadillac.

Djur Djura

VOICES OF SILENCE (Adventures In Afropea 2)
CD _____ 936245211-2
Luaka Bop / May '94 / Warner Music.

Djwahl Khul

SCHLACHTUNGSKIND
CD _____ EFA 121632
Apollyon / Aug '95 / SRD.

D'Leon, Oscar

KING OF THE SALSA LIVE
CD _____ CD 3531
Cameo / Aug '95 / Target/BMG.

TOITICO TUYO
Mentiras / Si fueras mia / Como olvidarte / Totico tuyo / Matematica sexual / Que raro / Casas de carton / De ti
CD _____ 66058038
Sonero / Jul '94 / New Note.

DMZ

WHEN I GET OFF
CD _____ VOXXCD 2004
Voxx / Jul '93 / Else / Disc.

DNA

DNA
CD _____ AVAN 006
Avant / Sep '93 / Harmonia Mundi / Cadillac.

Do Carmo, Lucilia

PORTUGAL - A SPIRIT OF FADO VOL.4
CD _____ PS 65704
Playasound / Oct '92 / Harmonia Mundi / ADA.

DO'A

ANCIENT BEAUTY (Do'A World Music Ensemble)
CD _____ CDPH 9004
Philo / Dec '86 / Direct / CM / ADA.

COMPANIONS OF THE CRIMSON COLOURED ARK (Do'A World Music Ensemble)
CD _____ CDPH 9009
Philo / Dec '86 / Direct / CM / ADA.

EARLY YEARS, THE (Do'A World Music Ensemble)
CD _____ CD 11539
Rounder / '88 / CM / Direct / ADA / Cadillac.

Dobbyn, Dave

TWIST
Lap of the gods / Naked / PC / It dawned on me / Protection / What do you really want / Gifted / Betrayal / Language / Umm / Rain on fire / I can't change my mind
CD _____ 4777922
Columbia / Jul '95 / Sony.

Dobkins, Carl Jr.

MY HEART IS AN OPEN BOOK
My heart is an open book / If you don't want my lovin' / Love is everything / My pledge to you / Lucky devil / Fool such as I / Promise me / Take time out / Chance to belong / In my heart / Ask me no questions / Sawdust Dolly / Pretty little girl in the yellow dress / Open up your arms / I'm sorry / Three little piggies / Class ring / Exclusively yours / For your love / True love / Raining in my heart / Sue / That's what I call true love / One little girl / Genie / Different kind of love / Lovelight / That's all I need to know
CD _____ BCD 15546
Bear Family / Feb '91 / Rollercoaster / Direct / CM / Swift / ADA.

Dobrogosz, Steve

FINAL TOUCH, THE
CD _____ DRAGONCD 195
Dragon / May '86 / Roots / Cadillac / Wellard / CM / ADA.

JADE
CD _____ DRCD 203
Dragon / Jul '87 / Roots / Cadillac / Wellard / CM / ADA.

TRIO
CD _____ 1232
Caprice / Dec '87 / CM / Complete/Pinnacle / Cadillac / ADA.

Dobson, Dobby

AT LAST
CD _____ ANGCD 22
Angella / Jul '94 / Jetstar.

GREATEST HITS
CD _____ SONCD 0072
Sonic Sounds / Nov '94 / Jetstar.

SWEET DREAMS
CD _____ PKCD 32993
K&K / Jul '93 / Jetstar.

Dobson, Richard

HEARTS & RIVERS (Dobson, Richard & State Of The Heart)
CD _____ BRAM 199014-2
Brambus / Nov '93 / ADA / Direct.

ONE BAR TOWN
CD _____ 199568CD
Brambus / Jul '95 / ADA / Direct.

RICHARD DOBSON SINGS TOWNES VAN ZANDT
CD _____ BRAMBUS 199450-2
Brambus / Jul '94 / ADA / Direct.

Dobson, Rudi

AUDREY HEPBURN - FAIR LADY OF THE SCREEN
Audrey Hepburn - Fair lady of the screen / Belgian rock / Fight for time / Dark city / Broadway melody / Little dog called 'Mr Famouse' / Sister Audrey / Moon river / Breakfast at Tiffany's / Charade / My fair lady (Medley) / Desert anthem / Lac Genieve (Lake Geneva) / Moon river (Requiem)
CD _____ PCOM 1136
President / Aug '94 / Grapevine / Target / BMG / Jazz Music / President.

Doc Holliday

SON OF THE MORNING SUN
CD _____ CDIRS 972190
Intercord / Aug '93 / Plastic Head.

Doc Houlind

TRIBUTE TO G. LEWIS (Doc Houlind Copenhagen Ragtime Band)
CD _____ MECCACD 1037
Music Mecca / Nov '94 / Jazz Music / Cadillac / Wellard.

Doc Ice

RELY ON SELPH
CD _____ WRA 8127CD
Wrap / Jun '94 / Koch.

Doc Wor Mirran

GARAGE PRETENSIONS
CD _____ EFA 11364-2
Musical Tragedies / Jan '94 / SRD.

Dodd, Ken

GREATEST HITS: KEN DODD (An Hour of Hits)
Happiness / Love is like a violin / Somewhere my love / River / Eight by ten / They didn't believe me / As time goes by / I wish you love / More than ever / So deep is the night / Tears / Still / Broken hearted / She / Old fashioned way / For all we know / What a wonderful world / Happy days and lonely nights / Just out of reach / Let me cry on your shoulder / Promises
CD _____ CC 202
Music For Pleasure / May '88 / EMI.

Dodds, Baby

BILL RUSSELL'S HISTORIC RECORDINGS
CD _____ AMCD 17
American Music / Feb '95 / Jazz Music.

Dodds, Johnny

1927
CD _____ CLASSICS 588
Classics / '91 / Discovery / Jazz Music.

BLUE CLARINET STOMP (1926-1928)
Weary blues / New Orleans Stomp / Wild man blues / Melancholy / Come on and stomp, stomp, stomp / After you've gone / Joe Turner blues / When Erastus plays his old kazoo / Blue clarinet stomp / Blue piano stomp / Bucktown stomp / Weary city / Bull fiddle blues / Blue washboard stomp / Sweet Lorraine / Pencil papa / My little Isabel-A / Heah' me talkin' / Goober dance / Too tight-A
CD _____ DGF 3
Frog / Oct '94 / Jazz Music / Cadillac / Wellard.

GREAT ORIGINAL PERFORMANCES
CD _____ RPCD 622
Robert Parker Jazz / Sep '93 / Conifer.

JOHNNY DODDS & JIMMY BLYTHE (Dodds, Johnny & Jimmy Blythe)
Little bits / Your folks / Struggling / Easy come, easy go blues / Struggling (2nd take) / Blues stampede / Bohunkus blues / I'm goin' huntin' / Buddy Barton's jazz / If you want to be my sugar Papa / Messin' around / Messin' around (2nd take) / Weary way blues / Adam's apple / Poutin' Papa / Idle hour special / Hot stuff / 47th Street stomp (2 takes) / My baby / Oriental man / Ape man
CD _____ CBC 1015
Chris Barber Collection / Nov '93 / New Note / Cadillac.

JOHNNY DODDS (1926)
CD _____ CLASSICS 589
Classics / Aug '91 / Discovery / Jazz Music.

JOHNNY DODDS (1926-28)
Perdido street blues / Gatemouth / Too tight / Papa dip / Mixed salad / I can't say / Flatfoot / Mad dog / Ballin' the Jack / Grandma's ball / My baby / Oriental man / Get 'em again blues / Brush stomp / My girl / Sweep 'em clean / Lady love / Brown bottom Bess
CD _____ JSPCD 319
JSP / Apr '92 / ADA / Target/BMG / Direct / Cadillac / Complete/Pinnacle.

JOHNNY DODDS - 1927-'28
CD _____ CLASSICS 617
Classics / '92 / Discovery / Jazz Music.

JOHNNY DODDS 1926-1940 (3CD Set)
What a man / Who's gonna do your lovin' / Nobody else will do / Bohunkus blues / Buddy Burton's jazz / Little bits / Struggling / Perdido street blues / Gate mouth / Too tight / Papa dip / Mixed salad / I can't say / Flat foot floogie / Mad dog / Messin' around / Adam's apple / East coast trot / pussy / Dogg day afternoon / 47th street stomp / Someday sweetheart / Stock yards strut / Salty dog / Ape man / Yours folks / House rent rag / Memphis shake / Carpet alley breakdown / Hen party blues / Stomp time blues / It must be the blues / Oh daddy / Loveless love / 19th street blues / San / Oh Lizzie (A lovers lament) / New St. Louis blues / Clarinet wobble / Easy come, easy go blues / Blues stampede / I'm goin' huntin' / If you want to be my sugar Papa / Weary blues / New Orleans stomp / Wild man blues / Melancholy / Wolverine blues / Mr. Jelly Lord / There'll come a day / Weary way blues / Cootie stomp / Poutin' papa / Hot stuff / Have mercy
CD Set _____ CDAFS 1023-3
Affinity / Jan '93 / Charly / Cadillac / Jazz Music.

JOHNNY DODDS 1926-40
CD _____ CD 14559
Jazz Portraits / Jul '94 / Jazz Music.

JOHNNY DODDS VOL 1
CD _____ VILCD 0022
Village Jazz / Sep '92 / Target/BMG / Jazz Music.

JOHNNY DODDS VOL. 2
CD _____ VILCD 0172
Village Jazz / Aug '92 / Target/BMG / Jazz Music.

KING OF THE NEW ORLEANS CLARINET (1926-1938)
CD _____ BLE 592352
Black & Blue / Dec '92 / Wellard / Koch.

MYTH OF NEW ORLEANS, THE (1926-40)
CD _____ GOJCD 53077
Giants Of Jazz / Mar '92 / Target/BMG / Cadillac.

Dodge City Productions

STEPPIN' UP AND OUT
CD _____ BRCD 587
4th & Broadway / May '93 / PolyGram.

Dodgy

DODGY ALBUM, THE
CD _____ 540082-2
A&M / Jun '93 / PolyGram.

HOMEGROWN
Staying out for the summer / Melodies haunt you / So let me in far / Crossroads / One day / We are together / Whole lot easier / Making the most of / Waiting for the day / What have I done wrong / Grassman
CD _____ 540 282 2
A&M / Oct '94 / PolyGram.

Doernberg, Ferdy

JUST A PIANO AND A HANDFUL OF DREAMS
CD _____ 08412112
SPV / Jan '96 / Plastic Head.

Dog Eat Dog

ALL BORO KINGS
CD _____ RR 90209
CD _____ RR 90202
Roadrunner / Apr '95 / Pinnacle.

WARRANT
It's like that / Dog eat dog / World keeps spinnin' / In the dog house / Psychorama / In the dog house (remix)
CD _____ RR 90712
Roadrunner / Jun '94 / Pinnacle.

Dog Faced Hermans

BUMP AND SWING
CD _____ K 153CD
Konkurrel / Jun '94 / SRD.

HUM OF LIFE
CD _____ K147D
Konkurrel / Mar '93 / SRD.

THOSE DEEP BUDS
CD _____ K 155C
Konkurrel / Oct '94 / SRD.

Dog, Tim

PENCILLIN IN WAX
Intro / Low down / Nigga / Robbin Harris shit / Fuck compton / D.J. quick beat down / Step to me / Phone conversation w/ porter / Bronx nigga / You ain't shit / I ain't takin' no shorts / NFL shit / I'll wax anybody / Michel'le conversation / Can't fuck around / Dog's gonna getcha / Goin' wild in the Penile / Get off the bitch / I ain't havin' it / Patriotic pimp / Secret fantasies
CD _____ 4053492
Ruff House / Feb '92 / Sony.

Dogg Pound

DOGG FOOD
Intro / Dogg pound gangstaz / Respect / New York, New York / Smooth / Cyco-ic-no (Bitch azz niggaz) / Ridin' slippin' and slidin' / Big pimpen'2 / Let's play house?? / don't like to dream about gettin' paid / Do what I feel / If we all fuc / Some bomb azz pussy / Dogg day afternoon / Reality / One by one / Soo much style
CD _____ 5241772
Death Row/Island / Oct '95 / PolyGram.

Doggett, Bill

AS YOU DESIRE ME
I hadn't anyone till you / Yesterdays / Alone / As time goes by / Dedicated to you / Sweet and lovely / Cottage for sale / As you desire me / Dream / Don't blame me / This love of mine / Fools rush in
CD _____ KCD 523
King/Paddle Wheel / Mar '90 / New Nule.

DAME DREAMING
Sweet Lorraine / Diane / Dinah / Kamona / Cherry / Cynthia / Jeannine / Tangerine / Nancy / Estrellita / Laura / Marcheta
CD _____ KCD 532
King/Paddle Wheel / Mar '93 / New Note.

DANCE A WHILE
Flying home / Misty moon / Bone tones / Tailor made / Chelsea bridge / Kid from Franklin Street / Pied piper of Islip / Passion flower / Song is ended (but the melody lingers on) / Autumn leaves / How could you / Smoochie
CD _____ KCD 585
King/Paddle Wheel / Mar '90 / New Note.

DOGGETT BEAT FOR HAPPY FEAT, THE
Soft / And the angels sing / Ding dong / Honey / Easy / Hammerhead / Ram-bunk-shush / Chloe / Hot ginger / King Bee / What a difference a day makes / Shinding
CD _____ KCD 557
King/Paddle Wheel / Mar '90 / New Note.

LEAPS AND BOUNDS
Bo-do rock / Honky tonk (pts 1 & 2) / Rainbow riot / Blue largo / Big boy / You ain't no good / Big dog / Hippy dippy / Backwards / Shindig / After hours / Peacock alley / In the wee hours / Leaps and bounds (pts 1 & 2) / Your kind of woman / Yocky dock (pts 1 & 2) / Wild oats
CD _____ CDCHARLY 281
Charly / Sep '91 / Charly / THE / Cadillac.

MANY MOODS OF BILL DOGGETT, THE
CD _____ KCD 778
King/Paddle Wheel / May '93 / New Note.

RIGHT CHOICE, THE
Fur piece / Roughneck / Warm breezes / Mush mouth / Du-da / Things ain't what they used to be / I'm ready / Wright choice / Honky tonk (pts 1 & 2) / Just a blues
CD _____ AFT 4112CD
Ichiban / Jun '94 / Koch.

Dogheimsgard

KRONET TIL KONGE
CD _____ MR 006CD
Malicious / Oct '95 / Plastic Head.

Dogpile

LIVE BUTT PLUGGED
CD _____ EL 100
Electrip / Dec '93 / Plastic Head.

Dogs D'Amour

DOG'S HITS AND THE BOOTLEG ALBUM
CD _____ WOLCD 1020
China / Aug '91 / Pinnacle.

ERROL FLYNN
Drunk like me / Hurricane / Errol Flynn / Princess valium / Trail of tears / Prettiest girl in the world / Goddess from the gutter / Satellite kid / Planetary pied piper / Dog's hair / Ballad of Jack / Girl behind the glass
CD _____ 8397002
China / Sep '89 / Pinnacle.

GRAVEYARD OF EMPTY BOTTLES, A
CD _____ WOLCD 1005
China / Mar '91 / Pinnacle.

MORE UNCHARTERED HEIGHTS OF DISGRACE
CD _____ WOLCD 1032
China / Apr '93 / Pinnacle.

Dolby, Thomas

STRAIGHT
CD _____ WOLCD 1007
China / Mar '91 / Pinnacle.

Dogstar

ILLUMINATE FABRICATI
CD _____ LALACD 3
La La Land / Apr '94 / Disc.

Doherty, John

BUNDLE AND GO
Hudie Gallagher's march / Black mare of Fanad / March of the meena toiten bull / Kiss the maid behind the bier/The bargain is over / 21 Highland / Paps o' Glencoe / Hare in the corn / Knights of St. Patrick / Dispute at the crossroads / Roaring Mary / Miss Patterson's slippers / Cat that kittled in Jamie's wig / Welcome home royal Charlie / Darby Gallagher / Teelin highland / Heathery breeze / Monaghan switch / Black haired lass / Paddy's rambles through the park
CD _____ OSS 17CD
Ossian / Jan '94 / ADA / Direct / CM.

Doherty, Tom

TAKE THE BULL BY THE HORNS
Three sisters reels / Donegal reel/The maid I daren't tell / Cathy Jones/The keel row / Road to the Isles/Auld Rigadoo / Maggie pickie / I've a polkie trimmed with blue/The gallope / Liverpool/Derry / Connaught man's rambles / Sally gardens/Cooley's / Humours of whiskey / Take the bull by the horns / Primrose lass / Corn rigs / Bridge O'Leary's / Paddy McGinty's goat/Green grow the rushes-o / Sweet cup of tea/Drowsy Maggie / Miss Drummond of Perth/Mollymusk / Silver spear/Mountain road/Maid behind the bar / Queen of the fair/Off she goes
CD _____ GLCD 1131
Green Linnet / Jul '93 / Roots / CM / Direct / ADA.

Dokken

BACK IN THE STREETS
CD _____ REP 4005-WG
Repertoire / Aug '91 / Pinnacle / Cadillac.

Dolan, Joe

BEST OF JOE DOLAN
CD _____ MATCD 277
Castle / Sep '93 / BMG.

DEFINITIVE COLLECTION, THE
Make me an island / You're such a good looking woman / Crazy woman / Gypsy lady / Home is where the heart is / Hush hush / Maria / Lady in blue / It's you, it's you, it's you / Little boy big man / Maybe someday my love / Don't set me free again / Sister Mary / Sixteen brothers / Most wanted man in the USA / This is my life / Dreaming (ghosts on the moon) / You belong to me / More and more
CD _____ KCD 390
Irish / Jan '96 / Target/BMG.

LOVE SONG COLLECTION
CD _____ DHCD 721
Outlet / Jan '95 / ADA / Duncans / CM / Ross / Direct / Koch.

MORE & MORE
CD _____ RITZSCD 416
Ritz / Apr '93 / Pinnacle.

Dolan, Michael

TRIBUTE TO MICHAEL DOLAN, A (Various Artists)
CD _____ GLCD 3097
Green Linnet / Jan '95 / Roots / CM / Direct / ADA.

Dolan, Packie

FORGOTTEN FIDDLE PLAYER OF THE 1920'S, THE
CD _____ VVCD 1
Viva Voce / Jul '94 / ADA / Direct.

PACKIE DOLAN
CD _____ VIVAVOCE 006CD
Viva Voce / Nov '94 / ADA / Direct.

Dolan's Acoustic Rangers

ACOUSTIC RANGERS
Nite hawkin' the dawn / Rhythm rider / Lost cargo / Tree moon and tide / So hard to be soft / Borrow love and dream / Playin' to win / First kiss / Corine Corina / Wish I was your river
CD _____ 900453
Line / Oct '94 / CM / Grapevine / ADA / Conifer / Direct.

Dolby, Thomas

ASTRONAUTS AND HERETICS
I love you, goodbye / Cruel / Silk pyjamas / I live in a suitcase / Eastern block (the sequel) / Close but no cigar / That's why people fall in love / Neon sister / Pudding of a dream
CD _____ CDV 2701
Virgin / Jul '92 / EMI.

DOLBY, THOMAS

FLAT EARTH, THE
Flat earth / Screen kiss / Mulu the rain forest / I scare myself / Hyperactive / White City / Dissidents
CD _____ CDP 746 028 2
Parlophone / Jul '84 / EMI.

GATE TO THE MIND, THE
CD _____ 74321233862
RCA / Mar '95 / BMG.

GOLDEN AGE OF WIRELESS, THE
She blinded me with science / Radio silence / Airwaves / Flying north / Weightless / Europa and the pirate twins / Windpower / Commercial break-up / One of our submarines is missing / Cloudburst at Shingle Street
CD _____ CDFA 3319
Fame / Apr '95 / EMI.

RETROSPECTACLE - THE BEST OF THOMAS DOLBY
Europa and the pirate twins / Urges / Leipzig / Windpower / Airwaves / She blinded me with science / One of our submarines is missing / Screen kiss / Hyperactive / I scare myself / Flat earth / Pulp culture / Budapest by Blimp / Cruel / Close but no cigar / I love you, goodbye
CD _____ CDEMC 3659
EMI / Feb '94 / EMI.

Doldinger, Klaus

DOLDINGER'S BEST
Blues for George / Two getting together / Minor kick / Quartenwaizer / Guachi guaro / Viva Brasilia / Fiesta / Raga up and down / Saragossa / Waltz of the jive cats / Comin' home baby / I feel free / Stormy Monday blues / Compared to what
CD _____ 92242
Act / Feb '96 / New Note.

Dole, Gerard

CO CO COLINDA (15 Original Songs)
CD _____ PS 65086
Playasound / Apr '92 / Harmonia Mundi / ADA.

Dollar

COLLECTION, THE
Overture / Shooting star / Tokyo / Star control / Who were you with in the moonlight / I need your love / Ring ring / Love Street / Love's gotta hold on me / I wanna hold your hand / Love tonight / Sugar sugar / Platinum rap / Living each day for you / Dia y noche / Oh l'amour
CD _____ CCSCD 320
Castle / Jan '92 / BMG.

SHOOTING STAR
Overture / Shooting star / Who were you with in the moonlight / Love's gotta hold on me / Oh l'amour / Sugar sugar / I need your love / B-beat / Ring ring / It's nature's way (No problem) / Star control / Tokyo / Dia y noche / Love street / Living each day for you / I wanna hold your hand
CD _____ 5507482
Spectrum/Karussell / Mar '95 / PolyGram / THE.

Dollface

GIANT
CD _____ KCCD 3
Kill City / Jul '95 / Pinnacle.

Dolphin, John

IRON LEGS
CD _____ MYSCD 001
BMG / Jan '96 / BMG.

Dolphy, Eric

1958-1961
CD _____ CD 53164
Giants Of Jazz / Nov '95 / Target/BMG / Cadillac.

AT THE FIVE SPOT VOLUME 1
CD _____ OJCCD 133
Original Jazz Classics / Feb '92 / Wellard / Jazz Music / Cadillac / Complete/Pinnacle.

BERLIN CONCERTS
CD _____ ENJACD 300792
Enja / Nov '94 / New Note / Vital/SAM.

CANDID DOLPHY
Reincarnation of a love bird / Stormy weather / African lady / Quiet please / Moods in free time / Hazy hues
CD _____ CCD 79033
Candid / Mar '90 / Cadillac / Jazz Music / Wellard / Koch.

ERIC DOLPHY & THE CHAMPS ELYSEES ALL STARS (Dolphy, Eric & The Champs Elysees All Stars)
Springtime / GW / 245 / Serene
CD _____ WWCD 016
West Wind / Dec '88 / Swift / Charly / CM / ADA.

ERIC DOLPHY 1961
CD _____ CD 14553
Jazz Portraits / Jul '94 / Jazz Music.

ERIC DOLPHY IN EUROPE VOL.2
CD _____ OJCCD 414-2
Original Jazz Classics / Mar '93 / Wellard / Jazz Music / Cadillac / Complete/Pinnacle.

ERIC DOLPHY QUARTET (1961) (Dolphy, Eric Quartet)
CD _____ GOJCD 53067
Giants Of Jazz / Mar '92 / Target/BMG / Cadillac.

ESSENTIAL, THE
GW / Les / Meetin' / Feathers / Eclipse / Ode to Charlie Parker / Bird's mother / Ralph's new blues / Status seeking
CD _____ FCD 60022
Fantasy / Apr '94 / Pinnacle / Jazz Music / Wellard / Cadillac.

FAR CRY (Dolphy, Eric & Booker Little)
CD _____ OJCCD 4002
Original Jazz Classics / Mar '93 / Wellard / Jazz Music / Cadillac / Complete/Pinnacle.

IN EUROPE VOLUME 1
Hi fly / Glad to be unhappy / God bless the child / Oleo
CD _____ OJCCD 413-2
Original Jazz Classics / Apr '93 / Wellard / Jazz Music / Cadillac / Complete/Pinnacle.

IN EUROPE VOLUME 3
Woody 'n' you / When lights are low / In the blues (takes 1, 2 & 3)
CD _____ OJCCD 416
Original Jazz Classics / Apr '93 / Wellard / Jazz Music / Cadillac / Complete/Pinnacle.

LAST DATE
CD _____ 5101242
Verve / Sep '92 / PolyGram.

MEMORIAL ALBUM (Dolphy, Eric & Booker Little)
CD _____ OJCCD 353
Original Jazz Classics / May '93 / Wellard / Jazz Music / Cadillac / Complete/Pinnacle.

MUSIC MATADOR
Jitterbug waltz / Music matador / Alone together / Love me
CD _____ LEJAZZCD 14
Le Jazz / Jun '93 / Charly / Cadillac.

OUT THERE
CD _____ OJCCD 023
Original Jazz Classics / May '93 / Wellard / Jazz Music / Cadillac / Complete/Pinnacle.

OUT TO LUNCH
Hat and beard / Something sweet, something tender / Gazzelloni / Out to lunch / Straight up and down
CD _____ CDP 7465242
Blue Note / Mar '95 / EMI.

OUTWARD BOUND
CD _____ OJCCD 022-2
Original Jazz Classics / Feb '91 / Wellard / Jazz Music / Cadillac / Complete/Pinnacle.

Dom Um Romao

DOM UM ROMAO
CD _____ MCD 6012
Muse / Sep '92 / New Note / CM.

SAUDADES
CD _____ WLACS 16CD
Waterlily Acoustics / Nov '95 / ADA.

Domain

CRACK IN THE WALL
CD _____ FT 30016CD
Flametrader / Jan '92 / Plastic Head.

Domancich, Sophia

L'ANNEE DES TREIZE LUNES
CD _____ A 15
Seventh / Oct '95 / Harmonia Mundi / Cadillac.

Dome

DOME 1 AND 2
CD _____ DOME 12CD
Grey Area / Aug '92 / Pinnacle.

DOME 3 AND 4
CD _____ DOME 34CD
Grey Area / Aug '92 / Pinnacle.

Domingo, Enrico

STRICTLY DANCING: MAMBO (Domingo, Enrico & His Big Band)
CD _____ 15335
Laserlight / May '94 / Target/BMG.

Domingo, Placido

AT THE NEW YORK STATE THEATRE
CD _____ MSCD 2
Magnum Music / May '94 / Magnum Music Group.

GOLDEN VOICE, THE
CD _____ MU 5041
Musketeer / Oct '92 / Koch.

Dominic Sonic

COLD TEARS
CD _____ CRAMCD 065
Southern / Nov '89 / SRD.

Dominique, Natty

NATTY DOMINIQUE 1953
CD _____ AMCD 18
American Music / Aug '94 / Jazz Music.

Domino

DOMINO
Diggady Domino / Ghetto jam / A.F.D. / Do you qualify / Jam / Money is everything / Sweet potato pie / Raincoat / Long beach thang / That's real
CD _____ 475759 2
Columbia / Feb '94 / Sony.

Domino, Anna

ANNA DOMINO
CD _____ TWI 600CD
Les Disques Du Crepuscule / '90 / Discovery / ADA.

Domino, Fats

16 GREATEST HITS: FATS DOMINO
Blueberry Hill / I'm in love again / Ain't that a shame / I'm walkin' / Blue Monday / Whole lotta lovin' / I want to walk you home / I'm ready / My blue Heaven / I'm gonna be a wheel someday / Jambalaya / So long / When the saints go marching in / Heartbreak Hill / Kansas City / Walking to New Orleans
CD _____ CD 32
Bescol / May '87 / CM / Target/BMG.

AUDIO ARCHIVE
Tring / Jun '92 / Tring / Prism.
CD _____ CDAA 048

BEST OF FATS DOMINO
Blueberry Hill / Whole lotta lovin' / Fat man / Blue Monday / I'm walkin' / I'm in love again / Be my guest / When my dreamboat comes home / Let the four winds blow / I'm gonna be a wheel someday / Walking to New Orleans / Ain't that a shame / I want to walk you home / My blue Heaven / Valley of tears
CD _____ CDMFP 6026
Music For Pleasure / Apr '88 / EMI.

BEST OF FATS DOMINO
CD _____ 399232
Koch / Nov '93 / Koch.

BEST OF FATS DOMINO VOL. 1 (My Blue Heaven)
My blue heaven / Fat man / Please don't leave me / Ain't that a shame / I'm in love again / When my dreamboat comes home / Blueberry Hill / Blue Monday / I'm walkin' / Valley of tears / Big beat / Yes my darling / Whole lotta lovin' / I'm ready / I'm gonna be a wheel someday / I want to walk you home / Be my guest / Walking to New Orleans / Let the four winds blow / What a party
CD _____ CZ 368
Liberty / Nov '90 / EMI.

BEST OF FATS DOMINO, THE
CD _____ MATCD 325
Castle / Feb '95 / BMG.

BLUEBERRY HILL
CD _____ KWEST 5400
Disky / Oct '94 / THE / BMG / Discovery / Pinnacle.

BLUEBERRY HILL (PICKWICK)
CD _____ PWK 021
Carlton Home Entertainment / '88 / Carlton Home Entertainment.

E.P. COLLECTION, THE
Ain't that a shame / All by myself / My blue heaven / Bo weevil / Coquette / Tired of crying / It must be love / Sick and tired / Telling lies / Please don't leave me / Margie / Blueberry Hill / I want to walk you home / I'm ready / I'm in the mood for love / So long / Walking to New Orleans / Don't come knocking / Let the four winds blow / I'm in love again / Poor me / Don't blame it on me / Blue Monday / Fat man
CD _____ SEECD 416
See For Miles/C5 / Nov '94 / Pinnacle.

FAT MAN SINGS, THE
Ain't that a shame / All by myself / Blueberry Hill / Margie / I hear you knocking / Don't blame it on me / You always hurt the one you love / Walking to New Orleans / Honey Chile / My happiness / Sick and tired / Country boy / Your cheatin' heart / You win again / One night / It keeps rainin' / Trouble blues / Nothing new (Same old thing) / My blue heaven / Fat man
CD _____ CDMFP 5938
Music For Pleasure / Apr '92 / EMI.

FATS DOMINO
CD _____ LECD 047
Dynamite / May '94 / THE.

FATS DOMINO (LIVE)
Introduction / Blueberry Hill / Please don't leave me / Domino twist / Let the four winds blow / Whole lotta lovin' / Blue Monday /

You win again / I'm walkin' / I'm gonna be a wheel someday / I'm in the mood for love / Jambalaya / O what a price / Ain't that a shame / So long / When the saints go marching in / Deep in the heart of Texas
CD _____ 15071
Laserlight / Aug '91 / Target/BMG.

FATS DOMINO 50 GREATEST HITS
CD Set _____ DBP 102006
Double Platinum / Feb '95 / Target/BMG.

FATS DOMINO IN CONCERT
CD _____ CDSGP 0162
Prestige / Aug '95 / Total/BMG.

HIS GREATEST HITS
CD _____ MU 5015
Musketeer / Oct '92 / Koch.

JAMBALAYA
Jambalaya / Ain't that a shame (live) / Let the four winds blow / Blue Monday / I'm walkin' / When the Saints go marching in / Blueberry Hill / Walking to New Orleans / My blue heaven / I left my heart in San Francisco / You win again / I done got over it / Mardi Gras in New Orleans
CD _____ 5501792
Spectrum/Karussell / Mar '94 / PolyGram / THE.

KINGS OF BEAT (STAR-CLUB)
CD _____ REP 4160-WZ
Repertoire / Aug '91 / Pinnacle / Cadillac.

ROCKIN' WITH FATS
I'm gonna be a wheel someday / I want to walk you home / Whole lotta lovin' / Fat man / Blueberry hill / Ain't that a shame / Be my guest / Blue Monday / Jambalaya / I'm in love again / Red sails in the sunset / Goin' home / Domino twist / Let the four winds blow / I'm in the mood for love / What a price
CD _____ CDCD 1015
Charly / Mar '93 / Charly / THE / Cadillac.

ROLLIN'
CD _____ 269663-2
Tomato / Apr '90 / Vital.

SPOTLIGHT ON FATS DOMINO
Ain't that a shame / Blueberry hill / Lawdy Miss Clawdy / Fat man / When the saints go marching in / Blue Monday / Domino twist / I'm in the mood for love / I'm in love again / Jambalaya / Lady Madonna / There goes my heart again / Honest papa's love their mama's / Oh what a price / Whole lotta lovin' / Be my guest
CD _____ HADCD 133
Javelin / Feb '94 / THE / Henry Hadaway Organisation.

THEY CALL ME THE FAT MAN
Fat man / She's my baby / Little Bee / Boogie woogie baby / Hey la bas boogie / Every night about this time / Careless love / Don't lie to me / Going home / Mardi Gras in New Orleans / Goin' to the river / Swanee river hop / Please don't leave me / Domino stomp / Rosemary / Where did you stay / You can pack your suitcase / Love me / I know / Don't you know / All by myself / Ain't it a shame / La la / Blue Monday / Poor me / I can't go on / I'm in love again / Bo weevil / Don't blame it on me / If you need me / So long / My blue heaven / Ida Jane / When my dreamboat comes home / What's the reason I'm not pleasin' you / Set me free (the twist set me free) / Blueberry Hill / Honey chile / I'm walkin' / What will I tell my heart / My happiness / Don't deceive me / Rooster / Telling lies / It's you I love / Valley of tears / Wait and see / Sailor boy / Big beat / Little Mary / When I see you / I still love you (wedding ring) / I want you to know / Yes my darling / Don't you know I love you / Sick and tired / No no (the river) / I'm gonna be a wheel someday / Whole lotta lovin' / At the Darktown strutter's ball / Margie / I hear you knocking / Li'l Liza Jane / When the saints go marching in / Country boy / I'm ready / I want to walk you home / I've been around / Be my guest / Tell me that you love me / Walking to New Orleans / Don't come knockin' / La la (version) / Put your arms around me honey / Three nights a week / Shu-rah / My girl Josephine / Natural born lover / Ain't that just like a woman / It keeps rainin' / What a price / Fell in love on Monday / Bad luck and trouble / Good hearted man / One night / You win again / Let the four winds blow / Your cheatin' heart / What a party / Rockin' bicycle / Did you ever see a dream walking / Birds and bees / Jambalaya / Do you know what it means to miss New Orleans / Stop the clock / My real name / Hum diddy doo / I want to go home / Dance with Mr. Domino / Nothing new (same old thing)
CD Set _____ CDS 7967842
EMI / Oct '91 / EMI.

WALKING TO NEW ORLEANS
Detroit City blues / Fat man / Hide away blues / She's my baby / Brand new baby / Little Bee / Boogie woogie baby / Hey la bas boogie / Korea blues / Every night about this time / Careless love / Hey man / Tired of crying / Tired of crying (2) / What's the matter baby / I've got eyes for you / Stay away / Don't you lie to me / My baby's gone / Rockin' chair / Sometimes I wonder / Right from wrong / You know I'll miss you / I'll be gone / No, no baby / Ree-

lin' and rockin' / Goin' home / Fat man's hop / How long / How long (2) / Long lonesome journey / Long lonesome journey (2) / Poor, poor me / Poor, poor me (2) / Trust in me / Cheatin' / Mardi Gras in New Orleans / I guess I'll be on my way / Nobody loves me / Dreaming / Going to the river / I love her / Second line jump / Goodbye / Swanee river hop / Rosemary / Please don't leave me / Domino stomp / You said you love me / Rosemary (2) / Fats Domino blues / Ain't it good / Girl I love / Don't leave me this way / Something's wrong / Fats' frenzy / Goin' back home / You left me / You left me (2) / 44 / Barrel house / Little school girl / If you need me / You done me wrong / Thinking of you / Baby please / Where did you stay / You can pack your stay / I lived my life / Little Mama / I know / Love me / Don't you hear me calling you / Don't you know / Helping hand / Help me / All by myself / Ain't it a shame / Oh ba-a-aby / La la (2) / Blue Monday / Troubles of my own / What's the matter / Poor me / I can't go on / I'm in love / Bo Weevil / Don't blame it on me / Howdy podner / So long / I can't go on / My blue heaven / Don't know what's wrong home / Ida Jane / When my dreamboat comes home / What's the reason / Twist set me free / Blueberry hill / Honey chile / I'm walkin' / What will I tell my heart / I'm in the mood for love / Would you / My happiness / Don't deceive me / Rooster song / Telling lies / As time goes by / Town talk / Twistin' the spots / It's you I love / Valley of tears / Valley of tears (2) / Wait and see / True confession / Sailor boy / It must be love / Big beat / Little Mary / Stack and Rilly / When I see you / Oh whee / I still love you / My love for her / I want you to know / Yes my darling / Don't you know I love you / Sick and tired / No, no / Prisoner's song / One of these days / (I'll be glad when you're dead) you rascal you / Young school girl / I'm gonna be a wheel someday / How can I be happy / Lazy woman / Isle of Capri / Coquette / Once in a while / Sheikh of Araby / Whole lotta lovin' / I miss you so / Margie / I'll always be in love with you / HAnds across the table / If you need me (2) / So glad / At the Darktown strutter's ball / Margie (2) / Sheikh of Araby (2) / My heart is bleeding / I hear you knocking / Li'l Liza Jane / Every night / When the saints go marching in / Country boy / I'm ready / I'm ready (2) / I want to walk you home / When I was young / When I was young (2) / Easter Parade / I've been around / Be my guest / Tell me that you love me / Before I grow too old / Walking to New Orleans / Walking to New Orleans (2) / Don't come knockin' / Don't come knockin' (2) / La la / Put your arms around me honey / Three nights a week / Shu Rah / Rising Sun / My girl Josephine / You always hurt the one you love / Magic Isles / Natural born lover / Am I blue / It's tha talk of the town / It keeps rainin' / What a price / Ain't that just like a woman / Fell in love on Monday / Fell in love on Monday (2) / Trouble in mind / Hold hands / Bad luck and trouble / I've been calling / I just cry / Ain't gonna do it / Won't you come on back / I can't give you anything but love / I'm alone because I love you / Good hearted man / (In) a shanty in old Shanty Town / Along the Navajo trail / One night / Let the four winds blow / Trouble blues / You win again / Your cheatin' heart / Let the four winds blow (2) / What a party / Rockin' bicycle / Did you ever see a dream walking / Birds and the bees / Wishing ring / Jambalaya / Do you know what it means to miss New Orleans / South of the border / Teenage love / Stop the clock / Didn't home (2) / My real name / Hum diddy doo / Those eyes / I want to go home / Domino / Nothing new (same old thing)
CD Set _____ BCD 15541
Bear Family / Oct '93 / Rollercoaster / Direct / CM / Swift / ADA.

WHEN I'M WALKING
CD _____ 12362
Laserlight / May '94 / Target/BMG.

Dominoes

DOMINOES MEET THE RAVENS (Dominoes & Ravens)
Take me back to heaven / Green eyes / On Chapel Hill / Stop you're sending me / Happy go lucky baby / Bells of San Raquel / We'll raise a ruckus tonight / Gimme gimme gimme / Rockin' at the record hop / She's fine, she's mine / Take me back to heaven (Faster version) / Boots and saddles / Ashamed / Come to me baby / Same sweet wonderful one / Sweethearts on parade / I'll always be in love with you / Unbeliever / Take me back to heaven (Unreleased version) / Bye bye baby blues
CD _____ NEMCD 716
Sequel / Mar '95 / BMG.

Dominus

VIEW TO THE DIM
CD _____ RRS 942CD
Lost & Found / Sep '95 / Plastic Head.

Domnerus, Arne

ANTIPHONE BLUES
CD _____ PCD 7744

Proprius / Dec '95 / Jazz Music / May Audio.

ARNE DOMNERUS
CD _____ NCD 8831
Phontastic / Aug '94 / Wellard / Jazz Music / Cadillac.

ARNE DOMNERUS SEXTET (Domnerus, Arne Sextet)
CD _____ PHONTCD 9303
Phontastic / Feb '95 / Wellard / Jazz Music / Cadillac.

DOMPAN AT THE SAVOY
Rombacksbotten / Morning glory / Nearness of you / Solitude / Honeysuckle rose / Take the train
CD _____ ND 8806
Phontastic / '93 / Wellard / Jazz Music / Cadillac.

DOWNTOWN MEETING (Domnerus, Arne & Bengt Hallberg)
Gone with the wind / Embraceable you / On the sunny side of the street / I cover the waterfront / Song from Utanmyra
CD _____ PHONT CD 7518
Phontastic / Apr '88 / Wellard / Jazz Music / Cadillac.

JAZZ AT THE PAWNSHOP
CD _____ PCD 7778
Proprius / Dec '95 / Jazz Music / May Audio.

JAZZ AT THE PAWNSHOP 2
CD _____ PCD 9044
Proprius / Dec '95 / Jazz Music / May Audio.

JAZZ AT THE PAWNSHOP 3
CD _____ PCD 9058
Proprius / Dec '95 / Jazz Music / May Audio.

PAWNSHOP 3
CD _____ PRCD 9058
Prestige / Aug '94 / Complete/Pinnacle / Cadillac.

SKETCHES OF STANDARDS
CD _____ PCD 9036
Proprius / Dec '95 / Jazz Music / May Audio.

Don & Dewey

JUNGLE HOP
Jungle hop / Little love / Hey Thelma / Baby gotta party / Miss Sue / Good morning / Leavin' it all up to you / Jelly bean / Sweet talk / Farmer John / Just a little lovin' / Letter / When the sun has begun to shine / Bim bam / Day by day / Koko Joe / Justine / Little Sally Walker / Kill me / Big boy Pete / Pink champagne / Jump awhile / Mammerjammer / Get your hat
CD _____ CDCHD 358
Ace / Nov '91 / Pinnacle / Cadillac / Complete/Pinnacle.

Don Caballero

DON CABALLERO II
CD _____ TG 143CD
Touch & Go / Sep '95 / SRD.

Don-E

CHANGING SEASONS
Introlude / Circles / Rhythm of life / Simple / Phat beats (reprise) / Don't she / Fakin' the funk / Stop (reprise) / Changin' seasons / D.O.G. / Good things / Patricia boom (parts 1 & 2) / Cirlces (reprise) / All in my mind / Get high on me / Pop / History / Outrolude
CD _____ BRCD 603
4th & Broadway / Aug '95 / PolyGram.

UNBREAKABLE
Intro / Welcome to my world / Oh my gosh / Love makes the world go round / Unbreakable / Someday somehow / Interlude / Undercover lover / Stop what you're doing / Me oh my / Emancipate our love / Peace in the world / Never ever / So fine / U don't have 2 cry
CD _____ BRCD 586
4th & Broadway / Jul '92 / PolyGram.

Donahue, Jerry

BRIEF ENCOUNTERS (Donahue, Jerry & Doug Morter)
CD _____ ARIS 883510CD
Hypertension / Sep '93 / Total/BMG / Direct / ADA.

NECK OF THE WOOD
CD _____ RGFCD 011
Road Goes On Forever / Mar '91 / Direct.

TELECASTING
CD _____ CMML 88001CD
Music Maker / Jul '94 / Grapevine / ADA.

Donahue, Miles

DOUBLE DRIBBLE
Squabbish / Stardust memories / Inner urge / Crackin' eyes / Double dribble / What's happening / Don't blame me / When I fall in love

---

CD _____ CDSJP 392
Timeless Jazz / Aug '93 / New Note.

Donahue, Sam

CONVOY 1945 VOL.1
Convoy / Deep night / I've found a new baby / Moten swing / Homeward bound / Lonesome nights / Saxophone Sam / Without a song / Bugle call rag / You was right, baby / Just you, just me / Out of this world / Take me in your arms / C jam blues / Gypsy love song / On the sunny side of the street / My silent love / Please get us out
CD _____ HEPCD 2
Hep / Jun '94 / Cadillac / Jazz Music / New Note / Wellard.

LST PARTY - 1945 VOL.2
World is waiting for the sunrise / Dinah / I can't give you anything but love / Play fiddle play / Cocktails for two / Mean to me / Minor de luxe / C jam blues / C jam blues (Breakdown) / Liza / My heart stood still / LST Party / St. Louis blues / Moten swing / Convoy take / Paradise / Dear Al / My melancholy baby / Bugle call rag
CD _____ HEPCD 5
Hep / Oct '94 / Cadillac / Jazz Music / New Note / Wellard.

Donaldson, Eric

KENT VILLAGE PLUS
CD _____ RNCD 2119
Rhino / Sep '95 / Jetstar / Magnum Music Group / THE.

LOVE OF COMMON PEOPLE
CD _____ JMC 200116
Jamaica Gold / Jun '95 / THE / Magnum Music Group / Jetstar.

VERY BEST OF ERIC DONALDSON
CD _____ RNCD 2054
Rhino / May '94 / Jetstar / Magnum Music Group / THE.

Donaldson, John

MEETING IN BROOKLYN
CD _____ BDV 9405
Babel / Mar '95 / ADA / Harmonia Mundi / Cadillac / Diverse.

Donaldson, Lou

BEST OF LOU DONALDSON, THE
CD _____ CDARC 509
Charly / Apr '94 / Charly / THE / Cadillac.

BIRDSEED
Cherry / Walkin' again / Pennies from heaven / Red top / Blue bossa / Black door blues / Dorothy / Bird seed
CD _____ MCD 9198-2
Milestone / Apr '94 / Jazz Music / Pinnacle / Wellard / Cadillac.

CARACUS
Hot dog / Just a dream / Ornithology / I don't know why (I just do) / Night train / I be blue / Caracus / Li'l darlin'
CD _____ MCD 9217-2
Milestone / Jul '94 / Jazz Music / Pinnacle / Wellard / Cadillac.

EVERYTHING I PLAY IS FUNKY
Everything I do gonh be funky / Hamp's hump / Over the rainbow / Donkey walk / West Indian daddy / Minor bash
CD _____ CDP 8312482
Blue Note / Mar '88 / EMI.

FORGOTTEN MAN (Donaldson, Lou Quartet)
CD _____ CDSJP 153
Timeless Jazz / Jan '88 / New Note.

RIGHTEOUS REED - BEST OF LOU DONALDSON
Alligator boogaloo / Reverend Moses / Peepin' / Midnight creeper / Say it loud, I'm black and I'm proud / Snake bone / Turtle walk / Everything I do gonh be funky / Hamp's hump / (Don't worry) If there's a hell below, we're all gonna go / Sassy soul strut / Gravy train (LP only) / Crosstown shuffle (LP only) / Who's making love (LP only) / Caterpillar (LP only)
CD _____ CDP 8307212
Blue Note / Sep '94 / EMI.

SCORPION, THE (Live At The Cadillac Club)
Alligator boogaloo / Laura / Alligator boogaloo / (I'm afraid) the masquerade is over / Peepin' / Footpattin' time
CD _____ CDP 8318762
Blue Note / Apr '95 / EMI.

SENTIMENTAL JOURNEY
What now my love / Sentimental journey / What'll I tell my heart / Messin' around with C.P. / My little suede shoes / Midnight creeper / Danny boy / Peck time
CD _____ 4781772
Sony Music / Apr '95 / Sony.

SUNNY SIDE UP
Blues for JP / Man I love / Politely / It's you or no one / Truth / Goose grease / Softly as in a morning sunrise
CD _____ CDP 8320952
Blue Note / Aug '95 / EMI.

Donatto, L.C.

TEXAS ZYDECO
CD _____ CD 52038
Blues Encore / Oct '95 / Target/BMG.

Done Lying Down

JOHN AUSTIN RUTLEDGE
CD _____ ABT 0992
Abstract / Oct '94 / Pinnacle / Total/BMG.

Doneda, Michel

OGOOUE OGOWAY (Live At Banlieu Blues Festival 1994)
CD _____ TE 003
Buda / Jul '95 / Discovery / ADA.

Donegan, Dorothy

DOROTHY DONEGAN
CD _____ ACD 281
Audiophile / Aug '95 / Jazz Music / Swift.

EXPLOSIVE, THE
CD _____ ACD 209
Audiophile / May '95 / Jazz Music / Swift.

LIVE AT THE WIDDER BAR
Lover / Tea for two / Autumn in New York / Makin' whoopee / Take the 'A' train / Prelude to a kiss / Like someone in love
CD _____ CDSJP 247
Timeless Jazz / Aug '90 / New Note.

MAKIN' WHOOPEE
Here's that rainy day / Lullaby in rhythm / Am I blue / These foolish things / All of me / Makin' whoopee / I can't get started (with you) / Poor butterfly
CD _____ BLE 591462
Black & Blue / Dec '90 / Wellard / Koch.

Donegan, Lonnie

BEST OF LONNIE DONEGAN
CD _____ KAZCD 21
Kaz / Jul '92 / BMG.

BEST OF LONNIE DONEGAN, THE
CD _____ GOLD 213
Disky / May '94 / BMG / Discovery / Pinnacle.

COLLECTION: LONNIE DONEGAN
Rock Island line / Lost John / Nobody's child / Bring a little water Sylvie / Frankie and Johnny / Cumberland gap / Mule skinner blues / Puttin' on the style / My Dixie darling / Ham 'n' eggs / Grand coulee dam / Tennies are getting hard boys / Long summer day / Does your chewing gum lose its flavour / Whoa Buck / Battle of New Orleans / Fancy talking tinker / Miss Otis regrets / Talking guitar blues / My old man's a dustman / Have a drink on me / Keep on the sunny side / Pick a bale of cotton / This train
CD _____ CCSCD 223
Castle / Feb '93 / BMG.

EP COLLECTION: LONNIE DONEGAN
Lost John / Stewball / Railroad Bill / Ballad of Jesse James / Little water, Sylvie / Dead or alive / Don't you rock me daddy-o / Cumberland Gap / Puttin' on the style / Gamblin' man / My dixie darling / Jack O'Diamonds / Grand coulee dam / Sally, don't you grieve / Betty, Betty, Betty / Tom Dooley / Does your chewing gum lose its flavour / Fort Worth jail / Battle of New Orleans / Sal's got a sugar lip / My old man's a dustman / I wanna go home / Have a drink on me / Michael, row the boat ashore / Lumbered
CD _____ SEECD 346
See For Miles/C5 / May '92 / Pinnacle.

EP COLLECTION: LONNIE DONEGAN VOL.2
Midnight special / Worried man blues / Railroad Bill / Ballad of Jesse James / Mule skinner blues / On a monday / Bewildered / It is no secret / Corine Corina / Nobody understands me / No hiding place / Lorelei / Party's over / New burying ground / When the sun goes down / Stagger Lee / Ol' Riley / Old Hannah / Glory / Kevin Barry / My lagan love / Junko partner / Sorry, but I'm gonna have to pass / Pick a bale of cotton / Losing by a hair
CD _____ SEECD 382
See For Miles/C5 / Oct '93 / Pinnacle.

FAVOURITE FLAVOURS
Cumberland gap / Battle of New Orleans / Pick a bale of cotton / Michael, row the boat ashore / Bring a little water Sylvie / Sorry, but I'm gonna have to pass / Comancheros / Frankie and Johnny / Lorelei / Nobody's child / Have a drink on me / Joshua Fit De Battle Of Jericho / Tom Dooley / Aunt Rhody (The old grey goose) / Mule skinner blues / Nobody knows the trouble I've seen / Miss Otis regrets / 500 miles away from home / Corine Corina / Does your chewing gum lose its flavour
CD _____ 5507612
Spectrum/Karussell / Mar '95 / PolyGram / THE.

LONNIE DONEGAN
CD _____ CDMFP 5917
Music For Pleasure / '91 / EMI.

MORE THAN 'PYE IN THE SKY
Rock Island line / John Henry / Nobody's child / Wabash cannonball / Hard time blues / You don't know my mind / Midnight special / Precious Lord lead me on / Passing stranger / On a christmas day / Take my hand, precious Lord / When the sun goes down / New burying ground / Worried man blues / Harmonica blues / Ballad of Jesse James / Ol' Riley / Railroad Bill / Lost John / Stewball / Stagger Lee / Bring a little water Sylvie / Dead or alive / Frankie and Johnny / How long, how long blues / I'm a ramblin' man / I'm Alabamy bound / Wreck of ol' 97 / Noddy's child / I shall not be moved / Don't you rock me Daddy-o / Cumberland Gap / Love is strange / Light fingers (film theme) / Gamblin' man / Puttin' on the style / My Dixie darling / I'm just a rolling stone / Jack O'Diamonds / Grand coulee dam / Hard travellin' / Ham 'n' eggs / Nobody loves like an Irishman / Sally don't you grieve / Ain't you glad you got religion / Lonesome traveller / Light from the lighthouse / I've got rocks in my bed / I've got rocks in my bed (alt.) / Long summer day / Sunshine of his love / Times are getting hard boys / Ain't no more cane on the Brazos / Lazy John / Betty, Betty, Betty / Whoa Buck / Shorty George / Baby don't you know that's love / Lonnie with Alan Freeman / Lonnie's skiffle party / Lonnie's skiffle party (part 2) / Darling Corey / Bewildered / It is no secret / My Lagan love / Rock of my soul / Aunt Rhody (the old grey goose) / Tom Dooley / Does your chewing gum lose its flavour / Kevin Barry / My only son was killed in Dublin / Chesapeake Bay / Ace in the hole / Fortworth Jail / Battle of New Orleans / Sal's got a sugar lip / Just a closer walk with thee / Ice cream / Fancy talking tinker / Gloryland / Gold rush is over / House of the rising sun / Miss Otis regrets / Take this hammer / San Miguel / Jimmie Brown the newsboy / John Hardy / John Hardy (alt.) / Mr. Froggie / You pass me by / Talking guitar blues (American version) / Talking guitar blues (British version) / Golden vanity / My old man's a dustman / I wanna go home / I wanna go home (alt.) / Corine Corina / In all my wildest dreams / Beyond the sunset / Nobody understands me / Junco partner / Lorelei / Wreck of the John B. / Sorry, but I'm gonna have to pass / Lively / Black cat (crossed my path today) / Banana split for my baby / Leave my woman alone / Bury me beneath the willow / When I was young / Virgin Mary / Just a wearyin' for you / Ramblin' round / Have a drink on me / Seven daffodils / Keep on the sunny side / Tiger rag / Michael, row the boat ashore / Lumbered / Michael, row the boat ashore (stereo) / Red berets / Comancheros / Party's over / Over the rainbow / I'll never fall in love again / It was a very good year / I'll never smile again / I'll never fall in love again (alt.) / His eye is on the sparrow / Nobody knows the trouble I've seen / Steal away / Good news, chariot's a-comin' / Born in Bethlehem / Joshua fit de battle of Jericho / No hiding place / Noah found grace in the eyes of the Lord / Sing hallelujah / This train / We shall walk through the valley / Pick a bale of cotton / Market song / Tit bits / Losing by a hair / Trumpet sounds / Rise up / I've got a girl so fine / It's a long road home / Lemon tree / 500 miles away from home / Cajun Joe (the bully of the bayou) / Fisherman's luck / Louisiana man / Interstate 40 / Bad news / There's a big wheel / Diamonds of dew / Nothing to gain / Lovey told me goodbye / Beans in my ears / Get out of my life / Blistered / Bound for Zion / Where in this world are we going / Doctor's daughter / Reverend Mr. Black / Farewell (fare thee well) / Wedding bells / Won't you tell me / My sweet Marie / After taxes / I'm gonna be a bachelor / She was a T-bone talking woman / World Cup Willie / Ding ding / Leaving blues / Auntie Maggie's remedy / Over in the new buryin' ground / Leavin' blues / Bury my body / Diggin' my potatoes / When I move to the sky / On a Monday / In the evening (when the sun goes down) / Old Hannah (go down old Hannah) / Mule skinner blues / Precious memories / Brother Moses smote the water / Ella speed / Glory (false start) / Black girl / Glory
CD _____ BCD 15700
Bear Family / Oct '93 / Rollercoaster / Direct / CM / Swift / ADA.

ORIGINALS
CD _____ SEECD 331
See For Miles/C5 / Sep '91 / Pinnacle.

PUTTING ON THE STYLE
CD Set _____ NXTCD 233
Sequel / Nov '92 / BMG.

Donna

MY HAPPINESS
CD _____ SPCD 12
Spindle / Nov '95 / Jetstar / Else.

Donna Maria

REGGAE LOVE MUSIC VOL.4
CD _____ PILCD 204
Pioneer / Nov '94 / Jetstar.

Donna Marie

NOW
CD _____ LDRCD 018
Londisc / Jul '95 / Jetstar.

Donnelly, Des

REMEMBER
CD _____ DDCD 001
Des Donnelly / Dec '94 / CM.

Donner, Ral

COMPLETE RAL DONNER 1959-1962, THE
CD Set _____ NEDCD 190
Sequel / Feb '92 / BMG.

Donohoe, Martin

FREE SPIRIT (Donohoe, Martin & Phil Cunningham)
CD _____ CICD 089
Clo Iar-Chonnachta / Dec '93 / CM.

Donovan

COLOURS - LIVE
Jennifer juniper / Catch the wind / Hurdy gurdy / Sunshine superman / Sadness / Universal soldier / Cosmic wheels / Atlantis / Wear our love like heaven / To Susan on the west coast waiting / Colours / Young girls blues / Young but growing / Stealing / Sailing homeward / Love will find a way / Lalena / Make up your mind to be happy
CD _____ MDCD 6
Magnum Music / May '94 / Magnum Music Group.

COSMIC WHEELS
Cosmic wheels / Earth sign man / Sleep / Maria Magenta / Wild witch lady / Music makers / Intergalactic laxative / I like you / Only the blues / Appearance
CD _____ 477378-2
Epic / Aug '94 / Sony.

DONOVAN IN CONCERT
Isle of Islay / Young girl blues / There is a mountain / Poor cow / Celeste / Fat angel / Guinevere / Widow with a shawl / Preachin' love / Lullaby of Spring / Writer in the sun / Pebble and the man / Rules and regulations / Mellow yellow
CD _____ BGOCD 90
Beat Goes On / Dec '90 / Pinnacle.

EARLY YEARS
CD _____ EARLD 3
Castle / Mar '93 / BMG.

EP COLLECTION: DONOVAN
CD _____ SEECD 300
See For Miles/C5 / '90 / Pinnacle.

FAIRYTALE
Colours / I'll try for the sun / Sunny Goodge Street / Oh deed I do / Circus of sour / Summer day reflection song / Candy man / Jersey Thursday / Belated of a crystal man / Little tin soldier / Ballad of Geraldine
CD _____ CLACD 226
Castle / Feb '91 / BMG.

GIFT FROM A FLOWER TO A GARDEN, A
Song of the naturalist's wife / Enchanted gypsy / Isle of Islay / Mandolin man and his secret / Lay of the last tinker / Tinker and the crab / Widow with shawl portrait / Lullaby of spring / Magpie / Starfish on the toast / Epistle to Derroll / Voyage into the golden screen / Wear your love like heaven / Mad John's escape / Skip-a-long Sam / Sun / There was a time / Oh gosh / Little boy in corduroy / Under the greenwood tree / Land of doesn't have to be / Someone's singing
CD _____ BGOCD 194
Beat Goes On / Jun '93 / Pinnacle.

GREATEST HITS AND MORE
Sunshine superman / Wear your love like heaven / Jennifer juniper / Barabajagal (with the Jeff Beck Group.) / Hurdy gurdy man / Epistle to dippy / To Susan on the west coast waiting / Catch the wind / Mellow yellow / There is a mountain / Happiness runs / Season of the witch / Colours / Superlungs My supergirl / Lalena / Atlantis / Preachin' love (CD only.) / Poor cow (CD only.) / Teen angel (CD only.) / Aye my love (CD only.)
CD _____ CZ 193
EMI / Oct '89 / EMI.

IN CONCERT
Jenifer juniper / Catch the wind / Hurdy gurdy man / Sunshine superman / Sadness / Universal soldier / Cosmic wheels / Atlantis / Wear your love like heaven / To Susan on the westcoast waiting / Colours / Young girl blues / Young but growing / Stealing / Sailing homeward / Love will find a way
CD _____ HP 93432
Happy Price / Jan '96 / Target/BMG.

INTROSPECTIVE: DONOVAN
CD _____ CINT 5007
Baktabak / Feb '92 / Baktabak.

ORIGINALS
Sunshine superman / Legend of a girl child Linda / Three King Fishers / Ferris wheel /

Bert's blues / Season of the witch / Trip / Guinevere / Fat angel / Celeste / Mellow yellow / Writer in the sun / Sand and foam / Observation / Bleak City woman / House of Jansch / Young girl blues / Museum / Hampstead incident / Sunny South Kensington / Hurdy gurdy man / Peregrine / Entertaining of a shy girl / As I recall it / Get thy bearings / Hi it's been a long time / West Indian lady / Jennifer Juniper / River song / Tangier / Sunny day / Sun is a very magic fellow / Teas / Barabajagal / Superlungs my supergirl / Where is she / Happiness runs / I love my shirt / Love song / To Susan on the West Coast waiting / Atlantis / Trudi / Pamela Jo
CD Set _____ DONOVAN 1
EMI / Oct '94 / EMI.

SUNSHINE SUPERMAN
CD _____ BGOCD 68
Beat Goes On / Feb '91 / Pinnacle.

SUNSHINE SUPERMAN
CD _____ HADCD 197
Javelin / Nov '95 / THE / Henry Hadaway Organisation.

SUNSHINE SUPERMAN
CD _____ RMB 75059
Remember / Sep '93 / Total/BMG.

UNIVERSAL SOLDIER
Colours / Catch the wind / Ballad of a crystal man / Josie / Do you hear me now / Candy man / Belated forgiveness plea / Tangerine puppet / Ballad of Geraldine / Universal soldier / Turquoise / I'll try for the sun / Summer day reflection song / Why do you treat me like you do / Hey gyp (Dig the slowness) / To sing for you / You're gonna need somebody on your bond / Little tin soldier
CD _____ 5507212
Spectrum/Karussell / Jan '95 / PolyGram / THE.

Donovan, Jason

BETWEEN THE LINES
CD _____ HFCD 14
PWL / May '90 / Warner Music / 3MV.

GREATEST HITS: JASON DONOVAN
CD _____ HFCD 20
PWL / Sep '91 / Warner Music / 3MV.

TEN GOOD REASONS
Too many broken hearts / Nothing can divide us / Every day (I love you more) / You can depend on me / Time heals / Sealed with a kiss / Question of pride / If I don't have you / Change your mind / Too late to say goodbye / Especially for you
CD _____ HFCD 7
PWL / May '89 / Warner Music / 3MV.

Doobie Brothers

BROTHERHOOD
Something you said / Is love enough / Dangerous / Our love / Divided highway / Under the spell / Excited / This train I'm on / Showdown / Rollin' on
CD _____ CDEST 2141
Capitol / Apr '91 / EMI.

CAPTAIN AND ME, THE
Natural thing / Long train runnin' / China grove / Dark eyed Cajun woman / Clear as the driven snow / Without you / South City midnight lady / Evil woman / Busted down around O'Connelly Corners / Ukiah / Captain and me
CD _____ K 246217
Warner Bros. / Feb '95 / Warner Music.

DOOBIE BROTHERS
Nobody / Slippery St. Paul / Greenwood Creek / It won't be right / Travellin' man / Feeling down farther / Master / Growin' a little each day / Beehive state / Closer every day / Chicago
CD _____ 7599262152
Warner Bros. / May '95 / Warner Music.

LISTEN TO THE MUSIC (The Very Best Of The Doobie Brothers)
Long train runnin' / China grove / Listen to the music / Takin' it to the streets / Black water / Jesus is just alright / Rockin' down the highway / Take me in your arms / Without you / South city midnight lady / It keeps you runnin' / Little darlin' / You belong to me / Minute by minute / Here to love you / Real love / What a fool believes / Long train runnin' (mix)
CD _____ 954832803-2
Warner Bros. / Mar '94 / Warner Music.

LIVIN' ON THE FAULT LINE
Nothin' but a heartache / Little darlin' / Livin' on the fault line / Larry the logger two-step / Need a lady / You're made that way / Chinatown / There's a light / You belong to me / Echoes of love
CD _____ K 9273152
Warner Bros. / Jun '89 / Warner Music.

MINUTE BY MINUTE
Here to love you / What a fool believes / Minute by minute / Dependin' on you / Don't stop to watch the wheels / Open your eyes / Sweet feelin' / Streamer lane breakdown / You never change / How do fools survive
CD _____ 256 486
Warner Bros. / '88 / Warner Music.

ONE STEP CLOSER
Dedicate this heart / Real love / No stoppin' us now / Thank you love / One step closer / Keep this train a rollin' / Just in time / South bay strut / One by one
CD _____ 7599266282
Warner Bros. / Jan '96 / Warner Music.

STAMPEDE
Sweet Maxine / Neal's fandango / Texas lullaby / Music man / Slat key rag / Take me in your arms / I cheat the hangman / Precis / Rainy day crossroad blues / I been workin' on you / Double dealin' four flusher
CD _____ 759927289-2
Warner Bros. / Apr '93 / Warner Music.

TAKIN' IT TO THE STREETS
Wheels of fortune / Takin' it to the streets / 8th Avenue shuffle / Losin' end / Rio / For someone special / It keeps you runnin' / Turn it loose / Carry me away
CD _____ 9273002
Warner Bros. / Jul '93 / Warner Music.

TOULOUSE STREET
Listen to the music / Rockin' down the highway / Mamaloi / Toulouse Street / Cotton mouth / Don't start me talkin' / Jesus is just alright / White sun / Disciple / Snakeman
CD _____ 759927263-2
Warner Bros. / May '93 / Warner Music.

WHAT WERE ONCE VICES ARE NOW HABITS
Another park another Sunday / Black water / Daughters of the sea / Down in the track / Eyes of silver / Flying cloud / Pursuit on 53rd street / Road angel / Song to see you through / Spirit / Tell me what you want (and I'll give you what you need) / You just can't stop it
CD _____ 759927802
Warner Bros. / Jul '93 / Warner Music.

Doom

GREATEST INVENTION, THE
CD _____ DISCCD 10
Discipline / Aug '93 / Pinnacle.

PEEL SESSIONS: DOOM (29.5.79)
Symptom of the universe / Multinationals / Expoitation / Circles / No religion / Relief / Sold out / War crimes / Means to an end / Dream to come true / Natural abuse / Days go by / Life lock / Bury the debt / Life in freedom / Money drug / Fear of the future
CD _____ SFPMCD 203
Strange Fruit / '89 / Pinnacle.

Doomstone

THOSE WHO SATAN HATH JOINED
CD _____ NOSF 002CD
Nosferatu / Jan '95 / Plastic Head.

Doonan Family

FENWICK'S WINDOW
CD _____ FSCD 12
Folksound / Jan '91 / Roots / CM.

Doonican, Val

CHRISTMAS ALBUM
CD _____ PWKS 4218
Carlton Home Entertainment / Oct '95 / Carlton Home Entertainment.

VERY BEST OF VAL DOONICAN, THE
Special years / Elusive butterfly / If the whole world stopped loving / Morning / For the good times / First time ever I saw your face / Heaven is my woman's love / Now / Paddy McGinty's goat / Walk tall / If I knew then what I know now / What would I be / O'Rafferty's motor car / Marvellous toy / Song sung blue / King of the road / Two streets / I'm just a country boy / Delaney's donkey
CD _____ MCCD 008
Music Club / Feb '91 / Disc / THE / CM.

Doors

AMERICAN PRAYER, AN (Music By The Doors) (Morrison, Jim/Doors)
Awake / To come of age / Poet's dreams / World on fire / American prayer
CD _____ 7559618122
Elektra / May '95 / Warner Music.

BEST OF THE DOORS, THE
Break on through / Light my fire / Crystal ship / People are strange / Strange days / Love me two times / Five to one / Waiting for the sun / Spanish caravan / When the music's over / Hello I love you / Roadhouse blues / L.A. Woman / Riders on the storm / Touch me / Love her madly / Unknown soldier / End
CD _____ 9603452
Elektra / Nov '85 / Warner Music.

CEREMONY CONTINUES, THE
CD P.Disc _____ CBAK 4052
Baktabak / Mar '92 / Baktabak.

DOORS
Break on through / Soul kitchen / Crystal ship / Twentieth Century Fox / Alabama song / Light my fire / Back door man / I looked at you / End of the night / Take it as it comes / End

CD _____ 9740072
Elektra / Feb '89 / Warner Music.

DOORS IN CONCERT, THE
House announcer / Who do you love / Medley / Alabama song / Backdoor man / Love hides / Five to one / Build me a woman / When the music's over / Universal mind / Petition the Lord with prayers / Dead cats / Dead rats / Break on through / Celebration of the lizard / Soul kitchen / Roadhouse blues / Gloria / Light my fire / You make me real / Texas radio and the big beat / End / Unkown soldier / Close to you / Moonlight drive / Little red rooster / Love me two times
CD _____ 7559610822
Elektra / May '91 / Warner Music.

GREATEST HITS: THE DOORS
CD _____ 7559618602
Elektra / Nov '95 / Warner Music.

L.A. WOMAN
Changeling / Love her madly / Cars hiss by my window / L.A. woman / L'America / Hyacinth house / Crawlin' kingsnake / Wasp / Riders on the storm
CD _____ 9750112
Elektra / Feb '89 / Warner Music.

MORRISON HOTEL
Roadhouse blues / Waiting for the sun / You make me real / Peace frog / Blue Sunday / Ship of fools / Land ho / Spy / Queen of the highway / Indian Summer / Maggie McGill
CD _____ 9750072
Elektra / Feb '89 / Warner Music.

OPENING THE DOORS OF PERCEPTION - INTERVIEWS
CD _____ RVCD 33
Raven / May '94 / Direct / ADA.

SOFT PARADE
Tell all the people / Touch me / Shaman's blues / Do it / Easy rider / Wild child / Running blue / Wishful sin / Soft parade
CD _____ 9750052
Elektra / Feb '89 / Warner Music.

STRANGE DAYS
Strange days / You're lost / Little girl / Love me two times / Unhappy girl / Horse latitudes / Moonlight drive / People are strange / My eyes have seen you / I can't see your face in my mind / When the music's over
CD _____ 9740142
Elektra / '89 / Warner Music.

WAITING FOR THE SUN
Hello I love you / Love street / Not to touch / Earth / Summer's almost gone / Winter time love / Unknown soldier / Spanish caravan / My wild love / We could be so good together / Yes the river knows / Five to one
CD _____ 9740242
Elektra / '89 / Warner Music.

Doran, Brigeen

BRIGHT MOMENTS
Bibi's birthday / Slow samba / Once upon a time / Tell me / Wooden yodels / Perfect for you / Berimbau / Sing and dance / Whirlpool
CD _____ BW 020
B&W / Sep '93 / New Note.

Doran, Christy

PLAYS THE MUSIC OF JIMI HENDRIX (Doran, Christy & Fredy Studer)
Foxy lady / Manic depression / Up from the skies / Purple haze / Hey Joe / Third stone from the sun / If six was nine / I don't live today / Are you experienced
CD _____ ANYVBR 21342
Vera Bra / Apr '94 / Pinnacle / New Note.

WHAT A BAND
CD _____ ARTCD 6105
Hat Art / May '92 / Harmonia Mundi / ADA / Cadillac.

Dorau, Andreas

ARGER MIT DER UNSTERBLICHKEIT
CD _____ EFA 037532
Atatak / Apr '95 / SRD.

ERNTE
CD _____ EFA 037642
Atatak / Apr '95 / SRD.

Dordán

IRISH TRADITIONAL & BAROQUE
CD _____ CEFCD 150
Gael Linn / Jan '94 / Roots / CM / Direct / ADA.

JIGS TO THE MOON
CD _____ CEFCD 168
Gael Linn / Oct '94 / Roots / CM / Direct / ADA.

Dore, Charlie

THINGS CHANGE
CD _____ BICD 1
Black Ink / Aug '95 / Grapevine.

Dorge, Christian

LYCIA
CD _____ DW 100
Isol / Feb '95 / Plastic Head.

Dorge, Pierre

BALLAD ROUND THE LEFT CORNER
CD _____ SCCD 31132
Steeplechase / Jul '88 / Impetus.

Dorham, Kenny

ARRIVAL OF KENNY DORHAM, THE
CD _____ FSRCD 200
Fresh Sound / Dec '92 / Jazz Music / Discovery.

HOT STUFF FROM BRAZIL
Wee dot / Red door / Autumn leaves / Halley's comet / Night in Tunisia / It's all right with me
CD _____ WWCD 015
West Wind / Dec '88 / Swift / Charly / CM / ADA.

JAZZ CONTRASTS
CD _____ OJCCD 028
Original Jazz Classics / Oct '92 / Wellard / Jazz Music / Cadillac / Complete/Pinnacle.

NEW YORK 1953-1956
CD _____ LS 2918
Landscape / Feb '93 / THE.

OSMOSIS
CD _____ BLCD 760146
Black Lion / May '91 / Jazz Music / Cadillac / Wellard / Koch.

QUIET KENNY
CD _____ OJCCD 250
Original Jazz Classics / Sep '93 / Wellard / Jazz Music / Cadillac / Complete/Pinnacle.

ROUND ABOUT MIDNIGHT AT THE CAFE BOHEMIA (2CD Set)
Monaco / Round midnight / Mexico City / Night in Tunisia / Autumn in New York / Hill's edge / KD's blues / Who cares (as long as you care for me) / Mexico City (alt. take) / Royal roost / My heart stood still / Prophet / KD's blues (alt. take) / Riffin' / Who cares (as long as you care for me) (alt. take) / Monaco (alt. take) / N.Y. theme
CD Set _____ CDP 8335762
Capitol Jazz / Sep '95 / EMI.

ROUND ABOUT MIDNIGHT AT THE CAFE BOHEMIA, VOL. 2
Royal roost / My heart stood still / Prophet / K.D.'s Blues / Riffin' / Who cares / Monaco / N.Y. (theme)
CD _____ BNZ 26
Blue Note / May '87 / EMI.

UNA MAS
Una mas / Straight ahead / Sao Paulo / If ever I would leave you
CD _____ BNZ 27
Blue Note / May '87 / EMI.

WEST 42ND STREET
CD _____ BLCD 760119
Black Lion / Oct '92 / Jazz Music / Cadillac / Wellard / Koch.

Doro

ANGELS NEVER DIE
CD _____ 514 309-2
Vertigo / Mar '93 / PolyGram.

Dorough, Bob

CLANKIN ON TIN PAN ALLEY
CD _____ BL 005
Bloomdido / Oct '93 / Cadillac.

DEVIL MAY CARE
Old devil moon / It would happen to you / I had the craziest dream / You're the dangerous type / Ow / Polka dots and moonbeams / Yardbird suite / Baltimore Oriole / Midnight sun / Johnny one note
CD _____ BL 008
Bloomdido / Nov '87 / Cadillac.

JUST ABOUT EVERYTHING
Don't think twice, it's alright / Baltimore Oriole / I've got just about everything / Message / Crawdad song / Better than anything / But for now / 'Tis autumn / Baby, you should know it / Lazy afternoon
CD _____ ECD 220942
Evidence / Jul '94 / Harmonia Mundi / ADA / Cadillac.

MEMORIAL CHARLIE PARKER (Dorough, Bob & Bill Takas)
CD _____ 214 W24-2
Philology / Aug '91 / Harmonia Mundi / Cadillac.

Dorset, Ray

COLD BLUE EXCURSION
Got to be free / Cold blue excursion / With me / Have pity on me / Time is now / Livin' ain't easy / Help your friends / I need it / Because I want / Nightime / Maybe that's the way / Always on my mind
CD _____ BGOCD 282
Beat Goes On / Jul '95 / Pinnacle.

Dorsey Brothers

BEST OF THE BIG BANDS
Somebody stole Gabriel's horn / Mood Hollywood / Sing (it's good for ya) / By heck / My dog loves your dog / Old man Harlem / She reminds me of you / Shim sham

shimmy / She's funny that way / Blue room / But I can't make a man / Judy / Nasty man / Annie's cousin Fanny / I'm getting sentimental over you
CD _____ 4716492
Columbia / Jun '92 / Sony.

CAFE ROUGE N.Y. (1954-56) (Dorsey Brothers Orchestra)
CD _____ 90 507 2
Jazz Archives / Aug '91 / Jazz Music / Discovery / Cadillac.

DORSEY BROTHERS ORCHESTRA JANUARY 1955
CD _____ EBCD 2123-2
Jazzband / Feb '95 / Jazz Music / Wellard.

HARLEM LULLABY
Somebody stole Gabriel's horn / Stay on the right side of the road / Here is my heart / Stormy weather / Love is the thing / Don't blame me / Shadows on the Swanee / I like a guy what takes his time / Easy rider / You've got me crying again / I got a right to sing the blues / Is that religion / Harlem lullaby / There's a cabin in the Pines / Lazy bones / Shoutin' in the Amen Corner / Snowball / Give me Liberty or give me love / Doin' the uptown lowdown
CD _____ HEPCD 1006
Hep / Dec '91 / Cadillac / Jazz Music / New Note / Wellard.

LIVE IN THE MEADOWBROOK, 28 OCTOBER 1955 (Dorsey Brothers Orchestra)
CD _____ JH 1003
Jazz Hour / Feb '91 / Target/BMG / Jazz Music / Cadillac.

Dorsey, Don

BACH BUSTERS
CD _____ CD 80123
Telarc / '87 / Conifer / ADA.

Dorsey, Jimmy

1939-40 (Dorsey, Jimmy Orchestra)
CD _____ CCD 30
Circle / May '93 / Jazz Music / Swift / Wellard.

1940 (Dorsey, Jimmy Orchestra)
CD _____ CCD 46
Circle / May '93 / Jazz Music / Swift / Wellard.

22 ORIGINAL BIG BAND RECORDINGS
CD _____ HCD 415
Hindsight / Sep '92 / Target/BMG / Jazz Music.

I REMEMBER YOU
Tangerine / Keep a knockin' / Dixieland begone / Begone / Cherokee / I remember you / Green eyes / Always in my heart / Tropical magic / Time was / You make me love you / Holiday for strings / My ideal / They're either too young or too old / Besame mucho / Amapola / Maria elena / Yours / Brazil / At the crossroads
CD _____ RAJCD 852
Empress / May '95 / THE.

JIMMY DORSEY
CD _____ 15759
Laserlight / Aug '92 / Target/BMG.

JIMMY DORSEY AT THE 400 RESTAURANT 1946 (Dorsey, Jimmy Orchestra)
All the things you ain't / Grand Central getaway / Sunset Strip / September / Opus no.1 / I've got a crush on you / Outer drive / Come to baby do / Town hall tonight / Lover / It's the talk of the town / Super chief / Lover man / King Porter stomp / Here I go again / I can't believe that you're in love with me / Man with the horn / This can't be love / Contrasts
CD _____ HEPCD 41
Hep / Dec '91 / Cadillac / Jazz Music / New Note / Wellard.

PENNIES FROM HEAVEN
It's the natural thing to do / Slap that bass / I love bug will bite you / Dorsey Dervish / Pink yourself up / Moon got in my eyes / In a sentimental mood / Rap tap on wood / I love to sing / All you want to do is dance / They can't take that away from me / Serenade to nobody in particular / Let's call a heart a heart / Swingin' the jinx away / Stompin' at the Savoy / After you / Listen to the mockingbird / Pennies from Heaven
CD _____ CD AJA 5052
Living Era / May '88 / Koch.

PERFIDIA (Dorsey, Jimmy Orchestra)
CD _____ 15768
Laserlight / Jul '92 / Target/BMG.

SHINE ON HARVEST MOON
I've got rhythm / Grand Central getaway / Sowing wild oats / Just you, just me / Sophisticated swing / Together hit the note / (I would do) anything for you / Three little words / Shine on harvest moon / Imagination / I'm stepping out with a memory tonight / Contrasts in the morning / Nearness of you / Moonlight on the river / Sunday sweetheart / Fools rush in / Begin the beguine / Sunset strip
CD _____ CDGRF 067
Tring / '93 / Tring / Prism.

THEN & NOW (Dorsey, Jimmy Orchestra)
CD _____ 7567818012
Atlantic / Jul '93 / Warner Music.

Dorsey, Lee

FREEDOM FOR THE FUNK
CD _____ CPCD 8068
Charly / Nov '94 / Charly / THE / Cadillac.

GREAT GOOGA MOOGA
Lottie mo / Ya ya / Do re mi / Hoodlum Joe / You're breaking me up / Messed around (and fell in love) / Ay aa ay / Great googa mooga / People sure act funny / Ride your pony / Can you hear me / Get out of my life woman / Confusion / Working in a coalmine / Holy cow / My old car / Go go girl / Love lots of lovin' / Four corners (part 1) / Lover was born
CD _____ CDNEV 3
Charly / Sep '91 / Charly / THE / Cadillac.

SOUL MINE
CD _____ CDCD 1115
Charly / Jul '93 / Charly / THE / Cadillac.

WORKING IN A COALMINE
CD _____ REP 4169-WZ
Repertoire / Aug '91 / Pinnacle / Cadillac.

WORKING IN A COALMINE
CD _____ RMB 75055
Remember / Nov '93 / Total/BMG.

WORKING IN A COALMINE
CD _____ QSCD 6007
Charly / Jan '05 / Charly / THE / Cadillac.

Dorsey, Leon Lee

WATCHER, THE
Watcher / Miles / In remembrance of him / I am with you always / New testament / River of the fire / Centre avenue shuffle / Cheek to cheek / Caravan / Misty / United
CD _____ LCD 15402
Landmark / Aug '95 / New Note.

Dorsey, Tommy

1940 MEADOWBROOK BROADCAST 24/2/40
CD _____ TAXCD 3705
Tax / Jun '89 / Jazz Music / Wellard / Cadillac.

1944- ALL TIME HIT PARADE
On the sunny side of the Street / April in Paris / What is this thing called love / I may be wrong, but I think you're wonderful / East of the sun and west of the moon / Embraceable you / Cheek to cheek / I'll be seeing you / Dancing in the dark / I can't give you anything but love / I'll walk alone / South of the border / Summertime / If you are but a dream / Amor / Lover come back to me / Top hat / Lamp is low / Boogie woogie / I'll never smile again / Song of India / As time goes by / Hawaiian war chant
CD _____ HEPCD 39
Hep / Apr '90 / Cadillac / Jazz Music / New Note / Wellard.

AT THE FAT MAN'S
Blue skies / Dawn on the desert / At the Fat Man's / Bingo, bango, boffo / Marie / Chloe / Well git it / At sundown / Opus one / Candy / Continental / Call you sweetheart / Feels so good / Pussy Willow / Broadcasts from 1945-1948
CD _____ HEPCD 43
Hep / Jun '93 / Cadillac / Jazz Music / New Note / Wellard.

BEST OF TOMMY DORSEY
Maria / Star dust / Little white lies / I'll never smile again / Yes indeed / Boogie woogie / Opus one / Song of India / Who / Royal Garden blues / Once in a while / I'm getting sentimental over you
CD _____ ND 90587
Bluebird / Aug '92 / BMG.

BEST OF TOMMY DORSEY
CD _____ DCD 5330
Disky / Dec '93 / THE / BMG / Discovery / Pinnacle.

BEST OF TOMMY DORSEY
CD _____ DLCD 4010
Dixie Live / Mar '95 / Magnum Music Group.

BIG BAND BASH (Dorsey, Tommy Orchestra)
Opus one / On the sunny side of the street / I'm getting sentimental over you / Boogie woogie / Blue skies / Royal garden blues / Chicago / Stardust / Sheet of Araby / Song of India / Song sang swing / There are such things / Well git it / Mane / What is this thing called love / Imagination / Weary blues / Yes indeed / Liebestraum / East of the sun and west of the moon / Hawaiian war chant / Whispering / Mendelssohn's spring song
CD _____ GOJCD 53082
Giants Of Jazz / Mar '90 / Target/BMG / Cadillac.

BOOGIE WOOGIE (Dorsey, Tommy Orchestra)
CD _____ CDJJ 614
Jazz & Jazz / Jan '92 / Target/BMG.

CARNEGIE HALL V-DISC SESSION APRIL 1944, THE (Dorsey, Tommy Orchestra)
Minor goes muggin' / I dream of you / Milkman keep those bottles quiet / I never knew / Song of India / Tess's torch song / Irresistible you / Losers weepers / Wagon wheels / Paramount on parade / TD chant / Then I'll be happy / Small fry / Pennies from heaven / Somebody loves me / Indian Summer / I'm in the mood to be loved / Sweet and lovely / Chicago / Lady in red / For all we know / I'm nobody's baby / Three little words
CD _____ HEPCD 40
Hep / Dec '90 / Cadillac / Jazz Music / New Note / Wellard.

CLASSICS 1928-35
CD _____ CLASSICS 833
Classics / Sep '95 / Discovery / Jazz Music.

COMPLETE RECORDINGS 1940-42, THE (4CD Set) (Dorsey, Tommy & Frank Sinatra)
CD Set _____ 852137
New Rose / May '94 / Direct / ADA.

DANCE WITH DORSEY
Opus One / Lamp Is Low / You grow sweeter as the years go by / How Am I To Know / All I remember is you / Well alright / Big Dipper / Tin Roof Blues / Sweet Sue, Just You / Copenhagen / Panama / Chinatown, my Chinatown / When the midnight choo choo leaves for Alabam' / Big Apple / Hawaiian War Chant / Song Of India / Chicago / Marie
CD _____ PAR 2068
Parade / Jul '94 / Koch / Cadillac.

DORSEY & SINATRA (Dorsey, Tommy & Frank Sinatra)
CD Set _____ 74321155182
Jazz Tribune / May '94 / BMG.

ESSENTIAL V-DISCS, THE
CD _____ JZCD 334
Suisa / Jan '93 / Jazz Music / THE.

GO THEIR SEPARATE WAYS (Dorsey, Tommy & Jimmy)
Sinner kissed an angel / Blue skies / What'cha know Joe / East of the sun and west of the moon / Too romantic / How about you / Lady is a tramp / Fools rush in / Hawaiian war chant / Be careful it's my heart / Night in Sudan / Six lessons from Madame La Zonga / Bogg it / Arthur Murray taught me dancing in a hurry / Not mine / If you build a better mousetrap / Whispering grass / Dolimite / Aurora / I can't resist you / So do I / Contrasts
CD _____ RAJCD 817
Empress / Feb '94 / THE.

GREAT TOMMY DORSEY, THE
Music maestro please / Stardust / Who / Marie / Song of India / Hawaiian war chant / East of the sun and west of the moon / Night in Sudan / That's a plenty / Night and day / Smoke gets in your eyes / Tea for two / Beale Street blues / Lonesome road / Turn off the moon / After you've gone / Lady is a tramp / Call of the canyon / After I say I'm sorry / Polka dots and moonbeams / Too romantic
CD _____ PASTCD 9740
Flapper / Mar '91 / Pinnacle.

GREATEST HITS
CD _____ CDCD 1183
Charly / Apr '94 / Charly / THE / Cadillac.

HAVING WONDERFUL TIME
At the codfish ball / Head on my pillow / When the midnight choo-choo leaves for Alabam / Sailing at midnight / Music goes round and round / Milkman's matinee / Day I let you get away / Chinatown, my Chinatown / Having wonderful time (wish you were here) / Don't be a baby, baby / All you want to do is dance / Alla en el rancho grande / Am I dreaming / After you've gone / You must have been a beautiful baby / Twilight in Turkey
CD _____ 74321218242
RCA / Jan '95 / BMG.

IRISH AMERICAN TROMBONE
Music goes round and round / Who / Royal garden blues / Stardust / This is no dream / Lonesome road / Imagination / Swanee river / Cocktails for two / Well alright / Posin' / Dipsy doodle / Music maestro please / Panama / Symphony in riffs / Boogie woogie / Tisket-a-tasket / After you've gone / Humoresque / Deep river / Yes indeed
CD _____ AVC 522
Avid / Apr '93 / Avid/BMG / Koch.

MASTERPIECES #15 1935-44
CD _____ 158342
Masterpieces / Mar '95 / BMG.

MOONLIGHT IN VERMONT
Marie / You're my everything / Song of India / Love for sale / Taking a chance on love / This love of mine / Opus one / Swanee river / I'm getting sentimental over you / Boogie woogie / Melancholy serenade / Autumn in New York / I should care / Oo do do / It started all over again / I dream of you / Moonlight in Vermont / There are such things / High and mighty / Who / In a little Spanish town / Little Joe / Granada

MUSIC GOES ROUND AND ROUND, THE (Dorsey, Tommy & His Clambake Seven)
Music goes round and round / Rhythm in my nursery rhymes / Rhythm saved the world / At the Codfish ball / Milkman's matinee / Twilight in Turkey / After you / Lady is a tramp / Nice work if you can get it / When the midnight choo choo leaves for Alabam' / Everybody's doin' it / Sheikh of Araby / Chinatown, my Chinatown / As long as you live / Vol vistu gailey star / Shoot the sherbert to me, Herbert / There's good blues tonight / Sweet Eileen / But I do mind if ya don't / Nothin' from nothin' leaves nothin'
CD _____ ND 83140
Bluebird / Oct '91 / BMG.

ONE NIGHT STAND 1940
CD _____ CDSH 2001
Derann Trax / Nov '91 / Pinnacle.

OPUS ONE (Dorsey, Tommy Orchestra & Frank Sinatra)
CD _____ CA 14526
Jazz Portraits / Jan '94 / Jazz Music.

POST-WAR ERA, THE
Come rain or come shine / Then I'll be happy / Song is you / Hollywood hat / Bingo, bango, boffo / Tom Foolery / Fresh money / Rest stop / At sundown / How are things in Glocca Morra / Trombonology / Puddle wump / Continental / Drumology / Pussy willow / Hucklebuck / I'm in the mood for love / Summertime / I get a kick out of you / Picalili Dilly / Comin' thro' the rye / Birmingham bounce
CD _____ DBCD 08
Dance Band Days / Jul '87 / Prism.

RADIO DAYS VOL.1
CD _____ CDSG 405
Starline / Aug '89 / Jazz Music.

SONG OF INDIA (Dorsey, Tommy Orchestra)
They didn't believe me / Cheek to cheek / Opus one / Tico-tico / Blue skies / I'll never smile again / Begin the beguine / There's no you / Midriff / Cuttin' out / Pussy willow / Hollywood hat / Then I'll be happy / Now weather for ducks / And the angels sing / Somebody loves me / Boogie woogie / Song of India / On the sunny side of the street / Non drastic / Swanee river
CD _____ DBCD 08
Dance Band Days / Jul '87 / Prism.

STARDUST (Dorsey, Tommy & Frank Sinatra)
I'll be seeing you / Polka dots and moonbeams / Fools rush in / Imagination / East of the sun and west of the moon / I'll never smile again / Stardust / Dolores / This love of mine / Everything happens to me / There are such things
CD _____ ND 90627
Bluebird / Apr '92 / BMG.

STOP, LOOK AND LISTEN
After you've gone / Beale Street blues / Boogie woogie / Chinatown, my Chinatown / Davenport blues / Easy does it / He's a gypsy from Poughkeepsie / Liebestraum / Lonesome road / Mandy, make up your mind / Maple leaf rag / Marie / Night and day / Royal Garden blues / Sheikh of araby / Song of India / Stomp it off / Stop, look and listen / Swanee river / Symphony in riffs / Tin roof blues / Twilight in Turkey / Weary blues
CD _____ CDAJA 5105
Living Era / May '93 / Koch.

SWEET & HOT
CD _____ TAX 37052
Tax / Aug '94 / Jazz Music / Wellard / Cadillac.

TOMMY DORSEY
CD _____ TAXS 42
Tax / Aug '94 / Jazz Music / Wellard / Cadillac.

TOMMY DORSEY
CD _____ 22709
Music / Nov '95 / Target/BMG.

TOMMY DORSEY & HIS ORCHESTRA 1940-43
CD _____ JH 1035
Jazz Hour / Oct '93 / Target/BMG / Jazz Music / Cadillac.

TOMMY DORSEY - 1942 (Dorsey, Tommy Orchestra)
CD _____ JH 1013
Jazz Hour / Feb '92 / Target/BMG / Jazz Music / Cadillac.

TOMMY DORSEY AND FRANK SINATRA (Dorsey, Tommy & Frank Sinatra)
CD _____ 901042
Jazz Archives / Oct '91 / Jazz Music / Discovery / Cadillac.

TOMMY DORSEY AND HIS GREATEST BAND
Boogie woogie / Amor / But she's my buddy's chick / Swing high / Like a leaf in the wind / Marie / Opus No.1 / Wagon wheels / Clarinet cascades / Land of dreams / Song of India / Swanee river / Losers weepers /

There is no breeze to cool the flames / Minor goes muggin' / We'll git it / On the sunny side of the street / Rest stop / I'm in love with someone / That's my home / I'm getting sentimental over you
CD _____ JASMCD 2537
Jasmine / Nov '94 / Wellard / Swift / Conifer / Cadillac / Magnum Music Group.

TOMMY DORSEY AND ORCHESTRA - 1935-1947 (Dorsey, Tommy Orchestra)
CD _____ TAX S-4
Tax / Oct '90 / Jazz Music / Wellard / Cadillac.

TOMMY DORSEY ORCHESTRA & THE CLAMBAKE SEVEN, THE (Dorsey, Tommy Orchestra & The Clambake Seven)
CD _____ 3801262
Jazz Archives / Oct '92 / Cadillac / Discovery / Cadillac.

TOMMY DORSEY ORCHESTRA/DAVID ROSE STRING ORCHESTRA (Dorsey, Tommy Orchestra & Dave Rose)
CD _____ 15777
Laserlight / Jul '93 / Target/BMG.

TOMMY DORSEY WITH FRANK SINATRA
Marie / Too romantic / Polka dots and moonbeams / This is the beginning of the end / Hear my song / i haven't time to be a millionaire / Head on my pillow / I'll never smile again / One I love / Call of the canyon / Shadows on the sand / Do you know why / Yearning / Not so long ago / Stardust / How am I to know / Oh look at me now / You lucky people you / Without a song / Everything happens to me / Let's get away from it all / Love me as I am / Love of mine / Blue skies / How do you do without me / Violets for your furs / How about you / My melancholy baby / Dig down deep / It started all over again / I'll take Tallulah / Song is you
CD _____ 743211518-2
Jazz Tribune / Jun '94 / BMG.

TOMMY DORSEY WITH FRANK SINATRA
CD _____ CD 56004
Jazz Roots / Aug '94 / Target/BMG.

TOMMY DORSEY, VOL. 1
CD _____ 15755
Laserlight / Aug '92 / Target/BMG.

TOMMY DORSEY, VOL. 2
CD _____ 15756
Laserlight / Aug '92 / Target/BMG.

WELL, GIT IT (Dorsey, Tommy Orchestra)
CD _____ JASSCD 14
Jass / Oct '91 / CM / Jazz Music / ADA / Cadillac / Direct.

YES INDEED
Lonesome road (part 1) / Lonesome road (part 2) / Well alright / Stomp it off / Easy does it / Quiet please / Swing high / Swanee river / Yes indeed / Loose lid special / Swingin' on nothin' / Moonlight on the Ganges / Well git it / Opus 1 / Chloe / Minor goes muggin'
CD _____ ND 90449
RCA / Apr '90 / BMG.

Dos

UNO CON DOS
CD _____ NAR 061 CD
New Alliance / May '93 / Pinnacle.

Dos Santos, Jovino

MORNAS & COLADERAS FROM CAPE VERDE
CD _____ PS 65127
Playasound / May '94 / Harmonia Mundi / ADA.

Dosta Crew

ALL TOGETHER
We got wayz.. / Right on time / Daddy's girl / I need a cheetah / Gotta good thing / All together / Ya gotta have bones / Two of a kind / Koko's kandy shop / That body / Suckers will scatter
CD _____ WRA 8103 CD
Wrap / Nov '91 / Koch.

Dots Will Echo

DOTS WILL ECHO
Everything in the world / Sandra / Rain / Someday / Dots will echo / Science fiction / She's never lonely / She's a girl / I will too / Heartland / Big jets
CD _____ 72902
High Street / Sep '91 / ADA.

Dotsero

JUBILEE
CD _____ NOVA 9136
Nova / Jan '93 / New Note.

OFF THE BEATEN PATH
CD _____ NOVA 9023
Nova / Jan '93 / New Note.

Double Exposure

TEN PERCENT
Ten percent / Gonna give my love away / Everyman / Baby I need your loving / Just can't say hello / My love is free / Pick me
CD _____ CPCD 8062
Charly / Nov '94 / Charly / THE / Cadillac.

Double Muffled Dolphin

MY LEFT SIDE IS OUT OF SYNC
CD _____ APR 004CD
April / Jan '95 / Plastic Head.

Double Nelson

CEUX QUI L'ONT FAIT
CD _____ 760255
Cobalt / Nov '90 / Grapevine.

Double Trio

GREEN DOLPHIN SUITE (Arcado String Trio/Trio De Clarinettes)
Green Dolphin Street / Cold water music / Clic / Bosnia / Muhu / Suite domestique
CD _____ ENJ 90112
Enja / Jul '95 / New Note / Vital/SAM.

Double Vision

DOUBLE VISION
Conscience / Somebody / Trouble / Torn to pieces / Time / Ain't never giving up / Should I stay / Shades / Dawning / Kickstart / Summer never ending
CD _____ JAZIDCD 104
Acid Jazz / Aug '94 / Pinnacle.

Doubt

PROFIT
CD _____ CD 7913003
Progress Red / Jun '93 / Plastic Head.

Doucet, David

QUAND J'AI PARTI
T'en as cru / Balfa waltz / Zydeco sont pas sales / J'ai passe / Bee la manche / Ton papa / French blues (Je m'endors) / J'etais au bal / Les bons temps rouler / Pacquent d'epingles / Coulee rodair / J'ai fait la tour / La valse des cajuns
CD _____ CD 6040
Rounder / '91 / CM / Direct / ADA / Cadillac.

Doucet, Michael

BEAU SOLO
CD _____ ARHCD 321
Arhoolie / Apr '95 / ADA / Direct / Cadillac.

GREAT CAJUN (Doucet, Michael & Cajun Brew)
CD _____ CDROU 6017
Rounder / Apr '93 / CM / Direct / ADA / Cadillac.

MAD REEL, THE (Doucet, Michael & Beausoleil)
CD _____ ARHCD 397
Arhoolie / Apr '95 / ADA / Direct / Cadillac.

MICHAEL DOUCET & CAJUN BREW (Doucet, Michael & Cajun Brew)
CD _____ CDROU 607
Rounder / May '93 / CM / Direct / ADA / Cadillac.

Doughboys

HAPPY ACCIDENTS
Countdown / Sorry wrong number / Deep end / Intravenous DeMilo / Happy home / Sunflower honey / Far away / Happy sad day / Wait and see / Every bit of nothing / Dream day / Apprenticeship of Lenny Kravitz / Tupperware party
CD _____ LC 9336 2
Restless / Nov '90 / Vital.

WHEN UP TURNS TO DOWN
CD _____ EM 92442
Roadrunner / Nov '91 / Pinnacle.

Doughnuts

AGE OF CIRCLE
CD _____ VR 025CD
Victory / Nov '95 / Plastic Head.

Douglas, Blair

BENEATH THE BERET
CD _____ SKYECD 02
Macmeanma / Jan '92 / Duncans / CM / ADA.

Douglas, Carl

KUNG FU FIGHTING
Kung fu fighting / Dance the kung fu / Changing times / Witchfinder General / Girl you're so fine / Too hot to handle / Keep on pleasing me / It's a shame / Shanghai'd / Gamblin' man / Blue eyed soul / Love peace and happiness / Preacher man / What's good for the goose / Run back / I'll keep on lovin' you / I want to give you my everything / Stop
CD _____ 5507462

Spectrum/Karussell / Jan '95 / PolyGram / TI IC.

Douglas, Craig

BEST OF THE EMI YEARS, THE
Teenager in love / My first love affair / Come softly to me / Dream lover / Riddle of love / Only sixteen / Thirty nine steps / Battle of New Orleans / Heart of a teenage girl / My hour of love / Where's the girl (I never met) / Oh what a day / Nine times out of ten / After all / Change of heart / Girl next door / Hundred pounds of clay (original) / Hundred pounds of clay (revised lyrics) / Hello spring / Another you / No greater love / Time / Ring-a-ding / When my little girl is smiling / Our favourite melodies / Rainbows / Painted smile / It all depends on you / Five foot two, eyes of blue / Walkin' my baby back home / Row row row
CD _____ CDEMS 1494
EMI / May '93 / EMI.

ONLY SIXTEEN
Our favourite melodies / Time / Hundred pounds of clay / Change of heart / Rainbows / Riddle of love / When my little girl is smiling / Pretty blue eyes / No greater love / Girl next door / Wish it were me / Sandy / Hello spring / Another you / Teenager in love / Only sixteen / Oh what a day / Dream lover / Ring-a-ding doo
CD _____ SEECD 34
See For Miles/C5 / Feb '90 / Pinnacle.

Douglas, Dave

CONSTELLATIONS (Douglas, Dave Tiny Bell Trio)
CD _____ ARTCD 6174
Hat Art / Oct '95 / Harmonia Mundi / ADA / Cadillac.

PARALLEL WORLDS
CD _____ 121226-2
Soul Note / Jan '94 / Harmonia Mundi / Wellard / Cadillac.

Douglas, Jerry

EVERYTHING'S GONNA WORK OUT FINE
CD _____ ROUNDER 11535
Rounder / '89 / CM / Direct / ADA / Cadillac.

SKIP, HOP & HOBBLE (Douglas, Jerry & Russ Barenburg/Edgar Meyer)
CD _____ SH 3817CD
Sugarhill / Jan '94 / Roots / CM / ADA / Direct.

SLIDE RULE
Ride the wild turkey / Pearlie Mae / When papa played the dobro / We hide and seek / Shoulder to shoulder / Uncle Sam / It's a beautiful life / I don't believe you've met my baby / Rain on Oliviatown / Hey Joe / New day medley / Shenendoah breakdown
CD _____ SHCD 3797
Sugarhill / '92 / Roots / CM / ADA / Direct.

UNDER THE WIRE
T.O.B. / Dhaka rock / Time gone by / Monroe's hornpipe / Before the blues / Trip to Kilkerrin / Grant's corner / Redhill / Two friends / New day
CD _____ SHCD 3831
Sugarhill / Apr '95 / Roots / CM / ADA / Direct.

Douglas, John

SCOTTISH LOVE SONGS
Until my heart stands still / My love is like a red red rose / Culzean Bay / Flow gently sweet Afton / Ye banks and braes o' bonnie Doon / Skye boat song / Loch Lomond / Roamin' in the gloamin' / Jean / Down in the glen / Bonnie lass o'Fyvie / Almost like being in love / Heather on the hill / Crooked bawbee
CD _____ LC CD 004
Lapwing / '89 / CM.

Douglas, Johnny

IT'S MAGIC (Douglas, Johnny Strings)
All the things you are / Only love / Music of the night / It's magic / At this time of year / Sleepy shores / Warsaw concerto / Dulcima / Secret love / Dream of Olwen / Birthday waltz / Time / Quiet nights and quiet stars / Moonlight serenade / Windows of Paris / I can tell by the look in your eye
CD _____ DLCD 115
Dulcima / Apr '95 / Savoy / THE.

MORE ROMANCE WITH THE CLASSICS (Douglas, Johnny Strings)
Swan / Eighteenth variation on a Rhapsody on a theme of Paganini / Serenade / Piano concerto no.2 / Adagio / Romance no. 2 / Dreaming / Intermezzo from Cavalleria Rusticana / Swan lake / Spring song / Requiem for a love affair / Moonlight sonata / Symphony No. 5 / Romeo and Juliet / Sonata in D
CD _____ DLCD 105
Dulcima / Sep '88 / Savoy / THE.

ON SCREEN (Douglas, Johnny Strings)
Days of wine and roses / Gigi / Call me irresponsible / Summer knows / Laura / Dungeons and dragons / Like someone in love

---

/ Affair to remember / Smile / Young at heart / Railway children / As time goes by / Dulcima / Somewhere in time / Way we were
CD _____ DLCD 110
Dulcima / May '91 / Savoy / THE.

ON STAGE (Douglas, Johnny Strings)
I could write a book / Bali Ha'i / Tap your troubles away / Hey there / All I ask of you / Ascot Gavotte / If I loved you / Sweetest sounds / I won't send roses / Stranger in paradise / Where or when / Heather on the hill / I have dreamed / Try to remember / Love changes everything
CD _____ DLCD 109
Dulcima / Oct '90 / Savoy / THE.

ROMANCING WITH THE CLASSICS
CD _____ DLCD 103
Dulcima / May '94 / Savoy / THE.

Douglas, K.C.

BIG ROAD BLUES
Big road blues / Buck dance / Tore your playhouse down / Whisky headed woman / Catfish blues / Howlin' blues / Kansas City blues / Bottle up and go / K.C. blues / Key to the highway
CD _____ OBCCD 569
Original Blues Classics / Oct '95 / Complete/Pinnacle / Wellard / Cadillac.

K.C.'S BLUES
CD _____ OBCCD 533
Original Blues Classics / Nov '92 / Complete/Pinnacle / Wellard / Cadillac.

Douglass, Greg

MAELSTROM
CD _____ TX 2007CD
Taxim / Jan '94 / ADA.

Dour, Yann

JOB DAOULAS
CD _____ CAR 013CD
Diffusion Breizh / Apr '95 / ADA.

Dove

WRECKING BALL
CD _____ LF 041CD
Lost & Found / Nov '92 / Plastic Head.

Dove Shack

THIS IS THE SHACK
CD _____ 5279332
RAL / Sep '95 / PolyGram.

Dover, Connie

SOMEBODY
CD _____ TPMD 0101CD
Taylor Park / '92 / ADA.

WISHING WELL
CD _____ TPMD 21CD
Taylor Park / Apr '94 / ADA.

Dowling, Leslie Rae

UNBOUNDED WATERS
CD _____ 450997108-2
Warner Bros. / Aug '94 / Warner Music.

Dowling, Mike

SWAMP DOG BLUES
CD _____ SCR 39
Strictly Country / Sep '95 / ADA / Direct.

Down By Law

BLUE
CD _____ E 86419 2
Epitaph / Nov '92 / Plastic Head / Pinnacle.

DOWN BY LAW/GIGANTOR (Down By Law/Gigantor)
CD _____ LF 064CD
Lost & Found / Aug '93 / Plastic Head.

PUNKROCKACADEMYFIGHTSONG
CD _____ E 864312
Epitaph / Jun '94 / Plastic Head / Pinnacle.

Downchild

GONE FISHING
CD _____ SP 1139CD
Stony Plain / Oct '93 / ADA / CM / Direct.

Downes, David

PAVILION
CD _____ WCL 11006
White Cloud / May '94 / Select.

RUSTED WHEEL OF THINGS, THE
CD _____ WCL 110112
White Cloud / May '95 / Select.

Downes, Geoffrey

EVOLUTION
CD _____ BP 215CD
Blueprint / Oct '95 / Pinnacle.

LIGHT PROGRAM, THE
Ethnic dance / East West / Urbanology / Symphonie electronique / Oceania electronique
CD _____ BP 216CD
Blueprint / Oct '95 / Pinnacle.

VOX HUMANA
Tears / Video killed the radio star / Roads of destiny / Plastic age / Ave Maria / Network / All of the time / Concerto / Satellite blues / England / Moon under the water / White car / Adagio
CD _____ BP 214CD
Blueprint / Oct '95 / Pinnacle.

Downing, Will

COME TOGETHER AS ONE
Come together as one / Sake of love / Sometimes / Cry / Love call / Love we share / Too soon / I'll wait / Rules of love / Test of time / Closer to you / Wishing on a star
CD _____ BRCD 538
4th & Broadway / Oct '89 / PolyGram.

DREAM FULFILLED, A
She / I'll wait / Giving my all to you / I try / For all we know / Something's going on / Don't make me wait / I go crazy / No love intended / World is a ghetto
CD _____ IMCD 212
Island / Mar '96 / PolyGram.

LOVE'S THE PLACE TO BE
CD _____ IMCD 218
Island / Mar '96 / PolyGram.

MOODS
CD _____ BRCD 612
4th & Broadway / Nov '95 / PolyGram.

WILL DOWNING
In my dreams / Do you / Free / Love supreme (12" & CD single only.) / Security / Set me free / Sending out an S.O.S. / Dancing in the moonlight / Do you remember
CD _____ IMCD 190
Island / Mar '94 / PolyGram.

Downliners Sect

BIRTH OF SUAVE, THE
CD _____ HOG2
Hangman's Daughter / Sep '94 / SRD.

SAVAGE RETURN
Bad girls looking for fun / Piccadilly run / Ain't I got you / Hard case / Midnight call / Pan American boogie / Eat pie memories / Down the road apiece / Talking 'bout you / Studio 51 / Bad penny / Who do you love / Cadillac / Bye bye Johnny / Some say they do / Before you accuse me
CD _____ CDKVL 9033
Kingdom / May '94 / Kingdom.

SINGLES A'S & B'S
Cadillac / Roll over Beethoven / Beautiful Delilah / Shame, shame, shame / Green onions / Nursery rhymes / Baby what's wrong / Be a sect maniac / Little Egypt / Sect appeal / Find out what's happening / Insecticide / Wreck of ol' 97 / Leader of the sect / I want my baby back / Midnight hour / Now she's dead / I don't mind / Waiting in heaven somewhere / Bad storm coming / Lonely and blue / All night worker / He was a square / Glendora / I'll find out / Cost of living / Everything I've got to give / I can't get away from you / Roses
CD _____ SEECD 398
See For Miles/C5 / May '95 / Pinnacle.

Dowsett, Janet

ENCORE
CD _____ CDGRS 1280
Grosvenor / Aug '95 / Target/BMG.

KALEIDOSCOPE
I could have danced all night / Groovy kind of love / Tea for two / Water fountain / Splanky / Pavanne / Elizabethan serenade / Disney medley / Dizzy fingers / Aranjuez mon amour / Walking in the sunshine / Adagio for organ and strings in G minor / Hello Dolly/Mame / West Side story medley / Prelude in classic style (CD only) / Forgotten dreams (CD only)
CD _____ CDGRS 1259
Grosvenor / Feb '95 / Target/BMG.

Doy, Carl

PIANO BY CANDLELIGHT VOL.1
CD _____ NELCD 101
Timbuktu / Aug '93 / Pinnacle.

PIANO BY CANDLELIGHT VOL.2
CD _____ NELCD 102
Timbuktu / Aug '93 / Pinnacle.

PIANO BY CANDLELIGHT VOL.3
CD _____ NELCD 103
Timbuktu / Aug '93 / Pinnacle.

Dp-Sol

LIVE IN OSLO
CD _____ TSF 9006
Play It Again Sam / Apr '95 / Vital.

Dr. Alban

HELLO AFRIKA
No coke / Groove machine II / Sweet reggae mujsic / China man / Alban prelude / Hello Afrika / Proud (to be Afrikan) / Our father / U and Mi / Thank you (CD only.)
CD _____ 261391
Arista / Aug '95 / BMG.

LOOK WHO'S TALKING
Hard pan of drums / Look who's talking / Free up Soweto / Away from home / Gimme dat loven / Let the beat go on / Fire / Home sweet home / Go see the dentist / Sweet little girl / Plastic smile / Awillawillawillaey / Stone radio
CD _____ 74321201532
Arista / Aug '94 / BMG.

SECOND EDITION
CD _____ 7432113565-2
Arista / Apr '93 / BMG.

Dr. Alimantado

BEST DRESSED CHICKEN IN TOWN, THE
Gimme mi gun / Plead I cause / Poison flour / Ride on / Just the other day / Best dressed chicken in town / Unitone skank
CD _____ KMCD 001
Keyman / Jan '94 / SRD / Jetstar / Greensleeves.

BORN FOR A PURPOSE.
Chant to Jah / Return of Muhammed Ali / Sons of thunder / Dreadlocks dread / Call on Jah / Born for a purpose / Careless Ethiopians repent / Oil crisis / Sitting in the park / Marriage licence
CD _____ GRELCD 22
Greensleeves / Jul '87 / Total/BMG / Jetstar / SRD.

IN THE MIX
CD _____ KMCD 003
Keyman / Oct '88 / SRD / Jetstar / Greensleeves.

KING'S BREAD
CD _____ ISDACD 5000
Keyman / Apr '94 / SRD / Jetstar / Greensleeves.

LOVE IS
CD _____ KMCD 1001
Keyman / Nov '83 / SRD / Jetstar / Greensleeves.

PRIVILEGED FEW
CD _____ KMCD 009
Keyman / Nov '94 / SRD / Jetstar / Greensleeves.

REGGAE REVUE PART 1
CD _____ KMCD 002
Keyman / Oct '88 / SRD / Jetstar / Greensleeves.

Dr. Clayton

DR. CLAYTON & HIS BUDDY
CD _____ SOB 035392
Story Of The Blues / Apr '93 / Koch / ADA.

Dr. Didg

OUT OF THE WOODS
Street music / Devon / Easy / King tut / Ever increasing circles / Brolga / Suntan / Rave on / Say what you like / Under the influence
CD _____ HNCD 1384
Hannibal / Apr '95 / Vital / ADA.

Dr. Dixie

BEST OF DOCTOR DIXIE JAZZ BAND (Dr. Dixie Jazz Band)
CD _____ CDTTD 521
Timeless Traditional / Jan '88 / New Note.

Dr. Dre

CHRONIC, THE
Chronic / Fuck wit Dre day (and everybody's celebratin') / Let me ride / Day the niggaz took over / Nuthin' but a G thang / Deeez nuuuts / Li'l ghetto boy / Niqqa witta gun / Rat-tat-tat-tat / Twenty dollar sack pyramid / Lyrical gangbang / High powered / Doctor's office / Stranded on death row / Roach (the chronic outro)
CD _____ 7567922332
WEA / Feb '93 / Warner Music.

Dr. Ease

PUT YOUR MIND AND BODY AT EASE (Dr. Ease & D.J. Mix)
Make U dance / Can't stand still / Make it last / Get fresh Eastown express / Give the people / Oh girl / Terminator
CD _____ CDBUL 4011
Bullseye / Sep '89 / Bullseye / ADA.

Dr. Feelgood

AS IT HAPPENS
Take a tip / Every kind of vice / Down at the doctors / Baby Jane / Sugar shaker / Things get better / She's a windup / Ninety nine and a half (won't do) / Buddy Buddy friends / Milk and alcohol / Matchbox / As long as the price is right / Night time / Riot in cell

block 9 / Blues had a baby and they named it rock 'n' roll
CD _____ GRANDCD 15
Grand / Sep '95 / Direct / Vital / ADA.

BE SEEING YOU
Ninety nine and a half (won't do) / She's a wind up / I thought I had it made / I don't wanna know / That's it I quit / As long as the price is right / Hi rise / My buddy buddy friends / Blues had a baby and they named it rock 'n' roll / Looking back / Sixty minutes
CD _____ GRANDCD 14
Grand / Sep '95 / Direct / Vital / ADA.

BRILLEAUX
I love you so you're mine / You've got my number / Big enough / Don't wait up / Get rhythm / Where is the next one / Play dirty / Grow too old / Rough ride / I'm a real man / Come over here / Take what you can get
CD _____ GRANDCD 04
Grand / Sep '95 / Direct / Vital / ADA.

CASE HISTORY - THE BEST OF DR. FEELGOOD
Going back home / Back in the night / Roxette / She does it right / Sneakin' suspicion / No mo do yakamo / She's a wind up / As long as the price is right / Down at the doctors / Milk and alcohol / Violent love / Jumping from love to love / Best in the world / Rat race / Close but no cigar / Play dirty / Don't wait up / See you later alligator
CD _____ CDP 7467112
Liberty / Apr '83 / EMI.

CASE OF THE SHAKES, A
Jumping from love to love / Going some place else / Best in the world / Punch drunk / King for a day / Violent love / No mo do yakamo / Love hound / Coming to you / Who's winning / Drives me wild / Case of the shakes
CD _____ GRANDCD 10
Grand / Sep '95 / Direct / Vital / ADA.

CLASSIC
Hunting shooting fishing / Break these chains / Heartbeat / (I wanna) make love to you / Hurricane / Quit while you're behind / Nothing like it / Spy Vs. spy / Highway 61 / Crack me up
CD _____ GRANDCD 11
Grand / Sep '95 / Direct / Vital / ADA.

DOCTOR'S ORDERS
Close but no cigar / So long / You don't love me / My way / Neighbour, neighbour / Talk of the devil / Hit, git and split / I can't be satisfied / Saturday night fish fry / Drivin' wheel / It ain't right / I don't worry about a thing / She's in the middle / Dangerous
CD _____ GRANDCD 06
Grand / Sep '95 / Direct / Vital / ADA.

DOWN AT THE DOCTORS
If my baby quit me / Styrofoam / Tanqueray / Roadrunner / Wolfman callin' / Double crossed / One step forward / Mojo workin' / Milk and alcohol / Down at the doctors / Freddie's footsteps / Heart of the city
CD _____ GRANDCD 018
Grand / Sep '95 / Direct / Vital / ADA.

DOWN BY THE JETTY
She does it right / Boom boom / More I give / One weekend / I don't mind / Twenty yards behind / Keep it out of sight / All through the city / Cheque book / Oyeh / Bony Moronie / Tequila
CD _____ GRANDCD 05
Grand / Sep '95 / Direct / Vital / ADA.

FAST WOMEN AND SLOW HORSES
She's the one / Sweet sweet lovin' (gone sour on me) / Trying to live my life without you / Rat race / Baby jump / Crazy about girls / Sugar bowl / Educated fool / Bum's rush / Baby why do you treat me this way / Beautiful Delilah / Monkey
CD _____ GRANDCD 03
Grand / Sep '95 / Direct / Vital / ADA.

FEELGOOD FACTOR, THE
Feelgood factor / Tanqueray / Tell me no lies / Styrofoam / I'm in the mood for you / Double crossed / Lying about the blues / She moves me / Wolfman callin' / One step forward / One to ten / Fool for you
CD _____ GRANDCD 017
Grand / Sep '95 / Direct / Vital / ADA.

LET IT ROLL
Java blues / Feels good / Put him out of your mind / Bend your ear / Hong Kong money / Keeka smeeka / Shotgun / Pretty face / Ridin' on the L and N / Drop everything and run
CD _____ GRANDCD 07
Grand / Sep '95 / Direct / Vital / ADA.

LIVE IN LONDON
King for a day / As long as the price is right / Baby Jane / See you later alligator / You upset me / She does it right / Back in the night
CD _____ GRANDCD 08
Grand / Sep '95 / Direct / Vital / ADA.

LOOKING BACK (5CD Set)
Roxette / All through the city / Cheque book / 20 yards behind / She does it right / Bonie moronie/Tequila / Going back home / You shouldn't call the doctor (if you can't afford the pills / I can tell / Back in the night / I'm a man (live) / I don't mind (live) / I'm a hog for you baby (live) / Checkin' up on my baby

(live) / Stupidity (live) / Johnny B. Goode (live) / Lights out / You'll be mine / Walking on the edge / Hey Mama keep your big mouth shut / Nothin' shakin' (but the leaves on the trees) / Sneakin' suspicion / She's a windup / Looking back / 99 & a half won't do / Baby Jane / As long as the price is right / Down at the doctors / Take a tip / Every kind of vice / Milk and alcohol / Sugar shaker / Night time / Riot in cell block 9 / My buddy buddy friends / Great balls of fire / Pretty face / Put him out of your mind / Java blue / Hong Kong money / No mo do Yakamo / Jumping from love to love / Violent love / Shotgun blues (live) / Waiting for Saturday night / Trying to live my life without love / She's the one / Crazy about girls / Monkey / Rat race / You don't love me / She's in the middle / Dangerous / I can't be satisfied / Close but no cigar / My way / Rock me baby / Tore down / Dust my broom / I love you so you're mine / Don't wait up / Come over here / Get rhythm / I'm a real man / See you later alligator / Quit while you're behind / Hunting shooting fishing / (I wanna) Make love to you / Mad man blues (live) / King for a day (live) / No time / Wolfman callin / Feelgood factor / If my baby quits me (live) / Roadrunner (live) / One step forward / Mojo workin' (live) / Route 66 / Keep it out of sight / Homeward (live) / You upset me baby / Down at the (other) doctor's / Love hound / Don't take but a few minutes / Eileen / Touch of class / She's got her eyes on you / Solitary blues / Looking at you
CD Set _____ ACDFEEL 195
Liberty / Oct '95 / EMI.

MAD MAN BLUES
Dust my broom / Something you got / Dimples / Living on the highway / Tore down / Madman blues / I've got news for you / My babe / Can't find the lady / Rock me baby
CD _____ GRANDCD 02
Grand / Sep '95 / Direct / Vital / ADA.

MALPRACTICE
I can tell / Going back home / Back in the night / Another man / Rollin' and tumblin' / Don't let your daddy know / Watch your step / Don't you just know it / Riot in cell block 9 / Because you're mine / You shouldn't call the doctor
CD _____ GRANDCD 09
Grand / Sep '95 / Direct / Vital / ADA.

ON THE JOB
Drives me wild / Java blues / Jumping from love to love / Pretty face / Nomo do yakamo / Love hound / Best in the world / Who's winning / Ridin' on the L 'n' N / Case of the shakes / Shotgun blues / Goodnight Vienna
CD _____ GRANDCD 16
Grand / Sep '95 / Direct / Vital / ADA.

PRIMO
Heart of the city / My sugar turns to alcohol / Going down / No time / World in a jug / If my baby quit me / Primo blues / Standing at the crossroads again / Been down so long / Don't worry baby / Down by the jetty blues / Two times nine
CD _____ GRANDCD 12
Grand / Sep '95 / Direct / Vital / ADA.

PRIVATE PRACTICE
Down at the doctors / Every kind of vice / Things get better / Milk and alcohol / Night time / Let's have a party / Take a tip / It wasn't me / Greaseball / Sugar shaker
CD _____ GRANDCD 01
Grand / Sep '95 / Direct / Vital / ADA.

SINGLES - THE UA YEARS
Roxette / She does it right / Back in the night / Ging back home / Riot in cell block 9 / Sneakin' suspicion / She's a wind up / Baby Jane / Down at the doctors / Milk and alcohol / As long as the price is right / Put him out of your mind / Hong Kong money / No mo do yakamo / Jumping from love to love / Violent love / Waiting for Saturday night / Monkey / Trying to live my life without you / Crazy about girls / My way / Madman blues / See you later alligator / Hunting shooting fishing / Don't wait up (Not on CD.) / Milk and alcohol (New recipe) (Not on CD.)
CD _____ CDEM 1332
Liberty / May '89 / EMI.

SNEAKIN' SUSPICION
Sneakin' suspicion / Paradise / Nothin' shakin' (but the leaves on the trees) / Time and the devil / Lights out / Lucky seven / All my love / She'll be mine / Walking on the edge / Hey mama keep your mouth shut
CD _____ GRANDCD 13
Grand / Sep '95 / Direct / Vital / ADA.

STUPIDITY PLUS (Live 1976-1990)
I'm taking about / Twenty yards behind / Stupidity / All through the city / I'm a man / Walking the dog / She does it right / Going back home / I don't mind / Back in the night / I'm a hog for you baby / Roxette / Riot in cell block 9 / Johnny B. Goode / Take a trip / Every kind of vice / She's a wind up / No mo do yakamo / Love hound / Shotgun blues / King for a day / Milk and alcohol / Down at the doctors
CD _____ CDP 795 934 2
Liberty / Mar '91 / EMI.

Dr. Fink

I'M IN THE MOOD FOR THE BEATLES (Dr. Fink & The Mystery Band)
CD _____ LPCD 1024
Disky / Apr '94 / THE / BMG / Discovery / Pinnacle.

Dr. Hector

EMERGENCY (Dr. Hector & The Groove Injectors)
Emergency / When did love let go / Woman like you / Don't be afraid / Downtown drinking / Southern fried groove / Bad news / 14 carat fool / Double trouble / Just to satisfy you
CD _____ ICH 9012 CD
Ichiban / Nov '91 / Koch.

Dr. Hook

COMPLETELY HOOKED - THE BEST OF DR. HOOK
Sylvia's mother / Cover of the Rolling Stone / Everybody's makin' it big but me / You make my pants want to get up and dance / Sleeping late / Only sixteen / Walk right in / Millionaire / More like the movies / When you're in love with a beautiful woman / Sexy eyes / If not you / Little bit more / Sharing the night together / I don't want to be alone tonight / Better love next time / In over my head / Years from now / Sweetest of all / Couple more years
CD _____ CDESTV 2
Capitol / May '92 / EMI.

DR. HOOK (Dr. Hook & The Medicine Show)
Sylvia's mother / Marie Lavaux / Sing me a rainbow / Hey Lady Godiva / Four years older than me / Kiss it away / Making it natural / I call that true love / When she cries / Judy / Mama I'll sing one song for you
CD _____ 4805222
Columbia / May '95 / Sony.

MAKING LOVE AND MUSIC - THE 1976-79 RECORDINGS
When you're in love with a beautiful woman / Little bit more / If not you / Up on the mountain / Bad eye Bill / Who dat / Let the loose and drag / I'm a lamb / Making love and music / Radio / Everybody loves me / Oh Jesse / Jungle in the zoo / More like the movies / I don't feel much like smilin' / Mountain Mary / Leviate / Dooley Jones / Sexy energy / Love monster
CD _____ CDMFP 5979
Music For Pleasure / Apr '93 / EMI.

SYLVIA'S MOTHER (2)
Queen of the silver dollar / Put a little bit on me / Get my rocks off / Cover of the Rolling Stone / Sing me a rainbow / Sylvia's mother / Lady Godiva / Turn on the world / Life ain't easy / I can't touch the sun / Carry me Carrie / Ballad of Lucy Jordan
CD _____ PWKS 4046
Carlton Home Entertainment / Apr '91 / Carlton Home Entertainment.

TAKE THE BAIT
Baby makes her blue jeans talk / Loveline / That didn't hurt too bad / Pity the fool / Crazy Rosie / Rings / Fire in the night / Hold me like you never had me / Do you right tonight / Body talking / Hearts like yours and mine / S.O.S. for love / Lady sundown / Girls can get it
CD _____ 5500552
Spectrum/Karussell / May '93 / PolyGram / THE.

Dr. John

AFTERGLOW
I know what I've got / Gee baby ain't I good to you / I'm just a lucky so and so / Blue skies / So long / New York City blues / Tell me you'll wait for me / There must be a better world somewhere / I still think about you / I'm confessin' that I love you
CD _____ GRB 70002
GRP / Jun '95 / BMG / New Note.

BABYLON
Babylon / Glowin' / Black widow spider / Barefoot lady / Twilight zone / Patriotic flag waver / Lonesome guitar strangler
CD _____ 7567804382
Atco / Feb '92 / Warner Music.

BRIGHTEST SMILE IN TOWN, THE
Saddled the cow / Boxcar boogie / Brightest smile in town / Waiting for a train / Monkey puzzle / Average kind of guy / Pretty libby / Marie Le Veau / Come rain or come shine / Suite home New Orleans
CD _____ FIENDCD 9
Demon / Oct '90 / Pinnacle / ADA.

CUT ME WHILE I'M HOT
CD _____ CDTB 128
Thunderbolt / Mar '95 / Magnum Music Group.

DESITIVELY BONNAROO
Quitters never win / Stealin' / What comes around (goes around) / Me, you, loneliness / Mos' scocious / Everybody wanna get rich) Rite away / Let's make a better world / R U 4 Real / Sing along song / Can't git enough / Go tell the people / Destitively bonnaroo

CD _____ 756780441-2
Atco / Dec '93 / Warner Music.

DOCTOR JOHN PLAYS MAC REBENNACK
Dorothy / Mac's boogie / Memories of Professor Longhair / Nearness of you / Delicado / Honey dripper / Big Mac / New island midnight / Saints / Pinetop / Silent night (Available on CD only) / Dance a la negres (Available on CD only) / Wade in the water (Available on CD only)
CD _____ FIENDCD 1
Demon / '88 / Pinnacle / ADA.

DR. JOHN
CD _____ GRP 7002
GRP / Jun '95 / BMG / New Note.

GOIN' BACK TO NEW ORLEANS
Litanie des saints / Careless love / My indian red / Milneburg joys / I thought I heard Buddy Bolden say / Basin Street blues / Didn't he ramble / Do you call that a buddy / How come my dog don't bark (when you come around) / Goodnight Irene / Fess up / Since I tell for you / (I'll be glad when you're dead) you rascal you / Cabbagehead / Come home tomorrow / Blue Monday / Scald dog medley / I can't go on / Goin' back to New Orleans
CD _____ 7599269402
Atco / Mar '94 / Warner Music.

GRIS GRIS
Gris gris gumbo ya ya / Danse Kalinda ba doom / Mama roux / Danse fambeaux / Croker courtbullion / Jump study / Walk on gilded splinters
CD _____ REP 4130-WZ
Repertoire / Aug '91 / Pinnacle / Cadillac.

GUMBO
Iko Iko / Blow wind blow / Big chief / Somebody changed the lock / Mess around / Let the good times roll / Junko partner / Stagger Lee / Tipitina / Those lonely lonely nights / Huey Smith medley (Including: High blood pressure/Don't you just know it/Well I'll be John Brown.) / Little Liza Jane
CD _____ 756780398-2
Atco / Mar '93 / Warner Music.

HOLLYWOOD BE THY NAME
New Island soiree / Reggae doctor / Way you do the things you do / Swanee river boogie / Yesterday / Babylon / Back by the river / Medley (It's alright with me; Blue skies; Will the circle be unbroken) / Hollywood be thy name / I wanna rock
CD _____ BGOCD 62
Beat Goes On / Oct '89 / Pinnacle.

IN A SENTIMENTAL MOOD
Makin' whoopee / Candy / Accentuate the positive / My buddy / In a sentimental mood / Black night / Don't let the sun catch you crying / Love for sale / More than you know
CD _____ K 9258892
Atco / Apr '89 / Warner Music.

IN THE RIGHT PLACE
Right place wrong time / Same old same old / Just the same / Qualified / Travelling mood / Peace brother peace / Life / Such a night / Shoo fly marches on / I been hoodood / Cold cold cold
CD _____ 756780360-2
Atco / Mar '93 / Warner Music.

LOSER FOR YOU, BABY
Time had come / Loser for you baby / Ear is on strike / Little closer to my home / I pulled the cover off you two lovers / New Orleans / Go ahead on / Just like a mirror / Bring your love / Bald head / Make your own
CD _____ CDTB 066
Thunderbolt / Nov '88 / Magnum Music Group.

MOS'SCOCIOUS (Dr. John Anthology)
Bad neighborhood / Morgus the magnificent / Storm warning / Sahara / Down the road / Gris gris gumbo ya ya / Mama Roux / Jump sturdy / I walk on gilded splinters / Black widow spider / Lop garoo / Wash Mama wash / Mardi gras day / Familiar reality / Opening / Zu zu mamou / Mess around / Somebody changed the lock / Iko iko / Junko partner / Tipitina / Huey Smith medley / Right place wrong time / Travelling mood / Life / Such a night / I been hoodood / Cold cold cold / Quitters never win / What comes around (goes around) / Mos' scocious / Let's make a better world / Back by the river / I wanna rock / Memories of Professor Longhair / Honey dripper / Pretty libby / Makin' whoopee / Accentuate the positive / More than you know
CD Set _____ 812271450-2
Atco / Feb '94 / Warner Music.

REMEDIES
Loop garoo / What goes around / Wash Mama wash / Chippy, chippy / Mardi gras day / Angola anthem
CD _____ 7567804392
Atco / Feb '94 / Warner Music.

SUN, MOON & HERBS, THE
Black John the conqueror / Where ya at mule / Craney crow / Familiar reality / Opening / Pots on fiyo (file gumbo) / Who I got to fall on / Zu zu mamou / Familiar reality (reprise)
CD _____ 7567804402
Atco / Jan '89 / Warner Music.

TELEVISION
Television / Lissen / Limbo / Witchy red / Only the shadow knows / Shut D. Fonk up / Spaceship relationship / Hold it / Money / U lie too much / Same day service
CD _____ GRM 40252
GRP / Jun '95 / BMG / New Note.

VERY BEST OF DR. JOHN
CD _____ 9548335532
Atco / May '95 / Warner Music.

ZU ZU MAN
Loser for you baby / Ear is on strike / Little closer to my home / I pulled the cover off you two lovers / Go ahead on / Just like a mirror / Bring your love / Make your own
CD _____ CDCD 1090
Charly / Apr '93 / Charly / THE / Cadillac.

ZU ZU MAN (2)
In the night / Tipitina / Grass is greener / Did she mention my name / Shoo ra / Zu zu man / One night late / She's just a square / Mean cheatin' woman / Helpin' hand
CD _____ CDTB 069
Thunderbolt / May '89 / Magnum Music Group.

Dr. K's Blues band

ROCK THE JOINT
I can't lose / Walkin' / Key to the highway / Crippled Clarence / Pet cream man / Feel so bad / Messin' with kid / Don't quit the man you love, for me / Rolty's banjo shuffle / Strobe lemming's lament / Lond distance call
CD _____ SEECD 361
See For Miles/C5 / Oct '92 / Pinnacle.

Dr. Mastermind

DOCTOR MASTERMIND
Domination / Right way / Man of the year / We want the world / Control / Abuser / Black leather maniac / I don't wanna die
CD _____ RR 9605 2
Roadrunner / Dec '87 / Pinnacle.

Dr. Nerve

ARMED OBSERVATION/OUT OT BOMB FRESH
CD _____ RUNE 38X
Cuneiform / Apr '86 / ReR Megacorp.

Dr. Phibes

HYPNOTWISTER (Dr. Phibes & The House Of Wax Equations)
Deadpan control freak / Real world / Anti-clockwise / Moment of time / Misdiagno-sedive / Hazy lazy hologram / Jugular junkie / Bearhug / Hypnotwister / Burning cross
CD _____ CDDRP 1
Quigley Records / Offside / May '93 / PolyGram.

Dr. Rain

KNIFE RAN AWAY WITH THE SPOON, THE
Suzanne / Turn your head around / It hurts to see you smiling / Go for your gun / Rat-tlin' blue / Heaven and hell / Wasted on you / Party girl / Wonderful lowlife / Between the Devil and the deep blue sea / What's your name
CD _____ 72787210032
RCA / Nov '92 / BMG.

Dr. Robert

REALMS OF DREAMS
CD _____ PERMCD 40
Permanent / Jan '96 / Total/BMG.

Dr. Strangely Strange

KIP OF THE SERENES
Strangely strange but oddly normal / Dr. Dim and Dr. Strange / Roy Rogers / Dark haired lady / On the West Cork hack / Tale of two orphanages / Strings in the earth and air / Ship of fools / Frosty mornings / Don-nybrook fair
CD _____ 3DCID 1004
Island / Jul '92 / PolyGram.

Dragon

FALLEN ANGEL
CD _____ CDFLAG 48
Under One Flag / Oct '90 / Pinnacle.

Dragonfly

ALMOST ABANDONES
CD _____ RTCD 901179
Line / Sep '92 / CM / Grapevine / ADA / Conifer / Direct.

DRAGONFLY
CD _____ 842970
EVA / May '94 / Direct / ADA.

Dragonsfire

ROYAL ARRAY, A
Sumer is y-cumen in / Earl of Salisbury's Pavan and Galliard / Boar's head carol / Courtly capers: English dance tunes / Greensleeves / Come again - Sweet love

doth now invite / Agincourt song / Woods so wilde / Now Is the month of Maying / Blame not my lute / Ampleforth / Green grow'th the holly
CD _____ URCD 102
Upbeat / Jul '90 / Target/BMG / Cadillac.

Drags

DRAGSPLOITATION
CD _____ ES 110CD
Estrus / Nov '95 / Plastic Head.

Draiocht

DRUID & THE DREAMER, THE
CD _____ CBM 006CD
Cross Border Media / Oct '93 / Direct / ADA.

Drake, Nick

BRYTER LAYTER
CD _____ IMCD 71
Island / '89 / PolyGram.

FIVE LEAVES LEFT
Time has told me / River man / Three hours / Day is done / Way to blue / Cello song / Thoughts of Mary Jane / Man in a shed / Fruit tree / Saturday Sun
CD _____ IMCD 8
Island / '89 / PolyGram.

FRUIT TREE (4CD BOX SET) (Five Leaves Left/Bryter Later/Pink Moon/Time Of No Reply)
CD Set _____ HNCD 5302
Hannibal / Nov '91 / Vital / ADA.

PINK MOON
Pink moon / Place to be / Road / Which will / Horn / Things behind the sun / Know / Parasite / Ride / Harvest breed / From the morning
CD _____ IMCD 94
Island / Feb '90 / PolyGram.

TIME OF NO REPLY
Joey / Clothes of sand / May fair / I was made to love magic / Strange meetings II / Been smoking too long
CD _____ HNCD 1318
Hannibal / May '89 / Vital / ADA.

WAY TO BLUE (An Introduction To Nick Drake)
Cello song / Hazey Jane (pts 1 & 2) / Way to blue / Things behind the sun / River man / Poor boy / Time of no reply / From the morning / One of these things first / Northern sky / Which will / Time has told me / Pink moon / Black eyed dog / Fruit tree
CD _____ IMCD 196
Island / May '94 / PolyGram.

Dramarama

10 FROM 5
Work for food / What are we gonna do / Last cigarette / Haven't got a clue / Sha-dowless heart / Some crazy dame / Would you like / Memo to Turner / It's still warm / Work for food (acoustic version)
CD _____ 3705615842
Chameleon / Sep '93 / Warner Music.

BOX OFFICE BOMB
Steve and Edie / New dream / Whenever I'm with her / Spare change / 400 blows / Pumpin (my heart) / It's still warm / Out in the rain / Baby rhino's eye / Worse than be-ing by myself / Modesty personified
CD _____ ROSE 138CD
New Rose / Jan '88 / Direct / ADA.

CINEMA VERITE
CD _____ ROSE 74CD
New Rose / Nov '85 / Direct / ADA.

Dramatics

ABC YEARS 1974-1980
CD _____ SCL 2108
Ichiban Soul Classics / Dec '95 / Koch.

WHATCHA SEE IS WHATCHA GET/DRAMATIC EXPERIENCE, A
Get up and get down / Thank you for your love / Hot pants in the summertime / What'cha see is what'cha get / In the rain / Good soul music / Fall in love, lady love / Mary don't cha wanna / Devil is dope / You could become the very heart of me / Now you got me loving you / Fell for you / Jim, what's wrong with him / Hey you get off my mountain / Beautiful people / Beware of the man (with the candy in his hand)
CD _____ CDSXD 963
Stax / Jan '91 / Pinnacle.

Drambuie Kirkliston Pipe.

LINK WITH THE '45 (Drambuie Kirkliston Pipe Band)
King has landed in Moidart / Glenfinnan highland gathering / March of the Cameron men / Johnny Cope / Southward bound / Wae's me for Prince Charlie / Forty five rev-olution / Link with the '45 / Young pretender / White rose of Culloden / Skye boat song / Fugitive / Tribute to the lost souls / Will ye no' come back again
CD _____ CDTRAX 084
Greentrax / Apr '95 / Conifer / Duncans / ADA / Direct.

Drame, Adama

MANDINGO DRUMS
CD _____ PS 65085
Playasound / Apr '92 / Harmonia Mundi / ADA.

MANDINGO DRUMS - VOL. 2 (Drame, Adama & Foliba)
CD _____ PS 65122
Playasound / Feb '94 / Harmonia Mundi / ADA.

Dranes, Arizona

ARIZONA DRANES 1926-1929
CD _____ DOCD 5186
Blues Document / Oct '93 / Swift / Jazz Music / Hot Shot.

Dransfield, Barry

BE YOUR OWN MAN
I once was a fisherman / John Barleycorn / Jezebel waltz / Farewell to Hong Kong/Mrs Wong's / Bonny boy / Grey funnel line / Be your own man / Betray me / Water is wide / La tete tie fancy / One for Jo / You can't change me now / Gossip Joan / Festus Burke / Bonny bunch of roses / Lily Bulero / Friendship reel/Welly reel / Daddy fox
CD _____ RHYD 5003
Rhiannon / Oct '94 / Vital / Direct / ADA.

Drax

TALES FROM THE MENTAL PLANE
CD _____ TROPE 013
Trope / May '95 / Vital / Plastic Head.

Dread & Fred

IRON WORK'S PART 3
CD _____ SHAKA 937CD
Jah Shaka / Mar '94 / Jetstar / SRD / Greensleeves.

Dread Flimstone

FROM THE GHETTO (Dread Flimstone & Modern Tone Age Family)
From the ghetto / Into u / Sitting / Knowl-edge / Tribute / fantasy / Justice / Roots / Slackness / Police
CD _____ 510870-2
Acid Jazz/FFRR / Nov '91 / PolyGram.

Dread, Mikey

BEST SELLERS
CD _____ RCD 20178
Rykodisc / Aug '91 / Vital / ADA.

DUB PARTY
CD _____ RUSCD 8208
Roir USA / Jul '95 / Plastic Head.

PAVE THE WAY
CD _____ CDHB 31
Heartbeat / Oct '95 / Greensleeves / Jetstar / Direct / ADA.

Dread, Sammy

ROADBLOCK
CD _____ JJCD 068
Jetstar / Sep '95 / Jetstar.

Dread Zeppelin

5,000,000
Fab (part 1) / Stir it up / Do the claw / When the levee breaks / Misty mountain top / Train kept a rollin' / Nobody's fault (butt-mon) / Big ol' gold belt / Fab (part 2) / Stair-way to heaven
CD _____ EIRSACD 1057
IRS / May '91 / PolyGram / BMG / EMI.

Dread Zone

360 DEGREES
CD _____ CRECD 162
Creation / Oct '93 / 3MV / Vital.

PERFORMANCE DEADZONE...LIVE
CD _____ TTPCD 002
Totem / Oct '94 / Grapevine / THE.

Dreadful Shadows

ESTRANGEMENT
CD _____ SPV 084-23612
SPV / Jul '94 / Plastic Head.

Dreadful Snakes

SNAKES ALIVE
CD _____ ROUNDER 177CD
Rounder / Jun '95 / CM / Direct / ADA / Cadillac.

Dreadie Knight

ELECTRONIC BAND
CD _____ TASTE 60CD
Taste / Aug '95 / Plastic Head.

Dreadzone

SECOND LIGHT
Life, love and unity / Little Britain / Canter-bury tale / Captain Dread / Cave of angels

/ Zion youth / One way / Shining path / Out of heaven
CD _____ CDV 2778
Virgin / May '95 / EMI.

Dream Academy

DREAM ACADEMY
Life in a northern town / Edge of forever / Johnny new light / In places on the run / This world / Bound to be / Moving on / Love parade / Party / One dream
CD _____ 7599252652
Blanco Y Negro / Jan '96 / Warner Music.

Dream Disciples

IN AMBER
In amber / Rememeber Bethany / Walk the wire / Mark 13 / Burn the sky / Dream is dead / Love letters / Sweet dreams / Where the weeping lie
CD _____ DDICK 007CD
Dick Bros. / May '95 / Vital.

Dream Machine

STEPS
CD _____ MSECD 013
Mouse / Jun '95 / Grapevine.

Dream Sequence

ENDLESS REFLECTION (Dream Sequence & Blake Baxter)
CD _____ EFA 017802
Tresor / Jun '95 / SRD.

Dream Syndicate

3 & 1/2
CD _____ NORM 156CD
Normal/Okra / Nov '93 / Direct / ADA.

DAY BEFORE WINE AND ROSES, THE
CD _____ NORMAL 176CD
Normal/Okra / Dec '94 / Direct / ADA.

DREAM SYNDICATE
Sure thing / That's what you always say / When you smile / Some kinda itch
CD _____ VEXCD 10
Demon / Jul '92 / Pinnacle / ADA.

GHOST STORIES
Side I'll never show / Loving the sinner, hat-ing the sin / Weathered and torn / I have faith / Black / My old haunts / Whatever you please / See that my grave is kept clean / Someplace better than this / When the cur-tain fails
CD _____ 727582
Restless / Sep '95 / Vital.

LIVE AT RAJI'S
Still holding on to you / Forest for the trees / Until lately / That's what you always say / Merrittville / Days of wine and roses / Medicine show / Halloween / Boston / John Coltrane stereo blues
CD _____ FIENDCD 176
Demon / Apr '90 / Pinnacle / ADA.

LOST TAPES 1985-88, THE
CD _____ NORMAL 156CD
Normal/Okra / Mar '94 / Direct / ADA.

Dream Theater

AWAKE
CD _____ 756790126-2
Warner Bros. / Oct '94 / Warner Music.

CHANGE OF SEASONS, A
CD _____ 7559618302
Warner Bros. / Sep '95 / Warner Music.

IMAGES AND WORDS
Pull me under / Another day / Take the time / Surrounded / Metropolis / Miracle and the sleeper / Under a glass moon / Wait for sleep / Learning to live
CD _____ 7567921482
Warner Bros. / Feb '92 / Warner Music.

LIVE AT THE MARQUEE
Metropolis / Miracle and the sleeper / For-tune in lies / Bombay vindaloo / Surrounded / Pull me under / Killing hand / Another hand
CD _____ 7567922862
Warner Bros. / Feb '92 / Warner Music.

Dream Warriors

AND NOW THE LEGACY BEGINS
Mr. Bibbinut spills his guts / My definition of a boombastic jazz style / Follow me not / Ludi / U never know a good thing till u lose it / And the legacy begins / Tune from the missing channel / Wash your face in my sink / Voyage through the multiverse / U could get arrested / Journey on / Face in the basin / Do not feed the alligators / Twelve sided dance / Maximum 60 lost in a dream
CD _____ IMCD 204
Island / Apr '95 / PolyGram.

SUBLIMINAL SIMULATION
Intro / Are we there yet / Day in, day out / Adventures of public man / It's a project thing / Paranoia - The P noise / I've lost my ignorance (and don't know where to find it) / Break the stereo / When I was at the jam / Burns 1 / Tricycles and kittens / California dreamin' / No dingbats allowed / You think

I don't know / Sink into the frame of the portrait / I wouldn't wanna be ya / Outro
CD _____ CDEMC 3690
EMI / Feb '95 / EMI.

Dreamfish

DREAMFISH
CD _____ RSNCD 9
Rising High / Sep '93 / Disc.

Dreamgrinder

AGENTS OF THE MIND
CD _____ CDBLEED 15
Bleeding Hearts / Nov '95 / Pinnacle.

Dreamlovers

BEST OF THE DREAMLOVERS
CD _____ NEMCD 673
Sequel / May '94 / BMG.

Dreams Of Ireland

22 SONGS OF HOME
CD _____ PLATCD 3930
Prism / May '94 / Prism.

Dreamside

PALE BLUE LIGHTS
CD _____ DW 0732
Deathwish / Jan '95 / Plastic Head.

Dresher, Paul

OPPOSITES ATTRACT
CD _____ 804112
New World / Aug '92 / Harmonia Mundi / ADA / Cadillac.

Dresser, Mark

CABINET OF DR. CALIGARI
CD _____ KFWCD 155
Knitting Factory / Feb '95 / Grapevine.

FORCE GREEN
CD _____ 1212732
Soul Note / Jan '96 / Harmonia Mundi / Wellard / Cadillac.

Drew, Kenny

AND FAR AWAY (Drew, Kenny Quartet)
CD _____ SNCD 1081
Soul Note / Jan '86 / Harmonia Mundi / Wellard / Cadillac.

KENNY DREW TRIO (Drew, Kenny Trio)
CD _____ OJCCD 065
Original Jazz Classics / Nov '95 / Wellard / Jazz Music / Cadillac / Complete/Pinnacle.

MORNING
CD _____ SCCD 31048
Steeplechase / Jul '88 / Impetus.

YOUR SOFT EYES (Drew, Kenny Trio)
CD _____ SNCD 1031
Soul Note / Jan '86 / Harmonia Mundi / Wellard / Cadillac.

Drew, Kenny Jr.

FLAME WITHIN, THE (Drew, Kenny Jr. & Bob Berg)
Flame within / Fly me to the moon / Las Palmas / Heather on the hill / Matrix / Three views of a secret / We see / House is not a home / Criss cross / Stella by starlight
CD _____ 66053017
Jazz City / May '91 / New Note.

LOOK INSIDE, A
CD _____ 514211-2
Antilles/New Directions / Feb '94 / PolyGram.

MAYBECK RECITAL HALL SERIES VOL.39
Stella by starlight / Peace / After you / Ugly beauty / Well you needn't / Coral sea / Images / Straight no chaser / Waitin' for my dearie / Autumn leaves
CD _____ CCD 4653
Concord Jazz / Jul '95 / New Note.

THIRD PHASE
Third phase / Falling in love with love / Soul eyes / I'm all smiles / I mean you / Alhambra / Lush life / Autumn leaves / Alone together
CD _____ 66053002
Jazz City / Dec '90 / New Note.

Drew, Ronnie

COLLECTION, THE
CD _____ CHCD 1053
Chyme / Feb '95 / CM / ADA / Direct.

Dribbling Darts

PRESENT PERFECT
CD _____ FNCD 247
Flying Nun / Jul '94 / Disc.

Drift Pioneer

METAL ELF BOY
CD _____ TEQM 95004
TEQ / May '95 / Plastic Head.

Drifters

70'S CLASSICS
Kissin' in the back row of the movies / You're more than a number in my little black book / Hello happiness / Like sister and brother / There goes my first love / Sweet Caroline / Harlem child / Like a movie I've seen before / Songs we used to sing / Love games / Down on the beach tonight / Every night's a Saturday night with you / Can I take you home little girl / Another lonely weekend / Summer in the city / Midnight cowboy
CD _____ SCCD 1
Music Club / Mar '93 / Disc / THE / CM.

BEST OF THE DRIFTERS
Save the last dance for me / Up on the roof / When my little girl is smiling / Dance with me / I've got sand in my shoes / There goes my baby / I'll take you home / Come on over to my place / Under the boardwalk / At the club / This magic moment / (If you cry) true love, true love / I count the tears / Saturday night at the movies / Some kind of wonderful / On Broadwalk
CD _____ PWKS 589
Carlton Home Entertainment / Jul '90 / Carlton Home Entertainment.

BEST OF THE DRIFTERS, THE
CD _____ 74321265062
RCA / Aug '95 / BMG.

BOOGIE WOOGIE ROLL (Greatest Hits 1953-58)
CD _____ 7567819272
Atlantic / Mar '95 / Warner Music.

COLLECTION, THE
CD _____ 74321292762
RCA / Jul '95 / BMG.

DRIFTERS
CD _____ LECD 039
Dynamite / May '94 / THE.

DRIFTERS COLLECTION, THE
CD _____ COL 011
Collection / Jun '95 / Target/BMG.

ESSENTIAL COLLECTION
CD Set _____ LECD 620
Wisepack / Apr '95 / THE / Conifer.

GOLDEN HITS: DRIFTERS
There goes my baby / True love, true love (If you cry) / Dance with me / This magic moment / Save the last dance for me / I count the tears / Some kind of wonderful / Up on the roof / On Broadway / Under the boardwalk / I've got sand in my shoes / Saturday night at the movies
CD _____ 9781440 2
Atlantic / Jul '88 / Warner Music.

GREATEST
Hello happiness / Kissin' in the back row of the movies / Always something there to remind me / Every night / Sweet Caroline / If it feels good do it / Save the last dance for me / There goes my first love / Like sister and brother / I can't live without you / Harlem child / You've got your troubles / Love games / Down on the beach tonight
CD _____ CDMFP 5734
Music For Pleasure / Oct '91 / EMI.

GREATEST HITS
CD _____ CDSGP 0153
Prestige / Apr '95 / Total/BMG.

GREATEST HITS & MORE 1959-65
There goes my baby / Oh my love / Baltimore / Hey senorita / Dance with me / (If you cry) True love, true love / This magic moment / Lonely winds / Nobody but me / Save the last dance for me / I count the tears / Sometimes I wonder / Please stay / Room full of tears / Sweets for my sweet / Some kind of wonderful / Loneliness of happiness / Mexican divorce / Somebody new dancing with you / Jackpot / She never talked to me that way / When my little girl do / Up on the roof / Another night with the boys / I feel good all over / Let the music play / On Broadway / I'll take you home / If you don't come back / Didn't it / One way love / He's just a playboy / Under the Boardwalk / I don't want to go on without you / I've got sand in my shoes / Saturday night at the movies / At the club / Come on over to my place
CD _____ 7567819312
Atlantic / Jul '93 / Warner Music.

GREATEST HITS LIVE
CD _____ CDCD 1243
Charly / Jun '95 / Charly / THE / Cadillac.

KISSING IN THE BACK ROW
CD _____ PWKS 4117
Carlton Home Entertainment / Sep '92 / Carlton Home Entertainment.

ON BROADWAY
CD _____ 15074
Laserlight / Aug '92 / Target/BMG.

PEARLS FROM THE PAST - THE DRIFTERS
CD _____ KLMCD 008
Scratch / Nov '93 / BMG.

SAVE THE LAST DANCE FOR ME
CD _____ AVC 511
Avid / Dec '92 / Avid/BMG / Koch.

SPOTLIGHT ON DRIFTERS
Under the boardwalk / I count the tears / Up on the roof / Please stay / On Broadway / When my little girl is smiling / (If you cry) true love, true love / There goes my baby / This magic moment / Some kind of wonderful / Dance with me / Save the last dance for me / Sweets for my sweet / Saturday night at the movies
CD _____ HADCD 122
Javelin / Feb '94 / THE / Henry Hadaway Organisation.

UNDER THE BOARDWALK
Under the boardwalk / Please stay / Twist / Some kinda wonderful / My girl / Sand in my shoes / This magic moment / I count the tears / Money honey / True, true love / Honey love / When my little girl is smiling / On broadway / Dance with me / Lonely winds / There goes my baby / Sweets for my sweet / Save the last dance for me
CD _____ MUCD 9016
Start / Apr '95 / Koch.

UP ON THE ROOF
CD _____ 8122712302
Carlton Home Entertainment / Oct '94 / Carlton Home Entertainment.

VERY BEST OF DRIFTERS
CD _____ 812271211-2
Atlantic / Jun '93 / Warner Music.

Driftwood, Jimmie

AMERICANA
Unfortunate man / Fair Rosamund's bower / Soldier's joy / Country Boy / I'm too young to marry / Pretty Mary / Sailor man / Zelma Lee / Rattlesnake song / Old Joe Clark / Tennesee stud / Razor back steak / First covered wagon / Maid of Argenta / Bunker Hill / Song of the cowboys / Peter Francisco / Four little girls in Boston / Slack your rope, hangman / Run Johnny run / Arkansas traveller / Damn Yankee lad / Chalamette / Battle of New Orleans / Land where the bluegrass grows / Widders of Bowling green / Get along boys / Sweet Betsy from pike / Shoot the buffalo / Song of the pioneer / I'm leavin' on the wagon train / Jordan am a hard road to travel / Marshall of Silver City / Wilderness road / Pony express / Mooshatonio / Shanty in the holler / Big river man / Big John Davy / On top of Pikes peak / Fi di diddle um-a-dazey / Song of creation / Battle of San Juan hill / Banjer pickin' man / Tucumcari / St. Brendan's isle / He had a long chain on / Big Hoss / Sal's got a sugar lip / Ox driving song / General Custer / What was your name in the States / Billy the kid / Jesse James / Billy Yank and Johnny Reb / Won't you come along and go / Rock of Chickamauga / How do you like the army / Git along little yearlings / Oh Florie / I'm a poor rebel soldier / My black bird has gone / Goodbye Reb, you all come / On top of Shiloh's hill / When I swim the Golden River / Giant of the Thunderhead / Shanghai'd / Santy Anno O-Roe / Bullies Row / Land of the Amazon / What could I do / Driftwood at sea / In a cotton shirt and a pair of dungarees / Davy Jones (Song of a dead soldier) / Sailor, sailor marry me / River boy / Ship that never returned / Sailing away on the ocean / John Paul Jones / Bear flew over the ocean
CD Set _____ BCD 15465
Bear Family / Apr '92 / Rollercoaster / Direct / CM / Swift / ADA.

Drill

PAROXYSM
CD _____ BLOODCD 001
Retribution / Oct '94 / Plastic Head.

SKIN DOWN
CD _____ ABT 092 CD
Abstract / May '91 / Pinnacle / Total/BMG.

WHITE FINGER
CD _____ ABT 039CD
Abstract / Jul '92 / Pinnacle / Total/BMG.

Driller Killer

BRUTALIZED
CD _____ DISTCD 8
Distortion / Jun '94 / Plastic Head.

L.I.F.E.
CD _____ DISTEP 20
Distortion / Nov '95 / Plastic Head.

Drink Small

BLUES DOCTOR, THE
Tittie man / Little red rooster / So bad / Something in the milk ain't clean / Rub my belly / Baby leave your panties home / Stormy Monday blues / I'm gonna move to the outskirts of town / John Henry Ford
CD _____ ICDICH 1062
Ichiban / Oct '93 / Koch.

ROUND TWO
D.U.I. / Steal away / Thank you, pretty baby / Don't let nobody know / Widow woman / I'm tired now / Honky tonk / They can't make me hate you / Bishopville women / Can I come over tonight
CD _____ ICH 9009CD
Ichiban / Jun '94 / Koch.

Dripping Goss

BLOWTORCH CONSEQUENCE
CD _____ AP 60052
Profile / Apr '95 / Pinnacle.

Driscoll, Julie

1969
CD _____ OW 30013
One Way / Sep '94 / Direct / ADA.

Driscoll, Phil

CLASSIC HYMNS
CD _____ MHD 001
Nelson Word / Jan '89 / Nelson Word.

Drive Like Jehu

YANK CRIME
CD _____ ELM 22CD
Elemental / May '94 / Disc.

Drive, She Said

DRIVE SHE SAID
If this is love / Don't you know / Love has no pride / Hold on / I close my eyes / Hard way home / But for you / Maybe it's love / If I told you / As she touches me
CD _____ MFNCD 100
Music For Nations / Apr '90 / Pinnacle.

DRIVIN' SHE SAID
CD _____ CDMFN 118
Music For Nations / Sep '91 / Pinnacle.

EXCELLERATOR
CD _____ CDMFN 149
Music For Nations / Oct '93 / Pinnacle.

D'Rivera, Paquito

LA HABANA
CD _____ MES 158202
Messidor / Nov '92 / Koch / ADA.

REUNION (D'Rivera, Paquito & Arturo Sandoval)
Mambo influenciado / Reunion / Tanga / Claudia / Friday morning / Part I, II, III / Body and soul / Caprichosos de la habana
CD _____ 158052
Messidor / Feb '91 / Koch / ADA.

WHO'S SMOKING (D'Rivera, Paquito & James Moody)
CD _____ CCD 79523
Candid / Jun '93 / Cadillac / Jazz Music / Wellard / Koch.

Drivin' N' Cryin'

FLY ME COURAGEOUS
CD _____ CID 9991
Island / Mar '92 / PolyGram.

Droge, Pete

NECKTIE SECOND
If you don't love me (I'll kill myself) / Northern bound train / Strayin street / Faith in you / Two steppin' monkey / Sunspot stopwatch / Hardest thing to do / So i am over you / Dog on a chain / Hampton Inn Room 306
CD _____ 74321242302
American / Apr '95 / BMG.

Drome

FINAL CORPORATE COLONIZATION OF THE UNCONSCIOUS
Age of the affordable retina / Hinterland, Kassler Kessel / Down at heels / Hoax what did you get / Steel lung, bye one / Nuzzling / Wonderland / Squirrel / Marathon/Texas / Party in the woods 4
CD _____ ZENCD 011
Ninja Tune / Feb '94 / Vital / Kudos.

Drone

FAT CONTROLLER, THE
CD _____ QDKCD 007
Normal/Okra / Mar '94 / Direct / ADA.

Drones

FURTHER TEMPTATION
CD _____ CDPUNK 20
Anagram / Oct '93 / Pinnacle.

Droney, Chris

FERTILE ROCK, THE
CD _____ CICD 110
CICD / Jul '95 / ADA.

Drop

WITHIN BEYOND
CD _____ CHAPMCD 061
Chapter 22 / Nov '91 / Vital.

Drop 19's

DELAWARE
CD _____ HUTCD 004
Hut / Aug '92 / EMI.

NATIONAL COMA
Limp / All swimmers are brothers / Skull / Cuban / Rot winter / Martini love / 7/8 /

Franco inferno / My hotel deb / Moses
brown / Superfeed / Dead / Royal
CD _____ CDHUT 14
Hut / Sep '93 / EMI.

Drop Acid

MAKING GOD SMILE
CD _____ LS 92502
Roadrunner / Nov '91 / Pinnacle.

Droste, Silvia

AUDIOPHILE VOICINGS
CD _____ BLR 84 004
L&R / May '91 / New Note.

Drovers

TIGHTROPE TOWN
CD _____ TX 2010CD
Taxim / Jan '94 / ADA.

Drowsey, Maggie

HOOKED ON IRISH
Miss MacLeods reel / Whiskey in the jar /
I'll tell me ma / Muirsheen durkin / Lord of
the dance / Gypsy rover / Boys of County
Armagh / Black velvet band / Wild rover /
Danny boy / Higgin's hornpipe / Lanigans
ball / Drowsy maggie / Leaving of Liverpool
/ Roddy McCorley / Irish rover / Patsy
McCann / Far away in Australia / Spancil hill
/ Molly Malone / Maggie / Red is the rose /
After all these years / Irish washerwoman /
Captain pugwash / Fields of athenry / Hills
of donegal / Holy ground / Mason's apron
/ Keel row / Scotland the brave / Minstrel
boy / McNamara's band / Peter street
CD _____ SOV 013CD
Sovereign / Jul '92 / Target/BMG.

Drug Free America

NARCOTICA
CD _____ CBKTB 21
Dreamtime / Jul '95 / Kudos / Pinnacle.

TRIP
Detroit walkabout / One Alien/Nation / Out
on the blue horizon / Orient pearl and cherry
blue / Drop zone (reprise,live) / Cygni X-1
CD _____ CYBERCD 001
Cybersound / Oct '92 / Vital.

TRIP - THE DREAMTIME REMIXES
Cyberspace / Detroit walkabout / One alien
nation under a groove / Out on the blue /
Horizon / Orient pearl and cherry blue / Can
you feel / Drop zone / Cygni X-1 / Drop zone
(free Yibet)
CD _____ CDKTB 14
Dreamtime / Apr '95 / Kudos / Pinnacle.

Drugstore

DRUGSTORE
Speaker 12 / Favourite sinner / Alive / Solitary party groover / If / Devil / Saturday
sunset / Fader / Super glider / Baby Astro-
lab / Gravity / Nectarine / Accelerate
CD _____ 8285562
Honey / Mar '95 / Disc.

Druid

TOWARD THE SUN/FLUID DRUID
Voices / Remembering / Theme / Toward
the sun / Red carpet for an evening / Dawn
of evening / Shangri la / Razor truth / Painters clouds / FM 145 / Crusade / Nothing
but morning / Barnaby / Kestrel / Left to find
/ Fisherman's menu
CD _____ BGOCD 285
Beat Goes On / Aug '95 / Pinnacle.

Drukpa Tibetan Monks

**TIBETAN BUDDHIST RITES FROM
BHUTAN MONASTRIES 1**
CD _____ LYRCD 7255
Lyrichord / Feb '94 / Roots / ADA / CM.

**TIBETAN BUDDHIST RITES FROM
BHUTAN MONASTRIES 2 (Drukpa &
Nyingmapa Tibetan Monks)**
CD _____ LYRCD 7256
Lyrichord / Feb '94 / Roots / ADA / CM.

**TIBETAN BUDDHIST RITES FROM
BHUTAN MONASTRIES 3**
CD _____ LYRCD 7257
Lyrichord / May '94 / Roots / ADA / CM.

**TIBETAN BUDDHIST RITES FROM
BHUTAN MONASTRIES 4**
CD _____ LYRCD 7258
Lyrichord / May '94 / Roots / ADA / CM.

**TIBETAN BUDDHIST RITES FROM
BHUTAN MONASTRIES BOX SET**
CD Set _____ LYRCD 9001
Lyrichord / May '94 / Roots / ADA / CM.

Drum Club

DRUMS ARE DANGEROUS
CD _____ BFLCD 10
Big Life / Aug '94 / Pinnacle.

LIVE IN ICELAND
Oscillate and infiltrate / Bug / Follow the sun
/ Reefer / Crystal express / De-lushed / Pla-
teau of wolves / U make me feel so good

CD _____ SBR 003
Sabres Of Paradise / Aug '95 / Vital.

Drummers Of Burundi

DRUMMERS OF BURUNDI
CD _____ RWMCD 1
Realworld / Mar '92 / EMI / Sterns.

Drummond, Bill

MAN, THE
CD _____ CRECD 14
Creation / May '94 / 3MV / Vital.

Drummond, Billy

GIFT, THE (Drummond, Billy Quartet)
CD _____ CRISS 1083CD
Criss Cross / May '94 / Cadillac /
Harmonia Mundi.

**NATIVE COLOURS (Drummond, Billy
Quintet)**
CD _____ CRISS 1057CD
Criss Cross / May '92 / Cadillac /
Harmonia Mundi.

Drummond, Don

BEST OF DON DRUMMOND, THE
CD _____ SOCD 9008
Studio One / Mar '95 / Jetstar.

GREATEST HITS: DON DRUMMOND
Corner stone / Musical communion / Mes-
opotamia / Cool smoke / Burning torch /
Alipang / Don memorial / Stampede /
Thorough fare
CD _____ TICD 004
Treasure Isle / May '89 / Jetstar / SRD.

MEMORIAL
CD _____ LG 21023
Lagoon / Jul '93 / Magnum Music Group /
THE.

Drummond, Ray

**CAMERA IN A BAG (Drummond, Ray
Quintet)**
CD _____ CRISS 1040CD
Criss Cross / Nov '90 / Cadillac /
Harmonia Mundi.

CONTINUUM
Blues from the sketchpad / Some serious
steppin' / Intimacy of the blues / Sakura /
Blues in the closet / Equipoise / Gloria's
step / Sail away / Sophisticated lady
CD _____ AJ 0111
Arabesque / Aug '94 / New Note.

EXCURSION
Susanita / Penta-major / Prelude / Quads /
Invitation / Well you needn't / Andei / Blues
African / Exscursion
CD _____ AJ 0106
Arabesque / Jun '93 / New Note.

Drumpact

(NEW MUSIC) LIVE
CD _____ EPC 886
European Music Production / Oct '92 /
Harmonia Mundi.

Drunken Boat

DRUNKEN BOAT
Tragic hands / New pop / Accidents / Home
skull crusher / Fury / Jubilee / Lluu'u dream
/ Shit suit / Uniform gold / Stacko / Spin
around / What's going on
CD _____ EFACD 6185
House In Motion / Oct '92 / SRD.

Dry Branch Fire Squad

FERTILE GROUND
Devil, take the farmer / Darling Nellie across
the sea / Where we'll never die / Turkey in
the straw / There's nothing between us /
Love has bought me to dispair / Honest
farmer / Great Titanic / Golden morning / Do
you ever dream of me / Old time way / Don-
aparte's crossing the Rhine
CD _____ CD 0258
Rounder / '89 / CM / Direct / ADA / Cadillac.

JUST FOR THE RECORD
CD _____ ROU 306CD
Rounder / Jan '94 / CM / Direct / ADA /
Cadillac.

TRIED AND TRUE
CD _____ CD 11519
Rounder / '88 / CM / Direct / ADA /
Cadillac.

Dry Throat Fellows

DO SOMETHING
CD _____ SOSCD 1226
Stomp Off / '92 / Jazz Music / Wellard.

D'Semble

D'SEMBLE
CD _____ BBCD 4001
Blue Black / Oct '93 / Cadillac.

DSL

DOIN' IT
CD _____ DMUT 1278
Multitone / Jul '94 / BMG.

Dub Addxx

DUB MISSION
CD _____ LRCD 004
Lush / Nov '95 / SRD.

DUD TO THE TRUTHSEEKERS
CD _____ LRCD 002
Lush / Jan '95 / SRD.

Dub Crusaders

UNIVERSAL SPIRIT WARRIOR
CD _____ JW 014D
Jah Works / Mar '95 / Roots Collective.

Dub Funk Association

PENDULUM VERSION
Good man's dub / Dub of spirits / Don't test
/ Return of the pharaohs / Influence / Jus-
tice dub / Version to die / Scientific wizard
/ House of trance / Restless breed / Pen-
dulum version / Ambience
CD _____ TNTYCD 002
Tanty / May '95 / Total/BMG / Jetstar / Fat
Shadow.

Dub Judah

BETTER TO BE GOOD
CD _____ DJCD 004
Dub Juckey / Aug '94 / Jetstar / SRD.

**DUB FACTOR 3 IN CAPTIVITY DUB
CHRONICLES**
Wipe away the tears / Warning / Burn the
wicked one / Conscious man / In captivity
/ Rise up / Remember / Jah people come /
Love your freedom / Driving on / Stand firm
(CD only) / Repatriation dub (CD only) /
Good, the dub and the free (CD only) /
Young pool (CD only)
CD _____ NRCD 011
Nubian / Mar '95 / Jetstar / Vital.

Dub Narcotic

INDUSTRIAL BREAKDOWN
CD _____ SOUL 8CD
Soul Static Sound / Jul '95 / SRD.

RIDING SHOTGUN
CD _____ KCD 50
K / Nov '95 / SRD.

Dub Specialist

17 DUB SHOTS
CD _____ CDHB 142
Heartbeat / Aug '95 / Greensleeves /
Jetstar / Direct / ADA.

DUB TO DUB, BREAK TO BREAK
CD _____ CP 001CD
Crispy / May '95 / SRD.

Dub Syndicate

CLASSIC SELECTION VOL 1
CD _____ ONUCD 5
On-U Sound / Jul '89 / SRD / Jetstar.

CLASSIC SELECTION VOL.3
CD _____ ONUCD 69
On-U Sound / Jul '94 / SRD / Jetstar.

ECHOMANIA
CD _____ ONUCD 24
On-U Sound / Sep '93 / SRD / Jetstar.

LIVE
CD _____ ONUCD 19
On-U Sound / Mar '93 / SRD / Jetstar.

ONE WAY SYSTEM
CD _____ DANCD 115
Danceteria / Nov '94 / Plastic Head / ADA.

STONED IMMACULATE
CD _____ ONUCD 15
On-U Sound / '93 / SRD / Jetstar.

Dub Teacher

DUB TEACHINGS LESSON 1
CD _____ PRCD 001
Progressive / Nov '95 / Jetstar / SRD.

Dub War

DUB WARNING
CD _____ WOWCD 37
Words Of Warning / '94 / SRD.

PAIN
CD _____ MOSH 121CD
CD _____ GMOSH 121CD
Earache / Feb '95 / Vital.

WORDS OF DUB WARNING
CD _____ WOWCD 47
Words Of Warning / Dec '95 / SRD.

XTRA PAIN
Why / Mental / Nar say a ting / Mad zone /
Strike it / Respected / Pain / Nations / Count
/ Spiritual warfare / Fool's gold / Over now
/ Psycho system / Words of warning / Orig-
inal murder

CD _____ MOSH 121CDF
Earache / Aug '95 / Vital.

Dube, Lucky

HOUSE OF EXILE
CD _____ SHCD 43094
Shanachie / Apr '92 / Koch / ADA /
Greensleeves.

Dublin City Ramblers

BEST OF THE DUBLIN CITY RAMBLERS
Ferryman / Rare ould times / Paddy lie back
/ O'Carolan's draught / Green hills of Kerry
/ Mary's song / John O'Dreams / Punch and
Judy man / Town of Ballybay / Nancy Spain
/ Belfast mill / Slievenamon / My green val-
leys / Crack was ninety in the Isle of Man
CD _____ DOCD 9005
Delmark / Nov '93 / Hot Shot / ADA / CM /
Direct / Cadillac.

**CRAIC AND THE PORTER BLACK, THE
(The Best Of Irish Pub Songs)**
CD _____ DOCDK 107
Dolphin / Nov '95 / CM / Koch /
Grapevine.

FLIGHT OF THE EARLS
CD _____ DOCD 9015
Delmark / Nov '93 / Hot Shot / ADA / CM
/ Direct / Cadillac.

HERE'S TO THE IRISH
CD _____ SOW 90143
Sounds Of The World / Apr '95 / Target/
BMG.

HOME AND AWAY
CD _____ DOCD 101
Delmark / Nov '93 / Hot Shot / ADA / CM
/ Direct / Cadillac.

Dubliners

20 GREATEST HITS: DUBLINERS
CD _____ CD 11
Sound / Jan '89 / Direct / ADA.

20 ORIGINAL GREATEST HITS
CD _____ CHCD 1028
Chyme / Dec '88 / CM / ADA / Direct.

20 ORIGINAL GREATEST HITS VOL.2
Monto / Black Velvet Band / Johnston's
motorcar / Drops of brandy/Lady Carberry
/ Button pusher / Old triangle / Downfall of
Paris / Johnny McGory / Spanish lady / Kil-
lieburne brae / Molly Malone / God save Ire-
land / Spancil hill / Peat bog soldiers / Joe
Hill / Molly Maguires / Hand me down me
bible / Musical priest/Blackthorn stick /
Schoolday's over / Wild Rover
CD _____ CHCD 1014
Chyme / Jul '93 / CM / ADA / Direct.

30 YEARS A-GREYING
Rose / Eileen oge / Three jigs / Death of the
bear / Galway shawl / Auld triangle / Will
the circle be unbroken / Sands of Sudan /
Manchester rambler / Drag that fiddle / Call
and the answer / Boots of spanish leather /
Two hornpipes / I'll tell me Ma / Sweet
Thames flow softly / Whiskey in the jar /
Deportees / Nora / Three reels / Liverpool
Lou / Whay will we tell the children / Man
you don't meet every day
CD _____ RTECD 157
Tara / Aug '94 / CM / ADA / Direct / Conifer.

40 TRADITIONAL IRISH TUNES
CD _____ CHCD 1052
Chyme / Dec '94 / CM / ADA / Direct.

ANTHOLOGY
CD _____ 900792
Line / Oct '94 / CM / Grapevine / ADA /
Conifer / Direct.

AT HOME WITH THE DUBLINERS
CD _____ EUCD 1093
ARC / '89 / ARC Music / ADA.

COLLECTION: DUBLINERS
Wild rover / Chief O'Neill's favourite / Glen-
dalough Saint / Off to Dublin in the green /
Love is pleasing / Nelson's farewell / Monto
/ Dublin fusiliers / Rocky road to Dublin /
Leaving of Liverpool / Old orange flute / Jar
of porter / Prefad san ol / High reel / Patriot
game / Swallow tail reel / McAlpine's fusil-
iers / Hot asphalt / Within a mile of Dublin /
Finnegan's wake / Banks of the roses / My
love in America / Foggy dew / Sea around
us
CD _____ CCSCD 164
Castle / Sep '87 / BMG.

COLLECTION: DUBLINERS VOLUME 2
Roddy McCorley / Twwang man / Sligo
maid/Colonel Rodney / Woman from Wex-
ford / Roisin Dubh / Air fa la la la lo / Peggy
Lettermore / Easy and slow / Kerry recruit /
Donegal reel / Longford collector / Tramps
and hawkers / Home boys home / Sunshine
hornpipe / Mountain road / Will you come to
the bower / I'll tell me ma / Mason's
apron / Holy ground / Boulavogue / Master
McGrath / Walking in the dew / Nightingale
/ Sea shanty
CD _____ CCSCD 270
Castle / Sep '90 / BMG.

DUBLIN
Finnegan's wake / Raglan Road / Zoo /
Logical Gardens / Sez she

197

CD _____ CLACD 337
Castle / Aug '93 / BMG.

DUBLINER'S IRELAND
CD _____ HCD 1005
Carlton Home Entertainment / Nov '92 /
Carlton Home Entertainment.

DUBLINERS COLLECTION
Biddy Mulligan / Springhill disaster / Doh-
erty's reel/Down the broom/The honey-
moon reel / Foggy dew / Weila weila weila
/ Kimmage / Donegal Danny / Queen of the
fair/Tongs by the fire / Louse house in Kilk-
enny / Home boys home / High Germany /
Whiskey in the jar / Champion at keeping
them rolling / Scholar/Teetotaler / Joe Hill /
Free the people / Son is burning / Monto /
Johnston's motorcar / Musical priest/Black-
thorn stick / Battle of the Somme / Smith of
Bristol / Button pusher / Molly Maguires /
Kid on the mountain / Parcel o' rogues /
School days's over / Jail of Claun Meala /
Skibereen / Ojos negros / Killieburne brae /
Saxon shilling / Lowlands of Holland / Holy
ground
CD Set _____ CHCD 1011
Chyme / Jul '93 / CM / ADA / Direct.

DUBLINERS LIVE
CD _____ CC 8235
Music For Pleasure / Jan '92 / EMI.

DUBLINERS, THE
Seven drunken nights / Galway races / Irish
navvy / I wish I were back in Liverpool /
Zoological gardens / Rising of the moon /
Whiskey on a Sunday / Dundee weaver /
Seven deadly sins / Leaving of Liverpool /
Maids. when you're young never wed an
old man / Dirty old town / Donkey reel /
Black velvet band / Pub with no beer /
Peggy Gordon / Net hauling song / Nancy
Whisky / Paddy's gone to France / Skylark
/ Tibby Dunbar / Go to sea no more
CD _____ CC 227
Music For Pleasure / Sep '88 / EMI.

FIFTEEN YEARS ON
CD _____ CHCD 1025
Chyme / Jan '95 / CM / ADA / Direct.

INSTRUMENTAL
CD _____ CH 1052CD
Outlet / Sep '94 / ADA / Duncans / CM /
Ross / Direct / Koch.

IRISH PUB SONGS
CD _____ CDPUB 027
Outlet / Oct '95 / ADA / Duncans / CM /
Ross / Direct / Koch.

IRISH REBEL BALLADS
Johnston's motorcar / Ould triangle / Four
green fields / God save Ireland / Charles
Stewart Parnell / Town I loved so well / Free
the people / Down by the glenside / Boul-
avogue / Take it down from the mast /
Rebel / Wrap the green flag 'round me /
West's awake / Nation once again
CD _____ CHCD 1055
Chyme / Oct '95 / CM / ADA / Direct.

LIVE AT THE ROYAL ALBERT HALL
Black velvet band / McAlpine's fusiliers /
Peggy Gordon / Wella walla / Monto / Cork
hornpipe / Leaving of Liverpool / Whisky on
a Sunday / I wish I were back in Liverpool
/ Flop eared mule (Donkey Reel) / Navvy
boots / Whiskey in the jar / Maids, when
you're young never wed an old man / Seven
drunken nights
CD _____ CDMFP 6127
Music For Pleasure / Sep '94 / EMI.

LIVE IN CARRE, AMSTERDAM
Sweets of May / Dicey Riley / Song for Ire-
land / Building up and tearing England
down / Dunphy's hornpipe / Leitrim fancy /
Down the broom / Dirty old town / Old tri-
angle / Whiskey in the jar / Humours of
Scariff / Flannel jacket / Galway races /
Prodigal son / Sick note / Wild rover / Seven
drunken nights
CD _____ 5509292
Spectrum/Karussell / Jul '95 / PolyGram /
THE.

MILESTONES
CD _____ TRACD 110
Transatlantic / Apr '95 / BMG / Pinnacle /
ADA.

OFF TO DUBLIN GREEN
CD _____ MATCD 211
Castle / May '93 / BMG.

ORIGINAL DUBLINERS
Seven drunken nights / Galway races / Old
alarm clock / Colonel Fraser and
O'Rourke's reel / Rising of the moon /
McCafferty / I'm a rover / Weila waila / Travelling people / Limerick rake / Zoological
gardens / Fairmoye lasses and sporting
Paddy / Black velvet band / Poor Paddy on
the railway / Seven deadly sins / Net hauling
song / Nancy Whiskey / Many young men
of twenty / Paddy's gone to France/Skylark
(instrumental medley) / Molly Bawn / Dundee weaver / Irish navvy / Tibby Dunbar /
Inniskillen Dragoons / I wish I were back in
Liverpool / Go to sea no more / instrumental
medley (inc. The piper's chair/Bill Hart's jig)
/ Darby O'Leary / Cork hornpipe / Peggy
Gordon / Maid of the sweet brown knowe /
Quare bungle rye / Flop eared mule (Donkey
reel) / Poor old Dicey Riley / Whiskey on a
Sunday / Gentleman soldier / Navvy boots

/ Maids, when you're young never wed an
old man / Rattlin' roarin' Willie / Mrs.
McGrath / Carolan concerto / Partin' glass
/ Muirsheen durkin / Nation once again /
Whiskey in the jar / Old triangle / Pub with
no beer / Kelly, the boy from Killane /
Croppy boy / Sullivan's John / Come and
join the British Army / Shoals of herring /
Mormon braes / Drink it up men / Maloney
wants a drink
CD Set _____ CDEM 1480
EMI / Mar '93 / EMI.

PARCEL OF ROGUES, A
Spanish lady / Foggy dew / Kid on the
mountain / Avondale / Acrobats / Village
bells / Blantyre explosion / False hearted
lover / Thirty foot trailer / Boulavogue / Doherty's reel / Down the broom / Honeymoon
reel / Killieburne brae
CD _____ EUCD 1061
ARC / '89 / ARC Music / ADA.

REVOLUTION
CD _____ CHCD 1002
Chyme / Jan '95 / CM / ADA / Direct.

SEVEN DRUNKEN NIGHTS
Seven Drunken nights / Finnegan's wake /
Monto / Auld triangle / Dirty old town / Sam
Hall / Holy ground / Black velvet ground /
Whiskey in the jar / McAlpine's fusileers /
All for me grog / Wild rover / Weila wallia /
Home boys home
CD _____ CHCD 1032
Chyme / '88 / CM / ADA / Direct.

SONGS FROM IRELAND
CD _____ SOW 90108
Sounds Of The World / Oct '95 / Target/
BMG.

SONGS OF DUBLIN
CD _____ CHCD 1054
Chyme / Oct '95 / CM / ADA / Direct.

THIRTY YEARS OF GREYING
CD _____ RTE 157-30CD
RTE / Feb '93 / ADA / Koch.

WILD ROVER, THE
CD _____ 295943
Ariola / Oct '94 / BMG.

Dubplate Vibe Crew

HORN OF AFRICA
CD _____ SOLDCD 002
Solardub / Mar '95 / Jetstar / SRD.

Dubrovniks

AUDIO SONIC LOVE AFFAIR
CD _____ NORMAL 127
Normal/Okra / May '94 / Direct / ADA.

DUBROVNIK BLUES
CD _____ NORMAL 117
Normal/Okra / May '94 / Direct / ADA.

MEDICINE WHEEL
CD _____ NORMAL 167CD
Normal/Okra / Dec '94 / Direct / ADA.

Dubstar

DISGRACEFUL
Stars / Anywhere / Just a girl she said / El-
evator song / Day I see you again / Week
in week out / Not so manic now / Popdorian
/ Not once, not ever / St. Swithin's day /
Disgraceful
CD _____ FOODCD 13
CD Set _____ FOODCDX 13
Food / Oct '95 / EMI.

Ducas, George

GEORGE DUCAS
Teardrops / Kisses don't lie / Hello cruel
world / My world stopped turning / Lipstick
promises / Shame on me / Waiting and
wishing / In no time at all / Only in my
dreams / It ain't me
CD _____ CDP 8283292
Liberty / Feb '95 / EMI.

Duchaine, Kent

JUST ME AND MY GUITAR
CD _____ CAD 01CD
Cadillac / Jun '94 / ADA.

LOOKIN' BACK
CD _____ CAD 1313CD
Cadillac / Jun '94 / ADA.

TAKE A LITTLE RIDE WITH ME
CD _____ CAD 1414CD
Cadillac / Apr '95 / ADA.

Duchesne, André

L' OU 'L
CD _____ VICTOCD 010
Victo / Nov '94 / These / ReR Megacorp /
Cadillac.

Ducks Deluxe

TAXI TO THE TERMINAL ZONE
Coast to coast / Nervous breakdown /
Daddy put the bomp / I got you / Please
please please / Fireball / Don't mind rockin'
tonite / Heart's on my sleeve / Falling on my
sleeve / Falling for the woman / West Texas
trucking board / It's all over now / Cherry

pie / It don't matter tonite / I'm crying / Lo-
ve's melody / Teenage head / Rio Grande /
My my music / Rainy night in Kilburn / Paris
9
CD _____ MAUCD 610
Mau Mau / Oct '91 / Pinnacle.

Dudley, Anne

ANCIENT AND MODERN
Canticles of the sun and the moon / Veni
sanct spiritus / Communion / Veni veni em-
manuel / Tallis canon / Holly and the ivy /
Coventry carol / Prelude / Vater unser im
himmelreich
CD _____ ECHCD 3
Echo / Feb '95 / Pinnacle / EMI.

SONGS FROM THE VICTORIOUS CITY
(Dudley, Anne & Jaz Coleman)
Awakening / Endless festival / Minarets and
memories / Force and fire / Habebe / Zig-
garats and Cinnamon / Hannah / Conqueror
/ Survivor's tale / In a timeless place
CD _____ WOLCD 1009
China / Apr '91 / Pinnacle.

Due Nueva America

**FIESTA LATINA - LATIN AMERICAN
SONGS**
Maria Paleta / Pampa Lirima / Brasileirinho
/ Patricia / El condor pasa / Delicado / LA
llorona / Candombe mulato / Seleccion san
juanitos / Del caribe a los Andes / Senora
tentacion / Camino real / La partida / Flor
de cacao / Aptao
CD _____ EUCD 1203
ARC / Sep '93 / ARC Music / ADA.

Duet Emmo

OR SO IT SEEMS
CD _____ CDSTUMM 11
Mute / Aug '92 / Disc.

Duff, Mary

COLLECTION
CD _____ RITZRCD 550
Ritz / Oct '95 / Pinnacle.

JUST LOVING YOU
She broke her promise / End of the world /
Moonlighter / What do they know / More
than I can say / Power of love / Secret love
/ When you're not a dream / If anything
should happen to you / What the eyes don't
see / Tonight we might fall in love again / You
/ Cliffs of Dooneen / Strangers / Just loving
you
CD _____ CD 0075
Ritz / Jun '95 / Pinnacle.

LOVE SOMEONE LIKE ME
Love someone like me / She's got you / Are
you teasing me / Crazy / Forever and ever
Amen / It's not over (if I'm not over you) /
Daddy's hands / Pick me up on your way
down / Dear God / Chicken every Sunday /
There won't be any patches in heaven / Do
me with love
CD _____ RITZCD 503
Ritz / '91 / Pinnacle.

SILVER AND GOLD
Your one and only / Picture of me (without
you) / Walk the way the wind blows / Deep
water / Silver and gold / Mama was a working man / Sunshine and rain / Homeland /
One you slip around with / Where would
that leave me / I'll be your San Antone rose
/ Fields of Athenry / Beautiful breath / Down
by the Sally gardens
CD _____ RITZCD 0066
Ritz / May '92 / Pinnacle.

WINNING WAYS
Goin' gone / Yellow roses / Eighteen wheels
and a dozen roses / Can I sleep in your
arms / Once a day / Does Fort Worth ever
cross your mind / One bird on a wing / Just
out of reach / Heartaches by the number /
I'm not that lonely yet / Come on in /
Maggie
CD _____ RITZCD 506
Ritz / '91 / Pinnacle.

Duffy, Stephen

**UPS AND DOWNS, THE (Duffy, Stephen
'Tin Tin')**
Kiss me / She makes me quiver / Master-
piece / But is it art / Wednesday Jones /
Icing on the cake / Darkest blues / Be there
/ Believe in me / World at large alone
CD _____ DIXCD 5
10 / Apr '85 / EMI.

Duffy, Waller

CLASSIC COUNTRY GENTS REUNION
(Duffy, Waller, Adcock, Gray)
Fare thee well / Stewball / I'll be there in the
morning / Champagne breakdown / Here
today, gone tomorrow / Gonna get there
soon / Hey Lala / Casey's last ride / Wild
side of life / Wait a little longer / Say won't
you be mine
CD _____ SHCD 3772
Sugarhill / '89 / Roots / CM / ADA / Direct.

Dufourcet, Marie

DUETS FOR ORGAN AND PIANO
**(Dufourcet, Marie Bernadette &
Francoise Dechico Cartier)**
CD _____ PRCD 347
Priory / Sep '92 / Priory.

Duggan Family

DUGGAN'S TRAD, THE
CD _____ CICD 090
Clo Iar-Chonnachta / Dec '93 / CM.

Duggan, John

MISSION, THE
Memories of the mission / Night the telly
blinked / Country boy / Michael mor agus
city Sue / Radioholic / Cigarettes / Barmaid
I met in Kinsale
CD _____ SUNCD 9
Sound / '93 / Direct / ADA.

Duh

BLOWHARD
CD _____ TUPCD 032
Tupelo / Feb '92 / Disc.

UNHOLY HAND JOB, THE
CD _____ K 163C
Konkurrel / Nov '95 / SRD.

Duhan, Johnny

FAMILY ALBUM
Room / Ordinary town / Trying to get the
balanace right / Young mothers / Couple of
kids / Corner stone / Well knit family / We
had our trouble then / Storm is passed /
Voyage
CD _____ RTMCD 16
Round Tower / Jul '90 / Pinnacle / ADA /
Direct / BMG / CM.

Duignan, Eoin

COUMINEOL
CD _____ CEFCD 163
Gael Linn / Jan '94 / Roots / CM / Direct /
ADA.

Duisit, Lorraine

**FEATHER RIVER (Duisit, Lorraine & Tom
Espinola)**
CD _____ CDPH 9012
Philo / '88 / Direct / CM / ADA.

Duke

RETURN OF THE DREAD 1
CD _____ DUKE 2 CD
Music Of Life / Sep '91 / Grapevine.

Duke, George

BRAZILIAN LOVE AFFAIR
Brazilian love affair / Summer breezin' /
Cravo E Canela / Alone / 6 a.m. / Brazilian
sugar / Sugar loaf mountain / Love reborn /
Up from the sea it arose and ate Rio in one
/ I need you now / Ao que vai Nascer
CD _____ 4712832
Sony Jazz / Jan '95 / Sony.

COLLECTION: GEORGE DUKE
Reach for it / Dukey stick / Party down /
Say that you will / Festival / I want you for
myself / Brazilian love affair / Up from the
sea it arose and ate Rio in one swift bite /
Sweet baby / Shine on / Son of reach for it
(the funky dream) / Born to love you / He-
roes / Better ways / Mothership connection
/ Finger prints
CD _____ CCSCD 298
Castle / Oct '91 / BMG.

GUARDIAN OF THE LIGHT
Overture / Light / Shane / Born to love you
/ Silly fightin' / You / War fugue interlude /
Reach out / Give me your love / Stand /
Soon / Celebrate / Fly away
CD _____ 4738692
Sony Jazz / Jul '95 / Sony.

ILLUSIONS
CD _____ 9362457552
Elektra / Jan '95 / Warner Music.

MASTER OF THE GAME
Look what you find / Every step I take /
Games / I want you for myself / In the dis-
tance / I love you more / Dog man / Ever-
ybody's talkin'
CD _____ 4712342
Sony Jazz / Jan '95 / Sony.

MUIR WOOD SUITE
CD _____ 9362461322
Elektra / Nov '95 / Warner Music.

REACH FOR IT
Beginning / Lemme at it / Hot fire / Reach
for it / Just for you / OMI (Fresh water) /
Searchin' my mind / Watch out baby / Di-
amonds / End / Bring it on home
CD _____ 4679662
Epic / Nov '94 / Sony.

RENDEZVOUS
CD _____ EK 39262
Sony Jazz / Jul '95 / Sony.

SNAPSHOT
From the void (intro) / History (I remember) / Snapshot / No rhyme, no reason / Six o'clock / Ooh baby / Fame / Geneva / Speak low / Keeping love alive / Until sunrise / Bus tours / In the meantime (interlude) / Morning after
CD _____ 9362450262
Elektra / Oct '92 / Warner Music.

Dukes Of Stratosphear

CHIPS FROM THE CHOCOLATE FIREBALL
Twenty five o'clock / Bike ride to the moon / My love explodes / What in the world... / Your gold dress / Mole from the ministry / Vanishing girl / Have you seen Jackie / Little lighthouse / You're a good man Albert Brown (curse you red barrel) / Collideascope / You're my drug / Shiny cage / Brainiac's daughter / Affiliated / Pale and precious
CD _____ COMCD 11
Virgin / Aug '87 / EMI.

Dukowski, Chuck

UNITED GANG MEMBERS (Dukowski & Cutler)
CD _____ NAR 094CD
SST / May '94 / Plastic Head.

Dulcimer

DULCIMER
Sonnet to the fall / Pilgrim from the city / Morman's casket / Ghost of the wandering minstrel boy / Gloucester City / Starlight / Caravan / Lisa's song / Time in my life / Fruit of the musical tree / While it lasted / Suzanne
CD _____ SEECD 266
See For Miles/C5 / Sep '89 / Pinnacle.

ROB'S GARDEN
Rob's garden / Across the fields / Silver on white / Smoke / Mean old girl / Creation (poet and the firebird) / Indiana Jones / Army boy / Martin Hussingtree / Come the day / Shining way / Ghost of England
CD _____ PCOM 1144
President / Oct '95 / Grapevine / Target/ BMG / Jazz Music / President.

ROOM FOR THOUGHT
CD _____ HBG 122/6
Background / Apr '94 / Background.

Dulfer, Candy

BIG GIRL
Wake me when it's over / I.L.U. / Tommygun / Jazz it's me / Miles / Funkyness / Capone / Get funky / Chains / September / Upstairs / I'll still be looking up to you / Big girl
CD _____ 74321315132
RCA / Nov '95 / BMG.

SAX-A-GO-GO
CD _____ 74321 11181-2
RCA / Mar '93 / BMG.

SAXUALITY
Pee wee / Saxuality / So what / Jazzid / Heavenly city / Donja / There goes the neighborhood / Mr. Lee / Get the funk / House is not a home
CD _____ 260696
RCA / Aug '95 / BMG.

Dummer, John

NINE BY NINE
CD _____ IGOCD 2021
Indigo / May '95 / Direct / ADA.

Dummies

DAY IN THE LIFE OF THE DUMMIES, A
CD _____ RRCD 155
Receiver / Mar '92 / Grapevine.

Dumpster Juice

GET THAT OUT OF YOUR MOUTH
Clown midget / D.D.S. / Hud / Bowl / Stockton / Pound / Chisel you weasel / Farmer gatherer / Living dead / Gerald / Mommy's sobbin' / Kwan tu
CD _____ 89271-2
Spanish Fly / May '94 / Vital.

Dunbar, Aynsley

AYNSLEY DUNBAR RETALIATION, THE (Dunbar, Aynsley Retaliation)
CD _____ MCAD 22101
One Way / May '94 / Direct / ADA.

DOCTOR DUNBAR'S PRESCRIPTION (Dunbar, Aynsley Retaliation)
CD _____ MCAD 22102
One Way / May '94 / Direct / ADA.

TO MUM FROM AYNSLEY AND THE BOYS (Dunbar, Aynsley Retaliation)
CD _____ MCAD 22069
One Way / May '94 / Direct / ADA.

Dunbar, Sly

SLY, WICKED AND SLICK
Rasta fiesta / Sesame Street / Lover's bop / Senegal market / Mr. Music / Queen of the minstrels / Dirty Harry / Oriental taxis
CD _____ CDFL 9018
Virgin / Jun '91 / EMI.

Dunbar, Valerie

SCARLET RIBBONS
CD _____ CDKLP 69
Klub / Sep '90 / CM / Ross / Duncans / ADA / Direct.

Duncan, Gordon

JUST FOR SEAMUS
CD _____ CDTRAX 075
Greentrax / Aug '94 / Conifer / Duncans / ADA / Direct.

Duncan, Hugo

IRISH COLLECTION, THE
CD _____ CDIRISH 005
Outlet / Oct '95 / ADA / Duncans / CM / Ross / Direct / Koch.

IRISH COUNTRY
By the light of the silvery moon / Sweet forget me not / Part of me / Boyle in the Co. Roscommon / Two little girls in blue / Clock in the tower / Little town in the ould County Down / Back home to Glenamaddy / Home to Donegal / Old pals are always the best / Black sheep / I can't help it / Old cross of Arboe / Killarney in my dreams
CD _____ DHCD 719
Homespun / May '89 / Homespun Records / Ross / Wellard.

Duncan, John

SEND
CD _____ TO 20
Touch / Oct '95 / These / Kudos.

Duncan, Stuart

STUART DUNCAN
Bushy fork of John Creek/Mason's apron / G Forces / Thai clips / Passing / Miles to go / Lee highway blues / Lonely moon / Whistling Rufus / Summer of my dreams / My dixie home / Two o'clock in the morning
CD _____ ROUCD 0263
Rounder / '92 / CM / Direct / ADA / CM.

Dundee Strathspey & Reel.

FIDDLE ME JIG (Dundee Strathspey & Reel Society)
CD _____ LCOM 9047
Lismor / Aug '91 / Lismor / Direct / Duncans / ADA.

Dunham, Sonny

SONNY DUNHAM
CD _____ CCD 085
Circle / Oct '93 / Jazz Music / Swift / Wellard.

Dunkley, Errol

DARLING OOH
You never know / Movie star / Created by the father / Little way different / Like to be boosted / Darling ooh / Baby I love you / You're gonna need me / I'm not the man for you / It was nice while it lasted
CD _____ CDAT 117
Attack / Jun '94 / Jetstar / Total/BMG.

EARLY YEARS, THE
CD _____ RNCD 2104
Rhino / May '95 / Jetstar / Magnum Music Group / THE.

OK FRED (Dunkley, Errol & Sly & Robbie)
CD _____ RNCD 2017
Rhino / Jul '93 / Jetstar / Magnum Music Group / THE.

Dunlap, Slim

OLD NEW ME
Rockin' here tonight / Just for the hell of it / Isn't it / Partners in crime / Taken on the chin / From the get go / Busted up / Ain't exactly good / King and Queen / Ballad of the opening band / Love lost
CD _____ 89231-2
Medium Cool / Nov '93 / Vital.

Dunmall, Paul

SOLILOQUY - 1986
CD _____ MR 15
Matchless / '90 / These / ReR Megacorp / Cadillac.

Dunn, Holly

GETTING IT DUNN
CD _____ 7599269492
WEA / Sep '92 / Warner Music.

Dunn, Larry

LOVER'S SILHOUETTE (Dunn, Larry Orchestra)
Lover's silhouette / 2000 SKY-5 / Don't it make you wanna cry / Italian lady (A song for Mama) / Heaven sent (Michael's song) / Where's the love / Between 7 and earth / Pure faith (guitar interlude) / Maybe in my dreams / Jahap / Enchanted
CD _____ 101S 870712
101 South / Nov '93 / New Note.

Dunn, Roy

KNOW'D THEM ALL
She cooked cornbread for her husband / Further on down the line / Everything I get a hold to / C.C. Rider / You're worrying me / Lost lover blues / Stranger's blues / Move to Kansas city / Red cross store / Don't tear my clothes / I changed the lock / Pearl Harbour blues / Mr. Charlie / Bachelor's blues / Roy's matchbox blues
CD _____ TRIX 3312
Trix / Nov '93 / New Note.

Dunn, Willie

AKWESASNE NOTES
CD _____ TRIK 032
Trikont / Oct '94 / ADA / Direct.

PACIFIC
CD _____ TRIK 075
Trikont / Oct '94 / ADA / Direct.

Dunn-Packer Band

LOVE AGAINST THE WALL
CD _____ TRCD 9905
Tramp / Nov '93 / Direct / ADA / CM.

Dunne, Mickey

LIMERICK LASSIES
CD _____ SD 001CD
SD Recordings / Apr '94 / ADA.

Dunnery, Francis

FEARLESS
American life in the summertime / Home grown / Fade away / Climbing up the love tree / What's he gonna say / Feel like kissing you again / King of the blues / Everyone's a star / Couldn't find a reason / New vibration / Good life
CD _____ 756782582-2
Warner Bros. / Jan '95 / Warner Music.

ONE NIGHT IN SAUCHIEHALL STREET
CD _____ COTINDCD 2
Cottage Industry / May '95 / Total/BMG.

Dunvant Male Choir

WELSH CELEBRATION
CD _____ BNA 5057
Bandleader / Sep '91 / Conifer.

Duo Bertrand

DUO BERTRAND
CD _____ AVPL 12CD
Diffusion Breizh / Apr '94 / ADA.

Duo Dre

(TRE)
CD _____ 837950-2
Amadeo / Oct '94 / PolyGram.

Duo Kassnerquer

FROZEN TREES
CD _____ PCOM 1106
President / Sep '90 / Grapevine / Target/ BMG / Jazz Music / President.

OUR SPANISH COLLECTION
Gran jota de concierto / Los peregrintos / Las morillas de jaen / Zorongo / Anda jaleo / Mortal tristura me dieron / Danza alta / Madre de deus / Santa maria strela do dia / Fandango
CD _____ PCOM 1145
President / Oct '95 / Grapevine / Target/ BMG / Jazz Music / President.

TAMBOR DE GRANADEROS
CD _____ PCOM 1120
President / Oct '93 / Grapevine / Target/ BMG / Jazz Music / President.

Duo Peylet-Cunilot

MUSIQUE DES KLEZMORIM
CD _____ 925672
Buda / Jun '93 / Discovery / ADA.

MUSIQUE KLEZMER
CD _____ 925682
Buda / Jun '93 / Discovery / ADA.

Dupa, Sangwa

BUDDHIST TANTRAS OF GYUTO
CD _____ 7559791982
Elektra Nonesuch / Jan '95 / Warner Music.

Dupree, Champion Jack

1945-53
CD _____ KKCD 08
Krazy Kat / Nov '92 / Hot Shot / CM.

BIGTOWN PLAYBOYS BURNLEY FESTIVAL
CD _____ JSPCD 231
JSP / Oct '89 / ADA / Target/BMG / Direct / Cadillac / Complete/Pinnacle.

BLUES FOR EVERYBODY
Heartbreaking women / Watchin' my stuff / Ain't no meat on de bone / Blues got me rockin' / Tongue tied blues / Please tell me baby / Harelip blues / Two below zero / Let the doorbell ring / Blues for everybody / That's my pa / She cooks me cabbage / Failing health blues / Stumbling block / Mail order woman / Silent partner / House rent party / Rub a little boogie / Walking the blues / Daybreak rock
CD _____ 52029
Blues Encore / Mar '93 / Target/BMG.

BLUES FROM THE GUTTER
Strollin' / T.B. Blues / Can't kick the habit / Evil woman / Nasty boogie / Junkers blues / Bad blood / Goin' down slow / Frankie and Johnny / Stack-o-lee
CD _____ 7567824342
Atlantic / Jul '93 / Warner Music.

CHAMPION JACK DUPREE 1945-1946
Rum cola blues / She makes good jelly / Johnson street boogie / I'm a doctor for women / Wet neck mama / Love strike blues / Gin Mill Sal / Fisherman's blues / F.D.R. blues
CD _____ FLYCD 22
Flyright / Sep '90 / Hot Shot / Wellard / Jazz Music / CM.

CHAMPION JACK DUPREE 1977-1983
CD _____ 157712
Blues Collection / Feb '93 / Discovery.

HOME (Charly Blues - Masterworks Vol. 40)
My baby's coming home / (I'll be glad when you're dead) you rascal you / No tomorrow / Heart of the blues is sound / Japanese special / Hard feeling / Blues from 1921 / Don't mistreat your woman
CD _____ CDBM 40
Charly / Jan '93 / Charly / THE / Cadillac.

NEW ORLEANS BARRELHOUSE 1960
CD _____ PYCD 53
Magpie / Oct '93 / Hot Shot.

NEW ORLEANS BARRELHOUSE BOOGIE
Gamblin' man blues / Warehouse man blues / Chain gang blues / New low down dog / Black woman swing / Cabbage greens No.1 / Cabbage greens no.2 / Angola blues / My cabin inn / Bad health blues / That's all right / Gibing blues / Dupree shake dance / My baby's gone / Wee head woman / Junkers blues / Oh red / All alone blues / Big time Mama / Shady lane / Hurry down sunshine / Jackie P. blues / Heavy heart blues / Morning tea / Black cow blues
CD _____ 472192 2
Columbia / May '93 / Sony.

ONE LAST TIME
CD _____ BB 9522CD
Bullseye Blues / Aug '93 / Direct.

SINGS THE BLUES
CD _____ ROD 100
King/Paddle Wheel / Mar '90 / New Note.

WON'T BE A FOOL NO MORE
Third degree / T.V. mama / He knows the rules / Ain't it a shame / Ooh-la-la / Big leg Emmas / Won't be a fool no more / Calcutta blues / Take it slow and easy / She's all in my life / Poor, poor me / Twenty four hours / Pigfoot and a bottle of beer / Down in the valley / Too early in the morning / Shamsham-shimmy
CD _____ SEECD 388
See For Miles/C5 / Oct '93 / Pinnacle.

Dupree, Cornell

BOP 'N' BLUE
Freedom jazz dance / Bag's groove / Manteca / Round Midnight / Huckleback / Now's the time / Love letter / My little suede shoes / Walkin' / Bop 'n' blues
CD _____ KOKO 1302
Kokopelli / Apr '95 / New Note.

CAN'T GET THROUGH
Can't get through / Southern comfort / Double clutch / Sweet thing / Slippin' in / Let the sun shine on me again / Duck soup / Could it be
CD _____ CDMT 020
Meteor / Mar '93 / Magnum Music Group.

CHILD'S PLAY
Bumpin' / Short stuff / Putt's pub / For blues sake / Child's play / Smooth sailin' / Ramona / Just what you need / Mr. Bojangles
CD _____ CDMT 024
Meteor / Jan '94 / Magnum Music Group.

Dupree, Robbie

ROBBIE DUPREE
Steal away / I'm no stranger / Thin line / It's a feeling / Hot rod hearts / Nobody else / We both tried / Love is a mystery / Lonely runner
CD _____ 7559609692
Elektra / Jan '96 / Warner Music.

STREET CORNER HEROES
Street corner heroes / Desperation / Brooklyn girls / All night long / Free fallin' / I'll be the fool again / Are you ready for love / Saturday night / Missin' you / Long goodbye
CD _____ 7559609702
Elektra / Jan '96 / Warner Music.

Dupree, Simon

KITES (Dupree, Simon & The Big Sound)
Kites / Like the sun like the fire / Sleep / For whom the bell tolls / Broken hearted pirates / Sixty minutes of your love / Lot of love / Love / Get off my Bach / There's a little picture playhouse / Daytime, nighttime / I see the light / What is soul / Amen / Who cares / She gave me the sun / Thinking about my life / It is finished / I've seen it all before / You need a man / Reservations
CD _____ SEECD 368
See For Miles/C5 / Mar '93 / Pinnacle.

Duprees

BEST OF THE DUPREES
You belong to me / Why don't you believe me / Check yourself / Save your heart for me / Carousel / Two different worlds / Hope / Goodnight my love / Sky's the limit / People / My own true love / Have you heard / Delicious / Groovin' is easy / My love, my love / Ring of love / One in a million / Beautiful / My special angel / Delicious (Disco version)
CD _____ NEMCD 674
Sequel / Apr '94 / BMG.

THEIR COMPLETE COED MASTERS
CD _____ CDCHD 617
Ace / Feb '96 / Pinnacle / Cadillac / Complete/Pinnacle.

Duran Duran

BIG THING
Big thing / I don't want your love / All she wants is / Too late Marlene / Drug (It's just a state of mind) / Do you believe in shame / Palomino / Interlude one / Land / Flute interlude / Edge of America / Lake shore driving / Drug (It's just a state of mind)(Daniel Abraham Mix)
CD _____ CDPRG 1007
Parlophone / Aug '93 / EMI.

DECADE
Planet Earth / Girls on film / Hungry like the wolf / Rio / Save a prayer / Is there something I should know / Union of the snake / Reflex / Wild boys / View to a kill / Notorious / Skin trade / I don't want your love / All she wants is
CD _____ CDDDX 10
Parlophone / Nov '89 / EMI.

DURAN DURAN
Girls on film / Planet Earth / Anyone out there / To the shore / Careless memories / Night boat / Sound of thunder / Friends of mine / Tel Aviv
CD _____ CDPRG 1003
Parlophone / Aug '95 / EMI.

DURAN DURAN - DOUBLE PACK
Ordinary world / Love voodoo / Drowning man / Shotgun / Come undone / Breath after breath / U.M.F. / Femme fatale / None of the above / Shelter / To whom it may concern / Sin of the city / Falling angel / Stop dead / Time for temptation / Come undone (mix) / Ordinary world (acoustic) / Too much information (Mixes)
CD Set _____ CDDDB 35
Parlophone / Jan '94 / EMI.

LIBERTY
Violence of summer / Liberty / Hothead / Serious / All along the water / My Antarctica / First impressions / Read my lips / Can you deal with it / Venice drowning / Downtown
CD _____ CDPRG 1009
Parlophone / Aug '93 / EMI.

NOTORIOUS
Notorious / American science / Skin trade / Hold me / Vertigo (do the demolition) / So misled / Meet el presidente / Winter marches on / Proposition / Matter of feeling
CD _____ CDPRG 1006
Parlophone / Aug '93 / EMI.

RIO
Rio / My own way / Lonely in your nightmare / Hungry like the wolf / Hold back the rain / New religion / Last chance on the stairway / Save a prayer / Chauffeur
CD _____ CDPRG 1004
Parlophone / Aug '93 / EMI.

SEVEN AND THE RAGGED TIGER
Reflex / New moon on Monday / I'm looking for cracks in the pavement / I take the dice / Of crime and passion / Union of the snake / Shadows on your side / Tiger tiger / Seventh stranger

---

CD _____ CDPRG 1005
Parlophone / Aug '93 / EMI.

THANK YOU
White lines (don't don't do it) / I want to take you higher / Perfect day / Watching the detectives / Lay lady lay / 911 is a joke / Success / Crystal ship / Ball of confusion / Thank you / Drive-by / I want to take you higher again
CD _____ CDDDB 36
Parlophone / Mar '95 / EMI.

WEDDING ALBUM, THE
Too much information / Ordinary world / Love voodoo / Drowning man / Shotgun / Stop dead / Breath after breath / U.M.F. / None of the above / Time for temptation / Shelter / To whom it may concern / Sin of the city
CD _____ CDDDB 34
Parlophone / Feb '93 / EMI.

Durante, Jimmy

AS TIME GOES BY (The best of Jimmy Durante)
As time goes by / If I had you / Smile / Hi lili hi lo / Make someone happy / Young at heart / Hello, young lovers / Try a little tenderness / Glory of love / I'll be seeing you / September song / I'll see you in my dreams
CD _____ 936245456-2
WEA / Dec '93 / Warner Music.

I SAY IT WITH MUSIC
CD _____ VN 169
Viper's Nest / Aug '95 / Direct / Cadillac / ADA.

SEPTEMBER SONG
CD _____ NI 4026
Natasha / Feb '94 / Jazz Music / ADA / CM / Direct / Cadillac.

Durao, Eduardo

TIMBILA
Ngono utane vuna kudima / Walamba kudja mundino / Haguma nguma tekenha / Eduardo Durao mauaia / Magueleguele / Nhantumbuane / Unichenguile
CD _____ CDORBD 065
Globestyle / Jan '91 / Pinnacle.

Durbin, Deanna

BEST OF DEANNA DURBIN
It's raining sunbeams / My own / Spring in my heart / One fine day / Love is all / Perhaps / Last rose of summer / Can't help singing / Blue Danube dream / california-i-ay / Because / Turntable song / Spring will be a little late this year / Home sweet home / Waltzing in the clouds / Ave Maria
CD _____ MCLD 19183
MCA / May '93 / BMG.

CAN'T HELP SINGING
CD _____ JASCD 101
Jasmine / Nov '95 / Wellard / Swift / Conifer / Cadillac / Magnum Music Group.

FAN CLUB, THE
Amapola / Because / When April sings / Waltzing in the clouds / My own / Brindisi / Beneath the lights of home / Spring in my heart / It's raining sunbeams / Musetta's waltz song / Love is all / Perhaps / One fine day / Home sweet home / Last rose of summer / Il bacio / Ave Maria / Loch Lomond / Alleluia
CD _____ PASTCD 971
Flapper / May '92 / Pinnacle.

WITH A SONG IN MY HEART
Waltzing in the clouds / My own / Brindisi / It's raining sunbeams / Beneath the lights of home / Love is all / Les filles de cadiz / Perhaps / One fine day / Spring in my heart / Amapola / Estrellita / When April sings / Musetta's waltz song / Because / Blue Danube dream / Poor butterfly / Last rose of summer / It's foolish but it's fun / Home sweet home
CD _____ PLCD 534
President / Mar '93 / Grapevine / Target/BMG / Jazz Music / President.

Durham Constabulary...

GENTLE TOUCH, THE (Durham Constabulary Brass Band)
CD _____ BNA 5079
Bandleader / Mar '93 / Conifer.

Durham, Mike

SHAKE 'EM LOOSE
CD _____ LACD 45
Lake / Feb '95 / Target/BMG / Jazz Music / Direct / Cadillac / ADA.

Durham School Chapel...

FLOREAT DUNELMIA (Durham School Chapel Choir)
CD _____ CDCA 929
SCS Music / Nov '93 / Conifer.

Durutti Column

LIVE AT THE BOTTOM LINE
CD _____ RE 512CD

Reach Out International / Nov '94 / Plastic Head.

SEX & DEATH
Anthony / Rest of my life / For Colette / Next time / Beautiful lies / My irascible friend / Believe in me / Fermina / Where should I be / Fado / Madre mio / Blue period
CD _____ FACD 201
Factory Too / Nov '94 / Pinnacle.

Dury, Ian

IAN DURY
CD Set _____ IAN 1
Demon / Aug '91 / Pinnacle / ADA.

IAN DURY AND THE BLOCKHEADS
Intro / Wake up and make love with me / Clevor Trever / If I was with a woman / Billericay dickie / Quiet / My old man / Spasticus autisticus / Plaistow Patricia / There ain't half been some clever bastards / Sweet Gene Vincent / What a waste / Hit me with your rhythm stick / Blockheads
CD _____ FIENDCD 777
Demon / Aug '91 / Pinnacle / ADA.

Dusk

DUSK
CD _____ CYBERCD 15
Cyber / Feb '95 / Plastic Head.

Duskin, Big Joe

CINCINNATI STOMP
CD _____ ARHCD 422
Arhoolie / Sep '95 / ADA / Direct / Cadillac.

DON'T MESS WITH THE BOOGIE MAN
CD _____ SPDCD 1017
Special Delivery / Nov '88 / ADA / CM / Direct.

Dust

DUST
CD _____ REP 4002-WZ
Repertoire / Aug '91 / Pinnacle / Cadillac.

HARD ATTACK
CD _____ REP 4030-WZ
Repertoire / Aug '91 / Pinnacle / Cadillac.

Dutch Swing College Band

40 YEARS, 1945-1985, AT ITS BEST
CD _____ CDTTD 516
Timeless Traditional / Sep '86 / New Note.

DUTCH SAMBA
Corro / Velas blancas / Girl from Ipanema / Samba de Orfeu / Menina flor meditacao / Manana / Corcovado / Poinciana / Samba de Quena / Eso es el amor / La adelita
CD _____ CDTTD 552
Timeless Traditional / Jun '89 / New Note.

DUTCH SWING COLLEGE BAND (Best of Dixieland)
CD _____ 838 765-2
Verve / May '90 / PolyGram.

JOINT IS JUMPIN', THE
Milenberg joys / Grandpa's spells / Squeeze me / Bugle call rag / Peg o' my heart / King Porter stomp / Ballin' the Jack / Clarinet marmalade / Drop me off in Harlem / Freeze and melt / Snowy morning blues / Limehouse blues / Keepin' out of mischief now / Joint is jumpin'
CD _____ CDTTD 594
Timeless Jazz / Jul '95 / New Note.

OLD FASHIONED WAY, THE
CD _____ JHR 73566
Jazz Hour / Nov '93 / Target/BMG / Jazz Music / Cadillac.

STOMPIN' THE HITS
CD _____ 15137
Laserlight / May '94 / Target/BMG.

WORLD RENOWN
Hello Mary Lou / Oh babe / Bad, Bad Leroy Brown / Can't buy me love / Georgie / Waterloom / I will wait for you / Rosetta / Blueberry hill / Girls, girls 'n' girls / Old fashioned way / Mah-nah / Winchester Cathedral / More I see you / Foxie foxtrot / What a difference a day makes / Stargazer / Chanson d'amour / Tie a yellow ribbon / You are the sunshine of my life / When you smile / Champs Elysees / I'd like to teach the world to sing / Que Sera / Matrimony
CD _____ 90794-2
PMF / Jul '94 / Kingdom / Cadillac.

Dutronc

DUTRONC
CD _____ DAMGOOD 70CD
Damaged Goods / Jan '96 / SRD.

Dwarves

HORROR STORIES
CD _____ VOXXCD 2037
Voxx / Aug '88 / Else / Disc.

SUGAR FIX
Anybody out there / Evil primeval / Reputation / Lies / Saturday night / New Orleans / Action man / Smack city / Cain novacaine / Underworld / Wish that I was dead

---

CD _____ SPCD 76/243
Sub Pop / Jul '93 / Disc.

Dwyer, Finbarr

PURE TRADITIONAL IRISH ACCORDIAN
CD _____ PTICD 1004
Pure Traditional Irish / Apr '94 / ADA.

Dyer, Johnny

LISTEN UP
CD _____ BT 1101CD
Black Top / Apr '94 / CM / Direct / ADA.

SHAKE IT
CD _____ BT 1114CD
Black Top / Apr '95 / CM / Direct / ADA.

Dyke & The Blazers

SO SHARP
Funky Broadway (part 1) / Funky Broadway (part 2) / Uhh (part 1) / Runaway people / We got more soul / It's your thing / Shot gun Slim / So sharp / Let a woman be a woman - let a man be a man / You are my sunshine / Funky walk (part 2) / Wrong house / Don't bug me (On CD only) / City dump (On CD only) / My sisters and my brothers (On CD only) / Funky walk (part 1) (On CD only) / Uhh part 2 (On CD only) / Broadway combination (On CD only) / Stuff (On CD only) / Funky bull part 1 (On CD only) / Funky bull part 2 (On CD only) / Wobble (On CD only) / Uhh (edit) (On CD only) / I'm so all alone (On CD only)
CD _____ CDKEND 004
Kent / Aug '91 / Pinnacle.

Dykes, Omar

MUDDY SPRINGS ROAD
CD _____ PRD 70602
Provogue / Mar '94 / Pinnacle.

Dylan, Bob

ANOTHER SIDE OF BOB DYLAN
All I really want to do / Black crow blues / Spanish Harlem incident / Chimes of freedom / I shall be free / To Ramona / Motorpsycho nightmare / My back pages / I don't believe you (she acts like we never have met) / Ballads in plain D / It ain't me babe
CD _____ CD 32034
CBS / Nov '89 / Sony.

BASEMENT TAPES (Dylan, Bob & The Band)
Odds and ends / Orange juice blues (blues for breakfast) / Million dollar bash / Yaroo Street scandal / Goin' to Acapulco / Kate's been gone / You ain't goin' nowhere / Don't ya tell Henry / Nothing was delivered / Open the door, Homer / Long distance operator / This wheel's on fire / Lo and behold / Bessie Smith / Clothes line saga / Apple suckling tree / Mrs. Henry / Tears of rage / Too much of nothing / Yea, heavy and a bottle of bread / Ain't no more cane / Crash on the levee (down in the flood) / Ruben Remus / Tiny Montgomery
CD _____ 4661372
CBS / Nov '89 / Sony.

BEFORE THE FLOOD
Most likely you'll go your way and I'll go mine / Lay lady lay / Rainy day women #s 12 & 35 / Knockin' on Heaven's door / It ain't me babe / Ballad of a thin man / Up on Cripple Creek / I shall be released / Endless highway / Night they drove old Dixie down / Stagefright / Don't think twice, it's alright / Just like a woman / It's alright Ma (I'm only bleeding) / Shape I'm in / When you awake / Weight / All along the watchtower / Highway 61 revisited / Like a rolling stone / Blowin' in the wind
CD Set _____ CD 22137
CBS / Jul '87 / Sony.

BIOGRAPH (3CD Set)
Lay lady lay / If not for you / Times they are a changin' / Blowin' in the wind / Masters of war / Percy's song / Like a rolling stone / Subterranean homesick blues / Mr. Tambourine man / It ain't me babe / Million dollar bash / It's all over now baby blue / Positively 4th Street / Heart of mine / I believe in you / Time passes slowly / Forever young / Baby let me follow you down / I'll be your baby tonight / I'll keep it with mine / Lonesome death of Hattie Carroll / Mixed-up confusion / Tombstone blues / Groom's still waiting at the altar / Most likely you'll go your way and I'll go mine / Jet pilot / Lay down your weary tune / I don't believe you (she acts like we never have met) / Visions of Johanna / Every grain of sand / Quinn the Eskimo / Dear landlord / You angel you / To Ramona / You're a big girl now / Abandoned love / Tangled up in blue / Can you please crawl out of your window / Isis / Caribbean wind / Up to me / Baby I'm in the mood for you / I wanna be your lover / I want you / On a night like this / Just like a woman / Romance in Durango / Senor (tales of Yankee power) / Gotta serve somebody / I shall be released / Knockin' on Heaven's door / All along the watchtower / Solid rock
CD Set _____ CD 66509
CBS / Jan '86 / Sony.

BLONDE ON BLONDE
Rainy day women #s 12 & 35 / Pledging my time / Visions of Johanna / One of us must know / I want you / Stuck inside a mobile with the Memphis blues again / Leopard-skin pillbox hat / Just like a woman / Most likely you'll go your way and I'll go mine / Temporarily like Achilles / Absolutely sweet Marie / Fourth time around / Obviously five believers / Sad eyed lady of the Lowlands

CD Set _____ CD 22130
CBS / Nov '89 / Sony.

CD Set _____ CK 64411
Columbia / Feb '95 / Sony.

CD _____ 4804172
Columbia / Jul '95 / Sony.

BLONDE ON BLONDE/JOHN WESLEY HARDING/SELF PORTRAIT (3CD Set)
CD Set _____ 4716212
Columbia / Jul '93 / Sony.

BLOOD ON THE TRACKS
Tangled up in blue / Simple twist of fate / You're a big girl now / Idiot wind / You're gonna make me lonesome when you go / Meet me in the morning / Lily Rosemary and the jack of hearts / If you see her / Say hello / Shelter from the storm / Buckets of rain

CD _____ 4678422
Columbia / Sep '93 / Sony.

BOB DYLAN
She's no good / Talkin' New York blues / In my time of dying / Man of constant sorrow / Fixing to die blues / Pretty Peggy-O / Highway 51 blues / Gospel plow / Baby let me follow you down / House of the rising sun / Freight train blues / Song to Woody / See that my grave is kept clean

CD _____ CD 32001
CBS / Nov '89 / Sony.

BOB DYLAN - THE 30TH ANNIVERSARY CONCERT CELEBRATION (2CD/2MC/3LP) (Various Artists)
Like a rolling stone / Leopardskin pillbox hat / Introduction / Blowin' in the wind / Masters of war / Foot of pride / Times they are a changin' / It ain't me babe / What was it you wanted / I'll be your baby tonight / Seven days / Playboy 61 / Just like a woman / Just like Tom Thumb's blues / All along the watchtower / When the ship comes in / I shall be released / Don't think twice, it's alright / Emotionally yours / When I paint my masterpiece / You ain't goin' nowhere / Absolutely sweet Marie / Licence to kill / Rainy day women #s 12 & 35 / Mr. Tambourine man / It's alright Ma (I'm only bleeding) / My back pages / Girl from the North Country / Knockin' on Heaven's door

CD Set _____ 4740002
Columbia / Sep '93 / Sony.

BOB DYLAN SONGBOOK (Various Artists)
All I really want to do / Girl on the North Country / Si tu dois partir / You ain't goin' nowhere / Wanted man / Absolutely sweet Marie / To Ramona / I pity the poor immigrant / Tears of rage / Love minus zero / Blowin' in the wind / Tomorrow is a long time / Too much of nothing / Knockin' on heaven's door / Wicked messenger / Ballad of Hollis Brown / You angel you / This wheel's on fire / Mighty quinn / Nothing was delivered / When the ship comes in / Highway 61 revisited / Maggie's farm

CD _____ VSOPCD 158
Connoisseur / Apr '91 / Pinnacle.

BOOTLEG SERIES, THE VOLUMES 1-3 (Rare & Unreleased) 1961-1991(3CD Set)
Hard times in New York Town (Live in a Minnesota hotel room (20/11/61)) / He was a friend of mine (Out-take from the album Bob Dylan (20/11/61)) / Man on the street (Out-take from the album Bob Dylan (22/11/61)) / No more auction block (Live at The Gaslight Cafe, Greenwich Village, New York City (1962)) / House carpenter (Out-take from the album Freewheelin' Bob Dylan (19/3/62)) / Talkin' Bear Mountain picnic massacre blues (Out-take from the album Freewheelin' Bob Dylan (25/4/62)) / Let me die in my footsteps (Out-take from the album Freewheelin' Bob Dylan (25/4/62)) / Rambling gambling Willie (Out-take from the album Freewheelin' Bob Dylan (24/4/62)) / Talkin' Hava negeilah blues (Out-take from the album Freewheelin' Bob Dylan (25/4/62)) / Quit your low down ways (Out-take from the album Freewheelin' Bob Dylan (9/7/62)) / Worried blues (Out-take from the album Freewheelin' Bob Dylan (9/7/62)) / Kingsport Town (Out-take from the album Freewheelin' Bob Dylan (14/11/62)) / Walkin' down the line (Publishing demo for Witmark Publishing Company (1963)) / Walls of red wing (Out-take from the album Freewheelin' Bob Dylan (24/2/63)) / Paths of victory (Out-take from the album Times They Are A-Changin' (12/8/63)) / Talkin' John Birch paranoid blues (Live at Carnegie Hall (26/10/63)) / Who killed Davey Moore (Live at Carnegie Hall (26/10/63)) / Only a hobo (Out-take from the album Times They Are A-Changin' (12/8/63)) / Moonshiner (Out-take from the album Times They Are A-Changin' (12/8/63)) / When the ship comes in (Piano demo for Witmark Music Publishing Company (1962)) / The times they are a changin' (Piano demo from Witmark Music Publishing Company (1963)) / Last thoughts

on Woody Guthrie (Poem recited live at Town Hall (12/4/63)) / Seven curses (Out-take from the album Times They Are A-Changin' (6/8/63)) / Eternal circle (Out-take from the album Times They Are A-Changin' (24/10/63)) / Suze (The cough song) (Out-take from the album Times They Are A-Changin' (24/10/63)) / Mama you been on my mind (Out-take from the album Bringing It All Back Home (9/6/64)) / Farewell, Angelina (Out-take from the album Bringing It All Back Home (13/1/65)) / Subterranean homesick blues (Alternate acoustic version (13/1/65)) / If you gotta go, go now (or else you got to stay all night) / Sitting on a barbed wire fence (Out-take from the album Highway 61 Revisited (15/6/65)) / Like a rolling stone (Rehearsal in studio (15/6/65)) / It takes a lot to laugh, it takes a train to cry (Alt. take) / I'll keep it with mine (Rehearsal in studio (27/1/66)) / She's your lover now (Out-take from the album Blonde On Blonde (21/1/66)) / I shall be released (Out-take from the album Basement Tapes (1967)) / Santa Fe (Out-take from the album Basement Tapes (1967)) / If not for you (Alternate version (1/5/70)) / Wallflower (Studio recording (4/11/71)) / Nobody 'cept you (Out-take from the album Planet Waves (2/11/73)) / Tangled up in blue (Original New York studio session for Blood On The Tracks (16/9/74)) / Call letter blues (Out-take from the album Blood On The Tracks (16/9/74)) / Idiot wind (Original New York session for Blood On The Tracks (16/9/74)) / If you see her (say hello) / Golden loom (Out-take from the album Desire (30/7/75)) / Catfish (Out-take from the album Desire (28/7/75)) / Seven days (Live performance, Tampa, Florida (21/4/76)) / Ye shall be changed (Out-take from the album Slow Train Coming (2/5/79)) / Every grain of sand (Publishing demo for Special Rider Music (23/9/80)) / You changed my life (Out-take from the album Shot Of Love (23/4/81)) / Need a woman (Out-take from the album (4/5/81)) / Angelina (Out-take from the album Shot Of Love (4/5/81)) / Someone's got a hold of my heart (Early version of the song 'Tight connection to my heart' (25/4/83)) / Tell me (Out-take from the album Infidels (21/4/83)) / Lord protect my child (Out-take from the album Infidels (3/5/83)) / Foot of pride (Out-takefrom the album Infidels (25/4/83)) / Blind Willie McTell (Out-take from the album Infidels (5/5/83)) / When the night comes falling from the sky (Original version (19/2/85)) / Series of dreams (Out-take from the album Oh Mercy (23/3/89))

CD Set _____ 4680862
Columbia / Apr '91 / Sony.

BRINGING IT ALL BACK HOME
Subterranean homesick blues / She belongs to me / Maggie's farm / Love minus zero / Outlaw blues / On the road again / Bob Dylan's 15th dream / Mr. Tambourine man / Gates of Eden / It's alright Ma (I'm only bleeding) / It's all over now baby blue

CD _____ CD 32344
CBS / Jun '88 / Sony.

DESIRE
Hurricane / Isis / Mozambique / One more cup of coffee / Oh sister / Joey / Romance in Durango / Black Diamond Bay / Sara

CD _____ CDCBS 86003
CBS / '88 / Sony.

DOWN IN THE GROOVE
Let's stick together / When did you leave Heaven / Sally Sue Brown / Death is not the end / Had a dream about you, baby / Ugliest girl in the world / Silvio / Ninety miles an hour (down a dead end street) / Shenandoah / Rank strangers to me

CD _____ 4602672
CBS / Jun '88 / Sony.

DYLAN (A Fool Such As I)
Lily of the west / Can't help falling in love / Sarah Jane / Ballad of Ira Hayes / Mr. Bojangles / Mary Ann / Big yellow taxi / Fool such as I / Spanish is the loving tongue

CD _____ CD 32286
Columbia / Feb '91 / Sony.

DYLAN AND THE DEAD (Dylan, Bob & Grateful Dead)
Slow train / I want you / Gotta serve somebody / Queen Jane approximately / Joey / All along the watchtower / Knockin' on Heaven's door

CD _____ 4633812
CBS / Apr '94 / Sony.

EMPIRE BURLESQUE
Tight connection to my heart (has anybody seen my love?) / Seeing the real you at last / I'll remember you / Clean cut kid / Emotionally yours / Dark eyes / Something's burning baby / Never gonna be the same again / Trust yourself / When the night comes / Falling from the sky

CD _____ 4678402
Columbia / Feb '91 / Sony.

FREEWHEELIN' BOB DYLAN, THE
Blowin' in the wind / Girl from the North Country / Masters of war / Down the highway / Bob Dylan's blues / Hard rain's gonna fall / Don't think twice, it's alright / Bob Dylan's dream / Oxford Town / Talking World War III blues / Corine Corina / Honey just allow me one more chance / I shall be free

CD _____ CDCBS 32390
CBS / Nov '89 / Sony.

FREEWHEELIN'/ANOTHER SIDE OF .../ TIMES THEY ARE (3CD Set)
CD Set _____ 4673902
CBS / Dec '90 / Sony.

GOOD AS I'VE BEEN TO YOU
Frankie and Albert / Jim Jones / Blackjack Davy / Canadee-I-O / Sittin' on top of the world / Little Maggie / Hard times / Step it up / Tomorrow night / Arthur McBride / You're gonna quit me / Diamond Joe / Froggie went a-courtin'

CD _____ 472710-2
Columbia / Nov '92 / Sony.

GOOD AS I'VE BEEN TO YOU / GREATEST HITS
CD Set _____ 4727102 D
Columbia / Feb '93 / Sony.

GREATEST HITS: BOB DYLAN
Blowin' in the wind / It ain't me babe / Times they are a changin' / Mr. Tambourine man / She belongs to me / It's all over now baby blue / Subterranean homesick blues / One of us must know / Like a rolling stone / Just like a woman / Rainy day women #s 12 & 35 / I want you

CD _____ 4609072
CBS / Mar '91 / Sony.

GREATEST HITS: BOB DYLAN VOL. 2
CD _____ 4712432
Columbia / Jul '93 / Sony.

GREATEST HITS: BOB DYLAN VOL. 3
Tangled up in blue / Changing the guards / Groom's still waiting at the altar / Hurricane / Forever young / Jokerman / Dignity / Silvio / Ring them bells / Gotta serve somebody / Series of dreams / Brownsville girl / I shall be the red sky / Knockin' on heaven's door

CD _____ 477805-2
Columbia / Nov '94 / Sony.

HARD RAIN'S A-GONNA FALL, A
Maggie's farm / One too many mornings / Stuck inside a mobile with the Memphis blues again / Oh sister / Lay lady lay / Shelter from the storm / You're a big girl now / I threw it all away / Idiot wind

CD _____ CD 32308
CBS / Nov '89 / Sony.

HIGHWAY '61 REVISITED
Like a rolling stone / Tombstone blues / It takes a lot to laugh, it takes a train to cry / From a Buick 6 / Ballad of a thin man / Queen Jane approximately / Highway 61 revisited / Just like Tom Thumb's blues / Desolation Row

CD _____ 4609532
CBS / Nov '89 / Sony.

HIGHWAY 61 REVISITED/JOHN WESLEY HARDING (2CD Set)
Like a rolling stone / Tombstone blues / It takes a lot to laugh, it takes a train to cry / From a Buick 6 / Ballad of a thin man / Queen Jane approximately / Highway 61 revisited / Just like Tom Thumb's blues / Desolation row / John Wesley Harding / As I went out one morning / I dreamed I saw St. Augustine / All along the watchtower / Ballad of Frankie Lee and Judas Priest / Drifter's escape / Dear landlord / I'm a lonesome hobo / I pity the poor immigrant / Wicked messenger / Down along the cove / I'll be your baby tonight

CD Set _____ 4668312
Columbia / Jul '92 / Sony.

INFIDELS
Jokerman / Sweetheart like you / Neighbourhood bully / Licence to kill / Man of peace / Union sundown / I and I / Don't fall apart on me tonight

CD _____ 4607272
CBS / Nov '89 / Sony.

JOHN WESLEY HARDING
John Wesley Harding / As I went out one morning / I dreamed I saw St. Augustine / Drifter's escape / All along the watchtower / I am a lonesome hobo / Ballad of Frankie Lee and Judas Priest / Dear landlord / I pity the poor immigrant / Wicked messenger / Down along cove / I'll be your baby tonight

CD _____ 4633592
CBS / Nov '89 / Sony.

KNOCKED OUT LOADED
You wanna ramble / They killed him / Drifting too far from the shore / Precious memories / Maybe someday / Brownsville girl / Got my mind made up / Under your spell

CD _____ 4670402
Columbia / Feb '91 / Sony.

LIVE AT THE BUDOKAN
Mr. Tambourine Man / Shelter from the storm / Love minus zero / No limit / Ballad of a thin man / Don't think twice, it's alright / Once more cup of coffee (valley below) / Like a rolling stone / I shall be released / Is your love in vain / Blowin' in the wind / Just like a woman / Oh sister / Simple twist of fate / All along the watchtower / I want you / All I really want to do / Knockin' on Heaven's door / It's alright ma (I'm only bleeding) / Forever young / Times they are a changin'

CD _____ CD 96004
CBS / Jul '87 / Sony.

MORE BOB DYLAN'S GREATEST HITS
Watching the river flow / Don't think twice, it's alright / Lay lady lay / Stuck inside a mobile with the Memphis blues again / I'll

be your baby tonight / All I really want to do / My back pages / Maggie's farm / Tonight I'll be staying here with you / Positively 4th Street / All along the watchtower / Mighty Quinn / Just like Tom Thumb's blues / Hard rain's gonna fall / If not for you / New morning / Tomorrow is a long time / When I paint my masterpiece / I shall be released / You ain't goin' nowhere / Down in the flood

CD Set _____ 4678512
Columbia / Apr '92 / Sony.

NASHVILLE SKYLINE
Girl from the North Country (With Johnny Cash) / Nashville skyline rag / To be alone with you / I threw it all away / Peggy Day / Lay lady lay / One more night / Tell me that it isn't true / Country pie / Tonight I'll be staying here with you

CD _____ CD 63601
CBS / Jan '86 / Sony.

NEW MORNING
If not for you / Day of the locusts / Time passes slowly / Went to see the gypsy / Winterlude / If dogs run free / New morning / Sign in the window / One more weekend / Man in me / Three angels / Father of night

CD _____ CD 32267
Columbia / Feb '94 / Sony.

OH MERCY
Political world / Where teardrops fall / Ring them bells / Man in the long black coat / Most of the time / What good am I / Disease of conceit / What was it you wanted / Shooting star

CD _____ 4658002
CBS / Sep '89 / Sony.

OUTLAW BLUES (A Tribute To Bob Dylan) (Various Artists)
Sitting on a barbed wire fence / Just like Tom Thumb's blues / Mama you've been on my mind / Tombstone blues / It ain't me babe / Poster children / Outlaw blues / Can you please crawl out of your window / This wheel's on fire / One of us must know (sooner or later)

CD _____ ILLCD 014
Imaginary / Apr '92 / Vital.

OUTLAW BLUES VOL.2 (A Tribute To Bob Dylan) (Various Artists)
Visions of Johanna / Every grain of sand / Motor psycho nitemare / Abandoned love / Highway 61 revisited / Rainy day women / Buckets of rain / Just like Tom Thumb's blues / Mr. Jones

CD _____ ILLCD 040
Imaginary / Mar '93 / Vital.

PLANET WAVES
On a night like this / Going going gone / Tough mama / Hazel / Something there is about you / Forever young / Dirge / You angel you / Never say goodbye / Wedding song

CD _____ CD 32154
CBS / Nov '89 / Sony.

SAVED
Satisfied mind / Saved / Covenant woman / What can I do for you / Solid rock / Pressing on / In the garden / Saving grace / Are you ready

CD _____ CD 32742
Columbia / Feb '91 / Sony.

SELF PORTRAIT
All the tired horses / Alberta no.1 / I've forgotten more than you'll ever know / Days of 49 / Early morning rain / In search of little Sadie / Let it be me / Woogie boogie / Belle Isle / Living the blues / Like a rolling stone / Copper kettle / Gotta travel on / Blue moon / Boxer / Mighty Quinn / Take me as I am / It hurts me too / Minstrel boy / She belongs to me / Wigwam / Alberta no.2

CD _____ 4601122
Columbia / Feb '91 / Sony.

SLOW TRAIN COMING
Gotta serve somebody / Precious angel / When you gonna wake me up / I believe in you / Slow train / Gonna change my way of thinkin' / Do right to me baby / When he returns / Man gave names to all the animals / Changing of the guard / New pony / No time to think / Baby stop crying / Is your love in vain / Senor / True love tends to forget / We better talk this over / Where are you tonight / Journey through dark heat

CD _____ CD 32524
CBS / Apr '89 / Sony.

SONGS OF BOB DYLAN, THE (Various Artists)
Blowin' in the wind / Hard rain's gonna fall / Don't think twice, it's alright / Tomorrow's a long time / Dusty old fairgrounds / It ain't me babe / Mama you been on my mind / If you gotta go, go now / Mr. Tambourine man / Farewell Angelina / It's all over now baby blue / It takes a lot to laugh, it takes a train to cry / From a Buick 6 / Just like Tom Thumb's blues / Absolutely sweet Marie / This wheel's on fire / I shall be released / I pity the poor immigrant / All along the watchtower / Lay lady lay / Tonight I'll be staying here with you / Wanted man / Champaign Illinois / When I paint my masterpiece / Watching the river flow / Knockin' on Heaven's door / Simple twist of fate / Rita Mae / Abandoned love / Seven days / Need a woman / Let's keep it between us

CD _____ SCD 20
Start / Mar '89 / Koch.

SONGS OF BOB DYLAN, THE (Various Artists)
Absolutely sweet Marie / Hard rain's gonna fall / Can you please crawl out of your window / Girl from the North Country / I shall be released / It ain't me Babe / It's all over now baby blue / Mr. Tambourine man / Farewell (Fare thee well) / Lay lady lay / Masters of war (old masters) / Times they are a changin' / Just like a woman / Ballad of Hollis Brown / She belongs to me / I'll be your baby tonight
CD _____ NEBCD 655
Sequel / Jun '93 / BMG.

STREET LEGAL
Changing of the guard / New pony / No time to think / Baby stop crying / Is your love in vain / Senor (tales of Yankee power) / True love tends to forget / We better talk this over / Where are you tonight / Journey through dark heat
CD _____ 403289
Columbia / Apr '95 / Sony.

SUBTERRANEAN/HIGHWAY 61/ NASHVILLE SKYLINE (3CD Set)
CD Set _____ 4673912
CBS / Dec '90 / Sony.

TIMES THEY ARE A-CHANGIN', THE
Times they are a changin' / Ballad of Hollis Brown / With God on our side / One too many mornings / North Country blues / Only a pawn in their game / Boots of Spanish leather / When the ship comes in / Lonesome death of Hattie Carroll / Restless farewell
CD _____ CD 32021
CBS / Nov '89 / Sony.

UNDER THE RED SKY
Wiggle wiggle wiggle / Under the red sky / Unbelievable / Born in time / TV talkin' song / 10,000 men / Two times two / God knows / Handy Dandy / Cat's in the well
CD _____ 4671882
CBS / Sep '90 / Sony.

UNPLUGGED
Tombstone blues / Shooting star / All along the watchtower / Times they are a-changin' / John Brown / Desolation row / Rainy day women #s 12 & 35 / Dignity / Love minus zero / No limit / Knockin' on heaven's door / Like a rolling stone / With God on our side
CD _____ 4783742
Columbia / Mar '95 / Sony.

WORLD GONE WRONG
World gone wrong / Love Henry / Ragged and dirty / Blood in my eyes / Broke down engine / Delia / Stagger Lee / Two soldiers / Jackaroe / Lone pilgrim
CD _____ 474857 2
Columbia / Nov '93 / Sony.

Dylans

SPIRIT FINGER
CD _____ BBQCD 144
Beggars Banquet / Apr '94 / Warner Music / Disc.

Dynametrix

MEASURE OF FORCE, A
Beginning of the end / Equator / Crack the mic / Abort the mission / Illin / Astrocubic / Time to release / Mind snatch / Planet k11 v the hyperfunk alien / Max to relax / Measure of force / Who gives a damn / Worms in the brain / I got the clout / For real / Your brain is hollow / Shadow
CD _____ KSCD 8
Kold Sweat / Feb '94 / 3MV.

Dynamics

WHAT A SHAME
What a shame / She's for real (Bless you) / Let me be your friend / You'll never find a man like me / Woe is me / Voyage through the mind / You're the only one funkey key / Count your chips / Shucks I love you / We're gonna be together / Show the world (we can do it) / Sweet games of love / Let's start all over / Baby, baby I love you / I've been blessed / I'm thinking / Beautiful music (makes you dance) (mixes) / Get myself high
CD _____ NEMCD 720
Sequel / Feb '95 / BMG.

Dynasty

BEST OF DYNASTY, THE
I don' want to be a freak (but I can't help myself) / I've just begun to love you / Do me right / Adventures in the land of music / Love in the fast lane / Check it out / Questions / Your piece of the rock / Satisfied / Here I am / Strokin' / Does that ring a bell / Only one
CD _____ NEMCD 679
Sequel / Oct '94 / BMG.

Dyoxen

FIRST AMONG EQUALS
CD _____ CDATV 17
Active / Jul '92 / Pinnacle.

Dysart & Dundonald Pipe..

IN CONCERT, BALLYMENA 1983 (Dysart & Dundonald Pipe Band)
CD _____ COMD 2053
Temple / Jan '94 / CM / Duncans / ADA / Direct.

PIPE BANDS OF DISTINCTION (Dysart & Dundonald Pipe Band)
CD _____ CDMON 803
Monarch / Dec '89 / CM / ADA / Duncans / Direct.

Dysney Moon

RUNAWAY
CD _____ WHALE 101CD
Christine / Aug '93 / Friendly Overtures.

Dyson, John

AQUARELLE
Power in the wave / Angel falls / Desert / Shadows / Colorado rainmaker / Analog / Lady aquarelle / Rio grande / Tall ships
CD _____ REAL 096
Surreal / Sep '91 / Surreal To Real / C & D Compact Disc Services.

EVOLUTION
CD _____ REAL 099
Surreal / Sep '89 / Surreal To Real / C & D Compact Disc Services.

Dystopia

HUMAN GARBAGE
CD _____ EFA 124032
Common Cause / Dec '94 / Plastic Head / SRD.

Dystrophy

SPIEGEL MEINER KALTE
CD _____ SR 0003CD
Serenades / Nov '95 / Plastic Head.

Dzintars

SONGS OF AMBER
Blow wind blow / Breaking flax / Sun moves quickly / Sleep my child / Song of the wind / Autumn landscape / Tomtit's message / Where have you been, brother / Orphan girl in white / Di raike / Christmas masquerade / Oi hanuke / So silent is the Ukranian night / Forest shook from dancing
CD _____ RCD 10130
Rykodisc / Sep '91 / Vital / ADA.

E

(E.C.) Nudes

VANISHING POINT
OD _____ ReR N1
ReR Megacorp / Jun '94 / These / ReR Megacorp.

E.C.P.

STRAIGHT LACE PLAYAZ
CD _____ WRA 8143
Wrap / Nov '95 / Koch.

E.L.O.

AFTERGLOW (3CD Set)
10538 Overture / Mr. Radio / Kuiama / In old England town (Boogie no.2) / Mama / Roll over beethoven / Bluebird is dead / Ma-ma-ma belle / Showdown / Can't get it out of my head / Boy blue / One summer dream / Evil woman / Tightrope / Strange magic / Do ya / Nightrider / Waterfall / Roackania / Telephone line / So fine / Livin' thing / Mr. Blue Sky / Sweet is the night / Turn to stone / Sweet talkin' woman / Steppin' out / Midnight blue / Don't bring me down / Twilight / Julie don't live here / Shine a little love / When time stood still / Rain is falling / Bouncer / Hello my old friend / Hold on tight / Four little diamonds / Mandalay / Buildings have eyes / So serious / Matter of fact / No way out / Getting to the point / Destination unkown / Rock 'n' roll is king
CD Set _____ CD 46090
Legacy / Jul '94 / Sony.

BALANCE OF POWER
Heaven only knows / So serious / Getting to the point / Secret lives / Is it alright / Sorrow about to fall / Without someone / Calling America / Endless lies / Send it
CD _____ 4685762
Epic / Jun '91 / Sony.

DISCOVERY
Shine a little love / Confusion / Need her love / Diary of Horace Wimp / Last train to London / Midnight blue / On the run / Wishing / Don't bring me down
CD _____ 4500832
Epic / Jun '91 / Sony.

EARLY ELO (1971-1973)
10538 overture / Look at me now / Nellie takes her bow / Battle of Marston Moor / First movement / Mr. Radio / Kuiama rumble (49th street massacre) / Queen of the hours / Whispers in the night / Roll over Beethoven / In old England town (Boogie no.2) / Momma / From the sun to the world / Whole / My woman / Bev's trousers
CD Set _____ CDEM 1419
EMI / Aug '91 / EMI.

ELDORADO
Eldorado overture / Can't get it out of my head / Boy blue / Laredo tornado / Poorboy (The Greenwood) / Mr. Kingdom / Nobody's child / Illusions in G Major / Eldorado / Eldorado (finale)
CD _____ 476831 2
Epic / May '94 / Sony.

ELDORADO/NEW WORLD RECORD/ OUT OF THE BLUE (3CD Set)
CD Set _____ 4722672
Epic / Oct '92 / Sony.

FACE THE MUSIC
Fire on high / Waterfall / Nightrider / Poker / Strange magic / Down home town / One summer dream
CD _____ EK 57184
Epic / Nov '95 / Sony.

GREATEST HITS I
Telephone line / Evil woman / Livin' thing / Can't get it out of my head / Showdown / Turn to stone / Rockaria / Sweet talkin' woman / Ma-ma-ma belle / Strange magic / Mr. Blue sky
CD _____ 4503572
Jet / Mar '91 / Total/BMG.

GREATEST HITS II
Rock 'n' roll is King / Hold on tight / All over the world / Wild West hero / Diary of Horace Wimp / Shine a little love / Confusion / Ticket to the moon / Don't bring me down / I'm alive / Last to train / Don't walk away / Here is the news / Calling America / Twilight / Secret messages
CD _____ 4719632
Epic / Jul '93 / Sony.

MOMENT OF TRUTH (E.L.O. Part 2)
CD _____ 0096102 ULT
Ultra Pop / Sep '94 / Grapevine / THE.

NEW WORLD RECORD, A
Tightrope / Telephone line / Rockaria / Mission (A new record) / So fine / Livin' thing / Above the clouds / Do ya / Shangri la
CD _____ 902198 2

Carlton Home Entertainment

Carlton Home Entertainment / Feb '90 / Carlton Home Entertainment.

OUT OF THE BLUE
Turn to stone / It's over / Sweet talkin' woman / Across the border / Night in the city / Starlight / Jungle / Believe me now / Steppin' out / Standing in the rain / Summer and lightning / Mr. Blue sky / Sweet is the night / Whale / Wild West hero
CD _____ 4508852
Epic / Jun '91 / Sony.

POWER OF A MILLION LIGHTS (E.L.O. Part 2)
CD _____ 96125 ULT
Ultra Pop / Aug '94 / Grapevine / THE.

SECRET MESSAGES
Secret messages / Loser gone wild / Take me on and on / Bluebird / Four little diamonds / Stranger / Danger ahead / Letter from Spain / Train of gold / Rock 'n' roll is king
CD _____ 4624872
Epic / Jun '91 / Sony.

TIME
Prologue / Twilight / Yours truly 2095 / Ticket to the moon / Way life's meant to be / Another heart breaks / Rain is falling / From the end of the world / Lights go down / Here is the news / 21st century man / Hold on tight / Epilogue
CD _____ 4602122
Epic / Jun '91 / Sony.

TIME/SECRET MESSAGE/DISCOVERY (3CD Set)
Prologue / twilight / Yours truly / Ticket to the moon / 2095 / Way life's meant to be / Another heart breaks / Rain is falling / From the end of the world / Lights go down / Here is the news / 21st Century man / Hold on tight / Epilogue / Secret messages / Loser gone wild / Bluebird / Take me on and on / Four little diamonds / Stranger / Danger ahead / Letter from Spain / Train of gold / Rock 'n' roll is king / Shine a little love / Confusion / Need her love / Diary of Horace Wimp / Last train to London / Midnight blue / On the run / Wishing / Don't bring me down
CD Set _____ 477526-2
Epic / Oct '94 / Sony.

VERY BEST OF E.L.O., THE
CD _____ DINCD 90
Dino / Jun '94 / Pinnacle / 3MV.

E.P.M.D.

BUSINESS AS USUAL
I'm mad / Hardcore / Rampage / Manslaughter / Jane 3 / For my people / Mr. Bozack / Gold digger / Give the people / Rap is outta control / Brothers on my jock / Underground / Hit squad heist / Funky piano
CD _____ 5235102
Def Jam / Jan '96 / PolyGram.

BUSINESS NEVER PERSONAL
Boon dox / Nobody's safe chump / Can't hear nothing but the music / Chill / Headbanger / Scratch bring it back / Crossover / Play the next man / It's going down / Who killed Jane
CD _____ 4719632
Def Jam/CBS / Sep '92 / Sony.

E.V.A.

EXTRA VEHICULAR ACTIVITY
CD _____ KICKCD 26
Kickin' / Jul '95 / SRD.

E.V.E.

GOOD LIFE
CD _____ MCD 11194
MCA / Feb '95 / BMG.

IN THE BEGINNING
Ichiban / Apr '94 / Koch. _____ THE 4177CD

Each Dawn I Die

NOTES FROM A ...
CD _____ DVLR 009CD
Dark Vinyl / Nov '95 / Plastic Head.

Eagles

COMMON THREAD (The Songs Of The Eagles) (Various Artists)
Take it easy / Peaceful easy feeling / Desperado / Heartache tonight / Saturday night / Take it to the limit / I can't tell you why / Lyin' eyes / New kid in town / Saturday night / Already gone / Best of my love / Sad cafe
CD _____ 74321166772
Giant / Oct '93 / BMG.

DESPERADO
Doolin Dalton / Twenty one / Out of control / Tequila sunrise / Desperado / Certain kind of fool / Outlaw man / Saturday night / Bitter Creek
CD _____ K 253008
Asylum / '89 / Warner Music.

EAGLES
Take it easy / Witchy woman / Chug all night / Most of us are sad / Nightingale / Train leaves here this morning / Take the devil / Earlybird / Peaceful easy feeling / Trying / Doolin Dalton / Twenty one / Out of control / Tequila sunrise / Desperado / Certain kind of fool / Outlaw man / Saturday night / Bitter creek
CD _____ 253 009-2
Asylum / Feb '87 / Warner Music.

EAGLES LIVE
Hotel California / Heartache tonight / I can't tell you why / Long run / New kid in town / Life's been good / Seven Bridges Road / Wasted time / Take it to the limit / Doolin Dalton / Desperado / Saturday night / All night long / Life in the fast lane / Take it easy
CD _____ 7559605912
Asylum / Feb '92 / Warner Music.

HELL FREEZES OVER
Get over it / Love will keep us alive / Girl from yesterday / Learn to be still / Tequila sunrise / Hotel California / Wasted time / Pretty maids all in a row / I can't tell you why / New York minute / Last resort / Take it easy / In the city / Life in the fast lane / Desperado
CD _____ GED 24725
Geffen / Nov '94 / BMG.

HOTEL CALIFORNIA
Hotel California / New kid in town / Life in the fast lane / Wasted time / Wasted time (reprise) / Pretty maids all in a row / Try and love again / Last resort / Victim of love
CD _____ 253 051
Asylum / May '87 / Warner Music.

LONG RUN, THE
Long run / I can't tell you why / In the city / Disco strangler / King of Hollywood / Heartache tonight / Those shoes / Teenage jail / Greeks don't want no freaks / Sad cafe
CD _____ 252 181
Asylum / '86 / Warner Music.

ON THE BORDER
Already gone / You never cry like a lover / Midnight flyer / My man (mon homme) / On the border / James Dean / 01 55 / Is it true / Good day in hell / Best of my love
CD _____ 243 005
Asylum / Jun '83 / Warner Music.

ONE OF THESE NIGHTS
One of these nights / Too many hands / Hollywood waltz / Journey of the sorcerer / Lyin' eyes / Take it to the limit / Visions / After the thrill is gone / I wish you peace
CD _____ K253014
Asylum / '89 / Warner Music.

VERY BEST OF THE EAGLES, THE
Take it easy / Witchy woman / Peaceful easy feeling / Doolin dalton / Desperado / Tequila sunrise / Best of my love / James Dean / I can't tell you why / Lyin' eyes / Take it to the limit / One of these nights / Hotel California / New kid in town / Life in the fast lane / Hertache tonight / Long run
CD _____ 954832375-2
Asylum / Jul '94 / Warner Music.

Eagles

SMASH HITS...PLUS
March of the Eagles / Dance on / Lonely bull / Desperados / Scarlett O'Hara / Stranger on the shore / Al di la / Exodus / Johnny's tune / Bristol express / Pipeline / Some people / Old Ned (theme from Steptoe and son) / Maigret / Happy Jap (theme from Comedy Playhouse) / Special agent / Hava nagila / Sukiyaki / Desafinado / Theme from Station Six Sahara / Wishin' and hopin' / Come on baby (to the Floral Dance) / Moonstruck (CD only) / Andorra (CD only) / Theme to Oliver Twist (CD only) / Telstar (CD only)
CD _____ SEECD 277
See For Miles/C5 / '89 / Pinnacle.

Eaglin, Snooks

BABY YOU CAN GET YOUR GUN
You give me nothing but the blues / Oh sweetness / Lavinia / Baby you can get your gun / Drop the bomb / That certain door / Mary Joe / Nobody knows / Pretty girls everywhere
CD _____ FIENDCD 96
Demon / Mar '92 / Pinnacle / ADA.

Country Boy Down in New Orleans

COUNTRY BOY DOWN IN NEW ORLEANS
CD _____ ARHCD 348
Arhoolie / Apr '06 / ADA / Direct / Cadillac.

NEW ORLEANS STREET SINGER
Alberta / That's alright / Malaguena / When they ring the golden bells / Remember me / Fly right back baby / I don't know / Mean old world / I must see Jesus / She's one black rat / Don't you lie to me / Well I had my fun / Brown skin woman / Mama don't you tear my clothes / Who's been fooin' you / When shadows fall / One more drink / I got a woman / Come back baby / Trouble in mind / I got my questionaire / Drifter
CD _____ STCD 8023
Storyville / Dec '94 / Jazz Music / Wellard / CM / Cadillac.

OUT OF NOWHERE
Oh lawdy, my baby / Lipstick traces / Young girl / Out of nowhere / You're so fine / Mailman blues / Well-a, well-a, baby-la / Kiss of fire / It's your thing / Playgirl / West side baby / Cheetah
CD _____ JJCD 13
Black Top / Apr '90 / CM / Direct / ADA.

SOUL'S EDGE
CD _____ BT 1112CD
Black Top / Apr '95 / CM / Direct / ADA.

TEASIN' YOU
CD _____ BT 1072CD
Black Top / '92 / CM / Direct / ADA.

THAT'S ALL RIGHT (Eaglin, Blind Snooks)
CD _____ OBCCD 568
Original Blues Classics / Jul '95 / Complete/Pinnacle / Wellard / Cadillac.

Ealey, Robert

IF YOU NEED ME (Texas Blues Legend)
CD _____ IMP 705
Iris Music / Jul '95 / Discovery.

Ealey, Theodis

IF YOU LEAVE ME, I'M GOING WHI CHA
CD _____ ICH 1164CD
Ichiban / Jan '94 / Koch.

STUCK BETWEEN RHYTHM AND BLUES
CD _____ ICH 1185
Ichiban / Dec '95 / Koch.

Earl 16

NOT FOR SALE
CD _____ NXXCD 01
Next Step / Dec '93 / Jetstar / SRD.

ROOTSMAN
CD _____ RNCD 2038
Rhino / Jan '94 / Jetstar / Magnum Music Group / THE.

Earl, Jimmy

JIMMY EARL
CD _____ SFA 100070
Hotwire / May '95 / SRD.

Earl, Johnny

AMERICAN DREAM, THE
CD _____ F 3020 P
Fury / Nov '91 / Magnum Music Group / Nervous.

GIVE ME THE RIGHT (Earl, Johnny & The Jordonaires)
CD _____ WCPCD 1007
West Coast / Sep '92 / Direct.

PRESLEY STYLE OF..., THE
CD _____ ROCKCD 9115
Rockhouse / Oct '91 / Charly / CM / Nervous.

Earl, Ronnie

BLUES & FORGIVENESS (Earl, Ronnie & The Broadcasters)
CD _____ CCD 11042
Crosscut / Jun '94 / ADA / CM / Direct.

DEEP BLUES (Earl, Ronnie & The Broadcasters)
CD _____ CD 1033
Black Top / '88 / CM / Direct / ADA.

I LIKE IT WHEN IT RAINS
CD _____ ANTCD 0002
Antones / Jan '93 / Hot Shot / Direct / ADA.

LANGUAGE OF THE SOUL (Earl, Ronnie & The Broadcasters)
CD _____ BBCD 9554
Bullseye Blues / Nov '94 / Direct.

EARL, RONNIE

PEACE OF MIND (Earl, Ronnie & The Broadcasters)
I want to shout about it / I wish you could see me now / Peace of mind / T-Bone boogie / Wayne's blues / Bonehead too / More than I deserve / Can't keep from cryin' / I cried my eyes out / No use crying / Stickin' / Wayward angel (Only on CD)
CD _____ FIENDCD 169
Demon / Jun '90 / Pinnacle / ADA.

SOUL SEARCHIN' (With Jerry Portnoy) (Earl, Ronnie & The Broadcasters)
CD _____ CD 1042
Black Top / '88 / CM / Direct / ADA.

STILL RIVER (Earl, Ronnie & The Broadcasters)
Blues for the west side / Time to remember / Kansas city monarch / Szeren / Soul serenade / Equinox / Chili ba hugh / Eyes that smile / Wenesday night at the Bull / Rego park blues / Derek's peace
CD _____ AQCD 1018
Audioquest / Sep '95 / New Note.

Earland, Charles

BLACK TALK
CD _____ OJCCD 335
Original Jazz Classics / Nov '95 / Wellard / Jazz Music / Cadillac / Complete/Pinnacle.

BLACK TALK/BLACK DROPS
Black talk / Mighty burner / Here comes Charlie / Aquarius / More today than yesterday / Sing a simple song / Don't say goodbye / Lazybird / Letha / Raindrops keep falling on my head / Buck green
CD _____ CDBGPD 093
BGP / Apr '95 / Pinnacle.

I AIN'T JIVIN I'M JAMMIN'
I ain't jivin' I'm jammin' / Thinking of you / City lights / One for Andre / World of competition / Sweetie pie / Tell it like it is / Cease the bombing
CD _____ MCD 5481
Muse / Jul '94 / New Note / CM.

LEAVING THIS PLANET
Leaving this planet / Red clay / Warp factor 8 / Brown eyes / Asteroid / Mason's galaxy / No me esqueca (Don't forget me) / Tyner / Van jay / Never ending melody
CD _____ PRCD 66002-2
Prestige / Jan '94 / Complete/Pinnacle / Cadillac.

READY 'N ABLE
Ready 'n able / Free (wanna be free) / Nick of time / Sheila's dream / I'm Rudy's blues / Always and forever / Knee deep / Giving praise
CD _____ MCD 5499
Muse / Dec '95 / New Note / CM.

WHIP APPEAL
CD _____ MCD 5409
Muse / Nov '91 / New Note / CM.

Earle, Steve

BBC RADIO 1 IN CONCERT
CD _____ WINCD 020
Windsong / Jun '92 / Pinnacle.

COPPERHEAD ROAD
Copperhead Road / Snake oil / Back to the wall / Devil's right hand / Johnny come lately / Even when I'm blue / You belong to me / Waiting on you / Once you love / Nothing but a child
CD _____ MCLD 19213
MCA / Sep '93 / BMG.

EXIT O
Nowhere road / Sweet little '66 / No. 29 / Angry young man / San Antonio girl / Rain came down / I ain't ever satisfied / Week of living dangerously / I love you too much / It's all up to you
CD _____ MCLD 19070
MCA / Oct '92 / BMG.

HARD WAY, THE (Earle, Steve & the Dukes)
Other kind / Promise you anything / Esmerelda / Hopeless romantics / This highway / Billy Austin / Justice in Ontario / Have mercy on me / When the people find out / Country girl / Regular guy / West Nashville
CD _____ DMCG 6095
MCA / Jun '90 / BMG.

SHUT UP AND DIE LIKE AN AVIATOR - LIVE
CD _____ MCAD 10315
MCA / Aug '91 / BMG.

THIS HIGHWAY'S MINE
This highway's mine (roadmaster) / Little rock and roller / Back to the wall / Close your eyes / Hopeless romantics / Copperhead Road / Nothing but a child / I ain't ever satisfied / My old friend the blues / Snake oil / It's all up to you / Goodbye's all we got left / Once you love / Fearless heart
CD _____ PWKS 4178
Carlton Home Entertainment / Oct '93 / Carlton Home Entertainment.

TRAIN A COMIN'
CD _____ TRACD 11
Transatlantic / Jun '95 / BMG / Pinnacle / ADA.

Earls

REMEMBER THEN (Best of the Earls)
Remember then / Life is but a dream / Eyes / Out in the cold again / Looking for my baby / Remember me baby / Never / Lookin' my way / All through our teens / Don't forget / Cry cry cry / Without you / Amor / Let's waddle / I believe / Oh what a time / Cross my heart / Kissing / Old man river / Never (alt take) / Ask anybody / Our day will come / I keep a tellin' you
CD _____ CDCHD 366
Ace / May '92 / Pinnacle / Cadillac / Complete/Pinnacle.

Earls Of Suave

BASEMENT BAR AT THE HEARTBREAK HOTEL, THE
Ain't that lovin' you baby / Cheat / Fool such as I / Ring of fire / Sea of love / She's my witch / Mondo moodo / Stranger in my own hometown / Nothing takes the place of you / Somebody buy me a drink / Really gone this time / You can call (But I won't answer) / Cheap wine / Yabba dabba doo (So are you) / One more beer / Little ole wine drinker me / Nobody loves
CD _____ ASKCD 042
Vinyl Japan / Jul '94 / Vital.

Earth

CAPSULAR EXTRACTION
CD _____ 8P123B
Sub Pop / Feb '94 / Disc.

EARTH 2
CD _____ SPCD 65/222
Sub Pop / Feb '93 / Disc.

Earth Christ

FIRESTORM
CD _____ VR 12-2
We Bite / Apr '94 / Plastic Head.

Earth Crisis

ALL OUT WAR
CD _____ VR 203
Victory / May '95 / Plastic Head.

DESTROY THE MACHINES
CD _____ VE 022CD
Victory / Aug '95 / Plastic Head.

Earth Nation

TERRA INCOGNITA
CD _____ EYEUKCD 005
Eye Q / Sep '95 / Disc / Warner Music.

THOUGHTS IN PAST FUTURE
Lord giveth / Falling tears / Revelation / In your mind / World in blue / Chilled dreams / Claim for passion / Alienated / Isolation / In retrospect / Lord taketh
CD _____ 450995557-2
Eye Q / May '94 / Disc / Warner Music.

Earth Water Air Fire

AVALON
Hydroscope / Red fish / Miditation / Nautical dream / Cumana / Thunderdome / Earthbound / Gemini / Moontribe / Stereogen / Nautical mix / Gothama
CD _____ SSR 128
SSR / Nov '93 / Grapevine.

Earth, Wind & Fire

ALL 'N' ALL
Serpentine fire / Fantasy / In the marketplace (interlude) / Jupiter / Love's holiday / Mastermind / Runnin' / Brazilian rhyme (interlude) / Be ever wonderful
CD _____ 982842 2
Pickwick/Sony Collector's Choice / Apr '94 / Carlton Home Entertainment / Pinnacle / Sony.

BEST OF EARTH, WIND AND FIRE VOL. 1, THE
Got to get you into my life / Fantasy / Saturday night / Love music / Getaway / That's the way of the world / September / Shining star / Reasons / Sing a song
CD _____ CD 32536
Columbia / Jun '89 / Sony.

BEST OF EARTH, WIND AND FIRE VOL. 2, THE
Turn on (the beat box) / Let's groove / After the love has gone / Fantasy / Devotion / Serpentine fire / Love's holiday / Boogie wonderland / Saturday nite / Mighty mighty
CD _____ 4632002
Columbia / May '91 / Sony.

EARTH, WIND & FIRE
Help somebody / Moment of truth / Love is life / Fan the fire / C'mon children / World today / Bad tune
CD _____ 7599268612
Warner Bros. / Jan '96 / Warner Music.

ETERNAL DANCE, THE (3CD/MC Set)
Fan the fire / Love is life / I think about lovin' you / Interlude / Time is on your side / Where have all the flowers gone / Power / Keep your head to the sky / Mighty mighty / Feelin' blue / Hey girl / Open our eyes /

Shining star / That's the way of the world / Kalimba story/Sing a message to you (goddess (live) / Mighty mighty (Live) / Can't hide love / Sing a song / Sunshine / Getaway / Saturday nite spirit / Ponta de areia / Fantasy / Saturday night spirit / Ponta de Area / Brazilian rhyme / Serpentine fire / I'll write a song for you / Beijo / Got to get you into my life / September / Boogie wonderland / After the love has gone / In the stone / Dirty / Let me talk / And love goes on / Pride demo / Let's groove / Wanna be with you / Little girl / Night dreamin' / Fall in love with me / Magnetic / System of survival / Thinking of you / I gotta find out
CD Set _____ 472614-2
Columbia / Jan '93 / Sony.

FACES
Let me talk / Turn it into something good / Pride / You / Sparkle / Back on the road / Song in my heart / You went away / Love goes on / Sailaway / Take it to the sky / Win or lose / Share your love / In time / Faces / Got to get you into my life
CD _____ 983316 2
Pickwick/Sony Collector's Choice / Mar '94 / Carlton Home Entertainment / Pinnacle / Sony.

HEAD TO THE SKY
Evil / Keep your head to the sky / Build your nest / World's a masquerade / Clover / Zanzibar / Turn it into something good / You / Sparkle / Back on the road / Song in my heart / You went away / And love goes on / Sailaway / Take it to the sky / Win or lose / Share your love / In time / Faces / Got to get you into my life
CD _____ 982997 2
Pickwick/Sony Collector's Choice / Aug '93 / Carlton Home Entertainment / Pinnacle / Sony.

I AM/ALL N' ALL/RAISE (3CD Set)
CD Set _____ 4673882
Columbia / Dec '90 / Sony.

LIVE AND UNPLUGGED
CD _____ AVEXCD 20
Avex / Nov '95 / 3MV.

LOVE SONGS, THE
After the love has gone / I'm in love / You / Reasons / Sailaway / Fantasy / Could it be right / All about love / Be ever wonderful / We're living in our own time / Daydreamin' / I'll write a song for you / Wait / That's the way of the world / You can't hide love / Miracles
CD _____ 4677682
Columbia / Oct '95 / Sony.

MILLENNIUM, YESTERDAY, TODAY
Even if you wonder / Sunday morning / Blood brothers / Kalimba interlude / Spend the night / Divine / Two hearts / Honor the magic / Love is the greatest story / L word / Just another lonely night / Super hero / Wouldn't change a thing about you / Love across the wire / Chicago (Chi-town) blues / Kalimba blues
CD Set _____ 9362452742
WEA / Sep '93 / Warner Music.

NEED OF LOVE, THE
CD _____ 7599268622
Warner Bros. / Jan '96 / Warner Music.

POWER LIGHT/ELECTRIC UNIVERSE/ SPIRIT (3CD Set)
CD Set _____ 4688042
Columbia / Jul '94 / Sony.

Earthling

RADAR
First Transmission / Ananada's theme / Nefisa / I still love Albert Einstein / Accident at injured strings / Soup or no soup / God's interlude / Echo on my mind / Infinite M / Planet of the apes / By means of beams / Freak, freak / I could just die
CD _____ CTCD 44
Cooltempo / May '95 / EMI.

Earthmen

FALL AND RISE OF MY FAVORITE SIXTIES GIRL
Figure 8 / Brittle / Fall and rise of my favorite sixties girl / Things that worry grown-ups / Tell the women we're going / Language of you and me
CD _____ 95888-2
Seed / Jul '94 / Vital.

TEEN SENSATIONS
Cool chick / Stacey's cupboard / Blonde / Momentum / Encouragement kiss / Roll / Too far down / In the south / Flyby / Elephant
CD _____ 142412
Seed / Nov '93 / Vital.

Earthrise

DEEPER THAN SPACE
CD _____ SR 9344
Silent / Mar '94 / Plastic Head.

Earwig

UNDER MY SKIN I AM LAUGHING
CD _____ LADIDA 024CD
La-Di-Da / Jul '94 / Vital.

East 17

STEAM
Steam / Let it all go / Hold my body tight / Stay another day / Around the world / Let it rain / Be there / M.F. Power / Generation XTC
CD _____ 828542-2
London / Oct '94 / PolyGram.

UP ALL NIGHT
CD _____ 8286992
London / Oct '95 / PolyGram.

WALTHAMSTOW
House of love / Deep / Gold / Love is more than a feeling / I disagree / Gotta do something / Slow it down / I want it / It's alright / Feel what u can't c / West End girls
CD _____ 8284262
London / Jul '93 / PolyGram.

East Down Septet

OUT OF GRIDLOCK
Claudia's car / Three views of a secret / Mothers of the veil / Suite from Taxi Driver / It smells good / Knew rhythm / Black Monday / Gray whale / Cowboy song / Dedication
CD _____ HEPCD 2063
Hep / Jun '95 / Cadillac / Jazz Music / New Note / Wellard.

East London Chorus

ESSENTIALLY CHRISTMAS
CD _____ 053030
Koch / Nov '92 / Koch.

East Meets West

DUBOLOGY PRESENTS MEGADUB
CD _____ DOR 100CD
Dubology / Sep '95 / SRD / Jetstar.

East Of Java

IMP AND THE ANGEL, THE
CD _____ PLASCD 018
Plastic Head / Jan '90 / Plastic Head.

East River Pipe

EVEN THE SUN WAS AFRAID
Here we go / Marty / Sleeping with tallboy / Hide my life away from you / Fan the flame / When the ground walks away / Powerful man / Fan the flames
CD _____ SARAH 407CD
Sarah / May '95 / Vital.

GOODBYE CALIFORNIA
Firing room / Silhouette town / Dogman / When will your friends all disappear / Bernie Shaw / Psychic whore / Forty miles / Make a deal with the city
CD _____ SARAH 405CD
Sarah / Mar '95 / Vital.

POOR FRICKY
Bring on the loser / Ah dictaphone / Crawl away / Metal detector / Put down / Superstar in France / Keep all your windows tight tonight / Nuke it real / Hey, where's your girl / Walking the dog / Million trillion
CD _____ SARAH 621CD
Sarah / Nov '94 / Vital.

East Village

DROPOUT
Silver train / Shipwrecked / Here it comes / Freeze out / Circles / When I wake tomorrow / Way back home / What kind of friend of this / Black autumn / Everybody knows
CD _____ HVNLP 003CD
Heavenly / Nov '93 / Vital.

East West Ensemble

ZURNA
CD _____ ITM 001478
ITM / Nov '92 / Tradelink / Koch.

Easterhouse

CONTENDERS
CD _____ ROUGHCD 94
Rough Trade / May '87 / Pinnacle.

WAITING FOR THE REDBIRD
CD _____ ROUGHCD 124
Rough Trade / Feb '89 / Pinnacle.

Eastman Symphonic Wind...

FAMOUS MARCHES (Eastman Symphonic Wind Ensemble)
CD _____ 90 523-2
PMF / Aug '92 / Kingdom / Cadillac.

Eastman, Madeline

ART ATTACK
CD _____ MKCD 1005
Mad Kat / Feb '95 / Vital/SAM.

Eastman-Dryden Orchestra

CHANSONETTE
Sometime / L'amour toujours l'amour / Gloriana / Firefly / Vagabond King / Adieu / High jinks / Katinka
CD _____ ABQCD 6562
Arabesque / Dec '86 / New Note.

VICTOR HERBERT SOUVENIR
Suite of serenades / Karma / Souvenir / Badinage / Panamericana / 22nd regiment march / Mlle modiste / Naughty Marietta / Fortune teller
CD _____ Z 6529
Arabesque / Nov '85 / New Note.

Easton, Sheena

WORLD OF SHEENA EASTON, THE - THE SINGLES COLLECTION
Morning Train (nine to five) / Modern girl / For your eyes only / You could've been with me / When he shines / Machinery / I wouldn't beg for water / We've got tonight / Telefone (Long distance love affair) / Almost over you / Devil in a fast car / Strut / Sugar walls / Swear / Do it for love / Jimmy Mack / Magic of love / So far, so good / Eternity
CD _____ CDEMS 1495
EMI / Jun '93 / EMI.

Easton, Ted

KIDNEY STEW (Easton, Ted & His Band)
CD _____ DD 631
Delmark / Nov '93 / Hot Shot / ADA / CM / Direct / Cadillac.

Eastwood, Clint

AFRICAN ROOTS
CD _____ LG2 1054
Rhino / Mar '93 / Jetstar / Magnum Music Group / THE.

TWO BAD DJ'S (Eastwood, Clint & General Saint)
Can't take another world war / Another one bites the dust / Talk about run / Sweet sweet Matilda / Special request to all prisoner / Dance have it nice / Gal pon the front line / Jack Spratt / Tribute to General Echo / Hey Mr. DJ
CD _____ GRELCD 24
Greensleeves / '89 / Total/BMG / Jetstar / SRD.

Easy Club

ESSENTIAL
Easy club reel - Janine's reel / Dirty old town / Diamond / Euphemia / Train journey north / Black is the colour of my true love's hair / Little cascade / Quiet man / Fause, fause hae ye been / Skirlie beat / Auld toon shuffle / Road to Gerenish / Innocent railway / Auchengech / North sea chimaeran / Desert march / This for that / Murdo Mackensie of Torridon / Collier's 8 hour day / Arnish light / Eyemouth disaster / Easy club reel
CD _____ ECLCD 9103
Eclectic / Jan '96 / Pinnacle.

ESSENTIAL EASY CLUB, THE
CD _____ ECL 9103CD
Eclectic / Jun '93 / Pinnacle.

Easy Riders

MARIANNE (2 CDs)
What'cha gonna do / So true blues / Marianne / U.S. Adam / Rollin' home / Everybody loves Saturday night / Lonesome rider / Goodbye Chiquita / Champagne wine / South coast / Hot crawfish / Red sundown / Yermo's nightmare and Yermo red / Sky is high / Send for the captain / Don't hurry worry me / True love and tender care / Tina / Sweet sugar cane / I won't tell / Strollin' blues / Fare thee well / Weary travellin' blues / Blues ain't nothin' / Times / Man about town / Shorty Joe / Green fields / Blue mountain / Windjammer / Kari waits for me / Delia (I heard that) Lonesome whistle / Wanderin' blues / Eddystone light / Drill ye tarriers drill / East Virginia / I ride an old paint / Mayfield mountain / Ravin' gambler / Gambler's blues / John Henry / Six wheel driver / I'm gonna leave you now / Saturday's child / Love is a golden ring / Ride away / Vaquero / Take off your old coat / I fait si beau / Glory glory / My pretty quadron / Forever new / Poor boy / Lights of town / Cry of the wild goose / Young in love / Ballad of the Alamo / Green leaves of summer / Remember the Alamo / Laredo / Green grow the lilacs / Long lean Deliah / Leina / Plain old plainsmen / Girl I left behind / He's to the ladies / Tennessee babe / Mi amor, mi corazon / Haven't we met before / Silver and gold / Go tell her for me / Brother Simon and sister Mary / Ten men from Tennessee / Deerfoot Dan / Sam Hall/ Nellie / Maggie Gonzales / Along comes me / 900 Miles / Bachelor's boy / Joe Bowers daughter / See all the people / Bill goat hill / Ta pedia tou zmea (Run come see Jerusalem / Adieu Cherie / Dead aye Sam / Devil cat / Speak a word of love (I wish, I wish) / Lady from Laramie / Little King / Oh

Brandy leave me alone / Boll weevil / Black eyed Cusie / Story of creation / Cotton eyed Joe / Billy boy / Roving gambler / Jennie Jenkins / Black is the color / I know where I'm going / Ev'ryone's crazy ceptin me / Running away / Secret / Nellie Lou / Last freight / Solitary singer / Mr. Buzzard / Tick tock song / Across the wild Missouri / Girl in the wood / East freight / Hoofbeat serenade / Stay a while / Rollin' stone / World belongs to me / Three jolly rogues of Lynne / Charmin' bbfit / Nine hundred miles / Greensleeves / John Hardy / Fond affection / Box of rosewood / Man you don't meet every day / Tom Jack / Wait by the willow / Golden minute / Mackerel feel / Sparrow grass and brown bread / Gypsy Davey / Tall timber / Come home Zelda / Ride away Vaquero / Quit kicking my dog around / Man of the sky / Christopher Columbus
CD Set _____ BCDFI 15780
Bear Family / Aug '95 / Rollercoaster / Direct / CM / Swift / ADA.

Easybeats

FRIDAY ON MY MIND
CD _____ 422126
New Rose / May '94 / Direct / ADA.

GOOD FRIDAY
CD _____ REP 4162-WZ
Repertoire / Aug '91 / Pinnacle / Cadillac.

LIVE - STUDIO AND STAGE
CD _____ RVCD 40
Raven / Sep '95 / Direct / ADA.

VERY BEST OF THE EASYBEATS
CD _____ BRCD 118
BR Music / Jan '95 / Target/BMG.

Eat

EPICURE
CD _____ 5191032
Fiction / Jun '93 / PolyGram.

Eat Static

ABDUCTION
CD _____ BARKCD 001
Ultimate / Jul '94 / 3MV / Vital.

IMPLANT
CD _____ BARKCD 005
Ultimate / May '94 / 3MV / Vital.

Eater

COMPLETE EATER, THE
You / Public toys / Room for one / Lock it up / Sweet Jane / I don't need it / Ann / Get raped / Space dreaming / Queen Bitch / My business / Waiting for the man / Fifteen / No more / No brains / Peace and love (H-Bomb) / Outside view (CD only) / Thinking of the USA (CD only) / Michael's monetary system (CD only) / She's wearing green (CD only) / Notebook (CD only) / Jeepster (CD only) / Debutante's ball (CD only) / Holland (CD only) / What she wants she needs (CD only) / Reach for the sky (CD only) / Point of view (CD only) / Typewriter babes (CD only)
CD _____ CDPUNK 10
Anagram / Apr '93 / Pinnacle.

Eaton, Nigel

MUSIC OF THE HURDY-GURDY, THE
Il Pastor Fido (Vivaldi) / Les Amusements d'une favour (Baton) / Carmagnole houmon / Lady Diamond/New Jig / Satins blanc / Kalashevska / Laride / Queen Adelaide
CD _____ CDSDL 374
Saydisc / Mar '94 / Harmonia Mundi / ADA / Direct.

Eazy E

EAZY-DUZ IT
CD _____ IMCD 124
4th & Broadway / Apr '91 / PolyGram.

ETERNAL E
Boyz-n-the hood (remix) / 8 ball / Eazy duz it / Eazy-er said than dunn / No more questions / We want Eazy / Nobody move / Radio / Only if you want it / Neighborhood sniper / I'd rather fuck you / Automobile / Niggaz my height don't fight / Eazy Street
CD _____ CDPTY 122
Priority/Virgin / Jan '96 / EMI.

Ebbage, Len

SAY IT WITH MUSIC (Ebbage, Len Band)
CD _____ CDTS 054
Maestro / Dec '95 / Savoy.

Eberhardt, Cliff

LONG ROAD, THE
My father's shoes / Long road / Your face / Right now / Always want to feel like this / That kind of love / (Just to) walk down the street with you / Voyeur / White lighting / I am the storm / Nowhere to go / Goodnight
CD _____ WD 1092
Windham Hill / Jun '91 / Pinnacle / BMG / ADA.

MONA LISA CAFE

CD _____ SHCD 8017
Shanachie / Oct '95 / Koch / ADA / Greensleeves.

NOW YOU ARE MY HOME
CD _____ SHAN 8008CD
Shanachie / Dec '93 / Koch / ADA / Greensleeves.

Eberle, Ray

GLENN MILLER MEN - 1943-47 (Eberle, Ray & His Orchestra)
CD _____ JH 1011
Jazz Hour / '91 / Target/BMG / Jazz Music / Cadillac.

Ebi

ZEN
CD _____ EFA 117572
Space Teddy / May '94 / SRD.

Ebogo, Ange

EXPLOSION
CD _____ DTC 027
Sterns / Jan '91 / Sterns / CM.

Ebony Band

MUSIC FROM THE SPANISH CIVIL WAR
CD _____ BVHAASTCD 9203
Bvhaast / Jan '86 / ADA.

EC8TOR

EC8TOR
Cocain duck / You will never find / Think about / Pick the best one / Vibrator / Overload / Discriminate / We are pissed / Lichterloh / Plastic creatures / Intro / Speed erection / Short circuit / Iche suche nichts / Cheap drops
CD _____ DHRCD 003
Digital Hardcore / Nov '95 / Vital.

Echo & The Bunnymen

CROCODILES
Going up / Stars are stars / Pride / Monkeys / Crocodiles / Rescue / Villiers Terrace / Pictures on the wall / All that jazz / Happy death man / Do it clean (Only on import LP.)
CD _____ 2423162
Korova / '89 / Warner Music.

CUTTER, THE
CD _____ 4509 918862
Carlton Home Entertainment / Jan '93 / Carlton Home Entertainment.

ECHO AND THE BUNNYMEN
Game / Over you / Bedbugs and ballyhoo / All in your mind / Bombers bay / Lips like sugar / Lost and found / New direction / Bue blue ocean / Satellite / All my life
CD _____ 2292421372
Korova / Nov '94 / Warner Music.

HEAVEN UP HERE
Show of strength / With a hip / Over the wall / It was a pleasure / Promise / Heaven up here / Disease / All my colours / No dark things / Turquoise days / All I want
CD _____ 2423172
Korova / Jul '88 / Warner Music.

LIVE IN CONCERT
CD _____ WINCD 006
Windsong / Nov '91 / Pinnacle.

OCEAN RAIN
Silver / Nocturnal me / Crystal days / Yo yo man / My kingdom / Thorn of crowns / Killing moon / Seven seas
CD _____ 2403882
Korova / Apr '84 / Warner Music.

PORCUPINE
Cutter / Back of love / My white devil / Clay / Porcupine / Heads will roll / Ripeness / Higher hell / Gods will be gods / In bluer skies
CD _____ 2400272
Korova / Jul '88 / Warner Music.

Echo Art

COREOGRAFIE
CD _____ NT 6712
Robi Droli / Jan '94 / Direct / ADA.

Echo City

SONIC SPORT 1983-88
Shirtful of ice / Tour tuns / Singaraja bemo ride / Night strike / On tarr catch / In the field / In aluminium / Red red red / Spiv / Song for the black economy / Engineer and more
CD _____ GR 001CD
Voice Print / Mar '95 / Voice Print.

Echobelly

EVERYONE'S GOT ONE
CD _____ FAUV 003CD
Fauve / Aug '94 / Vital / 3MV.
ON
CD _____ FAUV 6CD
Fauve / Sep '95 / Vital / 3MV.

Echoes Of Ellington

MAIN STEM
CD _____ TOCD 001
Toad / Feb '95 / BMG.

Echolyn

AS THE WORLD
All ways the same / As the world / Uncle / How long have I waited / Best regards / Cheese stands alone / Prose / Short essay / My dear wormwood / Entry 11/9/83 / One for the show / Wiblet / Audio verite / Settled land / Habit worth forming / Never the same
CD _____ CYCL 025
Cyclops / May '95 / Pinnacle.

Eckert, Rinde

FINDING MY WAY HOME
CD _____ DIW 859
DIW / Jun '92 / Harmonia Mundi / Cadillac.

Ecklund, Peter

IN ELKHART
CD _____ JCD 246
Jazzology / Aug '95 / Swift / Jazz Music.

Eckstine, Billy

BEST OF THE MGM YEARS, THE
CD Set _____ 8194422
Verve / May '94 / PolyGram.

BILLY ECKSTINE
CD _____ CD 325
Entertainers / Feb '95 / Target/BMG.

BILLY ECKSTINE AND QUINCY JONES (Eckstine, Billy & Quincy Jones)
CD _____ 8325922
Emarcy / Feb '94 / PolyGram.

BILLY'S BEST
CD _____ 5264402
PolyGram Jazz / Feb '95 / PolyGram.

JAZZ MASTERS
CD _____ 5166932
Verve / Feb '94 / PolyGram.

MISTER B AND THE BAND
Lonesome lover blues / Cottage for sale / I love the rhythm in a riff / Last night / Prisoner of love / I ain't like that / I'm in the mood for love / You call it madness / All I sing is blues / Long long journey / I only have eyes for you / You're my everything / Jitney man / Blue / Second balcony jump / Tell me pretty baby / Love is the thing / Without a song / Cool breeze / Don't take your love from me / Oop bop sh'bam / In the still of the night / Jelly jelly / My silent love / Time on my hands / All the things you are
CD _____ SV 0264
Savoy Jazz / Apr '95 / Conifer / ADA.

NO COVER, NO MINIMUM
Have a song on me / I've grown accustomed to her face / Lady luck / Lush life / Without a song / Moonlight in vermont / I want a little girl / I'm beginning to see the light / Fools rush in / In the still of the night / Prisoner of love / Little mama / I apologise / Till there was you / You're my everything / Alright O.K. you win / Deed I do / It might as well be Spring / That's for me / I told it never truth aluna / Misty
CD _____ CDROU 018
Roulette / Sep '92 / EMI.

Eclipse First

ECLIPSE FIRST
CD _____ IRCD 012
Integrity / Oct '90 / Vital.

NAMES AND PLACES (Eclipse First & Scotrail Vale Of Atholl Pipe Band)
Landing at roscoff / West wind / Isle de groix / La grande nuit du port de peche / Games / Road to copshie / Oban inn / Victoria bar / Craigdarroch arms
CD _____ IRCD 133
Iona / Sep '91 / ADA / Direct / Duncans.

Ecllerzie

MUSIQUES A DANSER
CD _____ CDUP 68
Diffusion Breizh / May '93 / ADA.

Econoline Crush

AFFLICTION
Nowhere now / Blunt / Wicked / Emotional stain / Close / Blood in the river / Cruel world / Lost / Slug / Sycophant / Affliction
CD _____ CDEMC 3725
EMI / Oct '95 / EMI.

Economist

NEW BUILT GHETTO
CD _____ MASSCD 030
Massacre / Jun '94 / Plastic Head.

Ecstasy Of St. Theresa

FREE D
CD _____ CDFRE 4
Free / Feb '94 / Disc.

Ecume

ECUME
CD _____ CDLLL 127
La Lichere / Aug '93 / Discovery / ADA.

Eddie & The Hot Rods

END OF THE BEGINNING - THE BEST OF, THE
Anything you wanna do / Quit this town / Telephone girl / Teenage depression / Kids are alright (live) / Get out of Denver (live) / Till the night is gone let's rock / Schoolgirl love / Hard drivin' man (live) / On the run (live) / Power and the glory / Ignore them still life / Life on the line / Circles / Take it or leave it / Echoes / We sing the cross / Beginning of the end / Gloria (live) / Satisfaction (live)
CD _____ IMCD 156
Island / Jul '94 / PolyGram.

LIVE AND RARE
CD _____ RRCD 177
Receiver / Aug '93 / Grapevine.

Eddy, Duane

20 TWANGY HITS
CD _____ CDSR 049
Telstar / May '94 / BMG.

BECAUSE THEY'RE YOUNG
CD _____ BR 1492
BR Music / May '94 / Target/BMG.

ESPECIALLY FOR YOU/GIRLS, GIRLS, GIRLS
Peter Gunn / Only child / Lover / Fuzz / Yep / Along the Navajo trail / Just because / Quiniela / Trouble in mind / Tuxedo junction (stereo) / Hard times / Along came Linda / Tuxedo junction (mono) / I want to be wanted / That's all you gotta do / I'm sorry / Sioux City Sue / Tammy / Big Liza / Mary Ann / Annette / Tuesday / Sweet Cindy / Patricia / Mona Lisa / Connie / Carol
CD _____ BCD 15799
Bear Family / Apr '94 / Rollercoaster / Direct / CM / Swift / ADA.

HIS TWANGY GUITAR AND THE REBELS
Kicking asphalt / Rockestra theme / Theme for something really important / Spies / Blue city / Trembler / Los Companeros / Lost innocence / Rockabilly holiday / Last look back
CD _____ SEECD 417
See For Miles/C5 / Nov '94 / Pinnacle.

THAT CLASSIC TWANG
Rebel rouser / Moovin 'n' groovin / Ramrod / Cannonball / Mason Dixon lion / Lonely one / 3.30 blues / Yep / Peter Gunn / Forty miles of bad road / Quiet three / Some kinda earthquake / Bonnie come back / First love, first tears / Shazam / Because they're young / Kommotion / Pete / Theme from Dixie / Ring of fire / Drivin' home / Gidget goes Hawaiian / Avenger / Shazam #2
CD _____ BCD 15702
Bear Family / Apr '94 / Rollercoaster / Direct / CM / Swift / ADA.

TWANG'S THE THANG/SONGS OF OUR HERITAGE
My blue heaven / Tiger love and turnip greens / Last minute of innocence / Route 1 / You are my sunshine / St. Louis blues / Night train to Memphis / Battle / Trambone / Blueberry hill / Rebel walk / Easy / Cripple creek / Riddle song / John Henry / Streets of Laredo / Prisoner's song / In the pines / Ole Joe Clark / Wayfaring stranger / On top of old smokey / Mule train / Scarlet ribbons
CD _____ BCD 15807
Bear Family / Apr '94 / Rollercoaster / Direct / CM / Swift / ADA.

TWANGIN' FROM PHOENIX TO L.A.: THE JAMIE YEARS (7 CDs)
I want some lovin' baby / Soda fountain girl / Ramrod (ford, version) / Caravan (ford version) / Up and down / Moovin 'n' groovin / Pretty jane / Want me / Rebel rouser / Stalkin' / Have love will travel / Look at me / Doo waddie / Dear 53310761 / Walker / Lonely one / Cannonball / Mason Dixon lion / Lonesome road / I almost lost my mind / Loving you (Basic track and master version) / Anytime / Three 30 blues / Yep / Yep (take 7) / Dixie, part 1 / Dixie, part 2 / Yep (master) / Raid / Quiet three (basic track) / Peter Gunn / Lover / Along the Navajo trail / Forty miles of bad road (Mixes) / Some kinda earthquake / Some kind of earthquake (UK version) / Route 1 / Tiger love and turnip greens / Trambone / My blue heaven / Secret seven / You are my sunshine / Last minute of innocence / Rebel walk without overdub) / Blueberry hill / Battle (without overdub) / St. Louis blues / Nightrain to Memphis / Bonnie came back / Lost island (master) / Kommotion #2 (Without strings) / Rebel walk (master) / Battle (master) / Easy / Lost island (lost flute version) / Cripple creek / Riddle song / John Henry / Streets

of Laredo / Prisoner's song / In the pines / Old Joe Clark / Old Joe Clark (take 27 master) / Wayfaring stranger / Top of old smokey / Mule train / Scarlet ribbons / Shazam / Kommotion (Strings) / Kommotion #3 (Female chorus) / Because they're young / Theme for moon children (take 1) / Because they're young (take 27 master) / Theme for moon children (take 4, master) / Back porch, part 1 / Back porch, part 2 / Words mean nothing / Girl on death row / Pepe / Lost friend / Runaway pony / Drivin' home / I want to be wanted / That's all you gotta do / I'm sorry / Mary Ann / Sioux City Sue / Sweet Cindy / Jo Ann / Big Liza / Mona Lisa / Patricia / Connie / Carol / Dixie / Gidget goes Hawaiian / Ring of fire / Bobbie / Avenger / Londonderry air / Just because / Caravan part 1 / Caravan part 2 / Stalkin / Along came Linda / Back porch / Battle / Trouble in mind
CD Set _____ BCD 15778
Bear Family / Nov '94 / Rollercoaster / Direct / CM / Swift / ADA.

Eddy, Nelson

AH, SWEET MYSTERY OF LIFE (Eddy, Nelson & Jeanette MacDonald)
Indian love call / Who are we to say (obey your heart) / Isn't it romantic / Hills of home / Rose Marie / Lover come back to me / Mounties / 'Neath the southern moon / Beyond the blue horizon / When I grow too old to dream / Italian street song / Song of love / Sylvia / Senorita / Farewell to dreams / I'm falling in love with someone / Goodnight / Trees / One kiss / Will you remember
CD _____ PASTCD 7026
Flapper / Nov '93 / Pinnacle.

LOVE'S OLD SWEET SONG
When I grow too old to dream / Rose Marie / 'Neath the southern moon / Deep river / Perfect day / Rosary / Thy beaming eyes / Sylvia / Dusty road / Auf wiedersehen / Smilin' through / Ah sweet mystery of life / Love's old sweet song / At dawning / Oh promise me / Hills of home / Mounties / Trees / Dream / Through the years
CD _____ CDHD 150
Happy Days / '89 / Conifer.

ROSE MARIE
CD _____ CD 23111
All Star / Sep '93 / BMG.

Eddy, Samuel

STRANGERS ON THE RUN
CD _____ SPV 08589422
SPV / Jan '96 / Plastic Head.

Edegran Orchestra

SHIM SHAM SHIMMY (Edegran Orchestra & New Orleans Jazz Ladies)
CD _____ BCD 323
GHB / Mar '95 / Jazz Music.

Eden 224

HOLOCAUSTIC SODA
CD _____ TOPYCD 075
Temple / May '94 / Pinnacle / Plastic Head.

Eden Burning

MIRTH & MATTER
CD _____ FFG 405CD
Free For Good / May '94 / Total/BMG / Free For Good.

Edge Of Sanity

NOTHING BY DEATH REMAINS
CD _____ BMCD 10
Black Mark / '92 / Plastic Head.

PURGATORY AFTERFLOW
CD _____ BMCD 061
Black Mark / Oct '94 / Plastic Head.

SPECTRAL SORROWS, THE
CD _____ BMCD 37
Black Mark / Nov '93 / Plastic Head.

UNORTHODOX
Unorthodox / Enigma / Incipience to the butchery / In the veins/Darker than black / Human aberration (Cassette only) / Everlasting / After afterlife / Beyond the unknown (CD only) / Nocturnal / Curfew for the damned / Cold sun / Day of maturity (CD only) / Requiscon by page / Dead but dreaming / When all is said
CD _____ BMCD 018
Black Mark / Jun '92 / Plastic Head.

Edison, Harry

EDISONS LIGHTS (Edison, Harry 'Sweets')
CD _____ OJCCD 8042
Original Jazz Classics / Jun '95 / Wellard / Jazz Music / Cadillac / Complete/Pinnacle.

HARRY 'SWEETS' EDISON (Edison, Harry 'Sweets')
CD _____ CD 53174
Giants Of Jazz / May '95 / Target/BMG / Cadillac.

SWING SUMMIT (Live at Birdland 1990) (Edison, Harry & Buddy Tate)
CD _____ CCD 79050
Candid / Jan '90 / Cadillac / Jazz Music / Wellard / Koch.

SWINGIN' "SWEETS" (Edison, Harry 'Sweets')
Dejection blues / 'S wonderful / Falling in love / Centrepiece / It don't mean a thing if it ain't got that swing / Lover man / Close your eyes / Bag's groove / On Green Dolphin Street
CD _____ CDLR 45076
L&R / Aug '93 / New Note.

SWINGING AT SKYLINE (Edison, Harry & Clark Terry)
CD _____ CCD 79724
Candid / Nov '95 / Cadillac / Jazz Music / Wellard / Koch.

Edith Strategy

EDITH STRATEGY
CD _____ ABB 19 CD
Big Cat / Jul '90 / SRD / Pinnacle.

Edmunds, Dave

BEST OF DAVE EDMUNDS
Something about you / I hear you knocking (Live) / Deep in the heart of Texas / Information / Breaking out / From small things, big things come (Live) / Shape I'm in / Some other guy / Bail you out / S.O.S. / Slippin' away / Generation rumble / Your true love (Live) / Steel claw / Queen of hearts (Live) / How could I be so wrong
CD _____ 74321 12540-2
Arista / Sep '93 / BMG.

CHRONICLES
Sabre dance / You can't catch me / I hear you knocking / Down down down / Baby I love you / Born to be with you / Warmed over kisses / From small things, big things come / Slippin' away / Something about you / Get out of Denver / I knew the bride / Trouble boys / Girls talk / Queen of hearts / Crawling from the wreckage / Singin' the blues / Almost Saturday / Race is on / Baby ride easy
CD _____ VSOPCD 209
Connoisseur / Nov '94 / Pinnacle.

COMPLETE EARLY EDMUNDS, THE
Morning dew / It's a wonder / Brand new woman / Stumble / Three o'clock blues / I believe to my soul / So unkind / Summertime / On the road again / Don't answer the door / Wang dang doodle / Come back baby / Shake your hips / Hands helping / In the land of the few / Seagull / Nobody's talking / Farandole / You can't catch me / Mars / Sabre dance (2) / Sabre dance / Why / People, people / Think of love / Down down down / I hear you knocking / Hell of a pain / It ain't easy / Promised land / dance, dance, dance / I'm a lover not a fighter / Egg or the hen / Sweet little rock 'n' roller / Outlaw blues / Black Bill / Country roll / I'm comin' home / Blue Monday / I'll get along
CD Set _____ CDEM 1406
EMI / Jul '91 / EMI.

PLUGGED IN
CD _____ 477333-2
Columbia / Aug '94 / Sony.

REPEAT WHEN NECESSARY
Girls talk / Crawling from the wreckage / Black lagoon / Sweet little Lisa / Dynamite / Queen of hearts / Home in my hand / Goodbye Mr. Good Guy / Take me for a little while / We were both wrong / Bad is bad
CD _____ 7567903372
WEA / Feb '92 / Warner Music.

Edsel Auctioneer

GOOD TIME MUSIC OF, THE
Summer hit / Simple / Filled / Stuntman / What's the use / Instrumental 2-1 / Hangover / Faces 1 / Haircut / Country song / Short changed / Just can't believe it
CD _____ A 078D
Alias / Apr '95 / Vital.

Edsels

EVERLASTING BEST CO
CD _____ GROW 12-2
Grass / Apr '94 / SRD.

Edward II

TWO STEPS TO HEAVEN (With the Mad Professor) (Edward II & The Red Hot Polkas)
Bjorn again polka / Swing easy / Untitled polka / Steamboats / Lover's two step / Pomp and pride / Queen's jig / Cliffhanger / Staffordshire hornpipe / Jenny Lind / Stack of wheat (CD only) / Brimfield hornpipe (CD only) / Swedish polka (CD only) / Two step to heaven (CD only)
CD _____ COOKCD 019
Cooking Vinyl / Jan '89 / Vital.

Edward, John

BLUE RIDGE (Edward, John & The Seldom Scene)
Don't that road look rough and rocky / How long have I been waiting for you / Blue ridge / Seven daffodils / Sunshine / Only a hobo / God gave you to me / Little hands / I don't believe I'll stay here anymore / Don't crawfish me baby
CD _____ SH CD 3747
Sugarhill / Mar '89 / Roots / CM / ADA / Direct.

Edwards, Al

GOSPELS & SPIRITUALS
CD _____ 79720
Laserlight / Jan '93 / Target/BMG.

Edwards, Cliff

SINGING IN THE RAIN
CD _____ ACD 17
Audiophile / Jun '95 / Jazz Music / Swift.

Edwards, Frank

DONE SOME TRAVELIN'
Throw your time away / Slide interlude / Good morning little school girl / When the saints go marching in / Goin' back and get her / Chicken raid / She is mine / Mini dress wearer / Mean ol' Frisco / Alcatraz blues / Key to the highway / Love me baby / I know he shed the blood / Put your arms around me
CD _____ TRIX 3303
Trix / Nov '93 / New Note.

Edwards, Honeyboy

DELTA BLUESMAN
Roamin' and ramblin' blues / You got to roll / Water Coast blues / Stagolee / Just a spoonful / Spread my raincoat down / Hellatakin' blues / Wind howlin' blues / Worried life blues / Tear it down rag / Army blues / Big Katie Allen / Black cat / Number 12 at the station / Rocks in my pillow / Decoration Day / Who may your regular be / Eye full of tears / Bad whiskey and cocaine
CD _____ IGOCD 2003
Indigo / Jun '95 / Direct / ADA.

I'VE BEEN AROUND
Pony blues / Sad and lonesome / Ham bone blues / Ride with me tonight / I'm a country man / Banty rooster / Take me in your arms / You're gonna miss me / I feel so good today / Things have changed / Big fat Mama / Eyes full of tears / Woman I'm loving / Big road blues
CD _____ TRIX 3319
Trix / Mar '95 / New Note.

WHITE WINDOWS
West Helena blues / Don't say I don't love you / Build myself a cave / Don't you lie to me / 61 Highway / Drop down Mama / It's been so long since I laughed and talked with you / Shake 'em on down / Take a walk with me / War is over / Roll and tumble / Goin' down slow / Lay my burden down
CD _____ EC 260392
Evidence / Sep '93 / Harmonia Mundi / ADA / Cadillac.

Edwards, Jackie

DO IT SWEET
CD _____ CSDSGP 074
Prestige / Apr '95 / Total/BMG.

IN PARADISE
CD _____ CDTR 344
Trojan / Jun '94 / Jetstar / Total/BMG.

MEMORIAL
CD _____ RNCD 2026
Rhino / Jan '94 / Jetstar / Magnum Music Group / THE.

Edwards, John

CAREFUL MAN
Cold hearted woman / How can I make it without you / Vanishing love / Tin man / Look on your face / It's those little things that count / It's got to be the real thing this time / Ain't that good enough / Time / We always come back strong / I had a love / Everybody don't get a second chance / Way we were / Stop this merry go round / Spread the news / Careful man / Claim jumpin / I'll be your puppet / You we're made for love / You're messing up a good thing / It's a groove / Exercise my love / Danny Boy
CD _____ CDKEND 127
Kent / Jan '96 / Pinnacle.

Edwards, Rupie

DUB BASKET
CD _____ RHCD 2014
Rhino / Jun '93 / Jetstar / Magnum Music Group / THE.

IRIE FEELINGS
Wanderer / Dub master / Rasta Dreadlocks / Free the wind / Wandering dub / Feeling horn / Dub master special / Spangy / Rasta Dreadlocks dub / What can I do / Feeling time / Ten dread commandment
CD _____ CDTRL 281
Trojan / May '90 / Jetstar / Total/BMG.

Edwards, Roy (continued, LET THERE BE VERSION)

LET THERE BE VERSION
CD _____ CDTRL 280
Trojan / May '90 / Jetstar / Total/BMG.

SWEET GOSPEL VOL. 4
CD _____ RECD 06
Rupie Edwards / Oct '94 / Jetstar.

Edwards, Scott

DISTANT HORIZONS
CD _____ CD 0001
Out Of Orbit / Jul '94 / SRD / Plastic Head.

Edwards, Terry

DORA SUAREZ (Edwards, Terry & James Johnston)
Dora / Empire Gate / Voice / Mourning / College Hill / Season of storms
CD _____ HUNKACDL 006
Clawfist / Nov '93 / Vital.

MY WIFE DOESN'T UNDERSTAND ME
CD _____ STIM 7CD
Stim / Sep '95 / SRD.

NO FISH IS TOO WEIRD FOR HER AQUARIUM
CD _____ STIM 005
Stim / Jul '94 / SRD.

PLAYS, SALUTES AND EXECUTES
CD _____ STIM 4
Stim / Oct '93 / SRD.

Edwards, Wilfred 'Jackie'

20 SUPER HITS
CD _____ SONCD 0026
Sonic Sounds / Apr '92 / Jetstar.

Eek-A-Mouse

MOUSE-A-MANIA
CD _____ RASCD 30616
Ras / '88 / Jetstar / Greensleeves / SRD / Direct.

U-NEEK
CD _____ CIDM 1092
Island / Jul '93 / PolyGram.

WA DO DEM
Ganja smuggling / Long time ago / Operation eradication / There's a girl in my life / Slowly but surely / Wa-do-dem / Lonesome journey / I will never leave my love / Noahs ark / Too young to understand
CD _____ GRELCD 31
Greensleeves / May '87 / Total/BMG / Jetstar / SRD.

Eerk & Jerk

DEAD BROKE
CD _____ PCD 1409
Profile / Nov '91 / Pinnacle.

Eero Mieho

ATHANORA
CD _____ MELSKE 002CD
Melske / Dec '93.

Effigies

REMAINS NONVIEWABLE
CD _____ TG 135CD
Touch & Go / Oct '95 / SRD.

Fg & Alice

24 YEARS OF HUNGER
Rockets / In a cold way / Mystery man / I have seen myself / So high, so low / New year's eve / Indian / Doesn't mean that much to me / Crosstown / I.O.U. / I wish
CD _____ 903175388-2
WEA / Aug '91 / Warner Music.

TURN ME ON, I'M A ROCKET
CD _____ 0630132962
East West / Feb '96 / Warner Music.

Egan, Mark

MOSAIC
CD _____ EFA 034512
Wavetone / Nov '95 / SRD.

Egan, Seamus

TRADITIONAL MUSIC FROM IRELAND
CD _____ SHCD 34015
Shanachie / Dec '95 / Koch / ADA / Greensleeves.

WHEN JUNIPER'S SLEEP
CD _____ SHCD 79097
Shanachie / Jan '96 / Koch / ADA / Greensleeves.

Egan, Walter

HI FI
I can't wait / That's that / Little miss it's you / Man B. Goode / I do / Hi fi love / Hurt again / Drive away / Love at last / Like you do / You're the one / Bad news
CD _____ BTCD 979413
Bear Family / Jul '91 / Rollercoaster / Direct / CM / Swift / ADA.

Ege Bam Yasi

HOW TO BOIL AN EGG
CD _____ UGTCD 001
UGT / Oct '95 / Plastic Head.

Eggs

BRUISER
CD _____ TEENBEAT 76CD
Teenbeat / Sep '94 / SRD.

HOW DO YOU LIKE YOUR LOBSTER
CD _____ TB 156CD
Teenbeat / Jul '95 / SRD.

Egmose, Willy Trio

BARE DET SWINGER
CD _____ MECCACD 1046
Music Mecca / Nov '94 / Jazz Music / Cadillac / Wellard.

Egypt

PRESERVING THE DEAD
Baby, please don't go / Coal train union / Egypt / Khartoom / Legend of the light-house / Ecccentric man / Pearl of the orient / Lady luck
CD _____ HTDCD 21
HTD / May '94 / Pinnacle.

Ehrlich, Marty

CAN YOU HEAR A MOTION
Black hat / Welcome / Pictures in a glass house / North star / Ode to Charlie Parker / Reading the river / One for Robin / Comme il faut
CD _____ ENJ 80522
Enja / May '94 / New Note / Vital/SAM.

EMERGENCY PEACE (Ehrlich, Marty & The Dark Woods Emsemble)
Emergency peace / Dusk / Painter / Tucked sleave of a one-armed boy / Unison / Double dance / Circle the heart / Charlie in the Parker / Tribute
CD _____ 804092
New World / Jun '91 / Harmonia Mundi / ADA / Cadillac.

JUST BEFORE THE DAWN (Ehrlich, Marty & The Dark Woods Emsemble)
CD _____ 804742
New World / Aug '95 / Harmonia Mundi / ADA / Cadillac.

PLIANT PLIANT
CD _____ ENJA 5065-48
Enja / Jul '88 / New Note / Vital/SAM.

Ehrling, Thore

JAZZ HIGHLIGHTS
CD _____ DRCD 236
Dragon / Sep '87 / Roots / Cadillac / Wellard / CM / ADA.

SWEDISH SWING (1945 & 1947)
CD _____ ANCHA 9503
Ancha / Jun '95 / Jazz Music / Wellard / Cadillac.

Eide, Khalifa Ould

MOORISH MUSIC FROM MAURITANIA (Eide, Khalifa Ould & Dimi Mint Abba)
CD _____ WCD 019
World Circuit / Oct '90 / New Note / Direct / Cadillac / ADA.

Eightball & MJG

COMIN' OUT HARD
CD _____ RAP 60142
Rapture / Oct '94 / Plastic Head.

ON THE OUTSIDE
CD _____ RAP 60152
Rapture / Nov '94 / Plastic Head.

Eikas, Sigmund

JOLSTRING
CD _____ HCD 7101
Musikk Distribujson / Apr '95 / ADA.

Éinniú

EINNIÚ
CD _____ CICD 086
Clo Iar-Chonnachta / Dec '93 / CM.

Einstein

THEORY OF EMCEES SQUARED, THE
CD _____ STEIN 1 CD
Music Of Life / Jun '90 / Grapevine.

Einsturzende Neubauten

KOLLAPS
CD _____ EFA 2517CD
Zick Zack / Dec '88 / SRD.

MALADICTION
CD _____ BETON 206CD
Mute / Mar '93 / Disc.

STRATEGIES AGAINST ARCHITECTURE
CD _____ CDSTUMM 14
Mute / Apr '88 / Disc.

Eire Apparent

TABULA RASA
CD _____ BETON 106CD
Mute / Jan '93 / Disc.

SUNRISE
CD _____ NEXCD 199
Sequel / Feb '92 / BMG.

Eisenvater

EISENVATER 2
CD _____ WB 101-2
We Bite / Aug '93 / Plastic Head.

III
CD _____ WB 1132CD
We Bite / Jul '95 / Plastic Head.

Eitzel, Mark

SONGS OF LOVE
Firefly / Channel No. 5 / Western sky / Blue and grey shirt / Gary's song / Outside this bar / Room above the club / Last harbour / Kathleen / Crabwalk / Jenny / Take courage / Nothing can bring me down
CD _____ FIENDCD 213
Demon / Apr '91 / Pinnacle / ADA.

El Din, Hamza

ECLIPSE
CD _____ RCD 10103
Rykodisc / Nov '91 / Vital / ADA.

LILY OF THE NILE
CD _____ WLAAS 11CD
Waterlilly Acoustics / Nov '95 / ADA.

El Flaco

THUB
CD _____ SECTOR 210016
Sector 2 / Aug '95 / Direct / ADA.

El Gato's Rhythm...

STRICTLY DANCING: CHA CHA (El Gato's Rhythm Orchestra)
CD _____ 15336
Laserlight / May '94 / Target/BMG.

El Ghiwan, Nass

CHANSONS DE NASS EL GHIWAN
CD _____ 824672
Buda / Nov '90 / Discovery / ADA.

CHANTS GNAWA DU MAROC
CD _____ 824682
Buda / Nov '90 / Discovery / ADA.

El Gran Encuentro

DEL COMBO SHOW
El gran encuentro / Si mi merenguito canta / Talento de TV / Canto a la guira / Consejo a las casadas / Diez anos de amores / Marcela la peligrosa
CD _____ 66058074
RMM / Nov '95 / New Note.

El Masry, Hussein

ARABIAN EMOTIONS
CD _____ 12455
Laserlight / Jul '95 / Target/BMG.

ZAGAL
CD _____ AUB 006781
Auvidis/Ethnic / Aug '93 / Harmonia Mundi.

El Mondao

FLAMENCO NUEVO
CD _____ EUCD 1116
ARC / '91 / ARC Music / ADA.

FLAMENCO TOTAL
CD _____ EUCD 1089
ARC / '89 / ARC Music / ADA.

El Mubarak, Abdel Aziz

ABDEL AZIZ EL MUBARAK
Tahrimni minnak / Ahla eyyoun / Ah'laa jarah / Tariq ash-shoag / Bitgooli la
CD _____ CDORB 023
Globestyle / Jan '89 / Pinnacle.

El Nino De Almaden

GREAT SINGERS OF FLAMENCO VOL.1
CD _____ LDC 274 830
La Chant Du Monde / '88 / Harmonia Mundi / ADA.

El Rumbero

EL RUMBERO
CD _____ CDGRUB 23
Food For Thought / Sep '92 / Pinnacle.

El Sonido De La Ciudad

GRAND TANGO, THE
CD _____ MVCD 1079
CBC / Jul '95 / Kingdom.

El Tachuela, Rafa

GIPSY FLAMENCO GUITARRAS
CD _____ EUCD 1330
ARC / Nov '95 / ARC Music / ADA.

Elastic Purejoy

ELASTIC PUREJOY
If Samuel Beckett had met Lenny Bruce / Soul and fire / Unchain my sister / Element of doubt / Stiff / Suburban yoke / You are my perfect PFM / Claxton vs the Fourth Estate / Monkey bone-walker / Witness
CD _____ WDOM 010CD
World Domination / Jun '94 / Pinnacle.

Elastica

ELASTICA
Line up / Annie / Connection / Car song / Smile / Hold me now / S.O.F.T. / Indian / Blue / All-nighter / Waking up / Two to one / Vaseline / Never here / Stutter / Cleopatra (LP only)
CD _____ BLUFF 014CD
Deceptive / Mar '95 / Vital.

Elbert, Donnie

LITTLE PIECE OF LEATHER, A
Run little girl / Who's it gonna be / Little piece of leather / Memphis / Do whatcha wanna / Your red wagon / Down home blues / Never again / That funky ol' feeling / Lilly Lou
CD _____ TKOCD 021
TKO / Apr '92 / TKO.

Elders, Betty

CRAYONS
CD _____ FF 642CD
Flying Fish / Nov '95 / Roots / CM / Direct / ADA.

Eldridge, Roy

1935-1941
CD _____ CD 56066
Jazz Roots / Jul '95 / Target/BMG.

ARCADIA SHUFFLE
CD _____ 3801142
Jazz Archives / Feb '93 / Jazz Music / Discovery / Cadillac.

BIG SOUND OF LITTLE JAZZ
CD _____ TPZ 1021
Topaz Jazz / May '95 / Pinnacle / Cadillac.

CLASSICS 1935-40
CD _____ OJCCD 725
Original Jazz Classics / Dec '93 / Wellard / Jazz Music / Cadillac / Complete/Pinnacle.

FIESTA IN JAZZ
Sittin' in / Sittin' in no.2 / Stardust / Body & soul / 46 West 52 / 46 West 52 no.2 / Gasser / Jump through the wind / Minor jive / Don't be that way / I want to be happy / Fiesta in brass / Fiesta in brass (2) / St. Louis blues / I can't get started / After you've gone / Fish market / Twilight time
CD _____ LEJAZZCD 46
Le Jazz / Oct '95 / Charly / Cadillac.

FRENCHIE ROY
CD _____ VGCD 655009
Vogue / Jan '93 / BMG.

HECKLERS HOP
I hope Gabriel likes my music / Mutiny in the parlour / I'm gonna clap my hands / Swing is here / Wabash stomp / Florida stomp / Heckler's hop / Where the lazy river goes by / That thing / After you've gone / Sittin' in / Stardust / Body and soul / Forty six, west fifty two / It's my turn now / You're a lucky guy / Pluckin' the bass / I'm gettin' sentimental over you / High society / Muskrat ramble / Who told you I cared / Does your heart beat for me
CD _____ HEPCD 1030
Hep / Mar '91 / Cadillac / Jazz Music / New Note / Wellard.

LITTLE JAZZ (1950-60)
CD _____ CD 53178
Giants Of Jazz / May '95 / Target/BMG / Cadillac.

LITTLE JAZZ
CD _____ 158362
Jazz Archives / Jul '95 / Jazz Music / Discovery / Cadillac.

LIVE AT THE THREE DEUCES CLUB
CD _____ 3801242
Jazz Archives / Oct '92 / Jazz Music / Discovery / Cadillac.

LIVE IN 1959 (Eldridge, Roy & Coleman Hawkins)
CD _____ STCD 531
Stash / Feb '91 / Jazz Music / CM / Cadillac / Direct / ADA.

MONTREUX '77 (With Oscar Peterson, Niels Pederson & Bobby Durham)
Between the Devil and the deep blue sea / Go for / I surrender Dear / Joie De Roy / Perdido / Bye bye blackbird
CD _____ OJCCD 373
Original Jazz Classics / Apr '93 / Wellard / Jazz Music / Cadillac / Complete/Pinnacle.

NIFTY CAT, THE
Jolly Hollis / Cotton / 5400 North / Ball of
fire / Wineola / Nifty cat
CD _____ 803492
New World / Jan '96 / Harmonia Mundi /
ADA / Cadillac.

**ROY & DIZ (Eldridge, Roy & Dizzy
Gillespie)**
CD _____ 521647-2
Verve / Jul '94 / PolyGram.

ROY ELDRIDGE (1935-41)
CD _____ CD 14571
Jazz Portraits / May '95 / Jazz Music.

ROY ELDRIDGE - LIVE 1957
CD _____ EBCD 21072
Jazzband / Oct '91 / Jazz Music / Wellard.

ROY ELDRIDGE VOLUME 1: NUTS
It don't mean a thing if it ain't got that swing
/ Man I love / Wrap your troubles in dreams
(and dream your troubles away) (2 Takes) /
Ain't no flies on me / Undecided (4 takes) /
King David / Wild driver (2 takes) / If I had
you / Nuts / Easter parade (2 Takes) / Go-
liath bounce / Someone to watch over you
CD _____ 74321154682
Vogue / Oct '93 / BMG.

**ROY ELDRIDGE VOLUME 2: FRENCH
COOKING**
Une petite laitue / Tu disais qu'tu m'aimais
/ L'isle Adam / Black and blues / Baby don't
be like that / I remember Harlem / Fireworks
/ Wild man blues / Hollywood pastime /
Heat is on / I'd love him so / Oh shut up /
Boogie boy / Liszt blues / Just fooling
CD _____ 74321154692
Vogue / Oct '93 / BMG.

Eldritch

SEEDS OF RAGE
CD _____ IOMCD 002
Cyclops / Nov '95 / Pinnacle.

Electra, Carmen

CARMEN ELECTRA
Go go dancer / Good Judy girlfriend / Go
on (Witcha back self) / Step to the mic / S.T.
/ Fantasia erotica / Everybody get on up /
Segue / Fun / Just a little lovin' / Segue (2)
/ All that / Segue (3) / This is my house
CD _____ 759925338-2
Paisley Park / Apr '93 / Warner Music.

Electrafixion

BURNED
CD _____ 0630112482
East West / Sep '95 / Warner Music.

Electric Band

VOLTAGE
CD _____ 92624
Oberoi / May '94 / Jetstar.

Electric Boys

FREEWHEELIN'
CD _____ 521722-2
Polydor / Mar '94 / PolyGram.

Electric Family

MARIOPAINT
CD _____ 55IRDCOM 3CD
Irdial / Oct '95 / Disc.

Electric Flag

GROOVIN' IS EASY
Spotlight / I was robbed last night / I found
out / Never be lonely again / Losing game
/ My baby wants to test me / I should have
left her / You don't realise / Groovin' is easy
CD _____ CDTB 1.006
Thunderbolt / Nov '88 / Magnum Music
Group.

**OLD GLORY (The Best Of The Electric
Boys)**
Killing floor / Groovin' is easy / She should
have just / Goin' down slow / Texas / Sittin'
in circles / You don't realize / Movie music
/ Improvisation / Another country / Easy
rider / Soul searchin' / See to your neighbor
/ With time there is change / Nothing to do
/ Hey little girl / Drinkin' wine / Night time is
the right time
CD _____ CK 57629
Columbia / Jul '95 / Sony.

Electric Hellfire Club

BURN, BABY, BURN
CD _____ CLEO 72692
Cleopatra / Mar '94 / Disc.

KISS THE GOAT
CD _____ CLEO 95502
Cleopatra / Aug '95 / Disc.

Electric Kings

NOT FOR SALE
CD _____ MWCD 2017
Music & Words / Dec '95 / ADA / Direct.

Electric Love Hogs

ELECTRIC LOVE HOGS
CD _____ 8283052
London / Jul '93 / PolyGram.

Electric Skychurch

KNOWONENESS
CD _____ MM 800322
Moonshine / Feb '96 / Disc.

Electric Wizard

ELECTRIC WIZARD
CD _____ RISE 009CD
Rise Above / Jan '96 / Vital / Plastic Head.

Electro Assassin

BIOCULTURE
CD _____ HY 39100692
Hyperium / Nov '93 / Plastic Head.

Electrocution

INSIDE THE UNREAL
CD _____ BABECD 6
Rosemary's Baby / Sep '93 / Plastic
Head.

Electroids

ELEKTRO WORLD
CD _____ WARPCD 35
Warp / Aug '95 / Disc.

Electronic

ELECTRONIC
CD _____ CDPRG 1012
EMI / Feb '94 / EMI.

Electronic Eye

IDEA OF JUSTICE, THE
CD _____ RBADCD 14
Beyond / Oct '95 / Kudos / Pinnacle.

Elektraws

SHOCK ROCK
CD _____ NERCD 083
Nervous / Jan '96 / Nervous / Magnum
Music Group.

Elektric Music

ESPERANTO
TV / Showbusiness / Kissing the machine /
Lifestyle / Crosstalk / Information / Espe-
ranto / Overdrive
CD _____ 450992999-2
East West / Jun '93 / Warner Music.

Elementales

AL BANO MARIA
CD _____ 21060CD
Sonifolk / Apr '95 / ADA / CM.

ELEMENTALES
CD _____ J 1030CD
Sonifolk / Jun '94 / ADA / CM.

Elements

FAR EAST
CD _____ LIP 890162
Lipstick / Feb '95 / Vital/SAM.

FAR EAST VOL.2
CD _____ EFA 034522
Wavetone / Nov '95 / SRD.

Elend

LECONS DE TENEBRES
CD _____ HOLY 8CD
Holy / Nov '94 / Plastic Head.

Elephant

ELEPHANT
CD _____ HB016-2
Heatblast / Feb '94 / SRD.

Elevate

BRONZEE
CD _____ FLOWCD 001
Flower Shop / Oct '94 / SRD.

Elevated

CYBER HUM
CD _____ CARTE 40627
Scratch / Nov '94 / BMG.

Eleven Years From...

**ELEVEN YEARS FROM YESTERDAY
(Eleven Years From Yesterday)**
CD _____ BEADCD 1
Bead / May '90 / Cadillac.

Eleventh Dream Day

EL MOODIO
Makin' like a rug / Figure it out / After this
time is gone / Murder / Honeyslide / That's
the point / Motherland / Raft / Bend bridge
/ Rubber band

CD _____ 756782480-2
East West / Mar '93 / Warner Music.

LIVED TO TELL
Rose of jericho / Dream of a sleeping sheep
/ I could be lost / It's not my world / You
know what it is / Frozen mile / Strung up
and/or out / North of wasteland / It's all a
game / Trouble / There's this thing / Dae-
dalus / Angels spread your wings
CD _____ 7567821792
East West / Jun '91 / Warner Music.

PRAIRIE SCHOOL FREAKOUT
CD _____ 422128
New Rose / May '94 / Direct / ADA.

URSA MAJOR
CD _____ EFA 049432
City Slang / Jan '95 / Disc.

Elf

ELF ALBUMS, THE
Carolina county ball / LA 59 / Ain't it all
amusing / Happy / Annie New Orleans /
Rockin' chair rock'n'roll blues / Rainbow /
Do the same thing / Blanche / Black
swampy water / Prentice wood / When she
smiles / Good time music / Liberty road /
Shotgun boogie / Wonderworld / Street
walker
CD _____ VSOPCD 167
Connoisseur / Sep '91 / Pinnacle.

GARGANTUAN ELF ALBUM, THE
CD _____ LONGCD 78
Safari / May '87 / Pinnacle.

Elfish Echo

MULTIPLE VOID ENJOYMENT
Deviation man / Itsuka / Kitchen window /
Dandelion lodge / Omoi Kokora / Denia /
Mangetsu / Some time on a train / Aya-she
CD _____ CD 941018
Source / Jun '95 / Vital.

Elgart, Charlie

BALANCE
On the breeze of a shadow / My sentiments
exactly / Balance / Bryanna / Sight unseen
/ Goodbye my friend / Sundance
CD _____ PD 83068
Novus / Dec '89 / BMG.

SIGNS OF LIFE
Float / Sojourn / This thing we share / Signs
of life / I cry for you / When I'm with Stu /
Summer dusk
CD _____ PD 83045
RCA / Mar '89 / BMG.

Elgart, Larry

**SENSATIONAL SWING (Six Medleys Of
Timeless Swing Favourites) (Elgart,
Larry & His Manhattan Swing Orchestra)**
Switched on swing / Switched on big bands
/ Switched on a star / Switched on Astaire
/ Switched on the blues / Switched on
Broadway
CD _____ ECD 3042
K-Tel / Jan '95 / K-Tel.

Elgart, Les

BEST OF THE BIG BANDS
CD _____ 4716552
Sony Jazz / Jan '95 / Sony.

Elias, Elaine

BEST OF ELAINE ELIAS
Choro / Cross current / Through the fire /
Illusions / Moments / Beautiful love / One
sid of you / Falling in love with love / Logo
motif / When you wish upon a star / Coming
and going / Chan's song
CD _____ DC 8592
Denon / Jun '95 / Conifer.

CROSS CURRENTS
Hallucinations / Cross currents / Beautiful
love / Campari and soda / One side of you
/ Another side of you / Peggy's blue skylight
/ Impulsive / When you wish upon a star /
East coasting / Coming and going
CD _____ CY 2180
Denon / '88 / Conifer.

ILLUSIONS
Choro / Through the fire / Illusions / Mo-
ments / Falling in love with love / Iberia /
Loco motif / Sweet Georgie Fame / Chan's
song
CD _____ CY 1569
Denon / Jan '89 / Conifer.

LONG STORY, A
Back it time / Long story / Horizonte / Just
kidding / Avida continua (life goes on) / Nile
/ Get it / Just for you / Karamura / Let me
go (vida real)
CD _____ CDP 7954762
Blue Note / Oct '91 / EMI.

SOLO'S & DUETS
Autumn leaves / Masquerade is over / In-
terlude / Way you look tonight / All the
things you are / Joy spring / Have you met
Miss Jones / Just enough / Messages /
Messages part 2 / Messages part 3 / Mes-
sages part 4 / Asa branca
CD _____ CDP 8320732
Blue Note / Oct '95 / EMI.

Elias Hulk

UNCHAINED
Anthology of dreams / Nightmare / Been
around too long / Yesterday's trip / We can
fly / Free / Delhi blues / Ain't got you
CD _____ SEECD 286
See For Miles/C5 / Jan '90 / Pinnacle.

Elite Syncopators

RAGTIME SPECIAL
CD _____ SOSCD 1286
Stomp Off / Mar '95 / Jazz Music /
Wellard.

Elkanger Bjorsvik...

**VIKINGS, THE (Elkanger Bjorsvik
Musikklag)**
CD _____ DOYCD 023
Doyen / Feb '93 / Conifer.

Elkin, A.P.

ARNHEM LAND
CD _____ LARRCD 288
Larrikin / Jun '94 / Roots / Direct / ADA /
CM.

Elkins-Payne Jubilee...

**ELKINS-PAYNE JUBILEE SINGERS
(1923-1929) (Elkins-Payne Jubilee
Singers)**
CD _____ DOCD 5356
Blues Document / Jun '95 / Swift / Jazz
Music / Hot Shot.

Ellefson, Art

AS IF TO SAY
CD _____ SKCD 2-2030
Sackville / Jun '93 / Swift / Jazz Music /
Jazz Horizons / Cadillac / CM.

Elles

AALLE KREKAJENTE
CD _____ ELLES 9401CD
Musikk Distribujson / Dec '94 / ADA.

Elling, Kurt

CLOSE YOUR EYES
Close your eyes / Dolores dream / Ballad of
the sad young men / (Hide the) Salome /
Married blues / Storyteller experiencing total confusion / Never say goodbye (for Jod)
/ Thos clouds are heavy you dig / Wait till
you see her / Hurricane / Now is the time
that the Gods came walking out / Never
never land / Never never land improvisational poem / Remembering Veronica
Blue Note / Jun '95 / EMI.

Ellington, Duke

16 MOST REQUESTED SONGS
It don't mean a thing if it ain't got that swing
/ In a sentimental mood / Solitude / Caravan
/ I let a song go out of my heart / Do nothin'
'til you hear from me / Don't get around
much anymore / Sophisticated lady / I got
it bad and that ain't good / Perdido / In a
mellow tone / Mood indigo / Prelude to a
kiss / Satin doll / I'm beginning to see the
light / Take the 'A' train
CD _____ 476719-2
Columbia / Aug '94 / Sony.

1927-41 (Ellington, Duke Orchestra)
East St. Louis toodle-oo / Blues I love to
sing / Black and tan fantasy / Washington
wobble / Creole love call / Black beauty /
Mooche / Misty mornin' / Hot and bothered
/ Jubilee stomp / Take it easy / Cotton club
stomp / Tiger rag / Ring dem bells / Old
man blues / Mood indigo / Dicty glide / Doing the voom voom / Hop head / Wall Street
wail / Saratoga swing / Echoes of the jungle
/ Rockin' in rhythm / Take the 'A' Train /
Don't get around much anymore / Cotton
tail / I got it bad and that ain't good / Conga
brava / Do nothin' 'til you hear from me /
Portrait of Bert Williams / Warm valley / Solitude / Country gal / Prelude to a kiss / I let
a song go out of my heart / Diminuedno in
blue / Crescendo in blue / Echoes of Harlem
/ Caravan / Clarinet lament / Merry go round
/ In a sentimental mood / Live and love to-
night / Sophisticated lady / Harlem speaks
/ Slippery horn / In a mellow tone / Koko /
Jack the bear / Harlem air shaft / Just a
sittin' and a rockin' / Sepia panorama /
Jumpin' punkins / Mr. J.B. blues / Body and
soul / Bojangles / Sidewalks of New York /
Pitter panther patter / Across the track
blues / Plucked again / Blues / Chloe / C
Blues / Weely / Junior hop / Dusk / Blue
Serge / Morning glory
CD Set _____ CDB 1201
Giants Of Jazz / '92 / Target/BMG /
Cadillac.

1931-1932 (Ellington, Duke Orchestra)
CD _____ GOJCD 53046
Giants Of Jazz / Mar '90 / Target/BMG /
Cadillac.

1952 SEATTLE CONCERT, THE
Skin deep / How could you do a thing like
that to me / Sophisticated lady / Perfido /
Caravan / Harlem suite / Hawk talks / Don't

get around much anymore / In a sentimental mood / Mood indigo / I'm beginning to see the light / Prelude to a kiss / It don't mean a thing if it ain't got that swing / Solitude / Let a song go out of my heart / Jam with Sam
CD _____ 7863665312
Bluebird / Apr '95 / BMG.

1954 LOS ANGELES CONCERT
CD _____ GNPD 9049
GNP Crescendo / May '89 / Silva Screen.

20 JAZZ CLASSICS
Thing's ain't what they used to be / Satin doll / Flamingo / Liza / In a sentimental mood / My old flame / If I give my heart to you / Caravan / Star dust / Harlem air shaft / Band call / Bakiff / In the mood / One-o'clock jump / Flying home / Warm valley / C jam blues / Black and tan fantasy / Reflections in D / Rockin' in rhythm
CD _____ CDMFP 6161
Music For Pleasure / May '95 / EMI.

22 ORIGINAL BIG BAND RECORDINGS
CD _____ HCD 410
Hindsight / Sep '92 / Target/BMG / Jazz Music.

70TH BIRTHDAY CONCERT (2CD Set)
Rockin' in rhythm / B.P. / Take the 'A' train / Tootie for Cootie / 4.30 blues / El Gato / Black butterfly / Things ain't what they used to be / Laying on mellow / Satin doll / Azure / In triplicate / Perdido / Fifi / Prelude to a kiss/I'm just a lucky so and so / I let a song go out of my heart (medley with Do nothin' til you hear from me & Just squeeze me (but don't tease me)) / Prelude to a kiss / I'm just a lucky so and so / Do nothin' til you hear from me / Just squeeze me / Don't get around much anymore / Mood indigo / Sophisticated lady / Caravan / Black swan / Final Ellington speech
CD Set _____ CDP 8327462
Blue Note / Sep '95 / EMI.

AFRO-EURASIAN ECLIPSE, THE
CD _____ OJCD 645
Original Jazz Classics / Mar '93 / Wellard / Jazz Music / Cadillac / Complete/Pinnacle.

ALL AMERICAN JAZZ
CD _____ 4691382
Sony Jazz / Jan '95 / Sony.

ANATOMY OF A MURDER
CD _____ 4691372
Sony Jazz / Jan '95 / Sony.

APRIL IN PARIS (Ellington, Duke Orchestra)
Rockin' in rhythm / Four-thirty blues / Take the 'A' train / Jam with Paul / Satin doll / April in Paris / El gato / Don't get around much anymore / Caravan / Mood indigo / Passion flower / Jive stomp / Diminuendo and crescendo in blue
CD _____ WW 2406
West Wind / Jul '93 / Swift / Charly / CM / ADA.

AT NEWPORT (Ellington, Duke & Buck Clayton)
Take the 'A' train / Sophisticated lady / I got it bad and that ain't good / Skin deep / You can depend on me / Newport jump / In a mellow tone
CD _____ 477320 2
Columbia / Nov '94 / Sony.

AT THE COTTON CLUB
CD _____ CDSH 2029
Derann Trax / Aug '91 / Pinnacle.

AT THE GREEK 1966 (Ellington, Duke & Ella Fitzgerald)
CD _____ DSTS 1013
Status / '94 / Jazz Music / Wellard / Harmonia Mundi.

BACK TO BACK (Ellington, Duke & Johnny Hodges)
Weary blues / St. Louis blues / Loveless love / Royal Garden blues / Wabash blues / Basin Street blues / Beale Street blues
CD _____ 823 637-2
Verve / '88 / PolyGram.

BEST OF DUKE ELLINGTON
CD _____ DLCD 4009
Dixie Live / Mar '95 / Magnum Music Group.

BEST OF DUKE ELLINGTON, THE
Satin doll / Warm valley / Flamingo / Just a sittin' and a rockin' / Black and tan fantasy / Things ain't what they used to be / Happy go lucky local / Rockin' and rhymin' / C jam blues / Bakiff / Harlem air shaft / Serious serenade / It don't mean a thing if it ain't got that swing
CD _____ CDP 8315012
Capitol Jazz / Apr '95 / EMI.

BEST OF EARLY ELLINGTON, THE
East St. Louis toodle-o / Birmingham breakdown / Black and tan fantasy / Take it easy / Jubilee stomp / Black beauty / Yellow dog blues / Tishomingo blues / Awful sad / Mooche / Doin' the voom voom / Rent party blues / Harlem flat blues / Jolly wog / Jazz convulsions / Sweet Mama / Cotton club stomp (take B) / Mood indigo / Rockin' in rhythm / Creole rhapsody parts 1 and 2
CD _____ GRP 16602

American Decca / Feb '96 / BMG / New Note.

BEST OF THE FORTIES VOL.1 1940-42
CD _____ BMCD 3019
Blue Moon / Sep '95 / Magnum Music Group / Greensleeves / Hot Shot / ADA / Cadillac / Discovery.

BLACK, BROWN & BEIGE
CD _____ ND 86641
Bluebird / Oct '95 / BMG.

BLACK, BROWN AND BEIGE
Part I / Part II / Part III / Part IV (Come Sunday) / Part V (Come Sunday interlude) / Part VI (23rd psalm)
CD _____ CK 64274
Columbia / Nov '95 / Sony.

BLANTON-WEBSTER YEARS, THE
You, you darlin' / Jack the bear / Koko / Morning glory / So far, so good / Conga brava / Do nothin' 'til you hear from me / Me and you / Cotton tail / Never no lament / Dusk / Bojangles / Portrait of Bert Williams / Blue goose / Harlem air shaft / At a Dixie roadside diner / All too soon / Rumpus in Richmond / My greatest mistake / Sepia panorama / There shall be no night / In a mellow tone / Five o'clock whistle / Warm valley / Flaming sword / Jumpin' punkins / Across the track blues / John Hardy's wife / Blue Serge / After all / Chloe / Bakiff / Are you sticking / I never felt this way before / Just a sittin' and a rockin' / Giddybug gallop / Sidewalks of New York / Chocolate shake / Flamingo / I got it bad and that ain't good / Clementine / Brown skin gal / Girl in my dreams tries to look like you / Jump for joy / Moon over Cuba / Take the 'A' train / Five o'clock drag / Rocks in my bed / Blip blip / Chelsea Bridge / Raincheck / What good would it do / I don't know what kind of blues I got / Perdido / C jam blues / Moon mist / What am I here for / I don't mind / Someone / My little brown book / Main stem / Johnny come lately / Hayfoot strawfoot / Sentimental lady / Slip of the lip (can sink a ship) / Sherman shuffle
CD Set _____ 7432113181-2
Bluebird / Mar '93 / BMG.

BLUE FEELING
Black and tan fantasy / Creole love call / Harlem twist / Black Beauty / Swampy river / Cotton club stomp / Shout 'em Aunt Tillie / Ring dem bells / Echoes of the jungle / Blue Harlem / Drop me off at Harlem / Bundle of blues / Harlem speaks / Hyde Park / Blue feeling / Merry go round / Clarinet lament / I'm slapping Seventh Avenue with the sole of my shoe / Riding on a blue note / I let a song go out of my heart / Blue light / Koko / Conga Brava / Jack the Bear
CD _____ PPCD 78103
Past Perfect / Feb '95 / THE.

BLUES IN ORBIT
Blues in orbit / Track 360 / Villes ville is the place, man / Brown penny / Three J's blues / Smada / Pie eye's blues / C jam blues / Sweet and pungent / In a mellow tone / Swingers get the blues too / Singer's jump
CD _____ 4608232
Sony Jazz / Jan '95 / Sony.

BRUNSWICK SESSIONS VOL.1 (1932-35)
CD _____ RBD 3001
Mr. R&B / Oct '91 / Swift / CM / Wellard.

BRUNSWICK SESSIONS VOL.2 (Ellington, Duke Orchestra)
Clouds in my heart / Blue mood / Ducky wucky / Jazz cocktail / Raisin' the rent / Happy as the day is long / Drop me off in Harlem / Blackbirds medley / Swing low, sweet chariot
CD _____ RBD 3002
Mr. R&B / Oct '91 / Swift / CM / Wellard.

CARNEGIE HALL 1948 (Ellington, Duke Orchestra)
CD Set _____ VJC 1024/25-2
Vintage Jazz Classics / '91 / Direct / ADA / CM / Cadillac.

CHEEK TO CHEEK 1935
CD _____ PHONTCD 7657
Phontastic / Apr '94 / Wellard / Jazz Music / Cadillac.

CLASSICS 1927-1928
CD _____ CLASSICS 542
Classics / Dec '90 / Discovery / Jazz Music.

CLASSICS 1930
CD _____ CLASSICS 586
Classics / Aug '91 / Discovery / Jazz Music.

CLASSICS 1930-31 (Ellington, Duke Orchestra)
CD _____ CLASSICS 605
Classics / Oct '92 / Discovery / Jazz Music.

CLASSICS 1931-32 (Ellington, Duke Orchestra)
CD _____ CLASSICS 616
Classics / '92 / Discovery / Jazz Music.

CLASSICS 1932-33 (Ellington, Duke Orchestra)
CD _____ CLASSICS 626
Classics / '92 / Discovery / Jazz Music.

CLASSICS 1936-37
CD _____ CLASSICS 666
Classics / Nov '92 / Discovery / Jazz Music.

CLASSICS 1937 VOL.2 (Ellington, Duke Orchestra)
CD _____ CLASSICS 687
Classics / Mar '93 / Discovery / Jazz Music.

CLASSICS 1938 (Ellington, Duke Orchestra)
CD _____ CLASSICS 700
Classics / Jul '93 / Discovery / Jazz Music.

CLASSICS 1938 VOL. 2
CD _____ CLASSICS 717
Classics / Jul '93 / Discovery / Jazz Music.

CLASSICS 1938-1939
CD _____ CLASSICS 747
Classics / Aug '94 / Discovery / Jazz Music.

CLASSICS 1939
CD _____ CLASSICS 765
Classics / Aug '94 / Discovery / Jazz Music.

CLASSICS 1939 VOL. 2
CD _____ CLASSICS 780
Classics / Nov '94 / Discovery / Jazz Music.

CLASSICS 1939-40
CD _____ CLASSICS 790
Classics / Jan '95 / Discovery / Jazz Music.

CLASSICS 1940
CD _____ CLASSICS 805
Classics / Mar '95 / Discovery / Jazz Music.

CLASSICS 1940 VOL. 2
CD _____ CLASSICS 820
Classics / Jul '95 / Discovery / Jazz Music.

CLASSICS 1940-41
CD _____ CLASSICS 837
Classics / Sep '95 / Discovery / Jazz Music.

COLLECTION, THE
CD _____ HBCD 501
Hindsight / Sep '92 / Target/BMG / Jazz Music.

CONNECTICUT JAZZ FESTIVAL
CD _____ IAJRCD 1005
IAJRC / Jun '94 / Jazz Music.

COOL ROCK (Ellington, Duke Orchestra)
CD _____ 15782
Laserlight / Aug '92 / Target/BMG / Cadillac.

COSMIC SCENE, THE
CD _____ 4720832
Sony Jazz / Jan '95 / Sony.

COTTON CLUB 1938 VOL. 1
CD _____ 3801102
Jazz Archives / Jun '92 / Jazz Music / Discovery / Cadillac.

COTTON CLUB 1938 VOL. 2
CD _____ 3801102
Jazz Archives / Feb '93 / Jazz Music / Discovery / Cadillac.

COTTON CLUB DAYS - LEGENDARY LIVE BROADCASTS
CD _____ JZCD 335
Suisa / Jan '93 / Jazz Music / THE.

COTTON CLUB STOMP (Ellington, Duke Orchestra)
CD _____ CD 14544
Jazz Portraits / Jan '94 / Jazz Music.

COTTON CLUB STOMP 1927-1931
CD _____ CD 56051
Jazz Roots / Mar '95 / Target/BMG.

COUNT MEETS THE DUKE, THE (Ellington, Duke Orchestra & Count Basie Orchestra)
CD _____ 4505092
Sony Jazz / Jan '95 / Sony.

CRYSTAL BALLROOM, FARGO VOL.2
CD _____ TAXCD 3721
Tax / Mar '94 / Jazz Music / Wellard / Cadillac.

DRUM IS A WOMAN, A
CD _____ 4713202
Sony Jazz / Jan '95 / Sony.

DUKE (The RCA Jazz Collection)
CD Set _____ 74321244612
RCA / Dec '94 / BMG.

DUKE ELLINGTON (2CD Set)
CD Set _____ R2CD 4019
Deja Vu / Jan '96 / THE.

DUKE ELLINGTON & HIS GREAT VOCALISTS
It don't mean a thing if it ain't got that swing / St. Louis blues / I can't give you anything but love / Diga diga doo / I must have that man / Solitude / Woman'll get you / Don't get around much anymore / Love you madly / On a turquoise cloud / Love you madly / Take the 'A' train / Sophisticated lady / Autumn leaves / Love (my everything)
CD _____ CK 66372
Columbia / Jul '95 / Sony.

DUKE ELLINGTON & HIS ORCHESTRA (1927-31) (Ellington, Duke Orchestra)
CD _____ GOJCD 53030
Giants Of Jazz / Aug '88 / Target/BMG / Cadillac.

DUKE ELLINGTON & HIS ORCHESTRA 1963
CD _____ CD 14564
Jazz Portraits / May '95 / Jazz Music.

DUKE ELLINGTON (1927-34)
Creole love call / Black beauty / Got everything but you / Duke steps out / Jungle nights in Harlem / Blue feeling
CD _____ HRM 6001
Hermes / Jan '89 / Nimbus.

DUKE ELLINGTON (1941)
CD _____ UCD 19003
Forlane / Jul '88 / Target/BMG.

DUKE ELLINGTON AND HIS ORCHESTRA 1941-51 (Ellington, Duke Orchestra)
CD _____ GOJCD 53057
Giants Of Jazz / Mar '92 / Target/BMG / Cadillac.

DUKE ELLINGTON AND HIS ORCHESTRA, 1930, VOL. 2 (Ellington, Duke Orchestra)
CD _____ CD 596
Classic Jazz Masters / Sep '91 / Wellard / Jazz Music / Jazz Music.

DUKE ELLINGTON AND JOHN COLTRANE (Ellington, Duke & John Coltrane)
In a sentimental mood / Take the Coltrane / Big Nick / Stevie / My little brown book / Angelica / Feeling of jazz
CD _____ IMP 11662
Impulse Jazz / Oct '95 / BMG / New Note.

DUKE ELLINGTON AND THE SMALL GROUPS (1936-50)
CD _____ CD 53070
Giants Of Jazz / May '92 / Target/BMG / Cadillac.

DUKE ELLINGTON COLLECTORS' EDITION
CD _____ DVX 08042
Deja Vu / Apr '95 / THE.

DUKE ELLINGTON GOLD (2CD Set)
CD _____ D2CD 4019
Deja Vu / Jun '95 / THE.

DUKE ELLINGTON IN CONCERT
CD Set _____ RTE 15032
RTE / Apr '95 / ADA / Koch.

DUKE ELLINGTON LIVE AT MONTEREY 1960 (The Unheard Recordings Part 1) (Ellington, Duke Orchestra)
Deep river/Take the 'A' train / Perdido / Overture: Nutcracker suite / Half the fun / Jeep's blues / Newport up / Sophisticated lady / Suite Thursday / Dance of the floreadores / Diminuendo in blue / Blow by blow
CD _____ DSTS 1008
Status / May '95 / Jazz Music / Wellard / Harmonia Mundi.

DUKE ELLINGTON LIVE AT MONTEREY 1960 (The Unheard Recordings Part 2) (Ellington, Duke Orchestra/Cannonball Adderley Quintet)
Big P / Blue Daniel / Chant / Old country / Dis here / Sunny side of the street / Goin' to Chicago / Sent for you yesterday / You can't run around / Red carpet
CD _____ DSTS 1009
Status / May '95 / Jazz Music / Wellard / Harmonia Mundi.

DUKE ELLINGTON VOL. 1 - 1927-31
CD _____ KJ 144FS
King Jazz / Oct '93 / Jazz Music / Cadillac / Discovery.

DUKE ELLINGTON VOL. 2 - 1931-38
CD _____ KJ 145FS
King Jazz / Oct '93 / Jazz Music / Cadillac / Discovery.

DUKE ELLINGTON VOL. 7 - WALL STREET WAIL 1929
CD _____ 152232
Hot 'n' Sweet / Dec '93 / Discovery.

DUKE ELLINGTON VOL. 8 - JUNGLE BLUES 1929-30
CD _____ 152242
Hot 'n' Sweet / Dec '93 / Discovery.

DUKE PLAYS ELLINGTON
CD _____ TPZ 1020
Topaz Jazz / May '95 / Pinnacle / Cadillac.

DUKE'S BIG FOUR (Ellington, Duke Quartet)
Cotton tail / Blues / Hawk talks / Prelude to a kiss / Love you madly / Just squeeze me / Everything but you
CD _____ CD 2310703
Pablo / Nov '95 / Jazz Music / Cadillac / Complete/Pinnacle.

DUKE'S MEN: SMALL GROUPS #1 (2CD Set)
CD _____ 4666182
Columbia / May '93 / Sony.

DUKE'S MEN: SMALL GROUPS #2 (2CD Set)
Jeep's blues / If you were in my place / I let a song go out of my heart / Rendezvous with rhythm / Lesson in C / Swingtime in Honolulu / Carnival in Caroline / Ol' man river / You walked out of the picture / Pyramid / Empty ballroom blues / Lost in meditation / Blue serenade / Love in swingtime / Swinging in the dell / Jitterbug's lullaby / Chasin' chippies / Blue in the evening / Sharpie / Swing Pan Alley / Prelude to a kiss / There's something about love
CD Set _____ 472994 2
Columbia / May '93 / Sony.

DUKE, FARGO 1940 VOL.1 , THE
CD _____ TAX 37202
Tax / Aug '94 / Jazz Music / Wellard / Cadillac.

DUKE, FARGO 1940 VOL.2 , THE
CD _____ TAX 37212
Tax / Aug '94 / Jazz Music / Wellard / Cadillac.

EARLY ELLINGTON
Black and tan fantasy / Creole love call / East St. Louis toodle-oo / Black beauty / Mooche / Flaming youth / Ring dem bells / Old man blues / Mood indigo / Rockin' in rhythm / Creole rhapsody / Creole rhapsody (part 2) / Echoes of the jungle / Daybreak express / Stompy Jones / Solitude
CD _____ ND 86852
Bluebird / Jul '89 / BMG.

ELLINGTON '56
East St. Louis toodle-oo / Creole love call / Stompy Jones / Jeep is jumpin' / Jack the bear / In a mellow tone / Koko / Midriff / Stomp, look and listen / Unbooted character / Lonesome lullaby / Upper Manhattan medical group / Cotton tail / Daydream / Deep purple / Indian Summer / Laura / Blues
CD _____ LEJAZZCD 17
Le Jazz / Aug '94 / Charly / Cadillac.

ELLINGTON AT NEWPORT (Ellington, Duke Orchestra)
CD _____ 4509862
Sony Jazz / Jan '95 / Sony.

ELLINGTON INDIGOS
CD _____ 4633422
Sony Jazz / Jan '95 / Sony.

ELLINGTON MEETS HAWKINS (Ellington, Duke & Coleman Hawkins)
Limbo jazz / Mood indigo / Ray Charles' place / Wanderlust / You dirty dog / Self portrait (of the bean) / Jeep is jumpin' / Ricitic / Solitude
CD _____ IMP 11622
Impulse Jazz / Oct '95 / BMG / New Note.

ELLINGTON SUITES, THE
Queen's suite (Sunset and the mockingbird/ Lightning bugs and frogs/Le sucrier velours/Northern lights/Single petal of a rose/ Apes and peacocks) / Goutelas suite (Fanfare/Goutelas/Get with it ness/Something/ Having at it) / Uwis suite (Uwis/Klop/Loco madi)
CD _____ OJCCD 446
Original Jazz Classics / Feb '92 / Wellard / Jazz Music / Cadillac / Complete/Pinnacle.

ESSENTIAL DUKE ELLINGTON, THE (4 CD Box Set)
CD _____ CDDIG 13
Charly / Apr '95 / Charly / THE / Cadillac.

ESSENTIAL DUKE ELLINGTON/COUNT BASIE (Ellington, Duke & Count Basie)
CD _____ 4737532
Sony Jazz / Jan '95 / Sony.

ESSENTIAL RECORDINGS, THE
CD _____ LEJAZZCD 2
Le Jazz / Mar '93 / Charly / Cadillac.

ESSENTIAL V-DISCS, THE
CD _____ JZ-CD301
Suisa / Feb '91 / Jazz Music / THE.

ETERNAL DUKE ELLINGTON
CD _____ PHONTCD 7666
Phontastic / Apr '94 / Wellard / Jazz Music / Cadillac.

FAR EAST SUITE - SPECIAL MIX, THE
Tourist point of view / Bluebird of Delhi / Ifashan / Depk / Mount Harissa / Blue pepper (Far East of the blues) / Agra / Amad / Ad lib on Nippon / Tourist point of view (Alt. Take) / Bluebird of Delhi (Alt. Take) / Isfahan (alt. take) / Amad (Alt. take)
CD _____ 7863665512
Bluebird / Jun '95 / BMG.

FAR EAST SUITE, THE
Tourist point of view / Bluebird of Delhi / Isfahan / Depk / Mount Harissa / Blue pep-

---

per (far east of the blues) / Agra / Amad / Ad lib on Nippon
CD _____ ND 87640
Bluebird / Nov '88 / BMG.

FARGO, NORTH DAKOTA 1940 (Ellington, Duke Orchestra)
CD Set _____ VJC 1019/20 2
Vintage Jazz Classics / Oct '91 / Direct / ADA / CM / Cadillac.

FEELING OF JAZZ, THE
CD _____ BLCD 760123
Black Lion / Feb '89 / Jazz Music / Cadillac / Wellard / Koch.

FESTIVAL SESSION (Ellington, Duke Orchestra)
Idiom '59 (parts 1-3) / Things ain't what they used to be / Launching pad / Perdido / Cop out extension / Duael fuel (parts 1-3)
CD _____ 4684022
Sony Jazz / Jan '95 / Sony.

FOUR SYMPHONIC WORKS BY DUKE ELLINGTON
Harlem / Three black kings / New world a comin' / Black, brown and beige
CD _____ MMD 60176L
Denon / '89 / Conifer.

GENEROSITY OF MOOD, A
Mood Indigo / It don't mean a thing if it ain't got that swing / East St. Louis toodle-oo / Black and tan fantasy / Rockin' in rhythm / Mooche / Solitude / Caravan / Wall Street wail / When your smiling / Cotton Club Stomp / Running wild / Wang wang blues / Twelfth street rag / Creole rhapsody / I like the religion / Hot and bothered / Old man blues / Ring dem bells
CD _____ PAR 2036
Parade / Oct '94 / Koch / Cadillac.

GIRL'S SUITE & THE PERFUME SUITE, THE
CD _____ 4691392
Sony Jazz / Jan '95 / Sony.

GITANES - JAZZ 'ROUND MIDNIGHT (Ellington, Duke & Billy Strayhorn)
CD _____ 5107072
Polydor / Oct '91 / PolyGram.

GREAT ELLINGTON UNITS, THE
Daydream / Good Queen Bess / That's the blues, old man / Junior hop / Without a song / My Sunday gal / Mobile bay / Linger awhile / Charlie the chulo / Lament for Javanette / Lull at dawn / Ready Eddy / Some Saturday / Subtle slough / Menelik, the lion of Judah / Poor bubber / Squatty roo / Passion flower / Things ain't what they used to be / Good queen bess / Brown suede / C jam blues
CD _____ ND 86751
Bluebird / Nov '88 / BMG.

GREAT LONDON CONCERTS, THE
CD _____ 518446-2
Limelight / Jan '94 / PolyGram.

GREAT PARIS CONCERT, THE
Kinda dukish / Rockin' in rhythm / On the sunny side of the street / Star crossed lovers / All of me / Asphalt jungle / Do nothin' 'til you hear from me / Tutti for cootie / Suite Thursday / Perdido / Eighth veil / Rose of the Rio Grande / Cop out / Bula / Jam with Sam / Happy go lucky local / Tone parallel to Harlem / Don't get around much anymore / Black and tan fantasy / Creole love call / Mooch / Things ain't what they used to be / Pyramid / Blues (from black brown and beige) / Echoes of Harlem / Satin doll
CD _____ 7567813032
Atlantic / Feb '92 / Warner Music.

GREAT TIMES (Ellington, Duke & Billy Strayhorn)
Cotton tail / C jam blues / Flamingo / Bangup blues / Tonk / Johnny come lately / In a blue summer garden / Great times / Perdido / Take the 'A' train / Oscarlypso / Blues for blanton
CD _____ OJCCD 108
Original Jazz Classics / Sep '93 / Wellard / Jazz Music / Cadillac / Complete/Pinnacle.

GREATEST HITS: DUKE ELLINGTON
Take the 'A' train / Sophisticated lady / Perdido / Prelude to a kiss / C jam blues / Mood indigo / Mooche / Satin doll / Solitude / What am I here for / I got it bad and that ain't good / Skin deep
CD _____ 4629592
Sony Jazz / Oct '93 / Sony.

HAPPY BIRTHDAY DUKE
CD Set _____ 15965
Laserlight / Oct '95 / Target/BMG.

HAPPY BIRTHDAY DUKE VOL. 1 (Ellington, Duke Orchestra)
CD _____ 15783
Laserlight / Jul '92 / Target/BMG.

HAPPY BIRTHDAY DUKE VOL. 2 (Ellington, Duke Orchestra)
CD _____ 15784
Laserlight / Jul '92 / Target/BMG.

HAPPY BIRTHDAY DUKE VOL. 3 (Ellington, Duke Orchestra)
CD _____ 15785
Laserlight / Jul '92 / Target/BMG.

HAPPY BIRTHDAY DUKE VOL. 4 (Ellington, Duke Orchestra)
CD _____ 15786
Laserlight / Aug '92 / Target/BMG.

HAPPY BIRTHDAY DUKE VOL. 5 (Ellington, Duke Orchestra)
CD _____ 15787
Laserlight / Aug '92 / Target/BMG.

HAPPY GO LUCKY LOCAL
CD _____ 1046700522
Discovery / May '95 / Warner Music.

HAPPY-GO-LUCKY LOCAL (Ellington, Duke Orchestra)
CD _____ MVSCD 52
Musicraft / Jul '88 / Warner Music.

HARLEM (Ellington, Duke Orchestra)
Blow by blow / Caravan / Satin doll / Harlem / Things ain't what they used to be / All of me / Prowling cat / Opera / Happy reunion / Tutti for cootie
CD _____ CD 2308245
Pablo / Oct '92 / Jazz Music / Cadillac / Complete/Pinnacle.

HIS ORCHESTRA AND HIS SMALL GROUPS
C jam blues / Perdido / Sultry sunset / Blue skies (trumpet no end) / It don't mean a thing if it ain't got that swing / Magenta haze / Things ain't what they used to be (times's-a-wastin') / I'm beginning to see the light / Moonmist / Chelsea bridge / Jump for joy / Main stem / What am I here for / Johnny come lately / Do nothin' 'til you hear from me / Snibor / On a turquoise cloud / Park at 106th / In a sentimental mood / Black and tan fantasy / Caravan / Creole love call / Great times / Brown Betty / Dancers in love / Clothed man / Charlie the chulo / Chasin' chippies / Rent party blues / Tonk / Tip toe topic / Frankie and Johnny / Subtle slough / Without a song / Blues for blanton / Doop woop / Oscarlypso / Jeep's blues / Things ain't what you used to be / Good Queen Bess / Squaty roo / Menelik, the Lion of Judah / Lull at dawn / Goin' out the back way / Who knows / In a mellow tone / East St. Louis toodle-oo / Koko / Sophisticated lady / Cotton tail / Mooche / Bensonality / Prelude to a kiss / Satin doll / Mood indigo / Just a sittin' and a rockin' / I got it bad and that ain't good / Harlem air shaft / Blues in orbit / Hawk talks / El gato / Trambean (Theme from) / Smada / Take the 'A' train
CD Set _____ CDB 1211
Giants Of Jazz / '92 / Target/BMG / Cadillac.

HIS PIANO & HIS ORCHESTRA AT THE BAL MASQUE
CD _____ 4691362
Sony Jazz / Jan '95 / Sony.

I'M BEGINNING TO SEE THE LIGHT
Ellington medley / Symphony for a better world / Blues a la Willie Cook / Slow blues ensemble / Three trumps / Basin Street blues / Body and soul / Once in a blue / Junior hop / Charlie the chulo / So long
CD _____ WW 2077
West Wind / Jul '93 / Swift / Charly / CM / ADA.

IN A MELLOTONE
Take the 'A' train / Portrait of Bert Williams / Main stem / Just a sittin' and a rockin' / I got it bad and that ain't good / Perdido / Blue Serge / Flaming sword / In a mellow tone / Cotton tail / I don't know what kind of blues I got / Rumpus in Richmond / All too soon / Sepia panorama / Rocks in my bed / What am I here for
CD _____ 74321 13029-2
RCA / Sep '93 / BMG.

IN CONCERT AT THE PLEYEL PARIS
CD _____ DAWE 39
Magic / Oct '92 / Jazz Music / Swift / Wellard / Cadillac / Harmonia Mundi.

IN CONCERT AT THE PLEYEL PARIS VOL.2 (1958)
El Gato / Take the 'A' train / M.B. blue / V.I.P. boogie / Jam with Sam / Stompy Jones / Hi fi fo fun / Medley / Hawkes talks
CD _____ DAWE 40
Magic / May '90 / Jazz Music / Swift / Wellard / Cadillac / Harmonia Mundi.

IN THE TWENTIES 1924-29
Jazz Archives / Jun '93 / Jazz Music / Discovery / Cadillac.
CD _____ 157932

IN THE UNCOMMON MARKET
Bula / Silk lace / Asphalt jungle / Star crossed lovers / Getting sentimental over you / E.S.P. (extra sensory perception) / Paris blues / Shepherd / Kinda Dukish
CD _____ CD 2308247
Pablo / Apr '94 / Jazz Music / Cadillac / Complete/Pinnacle.

INCOMPARABLE, THE (Ellington, Duke Orchestra)
Rockin' in rhythm / Such sweet thunder / Newport up / St. Louis blues / Walkin' and singin' the blues / Anatomy of a murder / El gato (The cat) / Hank cinq (hank sank) / Jam with Sam / Things ain't what they used to be / Don't get around much anymore / Do nothin' 'til you hear from me / I've got it bad, and that ain't good / I'm beginning to see

---

the light / Caravan / I let a song go out of my heart
CD _____ DBCD 11
Dance Band Days / Dec '88 / Prism.

INDISPENSABLE DUKE ELLINGTON
CD _____ 74321155252
RCA / Apr '94 / BMG.

INDISPENSABLE DUKE ELLINGTON VOLS.5 & 6
Koko #2 / Bojangles (II) / Pitter panther patter (II) / Body and soul (take 2) / Sophisticated lady (II) / Jack the bear / Koko / Morning glory / Conga brava / Do nothin' 'til you hear from me / Bojangles / Cotton tail / Never no lament / Dusk / Portrait of Bert Williams / Blue goose / Harlem air shaft / At a Dixie roadside diner / All too soon / Rumpus in Richmond / Sepia panorama / In a mellow tone / Five o'clock whistle / Warm valley / Across the track blues / Chloe / Sidewalks of New York / Pitter panther patter / Body and soul / Sophisticated lady / Mr. J.B. Blues
CD Set _____ ND 89750
Jazz Tribune / May '94 / BMG.

INDISPENSABLE DUKE ELLINGTON VOLS.7 & 8
Take the 'A' train / Jumpin' punkins / John Hardy's wife / Blue serge / After all / Are you sticking / Just a sittin' and a rockin' / Giddybug gallop / Chocolate shake / I got it bad and that ain't good / Clementine / Brown skin gal / Jump for you / Five o'clock drag / Rocks in my bed / Bli-blip / Raincheck / I don't know what kind of blues I got / Chelsea bridge / Perdido / C jam blues / Moon mist / What am I here for / I don't mind / Someone / My little brown book / Main stem / Johnny come lately / Hayfoot strawfoot / Sentimental lady / Slip of the lip (can sink a ship) / Sherman shuffle
CD _____ 74321115524-2
Jazz Tribune / Jun '94 / BMG.

INDISPENSABLE DUKE ELLINGTON VOLS.9 & 10 (The Small Groups)
Daydream / Good Queen Bess / That's the blues, old man / Junior hop / Without a song / My Sunday gal / Mobile Bay / Linger awhile / Charlie the Chulo / Lament for Javanette / Lull at dawn / Ready Eddy / Dear old Southland / Solitude / Some Saturday / Subtle slough / Menelik, the Lion of Judah / Poor bubber / Squattyroo / Passion flower / Things ain't what they used to be / Going out the back way / Brown suede / Noir blue / C jam blues / June / Frankie and Johnny / Jumpin' room only / Tonk / Drawing room blues
CD Set _____ 74321115232
RCA / Mar '94 / BMG.

INTRODUCTION TO DUKE ELLINGTON 1927-1941
CD _____ 4024
Best Of Jazz / Sep '95 / Discovery.

JAM-A-DITTY (Ellington, Duke Orchestra)
CD _____ CDJJ 602
Jazz & Jazz / Jul '89 / Target/BMG.

JAZZ AT THE PLAZA VOL. 2
CD _____ 4713192
Sony Jazz / Jan '95 / Sony.

JAZZ COCKTAIL (Ellington, Duke Orchestra)
Stevedore stomp / Creole love call / It don't mean a thing if it ain't got that swing / Hot and bothered / Rose room / Old man blues / Jungle nights in Harlem / Tiger Bay / Sweet jazz o'mine / Mood indigo / Sing you sinners / Limehouse blues / Double check stomp / Swing low, sweet chariot / Jazz cocktail / Creole rhapsody
CD _____ CD AJA 5024
Living Era / Oct '88 / Koch.

JAZZ MASTERS
CD _____ 516338-2
Verve / Feb '94 / PolyGram.

JAZZ PARTY
CD _____ 4600592
Sony Jazz / Jan '95 / Sony.

JAZZ PORTRAITS (Ellington, Duke Orchestra)
Take the 'A' train / Don't get around much anymore / Cotton tail / I got it bad and that ain't good / Conga brava / Do nothin' 'til you hear from me / Portrait of Bert Williams / Solitude / I let a song go out of my heart / Prelude to a kiss / Caravan / Merry go round / In a sentimental mood / In a mellow tone / Sophisticated lady / Koko / Harlem air shaft / Just a sittin' and a rockin'
CD _____ CD 14505
Jazz Portraits / May '94 / Jazz Music.

JUBILEE STOMP
Jubilee stomp / High life / Dicty glide / Sloppy Joe / Stevedore stomp / Misty mornin' / Saratoga swing / Mississippi / Swanee shuffle / Breakfast dance / Immigration blues / It's glory / Dinah / Bugle call rag / Rude interlude / Dallas doings / Dear old Southland / Ebony rhapsody / Cocktails for two / Troubled waters / My old flame / Blue feeling
CD _____ 74321101532
Bluebird / Jul '92 / BMG.

JUMP FOR JOY 2
CD _____ JHR 73511
Jazz Hour / May '93 / Target/BMG / Jazz Music / Cadillac.

JUMPIN'
Newport Jazz Festival suite / Jeep's blues / Take the 'A' train / Diminuendo and crescendo in blue / Segue in C / Battle royal / Jumpin' at the woodside
CD _____ ELITE 014CD
Elite/Old Gold / Aug '90 / Carlton Home Entertainment.

LATIN AMERICAN SUITE (Ellington, Duke Orchestra)
CD _____ OJCCD 469-2
Original Jazz Classics / Mar '93 / Wellard / Jazz Music / Cadillac / Complete/Pinnacle.

LIBERIAN SUITE
CD _____ 4694092
Sony Jazz / Jan '95 / Sony.

LIVE AT NEWPORT 1958 (2CD Set) (Ellington, Duke Orchestra)
Introduction / Take the 'A' train / Princess blue / Duke's place / Just scratchin' the surface / Happy reunion / June flip / Mr. Gentle and Mr. Cool / Jazz festival jazz / Feet bone / Hi fi fo fum / I got it bad and that ain't good / Bill Bailey, Won't you please come home / Won't you please come home / Prima bara dubla / El gato / Multicoloured blue / Introduction to Mahalia Jackson / Come Sunday / Keep your hands on the plow / Take the 'A' train (2) / Jones
CD Set _____ C2K 53584
Columbia / Oct '94 / Sony.

LIVE AT THE BLUE NOTE
Take the 'A' train / Newport up / Haupe (Polly's theme) / Flirtibird / Pie Eye's blues / Almost cried / Dual fuel (dual filter) / Sophisticated lady / Mr. Gentle and Mr. Cool / El Gato / C jam blues / Tenderly / Honeysuckle rose / Drawing room blues / Tonk / In a mellow tone / All of me / Things ain't what they used to be / Jeep's blues / Mood indigo / Perdido / Satin doll / A disarming visit / Medley (Black & tan fantasy; Creole love call; Mooche; Passion flower; On the sunny side of the street; El Gato)
Roulette / Feb '94 / EMI.
CD _____ CDS 8286372

LIVE AT THE RAINBOW GRILL (Ellington, Duke Octet)
CD _____ MCD 0492
Moon / Nov '93 / Harmonia Mundi / Cadillac.

LIVE AT THE SALLE PLEYEL
CD _____ JMY 1011-2
JMY / Aug '91 / Harmonia Mundi.

LIVE AT THE WHITNEY
Black and fantasy / Prelude to a kiss / Do nothing 'til you hear from me / Caravan / Meditation / Mural from two perspectives / Sophisticated lady / Solitude / Soda fountain rag / New world a-coming / Amour, amour / Soul soothing beach / Lotus blossom / Flamingo / Le sucrier velors / Night shepherd / C jam blues / Mood indigo / I'm beginning to see the light / Dancers in love / Kixx / Satin doll
CD _____ IMP 11732
Impulse Jazz / Oct '95 / BMG / New Note.

LIVE IN PARIS - 1959
Black and tan fantasy / Creole love call / Mooche / Newport up / Sonet in search of amour / Kinda duckish/Rockin in rhythm / El nato / All of me / Won't you come home, Bill Bailey / Walkin' and singin' the blues / V.I.P. boogie / Jam with Sam / Skin deep / Ellington medley
CD _____ CDAFF 777
Affinity / Sep '91 / Charly / Cadillac / Jazz Music.

MASTERPIECES BY ELLINGTON
CD _____ 4694072
Sony Jazz / Jan '95 / Sony.

MASTERS OF JAZZ VOL.6 (Ellington, Duke Orchestra)
CD _____ STCD 4106
Storyville / Feb '89 / Jazz Music / Wellard / CM / Cadillac.

MIDNIGHT IN PARIS
CD _____ 4684032
Sony Jazz / Jan '95 / Sony.

MONEY JUNGLE
Monkey jungle / Fleurette Africaine (the African flower) / Warm valley / REM blues / Little Max / Wig wise / Switchblade / Caravan / Backward country boy blues / Solitude
CD _____ CDP 7463982
Blue Note / Mar '95 / EMI.

MOOD INDIGO
CD _____ CDSGP 087
Prestige / Sep '94 / Total/BMG.

MOOD INDIGO
CD _____ HADCD 193
Javelin / Nov '95 / THE / Henry Hadaway Organisation.

MOOD INDIGO - THE BEST OF DUKE ELLINGTON
CD _____ TRTCD 194
TrueTrax / Jun '95 / THE.

MOOD INDIGO 1930 (vol.9)
CD _____ 152252
Hot 'n' Sweet / May '94 / Discovery.

MUSIC IS MY MISTRESS
C jam blues / All of me / Black and tan fantasy / Danske onje (Danish eyes) / Queenie pie reggae / Azure / Jack the bear / Sweet Georgia Brown / Flower is a lovesome thing / Music is my mistress suite
CD _____ CIJD 60185K
Music Masters / '89 / Nimbus.

MY PEOPLE (Ellington, Duke Orchestra)
Ain't but the one / Will you be there / Come Sunday / David danced before the Lord with all his might / My mother and my father / Montage / My people / Blues ain't / Workin' blues / My man sends me / Jail blues / Lovin' lover / King fit the battle of Alabam' / What colour is virtue
CD _____ 4722042
Sony Jazz / Nov '92 / Sony.

NEW ORLEANS SUITE
Blues for New Orleans / Bourbon Street jingling jollies / Portrait of Louis Armstrong / Thanks for the beautiful land on the delta / Portrait of Wellman Braud / Second line / Portrait of Sidney Bechet / Aristocracy of Jean Lafitte / Portrait of Mahalia Jackson
CD _____ 756781376-2
Atlantic / Mar '93 / Warner Music.

NEWPORT 1958
CD _____ 4684362
Sony Jazz / Jan '95 / Sony.

NUTCRACKER SUITE (Ellington, Duke Orchestra)
Nutcracker suite / Peer Gynt suite No. 1 / Peer Gynt suite No. 2
CD _____ 4723562
Sony Jazz / Jan '95 / Sony.

OKEH ELLINGTON, THE (2CD Set)
CD _____ 4669642
Sony Jazz / Jan '95 / Sony.

PASSION FLOWER
CD _____ MCD 0742
Moon / Aug '95 / Harmonia Mundi / Cadillac.

PEER GYNT SUITE/SUITE THURSDAY
CD _____ 4723542
Sony Jazz / Jan '95 / Sony.

PIANO IN THE BACKGROUND (Ellington, Duke Orchestra)
CD _____ 4684042
Sony Jazz / Jan '95 / Sony.

PIANO IN THE FOREGROUND (Ellington, Duke Orchestra)
CD _____ 4749302
Sony Jazz / Jan '95 / Sony.

PLAYING THE BLUES 1927-1939
CD _____ BLE 592322
Black & Blue / Nov '92 / Wellard / Koch.

PRESENTS THE SOLOISTS OF HIS ORCHESTRA (1951-58)
In a mellotone / East St. Louis toodle-oo / Koko / Sophisticated lady / Cotton tail / Mooche / Bensonality / Prelude to a kiss / Satin doll / Mood indigo / Just a-settin' and a-rockin' / I got it bad and that ain't good / Harlem air shaft / Perdido in orbit / Hawk talks / Jeep's blues / El Gato / Theme for Trambean / Smada / Take the 'A' train
CD _____ CD 53066
Giants Of Jazz / Mar '92 / Target/BMG / Cadillac.

PRIVATE COLLECTION VOL.1 (Studio Sessions Chicago 1956)
March 19th blues / Feet bone / In a sentimental mood / Discontented / Jump for joy / Just scratchin' the surface / Prelude to a kiss / Miss Lucy / Uncontrived / Satin doll / Do not disturb / Love you madly / Short sheet cluster / Moon mist / Long time blues
CD _____ MSCD 22
Music De-Luxe / Jul '95 / Magnum Music Group.

RECOLLECTIONS OF THE BIG BAND ERA
Minnie the moocher / For dancers only / It's a lonesome old town (when you're not around) / Cherokee / Midnight sun will never set / Let's get together / I'm getting sentimental over you / Chant of the weed / Cirbiribin / Contrasts / Christopher Columbus / Auld lang syne / Tuxedo junction / Smoke rings / Artistry in rhythm / Waltz you saved for me / Woodchopper's ball / Sentimental journey / When it's sleepy time down South / One o'clock jump / Goodbye / Sleep, sleep, sleep / Rhapsody in blue
CD _____ 7567900432
Atlantic / Feb '94 / Warner Music.

RING DEM BELLS
Mooche / Ring dem bells / Frustration / Colortura / Rose of the Rio Grande / Love you madly / Harlem speaks / Caravan / Primpin' at the prom / Jam with Sam / One O'clock jump / Take the 'A' train / Crosstown / Perdido / Pretty woman / 920 special / Moon mist / Just squeeze me / Prelude to a kiss (medley) / Tootie for cootie
CD _____ CDGRF 039
Tring / Jun '92 / Tring / Prism.

ROCKIN' IN RHYTHM (Ellington, Duke Orchestra)
Shoe shine boy / Trumpet in spades / Solitude / Happy as the day is long / Cootie's concerto / In a jam / Uptown beat / Yearning for love / Love is like a cigarette / Exposition swing / Showboat shuffle / Barney's concerto / It was a sad night in Harlem / East St. Louis toodle-oo / Mooche / It don't mean a thing if it ain't got that swing / Rockin' in rhythm / Black and tan fantasy
CD _____ CD AJA 305T
Living Era / Nov '88 / Koch.

ROCKIN' IN RHYTHM
CD _____ JHR 73504
Jazz Hour / May '93 / Target/BMG / Jazz Music / Cadillac.

ROCKIN' IN RHYTHM 1930-31
CD _____ 152312
Hot 'n' Sweet / May '95 / Discovery.

S.R.O
Take the 'A' train / I got it bad and that ain't good / Things ain't what they used to be / West Indian pancake / Black and tan fantasy / Creole love call / Mooche / Soul call / El gato / Open house / Rockin' in rhythm / Jam with Sam / Adlib on Nippon / C jam blues / Hawk talks
CD _____ DC 8540
Denon / Apr '89 / Conifer.

SALUTE TO DUKE ELLINGTON, A (Various Artists)
CD _____ 4755702
Sony Jazz / Jan '95 / Sony.

SARATOGA SWING (Ellington, Duke & His Cotton Club Orchestra)
Take the 'A' train / Perdido / Five o'clock whistle / Sidewalks of New York / At a Dixie roadside diner / Sophisticated lady / Harlem air shaft / Me and you / Do nothin' till you hear from me / My greatest mistake / Johnny come lately / Sepia panorama / Cotton tail / Don't get around much anymore / Blue goose / C jam blues / Pitter panther patter / Raincheck / Hayfoot strawfoot / Moon mist / Morning glory / Saratoga swing
CD _____ RAJCD 842
Empress / Feb '95 / THE.

SATIN DOLL
CD _____ 90105-2
Jazz Archives / Oct '92 / Jazz Music / Discovery / Cadillac.

SECOND SACRED CONCERT
CD _____ PCD 24045
Prestige / Nov '95 / Complete/Pinnacle / Cadillac.

SIDE BY SIDE (Ellington, Duke & Johnny Hodges)
Stompy Jones / Squeeze me / Big shoe / Going up / Just a memory / Let's fall in love / Ruin / Bend one / You need go rock
CD _____ 821 578-2
Polydor / Sep '93 / PolyGram.

SOLOS, DUETS AND TRIOS
Tonk / Frankie and Johnny / Dear old Southland / Pitter panther patter (take 1) / Body and soul (take 1) / Body and soul (take 3) / Sophisticated lady (take 2) / Mr. J.B. blues (take 2) / Drawing room blues / Jumpin' room only / Solitude / Pitter panther patter (take 2) / Body and soul (take 2) / Sophisticated lady (take 1) / Mr. J.B. Blues (take 1)
CD _____ ND 82178
Bluebird / Jul '90 / BMG.

SONNY LESTER COLLECTION
CD _____ CDC 9066
LRC / Nov '93 / New Note / Harmonia Mundi.

SOPHISTICATED LADY (Ellington, Duke Orchestra)
Sophisticated lady / Harlem speaks / In a sentimental mood / Merry go round / Echoes of Harlem / Caravan / Diminuendo in blue / Crescendo in blue / I let a song go out of my heart / Prelude to a kiss / Solitude / Do nothin' 'til you hear from me / Don't get around much anymore / Cotton tail / I got it bad and that ain't good / Take the 'A' train
CD _____ CDCD 1010
Charly / Mar '93 / Charly / THE / Cadillac.

SOPHISTICATED LADY (Ellington, Duke Orchestra)
CD _____ ENTCD 251
Entertainers / Mar '92 / Target/BMG.

STEREO REFLECTIONS
CD _____ NI 4016
Natasha / Jul '93 / Jazz Music / ADA / CM / Direct / Cadillac.

SUCH SWEET THUNDER
CD _____ 4691402
Sony Jazz / Jan '95 / Sony.

SWING 1930-1938
Rockin' in rhythm / It don't mean a thing if it ain't got that swing / Baby you ain't there / Bugle call rag / Blue Harlem / Jazz cocktail / Lightnin' / Slippery horn / Drop me off at Harlem / Bundle of blues / Jive stomp / Dear old Southland / Saddest tale / Truckin'

ROCKIN' IN RHYTHM (Ellington, Duke Orchestra)
CD _____ RPCD 625
Robert Parker Jazz / Aug '94 / Conifer.

TAKE THE 'A' TRAIN (1933-41) (Ellington, Duke Orchestra)
CD _____ CD 56012
Jazz Roots / Aug '94 / Target/BMG.

TAKE THE 'A' TRAIN
CD _____ EMPRCD 565
Emporio / May '06 / THE / Disc / CM

TAKE THE 'A' TRAIN
CD _____ MU 5035
Musketeer / Oct '92 / Koch.

TAKE THE 'A' TRAIN
CD _____ VJC 1003-2
Victorious Discs / Aug '90 / Jazz Music.

TIMON OF ATHENS
CD _____ VSD 5466
Varese Sarabande/Colosseum / Mar '94 / Pinnacle / Silva Screen.

TRANSBLUCENCY
CD _____ CDJJ 12
Jazz & Jazz / Jan '92 / Target/BMG.

TWO GREAT CONCERTS IN EUROPE
Take the 'A' train / Caravan / Do nothin' 'til you hear from me / Fancy dance / Hawk talks / Swamp drum / Main stern / Tattooed bride / Threesome / Take the 'A' train (version) / Satin doll/Sophisticated lady / Mooche, shorted encore / I got it bad and that ain't good / Harmony in Harlem / Things ain't what they used to be / Perdido / New concerto for Cootie / Carolina shout
CD _____ 302284
Accord / Dec '89 / Discovery / Harmonia Mundi / Cadillac.

TWO ON ONE (Ellington, Duke & Count Basie)
CD _____ CDTT 7
Charly / Apr '94 / Charly / THE / Cadillac.

UNKNOWN SESSION
Everything but you / Black beauty / All too soon / Something to live for / Mood indigo / Creole blues / Don't you know I care (or don't you care too) / Flower is a lovesome thing / Mighty like the blues / Tonight I shall sleep / Dual highway / Blues
CD _____ 472084 2
Columbia / Nov '93 / Sony.

UPTOWN (& The Controversial Suite)
Take the 'A' train / Mooche / Tone parallel to Harlem / Perdido / Controversial suite part I / Before my time / Controversial suite part 2 / Skin deep
CD _____ 4608302
Sony Jazz / Jan '95 / Sony.

UPTOWN DOWNBEAT
East St. Louis toodle-oo / Washington wobble / Diga diga doo / I can't give you anything but love / Saratoga swing / Accordeon Joe / I've got the world on a string / Raisin' the rent / Solitude / In a sentimental mood / Uptown downbeat / In a jam / Braggin' in brass / Dinah's in a jam / Battle of swing / Riding on a blue note / Smorgasbord and schnapps / Harlem air shaft / Sepia panorama / Koko / Dusk / Conga brava / Blue goose / Never no lament / Cotton tail
CD _____ AVC 546
Avid / Jun '95 / Avid/BMG / Koch.

WASHINGTON WOBBLE
CD _____ CDSVL 206
Saville / Mar '90 / Conifer.

YALE CONCERT
CD _____ OJCCD 664
Original Jazz Classics / Feb '92 / Wellard / Jazz Music / Cadillac / Complete/Pinnacle.

YOUNG DUKE, THE (1927-40) (Ellington, Duke Orchestra)
Jazz cocktail / Drop me off in Harlem / Slippery horn / Blue ramble / Merry go round / In the shade of the old apple tree / Raisin' the rent / Blue tune / Kissin' my baby goodnight / Bundle of blues / Stompy Jones / Baby, when you ain't there / Blue feeling / Rockin' chair / East St. Louis toodle-oo / Rockin' in rhythm / Awful sad / Jazz convulsions / Dusk / Blue goose / Girl in my dreams tries to look like you / Flamingo
CD _____ PASTCD 9771
Flapper / Jan '92 / Pinnacle.

AFTER DARK
Street beat / Song for her / As I sleep / After dark / El anio / Tonight / On the run / If tomorrow never comes / Hold me tight / Bridge over troubled water / Boys from the bay / Candlelight / So special / Slow it down
CD _____ CDP 8278382
Blue Note / Jan '95 / EMI.

TIM ELLIOT & THE TROUBLEMAKERS (Elliot, Tim & Troublemakers)
CD _____ TRCD 9918
Tramp / Nov '93 / Direct / ADA / CM.

Elliott, Bern

BEAT YEARS, THE (Elliott, Bern & The Fenmen)
Money / Nobody but me / New Orleans / Chills / I can tell / Do the mashed potato / Please Mr. Postman / Shake sherry shake / Talking about you (Live) / Everybody needs a little love / Shop around / Little Egypt (live) / Good times / What do you want with my baby / Guess who / Make it easy on yourself / Forget her / Voodoo woman / Lipstick traces / Be my girl / Rag doll / I've got everything you need babe / Every little day now
CD _____ SEECD 239
See For Miles/C5 / Oct '93 / Pinnacle.

Elliott, G.H.

GOLDEN AGE OF MUSIC HALL, THE
I'se a-waiting for yer Josie / If the man on the moon were a coon / There's a little cupid in the moon / Lou, Sue, Mary, Dinah / Chocolate Major / Hello Susie Green / On the Mississippi / She has such dreamy eyes / My southern maid / Waiting / Way down yonder / My picture girl / You'd never know that old home town of mine / When the sun goes down in dixie / Give her a great big kiss for me / My Michaelmas daisy / If you're going back to dixie / Mississippi honeymoon / In Carolina / Tickle the keys of your silvery saxophone / Maybe it's the moon / My gal's given me the go-bye / That's just like heaven to me / Sue, Sue, Sue / I used to sigh for the silvery moon
CD _____ PASTCD 7033
Flapper / Jan '94 / Pinnacle.

Elliott, Jack

HARD TRAVELLIN' (Songs by Woody Guthrie & others)
Hard travellin' / Grand coulee dam / New York Town / Tom Joad / Howdido / Dust bowl blues / This land is your land / Pretty Boy Floyd / Philadelphia lawyer / Talking Columbia blues / Dust storm disaster / Riding in my car / 1913 massacre / So long (it's been good to know yuh) / Sadie Brown / East Virginia blues / I belong to glasgow / Cuckoo / Rollin' in my sweet baby's arms / South coast / San Francisco Bay blues / Last letter / Candy man / Tramp on the street / Railroad Bill
CD _____ CDWIK 952
Big Beat / Aug '90 / Pinnacle.

KEROUAC'S LAST DREAM (Elliott, Ramblin' Jack)
CD _____ TUT 72163
Wundertute / Jan '94 / CM / Duncans / ADA.

ME AND BOBBY MCGEE
CD _____ ROUCD 0368
Rounder / Nov '95 / CM / Direct / ADA / Cadillac.

SOUTH COAST
CD _____ RHR 59
Red House / Jul '95 / Koch / ADA.

Ellis, Alton

BEST OF ALTON ELLIS
CD _____ SOCD 8019
Studio One / Mar '95 / Jetstar.

CRY TOUGH
CD _____ CDHB 106
Heartbeat / May '93 / Greensleeves / Jetstar / Direct / ADA.

DUKE REID COLLECTION
CD _____ RNCD 2083
Rhino / Dec '94 / Jetstar / Magnum Music Group / THE.

LEGENDARY ALTON ELLIS, THE
CD _____ ATCD 012
All Tone / Dec '93 / Jetstar.

SILVER JUBILEE VOL. 1
CD _____ SKYCD 53
Skynote / May '93 / Jetstar.

SILVER JUBILEE VOL. 2
CD _____ SKYCD 46
Skynote / May '93 / Jetstar.

SUNDAY COMING
CD _____ CDHB 3511
Heartbeat / Feb '95 / Greensleeves / Jetstar / Direct / ADA.

VALLEY OF DECISION
CD _____ CDSGP 071
Prestige / Sep '94 / Total/BMG.

Ellis, Big Chief

BIG CHIEF ELLIS
Prison bound / All down blues / Dices 2 / Louise / Fare you well, mistreater / How long blues / Let's talk it over / Rocky mountain blues / Hey baby / Sweet home Chicago / Chiefs E flat blues / Blues for moot
CD _____ TRIX 3316
Trix / Mar '95 / New Note.

Ellis, Don

AUTUMN
CD _____ 4726222
Sony Jazz / Jan '95 / Sony.

DON ELLIS
I'll remember April / Sweet and lovely / Out of nowhere / All things you are / You stepped out of a dream / My funny valentine / I love you / Just one of those things / Johnny come lately / Angel eyes / Lover / Form / Sallie / How time passes / Simplex one
CD _____ CD 53262
Giants Of Jazz / Jan '96 / Target/BMG / Cadillac.

ELECTRIC BATH (Ellis, Don Orchestra)
CD _____ 4726202
Sony Jazz / Jan '95 / Sony.

HOW TIME PASSES
How time passes / Sally / Simplex one / Waste / Improvisational suite
CD _____ CCD 9004
Candid / Sep '87 / Cadillac / Jazz Music / Wellard / Koch.

OUT OF NOWHERE
CD _____ CCD 9032
Candid / May '89 / Cadillac / Jazz Music / Wellard / Koch.

Ellis, Herb

DOGGIN' AROUND (Ellis, Herb & Red Mitchell)
CD _____ CCD 4372
Concord Jazz / Apr '89 / New Note.

JAZZ MASTERS, THE (Ellis, Herb/Ray Brown/Serge Ermoll)
CD _____ AIM 1039CD
Aim / Jun '95 / Direct / ADA / Jazz Music.

TEXAS SWINGS
CD _____ JR 10022
Justice / Apr '94 / Koch.

TOGETHER (Ellis, Herb & Stuff Smith)
CD _____ 378052
Koch / Jan '96 / Koch.

TWO FOR THE ROAD (Ellis, Herb & Joe Pass)
Love for sale / Am I blue / Seven come eleven / Guitar blues / Lady be good / Cherokee (concept 1) / Cherokee (concept 2) / Gee baby ain't I good to you / Try a little tenderness / I found a new baby / Angel eyes
CD _____ OJCCD 726-2
Original Jazz Classics / Jun '94 / Wellard / Jazz Music / Cadillac / Complete/Pinnacle.

Ellis, John

DANCIN' WI' CLAYMORES (Ellis, John & His Highland Country Band)
Twa bonnie reels / Pipe jig and march / G.S. Manclennan selection / Folk waltz / Grand march / Eva three step / Slow air and march / Strip the willow / Mackay's music medley / Pipe march / Locl Leven castle (Reel set) / March, strathspey and reel / Gaelic waltzes / Polka / Highland fair (jig set) / Highland hornpipes / Gay gordons / Braes of breadalbane / Queens bridge (reel set)
CD _____ LCOM 5210
Lismor / Mar '92 / Lismor / Direct / Duncans / ADA.

Ellis, Lisle

ELEVATIONS
CD _____ VICTOCD 027
Victo / Oct '94 / These / ReR Megacorp / Cadillac.

Ellis, Osian

CLYMAU CYTGERDD/DIVERSIONS
Caneuon plant / Tri dam byrfyfyr / Clymau cytgerdd i ddwy delyn / Consierto i'r delyn / Canu penillion / Gavotte / Caniadau llanelwy / Sonata yn f leiaf / Caneuon atgof
CD _____ SCD 4038
Sain / Jun '89 / Direct / ADA.

Ellis, Paul

STORIES
CD _____ CDPH 1181
Philo / Oct '95 / Direct / CM / ADA.

Ellis, Pee Wee

BLUES MISSION
Zig zag / Gotcha / Cold sweat/mother popcorn / Yellin' blue / One mint julep / Texas sweet / Ham / Fort apache / Blues mission
CD _____ R 279486
Gramavision / Jun '93 / Vital/SAM / ADA.

PEE WEE, FRED AND MACEO (J.B. Horns)
Sweet and tangy / Bumpin' / Step on you're watch (part II) / Mother's kitchen / Everywhere is out of town / Strut / We're rollin' / Let's play house / Blues a la L.S. / Frontal system / Slipstream
CD _____ GV 794622
Gramavision / Feb '91 / Vital/SAM / ADA.

SEPIA TONALITY
What are you doing the rest of your life / I should care / Stardust / Sepia tonality /

Cleaning windows / Cherry red / Body and soul / Prayer of love / Why not / Come rain or come shine
CD _____ MM 801040
Minor Music / Jun '94 / Vital/SAM.

TWELVE AND MORE BLUES
There is no greater love / Bye bye blackbird / I love you / Doxy / My neighbourhood / My wife, my friend / In a sentimental mood / Pistachio / Twelve and more blues / In the middle
CD _____ MM 801034
Minor Music / Nov '93 / Vital/SAM.

YELLIN BLUE
CD _____ MM 801049
Minor Music / May '95 / Vital/SAM.

Ellis, Tinsley

COOL ON IT (Ellis, Tinsley & Heartfixers)
Drivin' woman / Cool on it / Hong Kong Mississippi / Second thoughts / Sailor's grave on the prairie / Greenwood chainsaw boogie / Tulane / Time to quit / Sugaree / Wild weekend
CD _____ ALCD 3905
Alligator / May '93 / Direct / ADA.

FANNING THE FLAMES
CD _____ ALCD 4778
Alligator / May '93 / Direct / ADA.

GEORGIA BLUE
Can't you lie / You picked a good time / Crime of passion / Double eyed whammy / Look ka py py / Free manwells / Texas stomp / I've made nights by myself / Hot potato / She wants to sell my monkey / As the years go passing by / Lucky lot
CD _____ ALCD 4765
Alligator / Apr '93 / Direct / ADA.

STORM WARNING
CD _____ ALCD 4823
Alligator / Oct '94 / Direct / ADA.

TROUBLE TIME
Highway man / Hey hey baby / Sign of the blues / What have I done wrong / Big chicken / Axe / Come morning / Restless heart / Bad dream No.108 / Hulk / Now I'm gone / Red dress
CD _____ ALCD 4805
Alligator / May '93 / Direct / ADA.

Ellis, Tony

DIXIE BANNER
CD _____ FF 444CD
Flying Fish / Apr '94 / Roots / CM / Direct / ADA.

Ellison, John

WELCOME BACK
CD _____ AFT 6113CD
Ichiban / Jun '94 / Koch.

Ellison, Lorraine

STAY WITH ME - THE BEST OF LORRAINE ELLISON
CD _____ SCL 2106
Ichiban Soul Classics / Nov '95 / Koch.

Ellwood, William

NATURAL SELECTIONS
Half moon / First love / Laughing earth / Summer words / Elysain fields / Simpatico / Barefoot dance / Blue period / Night calling / Spirit river / Cotton wood / Gymnopedie No.1
CD _____ ND 61049
Narada / Aug '95 / New Note / ADA.

TOUCHSTONE
Touchstone / Gypsy wind / Whispering moon / At the world / Dreamwalk / Thousand smiles / Navy blue / California dreamin' / Sundown / Dakota
CD _____ ND 61038
Narada / Nov '93 / New Note / ADA.

Elman, Ziggy

ZIGGY ELMAN AND FRIENDS - 1947 (Elman, Ziggy & His Orchestra)
CD _____ CCD 70
Circle / '92 / Jazz Music / Swift / Wellard.

Elmerhassel

BILLYOUS
Dehydration / Nearing home / Business as usual / Calm and collected / Bare back / Pert host / Safeish / Simian / Almost at one / Exposure / Common flowers
CD _____ DPROMCD 18
Dirter Promotions / Mar '94 / Pinnacle.

Eloy

CHRONICLES 1
CD _____ SPV 08448182
SPV / Jul '94 / Plastic Head.

CHRONICLES 2
CD _____ SPV 08448192
SPV / Jun '94 / Plastic Head.

DESTINATION
CD _____ SPV 08448082
SPV / Jan '95 / Plastic Head.

METROMANIA
CD _____ HMIXD 21
Heavy Metal / Sep '84 / Sony.

RA
CD _____ SPV 08548022
SPV / Jan '95 / Plastic Head.

TIDES RETURN FOREVER
CD _____ SPV 08448202
SPV / Jan '95 / Plastic Head.

Els Cosins Del Sac

AL FINAL DELL BALL T'ESPERO
CD _____ 20057CD
Sonifolk / Dec '94 / ADA / CM.

Els Trobadors

ET ADES SERA L'ALBA
CD _____ F 1016CD
Sonifolk / Jun '94 / ADA / CM.

Elsdon, Alan

KEEPERS OF THE FLAME
CD _____ PARCD 504
Parrot / Dec '94 / THE / Wellard / Jazz Music.

Elsdon, Tracy

RELATIVELY SPEAKING
Half the moon / Relatively speaking / Only a woman's heart / Somewhere under the sun / Heaven / You were my lover / Lonely street / One careful owner / Just when I needed you most / Water is wide / Dream a little dream of me / Loving arms / Golden years / I'll walk beside you
CD _____ RCD 534
Ritz / Oct '93 / Pinnacle.

Elstak, Nedley

MACHINE, THE
CD _____ ESP 1076-2
ESP / Jan '93 / Jazz Horizons / Jazz Music.

Elvis Hitler

HELLBILLY
CD _____ LS 94362
Restless / Dec '89 / Vital.

Elwood, Michael

ROLLING VALENTINE (Elwood, Michael & Beth Galiger)
CD _____ DJD 3219
Dejadisc / Sep '95 / Direct / ADA.

Ely, Brother Claude

SATAN GET BACK
I'm crying holy unto the lord / There's a leak in this old building / Send down the rain / There ain't no grave gonna hold my body down / Talk about Jesus / I'm just a stranger here / Thank you Jesus / I want to rest / You've got to move / Farther on / Jesus is the rock / Little David play your harp / There's a higher power / Holy holy holy (That's all right) / Dip your finger in the water (And cool my thumb) / Do you want to study / Those prayers and words still guide me / My crucified one / Old fireside / Fare you well / I want to go to heaven / You took the wrong road again / Stop that train
CD _____ CDCHD 456
Ace / Sep '93 / Pinnacle / Cadillac / Complete/Pinnacle.

Ely, Joe

DIG ALL NIGHT
Settle for love / For your love / My eyes got lucky / Maybe she'll find me / Drivin' man / Dig all night / Grandfather blues / Jazz street / Rich man, poor boy / Behind the bamboo shade
CD _____ FIENDCD 130
Demon / Oct '88 / Pinnacle / ADA.

LETTER TO LAREDO
CD _____ TRACD 222
Transatlantic / Nov '95 / BMG / Pinnacle / ADA.

LORD OF THE HIGHWAY
Lord of the highway / (Don't put a) lock on my heart / Me and Billy The Kid / Letter to L.A. / No rope, Daisy-o / Thinks she's French / Everybody got hammered / Are you listening Lucky / Row of dominoes / Silver city
CD _____ FIENDCD 101
Demon / Sep '87 / Pinnacle / ADA.

NO BAD TALK OR LOUD TALK
CD _____ EDCD 418
Edsel / Mar '95 / Pinnacle / ADA.

Elysian Fields

ADELAIN
CD _____ USR 018CD
Unisound / Jan '96 / Plastic Head.

Elysium

DANCE FOR THE CELESTIAL BEINGS
CD _____ NZCD 039
Nova Zembla / Sep '95 / Plastic Head.

Emblow, Jack

ENJOY YOURSELF (Emblow, Jack & The French Collection)
CD _____ CDTS 001
Maestro / Aug '93 / Savoy.

PICK YOURSELF UP (Emblow, Jack & The French Collection)
Pick yourself up / Hot time in the old town tonight / Boiled beef and carrots / Don't dilly dally on the way / Any old iron / I don't want to walk without you / Little on the lonely side / Dance of the hours / Guantanamera / Yes, we have no bananas / Whilst strolling in the park / Lily of laguna / Narcissus / La cucuracha / I yi yi yi yi (I like you very much) / Black orpheus samba / No strings / I'm putting all my eggs in one basket / I'm a dreamer (aren't we all) / I double dare you / Moonstruck / Bill Bailey, won't you please come home / Question and answer / Dubarry waltz / Endearing young charms / Rose of tralee / Mother McChree / Slow rhumbas / La golondrina / Indian summer / Pokarekareana / Estrellita / Too marvellous for words / Chihuahua / Opus one
CD _____ GRCD 46
Grasmere / '91 / Target/BMG / Savoy.

Embryo

OPAL
Opal / You don't know what's happening / Revolution / Glockenspiel / Got no time / Call / End of soul / People from outer space / You better have some fun / Lauft
CD _____ MASOCD 90012
Materiali Sonori / May '95 / New Note.

Emerson, Keith

CHANGING STATES
CD _____ AMPCD 026
AMP / Apr '95 / Cadillac / Magnum Music Group.

Emerson, Lake & Palmer

BEST OF EMERSON, LAKE AND PALMER, THE
CD _____ ESSCD 296
Essential / Nov '95 / Total/BMG.

BRAIN SALAD SURGERY
Jerusalem / Toccata / Still you turn me on / Benny the bouncer / Karn evil 9 / First impression (part 1) / First impression / Second impression / Third impression
CD _____ 828468-2
Victory / Dec '93 / PolyGram.

EMERSON, LAKE AND PALMER
Barbarian / Take a pebble / Knife edge / Three fates / Clotho / Lachesis / Auropos / Tank / Lucky man
CD _____ 828264-2
Victory / Dec '93 / PolyGram.

IN THE HOT SEAT
Hand of truth / Daddy / One by one / Heart on ice / Thin line / Man in the long black coat / Change / Give me a reason to stay / Gone too soon / Street war / Pictures at an exhibition
CD _____ 828554-2
Victory / Aug '94 / PolyGram.

LIVE AT THE ROYAL ALBERT HALL
CD _____ 8289332
Victory / Jan '93 / PolyGram.

LOVE BEACH
All I want is you / Love beach / Taste of my love / Gambler / For you / Canario / Memoirs of an officer and a gentleman / Prologue / Education of a gentleman / Love at first sight / Letters from the front / Honourable company
CD _____ 828469-2
Victory / Dec '93 / PolyGram.

PICTURES AT AN EXHIBITION
Promenade / Gnome / Sage / Old castle / Blues variation / Hut of Baba Yaga / Curse of Baba Yaga / Great gate of Kiev / End (nutrocker)
CD _____ 828466-2
Victory / Dec '93 / PolyGram.

RETURN OF THE MANTICORE
Touch and go / Hang on to a dream / 21st Century schizoid man / Fire / Pictures at an exhibition / I believe in Father Christmas / Introductory Fanfare/Peter Gunn / Tiger in a spotlight / Toccata / Trilogy / Tank / Lucky man / Tarkus / From the beginning / Take a pebble / Knife edge / Paper blood / Hoedown / Rondo / Barbarian / Still ... you turn me on / Endless enigma / C'est la vie / Enemy God dances with the black spirits / Bo Diddley / Bitches crystal / Time and a place / Living sin / Karn evil 9 / Honky tonk train blues / Jerusalem / Fanfare for the common man / Black moon / Watching over you / Toccata con fuoco / For you / Prelude and fugue / Memoirs of an officer and a gentleman / Pirates / Affairs of the heart
CD Set _____ 828459-2
Victory / Dec '93 / PolyGram.

TARKUS

Tarkus / Eruption / Stones of years / Iconoclast / Mass / Manticore / Battlefield / Aquatarkus / Jeremy Bender / Bitches crystal / Only way / Infinite space (conclusion) / Time and a place / Are you ready Eddy
CD _____ 828465-2
Victory / Dec '93 / PolyGram.

TRILOGY
Endless enigma (part 1) / Fugue / Endless enigma (part 2) / From the beginning / Sheriff / Hoedown / Trilogy / Living sin / Aboddon's bolero
CD _____ 8284672
Victory / Dec '93 / PolyGram.

WORKS VOL. 2
Tiger in the spotlight / When the apple blossoms bloom in the windmills of your mind / I'll be your valentine / Bullfrogs / Brain salad surgery / Barrelhouse shake down / Watching over you / So far to fall / Maple leaf rag / I believe in Father Christmas / Close but not touching
CD _____ 8284732
Victory / Dec '93 / PolyGram.

Emery, James

TURBULENCE (Emery, James & Iliad Quartet)
CD _____ KFWCD 106
Knitting Factory / Nov '94 / Grapevine.

Emery, Jon

IF YOU DON'T BUY THIS I'LL FIND SOMEBODY WHO WILL
She was bad / I let the freight train carry me on / I'm the fool (who told you to go) / If you don't leave me / I bought her roses / Midnight, music city U.S.A. / Rockin' Rhonda ain't rockin' no more / Fool in El Paso / I'm comin' home / Old that train / Christy-Ann / Fiddlin' John Carson / God don't never change / Chicken pickin' (break song) / Man who never lies
CD _____ BCDAH 15897
Bear Family / Aug '95 / Rollercoaster / Direct / CM / Swift / ADA.

EMF

CHA CHA CHA
Perfect day / La plage / Day I was born / Secrets / Shining / Bring me down / Skin / Slouch / Bleeding you dry / Patterns / When will you come / West of the Cox / Ballad o' the Bishop / Glass Smash Jack
CD _____ CDPCSD 165
Parlophone / Mar '95 / EMI.

SCHUBERT DIP
Children / Long Summer days / When you're mine / Travelling not running / I believe / Unbelievable / Girl of an age / Admit it / Lies / Long time / Live at the Bilson
CD _____ CDPCS 7353
Parlophone / Feb '94 / EMI.

STIGMA
They're here / Arizona / It's you / Never know / Blue highs / Inside / Getting through / She bleeds / Dog / Light that burns twice as bright
CD _____ CDPCSD 122
Parlophone / Sep '92 / EMI.

Emler, Andy

HEAD GAMES (Emler, Andy Mega Octet)
CD _____ LBLC 6553
Label Bleu / Jan '93 / New Note.

Emmanuel, Tommy

JOURNEY, THE
Tailin' the invisible man / Big Brother / Somethin's goin' on / Hellos and goodbyes / Journey / If your heart tells you to / Like family / Don't hold me back / Villa Anita / White picket fences / Big swell / Initiation
CD _____ 4744892
Epic / Oct '94 / Sony.

Emmett, Rik

SPIRAL NOTEBOOK
CD _____ IRS 993515CD
Intercord / Jan '96 / Plastic Head.

Emotions

FLOWERS
I don't wanna lose your love / Me for you / You've got the right to know / We go through the changes / You're a special part of my life / No plans for tomorrow / How can you stop loving someone / Flowers / God will take care of you
CD _____ 982996 2
Pickwick/Sony Collector's Choice / Aug '93 / Carlton Home Entertainment / Pinnacle / Sony.

SO I CAN LOVE YOU/ UNTOUCHED
So I can love you / Somebody wants what I got / Going on strike / I found my man / Got to be the man / Best part of a love affair / I like it / My letter / Daydreams / It's not fair / Two lovers / Take me back / Nothing seems impossible / Boss love maker / It's been fun / Love ain't easy onesided / Blind

End Of Green

INFINITY
CD _____ NB 140CD
Nuclear Blast / Jan '96 / Plastic Head.

Alley / Show me how / If you think it (you may as well do it) / Love is the hardest thing to find / Tricks are for kids / Boy I need you
CD _____ CDSXD 947
Stax / Oct '89 / Pinnacle.

Emperor

ENSLAVED
CD _____ CANDLE 12CD
Candlelight / Jan '94 / Plastic Head.

IN THE NIGHTSIDE ECLIPSE
CD _____ CANDLE 008
Candlelight / Jan '95 / Plastic Head.

Emperor Sly

HEAVY ROTATION
CD _____ ZD 6 CD
Zip Dog / Nov '95 / Grapevine.

Emperor's New Clothes

WISDOM & LIES
Luke's idea / Mystery daydream / Missing the sea / What's gone has disappeared / Stone's throwing / Making photographs underwater / Wishing hues of green / Don't you / Nowhere / Colours make waves
CD _____ JAZIDCD 122
Acid Jazz / Apr '95 / Pinnacle.

Empire, Alec

GENERATION STAR WARS
CD _____ EFA 006612
Mille Plateau / Mar '95 / SRD.

LOW ON ICE
CD _____ EFA 006682
Mille Plateau / Oct '95 / SRD.

LTD EDITIONS
CD _____ EFA 006522
Mille Plateau / May '94 / SRD.

Empire Brass

EMPIRE BRASS ON BROADWAY
Phantom of the opera / Hello Dolly / Man of La Mancha / Macavity / Don't cry for me Argentina / Mambo / Easy Street / Till there was you / Seventy six trombones / Fugue for tinhorns / At the end of the day / Lonely goatherd / Night and day / Bali Ha'i / Put on a happy face / Big spender
CD _____ 80303
Telarc / Jun '92 / Conifer / ADA.

PASSAGE
CD _____ CD 80355
Telarc / Jan '95 / Conifer / ADA.

Empirion

ADVANCED TECHNOLOGY
CD _____ XLCD 117
XL / Feb '96 / Warner Music.

Empress Of Fur

HOW DOES THAT MAD BAD HAWAIIAN VOODOO GRAB YOU
CD _____ RAUCD 011
Raucous / Jan '95 / Nervous / Disc.

Empress Rasheda

HAIL HIM
CD _____ RRCD 011
Roots Collective / May '95 / SRD / Jetstar / Roots Collective.

En Vogue

BORN TO SING
Party / Strange / Lies / Hip hop bugle boy / Hold on / Part of me / You don't have to worry / Time goes on / Just can't stay away / Don't go / Luv lines / Waitin' on you
CD _____ 7567820842
Atlantic / Jun '90 / Warner Music.

FUNKY DIVAS
This is your life / My lovin' / Hip hop lover / Free your mind / Desire / Give him something he can feel / It ain't over till the fat lady sings / Give it up, turn it loose / Yesterday / Hooked on your love / Love don't love you / What is love / Runaway love (On Oct '93 reissues only) / Whatta man (On Oct '93 reissues only)
CD _____ 756792310-2
East West / Oct '93 / Warner Music.

Enchantment

DANCE THE MARBLE NAKED
CD _____ CM 77066-2
Century Media / May '94 / Plastic Head.

End

GUSTO
CD _____ GUSTCD 1
Expression / Aug '91 / Pinnacle.

Endino's Earthworm

ENDINO'S EARTHWORM
CD _____ CRZ 021 CD
Cruz / May '93 / Pinnacle / Plastic Head.

Endless

BEYOND THE ABYSS
CD _____ DISC 1886CD
Deathwish / Jan '96 / Plastic Head.

Endpoint

AFTERTASTE
CD _____ DOG 024CD
Doghouse / Nov '94 / Plastic Head.

LAST RECORD
CD _____ DOG 30CD
Doghouse / Aug '95 / Plastic Head.

Endraum

IN FLIMMANDER NACHT
CD _____ EFA 11229-2
Danse Macabre / Mar '94 / SRD.

Endresen, Sidsel

EXILE
Here the moon / Quest / Stages, I, II, III / Hunger / Theme I / Waiting train / Dreaming / Dust
CD _____ 5217212
ECM / Apr '94 / New Note.

Endsley, Melvin

I LIKE YOUR KIND OF LOVE
I like your kind of love / Is it true / I got a feeling / Keep a lovin' me baby / Let's fall out of love / Just want to be wanted / I ain't gettin' nowhere with you / Hungry eyes / Loving on my mind / Lonely all over again / There's bound to be / Gettin' used to the blues / Bringin' the blues to my door / I'd just be fool enough
CD _____ BCD 15595
Bear Family / May '93 / Rollercoaster / Direct / CM / Swift / ADA.

Endura

DREAMS OF DARK WAVES
CD _____ NACD 202
Nature & Art / Oct '95 / Plastic Head.

Energy Orchard

ENERGY ORCHARD
CD _____ MNMCD 2
M&M / Oct '95 / Total/BMG.

PAIN KILLER
Surrender to the city / She's the one I adore / Wasted / D F Dogs / Shipyard song / Past is another country / Remember my name / Sight for sore eyes / Pain killer / I hate to say goodbye
CD _____ TRACD 100
Transatlantic / Feb '95 / BMG / Pinnacle / ADA.

SHINOLA
Coming through / Madame George / Atlantic City / Stay away / Don't fail me now / In my room / Seven sisters / Star of the County Down / London Fields / Big town / I'm no angel
CD _____ TRACD 103
Transatlantic / Feb '95 / BMG / Pinnacle / ADA.

Engelotaub

IGNIS FATUUS: IRRLICHTER
CD _____ EFA 12154-2
Apollyon / Jul '94 / SRD.

Engin, Esin

BELLY DANCE MUSIC
CD _____ EUCD 1309
ARC / Jul '95 / ARC Music / ADA.

Engine

AUTOWRECK
CD _____ SPRAYCD 304
Making Waves / Oct '93 / CM.

Engine 54

54-95
CD _____ EFA 127682
Heatwave / Sep '95 / SRD.

Engine Kid

ANGEL'S WINGS
CD _____ REV 038CD
Revelation / May '95 / Plastic Head.

England

LAST OF THE JUBBLIES
CD _____ MABEL 1
Vinyl Tap / Jan '96 / Vinyl Tap.

England, Buddy

FATE'S A FIDDLER, LIFE'S A DANCE
CD _____ LARRCD 304

Larrikin / Nov '94 / Roots / Direct / ADA / CM.

England, Ty

TY ENGLAND
Redneck son / Smoke in her eyes / Should've asked her faster / Her only bad habit is me / New faces in the fields / Swing like that / You'll find somebody new / Blues ain't news to me / It's lonesome everywhere / Is that you
CD _____ 74321285932
RCA / Aug '95 / BMG.

England's Glory

LEGENDARY LOST ALBUM
Devotion / Wide waterway / City of fun / First time I saw you / Broken arrows / Bright lights / It's been a long time / Guest / Peter and the pets / Showdown / Predictably blonde / Weekend / Trouble in the world
CD _____ CDMGRAM 73
Anagram / Apr '94 / Pinnacle.

Englesstaub

ALLEUS MALEFICARUM
CD _____ AP 00310593
Apollyon / Dec '93 / SRD.

English Brass Ensemble

LYRIC BRASS
CD _____ CDDCA 660
ASV / Apr '89 / Koch.

English Dogs

BOW TO NONE
CD _____ IRC 023CD
Impact / Aug '94 / Plastic Head.

Enid

AERIE FAERIE NONSENSE
Prelude / Mayday galliard / Ondine / Childe Roland / Fand: first movement / Fand: second movement
CD _____ MNTLCD 6
Newt / May '94 / Plastic Head.

AT THE HAMMERSMITH
CD _____ MNTLCD 10
Newt / May '94 / Plastic Head.

FINAL NOISE
Childe Roland / Hall of mirrors / Song for Europe / Something wicked this way comes / Sheets of blue / Chaldean crossing / La rage / Earth born / Jerusalem
CD _____ MNTLCD 3
Newt / May '94 / Plastic Head.

IN THE REGION OF THE SUMMER STARS
Fool / Falling tower / Death the reaper / Lovers / Devil / Sun / Last judgement / In the region of the Summer stars
CD _____ MNTLCD 7
Newt / May '94 / Plastic Head.

SALOME
O Salome / Streets of blue / Change / Jack / Flames of power
CD _____ MNTLCD 9
Newt / May '94 / Plastic Head.

SEED AND THE SOWER, THE
Children crossing / Bar of shadow / La rage / Longhome / Earth born
CD _____ MNTLCD 2
Newt / Apr '94 / Plastic Head.

SIX PIECES
Sanctus / Once she was / Ring master / Punch and Judy man / Hall of mirrors / Dreamer / Joined by the heart (CD only.)
CD _____ MNTLCD 4
Newt / May '94 / Plastic Head.

SOMETHING WICKED THIS WAY COMES
Raindown / Jessica / And then there was none / Evensong / Bright star / Song for Europe / Something wicked this way comes
CD _____ MNTLCD 1
Newt / May '94 / Plastic Head.

SUNDIALER
CD _____ MNTLCD 12
Mantella / Oct '95 / Plastic Head.

TOUCH ME
Humoresque / Cortege / Elegy (touch me) / Gallevant / Albion fair / Joined by the heart
CD _____ MNTLCD 5
Newt / May '94 / Plastic Head.

TRIPPING THE LIGHT FANTASTIC
Ultraviolet cat / Little shiners / Gateway / Tripping the light fantastic / Freelance human / Dark hydraulic / Biscuit game
CD _____ MNTLCD 11
Newt / Nov '94 / Plastic Head.

Enigma

CROSS OF CHANGES
Second chapter / Eyes of truth / Return to innocence / I love you... I'll kill you / Silent warrior / Dream of the dolphin / Age of loneliness (Carly's song) / Out from the deep / Cross of changes / Return to innocence (mix) (Special edition CD only) / Age of lone-

liness (mix) (Special edition CD only) / Eyes of truth (mix) (Special edition CD only)
CD _____ CDVIR 20
Virgin / Jan '94 / EMI.

MCMXC AD
Voice of Enigma / Principles of lust / Sadness / Find love / Sadness (reprise) / Callas went away / Mea culpa / Voice and the snake / Knocking on forbidden doors / Back to the rivers of belief / Way to eternity / Hallelujah / Rivers of belief
CD _____ CDVIR 1
Virgin / Dec '90 / EMI.

Enja Band

LIVE AT SWEET BASIL
Unnameable / Purse / Lorietta / Snalking / Yvette / Clockwork / Duke and Mr. Strayhorn / Form an X
CD _____ ENJACD 80342
Enja / Aug '94 / New Note / Vital/SAM.

Ennis, Seamus

BEST OF IRISH PIPING
CD _____ TARACD 1002/9
Tara / Aug '95 / CM / ADA / Direct / Conifer.

PURE DROP/FOX CHASE
CD _____ TARA 1002/9CD
Tara / Jul '95 / CM / ADA / Direct / True.

WANDERING MINSTREL, THE
Wandering minstrel/Jackson's morning brush / Boys of Bluehill/Dunphy's hornpipe / Glennephin cuckoo/Littlefair Cannavans / Frieze breeches / Rags of Dublin/Wind that shakes the barley / Little stack of barley/Cronin's hornpipe / New Demesne / Blackbird / Gillan's apples / Walls of Liscarroll/Stone in the field / Molly O'Malone / Kiss the maid behind the barrel / Happy to meet and sorry to part
CD _____ OSS 12CD
Ossian / Mar '94 / ADA / Direct / CM.

Ennis, Skinnay

1956/57 LIVE IN STEREO
When summer is gone / Cheek to cheek / Got a date with an angel / Love for sale / You've got me crying again / I've got you under my skin / Breathless / Rhythm is our business / Whispers in the night / Scatterbrain / Josephine / I went out of my way / There ought to be a moonlight saving time / Foggy day (Mixes) / Untitled instrumental / Boy, a girl, and a lamplight / Girlfriend
CD _____ JH 1027
Jazz Hour / Feb '93 / Target/BMG / Jazz Music / Cadillac.

Eno, Brian

ANOTHER GREEN WORLD
Sky saw / Over fire island / St. Elmo's fire / In dark trees / Big ship / I'll come running / Another green world / Sombre reptiles / Little fishes / Golden hours / Becalmed / Zawinul/Lava / Everything merges with the night / Spirits drifting
CD _____ EGCD 21
EG / May '87 / EMI.

ANOTHER GREEN WORLD/BEFORE & AFTER SCIENCE/APOLLO (3CD Set)
CD Set _____ EGBC 7
EG / Nov '89 / EMI.

APOLLO (Atmospheres & Soundtracks)
Under stars / Secret place / Matta / Signals / Ending (ascent) / Under stars II / Drift / Silver morning / Deep blue day / Weightless / Always returning / Stars
CD _____ EGCD 53
EG / Jan '87 / EMI.

BEFORE & AFTER SCIENCE/WARM JETS/ANOTHER GREEN WORLD (Compact Collection 3CD Set)
CD Set _____ TPAK 36
Virgin / Jan '94 / EMI.

BEFORE AND AFTER SCIENCE
No one receiving / Spider and I / Through hollow lands / By this river / Julie with ... / Here he comes / King's lead hat / Energy fools the magician / Kurt's rejoinder / Backwater
CD _____ EGCD 32
EG / Jan '87 / EMI.

BEGEGNUNGEN (Eno, Brian & Moebius/Rodelius/Plank)
CD _____ SKYCD 3090
Sky / Nov '94 / Koch.

BEGEGNUNGEN 2 (Eno, Brian & Moebius/Rodelius/Plank)
CD _____ SKYCD 3095
Sky / Nov '94 / Koch.

BRIAN ENO 1 (3CD Set)
Another green world / Energy fools the magician / Dover beach / Slow water / Untitled / Chemin de fer / Empty landscape / Reactor / Secret / Don't look back / Marseilles / Two rapid formations / Sparrowfall (1) / Sparrowfall (2) / Sparrowfall (3) / Events in dense fog / There is nobody / Patrolling wire borders / Measured room / Task force / M 386 / Final sunset / Dove / Roman twilight / Dawn, marshland / Always returning I /

Signals / Drift study / Approaching train / Always returning II / Asian river / Theme of creation / St. Tom / Warszawa / Chemistry / Courage / Moss garden / Tension block / Strong flashes of light / More volts / Mist/rhythm / He nonono / Stream with bright fish / Her fleeting smile / Arc of doves / Stars / Index of metals (edit) / 1/1 / Ikebukero / Lost day / Thursday afternoon (edit) / Discreet music / Dunwich beach, autumn, 1960 / Neroli (edit)
CD Set _____ ENOBX 1
Virgin / Oct '93 / EMI.

BRIAN ENO 2 (3CD Set)
Needle in the camel's eye / Baby's on fire / Cindy tells me / On some faraway beach / Blank Frank / Dead finks don't talk / Some of them are old / Here come the warm jets / Seven deadly finns / Burning airlines... / Back in Judy's jungle / Great pretender / Third uncle / Put a straw... / True wheel / Taking tiger mountain / Lion sleeps tonight / Sky saw / Over fire island / St. Elmo's fire / In dark trees / Big ship / I'll come running / Sombre reptiles / Golden hours / Becalmed / Zawinul/Lava / Everything merges / Spirits drifting / No one receiving / Backwater / Kurt's rejoinder / King's lead hat / Here he comes / Julie with... / By this river / Through hollow lands / Spider and I / R.A.F. / America is waiting / Regiment / Jezebel spirit / Very very hungry / Spinning away / One word / Empty frame / River / Soul of Carmen Miranda / Belldog / I fall up / Stiff / Are they thinking of me / Some words / Under / Over
CD Set _____ ENOBX 2
Virgin / Oct '93 / EMI.

DISCREET MUSIC
Discreet music 1 and 2 / Fullness of wind (part 1) / French catalogues (part 2) / Brutal adour (part 3)
CD _____ EEGCD 23
EG / '87 / EMI.

HEADCANDY
CD Set _____ 6896400052
EG / Jan '95 / EMI.

HERE COME THE WARM JETS
Needles in camel's eye / Paw paw negro blowtorch / Baby's on fire / Cindy tells me / Driving me backwards / On some faraway beach / Black Frank / Dead finks don't talk / Some of them are old / Here come the warm jets
CD _____ EGCD 11
EG / Jul '93 / EMI.

MORE BLANK THAN FRANK (Desert Island Selection)
Here he comes / Everything merges with the night / On some faraway beach / I'll come running (to he your shoe) / Taking tiger mountain / Backwater / St. Elmo's fire / No one receiving / Great pretender / King's lead hat / Julie with ... / Back in Judy's jungle
CD _____ EGCD 65
EG / Jun '87 / EMI.

MUSIC FOR AIRPORTS (Ambient 1)
1/1 / 2/1 / 1/2 / 2/2
CD _____ EEGCD 17
EG / Jan '87 / EMI.

MUSIC FOR FILMS
M 386 / Aragon / From the same hill / Inland sea / Two rapid formations / Slow water / Sparrow fall 1 / Sparrow fall 2 / Sparrow fall 3 / Quartz / Events in dense fog / There is nobody / Patrolling wire borders / Task force / Strange light / Final sunset / Measured room / Alternative 3
CD _____ EEGCD 5
EG / '87 / EMI.

MY LIFE IN THE BUSH OF GHOSTS (Eno, Brian & David Byrne)
America is waiting / Mea culpa / Help me somebody / Regiment / Jezebel spirit / Moonlight in glory / Come with us / Carrier / Mountain of needles / Very very very hungry
CD _____ EGCD 48
EG / Jul '93 / EMI.

NEROLI
Neroli
CD _____ ASCD 015
All Saints / Jun '93 / Vital / Discovery.

NERVE NET
Fractal zoom / Wire shock / What actually happened / Pierre and mist / My squelchy life / Decentre / Juju space jazz / Roll the choke / Ali click / Distributed being
CD _____ 9362450332
WEA / Aug '92 / Warner Music.

ON LAND (Ambient 4)
Lizard point / Lost day / Tal coat / Shadow / Lantern marsh / Unfamiliar wind (Leeks hills) / Clearing / Dunwich Beach, Autumn 1960
CD _____ EEGCD 20
EG / Apr '82 / EMI.

PLATEAUX OF MIRRORS (Ambient 2) (Eno, Brian & Harold Budd)
First light / Steal away / Plateaux of mirror / Above Chiangmai / Arc of doves / Not yet remembered / Chill air / Among fields of crystal / Wind in lonely fences / Failing light
CD _____ EEGCD 18
EG / '87 / EMI.

SHUTOV ASSEMBLY, THE
Triennale / Alhondiga / Markgraph / Lanzarote / Francisco / Riverside / Innocenti / Stedelijk / Ikebukero
CD _____ 9362450102
WEA / Nov '92 / Warner Music.

SPINNER (Eno, Brian & Jah Wobble)
Where we lived / Like Organza / Steam / Garden recalled / Marine radio / Unusual balance / Space diary / Spinner / Transmitter and trumpet / Left where it fell
CD _____ ASCD 023
All Saints / Oct '95 / Vital / Discovery.

TAKING TIGER MOUNTAIN BY STRATEGY
Burning airlines give you so much more / Back in Judy's jungle / Fair lady of Limbourg / Mother whale eyeless / Great pretender / Third uncle / Put a straw under baby / True wheel / China my china / Taking tiger mountain
CD _____ EGCD 17
EG / Jul '93 / EMI.

THURSDAY AFTERNOON
Thursday afternoon
CD _____ EGCD 64
EG / Jul '93 / EMI.

WRONG WAY UP (Eno, Brian & John Cale)
CD _____ ASCD 12
All Saints / Jun '92 / Vital / Discovery.

Eno, Roger

BETWEEN TIDES
Out at dawn / Field of gold / Prelude for St. John / Ringinglow / Frost / One gull / Silent hours / Between tides / Winter music / While the city sleeps / Sunburst / Autumn / Almost dark
CD _____ ASCD 01
All Saints / Feb '96 / Vital / Discovery.

FAMILIAR, THE (Eno, Roger & Kate St. John)
CD _____ ASCD 013
All Saints / Oct '92 / Vital / Discovery.

ISLANDS
CD _____ SINE 001
Sine / Sep '95 / Grapevine.

LOST IN TRANSLATION
CD _____ ASCD 018
All Saints / Feb '95 / Vital / Discovery.

VOICES
Place in the wilderness / Day after / At the water's edge / Grey promenade / Paier sky / Through the blue / Evening tango / Recalling winter / Voices / Old dance / Reflections on I.K.B.
CD _____ EEGCD 42
EG / Jul '93 / EMI.

Enola Gay

F.O.T.H
CD _____ SHARK 105CD
Shark / Jun '95 / Plastic Head.

Enriquez, Bobby

WILDMAN RETURNS, THE
Pink Panther / Our love is here to stay / Groovin' high / Walkin' shoes / Starlight souvenirs / Easy living / I'm confessin' that I love you / As long as I live / Blue Hawaii / Misty
CD _____ ECD 22059
Evidence / Oct '93 / Harmonia Mundi / ADA / Cadillac.

Ensemble Berehinya

VOROTARCHILC: THE GATEKEEPER
CD _____ PAN 7002
Pan / Feb '94 / ADA / Direct / CM.

Ensemble De Cuivres

BRASS ENSEMBLE 1
Suite in A major / Fugue in G minor (little) / Choral prelude / Fugue in C minor / Contrapunctus / Fancies, toyes and dreams / Concerto in C minor
CD _____ C 377237
Denon / '88 / Conifer.

BRASS ENSEMBLE 2
Merle et pinson / Impression of a parade / Tritsch tratsch polka / Satirical dance / Greensleeves / Five rags / Harlem rag / Teddy trombone / Little brown jug
CD _____ C 377238
Denon / '88 / Conifer.

Ensemble Dede Gorgud

HEYVA GULU: DANCES & ASHUG MELODIES FROM NAKHICHEVAN (Anthology Of Azerbaijanian Music #3)
CD _____ PAN 2021CD
Pan / Mar '94 / ADA / Direct / CM.

Ensemble Del Doppio...

JESUS CHRIST WAS BORN (Ensemble Del Doppio Bordonne)
CD _____ NT 6722
Robi Droli / Jan '94 / Direct / ADA.

Ensemble Folk-Art

BULGARIA - WOMEN'S CHORUS
CD _____ PS 65102
Playasound / Mar '93 / Harmonia Mundi / ADA.

Ensemble Kolkheti

OH BLACK EYED GIRL
CD _____ PANCD 2006
Pan / May '00 / ADA / Direct / CM.

Ensemble Kutaisi

MAKRULI: POLYPHONIC SONGS FROM GEORGIA
CD _____ PAN 7001
Pan / Feb '94 / ADA / Direct / CM.

Ensemble Musica Criolla

MUSIQUE TRADITIONALE DU CHILI
CD _____ 824742
Buda / Nov '90 / Discovery / ADA.

Ensemble Nihon No Oto

TRADITIONAL CHAMBER MUSIC OF JAPAN
CD _____ AUB 6784
Auvidis/Ethnic / Feb '94 / Harmonia Mundi.

Ensemble Nipponia

KABUKI AND OTHER TRADITIONAL MUSIC
CD _____ 7559720842
Elektra Nonesuch / Jan '95 / Warner Music.

TRADITIONAL VOCAL AND INSTRUMENTAL MUSIC
CD _____ 7559720722
Elektra Nonesuch / Jan '95 / Warner Music.

Ensemble Of The...

HARVEST, A SHEPHERD, A BRIDE, A (Village Music Of Bulgaria/Original 1955 Recording) (Ensemble Of The Bulgarian Republic)
CD _____ 7559720112
Elektra Nonesuch / Jan '95 / Warner Music.

Ensemble Tzigane...

SERENADE (Ensemble Tzigane Chiokerly)
CD _____ PV 785092
Disques Pierre Verany / Jul '93 / Kingdom.

Enslaved

ENSLAVED
CD _____ ANTI-MOSH 008CD
Voices Of Wonder / Apr '94 / Plastic Head.

FROST
CD _____ OP 025
Osmose / Nov '94 / Plastic Head.

Enteli

ENTELI
CD _____ PSCD 77
Phono Suecia / Oct '94 / ADA / Cadillac.

Entombed

CLANDESTINE
CD _____ MOSH 037CD
Earache / Sep '94 / Vital.

LEFT HAND PATH
Left hand path / Drowned / Revel in flesh / When life has ceased / Supposed to rot / But life goes on / Bitter loss / Morbid devourment / Deceased / Truth beyond / Carnal leftovers
CD _____ MOSH 021CD
Earache / Sep '94 / Vital.

WOLVERINE BLUES
Eyemaster / Rotten soil / Wolverine blues / Demon / Contempt / Full of hell / Blood song / Hollowman / Heavens die / Out of hand
CD _____ MOSH 082CD
Earache / Sep '94 / Vital.

Enuff Z Nuff

TWEAKED
Stoned / Life is strange / If I can't have / Love song / Bullet from a gun / Without your love / Jesus closed his eyes / Mr Jones / We're all right / Style / My dear dream / My heroin / It's 2 late
CD _____ CDMFN 190
Music For Nations / Sep '95 / Pinnacle.

Enya

CELTS, THE
Celts / Aldebaran / I want tomorrow / March of the celts / Deireadh an tuath / Sun in the stream / To go beyond / Fairytale / Epona / Triad: St. Patrick cu chulainn oisin / Portrait / Boadicea / Bard dance / Dan y dwr / To go beyond (2)
CD _____ 4509911672
WEA / Nov '92 / Warner Music.

MEMORIES OF TREES
CD _____ 0630128792
WEA / Nov '95 / Warner Music.

SHEPHERD MOONS
Shepherd moons / Caribbean blue / How can I keep from singing / Ebudae / Angeles / No holly for Miss Quinn / Book of days / Evacuee / Lothlorien / Marble halls / After ventus / Smaointe
CD _____ 903175572-2
WEA / Nov '91 / Warner Music.

WATERMARK
Watermark / Cursum perfico / On your shore / Storms in Africa / Exile / Miss Clare remembers / Orinoco flow / Evening falls / River / Longships / Na laetha geal m'oige / Storms in Africa (part II)
CD _____ 246006 2
WEA / Sep '88 / Warner Music.

Eon

VOID DWELLER
CD _____ STEAM 45 CD
Vinyl Solution / Oct '92 / Disc.

Epic Soundtracks

SLEEPING STAR
CD _____ NORMAL 186CD
Normal/Okra / Aug '95 / Direct / ADA.

Epidemic

DECAMERON
CD _____ CDZORRO 50
Metal Blade / Sep '92 / Pinnacle.

EXIT PARADISE
CD _____ CDZORRO 79
Metal Blade / Aug '94 / Pinnacle.

TRUTH OF WHAT WILL BE, THE
CD _____ CORE 4CD
Metalcore / Oct '90 / Plastic Head.

Epidemics

EPIDEMICS, THE
Never take no for an answer / What would I do without you / Situations / You don't love me anymore / Love is alright / You can be anything / No cure / Don't I know you / Give an inch / Full moon
CD _____ 8275222
ECM / May '87 / New Note.

Epilepsy

BAPHOMET - TAROT OF THE UNDERWORLD (CD Box With Tarot Cards & Book)
CD Set _____ KK 144CD
KK / Jan '96 / Plastic Head.

ROZIS
CD _____ PA 09CD
Paragoric / Aug '95 / Plastic Head.

Epilogue

HIDE
Swords and knives / Hide / Wheel of love / Living a lie / In the city / Travelling man / No sign of life / Into the clock / Matthew / Flame
CD _____ CYCL 010
Cyclops / Oct '94 / Pinnacle.

Episode Six

COMPLETE PYE SESSIONS
CD _____ NEXCD 156
Sequel / Jul '91 / BMG.

Epitaph

SEEMING SALVATION
CD _____ THRO 17CD
Thrash / Nov '94 / Plastic Head.

Epstein Brothers

KINGS OF FREYLEKH
CD _____ SM 16112
Wergo / Dec '95 / Harmonia Mundi / ADA / Cadillac.

Equals

ALL THE HITS PLUS MORE
CD _____ CDPT 001
Prestige / Jun '92 / Total/BMG.

ULTIMATE HIT COLLECTION, THE
CD _____ REP 4214-WZ
Repertoire / Aug '91 / Pinnacle / Cadillac.

VERY BEST OF THE EQUALS, THE
Baby come back / Hold me closer / Viva Bobby Joe / Laurel and Hardy / Another sad and lonely night / Rub-a-dub dub / Softly, softly / Soul brother Clifford / I get so excited / Teardrops / You'd better tell her / I can see, but you don't know / Black skinned blue eyed boys / I won't there / I'm a poor man / Michael and his slipper tree / Cinderella / Christine / Friday night / Honey gum / No love can be sweeter / Ain't got

nothing to give you / Leaving you is hard to do / Put some rock 'n' roll in your soul / Diversion
CD _____ SEECD 374
See For Miles/C5 / Jul '93 / Pinnacle.

Equidad Bares

MES ESPAGNES
CD _____ Y 225049CD
Silex / Apr '95 / ADA.

Equipe 84

RACCOLTA DI SUCCESSI V2
CD _____ 182562
Ricordi / Aug '93 / Discovery.

Equomanthorn

NINDINUGGA NIMSHIM
CD _____ USR 009CD
Unisound / Jan '96 / Plastic Head.

Erasure

CHORUS
Chorus / Waiting for the day / Joan / Breath of life / Am I right / How I love to hate you / Turns the love to anger / Siren song / Perfect stranger / Home
CD _____ CDSTUMM 95
Mute / Oct '91 / Disc.

CIRCUS, THE
It doesn't have to be / Hideaway / Don't dance / If I could / Sexuality / Victim of love / Leave me to bleed / Sometimes / Circus / Spiralling
CD _____ CDSTUMM 35
Mute / '87 / Disc.

ERASURE
Guess I'm into feeling / Rescue me / Sono luminus / Fingers and thumbs (Cold summer's day) / Rock me gently / Grace / Stay with me / Love the way you do so / Angel / I love you / Long goodbye
CD _____ CDSTUMM 138
Mute / Oct '95 / Disc.

I SAY, I SAY, I SAY
CD _____ CDSTUMM 115
Mute / May '94 / Disc.

INNOCENTS, THE
Little respect / Ship of fools / Phantom bride / Chains of love / Hallowed ground / 65,000 / Heart of stone / Yahoo / Imagination / Witch in the ditch / Weight of the world
CD _____ CDSTUMM 55
Mute / Apr '88 / Disc.

POP - THE FIRST 20 HITS
Who needs love like that / Heavenly action / Oh l'amour / Sometimes / It doesn't have to be / Victim of love / Circus / Ship of fools / Chains of love / Little respect / Stop / Drama / You surround me / Blue savanna / Star / Chorus / Love to hate you / Am I right / Breath of life / Take a chance on me / Who needs love like that #2 (Mix)
CD _____ CDMUTEL 1
Mute / Nov '92 / Disc.

TWO RING CIRCUS
CD _____ CDSTUMM 35 R
Mute / '87 / Disc.

WILD
Piano song (instrumental) / Blue Savannah / Drama / How many times / Star / La Gloria / You surround me / Brother and sister / 2000 miles / Crown of thorns / Piano song
CD _____ CDSTUMM 75
Mute / Oct '89 / Disc.

WONDERLAND
Who needs love like that / Reunion / Cry so easy / Push me, shove me / Heavenly action / Say what / Love is a loser / Senseless / My heart... so blue / Oh l'amour / Pistol
CD _____ CDSTUMM 25
Mute / '86 / Disc.

Erazerhead

SHELLSHOCKED - BEST OF ERAZERHEAD
CD _____ AHOY 28
Captain Oi / Dec '94 / Plastic Head.

Erdmann, Dietrich

WORKS FOR STRING ORCHESTRA
CD _____ CTH 2145
Thorofon / Jul '92 / RRD.

Erguner, Kudsi

DERVISHES OF TURKEY - SUFI MUSIC
CD _____ PS 65120
Playasound / Feb '94 / Harmonia Mundi / ADA.

PESHREV & SEMAI OF TANBURI DJEMI BEY
Seddiaraban peshrev / Taksim on tanbur / Seddiaraban saz semasi / Muhayyer peshrev / Muhayyer saz semaisi / Taksim on oud and kanun / Ferarfeza peshrev / Taksim on the ney / Ferarfeza saz semaisi / Neva peshrev / Huseyni / Nikriz sirto
CD _____ CMPCD 3013
CMP / Oct '94 / Vital/SAM.

Eric & The Good Good...

FUNKY (Eric & The Good Good Feeling)
CD _____ EQNCD 1
Equinox / Nov '89 / Total/BMG.

Eric B & Rakim

PAID IN FULL
I ain't no joke / Eric B is on the cut / My melody / I know you got soul / Move the crowd / As the rhyme goes on / Chinese arithmetic / Eric B for president / Extended beat / Paid in full
CD _____ IMCD 9
4th & Broadway / '89 / PolyGram.

Erick

ESTRANGED
Progress / Terry / Anarchy / 4004 BC 9 a.m. / Beast / Martini 2000 / Egyptians in space / Half hearted Jon / 2 Ways 2 love U / Moral village / Death boll tell
CD _____ CLOD 14
Fragment / Aug '93 / Fragment Records.

Erickson, Eddie

ON EASY STREET
CD _____ ARCD 19111
Arbors Jazz / Nov '94 / Cadillac.

Erickson, Roky

ALL THAT MAY DO MY RHYME
CD _____ TR 33CD
Trance / Feb '95 / SRD.

CLICK YOUR FINGERS APPLAUDING THE PLAY
CD _____ 422130
New Rose / May '94 / Direct / ADA.

GREMLINS HAVE PICTURES
Night of the vampire / Interpreter / Song to Abe Lincoln / John Lawman / Anthem / Warning / Sweet honey pie / I am / Cold night for alligators / Heroin / I have always been here before / Before in the beginning
CD _____ FIENDCD 66
Demon / Oct '90 / Pinnacle / ADA.

LIVE DALLAS 1979 (Erickson, Roky & The Nervebreakers)
CD _____ 422404
New Rose / May '94 / Direct / ADA.

LOVE TO SEE YOU BLEED
CD _____ SFMDCD 2
Swordfish / Feb '93 / Disc.

MAD DOG
CD _____ SFMDCD 001
Swordfish / Feb '92 / Disc.

WHERE THE PYRAMID MEETS THE EYE (A Tribute To Roky Erickson) (Various Artists)
Reverberation (doubt) / If you have ghosts / I had to tell you / She lives in a time of her own / Slip inside this house / You don't love me yet / I have always been here before / You're gonna miss me / Cold night for alligators / Fire engine / Bermuda / I walked with a zombie / Earthquake / Don't slander me / Red temple prayer (two headed dog) / Burn the flames / Postures (leave your body behind) / Nothing in return / Splash 1 (MC only) / We sell soul (MC only) / White faces (MC only) / Reverberation (doubt) (2) (CD only)
CD _____ 7599264222
Sire / Feb '91 / Warner Music.

Eric's Trip

ALBUM
CD _____ SPCD 136336
Sub Pop / Oct '94 / Disc.

LOVE TARA
CD _____ SPCD 115-293
Sub Pop / Nov '93 / Disc.

PETER
CD _____ SPCD 102/274
Sub Pop / Jun '93 / Disc.

PURPLE BLUE
CD _____ SPCD 333
Sub Pop / Jan '96 / Disc.

Ericson, Rolf

STOCKHOLM SWEETNIN'
CD _____ DRCD 256
Dragon / Oct '94 / Roots / Cadillac / Wellard / CM / ADA.

Ericsson, Lena

DOODLIN'
Days of wine and roses / Doodlin' / Too long at the fair / Love for sale / My second home / Cheek to cheek / Hey John / But not for me / (I'm afraid) the masquerade is over
CD _____ NCD 8808
Phontastic / Dec '94 / Wellard / Jazz Music / Cadillac.

215

Erkose Ensemble

TURKISH TZIGANE MUSIC
CD _____ CMP CD 3010
CMP / Jul '92 / Vital/SAM.

Eroglu, Musa

INSTRUMENTAL MUSIC FROM ANATOLIA (Eroglu, Musa & Arif Sag)
CD _____ 926202
Buda / Jul '95 / Discovery / ADA.

Erosion III

EROSION III
CD _____ WB 095CD
We Bite / Nov '92 / Plastic Head.

MORTAL AGONY
CD _____ WEBITE 36CD
We Bite / Dec '88 / Plastic Head.

Erotic Dissidents

NAKED ANGEL
Introduction / Jack to the air / Sure beats are working / Right rhythm, right time / Off your ass / Mind fuck / T.W.A.T. / Body language / I wanna be loved by you / Move your ass / Shake your hips
CD _____ SD 4005 CD
SPV / Jul '89 / Plastic Head.

Erotic Suicide

ABUSEMENT PARK
CD _____ 341972
No Bull / Oct '95 / Koch.

Erquiaga, Steve

ERKIOLOGY
San Sebastian / Pick it up / Erkiology / Night light / Euzkadi (ooh-ska-dee) / Something old, something new / Afro centric / Three heats dancing
CD _____ WD 0127
Windham Hill / Jun '91 / Pinnacle / BMG / ADA.

Erraji, Hassan

IA DOUNIA (Erraji, Hassan & Arabesque/Sabra)
CD _____ TUGCD 002
Riverboat / Nov '90 / New Note / Sterns.

Errisson, King

GLOBAL MUSIC
Here I am (come and take me) / Street dance / Babalay / Any love / Say nothing / Goombay / Together in America / Jimbo (king of the dance floor) / Calypso woman
CD _____ ICHCD 1123
Ichiban / Oct '91 / Koch.

Erskine, Peter

MOTION POET
Erskoman / Not a word / Hero with a thousand faces / Dream clock / Exit up right / New regalia / Boulez / Mysery man / In walked Maya
CD _____ CY 72582
Denon / Oct '88 / Conifer.

PETER ERSKINE
Leroy Street / E.S.P. / All's well that ends / Coyote blues / In statu nascendi / Change of mind / My ship
CD _____ OJCCD 610
Original Jazz Classics / Feb '92 / Wellard / Jazz Music / Cadillac / Complete/Pinnacle.

SWEET SOUL
Touch her soft lips and part / Press enter / Sweet soul / To be or not to be / Ambivalence / Angels and devils / Speak low / Scholastic / Distant blossom / But is it art / In your own sweet way
CD _____ PD 90616
Novus / May '92 / BMG.

TIME BEING (Erskine, Peter & John Taylor/Palle Danielsson)
CD _____ 5217192
ECM / Sep '94 / New Note.

TRANSITION
Osaka castle / Rabbit in the moon / Corazon / Suite / King Richard II / Hard speaks hold / My foolish heart / Orson Welles and others
CD _____ CY 1484
Denon / '88 / Conifer.

Erstrand, Lars

DREAM DANCING
CD _____ OP 9101CD
Opus 3 / Sep '91 / May Audio / Pentacone.

LARS ERSTRAND AND FOUR BROTHERS (Erstrand, Lars & Four Brothers)
CD _____ OP 8402CD
Opus 3 / Sep '91 / May Audio / Pentacone.

TRIBUTE TO LIONEL HAMPTON (Erstrand, Lars & Wobbling Woollwinds)
CD _____ NCD 8835
Phontastic / Feb '95 / Wellard / Jazz Music / Cadillac.

Ervin, Booker

BLUES BOOK
Blues book / Eeerie dearie / One for Mort / No booze blooze / True blue
CD _____ OJCCD 780-2
Original Jazz Classics / Jan '94 / Wellard / Jazz Music / Cadillac / Complete/Pinnacle.

COOKIN'
Dee da do / Mr. Wiggles / You don't know what love is / Down in the dumps / Well well / Autumn leaves
CD _____ SV 0150
Savoy Jazz / Apr '93 / Conifer / ADA.

DOWN IN THE DUMPS
Down in the dumps / Well well / Mr. Wiggles / When you're smiling / Dee da do / You don't know what love is / Autumn leaves / Trolley song
CD _____ SV 0245
Savoy Jazz / Oct '94 / Conifer / ADA.

SONG BOOK, THE
Lamp is low / Come Sunday / All the things you are / Just friends / Yesterdays / Our love is here to stay
CD _____ OJCCD 779
Original Jazz Classics / Apr '94 / Wellard / Jazz Music / Cadillac / Complete/Pinnacle.

THAT'S IT
Mojo / Uranus / Poinciana / Speak low / Booker's blues / Boo
CD _____ CCD 79014
Candid / Jun '88 / Cadillac / Jazz Music / Wellard / Koch.

Eschete, Ron

CLOSER LOOK, A
Like someone in love / One for Pop / When it's sleepy time down South/Stars fell on Alabama / Do you know what it means to miss New Orleans / You stepped out of a dream / I'll be seeing you / Mona Lisa / Amazing Grace / Stardust / Coquette / My foolish heart / Manha De Carnaval / My blue heaven
CD _____ CCD 4607
Concord Jazz / Jul '94 / New Note.

COME RAIN OR COME SHINE
Azul serape / Some other time / Come rain or come shine / Theme for Jeff / Naima / Girl next door / Moanin' / Nuages / Loads of love / Goodbye
CD _____ CCD 4665
Concord Jazz / Sep '95 / New Note.

Escorts

FROM THE BLUE ANGEL
Dizzy Miss Lizzy / All I want is you / One to cry / Tell me baby / I don't want to go without you / Don't forget to write / C'mon home baby / You'll get no lovin' that way / Let it be me / Mad mad world / From head to toe / Night time
CD _____ EDCD 422
Edsel / May '95 / Pinnacle / ADA.

OLD SCHOOL HARMONY
CD _____ DGPCD 726
Deep Beats / May '95 / BMG.

Escoude, Christian

HOLIDAYS
CD _____ 514304-2
Emarcy / Feb '94 / PolyGram.

Escovedo, Alejandro

13 YEARS
CD _____ NR 422485
New Rose / Jan '94 / Direct / ADA.

GRAVITY
CD _____ 422409
New Rose / May '94 / Direct / ADA.

Escovedo, Pete

YESTERDAY'S MEMORIES - TOMORROW'S DREAMS
Charango sunrise / Moving pictures / Azteca Mozambique / Ah ah / Cueros / Modern dance / Zina's Zamba / Yesterday's memories, tomorrow's dreams / Revolt
CD _____ CCD 45002
Concord Jazz / Jul '87 / New Note.

Esen, Aydin

ANADOLU
CD _____ 4719982
Sony Jazz / Jan '95 / Sony.

Eshelman, Dave

DEEP VOICES (Eshelman, Dave Jazz Garden Big Band)
CD _____ CDSB 2039
Sea Breeze / '88 / Jazz Music.

Eskalte Gaeste

KUNSTSCHEISSE
_____ EFA 11891
EFA / Apr '93 / SRD.

Eskelin, Ellery

FIGURE OF SPEECH
CD _____ 121232-2
Soul Note / Apr '93 / Harmonia Mundi / Wellard / Cadillac.

Eskimos & Egypt

PERFECT DISEASE
CD _____ TPLP 37CD
One Little Indian / Sep '93 / Pinnacle.

Espacio, Cuarto

REENCUENTRO
Tumbania / Sancho / Reencuentro / Pantera / Tranquilidad / Polka and son / Reencuentro (reprise) / Hay gritos / Momo
CD _____ INT 30602
Intuition / Nov '93 / New Note.

Esperanto

ESPERANTO
You're the one / Are you the best / Only a miracle / Turning point / All good things / Love affair / Don't let love pass away / Something that you said / Glad that you were mine
CD _____ SJRCD 023
Soul Jazz / Mar '95 / New Note / Vital.

Esplendor Geometrico

VERITAS SPLENDOR
_____ GR 006
No CD / Dec '95 / Vital/SAM.

Esplin, Joss

SCOTLAND 'TIL I RETURN (Esplin, Joss & Sandra Wright)
CD _____ JJCD 1020
Beechwood / Jan '93 / Ross / Duncans.

Esposito, Gene

RHYTHM SECTION
CD _____ PS 004CD
P&S / Sep '95 / Discovery.

Esquerita

BEST OF ESQUERITA
CD _____ FC 053CD
Fan Club / Aug '89 / Direct.

SOCK IT TO ME BABY
Introduction by Little Richard / Sock it to me baby / Nobody want you when you're down and out / Mississippidod damn / Wig wearin' baby / I can't stand it anymore / Get along, honey, honey / I guess I'll go through life alone / Never again / Till then / At the Dewdrop Inn / (I don't want nobody gonna) steal my love from me / What's wrong with you
CD _____ BCD 15504
Bear Family / Nov '93 / Rollercoaster / Direct / CM / Swift / ADA.

Essence

DANCING IN THE RAIN (Best Of Essence)
Out of grace / Like Christ / Only for you / Cat / Everything / Drifting / Mirage / In your heart / Time / Forever in death / Waves of death / Burned in memory / Endless lakes / Ice / U 4 life / Angelic / How to make me hate / Mirage '94 / Afterworld / Thirty second song
CD _____ CDMGRAM 82
Anagram / Aug '94 / Pinnacle.

MONUMENT OF TRUST, A
Mirage / Drifting / In teats / Nothing / Waves of death / Happiness / Lollipop / Years of doubt / Fire / Death cell / Monument of trust
CD _____ CDMGRAM 96
Anagram / Sep '95 / Pinnacle.

PURITY
Last preach / Reflected dream / Cat / Blind / Never mine / Endless lakes / Forever in death / Salvation / Waving girl / Purity / Confusion / From my mouth / Swaying wind
CD _____ CDMGRAM 95
Anagram / Sep '95 / Pinnacle.

Essex

BEST OF THE ESSEX, THE
Easier said than done / Whenever I need my baby / Where is he / Every night / I love her / Come on to my party / Walkin' miracle / She's got everything / More than it would help / Marriage license / In my dreams / You talk too much / There's no fool like a young fool / Where there's a will / Make him feel like a man / Don't fight it baby / When somethin's hard to get / Just for the boy / I'm making it over / Everybody's got you (for their own) / Be my baby / Be sure / When the music stops / Real true lover
CD _____ NEMCD 714
Sequel / Nov '94 / BMG.

Essex, David

BACK TO BACK
Africa / Father and son / Fall at your feet / Awesome story / True love ways / Love train / Singin' the blues / Never meant to hurt you / You really got me / Really nice / Won't back down / Oh Father
CD _____ 523790-2
PolyGram / Oct '94 / PolyGram.

BEAUTY AND THE BEAST
CD Set _____ MBOCD 1
MBO / Dec '95 / Total/BMG.

BEST OF DAVID ESSEX, THE
Hold me close / Gonna make you a star / If I could / Lamplight / Coming home / Cool out tonight / Bring in the sun / For Emily, whenever I might find her / Rolling stone / City lights / Stardust / Good ol' rock and roll / Turn me loose / America / On and on
CD _____ 4810362
Columbia / Dec '95 / Sony.

BROADWAY COLLECTION, THE
CD _____ RLBTC 002
Realisation / Oct '93 / Prism.

COLLECTION, THE
Oh what a circus / Heart on my sleeve / No substitutes / Imperial wizard / Silver dream machine / Hot love / Ships that pass in the night / Me and my girl (Night-clubbing) / High flying, adored / Winter's tale / Smile / Won't change me now / Goodbye first love / Tahiti / Fishing for the moon / You're in my heart / Falling angels riding
CD _____ 5517952
Spectrum/Karussell / Nov '95 / PolyGram / THE.

COLLECTION: DAVID ESSEX
Lamplight / Ocean girl / On and on / Rock on / Tell him no / Window / I know / America / Gonna make you a star / Bring in the sun / Ooh darling / Stardust / Street fight / Turn me loose / For Emily / We all insane
CD _____ CCSCD 248
Castle / Jun '90 / BMG.

COVER SHOT
Everlasting love / Time after time / Waterloo sunset / First cut is the deepest / Here comes the night / Paint it black / Out of time / Horse with no name / Letter / I can't let Maggie go / New York mining disaster 1941 / Summer in the city
CD _____ 514 563-2
PolyGram TV / Mar '93 / PolyGram.

DAVID ESSEX
Gonna make you a star / Window / I know / There's something about you baby / Good ol' rock 'n roll / America / Dance little girl / Ooh Darling / Miss Sweetness / Stardust
CD _____ 982991 2
Pickwick/Sony Collector's Choice / Aug '93 / Carlton Home Entertainment / Pinnacle / Sony.

HIS GREATEST HITS
Rock on / Gonna make you a star / Hold me close / Winter's tale / Oh what a circus / Silver dream machine / My and my girl (nightclubbing) / Tahiti / Lamplight / Stardust / Cool out tonight / If I could / Myfanwy / Rollin' stone / You're in my heart / Sun ain't gonna shine anymore / Africa - you shine / Rock on (new version)
CD _____ 5103082
Mercury / Oct '91 / PolyGram.

MISSING YOU
CD _____ 5295822
PolyGram TV / Nov '95 / PolyGram.

SHOWSTOPPERS
Phantom of the opera / Bright eyes / Forty second street/Lullaby of Broadway / Summertime / Ghostbusters / Save the people / Out here on my own / I dreamed a dream / Corner on the sky / Tahiti
CD _____ MSCD 14
Music De-Luxe / Mar '95 / Magnum Music Group.

SPOTLIGHT ON DAVID ESSEX
CD _____ 8481812
Mercury / Jul '93 / PolyGram.

YOU'RE IN MY HEART
Me and my girl / You're in my heart / Heart on my sleeve / No substitutes / Sea of love / Sunshine girl / Silver dream machine / Cold as ice / Don't leave me this way / Come on little darlin' / Are you still my true love / You don't know like I know / Smile / Winter's tale
CD _____ 5500012
Spectrum/Karussell / May '93 / PolyGram / THE.

Essig, David

REBEL FLAG
CD _____ APCD 072
Appaloosa / '92 / ADA / Magnum Music Group.

Essix, Eric

FIRST IMPRESSIONS
CD _____ NOVA 8920
Nova / Sep '92 / New Note.

SECOND THOUGHTS
CD _____ NOVA 0138
Nova / Sep '92 / New Note.

Estefan, Gloria

ABRIENDOS
Abriendo puertas / Tres deseos / Mas alla / Dulce amor / Farolita / Nuevo dia / La parranda / Milagro de amor / Lejos de ti / Felicidad
CD _____ 4809922
Epic / Oct '95 / Sony.

ANYTHING FOR YOU (Estefan, Gloria & Miami Sound Machine)
Betcha say that / Let it loose / Can't stay away from you / Give it up / Surrender / Rhythm is gonna get you / Love toy / I want you so bad / 1-2-3 / Anything for you / Rhythm is gonna get you (12" mix) (CD only) / Betcha say that (Mix) (Only on CD.)
CD _____ 4631252
Epic / Oct '88 / Sony.

ANYTHING FOR YOU/CUTS BOTH WAYS
Betcha say that / Let it loose / Can't stay away from you / Give it up / Surrender / Rhythm is gonna get you / Love toy / I want you so bad / 1-2-3 / Anything for you / Rhythm is gonna get you (12" mix) / Betcha say that (Mix) / Ay ay ay / Here we are / Say / Think about you now / Nothin' new / Oye mi canto (Hear my voice) / Don't wanna lose you / Get on your feet / Your love is bad for me / Cuts both ways
CD Set _____ 4784852
Epic / Mar '95 / Sony.

CUTS BOTH WAYS
Ay ay ay / Here we are / Say / Think about you / Nothin' oye mi canto / Don't wanna lose you / Get on your feet / Your love is bad for me / Cuts both ways
CD _____ 4651452
Epic / Sep '94 / Sony.

EXITOS DE GLORIA ESTEFAN
Renacer / Conga / No sera facil / Dr. Beat / Regresa a mi / No lo olvidare / Dingue li bangue / No me vuelvo enamorar / Si voy a perderte / Oye mi canto (hear my voice)
CD _____ 4675202
Epic / Nov '90 / Sony.

EYES OF INNOCENCE (Miami Sound Machine)
Dr. Beat / Prisoner of love / OK / Love me / Orange express / I need a man / Eyes of innocence / When someone comes into your life / I need your love / Do you want to dance
CD _____ 983325 2
Pickwick/Sony Collector's Choice / Oct '93 / Carlton Home Entertainment / Pinnacle / Sony.

GLORIA ESTEFAN - THE 12" TAPE
Oye mi canto (hear my voice) / Bady boy / Get on your feet / Rhythm is gonna get you
CD _____ 4689892
Epic / Mar '93 / Sony.

GREATEST HITS
Dr. Beat / Can't stay away from you / Bad boy / 1-2-3 / Anything for you / Here we are / Rhythm is gonna get you / Get on your feet / Don't wanna lose you / Coming out of the dark / Christmas through your eyes / I see your smile / Go away / Always tomorrow
CD _____ 472332-2
Epic / Nov '92 / Sony.

HOLD ME, THRILL ME, KISS ME
Hold me, thrill me, kiss me / How can I be sure / Everlasting love / Traces / Don't let the sun catch you crying / You've made me so very happy / Turn the beat around / Breaking up is hard to do / Love on a two way street / Cherchez la femme / It's too late / Goodnight my love / Don't let the sun go down on me
CD _____ 477416-2
Epic / Oct '94 / Sony.

INTO THE LIGHT
Coming out of the dark / Seal our fate / What goes around / Nayib's song (I am here for you) / Remember me with love / Heart with your name on it / Sex in the '90s / Close my eyes / Language of love / Light of love / Can't forget you / Live for loving you / Mama you can't go / Desde la oscuridad
CD _____ 4677822
Epic / Apr '95 / Sony.

MI TIERRA
Con los anos que me quedan / Mi Tierra / Ayer / Mi buen Amor / Tus Ojos / No hay mal Que por bien no Venga / Si senor / Volveras / Montuno / Hablemos el Mismo Idioma / Hablas de mi / Tradicion
CD _____ 473799 2
Epic / Jun '93 / Sony.

PRIMITIVE LOVE (Miami Sound Machine)
Body to body / Primitive love / Words get in the way / Falling in love (Uh-oh) / Conga / Mucho money / You made a fool of me / Movies / Surrender paradise
CD _____ 4634002
Epic / Feb '94 / Sony.

Estes, Sleepy John

BROKE AND HUNGRY
CD _____ DE 608
Delmark / Dec '95 / Hot Shot / ADA / CM / Direct / Cadillac.

BROWNSVILLE BLUES
CD _____ DD 613
Delmark / Jan '93 / Hot Shot / ADA / CM / Direct / Cadillac.

ELECTRIC SLEEP
CD _____ DD 619
Delmark / Dec '88 / Hot Shot / ADA / CM / Direct / Cadillac.

I AIN'T GONNA BE WORRIED NO MORE
CD _____ CD 2004
Yazoo / Sep '92 / CM / ADA / Roots / Koch.

LEGEND OF SLEEPY JOHN ESTES, THE
CD _____ DD 603
Delmark / May '87 / Hot Shot / ADA / CM / Direct / Cadillac.

SLEEPY JOHN ESTES
Broken hearted ragged and dirty too / Girl I love she got long curly hair / Ticket agent blues / Bad luck's my buddy
CD _____ JSPCD 601
JSP / Mar '92 / ADA / Target/BMG / Direct / Cadillac / Complete/Pinnacle.

SLEEPY JOHN ESTES (1929-37)
CD _____ DOCD 5015
Blues Document / Aug '91 / Swift / Jazz Music / Hot Shot.

SLEEPY JOHN ESTES (1937-41)
CD _____ DOCD 5016
Blues Document / Aug '91 / Swift / Jazz Music / Hot Shot.

SLEEPY JOHN ESTES 1935-1938
CD _____ BLE 592542
Black & Blue / Dec '92 / Wellard / Koch.

Estevan, Pedro

NOCTURNOS Y ALLEVOSIAS
CD _____ 21050CD
Sonifolk / Jun '94 / ADA / CM.

Estragon, Vladimir

THREE QUARKS FOR MISTER MARK
CD _____ 888 803
Tiptoe / Nov '89 / New Note.

Estrand, Lars

BEAUTIFUL FRIENDSHIP, A
CD _____ SITCD 9204
Sittel / Feb '94 / Cadillac / Jazz Music.

SECOND SET: BEAUTIFUL FRIENDSHIP
Lady be good / Someone to watch over me / 'S wonderful / Our love is here to stay / Man I love / Tiger rag / Dream dancing / Between the devil and the deep blue sea / Things ain't what they used to be
CD _____ SITCD 9205
Sittel / Aug '94 / Cadillac / Jazz Music.

Etant Donnes

ROYAUME
Royaume / Matin / Quatre / Bleu
CD _____ SPL 2
Spiral / Mar '91 / President.

Etchingham Steam Band

ETCHINGHAM STEAM BAND, THE
CD _____ FLED 3002
Fledg'ling / Apr '95 / CM / ADA / Direct.

Eternal

ALWAYS AND FOREVER
Stay / Crazy / Save our love / Oh baby, I / I'll be there / Sweet funky thing / Never gonna give you up / Just a step from heaven / Let's stay together / This love's for real / So good / If you need me tonight / Don't say goodbye / Amazing grace
CD _____ CDEMD 1053
EMI / Nov '93 / EMI.

POWER OF A WOMAN
Power of a woman / I am blessed / Good thing / Telling you now / Hurry up / Redemption song / It will never end / Who are you / Secrets / Your smile / Don't make me wait / Up to you / Faith in love
CD _____ CDEMD 1090
EMI / Oct '95 / EMI.

Eternal Afflict

JAHWEH KDRESH
CD _____ EFA 11264-2
Danse Macabre / Mar '94 / SRD.

LUMINOGRAPHIC AGONY
CD _____ EFA 11252
Glasnost / Apr '93 / SRD.

NOW MIND REVOLUTION
CD _____ EFA 11258
Glasnost / Apr '93 / SRD.

WAR
CD _____ EFA 155762
Gymnastic / Dec '94 / SRD.

Eternal Basement

NERV
CD _____ HHCD 11
Harthouse / Apr '95 / Disc / Warner Music.

Eterne

STILL DREAMING
CD _____ CANDLE 009CD
Candlelight / Sep '95 / Plastic Head.

Ethereal

OMSANTHI
CD _____ USR 019CD
Unisound / Jan '96 / Plastic Head.

Ethereal Winds

FIND THE WAY
CD _____ CYBERCD 14
Cyber / May '95 / Plastic Head.

Etheridge, John

ASH
In / Ash / Venerable bede / Ugetsu / Baiere / Your own sweet way / Chips / Infant eyes / Nardis / You don't know what love is / No greater love / Little wing / 81 / Out
CD _____ VP 175CD
Voice Print / Sep '94 / Voice Print.

Etheridge, Melissa

BRAVE AND CRAZY
No souvenirs / Bravo and crazy life / You used to love to dance / Angels / You can sleep while I drive / Testify / Let me go / My back door / Skin deep / Royal station 4/16
CD _____ CID 9939
Island / Aug '89 / PolyGram.

MELISSA ETHERIDGE
Similar features / Chrome plated heart / Like the way I do / Precious pain / Don't need / Late September dogs / Occasionally / Watching you / Bring me some water / I want you
CD _____ CID 9879
Island / May '88 / PolyGram.

NEVER ENOUGH
2001 / It's for you / Letting go / Keep it precious / Boy feels strange / Meet me in the back / Must be crazy for me / Place your hand / Dance without sleeping / Ain't it heavy
CD _____ IMCD 214
Island / Sep '95 / PolyGram.

YES I AM
I'm the only one / If I wanted to / Come to my window / Silent legacy / I will never be the same / All American girl / Yes I am / Resist / Ruins / Talking to my angel
CD _____ CID 8010
Island / Apr '94 / PolyGram.

YOUR LITTLE SECRET
Your little secret / I really like you / Nowhere to go / Unusual kiss / I want to come over / All the way to heaven / I could have been you / Shriner's park / Change / War is over
CD _____ CID 8042
Island / Nov '95 / PolyGram.

Ethik

MUSIC FOR STOCK EXCHANGE
CD _____ DIGI 1001CD
Digitrax / Oct '95 / Plastic Head.

Ethik II

INDIVIDUAL TRAFFIC
CD _____ EAT 003CD
Eat Raw / Oct '95 / Plastic Head.

Ethiopians

CLAP YOUR HANDS
CD _____ LG 21086
Lagoon / Sep '93 / Magnum Music Group / THE.

LET'S SKA AND ROCK STEADY
CD _____ JMC 200103
Jamaica Gold / Nov '92 / THE / Magnum Music Group / Jetstar.

ORIGINAL REGGAE HIT SOUNDS
Free man / Train to Skaville / Engine 54 / Come on now / Train to glory / Whip / Everything crash / Things a get bad to worse / Well red / One / Hong Kong-flu / Gun man / What a fire / Woman capture man / Feel the spirit / Drop him / Good ambition / No baptism / Selah / Pirate / Word is love
CD _____ CDTRL 228
Trojan / Mar '94 / Jetstar / Total/BMG.

OWNER FE DE YARD
CD _____ HBCD 127
Heartbeat / Apr '94 / Greensleeves / Jetstar / Direct / ADA.

SIR JJ & FRIENDS
CD _____ LG 21088
Lagoon / Sep '93 / Magnum Music Group / THE.

Europa String Choir

SLAVE CALL
CD _____ HBCD 56
Heartbeat / Nov '92 / Greensleeves / Jetstar / Direct / ADA.

WOMAN CAPTURE MAN
CD _____ RB 3006
Reggae Best / Jul '94 / Magnum Music Group / THE.

WORLD GOES SKA, THE
I need you / Do it sweet / Stay loose mama / World goes ska / Give me your love / You get the dough / Sh-boom / Long time now / I'm not losing now / Everyday talking / Wreck it up / Hang on (don't let it go) / I'll never get burnt / So you look on it / He's not a rebel / Mothers tender care / Sad news / Rim bam bam / I need someone / Solid as a rock
CD _____ CDTRL 312
Trojan / Mar '94 / Jetstar / Total/BMG.

Ethyl Meatplow

HAPPY DAYS, SWEETHEART
Suck / Devil's johnson / Car / Queenie / Close to you / Tommy / Mustard requiem / Abazab / Ripened peach / Feed / Rise / For my sleepy lover / Sad bear / Coney island
CD _____ 3704613542
WEA / Oct '93 / Warner Music.

Etoile De Dakar

XALIS
CD _____ ADC 303
PAM / Feb '94 / Direct / ADA.

Etting, Ruth

LOVE ME OR LEAVE ME
CD _____ PASTCD 7061
Flapper / Jan '96 / Pinnacle.

TEN CENTS A DANCE
Ten cents a dance / Button up your overcoat / Funny, dear, what love can do / But I do, you know I do / Mean to me / I'm yours / If I could be with you one hour tonight / Don't tell him what happened to me / Body and soul / Sam, the old accordion man / Dancing with tears in my eyes / Hello baby / What wouldn't I do for that man / Could I, certainly could / Kiss waltz / Shakin' the blues away / You're the cream in my coffee / Lonesome and sorry / Laughing at life / Love me or leave me
CD _____ CD AJA 5008
Living Era / '88 / Koch.

Etzel, Roy

SERENADE
CD _____ INT 860 196
Interchord / '88 / CM.

Eubanks, Kevin

BEST OF KEVIN EUBANKS, THE
Moments aren't momoments / Sorrir / Smile / Wave / Cookin' / Face to face / Navigator / It's all the same to me / Essence / Forbidden romance / Hope / Songhouse
CD _____ GRP 98402
GRP / Jan '96 / BMG / New Note.

FACE TO FACE
Face to face / That's what friends are for / Essence / Silent waltz / Moments aren't moments / Wave / Relaxin' at Camarillo / Ebony surprise / Trick bag
CD _____ GRP 95392
GRP / Jan '93 / BMG / New Note.

GUITARIST
Novice bounce / Inner-vision / Yesterdays / Evidence / Urban heat / Thumb, The/Blues for Wes / Untitled shapes / Blue in green
CD _____ 1046710062
Discovery / May '94 / Warner Music.

SPIRITALK II: REVELATION
Faith / Like the wind / Whispers of life / Revelations / Earth / Sun / Moon / Being / Passing
CD _____ CDP 8301322
Blue Note / Mar '95 / EMI.

Eugenius

EUGENIUS
CD _____ PAPCD 011
Paperhouse / Aug '92 / Disc.

MARY QUEEN OF SCOTS
CD _____ RUST 008CD
Creation / Jan '91 / 3MV / Vital.

Eulogy

ESSENCE
CD _____ SPV 077-140782
SPV / Sep '94 / Plastic Head.

Europa String Choir

STARVING MOON, THE
Monkey never lies / Sermon on the Mount / Waltz / Mama Tequila / Delicate little me / Carol / Saving grace / Camomilla / La pasta / Prelude / Dancing bride / Little Sinfonie / Health food frenzy / Starving moon
CD _____ DGM 9509
Discipline / Nov '95 / Pinnacle.

Europe

EUROPE 1982-1992
In the future to come / Seven doors hotel / Stormwind / Open your heart / Scream of anger / Dreamer / Final countdown / On broken wings / Rock the night / Carrie / Cherokee / Superstitious / Ready or not / Prisoners in paradise (Single edit) / I'll cry for you (acoustic) / Sweet love child (Previously unreleased.) / Yesterday's news
CD _____ 473589 2
Epic / Apr '93 / Sony.

FINAL COUNTDOWN, THE
Love chaser / On the loose / Heart of stone / Time has come / Final countdown / Cherokee / Ninja / Danger on the track / Rock the night / Carrie
CD _____ 4663282
Epic / Mar '90 / Sony.

WINGS OF TOMORROW
Stormwind / Scream of anger / Open your heart / Treated bad again / Aphasia / Wings of tomorrow / Wasted time / Lyin' eyes / Dreamer / Dance the night away
CD _____ 9826502
Pickwick/Sony Collector's Choice / Nov '91 / Carlton Home Entertainment / Pinnacle / Sony.

European Concert...

EUROPEAN FAVOURITES (European Concert Orchestra)
European anthem / White cliffs of Dover / We'll keep a welcome / Skye boat song / La vie en rose / Luxembourg polka / Walk in the Black Forest / Granada / Portuguese washerwoman / Chanson des Scieurs de long / Tulips from Amsterdam / O sole mio / Wonderful Copenhagen / Zorba's dance / Danny boy
CD _____ CDEURO 1
Premier/MFP / Feb '92 / EMI.

European Music Orchestra

GUEST
CD _____ SN 121299-2
Soul Note / Oct '94 / Harmonia Mundi / Wellard / Cadillac.

Eurythmics

BE YOURSELF TONIGHT
It's alright (baby's coming back) / Would I lie to you / There must be an angel (playing with my heart) / I love you like a ball and chain / Sisters are doin' it for themselves / Conditioned soul / Adrian / Here comes that sinking feeling / Better to have lost in love than never to have loved at all
CD _____ ND 74602
RCA / May '90 / BMG.

BE YOURSELF TONIGHT/REVENGE
Would I lie to you / There must be an angel (playing with my heart) / I love you like a ball and chain / Sisters are doin' it for themselves / Conditioned soul / Adrian / Here comes that sinking feeling / Better to have lost in love (than never to have loved at all / Missionary man / Thorn in my side / When tomorrow comes / Last time / Miracle of love / Let's go / Take your pain away / Little of you / In this town / I remember you
CD Set _____ 74321264422
RCA / Mar '95 / BMG.

EURYTHMICS LIVE 1983-1989 (2CD Set)
Never gonna cry again / Love is a stranger / Sweet dreams (are made of this) / This city never sleeps / Somebody told me / Who's that girl / Right by your side / Here comes the rain again / Sexcrime (1984) / I love you like a ball and chain / There must be an angel (playing with my heart) / Thorn in my side / Let's go / Missionary man / Last time / Miracle of love / I need a man / We too are one / (My my) Baby's gonna cry / Don't ask me why / Angel / I need you (Ltd ed only) / You have placed a chill in my heart (Ltd ed only) / Here comes the rain again (acoustic) (Ltd ed only) / Would I lie to you (acoustic) (Ltd ed only) / It's alright (Baby's coming back) (Ltd ed only) / Right by your side (acoustic) (Ltd ed only) / When tomorrow comes (Ltd ed only)
CD Set _____ 74321177042
RCA / Aug '95 / BMG.

GREATEST HITS: EURYTHMICS
Love is a stranger / Sweet dreams (are made of this) / Who's that girl / Right by your side / Here comes the rain again / There must be an angel (playing with my heart) / Sisters are doin' it for themselves / It's alright (baby's coming back) / When tomorrow comes / You have placed a chill in my heart / Sexcrime (1984) / Thorn in my side / Don't ask me why / Angel (CD/MC only) / Would I lie to you (CD/MC only) / Missionary man (CD/MC only) / I need a man (CD/MC only) / Miracle of love (CD/MC only)
CD _____ PD 74856
RCA / Mar '91 / BMG.

IN THE GARDEN
English summer / Belinda / Take me to your heart / She's invisible now / Your time will come / Caveman head / Never gonna cry

again / All the young people (of today) / Sing, sing / Revenge
CD _____ ND 75036
RCA / Aug '91 / BMG.

REVENGE
Let's go / Take your pain away / Little of you / Thorn in my side / In this town / I remember you / Missionary man / Last time / When tomorrow comes / Miracle of love
CD _____ 74321 12529-2
RCA / Sep '93 / BMG.

SAVAGE
Beethoven (I love to listen to) / I've got a lover back in Japan / Do you want to break up / You have placed a chill in my heart / Shame / Savage / I need a man / Put the blame on me / Heaven / Wide eyed girl / I need you / Brand new day
CD _____ 74321134402
RCA / May '93 / BMG.

TOUCH DANCE
Cool blue / Paint a rumour / Regrets / First cut (Mixes) / Cool blue (instrumental) / Paint a rumour (instrumental)
CD _____ ND 75151
RCA / Jan '92 / BMG.

WE TOO ARE ONE
We too are one / King and Queen of America / (My my) Baby's gonna cry / Don't ask me why / Angel / Revival / You hunt me (I hate you) / Sylvia / How long / When the day goes down
CD _____ 74321 20898-2
RCA / Jun '94 / BMG.

Eva-lution

SOUL GLIDE
CD _____ SUNFCD 001
Sunflower / Jul '95 / Direct / ADA.

Evans, Bill

BLUE IN GREEN
Elsa / Detour ahead / Skidoo / Alfie / Peri's scope / Blue in green / Emily / Who can I turn to / Some other time / Waltz for Debbie
CD _____ LEJAZZCD 42
Le Jazz / Jun '95 / Charly / Cadillac.

NATIVE AND FINE
CD _____ ROUCD 0295
Rounder / Nov '95 / CM / Direct / ADA / Cadillac.

Evans, Bill

1960 BIRDLAND SESSIONS, THE (Evans, Bill Trio)
Cool 'n' Blue / Dec '92 / Jazz Music / Discovery.
CD _____ C&BCD 106

ALONE
CD _____ 8338012
Verve / Feb '94 / PolyGram.

AT SHELLY'S MANNE-HOLE (Evans, Bill Trio)
Isn't it romantic / Boy next door / Wonder why / Swedish pastry / Love is here to stay / Blues in F / Round Midnight / Stella by starlight
CD _____ OJCCD 263
Original Jazz Classics / Feb '92 / Wellard / Jazz Music / Cadillac / Complete/Pinnacle.

AT THE VILLAGE VANGUARD (Evans, Bill Trio)
My foolish heart / My romance (take 1) / Solar / Gloria's step (take 2) / My man's gone now / All of you / I loves you Porgy / Milestones / Waltz for Debbie (take 2) / Jade visions
CD _____ FCD 60017
Fantasy / Apr '94 / Pinnacle / Jazz Music / Wellard / Cadillac.

AUTUMN LEAVES
Emily / There will never be another you / Stairway to the stars / Someday my Prince will come / Blue in green / Round Midnight / Autumn leaves
CD _____ CD 53211
Giants Of Jazz / Nov '95 / Target/BMG / Cadillac.

BILL EVANS - HIS LAST CONCERT IN GERMANY
CD _____ WW 2022
West Wind / Mar '93 / Swift / Charly / CM / ADA.

BILL EVANS ALBUM, THE
Funkallero / Two lonely people / Sugar plum / Waltz for Debby / T.T.T.T. (Twelve tune tune) / Re: person I knew / Comrade Conrad
CD _____ 4809892
Sony Jazz / Dec '95 / Sony.

BLUE IN GREEN
CD _____ MCD 9185
Milestone / Oct '93 / Jazz Music / Pinnacle / Wellard / Cadillac.

BRILLIANT BILL EVANS, THE
Who can I turn to / My romance / Re: Person I knew / Laura / Very early / Peacocks / Green dolphin street / Morning glory / So- lar / M.A.S.H. (Suicide is painless) / Five
CD _____ WW 2058

West Wind / Jul '93 / Swift / Charly / CM / ADA.

BUENOS AIRES 1979 (Evans, Bill Trio)
CD _____ WWCD 2061
West Wind / Jan '91 / Swift / Charly / CM / ADA.

COMPLETE FANTASY RECORDINGS, THE
CD Set _____ FCD 1012-2
Fantasy / Nov '92 / Pinnacle / Jazz Music / Wellard / Cadillac.

EMPATHY
CD _____ 837 757-2
Verve / Jan '90 / PolyGram.

EVERYBODY DIGS BILL EVANS
Minority / Young and foolish / Lucky to be me / Night and day / Epilogue / Tenderly / Peace piece / What is there to say / Oleo
CD _____ OJCCD 068
Original Jazz Classics / Feb '92 / Wellard / Jazz Music / Cadillac / Complete/Pinnacle.

EXPLORATIONS
CD _____ OJCCD 037
Original Jazz Classics / Feb '92 / Wellard / Jazz Music / Cadillac / Complete/Pinnacle.

GAMBLER, THE (Live at the Blue Note Tokyo 2)
Gambler / Sun dried / Sea of fertility / Just a hunch / All logic / Gorgeous / Crest annexe
CD _____ 66053025
Jazz City / Jul '91 / New Note.

HIS LAST CONCERT IN GERMANY
CD _____ WWCD 0022
West Wind / Apr '90 / Swift / Charly / CM / ADA.

HOW DEEP IS THE OCEAN
CD _____ WWCD 2055
West Wind / Jan '91 / Swift / Charly / CM / ADA.

HOW MY HEART SINGS (Evans, Bill Trio)
CD _____ OJCCD 369
Original Jazz Classics / Feb '92 / Wellard / Jazz Music / Cadillac / Complete/Pinnacle.

I WILL SAY GOODBYE (Evans, Bill Trio)
I will say goodbye / Dolphin dance / Seascape / Peau douce / Nobody else but me / I will say goodbye (take 2) / Opener / Quiet light / House is not a home / Orson's theme
CD _____ OJCCD 761
Original Jazz Classics / Oct '93 / Wellard / Jazz Music / Cadillac / Complete/Pinnacle.

INTERMODULATION (Evans, Bill & Jim Hall)
CD _____ 8337712
Verve / Jan '93 / PolyGram.

INTERPLAY (Evans, Bill & Freddie Hubbard)
CD _____ OJCCD 308
Original Jazz Classics / Feb '92 / Wellard / Jazz Music / Cadillac / Complete/Pinnacle.

JAZZ MASTERS
CD _____ 519821-2
Verve / May '94 / PolyGram.

JAZZHOUSE
How deep is the ocean / How my heart sings / Goodbye / Autumn leaves / California here I come / Sleepin' bee / Polka dots and moonbeams / Stella by starlight / Five (theme)
CD _____ MCD 9151-2
Milestone / Apr '94 / Jazz Music / Pinnacle / Wellard / Cadillac.

LIVE AT THE BLUE NOTE TOKYO
Let the juice loose / Hobo / My favourite little sailboat / Let's pretend / In the hat / Ginza / Wait / Kwitchur Bellakin
CD _____ 66053001
Jazz City / Dec '90 / New Note.

LIVE IN EUROPE
How my heart sings / Time to remember / Twelve toned tune / Waltz for Debbie / Stella by starlight / Someday my Prince will come / Round Midnight
CD _____ LIP 890292
Lipstick / May '95 / Vital/SAM.

LIVE IN PARIS 1972 VOL 1
Re person I knew / Gloria's step / Waltz for Debbie / Turn out the stars / Two lonely people / What are you doing the rest of your life
CD _____ FCD 107
Esoldun / Jun '88 / Target/BMG.

LIVE IN PARIS VOL.1
CD _____ FCD 125
France's Concert / Jun '89 / Jazz Music / BMG.

LIVE IN PARIS VOL.2
Twelve tone tune / Sugar plum / Quiet now / Very early / Autumn leaves / Time remembered / My romance / Someday my Prince will come
CD _____ FCD 114
France's Concert / Jun '88 / Jazz Music / BMG.

LIVE IN STOCKHOLM 1965
CD _____ LS 2917
Landscape / Feb '93 / THE.

LIVE IN SWITZERLAND
CD _____ LS 2914
Landscape / Jun '93 / THE.

LIVE IN SWITZERLAND 1975
CD _____ JH 01
Jazz Helvet / Dec '90 / Magnum Music Group.

LIVE IN TOKYO
Mornin' glory / Up with the lark / On Green Dolphin Street / Gloria's step / Hullo bolinas / T.T.T.T. (Twelve tone two) / When autumn comes / My romance / Yesterday I heard the rain
CD _____ 4812652
Sony Jazz / Dec '95 / Sony.

LIVE SWITZERLAND 1975 (Evans, Bill Trio)
CD _____ 449142
Landscape / Jun '93 / THE.

LOOSE BLUES
Loose bloose / Time remembered / Funkallero / My bells / There came you / Fudgesickle built for four / Fun ride
CD _____ MCD 9200-2
Milestone / Aug '94 / Jazz Music / Pinnacle / Wellard / Cadillac.

MIDNIGHT MOOD
All That's Jazz / Oct '92 / THE / Jazz Music.
CD _____ ATJCD 54969

MONTREUX II
Very early / Alfie / 34 Skidoo / How my heart sings / Israel / I hear a rhapsody / Peri's scope
CD _____ 4812692
Sony Jazz / Dec '95 / Sony.

MONTREUX III (Evans, Bill & Eddie Gomez)
CD _____ OJCCD 644
Original Jazz Classics / Feb '92 / Wellard / Jazz Music / Cadillac / Complete/Pinnacle.

MOODS UNLIMITED (Evans, Bill/Hank Jones/Red Mitchell)
Yesterdays / There is no greater love / All the things you are / In a sentimental mood / Night and day
CD _____ ECD 220722
Evidence / Nov '93 / Harmonia Mundi / ADA / Cadillac.

MOONBEAMS (Evans, Bill Trio)
CD _____ OJCCD 434
Original Jazz Classics / Feb '92 / Wellard / Jazz Music / Cadillac / Complete/Pinnacle.

MY FOOLISH HEART (Evans, Bill Trio)
Beautiful Heart / My foolish heart / My romance / Two lovely people / T.T.T. / Yesterday I heard the rain / Waltz for Debbie
CD _____ WW 2075
West Wind / May '93 / Swift / Charly / CM / ADA.

NEW JAZZ CONCEPTIONS
I love you / Five / I got it bad and that ain't good / Conception / Easy living / Displacement / Speak low / Waltz for Debbie / Our delight / My romance / No cover, no minimum (2 takes)
CD _____ OJCCD 025
Original Jazz Classics / Feb '92 / Wellard / Jazz Music / Cadillac / Complete/Pinnacle.

PERSON I KNEW
Re: Person I knew / Sugar plum / Alfie / T.T.T. / Excerpt from Dolphin dance / Very early / 34 skidoo / Emily / Are you all the things
CD _____ OJCCD 749
Original Jazz Classics / Apr '93 / Wellard / Jazz Music / Cadillac / Complete/Pinnacle.

PORTRAIT IN JAZZ
Come rain or come shine / Autumn leaves / Witchcraft / When I fall in love / Peri's scope / What is this thing called love / Spring is here / Someday my Prince will come / Blue in green
CD _____ OJCCD 088
Original Jazz Classics / Feb '92 / Wellard / Jazz Music / Cadillac / Complete/Pinnacle.

PUSH
Push / Road to ruin / If only in your dreams / London House / Night wing / Stand up and do something / Hobo / You gotta believe / Life is dangerous / U R what U hear / Simple life / Matter of time
CD _____ LIP 890222
Lipstick / Feb '95 / Vital/SAM.

QUIET NOW
Very airy / Sleeping bee / Quiet now / Turn out the stars / Autumn leaves / Nardis
CD _____ LEJAZZCD 32
Le Jazz / Sep '94 / Charly / Cadillac.

RARE CONCERT RECORDINGS - 1962-65-69
CD _____ JZCD 359
Suisa / Feb '91 / Jazz Music / THE.

RIVERSIDE RECORDINGS (12CD Set)
CD Set _____ 12RCD 018
Original Jazz Classics / Sep '93 / Wellard / Jazz Music / Cadillac / Complete/Pinnacle.

SERENITY
CD _____ LEJAZZCD 5
Le Jazz / Mar '93 / Charly / Cadillac.

SINCE WE MET
Since we met / Midnight mood / See saw / Sareen jurer / Time remembered / Turn out the stars / But beautiful
CD _____ OJCCD 622-2
Original Jazz Classics / Aug '94 / Wellard / Jazz Music / Cadillac / Complete/Pinnacle.

SMALL HOTEL, A (Evans, Bill Trio)
CD _____ FDM 365612
Dreyfus / Jul '93 / ADA / Direct / New Note.

SOLO SESSIONS VOL. 1
CD _____ MCD 9170
Milestone / Oct '93 / Jazz Music / Pinnacle / Wellard / Cadillac.

SUMMERTIME
Chatterton bells / Let's pretend / Melvin's pond / My ship / Summertime / Arthur Avenue / All of you / These dreams / Jitterbug waltz / Red scarf / Kwitchur Bellakin
CD _____ 66053018
Jazz City / Mar '91 / New Note.

SUNDAY NIGHT AT THE VILLAGE VANGUARD
CD _____ OJCCD 140
Original Jazz Classics / Feb '92 / Wellard / Jazz Music / Cadillac / Complete/Pinnacle.

TIME TO REMEMBER
Natasha / Jun '93 / Jazz Music / ADA / CM / Direct / Cadillac.

TOKYO CONCERT, THE
CD _____ OJCCD 345
Original Jazz Classics / Feb '92 / Wellard / Jazz Music / Cadillac / Complete/Pinnacle.

TRIO '65 (Evans, Bill Trio)
Israel / Elsa / Round Midnight / Our love is here to stay / How my heart sings / Who can I turn to / Come rain or come shine / If you could see me now
CD _____ 519808-2
Verve / Dec '93 / PolyGram.

YOU'RE GONNA HEAR FROM ME
You're gonna hear from me / Waltz for Debbie / Time remembered / Emily / Someday my Prince will come / Round Midnight / Nardis / Who can I turn to / Love is here to stay
CD _____ MCD 9164-2
Milestone / Aug '94 / Jazz Music / Pinnacle / Wellard / Cadillac.

Evans, Bill

ALTERNATIVE MAN
Alternative man / Path of least resistance / Let the juice loose / Gardiners garden / Survival of the fittest / Jo Jo / Cry in her eyes / Miles away / Flight of the falcon
CD _____ BNZ 30
Blue Note / Jul '87 / EMI.

Evans, Ceri

HIDDEN TREASURE
CD _____ BLJCD 001
Big Life Jazz / Oct '95 / Pinnacle.

Evans, Delyth

DELTA
Taith ar y fferi / Pibddawns y sipsi newydd / Pibddawns y gof / Branle / Mwynder maldwyn / Merch megan / Pandeirada de nebra / Y maerdy/Pibddawns merthyr / Eleanor Plunkett / Bete a Lamentation / El sie Marley / Er gwell er gwaeth / A l'rntree de l'este / Carolan's receipt for drinking / Jackson's bottle of brandy / Baltimorn / Cariad pur / Gymnopedie III / Carolan's farewell to music / Ysbryd Kilvrough
CD _____ SAIN 4062CD
Sain / Aug '94 / Direct / ADA.

Evans, Doc

STOMP AND BLUES (Evans, Doc Jazzband)
CD _____ JCD 195
Jazzology / Oct '93 / Swift / Jazz Music.

Evans, Faith

FAITH
Faith (interlude) / No other love / Fallin' in love / Ain't nobody / You are my joy / Love don't live here anymore / Come over / Soon as I get home / All this love (Not on vinyl) / Thank you Lord (Not on vinyl) / You used to love me / Give it to me / You don't understand (Not on vinyl) / Reasons (On CD only)
CD _____ 78612730032
Arista / Aug '95 / BMG.

Evans, Gil

BRITISH ORCHESTRA, THE
Hotel me / Friday 13th / London / Little wing
CD _____ MOLECD 8
Mole Jazz / May '83 / Jazz Horizons / Jazz Music / Cadillac / Wellard / Impetus.

BUD AND BIRD (Evans, Gil & The Monday Night Orchestra)
CD _____ K32Y 6171
Electric Bird / Sep '88 / New Note.

FAREWELL (Evans, Gil & The Monday Night Orchestra)
CD _____ K32Y 6250
King/Paddle Wheel / Sep '88 / New Note.

GIL EVANS & TEN
Remember / Ella Speed / Big stuff / Nobody's heart / Just one of those things / If you could see me now / Jambangle
CD _____ OJCCD 346
Original Jazz Classics / Sep '93 / Wellard / Jazz Music / Cadillac / Complete/Pinnacle.

HONEY MAN
CD _____ RD 5022CD
Robi Droli / Apr '95 / Direct / ADA.

INDIVIDUALISM OF GIL EVANS, THE
CD _____ 8338042
Verve / Oct '93 / PolyGram.

JAZZ MASTERS
CD _____ 5218602
Verve / Feb '94 / PolyGram.

LITTLE WING (Evans, Gil & Orchestra)
Dr. Jekyll / Meaning of the blues / Little wing / For Bob's tuba
CD _____ WW 2042
West Wind / May '93 / Swift / Charly / CM / ADA.

LIVE AT SWEET BASIL (Evans, Gil & The Monday Night Orchestra)
Parabola / Voodoo chile / Orange was the colour of her dress / Prince of Darkness / Blues in C / Cheryl / Bird feathers / Relaxin' at Camarillo / Goodbye pork pie hat / Up from the skies
CD _____ K32Y 6017
King/Paddle Wheel / Oct '87 / New Note.

LIVE AT SWEET BASIL. VOL.2 (Evans, Gil & The Monday Night Orchestra)
CD _____ K32Y 6018
King/Paddle Wheel / Oct '87 / New Note.

LIVE AT THE PUBLIC THEATRE NEW YORK 1980 VOLUME 1
Anita's dance / Jelly roll / Alyrio / Variation on the misery / Orgone / Up from the skies
CD _____ ECD 220892
Evidence / Jun '94 / Harmonia Mundi / ADA / Cadillac.

LIVE AT THE PUBLIC THEATRE NEW YORK 1980 VOLUME 2
Copenhagen sight / Zee zee / Sirhan's blues / Stone free / Orange was the colour of her dress
CD _____ ECD 220902
Evidence / Jun '94 / Harmonia Mundi / ADA / Cadillac.

LUNAR ECLYPSE (Evans, Gil & His Orchestra)
CD _____ 129806711-2
Robi Droli / Jun '93 / Direct / ADA.

ORCHESTRA 1957-59
Giants Of Jazz / Sep '94 / Target/BMG / Cadillac.

PLAYS THE MUSIC OF JIMI HENDRIX (Evans, Gil Orchestra)
Angel / Crosstown traffic / Castles made of sand / Up from the skies (take 1) / 1983 / Voodoo chile / Gypsy eyes / Little wing / Up from the skies (take 2) / Little Miss Lover
CD _____ ND 88409
Bluebird / Nov '88 / BMG.

PRIESTESS
Priestess / Short visit / Lunar eclipse / Orange was the colour of her dress
CD _____ ANCD 8717
Antilles/New Directions / May '87 / PolyGram.

SVENGALI
Thoroughbred / Blues in orbit / Eleven / Cry of hunger / Summertime / Zee zee
CD _____ 92072
Act / Apr '94 / New Note.

TOKYO CONCERT
CD _____ WWCD 2056
West Wind / Jan '91 / Swift / Charly / CM / ADA.

Evans, Guy

LONG HELLO VOL.4 (RE-MASTERED), THE
Holsworthy market place / Trick or treat / Der traum von julius / Rock of riley / Caretaker's wife / Wonderful brothers / Martha's express wishes / Hamburg station / Solo kabine / Finger points / Haben sie waffen oder funk dabei? / Slow slither loop / My feet are freezing but my knees are warm
CD _____ VP 112CD
Voice Print / Mar '93 / Voice Print.

Evans, Paul

FABULOUS TEENS AND BEYOND, THE
Midnite special / Hushabye little guitar / I'm in love again / Hambone rock / Over the mountain, across the sea / Tutti frutti / Butterfly / Slippin' and slidin' / Honey love / I'm walkin' / Since I met you baby / 60 Minute man / Fool / Seven little girls sitting in the back seat / Worshipping an idol / Happy go lucky me / Fish in the ocean / Brigade of broken hearts / Blind boy / Twins / After the hurricane / Just because I love

---

you / Show folk / Why / Roses are red / Disneyland Daddy / Willie's sung with everyone (but me) / I lello, this io Joanne
CD _____ CDCHD 551
Ace / Nov '95 / Pinnacle / Cadillac / Complete/Pinnacle.

Evans, Terry

BLUES FOR THOUGHT
Too many cooks / Hey Mama, keep your big mouth shut / Shakespeare didn't quote that / Natcha bone lover / That's the way love turned out for me / So fine / Get your lies straight / Live, love and friends / Honey boy / I want to be close to you, God
CD _____ VPCD 16
Pointblank / Jan '93 / EMI.

PUTTIN' IT DOWN
Money in your pocket / Too many ups and downs / Walking in the same tracks / Down in Mississippi / In this day and time / Rooftop tomcat / Lover like you / One sided love affair / Nasty doll / Blues no more
CD _____ AQCD 1038
Audioquest / Nov '95 / New Note.

Evans, Tony

I WON'T SEND ROSES (Evans, Tony & His Orchestra)
CD _____ CDE 1025
Tema / May '93 / Target/BMG / Savoy.

Evelev, Yale

CUBA CLASSICS 3 (Diablo al Inferno - New Directions in Cuban Music)
Bacalao con pan / Asoyin / El baile del buey cansao / Tu no sabes de amor / Ikiri ada / Rompe saraguey / Congo yambumba / No me carezcas / Que viva chango / Homenaje / Guillermo tell / Diablo al infierno
CD _____ 9362 451072
Luaka Bop / Feb '93 / Warner Music.

Even As We Speak

FERAL POP FRENZY
Beelzebub / Beautiful day / Falling down the stairs / Zeppelins / Anybody anyway / Love is the answer / To see you smile / Straight as an arrow / Squid / One thing / Sailor's graves / Spirit of progress / Cripple creek / Swimming song / One step forward / Drown / O.G.T.T
CD _____ SARAH 614CD
Sarah / Mar '95 / Vital.

Everclear

WORLD OF NOISE
CD _____ FIRECD 46
Fire / Feb '95 / Disc.

Everett, Betty

LOVE RHYMES/HAPPY ENDINGS
Sweet Dan / I gotta tell somebody / I wanna be there / Be anything, but be mine / Wondering / Who will your next fool be / I'm your friend / Just a matter of time / I'm afraid of losing you / La la la / Try it you'll like it / Here's the gift / God only knows / Things I say to his shoulder / Bedroom eyes / Keep it up / Just a little piece of you / Don't let it end ('til you let it begin) / As far as we can go / Happy endings
CD _____ CDSEWD 085
Southbound / Jul '93 / Pinnacle.

Evergreen Classic Jazz...

EVERGREEN CLASSIC JAZZ BAND (Evergreen Classic Jazz Band)
CD _____ SOS 1202
Stomp Off / Oct '92 / Jazz Music / Wellard.

Evergreens

20 MOST REQUESTED IRISH SONGS
CD _____ EHCD 1
Emerald Hour / Nov '93 / BMG.

SONGS OF IRELAND
CD _____ EMPRCD 578
Emporio / Jul '95 / THE / Disc / CM.

Everly Brothers

BEST OF THE EVERLY BROTHERS
CD _____ DCD 5324
Disky / Dec '93 / THE / BMG / Discovery / Pinnacle.

BEST OF THE EVERLY BROTHERS, THE
CD _____ MCCD 209
MCI / Jul '95 / Disc / THE.

BYE BYE LOVE
CD _____ ENTCD 207
Entertainers / Sep '87 / Target/BMG.

CLASSIC EVERLY BROTHERS (1955-60)
Keep a lovin' me / Suns keeps shining / If here love isn't true / That's the life I have to live / I wonder if I care as much / Bye bye love / Should we tell him / Wake up little Susie / Hey doll baby / Maybe tomorrow / Brand new heartache / Keep a knockin' / Leave my woman alone / Rip it up / This little girl of mine / Be bop a lula / All I have to do is dream / Claudette / Devoted to you

---

/ Bird dog / Problems / Love of my life / Take a message to Mary / Poor Jenny (one o'clock version) / Oh true love / 'Til I kissed you / Oh what a feeling / Let it be me / Since you broke my heart / Like strangers / When will I be loved / Roving gambler / Who's gonna shoe your pretty little feet / Rockin' alone in an old rocking chair / Put my little shoes away / Down in the willow garden / Long time gone / Lightning express / That silver haired daddy of mine / Barbara Allen / Oh so many years / I'm here to get my baby out of jail / Kentucky
CD Set _____ BCD 15618
Bear Family / Feb '92 / Rollercoaster / Direct / CM / Swift & Jazz.

COLLECTION: EVERLY BROTHERS
Problems / When will I be loved / This little girl of mine / Be bop a lula / Leave my woman alone / Roving gambler / Lightning express / Rockin' alone in an old rocking chair / Like strangers / Wake up little Susie / Devoted to you / Bird dog / Rip it up / Brand new heartache / Should we tell him / Keep a knockin' / Put my little shoes away / Kentucky / Long time gone / Down in the willow garden / Take a message to Mary / Maybe tomorrow / Since you broke my heart / Let it be me
CD _____ CCSCD 139
Castle / '88 / BMG.

DREAMING
On the wings of a nightingale / Don't worry baby / You send me / Story of me / Amanda Ruth / Ride the wind / Lay lady lay / Arms of Mary / Why worry / Following the sun / Any single solitary heart / Wake up little Susie (Live) / All I have to do is dream / Cathy's clown (Live)
CD _____ 5500562
Spectrum/Karussell / May '93 / PolyGram / THE.

EVERLY BROTHERS AND THE FABULOUS STYLE OF...
This little girl of mine / Maybe tomorrow / Bye bye love / Brand new heartache / Keep a knockin' / Be bop a lula / Leave my woman alone / Poor Jenny / Rip it up / I wonder if I care as much / Wake up little Susie / Leave my woman alone / Should we tell him / Hey doll baby / Claudette / Like strangers / Since you broke my heart / Let it be me / Oh what a feeling / Take a message to Mary / Devoted to you / When will I be loved / Bird dog / Till I kissed you / Problems / Love of my life / Poor Jenny (2nd version) / All I have to do is dream
CD _____ CDCH 932
Ace / Apr '90 / Pinnacle / Cadillac / Complete/Pinnacle.

FABULOUS EVERLY BROTHERS, THE
Bye bye love / Wake up little Susie / All I have to do is dream / Bird dog / Problems / Till I kissed you / Let it be me / When will I be loved / Take a message to Mary / Claudette / Poor Jenny / Devoted to you
CD _____ CDFAB 006
Ace / Sep '91 / Pinnacle / Cadillac / Complete/Pinnacle.

GOLDEN YEARS OF THE EVERLY BROTHERS
Walk right back / Crying in the rain / Wake up little Susie / Love hurts / Claudette / Till I kissed you / Love is strange / Ebony eyes / Temptation / Let it be me / Don't blame me / Cathy's clown / All I have to do is dream / Lucille / So sad (to watch good love go bad) / Bird dog / When will I be loved / No one can make my sunshine smile / Ferris wheel / Price of love / Muskrat / Problems / How can I meet her / Bye bye love
CD _____ 954831992-2
Warner Bros. / May '93 / Warner Music.

GREATEST HITS LIVE
CD _____ 5147262
Mercury / Jul '93 / PolyGram.

GREATEST RECORDINGS
Wake up little Susie / Problems / Take a message to Mary / I wonder if I care as much / Poor Jenny / Love of my life / Bird dog / Like strangers / Hey doll baby / Leave my woman alone / Till I kissed you / Claudette / Should we tell him / All I have to do is dream / Rip it up / When will I be loved / Bye bye love / Let it be me
CD _____ CDCH 903
Ace / '88 / Pinnacle / Cadillac / Complete/Pinnacle.

HIT SINGLE COLLECTABLES
CD _____ DISK 4502
Disky / Apr '94 / THE / BMG / Discovery / Pinnacle.

MERCURY YEARS
CD _____ 5109092
Mercury / Jul '93 / PolyGram.

NICE GUYS
Trouble / What about me / Eden to Cainin / Chains / Meet me in the bottom / In the good old days / Nice guys / Stained glass morning / Dancing on my feet / Mr. Soul / Don't you even try / Kiss your man goodbye
CD _____ CDMF 1028
Magnum Force / Nov '88 / Magnum Music Group.

ORIGINAL BRITISH HIT SINGLES, THE
Bye bye love / I wonder if I care as much / Wake up little Susie / Maybe tomorrow / Should we tell him / This little girl of mine / All I have to do is dream / Claudette / Bird dog / Devoted to you / Problems / Love of my life / Poor Jenny / Take a message to Mary / Till I kissed you / Oh what a feeling / Let it be me / Since you broke my heart / When will I be loved / Be bop a lula / Like strangers / Leave my woman alone
CD _____ CDCHM 544
Ace / Nov '94 / Pinnacle / Cadillac / Complete/Pinnacle.

PASS THE CHICKEN AND LISTEN
Lay it down / Husbands and wives / Woman don't you try to tie me down / Sweet memories / Ladies love outlaws / Not fade away / Watchin' it go / Paradise / Somebody nobody knows / Good hearted woman / Nickel for the fiddler / Rocky top
CD _____ EDCD 319
Edsel / '91 / Pinnacle / ADA.

RE-UNION
Price of love / Walk right back / Claudette / Crying in the rain / Love is strange / (Take a) message to Mary / When will I be loved / Bird dog / Devoted to you / Ebony eyes / Love hurts / Gone gone gone / Cathy's clown / You send me / So sad (to watch good love go bad) / Bye bye love / All I have to do is dream / Wake up little Susie / Till I kissed you / Temptation / Be bop a lula / Lucille / Let it be me / Good golly Miss Molly
CD _____ MOCD 3002
More Music / Feb '95 / Sound & Media.

REUNION CONCERT
Price of love / Walk right back / Claudette / Crying in the rain / Love is strange / (Take a) message to Mary / Maybe tomorrow / I wonder if I care as much / When will I be loved / Bird dog / Devoted to you / Ebony eyes / Love hurts / For the love of Barbara Allen / Lightning express / Put my little shoes away / Long time gone / Down in the willow garden / Step it up and go / Cathy's clown / Gone gone gone / You send me / So sad (to watch good love go bad) / Blues (stay away from me) / Bye bye love / All I have to do is dream / Wake up little Susie / Till I kissed you / Temptation / Be bop a lula / Lucille / Let it be me / Good golly Miss Molly
CD Set _____ PLATCD 5901
Prism / Oct '93 / Prism.

REUNION CONCERT PART 1, THE
CD _____ CDCD 1226
Charly / Jun '95 / Charly / THE / Cadillac.

REUNION CONCERT PART 2, THE
CD _____ CDCD 1227
Charly / Jun '95 / Charly / THE / Cadillac.

ROOTS
CD _____ 7599269272
Warner Bros. / May '95 / Warner Music.

SIMPLY THE BEST
CD _____ WMCD 5704
Disky / Oct '94 / THE / BMG / Discovery / Pinnacle.

SONGS OUR DADDY TAUGHT US
Roving gambler / Down in the willow garden / Long time gone / Lightning express / That silver haired daddy of mine / Who's gonna shoe your pretty little feet / Barbara Allen / Oh so many years / I'm here to get my baby out of jail / Rockin' alone in an old rocking chair / Kentucky / Put my little shoes away
CD _____ CDCHM 75
Ace / Nov '90 / Pinnacle / Cadillac / Complete/Pinnacle.

SUSIE Q
Love with your heart / How can I meet her / Nothing but the best / Sheikh of Araby / To show I love you / Suzie Q / Am alone auf der heide / Sag su wiedersehenm / When snowflakes fall in the summer / Little Hollywood girl / He's got my sympathy / Silent treatment
CD _____ CDMF 052
Magnum Force / Jun '88 / Magnum Music Group.

SWEET MEMORIES
CD _____ 295 728
Ariola Express / Sep '92 / BMG.

VERY BEST OF THE EVERLY BROTHERS
CD _____ PWKS 515
Carlton Home Entertainment / Oct '88 / Carlton Home Entertainment.

VERY BEST OF THE EVERLY BROTHERS VOL.2
Cathy's clown / Price of love / Muskrat / Temptation / Love is strange / So sad (to watch good love go bad) / So it will always be / Crying in the rain / Walk right back / Lucille / Ebony eyes / How can I make my sunshine smile / How can I meet her / Don't blame me / Gone gone gone / Ferris wheel
CD _____ PWKS 4028
Carlton Home Entertainment / Oct '90 / Carlton Home Entertainment.

Everly, Don

BROTHER JUKE BOX
Love at last sight / So sad (to watch good love go bad) / Letting go / Since you broke my heart / Never like this / Deep water / Yesterday just passed my way again / Oh I'd like to go away / Oh what a feeling / Turn the memories loose again / Brother juke box
CD _____ CDSD 002
Sundown / Sep '94 / Magnum Music Group.

Everly, Phil

LONDON SESSIONS, THE
CD _____ NEXCD 164
Sequel / Apr '91 / BMG.

LOUISE
Louise / Sweet Suzanne / She means nothing to me / Man and a woman / Who's gonna keep me warm / One way love / Sweet pretender / Better than now / Oh baby oh / God bless older ladies / Never gonna dream again / I'll mend your broken heart / When I'm dead and gone
CD _____ CDMF 053
Magnum Force / Jan '88 / Magnum Music Group.

PHIL EVERLY
She means nothing to me / I'll mend your broken heart / God bless older ladies / Sweet pretender / Never gonna dream again / Better than now / Woman and a man / Oh baby oh (you're the star) / Sweet Suzanne / Oh baby oh (you're the star)
CD _____ BGOCD 199
Beat Goes On / Feb '95 / Pinnacle.

WILL I BE LOVED
When will I be loved / January butterfly / Three bells / Patiently / It's true / You and I are a song / Invisible man / Friends / Caroline / Too blue / Summershine / Better than now / Mystic line / Sweet music
CD _____ 5507622
Spectrum/Karussell / Mar '95 / PolyGram / THE.

Every New Dead Ghost

ENDLESS NIGHTMARE
CD _____ NIGHTCD 001
Plastic Head / Jul '92 / Plastic Head.

NEW WORLD, A
CD _____ PLASCD 024
Plastic Head / Nov '90 / Plastic Head.

RIVER OF SOULS
CD _____ APOREK 1110893
Apollyon / Feb '95 / SRD.

WHO'S SANE ANYWAY
CD _____ AJE 07
Alea Jacta Est / Jun '93 / Plastic Head.

Everyman Band

WITHOUT WARNING
Patterns which connect / Talking with himself / Multibluetonic blues / Celebration / Trick of the wool / Huh what he say / Al ur
CD _____ 8254052
ECM / '88 / New Note.

Everything But The Girl

AMPLIFIED HEART
Rollercoaster / Troubled mind / I don't understand anything / Walking to you / Get me / Missing / Two star / We walk the same line / 25th December / Disenchanted
CD _____ 450996482-2
Blanco Y Negro / Jun '94 / Warner Music.

BABY THE STARS SHINE BRIGHT
Come on home / Don't leave me behind / Country mile / Cross my heart / Don't let the teardrops rust your shining heart / Careless / Sugar Finney / Come hell or high water / Fighting talk / Little Hitler
CD _____ 2409662
Blanco Y Negro / Aug '86 / Warner Music.

EDEN
Each and every one / Bittersweet / Tender blue / Another bridge / Spice of life / Dust bowl / Crabwalk / Even so / Frost and fire / Fascination / I must confess / Soft touch
CD _____ 2403952
Blanco Y Negro / '84 / Warner Music.

HOME MOVIES (The Best of Everything But The Girl)
Driving / Each and every one / Another bridge / Fascination / Native land / Come on home / Cross my heart / Apron strings / I don't want to talk about it / Night I heard Caruso sing / Imagining America / Understanding / Twin cities / Love is strange / I didn't know I was looking for love / Only living boy in New York
CD _____ BYN 29CD
Blanco Y Negro / Apr '93 / Warner Music.

IDLEWILD
Love is here where I live / These early days / Oxford Street / Night I heard Caruso sing / Goodbye Sunday / Shadow on a harvest moon / Blue moon rose / Tears all over town / Lonesome for a place I know / Apron strings / I don't want to talk about it
CD _____ K 2438402
Blanco Y Negro / Nov '94 / Warner Music.

LANGUAGE OF LIFE, THE
Driving / Get back together / Meet me in the morning / Me and Bobby D / Language of life / Take me / Imagine America / Letting love go / My baby don't love me / Road
CD _____ 2462602
Blanco Y Negro / Jan '90 / Warner Music.

LOVE NOT MONEY
When all's well / Ugly little dreams / Shoot me down / Are you trying to be funny / Sean / Ballad of the times / Anytown / This love (not for sale) / Trouble and strife / Angel / Heaven help me (Available on cassette only) / Kid (Only on cassette.)
CD _____ 2406572
Blanco Y Negro / May '85 / Warner Music.

WORLDWIDE
Old friends / Understanding / You lift me up / Talk to me like the sea / British summertime / Twin cities / Frozen river / One place / Politics aside / Boxing and pop music / Feeling alright
CD _____ 9031753082
Blanco Y Negro / Oct '91 / Warner Music.

Eviction

WORLD IS HOURS AWAY, THE
CD _____ CDZORRO 14
Metal Blade / Nov '90 / Pinnacle.

Evil Dead

ANNIHILATION OF CIVILISATION
CD _____ 847603
Steamhammer / '90 / Pinnacle / Plastic Head.

RISE ABOVE
CD _____ 557590
Steamhammer / '88 / Pinnacle / Plastic Head.

Evil Mothers

CROSSDRESSER
CD _____ CDDVN 26
Under One Flag / Dec '93 / Pinnacle.

PITCHFORKS & PERVERTS
CD _____ CDDVN 30
Devotion / May '94 / Pinnacle.

Evil's Toy

HUMAN REFUSE
CD _____ HY 85921053
Hyperium / Jun '94 / Plastic Head.

Evol

SAGA, THE
CD _____ CDAR 026
Adipocre / May '95 / Plastic Head.

Evolution

THEORY OF EVOLUTION
CD _____ WARPCD 29
Warp / Apr '95 / Disc.

Evora, Cesaria

DIVA AUX PIEDS NUS
CD _____ 824532
Buda / Jun '93 / Discovery / ADA.

MUSIC FROM CAPE VERDE
CD _____ 824842
Buda / Nov '90 / Discovery / ADA.

Ewell, Don

DON EWELL MEETS PAMELA & LLEW HIRD
CD _____ BCD 342
GHB / Jun '95 / Jazz Music.

IN JAPAN 1975 (Ewell, Don & Yoshio Toyama)
CD _____ JCD 179
Jazzology / Oct '91 / Swift / Jazz Music.

LIVE AT THE 100 CLUB
CD _____ SACD 89
Solo Art / Jul '93 / Jazz Music.

Ex

BLUEPRINTS FOR A BLACKOUT
CD _____ EX 19D
Konkurrel / May '93 / SRD.

INSTANT
CD _____ EX 063064D
Konkurrel / Nov '95 / SRD.

JOGGERS AND SNOGGERS
CD _____ EX 40/41
Ex / Apr '92 / These / Pinnacle.

SCRABBLING AT THE LOCK (Ex & Tom Cora)
CD _____ EX 051D
Rec Rec / Mar '92 / Plastic Head / SRD / Cadillac.

SHRUG THEIR SHOULDERS (Ex & Tom Cora)
CD _____ EX 57CD
Rec Rec / Sep '93 / Plastic Head / SRD / Cadillac.

TUMULT
CD _____ EX 14D
Konkurrel / May '93 / SRD.

WEATHERMEN SHRUB
CD _____ EX 57CD
Ex / Feb '94 / These / Pinnacle.

Ex-Girlfriend

IT'S A WOMAN THANG
X in your sex / Can I get a nasty / You for me / Sexual chocolate / I want you / It's a woman thang (you wouldn't understand) / Yes I'm ready / Falling 4 U / Nobody like you / Bak together / Takes me away / Cost of love / X in your sex (X between the sheets F.F. Remix)
CD _____ 936245376-2
Warner Bros. / Aug '94 / Warner Music.

Exact Life

GERONIMO
CD _____ SOH 023CD
Suburbs Of Hell / Jan '96 / Pinnacle / Plastic Head / Kudos.

Excelsior Brass Band

EXCELSIOR NEW ORLEANS JAZZ BAND
CD _____ BARX 051CD
Bartrax / Nov '95 / Jazz Music.

Excessive Force

CONQUER YOUR WORLD
CD _____ CDDVN 2
Devotion / Jul '92 / Pinnacle.

Excidium

INNOCENT RIVER
CD _____ CDAR 034
Adipocre / Jan '96 / Plastic Head.

Exciter

BETTER LIVE THAN DEAD
Stand up and fight / Heavy metal maniac / Victims of sacrifice / Under attack / Sudden impacts / Delivering to the master / I am the beast / Blackwitch / Long live the loud / Rising of the dead / Cry of the banshee / Pounding metal / Violence and force
CD _____ CD BLEED 5
Bleeding Hearts / Mar '93 / Pinnacle.

KILL AFTER KILL
Rain of terror / No life no future / Cold blooded murder / Smashin' 'em down / Shadow of the cross / Dog eat dog / Anger, hate and destruction / Second coming / Born to kill (Live)
CD _____ N 01922
Noise/Modern Music / Apr '92 / Pinnacle / Plastic Head.

OTT
CD _____ 854603
Maze / '89 / Plastic Head.

Exciters

SOMETHING TO SHOUT ABOUT (Complete Roulette Sessions)
Something to shout about / I want you to be my boy / Stars are shining bright / Run mascara / I knew you would / Talkin' 'bout my baby / Tonight, tonight / I know, I know / Baby did you change your mind / Love, life, peace / There they go / Are you satisfied / That's how love starts / My father / Just not ready
CD _____ NEMCD 730
Sequel / May '95 / BMG.

Excrement

SCORCHED
CD _____ IR 012CD
Invasion / Apr '95 / Plastic Head.

Excrement Of War

CATHODE RAY COMA
CD _____ FINNREC 07CD
Finn / Jun '94 / Plastic Head / Cadillac.

Excruciate

PASSAGE OF LIFE
CD _____ THR 019
Thrash / Jul '93 / Plastic Head.

Executive Slacks

BEST OF EXECUTIVE SLACKS
CD _____ CLEO 94632
Cleopatra / Jul '94 / Disc.

Exeter Bramclean Boys...

MELODIES OF MEDITATION, THE (Exeter Bramclean Boys Choir)
CD _____ CDDSC 2
Golden Sounds / Jul '94 / Grapevine.

Exit 13

ETHOS MUSICK
CD _____ RR 69132
Roadrunner / Dec '94 / Pinnacle.

Exit 23

JUST A FEW MORE
CD _____ RR 6966CD
Relapse / Nov '95 / Plastic Head.

Exit EEE

EPIDEMIC
CD _____ NRR 018-5
No Respect / Nov '93 / Plastic Head.

Exmortem

LABYRINTHS OF HORROR
CD _____ PHONO 1001CD
Euphonious Metal / Aug '95 / Plastic
Head.

Exocet

CONFUSION
CD _____ MASSCD 068
Massacre / Sep '95 / Plastic Head.

Exodus

BONDED BY BLOOD
Bonded by blood / And then there were
none / Metal command / No love / Strike of
the beast / Exodus / Lesson in violence /
Piranha / Deliver us to evil
CD _____ CDMFN 44
Music For Nations / Apr '85 / Pinnacle.

FABULOUS DISASTER
CD _____ CDMFN 90
Music For Nations / Feb '09 / Pinnacle.

LESSONS IN VIOLENCE
CD _____ CDMFN 138M
Music For Nations / Jul '92 / Pinnacle.

PLEASURES OF THE FLESH
Deranged / Parasite / Faster than you'll ever
live to be / Thirty seconds / Chemi-kill / Till
death do us part / Brain dead / Pleasures
of the flesh / Seed of late / Choose your
weapon
CD _____ CDMFN 77
Music For Nations / Aug '89 / Pinnacle.

Experiment Fear

ASSUMING
CD _____ MASSCD 054
Massacre / Jun '95 / Plastic Head.

Experimental Flux

MODULATION RENOVATIO
CD _____ EFA 001
Clubscene / Oct '94 / Clubscene / Mo's
Music Machine / Grapevine.

Exploding White Mice

EXPLODING WHITE MICE
CD _____ NORMAL 119CD
Normal/Okra / Aug '90 / Direct / ADA.

Exploited

BEAT THE BASTARDS
If you are sad / They lie / Sea of blood / I
syrs / Fight back / Police TV / Law for the
rich / Don't blame me / Beat the bastards /
System fucked up / Massacre of innocents
/ Affected by them / Serial killer
CD _____ CDJUST 22
Rough Justice / Nov '95 / Pinnacle.

DEATH BEFORE DISHONOUR
CD _____ CDJUST 6
Rough Justice / Sep '90 / Pinnacle.

HORROR EPICS
Horror epics / Don't forget the chaos / Law
and order / I hate you / No more idols /
Maggie / Dangerous vision / Down below /
Treat you like shit / Forty odd years ago /
My life
CD _____ DOJOCD 184
Dojo / Feb '94 / BMG.

**LET'S START A WAR (SAID MAGGIE
ONE DAY)**
Let's start a war (said maggie one day) /
Insanity / Safe below / Eye's of the vulture /
Should we, can't we / Rival leaders / God
save the Queen / Psycho / Kidology / False
hopes / Another day to go nowhere /
Wankers
CD _____ DOJOCD 183
Dojo / Feb '94 / BMG.

LET'S START A WAR/HORROR EPICS
Let's start a war (Said Maggie one day) /
Insanity / Safe below / Eye's of the vulture

/ Should we, can't we / Rival leaders / God
saved the queen / Psycho / Kidology / False
hope / Another day to go nowhere / Horror
epics / Wankers / Don't forget the chaos /
Law and order / I hate you / No more idols
/ Maggie / Dangerous vision / Down below
/ Treat you like shit / Forty odd years ago /
My life
CD _____ LOMACD 3
Loma / Feb '94 / BMG.

LIVE AND LOUD
Law and order / Let's start a war (said Mag-
gie one day) / Horror epics / Cop cars /
Blown to bits / Hitler's in the charts again /
U.K. 82 / Rival leaders / Maggie / Troops
of tomorrow / Sex and violence / Daily news
/ Crashed out / S.P.G. / Exploited barmy
army / Dead cities / I believe in anarchy
CD _____ LINK CD 018
Street Link / Sep '93 / BMG.

LIVE IN JAPAN
Let's start a war (said Maggie one day) /
Scaling the Derry Walls / Dogs of war /
Massacre / U.K. 82 / About to die / Alter-
native / Rival leaders / Maggie / I still believe
in anarchy / Death before dishonour / Dead
cities / Troops of tomorrow / Army life /
U.S.A. / Punk's not dead / Exploited barmy
army / Sex and violence
CD _____ DOJOCD 109
Dojo / Feb '94 / BMG.

**LIVE ON STAGE 1981/LIVE AT THE
WHITEHOUSE 1985**
Cop cars / Crashed out / Dole Q / Dogs of
war / Army life / Out of control / Ripper /
Mod song / Exploited barmy army / Royalty
/ SPG / Sex and violence / Punk's not dead
/ I believe in anarchy / Let's start a war (said
Maggie one day) / Jimmy Boyle / Don't for-
get the chaos / God saved the Queen / Al-
ternative / Horror epics / Wankers / Dead
cities / Rival leaders / I hate you / Daily
news
CD _____ LOMACD 2
Loma / Feb '94 / BMG.

MASSACRE, THE
CD _____ CDJUST 15
Rough Justice / Sep '90 / Pinnacle.

PUNK'S NOT DEAD
Punk's not dead / Mucky pup / Cop cars /
Free flight / Army life / Blown to bits / Sex
and violence / S.P.G. / Royalty / Dole Q /
Exploited barmy army / Ripper / Out of con-
trol / Son of a copper / I believe in anarchy
/ Dogs of war / What you gonna do
CD _____ DOJOCD 106
Dojo / Mar '93 / BMG.

SINGLES COLLECTION, THE
Army life / Fuck the mods / Crashed out /
Exploited barmy army / I believe in anarchy
/ What you gonna do / Dogs of war / Blown
to bits (Live) / Dead cities / Hitler's in the
charts again / Class war / S.P.G. (Live) /
Cop cars (Live) / Yop / Attack / Alternative
/ Troops of tomorrow / Computers don't
blunder / Addiction / Rival leaders / Army
style / Singalongabushell
CD _____ DOJOCD 118
Dojo / Apr '93 / BMG.

SINGLES, THE
CD _____ CLEO 5000CD
Cleopatra / Jan '94 / Disc.

TOTALLY EXPLOITED
Punk's not dead / Army life / Fuck a mod /
Barmy army / Dogs of war / Dead cities /
Sex and violence / Yops / Daily news / Dole
Q / Delious in anarchy / God save the queen
/ Psycho / Blown to bits / Insanity / SPG /
Jimmy Boyle / U.S.A. / Attack / Rival
leaders
CD _____ DOJOCD 1
Dojo / Jun '86 / BMG.

TROOPS OF TOMORROW
Jimmy Boyle / Daily news / Disorder / Al-
ternative / Rapist / Troops of tomorrow /
U.K. 82 / Sid Vicious was innocent / War /
They won't stop / So tragic / Germs / U.S.A.
CD _____ DOJOCD 107
Dojo / Mar '93 / BMG.

Expresion

Q'EROS
CD _____ TUMICD 031
Tumi / '93 / Sterns / Discovery.

Expulsion

OVERFLOW
CD _____ GOD 011CD
Godhead / May '95 / Plastic Head.

Exquisite Corpse

INNER LIGHT
CD _____ KK 107CD
KK / Oct '93 / Plastic Head.

SEIZE
CD _____ KK 083CD
KK / Aug '92 / Plastic Head.

Extra Prolific

LIKE IT SHOULD BE
Intro / Brown sugar / In front of the kids / Is
this right / Sweet potato pie / Cash (cash
money) / One motion / Never changing /
First sermon / No what / It's alright / In 20
minutes / Go back to school / Fat outro
CD _____ CHIP 150
Jive / Sep '94 / BMG.

Extrema

POSITIVE PRESSURE
CD _____ FLY 190CD
Flying / Nov '95 / Plastic Head.

TENSION AT THE SEAMS
CD _____ BABECD 5
Rosemary's Baby / Sep '93 / Plastic
Head.

Extreme

EXTREME
Little girls / Wind me up / Kid ego / Watching waiting / Mutha (don't wanna go to
school today) / Teacher's pet / Big boys
don't cry / Smoke signals / Flesh and blood
/ Rock-a-bye bye
A&M / Mar '89 / PolyGram.   CDA 5238

III SIDES TO EVERY STORY
CD _____ 5400062
A&M / Sep '92 / PolyGram.

PORNOGRAFFITI
Decadance dance / Li'l Jack horny / When
I'm president / Get the funk out / More than
words / Money (In God we trust) / It's a
monster / Pornograffiti / When I first kissed
you / Suzi / He-man woman hater / Song
for love / Hole hearted
CD _____ CDMID 191
A&M / May '94 / PolyGram.

WAITING FOR THE PUNCHLINE
There is no God / Cynical / Tell me something I don't know / Hip today / Naked /
Midnight express / Leave me alone / No
respect / Evilangelist / Shadow boxing / Unconditionally / Fair-weather faith / Waiting
for the punchline
CD _____ 5403052
A&M / Jan '95 / PolyGram.

Extreme Noise Terror

**PEEL SESSIONS: EXTREME NOISE
TERROR (10.11.87-16.2.90)**
False profit / Use your mind / Human error
/ Only in it for the music / Subliminal music
/ Punk, fact and fiction / Deceived / Another
nail in the coffin / Carry on screaming /
Conned thru life / Work for never / Third
world genocide / I am a bloody fool / In it
for life / Shock treatment
CD _____ SFPSCD 208
Strange Fruit / Aug '90 / Pinnacle.

PRODUCT AND STRATEGY
CD _____ N 02012
Noise/Modern Music / Sep '92 / Pinnacle /
Plastic Head.

**RETROBUTION (TEN YEARS OF
TERROR)**
Raping the earth / Bullshit propaganda /
Love brain / Work for never / We the help-
less / Invisible war / Subliminal music / Hu-
man error / Murder / Think about it / Pray
to be saved / Conned thru life / Deceived /
Third World genocide
CD _____ MOSH 083CD
Earache / Jan '95 / Vital.

Exxplorer

RECIPE FOR POWER, A
CD _____ MASSCD 041
Massacre / Oct '94 / Plastic Head.

Eye Dance

PREFERRED HIM IN THE SMITHS
Squirm / Hurricane / Fear / Joke's on you /
Die / Life's mean / Peal harbour / Jim Mor-
rison / Never / Zed / Hilbre island / Smug /
Brilliant / Marine parade / My father's house

CD _____ PROBECD 037
Probe Plus / Aug '94 / Vital.

Eye Hate God

TAKE AS NEEDED FOR PAIN
CD _____ CM 77052-2
Century Media / Sep '93 / Plastic Head.

Eyeless In Gaza

BACK FROM THE RAINS
Between these dreams / Twilight / Back
from the rains / Lie still, sleep long / Catch
me / Evening music / She moved through
the fair / Sweet life longer / New love then
/ Welcome now / Your rich sky / Flight of
swallows / My last lost melody / New risen
/ Bright play of eyes / Scent on evening air
/ Drumming the beating heart
CD _____ CDBRED 69
Cherry Red / Jul '89 / Pinnacle.

TRANSIENCE IN BLUE
CD _____ IR 006CD
Integrity / Jan '90 / Vital.

**VOICE - THE BEST OF EYELESS IN
GAZA (Recollections 1980 - 1986)**
Kodak ghosts run amok / No noise / Seven
years / From A to B / Speech rapid fire /
Invisibility / Others / Rose petal knot / Out
from the day today / Transcience blues /
Picture the day / Two / Veil like calm / One
by one / Pencil sketch / Through eastfields
/ Changing stations / Corner of dusk /
Drumming the beating heart / New risen /
Sun bursts in / Welcome now / Back from
the rains / Lilt of music / Evening music /
Between these dreams
CD _____ CDBRED 104
Cherry Red / Oct '93 / Pinnacle.

Eyermann, Tim

**OUTSIDE INSIDE (Eyermann, Tim & East
Coast Offering)**
CD _____ R 279163
Rhino / Sep '91 / Warner Music.

Eyes Of The Nightmare...

FATE (Eyes Of The Nightmare Jungle)
CD _____ SPC 084-25152
SPV / Jan '94 / Plastic Head.

**INNOCENCE (Eyes Of The Nightmare
Jungle)**
CD _____ SPV 08461722
SPV / May '95 / Plastic Head.

Eyewitness

EYEWITNESS
CD _____ NTHEN 17
Now & Then / Apr '95 / Plastic Head.

Eyges, David

**LIGHTNIN' STRIKES (Eyges, David &
Byard Lancaster)**
CD _____ BLE 592212
Black & Blue / Feb '93 / Wellard / Koch.

Eyuphuro

MAMA MOSAMBIKI
Samukeha (the nostalgic man) / Mwanuni
(the bird) / Akakswela / We awaka (you are
mine) / Kihiyeny / Nifungo (the key of the
house) / Oh mama (oh mother) / Nana maa
Iani (single mother of a single mother
CD _____ CDRW 10
Realworld / '90 / EMI / Sterns.

Ezio

BLACK BOOTS ON LATIN FEET
Saxon street / Thirty and confused / Just to
talk to you again / Cancel today / Go / Steal
away / Further we stretch / Tuesday night /
1000 years / Agony / Wild side / Brave man
/ Angel song
CD _____ 74321240152
Arista / Jan '95 / BMG.

Ezra

SHAPES
Just a game / Smiled at me / Red sky /
Falling / Life and times / She cries / Rain-
gods / First light / Big world / Tea at cyrils
CD _____ CYCL 017
Cyclops / Nov '94 / Pinnacle.

F

F.F.W.

KILLER (Freaky Fukin Weirdoz)
CD _____ EFA 15525CD
Sub Up / Feb '92 / SRD.

F.M.

APHRODISIAC
CD _____ CDMFN 141
Music For Nations / Oct '92 / Pinnacle.

DEAD MAN'S SHOES
CD _____ RAWCD 107
Raw Power / Nov '95 / BMG.

INDISCREET
That girl / Other side of midnight / Love lies dying / I belong to the night / American girls / Hot wired / Face to face / Frozen heart / Heart of the matter
CD _____ BGOCD 184
Beat Goes On / Mar '93 / Pinnacle.

NO ELECTRICITY REQUIRED
CD _____ CDMFN 155
Music For Nations / Oct '93 / Pinnacle.

ONLY THE STRONG (The Best Of FM 1984-1994)
That girl / Other side of midnight / American girls / Face to face / Frozen heart / Tough it out / Don't stop / Bad luck / Burning my heart down / Let love be the leader / Heard it through the grapevine / Only the strong survive / Dangerous ground / Breathe fire / Blood and gasoline / All or nothing / Closer to heaven
CD _____ VSOPCD 203
Connoisseur / Aug '94 / Pinnacle.

TAKIN' IT TO THE STREETS
CD _____ CDMFN 119
Music For Nations / Oct '91 / Pinnacle.

F.U.'s

ORIGIN OF, THE
CD _____ LF 020CD
Lost & Found / Apr '92 / Plastic Head.

REVENGE
CD _____ LF 037CD
Lost & Found / Jun '92 / Plastic Head.

F/I

EARTHPIPE
CD _____ POT 2
PDCD / Aug '93 / Plastic Head.

Fab 5

BEST OF FAB 5, THE
CD _____ PKCD 32593
K&K / Jul '93 / Jetstar.

Fabares, Shelly

BEST OF SHELLY FABARES, THE
Johnny Angel / What did they do before rock n' roll / Johnny loves me / I'm growing up / Welcome home / Big star / Things we did last summer / I left a note to say goodbye / Telephone (Won't you ring) / Billy boy / Ronnie, call me when you get a chance / How lovely to be a woman / Bye bye birdie / Football seasons over / He don't love me
CD _____ NEMCD 695
Sequel / Aug '94 / BMG.

Fabian

HOLD THAT TIGER
CD _____ REP 4157-WZ
Repertoire / Aug '91 / Pinnacle / Cadillac.

THIS IS FABIAN
Tiger / Turn me loose / Got the feeling / Mighty cold (to a warm warm heart) / Tomorrow / I'm a man / Hypnotised / Come on and get me / Tongue tied / Gonna get you / Steady date / King of love / Stop thief / Hound dog man / Lilly Lou / Long before / Wild party / Shivers / This friendly world / I'm gonna sit right down and write myself a letter / String along / Girl like you / About this thing called love / Kissin' and twistin' / Love that I'm giving to you / Grapevine
CD _____ CDCHD 321
Ace / Jul '91 / Pinnacle / Cadillac / Complete/Pinnacle.

Fabric

BODY OF WATER
Failure / Value / A student baby / Stick colour / Trudgeth / Helpless / Carried away / Quilt / Instrumental / Wild place / Shake it / Truth / Freedom / March of the machines / Seven / Saturnalia / Without
CD _____ WCAR 004CD
Whole Car / Sep '94 / Vital.

LIGHTBRINGER
CD _____ WCAR 005CD
Whole Car / Oct '95 / Vital.

Fabulous Poodles

HIS MASTERS VOICE
CD _____ NEMCD 697
Sequel / Jun '95 / BMG.

Fabulous Sister Brothers

LIVE IN KEMP TOWN
Intro / Here I am / Let your love / I lift up my voice / I will comfort you / Capitol Hill / Lead me on / Glory day / That the world / Up jump shout
CD _____ FSB 01
FSB / Sep '95 / FSB.

Fabulous Thunderbirds

BUTT ROCKIN'/T-BIRD RHYTHM
I believe I'm in love / One's too many / Give me all your lovin' / Roll roll roll / Cherry pink and apple blossom white / I hear you knocking / Tip on in / I'm sorry / Mathilda / How do you spell love / You're humbuggin' me / My babe / Neighbour tend to your business / Monkey / Diddy wah diddy / Lover's crime / Poor boy / Tell me (pretty baby) / Gotta have some/Just got some
CD _____ BGOCD 193
Beat Goes On / Jun '93 / Pinnacle.

FABULOUS THUNDERBIRDS, THE/ WHAT'S THE WORD
Wait on time / Scratch my back / Rich woman / Full time lover / Pocket rockets / She's tuff / Marked deck / Walkin' to my baby / Rock with me / C-boy's blues / Let me in / Running shoes / You ain't nothing but fine / Low-down woman / Extra Jimmies / Sugar coated love / Last call for alcohol / Crawl / Jumpin' bad / Learn to treat me right / I'm a good man if you treat me right / Dirty work / That's enough of that stuff / Los Fabulosos Thunderbirds
CD _____ BGOCD 192
Beat Goes On / Jun '93 / Pinnacle.

ROLL OF THE DICE
Roll of the dice / Too many irons / How do I get you back / Here comes the night / Taking it too easy / I don't want to be / Mean love / I can't win / Memory from hell / Looking forward / Do as I say / Zip a dee do dah
CD _____ 1005 8210302
Private Music / Sep '95 / BMG.

Face To Face

DON'T TURN AWAY
CD _____ FAT 515CD
Fat Wreck Chords / Mar '94 / Plastic Head.

Face Value

CHOICES
CD _____ WB 2130CD
We Bite / Sep '95 / Plastic Head.

Faceless

ACHIEVEMENT
CD _____ NBX 010
Noisebox / May '95 / Disc.

Faces

FIRST STEP
Wicked messenger / Devotion / Shake shudder shiver / Stone / Around the plynth / Flying / Pinapple and the monkey / No-body knows / Looking out the window / Three button hand me down
CD _____ 7599263762
Warner Bros. / Sep '93 / Warner Music.

LONG PLAYER
Bad 'n' ruin / Tell everyone / Sweet Lady Mary / Richmond / Maybe I'm amazed / Had me a real good time / On the beach / I feel so good / Jerusalem
CD _____ 7599261912
Warner Bros. / Sep '93 / Warner Music.

NOD'S AS GOOD AS A WINK TO A BLIND HORSE, A
Miss Judy's farm / You're so rude / Love lived here / Last orders please / Stay with me / Debris / Memphis / Too bad / That's all you need
CD _____ 7599259292
Warner Bros. / Sep '93 / Warner Music.

OOH LA LA
Silicone grown / Cindy incidentally / Flags and banners / My fault / Borstal boys / Fly in the ointment / If I'm on the late side / Glad and sorry / Just another honky / Ooh la la
CD _____ 7599263682
Warner Bros. / Sep '93 / Warner Music.

Facil

FACIL
CD _____ IAE 004
Instinct Ambient Europe / May '95 / Plastic Head.

Faction

HEAVEN
CD _____ TMCD 056
Third Mind / Oct '90 / Pinnacle / Third Mind.

Faddis, Jon

JON AND BILLY (Faddis, Jon & Billy Harper)
Jon and Billy / Water bridge-mizu hashi san / Ballad for Jon Haddis / Two d's from Shinjyuku, dig and dug / Seventeen bar blues / This all-koredake
CD _____ ECD 22052
Evidence / Jul '93 / Harmonia Mundi / ADA / Cadillac.

Fagen, Donald

KAMAKIRIAD
Trans island skyway / Countermoon / Springtime / Snowbound / Tomorrow's girls / Florida room / On the dunes / Teahouse on the tracks
CD _____ 936245230-2
Warner Bros. / May '93 / Warner Music.

NIGHTFLY, THE
New frontier / I.G.Y. / Green Flower Street / Ruby baby / Maxine / Walk between raindrops / Goodbye look / Night fly
CD _____ 923696 2
WEA / Oct '82 / Warner Music.

ORIGINS OF STEELY DAN OLD REGIME (Fagen, Donald & Walter Becker)
CD _____ CDSGP 029
Prestige / Mar '94 / Total/BMG.

Fagin, Joe

BEST OF JOE FAGIN
Am I asking too much / Crazy in love / That's livin' adult / (Cry) for no one / Younger days / Forever now / Only love can show the way / Epitaph (for a drunk) / Why don't we spend the night / Put out the light / Get it right / Love hangs by a thread / As time goes by / So much for saying goodbye / Breaking away / She's leaving home / Annie
CD _____ CDWM 107
Westmoor / Jan '96 / Target/BMG.

Fahey, John

CHRISTMAS GUITAR VOLUME 1
CD _____ CDVR 002
Varrick / Dec '94 / Roots / CM / Direct / ADA.

FARE FORWARD VOYAGERS
CD _____ SHANCD 99005
Shanachie / '92 / Koch / ADA / Greensleeves.

I REMEMBER BLIND JOE DEATH
Evening mysteries of Ferry Street / You'll find her name written there / Minutes seem like hours, hours seem like days / Are you from Dixie / Minor blues / Steel guitar rag / Nightmare / Summertime / Let me call you sweetheart / Unknown tango / Improv in E minor / Lava on Waikiki / Gaucho
CD _____ FIENDCD 207
Demon / Apr '91 / Pinnacle / ADA.

OLD FASHIONED LOVE
In a Persian market / Jaya shiva shankaram / Marilyn / Assassination of Stefan Grossman / Old fashioned love / Boodle am shake / Keep your lamp trimmed and burning / I saw the light shining 'round and 'round
CD _____ SHCD 99001
Shanachie / Jun '91 / Koch / ADA / Greensleeves.

OLD GIRLFRIENDS AND OTHER HORRIBLE MEMORIES
CD _____ CDVR 031
Varrick / Feb '92 / Roots / CM / Direct / ADA.

POPULAR SONGS OF CHRISTMAS AND NEW YEAR
CD _____ VR 012CD
Varrick / Feb '95 / Roots / CM / Direct / ADA.

RAILROAD
CD _____ SHAN 99003CD
Shanachie / '92 / Koch / ADA / Greensleeves.

RAIN FORESTS, OCEANS AND OTHER THEMES
CD _____ CDVR 019
Rounder / Dec '86 / CM / Direct / ADA / Cadillac.

Faine Jade

INTROSPECTION: A FAINE JADE RECITAL
Tune up (Non-music work) / Dr. Paul overture / People games play / Cold winter sun symphony in D major / I lived tomorrow yesterday / Ballad of the bad guys (1956 A.D.) / Piano interlude / Introspection / In a brand new groove / On the inside there's a middle / Don't hassle me / Grand finale (Don't hassle me pt 2) / Stand together in the end (Theme from an imaginary Beatles reunion or Woodstock reprise) / Dr. Paul / People games play (2) / Don't hassle me (instrumental)
CD _____ CDWIKD 141
Big Beat / Mar '95 / Pinnacle.

Fair, Jad

I LIKE IT WHEN YOU SMILE
CD _____ PAPCD 009
Paperhouse / Feb '92 / Disc.

IT'S SPOOKY (Fair, Jad & Daniel Johnston)
CD _____ PAPCD 019
Paperhouse / Jul '93 / Disc.

Fairburn, Werly

EVERYBODY'S ROCKIN'
I'm a fool about your love / Everybody's rockin' / All the time / My heart's on fire / Speak to me baby / Telephone baby / No blues tomorrow / I'm jealous / I guess I'm crazy / That sweet love of mine / Nothin' but lovin' / Love spelled backwards is evol / Broken hearted me / Stay close to me / It's heaven / Old mem'ries come back / Good deal Lucille / Baby he's a wolf / Won't it be nice / Little bit of nothing / Prison cell of love / Spiteful heart / It's a cold weary world / I feel like cryin' / Camping with Marie / Let's live it over / Doggone that moon / Black widow spider woman / You are my sunshine
CD _____ BCD 15578
Bear Family / Nov '93 / Rollercoaster / Direct / CM / Swift / ADA.

Fairclough Group

SHEPHERD WHEEL
Jacob's ladder / Shepherd wheel / Yaller belly / Saint Monda / Rattening / Stoneburst / Racing / When there's nothing left to burn
CD _____ ASCCD 1
ASC / Jun '95 / New Note / Cadillac.

Fairer Sax

DIVERSIONS WITH THE FAIRER SAX
Arrival of the Queen of Sheba / Sixteenth century dances / Fugue in D minor (Bach) / Aria (From suite No.3 Bach) / Moment musicale (Schubert) / Something doing
CD _____ CDSDL 365
Saydisc / Oct '87 / Harmonia Mundi / ADA / Direct.

Fairey Engineering Works.

SPECTRUM - MUSIC OF GILBERT VINTER VOL 1 (Fairey Engineering Works Band)
CD _____ QPRL 058D
Polyphonic / Aug '93 / Conifer.

TRIUMPHANT RHAPSODY (Fairey Engineering Works Band)
CD _____ QPRL 068D
Polyphonic / Sep '94 / Conifer.

Fairfield Four

STANDING ON THE ROCK
Don't leave me by myself / Hope to shout in glory / I can tell you the time / My prayer / Come on to this altar / I love the name Jesus / Does Jesus care / Leave it there / Love like a river / Who is that knocking / His eye is on the sparrow / How I got over / This evening our father / Hear me when I pray / When the battle is over / Standing on the rock / Somebody touched me / On my journey now / Old time religion / Talking about Jesus / No room at the inn / When we bow / Let's go / Don't drive your children away / Packin' every burden / Poor pilgrim
CD _____ CDCHD 449
Ace / Aug '93 / Pinnacle / Cadillac / Complete/Pinnacle.

Fairground Attraction

AY FOND KISS
Jock O'Hazeldean / Walkin' after midnight / Trying times / Winter rose / Allelujah (live) / Watching the party / Game of love / You send me / Mystery train / Do you want to know a secret / Cajun band / Ae fond kiss
CD _____ 74321 19371-2
RCA / Apr '94 / BMG.

AY FOND KISS/FIRST OF A MILLION KISSES
Perfect / Moon in the rain / Find my love / Mythology / Falling backwards / Allelujah / Whispers / Station street / Moon is mine / Comedy waltz / Clare / Wind knows my name / Jock O'Hazeldean / Game of love / Walkin' after midnight / You send me / Trying times / Mystery train / Winter rose / Do you want to know a secret / Allelujah (live) / Cajun band / Watching the party / Ae fond kiss
CD Set _____ 74321259592
RCA / Mar '95 / BMG.

FIRST OF A MILLION KISSES
Smile in a whisper / Perfect / Moon on the rain / Find my love / Fairground attraction / Wind knows my name / Clare / Comedy waltz / Moon is mine / Station Street / Whispers / Allelujah / Falling backwards (Only on CD.) / Mythology (Only on CD.)
CD _____ 7432113439-2
RCA / May '93 / BMG.

PERFECT - THE BEST OF FAIRGROUND ATTRACTION
CD _____ 74321292772
RCA / Jul '95 / BMG.

Fairhurst, Richard

HUNGRY ANTS
CD _____ BDV 9504
Babel / Jan '96 / ADA / Harmonia Mundi / Cadillac / Diverse.

Fairies Fortune

SNOWFISH
CD _____ EFA 155852
Gymnastic / Aug '95 / SRD.

Fairport Convention

25TH ANNIVERSARY PACK (Rosie/John Babbacombe Lee/Nine/Rising For The Moon)
CD _____ FCBX 1
Island / Aug '92 / PolyGram.

5 SEASONS
CD _____ HTCD 48
HTD / Jan '96 / Pinnacle.

ANGEL DELIGHT
Lord Marlborough / Sir William Gower / Bridge over the river Ash / Wizard of the wordly game / Journeyman's grace / Angel delight / Banks of the sweet primroses / Instrumental medley / Bonnie black hare / Sickness and diseases
CD _____ IMCD 166
Island / Mar '93 / PolyGram.

BONNY BUNCH OF ROSES
Adieu adieu / Bonnie bunch of roses / Eynsham poacher / General Taylor / James O'Donnell's jig / Last waltz / Poor ditching boy / Royal selleccion number 13 / Run Johnny run
CD _____ WRCD 011
Woodworm / Oct '88 / Pinnacle.
CD _____ 5129882
Vertigo / Jan '92 / PolyGram.

EXPLETIVE DELIGHTED
CD _____ TRUCKCD 16
Terrapin Truckin' / Nov '95 / Total/BMG / Direct / ADA.

FAIRPORT CONVENTION
Time will show the wiser / I don't know where I stand / Decameron / Jack O'Diamonds / Portfolio / Chelsea morning / Sun shade / Lobster / It's alright ma, it's only witchcraft / One sure thing / M.I. breakdown
CD _____ 835 230-2
Polydor / Oct '90 / PolyGram.

FAIRPORT CONVENTION 9
Hexhamshire lass / Polly on the shore / Brilliancy medley and Cherokee shuffle / To Althea from prison / Tokyo / Bring 'em down / Big William / Pleasure and pain / Possibly parsons green
CD _____ IMCD 154
Island / Aug '92 / PolyGram.

FAREWELL, FAREWELL
Matty groves / Orange blossom special / John Lee / Bridge over the river Ash / Sir Patrick Spens / Mr. Lacey / Walk awhile / Bonnie black hare / Journeyman's grace / Meet on the ledge
CD _____ TRUCKCD 011
Terrapin Truckin' / Jun '94 / Total/BMG / Direct / ADA.

FIVE SEASONS, THE
CD _____ TRUCKCD 019
Terrapin Truckin' / Jul '95 / Total/BMG / Direct / ADA.

FULL HOUSE
Walk awhile / Dirty linen / Sloth / Sir Patrick Spens / Flatback caper / Doctor of physick / Flowers of the forest
CD _____ HNCD 4417
Hannibal / Nov '91 / Vital / ADA.

GLADYS LEAP
CD _____ TRUCKCD 15
Terrapin Truckin' / Aug '94 / Total/BMG / Direct / ADA.

HEYDAY (BBC Radio Sessions)
CD _____ HNCD 1329
Hannibal / Oct '87 / Vital / ADA.

HISTORY OF FAIRPORT CONVENTION, THE
Meet on the ledge / Fotheringay / Mr. Lacey / Book song / Sailor's life / Si tu dois partir / Who knows where the time goes / Matty Groves / Crazy man Michael / Now be thankful (Medley) / Walk awhile / Sloth / Bonnie black hare / Angel delight / Bridge over the river Ash / John Lee / Breakfast in Mayfair / Hanging song / Hen's march / Four poster bed
CD _____ IMCD 128
Island / Jun '91 / PolyGram.

HOUSE FULL (Live In Los Angeles)
Sir Patrick Spens / Banks of the sweet primroses / Toss the feathers / Sloth / Staines morris / Matty groves / Mason's apron / Battle of the Somme
CD _____ HNCD 1319
Hannibal / Jul '90 / Vital / ADA.

IN REAL TIME
CD _____ IMCD 10
Island / '90 / PolyGram.

JEWEL IN THE CROWN
CD _____ WRMCD 023
Woodworm / Jan '95 / Pinnacle.

JOHN BABBACOMBE LEE
CD _____ IMCD 153
Island / Aug '92 / PolyGram.

LIEGE AND LIEF
Come all ye / Reynardine / Matty groves / Farewell farewell / Deserter / Lark in the morning (medley) / Tamlin / Crazy man Michael / Rakish paddy / Foxhunters jigs / Toss the feathers
CD _____ IMCD 60
Island / '89 / PolyGram.

LIVE: FAIRPORT CONVENTION
Matty groves / Rosie / Fiddlestix / John the gun / Something you got / Sloth / Dirty linen / Down in the flood / Sir B MacKenzie
CD _____ IMCD 305
Island / Feb '90 / PolyGram.

RED AND GOLD
Set me up / Red and gold / Battle / London river / Noise club / Beggars song / Dark eyed Molly / Open the door Richard
CD _____ TRUCKCD 018
Terrapin Truckin' / Jul '95 / Total/BMG / Direct / ADA.

RISING FOR THE MOON
Rising for the moon / Restless / White dress / Let it go / Stranger to himself / What is true / Iron lion / Dawn / After halloween / Night-time girl / One more chance
CD _____ IMCD 155
Island / Aug '92 / PolyGram.

ROSIE
Rosie / Matthew, Mark, Luke and John / Knights of the road / Peggy's pub / Plainsman / Hungarian rhapsody / My girl / Me with you / Hen's march / Furs and feathers
CD _____ IMCD 152
Island / Aug '92 / PolyGram.

TIPPLERS' TALES
Ye mariners all / Jack orion / Banruptured / Hair of the dogma / Three drunken maidens / Reynard the fox / Widow of Westmorland / John Barleycorn
CD _____ BGOCD 72
Beat Goes On / '89 / Pinnacle.

UNHALFBRICKING
Genesis hall / Si tu dois partir / Autopsy / Cajun woman / Who knows where the time goes / Percy's song / Million dollar bash / Sailor's life
CD _____ IMCD 61
Island / Nov '89 / PolyGram.

WHAT WE DID ON OUR HOLIDAYS
Fotheringay / Mr. Lacey / Book song / Lord is in this place / No man's land / I'll keep it with mine / Eastern rain / Nottamun town / Tale in hard time / She moved through the fair / Meet me on the ledge / End of a holiday
CD _____ IMCD 97
Island / Feb '90 / PolyGram.

Fairweather, Digby

PORTRAIT OF DIGBY FAIRWEATHER
CD _____ BLCD 760505
Black Lion / Apr '91 / Jazz Music / Cadillac / Wellard / Koch.

WITH NAT IN MIND (Fairweather, Digby & His New Georgians)
CD _____ JCD 247
Jazzology / Aug '95 / Swift / Jazz Music.

Faitelson, Dalia

COMMON GROUND (Faitelson, Dalia Group)
Dahab / Eye of the morning / East west / My treasure / Trail of a trail / Captain / Mustafa / Common ground / Cheek to cheek / Alone with you
CD _____ STCD 4196
Storyville / Nov '94 / Jazz Music / Wellard / CM / Cadillac.

Faith, Adam

ADAM FAITH SINGLES COLLECTION (His Greatest Hits)
Got a heartsick feeling / What do you want / Poor me / Someone else's baby / When Johnny comes marching home / Made you / How about that / Who am I / Easy going / me / Don't you know it / Time has come / Lonesome / As you like it / Don't that beat all / What now / First time / We are in love / Message to Martha / Someone's taken Maria away / Cheryl's goin' home
CD _____ CZ 260
EMI / Jan '90 / EMI.

BEST OF ADAM FAITH (2)
What do you want / Poor me / Someone else's baby / Johnny comes marching home / Made you / How about that / Lonely pup (in a christmas shop) / This is it / Who am I / Easy going me / Don't you know it / Time has come / Lonesome / As you like it / Don't that beat all / What now / Walkin' tall / First time / We are in love / If he tells you (CD only) / I love being in love with you (CD only) / Message to Martha / Stop feeling sorry for yourself (CD only.) / Someone's taken Maria away (CD only.) / Cheryl's goin' home
CD _____ CDMFP 6048
Music For Pleasure / Jan '89 / EMI.

BEST OF THE EMI YEARS, THE
What do you want / (Got a) Heartsick feeling / From now until forever / Ah poor little baby / Poor me / Summertime / Wonderful time / Someone else's baby / When Johnny comes marching home / Made you / Hit the road to dreamland / I'm a man / How about that / With open arms / Singin' in the rain / Fare thee well my pretty maid / Lonely pup (in a christmas shop) / This is it / Who am I / So I know a lot about love / As long as you keep loving me / I'm gonna love you too / Easy going me / Wonderin' / Watch your step / Don't you know it / Time has come / Help each other romance / Lonesome / Ballad of a broken heart / (I'm) Knockin' on wood / As you like it / Learning to forget / You 'n' me / Face to face / You can do it if you try / Don't that beat all / Mix me a person / Baby take a bow / What now / What have I got / Walkin' tall / Forget me not / First time / So long baby / Made for me / We are in love / If he tells you / Come closer / Talk to me / It's alright / I love being in love with you / Message to Martha / I've gotta see my baby / Stop feeling sorry for yourself / I'll stop at nothing / Hand me down things / Talk about love / Someone's taken Maria away / I don't need that kind of lovin' / If you ever need me / Cheryl's goin' home / What more can anyone do / Cowman milk your cow / To hell with love / Close the door / You make my life worthwhile
CD _____ CDEM 1513
EMI / Feb '94 / EMI.

MIDNIGHT POSTCARDS
Body to body / Stuck in the middle / When I'm dead and gone / Once the love has gone / I'll be your baby tonight / Roxy roxy / Back on the road / Squeeze box / Why me / Promise / Not without you / All I ever need is you / Making up
CD _____ 821398-2
PolyGram TV / Nov '93 / PolyGram.

Faith, George

SOULFUL
CD _____ CDSGP 073
Prestige / Jul '95 / Total/BMG.

TO BE A LOVER (HAVE MERCY)
CD _____ RRCD 31
Reggae Refreshers / Sep '91 / PolyGram / Vital.

Faith Healers

IMAGINARY FRIEND
CD _____ PURECD 027
Too Pure / Oct '93 / Vital.

L
Pop song / Delores / Slag / Reptile smile / Lovely / Gorgeous blue / Not a God
CD _____ PEUR 002
Too Pure / Apr '92 / Vital.

LIDO
Love song / Don't Jones me / This time / Word of advice / Hippy hole / Mother sky / Spin 1/2 / Untitled
CD _____ PURECD 012
Too Pure / Jun '92 / Vital.

Faith, Michael

SUSPENDED ANIMATION
CD _____ CMMR 922
Music Maker / Oct '93 / Grapevine / ADA.

Faith No More

ANGEL DUST
CD _____ 828 401-2
Slash / Jan '93 / PolyGram.

INTRODUCE YOURSELF
Faster disco / Anne's song / Introduce yourself / Chinese arithmetic / Death march / We care a lot / R 'N' R / Crab song / Blood / Spirit
CD _____ 828 051 2
Slash / Apr '87 / PolyGram.

KING FOR A DAY, FOOL FOR A LIFETIME
Get out / Ricochet / Evidence / Gentle art of making enemies / Star A.D. / Cuckoo for caca / Caralho voador / Ugly in the morning / Digging the grave / Take this bottle / King for a day / What a day / Last to know / Just a man
CD _____ 8285602
Slash / Mar '95 / PolyGram.

LIVE AT THE BRIXTON ACADEMY
Epic / From out of nowhere / We care a lot / Falling to pieces / Real thing / Warriors / Zombie eaters / Edge of the world / Grade (Not on LP) / Cowboy song (Not on LP)
CD _____ 828 238 2
Slash / Feb '91 / PolyGram.

REAL THING, THE
From out of nowhere / Epic / Falling to pieces / Surprise you're dead / Zombie eaters / Real thing / Underwater love / Morning after / Woodpecker from Mars / War pigs (Not on LP) / Edge of the world (Not on LP)
CD _____ 828 154 2
Slash / Jun '89 / PolyGram.

Faith Over Reason

EYES WIDE SMILE
CD _____ ABBCD 027
Big Cat / Sep '91 / SRD / Pinnacle.

Faith, Percy

16 MOST REQUESTED SONGS
Swedish rhapsody / Moulin Rouge / Delicado / Baubles, bangles and beads / Rain in Spain / Show me / Malaguena / Summer place / I will follow you / There for young lovers / Sound of music / Tara's theme / Girl from Ipanema / Oscar / Love theme from Romeo and Juliet / MacArthur Park
CD _____ 472417 2
Columbia / Nov '92 / Sony.

Faithfull, Marianne

BLAZING AWAY
Les prisons du roy / Guilt / Sister Morphine / Why'd ya do it / Ballad of Lucy Jordan / Blazing away / Broken English / Strange weather / Working class hero / As tears go by / When I find my life / Times Square / She moved through the fair
CD _____ IMCD 207
Island / Apr '95 / PolyGram.

BROKEN ENGLISH
Working class hero / What's the hurry / Ballad of Lucy Jordan / Why d'ya do it / Broken English / Witch's song / Guilt / Brain drain
CD _____ IMCD 11
Island / Apr '95 / PolyGram.

CHILD'S ADVENTURE, A
CD _____ IMCD 206
Island / Apr '95 / PolyGram.

DANGEROUS ACQUAINTANCES
Sweetheart / Intrigue / Easy in the city / Strange one / Tenderness / For beauty's sake / So sad / Eye communication / Truth, bitter truth
CD _____ IMCD 205
Island / May '95 / PolyGram.

FAITHFULL - A COLLECTION OF HER BEST SONGS
Broken english / Ballad of Lucy Jordan / Working class hero / Guilt / Why'd ya do it / Ghost dance / Trouble in mind / Times Square / Strange weather / She / As tears go by
CD _____ CID 8023
Island / Aug '94 / PolyGram.

FAITHLESS
Dreamin' my dreams / Vanilla O'Lay / Wait for me down by the river / I'll be your baby tonight / Lady Madelaine / All I wanna do in life / Way you want me to be / Wrong road again / That was the day (Nashville) / This time / I'm not Lisa / Honky tonk angels
CD _____ CLACD 148
Castle / Apr '89 / BMG.

SECRET LIFE, A
Prologue / Sleep / Love in the afternoon / Flaming September / She / Bored by dreams / Losing / Wedding / Stars line up / Epilogue
CD _____ CID 8038
Island / Mar '95 / PolyGram.

STRANGE WEATHER
Stranger intro / Boulevard of broken dreams / I ain't goin' down to the well no more / Yesterdays / Sing of judgement / Strange weather / Love life and money / I'll keep it with mine / Hello stranger / Penthouse serenade / As tears go by / Stranger on earth
CD _____ IMCD 12
Island / '89 / PolyGram.

THIS LITTLE BIRD
This little bird / Morning sun / Monday Monday / Our love has come / Et maintenant / Blowin' in the wind / Portland town / Is this what I get for loving you / Black girl / Oh look around / What have they done to the rain / Young girl blues / You can't go where the roses go / Come and stay with me
CD _____ 5500972
Spectrum/Karussell / Oct '93 / PolyGram / THE.

VERY BEST OF MARIANNE FAITHFULL
As tears go by / Come and stay with me / Scarborough Fair / Monday, Monday / Yesterday / Last thing on my mind / What have they done to the rain / This little bird / In my time of sorrow / Is this what I get for loving you / Tomorrow's calling / Reason to believe / Sister Morphine / Go away from my world / Summer nights
CD _____ 8204822
London / Sep '87 / PolyGram.

Falco, Tav

BEHIND THE MAGNOLIA CURTAIN
(Falco, Tav Panther Burns)
Come on little mama / She's the one that got it / Hey high school baby / Brazil / You're undecided / Oo wee baby / River of love / Snake drive / Blind man / Where the Rio de Rosa flows / Snatch it back / Bourgeois blues / St. Louis blues / Moving on down the line
CD _____ FC 029CD
Fan Club / Feb '88 / Direct.

BEHIND THE MAGNOLIA CURTAIN/ BLOW YOUR TOP (Falco, Tav Panther Burns)
CD _____ 422135
New Rose / May '94 / Direct / ADA.

LIFE SENTENCE (Falco, Tav Panther Burns)
CD _____ 422136
New Rose / May '94 / Direct / ADA.

MIDNIGHT IN MEMPHIS (Falco, Tav Panther Burns)
CD _____ 422141
New Rose / May '94 / Direct / ADA.

RED DEVIL
CD _____ ROSE 140CD
New Rose / Feb '88 / Direct / ADA.

SUGAR DITCH REVISITED
CD _____ 422137
New Rose / May '94 / Direct / ADA.

UNRELEASED SESSIONS (Falco, Tav Panther Burns)
CD _____ FM 1011CD
Marilyn / Jul '92 / Pinnacle.

WORLD WE KNEW, THE (Falco, Tav Panther Burns)
CD _____ 422142
New Rose / May '94 / Direct / ADA.

Fall

27 POINTS - THE FALL LIVE
CD _____ PERMCD 36
Permanent / Jul '95 / Total/BMG.

458 AND 78 (The A Sides)
Oh brother / C.R.E.E.P. / No bulbs 3 / Rollin' dany / Couldn't get ahead / Cruiser's creek / L.A. / Living too late / Hit the North (pt 1) / Mr. Pharmacist / Hey Luciani / There's a ghost in my house / Victoria / Big new prinz / Wrong place right time / Jerusalem / Dead beat descendand
CD _____ BEGA 111 CD
Beggars Banquet / Sep '90 / Warner Music / Disc.

B SIDES
Oh brother / God box / C.R.E.E.P. / Pat-trip dispenser / Slang King 2 / Draygo's guilt / Clear off / No bulbs / Petty thief / Lucifer / Hot aftershave bop / Living too long / Lucifer over Lancashire / Auto-tech pilot / Entitled / Shoulder pads / Sleep debt snatches / Mark'll sink us / Haf found bormann / Australians in Europe / Northerns in Europe / Hit the North part 2 / Guest informant / Tuff like boogie / Twister / Bremen nacht run out / Acid priest 2088 / Cab it up / Kurious oranj / Hit the North
CD Set _____ BEGA 116CD
Beggars Banquet / Dec '90 / Warner Music / Disc.

BBC LIVE IN CONCERT
Australians in Europe / Shoulder pads / Ghost in my house / Hey Luciani / Terry Waite sez / Fiery Jack / Lucifer over Lancashire
CD _____ WINCD 038
Windsong / Jul '93 / Pinnacle.

BEND SINISTER
R.O.D. / Dr. Faustus / Shoulder pads / Mr. Pharmacist / Gross chapel / U.S. 80's - 60's

/ Terry Waite sez / Bournemouth runner / Riddler / Shoulder pads 2
CD _____ BEGA 75 CD
Beggars Banquet / Jan '88 / Warner Music / Disc.

CEREBRAL CAUSTIC
CD _____ PERMCD 30
Permanent / Feb '95 / Total/BMG.

CODE: SELFISH
Birmingham school of business school / Free range / Return / Time enough at last / Everything hurtz / Immortality / Two face / Just waiting / So called dangerous / Gentleman's agreement / Married two kids / Crew filth
CD _____ 5121622
Fontana / Mar '92 / PolyGram.

COLLECTION
CD _____ CCSCD 365
Castle / Mar '93 / BMG.

FRENZ EXPERIMENT
Frenz / Carry bag man / Get a hotel / Victoria / Athlete cured / In these times / Steak place / Bremen nacht / Guest informant / Oswald defence lawyer
CD _____ BEGA 91CD
Beggars Banquet / '88 / Warner Music / Disc.

GROTESQUE
Pay your rates / English scheme / New face in hell / C'N'Cs mithering / Container drivers / Impression of J Temperance / In the park / WMC blob 59 / Gramme Friday / NWRA
CD _____ CLACD 391
Castle / Sep '93 / BMG.

HIP PRIESTS AND KAMERADS
Lie dream of a casino soul / Classical / Fortress / Look, know / Hip priest / Who makes the nazis / Just step sideways / Room to love / Mere peasd mag ed / ED / Hard life in country / I'm into C.B. / Fantastic life / Jawbone and the air rifle / And this day
CD _____ SITL 13CD
Lowdown/Beggars Banquet / '88 / Warner Music / Disc.

I AM KURIOUS ORANJ
Overture from 'I am kurious oranj' / Dog is life / Jerusalem / Kurious oranj / Wrong place right time / Win fall CD / Van plague / Bad news girl
CD _____ BEGA 96 CD
Beggars Banquet / Nov '88 / Warner Music / Disc.

INFOTAINMENT SCAN, THE
Ladybird (Green grass) / Lost in music / Glam racket No.3 / I'm going to Spain / It's a curse / Paranoid man in cheap shit room / Service / League of bald headed men / Past gone mad / Light up-fireworks-legend / Why are people grudgeful (CD only) / League of bald headed men (mix) (CD only)
CD _____ PERMCD 12
Permanent / Apr '93 / Total/BMG.

MIDDLE CLASS REVOLT
CD _____ PERMCD 16
Permanent / May '94 / Total/BMG.

PALACE OF SWORDS REVERSED
CD _____ CDCOG 1
Cog Sinister / Dec '87 / PolyGram.

PERVERTED BY LANGUAGE
Eat y'self fitter / Neighbourhood of infinity / Garden / Hotel Bloedel / Smile / I feel voxish / Tempo house / Hexen definitive/Strife knot
CD _____ CLACD 392
Castle / Sep '93 / BMG.

SEMINAL LIVE
Dead beat descendant / Pinball machine / H.O.W. / Squid law / Mollusc in tory! / Kurious oranj / Frenz / Hit the North / Two times four / Elf prefix / L.A. / Victoria / Pay your rates / Cruiser's creek / In these times
CD _____ BBL 102CD
Lowdown/Beggars Banquet / Jun '89 / Warner Music / Disc.

SLATES/PART OF AMERICA THEREIN 1981
Middle mass / Older lover etc / Prole art threat / Fit and working / Slates, slags etc / Leave the capitol / NWRA / Hip priest / Totally wired / Lie dream of a casino soul / Cash 'n' carry / Older lover / Deep park / Winter
CD _____ LOMACD 10
Loma / Feb '94 / BMG.

THIS NATION'S SAVING GRACE
Mansion / Bombast / Barmy / What you need / Spoilt Victorian child / L.A. / Gut of the quantifier / My new house / Paintwork / I am Damo Suzuki / To Nkroachment : Yarbles
CD _____ BBL 67CD
Lowdown/Beggars Banquet / Feb '93 / Warner Music / Disc.

TOTALES TURN
Fiery Jack / Rowche rumble / Muzorewi's daughter / In my area / Choc stock / Spector vs Rector 2 / Cary Grant's wedding / That man / New puritan / No xmas for John Quays
CD _____ DOJOCD 83
Dojo / Nov '92 / BMG.

WONDERFUL AND FRIGHTENING WORLD OF THE FALL, THE
Lay of the land / Two times four / Copped it / Elves / Oh brother / Draygo's guilt / God box / Clear off / C.R.E.E.P. / Pat trip dispenser / Slang King / Bug day / Stephen song / Craigness / Disney's dream debased / No bulbs
CD _____ BBL 58 CD
Lowdown/Beggars Banquet / Jul '88 / Warner Music / Disc.

Falla Trio

WEST SIDE STORY/PULCINELLA/JAZZ SONATA
CD _____ CCD 42013
Concord Jazz / Feb '89 / New Note.

Fallen Angels

PRETTY THINGS
Fallen angels / California / Thirteenth floor suicide / Dance again / Shine on baby / My good Friday / Cold wind / I keep on / Dogs of war / Girl like you / When the Russians came back / Chance / Lazy days
CD _____ SRH 801
Start / Jan '96 / Koch.

Fallen Christ

ABDUCTION RITUAL
CD _____ POSH 005CD
Osmose / Nov '94 / Plastic Head.

Falling Joys

PSYCHOHUM
Black bandages / Incinerator / God in a dustbin / Challenger / Dynamite / Lullaby / Parachute / Natural scene / Fortune teller / Psychohum / Winter's tale / Ending or beginning
CD _____ VOLT 059CD
Volition / Jun '92 / Vital / Pinnacle.

WISH LIST
CD _____ VOLTCD 029
Volition / Jan '92 / Vital / Pinnacle.

False Virgins

INFERNAL DOLL
CD _____ OUT 107-2
Brake Out / Nov '94 / Vital.

SKIN JOB
CD _____ OUT 104-2
Brake Out / Nov '94 / Vital.

Faltskog, Agnetha

EYES OF A WOMAN
One way love / Eyes of a woman / Just one heart / I won't let you go / Angels cry / Click track / We should be together / I won't be leaving you / Save me / I keep turning off lights / We move as one
CD _____ 825 600-2
Polydor / Jan '93 / PolyGram.

WRAP YOUR ARMS AROUND ME
Heat is on / Can't shake loose / Shame / Stay / Once burned, twice shy / Mr. Persuasion / Wrap your arms around me / To love / I wish tonight could last forever / Man / Take good care of your children / Stand by my side
CD _____ 813 242-2
Polydor / Jan '93 / PolyGram.

Falu, Eduardo

RESOLANA
CD _____ NI 5281
Nimbus / Sep '94 / Nimbus.

Fambrough, Charles

BLUES AT BRADLEY'S
Duck feathers / Blues for Bu / Andrea / Better days are coming / Steve's blues
CD _____ ESJCD 236
Essential Jazz / Oct '94 / BMG.

CHARMER, THE
Charmer / Beautiful love / Alycia love / Oasis / Lullaby for Shana / Little man / Sparks
CD _____ ESJCD 232
Essential Jazz / Oct '94 / BMG.

KEEPER OF THE SPIRIT
Angels at play / Pop pop's song / Life above the means / Little this, a little that / Keeper of the spirit / Tears of romance / Save that time / Descent / Kaln / Secret hiding place
CD _____ AQCD 1033
Audioquest / Aug '95 / New Note.

PROPER ANGLE, THE
Don Quixote / Dreamer / Uncle Pete / Sand jewels / Broski / Dolores Carla Maria / Earthlings / Proper angle / Our father who Art Blakey / One for honor / Tonality of atonement
CD _____ R2 79476
CTI / May '92 / Sony.

Fame, Georgie

BEST OF GEORGIE FAME, THE
CD _____ MATCD 323
Castle / Feb '95 / BMG.

BLUES AND ME, THE
CD _____ GOJ 60052
Go Jazz / Sep '95 / Vital/SAM.

COOL CAT BLUES
Cool cat blues / Every knock is a boost / You came a long way from St. Louis / Big brother / It should have been me / Yeah yeah / Moondance / Cats' eyes / I love the life I live, I live the life I love / Survival / Little pony / Rockin' chair
CD _____ GOJ 60022
Go Jazz / Sep '95 / Vital/SAM.

FIRST THIRTY YEARS, THE
Do the dog / Yeh yeh / Getaway / Ballad of Bonnie and Clyde / Rosetta / Daylight / Samba (toda menina baiana) / In crowd / C'est la vie / Fully booked / That ol' rock and roll / Sitting in the park / Do re mi / Like we used to be / Sunny / Seventh son / Ali shuffle / Hurricane / Moody's mood for love / Dawn yawn / Mellow yellow / Woe is me / Funny how time slips away / Old music master
CD _____ VSOPCD 144
Connoisseur / Dec '89 / Pinnacle.

GEORGIE FAME & THE DANISH RADIO BIG BAND 1992-93 (Fame, Georgie & Danish Radio Big Band)
CD _____ MECCACD 1040
Music Mecca / Oct '93 / Jazz Music / Cadillac / Wellard.

GET AWAY WITH
Yeh yeh / Green onions / Let the good times roll / Sitting in the park / Funny how time slips away / Shop around / Baby, please don't go / Get away / Eso beso / In the meantime / Sunny / Ride your pony / Night train / I love the life I live, I live the life I love
CD _____ 5500152
Spectrum/Karussell / May '93 / PolyGram / THE.

NO WORRIES (Fame, Georgie & The Australian Blue Flames)
Lady be good / Ole buttermilk sky / Eros hotel / Little Samba / 'h ain't right / On a misty night / Cats' eyes / Parchman farm / Zulu / Saturday night fish fry / Try na get along with the blues / Yeh yeh / Get away
CD _____ FLCD 5099
Four Leaf Clover / May '88 / Wellard.

SELECTION OF STANDARDS... (Fame, Georgie, Hoagy Carmichael & Annie Ross)
CD _____ CDSL 5197
DRG / '88 / New Note.

THREE LINE WHIP
It happened to me / Kan tsukete / Vinyl / Mercy mercy mercy/Vanlose stairway / Since I fell for you / Zavalo / You are there / Declaration of love / Will Carling / It happened to me (reprise)
CD _____ TLW 001
Three Line Whip / May '94 / New Note.

TWO FACES OF FAME
Greenback dollar bill / Things ain't what they used to be / River's invitation / Bluesology / Don't try / Keep your big mouth shut / You're driving me crazy / C'est la vie / El pussy cat
CD _____ 477850 2
Columbia / Oct '94 / Sony.

Familia Valera Miranda

SON, THE
CD _____ NI 5421
Nimbus / Feb '95 / Nimbus.

Family

ANYWAY
Good news bad news / Willow tree / Holding the compass / Strange band / Normans / Part of the load / Lives and ladies / Anyway
CD _____ CLACD 375
Castle / May '94 / BMG.

AS & BS
CD _____ CCSCD 354
Castle / Nov '92 / BMG.

BANDSTAND
Burlesque / Bolero babe / Coronation / Dark eyes / Broken nose / My friend the sun / Glove / Ready to go / Top of the hill
CD _____ CLACD 322
Castle / Mar '94 / BMG.

BEST OF FAMILY/CLASSIC ROCK LINE
CD _____ 901238
Line / Oct '94 / CM / Grapevine / ADA / Conifer / Direct.

COLLECTION
CD _____ CCSCD 374
Castle / Mar '93 / BMG.

ENTERTAINMENT
Weaver's answer / Observations from a hill / Hung-up down / Summer '67 / How-hi-the-li / Second generation woman / From the past archives / Dim / Processions / Face in the crowd / Emotions
CD _____ SEECD 200
See For Miles/C5 / Apr '94 / Pinnacle.

FEARLESS
Between blue and me / Sat'dy barfly / Larf and sing / Spanish tide / Save some for

thee / Take your partners / Children / Crinkley grin / Blind / Burning bridges
CD _____ CLACD 324
Castle / Feb '93 / BMG.

IT'S ONLY A MOVIE
It's only a movie / Leroy / Buffet tea for two / Boom bang / Boots 'n' roots / Banger / Sweet desiree / Suspicion / Check out
CD _____ CLACD 323
Castle / Apr '93 / BMG.

MUSIC IN A DOLL'S HOUSE
Chase / Mellowing grey / Never like this / Me, my friend / Hey Mr. Policeman / See through windows / Variation on a theme of hey Mr. policeman / Winter / Old songs new songs / Variation on the theme of the breeze / Variation on a theme of me my friend / Peace of mind / Voyage / Breeze / Three times time
CD _____ SEECD 100
See For Miles/C5 / Apr '94 / Pinnacle.

PEEL SESSIONS
CD _____ DEI 8333-2
Dutch East India / Mar '93 / SRD.

SONG FOR ME, A
Drowned in wine / Some poor soul / Love is a slave / Stop for the traffic (through the heart of me) / Wheels / Song for sinking lovers / Hey let it rock / Cat and the rat / 93's OK J / Song for me
CD _____ CLACD 376
Castle / Nov '93 / BMG.

Family Cat

FURTHEST FROM THE SUN
CD _____ DEDCD 007
Dedicated / Jun '93 / Vital.

MAGIC HAPPENS
Wonderful excuse / Amazing hangover / Move over I'll drive / Your secrets will stay mine / Airplane gardens / Gone so long / Hamlet for now / Golden book / Rockbreaking / Spring the atom / Blood orange / Nowhere to go but down
CD _____ 74321 20466-2
Dedicated / May '94 / Vital.

TELL 'EM WE'RE SURFING
CD _____ BCRLCD 1
Big Cat / Mar '90 / SRD / Pinnacle.

Family Dogg

WAY OF LIFE, A
CD _____ BX 4532
BR Music / Oct '95 / Target/BMG.

Family Foundation

ONE BLOOD
One Blood / 10 Snide E / Tarzan / It's not over / Someday / Red hot interview
CD _____ MHFCD 1
380 / Jan '93 / Warner Music.

Famous Castle Jazz Band

FAMOUS CASTLE JAZZ BAND
CD _____ GTCD 10030
Good Time Jazz / Oct '93 / Jazz Music / Wellard / Pinnacle / Cadillac.

Famous Five

LOST IN FISHPONDS
CD _____ UNCCD 3
Uncle / Jun '95 / Direct.

Famous Monsters

SUMMERTIME EP
CD _____ BLAZE 90CD
Fire / Aug '95 / Disc.

Fancy

SOMETHING TO REMEMBER/WILD THING
Wild thing / Love for sale / Move on / I don't need your love / One night / Touch me / U.S. Surprise / Between the devil and me / I'm a woman / Feel good / Fancy / She's riding the rock machine / I was made to love him / You've been in love too long / Something to remember / Everybody's cryin' mercy / Tour song / Stop / Music maker / Bluebird
CD _____ SRH 802
Rock Heritage / Jan '96 / Koch.

Fania Allstars

LATIN SOUL & JAZZ
Viva tirado / Chanchullo / Smoke / There you go / Mama guelo / El raton / Soul makossa / Congo bongo
CD _____ CDHOT 504
Charly / Oct '93 / Charly / THE / Cadillac.

Fantastic Four

ALVIN STONE (BIRTH AND DEATH OF A GANGSTER)/NIGHT PEOPLE
Alvin Stone (birth and death of a gangster) / Have a little mercy / County line / Let this won't stop at nothing / Medley: Night people/Lies divided by jive / If I lose my job / Hideaway / By the river under the tree /

Don't risk your happiness on foolishness / They took the show on the road
CD _____ CDSEWD 057
Westbound / Jan '93 / Pinnacle.

GOT TO HAVE YOUR LOVE/BRING YOUR OWN FUNK
She'll be right for me / Mixed up moods and attitudes / There's fire down below / Ain't I been good to you / Cash money / I got to have your love / Disco pool blues / Give me all the love you got / Super lover / I just want to love ya baby / Shout (Let it all hang out) / Cold and windy night / Sexy lady / Realize (When you're in love) / B.Y.O.F. (Bring your own funk)
CD _____ CDSEWD 92
Westbound / Jun '94 / Pinnacle.

Farafina

FASO DENOU
Mama Sara / Kara mogo mousso / Dounouia / Nanore / Faso denou / Hereyo mibi / Ourodara sidiki / Lanaya / Bi mousso
CD _____ CDRW 35
Realworld / May '93 / EMI / Sterns.

Farah Dance Orchestra

TURKISH DELIGHT
CD _____ CNCD 5957
Disky / Jul '93 / THE / BMG / Discovery / Pinnacle.

Farber, Mitch

STARCLIMBER
Starclimber / Lonely promises / Chooser / Sky dance / Monuments / Time line
CD _____ MCD 5400
Muse / Sep '92 / New Note / CM.

Fardon, Don

INDIAN RESERVATION (Best Of Don Fardon)
Indian reservation / Gimme gimme good lovin' / Letter / Treat her right / I'm alive / Follow your drum / Delta queen / Running bear / Belfast boy / Take a heart / Lola / It's been nice loving you / Hudson Bay / On the beach / Tobacco Road / California maiden / Coming on strong / Mr. Station Master / Miami sunset / Riverboat / I need somebody (CD only) / For your love (CD only) / Girl (CD only) / Sunshine woman (CD only)
CD _____ C5 CD540
See For Miles/C5 / Oct '92 / Pinnacle.

Farian, Frank

HIT COLLECTION (Hits Of Frank Farian) (Various Artists)
CD _____ 74321199402
Arista / Jun '94 / BMG.

Farina, Mimi

SOLO
CD _____ CDPH 1102
Philo / Dec '86 / Direct / CM / ADA.

Farina, Richard

MEMORIES (Farina, Richard & Mimi)
CD _____ VND 79263
Vanguard / Oct '95 / Complete/Pinnacle / Discovery.

REFLECTIONS IN A CRYSTAL WIND (Farina, Richard & Mimi)
CD _____ VND 79204
Vanguard / Oct '95 / Complete/Pinnacle / Discovery.

Farjami, Hossein

PLAYS SANTOOR (Folk Music From Iran)
CD _____ EUCD 1100
ARC / '91 / ARC Music / ADA.

Farkas, Andras

FAMOUS HUNGARIAN GIPSY TUNES (Farkas, Andras & Budapest Ensemble)
CD _____ EUCD 1133
ARC / '91 / ARC Music / ADA.

POPULAR GIPSY MELODIES (Farkas, Andras & Budapest Ensemble)
CD _____ EUCD 1197
ARC / Sep '93 / ARC Music / ADA.

Farlow, Billy C.

GULF COAST BLUES
CD _____ AP 102
Appaloosa / Nov '95 / ADA / Magnum Music Group.

I AIN'T NEVER HAD TOO MUCH FUN
CD _____ APCD 074
Appaloosa / '92 / ADA / Magnum Music Group.

Farlow, Tal

CHROMATIC PALETTE
All alone / Nuages / I hear a rhapsody / If I were a bell / St Thomas / Blue art too / Stella by starlight / One for my baby (And one more for the road)

CD _____ CCD 4154
Concord Jazz / Mar '94 / New Note.

LEGENDARY TAL FARLOW, THE
You stepped out of a dream / When your lover has gone / I got it bad and that ain't good / When lights are low / Who cares / I can't get started (with you) / Prelude to a kiss / Everything happens to me
CD _____ CJ 266 390
Concord Jazz / '88 / New Note.

RETURN OF TAL FARLOW, THE/1969
Original Jazz Classics / Nov '95 / Wellard / Jazz Music / Cadillac / Complete/Pinnacle.
CD _____ OJCCD 356

SIGN OF THE TIMES
Fascinating rhythm / You don't know what love is / Put a happy face / Stompin' at the Savoy / Georgia on my mind / You are too beautiful / In your own sweet way / Bayside blues
CD _____ CCD 4026
Concord Jazz / May '92 / New Note.

TRINITY
CD _____ 476580 2
Sony Jazz / May '94 / Sony.

Farlowe, Chris

AS TIME GOES BY
CD _____ KDEC 4
KFG / Feb '96 / Total/BMG.

BEST OF CHRIS FARLOWE - OUT OF TIME
CD _____ CSL 6036
Immediate / Nov '93 / Charly / Target/ BMG.

EXTREMELY
CD _____ INAK 8905
In Akustik / Sep '95 / Magnum Music Group.

HIT SINGLE COLLECTABLES
CD _____ DISK 4509
Disky / Apr '94 / THE / BMG / Discovery / Pinnacle.

I'M THE GREATEST
Paint it black / Think / Satisfaction / Handbags and gladrags / Baby make it soon / Looking for you / My colouring book / Don't just look at me / Moanin' / It was easier to hurt her / What becomes of the broken hearted / In the midnight hour / North west south east / Out of time / Yesterdays papers / Ride on baby / My way of giving / Headlines / Don't play that song (You lied) / I just don't know what to do with myself / You're so good for me / Life is but nothing / Dawn / Reach out, I'll be there / Mr. Pitiful
CD _____ SEECD 396
See For Miles/C5 / Feb '94 / Pinnacle.

LONESOME ROAD
CD _____ IGOXCD 500
Indigo / Dec '95 / Direct / ADA.

OLYMPIC ROCK AND BLUES CIRCUS (Farlowe, Chris, Brian Auger & Pete York)
CD _____ BLR 84 013
L&R / May '91 / New Note.

OUT OF TIME
Try me / Rock 'n' roll soldier / Some mother's son / Hold on / Blues anthem / Waiting in the wings / Function to function / Working in a parking lot / Make it fly / On the beach / Out of time
CD _____ JHD 054
Thing / Jun '88 / Thing / Pilum.

R & B YEARS, THE
CD _____ CDRB 5
Charly / Apr '94 / Charly / THE / Cadillac.

WAITING IN THE WINGS
CD _____ LICD 901200
Line / Oct '92 / CM / Grapevine / ADA / Conifer / Direct.

Farm

HULLABALOO
Messiah / Shake some action / Comfort / Man who cried / Hateful / Golden vision / To the ages / All American world / Distant voices
CD _____ 936245588-2
Warner Bros. / Aug '94 / Warner Music.

Farmer, Art

ART FARMER & LEE KONITZ/JOE CARTER
CD _____ STCD 4
Stash / Mar '94 / Jazz Music / CM / Cadillac / Direct / ADA.

ART FARMER SEPTET (Farmer, Art Septet)
CD _____ OJCCD 054
Original Jazz Classics / Sep '93 / Wellard / Jazz Music / Cadillac / Complete/Pinnacle.

COMPANY I KEEP, THE
Sunshine in the rain / Song of the canopy / Santana / Beside myself / Beyond / TGTT / Who knows / Turn out the stars
CD _____ AJ 0112
Arabesque / Aug '94 / New Note.

Farnham, Allen

COMMON THREAD, THE
Common thread / Hamma-ron / Nocturne / Glide / Falling grace / Interlude / How deep is the ocean / In a sentimental mood / No more blues / Very early
CD _____ CCD 4634
Concord Jazz / Mar '95 / New Note.

FOOLISH
Larry's delight / Al-leu-cha / D's dilemma / In a sentimental mood / Foolish memories / Farmer's market
CD _____ CDLR 45008
L&R / Dec '88 / New Note.

GENTLE EYES
Time for love / Didn't we / Soulsides / So are you / Song of no regrets / Gentle rain / We've only just begun / God bless the child / Gloomy morning / Gentle eyes / Some other time
CD _____ 4744162
Sony Jazz / Dec '93 / Sony.

IN CONCERT
Half Nelson / Darn that dream / Barbados / I'll remember April
CD _____ ENJ 40882
Enja / Jul '95 / New Note / Vital/SAM.

LIVE AT THE HALF NOTE
CD _____ 7567906662
Atlantic / Apr '95 / Warner Music.

MANHATTAN (Farmer, Art Quintet)
CD _____ SNCD 1026
Soul Note / '86 / Harmonia Mundi / Wellard / Cadillac.

MEANING OF ART, THE
On the plane / Just the way you look tonight / Lift your spirit high / One day forever / Free verse / Home / Johnny one note
CD _____ AJO 118
Arabesque / Dec '95 / New Note.

MEETS MULLIGAN & HALL
CD _____ MCD 0512
Moon / Apr '94 / Harmonia Mundi / ADA.

MIRAGE (Farmer, Art Quintet)
CD _____ SNCD 1046
Soul Note / '86 / Harmonia Mundi / Wellard / Cadillac.

PH.D.
Ph.D. / Affaire d'amour / Mr. Day's dream / Summary / Blue wail / Like someone in love / Rise to the occasion / Ballade art
CD _____ CCD 14055-2
Contemporary / Apr '94 / Jazz Music / Cadillac / Pinnacle / Wellard.

SOMETHING TO LIVE FOR (The Music Of Billy Strayhorn)
Isfahan / Bloodcount / Johnny come lately / Something to live for / Upper Manhattan medical group / Raincheck / Daydream
CD _____ CCD 14029-2
Contemporary / Apr '94 / Jazz Music / Cadillac / Pinnacle / Wellard.

TWO TRUMPETS (Farmer, Art & Donald Byrd)
CD _____ OJCCD 018
Original Jazz Classics / Nov '95 / Wellard / Jazz Music / Cadillac / Complete/Pinnacle.

WARM VALLEY
Moose the mooche / And now there's you / Three little words / Eclypso / Sad to say / Upper Manhattan medical group / Warm valley
CD _____ CCD 4212
Concord Jazz / Mar '92 / New Note.

YOU MAKE ME SMILE (Farmer, Art Quintet)
CD _____ SNCD 1076
Soul Note / '86 / Harmonia Mundi / Wellard / Cadillac.

Farmer Boys

FLASH CRASH AND THUNDER
Flash crash and thunder / Cool down Mame / Yearnin' / Burning heart / Somehow, someway, someday / Flip flop / Charming Betsy / Lend a helpin' hand / It pays to advertise / Someone to love me / My baby done left me / Oh how it hurts / No one / You lied / You're a hungdinger / I'm just too lazy / Onions, onions
CD _____ BCD 15579
Bear Family / Mar '92 / Rollercoaster / Direct / CM / Swift / ADA.

Farmers

ROCK ANGEL
CD _____ FF 548CD
Flying Fish / '92 / Roots / CM / Direct / ADA.

Farmers Market

SPEED/BALKAN/BOOGIE
CD _____ FX 148CD
Musikk Distribusjon / Apr '95 / ADA.

Farnham, Allen

PLAY CATION
M'kashi b'nashi / Play cation / Long ago and far away / My man's gone now / Foot

225

prince / Alone together / Stablemates / Day-
dream / Cheek to Chico
CD _____ CCD 4521
Concord Jazz / Sep '92 / New Note.

Farnham, John

CHAIN REACTION
That's freedom / In days to come / Burn for
you / See the banners fall / I can do anything / All our sons and daughters / Chain
reaction / In your hands / New day / Time
has come / First step / Time and money
CD _____ PD 74768
RCA / Sep '90 / BMG.

WHISPERING JACK
Pressure down / You're the voice / One
step away / Reasons / Going going gone /
No one comes close / Love to shine / Trou-
ble / Touch of paradise / Let me out
CD _____ 74321 18720-2
RCA / Apr '94 / BMG.

Farnon, Robert

**AT THE MOVIES (Farnon, Robert & his
Orchestra)**
Moment I saw you / Early one morning /
Best things in life are free / Wouldn't it be
lovely / How beautiful is night / You're the
cream in my coffee / Pictures in the fire / I
guess I'll have to change my plan / Great
day / When I fall in love / Melody fair / Just
imagine / Lady Barbara / Trolley song / Way
we were / Sunny side up
CD _____ CDSIV 6111
Horatio Nelson / Jul '95 / THE / BMG / Avid/
BMG / Koch.

MELODY FAIR
Journey into melody / Tangerine / Jumping
bean / Nearness of you / Dancing in the
dark / Very thought of you / Melody fair /
Moonlight becomes you / Love walked in /
British Grenadiers / Portrait of a flirt / Georgia on my mind / Reflections in the water /
Secret love / Can I forget you / Where or
when / My foolish heart / You're the cream
in my coffee / You and the night and the
music / Comin' thro' the rye / My love is like
a red red rose
CD _____ TCPLE 526
President Evergreen / Apr '90 / President.

Farrell, Eileen

EILEEN FARRELL SINGS ALEC WILDER
Lady sings the blues / Where do you go /
Moon and sand / Worm has turned / Black-
berry winter / I'll be around
CD _____ RR 36-CD
Reference Recordings / '90 / May Audio.

**EILEEN FARRELL SINGS HAROLD
ARLEN**
Let's fall in love / Out of this world / I wonder what became of me / I've got the world
on a string / Like a straw in the wind / Down
with love / Happiness is a thing called Joe
/ Woman's prerogative / Come rain or come
shine / Little drops of rain / Over the rainbow / When the sun comes out / As long
as I live / My shining hour / Last night when
we were young
CD _____ RR 30-CD
Reference Recordings / '90 / May Audio.

**EILEEN FARRELL SINGS RODGERS
AND HART**
I could write a book / I wish I were in love
again / Wait 'til you see him / I didn't know
what time it was / Love me tonight / No-
body's heart / It never entered my mind /
Mountain greenery / Sing for your supper /
Can't you do a friend a favour / Lover / My
heart stood still / Little girl blue / You're
nearer
CD _____ RR 32-CD
Reference Recordings / '90 / May Audio.

**EILEEN FARRELL SINGS TORCH
SONGS**
Stormy weather / Round Midnight / End of
a love affair / Black coffee / When your lover
has gone / Don't explain / This time the
dream is on me / I get along without you
very well / Something cool ... and more
CD _____ RR 34-CD
Reference Recordings / '90 / May Audio.

I GOTTA RIGHT TO SING THE BLUES
CD _____ CD 47255
Sony Classical / Nov '91 / Sony.

LOVE IS LETTING GO
Just in time / Why did I choose you / Love
is letting go / I've never been in love before
/ Country boy / Where were you this afternoon / Everyday / I dream of you / Quiet
thing / Time after time / My love turned me
down today / I'll be tired of you / For Eileen
CD _____ DRGCD 91436
DRG / Oct '95 / New Note.

**WITH THE LOONIS McGLOHON
QUARTET**
CD _____ ACD 237
Audiophile / Apr '93 / Jazz Music / Swift.

Farren, Mick

**GRINGO MADNESS (Farren, Mick &
Tijuana Bible)**
Leader hotel / Mark of zorro / Lone sungu-
larity / Solitaire devil / Spider kissed / Jezebel / Long walk with the devil/Jumping

Jack flash / Movement of the whores on
revolution plaza / Hippie death cult / Last
night the alhambra burned down / Eternity
is a very long time / Memphis psychosis /
Riot in cell block 9
CD _____ CDWIK 117
Big Beat / Feb '93 / Pinnacle.

Farreyrol, Jacqueline

REUNION ISLAND TRADITIONS
CD _____ PS 65091
Playasound / Jul '92 / Harmonia Mundi /
ADA.

Farris, Dionne

WILD SEED, WILD FLOWER
I know / Reality / Stop to think / Passion /
Food for thought / Now or later / Don't ever
touch me (again) / Eleventh hour / Water
blackbird / Old ladies / Human / Find your
way / Audition
CD _____ 4777552
Columbia / Apr '95 / Sony.

Farside

RIGGED
CD _____ REVEL 033
Revelation / Aug '94 / Plastic Head.

Fasoli, Claudio

**CITIES (Fasoli, Claudio & Dalla Porta/
Elgart/Goodrick)**
CD _____ RMCD 4503
Ram / Nov '93 / Harmonia Mundi /
Cadillac.

Fassaert, Tammy

JUST PASSIN' THROUGH
CD _____ SCR 36
Strictly Country / Nov '95 / ADA / Direct.

Fast Freddies Fingertips

NEW TOWN SOUL
CD _____ 323184
Koch / Aug '94 / Koch.

WHAT'S MY NAME
CD _____ SCRCD 010
Scratch / Jun '95 / BMG.

Fastbacks

AND HIS ORCHESTRA
CD _____ PLCD 803
Pop Llama / Feb '95 / 3MV.

ANSWER THE PHONE DUMMY
CD _____ SPCD 259
Sub Pop / Nov '94 / Disc.

QUESTION IS NO
CD _____ SP 146B
Sub Pop / Mar '94 / Disc.

VERY VERY POWERFUL MOTOR
In the summer / Apologies / Trouble sleep-
ing / Better than before / What to except /
Dirk's car jam / Says who / Last night I had
a dream that I could fly / I won't regret / I
guess / I'll be okay
CD _____ PLCD 011
Pop Llama / Feb '95 / 3MV.

ZUCKER
CD _____ SP 231 CD
Sub Pop / Jan '93 / Disc.

Fat

AUTOMAT HIGHLIFE
CD _____ RERFATCD
Recommended / Apr '91 / These / ReR
Megacorp.

Fat & Frantic

QUIRK
Too late / Last night my wife hoovered my
head / Rise up / Who's your friend Eddy / I
don't want to say goodbye / Africa / It's you
/ If I could be your milkman / Aggressive
sunbathing / Senator's daughter / I'm sorry
I wish / Darling Doris / River
CD _____ 5018524 01102
I'll Call You / Aug '90 / Total/BMG.

Fat Boys

MACK DADDY
Gettin' hefty / Mack daddy / Fly car / Da
bump / Whip it on me / Let's make love 2
night / Tonite / You're da man / Negaza-
playa / Crazy / Love you down / Da-source
/ Sweet lovin' baby
CD _____ CDEMP 4118
Emperor / Jan '92 / Disc.

Fat Larry's Band

**CLOSE ENCOUNTERS OF A FUNKY
KIND**
Close encounters of a funky kind / Stand
up / Good time / Can't keep my hands to
myself / Last chance to dance / Everything
is disco / Hey Pancho, it's disco / Zoom /
Play with me / Boogie town / I love you so
/ Dirty words / Lookin' for love / You gotta
help yourself

CD _____ CDSEWD 095
Southbound / Jan '95 / Pinnacle.

OFF THE WALL
Sparkle / Peaceful journey / Castle of joy /
Passing time / Easy / Don't you worry about
tomorrow / Time / I love you so / In the
pocket
CD _____ CDSXE 069
Stax / Nov '92 / Pinnacle.

Fat Mattress

FAT MATTRESS 1
All nightdrinker / I don't mind / Bright new
way / Petrol pump assistant / Mr. Moonshine / Magic forest / She came in the
morning / Everything's blue / Walking
through a garden / How can I live / Little girl
in white / Marguerita / Which way to go /
Future days / Cold wall of stone
CD _____ NEXCD 196
Sequel / May '92 / BMG.

FAT MATTRESS II
Storm / Anyway you want / Leafy lane / Nat-
urally / Roamin' / Happy my love / Child-
hood dream / She / Highway / At the ball /
People / Hall of kings / Long red / Words /
River
CD _____ NEXCD 197
Sequel / May '92 / BMG.

Fat Tuesday

CALIFUNERAL
CD _____ CDZORRO 43
Metal Blade / Jul '92 / Pinnacle.

Fat Tulips

STARFISH
So unbelievable / World away from me /
Ribs / Sweetest child / Chainsaw / I promise
you / My secret place / Double decker bus
/ Clumsy / If God exists / Big toe / Nothing
less than you deserve / Letting go / Death
of me / Never
CD _____ ASKCD 034
Vinyl Japan / Jul '94 / Vital.

Fatal Opera

FATAL OPERA
CD _____ MASSCD 051
Massacre / Apr '95 / Plastic Head.

Fatala

GONGOMA TIMES
Timini / Yekeke / Maane / Gongoma times
/ Seoraba / Boke (N'yaraloum-ma) / Lim-
badji toko / Sohko / Soisisa
CD _____ RWMCD 4
Realworld / Jan '93 / EMI / Sterns.

Fatback Band

14 KARAT
Let's do it again / Angel / Backstrokin' /
Concrete jungle / Without your love / Gotta
get my hands on some (money) / Your love
is strange / Lady groove / Chillin' out
CD _____ CDSEWM 060
Southbound / Jun '93 / Pinnacle.

21 KARAT FATBACK
I found lovin' (CD only) / Girl is fine (CD only)
/ Night fever (CD only) / (Are you ready) Do
the bus stop / Double Dutch (CD only) /
King Tim III (Personality jock) / Wicky wacky
/ I like girls / Gotta get my hands on some
(money) / Let's do it again (CD only) / Mas-
ter Booty / Backstrokin' / Keep on steppin'
/ Freak the freak the funk (rock) (CD only) /
Take it any way you want it (CD only) /
Spanish hustle / Rockin' to the beat / On
the floor (CD only) / Booty (CD only) / Yum
yum (gimme some) / Is this the future (CD
only) / Party time (LP only)
CD _____ CDSEWD 101
Southbound / Mar '95 / Pinnacle.

BRITE LITES/ BIG CITY
Freak the freak the funk (rock) / Let me do
it to you / Big city / Do the boogie woogie
/ Hesitation / Wild dreams
CD _____ CDSEWM 045
Southbound / Jan '92 / Pinnacle.

FATBACK BAND LIVE
CD _____ SCD 12
Start / Jun '87 / Koch.

FIRED UP 'N' KICKIN'
I'm fired up / Boogie freak / Get out on the
dance floor / At last / I like girls / Snake /
Can't you see
CD _____ CDSEW 041
Southbound / Jul '91 / Pinnacle.

GIGOLO
Rockin' to the beat / Rub down / I'm so in
love / Higher / Do it / Gigolo / Oh girl / Na
na hey hey kiss her goodbye
CD _____ CDSEWM 081
Southbound / Nov '93 / Pinnacle.

HOT BOX
Hot box / Come and get the love / Love
spell / Gotta get my hands on some
(money) / Backstrokin' / Street band
CD _____ CDSEWM 056
Southbound / Sep '92 / Pinnacle.

IS THIS THE FUTURE.

Is this the future / Double love affair /
Spread love / Funky aerobics (Body move-
ment) / Up against the wall / Finger lickin'
good / Sunshine lady / Girl is fine
CD _____ CDSEWM 058
Southbound / Mar '94 / Pinnacle.

KEEP ON STEPPIN'
Mr. Bass man / Stuff / New York style /
Love / Can't stop the flame / Wicky wacky
/ Feeling / Keep on stepping / Breaking up
with someone you love is hard to do
CD _____ CDSEW 001
Southbound / Jun '89 / Pinnacle.

MAN WITH THE BAND
Man with the band / Master Booty / Funk
backin' / Mile high / I gotta thing for you /
Midnight freak / Zodiac man
CD _____ CDSEW 036
Southbound / Jan '91 / Pinnacle.

NIGHT FEVER
Night fever / Little funky dance / If that's the
way you want it / Joint (you and me) / Disco
crazy / Booty / No more room on the dancefloor / December 1963 (Oh what a night)
CD _____ CDSEW 008
Southbound / Aug '89 / Pinnacle.

NYCNYUSA
Double Dutch / Soul finger (gonna put on
you) / Spank the baby / Duke walk / NYC-
NYUSA / Love street / Changed man / Cos-
mic woman
CD _____ CDSEW 030
Southbound / Jul '90 / Pinnacle.

ON THE FLOOR
On the floor / U.F.O. (Unidentified funk ob-
ject) / Burn baby burn / She's my shining
star / Hip so slick / Do it to me now
CD _____ CDSEWM 091
Southbound / Mar '94 / Pinnacle.

RAISING HELL
(Are you ready) do the bus stop / All day /
Put your love (in my tender care) / Groovy
kind of day / Spanish hustle / I can't help
myself / Party time
CD _____ CDSEW 028
Southbound / Apr '90 / Pinnacle.

TASTY JAM
Take it any way you want it / Wanna dance
/ Keep your fingers out of the jam / Kool
whip / High steppin' lady / Get ready for the
night
CD _____ CDSEWM 088
Southbound / Feb '94 / Pinnacle.

TONITE'S ALL NIGHT PARTY
CD _____ SCD 16
Start / Jun '88 / Koch.

WITH LOVE
He's a freak undercover / Rastajam / I love
your body language / I found lovin' / I
wanna be your lover / Please stay / Wide
glide
CD _____ CDSEW 024
Southbound / Feb '90 / Pinnacle.

XII
You're my candy sweet / Disco bass /
Gimme that sweet, sweet lovin' / King Tim
III (personality jock) / Disco queen / Love in
perfect harmony
CD _____ CDSEWM 049
Southbound / Apr '92 / Pinnacle.

YUM YUM
Yum yum (gimme some) / Trompin' / Let the
drums speak / Put the funk on you / Feed
me your love / Boogie with Fatback / Got
to learn how to dance / If you could turn
into me / (Hey) I feel real good
CD _____ CDSEW 016
Southbound / Nov '89 / Pinnacle.

Fates Warning

CHASING TIME
CD _____ CDZORRO 84
Metal Blade / Feb '95 / Pinnacle.

INSIDE OUT
CD _____ MASSCD 037
Massacre / Jun '94 / Plastic Head.

NO EXIT
CD _____ RR 9558 2
Roadrunner / Apr '88 / Pinnacle.

NO EXIT/AWAKEN THE GUARDIAN
CD _____ CDZORRO 39
Metal Blade / Jul '90 / Pinnacle.

PARALLELS
CD _____ CDZORRO 31
Metal Blade / Nov '91 / Pinnacle.

PERFECT SYMMETRY
CD _____ CDMZORRO 73
Metal Blade / May '94 / Pinnacle.

**SPECTRE WITHIN/NIGHTS ON
BROCKEN**
CD _____ CDZORRO 38
Metal Blade / Jul '90 / Pinnacle.

Father Dom

FATHER DOM
I'm fed up / Father Dom story / Hard to handle / Grand pooba... / Letter to my listeners
/ U don't stop / I can't stay mad (at you
forever) / Everybody wants to be an M.C. /

Now we gotcha / Keep on doin' watcha doin'
CD _____ CDWRA 8105
Wrap / Feb '92 / Koch.

Father MC

THIS IS FOR THE PLAYERS
CD _____ CDMISH 3
Mission / Nov '95 / 3MV / Sony.

Fatima Mansions

COME BACK MY CHILDREN
Only losers take the bus / Day I lost everything / Wilderness on time / You won't get me home / Thirteenth Century boy / Bishop of babel / Valley of the dead cars / Big madness / What / Blues for Ceausescu / On suicide bridge / Hive / Holly mugger / Stigmata / Lady Godiva's operation
CD _____ CGCCD 001
Kitchenware / Feb '93 / Sony / PolyGram / BMG.

Fatman

FATMAN VS. SHAKA (First, Second & Third Generation Of Dub) (Fatman & Jah Shaka)
CD _____ FM 001CD
Fatman / May '95 / SRD / Jetstar / THE.

SAME SONG DUB (Fatman Riddim Section)
CD _____ LG 21103
Lagoon / Apr '95 / Magnum Music Group / THE.

Fat's Garden

BURIED IN EDEN
CD _____ TWI 8962
Les Disques Du Crepuscule / Jul '90 / Discovery / ADA.

Fattburger

GOOD NEWS
CD _____ 3287 2
Enigma / Oct '87 / EMI.

LIVIN' LARGE
CD _____ SHCD 5012
Shanachie / Mar '95 / Koch / ADA / Greensleeves.

Fatty George

FATTY'S SALON 1958
CD _____ RST 91425
RST / Sep '92 / Jazz Music / Hot Shot.

Faucett, Dawnett

TAKING MY TIME
Slow dancing / Don't stop to count the memories / Mama never told me / Bus won't be stopping / Heart heart / Cheap perfume / Good for you / Taking my time / As far as love can throw me / Dusty road / Two empty arms / Unwanted
CD _____ SORCD 0054
D-Sharp / Oct '94 / Pinnacle.

Faulk, Dan

FOCUSING IN (Faulk, Dan Quintet)
CD _____ CRISS 1076CD
Criss Cross / Nov '93 / Cadillac / Harmonia Mundi.

Faulkner, John

KIND PROVIDENCE
Sweet Thames flow softly / Walecatchers/ Drunken landlady / Planxty gan ainm / Wild rover / Johnny Coughlin / McCaffery / Banks of Newfoundland / Forger's farewell / Road to Cashel/Jackie Daly's reel / Newry town
CD _____ GLCD 1064
Green Linnet / Feb '93 / Roots / CM / Direct / ADA.

NOMADS/FANAITHE
MacCrimmon will never come back / MacCrimmon's lament / Sucah a Parcel of Rogues in a Nation / Farewell to Scotland/ In the mist / Young Munroe / La reel du Pendu / Cape Sky waltz/Joe Tom's reels / I am a little orphan/Two step too / I loved a lass / Jolly bold robber / Flowers of Finae / Child owlet/Erskine's folly / Nomads of the road/Pristina
CD _____ CIC 071CD
Clo Iar-Chonnachta / Jan '92 / CM.

Faust

71 MINUTES OF ...
CD _____ RERF 1CD
Recommended / '90 / These / ReR Megacorp.

FAUST IV
Krautrock / Sad skinhead / Jennifer / Jus' a second / Picnic on a frozen river, Deuxieme tableux / Giggy smile / Lauft... Heist das es lauft oder es kommt bald... Lauft / It's a bit of a pain
CD _____ CD 0501
Virgin / Oct '92 / EMI.

FAUST TAPES
CD _____ RERF 2CD
Recommended / '91 / These / ReR Megacorp.

OUTSIDE THE DREAM SYNDICATE (Faust & Tony Conrad)
CD _____ LITHIUM 3
Southern / Jan '94 / SRD.

Faux, George

TIME FOR A LAUGH AND A SONG
Birthday reel / Farewell to the building / Cultural dessert / Kellswater / Parker's fancy / Farewell to London / Artesian water / Leggett's reel - the old grey cat / Do me amma / Gallant brigantine / Dominic's march / Time for a laugh and a song
CD _____ HARCD 006
Harbour Town / Oct '93 / Roots / Direct / CM / ADA.

Favre, Pierre

WINDOW STEPS
Snow / Cold nose / Lea / Girimella / En passant / Aguilar / Passage
CD _____ 5293482
ECM / Feb '96 / New Note.

Fawkes, Wally

FIDGETY FEET
CD _____ SOSCD 1248
Stomp Off / Jul '93 / Jazz Music / Wellard.

Fay, Colin

DANCING ON THE CEILING
Snowbird / Walking the floor / Swanee / Please baby please / Ain't we got fun / Melody in F / Oh my Papa / Andantiono / Dancing on the ceiling / Silver threads among the gold / Rose room / Coppelia / Love theme from The Thorn Birds / Nocturne in Eb / If those lips could only speak / I'll be your sweetheart / Let the rest of the world go by / Pretty baby / Make mine love / Strollin' / Underneath the arches / Louise / Broken doll / Honeysuckle and the bee / Nola / Glory of love / Waiting at the church / Oh Mr Porter / Daddy wouldn't buy me a bow-wow / On the banks of wabash / Lily of Laguna / Man who broke the bank at Monte Carlo / Let's all go down the strand / Wot'cher (Knocked 'em in the Old Kent Road) / Fall in and follow me / Light of foot / Life on the ocean wave / Stephanie Gavotte / Kind regards / Tell me pretty maiden / Ascot gavotte / Ay ay ay / La concordia / Pablo the dreamer / Creole tango
CD _____ GRCD 52
Grasmere / Aug '92 / Target/BMG / Savoy.

Fay, Rick

GLENDENA FOREVER (Fay, Rick & Jackie Coon)
CD _____ ARCD 19104
Arbors Jazz / Nov '94 / Cadillac.

HELLO HORN
CD _____ ARCD 19102
Arbors Jazz / Nov '94 / Cadillac.

LIVE AT LONE PINE
CD _____ ARCD 19101
Arbors Jazz / Nov '94 / Cadillac.

LIVE AT THE STATE THEATRE
CD _____ ARCD 29102
Arbors Jazz / Nov '94 / Cadillac.

MEMORIES OF YOU
CD _____ ARCD 19103
Arbors Jazz / Nov '94 / Cadillac.

OH BABY
CD _____ ARCD 19105
Arbors Jazz / Nov '94 / Cadillac.

ROLLING ON
I double dare you / Blues (my naughtie sweetie gives to me) / Somebody loves me / Tishomingo blues / Manoir de mes reves / Come back Papa
CD _____ ARCD 19108
Arbors Jazz / Nov '94 / Cadillac.

SAX-O-POEM
CD _____ ARCD 19113
Arbors Jazz / Nov '94 / Cadillac.

THIS IS WHERE I CAME IN
CD _____ ARCD 19106
Arbors Jazz / Nov '94 / Cadillac.

Faye, Alice

ON THE AIR 1933-84
CD _____ CDSH 2020
Derann Trax / Nov '91 / Pinnacle.

Faye, Frances

CAUGHT IN THE ACT
CD _____ GNPD 41
GNP Crescendo / Jan '92 / Silva Screen.

Faye, Glenda

FLATPICKIN' FAVORITES
CD _____ FF 70432
Flying Fish / Oct '89 / Roots / CM / Direct / ADA.

Fays, Raphael

GIPSY TOUCH
CD _____ OMDCD 068
OMD / Sep '92 / Koch.

VOYAGES
CD _____ BEST 1015CD
Acoustic Music / Nov '93 / ADA.

Fear

HAVE ANOTHER BEER WITH FEAR
CD _____ SECT 10020
Sector 2 / Jan '96 / Direct / SRD.

LIVE FOR THE RECORD
CD _____ LS 92522
Roadrunner / Nov '91 / Pinnacle.

Fear Factory

DEMANUFACTURE
Demanufacture / Self bias resistor / Zero signal / Replica / New breed / Dog day sunrise / Body hammer / Flashpoint / H-K (Hunter killer) / Pisschrist / Therapy for pain
CD _____ RR 89562
CD _____ RR 89565
Roadrunner / Jun '95 / Pinnacle.

FEAR IS THE MINDKILLER
CD _____ RR 90822
Roadrunner / Apr '93 / Pinnacle.

SOUL OF A NEW MACHINE
CD _____ RR 91602
Roadrunner / Sep '92 / Pinnacle.

Fear Of God

TOXIC VOODOO
CD _____ CDVEST 24
Bulletproof / Jul '94 / Pinnacle.

Fearing, Stephen

ASSASSIN'S APPRENTICE, THE
CD _____ CSCCD 1001
CRS / Aug '95 / Direct / ADA.

BLUE LINE
CD _____ RUE CD 003
New Routes / Apr '90 / Pinnacle.

Fearon, Phil

BEST OF PHIL FEARON & GALAXY, THE (Fearon, Phil & Galaxy)
Dancing tight / Head over heels / What do I do / Nothing is too good for you / I can prove it / Everybody's laughing / Burning my bridges / Wait until tonight (my love) / All I give to you / You don't need a reason / This kind of love / Ain't nothing but a house party / If you're gonna fall in love / Fantasy real
CD _____ MCCD 150
Music Club / Feb '94 / Disc / THE / CM.

DANCING TIGHT (Fearon, Phil & Galaxy)
Dancing tight (mixes) / Wait until tonight (my love) / Head over heels / Ain't nothing but a house party / Fantasy real / This kind of love / You don't need a reason / I can prove it / Everybody's laughing / What do I do (mixes) / I can prove it (edit) (MC only)
CD _____ MOCD 3006
More Music / Feb '95 / Sound & Media.

DANCING TIGHT - THE BEST OF GALAXY (Fearon, Phil & Galaxy)
What do I do / Dancing tight / This kind of love / I don't care / Wait until tonight (my love) / reason / Wait until tonight (my love) / you're gonna fall in love / Everybody's laughing / I can prove it / All I give to you / Fantasy real / Ain't nothing but a house party / Nothing is too good for you / Anything you want
CD _____ CDCHEN 31
Ensign / Oct '92 / EMI.

Feathers, Charlie

CHARLIE FEATHERS
Man in love / When you come around / Pardon me mister / Fraulein / Defrost your heart / Mean woman blues / I don't care if tomorrow never comes / Cootzie coo / We can't seem to remember to forget / Long time ago / Seasons of my heart / Uh huh honey / Oklahoma hills
CD _____ 7559611472
Elektra Nonesuch / Jul '91 / Warner Music.

GONE GONE GONE
Peepin' eyes / I've been deceived / Defrost your heart / Wedding gown of white / We're getting closer to being apart / Bottle to the baby / One hand loose / Can't hardly stand it / Everybody's lovin' my baby / Too much alike / When you come around / When you decide / Nobody's woman / Man in love / I forgot to remember to forget / Uh huh honey / Mound of clay / Tongue tied Jill / Gone gone gone / Two to choose / Send me the pillow that you dream on / Folsom Prison blues
CD _____ CDCHARLY 278
Charly / Sep '91 / Charly / THE / Cadillac.

GOOD ROCKIN TONITE
CD _____ EDCD 355
Edsel / Sep '92 / Pinnacle / ADA.

Feinstein, Michael

HONKY TONK MAN
CD _____ ROSE 144CD
New Rose / Jun '88 / Direct / ADA.

ROCK-A-BILLY 1954 - 1973 (The Definitive Of Rare & Unissued Recordings)
Bottle to the baby / So ashamed / Honky tonk kind / Frankie and Johnny / Defrost your heart / Runnin' around / I've been deceived / Corine Corina / Wedding gown of white / Defrost your heart #2 / Bottle to the baby (2) / I can't hardly wait / One hand loose / Everybody's lovin' my baby / Dinky John / South of Chicago / I'm walking the dog / Today and tomorrow / Wild wild party / Where's she at tonight / Don't you know / Wild side of life / Long time ago / Tongue tied Jill / Folsom Prison blues / Gone gone gone
CD _____ CDZ 2011
Zu Zazz / Apr '94 / Rollercoaster.

THAT ROCKABILLY CAT
Gone gone gone / Tongue tied Jill / Wild side of life / Do you know / Rock me / Wide river / Crazy heart / Uh huh honey / Cold dark night / Rain / Mama oh Mama / Cherry wine / There will be three / I'm movin' on
CD _____ EDCD 348
Edsel / Jun '92 / Pinnacle / ADA.

Featureman

HOO-HAH
CD _____ RFCD 8
Red Flame / Sep '93 / Pinnacle.

Feddy, Jason

FISH ON THE MOON
CD _____ REDHEDCD 1
Redhead / Nov '94 / CM.

Federal Music Society

COME AND TRIP IT (Hyman, Dick & Gerard Schwarz Orchestras)
Prima donna waltz / Jenny Lind polka / Minuet and gavotte / Country fiddle music / Natilie polka-mazurka / Flying cloud / Victoria gallop / Flirt polka / La sonnambula / Eliza Jane McCue / Blaze-away / Hiawatha / Sweet man
CD _____ 802932
New World / Aug '94 / Harmonia Mundi / ADA / Cadillac.

Feed Your Head

AMBIENT COMPILATION
CD _____ BARKCD 002
Planet Dog / Aug '94 / 3MV / Vital.

Feedback Bleep

ENGRAM
CD _____ EFA 119712
Electro Smog / Apr '95 / SRD.

Feenjon/Avram

SALUTE TO ISRAEL
CD _____ MCD 71746
Monitor / Jun '93 / CM.

Feeny, Michael

MY OLD IRISH ROSE
CD _____ CNCD 5951
Disky / Jul '93 / THE / BMG / Discovery / Pinnacle.

Feetpackets

LISTEN FEETPACKETS
CD _____ DISCUS 01
Discus / Feb '86 / Cadillac.

Feidman, Giora

MAGIC OF THE KLEZMER, THE (Feidman, Giora & The Feidman Ensemble)
Song of rejoicing / Mr. Mizrion / Mothers in law / Happiness is a nigon / Cigarettes / With much sentiment / Frilling / Market place in jaffa / Hopkefe / Nigon / Dudele / Music for ghetto / Humoresque / Gershwin suite / Freilach
CD _____ DE 4005
Delos / Jan '94 / Conifer.

Feinstein, Michael

FOREVER
Time enough for love / My romance / Moondance / You are there / Wish you were here / Sophisticated swing / Soon / Little white lies / Song / Too marvelous for words / Whatever happened to melody / Half of April (Most of May) / And I'll be there
CD _____ 755961423-2
Elektra / '93 / Warner Music.

PURE IMAGINATION
Pure imagination / Swinging on a star / Teddy bears' picnic / Because we're kids / Ferdinand the bull / Not much of a dog / Lydia, the tattoed lady / Dressing song / Ugly bug ball / When you wish upon a star / Mole people / Alice in wonderland medley / Aren't you glad you're my / I like old people / Ten feet off the ground / Be kind to your parents / Jitterbug / Johnny Fedora

227

and Alice Blue Bonnet / Angels on your pillow
CD _____ 7559610462
Elektra / Jun '92 / Warner Music.

SUCH SWEET SORROW
CD _____ 7567827402
Atlantic / Sep '95 / Warner Music.

Felder, Wilton

FOREVER ALWAYS
Lillies of the nile / For lovers only / My way / My one and only love / Rainbow visions / Forever / Goin' crazy / Asian flower / African queen / Mr. Felder
CD _____ CPCD 8141
Charly / Nov '95 / Charly / THE / Cadillac.

NOCTURNAL MOODS
Feel so much better / Night moves / Southern pearl / If I knew then what I know now / Sugar loaf / Love stops / Out of sight not out of mind / Since I fell for you / Music of the night
CD _____ CPCD 8124
Charly / Oct '95 / Charly / THE / Cadillac.

Feldman, Morton

COMPOSITIONS 1952-75
CD _____ RZCD 1010
FMP / Oct '94 / Cadillac.

FOR CHRISTIAN WOLFF
CD Set _____ ARTCD 3-6120
Hat Art / Apr '93 / Harmonia Mundi / ADA / Cadillac.

FOR PHILIP GUSTON
CD _____ ARTCD 46104
Hat Art / Jul '92 / Harmonia Mundi / ADA / Cadillac.

FOR SAMUEL BECKETT
CD _____ ARTCD 6107
Hat Art / Jan '93 / Harmonia Mundi / ADA / Cadillac.

PIANO AND STRING QUARTETS
(Feldman, Morton & Aki Takahashi/ Kronos Quartet)
CD _____ 7559793202
Elektra Nonesuch / Jan '95 / Warner Music.

Feldman, Victor

ARTFUL DODGER, THE
Limehouse blues / Haunted ballroom / Walk on the heath / Isn't she lovely / Smoke gets in your eyes / Agitation / Artful Dodger / St. Thomas
CD _____ CCD 4038
Concord Jazz / Jun '89 / New Note.

Feleus, Pali

ZIGEUNERORKEST ZIGEUNERKAPELLE (Feleus, Pali & Gipsy Band)
CD _____ SYNCOOP 5755CD
Syncoop / Feb '95 / ADA / Direct.

Felice, Dee

DEE FELICE (Felice, Dee & The Sleep Cat Band)
CD _____ JCD 168
Jazzology / Feb '91 / Swift / Jazz Music.

Felice, John

NOTHING PRETTY (Felice, John & The Lowdowns)
Don't be telling me / Ain't we having fun / I'll never sing that song again / Not the one / Perfect love / Nowadaze kids / Nothing pretty / Dreams / Don't make me wait / Can't play it safe
CD _____ ROSE 141CD
New Rose / Mar '88 / Direct / ADA.

Feliciano, Jose

AND I LOVE HER
And I love her / Light my fire / For my love / You're no good / (There's) Always something there to remind me / Yesterday / Don't let the sun catch you crying / I want to learn a love song / Find somebody and the sun will shine / Rain / Twilight time
CD _____ 743213394626
Camden / Jan '96 / BMG.

BEST OF JOSE FELICIANO
Light my fire / California dreamin' / And the sun will shine / Windmills of your mind / Miss Otis regrets / Rain / First of May / Guantanamera / Che sara / Destiny / Suzie Q / Hi-heel sneakers / Cico and the man (theme) / Hitchcock railway / Malaguena / No dogs allowed
CD _____ ND 89561
RCA / Feb '90 / BMG.

CHE SARA
CD _____ WMCD 6544
Disky / May '94 / THE / BMG / Discovery / Pinnacle.

LIGHT MY FIRE
Light my fire / Sunny / California dreamin' / You're no good / Norwegian wood / Always something there to remind me / Hey Jude / Yesterday / Don't let the sun catch you crying / Don't think twice, it's alright / Here,

there and everywhere / Nature boy / Day in a life / Masters of war / Let it be
CD _____ KAZ CD 20
Kaz / Oct '91 / BMG.

TRIBUTE TO THE BEATLES, A
CD _____ 290810
RCA / Dec '92 / BMG.

Felix

ONE
Fastslow / Fools in love / You gotta work / Stars / It's me / Don't you want me / It will make me crazy (On CD only)
CD _____ 74321 13776-2
De-Construction / Mar '93 / BMG.

Felix Da Housecat

THEE ALBUM - 'METROPOLIS PRESENT DAY'
Some kinda special / Marine mood / Metropolis present day / Little bloo / Trippin' on a trip / Ano.Th.A. Level / Submarine / B4 wuz then / Cycle spin / Footsteps of rage / Thee dawn / Radikal thanx
CD _____ FEAR 011CD
Radikal Fear / May '95 / Vital.

Felix, Julie

EL CONDOR PASA
Amazing grace / Mr Tambourine man / Early morning rain / San Francisco / Vincent / Where have all the flowers gone / Going to the zoo / Scarborough fair / Blowing in the wind / Let it be / Dona Dona / Soldier from the 60's / If I could / Where you are / Last thing on my mind / Man gave names to all the animals / I miss you / Bring on Lucie (free da people) / So much trouble / Changing / We better talk this over / Steal away again / My preservation kit / Big bang / Yoko (we believe)
CD _____ SCD 26
Start / Sep '91 / Koch.

Fell, Simon H.

COMPILATION
CD _____ CDBF 01
Bruce's Fingers / Oct '93 / Cadillac.

COMPILATION II
CD _____ CDBF 04
Bruce's Fingers / Oct '93 / Cadillac.

Fell, Terry

TRUCK DRIVIN' MAN
Truck driving man / Caveman / Don't drop it / Play the music / I'm hot to trot / Mississippi River shuffle / Get aboard my wagon / You don't give a damn about me / He's in love with you / I believe my heart / What am I worth / Over and over / I nearly go crazy / That's the way the big ball bounces / Don't do it Joe / Consolation prize / Let's stay together till after Christmas / (We wanna see) Santa do the mambo / Wham bam hot ziggity zam / If I didn't have you / That's what I like / Fa-so-la / I can hear you cluckin' / What's good for the goose
CD _____ BCD 15762
Bear Family / Nov '93 / Rollercoaster / Direct / CM / Swift / ADA.

Fellinis, Broun

APHROKUBIST IMPROVISATIONS VOL.9
CD _____ MM 800222
Moonshine / Aug '95 / Disc.

Fellow Travellers

FEW GOOD DUBS, A
CD _____ OKRA 33023
Normal/Okra / Dec '94 / Direct / ADA.

JUST A VISITOR
CD _____ OK 33016CD
Normal/Okra / Mar '94 / Direct / ADA.

LOVE SHINES BRIGHTER
CD _____ RTS 4
Return To Sender / Nov '94 / Direct / ADA.

NO EASY WAY
CD _____ OK 010CD
Normal/Okra / Mar '94 / Direct / ADA.

THINGS AND TIME
CD _____ OKRACD 33020
Normal/Okra / Mar '94 / Direct / ADA.

Felony, Jayo

TAKE A RIDE
CD _____ 5282912
Island / Sep '95 / PolyGram.

Felt

ABSOLUTE CLASSIC MASTERPIECES VOL.2
CD Set _____ CRECD 150
Creation / Sep '93 / 3MV / Vital.

BUBBLEGUM PERFUME
I will die with my head in flames / I didn't mean to hurt you / Autumn / There's no such thing as victory / Final resting place of the ark / Don't die on my doorstep / Book

of swords / Gather up your wings and fly / Bitter end / Voyage to illumination / Stained glass windows / Space blues / Be still / Magellan / Sandman's on the rise again / Wave crashed on my doorstep / Declaration / Darkest ending / Rain of crystal spires / Ballad of the band
CD _____ CRECD 69
Creation / Apr '90 / 3MV / Vital.

FOREVER BREATHES THE LONELY WORD
CD _____ CRECD 011
Creation / Oct '90 / 3MV / Vital.

GOLDMINE TRASH
Something sends me to sleep / Trails of colours dissolve / Dismantled King is off the throne / Penelope tree / Sunlight bathed the golden glow / Crystal ball / Day the rain came down / Fortune / Vasco da Gama / Primitive painters
CD _____ CDMRED 79
Cherry Red / Sep '87 / Pinnacle.

KISS YOU KIDNAPPED CHARABANC/ DEAD MEN TELL NO TALES
CD _____ CRECD 8-62
Creation / May '88 / 3MV / Vital.

LET THE SNAKES CRINKLE THEIR HEADS TO DEATH
CD _____ CRECD 009
Creation / May '94 / 3MV / Vital.

PICTORIAL JACKSON REVIEW
CD _____ CRELP 030CD
Creation / Mar '88 / 3MV / Vital.

POEM OF THE RIVER
CD _____ CRECD 017
Creation / May '88 / 3MV / Vital.

POEM OF THE RIVER/FOREVER BREATHES THE LONELY WORD
CD _____ CRECD 6-53
Creation / May '88 / 3MV / Vital.

STRANGE IDOLS PATTERN & OTHER SHORT STORIES
Roman litter / Sempiternal darkness / Spanish house / Imprint / Sunlight bathed the golden glow / Vasco da Gama / Crucifix heaven / Dismantled King is off the throne / Crystal ball / Whirlpool vision of shame
CD _____ CD BRED 65
Cherry Red / Feb '93 / Pinnacle.

TRAIN ABOVE THE CITY
CD _____ CRECD 035
Creation / Oct '88 / 3MV / Vital.

Felten, Eric

GRATITUDE
CD _____ 1212962
Soul Note / Sep '95 / Harmonia Mundi / Wellard / Cadillac.

T-BOP (Felten, Eric & Jimmy Knepper)
CD _____ 121196-2
Soul Note / Sep '93 / Harmonia Mundi / Wellard / Cadillac.

Felts, Narvel

MEMPHIS DAYS
Night creature / Your true love / Blue darlin' / What you're doing to me / Sad and blue / She's in your heart to stay / Return / Welcome home / Love is gone / Tear down the wall / Four seasons of life / Come what may / Lola did a dance / Lovelight man / Mr. Pawnshop broker / Tongue tied Jill / All that heaven sent / I had a girl / Slippin' and slidin' / Larry and Joellen / You were mine / Get on the right track baby / Sweet sweet loving / Mountain of love / Private detective / One man at a table
CD _____ BCD 15515
Bear Family / Oct '90 / Rollercoaster / Direct / CM / Swift / ADA.

THIS TIME
This time / Since I met you baby / Butterfly / You're out of my reach / Chased by the dawn / No one will ever know / Endless love / Little bit of soap / Sound of the wind / All in the game / I'd trade all of my tomorrows / Greatest gift / I had to cry / Dee Dee / Eighty six Miles
CD _____ HIUKCD 123
Hi / Sep '92 / Pinnacle.

Fem 2 Fem

ANIMUS
CD _____ AHLCD 33
Hit / Aug '95 / PolyGram.

Fender, Freddy

14 GREAT TEX-MEX TRACKS (Fender, Freddy & Flaco Jimenez)
Elhijo de su / El corrido de carasco / Tu yu las nubes / Jambalaya / Indita mia / Tu corazon taridor / Se apago mi estrella / La comadre el muchacho afortunado vieja escaler / Noches eternas / Amor chiquito / Chiquitita / Fiches negras / Enamorado / Suena y quereme / Los barandeles del puente / San Quilmas Querido / Ella me dijo que no / Nichecita
CD _____ 90753-2
PMF / Jul '94 / Kingdom / Cadillac.

CANCIONES DE MI BARRIO
CD _____ ARHCD 366
Arhoolie / Apr '95 / ADA / Direct / Cadillac.

COLLECTION
CD _____ COL 013
Collection / Oct '95 / Target/BMG.

FREDDY FENDER
Before the next teardrop falls / Wasted days and wasted nights / Tiu y las nubes / Jambalaya / Six days on the road / Tu corazon traidor / Enamorado / Your cheatin' heart / Tell it like it is / Noches eternas / Amor chiquito / Chuquitta / Fiches negras / San Quilmas Querido / Ella me dijo que no / Nochecita
CD _____ 90848-2
PMF / Jul '94 / Kingdom / Cadillac.

GREATEST HITS, THE
Your cheatin' heart / These arms of mine / She's about a mover / Baby I want to love you / High school dance / Talk to me / Let the good times roll / In the still of the night / Man can cry / Wasted days and wasted nights / Crazy baby / Enter my heart / La Bamba / I'm leaving it all up to you / Wild side of life / Sweet summer day / Mathilda / Silver wings / Since I met you baby / Before the next teardrop falls
CD _____ HADCD 167
Javelin / May '94 / THE / Henry Hadaway Organisation.

WASTED DAYS & WASTED NIGHTS
Wasted days and wasted nights / Rains came / You'll lose a good thing / Almost persuaded / I'm leaving it all up to you / She's about a mover / Crazy baby / Girl who waits on tables / Before the next teardrop falls / Lovin' cajun style / But I do / Sweet summer day / Silver wings / Running back / Enter my heart / Going out with the tide / Baby I want to love you / Just because
CD _____ CDGRF 072
Tring / Feb '93 / Tring / Prism.

Fenech, Paul

DADDY'S HAMMER
Guitar slinger / Daddy's hammer / Hear me howl / Running back to you / Scrape your sanity / Snakin' with the bad guys / Locked in a room with Betty / Cold cold baby / (We're) not like you / One fine day / (Alone) In the killing room / 1000 Guns for Pablo
CD _____ CDGRAM 87
Anagram / Mar '95 / Pinnacle.

Fenton, George

TRAILS OF LIFE
CD _____ CDSGP 030
Prestige / Oct '92 / Total/BMG.

Fenton, Shane

I'M A MOODY GUY (Fenton, Shane & The Fentones)
I'm a moody guy / Five foot two / Eyes of blue / Why little girl / It's all over now / It's gonna take magic / Cindy's birthday / Too young for sad memories / Fallen leaves on the ground / You're telling me / Walk away / Don't do that / I'll know / Fool's paradise / You need love / Somebody else not me / I ain't got nobody / Hey Miss Ruby / Hey Lulu / I do, do you / Breeze and I
CD _____ SEECD 369
See For Miles/C5 / Mar '93 / Pinnacle.

Feon, Daniel

EVIT DANSAL (Feon, Daniel & Jil Lehart)
CD _____ 432CD
Diffusion Breizh / Jul '95 / ADA.

Ferber, Mordy

MR.X
CD _____ EFA 015052
Ozone / Jun '95 / SRD.

Ferguson, Maynard

AMERICAN MUSIC HALL 1972, THE
CD _____ DSTS 1004
Status / '94 / Jazz Music / Wellard / Harmonia Mundi.

BODY AND SOUL
Expresso / Body and soul / M.O.T. / Mira Mira / Last dive / Beautiful hearts / Central Park
CD _____ TJA 10027
Jazz Alliance / Feb '96 / New Note.

DUES
CD _____ 4744182
Sony Jazz / Dec '93 / Sony.

FOOTPATH CAFE
Get it to go / Footpath cafe / Brazil / That's my desire / Crusin' for a bluesin' / Poison ya' blues / Break the ice / Hit and run
CD _____ IOR 83122
In & Out / Sep '95 / Vital/SAM.

CD _____ TJA 10028
Jazz Alliance / Jan '96 / New Note.

HIGH VOLTAGE
CD _____ CDENV 517
Enigma / Feb '89 / EMI.

LIVE AT PEACOCK LANE (Ferguson, Maynard & His Orchestra)
CD _____ JH 1030
Jazz Hour / Jul '93 / Target/BMG / Jazz Music / Cadillac.

LIVE AT THE GREAT AMERICAN MUSIC HALL
CD _____ DSTS 1007
Status / May '95 / Jazz Music / Wellard / Harmonia Mundi.

MAYNARD FERGUSON ORCHESTRA 1967
CD _____ JAS 9504
Just A Memory / Dec '95 / Harmonia Mundi.

MAYNARD FERGUSON SEXTET 1967
CD _____ JAS 9503
Just A Memory / Dec '95 / Harmonia Mundi.

NEW SOUNDS OF...1964
CD _____ FSCD 2010
Fresh Sound / Nov '94 / Jazz Music / Discovery.

THESE CATS CAN SWING (Ferguson, Maynard & Bip Bop)
Sugar / Caravan / I don't wanna be a hoochie coochie man no mo' / Sweet bab suite (Bai Ravi) / I'll be around / He can't swing / It's the gospel truth
CD _____ CCD 4669
Concord Jazz / Oct '95 / New Note.

Fermenting Innards
MYST
CD _____ INV 016 CD
Invasion / Nov '95 / Plastic Head.

Fernandel
ETOILES DE LA CHANSON
CD _____ 878152
Music Memoria / Jun '93 / Discovery / ADA.

IGNACE
CD _____ CDCD 3011
Charly / Sep '94 / Charly / THE / Cadillac.

L'IRRESISTIBLE
CD _____ UCD 19028
Forlane / Jun '95 / Target/BMG.

Fernandez, Roberto
NEW YORK SESSIONS (Fernandez, Roberto 'Fats')
CD _____ CDCH 564
Milan / Feb '91 / BMG / Silva Screen.

Fernando, Alfredo
MILONGAS FROM URUGUAY
CD _____ EUCD 1098
ARC / '91 / ARC Music / ADA.

TRIBUTE TO CARLOS GARDEL
CD _____ EUCD 1134
ARC / '91 / ARC Music / ADA.

Ferrari, Luc
ACOUSMATRIX 3
CD _____ BVHAASTCD 9009
Bvhaast / Oct '93 / Cadillac.

Ferre, Boulou
TRINITY
CD _____ SCCD 31171
Steeplechase / Jul '88 / Impetus.

Ferre, Leo
PREMIERE CHANSON
CD _____ LDX 274967
La Chant Du Monde / Sep '93 / Harmonia Mundi / ADA.

Ferrell, Rachelle
FIRST INSTRUMENT
You send me / You don't know what love is / Bye bye blackbird / Prayer dance / Inchworm / With every breath I take / What is this thing called love / My funny valentine / Don't waste your time / Extensions / Autumn leaves
CD _____ CDP 8728202
Blue Note / Jun '95 / EMI.

RACHELLE FERRELL
I'm special / Welcome to my love / Waiting / It only took a minute / With open arms / Until you come back to me / You can't get (until you learn to start giving) / Nothing has ever felt like this / I know you love me / Sentimental
CD _____ CDEST 2177
Capitol / Sep '92 / EMI.

Ferrero, Medard
INOUBLIABLES DE L'ACCORDEON
CD _____ 882392
Music Memoria / Aug '93 / Discovery / ADA.

Ferrick, Melissa
MASSIVE BLUR
Honest eyes / Happy song / Hello dad / What have I got to lose / Love song / Ten friends / For once in my life / Blue sky night / Massive blur / Love me all / Wonder why / Meaning of love / In a world like this / Breaking vows
CD _____ 7567825022
Elektra / Dec '93 / Warner Music.

Ferris, Glenn
FLESH AND STONE
CD _____ ENJACD 80882
Enja / Jan '95 / New Note / Vital/SAM.

Ferron
PHANTOM CENTER
CD _____ 9425762
Earthbeat / Jan '96 / Direct / ADA.

Ferry, Bryan
ANOTHER TIME, ANOTHER PLACE
In crowd / Smoke gets in your eyes / Walk a mile in my shoes / Funny how time slips away / You are my sunshine / What a wonderful world / It ain't me babe / Finger poppin' / Help me make it through the night / Another time another place
CD _____ EGCD 14
EG / Sep '91 / EMI.

ANOTHER TIME/THESE FOOLISH THINGS/LET'S STICK TOGETHER (Compact Collection/3CD Set)
CD _____ TPAK 22
Virgin / Nov '92 / EMI.

BETE NOIRE
Limbo / Kiss and tell / New town / Day for night / Zamba / Right stuff / Seven deadly sins / Name of the game / Bete noire
CD _____ CDV 2474
Virgin / Nov '87 / EMI.

BOYS AND GIRLS
Sensation / Slave to love / Don't stop the dance / Wasteland / Windswept / Chosen one / Valentine / Stone woman / Boys and girls
CD _____ EGCD 62
EG / Sep '91 / EMI.

BRIDE STRIPPED BARE, THE
Sign of the times / Can't let go / Hold on I'm comin' / Same old blues / When she walks in the room / Take me to the river / What goes on / Carrickfergus / That's how strong my love is / This island Earth
CD _____ EGCD 36
EG / Sep '91 / EMI.

IN YOUR MIND
This is tomorrow / All night operator / One kiss / Love me madly again / Tokyo Joe / Party doll / Rock of ages / In your mind
CD _____ EGCD 27
EG / Sep '91 / EMI.

LET'S STICK TOGETHER
Let's stick together / Casanova / Sea breezes / Shame, shame, shame / 2HB / Price of love / Chance meeting / It's only love / You go to my head / Re-make/Remodel / Heart on my sleeve
CD _____ EGCD 24
EG / Jan '84 / EMI.

MAMOUNA
Don't want to know / N.Y.C. / Your painted smile / Mamouna / Only face / Thirty nine steps / Which way to turn / Wild cat days / Gemini moon / Chain reaction
CD _____ CDV 2751
Virgin / Sep '94 / EMI.

MORE THAN THIS (The Best Of Bryan Ferry & Roxy Music)
Virginia Plain / Hard rain's gonna fall / Street life / These foolish things / Love is the drug / Dance away / Let's stick together / Angel eyes / Slave to love / Oh yeah / Don't stop the dance / Same old scene / Is your love strong enough / Jealous guy / Kiss and tell / More than this / I put a spell on you / Avalon / Your painted smile / Smoke gets in your eyes
CD _____ CDV 2791
Virgin / Oct '95 / EMI.

TAXI
I put a spell on you / Will you still love me tomorrow / Answer me / Just one look / Rescue me / All tomorrow's parties / Girl of my best friend / Amazing grace / Taxi / Because you're mine
CD _____ CDV 2700
Virgin / Mar '93 / EMI.

THESE FOOLISH THINGS
Hard rain's gonna fall / River of salt / Don't ever change / Piece of my heart / Baby I don't care / It's my party / Don't worry baby / Sympathy for the devil / Tracks of my tears / You won't see me / I love how you love me / Loving you is sweeter than ever / These foolish things
CD _____ EGCD 9
EG / Jul '93 / EMI.

Fertile Crescent
FERTILE CRESCENT
CD _____ KFWCD 118
Knitting Factory / Nov '92 / Grapevine.

Fertilizer
PAINTING OF ANNOYANCE
CD _____ IR 008CD
Invasion / Apr '95 / Plastic Head.

Fervant, Thierry
LEGENDS OF AVALON
CD _____ QMCD 7042
Quartz / Sep '90 / SRD.

UNIVERSE
CD _____ QMCD 7012
Quartz / Sep '90 / SRD.

Fest, Manfredo
COMECAR DE NOVO
Fetuccini Manfredo / Voce e eu / You must believe in spring / Where's montgomery / Bonita / Seresta / Lush life / Morning / How insensitive / Brazilian divertimento # 2 / Comecar de novo / Vera cruz
CD _____ CCD 4660
Concord Jazz / Aug '95 / New Note.

Fester
WINTER OF SIN
CD _____ NFR 002
No Fashion / Oct '94 / Plastic Head.

Fesu
WAR WITH NO MERCY
CD _____ CDTURM 7
Continuum / Jul '94 / Pinnacle.

Fetish 69
ANTI-BODY
CD _____ NB 087
Nuclear Blast / Dec '93 / Plastic Head.

BRUTE FORCE
Void / Marooned / Stares to nowhere / Stomach turner / Tough center/harter ken / Hellville (pop. 7,000)
CD _____ SPASM 005CD
Intellectual Convulsion / Jul '93 / Vital.

Fever Tree
FEVER TREE/ANOTHER TIME ANOTHER PLACE
Imitation situation 1 / Where do you go / San Francisco girls (return of the natives) / Ninety nine and one half / Man who paints the pictures / Filigree and shadow / Sun also rises / Day tripper/We can work it out / Nowadays Clancy can't even sing / Unlock my door / Come with me / Man who paints the pictures (part 2) / What time did you say it was in salt lake city / Don't come crying to me girl / Fever / Grand candy young sweet / Jokes are for sad people / I've just seen evergreen / Peace of mind / Death is the dancer
CD _____ SEECD 364
See For Miles/C5 / Feb '93 / Pinnacle.

Few Good Men
TAKE A DIP
Tonite / Walk you thru / Let's take a dip / All of my love / Please baby don't cry / Have I never / Thang for you young girl / Don't say (behind my book) / Sexy day / Good man / 1-900-G-Man (How I say I love you)
CD _____ 73008260212
Arista / Nov '95 / BMG.

Feyer, George
GEORGE FEYER PLAYS COLE PORTER
Anything goes / In the still of the night / I love Paris / It's all right with me
CD _____ 08601471
Vanguard / Mar '92 / Complete/Pinnacle / Discovery.

FFA Coffi Pawb
HEI VIDAL
CD _____ AMKSTCD 036
Ankst / Mar '93 / SRD.

Fflaps
AMHERSAIN
CD _____ PROBE 21C
Probe Plus / Jul '89 / Vital.

FFWD
FFWD
CD _____ INTA 1CD
Intermodo / Aug '94 / Disc.

Fiahlo, Fransico
BEST OF FADO PORTUGUESE
CD _____ EUCD 1165
ARC / '91 / ARC Music / ADA.

MEU ALENTEJO
CD _____ EUCD 1113
ARC / '91 / ARC Music / ADA.

O Fadoal Latino
CD _____ EUCD 1075
ARC / '89 / ARC Music / ADA.

Fiction Factory
THROW THE WARPED WHEEL OUT
Feels like heaven / Heart and mind / Hanging gardens / All or nothing / Hit the mark / Ghost of love / Tales of tears / First step / Warped wheel
CD _____ 4805232
Columbia / May '05 / Sony.

Fiddle, Johnny
CAJUN GIRL
CD _____ RPCDS 001
Rivet Productions / Dec '94 / ADA.

Fiddle Puppets
LIFT UP YOUR WINGS
CD _____ HEE 009CD
Yodel-Ay-Hee / Jun '94 / ADA.

Fiddler, John
RETURN OF THE BUFFALO
CD _____ RMCCD 0197
Red Steel Music / Feb '95 / Grapevine.

Fiddler's Green
KING SHEPHERD
CD _____ EFA 127502
Deaf Shepherd / May '95 / SRD.

Fiddlers Five
FIDDLE MUSIC FROM SCOTLAND
CD _____ COMD 2044
Temple / Feb '94 / CM / Duncans / ADA / Direct.

Fiedler, Arthur
POPS CHRISTMAS PARTY (Boston Pops Orchestra)
CD _____ 09026616852
RCA Victor / Nov '95 / BMG.

Field Day
FRICTION
CD _____ AGO 742
Noise/Modern Music / Jul '95 / Pinnacle / Plastic Head.

Field Mice
FOR KEEPS
CD _____ SARAH 607CD
Sarah / Mar '95 / Vital.

Fields, Brandon
OTHER PLACES
CD _____ NOVA 9025
Nova / Sep '92 / New Note.

OTHER SIDE OF THE STORY, THE
CD _____ NOVA 8602
Nova / Jan '93 / New Note.

TRAVELER
CD _____ NOVA 8811
Nova / Sep '92 / New Note.

Fields, Gracie
GRACIE FIELDS
Looking on the bright side / Isle of Capri / Painting the clouds with sunshine / Biggest aspidistra in the world / Sing as we go / Body and soul / Sally / You're more than all the world to me / Love in bloom / Stormy weather / Ring down the curtain / I give my heart / Oh mamma! (The butchers boy) / Where are you / Turn 'Erbert's face to the wall mother / OLd violin / Snow White / Holy city / Now it can be told / Gracie's hit medley / Alexander's ragtime band / Love is everywhere / Melody at dawn
CD _____ PASTCD 9710
Flapper / '90 / Pinnacle.

GRACIE FIELDS COLLECTORS EDITION
CD _____ DVX 08052
Deja Vu / Apr '95 / THE.

QUEEN OF HEARTS - BEST OF 1930S
Queen of hearts / First time I saw you / It looks like rain in Cherry Blossom Lane / Did your mother come from Ireland / One of the little orphans of the storm / Song in your heart / Gypsy lullaby / In the chapel in the moonlight / We're all good pals together / When my dreamboat comes home / September in the rain / Little old lady / Giannina mia / Clogs and shawl / Would you / My love for you / Laughing Irish eyes / Where is the sun / When the harvest moon is shining / Feather in her Tyrolean hat / Organ, the monkey and me / Smile when you say goodbye
CD _____ CDHD 144
Happy Days / Feb '89 / Conifer.

SING AS WE GO
Sally / Oh sailor behave / Just one more chance / It isn't fair / Bargain hunter / Mary Rose / My lucky day / There's a lovely lake in London / Walter, Walter, lead me to the altar / Chapel in the moonlight / Sing as we

go / It's a sin to tell a lie / I'll never say Never Again again / Pity the poor goldfish / In my little bottom drawer / Laugh at life / I took my harp to a party / Mocking bird went cuckoo / Fred Fanna / Stop and shop at the Co-op shop / We've got to keep up with the Joneses / Have you forgotten so soon / Roll along prairie moon / Goody goody / Daisy daisy / Light in the window
CD _____ RAJCD 833
Empress / Jul '94 / THE.

THAT OLD FEELING
Sweetest song in the world / Turn 'Erbert's face to the wall mother / Home / Remember me / Round the bend of the road / Will you remember / When I grow too old to dream / That old feeling / Fred Fannakapan / My first love song / Walter, Walter, lead me to the altar / Goodnight my love / Red sails in the sunset / Ah sweet mystery of life / Smilin' through / Giannina mia / There's a lovely lake in London / We've got to keep up with the Joneses / I never cried so much in all my life / First time I saw you / Fall in and follow the band / Sally
CD _____ CD AJA 5062
Living Era / Jun '89 / Koch.

THAT OLD FEELING
CD _____ PASTCD 7050
Flapper / Sep '94 / Pinnacle.

Fields Of The Nephilim

BBC RADIO 1 IN CONCERT
CD _____ WINCD 023
Windsong / Jun '92 / Pinnacle.

BURNING THE FIELDS
CD _____ MOO 1CD
Jungle / Dec '93 / Disc.

DAWNRAZOR
Intro / Slow kill / Volcane / Vet for the insane / Dust / Reanimator / Dawnrazor / Sequel / Power (Not on LP) / Preacher man (Not on LP) / Secrets (CD only) / Tower (CD only)
CD _____ SITL 18CD
Lowdown/Beggars Banquet / '88 / Warner Music / Disc.

EARTH INFERNO
Intro (dead but dreaming) / For her light / At the gates of silent memory (paradise regained) / Moonchild / Submission / Preacher man / Love under will / Summer land / Last exit for the lost / Psychonaut / Dawnrazor
CD _____ BEGA 120CD
Beggars Banquet / Apr '91 / Warner Music / Disc.

ELIZIUM
(Dead but dreaming) for her light / At the gates of silent memory (paradise regained) / Submission / Summer land / Wail of summer.. and will your heart be also
CD _____ BEGA 115CD
Beggars Banquet / Oct '90 / Warner Music / Disc.

LAURA
CD _____ CONTECD 196
Contempo / Oct '91 / Plastic Head.

NEPHILIM, THE
Endemoniada / Celebrate / Watchman / Moonchild / Chords of souls / Last exit for the lost / Phobia
CD _____ SITU 22 CD
Situation 2 / Sep '88 / Pinnacle.

REVELATIONS
CD _____ BEGA 137CD
Beggars Banquet / Jul '93 / Warner Music / Disc.

Fier, Anton

DREAMSPEED
CD _____ AVAN 009
Avant / Nov '93 / Harmonia Mundi / Cadillac.

Fiestas

OH SO FINE
So fine / Dollar bill / That was me / Mr. Dillon, Mr. Dillon / Come on and love me / Mexico / Last night I dreamed / Lawman / Our anniversary / Railroad song / Try it one more time / Mama put the law down / Fine as wine / You can be my girlfriend / Anna / I'm your slave
CD _____ CDCHD 382
Ace / Feb '93 / Pinnacle / Cadillac / Complete/Pinnacle.

Fifteen

BUZZ
CD _____ GROW 15-2
Grass / Nov '94 / SRD.

Fifty Lashes

HARDER
CD _____ CDVEST 36
Bulletproof / Oct '94 / Pinnacle.

Fight

SMALL DEADLY SPACE, A
I am alive / Mouthpiece / Legacy of hate / Blowout in the radio room / Never again /

Small deadly space / Gretna Green / Beneath the violence / Human crate / In a world of my own making
CD _____ 4784002
Epic / Apr '95 / Sony.

Figlin, Arkadi

PARTS OF A WHOLE (A Jazz Portrait)
CD _____ MK 437061
Mezhdunarodnaya Kniga / Jul '92 / Complete/Pinnacle.

Filarfolket

SMUGGLE
CD _____ CDAM 71
Temple / Jul '95 / CM / Duncans / ADA / Direct.

VINTERVALS
CD _____ RESCD 504
Resource / Oct '94 / ADA.

File

2 LEFT FEET
CD _____ FF 507CD
Flying Fish / '92 / Roots / CM / Direct / ADA.

Filipinos

PEEL BACK THE SKIN
CD _____ TWIST 003CD
Wild / Jun '92 / Pinnacle.

Filter

SHORT BUS
CD _____ 9362458642
Warner Bros. / Apr '95 / Warner Music.

Filthy Christians

MEAN
CD _____ MOSH 017CD
Earache / Apr '90 / Vital.

Fin

POSITIVE
CD _____ FROMCD 005
Fromage Rouge / Sep '95 / 3MV.

Finchley Boys

EVERLASTING TRIBUTES
CD _____ 852127
EVA / Jun '94 / Direct / ADA.

Fine Arts Brass Ensemble

LIGHTER SIDE OF FINE ARTS BRASS ENSEMBLE, THE
CD _____ CDSDL 381
Saydisc / Aug '90 / Harmonia Mundi / ADA / Direct.

Fine Young Cannibals

FINE YOUNG CANNIBALS
Johnny come home / Couldn't care more / Don't ask me to choose / Funny how love is / Suspicious minds / Blue / Move to work / On a promise / Time isn't kind / Life is a stranger
CD _____ 828 004 2
London / Jan '86 / PolyGram.

RAW AND THE COOKED, THE
She drives me crazy / Good thing / I'm not the man I used to be / I'm not satisfied / Tell me what / Don't look back / It's OK (It's alright) / Don't let it get you down / As hard as it is / Ever fallen in love
CD _____ 828 069 2
London / Jan '89 / PolyGram.

RAW AND THE REMIX, THE
I'm not satisfied (Matt Dike/New York rap mixes) / Good thing (12" mix) / Johnny come home / I'm not the man I used to be (Jazzie B & Nellee Hooper/Smith & Mighty mixes) / She drives me crazy (mixes) / It's OK (it's alright) (Ploeg club mix) / Johnny takes a trip / Tired of getting pushed around (mixes/not on LP) / Don't look back (12" mix/not on LP)
CD _____ 828 221 2
London / Nov '90 / PolyGram.

Finger, Peter

BETWEEN THE LINES
CD _____ BEST 1079CD
Acoustic Music / Nov '95 / ADA.

INNERLEBEN
CD _____ BEST 1019CD
Acoustic Music / Nov '93 / ADA.

NIEMANDSLAND
CD _____ BEST 1001CD
Acoustic Music / Nov '93 / ADA.

SOLO
CD _____ BEST 1032CD
Acoustic Music / Nov '93 / ADA.

Fingers, Eddie

TILL DEATH DO US DISCO (Fingers, Eddie Music)

Till death do us disco / Silicon mysteries / Long hard funky dreams / Midnight safari / Graveyard shuffle / Transilvania transcendental / Hot summer dreams / Apres minuit / Infinite Mass / Nov '94 / Pinnacle
CD _____ MASSCD 022
Infinite Mass / Nov '94 / Pinnacle.

Fini Tribe

GROSSING 10K
CD _____ TPLP 24 CD
One Little Indian / Dec '89 / Pinnacle.

NOISE LUST AND FUN
CD _____ TPCD 21
One Little Indian / Nov '89 / Pinnacle.

SHEIGRA
Dark / Sunshine / Brand new (tip-top tune) / Mushroom-shaped / Sheigra 5 / Truth / Catch the whistle / We have come / Mesmerise / Off on a slow one / Love above
CD _____ 8286152
FFRR / Jun '95 / PolyGram.

UNEXPECTED GROOVY TREAT, AN
CD _____ TPLP 34CD
One Little Indian / Aug '92 / Pinnacle.

Fink, Cathy

CATHY FINK & MARCY MARXER (Fink, Cathy & Marcy Marxer)
Last night I dreamed / Love's last chance / Freight train blues / My prairie home / I'm not alone anymore / Names / Walking in the glory / Are you tired of me / Tune medley (CD only) / Crawdad song (CD only)
CD _____ SHCD 3775
Sugarhill / '89 / Roots / CM / ADA / Direct.

COLLECTION FOR KIDS, A (Fink, Cathy & Marcy Marxer)
CD _____ ROU 8029CD
Rounder / Apr '94 / CM / Direct / ADA / Cadillac.

DOGGONE MY TIME
Where the west begins / I'm so lonesome I could cry / Cuckoo / Sara McCutcheon / Cat's got the measles / Coal mining woman / Monkey medley / Midnight prayerlight / No tell motel / When it's darkness on the delta / Cotton patch rag / Coming home / Little Billy Wilson / Shenandoah Falls / My old Kentucky home
CD _____ SHCD 3783
Sugarhill / '90 / Roots / CM / ADA / Direct.

GRANDMA SLID DOWN THE MOUNTAIN
CD _____ CD 8010
Rounder / Oct '88 / CM / Direct / ADA / Cadillac.

PARENTS' HOME COMPANION, A (Fink, Cathy & Marcy Marxer)
CD _____ ROUCD 8031
Rounder / Feb '95 / CM / Direct / ADA / Cadillac.

WHEN THE RAIN COMES DOWN
CD _____ CD 8013
Rounder / '88 / CM / Direct / ADA / Cadillac.

Finlayson, Willy

VERY MUCH ALIVE
CD _____ BRGCD 03
Music Maker / Jul '94 / Grapevine / ADA.

Finley, Karen

CERTAIN LEVEL OF DENIAL, A (2CD Set)
CD Set _____ RCD 40317
Rykodisc / Feb '95 / Vital / ADA.

Finn

FINN
Only talking sense / Eyes of the world / Mood swinging man / Last day of June / Suffer never / Angel's heap / Niwhai / Where is my soul / Bullets in my hairdo / Paradise (wherever you are) / Kiss the road of Raratonga
CD _____ CDFINN 1
Parlophone / Oct '95 / EMI.

Finn, Alec

BLUE SHAMROCK
CD _____ 7567827352
Warner Bros. / Apr '95 / Warner Music.

Finn, Tim

BEFORE AND AFTER
Hit the ground running / Protected / In love with it all / Persuasion / Many's the time (in Dublin) / Funny way / Can't do both / in your sway / Strangeness and charm / Always never now / Walk you home / I found it
CD _____ CDEST 2202
Capitol / Jun '93 / EMI.

ESCAPADE
Fraction too much friction / Staring at the embers / Through the years / Not for nothing / In a minor key / Made my day / Wait and see / Below the belt / I only want to know / Growing pains

CD _____ 474610 2
Epic / May '94 / Sony.

Finnegan, Brian

WHEN THE PARTY'S OVER
CD _____ ARADCD 101
Acoustic Radio / Mar '94 / CM.

Finnegans

FINNEGANS, THE
CD _____ CDMANU 1439
Manu / Dec '93 / Discovery / ADA.

Finnerty, Barry

STRAIGHT AHEAD
Count up / Straight ahead / Outness / I can't make you love me / Sheer lunacy / OD / Inner urge / Elvinesque / Carnaval / Bells
CD _____ AJ 0116
Arabesque / Jun '95 / New Note.

Finnigan, Jim

IRISH HARVEST DAY
CD _____ DHCD 722
Outlet / Jan '95 / ADA / Duncans / CM / Ross / Direct / Koch.

Firat, Ozan

TURKEY: MUSIC OF THE TROUBADORS
CD _____ AUB 006771
Auvidis/Ethnic / Jun '93 / Harmonia Mundi.

Fire

MAGIC SHOEMAKER
Children of immagination / Tell you a story / Magic shoes / Reason for everything / Only a dream / Flies like a bird / Like to help you if I can / I can see the sky / Shoemaker / Happy man am I
CD _____ SEECD 294
See For Miles/C5 / '90 / Pinnacle.

Fire Escape

PSYCHOTIC REACTION/RAW AND ALIVE (Fire Escape & The Seeds)
Psychotic reaction / Talk talk / Love special delivery / Trip / 96 tears / Blood beat / Trip maker / Journey's end / Pictures and designs / Fortune teller / No escape / Satisfy you / Night time girl / Up in her room / Gypsy plays his drums / Can't seem to make you mine / Mumble and bumble / Forest outside your door / 900 million people daily (all making love) / Pushin' too hard
CD _____ DOCD 1990
Drop Out / Oct '91 / Pinnacle.

Fire Facts

REMAND CENTRE
CD _____ SHCD 6016
Sky High / Jul '95 / Jetstar.

Fire House Crew

STARS IN THE ARENA VOL.1
CD _____ FCCD 001
Roots Collective / Jul '94 / SRD / Jetstar / Roots Collective.

Fire, Jack

DESTRUCTION OF SUARESILLE, THE
CD _____ ESD 1213
Estrus / Sep '95 / Plastic Head.

Fire Merchants

IGNITION
CD _____ MD 94352
Roadrunner / Dec '89 / Pinnacle.

LANDLORDS OF ATLANTIS
CD _____ EFA 130012
Ozone / May '94 / SRD.

Fire Next Time

NORTH AND SOUTH
Fields of France / Can't forgive / Stay with me now / Supasave / We've lost too much / Too close / St. Mary's steps / Following the hearse / North and South
CD _____ 835 855-2
Polydor / Oct '88 / PolyGram.

Fireballs

BEST OF THE FIREBALLS, THE (The Original Norman Petty Masters)
Torquay / Bulldog / Carioca / Yacky doo / Foot patter / Dumbo / Vaquero / Long long ponytail / Gunshot / Nearly sunrise / Rik-atik / Quite a party / Really big time / Peg leg / Fireball / Panic button / Cry baby / Tuff-a-nuff / Find me a golden street / Blacksmith blues / Daytona drag / Kissin' / Chief whoopin' koff / El ringo / Torquay (2)
CD _____ CDCHD 418
Ace / Sep '92 / Pinnacle / Cadillac / Complete/Pinnacle.

BEST OF THE FIREBALLS, THE
Do you think / Wishing / True love ways / Call in the sheriff / Don't stop / Good good

lovin' / Won't be long / Sugar shack / Ain't gonna tell anybody / Daisy petal pickin' / When my tears have dried / Look at me / I'll send for you / What kind of love / Cry baby / Bull moose / Lonesome tears / Indian giver / Red Cadillac and a black moustache / Almost eighteen / Pretend / I wonder why / Maybe baby / Everyday / Little baby / It's so easy / Bottle of wine / Come on react / Goin' away / Can't you see I'm trying
CD _____ CDCHD 468
Ace / Oct '91 / Pinnacle / Cadillac / Complete/Pinnacle.

BLUE FIRE / RARITIES
Blue fire / Blues in the night / Bluesday / Wang wang blues / Birth of the blues / Blacksmith blues / Blue tinted blues / Wabash blues / Big daddy blues / Basin Street blues / Bye bye blues / St. Louis blues / Almost paradise / Sweet talk / Sneakers / I doubt it / La golondrina / Tequila / Spur / Spanish legend / Jesusita en chihuahua / La borachita / Gay ranchero / El rancho grande
CD _____ CDCHD 472
Ace / Oct '93 / Pinnacle / Cadillac / Complete/Pinnacle.

FIREBALLS & VAQUERO
Torquay / Guess what / Panic button / Let there be love / Nearly sunrise / Long long ponytail / Bulldog / I wonder why / Foot patter / Blind date / Kissin' / Cry baby / Vaquero / La raspa / In a little Spanish town / Cielito lindo / La golondrina / Tequila / Spur / Spanish legend / Jesusita en chihuahua / La borachita / Gay ranchero / El rancho grande
CD _____ CDCHD 447
Ace / Mar '93 / Pinnacle / Cadillac / Complete/Pinnacle.

TORQUAY/CAMPUSOLOGY
Torquay / Alone / Joey's song / Last date / Chief whoopin' koff / El ringo / Wheels / Honey / Rawhide / Tuff-a-nuff / Dumbo / Quite a part / Ahhh soul / Campusology / Daytona drag / Evermore / Peg leg / Sheezburger / In the mood / Mr. Mean / Mrs. Mean / Gently, gently / Mr. Reed / Find me a golden street
CD _____ CDCHD 452
Ace / Apr '93 / Pinnacle / Cadillac / Complete/Pinnacle.

Firebirds

TAKING BY STORM
CD _____ FBCD 101
Pollytone / Jan '95 / Pollytone.

THIS IS IT
CD _____ PEPCD 105
Pollytone / Mar '95 / Pollytone.

TOO HOT TO HANDLE
CD _____ PEPCD 103
Pollytone / Jan '95 / Pollytone.

Firefall

FIREFALL
It doesn't matter / Love isn't all / Livin' ain't livin' / No way out / Dolphin's lullaby / Cinderella / Sad ol' love song / You are the woman / Mexico / Do what you want
CD _____ 812270379-2
WEA / Mar '93 / Warner Music.

GREATEST HITS, THE
CD _____ 8122710552
WEA / Jul '93 / Warner Music.

Firehose

FROMOHIO
CD _____ SST 235 CD
SST / Feb '89 / Plastic Head.

IF'N
Sometimes / Honey please / For the singer of REM / Anger / Hear me / Backroads / From one comes one / Making the freeway safe for the freeway / Operation solitaire / Windmilling / Me and you remembering / In memory of Elizabeth Cotton / Soon / Thunderchild
CD _____ SST 115 CD
SST / May '93 / Plastic Head.

RAGIN' FULL ON
Locked in / Brave captain / Under the influence of meat puppets / Chemical wire / Another theory shot to shit on your ... / It matters / On your knees / Candle and the flame / Choose any memory / Perfect pairs / This / Caroms / Relatin' dudes to jazz / Things could turn around
CD _____ SST 079 CD
SST / May '93 / Plastic Head.

Firehouse

3
Love is a dangerous thing / What's wrong / Something 'bout your body / Trying to make a living / Here for you / Get a life / Two sides / No one at all / Temptation / I live my life for you
CD _____ 4783802
Epic / Jul '95 / Sony.

MR MACHINERY OPERATOR
Formal introduction / Blaze / Herded into pools / Witness / Number seven / Powerful

hankerin' / Rocket sled/Fuel tank / Quicksand / Disciples of the 3-way / More famous quotes / Sincerely / Hell-hole / 4.29.92 / Cliffs thrown down
CD _____ 472967 2
Columbia / Mar '93 / Sony.

Firehouse Five

AT DISNEYLAND
CD _____ GTCD 10049
Good Time Jazz / Oct '93 / Jazz Music / Wellard / Pinnacle / Cadillac.

DIXIELAND FAVOURITES (Firehouse Five Plus Two)
CD _____ FCD 60008
Fantasy / May '95 / Pinnacle / Jazz Music / Wellard / Cadillac.

GOES SOUTH
CD _____ GTCD 12018
Good Time Jazz / Oct '93 / Jazz Music / Wellard / Pinnacle / Cadillac.

Fireworks

SET THE WORLD ON FIRE
CD _____ EFA 11573-2
Crypt / Apr '94 / SRD.

Firk, Backwards Sam

TRUE BLUES & GOSPEL
CD _____ STCD 0002
Stella / Aug '94 / ADA.

First Choice

BEST OF FIRST CHOICE
Armed and extremely dangerous / Smarty pants / One step away / Newsy neighbours / This little woman / This is the house (where love is) / Love and happiness / Runnin' out of fools / Wake up to me / Player / Guilty / Love freeze / Boy named Junior / All I need / You've been doing wrong for so long / Don't fake it / Why can't I touch you (if you let me make love to you) / This is the house
CD _____ CDSEWD 096
Southbound / Aug '94 / Pinnacle.

DELUSIONS
CD _____ CPCD 8060
Charly / Nov '94 / Charly / THE / Cadillac.

HOLD YOUR HORSES
Let me down easy / Good morning midnight / Great expectations / Hold your horses / Love thang / Double cross
CD _____ CPCD 8096
Charly / Apr '95 / Charly / THE / Cadillac.

First Class Bluesband

FIRST CLASS BLUES
CD _____ BEST 1031CD
Acoustic Music / Nov '93 / ADA.

First Down

WORLD SERVICE
CD _____ EFA 610092
Blitzvinyl / Apr '95 / SRD.

First House

ERINDIRA
Day away / Innocent erendira / Journeyers to the east / Bracondale / Grammenos / Stranger than paradise / Bridge call / Doubt / Further away
CD _____ 8275212
ECM / Apr '86 / New Note.

First Star

MY GRIP IS LIKE A COBRA
Explode / All I want to do / Ladies night out / Diss is for the suckas / Duce / My grip is like a cobra / Stop jockin / It's on you / Why you want to talk about me / Calling shouts
CD _____ ICHCD 1121
Ichiban / Oct '91 / Koch.

Fisc

HANDLE WITH CARE
Come run riot / Won't let go / Love fight / Hold your head up / Let me leave / Live it up / Lover under attack / Handle with care / Got to beat the clock / Speed limit 55
CD _____ CDMFN 91
Music For Nations / Mar '89 / Pinnacle.

Fischbacher Group

MYSTERIOUS PRINCESS (Fischbacher Group & Adam Nussbaum)
CD _____ BEST 1025
Acoustic Music / Nov '93 / ADA.

Fischer, Clare

JUST ME - SOLO PIANO EXCURSIONS
Autumn leaves / Pra braden / Round midnight / I'm gettin' sentimental over you / I'd do anything for you / Liebesleid / After you've gone / Guajira / Ill wind / Pensativa / Topsy
CD _____ CCD 4679
Concord Jazz / Feb '96 / New Note.

LEMBRANCAS (REMEMBRANCES)
C.P. (Charlie Palmieri) / Fina / Coco B. / Curumim / Endlessly / On Green Dolphin Street / Xapun / Gilda / Pan pipe dance / And miss you go / Strut (CD only.)
CD _____ CCD 4404
Concord Jazz / Mar '90 / New Note.

Fischer, Frank

MULLUMBIMBY
CD _____ 710115
Innovative Communication / Apr '90 / Magnum Music Group.

Fischer-Z

KAMIKAZE SHIRT
CD _____ WELFD 6
Welfare / Apr '94 / Total/BMG.

STILL IN FLAMES
CD _____ WELFD 7
Welfare / Jun '95 / Total/BMG.

Fish

SUITS
1470 / Lady let it lie / Emperor's song / Fortunes of war / Somebody special / No dummy / Pipeline / Jumpsuit city / Bandwagon / Raw meat
CD _____ DDICK 004CD
Dick Bros. / May '94 / Vital.

SUSHI
Fearless / Big wedge / Boston tea party / Credo / Family business / View from a hill / He knows you know / She chameleon / Kayleigh / White Russian / Company / Just good friends / Jeepster / Hold your head up / Lucky / Internal exile / Cliche / Last straw / Poets moon / Five years
CD Set _____ DDICK 002CD
Dick Bros. / Mar '94 / Vital.

VIGIL IN THE WILDERNESS OF MIRRORS
Vigil / Big wedge / State of mind / Company / Gentlemen's excuse me / Voyeur (Not on LP) / Family business / View from the hill / Cliche
CD _____ CDEMD 1015
EMI / Feb '90 / EMI.

YANG
Lucky / Big wedge / Lady let it lie / Lavender / Credo / Gentlemen's excuse me / Kayleigh / State of mind / Somebody special / Sugar mice / Punch and Judy / Fortunes of war / Internal exile
CD _____ DDICK 012CD
Dick Bros. / Sep '95 / Vital.

YIN
Incommunicado / Family business / Just good friends / Pipeline / Institution waltz / Tongues / Time and a word / Company / Incubus / Solo / Favourite stranger / Boston tea party / Raw meat
CD _____ DDICK 011CD
Dick Bros. / Sep '95 / Vital.

Fish Karma

SUNNYSLOPE
CD _____ 422433
New Rose / May '94 / Direct / ADA.

Fish Out Of Water

LUCKY SCARS
Just like in the movies (Part 1) / Once in a lifetime / Take it easy / Cry from the city / Belfast boy / Her old man / Parisienne pretude / Persistence of memory / M.G. Mad ness / He like a drink / Take it easy (Instrumental) / Cry from the city (Dub) / Lucky scars / Just like the movies (Part 2)
CD _____ SRCD 004
Stream / Aug '95 / Stream / Vital.

Fish, R. A.

RHYTHMIC ESSENCE (The Art of the Dumbek)
CD _____ LYRCD 7411
Lyrichord / Jan '92 / Roots / ADA / CM.

Fishbelly Black

FISHBELLY BLACK
CD _____ BBCD 72107
Backbeat / Dec '93 / Jetstar.

Fishbone

GIVE A MONKEY A BRAIN AND HE'LL SWEAR HE'S THE CENTRE...
Swim / Servitide / Black flowers / Unyielding conditioning / Properties of propaganda / Warmth of your breath / Lemon meringue / They have all abandoned their hopes / End the reign / Drunk skitzo / No fear / Nutt megalomaniac
CD _____ 473875 2
Columbia / Jun '93 / Sony.

REALITY OF MY SURROUNDINGS, THE
Fight the youth / If I were a... I'd / So many millions / Asswhippin' / Housework / Death march / Behaviour control technician / Pressure / Junkie's prayer / Prayer to the junkiemaker / Everyday sunshine / Naz-tee may'en / Babyhead / Those days are gone / Sunless Saturday

CD _____ 4676152
Columbia / Jul '91 / Sony.

TRUTH AND SOUL
Freddie's dead / Ma and pa / Might long way / Pouring rain / Deep inside / Question of life / Bonin' in the boneyard / One day / Subliminal fascism / Slow bus movin' (Howard beach party) / Ghetto soundwave / Change
CD _____ 4611732
Columbia / Oct '88 / Sony.

Fisher, Andy

MAN IN THE WOODS, A
CD _____ BTCD 971407
Beartracks / Aug '89 / Rollercoaster.

Fisher, Archie

SUNSET'S I'VE GALLOPED INTO... (Fisher, Archie & Garnet Rogers)
Ashfields and Brine / Yonder banks / Shipyard apprentice / Cuillins of Home / Southside blues / Silver coin / Prescence / Guns and whiskey / Bill Hosie / I wandered by a brookside / Merry England / Great North road / Eastfield / Black horse / All that you ask
CD _____ CDTRAX 020
Greentrax / Apr '92 / Conifer / Duncans / ADA / Direct.

WILL YE GANG, LOVE
CD _____ GLCD 3076
Green Linnet / May '9 / Roots / CM / Direct / ADA.

Fisher, Eddie

EDDIE FISHER
CD _____ DVAD 6062
Deja Vu / May '95 / THE.

Fisher, Jay

VELVETINE EAR, THE
Twitching man / Head / She's running / Fairweathered friend / Old man McKeensley / St. Judith's hill / Little face / Home / Hallowed day / Do you fill the room / Shore
CD _____ MAUVED 001
Mauve / Feb '94 / Pinnacle.

Fisher, Matthew

SALTY DOG RETURNS, A
Sabre Band on the Titanic / Salty dog returns / Nutcracker / Whiter shadow of pale / Pilgrimage / Rathurter / Strange conversation continues / G String / Sax and violence / Green onions / Linda theme / Downliners Sect manifesto / Peter Grump
CD _____ CDKVL 9032
Kingdom / May '94 / Kingdom.

STRANGE DAYS
CD _____ BGOCD 308
Beat Goes On / Feb '96 / Pinnacle.

Fisher, Natalie

NATALIE FISHER
CD _____ 450996641-2
Warner Bros. / Aug '94 / Warner Music.

Fisher, Ray

TRADITIONAL SONGS OF SCOTLAND (Fisher, Ray & Colin Ross/Martin Carthy/John Kirkpatrick)
Night riding song / Wash it / The unquorn / Laddie's lament / Gallowa' hills / Coulter's candy / Willie's fatal visit / Twa recruiting sergeants / Floo'ers o' the forest / MacGinty's meal and ale / Baron o'Brackley / Gypsy laddie / Lang biding here / Jute mill song / Hie, Jeannie hie / Johnny my man / My laddie's bedside / What can a young Lassie / Nicky Tams
CD _____ CDSDL 391
Saydisc / Mar '94 / Harmonia Mundi / ADA / Direct.

Fisher-Turner, Simon

EDWARD 2 (Fisher-Turner 5)
CD _____ IONICD 8
Mute / Nov '91 / Disc.

LIVE BLUE ROMA (The Archaeology Of Sound)
CD _____ CDMUTE 149
Mute / Jun '95 / Disc.

LIVE IN JAPAN
CD _____ BAH 7
Humbug / May '93 / Pinnacle.

REVOX
Scott / I just woke up man, is it too early / Miaw / Blackouts / Sappora sky / Pop song 93 / Fall / Boxer / Luch at Great Rissington / Recover / Where are we going / Iona / Stuck inside lady / Mr. Davidson's tube / Moist
CD _____ BAH 16
Humbug / Feb '94 / Pinnacle.

SEX APPEAL
CD _____ MONDE 7 CD
Cherry Red / Oct '92 / Pinnacle.

SIMON TURNER
CD _____ CRECD 64
Creation / May '94 / 3MV / Vital.

Fisherstreet

OUT IN THE NIGHT
CD _____ CLUNCD 057
Mulligan / Feb '86 / CM / ADA.

Fisk, Steve

448 DEATHLESS DAYS
CD _____ SST 159 CD
SST / May '93 / Plastic Head.

Fitz Of Depression

LET'S GIVE IT A TWIST
CD _____ FIRECD 44
Fire / Jan '95 / Disc.

Fitzgerald, Ella

70 MINUTES OF JAZZ WITH THE UNIQUE ELLA FITZGERALD
CD _____ ENTCD 226
Entertainers / '88 / Target/BMG.

75TH BIRTHDAY SALUTE
Tisket-a-tasket / Undecided / Don't worry 'bout me / Stairway to the stars / Five o'clock whistle / Cow cow boogie / Flying home / Oh lady be good / How high the moon / My happiness / Black coffee / Dream a little dream of me / Smooth sailin' / Rough ridin' / Goody goody / Angel eyes / Preview / Blue Lou / Lullaby of birdland / If you can't sing it, you'll have to swing it (Mr. Paganini) / I wished on the moon / Until the real thing comes along / Ol' devil moon
CD _____ GRP 26192
GRP / Apr '93 / BMG / New Note.

ALL THAT JAZZ
Dream a little dream of me / My last affair / Baby don't you get now / Oh look at me now / Jersey bounce / When your lover has gone / That ole devil called love / All that jazz / Just when we're falling in love / Good morning heartache / Little jazz / Nearness of you
CD _____ CD 2310938
Pablo / Nov '95 / Jazz Music / Complete/Pinnacle.

AT THE MONTREUX JAZZ FESTIVAL 1975
Caravan / Satin doll / Teach me tonight / Wave / It's all right with me / Let's do it / How high the moon / Girl from Ipanema / T'ain't nobody's business if I do
CD _____ OJCCD 789
Original Jazz Classics / May '94 / Wellard / Jazz Music / Cadillac / Complete/Pinnacle.

AT THE OPERA HOUSE
It's all right with me / Don't cha go 'way mad / Bewitched, bothered and bewildered / Stompin' at the Savoy / These foolish things / Ill wind / Goody goody / Moonlight in Vermont / Lady be good
CD _____ 831 269-2
Verve / Jan '94 / PolyGram.

BASIN STREET BLUES
Basin Street blues / Starlit hour / We can't go on this way / Stairway to the stars / Lover come back to me / Is there somebody else / Tisket-a-tasket / Sing song swing / That old black magic / Sugar blues / It's a blue world / Flying home / Who ya hunchin' / Chewing gum / Goin' and gettin' it / I wanna be a rug cutter / Don't be that way / Can't we be friends / Cheek to cheek / Fine romance / Moonlight in Vermont / Foggy day
CD _____ CDGRF 064
Tring / Jun '92 / Tring / Prism.

BEST IT'S YET TO COME (Fitzgerald, Ella & Nelson Riddle)
I wonder where our love has gone / Don't be that way / God bless the child / You're driving me crazy / Goodbye / Any old time / Autumn in New York / Best is yet to come / Deep purple / Somewhere in the night
CD _____ CD 2312138
Pablo / Apr '92 / Jazz Music / Cadillac / Complete/Pinnacle.

BEST OF ELLA FITZGERALD
Tisket-a-tasket / Stairway to the stars / Into each life some rain must fall / it's only a paper moon / Flying home / (I love you) for sentimental reasons / Lady be good / How high the moon / Basin Street blues / My one and only love / I've got the world on a string / Walkin' by the river / Lover come back to me / Mixed emotions / Smooth sailin' / If you can't sing it, you'll have to swing it (Mr. Paganini) / I wished on the moon / That old black magic / It's too soon to know / Tender trap
CD _____ MCBD 19521
MCA / Apr '95 / BMG.

BEST OF ELLA FITZGERALD
Dreamer / Fine and mellow / Street of dreams / This love that I've found / How long has this been going on / You're blase / Honeysuckle rose / I'm walkin' / I'm gettin' sentimental over you / Don't be that way
CD _____ PACD 24054212

Pablo / Apr '94 / Jazz Music / Cadillac / Complete/Pinnacle.

BEST OF ELLA FITZGERALD
CD _____ DLCD 4005
Dixie Live / Mar '95 / Magnum Music Group.

BEST OF THE SONGBOOKS - BALLADS
CD _____ 521867-2
Verve / Aug '94 / PolyGram.

BEST OF THE SONGBOOKS, THE
CD _____ 519804-2
Verve / Dec '93 / PolyGram.

BIG BOY BLUE
Big boy blue / Dedicated to you / You showed me the way / Cryin' mood / Love is the thing so they say / All over nothing at all / If you ever should leave / Everyone's wrong but me / Deep in the heart of the south / Just a simple melody / I got a guy / Holiday in Harlem / Rock it for me / I want to be happy / Dipsy doodle / If dreams come true / Hallelujah / Bei mir bist du schon / It's my turn now / 'S wonderful / I was doing all right / Tisket-a-tasket
CD _____ CDGRF 091
Tring / '93 / Tring / Prism.

CHRONOLOGICAL ELLA FITZGERALD 1937-38
Big boy blue / Dedicated to you / You showed me the way / Cryin' mood / Love is the thing so they say / All over nothing at all / If you ever should leave / Everyone's wrong but me / Deep in the heart of the south / Just a simple melody / I've got a guy / Holiday in Harlem / Rock it for me / I want to be happy / Dipsy doodle / If dreams came true / Hallelujah / Bei mir bist du schon / It's my turn now / 'S wonderful / I was doing all right / Tisket-a-tasket
CD _____ CLASSIC 506
Classics / Apr '90 / Discovery / Jazz Music.

CLAP HANDS, HERE COMES CHARLIE
CD _____ 835 646-2
Verve / Mar '90 / PolyGram.

CLASSICS 1941-44
CD _____ CLASSICS 840
Classics / Nov '95 / Discovery / Jazz Music.

CLASSY PAIR, A (Fitzgerald, Ella & Count Basie)
I'm getting sentimental over you / Organ grinder swing / Just a sittin' and a rockin' / My kind of trouble is you / Ain't misbehavin' / Some other Spring / Teach me tonight / Don't worry 'bout me / Honeysuckle rose / Sweet Lorraine / Please don't talk about me when I'm gone
CD _____ J33J 20057
Pablo / Apr '86 / Jazz Music / Cadillac / Complete/Pinnacle.

COLE PORTER SONG BOOK VOLS. 1 AND 2 (2CD Set)
All through the night / Anything goes / Miss Otis regrets / Too darn hot / In the still of the night / I get a kick out of you / Do I love you / Always true to you in my fashion / Let's do it / Just one of those things / Every time we say goodbye / All of you / Begin the beguine / Get out of town / I am in love / From this moment on / I love Paris / You do something to me / Riding high / Easy to love / It's all right with me / Why can't you behave / What is this thing called love / You're the top / Love for sale / It's de-lovely / Night and day / Ace in the hole / So in love / I've got you under my skin / I concentrate on you / Don't fence me in
CD Set _____ 8219892/9902
Verve / Mar '93 / PolyGram.

COLE PORTER SONGBOOK VOL.1
CD _____ 8219892
Verve / Feb '93 / PolyGram.

COLE PORTER SONGBOOK VOL.2
CD _____ 8219902
Verve / Feb '93 / PolyGram.

COLLECTION
CD _____ COL 014
Collection / Apr '95 / Target/BMG.

COMPLETE RECORDINGS 1933-40, THE (3CD Set)
I'll chase the blues away / Love and kisses / Rhythm and romance / Crying my heart out for you / Under the spell of the blues / When I get low I get high / Sing me a swing song / Little bit later on / Love you're just a laugh / Devoting my time to you / If you can't sing it, you'll have to swing it (Mr. Paganini) / Swinging on the reservation / I've got the spring fever blues / Vote for Mr. Rhythm / My melancholy baby / All my life / Goodnight my love / Oh yes take another guess / Did you mean it / My last affair / Organ grinder swing / Shine / Darktown strutter's ball / Big boy blues / Dedicated to you / Wake up and live / You showed me the way / Cryin' mood / Love is the thing so they say / Just a simple melody / I got a guy / Holiday in Harlem / Rock it for me / I want to be happy / Hallelujah / Tisket-a-tasket / Heart of mine / I'm just a jitterbug / All over nothing at all / If you ever should leave / Everyone's wrong but me / Deep in the heart of the south / Bei mir bist du schon / It's my turn now / 'S Wonderful / I

was doing all right / This time it's real / What do you know about love / You can't be mine (and someone else's too) / We can't go on this way / Saving myself for you / If you only knew / Strictly from Dixie / Woe is me / Pack up your sins and go to the devil / Mac-Pherson is rehearsin' / Everybody step / Ella / Wacky dust / Gotta pebble in my shoe / I can't stop loving you / I let a tear fall in the river / FDR Jones / I take each move you make / It's foxy / I found my yellow basket / Undecided / T'aint what you do / One side of me / My heart belongs to Daddy
CD Set _____ CDAFS 1020-3
Affinity / Oct '93 / Charly / Cadillac / Jazz Music.

COMPLETE SONGBOOKS, THE
CD Set _____ 519832-2
Verve / Dec '93 / PolyGram.

CONCERT YEARS, THE (4 CDST)
CD Set _____ 4 PACD 4414
Pablo / May '95 / Jazz Music / Cadillac / Complete/Pinnacle.

DAYDREAM: THE BEST OF THE DUKE ELLINGTON SONGBOOK
CD _____ 5272232
Verve / Jun '95 / PolyGram.

DIGITAL III AT MONTREUX (Fitzgerald, Ella/Count Basie/Joe Pass)
I can't get started (with you) / Good mileage / Ghost of a chance / Flying home / I cover the waterfront / Li'l darlin' / In your own sweet way / Oleo
CD _____ CD 2308223
Pablo / May '94 / Jazz Music / Cadillac / Complete/Pinnacle.

DREAM DANCING (Fitzgerald, Ella & Cole Porter)
Dream dancing / I've got you under my skin / I concentrate on you / My heart belongs to Daddy / Love for sale / So near and yet so far / Down in the depths / After you / Just one of those things / I get a kick out of you / All of you / Anything goes / At long last love / C'est magnifique / Without love
CD _____ CD 2310 814
Pablo / May '94 / Jazz Music / Cadillac / Complete/Pinnacle.

EASY LIVIN' (Fitzgerald, Ella & Joe Pass)
CD _____ CD 2310921
Pablo / Oct '92 / Jazz Music / Cadillac / Complete/Pinnacle.

ELLA A NICE
Night and day / Get out of town / Easy to love / You do something to me / Body and soul / Man I love / Porgy / Bossa scene / Girl from Ipanema / Fly me to the moon / O nosso amor / Cielito lindo / Magdalena / Aqua de beber / Summertime / They can't take that away from me / Mood indigo / Do nothin' 'til you hear me / It don't mean a thing if it ain't got that swing / Something / St. Louis blues / Close to you / Put a little love in your heart
CD _____ OJCCD 442
Original Jazz Classics / Feb '92 / Wellard / Jazz Music / Cadillac / Complete/Pinnacle.

ELLA ABRAÇA JOBIM
CD _____ CD 2630201
Pablo / Oct '92 / Jazz Music / Cadillac / Complete/Pinnacle.

ELLA AND LOUIS (Fitzgerald, Ella & Louis Armstrong)
Can't we be friends / Isn't this a lovely day (to be caught in the rain) / Moonlight in Vermont / They can't take that away from me / Under a blanket of blue / Foggy day / Tenderly / Stars fell on Alabama / Nearness of you / April in Paris / Cheek to cheek
CD _____ 825 373-2
Verve / Sep '85 / PolyGram.

ELLA AND LOUIS AGAIN (Fitzgerald, Ella & Louis Armstrong)
CD _____ 825 374-2
Verve / Feb '93 / PolyGram.

ELLA AND OSCAR (Fitzgerald, Ella & Oscar Peterson)
Mean to me / How long has this been going on / When your lover has gone / More than you know / There's a lull in my life / Midnight sun / I hear music / Street of dreams / April in Paris / Hear music
CD _____ CD 2310759
Pablo / '94 / Jazz Music / Cadillac / Complete/Pinnacle.

ELLA FITZGERALD
Timeless Treasures / Oct '94 / THE. CD 109

ELLA FITZGERALD
CD _____ 22708
Music / Nov '95 / Target/BMG.

ELLA FITZGERALD
Ain't nobody's business but mine / Smooth sailing / A-tisket-a-tasket / Ver mir du schoen / Airmail special / Stardust / But not for me / Flying home / Basin Street blues / How high the moon
CD _____ MCD 33682
MCA / Nov '95 / BMG.

ELLA FITZGERALD (2CD Set)
CD Set _____ R2CD 4018
Deja Vu / Jan '96 / THE.

ELLA FITZGERALD & HER FAMOUS ORCHESTRA
CD _____ JZCD 332
Suisa / Jan '93 / Jazz Music / THE.

ELLA FITZGERALD & JOE PASS AGAIN (Fitzgerald, Ella & Joe Pass)
I ain't got nothin' but the blues / 'Tis autumn / My old flame / That old feeling / Rain / I didn't know about you / You took advantage of me / I've got the world on a string / All too soon / One I love (belongs to somebody else) / Solitude / Nature boy / Tennessee waltz / One note samba
CD _____ CD 2310722
Pablo / Oct '93 / Jazz Music / Cadillac / Complete/Pinnacle.

ELLA FITZGERALD & THE CHICK WEBB ORCHESTRA
CD _____ JZCD 331
Suisa / Jan '93 / Jazz Music / THE.

ELLA FITZGERALD 1957-58
CD _____ CD 53159
Giants Of Jazz / Jan '94 / Target/BMG / Cadillac.

ELLA FITZGERALD COLLECTOR'S EDITION
CD _____ DVAD 6032
Deja Vu / Apr '95 / THE.

ELLA FITZGERALD GOLD (2CD Set)
CD Set _____ D2CD 4018
Deja Vu / Jun '95 / THE.

ELLA FITZGERALD SINGS THE ELLINGTON SONGBOOK (3CD Set)
CD _____ 837 035-2
Verve / Apr '89 / PolyGram.

ELLA FITZGERALD WITH THE CHICK WEBB BAND
Harlem Congo (white) / I gotta guy / I'll chase the blues away / If you can't sing it, you'll have to swing it (Mr. Paganini) / Squeeze me / Vote for Mr. Rhythm / If dreams come true / Down home rag (sweatman) / Crying my heart out for you / Sing me a swing song / Liza (all the clouds'll roll away) / Tisket-a-tasket / Little bit later on / Strictly love / Rock it for me / Everybody step / Sweet Sue, just you / Pack up your sins and go to the devil / When I get low I get high / Midnite in Harlem / Love you're just a laugh / Take another guess
CD _____ PASTCD 9762
Flapper / Aug '91 / Pinnacle.

ELLA IN LONDON
Sweet Georgia Brown / They can't take that away from me / Every time we say goodbye / It don't mean a thing if it ain't got that swing / You've got a friend / Lemon drop / Very thought of you / Happy blues / Man I love
CD _____ CD 2310711
Pablo / Apr '94 / Jazz Music / Cadillac / Complete/Pinnacle.

ELLA IN ROME 1958
CD _____ 8354542
Verve / Mar '93 / PolyGram.

ELLA SWINGS BRIGHTLY WITH NELSON
CD _____ 5193472
Verve / Mar '93 / PolyGram.

ELLA SWINGS EASY
CD _____ CDMOIR 508
Memoir / Jan '95 / Target/BMG.

ELLA SWINGS GENTLY WITH NELSON
CD _____ 5193482
Verve / Mar '93 / PolyGram.

ELLA SWINGS LIGHTLY
Little white lies / You hit the spot / What's your story Morning Glory / Just you, just me / As long as I live / Teardrops from my eyes / Gotta be this or that / Moonlight on the Ganges / My kinda love / Blues in the night / If I were a bell / You're an old smoothie / Little Jazz / You brought a new kind of love to me / Knock me a kiss / 720 in the books
CD _____ 5175352
Verve / Feb '88 / PolyGram.

ELLA WITH... (Feat. Mills Brothers/Chick Webb/Benny Goodman)
All over nothing at all / If you ever should leave / It's my turn now / Everyone's wrong but me / Bei mir bist du schon / Little bit later on / I want to be happy / Hallelujah / Crying my heart out for you / If you can't sing it, you'll have to swing it (Mr. Paganini) / Holiday in Harlem / Cryin' mood / Devoting my time to you / Rock it for me / At the Darktown strutter's ball / Sing me a swing song / Vote for Mr. Rhythm / Just a simple melody / Swinging on the reservation / Under the spell of the blues / I got the spring fever blues / Rhythm and romance / If dreams come true / Take another guess / Dipsy doodle / I've got a guy / When I get low I get high / Did you mean it / Dedicated to you / Big boy blues / Goodnight my love
CD Set _____ CD AJD 055
Living Era / Feb '88 / Koch.

ELLA, BILLIE, SARAH (Fitzgerald, Ella/Billie Holiday/Sarah Vaughan)
Oh Johnny oh Johnny oh / Blue Lou / Diga diga doo / I want the waiter (with the water) / Limehouse blues / T'aint what you do / Traffic jam / I'm confessin' that I love you / Breakin' down / Swing out / Swing brother

swing / Do nothin' 'til you hear from me /
You're driving me crazy / Lover man / Nobody's business / My man (mon homme) /
They can't take that away from me / He's
funny that way / Don't be late / God bless
the child / Lover come back to me / Don't
explain / Same old story / Detour ahead /
Billie's blues / Miss Brown top you / It's you
or no one / Tenderly / Lord's prayer / What
a difference a day makes / Gentleman
friend / East of the sun and west of the
moon / Motherless child / One I love belongs somebody else / September / Time
after time / Hundred years from today /
Signing off / I cover the waterfront / Them
there eyes / No smokes / What more can a
woman do / Man to me
CD Set _____ TKOCDB 026
TKO / May '92 / TKO.

FINE AND MELLOW
Fine and mellow / I'm just a lucky so and
so / Ghost of a chance / Rockin' in rhythm
/ I'm in the mood for love / Round Midnight
/ I can't give you anything but love / Man I
love / Polka dots and moonbeams
CD _____ CD 2310829
Pablo / May '94 / Jazz Music / Cadillac /
Complete/Pinnacle.

FIRST LADY OF JAZZ
Tisket-a-tasket / Darktown Strutter's Ball / I
want to be happy / Everybody sing / If you
can't sing it, you'll have to swing it (Mr. Paganini) / Crying my heart out for you / Little
bit later on / If dreams come true / Rock it
for me / All over nothing at all / Sing me a
swing song / Where have I got to get high / I'll
chase the blues away / Holiday in Harlem /
I gotta guy / Everyone's wrong but me
CD _____ HADCD 154
Javelin / May '94 / THE / Henry Hadaway
Organisation.

FLYING HOME
CD _____ CDSGP 084
Prestige / Oct '93 / Total/BMG.

FOREVER GOLD
CD _____ ST 5008
Star Collection / Apr '95 / BMG.

FOREVER YOUNG
Shine / Dedicated to you / I want to be
happy / If dreams come true / Hallelujah /
Bei mir bist du schon / Tisket-a-tasket /
Saving myself for you / Ella / Undecided /
T'ain't what you do it's the way that you do
it) / My heart belongs to daddy / 'S Won-
derful / Goodnight my love / Organ grinders
swing / My last affair
CD _____ CDCD 1003
Charly / Mar '93 / Charly / THE / Cadillac.

HALLELUJAH
Hallelujah / Coochi coochi coo / Sing song
swing / Little white lies / I'm up a tree / Tis-
ket-a-tasket / Undecided / One side of me
/ Baby, what else can I do / Sugar pie / Ella
/ Dipsy doodle
CD _____ SMS 49
Carlton Home Entertainment / Apr '92 /
Carlton Home Entertainment.

IN STOCKHOLM 1957
CD _____ TAX 37032
Tax / Aug '94 / Jazz Music / Wellard /
Cadillac.

INCOMPARABLE ELLA, THE
Lady is a tramp / Manhattan / Very thought
of you / From this moment on / I've got you
under my skin / Foggy day / With a song in
my heart / Cheek to cheek / I've got a crush
on you / Night and day / Every time we say
goodbye / It's only a paper moon / I get a
kick out of you / I got rhythm / My funny
valentine / That old black magic
CD _____ 835610-2
PolyGram TV / Apr '94 / PolyGram.

INTIMATE ELLA, THE
CD _____ 839 838-2
Verve / Mar '90 / PolyGram.

JAZZ AT THE PHIL
CD _____ TAXCD 3703
Tax / Feb '89 / Jazz Music / Wellard /
Cadillac.

**JAZZ COLLECTOR EDITION (5CD/MC
Set) (Fitzgerald, Ella/Louis Armstrong)**
CD Set _____ 15910
Laserlight / Jan '92 / Target/BMG.

JAZZ MASTERS
CD _____ 5198222
Verve / Apr '93 / PolyGram.

**JAZZ MASTERS (Fitzgerald, Ella & Louis
Armstrong)**
CD _____ 5218512
Verve / Feb '94 / PolyGram.

JAZZ PORTRAITS
If you can't sing it, you'll have to swing it
(Mr. Paganini) / You're just a laugh /
Swinging on the reservation / I got the
spring fever blues / Rock it for me / Holiday
in Harlem / Cryin' mood / Just a simple melody / Love is the thing so they say / You
showed me the way / All my life / If dreams
come true / Take another guess / Pack up your
sins and go to the devil / I can reach even you make /
Sugar pie / I got a guy
CD _____ CD 14524
Jazz Portraits / May '94 / Jazz Music.

JEROME KERN SONGBOOK
Let's begin / Fine romance / All the things
you are / I'll be hard to handle / You
couldn't be cuter / She didn't say yes / I'm
old fashioned / Remind me / Way you look
tonight / Yesterdays / Can't help lovin' dat
man / Why was I born
CD _____ 825 669-2
Verve / Oct '92 / PolyGram.

JOHNNY MERCER SONGBOOK, THE
Too marvellous for words / Early Autumn /
Day in, day out / Laura / This time the
dream is on me / Skylark / Single-o / Something's gotta give / Travellin' light / Midnight sun / Dream / I remember you / Have
a woman loves a man
CD _____ 823 247-2
Verve / '92 / PolyGram.

LADY TIME
I'm walkin' / All or nothing at all / I never
had a chance / I cried for you / What will I
tell my heart / Since I fell for you / And the
angels sing / I'm confessin' that I love you
/ Mack the knife / That's my desire / I'm in
the mood for love
CD _____ OJCCD 864
Original Jazz Classics / Nov '95 / Wellard /
Jazz Music / Cadillac / Complete/Pinnacle.

**LEGENDARY DECCA RECORDINGS
1935-1955 (4 CDs)**
Undecided / Stairway to the stars / Five
o'clock whistle / Cow cow boogie / Flying
home / Stone cold dead in the market / You
won't be satisfied until you break my heart
/ I'm just a lucky so and so / I didn't mean
a word I said / Oh, lady be good / How high
the moon / My happiness / In the evening
when the sun goes down / Smooth sailing
/ Airmail special / You'll have to swing it /
Blue Lou / Lullaby of birdland / Hard
hearted Hannah / Frim fram sauce / Dream
a little dream of me / Can anyone explain /
Would you like to take a walk / Who walks
in when I walk out / Each life some rain
must fall / I'm making believe / I'm beginning to see the light / I still feel the same
about you / Petootie pie / Baby it's cold
outside / Don't cry, cry baby / Ain't nobody's business but my own / I'll never be free
/ It's only paper moon / (Gonna) Cry you out
of my heart / (I love you) For sentimental
reasons / It's a pity to say goodnight / Fairy
tales / I gotta have my baby back / Someone to watch over me / My one and only /
But not for me / Looking for a boy / I've got
a crush on you / Maybe / Soon / I'm glad
there is you / What is there to say / People
will say we're in love / Please be kind / Until
the real thing comes along / Makin
whoopee / Imagination / Stardust / My heart
belongs to Daddy / You leave me breathless / Baby, what else can I do / Nice work
if you can get it / Basin street blues / I've
got the world on a string / Goody goody /
Angel eyes / Gordon Jenkins / Happy talk /
I'm gonna wash that man right out of my
hair / Black coffee / I wished on the moon
/ Bob Haggart / Sunday kind of love / That's
my desire / Thanks for the Memory / It
might as well be spring / You'll never know
/ I can't get started / That old black magic
/ Between the devil and the deep blue sea
/ Toots camarata / (Love is) the tender trap
/ My one and only love
CD Set _____ GRP 46482
GRP / Nov '95 / BMG / New Name.

**LEGENDS IN MUSIC - ELLA
FITZGERALD**
CD _____ LECD 090
Wisepack / Sep '94 / THE / Conifer.

LET'S GET TOGETHER
CD _____ 17003
Laserlight / Jul '94 / Target/BMG.

LOVE & KISSES
CD _____ 17009
Laserlight / Aug '93 / Target/BMG.

**MY HAPPINESS (Fitzgerald, Ella & Bing
Crosby)**
CD _____ PARCD 002
Parrot / Jan '96 / THE / Wellard / Jazz
Music.

MY HEART BELONGS TO DADDY
CD _____ MU 5040
Musketeer / Oct '92 / Koch.

**NEWPORT JAZZ FESTIVAL LIVE AT
CARNEGIE HALL, JULY 5, 1973 (2CD
Set)**
I've gotta me / Good morning heartache
/ Miss Otis regrets / Medley: Don't worry
about me/These foolish things / Any old
blues / Tisket-a-tasket / Indian summer /
Smooth sailin' / You turned the tables on
me / Nice work if you can get it / I've got a
crush on you / Medley: I can't get started /
Young man with the horn / Round Midnight
/ Star dust / C Jam blues / Medley: Taking
a chance on love / I'm in the mood for love
/ Lemon drop / Some of these days /
People
CD Set _____ C 2K66809
Sony Jazz / Aug '95 / Sony.

**NICE WORK IF YOU CAN GET IT
(Fitzgerald, Ella & Andre Previn)**
Let's call the whole thing off / How long has
this been going on / Who cares / I've got a
crush on you / Someone to watch over me

/ Embraceable you / They can't take that
away from me / Foggy day / But not for me
/ Nice work if you can get it
CD _____ CD 2312140
Pablo / '94 / Jazz Music / Cadillac / Com-
plete/Pinnacle.

PABLO YEARS, THE (20 CD Box Set)
CD Set _____ PACD 020
Pablo / Jun '93 / Jazz Music / Cadillac /
Complete/Pinnacle.

**PERFECT MATCH, A (Fitzgerald, Ella &
Count Basie)**
Please don't talk about me when I'm gone
/ Sweet Georgia Brown / Some other Spring
/ Make me rainbows / After you've gone /
Round Midnight / Fine and mellow / You've
changed / Honeysuckle rose / St. Louis
blues / Basella
CD _____ CD 2312110
Pablo / Apr '94 / Jazz Music / Cadillac /
Complete/Pinnacle.

ROCK IT FOR ME
CD _____ JTM 8104
Jazztime / Apr '94 / Discovery / BMG.

RODGERS AND HART SONGBOOK
Have you met Miss Jones / You took advantage of me / Ship without a sail / To
keep my love alive / Dancing on the ceiling
/ Lady is a tramp / With a song in my heart
/ Manhattan / Johnny One Note / I wish I
were in love again / Spring is here / I never
entered my mind / This can't be love / Thou
swell / My romance / Where or when / Little
girl blue / Give it back to the Indians / Ten
cents a dance / There's a small hotel / I
didn't know what time it was / Everything
I've got / I could write a book / Blue room
/ My funny valentine / Bewitched / Mountain greenery / Wait till you see her / Lover
/ Isn't it romantic / Here in my arms / Blue
moon / My heart stood still / I've got five
dollars
CD _____ 8215792
Verve / Feb '92 / PolyGram.

RODGERS AND HART SONGBOOK II
CD _____ 8215802
Verve / Feb '92 / PolyGram.

**ROYAL ROOST (Fitzgerald, Ella & Ray
Brown)**
CD _____ C&BCD 112
Cool 'n' Blue / Oct '93 / Jazz Music /
Discovery.

**SING ME A SWING SONG (Fitzgerald,
Ella & Chick Webb Orchestra)**
CD _____ JHR 73512
Jazz Hour / '91 / Target/BMG / Jazz
Music / Cadillac.

SING SONG SWING
CD _____ 17008
Laserlight / Jul '93 / Target/BMG.

SING SONG SWING
CD _____ CDCD 1203
Charly / Sep '94 / Charly / THE / Cadillac.

SOMEONE IN LOVE
CD _____ 5115242
Verve / Sep '93 / PolyGram.

**SONGBOOKS, THE (The Silver
Collection)**
Lady be good / Nice work if you can get it
/ Fascinating rhythm / All the things you are
/ Yesterdays / Can't help lovin' dat man /
Come rain or come shine / It's only a paper
moon / Over the rainbow / Laura / Skylark
/ This time the dream is on me / Puttin' on
the Ritz / Alexander's ragtime band / Cheek
to cheek / My funny Valentine / Lady is a
tramp / Have you met Miss Jones /
Manhattan
CD _____ 823 445-2
Verve / Nov '84 / PolyGram.

SPEAK LOVE
Speak love / Come love / There's no you /
I may be wrong, but I think you're wonderful
/ At last / Thrill is gone / Gone with the wind
/ Blue and sentimental / Girl talk / Georgia
on my mind
CD _____ CD 2310888
Pablo / Apr '94 / Jazz Music / Cadillac /
Complete/Pinnacle.

**STOCKHOLM CONCERT, 1966
(Fitzgerald, Ella & Duke Ellington)**
Imagine my frustration / Duke's place /
Satin doll / Something to live for / Wives and
lovers / So dance samba / Let's do it / Lover
man / Cotton tail
CD _____ CD 2308242
Pablo / May '94 / Jazz Music / Cadillac /
Complete/Pinnacle.

SWINGS
You got me singin' the blues / Angel eyes /
Lullaby of birdland / Tenderly / Do nothin'
'til you hear from me / April in Paris / I can't
give you anything but love / For sale /
Papa loves mambo / Lover come back to
me / Just one of those things / Air mail spe-
cial / I'm beginning to see the light / So-
phisticated lady / Old mother hubbard /
How high the moon
CD _____ BSTCD 9111
Best Compact Discs / Apr '94 / Complete/
Pinnacle.

**TAKE LOVE EASY (Fitzgerald, Ella & Joe
Pass)**
Take love easy / Once I loved / Don't be
that way / You're blase / Lush life / Foggy
day / Gee baby ain't I good to you / You go
to my head / I want to talk about you
CD _____ CD 2310702
Pablo / Jan '92 / Jazz Music / Cadillac /
Complete/Pinnacle.

**THANKS FOR THE MEMORY (50th
Anniversary Collection)**
I'm beginning to see the light / Stardust /
Nice work if you can get it / My heart be-
longs to daddy / Guy is a guy / Happy talk
/ Crying in the chapel / That old black magic
/ My man (mon homme) / How high the
moon / Oh Lady be Good / I'm gonna wash
that man right outa my hair / Can't help
lovin' dat man / It might as well be spring /
Imagination / Thanks for the memory
CD _____ PWKS 573
Carlton Home Entertainment / Apr '90 /
Carlton Home Entertainment.

WAR YEARS (1941-1947), THE
Jim / This love of mine / Somebody loves
me / You don't know what love is / Make
love to me / Mama come home / My heart
and I decided / He's my guy / Cow cow
boogie / Time alone will tell / Once too often
/ Into each life some rain must fall / I'm
making believe / Tears flowed like wine / I'm
confessin' that I love you / I'm beginning to
see the light / That's the way it is / It's only
a paper moon / Cry you out of my heart /
Kiss goodnight / Benny's coming home on
Saturday
CD _____ GRP 26282
GRP / Sep '94 / BMG / New Name.

WITH TOMMY FLANAGAN
CD _____ OJCCD 376
Original Jazz Classics / Feb '92 / Wellard /
Jazz Music / Cadillac / Complete/Pinnacle.

YOU'LL HAVE TO SWING
CD _____ JTM 8103
Jazztime / Apr '94 / Discovery / BMG.

YOUNG ELLA (4 CD Box Set)
Charly / Apr '95 / Charly / THE / Cadillac.

Fitzgerald, Patrick

**SAFETY PINS STUCK IN MY HEART
(The Very Best Of Patrik Fitzgerald)**
Banging and shouting / Safety pin stuck in
my heart / Work rest play reggae / Set we
free / Optimism reject / Buy me sell me /
Little dippers / Trendy / Backstreet boys /
Babysitter / Irrelevant battles / Cruellest
crime / Paranoid ward / Bingo crowd / Life
at the top / Ragged generation for real / Live
out my stars / George / All sewn up (Demo
Version) / Improve myself / Tonight 22 / Mr.
and Mrs. / Animal mentality / Mr. and Mrs.
23 / Superbeing / Waiting for the final cue /
Without sex / Pop star pop star
CD _____ CDPUNK 31
Anagram / Apr '94 / Pinnacle.

Fiuczynski, David

LUNAR CRUSH
Vog / Pacifica / Gloria ascending / Pineapple / Guest / Freelance Brown / Slow
blues for Fuzy's Mama / Lillies that fester /
122 St. Marks / Fima's sunrise
CD _____ R 279498
Gramavision / Jun '94 / Vital/SAM / ADA.

Five Americans

I SEE THE LIGHT
I see the light / Losing game / Goodbye / I
know they lie / Twist and shout / She's a-
my-own / Train / It's a crying shame / I'm
so glad / Don't blame me / Outcast / What'd
I say / Train (unissued version) / Good times
(unissued version)
CD _____ CDSC 6018
Sundazed / Apr '94 / Rollercoaster.

Five Blind Boys Of...

**DEEP RIVER (Five Blind Boys Of
Alabama & Clarence Fountain)**
Deep river (part one) / Don't play with God
/ Reminiscing / God said it / Look where he
brought me from / Down on bended knees
/ I believe in you / I'm getting better all the
time / Brother Moses / Every time I feel the
spirit / Just a closer walk with thee / Joy of
the love of Jesus / Deep river (part two)
CD _____ 7559614412
Elektra Nonesuch / Nov '92 / Warner Music.

**I BROUGHT HIM WITH ME (Five Blind
Boys Of Alabama)**
Rain / He's got what I want / Do Lord / Better all the time / Listen to the lambs / If I
had a hammer / No dope / Hush / King Jesus / Walking Jerusalem / Lord will make a
way / Praying time / Amazing grace / Looking back
CD _____ 70010 870032
Private Music / Nov '95 / BMG.

**OH LORD STAND BY ME/ MARCHING
UP TO ZION (Five Blind Boys Of
Alabama)**
Oh Lord / Stand by me / You got to move
/ Lord have mercy / Living for Jesus / Take
my hand, precious Lord / I'll fly away / This

may be the last time / Alone and motherless / Since I met Jesus / Our father's praying ground / Broken hearts of mine / Here am I / Marching up to Zion / Servant's prayer amen / Count me in / When I lost my mother / There is a fountain / I've been born again / He'll be there / Think about me / Does Jesus care / Fix it Jesus / Goodbye mother / I've got a home
CD _____ CDCHD 341
Ace / Nov '93 / Pinnacle / Cadillac / Complete/Pinnacle.

SERMON, THE (Five Blind Boys Of Alabama)
Sermon / All the way / I'll fly away / Without the help of Jesus / I'm on the battlefield / Heavenly light / Sit down servant / Standing by the bedside / When I need him most / Precious Lord / This may be the last time / Our father's praying ground / Marching up to Zion / God's promise / You got to move / Old time religion / Does Jesus care / Swingin' on the golden gate / I cried / Hallelujah / Golden bells / Heaven on my mind / I'm going through / Fix it Jesus / I've been born again / When death comes / In the garden
CD _____ CDCHD 479
Ace / Jul '93 / Pinnacle / Cadillac / Complete/Pinnacle.

Five Blind Boys Of...
JESUS IS A ROCK (Five Blind Boys Of Mississippi)
Let's have a church / I'm willing to run / Leave you in the hands of the Lord / Where there's a will / You don't know / I'm a soldier / Jesus loves me / I'm a-rolling / My robe will fit me / All over me / Somebody's mother / No need to cry / I never heard a man / Oh why / Don't forget the bridge / Waiting at the river / Jesus is a rock in a weary land / I've been weeping for a mighty long time / One talk with Jesus / I haven't been home in a mighty long time
CD _____ CPCD 8086
Charly / Apr '95 / Charly / THE / Cadillac.

Five Day Train
ROUGH MARMALADE
CD _____ HBG 123/1
Background / Apr '93 / Background.

Five Eight
ANGRIEST MAN, THE
CD _____ SKY 3101CD
Sky / Sep '94 / Koch.

WEIRDO
CD _____ SKY 3102CD
Sky / May '94 / Koch.

Five Keys
DREAM ON
I burned your letter / How can I forget you / Gonna be too late / I took your love for a toy / Dancing senorita / Dream on / Your teeth and your tongue / I've always been a dreamer / You broke the nest / Maw / Rosetta / Ziggus / I can't escape from you / Will you / Wrapped in a dream / Do something for me / Valley of love / No say's my heart / That's what you're doing to me / Now I know I love you / Stop your crying / Girl you better stop it / I'll never stop loving you / Bimbo
CD _____ CDCHARLY 265
Charly / Mar '91 / Charly / THE / Cadillac.

Five Knuckle Chuckle
CHARLIE HORSE
CD _____ BMCD 079
Black Mark / Dec '95 / Plastic Head.

Five Royales
FIVE ROYALES, THE
I know it's hard but it's fair / Miracle of love / My sugar sugar / When you walked through the door / School girl / Get som.thing out of it / Tell me you care / Wonder where your love has gone / It hurts inside / Mine forever more / One mistake / Women about to make me go crazy
CD _____ KCD 678
King/Paddle Wheel / Mar '90 / New Note.

REAL THINGS, THE
Baby don't do it / Come over here / Laundromat blues / All righty / I want to thank you / Send me somebody
CD _____ RBD 802
Mr. R&B / Apr '91 / Swift / CM / Wellard.

SING FOR YOU
Your only love / Real thing / Don't let it be in vain / Do the cha cha cherry / Double or nothing / Mohawk squaw / How I wonder / I need your lovin' baby / Feeling is real / Tell the truth / My wants for love / Slummer the slum / Do unto you / I ain't getting caught / When I get like this / Monkey hips and rice
CD _____ KCD 0616
King/Paddle Wheel / Mar '93 / New Note.

Five Stairsteps
BEST OF THE FIVE STAIRSTEPS
You waited too long / Come back / Behind curtains / Under the spell of your love /

Baby make me feel so good / Love's happening / Little young lover / Ooh child / Because I love you / I love you stop / I feel a song in my heart / Hush child / Look out / World of fantasy / Danger, she's a stranger / Ooo baby baby / Don't change your love / We must be in love / Stay close to me / I'm the one who loves you / Dear Prudence / Didn't it look so easy / Peace is gonna come / Easy way / Snow
CD _____ NEMCD 696
Sequel / Oct '94 / BMG.

Five Star
FIVE STAR
Slightest touch / System addict / Can't wait another minute / Another weekend / With every heartbeat / Stay out of my life / Rain or shine / Find the time / R.S.V.P. / Love take over / If I say yes / Let me be the one / Strong as steel / There's a brand new world / Rock my world / All fall down
CD _____ 74321 18325-2
Ariola Express / Feb '94 / BMG.

HEART AND SOUL
CD _____ TRIFSCD 2
Tent / Nov '95 / Total/BMG.

Five-a-Slide
STRIKE UP THE BAND
CD _____ BLCD 760509
Black Lion / Oct '93 / Jazz Music / Cadillac / Wellard / Koch.

Five-O
IF U R NOT PART OV DA SOLUTION
CD _____ WRA 8129CD
Wrap / Apr '94 / Koch.

Fix
COLD DAYS
CD _____ LF 078
Lost & Found / Mar '94 / Plastic Head.

Flack, Roberta
BEST OF ROBERTA FLACK - SOFTLY WITH THESE SONGS
First time ever I saw your face / Will you still love me tomorrow / Where is the love / Killing me softly / Feel like makin' love / Closer I get to you / More than everything / Only heaven can wait (for love) / Back together again / Making love / Tonight, I celebrate my love / Oasis / And so it goes / You know what it's like / Set the night to music / My foolish heart / Uh-uh ooh-ooh look out (here it comes)
CD _____ 756782498-2
Atlantic / Feb '94 / Warner Music.

BORN TO LOVE (Flack, Roberta & Peabo Bryson)
Tonight, I celebrate my love / Blame it on me / Heaven above / Born to love / Maybe You're lookin' like love to me / Can we find love again
CD _____ MUSCD 508
MCI / Nov '94 / Disc / THE.

CHAPTER TWO
Reverend Lee / Do what you gotta do / Just like a woman / Let it be me / Gone away / Until it's time for you to go / Impossible dream / Business goes on as usual
CD _____ 7567813732
Atlantic / Jan '96 / Warner Music.

FEEL LIKE MAKIN' LOVE
Feeling that glow / I wanted it too / I can see the sun in late December / Some gospel according to Mathew / Feel like makin' love / Mr. Magic / Early every midnight / Old heart break top ten / She's not blind
CD _____ 7567803332
Atlantic / Feb '91 / Warner Music.

FIRST TAKE
Compared to what / Angelitos negros / Our ages or our hearts / I told Jesus / Hey, that's no way to say goodbye / First time ever I saw your face / Tryin' times / Ballad of the sad young man
CD _____ 7567814462
Atlantic / Feb '91 / Warner Music.

I'M THE ONE
I'm the one / Till the morning comes / Love and let love / Never loved before / In the name of love / Ordinary man / Making love / Happiness / My love for you
CD _____ 7567815932
Atlantic / Jan '96 / Warner Music.

KILLING ME SOFTLY
Killing me softly / Jesse / No tears (In the end) / I'm the girl / River / Conversation love / When you smile / Suzanne
CD _____ 7567815402
Atlantic / Feb '91 / Warner Music.

QUIET FIRE
Go up Moses / Bridge over troubled water / Sunday and Sister Jones / See you then / Will you still love me tomorrow / To love somebody / Let them talk / Sweet bitter love
CD _____ 7567813782
Atlantic / Feb '91 / Warner Music.

ROBERTA
CD _____ 7567825972
Atlantic / Nov '94 / Warner Music.

SET THE NIGHT TO MUSIC
Waiting game / Set the night to music / When someone tears your heart in two / Something your heart has been telling me / You make me feel brand new / Unforgettable / Summertime / Natural thing / My foolish heart / Friend / Always
CD _____ 7567823212
Atlantic / Nov '91 / Warner Music.

Flacke, Ray
UNTITLED ISLAND
Squeeze the weazel / Untitled island / Wring that neck / Devoted to the dog / Main Street breakdown / Bandits on Bordbon / South Downs gallop / Raison d'etre / Going on after the theatre / Blarney's stoned / New land shining
CD _____ INCD 901149
Line / Mar '92 / CM / Grapevine / ADA / Conifer / Direct.

Flag Of Convenience
BEST OF STEVE DIGGLE & FLAG OF CONVENIENCE (The Secret Public Years 1981-1989) (Diggle, Steve & Flag Of Convenience)
Fifty Years comparative wealth / Shut out the light / Here comes the fire brigade / Life on the telephone / Picking up on audio sound / Other mans sin / Men from the city / Who is innocent / Drift away / Change / Longest life / Arrow has come / Keep on pushing (live) / Pictures in my mind / Last train to safety / Exiles / Can't stop the world / Shot down with a gun / Tragedy in Market Street / Tomorrows sunset / Life with the lions
CD _____ CDMGRAM 74
Anagram / Feb '94 / Pinnacle.

Flamin' Groovies
BUCKETFUL OF BRAINS
Shake some action / Talahassie lassie / Married woman / Get a shot of rhythm and blues / Little Queenie / You tore me down / Slow death / Get a shot rhythm and blues
CD _____ CZ 542
EMI / Apr '95 / EMI.

FLAMINGO
Gonna rock tonite / Comin' after me / Headin' for the Texas border / Sweet roll on down / Keep a knockin' / Second cousin / Childhood's end / Jailbait / She's falling apart / Roadhouse / Walking the dog / Something else / Hello / Josephine / Louie Louie / Rockin' pneumonia and the boogie woogie flu / Going out theme II
CD _____ REP 4020-WZ
Repertoire / Aug '91 / Pinnacle / Cadillac.

GROOVE IN
CD _____ 890011
New Rose / May '94 / Direct / ADA.

GROOVIES GREATEST, THE
CD _____ 7599259482
Sire / Jan '96 / Warner Music.

LIVE 1968/1970
CD _____ 842070
EVA / May '94 / Direct / ADA.

LIVE AT THE FESTIVAL OF THE SUN BARCELONA
CD _____ AIM 1051
Aim / Apr '95 / Direct / ADA / Jazz Music.

ONE NIGHT STAND
CD _____ AIM 1008CD
Aim / Oct '93 / Direct / ADA / Jazz Music.

SHAKE SOME ACTION
Shake some action / Sometimes / Yes it's true / St. Louis blues / You tore me down / Please please girl / Let the boy rock 'n' roll / Don't you lie to me / She said yeah / I'll cry alone / Misery / I say her / Teenage confidential / I can't hide
CD _____ AIM 1017CD
Aim / Oct '93 / Direct / ADA / Jazz Music.

SNEAKERS/ROCKFIELD SESSIONS
CD _____ COLLECT 12
Aim / Oct '93 / Direct / ADA / Jazz Music.

STEP UP
CD _____ AIM 1030CD
Aim / Oct '93 / Direct / ADA / Jazz Music.

TEENAGE HEAD LP
Teenage head / Evil hearted Ada / Dr. Boogie / Whiskey woman / High flyin' baby / City lights / Have you seen my baby / Yesterday's numbers / Rumble / Shakin' all over / That'll be the day / Around and around / Going out theme
CD _____ REP 4042-WZ
Repertoire / Aug '91 / Pinnacle / Cadillac.

Flaming Ember
WESTBOUND NO.9
Spinning wheel / Westbound no.9 / Mind, body and soul / Shades of green / Going in circles / Why don't you stay / Flashbacks and re-runs / This girl is a woman now / Stop the world (and let me off) / Heart on (loving you) / Where's all the joy / Empty

crowded room / I'm not my brother's keeper
CD _____ HDHCD 503
HDH / Apr '92 / Pinnacle.

Flaming Lips
CLOUDS TASTE METALLIC
CD _____ 9362459112
Warner Bros. / Sep '95 / Warner Music.

TELEPATHIC SURGERY
Drug machine / Michael time to wake up / Miracle on 42nd Street / U.F.O. story / Shaved gorilla / Begs and achin' / Right now / Hare Krishna stomp wagon / Chrome plated suicide / Redneck school of technology / Spontaneous combustion of John / Last drop of morning dew
CD _____ CDENV 523
Enigma / Feb '89 / EMI.

TRANSMISSIONS FROM THE SATELLITE HEART
Turn it on / Pilot can at the queer of God / Oh my pregnant head (Labia in the sunlight) / She don't use jelly / Chewin' the apple of your eye / Superhumans / Be my head / Moth in the incubator / #@#@#@ (Plastic Jesus) / When yer twenty two / Slow nerve action
CD _____ 936245334-2
Warner Bros. / Jun '93 / Warner Music.

Flamingoes
PLASTIC JEWELS
Disappointed / Teenage emergency / Safe / Try it on / Absent Fathers, violent sons / Winter / Scenester / Chosen few / Unstable / Suicide bridge / Last of the big spenders / It's been a thrill
CD _____ PANNCD 007
Pandemonium / Feb '95 / Vital.

Flamingos
I ONLY HAVE EYES FOR YOU
CD _____ NEMCD 609
Sequel / Apr '91 / BMG.

I'LL BE HOME
Someday someway / Golden teardrops / Cross over the bridge / Carried away / You ain't ready / Hurry home baby / Blues in the letter / On my merry way / Dream of a lifetime / If I could love you / I really don't want to know / I found a new baby / Kokomo / That's my baby (chicka boom) / Whispering stars / Chickie-um-bah / I'll be home / Kiss from your lips / Get with it / Nobody's love / Would I be crying / Shilly dilly / Stolen love
CD _____ CDINS 5072
Charly / Jun '93 / Charly / THE / Cadillac.

Flanagan & Allen
ARCHES AND UMBRELLAS
Music, maestro please / Umbrella song / Oi / Milking time in Switzerland / Nice people / New M.P. / Run rabbit run / (We're gonna hang out the) washing on the Siegfried Line / Sending out an S.O.S. for you / Down and out blues / Sport of kings / Home town / If a grey-haired lady says How's yer father / Free / Digging holes / F.D.R. Jones / Dreaming / How do you do Mr. Right / Crazy Gang at sea / Underneath the arches / Flanagan and Allen memories
CD _____ PASTCD 9720
Flapper / '90 / Pinnacle.

DOWN FORGET-ME-NOT LANE
Down Forget-me-not lane / I don't want to walk without you / Sierra Sue / We're gonna hang out the washing on the Siegfried Line / Let's be buddies / On the outside looking in / We'll smile again / There's a boy coming home on leave / Down every street / Are you having any fun / Rose O'Day / If a grey-haired lady says How's yer father / Don't ever walk in the shadows / Miss you / Round the back of the arches / I'm nobody's / F.D.R. Jones / What more can I say / Run rabbit run / Medley: Can't we meet again/A million tears/Underneath the a
CD _____ PLCD 533
President / Mar '93 / Grapevine / Target/ BMG / Jazz Music / President.

LET'S BE BUDDIES
Are you having any fun / Round the back of the arches / Let's be buddies / Smiths and the Jones / Don't ever walk in the shadows / Why don't you fall in love with me / Down forget-me-not lane / Corn silk / We'll smile again / What more can I say / Yesterday's dreams / Down every street / I don't want to walk without you / If a grey-haired lady says How's yer father / Umbrella man / Can't we meet again / Underneath the arches / Rose o'day / I'm nobody's baby / In a little rocky valley / On the outside looking in / Miss you / Washing on siegfried line / Million years
CD _____ RAJCD 832
Empress / Jul '94 / THE.

ORIGINAL PERFORMANCES 1932 - 1942
World War II air raid / We'll smile again / Don't ever walk in the shadows / Sport of kings / Memories / Wanderer, dreaming / Underneath the arches used to be / Memories #2 / Can't we meet again / Million tears / Un-

derneath the arches / Run rabbit run / We're gonna hang out the washing on the Siegfried Line / FDR Jones / If a grey-haired lady says How's yer father / There's a boy coming home on leave / In a little rocky valley/ Sierra Sue / I'm nobody's baby / Yesterday's dreams / Down forget-me-not-lane / Rose O'day / What more can I say / I don't want to walk without you / Miss you / Oi
CD _____ RPCD 322
Robert Parker Jazz / Nov '93 / Conifer.

UNDERNEATH THE ARCHES
Run rabbit run / Miss you / Smiths and the Jones / In a little rocky valley / Two very ordinary people / Down every street / Flying through the rain / F.D.R. Jones / On the outside looking in / Roll on tomorrow / There's a boy coming home on leave / Shine on harvest moon / We'll smile again / Underneath the arches
CD Set _____ CDDL 1209
Music For Pleasure / Jun '91 / EMI.

Flanagan, Kevin

ZANZIBAR (Flanagan, Kevin & Chris Ingham Quartet)
Don't look what we like that / Po-town / Walk between raindrops / Born to be blue / Pent-up house / Waiting for dusko / It's your dance / Gloryhound / Sleepin' bee / Zanzibar
CD _____ GBCD 2
Gray Brothers / Sep '95 / Pinnacle.

Flanagan, Ralph

LET'S DANCE WITH RALPH FLANAGAN (Flanagan, Ralph Orchestra)
CD _____ DAW 74
Magic / Jan '96 / Jazz Music / Swift / Wellard / Cadillac / Harmonia Mundi.

Flanagan, Tommy

3
CD _____ CD 20036
Pablo / May '86 / Jazz Music / Cadillac / Complete/Pinnacle.

3 FOR ALL (Flanagan, Tommy/Red Mitchell/Phil Woods)
Enja / Jan '95 / New Note / Vital/SAM. _____ ENJACD 308167

CATS, THE (Flanagan, Tommy, John Coltrane, Kenny Burrell)
Minor mishap / How long has this been going on / Eclypso / Solacium / Tommy's time
CD _____ OJCCD 079-2
Original Jazz Classics / Jun '86 / Wellard / Jazz Music / Cadillac / Complete/Pinnacle.

JAZZ POET
Raincheck / Lament / Willow weep for me / Caravan / That tired routine called love / Glad to be happy / St. Louis blues / Mean streets
CD _____ CDSJP 301
Timeless Jazz / Nov '89 / New Note.

LADY BE GOOD...FOR ELLA
CD _____ 521617-2
Groovin' High / Jun '94 / PolyGram.

LET'S
Let's / Mean what you say / To you / Bird song / Scratch / Thadrack / Child is born / Three in one / Quietude / Zec / Elusive
CD _____ ENJ 80402
Enja / Nov '93 / New Note / Vital/SAM.

MAGNIFICENT TOMMY FLANAGAN, THE
■■ _____ RCD 7059
Progressive / Oct '91 / Jazz Music.

MASTER TRIO
CD _____ PRCDSP 204
Prestige / May '94 / Total/BMG.

MONTREUX '77 (Flanagan, Tommy Trio)
CD _____ OJCCD 372
Original Jazz Classics / Nov '95 / Wellard / Jazz Music / Cadillac / Complete/Pinnacle.

YOU'RE ME (Flanagan, Tommy & Red Mitchell)
You're me / Darn that dream / What am I here for / When I have you / All the things you are / Milestones / Whisper not / There'll never be another you
CD _____ PHONTCD 7528
Phontastic / Apr '94 / Wellard / Jazz Music / Cadillac.

Flanders & Swann

AT THE DROP OF A HAT
Transport of delight / Song of reproduction / Gnu song / Design for living / Je suis les tenebreux / Songs for our time / Song of the weather / Reluctant cannibal / Greensleeves / Misalliance / Kokoraki (CD only) / Madeira m'dear / Too many cookers (CD only) / Vanessa (CD only) / Tried by the centre court (CD only) / Youth of the heart (CD only) / Hippopotamus song / Happy song (Not on CD) / Satellite moon (Not on CD) / Philogical waltz (Not on CD)
CD _____ CZ 515
EMI / Sep '92 / EMI.

AT THE DROP OF ANOTHER HAT
Gas man cometh / Sounding brass / Los Olivados / In the desert / Ill wind / First and

second law / All gall / Horoscope / Friendly duet / Bedstead men / By air / Slow train / Song of patriotic prejudice / Built up area (CD only) / In the bath (CD only) / Sea fever (CD only) / Hippo encore
CD _____ CZ 517
EMI / Sep '92 / EMI.

BESTIARY OF FLANDERS & SWANN, THE (2)
Warthog / Sea horse / Chameleon / Whale / Sloth / Rhinoceros / Twosome - Kang and Jag (Kangaroo tango and jaguar) / Dead ducks / Elephant / Armadillo / Spider / Duck billed Platypus/Humming bird/Portuguese man-o'war / Wild boar / Ostrich / Wompom / Twice shy / Commonwealth fair / P''P''B''''B''D'''''' / Paris / Ein kleine nachtmusik cha cha cha / Hundred song / Food for thought / Bed / Twenty tons of TNT / War of 14-18
CD _____ CZ 516
EMI / Sep '92 / EMI.

COMPLETE FLANDERS AND SWANN
Transport of delight / Song of reproduction / Gnu song / Design for living / Je suis les tenebreux / Songs for our time / Song of the weather / Reluctant cannibal / Greensleeves / Misalliance / Kokoraki / Madeira m'dear / Too many cookers / Vanessa / Tried by the centre court / Youth of the heart / Hippopotamus song / Gas man cometh / Sounding brass / Los olivados / In the desert / Ill wind / First and second law / All gall / Horoscope / Friendly duet / Bedstead men / By air / Slow train / Song of patriotic prejudice / Built up area / In the bath / Sea fever / Hippo encore / Warthog / Sea horse / Chameleon / Whale / Sloth / Rhinoceros / Twosome - Kang and Jag / Dead ducks / Elephant / Armadillo / Spider / Threesome / Wild boar / Ostrich / Wompom / Twice shy / Commonwealth fair / Paris / Eine kleine nachtmusik cha cha cha / Hundred song / Food for thought / Bed / Twenty tons of TNT / War of 14-18
CD Set _____ CDFSB 1
EMI / Aug '91 / EMI.

TRANSPORT OF DELIGHT, A (The Best Of Flanders & Swann) (Flanders, Michael & Donald Swann)
act 1: Introduction / Transport of delight / Song of reproduction / Gnu song / Songs for our time, Philological waltz, Satellite moon, Happy / Song of the weather / Greensleeves / Misalliance / Madeira m'dear / Hippopotamus song / Act 2: introduction / All gall / Horoscope / Gas man cometh / Sounding brass / Ill wind / First and second law / By air / Song of patriotic prejudice / Hippo encore / Encore / Wompon
CD _____ CDGO 2061
EMI / Aug '94 / EMI.

Flash

FLASH
CD _____ OW S2117796
One Way / Sep '94 / Direct / ADA.

IN THE CAN
CD _____ OW S2156841
One Way / Sep '94 / Direct / ADA.

OUT OF OUR HANDS
CD _____ OW S2117414
One Way / Sep '94 / Direct / ADA.

Flat Duo Jets

FLAT DUO JETS
CD _____ DOG 004CD
Wild Dog / Sep '94 / Koch.

GO GO HARLEM BABY
CD _____ SKY 75031
Sky / Sep '94 / Koch.

IN STEREO
CD _____ SKY 75032CD
Sky / Sep '94 / Koch.

WHITER TREES
CD _____ SKY 75033
Sky / Sep '94 / Koch.

Flatischler, Reinhard

KETU
Opening the clyde / Primal forces / Ketu / Rhythm changes / Reunion of cultures / Suar agung / Taiko convocation / Dance of the magic / Closing the cycle
CD _____ VBR 21172
Vera Bra / Feb '94 / Pinnacle / New Note.

Flatlanders

MORE A LEGEND THAN A BAND
Dallas / Tonight I'm gonna go downtown / You've never seen me cry / She had everything / Rose from the mountain / One day at a time / Jolie blon / Down in my home-town / Bhagavan decreed / Heart you left behind / Keeper of the mountain / Stars in my life / One more road
CD _____ SSCD 34
Rounder / '90 / CM / Direct / ADA / Cadillac.

Flatley, Michael

MICHAEL FLATLEY
CD _____ BUA 9501CD
BUA / Apr '95 / ADA.

Flatt & Scruggs

DON'T GET ABOVE YOUR RAISIN' (Flatt, Lester & Earl Scruggs)
CD _____ SSCD 08
Rounder / Feb '94 / CM / Direct / ADA / Cadillac.

FLATT AND SCRUGGS 1948-1959 (4CD Set) (Flatt, Lester & Earl Scruggs)
God loves his children / I'm going to make Heaven my home / We'll meet again sweetheart / My cabin in Caroline / Baby blue eyes / Bouquet in Heaven / Down the road / Why don't you tell me so / I'll never shed another tear / No mother or dad / Is it too late now / Foggy mountain breakdown / Cora is gone / Preaching, praying, singing / Pain in my heart / Rollin' in my sweet baby's arms / Back to the cross / Farewell blues / Old salty dog blues / Take me in a lifeboat / Will the roses bloom / I'm head over heels in love / I'm waiting to hear you call me darling / Old home town / I'll stay around / We can't be darlings anymore / Jimmie Brown the newsboy / Somehow tonight / Don't get above your raising / I'm working on a road / He took your place / I've lost you / Tis sweet to be remembered / I'm gonna settle down / Earl's breakdown / I'm lonesome and blue / Over the hills to the poorhouse / My darling's last goodbye / Get in Line with brother / Brother I'm getting ready to go / Why did you wander / Flint Hill special / Thinking about you / If I should wander back tonight / Dim lights, thick smoke / Dear old Dixie / Reunion in Heaven / Pray for the boys / I'll go stepping too / I'd rather be alone / Foggy mountain chimes / Some one took my place with you / Mother prays loud in her sleep / That old book of mine / Your love is like a flower / Be ready for tomorrow may never come / Till the end of the world rolls around / You're not a drop in the bucket / Don't that road look rough and rocky / Foggy mountain special / You can feel it on your soul / Old fashioned preacher / Before I met you / I'm gonna sleep with one eye open / Randy Lynn rag / On my mind / Blue Ridge cabin home / Some old day / It won't be long / No mother in this world / Gone home / Bubbling in my soul / Joy bells / What's good for you / No doubt about it / Who will sing for me / Give mother my crown / Six white horses / Shuckin' the corn / I'll take the blame / Don't let your deal go down / Hundred years from now / Give me the flowers while I'm living / Is there room for me / Let those brown eyes smile at me / I won't be hanging around / I don't care anymore / Big black train / Mama's and daddy's little girl / Crying alone / Million years ago
CD Set _____ BCD 15472
Bear Family / Jan '94 / Rollercoaster / Direct / CM / Swift / ADA.

FLATT AND SCRUGGS 1959-1963 (5CD Set) (Flatt, Lester & Earl Scruggs)
Angel band / When the angels carry me home / I'll never be lonesome again / Get on the road to glory / Take me in your lifeboat / Bubbling in my soul / Heaven / Joy bells / Give me flowers while I'm living / You can feel it in your soul / Give mother my crown / Great historical bum / I've lost you forever / Polka on a banjo / All I want is you / I still miss someone / Momma sweet home (Instrumental) / Fireball mail / Cripple creek (Instrumental) / Reuben (Instrumental) / John Henry (Instrumental) / Cumberland gap (Instrumental) / Lonesome road blues (Instrumental) / Sally Goodin (Instrumental) / Little darlin', pal of mine (Instrumental) / Sally Ann (Instrumental) / Bugle call rag (Instrumental) / I ain't gonna work tomorrow / If I should wander back tonight / Cold, cold loving / Welcome to the club / False hearted lover (Instrumental) / Picking in the wildwood (Instrumental) / Homestead on the farm / Foggy mountain top / You are my flower / Forsaken love / Storms are on the ocean / Gathering flowers from the hillside / Worried man blues / On the rock where Moses stood / Keep on the sunny side / Jimmie brown the newsboy / Just ain't / Where will I shelter my sheep / I saw mother with God last night / Go home / Old Joe Clark / Sally Goodin / Black mountain rag / Billy in the lowground / Twinkle little star / Old fiddler / Soldier's joy / Georgia shuffle / Golden slippers / Tennessee Wagner / Handsome Molly / Coal loadin' Johnny / Hear that whistle blow (a hundred miles) / Too old for a broken heart / Legend of the Johnson boys / All the good times are past and gone / George Ailey's F.F.V. / This land is your land / Philadelphia lawyer / Sun's gonna shine in my back door some day / Hear the wind blow / I'll be no man's wife / McKinley's gone / Nine pound hammer / Ellen Smith / Life of trouble / Hand travellin' / Wreck of ol' 97 / Ninety nine years is almost for life / Over the hills to the poorhouse / New York town / Dixie home / Pastures of plenty / Bound to ride / When I left East Virginia / Drowned in the deep blue sea / My native home / Coal miner's blues

/ Salty dog blues / Durham's reel / Down the road / Rainbow / Big ball in Brooklyn / Flint Hill special / Dig a hole in the meadow / I hung my head and cried / Hot corn, cold corn / Little darlin', pal of mine / Mama don't allow it / Footprints in the snow / Martha White theme / I wonder where you are tonight / Old Macdonald / He will set your fields on fire / Let the church roll on / Picking the wildwood flower / Fiddle and banjo / Old leather britches / Ballad of Jed Clampett / Yonder stands little Maggie / Reuben / Mama blues / I know what it mean to be lonesome / Foggy mountain rock / Take this hammer / Rollin' in my sweet baby's arms / Gotta travel on / Mountain dew / Pearl, Pearl, Pearl / What about you / Rambling gambler / I'm troubled / My Sarah Jane / Train that carried my girl from town / Little birdy / Po' rebel soldier
CD Set _____ BCD 15559
Bear Family / Jun '92 / Rollercoaster / Direct / CM / Swift / ADA.

FLATT AND SCRUGGS 1964-1969 (6CD Set) (Flatt, Lester & Earl Scruggs)
Petticoat junction / Have you seen my dear companion / Good things (outweigh the bad) / Working it out / Amber tresses (tied in blue) / Jimmie Brown / Newsboy / When Papa played the dobro / Fireball / Father's table grace / I'm walking with him / My wandering boy / Sally don't you grieve / Faded red ribbon / Bummin' an old freight train / Georgia Buck / Hello stranger / Please don't wake me / You're gonna miss me when I'm gone / I still miss someone / Wabash cannonball / Rose conelly / You've been fooling my baby / Will you be lonesome too / Big shoes to fill / Branded wherever I go / Starlight on the rails / Loafer's glory / I'll be on the good road some day / Confessing / Gonna have myself a ball / Rock, salt and nails / Soldier's return / Memphis / Jackson / Colours / For lovin' me / Houston / Detroit city / Foggy mountain breakdown / Kansas city / Nashville blues / Take me back to Tulsa / Last public hanging in West Virginia / Boys form Tennessee / Ten miles from Natchez / Seattle town / Green acres / I had a dream / When the saints go marching in / God gave Noah the rainbow sign / Call me on home / Stone that builders refused / Wait for the sunshine / No Mother in this world / Thank God I'm on my way / Troublesome waters / Last thing on my mind / Mama, you been on my mind / It was only the wind / Why can't I find myself with you / Southbound / I'm gonna ride the steamboat / Roust-a-bout / Nashville cats / Train number 1262 / Bringin in the Georgia mail / Going across the sea / Atlantic coastal line / East bound train / Orange blossom special / Last train to Clarksville / California up tight band / Don't think twice it's alright / Four strong winds / Blowin' in the wind / It ain't me babe / Down in the flood / Buddy don't you roll so slow / Where have all the flowers gone / This land is your land / Mr. Tambourine man / Ode to Billie Joe / Like a rolling stone / I'd like to say a word for Texas / I'll be your baby tonight / Folsom prison blues / Gentle on my mind / Times they are a-changin' / If I were a carpenter / Universal soldier / Long road to Houston / Catch the wind / Rainy day women / Frieda Florentine / Nashville skyline rag / I walk the line / Ruby, don't take your love to town / Boy named Sue / Maggie's farm / Wanted man / One more night / One too many mornings / Girl from the north country / Honey, just allow me one more chance / Tonight will be fine / Story of Bonnie and Clyde / Another ride with Clyde / Picture of Bonnie / Barrow gang will get you little man / Bang you're alive / See Bonnie die, see City ole / Get away / Chase / Highway's end / Pick along / John Hardy was a desperate little man / Jazzing / Evelina / Tommy's song / Lonesome Ruben / Spanish two step / Careless love / Liberty / Bill Cheatham / Nothin' to it / Lost all my money / Maggie blues / Steamboat whistle blues / Paul and Silas / Cannonball blues / You are my flower / Old leather britches / Across the blue ridge mountains / Old folks / Going back to Harlan / Poor rebel soldier / No hiding place down here / Going up cripple creek / Foggy mountain special / Bile them cabbage down / Old Joe Clark / Sally goodin / Black mountain rag / Billy in the lowground / Twinkle little star / Old fiddler / Soldier's joy / Cheyenne / Down yonder / Georgia shuffle / Golden slippers / Tennessee Wagner / Chicken reel / Theme from Beverly Hillibillies / Beverly Hills / Vittles / Long talk with that boy / Jethro's a powerful man / Elly's spring song / Back home U.S.A. / Critters / What a great doctor Granny is / Lady lessons / Birds and the bees / Love or money / Close
CD _____ BCDFI 15879
Bear Family / Nov '95 / Rollercoaster / Direct / CM / Swift / ADA.

GOLDEN ERA, THE (Flatt, Lester & Earl Scruggs)
Flint Hill special / Your love is like a flower / I'm waiting to hear you call me darling / I'm head over heels in love / I'm working on a road (to Glory Land) / Till the end of the world rolls around / Jimmie Brown the newsboy / Earl's breakdown / Someone took my place with you / I'm gonna sleep with one eye open / Dim lights, thick smoke

/ Don't that road look rough and rocky / Randy lynn rag / Old home town / Brother I'm getting ready to go
CD _____ SSCD 05
Rounder / '92 / CM / Direct / ADA / Cadillac.

MERCURY SESSIONS VOL. 1 (Flatt, Lester & Earl Scruggs)
CD _____ SSCD 18
Rounder / Dec '87 / CM / Direct / ADA / Cadillac.

MERCURY SESSIONS VOL. 2 (Flatt, Lester & Earl Scruggs)
My little girl in Tennessee / Will the roses bloom / I'll never shed another tear / Bouquet in heaven / Cabin in Caroline / I'll never love another / God loves his children / Pain in my heart / Baby blue eyes / Doing my time / Preaching, praying, singing / Why don't they tell me so / Foggy mountain breakdown / I'm going to make heaven my home
CD _____ SSCD 17
Rounder / Dec '87 / CM / Direct / ADA / Cadillac.

Flatville Aces

CRAWFISHTROMBONES
CD _____ FLATCD 123
Flat / Apr '94 / Direct / Else / ADA.

Flavin, Mick

COUNTRY SOUNDS
In the echoes of my mind / You're the reason / Walk softly on the bridges / Love bug / I wish it was that easy going home / County of Fermanagh / Can you feel it / Yours to hurt tomorrow / Life's too short to be unhappy / Grand tour / Dreams of Donegal / If you remember me / Maria's heading out to California / Take my back home to Mayo
CD _____ RITZRCD 545
Ritz / Nov '94 / Pinnacle.

LIGHTS OF HOME, THE
Someday you'll love me / I see an angel every day / On the wings of love / It started all over again / For a minute there / One of these days (I want to be in your nights) / I never loved you more / Little things in life / Lights of home / Connemara rose / Keeper of my heart / You done me wrong / Old home in Mayo / Table in the corner / Little mountain church mouse / Longford on my mind
CD _____ RITZRCD 533
Ritz / Aug '93 / Pinnacle.

SWEET MEMORY
If you're going do me wrong (do it right) / Gonna have love / What she don't know won't hurt her / Way down deep / I took a memory to lunch / Old school yard / She's my rose / Haven't you heard / Wine flowed freely / Lady Jane / Hills of Tyrone / All I can be (is a sweet memory)
CD _____ RITZRCD 517
Ritz / Jun '92 / Pinnacle.

TRAVELLIN' LIGHT
Jennifer Johnson and me / Blue blue day / Hard times lovin' can bring / Where have all the lovers gone / Home to Donegal / Old side of town / Roads and other reasons / Travellin' light / There is no other way / Rarest flowers
CD _____ RITZCD 507
Ritz / '91 / Pinnacle.

Fleck, Bela

DAYBREAK
CD _____ CD 11518
Rounder / '88 / CM / Direct / ADA / Cadillac.

DEVIATION (Fleck, Bela & The New Grass Revival)
CD _____ ROUCD 0196
Rounder / Jul '95 / CM / Direct / ADA / Cadillac.

DRIVE
Whitewater / Slipstream / Up and around the bend / Natchez trace / See rock city / Legend / Lights of home / Down in the swamp / Sanctuary / Open road
CD _____ CD 0255
Rounder / Aug '88 / CM / Direct / ADA / Cadillac.

INROADS
Tonino / Somerset / Cecata / Four wheel drive / Ireland / Perplexed / Old country / Hudson's bay / Close to home
CD _____ ROU 0219CD
Rounder / May '93 / CM / Direct / ADA / Cadillac.

PLACES
CD _____ CD 11522
Rounder / '88 / CM / Direct / ADA / Cadillac.

THREE FLEW OVER THE CUCKOO'S NEST
Vix 9 / At last we meet again / Spunky and Clorissa / Bumbershoot / Blues for Gordon / Monkey see / Message / Interlude (return of the ancient ones) / Drift / Celtic melody / Peace, be still / Longing / For now

CD _____ 936245328-2
Warner Bros. / Jun '94 / Warner Music.

Flecknor, Gregory

MONKEY BOOTS (Flecknor, Gregory Quartet)
CD _____ CLR 419CD
Clear / Oct '95 / Disc.

Flee-Rekkers

JOE MEEK'S FABULOUS FLEE REKKERS
CD _____ C5CD 564
See For Miles/C5 / Jun '91 / Pinnacle.

Fleetwood Mac

25 YEARS - SELECTIONS FROM THE CHAIN (2CD Set)
Paper doll / Love shines / Love in store / Goodbye angel / Heart of stone / Silver springs / Oh Diane / Big love / Rhiannon / Crystal / Chain / Over my head / Dreams / Go your own way / Sara / Hold me / Gypsy / Make me a mask / Don't stop / Everywhere / Tusk / Not funny / Beautiful child / Teen beat / Need your love so bad / Did you ever love me / Oh well, part 1 / I believe my time ain't long / Bermuda triangle / Why / Station man / Albatross / Black magic woman / Stop messin' around / Trinity / Heroes are hard to find / Green manalishi
CD _____ 9362-45188-2
WEA / Feb '93 / Warner Music.

25 YEARS - THE CHAIN (4CD Set)
Paper doll / Love shines / Stand back / Crystal / Isn't it midnight / Big love / Everywhere / Affairs of the heart / Heart of stone / Sara / That's all for everyone / Over my head / Little lies / Eyes of the world / Oh Diane / In the back of my mind / Make me a mask / Save me / Goodbye angel / Silver springs / What makes you think you're the one / Think about me / Gypsy / You make loving fun / Second hand news / Love in store / Chain / Teen beat / Dreams / Only over you / I'm so afraid / Love is dangerous / Gold dust woman / Not that funny / Warm ways / Say you love me / Don't stop / Rhiannon / Walk a thin line / Storms / Go your own way / Sisters of the moon / Monday morning / Landslide / Hypnotised / Lay it all down / Angel / Beautiful child / Brown eyes / Save me a place / Tusk / Never go back again / Songbird / I believe my time ain't long / Need your love so bad / Rattlesnake shake / Oh well, part 1 / Stop messin' around / Green manalishi / Albatross / Man of the world / Love that burns / Black magic woman / Watch out / String-a-long / Station man / Did you ever love me / Sentimental lady / Come a little bit closer / Heroes are hard to find / Trinity / Why
CD Set _____ 9362-45129-2
WEA / Feb '93 / Warner Music.

ALBATROSS (Fleetwood Mac & Christine Perfect)
Albatross / Rambling pony / I believe my time ain't long / Dr. Brown / Stop messin' around / Love that burns / Jigsaw puzzle blues / Need your love tonight / I'd rather go blind / Crazy about you baby / And that's saying a lot / I'm on my way / No road is the right road / Let me go (leave me alone) / I'm too far gone (to turn around) / When you say
CD _____ CD 31569
Columbia / Feb '91 / Sony.

BARE TREES
Child of mine / Ghost / Homeward bound / Sunny side of heaven / Bare trees / Sentimental lady / Danny's chant / Spare me a little of your love / Dst / Thoughts on a grey day
CD _____ 7599272242
WEA / Feb '93 / Warner Music.

BEHIND THE MASK
Skies the limit / Love is dangerous / In the back of my mind / Do you know / Save me / Affairs of the heart / When the sun goes down / Behind the mask / Stand on the rock / Hard feelings / Freedom / When it comes to love / Second time
CD _____ 7599261112
WEA / Feb '95 / Warner Music.

BLUES COLLECTION, THE
CD _____ CCSCD 216
Castle / Apr '89 / BMG.

BLUES YEARS, THE
CD _____ MATCD 266
Castle / May '94 / BMG.

BOSTON LIVE
Oh well / Like it this way / World in harmony / Only you / Black magic woman / Jumping at shadows / Can't hold on
CD _____ CLACD 152
Castle / Oct '89 / BMG.

CLASSIC MAC (Plays Fleetwood Mac Classics) (London Rock Orchestra)
Oh well (Part one) / Black magic woman / Future games / Green manalishi / Dragonfly / Need your love so bad / Tusk / Albatross / Jigsaw puzzle blues / Sentimental lady / Man of the world / Oh well (Part two) / Hypnotised / Don't stop
CD _____ DCD 5368

Disky / Apr '94 / THE / BMG / Discovery / Pinnacle.

EARLY YEARS, THE (Live)
Black magic woman / Oh well / Madison blues / Stranger blues / Great balls of fire / Jenny Jenny / Like it this way / Oh baby / Loving kind / Tutti frutti / Keep a knockin' / Green manalishi
CD _____ EARL D 5
Castle / Aug '92 / BMG.

FAMILY ALBUM
CD _____ VSOPCD 222
Connoisseur / Jan '96 / Pinnacle.

FLEETWOOD MAC
Monday morning / Warm always / Blue letter / Rhiannon / Over my head / Crystal / Say you love me / Landslide / I'm so afraid / World turning / Sugar daddy
CD _____ 254043
WEA / Dec '85 / Warner Music.

FLEETWOOD MAC
My heart beats like a hammer / Merry go round / Long grey mare / Hellhound on my trail / Shake your moneymaker / Looking for somebody / No place to go / My baby's good to me / I loved another woman / Cold black night / World keeps on turning / Got to move
CD _____ 477358-2
Columbia / Aug '94 / Sony.

FLEETWOOD MAC LIVE
CD _____ SSLCD 207
Savanna / Jun '95 / THE.

FUTURE GAMES
Woman of 1000 years / Morning rain / What a shame / Future games / Sands of time / Sometimes / Lay it all down / Show me a smile
CD _____ 7599274582
WEA / Jan '93 / Warner Music.

GREATEST HITS: FLEETWOOD MAC
Green Manalishi (with the two pronged crown) / Oh well (pts 1 & 2) / Shake your moneymaker / Need your love so bad / Rattlesnake shake / Dragonfly / Black magic woman / Albatross / Man of the world / Stop messin' around / Love that burns
CD _____ 4607042
CBS / Apr '89 / Sony.

GREATEST HITS: FLEETWOOD MAC
As long as you follow / No questions asked / Rhiannon / Don't stop / Go your own way / Hold me / Everywhere / Gypsy / Say you love me / Dreams / Little lies / Sara / Tusk / Oh Diane (Not on LP) / Big love (Not on LP) / You make loving fun (Not on LP) / Seven wonders (Not on LP)
CD _____ 925838 2
WEA / Nov '88 / Warner Music.

HEROES ARE HARD TO FIND
Heroes are hard to find / Coming home / Angel / Bermuda Triangle / Come a little bit closer / She's changing me / Bad loser / Silver heels / Prove your love / Born enchanter / Safe harbour
CD _____ 7599272162
WEA / Jan '93 / Warner Music.

KILN HOUSE
This is the rock / Station man / Blood on the floor / Hi ho silver / Jewel eyed Judy / Buddy's song / Earl Grey / One together / Tell me all the things you do / Mission bell
CD _____ 7599274532
WEA / Jul '93 / Warner Music.

LIKE IT THIS WAY
Lazy poker blues / Something inside of me / Evenin' boogie / Rockin' boogie / Dust my broom / Rollin' man / Merry go round / Hellhound on my trail / Last night / Need your love tonight / Rambling pony / I can't hold out / Like it this way / Homework / Cold black night / Big boat / Just the blues / Dragonfly / Trying so hard to forget
CD _____ ELITE 008CD
Elite/Old Gold / Aug '93 / Carlton Home Entertainment.

LIVE AT THE BBC
CD Set _____ EDFCD 297
Essential / Sep '95 / Total/BMG.

LIVE IN BOSTON
CD _____ IMCD 900129
Line / Sep '94 / CM / Grapevine / ADA / Conifer / Direct.

LONDON LIVE '68
Got to move / I held my baby last night / My baby's sweet / My baby's a good un / Don't know which way to go / Buzz me / Dream / World keeps turning / How blue can you get / Bleeding heart
CD _____ CDTB 11038
Thunderbolt / Mar '95 / Magnum Music Group.

LOOKING BACK AT FLEETWOOD MAC
Albatross / Looking for somebody / My baby's good to me / I loved another woman / Rambling pony / Oh well / Jigsaw puzzle blues / Black magic woman / Need your love so bad / Love that burns / My heart beats like a hammer / I believe my time ain't long / Shake your moneymaker / World keep on turning / Stop messin' around / Coming home

CD _____ PWKS 533
Carlton Home Entertainment / May '90 / Carlton Home Entertainment.

MIRAGE
Love in store / Can't go back / That's alright / Book of love / Gypsy / Only over you / Empire State / Straight back / Hold me / Oh Diane / Eyes of the world / Wish you were here
CD _____ K 256952
WEA / '89 / Warner Music.

MYSTERY TO ME
Emerald eyes / Believe me / Just crazy love / Hypnotised / Forever / Keep on going / City / Miles away / Somebody / Way I feel / Good things to those who wait / Why
CD _____ 7599259822
WEA / Jan '93 / Warner Music.

ORIGINAL FLEETWOOD MAC, THE
Drifting / Leavin' town blues / Watch out / Fool no more / Mean old fireman / Can't afford to do it / Fleetwood Mac / Worried dream / Love that woman / Allow me one more show
CD _____ CLACD 344
Castle / Jun '94 / BMG.

PIOUS BIRD OF GOOD OMEN, THE
Need your love so bad / Coming home / Rambling pony / Big boat / I believe my time ain't long / Sun is shining / Albatross / Black magic woman / Just the blues / Jigsaw puzzle blues / Looking for somebody / Stop messin' around
CD _____ 4805242
Columbia / May '95 / Sony.

RUMOURS
Second hand news / Dreams / Never going back again / Don't stop / Go your own way / Songbird / Chain / You make loving fun / I don't want to know / Oh daddy / Gold dust woman
CD _____ 256344
WEA / Dec '83 / Warner Music.

TANGO IN THE NIGHT
Big love / Seven wonders / Everywhere / Caroline / Tango in the night / Mystified / Little lies / Family man / Welcome to the room...Sara / Isn't it midnight / When I see you again / You and I (part 2)
CD _____ 925471 2
WEA / Apr '87 / Warner Music.

THEN PLAY ON
Coming your way / Closing my eyes / Fighting for Madge / When you say / Showbiz blues / Underway / One sunny day / Although the sun is shining / Rattlesnake shake / Without you / Searching for Madge / My dream / Like crying / Before the beginning
CD _____ 927448 2
WEA / '88 / Warner Music.

TIME
CD _____ 9362459202
WEA / Oct '95 / Warner Music.

TUSK
Over and over / Ledge / Think about me / Save me a place / Sara / What makes you think you're the one / Storms / That's all for everyone / Not that funny / Sisters of the moon / Angel / That's enough for me / Brown eyes / Never make me cry / I know I'm not wrong / Honey hi / Beautiful child / Walk a thin line / Tusk / Never forget
CD _____ K2 66088
WEA / Mar '87 / Warner Music.

Fleming & John

DELUSIONS OF GRANDEUR
CD _____ REX 460122
Rex / Nov '95 / Cadillac.

Flesh Eaters

DRAGSTRIP RIOT
CD _____ SST 273 CD
SST / May '93 / Plastic Head.

PREHISTORIC FITS
CD _____ SST 264 CD
SST / May '93 / Plastic Head.

SEX DIARY OF MR. VAMPIRE
CD _____ SST 292 CD
SST / May '93 / Plastic Head.

Flesh For Lulu

LONG LIVE THE NEW FLESH
Lucky day / Postcards from paradise / Hammer of love / Siamese twist / Sooner or later / Good for you / Crash / Way to go / Sleeping dogs / Dream on cowboy
CD _____ BBL 82CD
Beggars Banquet / Feb '90 / Warner Music / Disc.

PLASTIC FANTASTIC
Decline and fall / House of cards / Time and space / Every little word / Slowdown / Highwire / Slide / Day one / Choosing you / Stupid on the street / Avenue / Plastic fantastic
CD _____ BEGA 100CD
Beggars Banquet / '88 / Warner Music / Disc.

Fleshcrawl

DESCEND INTO THE ABSURD
Between the shadows they crawl / Phrenetic Tendencies / Perpetual damnation / Purulent bowel erosion / Lost in a grave / Never to die again / Festering flesh / Infected subconscious / Evoke the excess
CD _____ BMCD 027
Black Mark / Oct '92 / Plastic Head.

IMPURITY
CD _____ BMCD 48
Black Mark / Mar '94 / Plastic Head.

Fleshold

PATHETIC
CD _____ MASSCD 049
Massacre / May '95 / Plastic Head.

Fleshtones

BEAUTIFUL LIGHT
CD _____ NAK 6116-2
Naked Language / Jan '94 / Koch.

BLAST OFF
CD _____ RE 107CD
Reach Out International / Nov '94 /
Jetstar.

LABORATORY OF SOUND
Let's go / High on drugs / Sands of our lives / Nostradamus Jr / Sweetest thing / Hold you / Accelerated emotion / Train of thought / One step less / Motor needs gas / Psychedelic swamp / Fading away / We'll never forget
CD _____ 118542
Musidisc / Oct '95 / Vital / Harmonia Mundi / ADA / Cadillac / Discovery.

POWERSTANCE
Armed and dangerous / I'm still thirsty / Waiting for a message / Let it rip / Three fevers / Living legends / I can breathe / Mod teepee / House of rock / Irresistible / Candy ass
CD _____ NAK 6101
Naked Language / Jan '94 / Koch.

Fleshy Ranks

BUSTIN' OUT
CD _____ HBCD 163
Heartbeat / Oct '94 / Greensleeves /
Jetstar / Direct / ADA.

Fleurety

MIN TID SKAL KOMME
CD _____ AMAZON 005CD
Misanthropy / Jul '95 / Plastic Head.

Flight 16

AGAINST THE WIND
CD _____ PHMCD 001
BMG / Apr '95 / BMG.

Flint, Tim

FLINTASIA
CD _____ CDGRS 1279
Grosvenor / Aug '95 / Target/BMG.

SHOW TUNES - AND THEN SOME
Overture / All I need is the girl / We kiss in a shadow / I have dreamed fugue for tin horns / Anything goes / On the street where you live / This can't be love / I've never been in love before / They say that falling in love is wonderful / Once in love with Amy / Give my regards to Broadway / Bandology / La Calinda / Love walked in/Forgotten dreams / Autumn concerto / April in Paris / Thunder and lightning polka (CD only) / Tritsch tratsch polka (CD only) / Special
CD _____ CDGRS 1264
Grosvenor / Sep '93 / Target/BMG.

TOO MARVELLOUS FOR WORDS
Moment of truth / Where are you / Too marvellous for words / Sweet Lorraine / Shiny stockings / Somewhere along the way / Bahn frei / Rook revolution / Disney selection / When you wish upon a star / Heigh ho / Whistle while you work / Party gras / Jolly holiday / With a smile and a song / So this is love / Unbirthday song / It's a small world / Pomp and circumstance No.1
CD _____ KGRS 1242
Grosvenor / '91 / Target/BMG.

Flippen, Benton

OLD TIMES, NEW TIMES
CD _____ ROUCD 0326
Rounder / Oct '94 / CM / Direct / ADA /
Cadillac.

Flipper

AMERICAN GRAFISHY
CD _____ DABCD 1
Beggars Banquet/Def America / May '93 /
Pinnacle.

BLOW'N CHUNKS
CD _____ RE 126CD
Reach Out International / Nov '94 /
Jetstar.

Generic Flipper

CD _____ DABCD 3
Beggars Banquet / Jun '93 / Warner
Music / Disc.

SEX BOMB BABY
Sex bomb / Love canal / Ha ha ha / Sacrifice / Falling / Ever get away / Earthworm / Games' got a price / Old lady who swallowed a fly / Brainwash / Lowrider / End the game
CD _____ 74321298982
Infinite Zero / Oct '95 / BMG.

Flitcroft, Iain

GRANADALAND WURLITZER
Wurlitzer march / Reilly, ace of spies / Rose medley / Cavaquinho / Waltz medley / Tango Havana / Musetta's waltz song / White Horse Inn / Granada television medley / Masterpiece / Quickstep / City of Chester / Vija / Ballet Egyptien / Paris medley / Samba incognito / Medley / Buffoon / Granada connection
CD _____ OS 213
Bandleader / Aug '95 / Conifer.

Flock

FLOCK
Clown / I am the tall tree / Tired of waiting / Store brought / Store thought / Truth
CD _____ 4694432
Epic / Feb '95 / Sony.

Flock Of Seagulls

20 CLASSICS OF THE 80'S
CD _____ EMPRCD 562
Emporio / Mar '95 / THE / Disc / CM.

BEST OF A FLOCK OF SEAGULLS
I ran / Space age love song / Telecommunication / More you live, the more you love / Nightmares / Wishing (if I had a photograph of you) / It's not me talking / Transfer affection / Who's that girl / D.N.A. I ran
CD _____ CHIP 41
Jive / Jun '91 / BMG.

TELECOMMUNICATIONS
Wishing (if I had a photograph of you) / Modern love is automatic / (It's not me) talking / I ran / Nightmares / Heartbeat like a drum / Committed / Transfer affection / More you live, the more you love / Never again / Who's that girl / Space age love song / Living in heaven / D.N.A. / Telecommunications
CD _____ ELITE 024 CD
Carlton Home Entertainment / Oct '92 /
Carlton Home Entertainment.

Floppy Sounds

DOWNTIME
Actual footage / Durexx / Daisy / Since I split / Superhype / Ultrasong / Oblivion / Excursions / Deliverance / Sprawl / Weird
CD Set _____ SLIPCD 040
Slip 'n' Slide / Nov '95 / Vital / Disc.

Florence

DOMINIONS
CD _____ ELEC 2CD
New Electronica / Oct '93 / Pinnacle /
Plastic Head.

Florence, Bob

BOB FLORENCE & HIS BIG BAND
(Florence, Bob Big Band)
Party harty / Trinity fair / BBC / Jewels / Willowcrest / Invitation / Forgetful / Samba de rollins / Collage
CD _____ HEPCD 2064
Hep / Jun '95 / Cadillac / Jazz Music / New
Note / Wellard.

STATE OF THE ART (Florence, Bob Limited Edition)
Just friends / Moonlight serenade / Silky / Crunch / Stella by starlight / All the things you are / Mr. Paddington / BBC / Auld lang syne
CD _____ CDPC 797
Prestige / Oct '90 / Total/BMG.

Flores, Pedro

1938-1942
CD _____ HQCD 49
Harlequin / May '95 / Swift / Jazz Music /
Wellard / Hot Shot / Cadillac.

Flores, Rosie

AFTER THE FARM
CD _____ HACD 8033
Hightone / Jul '94 / ADA / Koch.

ONCE MORE WITH FEELING
CD _____ HCD 8047
Hightone / Jun '94 / ADA / Koch.

ROCKABILLY FILLY
CD _____ HITCD 8067
Hightone / Oct '95 / ADA / Koch.

Florida

BRASS ROOTS
CD _____ FLP 003CD
Florida / Nov '95 / ADA.

Flory, Chris

CITY LIFE
Alexandria, VA / Besame mucho / s'posin' / Tin tin por tin tin / Good morning heartache / J.A. Blues / My shining hour / So dance samba / Drafting / Come back to me / New York / Penthouse serenade / Cafe solo
CD _____ CCD 4589
Concord Jazz / Feb '94 / New Note.

FOR ALL WE KNOW
Soft winds / T'aint me / Avalon / Tenderly / Close your eyes / Lee's blues / It had to be you / For all we know / Airmail special / Ninth Avenue shuffle / Lullaby of the leaves
CD _____ CCD 4403
Concord Jazz / Jun '94 / New Note.

Flotsam & Jetsam

DOOMSDAY FOR THE DECEIVER
CD _____ ZORRO 36CD
Music For Nations / Sep '91 / Pinnacle.

Flotsam & Jetsam

FLOTSAM & JETSAM/MALCOLM MCEACHERN
Introduction / Maud Marie / Drinking / Businessman's love song / Aylesbury ducks / Changing of the guard / Song of love / My grandfather's clock / Little Betty Bouncer / Roman road / More into my house / I am friar of orders grey / Alsatian and the pekinese / Devonshire cream and cider / Musical confession / Rocked in the cradle of the deep / We never know what to expect / Merry peasant / Cobbler's song / Ghost of an old King's jester / Lucy Long / King Canute / Gendarmes duet / I am Roamer / Melodrama of the mice / Gentlemen, good-night / Is 'e an Aussie Lizzie, is 'e / Postscript
CD _____ CDHD 228
Happy Days / Aug '93 / Conifer.

FLOTSAM AND JETSAM
Introduction / King Canute / Mrs. Peer Gynt / P.C. Lamb / Maude-Marie / Optimist and pessimist / Polonaise in the Mall / Melodrama of the mice / Only a few of us left / Businessman's love song / Simon the bootlegger / Song of the air / Move into my house / Little Betty Bouncer / Weather reports / We never know what to expect / Schubert's toy shop / Village blacksmith / Alsation and the pekinese / Maiden diver / Little Joan / What was the matter with Rachmaninov / British pantomime / Ghost of old king's jester / High-brow sailor / When I grow old, dad / Postscript
CD _____ PASTCD 9723
Flapper / '90 / Pinnacle.

FLOTSAM AND JETSAM, VOL. 2
CD _____ PASTCD 9749
Flapper / Jul '91 / Pinnacle.

Flour

FOURTH AND FINAL
CD _____ TG 125CD
Touch & Go / Apr '94 / SRD.

Flouride, Klaus

BECAUSE I SAY SO
CD _____ VIRUS 67CD
Alternative Tentacles / Jul '89 / Pinnacle.

LIGHT IS FLICKERING, THE
CD _____ VIRUS 95CD
Alternative Tentacles / '92 / Pinnacle.

Flower

HOLOGRAM SKY
CD _____ SR 330491CD
Semaphore / Jul '91 / Plastic Head.

Flowered Up

LIFE WITH BRIAN, A
Sunshine / Take it / Mr. Happy reveller / Hysterically blue / It's on / Silver plan / Phobia / Egg rush / Doris... is a little bit partial / Crackerjack
CD _____ 8282442
London / Jun '92 / PolyGram.

Flowerpot Men

LET'S GO TO SAN FRANCISCO
Let's go to San Francisco (Part two) / Walk in the sky / Am I losing you / You can never be wrong / Man without a woman / In a moment of madness / Young birds fly / Journey's end / Mythological Sunday / Blow away / Piccolo man / Silicon City
CD _____ C5CD 529
See For Miles/C5 / Jul '95 / Pinnacle.

Floyd, Eddie

CALIFORNIA GIRL/DOWN TO EARTH
California girl / Didn't I blow your mind this time / Why is the wine sweeter (on the other

side) / Rainy night in Georgia / Love is you / People, get it together / Laurie / Hey there lonely girl / I feel good / Too much is too little for me / You got that kind of love / People get ready / Linda Sue Dixon / My mind was messed around at the time / When the sun goes down / Salvation / I only have eyes for you / Tears of joy / Changing love
CD _____ CDSXD 087
Stax / Jul '95 / Pinnacle.

I'VE NEVER FOUND A GIRL
Bring it on home to me / Never gonna give you up / Girl I love you / Hobo / I need you woman / I've never found a girl / I'll take her / Slip away / I'm just the kind of fool / Water / Sweet things you do
CD _____ CDSXE 059
Stax / Jul '92 / Pinnacle.

KNOCK ON WOOD
Knock on wood / Something you got / But it's alright / I stand accused / If you gotta make a fool of somebody / I don't want to cry / Raise your hand / Got to make a comeback / 634 5789 / I've just been feeling bad / Hi-heel sneakers / Warm and tender love
CD _____ 7567802832
Pickwick/Warner / Oct '94 / Pinnacle / Warner Music / Carlton Home Entertainment.

KNOCK ON WOOD - THE BEST OF EDDIE FLOYD
Knock on wood / Raise your hand / Big bird / On a Saturday night / Things get better / Love is a doggone good thing / I've never found a girl / Consider me / Bring it on home to me / I've got to have your love / Blood is thicker than water / Baby, lay your head down / Too weak to fight / Oh how it rained / Why is the wine sweeter (on the other side) / Soul Street / Don't tell your mama (On CD only) / Girl, I love you (On CD only) / People, get it together (On CD only) / Something to write home about (On CD only) / Check me out (On CD only) / Stealing love (On CD only)
CD _____ CDSX 010
Stax / Mar '88 / Pinnacle.

RARE STAMPS/I'VE NEVER FOUND A GIRL
Bring it on home to me / Never give you up / Girl I love you / Hobo / I need you woman / I've never found a girl / I'll take her / Slip away / I'm just the kind of fool / Water / Sweet things you do / Knock on wood / Raise your hand / Love's a doggone good thing / On a Saturday night / Things get better / Big bird / Got to make a comeback / I've just been feeling bad / This house / I've got to have your love / Consider me / Never let you go / Ain't that good / Laurie
CD _____ CDSXD 096
Stax / Jul '93 / Pinnacle.

Floyd, Gary

BROKEN ANGELS
CD _____ GRCD 367
Glitterhouse / Jun '95 / Direct / ADA.

WORLD OF TROUBLE
CD _____ GRCD 316
Glitterhouse / Sep '94 / Direct / ADA.

Flue

SOMETIMES
CD _____ TORSO 12031
Torso / May '87 / SRD.

Flugschädel

FLUGSCHADEL
CD _____ EFA 800232
Platten Meister / Mar '94 / SRD.

OTHNIEL
CD _____ EFA 800312
Platten Meister / Apr '95 / SRD.

Fluke

OTO
Bullet / Tosh / Cut / Freak / Wobbler / Squirt / O.K. / Setbook
CD _____ CTRCD 31
Circa / Jul '95 / EMI.

PEEL SESSIONS: FLUKE
CD _____ SFMCD 215
Strange Fruit / Oct '94 / Pinnacle.

SIX WHEELS ON MY WAGON
Groovy feeling / Love letters / Glidub / Electric guitar / Top of the world / Slud / Slow motion / Spacey (catch 22 dub) / Astrosapiens / Oh yeah / Exo / Life support / Philly (Not on CD/MC) / Glorious (Not on CD/MC) / Cool hand flute (Not on CD/MC) / Joni (Not on CD/MC) / Easy peasey (Not on CD/MC) / Phin (Not on CD/MC) / Electric guitar (Not on CD/MC) / Taxi (Not on CD/MC) / Coolest (Not on CD/MC)
CD _____ CIRCD 27
Circa / Oct '95 / EMI.

Flush

LOCUST FUDGE
CD _____ GRCD 280
Glitterhouse / Aug '93 / Direct / ADA.

Flux Of Pink Indians

FUCKING CUNTS TREAT US LIKE PRICKS
CD _____ TPCD 3
One Little Indian / Jun '88 / Pinnacle.

STRIVE TO SURVIVE CAUSING THE LEAST SUFFERING POSSIBLE
Progress / They lie, we die / Myxomatosis / Is there anybody there / Fun is over / Song for them / Charity hilarity / Some of us scream / Some of us shoot / Take heed / T.V. dinners / Tapioca sunrise
CD _____ TPCD 2
One Little Indian / Jun '88 / Pinnacle.

UNCARVED BLOCK
CD _____ TPCD 1
One Little Indian / Jun '88 / Pinnacle.

Fly Ashtray

CLUMPS TAKES A RIDE
Second song / Soft pack / L'age-nt-sno-pee / Dolphin brain / Sink / Man who stayed in ed all day / Ssssssss / Do what you can / Best boy / Hypoblast / Ignells 2 / Crows / It doesn't matter / Hoafie hoafie / Ostrich atmosphere / Bad head park (Theme from) / Anyway / Head park rev. / Non-ignells
CD _____ WORD 004-2
See Eye / Aug '92 / Vital.

Fly Right Trio

WILD ABOUT
CD _____ TBCD 2008
Nervous / Mar '93 / Nervous / Magnum Music Group.

Flying Burrito Brothers

BACK TO THE SWEETHEART OF THE RODEO (Burrito Brothers)
CD Set _____ AP 054552
Appaloosa / Jun '95 / ADA / Magnum Music Group.

BURRITO DELUXE
Lazy days / Image of me / High fashion queen / If you gotta go, go now / Man in the fog / Farther along / Older guys / Cody, Cody / God's own singer / Down in the churchyard
CD _____ EDCD 194
Edsel / Jun '90 / Pinnacle / ADA.

CHRONICLES
CD Set _____ 5404082
A&M / Sep '95 / PolyGram.

COLLECTION
CD _____ CCSCD 366
Castle / Mar '93 / BMG.

DIM LIGHTS, THICK SMOKE AND LOUD MUSIC
Train song / Close all the honky tonks / Sing me back home / Tonight the bottle let me down / Your angel steps out of heaven / Crazy arms / Together again / Honky tonk women / Green green grass of home / Bony Moronie / To love somebody / Break my mind / Dim lights, thick smoke
CD _____ EDCD 197
Edsel / Mar '87 / Pinnacle / ADA.

ENCORE (LIVE 1990) (Burrito Brothers)
Dim lights, thick smoke / You ain't goin' nowhere / Hickory wind / White line fever / Sweet little Colette / Big bayou / Sweet Suzanna / Wild horses / Silverwings / Help wanted / Cannonball rag / When it all comes down to love / Wheels
CD _____ CDSD 069
Sundown / Nov '90 / Magnum Music Group.

EYE OF A HURRICANE
Wheel of love / Like a thief in the night / Bayou blues / Angry words / Rosetta knows / Heart highway / I sent your saddle home / Jukebox Saturday night / Arizona moon / Wild wild West / Eye of a hurricane / Sunset boulevard / Smile
CD _____ CDSD 075
Magnum Music / Nov '93 / Magnum Music Group.

EYE OF THE HURRICANE
CD _____ OW 30330
One Way / Jul '94 / Direct / ADA.

FLYING AGAIN
Easy to get on / Wind and rain / Why baby why / Dim lights / Thick smoke / You left the water running / Building fires / Sweet desert childhood / Bon soir blues / River road / Hot burrito (no.3)
CD _____ 900931
Line / Oct '94 / CM / Grapevine / ADA / Conifer / Direct.

FROM ANOTHER TIME
Diggi diggi li / Wheels / Dim lights, thick smoke / Faded love / Devil in disguise / Building fires / Bon soir blues / White line fever / Sin City / She thinks I still care / Why baby why / Close all the honky tonks
CD _____ CDSD 072
Sundown / Apr '91 / Magnum Music Group.

GILDED PALACE OF SIN, THE
Christine's tune / Sin City / Do right woman, do right man / Dark end of the street / My uncle / Wheels / Juanita / Hot burrito no.1

& 2) / Do you know how it feels to be lonesome / Hippie boy
CD _____ EDCD 191
Edsel / '88 / Pinnacle / ADA.

HOLLYWOOD NIGHTS 79-82
She belongs to everyone but me / Somewhere tonight / Baby, how'd we ever get this way / Too much honky tonkin' / My abandoned heart / She's a friend of mine / Louisiana / Why must the ending always be so sad / That's when you know it's over / She's a hell of a deal / Another shade of grey / Damned if I'll be lonely tonight / If something should come between us / Run to the night / Coast to coast / Closer to you / True love never runs dry / Tell me it ain't so
CD _____ CDSD 067
Sundown / May '90 / Magnum Music Group.

IN CONCERT
CD _____ HP 93422
Start / Nov '94 / Koch.

LIVE FROM TOKYO
Big bayou / White line fever / Dim lights, thick smoke / There'll be no teardrops tonight / Rollin' in my sweet baby's arms / Hot burrito (no.2) / Colorado / Rocky top / Six days on the road / Truck drivin' man
CD _____ CDSD 025
Sundown / '86 / Magnum Music Group.

WHEELS: TRIBUTE TO CLARENCE WHITE & GRAM PARSONS (Burrito Brothers & CO)
Six white horses / Emmy / Bugler / Promised land / Freeborn man / Games people play / Detroit city / 500 miles away from home / Four strong winds / Shame on me / Streets of Baltimore / Millers cave / Christine's tune / Wheels
CD _____ APCD 049
Appaloosa / '88 / ADA / Magnum Music Group.

Flying Medallions

WE LOVE EVERYBODY
CD _____ JIZCD 1
Big Life / Sep '94 / Pinnacle.

Flying Nun

PILOT
Submarine / Frank / Shades / Carousel of freaks / Life on the ground
CD _____ OLE 1512
Matador / Sep '95 / Vital.

Flying Pickets

LOST BOYS
Remember this / I heard it through the grapevine / Disco down / So close / Tears of a clown / When you're young and in love / You've lost that lovin' feelin' / Psycho killer / Wide boy / Factory / Monica engineer / Only you / Masters of war / Who's that girl
CD _____ MTD 021
Moving Target / Dec '93 / CM.

ONLY YOU - THE BEST OF THE FLYING PICKETS
Only you / I heard it through the grapevine / Tears of a clown / You've lost that lovin' feelin' / Sealed with a kiss / Only the lonely / Space oddity (Live) / Who's that girl / When you're young and in love / Groovin' / Coral island / Buffalo soldier / I got you babe (live) / Summer in the city / Get off my cloud / Higher and higher
CD _____ CDVIP 115
Virgin VIP / Mar '94 / Carlton Home Entertainment / THE / EMI.

ORIGINAL FLYING PICKETS, THE
CD _____ 4509982452
WEA / Dec '94 / Warner Music.

Flying Saucer Attack

CHORUS
Feedback song / Light in the evening / Popul vuh III / Always / Feedback song demo / Second hour / Beach red lullaby / There, but not there / February 8th / There dub
CD _____ WIGCD 22
Domino / Nov '95 / Pinnacle.

DISTANCE
CD _____ WIGCD 12
Domino / Oct '94 / Pinnacle.

FURTHER
CD _____ WIGCD 20
Domino / Apr '95 / Pinnacle.

Flyscreen

COUNCIL POP
CD _____ WOWCD 42
Words Of Warning / May '95 / SRD.

Flyte Reaction

CREATE A SMILE
CD _____ SPLENCD 3
Backs / Jun '95 / Disc.

FM Sound Lab

LET'S DO LUNCH (Rave Jazz)
Let's do lunch / Say what / Transilvania / Superleggera / Planet cricklewood / Save the whales, eat a Viking / Heat seeker / Just desserts / Let's do lunch (B) / Let's do lunch (C)
CD _____ VCIJD 3
Vocal Cords / Nov '93 / Grapevine.

Focus

HOCUS POCUS: THE BEST OF FOCUS
Hocus pocus / Anonymus / House of the king / Focus (Mixes) / Janis / Focus II / Tommy / Sylvia / Focus III / Harem scarum / Mother focus / Focus IV / Bennie Helder / Glider / Red sky at night / Hocus pocus (U.S. single version)
CD _____ CDP 8281622
EMI / May '94 / EMI.

Foetus

GASH
CD _____ ABB 88CD
Big Cat / May '95 / SRD / Pinnacle.

MALE (Foetus Corruptus)
CD _____ ABB 31/2CD
Big Cat / Feb '92 / SRD / Pinnacle.

NAIL (Scraping Foetus Off The Wheel)
CD _____ WOMBFIP 004CD
Some Bizarre / Apr '86 / Pinnacle.

Fogelberg, Dan

HOME FREE
To the morning / Stars / More than ever / Be on your way / Hickory groove / Long way home / Anyway I love you / Wysteria / River / Looking for a lady
CD _____ 982989 2
Pickwick/Sony Collector's Choice/ Aug '93 / Carlton Home Entertainment / Pinnacle / Sony.

Fogerty, John

CENTERFIELD
Old man down the road / Rock 'n' roll girls / Big train / I saw it on T.V. / Mr. Greed / Searchlight / Centerfield / I can't help myself / Zanz kant danz
CD _____ 9252032
WEA / Feb '85 / Warner Music.

JOHN FOGERTY
Rockin' all over the world / (I'll be glad when you're dead) you rascal you / Wall / Travellin' high / Lonely teardrops / Almost Saturday night / Where the river flows / Sea cruise / Dream song / Flying away / Comin' down the road / Ricochet
CD _____ CDFE 507
Fantasy / Sep '87 / Pinnacle / Jazz Music / Wellard / Cadillac.

Foghat

AKA ROCK & ROLL
CD _____ 812270890-2
WEA / Mar '93 / Warner Music.

BEST OF FOGHAT
I just want to make love to you / Maybellene / Ride ride ride / Take it or leave it / Home in my hand / Drivin' wheel / Fool for the city / Slow ride / Stone blue / Honey hush / Night shift / Wild cherry / Third time lucky (first time I was a fool) / Easy money / Chateau lafitte '59 boogie / Eight days on the road
CD _____ 8122700882
WEA / Jul '93 / Warner Music.

BEST OF FOGHAT - VOL.2, THE
CD _____ 8122705162
WEA / Jul '93 / Warner Music.

ENERGIZED
Honey hush / Step outside / Golden arrow / Home in my hand / Wild cherry / That'll be the day / Fly by night / Nothin' I won't do
CD _____ 812270883-2
WEA / Mar '93 / Warner Music.

FOGHAT
I just want to make love to you / Trouble trouble / Leavin' again / Fools hall of fame / Sarah Lee / Highway (killing me) / Maybellene / Hole to hide in / Gotta get to know you
CD _____ 812270887-2
WEA / Mar '93 / Warner Music.

FOGHAT (LIVE)
Fool for the city / Home in my hand / I just want to make love to you / Road fever / Honey hush / Slow ride
CD _____ 812270884-2
WEA / Mar '93 / Warner Music.

FOOL FOR THE CITY
Fool for the city / My babe / Slow ride / Terraplane blues / Save your sowing (for me) / Drive me home / Take it or leave it
CD _____ 812270882-2
WEA / Mar '93 / Warner Music.

NIGHTSHIFT
Drivin' wheel / Don't run me down / Burning the midnight oil / Nightshift / Hot shot love / Take me to the river / I'll be standing by

FM Sound Lab

CD _____ 812270888-2
WEA / Mar '93 / Warner Music.

ROCK & ROLL OUTLAW
CD _____ 812270889-2
WEA / Mar '93 / Warner Music.

STONE BLUE
CD _____ 812270881-2
WEA / Mar '93 / Warner Music.

Fol, Raymond

PARIS SWINGS THE 60'S (Fol, Raymond & Pierre Michelot)
Le printemps / L'ete / L'automne / L'hiver / Cherokee / Gavotte / Akkilino / Elephant green / Sous les ponts de Paris / Chet / Bye bye blackbird / Sweet feeling / Klook's shadow
CD _____ 8326572
ECM / Mar '88 / New Note.

Folds, Chuck

HITTING HIS STRIDE
CD _____ ARCD 19117
Arbors Jazz / Nov '94 / Cadillac.

Foley, Sue

WITHOUT A WARNING
CD _____ ANTCD 0025
Antones / May '94 / Hot Shot / Direct / ADA.

YOUNG GIRL BLUES
Queen Bee / (Me and my) Chauffeur blues / Cuban getaway / Mean old lonesome train / Gone blind / Walkin' home / But I forgive you / Off the hook / Hooked on love / Little mixed up / Time to travel
CD _____ ANTCD 0019
Alligator / Jun '92 / Direct / ADA.

Folk Friends

1
CD _____ TUT 72160
Wundertute / Jan '94 / CM / Duncans / ADA.

2
CD _____ CDTUT 72150
Wundertute / '89 / CM / Duncans / ADA.

Folkloyuma

MUSIC FROM THE ORIENTE DE CUBA: THE RUMBA
CD _____ NI 5425
Nimbus / Apr '95 / Nimbus.

Foly, Liane

REVE ORANGE
Au fur et a mesure / Nuit halogene / Goodbye lover / Reve orange / Blue notes / Va savoir / Be my boy / Sun / S'en balancer
CD _____ CDVIR 7
Virgin / Jun '91 / EMI.

SWEET MYSTERY
CD _____ CDVIR 19
Virgin / Apr '94 / EMI.

Fong Naam

ANCIENT MUSIC FROM THAILAND
CD _____ 140982
Celestial Harmonies / Nov '95 / ADA / Select.

Fonsea

ET SE ANGES NOIRS
CD _____ CNCD 5981
Disky / Apr '94 / THE / BMG / Discovery / Pinnacle.

Fonseca

MELODIES FROM PORTUGAL
CD _____ EUCD 1087
ARC / '89 / ARC Music / ADA.

Fontana, Wayne

GAME OF LOVE (Fontana, Wayne & The Mindbenders)
Game of love / She's got the power / You don't know me / Girl it / Jaguar and the thunderbirds / Certain girl / One more time / Um um um um um um / Where have you been / Keep your hands off my baby / Too many tears / Girl can't help it / Cops and robbers / I'm gonna be a wheel someday / Since you've been gone / It's just a little bit too late
CD _____ 8322602
Mercury / May '88 / PolyGram.

Fontane Sisters

HEARTS OF STONE - THE BEST OF THE FONTANE SISTERS
CD _____ VSD 5526
Varese Sarabande/Colosseum / Nov '94 / Pinnacle / Silva Screen.

Fontenot, Canray

LOUISIANA HOT SAUCE CREOLE STYLE
CD _____ ARHCD 381

Arhoolie / Apr '95 / ADA / Direct / Cadillac.

Foo Fighters

FOO FIGHTERS
This is a call / I'll stick around / Big me / Alone and easy target / Good grief / Floaty / Weenie beenie / Oh George / For all the cows / X-static / Watershed / Exhausted
CD _____ CDEST 2266
Roswell / Jul '95 / EMI.

Fool Proof

NO FRICTION
CD _____ 188804 2
Gramavision / Feb '89 / Vital/SAM / ADA.

For Love Not Lisa

MERGE
Softhand / Slip slide melting / Lucifer for now / Daring to pick up / Simple line of decline / Travis Hoffman / Just a phase / Traces / Mother's faith / Swallow / More than a girl / Merge
CD _____ 756792283-2
WEA / Oct '93 / Warner Music.

For Real

IT'S A NATURAL THANG
Easy to love / Where did your love go / You don't wanna miss / Just a matter of time / You don't wanna love you now / You don't know nothin' / With this ring (say yes) / D'yer mak'er / Harder I try / I like / Thinking of you / Prayer
CD _____ 5401562
A&M / Feb '95 / PolyGram.

Forbert, Steve

MISSION OF THE CROSS
CD _____ 74321259902
RCA / Apr '95 / BMG.

Forbes, Roy

LOVE TURNS TO ICE
CD _____ FF 70499
Flying Fish / Jul '89 / Roots / CM / Direct / ADA.

Forbes, Sandy

NIGHTINGALE SANG IN BERKELEY SQUARE, A
You'd be so nice to come home to / Nightingale sang in Berkeley Square / Jersey bounce / Room 504 / Tag und nacht / Run rabbit run / White cliffs of Dover / Que reste t'il de nos amours / Blues in the night / Deep purple / Cherokee / Seul ce soir / Begin the beguine / Lambert's nachtlokal / Tuxedo junction / Last time I saw Paris / Deep in a dream / It's a lovely day today
CD _____ PWKS 659
Carlton Home Entertainment / Dec '89 / Carlton Home Entertainment.

Forbidden

FORBIDDEN EVIL
CD _____ CDFLAG 27
Under One Flag / Aug '89 / Pinnacle.

POINT OF NO RETURN - THE BEST OF FORBIDDEN
Chalice of blood / Out of body (out of mind) / Feel no pain / Step by step / Off the edge / One foot in hell / Through the eyes of glass / Tossed away / March into fire / Victim of changes
CD _____ CDMFLAG 73
Under One Flag / Nov '92 / Pinnacle.

TWISTED INTO FORM
CD _____ CDFLAG 43
Under One Flag / Jul '89 / Pinnacle.

Force Dimension

DEUS EX MACHINA
CD _____ KK 049 CD
KK / Aug '90 / Plastic Head.

FORCE DIMENSION
CD _____ KK 020CD
KK / '90 / Plastic Head.

Forcefield

FORCEFIELD
Set me free / Best shot / Runaway / Sunshine of your love / Shine it on me / Whole lotta love / Black cat / White room / You really got me / Fire in the city / Keep on running / Smoke on the water
CD _____ PCOM 1088
President / Aug '93 / Grapevine / Target / BMG / Jazz Music / President.

FORCEFIELD IV - LET THE WILD RUN FREE
Let the wild run free / Can't get enough of your love / Money talks / I will not go quietly / Ball of confusion / Wind cries mary / Living by numbers / In a perfect world
CD _____ PCOM 1110
President / Nov '90 / Grapevine / Target / BMG / Jazz Music / President.

INSTRUMENTALS

Tokyo / Talisman / Perfect world / I lose again / Secret waters / Look don't touch / Three card shuffle / Rendezvous / Osaka
CD _____ PCOM 1121
President / Jun '92 / Grapevine / Target / BMG / Jazz Music / President.

TALISMAN, THE

Talisman / Year of the dragon / Tired of waiting for you / Heartache / Good is good / Carrie / Without your love / I lose again / Mercenary / Black night (CD only) / I lose again (instrumental) (CD only)
CD _____ PCOM 1095
President / Aug '88 / Grapevine / Target / BMG / Jazz Music / President.

Forces Of Music

KINGS & QUEENS OF DUB
CD _____ TWCD 1017
Tamoki Wambesi / Oct '94 / Jetstar / SRD / Roots Collective / Greensleeves.

Ford Blues Band

FORD BLUES BAND, THE
CD _____ CCD 11024
Crosscut / '92 / ADA / CM / Direct.

HOTSHOTS
CD _____ CCD 11041
Crosscut / Nov '95 / ADA / CM / Direct.

LIVE AT THE BREMINALE '92
CD _____ CCD 11038
Crosscut / Jul '93 / ADA / CM / Direct.

Ford, Charles

CHARLES FORD BAND, THE (Ford, Charles Band)
CD _____ ARHCD 353
Arhoolie / Apr '95 / ADA / Direct / Cadillac.

REUNION - LIVE
CD _____ CCD 11043
Crosscut / Nov '94 / ADA / CM / Direct.

Ford, Douglas

PIPES & DRUMS OF SCOTLAND (Ford, Douglas & The Gordon Highlanders)
Amazing grace / My home in the hills / Conund rum / Miss Kirkwood / Scotland the brave / Reveille / Rustic bridge by the mill / Miss McLeod O'Raasey / Cock of the north / Skye boat song / Bonnie Dundee
CD _____ SOW 90149
Sounds Of The World / Jan '96 / Target / BMG.

Ford, Emile

EMILE FORD AND THE CHECKMATES (Ford, Emile & The Checkmates)
CD _____ REP 4097-WZ
Repertoire / Aug '91 / Pinnacle / Cadillac.

GREATEST HITS
CD _____ SSLCD 201
Savanna / Jun '95 / THE.

VERY BEST OF EMILE FORD & THE CHECKMATES (Ford, Emile & The Checkmates)
What do you want to make those eyes at me for / After you've gone / Hold me, thrill me, kiss me / Keep on doin' what you're doin' / Them there eyes / Questions / Still / You'll never know what you're missing / Trouble / Lawdy Miss Clawdy / Joker / Yellow bird / Buona sera / I don't / Danny boy / That lucky old sun / Counting teardrops / Heavenly / What am I gonna do / On a slow boat to China / Don't tell me your troubles / Red sails in the sunset / Send for me (CD only) / Too-ra-loo-ra-loo-ral (CD only) / Scarlet ribbons (CD only) / Vaya con dios (CD only) / Move along (CD only)
CD _____ SEECD 309
See For Miles/C5 / Jan '91 / Pinnacle.

VERY BEST OF EMILE FORD, THE
CD _____ SOW 703
Sound Waves / May '94 / Target/BMG.

Ford, Gerry

BETTER MAN
On second thought / If tomorrow never comes / Somebody up there / What God has joined together / It don't hurt to dream / Fourteen minutes old / Better man / It's our anniversary / Lonely farmer's daughter / Alone / Don't play faded love
CD _____ CDTT 117
Trimtop / Mar '91 / Ross.

CAN I COUNT ON YOU
Cottage in the country / Can I count on you / Twice the speed of love / Whispering Bill / Tell me again / Where are you / If you want to find love / Heckle and Jeckel / All the time / (If it weren't for country music) I'd go crazy / After the storm / Look at us
CD _____ CDTT 118
Trimtop / '93 / Ross.

SIXTEEN COUNTRY FAVOURITES
Thank God for the radio / Heartache following me / Storms never last / Let's hear it for the working man / Blue eyes cryin' in the rain / Daddy's farm / I wouldn't change you

if I could / Daisy a day / Rainbows and roses / Amazing love / I'll never need another you / Teardrop on a rose / I don't care / I came so close to calling you last night / On the road to loving me again / Sweet dreams
CD _____ CDTT 113
Trimtop / '90 / Ross.

Ford, Lita

BEST OF LITA FORD, THE
What do ya know about love / Kiss me deadly / Shot of poison / Hungry / Gotta let / Larger than life / Only women bleed / Playin' with fire / Back to the cave / Lisa / Close my eyes forever
CD _____ 7863 66047-2
RCA / Aug '92 / BMG.

DANGEROUS CURVES
Larger than life / What do ya know about love / Shot of poison / Bad love / Playin' with fire / Hellbound train / Black widow / Little too early / Holy man / Tambourine dream / Little black spider
CD _____ 74321 16000-2
RCA / Feb '94 / BMG.

INTERVIEW COMPACT DISC: LITA FORD
CD P.Disc _____ CBAK 4020
Baktabak / Nov '89 / Baktabak.

LITA
Back to the cave / Can't catch me / Blueberry / Kiss me deadly / Falling in and out of love / Fatal passion / Under the gun / Broken dreams / Close my eyes forever
CD _____ 74321 13887-2
RCA / Feb '94 / BMG.

Ford Pier

MECONIUM
CD _____ WRONG 15
Wrong / Nov '95 / SRD.

Ford, Ricky

AMERICAN - AFRICAN BLUES
CD _____ CCD 79528
Candid / Jul '93 / Cadillac / Jazz Music / Wellard / Koch.

EBONY RHAPSODY
CD _____ CCD 79053
Candid / May '91 / Cadillac / Jazz Music / Wellard / Koch.

HOT BRASS
CD _____ CCD 79518
Candid / Oct '93 / Cadillac / Jazz Music / Wellard / Koch.

MANHATTAN BLUES
In walked Bud / Misty / Ode to crispus attacks / Bop nouveau / My little strayhorn / Manhattan blues / Half nelson
CD _____ CCD 79036
Candid / Mar '90 / Cadillac / Jazz Music / Wellard / Koch.

SAXOTIC STOMP
CD _____ MCD 5349
Muse / Sep '92 / New Note / CM.

TENOR MADNESS TOO
Summer summit / Ballad de jour / Blues abstractions / Up a step / Con alma / Soul eyes / Rollin' and strollin' / I got it bad and that ain't good / Nigeria blues
CD _____ MCD 5478
Muse / Jul '95 / New Note / CM.

Ford, Robben

HANDFUL OF BLUES (Ford, Robben & The Blue Line)
Rugged road / Chevrolet / When I leave here / Strong will to live / I just want to make love to you / Think twice / Good thing / Tired of talking / Running out on me / Top of the hill / Don't let me be misunderstood / Miller's son
CD _____ BTR 70042
Blue Thumb / Aug '95 / BMG / New Note.

INSIDE STORY, THE
CD _____ 7559610212
Elektra / Jan '96 / Warner Music.

MYSTIC MILE
He don't play nothin' but the blues / Busted up / Politician / Worried life blues / Misdirected blues / Trying to do the right thing / Say what's on your mind / Plunge / I don't play / Mystic mile
CD _____ GRS 00082
GRP / Oct '93 / BMG / New Note.

ROBBEN FORD AND BLUE TRAIN
Brother / You cut me to the bone / Real man / My love will never die / Prisoner of love / Tell me I'm your man / Start it up / Life song
CD _____ GRS 10022
GRP / Aug '92 / BMG / New Note.

Ford, Tennessee Ernie

SHOWTIME
Night train to Memphis / Catfish boogie / You gotta see Mama tonight / Cool water / Just because / My little red wagon / Do the hucklebuck / Up the lazy river
CD _____ DATOM 7

A Touch Of Magic / Apr '94 / Harmonia Mundi.

SIXTEEN TONS
Milk 'em in the morning blues / Country junction / Smoky mountain boogie / Anticipation blues / Mule train / Cry of the wild goose / My hobby / Feed 'em in the morning blues / Shot gun boogie / Tailormade woman / You're my sugar / Rock City boogie / Kissin' bug boogie / Hey good lookin' / Ham bone / Everybody's got a girl but me / Snow shoe Thomoson / Blackberry boogie / Hey Mr. Cotton Picker / Kiss me big / Catfish boogie / Ballad of Davy Crockett / Sixteen tons / Roving gambler / Black eyed Susan Brown
CD _____ BCD 15487
Bear Family / Feb '90 / Rollercoaster / Direct / CM / Swift / ADA.

Fordham, Julia

FALLING FORWARD
I can't help myself / Caged bird / Falling forward / River / Blue sky / Different time, different place / Threadbare / Love and forgiveness / Honeymoon / Hope, prayer and time / Safe
CD _____ CIRCD 28
Circa / May '94 / EMI.

JULIA FORDHAM
Happy ever after / Comfort of strangers / Few too many / Invisible war / My lover's keeper / Cocooned / Where does the time go / Woman of the 80's / Other woman / Behind closed doors / Unconditional love
CD _____ CIRCD 4
Circa / Apr '92 / EMI.

PORCELAIN
Lock and key / Porcelain / Girlfriend / For you only for you / Genius / Did I happen to mention / Towerblock / Island / Your lovely face / Prince of peace
CD _____ CIRCD 10
Circa / Sep '89 / EMI.

SWEPT
CD _____ CIRCD 18
Circa / Oct '91 / EMI.

Foreheads In A Fishtank

STRIPPER
CD _____ TOAD 5CD
Newt / Jun '94 / Plastic Head.

Foreigner

AGENT PROVOCATEUR
Tooth and nail / That was yesterday / I want to know what love is / Growing up the hard way / Reaction to action / Stranger in my own house / Love in vain / Down on love / Two different worlds / She's too tough
CD _____ 781 999-2
Atlantic / Jan '85 / Warner Music.

CLASSIC HITS LIVE
Double vision / Cold as ice / Damage is done / Women / Dirty white boy / Fool for you anyway / Head games / Not fade away / Waiting for a girl like you / Jukebox hero / Urgent / Love maker / I want to know what love is / Feels like the first time
CD _____ 7567825252
Atlantic / Dec '93 / Warner Music.

DOUBLE VISION
Hot blooded / Blue morning, blue day / You're all I am / Back where you belong / Love has taken it's toll / Double vision / Tramontane / I have waited so long / Lonely children / Spellbinder
CD _____ K250 476
Atlantic / Aug '83 / Warner Music.

FOREIGNER
Feels like the first time / Cold as ice / Starrider / Headknocker / Damage is done / Long long way from home / Woman oh woman / At war with the world / Fool for the anyway / I need you
CD _____ 250 356
Atlantic / Apr '83 / Warner Music.

FOREIGNER 4
Night life / Jukebox hero / Break it up / Waiting for a girl like you / Luanno / Urgont / I'm gonna win / Woman in black / Girl on the moon / Don't let go
CD _____ 250796
Atlantic / '88 / Warner Music.

HEAD GAMES
Dirty white boy / Love on the telephone / Women I'll get even with you / Seventeen / Head games / Modern day / Blinded by science / Do what you like / Rev on the red line
CD _____ 250 651
Atlantic / Nov '85 / Warner Music.

INSIDE INFORMATION
Heart turns to stone / Can't wait / Say you will / I don't want to live without you / Night to remember / Inside information / Beat of my heart / Face to face / Out of the blue / Counting every minute
CD _____ 7818082
Atlantic / Dec '87 / Warner Music.

MR MOONLIGHT
White lie / Rain / Until the end of time / All I need to know / Running the rise / Real

world / Big dog / Hole in my soul / I keep hoping / Under the gun / Hand on my heart
CD _____ 74321232852
Arista / Oct '94 / BMG.

RECORDS
Cold as ice / Double vision / Head games / Waiting for a girl like you / Feels like the first time / Urgent / Dirty white boy / Jukebox hero / Long long way from home / Hot blooded
CD _____ 7567828002
Atlantic / Nov '95 / Warner Music.

UNUSUAL HEAT
Only heaven knows / Lowdown and dirty / I'll fight for you / Moment of truth / Mountain of love / Ready for the rain / When the night comes down / Safe in my heart / No hiding place / Flesh wound / Unusual heat
CD _____ 7567822992
Atlantic / Jun '91 / Warner Music.

VERY BEST OF FOREIGNER...AND BEYOND
Soul doctor / Prisoner of love / With heaven on our side / Jukebox hero / Hot blooded / Cold as ice / Head games / Waiting for a girl like you / Urgent / Double vision / I want to know what love is / Say you will / That was yesterday / I don't want to live without you / Rev on the red line / Dirty white boy / Feels like the first time
CD _____ 7567899992
Atlantic / Dec '92 / Warner Music.

Foreman, Bruce

THERE ARE TIMES (Foreman, Bruce Quartet)
CD _____ CCD 4332
Concord Jazz / Dec '87 / New Note.

Forest

FOREST/FULL CIRCLE
Bad penny / Glade somewhere / Lovemaker's ways / While you're gone / Sylvie / Fantasy you / Fading light / Do you want some smoke / Don't want to go / Nothing else will matter / Mirror of life / Rain is on my balcony / Hawk the hawker / Bluebell dance / Midnight hanging of a runaway serf / To Julie / Gypsy girl and rambleaway / Do not walk in the rain / Much ado about nothing / Graveyard / Famine song / Autumn child
CD _____ BGOCD 206
Beat Goes On / Sep '94 / Pinnacle.

Forest, Andy J.

HOG WILD
CD _____ APCD 036
Appaloosa / '92 / ADA / Magnum Music Group.

HOGSHEAD CHEESE (Forest, Andy & Kenny Holladay)
CD _____ AP 118
Appaloosa / Oct '95 / ADA / Magnum Music Group.

LIVE (Forest, Andy J. Band)
CD _____ APCD 066
Appaloosa / '92 / ADA / Magnum Music Group.

Forest, Helen

ON THE SUNNY SIDE OF THE STREET
CD _____ ACD 047
Audiophile / Oct '93 / Jazz Music / Swift.

Forever Amber

LOVE CYCLE
CD _____ HBG 122/7
Background / Apr '94 / Background.

Forgodsake

BLASTHEAD
Armchair enthusiast / Wake up now / If this is what it takes / Bad sex / Half past anything / Blasthead / Strange / Negative / In front of me / Crash / This one (CD only) / Not today (CD only) / Sky high (CD only) / Dumbtown (CD only)
CD _____ CDBLEED 3
Bleeding Hearts / Apr '93 / Pinnacle.

Forkeye

P.I.8
CD _____ HCCD 001
Human Condition / Sep '93 / Disc.

Forman, Bruce

PARDON ME (Forman, Bruce Quartet)
CD _____ CCD 4368
Concord Jazz / Feb '89 / New Note.

Forman, Mitchel

CHILDHOOD DREAMS
CD _____ 1210502
Soul Note / Jan '93 / Harmonia Mundi / Wellard / Cadillac.

NOW AND THEN - A TRIBUTE TO BILL EVANS
Waltz for Debbie / Very early / Nardis / My romance / My foolish heart / Perc jazz / Glo-

ria's step / Now and then / How my heart sings / But beautiful
CD _____ 01241631652
Novus / Mar '94 / BMG.

WHAT ELSE?
What else / Mr. Smarty Pants / End of the tunnel / Just ideas / Beauty and the beast / Gorgeous P.D. / Near miss / We start again / Alley / One design
CD _____ PD 90664
Novus / Jun '92 / BMG.

Formanek, Michael

LOW PROFILE
Groogly / Immaculate deception / Rivers / Great plains / Paradise revisited / Isonychia / Shuddawuddacudda / Uncommon ground / Signs of life / Black rose / Big spirit people
CD _____ ENJ 80502
Enja / Jul '94 / New Note / Vital/SAM.

Formby, George

BELL-BOTTOM GEORGE (George Formby Vol. 2)
Bell bottom George / When the lads of the village get crackin' / When the waterworks caught fire / It serves you right (You shouldn't have joined) / Got to get your photo in the press / If I had a girl like you / Thirty thirsty sailors / I'd do it with a smile / Home guard blues / Swim little fish / At the baby show / Hold your hats on / Mr. Wu's an air raid warden now / Bar maid at the Rose and Crown / I wish I was back on the farm / Delivering the morning milk / Grandad's flannelette nightshirt / Guarding the homes of the Home Guard / Our Sergeant Major / Baby / She's never been seen since then / Swimmin' with the wimmin'
CD _____ PASTCD 7043
Flapper / May '94 / Pinnacle.

BEST OF GEORGE FORMBY, THE
CD _____ MU 3006
Musketeer / Oct '92 / Koch.

EASY GOING CHAP
Pleasure cruise / You can't stop me from dreaming / You're a li-a-ty / Noughts and crosses / It ain't nobody's biz'ness what I do / Goody goody / I like bananas / Biceps, muscle and brawn / I'm a froggie / Radio bungalow town / I don't like / Wunga bunga boo / Somebody's wedding day / Tan-tantivvy tally ho / My little goat and me / Five and twenty years / Like the big pots do / My plus fours / Ring your little bell / Farmer's boy / Trailing around in a trailer / Easy going chap
CD _____ CMSCD 003
Movie Stars / Jun '88 / Conifer.

FORMBY AT WAR - LIVE
Auntie Maggie's remedy / Frank on his tank / Guarding the homes of the home guard / Chinese laundry blues / Cleaning windows / Little stick of Blackpool rock / Imagine me in the maginot line / When the lads of the village get crackin' / Thirty thirsty sailors / Out in the Middle East / Mr. Wu's an air raid warden now / It's in the air / Little ukulele / Down the old coal hole / Bless 'em all
CD _____ CDGRS 1224
Grosvenor / '91 / Target/BMG.

HIS GREATEST FAVOURITES
I'm the ukelele man / Leaning on a lamppost / Auntie Maggie's remedy / With my little stick of Blackpool rock / Window cleaner / Mr. Wu's a window cleaner now / Chinese laundry blues / Do de o do / Blue eyed blonde next door / Like the big pots do / Window cleaner (2) / I don't like / Easy going chap / Noughts and crosses / Lancashire hot pot swingers / You can't go wrong in these / Who are you a-shoving off / I'm the husband of the wife of Mr.Wu / Hitting the high spots / Kiss your mamsy pansy / I can tell it by my horoscope / I'm the emperor of Lancashire
CD _____ PASTCD 7001
Flapper / Feb '93 / Pinnacle.

I'M THE UKELELE MAN
Window cleaner / Auntie Maggie's remedy / Leaning on a lamp-post / In my little snapshot album / With my little stick of Blackpool rock / Mr. Wu's a window cleaner now / Our Sergeant Major / I'm the ukelele man / Bless 'em all / I don't like / Joo-jah tree / Chinese laundry blues / Baby / Why don't women like me / Running round the fountains in Trafalgar Square / My ukelele / De do do / Believe it or not / I went all hot and cold / Wedding of Mr. Woo / In a little Wigan garden / Alexander's ragtime band
CD _____ RAJCD 801
Empress / Jul '94 / THE.

IT'S TURNED OUT NICE AGAIN
Keep your seats please (Trailer) / On the beat / It ain't nobody's biz'ness what I do (in medley) / Goody goody (in medley) / I like bananas (in medley) / Sitting on the sands all night / On the Wigan Boat Express / Talking to the moon about you / Some of these days (in medley) / Hard hearted Hannah / Sweet Georgia Brown (in medley) / Sweet Sue, just you (in medley) / Dinah (in medley) / Tiger rag (in medley) / Hitting the high spots / Home guard blues / Goodnight little fellow, goodnight / Window cleaner / Lad from Lancashire / Oh you have no idaea / Riding in the TT races / They can't

fool me / Under the blasted oak / I always get to bed by half-past nine / Down the old coal hole / I wonder who's under her balcony now / Delivering the morning milk / Leaning on a lamp-post / It's turned out nice again
CD _____ PPCD 78105
Past Perfect / Feb '95 / THE.

LEGENDARY GEORGE FORMBY, THE
Leaning on a lamp-post / Auntie Maggie's remedy / In my little snapshot album / With my little stick of Blackpool rock / Window cleaner / Window cleaner (2) / Mr. Wu's a window cleaner now / Our Sergeant Major / Mother, what'll I do now / Grandad's flannelette nightshirt / I'm the ukelele man / Mr. Wu in the Air Force / Unconditional surrender / Home guard blues / Cook house serenade / Spotting on the top of Blackpool Tower / I wonder who's under her balcony now / It serves you right / I don't like / Bless 'em all
CD _____ CC 8234
Music For Pleasure / Dec '93 / EMI.

V FOR VICTORY
CD _____ RKD 23
Redrock / Mar '95 / THE / Target/BMG.

VERY BEST OF GEORGE FORMBY, THE (20 Great Songs)
Leaning on a lamp-post / With my little stick of Blackpool rock / Chinese laundry blues / Window cleaner / Swimmin' with the wimmin' / With my little ukelele in my hand / Why don't women like me / You can't keep a growing lad down / Mother, what'll I do now / There's nothing proud about me / In my little snapshot album / Old kitchen kettle / Isle of Man / Lancashire toreador / Our sergeant major / Believe it or not / Madame moscovitch / As the hours and the days and the months and the years roll / Sitting on the ice in the ice rink / I told my baby with the ukelele
CD _____ PLATCD 28
Platinum Music / Aug '90 / Prism / Ross.

WHEN I'M CLEANING WINDOWS
When I'm cleaning windows / Oh don't the wind blow cold / It's turned out nice again / With my little stick of Blackpool rock / Hi tiddly hi ti island / It's in the air / Count your blessings and smile / Easy going chap / Grandad's flannelette nightshirt / Hillbilly Willie / Hitting the high spots / I don't like / I'm a froggie / Keep your seats please / Lancashire hot pot swingers / Leaning on a lamp-post / Like the big pots do / Mr. Wu's a window cleaner now / My plus fours / Our sergeant major / Rhythm in the alphabet / Somebody's wedding day / They can't fool me / You can't stop me from dreaming
CD _____ CD AJA 5079
Living Era / Apr '91 / Koch.

WHEN I'M CLEANING WINDOWS
Sitting on the ice in the ice rink / Do de o do / Chinese laundry blues / You can't stop me from dreaming / Pleasure cruise / Keep fit / Riding in the TT races / Hindoo man / It ain't nobody's biz'ness what I do / Goody goody / I like bananas / Lancashire Toreador / Farmer's boy / You can't keep a growing lad down / You're a li-a-ty / With my little stick of Blackpool rock / Trailing around in a trailer / Why don't women like me / Dare devil Dick / Somebody's wedding day / Sitting on the sands all night / Madame Moscovitch / With my little ukelele in my hand / Fanlight Fanny / When I'm cleaning windows / Leaning on a lamp-post
CD _____ PLCD 538
President / Jul '95 / Grapevine / Target/BMG / Jazz Music / President.

Formell, Juan

SANDUNGUERA (Formell, Juan & Los Van Van)
CD _____ MES 159892
Messidor / Jun '93 / Koch / ADA.

Formerly Brothers

RETURN OF THE FORMERLY BROTHERS
Smack dab in the middle / Big mamou / Teardrops on your letter / Drunk / Don't tell me / Coming back home / Sure is a good thing / Amarillo highway / Banks of the old Ponchartrain / Just like a woman / Gene's boogie / Queen of the Okanagan
CD _____ BTCD 971408
Beartracks / Jun '89 / Rollercoaster.

Forrest, Helen

CREAM OF HELEN FORREST
CD _____ PASTCD 7062
Flapper / May '95 / Pinnacle.

DOUBLE DATE WITH HELEN FORREST AND CHRIS CONNOR (Forrest, Helen & Chris Connor)
CD _____ STCD 14
Stash / Oct '91 / Jazz Music / CM / Cadillac / Direct / ADA.

EMBRACEABLE YOU (Previously Unreleased 1949-1950)
CD _____ HCD 257
Hindsight / Jul '95 / Target/BMG / Jazz Music.

I WANNA BE LOVED
CD _____ HCD 250
Hindsight / Mar '94 / Target/BMG / Jazz Music.

Forrest, Jimmy

ALL THE GIN IS GONE
CD _____ DD 404
Delmark / Jan '87 / Hot Shot / ADA / CM / Direct / Cadillac.

BLACK FORREST
CD _____ DD 427
Delmark / Oct '86 / Hot Shot / ADA / CM / Direct / Cadillac.

FORREST FIRE
Forrest fire / Remember / Dexter's deck / Jim's jam / Bag's groove / When your love has gone / Help
CD _____ OJCCD 199-2
Original Jazz Classics / Jan '91 / Wellard / Jazz Music / Cadillac / Complete/Pinnacle.

HONKERS AND BAR WALKERS VOL.1 (Forrest, Jimmy/Tab Smith/Etc)
CD _____ DD 438
Delmark / Nov '92 / Hot Shot / ADA / CM / Direct / Cadillac.

MOST MUCH
CD _____ OJCCD 350
Original Jazz Classics / Jan '95 / Wellard / Jazz Music / Cadillac / Complete/Pinnacle.

NIGHT TRAIN
CD _____ DD 435
Delmark / Apr '86 / Hot Shot / ADA / CM / Direct / Cadillac.

Forrester, Sharon

THIS TIME
CD _____ VPCD 1434
VP / Oct '95 / Jetstar.

Forsen, Arne

UR HJARTANS DJUP (Forsen, Arne & Pia Olby)
CD _____ DRCD 198
Dragon / Apr '87 / Roots / Cadillac / Wellard / CM / ADA.

Forsmark Tre

VASTGOTALATAR
CD _____ FMPCD 001
FMP / May '93 / Cadillac.

Forster, John

ENTERING MARION
CD _____ PH 1164CD
Philo / Jan '94 / Direct / CM / ADA.

Forster, Robert

CALLING FROM A COUNTRY PHONE
CD _____ BBL 127CD
Beggars Banquet / Sep '95 / Warner Music / Disc.

DANGER IN THE PAST
Baby stones / Leave here satisfied / Is this what you call change / Danger in the past / Justice / River people / Heart out to tender / Dear black dream / I've been looking for somebody
CD _____ BEGA 113 CD
Beggars Banquet / Sep '90 / Warner Music / Disc.

I HAD A NEW YORK GIRLFRIEND
CD _____ BBQCD 161
Beggars Banquet / Aug '94 / Warner Music / Disc.

Forsythe, Guy

HIGH TEMPERATURE (Forsythe, Guy Band)
CD _____ LDCD 80001
Lizard / Aug '94 / Direct / Disc.

Fortaleza

SOY DE SANGRE KOLLA
CD _____ FF 529CD
Flying Fish / '92 / Roots / CM / Direct / ADA.

Forte

DIVISION
CD _____ MASSCD 035
Massacre / Jun '94 / Plastic Head.

Forthcoming Fire

ILLUMINATION
CD _____ HY 39100702
Hyperium / Jan '94 / Plastic Head.

Fortran 5

BAD HEAD PARK
CD _____ CDSTUMM 104
Mute / Jun '93 / Disc.

BLUES, THE
CD _____ STUMMCD 79
Mute / Sep '91 / Disc.

Fortune, Jesse

FORTUNE TELLIN' MAN
CD _____ DD 658
Delmark / Jul.'93 / Hot Shot / ADA / CM /
Direct / Cadillac.

Fortune, Sonny

MONK'S MOOD
Little rootie tootie / Mysterioso / Nutty / I
mean you / Monk's wood / Ruby my dear /
In walked bud / Off minor
CD _____ KCD 5048
Konnex / Nov '93 / SRD.

Fortunes

FORTUNES
CD _____ GRF 186
Tring / Jan '93 / Tring / Prism.

FORTUNES, THE
CD _____ KLMCD 037
Scratch / Jan '95 / BMG.

GREATEST HITS
CD _____ RC 83118
Royal Classics / Mar '93 / Complete/
Pinnacle.

SPOTLIGHT ON FORTUNES
You've got your troubles / Here comes that
rainy day feeling again / Caroline / Seasons
in the sun / Don't throw your love away /
When your heart speaks to you / Anna Ma-
ria / Storm in a teacup / Mumba Sarah / Half
way to paradise / It's a beautiful dream /
Funny how love can be
CD _____ HADCD 113
Javelin / Feb '94 / THE / Henry Hadaway
Organisation.

Foster & Allen

100 GOLDEN GREATS
CD Set _____ TCD 2791
Telstar / Oct '95 / BMG.

AFTER ALL THESE YEARS
Old Dungarvan oak / When I dream / Bluebell polka / Do you think you could love
again / Leaving of Liverpool / Rose of Allendale / I still love you / Cottage by the sea /
Old Ardboe / Scots polka / Rose of Mooncoin / Six foot seven woman / When my
blue moon turns gold again / After all these
years
CD _____ RITZSCD 420
Ritz / Jun '92 / Pinnacle.

BUNCH OF THYME
Bunch of thyme / Fiddler / Come back
Paddy Reilly / Drink up the cider / Green
willow / Living here London / Blacksmith /
Alice Benbolt / Benbulben of Sligo / Wise
maid / Cooley's reel / Foster's fancy /
Nancy Miles / Courtin' in the kitchen
CD _____ RITZSCD 408
Ritz / Apr '93 / Pinnacle.

BY REQUEST
CD _____ TCD 2670
Telstar / Oct '93 / BMG.

CHRISTMAS ALBUM
CD _____ TCD 2459
Telstar / Nov '90 / BMG.

FOSTER & ALLEN SELECTION, THE
Blind / Green willow / Jacqueline waltz /
Cocky farmer / Polkas / Fagins wake / Sligo
maid / Nancy Myles / Old flames / Oslo
waltz / Salonika / Boys of Bluehill / Bally
James Duff / Green groves of Erin / Gentle
Annie / Sweets of May
CD _____ RITZSCD 409
Ritz / Apr '93 / Pinnacle.

HEARTSTRINGS
CD _____ TCD 2608
Telstar / Oct '92 / BMG.

I WILL LOVE YOU ALL OF MY LIFE
I will love you all my life / Whiskey on a Sunday / Birdie song / Mull of Kintyre / Swedish
rhapsody / Forever and ever / I'll take you
home again Kathleen / Cock o' the North /
If those lips could only speak / Mountains
of Mourne / Happy hour / When I grow too
old to dream
CD _____ RITZSCD 419
Ritz / Jun '92 / Pinnacle.

MAGGIE
Maggie / Old rustic bridge by the mill / Har-
vest moon / Isle of Innisfree / Mist upon the
morning / Hornpipes / Sweethearts in the
spring / Blue eyes cryin' in the rain / Molly
my lovely Molly / Seasons of my heart /
Reels / Nell Flaherty's drake / Farewell to
Derry / Johnny Brown
CD _____ RITZSCD 418
Ritz / Jun '92 / Pinnacle.

MEMORIES
CD _____ CDSR 037
Telstar / Oct '93 / BMG.

SONGS WE LOVE TO SING
CD _____ TCD 2741
Telstar / Oct '94 / BMG.

VERY BEST OF FOSTER & ALLEN, THE
Bunch of thyme / Old flames / Maggie / I
will love you all my life / Blacksmith / Oslo
waltz / Place in the choir / Just for old times
sake / Job of journeywork / Spinning wheel

/ We will make love / Maid behind the bar /
My love is in America / Molly darling / Be-
fore I met you / Gentle mother
CD _____ RITZRCD 523
Ritz / Apr '93 / Pinnacle.

**VERY BEST OF THE LOVE SONGS
VOL.2**
CD _____ RITZRCD 524
Ritz / Apr '93 / Pinnacle.

WORLD OF FOSTER & ALLEN, THE
CD _____ TCD 2478
Telstar / Apr '91 / BMG.

Foster, David

**CHRISTMAS ALBUM, THE (Various
Artists)**
Carol of the bells / Blue Christmas / First
Noel / It's the most wonderful time of the
year / Grown up christmas list / O Holy night
/ Go tell it on the mountain/Mary had a baby
/ I'll be home for Christmas / Mary's boy
child / Christmas song / Away in a manger
/ White Christmas
CD _____ 654492295-2
Atlantic / Dec '93 / Warner Music.

CHRISTMAS ALBUM, THE
Carol of the bells / Blue Christmas / First
Noel / It's the most wonderful time of the
year / Grown up Christmas list / O holy
night / Go tell it on the mountain / Mary had
a baby / I'll be home for Christmas / Mary's
boy child / Christmas song / Away in a
manger / White Christmas
CD _____ 6544922952
Atlantic / Feb '93 / Warner Music.

Foster, Frank

**FRANKLY SPEAKING (Foster, Frank &
Frank Weiss)**
When did you leave Heaven / Up and com-
ing / One morning in May / Two Franks /
This is all I ask / Blues backstage / An' all
such stuff as dat / Summer knows
CD _____ CCD 4276
Concord Jazz / Sep '86 / New Note.

NO COUNT
Stop gap / Excursion / Casa de marcel /
Apron strings / Alternative / Serenata
CD _____ SV 0114
Savoy Jazz / Apr '93 / Conifer / ADA.

**SHINY STOCKINGS (Foster, Frank &
Loud Minority)**
Shiny stockings / Love scene / Tomorrow's
blues today / Day spring / Hills of the north
rejoice
CD _____ DC 8545
Denon / Jun '89 / Conifer.

Foster, Gary

MAKE YOUR OWN FUN
Alone together / Peacocks / Warne-ing / Nica's dream / What a life (Only on CD) / I
concentrate on you (Only on CD) / Some
other Spring (Only on CD) / Teef / I'll close
my eyes / Easy living / Sweet lips
CD _____ CCD 4459
Concord Jazz / May '91 / New Note.

Foster, John

**ESSENCE OF TIME, THE (Foster, John
Band)**
CD _____ QPRL 047D
Polyphonic / Sep '91 / Conifer.

Foster, Mo

BEL ASSIS (Foster, Mo & Gary Moore)
Light in your eyes / Walk in the country /
Gaia / Crete re-visited / So far away / An-
alytical engine / Pump II / Jaco / Bel assis
/ And then there were ten / Nomad
CD _____ INAK 11003
In Akustik / Mar '95 / Magnum Music
Group.

**SOUTHERN REUNION (Foster, Mo &
Gary Moore)**
CD _____ INAK 11006
In Akustik / Aug '95 / Magnum Music
Group.

Foster, Radney

DEL RIO, TX 1959
Just call me lonesome / Don't say goodbye
/ Easier said than done / Fine line / Went
for a ride / Nobody wins / Louisiana blue /
Closing time / Hammer and nails / Old silver
line
CD _____ 07822187132
Arista / Jun '94 / BMG.

LABOR OF LOVE
Willing to talk / Labor of love / My whole
wide world / Never say die / Jesse's soul /
Everybody gets the blues / It it went done /
Broke down / Precious pearl / Last chance
for love / Fine line / Nobody wins / Making
it up as I go along / Walkin' talkin' woman
CD _____ 74321229842
Arista / Apr '95 / BMG.

Foster, Ronnie

TWO HEADED FREAP
Chunky / Drowning in the sea of love / Two
headed freap / Summer song / Let's stay

together / Don't knock my love / Mystic
brew / Kentucky fried chicken
CD _____ CDP 8320822
Blue Note / Mar '95 / EMI.

Fotheringay

**FOTHERINGAY (Fotheringay & Sandy
Denny)**
Nothing more / Sea / Ballad of Ned Kelly /
Winter winds / Peace in the end / Way I feel
/ Pond and the stream / Too much of noth-
ing / Banks of the Nile
CD _____ HNCD 4426
Hannibal / May '89 / Vital / ADA.

Foulplay

SUSPECTED
CD _____ ASHADOW 2 CD
Moving Shadow / Oct '95 / SRD.

Foundations

BUILD ME UP
Baby, now that I've found you / That same
old feeling / Back on my feet again / Take
a girl like you / In the bad bad old days /
Let the heartaches begin / Tomorrow / Mr.
Personality man / Harlem shuffle / Build me
up buttercup / Give me love / Waiting on
the shores of nowhere / Any old time you're
lonely and sad / Come on back to me /
Baby I couldn't see / I can take or leave
your loving / I'm gonna be a rich man / Born
to live, born to die
CD _____ 5507492
Spectrum/Karussell / Sep '94 / PolyGram
THE.

DIGGIN' THE FOUNDATIONS
CD _____ REP 4183-WZ
Repertoire / Aug '91 / Pinnacle / Cadillac.

FOUNDATIONS, THE
CD _____ KLMCD 032
Scratch / Nov '94 / BMG.

FROM THE FOUNDATIONS
Baby now I found you / Take or leave your
loving / Just a little while longer / Come on
back to me / Call me / Etc
CD _____ REP 4182-WZ
Repertoire / Aug '91 / Pinnacle / Cadillac.

Foundry Bar Band

ROLLING HOME
Conundrum / Rollin' home / Murdo's wed-
ding / Weaver / Braes of Castlegrant /
Come by the hills / Dashing white sergeant
/ Muckin' O' Geordie's byre / How her in
ma plaide / Barren rocks of Aden / Aince
upon a time / Skye gathering / Angus
MacLeod / All for me grog / Scotland the
brave
CD _____ SPRCD 1026
Springthyme / Dec '88 / Direct / Roots / CM
/ Duncans / ADA.

Fountain, Pete

DO YOU KNOW WHAT IT MEANS
CD _____ BCD 300
GHB / Aug '94 / Jazz Music.

HIGH SOCIETY
High society / Farewell blues / At the Darktown strutter's ball / Ballin' the Jack / Muskrat ramble / Twelth street rag / Tin roof
blues / Won't you come home, Bill Bailey
CD _____ 07863660712
Bluebird / Oct '92 / BMG.

PETE FOUNTAIN
Waiting for the Robert E. Lee / South Rampart Street Parade / Angry / Bonaparte's retreat / Original dixieland one-step / Land of
dreams / Mahogany Hall Stomp / Royal
Garden blues / Sailing down the Chesea-
peake Bay / Up a lazy river / Milenburg joys
/ Margie / High society / I'm going home /
Farewell blues
CD _____ 504CD 16
504 / Aug '94 / Wellard / Jazz Music / Tar-
get/BMG / Cadillac.

**PETE FOUNTAIN AT PIPER'S OPERA
HOUSE**
CD _____ JCD 217
Jazzology / Aug '94 / Swift / Jazz Music.

SWINGIN' BLUES
CD _____ RDS 1002
Start / Oct '92 / Koch.

Fountainhead

DRAIN
CD _____ DOG 021
Doghouse / Nov '94 / Plastic Head.

Four Aces

20 GREATEST HITS: FOUR ACES
CD _____ CD 44
Bescol / '87 / CM / Target/BMG.

FOUR ACES
CD _____ CD 113
Timeless Treasures / Oct '94 / THE.

GREATEST HITS
CD _____ CD 338
Entertainers / Feb '95 / Target/BMG.

Four Preps

**LOVE IS A MANY SPLENDOURED
THING**
CD _____ RMB 75060
Remember / Aug '92 / Total/BMG.

Four Bitchin' Babies

BUY ME, BRING ME, TAKE ME
CD _____ PHCD 1150
Philo / May '93 / Direct / CM / ADA.

Four Brothers

MAKOROKOTO
Makorokoto / Rugare / Wapenga nayo bonus / Ndakatadzeiko / Sara Tasangana /
Pamusoroi / Nhaka yemusiiranwa / Uchan-
difunga / Guhwa uri mwana waani / Ndak-
atambura / Vimbayi (CD only) / Rumbidzai
(CD only) / Rudo imoto (CD only) / Pasi
pano pane zviedzo (CD only) / Maishoko
ababa namai (CD only) / Siya zviriko (CD
only)
CD _____ BAKECD 004
Cooking Vinyl / May '90 / Vital.

TOGETHER AGAIN!
Four and one moore / So blue / Swinging
door / Four in hand / Quick one / Four
brothers / Ten years later / Pretty one /
Aged in wood / Here we go again
CD _____ 74321 13040-2
RCA / Sep '93 / BMG.

Four Courts

**TRADITIONAL IRISH MUSIC AND SONG
FROM COUNTY CLARE**
CD _____ TRADCD 001
GTD / Feb '91 / Else / ADA.

Four Freshmen

DAY BY DAY
CD _____ HCD 604
Hindsight / Feb '95 / Target/BMG / Jazz
Music.

GRADUATION DAY
CD _____ 12120
Laserlight / Jan '94 / Target/BMG.

**LIVE AT BUTLER UNIVERSITY (Four
Freshmen & The Stan Kenton
Orchestra)**
There will never be another you / After you
/ Byrd Avenue / Surfer girl / Girl talk / When
the feeling hit you / Walk on by / What are
you doing the rest of your life / Brand new
key / Teach me tonight / Beautiful friendship
/ Summer has gone / Hymn to her / Come
back to me / It's not unusual / Coming
round the mountain / Walk softly / Artistry
in rhythm
CD _____ GNPD 1059
GNP Crescendo / Aug '95 / Silva Screen.

Four Lovers

JOYRIDE
What is a thing called love / Joyride / Such
a night / Girl in my dreams / Diddilly diddilly
baby / Shake a hand / Please don't leave
me / You're the apple of my eye / Stranger
/ White Christmas / It's too soon to know /
San Antonio rose / Night train / Cimarron /
Lawdy Miss Clawdy / This is my story / (I
love you) for sentimental reasons / I want a
girl - just like the girl that married dear old
Dad / Memories of you / Jambalaya / Be
lovey lovey / Love sweet love / Happy am I
/ Never never / Honey love / (I love you) for
sentimental reasons #2 / White Christmas
(2) / Girl in my dreams (2) / Diddilly diddilly
baby (2) / Don't leave me (2) / Honey love (2)
CD _____ BCD 15424
Bear Family / Apr '89 / Rollercoaster / Direct
/ CM / Swift / ADA.

Four Men & A Dog

BARKING MAD
Hidden love/Sheila Coyles / Wee Johnny
set / Wrap it up / Foxhunters / Waltzing for
dreamers / Reel / Polkas / Swing set / Short
fat Fanny / Jigs / Cruel father / High on a
mountain / McFadden's reels
CD _____ CBMMCCD 001
Special Delivery / Sep '91 / ADA / CM /
Direct.

DR. A'S SECRET REMEDIES
Papa Genes Tree / Bertha / Last month of
Summer / Mother of mercy / Punch in the
dark / Take it on back / Samba / Hollow
time / Last nite / Woodstock set / Heading
West / Hector the hero
CD _____ TRACD 106
Transatlantic / Feb '95 / BMG / Pinnacle /
ADA.

SHIFTING GRAVEL
CD _____ SPDCD 1047
Special Delivery / May '93 / ADA / CM /
Direct.

Four Preps

THREE GOLDEN GROUPS IN ONE
Hello again / Big man / Summer place /
Church bells may ring / Can't take my eyes
off you / Got a girl / Graduation day / Hurt
so bad / I'll sing for you / MacArthur Park /
I heard it through the grapevine / You've
lost that lovin' feelin' / Hard habit to break

FOUR PREPS

/ Why do fools fall in love / When I fall in love / Stroll / Little darlin' / Put your head on my shoulder / Ride like the wind / Stand by me / Love love love / Down by the station / Going out of my head / Lazy summer night / Silhouettes / Twenty six miles (Santa Catalina) / Shangri la / Over the rainbow / I'll still be loving you / Somewhere
CD _____ C5MCD 588
See For Miles/C5 / Aug '92 / Pinnacle.

Four Tops

ANTHOLOGY - FOUR TOPS
Baby I need your loving / Without the one you love / Ask the lonely / I can't help myself / It's the same old story / Something about you / Shake me, wake me / Loving you is sweeter than ever / Reach out, I'll be there / Standing in the shadows of love / I got a feeling / Bernadette / Seven rooms of gloom / (You keep) running away / Walk away Renee / If I were a carpenter / Yesterdays dreams / I'm in a different world / Can't seem to get you out of my mind / It's all in the game / Still water (love) / I can't seem to get you out of my mind / In these changing times / I can't quit your love / Nature planned it / You gotta have love in your heart / What is a man / Do what you gotta do / MacArthur Park part 2 / Simple game / So deep within you / Hey man / We gotta get you a woman
CD Set _____ 5301902
Motown / Jan '92 / PolyGram.

FOUR TOPS SINGLES COLLECTION
Reach out, I'll be there / Standing in the shadows of love / Bernadette / Walk away Renee / If I were a carpenter / Simple game / Seven rooms of gloom / Loving you is sweeter than ever / You keep running away / Yesterday's dreams / I'm in a different world / What is a man / Loco in Acapulco / Indestructible / When she was my girl / It's all in the game / Still water (love) / I can't help myself / Do what you gotta do / Keeper of the castle / Don't walk away
CD _____ 5157102
Motown / Sep '92 / PolyGram.

LOOK OF LOVE, THE
Standing in the shadows of love / Look of love / Seven rooms of gloom / Where did you go / Sunny / Honey / Loving you is sweeter than ever / Daydream believer / I'm grateful / This guy's in love with you / Key / Light my fire
CD _____ 5500772
Spectrum/Karussell / May '93 / PolyGram / THE.

MOTOWN'S GREATEST HITS: FOUR TOPS
CD _____ 5300162
Motown / Jan '92 / PolyGram.

UNTIL YOU LOVE SOMEONE - MORE BEST OF THE FOUR TOPS (1965-1970)
Teahouse in your kitchen / Your love is amazing / Since you've been gone / Helpless / Love feels like fire / I like everything about you / Stay in my lonely arms / Darling I hum our song / I got a feeling / Brenda / Until you love someone / You can't hurry love / Wonderful baby / What else is there to do (but think about you) / What is a man / Nothing / L.A. (My town) / Reflections
CD _____ 812271183-2
WEA / Jan '93 / Warner Music.

WITH LOVE
Don't walk away / Sweet understanding love / When she was my girl / I believe in you and me / Tonight I'm gonna love you all over / Ain't no woman (like the one I've got) / One more mountain to climb / Keeper of the castle / Let me set you free / Sad hearts / Are you man enough / Seven lonely nights / Catfish / We all gotta stick together
CD _____ 5501352
Spectrum/Karussell / Oct '93 / PolyGram / THE.

Four Tunes

COMPLETE JUBILEE SESSIONS
CD _____ NEDCD 229
Sequel / Nov '92 / BMG.

Fourplay

BETWEEN THE SHEETS
Chant / Monterrey / Between the sheets / Li'l darlin' / Flying east / One in the A.M. / Gulliver / Amoroso / Summer child / Anthem / Song for Somalia
CD _____ 9362452402
WEA / Aug '93 / Warner Music.

FOURPLAY
Bali run / 101 eastbound / Foreplay / Moonjogger / Max-o-man / After the dance / Quadrille / Midnight stroll / October morning / Wish you were here / Rainforest
CD _____ 7599266562
WEA / Mar '94 / Warner Music.

Fourth Way

FOURTH WAY, THE
CD _____ COD 022
Jazz View / Aug '92 / Harmonia Mundi.

Fourth World

ENCOUNTERS OF THE FOURTH WORLD
Burning money / What you see / Canja na cavaca / Pandeiro solo/Seven seeds / Yara/Firewalk / Scorpio rising / Final celebration
CD _____ BW 045
B&W / Jan '96 / New Note.

FOURTH WORLD
Esperanza / River Sao Francisco / Starfish / Povo da Lira / Africa / Earthquake / Lua / Seven steps / Firewater - Jive talk / Santa Anita
CD _____ JHCD 026
Ronnie Scott's Jazz House / Jan '94 / Jazz Music / Magnum Music Group / Cadillac.

Fowler, Lemuel

LEM FOWLER (1923-27) (Fowler, Lem/Helen Baxter/H. McDonald)
CD _____ JPCD 1520
Jazz Perspectives / May '95 / Jazz Music / Hot Shot.

Fowley, Kim

KINGS OF SATURDAY NIGHT (Fowley, Kim & Ben Vaughn)
CD _____ SECTOR2 1002
Sector 2 / Jul '95 / Direct / ADA.

LET THE MADNESS IN
CD _____ RRCD 203
Receiver / Aug '95 / Grapevine.

MONDO HOLLYWOOD
CD _____ CREV 36CD
Rev-Ola / Nov '95 / 3MV / Vital.

OUTRAGEOUS/GOOD CLEAN FUN
CD _____ CREV 033CD
Rev-Ola / Feb '95 / 3MV / Vital.

WHITE NEGROES IN DEUTSCHLAND
CD _____ USMCD 1021
Marilyn / Jul '93 / Pinnacle.

Fowlkes, Eddie

TECHNOSOUL (Fowlkes, Eddie 'Flashin' & 3MB)
My soul / Computee / Move me / Tribal joy / Hoodlum child / Golden apple / Image-a-nation
CD _____ TRESOR 8CD
Tresor / Apr '93 / SRD.

Fox, Donal

UGLY BEAUTY (Fox, Donal & David Murray)
Ugly beauty / Vamping with T.T. / Round Midnight / Hope scope / Song for Murray / Icarus / Becca's ballad / Picasso / Golden ladders / Hope scope (Live)
CD _____ ECD 221312
Evidence / Dec '95 / Harmonia Mundi / ADA / Cadillac.

Fox, Paul

TRIBULATION DUB VOL.1
CD _____ WSPCD 002
WSP / Nov '93 / Jetstar.

Fox, Roy

ROY FOX
CD _____ PASTCD 9745
Flapper / Aug '91 / Pinnacle.

Fox, Samantha

GREATEST HITS - SAMANTHA FOX
CD _____ CHIP 122
Jive / Sep '92 / BMG.

HITS ALBUM, THE
CD _____ EMPRCD 557
Emporio / Mar '95 / THE / Disc / CM.

HITS COLLECTION: SAMANTHA FOX
Touch me (I want your body) / Hot for you / I promise you / Best is yet to come / True devotion / Baby I'm lost for words / Naughty girls / Hold on tight / One in a million / That sensation / I surrender (to the spirit of the night) / Confession / It's only love / Do ya do ya (wanna please me)
CD _____ PWKS 541
Carlton Home Entertainment / Sep '89 / Carlton Home Entertainment.

INTERVIEW COMPACT DISC: SAM FOX
CD P.Disc _____ CBAK 4023
Baktabak / Nov '89 / Baktabak.

SAM
Nothing's gonna stop me now / Want you to want to / Tonight's the night / Best is yet to come / Ready to fly / Dream city / Satisfaction / Do ya do ya (wanna please me) / I promise you / Lovehouse / Hold on tight / Suzie don't leave me with your boyfriend / One in a million / Never gonna fall in love again
CD _____ 5501162
Spectrum/Karussell / Oct '93 / PolyGram / THE.

Foxley, Ray

PROFESSOR FOXLEY'S SPORTING HOUSE MUSIC
CD _____ BLR 84 021
L&R / May '91 / New Note.

RAY FOXLEY & BLACK EAGLE JAZZBAND (Foxley, Ray & Black Eagle Jazzband)
Stomp Off / Oct '93 / Jazz Music / Wellard.
CD _____ SOSCD 1257

Foxx, Inez

AT MEMPHIS AND MORE
There's a hand that's reaching out / Let me down easy / Crossing over the bridge / I had a talk with my man / You're saving me for a rainy day / You don't want my love / Lady, the doctor and the prescription / Time / Mousa muse / Circuits overloaded / I just want to know (before you go) / He ain't all good but he ain't all bad / One woman's man / Watch the dog / You hurt me for the last time
CD _____ CDSXD 034
Stax / Oct '90 / Pinnacle.

COUNT THE DAYS (Foxx, Inez & Charlie)
CD _____ CDRB 26
Charly / Aug '95 / Charly / THE / Cadillac.

Foxx, John

ASSEMBLY
CD _____ CDVM 9002
Virgin / Jun '92 / EMI.

GARDEN, THE
Europe after the rain / Systems of romance / When I was a man and you were a woman / Dancing like a gun / Pater Noster / Night suit / You were there / Fusion / Walk away / Garden / Fission
CD _____ CDV 2194
Virgin / Jul '93 / EMI.

METAMATIC
Plaza / He's a liquid / Underpass / Metal beat / No-one driving / New kind of man / Blurred girl / 030 / Tidal wave / Touch and girl
CD _____ CDV 2146
Virgin / Jul '93 / EMI.

Foyer Des Arts

DIE UNFAEHIGKEIT ZU FRUEHSTUECKEN
CD _____ EFA 4522 CD
Funfundvierzig / Jun '89 / SRD.

Fracasso, Michael

LOVE AND TRUST
CD _____ DJD 3205
Dejadisc / May '94 / Direct / ADA.

WHEN I LIVED IN THE WILD
CD _____ BOHB 003
Bohemia Beat / Feb '95 / Direct / CM / ADA.

Fracus, Dimitru

IMPROVISATIONS ON FAMOUS ROMANIAN THEMES (Fracus, Dimitru & Marcel Cellier)
Marie Polaie ciurate / Cinrec de unstrainare / Quand dieu crea les montagnes / Les moutons, les bergers / Dooina prieteniei / Doina Cind aram copil d-un an / Bruil lui cepzan / Doina Cresta frunza / Entre ciel et terre / Appels des sommets et danse du berger / Doina lui constantin gherghina / Poarga din pomezau / Doina au sommet de la collins / Suite: Un soir en transylvanie / Doina: Les plaines du banat / Duex danses dominicales / Oh montagnes aux sapins majesteux / Ardaean de la zarvesti / Cind s a pierduit ciobanul oile
CD _____ PV 750003
Disques Pierre Verany / Jul '94 / Kingdom.

Fradon, Amy

TAKE ME HOME (Fradon, Amy & Leslie Ritter)
CD _____ SHCD 8013
Shanachie / Dec '94 / Koch / ADA / Greensleeves.

Fraley, J.P.

MAYSVILLE (Fraley, J.P. & Annadeene)
CD _____ ROUCD 0351
Rounder / Nov '95 / CM / Direct / ADA / Cadillac.

Frampton, Peter

FRAMPTON COMES ALIVE
Something's happening / Doobie wah / Show me the way / It's a plain shame / All I want to be (is by your side) / Wind of change / Baby, I love your way / I wanna go to the sun / Penny for your thoughts / (I'll give you) money / Shine on / Jumpin' Jack Flash / Lines on my face / Do you feel like we do
CD _____ CDMID 164
A&M / Oct '92 / PolyGram.

FRAMPTON COMES ALIVE II
Day in the sun / Lying / For now / Most of all / You / Waiting for your love / I'm in you / Talk to me / Hang on to a dream / Can't take that away / More ways than one / Almost said goodbye / Off the hook / Show me the way (On CD set only) / Baby I love your way (On CD set only) / Lines on my face (On CD set only) / Do you feel like we do (On CD set only)
CD _____ EIRSCD 1074
CD Set _____ EIRSCDX 1074
IRS/EMI / Oct '95 / EMI.

LOVE TAKER
CD _____ HADCD 199
Javelin / Nov '95 / THE / Henry Hadaway Organisation.

Peter Frampton

Day in the sun / You can be sure / It all comes down to you / You / I can't take that away / Young island / Off the hook / Waiting for your love / So hard to believe / Out of the blue / Shelter through the night / Changing all the time
CD _____ 474876 2
Relativity / Apr '94 / Sony.

SHINE ON
CD _____ CDMID 174
A&M / Oct '92 / PolyGram.

SHOWS THE WAY
Friday on my mind / Signed, sealed, delivered (I'm yours) / Baby, I love your way / I can't stand it no more / You don't know like I know / Wind of change / Show me the way / We've just begun / (I'll give you) money / Breaking all the rules / All night long / Jumpin' Jack Flash
CD _____ 5501032
Spectrum/Karussell / Mar '94 / PolyGram / THE.

Fran, Carol

SEE THERE (Fran, Carol & Clarence Holliman)
CD _____ BT 1100CD
Black Top / Apr '94 / CM / Direct / ADA.

SOUL SENSATION (Fran, Carol & Clarence Holliman)
CD _____ BT 1071CD
Black Top / Feb '92 / CM / Direct / ADA.

Francis, Connie

24 GREATEST HITS
Where the boys are / If I didn't care / Hurt / Vacation / Are you lonesome tonight / Together among my souvenirs / Everybody's somebody's fool / Old time rock 'n' roll / My heart has a mind of its own / Crying time / My happiness / Lipstick on your collar / Who's sorry now / Stupid cupid / Misty blue / Torn between two lovers / Breakin' in a brand new broken heart / Many tears ago / Don't break the heart that loves you / Cry / Frankie / Second hand love / Something stupid
CD _____ PLATCD 3910
Prism / Nov '90 / Prism.

COLLECTION, THE
Stupid Cupid / Lipstick on your collar / Don't break the heart that loves you / Jealous heart / Where the boys are / Breakin' in a brand new broken heart / Plenty good lovin' / Singing the blues / Valentino / You always hurt the one you love / My heart has a mind of its own / Heartaches by the number / Bye bye love / Your cheatin' heart / I can't stop loving you / Walk on by / Among my souvenirs / My happiness
CD _____ 5518222
Spectrum/Karussell / Nov '95 / PolyGram / THE.

CONNIE FRANCIS - 24 GREATEST HITS
CD _____ RMB 75069
Remember / Jan '94 / Total/BMG.

LOVE SONGS
Carolina moon / My happiness / I can't stop loving you / Breakin' in a brand new broken heart / True love / Make it easy on yourself / I say a little prayer / It's only make believe / What the world needs now is love / Don't break the heart that loves you / All by myself / Moon river / Love is a many splendoured thing / La vie en rose
CD _____ 5500862
Spectrum/Karussell / Oct '93 / PolyGram / THE.

LOVE SONGS: CONNIE FRANCIS
Who's sorry now / Carolina Moon / Jealous heart / He thinks I still care / Fallin' / I don't hurt anymore / Bye bye love / When the boy in your arms (is the boy in your heart) / My heart has a mind of its own / Half as much / Make it easy on yourself / Walk on by / Oh lonesome me / Among my souvenirs
CD _____ PWKS 540
Carlton Home Entertainment / Sep '89 / Carlton Home Entertainment.

LOVE'N'COUNTRY
My happiness / This girl's in love with you / I'm sorry I made you cry / What's wrong with my world / I fall to care / Please help me, I'm falling / Many tears ago / I can't stop loving you / You always hurt the one you love / Look of love / If I didn't care / Breaking in a brand new broken heart / If

242

you ever change your mind / Send me the pillow that you dream on / Everybody's somebody's fool / My heart cries for you
CD _____ **PWK 113**
Carlton Home Entertainment / Jun '89 / Carlton Home Entertainment.

PORTRAIT OF A SONG STYLIST
Come rain or come shine / All by myself / Song is ended (but the melody lingers on) / Moon river / Mack the knife / Love is a many splendoured thing / True love / All the way / Second time around / Lili Marlene / Milord / Am I blue / La vie en rose / Take me to your heart again / Fascination
CD _____ **HARCD 108**
Masterpiece / Apr '89 / BMG.

SING GREAT COUNTRY FAVORITES
(Francis, Connie & Hank Williams Jr)
Bye bye love / Send me the pillow that you dream on / Wolverton mountain / No letter today / Please help me, I'm falling / Singin' the blues / Walk on by / If you've got the money, I've got the time / Mule skinner blues / Making believe / Blue blue day / No letter today (alt) / Wabash cannonball / Mule skinner blues (alt.take)
CD _____ **BCD 15737**
Bear Family / Aug '93 / Rollercoaster / Direct / CM / Swift / ADA.

SINGLES COLLECTION, THE
Lipstick on your collar / Everybody's somebody's fool / I'm sorry I made you cry / I'm gonna be warm this winter / Together / V-A-C-A-T-I-O-N / If by Frankie / Many tears ago / Mama/Hobot man / Fallin' / Among my souvenirs / In the valley of love / Who's sorry now / Stupid cupid/Carolina moon / Breakin' in a brand new broken heart / Plenty good lovin' / Baby's first Christmas / You always hurt the one you love / Don't break the heart that loves you / My happiness / Valentino / Where the boys are/Baby Roo / My heart has a mind of its own / Senza fine / Jealous heart / My child
CD _____ **519 131-2**
PolyGram TV / Apr '93 / PolyGram.

WHITE SOX, PINK LIPSTICK & STUPID CUPID (5 CDs)
Didn't I love you enough / Freddy / (Oh please) Make him jealous / Goody goodbye / Are you satisfied / My treasure / My first real love / Believe in me / Forgetting / Send for my baby / I never had a sweetheart / Little blue wren / Everyone needs someone / My sailor boy / No other one / I leaned on a man / Faded orchid / Eighteen / My sisters clothes / Majesty of love / You my darling you / Who's sorry now / You were only fooling (while I was falling in love) / I'm beginning to see the light / Rudolph the red nosed reindeer / Wheel of fortune / How can I make you believe in me / You belong to me / Daddy's little girl / I'm sorry I made you cry / I cried for you / You always hurt the one you love / I'll get by / Lock up your heart / Heartaches / I'm nobody's baby / My melancholy baby / I miss you so / It's the talk of the town / If I had you / How deep is the ocean / Carolina moon / Stupid Cupid / Happy days and lonely nights / Fallin' / You're my everything / My happiness / Don't speak of love / Love eyes / Never before / In the valley of love / Time after time / Blame it on my youth / How did he look / That's all / Toward the end of the day / I really don't want to know / No-one to cry to / If I didn't care / If you love me tonight (2 takes) / Come rain or come shine / All by myself / Hold me, thrill me, kiss me / Song is ended (but the melody lingers on) / There will never be another you / Melancholy serenade / Rock-a-bye your baby with a Dixie melody / Hallelujah, I love him so / My thanks to you / Bells of St. Mary's / Good luck, good health, God bless you / Garden in the rain / Try a little tenderness / Goodnight sweetheart / Cruising down the river / I'll close my eyes (American/British versions) / Very thought of you / These foolish things / Tree in the meadow / Gypsy / Now is the hour / You're gonna miss me / Frankie / Lipstick on your collar / Oh, Frankie / I almost lost my mind / I'm walkin' / Just a dream / Heartbreak hotel / I hear you knocking / Tweedle dee / Ain't that a shame / It's only make believe / Sincerely / Don't be cruel / Bye bye love / Earth angel / Hearts of stone / Silhouettes / Plenty good lovin' / Singin' the blues / My special angel / Tennessee waltz / Let me go, Lover / Young love / Half as much / Anytime / Your cheatin' heart / Cold cold heart / Peace in the valley / Too young / Temptation / You made me love you / Prisoner of love / Young at heart / It's not for me to say / Thinking of you / That's my desire / Because of you / Where the blue of the night meets the gold of the day / April love / Cry / God bless America / Among my souvenirs / Snapdragon / No one / Tiger and the mouse / Fascination (take 10) / Look up the heart (slow version) / My melancholy baby (take 2) / No one (take 2) / Tiger and the mouse, The (take 4)
CD Set _____ **BCD 15616**
Bear Family / Jul '93 / Rollercoaster / Direct / CM / Swift / ADA.

Francis, Dean

THIS GROOVE'S FOR YOU
This groove's for you / Just funkin' around / Without guns / I got the hots / It's okay / Got a funky disposition / Dancefloor jazz / In the rain / Know when to leave it alone
CD _____ **ME 000332**
Souloicty/Bassism / Sep '95 / EWM.

Francis, Panama

GET UP AND DANCE (Francis, Panama & The Savoy Sultans)
CD _____ **STCD 5**
Stash / '88 / Jazz Music / CM / Cadillac / Direct / ADA.

GETTIN' IN THE GROOVE (Francis, Panama & The Savoy Sultans)
Song of the islands / Stitches / Rhythm Dr Man / Frezey / Chequered had / Second balcony jump / Nuages / Little John special
CD _____ **BLE 233320**
Black & Blue / Dec '90 / Wellard / Koch.

Francis, W.J.

RAGGA LOVE
CD _____ **MRCD 002**
Metronome / Dec '92 / Jetstar.

Franck, Albert

UN PARISIEN A PARIS
CD _____ **ROSE 236CD**
New Rose / Feb '91 / Direct / ADA.

Franck, Thomas

THOMAS FRANCK IN NEW YORK (Franck, Thomas Quartet)
CD _____ **CRISS 1052CD**
Criss Cross / Nov '91 / Cadillac / Harmonia Mundi.

Franco, Gian

SEA, THE (Franco, Gian Reverberi)
CD _____ **CDPM 6001**
Prestige / Mar '90 / Total/BMG.

Frank & Walters

TRAINS AND BOATS AND PLANES
CD _____ **8284022**
Go Discs / Jul '93 / PolyGram.

Frank, Ed

NEW NEW ORLEANS MUSIC, VOL. 1 (Frank, Ed Quintet)
CD _____ **CD 2065**
Rounder / '88 / CM / Direct / ADA / Cadillac.

Franke, Bob

HEART OF THE FLOWER, THE
CD _____ **DARINGCD 3016**
Daring / Oct '95 / Direct / CM / ADA.

Franke, Christopher

KLEMANIA
Scattered thoughts of a canyon flight / Inside a morphing space / Silent waves
CD _____ **SI 85042**
Sonic Images / Sep '95 / Pinnacle.

Frankel, Judy

SEPHARDIC SONGS OF LOVE & HOPE
CD _____ **GVMCD 157**
Global Village / May '93 / ADA / Direct.

Frankfurt Jazz Ensemble

ATMOSPHERIC CONDITIONS PERMITTING
CD _____ **5173542**
ECM / Dec '95 / New Note.

Frankie Goes To Hollywood

BANG (Greatest Hits)
Relax / Two tribes / War / Ferry 'cross the Mersey / Warriors of the wasteland / For heaven's sake / World is my oyster / Welcome to the pleasure dome / Watching the wildlife / Born to run / Rage hard / Power of love / Bang
CD _____ **450993912-2**
ZTT / Oct '93 / Warner Music.

LIVERPOOL
Warriors of the wasteland / Rage hard / Kill the pain / Maximum joy / Watching the wildlife / Lunar bay / For heaven's sake / Is anybody out there
CD _____ **450994744-2**
ZTT / Mar '94 / Warner Music.

WELCOME TO THE PLEASURE DOME
World is my oyster / Welcome to the pleasure dome / Relax / War / Two tribes / Happy hi / Born to run / Wish the lads were here (inc. ballad of '32) / Krisco kisses / Black night white light / Only star in heaven / Power of love / Bang...
CD _____ **4509947452**
ZTT / Feb '95 / Warner Music.

WHOLE TWELVE INCHES, THE
Relax / Two tribes / Welcome to the pleasure dome / Rage hard / Warriors of the wasteland
CD _____ **450995292-2**
ZTT / Apr '94 / Warner Music.

Franklin, Aretha

30 GREATEST HITS
I never loved a man (the way I love you) / Respect / Do right woman, do right man / Dr. Feelgood / Save me / Baby I love you / (You make me feel like) a natural woman / Chain of fools / Since you've been gone / Ain't no way / Think / I say a little prayer / House that Jack built / See saw / Weight / Share your love with me / Eleanor Rigby / Call me / Spirit in the dark / Don't play that song (You lied) / You're all I need to get by / Bridge over troubled water / Spanish harlem / Rock steady / Oh me oh my (I'm a fool for you baby) / Daydreaming / Wholly holy / Angel / Until you come back to me / I'm in love
CD _____ **756781668-2**
Atlantic / Mar '93 / Warner Music.

AFTER HOURS
Bitter earth / Once in a lifetime / Misty / There is no greater love / Unforgettable / If I should lose you / Don't cry baby / Just for a thrill / I'm wanderin' / Don't say you're sorry again / Look for the silver lining
CD _____ **983300.2**
Pickwick/Sony Collector's Choice / Oct '93 / Carlton Home Entertainment / Pinnacle / Sony.

AMAZING GRACE
Mary don't you weep / Precious Lord, take my hand / You've got a friend / Old landmark / Give yourself to Jesus / How I got over / What a friend we have in Jesus / Amazing grace / Precious memories / Climbing higher mountains / God will take care of you / Wholy holy / You'll never walk alone / Never grow old
CD _____ **756781324-2**
Atlantic / Jun '93 / Warner Music.

ARETHA ARRIVES
Satisfaction / You are my sunshine / Never let me go / 96 tears / Prove it / Night life / That's life / Ronettes / Ain't nobody / Going down slow / Baby I love you
CD _____ **8122712742**
Atlantic / Jan '93 / Warner Music.

ARETHA IN PARIS
Satisfaction / Don't let me lose this dream / Soul serenade / Night life / Baby I love you / Groovin' / Natural woman / Come back baby / Dr. Feelgood / Respect / Since you've been gone / I never loved a man (the way I love you) / Chain of fools
CD _____ **8122718522**
Atlantic / Dec '94 / Warner Music.

ARETHA NOW
Think / I say a little prayer / See saw / Night time is the right time / You send me / You're a sweet sweet man / I take what I want / Hello sunshine / Change / I can't see myself leaving you
CD _____ **8122712732**
Atlantic / Feb '93 / Warner Music.

ARETHA'S GOLD
I never loved a man (the way I love you) / Do right woman, do right man / Respect / Dr. Feelgood / Baby I love you / (You make me feel like) a natural woman / Chain of fools / Since you've been gone / Ain't no way / Think / You send me / House that Jack built / I say a little prayer / Don't
CD _____ **756781445-2**
Atlantic / Jun '93 / Warner Music.

ARETHA'S GREATEST HITS
Spanish Harlem / Chain of fools / Don't play that song (You lied) / I say a little prayer / Dr. Feelgood / Let it be / Do right woman, do right man / Bridge over troubled water / Respect / Baby I love you / (You make me feel like) a natural woman / I never loved a man (the way I love you) / You're all I need to get by / Call me
CD _____ **756781451-2**
Atlantic / Jun '93 / Warner Music.

ARETHA'S JAZZ
Ramblin' / Today I sing the blues / Pitiful / Crazy he calls me / Bring it on home to me / Somewhere / Moody's mood for love (Moody's love) / Just right tonight
CD _____ **756781230-2**
Atlantic / Jun '93 / Warner Music.

BACK2BACK
CD Set _____ **74321291442**
RCA / Sep '95 / BMG.

COLLECTION: ARETHA FRANKLIN
Walk on by / It ain't necessarily so / What a difference a day makes / Once in a lifetime (Love) / Over the rainbow / You made me love you / Say it isn't so / Unforgettable / My guy / Exactly like you / Try a little tenderness / I'm sitting on top of the world / Skylark / Solitude / Where are you / Love for sale (Live) / Swanee / I surrender dear / Look for the silver lining / Lover come back to me / Make someone happy / Ol' man river / I apologise
CD _____ **CCSCD 152**
Castle / Jul '87 / BMG.

GOSPEL ROOTS
CD _____ **CDCD 1164**
Charly / Apr '94 / Charly / THE / Cadillac.

GREAT ARETHA FRANKLIN, THE
Won't be long / Over the rainbow / Love is the only thing / Sweet lover / All night long / Who needs you / Right now / Are you sure / Maybe I'm a fool / It ain't necessarily so / Blue my myself / Today I sing the blues
CD _____ **9022912**
Pickwick/Sony Collector's Choice / Mar '94 / Carlton Home Entertainment / Pinnacle / Sony.

GREATEST HITS: ARETHA FRANKLIN (1960-1965)
Soulville / Lee Cross / Skylark / Take it like you give it / Try a little tenderness / Take a look / Runnin' out of fools / Sweet bitter love / Rock-a-bye your baby with a Dixie melody / Cry like a baby / God bless the child
CD _____ **9825842**
Pickwick/Sony Collector's Choice / Oct '91 / Carlton Home Entertainment / Pinnacle / Sony.

HEY NOW HEY (The Other Side Of The Sky)
CD _____ **8122718532**
Atlantic / Dec '94 / Warner Music.

I NEVER LOVED A MAN THE WAY I LOVE YOU
Respect / Drown in my own tears / I never loved a man (the way I love you) / Soul serenade / Don't let me lose this dream / Baby baby baby / Dr. Feelgood / Good times / Do right woman, do right man / Save me / Change is gonna come
CD _____ **756781439-2**
Atlantic / Mar '93 / Warner Music.

JAZZ TO SOUL
Today I sing the blues / (Blue) by myself / Maybe I'm a fool / All night long / Blue holiday / Nobody like you / Sweet lover / Just for a thrill / If ever I would leave you / Once in a while / This bitter earth / God bless the child / Skylark / Muddy water / Drinking again / What a difference a day makes / Unforgettable / Love for sale / Misty / Impossible / This could be the start of something / Won't be long / Operation heartbreak / Soulville / Runnin' out of fools / Trouble in mind / Walk on by / Every little bit hurts / Mockingbird / You'll lose a good thing / Cry like a baby / Take it like you give it / Land of dreams / Can't you just see me / (No no) I'm losing you / Bit of soul / Why was I born / Until you were gone / Lee cross
CD Set _____ **CD 48515**
Legacy / Nov '93 / Sony.

LADY SOUL
Chain of fools / Money won't change you / People get ready / Niki Hoeky / Natural woman / Since you've been gone / Good to me as I am to you / Come back baby / Groovin' / Ain't no way
CD _____ **756781818-2**
Atlantic / Mar '93 / Warner Music.

LET ME IN YOUR LIFE
Let me into your life / Every natural thing / Ain't nothing like the real thing / I'm in love / Until you come back to me / I'm afraid / the masquerade is over / With pen in hand / Oh baby / Eight days on the road / If you don't think / Song for you
CD _____ **8122718542**
Atlantic / Dec '94 / Warner Music.

LIVE AT FILLMORE WEST
Respect / Love the one you're with / Bridge over troubled water / Eleanor Rigby / Make it with you / Don't play that song (You lied) / Dr. Feelgood / Spirit in the dark / Reach out and touch
CD _____ **812271526-2**
Atlantic / Feb '94 / Warner Music.

QUEEN OF SOUL
I never loved a man (the way I love you) / Do right woman, do right man / Dr. Feelgood / Baby I love you / (You make me feel like) a natural woman / Chain of fools / Since you've been gone / Ain't no way / Save me / House that Jack built / Think / I say a little prayer / See saw / Daydreaming / Call me / Don't play that song (You lied) / Border song (Holy Moses) / You're all I need to get by / I'm in love / Spanish Harlem / Rock steady / Angel / Until you come back to me
CD _____ **756780606-2**
Atlantic / Oct '94 / Warner Music.

QUEEN OF SOUL - THE ATLANTIC RECORDINGS (4CD Set)
CD Set _____ **8122710632**
Atlantic / Nov '92 / Warner Music.

SOUL '69
Ramblin' / Today I sing the blues / River's invitation / Pitiful / Crazy he calls me / Bring it on home to me / Tracks of my tears / If you gotta make a fool of somebody / Gentle on my mind / So long / I'll never be free / Elusive butterfly
CD _____ **812271523-2**
Atlantic / Feb '94 / Warner Music.

SOUL QUEENS VOL.1
Power / He's alright / Day is past / White as snow / Yield not to temptation / Jesus on the main line / This little girl of mine /

There is a fountain / Precious lord / You
grow closer
CD _____ SMS 059
Carlton Home Entertainment / Oct '92 /
Carlton Home Entertainment.

SPIRIT IN THE DARK
Don't play that song (You lied) / Thrill is
gone / Pullin' / You and me / Honest I do /
Spirit in the dark / When the battle is over /
One way ticket / Try Matty's / That's all I
want from you / Oh no, not my baby / Why
I sing the blues
CD _____ 8122715252
Atlantic / Feb '94 / Warner Music.

THIS GIRL'S IN LOVE WITH YOU
Son of a preacher man / Share your love
with me / Dark end of the street / Let it be
/ Eleanor Rigby / This girl's in love with you
/ It ain't fair / Weight / Call me / Sit down
and cry
CD _____ 8122715242
Atlantic / Feb '93 / Warner Music.

**UNFORGETTABLE (A Tribute To Dinah
Washington)**
Unforgettable / Cold cold heart / What a dif-
ference a day makes / Drinking again / No-
body knows the way I feel this morning /
Evil gal blues / Don't say you're sorry again
/ This bitter earth / If I should lose you /
Soulville / Lee cross
CD _____ 4805082
Columbia / May '95 / Sony.

WHAT YOU SEE IS WHAT YOU SWEAT
Everyday people / Everchanging time /
What you see is what you sweat / Mary
goes round / I dreamed a dream / Someone
else's eyes / Doctor's orders / You can't
take me for granted /What did you give
CD _____ 261724
Arista / Feb '94 / BMG.

WHO'S ZOOMIN' WHO?
Freeway of love / Another night / Sweet bitter love / Who's zoomin' who / Sisters are
doin' it for themselves / Until you say you
love me / Push / Ain't nobody ever loved
you / Integrity
CD _____ 259053
Arista / Aug '88 / BMG.

YOUNG, GIFTED AND BLACK
Oh me oh my / Daydreaming / Rock steady
/ Young, gifted and black / All the king's
horses / Brand new me / April fools / I've
been loving you too long / First snow in Ko-
komo / Long and winding road / Didn't I /
Border song
CD _____ 812271527-2
Atlantic / Feb '94 / Warner Music.

Franklin, Kirk

**KIRK FRANKLIN AND FAMILY (Franklin,
Kirk & The Family)**
Why we sing / He's able / Silver and gold /
Call on the lord / Real love / He can handle
it / Letter from my friend / Family worship /
Speak to me / Till we meet again
CD _____ GCD 2119
Alliance Music / Jun '95 / EMI.

Franko, Mladen

**FUN AND ROMANCE (Franko, Mladen &
Norman Candler)**
CD _____ ISCD 123
Intersound / '91 / Jazz Music.

Franks, Michael

ART OF TEA
Nightmoves / Egg plant / Monkey see,
Monkey do / St. Elmo's fire / Don't know
why I'm so happy I'm sad / Jive / Popsicle
toes / Mr. Blue / Sometimes I just forget to
smile
CD _____ 7599272242
WEA / Aug '81 / Warner Music.

BLUE PACIFIC
Art of love / Woman in the waves / All I need
/ Long slow distance / Vincent's ear / Speak
to me / On the inside / Chez nous / Blue
pacific / Crayon sun
CD _____ 7599261832
WEA / Jun '90 / Warner Music.

DRAGONFLY SUMMER
Coming to life / Soul mate / Dragonfly summer / Monk's new tune / Learning what love
means / I love Lucy / Practice makes perfect / String of pearls / Keeping my eye on
you / Dream / You were meant for me / How
I remember you
CD _____ 936245227-2
Warner Bros. / May '93 / Warner Music.

ONE BAD HABIT
Baseball / Inside you / All dressed up with
nowhere to go / Lotus blossom / On my
way home / One bad habit / Loving you
more and more / Still life / He tells himself
he's happy
CD _____ 7599234272
WEA / Feb '94 / Warner Music.

SKIN DIVE
Read my lips / Let me count the ways /
Your secret's safe with me / Don't be shy /
When I give my love to you / Queen of the
underground / Now I know why they call it
falling / Please don't say goodnight / When
she is mine

CD _____ 7599252752
WEA / Feb '94 / Warner Music.

Franks, Rebecca

**ALL OF A SUDDEN (Franks, Rebecca
Coupe)**
CD _____ JR 009022
Justice / Sep '92 / Koch.

**SUIT OF ARMOUR (Franks, Rebecca
Coupe)**
CD _____ JR 009012
Justice / Nov '92 / Koch.

Frantic Flintstones

ENJOY YOURSELF
Enjoy yourself / Cradle baby / Black Caddi
/ I gotta baby / You don't love me anymore
/ Tip of my tongue / Ain't got a / Draw your
breaks / She done me wrong / Mummy's
boy / Sunset of my tears / Up your nose /
Crazy Clems dream / Chop one up Chuck
CD _____ CDGRAM 86
Anagram / Sep '94 / Pinnacle.

JAMBOREE
Detroit dirt box / Love for a nutter / Your
time is up / Mean mean woman / Diablo /
Saty with me / Sweet Georgia Brown / Lu-
natics (are raving) / Busted / Mindkill / (To
the Devil) a son / Oh 888 / Candy man /
He's waiting / Sad 'n' lonely / Suspended /
Chop chop splash splash / Honeychild /
Hey Chuck / Detroit blood box
CD _____ CDGRAM 65
Anagram / Sep '93 / Pinnacle.

MY WOMAN IS...
CD _____ TBCD 2006
Nervous / Mar '93 / Nervous / Magnum
Music Group.

**NIGHTMARE CONTINUES/
SCHLACHTOFF BOOGIE WOOGIE, THE**
Five clawed talon / Angel / Lost love / Astral
cowboy / Waste of life / Smack, smack /
Dog rip / Bone rest / Twisted retard / Rasp-
pin' grasses / Burned 'n' turned / Dustbin
case / Drugs in the valley / Holy sisters /
Please cool baby / Absolution / Endless
sleep / Hang 10 / Trips / Pantman / Breakout Mania / Gonna miss ya / Sexy red number / West of London / Race is on / Legions
song / Drug squad / Pantman (vocal)
CD _____ SLOG CD 8
Street Link / Oct '92 / BMG.

**ROCKIN' OUT/ NOT CHRISTMAS
ALBUM**
Rockin' out / What the hell / One night
stand / Hot head baby / Chuck blows a fuse
/ Rockin' bones / Let's go somewhere / No
one stays / Frantic / Wider road to hell /
Honey maker / Necro blues / Oh little town
of Bedrock / Gone gone well gone / Alone
again / Round Midnight / Just because /
Santa Claus bring my baby back to me /
Santa Claus is back in town / Blue Christ-
mas / Ole black joe
CD _____ CDMPSYCHO 6
Anagram / Jun '95 / Pinnacle.

Fraser, Alasdair

DAWN DANCE
CD _____ CUL 106CD
Culburnie / Jul '95 / Ross / ADA.

**DRIVEN BOW, THE (Fraser, Alasdair &
Jody Stretcher)**
CD _____ CUL 102CD
Culburnie / Jul '95 / Ross / ADA.

PORTRAIT OF A SCOTTISH FIDDLER
CD _____ CUL 109CD
Culburnie / Jul '95 / Ross / ADA.

**SKYEDANCE (Fraser, Alasdair & Paul
Machlis)**
CD _____ CUL 101D
Culburnie / Oct '95 / Ross / ADA.

Fraser, Dean

CLASSICS
CD _____ RNCD 2080
Rhino / Dec '94 / Jetstar / Magnum Music
Group / THE.

PUMPIN' AIR
Redemption song / Rent a car / I'll always
love you / Moody's mood for love / Stop,
look, listen (for your heart) / For the love of
you / To Sir with love / His house and me /
Always and forever
CD _____ RRCD 38
Island / Jul '92 / PolyGram.

RAW SAX
CD _____ GRELCD 129
Greensleeves / Sep '89 / Total/BMG /
Jetstar / SRD.

SINGS AND BLOWS
Falling in love / Jamaican lady / Girlfriend /
Magnet and steel / Voyage to Atlantis
CD _____ GRELCD 113
Greensleeves / Jun '88 / Total/BMG / Jets-
tar / SRD.

TAKING CHANCES
CD _____ RASCD 3106
Ras / Jun '93 / Jetstar / Greensleeves /
SRD / Direct.

Fraser, Donald

**WORLD ANTHEMS (Fraser, Donald &
English Chamber Orchestra)**
Olympic theme / Marcha real / Advance
Australia fair / Jeszche Polska / Patra
amada, Brasil / King Christian / Ee mungu
nguvu ye tu / O Canada / God save the
Queen / Ch'i lai / La brabanconne /
Maamme laulu / Isten aldd meg a Magyard
/ Ja vi elsker dette landet / Einigkeit und
recht und freiheit / Kde domov kuj / Star
spangled banner / Segnorees apo tin kopsi
/ Wilhelmus Van Nassouwe / Peaceful reign
/ Hatikvah (Israel) / Walla zaman algunud /
La Marseillaise / Sean eternos los laurales /
Du camla, du fria / Mexicanos al grito de
guerra / Ethiopia / Land der berge / Lietuva
/ Inno di mameli
CD _____ 09026613442
RCA / Jul '92 / BMG.

Fraser Highlanders

LIVE IN CONCERT IN IRELAND
Lord Lovat's lament / Beverley's wedding /
Ishabel T MacDonald / Catrina Baker / Gor-
don MacRae's favourite / Cliffs of Dooneen
/ Brig. Gen. Ronald Cheape of Tiroran /
Laggan love song / Lament for the children
/ Up to the line / John MacColl's farewell to
the Scottish / Farewell to Erin / Journey to
Skye / Mason's apron / Fair maid of Barra
CD Set _____ LCDM 8003
Lismor / '89 / Lismor / Direct / Duncans /
ADA.

MEGANTIC OUTLAW CONCERT, THE
4/4 marches / Medley / Solo piping / Drum
fanfare / Waulking songs / Hornpipes / Megantic outlaw / Piping duet / Airs / Jigs
CD _____ LCOM 8014
Lismor / Sep '92 / Lismor / Direct / Duncans
/ ADA.

Fraser, Iain

NORTHLINS
Old fincastle / Northlins / Pride of the north
/ Blue bonnets / Devil in the kitchen /
Golden mile / Walnut grove / Valparaiso /
Loup / Tummelside / Drummossie moor /
North wall / Farewell to whiskey / Am bal-
achan siubhlach / Merry making / Last light
CD _____ IRCD 027
Iona / Aug '94 / ADA / Direct / Duncans.

Fraser, Simon

**DO MO CHARA MAITH (Fraser, Simon
University Pipe Band)**
Iochanside / McPhedran's Strathspey / A.A.
Cameron's Strathspey / Lexy McAskill /
Blackberry bush / Our ain fireside / Mac-
Leod medley / Compound / 420 Byng
Street / Buskin' / Flowers of Edinburgh /
Drops / Highland Set / Maestro and the
minions / Sorcerer Set / Three Fours / Boys
/ Do mo chara maith / Three stripes / Gut-
leach an Dudain
CD _____ LCOM 5236
Lismor / Jul '94 / Lismor / Direct / Duncans
/ ADA.

Fraser-Myers Band

**FAST JAZZ, FAST WOMEN AND
ASTONS**
Sweet lullaby / Miss Mayhew / Zagato /
Lunch at Langan's / Say what / Project 215
/ Volante / D.B. 2 Mark 3 / Salvadori /
Superleggera
CD _____ VCTMD 4
Vocal Cords / Aug '94 / Grapevine.

Fraternity Of Man

FRATERNITY OF MAN
CD _____ EDCD 437
Edsel / Oct '95 / Pinnacle / ADA.

GET IT ON
CD _____ EDCD 438
Edsel / Oct '95 / Pinnacle / ADA.

Fraunhofer Saitenmusik

VOLSMUSIK
CD _____ TRIK 0107
Trikont / Oct '94 / ADA / Direct.

Frazier Chorus

SUE
Dream kitchen / Forty winks / Sloppy heart
/ Sugar high / Typical / Little chef / Storm /
Ha ha happiness / Living room / Forgetful /
Shi-head
CD _____ CDV 2578
Virgin / Dec '88 / EMI.

WIDE AWAKE
CD _____ PINKCD 1
Pinkerton / Jul '95 / 3MV.

Freak Of Nature

FREAK OF NATURE
CD _____ CDMFN 146
Music For Nations / Mar '93 / Pinnacle.

GATHERING OF FREAKS
CD _____ CDMFN 169
Music For Nations / Sep '94 / Pinnacle.

Freakpower

DRIVE-THRU BOOTY
Moonbeam woman / Turn on, tune in, cop
out / Get in touch / Freak power / Running
away / Change my mind / What it is / Waiting for the story to end / Rush / Big time /
Whip
CD _____ BRCD 606
4th & Broadway / Apr '95 / PolyGram.

Freakwater

FEELS LIKE THE THIRD TIME
CD _____ EFA 049202
City Slang / Oct '93 / Disc.

OLD PAINT
CD _____ EFAO 49652
City Slang / Oct '95 / Disc.

Freaky Realistic

FREALISM
Frealism / Something new/Cosmic love
vibes / Koochie ryder / Love that loves /
Leonard Nimoy / Reach / Salivate spacial /
Trickle in / Imaginary pavillions / Make it
happen / Sooner / Most / This is freaky re-
alistic / Reprise/Frealism
CD _____ 5179192
Polydor / Oct '93 / PolyGram.

Fred, John

**AGNES ENGLISH (Fred, John & His
Playboy Band)**
CD _____ REP 4153-WZ
Repertoire / Aug '91 / Pinnacle / Cadillac.

Freddie & The Dreamers

**EP COLLECTION: FREDDIE & THE
DREAMERS**
See For Miles/C5 / '90 / Pinnacle.
CD _____ SEECD 299

**VERY BEST OF FREDDIE & THE
DREAMERS, THE**
If you gotta make a fool of somebody / I
understand (just how you feel) / It doesn't
matter anymore / Jailer bring me water / I
think of you / If you've got a minute, baby
/ Feel so blue / Do the Freddie / Thou shalt
not steal / See you later alligator / I'm telling
you now / I don't love you anymore / Viper
/ You were made for me / Over you / Money
(that's what I want) / Tell me when / Playboy
/ Don't make me cry / Little you
CD _____ CDSL 8261
Music For Pleasure / Jul '95 / EMI.

Freddie & The Screamers

DEATH LETTER BLUES
CD _____ APP 6105CD
Appaloosa / Jun '94 / ADA / Magnum
Music Group.

Freddy K

RAGE OF AGE
CD _____ ACVCD 8
ACV / Jun '95 / Plastic Head / SRD.

Frederick The Great

BROADWAY USA
CD _____ HIICD 804
Hard Hat / Oct '94 / Else.

Frederiksen/Phillips

FREDERIKSEN/PHILLIPS
CD _____ ERCD 1021
Now & Then / Jul '95 / Plastic Head.

Fredrix, Dee

GRACE
Dirty money / And so I will wait for you /
Whatever it takes / Hold on to what we've
got / How can this be wrong / There but for
the grace / If I could relive your love / Don't
get in my way / Buried treasure / Look my
way
CD _____ 450991788-2
East West / Mar '93 / Warner Music.

Free

ALL RIGHT NOW
Wishing well / All right now / Little bit of love
/ Come together in the morning / Stealer /
Sail on / Mr. Big / My brother Jake the
hunter / Be my friend / Travellin' in style /
Fire and water / Travelling man / Don't say
you love me
CD _____ CIDTV 2
Island / Feb '91 / PolyGram.

FIRE & WATER/ HEARTBREAKER
CD Set _____ ITSCD 3
Island / Nov '92 / PolyGram.

FIRE AND WATER
Oh I wept / Remember / Heavy load / Fire
and water / Mr. Big / Don't say you love me
/ All right now
CD _____ IMCD 80
Island / Apr '90 / PolyGram.

FREE
I'll be creepin' / Songs of yesterday / Lying
in the sunshine / Trouble on double time /

Mouthful of grass / Woman / Free me /
Broad daylight / Mourning sad mourning
CD _____ IMCD 64
Island / '89 / PolyGram.

FREE AT LAST
Catch a train / Soldier boy / Magic ship /
Sail on / Travelling man / Little bit of love /
Guardian of the Universe / Child / Goodbye
CD _____ IMCD 82
Island / Feb '90 / PolyGram.

FREE LIVE
All right now / I'm a mover / Be my friend /
Fire and water / Ride on pony / Mr. Big /
Hunter / Get where I belong
CD _____ IMCD 73
Island / Jan '89 / PolyGram.

FREE STORY, THE
I'm a mover / I'll be creepin' / Mourning sad
morning / All right now / Heavy load / Fire
and water / Be my friend / Stealer / Soon I
will be gone / Mr. Big / Hunter / Get where
I belong / Travelling man / Just for the love
/ Lady / My brother Jake / Little bit of love
/ Sail on / Come together in the morning
CD _____ CID 9945
Island / Oct '89 / PolyGram.

FREE THE FREE
I'll be creepin' / Songs of yesterday / Lying
in the sunshine / Trouble on double time /
Mouthfull of grass / Woman / Free me /
Broad daylight / Mourning sad morning
CD _____ 842 782-2
Island / Sep '89 / PolyGram.

HEARTBREAKER
Wishing well / Come together in the morn-
ing / Travellin' in style / Heartbreaker /
Muddy water / Common mortal man / Easy
on my soul / Seven angels
CD _____ IMCD 81
Island / Feb '90 / PolyGram.

HIGHWAY
Highway song / Stealer / On my way / Be
my friend / Sunny day / Ride on pony / Love
you so / Bodies / Soon I will be gone
CD _____ IMCD 63
Island / '89 / PolyGram.

MOLTEN GOLD
I'm a mover / Hunter / Walk in my shadow
/ I'll be creepin' / Songs of yesterday /
Woman / Broad daylight / Mouthful of grass
/ All right now / Oh I wept / Heavy load /
Don't say you love me / Stealer / Highway
song / Be my friend / Soon I will be gone /
My brother Jake / Fire and water / Ride on
pony / Mr. Big / Time away / Molten gold /
Catch a train / Travelling man / Little bit of
love / Sail on / Wishing well / Come together
in the morning / Travellin' in style /
Heartbreaker
CD _____ CRNCD 2
Island / May '94 / PolyGram.

TONS OF SOBS
Over the green hills (part 1) / Worry / Walk
in my shadow / Wild Indian woman / Going
down slow / I'm a mover / Hunter / Moon-
shine sweet tooth / Over the green hills
(Part 2)
CD _____ IMCD 62
Island / '89 / PolyGram.

Free Hot Lunch

EAT THIS
CD _____ FF 540CD
Flying Fish / '92 / Roots / CM / Direct /
ADA.

Free Jazz Quartet

PREMONITIONS - 1989
CD _____ MR 18
Matchless / '90 / These / ReR Megacorp /
Cadillac.

Free Kitten

NICE ASS
Harvest spoon / Rock of ages / Proper band
/ What's fair / Kissing well / Call back /
Blindfold test / Greener pastures / Revlon
liberation orchestra / Boasta / Scratch tha
D.J. / Secret sex fiend / Royal flush / Feelin'
/ Alan Licked has ruined music for an entire
generation
CD _____ WIJ 041CD
Wiiija / Jan '95 / Vital.

UNBOXED
Skinny butt / Platinumb / Smack / Falling
backwards / Oneness / Dick / Yoshimi Vs.
Mascis / Oh bondage up yours / 1-2-3 /
Party with me punker / John stark blues /
Guilty pleasure / Sex boy / Cleopatra /
Loose lips / Oh baby
CD _____ WIJ 036CD
Wiiija / Jun '94 / Vital.

Free The Spirit

PAN PIPE MOODS
I will always love you / Everything I do (I do
it for you) / Holding back the years / Love
theme from Bladerunner / Sacrifice/Nikita /
From a distance / Wonderful tonight / Without you / Circle of life / Love is all around /
Can you feel the love tonight / Mission /
Careless whisper / Cockeye's song / Wonderful life / It must have been love / Evergreen / World in union

CD _____ 5271972
PolyGram TV / Jan '95 / PolyGram.

Freedom

THROUGH THE YEARS
CD _____ REP 4226-WP
Repertoire / Aug '91 / Pinnacle / Cadillac.

Freeez

FREEEZ FRAME (The Best Of Freeez)
CD _____ MCCD 131
Music Club / Sep '93 / Disc / THE / CM.

Freelon, Nnenna

HERITAGE
Girl blue / 'Tis Autumn / Heritage / Comes
love / Prelude to a kiss / It's you I like /
Infant eyes / Young and foolish / Never let
me go / All of nothing at all / So wrong /
Something to live for / Bewitched, bothered
and bewildered
CD _____ 473950 2
Columbia / Apr '94 / Sony.

LISTEN
CD _____ 4772852
Sony Jazz / Jan '95 / Sony.

NNENNA FREELON
CD _____ 4719992
Sony Jazz / Jan '95 / Sony.

Freeman

ROUGH ROADS
CD _____ NAR 116CD
SST / Dec '94 / Plastic Head.

Freeman, Bud

BUD FREEMAN 1927 - 1928
CD _____ RPCD 604
Moidart / Aug '92 / Conifer / ADA.

**CHICAGO/AUSTIN HIGH SCHOOL JAZZ
IN HI-FI (Freeman, Bud Summa Cum
Laude)**
China boy / Sugar / Liza / Nobody's sweet-
heart / Chicago / At sundown / Prince of
wails / Jack hits the road / Forty seventh
and state / There'll be some changes made
/ At the jazz band ball
CD _____ 74321 13031-2
RCA / Sep '93 / BMG.

CLASSICS 1928-38
CD _____ CLASSICS 781
Classics / Nov '94 / Discovery / Jazz
Music.

CLASSICS 1939-1940
CD _____ CLASSICS 811
Classics / May '95 / Discovery / Jazz
Music.

SOMETHING TO REMEMBER YOU BY
CD _____ BLCD 760153
Black Lion / Jul '91 / Jazz Music / Cadillac
/ Wellard / Koch.

Freeman, Chico

DESTINY'S DANCE
CD _____ OJCCD 799
Original Jazz Classics / Nov '95 / Wellard /
Jazz Music / Cadillac / Complete/Pinnacle.

GROOVIN' LATE (Live at Ronnie Scott's)
Going places / Groovin' late / Free associa-
tion / In a sentimental mood / What if /
Traveller
CD _____ CLACD 336
Castle / '93 / BMG.

**LUMINOUS (Freeman, Chico & Arthur
Blythe)**
Footprints / Luminous / Naima's love song
/ Avotja / You are too beautiful
CD _____ JHCD 010
Ronnie Scott's Jazz House / Jan '94 / Jazz
Music / Magnum Music Group / Cadillac.

**MYSTICAL DREAMER (Freeman, Chico
& Drainstorm)**
Footprints / Do I say anything (prelude) /
On the Nile / Sojourn / Mystical dreamer /
I'll be there / Do I say anything (CD only.)
CD _____ 70062
In & Out / Jan '90 / Vital/SAM.

**NO TIME LEFT (Freeman, Chico
Quartet)**
CD _____ BSR 0036CD
Black Saint / '86 / Harmonia Mundi /
Cadillac.

**SWEET EXPLOSION (Freeman, Chico &
Brainstorm)**
Peaceful heart / Exotic places / Afro tang /
My heart / Pacifica 1 / Pacifica 2 / Pacifica
3 / Read the signs / On the Nile
CD _____ 70102
In & Out / Dec '90 / Vital/SAM.

THRESHOLD
Trespasser / Duet / Mist / Subway / blues
for Miles / Chejudo / Oleo / Chant / Lena's
lullaby / Awakening
CD _____ IOR 70222
In & Out / Sep '95 / Vital/SAM.

**UNSPOKEN WORD, THE (Freeman,
Chico Quintet)**
Unspoken word / Gano club / Playpen / In-
fant eyes / Peace maker / Misty / Rhythm-
a-ning
CD _____ JHCD 030
Ronnie Scott's Jazz House / Aug '94 / Jazz
Music / Magnum Music Group / Cadillac.

**UP AND DOWN (Freeman, Chico & Mal
Waldron)**
CD _____ 120136-2
Black Saint / Sep '92 / Harmonia Mundi /
Cadillac.

Freeman, George

BIRTH SIGN
CD _____ DD 424
Delmark / Aug '94 / Hot Shot / ADA / CM
/ Direct / Cadillac.

Freeman, Ken

TRIPODS
CD _____ GERCD 1
GR Forrester / Nov '95 / Pinnacle.

Freeman, Louise

LISTEN TO MY HEART
When push comes to shove / Save your
love / Nothin's gonna win me (but love) /
Love is gone / Back in stride / I don't want
to talk about it / Fever / Unchained melody
CD _____ CDICH 1111
Ichiban / Oct '93 / Koch.

Freeman, Russ

HOLIDAY
Carol of the bells / Faith / O come' all ye
faithful / Hark the herald angels sing / God
rest ye merry gentlemen / Angels we have
heard on high / Hymn / Holiday / My fa-
vourite things / Jesu, joy of man's desiring
/ Merry Christmas, baby / This Christmas /
Have yourself a merry little Christmas
CD _____ GRP 98262
GRP / Oct '95 / BMG / New Note.

**SAHARA (Freeman, Russ & The
Rippingtons)**
Native sons of a distant land / True com-
panion / I'll be around / Principles of desire
/ Sahara / Till we're together again / Best is
yet to come / Journey's end / Girl with the
indigo eyes / Porscha
CD _____ GRP 97812
GRP / Sep '94 / BMG / New Note.

Freeman, Von

SERENADE AND BLUES
Serenade in blue / After dark / Time after
time / Von Freeman's blues / I'll close my
eyes
CD _____ CHIEFCD 3
Chief / Jun '89 / Cadillac.

Freestyle Fellowship

INTERCITY GRIOTS
Blood / Bullies of the block / Everything's
everything / Shammy's / Heat mizer / Six
tray / Danger / Inner city boundaries / Bomb
zombies / Cornbread / Way cool / Hot potato / Mary / Park bench people
CD _____ BRCD 595
4th & Broadway / Apr '93 / PolyGram.

Freeze

CRAWLING BLIND
CD _____ LF 075
Lost & Found / Mar '94 / Plastic Head.

FIVE WAY FURY
CD _____ LF 132CD
Lost & Found / Apr '92 / Plastic Head.

FREAKSHOW
CD _____ LF 198CD
Lost & Found / Jan '96 / Plastic Head.

**FREEZE/KILLRAYS (Split CD) (Freeze/
Killrays)**
CD _____ LF 143CD
Lost & Found / Jul '95 / Plastic Head.

Frehel

CHANSOPHONE 1933-39
CD _____ 701252
Chansophone / Jun '93 / Discovery.

Frehley, Ace

FREHLEY'S COMET (Frehley's Comet)
Rock soldiers / Breakout / Into the night /
Something moved / We got your rock /
Love me right / Calling to you / Dolls /
Stranger in a strange land / Fractured too
CD _____ 7567817492
Atlantic / Jan '96 / Warner Music.

LIVE PLUS ONE (Frehley's Comet)
Rip it out / Breakout / Something / Some-
thing moved / Rocket ride / Words are not
enough
CD _____ 7567818262
Atlantic / Jan '96 / Warner Music.

SECOND SIGHTING (Frehley's Comet)
Insane / Time ain't runnin' out / Dancin' with
danger / It's over now / Loser in a fight /

Juvenile delinquent / Fallen angel / Sepa-
rate / New kind of lover / Acorn is spinning
CD _____ 7567818622
Atlantic / Jan '96 / Warner Music.

TROUBLE WALKING (Frehley's Comet)
Shot full of rock / Do ya / Five card stud /
Hide your heart / Lost in limbo / Trouble
walkin' / 2 young 2 die / Back to school /
Remember me / Fractured III
CD _____ 7567820422
Atlantic / Jan '96 / Warner Music.

Frejlechs

YIDDISH KLEZMER MUSIC
CD _____ EUCD 1185
ARC / Apr '92 / ARC Music / ADA.

Frej's Jazz

NORDLYD
CD _____ MECCACD 1039
Music Mecca / Nov '94 / Jazz Music /
Cadillac / Wellard.

French Alligators

SOUS LA GALLERIE
CD _____ FA 003CD
French Alligator / Jan '95 / ADA.

French Charleston...

**STRICTLY DANCING: CHARLESTON
(French Charleston Orchestra)**
CD _____ 15339
Laserlight / May '94 / Target/BMG.

French, John

**INVISIBLE MEANS (French, Frith, Kaiser
& Thompson)**
Peppermint rock / To the rain / Lizard's tail
/ March of the cosmetic surgeons / Suz-
anne / Quick sign / Invisible means / Book
of lost dreams
CD _____ FIENDCD 199
Demon / Oct '90 / Pinnacle / ADA.

**LIVE, LOVE, LARF, LOAF (French, Frith,
Kaiser & Thompson)**
Wings a la mode / Killerman gold posse /
Where's the money / Hai sai oji-san /
Drowned dog black night / Surfin' USA /
Blind step away / Second time / Tir-nan
darag / Disposable thoughts / Bird in god's
garden/Lost and found
CD _____ FIENDCD 102
Demon / '88 / Pinnacle / ADA.

WAITING ON THE FLAME
CD _____ FIENDCD 759
Demon / Nov '94 / Pinnacle / ADA.

French, Robert

**ROBERT FRENCH, HEAVY D &
FRIENDS (French, Robert & Heavy D)**
Ras / Aug '95 / Jetstar / Greensleeves /
SRD / Direct.
CD _____ RASCD 3148

Frente

MARVIN THE ALBUM
CD _____ TVD 93367
Mushroom / May '94 / BMG / 3MV.

Frenzy

(IT'S A) MAD, MAD WORLD
(It's a) mad mad world / So far away / Part
of my mind / C.C. rider / Brenzure / Not red cat-
ellite / Rock hard / Brand new gun / Crunch
/ I can't tell you / Ready or not / Draw me
the way / This is the fire / Can't stop thinkin'
about you / Reward / Scandalous / Forever
young / Wild night / Ready or not (mix)
CD _____ RAGECD 111
Rage / Mar '93 / Nervous / Magnum Music
Group.

BEST OF FRENZY
Hall Of Mirrors / Robot Riot / Misdemean-
our / Clockwork Toy / I See Red / Schitzo-
phrenic / Emotions / Hot Rod Satellite /
Gotta Go / Cry Or Die / Long Gone / Sweet
Money / Wound up / Aftermath / Nobody's
Business / Don't Give Up / House On Fire
/ Hunt / Howard Hughes / Can't Stop Think-
ing About You
CD _____ RAGECD 107
Rage / Nov '90 / Nervous / Magnum Music
Group.

CLOCKWORK TOY
CD _____ NERCD 065
Nervous / '91 / Nervous / Magnum Music
Group.

HALL OF MIRRORS
One last chance / Schizophrenic emotions
/ Choice / Hall of mirrors / frenzy / Asylum
moves / Skeleton rock / Sweet money /
Ghost train / Long gone / Surfin' bird / Was
it me / Wound up / Frustration
CD _____ NERDCD 016
Nervous / Jul '90 / Nervous / Magnum Mu-
sic Group.

THIS IS THE FIRE
Ready Or Not / Robot Riot / This Is The Fire
/ Come back my love / Wild Night / Can't
Stop Thinking About You / Another Day / I

Want Your Lovin' / Scandalous / Forever
Young / Reward
CD _____ RAGECD 101
Rage / Aug '92 / Nervous / Magnum Music
Group.

Frequenzia Mod

SONG AUS LATCHINAMERIKA
CD _____ REP 4193-WZ
Repertoire / Aug '91 / Pinnacle / Cadillac.

Fresh Claim

BROKEN
Broken man / Pillar sways / Morning ashtray
blues / Wayfaring stranger (CD only.) / Driving through the rain / Defiled / Slow burning
candle / Broken jam
CD _____ PCDN 146
Plankton / Nov '95 / Plankton.

ROCK COMMUNION, THE
What a friend we have in Jesus / Peruvian
Gloria / Father hear the prayer we offer /
Sanctus (Holy, holy, holy) / Blessed is he /
Christ has died / Agnus dei (Lamb of God)
/ Purple robe / Broken by / Jesus light of
the world / Eternal love / Father on high /
Swing low, sweet chariot / Oh sacred head
/ Crown him with many crown
CD _____ PCN 142
Plankton / Aug '94 / Plankton.

Fresh, Doug E

PLAY
Where's da party at / It's on / Take 'em uptown / I-ight / Original old school / Freaks /
Freak it out / It's really goin' on here / Who's
got all the money / Get da money / Hands
in the air / Doug. E got it going on / Keep it
going / Breath of fresh air
CD _____ GEECD 17
Gee Street / Oct '95 / PolyGram.

Fretblanket

JUNK FUEL
CD _____ 5219972
Polydor / Aug '94 / PolyGram.

Frevo

FREVO
Events / Joy / Dee tee / Victory / Into the
night / Songlines / Thanks / Touched
CD _____ TJL 002CD
The Jazz Label / Jan '94 / New Note.

Frey, Glenn

ALLNIGHTER, THE
Allnighter / Sexy girl / I got love / Somebody
else / Lover's moon / Smuggler's blues /
Let's go home / Better in the USA / Living
in darkness / New love
CD _____ MCLD 19009
MCA / Apr '92 / BMG.

SOLO CONNECTION
This way to happiness / Who's been sleep-
ing in my bed / Common ground / Call on
me / One you love / Sexy girl / Smuggler's
blues / Heat is on / You belong to the city
/ True love / Soul searchin' / Part of me, part
of you / I've got mine / River of dreams /
Rising high / Brave new world
CD _____ MCD 11227
MCA / Apr '89 / BMG.

STRANGE WEATHER
Silent spring / Long hot summer / Strange
weather / Agua tranquilo / Love in the 21st
century / He took advantage / River of
dreams / Before the ship goes down / I've
got mine / Rising sun / Brave new world /
Delicious / Walk in the dark / Big life / Part
of me, part of you
CD _____ MCAD 10599
MCA / Jul '92 / BMG.

Freya, Jo

LUSH (Freya, Jo & Kathryn Locke)
CD _____ NMV 5CD
No Master's Voice / Jan '94 / ADA.

TRADITIONAL SONGS OF ENGLAND
All things are quite silent / As I set off to
Turkey / As Sylvie was walking / General
Wolfe / Though I live not where I love / Sai-
lor's life / Rounding the Horn / Lord Franklin
/ Unquiet grave / Broomfield wager / There
was a lady all skin and bone / Geordie /
Maids, when you're young never wed an
old man / Bold William Taylor / Lovely Joan
/ Blacksmith courted me / Carnal and the
crane / Green Cockade / Fourpence a day
/ Streams of lovely Nancy / Sweet England
CD _____ CDSDL 402
Saydisc / Mar '94 / Harmonia Mundi / ADA
/ Direct.

Freyda

GLOBALULLABIES
CD _____ 9425712
Music For Little People / Jan '96 / Direct.

Friction

REPLICANT WALK
CD _____ EMY 109-2
Enemy / Jan '90 / Grapevine.

Frida

SHINE
Shine / One little lie / Face / Twist in the
dark / Slowly / Heart of the country / Come
to me / Chemistry tonight / Don't do it /
Comfort me
CD _____ 823 580-2
Polydor / Jan '93 / PolyGram.

SOMETHING'S GOING ON
Tell me it's over / I see red / I got something
/ Strangers / To turn the stone / I know the-
re's something going on / Threnody / Baby
don't you cry no more / Way you do / You
know what I mean / Here we'll stay
CD _____ 800 102-2
Polydor / Jan '93 / PolyGram.

Friday, Gavin

ADAM 'N' EVE
I want to live / Falling off the edge of the
world / King of trash / Why say goodbye /
Saint divine / Melancholy baby / Fun and
experience / Big no no / Where in the world
/ Wind and rain / Eden
CD _____ CID 9984
Island / Mar '92 / PolyGram.

**EACH MAN KILLS THE THING HE
LOVES**
Each man kills the thing he loves / He got
what he wanted / Tell tale heart / Man of
misfortune / Apologia / Rags to riches /
Dazzle and delight / Next thing to murder /
Next / Love is just a word / You take away
the sun / Another blow on the bruise / Death
is not the end
CD _____ IMCD 175
Island / Jul '93 / PolyGram.

SHAG TOBACCO
CD _____ CID 8036
Island / Aug '95 / PolyGram.

Fried Funk Food

REAL SHIT VOL. 2
Real shit / Frame of da week / George /
Rhapsody in loop / B boys on acid / Real
bonus beats
CD _____ BVMCD 1
Blunted Vinyl / May '95 / Vital / PolyGram.

Friedlander, Erik

CHIMERA
CD _____ AVAN 057
Avant / Jan '96 / Harmonia Mundi /
Cadillac.

Friedman, Dean

**DEAN FRIEDMAN / WELL WELL SAID
THE ROCKING CHAIR**
Company / Ariel / Solitaire / Woman of mine
/ Song for my mother / Letter / I may be
young / Humor me / Funny papers / Love
is not enough / Rocking chair / I've had
enough / Lucky stars / Shopping bag ladies
/ Don't you ever dare / Deli song (corned
beef on wry) / Lydia / S and M / Let down
your hair
CD _____ CDWIKD 98
Chiswick / Apr '91 / Pinnacle.

RUMPLED ROMEO
First date / McDonald's girl / Are you ready
yet / Hey Larry / Love is real / Buy my baby
a car / Special effects / I depend on you,
Jesus / Marginal middle class / I will never
leave you
CD _____ CDWIK 106
Chiswick / May '92 / Pinnacle.

VERY BEST OF DEAN FRIEDMAN
Lucky stars / Company / Solitaire / Letter /
Humor me / Love is not enough / Woman
of mine / Lydia / Ariel / Rocking chair / I've
had enough / Shopping bag ladies / Deli
song (corned beef on wry) / S and M /
Funny papers / I may be young
CD _____ MCCD 036
Music Club / Sep '91 / Disc / THE / CM.

Friedman, Don

**FRIEDMAN/PEPPER/KNEPPER
(Friedman, Don/Pepper Adams/Jimmy
Knepper)**
CD _____ PCD 7036
Progressive / Jun '93 / Jazz Music.

I HEAR A RHAPSODY
CD _____ ST 577
Stash / Jul '94 / Jazz Music / CM /
Cadillac / Direct / ADA.

**LIVE AT MAYBECK RECITAL HALL,
VOL. 33**
In your own sweet way / Alone together /
Prelude to a kiss / Invitation / Memory for
Scotty / I concentrate on you / How deep
is the ocean / Sea's breeze
CD _____ CCD 4608
Concord Jazz / Aug '94 / New Note.

Friedman, Kinky

KINKY FRIEDMAN
CD _____ VSD 5488
Varese Sarabande/Colosseum / Dec '94 /
Pinnacle / Silva Screen.

Friedman, Maria

MARIA FRIEDMAN
I happen to like New York / Man with the
child in his eyes / Golden days / If you go
away / I'm gorgeous / My romance / In the
sky / Paris in the rain / Toby's song / Man
that got away / Guess who I saw today /
Play the song again / Finishing the hat /
Now and then / Broadway baby
CD _____ 30360 00012
Carlton Home Entertainment / Oct '95 /
Carlton Home Entertainment.

Friedman, Marty

DRAGON'S KISS
CD _____ RR 9529 2
Roadrunner / '89 / Pinnacle.

INTRODUCTION
Arrival / Bittersweet / Be / Escapism / Luna
/ Mama / Loneliness / Siberia
CD _____ RR 8950 2
Roadrunner / Dec '94 / Pinnacle.

SCENES
Tibet / Angel / Valley of enternity / Night /
Realm of the senses / West / Trance /
Triumph
CD _____ CDRR 9104 2
Roadrunner / Nov '92 / Pinnacle.

Friedmann

INDIAN SUMMER
CD _____ BIBERCD 66301
In Akustik / '88 / Magnum Music Group.

LEGENDS OF LIGHT
Fairies of sternsea / Mount belenos / Joy of
Beltane / Seven silver stars / Spring has
come to wiesental / Sunday in Alsace /
Memories of Lugnasad / Black cherries,
white wine / Lament of the white goddess /
Sun at midnight
CD _____ ND 63033
Narada / Oct '95 / New Note / ADA.

VOYAGER IN EXPANSE
CD _____ INAK 860 CD
In Akustik / '88 / Magnum Music Group.

Friedmann, Bernd

LEISURE ZONES
CD _____ ASH 2.5
Ash International / Jan '96 / These /
Kudos.

Friends Of Dean Martinez

SHADOW OF YOUR SMILE, THE
CD _____ SPCD 306
Sub Pop / Sep '95 / Disc.

Friesen, David

LONG TRIP HOME
CD _____ ITM 970073
ITM / Sep '92 / Tradelink / Koch.

OTHER TIMES, OTHER PLACES
Festival dance / Tyrone's dedication / Song
for my daughter / Father's delight / Song for
my family / Our 25th year / Childhood walk
/ Years through time
CD _____ 66052001
Global Pacific / Feb '91 / Pinnacle.

THREE TO GET READY
CD _____ ITMP 970084
ITM / Oct '95 / Tradelink / Koch.

TWO FOR THE SHOW
CD _____ ITM 960079
ITM / Oct '95 / Tradelink / Koch.

UPON THE SWING
CD _____ SHAM 1020CD
Shamrock / Nov '95 / Wellard / ADA.

Frijid Pink

DEFROSTED
CD _____ REP 4172-WZ
Repertoire / Aug '91 / Pinnacle / Cadillac.

FRIJID PINK
CD _____ REP 4156-WZ
Repertoire / Aug '91 / Pinnacle / Cadillac.

Fringe

IT'S TIME FOR THE FRINGE
CD _____ 121205-2
Soul Note / Sep '93 / Harmonia Mundi /
Wellard / Cadillac.

Fripp, Robert

**BLESSING OF TEARS, A (1995
Soundscape)**
Cathedral of tears / First light / Midnight
blue / Reflection 1 / Second light / Blessing
of tears / Returning 1 / Returning 2
CD _____ DGM 9506
Discipline / Aug '95 / Pinnacle.

BRIDGE BETWEEN
Kan-non power / Yamanashi blues / Hope
/ Chromatic fantasy / Contrapunctus / Bi-
cycling to Afghanistan / Blue / Blockhead /
Passacaglia / Threnody for souls in
torment
CD _____ DGM 9303
Discipline / Sep '94 / Pinnacle.

CHEERFUL INSANITY (Giles, Giles &
Fripp)
Saga of Rodney Toady / North meadow /
Newly weds / One in a million / Call tomor-
row / Digging my lawn / Little children /
Crukster / Thursday morning / Just George
/ How do they know / Elephant song / Sun
is shining / Suite No.1 / Erudite eyes
CD _____ 8209652
London / Jul '93 / PolyGram.

**ESSENTIAL FRIPP & ENO, THE (Fripp,
Robert & Brian Eno)**
Heavenly music corporation / Swastika girls
/ Wind on water / Evening star / Healthy
colours (pts I-IV)
CD _____ CDVE 920
Virgin / Apr '94 / EMI.

**EVENING STAR (Fripp, Robert & Brian
Eno)**
Wind on water / Evening star / Evensong /
Wind on wind / Index of metals
CD _____ EEGCD 3
EG / '87 / EMI.

EXPOSURE
Breathless / Chicago / Disengage / Expo-
sure / First inaugural address to the I.A.C.E.
Sherbourne House / Here comes the flood
/ I may not have had enough of me but I've
had enough of you / Mary / North star / NY3
/ Urban landscape / Water music 1 / You
burn me up I'm a cigarette / Preface / Post-
script / Haaden two / Water music 2
CD _____ EEGCD 41
EG / Jan '87 / EMI.

GOD SAVE THE KING
God save the King / Under heavy manners
/ Heptaparaparshinokh / Inductive reson-
ance / Cognitive dissonance / Dislocated /
H.G. Wells / Eye needles / Trap
CD _____ EEGCD 9
EG / Jun '85 / EMI.

**INTERGALACTIC BOOGIE EXPRESS
LIVE**
Connecticut yankee in the court of King Arth-
ur / Rhythm of the universes / Lark's thrak
/ Circulation I / Intergalactic boogie express
/ G Force / Eye of the needle / Corrente /
Driving force / Groove penetration / Flying
home / Circulation II / Fireplace / Fragments
of skylab / Asturias / Prelude circulation /
Cheeseballs / Prelude in C minor / Wabash
cannonball
CD _____ DGM 9502
Discipline / Sep '95 / Pinnacle.

**LET THE POWER FALL (An album of
Frippertronics)**
1984 / 1985 / 1986 / 1987 / 1988 / 1989
CD _____ EEGCD 10
EG / '87 / EMI.

**NO PUSSY FOOTING (Fripp, Robert &
Brian Eno)**
Heavenly music corporation / Swastika girls
CD _____ EEGCD 2
EG / Jan '87 / EMI.

**ROBERT FRIPP AND THE LEAGUE OF
CRAFTY GUITARISTS - LIVE**
Guitar craft theme 1: Invocation / Tight
muscle party at love beach / Chords that
bind / Guitar craft theme 3: Eye of the nee-
dle / All or nothing (2) / Crafty march / Guitar
craft theme 2: Aspiration / All or nothing (1)
/ Circulation / Fearful symmetry / New world
CD _____ EEGCD 43
EG / Nov '86 / EMI.

**SHOW OF HANDS (Fripp, Robert & The
League Of Crafty Guitarists)**
CD _____ EEG 21022
EG / Jul '93 / EMI.

Frisco Syncopators

SAN FRANCISCO BOUND
CD _____ SOSCD 1211
Stomp Off / Oct '92 / Jazz Music /
Wellard.

Frisell, Bill

BEFORE WE WERE BORN
Before we were born / Pip squeak / Hard
plains drifter / Steady girl / Some song and
dance / Goodbye / Lone ranger
CD _____ 7559608432
Elektra Nonesuch / Jan '94 / Warner Music.

HAVE A LITTLE FAITH
CD _____ 7559793012
Elektra Nonesuch / Jan '94 / Warner
Music.

IN LINE
Start / Throughout / Two arms / Shorts /
Smile on you / Beach / In line / Three / God-
son song
CD _____ 8370192
ECM / Jul '91 / New Note.

IS THAT YOU
CD _____ 7559609562
Elektra Nonesuch / Jan '94 / Warner
Music.

LIVE
CD _____ GCD 79504
Gramavision / Oct '95 / Vital/SAM / ADA.

LOOKOUT FOR HOPE (Frisell, Bill Band)
Lookout for hope / Little brother Bobby /
Hangdog / Remedios / Beauty / Lonesome

/ Melody for Jack / Hackensack / Little big-
ger / Animal race / Alien prints (for D
Sharpe)
CD _____ 8334952
ECM / Feb '88 / New Note.

RAMBLER
Tone / Music I heard / Rambler / When we
go / Resistor / Strange meeting / Wizard of
odds
CD _____ 8252342
ECM / May '85 / New Note.

**SAFETY BY NUMBERS - AMERICAN
BLOOD** (Frisell, Bill & Victor Godsey)
CD _____ VBR 20642
Vera Bra / Oct '94 / Pinnacle / New Note.

THIS LAND
CD _____ 755979316-2
Elektra Nonesuch / Jun '94 / Warner
Music.

WHERE IN THE WORLD
CD _____ 7559611812
Elektra Nonesuch / Jan '94 / Warner
Music.

WORKS: BILL FRISELL
Monica Jane / Beach / When we go
throughout / Black is the colour of my true
love's hair / Wizard of odds / Conception
vessel / Etude
CD _____ 8372732
ECM / Jun '89 / New Note.

Frishberg, Dave

**DOUBLE PLAY (Frishberg, Dave & Jim
Goodwin)**
CD _____ ARCD 19118
Arbors Jazz / Nov '94 / Cadillac.

LET'S EAT HOME
Brenda Starr / Let's eat home / Mr. George
/ Matty / Mooche / I was ready / Strange
music / Ship without a sail / Lookin' good /
Underdog
CD _____ CCD 4402
Concord Jazz / Jan '90 / New Note.

WHERE YOU AT
CD _____ BL 010
Bloomdido / Oct '93 / Cadillac.

Frith, Fred

GRAVITY
CD _____ DEC 901
ReR Megacorp / May '93 / These / ReR
Megacorp.

GUITAR SOLOS
CD _____ DEC 904
ReR Megacorp / May '93 / These / ReR
Megacorp.

**NOUS AUTRES (Frith, Fred & Rene
Luiser)**
CD _____ VICTOCD 01
Victo / Nov '94 / These / ReR Megacorp /
Cadillac.

STEP ACROSS THE BORDER
CD _____ DEC 30
ReR Megacorp / May '93 / These / ReR
Megacorp.

TECHNOLOGY OF TEARS
CD _____ SST 172 CD
SST / May '93 / Plastic Head.

**WITH ENEMIES LIKE THESE, WHO
NEEDS FRIENDS (Frith & Kaiser)**
CD _____ SST 147 CD
SST / May '93 / Plastic Head.

Frizzell, Lefty

LIFE'S LIKE POETRY (12CD Set)
I love you a thousand ways / If you've got
the money, I've got the time / Shine, shave
shower / Cold feet / Don't think it ain't been
fun dear / When payday comes around / My
baby's just like money / Look what
thoughts will do / You want everything but
me / I want to be with you always / Give
me more more more (of your kisses) / How
long will it take (to stop loving you) / Always
late (with your kisses) / Mom and dad's
waltz / You can go on your way now /
Treasure untold / Blue yodel / Travellin'
blues / My old pal / Lullaby yodel / Break-
man's blues / My rough and rowdy ways /
I love you (Though you're no good) / It's just
you (I could love always) / (Darling now)
you're here so everything's alright / I've got
reasons to hate you / Don't stay away / If
you can spare the time (I won't miss the
money) / King without a Queen / Forever
(and always) / I know you're lonesome
(while waiting for me) / Lost love blues /
That's me without you / Send her here to
be mine / I won't be good for nothin' / If I
lose you (I'll lose my world) / I'm an old old
man (Tryin' to love while I can) / You're just
mine (Only in my dreams) / I'll try / Bring
your sweet self back / Time changes things
/ All of me (loves all of you) / California blues
/ Never no' mo' blues / We crucified our
Jesus / When it comes to measuring love /
Sleep, baby, sleep / I'm Lonely and blue /
Before you go, make sure you know / Two
friends of mine in love / Hopeless love /
Then I'll come back to you / Tragic letter
(The letter that you left) / You can always
count on me / I've been away way too long

/ Run 'em off / Darkest moment (Is just before the light of da / You're too late / My
little her and him / I love you mostly / You're
there, I'm ere / Let it be so / Mama / Making
believe / Moonlight, Darling and you / I'll sit
alone and cry / Forest fire (Is in your heart)
/ Sweet lies / Your tomorrows will never
come / It gets late so early / I'm lost between right and wrong / Promises (promises, promises) / My love and baby's gone
/ Today is that tomorrow (I dreamed of yesterday) / First to have a second chance /
Those hands / You ain't diverse my heart
/ Treat her right / Heart's highway / I'm a
boy left alone / Just can't live that fast (anymore) / Waltz of the angels / Lullaby waltz
/ Glad I found you / Now that you are gone
/ From an angel to a devil / Lover by appointment / Sick, sober and sorry / No one
to talk to (but the blues) / Is it only that
you're lonely / Mailman bring me no more
blues / You've still got it / Tell me dear / To
stop loving you (means cry) / Torch within
my heart / Time out for the blues / (Darling)
let's turn back the years / You win again /
Why should I be lonely / Signed, sealed,
delivered (I'm yours) / Nobody knows but
me / If you're ever lonely darling / Silence /
Release me / Our love's no bluff / You're
humbuggin' me / She's gone / Cigarettes
and coffee blues / I need your love / My
bucket's got a hole in it / Sin will be the
chaser for the wine / Knock again, true love
/ Long black veil / One has been to another
/ Farther than my eyes can see / My blues
will pass / Ballad of the blue and grey /
That's all I can remember / So what, let it
rain / What you gonna do, Leroy / I feel
sorry for me / Heaven's plan / Looking for
you / Stranger / Few steps away / I forbidden lovers / Just passing through / That re-
minds me of me / Don't let her see me cry
/ Through the eyes of a fool / James river /
Preview of coming attractions / Lonely heart
/ What good did you get (out of breaking
my heart) / When it rains the blues / I'm not
the man I'm supposed to be / Saginaw
Michigan / There's no food in this house /
Rider / Nester / I was coming home to you
/ Hello to him (goodbye to me) / I can tell /
Make that one for the road a cup of coffee
/ Gator hollow / It costs too much to die /
She's gone, gone, gone / Confused / How
far down can I go / It's bad (when it's that
way) / I don't trust you anymore / Little unfair / Woman let me sing you a song / Preparations to be blue / Love looks good on
you / It's hard to please you / You don't
want me to get well / Writing on the wall / I
just couldn't see the forest (for the trees) /
I'm not guilty / It couldn't happen to a nicer
guy / Everything keeps coming back (but
you) / Heart (don't love her anymore) / You
don't have to be present to win / My feet
are getting cold / Is there anything I can do
/ Old gang's gone / Song from a lonely
heart / You gotta me puttin' me on / There
in the mirror / Get this stranger out of me /
Money tree / Hobo's pride / When the
rooster leaves the yard / Anything you can
spare / Only way to fly / Only way to fly
(Laughing version) / Prayer on your lips is
like freedon in your hands / Little ole wine
drinker me / Word or two to Mary / Almost
persuaded / Have you ever been untrue /
When the grass grows green again / Marriage bit / I'll remember you / Wasted way
of live / Blind street singer / Honky tonk hill
/ My baby is a tramp / She brought love
sweet love / Watermelon time in Georgia / I
must be getting over you / Out of you / It's
raining all over the world / There's something loiney in this house / Three cheers for
the good guys / Article from life / Honky
tonk hill (without overdub) / Honky tonk
stardust cowboy / What am I gonna do /
Give me more, more, more (of your kisses)
/ You babe / This just ain't a good day for
leavin' / Down by the railroad track / Let me
give her the flowers / If I had half the sense
/ The wine / If she just helps me to get over
you / Failing / Railroad lady / I can't get over
you to save my life / I never go around mirrors (I've got heartache to hide) / That's the
way love goes / She found the key / I wonder who's building the bridge / My wishing
room / I'm gonna hang out my mind today
/ Sittin' and thinkin' / I'm not that good at
goodbye / Yesterday just passed my way
again / Life's like poetry / Darling I'm missing you / I'll never cry over you / My confession / I hope you're not lonely when I'm
gone / My baby and my wife / It's all over
now / Worried mind / Maiden's prayer / I'm
wasting my life away / You nearly lose your
mind / Just can't live that fast (anymore) #3 /
Honey baby, you were wrong / Please me
mine, dear blue eyes / I'm yours if you want
me / I'll be a bachelor till I die / Yesterday's
mail / Shine, shave and shower / I want to
be with you / Always / Ida red (likes the
boogie) / Always late / Theme and If you've
got the money / Make the one for the road
a cup of coffee / Darling let's turn back the
years / Things / At the woodchoppers' ball
/ Stay all night / Somebody's pushing /
Mona Lisa / Sunday down in Tennessee /
I'll make it up to you / Too much love / My
abandoned heart / Wait till I'm asleep / Not
this time / Why didn't you tell me our love
was wrong / Forever and always / Please

don't stay away so long (1) / Please don't
stay away so long (2) / You have never
known to be wrong / Reason why my
heart's in misery / Just little things like that
/ I love you so / Fool's advice / When me
and my baby go steppin' out (1) / When me
and my baby go steppin' out (2) / Brakeman's blues
CD Set _____ BCD 15550
Bear Family / Feb '92 / Rollercoaster /
Direct / CM / Swift / ADA.

Froboess, Conny

DIE SINGLES 1958-59
Diana / Teenager Susan / I love you baby /
Schicke schicke schuh / Auch du hast dein
schicksal in der hand / Glockergiesser rock
/ Blue jean boy / Sunshine / Hey boys, how
do you do / Jolly joker / Teenager melodie
/ Ich mocht mit dir traumen / Holiday in
Honolulu / Ob 15, ob 16, ob 17 jahre alt /
Mr. Music / Wenn das mein grosser bruder
wusste / Kleine Lucienne / Such das gluck
des lebens / Little girl / Ein madchen mit
sechzehn / Lieber disc jockey / Billy, Jack
and Joe / Een meisje ven zestien / Liefde
als zonnenschjn
CD _____ BCD 15410
Bear Family / Dec '87 / Rollercoaster /
Direct / CM / Swift / ADA.

DIE SINGLES 1960-62
Yes my darling / Lippenstift am jacket / Midi
midinette / Wer wird der erste sein / Lago
maggiore / Junge mach musik / Sag mir
was du denkst / Das geht di leute gar nichts
an / Papa liebt mama / Nicht so schuchtern,
junger mann / Ich ben tur die liebe nicht zu
jung / Mein vater war ein cowboy / Firulin /
Oky doky / Mariandl / Nur ein kleines me-
daillon / Einen kuss und noch einen kuss /
Tanz noch einmal mit mir / Zwei kleine It-
aliener / Hallo, hallo, hallo / Das tu' ich alles
nur fur dich / Italien / Un bacio al' Italiano
(Italian) / Hallo, hallo, hallo (Italian) / Twe
kleine Italianen (Dutch) / Hallo, hallo, hallo
(Dutch)
CD _____ BCD 15411
Bear Family / Dec '87 / Rollercoaster /
Direct / CM / Swift / ADA.

DIE SINGLES 1962-64
CD _____ BCD 15452
Bear Family / Feb '90 / Rollercoaster /
Direct / CM / Swift / ADA.

DIE SINGLES 1964-1967
Diese nacht hat viele lichter / Ist es wahr /
Meine hochzeitsreise mach'ich auf den
mond / Schone manner sind nicht sehr ge-
fahrlich / Gestern um dreiviertel zehn / Es
muss nicht dies sein / Ich geh' durch den
regen / Tausend und noch ein paar traume
/ Der sommer geht / Und das leben geht
weiter / Schreib' es in den sand / So ist das
leben / Ich komme nie mehr los von dir / Oh
Gloria / Georgy girl / Frage und antwort /
Adios, adios / Arme kleine sterne / Mein
herz schlagt daba daba dab / Liverpool
waltz / Die sommerballade von der armen
Louise / Folg dem sonnenschein / Um die
welt geht die reise / L'amourette / Dis moi
si tu veux / Les yeux de Paris / On peux
bien dire / Jolly Joker / Hey boys / How do
you do
CD _____ BCD 15491
Bear Family / Aug '91 / Rollercoaster /
Direct / CM / Swift / ADA.

Froese, Edgar

AQUA
Upland / Panorphelia / NGC / Aqua
CD _____ CDV 2016
Virgin / Jun '87 / EMI.

**AQUA/BLACKOUTS/TIMEWIND (Froese,
Edgar/Ashra/Klaus Schulze)**
CD Set _____ TPAK 12
Virgin / Oct '90 / EMI.

BEYOND THE STORM
Heatwave city / Dome of yellow turtles /
One fine day in Siberia / Magic lantern /
Walkabout / Genesta in the afternoon glow
/ Moonlight on a crawler lane / Scarlet score
for Mescalero / Upland / Santa Elena Mar-
isal / Macula transfer / Drunken Mozart in
the desert / Descent like a hawk / Cannoi
/ Light cone / Detroit snackbar dreamer /
Epsilon in Malaysian pale / Tierra del fuego
/ Bobcats in the sun / Metropolis / Year of
the falcon / Juniper mascara / Shores of
Guam / Pinnacles / Stuntman / Days of
camouflage / Tropic of Capricorn / Vault of
the heaven
CD _____ AMBT 5
Virgin / Jun '95 / EMI.

PINNACLES
Specific gravity of smile / Light cone / Walk-
about / Pinnacles
CD _____ CDV 2277
Virgin / May '88 / EMI.

STUNTMAN
Stuntman / It would be like Samoa / Detroit
snackbar dreamer / Drunken Mozart in the
desert / Dali-esque sleep fuse / Scarlet
score for Mescalero
CD _____ CDV 2139
Virgin / '87 / EMI.

Froggatt, Raymond

SOMEDAY
CD _____ RBMCD 0016
Red Balloon / Oct '95 / Koch.

Frohmader, Peter

GATES
CD _____ EFA 127612
Atonal / Sep '95 / SRD.

HOMUNCULUS (2 CDs)
CD Set _____ MRC 020
Staalplaat / Dec '95 / Vital/SAM.

From The Fire

30 DAYS & DIRTY NIGHTS
CD _____ CDATV 22
Active / Jul '92 / Pinnacle.

Frongia, Enrico

ARGIA (Frongia, Enrico & Alberto Balia)
CD _____ NT 6713
Robi Droli / Jan '94 / Direct / ADA.

Front 242

LIVE CODE 5413356424225
Der verfluchte engel / Motion / Masterhit /
Flag / Tragedy for you / Im rhythmus blei-
ben / Skin / Headhunter / Welcome to para-
dise / Crapage / Soul manager / Punish
your machine / Religion
CD _____ BIAS 242CD
Play It Again Sam / Oct '94 / Vital.

LIVE TARGET
Rhythm of time / Soul manager / Don't
crash / Im rhythmus bleiben / DSM 123 and
Moldavia / No shuffle / Gripped by fear /
Never stop / Headhunter / Tragedy for you
/ Welcome to paradise / Punish your ma-
chine / Intro/Circling overland
CD _____ GUZZ 1888
Guzzi Records / Dec '92 / Vital.

MUT@GE MIX@GE
Rhythm of time (Mixes) / Happiness (Mixes)
/ Gripped by fear / Mixed by fear / Crapage
/ Junkdrome / Religion / Break me /
Dancesoundtrackmusic
CD _____ RRE 020CD
Play It Again Sam / Feb '96 / Vital.

NO COMMENT (1984-1985)
Commando mix / S. fr. nomenklatura pt 1 /
2 / Deceit / Lovely day / No shuffle / Special
forces / See the future (live) (June 1992 CD
release only) / In November (live/June '92
CD only) / Body to body (June 1992 CD release only)
CD _____ MK 002CD
Mask / Jun '92 / Vital.

Front Range

BACK TO RED RIVER
CD _____ SH 3811CD
Sugarhill / Jan '94 / Roots / CM / ADA /
Direct.

NEW FRONTIER, THE
Waiting for the real thing / Chains of dark-
ness / Down in Caroline / Without you / Why
don't you leave me baby / Lonesome night
/ When I still needed you / So far away /
Burning the breakfast / Shady river / Build-
ing on the rock / Happy after all
CD _____ SHCD 3801
Sugarhill / '92 / Roots / CM / ADA / Direct.

ONE BEAUTIFUL DAY
CD _____ SHCD 3830
Sugarhill / Mar '95 / Roots / CM / ADA /
Direct.

Frontline Assembly

BLADE, THE
CD _____ TM 91192
Roadrunner / Sep '92 / Pinnacle.

CAUSTIC GRIP
CD _____ TM 91162
Roadrunner / Sep '92 / Pinnacle.

CORRODED DISORDER
CD _____ 08422332CD
Westcon / Jan '96 / Pinnacle.

GASHED SENSES AND CROSSFIRE
No limit / Hypocrisy / Prayer / Big money /
Sedation / Anti-social / Shut down / Digital
tension dementia / Fools game
CD _____ TM 91152
Roadrunner / Sep '92 / Pinnacle.

HARD WIRED
CD _____ 08622290CD
CD _____ 08522292CD
Westcon / Nov '95 / Pinnacle.

INITIAL COMMAND
Initial command
CD _____ KK 006CD
KK / '88 / Plastic Head.

MILLENNIUM
CD _____ RR 90192
Roadrunner / Oct '94 / Pinnacle.

STATE OF MIND
CD _____ DCD 9005
Dossier / Aug '88 / SRD.

TACTICAL NEURAL IMPLANT
CD _____ TM 91882
Third Mind / Apr '92 / Pinnacle / Third Mind.

TOTAL TERROR VOL 1
CD _____ EFA 08451CD
Dossier / Nov '93 / SRD.

TOTAL TERROR VOL 2
CD _____ EFA 08452CD
Dossier / Nov '93 / SRD.

Frost, Frank

JELLY ROLL KING
CD _____ CDCHARLY 223
Charly / Jul '90 / Charly / THE / Cadillac.

JELLY ROLL KING (Charly Blues - Masterworks Vol. 36)
Everything's alright / Lucky to be living / Jelly roll king / Bay you're so kind / Gonna make you mine / Now twist / Big boss man / Jack's jump / So tired of living by myself / Now what you gonna do / Pocket full of shells / Just come on home / Crawlback / My back scratcher / Things you do / Ride with your daddy tonight / Pocket full of money / Didn't mean no harm
CD _____ CDBM 36
Charly / Jan '93 / Charly / THE / Cadillac.

Frostbite

SECOND COMING
CD _____ TPLP 666CD
One Little Indian / Aug '93 / Pinnacle.

Frozen Brass

ASIA
CD _____ PANCD 2020
Pan / May '93 / ADA / Direct / CM.

Frozen Doberman

BONZAI
CD _____ FD 019CD
Modern Invasion / Jul '95 / Plastic Head.

Frugivore

BIONAUT, THE
CD _____ DIGI 1002CD
Digitrax / Oct '95 / Plastic Head.

Fruitcake

HOW TO MAKE IT
How to make it / Inside our place / Fly away / Whims of time / Play my part / Whatever / Sky is dark / Stone of light / Earl grey / Mountain queen / Infalated man / Never really learn
CD _____ CYCL 016
Cyclops / Oct '94 / Pinnacle.

Frumpy

ALL WILL BE CHANGED
CD _____ REP 4146-WP
Repertoire / Aug '91 / Pinnacle / Cadillac.

BY THE WAY
CD _____ REP 4231-WP
Repertoire / Aug '91 / Pinnacle / Cadillac.

Fruscella, Tony

TONY'S BLUES
CD _____ C&BCD 107
Cool 'n' Blue / Dec '92 / Jazz Music / Discovery.

Frusciante, John

NIANDRA LADES AND USUALLY JUST A T-SHIRT
CD _____ 74321236792
American / Nov '95 / BMG.

Frustrated

ANTHOLOGY OF EXPERIMENTAL MUSIC
CD _____ DIS 011CD
Disturbance / Jun '94 / Plastic Head.

Fry, Albert

THIAR I DTIR CHONAILL
CD _____ CIC 081CD
Clo Iar-Chonnachta / Nov '93 / CM.

Frye, Howard

GYPSY MANDOLIN
CD _____ MCD 71463
Monitor / Jun '93 / CM.

FSK

PEEL SESSIONS:FSK (3.8.86-21.5.87)
I wish I could sprechen sie Deutch / Die musik finik findet immer nach haus / Dr. Arnold Fanck / Am tafelberg von kepstadt / Komm gib mir deine hand / Girl / Birthday / Don't pass me by
CD _____ SFPMCD 204
Strange Fruit / '89 / Pinnacle.

Fu-Schnickens

NERVOUS BREAKDOWN
Breakdown / Sum dum monkey / Visions (20/20) / Watch ya back door / Aaahh ooohhh / Sneakin' up on ya / Got it covered / Who stole the pebble / Hi Lo / What's up doc (Can we rock) / Breakdown (remix)
CD _____ CHIP 153
Jive / Oct '94 / BMG.

Fuchs, Wolfgang

FINKFARKER (Fuchs, Wolfgang & George Katzer)
CD _____ FMPCD 26
FMP / Nov '86 / Cadillac.

Fudge

FEROCIOUS RHYTHM OF PRECISE LAZINESS, THE
Oreo dust / Jr. high blur / Peanut butter / Mystery machine / Mull / Wayside / Pez / Astronaut / 20-Nothing dub / Drive / Snowblind
CD _____ QUIGD 2
Quigley / Mar '93 / EMI.

Fudge Tunnel

COMPLICATED FUTILITY OF IGNORANCE, THE
Random acts of cruelty / Joy of irony / Backed down / Cover up / Six eight / Long day / Excuse / Find your fortune / Suffering makes great stories / Circle of friends, circle of trends / Rudge with A G
CD _____ MOSH 119CD
Earache / Sep '94 / Vital.

CREEP DIETS
Grey / Tipper Gore / Ten percent / Face down / Grit / Don't have time for you / Good kicking / Hot salad / Creep diets / Stuck / Always
CD _____ MOSH 064CD
Earache / Apr '93 / Vital.

HATE SONGS IN E
CD _____ MOSH 036CD
Earache / Jan '93 / Vital.

IN A WORD
Sex mammoth / Bed crumbs / Boston baby / Sweet meat / Grey / Spanish fly / Ten percent / Good kicking / Stuck / Tipper Gore / Gut rot / SRT / Kitchen belt / For madmen only / Changes
CD _____ MOSH 099CD
Earache / Jun '95 / Vital.

Fugazi

FUGAZI
Waiting room / Bulldog front / Bad mouth / Burning / Give me the cure / Suggestion / Glue man
CD _____ DIS 30CD
Dischord / Dec '88 / SRD.

IN ON THE KILLTAKER
Facet squad / Public witness programme / Returning the screw / Smallpox champion / Rend it / Twenty three beats off / Sweet and low / Cassavetes / Great cop / Walken's syndrome / Instrument / Last chance for a sow dance
CD _____ DIS 70D
Dischord / Jun '93 / SRD.

MARGIN WALKER
Margin walker / And the same / Burning too / Provisional / Lockdown / Promises
CD _____ DIS 35CD
Dischord / Jul '89 / SRD.

RED MEDICINE
Do you like me / Bed for the scraping / Latest disgrace / Birthday bony / Forensic scene / Combination lock / Fell, destroyed / By you / Version / Target / Back to base / Downed city / Long distance runner
CD _____ DIS 90CD
Dischord / May '95 / SRD.

REPEATER
Turnover / Repeater / Brendan No.1 / Merchandise / Blueprint / Sieve-fisted find / Greed / Two beats off / Styrofoam / Reprovisional / Shut the door
CD _____ DIS 44CD
Dischord / Mar '90 / SRD.

STEADY DIET OF NOTHING
Exit only / Reclamation / Nice new outfit / Stacks / Latin roots / Steady diet of nothing / Long division / Runaway return / Polish / Dear justice letter / KYEO
CD _____ DISCHORD 60CD
Dischord / Sep '91 / SRD.

Fugees

BLUNTED ON REALITY
Introduction / Nappy heads / Blunted interlude / Recharge / Free-style interlude / Vocab / Special new bulletin interlude / Boof baf / Temple / How hard is it / Harlem chit chat interlude / Some seek stardom / Giggles / Da kid from Haiti interlude / Refugees on the mic / Living like there's not no tomorrow / Shouts out from the block
CD _____ 474713-2
Columbia / Mar '94 / Sony.

Fugs

FIRST ALBUM
Slum Goddess / Ah sunflower weary of time / Supergirl / Swinburne stomp / I couldn't get high / How sweet I roamed / Carpe diem / My baby done left me / Boobs a lot / Nothing / We're the fugs / Defeated / Ten commandments / CIA man / In the middle of their first recording session The Fugs sign / I saw the best minds of my generation rock / Spontaneous salute at Andy Warhol / War kills babies / Fugs national anthem / Fugs spaghetti death / Rhapsody of Tuli
CD _____ CDWIKD 119
Fugs/Big Beat / Jun '93 / Pinnacle.

FUGS LIVE FROM THE 60'S
Doin' alright / Swedish nada / Homage to Catherine and William Blake / I couldn't / Johnny pissoff and the red angel / J.O.B. / My baby done left me / Garden is open / Exorcism of the grave of Senator Joseph McCarthy / Yodeling yippie / Ten commandments / Swinburne stomp
CD _____ CDWIKD 125
Fugs/Big Beat / May '94 / Pinnacle.

NO MORE SLAVERY
CD _____ ROSE 79CD
New Rose / Jul '86 / Direct / ADA.

REAL WOODSTOCK FESTIVAL, THE (Byrdcliffe Barn, Woodstock NY - 14th August 1994/2CD Set) (Fugs & Allen Ginsberg/Friends)
Nova slum goddess / Poe job / Cia man / Crystal liason / Golden age / Rock 'n' roll hall of fame / Frenzy / Sonnet 29: Fortune and men's eyes / Postmodern nothing / Ramses the II is dead, my love / When the mode of the music changes / Ten commandments, together with the ten amendments / Woodstock nation / Augries of innocence / They're closing up the loudspeakers of life / Einstein never wore socks / Shadows of paradise / I want to know / Song for Janis Joplin / Cave 64 / Down by the Salley Gardens / Coming down / Wide wide river / How sweet I roamed from field to field / Morning morning / Nurse's song and all the hills echoed)
CD _____ CDWIK2 160
Fugs/Big Beat / Sep '95 / Pinnacle.

REFUSE TO BE BURNT-OUT (Live in the 1980s)
Five feet / If you want to be President / Nova slum goddess / Nicaragua / Fingers of the sun / Wide wide river / How sweet I roamed / Refuse to be burnt-out / Country punk / CIA man / Ban the bomb / Keeping the issues alive / Dreams of sexual perfection (Gratified desire/Emily Dickinson/Party, party, party/Golden Bard Retirement Home/Little Lydia/Healing river/Chaos, earth and Eros) / Summer of love
CD _____ CDWIKD 139
Fugs/Big Beat / Mar '95 / Pinnacle.

SECOND ALBUM
Frenzy / I want to know / Skin flowers / Group grope / Coming down / Dirty old man / Kill for peace / Morning morning / Doin' alright / Virgin forest / Mutant stomp / Carpe diem / Wide wide river / Nameless voices crying for kindness
CD _____ CDWIKD 121
Fugs/Big Beat / Sep '93 / Pinnacle.

STAR PEACE
CD _____ ROSE 115CD
New Rose / Jun '87 / Direct / ADA.

Fukushima, Kazuo

WORKS FOR FLUTE AND PIANO
CD _____ ARTCD 6114
Hat Art / Oct '92 / Harmonia Mundi / ADA / Cadillac.

Full Moon

EUPHORIA
CD _____ DMCD 1031
Demi-Monde / Feb '92 / Disc / Magnum Music Group.

Full Moon Scientists

MEN IN WHITE COATS
CD _____ HANDCD 1
Hard Hands / Oct '94 / Sony / Disc.

Fuller, Blind Boy

1935-1940
Baby you gotta change your mind / Baby I don't have to worry / Looking for my woman / Precious lord / Jesus is a holy man / Bye bye baby / You got to have your dollar / Shake that shimmy / Truckin' my blues away
CD _____ TMCD 01
Travellin' Man / Apr '90 / Wellard / CM / Jazz Music.

BLIND FULLER BOY, VOL. 1 (1935-36)
CD _____ DOCD 5091
Blues Document / '92 / Swift / Jazz Music / Hot Shot.

BLIND FULLER BOY, VOL. 2 (1937)
CD _____ DOCD 5092
Blues Document / '92 / Swift / Jazz Music / Hot Shot.

BLIND FULLER BOY, VOL. 3 (1937)
CD _____ DOCD 5093
Blues Document / '92 / Swift / Jazz Music / Hot Shot.

BLIND FULLER BOY, VOL. 4 (1937-38)
CD _____ DOCD 5094
Blues Document / '92 / Swift / Jazz Music / Hot Shot.

BLIND FULLER BOY, VOL. 5 (1938-40)
CD _____ DOCD 5095
Blues Document / '92 / Swift / Jazz Music / Hot Shot.

BLIND FULLER BOY, VOL. 6 (1940)
CD _____ DOCD 5096
Blues Document / '92 / Swift / Jazz Music / Hot Shot.

BULL CITY BLUES
CD _____ ALB 1010CD
Aldabra / Mar '94 / CM / Disc.

EAST COAST PIEDMONT BLUES
Rag mama rag / Baby you gotta change your mind / My brownskin sugar plum / I'm a rattlesnakin' daddy / I'm climbin' on top of the hill / Baby I don't have to worry / Looking for my woman / Ain't It a cryin' shame / Walking my troubles away / Sweet honey hole / Somebody's been playing with that thing / Log cabin blues / Keep away from my woman / Cat man blues / Untrue blues / Black and tan fantasy / Big leg woman gets my pay / You've got something there / I'm a stranger here / Evil hearted woman
CD _____ 4679232
Columbia / May '91 / Sony.

TRUCKIN' MY BLUES AWAY
CD _____ YAZCD 1060
Yazoo / Apr '91 / CM / ADA / Roots / Koch.

Fuller, Bobby

BEST OF THE BOBBY FULLER FOUR (Fuller, Bobby Four)
I fought the law / Love's made a fool of you / Another sad and lonely night / She's my girl / New shade of blue / My true love / Pamela / Let her dance / Never to be forgotten / Thunder reef / Baby my heart / Fool of love / Only when I dream / Don't ever let me know / King of the wheels / Think it over / Magic touch / Keep a knockin'
CD _____ CDCHM 388
Ace / Mar '92 / Pinnacle / Cadillac / Complete/Pinnacle.

I FOUGHT THE LAW (Fuller, Bobby Four)
CD _____ 842614
EVA / May '94 / Direct / ADA.

I FOUGHT THE LAW AND THE KRLA KING OF THE WHEELS (Fuller, Bobby Four)
Thunder reef / Wolfman / She's my girl / King of the wheels / Lonely dragster / Phantom dragster / KRLA top eliminator / Let her dance / Julie / New shade of blue / Only when I dream / You kiss me / Little Annie Lou / I fought the law / Another sad and lonely night / Saturday night / Take my word / Fool of love / Never to be forgotten / Love's made a fool of you / Don't ever let me know / My true love / Magic touch / I'm a lucky guy
CD _____ CDCHD 956
Ace / Nov '90 / Pinnacle / Cadillac / Complete/Pinnacle.

LIVE AT PJ'S PLUS! (Fuller, Bobby Four)
Anytime at all / Wooly bully / Gloria / Oh boy / Think it over / Thunder reef / Hi-heel sneakers / Slow down / I fought the law / New shade of blue / Let her dance / C.C. Rider / My babe / Keep a knockin' / Long tall Sally / Baby my heart / Pamela / My true love / Our favourite Martian / Never to be forgotten
CD _____ CDCHD 314
Ace / Jul '91 / Pinnacle / Cadillac / Complete/Pinnacle.

Fuller, Curtis

BLUES-ETTE
Five spot after dark / Undecided / Bluesette / Minor vamp / Love your spell is everywhere / Twelve inch
CD _____ SV 0127
Savoy Jazz / Apr '93 / Conifer / ADA.

BLUES-ETTE PART II (Fuller, Curtis Quintet)
Love your spell is everywhere / Sis / Bluesette / Is it all a game / Captain Kidd / Five spot after dark / How am I to know / Along came Betty / Autumn in New York / Manhattan serenade
CD _____ CY 75624
Savoy Jazz / Sep '93 / Conifer / ADA.

CURTIS FULLER JAZZTETTE, THE
It's all right with me / Wheatleigh Hall / I'll walk alone / Arabia / Judy's dilemma
CD _____ SV 0134
Savoy Jazz / Apr '93 / Conifer / ADA.

IMAGES OF CURTIS FULLER
Accident / Darryl's mirror / Be back / Tareckla / Judyful / New date

CD _____ SV 0129
Savoy Jazz / Aug '93 / Conifer / ADA.

IMAGINATION
Kachin / Bang bang / Imagination / Blues
de funk / Lido Road
CD _____ CY 78996
Savoy Jazz / Nov '95 / Conifer / ADA.

JAZZ...IT'S MAGIC
Two Tom / It's magic / My one and only love
/ They didn't believe me / Soul station /
Club oar / Upper berth
CD _____ SV 0153
Savoy Jazz / Apr '93 / Conifer / ADA.

Fuller, Jesse

FRISCO BOUND
CD _____ ARHCD 360
Arhoolie / Apr '95 / ADA / Direct /
Cadillac.

FULLER'S FAVOURITES
Red river blues / How long blues / You can't
keep a good man down / Key to the highway / Tickling the strings / Midnight special
/ Stranger blues / Fables aren't nothing but
doggone lies / Brown skin gal I got my eyes
on you / Cincinnati blues / Hump in your
back / Trouble if I don't use my head
CD _____ OBCCD 528
Original Blues Classics / Nov '92 / Com-
plete/Pinnacle / Wellard / Cadillac.

**JAZZ, FOLK SONGS, SPIRITUALS &
BLUES**
CD _____ OBCCD 564
Original Blues Classics / Jan '94 /
Complete/Pinnacle / Wellard / Cadillac.

LONE CAT, THE
Leavin' Memphis, Frisco bound / Take it
slow and easy / Monkey and the engineer /
New Corrine / Guitar blues / Running wild /
Hey hey / In that great land / Way you treat
me / Down home waltz / Beat it on down
the line / Buck and wing
CD _____ OBCCD 526
Original Blues Classics / Nov '92 / Com-
plete/Pinnacle / Wellard / Cadillac.

RAILROAD WORKSONG
Move on down the line / Stealing / Ninety
nine years and one dark day / Animal fair /
Sleeping in the midnight cold / Stagolee /
Bill Bailey, Won't you please come home /
San Francisco Bay blues / Crazy waltz /
Railroad worksong / Meet my loving mother
/ I love my baby / Tune (Creole love call) /
Running wild / Stranger blues / Hanging
around a skin game / Monkey and the
engineer / Buck dancer's jump
CD _____ LACD 24
Fellside / Jan '93 / Target/BMG / Direct /
ADA.

SAN FRANCISCO BAY BLUES
San Francisco Bay blues / Jesse's new
midnight special / Morning blues / Little
black train / Midnight cold / Whoa mule /
John Henry / I got a mind to ramble / Crazy
about a woman / Where could I go but to
the Lord / Stealin' blues / All day long used
to be / Brown skin gal
CD _____ OBCCD 537
Original Blues Classics / Nov '92 / Com-
plete/Pinnacle / Wellard / Cadillac.

Fuller, Johnny

FULLER'S BLUES
CD _____ DDCD 4311
Diving Duck / '88 / Impetus / CM /
Duncans.

Fulson, Lowell

HOLD ON
CD _____ BBCD 9525
Bullseye Blues / Jan '93 / Direct.

IT'S A GOOD DAY
CD _____ ROUNDERCD 2088
Rounder / '88 / CM / Direct / ADA /
Cadillac.

OL' BLUES SINGER, THE
CD _____ IGOCD 2022
Indigo / May '95 / Direct / ADA.

ONE MORE BLUES
CD _____ BLE 597242
Black & Blue / Dec '90 / Wellard / Koch.

**RECONSIDER BABY (Charly Blues -
Masterworks Vol. 48)**
Reconsider baby / Lonely hours / Loving
you / Trouble trouble / It's a long time / Rollin' blues / Took a long time / Someday
baby / I want to make love to you / Rock
this morning / That's all right / Worry worry
/ Comin' home someday / Have you
changed your mind / K.C. Bound / I'm glad
you reconsidered / Blue shadows / I want
to know / So many tears / Why don't you
write me / Hung down head / Pay day blues
/ Shed no tears / Trouble with the blues
CD _____ CDBM 48
Charly / Jun '93 / Charly / THE / Cadillac.

SAN FRANCISCO BLUES
CD _____ BLC 760176
Black Lion / Dec '92 / Jazz Music /
Cadillac / Wellard / Koch.

SWINGIN' PARTY
CD _____ FC 90CD
Fan Club / Feb '92 / Direct.

THEM UPDATE BLUES
CD _____ CDBB 9558
Bullseye Blues / Aug '95 / Direct.

THINK TWICE BEFORE YOU SPEAK
Parachute woman / I'm tough / Think twice
before you speak / Well oh well / Come
back baby / Sinner's prayer / One-room
country shack / Meet me in the bottom /
Come on / You're gonna miss me
CD _____ JSPCD 207
JSP / Oct '92 / ADA / Target/BMG / Direct
/ Cadillac / Complete/Pinnacle.

TRAMP/ SOUL
Tramp / I'm sinking / Get your game up tight
/ Back door key / Two way wishing / Lonely
day / Black nights / Year of 29 / No hard
feelings / Hustlers game / Goin' home / Pico
/ Talkin' woman / Shattered dreams / Sittin'
here thinkin' / Little angel / Change your
ways / Blues around midnight / Everytime it
rains / Just one more time / Ask at any door
in town / Too many drivers / My aching
back
CD _____ CDCHD 339
Ace / Nov '93 / Pinnacle / Cadillac / Com-
plete/Pinnacle.

Fun Boy Three

BEST OF FUN BOY THREE
T'ain't what you do (it's the way that you do
it) / Really saying something / Summertime
/ Lunatics (have taken over the asylum) /
More I see (the less I believe) / Telephone
always rings / Our lips are sealed / Tunnel
of love / We're having all the fun / Farmyard
connection / Pressure of life (takes weight
off the body)
CD _____ CPCD 1469
Chrysalis / Jun '87 / EMI.

LIVE ON THE TEST
CD _____ WHISCD 003
Windsong / May '94 / Pinnacle.

SINGLES (Fun Boy Three/Colourfield)
CD _____ VSOPCD 196
Connoisseur / Apr '94 / Pinnacle.

Fun Factory

NONSTOP
CD _____ 0041062REG
Edel / May '95 / Pinnacle.

Fun Republic

**HAPPY PEOPLE AND MORE REALITY
TV**
CD _____ EFA 046212
Pork Pie / Oct '95 / SRD.

Fun-Da-Mental

SEIZE THE TIME
CD _____ NATCD 33
Nation / May '94 / Disc.

**WITH INTENT TO PERVERT THE
COURSE OF JUSTICE**
CD _____ NATCD 56
Nation / Jul '95 / Disc.

Funbug

SPUNKIER
CD _____ CDHOLE 006
Golf / Oct '95 / Plastic Head.

Fundeburgh, Anson

**ANSON FUNDEBURGH AND THE
ROCKETS (Featuring Sam Myers)
(Fundeburgh, Anson & The Rockets)**
CD _____ CD 1038
Black Top / '88 / CM / Direct / ADA.

**BLACK TOP BLUES-A-RAMA VOL.1
(Live At Tipitina's) (Fundeburgh, Anson
& The Rockets)**
CD _____ CD 1044
Black Top / '88 / CM / Direct / ADA.

HARPOON MAN
CD _____ AP 117
Appaloosa / Oct '95 / ADA / Magnum
Music Group.

LIVE AT THE GRAND
CD _____ BT 1111CD
Black Top / Apr '95 / CM / Direct / ADA.

**LIVE AT THE GRAND EMPORIUM
(Fundeburgh, Anson & The Rockets)**
CD _____ BT 1111CD
Black Top / Feb '95 / CM / Direct / ADA.

RACK 'EM UP
Tell me what I have done wrong / Since we-
've been together / Rack 'em up / Mama
and poppa / Twenty miles / Hold that train,
conductor / I'm your professor / I'll keep on
trying / All your love / Are you out there /
Lemonade / Meanstreak
CD _____ FIENDCD 147
Demon / Oct '89 / Pinnacle / ADA.

**SINS (With Sam Myers) (Fundeburgh,
& The Rockets)**
Man needs his loving / I'll be true / Don't
want no leftovers / Walked all night / My

kind of baby / Changing neighbourhoods /
I can't stop loving you / Chill out / My heart
/ Trying to make you mine / Sleeping in the
ground / Hard hearted woman
CD _____ DIAB 804
Diabolo / Feb '94 / Pinnacle.

Funeral Nation

AFTER THE BATTLE
CD _____ TURBOCD 003
Turbo Music / Jan '92 / Plastic Head.

Funeral Oration

FUNERAL ORATION
CD _____ HR 606CD
Hopeless / Nov '95 / Plastic Head.

Funk Inc.

ACID INC - THE BEST OF FUNK INC
Chicken lickin' / Sister Jane / Jung bongo /
Where are we going / Smokin' at Tiffany's /
Kool's back again / Give me your love /
Let's make love and stop the war / Better
half (On CD only) / Bowlegs (On CD only)
CD _____ CDBGP 1011
BGP / Oct '91 / Pinnacle.

FUNK INC./CHICKEN' LICKIN'
Kool is back / Bowlegs / Sister Janie / Thrill
is gone / Whipper / Chicken lickin' / Run-
ning away / They trying to get me / Better
half / Let's make peace and stop the war /
Jung bongo
CD _____ CDBGPD 040
BGP / Sep '92 / Pinnacle.

HANGIN' OUT/SUPERFUNK
Smokin' at Tiffany's / Give me your love /
We can be friends / Dirty red / I can see
clearly now / I'll be around / Message from
the Meters / Goodbye so long / Hill where
the lord hides / Honey, I love you / Just
don't mean a thing / I'm gonna love you just
a little bit more baby
CD _____ CDBGPD 058
BGP / Feb '93 / Pinnacle.

PRICED TO SELL
It's not the spotlight / Priced to sell / God
only knows / Where are we going / Gimme
some lovin' / Somewhere in my mind / Girl
of my dreams
CD _____ CDBGPM 075
BGP / Jun '93 / Pinnacle.

Funk Master Flex

**MIX TAPE VOL.1 - 60 MINUTES OF
FUNK**
CD _____ 07863668052
RCA / Nov '95 / BMG.

Funkadelic

AMERICA EATS ITS YOUNG
You hit the nail on the head / If you don't
like the effects, don't produce the cause /
Everybody is going to make it this time /
Joyful process / We hurt too / Loose booty
/ Philmore / I call my baby pussycat / Amer-
ica eats its young / Biological speculation /
That was my girl / Balance / Miss Lucifer's
love / Wake up
CD _____ CDSEWD 029
Westbound / Jul '90 / Pinnacle.

BEST OF FUNKADELIC 1976-1981, THE
One nation under a groove / Cholly (funk
getting ready to roll) / Who says a funk band
can't play rock / Coming round the mountain / Smoky / Cosmic slop (live) / Electric
spanking of war babies / Funk gets stronger
(pt 1) / Undisa Jam (edit) / Icka prick / (Not
just) knee deep
CD _____ CDGR 104
Charly / Feb '94 / Charly / THE / Cadillac.

ELECTRIC SPANKING OF WAR BABIES
Electric spanking of war babies / Electro-
cuties / Funk gets stronger / Brettino's
bounce / She loves you / Shockwaves / Oh,
I / Icka prick
CD _____ CDGR 102
Charly / Jun '93 / Charly / THE / Cadillac.

FUNKADELIC LIVE
Funkentelechy / Cosmic slop / Maggot
brain / Bop gun / Funk gettin' ready to roll
/ It ain't legal / Flashlight / Mothership connection / Give up the funk / Let's take it to
the stage / Do that stuff / Undisa (edit) /
Children of production / Atomic dog / Maceo, not Charlie / Red hot Mama / Into you
/ Standing on the verge of getting it on /
One nation under a groove / Coming round
the mountain / Won't you dance / Quickie /
Aquaboogie / I wanna know if it's good to
you / Up for the down stroke / Hit it and
quit it / Gamin' on ya / Put your hands together / Dog you out / P-funk / You do me
/ Nickel bag o'solos / Dope dog / I call my
baby pussycat / Lampin / Microphone fiend
underground angel / Yank my doodle su-
m'else / I got a thing, you got a thing, everybody got a thing / All your goodies are gone
/ Lifted
CD Set _____ NEFCD 273
Sequel / Oct '94 / BMG.

FUNKADELIC PICTURE DISC BOX SET
CD Set _____ WBOXPD 1
Westbound / Aug '90 / Pinnacle.

**FUNKADELIC PICTURE DISC BOX SET
2 (Cosmic slop/Tales of.../Let's take it.../
Standing on...)**
CD Set _____ WBOXPD 5
Westbound / Feb '94 / Pinnacle.

HARDCORE FUNK JAM
CD _____ CPCD 8064
Charly / Nov '94 / Charly / THE / Cadillac.

HARDCORE JOLLIES
Osmosis phase one / Coming round the
mountain / Smoky / If you got funk, you got
style / Hardcore jollies / Terribitus phase
two / Soul mate / Cosmic slop / You scared
the lovin outta me / Adolescent funk
CD _____ CDGR 101
Charly / Jun '93 / Charly / THE / Cadillac.

MUSIC FOR YOUR MOTHER
Music for my mother / Music for my mother
(instrumental) / Can't shake it loose / As
good as I can feel / I'll bet you / Qualify and
satisfy / Open our eyes / I got a thing, you
got a thing, everybody got a thing / Fish,
chips and sweat / I wanna know if it's good
to you (instrumental) / You and your folks,
me and my folks / Funky dollar bill / Can
you get to that / Back in our minds / I miss
my baby / Baby I owe you something good
/ Hit it and quit it / Whole lot of BS / Loose
booty / Joyful process / Cosmic slop / If you
don't like the effects, don't produce the
cause / Standing on the verge of getting it
on / Jimmy's got a little bit of bitch in him /
Red hot Mama / Vital juices / Better by the
pound / Stuffs and things / Let's take it to
the stage / How do yeaw view you
CD Set _____ CDSEW2 055
Southbound / Oct '92 / Pinnacle.

ONE NATION UNDER A GROOVE
One nation under a groove / Groovallegci-
ance / Who says a funk band can't play
rock / Promentalshitbackwashpsychosise-
nema squad / Into you / Cholly (funk getting
ready to roll) / Lunchmeataphobia / P.E.
squad / Doodoo chasers / Maggot brain
CD _____ CDGR 100
Charly / Jul '93 / Charly / THE / Cadillac.

UNCLE JAM WANTS YOU
Freak of the week / (Not just) knee deep /
Uncle Jam / Field manoeuvers / Holly wants
to go to California / Foot soldiers
CD _____ CDGR 103
Charly / Jun '93 / Charly / THE / Cadillac.

Funkdoobiest

BROTHERS DOOBIE
This it it (interlude) / Rock on / What the deal
/ Lost in thought / Dedicated / Ka sera sera
/ Pussy ain't shit / XXX Funk / It ain't going
down / You're dommin' / Tomahawk bang
/ Super hoes / Who ra ra
CD _____ 4783812
Epic / Jul '95 / Sony.

WHICH DOOBIE U B
Funkiest / Bow wow wow / Freak mode /
I'm shittin' on 'em / Who's the doobiest /
Doobie to the head / Where's it at / Wop-
babalubop / Porno King / Uh c'mon yeah /
Here I am / Funks on me
CD _____ 473648 2
Epic / Jul '93 / Sony.

Funki Porcini

HED PHONE SEX
Word of vice / B Monkey / Dubble / King
ashababapal part 1 / Deep / King Ashaban-
apal part 2 / Michael's little friend / White
slave / Poseathon / Wicked, cruel, nasty
and hard / Redi plimmin / Softest thing in the
world (motorway accident) / Tiny kangeroo
dolphin (from hell) / Long road / Mushroom
head (LP only.) / Pork kiss head (LP only.)
CD _____ ZENCD 017
Ninja Tune / May '95 / Vital / Kudos.

Funky New Orleans Jazz...

**FUNKY NEW ORLEANS JAZZ BAND
(Funky New Orleans Jazz Band)**
CD _____ MMRC CD 3
Merry Makers / Feb '94 / Jazz Music.

Funky Poets

TRUE TO LIFE
Born in the ghetto / 1975 / Lessons learned
/ It doesn't have to be this way / Never say
never / Set it off / We as a people / Can
you feel the love / When will we learn / How
can you leave me now / I only have eyes
for you
CD _____ 474211 2
Epic / May '94 / Sony.

Funny Hill

COWBOY BOOTS
CD _____ BRAM 198906-2
Brambus / Nov '93 / ADA / Direct.

LIVE IN NASHVILLE
CD _____ BRAM 199015-2
Brambus / Nov '93 / ADA / Direct.

Fur

FUR
Beautiful wreck / Brazil / They say / Ocelot
/ Beauty and speed / Devil to the lamb / I'm

not coming / James Brown / X-offender /
Sex drive
CD _____ BLK 026ECD
Blackout / Dec '95 / Vital.

Furbowl

AUTUMN YEARS
CD _____ BMCD 47
Black Mark / Mar '94 / Plastic Head.

Furey, Finbar

DAWNING OF THE DAY
CD _____ BGOCD 291
Beat Goes On / Oct '95 / Pinnacle.

Fureys

7 CLADDAGH ROAD
Sound of thunder / Donegal / Mary Skeffington / Liffey walls / Roy's tribute / Living
on the edge of your town / America cried /
6000 lonely miles / I remember Mary / Ama-
dan / Cross me heart / Mo Chuileann
CD _____ CDDPR 132
Premier/MFP / Jan '96 / EMI.

BEST OF THE FUREYS
Spanish cloak / dainty Davie / Castle Ter-
race / Roy's hands / Dance around the
spinning wheel / Let me go to the moun-
tains / McShane / Colonel Fraser / Carron
Lough Bay / Prickly bush / Fox chase / Bill
Hart's favourite / Silver spear / Tattered
Jack Welch / Pigeon on the gate / Fin's fa-
vourite / Peter Byrne's fancy / Bonny bunch
of roses / Eddie's fancy / O'Rourke's reel
CD _____ TRTCD 137
TrueTrax / Dec '94 / THE.

**BEST OF THE FUREYS AND DAVEY
ARTHUR (Fureys & Davey Arthur)**
When you were sweet sixteen / Maggie /
Morning has broken / Twelfth of never / Annie's song / I'll take you home again Kathleen / Love is pleasin' / Beautiful dreamer /
Bonnie Mary of Argyle / Just a song at
twilight / Bless this house / I'll be your
sweetheart / Last rose of summer / If I had
my life to live over / Wait till the clouds roll
by / Scarlet ribbons / Perfect day / When I
grow too old to dream / Come by the hills
/ Anniversary waltz
CD _____ MCCD 010
Music Club / Feb '91 / Disc / THE / CM.

**COLLECTION: FUREYS (Furey, Finbar &
Eddie)**
Rakish Paddy / Hag with the money / Bill
Hart's favourite / Dance around the spin-
ning wheel / Fin's favourite / Spanish cloak
/ Young girl milking the cow / Piper in the
meadow straying / Castle terrace / Madam
Bonaparte / Grahams flat / Fox chase /
McShane / Colonel Fraser / Lonesome
boatman / Carron Lough bay / Come by the
hills / Sliabh na mBan / Flowers in the valley
/ Pigeon on the gate / Eamonn an chnuic
(Ned of the hills) / This town is not their own
/ Rocking the baby
CD _____ CCSCD 165
Castle / Apr '94 / BMG.

**COLLECTION: FUREYS AND DAVEY
ARTHUR (Fureys & Davey Arthur)**
Paddy in Paris / Reason I left Mullingar /
Mountains of Mourne / Irish eyes / Who do
you think you are / Lovers / Ted Furey's
selection / Evening falls / Night Ferry / Port-
land town / Ned of the hill / October song /
Leaving Nancy / Garrett Barry's jig / Sitting
alone / Big ships / From where I stand /
Morning cloud
New copperplate etc. / Dreaming my
dreams / Lament / I'll be there / First leaves
of Autumn
CD _____ CCSCD 231
Castle / Oct '89 / BMG.

FINEST (Fureys & Davey Arthur)
When you were sweet sixteen / Dublin /
When I leave behind Neidin / Green fields
of France / Lonesome boatman / I will love
you ev'ry time / Stealaway / Red rose cafe
/ Maggie
CD _____ CLACD 319
Castle / '92 / BMG.

**FOUR GREEN FIELDS (Furey, Finbar &
Eddie)**
CD _____ TUT 72166
Wundertute / Jan '94 / CM / Duncans /
ADA.

**FUREYS & DAVEY ARTHUR,THE (Fureys
& Davey Arthur)**
CD _____ EMPRCD 518
Emporio / Jul '94 / THE / Disc / CM.

**SOUND OF THE FUREYS & DAVEY
ARTHUR, THE (Fureys & Davey Arthur)**
Green fields of France / Gypsy Davey /
Reason I left Mullinger / Clare to here / Ask
me father / Finbar Dwyers / Old man /
Lark on the strand / Her father didn't like
me anyway / Shipyard slips / Leaving
Nancy / O'Carolans tribute / Roster / Night
ferry / Lament / Beer, beer, beer / Lone-
some boatman

CD _____ RGCD 11
Polydor / '88 / PolyGram.

STEAL AWAY (Fureys & Davey Arthur)
Steal away / Ladybird / Alcohol holidays:
last orders / Katriona / Dublin / Now is the
hour / Silver threads among the gold /
Jenny
CD _____ CLACD 259
Castle / Oct '91 / BMG.

**WHEN YOU WERE SWEET SIXTEEN
(Fureys & Davey Arthur)**
Green fields of France / When you were
sweet sixteen / My love is like a red red rose
/ Anniversary song / I will love you ev'ry time
/ Yesterdays people / Lonesome boatman /
Old man / Oh Babushka / Belfast mill /
Siege of a nation / Yesterdays men
CD _____ CLACD 171
Castle / Feb '90 / BMG.

WINDS OF CHANGE
Oro oro / It's good to see you / Sweet and
gentle love / Old george / Didn't It rain /
North by north / Mary and me / Campfire in
the dark / Travelling lady / If I don't bring
you flowers / Cry of the celts / Man of our
times / Noraleen / Song for the fox / Goodbye booze
CD _____ RITZLCD0069
Ritz / Oct '92 / Pinnacle.

Furic, Stephane

STEPHANE FURIC
CD _____ 121215-2
Soul Note / May '91 / Harmonia Mundi /
Wellard / Cadillac.

Furioso

FURIOSO
CD _____ CDGRUB 24
Food For Thought / Sep '92 / Pinnacle.

Furniture

FURNITURE SCRAPBOOK, THE
CD _____ SURCD 013
Survival / Sep '91 / Pinnacle.

Furtado, Tony

FULL CIRCLE
CD _____ ROUCD 0323
Rounder / Oct '94 / CM / Direct / ADA /
Cadillac.

WITHIN REACH
Ralph Trischka / St. John's fire / I will / Wait-
ing for Guiteau/President Garfield's Horn-
pipe / Queen Anne's lace / Sao Miguel /
Julia Dealaney/The Drunken landiady / Dra-
ke's bay / Magpie on the gallows / Duskus
CD _____ CDROU 0290
Rounder / '92 / CM / Direct / ADA / Cadillac.

Further

5 FURTHER JOURNEYS
CD _____ FUR 100CD
Abstract / Sep '94 / Pinnacle / Total/BMG.

SUPER GRIP TAPE
CD _____ SHED 003CD
Creation / Aug '93 / 3MV / Vital.

Furudate, Tetsuo

AUTREMENT QU'ETRE
CD _____ DSA 54040
Les Disques Du Soleil / Dec '95 /
Harmonia Mundi.

Fury, Billy

ALL THE BEST
I will / Like I've never been gone / Last night
was made for love / I'm lost without you /
Stand up / My say / Love you / Run to my
lovin' arms / It's only make believe / Maybe
tomorrow / In thoughts of you / Give me
your word / That's love / Once upon a
dream / Colette / Wondrous place / Thousand stars / I'll never find another you /
Fools errand (Do you really love me) / Jealousy / Someone else's girl / Halfway to
paradise
CD _____ ECD 3041
K-Tel / Jan '95 / K-Tel.

AM I BLUE
CD _____ 8289022
London / Jul '93 / PolyGram.

BILLY FURY HIT PARADE, THE
Maybe tomorrow / Colette / That's love /
Thousand stars / Halfway to paradise /
Jealousy / I'd never find another you / Last
night was made for love / Like I've never
been gone / When will you say I love you /
In summer / Somebody else's girl / Do you
really love me too / I will / It's only make
believe / Lost without you / In thoughts of
you / Run to my lovin' arms
CD _____ 820 503-2
London / Jan '87 / PolyGram.

EP COLLECTION: BILLY FURY
Turn your lamp down low / Don't walk away
/ You're having the last dance with me /
Wonderous place / What am I living for /
That's enough / You got me dizzy / Saved
/ Keep away / My Christmas prayer / I can
feel it / I love how you love me / Would you
stand by me / Margo / Play it cool / Don't
jump / Please don't go / What did I do / I'll
never quite get over you / Nobody's child
CD _____ SEECD 59
See For Miles/C5 / Oct '89 / Pinnacle.

HALFWAY TO PARADISE
Halfway to paradise / Don't worry / You're
having the last dance with me / Push push
/ Fury's tune / Talkin' in my sleep / Stick
around / Thousand stars / Cross my heart
/ Comin' up in the world / He will break your
heart / Would you stand by me
CD _____ 8209242
London / Aug '90 / PolyGram.

**IN THOUGHTS OF YOU (The Best Of
Billy Fury)**
It's only make believe / Jealousy / Thou-
sand stars / Push push / Angel face / I will
/ Letter full of tears / I'll never quite get over
you / In thoughts of you / Wonderous place
/ Nobody's child / Kansas City / Candy
kisses / Glad all over / If I lose you / Give
me your word
CD _____ PWKS 4053P
Carlton Home Entertainment / May '91 /
Carlton Home Entertainment.

LEGENDS IN MUSIC - BILLY FURY
CD _____ LECD 086
Wisepack / Sep '94 / THE / Conifer.

OTHER SIDE OF BILLY FURY
Cross my heart / King for tonight / What do
you think you're doing of / All I wanna do is
cry / I'll never fall in love again / Don't you
see the real thing come along / If I lose you
/ Alright goodbye / Where do you run /
Away from you / She's so far out she's in /
Baby, what you want me to do / Talkin in
my sleep / Running around / You don't
know / Last kiss / What am I gonna do /
Gonna type a letter / Don't knock upon my
door / Nothin' shakin' / Go ahead and ask
her / Glad all over
CD _____ SEECD 383
See For Miles/C5 / Oct '93 / Pinnacle.

PARADISE
Halfway to paradise / It's only make believe
/ Last night was made for love / I will / Wonderous place / Don't worry / We were meant
for each other / Our day will come / I'll never
fall in love again / Forget him / Love or
money / Begin the beguine / Be mine tonight / Don't leave me this way
CD _____ 5500112
Spectrum/Karussell / May '93 / PolyGram /
THE.

ROUGH DIAMONDS AND PURE GEMS
Sticks 'n' stones / Things are changing /
Loving you / I'll go along with it / Suzanne
in the mirror / Phone box / Any morning now
/ Lady / Certain things / All the way to the
USA / Well alright / Baby get yourself to-
gether / Driving nicely / Your words / Maybe
baby / Sheila / Lazy life / I'm gonna love
you too / In my room / I love you / Lyanna
/ Going back to Germany / Come outside
and play / Easy living / Day by day / Dream-
ing of St. Louis
CD _____ CDMF 072
Magnum Force / Apr '91 / Magnum Music
Group.

SOUND OF FURY + 10
That's love / My advice / Phone call / You
don't know / Turn my back on you / Don't
say it's over / Since you've been gone / It's
you I need / Alright, goodbye / Don't leave
me this way / Gonna type a letter / Margo
/ Don't knock upon my door / Time has
come / Angel face / Last kiss / My Christmas prayer / Baby how I cried / I got someone / Don't jump
CD _____ 8206272
London / Jul '93 / PolyGram.

VERY BEST OF BILLY FURY
CD _____ SOW 709
Sound Waves / Jul '93 / Target/BMG.

WE WANT BILLY/BILLY
Sweet little sixteen / Wedding bells / I'm
movin' on / I'd never find another you / Like
I've never been gone / How many nights,
how many days / She cried / Our day will
come / One kiss / Baby come on / Sticks
and stones / Just because / Once upon a
dream / When will you say I love you / Willow weep for me / Let me know / Million
miles from nowhere / All my hopes / Hard
times / That's alright / Unchain my heart /
Halfway to paradise / Last night was made
for love / We were meant for each other /
Bumble bee / Chapel on the hill / I'll show
you / One step from heaven / (Here I am)
Broken hearted
CD _____ BGOCD 258
Beat Goes On / Feb '95 / Pinnacle.

Fuse

DIMENSION INTRUSION
CD _____ WARPCD 12
Warp / May '93 / Disc.

Fuster, Francis

NINKIRIBI - LISTEN EVERYBODY
CD _____ FMFD 0193
4th & Broadway / Sep '93 / PolyGram.

Future

1998
CD _____ RRCD 1998
Receiver / May '90 / Grapevine.

FUTURE
CD _____ APR 010CD
April / Nov '95 / Plastic Head.

Future Sound Of London

ISDN
Just a fuckin' idiot / Far out son of lung and
the ramblings of a madman / Appendage /
Slider / Smokin' Japanese babe / You're
creeping me out / Eyes pop - skin explodes
- everybody dead / It's my mind that works
/ Dirty shadows / Tired / Egypt / Are they
fighting us / Kai / Amoeba / Study of six
guitars / Snake hips
CD _____ CDV 2755
Virgin / Dec '94 / EMI.
CD _____ CDVX 2755
Virgin / Jun '95 / EMI.

LIFEFORMS
Cascade / Ill flower / Flak / Bird wings /
Dead skin cells / Lifeforms / Eggshell /
Among myselves / Domain / Spineless jelly
/ Interstat / Vertical pig / Cerebral / Life.
Form. Ends / Vit / Omnipresence / Room
208 / Elaborate burn / Little brother
CD _____ CDV 2722
Virgin / May '94 / EMI.

Futuresound

BEST OF FUTURESOUND, THE
CD _____ CAT 025CD
Rephlex / Jan '96 / Disc.

Fuzzbox

BIG BANG
Pink sunshine / Jamaican sunrise / Versatile
for discos and parties / Self / Do you know
/ Fast forward futurama / Walking on thin
ice / International rescue / Irish bride /
Beauty
CD _____ 2292460662
WEA / Jan '96 / Warner Music.

Fuzztones

IN HEAT
In heat / Chedenne rider / Black box / It
came in the mail / Heathen set / What you
don't know / Nine months later / Everything
you got / Shame on you / Ne Tarzan, you
Jane / Hurt on hold / Charlotte's remains
CD _____ SITUCD 23
Situation 2 / Jun '89 / Pinnacle.

Fuzzy

FUZZY
Flashlight / Bill / Postcard / Now I know /
Four Wheel friend / Almond / Lemon ring /
Rock song / Intro / Sports / Severe / Got it
/ Surfing / Girlfriend
CD _____ 14254-2
Seed / Jul '94 / Vital.

Fuzzy Mountain String...

**FUZZY MOUNTAIN STRING BAND
(Fuzzy Mountain String Band)**
CD _____ ROUCD 11571
Rounder / Jul '95 / CM / Direct / ADA /
Cadillac.

Fyffe, Will

**WILL FYFFE (Legendary Scottish Singer
Performs His Best Songs)**
It isn't the hen that cackles the most / Spirit
of a man from Aberdeen / Wedding of Mary
Maclean / I'm the landlord at the inn at
Aberfoyle / He's been on the bottle since a
baby / She was the belle of the ball / Rail-
way guard / Train that's taking you home /
Twelve and a tanner a bottle / Will Fyffe's
war-time sketch: Clyde built / I belong to
Glasgow / I'm 94 today
CD _____ LCOM 5234
Lismor / May '94 / Lismor / Direct / Duncans
/ ADA.

Fygi, Laura

LADY WANTS, THE
CD _____ 518924-2
PolyGram Jazz / Nov '94 / PolyGram.

G

G & K Ceili Band

SONGS JIGS & REELS
CD _____ MATCD 219
Castle / Dec '92 / BMG.

G-Love & Special Sauce

COAST TO COAST MOTEL
Sweet sugar Mama / Leaving the city / Nancy / Kiss and tell / Chains no.3 / Sometimes / Everybody / Soda pop / Bye bye baby / Tomorrow night / Small fish / Coming home
CD _____ 4809792
Okeh/Epic / Jan '96 / Sony.

G-LOVE & SPECIAL SAUCE
Things I used to do / Blues music / Garbage man / Eyes have miles / Baby's got sauce / Rhyme for the summertime / Cold beverage / Fatman / This ain't living / Walk to slide / Shooting hoops / Some peoples like that / Town to town / I love you
CD _____ 476632 2
Epic / Jul '94 / Sony.

G.B.H.

ATTACK AND REVENGE
CD _____ RR 349678
Roadrunner / '89 / Pinnacle.

CLAY YEARS 81-84, THE
Necrophilia / Generals / No survivors / Sick boy / Time bomb / I am the hunted / City baby attacked by rats / Give me fire / Catch 23 / Diplomatic immunity / Womb with a view / City baby's revenge / Christianised cannibals / Four men
CD _____ CLAYCD 21
Clay / Apr '93 / Cargo.

FRIDGE TOO FAR, A
Go home / Twenty floors below / Checking out / Needle inna haystack / See you bleed / Pass the axe / Crossfire / Captain Chaos / Fist of regret / Nocturnal journal
CD _____ CDJUST 13
Rough Justice / Oct '89 / Pinnacle.

FROM HERE TO REALITY
CD _____ CDJUST 16
Music For Nations / Oct '90 / Pinnacle.

LIVE IN JAPAN
Give me fire / New decade / Seed of madness / Checkin' out / Mass production / Just in time for the epilogue / C U Bleed / Drugs party in 526 / I am the hunter / Sick boy / City baby attacked by rats / City baby's revenge / Race against time / Knife edge / Necrophilia / Moonshine / Freak
CD _____ DOJOCD 112
Dojo / Feb '94 / BMG.

MIDNIGHT MADNESS AND BEYOND
CD _____ CDJUST 2
Rough Justice / Aug '87 / Pinnacle.

NO NEED TO PANIC
CD _____ CDJUST 7
Rough Justice / '89 / Pinnacle.

G.E.N.E.

DIVING DREAMS
CD _____ 720155
Magnum Music / Oct '92 / Magnum Music Group.

KATCHINA
CD _____ 720143
Magnum Music / Feb '93 / Magnum Music Group.

G.G.F.H.

HALLOWEEN
Little Missy / Blood is thicker / Chainsaw / She comes to you / Curiosity killed the cat / Thorns / Night stalker / As I touch you / Plaster Christ '88 / Ireland / Fetal infection / Dread / Missy '84 / Go away / Missy's revenge
CD _____ KTB 012
Dreamtime / Oct '94 / Kudos / Pinnacle.

G.P.'s

SATURDAY ROLLING AROUND
CD _____ WRCD 014
Woodworm / May '92 / Pinnacle.

Gaard Quintet

GAARD QUINTET
CD _____ MECCACD 1036
Music Mecca / Nov '94 / Jazz Music / Cadillac / Wellard.

Gaberlunzie

FOR AULD LANG SYNE
CD _____ CDLDL 1224

Lochshore / Oct '95 / ADA / Direct / Duncans.

HIGHLAND LINES
CD _____ CDLOC 1056
Lochshore / Jul '90 / ADA / Direct / Duncans.

Gabin, Jean

LA COMPILATION
CD _____ UCD 19033
Forlane / Jun '95 / Target/BMG.

QUAND ON S'PROMENE AU BORD DE L'EAU
CD _____ CDCD 3009
Charly / Sep '94 / Charly / THE / Cadillac.

Gable, Bill

THERE WERE SIGNS
Go ahead and run / Who becomes the slave / All the posters come down / Three levels of Nigeria / Cape Horn / High trapeze / There were signs / Letting the jungle in / Leaving Venice to the rain
CD _____ 259 759
Private Music / Apr '89 / BMG.

Gable, Eric

PROCESS OF ELIMINATION
Process of elimination / Don't wanna hurt nobody / Driving me crazy / Call me / I'll be around / I'm not the one / Try again / Let me rock / Don't stop / This time
CD _____ 474266 2
Epic / Apr '94 / Sony.

Gable, Tony

TONY GABLE & 206
Slip / Tailwind / Island lady / Bus song / Camano island / Pockets / Lake Union / Homeport / Futon fun
CD _____ 101S 71462
101 South / Nov '93 / New Note.

Gabrels, Reeves

SECRET SQUALL OF NOW, THE
CD _____ UPSTART 020
Upstart / Sep '95 / Direct / ADA.

Gabriel, Peter

PASSION SOURCES (Various Artists)
Shamus ud doja / Call to prayer / Sankarabaranam pancha nadai pallavi / Ulvi / Fallahi / Sabahiva / Atejbeit / Prelude in tchahargah / Wedding song / Magdelene's house / Yoky / Nass el ghiwane / Song of complaint
CD _____ RWCD 2
Virgin / Jun '89 / EMI.

PETER GABRIEL 1
Moribund the burgermeister / Solsbury Hill / Modern love / Excuse me / Humdrum / Slowburn / Waiting for the big one / Down the dolce vita / Here comes the flood
CD _____ PGCD 1
Charisma / May '87 / EMI.

PETER GABRIEL 1/2/3 (Compact Collection/3CD Set)
CD Set _____ TPAK 9
Virgin / Oct '90 / EMI.

PETER GABRIEL 2
On the air / D.I.Y. / Mother of violence / Wonderful day in a one way world / White shadow / Indigo / Animal magic / Exposure / Flotsam and jetsam / Perspective / Home sweet home
CD _____ PGCD 2
Charisma / May '87 / EMI.

PETER GABRIEL 3
Intruder / No self control / I don't remember / Family snapshot / And through the wire / Games without frontiers / Not one of us / Lead a normal life / Biko
CD _____ PGCD 3
Charisma / May '87 / EMI.

PETER GABRIEL 3/DEUTSCHES ALBUM
Eindringling / Keine selbstkontrolle / Frag mich nicht immer / Schnappshub (ein familienfoto) / Und durch den draht / Spiel ohne grenzen / Du bist nicht wie wir / Ein normales leben / Biko
CD _____ XCDSD 4019
Virgin / '88 / EMI.

PETER GABRIEL 4 (Deutsches album)
Der rythmus der hitze / Das fischernetz / Kon takt / San Jacinto / Schock den affen

---

/ Handauflegen / Nicht die erde hat dich verschluckt / Mundzumundeatmung
CD _____ XPGCD 4
Virgin / Apr '88 / EMI.

PLAYS LIVE (2CD Set)
San Jacinto / Solsbury Hill / No self control / Shock the monkey / I don't remember / Humdrum / On the air / Biko / Rhythm of the heat / I have the touch / Not one of us / Family snapshot / D.I.Y. / Family and the fishing net / Intruder / I go swimming
CD Set _____ CDPGD 100
Virgin / '88 / EMI.

SECRET WORLD LIVE
Come talk to me / Steam / Across the river / Slow marimbas / Shaking the tree / Red rain / Blood of Eden / Kiss that frog / Washing of the water / Solsbury Hill / Digging in the dirt / Sledgehammer / Secret world / Don't give up / In your eyes
CD Set _____ PGDCD 8
Virgin / Aug '94 / EMI.

SHAKING THE TREE
Solsbury Hill / I don't remember / Sledgehammer / Family snapshot / Mercy Street / Shaking the tree / Don't give up / Here comes the flood / Games without frontiers / Shock the monkey / Big time / Biko / San Jacinto (Not on LP) / Zaar (Not on LP) / Red rain (Not on LP) / I have the touch (Not on LP)
CD _____ PGTVD 6
Virgin / Nov '90 / EMI.

SO
Red rain / Sledgehammer / Don't give up / That voice again / In your eyes / Mercy street / Big time / We do what we're told (Milgram's 37) / This is the picture (excellent birds) (Not on LP)
CD _____ PGCD 5
Charisma / '86 / EMI.

US
Come talk to me / Love to be loved / Blood of Eden / Steam / Only us / Washing of the water / Digging in the dirt / Fourteen black paintings / Kiss that frog / Secret world
CD _____ PGCD 7
Virgin / Sep '92 / EMI.

Gabrielle

FIND YOUR WAY
Going nowhere / Who could love you / Find your way / I wanna know / Dreams / I wish / We don't talk / Second chance / Say what you gotta say / Because of you / Inside your head
CD _____ 8284412
Go Beat / Oct '93 / PolyGram.

Gad, Pablo

BEST OF PABLO GAD
CD _____ ROTCD 1
Reggae On Top / Nov '93 / Jetstar / SRD.

EPISTLES OF DUB CHAPTER 1 (Gad, Pablo & Conscious Sounds)
CD _____ ROTCD 002
Reggae On Top / Nov '94 / Jetstar / SRD.

LIFE WITHOUT DEATH
CD _____ ROTCD 005
Reggae On Top / Jul '95 / Jetstar / SRD.

Gadd, Eric

DO YOU BELIEVE IN GADD
CD _____ 450996777-2
East West / Oct '94 / Warner Music.

Gade, Jacob

TANGO JALOUSIE
CD _____ MECCACD 1005
Music Mecca / Nov '94 / Jazz Music / Cadillac / Wellard.

Gadgets

BLUE ALBUM, THE
CD _____ PLASCD 16
Plastic Head / May '89 / Plastic Head.

GADGETREE
CD _____ PLASCD 013
Plastic Head / May '89 / Plastic Head.

INFANTREE/FRUITS OF AKELDAMA
CD _____ PLASCD 012
Plastic Head / Jul '89 / Plastic Head.

LOVE, CURIOSITY, FRECKLES AND DOUBT
CD _____ PLASCD 014
Plastic Head / Jul '89 / Plastic Head.

Gaelforce Orchestra

ABIDE WITH ME
Lord's my shepherd / By cool siloam's shady rill / There is a green hill faraway /

When I survey the wondrous cross / O worship the king (all glorious above) / Lead kindly light / Praise my soul the king of heaven / Day thou gavest Lord is ended / O for a closer walk with God / O God of Bethel by whose hand / I to the hills will lift mine eyes / All people that on earth do dwell / Behold the mountain to the lord / Holy holy holy, Lord God almighty / Child in a manger
CD _____ LCOM 5230
Lismor / Oct '93 / Lismor / Direct / Duncans / ADA.

FROM HIGHLANDS TO LOWLANDS
Maciain of Glencoe / Dream Angus / Ca' the yowes / Crimond / Green grow the rushes-o / Mingulay boat song / Aye waukin' o / Queen's Maries / Mo mathair (my mother) / Bluebells of Scotland / Jock O'Hazeldean / Cradle song / Proud lion rampant / Old Scots songs
CD _____ LCDM 9025
Lismor / '90 / Lismor / Direct / Duncans / ADA.

FROM THE GREEN ISLAND TO THE LAND OF THE EAGLE
Green Island / Pat Murphy's meadow / Meeting of the waters / After all these years / Rose of Tralee / My cavan girl / Danny boy / Song for Ireland / Boolavogue / Flight of Earls / Little grey home in the west / Banks of my own lovely Lee / Green glens of Antrim / shores of Amerikay
CD _____ LCDM 9029
Lismor / '90 / Lismor / Direct / Duncans / ADA.

SKYE HIGH
Of a' the airts / Abide with me / Northern lights of old Aberdeen / Afton water / Skye high / Bonnie wee thing / Durisdeer / Annie McKelvie / Cuillin / Fair maid of Barra / Broom o'the cowdenknowes / Isle of Mull / Clearcall a'chuain / Amazing grace
CD _____ LCOM 5215
Lismor / Oct '91 / Lismor / Direct / Duncans / ADA.

STOIRM (Gaelforce)
CD _____ GH 002CD
Goatshed / Oct '94 / ADA.

Gaffney, Chris

LOSER'S PARADISE
CD _____ HCD 8062
Hightone / Aug '95 / ADA / Koch.

Gaillard, Slim

AT BIRDLAND 1951
Flat foot floogie, no 1 / Cement mixer / Laughin' in rhythm / Imagination / Oh, lady be good / Sabroso / Flat foot floogie, No.2 / Fire and dandy / Srenade in vout / Ya ha ha
CD _____ HEPCD 21
Hep / Jan '96 / Cadillac / Jazz Music / New Note / Wellard.

BEST OF THE VERVE YEARS, THE
CD _____ 521651-2
Verve / Aug '94 / PolyGram.

CLASSICS 1939-40
CD _____ OJCCD 724
Original Jazz Classics / Dec '93 / Wellard / Jazz Music / Cadillac / Complete/Pinnacle.

CLASSICS 1940-42
CD _____ CLASSICS 753
Classics / May '94 / Discovery / Jazz Music.

LEGENDARY MCVOUTY
Voutoreene / Operatic aria / Hey stop that dancing up there / Chicken rhythm / Yep roc heresi / Gaillard special / Matzoh balls / Advocado seed soup symphony / Sonny boy / Cement mixer / Fried chicken o routie / African jive / Ya ha ha / Advocado seed soup symphony (part 2)
CD _____ HEPCD 6
Hep / Jul '90 / Cadillac / Jazz Music / New Note / Wellard.

SHUCKIN' & JIVIN'
Vout orenee / Please wait for me / Sighing boogie / Vout boogie / Nightmare boogie / Slim Gaillard's boogie / Harlem hunch / Tutti frutti / Travelin' blues / Sightseeing boogie / Central avenue boogie / Boogie / Slim's cement boogie / Still wailin' / Shuckin' and jivin' / House rent party / She's just right for me / Be bop Santa Claus / Watch them resolutions
CD _____ CDCHARLY 279
Charly / Nov '94 / Charly / THE / Cadillac.

SLIM & SLAM - COMPLETE RECORDINGS 1938-1942 (3CD Set) (Gaillard, Slim & Slam Stewart)
Flat foot floogie / Chinatown, my Chinatown / That's what you call romance / Ti-pi-tin / Eight, nine and ten / Dancing on the beach

/ Oh Lady be good / Ferdinand the bull / Tutti frutti / Look-a-there / Humpty dumpty / Dark eyes / Bei mir bist due schoen / Jump session / Laughin' in rhythm / Voi vistu gailey star / Dopey Joe / Sweet Safronia / It's gettin' kinda chilly / Buck dance rhythm / I got rhythm / Lady's in love with you / Caprice paganini / That's a bringer / A-well-a-take-um-a-Joe / Chicken rhythm / Swingin' in C / Boot-ta-la-za / It's you, only you / Beatin' the board / Look out / Matzoh balls / Early in the morning / Chitlin' switch blues / Huh uh-huh / Windy city hop / Baby be mine / Splogjhm / Fitzwater Street / Don't let us say goodbye / Rhythm mad / Bongo / Broadway jump / Put your arms around me / Baby / Lookin' for a place to park / Hit that mess / Hey chef / Ah now / Tip on the numbers / Slim slam boogie / Bassology / Bingie-bingie-scootie / B-19 / Champagne lullaby / African jive / Palm springs jump / Groove juice special-1 / Ra-da-da-da
CD Set _____ **CDAFS 1034-3**
Affinity / Jun '93 / Charly / Cadillac / Jazz Music.

SLIM & SLAM 1938 (Gaillard, Slim & Slam Stewart)
CD _____ **TAXS 12**
Tax / Aug '94 / Jazz Music / Wellard / Cadillac.

SLIM & SLAM 1938-39 (Gaillard, Slim & Slam Stewart)
CD _____ **TAXS 22**
Tax / Aug '94 / Jazz Music / Wellard / Cadillac.

SLIM & SLAM 1940-42 (Gaillard, Slim & Slam Stewart)
CD _____ **TAXS 72**
Tax / Aug '94 / Jazz Music / Wellard / Cadillac.

SLIM GAILLARD 1937-38
CD _____ **CLASSICS 705**
Classics / Jul '93 / Discovery / Jazz Music.

SLIM GAILLARD ORIGINAL 1938 RECORDING, VOL.1
CD _____ **TAXCD S-1**
Tax / Aug '89 / Jazz Music / Wellard / Cadillac.

SLIM GAILLARD ORIGINAL 1938 RECORDING, VOL.2
CD _____ **TAXCD S-2**
Tax / Jan '93 / Jazz Music / Wellard / Cadillac.

Gailmor, Jon
GENERATIONS
CD _____ **GLCD 1082**
Green Linnet / Jul '88 / Roots / CM / Direct / ADA.

Gaines, Earl
I BELIEVE IN YOUR LOVE
CD _____ **AP 119**
Appaloosa / Oct '95 / ADA / Magnum Music Group.

Gaines, Grady
FULL GAIN (Gaines, Grady & The Texas Upsetters)
Mr. Blues in the sky / I've been out there / If I don't get involved / Full gain / Shaggy dog / Soul twist / If I loved you a little easy / Your girlfriend / Stealing love / There is something on your mind / Gangster of the blues / Miss Lucy Brown
CD _____ **FIENDCD 148**
Demon / '88 / Pinnacle / ADA.

HORN OF PLENTY (Gaines, Grady & The Texas Upsetters)
CD _____ **BT 1084CD**
Black Top / Jan '93 / CM / Direct / ADA.

Gaines, Rosie
CLOSER THAN CLOSE
CD _____ **5305782**
Polydor / Oct '95 / PolyGram.

Gaither, Bill
BILL GAITHER VOL. 1 1935-1941
CD _____ **DOCD 5251**
Blues Document / May '94 / Swift / Jazz Music / Hot Shot.

BILL GAITHER VOL. 2 1935-1941
CD _____ **DOCD 5252**
Blues Document / May '94 / Swift / Jazz Music / Hot Shot.

BILL GAITHER VOL. 3 1935-1941
CD _____ **DOCD 5253**
Blues Document / May '94 / Swift / Jazz Music / Hot Shot.

BILL GAITHER VOL. 4 1935-1941
CD _____ **DOCD 5254**
Blues Document / May '94 / Swift / Jazz Music / Hot Shot.

BILL GAITHER VOL. 5 1940-1941
CD _____ **DOCD 5255**
Blues Document / Dec '94 / Swift / Jazz Music / Hot Shot.

Galactic Cowboys
MACHINE FISH
CD _____ **3984114105CD**
Metal Blade / Jan '96 / Plastic Head.

Galahad
SLEEPERS
Sleepers / Julie Anne / Live and learn / Dentist song / Picture of bliss / Before, after and beyond / Exorcising demons / Middleground / Amaranth
CD _____ **GHCD 4**
Avalon / Aug '95 / Pinnacle.

VOICEPRINT RADIO SESSION
CD _____ **VPR 018CD**
Voice Print / Oct '94 / Voice Print.

Galahad Acoustic Quintet
NOT ALL THERE
Sir Galahad / Mother mercy / Club 18-30 / Dreaming from the inside / Melt / White lily / Through the looking glass / Looking up at the apple trees / Shrine / Legless in Gaza / Iceberg / Where there's all or nothing
CD _____ **GAQ 001CD**
Avalon / Jan '95 / Pinnacle.

Galas, Diamanda
LITANIES OF SATAN
CD _____ **CDIS 001**
Mute / Apr '89 / Disc.

MASQUE OF THE RED DEATH
CD _____ **GALAS 001**
Mute / Dec '88 / Disc.

SAINT OF THE PIT/DIVINE PUNISHMENT
La treizieme revient / E-eaoyme / L'heau-tontimouroumenos / Artemis / Cris d'aveugle
CD _____ **CDSTUMM 33**
Mute / Apr '88 / Disc.

SINGER, THE
CD _____ **CDSTUMM 103**
Mute / Apr '92 / Disc.

SPORTING LIFE (Galas, Diamanda & John Paul Jones)
CD _____ **CDSTUMM 127**
Mute / Sep '94 / Disc.

VENA CAVA
CD _____ **CDSTUMM 119**
Mute / Sep '93 / Disc.

YOU MUST BE CERTAIN OF THE DEVIL
Swing low, sweet chariot / Let's not chat about despair / You must be certain of the devil / Malediction / Double barrel prayer / Birds of death / Let my people go / Lord's my shepherd
CD _____ **CDSTUMM 46**
Mute / Jun '88 / Disc.

Galaxie 500
ON FIRE
CD _____ **ROUGHCD 146**
Rough Trade / Oct '89 / Pinnacle.

THIS IS OUR MUSIC
CD _____ **ROUGHCD 156**
Rough Trade / Oct '90 / Pinnacle.

TODAY
Flowers / Pictures / Parking lot / Don't let our youth go to waist / Temperature's rising / Oblivious / It's getting late / Instrumental / Tugboat / King of Spain (CD only.) / Crazy (CD only.)
CD _____ **SDE 8908**
Shimmy Disc / Oct '89 / Vital.

Galaxy P
OLD FRIENDS
CD _____ **CRCD 23**
Charm / Sep '93 / Jetstar.

Galaxy Trio
IN THE HAREM
CD _____ **ES 107CD**
Estrus / Jun '95 / Plastic Head.

Gales, Larry
MESSAGE FROM MONK, A
CD _____ **CCD 79503**
Candid / Jul '91 / Cadillac / Jazz Music / Wellard / Koch.

Gall, Gunter
TIVOLI
CD _____ **BEST 1007CD**
Acoustic Music / Nov '93 / ADA.

Gallagher & Lyle
BEST OF GALLAGHER & LYLE, THE
Heart on my sleeve / I wanna stay with you / Showdown / You're the one / Song and dance man / I believe in you / Willie / Mhairu / Love on the airwaves / Runaway / Breakaway / Heartbreaker / All grown up / I'm amazed / Country morning / Never give up on love / Hurts to learn / We / Sittin' down music / Every little teardrop
CD _____ **5518302**

Spectrum/Karussell / Nov '95 / PolyGram / THE.

BREAKAWAY
CD _____ **5500642**
Spectrum/Karussell / May '93 / PolyGram / THE.

HEART ON MY SLEEVE - VERY BEST OF GALLAGHER & LYLE
Breakaway / I wanna stay with you / Every little teardrop / Heart on my sleeve / Stay young / Fifteen summers / Heart in New York / You put the heart back in the city / When I'm dead and gone / Malt and barley blues / Willie / Layna / We / Keep the candle burning / Runaway / I believe in you
CD _____ **CDMID 172**
A&M / Oct '92 / PolyGram.

Gallagher, Rory
AGAINST THE GRAIN
Let me in / Cross me off your list / Ain't too good / Souped up Ford / Bought and sold / I take what I want / Lost at sea / All around man / Out on the Western Plain / At the bottom
CD _____ **CLACD 233**
Castle / May '91 / BMG.

BLUEPRINT
Walk on hot coals / Daughter of the Everglades / Banker's blues / Hands off / Race the breeze / Seventh son of a seventh son / Unmilitary two step / If I had a reason
CD _____ **CLACD 316**
Castle / Feb '94 / BMG.

CALLING CARD
Do you read me / Country mile / Moonchild / Calling card / I'll admit your gone / Secret agent / Jack knife beat / Edged in blue / Barley and grape rag
CD _____ **CLACD 352**
Castle / Mar '94 / BMG.

DEFENDER
Kick back city / Loan shark blues / Continental op / I ain't no saint / Failsafe day / Road to hell / Doin' time / Smear campaign / Don't start me talkin' / Seven days / Seems to me (Not on LP) / No peace for the wicked (Not on LP)
CD _____ **FIENDCD 98**
Demon / Jul '87 / Pinnacle / ADA.

EDGED IN BLUE
Don't start me talkin' / Loop / Calling card / Heaven's gate / At the deopt / Brute force and ignorance / Loan shark blues / I could have had religion / Ride on red, ride on / I wonder who / Seven days
CD _____ **FIENDCD 719**
Demon / Jun '92 / Pinnacle / ADA.

G-MEN (THE BOOTLEG SERIES)
CD _____ **ESBCD 187**
Castle / Nov '92 / BMG.

IRISH TOUR '74...
Cradle rock / I wonder who (who's gonna be your sweet man) / Tattoo'd lady / Too much alcohol / As the crow flies / Million miles away / Walk on hot coals / Whose that comin' / Stomping ground / Just a little bit
CD Set _____ **FIENDCD 120**
Demon / May '88 / Pinnacle / ADA.

JINX
Big guns / Bourbon / Double vision / Devil made me do it / Hellcat / Signals / Jinxed / Easy come, easy go / Ride on red, ride on / Loose talk
CD _____ **FIENDCD 126**
Demon / May '88 / Pinnacle / ADA.

LIVE IN EUROPE
Messin' with the kid / Laundromat / I could've had religion / Pistol slapper blues / Going to my home town / In your town / Bullfrog blues
CD _____ **CLACD 406**
Castle / '95 / BMG.

RORY GALLAGHER
CD Set _____ **RORY G. 1**
Demon / '91 / Pinnacle / ADA.

STAGE STRUCK
Shin kicker / Wayward child / Brute force and ignorance / Moonchild / Follow me / Bought and sold / Last of the independents / Shadow play
CD _____ **CLACD 407**
Castle / '95 / BMG.

TATTOO
Tattoo'd lady / Cradle rock / 20/20 vision / They don't make them like you any more / Livin' like a trucker / Sleep on a clothes-line / Who's that coming / Million miles away / Admit it
CD _____ **CLACD 315**
Castle / Jan '94 / BMG.

TOP PRIORITY
Follow me / Philby / Wayward child / Keychain / At the depot / Bad penny / Just hit town / Off the handle / Public enemy no.1
CD _____ **FIENDCD 123**
Demon / May '88 / Pinnacle / ADA.

Galli, Sandro
SPECTRUM
CD _____ **ACVCD 9**
ACV / Oct '95 / Plastic Head / SRD.

Galliano
IN PURSUIT OF THE 13TH NOTE
Leg in the sea of history / Welcome to the story / Coming on strong / Sweet you like your favourite gears / Cemetary of drums (Theme from Buhaina) / Five sons of the Mother / Storm clouds gather / Nothing has changed / Fifty seventh minute of the twenty third hour / Power and glory / Stoned again / Reviewing the situation / Little ghetto boy / Me, my Mike, my lyrics / Love bomb / Welcome to the story (summer breeze)
CD _____ **8484932**
Talkin' Loud / Apr '91 / PolyGram.

JOYFUL NOISE UNTO THE CREATOR, A
Grounation part 1 / Jus' reach / Skunk funk / Earth boots / Phantom / Jazz / New world order / So much confusion / Totally together / Golden flower / Prince of peace / Grounation part 2
CD _____ **848 080-2**
Talkin' Loud / Jun '92 / PolyGram.

PLOT THICKENS, THE
Was this the time / Blood lines / Rise and fall / Travels the road / Twyford down / Little one / Down in the gulley / Long time gone / Believe / Do you hear them / Better all the time / What colour our flag / Cold wind
CD _____ **5224502**
Talkin' Loud / May '94 / PolyGram.

THICKER PLOT, A (remixes)
Long time gone (mix) / Bloodlines / Believe / Twyford down / Travels the road / Long time gone / Twyford down / Rise and fall / Better all the time
CD _____ **5264262**
Talkin' Loud / Oct '94 / PolyGram.

Galliano, Richard
NEW MUSETTE (Galliano, Richard Quartet)
CD _____ **LBLC 6547**
Label Bleu / Jan '92 / New Note.

VIAGGIO
Waltz for Nicky / Java indigo / Viaggio / Billie / Tango pour claude / Christopher's bossa / Coloriage / Romance / Little muse / La liberte est une fleur
CD _____ **FDM 365622**
Dreyfus / Mar '94 / ADA / Direct / New Note.

Galliard Brass Ensemble
CAROLS FOR BRASS
Joy to the world / Rejoice and be merry / It came upon a midnight clear / O come, all ye faithful / Once in royal David's city / Deck the halls with boughs of holly / Wexford carol / Ding dong merrily on high / Hosanna to the Son of David / Rejoice in the Lord always / Queum vidistis pastores / Boston and Judea / Puer natus in Bethlehem / Hodie Christus natus est / In dulci jubilo
CD _____ **CD QS 6035**
Quicksilva / Oct '89 / Koch.

Galliards
STRANGE NEWS
CD _____ **HOP 941CD**
Grasshopper / Apr '95 / ADA.

Gallon Drunk
GALLON DRUNK
Rev up, TPA / Some fools mess / Just one more / Two wings mambo / You, the night, and the music / Gallon Drunk / Night tide / Eye of the storm / Thundering away
CD _____ **HÜNKACDL 001**
Clawfist / Feb '92 / Vital.

TONITE... THE SINGLES BAR
Last gasp (safty) / Rollin' home / Snakepit / Miserlou / Ruby / Draggin' along / May the earth open here / Please give me something / Whirlpool / Gallon drunk
CD _____ **HUNKACD 002**
Clawfist / Apr '92 / Vital.

Galloway, Jim
JIM GALLOWAY
CD _____ **SKCD 3057**
Sackville / Aug '94 / Swift / Jazz Music / Jazz Horizons / Cadillac / CM.

Galper, Hal
JUST US
Just us / Unforgettable / Moon glaze / Stablemates / Bye bye blackbird / Lover man / I'll never be the same
CD _____ **ENJACD 80582**
Enja / Jun '94 / New Note / Vital/SAM.

PORTRAIT: HAL GALPER TRIO (Galper, Hal Trio)
After you've gone / Giant steps / In your own sweet way / I'll be seeing you / What is this thing called love / I didn't care / I should care
CD _____ **CCD 4383**
Concord Jazz / Jun '89 / New Note.

REBOP
All the things you aren't / Laura / It's magic / Jackie-ing / Ghost of a chance / Take the Coltrane
CD _____ ENJ 90292
Enja / Oct '95 / New Note / Vital/SAM.

Galvin, Mick

AT HOME IN IRELAND
CD _____ FRCD 031
Foam / Oct '04 / CM.

Galway, James

CHRISTMAS CAROL
CD _____ 902661233-2
RCA / Oct '92 / BMG.

CHRISTMAS WITH JAMES GALWAY
CD _____ RD 60736
RCA / Oct '91 / BMG.

ENCHANTED FOREST, THE (Melodies of Japan)
Enchanted forest / Lyrical shortpiece / Na-kasendo (The old road) / Zui zui zukkoro-bashi (Children's play song) / Star children / Song of the deep forest (Improvisation) / Tokuyama lullaby / Hietsuki bushi (Love song) / Usuhiki uta (Song of the mill) / Love song / Echoes / Song of clay / Harukoma (Spring horse-dance) / Sakura / Romantic world
CD _____ RD 87893
RCA / Sep '90 / BMG.

GALWAY AT THE MOVIES
CD _____ 0926613262
RCA / Sep '93 / BMG.

GREATEST HITS: JAMES GALWAY
Annie's song / Thorn birds / Memory / Danny boy / Perhaps / Kanon in D / Pink panther / Sabre dance / Clair de Lune
CD _____ RD 87778
RCA / Jul '88 / BMG.

I WILL ALWAYS LOVE YOU
Wind of change / I will always love you / Here, there and everywhere / Tears in heaven / Whole new world / Dreamlover / Belle-ile-en-Mer / Holding back the years / When a man loves a woman / Last song / Golden slumbers / Little Jeannie / Always on my mind / If you leave me now / Caruso / Can't help falling in love / I just called to say I love you / Tu
CD _____ 74321262212
RCA Victor / Feb '95 / BMG.

IN THE PINK (Galway, James & Henry Mancini)
Pink panther / Thorn birds / Breakfast at Tiffany's / Penny whistle jig / Crazy world / Pie in the face polka / Baby elephant walk / Two for the road / Speedy Gonzalez / Molly McGuires / Cameo for flute / Days of wine and roses / Roses / Charade / Moon River
CD _____ RD 85315
RCA / Jan '85 / BMG.

JAMES GALWAY & THE CHIEFTANS IN IRELAND (Galway, James & The Chieftains)
Roche's favourite / Down by the Sally Gardens / She moved through the fair / O'Carolan's concerto / Danny boy / Crowley's reels / Avondale / Up and about / Humours of Kilfenora / Carrickfergus
CD _____ RD 85798
RCA Victor / Apr '87 / BMG.

LARK IN THE CLEAR AIR
CD _____ 09026619552
RCA / Apr '94 / BMG.

OVER THE SEA TO SKYE (Galway, James & The Chieftains)
Carolan's quarrel with the landlady / Three hornpipes / Eugene Stratton / Banks / Arthur Seat / Over the sea to Skye / Slip and double jig / Cath cheim an fhia / Rowan tree / Bonnie Prince Charlie / Lilliburlero / Dark island / Skibbereen / Fanfare / Last rose of summer / Dance in the morning early / Three sea captains / Full of joy (Chinese folk tune) / Solo salutes
CD _____ RD 60424
RCA / Jun '90 / BMG.

WIND BENEATH MY WINGS, THE
CD _____ RD 60862
RCA / Oct '91 / BMG.

Gambale, Frank

GREAT EXPLORERS, THE
Frankly speaking / Final frontier / Jaguar / Great explorers / Duet tuet / She knows me well / Thunder current / Dawn over the Nullarbor / Cruising altitude / Naughty business
CD _____ JVC 20202
JVC / Jun '93 / New Note.

PASSAGES
Little charmer / 6.8 shaker / Passages / White room / D-Day / Nuncios near / Free spirit / One with everything / Romania / Ulura / Another alternative
CD _____ JVC 20362
JVC / Aug '94 / New Note.

THINKING OUT LOUD
Magritte / Bondi beach / No-neck Louie / Gaudi / Felicidad / Dali / Infinity / Lover's night / Avengers suite / My little viper

CD _____ JVC 20452
JVC / Oct '95 / New Note.

THUNDER FROM DOWN UNDER
Humid being / Faster than an arrow / Samba di somewhere / Kuranda / Obsessed for life / Leave ozone alone / Land of wonder / Obrigado fukuoka / Robo roo / Forgotten but not gone / Mambo jambo / One not two
CD _____ JVC 20242
JVC / Apr '94 / New Note.

Gambetta, Beppe

DIALOGS
CD _____ BRAM 199122-2
Brambus / Nov '93 / ADA / Direct.

GOOD NEWS FROM HOME
CD _____ GLCD 2117
Green Linnet / Mar '95 / Roots / CM / Direct / ADA.

Gambit Jazzmen

KING OF THE MARDI GRAS
CD _____ LACD 54
Lake / Oct '95 / Target/BMG / Jazz Music / Direct / Cadillac / ADA.

Game Theory

BIG SHOT CHRONICLES
Here it is tomorrow / Where you going northern / I've tried subtlety / Erica's world / Make any vows / Regenisraen / Crash into June / Ronk of millionaires / Only lesson learned / Too closely / Never mind / Like a girl Jesus / Girl with a guitar / Come home with me / Seattle / Linus and Lucy / Faithless
CD _____ A 046D
Alias / Feb '94 / Vital.

DISTORTION OF GLORY
Something to show / Tin scarecrow / White blues / Date with an angel / Mary Magdalene / Young drug / Bad year at U.C.L.A. / All I want is everything / Stupid heart / Sleeping through heaven / It gives me chills / T.G.A.R.T.G. / Dead center / Penny, things won't / Metal and glass exact / Selfish again / Life in July / Shark pretty / Nine lives to rigel five / Red baron / Kid convenience / Too late for tears
CD _____ A 048D
Alias / Feb '94 / Vital.

REAL NIGHTIME
Here comes everybody / Twenty four / Waltz the halls always / I mean it this time / Friend of the family / If and when it all falls apart / Curse of the frontierland / Rayon drive / She'll be a verb / Real nightime / You can't have me / I turned her away / Any other hand / I want to hold your hand / Couldn't I just tell you
CD _____ A 047D
Alias / Feb '94 / Vital.

TWO STEPS FROM THE MIDDLE AGES
Room for one more, honey / What the whole world wants / Picture of agreeability / Amelia have you lost / Rolling with the moody girls / Wyoming / In a delorean / You drive / Leilian / Wish I could stand or have / Don't entertain me twice / Throwing the election / Initiations week
CD _____ CDENV 007
Enigma / Oct '88 / EMI.

Gameface

THREE TO GET READY
CD _____ DSR 038CD
Dr. Strange / Nov '95 / Plastic Head.

Gamil, Soliman

ANKH
CD _____ TO 14CD
Touch / Apr '90 / These / Kudos.

EGYPTIAN MUSIC
CD _____ TO 7
Touch / Apr '90 / These / Kudos.

Gamma Ray

FUTURE MADHOUSE
CD _____ NO 2033
Noise/Modern Music / Jun '93 / Pinnacle / Plastic Head.

HEADING FOR TOMORROW
CD _____ N 0151-2
Noise/Modern Music / '91 / Pinnacle / Plastic Head.

INSANITY & GENIUS
Tribute to the past / No return / Last before the storm / Cave principle / Future madhouse / Gamma ray (edited version) / Insanity and genius / Eighteen years / Your torn is over / Heal me / Brothers
CD _____ N 0203-2
Noise/Modern Music / Jun '93 / Pinnacle / Plastic Head.

LAND OF THE FREE
CD _____ NO 2272
Noise/Modern Music / May '95 / Pinnacle / Plastic Head.

SIGN NO MORE
CD _____ NO 1782
Noise/Modern Music / Oct '91 / Pinnacle / Plastic Head.

Gandalf

COLOURS OF THE EARTH
CD _____ SKV 080CD
Sattva Art / Jul '95 / THE.

GANDALF
Golden earrings / Hang on to a dream / Never to far / Scarlet ribbons / You upset the grace of living / Can you travel alone / Nature boy / Tiffany rings / Me about you / I watch the moon
CD _____ SEECD 326
See For Miles/C5 / Jul '91 / Pinnacle.

Gandy, Bruce

COMPOSER'S SERIES VOL.2
CD _____ LCOM 5242
Lismor / Aug '95 / Lismor / Direct / Duncans / ADA.

COMPOSERS SERIES VOL.2
CD _____ LC 5242CD
Lismor / Nov '95 / Lismor / Direct / Duncans / ADA.

Ganelin Trio

ENCORES
CD _____ CDLR 106
Leo / Oct '94 / Wellard / Cadillac / Impetus.

OPUSES
CD _____ CDLR 171
Leo / '90 / Wellard / Cadillac / Impetus.

POCO A POCO
CD _____ CDLR 101
Leo / Feb '89 / Wellard / Cadillac / Impetus.

Gang Green

ANOTHER WASTED NIGHT
Another wasted night / Skate to hell / Last chance / Alcohol / Have fun / Nineteenth hole / Skate hate / Let's drink some beer / Protect and serve / Another bomb / Voices carry / Sold out Alabama
CD _____ TAANG 131CD
Taang / Nov '92 / Plastic Head.

KING OF BANDS
CD _____ RR 92542
Roadrunner / Nov '91 / Pinnacle.

YOU GOT IT
CD _____ RR 349591
Roadrunner / '89 / Pinnacle.

Gang Of Four

BRIEF HISTORY OF THE 20TH CENTURY (The EMI Compilation)
At home he's a tourist / Damaged goods / Ntur's not in it (Not on LP.) / Not great men / Anthrax / Return the gift / It's her factory (Not on LP.) / What we all want / Paralysed / Hole in the wallet (Not on LP.) / Cheeseburger (Not on LP.) / To hell with poverty / Capital (it fails us now) / Call me up (If I'm home) / I will be a good boy / History of the world / I love a man in a uniform / Is it love / Woman town / We live as we dream, alone
CD _____ CDEMC 3583
EMI / Oct '90 / EMI.

ENTERTAINMENT
Ether / Naturals not in it / Damaged goods / Return the gift / Guns before butter / I found that essence rare / Glass / Contract / At home he's a tourist / 5-45 / Love like anthrax / Not great men / Outside the trains don't run on time / He'd send in the army / It's her factory
CD _____ CZ 541
EMI / Jan '95 / EMI.

PEEL SESSIONS: GANG OF FOUR. (Complete Sessions 1979-1981)
I found that essence rare / Return the gift / 5.45 / At home he's a tourist / natural's not in it / Not great men / Ether / Guns before butter / Paralysed / History's bunk / To hell with poverty
CD _____ SFRCD 107
Strange Fruit / Jun '90 / Pinnacle.

SHRINKWRAPPED
CD _____ WENCD 003
When / Oct '95 / BMG / Pinnacle.

Gang Starr

DAILY OPERATION
Daily operation (intro) / Place where we dwell / Flip the script / Ex girl to next girl / Soliloquy of chaos / I'm the man / Interlude / Take it personal / 2 deep / 24-7-365 / No shame in my game / Conspiracy / Illest brother / Hardcore composer / B.Y.S. / Much too much (Mack A Mil) / Take two and pass / Stay tuned
CD _____ CCD 1910
Cooltempo / May '92 / EMI.

HARD TO EARN
Intro (the first steps) / Alongwaytogo / Code of the streets / Brainstorm / Tonz 'o' guez / Planet / Aiiight chill... / Speak ya clout /

Dwyck / Words from the Nutcracker / Mass appeal / Blowin' up the spot / Suckas need bodyguards / Now you're mine / Mostly the voice / F.A.L.A. / Comin' for the datazz
CD _____ CTCD 38
Cooltempo / Feb '94 / EMI.

STEP IN THE ARENA
Name tag (Premier and The Guru) / Step in the arena / Form of intellect / Execution of a chump (No more Mr. Nice Guy Pt. 2) / Who's gonna take the weight / Beyond comprehension / Cheek the technique / Lovesick / Here today, gone tomorrow / Game plan / Take a rest / What you want this time / Street ministry / Just to get a rep / Say your prayers / As I read my S-A / Precisely the right rhymes / Meaning of the name
CD _____ CCD 1798
Cooltempo / Jan '91 / EMI.

Ganksta C

STEPCHILD
CD _____ FILECD 455
Profile / Jan '95 / Pinnacle.

Gant, Cecil

CECIL GANT
Cecil boogie / Hit that jive Jack / Hogan's alley / I gotta girl / Boogie blues / Sloppy Joe / Playing myself the blues / Time will tell / Cecil's mop top / Train time blues
CD _____ KKCD 03
Krazy Kat / Apr '90 / Hot Shot / CM.

Gantry, Elmer

VERY BEST OF ELMER GANTRY/ VELVET OPERA, THE (Gantry, Elmer & Velvet Opera)
Mother writes / Long nights of summer / Mary Jane (Single version) / Air / Looking for a happy life / Reactions of a young man / Flames (single version) / Dreamy / Talk of the devil / And I remember / To be with you / Painter / Volcano / Raga / Eleanor Rigby / Money by / Raise the light / Warm day in July / Black Jack Davy / Anna Dance square / Statesboro blues / There's a hole in my pocket
CD _____ SEECD 437
See For Miles/C5 / Jan '96 / Pinnacle.

Ganxsta Rid

OCCUPATION HAZARDOUS
If I die, let me roll / Chilling on the west side / One life, last breath / Happy feelings / Karson makes u bounce / Gs from the otha side / Born May 1st / Occupation hazardous / Rid is coming / Operation green light / Tell em who sent yo ass / Once upon a mossburg
CD _____ CDVEST 65
Bulletproof / Nov '95 / Pinnacle.

Gap Band

BEST OF THE GAP BAND, THE
Early in the morning / Shake / Outstanding / Why you wann hurt me / Yearning / Open your mind / You dropped a bomb on me / You can always count on me / Don't believe you want to get up and dance / Steppin' out / Humping around / Boys are back in town / Party train
CD _____ 522 457-2
Mercury / Jun '94 / PolyGram.

OOPS UPSIDE YOUR HEAD
Oops upside your head / Outstanding / Burn rubber on me (why you wanna hurt me) / Party lights / Jammin' in America / You dropped a bomb on me / Boys are back in town / Baby baba boogie / Steppin' (out) / Humpin' (edit version) / When I look in your eyes / Yearning for your love / Sweet Caroline / You can count on me / Open your mind (wide) / I don't believe you want to get up and dance (oops)
CD _____ 5511722
Spectrum/Karussell / Aug '95 / PolyGram / THE.

Garbage

GARBAGE
CD _____ D 31450
Mushroom / Oct '95 / BMG / 3MV.

Garbage Collectors

GARBAGE COLLECTORS
CD _____ PER 029
Semantic / Feb '94 / Plastic Head.

Garbarek, Jan

AFTENLAND
CD _____ 8393042
ECM / Nov '89 / New Note.

ALL THOSE BORN WITH WINGS
Last clown / Yellow fever / Soulful Bill / La divetta / Cool train / Loop
CD _____ 8313942
ECM / Mar '87 / New Note.

DANSERE
CD _____ 8291932
ECM / Oct '86 / New Note.

DIS
Vandrere / Krusning / Viddene / Skygger / YR / Dis
CD _____ 8274082
ECM / Feb '86 / New Note.

ESOTERIC CIRCLE
Traneflight / Rabalder / Esoteric circle / VIPs / S.A.S. 644 / Nefertiti / Gee / Karin's mode / Breeze ending
CD _____ FCD 41031
Freedom / Dec '87 / Jazz Music / Swift / Wellard / Cadillac.

EVENTYR
CD _____ 8293842
ECM / Aug '88 / New Note.

GRAY VOICE, THE
CD _____ 8254062
ECM / Aug '88 / New Note.

I TOOK UP THE RUNES
Gula gula / Molde canticle (parts 1-5) / His eyes were suns / I took up the runes / Buena hora, buenos vientos
CD _____ 8438502
ECM / Nov '90 / New Note.

LEGENDS OF THE SEVEN DREAMS
He comes from the North / Aichuri, the song man / Tongue of secrets / Brother wind / It's name is secret road / Send word / Voy cantando / Mirror store
CD _____ 8373442
ECM / Oct '88 / New Note.

OFFICIUM (Garbarek, Jan & The Hilliard Ensemble)
CD _____ 4453692
ECM / Sep '94 / New Note.

PHOTO WITH BLUE SKY (Garbarek, Jan Group)
Blue sky / White cloud / Windows / Red roof / Wives / Picture
CD _____ 843 168 2
ECM / Oct '90 / New Note.

PLACES
CD _____ 8291952
ECM / Oct '86 / New Note.

ROSENSFOLE (Garbarek, Jan & Maria Buen-Garnas)
CD _____ 8392932
ECM / Jun '89 / New Note.

STAR
Star / Jumper / Lamenting / Anthem / Roses for you / Clouds in the mountain / Snowman / Music of my people
CD _____ 8496492
ECM / Oct '91 / New Note.

TRIPTYKON
Rim / Selji / J.E.V. / Sang / Triptykon / Etu hei / Bruremarsi
CD _____ 8473212
ECM / Jun '92 / New Note.

TWELVE MOONS
Twelve moons / Psalm / Brother wind march / There were swallows / Tall tear trees / Arietta / Gautes-Margrit / Darvanan / Huhai / Witch-tai-to
CD _____ 519500-2
ECM / May '93 / New Note.

USTAD SHAUKAT HUSSAIN-MADAR (Garbarek, Jan & Anouar Brahem)
Sull lull / Madar / Sebika / Bahia / Ramy / Jaw / Joron / Qaws / Epilogue
CD _____ 5190752
ECM / Feb '94 / New Note.

WAYFARER
Gesture / Wayfarer / Gentle / Pendulum / Spor / Singsong
CD _____ 8119682
ECM / Aug '86 / New Note.

WITCHI-TAI-TO
A.I.R. / Kukka / Hasta siempre / Witchi-tai-to / Desireless
CD _____ 8333302
ECM / Mar '88 / New Note.

WORKS: JAN GARBAREK
Folk songs / Skirk and hyl / Passing / Selje / Viddene / Snipp, snapp, snute / Beast of Kommodo / Svevende
CD _____ 8232662
ECM / Jun '89 / New Note.

Garber, Jan

22 ORIGINAL BIG BAND RECORDINGS (Garber, Jan & His Orchestra)
CD _____ HCD 403
Hindsight / Oct '92 / Target/BMG / Jazz Music.

Garbo, Chuck

DRAWERS TROUBLE
CD _____ ROU 2123CD
Rounder / Aug '93 / CM / Direct / ADA / Cadillac.

Garcia, Jerry

ALMOST
CD _____ 9006480
Line / Jun '94 / CM / Grapevine / ADA / Conifer / Direct.

ALMOST ACOUSTIC (Garcia, Jerry Acoustic Band)
Swing low, sweet chariot / Blue yodel no. 9 (Standing on the corner) / I'm troubled / Oh babe, it ain't no lie / Casey Jones / Ripple / Deep elem blues / I'm here to get my baby out of jail / Girl at the crossroads bar / Diamond Joe / Spike diver blues (CD only) / I've been all around this world (CD only) / In the wind and the rain (CD only) / Gone home (CD only)
CD _____ GDCD 4005
Grateful Dead / Feb '89 / Pinnacle.

COMPLIMENTS OF GARCIA
Let it rock / That's what love will make us do / Turn on the bright lights / What goes around / Mississippi moon / Hunter gets captured by the game / Russian lullaby / He ain't give you none / Let's spend the night together / Midnight town
CD _____ GDCD 4011
Grateful Dead / Mar '89 / Pinnacle.

HOOTEROLL (Garcia, Jerry & Howard Wales)
CD _____ RCD 10052
Rykodisc / Oct '87 / Vital / ADA.

OLD IN THE WAY (Garcia, Jerry/David Grisman/Peter Rowan)
Pig in a pen / Midnight moonlight / Old and in the way / Knockin' on your door / Hobo song / Panama red / Wild horses / Kissimmee kid / White dove / Land of the Navajo
CD _____ SHCD 3746
Sugarhill / Feb '85 / Roots / CM / ADA / Direct.

REFLECTIONS
Might as well / Mission in the rain / They love each other / I'll take a melody / It must have been the roses / Tore up (over you) / Catfish John / Comes a-time
CD _____ GDCD 4008
Grateful Dead / May '89 / Pinnacle.

WHEEL, THE
Deal / Sugaree / Late for supper / Eep hour / Odd little place, An / Bird song / Loser / Spidergawd / To lay me down / Wheel
CD _____ GDCD 4003
Grateful Dead / Feb '89 / Pinnacle.

Garcia-Fons, Renaud

ALBOREA
Al Cameron / Alborea / Natgo / Secret zambra / Eosine / Gus's smile / Amadu / Sacre coeur / Tropea / Fort apache / Rue de buci
CD _____ ENJ 90572
Enja / Feb '96 / New Note / Vital/SAM.

Gardel, Carlos

COLLECTION, THE
CD _____ ND 75000
RCA / Jul '94 / BMG.

TANGO
CD _____ CD 62027
Saludos Amigos / Oct '93 / Target/BMG.

Garden, Bill

BILL GARDEN'S HIGHLAND FIDDLE ORCHESTRA (Garden, Bill & His Highland Fiddle Orchestra)
French Canadian special (Porteau blanc/ Snowshoers reel/Quintuplets reel) / Stings to the bow (reels and jigs) (Masons apron/ Fairy dance) / De'il among the tailors / Blackthorn stick / Roaring jelly / Brumley brae / Slow air, strathspey and reel (Bonnie Mary of Argyle/Highland whiskey/Laird of Drumblair/Kate Dalrymple) / Hornpipes (Jans dance/Mathematician/High level) / Reel of Tulloch / Robert Burns waltz (Comin' thro' the rye/Scots wha' hae/The banks and braes) / March, strathspey and reel (Marie's wedding/Vist tramping songs/ Marquis of Huntly/Scotland the Brave) / Scots and Irish (reels and jigs) (Phil the fluter's ball/Flannel jacket/March hare/Mrs McLeod/Speed the plough/Rollicking Irishman/Pet of the pipers/Irish washerwoman/ Rowan tree) / Polka (Jigtime/McFlannels/ Para handy) / Country hoedown (Turkey in the straw/Arkansas traveller/Smiths reel/Orange blossom special) / Intercity waltz (Road and the miles to Dundee/Northern lights of old Aberdeen/I belong to Glasgow) / Schottische reel (Lady Madeline Sinclair/ Jelly bawbee/Lord Moira/Orange and blue/ Drunken piper) / Sir Harry Lauder selection (Roamin' in the gloamin'/I love a lassie/Stop your ticklin' Jock/Wee Deoch an' Doris)
CD _____ CD ITV 423
Scotdisc / May '87 / Duncans / Ross / Conifer.

IOLAIRE (Garden, Bill Fiddle Orchestra)
CD _____ CDITV 514
Scotdisc / Jul '90 / Duncans / Ross / Conifer.

TRAVEL THE LAKES (Garden, Bill Fiddle Orchestra)
CD _____ CDITV 577
Scotdisc / Sep '94 / Duncans / Ross / Conifer.

Gardiner, Bobby

MASTER'S CHOICE, THE
Fermoy lassies, Doon reel, concertina reel / Paul Halfpenny, Mulvihills / Reel of Rio, the thacoir an phíobaire, Chorus jig / Blind Mary / Tailor's thimble, Lilies in the field, Take your choice / McDermotts, Humours of Lissadell / Colleys delight / Banbridge town, Mr. McGuire, Pride of the Bronx / Jack Gorman's favourite showjumper drinking whiskey / Road to Ballymac/Silver birch / Johnson's / Kilty town, The lobster / Gentian waltz / Sporting nell/Earl's chair
CD _____ OSS 86CD
Ossian / Aug '93 / ADA / Direct / CM.

Gardiner, Boris

IT'S WHAT'S HAPPENING
CD _____ RNCD 2125
Rhino / Nov '93 / Jetstar / Magnum Music Group / THE.

REGGAE HAPPENING
CD _____ JMC 200110
Jamaica Gold / Sep '93 / THE / Magnum Music Group / Jetstar.

THIS IS BORIS GARDINER
CD _____ RNCD 2006
Rhino / May '93 / Jetstar / Magnum Music Group / THE.

Gardiner, Paula

TALES OF INCLINATION
CD _____ SCDC 2103
Sain / Nov '95 / Direct / ADA.

Gardiner, Ronnie

MY SWEDISH HEART
CD _____ SITCD 9225
Sittel / Aug '95 / Cadillac / Jazz Music.

Gardner, Dave

EMPTY DREAMS
CD _____ PLAN 006CD
Planet / Jul '95 / Grapevine / ADA / CM.

Gardner, Freddy

VALAIDA 1935-37, VOL. 1
CD _____ HQCD 12
Harlequin / '92 / Swift / Jazz Music / Wellard / Hot Shot / Cadillac.

VALAIDA VOL. 2
CD _____ HQCD 18
Harlequin / Feb '94 / Swift / Jazz Music / Wellard / Hot Shot / Cadillac.

Gardner, Jeff

SKY DANCE
CD _____ 500332
Musidisc / Nov '93 / Vital / Harmonia Mundi / ADA / Cadillac / Discovery.

Garfunkel, Art

ANGEL CLARE
Travelin' boy / Down in the willow garden / I shall sing / Old man / Feuilles-oh / Do space men pass dead souls on their way to... / All I know / Harry was an only child / Woyaya / Barbara Allen / Another lullaby
CD _____ 9821852
Pickwick/Sony Collector's Choice / Jul '89 / Carlton Home Entertainment / Pinnacle / Sony.

ART GARFUNKEL ALBUM, THE
Bright eyes / Breakaway / Heart in New York / I shall sing / Watermark / Sometimes when I'm dreaming / Travellin boy / Same old tears on a new background / What a wonderful world / I believe / Scissors cut
CD _____ 4663332
CBS / Oct '90 / Sony.

BREAKAWAY
I believe / Rag doll / Breakaway / Disney girls / My little town / Waters of March / I only have eyes for you / Looking for the right one / Ninety nine miles from L.A. / Same old tears on a new background
CD _____ 982199 2
Pickwick/Sony Collector's Choice / Mar '94 / Carlton Home Entertainment / Pinnacle / Sony.

FATE FOR BREAKFAST
In a little while / Since I don't have you / I know / Sail on a rainbow / Miss you nights / Bright eyes / Finally found a reason / Beyond the tears / Oh how happy / When someone doesn't want you / Take me away
CD _____ 982634 2
Pickwick/Sony Collector's Choice / Aug '91 / Carlton Home Entertainment / Pinnacle / Sony.

UP 'TIL NOW
Crying in the rain (A duet with James Taylor) / All I know / Just over the Brooklyn Bridge / Sound of silence / Breakup / Skywriter / Decree / It's all in the game / One less holiday / Since I don't have you / Two sleepy people / Why worry / All my love's laughter

---

CD _____ 474853 2
Columbia / Nov '93 / Sony.

WATERMARK
Crying in my sleep / Marionette / Shine it on me / Watermark / Saturday suit / All my love's laughter / What a wonderful world / Mr. Shuck 'n' jive / Paper chase / She moved through the fair / Someone else / Wooden planes / (What a) wonderful world
CD _____ 982984-2
Pickwick/Sony Collector's Choice / Mar '94 / Carlton Home Entertainment / Pinnacle / Sony.

Garibian, Luidvig

ARMENIA (Garibian, Ludwig Trio & Folk Lab)
CD _____ MWCD 9303
Music & Words / Jul '93 / ADA / Direct.

Garland, Hank

HANK GARLAND AND HIS SUGAR FOOTERS
Sugarfoot rag / Third man theme / Flying eagle polka / Sugarfoot boogie / Hillbilly express / Seventh and union / Lowdown Billy / Sentimental journey / Doll dance / Chic, No. 1 / Chic, No. 2 / E string rag / Guitar shuffle / I'm movin' on / This cold war with you / I'll never slip around again / Some other world / I'm crying
CD _____ BCD 15551
Bear Family / Apr '92 / Rollercoaster / Direct / CM / Swift / ADA.

Garland, Judy

25TH ANNIVERSARY - RETROSPECTIVE
Over the rainbow / Be a clown / Easter parade / I wish I were in love again / Merry Christmas / Get happy / Medley / You made me love you (I didn't want to do it) / For me and my gal / Boy next door / Trolley song / Rock-a-bye your baby with a Dixie melody / Just imagine / I feel a song comin' on / How about me / Do it again / I am loved / Purple people eater / It never was you / It's a great day for the Irish / Man that got away / San Francisco / Swanee / Never will I marry / By myself / Jamboree Jones / Hello Dolly / What now my love / Chicago
CD _____ CDEST 2273
Premier / Jan '96 / EMI.

ALL THE THINGS YOU ARE
CD _____ VJCD 1043
Vintage Jazz Classics / May '93 / Direct / ADA / CM / Cadillac.

ALWAYS CHASING RAINBOWS (The young Judy Garland)
All God's chillun got rhythm / Buds won't bud / Cry baby cry / Embraceable you / End of the rainbow / Everybody sing / F.D.R. Jones / I'm always chasing rainbows / I'm just wild about Harry / I'm nobody's baby / In between / It never rains but it pours / Oceans apart / Our love affair / Over the rainbow / Sleep my baby sleep / Stompin' at the Savoy / Sweet sixteen / Swing Mister Charlie / Ten pins in the sky / You can't have everything / Zing went the strings of my heart
CD _____ CDAJA 5093
Living Era / Jul '92 / Koch.

BEST OF JUDY GARLAND
On the Atchison, Topeka and The Santa Fe / I'm always chasing rainbows / But not for me / Meet me in St. Louis / For me and my gal / In between / Dear Mr. Gable / F.D.R. Jones / Embraceable you / Trolley song / I'm nobody's baby / Over the rainbow
CD _____ DCD 5332
Disky / Dec '93 / THE / BMG / Discovery / Pinnacle.

BEST OF JUDY GARLAND, THE
That's entertainment / More / Come rain or come shine / It's yourself / Lucky day / I could go on singin' (till the cows come home) / Day in, day out / Foggy day / Almost like being in love/This can't be love (medley) / Fly me to the moon / Battle Hymn of the Republic / Zing went the strings of my heart / You'll never walk alone / Old devil moon / Maggie May / You made me love you/For me and my girl/The trolley song / Man that got away / Rock-a-bye your baby with a Dixie melody / As long as he needs me / Over the rainbow
CD _____ CDSL 8258
Music For Pleasure / Sep '95 / EMI.

CAPITOL YEARS: JUDY GARLAND
That's entertainment / You made me love you / For me and my girl / Trolley song / Man that got away / Lucky day / I can't give you anything but love / Zing went the strings of my heart / I hadn't anyone till you / Come rain or come shine / Shine on harvest moon / Some of these days / Mine (mon homme) / I don't care / Do I love you / If I love again / Old devil moon / This is it / Do it again / Who cares / Over the rainbow
CD _____ CZ 247
Capitol / Nov '89 / EMI.

CHASING RAINBOWS
I never knew / Oceans apart / Love / But not for me / Embraceable you / Over the

rainbow / Blues in the night / How about you / Poor little rich girl / No lover no nothing / For me and my gal / Trolley song / This heart of mine / You made me love you
CD _____ RMB 75007
Remember / Nov '93 / Total/BMG.

CHILD OF HOLLYWOOD
Over the rainbow / Stompin' at the Savoy / Swing Mister Charlie / (Dear Mr. Gable) You made me love you / You can't have everything / All God's chillun got rhythm / In between / Figaro / Oceans apart / Friendship / I'm nobody's baby / Alone / Singin' in the rain / It's a great day for the Irish / Minnie from Trinidad / Chin up, cheerio, carry on / F.D.R. Jones / How about you / Hoedown / On the sunny side of the street / I'm always chasing rainbows
CD _____ RPCD 321
Robert Parker Jazz / Nov '93 / Conifer.

EARLY YEARS, THE
CD _____ AVC 536
Avid / May '94 / Avid/BMG / Koch.

HER 25 GREATEST HITS
CD _____ ENTCD 271
Entertainers / Mar '92 / Target/BMG.

JUDY AT CARNEGIE HALL
When you're smiling / Almost like being in love (medley) (Includes: Almost like being in love/This can't be love/You go to my head) / Who cares / Puttin' on the Ritz / How long has this been going on / Just you, just me / Man that got away / San Francisco / That's entertainment / Come rain or come shine / You're nearer / Foggy day / If love were all / Zing went the strings of my heart / Stormy weather / You made me love you / For me and my gal/The trolley song.) / Rock-a-bye my baby with a Dixie melody / Over the rainbow / Swanee / After you've gone / Chicago / Trolley song, The (over-ture) / Over the rainbow (overture) (Not on CD) / Man that got away #2 / This can't be love (medley) / Do it again (Not on CD.) / You go to my head / Alone together / I can't give you anything but love
CD _____ CZ 76
Capitol / Jun '87 / EMI.

JUDY GARLAND
CD _____ DVGH 7062
Deja Vu / May '95 / THE.

JUDY GARLAND - HER GREATEST HITS
CD _____ PMCD 7007
Pure Music / Nov '94 / BMG.

JUDY GARLAND SHOW, THE
Laserlight / Oct '95 / Target/BMG. 15942

LEGENDS IN MUSIC - JUDY GARLAND
CD _____ LECD 094
Wisepack / Sep '94 / THE / Conifer.

MAIL CALL (Garland, Judy & Bing Crosby)
CD _____ 15413
Laserlight / Jan '93 / Target/BMG.

MISS SHOWBUSINESS
Zing went the strings of my heart / Stompin' at the savoy / All God's chillun got rhythm / Everybody sing / You made me love you / Over the rainbow / Sweet sixteen / Embraceable you / (Can this be) The end of the rainbow / I'm nobody's baby / Pretty girl milking her cow / It's a great day for the Irish / Sunny side of the street / For me and my gal / That old black magic / When you were a tulip
CD _____ HADCD 156
Javelin / May '94 / THE / Henry Hadaway Organisation.

ON THE RADIO 1936-1944
CD _____ VJC 1043
Vintage Jazz Classics / Feb '93 / Direct / ADA / CM / Cadillac.

OVER THE RAINBOW
Over the rainbow / Foggy day / Make someone happy / What'll I do / Man that got away / Couple of swells / I'm always chasing rainbows / How about me / Free and easy / Alexander's ragtime band
CD _____ CDCD 1137
Charly / Mar '93 / Charly / THE / Cadillac.

OVER THE RAINBOW
CD _____ PWK 022
Carlton Home Entertainment / '88 / Carlton Home Entertainment.

SONGS FROM THE MOVIES
Somewhere over the rainbow / Come rain or come shine / Give my regards to Broadway / Carolina in the morning / Rock-a-bye baby
CD _____ BSTCD 9110
Best Compact Discs / May '92 / Complete/Pinnacle.

SWEET SIXTEEN
CD _____ CD 23123
All Star / Sep '92 / BMG.

WHEN YOU'RE SMILING (Garland, Judy & Bing Crosby)
CD _____ PARCD 003
Parrot / Jan '96 / THE / Wellard / Jazz Music.

YOUNG JUDY GARLAND
Swanee / Friendship / Embraceable you / Pretty girl milking her cow / It's a great day for the Irish / Zing went the strings of my heart / Oceans apart / F.D.R. Jones / I'm just wild about Harry / How about you / In between / Figaro / Sweet sixteen / Jitterbug / Over the rainbow / Dear Mr. Gable / You can't have everything / It never rains but it pours / Ten pins in the sky / Buds won't bud / Our love affair / I'm always chasing rainbows / Everybody sing / All God's chillun got rhythm / I'm nobody's baby
CD _____ PASTCD 7014
Flapper / Jun '93 / Pinnacle.

Garland, Peter

NANA & VICTORIO
CD _____ AVAN 012
Avant / Nov '92 / Harmonia Mundi / Cadillac.

Garland, Red

ALL MORNIN' LONG (Garland, Red Trio)
CD _____ OJCCD 293-2
Original Jazz Classics / Feb '92 / Wellard / Jazz Music / Cadillac / Complete/Pinnacle.

GROOVY (Garland, Red Trio)
CD _____ OJCCD 061
Original Jazz Classics / Nov '95 / Wellard / Jazz Music / Cadillac / Complete/Pinnacle.

RED GARLAND TRIO & EDDIE 'LOCKJAW' DAVIS (Garland, Red Trio & Eddie 'Lockjaw' Davis)
CD _____ OJCCD 360
Original Jazz Classics / Nov '95 / Wellard / Jazz Music / Cadillac / Complete/Pinnacle.

RED IN BLUESVILLE
CD _____ OJCCD 295
Original Jazz Classics / Sep '93 / Wellard / Jazz Music / Cadillac / Complete/Pinnacle.

ROJO
Rojo / We kiss in a shadow / Darling je vous aime beaucoup / Ralph J. Gleason blues / You better go now / Mr. Wonderful
CD _____ OJCCD 772
Original Jazz Classics / Jun '94 / Wellard / Jazz Music / Cadillac / Complete/Pinnacle.

SOUL JUNCTION (Garland, Red Quintet & John Coltrane)
CD _____ OJCCD 481
Original Jazz Classics / Jan '95 / Wellard / Jazz Music / Cadillac / Complete/Pinnacle.

Garland, Terry

TROUBLE IN MIND
Kokomo / Wang dang doodle / Upside your head / Hospital bill blues / Forty four / Trouble in mind / Ain't long afore day / Aberdeen / Trouble on the way / Bad luck and trouble / Hard time killing floor
CD _____ PD 90666
First Warning / May '92 / BMG.

Garland, Tim

POINTS ON THE CURVE - NORTH SHIP SUITE
CD _____ FMRCD 01
Future / Oct '87 / Harmonia Mundi / ADA.

TALES FROM THE SUN
CD _____ EFZ 1014
EFZ / Sep '95 / Vital/SAM.

Garmarna

GARMARNA
CD _____ MASS 54CD
Mass Productions / Jul '95 / ADA.

VITTRAD
CD _____ MASS 61CD
Mass Productions / Jul '94 / ADA.

Garner, Erroll

1950-1951
CD _____ CD 53216
Giants Of Jazz / Nov '95 / Target/BMG / Cadillac.

BODY AND SOUL
Way you look tonight / Body and soul / (Back home again in) Indiana / Honeysuckle rose / I'm in the mood for love / I can't get started (with you) / Play piano play / Undecided / You're blase / Sophisticated lady / Ain't she sweet / I don't know / Fine and dandy / Robbin's nest / Please don't talk about me when I'm gone / It's the talk of the town / You're driving me crazy / Ja da / Summertime / I never knew
CD _____ 4679162
Sony Music / '91 / Sony.

BOUNCE WITH ME
CD _____ JHR 73575
Jazz Hour / Nov '93 / Target/BMG / Jazz Music / Cadillac.

CLASSICS 1944 VOL. 2
CD _____ CLASSICS 818
Classics / May '95 / Discovery / Jazz Music.

CONCERT BY THE SEA
I'll remember April / Teach me tonight / Mambo Carmel / It's all right with me / Red top / April in Paris / They can't take that away from me / Where or when / Erroll's theme
CD _____ 4510422
CBS / Oct '93 / Sony.

ENCORES IN HI FI
Moonglow / Sophisticated Lady / Robbin's nest / Creme De Menthe / Humoresque / I low high the moon / Fancy / Groovy day / Man I love
CD _____ 4677072
Sony Jazz / Jan '95 / Sony.

ERROLL GARNER (Garner, Erroll & Friends)
CD _____ GOJCD 53103
Giants Of Jazz / Mar '92 / Target/BMG / Cadillac.

ERROLL GARNER - LIVE
CD _____ EBCD 21042
Jazzband / Feb '92 / Jazz Music / Wellard.

ERROLL GARNER 1944
CD _____ CLASSICS 802
Classics / Mar '95 / Discovery / Jazz Music.

IN THE BEGINNING
CD _____ CDJJ 615
Jazz & Jazz / Jan '92 / Target/BMG.

JAZZ MASTERS
CD _____ 518197-2
Verve / Feb '94 / PolyGram.

JAZZ PORTRAITS
Misty / Play piano play / Pastel / Trio / Turquoise / Frankie and Johnny Fantasy / Impressions / This can't be love / Moonglow / I can't give you anything but love / Blue and sentimental / Way you look tonight / She's funny that way / I can't believe that you're in love with me / Cool blues / Bird's nest / Frantonality / Man I love
CD _____ CD 14508
Jazz Portraits / May '94 / Jazz Music.

LIVE AT CARMEL, CALIFORNIA SEPT. 1955
CD _____ GOJCD 53034
Giants Of Jazz / Jan '89 / Target/BMG / Cadillac.

LONG AGO AND FAR AWAY
When Johnny comes marching home / It could happen to you / I don't know why / It could happen to you (2) / My heart stood still / When you're smiling / Long ago and far away / Poor butterfly / Spring is here / Petite waltz / Petite waltz bounce / Lover / How high the moon / People will say we're in love / Laura / I cover the waterfront / Penthouse serenade
CD _____ 4606142
Sony Jazz / Jan '95 / Sony.

MAGICIAN & GERSHWIN & KERN
Close to you / It gets better every time / Someone to watch over me / Nightwind / One good turn / Watch what happens / Yesterdays / I only have eyes for you / Mancho gusto / Strike up the band / Love walked in / I can't help lovin' dat man / Nice work if you can get it / Lovely to look at / I can't help lovin' dat man / Only make believe / Old man river / Dearly beloved / Why do I love you / Fine romance
CD _____ CD 83337
Telarc / Apr '95 / Conifer / ADA.

MISTY
Misty / Very thought of you / It might as well be spring / Dreamy / I didn't know what time it was / Moment's delight / On the street where you live / Other voices / This is always / Solitaire / St. Louis blues / Summertime / S wonderful / Easy to love / Way you look tonight / I'm in the mood for love
CD _____ CD 56019
Jazz Roots / Aug '94 / Target/BMG.

MOON GLOW
CD _____ TCD 1010
Rykodisc / Feb '96 / Vital / ADA.

MOONGLOW
CD _____ CDSGP 098
Prestige / May '94 / Total/BMG.

ORIGINAL MISTY, THE
CD _____ 8349102
Mercury / Feb '94 / PolyGram.

OVERTURE TO DAWN
CD _____ LEJAZZCD 49
Le Jazz / Nov '95 / Charly / Cadillac.

PARIS IMPRESSIONS
CD _____ 4756242
Sony Jazz / Jan '95 / Sony.

PENTHOUSE SERENADE
(Back home again in) Indiana / Love walked in / Body and soul / Penthouse serenade / Stompin' at the Savoy / Stardust / More than you know / Over the rainbow
CD _____ SV 0162
Savoy Jazz / Apr '93 / Conifer / ADA.

PLAY, PIANO, PLAY
Way you look tonight / Sophisticated lady / Fine and Dandy / Petite waltz bounce / Body and soul / I never knew / Please don't talk about me when I'm gone / Play, piano,

---

play / Ain't she sweet / Groovy day / Frenesi / Robbin's nest / St. Louis blues / S'wonderful / You're driving me crazy / Summertime / Undecided / It's the talk of the town / You're blase / I didn't know / Ja-da
CD _____ CD 53221
Giants Of Jazz / Jan '96 / Target/BMG / Cadillac.

PLAYS GERSHWIN AND KERN
Strike up the band / Love walked in / I got rhythm / Someone to watch over me / Foggy day / Nice work if you can get it / Lovely to look at / Can't help lovin' dat man / Only make believe / Ol' man river / Dearly beloved / Why do I love you / Fine romance
CD _____ 826 224-2
Mercury / Jun '86 / PolyGram.

SEPARATE KEYBOARDS (Garner, Erroll & Billy Taylor)
Cottage for sale / Rosalie / Everything happens to me / Stairway to the stars / September song / All the things you are / Mad Monk / Solace / Night and day / Alexander's ragtime band / Misty blues / Bug
CD _____ SV 0223
Savoy Jazz / Aug '93 / Conifer / ADA.

SERENADE TO LAURA
Laura / This can't be love / Man I love / Moonglow / I want a little girl / It's easy to remember / Goodbye / She's funny that way / Until the real thing comes along / Confessin' / Stormy weather / I surrender dear / I'm in the mood for love / All of me
CD _____ SV 0221
Savoy Jazz / Oct '93 / Conifer / ADA.

SOLILOQUY - AT THE PIANO
Caravan / No greater love / Avalon / Lullaby of Birdland / Memories of you / Will you still be mine / You'd be so nice / You's be so nice to come home to / No more time / I surrender dear / If I had you / Don't take your love from me
CD _____ 4656312
Sony Jazz / Jan '95 / Sony.

SOLITAIRE
CD _____ 518279-2
Mercury / May '94 / PolyGram.

THAT'S MY KICK/GEMINI
That's my kick / Shadow of your smile / Like it is / It ain't necessarily so / Autumn leaves / Blue moon / More / Gaslight / Nervous waltz / Passing through / Afinidad / How high the moon / It could happen to you / Gemini / When a gypsy makes his violin cry / Tea for two / Something / Eldorado / These foolish things
CD _____ CD 83332
Telarc / Sep '94 / Conifer / ADA.

YESTERDAYS
Play fiddle play / Dark eyes / Laff slam laff / Jumpin' at the Deuces / September song / Everything happens to me / I only have eyes for you / Cottage for sale / On the sunny side of the street / All the things you are / Rosalie / Stairway to the stars / Yesterdays
CD _____ SV 0244
Savoy Jazz / Oct '94 / Conifer / ADA.

Garner, Larry

TOO BLUES
CD _____ JSP 249CD
JSP / May '93 / ADA / Target/BMG / Direct / Cadillac / Complete/Pinnacle.

Garner, Lynn

KEEP THE CIRCLE TURNING
CD _____ DLD 1063
Dance & Listen / Dec '95 / Savoy.

Garnet Silk

GARNET SILK & THE DJ's RULE THING
CD _____ RNCD 2035
Rhino / Oct '93 / Jetstar / Magnum Music Group / THE.

GARNET SILK GOLD
CD _____ CRCD 20
Charm / Aug '93 / Jetstar.

IT'S GROWING
CD _____ NWSCD 1
New Sound / Mar '93 / Jetstar.
CD _____ VYDCD 4
Vine Yard / Sep '95 / Grapevine.

LORD WATCH OVER OUR SHOULDERS
CD _____ GRELCD 219
Greensleeves / Aug '95 / Total/BMG / Jetstar / SRD.

LOVE IS THE ANSWER
CD _____ SCCD 3
Steely & Cleevie / Nov '94 / Jetstar.

NOTHING CAN DIVIDE US
CD _____ CRCD 38
Charm / Apr '93 / Jetstar.

Garnier, Laurent

SHOT IN THE DARK
Shapes under water / Astral dreams (Speahers Mix (CD & MC)) / Bouncing metal / Rising spirit / Harmonic grooves / Force / Geometric world / 022 / Rex attitude / Raw cut / Track for Mike / Silver string (LP & MC)

CD _____ **F 014CD**
F-Communications / Oct '94 / Vital.

Garrett, Amos

AMOSBEHAVIN'
CD _____ **SP 1189CD**
Stony Plain / Oct '93 / ADA / CM / Direct.

BURIED ALIVE IN THE BLUES
Home in my shoes / Move on down the line / Don't tell me / Smack dab in the middle / Ha ha in the daytime / Stanley Street / Hair of the dog / Too many rivers / Buried alive in the blues / What a fool I was / Lost love / All my money / Bert's boogie / Got to get you off my mind
CD _____ **VDCD 110**
Voodoo / Jun '94 / Vital.

I MAKE MY HOME IN MY SHOES
CD _____ **SP 1132CD**
Stony Plain / Oct '93 / ADA / CM / Direct.

LIVE IN JAPAN (Garrett, Amos & Doug Sahm)
CD _____ **FM 1008CD**
Marilyn / Jul '92 / Pinnacle.

RETURN OF THE FORMERLY BROTHERS, THE (Garrett, Amos/Doug Sahm/Gene Taylor)
CD _____ **RCD 10127**
Rykodisc / Aug '92 / Vital / ADA.

THIRD MAN IN
CD _____ **SP 1179CD**
Stony Plain / Oct '93 / ADA / CM / Direct.

Garrett, Kenny

GARRETT FIVE
Feeling good / But beautiful / Computer G / Lee Hall's blues / Odoriko / Little Dixie / Little melonae / La Bamba / Tokyo tower / United we waltz
CD _____ **K32Y 6280**
King/Paddle Wheel / Jun '89 / New Note.

Garrett, Lesley

ALBUM, THE
CD _____ **TCD 2709**
Telstar / Jan '94 / BMG.

SOPRANO IN RED
Waltz of my heart / If love were all / Vilja / Softly as in a morning sunrise / Why did you kiss my heart awake / We'll gather lilacs / Romance / Lover come back to me / Nun's chorus / Laura's song / Final aria / Can-can
CD _____ **SILKTVCD 1**
Silva Classics / Nov '95 / Conifer / Silva Screen.

Garrett, Vernon

CAUGHT IN THE CROSSFIRE
Lonely, lonely nights / Bottom line / Drifting apart / Love me right / If you can't help me baby / Somebody done messed up / Don't make me pay for his mistakes / Walkin' the back streets and crying / Caught in the crossfire
CD _____ **CDICH 1128**
Ichiban / Oct '93 / Koch.

TOO HIP TO BE HAPPY
Are you the one / You just call me / You don't know nothin' about love / Too hip to be happy / Doors of my heart / Special kind of lady / She's a burgular / I'll be doggone / Gonna have to use my head / Li'l black woman
CD _____ **ICH 1169CD**
Ichiban / May '94 / Koch.

Garrick, David

BOY CALLED DAVID, A
CD _____ **REP 4091-WZ**
Repertoire / Aug '91 / Pinnacle / Cadillac.

Garrick, Michael

LADY IN WAITING, A (Garrick, Michael Trio)
CD _____ **JAZA 1**
Jazz Academy / Oct '94 / Cadillac.

METEORS CLOSE AT HAND (2CD Set)
CD _____ **JAZA 2**
Jazz Academy / Dec '95 / Cadillac.

Garrido, David

EL SONIDO DEL TIEMPO
CD _____ **20051CD**
Sonifolk / Dec '94 / ADA / CM.

Garside, Robin

RAGMAN'S TRUMPET, THE
CD _____ **GET 2CD**
Get / Aug '94 / ADA.

Garson, Michael

OXNARD SESSIONS
CD _____ **RR 37CD**
Reference Recordings / Sep '91 / May Audio.

SERENDIPITY
Serendipity / Lady / Autumn leaves / I should care / Spirit of play / Trio blues / My romance / Promise / Tam's jam / Searching / My one and only love
CD _____ **RR 20CD**
Reference Recordings / Sep '91 / May Audio.

Gary, John

SINGS COLE PORTER
CD _____ **ACD 274**
Audiophile / Apr '95 / Jazz Music / Swift.

Garzone, George

ALONE
Spring can really hang you up the most / Night and day / Moonlight in Vermont / Insensatez / Ballad for Lana / What is this thing called love / Alone / Lush life / Con Alma / Nature boy / Anytime tomorrow
CD _____ **NYC 60182**
NYC / Oct '95 / New Note.

Gas 0095

EMIT 0095
CD _____ **EMIT 0095**
Time Recordings / Feb '95 / Pinnacle.

Gas Huffer

BEER DRINKING
CD _____ **EFA 11396D**
Musical Tragedies / Apr '93 / SRD.

INTERGRITY TECHNOLOGY AND SERVICE
CD _____ **MT 181CD**
Burning Heart / Sep '95 / Plastic Head.

M.T.I.
CD _____ **E 11373 CD**
Musical Tragedies / Jan '93 / SRD.

ONE INCH MASTERS
CD _____ **E 86439-2**
Epitaph / Aug '94 / Plastic Head / Pinnacle.

Gas Mark 5

GUIZERS
CD _____ **REGULO 3**
Regulo / Oct '94 / ADA.

JUMP
CD _____ **REGULO 2**
Regulo / Oct '94 / ADA.

Gaskin, Ray

SOUL CRUSADE
CD _____ **MTRCD 1002**
MT / Feb '95 / Grapevine.

Gaslini, Giorgio

AYLER'S WINGS
CD _____ **121270-2**
Soul Note / Apr '91 / Harmonia Mundi / Wellard / Cadillac.

GASLINI PLAYS MONK
CD _____ **121020-2**
Soul Note / May '92 / Harmonia Mundi / Wellard / Cadillac.

LAMPI (LIGHTNINGS)
CD _____ **121290-2**
Soul Note / May '94 / Harmonia Mundi / Wellard / Cadillac.

SCHUMANN REFLECTIONS
Von fremden landern und menschen / Kuriose geschichte / Hasche-mann / Schmann reflections / Bittendes kind / Gluckes genius / Wichtige begebenheit / Traumerei / Am kamin / Ritter vom steckenpferd / Fast zu ernst / Furchtenmachen / Kind im einschlummern / De ditcher spricht
CD _____ **121120-2**
Soul Note / May '92 / Harmonia Mundi / Wellard / Cadillac.

Gasparyan, Djivan

I WILL NOT BE SAD IN THIS WORLD
CD _____ **ASCD 06**
All Saints / Jun '92 / Vital / Discovery.

MOON SHINES AT NIGHT
Lovely spring / Sayat nova / 7th December 1988 / Don't make me cry / You have to come back home / Tonight / They took my love away / Moon shines at night / Apricot tree / Mother of mine
CD _____ **ASCD 016**
All Saints / Sep '93 / Vital / Discovery.

Gates, David

FIRST ALBUM
CD _____ **7559609102**
Elektra / Jan '96 / Warner Music.

GOODBYE GIRL
Goodbye girl / Took the last train / Overnight sensation / California lady / Ann / Drifter / Her don't know how to love you / Clouds suite / Lorilee / Part time love / Sunday rider / Never let her go
CD _____ **7559611722**
Elektra / Jan '96 / Warner Music.

LOVE IS ALWAYS SEVENTEEN

Avenue of love / Love is always seventeen / Ordinary man / I will wait for you / Save this dance for me / No secrets in a small town / Heart, it's all over / I don't want to share your love / I can't find the words to say goodbye / Dear world / Thankin' you sweet baby James
CD _____ **1046770122**
Discovery / May '95 / Warner Music.

Gateway Jazz Band

HOMECOMING
Homecoming / Waltz new / Modern times / Calypso falto / Short cut / How's never / In your arms / 7th D / Oneness
CD _____ **5276372**
ECM / Oct '95 / New Note.

Gathering

ALMOST A DANCE
CD _____ **FDN 2008-2**
Foundation 2000 / Dec '93 / Plastic Head.

ALWAYS
CD _____ **FDN 2004 CD**
Foundation 2000 / Jul '92 / Plastic Head.

MANDYLION
CD _____ **CM 77098**
Century Media / Sep '95 / Plastic Head.

Gatica, Lucho

HISTORIA DE UN AMOR
CD _____ **CD 62035**
Saludos Amigos / Apr '94 / Target/BMG.

Gatton, Danny

CRUISIN' DEUCES
Fun house / Sun medley / Harlem nocturne / Thirteen women / Sky king / Beat of the night / So good / It doesn't matter anymore / Puddin' and pie / Tragedy / Cruisin' deuce / Satisfied mind
CD _____ **755961465-2**
Elektra / May '93 / Warner Music.

RELENTLESS (Gatton, Danny & Joey DeFrancesco)
CD _____ **BIGMO 2023**
Big Mo / Aug '94 / Direct / ADA.

Gaudreau, Jimmy

LIVE IN HOLLAND (Gaudreau, Jimmy Bluegrass Unit)
CD _____ **SCR 21**
Strictly Country / Jul '95 / ADA / Direct.

Gaughan, Dick

COPPERS AND BRASS (Scots & Irish Dance Music on Guitar)
Coppers and brass / Gander in the pratie hole / O'Keefe's / Foxhunter's / Flowing tide / Fairies hornpipe / Oak tree / Music in the glen / Planxty Johnson / Gurty's frolics / Spey in spate / Hurricane / Alan MacPherson of Mosspark / Jig of slurs / Thrush in the storm / Flogging reel pipes / Ask my father / Lads of Laois / Connaught heifers / Bird in the bush / Boy in the gap / MacMahon's reel / Strike the gay harp / Shores of Lough Gowna / Jack broke da prison door / Donald blue / Wha'll dance wi' wattie
CD _____ **GLCD 3064**
Green Linnet / Oct '93 / Roots / CM / Direct / ADA.

HANDFUL OF EARTH
Bonnie Jeannie O'Bethelnie / Bonnie lass among the heather / Crooked Jack / Recruited colliers / Pound a week rise / My Donald / Willie o' Winsbury / Such a parcel of rogues in a nation / Gillie Mor
CD _____ **TSCD 384**
Topic / Nov '90 / Direct / ADA.

PARALLEL LINES (Gaughan, Dick & Andy Irvine)
CD _____ **CDTUT 724007**
Wundertute / Oct '89 / CM / Duncans / ADA.

WOODY LIVES
Hard travellin' / Vigilante man / deportees / Do re mi / Tom Joad / This land is your land / Pretty boy Floyd / Philadelphia lawyer / Pastures of plenty / Will you miss me
CD _____ **CROCD 217**
Black Crow / Jun '88 / Roots / Jazz Music / CM.

Gaunt

I CAN SEE YOUR MOM FROM HERE
CD _____ **EFACD 115872**
Crypt / Nov '94 / SRD.

YEAH, ME TOO
CD _____ **ARRCD 66009**
Amphetamine Reptile / Dec '95 / SRD.

Gauthe, Jacques

CASSOULET STOMP (Gauthe, Jacques & His Creole Rice Jazzband)
CD _____ **SOSCD 1170**
Stomp Off / Feb '89 / Jazz Music / Wellard.

CLARINET SERENADERS (Gauthe, Jacques & Alain Marquet Clarinet Serenaders)

CD _____ **SOSCD 1216**
Stomp Off / Oct '92 / Jazz Music / Wellard.

JACQUES GAUTHE & CREOLE RICE YERBA BUENA JAZZBAND

CD _____ **SOSCD 1256**
Stomp Off / Apr '94 / Jazz Music / Wellard.

Gauty, Lys

1932-33
CD _____ **122**
Chansophone / Nov '92 / Discovery.

Gavin, Frankie

BEST OF FRANKIE GAVIN, THE
CD _____ **RTE 187CD**
RTE / Dec '95 / ADA / Koch.

FRANKIE GAVIN & ALEC FINN (Gavin, Frankie & Alec Finn)
CD _____ **SHANCD 34049**
Shanachie / Jan '95 / Koch / ADA / Greensleeves.

FRANKIE GOES TO TOWN
CD _____ **GLCD 3051**
Green Linnet / Oct '93 / Roots / CM / Direct / ADA.

IRISH CHRISTMAS
CD _____ **BK 003CD**
Bee's Knees / Jan '94 / Roots / ADA.

IRLANDE (Gavin, Frankie & Arty McGlynn)
CD _____ **C 560021CD**
Oscora / Apr '94 / ADA.

TRIBUTE TO JOE COOLEY (Gavin, Frankie & Paul Brock)
CD _____ **CEFCD 115**
Gael Linn / Jan '94 / Roots / CM / Direct / ADA.

UP AND AWAY
CD _____ **CEFCD 103**
Gael Linn / Jan '94 / Roots / CM / Direct / ADA.

Gavioli Fair Organ

TWELFTH STREET RAG
CD _____ **GRCD 63**
Grasmere / May '94 / Target/BMG / Savoy.

Gay, Noel

SONGS OF NOEL GAY, THE
CD _____ **PASTCD 7035**
Flapper / Jan '95 / Pinnacle.

Gaye Bykers On Acid

GAYE BYKERS ON ACID
CD _____ **RRCD 160**
Receiver / Jul '93 / Grapevine.

Gaye, Marvin

ANTHOLOGY: MARVIN GAYE
CD _____ **530181-2**
Motown / Jan '92 / PolyGram.

BEST OF MARVIN GAYE
CD _____ **530292-2**
Motown / Mar '94 / PolyGram.

DIANA & MARVIN (Gaye, Marvin & Diana Ross)
You are everything / Love twins / Don't knock my love / You're a special part of me / Pledging my love / Just say just say / Stop, look, listen (to your heart) / I'm falling in love with you / My mistake (was to love you) / Include me in your life
CD _____ **530048-2**
Motown / Jan '93 / PolyGram.

DISTANT LOVER
Third World girl / I heard it through the grapevine / Come get to this / Let's get it on / God is my friend / What's going on / Inner city blues / Joy / Ain't nothing like the real thing / Heaven must have sent you / If this world were mine / Rockin' after midnight / Distant lover / Sexual healing
CD _____ **MU 3003**
Musketeer / Oct '92 / Koch.

DISTANT LOVER
CD _____ **HADCD 165**
Javelin / May '94 / THE / Henry Hadaway Organisation.

DREAM OF A LIFETIME
Sanctified lady / Savage in the sack / Masochistic beauty / It's madness / Ain't it funny / Symphony / Life's opera / Dream of a lifetime
CD _____ **9825912**
Pickwick/Sony Collector's Choice / Jun '94 / Carlton Home Entertainment / Pinnacle / Sony.

DREAM OF A LIFETIME/ ROMANTICALLY YOURS/MIDNIGHT LOVE (3CD Set)
Sanctified lady / Savage in the sack / Masochistic beauty / It's madness / Ain't it

funny (how things turn around) / Symphony / Life's opera / Dream of a lifetime / More / Why did I choose you / Maria / Shadow of your smile / Fly me to the moon / I won't cry anymore / Just like / Walkin' in the rain / I live for you / Stranger in my life / Happy go lucky / Midnight lady / Sexual healing / Rockin' after midnight / Till tomorrow / Turn on some music / Third world girl / Joy / My love is waiting
CD Set _____ 477525 2
Columbia / Oct '94 / Sony.

FOR THE VERY LAST TIME
I heard it through the grapevine / Come get to this / Let's get it on / God is love / What's going on / Inner city blues / Joy / Ain't nothing like the real thing / Your precious love / If this world were mine / Rockin' after midnight / Distant lover / Percussian suite / Sexual healing
CD _____ MDCD 1
MMG Video / Jan '94 / Magnum Music Group.

HERE, MY DEAR
Here my dear / I met a little girl / When did you stop loving me, when did I stop loving you / Anger / Funky space reincarnation / You can leave but it's goin' to cost you / Falling in love again / Is that enough / Everybody needs love / Time to get it together / Sparrow / Anna's song
CD _____ 530253-2
Motown / Feb '92 / PolyGram.

I WANT YOU
I want you / Come live with me angel / Angel / After the dance (Instrumental.) / Feel all my love inside / I wanna be where you are / All the way round / Since I had you / Soon I'll be loving you again / I want you (intro jam) / After the dance (plus instrumental)
CD _____ 5300212
Motown / Jul '94 / PolyGram.

INNER CITY BLUES (A Tribute To Marvin Gaye) (Various Artists)
Save the children / Let's get it on / Trouble man / You're the man / Inner city blues / I want you / God is love/Mercy mercy me / What's going on / Just to keep you satisfied / Stubborn kind of fellow
CD _____ 5304522
Polydor / Sep '95 / PolyGram.

LET'S GET IT ON
Let's get it on / Please don't stay (once you go away) / If I should die tonight / Keep gettin' it on / Distant lover / You sure love to ball / Just to keep you satisfied / Come get to this
CD _____ 530055-2
Motown / Jul '92 / PolyGram.

LIVE
CD _____ STACD 082
Wisepack / Jul '93 / THE / Conifer.

LIVE
CD _____ 112007-2
Scratch / Oct '94 / BMG.

M.P.G.
Too busy thinking about my baby / This magic moment / That's the way love is / End of our road / Seek and you shall find / Memories / Only a lonely man would know / It's a bitter pill to swallow / More than a heart can stand / Try my true love / I got to get to California / It don't take much to keep me
CD _____ 5302102
Motown / Aug '93 / PolyGram.

MARVIN GAYE - LIVE
CD Set _____ STADD 536
Stardust / Apr '93 / Carlton Home Entertainment.

MARVIN GAYE IN CONCERT
CD _____ CDSGP 0152
Prestige / Apr '95 / Total/BMG.

MASTER 1961 - 1984, THE (4CD Box Set)
CD Set _____ 5304922
Motown / May '95 / PolyGram.

MIDNIGHT LOVE
Joy / My love is waiting / Midnight lady / Sexual healing / Rockin' after midnight / Till tomorrow / Turn on some music / Third world girl
CD _____ CD 85977
Columbia / Jul '94 / Sony.

MOTOWN'S GREATEST HITS: MARVIN GAYE
I heard it through the grapevine / Let's get it on / Too busy thinking about my baby / How sweet it is (to be loved by you) / You're all I need to get by / Got to give it up (pt. 1) / That's the way love is / Are you everything / Can I get a witness / If I'm are everything / What's going on / Abraham, Martin and John / It takes two / Stop, look, listen (to your heart) / Chained / Trouble man / I want you / You ain't livin' till you're lovin' / Onion song / Wherever I lay my hat
CD _____ 5300122
Motown / Jan '92 / PolyGram.

NIGHTLIFE
Nightlife / I'll be doggone / Little darlin' / Take this heart of mine / Hey diddle diddle / One more heartache / Too busy thinking

about my baby / How sweet it is (to be loved by you) / You've been a long time coming / Your unchanging love / You're the one for me / I worry 'bout you / One for my baby (and one more for the road)
CD _____ 5500722
Spectrum/Karussell / May '93 / PolyGram / THE.

ROMANTICALLY YOURS
More / Why did I choose you / Maria / Shadow of your smile / Fly me to the moon / I won't cry anymore / Just like / Walking in the rain / I live for you / Stranger in my life / Happy go lucky
CD _____ 902121-2
Pickwick/Sony Collector's Choice / Jun '94 / Carlton Home Entertainment / Pinnacle / Sony.
CD _____ 4631582
Columbia / Dec '95 / Sony.

SEEK AND YOU SHALL FIND - MORE BEST OF MARVIN GAYE (1963-81)
Wherever I lay my hat / Get my hands on some lovin' / Is that enough / You've been a long time coming / When I had your love / You're what's happening (in the world today) / Loving you is sweeter than ever / It's a bitter pill to swallow / Seek and you shall find / Gonna keep on tryin' till I win your love / Gonna give her all the love I've got / I wish it would rain / Abraham, Martin and John / Save the children / You sure love to ball / Ego tripping out / Praise / Heavy love affair
CD _____ 812271182-2
WEA / Jun '93 / Warner Music.

THAT'S THE WAY LOVE IS
Gonna give her all the love I've got / Yesterday / Groovin' / I wish it would rain / That's the way love is / How can I forget / Abraham, Martin and John / Gonna keep on tryin' till I win your love / No time for tears / Cloud 9 / Don't you miss me a little bit baby / So long
CD _____ 5302142
Motown / Aug '93 / PolyGram.

TRIBUTE TO THE GREAT NAT KING COLE, A
Nature boy / Ramblin' rose / Too young / Pretend / Straighten up and fly right / Mona Lisa / Unforgettable / To the ends of the earth / Sweet Lorraine / It's only a paper moon / Send for me / Calypso blues
CD _____ 530054-2
Motown / Jul '92 / PolyGram.

TROUBLE MAN
Trouble man main theme (2) / T plays it cool / Poor Abbey Walsh / Break in (police shoot big) / Cleo's apartment / Trouble man / Trouble man, Theme from / T stands for trouble / Trouble man main theme (1) / Life is a gamble / Deep in it / Don't mess with Mr. T / There goes mister 'T'
CD _____ 530097-2
Motown / Jan '92 / PolyGram.

WHAT'S GOING ON?
What's going on / What's happening brother / Flyin' high / Save the children / God is love / Mercy mercy me / Right on / Wholly holy / Inner city blues
CD _____ 5300222
Motown / Jul '94 / PolyGram.

YOU'RE ALL I NEED (Gaye, Marvin & Tammi Terrell)
Ain't nothing like the real thing / Keep on lovin' me, honey / You're all I need to get by / Baby dontcha worry / You ain't livin' till you're lovin' / Give in, you just can't win / When love comes knocking at my heart / I can't help but love you / That's how it is (since you've been gone) / I'll never stop loving you, baby / Memory chest
CD _____ 5302162
Motown / Sep '93 / PolyGram.

Gaylads

AFTER STUDIO ONE
CD _____ MRCD 001
Metronome / May '95 / Jetstar.

OVER THE RAINBOW'S END
CD _____ CDTRL 351
Trojan / Apr '95 / Jetstar / Total/BMG.

SOUL BEAT
CD _____ SOCD 001
Studio One / Mar '95 / Jetstar.

Gayle, Charles

CONSECRATION
CD _____ 120138-2
Black Saint / Nov '93 / Harmonia Mundi / Cadillac.

KINGDOM COME (Gayle, Charles Trio)
CD _____ KFWCD 157
Knitting Factory / Feb '95 / Grapevine.

MORE LIVE AT THE KNITTING FACTORY (Gayle, Charles Quartet)
CD _____ KFWCD 137
Knitting Factory / Feb '95 / Grapevine.

RAINING FIRE
CD _____ SHCD 137
Silkheart / Oct '94 / Jazz Music / Wellard / CM / Cadillac.

REPENT
CD _____ KFWCD 122
Knitting Factory / Nov '94 / Grapevine.

TOUCHIN' ON TRANE
CD _____ FMPCD 48
FMP / Oct '86 / Cadillac.

TRANSLATION VOL.1
CD _____ SHCD 134
Silkheart / Oct '94 / Jazz Music / Wellard / CM / Cadillac.

Gayle, Crystal

20 LOVE SONGS
Hello I love you / Cry me a river / Dreaming my dreams with you / Someday soon / I'll do it all over again / I wanna come back to you / Somebody loves you / It's all right with me / Coming closer / Don't it make my brown eyes blue / When I dream / I'll get over you / Heart mender / Funny / I still miss someone / Talking in your sleep / Right in the palm of your hand / Beyond you / Going down is slow / Woman's heart (is a handy place to be) (CD only.)
CD _____ CDMFP 5629
Music For Pleasure / Apr '91 / EMI.

BEST ALWAYS
Ready for the times to get better / Crazy / For the good times / Silver threads and golden needles / When I dream / Talkin' in your sleep / Oh Lonesome me / I fall to pieces / Beyond you / Don't it make my brown eyes blue / Break my mind
CD _____ RITZRCD 530
Ritz / Jun '93 / Pinnacle.

COUNTRY GIRL
Why have you left the one you left me for / Wrong road again / When I dream / They come out at night / Wayward wind / You never miss a real good thing ('til he says goodbye) / Forgettin' 'bout you / I'll do it all over again / Someday soon / Ready for the times to get better / I still miss someone / Sweet baby on my mind / Somebody loves you / We should be together / River road / This is my year for Mexico
CD _____ CDMFP 6037
Music For Pleasure / Nov '88 / EMI.

EMI COUNTRY MASTERS
Somebody loves you / High time / I'll get over you / Woman's heart (Is a handy place to be) / Restless / You / Wrong road again / Beyond you / Hands / Counterfeit love / This is my year for Mexico / Dreaming my dreams with you / One more time (Karneval) / Oh my soul / Come home Daddy / You never miss a real good thing ('til he says goodbye) / I'll do it all over again / It's all right with me / Going down slow / Make a dream come true / Funny / We must believe in magic / Cry me a river / Wayward wind / Why have you left the one you left me for / Don't it make my brown eyes blue / Ready for the times to get better / Someday soon / I still miss someone / Talking in your sleep / Green door / Paintin' this old town blue / All I wanna do in life / When I dream / Time will prove I'm right / Your kisses will / Your old cold shoulder / Too deep for tears / We should be together / River road / I wanna come back to you / Heart mender / Everybody's reaching out for someone / Just an old love / Never ending song of love / Once in a very blue moon / Trouble with me is you / Love to, can't do / 99% Of the time / Faithless love
CD _____ CDEM 1499
EMI / May '93 / EMI.

LOVE SONGS: CRYSTAL GAYLE
Other side of me / I just can't leave your love alone / What a little moonlight can do / It's like we never said goodbye / You've almost got me believin' / Help yourselves to each other / If you ever change your mind / Miss the Mississippi and you / Don't go, my love / Too many lovers / Half the way / Blue side
CD _____ PWKS 521
Carlton Home Entertainment / '88 / Carlton Home Entertainment.

SINGLES ALBUM
Somebody loves you / Wrong road again / I'll get over you / High time / Ready for the times to get better / You never miss a real good thing (Til he says goodbye) / River road / Don't it make my brown eyes blue / When I dream / Talking in your sleep / Why have you left the one you left me for / All I wanna do in life / We should be together / Too deep for tears
CD _____ CZ 204
Liberty / Jul '89 / EMI.

Gayle, Michelle

MICHELLE GAYLE
Get off my back / Happy just to be with you / Walk with pride / Looking up / Girlfriend / Freedom / Personality / It doesn't matter / Your love / Sweetness / One day / Say what's on your mind / Rise up / Baby don't go / All night long
CD _____ 74321234122
RCA / Dec '95 / BMG.

Gaynor, Gloria

GLORIA GAYNOR - THE HITS
CD _____ OVCCD 003
Satellite Music / Mar '94 / THE.

HIT COLLECTION
CD _____ 3082
Scratch / Oct '94 / BMG.

I AM WHAT I AM
CD _____ MU 5045
Musketeer / Apr '92 / Koch.

I WILL SURVIVE
CD _____ LMCD 001
Wisepack / Sep '93 / THE / Conifer.

REACH OUT
Reach out, I'll be there / Can't fight the feelin' / How high the moon / Tonight / Don't stop us / One number one / This love affair / I've got you under my skin / Substitute / Anybody wanna party / Let me know (I have a right) / Honey bee / Goin' out of my head
CD _____ 5502012
Spectrum/Karussell / Mar '94 / PolyGram / THE.

Geckoes

ART GECKO
CD _____ OCK 003CD
Ock / Jul '95 / ADA.

Geesin, Ron

HYSTERY - THE RON GEESIN STORY
Ron's address to a notion / Parallel bar / Mental passage / Coughsemble / Whistling heart / Go / Fore-teases / Twisted pair / Big imp / Morecambe bay / Sit down, Mamma / T'mith / Throb thencewards thrill / Chromatic essence and smoked hips (the time dance) / Frenzy / Animal autos / Where daffodils do thrive / Vocal chords / Upon composition / Can't you stop that thing / Syncopot / Song of the wire / Affections for string quartet / With a smile up his nose they entered / Three vignettes / Certainly random / Raise of eyebrows / No.8 Scalpel incision
CD _____ CDBRED 110
Cherry Red / Dec '93 / Pinnacle.

RAISE OF EYEBROWS/AS HE STANDS
Raise of eyebrows / Freedom for four voices and me / Psychedelia / Positives / It's all very new, you know / Female / Certainly random / Eye that nearly saw / Two fifteen string guitars for nice poeple / From an electric train / World of too much sound / Another female / We're all going to Liverpool / Ha ha but reasonable / Can't stop that thing / Looming view / Rise up Sebastian / Concrete line up / Upon composition / Mr. Peugeot's trot / To Roger Waters wherever you are / Cymbal and much electronics / Up above my heart / Twist and knit for two guitars / Wrap a keyboard round a plant / Middle of whose night / Waiting for life / On-through-out-up
CD _____ SEECD 433
See For Miles/C5 / Aug '95 / Pinnacle.

Geet

NO PROBLEM
CD _____ CDSR 012
Star / May '90 / Pinnacle / Sterns.

Gehrman, Shura

ENGLISH SONGS
Songs of travel / Shropshire lad / Selected songs
CD _____ NI 5033
Nimbus / '88 / Nimbus.

FOLKSONGS OF THE BRITISH ISLES
CD _____ NI 5082
Nimbus / '88 / Nimbus.

Geils, J. Band

BEST OF THE J.GEILS BAND
Southside shuffle / Give it to me / Where did our love go / Ain't nothing but a house party / Detroit breakdown / Whammer jammer / I do / Must of got lost / Looking for a love
CD _____ 7567815572
WEA / Feb '84 / Warner Music.

BLOW YOUR FACE OUT
Southside shuffle / Back to get ya / Shoot your shot / Must have got lost / Where did our love go / Truck driving man / Love this / Looking for a love / Ain't nothing but a house party / So sharp / Detroit breakdown / Chimes / Sno-cone / Wait / Raise your hand / Start all over again / Give it to me
CD _____ 812271278-2
WEA / Oct '93 / Warner Music.

FREEZE FRAME
Freeze frame / Rage in the cage / Centrefold / Do you remember when / Insane, insane again / Flamethrower / River blindness / Angel in blue / Piss on the wall
CD _____ BGOCD 196
Beat Goes On / Jul '93 / Pinnacle.

LADIES INVITED
Chimes / Did you no wrong / Diddyboppin' / I can't go on / Lady makes demands / Lay your good thing down / My baby don't love

me / No doubt about it / Take a chance (on romance) / That's why I'm thinking of you
CD _____ 7567814312
Pickwick/Warner / Feb '95 / Pinnacle / Warner Music / Carlton Home Entertainment.

LOVE STINKS
Just can't wait / Come back / Takin' you down / Night time / No anchovies, please / Love stinks / Tryin' not to think about it / Desire / Till the walls come tumblin' down
CD _____ BGOCD 254
Beat Goes On / Dec '94 / Pinnacle.

SANCTUARY
I could hurt you / One last kiss / Take it back / Sanctuary / Teresa / Wild man / I can't believe you / I don't hang around much anymore / Jus' can't stop me
CD _____ BGOCD 262
Beat Goes On / May '95 / Pinnacle.

SHOWTIME
Jus' can't stop me / Just can't wait / Till the walls come tumblin' down / Sanctuary / I'm falling / Love rap / Love stinks / Stoop down 39 / I do / Centrefold / Land of 1000 dances
CD _____ BGOCD 264
Beat Goes On / Nov '95 / Pinnacle.

Geins't Nait

FRIGO
CD _____ PPP 109
PDCD / Sep '93 / Plastic Head.

Gelato, Ray

FULL FLAVOUR, THE (Gelato, Ray's Giants Of Jive)
CD _____ AKD 034
Linn / Mar '95 / PolyGram.

Geldof, Bob

LOUD MOUTH (The Best Of Bob Geldof/ Boomtown Rats)
I don't like Mondays / This is the world calling / Rat trap / Great song of indifference / Love or something / Banana republic / Crazy / Elephant's graveyard / Someone's looking at you / She's so modern / House on fire / Beat of the night / Diamond smiles / Like clockwork / Room 19 (Sha la la la lee) / Mary of the 4th form / Looking after no. 1
CD _____ 522283-2
Vertigo / Apr '94 / PolyGram.

Geller, Herb

JAZZ SONG BOOK, A
CD _____ 6006-2
Tiptoe / Nov '89 / New Note.

THAT GELLER FELLER
CD _____ FSRCD 091
Fresh Sound / Jul '92 / Jazz Music / Discovery.

Gemini Gemini

FLAVOURS OF THELONIUS MONK, THE
CD _____ ITMP 970082
ITM / Oct '95 / Tradelink / Koch.

GEMINI GEMINI
CD _____ ITMP 970063
ITM / Oct '95 / Tradelink / Koch.

Genaro, Tano

PIONNIER DU TANGO ARGENTIN
CD _____ 883142
Music Memoria / Aug '93 / Discovery / ADA.

Gene

OLYMPIAN
Haunted by you / Your love, it lies / Truth, rest your head / Car that sped / Left-handed / London, can you wait / To the city / Still can't find the phone / Sleep well tonight / Olympian / We'll find our own way
CD _____ GENE 1CD
Costermonger / Mar '95 / Vital / PolyGram.

TO SEE THE LIGHTS
Be my light, be my guide / Sick, sober and sorry / Her fifteen years / Haunted by you / I can't decide if she really love me / Car that sped / For the dead (version) / Sleep well tonight / How much for love / London, can you wait / I can't help myself / City boy / Don't let me down / I say a little prayer / Do you want to hear it from me / This is not my crime / Olympian / For the dead
CD _____ GENE 002CD
Costermonger / Jan '96 / Vital / PolyGram.

Gene Loves Jezebel

DISCOVER
Heartache / Over the rooftops / Kicks / White horse / Wait and see / Desire / Beyond doubt / Sweetest thing / Maid of Sker / Brand new moon
CD _____ BEGA 73 CD
Beggars Banquet / Oct '86 / Warner Music / Disc.

HEAVENLY BODIES
CD _____ 74785502102
Arista / Jun '93 / BMG.

HOUSE OF DOLLS, THE
Gorgeous / Motion of love / Set me free / Suspicion / Every door / Twenty killer hurts / Treasure / Message / Drowning crazy / Up there
CD _____ BEGA 87CD
Beggars Banquet / Oct '87 / Warner Music / Disc.

IN THE AFTERGLOW
CD Set _____ PINKGCD 1
Pink Gun / Oct '95 / Total/BMG.

KISS OF LIFE
Jealous / Kiss of life / Szyzygy / Tangled up in you / Evening star / It'll end in tears / Why can't I / Walk away / Two shadows / I die for you
CD _____ BEGA 109 CD
Beggars Banquet / Aug '90 / Warner Music / Disc.

General Lafayette

JESTER
Oh my beloved Father / Power of music / Love in the eyes of a child / Blow the trumpet at the new moon / Trumpet on fire / Going back to Scotland / Jester / Gentle to the soul / Lizzie's song (Is on the radio) / Sentimental value / Jupiter / Burn's theme / Silent anguish / Country barn dance
CD _____ PZA 003CD
Plaza / Mar '93 / Pinnacle.

KING OF THE BROKEN HEARTS
CD _____ PZA 007CD
Plaza / Nov '89 / Pinnacle.

LOVE IS A RHAPSODY
Angel in blue / For the girl who couldn't find love / Melody for you / Florence serenade / Love is a rhapsody / Life is for loving / Lonely trumpet / Love you love me Aloha
CD _____ PZA 001CD
Plaza / Jul '88 / Pinnacle.

PIERROT
CD _____ PZA 009CD
Plaza / Apr '91 / Pinnacle.

General Levy

RUMBLE IN THE JUNGLE VOL.1
(General Levy & Top Cat)
CD _____ JFCD 001
Fashion / Jan '95 / Jetstar / Grapevine.

WICKEDER GENERAL, THE
CD _____ FADCD 024
Fashion / Dec '92 / Jetstar / Grapevine.

WICKEDNESS INCREASE
Champagne body / Tight like a vice / Diamonds and pearls / Grudge me / Monkey man / Mr. Push it good / Guidance / Moonlight lover / Mad them / Heat / Wig
CD _____ 8284302
FFRR / Sep '93 / PolyGram.

General Pecos

BACK WITH A VENGEANCE
CD _____ WRCD 10
World / Aug '95 / Jetstar / Total/BMG.

TALK BOUT GUN
CD _____ GRELCD 185
Greensleeves / Jun '93 / Total/BMG / Jetstar / SRD.

General Public

RUB IT BETTER
Tough / Rainy days / Hold it deep / Big bed / Punk / Friends again / It's weird / Never not alone / Handgun / Blowhard / Warm love / Rub it better
CD _____ 4783582
Epic / Oct '95 / Sony.

General Trees

BATTLE OF THE GENERALS (General Trees & General Degree)
CD _____ 790042
Pippers / Nov '92 / Jetstar.

RAGGA RAGGA RAGAMUFFIN
CD _____ RRTGCD 7702
Rohit / Aug '88 / Jetstar.

General, Mikey

XTERMINATOR
Sinners / I'm going home / Women of Israel / Tired of it / I'm wondering / I know I love you / New name / I'll never be / Rastaman have to be strong / Black and comey / Deh pon derm (CD only.) / Many have fallen (CD only.)
CD _____ CRCD 43
Charm / Sep '95 / Jetstar.

Generation

BRUTAL REALITY
CD _____ CDZORRO 82
Metal Blade / Nov '94 / Pinnacle.

Generation X

GENERATION X
Hundred punks / Listen / Ready steady go / Kleenex / Promises, promises / Day by day / Invisible man / Kiss me deadly / Too

personal / Valley of the dolls / Running with the boss sound / Night of the cadillacs / Friday's angels / King rocker / Wild youth / Dancing with myself / Triumph / Revenge / Youth youth youth / From the heart
CD _____ CD25CR 14
Chrysalis / Mar '94 / EMI.

PERFECT HITS
Dancing with myself / Your generation / Ready steady go / Untouchables / Day by day / Wild youth / Wild dub / Hundred punks / King Rocker / Kiss me deadly / Gimme some truth / New order / English dream / Triumph / Youth youth youth
CD _____ CCD 1854
Chrysalis / Oct '91 / EMI.

Genesis

ABACAB
No reply at all / Me and Sarah Jane / Keep it dark / Dodo / Lurker / Man on the corner / Who dunnit / Like it or not / Another record / Abacab
CD _____ CBRCDX 102
Charisma / Oct '94 / EMI.

AND THEN THERE WERE THREE
Scenes from a night's dream / Snowbound / Ballad of big / Burning rope / Deep in the motherlode / Down and out / Follow you follow me / Lady lies / Many too many / Say it's alright Joe / Undertow
CD _____ CDSCDX 4010
Charisma / Oct '94 / EMI.

DUKE
Behind the lines / Duchess / Guide vocal / Man of our times / Misunderstanding / Heathaze / Turn it on again / Alone tonight / Cul-de-sac / Please don't ask / Duke's end / Duke's travels
CD _____ CBRCDX 101
Charisma / Oct '94 / EMI.

FOXTROT
Watcher of the skies / Time table / Get 'em out by Friday / Can-utility and the coastliners / Horizon / Supper's ready
CD _____ CASCDX 1058
Charisma / Aug '94 / EMI.

GENESIS
Mama / Illegal alien / That's all / Taking it all too hard / Just a job to do / Home by the sea / Second home by the sea / It's gonna get better / Silver rainbow
CD _____ GENCD 1
Charisma / Dec '83 / EMI.

GENESIS LIVE
Watcher of the skies / Get 'em out by friday / Knife / Return of the giant hogweed / Musical box
CD _____ CLACDX 1
Charisma / Aug '94 / EMI.

INTERVIEW COMPACT DISC
CD P.Disc _____ CBAK 4028
Baktabak / Sep '90 / Baktabak.

INVISIBLE TOUCH
Invisible touch / Tonight tonight tonight / Land of confusion / In too deep / Anything she does / Domino (In the glow of the night/ The last domino) / Throwing it all away / Brazilian
CD _____ GENCD 2
Charisma / Dec '86 / EMI.

LAMB LIES DOWN ON BROADWAY, THE
Lamb lies down on Broadway / Riding the scree / In the rapids / It / Fly on a windshield / Broadway melody of 1974 / Cuckoo cocoon / In the cage / Grand parade of lifeless packaging / Back in N.Y.C. / Hairless heart / Counting out time / Carpet crawlers / Chamber of 32 doors / Lilywhite lilith / Waiting room / Anyway / Here comes the supernatural anaesthetist / Lamia / Silent sorrow in empty boats / Colony of slippermen (The arrival) / Colony of slippermen (The-Raven) / Ravine / Light dies down on Broadway
CD _____ CGSCDX 1
Charisma / Aug '94 / EMI.

NURSERY CRYME
Musical box / For absent friends / Return of the giant hogweed / Seven stones / Harold the barrel / Harlequin / Fountain of Salmacis
CD _____ CASCDX 1052
Charisma / Aug '94 / EMI.

SECONDS OUT
Squonk / Carpet crawlers / Robbery, assault and battery / Afterglow / Firth of fifth / I know what I like (in your wardrobe) / Lamb lies down on Broadway / Musical box (closing section) / Supper's ready / Cinema show / Dance on a volcano / Los Endos
CD Set _____ GECDX 2001
Virgin / Sep '94 / EMI.

SELLING ENGLAND BY THE POUND
Dancing with the moonlit knight / I know what I like (in your wardrobe) / Firth of fifth / More fool me / Battle of Epping Forest / After the ordeal / Cinema show / Aisle of plenty
CD _____ CASCDX 1074
Charisma / Aug '94 / EMI.

SELLING ENGLAND BY THE POUND/ THE LAMB LIES DOWN ON BROADWAY (3CD Set)
CD Set _____ TPAK 17
Virgin / Nov '91 / EMI.

SUPPER'S READY (A Tribute To Genesis) (Various Artists)
CD _____ RR 89122
Roadrunner / Nov '95 / Pinnacle.

THREE SIDES LIVE
Behind the lines / Duchess / Me and Sarah Jane / Follow you follow me / One for the vine / Fountain of Salmacis / Watcher of the skies / Turn it on again / Dodo / Abacab / Misunderstanding / In the cage (Medley: Cinema show/Slippermen) / Afterglow / Paperlate (CD only) / You might recall (CD only) / Me and Virgil (CD only) / Evidence of autumn (CD only) / Open door (CD only)
CD Set _____ GECDX 2002
Virgin / Oct '94 / EMI.

TRESPASS
Looking for someone / White mountain / Visions of angels / Stagnation / Dusk / Knife
CD _____ CASCDX 1020
Charisma / Aug '94 / EMI.

TRESPASS/NURSERY CRYME/ FOXTROT (3CD Set)
CD Set _____ TPAK 1
Virgin / Oct '90 / EMI.

TRICK OF THE TAIL, A
Dance on a volcano / Entangled / Squonk / Madman moon / Robbery, assault and battery / Ripples / Trick of the tail / Los Endos
CD _____ CDSCDX 4001
Charisma / Oct '94 / EMI.

WAY WE WALK, THE (The Shorts)
Land of confusion / No son of mine / Jesus he knows me / Throwing it all away / I can't dance / Mama / Hold on my heart / That's all / In too deep / Tonight tonight tonight / Invisible touch
CD _____ GENCD 4
Virgin / Nov '92 / EMI.

WAY WE WALK, THE (The Longs)
Drum duet / Dance on a volcano / Lamb lies down on broadway / Musical box / Firth of fifth / I know what I like (in your wardrobe) / Driving the last spike / Domino (In the glow of the night/The last domino) / Fading lights / Home by the sea / Second home by the sea
CD _____ GENCD 5
Virgin / Jan '93 / EMI.

WE CAN'T DANCE
No son of mine / Jesus he knows me / Driving the last spike / I can't dance / Never a time / Dreaming while you sleep / Tell me why / Living forever / Hold on my heart / Way of the world / Since I lost you / Fading lights
CD _____ GENCD 3
Virgin / Nov '91 / EMI.

WIND AND WUTHERING
Eleventh Earl of Mar / One for the vine / Your own special way / Wot gorilla / All in a mouse's night / Blood on the rooftops / Unquiet slumbers for the sleepers / In that quiet earth / Afterglow
CD _____ CDSCDX 4005
Charisma / Oct '94 / EMI.

Genetic Control

FIRST IMPRESSIONS
First impressions
CD _____ LF 069
Lost & Found / Jan '94 / Plastic Head.

Genitorturers

120 DAYS OF GENITORTURE
CD _____ CDFLAG 81
Under One Flag / Oct '93 / Pinnacle.

Gentle Giant

CIVILIAN
CD _____ TRUCKCD 8
Terrapin Truckin' / Jul '94 / Total/BMG / Direct / ADA.

FREE HAND
Just the same / On reflection / Free hand / Time to kill / His last voyage / Talybont / Mobile
CD _____ TRUCKCD 4
Terrapin Truckin' / Jul '94 / Total/BMG / Direct / ADA.

GIANT FOR A DAY
CD _____ TRUCKCD 7
Terrapin Truckin' / Jul '94 / Total/BMG / Direct / ADA.

INTERVIEW
Interview / Give it back / Design / Another show / Empty city / Timing / I lost my head
CD _____ TRUCKCD 005
Terrapin Truckin' / Jul '94 / Total/BMG / Direct / ADA.

LAST TIME - LIVE 1980, THE
CD _____ TRUCKCD 1010
Terrapin Truckin' / Apr '94 / Total/BMG / Direct / ADA.

LIVE - PLAYING THE FOOL
Just the song / Proclamation / On reflection / Excerpts from Octopus / Funny ways / Runaway / Experience / So sincere / Freehand / Breakdown in Brussels / The fee paint / I lost my head
CD _____ TRUCKCD 1009
Terrapin Truckin' / Dec '94 / Total/BMG / Direct / ADA.

LIVE IN CONCERT
Two weeks in Spain / Free hand / On reflection / Just the same / Playing the game / Memories of old days / Betcha thought we couldn't do it / I'm turning around / For nobody / Mark time
CD _____ WINCD 066
Windsong / Oct '94 / Pinnacle.

Gentlemen Of Jazz

THIRD TIME ROUND
CD _____ MECCACD 130591
Music Mecca / Nov '94 / Jazz Music / Cadillac / Wellard.

WE'LL MEET AGAIN
CD _____ MECCACD 1026
Music Mecca / Nov '94 / Jazz Music / Cadillac / Wellard.

Gentry, Bobbie

BEST OF BOBBIE GENTRY, THE
Ode to Billie Joe / All I have to do is dream / I'll never fall in love again / Raindrops keep falling on my head / Mississippi delta / Little green apples / Natural to be gone / Son of a preacher man / Season come, seasons go / Gentle on my mind / Touch 'em with love / Where's the playground Johnny / My elusive dreams / Grey hound goin' somewhere / You've made me so very happy / Mornin' glory / I wouldn't be surprised / Ace insurance man / Glory hallelujah, how they'll sing / Let it be me
CD _____ CDMFP 6115
Music For Pleasure / Mar '94 / EMI.

TOUCH 'EM WITH LOVE
CD _____ CREV 38CD
Rev-Ola / Nov '95 / 3MV / Vital.

Genty, Alain

LA COULEUR DU MILIEU
CD _____ GWP 006CD
Gwerz Productions / Jul '94 / ADA.

Geordie

DON'T BE FOOLED BY THE NAME
CD _____ REP 4124-WZ
Repertoire / Aug '91 / Pinnacle / Cadillac.

HOPE YOU LIKE IT
CD _____ REP 4033-WZ
Repertoire / Aug '91 / Pinnacle / Cadillac.

George, Lowell

THANKS I'LL EAT IT HERE
What do you want the girl to do / Honest man / Two trains / Can't stand the rain / Cheek to cheek / Easy money / Twenty million things / Find a river / Himmler's ring
CD _____ 7599267552
WEA / Jul '93 / Warner Music.

George, Siwsann

CANEUON TRADDODIADOL CYMRU (Traditional Songs Of Wales)
Adar mân y mynydd / Y gwnwr foch / Can Merthyr / Miner's life / Blodau'r flwyddyn / Hen ferchetan / Hiraeth / Can y Cardi / Cainc yr aradwr / Titrwm tatrwm / Yr hen wr mwyn / Yr eneth gadd ei gwrthod / Bachgen bach o dincer / Mae'r ddaear yn glasu / Ar fore Dydd Nadolig / Clywch clywch / Llangollen market / Can y bugail / Lisa lan / Marwnad yr ehedydd / Llongau Caernarfon / Yr insiwrans agent / Rhybudd i'r carwr
CD _____ CDSDL 406
Saydisc / Sep '94 / Harmonia Mundi / ADA / Direct.

George, Sophia

LATEST SLANG
CD _____ RNCD 2004
Rhino / May '93 / Jetstar / Magnum Music Group / THE.

Georgia Satellites

GEORGIA SATELLITES
Keep your hands to yourself / Railroad steel / Battleship chains / Red lights / Myth of love / I can't stand the pain / Golden lights / Over and over / Nights of mystery / Every picture tells a story
CD _____ 7559 604962
Elektra / Jan '93 / Warner Music.

LET IT ROCK (The Best Of Georgia Satellites)
Don't pass me by / Keep your hands to yourself / Battleship chains / Myth of love / Can't stand the rain / Nights of mystery / Let it rock (live) / Open all night / Sheila / Mon cheri / Down and down / Saddle up / Hippy hippy shake / I dunno / All over but the crying / Six years gone / Hard luck boy

/ Almost Saturday night/Rockin' all over the world / Dan takes five / Another chance
CD _____ 7559613362
Elektra / Feb '93 / Warner Music.

Geraci, Little Anthony

TAKE IT FROM ME (Geraci, Little Anthony & Sugar Ray Norcia)
CD _____ TONECOOLCD 1149
Tonecool / Nov '94 / Direct / ADA.

Geraldine Fibbers

GERALDINE FIBBERS, THE
Marmalade / Get thee gone / Grand tour / Outside of town / They suck / Fancy / Blue cross
CD _____ DGHUTM 22
Hut / Jan '95 / EMI.

LOST SOMEWHERE BETWEEN THE EARTH AND MY HOME
Lily Belle / Small song / Marmalade / Dragon lady / Song about walls / House is falling / Outside of town / French song / Dusted / Richard / Blast of baby / Get thee gone
CD _____ CDHUT 28
Hut / Jul '95 / EMI.

Geraldo

DANCING IN THE BLITZ
Good morning / I'm nobody's baby / Whose little what is it are you / I've got my eyes on you / Where or when / When night is through / Don't worry bout me / Sierra Sue / Singing hills / I can't love you anymore / Let's top the clock / Ferryboat serenade / Sweetheart it's you / Don't you ever cry / Love stay in my heart / World is waiting for the sunrise / Blue orchids / We'll go smiling along / Nightingale sang in berkely square / Goodnight again
CD _____ PAR 2009
Parade / Apr '95 / Koch / Cadillac.

GERALDO AND HIS ORCHESTRA
CD _____ PASTCD 7070
Flapper / Jul '95 / Pinnacle.

JOURNEY TO A STAR, A (Geraldo & His Orchestra)
Sweet Sue, just you / Goodnight again / World is waiting for the sunrise / I can't love you anymore / Singing hills / Don't you ever cry / Breathless / Elmer's tune / Hey Mabel / Jim / Jingle jangle jingle / My devotion / Canzonetta / Russian rose / Waiter and the porter and the upstairs maid / There's this thing called love / Journey to a star / Don't ask me why
CD _____ RAJCD 811
Empress / Nov '93 / THE.

TIP-TOP TUNES
In a little Spanish town / Nearness of you (Featuring Carole Carr) / Top hat / Autumn concerto (Featuring Roy E.) / Hallelujah (Featuring Carole Carr) / Signature tune / My heart stood still / There's a small hotel (Featuring Dick Ja) / Heather on the hill (Featuring Neville Williams and Joy Hoodles) / Rockin' through Dixie / Nature boy (Featuring Archie Lewis) / What is this thing called love / I'm on a see-saw (Featuring Dick Ja) / So many times I have cried over you (Featuring Derrick Francis) / When Johnny comes marching home / Begin the beguine / Isle of Innisfree (Featuring Bob Dale) / Arkansas traveller
CD _____ CDHD 135
Happy Days / '89 / Conifer.

Geremia, Paul

REALLY DON'T MIND/MY KIND OF PLACE
CD _____ FF 395CD
Flying Fish / May '93 / Roots / CM / Direct / ADA.

SELF PORTRAIT IN BLUES
CD _____ RHRCD 77
Red House / '95 / Koch / ADA.
CD _____ SHAM 1024CD
Shamrock / Apr '95 / Wellard / ADA.

Germ

GONE
CD _____ GPRCD 6
General Production Recordings / Aug '94 / Pinnacle.

Germano, Lisa

GEEK THE GIRL
CD _____ CAD 4017CD
4AD / Oct '94 / Disc.

HAPPINESS
CD _____ CAD 4005CD
4AD / Apr '94 / Disc.

Germs

GERMICIDE: LIVE AT THE WHISKEY
CD _____ RE 108CD
Reach Out International / Nov '94 / Jetstar.

Media Blitz

CD _____ CLEO 3736CD
Cleopatra / Jan '94 / Disc.

Geronimo

PEACE TO THE CHIEF
CD _____ TRP 002CD
Trechoma / Sep '95 / Plastic Head.

Gerrard, Lisa

MIRROR POOL, THE
Violina: The last embrace / La bas: Song of the drowned / Persian love song : The silver gun / Sanvean: I am your shadow / Rite / Ajhon / Glorafin / Majhnavea's music box / Largo / Werd / Laurelei / Celon / Ventelas / Swans / Nilleshna / Gloradin
CD _____ CAD 5009CD
4AD / Aug '95 / Disc.

Gerry & The Pacemakers

50 NON-STOP PARTY HITS
Let's dance / Let's twist again / Locomotion / Simon says / Singin' the blues / Y.M.C.A. / My old man's a dustman / Agadoo / Knock three times / Da doo ron ron / Hi ho silver lining / Do wah diddy diddy / Keep on running / Glad all over / I like it / How do you do it / Save the last dance / You can't get me / Young girl / Ob la di ob la da / Ticket to ride / Do you love me / I'm the one / Might as well rain until September / Most beautiful girl in the world / Raining in my heart / Roses are red / All you have to do is dream / If you leave me now / Don't let the sun catch you crying / Ferry across the Mersey / Leader of the gang / Sweet Caroline / It's a heartache / Na na hey hey / I hear you knocking / Get it on / Rockin' all over the world / Radio ga ga / Lucille / Peggy Sue / (We're gonna) Rock around the clock / Jailhouse rock / Let's have a party / Gonna be alright / Long tall Sally / C'mon everybody / Rock 'n' roll music / Great balls of fire / You'll never walk alone
CD _____ DSHCD 7011
D-Sharp / Nov '94 / Pinnacle.

EMI YEARS: GERRY & THE PACEMAKERS
How do you do it / Maybellene / I like it / Chills / Pretend / Jambalaya / You're the reason / Hello little girl / You'll never walk alone / Shot of rhythm and blues / Slow down / It's all right / I'm the one / Don't let the sun catch you crying / What would I say / I like / It's just because / You, you, you / It's gonna be alright / Ferry 'cross the Mersey / I'll wait for you / Hallelujah, I love her so / Reelin' and rockin' / Why oh why / Baby you're so good to me / Walk hand in hand / Dreams / Give all your love to me / I'll be there / La la la / Fool to myself / Girl on a swing
CD _____ CDEMS 1443
EMI / May '92 / EMI.

EP COLLECTION: GERRY & THE PACEMAKERS
How do you do it / Away from you / I like it / Chills / You'll never walk alone / Shot of rhythm and blues / You've got what I like / I'm the one / Don't let the sun catch you crying / Where have you been all my life / Maybellene / You're the reason / It's gonna be alright / I'll wait for you / Ferry 'cross the Mersey / You win again / Reelin' and rockin' / Whole lotta shakin' goin' on / Skinny Lizzie / My babe / What'd I say
CD _____ SEECD 95
See For Miles/C5 / Mar '95 / Pinnacle.

GERRY & THE PACEMAKERS
CD _____ GRF 191
Tring / Jan '93 / Tring / Prism.

GERRY & THE PACEMAKERS
CD _____ KLMCD 045
Scratch / Nov '94 / BMG.

VERY BEST OF GERRY & THE PACEMAKERS
How do you do it / I like it / It's gonna be alright / I'll be there / Girl on a swing / Come back to me / When, oh when / Don't let the sun catch you crying / You'll never walk alone / I'm the one / Walk hand in hand / La la la / It's all right / Give all your love to me / Hallelujah, I love her so / Ferry 'cross the Mersey
CD _____ CDMFP 5654
Music For Pleasure / Mar '94 / EMI.

Gershwin, George

20 INTRUMENTAL GREATS
But not for me / Embraceable you / Fascinating rhythm / Foggy day / I got rhythm / It ain't necessarily so / Let's call the whole thing off / Liza (all the clouds'll roll away) / Man I love / Nice work if you can get it / Shall we dance / Someone to watch over me / 'S wonderful / They can't take that away from me / Who cares / Long ago and far away / Summertime / There's a boat dat's leavin' soon for New York / Oh I can't sit down / Somebody loves me
CD _____ CDGRF 108
Tring / '93 / Tring / Prism.

GEORGE GERSHWIN PLAYS GEORGE GERSHWIN

Rhapsody in blue / Hang on to me / Fascinating rhythm / Half of it dearie blues / I'd rather charleston / Sweet and low down / That certain feeling / Looking for a boy / Then do we dance / Do do do / Someone to watch over me / Clap yo' hands / Maybe / My one and only / Three preludes / Andante / 'S wonderful/Funny face / Rhapsody in blue (2) / American in Paris / It ain't necessarily so / Buzzard song / Summertime / Bess, you is my woman now / My man's gone now / Concerto in F (Third movement) / I got rhythm/Of thee I sing
CD Set _____ GEMM CDS 9483
Pearl / Mar '91 / Harmonia Mundi.

GEORGE GERSHWIN, THE ONE & ONLY (Various Artists)
When do we dance / I got plenty o' nuttin' / Embraceable you / Half of it dearie blues / 'S Wonderful / Man I love / Swanee / I'll build a stairway to paradise / I was doing all right / I got rhythm / Someone to watch over me / Liza (All the clouds'll roll away) / Love walked in / Nice work if you can get it / They can't take that away from me / Oh Lady be good / But not for me / Let's call the whole thing off / Summertime / Somebody loves me / Andante
CD _____ PAR 2033
Parade / Sep '94 / Koch / Cadillac.

GERSHWIN PLAYS GERSHWIN: THE PIANO ROLLS #1
CD _____ 7559792872
Elektra Nonesuch / Jul '94 / Warner Music.

GERSHWIN PLAYS GERSHWIN: THE PIANO ROLLS #2
CD _____ 7559793702
Elektra Nonesuch / Nov '95 / Warner Music.

RHAPSODY IN BLUE
Rhapsody in blue / American in Paris / Swanee / Walking the dog / Let's call the whole thing off / Somebody loves me / Our love is here to stay / 'S Wonderful / Embraceable you / Oh Lady be good
CD _____ BCD 106
Biograph / Jul '91 / Wellard / ADA / Hot Shot / Jazz Music / Cadillac / Direct.

S'MARVELLOUS (Gershwin, George & Ira)
CD _____ 5216582
Verve / Feb '94 / PolyGram.

S'WONDERFUL
CD _____ 5139282
Verve / Apr '92 / PolyGram.

TRIBUTE TO GEORGE GERSHWIN, A (Various Artists)
CD _____ 4716812
Sony Jazz / Jan '95 / Sony.

TWO SIDES OF GEORGE GERSHWIN, THE
Rhapsody in blue / Three piano preludes / Andante / American in Paris / Sweet and low down / That certain feeling / Looking for a boy / When do we dance / Do do do / Someone to watch over me / Clap yo' hands / Maybe / My one and only / 'S wonderful / Funny face
CD _____ DHDL 101
Halcyon / Oct '91 / Jazz Music / Wellard / Swift / Harmonia Mundi / Cadillac.

Gertz, Bruce

BLUEPRINT (Gertz, Bruce Quartet)
CD _____ FRLCD 017
Freelance / Nov '92 / Harmonia Mundi / Cadillac / Koch.

Gessinger, Nils

DUCKS 'N' COOKIES
Duck 'n' cookies / Angel / Late nite / Mind overload / Nighttalk / Pem pem / Central Park / Casacajun girl / Smoothin' / Nilas / Afif / Bobo's blues / Almost seven / Friends and gloves
CD _____ GRP 96302
GRP / Jan '96 / BMG / New Note.

Gettel, Michael

ART OF NATURE, THE
Light of the land / When all is quiet (she dreams if horses) / Watershed / Shelter / Fire from the sky / Solace / Where eagles soar / Midsummer / Crosswind
CD _____ ND 63032
Narada / Jul '95 / New Note / ADA.

KEY, THE
Waiting / Turning of a key / Breaking the silence / When hearts collide / Search / Glimmer of hope / Broken / Light of a candle / Letting go / Awakening / Through the doorway
CD _____ ND 63027
Narada / Jun '94 / New Note / ADA.

SKYWATCHING
Anasazi Roads / Skywatching / Windows and walls / Prelude / Sacred side (in ruins) / Wellspring / Prelude: Kiva / Sipapu / Tekohananae (to the morning) / Prelude: Stillness / Scent of rain / Where the road meets the sky

CD _____ ND 63025
Narada / May '93 / New Note / ADA.

Getz, Stan

'ROUND MIDNIGHT
CD _____ JHR 73542
Jazz Hour / May '93 / Target/BMG / Jazz
Music / Cadillac.

ACADEMY OF JAZZ (Getz, Stan & Bob Brookmeyer)
CD _____ COD 024
Jazz View / Mar '92 / Harmonia Mundi.

ANOTHER WORLD
Pretty city / Keep dreaming / Sabra / Anna
/ Another world / Sum, sum / Willow weep
for me / Blue Serge / Brave little Pernille /
Club Seven and other places
CD _____ 4715132
Sony Jazz / Jan '95 / Sony.

APASIANADO
Apasionado / Coba / Waltz for Stan / Es-
panola / Madrugada / Amorous cat / Mid-
night ride / Lonely Lady
CD _____ 3952972
A&M / Aug '90 / PolyGram.

ARTISTRY OF STAN GETZ VOL. 2, THE
CD Set _____ 5173302
Verve / Jan '93 / PolyGram.

AT LARGE VOL.1
CD _____ JUCD 2001
Jazz Unlimited / Jan '89 / Wellard /
Cadillac.

AT LARGE VOL.2
CD _____ JUCD 2002
Jazz Unlimited / Dec '91 / Wellard /
Cadillac.

AT THE OPERA HOUSE (Getz, Stan & J J Johnson)
Billie's bounce / My funny valentine / Crazy
rhythm / Blues in the closet / Yesterdays /
It never entered my mind
CD _____ 831 272-2
Verve / Jan '93 / PolyGram.

BEST OF TWO WORLDS
CD _____ 4715112
Sony Jazz / Jan '95 / Sony.

BIG BAND BOSSA NOVA
CD _____ 8257712
Verve / Jan '93 / PolyGram.

BIRDLAND SESSIONS 1952 (Getz, Stan Quintet)
CD _____ FSRCD 149
Fresh Sound / Dec '90 / Jazz Music /
Discovery.

BLUE SKIES
Spring is here / Antigny / Easy living / There
we go / Blue skies / How long has this been
going on
CD _____ CCD 4676
Concord Jazz / Dec '95 / New Note.

BOSSA NOVA YEARS
CD Set _____ 8236112
Verve / Jan '90 / PolyGram.

BROTHERS, THE
CD _____ OJCCD 008
Original Jazz Classics / Apr '87 / Wellard /
Jazz Music / Cadillac / Complete/Pinnacle.

CAPTAIN MARVEL
CD _____ 4684122
Sony Jazz / Jan '95 / Sony.

CHILDREN OF THE WORLD
Don't cry for me Argentina / Children of the
world / Livin' it up / Street tattoo / Hop
scotch / On rainy afternoons / You, me and
the spring / Summer poem / Dreamer /
Around the day in eighty minutes
CD _____ 4688112
Sony Jazz / Jan '95 / Sony.

DOLPHIN,THE (Getz, Stan Quartet)
Time for love / Joy Spring / Dolphin / Close
enough for love (Theme for the film
'Agatha'.)
CD _____ CCD 4158
Concord Jazz / Jul '87 / New Note.

DYNASTY
Dum dum / Ballad for Leo / Our kind of Sabi
/ Mona / Emmanuelle theme / Invitation /
Ballad for my dad / Song Martine / Dynasty
CD Set _____ 839 117-2
Verve / Jan '93 / PolyGram.

EARLY STAN (With Jimmy Raney & Terry Gibbs)
Motion / Lee / Michelle / T and S / Signal /
Round Midnight / Terry's tune (original, al-
ternate and alternate two) / Cuddles
(Speedway)
CD _____ OJCCD 654-2
Original Jazz Classics / Apr '93 / Wellard /
Jazz Music / Cadillac / Complete/Pinnacle.

ESSENTIAL STAN GETZ, THE
Ligia / Lester left town / Blue Serge / Hop-
scotch / Anna / Captain Marvel / What am
I here for / Lush life / Double rainbow / Pea-
cocks / La Fiesta
CD _____ 4715182
Columbia / Jul '93 / Sony.

GETZ/GILBERTO 2 (Getz, Stan & Joao Gilberto)
CD _____ 519800-2
Verve / Dec '93 / PolyGram.

HIGHLIGHTS
Stella by starlight / Exactly like you / It don't
mean a thing if it ain't got that swing /
Handful of stars / Wee (Allen S Alley) / Bal-
lad / You're blase / My funny valentine /
Round Midnight / Desafinado / Manha de
carnaval / Girl from Ipanema / Corcovado /
Melinda
CD Set _____ 847 430-2
Polydor / May '91 / PolyGram.

IMMORTAL CONCERTS (Stan Getz meets Joao & Astrud Gilberto) (Getz, Stan, Joao Gilberto & Astrud Gilberto)
Corcovado / O Pato / It might as well be
Spring / Samba da minha terra / One note
samba / Tonight I shall sleep / Bim bom /
Singing song / Telephone song / Here's that
rainy day / Eu e voce / Rosa moreno /
Grandfather's waltz / Only trust your heart
/ Um abraco no bonfa / Stan's blues / Med-
itation / Summertime / Six mix pix flix
CD _____ GOJCD 53021
Giants Of Jazz / Jun '88 / Target/BMG /
Cadillac.

IN CONCERT (Getz, Stan, Joe Farrell, Paul Horn & Mike Garson)
Heartplace / Kali-au / Chappaqua / Nature
boy / 500 miles high / Lady Day / Autumn
leaves / Billie's bounce
CD _____ CDGATE 7022
Kingdom Jazz / '89 / Kingdom.

JAZZ MASTERS
CD _____ 519823-2
Verve / May '94 / PolyGram.

JAZZ MASTERS (Getz, Stan & Dizzy Gillespie)
CD _____ 5218522
Verve / Feb '94 / PolyGram.

JAZZ PORTRAITS (Getz, Stan, Joao Gilberto & Astrud Gilberto)
Corcovado / It might as well be spring / Eu
e voce / Girl from Ipanema (Garota de Ipa-
nema) / O pato (the duck) / Um abraco no
bonfa / Meditation / Here's that rainy day /
Samba de minha terra / One note samba /
Telephone song / Only trust your heart /
Stan's blues / Bim bom / Rosa morena /
Singing song
CD _____ CD 14514
Jazz Portraits / May '94 / Jazz Music.

JAZZ SAMBA (Getz, Stan & Charlie Byrd)
Desafinado / Samba dees days / O Pato /
Samba triste / Samba de uma nota so / E
luxo so / Baia
CD _____ 810 061-2
Verve / Apr '89 / PolyGram.

LIVE AT MONTMARTRE VOL. 1
CD _____ SCCD 31073
Steeplechase / '90 / Impetus.

LIVE AT MONTMARTRE VOL. 2
CD _____ SCCD 31074
Steeplechase / '90 / Impetus.

LIVE FROM 1952-1955
CD _____ LS 2911
Landscape / Nov '92 / THE.

LIVE IN EUROPE
CD Set _____ JWD 102304
JWD / Nov '94 / Target/BMG.

LIVE, VOL. 1
CD _____ CDJJ 617
Jazz & Jazz / Jan '92 / Target/BMG.

LYRICAL STAN GETZ, THE
Willow weep for me / La fiesta / Captain
Marvel / Ligia / Misty / Lover man
CD _____ 4608192
Sony Jazz / Jan '95 / Sony.

MASTER OF SAX
Autumn leaves / Billie's bounce / Heart
place / Kali-au / Chappaqua
CD _____ 722009
Scorpio / Sep '92 / Complete/Pinnacle.

MASTER, THE
Summer night / Raven's wood / Lover man
/ Invitation
CD _____ 471512 2
Columbia / Nov '93 / Sony.

MOVE
CD _____ NI 4005
Natasha / Jun '93 / Jazz Music / ADA /
CM / Direct / Cadillac.

NATURE BOY VOL.2
CD _____ JHR 73554
Jazz Hour / Jan '93 / Target/BMG / Jazz
Music / Cadillac.

NEW COLLECTION
Four brothers / Lush life / I've grown ac-
customed to your face / Sum Sum / Skylark
/ Captain Marvel / Willow weep for me /
Who cares
CD _____ 472993 2
Columbia / May '93 / Sony.

NOBODY ELSE BUT ME
CD _____ 521660-2
Verve / Nov '94 / PolyGram.

OPUS DE BOP
Opus de bop / Running water / Don't worry
'bout me / And the angels swing / Fool's
fancy / Be bop in pastel / Ray's idea / Bom-
bay / Eb bob / Goin' to Minton's / Fat girl /
Ice freezes red
CD _____ CY 78993
Savoy Jazz / Nov '95 / Conifer / ADA.

PEACOCKS, THE (Stan Getz Presents Jimmy Rowles) (Getz, Stan & Jimmy Rowles)
I'll never be the same / Lester left town /
Body and soul / What am I here for / Ser-
enade to Sweden / Chess players / Mosaic
/ Peacocks / My buddy / Hour of parting /
Rose Marie / This is all I ask / Skylark /
Would you like to take a walk
CD _____ 475697 2
Columbia / Feb '94 / Sony.

PEOPLE TIME (Getz, Stan & Kenny Barron)
East of the sun and west of the moon /
Night and day / I'm okay / Like someone in
love / Stablemates / I remember Clifford /
Gone with the wind / First song / There is
no greater love / Surrey with the fringe on
top / People time / Softly as in a morning
sunrise / Hush-a-bye / Soul eyes
CD Set _____ 5101342
Verve / Mar '92 / PolyGram.

PURE GETZ (Getz, Stan Quartet)
On the up and up / Blood count / Very early
/ Sippin' at bells / I wish I knew / Come rain
or come shine / Tempus fugit
CD _____ CCD 4188
Concord Jazz / Dec '86 / New Note.

QUARTETS
CD _____ OJCCD 121
Original Jazz Classics / Feb '93 / Wellard /
Jazz Music / Cadillac / Complete/Pinnacle.

RARE DAWN SESSIONS
CD _____ BCD 132
Biograph / Oct '94 / Wellard / ADA / Hot
Shot / Jazz Music / Cadillac / Direct.

RARE RECORDINGS AND COLLECTIBLES (The Golden Age of Jazz)
CD _____ JZCD 363
Suisa / May '92 / Jazz Music / THE.

ROOST YEARS, THE (The Best Of Stan Getz)
Gone with the wind / Yesterdays / Hershey
Bar / Imagination / Split kick / It might as
well be Spring / Parker '51 / Signal / Every-
thing happens to me / Budo / Potter's luck
/ Wild wood / Autumn leaves / Lullaby of
Birdland / Moonlight in Vermont / Some-
times I'm happy
CD _____ CDROU 1047
Roulette / Oct '91 / EMI.

ROUND MIDNIGHT
CD _____ JD 1266
Koch / Nov '94 / Koch.

SILVER COLLECTION, THE (Getz, Stan & Oscar Peterson)
I want to be happy / Pennies from heaven
/ Ballad medley: Bewitched bothered and
bewildered / Ballad medley: I don't know
why I just do / Ballad medley: How long has
this been going on / Ballad medley: I can't
get started / Ballad medley: Polka dots and
moonbeams / I'm glad there is you / Tour's
end / I was doing all right / Bronx blues /
Three little words / Detour ahead / Sunday
CD _____ 827 826-2
Polydor / '86 / PolyGram.

SONG AFTER SUNDOWN, A (Getz, Stan & Arthur Fiedler)
Love is for the very young / Song after sun-
down / Three ballads for Stan / Where do
you go / Tanglewood concerto / Girl from
Ipanema
CD _____ ND 86284
Bluebird / Oct '94 / BMG.

SPRING IS HERE
How about you / You're blase / Easy living
/ Sweet Lorraine / Old devil moon / I'm old
fashioned / Spring is here
CD _____ CCD 4500
Concord Jazz / Mar '92 / New Note.

STAN GETZ (2) (Getz, Stan/Jimmy Raney/Al Haig/Teddy Kotick)
CD _____ CD 53113
Giants Of Jazz / Jun '92 / Target/BMG /
Cadillac.

STAN GETZ AT THE SHRINE
CD _____ 5137532
Verve / Jan '93 / PolyGram.

STAN GETZ PLAYS
CD _____ 8335352
Verve / Sep '93 / PolyGram.

STAN GETZ QUARTET & QUINTET: 1950-52
CD _____ CD 53137
Giants Of Jazz / Nov '92 / Target/BMG /
Cadillac.

STAN GETZ WITH LAURINDO ALMEIDA
CD _____ 8231492
Verve / Jan '93 / PolyGram.

SWEET RAIN
Litha / O grande amor / Sweet rain / Con
Alma / Windows / There will never be an-
other you
CD _____ 8150542
Verve / Jan '93 / PolyGram.

WITH CAL TJADER SEXTET (Getz, Stan Sextet)
CD _____ OJCCD 275-2
Original Jazz Classics / Feb '92 / Wellard /
Jazz Music / Cadillac / Complete/Pinnacle.

Ghetto Mafia

DRAW THE LINE
CD _____ FTR 4184CD
Ichiban / May '94 / Koch.

Ghiglioni, Tiziana

CANTA LUIGI TENCO
CD _____ W 60-2
Philology / Apr '94 / Harmonia Mundi /
Cadillac.

I'LL BE AROUND (Ghiglioni, Tiziana, Enrico Rava & Mal Waldron)
CD _____ 121256-2
Soul Note / Jun '91 / Harmonia Mundi /
Wellard / Cadillac.

SOUNDS OF LOVE
Beautiful singing / My old flame / All of me
/ Ruby my dear / Naima / Sound of love / I
remember you / My funny valentine /
Straight no chaser
CD _____ 1210562
Soul Note / Nov '90 / Harmonia Mundi /
Wellard / Cadillac.

Ghorwane

MAJURUGENTA
Muthimba / Majurugenta / Matarlatanta /
Xai-xai / Mavabwyi / Sathuma / Rukuku /
Terehuma / Akuhanha
CD _____ CDRW 29
Realworld / Jul '93 / EMI / Sterns.

Ghost

WHEN YOU'RE DEAD
CD _____ BFTP 005CD
UFO / May '91 / Pinnacle.

Ghostings

LIPS LIKE RED
CD _____ SPV 08561772
SPV / Aug '95 / Plastic Head.

Ghoststorm

FROZEN IN FIRE
CD _____ BMCD 65
Black Mark / May '95 / Plastic Head.

Ghriallais, Nora

NATIVE CONNEMARA IRISH SINGING
CD _____ NGCD 001
Claddagh / May '94 / ADA / Direct.

Giammarco, Maurizio

HORNITHOLOGY (Giammarco, Maurizio Quartet)
Old home / Sky walker / End of a bop affair
/ No Spanish night / Arboreal code / Un-
expected flight / Voce vai ver
CD _____ CDSGP 040
Prestige / Feb '93 / Total/BMG.

INSIDE (Giammarco, Maurizio Quartet)
CD _____ 121254-2
Soul Note / Jan '94 / Harmonia Mundi /
Wellard / Cadillac.

Gianelli, Fred

TELEPATHIC WISDOM VOLUME 1
Acid diji 3 / Salacious / Fox hunt / Precog-
nition / Eloquence / Clairvoyance / Fingered
/ Kooky scientist / Painkiller / E.O.D. / Ex-
celsior / Sleeps with the foxes / Acid diji 2
CD _____ SUPER 2025CD
Superstition / Feb '95 / Vital / SRD.

Giant

LAST OF THE RUNAWAYS
I'm a believer / Innocent days / I can't get
close enough / I'll see you in my dreams /
No way out / Shake me up / It takes two /
Stranger to me / Hold back the night / Love
welcome home / Big pitch
CD _____ CDA 5272
A&M / Apr '90 / PolyGram.

Giant Sand

BACKYARD BARBECUE BROADCAST
CD _____ 379142
Koch International / Jan '96 / Koch.

BEST OF GIANT SAND VOLUME 2, THE
Can't find love / Get to leave / Town with a
little or no pity / Dreamville New Mexico /
October anywhere / Almost the politicians
wife / Badlands / Christmas Day (maybe it'll
snow) / Is anyone in a cage / Who am I /
Death dying and channel 5 / Sandman / Sisters
and brothers / Sage advice / Love like a
train / Trickle down system

CD _____ **GSCD 2**
Demon / Jul '95 / Pinnacle / ADA.

CENTRE OF THE UNIVERSE
CD _____ **OUT 1092**
Brake Out / Nov '92 / Vital.

GIANT SONGS (Best Of Giant Sand)
Down on town / Valley of rain / Thin line man / Body of water / Moon over Memphis / Uneven light of day / Big rock / One man's woman, no man's land / Mountain of love / Curse of a thousand flames / Barrio / Graveyard / Heartland / Underground train / Bigger than that / Wearing the robes of bible black / Fingernail moon, barracuda and me
CD _____ **GSCD 1**
Demon / Jul '89 / Pinnacle / ADA.

LONG STEM RANT
Unfinished love / Sandman / Bloodstone / Searchlight / Smash jazz / Sucker in a cage / Patsy does Dylan / It's long 'bout now / Lag craw / Loving cup / Paved road to Berlin / Anthem / Picture shows / Drum and guitar / Get to leave / Searchlight cha cha (CD only) / Return of the big red guitar (CD only) / Stuck dog (CD only) / Real gone blue guitar (CD only) / Jig is up (CD only)
CD _____ **HMS 148 2**
Homestead / May '93 / SRD.

LOVE SONGS
CD _____ **FIENDCD 129**
Demon / Sep '90 / Pinnacle / ADA.

PURGE & SLOUCH
CD _____ **OUT 115-2**
Brake Out / Nov '94 / Vital.

RAMP
CD _____ **R 2762**
Rough Trade / Oct '91 / Pinnacle.

STORM
Town where no town belongs / Back to black and grey / Bigger than that / Right makes right / Three sixes / Replacement / Storm / Was is a big word / Town with little or no pity / Weight
CD _____ **FIENDCD 115**
Demon / Sep '90 / Pinnacle / ADA.

STROMAUSFALL
CD _____ **RTS 7**
Return To Sender / Nov '94 / Direct / ADA.

SWERVE
Trickle down system / Dream stay / Former versions of ourselves / Angels at night / Can't find love / Swerver / Sisters and brothers / Swerving / Every grain of sand / Some kind of (cd only) / Swervette (cd only) / Final swerve (CD only)
CD _____ **FIENDCD 204**
Demon / Oct '90 / Pinnacle / ADA.

Giants Causeway

IS THERE ANYWAY
CD _____ **MASSCD 070**
Massacre / Aug '95 / Plastic Head.

Gibb, Andy

GREATEST HITS: ANDY GIBB
I just want to be your everything / Thicker than water / Shadow dancing / Everlasting love / Don't throw it all away / Time is time / Me / Will you still love me tomorrow / After dark / Desire
CD _____ **5115852**
Polydor / Jul '94 / PolyGram.

Gibb, Robin

HOW ALONG ARE YOU
Juliet / How old are you / In and out of love / Kathy's gone / Don't stop the night / Another lonely night in New York / Danger / He can't love you / Hearts on fire / I believe in miracles
CD _____ **810896-2**
Polydor / Apr '94 / PolyGram.

SECRET AGENT
Boys (do fall in love) / In your diary / Rebecca / Secret agent / Living in another world / X-ray eyes / King of fools / Diamonds
CD _____ **821 797-2**
Polydor / Jul '84 / PolyGram.

Gibbons, Carroll

BRIGHTER THAN THE SUN (Gibbons, Carroll & Savoy Hotel Orpheans)
You're gonna lose your gal / One morning in May / May I / Beat o' my heart / So help me / I saw stars / For all we know / All my life / You're the kind of a baby for me / Kiss by kiss / Sailin' on the Robert E. Lee / One hour with you / What makes you so adorable / After tonight we say goodbye / I wish I knew a bigger word than love / What more can I ask / Brighter than the sun / It's gonna be you / Oceans of time
CD _____ **CDSVL 174**
Saville / Apr '93 / Conifer.

CARROLL GIBBONS WITH THE SAVOY HOTEL ORPHEANS
On the air / Sweet as a song / With thee I swing / Let me give my happiness to you / Three wishes / I need you / Certain age /

Gibbs, Mike

BIG MUSIC (Gibbs, Mike Orchestra)
Wall to wall / Pride aside / Kosasa / Almost ev'ry day / Watershed / Mopsus / Adult / Pride outside
CD _____ **CDVE 27**
Venture / Oct '88 / EMI.

BY THE WAY (Gibbs, Mike Orchestra)
Beauteous being / Blueprint / To Lady Mac: In sympathy / Something similar / World without / Rain before it falls / Jeunesse / Roses are red / Turn of the century / Out of the question / Just a head/Fanfare
CD _____ **AHUM 016**
Ah-Um / Nov '93 / New Note / Cadillac.

ONLY CHROME WATER FALL ORCHESTRA (Gibbs, Mike Orchestra)
To Lady Mac: In retrospect / Nairam / Blackgang / Antique / Undergrowth / Tunnel of love / Unfinished sympathy
CD _____ **BGOCD 273**
Beat Goes On / May '95 / Pinnacle.

Gibbs, Terry

DREAM BAND
CD _____ **CCD 76472**
Contemporary / Jun '95 / Jazz Music / Cadillac / Pinnacle / Wellard.

DREAM BAND #2 (The Sundown Sessions)
CD _____ **CCD 7652**
Contemporary / Jun '95 / Jazz Music / Cadillac / Pinnacle / Wellard.

DREAM BAND #3 (Flying Home)
CD _____ **CCD 7654**
Contemporary / Jun '95 / Jazz Music / Cadillac / Pinnacle / Wellard.

DREAM BAND #4 (The Main Stem)
CD _____ **CCD 7656**
Contemporary / Jun '95 / Jazz Music / Cadillac / Pinnacle / Wellard.

DREAM BAND #5 (The Big Cat)
CD _____ **CCD 7657**
Contemporary / Nov '95 / Jazz Music / Cadillac / Pinnacle / Wellard.

KINGS OF SWING (Gibbs, Terry & Buddy De Franco/Herb Ellis)
Seven come eleven / Soft winds / Man I love / Undecided / Body and soul / Just one of those things / Stompin' at the savoy / These foolish things (Remind me of you) / Air mail special
CD _____ **CCD 140672**
Pablo / Jan '94 / Jazz Music / Cadillac / Complete/Pinnacle.

MEMORIES OF YOU (Gibbs, Terry & Buddy De Franco/Herb Ellis)
Flying home / Rose room / I surrender dear / Dizzy spells / Don't be that way / Poor butterfly / Avalon / Memories of you / After you've gone
CD _____ **CCD 14066**
Contemporary / Apr '94 / Jazz Music / Cadillac / Pinnacle / Wellard.

Gibson, Andy

MAINSTREAM JAZZ
Blueprint / I got nothing but you / Bedroom eyes / Give the lady what she wants most
CD _____ **74321218322**
RCA / Jan '95 / BMG.

Gibson, Anthony T

COMPLETE ANTHONY T. GIBSON, THE
Aint no way / Say it isn't so / Special kinda woman / My heart is in your hands / Sitting in the park / I want a lover / If you need someone / Girl on the sidelines / Is it for real / Take the money and run / At this moment / Searching for romance
CD _____ **AT CD-016**
About Time / Apr '93 / Target/BMG.

Gibson Brothers

HITS
CD _____ **KWEST 5408**
Disky / Feb '93 / THE / BMG / Discovery / Pinnacle.

Gibson, Banv

JAZZ BABY (Gibson, Banv & NOR Hot Jazz)
CD _____ **SOSCD 1073**
Stomp Off / Aug '90 / Jazz Music / Wellard.

Gibson, Bob

REVISITED (Gibson, Bob & Hamilton Camp)
CD _____ **FE 1413**
Folk Era / Dec '94 / CM / ADA.

Gibson, Clifford

BEAT YOU DOING IT
CD _____ **YAZCD 1027**
Yazoo / Mar '92 / CM / ADA / Roots / Koch.

Gibson, Debbie

ANYTHING IS POSSIBLE
Another brick falls / Anything is possible / Reverse psychology / One step ahead / It wasn't been my boy / Can't hear me now / One hand, one heart / Sure / Negative energy / Mood swings / Where have you been / (This so called) Miracle / Stand your ground (MC, CD only) / Deep down (MC, CD only) / Try (MC, CD only) / In his mind (MC, CD only)
CD _____ **7567821627**
Atlantic / Mar '91 / Warner Music.

BODY MIND SOUL
Love or money / Do you have it in your heart / Free me / Shock your mama / Losin' myself / How can this be / When I say no / Little birdy / Kisses 4 one / Tear down these walls / Goodbye
CD _____ **756782451-2**
Atlantic / Apr '93 / Warner Music.

OUT OF THE BLUE
Out of the blue / Staying together / Only in my dreams / Foolish beat / Red hot / Wake up to love / Shake your love / Fallen angel / Play the field / Between the lines
CD _____ **K 781 780 2**
Atlantic / Sep '87 / Warner Music.

Gibson, Don

BEST OF DON GIBSON
CD _____ **7432121848-2**
Arista / Jun '94 / BMG.

COLLECTION: DON GIBSON
Oh lonesome me / Snap your fingers / Just one time / Take these chains from my heart / Sweet dreams / Release me / Blue blue day / Funny familiar forgotten feelings / Kaw-liga / There goes my everything / Touch the morning / Too soon to know / Cold cold heart / I'm all wrapped up in you / You've still got a place in my heart / Sweet sensuous sensation / Why you been gone so long / I can't stop loving you / Lonesome number one / You win again / Mansion on the hill / Legend in my time / Yesterday just passed my way again / Fan the flame feed the fire
CD _____ **CCSCD 158**
Castle / Feb '93 / BMG.

DON GIBSON THE SINGER, THE SONGWRITER (1949-1960)
I lost my love / Why am I so lonely / Automatic mamma / Cloudy skies / I love no one but you / Carolina breakdown / Roses are red / Wiggle wag / Dark future / Just let me love you / Blue million tears / Red lips, white lies and blue hours / Sample kisses / No shoulder to cry on / Let me stay in your arms / We're stepping out tonight / Waitin' down the road / Walkin' in the moonlight / I just love the way you tell a lie / You cast me out (forevermore) / Symptoms of love / Selfish with your kisses / Ice cold heart / Many times I've waited / Road of life alone / Run boy / Sweet dreams / I must forget you / Taller than trees / Satisfied / Wait for the light to shine / Cannan's land / Faith unlocks the door / Evening prayer / Lord I'm coming home / Climbing up the mountain / Where no one stands alone / Known only to him / My God is real / The lonesome valley / Who cares (for me) / When will this ever end / Sweet sweet girl / Stranger to me / Won't cha come back to me / Stranger to me #2 / As much / Who cares (for me) (2) / I wish it had been a dream / Ages and ages ago / Even tho' / Didn't work out did it / It's my way / Almost / Do you think / Foggy river / Midnight / Lonesome old house / Ah-ha / It happens every time / I ain't gonna waste my time / I ain't a-studyin' you baby / I'm gonna fool everybody / I believed in you / What a fool I was for you / You're the only one for me / I love you still / Everything turns out for the best / I can't leave / Sittin' here cryin' / Too soon to know / Pretty rainbow / Blue blue day / Tell it like it is / Oh lonesome me / I can't stop loving you / It has to be / Give myself a party / Look who's blue / Bad bad day / Take me as I am / Heartbreak Avenue / We could / If you don't know it / Blues in my heart / Give myself a party (2) / Don't tell me your troubles / I couldn't care less / Don't tell me your troubles (2) / Heartbreak Avenue (2) / Big hearted me / Maybe tomorrow / Everybody but me / I'm movin' on / Just one time / I may never get to heaven / Lonely Street / On the banks of the old Ponchartrain / Why don't you love me / If I can stay away / Never love again / Streets of Laredo / My love for you / My hands are tied / It only hurts for a little while / Legend in my time / Far far away / Foolish me / My tears don't show / World is waiting for the sunrise / What about me / Next voice you hear / Hurtin' inside / Time hurts (as well as it heals) / What's the reason I'm not pleasin' you / Sweet dreams (2) / Same street
CD Set _____ **BCD 15475**
Bear Family / Jan '92 / Rollercoaster / Direct / CM / Swift / ADA.

LEGEND IN MY TIME, A
Sittin' here cryin' / Blue blue day / Oh lonesome me / I can't stop loving you / Look who's blue / If you don't know it / Bad bad day / Sweet sweet girl / Give myself a party / Who cares / Didn't work out did it / Lone-

Gibbons, Steve

BIRMINGHAM TO MEMPHIS
CD _____ **AKD 019**
Linn / Apr '93 / PolyGram.

CAUGHT LIVE IN THE ACT (Gibbons, Steve Band)
CD _____ **REP 4048-WZ**
Repertoire / Aug '91 / Pinnacle / Cadillac.

DOWN IN THE BUNKER
CD _____ **REP 4047-WZ**
Repertoire / Aug '91 / Pinnacle / Cadillac.

ON THE LOOSE (Gibbons, Steve Band)
Down the road apiece / Chuck in my car / absolutely gone / Love part one / Trucker / On the loose / To be alone with you / Love 'n' peace / Like a rolling stone
CD _____ **CDMF 041**
Magnum Force / May '92 / Magnum Music Group.

STEVE GIBBONS- LIVE
CD _____ **848829**
SPV / Sep '90 / Plastic Head.

Gibbs, Joe

EXPLOSIVE ROCKSTEADY (Joe Gibbs Amalgamated '67-'73) (Various Artists)
CD _____ **CDHB 72**
Heartbeat / May '92 / Greensleeves / Jetstar / Direct / ADA.

JOE GIBBS RARE GROOVES (Various Artists)
CD _____ **RGCD 014**
Rocky One / Nov '94 / Jetstar.

MIGHTY TWO, THE (Gibbs, Joe & Errol Thompson)
CD _____ **HBCD 73**
Heartbeat / Nov '92 / Greensleeves / Jetstar / Direct / ADA.

REGGAE TRAIN, THE (1968 - 1971) (Gibbs, Joe & Friends)
CD _____ **CDTRL 261**
Trojan / Sep '94 / Jetstar / Total/BMG.

Gibbs, Michael

CENTURY/CLOSE MY EYE
CD _____ **IONIC 10CD**
Mute / Jan '94 / Disc.

HARDBOILED
CD _____ **IONIC 11 CD**
Mute / Jul '93 / Disc.

IRON AND SILK
CD _____ **IONIC 7 CD**
Mute / Nov '91 / Disc.

Gibbs, Michael

EUROPEANA - JAZZPHONY NO.1 (Gibbs, Michael & Joachim Kuhn)
Castle in heaven / Black is the colour of my true love's hair / Shepherd of Breton / Ingrian rune song / Groom's sister / Norwegian psalm / There angels / Heaven has created / She moved through the fair / Crebe de chet / Midnight sun / Londonderry air / Otra jazzpana
CD _____ **92202**
Act / Mar '95 / New Note.

261

some old house / Don't tell me your troubles / I couldn't care less / Just one time /
Legend in my time / Far far away / Sweet
dreams / Sea of heartbreak / I sat back and
let it happen / Lonesome number one / I
can mend your broken heart / If you knew
me / If you don't know the sorrow / Think
of me / I'm crying inside
CD _____ BCD 15401
Bear Family / Nov '87 / Rollercoaster /
Direct / CM / Swift / ADA.

SINGER SONGWRITER 1961 – 1966
Sweet dreams / I think it's best (To forget
me) / That's how it goes / Sea of heartbreak
/ No one will ever know / Born to lose /
Beautiful dreamer / Camptown races / Fireball mail / Last letter / White silver sands /
Driftwood on the river / Lonesome road /
Above and beyond / I sat back and let it
happen / I know the score / Same old trouble / So how come (no one loves me) /
Lonesome number one / Let's fall out of
love (Tonight) / I let her get lonely / I can
mend your broken heart / For a little while /
It makes no difference now / Settin' the
woods on fire / Baby we're really in / I love
you so much it hurts / It's a sin / I'm
sorry for you my friend / This cold war with
you / Where is your heart tonight / Blue
dream / How's the world treating you / May
you never be alone / We live in two different
worlds / Old ship of zion / Then I met the
master / I'd rather have Jesus / Be ready /
Can't see myself / For old time's sake / It
was worth it all / Head over heels in love
with you / I can't stop loving you / Legend
in my time / Give myself a party / Oh lonesome me / Don't tell me your troubles /
Love has come my way / Blue blue day /
Just one time / Oh such a stranger / After
the heartache / Anything new gets old (Except my love for you) / God walks these hills
/ Do you know my Jesus / Hide me rock of
ages / Where else would I want to be / If I
can help somebody / He's everywhere /
You don't knock / When they ring the
golden bells / There she goes (Let her go) /
If you knew me / If you don't know the sor-
row / Mixed up love / There she goes /
Think of me / 'Cause I believe in you / Then
I'll be free / Love that can't be / Waltz of
regret / When your house is not a home /
Watch where you're going / You're going
away / Again / Too much hurt / Born loser
/ Wound time can't erase / Around the town
/ I'm crying inside / Dark as a dungeon /
Right away / Lovin' lies / All the world is
lonely now / Worried mind / There's a big
wheel / Take these chains from my heart /
Singin' the blues / With your love on my
mind / Address unknown / My adobe hacienda / Lonely street / Cryin' heart blues /
I can't tell my heart that / (Yes) I'm hurting
/ My whole world is hurt / You can't laugh
(At a fool) / My tomorrows (They don't come
easy) / Don't you ever get tired of hurting
me / Once a day / My friends are gonna be
strangers / Vaya con dios / Just call me
lonesome / With love on my mind / Stranger
to me / Maria Elena / Blues in my mind /
Making believe / Somebody loves you darlin' / I'd just be fool enough / Lost highway
/ Let's fall out of love / I thought I heard you
calling my name / Don't touch me / How do
you tell someone / Just out of reach / When
I stop dreaming / Cute little girls
CD Set _____ BCD 15664
Bear Family / Nov '93 / Rollercoaster /
Direct / CM / Swift / ADA.

SINGS COUNTRY FAVOURITES
Green green grass of home / There goes my
everything / Release me / (I heard that)
lonesome whistle / Cold cold heart / Kaw-
liga / She even woke me up to say goodbye
/ Sea of heartbreak / My elusive dreams /
You win again / I love you because / Window shopping / Legend in my time / Too
soon to know / Take these chains from my
heart / Lonesome number one / Sweet
dreams / I can't stop loving you / Oh, lonesome me / Funny familiar forgotten feelings
CD _____ PWK 4049
Carlton Home Entertainment / Feb '91 /
Carlton Home Entertainment.

Gibson, Lee

YOU CAN SEE FOREVER
Child is born - part 1 / Child is born - part
2 / Honeysuckle rose / Get out of town /
Love dance / He loves you / Not like this /
Lover man / It was a lover and his lass / Joy
spring / London at midnight / On a clear day
/ Authropology / Bird / Some other time /
After you've gone
CD _____ D 6005
D6 / Mar '94 / New Note.

Gibson, Steve

**BOOGIE WOOGIE ON A SATURDAY
NIGHT (Gibson, Steve & The Red Caps)**
Sidewalk shuffle / Bobbin' / Would I mind /
Always / Freehearted / How I cry / Three
dollars and ninety nine cents / D'ya eat yet,
Joe / Boogie woogie on a Saturday night /
I went to your wedding / My tzatskele (my
little darling) / Feeling kinda happy / half of
that stuff / Win or lose / Two little kisses / I
may hate myself in the morning / Wait / Big
game hunter / Shame / Do I, do I, do I /
Why don't you love me / Truthfully / When
you come to love / Fussing and fighting

(unissued) / Thing / Am I to blame / I'm to
blame / Sleepy little cowboy
CD _____ BCD 15490
Bear Family / Jul '90 / Rollercoaster / Direct
/ CM / Swift / ADA.

Gift

MULTUM IN PARVA
Little deranged puppet Pt.1 / Sinking ship /
OK this is the pops / Don't need a reason /
Restless spirit / Little deranged puppet Pt.2
/ Never too young / Social cleansing / Date
with failure / Bayond the tears / Kelly K. /
Jezebel / Little deranged puppet Pt.3
CD _____ TK 93CD068
T/K / Oct '94 / Pinnacle.

Gigantic

ANSWER
CD _____ HB 12CD
Heatblast / Mar '93 / SRD.

Gigantor

ATOMIC
CD _____ LF 186CD
Lost & Found / Nov '95 / Plastic Head.

MAGIC BOZO SPIN
CD _____ LF 074CD
Lost & Found / May '94 / Plastic Head.

SINGLES AND MORE, THE
CD _____ LF 129CD
Lost & Found / Jan '95 / Plastic Head.

Giger, Paul

SCHATTENWELT
CD _____ 4377762
ECM / Jun '93 / New Note.

Giger, Peter

JAZZZ.. (Giger, Peter Trio)
Jones bones / Sweet and short / Rue de la
tour / Frankfurt - Maputo / Zbigi / Henrick's
choice / Gaba / Sweet maya / Some drum
samba
CD _____ BW 029
B&W / Oct '93 / New Note.

Gigolo Aunts

FLIPPIN' OUT
CD _____ FIRECD 35
Fire / May '95 / Disc.

Gil, Gilberto

ACOUSTIC
A novidade / Tenho sede / Refazenda /
Realce / Esoterico / Drao / A paz (leila IV) /
Beira mar / Sampa / Parabolicamara / Se-
cret life of plants / Tenmpo rei / Expresso
2222 / Aquele abraco / Palco / Toda men-
iina baiana
CD _____ 450995324-2
Warner Bros. / May '94 / Warner Music.

ORIENTE - LIVE IN TOKYO
CD _____ WW 2211
West Wind / Feb '93 / Swift / Charly / CM
/ ADA.

PARABOLICAMARA
Madalena / Parabolicamara / Un sonho /
Buda nago / Serafim / Quero ser teu funk /
Neve na bahia / Ya olokum / O fim da his-
toria / De onde vem o baiao / Falso toureiro
/ Sina
CD _____ 9031762922
Warner Bros. / Mar '92 / Warner Music.

SOUNDS OF BRAZIL
CD _____ SOW 90121
Sounds Of The World / Jun '94 / Target/
BMG.

Gilbert & Lewis

8 TIME
CD _____ CAD 16 CD
4AD / May '88 / Disc.

Gilbert, Bruce

AB OVO
CD _____ CDSTUMM 117
Mute / Jan '96 / Disc.

SONGS FOR FRUIT
CD _____ CDSTUMM 77
Mute / Sep '91 / Disc.

THIS WAY TO THE SHIVERING MAN
Work for 'do you me? I did' / Hommage /
Shivering man / Here visit / Epitaph for Hen-
ran Brenlar / Angelfood
CD _____ STUMM 18 CD
Mute / Aug '84 / Disc.

Gilbert, Vance

EDGEWISE
CD _____ PH 1156CD
Philo / Mar '94 / Direct / CM / ADA.

FUGITIVES
CD _____ CDPH 1186
Philo / Aug '95 / Direct / CM / ADA.

Gilberto, Astrud

JAZZ MASTERS
CD _____ 5198242
Verve / Apr '93 / PolyGram.

LOOK TO THE RAINBOW
Berimbau / Once upon a summertime / Fel-
icidade / I will wait for you / Frevo / Maria
Quiet (Marie Moita) / Look at the rainbow /
Bim bom / Lugar bonito / El preciso apren-
der a ser so (learn to live alone)
CD _____ 8215562
Polydor / Sep '93 / PolyGram.

MUSIC FOR THE MILLIONS
Once I loved / Auga de beber / Meditation
/ And roses and roses / How insensitive / O
morro / Dindi / Photograph / Dreamer / So
tinha de ser com voce / All that's left is to
say goodbye
CD _____ 8234512
Verve / Feb '92 / PolyGram.

**SO AND SO (Mukai Meets Gilberto)
(Gilberto, Astrud & Shigeharu, Mukai)**
Champagne and caviar / Velas / Noos dois
/ Berimbau / Miracle of the fishes / Terra-
firme / Keep on riding / Hold me
CD _____ DC 8569
Denon / Oct '90 / Conifer.

THIS IS ASTRUD GILBERTO
Girl from Ipanema / How insensitive / Beach
samba / Fly me to the moon / Without him
/ Face I love / It's a lovely day today / Pa-
rade (A banda) / Bim bom / Shadow of your
smile / I haven't got anything better to do /
Look at the rainbow / Agua de beber / (Take
me to) Arunda
CD _____ 8250642
Verve / Sep '92 / PolyGram.

Gilberto, Joao

DESAFINADO
CD _____ CD 62024
Saludos Amigos / Jan '93 / Target/BMG.

Gildo, Rex

REX GILDO
CD _____ 16010
Laserlight / Aug '91 / Target/BMG.

Giles, Angie

SURFACE
CD _____ CID 9986
Island / Apr '92 / PolyGram.

Gill, John

CAROLINA SHOUT
CD _____ RQCD 1403
Request / Mar '94 / Jazz Music.

DOWN HOME FIVE
CD _____ SDSCD 1364
Stomp Off / Jun '94 / Jazz Music /
Wellard.

**JOHN GILL & HIS NOVELTY
ORCHESTRA OF NEW ORLEANS**
CD _____ SOSCD 1270
Stomp Off / Apr '94 / Jazz Music /
Wellard.

RAGTIME DYNASTY, THE
Original rags / Charleston rag / Sensation
rag / Pork and beans / Evergreen rag /
Pearls / Wildcat blues / Jingles / Keep your
temple / Hobson Street blues / Root beer
rag / Heliotrope bouquet / Grace and
beauty / Silver swan rag / Reindeer rag /
Chicago breakdown / Echo of spring /
Crave / Piccadilly / Eubie's classical rag
CD _____ RQCD 1405
Request / Jul '94 / Jazz Music.

Gill, Johnny

PROVOCATIVE
CD _____ 530206-2
Motown / Jan '93 / PolyGram.

Gill, Vince

I STILL BELIEVE IN YOU
Don't let our love start slippin' away / No
future in the past / Nothin' like a woman /
Tryin' to get over you / Say hello / One more
last chance / Under these conditions /
Pretty words / Love never broke anyone's
heart / I still believe in you
CD _____ MCD 10630
MCA / Sep '92 / BMG.

POCKET FULL OF GOLD
I quit / Look at us / Take your memory with
you / Pocket full of gold / Strings that tie
you down / Liza Jane / If I didn't have you
in my world / Little left over / What's a man
to do / Sparkle
CD _____ MCAD 10140
MCA / May '92 / BMG.

SOUVENIRS
CD _____ MCD 11394
MCA / Dec '95 / BMG.

WHEN LOVE FINDS YOU
Whenever you come around / You better
think twice / Real lady's man / What the
cowgirls do / When love finds you / If there's anything I can do / South side of Dixie
/ Maybe tonight / Which bridge to cross

(which bridge to burn) / If I had my way /
Go rest high on that mountain / Ain't noth-
ing like the real thing / I can't tell you why
CD _____ MCD 11078
MCA / May '94 / BMG.

Gillan, Ian

**ACCIDENTALLY ON PURPOSE (Gillan,
Ian & Roger Glover)**
Clouds and rain / Evil eye / She took my
breath away / Distocated / Via Miami / I
can't dance to that / Can't believe you
wanna leave / Lonely Avenue / Telephone
box / I thought no / Cayman Island (CD
only) / Purple people eater (CD only) / Chet
(CD only)
CD _____ CDV 2498
Virgin / Feb '88 / EMI.

CHERKAZOO & OTHER STORIES
CD _____ RPM 104
RPM / Jul '93 / Pinnacle.

CHILD IN TIME (Gillan)
Lay me down / You make me feel so good
/ Shame / My baby loves me / Down the
road / Child in time / Let it slide
CD _____ CDVM 2606
Virgin / Apr '90 / EMI.

DOUBLE TROUBLE (Gillan)
I'll rip your spine out / Restless / Men of war
/ Sunbeam / Nightmare / Hadely bop bop /
Life goes on / Born to kill / No laughing in
Heaven / No easy way / Trouble / Mutually
assured destruction / If you believe me /
New Orleans
CD _____ CDVM 3506
Virgin / Nov '89 / EMI.

FUTURE SHOCK (Gillan)
Future shock / Night ride out of Phoenix /
Ballad of the Lucitania Express / No laughing in Heaven / Sacre bleu / New Orleans /
Bite the bullet / If I sing softly / Don't want
the truth / For your dreams / One for the
road (CD only) / Bad news (CD only) / Take
a hold of yourself (CD only) / M.A.D. (CD
only) / Maelstrom (CD only) / Trouble (CD
only) / Your sister's on my list (CD only) /
Handles on her hips (CD only) / Higher and
higher (CD only) / I might as well go home
(mystic) (CD only)
CD _____ CDVIP 131
Virgin / Apr '95 / EMI.

GLORY ROAD (Gillan)
Unchain your brain / Are you sure / Time
and again / No easy way / Sleeping on the
job / On the rocks / If you believe me / Running white face city boy / Nervous / Your
mother was right (CD only) / Red watch (CD
only) / Abbey of Thelema (CD only) / Trying
to get to you (CD only) / Come tomorrow
(CD only) / Dragon's tongue (CD only) /
Post-fade brain damage (CD only)
CD _____ CDVM 2171
Virgin / Nov '89 / EMI.

**IAN GILLAN'S GARTH ROCKETT & THE
MOONSHINERS STORY (Rockett, Garth
& The Moonshiners)**
CD _____ ROHACD 3
EMI / Feb '90 / EMI.

JAPANESE ALBUM (Gillan)
CD _____ RPM 113
RPM / Jul '93 / Pinnacle.

**LIVE AT READING ROCK FESTIVAL
1980 (Gillan)**
CD _____ FRSCD 002
Raw Fruit / Dec '90 / Pinnacle.

MAGIC (Gillan)
What's the matter / Bluesy blue sea /
Caught in a trap / Long gone / Driving me
wild / Demon driver / Living a lie / You're so
right / Living for the city / Demon driver (reprise) / Breaking chains (CD only) / Fiji (CD
only) / Purple sky (CD only) / South Africa
(CD only mixes.) / John (CD only) / Helter
skelter (CD only) / Smokestack lightnin' (CD
only)
CD _____ CDVM 2238
Virgin / Nov '89 / EMI.

MR. UNIVERSE (Gillan)
Mr. Universe / Second sight / Secret of the
dance / She tears me down / Roller / Ven-
geance / Puget sound / Dead of night /
Message in a bottle / Fighting man / On the
rocks (CD only) / Bite the bullet (CD only) /
Mr. Universe (version) (CD only) / Smoke on
the water (CD only) / Lucille (CD only)
CD _____ CDVM 2589
Virgin / Mar '83 / EMI.

ROCK PROFILE
CD _____ VSOPCD 214
Connoisseur / Jul '95 / Pinnacle.

**SOLE AGENCY & REPRESENTATION
(Gillan, Ian & The Javelins)**
Too much monkey business / It'll be me /
You really got a hold on me / It's only make
believe / Can I get a witness / Poison Ivy /
Rave on / Blue Monday / You better move
on / Something else / Money / Love potion
no.9 / Let's dance / Roll over Beethoven
CD _____ RPM 132
RPM / Aug '94 / Pinnacle.

**TROUBLE - THE BEST OF GILLAN
(Gillan)**
Trouble / New Orleans / Fighting man / Liv-
ing for the city / Helter skelter / Mr. Universe

/ Telephone box / Dislocated / Sleeping on the job / M.A.D. (Mutually Assured Destruction) / No laughing in heaven / Nightmare / Restless / Purple sky / Born to kill (Live) / Smoke on the water (Live)
CD _____ CDVIP 108
Virgin VIP / Nov '93 / Carlton Home Entertainment / THE / EMI.

VERY BEST OF GILLAN (Gillan)
Sleeping on the job / Secret of the dance / Time and again / Vengeance / Roller / M.A.D. / Dead of night / Nightmare / Don't want the truth / If you believe me / Trouble / New Orleans / Living for the city / Restless / No laughing in heaven / Smoke on the water (live)
CD _____ MCCD 032
Music Club / Sep '91 / Disc / THE / CM.

Gillespie, Dana

ANDY WARHOL
CD _____ GY 001
Trident / Mar '94 / Pinnacle.

BLUES IT UP
Lotta what you got / My man stands out / Fat Sam from Birmingham / Sweet meat / Ugly papa / Sweets / King size papa / One hour mama / 300 pounds of joy / Don't you make me high / Big ten inch record / Below the belt / Long lean baby / Tongue in cheek / Meat balls / Wasn't that good / Joe's joint / Organ grinder / Come on (if you're coming) / Nosey Joe / It ain't the meat / Sixty minute man / Snatch and grab it
CD _____ CDCHD 950
Ace / Aug '00 / Pinnacle / Cadillac / Complete/Pinnacle.

HOT STUFF
Lovin' machine / Pencil thin Papa / Easy does it / Meat on their bones / Raise a little hell / Empty bed blues / Play with your poodle / Big fat Mamas are back in style again / Too many drivers / Sailor's delight / Built for comfort / Fat meat is good meat / Hot stuff / Tall skinny Papa / Big car / Spoonful / Diggin' my potatoes / Mainline baby / Pint size Papa / Horizontal boogie
CD _____ CDCHD 605
Ace / Nov '95 / Pinnacle / Cadillac / Complete/Pinnacle.

METHODS OF RELEASE
Politics of ecstasy / Overseas male / Oh what a night / Your love is in me / Method of release / Love is a strange thing / Sun arise / Let's get wet / Divine romance / Still around / Circle is complete
CD _____ 29031022
Bellaphon / Mar '94 / New Note.

Gillespie, Dizzy

AFRO-CUBAN JAZZ MOODS (Gillespie, Dizzy & Machito)
Oro, incienso y mirra / Calidoscopico / Pensativo / Exuberante
CD _____ OJCCD 447
Original Jazz Classics / Oct '92 / Wellard / Jazz Music / Cadillac / Complete/Pinnacle.

AT MONTREUX '75 (Gillespie, Dizzy Big Seven)
CD _____ OJCCD 739
Original Jazz Classics / May '93 / Wellard / Jazz Music / Cadillac / Complete/Pinnacle.

BEBOP & BEYOND PLAYS DIZZY GILLESPIE... (Gillespie, Dizzy & Benny Carter)
Win na high Hell / Manteca / I waited for you / That's Earl, brother / Con Alma / Diddy wah diddy / Father time / Rhythm man
CD _____ R2 79170
Bluemoon / Feb '92 / New Note.

BEST OF DIZZY GILLESPIE
Unicorn / Free ride / Pensavito / Exuberante / Behind the moonbeam / Shim-sham-shimmy
CD _____ CD 2405411
Pablo / Apr '94 / Jazz Music / Cadillac / Complete/Pinnacle.

BEST OF DIZZY GILLESPIE
CD _____ DLCD 4019
Dixie Live / Mar '95 / Magnum Music Group.

CHAMP, THE
Champ / Birk's works / Caravan / Time on my hands / On the sunny side of the street / Tin tin deo / Stardust / They can't take that away from me / Bluest blues / Swing low, sweet cadillac / Ooh-shoo-be-doo-bee
CD _____ SV 0174
Savoy Jazz / Apr '93 / Conifer / ADA.

COMPLETE RCA VICTOR RECORDINGS (1947-1949), THE
Manteca / Anthropology / King Porter stomp / Yours and mine / Blue rhythm fantasy / Hot mallets / 52nd Street (theme) / Night in Tunisia / Ol' man rebop / Ow / Oop-bop-a-da / Stay on it / Algo bueno (Woody 'n you) / Cool breeze / Cubana be, cubana bop / Ool-ya-koo / Minor walk / Good bait / Guarachi guaro / Duff capers / Lover come back to me / I'm beboppin' too / Swedish suite / St. Louis blues / I should care / That old black magic / You go to my head / Jump di-le ba / Dizzier and dizzier / Hey Pete / Let's eat more meat / Jumpin' and

symphony Sid / If love is trouble / In the land of oo-bla-dee / Overtime / Victory ball
CD _____ 786366528
Bluebird / Apr '95 / BMG.

DEEGEE DAYS (Savoy Sessions)
Tin tin deo / Birk's works / We love to boogie / Lady be good / Champ / I'm in a mess / School days / Swing low, sweet cadillac / Bopsie's blues / I couldn't beat the rap / Caravan / Nobody knows / Bluest blues / On the sunny side of the street / Stardust / Time on my hands / Blue skies / Umbrella man / Confessin' / Ooh-shoo-be-doo-bee / They can't take that away from me
CD _____ VGCD 650101
Vogue / Jan '93 / BMG.

DIGITAL AT MONTREUX
Christopher Columbus / I'm sitting on top of the world / Manteca / Get the booty / Kisses
CD _____ CD 2308226
Pablo / Oct '92 / Jazz Music / Cadillac / Complete/Pinnacle.

DIZ AND GETZ (Getz, Stan & Dizzy Gillespie)
It don't mean a thing if it ain't got that swing / I let a song go out of my heart / Exactly like you / It's the talk of the town / Impromptu / One alone / Girl of my dreams / Siboney (Part 1) / Siboney (Part 2)
CD _____ 833 559-2
Verve / Aug '90 / PolyGram.

DIZ MEETS STITT (Gillespie, Dizzy & Sonny Stitt)
Moon / Aug '02 / Harmonia Mundi / Cadillac.

DIZZY (Gillespie, Dizzy Big Seven)
CD _____ CD 20038
Pablo / May '86 / Jazz Music / Cadillac / Complete/Pinnacle.

DIZZY & MITCHELL-RUFF DUO (Gillespie, Dizzy & Mitchell-Ruff Duo)
CD _____ 4744172
Sony Jazz / Dec '93 / Sony.

DIZZY GILLESPIE
CD _____ CD 14554
Jazz Portraits / Jul '94 / Jazz Music.

DIZZY GILLESPIE & HIS ORCHESTRA 1928-49
CD _____ CD 53119
Giants Of Jazz / Jan '94 / Target/BMG / Cadillac.

DIZZY GILLESPIE (1946-1949)
Manteca / Good bait / Ool-ya-koo / 52nd Street (theme) / Night in Tunisia / Ol' man rebop / Anthropology / Owl / Oop-bop-a-da / Cool breeze / Cubana be, Cubana bop / Minor walk / Guarachi guaro / Duff capers / Lover come back to me / I'm beboppin' / Overtime / Victory ball / Swedish suite / St. Louis blues / Katy mo' meat / Jumpin' with Symphony Sid / In the land of oo-bla-dee
CD Set _____ ND 89763
Jazz Tribune / May '94 / BMG.

DIZZY GILLESPIE AND HIS BAND IN CONCERT (Pasadena Civic Auditorium, 1948) (Gillespie, Dizzy & His Band)
Emanon / Oll-ya-koo / Round Midnight / Stay on it / Good bait / One bass hit / I can't get started (with you) / Manteca
CD _____ GNPD 23
GNP Crescendo / Jul '95 / Silva Screen.

DIZZY GILLESPIE MEETS PHIL WOODS QUARTET
CD _____ CDSJP 250
Timeless Jazz / Jan '88 / New Note.

DIZZY GILLESPIE SEXTET (Gillespie, Dizzy Sextet)
CD _____ GOJCD 53099
Giants Of Jazz / Mar '92 / Target/BMG / Cadillac.

DIZZY GILLESPIE STORY, THE
Swing low, sweet chariot / Alone together / These are the things I love / Lullaby of the leaves / Boppin' the blues / Smoky hollow jump / On the Alamo / I found a million dollar baby / What is there to say / Interlude in C / Moody speaks / For heckiers only
CD _____ SV 0177
Savoy Jazz / Apr '93 / Conifer / ADA.

DIZZY SONGS
Afro Paris (2 Takes) / Hurry home (2 takes) / I cover the waterfront / Cripple crapple crutch / Dizzy song (Lady Bird) / Somebody loves me / She's funny that way / Wrap your troubles in dreams (2 Takes) / Sweet Lorraine / Everything happens to me / I don't know why / Always / Mon homme / Clappin' rhythm / Fais gaffe (Watch out) / Moon nocturne / This is the way / 'S Wonderful / Oo-bla-dee
CD _____ 74321154642
Vogue / Oct '93 / BMG.

DIZZY'S DIAMONDS
CD _____ 5138752
Verve / Apr '92 / PolyGram.

FREE RIDE
Unicorn / Incantation / Wrong number / Free ride / Ozone madness / Love poem for Donna / Last stroke of midnight
CD _____ OJCCD 784

Original Jazz Classics / Jun '94 / Wellard / Jazz Music / Cadillac / Complete/Pinnacle.

GIANT, THE
CD _____ 139 217
Accord / '86 / Discovery / Harmonia Mundi / Cadillac.

GILLESPIANA
CD _____ 519609-2
Verve / Dec '93 / PolyGram.

GITANES - JAZZ 'ROUND MIDNIGHT
Don't try to keep up with the Joneses / Poor Joe / Then she stopped / Barbados carnival / Jambo / Lorraine / Rumbola / Tangorine / Confusion / I can't get started (with you) / Whisper not / (There is) No greater love / Constantinople / Sea breeze
CD _____ 5100882
Verve / Oct '91 / PolyGram.

GROOVIN' HIGH
CD _____ JHR 73550
Jazz Hour / Jan '93 / Target/BMG / Jazz Music / Cadillac.

GROOVIN' HIGH
Blue 'n' boogie / Groovin' high / Dizzy atmosphere / All the things you are / Salt peanuts / Hot house / Oop bop sh'bam / That's Earl brother / Our delight / One bass hit Pt. 2 / Things to come / Ray's idea / Emanon
CD _____ SV 0152
Savoy Jazz / Apr '92 / Conifer / ADA.

IN CONCERT (24.11.65) (Gillespie, Dizzy Quintet)
CD _____ RTE 710465
RTE / May '95 / ADA / Koch.

IT DON'T MEAN A THING
It don't mean a thing if it ain't got that swing / I let a song go out of my heart / It's the talk of the town / Impromptu / Siboney / Exactly like you / Girl of my dreams
CD _____ CDSGP 062
Prestige / May '93 / Total/BMG.

JAM AT MONTREUX '77
CD _____ OJCCD 381-2
Original Jazz Classics / Feb '92 / Wellard / Jazz Music / Cadillac / Complete/Pinnacle.

JAZZ MASTERS
CD _____ 5163192
Verve / Apr '93 / PolyGram.

JAZZ MATURITY...WHERE IT'S COMING FROM (Gillespie, Dizzy & Roy Eldridge)
CD _____ OJCCD 807
Original Jazz Classics / Oct '95 / Wellard / Jazz Music / Cadillac / Complete/Pinnacle.

JIVIN' IN BEBOP
CD _____ MCD 0452
Moon / Nov '93 / Harmonia Mundi / Cadillac.

LEGENDARY BIG BAND CONCERT 1948, THE
Emanon / O ol-ua-koo / Round Midnight / Stay on it / Good bait / One bass hit / I can't get started (with you) / Manteca / Algo bueon / Afro Cuban suite / Things to come
CD _____ 655612
GNP Crescendo / Jul '91 / Silva Screen.

LIVE AT CHESTER (Gillespie, Dizzy Big Band)
CD _____ JH 1029
Jazz Hour / Jul '93 / Target/BMG / Jazz Music / Cadillac.

MANTECA
CD _____ CD 14575
Complete / Nov '95 / THE.

MEMORIAL ALBUM
CD _____ NI 4018
Natasha / May '93 / Jazz Music / ADA / CM / Direct / Cadillac.

MOST IMPORTANT RECORDINGS
CD _____ CD OFF 83056-2
Ogun / Mar '90 / Cadillac / Jazz Music / Charly.

NIGHT IN TUNISIA
CD _____ CD 53122
Giants Of Jazz / Nov '92 / Target/BMG / Cadillac.

ON THE SUNNY SIDE OF THE STREET
CD _____ MCD 077
Moon / Dec '95 / Harmonia Mundi / Cadillac.

PLEYEL CONCERT 1948 (Gillespie, Dizzy & Max Roach)
CD _____ 74321134152
Vogue / Jul '93 / BMG.

PLEYEL CONCERT 1953
Intro / Champ / Good bait / Swing low, sweet cadillac / Lady be good / Mon homme / Bluest blues / Birk's works / Ooh-shoo-bee-doo-be / They can't take that away from me / Play fiddle play / I can't get started (with you) / Embraceable you / Tin tin deo / On the sunny side of the street / School days
CD _____ 74321154662
Vogue / Oct '93 / BMG.

PROFESSOR BOP
Blue 'n' boogie / Groovin' high / Dizzy atmosphere / All the things you are / Hot

house / Oop bop sh'bam / Our delight / Things to come / Ray's idea / Emanon / Good dues blues
CD _____ LEJAZZCD 25
Le Jazz / Feb '94 / Charly / Cadillac.

QUINTET, THE
CD _____ OJCCD 044-2
Original Jazz Classics / Feb '92 / Wellard / Jazz Music / Cadillac / Complete/Pinnacle.

S'WONDERFUL
CD _____ VGCD 670508
Vogue / Jan '93 / BMG.

SCHOOL DAYS
Lady be good / Pop's confessin' / Nobody knows the trouble / Bopsie's blues / I couldn't beat the rap / School days / I'm in a mess / Umbrella man / Love me pretty baby / We love to boogie
CD _____ SV 0157
Savoy Jazz / Apr '92 / Conifer / ADA.

SHAW NUFF
CD _____ 1046700532
Discovery / May '95 / Warner Music.

SMALL GROUPS 1945-1946
CD _____ CD 56055
Jazz Roots / Mar '94 / Target/BMG.

SONNY SIDE UP (Gillespie, Dizzy & Sonny Rollins)
On the sunny side of the street / Eternal triangle / After hours / I know that you know
CD _____ 825 674-2
Polydor / Feb '87 / PolyGram.

SOUL TIME
Slewfoot / Soul Mama / Azure / Sweet stuff / Dirty dude / Partyman / Get to that / Soul time / Rutabaga pie / Gettin' down
CD _____ AAOHP 93312
Start / Dec '94 / Koch.

SUMMERTIME (Gillespie, Dizzy & Mongo Santamaria)
Virtue / Afro blue / Summertime / Mambo Mongo
CD _____ OJCCD 626-6
Original Jazz Classics / Feb '92 / Wellard / Jazz Music / Cadillac / Complete/Pinnacle.

SWING LOW SWEET CADILLAC
Swing low. sweet cadillac / Mas que nada / Something in your smile / Kush / Bye
CD _____ IMP 11782
Impulse Jazz / Feb '96 / BMG / New Note.

TO BIRD WITH LOVE
Billie's bounce / Be bop / Ornithology / Anthropology / Oo pa pa da / Diamond jubilee blues / Theme
CD _____ CD 83316
Telarc / Nov '92 / Conifer / ADA.

TO DIZ, WITH LOVE (Diamond Jubilee recordings)
Billie's bounce / Confirmation / Mood indigo / Straight no chaser / Night in Tunisia
CD _____ 83307
Telarc / May '92 / Conifer / ADA.

TRUMPET ROYALTY (25 un-released tracks)
CD _____ VJC 1009-2
Victorious Discs / Aug '90 / Jazz Music.

Gillespie, Hugh

CLASSIC
CD _____ GLCD 3066
Green Linnet / Jun '92 / Roots / CM / Direct / ADA.

Gillet & Groitor

TERRACOTA
CD _____ BEST 1056
Acoustic Music / Oct '94 / ADA.

Gillette, Steve

LIVE IN CONCERT (Gillette, Steve & Cindy Mangsen)
CD _____ BRAMBUS 199231
Brambus / Oct '94 / ADA / Direct.

Gilley, Mickey

THAT HEART BELONGS TO ME
I'm to blame / Night after night / Suzie Q / I'll make it all up to you / Breathless / Is it wrong / Lonely wine / Forgive / My babe / Turn around and look at me / She's still got a hold on you / Running out of reasons / World of our own / That heart belongs to me / I'm gonna put my love in the want ads / Without you / It's just a matter of making up my mind / New way to live / There's no one like you / You can count me missing / Still care about you / Grapevine / That's how it's gotta be / Boy who didn't pass / Fraulein / I miss you so / Just out of reach / Keepin' on / Watching the way
CD _____ CDGRF 074
Tring / Feb '93 / Tring / Prism.

Gillies, Alasdair

AMONG MY SOUVENIRS
Take me home / I dream of Jeannie with the light brown hair / Among my souvenirs / I will love you all my life / Dark o' dram / Scarlet ribbons / Scotland my home / Banners of Scotland / Bonnie Mary of Argyle / Say

you'll stay until tomorrow / Beautiful dreamer / More than yesterday / Maggie / Messin' about on the river
CD _____ CD ITV 416
Scotdisc / Dec '86 / Duncans / Ross / Conifer.

WORLD'S GREATEST PIPERS VOL. 12
2/4 Marches / Strathspey and Reel / Gaelic airs and hornpipes / 6/8 Marches / March, Strathspey and Reel / Gaelic Air and Jigs / Strathspeys and Reels / 2/4 Marches (2) / Jigs / Gaelic Airs, Strathspeys and Reels
CD _____ LCOM 5231
Lismor / Jul '94 / Lismor / Direct / Duncans / ADA.

Gillis, Brad

GILROCK RANCH
Gilrock ranch / Lions, tigers and bears / Honest to god / Slow blow / Monster breath / Shades of pomposity / Gospel / Opus win-frus / Afterthought / If looks could kill
CD _____ CDGRUB 27
Food For Thought / Jan '93 / Pinnacle.

Gillman, Jane

ONE LOOK BACK
Howlin' at the moon / Song on the radio / Song of Baltimore / Ready for the time to come / Open up / Three quarters / Falling in place / One look back / What tomorrow finds / Tell the rooster / Listen to the thunder / Elsa's tune
CD _____ GLCD 2101
Green Linnet / Oct '93 / Roots / CM / Direct / ADA.

PICK IT UP
CD _____ GLCD 1068
Green Linnet / Feb '92 / Roots / CM / Direct / ADA.

Gillum, Bill 'Jazz'

HARMONICA & WASHBOARD BLUES (1937-1940) (Gillum, Bill 'Jazz' & Washboard Sam)
CD _____ BLE 592522
Black & Blue / Dec '92 / Wellard / Koch.

JAZZ GILLUM VOL.1 - 1936-38
CD _____ DOCD 5197
Blues Document / Oct '93 / Swift / Jazz Music / Hot Shot.

JAZZ GILLUM VOL.2 - 1938-41
CD _____ DOCD 5198
Blues Document / Oct '93 / Swift / Jazz Music / Hot Shot.

JAZZ GILLUM VOL.3 - 1941-46
CD _____ DOCD 5199
Blues Document / Oct '93 / Swift / Jazz Music / Hot Shot.

JAZZ GILLUM VOL.4 - 1946-49
CD _____ DOCD 5200
Blues Document / Oct '93 / Swift / Jazz Music / Hot Shot.

KEY TO THE HIGHWAY 1935-42
CD _____ 158402
Blues Collection / Sep '95 / Discovery.

Gilmore, Jimmie Dale

AFTER AWHILE
Tonight I think I'm gonna go downtown / My mind's got a mind of its own / Treat me like a Saturday night / Chase the wind / Go to sleep alone / After a while / Number 16 / Don't be a stranger to your heart / Blue moon waltz / These blues / Midnight train / Story of you
CD _____ 7559611482
Elektra Nonesuch / Sep '91 / Warner Music.

SPINNING AROUND THE SUN
Where are you going / Santa fe thief / So I'll run / I'm so lonesome I could cry / Mobile line (France blues) / Nothing of the kind / Just a wave, reunion / I'm gonna love you / Another colorado / Thinking about you
CD _____ 7559615022
Elektra / Sep '93 / Warner Music.

Gilmore, Joey

JUST CALL ME JOEY
CD _____ WIL 4214
Wilbe / Aug '95 / Koch.

Gilmour, David

ABOUT FACE
Until we sleep / Murder / Love on the air / Blue light / Out of the blue / You know I'm right / Cruise / Let's get metaphysical / Near the end / All lovers are deranged
CD _____ CDP 746 031 2
Harvest / Aug '84 / EMI.

Gilstrap, Jim

SWING YOUR DADDY
CD _____ CHELD 1005
Start / May '89 / Koch.

SWING YOUR DADDY/LOVE TALK
Put out the fire / Special occasion / Ain't that peculiar / One more heartache / House of strangers / Take your daddy for a ride / Swing your daddy / Love talk / Hello it's me

/ Move me / Never stop your loving me (Never stop)
CD _____ NEMCD 702
Sequel / Nov '94 / BMG.

Giltrap, Gordon

BEST OF GORDON GILTRAP, THE
CD _____ CDSGP 005
Prestige / Sep '91 / Total/BMG.

GORDON GILTRAP/PORTRAIT
Gospel song / Fast approaching / Don't you feel good / Birth of spring / Won't you stay awhile Suzanne / Wilderness / Adolescent years / Saturday girl / Don't you hear your mother's voice / Ives horizon / Blyth Hill / Willow pattern / Portrait / Thoughts in the rain / Never ending solitude / Tuxedo / All characters ficticious / Lucifer's cage / Care-ful as you go / Free for all / William Taplin / Hands of fate / Confusion / Young love
CD _____ TDEM 15
Trandem / Apr '94 / CM / ADA / Pinnacle.

GUITARIST
CD _____ CMML 88006CD
Music Maker / Jul '94 / Grapevine / ADA.

LIVE ON THE TEST
CD _____ WHISCD 009
Windsong / Mar '95 / Pinnacle.

MATTER OF TIME, A (Giltrap, Gordon & Martin Taylor)
CD _____ CDSGP 007
Prestige / Aug '91 / Total/BMG.

MUSIC FOR THE SMALL SCREEN
CD _____ MRCD 1
Munchkin / May '95 / Grapevine.

ON A SUMMER'S NIGHT
CD _____ CMMR 924CD
Music Maker / Jul '94 / Grapevine / ADA.

ONE TO ONE
CD _____ NP 002CD
Nico Polo / Sep '89 / Roots / Direct / ADA.

PEACOCK PARTY
Headwind - the eagle / Magpie rag / Hocus pocus / Turkey trot - a country bluff / Tailor bird / Black rose - the raven / Birds of a feather / Jester's jig / Gypsy Lane / Party piece / Chanticleer / Dono's dream
CD _____ CDPT 507
Prestige / Jul '90 / Total/BMG.

PERILOUS JOURNEY/ELEGY
CD Set _____ CDPM 850
Prestige / Jun '92 / Total/BMG.

SOLO ALBUM
CD _____ CDSGP 021
Prestige / Jun '92 / Total/BMG.

VISIONARY/FEAR OF THE DARK
CD Set _____ CDPM 851
Prestige / Jun '92 / Total/BMG.

Gin Blossoms

CONGRATULATIONS, I'M SORRY
CD _____ 5404702
A&M / Feb '96 / PolyGram.

Gin On The Rocks

COOLEST GROOVE
CD _____ 847025
Steamhammer / Dec '90 / Pinnacle & Plastic Head.

Ginn, Greg

DICK
Never change, baby / I want to believe / You wanted it / I won't give in / Creeps / Strong violent type / Don't tell me / You dirty rat / Disgusting reference / Walking away / Ignorant order / Slow fuse / You're going to get it
CD _____ CRZ 032 CD
Cruz / Sep '93 / Pinnacle / Plastic Head.

GETTING EVEN
CD _____ CRZ 029 CD
Cruz / May '93 / Pinnacle / Plastic Head.

LET IT BURN BECAUSE
CD _____ CRZ 036CD
SST / Jul '94 / Plastic Head.

PAYDAY
CD _____ CRZ 028 CD
Cruz / May '93 / Pinnacle / Plastic Head.

Giordand, Vince

QUALITY SHOUT
CD _____ SOSCD 1260
Stomp Off / Apr '94 / Jazz Music / Wellard.

Giorgia T

NATURAL WOMAN
Taking it to the streets / Ain't no sunshine / Chain of fools / (You make me feel like a natural woman / Love of my life / You don't know what love is / Wind cries Mary / Man in the mirror / Bridge over troubled water
CD _____ VBR 21322
Go Jazz / Feb '94 / Vital/SAM.

NATURAL WOMAN/LIVE IN ROME
CD _____ GOJ 60122
Go Jazz / Sep '95 / Vital/SAM.

Gipsy Family

LOS REYES
CD _____ 15490
Laserlight / Aug '92 / Target/BMG.

Gipsy Fire

GIPSY FIRE
CD _____ INT 845149
Interchord / Feb '91 / CM.

Gipsy Kings

ALLEGRIA
Tena tinita / La dona / Sueno / Un amor / Pharoan / Recuerdo / Allegria / Solituda / Papa, no pega la mama / Tristessa / Pena Penita / Djobi djoba / Papa / No pega la mama / Pharaon
CD _____ 466762 2
Columbia / Jul '93 / Sony.

ESTE MUNDO
Baila me / Sin ella / Habla me / Lagrimas / Oy / Mi vida / El mauro / Non Volvere / Furia / Oh mai / Ternuras / Ests mundo
CD _____ 4686482
Columbia / Jul '91 / Sony.

ESTRELLAS
La rumba / A ti a ti / Siempre acaba tu vida / Forever / Mujer / Campesino / Cata luna igual se entonces / Pararito / Tierra gitana / A tu vera / Mi carazon / Estrellas
CD _____ 4813452
Columbia / Nov '95 / Sony.

GIPSY KINGS
Tu quieres volver / Moorea / Bem bem Ma-ria / Un amor / Inspiration / Mi minera / Djobi djoba / Faena / Quiero saber / Amor amor / Duende / Bamboleo
CD _____ 469123 2
Columbia / Jul '93 / Sony.

GIPSY KINGS/LUNA DE FUEGO/ALLEGRIA
Bamboleo / Tu quieres volver / Moorea / Bem bem Maria / Un amor / Inspiration / A mi manera (Comme d'habitude) / Djobi djoba / Faena / Quiero saber / Amor amor / Duende / Amor d'un dia / Luna de fuego / Caliente / Pena penita / Allegria / La Dona / Solituda / Suena / Papa, no pega la Mama / Pharaon / Triestessa / Recuerdo
CD Set _____ 477524 2
Columbia / Oct '94 / Sony.

GREATEST HITS
Djobi djoba / Baila me / Bamboleo / Pida me la / Bem bem Maria / Voalre (Nel blu di pinto di blue) / Moorea / A mi manera (Comme d'habitude) / Un amor / Galaxia / Escucha me / Tu quieres volver / Soy / La quiero / Allegria / Vamos a bailar / La Dona
CD _____ 477242 2
Columbia / Jul '94 / Sony.

LIVE
Intro / Allegria / La dona / El mauro / Bem bem Maria / Trista pena / Odeon / Sin ella / Quiero saber / Habla me / Galaxia / Fandango / Tu quieres volver / Oh mai / Djobi djoba / Bamboleo
CD _____ 472648-2
Columbia / Oct '92 / Sony.

LIVE/ESTE MUNDO
CD Set _____ 4726482 D
Columbia / Feb '93 / Sony.

LOVE & LIBERTE
Escucha me / Montana / Michael / Pedir a tu Corazon / Queda te aqui / Guitarra negra / Non vivire / Madre mia / Ritmo de la noche / Navidad / Campana / Love and liberte / La quiero
CD _____ 474950 2
Columbia / Nov '93 / Sony.

LUNA DE FUEGO
Amor d'un dia / Luna de fuego / Calaverada / Galaxia / Ruptura / Gypsy rock / Viento del arean / Princessa / Olvidado / Ciento
CD _____ 4667632
Columbia / Feb '91 / Sony.

MOSAIQUE
Caminando por la calle / Viento del arena / Mosaique / Camino / Passion / Soy / Volare / Trista pena / Liberte / Serana / Bossamba / Vamos a Bailar
CD _____ 466213 2
Columbia / Jul '93 / Sony.

Gira, Michael

DRAINLAND
You see through me / Where does your body begin / I see them all lined up / Unreal / Fan letter / Your naked body / Low life form / If you... / Why I ate my wife / Blind
CD _____ SR 086
Young God / Jun '95 / Vital.

Girl

BLOOD, WOMEN, ROSES
CD _____ PRODCD 4
Product Inc. / May '87 / Vital.

Sheer Greed

SHEER GREED
Hollywood tease / Things you say / Lovely Lorraine / Strawberries / Little Miss Ann / Doctor doctor / Do you love me / Take me dancing / What's up / Passing clouds / My number / Heartbreak America
CD _____ JETCD 1009
Jet / Sep '94 / Total/BMG.

WASTED YOUTH
Thru the twilight / Old dogs / Ice in the blood / Wasted youth / Standard romance / Nice 'n' nasty / McKitty's back / Nineteen / Overnight angels / Sweet kids
CD _____ JETCD 1010
Jet / Oct '94 / Total/BMG.

Girl Trouble

GIRL TROUBLE LIVE
CD _____ EFA 12355-2
Empty / Jan '94 / Plastic Head / SRD.

NEW AMERICAN SHAME
CD _____ EFA 11390CD
Musical Tragedies / Jun '93 / SRD.

Girlandia

CELTIC HEIR
CD _____ BRAM 199346-2
Brambus / Mar '94 / ADA / Direct.

Girlfriend

MAKE IT COME TRUE
CD _____ 7432115217-2
Arista / May '93 / BMG.

Girls Against Boys

CRUISE YOURSELF
CD _____ TG 134CD
Touch & Go / Oct '94 / SRD.

NINETIES VS. EIGHTIES
CD _____ AS 3CD
Touch & Go / '93 / SRD.

TROPIC OF SCORPIO
CD _____ AS 4CD
Touch & Go / '94 / SRD.

VENUS LUXURE NO.1 BABY
CD _____ TG 117CD
Touch & Go / '94 / SRD.

Girls At Our Best

PLEASURE
Getting nowhere fast / Warm girls / Politics / It's fashion / Go for gold / Pleasure / Too big for your boots / I'm beautiful now / Wa-terbed babies / Fun city teenagers / 600,000 / Heaven / China blue / Fast boy-friends / She flipped / Goodbye to that jazz / This train
CD _____ ASKCD 047
Vinyl Japan / Oct '94 / Vital.

Girlschool

BEST OF GIRLSCHOOL, THE
Take it all away / It could be better / Emer-gency / Nothing to lose / Race with the devil / Demolition boys / C'mon let's go / Yeah right / Hit and run / Tonight (Live) / Kick it down / Please don't touch / Bomber / Wild-life / Don't call it love / Screaming blue mur-der / 1-2-3-4 Rock 'n' roll / Burning in the heat / Twentieth century boy / Play dirty / I'm the leader of the gang (I am) / Play dirty / Fox on the run / Head over heels
CD _____ DOJOCD 103
Dojo / Feb '94 / BMG.

COLLECTION: GIRLSCHOOL
1-2-3-4 Rock 'n' roll / Furniture fire / Take it all away / Kick it down / Midnight ride / Race with the devil / Play dirty / Yeah right / Emergency / Breakout (Knob in the media) / Victim / Flesh and blood / Tush / Don't stop / Future flash / Rock me shock me / Screaming blue murder / Wild life / Bomber / Nothing to lose / Live with me / Like it like that / Tonight / Take it from me
CD _____ CCSCD 314
Castle / Dec '91 / BMG.

DEMOLITION/HIT AND RUN
Demolition boys / Not for sale / Race with the devil / Take it all away / Nothing to lose / Breakdown / Midnight ride / Emergency / Baby doll / Deadline / C'mon let's go / Hun-ter / Victim / Kick it down / Following the crowd / Tush / Hit and run / Watch your step / Back to start / Yeah right / Future flash
CD _____ LOMACD 1
Loma / Feb '94 / BMG.

FROM THE VAULTS
Nothing to lose / Furniture fire / Bomber / Demolition boys (Live) / 1-2-3-4 Rock 'n' roll / Tush (New version) / I'm the leader of the gang (I am) / Not for sale / Please don't touch / Midnight (Mixes) / Don't stop / Don't call it love / Like it like that
CD _____ NEMCD 642
Sequel / Apr '94 / BMG.

GIRLSCHOOL
CD _____ CMGCD 006
Communique / Nov '92 / Plastic Head.

LIVE
CD _____ CMGCD 013
Communique / Nov '95 / Plastic Head.

Gisbert, Greg

HARCOLOGY (Gisbert, Greg Quintet)
CD _____ CRISS 1084CD
Criss Cross / May '94 / Cadillac /
Harmonia Mundi.

Giscombe, Junior

BEST OF JUNIOR, THE
CD _____ 5269722
Mercury / Sep '95 / PolyGram.

Gismonti, Egberto

ACADEMIA DE DANCAS
CD _____ 5112022
Carmo / Feb '92 / Pinnacle / New Note.

AMAZONIA
Dois Curumins na floresta / O senhor dos
caminhos / Trenzinho amazonico / Forro na
beira da mata / Os deuses da selva 1 / O
baile dos caraibas / O coracao das trevas /
Danca das amazonas / Todos os fogos. O
fogo / Ciranda no ceu / Os deuses da selva
II / Sertao/Forrobodo / Ao redor da fogueira
/ Turma do mercado / Fuga and destruicao
/ Floresta (Amazonia) / Forro Amazonico /
Ruth / No coracao dos homens
CD _____ 517716-2
Carmo / Jun '93 / Pinnacle / New Note.

ARVORE
Luzes da ribalta / Memoria e fado /
Academio de danca / Tango / Encontro no
bar / Adagio / Variacoes sombre um tema
de leo brouwer / Salvador
CD _____ 8490762
Carmo / May '91 / Pinnacle / New Note.

CIRCENSE
Karate / Cego aderaldo / Magico / Palhaco
/ Ta boa, santa / Equilibrista / Ciranda /
Mais que a paixao
CD _____ 8490772
Carmo / May '91 / Pinnacle / New Note.

DANCA DOS ESCARVOS
CD _____ 8377532
ECM / Nov '89 / New Note.

**DUAS VOZES (Gismonti, Egberto &
Nana Vasconcelos)**
Rio De Janeiro / Tomarapeba / Dancando /
Fogueira / Bianca / Don Quixote / O dia / A
noite
CD _____ 8236402
ECM / Apr '86 / New Note.

INFANCIA
CD _____ 8478892
ECM / Sep '91 / New Note.

KUARUP
Senhores da Terra / Ossuario / Valsa de
Francisca #2 / Anta / Urucum / A Forca da
Floresta / A Danca da Floresta / Aguas /
Sonia / A Morte da Floresta / Valsa de Fran-
cisca / O Som da Floresta / Jogos da Flo-
resta 1 / Jogos da Floresta 2 / Mutacao
CD _____ 8431992
Carmo / May '91 / Pinnacle / New Note.

NO CAIPIRA
Saudacoes / No caipira and zambumba /
Noca and Garrafas / Pira and Bambuzal /
Palacio de pinturas / Maracatu, sapo, quei-
mada and Grilo / Frevo / Esquenta muie and
banda de pffanos / Frevo rasgado / Sertao
Brasilero / Selva Amazonica / Uana Lua
and Kalimbas / Cancao da espera / Danca
das cambiral
CD _____ 517715-2
Carmo / Jun '93 / Pinnacle / New Note.

SANFONA
CD _____ 8293912
ECM / Aug '88 / New Note.

SOL DO MEIO DIA
Palacio de pinturas / Raga / Kalimba / Cor-
acao / Cafe / Sapain / Dance solitaria No.2
/ Baiao Malandro
CD _____ 8291172
ECM / Jun '86 / New Note.

SOLO
Selva Amazonica / Pau Rolou / And zero /
Frevo / Salvador / Ciranda Nordestina
CD _____ 8271352
ECM / Dec '85 / New Note.

TREM CAIPIRA
Trenzinho do Caipira / Dansa / Bachianas
brasileiras No.5 / Desejo / Cantiga / Cancao
de Carreiro / Preludio / Pobre cega
CD _____ 8417752
Carmo / Feb '92 / Pinnacle / New Note.

WORKS: EGBERTO GISMONTI
Loro / Gismonti / Mauro senise / Zeca as-
sumpcao / Nene raga / Vasconcelos / Colin
Walcott / Ciranda nordestina / Magico /
Garbarek / Charlie Haden / Maracutu / Nene
salvador
CD _____ 8232692
ECM / Jun '89 / New Note.

Gitbox

TOUCH WOOD
Engagement / Wedlock / Sipho / Les bou-
che du monde / Elfwalk / Springscape /

Journey / Oceanscape / Be longing / Mor-
man X and the Major's cheque / Icescape /
Neither a candle for the angel nor a poker
for the devil / Autumnscape / In vocation /
Rajasthani heart / Panda miracle / Touch
wood
CD _____ DGM 9511
Discipline / Nov '95 / Pinnacle.

Gits

FRENCHING THE BULLY
CD _____ CZ 051CD
C/Z / Dec '92 / Plastic Head.

Giuffre, Jimmy

FLIGHT, BREMEN 1961
CD _____ ARTCD 6071
Hat Art / Oct '92 / Harmonia Mundi / ADA
/ Cadillac.

FREE FALL
Propulsion / Threewe / Ornothoids / Di-
chotomy / Man alone / Spasmodic / Yggd-
rasill / Divided man / Primordial call / Five
ways
CD _____ 44807082
Sony Jazz / Dec '95 / Sony.

**JIMMY GIUFFRE 3, 1961 (Giuffre, Jimmy
Trio)**
Jesus Maria / Emphasis / In the mornings
out there / Scootin' about / Cry want / Brief
hesitation / Venture / Afternoon / Trudgin' /
Ictus / Carla / Sonic / Whirrr / That's true,
that's true / Goodbye / Flight / Gamut / Me
too / Temporarily / Herb and Ictus
CD Set _____ 8496442
ECM / Mar '02 / Now Note.

JIMMY GIUFFRE THREE, THE
CD _____ 7567909812
Atlantic / Apr '95 / Warner Music.

**LIFE OF A TRIO VOL. 1, THE (Giuffre,
Jimmy, Paul Bley & Steve Swallow)**
CD _____ OWL LC 059
Owl / Mar '91 / Harmonia Mundi (USA).

LIQUID DANCERS
CD _____ 121158-2
Soul Note / Apr '91 / Harmonia Mundi /
Wellard / Cadillac.

**RIVER STATION (Giuffre, Jimmy &
Andre Jaume)**
CD _____ CELPC 26
CELP / Nov '93 / Harmonia Mundi /
Cadillac.

TRIO AND QUARTET
Song is you / Gotta dance / Train and the
river / Train and river / Two kinds of blues
/ Voodoo / Crazy she calls me / That's the
way it is / My all / Crawdad suite / Green
country (New England mood) / Little melody
/ Careful / Crab / Four brothers
CD _____ CD 53252
Giants Of Jazz / Jan '96 / Target/BMG /
Cadillac.

Glacial Fear

ATLASPHERE
CD _____ NOSFVS 007
Nosferatu / Nov '95 / Plastic Head.

Glackin, Kevin

**NORTHERN LIGHTS (Na saighneain)
(Glackin, Kevin & Seamus)**
CD _____ CEFCD 140
Gael Linn / Jan '94 / Roots / CM / Direct /
ADA.

Glackin, Paddy

IN FULL SPATE
CD _____ CEFCD 153
Gael Linn / Jan '94 / Roots / CM / Direct /
ADA.

SEIDEAN SI
CD _____ CEFCD 171
Gael Linn / Aug '95 / Roots / CM / Direct /
ADA.

**WHIRLWIND, THE (Glackin, Paddy &
Robbie Hannon)**
CD _____ SHCD 79093
Shanachie / Oct '95 / Koch / ADA /
Greensleeves.

Gladiators

DREADLOCKS THE TIME IS NOW
Mix up / Bellyfull / Looks is deceiving /
Chatty chatty mouth / Soul rebel / Eli Eli /
Hearsay / Rude boy ska / Dreadlocks the
time is now / Jah works / Pocket money /
Get ready / Stick a bush / Write to me /
Naturality / Struggle / Day we go / Sweet
so till / Hello Carol
CD _____ CDFL 9001
Frontline / Jul '90 / EMI / Jetstar.

STORM, THE
Lovin' you / Cuss cuss / Community / Fools
rush in / Reggae music / Storm / Hello my
love / Love got the power / Rewind / Sun
comes out
CD _____ 111222
Musidisc / Jul '95 / Vital / Harmonia Mundi
/ ADA / Cadillac / Discovery.

TRUE RASTAMAN, A
No rice and peas / Let's face it / Think twice
(A wise saying) / Sea breeze / Hearts on fire
/ South Africa / True Rastaman / Galdhe
head / Every moment / One way ticket
CD _____ 109632
Musidisc / Feb '94 / Vital / Harmonia Mundi
/ ADA / Cadillac / Discovery.

Glaser, Tompall

OUTLAW, THE
It never crossed my mind / Bad times /
What are we doing with our lives / How I
love them old songs / On second thought /
Drinkin' them beers / My mother was a lady
/ Duncan and Brady / Easy on my mind /
Wonder of it all / You can have her / Re-
lease me / Tennessee blues / Come back
Shane / It'll be her / It ain't fair (medley) /
Sweethearts or strangers / Late nite show /
I just want to hear the music / Storms never
last
CD _____ BCD 15605
Bear Family / Jun '92 / Rollercoaster / Direct
/ CM / Swift / ADA.

ROGUE, THE
Rogue / Tears on my pillow / Forever and
ever / Shackles and chains / My pretty
quadron / Lean on me / I'll hold you in my
heart / True love / Open arms / I love you
so much it hurts / Chattanooga shoe shine
boy / You can't borrow back any time / Like
an old country song / Sad country songs /
What a town / Don't think you're too good
for country music / Unwanted outlaw / Man
you think you see / When I dream / Burn
Georgia burn / Billy Tyler / Carry me on
CD _____ BCD 15596
Bear Family / Apr '92 / Rollercoaster / Direct
/ CM / Swift / ADA.

Glasgow Gaelic Musical...

**CENTENARY SELECTION, A (Glasgow
Gaelic Musical Association)**
CD _____ LCOM 5220
Lismor / Jun '93 / Lismor / Direct /
Duncans / ADA.

**GAELIC GALORE (Glasgow Gaelic
Musical Association)**
Tuireadh nan treun / 'S olc a dh' fhag an
uiridh mi / O hi ri ri, tha e tighinn / Maighdeanan na h-airidh / Tir an airm / Seoladh
dhachaidh / An ataireachd ard / Allt an t-
siucair / An ubhal as airde / Nuair bha mi
og / Strathspeys and reels / O righ nan dul
/ 'S cian bho dh'fhag mi leodhas / An t-Iarla
diurach / Cathair a chuilchinn / Cearcall a'
chuain / Oran an lennaibh og / Och nan
och, tha mi fo mhulad / Caberfeidh
CD _____ LCOM 9037
Lismor / Oct '90 / Lismor / Direct / Duncans
/ ADA.

Glasgow Orpheus Choir

20 CLASSIC RECORDINGS
All in the April evening /.Belmont peat / Fire
smoothing prayer / Bonnie Dundee Orling-
ton / Eriskay love lilt / Lilt / Ca the Yowes
/ Crimond / Hark, hark the echo falling /
Bluebird / Ellan Vannin / Jesu joy of man's
desiring / Cloud capp'd towers / Faery song
/ Campbells are coming / Far away / Iona
boat song / Cradle song / Sea sorrow / All
through the night
CD _____ MOICD 007
Moidart / Nov '92 / Conifer / ADA.

Glasgow Phoenix Choir

FEEL GOOD
CD _____ CDLOC 1080
Klub / Jul '94 / CM / Ross / Duncans /
ADA / Direct.

WITH VOICES RISING
Scots wha hae / In the Wheatfield / When
the saints go marching in / Annie Laurie /
Time for man go home / Brother James' air
/ Duncan and Brady / John Anderson, my Jo /
Tumbalalaika / Little cherry tree / Corn rigs
/ Dream angus / Death o' death oh me lawd
/ Loch Lomond / Campbells are coming /
All my trials / Lament of Mary Queen Of
Scots / Battle of the republic
CD _____ LCOM 9024
Lismor / Aug '90 / Lismor / Direct / Duncans
/ ADA.

Glasgow, Alex

SONGS OF ALEX GLASGOW VOL. 1 & 2
CD _____ MWMCDSP 14
Mawson & Wareham / Nov '94 / BMG /
THE.

Glasgow, Deborahe

GIMME YOUR LOVE
CD _____ WRCD 011
World / Sep '94 / Jetstar / Total/BMG.

Glass House

CRUMBS OFF THE TABLE
Crumbs off the table / If it ain't love (it don't
matter) / Touch me Jesus / I surrendered /
You ain't livin' (unless you're in love) / Steal-
ing moments (from another woman's life) /
Let it flow / Giving up the ghow / Thanks I

---

needed that / I don't see me in your eyes
anymore / Hotel / I can't be you, you can't
be me / He's in my life / V.I.P. / Look what
we've done to love / Heaven is there to
guide us / Don't go looking for something
(you don't want to see)
CD _____ HDHCD 505
HDH / Apr '92 / Pinnacle.

Glass, Philip

1000 AIRPLANES ON THE ROOF
1000 airplanes on the roof / City walk / Girlfriend / My building disappeared / Screeno
of memory / What time is grey / Labyrinth /
Return to the hive / Three truths / Encounter
/ Grey cloud over New York / Where have
you been as the doctor / Normal man
running
CD _____ CDVE 39
Venture / Feb '89 / EMI.

ESSENTIAL PHILIP GLASS, THE
CD _____ SK 64133
Sony Music / Dec '93 / Sony.

**HYDROGEN JUKEBOX (Glass, Philip &
Allen Ginsberg)**
CD _____ 7559792862
Elektra Nonesuch / Jan '95 / Warner
Music.

**LOW SYMPHONY, THE (From music by
David Bowie & Brian Eno)**
CD _____ 4381502
Philips / Mar '93 / PolyGram.

NORTH STAR
Etoile polaire (North star) / Victor's lament /
River run / Mon pere, mon pere / Are years
what? (for Marianne Moore) / Lady Day /
Ange des orages / Ave / Ik-ook / Montage
CD _____ CDV 2085
Virgin / Jun '88 / EMI.

**PASSAGES (Glass, Philip & Ravi
Shankar)**
Offering / Channels and winds / Meetings
along the edge / Sadhanipa / Ragas in mi-
nor scale / Prashanti
CD _____ 260947
Private Music / Sep '90 / BMG.

Glasse, Paul

ROAD TO HOME, THE
CD _____ DOSCD 7004
Dos / May '94 / CM / Direct / ADA.

Glaz

GLAZ
CD _____ CD 848
Escalibur / Aug '93 / Roots / ADA /
Discovery.

Gledhill, Simon

SHALL WE DANCE
Shall we dance / Fleurette / El relicario /
These foolish things / Garland of Judy /
Canyon caballero / No matter what hap-
pens / Veradero / Dancing in the dark / Au-
tumn crocus / June night on marlow reach
/ Swing time / My silent love / Themes from:
Skyscraper fantasy / Haunted ballroom
CD _____ OS 205
Valentine / Jul '94 / Conifer.

Glee Club

MINE
Need / Blame / No reason / Bad child's
dolly / Already there / Free to believe /
Drives you away / Remember the years / All
the promises / Take you there / Icy blue
CD _____ SETCD 012
Setanta / Jan '94 / Vital.

Gleeson, Barry

PATH ACROSS THE OCEAN
CD _____ CD 001
Wavelength / Sep '94 / CM / Direct / ADA.

Gleeson, Patrick

FOUR SEASONS
Spring / Summer / Autumn / Winter
CD _____ VCD 47212
Varese Sarabande/Colosseum / '87 / Pin-
nacle / Silva Screen.

Glenfiddle

NEVERTHELESS
CD _____ EFA 800392
Twah / Dec '95 / SRD.

Glenn, Glen

**GLEN GLENN STORY/EVERYBODY'S
MOVIN' AGAIN**
If I had me a woman / One cup of coffee /
Hold me baby / Baby let's play house / Laurie Ann / Be bop a lula / Kitty Kat / Everybody's movin' / Shake, rattle and roll / Treat
me nice / Blue jeans and a boy's shirt / I
got a woman / Kathleen / Would ja' / I'm
glad my baby's gone away / Down the line
/ Come on / Flip flop and fly / Jack and Jill
boogie / I so glad to love you baby / Bony
Moronie / Mean woman blues / Rock 'n' roll
Ruby / Sick and tired / Rockin' around the
mountain / Why don't you love me / Ugly

---

and slouchy / You win again / Everybody's movin' again
CD _____ CDCHD 403
Ace / Jun '92 / Pinnacle / Cadillac / Complete/Pinnacle.

Glenn Miller Orchestra...

LEGEND LIVES ON, THE (Glenn Miller Orchestra U.K.)
CD _____ OVCCD 001
Satellite / Jun '93 / Disc.

Glinn, Lillian

LAST SESSION 1929 (Glinn, Lillian & Mae Glover)
CD _____ SOB 035372
Story Of The Blues / Oct '92 / Koch / ADA.

LILLIAN GLINN 1927-1933
CD _____ DOCD 5184
Blues Document / Oct '93 / Swift / Jazz Music / Hot Shot.

Glitter, Gary

BACK AGAIN - THE VERY BEST OF GARY GLITTER/GLITTER BAND (Glitter, Gary & Glitter Band)
Hello hello I'm back again / Do you wanna touch me (oh yeah) / I'm the leader of the gang (I am) / Rock 'n' roll (Part 2) / I love you love me love / Always yours / Remember me this way / Love in the sun / Angel face / People like you and people like me / Tears I cried / Goodbye my love / Just for you
CD _____ PWKS 4052
Carlton Home Entertainment / Apr '91 / Carlton Home Entertainment.

GARY GLITTER
CD _____ GRF 200
Tring / Jan '93 / Tring / Prism.

GARY GLITTER'S GANGSHOW
Rock 'n' roll (part 2) / I didn't know I loved you (till I saw you rock 'n' roll) / When I'm on I'm on / Do you wanna touch me (Oh yeah) / Alright with the boys / Hello hello I'm back again / Shake it up / Always yours / Frontiers of style / Only way to survive / Rock 'n' roll (part 1) / Good rockin' tonight / Baby let's play mama / Be bop a lula / Another rock'n'roll Christmas / I love you love me love / Leader of the gang
CD _____ CCSCD 234
Castle / Nov '89 / BMG.

LEADER, THE
CD Set _____ TFP 026
Tring / Nov '92 / Tring / Prism.

MANY HAPPY RETURNS - THE HITS
Rock 'n' roll (part 1) / Rock 'n' roll (part 2) / I didn't know I loved you (till I saw you rock 'n' roll) / Ready to rock / Rock on / Doing alright with the boys / I'm the leader of the gang (I am) / Wanderer / Do you wanna touch me (Oh yeah) / Hello hello I'm back again / I love you love me love / You belong to me / It takes all night long / Oh yes, you're beautiful / Love like you and me / Little boogie woogie (in the back of my mind) / Dance me up / Through the years / Always yours / Remember me this way / And the leader rocks on / Another rock and roll Christmas
CD _____ CDFA 3303
Fame / Jan '94 / EMI.

GLO

EVEN AS WE
Deiea / I'm in your gravity / Travellers stargate / Crystal world / Doom ghosts / And / Pagli herbus / Spirit lover / Walk the streets / Goddesses love oranges / Let's GLO / Back to the sea
CD _____ AGASCD 009
Gas / Oct '95 / Vital.

Global Communication

76.14
CD _____ DEDCD 014
Dedicated / Jul '94 / Vital.

REMOTION
CD _____ DEDCD 21
Dedicated / Nov '95 / Vital.

Globe Unity Orchestra

20TH ANNIVERSARY
CD _____ FMPCD 45
FMP / Nov '89 / Cadillac.

RUMBLING - 1975
CD _____ FMPCD 40
FMP / Dec '89 / Cadillac.

Glod

GLOD
CD _____ EEE 22CD
Audioglobe / Sep '94 / Plastic Head.

Glommin Geek

DIG A HOLE IN THE SKY
CD _____ WD 014CD
Wide / Aug '92 / Plastic Head.

Gloria

20 SONGS
CD _____ PHCD 535
Outlet / Jan '95 / ADA / Duncans / CM / Ross / Direct / Koch.

Gloucester Cathedral...

MUSIC FOR CHRISTMAS (Gloucester Cathedral Choir)
There is no rose / O little one sweet / See amid the winter's snow / I sing of a maiden / Three mummers / Sing lullaby / Carol of praise / New Year carol / Hymn of the Nativity / Carol for today / Tomorrow shall be my dancing day / Lamb / O little town of Bethlehem / Silent night / Blessed be that maid Mary / Whence is that goodly fragrance / Ding dong merrily on high / It came upon a midnight clear / Once in royal David's City
CD _____ CDCA 917
Alpha / Nov '91 / Abbey Recording.

Glove

BLUE SUNSHINE
Like an animal / Looking glass girl / Sexeye-make-up / Blues in drag / Mr. Alphabet says / Punish me with kisses / This green city / Orgy / Perfect murder / Relax
CD _____ 815 019-2
Polydor / Aug '90 / PolyGram.

Glover, May

MAY GLOVER 1927-1931
CD _____ DOCD 5185
Blues Document / Oct '93 / Swift / Jazz Music / Hot Shot.

Glover, Roger

BUTTERFLY BALL, THE/WIZARD'S CONVENTION (Glover, Roger & Deep Purple)
Dawn / Get ready / Saffron dormouse and Lizzy bee / Harlequin hare / Old blind mole / Magician moth / No solution / Behind the smile / Fly away / Aranea / Sitting in a dream / Waiting / Sir Maximus mouse / Dreams of Sir Bedivere / Together again / Watch out for the bat / Little chalk blue / Feast / Love is all / Homeward / Craig song / When the sun stops shining / Loose ends / Money to burn / Who's counting on me / Make it soon / Until tomorrow / Light of my life / She's a woman / Swanks and swells
CD _____ VSOPCD 139
Connoisseur / Oct '89 / Pinnacle.

MASK & THE ELEMENTS
First a ring of clay / Next a ring of fire / Third rings watery flow / Fourth rings with the wind / Finale / Divided world / Getting stranger / Mask / Fake it / Dancin' again / (You're so) Remote / Hip level / Don't look down
CD _____ VSOPCD 183
Connoisseur / Apr '93 / Pinnacle.

Glover, Tony

ASHES IN MY WHISKEY (Glover, Tony & Dave Ray)
CD _____ ROUGHCD 152
Rough Trade / Sep '90 / Pinnacle.

Glu Gun

JUST GLU IT
CD _____ EFA 11389-2
Poshboy / May '94 / Disc.

Glue

MACHINE KEEP ME WARM
CD _____ FAN 1012
Fantastick / Jun '94 / SRD.

GMT

WAR GAMES
CD _____ 367 0004.3
Mausoleum / Oct '91 / Grapevine.

Go To Blazes

ANY TIME
CD _____ GRCD 374
Glitterhouse / Aug '95 / Direct / ADA.

Go West

ACES & KINGS - BEST OF
We close our eyes / King of wishful thinking / Tracks of my tears / Call me / Faithful / Don't look down (the sequel) / One way street / What you won't do for love / From Baltimore to Paris / Goodbye girl / I want to hear it from you / Tell me / King is dead
CD _____ CDCHR 6050
Chrysalis / Oct '93 / EMI.

BANGS AND CRASHES
We close our eyes (mix) / Man in my mirror / Goodbye girl / S.O.S. (mix) / Eye to eye (mix) / Ball of confusion (live) / Call me (mix) / Haunted / Missing persons (mix) / Don't look down (mix) / One way street / Innocence (mix)
CD _____ CCD 1536
Chrysalis / Aug '86 / EMI.

GO WEST
We close our eyes / Don't look down / Call me / Eye to eye / Haunted / S.O.S. / Goodbye girl / Innocence / Missing persons
CD _____ CD25CR 10
Chrysalis / Mar '94 / EMI.

INDIAN SUMMER
Faithful / Still in love / Tell me / That's what love can do / What you won't do for love / King of wishful thinking / Sun and the moon / Count me out / Crystal ball / Forget that girl / Bluebeat / I want you back / Taste of things to come
CD _____ CDCHR 1964
Chrysalis / Oct '92 / EMI.

Go-Betweens

16 LOVERS LANE
Love goes on / Quiet heart / Love is a sign / You can't say no forever / Dive for your memory / Devil's eye / Streets of your town / Clouds / Was there anything I could do / I'm alright
CD _____ BEGA 95 CD
Beggars Banquet / Aug '88 / Warner Music / Disc.

1978-1990
Karen / Eight pictures / Hammer the hammer / I need two heads / Cattle and cane / When people are dead / Man o'sand to girl o'sea / Sound of the rain / Bachelor kisses / People say / Draining the pool for you / World weary / Spring rain / Rock 'n' roll friend / Wrong road / Dusty in here / The Clarke sisters / King in mirrors / Right here / Second hand furniture / Bye bye pride / girl, black girl / House that Jack Kerouac built / Don't call me gone / Streets of your town / Mexican postcard / Love is a sign / You won't find it again
CD _____ BEGA 104 CD
Beggars Banquet / Mar '90 / Warner Music / Disc.

BEFORE HOLLYWOOD
Bad debt follows you / Two steps step out / Before Hollywood / Dusty in here / Ask / Cattle and cane / By chance / As long as that / On my block / That way
CD _____ LCD 54
Rough Trade / Jun '90 / Pinnacle.

LIBERTY BELLE AND THE BLACK DIAMOND EXPRESS
Spring rain / Ghost and the black hat / Wrong road / To reach me / Twin layers of lightning / In the core of a flame / Head full of steam / Bow down / Palm down / Apology accepted
CD _____ BBL 72CD
Lowdown/Beggars Banquet / Feb '89 / Warner Music / Disc.

TALLULAH
Right here / You tell me / Someone else's wife / I just get caught out / Cut it out / House that Jack Kerouac built / Bye bye pride / Spirit of a vampyre / Clarke sisters / Hope then strife
CD _____ BBL 81CD
Lowdown/Beggars Banquet / Feb '90 / Warner Music / Disc.

Go-Go's

RETURN TO THE VALLEY OF THE GO-GO'S
Living at the Canterbury/Party pose / Fashion seekers (live) / He's so strange / London boys (live) / Beatnik beach (live) / Cool jerk / We got the beat / Our lips are sealed / Surfing and spying / Vacation / Speeding / Good for gone / Head over heels / Can't stop the world (live) / Mercenary (live) / Good girl / Beautiful / Whole world lost its head
CD _____ EIRSCD 1071
IRS/EMI / Mar '95 / EMI.

Goat

AS YOU LIKE
Don't cry / Fallen over you / Mother / Zombie break out / D'ya like it / How long
CD _____ BBL 110 CD
Beggars Banquet / Sep '90 / Warner Music / Disc.

MEDICATION TIME
Sexman / Everybody wants to be there / Good times / Bug / Falling / Lying in the flowers / Something wrong / In the fields / Is this me / I want you back / Beneath the skin
CD _____ BEGACD 119
Beggars Banquet / Jun '91 / Warner Music / Disc.

Goats

NO GOATS, NO GLORY
Wake 'n' bake / Philly Blunts / Boom / Lincoln Drive / Butcher countdown / Mutiny / Rumblefish / Blind with anger / Revolution 94 / Times runnin' up / Idiot Business
CD _____ 476937-2
Columbia / Aug '94 / Sony.

TRICKS OF THE SHADE
We got freaks / Typical American / Hangerhead is born / What'cha got is what'cha gettin' / Columbus boat ride / R U down wit da goats / Cummin in ya ear / Noriega's

coke stand / Wrong pot 2 piss in / Leonard Peltier in a cage / Do the digs dug / TV cops / Tattooed lady / Rovie Wade, The sword swallower / Aaah d yaaa / Drive-by bumper cars / Burn the flag / Hip hopola
CD _____ 472680 2
Columbia / Mar '93 / Sony.

Goats Don't Shave

OUT IN THE OPEN
Coming home / Keep / Children of the highway / Rose street / Arranmore / This world / She's leaving / Song for Fionula / War / Let it go / Lock it in
CD _____ COOKCD 075
Cooking Vinyl / Sep '94 / Vital.

RUSTY RAZOR
Let the world keep on turning / Las Vegas (In the hills of Donegal) / Eyes / John Cherokee / Evictions / Biddy from Sligo/Connaught man's rambles / Ranger / Mary Mary / Closing time / What she means to me / Crooked Jack / When you're dead
CD _____ COOKCD 074
Cooking Vinyl / Jul '94 / Vital.

God

APPEAL TO HUMAN GREED
CD _____ ABB 79XCD
Big Cat / Jun '95 / SRD / Pinnacle.

GOD
CD _____ PPP 106
PDCD / Jan '94 / Plastic Head.

POSSESSION
Pretty / Fucked / Return to hell / Soul fire / Hate meditation / Lord I'm on my way / Love / Black Jesus
CD _____ CDVE 910
Venture / Mar '92 / EMI.

God & Texas

CRIMINAL ELEMENT
Incoming / Bury magnets / D 2 / Cold bringer / Chromalox / Breach / Drive time / In the blast furnace / Flat black wide / Cruel andunusual
CD _____ 72900-2
Restless / Nov '93 / Vital.

DOUBLE SHOT
Confidential scrape / Codename: Soul albino / In the flesh again / Lower / Meet me at the inversion layer / Zappatos del diablo / Red room / Back on the downside / Profiteerings / Goodbye blacksheep / Chevalier / Outro
CD _____ 72902-2
Restless / Sep '94 / Vital.

God Bullies

KILL THE KING
CD _____ VIRUS 152CD
Alternative Tentacles / Oct '94 / Pinnacle.

God Forsaken

DISMAL GLEAMS OF DESOLATION
CD _____ CDAR 008
Adipocre / Mar '94 / Plastic Head.

DREAMS OF DESOLATION
CD _____ CDAR 08
Adipocre / Feb '94 / Plastic Head.

TIDE HAS TURNED
CD _____ CDAR 025
Adipocre / May '95 / Plastic Head.

God Is My Co-Pilot

PUSS 02
CD _____ DSA 54041
Les Disques Du Soleil / Dec '95 / Harmonia Mundi.

TIGHT LIKE FIST
CD _____ KFWCD 148
Knitting Factory / Feb '95 / Grapevine.

God Lives Underwater

EMPTY
Still / All wrong / Empty / Don't know how to be / No more love / 23 / Weaken / Tortoise / Scared / Lonely again / Nothing / Try / Waste of time / Drag me down
CD _____ 74321295182
American / Oct '95 / BMG.

God Machine

ONE LAST LAUGH IN A PLACE OF DYING
Tremelo song / Mama / Alone / In bad dreams / Painless / Love song / Life song / Devil song / Hunter / Evol / Train song / Flower song / Boy by the roadside / Sunday song
CD _____ FIXCD 27
Fiction / Oct '94 / PolyGram.

SCENES FROM A 2ND STOREY
Dream machine / Seed / Blind man / I've seen the man / Desert song / Home / It's all over / Temptation / Out / Ego / Seven / Purity / Piano song
CD _____ 5171542
Fiction / Jan '93 / PolyGram.

Godard, Michel

ABORIGENE
CD _____ HOP 200002
Label Hopi / May '94 / Harmonia Mundi.

LE CHANT DU SERPENT
CD _____ CDLLL 37
La Lichere / Oct '93 / Discovery / ADA.

Godard, Vic

END OF THE SURREY PEOPLE
Imbalance / Johnny Thunders / Water was bad / Malicious love / On the shore / Nullify my reputation (I'm gonna) / Won't turn back / Talent to follow / Same mistakes / Pain barrier / I can't stop you / End of the Surrey people
CD _____ DUBH 936CD
Postcard / Jun '93 / Vital.

Godchildren Of Soul

GODCHILDREN OF SOUL, THE
CD _____ TOTCD 4
Total / Sep '95 / Total/BMG.

Goddess

SEXUAL ALBUM, THE
Sexual / Lingerie / X-rated / Cleopatra / Erotic / In my bed / Boyz / Je t'aime / She's wild / Sexual (safe sex version)
CD _____ 472488-2
Epic / Nov '92 / Sony.

Godfathers

ORANGE
CD _____ 986974
Intercord / Oct '93 / Plastic Head.

Godflesh

GODFLESH
CD _____ MOSH 020CD
Earache / Feb '94 / Vital.

PURE
CD _____ MOSH 032CD
Earache / Sep '94 / Vital.

SELFLESS
Xnoybis / Bigot / Black bored angel / Anything is mine / Empyreal / Crush my soul / Body dome light / Toll / Heartless / Mantra / Go spread your wings (On CD only.)
CD _____ MOSH 085CD
Earache / Sep '94 / Vital.

STREETCLEANER
CD _____ MOSH 015CD
Earache / Sep '94 / Vital.

Godley & Creme

IMAGES
Englishman in New York / Get well soon / Wedding bells / Power behind the throne / Out in the cold / My body the car / Bits of blue sky / Cry / Little piece of heaven / Save a mountain for me / Wide boy / Party / Submarine / Last weekend
CD _____ 5500072
Spectrum/Karussell / May '93 / PolyGram THE.

Godplow

RED GIANT JUDAS
CD _____ GROW 042
Grass / May '95 / SRD.

God's Little Monkeys

LIP
Hollywood or the Humber / You win some but lose more / True colour / Too many flesh suppers / Reynard / Ball of confusion / Defence of the wicked / Barefloor blues / Calgary cross / Greed creed
CD _____ COOKCD 043
Cooking Vinyl / Sep '91 / Vital.

NEW MAPS OF HELL
Pay that money down / Hangman Botha / Underneath the arches / Sound out the symbols / Minister for motivation / New Year's honours / Sea never dry / Tory heart / Where were you / New statesman / Gas town / Whistle, daughter, whistle
CD _____ COOKCD 022
Cooking Vinyl / Sep '89 / Vital.

Godsend

AS THE SHADOWS FALL
CD _____ HOLY 3CD
Holy / May '94 / Plastic Head.

Godspeed

RIDE
Ride / Not enough / Hate / Abstract life / Stubborn ass / Downtown / Born and raised / Houston St. / Mind blaster / Christ / My brother
CD _____ 756782573-2
WEA / Mar '94 / Warner Music.

Godstar

SLEEPER
CD _____ TAANG 79CD
Taang / Dec '93 / Plastic Head.

Godzilla

VOLUME
CD _____ TOPYCD 073
Temple / May '94 / Pinnacle / Plastic Head.

Goebbels, Heiner

DISASTROUS LANDING
CD _____ 5279302
ECM / Dec '95 / New Note.

HORSTUCKE
CD _____ 5133682
ECM / Jun '94 / New Note.

LIVE À VICTORIAVILLE (Goebbels, Heiner & Alfred Harth)
CD _____ VICTOCD 04
Victo / Nov '94 / These / ReR Megacorp / Cadillac.

MAN IN THE ELEVATOR, THE (Goebbels, Heiner & Heiner Muller)
CD _____ 8371102
ECM / Nov '88 / New Note.

Gogh Van Go

GOGH VAN GO
Bed where we hide / Say you will / Vinyl / Long story short / Tunnel of trees / Call it romance / 97 / Have a whirl / Instant karma / Kiss the ground / Say you will (2)
CD _____ ATLASCD 005
Equator / Apr '94 / Pinnacle.

Goins, Herbie

SOULTIME (Goins, Herbie & The Nightimers)
Outside of heaven / Look at Granny run run / I don't mind / Pucker up buttercup / Coming home to you / No. 1 in your heart / Satisfaction / Good good lovin' / Cruisin' / Knock on wood / 36-22-36 / Turn on your love light / Coming home to you (Live)
CD _____ SEECD 362
See For Miles/C5 / Oct '92 / Pinnacle.

Gold, Andrew

ANDREW GOLD
That's why I love you / Heartaches, heartaches / Love hurts / Resting in your arms / I'm a gambler / Endless flight / Hang my picture straight / Ten years behind me / I'm
CD _____ 7559606052
Elektra / Jan '96 / Warner Music.

NEVER LET HER SLIP AWAY
CD _____ 9548 316152
Carlton Home Entertainment / Jan '93 / Carlton Home Entertainment.

WHAT'S WRONG WITH THIS PICTURE
Hope you feel good / Passing thing / Do wah diddy diddy / Learning the game / Angel woman / Must be crazy / Lonely boy / Firefly / Stay / Go back home again / One of them is me
CD _____ 7559611662
Elektra / Jan '96 / Warner Music.

Gold, Brian

BULLSEYE (Gold, Brian & Tony)
CD _____ VPCD 1435
VP / Oct '95 / Jetstar.

Goldberg, Barry

BARRY GOLDBERG AND FRIENDS
CD _____ NEXCD 160
Sequel / May '91 / BMG.

REUNION
CD _____ OW 24833
One Way / Jul '94 / Direct / ADA.

TWO JEWS BLUES
CD _____ OW 27672
One Way / Jul '94 / Direct / ADA.

Goldberg, Ben

BEN GOLDBERG & TREVOR DUNN/ JOHN SCOTT/KENNY WOLLESEN PROJECT
CD _____ KFWCD 160
Knitting Factory / Feb '95 / Grapevine.

Goldberg, Stu

FANCY GLANCE
CD _____ INAK 8614 CD
In Akustik / Dec '87 / Magnum Music Group.

Golden & Carillo

FIRE IN NEW TOWN, A
CD _____ 9070822
Silenz / Aug '92 / BMG.

Golden Bough

BEST OF GOLDEN BOUGH
CD _____ EUCD 1145
ARC / '91 / ARC Music / ADA.

BEYOND THE SHADOWS
CD _____ EUCD 1092
ARC / '89 / ARC Music / ADA.

BOATMAN'S DAUGHTER
CD _____ EUCD 1037
ARC / '89 / ARC Music / ADA.

FAR FROM HOME
CD _____ EUCD 1065
ARC / '89 / ARC Music / ADA.

FLIGHT OF FANTASY
CD _____ EUCD 1045
ARC / '89 / ARC Music / ADA.

GOLDEN BOUGH
CD _____ EUCD 1123
ARC / '91 / ARC Music / ADA.

WINDING ROAD
CD _____ EUCD 1051
ARC / '89 / ARC Music / ADA.

WINTER'S DANCE
CD _____ EUCD 1046
ARC / '89 / ARC Music / ADA.

Golden Claw Music

ALL BLUE REVIEW
CD _____ INFECT 7CD
Infectious / Jul '94 / Disc.

Golden Dawn

POWER PLANT
Evolution / This way please / Starvation / I'll be around / Seeing is believing / My time / Nice surprise / Everyday / Tell me why / Reaching out to you
CD _____ 842969
EVA / May '94 / Direct / ADA.

Golden Eagle Jazz Band

MOROCCO BLUES
Stomp Off / Aug '90 / Jazz Music / Wellard.
CD _____ SOSCD 1192

Golden Eagles

LIGHTNING AND THUNDER (ROUNDER) (Golden Eagles & Monk Boudreaux)
CD _____ CD 2073
Rounder / '88 / CM / Direct / ADA / Cadillac.

Golden Earring

ANGEL
CD _____ 4776502
Sony Music / Jul '93 / Sony.

BEST OF GOLDEN EARRING, THE
CD _____ VSOPCD 171
Connoisseur / Mar '92 / Pinnacle.

Golden Gate Quartet

FROM SPIRITUALS TO SWING VOL.2
CD _____ 7805732
Jazztime / Aug '93 / Discovery / BMG.

GOSPEL TRAIN (Golden Gate Jubilee Quartet)
CD _____ JSPCD 602
JSP / Jul '93 / ADA / Target/BMG / Direct / Cadillac / Complete/Pinnacle.

GREATEST HITS 1946-50
CD _____ BMCD 3016
Blue Moon / Sep '95 / Magnum Music Group / Greensleeves / Hot Shot / ADA / Cadillac / Discovery.

THEIR EARLY YEARS 1937-39
CD _____ BMCD 3015
Blue Moon / Sep '95 / Magnum Music Group / Greensleeves / Hot Shot / ADA / Cadillac / Discovery.

TRAVELIN' SHOES
Golden gate gospel train / Beside of a neighbor / Job / Motherless child / Travelin' shoes / Dipsy doodle / Lead me on and on / Sampson / Take your burdens to God / Bye and bye little children / God almighty said / Let that liar alone / To the rock / Cheer the weary traveler / I heard Zion moan / Packing up, getting ready to go / Noah / Ol' man Mose / Hide me in thy bosom / If I had my way / I looked down the road and I wondered / Way down in Egypt land / I'm a pilgrim / Stormy weather / My walking stick
CD _____ 7863 66063-2
Bluebird / Oct '92 / BMG.

Golden Palaminos

HISTORY OF THE GOLDEN PALAMINOS VOL.2 (1986-1989)
CD _____ MAUCD 626
Mau Mau / Aug '92 / Pinnacle.

NO THOUGHT, NO BREATH, NO EYES, NO HEART (The pure remix E.P.)
Heaven (you have to be in hell to see heaven) / No skin (tempting fate) / Gun/Little

---

suicides (brown stainwalls, red jelly corners) / No skin (cold spells) / No skin (aural circumcision) / No skin (funky hornsey)
CD _____ 727902
Restless / Mar '95 / Vital.

PURE
Little suicides / Heaven / Anything / Wings / Pure / No skin / Gun / Break in the road / Touch you
CD _____ 77276-2
Restless / Oct '94 / Vital.

THIS IS HOW IT FEELS
Sleepwalk / Prison of the rhythm / I'm not sorry / This is how it feels / To a stranger / Wonder / Breakdown / These days / Rain holds / Twist the knife / Bird flying / Divine kiss
CD _____ 72735-2
Restless / Nov '93 / Vital.

VISIONS OF EXCESS
CD _____ CPCD 8151
Celluloid / Nov '95 / Charly.

Golden Smog

DOWN BY THE OLD MAINSTREAM
V / Ill-fated / Pecan pie / Yesterday I cried / Glad and sorry / Won't be coming home / He's a dick / Walk where he walked / Nowhere bound / Friend / She don't have to see you / Red headed stepchild / Williamton angel / Radio King
CD _____ RCD 10325
Rykodisc / Jan '96 / Vital / ADA.

Golden Star

DHOOTAKADA BAI DHOOTAKADA
CD _____ CDSR 019
Star / Aug '90 / Pinnacle / Sterns.

Goldie

TIMELESS
Timeless / Saint Angel / State of mind / This is a bad / Sea of tears / Jah the seventh seal / Sense of rage / Still life / Angel / Adrift / Kemistry / You and me
CD _____ 8286462
FFRR / Sep '95 / PolyGram.

Goldings, Larry

CAMINHOS CRUZADOS
So dance samba / Caminhos cruzados / Ho-ba-la-la / O amor en paz / Where or when / Manine / Avaraundado / Serenata / Menina-moca / Words / Una mas
CD _____ 01241631842
Novus / Jun '95 / BMG.

Goldsboro, Bobby

HONEY (22 Greatest Hits)
See the funny little clown / Whenever he holds you / Me japanese boy, I love you / Summer (the first time) / Brand new kind of love / Watching scotty grow / Can you feel it / I'm a drifter / Glad she's a woman / Straight life / Autumn of my life / Blue Autumn / It hurts me / It's too late / Voodoo woman / Little things / I don't know you anymore
CD _____ RMB 75084
Remember / Jan '96 / Total/BMG.

HONEY - THE BEST OF BOBBY GOLDSBORO
See the funny little clown / Hello loser / Whenever he holds you / My Japanese boy, i love you / I don't know you anymore / Little things / Voodoo woman / It hurts me heart / If you wait for love / If you've got a heart / Broomstick cowboy / It's too late / It hurts me / Blue Autumn / Honey / Autumn of my life / Straight life / Glad she's a woman / I'm a drifter / Can you feel it / Watching Scotty grow / Brand new kind of love / Summer (the first time)
CD _____ 295898
RCA / Jul '93 / BMG.

VERY BEST OF BOBBY GOLDSBORO, THE
Honey / Straight life / With pen in hand / Muddy Mississippi line / Blue Autumn / Little things / Summer (the first time) / Watchin' Scotty grow / See the funny little clown / Cowboy and the lady / Broomstick cowboy / It's too late / Autumn of my life / Hello summertime / I'm a drifter / Love divine / Payin' for the good times / Street dancin'
CD _____ C5CD-534
See For Miles/C5 / Dec '89 / Pinnacle.

Goldsby, John

TALE OF THE FINGERS (Goldsby, John Quartet)
Op / Terrace / Three short stories for contrabass and piano / Tale of the fingers / Twilight time / Tricotism / Time and again / Beautiful / Seven minds / Pitter, panther, patter
CD _____ CCD 4632
Concord Jazz / Feb '95 / New Note.

Goldschmidt, Per

FRAME, THE
Blues for Trane / Snowgirl / Frame / Lone-
liness / Bermuda triangle
CD _____ CDSJP 290
Timeless Jazz / Aug '90 / New Note.

Goldstein, Gil

SANDS OF TIME
Sands of time / Wishing well / Finding your
own way / Singing rhythm / Wrapped in a
cloud / Beantown (revisited)
CD _____ MCD 5471
Muse / Jun '93 / New Note / CM.

Goldy, Craig

**HIDDEN IN PLAIN SIGHT (Craig Goldy's
Ritual)**
CD _____ CDMFN 125
Music For Nations / Mar '92 / Pinnacle.

Golgotha

MELANCHOLY
CD _____ RPS 011CD
Repulse / Jan '96 / Plastic Head.

SYMPHONY IN EXTREMIS
CD _____ CMGCD 009
Communique / Jul '93 / Plastic Head.

UNMAKER OF WORLDS
CD _____ CMGCD 003
Communique / Nov '90 / Plastic Head.

Golia, Vinny

**HAUNTING THE SPIRITS INSIDE THEM
(Golia, Vinny & Joelle Leandre/Ken
Filiano)**
CD _____ CD 893
Music & Arts / Jan '96 / Harmonia Mundi /
Cadillac.

REGARDS FROM NORMAN DESMOND
CD _____ FSNT 008CD
Fresh Sound / Mar '95 / Jazz Music /
Discovery.

Golson, Benny

BENNY GOLSON IN PARIS
CD _____ CDSW 8418
DRG / Jan '89 / New Note.

BENNY GOLSON QUARTET - LIVE
Sweet and lovely / Along came Betty / I re-
member Clifford / Cup bearers / Jam the
avenue
CD _____ FDM 365522
Dreyfus / Aug '94 / ADA / Direct / New Note.

GROOVIN' WITH GOLSON
CD _____ OJCCD 226
Original Jazz Classics / Sep '93 / Wellard /
Jazz Music / Cadillac / Complete/Pinnacle.

**STARDUST (Golson, Benny & Freddie
Hubbard)**
Stardust / Double bass / Gypsy jingle-jangle
/ Povo / Love is a many splendoured thing
/ Sad to say / Far away
CD _____ CY 1838
Denon / Oct '88 / Conifer.

THIS IS FOR YOU JOHN
Jam the avenue / Greensleeves / Origin /
Change of heart / Times past (this is for you,
John) / Page 12 / Vilia
CD _____ CDSJP 239
Timeless Jazz / Jan '88 / New Note.

TIME SPEAKS
I'll remember April / Time speaks / No dan-
cin' / Jordu / Blues for Duane / Theme for
Maxine
CD _____ CDSJP 187
Timeless Jazz / Jan '87 / New Note.

Golub, Jeff

UNSPOKEN WORDS
CD _____ 139008-2
Gaia / May '89 / New Note.

Gomez, Eddie

GOMEZ (Gomez, Eddie & Chick Corea)
Dabble vision / Santurce / Japanese waltz
/ Zimmermann (for Toru Takemitsu) / Mez-
ga / Ginkakuji / Pops and Alma / Row row
row your tones / We will meet again
CD _____ DC 8562
Denon / Aug '90 / Conifer.

LIVE IN MOSCOW
Alice in wonderland / Stella by starlight /
Someday my prince will come / Dabble ver-
sion / Spartacus love theme / Nardis / Solar
CD _____ BW 038
B&W / Mar '94 / New Note.

STREET SMART
Street smart / Lorenzo / I'caramba / It was
you all along / Blues period / Double entendre / Carmen's song / Bella horizonte / Besame mucho
CD _____ 4662252
Epic / Apr '90 / Sony.

Gomez, Jill

**CABARET CLASSICS (Gomez, Jill &
John Constable)**

CD _____ DKPCD 9055
Unicorn-Kanchana / Aug '88 / Harmonia
Mundi.

**SOUTH OF THE BORDER...DOWN
MEXICO WAY**
CD _____ CDA 66500
Hyperion / Dec '90 / Select.

Gomorrah

**REFLECTIONS OF AN INANIMATE
MATTER**
CD _____ BMCD 067
Black Mark / Aug '95 / Plastic Head.

Gone

ALL THE DIRT THAT'S FIT TO PRINT
CD _____ SST 306CD
SST / Sep '94 / Plastic Head.

CRIMINAL MIND
CD _____ SST 300 CD
SST / Jan '94 / Plastic Head.

GONE II, BUT NEVER TOO GONE
CD _____ SST 086 CD
SST / May '93 / Plastic Head.

**LET'S GET REAL, REAL GONE FOR A
CHANGE**
CD _____ SST 061 CD
SST / May '93 / Plastic Head.

Gonella, Nat

**CRAZY VALVES (Gonella, Nat & His
Georgians)**
How'm I doin / Capri caprice / Skeleton in
the cupboard / I can't dance / Crazy valves
/ Bessie couldn't help it / Take another
guess / Nagasaki / Just a crazy song /
Sheikh of Araby / Tiger rag / Copper col-
oured gal / Ol' man mose / Trumpetuous /
I'm gonna clap my hands / Makin' a fool of
myself / Bill Tell / Georgia on my mind
CD _____ CD AJA 5055
Living Era / Sep '88 / Koch.

CREAM OF NAT GONELLA, THE
CD _____ PASTCD 9750
Flapper / Aug '91 / Pinnacle.

NATURALLY GONELLA
Yeah man / Truckin' / Hot lips / Sheikh of
Araby / Black coffee / Blow Gabriel blow /
Capri caprice / Oh Peter (you're so nice) /
Georgia rockin' chair / Lazy river / Sweet
and hot / Pidgin English hula / Squareface
/ Japanese sandman / Ghost of Dinah / Jig
time / Gonna wed that gal o' mine / Peanut
vendor / Sophisticated lady / Georgia on my
mind / Tuxedo Junction / Big noise from
Winnetka / I understand / At the wood-
choppers' ball / South with the boarder /
Hep hep the jumpin' jive / Johnson rag / If
you were the only girl in the world / Beat
me Daddy, eight to the bar / In the mood /
Ay ay ay / No Mama no / I haven't time to
be a millionaire / Vox poppin' / Oh Buddy
I'm in love / It's a pair of wings for me / Eep
ipe wanna piece of pie / Sunrise serenade
/ Yes my darling daughter / Plucking on the
golden harp
CD _____ RAJCD 804
Empress / Oct '93 / THE.

Gong

25TH BIRTHDAY PARTY (2 CDST)
Thom intro / Floating into a birthday gig /
You can't kill me / Radio gnome 25 / I am
you pussy / Pot head pixies / Never glid
before / Eat that phonebook / Gnomic gard-
dress / Flute salad / Oily way
CD Set _____ VPGAS 101CD
Gas / Sep '95 / Vital.

ANGELS EGGS
Other side of the sky / Sold to the highest
Buddha / Castle in the clouds / Prostitute
poem / Givin' my luv to you / Selene / Flute
salad / Oily way / Outer temple / Inner temple / Love is how you make it / I never glid
before / Eat that phonebook code
CD _____ CDLIK 75
Decal / May '91 / Charly / Swift.

BEST OF GONG
Wet cheese delirum / Tropical fish / Seline
/ Flying teapot / Pot head Pixies / Outer
temple / Eat the phone book coda / Magick
mother invocation / Master builder / Mister
long shanks / O Mother I am your fantasy /
Squeezing sponges over policemen's
heads / Octave doctors and the crystal ma-
chine / Zero the hero and the witches spell
/ Castle in the clouds / Inner temple /
Sprinkling of clouds / Much too old
CD _____ NTMCD 517
Nectar / Oct '95 / Pinnacle.

BREAKTHROUGH
CD _____ EUCD 1053
ARC / '89 / ARC Music / ADA.

CAMEMBERT ELECTRIQUE
Radio gnome predection / You can't kill me
/ I've bin stone before / Mr. Long Shanks:
O Mother! am your fantasy / Dynamite: I
am your animal / Wet cheese delirium /
Squeezing sponges over policemen's
heads / Fohat digs holes in space / And you
tried so hard / Tropical fish: Selene / Gnome
the second

CD _____ CDLIK 64
Decal / Apr '90 / Charly / Swift.

CAMEMBERT ELECTIQUE
Cafe monjalilieu demos / Garcon ou fille /
Dynamite/Goldilocks / Rock 'n' roll angel /
Hyp hypnotise you / Haunted chateau re-
hersals / Big city energy intro / Gongwash
indelible
CD _____ GAS 001CD
Gas / Nov '94 / Vital.

EXPRESSO 2
Heavy tune / Golden dilemma / Sleepy / Soli
/ Boring / Three blind mice
CD _____ CDV 2099
Virgin / Jun '90 / EMI.

EYE (Mother Gong)
Fanfare / She's the mother of / Sunday /
Beds / Time is a hurrying dog / Ancient /
Zen / Quantum / Spirit canoe / What if we
were gods and goddesses / Auction / Little
boy / Magic stories / Excuses / Sax canoe
/ Fairy laughter / Virtual reality
CD _____ VP 176CD
Voice Print / Sep '94 / Voice Print.

FLOATING ANARCHY (LIVE)
CD _____ CDLIK 68
Decal / Oct '90 / Charly / Swift.

GAZEUSE
Expresso / Night illusion / Percolations (part
1) / Percolations (part 2) / Shadows of Mir-
eille / Esnuria
CD _____ CDV 2074
Virgin / Jun '90 / EMI.

GONG MAISON (Gong Maison)
CD _____ DMCD 1024
Demi-Monde / Feb '90 / Disc / Magnum
Music Group.

**HISTORY AND THE MYSTERY OF THE
PLANET GONG, THE**
Concert intro / Captain Shaw and Mr. Gilbert / Love makes sweet music /
D.L.T.interview / Riot 1968 / Dreaming it / I
feel so lazy / And I tried so hard / Radio
gnome pre-mix / Pot head pixies / Majick
brother / Line up / Clarence in Wonderland
/ Breakthrough interview / Where have all
the hours gone / Gong poem / Dey a Goddess / Opium for the people / Red alert /
13/8 / Gliss-u-well / Future / Dream / Chernobyl rain / Let me be one
CD _____ CDTB 116
Thunderbolt / '91 / Magnum Music Group.

HOW TO NUKE THE EIFFEL TOWER
Away away / Nuclear mega waste / Cher-
nobyl rain
CD _____ VPGASCD 102
Gas / Sep '95 / Vital.

LIVE 1990
CD _____ NINETY 1
Demon / Mar '93 / Pinnacle / ADA.

LIVE ETC
You can't kill me / Zero the hero and the
witches spell / Flying teapot / Dynamite: I
am your animal / 6/8 / Est-ce que je suis /
Ooby-scooby doomsday or the D-day DJ's
got the / Radio gnome invisible / Oily way /
Outer temple / Inner temple / Where have
all the flowers gone / Isle of everywhere /
Get it inner / Master Builder / Flying teapot
(reprise)
CD _____ CDVM 3501
Virgin / '90 / EMI.

OWL AND THE TREE, THE
CD _____ CDTB 118
Thunderbolt / Feb '92 / Magnum Music
Group.

PRE MODERNIST WIRELESS ON RADIO
Magick brother / Clarence in wonderland /
Tropical fish / Selene / You can't kill me /
Radio gnome direct broadcast / Crystal ma-
chine / Zero the hero and the orgasm witch
/ Captain capricorns dream saloon / Radio
gnome invisible / Oily way / Sleepy
CD _____ SFRCD 137
Strange Fruit / Dec '95 / Pinnacle.

**RADIO GNOME INVISIBLE, PART 2
(Angel's Egg)**
Other side of the sky / Sold to the highest
Buddha / Castle in the clouds / Prostitute
poem / Givin' my luv to you / Selene / Flute
salad / Oily way / I never glid before / Eat
that phonebook code / Outer temple / Inner
temple / Percolations / Love is how you
make it
CD _____ CDV 2007
Virgin / Jun '90 / EMI.

SECOND WIND (Pierre Moelen's Gong)
Second wind / Time and space / Say no
more / Deep end / Crystal funk / Exotic /
Beton / Alan Key / Crash and Co. #1 / Crash
and Co. #2 / Crash and Co. #3
CD _____ LICD 900698
Line / Nov '92 / CM / Grapevine / ADA /
Conifer / Direct.

SHAMAL
Wingful of eyes / Chandra / Bambooji / Cat
in Clark's shoes / Mandrake / Shamal
CD _____ CDV 2046
Virgin / Jun '90 / EMI.

SHE MADE THE WORLD MAGENTA
Magenta / Water / She made the world /
Weather / Malicious sausage / Sea horse /
Spirit calling / Tattered jacket / Warn / When

---

the show is over / I am a witch / Spirit of
the bush / Blessed be
CD _____ VP 134CD
Voice Print / May '93 / Voice Print.

**VOICEPRINT RADIO SESSION (Mother
Gong)**
CD _____ VPR 007CD
Voice Print / Oct '94 / Voice Print.

WILD CHILD (Mother Gong)
CD _____ DMCD 1026
Demi-Monde / Jul '94 / Disc / Magnum
Music Group.

WINGFUL OF EYES, A
Heavy tune / Cat in Clark's shoes / Night
illusion / Golden dilemma / Wingful of eyes
/ Three blind mice / Expresso / Soli / Shad-
ows of / Mandrake / Bambouji
CD _____ CDOVD 462
Virgin / Jan '96 / EMI.

YOU
A.P.H.P's advice / Thoughts for nought /
Magick mother invocation / Master builder
/ Sprinkling of clouds / Perfect mystery / Isle
of everywhere / You never blow your trip
forever
CD _____ CDV 2019
Virgin / Jun '90 / EMI.

Gonnella, Ron

**RON GONNELLA'S INTERNATIONAL
FRIENDSHIP TUNE**
BBC echoes / Cape Breton ceudh / Hector
MacAndrews favourites / Congratulations
all round / Sounds of Strathearn / Touch of
Gaelic / Bonnie Dundee / Boston tea party
/ Jimmy Shand special / Strathspey king
and friends / Scottish dance music corner /
Canadian connection / Fiddlers two / My
friend Adam Rennie / New York, New York
/ Music of William Marshall
CD _____ CDITV 453
Scotdisc / Aug '88 / Duncans / Ross /
Conifer.

Gonsalves, Paul

GETTIN' TOGETHER
CD _____ OJCCD 203-2
Original Jazz Classics / Feb '92 / Wellard /
Jazz Music / Cadillac / Complete/Pinnacle.

**JAZZ TILL MIDNIGHT (Gonsalves, Paul
& Eddie 'Lockjaw' Davis)**
CD _____ STCD 4123
Storyville / Feb '90 / Jazz Music / Wellard
/ CM / Cadillac.

**JUST A-SITTIN' AND A-ROCKIN'
(Gonsalves, Paul & Ray Nance)**
BP blues / Lotus blossom / Don't blame me
/ Just a sittin' and a rockin' / Hi ya, Sue /
Angel eyes / I'm in the market for you / Tea
for two
CD _____ BLCD 760148
Black Lion / May '91 / Jazz Music / Cadillac
/ Wellard / Koch.

**PAUL GONSALVES MEETS EARL HINES
(Gonsalves, Paul & Earl Hines)**
CD _____ BLCD 760177
Black Lion / Mar '93 / Jazz Music /
Cadillac / Wellard / Koch.

Gonzalez, Celina

FIESTA GUAJIRA
Yo soy el punto Cubana / Muero de olvido
/ Santa Barbara / Oye mi le lo ley / Guajiro
Guacarono / Paisajes naturales / El refran
se te Olivido / Aguacero aguacerito / Mi
tierra es asi
CD _____ WC 34CD
World Circuit / Oct '93 / New Note / Direct
/ Cadillac / ADA.

QUE VIVA CHANGO
Santa Barbara / Oye mi la lo lei / El refran
se te olvido / Aurora / Mi tierra es asi / El
reto / Yo soy el punto Cubana / Camina y
ven / Aguacero aguacerito / Guateque campesino / Paisajes / El hijo del sibony
CD _____ PSCCD 1002
Pure Sounds From Cuba / Feb '95 / Henry
Hadaway Organisation / THE.

Gonzalez, Dennis

DEBENGE DEBENGE
CD _____ SHCD 112
Silkheart / May '89 / Jazz Music / Wellard
/ CM / Cadillac.

**NAMESAKE (Gonzalez, Dennis New
Dallas Quartet)**
CD _____ SHCD 106
Silkheart / May '88 / Jazz Music / Wellard
/ CM / Cadillac.

Gonzalez, Jerry

**EARTH DANCE (Gonzalez, Jerry & Fort
Apache Band)**
CD _____ SSC 1050D
Sunnyside / May '91 / Pinnacle.

**RIVER IS DEEP, THE (Gonzalez, Jerry &
Fort Apache Band)**
CD _____ 4040-2
Enja / Apr '91 / New Note / Vital/SAM.

Goo Goo Dolls

BOY NAMED GOO, A
CD _____ 9362457502
Warner Bros. / Apr '95 / Warner Music.

GOO GOO DOLLS
CD _____ 14079-2
Metal Blade / Oct '95 / Plastic Head.

JED
Out of sight / No way out / Down the corner / Road To Salinas / Misfortune / Gimme shelter / Up yours / Sex maggot / Had enough / Em elbmuh / Artie / James Dean
CD _____ CDZORRO 70
Metal Blade / Feb '94 / Pinnacle.

Good Fellas

GOOD FELLAS
Rap city / Witches / Head and out / Candy / Almost always / Secret love / Bossami / Cherokee / Taxi driver (theme)
CD _____ ECD 22050
Evidence / Jul '93 / Harmonia Mundi / ADA / Cadillac.

GOOD FELLAS 2
Look out / Dr. Jamie / It's you or no one / In the dream / Anti-calypso / I'll miss you / Welcome / Pop gun / Quick way / Breezi-lee
CD _____ ECD 220772
Evidence / Mar '94 / Harmonia Mundi / ADA / Cadillac.

GOOD FELLAS 3
Spacing / Twice around / Tribeca / Moon in Rio / Fabiophobia / Folklore / Old fisherman's daughter / Koba's fax / Natalie / Snowflakes
CD _____ KICJ 166
King/Paddle Wheel / Nov '93 / New Note.

Good Morning Blues

NEVER MAKE A MOVE TO SOON
CD _____ SITCD 9201
Sittel / Aug '94 / Cadillac / Jazz Music.

Good Ol' Persons

GOOD 'N' LIVE
CD _____ SHCD 2208
Sugarhill / Jan '96 / Roots / CM / ADA / Direct.

Good Rats

GOOD RATS
CD _____ REP 4034-WZ
Repertoire / Aug '91 / Pinnacle / Cadillac.

Good Riddance

FOR GOD AND COUNTRY
CD _____ FAT 23
Fat Wreck Chords / Mar '95 / Plastic Head.

Good Sons

SINGING THE GLORY DOWN
Help me to find / Leaving time / When the night comes / Gospel Hall / Riding the range / You are everything / God's other son / Tower of strength / Watch my dreamboat sail / Day to day / My own prayers / When I turn out the light
CD _____ GRCD 379
Glitterhouse / Dec '95 / Direct / ADA.

Goodbye Harry

FOOD STAMP BBQ
CD _____ CRZ 037CD
Cruz / Jan '95 / Pinnacle / Plastic Head.

Goodbye Mr. Mackenzie

FIVE
CD _____ BLOKCD 002
Blokshok / Oct '93 / Pinnacle.

JEZEBEL
CD _____ BLOKCD 004
Blokshok / Jul '95 / Pinnacle.

LIVE: ON THE DAY OF STORMS
Goodwill city / Blacker than black / Face to face / Diamonds / Pleasure search / Sick baby / Goodbye Mr. Mackenzie / Dust
CD _____ BLOKCD 001
Blokshok / Mar '93 / Pinnacle.

Goode, B.

SHOCK OF THE NEW
CD _____ DD 440
Delmark / Nov '92 / Hot Shot / ADA / CM / Direct / Cadillac.

Gooding, Cuba

MEANT TO BE IN LOVE
CD _____ TRI 4162CD
Ichiban / Feb '94 / Koch.

Goodman, Benny

16 MOST REQUESTED SONGS
Let's dance / Don't be that way / Avalon / Flying home / Memories of you / Somebody stole my gal / Clarinet a la King / Jersey bounce / Why don't you do right / After you've gone / Stompin' at the Savoy / Sing, sing, sing / Symphony / Liza (All the clouds'll roll away) / How am I to know / Goodbye
CD _____ 474396 2
Columbia / Feb '94 / Sony.

1928-31 (Goodman, Benny Orchestra)
CD _____ CLASSICS 693
Classic Jazz Masters / May '93 / Wellard / Jazz Music / Jazz Music.

1935 RADIO TRANSCRIPTS (Goodman, Benny & His Rhythm Makers)
Makin' whoopee / Poor butterfly / Between the Devil and the deep blue sea / Farewell blues / I would do almost anything for you / Bugle call rag
CD _____ TAXCD 3708
Tax / Apr '90 / Jazz Music / Wellard / Cadillac.

1935 RADIO TRANSCRIPTS VOLUME 2 (Goodman, Benny & His Rhythm Makers)
Royal Garden blues / Down South camp meeting / Lovely to look at / Stardust / Sugarfoot stomp / Wrappin' it up
CD _____ GRV 74602
Gramavision / Sep '91 / Vital/SAM / ADA.

1935 VOLUME 1 (Goodman, Benny & His Rhythm Makers)
CD _____ TAX 37082
Tax / Aug '94 / Jazz Music / Wellard / Cadillac.

1935 VOLUME 2 (Goodman, Benny & His Rhythm Makers)
CD _____ TAX 37192
Tax / Aug '94 / Jazz Music / Wellard / Cadillac.

1935-1938
CD _____ CD 56060
Jazz Roots / Mar '95 / Target/BMG.

1946/49/61
CD _____ 90510-2
Jazz Archives / Oct '92 / Jazz Music / Discovery / Cadillac.

AIR CHECKS 1937 - 1938
Let's dance / Moten swing / Vibraphone blues / Peckin' / Nagasaki / St. Louis blues / Sugarfoot stomp / I'm a ding dong daddy from Dumas / Bumble Bee stomp / Naughty waltz / Vieni vieni / Roll 'em / Have you met Miss Jones / Shine / When Buddha smiles / Laughing at life / You turned the tables / My gal Sal / Mama that moon is here again / Time on my hands / In the shadow of the old apple tree / Benny sent me / Moonlight on the highway / Killer diller / Someday sweetheart / Goodbye / Riding high / Nice work if you can get it / Sheikh of Araby / Sunny disposish / Whispers in the dark / Life goes to a party / Moonglow / I hadn't anyone till you / Down south camp meeting / Sweet leilani / Sometimes I'm happy / King Porter stomp / Limehouse blues / Minnie The Moocher's wedding day / Running wild / At the Darktown strutter's ball / Bugle call rag / Clarinet marmalade / Stardust / Everybody loves my baby / Josephine / Caravan
CD Set _____ 472990 2
Columbia / Oct '93 / Sony.

ALL THE CATS JOIN IN
Clarinade / All the cats join in / Mad boogie / Remember / Somebody stole my gal / At the Darktown strutter's ball / Lucky / Rattle and roll / Body and soul / Lady be good
CD _____ TII 088 018
TKO / '92 / TKO.

ALL THE CATS JOIN IN (Goodman, Benny Orchestra)
CD _____ CDCD 1237
Charly / Jun '95 / Charly / THE / Cadillac.

AVALON - THE SMALL BANDS (Goodman, Benny Quartet)
Avalon / Handful of keys / Man I love / Smiles / Liza / Where or when / Vieni vieni / I'm a ding dong daddy from Dumas / Sweet Lorraine / Blues in your flat / Sugar / Dizzy spells / Opus 1/2 / I must have that man / Sweet Georgia Brown / 'S wonderful / Pick-a-rib (part 1) / Pick-a-rib (part 2) / I cried for you / I know that you know / Opus 3/4
CD _____ ND 82273
Bluebird / Oct '90 / BMG.

BENNY GOODMAN
CD _____ 295715
Ariola / Apr '93 / BMG.

BENNY GOODMAN
CD _____ CWNCD 2006
Javelin / Jun '95 / THE / Henry Hadaway Organisation.

BENNY GOODMAN & HIS GREAT VOCALISTS
Riffin' the scotch / Blue moon / Gal in Calico / Blue skies / Symphony / It's only a paper moon / Gotta this or that / Close a pages in a book / Every time we say goodbye / Serenade in blue / Somebody else is taking my place / I got it bad and that ain't good / Taking a chance on love / Peace, brother / There'll be some changes made / Loch Lomond
CD _____ CK 66198
Columbia / Jul '95 / Sony.

BENNY GOODMAN - 1934
CD _____ CCD 111
Circle / Oct '91 / Jazz Music / Swift / Wellard.

BENNY GOODMAN AND HIS ORCHESTRA (Goodman, Benny Orchestra)
CD _____ 11042
Lacerlight / '86 / Target/BMG.

BENNY GOODMAN AND HIS ORCHESTRA 1935 - 1939 (Goodman, Benny Orchestra)
CD _____ GOJCD 53042
Giants Of Jazz / Jan '89 / Target/BMG / Cadillac.

BENNY GOODMAN AND HIS ORCHESTRA 1935-1939 (Goodman, Benny Orchestra)
Don't be that way / King Porter stomp / Roll 'em / Down south camp meeting / Goodbye / Christopher Columbus / One o'clock jump / Bugle call rag / Sing, sing, sing / I want to be happy / Smoke house rhythm / Stompin' at the Savoy / Topsy / Sugarfoot stomp / Kingdom of swing / Bach goes to town / Sent for you yesterday / Sing me a swing song
CD _____ CD 56005
Jazz Roots / Aug '94 / Target/BMG.

BENNY GOODMAN CLASSICS 1935-1941
CD _____ NEOVOX 879
Neovox / Oct '93 / Wellard

BENNY GOODMAN IN STOCKHOLM (1959) (Goodman, Benny & Flip Phillips)
CD _____ PHONTCD 8801
Phontastic / '88 / Wellard / Jazz Music / Cadillac.

BENNY GOODMAN ORCHESTRA & SEXTET (Goodman, Benny Orchestra)
CD _____ CD 14562
Jazz Portraits / May '95 / Jazz Music.

BENNY GOODMAN SEXTET FEATURING CHARLIE CHRISTIAN 1939-1941
CD _____ 4656792
Sony Jazz / Jan '95 / Sony.

BENNY GOODMAN STORY, THE
Down South camp meetin' / And the angels sing / Goodbye / Sing, sing, sing / Shine / One o'clock jump / Bugle call rag / King Porter stomp / Let's dance / Don't be that way / It's been so long / Sometimes I'm happy / Goody goody / Avalon / Moonglow / Alicia's blues / Memories of you / China boy / Seven come eleven
CD _____ CDP 8335692
Capitol Jazz / Nov '95 / EMI.

BENNY GOODMAN SWINGS AGAIN
CD _____ 4756252
Sony Jazz / Jan '95 / Sony.

BENNY GOODMAN TRIO AND QUARTET SESSIONS, VOL 1 (Goodman, Benny Trio & Quartet)
After you've gone / Body and soul / Who / Someday, sweetheart / China boy / More than you know / All my life / Lady be good / Nobody's sweetheart / Too good to be true / Moonglow / Dinah / Exactly like you / Vibraphone blues / Sweet Sue, just you / My melancholy baby / Tiger rag / Stompin' at the Savoy / Whispering / Ida / Tea for two / Running wild
CD _____ ND 85631
Bluebird / Apr '88 / BMG.

BENNY GOODMAN VOL.1
Sweet Georgia Brown / Broadway / Blue room
CD _____ CIJ 60142 Z
Music Masters / Jan '89 / Nimbus.

BENNY GOODMAN VOLS.3 & 4
Smiles / Liza (All the clouds'll roll away) / Where or when / Silhouetted in the moonlight / Vieni vieni / I'm a ding dong daddy from Dumas (2 versions) / Bei mir bist du schon (Parts 1 & 2) / Sweet Lorraine / Blues in your flat (2 versions) / Sugar (2 versions) / Dizzy spells / Opus onen half / I must have that man / Sweet Georgia Brown / 'S wonderful (2 versions) / Pick-a-rib (Parts 1 & 2) / I cried for you (2 versions) / I know that you know and you know that I know (2 versions)
CD _____ ND 89754
Jazz Tribune / Jun '94 / BMG.

BENNY'S BOP
Mary's idea / Bye bye blues bop / There's a small hotel / Blue views / I can't give you anything but love / You took advantage of me / Where oh where has my little dog gone / Pepper (Patsy's idea) / String of pearls / I'll see you in my dreams / Undercurrent blues
CD _____ HEPCD 36
Hep / Oct '93 / Cadillac / Jazz Music / New Note / Wellard.

BEST OF BENNY GOODMAN
Don't be that way / Sing, sing, sing / And the angels sing / Loch Lomond / King Porter stomp / Stompin' at the Savoy / One

o'clock jump / After you've gone / Goodnight my love / Goodbye
CD _____ DCD 5331
Disky / Dec '93 / THE / BMG / Discovery / Pinnacle.

BEST OF BENNY GOODMAN
CD _____ DLCD 4011
Dixie Live / Mar '95 / Magnum Music Group.

BEST OF THE BIG BANDS
Don't be that way / What's new / Taking a chance on love / My old flame / Shake down the stars / Tangerine / How high the moon / Air mail special / How long has this been going on / Why don't you do right / Symphony / I'm nobody's baby / Close as pages in a book / Something new / My guy's come back / Somebody stole my gal
CD _____ 4666202
CBS / '91 / Sony.

BEST OF THE BIG BANDS (Goodman, Benny & Helen Forrest)
Yours is my heart alone / Mr. Meadowlark / Dreaming out loud / Nobody / Man I love / I'm always chasing rainbows / I hear a rhapsody / Corn silk / You're dangerous / This is new / Perfidia / Lazy river / Yours / Oh look at me now / Amapola / Smoke gets in your eyes
CD _____ 4716582
Columbia / Jun '92 / Sony.

BEST OF THE BIG BANDS (Goodman, Benny & Peggy Lee)
Elmer's tune / I see a million people / That's the way it goes / I got it bad and that ain't good / My old flame / How deep is the ocean / Shady ladybird / Let's do it / Somebody else is taking my place / Somebody nobody loves me / How long has this been going on / That did it, Marie / Winter weather / Everything I love / Not mine / Not a care in the world
CD _____ 473661 2
Columbia / Aug '93 / Sony.

BIG BAND EUROPE (Benny Goodman vol. 3)
Pennies from Heaven / Fine romance
CD _____ CIJ 60157X
Music Masters / '89 / Nimbus.

BIRTH OF SWING (1935-1936), THE
Hunkadola (takes 1 & 2) / I'm livin' in a great big way / Hooray for love / Dixieland band / Japanese sandman / You're a heavenly thing / Restless / Always / Get rhythm in your feet / Ballad in blue / Blue skies / Dear old Southland / Sometimes I'm happy / King Porter stomp / Devil and the deep blue sea / Jingle bells / Santa Claus came in the spring / Goodbye / Madhouse (take 1) / Madhouse (take 2) / Sandman / Yankee Doodle never went to town / No other one / Eeny meeny miney mo / Basin Street blues / If I could be with you one hour tonight / When Buddha smiles / It's been so long / Stompin' at the Savoy / Goody goody / Breakin' in a pair of shoes / Get happy / Christopher Columbus / I know that you know / Star dust / You can't pull the wool over my eyes / Glory of love / Remember / Walk Jennie walk / House hop (takes 2 & 3) / Sing me a swing song / (I would do) anything for you / In a sentimental mood / I've found a new baby / Swingtime in the Rockies / These foolish things / There's a small hotel / You turned the tables on me / Here's love in your eyes / Pick yourself up / Down South camp meeting / St. Louis blues (takes 1 & 2) / Bugle call rag (take 1) / When a lady meets a gentleman down South / You're giving me a song and a dance / I'm gan grinder swing / Peter Piper / Riffin' at the Ritz / Alexander's ragtime band / Somebody loves me / T'aint no use / Bugle call rag (take 2) / Jam session / Goodnight my love / Take another guess / Did you mean it
CD Set _____ ND 90601(3)
Bluebird / Jan '92 / BMG.

BODY & SOUL (Goodman, Benny Quartet)
CD _____ CDSGP 0209
Prestige / Apr '94 / Total/BMG.

BREAKFAST BALL
CD _____ TQ 201
Happy Days / Jan '93 / Conifer.

BREAKFAST BALL, 1934 (Goodman, Benny Orchestra)
Georgia jubilee / Junk man / Ol' pappy / Emaline / I ain't lazy / I'm just dreaming / As long as I live / Moon glow / Breakfast ball / Take my word / It happens to the best of friends / Nitwit serenade / Bugle call rag / Learning / Stars fell on Alabama / Solitude / I'm getting sentimental over you / I'm 100% for you / Cokey / Like a bolt from the blue / Music hall rag
CD _____ CDSVL 172
Saville / Mar '93 / Conifer.

CAMEL CARAVAN BROADCASTS 1939 VOL.1
Jeepers creepers / Hold tight / I cried for you / Undecided / Angels sing / Basin Street blues / Roll 'em
CD _____ NCD 8817
Phontastic / '93 / Wellard / Jazz Music / Cadillac.

CAMEL CARAVAN BROADCASTS 1939 VOL.2
CD _____ NCD 8818
Phontastic / '93 / Wellard / Jazz Music / Cadillac.

CAMEL CARAVAN BROADCASTS, VOL 3 (Goodman, Benny Orchestra)
CD _____ NCD 8819
Phontastic / '93 / Wellard / Jazz Music / Cadillac.

CARNEGIE HALL CONCERT 1938 PART 1
Don't be that way / One o'clock jump / Shine / Honeysuckle rose / Body and soul / Avalon
CD _____ CD 53101
Giants Of Jazz / May '92 / Target/BMG / Cadillac.

CARNEGIE HALL CONCERT 1938 PART 2 (And second Carnegie Hall concert 1939)
Loch Lomond / Stompin' at the Savoy / Dizzy spells / Don't be that way / Stardust
CD _____ CD 53102
Giants Of Jazz / May '92 / Target/BMG / Cadillac.

CLASSICS 1931-33
CD _____ CLASSICS 719
Classics / Jul '93 / Discovery / Jazz Music.

CLASSICS 1934-35
CD _____ CLASSICS 744
Classics / Feb '94 / Discovery / Jazz Music.

CLASSICS 1935
CD _____ CLASSICS 769
Classics / Aug '94 / Discovery / Jazz Music.

CLASSICS 1935-36
CD _____ CLASSICS 789
Classics / Nov '94 / Discovery / Jazz Music.

CLASSICS 1936
CD _____ CLASSICS 817
Classics / May '95 / Discovery / Jazz Music.

CLASSICS 1936 VOL.2
CD _____ CLASSICS 836
Classics / Sep '95 / Discovery / Jazz Music.

COMPLETE CAMEL CARAVAN SHOWS 20 & 28/9/1938
CD _____ JH 1025
Jazz Hour / Feb '93 / Target/BMG / Jazz Music / Cadillac.

COMPLETE VAMEL CARAVAN SHOWS 1938 (Goodman, Benny Orchestra)
CD _____ JH 1038
Jazz Hour / Feb '95 / Target/BMG / Jazz Music / Cadillac.

CREAM SERIES, THE
Stompin' at the Savoy / Sing, sing, sing / My melancholy baby / Louise / 'S Wonderful / Avalon / Who / Make believe / When a lady meets a gentleman down South / Chloe / Bach goes to town / Handful of keys / Take another guess / Dear old Southland / Sandman / Goodnight my love / Nobody's sweetheart / He ain't got rhythm / Japanese sandman / Vibraphone blues / Did you mean it
CD _____ PASTCD 9743
Flapper / Sep '91 / Pinnacle.

DIFFERENT VERSION VOL.I (1939-42)
CD _____ NCD 8821
Phontastic / Apr '94 / Wellard / Jazz Music / Cadillac.

DIFFERENT VERSION VOL.II
CD _____ NCD 8822
Phontastic / Jun '94 / Wellard / Jazz Music / Cadillac.

DIFFERENT VERSION VOL.III
CD _____ NCD 8823
Phontastic / Jun '94 / Wellard / Jazz Music / Cadillac.

DIFFERENT VERSION VOL.IV (1942-45)
CD _____ NCD 8824
Phontastic / Apr '94 / Wellard / Jazz Music / Cadillac.

DIFFERENT VERSION VOL.V
CD _____ NCD 8825
Phontastic / Jun '94 / Wellard / Jazz Music / Cadillac.

DON'T BE THAT WAY (Goodman, Benny Orchestra)
CD _____ CD 14527
Jazz Portraits / Jan '94 / Jazz Music.

EARLY YEARS
Old man Harlem / Keep on doin' what you're doin' / Nobody's sweetheart now / Ain't cha glad / Dr. Heckle and Mr. Jibe / Georgia jubilee / Texas tea party / Honeysuckle rose / Sweet Sue, just you / Hundred years from today / Riffin' the scotch / Your mother's son-in-law / Love me or leave me / I can't give you anything but love / Baby / I gotta right to sing the blues
CD _____ BCD 109

Biograph / Jul '91 / Wellard / ADA / Hot Shot / Jazz Music / Cadillac / Direct.

ESSENTIAL BENNY GOODMAN, THE
Let's dance / Flying home / Good enough to keep / Sm-o-o-oth one / Scarecrow / Clarinet a la King / Jersey bounce / Mission to Moscow / Body and soul / After you've gone / Liza / King Porter stomp / Down South camp meeting / South of the border / Wrappin' it up
CD _____ 467151 2
Columbia / Jul '93 / Sony.

ESSENTIAL V-DISCS, THE
CD _____ JZ-CD304
Suisa / Feb '91 / Jazz Music / THE.

GET HAPPY, GET HOT
CD _____ AVC 542
Avid / May '94 / Avid/BMG / Koch.

GREAT JAZZ ORCHESTRAS (5CD Set) (Goodman, Benny/Duke Ellington/Glenn Miller/Artie Shaw)
Blue skies / Dear old Southland / Sometimes I'm happy / King Porter stomp / Goodbye / When buddha smiles / Goody goody / Get happy / Christopher Columbus / I know that you know / Stardust / I've found a new baby / Swingtime in the Rockies / Somebody loves me / Bugle call rag / Sophisticated lady / Harlem speaks / In a sentimental mood / Merry go round / Echoes of harlem / Caravan / Dominuendo in blue / Crescendo in blue / I let a song go out of my heart / Prelude to a kiss / Solitude / Do nothin' 'til you hear from me / Cotton tail / I got it bad and that ain't good / Take the 'A' train / Wishing (will make it so) / Stairway to the stars / Moon love / Over the rainbow / In the mood / Careless / Tuxedo junction / When you wish upon a star / Imagination / Fools rush in (where angels fear to tread) / Song of the Volga boatmen / You and I / Chattanooga choo choo / El-mer's tune / String of pearls / Moonlight cocktail / Begin the beguine / Back bay shuffle / Indian love call / Nightmare / What is this thing called love / Deep purple / Traffic jam / Comes love / Serenade to savage / Oh lady be goode / Frenesi / Special delivery stomp / Summit ridge drive / Temptation / Moonglow / Swinging at the Daisy Chain / Honeysuckle rose / Roseland shuffle / One o'clock jump / John's idea / Time out / Topsy / Swingin' the blues / Blue and sentimental / Texas shuffle / Jumpin' the woodside / Pannasie stomp / Cherokee (parts 1and2) / You can depend on me / Jive at five / Oh lady be good
CD Set _____ CDPAK 4
Charly / Jan '93 / Charly / THE / Cadillac.

GREAT ORIGINAL PERFORMANCES 1934-1938
Nitwit serenade / Cokey / Music hall rag / Blue skies / Dear old Southland / Mad house / Breakin' in a pair of shoes / Get happy / Christopher Columbus / Walk Jennie walk / Bugle call rag / Jam session / Sing, sing, sing / Bumble bee stomp / Topsy / Smoke house / My honey's lovin' arms / Farewell blues
CD _____ RPCD 634
Robert Parker Jazz / Jul '94 / Conifer.

HAPPY SESSION (Goodman, Benny Orchestra)
CD _____ 476523 2
Sony Jazz / May '94 / Sony.

HARRY JAMES YEARS VOL.1
I want to be happy / Chloe / Rosetta / Peckin' / Let's we be friends / Sing, sing, sing / Roll 'em / When it's sleepy time down South / Changes / Sugarfoot stomp / I can't give you anything but love / Minnie the moocher's wedding day / Camel hop - Take 1/2 / Life goes to a party (takes 2/3) / Don't be that way (Takes 1/2)
CD _____ 07863 66155-2
Bluebird / Apr '93 / BMG.

HARRY JAMES YEARS VOL.2 (Wrappin' It Up) (Goodman, Benny Orchestra)
Ti-pi-ti / Blue room / Lullaby in rhythm / Sweet Sue, just you / Big John special / Wrappin' it up / Could you pass in love / Margie Russian lullaby / Bumble bee stomp / Topsy / Smoke house / My honey's lovin' arms / Farewell blues / It had to be you / Louise whispering / I'll always be in love with you / Undecided / Estrellita / Siren's song / You and your love
CD _____ 7863665492
Bluebird / Jun '95 / BMG.

I'M NOT COMPLAININ' (Goodman, Benny & His Band)
Clarinet a la King / My old flame / Cornsilk / Birds of a feather / I'm not complainin' / Time on my hands / I can't give you anything but love / Gilly / Yes my darling daughter / I'm always chasing rainbows / Let the door knob hitcha / Good evenin' good lookin' / Something new / I found a million dollar baby / When the sun comes out / Smoke gets in your eyes / I hear a rhapsody / It's always a new day / Elmer's tune / Down down down / Cherry
CD _____ RAJCD 813
Empress / Feb '94 / THE.

IN MOSCOW 1962
CD _____ CD 53195
Giants Of Jazz / Nov '95 / Target/BMG / Cadillac.

IN STOCKHOLM 1958
CD _____ NCD 8801
Phontastic / Apr '94 / Wellard / Jazz Music / Cadillac.

INDISPENSABLE BENNY GOODMAN VOLS.1 & 2 (1935-36) (Goodman, Benny Orchestra)
Blue skies / Dear old Southland / Sometimes I'm happy / King Porter stomp / Between the Devil and the deep blue sea / Mad house / If I could be with you one hour tonight / When Buddha smiles / Stompin' at the Savoy / Breakin' in a pair of shoes / I hope Gabriel likes my music / Mutiny in the parlour / I'm gonna clap my hands / Swing is here / Get happy / Christopher Columbus / I know that you know / Stardust / You forgot to remember / House hop / (I could do anything for you) I've found a new baby / Swingtime in the Rockies / Pick yourself up / Down south camp meeting / St. Louis blues / Love me or leave me / Bugle call rag (2 Takes) / Organ grinder swing / Riffin' at the Ritz / Somebody loves me
CD Set _____ 74321155212
RCA / Mar '94 / BMG.

INTRODUCTION TO BENNY GOODMAN 1928-41
CD _____ 4007
Best Of Jazz / May '94 / Discovery.

JAZZ PORTRAIT
CD _____ CD 14573
Complete / Nov '95 / THE.

JAZZ PORTRAITS (Goodman, Benny Trio & Quartet)
Dinah / Sweet Sue, just you / Moonglow / After you've gone / Body and soul / Who / Exactly like you / Tiger rag / Stompin' at the Savoy / Whispering / China boy / Oh lady be good / Nobody's sweetheart / Tea for two / Running wild / Avalon / Sugar / Blues in my flat
CD _____ CD 14520
Jazz Portraits / May '94 / Jazz Music.

KING OF SWING (1935-55)
Don't be that way / King Porter stomp / Roll 'em / Down South camp meeting / Goodbye / Christopher Columbus / One o'clock jump / If I could be with you one hour tonight / Bugle call rag / Goody goody / Sing, sing, sing / I want to be happy / Smoke house rhythm / Stompin' at the Savoy / Topsy / Sugarfoot stomp / Kingdom of swing / Bach goes to town / St. Louis blues / Sent for you yesterday / He ain't got rhythm / Sing me a swing song / After you've gone / Body and soul / Who / China boy / Oh Lady be good / Nobody's sweetheart / Moonglow / Dinah / Exactly like you / Sweet Sue, just you / Just you / Tiger rag / Whispering / Tea for two / Running wild / Avalon / Sugar / Blues in my flat / Pick a rib / Shivers / Rose room / Boy meet god / On the Alamo / Let's dance / Jumpin' at the woodside / Get happy / Blue Lou / Seven come eleven / Memories of you / Somebody stole my gal / Rock Rimmon / And the angels sing / Air mail special / Jersey bounce / Lullaby of the leaves / What can I say after I say I'm sorry / East of the sun and west of the moon / Temptation rag / You brought a new kind of love to me / Four or five times / Big John special / I got rhythm / Loved walked in / Stealin' apples / Undercurrent blues / Clarinet a la King
CD Set _____ CDB 1206
Giants Of Jazz / '92 / Target/BMG / Cadillac.

KING OF SWING
CD _____ 300154
Accord / Dec '89 / Discovery / Harmonia Mundi / Cadillac.

KING OF SWING
CD _____ PWK 027
Carlton Home Entertainment / '88 / Carlton Home Entertainment.

KING OF SWING
Don't be that way / Stompin' at the Savoy / One o'clock jump / Bach goes to town / Bugle call rag / St. Louis blues / Kingdom of swing
CD _____ BSTCD 9106
Best Compact Discs / May '92 / Complete/ Pinnacle.

KING OF SWING, THE
Blue skies / Dear old southland / Sometimes I'm happy / King Porter stomp / Goodbye / When buddha smiles / Goody / Get happy / Christopher Columbus / I know that you know / Stardust / I've found a new baby / Swingtime in the Rockies / Somebody loves me / Bugle call rag
CD _____ CDCD 1001
Charly / Mar '93 / Charly / THE / Cadillac.

KING PORTER STOMP
Someday, sweetheart / Mad house / Sandman / If I could be with you one hour tonight / When Buddha smiles / Hunkadola / I'm living in a great big way / Dixieland band / Japanese Sandman / You're a heavenly thing / Restless / Always / Ballad in Blue / Dear old Southland / Sometimes I'm happy

KING PORTER STOMP
King Porter stomp / Clarinade / And the angels sing / All the cats join in / Mad boogie / One o'clock jump / Clarinet a la King / 'S Wonderful / Jealousy / Rattle and roll / I want to be loved / Remember / Somebody stole my gal / Don't be that way / Tattle tale / Blue skies / Mahzel / Moon-faced and starry eyed / Old buttermilk / Oh baby / Theme (goodbye)
CD _____ DBCD 22
Dance Band Days / Jun '86 / Prism.

KING SWINGS, THE
CD _____ SLCD 9007
Starline / Jun '94 / Jazz Music.

LET'S DANCE (Goodman, Benny Orchestra)
Blue Hawaii / Vieni vieni / All of me / Yam / Moten swing / Clap hands, here comes Charlie / Sly mongoose / Hot foot shuffle / Hold tight / Hartford stomp / Trees / Begin the beguine / Let's dance / I know that you know
CD _____ MM 60112 X
Music Masters / Jan '89 / Nimbus.

LET'S DANCE
CD _____ 15780
Laserlight / Jan '93 / Target/BMG.

LIVE AT BASIN STREET (Benny Goodman vol 2)
Let's dance / Memories of you / Airmail special
CD _____ CIJ 60156 Z
Music Masters / Jan '89 / Nimbus.

LIVE AT CARNEGIE HALL (40th Anniversary Concert/2CD Set)
Let's dance / I've found a new baby / Send in the clowns / Loch Lomond / Stardust / I love a piano / King Porter stomp / Rocky raccoon / Yesterday / That's a plenty / How high the moon / Moonglow / Oh lady be good / Jersey bounce / Someone to watch over me / Please don't talk about me when I'm gone / Benny Goodman Medley / Sing, sing, sing / Goodbye
CD Set _____ 4509832
CBS / Oct '93 / Sony.

LIVE AT THE CARNEGIE HALL 6 OCTOBER 1939 (Goodman, Benny & Glenn Miller)
CD _____ EBCD 21032
Flyright / Dec '90 / Hot Shot / Wellard / Jazz Music / CM.

LIVE AT THE INTERNATIONAL WORLD EXHIBITION (Brussels 1958: Unissued Recordings) (Goodman, Benny Orchestra)
Let's dance / When you're smiling / Sent for you yesterday / Pennies from Heaven / Goin' to Chicago / Soon / Who cares / Deed I do / I hadn't anyone till you / I've got you under my skin / There's no fool like an old fool / Sometimes I'm happy / Oh boy I'm lucky / Song is ended (but the melody lingers on) / I'm coming Virginia / Fine romance / Harvard blues / If I had you / Goodbye theme
CD _____ DAWE 36
Magic / Sep '93 / Jazz Music / Swift / Wellard / Cadillac / Harmonia Mundi.

MANHATTAN ROOM 1937 VOL.1 SATAN TAKES A RIDE
CD _____ VN 171
Viper's Nest / Aug '95 / Direct / Cadillac / ADA.

MANHATTAN ROOM 1937 VOL.2 ONE O'CLOCK JUMP
CD _____ VN 172
Viper's Nest / Aug '95 / Direct / Cadillac / ADA.

MANHATTAN ROOM 1937 VOL.3: JAM SESSION
CD _____ VN 173
Viper's Nest / Aug '95 / Direct / Cadillac / ADA.

MASTERPIECES 1935-42
CD _____ 158172
Masterpieces / Mar '94 / BMG.

PERMANENT GOODMAN-KING OF SWING (VOL. 1) (1926-38)
CD _____ PHONTCD 7659
Phontastic / Feb '89 / Wellard / Jazz Music / Cadillac.

PERMANENT GOODMAN-KING OF SWING (VOL. 2) (1939-45)
CD _____ PHONTCD 7660
Phontastic / Apr '94 / Wellard / Jazz Music / Cadillac.

PLAYS FLETCHER HENDERSON
Japanese sandman / Get rhythm in your feet / Blue skies / Sometimes I'm happy / King Porter stomp / Devil and the deep blue sea / Sandman / Basin Street blues / If I could be with you one hour tonight / When Buddha smiles / Christopher Columbus / Down south camp meeting / St. Louis blues / Alexander's ragtime band / I want to be happy / Chloe (song of the swamp) / Ro-

/ King Porter stomp / Between the Devil and the deep blue sea / After you've gone / Body and soul
CD _____ CDSVL 176
Saville / Oct '87 / Conifer.

setta / Can't we be friends / Sugarfoot stomp / Wrappin' it up / Bumble bee stomp / Rose of Washington square
CD _____ HEPCD 1038
Hep / Nov '93 / Cadillac / Jazz Music / New Note / Wellard.

PLAYS JIMMY MUNDY
Mad house / You can't pull the wool over my eyes / House hop / Sing me a swing song / In a sentimental mood / Swingtime in the rockies / These foolish things / There's a small hotel / Bugle call rag / Jam session / Did you mean it / When you and I were young / Swing low, sweet chariot / He ain't got rhythm / Sing, sing, sing / I'm like a fish out of water / Sweet stranger / Margie / Farewell blues / Roll' em / Camel hop
CD _____ HEPCD 1039
Hep / Feb '94 / Cadillac / Jazz Music / New Note / Wellard.

ROLL 'EM (Goodman, Benny & Sid Catlett)
CD _____ VJC 1032-2
Vintage Jazz Classics / Oct '92 / Direct / ADA / CM / Cadillac.

RUNNIN' WILD (Goodman, Benny Quartet)
CD _____ CDSGP 099
Prestige / Mar '94 / Total/BMG.

SEXTET
CD _____ 4504112
Sony Jazz / Jan '95 / Sony.

SING SING SING (Goodman, Benny Orchestra)
King Porter stomp / Sometimes I'm happy / Basin Street blues / If I could be with you one hour tonight / Goody goody / Christopher Columbus / Sing me a swing song / I would do) anything for you / These foolish things / Down south camp meeting / Bugle call rag / Goodnight my love / He ain't got rhythm / I want to be happy / Roll 'em / Thanks for the memory / Don't be that way / One o'clock jump / Ti-pi-tin / Sing, sing, sing / Goodbye
CD _____ CDSVL 218
Saville / Jun '91 / Conifer.

SMALL COMBOS 1935-41
CD _____ GOJCD 53039
Giants Of Jazz / Mar '92 / Target/BMG / Cadillac.

SMALL GROUPS 1941/45
If I had you / Limehouse blues (part 1) / Limehouse blues (part 2) / Blues in the night / Where or when / On the sunny side of the street / Wang wang blues / World is waiting for the sunrise / Way you look tonight / St. Louis blues / Every time we say goodbye / After you've gone / Only another boy and girl / Rachel's dream / Body and soul
CD _____ 4633412
Sony Jazz / Jan '95 / Sony.

SMALL GROUPS, THE
After you've gone / Avalon / Exactly like you / Flying home / Gone with "what" wind / Good enough to keep / Limehouse blues / Moon glow / More than you know / Oh Lady be good / On the Alamo / On the sunny side of the street / Opus 1/2 / Opus 3/4 / Pick-a-rib (pts 1 & 2) / Running wild / Sheikh of araby / Smo-o-o-o-th one / Someday sweetheart / Stardust / Sweet Georgia Brown / Wang wang blues / Wholly cats / World is waiting for the sunrise
CD _____ CDAJA 5144
Living Era / Dec '94 / Koch.

STOMPIN AT THE SAVOY
CD _____ CDJJ 609
Jazz & Jazz / Jul '89 / Target/BMG.

STOMPIN' AT THE SAVOY
King Porter stomp / Goodbye / Goody goody / Stompin' at the Savoy / These foolish things / Bugle call rag / Goodnight my love / Don't be that way / One o'clock jump / Sing, sing, sing
CD _____ JHR 73518
Jazz Hour / Oct '92 / Target/BMG / Jazz Music / Cadillac.

SWING IS THE THING
CD _____ CDCD 1178
Charly / Apr '94 / Charly / THE / Cadillac.

SWING KING
Let's dance / Don't be that way / When Buddha smiles / Down south camp meeting / You turned the tables on me / King Porter stomp / Sometimes I'm happy / Blue skies / Sugarfoot stomp / I know that you know / Why don't you do right / Perfidia / Smoke gets in your eyes / Stardust / Clarinet a la King / After you've gone / Someday sweetheart / Big John special
CD _____ PAR 2029
Parade / Sep '94 / Koch / Cadillac.

SWING SESSIONS - PREMIERE RELEASE
CD _____ HCD 254
Hindsight / Sep '94 / Target/BMG / Jazz Music.

UNDERCURRENT BLUES
Lonely moments / Whistle blues / Shirley steps out / Stealin' apples / Undercurrent blues / Shishkabop / Huckle buck / Bop hop / Trees / Dreazag / Bedlam / In the land

of oo-bla-dee / Blue Lou / Fiesta time / Egg head
CD _____ CDP 8320862
Capitol Jazz / Aug '95 / EMI.

WAY DOWN YONDER (V-Discs)
CD _____ VJC 1001-2
Victorious Discs / Aug '90 / Jazz Music.

WHEN BUDDHA SMILES
Music Hall rag / Always / Blue skies / Down home rag / Ballad in blue / Devil and the deep blue sea / Mad house / Down South Camp meeting / Can't we be friends / Sugarfoot stomp / Big John special / Jumpin' at the woodside / Night and day / Board meeting / When Buddha smiles / Take an other guess / Roll 'em / Don't be that way / Wrappin' it up / Stealin' apples / Honeysuckle rose / Zaggin' with Zig.
CD _____ CDAJA 5071
Living Era / May '90 / Koch.

WORLD WIDE
CD Set _____ TCB 43012
TCB / Jan '94 / New Note.

YALE ARCHIVES VOLS. 1 - 5 (6 CD Box Set)
CD Set _____ 650952
Music Masters / May '95 / Nimbus.

YALE UNIVERSITY LIBRARY TAPES VOL. 4
CD _____ CIJ 60201 Z
Music Masters / '89 / Nimbus.

Goodman, Gabrielle

UNTIL WE LOVE
CD _____ 5140152
JMT / Dec '94 / PolyGram.

Goodman, Jerry

ARIEL
Going on 17 / Tears of joy / Lullaby for Joey / Topanga waltz / Broque / Rockers / Once only
CD _____ 259.961
Private Music / Nov '89 / BMG.

IT'S ALIVE
Goin' on / Tears of joy / Too cool / Endless / November / Topanga waltz / I hate you / Orangutango / Outcast islands / Heart's highway / Perry Mason (theme from)
CD _____ 259642
Private Music / May '89 / BMG.

Goodman, Steve

SOMEBODY ELSE'S TROUBLES
Dutchman / Six hours ahead of the sun / Song for David / Chicken Gordon blues / Somebody else's troubles / Loving of the game / I ain't heard you play no blues / Don't do me any favours anymore / Vegetable song / Lincoln Park pirates / Ballad of Penny Evans / Election year rag
CD _____ OW 28560
One Way / May '94 / Direct / ADA.

STEVE GOODMAN
I don't know where I'm going / Rainbow road / Donald and Lydia / You never even called me by my name / Mind your own business / Eight ball blues / City of New Orleans / Turnpike Tom / Yellow coat / So fine / Jazzman / Would you like to learn to dance
CD _____ OW 28559
One Way / May '94 / Direct / ADA.

Goodrick, Mick

IN PAS(S)ING
Feebles, fables and ferns / In the tavern of ruin / Summer band camp / Pedal pusher / In passing
CD _____ 8473272
ECM / Mar '92 / New Note.

RARE BIRDS (Goodrick, Mick & Joe Diorio)
Ram / Nov '93 / Harmonia Mundi
CD _____ RMCD 4505

SUNSCREAMS (Goodrick, Mick Quartet)
Ram / Apr '94 / Harmonia Mundi / Cadillac.
CD _____ RMCD 4507

Goodwin, Bill

NO METHOD (Goodwin, Bill/ Hal Galper/ Billy Peterson)
CD _____ FSRCD 136
Fresh Sound / Dec '90 / Jazz Music / Discovery.

THREE IS A CROWD (Goodwin, Bill Trio)
Loose change / After the storm / Limbo / Sim / Tonight I shall sleep / Bessie's blues / Samba du jour
CD _____ TCB 93402
TCB / Nov '93 / New Note.

Goodwin, Ron

MY KIND OF MUSIC (Goodwin, Ron & Bournemouth Symphony Orchestra)
Trap, The (London marathon theme) / Here where are / Kojak / Hill Street Blues / Star Trek / Dynasty / Dallas / Here's that rainy day / Tribute to Miklos Rosza / Ben

Hur (Love theme) / Red house / Four feathers / Parade of the Charioteers / Trolley song / Zip a dee doo dah / Someday my Prince will come / I wanna be like you / Little April showers / When you wish upon a star / Caravan - the girl from Corsica / Stephen Foster tribute / Oh Susanna / Swanee River / Beautiful dreamer / Camptown races / Drake 400 suite / Battle finale
CD _____ CHAN 8797
Chandos / '89 / Chandos.

Goofus Five

1926-27
Poor Papa (he's got nothin' at all) / I wonder what's become of Joe / Ya gotta know how to love / Where'd you get those eyes / Mary Lou / Someone is losin' Susan / Crazy quilt / Sadie Green the vamp of New Orleans / Heebie jeebies / Tuck in Kentucky and smile / I need lovin' / I've got the girl / Farewell blues / I wish I could shimmy like my sister Kate / Muddy water / Wang wang blues / Whisper song / Arkansas blues / Lazy weather / Vo-do-do-de-o blues / Ain't that a grand and glorious feeling / Clementine / Nothin' doe-does like it used to do-do-do / I left my sugar standing in the rain (and she melted away)
CD _____ CBC 1017
Timeless Historical / Aug '94 / New Note / Pinnacle.

Goops

GOOPS, THE
Dead/Alive / I don't care / Day I met Iggy / City slang / Use no hooks / Nobodys goes to waste / Never live it down / Island earth / Booze cabana / I am legend
CD _____ BLK 018ECD
Blackout / Oct '95 / Vital.

Gopalakrishnan, K.S.

CARNATIC FLUTE
CD _____ SM 15022
Wergo / Nov '91 / Harmonia Mundi / ADA / Cadillac.

Gordon, Bobby

DON'T LET IT END
CD _____ ARCD 19112
Arbors Jazz / Nov '94 / Cadillac.

Gordon, Dexter

AFTER HOURS
CD _____ SCCD 31224
Steeplechase / '88 / Impetus.

AMERICAN CLASSIC
Jumpin' blues / Besame mucho / For soul sister / Sticky wicket / Skylark / Interview with Dexter Gordon
CD _____ 1046710092
Discovery / May '95 / Warner Music.

BALLADS
Darn that dream / Don't explain / I'm a fool to want you / Ernie's tune / You've changed / Willow weep for me / Guess I'll hang my tears out to dry / Body and soul
CD _____ BNZ 275
Blue Note / Sep '92 / EMI.

BEST OF DEXTER GORDON (Blue Note Years)
It's you or no one / Society red / Smile / Cheesecake / Three o'clock in the morning / Soy califa / Don't explain / Tanya (CD only.)
CD _____ BNZ 142
Blue Note / Sep '92 / EMI.

BODY AND SOUL
CD _____ BLCD 760118
Black Lion / Feb '89 / Jazz Music / Cadillac / Wellard / Koch.

BOTH SIDES OF MIDNIGHT
CD _____ BLCD 760103
Black Lion / Dec '88 / Jazz Music / Cadillac / Wellard / Koch.

CHASE, THE
Chase / Mischievous lady / Lullaby in rhythm / Horning in / Chromatic aberration / Talk of the town / Blues bikini / Ghost of a chance / Sweet and lovely / Daddy plays the horn
CD _____ GOJCD 53064
Giants Of Jazz / Mar '92 / Target/BMG / Cadillac.

CHASE, THE
CD _____ STB 613
Stash / Aug '95 / Jazz Music / CM / Cadillac / Direct / ADA.

CLUBHOUSE
Hanky panky / I'm a fool to want you / Devilette / Clubhouse / Jody / Lady Iris B
CD _____ CDP 7844452
EMI / Sep '92 / EMI.

COME RAIN OR COME SHINE
CD _____ JHR 73508
Jazz Hour / May '93 / Target/BMG / Jazz Music / Cadillac.

COMPLETE SESSIONS ON DIAL, THE
Mischievious lady / Lullaby in rhythm / Chase / Chromatic abberation / It's the talk of the town / Blue bikini / Ghost of a chance

/ Sweet and lovely / Horning in / Duel / Blues in Teddy's flat
CD _____ SPJCD 130
Spotlite / Apr '95 / Cadillac / Jazz Horizons / Swift.

DEXTER BLOWS HOT AND COOL
Silver plated / Cry me a river / Rhythm mad / Don't worry 'bout me / I hear music / Bonna Rue / I should care / Blowin' for Dootsie / Tenderly
CD _____ CDBOP 006
Boplicity / Feb '89 / Pinnacle / Cadillac.

DEXTER GORDON QUARTET (1955-67) (Gordon, Dexter Quartet)
CD _____ GOJCD 53065
Giants Of Jazz / Mar '92 / Target/BMG / Cadillac.

DEXTER RIDES AGAIN
Dexter's riff / Settin' the pace Pts 1 and 2 / So easy / Long tall Dexter / Dexter rides again / I can't escape from you / Dexter digs in / Dexter's minor mad / Blow Mr. Dexter / Dexter's deck / Dexter's cuttin' out
CD _____ SV 0120
Savoy Jazz / Apr '92 / Conifer / ADA.

DEXTERITY - NEW YORK 1977 & COPENHAGEN 1967
CD Set _____ JWD 102303
JWD / Oct '94 / Target/BMG.

GO
Cheesecake / Guess I'll hang my tears out to dry / Second balcony jump / Love for sale / Where are you / Three o'clock in the morning
CD _____ CDP 7460942
EMI / Mar '95 / EMI.

GREAT ENCOUNTERS
Blues up and down / Cake / Diggin' in / Ruby my dear / It's only a paper moon
CD _____ 4718762
Sony Jazz / Jan '95 / Sony.

HOMECOMING (2CD Set)
CD _____ 4718762
Sony Jazz / Jan '95 / Sony.

HOT AND COOL
CD _____ WWCD 2004
West Wind / Mar '93 / Swift / Charly / CM / ADA.

LIVE AT THE AMSTERDAM PARADISO
Fried bananas / What's new / Good bait / Rhythm-a-ning / Willow weep for me / Junior / Scrapple from the apple / Closing announcement / Introduction
CD _____ LEJAZZCD 28
Le Jazz / Aug '94 / Charly / Cadillac.

LONG TALL DEXTER
Blow Mr. Dexter / Dexter's deck / Dexter's cuttin' out / Dexter's minor mad / Long tall Dexter / Dexter rides again / I can't escape from you / Dexter digs in / Settin' the pace / So easy so easy / Dexter's riff / Dexter's mood / Dextrose index / Dextivity / Wee dot / Lion roars / After hours bop
CD _____ VGCD 650117
Vogue / Oct '93 / BMG.

LULLABY OF BIRDLAND
CD _____ JHR 73556
Jazz Hour / Jan '93 / Target/BMG / Jazz Music / Cadillac.

MANHATTAN SYMPHONIE
As time goes by / Moment's notice / Tanya / Body and soul / LTD
CD _____ 4718752
Sony Jazz / Jan '95 / Sony.

MASTER OF BALI
Cute / They say that falling in love is wonderful / Lullaby of Birdland / I should care / Seven come eleven / Blues for gates
CD _____ 722007
Scorpio / Sep '92 / Complete/Pinnacle.

MORE THAN YOU KNOW
CD _____ SCCD 31030
Steeplechase / Jul '88 / Impetus.

OUR MAN IN PARIS
Scrapple from the apple / Willow weep for me / Stairway to the stars / Night in Tunisia / Our love is here to stay / Like someone in love / Broadway
CD _____ BNZ 34
Blue Note / Jun '87 / EMI.

SOMETHING DIFFERENT
CD _____ SCCD 31136
Steeplechase / Jul '88 / Impetus.

SOPHISTICATED GIANT
Laura / Moontrane / Red top / Fried bananas / You're blase / How insensitive
CD _____ 4718742
Sony Jazz / Jan '95 / Sony.

STABLE MABLE (Gordon, Dexter Quartet)
CD _____ SCCD 31040
Steeplechase / Oct '90 / Impetus.

TAKE THE A TRAIN
But not for me / Take the 'A' train / For all we know / Blues walk / I guess I'll hang my tears out to dry / Love for sale
CD _____ BLC 760133
Black Lion / Oct '94 / Jazz Music / Cadillac / Wellard / Koch.

GORDON, DEXTER

TOWER OF POWER
Montmartre / Rainbow people / Stanley the steamer / Those were the days
CD _____ OJCCD 299
Original Jazz Classics / Sep '93 / Wellard / Jazz Music / Cadillac / Complete/Pinnacle.

TOWER OF POWER AND MORE POWER, THE
Tower of power / Rainbow people / Stanley the steamer / Those were the days / More power / Ladybird / Meditation / Fried bananas / Boston Bernie / Sticky wicket
CD _____ CDJZD 004
Prestige / Jan '91 / Complete/Pinnacle / Cadillac.

WE THREE (Gordon, Dexter/Zoot Sims/Al Cohn)
CD _____ BCD 137
Biograph / Aug '95 / Wellard / ADA / Hot Shot / Jazz Music / Cadillac / Direct.

Gordon, Frank

CLARION ECHOES
CD _____ SNCD 1096
Soul Note / '86 / Harmonia Mundi / Wellard / Cadillac.

Gordon Highlanders

BAGPIPES AND DRUMS OF SCOTLAND, THE
CD _____ 15159
Laserlight / May '94 / Target/BMG.

COCK 'O' THE NORTH
CD _____ BNA 5077
Bandleader / Jan '93 / Conifer.

HOUR OF THE GORDON HIGHLANDERS, A
CD _____ CC 294
EMI / May '93 / EMI.

MARCHES ECOSSAISES
CD _____ 824922
Buda / Nov '90 / Discovery / ADA.

Gordon, Jimmie

MISSISSIPPI MUDDER 1934-1941
CD _____ SOB 035182
Story Of The Blues / Feb '93 / Koch / ADA.

Gordon, Joe

GORDON FAMILY, THE (Gordon, Joe & Sally Logan)
Rose of Allendale / Craigieburn woods / Band boys / Holy City / Wee toon clerk / Faraway land / Jig selection / Dark lochnagar / Medley of reels / Hunting tower / Bonnio gallows / Charness waltz / My ain folk / Dantesque / Darvol dam
CD _____ CDGR 142
Ross / Oct '92 / Ross / Duncans.

JOE GORDON & SCOTT LA FARO (Gordon, Joe & Scott La Faro)
CD _____ FSCD 1030
Fresh Sound / Jan '93 / Jazz Music / Discovery.

Gordon, Lonnie

IF I HAVE TO STAND ALONE
CD _____ CDSU 6
Supreme / Apr '91 / Pinnacle.

Gordon, Rob

COMPLETE CALEDONIAN BALL (Gordon, Rob & His Band)
Circassian circle / Brisk young lad / Byron strathspey / Saltire society reel / Hebridean weaving lilt / Johnnie Walker / Crammond Bridge / Silver star / Cumberland reel / New Scotia quadrille / Dundee whaler / Bannestane / Lomond waltz / Angus reel / Belle of Bon Accord / Rab the ranter / C'est l'amour / Wind on Loch Fyne / Seton's ceilidh band / New petronella / Bonnie lass o'Bon Accord / Bank Street reel / Joe McDiarmid's jig / Breon's reel / Rothesay rant
CD Set _____ LCDM 8005
Lismor / Dec '88 / Lismor / Direct / Duncans / ADA.

OLD TIME AND SEQUENCE BALL
Quadrilles (patience) / Flirtation / Chrysanthemum waltz / Silver wedding waltz / Mississippi dip / Dinkie one step / Ideal schottische / Ken and Cathy Jamieson Barn dance / Marine four step / Southern two step / Stanley and Vera Carson's polka / Swedish masquerade / Foxtrots and saunters / Moonlight saunter / Heather mixture polka / Waltz cotillion (half figure) / Lancers / Waltzmanze / Honeysuckle waltz
CD _____ LCDM 9014
Lismor / '89 / Lismor / Direct / Duncans / ADA.

Gordon, Robert

ALL FOR THE LOVE OF ROCK 'N' ROLL
CD _____ 422506
New Rose / Mar '95 / Direct / ADA.

BLACK SLACKS
Summertime blues / I just found out / Boppin' the blues / Picture of you / I just met a memory / Am I blue / Walk on by / Blue

Christmas / Fire / Twenty flight rock / But, but / Sea cruise / Bad boy / Red cadillac and a black moustache / Uptown / Five days, five days / Are you gonna be the one / Standing on the outside of her door / Loverboy / Take me back / Too fast to live, too young to die / Born to lose / Is it wrong / Torture / Black slacks (live)
CD _____ BCD 15489
Bear Family / Apr '90 / Rollercoaster / Direct / CM / Swift / ADA.

GREETINGS FROM N.Y. CITY
CD _____ 422155
New Rose / May '94 / Direct / ADA.

LIVE AT THE LONE STAR
CD _____ 422156
New Rose / May '94 / Direct / ADA.

ROBERT GORDON IS RED HOT
Red hot / Fool / I sure miss you / Flyin' saucer rock 'n' roll / Way I walk / Lonesome train / I want to be free / Rockabilly boogie / All by myself / Catman / Wheel of fortune / Love baby / It's only make believe / Crazy man crazy / Worryin' kind / Nervous / Sweet love on my mind / Need you / Someday, someway / Look who's blue / Drivin' wheel / Something's gonna happen / Fire / Black slacks
CD _____ BCD 15446
Bear Family / Apr '89 / Rollercoaster / Direct / CM / Swift / ADA.

Gordons

FIRST ALBUM AND FUTURE SHOCK
CD _____ FNE 16 CD
Flying Nun / '88 / Disc.

Gore

CRUEL PLACE, THE
Breeding / Cruel place / Garden of evil / Death has come
CD _____ MD 7905CD
Megadisc / Apr '89 / Vital.

LIFELONG DEADLINE
CD _____ MM1
Barooni / Mar '93 / SRD.

Gore, Lesley

IT'S MY PARTY
Hello, young lovers / Something wonderful / It's my party / Danny / Party's over / Judy's turn to cry / Just let me cry / Misty / Cry me a river / I would / No more tears / Cry and you cry alone / I understand / Cry / Sunshine, lollipops, and rainbows / What kind of fool am I / If that's the way you want it / She's a fool / I'll make it up to you / Old crowd / I struck a match / Consolation prize / Run Bobby run / Young and foolish / Fools rush in (Where angels fear to tread) / My foolish heart / That's the way the ball bounces / After he takes me home (1 Voice) / After he takes me home (2 Voices) / You don't own me (Mono) / You don't own me (Stereo) / Time to go / You name it / That's the way boys are / Boys / I'm coolin', no foolin' / Don't deny it / I don't wanna be a loser / It's gotta be you / Leave me alone / Don't call me / Look of love / Wonder boy / Secret love / Maybe / Live and learn / Sometimes I wish I were a boy / Hey now / Died inside / Movin' away / It's about that time / Little girl go home / Say goodbye / You've come back / I just don't know if I can / That's the boy / All of my life / What's a girl supposed to do / Before and after / I cannot hope for anyone / I don't care / You didn't look around / Baby that's me / No matter what you do / Sunshine and lollipops / What am I gonna do with you / Girl in love / Just another fool / My town, my guy and me / Let me dream / Things we did last summer / Start the party again / I can tell / I won't love you anymore / I just can't get enough of you / Only last night / Any other girl / To know him is to love him / Young love / Too young / Will you still love me tomorrow / We know we're in love / Yeah yeah yeah that boy of mine / That's what I'll do / Lilacs and violets / Off and running / Happiness is just around the corner / Hold me tight / Cry like a baby / Treat me like a lady / Maybe now / Bubble broke / California nights / I'm going out the same way I came in / Bad / Love goes on forever / Summer and Sandy / I'm falling down / Where can I go / You sent me silver bells / He won't see the light / Magic colours / How can I be sure / To Sir with love / It's a happening world / Small talk / Say what you see / He gives me love (La la la) / Brand new me / I can't make it without you / Look the other way / Take good care (Of my heart) / I'll be standing by / Ride a tall white horse / 98.6 / Summer symphony / All cried out / One by one / Wedding bell blues / Got to get you into my life / Goodbye Tony (You don't own me) / Musikant (Time to go) / So sind die boys alle / Nur du allein / Hab ich das verdient / Der erste tanz / Little little liebling / Sieben girls / Tu t'en vas / Je ne sais plus / Je n'ose pas / Si ton coeur le desire / Je sais qu'en jour / C'est trop tard / Eh non / Te voila / Judy's turn to cry (Italian) / You don't own me (Italian) / Lazy day
CD Set _____ BCDEI 15742

START THE PARTY AGAIN
CD _____ RVCD 31
Raven / Jan '94 / Direct / ADA.

Gore, Martin L

COUNTERFEIT
Compulsion / In a manner of speaking / Smile in the crowd / Gone / Never turn your back on mother earth / Motherless child
CD _____ CDSTUMM 67
Mute / Apr '89 / Disc.

Gorefést

EINDHOVEN INSANITY
CD _____ NB 091
Nuclear Blast / Aug '93 / Plastic Head.

ERASE
CD _____ NBCD 110
Nuclear Blast / Jul '94 / Plastic Head.
CD _____ NB 110BOX
Nuclear Blast / Oct '95 / Plastic Head.

MINDLOSS
CD _____ NB 086
Nuclear Blast / Aug '93 / Plastic Head.

Gorgoroth

PENTAGRAM
CD _____ TE 001CD
Embassy / Oct '94 / Plastic Head.

Gories

HOUSEROCKIN
CD _____ EFA 11577 2
Crypt / Sep '94 / SRD.

Gorilla Biscuits

START TODAY
New direction / Degradation / Forgotten / Start today / First failure / Time flies / Stand still / Good intentions / Things we say / Two sides / Competition / Cats and dogs
CD _____ 846104
We Bite / '90 / Plastic Head.

Gorillas

MESSAGE TO THE WORLD
CD _____ DAMGOOD 49
Damaged Goods / Nov '94 / SRD.

Gorka, John

I KNOW
CD _____ RHR 18CD
Red House / Jul '95 / Koch / ADA.

OUT OF THE VALLEY
Good noise / That's why / Carnival knowledge / Talk about love / Big time lonesome / Furniture / Mystery to me / Out of the valley / Thoughtless behaviour / Always going home / Flying red horse / Up until then
CD _____ 72902 10325-2
Windham Hill / Aug '94 / Pinnacle / BMG / ADA.

Gorky's Zygotic Mynci

BWYD TIME
CD _____ ANKST 059CD
Ankst / Jul '95 / SRD.

PATIO
CD _____ ANKSTCD 055
Ankst / Jan '95 / SRD.

TATAY
CD _____ ANKST 47CD
Ankst / Apr '95 / SRD.

Gorman, Skip

GREENER PRAIRIE, A
CD _____ ROUCD 0329
Rounder / Oct '94 / CM / Direct / ADA / Roots.

Gorme, Eydie

20 LOVE SONGS
CD _____ RMB 75025
Remember / Jan '92 / Total/BMG.

EYDIE GORME COLLECTOR'S EDITION
CD _____ DVAD 6052
Deja Vu / Apr '95 / THE.

SINCE I FELL FOR YOU
Charly / Apr '93 / Charly / THE / Cadillac.
CD _____ CDCD 1079

Gospel Hummingbirds

TAKING FLIGHT
CD _____ BPCD 5023
Blind Pig / Dec '95 / Hot Shot / Swift / CM / Roots / Direct / ADA.

Gospellers

WE'VE GOT THE POWER
CD _____ VSCD 100
Vision UK / Dec '95 / Jetstar.

Goss, Kieran

BRAND NEW STAR
CD _____ DARA 047CD
Dara / Jul '92 / Roots / CM / Direct / ADA / Koch.

NEW DAY
CD _____ DARA 064CD
Dara / Dec '94 / Roots / CM / Direct / ADA / Koch.

Goss, Matt

KEY, THE
CD _____ 5403892
Polydor / Feb '96 / PolyGram.

Gostanzo, Sonny

SONNY'S ON THE MONEY
CD _____ STCD 555
Stash / Jan '93 / Jazz Music / CM / Cadillac / Direct / ADA.

Gota

LIVE WIRED ELECTRO (Gota & The Low Dog)
CD _____ RPLCD 2
Respect / Oct '95 / Total/BMG.

SOMETHING TO TALK ABOUT
Move / It's so different here / European comfort / Someday / Changes / Play fair / Someday reprise / Take you anywhere / All alone / Chillin' chil'ren / Groove ride / Easy when you want it
CD _____ RPLCD 1
Respect / Jul '94 / Total/BMG.

Gotham Gospel

BEST OF GOTHAM GOSPEL
Harmonizing four / Dixie hummingbird / Echo gospel singers / Edna Gallmon Cook / Zion harmonizers / Harmony kings / Rugged cross singers
CD _____ HTCD 04
Heritage / Oct '90 / Swift / Roots / Wellard / Direct / Hot Shot / Jazz Music / ADA.

Gottlieb, Danny

NEW AGE OF CHRISTMAS
CD _____ 7567820542
Atlantic / Jul '93 / Warner Music.

Goubert, Simon

HAITI
CD _____ A 7
Seventh / Apr '93 / Harmonia Mundi / Cadillac.

L'ENCIERRO
CD _____ A XVIII
Seventh / Dec '95 / Harmonia Mundi / Cadillac.

Goulder, Dave

STONE, STEAM AND STARLINGS
Clearing place / Corter / Stone on stone / These dry stone walls / Go from my window / Proper little gent / Colours / Seven summers / Friar in the well / Sally gardens / Follower / I will go with my father / Footplate cuisine
CD _____ HARCD 017
Harbour Town / Oct '93 / Roots / Direct / CM / ADA.

Gouldman, Graham

GRAHAM GOULDMAN THING, THE
CD _____ EDCD 346
Edsel / Apr '92 / Pinnacle / ADA.

Goulesco, Lido

CHANTS FOLKLORIQUES TZIGANES
CD _____ 824412
Buda / Nov '90 / Discovery / ADA.

Goulet, Robert

ROBERT GOULET
CD _____ DVAD 6102
Deja Vu / May '95 / THE.

Gourlay, James

GOURLAY PLAYS TUBA (Gourlay, James & The Britannia Building Society Band)
CD _____ DOYCD 028
Doyen / Apr '94 / Conifer.

Gourley, Jimmy

GOOD NEWS
CD _____ BL 007
Bloomdido / Oct '93 / Cadillac.

Gouzil, Denis

LE P'TIT GROUILLOT QUI DANSE (Gouzil, Denis Groupe)
CD _____ EPC 885
European Music Production / Feb '92 / Harmonia Mundi.

Government Issue

CRASH
CD _____ WEBITE 42CD
We Bite / Dec '88 / Plastic Head.

FINALE
CD _____ LF 012CD
Lost & Found / Apr '92 / Plastic Head.

MAKE AN EFFORT
CD _____ LF 114CD
Lost & Found / Oct '94 / Plastic Head.

YOU
CD _____ WB 3041-2
We Bite / Sep '93 / Plastic Head.

Goykovich, Dusko

BEBOP CITY
Sunrise in St. Petersburg / In the sign of
Libra / Be bop city / Lament / Bop town /
No love without tears / One for klook / Day
by day / Brooklyn blues
CD _____ ENJ 90152
Enja / Jul '95 / New Note / Vital/SAM.

BELGRADE BLUES
CD _____ HHCD 1008
Hot House / Jan '91 / Cadillac / Wellard /
Harmonia Mundi.

SOUL CONNECTION
Soul connection / Ballad for miles / Inga /
I'll close my eyes / Blues time / Adriatica /
NYC / Blues valse / Teamwork song
CD _____ ENJ 80442
Enja / Mar '94 / New Note / Vital/SAM

Goz Of Kermeur

IRONDELLES
CD _____ CDRECDE 61
Rec Rec / Apr '94 / Plastic Head / SRD /
Cadillac.

Grabowsky, Paul

VIVA VIVA
CD _____ 450994167-2
East West / Aug '94 / Warner Music.

Grace

POET, THE PIPER AND THE FOOL, THE
Piper / Field / Poet / Raindance / Success
/ Lullaby / Holy man
CD _____ GCD 1
Cyclops / Jun '96 / Pinnacle.

PULLING STRINGS & SHINY THINGS
Fool / Lean on me / Earth bites back / Every
cloud has a silver lining / Architecht of war
/ Hanging Rock / Gift
CD _____ CYCL 002
Cyclops / Feb '94 / Pinnacle.

Grace, Teddy

TEDDY GRACE 1937-40
I've taken a fancy to you / Oh Daddy blues
/ I'll never let you cry / You don't know my
mind / Goodbye Jonah / Low down blues /
Ears in my heart / Graveyard blues / Love
me or leave me / Hey lawdy Papa / Crazy
blues / Mama doo-shee (blues) / Monday
morning / Gee but I hate to go home alone
/ Betty and Dupree / Sing (It's good for ya)
/ Arkansas blues / See what the boys in the
backroom will have / Down home blues /
Gulf coast blues / I'm the lonesomest gal in
town
CD _____ CBC 1016
Chris Barber Collection / Nov '93 / New
Note / Cadillac.

Gracenotes

DOWN FALLS THE DAY
CD _____ GN 001CD
Gracenotes / Jan '94 / ADA.

Gracie, Charlie

IT'S FABULOUS
CD _____ CTOD 2
Stomper Time / May '95 / Magnum Music
Group.

Gracious

GRACIOUS
CD _____ REP 4060-WP
Repertoire / Aug '91 / Pinnacle / Cadillac.

GRACIOUS/THIS IS GRACIOUS
Introduction / Hell / Dream / Blood red sun
/ Prepare to meet thy maker / What's come
to be / Hold me down / Heaven / Fugue in
D minor / Supernova / Arrival of the traveller
/ Say goodbye to love / C.B.S. / Blue skies
and alibis
CD _____ BGOCD 256
Beat Goes On / Feb '95 / Pinnacle.

Graf, Bob

AT WESTMINSTER
CD _____ DD 401
Delmark / Nov '92 / Hot Shot / ADA / CM
/ Direct / Cadillac.

Graham Central Station

AIN'T NO BOUT A DOUBT IT
Jam / Your love / It's alright / I can't stand
the rain / Ain't nothing but a Warner Brothers party / Ole Smokey / Easy rider / Water
luckiest people
CD _____ 7599263462
WEA / Jan '96 / Warner Music.

GRAHAM CENTRAL STATION
We've been waiting / It ain't no fun to me /
Hair / We be's getting down / Tell me what
it is / Can you handle it / People / Why /
Ghetto
CD _____ 7599263392
WEA / Jan '96 / Warner Music.

MIRROR
CD _____ 7599263472
WEA / Jan '96 / Warner Music.

RELEASE YOURSELF
CD _____ 7599263522
WEA / Jan '96 / Warner Music.

Graham, Davey

**FOLK BLUES AND ALL POINTS IN
BETWEEN**
Leaving blues / Cocaine / Rock me baby /
Moanin' / Skillet / Ain't nobody's business
/ Maajun / I can't keep from crying some-
times / Going down slow / Better git it in
your soul / Freight train blues / Both sides
now / No prouder blues / Bad boy blues /
I'm ready / Hoochie coochie man / Blue
raga
CD _____ SEECD 48
See For Miles/C5 / May '00 / Pinnacle.

GUITAR PLAYER...PLUS, THE
Don't stop the carnival / Sermonette / Take
five / How long, how long blues / Sunset
eyes / Cry me a river / Angie / 3/4 AD / Ruby
and the pearl / Buffalo / Exodus / Yellow
bird / Blues for Betty / Hallelujah, I love her
so / Davy's train blues
CD _____ SEECD 351
See For Miles/C5 / Jun '92 / Pinnacle.

Graham, David

VERY THOUGHT OF YOU, THE
West side story / Jumpin' Charlie / Slow
foxtrot / Bossa nova / Let it be me / Quickstep / Love changes everything / Tango Havana / Miranda's theme / Swingin' shepherd blues / Ave Maria
CD _____ OS 216
Valentine / Nov '95 / Conifer.

Graham, Len

DO ME JUSTICE
CD _____ CC 37CD
Claddagh / Dec '94 / ADA / Direct.

YE LOVERS ALL
CD _____ CC 41CD
Claddagh / Dec '94 / ADA / Direct.

Grahamophones

**LET'S DO IT AGAIN (Dalby, Graham &
Grahamophones)**
Let's do it again / / Charleston / Hair of the
dog / Crazy weather / Thinking of you /
Jealousy / Breakaway / Sheikh of Araby /
Minnie the moocher / I wasn't there / Dance
little lady / Steppin' out with my baby / I
wonder if you know what it means / Love's
melody / Is you is or is you ain't my baby
CD _____ PCOM 1108
President / Jul '91 / Grapevine / Target/
BMG / Jazz Music / President.

MAD DOGS AND ENGLISHMEN
CD _____ PCOM 1097
President / Feb '89 / Grapevine / Target/
BMG / Jazz Music / President.

**TRANSATLANTIQUE (Dalby, Graham &
Grahamophones)**
Jeeves and Wooster / La mer / Anything
goes / Easy come, easy go / Mackie Messer
/ My canary has circles under his eyes / Top
hat, white tie and tails / Ces petites choses
(These foolish things) / Forty second street
/ Once in a while / Crazy words crazy tune
/ I would sooner be a crooner / Ill wind /
Hollywood's got nothing on you / Let's
misbehave
CD _____ PCOM 1128
President / Aug '93 / Grapevine / Target/
BMG / Jazz Music / President.

Grainger, Richard

THUNDERWOOD
Silent spring / Old Whitby town / Golden
Grove/Mallaig moorings / Northern town
bay / Foxhunting song / Streets of Kings
Cross / Mermaid / Polly on the shore / Glas-
gow wedding/Far from home / Grove fisher-
man / Ghost of Old Solem / From Mulgrave
to Eskside / Thunderwood
CD _____ FSCD 27
Folksound / Aug '94 / Roots / CM.

Gramm, Lou

FOREIGNER IN A STRANGE LAND
Won't somebody take me home / Don't you
know me, my friend / Better know your
heart / I can't make it alone / How do you

tell someone / Society's child / I wish today
was yesterday / My baby / Headin' home /
Watch you walk away
CD _____ CDTB 065
Thunderbolt / '88 / Magnum Music Group.

READY OR NOT
Ready or not / Heartache / Midnight blue /
Time / Not if I don't have you / She's got to
know / Arrow thru your heart / Until I make
you mine / Chain of love / Lover come back
CD _____ 7817282
Atlantic / Feb '87 / Warner Music.

Grampian Police Pipe Band

PIPES & DRUMS
CD _____ EUCD 1261
ARC / Mar '94 / ARC Music / CM.

Grand Dominion Jazz Band

GRAND DOMINION JAZZBAND VOL.2
CD _____ SOSCD 1268
Stomp Off / Oct '93 / Jazz Music /
Wellard.

Grand Funk Railroad

COLLECTION: GRAND FUNK RAILROAD
CD _____ CCSCD 332
Castle / Jan '96 / BMG.

Grand, Otis

**ALWAYS HOT! (Grand, Otis & the Dance
Kings)**
CD _____ SPCD 1019
Special Delivery / Oct '88 / ADA / CM /
Direct.

HE KNOWS THE BLUES
Things are getting harder to do / You hurt
me / Jumpin' for Jimmy / Grand style / Real
gone lover / SRV (My mood too) / Leave
that girl / Ham / Your love pulls no punches
/ Swing turn / Teach me how to love you /
He knows the blues
CD _____ NEX CD 219
Sequel / Jul '92 / BMG.

NOTHING ELSE MATTERS
CD _____ NEXCD 272
Sequel / Sep '94 / BMG.

Grand Puba

2000
CD _____ 7559616192
Elektra / Jun '95 / Warner Music.

REEL TO REEL
Check tha resume / 360 degrees (what
goes around) / That's how we move it /
Check it out / Big kids don't play / Honey
don't front / Lick shot / Ya know how it goes
/ Reel to reel / Soul controller / Proper ed-
ucation / Back it up / Baby what's your
name
CD _____ 7559613142
Elektra / Nov '92 / Warner Music.

Grandjean, Etienne

CIRCUS VALSE
CD _____ CD 842
Diffusion Breizh / May '93 / ADA.

Grandmaster Flash

**GREATEST HITS: GRANDMASTER
FLASH... (Grandmaster Flash & Melle
Mel)**
White lines (don't don't do it) / Step off /
Bump mo up / Jesse / Reat street / Vice /
Freedom / Birthday party / Flash to the beat
/ It's nasty (genius of love) / Message /
Scorpio / Message II (survival) / New York,
New York
CD _____ NEMCD 622
Sequel / May '92 / BMG.

Grandmothers

DREAMS IN LONG PLAY
CD _____ CD 986970
Intercord / Aug '93 / Plastic Head.

DREAMS ON LONGPLAY
CD _____ EFAO 34032
Muffin / Apr '95 / SRD.

WHO COULD IMAGINE
CD _____ NETCD 53
Munich / Nov '94 / CM / ADA /
Greensleeves / Direct.

Granelli, Jerry

FORCES OF FLIGHT
CD _____ ITMP 970061
ITM / Apr '93 / Tradelink / Koch.

KOPUTAI
Koputai / Pillars / Haiku / I could see forever
/ Julia's child / In the moment
CD _____ ITMP 970058
ITM / Jan '94 / Tradelink / Koch.

NEWS FROM THE STREET
Honey boy / Big love / Rainbow's cadillac /
Swamp / Sad hour / Akicita / Ellen waltzing
/ Brilliant corners / Blue Spanish eyes /
News from the street / Little wing
CD _____ VBR 2146
Vera Bra / Sep '95 / Pinnacle / New Note.

Graney, Dave

MY LIFE ON THE PLAINS
CD _____ FIRE 33020
Fire / Oct '91 / Disc.

Grant, Amy

AGE TO AGE
In a little while / I have decided / I love a
lonely day / Don't run away / Fat baby /
Sing your praises to the Lord / El-Shaddai /
Raining on the inside / Got to let it go /
Arms of love
CD _____ MYRCD 6697
Myrrh / '88 / Nelson Word.

AMY GRANT
CD _____ MYRCD 6586
Myrrh / '88 / Nelson Word.

AMY GRANT IN CONCERT VOL 1
CD _____ MYRCD 6668
Myrrh / '88 / Nelson Word.

AMY GRANT IN CONCERT VOL 2
CD _____ MYRCD 6677
Myrrh / '88 / Nelson Word.

CHRISTMAS ALBUM, A
Tennessee Christmas / Hark the herald an-
gels sing / Preiset dem Konig (Praise the
King) / Emmanuel / Little town / Christmas
hymn / Love has come / Sleigh ride / Christ-
mas song / Heirlooms / Mighty fortress /
Angels we have heard on high
CD _____ MYRCD 6768
Myrrh / '88 / Nelson Word.

COLLECTION: AMY GRANT
Old man's rubble / My father's eyes / El
Shaddai / Stay for a while / Find a way /
Angels / Love can do / Sing your praises to
the Lord / Thy word / Emmanuel
CD _____ GEFD 24340
Geffen / Sep '91 / BMG.

FATHER'S EYES
CD _____ MYRCD 6625
Myrrh / '88 / Nelson Word.

HEART IN MOTION
Good for me / Baby baby / Every heartbeat
/ That's the way love is / Ask me / Galileo /
You're not alone / Hats / I will remember
you / How can we see that far / Hopes set
high
CD _____ 3953212
A&M / Apr '91 / PolyGram.

**HEART IN MOTION/LEAD ME ON (2CD
Set)**
CD Set _____ CDA 24123
A&M / Jul '94 / PolyGram.

HOME FOR CHRISTMAS
Have yourself a merry little Christmas / It's
the most wonderful time of the year / Joy
to the world / Breath of heaven (Mary's
song) / O'come all ye faithful / Grown up
Christmas list / Rockin' around the Christmas tree / Winter wonderland / Night before
for Christmas / Night before Christmas /
Emmanuel, God with us / Jesu joy of man's
desiring
CD _____ 5400012
A&M / Nov '95 / PolyGram.

HOUSE OF LOVE
Lucky one / Say you'll be mine / Whatever
it takes / House of love / Power / Oh how
the years go by / Big yellow taxi / Helping
hand / Politics of kissing / Love has a hold
on me / Our love / Children of the world
CD _____ 5402882
A&M / Jul '95 / PolyGram.

NEVER ALONE
Look what has happened to me / So glad /
Walking away with you / Family / Don't give
up on me / That's the day / If I have to die
/ All I ever have to be / It's a miracle / Too
late / First love / Say once more
CD _____ MYRCD 6645
Myrrh / '88 / Nelson Word.

STRAIGHT AHEAD
CD _____ MYRCD 6757
Myrrh / '88 / Nelson Word.

UNGUARDED
Love of another kind / Find a way / Every
where I go / I love you / Stepping in your
shoes / Fight / Wise up / Who to listen to /
Sharayah / Prodigal
CD _____ MYRCD 6806
Myrrh / '88 / Nelson Word.

Grant, Darrell

BLACK ART
CD _____ CRISS 1987CD
Criss Cross / Sep '95 / Cadillac /
Harmonia Mundi.

NEW BOP, THE
CD _____ CRISS 1106
Criss Cross / Dec '95 / Cadillac /
Harmonia Mundi.

Grant, David

BEST OF DAVID GRANT & LYNX
Mated / So this is romance / Watching you
watching me / Rock the midnight / Where
our love begins / Organize (remix) / Love will
find a way / Intuition / Could it be I'm falling

in love / Stop and go / Plaything / Can't help
myself / Throw away the key / You're lying
CD _____ CDCHR 6051
Chrysalis / Oct '93 / EMI.

Grant, Della

BLACK ROSE
CD _____ RG 5803
Twinkle / Feb '95 / SRD / Jetstar /
Kingdom.

DAWTA OF THE DUST
CD _____ RGCD 5804
Twinkle / Oct '95 / SRD / Jetstar /
Kingdom.

ROOTICALLY YOURS
CD _____ NGCD 542
Twinkle / Feb '94 / SRD / Jetstar /
Kingdom.

Grant, Eddy

BEST OF EDDY GRANT, THE
I don't wanna dance / Gimme hope Jo'anna
/ Electric Avenue / Walking on sunshine /
Do you feel my love / Symphony for Michael
opus 2 / Living on the front line / Front line
symphony / Can't get enough of you /
Nightjcar, neighbour / I love you, yes I love
you / It's our time / Romancing the stone /
Till I can't take love no more / War party /
Say I love you
CD _____ CDMFP 6203
Music For Pleasure / Nov '95 / EMI.

FILE UNDER ROCK
Harmless piece of fun / Don't talk to strang-
ers / Hostile country / Win or lose / Gimme
hope Jo'Anna / Another riot / Say hello to
Fidel / Chuck (is the king) / Long as I'm
wanted by you / Put a hold on it
CD _____ CDFA 3232
Fame / Aug '89 / EMI.

GOING FOR BROKE
Romancing the stone / Boys in the street /
Come on let me know / Till I can't take love
no more / Political bassa bassa / Telepathy
/ Only heaven knows / Irie Harry / Rock you
good / Blue wave
CD _____ 920412
Ice / Jun '92 / Pinnacle / Jetstar.

PAINTINGS OF THE SOUL
CD _____ 90202
Ice / Mar '92 / Pinnacle / Jetstar.

Grant, Julie

**HERE COME THE GIRLS VOL.2 (Take 3
Girls) (Grant, Julie/Billie Davis/Helen
Shapiro)**
CD _____ NEXCD 177
Sequel / '92 / BMG.

YOU CAN COUNT ON ME
Somebody tell him / Every letter you write /
So many ways / Unimportant things / When
you're smiling / Lonely sixteen / Up on the
roof / When you ask about love / Count on
me / Then only then / That's how heartaches are made / Cruel world / Don't ever
let me down / Somebody cares / Hello love
/ It's all right / Every day I have to cry / What
what you do with my baby / You're nobody
'til somebody loves you / I only care about
you / Come to me / Can't get you out of my
mind / Baby baby / My world is empty without you / Giving up / 'Cause I believe in you
/ Lonely without you / As long as I know
he's mine / Stop / When the loving ends
CD _____ RPM 133
RPM / Aug '94 / Pinnacle.

Grant Lee Buffalo

FUZZY
Shining hour / Jupiter and Teardrop / Fuzzy
/ Wish you well / Hook / Soft wolf tread /
Stars 'n' stripes / Dixie drugstore / America
snoring / Grace / You just have to be crazy
CD _____ 8283892
Slash / Jun '93 / PolyGram.

MIGHTY JOE MOON
Lone star song / Mockingbirds / It's the life
/ Sing along / Mighty Joe Moon / Demon
called deception / Lady Godiva and me /
Drag / Last days of Tecumseh / Happiness
/ Honey don't think / Side by side / Rock of
ages
CD _____ 8285412
Slash / Aug '94 / PolyGram.

Grant, Tom

INSTINCT
CD _____ SHCD 5015
Shanachie / Oct '95 / Koch / ADA /
Greensleeves.

Grappelli, Stephane

85 AND STILL SWINGING
CD _____ CDC 754918-2
Angel / Jun '94 / EMI.

AT THE WINERY VOL.1
You took advantage of me / So dance
samba / Sheikh of Araby / Straighten up
and fly right / Just in time / Talk of the town
/ Body and soul
CD _____ CCD 4131
Concord Jazz / Sep '86 / New Note.

AT THE WINERY VOL.2
You are the sunshine of my life / Love for
sale / Angel's camp / Willow weep for me /
Chicago / Talking a chance on love / Minor
swing / Let's fall in love / Just you, just me
CD _____ CCD 4139
Concord Jazz / Jul '87 / New Note.

**BLUE SKIES (Grappelli, Stephane &
Eddy Louiss)**
CD _____ 500552
Musidisc / Jan '94 / Vital / Harmonia
Mundi / ADA / Cadillac / Discovery.

COLLECTION: STEPHANE GRAPPELLI
CD _____ CCSCD 274
Castle / Oct '90 / BMG.

CRAZY RHYTHM
CD _____ MATCD 232
Castle / Dec '92 / BMG.

EMOTION
CD _____ ATJCD 5960
All That's Jazz / Jun '92 / THE / Jazz
Music.

FEELING + FINESSE = JAZZ
Django / Nuages / Alabamy bound / You
better go now / Daphne / Le tien / Minor
swing / Makin' whoopee / How about you /
Soft winds
CD _____ 7567901402
Atlantic / Jul '93 / Warner Music.

GRAPPELLI STORY, THE
CD _____ 515807-2
Verve / May '94 / PolyGram.

HOT 'N' SWEET
CD _____ TRTCD 179
TrueTrax / Jun '95 / THE.

I HEAR MUSIC
I hear music / All God's chillun got rhythm
/ Honeysuckle rose / Do you know what it
means to miss New Orleans / It's you or no
one / If I were a bell / Chicago / Nuages -
Daphne / La chanson des rues / Fascinating
rhythm / Them their eyes / You are the sunshine of my life / I won't dance / Old man
river / Someone to watch over me / I got
rhythm / How high the moon
CD _____ JHR 73586
Jazz Hour / Apr '95 / Target/BMG / Jazz
Music / Cadillac.

**IN CONCERT (Grappelli, Stephane &
McCoy Turner)**
CD _____ GATE 7025
Kingdom Jazz / Sep '95 / Kingdom.

IT MIGHT AS WELL BE SWING
CD _____ JWD 102216
JWD / Jul '95 / Target/BMG.

JAZZ MASTERS
CD _____ 5167582
Verve / Apr '93 / PolyGram.

**JEALOUSY (Hits Of The Thirties)
(Grappelli, Stephane & Yehudi Menuhin)**
Jealousy / Blue room / Fine romance / Billy
up / Night and day / I can't believe that
you're in love with me / These foolish things
/ Errol / Lady be good / Jermyn Street /
Cheek to cheek / Lady is a tramp
CD _____ CDCFP 4576
Classics For Pleasure / Oct '90 / EMI.

**JOUE GEORGE GERSHWIN ET COLE
PORTER (Plays Gershwin and Porter)**
CD _____ MCD 139 004
Accord / '88 / Discovery / Harmonia
Mundi / Cadillac.

JUST ONE OF THOSE THINGS
Cheek to cheek / Are you in the mood / Just
one of those things / There's a small hotel
/ Pent-up house / I'll remember April / Surrey with the fringe on top / I get a kick out
of you / Blue moon / Them there eyes / I
can't give you anything but love / How high
the moon / Waltz du passe / My one and
only love
CD _____ CDM 769 172 2
EMI / Feb '88 / EMI.

**JUST ONE OF THOSE THINGS
(Recorded Live at the Montreux Festival
1973)**
CD _____ BLCD 760180
Black Lion / Apr '93 / Jazz Music /
Cadillac / Wellard / Koch.

**LA GRANDE REUNION (Grappelli,
Stephane & Baden Powell)**
CD _____ 557322
Accord / Nov '93 / Discovery / Harmonia
Mundi / Cadillac.

**LIVE IN COPENHAGEN (Grappelli,
Stephane & Joe Pass)**
CD _____ J33J 20041
Pablo / Aug '86 / Jazz Music / Cadillac /
Complete/Pinnacle.

LIVE IN LONDON
This can't be love / Flamingo / Them there
eyes / After you've gone / Nuages / Tea for
two
CD _____ BLCD 760139
Black Lion / Oct '90 / Jazz Music / Cadillac
/ Wellard / Koch.

MAKIN' WHOOPEE
Crazy rhythm / Sweet Georgia Brown / Peanut vendor / Ain't misbehavin' / I can't give

you anything but love / Nearness of you /
Avalon / Makin' whoopee / It don't mean a
thing if it ain't got that swing / Oh lady be
good / Ol' man river / What are you doing
the rest of your life / Folks who live on the
hill / I've got the world on a string / Birth of
the blues
CD _____ 5507632
Spectrum/Karussell / Mar '95 / PolyGram /
THE.

MASTER OF VIOLIN
All of me / Star eyes / Anything goes / Caravan / Don't blame me / Moonlight in Vermont / It might as well be spring / Have you
met Miss Jones
CD _____ 722010
Scorpio / Sep '92 / Complete/Pinnacle.

**NUAGES (Grappelli, Stephane & Django
Reinhardt)**
Billets doux / Nuages / Exactly like you /
China boy / Swing '39 / Them there eyes /
St. Louis blues / Appel direct / I've found a
new baby / Ultrafox / Twelfth year / Japa-
nese sandman / I wonder where my baby
is tonight / Chasing shadows / Djangology
/ Lady be good / Charleston / I'll see you in
my dreams
CD _____ TRTCD 148
TrueTrax / Oct '94 / THE.

NUAGES LIVE IN WARSAW
I hear music / All God's chillun got rhythm
/ Honeysuckle rose / Do you know what it
means to miss New Orleans / It's you or no
one / If I were a bell / Chicago / Nuages /
Chanson des rues / Fascinating rhythm / I
won't dance / Someone to watch over me
/ I didn't know what time it was / How high
the moon
CD _____ AAOHP 93382
Start / Dec '94 / Koch.

ONE AND ONE
CD _____ MCD 9181
Milestone / Oct '93 / Jazz Music /
Pinnacle / Wellard / Cadillac.

PARISIAN THOROUGHFARE
Love for sale / Perugia / Two cute / Parisian
thoroughfare / Improvisation on prelude in
E minor / Wave / Hallelujah
CD _____ BLCD 760132
Black Lion / Oct '94 / Jazz Music / Cadillac
/ Wellard / Koch.

**PORTRAIT OF STEPHANE GRAPPELLI,
THE**
CD _____ EMPRCD 567
Emporio / May '95 / THE / Disc / CM.

**REUNION (Grappelli, Stephane & Martin
Taylor)**
Jive at five / Willow weep for me / Drop me
off in Harlem / Miraval / Jenna / Reunion /
Emily / Hotel splendid / La dame du lac / I
thought about you / It's only a paper moon
CD _____ AKD 022
Linn / Oct '93 / PolyGram.

SATIN DOLL
CD _____ 440162CD
Musidisc / Jul '94 / Vital / Harmonia Mundi
/ ADA / Cadillac / Discovery.

**SPECIAL STEPHANE GRAPPELLI (1947-
1961)**
Qui, pour vous revoir / Tea for two / Pennies
from Heaven / Can't help lovin' dat man /
Girl in Calico / World is waiting for the sunrise / I can't recognize the tune / You took
advantage of me / Folks who live on the hill
/ Looking at you / Swing '39 / Belleville /
Manoir de mes reves / Djangology / Have
you met Miss Jones / This can't be love /
Alemberts / Marno / Blue moon (With Sextette Pierre Spiers.) / Foggy day (With Sextette Pierre Spiers.)
CD _____ CZ 317
EMI / Jun '90 / EMI.

STARDUST
CD _____ BLC 760117
Black Lion / Apr '91 / Jazz Music /
Cadillac / Wellard / Koch.

**STEFF AND SLAM (Grappelli, Stephane
& His Trio)**
CD _____ 233076
Black & Blue / '86 / Wellard / Koch.

**STEPHANE GRAPPELLI & JEAN-LUC
PONTY (Grappelli, Stephane & Jean-Luc
Ponty)**
CD _____ 556552
Accord / Nov '93 / Discovery / Harmonia
Mundi / Cadillac.

STEPHANE GRAPPELLI 1935-40
CD _____ CLASSICS 708
Classics / Jul '93 / Discovery / Jazz
Music.

STEPHANE GRAPPELLI 1941-43
CD _____ CLASSICS 779
Classics / Mar '95 / Discovery / Jazz
Music.

STEPHANE GRAPPELLI IN TOKYO
I'm coming Virginia / Honeysuckle rose / Do
you know what it means to miss New Orleans / Just one of those things / Nuages /
Daphne / As time goes by / Embraceable
you / Liza / Them there eyes / You are the
sunshine of my life / Time after time / Two
sleepy people / Satin doll / Double Scotch

/ Pent-up house / Ol' man river / Sweet
Georgia Brown / Valse du passe
CD _____ CY 77130
Denon / Apr '91 / Conifer.

**STEPHANE GRAPPELLI MEETS
BARNEY KESSEL (Grappelli, Stephane
& Barney Kessel)**
CD _____ BLC 760150
Black Lion / Apr '91 / Jazz Music /
Cadillac / Wellard / Koch.

**STEPHANE GRAPPELLI MEETS EARL
HINES**
CD _____ BLCD 760168
Black Lion / Oct '93 / Jazz Music /
Cadillac / Wellard / Koch.

STEPHANE GRAPPELLI TRIO
Honeysuckle rose / Chicago / Nuages / I
won't dance / I got rhythm / Fascinatin'
rhythm
CD _____ 66050007
Bellaphon / Jul '93 / New Note.

**STEPHANE GRAPPELLI WITH JEAN
LUC PONTY (Grappelli, Stephane &
Jean-Luc Ponty)**
CD _____ MCD 139 139
Accord / '88 / Discovery / Harmonia
Mundi / Cadillac.

**STEPHANE GRAPPELLI/JEAN-LUC
PONTY VOL.2 (Grappelli, Stephane &
Jean-Luc Ponty)**
CD _____ 139 210
Accord / '86 / Discovery / Harmonia
Mundi / Cadillac.

STEPHANOVA
Tune up / Thou swell / Norwegian dance /
Fulton Street samba / My foolish heart /
Lover / Way you look tonight / Stephanova
/ Smoke rings and wine / Tangerine / Waltz
for Queenie / Sonny boy
CD _____ 292E 6033
Concord Jazz / Jan '90 / New Note.

**TOGETHER AT LAST (Grappelli,
Stephane & Vassar Clements)**
CD _____ FF 70421
Flying Fish / Oct '89 / Roots / CM / Direct
/ ADA.

**VENUPELLI BLUES (Grappelli, Stephane
& Joe Venuti)**
I can't give you anything but love / My one
and only love / Undecided / Venupelli blues
/ I'll never be the same / Tea for two
CD _____ LEJAZZCD 18
Le Jazz / Jun '93 / Charly / Cadillac.

VINTAGE 1981
If I had you / I can't get started (with you) /
Blue moon / But not for me / It's only a
paper moon / Jamie / I'm coming Virginia /
Do you know what it means to miss New
Orleans / Isn't she lovely / Swing '42 / Hon-
eysuckle rose
CD _____ CCD 4169
Concord Jazz / Nov '92 / New Note.

Grass Roots

**WHERE WERE YOU WHEN I NEEDED
YOU**
CD _____ VSD 5511
Varese Sarabande/Colosseum / Jul '95 /
Pinnacle / Silva Screen.

Grasson, Mathias

IN SEARCH OF SANITY
CD _____ CDNO 005
No CD / Dec '95 / Vital/SAM.

Grassy Knoll

GRASSY KNOLL
Culture of complaint / March eighteenth /
Unbelievable truth / Altering the gates of the
mind / Conversations with Julian Dexter /
Floating above the earth / Less than one /
Low / Evolution #9 / Beauty within / Illusions
of peace
CD _____ NET 059CD
Nettwerk / Oct '94 / Vital / Pinnacle.

Grateful Dead

AMERICAN BEAUTY
Box of rain / Friend of the Devil / Operator
/ Sugar magnolia / Ripple / Brokedown pal-
ace / Till the morning comes / Attic of my
life / Truckin
CD _____ K2 46 074
WEA / Jun '89 / Warner Music.

ANTHEM OF THE SUN
That's it for the other one / Cryptical envel-
opment / Quadlibet / For tender feet / Faster we go, the rounder we get / We leave
the castle / Alligator / Caution (do not stop
on the tracks)
CD _____ 7599271732
WEA / Feb '94 / Warner Music.

BLUES FOR ALLAH
Help on the way / Slipknot / Franklin's tower
/ King Solomon's marbles (Stronger than/
Milkin' the turkey) / Music never stopped /
Crazy fingers / Sage and spirit / Blues for
Allah / Sand castles and glass camels / Un-
usual occurrences in the desert
CD _____ GDCD 4001
Grateful Dead / Feb '89 / Pinnacle.

DICK'S PICKS (2CD Set)
CD Set _____ GDCD 24019
Grateful Dead / Jan '96 / Pinnacle.

DICK'S PICKS VOL. 3 (Pembroke Pines, Florida 22/5/77 - 2CD Set)
Funiculi funicula / Music never stopped / Sugaree / Lazy lightning / Supplication / Dancin' in the streets / Help on the way / Slipknot / Franklin's tower / Samson and Delilah / Sunrise / Estimated prophet / Eyes of the world / Wharf rat / Terrapin station / (Walk me out in the) Morning dew
CD Set _____ GDCD 24022
Grateful Dead / Dec '95 / Pinnacle.

FROM THE MARS HOTEL
U.S. blues / Unbroken chain / Scarlet begonias / Money money / China doll / Loose Lucy / Pride of cucamonga / Ship of fools
CD _____ 900646
Line / Oct '94 / CM / Grapevine / ADA / Conifer / Direct.

GRATEFUL DEAD, THE
Bertha / Mama tried / Big railroad blues / Playing in the band / Other one / Me and my uncle / Big boss man / Me and Bobby McGee / Johnny B. Goode / Wharf rat / Not fade away / Goin' down the road / Feelin' bad
CD _____ 7599271922
WEA / Feb '93 / Warner Music.

GRATEFUL DEAD: INTERVIEW PICTURE DISC
CD P.Disc _____ CBAK 4039
Baktabak / Apr '90 / Baktabak.

HUNDRED YEAR HALL
Bertha / Me and my uncle / Next time you see me / China cat sunflower / I know you rider / Jack straw / Big railroad / Playing in the band / Turn on your lovelight / Going down the road feeling bad / One more Saturday night
CD _____ GDCD 24021
Grateful Dead / Oct '95 / Pinnacle.

INFRARED ROSES
Crowd sculpture / Parallelogram / Little Nemo in Nightland / Riverside rhapsody / Post-modern highrise table top stomp / Infrared roses / Silver apples of the moon / Speaking in swords / Magnesium night light / Sparrow hawk row / River of nine sorrows / Apollo at the Ritz
CD _____ GDCD 4016
Grateful Dead / Jan '92 / Pinnacle.

LIVE DEAD
Dark star / Death don't have no mercy / Feedback / And we bid you goodnight / St. Stephen / Eleven / Turn on your love / Light
CD _____ K 9271812
WEA / Jun '89 / Warner Music.

ONE FROM THE VAULT
Introduction / Help on the way / Franklin's tower / Music never stopped / It must have been the roses / Eyes of the world / King Solomon's marbles / Around and around / Sugaree / Big river / Crazy fingers / Other one / Sage and spirit / Goin' down the road feeling bad / U.S. blues / Blues For Allah
CD Set _____ GDCD2 4015
Grateful Dead / May '91 / Pinnacle.

RISEN FROM THE VAULTS
CD _____ DILCD 1001
Dare International / Jan '94 / Total/BMG.

SHAKEDOWN STREET
Good lovin' / France / Shakedown Street / Serengeti / Fire on the mountain / I need a miracle / From the heart of me / Stagger Lee / All new minglewood blues / If I had the world to give
CD _____ 251133
Arista / Jun '91 / BMG.

SKELETONS FROM THE CLOSET
Golden road (to unlimited devotion) / Truckin' / Rosemary / Sugar magnolia / St. Stephen / Uncle John's band / Casey Jones / Mexicali blues / Turn on your love light / One more Saturday night / Friend of the devil / Don't fall in love (feel 'n' roll) / Do you believe / Creeper / Wednesday / Remember (walkin' in the sand) / Call your name / Take you home / Halloween / Rollercoaster / Blizzard / On the run
CD _____ CDTB 018
Thunderbolt / '87 / Magnum Music Group.

STEAL YOUR FACE
Promised land / Cold rain and snow / Around and around / Stella blue / Mississippi half step uptown toodeloo / Ship of fools / Beat it on down the line / Big river / Black throated wind / U.S. blues / El Paso / Sugaree / It must have been the roses / Casey Jones
CD Set _____ GDCD 24006
Grateful Dead / Mar '89 / Pinnacle.

TERRAPIN STATION
Estimated prophet / Dancing in the street / Passenger / Samson and Delilah / Sunrise / Lady with the fan / Terrapin station / Terrapin / Terrapin transit / At a siding / Terrapin fever / Refrain
CD _____ 260175
Arista / Nov '90 / BMG.

TWO FROM THE VAULT
CD Set _____ GDCD2 4018
Grateful Dead / Apr '92 / Pinnacle.

WAKE OF THE FLOOD
Mississippi half step uptown toodeloo / Row Jimmy / Here comes sunshine / Weather report / Let me sing your blues away / Stella blue / Eyes of the world
CD _____ GDCD 4002
Grateful Dead / Nov '87 / Pinnacle.

WORKINGMAN'S DEAD
Uncle John's band / High time / Dire wolf / New speedway boogie / Cumberland blues / Black Peter / Easy wind / Casey Jones
CD _____ K 246049
WEA / Jun '89 / Warner Music.

Gratz, Wayne

BLUE RIDGE
Blue ridge part 1 / Blue ridge part II / Heart in the clouds / Sacred river / Dancing lights / Waterfall / Trail of tears / Fields are burning / Scenes of reflection / Past time / Peaks of otter / Pathway to waterrock / White on white / Endless mountains
CD _____ ND 61047
Narada / May '95 / New Note / ADA.

FOLLOW ME HOME
Southlands / Imaginary friend / Water song / Lighthouse / Time in a forgotten cavern / Follow me home / Northern harvest / Dancer / Good question / Off the sidelines / Friend in L.A.
CD _____ ND 61034
Narada / Jul '93 / New Note / ADA.

Grave

AND HERE I DIE
CD _____ MC 770622
Century Media / Feb '94 / Plastic Head.

DEVOLUTION
CD _____ PRO 006CD
Prophet / Nov '92 / Pinnacle.

INTO THE GRAVE
CD _____ CM 97212
Century Media / Sep '94 / Plastic Head.

SOULLESS
CD _____ CM 770702
Century Media / Jun '94 / Plastic Head.

Gravediggaz

NIGGAMORTIS
Just when you thought it was over (intro) / Constant elevation / Nowhere to run, nowhere to hide / Defective trip (trippin') / Two cups of blood / Blood brothers / 360 questions / 1-800 suicide / Diary of a madman / Mommy what's a gravedigga / Bang your head / Here comes the Gravediggaz / Graveyard chamber / Death trap / Six feet deep / Rest in peace (outro)
CD _____ GEECD 14
Gee Street / Jun '94 / PolyGram.

Gravedigger

WITCH HUNT
CD _____ NCD 002
Noise/Modern Music / '88 / Pinnacle / Plastic Head.

Gravedigger V

ALL BLACK & HAIRY/THE MIRROR CRACKED
CD _____ VOXXCD 2025
Voxx / Oct '94 / Else / Disc.

Graves, Blind Roosevelt

1929-36
CD _____ DOCD 5105
Blues Document / Nov '93 / Swift / Jazz Music / Hot Shot.

Graveyard Rodeo

ON THE VERGE
CD _____ CM 77069-2
Century Media / Aug '94 / Plastic Head.

Gravy Train

DALLAD OF A PEACEFUL MAN
CD _____ REP 4122-WZ
Repertoire / Aug '91 / Pinnacle / Cadillac.

GRAVY TRAIN
CD _____ REP 4063-WP
Repertoire / Aug '91 / Pinnacle / Cadillac.

Grawe, George

SIX STUDIES FOR PIANO SOLO
CD _____ WWCD 012
West Wind / Jul '88 / Swift / Charly / CM / ADA.

Gray, David

CENTURY ENDS, A
Shine / Century ends / Debauchery / Let the truth sing / Gathering dust / Wisdom / Lead me upstairs / Living room / Birds without wings / It's all over
CD _____ CDHUT 9
Hut / Apr '93 / EMI.

FLESH
What are you / Light / Coming down / Falling free / Made up my mind / Mystery of

---

love / Lullaby / New horizons / Love's old song / Flesh
CD _____ CDHUT 17
Hut / Sep '94 / EMI.

Gray, Dobie

DRIFT AWAY
CD _____ CDCOT 106
Cottage / Jan '94 / THE / Koch.

Gray, Glen

CONTINENTAL, THE
CD _____ HCD 261
Hindsight / Oct '95 / Target/BMG / Jazz Music.

UNCOLLECTED 1939-1940, THE (Gray, Glen & The Casa Loma Orchestra)
CD _____ HCD 104
Hindsight / Jan '95 / Target/BMG / Jazz Music.

Gray, Kellye

STANDARDS
CD _____ JR 001012
Justice / Sep '92 / Koch.

Gray Matter

THOG
CD _____ DIS 68VCD
Dischord / Sep '92 / SRD.

Gray, Owen

CALL ON ME
CD _____ WRCD 0020
Techniques / Nov '95 / Jetstar.

LET'S GO STEADY
CD _____ FECD 21
First Edition / Dec '95 / Jetstar.

MISS WIRE WAIST
CD _____ PICD 209
Body Music / Jun '95 / Jetstar.

Gray, Russell

SOLO
From the shores of the mighty pacific / Traumerei / Chablis / Caro nome / Fantasia on themes from Carmen / Salut d'amour / Concerto for cornet and brass bands / Bess, you is my woman now / Sunshine of your smile / Aye waukin' o / Una furtiva lagrima / Song and dance / Londonderry air
CD _____ QPRL 070D
Polyphonic / Jan '95 / Conifer.

Gray, Simon

VANISHING POINT
CD _____ KLB 30012
Extreme / Nov '94 / Vital/SAM.

Gray, Wardell

HOW HIGH THE MOON
CD _____ MCD 076
Moon / Dec '95 / Harmonia Mundi / Cadillac.

MEMORIAL VOL.1
CD _____ OJCCD 050
Original Jazz Classics / Nov '95 / Wellard / Jazz Music / Cadillac / Complete/Pinnacle.

ONE FOR PREZ
CD _____ BLCD 760106
Black Lion / Feb '89 / Jazz Music / Cadillac / Wellard / Koch.

WAY OUT WARDELL
Blue Lou / Sweet Georgia Brown / Tenderly / Just you, just me / One o'clock jump
CD _____ CDBOP 014
Boplicity / Jul '91 / Pinnacle / Cadillac.

Greaney, Con

ROAD TO ATHEA
CD _____ CIC 082CD
Clo Iar-Chonnachta / Nov '93 / CM.

Great British Jazz Band

JUBILEE
Jubilee / Jazz me blues / Original Dixieland one-step / Washboard blues / Prelude to a kiss / Idaho / Imagination / Beautiful friendship / Petite fleur / Someday sweetheart / Apex blues / All I do is dream of you / Chelsea bridge / Tiger rag
CD _____ CCD 79720
Candid / Jan '95 / Cadillac / Jazz Music / Wellard / Koch.

Great Guitars

STRAIGHT TRACKS
I'm putting all my eggs in one basket / Clouds / Gravy waltz / Um abraco no bonfa / Little rock getaway / It might as well be Spring / Kingston cutie / Favela
CD _____ CCD 4421
Concord Jazz / Nov '90 / New Note.

Great Jazz Trio

CLUB NEW YORKER, THE
'S wonderful / Autumn in New York / Our love is here to stay / I've got a crush on you / Manhattan / Someone to watch over me / They can't take that away from me / Isn't it romantic / Embraceable you / But not for me
CD _____ DC 8567
Denon / Oct '90 / Conifer.

N.Y. SOPHISTICATE (Tribute to Duke Ellington)
In a sentimental mood / C jam blues / Mood indigo / Satin doll / Lush life / Sophisticated lady / Take the 'A' train / I got it bad and that ain't good / Caravan / Solitude
CD _____ DC 8575
Denon / '90 / Conifer.

STANDARD COLLECTION
Autumn in New York / Caravan / 'S wonderful / Our love is here to stay / Someone to watch over me / Isn't it romantic / Embraceable you / In a sentimental mood / Satin doll / Lush life / Sophisticated lady / Take the 'A' train / Blue monk / Ruby my dear / Monk's dream / Monk's mood
CD _____ DC 8564
Denon / Aug '90 / Conifer.

STANDARD COLLECTION VOL. 1
After you've gone / Summertime / Days of wine and roses / As time goes by / You'd be so nice to come home to / Summer knows / Georgia on my mind / Prelude to a kiss / St. Louis blues / Danny boy
CD _____ MCD 0031
Limetree / Dec '06 / New Note.

STANDARD COLLECTION VOL.2
Angel eyes / Autumn leaves / Black orpheus / Gone with the wind / Over the rainbow / Softly as in a morning sunrise / Misty / On Green Dolphin Street / Alone together / Dark eyes
CD _____ MCD 0032
Limetree / Jul '95 / New Note.

Great Speckled Bird

GREAT SPECKLED BIRD
CD _____ SPCD 1200
Stony Plain / Dec '94 / ADA / CM / Direct.

Great White

ONCE BITTEN
Lady red light / Gonna getcha / Rock me / All over now / Fast road / What do you do / Face the day (US radio blues version) / Gimme some lovin'
CD _____ NSPCD 515
Connoisseur / Jun '95 / Pinnacle.

SAIL AWAY
Short overture / Mothers eyes / Cryin' / Momma don't stop / Alone / All night / Sail away / Gone with the wind / Livin' in the USA / If I ever saw a good thing / Call it rock 'n' roll (live) / All over now (live) / Babe I'm gonna leave you (live) / Rock me (live) / Once biten twice shy (live)
CD Set _____ 72445110802
Zoo Entertainment / Aug '94 / BMG.

Greater Than One

G-FORCE
CD _____ TORSOCD 149
Torso / Jun '89 / SRD.

Greaves, John

SONGS
Old kinderhook / Song / Swelling valley / Green fuse / Kew.Rhone / Eccentric waters silence / Piece of my / L'aise aux en-sans trique / Back where we began / Gegenstand
CD _____ RES 112CD
Resurgence / Nov '95 / Vital.

Greaves, M.C.

DIAMONDS ALWAYS SHINE (M.C. Greaves & The Lonesome Too)
CD _____ MGLON 3CD
Lonesome Trail / Jul '93.

Greco, Buddy

16 MOST REQUESTED SONGS
Lady is a tramp / Like young / Something's gotta give / This could be the start of something / I love being here with you / Around the world / Roses of Picardy / Teach me tonight / My kind of girl / At long last love / Mr. Lonely / Most beautiful girl in the world / Call me Irresponsible / She loves me / You win again / It had better be tonight
CD _____ 474400 2
Columbia / Feb '94 / Sony.

BUDDY GRECO
CD _____ DVAD 6082
Deja Vu / May '95 / THE.

I HAD A BALL
CD _____ CDCD 1083
Charly / Apr '93 / Charly / THE / Cadillac.

IT'S MY LIFE/MOVING ON
It's gonna take some time / October 4th 1971 / If / Power and the glory / You've got a friend / Without you / Your song / As long

as she will stay / Song for you / It's my life / Macarthur park / Movin' on / Touch me in the morning / Maggi / Baby lean on me / I know where I belong / What's going on / Beautiful friendship / Neither one of us (wants to be first to say go) / If I could live my life again / I could be the one / Cardboard California
CD _____ C5CD 634
See For Miles/C5 / Oct '95 / Pinnacle.

Greedsville

CASINO ROYALE COLLECTION
Disco queen / Casino / Simple moonshine / Du cats / Jazz the spanish fly / Caller 38 / Stroll by the sea / It's a gas / Splash
CD _____ CDBLEED 9
Bleeding Hearts / Mar '94 / Pinnacle.

Greedy Beat Syndicate

MY MAN/SOMETHING TO SAY
CD _____ BUMPD 003
Bumpin' / Oct '95 / EWM.

Green, Al

AL
Tired of being alone / Call me / I'm still in love with you / Here I am (come and take me) / Let's stay together / Sha la la (make me happy) / L.O.V.E. Love / Look what you done for me / Love and happiness / Take me to the river / I can't get next to you / How can you mend a broken heart / I tried to tell myself / I've never found a girl / Oh me, oh my (Dreams in my arms) / You ought to be with me
CD _____ AGREECD 1
Beechwood / Oct '92 / BMG / Pinnacle.

CALL ME/I'M STILL IN LOVE WITH YOU
CD _____ HIUKCD 111
Hi / Mar '91 / Pinnacle.

CHRISTMAS ALBUM PLUS
CD _____ HILOCD 21
Hi / Oct '95 / Pinnacle.

CHRISTMAS ALBUM/CHRISTMAS CHEERS (Green, Al & Ace Cannon)
White Christmas / Christmas song / Winter wonderland / I'll be home for Christmas / Jingle bells / What Christmas means to me / Oh holy night / Silent night / Feels like Christmas / Santa Claus is coming to town / Rudolph the red nosed reindeer / Here comes Santa Claus / Frosty the snowman / Blue Christmas / I saw Mommy kissing Santa Claus / Let it snow, let it snow, let it snow / Jingle bell rock / Rockin' around the Christmas tree
CD _____ HIUKCD 126
Hi / Oct '91 / Pinnacle.

COVER ME GREEN
I want to hold your hand / My girl / The letter / Light my fire / I say a little prayer / Summertime / Get back / For the good times / Oh pretty woman / I'm so lonesome I could cry / Lean on me / Unchained melody / Ain't no mountain high enough / People get ready / Amazing grace
CD _____ HIUKCD 107
Hi / Apr '91 / Pinnacle.

DON'T LOOK BACK
Best love / Love is a beautiful thing / Waiting on you / What does it take / Keep on pushing love / You are my everything / One love / People in the world / Give it everything / Your love / Fountain of love / Don't look back / Love in motion
CD _____ 74321 16310-2
RCA / Oct '93 / BMG.

EXPLORES YOUR MIND
Sha la la / Take me to the river / God blessed our love / City / One night stand / I'm hooked on you / Stay with me forever / Hangin' on / School days
CD _____ HIUKCD 413
Hi / Sep '86 / Pinnacle.

FLIPSIDE OF AL GREEN, THE
CD _____ HIUKCD 141
Hi / May '93 / Pinnacle.

GREATEST HITS
Let's stay together / I can't get next to you / You ought to be with me / Look what you done for me / Let's get married / Tired of being alone / Call me / I'm still in love with you / Here I am (come and take me) / How can you mend a broken heart
CD _____ HIUKCD 425
Hi / Feb '87 / Pinnacle.

GREATEST HITS #2 (Take me To The River)
Drivin' wheel / I've never found a girl / Love and happiness / Living for you / Sha la la / L.O.V.E. Love / One woman / Take me to the river / Rhymes / Oh me, oh my (dreams in my arms) / Glory glory / Full of fire / Keep me cryin' / Belle
CD _____ HIUKCD 438
Hi / Oct '87 / Pinnacle.

GREEN IS BLUES/AL GREEN GETS NEXT TO YOU
One woman / Talk to me / My girl / Letter / I stand accused / Gotta find a new world / What am I gonna do with myself / Tomorrow's dream / Get back baby / Get back / Summertime / I can't get next to you / Are

you lonely for me baby / God is standing by / Tired of being alone / I'm a ram / Drivin' wheel / Light my fire / You say it / Right now, right now / All because
CD _____ HIUKCD 106
Hi / Aug '90 / Pinnacle.

HAVE A GOOD TIME/THE BELLE ALBUM
CD _____ HIUKCD 119
Hi / Sep '91 / Pinnacle.

IS LOVE / FULL OF FIRE
L.O.V.E. Love / Rhymes / Love sermon / There is love / Could I be the one / Love ritual / I didn't know / Oh me, oh my (dreams in my arms) / I gotta be more (take me higher) / I wish you were here / Glory glory / That's the way it is / Always / There's no way / I'd fly away / Full of fire / Together again / Soon as I get home / Let it shine
CD _____ HIUKCD 114
Hi / May '91 / Pinnacle.

LET'S STAY TOGETHER
Let's stay together / I've never found a girl / So you're leaving / It ain't no fun to me / What is this feelin' / Tomorrow's dream / How can you mend a broken heart / La for you
CD _____ HIUKCD 405
Hi / Jul '86 / Pinnacle.

LIVIN' FOR YOU / EXPLORES YOUR MIND
Livin' for you / Home again / Free at last / Let's get married / So good to be here / Sweet sixteen / Unchanged malady / My God is real / Beware / Sha la la / Take me to the river / God blessed our love / City / One nite stand / I'm hooked on you / Stay with me forever / Hangin' on / School days
CD _____ HIUKCD 113
Hi / May '91 / Pinnacle.

LOVE IS REALITY
Just can't let you go / I can feel it / Love is reality / Positive attitude / Again / Sure feels good / I like it / You don't know me / Long time / Why
CD _____ 701927160X
Nelson Word / Apr '92 / Nelson Word.

LOVE RITUAL (Rare & Previously Unreleased 1968-1972)
Love ritual / So good to be here / Ride Sally ride / Surprise attack / Love is real / I think it's for the feeling / Up above my head / Strong as death / Mimi / I want to hold your hand
CD _____ HIUKCD 443
Hi / '89 / Pinnacle.

SUPREME AL GREEN, THE
Tired of being alone / I can't get next to you / Let's stay together / How can you mend a broken heart / Love and happiness / I'm still in love with you / Simply beautiful / What a wonderful thing love is / Call me / My God is real / Let's get married / Sha la la (make me happy) / Take me to the river / Love ritual / L.O.V.E. Love / I didn't know / Full of fire / Belle
CD _____ HIUKCD 130
Hi / Apr '92 / Pinnacle.

TOKYO - LIVE
L.O.V.E. Love / Tired of being alone / Let's stay together / How can you mend a broken heart / All 'n' all / God blessed our love / You ought to be with me / For the good times / Belle / Sha la la / Let's get married / Dream / I feel good / Love and happiness
CD _____ HIUKCD 104
Hi / Apr '90 / Pinnacle.

TRUST IN GOD
Don't make you wanna go home / No not one / Trust in God / Lean on me / Ain't no mountain high enough / Up the ladder to the roof / Never met nobody like you / Holy spirit / All we need is a little more love
CD _____ HIUKCD 423
Hi / May '91 / Pinnacle.

YOU SAY IT
You say it / I'll be standing by / True love / Right now, right now / Memphis, Tennessee / I'm a ram / Listen / Baby what's wrong with you / Ride Sally ride / Eli's game / Sweet song / Everything to me / Starting all over again
CD _____ HIUKCD 444
Hi / Jun '90 / Pinnacle.

Green, Bennie

BENNIE GREEN WITH ART FARMER (Green, Bennie & Art Farmer)
CD _____ OJCCD 1800
Original Jazz Classics / Jan '94 / Wellard / Jazz Music / Cadillac / Complete/Pinnacle.

BLOWS HIS HORN
CD _____ OJCCD 1728
Original Jazz Classics / Jan '94 / Wellard / Jazz Music / Cadillac / Complete/Pinnacle.

WALKING DOWN
CD _____ OJCCD 1752
Original Jazz Classics / Jan '94 / Wellard / Jazz Music / Cadillac / Complete/Pinnacle.

Green, Benny

ELLINGTON LEGACY, THE (Green, Benny & Joe Van Enkhuizen)

Blues at sundown / Do not disturb / Jeeps blues / Isfahan / Take it easy / In the stands / Country gal / Gypsy without a song / Blue light / I'm just a lucky so and so / Timon of Athens / Fontainebleau forest
CD _____ CD 5115
September / Feb '94 / Kingdom / Cadillac.

POETRY OF JOHNNY MERCER, THE (Too Marvellous For Words)
Too marvellous words / Strip polka / When a woman loves a man / Something tells me / Swing is the thing / Jeepers creepers / Arthur Murray taught me dancing in a hurry / Mr. Meadowlark / I'll dream tonight / (I ain't hep to that step, but I'll) Dig it / Tangerine / Fools rush in / Say it with a kiss / That old black magic / OLd music master / If I had a million dollars / Blues in the night / On behalf of the visiting fireman / I'm old fashioned / I thought about you / Dearly beloved / Goody goody / I'd know you anywhere
CD _____ AVC 548
Avid / Jun '95 / Avid/BMG / Koch.

Green Bullfrog

GREEN BULLFROG SESSIONS, THE
My baby left me / Making time / Lawdy Miss Clawdy / By Bullfrog / I want you / I'm a free man / Walk a mile in my shoes / Lovin' you is good for me baby / Who do you love / Ain't nobody home / Louisiana man
CD _____ NSPCD 503
Connoisseur / Nov '91 / Pinnacle.

Green Day

DOOKIE
Burnout / Having a blast / Chump / Longview / Welcome to paradise / Pulling teeth / Basket case / She / Sassafras roots / When I come around / Coming clean / Emenius sleepus / In the end / F.O.D.
CD _____ 936245529-2
Warner Bros. / Feb '94 / Warner Music.

KERPLUNK
CD _____ LOOKOUT 46CD
Lookout / Aug '94 / SRD.

SMOOTH
CD _____ LOOKOUT 22CD
Lookout / Aug '94 / SRD.

Green, Grant

BEST OF GRANT GREEN, THE (Street Funk & Jazz Grooves)
Grantstand / Jazz jumpin' / Sookie sookie / Talkin' about JC / Jean de Fleur / Windjammer / Walk in the night / I don't want nobody / Cease the bombing / Final comedown / In the middle / Wives and lovers (On LP only) / My favourite things (On LP only) / Ain't it funky now (On LP only)
CD _____ BNZ 317
Blue Note / Jun '93 / EMI.

CARRYIN' ON
Ease back / Hurt so bad / I don't want nobody to give me nothing (Open up the door I'll get it myself) / Upshot / Cease the bombing
CD _____ CDP 8312472
Blue Note / Mar '95 / EMI.

GRANT GREEN
Reaching out / Our Miss Brooks / Flick of a prick / One for Blena / Baby, you should know it / Falling in love with love
CD _____ BLCD 760129
Black Lion / May '90 / Jazz Music / Cadillac / Wellard / Koch.

GREEN STREET
No.1 Green Street / Round Midnight / Grant's dimensions / Green with envy / Alone together
CD _____ CDP 8320882
Blue Note / May '95 / EMI.

SOLID
Minor league / Ezz-thetic / Grant's tune / Solid / Kicker / Wives and lovers (CD only)
CD _____ CDP 8335802
Blue Note / Oct '95 / EMI.

Green Jelly

333
Carnage rules / Orange krunch / Pinata head / Fixation / Bear song / Fight / Super elastic / Jump jerk / Anthem / Slave boy
CD _____ 74321235362
Zoo Entertainment / May '95 / BMG.

CEREAL KILLER
Obey the cowgod / Three little pigs / Ugly truth / Cereal killer / Rock 'n' roll pumpkin / Anarchy in the U.K. / Electric harley house (of love) / Trippin' on XTC / Mis-adventures of Shit man / House me teenage rave / Fight of the Skajaquada / Green Jelly theme song
CD _____ 72445110382
Zoo Entertainment / Jun '93 / BMG.

Green, Jesse

ROUND TRIP
CD _____ BHCD 00032
Bad Habits / Jul '95 / BMG.

SEA JOURNEY (Green, Jesse Trio)
CD _____ CRD 328
Chiara Scuro / Nov '95 / Jazz Music / Kudos.

Green, Lee

LEE GREEN VOL.1 - 1929-1930
CD _____ DOCD 5187
Blues Document / Oct '93 / Swift / Jazz Music / Hot Shot.

LEE GREEN VOL.2 - 1930-1937
CD _____ DOCD 5188
Blues Document / Oct '93 / Swift / Jazz Music / Hot Shot.

Green, Lloyd

STEELS THE HITS
Misty moonlight / Ruby, don't take your love to town / My elusive dream / Crazy arms / Too much of you / There goes my everything / Take these chains from my heart / Moody river / No another time / Moon river / Feelings / My love / Little bit more / You and me / Amie / Desperado / Kiss the moonlight / Edgewater beach / Stainless steel
CD _____ PLATCD 33
Platinum Music / Jul '92 / Prism / Ross.

Green On Red

BEST OF GREEN ON RED
CD _____ WOLCD 1047
China / Jun '94 / Pinnacle.

GAS FOOD LODGING
That's what dreams / Black river / Hair of the dog / This I know / Fading away / Easy way out / Sixteen ways / Drifter / Sea of Cortez / We shall overcome
CD _____ MAUCD 612
Mau Mau / Jun '92 / Pinnacle.

HERE COME THE SNAKES
Keith can't read / Morning blue / Broken radio / Tenderloin / D.T. blues / Rock 'n' roll disease / Zombie for love / Change / Way back home
CD _____ WOLCD 1013
China / Mar '91 / Pinnacle.

LITTLE THINGS IN LIFE (1987-91)
Gold in the graveyard / Shed a tear (for the lonesome) / Broken radio / Rock 'n' roll disease / Good patient woman / Little things in life / Quarter / Pills and booze / We had it all / Hector's out / Zombie for love (Live) / Sixteen ways (Live) / Change (Live) / Fading away (Live) / Are you sure Hank done it this way (Live) / Hair of the dog (Live)
CD _____ MCCD 037
Music Club / Sep '91 / Disc / THE / CM.

NO FREE LUNCH
CD _____ OW 30015
One Way / Sep '94 / Direct / ADA.

SCAPEGOATS
CD _____ WOLCD 1001
China / Apr '91 / Pinnacle.

THIS TIME AROUND
This time around / Cool million / Reverend Luther / Good patient woman / You couldn't get arrested / Quarter / Foot / Hold the line / Pills and booze / We're all waiting
CD _____ WOLCD 1019
China / Jul '91 / Pinnacle.

TOO MUCH FUN
CD _____ WOLCD 1029
China / Sep '92 / Pinnacle.

Green Pajamas

GHOSTS OF LOVE
CD _____ BCD 4033
Bomp / Jul '90 / Pinnacle.

Green, Peter

END OF THE GAME, THE
Bottoms up / Timeless time / Descending scale / Burnt foot / Hidden depth / End of the game
CD _____ 7599267582
Reprise / Jan '96 / Warner Music.

LAST TRAIN TO SAN ANTONE
Proud pinto / Clown / In the skies / Rubbing my eyes / Bandit / Funky jam / Black woman / Just for you / Tribal dance / One woman love / Momma don't cha cry / Lost my love / Last train to San Antone / Promised land
CD _____ FG 2801
Frog / Dec '95 / Total/BMG.

ONE WOMAN LOVE
CD _____ PACD 7013
Disky / Feb '93 / THE / BMG / Discovery / Pinnacle.

RARITIES
CD _____ AP 052
Appaloosa / Jan '96 / ADA / Magnum Music Group.

WHATCHA' GONNA DO
CD _____ RNCD 1006
Rhino / Feb '93 / Warner Music.

WHITE SKY
Time for me to go / Shining star / Clown / White sky (love that evil woman) / It's gonna be me / Born on the wild side / Falling apart / Indian lover / Just another guy
CD _____ RNCD 1004

Rhino / Nov '92 / Jetstar / Magnum Music Group / THE.

Green River

COME ON DOWN
CD _____ HMS 031-2
Homestead / May '94 / SRD.

DRY AS A BONE/REHAB DOLL
This town / P.C.C. / Ozzie / Unwind / Baby takes / Searchin' / Ain't nothing to do / Queen bitch / Forever means / Rehab doll / Swallow my pride / Together we'll never / Smilin' and dyin' / Porkfist / Take a dive / One more stitch
CD _____ SPCD 72
Sub Pop / May '94 / Disc.

Greenberg, Rowland

HOW ABOUT YOU
Seven up / I don't stand a ghost of a chance with you / Have you met Miss Jones / Georgia on my mind / Stella by starlight / Gone with the wind / Basin Street blues / Strike up the band / On the sunny side of the street / Taps Miller / Sweet and lovely
CD _____ GECD 155
Gemini / Jan '88 / Cadillac.

Greenberry Woods

RAPPLE DAPPLE
Trampoline / No 37 (Feels so strange) / Sentimental role / I'll send a message / Oh Christine / I knew you would / Waiting for dawn / That's what she said / Sympathy song / Adieu / Dusted / More and more / Nowhere to go / Hold on
CD _____ 9362454952
WEA / May '94 / Warner Music.

Greenbriar Boys

BEST OF THE GREENBRIAR BOYS
(Greenbriar Boys & John Herald)
CD _____ VND 79317
Vanguard / '89 / Complete/Pinnacle / Discovery

Greene, Burton

BURTON GREENE TRIO ON TOUR
CD _____ ESP 1074-2
ESP / Jan '93 / Jazz Horizons / Jazz Music.

Greene String Quartet

MOLLY ON THE SHORE
CD _____ HNCD 1333
Hannibal / Nov '88 / Vital / ADA.

Greenfield, Haze

PROVIDENCE
CD _____ 260692
Owl / Nov '92 / Harmonia Mundi (USA).

Greenfields

HOBO BY MY SIDE, A
Stay away / Broken heart / Who's that guy called Tom T. Hall / Riverboat queen / Moonlight rider / San Bernardino / Come home with me tonight / Baby's gone / Rollin' down / What a wonderful world / Hobo blues
CD _____ BCD 15698
Bear Family / Jul '93 / Rollercoaster / Direct / CM / Swift / ADA.

Greenfields of America

LIVE IN CONCERT
CD _____ GLCD 1096
Green Linnet / Aug '92 / Roots / CM / Direct / ADA.

Greenslade

BEDSIDE MANNERS ARE EXTRA
Bedside manners are extra / Pilgrims progress / Time to dream / Drum folk / Sunkissed you're not / Chalkhill
CD _____ 7599268662
WEA / Jan '96 / Warner Music.

GREENSLADE
Feathered friends / English western / Drowning man / Temple song / Melange / What are you doin' to me / Sundance
CD _____ 7599268122
WEA / Jan '96 / Warner Music.

SPYGLASS GUEST
Spirit of the dance / Little red fry up / Rainbow / Siam seesaw / Joie de vivre / Red light / Melancholic race / Theme for an imaginary western
CD _____ 7599268672
WEA / Jan '96 / Warner Music.

TIME AND TIDE
Animal farm / Newsworth / Time / Tide / Catalan / Flatery stakes / Waltz for a fallen idol / Ass's ears / Doldrums / Gangsters
CD _____ 7599268682
WEA / Jan '96 / Warner Music.

Greenslade, Dave

PENTATEUCH OF THE COSMOLOGY, THE

Intriot / Moondance / Beltempest / Glass / Three brides / Birds and bats and dragonflies / Nursery hymn / Minstrel / Fresco / Kashrinn / Barcarolle / Dry land / Forest kingdom / Vivat regina / Scream but not / married / Mischief / War / Lament for the sea / Miasma generator / Exile / Jubilate / Tiger the dove
CD _____ BGOCD 170
Beat Goes On / Jul '94 / Pinnacle.

Greenwich, Sonny

LIVE AT SWEET BASIL
CD _____ JUST 262
Justin Time / Jul '92 / Harmonia Mundi / Cadillac.

Greer, Big John

BIG JOHN'S ROCKIN' (3CD Set)
CD Set _____ BCD 15554
Bear Family / Feb '92 / Rollercoaster / Direct / CM / Swift / ADA.

Greeson, Ron

BLUEFUSE
CD _____ HEDC 002
Headscope / Jun '93 / Magnum Music Group.

Gregory, Michael

WHAT TO WHERE
Jubilee / One / Still waiting / Heart of happiness / Superstitious game / Lost home at / Where / What / Falling down / Fan the flame / Slow burn (there's more) / Elan
CD _____ PD 83023
Novus / Dec '88 / BMG.

Gregory, Steve

BUSHFIRE
CD _____ LJKCD 011
LKJ / Mar '95 / Jetstar / Grapevine.

Gregson & Collister

LOVE IS A STRANGE HOTEL
For a dancer / Move away Jimmy Blue / How men are / Love is a strange hotel / Even a fool would let go / One step up / Things we do for love / (I heard that) Lonesome whistle / Same situation / Always better with you / Today I started loving you again / Most beguiling eyes
CD _____ SPCD 1035
Special Delivery / Oct '90 / ADA / CM / Direct.

MISCHIEF
CD _____ SPCD 1010
Special Delivery / Sep '87 / ADA / CM / Direct.

Gregson, Clive

CAROUSEL OF NOISE (Live/Unreleased Tracks)
CD _____ CGCD 9401
Gregsongs / May '95 / Direct / ADA.

PEOPLE AND PLACES
CD _____ FIENDCD 764
Demon / Apr '95 / Pinnacle / ADA.

STRANGE PERSUASIONS
Summer rain / Jewel in your crown / I still see her face / Home is where the heart is / Play the fool / Poor relation / This town / Safety net / American car / I fell apart
CD _____ FIENDCD 45
Demon / Jan '90 / Pinnacle / ADA.

Grenadier Guards Band

BRITISH GRENADIERS, THE
British Grenadiers / Scipio / First battalion bugle call / Queens company / Second battalion bugle call / Nilimegen / Third battalion bugle call / Inkerman / Rule Brittania / Grenadiers march / Duke of York / Gloster's march / Belle Isle / Portsmouth / Wargramer grenadier march / Last post / Grenadiers return / Reveille / Musick marziale
CD _____ BNA 5015
Bandleader / Oct '87 / Conifer.

DRUMS AND FIFES (The 1st & 2nd Battalion of Grenadier Guards)
British Grenadiers / Girl I left behind me / Goodbye Dolly Gray / Garry Owen / Pack up your troubles in your old kit bag / Lilliburlero / Great escape / Hazlemere / Old grey mare / Brazil / See the conquering hero comes / Scipio / Red cloak / Army and Marine / Bugle calls / Marching down the years / Potpourri / Regimental music of the 18th century / First battalion bugle call / Parade flute call / Second battalion bugle call / Drummer's call / Third battalion bugle call / Grenadiers march / Flag and empire / Prussia's glory / Eton boating song / After reflection / Belle Isle march / Prince Rupert's march / Duke of York / Captain Morley's march / Fanfare
CD _____ BNA 5003
Bandleader / Nov '86 / Conifer.

MARCH SPECTACULAR (Bands Of The Grenadier, Coldstream & Irish Guards)
British Grenadiers / Scipio / Grenadiers march / Milanollo / Gigaro / St. Patrick's day / Let erin remember / Through bolts and bars / Army and marine / Furchtlos und treu / Red men's march / Nijmegen / Dunedin / Badenviller / Carry on / Bond of friendship / Independentia / King's troop / Luftwaffe March / Imperial echoes / Admiral of the air / Trafalgar / Frensham / Pioneer spirit / quis separabit / Wellington / San Lorenzo / Sons of the brave / Star of St Patrick
CD _____ BNA 5040
Bandleader / '91 / Conifer.

MARCHING WITH THE GRENADIER GUARDS
British Grenadiers / Tour of duty / Imperial echoes / Zapfenstreich nr.1 / Old comrades / Scipio march / Blaze away / Troop 'Les Huguenots' / Hands across the sea / Colonel Bogey / Grenadiers slow march / Liberty bell / Purple pageant / Radetzky march / Duke of York / Europe united / Coronation bells / New colonial march
CD _____ CDGUARDS 1
Premier/MFP / Oct '90 / EMI.

NEW WORLD SALUTE (Grenadier Guards & Gordon Highlanders)
New world salute / General Mitchell / Stabat Mater / Arromanches / Green hills of Tyrol / Battle's o'er / Lochanside / See the conquering hero comes / Edinburgh Castle / Soldier's return / Crusader's march / Bonnie lass o'Fyvie / Kumbaya / Barren rocks of Aden / Piping hot / Highland Cathedral / Westminster chimes / Oranges and lemons / Let's all go down the Strand / London pride / Maybe it's because I'm a Londoner / Scottish division / Braes o'mar / Aspin bank / High road to Linton / Piper of Drummond / Also Sprach Zarathustra / Superman / 633 Squadron / Day thou gavest Lord is ended / America the beautiful / Amazing grace / British Grenadiers / Cock o' the North
CD _____ BNA 5019
Bandleader / Sep '88 / Conifer.

ON STAGE
Fanfare - stage presence / Full speed ahead / Grenadiers waltz / Overture on themes of Offenbach / Love changes everything / Carnival of Venice / Debutante / Prelude to romance / Send in the clowns / Portrait in time / Me and my girl / March and dance of the comedians / Les miserables / Spanish rhapsody fiesta / March: Atlantis (Tape only.) / Three bavarian dances (Tape only.)
CD _____ BNA 5032
Bandleader / Aug '89 / Conifer.

WHEN THE GUARDS ARE ON PARADE
British grenadiers / Scorpio / Duke of York / Grenadiers return / Queen's company / Inkerman / Royal salute / Army and marine / Glorious victory / Army of the nile / Great little army / Royal standard / Steadfast and true / King's guard / National emblem / Birdcake walk / Old grenadier / Namur / brave / On the square / Contemptibles
CD _____ BNA 5104
Bandleader / Mar '91 / Conifer.

Grenadine

NOPALITOS
CD _____ SMR 23CD
Simple Machines / Oct '94 / SRD.

Gretsy, Alan

BOBCATS RECAPTURED
CD _____ JCD 258
Jazzology / Dec '95 / Swift / Jazz Music.

Grey, Al

CENTER PIECE - LIVE AT THE BLUE NOTE
Diz related / South side / I wish I knew / Homage to Norman / Nascimento / S.W.B. Blues / Lester leaps in / Bewitched / Center piece
CD _____ CD 83379
Telarc / Sep '95 / Conifer / ADA.

CHRISTMAS STOCKIN' STUFFER
CD _____ 74039
Capri / Nov '93 / Wellard / Cadillac.

FAB
CD _____ 74038
Capri / Nov '93 / Wellard / Cadillac.

NEW AL GREY QUINTET, THE
Bluish grey / Sonny's tune / Don't blame me / Syrup and bisquits / T'aint no use / Al's rose / Night and day / Call it whatchawanna / Underdog / Stompin' at the Savoy / Al's blues / Rue prevail / Soap gets in your eyes
CD _____ CRD 305
Chiara Scuro / Oct '91 / Jazz Music / Kudos.

TRULY WONDERFUL (Grey, Al & Jimmy Forrest)
CD _____ STCD 552
Stash / '92 / Jazz Music / CM / Cadillac / Direct / ADA.

Grey, Jerry

SOUND OFF
CD _____ DAWE 73
Magic / Oct '95 / Jazz Music / Swift / Wellard / Cadillac / Harmonia Mundi.

Grey Lady Down

12.02 / All join hands / Thrill of it all / Ballad of Billy Grey / Circus of thieves / Annabez / Fugitive / I believe
CD _____ CYCL 001
Cyclops / Feb '94 / Pinnacle.

FORCES
Paradise lost / Battlefields of counterpane / Without a trace / Cold stage / I believe / Flyer
CD _____ CYCL 020
Cyclops / Jun '95 / Pinnacle.

Grey, Michael

COMPOSERS SERIES VOL.1
CD _____ LCOM 5217
Lismor / Sep '94 / Lismor / Direct / Duncans / ADA.

Grey, Owen

ON TOP
CD _____ RNCD 2073
Rhino / Oct '94 / Jetstar / Magnum Music Group / THE.

Greyhound

BLACK AND WHITE
Black and white / Dream lover / Stand for our rights / Jamaica rum / Sky high / Wily / Only love can win / Mango rock / Unchained melody / Hold on to your happiness / Wappadusa / Some dark city
CD _____ CSCD 539
See For Miles/C5 / Oct '92 / Pinnacle.

Grianan

MAID OF EIRIN
CD _____ WWCD 14
West Wind / Jan '94 / Swift / Charly / CM / ADA.

Grid

456
Face the sun / Ice machine / Crystal clear / Aquarium / Instrument / Heartbeat / Oh six one / Figure of eight / Boom / Leave your body / Fire engine red
CD _____ CDV 2696
Virgin / Oct '92 / EMI.

ELECTRIC HEAD
One giant step / Interference / Are you receiving / Islamatron / Traffic / Driving instructor / Beat called love / Friend of the devil / Sugar magnolia / Operator / Candy man / Ripple / Brokedown palace / Till the morning comes / Attics of my life / Truckin' / Floatation / Strange electric sun / Typical Waterloo sunset / Dr. Celine / Machine delay / This must be heaven / Beautiful and profound / Intergalactica / Central locking / First stroke
CD _____ 9031715572
East West / Sep '90 / Warner Music.

EVOLVER
Wake up / Rollercoaster / Swamp thing / TIROB / Rise / Shades of sleep / Higher peaks / Texas cowboys / City scape / Golden dawn
CD _____ 74321 22718-2
De-Construction / Sep '94 / BMG.

MUSIC FOR DANCING
Floatation / Crystal clear / Boom / Figure of 8 / Rollercoaster / Texas cowboys / Swamp thing / Crystal clear (remix) / Figure of 8 (remix) / Diablo / Rollercoaster (remix)
CD _____ 74321276702
De-Construction / Sep '95 / BMG.

Grief

AU DELA
CD _____ DANCD 023
Danceteria / Jan '90 / Plastic Head / ADA.

KITTYSTRA QUATRE
CD _____ DANCD 024
Danceteria / Jan '90 / Plastic Head / ADA.

Grief

COME TO GRIEF
CD _____ CM 77087
Century Media / Jan '95 / Plastic Head.

Grier, David

FREEWHEELING
Wheeling / Shadowbrook / Old hotel rag / Angeline the baker / Bluegrass itch / Alabama jubilee / Blue midnite star / Roanoke / If I knew her name / Gold rush / Fog rolling over the Glen / New soldier's joy
CD _____ CDROU 0250
Rounder / '91 / CM / Direct / ADA / Cadillac.

LONE SOLDIER
CD _____ ROUCD 0309
Rounder / Apr '95 / CM / Direct / ADA / Cadillac.

Grievous Angels

ONE JOB TOWN
CD _____ SP 1162CD
Stony Plain / Oct '93 / ADA / CM / Direct.

Griffin, Buck

LET'S ELOPE BABY
Pretty Lou / Girl in 1209 / You'll never come back / Stutterin' Papa / Watchin' the 7:10 roll by / Broken heart with alimony / Jessie Lee / Bow my back / Old bee tree / Every night / Party / Little Dan / Neither do I / Cochise / Go-stop-go / Bawlin' and squalin' / Let's elope baby / It don't make no never mind / Meadow lark boogie / Rollin' tears / One day after payday / Going home all alone / Twenty six steps / First man to stand on the moon / Sorry I never knew you / Lord give me strength / Next to mine / Lookin' for the green
CD _____ BCDAH 15811
Bear Family / Jun '95 / Rollercoaster / Direct / CM / Swift / ADA.

Griffin, Della

TRAVELIN' LIGHT
Smile / Travelin' light / Out of nowhere / Some other Spring / Second time around / Easy living / Trouble in mind / Trust in me / Blue gardenia
CD _____ MCD 5496
Muse / Jul '94 / New Note / CM.

Griffin, Johnny

DANCE OF PASSION
CD _____ 5126042
Antilles/New Directions / Jan '93 / PolyGram.

MAN I LOVE, THE
Man I love / Hush-a-bye / Blues for Harvey / (I'm afraid) the masquerade is over / Sophisticated lady / Wee / I'll get by / Mean to me / I'll never be the same / Easy living / Foolin' myself / Without your love / Me, myself and I / Sailboat in the moonlight / trav'lin all alone / She's funny that way / Getting some fun out of life / I can't believe that you're in love with me / Back in your own backyard / You can't be mine (and someone else's too) / Say it with a kiss
CD _____ BLCD 760107
Black Lion / Jun '88 / Jazz Music / Cadillac / Wellard / Koch.

MASTER OF SAX
Isfahan / Take my hand / All through the night / Coming on the hudson / Woe is me / Hush-a-bye / Out of this world / If i should lose you
CD _____ 722011
Scorpio / Sep '92 / Complete/Pinnacle.

WOE IS ME
CD _____ JHR 73559
Jazz Hour / Oct '92 / Target/BMG / Jazz Music / Cadillac.

Griffith, Nanci

BEST OF NANCI GRIFFITH
Trouble in the fields / From a distance / Speed of the sound of loneliness / Love at the five and dime / Listen to the radio / Gulf coast highway / I wish it would rain / Ford Econoline / If wishes were changes / Wing and the wheel / Late night Grand hotel / From Clare to here / It's just another morning here / Tumble and fall / There's a light beyond these woods (Mary Margaret) / Outbound plane / Lone star state of mind / It's a hard life wherever you go / Road to Aberdeen
CD _____ MCD 10966
MCA / Oct '93 / BMG.

FLYER
Flyer / Nobody's angel / Say it isn't so / Southbound train / These days in a open book / Time of inconvenience / Don't forget about me / Always will / Going back to Georgia / Talk to me while I'm listening / Fragile / On Grafton street / Anything you need but me / Goodnight to a Mothers dream / This heart
CD _____ MCD 11155
MCA / Sep '94 / BMG.

LAST OF THE TRUE BELIEVERS
Last of the true believers / Love at the five and dime / St. Olav's gate / More than a whisper / Banks of the old Pontchartrain / Looking for the time / Goin' gone / One of these days / Love's found a shoulder / Fly by night / Wing and the wheel
CD _____ REUCD 1013
Rounder / Jun '88 / CM / Direct / ADA / Cadillac.

LATE NIGHT GRANDE HOTEL
CD _____ MCLD 19304
MCA / Oct '95 / BMG.

LITTLE LOVE AFFAIRS
Anyone can be somebody's fool / I knew love / Never mind / Love wore a halo / So long ago / Gulf coast highway / Little love

affairs / I wish it would rain / Outbound plane / I would change my life / Sweet dreams will come
CD _____ MCLD 19211
MCA / Aug '93 / BMG.

LONE STAR STATE OF MIND
Lone star state of mind / Cold hearts, closed minds / From a distance / Beacon Street / Nickel dreams / Sing one for sister / Ford econoline / Trouble in the fields / Love in a memory / Let it shine on me / There's a light beyond these woods (Mary Margaret)
CD _____ MCLD 19176
MCA / Oct '92 / BMG.

ONCE IN A VERY BLUE MOON
Ghost in the music / Love is a hard waltz / Roseville fair / Mary and Omie / Friend out in the madness / I'm not drivin' these wheels / Ballad of Robin Winter-Smith / Daddy said / Once in a very blue moon / Year down in New Orleans / Spin on a red brick floor
CD _____ MCLD 19039
MCA / Apr '92 / BMG.

OTHER VOICES, OTHER ROOMS
Across the great divide / Woman of the phoenix / Tecumseh valley / Three fights up / Boots of Spanish leather / Speed of the sound of loneliness / From Clare to here / I can't help but wonder where I'm bound / Do re mi / This old town / Comin' down in the rain / Ten degrees and getting colder / Morning song to Sally / Night rider's lament / Are you tired of me darling / Turn around / Wimoweh
CD _____ MCD 10796
MCA / Mar '93 / BMG.

THERE'S A LIGHT BEYOND THESE WOODS
Michael's song / West Texas sun / Dollar matinee / Alabama soft spoken blues / Song for remembered heroes / There's a light beyond these woods (Mary Margaret) / Montana backroads
CD _____ MCLD 19112
MCA / Jul '93 / BMG.

Griffiths, Albert

WHOLE HEAP, A (Griffiths, Albert & The Gladiators)
CD _____ HBCD 11554
Heartbeat / '88 / Greensleeves / Jetstar / Direct / ADA.

Griffiths, Marcia

DREAMLAND
CD _____ CDSGP 0148
Prestige / Oct '95 / Total/BMG.

INDOMITABLE
CD _____ PHCD 26
Penthouse / Sep '93 / Jetstar.

MARCIA
CD _____ DGCD 7
Germaine / Apr '89 / Jetstar.

MARCIA GRIFFITHS AND FRIENDS
CD _____ RNCD 2040
Rhino / Jan '94 / Jetstar / Magnum Music Group / THE.

PUT A LITTLE LOVE IN YOUR HEART (The Best Of Marcia Griffiths)
Toil (my ambition) / Don't let me down / Put a little love in your heart / Young, gifted and black / We've got to get ourselves together / Private number / Band of gold / Pied piper / But I do / Your love / I don't care / You're mine / Help me up / First time ever I saw your face / Play me / There's no me without you / Sweet bitter love / When will I see you again
CD _____ CDTRL 325
Trojan / Mar '94 / Jetstar / Total/BMG.

STEPPIN'
CD _____ SHCD 44007
Shanachie / Jun '91 / Koch / ADA / Greensleeves.

Grifters

CRAPPIN YOU NEGATIVE
CD _____ 185192
Southern / May '94 / SRD.

EYES FULL OF GOLD
CD _____ SPCD 327
Sub Pop / Feb '96 / Disc.

ONE SOCK MISSING
CD _____ 185112
Southern / Jun '93 / SRD.

Grill

LIGHT
CD _____ CDPPP 111
PDCD / Feb '94 / Plastic Head.

Grillo, Alex

VIBRAPHONE ALONE
CD _____ CELPC 24
CELP / Nov '93 / Harmonia Mundi / Cadillac.

Grimes, Carol

ALIVE AT RONNIE SCOTT'S
Solitude / Never say never / Give me liberty / Wild women / Lush life / Who do you want / Where are you / Life is dangerous / Your shoes are hot / We said yes
CD _____ JHCD 034
Ronnie Scott's Jazz House / '91 / Jazz Music / Magnum Music Group / Cadillac.

LAZY BLUE EYES (Grimes, Carol & Ian Shaw)
I got it bad and that ain't good / You always miss the water (when the well runs dry) / I'm scared / Don't explain / Lush life / In a sentimental mood / Lover man / I ain't got nothin' but the blues / I cover the waterfront / I love you / Spring can really hang you up the most / Lazy blue eyes / Snake / Misty / Body and soul
CD _____ CDWIK 93
Big Beat / Oct '90 / Pinnacle.

Grimes, Tiny

TINY GRIMES AND THE ROCKIN' HIGHLANDERS (Grimes, Tiny & His Rockin' Highlanders)
Call of the wild / St. Louis blues / Tiny's jump / Howlin' blues / Frankie and Johnny boogie / My baby's cool / Pert skirt / Hey Mr. J.B. / Drinking beer / Marie
CD _____ KKCD 01
Krazy Kat / Apr '89 / Hot Shot / CM.

Grimethorpe Colliery Band

CLASSIC BRASS
Florentiner march / William Tell overture / Sweet Georgia Brown / Serenade / Sugar blues / Lovers / Mr. Jums / Valdres march / MacArthur Park / Gymnopedie No.1 / Mr. Lear's carnival / Misty / Procession to the Minster / Irish tune from County Derry (Danny boy). (CD only.) / Finale from Faust (CD only.)
CD _____ CDMFP 6058
Music For Pleasure / May '89 / EMI.

FIREBIRD (Conducted By Ray Farr)
Midnight sleighride / On with the motley / Songs of the quay / In a sentimental mood / Pictures at an exhibition / Festive prelude / Scherzo / Berne patrol / Why did I choose you / Firebird
CD _____ QPRL 010
Polyphonic / May '94 / Conifer.

GRIMETHORPE COLLIERY BAND
Red sky at night / Hogarth's hoe down / I dream of Jeannie with the light brown hair / Barney's tune / Cornet concerto / Chinese takeaway / Parade / Paris le soir / Mosaic / Stars and stripes forever / Moorside suite / Severn suite
CD _____ 450023-2
Decca / Aug '93 / PolyGram.

PAGANINI VARIATIONS FOR BRASS BAND
Raven's wood / Journey into freedom / Queen of the night's aria / Ruby Tuesday / Buster strikes back / Finale from organ symphony No. 3 / President / Girl with the flaxen hair / Blue John / Blue rondo a la Turk / Panagini variations
CD _____ DOYCD 015
Doyen / May '92 / Conifer.

POPULAR HYMNS
CD _____ MATCD 268
Castle / Apr '93 / BMG.

WILBY
CD _____ DOYCD 029
Doyen / Mar '94 / Conifer.

Grimetime

SPIRIT OF DISGUST
CD _____ KCCD 1
Kill City / Jun '94 / Pinnacle.

Grimms

ROCKING DUCK
Interruption at the Opera House / Three times corner / Sex maniac / Galatic love poem / Chairman Shankly / Italian job / Albatross ramble / Humanoid boogie / Short blues / Summer with the Monarch / Twyfords vitromant / Following you / Newly pressed suit / Eleventh hour / Conservative government figures / Brown paper carrier bag / Soul song / Rockin' duck / Songs of the stars / Right mask / Policeman's lot / Question of habit / Take it while you can / Poetic license / Masked poet / Hiss and boo / Gruesome / FX / Blab blab blab / Backwards thru space / Do chuck a mao mao
CD _____ EDCD 370
Edsel / Jun '93 / Pinnacle / ADA.

Grin

ALL OUT
Sad letter / Heavy chew / Don't be long / Love again / She ain't right / Love or else / Ain't love nice / Heart on fire / All out / Rusty gun
CD _____ 477847 2
Epic / Oct '94 / Sony.

Grip Inc.

POWER OF INNER STRENGTH
CD _____ SPV 08576922
SPV / Feb '95 / Plastic Head.

Grisman, David

ACOUSTIC CHRISTMAS
CD _____ CD 0190
Rounder / '88 / CM / Direct / ADA / Cadillac.

DAVID GRISMAN ROUNDER ALBUM
Hello / Sawing on the strings / Waiting on Vasser / I ain't broke but I'm badly bent / Op 38 / Hold to God's unchanging hand / Boston boy / Cheyenne / Till the end of the world rolls around / You'll find her name written there / On and on / Bob's Brewin / So long
CD _____ CD 0069
Rounder / '88 / CM / Direct / ADA / Cadillac.

DAWGANOVA
CD _____ AC 017CD
Acoustic Disk / Nov '95 / ADA.

EARLY DAWG
CD _____ SH 3713CD
Sugarhill / Jan '94 / Roots / CM / ADA / Direct.

HERE TODAY (Grisman, David & Various Artists)
I'll love nobody but you / Once more / Foggy mountain chimes / Children are cryin' / Hot corn / Cold corn / Lonesome river / My walking shoes / Love and wealth / Billy in the lowground / Making plans / Sweet little Miss blue eyes / Going up home to live in green pastures
CD _____ ROU 0169CD
Rounder / Aug '93 / CM / Direct / ADA / Cadillac.

HOME IS WHERE THE HEART IS
True life blues / Down in the willow garden / My long journey home / Little Willie / Highway of sorrow / Sophronie / My aching heart / Close by / Feast here tonight / Leavin' home / Little cabin home on the hill / Salty Dawg blues / If I lose / Sad and lonesome day / My little Georgia rose / Foggy mountain top / I'm my own grandpa / Pretty Polly / Home is where the heart is / Nine pound hammer / Memories of mother and day / Teardrops in my eyes / House of gold
CD Set _____ CD 0251/2
Rounder / Aug '88 / CM / Direct / ADA / Cadillac.

TONE POEMS 2
CD _____ AC 018CD
Acoustic Disk / Nov '95 / ADA.

Grolnick, Don

HEARTS AND NUMBERS (Grolnick, Don & Michael Brecker)
Pointing at the moon / More pointing / Pools / Regrets / Four sleepers / Human bites / Act natural / Hearts and numbers
CD _____ WD 0106
Windham Hill Jazz / Mar '92 / New Note.

Groon

REFUSAL TO COMPLY
CD _____ DIS 002
FMR/Dissenter / Oct '95 / Harmonia Mundi / Cadillac.

Groove Collective

GROOVE COLLECTIVE
Restrike / Balimka / Nerd / Rahsaanasong / Ms. Grier / Whatugot / El golpe avisa / Genji monogatari / Buddha head / Saturday afternoon
CD _____ 9362455412
WEA / Mar '94 / Warner Music.

Groove Corporation

CO-OPERATION
CD _____ CORPCD 1
Network / Sep '95 / Sony / 3MV.

Groove Theory

GROOVE THEORY
10 minute high / Time flies / Ride / Come home / Baby love / Tell me / Hey you / Hello it's me / Good 2 me / Angel / Keep tryin' / You're not the one / Didja know / Boy at the window
CD _____ 4783822
Epic / Nov '95 / Sony.

Grooverider

GROOVERIDER'S HARDSTEP SELECTION (Various Artists)
CD _____ KICKCD 15
Kickin' / Nov '94 / SRD.

GROOVERIDER'S HARDSTEP SELECTION 2 (Various Artists)
CD _____ KICKCD 24
Kickin' / Jul '95 / SRD.

Groovezilla

GROOVEZILLA
CD _____ 9040232
Mausoleum / Mar '95 / Grapevine.

Groovy

GROOVY
CD _____ XCD 033
Extreme / Dec '95 / Vital/SAM.

Groovy, Winston

AFRICAN GIRL
African girl / Moving on / You keep me hangin' on / From we met / Please don't go / Lay back in the arms of someone / Girl, without you / So in love with you / Be because of you / Give me time / Please don't make me cry / Am I a dreamer / Oh little darling / Dear mama / Black hearted woman / Midnight train / Can't stand the morning / Anything goes with me / Old rock 'n' roller / Don't wanna hear that song again / Sea of dreams
CD _____ BRCD 3000
Blue Moon / Apr '92 / Magnum Music Group / Greensleeves / Hot Shot / ADA / Cadillac / Discovery.

COME ROCK WITH ME
CD _____ WGCD 009
Winston Groovy / Nov '95 / Jetstar.

COMING ON STRONG
CD _____ WGCD 007
WG / Oct '92 / Jetstar.

Grope

PRIMATES
CD _____ RRS 941CD
Lost & Found / Sep '95 / Plastic Head.

Gross, Henry

RELEASE/SHOW ME TO THE STAGE
CD _____ CDWIKD 104
Chiswick / Apr '92 / Pinnacle.

Grossman, Stefan

HOT DOGS
CD _____ 9012370
Line / Jun '94 / CM / Grapevine / ADA / Conifer / Direct.

Grossman, Steve

MY SECOND PRIME
CD _____ 1232462
Red / Nov '91 / Harmonia Mundi / Jazz Horizons / Cadillac / ADA.

REFLECTIONS (Grossman, Steve & Alby Cullaz/Simon Goubert)
CD _____ 500212
Musidisc / Nov '93 / Vital / Harmonia Mundi / ADA / Cadillac / Discovery.

SOME SHAPES TO COME
CD _____ OW 30329
One Way / Sep '94 / Direct / ADA.

TIME TO SMILE
415 Central Park West / Circus / I'm confessin' that I love you / Extemporaneous / This time the dreams on me / Time to smile / Till there was you / EJ's blues
CD _____ FDM 365662
Dreyfus / Dec '94 / ADA / Direct / New Note.

WAY OUT FAST VOL.1
CD _____ 123176-2
Red / Apr '93 / Harmonia Mundi / Jazz Horizons / Cadillac / ADA.

WAY OUT EAST VOL.2
CD _____ 123183-2
Red / Apr '93 / Harmonia Mundi / Jazz Horizons / Cadillac / ADA.

Grosz, Marty

LIVE AT THE L.A. CLASSIC (Grosz, Marty & His Orphan Newsboys)
CD _____ JCD 230
Jazzology / Jan '94 / Swift / Jazz Music.

MARTY GROSZ & HIS ORPHAN NEWSBOYS
CD _____ SOSCD 1225
Stomp Off / Oct '92 / Jazz Music / Wellard.

MARTY GROSZ & KEITH INGHAM (Grosz, Marty & Keith Ingham & Their Paswonky Serenaders)
CD _____ SOSCD 1214
Stomp Off / Oct '92 / Jazz Music / Wellard.

SINGS OF LOVE (Grosz, Marty & Tiny Signa)
CD _____ JCD 210
Jazzology / Oct '93 / Swift / Jazz Music.

SWING IT (Grosz, Marty & Destiny's Tots)
Let's swing it / Skeleton in the closet / Emaline / Old man harlem / Love dropped in for tea / Little girl / Sunrise serenade / I've got a feeling / You're foolin' / What's the use / Eye opener / Sun will shine tonight / It's been so long / I surrender dear / It's the last

time / Sonny boy / High hat, a piccolo and a cane
CD _____ JCD 180
Jazzology / Apr '89 / Swift / Jazz Music.

Grotus

SLOW MOTION APOCALYPSE
CD _____ VIRUS 118CD
Alternative Tentacles / Mar '93 / Pinnacle.

Groundhogs

BACK AGAINST THE WALL
Back against the wall / No to submission / Blue boar blues / Waiting in the shadows / Ain't no slaver / Stick to your grass / in the meantime 54156
CD _____ CDTB 111
Thunderbolt / '91 / Magnum Music Group.

BBC RADIO 1 LIVE IN CONCERT
Split part 1 / Cherry red / Split part 2 / Ground hog blues / Still a fool / Ship on the ocean / Free from all alarm / Dog me bitch / Light my light / Sins of the father
CD _____ WINCD 064
Windsong / Aug '94 / Pinnacle.

BLACK DIAMOND/CROSSCUT SAW
CD _____ BGOCD 131
Beat Goes On / Feb '92 / Pinnacle.

BLUES OBITUARY
B.D.D. / Daze of the weak / Times / Mistreated / Express man / Natchez burning / Light was the day
CD _____ BGOCD 6
Beat Goes On / Jan '89 / Pinnacle.

GROUNDHOG NIGHT
Shake for me / No more doggin' / Eccentric man / 3744 James Road / I want you to love me / Garden / Split part 1 / Split part 2 / Still a fool / I love you misogyny / Thank Christ for the bomb / Soldier / Mistreated / Me and the devil / Cherry red / Ground hog blues / Been there, done that / Down in the bottom
CD _____ HTDCD 1
HTD / Jun '93 / Pinnacle.

GROUNDHOGS
CD _____ CSAPCD 112
Connoisseur / Oct '92 / Pinnacle.

GROUNDHOGS BEST 1969-1972
Ground hog / Strange town / Bog roll blues / You had a lesson / Eccentric man / Earth is not room enough / BDD / Split part 1 / Cherry red / Mistreated / 3744 James Road / Soldier / Sad is the hunter / Garden / Split part 4
CD _____ CZ 282
EMI / Mar '90 / EMI.

HOG WASH
CD _____ BGOCD 44
Beat Goes On / '89 / Pinnacle.

HOGGIN' THE STAGE
CD _____ RRCD 207
Receiver / Sep '95 / Grapevine.

HOGS ON THE ROAD
Ground hogs / Hogs in the road / Express man / Strange town / Eccentric man / 3744 James Road / I want you to love me / Split IV / Soldier / Back against the wall / Garden / Split / Waiting in the shadows / Light my light / Me and the devil / Mistreated / Ground hogs blues / Cherry red
CD _____ CDTB 112
Thunderbolt / '91 / Magnum Music Group.

NO SURRENDER
Razor's edge / 3744 James Road / Superseded / Light my light / One more chance / Garden / Split Pt. 2 / Eccentric man (CD only.) / Strange town (CD only.) / Cherry red (CD only.)
CD _____ HTDCD 2
HTD / Dec '90 / Pinnacle.

RAZOR'S EDGE
Razor's edge / I confess / Born to be with you / One more chance / Protector / Superseded / Moving fast standing still / I want you to love me
CD _____ BUT CD 005
Hound Dog / Oct '92 / Street link.

SCRATCHING THE SURFACE
CD _____ BGOCD 15
Beat Goes On / '89 / Pinnacle.

SOLID
CD _____ CLACD 266
Castle / Jun '92 / BMG.

SPLIT
Split (pt 1) / Cherry red / Year in the life / Junk man groundhog / Split (pts 2-4)
CD _____ BGOCD 76
Beat Goes On / Dec '89 / Pinnacle.

THANK CHRIST FOR THE BOMB
Strange town / Darkness is no friend / Soldier / Thank Christ for the bomb / Ship on the ocean / Garden / Status people / Rich man, poor man / Eccentric man
CD _____ BGOCD 67
Beat Goes On / '89 / Pinnacle.

WHO WILL SAVE THE WORLD
CD _____ BGOCD 77
Beat Goes On / Apr '91 / Pinnacle.

Group Called Smith

SMITH
CD _____ VSD 5489
Varese Sarabande/Colosseum / Mar '95 / Pinnacle / Silva Screen.

Groupe Kalyi Jag

GYPSY SONGS OF HUNGARY
CD _____ PS 65112
Playasound / Nov '93 / Harmonia Mundi / ADA.

Growing Movement

CIRCLE OF TORTURE
CD _____ WB1 107-2
We Bite / Apr '94 / Plastic Head.

GRP All Star Big Band

ALL BLUES
Cookin' at the continental / Stormy Monday blues / All blues / Birks work / Goodbye pork pie hat / Senor blues / Blue miles / Mysterioso/Ba-lue bottana / Some other blues / Aunt Hagar's blues
CD _____ GRP 98002
GRP / Feb '95 / BMG / New Note.

ALL-STAR BIG BAND
Airegin / Blue train / Donna Lee / Maiden voyage / Sister Sadie / Sidewinder / Seven steps to heaven / I remember Clifford / Footprints / Manteca / Round Midnight / Spain
CD _____ GRP 96722
GRP / May '92 / BMG / New Note.

Gruberova, Edita

CHILDREN'S SONGS OF THE WORLD
Poesje mauw / D'esos caballos / Si toutes les filles / Che baccan / Es klappert die muhle / Spi mladjenec / Miala kasienka / Numi numi / Tancuj tancuj / Una flor de la cantuta / Three blind mice / Aa aa alin lasta / Haragszik / Pridi ty suhajko / Yuyake koyake / Heidschi bumbeidschi / Pera ston pera kambo / L'inverno e passato / Mi jachol lassim / Sakura / Dolina dolina / Humpty dumpty / Kumbaya / Nana mara haath / Katten og killingen / Ciobanas / Schyau / Joli tambour / Ba ba vita lamm / Itsy bitsy spider / Tala al-badru 'alaina / Alle voglein
CD _____ NC 706602
Nightingale Classics / Feb '94 / Complete/ Pinnacle.

Gruntruck

INSIDE YOURS
CD _____ RO 92602
Roadrunner / May '92 / Pinnacle.

Gruntz, George

BEYOND ANOTHER WALL
Literary lizard / All day, all night / Guiseppi / Anabel at two / Carl / Billy / Farewell to China
CD _____ TCB 94102
TCB / Aug '94 / New Note.

HAPPENING NOW! (Gruntz, George Concert Jazz Band '87)
CD _____ ARTCD 6008
Hat Art / '88 / Harmonia Mundi / ADA / Cadillac.

MOCK-LO-MOTION
Mock-lo-motion / You should know by now / One for kids / Annalisa / Giuseppi's blues / Vodka-pentatonic
CD _____ TCB 95552
TCB / Feb '96 / New Note.

Grupo ABC

AMOR DE MACARADA
Grupo ABC / Que lastima / Amore de mascarada / No quiero problema / Macario / Que he de hacer / Mesie bombe / Princelda de amor
CD _____ 66058086
RMM / Feb '96 / New Note.

Grupo Belen De Tarma

CHICHA
CD _____ TUMICD 045
Tumi / '94 / Sterns / Discovery.

Grupo Caneo

FASE IV
La rutina / Te recuerdo iqual que ayer / Sacala a bailar / Con el corazon en la mano / Mujeres divinas / Negrita / No te vayas a marchar / Aunque so amo
CD _____ 66058041
RMM / Jul '94 / New Note.

Grupo Chicontepec

MEXICAN LANDSCAPES VOL. 2
CD _____ PS 65902

Playasound / Jan '92 / Harmonia Mundi / ADA.

Grupo Mandarina

DISPUESTAS A TODO
La boquita / Cada vez / Lo quiero a morir / El hueso / El falsante / Tu jeego se acabo / Me nacio del alma / Mandarina navidena / Pena solo pena
CD _____ 66058073
RMM / Oct '95 / New Note.

Grupo Mantaza

MAMBORAMA
CD _____ UCD 19076
Forlane / Jul '95 / Target/BMG.

Grupo Merecumbe

MUSIC FROM COLOMBIA, CUMBIA, MERENGUE...
CD _____ EUCD 1253
ARC / Mar '94 / ARC Music / ADA.

Grusin, Dave

GRUSIN COLLECTION, THE
CD _____ GRP 95792
GRP / Aug '91 / BMG / New Note.

MIGRATION
CD _____ GRP 95922
GRP / Sep '89 / BMG / New Note.

ORCHESTRAL ALBUM, THE
Cuba libre / Santa Clara suite (Four movements) / Throo cowboy songs (Three movements) / Medley: Bess you is my woman/I loves you Porgy / Suite from the Milagro Beanfield War (Five movements) / Heart is a lonely hunter / Summer sketches / Condor / On Golden Pond
CD _____ GRP 97972
GRP / Oct '94 / BMG / New Note.

Grusin, Don

DON GRUSIN
Number eight / Hot / Shuffle city / Cuidado / Nice going / Cowboy reggae / Kona / What a friend we have in Jesus
CD _____ JMI 20102
JVC / Nov '93 / New Note.

Gryce, Gigi

NICA'S TEMPO
Speculation / In a meditating mood / Social call / Smoke signal / You'll always be the one I love / Kerry dance / Shuffle boil / Brake's sake / Gallop's gallop / Nica's tempo
CD _____ SV 0126
Savoy Jazz / Apr '93 / Conifer / ADA.

Gryphon

COLLECTION II, THE
CD _____ ITEMCD 3
Curio / May '95 / Plastic Head.

COLLECTION: GRYPHON
CD _____ ITEM CD1
Progress / Jul '92 / Vital.

GRYPHON
CD _____ ITEMCD 4
Curio / May '95 / Plastic Head / ADA.

GRYPHON MIDNIGHT MUSIC
CD _____ ESMCD 356
Essential / Jan '96 / Total/BMG.

MIDNIGHT MUSHROOMS
Midnight mushrumps / Ploughboys dream / Last flash of gaberdine tailor / Gulland rock / Dubbel dutch / Ethelion
CD _____ ITEMCD 5
Curio / May '95 / Plastic Head / ADA.

RAINDANCE
CD _____ ITEMCD 7
Curio / May '95 / Plastic Head / ADA.

RED QUEEN TO GRYPHON THREE
CD _____ ITEMCD 6
Curio / May '95 / Plastic Head / ADA.

TREASON
Spring song / Flash in the pantry / Snakes and ladders / Major disaster / Round and round / Falero lady / Fall of the leaf
CD _____ C5CD 602
See For Miles/C5 / May '93 / Pinnacle.

Guadalquivir

FLAMENCO INSTRUMENTAL
CD _____ PS 65100
Playasound / Feb '93 / Harmonia Mundi / ADA.

Guana Batz

GUANA BATZ 1985 - 1990, THE
Down the line / Can't take the pressure / Nightwatch / King rat / Please give me something / Seethrough / Batman / My way / Radio sweetheart / Lose shark / Shake your moneymaker / I'm on fire / Rock this town / Dynamite / Street wise / Spycatcher / Love generator / Bring my cadillac back / You can run / Two shadows / Electric glide in blue / Texas eyes / No matter how / Now

matter how / Who needs it / Lights out / Johnny B. Goode
CD _____ DOJOCD 120
Dojo / Mar '93 / BMG.

HELD DOWN AT LAST/LOAN SHARK
Down on the line / Get no money / Can't take the pressure / Nightwatch / Lady babcon / King rat / You're my baby / Nightmare fantasy / Please give me something / Bust out / Pile driver boogie / My way / Slippin' in / Tiny minds / Radio sweetheart / Life's a beech / Loan shark / Shake your moneymaker / I'm weird / Hippy hippy shake / Live for the day / No particular place to go / I'm on fire
CD _____ LOMCD 13
Loma / Feb '94 / BMG.

KLUB FOOT CONCERTS, THE
Can't take the pressure / Rockin' in the graveyard / My way / Live for the day / Rocky road blues / See through / Loan sharks / Baby blue eyes / I'm on fire / Dynamite / Rock this town / Endless sleep / King rat / Shake your moneymaker / Joe 90 / Train kept a rollin' / Please give me something / Devil's guitar / You're so fine / No particular place to go / Cave
CD _____ STR CD 033
Street Link / Oct '92 / BMG.

ROUGH EDGES/ELECTRA GLIDE IN BLUE
Street wise / Open your mouth / One night / Good news / Rocking on creek road / Fight back / Spy catcher / Love generator / Bring my cadillac back / Rocking with ollie vee / Two shadows / You can run / Electra glide in blue / Green eyes / Texas eyes / No matter how / Wonderous place / Katherine / Sylin / Spector love / Self made prison / Who needs it / Lover man / Take a rocket
CD _____ LOMCD 14
Loma / Feb '94 / BMG.

UNDER COVER
You're my baby / Please give me something / Bust out / My way / Slippin' in / Radio sweetheart / Shake your moneymaker / Hippy hippy shake / No particular place to go / I'm on fire / Baby blue eyes / Batman / One night / Bring my cadillac back / Rock around with Ollie Vee / Wonderous place / Lights out / Johnny B. Goode / Joe 90 / Rockin' in the graveyard / Rocky road blues / Dynamite (live) / Rock this town / Endless sleep (live)
CD _____ CDMPSYCHO 7
Anagram / Sep '95 / Pinnacle.

Guaraldi, Vince

CHARLIE BROWN CHRISTMAS, A
CD _____ FCD 8431
Fantasy / Nov '95 / Pinnacle / Jazz Music / Wellard / Cadillac.

JAZZ IMPRESSIONS OF BLACK ORPHEUS (Guaraldi, Vince Trio)
CD _____ OJCCD 437
Original Jazz Classics / Nov '95 / Wellard / Jazz Music / Cadillac / Complete/Pinnacle.

VINCE GUARALDI TRIO
CD _____ OJCCD 149
Original Jazz Classics / Nov '95 / Wellard / Jazz Music / Cadillac / Complete/Pinnacle.

Guards Division

BANDS OF PARADE (Massed Bands Of Guards Division)
CD _____ BNA 5063
Bandleader / Jun '91 / Conifer.

DRUM MAJOR GENERAL, THE (Combined Corps Of Drums Of The Guards Division)
CD _____ BNA 5076
Bandleader / Feb '93 / Conifer.

SCARLET AND GOLD (Massed Bands Of Guards Division)
National anthem / Duke of Cambridge / Me and my girl / Slave's chorus / Radetzky march / Strauss garland / Universal judgement / Procession of the nobles / Anvil chorus / American patrol / William Tell overture / Il silenzio / Trombones to the fore / March to the scaffold / Cockles and mussels / Crown imperial
CD _____ BNA 5016
Bandleader / Apr '88 / Conifer.

Guem

DANSE-PERCUSSIONS
CD _____ LDX 274968
La Chant Du Monde / Sep '93 / Harmonia Mundi / ADA.

Guerouabi, Hachemi

LE CHAABI
CD _____ AAA 119
Club Du Disque Arabe / Oct '95 / Harmonia Mundi / ADA.

Guerra, Juan Luis

AREITO
Areito / El costo de la vida / Senales de humo / Ayer / Frio frio rompieno fuente / Mal de amor / Si saliera amor / Coronita de flores / Cuando te beso / Cuando te beso #2 / NAboria/Daca mayanimancana
CD _____ 74321128972
Arista / Mar '93 / BMG.

BACHATA ROSA (Guerra, Juan Luis & 4.40)
Rosalia / Como abeja al panal / Carta de amor / Estrelitas y duendes / Pedir su mano / La bilirrubina burbujas de amor / Bachata rosa / Reforestame / Acompaneme civil
CD _____ 261 927
Ariola / Nov '91 / BMG.

Guerrero, Tony

ANOTHER DAY, ANOTHER DREAM
CD _____ NOVA 9137
Nova / Jan '93 / New Note.

Guesch Patti

NOMADE
L'homme au tablier vert -(Fleurs carnivores) / Dans l'enfer / Comment dire / Il va loin le malheur / Et meme (CD only.) / Nomade / J'veux pas m'en meler / Opera / Raler / Piege de lumiere / Libido (CD only.) / Encore / Merci (CD only.)
CD _____ CDEMC 3575
EMI / May '90 / EMI.

Guests

BOTTLE GREEN
CD _____ MSECD 015
Mouse / Oct '95 / Grapevine.

Guetary, Georges

GEORGES GUETARY IN PARIS
CD _____ CDXP 605
DRG / Jan '89 / New Note.

Guianko

ILLAMAME "YANKO"
Temes / El amor no miente / Dime / Busco un amor / Caminaria / Y me acusas / Te quiero asi / Los ojos de ana
CD _____ 66058058
RMM / Jul '95 / New Note.

Guided By Voices

ALIEN LANES
Salty salute / Evil speakers / Watch me jumpstart / They're not witches / As we go up we go down / (I wanna be a) Dumbcharger / Game of pricks / Ugly vision / Good flying bird / Cigaretter tricks / Pimple zoo / Big chief chines restaurant / Closer you are / Auditorium / Motor away / Hit / My valuable hunting knife / Gold hick / King and Caroline / Striped white jets / Ex-supermodel / Blimps go 90 / Straw dogs / Chicken blows / Little whirl / My son cool / Always crush me / Alright
CD _____ OLE 1232
Matador / Apr '95 / Vital.

BEE THOUSAND
Hardcore UFO's / Buzzards and dreadful crows / Tractor rape chain / Golden heart mountain top queen directory / Hot freaks / Smothered in hugs / Yours to keep / Echos myron / Awful bliss / Mincer Ray / Big fan of pigeon / Queen of cans and jars / Her psychology today / Kicker of elves / Ester's day / Demons are real / I am a scientist / Peep-Hole / You're not an airplane
CD _____ OLE 084-2
Matador / Jul '94 / Vital.

BOX
CD Set _____ SCT 0402
Scat / Feb '95 / Vital.

VAMPIRE ON TITUS/PROPELLER
Wished I was a giant / No.2 In the model home / Expecting brainchild / Superior sector janitor / Donkey school / Dusted / Marches in orange / Sot / World of fun / Jar of cardinals / Unstable journey / E 5 / Cool off kid kiolowatt / Gleemer / Wondering boy poet / What about it / Perhaps now the vultures
CD _____ OLE 083-2
Matador / Oct '94 / Vital.

Guilbert, Yvette

LE FIACRE
Le fiacre / Madame Arthur / Ecoute dans le jardin / Enfance / Les caquets de la couchee / L'hotel de numero trois / Les ingenues / Les quatz etudiants / La soularde / A grenelle / Je suis pocharde / La pierreuse / I want yer, ma honey / Keys of heaven / A la villette / Pourquoi me bat. mon mari / Dites moi si je suis belle / Elle etait tres bien / Je m'embrouille / Le voyage a Bethlahem
CD _____ PASTCD 9773
Flapper / Nov '91 / Pinnacle.

Guild Of Ancient Fifes &.

BY BEAT OF DRUM (Guild Of Ancient Fifes & Drums)
Drummer's call / Drum demonstration / English march / 1775 medley / Chester Castle / Downfall of Paris / To danton me / Rogue's march / Grenadiers march / See the conquering hero comes / Toledo / It's a long way to Tipperary / San Lorenzo / Won-

dermarsch / Basle drum and fife display / Der morgenstreich / Sans Gene / Come lasses and lads / Glopfgaisht / Stenlemmer / Windschi / Dtitt vars / Arabi / Guards / Der vaudois / S'laggerli
CD _____ BNA 5013
Bandleader / Feb '88 / Conifer.

Guildford Cathedral Choir

EVENING AT GUILDFORD CATHEDRAL, AN
CD _____ WSTCD 9705
Nelson Word / Nov '89 / Nelson Word.

Guillory, Isaac

EASY...
CD _____ PRCD 003
Personal / Feb '95 / Ross / Jazz Music / Duncans / CM.

Guillot, Olga

CON LA ORQUESTA HERMANOS CASTRO
CD _____ CCD 802
Caney / Nov '95 / ADA / Discovery.

Guilt

BARDSTWON UGLY BOX
CD _____ VR 029CD
Victory Europe / Jan '96 / Plastic Head.

Guinness Choir

CLASSIC IRISH SONGS
CD _____ CHCD 1096
Chyme / Oct '95 / CM / ADA / Direct.

Guitar, Bonnie

DARK MOON
Mr. Fire eyes / Dark moon / Open the door / Half your heart / If you see my heart dancing / Johnny Vagabond / Making believe / Down where the tradewinds blow / Letter from Jenny / There's a new moon over my shoulder / Moonlight and shadows / Carolina moon / By the light of the silvery moon / Shine on harvest moon / Moon is low / Get out and get under the moon / Moonlight on the Colorado / Moonlight and roses / It's only a paper moon / Prairie moon / Roll along Kentucky moon / Love is over / Love is done / Stand there mountain / I found you out / Love by the jukebox light / Big Mike / Very precious love / If you'll be the teacher
CD Set _____ BCD 15531
Bear Family / Feb '92 / Rollercoaster / Direct / CM / Swift / ADA.

Guitar Crusher

MESSAGE TO MAN (Guitar Crusher & Alvin Lee)
CD _____ INAK 9034
In Akustik / Aug '95 / Magnum Music Group.

Guitar Johnny

GUITAR JOHNNY & THE RHYTHM ROCKERS (Guitar Johnny & The Rhythm Rockers)
CD _____ 422160
New Rose / May '94 / Direct / ADA.

Guitar Junior

CRAWL, THE (Charly Blues - Masterworks Volume 1)
Crawl / Family rules (Angel Child) / I got it made (when I marry Shirley Mae) / Tell me baby / Now you know / Roll roll roll / Roll roll roll (ait. take) / Broken hearted rollin' tears / Please / Pick me up on your way down / Love me love me / Knocks me out fine, fine, fine / Love me love Mary Ann / Oo wee baby
CD _____ CD BM 1
Charly / Apr '92 / Charly / THE / Cadillac.

Guitar Orchestra

GUITAR ORCHESTRA, THE
Really / Pernod for the bamboo man (aperitif) / First kiss / Closer to the heart / Ocean / Pernod for the bamboo man
CD _____ PRKCD 6
Park / Jun '91 / Pinnacle.

INTERPRETATIONS
Africa / Fool on the hill / Space oddity / Strawberry fields forever / (Don't fear) the reaper / Stranger on the shore / Don't give up / Do it again / I am the walrus / Day in the life
CD _____ PRKCD 18
Park / May '94 / Pinnacle.

Guitar Shorty

ALONE IN HIS FIELD
Easter blues / Boogie now / Don't cry baby / Like a damn fool / Jessie jones / Whistlin' blues / Near the cross / Pull your dress / Working hard / Now tell me baby / Shorty's talking boogie
CD _____ TRIX 3306
Trix / Jun '94 / New Note.

MY WAY ON THE HIGHWAY (Guitar Shorty & The Otis Grand Blues Band)
CD _____ JSPCD 245
JSP / Apr '91 / ADA / Target/BMG / Direct / Cadillac / Complete/Pinnacle.

TOPSY TURVY
CD _____ BT 1094CD
Black Top / Oct '93 / CM / Direct / ADA.

Guitar Slim

THINGS THAT I USED TO DO, THE
Well I done got over it / Trouble don't last / Guitar Slim / Story of my life / Quicksand / Bad luck blues / Think it over / Our only child / I got sumpin' for you / Sufferin' mind / Twenty five lies / Something to remember you by
CD _____ CD 52033
Blues Encore / May '94 / Target/BMG.

Guitar Zeus

GUITAR ZEUS
CD _____ 343362
CD _____ 342622
Koch International / Dec '95 / Koch.

Guitaresque

GUITARESQUE
CD _____ HCRCD 81
Hot Club / Oct '94 / Cadillac.

Gulabi Sapera

MUSIQUE DU RAJASTHAN
CD _____ Y 225213CD
Silex / Jul '95 / ADA.

Gullin, Lars

LARS GULLIN & CHET BAKER
CD _____ DRAGONCD 224
Dragon / Feb '89 / Roots / Cadillac / Wellard / CM / ADA.

LATE SUMMER
CD _____ DRCD 244
Dragon / Nov '94 / Roots / Cadillac / Wellard / CM / ADA.

MODERN SOUNDS
CD _____ DRCD 234
Dragon / Nov '94 / Roots / Cadillac / Wellard / CM / ADA.

Gullin, Peter

TENDERNESS
CD _____ DRAGONCD 222
Dragon / Jul '87 / Roots / Cadillac / Wellard / CM / ADA.

TRANSFORMED EVERGREEN (Gullin, Peter Trio)
CD _____ DRCD 266
Dragon / Oct '94 / Roots / Cadillac / Wellard / CM / ADA.

Gumball

REVOLUTION ON ICE
Revolution on the rocks / Free grazin' / With a little rain / Nights on fire / What'cha gonna do / Breath away / Gone to the moon / I ain't nothin' / Read the news / Boat race / Trudge / She's as beautiful as a foot
CD _____ 475927 2
Columbia / Sep '94 / Sony.

Gumede, Sipho

DOWN FREEDOM AVENUE
Down freedom avenue / Godfather special / Ngiyabonga (thanking you) / Song for Johnny Dyani / Please don't dance / Nozipho the dancer / Nlabelela (just sing) / Village lullaby / African wedding / Country side
CD _____ BW 051
B&W / Oct '94 / New Note.

Gun

GALLUS
Steal your fire / Money to burn / Long road / Welcome to the real world / Higher ground / Borrowed time / Freedom / Won't back down / Reach out for love / Watching the world go by
CD _____ 3953832
A&M / Mar '95 / PolyGram.

SWAGGER
Stand in line / Find my way / Word up / Don't say it's over / Only one / Something worthwhile / Seems like I'm losing you / Crying over you / One reason / Vicious heart
CD _____ 540254-2
A&M / Jul '94 / PolyGram.

TAKING ON THE WORLD
Better days / Feeling within / Inside out / Money (Everybody loves her) / Taking on the world / Shame on you / Can't get any lower / Something to believe in / Girls in love / I will be waiting
CD _____ 3970072
A&M / Mar '95 / PolyGram.

Gun Club

AHMED'S WILD DREAM
Masterplan / Walkin' with the beast / I hear your heart singin' / Another country's song / Sexbeast / Lupita screams / Go tell the mountain / Preachin' the blues / Stranger in town / Port of souls / Black hole / Little wing / Yellow eyes
CD _____ 527500220
Solid / Jun '93 / Vital.

DEATH PARTY
CD _____ 890012
New Rose / May '94 / Direct / ADA.

DIVINITY
CD _____ 527900920
Solid / Jun '93 / Vital.

FIRE OF LOVE
Sex beat / Preachin' the blues / Promise me / She's like heroin to me / For the love of Ivy / Fire spirit / Ghost on the highway / Jack on fire / Black train / Cool drink of water / Goodbye Johnny / Walking with the beast
CD _____ 422162
New Rose / May '94 / Direct / ADA.

MOTHER JUNO
Bill Bailey, won't you please come home / Thunderhead / Lupita screams / Yellow eyes / Breaking hands / Araby / Hearts / My cousin Kim / Ports of souls
CD _____ 527500420
Solid / Nov '92 / Vital.

PASTORAL HIDE AND SEEK
CD _____ 527900020
Solid / Jun '93 / Vital.

Gunjah

HEREDITY
CD _____ M 02082
Noise/Modern Music / Feb '93 / Pinnacle / Plastic Head.

POLITICALLY CORRECT
CD _____ NO 2552
Noise/Modern Music / May '95 / Pinnacle / Plastic Head.

Gunn, Douglas

O'CAROLAN'S FEAST (Gunn, Douglas Ensemble)
Carolan's welcome / Planxty Connor / Cupan ui eaghra / John Kelly / Sir Arthur Shaen / Madam Cole / Plearaca na ruarcach / Carolan's receipt for drinking / Charles O'Connor / Thomas O'Burke / Lament for Charles MacCabe / John Nugent / Dr. Sean O'Hairt / O'Rourke's feast
CD _____ CDOSS 69
Ossian / Apr '93 / ADA / Direct / CM.

Gunn, Russell

YOUNG GUNN
East St Louis / Fly me to the moon / Wade in the water / DJ / You don't know what love is / Concept / Message / There is no greater love / Blue Gene / Pannonica
CD _____ MCD 5539
Muse / Dec '95 / New Note / CM.

Gunn, Trey

ONE THOUSAND YEARS
Night air / Screen door and the flower girl / Killing for London / Real life / Into the wood / Gift / Take this wish / 1000 years
CD _____ DGM 9302
Discipline / Sep '94 / Pinnacle.

Gunness, Lee

LEE GUNNESS SINGS THE BLUES
CD _____ BCD 314
GHB / Oct '93 / Jazz Music.

Guns N' Roses

APPETITE FOR DESTRUCTION
Welcome to the jungle / It's so easy / Nightrain / Out ta get me / Mr. Brownstone / Paradise city / My Michelle / Think about you / Sweet child o' mine / You're crazy / Anything goes / Rocket queen
CD _____ GFLD 19286
Geffen / Oct '95 / BMG.

GN'R LIES
Reckless life / Patience / Nice boys / Used to love her / Move to the city / You're crazy / Mama kin / One in a million
CD _____ GFLD 19287
Geffen / Oct '95 / BMG.

INTERVIEW COMPACT DISC: GUNS 'N' ROSES
CD P.Disc _____ CBAK 4015
Baktabak / Nov '89 / Baktabak.

SPAGHETTI INCIDENT, THE
Since I don't have you / New Rose / Down on the farm / Human being / Raw power / Ain't it fun / Buick Mckane / Hair of the dog / Attitude / Black leather / You can't put your arms around a memory / Look at your game girl
CD _____ GED 24617
Geffen / Nov '93 / BMG.

TRUTH OR LIES THE INTERVIEW
CD P.Disc _____ CBAK 4077
Baktabak / Feb '94 / Baktabak.

USE YOUR ILLUSION I
Right next door to hell / Dust and bones / Live and let die / Don't cry / Perfect crime / You ain't the first / Bad obsession / Back off bitch / Double talkin' jive / November rain / Garden / Garden of Eden / Don't damn me / Bad apple / Dead horse / Coma
CD _____ GEFD 24415
Geffen / Sep '91 / BMG.

USE YOUR ILLUSION II
Civil war / Fourteen years / Yesterdays / Knockin' on heaven's door / Get in the ring / Shotgun blues / Breakdown / Pretty tied up / Locomotive / So fine / Estranged / You could be mine / Don't cry / My world
CD _____ GEFD 24420
Geffen / Sep '91 / BMG.

Guns N' Wankers

WANCHOR
Help / Skin deep / Raise your glass / Sunstroke / Nervous / Blows away / Blah blah blah / Surprise / 668 / Evergreen / Incoming
CD _____ SEEP 008
Rugger Bugger / Aug '94 / Vital.

Gunshot

PATRIOT GAMES
CD _____ STEAM 43CD
Vinyl Solution / Jun '93 / Disc.

SINGLES, THE
CD _____ STEAM 92CD
Vinyl Solution / Nov '94 / Disc.

Gunter, Hardrock

GONNA ROCK 'N' ROLL, GONNA DANCE ALL NIGHT
Birmingham bounce / Lonesome blues / Gonna dance all night #2 / How can I believe you love me / My bucket's been fixed / Rifle belt and bayonet / Maybe baby / Birmingham bounce #2 / Boppin' to Grandfather's clock / Beggars can't be choosers / It can't be right / Rock-a-bop baby / Whoo, I mean whee / We three / Jukebox help me find my baby / Fiddle bop / Hardrock rocks the moon (How high the moon) / Bloodshot eyes / Take away your rosy lips / Right key but the wrong keyhole / Mountain dew / I'll go chasin' women / Spring has sprung / Tico tico / Go low boogie / Bonaparte's retreat / Chattanooga sunshine boy / Dad gave my hog away / Guitar on the moon / Fallen angel / Gonna dance all night
CD _____ RCCD 3031
Rollercoaster / Jul '95 / CM / Swift.

Gunther, John

BIG LUNAGE (Gunther, John & Greg Gisbert)
CD _____ 74035-2
Capri / Oct '94 / Wellard / Cadillac.

QUINTET (Gunther, John & Greg Gisbert)
CD _____ 74035
Capri / Nov '93 / Wellard / Cadillac.

Guo Ye

RED RIBBON
CD _____ TUG 1010CD
Tugboat / Feb '95 / ADA.

Gupta, Buddhadev Das

RAGA JAIJAIVANTI
CD _____ NI 5314
Nimbus / Sep '94 / Nimbus.

Gurd

ADDICTED
CD _____ CC 035016CD
Major / Jan '96 / Plastic Head.

GURD
CD _____ CC 026053CD
Shark / Jun '95 / Plastic Head

Gurtu, Trilok

BELIEVE
CD _____ CMPCD 67
CMP / Jan '95 / Vital/SAM.

CRAZY SAINTS
Manini / Tillana / Ballad for 2 musicians / Other tune / Blessing in disguise / Crazy saints / No discrimination
CD _____ CMPCD 66
CMP / Oct '93 / Vital/SAM.

LIVING MAGIC
Baba / Once I wished a tree upside down / From scratch / TMNOK / Living magic / Transition / Tac, et demi
CD _____ CMPCD 50
CMP / Jun '93 / Vital/SAM.

Guru

JAZZMATAZZ - VOL.1
Intro / Loungin' / When you're near / Transit ride / No time to play / Down the backstreets / Respectful dedications / Take a

---

look at yourself / Trust me / Slicker than most / Le bien, le mal / Sights in the city
CD _____ CTCD 34
Cooltempo / Jun '93 / EMI.

JAZZMATAZZ - VOL.2
Intro (into the light) / Jazzalude I / New reality style / Lifesaver / Living in this world / Looking through darkness / Skit A (Interview) / Watch what you say / Jazzalude II / Defining purpose / For you / Insert A (Mental relaxation) / Medicine / Lost souls / Insert B (Mental relaxation) / Nobody knows / Jazzalude III / Hip hop as a way of life / Respect the artitect / Feel the music / Young ladies / Travelor / Jazzalude IV / Count your blessings / Choice of weapons / Something in the past / Skit B (A lot on my mind) / Revelation
CD _____ CTCD 47
Cooltempo / Jul '95 / EMI.

Guru Guru

LIVE
CD _____ EFA 03501-2
Think Progressive / Jan '96 / SRD.

WAH WAH
CD _____ EFA 035002
Think Progressive / Dec '95 / SRD.

Gus

PROGRESSIVE SCIENCE OF BREEDING IDIOTS FOR A DUMB SOCIETY
CD _____ WRONG 14CD
Wrong / Jun '95 / SRD.

Gush

FROM SOUNDS TO THINGS
CD _____ DRCD 204
Dragon / Apr '87 / Roots / Cadillac / Wellard / CM / ADA.

Gustafsson, Mats

PARROT FISH EYE
CD _____ OD 12006
Okka Disk / Aug '95 / Harmonia Mundi / Cadillac.

Gustavson, Jukka

KADONNUT HAVIAMATTOMLIN
CD _____ BECD 4032
Beta / May '95 / Direct.

Guthrie, Arlo

BEST OF ARLO GUTHRIE
Alice's restaurant massacre / Gabriel's mother's highway ballad / Sixteen blues / Coopers lament / Motor cycle song / Coming into Los Angeles / Last train / City of New Orleans / Darkest hour / Last to leave
CD _____ 7599273402
WEA / Jan '93 / Warner Music.

MORE TOGETHER AGAIN (Guthrie, Arlo & Pete Seeger)
CD _____ RSR 0007/8
Rising Sun / Oct '94 / ADA.

Guthrie, Jack

OKLAHOMA HILLS
Oklahoma hills / When the cactus is in bloom / Next to the soil / Shame on you / I'm branding my darlin' / With my heart / Guitars datin' / Oakie boogie / In the shadows of my heart / For Oklahoma / I'm yearning / No need to knock on my door / Shut that gate / I'm tellin' you / Chained to a memory / Look out for the crossing / Dallas darlin' / Colorado blues / Welcome home stranger / I still love you as I did in yesterday / Oklahoma's calling / Clouds rain trouble down / Answer to Moonlight / Please, oh please / I loved you once but I can't trust you now / Out of sight / I'm building a stairway to heaven / Ida Red / I told you once / San Antonio rose / You laughed and I cried
CD _____ BCD 15580
Bear Family / Nov '91 / Rollercoaster / Direct / CM / Swift / ADA.

Guthrie, Woody

COLUMBIA RIVER COLLECTION
CD _____ CD 1036
Rounder / Aug '88 / CM / Direct / ADA / Cadillac.

DUST BOWL BALLADS
CD _____ CD 1040
Rounder / '88 / CM / Direct / ADA / Cadillac.

LIBRARY OF CONGRESS RECORDINGS VOL. 1
CD _____ CD 1041
Rounder / '88 / CM / Direct / ADA / Cadillac.

LIBRARY OF CONGRESS RECORDINGS VOL.2
CD _____ CD 1042
Rounder / '88 / CM / Direct / ADA / Cadillac.

LIBRARY OF CONGRESS RECORDINGS VOL.3
CD _____ CD 1043
Rounder / '88 / CM / Direct / ADA / Cadillac.

LONG WAYS TO TRAVEL (Unreleased Folkways masters 1944-1949)
CD _____ SFWCD 40046
Smithsonian Folkways / Jun '94 / ADA / Direct / Koch / CM / Cadillac.

NURSERY DAYS
CD _____ SFWCD 45036
Smithsonian Folkways / Dec '94 / ADA / Direct / Koch / CM / Cadillac.

PASTURES OF PLENTY - WOODY GUTHRIE TRIBUTE (Various Artists)
CD _____ DJD 3207
Dejadisc / May '94 / Direct / ADA.

SONGS TO GROW ON FOR MOTHER & CHILD
CD _____ SFWCD 45035
Smithsonian Folkways / Mar '95 / ADA / Direct / Koch / CM / Cadillac.

VERY BEST OF WOODY GUTHRIE, THE
This land is your land / Pastures of plenty / Pretty boy Floyd / Take a whiff on me / Do re mi / Put my little shoes away / Hard travellin' / Jesus Christ / Whoopee ti yi yo / Grand coulee dam / Picture from life's other side / Talkin' hard luck blues / Philadelphia lawyer / I ain't got no home / Wreck of old 97 / Keep your skillet good and greasy / Dust pneumonia blues / Going down that road feeling bad / Goodnight little arlo (Goodnight little darlin') / So long (it's been good to know yuh)
CD _____ MCCD 067
Music Club / Jun '92 / Disc / THE / CM.

WE AIN'T DOWN YET - WOODY GUTHRIE'S FRIENDS (Various Artists)
CD _____ DIAB 812
Diabolo / Aug '94 / Pinnacle.

WOODY GUTHRIE
CD _____ DVBC 92102
Deja Vu / May '95 / THE.

Gutierrez, Alfredo

EL PALITO
CD _____ TUMICD 021
Tumi / '93 / Sterns / Discovery.

FIESTA
CD _____ 12454
Laserlight / Jul '95 / Target/BMG.

Gutterball

GUTTERBALL
Trial seperation blues / Top of the hill / Lester Young / Motorcycle boy / One by one / When you make up your mind / Think it over / Falling from the sky / Please don't hold back / Preacher and the prostitute / Patent leather shoes / Blessing in disguise
CD _____ OUT 113-2
Brake Out / Jan '94 / Vital.

TURNYOR HEDINKOV
Return To Sender / Aug '95 / Direct / ADA.
CD _____ RTS 17

Guttermouth

FRIENDLY PEOPLE
CD _____ NITRO 158012
Nitro / Mar '95 / Plastic Head

PUKE BALLS
CD _____ DSR 09CD
Dr. Strange / Sep '95 / Plastic Head.

Guv'ner

HARD FOR MEASY FOR YOU
No big deal / Her velvet chair / Little bitch on the phone / Bridge under water / Almond roca / Making headlines / Go to sleep / Wild couple / Touch wood / Amplituden / I will get you (CD only) / Thespian girl (CD only) / She dog stop (CD only)
CD _____ WIJ 039CD
Wiija / Nov '94 / Vital.

Guy, Barry

AFTER THE RAIN
CD _____ NMCD 013
Maya / Oct '94 / Complete/Pinnacle / Direct / Cadillac.

STUDY-WITCH GONE GAME (Guy, Barry & Now Orchestra)
CD _____ MCD 9402
Maya / Oct '94 / Complete/Pinnacle / Direct / Cadillac.

Guy, Buddy

ALONE AND ACOUSTIC (Guy, Buddy & Junior Wells)
CD _____ ALCD 4802
Alligator / May '93 / Direct / ADA.

BLUES GIANT
CD _____ BLE 599002
Black & Blue / Jan '90 / Wellard / Direct.

BREAKIN' OUT
CD _____ JSPCD 215
JSP / Jul '88 / ADA / Target/BMG / Direct / Cadillac / Complete/Pinnacle.

COMPLETE CHESS STUDIO RECORDINGS, THE
CD Set _____ CHD 29337
Chess/MCA / Mar '92 / BMG / New Note.

D.J. PLAY MY BLUES
CD _____ JSPCD 256
JSP / Feb '95 / ADA / Target/BMG / Direct / Cadillac / Complete/Pinnacle.

DRINKIN' TNT 'N' SMOKIN' DYNAMITE (Guy, Buddy/Junior Wells & others)
Ah'w baby / Everything gonna be alright / How can one woman be so mean / Checking on my baby / When you see the little tears from my eyes / My younger days
CD _____ NEMCD 687
Sequel / Apr '94 / BMG.

FEELS LIKE RAIN
CD _____ ORECD 525
Silvertone / Mar '93 / Pinnacle.

FIRST TIME I MET THE BLUES
First time I met the blues / Slop around / Let me love you baby / Got to use your head / I dig your wig / My time after a while / Stick around / No lie / Night flight / My mother / Ten years ago / Don't know which way to go / Gully hully / I got a hully / I got a strange feeling / This is the end / Broken heart / Ed blues / You sure can't do / Try to quit you baby / I got my eyes on you / Sit and cry / Untitled instrumental / Drinking muddy water
CD _____ CD 52015
Blues Encore / '92 / Target/BMG.

HOLD THAT PLANE
Watermelon man / I'm ready / You don't love me / Hello San Francisco / Hold that plane / My time after a while / Come see about me
CD _____ VND 79323
Vanguard / Oct '95 / Complete/Pinnacle / Discovery.

I CRY AND SING THE BLUES (Charly Blues - Masterworks Vol. 27)
I got my eyes on you / Slop around / Broken hearted blues / Let me love you baby / My love is real / Untitled instrumental / Crazy love / Too many ways / Buddy's groove / Going to school / I cry and sing the blues / Lip lap Louie / My time after awhile / Too many ways (Alt. take) / Keep it to myself / I didn't know my mother
CD _____
Charly / Sep '92 / Charly / THE / Cadillac.

LIVE AT THE CHECKERBOARD LOUNGE, CHICAGO 1979
Buddy's blues (parts 1 and 2) / I've got a right to love my woman / Tell me what's inside of you (2 versions) / Done gone over you / Things I used to do / You don't know how I feel / Dollar done sell / Don't answer the door
CD _____ JSPCD 262
JSP / Oct '95 / ADA / Target/BMG / Direct / Cadillac / Complete/Pinnacle.

LIVE IN MONTREUX (Guy, Buddy & Junior Wells)
CD _____ ECD 20002-2
Everybody's / Jan '92 / Wellard.

MAN & BLUES/THIS IS BUDDY GUY/ HOLD THAT PLANE
CD Set _____ 662915
Vanguard / Jan '94 / Complete/Pinnacle / Discovery.

ORIGINAL BLUES BROTHERS - LIVE (Guy, Buddy & Junior Wells)
Buddy's blues / Blue Monday / Everyday I have the blues / Woman blues / Satisfaction / Messin' with the kid / No use cryin' / Just to be with you / Junior's shuffle / Out of sight
CD _____ CDBM 007
Blue Moon / Feb '89 / Magnum Music Group / Greensleeves / Hot Shot / ADA / Cadillac / Discovery.

PLAY THE BLUES (Guy, Buddy & Junior Wells)
Man of many words / My baby left me / Come on in this house / Have mercy baby / T-bone shuffle / Poor man's plea / Messin' with the kid / This old fool / I don't know / Bad bad whiskey / Honeydripper
CD _____ 812270299-2
WEA / Mar '93 / Warner Music.

SLIPPIN' IN
CD _____ ORECD 533
Silvertone / Oct '94 / Pinnacle.

STONE CRAZY
Slop around / Broken hearted blues / I got my eyes on you / First time I met the blues / Let me love you baby / I got a strange feeling / Hully gully / Ten years ago / Watch yourself / Stone crazy / Hard but fair / Baby (baby, baby) / When my left eye jumps / That's it no lie / Every girl I see / Leave my girl alone / She suits me to a tee / Mother in law blues / Going home / I suffer with the blues
CD _____ ALCD 4723
Alligator / May '93 / Direct / ADA.

TREASURE UNTOLD, THE (Charly Blues - Masterworks Volume 11)
I found a true love / Skippin' / Treasure untold / American bandstand / Don't know which way to go / Buddy's boogie / Worried blues / Moanin' / I dig your wig / My time after awhile / Night flight / You got to use your head / Keep it to yourself / My mother
CD _____
Charly / Apr '92 / Charly / THE / Cadillac.

Guy Called Gerald

BLACK SECRET TECHNOLOGY
CD _____ JBCD 25
Juice Box / Mar '95 / SRD.

Guy, Charles Lee

PRISONER'S DREAMS, THE
There goes a lonely man / This ole dog / You just don't know your man / Rich man's gold / Unhappy people / Prisoner's dream / Shackles and chains / They're all goin' home but one / Wall / Twenty one years /

Folsom prison blues / Prisoner's song "Cigarettes, whisky and will" / Send a picture of Mother / Cold gray bars / Wishin' she was here (instead of me) / Doin' my time
CD _____ BCD 15581
Bear Family / Apr '92 / Rollercoaster / Direct / CM / Swift / ADA.

Guy, Phil

BREAKING OUT ON TOP
CD _____ JSPCD 260
JSP / Oct '95 / ADA / Target/BMG / Direct / Cadillac / Complete/Pinnacle.

TINA NU
CD _____ JSPCD 226
JSP / Apr '89 / ADA / Target/BMG / Direct / Cadillac / Complete/Pinnacle.

Guzzard

QUICK, FAST, IN A HURRY
CD _____ AMREP 037CD
Amphetamine Reptile / Mar '95 / SRD.

Gwalarn

A-HED AN AMZER
CD _____ KMCD 10
Keltia Musique / '91 / ADA / Direct / Discovery.

GWAR

AMERICA MUST BE DESTROYED
CD _____ CDZORRO 037
Metal Blade / Mar '92 / Pinnacle.

HELL-O
Time for death / Americanized / Slutman city / War toy / Pure as the artic snow / Gwar theme / Ollie North / U ain't shit / Black and huge / A.E.I.O.U. / I'm in love with a dead dog / World o' filth / Captain crunch / Je m'appelle J. Cousteau / Bone meal / Techno's song / Rock 'n' roll party theme
CD _____ CDZORRO 35
Metal Blade / Sep '92 / Pinnacle.

RAG NA ROCK
CD _____ 17001-2
Metal Blade / Oct '95 / Plastic Head.

ROAD BEHIND, THE
CD _____ 398414004CD
Metal Blade / Nov '95 / Plastic Head.

SCUMDOGS OF THE UNIVERSE
CD _____ 398417003CD
Metal Blade / Sep '95 / Plastic Head.

THIS TOILET EARTH
CD _____ CDZORRO 63
Metal Blade / Mar '94 / Pinnacle.

Gwerinos

DI-DIDL-LAN
CD _____ SCD 2075
Sain / Jun '95 / Direct / ADA.

Gwernig, Youenn

JUST A TRAVELLER
CD _____ KM 49
Keltia Musique / Sep '94 / ADA / Direct / Discovery.

Gwerz

AU DELA
CD _____ CD 821
Diffusion Breizh / May '93 / ADA.

AUDELA
CD _____ BUR CD 821
Escalibur / '88 / Roots / ADA / Discovery.

LIVE
CD _____ GWP 001CD
Gwerz Productions / Aug '93 / ADA.

Gygafo

LEGEND OF THE KINGFISHER
CD _____ HBG 122/2
Background / Jan '93 / Background.

Gypsy

SOUNDTRACKS
CD _____ LIMB 37CD
Limbo / Oct '94 / Pinnacle.

Gypsy Kyss

WHEN PASSION MURDERED INNOCENCE
CD _____ 972210
FM / May '91 / Sony.

Gypsy Orchestra

JEWISH WEDDING
CD _____ RCD 10105
Rykodisc / Nov '91 / Vital / ADA.

Gyuto Monks

FREEDOM CHANTS FROM THE ROOF OF THE WORLD
Yamantaka / Mahakala / Number 2 for Gaia
CD _____ RCD 20113
Rykodisc / Sep '91 / Vital / ADA.

GZA The Genius

LIQUID SWORDS
Liquid swords / Duel of the iron mic / Living in the world today / Gold / Cold world / Labels / 4th Chamber / Shadowboxin' / Hell's wind staff / Killah hills 10304 / Investigate reports / Swordsman / I gotcha back / Basic instructions / Before leaving earth
CD _____ GED 24813
Geffen / Nov '95 / BMG.

GZR

PLASTIC PLANET
CD _____ RAWCD 105
Raw Power / Oct '95 / BMG.

H

H Block X

TIME TO MOVE
CD _____ 74321187512
RCA / Jan '96 / BMG.

H-Town

BEGGIN' AFTER DARK
H-Town intro '94 / Sex bowl / One night
gigolo / Prelude to emotion (CD only) / Emo-
tions / Cruisin' fo' honeys (CD only) / Full
time / 1-9800 Call GI (CD only) / Tumble and
rumble / Much feeling (and it tastes great)
(CD only) / Beggin' after dark / Indo love /
Back seat (wit no sheets) / Buss one / Baby
I love ya (CD only) / Rockit steady (CD only)
/ Last record
CD _____ 116312
Musidisc / Jan '95 / Vital / Harmonia Mundi
/ ADA / Cadillac / Discovery.

FEVER FOR DA FLAVOR
Introduction / Can't fade da H / Treat U right
/ Fever for da flavor / Sex me / H-town
bounce / Keepin' my composure / Interlude
/ Lick U up / Knockin' da boots / Won't U
come back / Baby I wanna
CD _____ 110702
Musidisc / May '95 / Vital / Harmonia Mundi
/ ADA / Cadillac / Discovery.

H. Oilers

**INNOCENT CATHOLIC COMBAT
WALTZ, THE**
CD _____ EFA 11968-2
Crippled Dick Hot Wax / Nov '94 / SRD.

H.F.L.

FIX
CD _____ AGO 722
Noise/Modern Music / Apr '95 / Pinnacle /
Plastic Head.

H.P. Zinker

AND THEN THERE WAS LIGHT
CD _____ NECKCD 004
Roughneck / Jul '91 / Disc.

HOVERING
CD _____ NECKCD 006
Roughneck / Sep '91 / Disc.

Habichuela, Pepe

A MANDELI
Resuene / Al aire / El dron / Guadiana / Del
cerro / Mi tierra / Boabdil / A mandeli /
Mandeli
CD _____ HNCD 1315
Hannibal / May '89 / Vital / ADA.

Hachig, Kazarian

ARMENIA ARMENIA
CD _____ MCD 61452
Monitor / Jun '93 / CM.

Hackberry Ramblers

CAJUN BOOGIE
CD _____ FF 629CD
Flying Fish / Dec '93 / Roots / CM / Direct
/ ADA.

JOLIE BLONDE
CD _____ ARHCD 399
Arhoolie / Apr '95 / ADA / Direct /
Cadillac.

Hacke, Alexander

FILMARBEITEN
CD _____ RTD 19713402
Our Choice / Jun '93 / Pinnacle.

Hackett, Bobby

**MILTON JAZZ CONCERT 1963 (Hackett,
Bobby & Vic Dickenson/Maxine Sullivan)**
CD _____ IAJRCD 1004
IAJRC / Jun '94 / Jazz Music.

**OFF MINOR (Hackett, Bobby & Jack
Teagarden)**
CD _____ VN 162
Viper's Nest / May '95 / Direct / Cadillac /
ADA.

Hackett, Steve

BLUES WITH FEELING
CD _____ PERMCD 27
Permanent / Oct '94 / Total/BMG.

CURED
Hope I don't wake / Picture postcard / Can't
let go / Air-conditioned nightmare / Funny
feeling / Cradle of swans / Overnight
sleeper / Turn back time
CD _____ CDSCD 4021
Virgin / Apr '89 / EMI.

DEFECTOR
Steppes / Time to get out / Slogans / Leav-
ing / Two vamps as guests / Jacuzzi / Ham-
mer in the sand / Toast / Show /
Sentimental
CD _____ CDSCD 4018
Virgin / '89 / EMI.

GUITAR NOIR
CD _____ PERMCD 13
Permanent / May '93 / Total/BMG.

HIGHLY STRUNG
Casino royale / Cell 151 / Always somewhere else / Walking through walls / Give it
away / Weightless / Group therapy / India
rubber man / Hackett to pieces
CD _____ HACKCD 1
Virgin / Apr '89 / EMI.

MOMENTUM
CD _____ PERMCDL 21
Permanent / May '94 / Total/BMG.

PLEASE DON'T TOUCH
Narnia / Carry on up the vicarage / Racing
in A / Kim / How can I / Icarus ascending /
Hoping love will last / Land of 1000 au-
tumns / Please don't touch / Voice of
Necam
CD _____ CDSCD 4012
Charisma / '89 / EMI.

SPECTRAL MORNINGS
Everyday / Virgin and the gypsy / Red
flower of Tachai blooms everywhere /
Clocks - The angel of Mons / Ballad of the
decomposing man / Lost time in Cordoba /
Tigermoth / Spectral mornings
CD _____ CDSCD 4017
Charisma / '87 / EMI.

UNAUTHORISED BIOGRAPHY
Narnia / Hackett to pieces / Don't fall away
from me / Spectral mornings / Steppes /
Virgin and the gypsy / Cell 151 / Slogans /
Icarus ascending / Prayers and dreams /
Star of Sirius / Hammer in the sand / Ace
of wands / Hoping love will last
CD _____ CDVM 9014
Charisma / Oct '92 / EMI.

VOYAGE OF THE ACOLYTE
Ace of wands / Hands of the priestess-part
1 / Tower struck down / Hands of the
priestess-part 2 / Hermit / Star of Sirius /
Lovers / Shadow of the Hierophant
CD _____ CASCD 1111
Charisma / '87 / EMI.

Hada To Hada

MY GERMAN LOVER
CD _____ SCD 294CD
Starc / Apr '94 / ADA / Direct.

Hadad, Astrid

AYI (Hadad, Astrid & Los Tarzanes)
CD _____ ROUCD 5066
Rounder / Nov '95 / CM / Direct / ADA /
Cadillac.

Haddaway

ALBUM, THE
CD _____ 74321183202
Arista / Aug '95 / BMG.

DRIVE, THE
Fly away / Breakaway / Lover by thy name
/ Waiting for a better world / Give it up /
Catch a fire / Desert prayer / First cut is the
deepest / Baby don't go / Another day with-
out you
CD _____ 74321306662
Arista / Sep '95 / BMG.

Haddix, Travis

BIG OLE GOODUN, A
CD _____ ICH 1168CD
Ichiban / Jan '94 / Koch.

WHAT I KNOW RIGHT NOW
CD _____ CDICH 1132
Ichiban / Oct '93 / Koch.

WINNERS NEVER QUIT
Homeslice / Bag lady / She's not the kind
of girl / Better than nothing / Winners never
quit / Something in the milk ain't clean /
Beggin' business / Abused / Someone to
love / I'm mean
CD _____ CDICH 1101
Ichiban / Oct '93 / Koch.

Haden, Charlie

BALLAD OF THE FALLEN
El Segardors / If you want to write me / Bal-
lad of the fallen / Grandola vila morena /
Introduction to people / People united will
never be defeated / Silence / Too late / La
pasionaria / La santa espina
CD _____ 8115462
ECM / Sep '84 / New Note.

CLOSENESS DUETS
Ellen David / O.C. / For Turiya / For a free
Portugal
CD _____ CDA 0808
A&M / Jul '89 / PolyGram.

**DREAM KEEPER (Haden, Charlie & The
Liberation Music Orchestra)**
Dream keeper / Rbo de nube / Nkosi sikelel
Afrika / Sandino / Spiritual
CD _____ DIW 844
DIW / Jan '92 / Harmonia Mundi / Cadillac.

GOLDEN NUMBER, THE
CD _____ 3908252
A&M / Feb '94 / PolyGram.

HAUNTED HEART
CD _____ 5130782
Verve / Mar '92 / PolyGram.

LIBERATION MUSIC ORCHESTRA
Introduction / Song of the united front / El
quinto regimento / Los cuatro generals (the
four generals) / Ending of the first side /
Song for Che / War orphans / Interlude /
Circus 68, 69 / We shall overcome
CD _____ MCAD 39125
Impulse Jazz / Jun '89 / BMG / New Note.

**MAGICO (Haden, Charlie & Jan
Garbarek/Egberto Gismonti)**
CD _____ 8234742
ECM / '88 / New Note.

QUARTET WEST
Hermitage / Body and soul / Good life / In
the moment / Bay city / My foolish heart /
Passport / Taney county / Blessing / Pas-
sion flower
CD _____ 831 673-2
Verve / Aug '87 / PolyGram.

**STEAL AWAY (Haden, Charlie & Hank
Jones)**
CD _____ 5272492
Verve / Sep '95 / PolyGram.

Hades

AGAIN SHALL BE FREE
CD _____ FMP 002
Misanthropy / Mar '95 / Plastic Head.

IF AT FIRST YOU DON'T SUCCEED
CD _____ RR 95332
Roadrunner / Oct '88 / Pinnacle.

Hadidjah, Idhah

TONGGERET
Tonggert / Bayu bayu / Mahoni / Hiji / Ca-
tetan / Arum / Bandung / Daun / Pulus /
Keser / Bojong / Serat / Sahara
CD _____ 7559791732
Elektra Nonesuch / Jan '95 / Warner Music.

Hadley, Tony

STATE OF PLAY, THE
Lost in your love / Just the thought of you
/ You keep me coming back for more / For
your blue eyes only / Fever / Riverside /
Never give up on love / This time / Game of
love / Freewheel / One good reason /
Somebody up there
CD _____ CDEMC 3619
EMI / Feb '92 / EMI.

Hafler Trio

ALL THAT RISES MUST CONVERGE
CD _____ KUT 5
Grey Area / May '93 / Pinnacle.

BANG! AN OPEN LETTER
CD _____ KUT 1CD
Grey Area / Jun '94 / Pinnacle.

BOOTLEG
CD _____ ASH 1.3CD
Ash International / Jan '95 / These /
Kudos.

FOUR WAYS OF SAYING FIVE
CD _____ KUT 4
Grey Area / Oct '93 / Pinnacle.

FUCK
CD _____ TONE 3
Touch / Oct '95 / These / Kudos.

**HAFLER TRIO PLAYS MURRAY
FONTANA ORCHESTRA**
CD _____ STCD 028
Staalplaat / Sep '95 / Vital/SAM.

HOW TO REFORM MANKIND
CD _____ TO 24
Touch / Oct '95 / These / Kudos.

INPUTOF
CD _____ KK 008CD
KK / '88 / Plastic Head.

MASTERY OF MONEY
CD _____ TO 18
Touch / Mar '91 / These / Kudos.

**RESURRECTION (Hafler Trio & The
Sons Of God)**
CD _____ TO 22
Touch / Oct '95 / These / Kudos.

SEVEN HOURS SLEEP
CD _____ KUT 3CD
Grey Area / Jun '94 / Pinnacle.

THIRSTY FISH, A
CD _____ KUT 6
Grey Area / May '93 / Pinnacle.

WALK GENTLY THROUGH
CD _____ KUT 2CD
Grey Area / Jun '94 / Pinnacle.

Hagar, Sammy

ANTHOLOGY
CD _____ VSOPCD 207
Connoisseur / Oct '94 / Pinnacle.

BEST OF SAMMY HAGAR, THE
Red / (Sittin' on) the dock of the bay / I've
done everything for you / Rock 'N' Roll
weekend / Cruisin' and boozin' / Turn up
the music / Reckless / Trans am (highway
wonderland) / Love or money / This planet's
on fire / Plain Jane / Bad reputation / Bad
motor scooter / You make me crazy
CD _____ C2 80262
Capitol / Apr '93 / EMI.

DANGER ZONE
Love or money / Twentieth century man /
Miles from boredom / Mommy says / In the
night / Iceman / Bad reputation / Heartbeat
/ Run for your life / Danger zone
CD _____ BGOCD 281
Beat Goes On / Jul '95 / Pinnacle.

LOUD 'N' CLEAR
Rock 'n' roll weekend / Make it last / Reckless / Turn up the music / I've done everything for you / Young girl blues / Bad motor
scooter / Space station no. 5
CD _____ BGOCD 149
Beat Goes On / Aug '92 / Pinnacle.

MUSICAL CHAIRS
Turn up the music / It's gonna be alright kid
/ You make me crazy / Reckless / Try /
Don't stop me now / Straight from the hip
kid / Hey boys / Someone out there / Crack
in the world
CD _____ BGOCD 201
Beat Goes On / May '94 / Pinnacle.

NINE ON A TEN SCALE
Keep on rockin' / Urban guerilla / Flamingos
fly / China / Silver lights / All American /
Confession (please come back) / Young girl
blues / Rock 'n' roll Romeo
CD _____ BGOCD 182
Beat Goes On / Apr '93 / Pinnacle.

RED
Red / Catch the wind / Cruisin' and boozin'
/ Free money / Rock 'N' Roll weekend / Fill-
more shuffle / Hungry / Pits / Love has
found me / Little star/Eclipse
CD _____ BGOCD 181
Beat Goes On / Apr '93 / Pinnacle.

STREET MACHINE
Never say die / This planet's on fire /
Wounded in love / Falling in love / Growing
pains / Child to man / Trans am (Highway
wonderland) / Feels like love / Plain Jane
CD _____ BGOCD 150
Beat Goes On / Apr '93 / Pinnacle.

**THROUGH THE FIRE (Hagar, Sammy/
Neil Schon/Kenny Aaronson/Michael
Shrieve)**
Top of the rock / Missing you / Animation /
Valley of the kings / Giza / Whiter shade of
pale / Hot and dirty / He will understand /
My home town
CD _____ RETRO 50059CD
Retroactive / Jan '96 / Plastic Head.

Hagen, Nina

NINA HAGEN
Move over / Super freak family / Love heart
attack / Hold me / Las Vegas / Live on Mars
/ Dope sucks / Only seventeen / Where's
the party / Ave Maria
CD _____ 8385052
Mercury / Jan '96 / PolyGram.

REVOLUTION BALLROOM
CD _____ ACTIVCD 3
Activ / Oct '95 / Total/BMG.

STREET
Blumen fur die damen / Divine love, sex and
romance / Ruler of my heart / Nina 4 presi-
dent / Keep it live / Berlin / In my world /
Gretchen / Erfurt and Gera / All 4 franckie
CD _____ 8487162
Mercury / Jan '96 / PolyGram.

Hagfish

ROCK YOUR LAME ASS
Happiness / Stamp / Flat / Bullet / Crater / Minite maid / White food / Disappointed / Plain / Buster / Trixi / Did you notice / Gertrude / Hose / Teenage kicks
CD _____ 8286842
London / Sep '95 / PolyGram.

Haggard, Merle

20 COUNTRY NO.1'S
Okie from Muskogee / I'm a lonesome fugitive / Branded man / Sing me back home / Legend of Bonnie and Clyde / Mama tired / Hungry eyes / Workin' man blues / Always wanting you / It's not love (but it's not bad) / Old man from the mountain / Everybody's had the blues / Movin' on / Roots of my raising / Fightin' side of me / Carolyn / I wonder if they ever think of me / Daddy Frank (the guitar man) / Grandma Harp / Kentucky gambler
CD _____ CDMFP 6114
Music For Pleasure / Mar '94 / EMI.

ALL NIGHT LONG
All night long / Honky tonk / Night-time man / I'm a white boy / Holding things together / Uncle Lem / Farmer's daughter / Man's got to give up a lot / I've done it all / Goodbye lefty / If you've got time (to say goodbye) / September in Miami / Bar in Bakersfield
CD _____ D2-77410
Curb / '91 / PolyGram.

CAPITOL COLLECTORS SERIES: MERLE HAGGARD
Swinging doors / Bottle let me down / I'm a lonesome fugitive / Sing me back home / I take a lot of pride in what I am / Hungry eyes / Workin' man blues / Okie from Muskogee / Fightin' side of me / Soldier's last letter / Daddy Frank / I wonder if they ever think of me / Emptiest arms in the world / Things aren't funny anymore / Old man from the mountain
CD _____ CZ 301
Capitol / Apr '90 / EMI.

COUNTRY LEGEND
Twinkle twinkle lucky star / If you want to be my woman / Workin' man blues / Always late / T.B. blues / Folsom prison blues / Footlights / Big city / Mama tried / Brain Cloudy blues / Milk cow blues / Begging to you / Bottle let me down / What am I gonna do (with the rest of my life) / Ida Red / San Antonio rose / Corine Corina / Take me back to Tulsa / Faded love / Maiden's prayer / Fiddle breakdown / Flight or wrong / Ramblin' fever / That's the way love goes / Today I started loving you again / Okie from Muskogee / Fightin' side of me
CD _____ PLATCD 358
Platinum Music / May '91 / Prism / Ross.

HITS & MORE, THE
Okie from Muskogee / If you want to be my woman / Games people play / Workin' man blues / Corine Corina / Bottle let me down / What am I gonna do / Mama tried / That's the way love goes / San Antonio rose / Ramblin' fever / Take me back to Tulsa / Ida Red / Begging to you / Always late / Big city / Folsom prison blues / Medley / Footlights / Today I started loving you again
CD _____ HADCD 168
Javelin / May '94 / THE / Henry Hadaway Organisation.

IN CONCERT
CD _____ CDCD 1263
Charly / Nov '95 / Charly / THE / Cadillac.

SAME TRAIN, A DIFFERENT TIME
California blues / Waiting for a train / Train whistle blues / Why should I be lonely / Blue yodel No. 6 / Miss the Mississippi and you / Mule skinner blues / Frankie and Johnny / Hobo Bill's last ride / Travelin' blues / Peach pickin' time in Georgia / No hard times / Down the old road to home / Jimmie Rodgers' last blue yodel / Jimmie the kid (CD only) / My rough and rowdy ways (CD only) / Hobo's meditation (CD only) / Mother, the Queen of my heart (CD only) / My Carolina sunshine girl (CD only) / My old pal (CD only) / Nobody knows but me (CD only) / Delta blues (CD only) / Mississippi delta blues (CD only) / Gambling polka dot blues (CD only)
CD _____ BCD 15740
Bear Family / Oct '93 / Rollercoaster / Direct / CM / Swift / ADA.

SAME TRAIN, A DIFFERENT TIME
CD _____ 340512
Koch / Jul '95 / Koch.

SING ME BACK HOME
CD _____ 340542
Koch International / Nov '95 / Koch.

STARS OVER BAKERSFIELD (Haggard, Merle & Buck Owens)
CD _____ CTS 55418
Country Stars / Jun '94 / Target/BMG.

STRANGERS
CD _____ 340532
Koch International / Nov '95 / Koch.

Haggart, Bob

WORLD'S GREATEST JAZZBAND (Haggart, Bob & Yank Lawson)
CD _____ CDTTD 533
Timeless Traditional / Jul '94 / Koch.

Hagiopian, Richard

ARMENIAN MUSIC THROUGH THE AGES
CD _____ SFCD 40414
Smithsonian Folkways / Jun '93 / ADA / Direct / Koch / CM / Cadillac.

BEST OF ARMENIAN FOLK MUSIC
CD _____ EUCD 1222
ARC / Sep '93 / ARC Music / ADA.

Hahn, Jerry

TIME CHANGES
Time changes / 245 / Method / Quiet now / Blues for allyson / Oregon / Goodbye pork pie hat / Hannah bear / Stolen moments / Chelsea rose
CD _____ ENJ 90072
Enja / May '95 / New Note / Vital/SAM.

SWINGING DOORS/THE BOTTLE LET ME DOWN
CD _____ 340522
Koch International / Nov '95 / Koch.

TRIBUTE TO THE BEST DAMN FIDDLE PLAYER IN THE WORLD (My Salute To Bob Wills)
Brown skin gal / Right or wrong / Brain cloudy blues / Stay a little longer / Misery / Time changes everything / San Antonio rose / I knew the moment I lost you / Roly poly / Old fashioned love / Corine Corina / Take me back to Tulsa
CD _____ 379002
Koch / Aug '95 / Koch.

TULARE DUST - THE SONGS OF MERLE HAGGARD (Various Artists)
CD _____ HCD 8058
Hightone / Dec '94 / ADA / Koch.

UNTAMED HAWK
Sing a sad song / You don't even try / Life in prison (false start) / Life in prison / You don't have far to go / Sam Hill / Please Mr. DJ / I'd trade all of my tomorrows / Strangers / Slowly but surely / Just between the two of us / Falling for you / I wanta live again / House without love (is not a home) / Walking the floor over you / Worst is yet to come / Piedras negras (go home) / Singin' my heart out / Skid row / If I had left it up to you / I'm gonna break every heart I can / Stranger in my arms / If I could be him / Shade tree (fix it man) / This town's not big enough / I'll take a chance / Our hearts are holding hands / Too used to being with you / That makes two of us / Forever and ever / Wait a little longer, please Jesus / Swinging doors / Girl turned ripe / I threw away the rose / Fugitive / Loneliness is eating me alive / Someone told my story / Hang up my gloves / Longer you wait / Bottle let me down / I can't stand me / Someone else you've known / High on a hilltop / I'll look over you / No more you and me / Mixed up mess of a heart / I'm a lonesome fugitive / House of memories / All of me belongs to you / Mary's mine / If you want to be my woman / Whatever happened to me / Drink up and be somebody / Gone crazy / Some of us never learn / Branded man / You don't have very far to go / Wine take me away / If you see my baby / Somewhere between / Don't get married / My hands are tied / I made the prison band / Look over me / Long black limousine / I'll leave the bottle on the bar / Sing me back home / Son of Hickory Holler's tramp / Seeing eye dog / Will you visit me on Sundays / Home is where a kid grows up / Where does the good times go / Good times / News break / My past is present / Mom and Dad's waltz / My Ramona / Because you can't be mine / Train never stops / You still have a place in my heart / Money tree / Picture from two sides of life / Legend of Bonnie and Clyde / I started loving you again / Love has a mind of it's own / Fool's castle / Is this the beginning of the end / Sunny side of my life / Run em off / I'll always know / You'll never love me now / Mama tried / In the good old days (when times were bad) / Little ole wine drinker me / Teach me to forget / Lookin' for my mind / Green green grass of home / I could have gone right / Day the rains came / I think we're living in the good old days / Somewhere on Skid Row / Who do I know in Dallas / Folsom prison blues / You're not home yet / Too many bridges to cross over / I take a lot of pride in what I am / I just want to look at you one more time / I'm bringin' home good news / Keep me from cryin' today / I can't hold myself in tune / I'll free / It meant goodbye to me when you said hello / Who'll buy the wine / She thinks I still care / What's wrong with stayin' home / When no flowers grow / Every fool has a rainbow / Hungry eyes / Silver wings
CD Set _____ BCD 15744
Bear Family / Mar '95 / Rollercoaster / Direct / CM / Swift / ADA.

Hahn, John

OUT OF THE SHADOWS
Rhino stomp / Captain Courageous / Outward bound / Looking glass / Warm summer rain / Cut to the chase / Let it ride / Deadly spell / Pickin' your seat / Second sight / Heat of the night / Inherit the wind
CD _____ KILCD 1004
Killerwatt / Oct '93 / Kingdom.

Haig, Al

ORNITHOLOGY
CD _____ PCD 7024
Progressive / Oct '91 / Jazz Music.

Hail

TURN OF THE SCREW
Another day / Honey smothered / Good luck / Sicko God / Tape hiss / Rusty old ring / Take me back / Burlesque egg / Racer hero / Tar pits / Suspended / Down the road / Star in the sky / Fifteen seconds of silence / My friend / Did you listen to this
CD _____ RERHCD
ReR Megacorp / Apr '91 / These / ReR Megacorp.

Haine Et Ses Amours

HAINE ET SES AMOURS
CD _____ 760486
Eurobon / Nov '90 / Triple Earth.

Haines, Paul

DARN IT
Threats that matter / There aren't these things / Curtsy / Les paramedicaux erotiques / What is going to supposed to mean / Jubilee / On the way to here and elsewhere / Funny bird song / Inexplicably / Outside the city / Poem for Gretchen Ruth / Art in heaven / Rawilpindi blues / Sticks in the mud
CD _____ AMCL 10142
American Clave / Nov '93 / New Note / ADA / Direct.

Haino, Keiji

21ST CENTURY HARDY-GUIDE-Y MAN, THE
CD _____ PSFD 68
PSF / Jan '96 / Harmonia Mundi.

Hair & Skin Trading...

JO IN NINE G HELL (Hair & Skin Trading Company)
CD _____ SITU 40 CD
Situation 2 / Apr '92 / Pinnacle.

OVER VALANCE (Hair & Skin Trading Company)
CD _____ BBQCD 141
Beggars Banquet / Sep '93 / Warner Music / Disc.

PSYCHEDLISCHE MUSIQUE (Hair & Skin Trading Company)
CD _____ FRR 11CD
Freek / May '95 / SRD.

Haircut 100

PELICAN WEST PLUS
Favourite shirts (boy meets girl) (Mixes) / Love plus one / Lemon firebrigade / Marine boy / Milk film / King size / Fantastic day / Baked beans / Snow girl / Love's got me in triangles / Surprise me again / Calling captain Autumn / Boat party / Ski club / Nobody's fool / October is orange
CD _____ 74321100782
Arista / Oct '92 / BMG.

VERY BEST OF HAIRCUT 100, THE
CD _____ 74321206522
Arista / May '94 / BMG.

Haiti Cherie

CREOLE - TRADITIONAL & VOODOO SONGS
CD _____ 995302
EPM / Aug '93 / Discovery / ADA.

Hajra Gipsy Orchestra

EVENING OF GIPSY SONGS, AN
CD _____ SOW 90129
Sounds Of The World / Sep '94 / Target/BMG.

Hakansson, Kenny

SPELAR SPRINGLEKAR
CD _____ SRS 3620CD
Silence / Jul '95 / ADA.

Hakim, Sadik

LADYBIRD
CD _____ STCD 4156
Storyville / Feb '90 / Jazz Music / Wellard / CM / Cadillac.

Hakmoun, Hassan

FIRE WITHIN, THE
CD _____ CDT 135CD

Music Of The World / Nov '95 / Target/ BMG / ADA.

TRANCE (Hakmoun, Hassan & Zahar)
Bania / Only one god (Maaboud alah) / Soudan minitara (Bum bastic mix) / Challaban / Soutanbi / Soulalahoalith / Alal wahya alal (Trance mix) / Sun is gone / Soudan minitara
CD _____ CDRW 38
Realworld / Aug '93 / EMI / Sterns.

Halcox, Pat

SONGS FROM TIN PAN ALLEY (Halcox, Pat & Friends)
CD _____ JCD 186
Jazzology / Oct '91 / Swift / Jazz Music.

Hale, Terry Lee

FRONTIER MODEL
CD _____ GRCD 311
Glitterhouse / Apr '94 / Direct / ADA.

OH WHAT A WORLD
CD _____ NORMAL 152CD
Normal/Okra / Mar '94 / Direct / ADA.

TORNADO ALLEY
CD _____ GRCD 359
Glitterhouse / Apr '95 / Direct / ADA.

Haley, Bill

16 GREATEST HITS: BILL HALEY (Haley, Bill & The Comets)
(We're gonna) Rock around the clock / See you later alligator / Shake, rattle and roll / Razzle dazzle / Saints rock 'n' roll / Skinny Minnie / Rock-a-beatin' boogie / Rip it up / Rudy's rock / Jenny jenny / Kansas City / Rock the joint / Yakety sax / Johnny B. Goode / Whole lotta shakin' goin' on / What'd I say
CD _____ CD 39
Bescol / May '87 / CM / Target/BMG.

BILL HALEY
CD _____ LECD 034
Dynamite / May '94 / THE.

BILL HALEY & THE COMETS (Haley, Bill & The Comets)
(We're gonna) Rock around the clock / Skinny Minnie / Ling ting tong / See you later alligator / Whole lotta shakin' goin' on / Rudy's rock / Caravan / Rock the joint / Johnny B. Goode / Lucille / Kansas City / Shake, rattle and roll / Flip flop and fly / Malaguena / New Orleans / What'd I say / Razzle dazzle / Rip it up / Rock-a-beatin' boogie / Saints rock 'n' roll
CD _____ PCD 838
Carlton Home Entertainment / '88 / Carlton Home Entertainment.

BILL HALEY & THE COMETS (Haley, Bill & The Comets)
CD _____ CD 114
Timeless Treasures / Oct '94 / THE.

BILL HALEY & THE COMETS (Haley, Bill & The Comets)
CD _____ 12396
Laserlight / Mar '95 / Target/BMG.

BILL HALEY AND THE COMETS
CD _____ ENTCD 283
Entertainers / Mar '92 / Target/BMG.

BILL HALEY/LITTLE RICHARD ESSENTIALS (Haley, Bill & Little Richard)
CD _____ LECD 624
Wisepack / Aug '95 / THE / Conifer.

MR ROCK 'N' ROLL
CD _____ CDCD 1080
Charly / Apr '93 / Charly / THE / Cadillac.

ORIGINAL HITS 1954-57 (Haley, Bill & The Comets)
(We're gonna) Rock around the clock / Rock the joint / Saints rock 'n' roll / Mambo rock / Rockin' rollin' rover / Don't knock the rock / Calling all Comets / Rockin' through the rye / Choo choo ch' boogie / Razzle dazzle / Rudy's rock / Hot dog buddy buddy / Rocking little tune / R.O.C.K.
CD _____ PWKS 575
Carlton Home Entertainment / Mar '90 / Carlton Home Entertainment.

RIP IT UP, ROCK'N'ROLL (Haley, Bill & The Comets)
(We're gonna) Rock around the clock / Saints rock 'n' roll / You hit the wrong note Billy Goat / Goofin' around / Thirteen women (and only one man in town) / Caldonia / Shake, rattle and roll / Choo choo ch' boogie / Burn that candle / Happy baby / Hook, line and sinker / Rock Lomond / See you later alligator / Mambo rock / Dim, dim the lights / Lean Jean / Tonight's the night / Calling all Comets / Rip it up / Hide and seek / Mary Lou / Teenage mothers / Move it on over / Viva la rock 'n' roll
CD _____ VSOPCD 116
Connoisseur / '88 / Pinnacle.

ROCK 'N' ROLL SCRAPBOOK
CD _____ NEMCD 600
Sequel / Apr '90 / BMG.

ROCK AROUND THE CLOCK (Haley, Bill & The Comets)
Shake, rattle and roll / R.O.C.K. / Calling all comets / See you later alligator / Saints love 'n' roll / Razzle dazzle / ABC Boogie / Don't knock the rock / Rip it up / Rockin' thru the rye / Birth of the boogie / Rock-a-beatin' boogie / Dim, dim the lights / Mambo rock / Rudy's rock / Skinny Minnie / Thirteen women / Corine Corina / Forty cups of coffee / (We're gonna) rock around the clock
CD _____ MOOD 0016
More Music / Feb '95 / Sound & Media.

ROCK THE JOINT (Haley, Bill & The Comets)
Rocket 88 / Tearstains on my heart / Green tree boogie / Jukebox cannonball / Sundown boogie / Icy heart / Rock the joint / Dance with a dolly / Rockin' chair on the moon / Stop beatin' around the mulberry bush / Real rock drive / Crazy man crazy / What'cha gonna do / Pat-a-cake / Fractured / Live it up / Farewell, so long, goodbye / I'll be true / Ten little Indians / Chattanooga choo choo / Straight jacket / Yes indeed
CD _____ RCCD 3001
Rollercoaster / Aug '90 / CM / Swift.

ROCKIN' AND ROLLIN' (Haley, Bill & The Comets)
Shake, rattle and roll / Skinny Minnie / Rip it up / See you later alligator / (We're gonna) Rock around the clock / Razzle dazzle / Crying time / Saints rock 'n' roll (When the saints go marchin' in) / Rock-a-beatin' boogie / Rock the joint / I'm walkin' / Hi-heel sneakers / Blue suede shoes / C.C. rider / Lawdy Miss Clawdy / Personality / Hail hail rock 'n' roll / Let the good times roll again / Battle of New Orleans / Heartaches by the number
CD _____ 5509552
Spectrum/Karussell / Mar '95 / PolyGram THE.

ROCKIN' ROLLIN' HALEY (Haley, Bill & The Comets)
(We're gonna) Rock around the clock / Thirteen women / Shake, rattle and roll / ABC Boogie / Happy baby / Dim, dim the lights / Birth of the boogie / Mambo rock / Two hound dogs / Razzle dazzle / R.O.C.K. / Rock-a-beatin' boogie / Saints rock 'n' roll / Burn that candle / See you later alligator / Paper boy / Goofin' around / Rudy's rock / Hide and seek / Hey then, there now / Tonight's the night / Hook, line and sinker / Blue comet blues / Calling all comets / Choo choo ch' boogie / Rocking little tune / Hot dog buddy buddy / Rockin' through the rye / Teenager's mother / Rip it up / Don't knock the rock / Forty cups of coffee / Miss you / You hit the wrong note Billy Goat / Rockin' rollin' rover / Please don't talk about me when I'm gone / You can't stop me from dreaming / I'm gonna sit right down and write myself a letter / Rock Lomond / Is it true what they say about Dixie / Carolina in the morning / Dipsy doodle / Ain't misbehavin' / Beak speaks / Moon over Miami / One sweet letter from you / I'll be with you in apple blossom time / Somebody else is taking my place / How many / Move it on over / Rock the joint / Me rock a hula / Rockin' Rita / Jamaica D.J. / Piccadilly rock / Pretty alouette / Rockin' rollin' schnitzlebank / Rockin' Matilda / Viva la rock 'n' roll / It's a sin / Mary Mary Lou / El rocko / Come rock with me / Oriental rock / Woodenshoe rock / Walkin' beat / Skinny Minnie / Sway with me / Lean Jean / Don't nobody move / Jean's song / Chiquita Linda / Dinah / Ida, sweet as apple cider / Whoa Mabel / Marie / Eloise / Corine Corina / BB. Betty / Sweet Sue, just you / Charmaine / Dragon rock / A.C. rock / Catwalk / I got a woman / Fool such as I / By by me / Where did you go last night / Caldonia / Shaky / Ooh, look a there, ain't she pretty / Summer souvenir / Puerto Rican peddler / Music music music / Skokiaan / Drowsy waters / Two shadows / In a little Spanish town / Strictly instrumental / Mack The Knife / Green door / Yeah, she's evil
CD Set _____ BCD 15506
Bear Family / Oct '90 / Rollercoaster / Direct / CM / Swift / ADA.

SEE YOU LATER ALLIGATOR (Haley, Bill & The Comets)
CD _____ 301374
Accord / Dec '89 / Discovery / Harmonia Mundi / Cadillac.

VERY BEST OF BILL HALEY & THE COMETS (Haley, Bill & The Comets)
(We're gonna) Rock around the clock / Shake, rattle and roll / See you later alligator / Saints rock 'n' roll / Rock-a-beatin' boogie / Rockin' thru the Rye / Rip it up / Don't knock the rock / Mambo rock / Rudy's rock / Razzle dazzle / Skinny Minnie / R.O.C.K. / Thirteen women / ABC boogie / Birth of the boogie / Forty cups of coffee / Burn that candle / Calling all comets
CD _____ MCCD 068
Music Club / Jun '92 / Disc / THE / CM.

Half Hour To Go

ITEMS FOR THE FULL OUTFIT
CD _____ GROW 0572
Grass / Aug '95 / SRD.

Half Japanese

BAND THAT WOULD BE KING, THE
CD _____ PAPCD 018
Paperhouse / Jul '93 / Disc.

CHARMED LIFE
CD _____ PAPCD 016
Paperhouse / Jul '93 / Disc.

FIRE IN THE SKY
CD _____ PAPCD 010
Paperhouse / Mar '92 / Disc.

HOT
CD _____ FIRECD 047
Fire / Jun '95 / Disc.

MUSIC TO STRIP BY
CD _____ PAPCD 017
Paperhouse / Jul '93 / Disc.

Half Man Half Biscuit

ACD
Best things in life / D'ye ken ted moult / Reasons to be miserable - part 10 / Rod Hull is alive - why / Dickie Davies eyes / Bastard son of Dean Friedman / I was a teenage armchair honved fan / Arthur's farm / Carry on cremating / Albert Hammond bootleg / Reflections in a flat / Sealclubbing / Architecture and morality Ted and Alice / Fuckin' 'ell it's Fred Titmus / Time flies by (when you're the driver of the train) / All I want for Christmas is a Dukla Prague away kit / Trumpton riots
CD _____ PROBE 008CD
Probe Plus / Apr '94 / Vital.

BACK AGAIN IN THE DHSS
Best things in life are free / D'ye Ken Ted Moult / Reasons to be miserable - part 10 / Rod Hull is alive - Why / Dickie Davies eyes / Bastard son of Dean Friedman / I was a teenage armchair Honved fan / Fan / Arthur's farm / All I want for Christmas is a Dukla Prague away kit / Trumpton riots
CD _____ PROBE 8CD
Probe Plus / Nov '88 / Vital.

BACK IN THE D.H.S.S./THE TRUMPTON RIOTS EP
Busy little market town / God gave us life / Fuckin' 'ell it's Fred Titmus / Sealclubbing / 99% of gargoyles look like Bob Todd / Time flies by (when you're the driver of a train) / I hate Nerys Hughes / Len Ganley stance / Venus in flares / I love you because (you look like Jim Reeves) / Reflections in a flat / I left my heart in Papworth General / Trumpton riots / Architecture and morality Ted and Alice / 1966 and all that / Albert Hammond Bootleg / All I want for Christmas is a Dukla Prague away kit
CD _____ PROBE 004CD
Probe Plus / Apr '94 / Vital.

MCINTYRE, TREADMORE & DAVITT
Outbreak of vitas gerulaitas / Prag vec at the Melkweg / Christian rock concert / Let's not / Yipps (my baby got the) / Hedley veriityesque / Lilac Harry Quinn / Our tune / Girlfriend's finished / With him / Everything's A.O.R.
CD _____ PROBE 030CD
Probe Plus / Apr '94 / Vital.

SOME CALL IT GODCORE
Sensitive outsider / Fretwork homework / Faithlift / Song for Europe / Even men with steel hearts / 24.99 from Argos / Sponsoring the Mospits / Fear my wraith / Styx gig (Seen by my mates coming out of a) / Friday night and the gates are low / I, trog / Tour jacket with detachable sleeves
CD _____ PROBE 041CD
Probe Plus / May '95 / Vital.

THIS LEADEN PALL
M 6ster / 4AD 3D CD / Running order squabble fest / Whiteness thy name is meltonian / This leaden pall / Turned up clocked on laid off / Eno's little eggs / meshow gobeshite / Thirteen Eurogoths floating in the dead sea / Whit week malarkey / Doreen / Quality janitor / Floreat inertia / Malayan jelutong / Numanoid hang glide / Footprints
CD _____ PROBE 036CD
Probe Plus / Oct '93 / Vital.

Half Pint

20 SUPER HITS
CD _____ SONCD 0001
Sonic Sounds / Oct '90 / Jetstar.

CLASSICS
CD _____ HCD 7009
Hightone / Aug '94 / ADA / Koch.

CLASSICS IN DUB
CD _____ HCD 7014
Hightone / Mar '95 / ADA / Koch.

VICTORY
Victory / Level the vibes / Come alive / Night life lady / She's mine / Desperate lover / Cost of living / When one gone / Mama / She's gone
CD _____ RASCD 3031
Ras / Feb '88 / Jetstar / Greensleeves / SRD / Direct.

Halfway House Orchestra

HALFWAY HOUSE ORCHESTRA (New Orleans 1925-28)
CD _____ BDW 8001
Jazz Oracle / Jun '95 / Jazz Music.

Halibuts

CHUMMING
CD _____ UPST 009
Upstart / Oct '94 / Direct / ADA.

Hall & Oates

ABANDONED LUNCHEONETTE
When the morning comes / Had I known you better then / Las Vegas turnaround / Stewardess song / She's gone / I'm just a kid (Don't make me feel like a man) / Abandoned luncheonette / Lady rain / Laughing boy / Everytime I look at you
CD _____ 7567815372
Atlantic / Mar '93 / Warner Music.

CHANGE OF SEASON
So close / Starting all over again / Sometimes a mind changes / Change of seasons / Ain't gonna take it this time / Everywhere I look / Give it up / Don't hold back your love / Halfway there / Only love / Heavy rain / So close (Un-plugged)
CD _____ 260548
Atlantic / Feb '93 / BMG.

H20
Maneater / Crime pays / Art of heartbreak / One on one / Open all night / Family man / Italian girls / Guessing games / Delayed reaction / At tension / Go solo
CD _____ ND 90080
Arista / Jan '89 / BMG.

HALL & OATES
CD _____ KLMCD 034
Scratch / Nov '94 / BMG.

HALL & OATES/HERMAN'S HERMITS ESSENTIALS (Hall & Oates/Herman's Hermits)
CD _____ LECDD 632
Wisepack / Aug '95 / THE / Conifer.

LEGENDS IN MUSIC - HALL & OATES
CD _____ LECD 084
Wisepack / Sep '94 / THE / Conifer.

LIVE AT THE APOLLO
Get ready / Ain't too proud to beg / Way you do the things you do / When something is wrong with my baby / Every time you go away / I can't go for that (no can do) / One by one / Possession obsession / Adult education
CD _____ 74321 16003-2
RCA / Sep '93 / BMG.

LOOKING BACK (The Best Of Daryl Hall And John Oates)
She's gone / Sara smile / Rich girl / You've lost that lovin' feelin' / Kiss on my list / Every time you go away / Private eyes / I can't go for that (no can do) / Maneater / One on one / Family man / Adult education / Out of touch / Method of modern love / Starting all over again / Back together again (CD only) / So close (CD only) / Everything your heart desires (CD only)
CD _____ PD 90388
RCA / Oct '91 / BMG.

LOT OF CHANGES COMIN'
CD _____ CDSGP 0128
Prestige / Dec '94 / Total/BMG.

OOH YEAH
Downtown life / I'm in pieces / Talking all night / Rocket to God / Real love / Everything your heart desires / Missed opportunity / Rockability / Soul love / Keep on pushin' love
CD _____ 74321116292
Arista / Feb '93 / BMG.

REALLY SMOKIN'
Past times behind / Everyday's a lovely day / Rose come home / Flo gene / Seventy / I'm really smokin' / Christine / Over the mountain / Lemon road / Truly good song
CD _____ CDTB 122
Thunderbolt / Jul '93 / Magnum Music Group.

ROCK 'N' SOUL PART 1
Sara smile / She's gone / Rich girl / Kiss in my list / You make my dreams / Private eyes / I can't go for that (no can do) / Maneater / One on one / Wait for me / Say it isn't so / Adult education
CD _____ 74321289832
RCA / Aug '95 / BMG.

SPOTLIGHT ON HALL & OATES
Lot of changes comin' / Drying in the sun / I'll be by / Perkiomen / Fall in Philadelphia / They need each other / Provider / Back in love again / Past times behind / Deep river blues / Goodnight and good morning / In honour of a lady / Angelina / Months, weeks, days / If that's what makes you happy
CD _____ HADCD 107
Javelin / Feb '94 / THE / Henry Hadaway Organisation.

WHOLE OATS
I'm sorry / All our love / Georgie / Fall in Philadelphia / Waterwheel / Lazy man /

Goodnight and good morning / They needed each other / Southeast city window / Thank you for... / Lilly (are you happy)
CD _____ 7567814232
Atlantic / Jan '93 / Warner Music.

Hall, Aaron

TRUTH, THE
Prologue - Do anything / Open up / Get a little freaky with me / Pick up the phone / Don't be afraid / Until I found you / You keep me crying (interlude) / Let's make love / When you need me / I miss you / Until the end of time / Epilogue
CD _____ MCD 10810
MCA / Nov '93 / BMG.

Hall, Adelaide

ADELAIDE HALL (Live At The Riverside Studios)
CD _____ CDVIR 8312
TER / Aug '90 / Koch.

AS TIME GOES BY
Rhapsody in love (unissued take) / I'll never be the same (unissued take) / This time it's love (unissued take) / I must have that man (unissued take) / Baby (unissued take) / I'm in the mood for love / Truckin / East of the sun and west of the moon / Solitude / I can't give you anything but love / Deep purple / Transatlantic lullaby / Lady is a tramp / Chloe / This can't be love / No souvenirs / Our love affair / Mist on the river / Ain't it a shame about Mame / It's always you / How did he look / Tes, my darling daughter / I hear a rhapsody / I yi yi yi yi (like you very much) / Sand in my shoes / As time goes by
CD _____ CDHD 248
Happy Days / Jan '94 / Conifer.

HALL OF FAME
Ain't it a shame about Mame / Baby mine / Begin the beguine / Creole love call / Doin' as I please / Don't worry 'bout me / Drop me off at Harlem / I can't give you anything but love / I get along without you very well / I got rhythm / I have eyes / I hear a rhapsody / I poured my heart into a song / Mississippi mamma / Moon love / No souvenirs / Rhapsody in love / Shake down the stars / T'aint what you do / That old feeling / Transatlantic lullaby / Who told you I cared
CD _____ CDAJA 5098
Living Era / Nov '92 / Koch.

HALL OF MEMORIES (1927-39)
CD _____ CDHD 169
Happy Days / Aug '90 / Conifer.

RED HOT FROM HARLEM
This time it's love / You gave me everything but love / Rhapsody in love / Baby mine / I'll never be the same / I must have that man / Minnie the moocher / Too darn hot / I'm red hot from Harlem / Doin' what I please / I got rhythm / Strange as it seems / Chlo-e / Solitude / Say you're mine / I get along without you very well / Don't worry 'bout me / T'ain't what you do / Shake down the stars / Who told you I cared / No souvenirs / This can't be love
CD _____ PASTCD 7029
Flapper / Jan '94 / Pinnacle.

Hall, Ben

COUNTRY WAYS AND ROCKIN' DAYS (Hall, Ben & The Ramblers/Weldon Myrick)
Blue days black nights / Even tho' / Hangin' around / Crying on my shoulder / Maria Elieve / Sleepless nights / Gunfighter's fame / Late hours / Don't ask me why / I'd give anything / All from loving you / Rose of Monterey / Drifting along with the wind / Driftwood on the river / Stormy skies / Season for love / Only 17 / That's the way dreams go / I don't wanna go home / You're here in my mind / Weeping willow / Before you begin / Johnny Law / Hiding alone / So close / Won't you be mine / I'll never be the same / I'll still be hanging around
CD _____ RCCD 3004
Rollercoaster / Oct '93 / CM / Swift.

Hall, Bob

ALONE WITH THE BLUES (Hall, Bob & Tom McGuinness)
CD _____ LACD 44
Lake / Mar '95 / Target/BMG / Jazz Music / Direct / Cadillac / ADA.

AT THE WINDOW
Detroit rocks / All I got is you / Beehive blues / Mr. Freddie Blues / How long blues / She's gone / Axel's wheel / Goin' down slow / Red river boogie / Gone fishing / Somebody watching me / Blues before sunrise / At the window
CD _____ LACD 23
Lake / Oct '94 / Target/BMG / Jazz Music / Direct / Cadillac / ADA.

Hall, Daryl

SOUL ALONE
Power of seduction / This time / Love revelation / I'm in a Philly mood / Borderline / Stop loving me, stop loving you / Help me find a way to your heart / Send me / Wildlife

/ Money changes everything / Written in stone
CD _____ 473921 2
Epic / Feb '94 / Sony.

Hall, Edmond

1941-57
CD _____ CD 53199
Giants Of Jazz / Jan '95 / Target/BMG / Cadillac.

CLASSICS 1937-44
CD _____ CLASSICS 830
Classics / Sep '95 / Discovery / Jazz Music.

EDMOND HALL/ALAN ELSDON BAND 1966 (Hall, Edmond & Alan Elsdon)
CD _____ JCD 240
Jazzology / Mar '95 / Swift / Jazz Music.

JAZZ PORTRAIT
CD _____ CD 14578
Complete / Nov '95 / THE.

Hall, Gary

WHAT GOES AROUND
CD _____ RTMCD 57
Round Tower / Jan '94 / Pinnacle / ADA / Direct / BMG / CM.

Hall, Henry

HENRY HALL & BBC DANCE ORCHESTRA (Hall, Henry & The BBC Dance Orchestra)
Five-fifteen / Have you ever been lonely / Goody goody / Wagon wheels / Waltz in swingtime / Mine for keeps / Sun has got his hat on / Wild ride / It's just the time for dancing / Elephant never forgets / I'm putting all my eggs in one basket / Teddy bears' picnic / Life begins when you're in love / I heard a song in a taxi / 1-2 Button your shoe / It's time to say goodnight / Here's to the next time
CD _____ RGM 001
Radiogram / Oct '90 / Club 50/50.

HENRY HALL & THE BBC DANCE ORCHESTRA (Hall, Henry & The BBC Dance Orchestra)
Come ye back to bonnie Scotland / Mrs. Henry Hall / It's just the time for dancing / Songs that are old live forever / Love / Moon country / Curly head / Phantom of a song / Rusticanella / Little Dutch mill / Viennese memories of Lehar / By the sycamore tree / OLd violin / Red sails in the sunset / Sidewalks of Cuba / Dreaming / Someday we'll meet again / Samum / I bought myself a bottle of ink / Hits of the day (1932) / Here's to the next time
CD _____ PASTCD 9725
Flapper / '90 / Pinnacle.

HENRY HALL'S HOUR (Hall, Henry & The BBC Dance Orchestra)
It's just the time for dancing / Keep a twinkle in your eye / If I had a million dollars / I'm building up to an awful let-down / Lot / Eeny meeny miney mo / Lazybones / Goody goody / Dream awhile / I'm an old cowhand (from the Rio Grande) / Your heart and mine / This'll make you whistle / Oliver Wakefield (2) / Bye bye baby / Business game / Sing me a swing song
CD _____ CDRGM 001
Radiogram / Oct '92 / Club 50/50.

HENRY HALL'S HOUR VOL. 2 (Hall, Henry & The BBC Dance Orchestra)
It's just the time for dancing / It had to be you / Fairy on the Christmas tree / Serenade in the night / Jimmy Kennedy and Michael Carr / Rusty and dusty / Oliver Wakefield / Serenade in the night (2) / Three brass bells / When did you leave Heaven / Oliver Wakefield (2) / Balkan Princess / From the bottom of my heart I thank you / Oliver Wakefield (3) / Across the great divide / Love bug will bite you / With plenty of money and you / Let's put our heads together
CD _____ RGM 002
Radiogram / Mar '94 / Club 50/50.

MY DANCE
CD _____ 2 BUR 009
Burlington / Sep '88 / CM.

WHAT A PERFECT COMBINATION (Hall, Henry & The BBC Dance Orchestra)
Twenty million people / In a little second hand store / Day you came along / Thanks / Thats another Scottish story / Roaming / On a steamer over / I'll string along with you / Little valley in the mountains / Love in bloom / With my eyes wide open / I'm dreaming / How's chances / What a perfect combination / In the moonlight / My darling / Just so you'll remember
CD _____ CDSVL 178
Saville / Mar '93 / Conifer.

Hall, Herb

OLD TYME MODERN (Hall, Herb Quartet)
Old-fashioned love / All of me / Buddy Bolden's blues / Crying my heart out for you / Swinging down Shaw's Hall / Beale Street blues / How come you do me like you do / Willow weep for me / Do you know what it

means to miss New Orleans / Sweet Georgia Brown
CD _____ SKCD 2-3003
Sackville / Jun '93 / Swift / Jazz Music / Jazz Horizons / Cadillac / CM.

Hall, James

MY LOVE, SEX AND SPIRIT
CD _____ ENDLCD 1000
CD _____ ENDXCD 1000
Endangered / May '95 / Pinnacle.

Hall, Jim

ALL ACROSS THE CITY (Hall, Jim Quartet)
Beija fior / Young one (for Debra) / All across the city / Something tells me / Prelude to a kiss / How deep is the ocean / Bemsha swing / R.E.M. State / Drop shot / Big blues / Jane
CD _____ CCD 4384
Concord Jazz / Sep '89 / New Note.

CIRCLES
(All of a sudden) My heart sings / Love letters / Down from Antigua / Echo / I can't get started (with you) / T.C. Blues / Circles / Aruba
CD _____ CCD 4161
Concord Jazz / Nov '92 / New Note.

CONCIERTO
Two's blues / Answer is yes / Concierto de Aranjuez / You'd be so nice to come home to
CD _____ 813 661 2
CTI / Feb '84 / Sony.

DEDICATIONS & INSPIRATIONS
Whistle stop / Hawk / Canto nostalgico / Why not dance / Joao / Seseragi / All the things you are / Bluesography / Miro / Money / Matisse / In a sentimental mood / Street dance
CD _____ CD 83365
Telarc / May '94 / Conifer / ADA.

JIM HALL
Stella by starlight / Stompin' at the Savoy / Things ain't what they used to be / Thanks for the memory / I'm getting sentimental over you / My funny valentine / Time after time / Polka dots and moonbeams / Tangerine / Romain / Seven come eleven / When you wish upon a star / Funkallero / Off center / Time enough / Abstraction
CD _____ CD 53218
Giants Of Jazz / Jan '96 / Target/BMG / Cadillac.

JIM HALL'S THREE (Hall, Jim Trio)
Hide and seek / Skylark / Bottlenose blues / And I do / All the things you are / Poor butterfly / Three
CD _____ CCD 4298
Concord Jazz / Mar '87 / New Note.

SOMETHING SPECIAL
CD _____ 518445-2
Limelight / May '94 / PolyGram.

THESE ROOMS (Hall, Jim Trio & Tom Harrell)
With a song in my heart / Cross court / Something tells me / Bimini / All too soon / These rooms / Darn that dream / My funny valentine / Where or when / From now on
CD _____ CY 30002
Denon / '88 / Conifer.

Hall, Michael

ADEQUATE DESIRE
CD _____ DJD 3212
Dejadisc / Dec '94 / Direct / ADA.

Hall, Pam

MISSING YOU BABY
CD _____ JFRCD 002
Joe Frazier / Jul '95 / Jetstar.

Hall, Sandra

SHOWIN' OFF
CD _____ ICH 1179
Ichiban / Mar '95 / Koch.

Hall, Terry

HOME
Forever J / You / Sense / I drew a lemon / Moon on your dress / No no no / What's wrong with me / Grief disguised as joy / First attack the love / I don't got you
CD _____ 450997269-2
Anxious / Sep '94 / Warner Music.

TERRY HALL - THE COLLECTION
Gangsters / Nite club / Ghost town / Friday night, Saturday morning / Lunatics (Have taken over the asylum) / T ain't what you do (it's the way that you do it) / Summertime / Tunnel of love / Our lips are sealed / Colourfield / Take / Thinking of you / Castles in the air / From dawn to distraction / She / Ultra modern nursery rhymes / Missing / Beautiful people
CD _____ CDCHR 1974
Chrysalis / Nov '92 / EMI.

Hall, Tom T.

BALLADS OF FORTY DOLLARS/ HOMECOMING
That's how I got to Memphis / Cloudy day / Shame on the rain / Highways / Forbidden flowers / Ain't got the time / Ballad of forty dollars / I washed my face in the morning dew / Picture of your mother / World the way I want / Over and over again / Beauty is a fading flower / Week in the country jail / Strawberry farms / Shoe shine man / Kentucky in the morning / Nashville is a groovy little town / Margie's at the Lincoln Park Inn / Homecoming / Carter boys / Flat-footin' it / George (and the Northwoods) / I miss a lot of trains
CD _____ BCD 15631
Bear Family / Jul '93 / Rollercoaster / Direct / CM / Swift / ADA.

I WITNESS LIFE/ 100 CHILDREN
Salute to a switchblade / Thankyou Connersville, Indiana / Do it to someone you love / Ballad of Bill Crump / All you want when you please / Chattanooga dog / Girls in Saigon city / Hang them all / Coming to the party / America the ugly / That'll be alright with me / Hundred children / I can't dance / I want to see the parade / Sing a little baby to sleep / Mama bake a pie (Papa kill a chicken) / Ode to half a pound of ground round / Pinto the wonder horse is dead / I hope it rains at my funeral / I took a memory to lunch / Hitch hiker / Old enough to want you
CD _____ BCD 15658
Bear Family / Jul '93 / Rollercoaster / Direct / CM / Swift / ADA.

Hall, Tony

MR UNIVERSE
CD _____ OSMOCD 003
Osmosys / Nov '95 / Direct / ADA.

Hallberg, Bengt

HALLBERG TOUCH, THE
You do something to me / Little white lies / When lights are low / Lady be good / Co-quette / Fascinating rhythm / Sometimes I'm happy / Sonny boy / In a little Spanish town / You and the night and the music / Charleston / You brought a new kind of love to me
CD _____ PHONTCD 7525
Phontastic / '93 / Wellard / Jazz Music / Cadillac.

HALLBERG TREASURE CHEST, THE
CD _____ PHONTNCD 8828
Phontastic / '93 / Wellard / Jazz Music / Cadillac.

HALLBERG'S HAPPINESS
CD _____ PHONTCD 7544
Phontastic / May '95 / Wellard / Jazz Music / Cadillac.

HALLBERG'S HOT ACCORDION (In the foreground)
Tiger rag / Bye bye blues / Farewell blues / St. Louis blues / Limehouse blues / Tva solroda segel / How high the moon / Sweet Sue, just you / Blue moon / Some of these days
CD _____ PHONTCD 7532
Phontastic / '93 / Wellard / Jazz Music / Cadillac.

HALLBERG'S SURPRISE (Not even the Old Masters are safe!)
CD _____ PHONT CD 7581
Phontastic / Apr '88 / Wellard / Jazz Music / Cadillac.

HALLBERG'S YELLOW BLUES
CD _____ PHONTCD 7583
Phontastic / '88 / Wellard / Jazz Music / Cadillac.

POWERHOUSE-KRAFTVERK (Hallberg, Bengt & Arne Dommerus)
CD _____ PHONTCD 7553
Phontastic / '93 / Wellard / Jazz Music / Cadillac.

TREASURE CHEST
CD _____ NCD 8828
Phontastic / Apr '94 / Wellard / Jazz Music / Cadillac.

Hallett, Sylvia

LET'S FALL OUT
CD _____ MASHCD 003
Mash / Oct '94 / Cadillac.

Halley, David

BROKEN SPELL
CD _____ DOSCD 7003
Dos / Nov '93 / CM / Direct / ADA.

STRAY DOG TALK
Live and learn / Rain just falls / Opportunity knockin' / It ever you need me / Tonight / Darlene / When it comes to you / Further / Walk the line / Dream life
CD _____ FIENDCD 187
Demon / Jun '90 / Pinnacle / ADA.

Halliday, Lin

DELAYED EXPOSURE
CD _____ DD 449
Delmark / Apr '84 / Hot Shot / ADA / CM / Direct / Cadillac.

EAST OF THE SUN
CD _____ DD 458
Delmark / Jan '93 / Hot Shot / ADA / CM / Direct / Cadillac.

Hallucination Generation

BLACK HOLE & BABY UNIVERSES
CD _____ THPCD 98
Thunderpussy / Feb '94 / SRD.

Hallucinogen

TWISTED
CD _____ BFLCD 15
Big Life / Oct '95 / Pinnacle.

Hallyday, Johnny

COLLECTION, THE
Souvenirs, souvenirs / Oh oh baby / Je cherche une fille / Je suis mordue / Pourquoi cet amour / Itsy bitsy petite bikini / Depuis qu'ma mome / Le plus beau des jeux / Le veux me promener / Tu es la / Ton fetiche d'amour / Sentimental (baby I don't care) / New Orleans / Mon vieux copain / Hey pony (pony time) / Si tu restes avec moi
CD _____ 74321145182
Vogue / Apr '94 / BMG.

NASHVILLE SESSIONS VOL.2
Hey baby / Tout bas, tout bas, tout bas / Shout / Quitte moi doucement / Oui, je veux / Ce n'est pas just apres tout / Les bras en croix / C'est une fille comme toil / Qui autrait dit ca / Pas cette chanson
CD _____ BCD 15497
Bear Family / Oct '90 / Rollercoaster / Direct / CM / Swift / ADA.

TRIFT DIE RATTLES
Mein leben fangt erst richtig an / Lass die leute doch reden (Keep searching) / Wilde boys / House of the rising sun / Ma guitare / Ja der elefant (wap dou wap) / It's monkey time / Vieleicht bist du fur mich noch night die / J'ai un probleme
CD _____ BCD 15492
Bear Family / Feb '90 / Rollercoaster / Direct / CM / Swift / ADA.

Halo Benders

DON'T TELL ME NOW
CD _____ KLP 46CD
K / Jan '96 / SRD.

GOD DON'T MAKE NO JUNK
CD _____ FIRECD 43
Fire / Jan '95 / Disc.

Halpin, Kieran

MISSION STREET
Refugee from heaven / Foreigners / Mission street / Berlin calling / China rose / Heart and soul / Nothing to show for it all / Celtic myth / Salt into the wound / Farewell to pride / Chase the dragon / Rolling the dice / Child bearing child
CD _____ RTMCD 31
Round Tower / Jul '91 / Pinnacle / ADA / Direct / BMG / CM.

RITE HAND, THE
Just a game without you / Blue tinted glasses / When the water turns to wine / Ghost in the song / Angel of paradise / Zodiac sign / Crucifix / Wind that rocks my cradle / Mirror town / Child lies sleeping
CD _____ RTMCD 56
Round Tower / Jan '94 / Pinnacle / ADA / Direct / BMG / CM.

Ham

BUFFALO VIRGIN
CD _____ TP016CD
One Little Indian / Sep '89 / Pinnacle.

Hamburg Dance Orchestra

ORCHESTRAL GOLD - THE MUSIC OF FAMOUS FILM THEMES
Warsaw concerto / Dream of Olwen / Tale of two cities / Slaughter on 10th avenue / Night has eyes / Legend of the glass mountain / Jealous lover / Cornish rhapsody / Spellbound
CD _____ STACD 033
Stardust / Oct '92 / Carlton Home Entertainment.

ORCHESTRAL GOLD - THE MUSIC OF GERSHWIN & LERNER & LOEWE
I've grown accustomed to her face / Gigi / Wouldn't it be loverly / Almost like being in love / I talk to the trees / They call the wind Maria / On the street where you live / Waltz at Maxim's / Get me to the church on time / If ever I would leave you / Rain in Spain / Thank heavens for little girls / Fascinating rhythm / 'S Wonderful / Summertime / Embraceable you / Foggy day / Liza / It ain't necessarily so / Nice work / Man I love / Somebody loves me / They can't take that away from me / I got rhythm

CD _____ STACD 032
Stardust / Oct '92 / Carlton Home Entertainment.

ORCHESTRAL GOLD - THE MUSIC OF IRVING BERLIN & COLE PORTER
Cheek to cheek / Anything you can do / Top hat, white tie and tails / Let's face the music and dance / Easter parade / Heatwave / There's no business like show business / You're just in love / Girl that I marry / Always / White Christmas / They say it's wonderful / I love Paris / So in love / Begin the beguine / I can can / My heart belongs to Daddy / Night and day / True love / C'est magnifique / From this moment on / It's all right with me / Wunderbar / What is this thing called love
CD _____ STACD 030
Stardust / Oct '92 / Carlton Home Entertainment.

ORCHESTRAL GOLD - THE MUSIC OF RODGERS & HAMMERSTEIN & HART
Lover / Oh what a beautiful morning / Hello, young lovers / Carousel waltz / Climb every mountain / It might as well be spring / There is nothin' like a dame / Keyboard medley / No other love / Blue moon / Oklahoma / If I loved you / Bali Ha'i / Shall we dance / You'll never walk alone / Sound of music / Slaughter on 10th avenue
CD _____ STACD 031
Stardust / Oct '92 / Carlton Home Entertainment.

Hamel, Peter Michael

LET IT PLAY (1979-83 selected pieces)
CD _____ CDKUCK 078
Kuckuck / Sep '87 / CM / ADA.

Hamill, Claire

LOVE IN THE AFTERNOON
CD _____ NAGE 18CD
Art Of Landscape / May '88 / Sony.

VOICES
CD _____ NAGE 8 CD
Art Of Landscape / Apr '86 / Sony.

Hamilton, Andy

JAMAICA BY NIGHT
Give me the highlife / Nobody knows / Port Antonio / Mango time / Every day / Jamaica by night / Otrum / Come back girl
CD _____ WCD 039
World Circuit / Sep '94 / New Note / Direct / Cadillac / ADA.

SILVERSHINE (Hamilton, Andy & The Blue Notes)
I can't get started (with you) / Body and soul / Old folks / You are too beautiful / Andy's blues / Uncle Joe / Silvershine
CD _____ WCD 025
World Circuit / Oct '91 / New Note / Direct / Cadillac / ADA.

Hamilton, Chico

EUPHORIA
CD _____ CHECD 7
Master Mix / Sep '89 / Wellard / Jazz Music / New Note.

MASTER, THE
One day five months ago / Feels good / Fancy / Stu / Gengis / Conquistadors '74 / Stacy / I can hear the grass grow
LD _____ ODORE 6T1
Stax / Nov '92 / Pinnacle.

MY PANAMANIAN FRIEND (Hamilton, Chico & Euphoria)
CD _____ 121265-2
Soul Note / May '94 / Harmonia Mundi / Wellard / Cadillac.

TRIO
CD _____ 121246-2
Soul Note / Apr '93 / Harmonia Mundi / Wellard / Cadillac.

Hamilton, Colbert

COLBERT HAMILTON & THE HELL RAZORS (Hamilton, Colbert & the Hell Razors)
Wow / Mystery train / H.lf hearted love / Woman love / Rock therapy / Long blonde hair / Ice cold / Long black shiny car / Nervous breakdown / Love me (the way that I love you) / I'm so high / Good rockin' tonight / I'll never let you go / Don't knock upon my do..r / Love me
CD _____ NERCD 071
Nervous / Mar '93 / Nervous / Magnum Music Group.

WILD AT HEART (Hamilton, Colbert & The Nitros)
Lucille / Wild at heart / Still rockin' after all these beers / Bad reputation / Too late / Boom boom / Do you wanna rock / Abused by you / High-flyin' cat / Boogaville / Pass the bottle to the baby / Boys are back in town / Big in the world / Ninety nine girls
CD _____ NERCD 076
Nervous / Mar '94 / Nervous / Magnum Music Group.

Hamilton, Dirk

GO DOWN SWINGIN
CD _____ APCD 071
Appaloosa / '92 / ADA / Magnum Music Group.

TOO TIRED TO SLEEP
CD _____ APCD 061
Appaloosa / '92 / ADA / Magnum Music Group.

YEP
CD _____ AP 107CD
Appaloosa / Jun '94 / ADA / Magnum Music Group.

Hamilton, George IV

AMERICAN COUNTRY GOTHIC
If I never see midnight again / My hometown / This is our love / Little country county fairs / Farmer's dream ploughed under / Never mind / I will be your friend / More about love / Heaven knows / Back up grinnin' again / Carolina sky / I believe in you
CD _____ CDRR 304
Request / Jan '90 / Jazz Music.

COUNTRY CHRISTMAS, A
I wonder as I wander / C-H-R-I-S-T-M-A-S / Christmas in the trenches / See amid the winter's snow / Friendly beast / Joy to the world / Little Grave / Silent night / Away in a manger / Natividad / Morning star / I'm the bleak midwinter
CD _____ WSTCD 9707
Nelson Word / Sep '93 / Nelson Word.

GEORGE HAMILTON IV 1954-1965 (6CD Set)
Beer, wine and whiskey / Sleeping at the foot of the bed / Caribbean / Satisfaction guaranteed / Satisfied mind / Out behind the barn / Serenader's swing / It's my way / I'll always remember you / Jalopy Jane / Driftin' / Daniel Boone / Driftin' (2) / I've got a secret / Verdict / Sam / Jamaica farewell / He's movin' on / Rose and a baby Ruth / I've got a secret (2) / It was me / If you don't know, I ain't gonna tell you / Everybody's body / I've got a secret (3) / Sam (2) / Rose and a baby Ruth (2) / If you don't, I ain't gonna tell you / If I possessed a printing press / Only one love / Everybody's body (2) / High school romance / Everybody's body (3) / Why don't they understand / Little Tom / Even tho' / You tell me your dream / Carolina moon / Let me call you sweetheart / When I grow too old to dream / Tell me why / Aura Lee / Girl of my dreams / Drink to me only with these eyes / Love's old sweet song / Auld lang syne / Ivy Rose / Clementine / One heart / May I / Now and for always / House of gold / I can't help it / How can you refuse him now / Your cheatin' heart / Half as much / I could never be ashamed of you / I'm so lonesome I could cry / Cold, cold heart / (I heard that) Lonesome whistle / Wedding bells / Who's taking you to the prom / I know where I'm goin' / You win again / Take these chains from my heart / So soon / When will I know / Lucy, Lucy / House a car and a wedding ring / Two of us / Steady game / Last night we fell in love / Can you blame us / Love has come to our house / Gee / One little acre / I know your sweetheart / Tremble / Why I'm walkin' / Loneliness is all around me / Before this day ends / Wrong side of the tracks / It's just the idea / Walk on the wild side of life / That's how it goes / Can't let her see me cry / To you and yours (from me and mine) / Three steps to the phone (millions of miles) / Railan id Widrier Jones / I want a girl / Those brown eyes / Where did the sunshine go / Baby blue eyes / Life's railway to heaven / East Virginia / Wall / If you don't, somebody else will / Rainbow / I miss you when you go (2) / Life is too short / China do' / Tender hearted baby / Commerce street and sixth avenue north / If you don't know ain't gonna tell you / (I want to go) Whe:n nobody knows me / Roving gambler / Oh so many years / Jimmy Brown the newsboy / Little lunch box / Come on home boy / Everglades / You are my sunshine / Last letter / If you want me to / Linda with the lonely eyes / In this very same room / Abilene / Mi.ne / Oh so many years (2) / Remember M, remember E, remember me / There's more pretty girls than one / You're easy to love / Fort Worth, Dallas or Houston / Fair and tender ladies / Kentucky / Candy apple red / Tag along / Little grave / Texarkana, Pecos or Houston / Truck driving man / Rose and a baby Ruth (3) / Roll muddy river / That's all right / Driftwood on the river / Let's say goodbye like we said hello / Rainbow at midnight / It's been so long darlin' / Letters have no arms / Walking the floor over you / I will miss you when you go (2) / Half a mind / You nearly lose your mind / Fortunes in memories / Soldier's last letter / Twist of the wrist / Nice place to visit / (You don't love me) Anymore / Late Mister Jones / Write me a picture / Something special to me / I've got a secret (4) / Slightly used / Under your spell again / Above and beyond / Excuse me (I think I've got a heartache) / Wishful thinking / I don't believe I'll fall in love today / Foolin around / Another day, another dollar / Keep those cards and letters coming in / Under the influence of love / Big, big love / You

better not do that / Long black limousine / Together again / Abilene (2) / Three steps to the phone (millions of miles) (2) / Rose and a baby Ruth (4) / Fort Worth, Dallas or Houston (2) / Before this day ends (2) / Truck driving man (2) / Walking the floor over you (2) / Write me a picture (2) / If you don't know, I ain't gonna tell
CD Set _____ BCD 15773 FK
Bear Family / Nov '95 / Rollercoaster / Direct / CM / Swift / ADA.

Hamilton, Scott

CLOSE UP
All of you / I remember you / Mad about you / Robbin's nest / Was I to blame for falling in love with you / Blue City / Mr. Big and Mr. Modern / Portrait of Jennie / Soft
CD _____ CCD 4197
Concord Jazz / Jun '91 / New Note.

EAST OF THE SUN
Autumn leaves / Stardust / It could happen to you / Bernie's tune / East of the sun and west of the moon / Time after time / Setagaya serenade / That's all / All the things you are / (Back home again in) Indiana
CD _____ CCD 4583
Concord Jazz / Dec '93 / New Note.

GROOVIN' HIGH (Hamilton, Scott/ Ken Peplowski/ Spike Robinson)
Blues up and down / You brought a new kind of love to me / That ole devil called love / Shine / Goof and I (CD only) / What's new / I'll see you in my dreams / Groovin' high (CD only) / Body and soul / Jeep is jumpin'
CD _____ CCD 4509
Concord Jazz / Jun '92 / New Note.

IS A GOOD WIND WHO IS BLOWING US NO ILL
CD _____ CDD 4042
Concord Jazz / Jul '92 / New Note.

LIVE AT BRECON JAZZ FESTIVAL
Way down yonder in New Orleans / I can't give you anything but love / My old flame / Ow / But beautiful / Fascinatin' rhythm / Nightingale sang in Berkley Square / Come rain or come shine / Blue wales
CD _____ CCD 4649
Concord Jazz / Jun '95 / New Note.

MAJOR LEAGUE (Hamilton, Scott, Jake Hanna, Dave McKenna)
Swinging at the Copper Rail / Pretty girl is like a melody / Cocktails for two / I'm through with love / Linger awhile / September in the rain / This is all I ask / It all depends on you / April in Paris
CD _____ CCD 4305
Concord Jazz / '86 / New Note.

ORGANIC DUKE
Jump for joy / Blue hodge / Moon mist / Paris blues / Castle rock / Just a sittin' and a rockin' / Rockin' in rhythm / Isfahan / Love you madly / Old circus train turn around blues
CD _____ CCD 4623
Concord Jazz / Nov '94 / New Note.

RACE POINT
Groove yard / Chelsea Bridge / Race point / Close enough for love / Oh, look at me now / Alone together / I've just seen her / Limehouse blues / You're my thrill / You say you care (CD only) / Song is you (CD only)
CD _____ CCD 4492
Concord Jazz / Jan '92 / New Note.

RADIO CITY
Apple honey / Yesterdays / I'll be around / Touch of your lips / Cherokee / Tonight I shall sleep with a smile on my face / Radio city / My ideal / Wig's blues / Remember
CD _____ CCD 4428
Concord Jazz / Aug '90 / New Note.

RIGHT TIME, THE (Hamilton, Scott Quintet)
Just in time / If I love again / Sleep / Eventide / All through the night / Skylark / Stealing port / Dropsy
CD _____ CCD 4311
Concord Jazz / Jul '87 / New Note.

SCOTT HAMILTON 2
East of the sun and west of the moon / There is no greater love / Rough ridin' / These foolish things remind me of you / I want to be happy / Everything happens to me / Love me or leave me / Blues for the players / Very thought of you / It could happen to you
CD _____ CCD 4061
Concord Jazz / Jun '94 / New Note.

SCOTT HAMILTON PLAYS BALLADS
CD _____ CCD 4386
Concord Jazz / Sep '89 / New Note.

SCOTT HAMILTON QUINTET IN CONCERT, THE (Hamilton, Scott Quintet)
I can't believe that you're in love with me / Wrap your troubles in dreams (and dream your troubles away) / I've found a new baby / When I fall in love / Whispering / Sultry serenade / Stardust / One o'clock jump
CD _____ CCD 4233
Concord Jazz / Feb '91 / New Note.

SECOND SET (Hamilton, Scott Quintet)
All the things you are / Time after time / Taps Miller / All too soon / How insensitive

/ I never knew / For all we know / Jumpin' the blues
CD _____ CCD 4254
Concord Jazz / May '85 / New Note.

TENOR SHOES
I should care / Falling in love with love / Shadow of your smile / Nearness of you / How high the moon / Our delight / My foolish heart / O.K.
CD _____ CCD 4127
Concord Jazz / Apr '90 / New Note.

Hamkin, Larry

POEMS AND STORIES
CD _____ NAR 114CD
SST / Jul '95 / Plastic Head.

Hamm, Stuart

KINGS OF SLEEP
Black ice / Surely the best / Call of the wild / Terminal beach / Count zero / I want to know / Prelude in C / Kings of sleep
CD _____ CDGRUB 13
Food For Thought / Oct '89 / Pinnacle.

Hammer

TERROR
CD _____ SHARK 028
Shark / Jul '92 / Plastic Head.

Hammer, Artie

JOY SPRING
CD _____ GECD 149
Gemini / Jan '89 / Cadillac.

Hammer, Jan

DRIVE
Peaceful sundown / Knight rider / Underground / Island dreamer / Drive / Lucky Jane / Up or down / Curiosity kills / Don't you know / Coming back home / Capital news / Nightglow
CD _____ MPCD 2501
Miramar / Dec '94 / New Note.

ESCAPE FROM TELEVISION
Crockett's theme / Theresa / Colombia / Rum cay / Trial and the search / Tubbs and Valerie / Forever tonight / Last flight / Rico's blues / Before the storm / Night talk / Miami vice
CD _____ MCLD 19133
MCA / Oct '92 / BMG.

Hammerbox

HAMMERBOX
CD _____ CZ 029CD
C/Z / Oct '91 / Plastic Head.

Hammerhead

ETHEREAL KILLER
CD _____ ARRCD 36/266
Amphetamine Reptile / Feb '93 / SRD.

EVIL TWIN
CD _____ ARRCD 47 306
Amphetamine Reptile / Nov '93 / SRD.

INTO THE VORTEX
CD _____ ARR 50/323CD
Amphetamine Reptile / Mar '94 / SRD.

Hammill, Peter

AFTER THE SHOW
CD _____ CDOVD 460
Virgin / Jan '96 / EMI.

AND CLOSE AS THIS
Too many of my yesterdays / Faith / Empire of delight / Silver / Beside the one you love / Other old cliches / Confidente / Sleep now
CD _____ CDV 2409
Virgin / Nov '88 / EMI.

BLACK BOX
Golden promises / Losing faith in words / Jargon king / Fogwalking / Spirit / In slow time / Wipe / Flight (Flying blind/White cave fandango/Control/Cockpit/Silkworm wings/Nothing is nothing/A black box)
CD _____ CDOVD 140
Virgin / Nov '88 / EMI.

CALM (AFTER THE STORM), THE
Shell / Not for Keith / Birds / Rain 3 AM / Just good friends / (On Tuesdays she used to do) yoga / Shingle song / Faith / Dropping the torch / After the show / Stranger still / If I could / Wilhelmina / Again / Been alone so long / Ophelia / Autumn / Sleep now
CD _____ CDVM 9017
Virgin / Jul '93 / EMI.

CHAMELEON IN THE SHADOW OF NIGHT
German overalls / Slender threads / Rock and role / In the end / What's it worth / Easy to slip away / Dropping the torch / (In the) black room / Tower
CD _____ CASCD 1067
Charisma / '89 / EMI.

ENTER K
Paradox Drive / Unconscious life / Accidents / Great experiments / Don't tell me / She wraps it up / Happy hour / Seven wonders

CD _____ FIE 9101
Fie / Apr '92 / Vital.

FIRESHIPS
I will find you / Curtains / His best girl / Oasis / Incomplete surrender / Fireship / Given time / Reprise / Gaia
CD _____ FIE 9103
Fie / Mar '92 / Vital.

FOOLS MATE
Imperial zeppelin / Candle / Happy / Solitude / Vision / Reawakening / Sunshine / Child / Summer song (in the Autumn) / Viking / Birds / I once wrote some poems
CD _____ CASCD 1037
Charisma / Oct '88 / EMI.

FUTURE NOW, THE
Pushing thirty / Second hand / Trappings / Mousetrap (caught in) / Energy vampires / If I could / Future now / Still in the dark / Mediaevil / Motor-bike in Afrika / Cut / Palinurus (castaway)
CD _____ CASCD 1137
Charisma / Nov '88 / EMI.

IN CAMERA
Ferret and featherbed / (No more) the submariner / Tapeworm / Again / Faint heart and the sermon / Comet, the course, the tail / Gog magog (in bromine chambers)
CD _____ CASCD 1089
Charisma / Nov '88 / EMI.

LOOPS & REELS
Ritual speak / Critical mass / Moebius loop / Endless breath / In slow time / My pulse / Bells, The Bells
CD _____ FIE 9105
Fie / Nov '93 / Vital.

LOVE SONGS: PETER HAMMILL
Just good friends / My favourite / Been alone so long / Ophelia / Again / If I could / Vision / Don't tell me / Birds / (This side of) the looking glass
CD _____ CASCD 1166
Charisma / Nov '88 / EMI.

MARGIN, THE (LIVE)
Future now / Porton down / Stranger still / Sign / Jargon king / Empress's clothes / Sphinx in the face / Labour of love / Sitting targets / Patient / Flight
CD _____ CDOVD 345
Virgin / Jun '91 / EMI.

NADIR'S BIG CHANCE
Nadir's big chance / Institute of mental health / Open your eyes / Nobody's business / Been alone so long / Pompeii / Shingle / Airport / People you were going to / Birthday special / Two or three spectres / Burning
CD _____ CASCD 1099
Charisma / Nov '88 / EMI.

NOISE, THE
Kick to kill the kiss / Like a shot, The entertainer / Noise / Celebrity kissing / Where the mouth is / Great european department store / Planet coventry / Primo on the parapet
CD _____ FIE 9104
Fie / Mar '93 / Vital.

OFFENSICHTLICH GOLDFISCH
Offensichtlich goldfisch / Dich zu finden / Die Kafte kilt den kuss / Favorit / Kaufhaus Europa / Der larm / Oase / Die prominenz kusst sich / Die tinte verlischt / Auto / Gaia / Schlaft nun
CD _____ GH 112012
Golden Hind / Jan '95 / Voice Print.

OVER
Crying wolf / Autumn / Time heals / Alice (letting go) / This side of the looking glass / Betrayed / (On Tuesdays she used to do) Yoga / Lost and found
CD _____ CASCD 1125
Charisma / Jun '91 / EMI.

PATIENCE
Labour of love / Film noir / Just good friends / Juenesse Doree / Traintime / Now more than ever / Comfortable / Patient
CD _____ FIE 9102
Fie / Apr '92 / Vital.

PEEL SESSIONS
CD _____ SFRCD 136
Strange Fruit / Nov '95 / Pinnacle.

PH7
My favourite / Careering / Porton down / Mirror images / Handicap / Equality / Not for Keith / Old school tie / Time for a change / Imperial walls / Mr. X gets tense / Faculty X
CD _____ CASCD 1146
Charisma / Apr '89 / EMI.

ROARING FORTIES
Sharply unclear / Gift of fire / You can't want what you always get / Headlong stretch / Tour ball ship
CD _____ FIE 9107
Fie / Sep '94 / Vital.

ROOM TEMPERATURE LIVE
Wave / Just good friends / Vision / Time to burn / Four pails / Comet, the course, the tail / Ophelia / Happy hour / If I could / Something about Ysabel's dance / Patient / Cat's eye, yellow fever (running) / Running / Skin / Hemlock / Our oyster / Unconscious

life / After the snow / Way out / Future now / Traintime / Modern
CD _____ FIE 9110
Fie / Jun '95 / Vital.

SILENT CORNER AND THE EMPTY STAGE, THE
Modern / Wilhelmina / Lie (Bernini's Saint Theresa) / Forsaken gardens / Red shift / Rubicon / Louse is not a home
CD _____ CACSD 1083
Charisma / Nov '88 / EMI.

SITTING TARGETS
Breakthrough / My experience / Ophelia / Empress's clothes / Glue / Hesitation / Sitting targets / Stranger still / Sign / What I did for love / Central hotel
CD _____ CDV 2203
Virgin / Oct '88 / EMI.

SKIN
Skin / After the show / Painting by numbers / Shill / All said and done / Perfect date / Four pails / Now lover
CD _____ CDOVD 344
Virgin / '89 / EMI.

SPUR OF THE MOMENT (Hammill, Peter & Guy Evans)
Sweating it out / Surprise / Little did he know / Without a glitch / Anatol's proposal / Multiman / Deprogramming Archie / Always so polite / Imagined brother / Bounced / Roger and out
CD _____ CDR 102
Red Hot / Mar '94 / THE.

STORM (BEFORE THE CALM), THE
Nadir's big chance / Golden promises / Perfect date / Spirit / Sitting targets / Tapeworm / Nobody's business / Crying wolf / You hit me where I live / My experience / Breakthrough / Skin / Energy vampires / Porton down / Birthday special / Lost and found / Central hotel
CD _____ CDVM 9018
Virgin / Jul '93 / EMI.

THERE GOES THE DAYLIGHT
Sci finance (revisited) / Habit of a broken heart / Sign / I will find you / Lost and found / Planet Coventry / Empress's clothes / Cat's eye, yellow fever (running) / Primo on the parapet / Central hotel
CD _____ FIE 9106
Fie / Nov '93 / Vital.

Hammond, Albert

GREATEST HITS
Free electric band / Peacemaker / Down by the river / When I need you / Rebecca / 99 Miles from LA / It never rains in southern California / Everything I want to do / We're running out / If you gotta break another heart / Moonlight lady / These are the good old days / I'm a train / New York city here I come / Half a million miles from home / Air that I breathe
CD _____ 4631852
Columbia / Oct '95 / Sony.

VERY BEST OF ALBERT HAMMOND, THE
Free electric band / Peacemaker / Down by the river / When I need you / Rebecca / Ninety nine miles from L.A. / It never rains in Southern California / Everything I want to do / We're running out / If you gotta break another heart / Moonlight lady / These are the good olddays / I'm a train / New York City here I come / Half a million miles from home / Air that I breathe
CD _____ 902292-2
Pickwick/Sony Collector's Choice / Apr '94 / Carlton Home Entertainment / Pinnacle / Sony.

Hammond, Beres

BERES HAMMOND
CD _____ CRCD 1
Charm / '88 / Jetstar.

EXPRESSION
CD _____ CBHB 166
Heartbeat / Jun '95 / Greensleeves / Jetstar / Direct / ADA.

FROM MY HEART WITH LOVE
CD _____ RGCD 026
Rocky One / Mar '94 / Jetstar.

FULL ATTENTION
CD _____ CRCD 17
Charm / Apr '93 / Jetstar.

IN CONTROL
CD _____ 755961656-2
Warner Bros. / Oct '94 / Warner Music.

IRIE AND MELLOW
CD _____ RNCD 2025
Rhino / Aug '93 / Jetstar / Magnum Music Group / THE.

MEET IN JAMAICA (Hammond, Beres & Mikey Zappow)
CD _____ RNCD 2115
Rhino / Jul '95 / Jetstar / Magnum Music Group / THE.

PUTTING UP A RESISTANCE
CD _____ CDTZ 001
Tappa / Aug '93 / Jetstar.

SOUL REGGAE
CD _____ CY 75336
Denon / Aug '93 / Conifer.

Hammond, Doug

SPACES
CD _____ DIW 359
DIW / Jul '92 / Harmonia Mundi / Cadillac.

Hammond, John

FOOTWORK
CD _____ 662219
Vanguard / Jan '94 / Complete/Pinnacle / Discovery.

FROGS FOR SNAKES
You don't love me / Got to find my baby / Step it up and go / Fattenin' frogs for snakes / Gypsy woman / Key to the highway / My baby left me / Louisiana blues / Mellow down easy / Your funeral and my trial / Mellow peaches / Gone so long
CD _____ ROUCD 3060
Rounder / Aug '94 / CM / Direct / ADA / Cadillac.

GOT LOVE IF YOU WANT IT
Got love if you want it / Driftin' blues / Dreamy eyed girl / Mattie Mae / You don't love me / Nadine / No one can forgive me but my baby / You're so fine / No place to go / Preachin' blues
CD _____ VPBCD 7
Pointblank / Mar '92 / EMI.

JOHN HAMMOND
CD _____ VMD 2148
Start / Oct '92 / Koch.

JOHN HAMMOND LIVE
CD _____ CDROU 3074
Rounder / Feb '92 / CM / Direct / ADA / Cadillac.

MILEAGE
My babe / Standing around crying / Riding in the moonlight / Big 45 / Seventh son / Red hot kisses / Help me / It hurts me too / 32-20 blues / You'll miss me / Hot tamales / Diddley daddy
CD _____ ROUCD 3042
Rhiannon / Aug '95 / Vital / Direct / ADA.

NOBODY BUT YOU
Ride till I die / Sail on / Diddley daddy / Memphis town / Lost lover blues / Nobody but you / Papa wants a cookie / If I get lucky / Cuttin' out / Killing me on my feet / Mother in law blues
CD _____ FF 502CD
Flying Fish / May '93 / Roots / CM / Direct / ADA.

SO MANY ROADS
CD _____ VND 79178
Vanguard / Oct '95 / Complete/Pinnacle / Discovery.

TROUBLE NO MORE
Just your fool / Who will be next / I'll change my style / Too tired / That nasty swing / Trouble blues / Love changin' blues / It's too late brother / Wild man on the loose / Homely girl / Baby how long / Fool's paradise
CD _____ VPBCD 15
Pointblank / Jul '93 / EMI.

YOU CAN'T JUDGE A BOOK BY THE COVER
CD _____ VCD 79472
Vanguard / Oct '95 / Complete/Pinnacle / Discovery.

Hamon/Le...

GWERZIOU ET CHANTS DE HAUTE VOIX (Hamon/Le Buhe/Marie/Vassallo)
CD _____ KMRS 211CD
Keltia Musique / Feb '94 / ADA / Direct / Discovery.

Hampel, Gunter

8TH OF JULY 1969, THE
CD _____ BIRTHCD 001
Birth / Oct '93 / Cadillac.

CELESTIAL GLORY
CD _____ BIRTHCD 040
Birth / Oct '93 / Cadillac.

DIALOG
CD _____ BIRTHCD 041
Birth / Oct '93 / Cadillac.

JUBILATION
CD _____ BIRTHCD 038
Birth / Oct '93 / Cadillac.

MUSIC FROM EUROPE
CD _____ ESP 1042-2
ESP / Jan '93 / Jazz Horizons / Jazz Music.

TIME IS NOW
CD _____ BIRTHCD 042
Birth / Oct '93 / Cadillac.

Hampton Callaway, Ann

ANN HAMPTON CALLAWAY
Lush life / Gaze in your eyes / Perfect / I live to love you / My romance / My foolish heart / But beautiful / Like someone I love

/ How deep is the ocean / Here's that rainy day / All the things you are / Time for love / I've got the world on a string / Our love is here to stay / Too late now / I've got just about everything
CD _____ DRGCD 91411
DRG / Aug '92 / New Note.

BRING BACK ROMANCE
Music / How long has this been going on / This might be forever / My one and only / Affair to remember / Bring back romance / You can't rush spring / Out of this world / Quiet thing / There will never be another you / Where does love go / You go to my head / It could happen to you / My shining hour/ I'll be seeing you
CD _____ DRGCD 91417
DRG / Sep '94 / New Note.

Hampton, Lionel

AIR MAIL SPECIAL (Holland, 1983) (Hampton, Lionel Big Band)
West Wind / Mar '93 / Swift / Charly / CM / ADA.
CD _____ WWCD 2401

ANTHOLOGY 1937-44
CD _____ EN 516
Encyclopaedia / Sep '95 / Discovery.

AT MALIBU BEACH
Flying home / Malibu swing / Autumn / Stellar P.M. / Breathless vibes / Short of breath
CD _____ JASMCD 2535
Jasmine / Jul '95 / Wellard / Swift / Conifer / Cadillac / Magnum Music Group.

AT NEWPORT '78 (Hampton, Lionel All Stars)
Stompin' at the Savoy / Hamp's the champ / Flying home / On the sunny side of the street / Carnegie hall blues
CD _____ CDSJP 142
Timeless Jazz / Jun '89 / New Note.

BEULAH'S SISTER (1942-49) (Hampton, Lionel Big Band)
Jazz Portraits / May '95 / Jazz Music.
CD _____ CD 14565

COMPLETE LIONEL HAMPTON (Volume 1 & 2)
Rhythm rhythm / Chinatown, my Chinatown / I know that you know / Confessin' / Drum stomp / Piano stomp / I surrender dear / Object of my affection / Ring dem bells / Don't be that way / I'm in the mood for swing / Shoe shiner's drag / Anytime at all / Muskrat ramble / Down home jump / Rock hill special / Fiddle diddle / My last affair / Jivin' the vibes / Mood that I'm in / Hampton stomp / Buzzin' round with the bees / Whoa babe / Stompology / On the sunny side of the street / Judy / Baby wont you please come home / Everybody loves my baby / After you've gone / I just couldn't take it baby / You're my ideal / Sun will shine tonight
CD Set _____ 7432115525-2
Jazz Tribune / May '94 / BMG.

EARLY HAMP
Ramble / Moonlight blues / Charlie's idea / Over night blues / Quality shout / Stuff / Harlem / Cuttin' up / New kinda blues / California swing / Burmah girl / Gettin' ready blues / To you, sweetheart / Alboa / On a cocoanut island / You came to my rescue / Here's love in your eyes / You turned the tables on me / Sing baby sing / Sunday / California here I come
CD _____ CDAFS 1011
Affinity / Oct '93 / Charly / Cadillac / Jazz Music.

FLYING HOME
Hammo's jive / On the sunny side of the street / Summertime / Blue boy / Swanee River / Flying home / Stardust / How high the moon / I only have eyes for you / Lady be good
CD _____ JW 77027
JWD / Nov '93 / Target/BMG.

FLYING HOME
Hot mallets / Shufflin' at the Hollywood / Central avenue breakdown / Save it pretty Mama / Dinah / Four of five times / Twelfth street rag / Chasin' with chase / Rhythm, rhythm / China stomp / Blue / Pig foot sonata / Three quarter boogie / Bouncing at the Beacon / Aint'cha comin' home / Munson street breakdown / When the lights are low / Shoe shiners drag / Ring dem bells / I've found a new baby / Singin' the blues / Flying home
CD _____ RAJCD 858
Empress / Oct '95 / THE.

FOR THE LOVE OF MUSIC
CD _____ 5305542
Mo Jazz / Oct '95 / PolyGram.

HAMP - THE LEGENDARY DECCA RECORDINGS (2CD Set)
Flying home / Hamp's boogie woogie / Million dollar smile / Red cross / Hamp's blues / Evil gal blues / Stardust / Ribs and hot sauce / Blow top blues / Hey ba-ba-re bop / Rockin' in rhythm, parts 1 and 2 / Limehouse blues / Tempo's blues / Jack the fox boogie / How high the moon / Three minutes in 52nd street / Red top / Mingus fingers / Midnight sun / Chicken shack boogie / Central Avenue breakdown / Drinkin'

wine, spo-dee-o-dee / Moonglow / Hucle-buck / Lavender coffin / Rag mop / I wish I knew / There will never be another you / Pink champagne / Memories of you / Time on my hands / Easy to love / Twentieth century boogie / Dancing on the ceiling
CD Set _____ GRD 2652
American Decca / Feb '96 / BMG / New Note.

HAMP IN HARLEM (Hampton, Lionel & His Jazz Giants)
CD _____ CDSLP 168
Timeless Jazz / Jan '88 / New Note.

HAMP'S BIG BAND (Hampton, Lionel & His Orchestra)
Flying home / Hey ba ba re bop / Hamp's boogie woogie / Kidney stew / Hamp's mambo / Airmail special / Big brass / Red top / Night train / Elaine and Duffy / Cutter's corner / Le chat noir
CD _____ 74321218212
RCA Victor / Nov '94 / BMG.

HAMP'S BLUES
Airmail special / E.G. / Psychedelic Sally / Raunchy Rita / Fum / Ham hock blues / Ring them bells / Lion's den / Here's that rainy day / Killer joe
CD _____ DC 8538
Denon / Apr '98 / Conifer.

HAMP'S BOOGIE WOOGIE
CD _____ CD 56014
Jazz Roots / Aug '94 / Target/BMG.

I'M IN THE MOOD FOR SWING
Buzzin' round with the bees / China stomp / Everybody loves my baby / For swing / Hampton stomp / I can't get started (with you) / I'm in the mood / Jivin' the vibes / Liza / Man I love / Memories of you / My last affair / New kinda blues / Object of my affection / On the sunny side of the street / Rhythm rhythm / Ring dem bells / Running wild / Sing baby sing / Stompology / Sweet Sue, just you / Vibraphone blues / Whoa babe / You turned the tables on me
CD _____ CDAJA 5090
Living Era / Feb '92 / Koch.

IN VIENNA 1954 VOL. 1
CD _____ RST 91423
RST / Oct '92 / Jazz Music / Hot Shot.

JAZZ MASTERS (Hampton, Lionel & Oscar Peterson)
CD _____ 5218532
Verve / Feb '94 / PolyGram.

JAZZ PORTRAITS
Ring dem bells / I know that you know / On the sunny side of the street / Divan / Sheikh of Araby / Shoe shiner's drag / House of morgan / Singin' the blues / Memories of you / Dough re mi / I've found a new baby / Jivin' with Jarvis / Twelfth street rag / After you've gone / Muskrat ramble / High society / It don't mean a thing if it ain't got that swing / Drum stomp
CD _____ CD 14519
Jazz Portraits / May '94 / Jazz Music.

JIVIN' THE VIBES (Hampton, Lionel & His Orchestra)
CD _____ JHR 73537
Jazz Hour / May '93 / Target/BMG / Jazz Music / Cadillac.

JIVIN' THE VIBES
CD _____ LEJAZZCD 1
Le Jazz / May '93 / Charly / Cadillac.

JUMPIN' JIVE ALL STAR GROUP 1937-1939
Jivin' the vibes / Stomp / Rhythm rhythm / Chinatown, my Chinatown / I know that you know / Drum stomp / I surrender / After you've gone / You're my deal / Rock Hill special / High society / Sweethearts on parade / Shufflin' at the Hollywood (take 1) / Wizzin' the wizz / Memories of you / Jum-pin' jive / When lights are low / Haven't named it yet
CD _____ ND 82433
Bluebird / Dec '90 / BMG.

JUST JAZZ - LIVE AT THE BLUE NOTE (Hampton, Lionel & The Golden Men Of Jazz)
CD _____ CD 83313
Telarc / Jan '93 / Conifer / ADA.

LIONEL HAMPTON & HIS ORCHESTRA 1942-44
CD _____ CLASSICS 803
Classics / Mar '95 / Discovery / Jazz Music.

LIONEL HAMPTON & LARS ERSTRAND
CD _____ NCD 8807
Phontastic / Apr '94 / Wellard / Jazz Music / Cadillac.

LIONEL HAMPTON - 1940-41 (Hampton, Lionel & His Orchestra)
CD _____ CLASSICS 624
Classics / '92 / Discovery / Jazz Music.

LIONEL HAMPTON AND FRIENDS
CD _____ JHR 73560
Jazz Hour / Oct '92 / Target/BMG / Jazz Music / Cadillac.

LIONEL HAMPTON AND HIS JAZZ GIANTS (Hampton, Lionel & His Jazz Giants)
CD _____ BLE 591072
Black & Blue / Apr '91 / Wellard / Koch.

LIONEL HAMPTON AND HIS ORCHESTRA (Hampton, Lionel & His Orchestra)
Stompology / Ring dem bells / Shuffin' at the Hollywood / Hot mallets / I just couldn't take it baby / Rhythm rhythm / I can't get started (with you) / I surrender dear / Handful of keys / Make believe / China stomp / 12th Street rag / Ain't cha comin' home / Four of five times / I've found a new baby / Moonglow / Running wild / On the sunny side of the street / Shoe shiner's drag / Jivin' the vibes / Gin for christmas
CD _____ PASTCD 9789
Flapper / May '92 / Pinnacle.

LIONEL HAMPTON AND ORCHESTRA (1911) (Hampton, Lionel & His Orchestra)
CD _____ 90 506 2
Jazz Archives / Aug '91 / Jazz Music / Discovery / Cadillac.

LIONEL HAMPTON BIG BAND, THE (Hampton, Lionel Big Band)
CD Set _____ WW 2404
West Wind / Dec '92 / Swift / Charly / CM / ADA.

LIONEL HAMPTON IN PARIS
CD _____ CDSW 8415
DRG / '88 / New Note.

LIONEL HAMPTON PRESENTS GERRY MULLIGAN (Hampton, Lionel & Gerry Mulligan)
Apple core / Song for Johnny Hodges / Blight of the fumble bee / Gerry meets Hamp / Blues for Gerry / Line for Lyons / Walking shoes / Limelight
CD _____ CDGATE 7014
Kingdom Jazz / Jun '87 / Kingdom.

LIVE AT MUZEVAL (Hampton, Lionel Big Band)
CD _____ CDSJP 120
Timeless Jazz / Mar '90 / New Note.

LIVE AT THE BLUE NOTE (Hampton, Lionel & His Orchestra)
CD _____ CD 83308
Telarc / Oct '91 / Conifer / ADA.

LIVE AT THE METROPOLE CAFE
CD _____ HCD 242
Hindsight / Feb '95 / Target/BMG / Jazz Music.

LIVE IN CANNES
CD _____ JHR 73584
Jazz Hour / Dec '94 / Target/BMG / Jazz Music / Cadillac.

LIVE IN SWEDEN
CD _____ NI 4010
Natasha / Jun '93 / Jazz Music / ADA / CM / Direct / Cadillac.

MADE IN JAPAN
Airmail special / Advent / Stardust / Mess is here / Interpretations, opus 5 / Minor the-sis / Jodo / Valve job
CD _____ CDSJP 175
Timeless Jazz / Mar '91 / New Note.

MASTER OF VIBES
Blues for Oliver / It don't mean a thing if it ain't got that swing / Basin Street blues / Oliver Twist / I hand naught / Bunny side of the street / When the saints go marching in
CD _____ 722006
Scorpio / Sep '92 / Complete/Pinnacle.

MOSTLY BLUES
Bye bye blues / Someday my Prince will come / Take the 'A' train / Blues for jazz beaux / Wailin' uptown / Honeysuckle rose / Mostly blues / Limehouse blues / Gone with the wind
CD _____ 8208052
Limelight / Nov '89 / PolyGram.

MUSKRAT RAMBLE
Muskrat ramble / Fiddle diddle / Shoe shi-ner's drag / Johnny get your horn and blow / Sweethearts on parade / Stand by for further announcements / Ain't cha comin' home / Denison swing / Jumpin' jive / 12th Street rag / Down home jump / Anytime at all / Wizzin' the wiz / If it's good (then I want it) / Shufflin' at the Hollywood / Don't be that way / I'm in the mood for swing / Big wig in the wigwam / I can give you love / It don't mean a thing if it ain't got that swing / High society / Rock hill special / Memories of you
CD _____ CDGRF 090
Tring / '93 / Tring / Prism.

REAL CRAZY
September in the rain / Blue panassie / Al-ways / Free press oui / I only have eyes for you / Walking at the Trocadero / Real crazy / More crazy / More and more crazy
CD _____ 74321134092
Vogue / Jul '93 / BMG.

SENTIMENTAL JOURNEY
CD _____ 756781644-2
Atlantic / Jun '93 / Warner Music.

SMALL COMBOS 1937-1940
CD _____ CD 56058
Jazz Roots / Mar '95 / Target/BMG.

SMALL COMBOS 1937-40 (Hampton, Lionel & Friends)
CD _____ GOJCD 53050
Giants Of Jazz / Mar '92 / Target/BMG / Cadillac.

SONNY LESTER COLLECTION
CD _____ CDC 9068
LRC / Nov '93 / New Note / Harmonia Mundi.

TEMPO AND SWING
Munson Street breakdown / I've found a new baby / I can't get started (with you) / Four or five times / Gin for Christmas / Di-nah (Takes 1 & 2) / My buddy / Swingin' the blues / Shades of jade / Till Tom special / Flying home / Save it pretty Mama / Tempo and swing / House of Morgan / I'd be lost without you / Central Avenue breakdown / Jack the bellboy / Dough re mi / Jivin' with Jarvis / Blue because of you / Martin on every block / Pig foot sonata
CD _____ 74321101612
Bluebird / Jul '92 / BMG.

TRIBUTE TO LOUIS ARMSTRONG
Cabaret / Hello Dolly / Do you know what it means to miss New Orleans / Someday you'll be sorry / Mack the knife / Louis dream / Black and blue / Jeepers creepers / Short ribs / Sleepy time down South / Saturday night function and Indiana
CD _____ JWD 102215
JWD / Apr '95 / Target/BMG.

VIBES BOOGIE (Live 1955)
CD _____ CDJJ 605
Jazz & Jazz / Jul '89 / Target/BMG.

VINTAGE HAMPTON
Telarc / Jan '94 / Conifer / ADA.
CD _____ CD 83321

Hampton, Slide

DEDICATED TO DIZ (Hampton, Slide & The Jazz Masters)
CD _____ CD 83323
Telarc / Jun '93 / Conifer / ADA.

MELLOW-DY
CD _____ CDC 9053
LRC / Nov '92 / New Note / Harmonia Mundi.

WORLD OF TROMBONES
CD _____ BLCD 760113
Black Lion / Oct '90 / Jazz Music / Cadillac / Wellard / Koch.

Hamsters

HAMSTER JAM
CD _____ HAMSTERCD 7
Hamsters / Jul '93 / Pinnacle.

HAMSTERS
CD _____ HAMSTERCD 8
Hamsters / Jul '93 / Pinnacle.

PURPLE HAZE
CD _____ 12372
Laserlight / Aug '94 / Target/BMG.

ROUTE 666
CD _____ HAMSTERCD 9
Hamsters / Feb '95 / Pinnacle.

Hancock, Butch

EATS AWAY THE NIGHT
CD _____ GRCD 341
Glitterhouse / Sep '94 / Direct / ADA.

JUNKYARD IN THE SUN
CD _____ GR 341
Glitterhouse / Oct '94 / Direct / ADA.

ON THE WAY OVER HERE
Talkin' about this Panama Canal / Only born / Smokin' in the rain / Corona del mar / Like the light at dawn / Gift horse of mercy / Neon wind / Perfection in the mud / Only makes me love you more / Already gone / Away from the mountain
CD _____ SH 1038CD
Sugarhill / May '93 / Roots / CM / ADA / Direct.

OWN & OWN
CD _____ GRCD 364
Glitterhouse / Apr '95 / Direct / ADA.

OWN AND OWN
Dry land farm / Wind's dominion / Diamond hill / 1981 - A spare odyssey / Fire water / West Texas waltz / Horseflies / If you were a bluebird / Own and own / Leo and Leona (Not on CD) / Fools in love / Split and slide (Not on CD) / Yellow rose / Like a kiss on the mouth / Ghost of Give and Take Av-enue / Tell me what you want to know / Just a storm / Just tell me that / When will you hold me again
CD _____ FIENDCD 150
Demon / Oct '89 / Pinnacle / ADA.

Hancock, Herbie

BEST OF HERBIE HANCOCK - THE BLUE NOTE YEARS
Watermelon man / Driftin' (CD only.) / Maiden voyage / Dolphin dance / One finger

snap / Cantaloupe island / Riot / Speak like a child / King cobra (CD only.)
CD _____ BNZ 143
Blue Note / Dec '88 / EMI.

CANTALOUPE ISLAND
Cantaloupe island / Watermelon man / Drif-tin' / Blind man / What it I don't / Maiden voyage
CD _____ CDP 8293312
Blue Note / Jul '94 / EMI.

COMPLETE WARNER RECORDINGS, THE
CD _____ 2457322
Warner Bros. / Feb '95 / Warner Music.

DIS IS DA DRUM
CD _____ 5281852
Mercury / Jun '95 / PolyGram.

EVENING WITH HERBIE HANCOCK AND CHICK COREA, AN (2CD Set) (Hancock, Herbie & Chick Corea)
Someday my Prince will come / Liza / But-ton up / February moments / Maiden voy-age / La fiesta
CD Set _____ 477296 2
Columbia / Nov '94 / Sony.

FUTURE SHOCK
Rockit / Future shock / TFS / Earthbeat / Autodrive / Rough
CD _____ 4712372
Sony Jazz / Jan '95 / Sony.

HEADHUNTERS
Chameleon / Watermelon man / Sly / Vein melter
CD _____ 4712392
Sony Jazz / Jan '95 / Sony.

JAZZ COLLECTION, A
Liza / I fall in love too easily / Nefertiti / Someday my Prince will come / Round Mid-night / Well you needn't / Parade / Eye of the hurricane / Maiden voyage
CD _____ 4679012
Columbia / Nov '93 / Sony.

MAIDEN VOYAGE
Maiden voyage / Eye of the hurricane / Little one / Survival of the fittest / Dolphin dance
CD _____ CDP 7463392
Blue Note / Mar '95 / EMI.

MANCHILD
CD _____ 4712352
Sony Jazz / Jan '95 / Sony.

MR. HANDS
Spiralling prism / Calypso / Just around the corner / 4 a.m. / Shifless shuffle / Textures
CD _____ 4712402
Sony Jazz / Jan '95 / Sony.

MWANDISHI
Ostinato (suite for Angela) / You'll know when you get there / Wandering spirit song
CD _____ 9362457322
Warner Bros. / Dec '94 / Warner Music.

QUARTET with WYNTON MARSALIS
Well you needn't / Round Midnight / Clear ways / Quick sketch / Eye of the hurricane / Parade / Sorcerer / Pee wee / I fall in love too easily
CD _____ 465626 2
Columbia / Nov '93 / Sony.

TAKIN' OFF/INVENTIONS AND DIMENSIONS/EMPRYEAN ISLES (3 CDs)
Watermelon man / Three bags full / Empty pockets / Maze / Driftin' / Alone & I / Suc-cotash / Triangle / Jack rabbit / Mimosa / Jump ahead / One finger snap / Oliloqui valley / Cantaloupe Island / Egg
CD Set _____ CDOMB 009
Blue Note / Oct '95 / EMI.

Hancock, Keith

COMPASSION
CD _____ HY 200133CD
Hypertension / Feb '95 / Total/BMG / Direct / ADA.

MADHOUSE
CD _____ HY 200107CD
Hypertension / Feb '95 / Total/BMG / Direct / ADA.

Hancock, Wayne

THUNDERSTORMS AND NEON LIGHTS
Dejadisc / Nov '95 / Direct / ADA.
CD _____ DJD 3221

Hand, Frederic

HEART'S SONG
CD _____ MM 5018
Music Masters / Oct '94 / Nimbus.

Handraizer UK

IN THE MIX WITH TALL PAUL
CD _____ MM 800102
Moonshine / Oct '94 / Disc.

Handsome Family

ODESSA
CD _____ SR1 004
Scout / Jan '96 / Koch.

Handy, John

CAPT. JOHN HANDY & EASY RIDERS JAZZBAND (Handy, Captain John)
CD _____ BCD 325
GHB / Apr '94 / Jazz Music.

CAPT. JOHN HANDY & HIS NEW ORLEANS STOMPERS VOL.1 (Handy, Captain John)
CD _____ BCD 41
GHB / Aug '94 / Jazz Music.

CAPT. JOHN HANDY & HIS NEW ORLEANS STOMPERS VOL.2 (Handy, Captain John & His New Orleans Stompers)
CD _____ BCD 42
GHB / Aug '94 / Jazz Music.

VERY FIRST RECORDINGS (Handy, Captain John)
CD _____ AMCD 51
American Music / Apr '94 / Jazz Music.

Handy, John

CENTERPIECE
CD _____ MCD 9173
Milestone / Jan '95 / Jazz Music / Pinnacle / Wellard / Cadillac.

HANDY DANDY MAN
CD _____ INAK 8618
In Akustik / Jun '95 / Magnum Music Group.

WHERE GO THE BOATS (Handy, John & Lee Ritenour)
CD _____ INAK 861 CD
In Akustik / '88 / Magnum Music Group.

Handy, W.C.

FATHER OF THE BLUES
CD _____ CD 14581
Complete / Nov '95 / THE.

Hangal, Gangubai

VOICE OF TRADITION, THE
CD _____ SM 15012
Wergo / Jan '91 / Harmonia Mundi / ADA / Cadillac.

Hanly, Mick

CONCERT HALL
Happy like this / Nobody told me / I feel I should be calling on you / Geronimo's child / One more from the Daddy / Fagan place / These days / Blessed / No mercy / Medicine man / Piano tuner / Writing on the wall / I could have missed her by a whisker
CD _____ RTMCD 61
Round Tower / Feb '92 / Pinnacle / ADA / Direct / BMG / CM.

HAPPY LIKE THIS
CD _____ RTM 61CD
Round Tower / Jan '94 / Pinnacle / ADA / Direct / BMG / CM.

WARTS AND ALL
Nothing in the can / What's his name / Don't try to cushion the blow / Fabulous thunderbirds / On vocals and guitar / Wherever you go / Joan / Warts and all / Let's not fight / Words and the bottle / Uncle John / Art and reality / My body and me / Happy to be here
CD _____ RTMCD 32
Round Tower / Sep '91 / Pinnacle / ADA / Direct / BMG / CM.

Hanna, Roland

DUKE ELLINGTON PIANO SOLOS
In my solitude / Something to live for / In a sentimental mood / Portrait of Bert Williams / Warm valley / Isfahan / Single petal of a rose / I got it bad and that ain't good / Reflections in D / Come Sunday / Caravan
CD _____ MM 5045
Music Masters / Oct '94 / Nimbus.

GLOVE
CD _____ STCD 4148
Storyville / Feb '90 / Jazz Music / Wellard / CM / Cadillac.

LIVE AT MAYBECK RECITAL HALL, VOL. 12
Love walked in / They can't take that away from me / Softly as in a morning sunrise / Gershwin medley: Fascinating rhythm/Man I love / Let's call the whole thing off / How long has this been going on / Oleo / Lush life / This can't be love
CD _____ CCD 4604
Concord Jazz / Jul '94 / New Note.

PERUGIA
Take the 'A' train / I got it bad and that ain't good / Time dust gathered / Perugia / Child is born / Wistful moment
CD _____ FCD 41010
Freedom / Sep '87 / Jazz Music / Swift / Wellard / Cadillac.

REMEMBERING CHARLIE PARKER
CD _____ PCD 7031
Progressive / Oct '91 / Jazz Music.

THIS TIME IT'S REAL
CD _____ STCD 4145
Storyville / Feb '90 / Jazz Music / Wellard / CM / Cadillac.

Hannah, Marcus

WEEDS AND LILIES
CD _____ RTS 10
Return To Sender / Nov '94 / Direct / ADA.

Hannan, Robert

TRADITIONAL IRISH MUSIC PLAYED ON UILLEANN PIPES
Flood on the Holm/Miss Monahan reel / Amhran an Tae / Liz King's jig / Stay another while/College groves / Derry hornpipe / Do you want anymore/Gallowglass / Rainy day/Shaskeen / Dark woman of the Glen / Boys of Tanderagee / Jackson's morning brush / Jenny picking cockles/My love is in America / Darby Gallagher's/An Buachaillin bui / Salamanca/Jenny's welcome to Charlie / Dark Lochnagar / Rambles of Kitty/When sick is it tea you want / Curragh races/Trim the velvet / Chief O'Neill/Plains of Boyle / Pipe on the hob / Merry Blacksmith/Bonnie Kate/Gorman's reel
CD _____ CC 53CD
Claddagh / Jan '91 / ADA / Direct.

Hanoi Rocks

BACK TO MYSTERY CITY
Strange boys play weird openings / Mental beat / Until I get you / Lick summer lover / Ice cream summer / Malibu beach nightmare / Tooting Bec wreck / Sailing down the years / Beating gets faster / Back to Mystery City
CD _____ ESMCD 272
Essential / Mar '95 / Total/BMG.

BANGKOK SHOCKS SAIGON SHAKES
CD _____ ESMCD 273
Essential / Mar '95 / Total/BMG.

LEAN ON ME
CD _____ ESMCD 282
Essential / Apr '95 / Total/BMG.

ORIENTAL BEAT
CD _____ ESMCD 274
Essential / Mar '95 / Total/BMG.

SELF DESTRUCTION BLUES
CD _____ ESMCD 271
Essential / Mar '95 / Total/BMG.

Hanrahan, Kip

ALL ROADS ARE MADE OF THE FLESH
CD _____ AMCL 10292
American Clave / Aug '95 / New Note / ADA / Direct.

ANTHOLOGY
CD _____ AMCL 10202
American Clave / Nov '93 / New Note / ADA / Direct.

DAYS AND NIGHTS OF BLUE LUCK INVERTED
Love is like a cigarette / Poker game / Luck inverts itself / Four swimmers / Gender / Marriage / American clave / Model Bronx childhood / Ah intruder (female) / Lisbon: blue request / My life outside of power / Road song / First and last to love me / Unobtainable days; unobtainable nights
CD _____ AMCL 10122
American Clave / Nov '90 / New Note / ADA / Direct.

DESIRE DEVELOPS AN EDGE
CD _____ AMCL 1009/8
American Clave / Aug '94 / New Note / ADA / Direct.

Hanrahan, Mike

MIKE HANRAHAN
CD _____ TUT 168
Wundertule / Oct '94 / CM / Duncans / ADA.

Hanselmann, David

LET THE MUSIC CARRY ON
CD _____ 845158
FM / May '91 / Sony.

Hansen, Ole Kock

PA EN GREN BAKKETOP
CD _____ MECCACD 1002
Music Mecca / Nov '94 / Jazz Music / Cadillac / Wellard.

Hansen, Randy

TRIBUTE TO JIMI HENDRIX
CD _____ 1890692
Trident / Nov '92 / Pinnacle.

Hanshaw, Annette

TWENTIES SWEETHEART, THE
Black bottom / Six feet of Papa / Don't take that bottom away / Here or there / I gotta get somebody to love / Wistful and blue / What do I care / Nuthin' / I'm somebody's somebody now / I like what you like / Ain't

---

that a grand and glorious feeling / Who-oo you-oo, that's who / Under the moon / It was only a sun shower / Who's that knocking at my door / We love it / Get out and get under the moon / There must be somebody else / Mine all mine / Thinking of you / Song is ended (but the melody lingers on)
CD _____ JASMCD 2542
Jasmine / May '95 / Wellard / Swift / Conifer / Cadillac / Magnum Music Group.

Hanson Brothers

GROSS MISCONDUCT
CD _____ VIRUS 116CD
Alternative Tentacles / Nov '92 / Pinnacle.

Hansson, Bo

ATTIC THOUGHTS
CD _____ SRS 3625CD
Silence / Jul '95 / ADA.

LORD OF THE RINGS
Leaving shire / Old forest / Tom Bombardil / Fog on the barrow / Downs / Black riders / Flight to the ford / At the house of Elrond / Ring goes South / Journey in the dark / Lothlorien / Horns of Rohan / Shadowfax / Battle of the Pelennor Fields / Dreams in the house of healing / Homeward bound / Scouring of the Shire / Grey havens
CD _____ RESCD 508
Resource / Oct '93 / ADA.

MAGICIAN'S HAT
City / Divided reality / Elidor / Fylke / Before the rain / Findhorn's song / Playing downhill into the downs / Awakening / Wandering song / Sun (Parallel or 90 degrees) / Excursion with complications
CD _____ RESCD 509
Resource / Oct '93 / ADA.

Happenings

BEST OF THE HAPPENINGS, THE
CD _____ NEMCD 690
Sequel / Aug '94 / BMG.

Happy Family

MAN ON YOUR STREET
CD _____ CAD 214CD
4AD / Nov '92 / Disc.

Happy Flowers

OOF
CD _____ HMS 136 2
Homestead / May '89 / SRD.

Happy Larry

MUSIC BY NUMBERS (Happy Larry's Big Beat Orchestra)
CD Set _____ 0090602DDX
Edel / Jun '95 / Pinnacle.

Happy Mondays

LOADS
Step on / WFL / Kinky Afro / Hallelujah / Mad Cyril / Lazyitis / Tokoloshe man / Loose fit / Bob's yer uncle / Judge Fudge / Stinkin' thinkin' / Sunshine and love / Angel / Tart tart / Kuff dam / 24 hour party people
CD _____ 5200362
London / Jul '95 / PolyGram.

UP ALL NIGHT
CD P.Disc _____ CBAK 4046
Baktabak / Apr '91 / Baktabak.

Har-El

PAGAN MOON CHILD
CD _____ EFA 009512
Nephilim / Aug '95 / SRD.

Haran, Mary Cleere

FUNNY WORLD (Mary Cleere Hart Sings Lyrics By Hart)
CD _____ VSD 5584
Varese Sarabande/Colosseum / Jul '95 / Pinnacle / Silva Screen.

Harbour Kings

SUMMERCOLTS
Tattoo / Grassfires / Roads to freedom / Forsyth C / Rosemary Road / Sleepers / Searchlight / Flood dream
CD _____ FIRE 33025
Fire / Oct '91 / Disc.

Hard Skin

HARD SKIN
CD _____ HSPCD 2000
Almanac / Jan '94 / Jetstar.

Hard-Ons

YUMMY
CD _____ SOL 26CD
Vinyl Solution / Feb '91 / Disc.

Hardcastle, Paul

HARDCASTLE
Can't stop now / Driftin' away / Forever dreamin' / Never let you go / You may be

---

gone / Feel the breeze / Only one / Lazy days / Do it again / Don't be shy / Cruisin' to midnight / It must be love / Rainforest / Nineteen ('95 jazzman melody)
CD _____ TOCO 37CD
Total Control / Sep '95 / Pinnacle.

Hardelin

UNION (Hardelin, Thore & Oline)
CD _____ CCD 10005CD
Musikk Distribujon / Apr '95 / ADA.

Harden, Wilbur

JAZZ WAY OUT
Dial Africa / Oomba / Gold coast
CD _____ SV 0122
Savoy Jazz / Apr '93 / Conifer / ADA.

KING AND I, THE (Harden, Wilbur & Tommy Flanagan)
Getting to know you / My Lord and Master / Shall we dance / We kiss in a shadow / I have dreamed / I whistle a happy tune / Hello, young lovers / Something wonderful
CD _____ SV 0124
Savoy Jazz / Apr '93 / Conifer / ADA.

MAINSTREAM 1958 (The East Coast Jazz Scene) (Harden, Wilbur & John Coltrane)
Wells Fargo / West 42nd Street / E.F.F.P.H. / Snuffy / Rhodomagnetics
CD _____ SV 0121
Savoy Jazz / Apr '92 / Conifer / ADA.

TANGANYIKA STRUT (Harden, Wilbur & John Coltrane)
Tanganyika strut / B.J. / Anedac / Once in a while
CD _____ SV 0125
Savoy Jazz / Apr '93 / Conifer / ADA.

Hardfloor

RESPECT
CD _____ HHCD 10
Harthouse / Dec '94 / Disc / Warner Music.

TB RESUSCITATION
CD _____ HARTUKCD 1
Harthouse / Jun '93 / Disc / Warner Music.

Hardie, Alastair

COMPLIMENTS TO THE KING
CD _____ HPMCD 002
Hardie Press / Jan '95 / ADA.

Hardie, Ian

BREATH OF FRESHER AIRS, A
Mrs. Elspeth Hardie / Goat in the boat / Fiona's jig / New 19th / Mellerstain House / Knock of Braemordy / Andrew James Hardie / Cawdor wood / Palpitation reel / Mrs. Willie Wastle / Compose yourself waltz / Segs hornpipe / Macbeaths of Tulloch Castle / Invernairn two-step / Lochindorb / Lochdhu waltz / Grand slam / Horsbrugh Castle / Vivianae / Helsinki Harbour / Lethen bar / White in the heather / Suitor's waltz / Bonnie lass o wark / Lights of balintore / Liathach / Duisie bridge / Locked bucket / Shifting sands / Esther Stephenson of Embleton / Chatterin' teeth / Nigg rigs jig / Oystercatcher / Drumochter sun / Crown knot / Snow on the ben / Up an' doon reel / Lost village of Culbin / Tarbat ness light / Drummossie muir
CD _____ CDTRAX 049
Greentrax / Jan '92 / Conifer / Duncans / ADA / Direct.

Hardie, Jonny

UP IN THE AIR (Hardie, Jonny & Gavin Marwick)
CD _____ LDLCD 1226
Lochshore / Jan '95 / ADA / Direct / Duncans.

Hardiman, Ronan

WATERWAYS
CD _____ HB 005
Hummingbird / Oct '94 / ADA / Direct.

Hardin & York

LIVE AT THE MARQUEE VOL.3
CD _____ RPM 135
RPM / Aug '94 / Pinnacle.

STILL A FEW PAGES LEFT
CD _____ CSA 106
Thunderbird / Oct '95 / Pinnacle.

Hardin, Eddie

DAWN TIL DUSK
CD _____ NAGE 9 CD
Art Of Landscape / Jul '86 / Sony.

SURVIVAL
Innocent victims / Lost childhood / Seeds of suspicion / Schools of thought / Perfect survivor / Lessons to learn / Where do we go from here / Slice of paradise / Never again / Rules we can't ignore
CD _____ NAGE 19CD
Art Of Landscape / Sep '88 / Sony.

Hardin, Tim

NINE
Shiloh town / Rags and old iron / Person to person / Blues on my ceiling / Fire and rain / Judge and jury / Never too far / Look our love over / Darling girl / Is there no rest for the weary / While you're on your way
CD _____ SEECD 335
See For Miles/C5 / Feb '92 / Pinnacle.

TIM HARDIN 1
CD _____ LMCD 951113
Line / Sep '92 / CM / Grapevine / ADA / Conifer / Direct.

TIM HARDIN 2
CD _____ LMCD 951069
Line / Sep '92 / CM / Grapevine / ADA / Conifer / Direct.

TIM HARDIN 3
CD _____ LMCD 951073
Line / Sep '92 / CM / Grapevine / ADA / Conifer / Direct.

TIM HARDIN 4
CD _____ LMCD 951091
Line / Sep '92 / CM / Grapevine / ADA / Conifer / Direct.

TOMORROW TODAY
CD _____ RPMCD 128
RPM / May '94 / Pinnacle.

WORLD'S SMALLEST BIG BAND
CD _____ RPMCD 129
RPM / May '94 / Pinnacle.

Harding, John Wesley

IT HAPPENED ONE NIGHT
Headful of something / Devil in me / Who you really are / Famous man / July 13th 1985 / One night only / Affairs of the heart / Humankind / Night he took her to the fairground / Careers service / Biggest monument / Roy Orbison knows (the best man's song) / You and your career / Bastard son
CD _____ LFIENDCD 137
Demon / Dec '88 / Pinnacle / ADA.

WHY WE FIGHT
Kill the messenger / Ordinary weekend / Truth / Dead centre of town / Into the wind / Hitler's tears / Get back down / Me against me / Original Miss Jesus / Where the bodies are / Millionaire's dream / Come gather round
CD _____ 936245032-2
WEA / Apr '93 / Warner Music.

Harding, Mike

CLASSIC TRACKS VOL.1
Cubs camp / Arnold my frog (Pamela Dolmen's song) / Fourteen and a half pound budgie / Captain Legless meets superdrunk / Ghost of the cafe Gungha Din / Beaky knucklewart / Talkin' Blackpool blues
CD _____ MOOCD 13
Moonraker / Mar '94 / ADA.

PLUTONIUM ALLEY
CD _____ MOOCD 9
Moonraker / Mar '94 / ADA.

Hardkiss

DELUSIONS OF GRANDEUR
Out of body experience / 3 Nudes in a purple garden / Raincry / Pacific coastal highway / Daylight / Phoenix / Someday my plane will crash
CD _____ 5283862
L'Attitude / Aug '95 / PolyGram / Vital.

Hardship Post

SOMEBODY SPOKE
CD _____ SPCD 289
Sub Pop / Jul '95 / Disc.

Hardvark

MEMORY BARGE
CD _____ ENDLOD 10001
Endangered / Jul '95 / Pinnacle.

Hardware

THIRD EYE OPEN
Got a feeling / Waiting on you / What's goin' down / Love obsession / Hard look / Shake it / Walls came down / 500 Years / Tell me / Leakin'
CD _____ RCD 10304
Black Arc / Jun '94 / Vital.

Hardy, Francoise

COLLECTION, THE
Tous les garcons les filles / Oh oh cheri / Ton meilleur ami / J'suis d'accord / Va pas prendre un tambour / Le temps de l'amour / Je n'attend plus personne / Ce petit coeur / Je veux qu'il revienne / Le temps des souvenirs / Je changerais d'avis (se telefonado) / Il est des choses / Comme / Je ne suis la pour presonne / Ma jeunesse fout le camp / Il n'ya pas d'amour hereux
CD _____ 74321145202
Vogue / Apr '94 / BMG.

GREATEST RECORDINGS
Tous le garcons et les filles / Le temps de l'amour / Le premier bonheur du jour / Mon amie la rose / All over the world / L'amitie / Ce petit coeur / Je ne suis la pour personne / Il est des chose / La maison ou j'ai grand / Comme / Voila
CD _____ 74321203912
Vogue / May '95 / BMG.

IN VOGUE VOL. 2
CD _____ VGCD 600145
Vogue / Oct '93 / BMG.

TOUS LES GARCONS ET LES FILLES
CD _____ CD 352060
Duchesse / May '93 / Pinnacle.

YEH-YEH GIRL FROM PARIS
Tous les garcons et les filles / Ca a rate / La fille avec toi / Oh oh mon coeur / Le temps de l'amour / Il est tout pour moi / On se plait / Ton meilleur ami / J'suis d'accord / C'est a la amour auquel je pense
CD _____ 74321264702
Vogue / May '94 / BMG.

Hardy, Hagood

MOROCCO (Hardy, Hagood Sextet)
CD _____ SCD 2-2018
Sackville / Jun '93 / Swift / Jazz Music / Jazz Horizons / Cadillac / CM.

Hardy, Jack

RETROSPECTIVE
CD _____ BRAM 198907-2
Brambus / Nov '93 / ADA / Direct.

THROUGH
CD _____ BRAM 199012-2
Brambus / Nov '93 / ADA / Direct.

TWO OF SWORDS
CD _____ 422166
New Rose / May '94 / Direct / ADA.

Hare, Colin

MARCH HARE...PLUS
Get up the road / Bloodshot eyes / For where have you been / Fine me / Underground girl / To my maker / Grannie, grannie / Alice / Nothing to write home about / New day / Cowboy Joe (saga) / Just like me / Charlie Brown's time / Fighting for peace
CD _____ SEECD 261
See For Miles/C5 / Sep '89 / Pinnacle

Harem Scarem

LOW AND BEHOLD
CD _____ CGAS 805CD
Citadel / Apr '89 / ADA.

Harewood, Dorian

LOVE WILL STOP CALLING
CD _____ CDER 1001
Ichiban / Nov '88 / Koch.

Hargrove, Roy

APPROACHING STANDARDS
Easy to remember / Ruby my dear / Whisper not / What's new / September in the rain / You don't know what love is / End of a love affair / Things we did last summer / Everything I have is yours / Dedicated to you / My shining hour
CD _____ 01241081709
Novus / Sep '94 / BMG.

DIAMOND IN THE ROUGH
Proclamation / Ruby my dear / New joy / Confidentially / Broski / All over again / Easy to remember / Premonition / BHG / Wee
CD _____ PD 90471
Novus / Jun '90 / BMG.

OF KINDRED SOULS
CD _____ 01241631542
Novus / Jul '93 / BMG.

PUBLIC EYE
Public eye / Spiritual companion / September in the rain / Lada / Once in awhile / Heartbreaker / End of a love affair / Night watch / You don't know what love is / Little Bennie / What's new (CD only)
CD _____ PD 83113
Novus / Jun '91 / BMG.

TOKYO SESSIONS, THE
Bohemia after dark / I love your spell is everywhere / Work song / I remember Clifford / Straight no chaser / But not for me / Alone together / Lotus blossom / Easy to love
CD _____ 01241631642
Novus / Mar '94 / BMG.

VIBE, THE
Vibe / Caryisms / Where were you / Alter ego / Thang / Pinocchio / Milestones / Things we did last summer / Blues for booty greens / Running out of time
CD _____ PD 90668
Novus / Jun '92 / BMG.

WITH THE TENORS OF OUR TIME
CD _____ 523019-2
Verve / Jun '94 / PolyGram.

Harket, Morten

WILD SEED
CD _____ 9362459122
Warner Bros. / Sep '95 / Warner Music.

Harle, John

SHADOW OF THE DUKE, THE
CD _____ CDC 754 298 2
Blue Note / Sep '90 / EMI.

Harlem Gospel Singers

HARLEM GOSPEL SINGERS
CD _____ 0028702
Edel / Apr '95 / Pinnacle.

Harlem Hamfats

HARLEM HAMFATS 1936 VOL. 1
CD _____ DOCD 5271
Blues Document / Aug '94 / Swift / Jazz Music / Hot Shot.

HARLEM HAMFATS 1936-1937 VOL. 2
CD _____ DOCD 5272
Blues Document / Aug '94 / Swift / Jazz Music / Hot Shot.

HARLEM HAMFATS 1937-1938 VOL. 3
CD _____ DOCD 5273
Blues Document / Aug '94 / Swift / Jazz Music / Hot Shot.

HARLEM HAMFATS 1938-1939 VOL. 4
CD _____ DOCD 5274
Blues Document / Aug '94 / Swift / Jazz Music / Hot Shot.

Harlem Jazz Camels

DROP ME OFF IN HARLEM
CD _____ NCD 8832
Phontastic / Mar '94 / Wellard / Jazz Music / Cadillac.

Harley, Steve

BEST YEARS OF OUR LIVES (Harley, Steve & Cockney Rebel)
Introducing 'The Best Years' / Mad mad moonlight / Mr. Raffles (man it was mean) / It wasn't me / Panorama / Make me smile (come up and see me) / Back to the farm / 49th parallel / Best years of our lives / Another journey / Sebastian
CD _____ CZ 385
EMI / Feb '91 / EMI.

IN CONCERT
Mr. Soft / Mr. Raffles (man it was mean) / When I'm with you / Star for a week / Riding the waves / Lighthouse / Best years of our life / Sweet dreams / Pyschomodo / Sling it / Sebastian / Make me smile (come up and see me) / Love's a prima donna
CD _____ HP 93442
Happy Price / Jan '96 / Target/BMG.

LIVE IN THE UK
CD _____ RLBTC 005
Realisation / Oct '93 / Prism.

MAKE ME SMILE (The best of Steve Harley & Cockney Rebel) (Harley, Steve & Cockney Rebel)
Mr. Soft / Riding the waves (for Virginia Woolf) / Irresistible (remix) / Mr. Raffles (man it was mean) / Freedom's prisoner / Hideaway / Judy Teen / Best years of our lives (live) / Make me smile (come up and see me) / If this is love (give me more) (live) / Here comes the sun / Sebastian / Roll the dice / Understand / I believe (love's a prima donna) / Tumbling down
CD _____ CDGO 2036
EMI / Apr '92 / EMI.

MAKE ME SMILE (Live 1989)
Dancing on the telephone / Mr. Soft / When I'm with you / Star for a week / Riding the waves (for Virginia Woolf) / Lighthouse / Best years of our lives / Sweet dreams / Pychomodo / Swing it / Sebastian / Make me smile (come up and see me) / Love's a prima donna
CD _____ MDCD 5
Magnum Music / May '94 / Magnum Music Group.

YES YOU CAN
CD _____ 08431802
CTE / Dec '95 / Koch.

Harman, James

BLACK AND WHITE
CD _____ BT 1118CD
Black Top / Aug '95 / CM / Direct / ADA.

CARDS ON THE TABLE (Harman, James Band)
CD _____ BT 1104CD
Black Top / Jul '94 / CM / Direct / ADA.

TWO SIDES TO EVERY STORY (Harman, James Band)
CD _____ BT 1091CD
Topic / Jul '93 / Direct / ADA.

Harmful

HARMFUL
CD _____ EFA 127902
Blu Noise / Dec '95 / SRD.

Harmonica Man

HARMONICA MAN
Blues brother medley / Stevie Wonder medley / Once upon a time / Orange blossom special / Midnight cowboy / Baker Street / Desperado / She's coming back / Misty / Georgia / Bridge over troubled water / Feel like making love
CD _____ 90792-2
PMF / May '94 / Kingdom / Cadillac.

Harmonica Slim

BACK BOTTOM BLUES
Back bottom soul / 2 Trains runnin' / Whiskey headed woman / Louise Ann / Baby please don't go / Tijuana blues / Shake yo' booty / Gonna move back to town / Dust my broom / Stoop down / Drunk woman / Back bottom blues
CD _____ TRIX 3323
Trix / Nov '95 / New Note.

Harmonizing Four

1950-1955
CD _____ HTCD 29
Heritage / May '95 / Swift / Roots / Wellard / Direct / Hot Shot / Jazz Music / ADA.

I SHALL NOT BE MOVED
All things are possible / Farther along / Motherless child / Where would I go / But to the Lord / I shall not be moved / Lived and he loved me / His eye is on the sparrow / When I've done my best / Go down / Moses / Will he welcome me / I love to call his name / Pass me not / Close to thee / God will take care of you / Mary don't you weep / Faith of our fathers / My Lord what a morning / Live like Jesus / Lord's prayer
CD _____ CPCD 8112
Charly / Jul '95 / Charly / THE / Cadillac.

Harmony

FRIENDSHIP
CD _____ EDM 41872
EDM / Oct '95 / EWM.

Harmony Rockets

PARALYZED MIND OF THE ARCHANGEL
CD _____ ABB 90CD
Big Cat / Oct '95 / SRD / Pinnacle.

Harp, Everette

COMMON GROUND
Strutt / Feel so right / Jeri's song / You make me feel brand new / Stay with me / I'm sorry / Sending my love / Love you to the letter / Perfect day (Tessa's smile) / Where do we go / Coming home / Common ground / Song for Toots
CD _____ CDP 7892972
Blue Note / Aug '94 / EMI.

Harper Brothers

YOU CAN HIDE INSIDE THE MUSIC
Segment / She's got the blues for sale / Round Midnight / For my children Quamara and Scott / Since I fell for you / Kahlil / I wish I knew / I ain't got nothin' but the blues / You can hide inside the music / That's the question / PS I love you / H D H Jr. (Big Brother)
CD _____ 5118202
Verve / Jan '93 / PolyGram

Harper, Ben

FIGHT FOR YOUR MIND
Oppresion / Ground on down / Another lonely day / Please me like you want to / Gold to me / Burn one down / Excuse me Mr / People lead / Fight for your mind / Give a man a home / By my side / Power of the gospel / God fearing man / End of the freedom
CD _____ CDVUS 93
Virgin / Jul '95 / EMI.

WELCOME TO THE CRUEL WORLD
CD _____ CDVUS 69
Virgin / Jul '94 / EMI.

Harper, Billy

CAPRA BLACK
Capra black / Sir Galahad / New breed / Soulfully, I love you/Black spiritual of love / Cry of hunger
CD _____ 66051022
Strata East / Nov '93 / New Note.

SOMALIA
Somalia / Thy will be done / Quest / Light within / Quest in 3
CD _____ ECD 221332
Evidence / Dec '95 / Harmonia Mundi / ADA / Cadillac.

Harper, Don

SYDNEY SUNDAY
St. Thomas / Polka dots and moonbeams / Honeysuckle Rose / Falling in love with love / Greensleeves / Sydney Sunday / Afternoon in the art gallery / Sunday morning /

Them there eyes / Air on a G string / Softly as in a morning sunrise
CD _____ CLGCD 024
Calligraph / Jun '92 / Cadillac / Wellard / Jazz Music.

Harper, Nick

LIGHT AT THE END OF THE KENNEL
CD _____ SG 094CD
Sangraal / Dec '94 / ADA.

Harper, Philip

SOULFULL SIN
Soulfull sin / Old country / Mellow afternoon / Songbird / Juicy fruit / Survival / Weaver of dreams / New endings / Blue jay
CD _____ MCD 5505
Muse / Aug '93 / New Note / CM.

THIRTEENTH MOON, THE
Amanda / Bella Maria de mi alma / Voices / Lotus blossom / Almost blue / Windmill / Thirteenth moon / Candy / I've never been in love
CD _____ MCD 5520
Muse / Feb '95 / New Note / CM.

Harper, Roy

BORN IN CAPTIVITY/WORK OF HEART (Two albums on one CD)
Stan / Drawn to the flames / Come to bed eyes / No woman is safe / I am a child / Elizabeth / No one ever gets out alive / Two lovers in the moon / We are the people / All of us children / We are the people (reprise)
CD _____ HUCD 008
Science Friction / Nov '94 / Vital.

BURN THE WORLD
CD _____ HUCD 013
Science Friction / Oct '94 / Vital.

COME OUT FIGHTING GHENGIS SMITH
Freak street / You don't need money / Ageing raver / In a beautiful rambling mess / All you need is what you have / Circle / Highgate cemetary / Come out fighting Ghengis Smith / Zaney Janey / Ballad of songwriter / Midspring dithering / Zenjam / It's tomorrow and today is yesterday / Francesca / She's the one
CD _____ HUCD 006
Science Friction / Nov '94 / Vital.

COMMERCIAL BREAKS
My little girl / I'm in love with you / Ten years ago / Sail away / I wanna be part of the news / Cora / Come up and see me / Fly catcher / Too many movies / Square boxes / Burn the world (part 1) / Playing prisons
CD _____ HUCD 016
Science Friction / Oct '94 / Vital.

DEATH OR GLORY
Death or glory / War came home / Tonight duty / Waiting for Godot / Part zed next to me / Man kind / Tallest tree / Miles remains / Fourth world / Why / Cardboard city / One more tomorrow / Plough / On summer day / If I can
CD _____ HUCD 012
Science Friction / Oct '94 / Vital.

FLASHES FROM THE ARCHIVES OF OBLIVION
Commune / Don't you grieve / Twelve hours of sunset / Kangaroo blues / All Ireland / Me and my woman / South Africa / Highway blues / One man rock and roll band / Another day / M.C.P. Blues
CD _____ HUCD 010
Science Friction / Sep '94 / Vital.

FLAT, BAROQUE AND BERSERK
Don't you grieve / I hate the white man / Feeling all the Saturday / How does it feel / Goodbye / Another day / Davey / East of the sun and west of the moon / Tom Tiddler's ground / Francesca / Song of the ages / Hell's angels
CD _____ HUCD 3
Science Friction / Oct '94 / Vital.

FOLKJOKEOPUS
Sgt. Sunshine / She's the one / In the time of water / Composer of life / One for all / Exercising some / Control / McGoohan's blues / Manana
CD _____ HUCD 009
Science Friction / Oct '94 / Vital.

GARDEN OF URANIUM (New version of Descendants Of Smith)
Laughing inside / Garden of uranium / Still life / Pinches of salt / Desert island / Government surplus / Surplus liquorice / Liquorice alltime / Maile Lei / Same shoes / Descendants of Smith / Laughing inside (Demo version)
CD _____ HUCD 014
Science Friction / Sep '94 / Vital.

H.Q
Game / Spirit lives / Grown ups are just silly children / Referendum / Forget me not / Hallucinating light / When an old cricketer leaves the crease
CD _____ HUCD 019
Science Friction / Jul '95 / Vital.

IN BETWEEN EVERY LINE

story / Game / One man rock and roll band / Hangman
CD _____ HUCD 018
Science Friction / Nov '94 / Vital.

INTRODUCTION TO ROY HARPER, AN
Legend / She's the one / Tom fiddler's ground / Highway blues / Che / Hallucinating light / One of those days in England / You / Nineteen forty-eightish / Pinches of salt / Ghost dance / Tallest tree / Miles remains
CD _____ HUCD 017
Science Friction / Feb '95 / Vital.

LEGEND
CD _____ JHD 064CD
JHD / Oct '94 / ADA.

LIFEMASK
Highway blues / All Ireland / Little lady / Bank of the dead / South Africa / Lord's prayer / Ballad of songwriter / Zaney Janey / Midspring dithering / Zenjam
CD _____ HUCD 005
Science Friction / Sep '94 / Vital.

LOONY ON THE BUS
No change / Playing prisons / I wanna be part of the news / Burn the world / Casualty / Cora / Loony on the bus / Come up and see me / Flycatcher / Square boxes
CD _____ AWCD 1011
Awareness / Nov '88 / ADA.

ONCE
Once / Once in the middle of nowhere / Nowhere to run to / Black cloud of Islam / If / Winds of change / Berliners / Sleeping at the wheel / For longer than it takes / Ghost dance
CD _____ HUCD 011
Science Friction / Oct '94 / Vital.
CD _____ 900892
Line / Oct '94 / CM / Grapevine / ADA / Conifer / Direct.

SOPHISTICATED BEGGAR
Goldfish bowl / Sophisticated beggar / Big fat silver aeroplane / Legend / Girlie / October 12th / Black clouds / Mr. Station Master / My friend / China girl
CD _____ HUCD 007
Science Friction / Oct '94 / Vital.

STORMCOCK
Hors d'oeuvres / One man rock and roll band / Same old rock / Me and my woman
CD _____ HUCD 004
Science Friction / Oct '94 / Vital.

UNHINGED
Descendants of Smith / Legend / North Country / When an old cricketer leaves the crease / Three hundred words / Hope / Naked flame / Commune / South Africa / Back to the stones / Frozen moment / Highway blues / Same old rock
CD _____ HUCD 020
Science Friction / Dec '95 / Vital.

VALENTINE
Forbidden fruit / Male chauvinist pig blues / I'll see you again / Twelve hours of sunset / Acapulco gold / Commune / Magic woman / Che / North country / Forever / Home (studio) (on CD only) / Too many movies (CD only) / Home (CD only)
CD _____ HUCD 015
Science Friction / Oct '94 / Vital.

WHATEVER HAPPENED TO JUGULA? (Harper, Roy & Jimmy Page)
Nineteen forty-eightish / Hangman / Elizabeth / Advertisement / Bad speech / Hope / Twentieth century man
CD _____ BBL 60 CD
Lowdown/Beggars Banquet / Aug '88 / Warner Music / Disc.

Harper, Winard

BE YOURSELF
Night watch / Li'l Willie / My shell / Trane stop / Last dance / Hi fly / Quiet as it's kept / Lonesome head / You're looking at me / Toku-do / Poon
CD _____ 4781972
Epicure / Feb '95 / Sony.

Harpo, Slim

BEST OF SLIM HARPO, THE
Baby scratch my back / Got love if you want it / I'm a king bee / Little queen bee (got a brand new king) / Shake your hips / Te-ni-nee-ni-nu / Buzz me baby / Buzzin' / Raining in my heart / Still rainin' in my heart / Late night / Tip on in, Part 1 / Bobby sox baby / Don't start cryin' now / I need money (keep your alibis) / Strange love / Rock me baby / Blues hangover
CD _____ CDCHM 410
Ace / Jul '92 / Pinnacle / Cadillac / Complete/Pinnacle.

I'M A KING BEE
I'm a king bee / I love the life I'm livin' / Moody blues / Buzzin' / Dream girl / Got love if you want it / Wonderin' and worryin' / Strange love / You'll be sorry one day / One more day / Bobby sox baby / Late last night / Buzz me baby / Yeah yeah baby / What a dream / Don't start cryin' now / Blues hangover / My home is a prison / Please don't turn me down / Snoopin'

around / raining in my heart / That's alright baby / Lover's confession / Boogie chillun
CD _____ CDCHD 510
Ace / Oct '93 / Pinnacle / Cadillac / Complete/Pinnacle.

RAININ' IN MY HEART
Raining in my heart / Blues hangover / Bobby sox baby / Got love if you want it / Snoopin' around / Buzz me baby / I'm a King Bee / What a dream / Don't start cryin' now / Moody blues / My home is a prison / Dream girl / Wonderin' and worryin' / Strange love / You'll be sorry one day / One more day / Late last night / Still rainin' in my heart
CD _____ ELDIABLO 8037
El Diablo / Mar '94 / Vital.

SHAKE YOUR HIPS
Shake your hips / Little queen bee (got a brand new king) / Still rainin' in my heart / I need money (keep your alibis) / What's goin' on baby / Harpo's blues / Sittin' here wonderin' / We're two of a kind / I'm gonna miss you (like the devil) / Baby scratch my back / I don't want no-one (to take me away from you) / Midnight blues / Lovin' you (the way I do) / Baby you got what I want / Your love for me is gone / I'm your bread maker, baby / Stop working blues / I'm waiting on you baby / You'll never find a love as true as mine / Little Sally Walker / I gotta stop lovin' you / Blueberry Hill / Something inside of me / Tonite I'm lonely / Man is crying / Still rainin' in my heart (2)
CD _____ CDCHD 558
Ace / Mar '95 / Pinnacle / Cadillac / Complete/Pinnacle.

TE-NI-NEE-NI-NU (The Best Of Slim Harpo)
CD _____ REP 4206-WZ
Repertoire / Aug '91 / Pinnacle / Cadillac.

Harrell, Tom

FORM
Vista / Brazilian song / Scene / January spring / Rhythm form / For heaven's sake
CD _____ CCD 14059
Contemporary / Oct '93 / Jazz Music / Cadillac / Pinnacle / Wellard.

SAIL AWAY
Eons / Glass mystery / Dream in June / Sail away / Buffalo wings / It always is / Dancing trees / Hope Street
CD _____ CCD 14043
Contemporary / Oct '93 / Jazz Music / Cadillac / Pinnacle / Wellard.

STORIES
Rapture / Song flower / Mountain / Waters edge / Story / Viable blues / Touchstone
CD _____ CCD 14043
Contemporary / Oct '93 / Jazz Music / Cadillac / Pinnacle / Wellard.

Harries, Mike

DR. ROOTS GUMBO KINGS
CD _____ CJC 008CD
CJC / Apr '94 / Jazz Music.

Harriet

WOMAN TO MAN
Temple of love / Magic bed / Takes a little time / Only the lonely/Good girl / Woman to man / Fool am I / Wish
CD _____ 9031721102
WEA / Oct '90 / Warner Music.

Harrington, Gerry

SCEAL EILE (Harrington, Gerry & Eoin O'Sullivan)
CD _____ LUN 059CD
Mulligan / Jan '94 / CM / ADA.

Harrington, Jan

MY GOD IS REAL
CD _____ MECCACD 1042
Music Mecca / Feb '94 / Jazz Music / Cadillac / Wellard.

Harriott, Derrick

16 ROCKSTEADY HITS
CD _____ JMC 200214
Jamaica Gold / Jul '94 / THE / Magnum Music Group / Jetstar.

DONKEY YEARS, THE
CD _____ JMC 20012
Jamaica Gold / Apr '94 / THE / Magnum Music Group / Jetstar.

RIDING THE MUSICAL CHARIOT
CD _____ CDHB 58
Heartbeat / May '93 / Greensleeves / Jetstar / Direct / ADA.

SINGS ROCKSTEADY
CD _____ JMC 200213
Jamaica Gold / May '94 / THE / Magnum Music Group / Jetstar.

SONGS FOR MIDNIGHT LOVERS
Eighteen with a bullet / Born to love you / Message from a black man / Groovy situation / Loser
CD _____ CDTRL 198
Trojan / May '90 / Jetstar / Total/BMG.

Harris, Barry

CONFIRMATION (Harris, Barry & Kenny Barron)
CD _____ CCD 79519
Black & Blue / Sep '92 / Wellard / Koch.

LIVE AT MAYBECK RECITAL HALL, VOL. 12
It could happen to you / All God's chillun got rhythm / I'll keep loving you / She / Cherokee / Gone again / Lucky day / It never entered my mind / Meet the flintstones / I love Lucy / Parker's mood / Would you like to take a walk
CD _____ CCD 4476
Concord Jazz / Aug '91 / New Note.

Harris, Beaver

BEAUTIFUL AFRICA
CD _____ 121002-2
Soul Note / May '92 / Harmonia Mundi / Wellard / Cadillac.

Harris, Corey

BETWEEN MIDNIGHT AND DAY
CD _____ ALCD 4837
Alligator / Nov '95 / Direct / ADA.

Harris, Craig

BLACKOUT IN THE SQUARE ROOT OF SOUL (Harris, Craig & Tailgater's Tales)
Blackout in the square root of soul (phase 1 and 2) / Generations / Free 1 / Love joy / Blue dues / Dingo / Awakening ancestors
CD _____ 8344152
JMT / May '91 / PolyGram.

Harris, Eddie

BEST OF EDDIE HARRIS, THE
Shadow of your smile / Freedom jazz dance / Sham time / Theme in search of a movie / Listen here / Live right now / 1974 Blues / Movin' on out / Boogie woogie / Bosa nova / Child is born / Is it in
CD _____ 756781370-2
Atlantic / Jun '93 / Warner Music.

DANCING BY A RAINBOW
CD _____ ENJACD 90812
Enja / Oct '95 / New Note / Vital/SAM.

EDDIE HARRIS ANTHOLOGY, THE
Exodus / Listen here / Cold duck time / Shadow of your smile / Theme in search of a movie / Sham time / Boogie woogie bosa nova / Is it in / Get on down / Funkaroma / It's alright now / 1974 Blues / Live right now / Freedom jazz dance / Yeah yeah yeah / Hey wado / Free speech / Cryin' blues / Gi-ant steps / Without you / Mean greens / Recess / Steps up / Love for sale
CD _____ 8122715142
Atlantic / Mar '94 / Warner Music.

LISTEN HERE
Funkaroma / I need some money / Listen here / People get funny when they get a little money / Is it in / How can I find some way to show you / Walkin' the walk / Fusion jazz dance
CD _____ ENJACD 70792
Enja / Jun '93 / New Note / Vital/SAM.

LIVE IN BERLIN
CD _____ CDSJP 289
Timeless Jazz / May '89 / New Note.

SWISS MOVEMENT (Harris, Eddie & Les McCann)
Compared to what / Cold duck time / Kathleen's theme / You got it in your soulness / Generation gap
CD _____ 756781365-2
Atlantic / Apr '94 / Warner Music.

YEAH, YOU RIGHT
CD _____ LAKE 2023
Lakeside / Aug '95 / Magnum Music Group.

Harris, Emmylou

AT THE RYMAN
Guitar town / Half as much / Cattle call / Guess things happen that way / Hard times / Mansion on the hill / Scotland / Montana cowgirl / Like strangers / Lodi / Calling my children home / If I could be there / Walls of time / Get up John / It's a hard life wherever you go/Abraham, Martin and John / Smoke along the track
CD _____ 759926662
WEA / Feb '95 / Warner Music.

BALLAD OF SALLY ROSE
Ballad of Sally Rose / Rhythm guitar / I think I love him / You are my flower heart to heart / Woman walk the line / Bad news / Timberline / Long tall Sally Rose / White line / Diamond in my crown / Sweetheart of the Rodeo / K-S-O-S (Instrumental medly) / Ring of fire / Wildwood flower / Six days on the road / Swing low, sweet chariot
CD _____ 7599252052
Reprise / Jan '96 / Warner Music.

BLUE KENTUCKY GIRL
Sister's coming home / Beneath still waters / Rough and rocky / Hickory wind / Save the last dance for me / Sorrow in the wind / They'll never take his love from me / Every

time you leave / Blue Kentucky girl / Even cowgirls get the blues
CD _____ 7599293922
WEA / Jan '93 / Warner Music.

BRAND NEW DANCE
Wheels of love / In his world / Easy for you to stay / Better off without you / Brand new dance / Tougher than the rest / Sweet dreams of you / Rollin' and ramblin' / Never be anyone else but you / Red red rose
CD _____ 7599263092
WEA / Oct '90 / Warner Music.

COWGIRL'S PRAYER
CD _____ GRA 101CD
Grapevine / Aug '94 / Grapevine.

DUETS
Price I pay (with Desert Rose Band) / Love hurts (with Gram Parsons) / Thing about you (with Southern Pacific) / That lovin' feelin' again (with Roy Orbison) / We believe in happy endings (with Earl Thomas Conley) / Star of Bethlehem (with Neil Young) / All fall down (with Ricky Skaggs) / Wild Montana skies (with John Denver) / Green pastures (with Ricky Skaggs) / Gulf Coast highway (with Willie Nelson) / If I needed you (with Don Williams) / Evangeline (with The Band)
CD _____ 7599257912
WEA / Aug '90 / Warner Music.

ELITE HOTEL
Amarillo / Together again / Feeling single / Seeing double / Sin City / One of these days / Till I gain control again / Here, there and everywhere / Ooh Las Vegas / Sweet dreams / Jambalaya / Satan's jewelled crown / Wheels
CD _____ K 254060
WEA / '88 / Warner Music.

LUXURY LINER
Luxury liner / Poncho and Lefty / Making believe / You're supposed to be feeling good / I'll be your San Antone Rose / C'est la vie / When I stop dreaming / Hello stranger / She / Tulsa queen
CD _____ 927338 2
WEA / Jun '89 / Warner Music.

NASHVILLE COUNTRY DUETS (Harris, Emmylou & Carl Jackson)
CD _____ CDSD 074
Sundown / Jun '93 / Magnum Music Group.

PIECES OF THE SKY
Bluebird wine / Too far gone / If I could only win your love / Boulder to Birmingham / Before believing / Bottle let me down / Sleepless nights / Coat of many colours / For no one / Queen of the silver dollar
CD _____ 7599272442
WEA / Feb '89 / Warner Music.

PROFILE: EMMYLOU HARRIS (The Best Of Emmylou Harris)
One of these days / Sweet dreams / To daddy / C'est la vie / Making believe / Easy from now on / Together again / If I could only win your love / Too far gone / Two more bottles of wine / Boulder to Birmingham / Hello stranger / You never can tell
CD _____ 256570
WEA / Jun '84 / Warner Music.

PROFILE: EMMYLOU HARRIS #2 (The Best Of Emmylou Harris)
Blue Kentucky girl / Wayfaring stranger / Beneath still waters / Born to run / Someone like you / Mister Sandman / Pledging my love / I'm moving on / I don't live on our last date / Save the last dance for me
CD _____ 7599251612
WEA / Feb '94 / Warner Music.

QUARTER MOON IN A TEN CENT TOWN
Easy from now on / Two more bottles of wine / To Daddy / My songbird / Leaving Louisiana in the broad daylight / Defying / Gravity / I ain't living long like this / One paper kid / Green rolling hills / Burn that candle
CD _____ 927345 2
WEA / Jun '89 / Warner Music.

SONGS OF THE WEST
I'll be your San Antone rose / Even cowgirls get the blues / Amarillo / Sweetheart of the rodeo / Queen of the silver dollar / One paper kid / Rose of Cimarron / Spanish is a loving tongue / Cattle call / Montana waltz
CD _____ 9362445725-2
WEA / Nov '94 / Warner Music.

WHITE SHOES
Drivin' wheel / Pledging my love / In my dreams / White shoes / On the radio / It's only rock 'n' roll / Diamonds are a girl's best friend / Good news / Baby, better start turning 'em down / Like an old fashioned waltz
CD _____ 7599239612
Reprise / Jan '96 / Warner Music.

WRECKING BALL
CD _____ GRACD 102
Grapevine / Sep '95 / Grapevine.

Harris, Gene

AT LAST (Harris, Gene & Scott Hamilton Quintet)
You are my sunshine / It never entered my mind / After you've gone / Angel eyes / At last / Blues for Gene / I fall in love too easily

/ Some of these days / Stairway to the stars / Sittin' in the sandtrap
CD _____ CCD 4434
Concord Jazz / Nov '90 / New Note.

BLACK AND BLUE (Harris, Gene Quartet)
Another star / Black and blue / C.C. rider / Hot toddy / Best things in life are free / Nobody knows you (when you're down and out) / It might as well be Spring / Blue bossa / Song is you / Will you still be mine
CD _____ CCD 4482
Concord Jazz / Oct '91 / New Note.

BROTHERHOOD
I remember you / For once in my life / Brotherhood of man / When you wish upon a star / Sidewinder / I told you so / September song / This little light of mine / Beautiful friendship
CD _____ CCD 4640
Concord Jazz / May '95 / New Note.

FUNKY GENE'S
Blues for Basie / Trouble with hello is goodbye / Old funky Gene's / Everything happens to me / Nice 'n' easy / Ahmad's blues / Bye bye blues / Children of Sanchez / Blues in Hoss's flat
CD _____ CCD 4609
Concord Jazz / Sep '94 / New Note.

GENE HARRIS & THE PHILIP MORRIS SUPERBAND (Harris, Gene & The Philip Morris Superband)
Surrey with the fringe on top / Creme de menthe (CD only) / When it's sleepy time down South / Love is here to stay / I'm just a lucky so and so / Serious grease (CD only) / Like a lover (CD only) / Old man river / Do you know what it means to miss New Orleans (LP only) / Porgy and Bess (medley) / You're my everything / There is no greater love / Things ain't what they used to be
CD _____ CCD 4397
Concord Jazz / Nov '89 / New Note.

GENE HARRIS TRIO PLUS ONE, THE
Gene's lament / Uptown sop / Things ain't what they used to be / Yours is my heart alone / Battle hyrnn of the Republic
CD _____ CCD 4303
Concord Jazz / Sep '90 / New Note.

LIKE A LOVER (Harris, Gene Quartet)
Like a lover / Misterioso / Strollin' / Until the real thing comes along / Jeannie / I can't stop loving you / You make me feel so young / Oh, look at me now / Wrap your troubles in dreams (and dream your troubles away)
CD _____ CCD 4526
Concord Jazz / Oct '92 / New Note.

LISTEN HERE (Harris, Gene Quartet)
His masquerade / I've got a feeling I'm falling in love / Blues for Jezebel / Lullaby / This can't be love / Don't be that way / Listen here / Sweet and lovel; / Song is ended (but the melody lingers on) / To you
CD _____ CCD 4385
Concord Jazz / Sep '90 / New Note.

LITTLE PIECE OF HEAVEN, A (Harris, Gene Quartet)
Blues in baxter's pad / Scotch and soda / Take the 'A' train / My little suede shoes / Blues for ste chapelle / Ma, he's making eyes at me / Pensativa / How long has this been going on / Old dog blues / Ode to Billy Joe / Sentimental journey
CD _____ CCD 4578
Concord Jazz / May '93 / New Note.

TRIBUTE TO COUNT BASIE (Harris, Gene All Star Big Band)
Captain Bill / Night mist blues / Swingin' the blues / When did you leave Heaven / Blue and sentimental / Riled up / (I'm afraid) the masquerade is over / Dejection blues
CD _____ CCD 4337
Concord Jazz / May '88 / New Note.

WORLD TOUR 1990 (Harris, Gene & The Philip Morris Superband)
Airmail special / Lonely bottles / Child is born / Buhaina Buhaina / Don't get around much anymore / Lover (CD only.) / In the wee small hours of the morning / Tricrotism (CD only.) / Centerpiece (CD only.) / Dear blues / Nica's dream / Girl talk / Battle royal / Warm valley
CD _____ CCD 4443
Concord Jazz / Feb '91 / New Note.

Harris, Greg

ELECTRIC
CD _____ AP 024CD
Appaloosa / Jun '94 / ADA / Magnum Music Group.

THINGS CHANGE
CD _____ APCD 047
Appaloosa / '92 / ADA / Magnum Music Group.

Harris, Jerome

IN PASSING
CD _____ MCD 5386
Muse / Sep '92 / New Note / CM.

Harris, Jet

ANNIVERSARY ALBUM : JET HARRIS
CD _____ CDMM 1038
Q / '88 / Pinnacle / BMG.

Harris, Kim

IN THE HEAT OF THE SUMMER (Harris, Kim & Reggie)
CD _____ FE 1412
Folk Fra / Nov '94 / CM / ADA.

Harris, Lafayette Jr

LAFAYETTE IS HERE
Monique and Andrea / Chan's song / Dearly beloved / Dance cadaverous / For the love of you / Little Kevin's embrace / Satin doll / A.L.C. / Geneva / Gingerbread boy / Escapade
CD _____ MCD 5507
Muse / Feb '94 / New Note / CM.

Harris, Larnelle

CHRISTMAS (LARNELLE HARRIS)
CD _____ CD 02474
Nelson Word / Dec '88 / Nelson Word.

I CAN BEGIN AGAIN
Mighty Spirit
CD _____ CD 02506
Nelson Word / Nov '89 / Nelson Word.

Harris, M.J.

M.J. HARRIS/BILL LASWELL (Harris, M.J./Bill Laswell)
CD _____ SNT 2080
Sentrax Corporation / Oct '95 / Plastic Head.

Harris, Marion

VOLUME IV 1922-33
Dixie highway / Carolina in the morning / Homesick / Hot lips / Aggravatin' papa / Who cares / Mississippi choo-choo / I wish you up just before you threw me down / Rose of the rio grande / St. Louis blues / I ain't got nobody / Running wild / You've got to see mama ev'ry night / Dearest / Beside a babbling brook / Two time Dan / That redhead gal / Who's sorry now
CD _____ NEO 957
Neovox / Mar '94 / Wellard.

Harris, Michael

WIDOR TRADITION, THE (French Organ Music From Canterbury Cathedral)
Marche Pontificale / Suite bretonne / Berceuse / Fleurise / Les cloches de perros-guirec / Suite Francaise / Variations sur un Noel Angevin / Variations sur un theme de Clement Jannequin / Prelude et Danse Fuguee
CD _____ YORK CD 112
York Ambisonic / Oct '91 / Target/BMG.

Harris, Michael

DEFENSE MECHANIZMS
CD _____ BD 051CD
Black Dragon / Dec '91 / Else.

Harris, R.H.

SHINE ON ME (Harris, R.H. & The Soul Stirrers)
By and by / I'm still living on mother's prayer / Feel like my time ain't long / Today / I have a right to the tree of life / In that awful hour / Jesus hits like the atom bomb / Shine on me / Faith and grace / Everybody ought to love their soul / Blessed by the name of the Lord / By himself am waiting for me (waiting and watching) / How long Who'll be the one / Lord's my shepherd / Christ is all / By and by Pts. 1 - 3
CD _____ CDCHD 415
Ace / Nov '93 / Pinnacle / Cadillac Complete/Pinnacle.

Harris, Rhonda

RHONDA HARRIS
CD _____ RAIN 014CD
Cloudland / Nov '95 / Plastic Head / SRD.

Harris, Rolf

DIDGEREELY-DOO ALL THAT (The Best Of Rolf Harris)
Tie me kangaroo down sport / Sun arise / I've lost my Mummy / Carra barra wirra canna / Nick Teen and Al K.Hall / Maximillian mouse / Court of King Caractacus / Six white boomers / Jake the peg / Bid dog / Fijian girl / Hurry home / Two little boys / Jindabyne / She'll be right / Come and see my land (Jimmy my boy) / Lazy day / Yarrabangee / Northern territorani / Bargin' down the Thames / Pavlova / Raining on the rock / Stairway to heaven
CD _____ CDGO 2062
EMI / May '94 / EMI.

ROLF RULES OK
CD _____ ROLFCD 001
Music Club / Jun '95 / Conifer.

Harris, Simon

BEATS, BREAKS & SCRATCHES VOL. 10
CD _____ MOLCD 027
Music Of Life / Mar '93 / Grapevine.

BEATS, BREAKS & SCRATCHES VOL. 11
CD _____ MOLCD 31
Music Of Life / Oct '93 / Grapevine.

BEATS, BREAKS & SCRATCHES VOL. 7
CD _____ MOMIX 7CD
Music Of Life / Jun '91 / Grapevine.

BEATS, BREAKS & SCRATCHES VOL. 8
CD _____ MOMIX 8CD
Music Of Life / Nov '91 / Grapevine.

BEATS, BREAKS & SCRATCHES VOL.12
CD _____ MOLCD 37
Music Of Life / Sep '95 / Grapevine.

BEATS, BREAKS & SCRATCHES VOLS. 1 & 2
CD Set _____ MOMIX 1/2CD
Music Of Life / '89 / Grapevine.

BEATS, BREAKS & SCRATCHES VOLS. 3 & 4
CD Set _____ MOMIX 3/4CD
Music Of Life / Sep '89 / Grapevine.

BEST OF BEATS, BREAKS AND SCRATCHES
CD _____ MOBEST 1CD
Music Of Life / Jun '92 / Grapevine.

DISTURBING THE PEACE
Theme from disturbing the peace / Time / Rock right now / Ragga house (All night long) / This is serious / Don't stop the music / Shock the house / Right here, right now / Twilight / Runaway love / Ragga house
CD _____ DISTURB 1CD
Living Beat / Nov '90 / Grapevine.

FOR YOUR EARS ONLY
CD _____ MOLCD 39
Living Beat / Jan '96 / Grapevine.

Harris, Wynonie

BATTLE OF THE BLUES (Harris, Wynonie & Roy Brown)
Mr. Blues is coming to town / Good rockin' tonight / Rock Mr. Blues / Bloodshot eyes / Just like two drops of water / Luscious woman / Lovin' machine / Keep on churnin' (till the butter comes) / Good morning judge / Quiet whiskey / Down boy down / Cadillac baby / Too much lovin' ain't no good / Hard luck blues / My gal from Kokomo / Big town / Rock-a-bye baby / Black diamond / Ain't no rockin' no more / Fannie Brown got married / Shake 'em up baby / Good lookin, and foxy too
CD _____ KCD 607
King/Paddle Wheel / Mar '90 / New Note.

GOOD ROCKING TONIGHT
Good rockin' tonight / She just won't sell no more / Blow your brains out / I want my Fanny Brown / All she wants to do is rock / Lollipop mama / Baby, shame on you / I like my baby's pudding / Wynonie's boogie / Sittin' on it all the time / Good morning judge / I feel that old age coming on / Lovin' machine / Mr. Blues is coming to town / Quiet whiskey / Rock Mr. Blues / Bloodshot eyes / Luscious woman / Down boy down / Keep on churnin' (till the butter comes)
CD _____ CDCHARLY 244
Charly / Apr '91 / Charly / THE / Cadillac.

WEST COAST JIVE
CD _____ DD 657
Delmark / Jul '93 / Hot Shot / ADA / CM / Direct / Cadillac.

WOMEN, WHISKEY AND FISH TAILS
Greyhound / Deacon don't like it / Christina / Shake that thing / Don't take my whiskey away / Drinkin' sherry wine / Fish tail blues / Big old country fool / Shotgun wedding / Wine wine sweet wine / Git to gittin' baby / Mr. Dollar / Bad news baby (There'll be no rockin' tonite) / Bring it back / I don't know where to go / Man's best friend / Page a talking / Please Louise / I get a thrill / There's no substitute for love / Mama your daughter done lied to me
CD _____ CDCHD 457
Ace / Sep '93 / Pinnacle / Cadillac / Complete/Pinnacle.

Harrison, Donald

FOR ART'S SAKE (Harrison, Donald Quintet)
CD _____ CCD 79501
Candid / Jul '91 / Cadillac / Jazz Music / Wellard / Koch.

FULL CIRCLE
Force / My little suede shoes / Call me / Bye bye blackbird / Nature boy / Hold it right there / Good morning heartache / Evidence of things not seen / Infinite heart / Let's go off
CD _____ 66055003
Sweet Basil / Jul '91 / New Note.

INDIAN BLUES
CD _____ CCD 79514
Candid / Apr '92 / Cadillac / Jazz Music / Wellard / Koch.

Harrison, George

POWER OF COOL, THE
Tropic of cool / Wind cries Mary / Shadowbrook / All I want is you / Till U comeback / Close the door / Power of cool / Too fast / Ceora / Four
CD _____ ESJCD 238
Essential Jazz / Oct '94 / BMG.

Harrison, George

ALL THINGS MUST PASS
I'd have you anytime / My sweet Lord / Wah wah / Isn't it a pity / What is life / If not for you / Behind that locked door / Let it down / Run of the mill / Beware of darkness / Apple scruffs / Ballad of Sir Frankie Crisp (Let it roll) / Awaiting on you all / All things must pass / I dig love / Art of dying / Hear me Lord / Out of the blue / It's Johnny's birthday / Plug me in / I remember jeep / Thanks for the pepperoni
CD Set _____ CDS 746 688 8
EMI / May '87 / EMI.

BEST OF DARK HORSE 1976-1989
Poor little girl / Blow away / That's the way it goes / Cockamamie business / Wake up my love / Life itself / Got my mind set on you / Crackerbox palace / Cloud 9 / Here comes the moon / Gone troppo / When we was fab / Love comes to everyone / All those years ago / Cheer down
CD _____ 9257262
Dark Horse / Oct '89 / Warner Music.

BEST OF GEORGE HARRISON
Something / If I needed someone / Here comes the sun / Taxman / Think for yourself / For you blue / While my guitar gently weeps / My sweet Lord / Give me love (give me peace on earth) / You / Bangladesh / Dark horse / What is life
CD _____ CDP 746 682 2
Parlophone / May '87 / EMI.

CLOUD NINE
Cloud 9 / That's what it takes / Fish on the sand / Just for today / This is love / When we was fab / Devil's radio / Someplace else / Wreck of the Hesperus / Breath away from heaven / Got my mind set on you
CD _____ 925 643-2
Dark Horse / Sep '87 / Warner Music.

DARK HORSE
Hari's on tour / Simply shady / So sad / Bye bye love / May a love / Ding dong ding dong / Dark horse / Far east man / Is it he (Jai Sri Krishna)
CD _____ CDPAS 10008
Parlophone / Oct '91 / EMI.

EXTRA TEXTURE (READ ALL ABOUT IT)
You / Answer's at the end / This guitar (can't keep from crying) / Ooh baby (you know that I love you) / World of stone / Bit more of you / Can't stop thinking about you / Tired of midnight blue / Grey cloudy lies / His name is legs
CD _____ CDPAS 10009
Parlophone / Oct '91 / EMI.

LIVE IN JAPAN
I want to tell you / Old brown shoe / Taxman / Give me love (give me peace on earth) / If I needed someone / Something / What is life / Dark horse / Piggies / Got my mind set on you / Cloud 9 / Here comes the sun / My sweet lord / All those years ago / Cheer down / Devil's radio / Isn't it a pity / While my guitar gently weeps / Roll over Beethoven
CD _____ 7599269642
Dark Horse / Jul '92 / Warner Music.

LIVING IN THE MATERIAL WORLD
Give me love (give me peace on Earth) / Sue me, sue you blues / Light that has lighted the world / Don't let me wait too long / Who can see it / Living in the material world / Lord loves the one (that loves to kill) / Be here now / Try some buy some / Day the world gets 'round / That's all
CD _____ CDPAS 10006
Parlophone / Oct '91 / EMI.

WONDERWALL MUSIC
Microbes / Red lady too / Table and Pakavaj / In the park / Drilling a home / Guru vandana / Greasy legs / Ski-ing / Gat kirwani / Dream scene / Party seacombe / Love scene / Crying / Cowboy music / Fantasy sequins / On the bed / Glass box / Wonderwall to be here / Singing om
CD _____ CDSAPCOR 1
Apple / Jun '92 / EMI.

Harrison, Jerry

RED & THE BLACK, THE
CD _____ 7599236312
East West / Jan '96 / Warner Music.

Harrison, John

GOING PLACES
You say you care / I have dreamed / Three views of a street / Never let me go / I hear a rhapsody / When I'm with you / On the street where you live / Nightingale sang in Berkley Square / Alone too long / If I should lose you / I'll remember April / Cedar's blues
CD _____ TCB 95702
TCB / Sep '95 / New Note.

Harrison, Michael A.

MOMENTS IN PASSION
CD _____ 101 S 7078 2
101 South / Nov '92 / New Note.

Harrow

PYLON OF INSANITY
CD _____ NO 2452
Noise/Modern Music / Aug '94 / Pinnacle / Plastic Head.

Harrow, Nancy

ANYTHING GOES
CD _____ ACD 142
Audiophile / '91 / Jazz Music / Swift.

LOST LADY
CD _____ SN 121263-2
Soul Note / Oct '94 / Harmonia Mundi / Wellard / Cadillac.

SECRETS
CD _____ 1212332
Soul Note / Jan '92 / Harmonia Mundi / Wellard / Cadillac.

WILD WOMEN DON'T HAVE THE BLUES
Take me back baby / All too soon / Can't we be friends / On the sunny side of the street / Wild women don't get the blues / I've got the world on a string / I don't know what kind of blues I got / Blues for yesterday
CD _____ CCD 9008
Candid / Sep '87 / Cadillac / Jazz Music / Wellard / Koch.

Harrup, Albie

PRAISE HIM ON THE GUITAR
I just want to praise you / In moments like these / Jesus all for Jesus / Father I adore you / More love, more power / You are my God / Sing hallelujah to the Lord / When I feel the touch / Jesus shall take the highest honour / When I look into your Holiness / Meekness and majesty / Send the rain
CD _____ SOPD 2051
Spirit Of Praise / Apr '92 / Nelson Word.

Harry Crews

NAKED IN GARDEN HILLS
About the author / Distopia / Gospel singer / (She's in a) bad mood / Bring me down / S.O.S. / Man hates a man / You're it / Knockout artist / Way out / Car / Orphans
CD _____ ABBCD 21
Big Cat / Apr '90 / SRD / Pinnacle.

Harry, Deborah

COMPLETE PICTURE, THE (The Best Of Deborah Harry & Blondie) (Harry, Deborah & Blondie)
Heart of glass / I want that man / Call me / Sunday girl / French kissin' in the USA / Denis / Rapture / Brite side / (I'm always touched by your) presence dear / Well did you evah / Tide is high / In love with love / Hanging on the telephone / Island of lost souls / Picture this / Dreaming / Sweet and low / Union City Blue / Atomic / Rip her to shreds
CD _____ CCD 1817
Chrysalis / Mar '91 / EMI.

DEF, DUMB AND BLONDE
I want that man / Lovelight / Kiss it better / Bike boy / Get your way / Maybe for sure / I'll never fall in love / Calmarie / Sweet and low / He's so / Bugeye / Comic books / Forced to live / Brite side / End of the run
CD _____ CCD 1650
Chrysalis / Sep '94 / EMI.

KOO KOO
Jump jump / Chrome / Under arrest / Jam was moving / Surrender / Inner city spillover / Oasis / Military rap / Backfired / Now I know you know
CD _____ CDCHR 6082
Chrysalis / Sep '94 / EMI.

ROCKBIRD
I want you / French kissin' in the USA / Buckle up / In love with love / You got me in trouble / Free to fall / Rockbird / Secret life / Beyond the limit
CD _____ CCD 1540
Chrysalis / Sep '94 / EMI.

Harry J All Stars

RETURN OF THE LIQUIDATOR
CD _____ CDTRD 412
Trojan / Mar '94 / Jetstar / Total/BMG.

Hart, Antonio

DON'T YOU KNOW I CARE
Zero grade reliance / Black children / At the closet inn / Don't you know I care (or don't you care to) / Mandela heart / Do what you want / Jessica's day / Black and gold / From across the ocean
CD _____ 01241631422
Novus / Aug '97 / BMG.

FOR CANNONBALL AND WOODY
Sticks / Sack o' woe / Organ grinder / Theme for Ernie / Woody I (on the new ark)

/ Cannonball / Big P / Nine weeks / Reflections of Woody / Rose wood
CD _____ 01241631622
Novus / Nov '93 / BMG.

IT'S ALL GOOD
91st miracle / Great Grandmother's song / Puerto Rico / Through the clouds / Bartzology / Sounds in the street / Lunch time again / Uptown traveller / Forever in love / Cappuccini / Missin' Miles
CD _____ 01241631832
Novus / Jun '95 / BMG.

NOT FOR THE FIRST TIME
Majority / Big H.M. / Embraceable you / Del Sasser / Self evaluation / K.Y.H. / Bewitched, bothered and bewildered / Where of when / For the first time / I've never been in love before / Straight ahead
CD _____ PD 83120
Novus / Aug '91 / BMG.

Hart, Billy

RAH
Motional / Naaj / Renedap / Dreams / Reflections / Breakup / Reminder / Jungu
CD _____ 1888022
Gramavision / Dec '88 / Vital/SAM / ADA.

Hart, Grant

ECCE HOMO
Ballad number 19 / 2541 / Evergreen memorial drive / Come come / Pink turns to blue / She floated away / Girl who lives on Heaven Hill / Admiral of the sea / Back somewhere / Last days of Pompeii / Old empire / Never talking to you again / Please don't ask / Main
CD _____ RTD 15730962
World Service / Nov '95 / Vital.

Hart, Kathy

TONIGHT I WANT IT ALL (Hart, Kathy & The Bluestars)
Tonight I want it all / Blue reverie / Get in / Get the money and get out / Two plays for a quarter / Good rockin' daddy / It seemed like such a good idea / Monkey ain't made outa gold
CD _____ BCD 119
Biograph / Jul '91 / Wellard / ADA / Hot Shot / Jazz Music / Cadillac / Direct.

Hart, Mickey

AT THE EDGE
Four for Garcia / Sky water / Slow sailing / Lonesome hero / Fast sailing / Cougar run / Eliminators / Brainstorm / Pigs in space
CD _____ RCD 10124
Rykodisc / Jul '91 / Vital / ADA.

DAFOS (Hart, Mickey & Flora Purim/Airto Moreira)
CD _____ RCD 10108
Rykodisc / Dec '94 / Vital / ADA.

MUSIC TO BE BORN BY
CD _____ RCD 0112
Rykodisc / Nov '91 / Vital / ADA.

PLANET DRUM (Hart, Mickey & Planet Drum)
CD _____ RCD 80206
Rykodisc / Dec '94 / Vital / ADA.

Hart, Mike

MIKE HART BLEEDS/BASHER, CHALKY, PONGO & ME
Yawny morning song / Ring song / Arty's wife / Aberfan / Almost Liverpool 6 / Intro / Interlude / Pocket full of dough / Bitchin' on a train / Sing song / Jousters / Epilogue / Shelter song / Please bring back the birch for the milkman / Disbelief blues / Dance Mr. Morning Man / Joke / Nell's song / Dear Bathseeba Everdene / Influences / I have been a rover / Christmas / War, violence, heroism and such like stupidity
CD _____ SEECD 419
See For Miles/C5 / May '95 / Pinnacle.

ROLLING THUNDER
Rolling thunder / Shoshone invocation / Fletcher carnaby / Blind John / Deep, wide and frequent / Granma's cookies / Main ten / Chase / Young man / Pump song / Hangin' on
CD _____ GDCD 4009
Grateful Dead / Mar '89 / Pinnacle.

Hart Rouge

INCONDITIONNEL
CD _____ HYCD 200143
Hypertension / Mar '95 / Total/BMG / Direct / ADA.

Hart, Tim

TIM HART
Keep on travelling / Tuesday afternoon / Hillman Avenger / Lovely lady / Come to my window / Nothing to hide / Overseas / Time after time / As I go my way
CD _____ BGOCD 305
Beat Goes On / Oct '95 / Pinnacle.

Harte, Fin

IRELAND CALLING
CD _____ CDPLAY 1035
Play / Oct '95 / Avid/BMG.

Harter Attack

HUMAN HELL
Death bells of the apocalypse / Last temptation / Slaves of conformity / Message from God / Nuclear attack / Human hell / Culture decay / Thugs against drugs / Symbol of hate / Let the sleeping dogs die
CD _____ CORE 1CD
Metalcore / Jul '89 / Plastic Head.

Hartford, John

DOWN ON THE RIVER
Here I am again in love / Bring your clothes back home / Wish I had our time again / All I got is gone away / Delta queen waltz / Old time river man / Men all want to be hobos / Right in the middle of falling for you / There'll never be another you / Little boy / General Jackson
CD _____ FF 70514
Flying Fish / '88 / Roots / CM / Direct / ADA.

HARTFORD & HARTFORD
CD _____ FF 566CD
Flying Fish / Jun '94 / Roots / CM / Direct / ADA.

MARK TWANG
Skippin' in the Mississippi dew / Long hot summer days / Let him go on Mama / Don't leave your records in the sun / Tater Tate and Allen Mundy / Julia Belle Swain / Little cabin home on the hill Waugh Waugh / Austin minor sympathy / Lowest pair / Tryin' to do something to get your attention
CD _____ FF 70020
Flying Fish / Oct '89 / Roots / CM / Direct / ADA.

ME OH MY, HOW TIME DOES FLY
CD _____ FF 440CD
Flying Fish / Jun '94 / Roots / CM / Direct / ADA.

MORNING BUGLE
CD _____ ROUCD 03656
Rounder / Aug '95 / CM / Direct / ADA / Cadillac.

Hartley, Pete

CLASSICS
Ave Maria / Danny boy / Killing me softly / Jesu joy of man's desiring / Lately / Air on a G string / Georgia / Nimrod / Moon dance / Bridge over troubled water / Walking in the air / And I love her / Way we were / Cavatina
CD _____ CDGRS 1226
Grosvenor / '91 / Target/BMG.

JAZZ PROJECT, THE
Autumn leaves / One note samba / Body and soul / Yardbird suite / Shoddy bop / Take the 'A' train / Gypsy with spots / Mr. P.C. / Ninth floor tasman / Night and day / Ornithology / Night in Tunisia / Birdland / Pent-up house / Spain
CD _____ CDGRS 1236
Grosvenor / '91 / Target/BMG.

MORE CLASSICS
We've only just begun / Goodbye to love / Chi mai / Lyin' eyes / Midnight train to Georgia / Aria / I shot the sheriff / Desperado / Deacon blues / Laughter in the rain / Stairway to heaven / Just the two of us / Wedding of Kevin and Claire / Nessun Dorma / Gymnopedie No.1 / Oye como va / Everything I do (I do it for you)
CD _____ CDGRS 1251
Grosvenor / '91 / Target/BMG.

Hartley, Trevor

HARTICAL
CD _____ JOVECD 2
Love Music / May '94 / Jetstar.

Hartman, Dan

INSTANT REPLAY
Instant replay / Countdown this is it / Double O Love / Chocolate box / Love is a natural / Time and space
CD _____ 983383 2
Carlton Home Entertainment / Feb '94 / Carlton Home Entertainment.

KEEP THE FIRE BURNIN'
Keep the fire burnin' / Love in your eyes / Living in America / I can dream about you / Name of the game / We are the young / Free ride / Vertigo / Relight my fire / Instant reply / Countdown / This is it
CD _____ 4777592
Columbia / Apr '95 / Sony.

Hartman, Johnny

I JUST DROPPED BY TO SAY HELLO
Charade / Our time / In the wee small hours of the morning / Sleeping bee / Don't you care / Kiss and run / If I'm lucky / I just dropped by to say hello / Stairway to the stars / Don't call it love / How sweet it is to be in love
CD _____ IMP 11762
Impulse Jazz / Oct '95 / BMG / New Note.

THIS ONE'S FOR TED
CD _____ ACD 181
Audiophile / Feb '91 / Jazz Music / Swift.

UNFORGETTABLE
Almost like being in love / Once in a while / Isn't it romantic / Our love is here to stay / More I see you / What do I owe you / Bidin' my time / Down in the depths / Fools rush in (where angels fear to tread) / Very thought of you / Unforgettable / Ain't misbehavin' / Today I love everybody / T'aint no need / For the want of a kiss / Girl talk / That old black magic
CD _____ IMP 11522
GRP / Aug '95 / BMG / New Note.

VOICE THAT IS
My ship / More I see you / These foolish things / Waltz for Debbie / It never entered my mind / Day the world stopped turning / Slow hot wind / Funny world / Joey Joey Joey / Let me love you / Sunrise sunset
CD _____ GRP 11442
GRP / Nov '95 / BMG / New Note.

Hartsman, Johnny

MADE IN GERMANY (Hartsman, Johnny & The Blues Company)
CD _____ INAK 9025
In Akustik / Jul '95 / Magnum Music Group.

Hartz, Hans

GNADENIOB
CD _____ 810 727 2
Mercury / '00 / PolyGram.

MORGENGRAUEN
CD _____ 818 352 2
Mercury / '88 / PolyGram.

Harvest Ministers

FEELING MISSION, THE
That won't wash / I've a mind / Drowning man / Temple to love / Dealing with a kid / Cleaning out the store / Only seat of power / Innoportune girl / She's burned / Modernising the new you / Mental charge / Secret way / Out of costume (Features only on CD.) / Happy to abort (Features on CD & MC only.)
CD _____ SETCD 019
Setanta / Apr '95 / Vital.

LITTLE DARK MANSION
Grey matters / Railroaded / Forfeit trials / Little dark mansion / Silent house / I gotta lie down / Fictitious Christmas / River wedding / Rug / When you have a faint heart / I hang from a great big oak / Dominique / Don't you ever
CD _____ SARAH 616CD
Sarah / Sep '93 / Vital.

Harvest Theory

HARVEST THEORY
CD _____ SBR 0072
Spring Box / Aug '95 / SRD.

Harvey, Alex

ALEX HARVEY BAND IN CONCERT (Harvey, Alex Band)
CD _____ WINCCD 002
Windsong / Sep '91 / Pinnacle.

ALL SENSATIONS (Harvey, Alex Sensational Band)
Midnight moses / Action strasse / Delilah / St. Anthony / Sgt. Fury / Next / Give my compliments to the chef / Gang bang / Framed / Faith healer / Vambo marble eye / Anthem
CD _____ 512 201-2
Vertigo / Jun '92 / PolyGram.

BBC LIVE IN CONCERT (Harvey, Alex Sensational Band)
Next / Faith healer / Give my compliments to the chef / Delilah / Boston tea party / Pick it up and kick it / Smouldering
CD _____ WHISCD 004
Windsong / Oct '94 / Pinnacle.

BEST OF THE SENSATIONAL ALEX HARVEY BAND, THE (Harvey, Alex Sensational Band)
Delilah (Live) / Cheek to cheek (Live) / Jungle ruboot / Man in the jar / Weights made of lead / Sgt. Fury / Boston tea party / Next / Gamblin' bar room blues / Tomorrow belongs to me (Live) / Snakebite / School's out / Love story / Faith healer / Framed
CD _____ MCCD 001
Music Club / Feb '91 / Disc / THE / CM.

DELILAH (Harvey, Alex Sensational Band)
Delilah / Money honey / Impossible dream / Last of the teenage idols / Shake that thing / Framed / Anthem / Gamblin' bar room blues / Tomorrow belongs to me / There's no light on the Christmas tree Mother, they're burni / Cheek to cheek / Runaway / School's out / Faith healer
CD _____ 5506332
Spectrum/Karussell / Aug '94 / PolyGram / THE.

LIVE IN GLASGOW 1993 (Harvey, Alex Band)
Faithhealer / St. Anthony / Framed / Gang bang / Amos moses / Boston tea party / Midnight moses / Vambo marble eye / Armed and ready / Delilah
CD _____ JIMBO 001
Grapevine / Apr '94 / Grapevine.

MAFIA STOLE MY GUITAR (Harvey, Alex New Band)
Don's delight / Back in the depot / Wait for me Mama / Mafia stole my guitar / Shakin' all over / Whalers / Oh spartacus / Just a gigolo / I ain't got nobody
CD _____ MAUCD 608
Mau Mau / Sep '91 / Pinnacle.

PORTRAIT: SAHB (Harvey, Alex Sensational Band)
CD _____ STFCD 1
Start / Sep '87 / Koch.

Harvey, Bobby

CEILIDH DANCES (Harvey, Bobby & His Ceilidh Band)
CD _____ CDLOC 1058
Lochshore / Dec '90 / ADA / Direct / Duncans.

Harvey, 'Kike

LA ISLA BONITA
CD _____ TUMICD 048
Tumi / '95 / Sterns / Discovery.

SALSA PACHANGA Y AMOR
CD _____ TUMICD 039
Tumi / Jun '93 / Storno / Discovery.

Harvey, Mick

INTOXICATED MAN
CD _____ CDSTUMM 144
Mute / Oct '95 / Disc.

Harvison, Jon

LONELY AS THE MOON
CD _____ D 001CD
Drive On / Jul '95 / ADA.

Hash

BASH
Twilight ball / Ghetto / Mr. Hello / I forgot my blanket / Operation herve / 4.30 a.m. hikes / Kit and kaboodle / In the grass / Mary I wanna / Orchard moons / Travelling / I'm down / American chorus / My icy death
CD _____ 755961513-2
Elektra / Nov '93 / Warner Music.

Hashim, Michael

BLUE STREAK, A
CD _____ STCD 546
Stash / '92 / Jazz Music / CM / Cadillac / Direct / ADA.

GUYS AND DOLLS
CD _____ STCD 558
Stash / Jun '93 / Jazz Music / CM / Cadillac / Direct / ADA.

TRANSATLANTIC AIRS
Have you met Miss Jones / Love song from threepenny opera / Speak low / Corn squeezin's / Charade / Play the notes you like the loudest / My ship / Pleasures and regrets / Do everything / Born to be blue / Tickle toe
CD _____ 33 JAZZ 023
33 Jazz / Jul '95 / Cadillac / New Note.

Haskell, Gordon

IT IS AND IT ISN'T
CD _____ 7567805522
Atlantic / Jan '96 / Warner Music.

IT'S JUST ANOTHER PLOT TO DRIVE YOU CRAZY
CD _____ VP 118CD
Voice Print / Jan '93 / Voice Print.

VOICEPRINT RADIO SESSION
CD _____ VPR 001CD
Voice Print / Oct '94 / Voice Print.

Haskins, Fuzzy

WHOLE NOTHER/RADIO ACTIVE THANG
Tangerine green / Cookie jar / Mr. Junk man / I can see myself in you / Fuz and da boog / Which way do I disco / Love's now is for ever / Sometimes I rock and roll / I'll be loving you / Right back where I started from / Not yet / I think I got my thang together / This situation called love / Gimme back (Some of the love you got from me) / Things we used to do / Woman / Sinderella / Silent day
CD _____ CDSEWD 093
Westbound / Sep '94 / Pinnacle.

Haslam, Annie

ANNIE IN WONDERLAND
Introlise / If I were made of music / I never believed in love / If I loved you / Hunioco / Rockalise / Nature boy / Inside my life / Going home
CD _____ INT 30092
Intuition / May '91 / New Note.

CD _____ 7599265152
WEA / Jan '96 / Warner Music.

Haslinger

FUTURE PRIMITIVE
CD _____ WLD 9211
Varese Sarabande/Colosseum / Apr '95 / Pinnacle / Silva Screen.

Haslip, Jimmy

ARC
Outland / Old town / Ninos / Leap / Orange guitars / I dreamt of you / Mafia / Red cloud / Market street / Hannah's house
CD _____ GRP 97262
GRP / Aug '93 / BMG / New Note.

Hasni, Cheb

CHEB HASNI
CD _____ CDSB 107
Club Du Disque Arabe / Sep '95 / Harmonia Mundi / ADA.

LATBKICHE
CD _____ CDSB 103
Club Du Disque Arabe / Sep '95 / Harmonia Mundi / ADA.

TALGHIYABEK YA GHOZAZI
CD _____ CDSB 102
Club Du Disque Arabe / Sep '95 / Harmonia Mundi / ADA.

Hassan, Chalf

SONGS AND DANCES FROM MOROCCO
CD _____ EUCD 1170
ARC / '91 / ARC Music / ADA.

Hassan, Nazia

HOT LINE
CD _____ DMUT 1043
Multitone / Mar '88 / BMG.

Hassan, Umar Bin

BE BOP OR BE DEAD
Niggers are scared of revolution / A.M. / Bum rush / Malcolm / Pop / Love / 40 Deuce Street / Personal things / This is madness (Mixes)
CD _____ 5180482
Axiom / Nov '93 / PolyGram / Vital.

Hasselgard, Ake 'Stan'

PERMANENT HASSELGARD, THE
Hallelujah / All the things you are / Am I blue / Lullaby in rhythm / Swedish pastry / Mel's idea
CD _____ NCD 8802
Phontastic / '93 / Wellard / Jazz Music / Cadillac.

PERMANENT STAN HASSELGARD WITH THE AMERICANS (1945-48)
CD _____ PHONTCD 8802
Phontastic / '88 / Wellard / Jazz Music / Cadillac.

Hasselhoff, David

MIRACLE OF LOVE
CD _____ 74321176182
Arista / Nov '93 / BMG.

NIGHT ROCKER
CD _____ WMSD 8878
Woodford Music / Feb '93 / THE.

Hassell, Jon

AKA/DARBARI/JAVA (Magic Realism)
Empire / Darbari extension
CD _____ EEGCD 31
EG / Feb '91 / EMI.

CITY: WORKS OF FICTION
Voiceprint / Mombasa / In the city of red dust / Ba ya d / Out of Adedara / Pagan / Tikal / Rain / Warriors
CD _____ ASCD 11
All Saints / Aug '92 / Vital / Discovery.

DREAM THEORY IN MALAYA
Chor moire / Courage / Dream theory / Datu bintung at jelong / Malay / These times / Gift of fire
CD _____ EEGCD 13
EG / Feb '91 / EMI.

DRESSING FOR PLEASURE
CD _____ 936245523-2
Warner Bros. / Nov '94 / Warner Music.

EARTHQUAKE ISLAND
CD _____ 269 612 2
Tomato / Mar '90 / Vital.

FLASH OF THE SPIRIT (Hassell, Jon & Farafina)
Flash of the spirit (laughter) / Night moves (fear) / Air Afrique (wind) / Out pours (body) / Blue (prayer) / Tango (play) / Like warriors everywhere (courage) / Dreamworld (dance) / Tales of the near future (clairvoyance) / Vampire dances / Masque
CD _____ INT 30092
Intuition / May '91 / New Note.

FOURTH WORLD MUSIC (Hassell, Jon & Brian Eno)
Chemistry / Delta rain dream / Griot (over Contagious Magic) / Ba-benzele / Rising thermal / Charm
CD _____ EEGCD 7
EG / Jan '87 / EMI.

POWER SPOT (Hassell, Jon & Brian Eno)
Power spot / Passage D E / Solaire / Miracle steps / Wing melodies / Elephant and the orchid / Air
CD _____ 8294662
ECM / Oct '86 / New Note.

SULLA STRADA
Sotto Il cielo, in un punto / Passaggio a nord-ovest / Ho avuto una visione, anch'io / Temperature variabili / Camminavo nella sera piena di lilla / Tenera e la notte / Frontiera a sud est / Tramonto caldo umido / Notte umidita crescente
CD _____ MASOCD 90066
Materiali Sonori / May '91 / New Note.

SURGEON OF THE NIGHTSKY, THE
Ravinia/Vancouver / Paris 1 / Hamburg / Brussels / Paris 2
CD _____ INT 30042
Intuition / May '91 / New Note.

Hatchett's Swingtette

HATCHETT'S SWINGTETTE FEATURING STEPHANE GRAPELLI (Hatchett's Swingtette & Stephane Grapelli)
Alexander's ragtime band / Ting a ling / Beat me Daddy, eight to the bar / Playmates / Oh Johnny! Oh Johnny! Oh / Sweet potato piper / Sheikh of Araby / Oh how he misses his missus / I hear bluebirds / Wrap yourself in cotton wool / Scrub me Mama with a boogie beat / Blue ribbon rag / Twelfth Street rag / She had those dark and dreamy eyes / Scatterbrain / In the mood / I got rhythm / It's a hap-hap-happy day / Papa's in bed with his breeches on / Mind the Handel's hot / Ma, he's making eyes at me / Bluebirds in the moonlight
CD _____ PASTCD 9785
Flapper / Mar '92 / Pinnacle.

Hater

HATER
CD _____ 5401372
A&M / Apr '95 / PolyGram.

Hatfield & The North

HATFIELD AND THE NORTH
Stubbs effect / Big jobs (poo poo extract) / Going up to people and tinkling / Calyx / Son of "There's no place like Homerton" / Aigrette / Rifferama / Fol de rol / Shaving is boring / Licks for the ladies / Bossa nochance / Big jobs No.2 / Lobster in cleavage probe / Gigantic land crabs in Earth takeover bid / Other Stubbs effect / Let's eat (real soon) (CD only) / Fitter Stoke has a bath (CD only)
CD _____ CDV 2008
Virgin / Jul '87 / EMI.

LIVE
CD _____ NINETY 6
Demon / Feb '93 / Pinnacle / ADA.

ROTTERS CLUB, THE
Share it / Lounging there trying / (Big) John Wayne socks psychology on the jaw / Chaos at the greasy spoon / Yes no interlude / Fitter Stoke has a bath / Didn't matter anyway / Underdub / Mumps (Your Majesty, is like a cream donut-quiet) / Mumps (lumps) / Mumps (prenut) / Mumps (your majesty is like a cream donut-loud) / Halfway between heaven and earth (CD only) / Oh Len's nature (CD only) / Lying and gracing (CD only)
CD _____ CDV 2030
Virgin / Jun '88 / EMI.

Hatfield, Juliana

BECOME WHAT YOU ARE
Supermodel / My sister / This is the sound / For the birds / Mabel / Dame with a rod / Addicted / Feelin' Massachusetts / Spin the bottle / President Garfield / Little pieces / I got no idols
CD _____ 4509935292
East West / Aug '93 / Warner Music.

ONLY EVERYTHING
CD _____ 4509998862
East West / Mar '95 / Warner Music.

Hathaway, Donny

DONNY HATHAWAY COLLECTION, A
Song for you / I love you more than you'll ever know / You were meant for me / Back together again / Where is the love / For all we know / Someday we'll all be free / Giving up / Closer I get to you / You are my heaven / What's goin' on / Ghetto / To be young, gifted and black / You've got a friend / This Christmas
CD _____ 7567820922
Atlantic / Apr '93 / Warner Music.

DONNY HATHAWAY IN PERFORMANCE
CD _____ 7567815692
Atlantic / Jan '96 / Warner Music.

EVERYTHING IS EVERYTHING
Voices inside / Je vous aime / I believe to my soul / Misty / Sugar Lee / Tryin' times / Thank you master / Ghetto / To be young, gifted and black
CD _____ 7567903982
Atlantic / Jan '96 / Warner Music.

Hato De Foces

CANTAR DE CAMINO
CD _____ J 1017CD
Sonifolk / Jun '94 / ADA / CM.

Hatoba, Omoide

KINSEI
Kinsei / Alternative funkaholic / Gion / Amen / We are hello / Mashroom airline / Sweet pea / Rock noodle / Oyaji / Touch / Theme from the ghost mountains / Good by Submarine / Japan dissolution / Human tornado / Satelite groove / Go
CD _____ EN 003
Earthnoise / Feb '96 / Vital.

Hatrix

COLLISIONCOURSSE
CD _____ MASSCD 040
Massacre / Nov '94 / Plastic Head.

Haujobb

FREEZE FRAME FACILITY
CD _____ SPV 08422192
SPV / May '95 / Plastic Head.

Haunted

HAUNTED, THE
CD _____ VOXXCD 2011
Voxx / Aug '95 / Else / Disc.

Haunted Garage

POSSESSION PARK
CD _____ CDZORRO 27
Metal Blade / Aug '91 / Pinnacle.

Hause, Alfred

STRICTLY DANCING: TANGO (Hause, Alfred & Big Tango Orchestra)
CD _____ 15340
Laserlight / May '94 / Target/BMG.

Have Mercy

HAVE MERCY
CD _____ CCD 11039
Crosscut / Jan '94 / ADA / CM / Direct.

Havel, Vaclav

TWO PRESIDENTS JAM SESSION (Havel, Vaclav & Bill Clinton)
CD _____ CR 0001-2
Czech Radio / Nov '95 / Czech Music Enterprises.

Havens, Bob

IN NEW ORLEANS
CD _____ BCD 126
GHB / Jun '95 / Jazz Music.

Havens, Richie

CUTS TO THE CHASE
They dance alone / Times they are a' changin / Lives in the balance / Hawk / Old love / At a glance
CD _____ ESSCD 212
Essential / Jun '94 / Total/BMG.

RICHIE HAVENS SINGS BEATLES AND DYLAN
CD _____ RCD 20035
Rykodisc / May '92 / Vital / ADA.

SIMPLE THING
CD _____ RBD 400
Start / Jun '87 / Koch.

Havoc Mass

KILLING THE FUTURE
CD _____ MASSCD 019
Massacre / Dec '93 / Plastic Head.

Havohej

DETHRONE THE SON OF GOD
CD _____ CANDLE 004CD
Candlelight / Oct '93 / Plastic Head.

Hawes, Hampton

BLUES FOR BUD (1968)
Blues enough / Sonora / They say it's wonderful / Black forest / Spanish steps / My romance / Dangerous / Blues for Bud
CD _____ BLCD 760126
Black Lion / '92 / Jazz Music / Cadillac / Wellard / Koch.

FOUR
Four / Yardbird suite / There will never be another you / Bow jest / Sweet Sue, just you / Up blues / Like someone in love / Love is just around the corner / Thou swell / Awful truth
CD _____ OJCCD 165-2

Original Jazz Classics / May '93 / Wellard / Jazz Music / Cadillac / Complete/Pinnacle.

HAMPTON HAWES TRIO VOL. 1
CD _____ OJCCD 316
Original Jazz Classics / Nov '95 / Wellard / Jazz Music / Cadillac / Complete/Pinnacle.

HIGH IN THE SKY
CD _____ FSCD 59
Fresh Sound / Oct '90 / Jazz Music / Discovery.

MONTREUX '71 (Hawes, Hampton Trio)
CD _____ FSCD 133
Fresh Sound / Jan '91 / Jazz Music / Discovery.

Hawkes, Chesney

GET THE PICTURE
Tell me something I don't know / What's wrong with this picture / Help me to help myself / Sometimes / Black or white people / Missing you already / One of those days / Fairweather Christian / Family way / Every little tear
CD _____ CDCHR 6011
Chrysalis / Jun '93 / EMI.

Hawkins, Coleman

APRIL IN PARIS
Body and soul / When day is done / Bouncing with Bean / April in Paris / Angel face / I love you / There will never be another you / Little girl blue / Bean stalks again / Have you met Miss Jones
CD _____ ND 90636
Bluebird / Apr '92 / BMG.

AT EASE WITH COLEMAN HAWKINS
CD _____ OJCCD 181
Original Jazz Classics / Nov '95 / Wellard / Jazz Music / Cadillac / Complete/Pinnacle.

AT THE OPERA HOUSE (Hawkins, Coleman & Roy Eldridge)
CD _____ 521641-2
Verve / Oct '94 / PolyGram.

BEAN AND BEN (Hawkins, Coleman & Ben Webster)
In the hush of the night / Out to lunch / Every man for himself / Look out, Jack / On the bean / Recollections / Flyin' Hawk / Drifting on a reed / Broke but happy / Blues on the bayou / Jumpin' with Judy / Blues on the delta / Bottle's only / Save it pretty Mama / For lovers only / Peach Tree Street blues
CD _____ HQCD 04
Harlequin / Oct '90 / Swift / Jazz Music / Wellard / Hot Shot / Cadillac.

BEAN AND THE BOYS
In the hush of the night / Out to lunch / Every man for himself / Look out Jack / On the bean / Recollections / Flyin' hawk / Drifting on a reed / I mean you / Bean and the boys / Bean and the boys (take 2) / Cocktails for two / You go to my head / Stasch / Trust in me / Roll 'em Pete / Skrouk / Since I fell for you / My babe
CD _____ LEJAZZCD 12
Le Jazz / Jun '93 / Charly / Cadillac.

BEAN AND THE BOYS
CD _____ PRCD 24124
Prestige / Oct '93 / Complete/Pinnacle / Cadillac.

BEAN STALKIN' (Hawkins, Coleman & Friends)
Bean stalkin' / Stompin' at the Savoy / Take the 'A' train / Indian Summer / Crazy rhythm / (Back home again in) Indiana
CD _____ CD 2310933
Pablo / Jun '93 / Jazz Music / Cadillac / Complete/Pinnacle.

BEAN, THE
CD _____ CD 53168
Giants Of Jazz / Jan '94 / Target/BMG / Cadillac.

BIG BANDS 1940 (Hawkins, Coleman & Erskine Hawkins)
Tuxedo junction / I'll be faithful / Whispering grass / Gin mill blues / Junction blues / Gabriel meets the Duke / Leanin' on the old top rail / Midnight stroll / Body and soul / Chant of the groove / Forgive a fool / Asleep in the deep / Can't get Indiana off my mind / Passin' it around / When a congresman meets a senator down South / I can't believe that you're in love with me
CD _____ TAXCD 3707
Tax / Apr '90 / Jazz Music / Wellard / Cadillac.

BODY AND SOUL
Meet Dr. Foo / Fine dinner / She's funny that way / Body and soul / When day is done / Sheikh of araby / My blue Heaven / Bouncing with Bean / Say it isn't so / Spotite / April in Paris / How strange / Half step down please / Angel face / Jumping for Jane / I love you / There will never be another you / Little girl blue / Dinner for one please James / I never knew / His very own blues / Thirty nine inches / Bean stalks again / I'm shooting high / Have you met Miss Jones / Day you came along / Essence of you
CD _____ ND 85717
Bluebird / '91 / BMG.

BODY AND SOUL
Rifftide / Man I love / Body and soul / Caravan / Love for sale / Love come back to me
CD _____ WW 2018
West Wind / May '93 / Swift / Charly / CM / ADA.

BODY AND SOUL
CD _____ CDCD 1121
Charly / Jul '93 / Charly / THE / Cadillac.

BODY AND SOUL
CD _____ TPZ 1022
Topaz Jazz / Jun '95 / Pinnacle / Cadillac.

CLASSICS 1943-44
CD _____ CLASSICS 807
Classics / Mar '95 / Discovery / Jazz Music.

CLASSICS 1944
CD _____ CLASSICS 842
Classics / Nov '95 / Discovery / Jazz Music.

COLEMAN HAWKINS
Jazz Portraits / Jul '94 / Jazz Music. _____ CD 14560

COLEMAN HAWKINS 1927/39
CD _____ RPCD 600
Moidart / Jul '92 / Conifer / ADA.

COLEMAN HAWKINS 1929-34
CD _____ CLASSICS 587
Classics / Aug '91 / Discovery / Jazz Music.

COLEMAN HAWKINS 1934-37
CD _____ CLASSICS 602
Classics / '91 / Discovery / Jazz Music.

COLEMAN HAWKINS 1937-39
CD _____ CLASSICS 613
Classics / Feb '92 / Discovery / Jazz Music.

COLEMAN HAWKINS 1939-40
CD _____ CLASSICS 634
Classics / '92 / Discovery / Jazz Music.

COLEMAN HAWKINS 1959-62 (Hawkins, Coleman, Roy Eldridge & Mickey Baker)
CD _____ STCD 538
Stash / '91 / Jazz Music / CM / Cadillac / Direct / ADA.

COLEMAN HAWKINS AND BENNY CARTER (Hawkins, Coleman & Benny Carter)
CD _____ UCD 19011
Forlane / Jun '95 / Target/BMG.

COLEMAN HAWKINS MEETS THE BIG SAX SECTION (Hawkins, Coleman & The Big Sax Section)
Ooga dooga / I've grown accustomed to your face / Thanks for the misery / Evening at Papa Joe's / There is nothing like a dame / Thanks for the misery (2)
CD _____ SV 0248
Savoy Jazz / Oct '94 / Conifer / ADA.

COLEMAN HAWKINS WITH THE SECTION
CD _____ VG 650134
Vogue / Oct '92 / BMG.

COMPLETE RECORDINGS 1929-1940, THE (6CD Set)
Hello Lola / One hour (If I could be with you one hour tonight) / Dismal Dan / Down Georgia way / Girls like you were meant for boys like me / Georgia on my mind / I can't believe that you're in love with me / Darktown strutter's ball / (I'll be glad when you're dead) you rascal you / Someday sweetheart / I wish I could shimmy like my sister Kate / River's takin' care of me / Ain't cha got music / Stringin' along on a shoe string / Shadows on the Swanee / Day you came along / Jamaica shout / Heartbreak blues / Blues rhapsody / Happy feet / I'm rhythm crazy now / Ol' man river / Minnie the moocher's wedding day / Ain't cha glad / I've got to sing a torch song / Hush my mouth / You're gonna lose your gal / Dark clouds / My Galveston gal / Georgia jubilee / Junk man / Ol' pappy / Emaline / I ain't got nobody / It sends me / On the sunny side of the street / Lullaby / Lady be good / Lost in a fog / I wish I were twins / I only have eyes for you / After you've gone / Some of these days / Honeysuckle rose / Hands across the table / Blue moon / Avalon / What a difference a day makes / Star dust / Chicago / Meditation / What Harlem is to me / Netcha's dream / Love cries / Sorrow / Tiger rag / It may not be true / I'm in the mood for love / I wanna go back to Harlem / Consolation / Strange fact / Original Dixieland one-step / Smiles / Something is gonna give me away / Crazy rhythm / Out of nowhere / Sweet Georgia brown / Lamentation / Devotion / Somebody loves me / Mighty like the blues / Pardon me pretty baby / My buddy / Well alright then / Blues evermore / Dear old Southland / Way down yonder in New Orleans / I know that you know / When buddha smiles / Swinging in the groove / My melancholy baby / Meet Dr. Foo / Fine dinner / She's funny that way / Body and soul / When day is done / Sheikh of araby / My blue heaven / Bouncing with Bean / Smack / I surrender dear / Dedication / Passin' it around / Serenade to a sleeping beauty / Rocky comfort / Forgive

a fool / Bugle call rag / One o'clock jump / 9-20 special / Feedin' the bean
CD Set _____ CDAFS 1026-6
Affinity / Sep '92 / Charly / Cadillac / Jazz Music.

DESAFINADO (Hawkins, Coleman Sextet)
Desafinado / I'm looking over a four leaf clover / Samba para bean / I remember you / One-note samba / O pato / Um abraco no bonfa / Stumpy bossa nova
CD _____ MCAD 33118
Impulse Jazz / Apr '90 / BMG / New Note.

EARLY YEARS, THE
CD _____ CDSGP 0158
Prestige / Sep '95 / Total/BMG.

ENCOUNTERS (Hawkins, Coleman & Ben Webster)
Blues for Yolande / It never entered my mind / La Rosita / You'd be so nice to come home to / Prisoner of love / Tangerine / Shine on harvest moon
CD _____ 8231202
Verve / Nov '91 / PolyGram.

GENIUS OF COLEMAN HAWKINS, THE
I'll never be the same / You're blase / I wished on the moon / How long has this been going on / Like someone in love / Melancholy baby / Ill wind / In a mellow tone / There's no you / World is waiting for the sunrise / Somebody loves me / Blues for Rene
CD _____ 825 673-2
Verve / Jan '86 / PolyGram.

HAWK EYES
CD _____ OJCCD 294-2
Original Jazz Classics / Feb '92 / Wellard / Jazz Music / Cadillac / Complete/Pinnacle.

HAWK FLIES HIGH, THE
Chant / Juicy fruit / Think deep / Laura / Blue lights / Sanctity
CD _____ OJCCD 027
Original Jazz Classics / Oct '92 / Wellard / Jazz Music / Cadillac / Complete/Pinnacle.

HAWK IN EUROPE, THE (1934-1937)
Lullaby / Lost in a fog / Lady be good / Avalon / What a difference a day makes / Stardust / Meditation / Netcha's dream / Strange fact / Crazy rhythm / Honeysuckle rose / Out of nowhere / Sweet Georgia Brown / Mighty like the blues / Pardon me pretty baby / Somebody loves me / My buddy / Well alright then
CD _____ CD AJA 5054
Living Era / Jul '88 / Koch.

HAWK IN PARIS, THE
CD _____ 07863 51059-2
Bluebird / Jul '93 / BMG.

HAWK RETURNS, THE
Flight eleven / Modern fantasy / Confessin' / September song / They can't take that away from me / Should I / I'll follow my secret heart / I'll tell you later / What a difference a day makes / On my way / Last stop / Goin' down home
CD _____ SV 0182
Savoy Jazz / Oct '92 / Conifer / ADA.

HAWK SWINGS, THE
Cloudy / Almost dawn / Stake out / Crosstown / Shadows
CD _____ CDBOP 015
Boplicity / Jul '91 / Pinnacle / Cadillac.

HAWK TAKES FLIGHT, THE
Jamaica shout / Heartbreak blues / I ain't got nobody / On the sunny side of the street / Lullaby / Lady be good / After you've gone / I wish I were twins / Blue moon / Avalon / What a difference a day makes / Star dust / Chicago / Meditation / Something is gonna give me away / Honeysuckle rose / Crazy rhythm / Out of nowhere / Sweet Georgia Brown / Devotion / I know that you know / Swinging in the groove / My melancholy baby / At the Darktown strutter's ball / Body and soul
CD _____ CDHD 230
Happy Days / Aug '93 / Conifer.

HAWK TALKS
Lucky duck / I can't get started (with you) / Foolin' around / Man I love / Trust in me / Where is your heart / Wishing / Carioca / If I could be with you one hour tonight / Ruby / Sin / Midnight sun / And so to sleep again / Lonely wine
CD _____ FSCD 130
Fresh Sound / Jan '91 / Jazz Music / Discovery.

HAWK TAWK
CD _____ TCD 1007
Rykodisc / Feb '96 / Vital / ADA.

IN A MELLOW TONE
You blew out the flame in my heart / I want to be loved / In a mellow tone / Greensleeves / Through for the night / Until the real thing comes along / Sweetest sounds / Then I'll be tired of you / Jammin' in swingville
CD _____ OJCCD 6001
Original Jazz Classics / Apr '93 / Wellard / Jazz Music / Cadillac / Complete/Pinnacle.

IN EUROPE 1934-39 (VOLUMES 1, 2 & 3)
CD _____ CBC 1006
Bellaphon / Jun '93 / New Note.

JAZZ MASTERS
CD _____ 5218562
Verve / Apr '94 / PolyGram.

LADY BE GOOD
Lullaby / Lady be good / Lost in a fog / Honeysuckle rose / Some of these days / After you've gone / After you've gone (alternative take) / I only have eyes for you / I only have eyes for you (alternative take) / I wish I were twins / I wish I were twins (alternative takes) / Hands across the table / Hands across the tables (alternative take) / Blue moon / Avalon / What a difference a day makes / Stardust / Chicago / Chicago (alternate take) / Meditation / What Harlem is to me / What Harlem is to me (alternate take) / Netcha's dream
CD _____ CDGRF 093
Tring / '93 / Tring / Prism.

LIVE FROM THE LONDON HOUSE (Chicago 1963) (Hawkins, Coleman Quartet)
CD _____ JASMCD 2521
Jasmine / Nov '93 / Wellard / Swift / Conifer / Cadillac / Magnum Music Group.

MASTER, THE
I only have eyes for you / 'S wonderful / I'm in the mood for love / Bean at the met / Flame thrower / Imagination / Night and day / Cattin' at the Keynote / On the sunny side of the street / Three little words / Battle of the saxes / Louise / Make believe / Don't blame me / Just one of those things / Hallelujah / I'm yours / Under a blanket of blue / Beyond the blue horizon / (In) a shanty in old Shanty Town
CD _____ LEJAZZCD 37
Le Jazz / May '95 / Charly / Cadillac.

MASTERS OF JAZZ VOL.12
CD _____ STCD 4112
Storyville / Feb '89 / Jazz Music / Wellard / CM / Cadillac.

PASSIN' IT AROUND
CD _____ JHR 73515
Jazz Hour / '91 / Target/BMG / Jazz Music / Cadillac.

PICASSO
CD _____ CD 53117
Giants Of Jazz / Nov '92 / Target/BMG / Cadillac.

QUINTESSENCE 1926-44, THE (2 CD)
CD Set _____ FA 213
Fremeaux / Nov '95 / Discovery / ADA.

RAINBOW MIST
CD _____ DDCD 459
Delmark / Aug '93 / Hot Shot / ADA / CM / Direct / Cadillac.

RARE RECORDINGS AND SOUNDTRACKS (The Golden Age of Jazz)
CD _____ JZCD 362
Suisa / May '92 / Jazz Music / THE.

SAVOY BROADCASTS 1940 (Hawkins, Coleman & Erskine Hawkins)
CD _____ TAX 37072
Tax / Aug '94 / Jazz Music / Wellard / Cadillac.

SIRIUS
Man I love / Don't blame me / Just a gigolo / One I love / Time on my hands / Sweet and lovely / Exactly like you / Street of dreams / Sugar
CD _____ OJCCD 861
Original Jazz Classics / Nov '95 / Wellard / Jazz Music / Complete/Pinnacle.

SONG OF THE HAWK
Rhythm crazy / Lady be good / It sends me / Old man river / Heartbreak blues / Day you came along / When day is done / Sweet Georgia Brown / Out of nowhere / Passin' it around / Rocky comfort / My blue heaven / Meet Dr. Foo / Blue moon / What a difference a day makes / Bouncing with bean / He's funny that way / Fine dinner / Star dust / Love cries / I ain't got nobody
CD _____ PASTCD 7032
Flapper / Jan '94 / Pinnacle.

SOUL
CD _____ OJCCD 096
Original Jazz Classics / Oct '92 / Wellard / Jazz Music / Cadillac / Complete/Pinnacle.

STANDARDS AND WARHORSES (Hawkins, Coleman & Red Allen)
CD _____ JASSCD 2
Jass / Oct '91 / CM / Jazz Music / ADA / Cadillac / Direct.

SUPREME
Lover come back to me / Body and soul / In walked bud / Quintessence / Fine and dandy / Ow
CD _____ ENJ 90092
Enja / Apr '95 / New Note / Vital/SAM.

SWINGVILLE 2001 (Hawkins, Coleman & the Red Garland Trio)
It's a blue world / I want to be loved / Red beans and rice / Bean's blues / Blues for Ron

CD _____ OJCCD 418
Original Jazz Classics / Apr '93 / Wellard / Jazz Music / Cadillac / Complete/Pinnacle.

VOGUE RECORDINGS, THE (Hawkins, Coleman & Johnny Hodges)
CD _____ 74321115112
Vogue / Jul '93 / BMG.

WITH HENRY RED ALLEN & HORACE HENDERSON 1933/34 (Hawkins, Coleman/Henry Allen/Horace Henderson)
Someday sweetheart / I wish I could shimmy like my sister Kate / River's takin' care of me / Ain'tcha got music / Stringin' along on a shoe string / Shadows on the Swanee / Day you come along / Jamaica shout / Heartbreak blues / Hush my mouth / You're gonna lose your gal / Dark clouds / My galveston gal / Happy feet / I'm rhythm crazy now / Ol' man river / Minnie the moocher's wedding day / Ain't cha glad / I've got to sing a torch song
CD _____ HEPCD 1028
Hep / Apr '90 / Cadillac / Jazz Music / New Note / Wellard.

Hawkins, Dale

LET'S ALL TWIST
CD _____ EDCD 385
Edsel / Aug '94 / Pinnacle / ADA.

OH SUZY-Q
Suzie Q / Don't treat me this way / Juanita / Tornado / Little pig / Hot dog / Baby baby / Mrs. Mergritory's daughter / Take my heart / Wild wild world / See you soon baboon / Four letter word R.O.C.K.
CD _____ MCD 3063
MCA / Apr '93 / BMG.

Hawkins, Edwin

OH HAPPY DAY (Best of Edwin Hawkins) (Hawkins, Edwin Singers)
Oh happy day / To my father's house / Lord don't move that mountain / Children get together / I heard the voice of Jesus say / Precious memories / Joy joy / He's a friend of mine / I'm going through / Footprints of Jesus / All you need / Jesus / I shall be free / Mine all mine / My Lord is coming back
CD _____ NEMCD 636
Sequel / Jun '93 / BMG.

OH HAPPY DAY (Hawkins, Edwin Singers)
CD _____ MATCD 280
Castle / Feb '95 / BMG.

OH HAPPY DAY (Hawkins, Edwin Singers)
CD _____ TRTCD 149
TrueTrax / Jun '95 / THE.

Hawkins, Erskine

CLASSICS 1938-39
CD _____ CLASSICS 667
Owl / Sep '92 / Harmonia Mundi (USA).

ERSKINE HAWKINS 1940-1941 (Hawkins, Erskine & His Orchestra)
CD _____ CLASSICS 701
Classics / Jul '93 / Discovery / Jazz Music.

TUXEDO JUNCTION
Rockin' rollin' jubilee / Easy rider / Swing out / Tuxedo junction / Sweet Georgia Brown / After hours / Soft winds / Blackout / Don't cry baby / Bear mash blues / Tippin' in
CD _____ ND 90635
Bluebird / Apr '92 / BMG.

Hawkins, Hawkshaw

HAWK 1953-1961 (3CD Set)
I'll trade yours for mine / Heap of lovin' / Mark round your finger / Long way / When you say yes / I'll take a chance with you / I'll never close my heart to you / Why don't you leave this town / Rebound / One white rose / I wanna be hugged to death by you / Why didn't I hear from you / Flashing lights / Waitin' for my baby / Kokomo / Ling ting tong / Pedro Gonzales Tennessee Lopez / How could anything so pretty / Car hoppin' mama / Love you steal / Oh how I cried / Borrowing / If it ain't on the menu / I gotta have you / Standing at the end of the world / I've got it again / Sunny side of the mountain / You just stood there / Dark moon / I'll get even with you / Guilty of dreaming / Are you happy / She was here / Freedom / It's easier said than done / Sensation / Ring on your finger / It would be a doggone lie / My fate is in your hands / I'll be gone / Best of company / Action / You can't find happiness that way / I don't apologise for loving you / With this pen / Thank you for thinking of me / Twenty miles from shore / Big ole heartache / Big red benson / Soldier's joy / Patanio, the pride of the plains / Alaska Lil and Texas Bill / Darkness on the face of the earth / Put a nickel in the jukebox / I can't seem to say goodbye / No love for me / You know me much too well / My story / Love I have for you / Your conscience
CD Set _____ BCD 15539
Bear Family / Aug '91 / Rollercoaster / Direct / CM / Swift / ADA.

HAWKSHAW HAWKINS
CD _____ KCD 587
King/Paddle Wheel / Apr '93 / New Note.

Hawkins, Ronnie

FOLK BALLADS OF RONNIE HAWKINS
Summertime / Sometimes I feel like a motherless child / I gave my love a cherry / Brave man / Poor wayfaring stranger / Virginia bride / Mister and Mississippi / John Henry / Fare thee well / Out of a hundred / Death of Floyd Collins / Love from afar
CD _____ EDCD 386
Edsel / Aug '94 / Pinnacle / ADA.

HELLO AGAIN, MARY LOU (Hawkins, Ronnie & The Hawks)
CD _____ PRD 70242
Provogue / Feb '91 / Pinnacle.

ROULETTE YEARS, THE
Ruby baby / Forty days / Horace / One of these days / What'cha gonna do when the creek runs dry / Wild little Willie / Mary Lou / Oh sugar / Odessa need your lovin' / My girl is red hot / Dizzy Miss Lizzy / Hayride / C riff rock / Baby Jean / Southern love / Someone like you / Hey Boba Lou / Love me like you can / You cheated, you lied / Dreams do come true / Lonely hours / Clara / Honey don't / Sick and tired / Ballad of Caryl Chessman / Summertime / You know I love you / Sexy ways / Come come / Searchin' / Honey love / I feel good / Suzie Q / Matchbox / What a party / Bo Diddley / Who do you love / Bossman / High blood pressure / There's a screw loose / Arkansas / Mojo man / Further on up the road / Nineteen years old / Cathy Jean / Mojo man take 1 / Hayride No.1 / Light in your window / My heart cries / Look for me / Love it up / Your love is what I need / Kansas City / Going to Moscow
CD Set _____ NEDCD 266
Sequel / Oct '94 / BMG.

SINGS THE SONGS OF HANK WILLIAMS
CD _____ EDCD 387
Edsel / Aug '94 / Pinnacle / ADA.

Hawkins, Screamin' Jay

BLACK MUSIC FOR WHITE PEOPLE
Is you is or is you ain't my baby / I feel alright / I put a spell on you / I hear you knocking / Heart attack and vine / Ignant and shit / Swamp gas / Voodoo priestess / Ice cream man / I want your body / Ol' man river / Strokin'
CD _____ FIENDCD 211
Demon / Mar '91 / Pinnacle / ADA.

COW FINGERS AND MOSQUITO PIE
Little demon / You ain't fooling me / I put a spell on you / You made me love you / Yellow coat / Hong Kong / There's something wrong with you / I love Paris / Orange coloured sky / Alligator wine / Darling please forgive me / Take me back to my boots and saddle / Temptation / Frenzy / Person to person / Little demon (2) / I put a spell on you (2) / There's something wrong with you (2) / Alligator wine (2)
CD _____ 4712702
Legacy / Mar '92 / Sony.

I PUT A SPELL ON YOU
Portrait of a man / Itty bitty pretty one / Don't deceive me / What's gonna happen on the 8th day / Ashes / We love / It's only make believe / Please don't leave me / I put a spell on you / I don't know / Guess who / What good is it
CD _____ CDINS 5078
Charly / Jun '93 / Charly / THE / Cadillac.

I SHAKE MY STICK AT YOU
CD _____ AIM 1031CD
Aim / Oct '93 / Direct / ADA / Jazz Music.

LIVE & CRAZY
CD _____ ECD 260032
Evidence / Jan '92 / Harmonia Mundi / ADA / Cadillac.

PORTRAIT OF A MAN
CD _____ EDCD 414
Edsel / Jan '95 / Pinnacle / ADA.

REAL LIFE
Deep in love / Get down France / Serving time / Feast of the Mau-Mau / Poor folks / Constipation blues / Your kind of love / All night / Alligator wine / I feel alright / Mountain jive
CD _____ CDCHARLY 163
Charly / Feb '89 / Charly / THE / Cadillac.

REAL LIFE-1983
CD _____ 157552
Blues Collection / Feb '93 / Discovery.

SOMETHIN' FUNNY GOIN' ON
Somethin' funny goin' on / I am the cool / Whistlin' past the graveyard / Rock the house / Scream the blues / Brujo / You make me sick / Give it a break / When you walked out the door / Fourteen wives
CD _____ FIENDCD 750
Demon / Feb '94 / Pinnacle / ADA.

SPELLBOUND 1955-1974
Voodoo / You put a spell on me / Makaha waves / There's too many teardrops / Two can play this game / Shattered / You're an exception to the rule / I'm not made of clay

/ All night / Mountain jive (unissued) / I'll be there / You're all of my life to me / Well I tried / Even though / Talk about me / In my front room (unissued) / This is all / What that is (unissued) / Put the whamee on me / I put a spell on you / Two can play this game (unissued) / Shattered (unissued) / You're an exception to the rule (unissued) / What that is / Feast of the Mau-Mau / Do you really love me / Stone crazy / I love you / Constipation blues / I'm lonely / Thing called woman / Dig / I'm your man / Ask him / Reprise / Please don't leave me / I want to know / I need you / My Marion / Bit it / Move me / Goodnight my love / Our love is not for three / Ain't nobody business / Take me back / Trying to reach my goal / So long
CD Set _____ BCD 15530
Bear Family / Oct '90 / Rollercoaster / Direct / CM / Swift / ADA.

Hawkins, Sophie B.

TONGUES AND TAILS
Damn, I wish I was your lover / California here I come / Mysteries we understand / Saviour child / Carry me / I want you / Before I walk on fire / We are one body / Listen / Live and let love / Don't stop swaying
CD _____ 4688232
Columbia / Sep '94 / Sony.

WHALER
Right beside you / Did we not choose each other / Don't don't tell me no / As I lay me down / Swing from limb to limb (my home is in your jungle) / True romance / Let me love you up / Ballad of sleeping beauty / I need nothing else / Sometimes I see / Mr. Tugboat Hello
CD _____ 476512-2
Columbia / Aug '94 / Sony.

Hawkins, Ted

BEST OF THE VENICE BEACH TAPES, THE
I got what I wanted / Ladder of success / Gypsy woman / He will break your heart / There stands a glass / Country roads / (Sittin' on) the dock of the bay / Crystal chandeliers / Don't ever leave me / Let the good times roll / Chain gang / San Francisco / Bring it on home to me / Green green grass of home / Part time love / North to Alaska / Quiet place / Your cheatin' heart / Too busy thinking about my baby / Blowin' in the wind / Searchin' for my baby / Just my imagination / I love you most of all
CD _____ UACD 101
UnAmerican Activities / Jul '89 / Hot Shot / Swift.

HAPPY HOUR
CD _____ ROU 2033CD
Rounder / Jul '94 / CM / Direct / ADA / Cadillac.

KERSHAW SESSIONS
CD _____ ROOTCD 006
Strange Fruit / May '95 / Pinnacle.

NEXT HUNDRED YEARS
Strange conversation / Big things / There stands the glass / Biloxi / Groovy little things / Good and the bad / Afraid / Greeneyed girl / Ladder of success / Long as I can make you happy
CD _____ GED 24627
Geffen / Apr '94 / BMG.

ON THE BOARDWALK
CD _____ MRCD 123
Munich / '88 / CM / ADA / Greensleeves / Direct.

ON THE BOARDWALK VOL 2
CD _____ MRCD 126
Munich / '88 / CM / ADA / Greensleeves / Direct.

WATCH YOUR STEP
Watch your step (Acoustic Version) / Bring it home Daddy / If you love me / Don't lose your cool / Lost ones / Who got my natural comb / Peace and Happiness / Sweet baby / Stop your crying / Put in a cross / Sorry you're sick / Watch your step (2) / T.W.A. / I gave up all I had / Stay close to me
CD _____ ROU 2024CD
Rounder / Jul '94 / CM / Direct / ADA / Cadillac.

Hawkins, Tramaine

ALL MY BEST TO YOU
Praise the name of Jesus / Potter's house / What shall I do / Goin' up yonder / All things are possible / Changed / Coming home / Highway / He loves me / Who is he / We're all in the same boat together
CD _____ SPD 1429
Alliance Music / Aug '95 / EMI.

TO A HIGHER PLACE
Amazing grace / Who's gonna carry you / That's why I love you like I do / Trees / I found the answer
CD _____ 4777542
Columbia / Jul '95 / Sony.

Hawkwind

ACID DAZE
CD Set _____ RRCD 1X
Receiver / May '90 / Grapevine.

ACID DAZE VOLUME 1
CD _____ RRCD 125
Receiver / Aug '93 / Grapevine.

ACID DAZE VOLUME 2
CD _____ RRCD 126
Receiver / Aug '93 / Grapevine.

ACID DAZE VOLUME 3
CD _____ RRCD 127
Receiver / Aug '93 / Grapevine.

ALIEN
CD _____ EBSCD 118
Emergency Broadcast System / Sep '95 / Vital.

ANTHOLOGY - HAWKWIND
CD Set _____ ESBCD 168
Essential / Mar '92 / Total/BMG.

BBC LIVE IN CONCERT
CD _____ WINCD 007
Windsong / Nov '91 / Pinnacle.

BEST OF FRIENDS AND RELATIONS
CD _____ SHARP 1724CD
Flicknife / Nov '88 / Pinnacle.

BEST OF HAWKWIND, THE
CD _____ MATCD 293
Castle / Mar '94 / BMG.

BRING ME THE HEAD OF YURI GAGARIN (Live At The Empire Pool - 1973)
Ga ga / Egg / Orgone accumulator / Wage war / Urban guerilla / Master of the universe / Welcome to the future / Sonic attack / Silver machine
CD _____ CDTB 101
Magnum Music / Dec '92 / Magnum Music Group.

BRITISH TRIBAL MUSIC
CD _____ STFCD 2
Start / Sep '87 / Koch.

BUSINESS TRIP, THE
Altair / Quark, strangeness and charm / LSD / Camera that could lie / Green finned demon / Do that / Day a wall came down / Berlin axis / Void of golden light / Right stuff / Wastelands / Dream goes on / Right to decide / Dream has ended / Future / Terra mystica (Features on DLP only.)
CD _____ EBSCD 111
Emergency Broadcast System / Sep '94 / Vital.

CALIFORNIA BRAINSTORM
CD _____ ILCD 1014
Iloki / Aug '94 / Plastic Head.

CHRONICLE OF THE BLACK SWORD
Song of the swords / Shade gate / Sea king / Pulsing cavern / Eric the enchanter / Needle gun / Zarzinia / Demise / Sleep of a thousand tears / Chaos army / Horn of destiny
CD _____ DOJOCD 72
Dojo / Feb '94 / BMG.

CHURCH OF HAWKWIND
Angel voices / Nuclear drive / Star cannibal / Phenomeno of luminosity / Fall of Earth City / Church / Joker at the gate / Some people never die / Light specific data / Experiment with destiny / Last Messiah / Looking in the future
CD _____ DOJOCD 86
Dojo / Jun '94 / BMG.

EARLY DAZE BEST OF
Hurry on sundown / Dreaming / Master of the universe / In the egg / Orgone accumulator / Sonic attack / Silver machine
CD _____ CDTB 044
Thunderbolt / Jun '88 / Magnum Music Group.

ELECTRIC TEPEE
CD _____ DOJOCD 244
Dojo / Jul '95 / BMG.

HALL OF THE MOUNTAIN GRILL
Psychedelic warlords (disappear in smoke) / Wind of change / D rider / Webb weaver / You'd better believe it / Hall of the mountain grill / Lost Johnny / Goat willow / Paradox
CD _____ CDFA 3133
Fame / May '89 / EMI.

HAWKWIND - FRIDAY ROCK SHOW SESSIONS
Magnu/ Angels of death / Pulsing Cavern / Assault and battery / Needle gun / Master of the universe / Utopia / Dream worker / Assassins of Allah / Silver machine
CD _____ FRSCD 006
Raw Fruit / Mar '92 / Pinnacle.

HAWKWIND FAMILY ALBUM
CD _____ EMPRCD 507
Emporio / Nov '94 / THE / Disc / CM.

HAWKWIND, FRIENDS & RELATIONS
Aimless flight / Psychedelia lives / Working time / Rainbow warrior / Brothel in Rosenstrasse / Toad on the Earth / Earth calling / Changing / Widow song / Starcruiser / I.C.U. / I see you / Human beings / Atom bomb / Phone home Elliot

CD _____ CDMGRAM 91
Anagram / Mar '95 / Pinnacle.

IN AND OUTTAKE
CD _____ DOJOCD 153
Dojo / Nov '94 / BMG.

IN SEARCH OF SPACE
You shouldn't do that / You know you're only dreaming / Master of the universe / We took the wrong step years ago / Adjust me / Children of the sun
CD _____ CDFA 3192
Fame / May '89 / EMI.

IN THE BEGINNING
Master of the universe / Dreaming / Shouldn't do that / Hurry on sundown / Paranoia / See it as you really are / I do it / Came home
CD _____ CDCD 1131
Charly / Feb '94 / Charly / THE / Cadillac.

INDEPENDENT DAYS VOLS 1 & 2
Night of the hawks / Motorway city / Motorhead / Angels of death / Who's gonna win the war / Watching the grass grow / Over the top / Hurry on sundown / Kiss of the velvet whip / Kings of speed / Social alliance / Dream dancers / Dragons and fables
CD _____ CDMGRAM 94
Anagram / Sep '95 / Pinnacle.

IT'S THE BUSINESS OF THE FUTURE TO BE DANGEROUS
CD _____ ESSCD 196
Essential / Oct '93 / Total/BMG.

LEVITATION
Levitation / Motorway city / Psychosis / World of tiers / Prelude / Who's gonna win the war / Space chase / Fifth second of forever / Dust of time
CD _____ CLACD 129
Castle / Jul '87 / BMG.

LIVE '79
Shotdown in the night / Motorway city / Spirit of the age / Brainstorm / Lighthouse / Master of the universe / Silver machine
CD _____ CLACD 243
Castle / Jul '94 / BMG.

LIVE COLLECTION
Song of the sword / Dragons and fables / Narration / Sea king / Angels of death / Choose your mesques / Flight sequence / Needle gun / Zarozinia / Lords of chaos / Dark Lords / Wizard of Pan Tang / Shade gate / Rocky paths / Pulsing cavern / Master of the universe / Dreaming city / Moonglum (Friend without a cause) / Elric the enchanter / Conjuration of magnu / Magnu dust of time / Horn of fate
CD _____ CCSCD 321
Castle / Apr '92 / BMG.

MASTERS OF THE UNIVERSE
Masters of the universe / Brainstorm / Sonic attack / Orgone accumulator / It's so easy / Lost Johnny
CD _____ CDFA 3220
Fame / May '89 / EMI.

MIGHTY HAWKWIND CLASSICS 1980-85
Hurry on sundown / Sweet mistress of pain / King of speed (live) / Motorhead / Valium ten / Night of the hawks / Green finned demon / Dream dancers / Dragons and fables / Over the top / Free fall / Death trap
CD _____ CDMGRAM 86
Anagram / Apr '92 / Pinnacle.

OUT AND INTAKE
Turning point / Waiting for tomorrow / Cajun jinx / Solitary mind games / Starflight / Ejection / Assassins of Allah / Flight to Maputo / Confrontation / Five to four / Ghost dance
CD _____ SHARP 040CD
Flicknife / Apr '87 / Pinnacle.

PALACE SPRINGS
Back in the box / Treadmill / Void of golden light / Lives of great men / Time we left / Heads / Acid test / Damnation alley
CD _____ CLACD 303
Castle / '92 / BMG.

PSYCHEDELIC WARLORDS
CD _____ CLEO 57412
Cleopatra / Oct '94 / Disc.

RARITIES (Hawkwind Friends & Relations)
Brothel in Rosenstrasse / Starcruiser / Earth calling / Psychedelia lives / Aimless flights / Rainbow warrior / Human beings / Changing / Toad on the road / Widow song / Phone home Elliot / Atom bomb / I see you / ICU 16 / Working time
CD _____ CDMGRAM 91
Anagram / Mar '95 / Pinnacle.

SILVER MACHINE
Prelude / Silver machine (live) / Shot down in the night (live) / Dust of time / Psychosis / Ghost dance (live) / You shouldn't do that (live) / Urban guerilla (live) / Who's gonna win the war / Fifth second of forever / Nuclear toy / Levitation / Space chase / Motorway city
CD _____ 5507642
Spectrum/Karussell / Mar '95 / PolyGram / THE.

SPACE BANDITS
Images / Black Elk speaks / Wings / Out of the shadow / Realms / Ship of dreams / TV suicide
CD _____ CLACD 282
Castle / Jul '92 / BMG.

SPACE IS DEEP
CD _____ RRCD 206
Receiver / Sep '95 / Grapevine.

SPACE RITUAL VOL.2
Space / Accumulator / Upside down sonic attack / Time we left / Ten seconds of forever / Brainstorm / Seven by seven / Master of the universe / Welcome to the future
CD _____ CDTB 099
Thunderbolt / Jan '91 / Magnum Music Group.

STASIS (The UA years 1971-1975)
Urban guerilla / Psychedelic warlords (disappear in smoke) / Brainbox pollution / Seven by seven / Paradox / Silver machine / You'd better believe it / Lord of light / Black corridor (live) / Earth calling (live/CD only) / Born to go (live/CD only) / Down through the night (live/CD only) / Awakening (live/CD only) / You shouldn't do that
CD _____ CDFA 3267
Fame / Apr '92 / EMI.

TEXT OF THE FESTIVAL, THE
Master of the universe / Dreaming / Shouldn't do that / Hurry on sundown / Paranoia / See it as you really are / I do it / Came home / Sound shouldn't / Improvise / Improvise...compromise / Reprise
CD _____ CDTB 2068
Thunderbolt / Nov '88 / Magnum Music Group.

THIS IS HAWKWIND... DO NOT PANIC
PSY power / Levitation / Circles / Space chase / Death trap / Angel of death / Show down in the night / Stonehenge decoded / Watching the grass grow
CD _____ CDMGRAM 54
Anagram / Jun '92 / Pinnacle.

TRAVELLERS AID TRUST, THE
CD _____ SHARP 2045CD
Flicknife / Dec '88 / Pinnacle.

UNDISCLOSED FILES - ADDENDUM
Orctone accumulator / Ghost dance / Sonic attack / Watching the grass grow / Coded language / Damned by the curse of man / Ejection / Motorway city / Dragons and fables / Heads / Angels of death
CD _____ EBSCD 114
Emergency Broadcast System / Feb '95 / Vital.

WARRIOR BOXSET
CD _____ CYCL 015
Cyclops / Sep '94 / Pinnacle.

WARRIOR ON THE EDGE OF TIME
Assault and battery / Golden void / Wizard blew his horn / Opa-loca / Demented king / Magno / Standing at the edge / Spiral galaxy 28948 / Warriors / Dying seas / Kings of speed / Motorhead
CD _____ DOJOCD 84
Dojo / Feb '94 / BMG.

XENON CODEX, THE
War I survived / Wastelands of sleep / Neon skyline / Lost chronicles / Tides / Heads / Mutation zone / EMC / Sword of the East / Good evening
CD _____ CLACD 281
Castle / Mar '93 / BMG.

ZONES
Zones / Dangerous vision / Running through the back brain / Island / Motorway city / Utopia 84 / Social alliance / Sonic attack / Dream worker / Brainstorm
CD _____ CDMGRAM 57
Anagram / Jun '88 / Pinnacle.

ZONES/STONEHENGE
CD _____ SHARP 1422CD
Flicknife / Nov '88 / Pinnacle.

Hawley, Jane

AS WE WALK ON THIN ICE
CD _____ TX 3004CD
Taxim / Jan '94 / ADA.

Haworth, Bryn

LIVE (Haworth, Bryn Band)
CD _____ KMCD 683
Kingsway / Oct '94 / Total/BMG / Complete/Pinnacle.

Hay, Colin James

TOPANGA
CD _____ 901304
Line / Jan '96 / CM / Grapevine / ADA / Conifer / Direct.

Haycock, Pete

LIVIN' IT UP (Haycock, Peter Band)
Liberty / So many roads / Communication / Medley (Includes Come on my kitchen, Country hat, Slide solo.) / Thrill is gone / Luvienne / Dr. Brown, I presume / Blackjack and me

CD _____ CDLR 42073
L&R / Nov '92 / New Note.

Hayden, Cathal

CATHAL HAYDEN
CD _____ CBM 012CD
Cross Border Media / Mar '94 / Direct / ADA.

Hayes, Clifford

CLIFFORD HAYES AND THE DIXIELAND JUG BLOWERS (Hayes, Clifford & The Dixieland Jug Blowers)
CD _____ YAZCD 1054
Yazoo / Apr '91 / CM / ADA / Roots / Koch.

CLIFFORD HAYES AND THE LOUISVILLE JUG BANDS VOL. 1 1924/26 (Hayes, Clifford & The Louisville Jug Bands)
CD _____ JPCD 1501-2
Jazz Perspectives / May '94 / Jazz Music / Hot Shot.

CLIFFORD HAYES AND THE LOUISVILLE JUG BANDS VOL. 2 1926/27 (Hayes, Clifford & The Louisville Jug Bands)
CD _____ JPCD 1502-2
Jazz Perspectives / May '94 / Jazz Music / Hot Shot.

CLIFFORD HAYES AND THE LOUISVILLE JUG BANDS VOL. 3 1927/29 (Hayes, Clifford & The Louisville Jug Bands)
CD _____ JPCD 1503-2
Jazz Perspectives / May '94 / Jazz Music / Hot Shot.

CLIFFORD HAYES AND THE LOUISVILLE JUG BANDS VOL. 4 1929/31 (Hayes, Clifford & The Louisville Jug Bands)
CD _____ JPCD 1504-2
Jazz Perspectives / May '94 / Jazz Music / Hot Shot.

Hayes, Edgar

EDGAR HAYES 1937-8
CD _____ CLASSICS 730
Classics / Jan '94 / Discovery / Jazz Music.

Hayes, Harry

HARRY HAYES & HIS BAND #1 - 1944-1946
CD _____ HH 01CD
Harry Hayes Musicals / Nov '95 / Harry Hayes Musicals.

HARRY HAYES & HIS BAND #2 - 1946-1947
CD _____ HH 02CD
Harry Hayes Musicals / Nov '95 / Harry Hayes Musicals.

Hayes, Isaac

BLACK MOSES
Never can say goodbye / Close to you / Nothing takes the place of you / Man's temptation / Part time love / Ike's rap IV / Brand new me / Going in circles / Never gonna give you up / Ike's rap II / Help me love / Need to belong / Good love / Ike's rap III / Your love is so doggone good / For the good times / I'll never fall in love again
CD Set _____ CDSXE2 033
Stax / Aug '90 / Pinnacle.

BRANDED
Ike's plea / Life's mood / Fragile / Life's mood II / Summer in the city / Let me love you / I'll do anything (to turn you on) / Thanks to the fool / Branded / Soulsville / Hyperbolicsyllabicsesquedalymistic
CD _____ VPBCD 7
Pointblank / May '95 / EMI.

COLLECTION: ISAAC HAYES, THE
Shaft / Joy / Never can say goodbye / Walk on by / I stand accused / (If loving you is wrong) I don't want to be right / I just don't know what to do with myself / By the time I get to Phoenix
CD _____ VSOPCD 210
Connoisseur / Feb '95 / Pinnacle.

HOT BUTTERED SOUL
Walk on by / Hyperbolicsyllabicsesqueda-lymistic / One woman / By the time I get to Phoenix
CD _____ CDSXE 005
Stax / May '91 / Pinnacle.

HOTBED
Use me / I'm gonna have to tell her / Ten commandments of love / Feel like makin' love / Hobosac and me
CD _____ CDSXE 105
Stax / Jul '94 / Pinnacle.

ISAAC HAYES MOVEMENT, THE
I stand accused / One big unhappy family / I just don't know what to do with myself / Something
CD _____ CDSXE 025
Stax / Feb '90 / Pinnacle.

ISAAC'S MOODS
Ike's mood / Soulsville / Joy / (If loving us is wrong) I don't want to be right / Never can say goodbye / Shaft / Ike's rap IV / Brand new me / Do your thing / Walk on by / I stand accused / Ike's rap I (On CD only) / Hyperbolicsyllabicsesquedalymystic (On CD only) / Ike's rap III (On CD only) / Ike's rap II (On CD only)
CD _____ CDSX 011
Stax / Apr '88 / Pinnacle.

JOY
Joy / I love you that's all / Man will be a man / Feeling keeps on coming / I'm gonna make it (without you)
CD _____ CDSXE 047
Stax / May '92 / Pinnacle.

LIVE AT THE SAHARA TAHOE
Shaft / Come on / Light my fire / Ike's rap / Never can say goodbye / Windows of the world / Look of love / Ellie's love theme / Use me / Do your thing / Men / It's too late / Rock me baby / Stormy Monday blues / Type thang / First time ever I saw your face / Ike's rap VI / Ain't no sunshine / Feelin' alright
CD Set _____ CDSXE 2053
Stax / Jul '92 / Pinnacle.

PRESENTING ISAAC HAYES
Precious memories (Mixes) / When I fall in love / I just want to make love to you / Rock me baby / Going to Chicago Blues / Misty / You don't know like I know
CD _____ SCD 8596
Stax / Jan '96 / Pinnacle.

RAW AND REFINED
Birth of Shaft / Urban nights / Funkalicious / Tahoe Spring / Night before / Memphis trax / Soul fiddle / Funky junky / You made me live / Making love at the ocean / Southern breeze / Didn't know love was so good / 405
CD _____ VPBCD 25
Pointblank / Jul '95 / EMI.

TO BE CONTINUED
Ike's rap 1 / Our day will come / Look of love / Ike's mood (1) / You've lost that lovin' feelin' / Runnin' out of fools
CD _____ CDSXE 030
Stax / Feb '91 / Pinnacle.

Hayes, Louis

CRAWL, THE
CD _____ CCD 79045
Candid / Oct '91 / Cadillac / Jazz Music / Wellard / Koch.

SUPER QUARTET, THE (Hayes, Louis & Company)
Bolivia / Song is you / Up jumped spring / On your own sweet way / Chelsea Bridge / Epistrophy / Blue Lou / Fee fi fo fum
CD _____ CDSJP 424
Timeless Jazz / Feb '95 / New Note.

Hayes, Martin

MARTIN HAYES
Morning star/The Caoilte mountains / Paddy Fahy's jig/Sean Ryan's jig / Whistler from Rosslea/Connor Dunn's / Golden castle / Star of munster / Colliers/Johnny's wedding / Brown coffin/Good natured man / Green gowned lass / I buried my wife and danced on her grave / Rooms of Doogh / Mist covered mountain / Britches / Tommy Coen's reel/The swallow
CD _____ GLCD 1127
Green Linnet / Jul '93 / Roots / CM / Direct / ADA.

UNDER THE MOON
CD _____ GL 1155CD
Green Linnet / Jul '95 / Roots / CM / Direct / ADA.

Hayes, Tommy

AN RAS
CD _____ LUNCD 055
Mulligan / Jan '95 / CM / ADA.

Hayes, Tubby

200% PROOF
CD _____ CHECD 00105
Master Mix / Jul '92 / Wellard / Jazz Music / New Note.

FOR MEMBERS ONLY (Live -1967) (Hayes, Tubby, Quartet)
Dear Johnny B / This is all I ask / Dolphin dance / Mexican green / Finky minky / For members only / You know I care / Conversations at dawn / Nobody else but me / Dedication to Joy / Off the wagon / Second city steamer
CD _____ CDCHE 10
Master Mix / Jan '91 / Wellard / Jazz Music / New Note.

JAZZ TETE A TETE (Hayes, Tubby & Tony Coe)
CD _____ PCD 7079
Progressive / Jan '94 / Jazz Music.

LIVE 1969 (Hayes, Tubby, Quartet)
CD _____ HQCD 05
Harlequin / Oct '91 / Swift / Jazz Music / Wellard / Hot Shot / Cadillac.

NIGHT AND DAY
Half a sawbuck / Spring can really hang you up the most / Simple waltz / I'm old fashioned / Night and day
CD _____ JHAS 602
Ronnie Scott's Jazz House / Oct '95 / Jazz Music / Magnum Music Group / Cadillac.

Haymes, Dick

BALLAD SINGER, THE
Oh look at me now / On a slow boat to China / What's new / Cheek to cheek / This time the dream's on me / Very precious love / You're my girl / Long hot summer / So far / Moonlight becomes you / You stepped out of a dream / Sinner kissed an angel / My heart stood still
CD _____ JASMCD 2525
Jasmine / Jul '89 / Wellard / Swift / Conifer / Cadillac / Magnum Music Group.

CAPITOL YEARS: DICK HAYMES
It might as well be spring / More I see you / Very thought of you / You'll never know / If there is someone lovelier than you / How deep is the ocean / Nearness of you / Where or when / Little white lies / Love is here to stay / Love walked in / Come rain or come shine / If I should lose you / You don't know what love is / Imagination / Skylark / Isn't this a lovely day (to be caught in the rain) / What's new / Way you look tonight / Then I'll be tired of you / I like the likes of you / Moonlight becomes you / Between the Devil and the deep blue sea / When I fall in love
CD _____ CDEMS 1364
Capitol / Jun '90 / EMI.

FOR YOU, FOR ME, FOR EVERMORE
CD _____ ACD 130
Audiophile / May '95 / Jazz Music / Swift.

HOW HIGH THE MOON (Haymes, Dick & Harry James & his Orchestra)
Cherry / My silent love / All or nothing at all / Fools rush in / Maybe / Skylark / Daydreaming / Mr. Meadowlark / Things I love / Yes indeed / How high the moon / He's my guy / Montevideo / Dolores / Walkin' by the river / Spring will be so sad / Ol' man river / You've got me out on a limb / I don't want to walk without you / Maria Elena / I've got a gal in Kalamazoo (With Benny Goodman & his Orchestra) / Aurora / Sinner kissed an angel / You've changed
CD _____ CDMOIR 510
Memoir / May '94 / Target/BMG.

IT HAD TO BE YOU
CD _____ CDMOIR 512
Memoir / Nov '95 / Target/BMG.

IT'S MAGIC (featuring Helen Forrest)
It might as well be spring / What a difference a day makes / Breeze and I / I surrender dear / It's de-lovely / It's magic / Best things in life are free / You'd be so nice to come home to / They didn't believe me / Summertime / You send me / I had to be you / Did you ever see a dream walking / Where or when / I'll be seeing you / One I love / Blue skies / To each his own
CD _____ PWKM 4043
Carlton Home Entertainment / Feb '91 / Carlton Home Entertainment.

KEEP IT SIMPLE (Haymes, Dick & Loonis McGlohon Trio)
More I see / I get along without you very well / Little white lies / Almost like being in love / Stella by starlight / Very thought of you / I'll remember April / That's for me / It might as well be spring / Who cares / Love is here to stay / Love walked in / You'll never know / There will never be another you
CD _____ ACD 200
Audiophile / Mar '95 / Jazz Music / Swift.

SONGBOOK (Haymes, Dick & Helen Forrest)
CD _____ MCCD 208
MCI / Jul '95 / Disc / THE.

STAR EYES
CD _____ JCD 633
Jass / Dec '89 / CM / Jazz Music / ADA / Cadillac / Direct.

SWINGIN' SESSION
CD _____ CDSG 404
Starline / Aug '89 / Jazz Music.

Haymes, Graham

GRIOT'S FOOTSTEPS, THE
CD _____ 5232622
Verve / Jan '95 / PolyGram.

TRANSITION
CD _____ 5290392
Verve / Dec '95 / PolyGram.

Haymes, Roy

HOMECOMING
Evidence / Green chimneys / You're blase / Bud Powell / Star eyes / Anniversary song
CD _____ ECD 220922
Evidence / Jul '94 / Harmonia Mundi / ADA / Cadillac.

MY SHINING HOUR (Haynes, Roy & Thomas Clausen's Jazzparticipants)
My shining hour / I fall in love too easily / Bessie's blues / All blues / Skylark / Rhythm-a-ning / A la blues / Bright
CD _____ STCD 4199
Storyville / Mar '95 / Jazz Music / Wellard / CM / Cadillac.

OUT OF THE AFTERNOON (Haynes, Roy Quartet)
Moon ray / Fly me to the moon / Raoul / Snap crackle / If I should lose you / Long wharf / Some other Spring
CD _____ IMP 11802
Impulse Jazz / Jan '96 / BMG / New Note.

TE-VOU
Like this / If I could / Blues M45 / Trinkle twinkle / Trigonometry / Good for the soul
CD _____ FDM 365692
Dreyfus / Nov '94 / ADA / Direct / New Note.

TRANSATLANTIC MEETINGS (Haynes, Roy & Kenny Clarke)
Red rose / Minuation sunset / Laffin' and crying / Minor encamp / Subscription / Dillon / Trianon / Kenny's special / Illusion / Love me or leave me / Cinerama / Vogue / Buyer's blues
CD _____ 74321115122
Vogue / Jul '93 / BMG.

TRUE OR FALSE
CD _____ FRLCD 007
Freelance / Oct '92 / Harmonia Mundi / Cadillac / Koch.

Haynes, Victor

OPTIMISTIC
Who isn't nobody else / This is love / Turn out the light / Breakin' my heart / Respect / Optimistic / Tell me where you are / Don't stop / Do you regret / First time / Tonight / Stand up
CD _____ EXCDP 7
Expansion / Nov '94 / Pinnacle / Sony / 3MV.

Haywains

GET HAPPY WITH...
Bythesea Road / Tobe's gone west / Fisherman's friends / Summer madness / I'm not really as foolish as you think / Billy Corknill's better / Side / Kicked in the teeth / Now I've got one up on you / Emily's shop / Really (Bee) / Last pancake / Surfin' in my sleep / I wouldn't want that / Forget me not / Please don't let me get hurt / Rosanna / Boy called Burden / You laughing at me laughing at you / Boy racers a go-go
CD _____ ASKCD 024
Vinyl Japan / Sep '93 / Vital.

NEVER MIND MANCHESTER, HERE'S ...THE HAYWAINS
Kill karaoke / Dusty Springfield / I hate to disappoint you / New kids on the block / Your point of view doesn't count / Money-go-round / Now I've got one up on you / I'm still waiting / Always the same / Somebody loves you / Why did I ever turn you down / Bythesea road / Hold on me / Time bomb baby / Forget me not
CD _____ ASKCD 014
Vinyl Japan / Mar '93 / Vital.

Hayward, Dennis

50'S IN SEQUENCE
CD _____ CDTS 037
Maestro / Aug '93 / Savoy.

DANCING FOR PLEASURE
Slow 'em all / And the band played on / Hello hello, who's your lady friend / Ship ahoy (all the nice girls love a soldier) / My bonnie lies over the ocean / Jolly good company / Darling buds of May / Forever green / Dying swan / Jupiter / Love theme from Spartacus / Morning: Peer Gynt / One fine day / Mr. Wonderful / On a clear day / Misty / Can't smile without you / I don't want to walk without you / Man I love / Can't help lovin' dat man / Nellie Dean / K-K-Katy / All by yourself in the moonlight / Dickie bird hop / Tchip tchip (birdie song) / Tonight / Lara's theme / Spanish eyes / Spanish harlem / Czardas / Sandie's shawl / Raindrops keep falling on my head / Raining in my heart / I'm confessin' that I love you / When somebody thinks you're wonderful
CD _____ CDTS 034
Maestro / Aug '93 / Savoy.

DENNIS HAYWARD'S PARTY DANCES (2CD Set)
Barn dance / Paul Jones / Blackpool belle / Blame it on the Bossa Nova / Chanson d'amour / Island of dreams / Knees up Mother Brown / Clap clap sound / Alley cat / Agadoo / Hands up / Atmophere / Y viva Espana / I just called to say I love you / Conga / Simon says / Birdie song / Brown girl in the ring / Rivers of Babylon / It's a holi holiday / Let's twist again / Loco-motion / Pal of my cradle days / Cokey cokey / Sailing / You'll never walk alone / We'll meet again / Fiona's polka / Lambeth walk / St. Bernard's waltz / Virginia reel / Farmer's wife / Have a drink on me / (Hands knees and) Bomps a daisy / Charleston and the black bottom / I am the music man /

Chestnut tree / Sons of the sea / Match of the day / Hip hip hip hooray / Zorba's dance / Fanfare #1/2 / March of the mods / This is your life #1/2 / Sand dance / Dosh / Harry Lime / Teddy bear's picnic / Gay Gordons / Havah nagilah / Mod rock barn dance / Chord
CD Set _____ SAV 220CD
Savoy / Dec '95 / THE / Savoy.

HAPPY DANCING FOR CHRISTMAS (2CD Set)
Santa Claus is coming to town / God rest ye merry gentlemen / We wish you a merry Christmas / Twelve days of Christmas / Deck the hall / Good King Wenceslas / Christmas song / Have yourself a merry little Christmas / Winter wonderland / White Christmas / When a child is born / Mary's boy child / Little donkey / Do you hear what I hear / Little boy that Santa Claus forgot / Let it snow, let it snow / I'm sending a letter to Santa Claus / Sleigh ride / Jingle bells / Midnight sleigh ride / Ding dong merrily on high / Silver bells / Away in a manger / We three kings / Silnet night / Holiday for bells / Snow coach / Snowy white and jingle bells / Here comes Santa Claus / Where did my snowman go / On Christmas island / Once upon a wintertime / I'll be home for Christmas / Fairy on the Christmas tree / Frosty the snowman / Rudolf the red nosed reindeer / O little town of Bethlehem / Jingle bell rock / Rockin' around the Christmas tree / I heard the bells on Christmas day / In the bleak mid-Winter / Christmas awake / Salute the happy morn / Angels from the realms of glory / C.H.R.I.S.T.M.A.S. / Caroling caroling / Santa Natale / Scarlet ribbons / Miners dream of home / Auld lang syne
CD Set _____ SAV 199CD
Savoy / Dec '95 / THE / Savoy.

HAPPY DANCING VOL.1 (Hayward, Dennis Organisation)
Every little while / Dancing with my shadow / Broken doll / Glad rag doll / Peg o' my heart / She's funny that way / I don't know why / Don't blame me / White cliffs of Dover / Love is the sweetest thing / It's a sin to tell a lie / Sally / Girl of my dreams / It happened in Monterey / Where the blue of the night meets the gold of the day / I'll see you again / Chinatown, my Chinatown / Waiting for the Robert E. Lee / I'm looking over a four leaf clover / Alabamy bound / Yankee doodle boy / Swanee / Can't help lovin' dat man / By the fireside / Seems to me, I've heard that song before / Two sleepy people / What more can I say / Play to me Gipsy / Goodnight Vienna / Alabama Jubilee / Is it true what they say about Dixie / California here I come / Sittin' on top of the world / Give my regards to Broadway / When the midnight choo choo leaves for Alabam' / As time goes by / It's the talk of the town / It had to be you / These foolish things / Blue room / Annapola / Marta / Mairzy doats and dozy doats / Give me five minutes more / Heart of my heart / Arm in arm together / We'll meet again / I'm a dreamer (aren't we all) / All I do is dream of you / Little on the lonely side / If I had my life to live over / Falling in love again / Carolina moon / Let the rest of the world go by / Let bygones be bygones
CD _____ SAV 132CD
Savoy / Mar '92 / THE / Savoy.

HAPPY DANCING VOL.3
CD _____ SAV 189CD
Savoy / May '93 / THE / Savoy.

IT'S SEQUENCE TIME
Hello jolly/Miss Anna Belle Lee/Don't bring LuLu / Keep your sunny side up/You are my sunshine / Spread a little happiness/Smoke gets in your eyes / You are my heart's delight / Waltzing in the clouds / Sindy / All I ask of you / Always there / Tango melodica / Perhaps, perhaps, perhaps / Unforgettable/Never say goodbye / With a song in my heart/Be careful it's my heart / South of the border / Ay ay ay / Hernando's hideaway / Whatever Lola wants (Lola gets) / Let's put out the lights and go to sleep / Shine through my dreams/My heart and I / Roses from the south / Les patineurs (skaters waltz)
CD _____ SAV 177CD
Savoy / Jul '92 / THE / Savoy.

LET'S DANCE (Hayward, Dennis & The Savoy Orchestra)
CD _____ SAV 128CD
Savoy / Feb '92 / THE / Savoy.

MUSIC FOR CELEBRATION AND SPECIAL OCCASIONS
Fanfare / Happy birthday / Barn dance medley / Congratulations / St. Bernard waltz / Wedding march / Get me to the church / My old Dutch / Anniversary waltz / Mayfair quickstep / Balmoral blues / Modern waltz / Saunter together / Saunter medley / Tango serida / Lilac waltz medley / Stripper / Can can / Four hand star / Conga / Virginia reel / Chimes of Big Ben / Auld lang syne / Gay Gordons / Easter parade / Wish me luck / Rule Britannia / Land of hope and glory / God save the Queen
CD _____ SAV 152CD
Savoy / Dec '95 / THE / Savoy.

RECALL
If I were a bell/This can't be love / There will never be another you / How am I to know/ Time was / All or nothing at all / Beautiful lady in blue / Dream lover/I'll follow my secret heart / My boy lollipop / He's a tramp / Something stupid / Cherry pink and apple blossom white / Strangers on the shore / Strangers in the night/Tonight / Women in love / Falling in love with you / Mr. Sandman/Lady be good/Baby face / Good old bad old days/Some of these days / Softly, softly/At the end of the day / Who's taking you home tonight / September in the rain/ Pennies from heaven / Embraceable you/ How about you
CD _____ SAV 178CD
Savoy / Jul '92 / THE / Savoy.

SEQUENCE TIME, VOL 2
CD _____ SAV 185CD
Savoy / May '93 / THE / Savoy.

SHALL WE DANCE 2 (Hayward, Dennis & His Orchestra)
On a little street in Singapore / New York, New York / Lover / Just the way you look tonight / London by night / Hi Lili hi lo / And I love you so/How soon / Yesterday/My way / Isle of Capri / What a difference a day makes / Ecstacy / Serenata / Lover come back / Dream / Indian summer/Stormy weather / Have you ever been lonely / If ever I would leave you / Stranger in Paradise / La cucaracha / Carioca / Copacabana / Tico-tico
CD _____ SAV 174CD
Savoy / Jun '92 / THE / Savoy.

SHOWTIME
CD _____ SAV 239CD
Savoy / Dec '95 / THE / Savoy.

STEP BY STEP
CD _____ CDTS 036
Maestro / Aug '93 / Savoy.

TEA DANCE 2
Jeepers creepers / Be mir bist do schoen / Goody goody / Tisket-a-tasket / Don't sit under the apple tree / Undecided / Dance in the old-fashioned way / Didn't we / You'd be so nice to come home to / Wrong (It must be right) / Romanesca / Italian fiesta / Nocturn in eb / Gymnopedie No.1 / Swan / Oh my beloved daddy / Cavatina (Deerhunter) / How wonderful to know / Hey there / Yours / I won't send roses / Portrait of my love / Magic moments / Finger of suspicion / Love and marriage / I ain't got nobody / Little bit independant / Birth of the blues / My blue heaven (CD only) / Room with a view (CD only) / I should care (CD only) / But not for me (CD only) / Tango erotique (CD only) / Song of the rose (CD only) / Charmaine (CD only) / Edelweiss (CD only) / Bless you (CD only) / Linger awhile (CD only) / Small fry (CD only) / Brother can you spare a dime (CD only) / You'll never walk alone (CD only) / Sleepy shores (CD only)
CD _____ SAV 170CD
Savoy / Mar '92 / THE / Savoy.

Hayward, Justin

BLUE JAYS (Hayward, Justin & John Lodge)
This morning / Remember me (my friend) / My brother / You / Nights winters years / Saved by the music / I dreamed last night / Who are you now / Maybe / When you wake up
CD _____ 8204912
London / '88 / PolyGram.

CLASSIC BLUE
Tracks of my tears / Blackbird / MacArthur Park / Vincent / God only knows / Bright eyes / Whiter shade of pale / Scarborough Fair / Railway hotel / Man of the world / Forever autumn / As long as the moon can shine / Stairway to Heaven
CD _____ CLACD 385
Castle / '93 / BMG.

NIGHT FLIGHT
Night flight / Maybe it's just love / Crazy lovers / Penumbra moon / Nearer to you / Face in the crowd / Suitcase / I'm sorry / It's not on / Bedtime stories
CD _____ 8205552
Threshold / Jan '89 / PolyGram.

Haywire

PRIVATE SPELL
CD _____ 846121
We Bite / Jul '90 / Plastic Head.

Hayworth, Rita

RITA HAYWORTH
CD _____ LCD 6002/3
Fresh Sound / Jan '93 / Jazz Music / Discovery.

RITA HAYWORTH COLLECTOR'S EDITION
CD _____ DVGH 7052
Deja Vu / Apr '95 / THE.

Haza, Ofra

KIRYA
Kirya / Innocent-a requiem for refugees / Daw da hiya / Mystery, fate and love / Hor-

ashoot - the bridge / Don't foresake me / Barefoot / Trains of no return / Take 7/8
CD _____ 9031761272
East West / Apr '92 / Warner Music.

YEMENITE SONGS
Im nin' alu / Yachilvi veyachail / A salk / Galbi / Ode le 'eli / Lefelach / Ayelet chen
CD _____ CDORB 006
Globestyle / May '87 / Pinnacle.

Haze

WORLD TURTLE
Ember / See her face / Ship of fools / Edge of heaven / Don't leave me here / Epitaph / Under my skin / New dark ages / Safe harbour / Autumn / Another country / Straw house / Wooden house / Stone house
CD _____ CYCL 008
Cyclops / Jun '94 / Pinnacle.

Hazel

ARE YOU GOING TO EAT THAT
CD _____ SPCD 144358
Sub Pop / Feb '95 / Disc.

TOREADOR OF LOVE
CD _____ SPCD 284
Sub Pop / Aug '93 / Disc.

Hazelby, Brian

ON THE SUNNY SIDE
Strauss medley / War years medley / La danza / Chi mai / Theatre organ tribute / Badinerie / This can't be love / Intermezzo karelia suite / Nimrod / Root beer rag / Sweet Georgia Brown / Speak low / Georgia / Sunny side of the street / Nat King Cole medley / Misty / When you wish upon a star / St. Louis blues / Devils gallop
CD _____ CDGRS 1283
Grosvenor / Nov '95 / Target/BMG.

He Said

HAIL
CD _____ CDSTUMM 29
Mute / Nov '86 / Disc.

TAKE CARE
CD _____ CDSTUMM 57
Mute / Sep '88 / Disc.

Head

HEAD
CD _____ VOXXCD 2061
Voxx / Jan '93 / Else / Disc.

INTOXICATOR
Walk like an angel / Stalemate / Ice cream skin / All the boyz / Party's over / Under the influence of books / Two or three things / Soakin' my pillow / Ships in the night / B'goode or be gone / You're so vain
CD _____ CDV 2595
Virgin / Jul '89 / EMI.

SNOG ON THE ROCKS,A
Out of the natch / Sex cattle man / Captain, the sailor and the dirty heartbreaker / I can't stop / Crackers (fer yer knackers) / I am the king / Don't wash your hair about it / Crazy racecourse crowd / Let's snog / Me and Mrs. Jones
CD _____ FIENDCD 95
Demon / Jun '87 / Pinnacle / ADA.

Head, Hands & Feet

HOME FROM HOME
Bring it all back home / Ain't gonna let it get me down / How does it feel to be right all the time / Achmed / Precious stone / Friend of a friend / Windy and warm / Who turned off the dark / Can you see me / Home from home / Make me feel much better
CD _____ C5CD 633
See For Miles/C5 / Oct '95 / Pinnacle.

Head, Jowe

UNHINGED
CD _____ OVER 35CD
Overground / Oct '94 / SRD.

Head Like A Hole

13
CD _____ N 02162
Noise/Modern Music / Aug '94 / Pinnacle / Plastic Head.

FLIK Y'SELF OFF Y'SELF
Chalkface / Spanish goat dancer / Oily rag / Kissy kissy / Faster hooves / One pound two pound / Raw sock / Dirt eater / Pops pox 'n' vox / Spitbag / Rabbit / Nosferatoo / Theme to Nincomjool / Velvet kushin
CD _____ N 02252
Noise/Modern Music / Feb '95 / Pinnacle / Plastic Head.

Head, Murray

SAY IT ISN'T SO
Say it ain't so Joe / Boats away / Someone's rocking my dreamboat / Never even thought / Don't forget me now / Boy on the bridge / When I'm yours / She's such a drag / Silence is a strong reply / No taste

CD _____ IMCD 83
Island / Feb '90 / PolyGram.

Head Of David

DUSTBOWL
CD _____ BFFP 18CD
Blast First / Apr '88 / Disc.

Head Or Tales

ETERNITY BECOMES A LIE
CD _____ BMCD 069
Black Mark / Sep '95 / Plastic Head.

Headbutt

PISSING DOWN
Sandyard / Duffle bag / Through the slides / Adding insult.... / Always scraping shit / Barbie skin
CD _____ OINK 031 CD
Pigboy / Jan '93 / Vital.

TIDDLES
CD _____ DPROMCD 25
Dirter Promotions / Oct '94 / Pinnacle.

Headcandy

STARCASTERS
CD _____ LNKCD 2
Street Link / Oct '91 / BMG.

Headcleaner

AUFOU
CD _____ EVRCD 15
Eve / Oct '92 / Grapevine.

NO OFFENCE MEANT, PLENTY TAKEN
Aperetif / Oscar / Understanding / Guff / Downer / Comet / Half life / Jack / Ampallang / Big D / Mix
CD _____ 118612
Musidisc / Nov '95 / Vital / Harmonia Mundi / ADA / Cadillac / Discovery.

Headcrash

HEADCRASH
CD _____ 450995540-2
Warner Bros. / Oct '94 / Warner Music.

Headhunter

REBIRTH
CD _____ CC 025050
Major / May '95 / Plastic Head.

Headless Chickens

HEADLESS CHICKENS E.P.
CD _____ D 19853
Mushroom / Oct '94 / BMG / 3MV.

Headlock

IT FOUND ME
CD _____ CDVEST 31
Bulletproof / Sep '94 / Pinnacle.

Headman

PHILADELPHIA EXPERIENCE, THE
CD _____ MILL 007CD
Millenium / Oct '94 / Plastic Head.

Headrush

FIVE
Easy / Crazy religion / Some people / Mountsorrel to venus / Trainer boy
CD _____ STAY 005CD
Stay Free / Aug '94 / Vital.

Heads Up

DUKE
CD _____ EM 93192
Roadrunner / Mar '91 / Pinnacle.

Headswim

PRECIPITY FLOOD
Gone to pot / Soup / Try disappointed / Crawl / Dead / Years on me / Apple of my eye / Down / Stinkhorn / Safe harvest / Beneath a black moon
CD _____ 477878 2
Epic / Oct '94 / Sony.

TENSE MOMENTS
Violent my life (Is driving me crazy) / One red eye / Chains and nails / Dead / Proud / Freedom from faith / Inside of us
CD _____ 4769902
Epic / Jun '94 / Sony.

Healey, Jeff

COVER TO COVER (Healey, Jeff Band)
Shapes of things / Freedom / Yer blues / Stop breakin' down / Angel / Evil / Stuck in the middle with you / I got the line on you / Run through the jungle / As the years go passing by / I'm ready / Communication breakdown / Me and my crazy self / Badge
CD _____ 74321238882
Arista / Mar '95 / BMG.

FEEL THIS (Healey, Jeff Band)
Cruel little number / Leave the light on / Baby's lookin' hot / Lost in your eyes / House that love built / Evil and here to stay / Feel

this / My kinda lover / It could all get blown away / You're coming home / Heart of an angel / Live and love / Joined at the heart / Dreams of love
CD _____ 74321120872
Arista / Aug '95 / BMG.

HELL TO PAY (Healey, Jeff Band)
Full circle / I think I love you too much / I can't get my hands on you / How long can a man be strong / Let it all go / Hell to pay / While my guitar gently weeps / Something to hold on to / How much / Highway of dreams / Life beyond the sky
CD _____ 260815
Arista / Jun '90 / BMG.

SEE THE LIGHT (Healey, Jeff Band)
Confidence man / River of no return / Don't let your chance go by / Angel eyes / Nice problem to have / Someday, someway / I need to be loved / Blue jean blues / That's what they say / Hideaway / See the light
CD _____ 259441
Arista / Aug '95 / BMG.

Healy, Linda

PLANT Y MOR
CD _____ SCD 2072
Sain / Feb '95 / Direct / ADA.

Heaney, Joe

COME ALL YE GALLANT IRISHMEN
CD _____ CIC 020CD
Clo Iar-Chonnachta / Jan '90 / CM.

JOE HEANEY
CD _____ OSS 22CD
Ossian / Dec '93 / ADA / Direct / CM.

Heap, Jimmy

RELEASE ME (Heap, Jimmy & The Melody Mastg)
Release me / Love in the valley / Just to be with you / Then I'll be happy / Heartbreaker / You're in love with you / Just for tonight / Girl with a past / Lifetime of shame / You don't kiss me 'cause you love me / One that I won / Ethyl in my gas tank (no gal in my arms) / My first love affair / Love can move mountains / Conscience / I'm guilty / This song is just for you / You ought to know / I told you so / Butternut / Long John / Mingling / Heap of boogie / You're nothin' but a nothin' / That's all I want from you / I'll follow the crowd / It takes a heap of lovin' / Cry cry darlin' / You didn't have time / Let's do it just once / This night won't last forever
CD _____ BCD 15617
Bear Family / Apr '92 / Rollercoaster / Direct / CM / Swift / ADA.

Heart

BAD ANIMALS
Who will you run to / Alone / There's the girl / I want you so bad / Wait for an answer / Bad animals / You ain't so tough / Strangers of the heart / Easy target / R.S.V.P.
CD _____ CDEST 2032
Capitol / Jul '94 / EMI.

BRIGADE
Wild child / All I wanna do is make love to you / Secret / Tall, dark handsome stranger / I didn't want to need you / Night / Fallen from grace / Under the sky / Cruel nights / Stranded / Call of the wild / I want your world to turn / I love you
CD _____ CDESTU 2121
Capitol / Feb '94 / EMI.

DESIRE WALKS ON
Desire / Black on black II / Back to Avalon / Woman in me / Rage / In walks the night / My crazy head / Ring them bells / Will you be there (in the morning) / Voodoo doll / Anything is possible / Avalon (Reprise) / Desire walks on / La mujer que hay en mi / Te quedaras (en la manana)
CD _____ CDEST 2216
Capitol / Nov '93 / EMI.

DOG AND BUTTERFLY
Cook with fire / High time / Hijinx / Straight on / Dog and butterfly / Lighter touch / Nada one / Mistral wind
CD _____ 9826492
Pickwick/Sony Collector's Choice / Nov '91 / Carlton Home Entertainment / Pinnacle / Sony.

GREATEST HITS: HEART
Tell it like it is / Barracuda / Straight on / Dog and butterfly / Even it up / Bebe le strange / Sweet darlin' / I'm down/Long tall Sally / Unchained melody / Rock and roll
CD _____ 4601742
CBS / Apr '94 / Sony.

HEART
If looks could kill / What about love / Never / These dreams / Wolf / All eyes / Nobody home / Nothin' at all / What he don't know / Shellshock
CD _____ CDLOVE 1
Capitol / Feb '86 / EMI.

INTERVIEW, THE
CD P.Disc _____ CBAK 4073
Baktabak / Feb '94 / Baktabak.

PRIVATE AUDITION

City's burning / Bright little girl / Perfect stranger / private audition / Angela / This man is mine / Situation / Hey darlin darlin / One word / Fast times / America
CD _____ 983429-2
Pickwick/Sony Collector's Choice / Apr '94 / Carlton Home Entertainment / Pinnacle / Sony.

ROCK THE HOUSE "LIVE"

Wild child / Fallen from grace / Call of the wild / How can I refuse / Shell shock / Love alive / Under the sky / Night / Tall, dark handsome stranger / If looks could kill / Who will you run to / You're the voice / Way back machine / Barracuda
CD _____ CDESTU 2154
Capitol / Aug '91 / EMI.

Heart Throbs

CLEOPATRA GRIP
CD _____ TPLP 23CD
One Little Indian / Jun '90 / Pinnacle.

JUBILEE GRIP
CD _____ TPLP 33CD
One Little Indian / Apr '92 / Pinnacle.

VERTICAL SMILE
CD _____ TPLP 43CD
One Little Indian / May '93 / Pinnacle.

Heartbeats

SPINNING WORLD
Ocean / Hollywood dream / All I want to do / Living in Babylon / Black mountain rag / Blue diamond mines / Signs of rain / Another day / Nine mile view of / Spinning world / They don't know you / Hand of man / Cotton eyed Joe / Power to run / Whole bunch of keys
CD _____ GLCD 2111
Green Linnet / Jul '93 / Roots / CM / Direct / ADA.

Heartbeats

BEST OF THE HEARTBEATS
Thousand miles away / Darling how long / People are talking / Everybody's somebody's fool / After New Year's Eve / 500 Miles to go / I found a job / Lonely lover / Three steps from the alter / Ready for your love / Crazy for you / Your way / I won't be the fool anymore / I want to know / Daddy's home / Down on my knees / One day next year / Sometimes I wonder / What did daddy do / Our Anniversary
CD _____ NEMCD 643
Sequel / Sep '93 / BMG.

Heartland

KICK, THE
Do you know the feeling / This can't be love / She's got it all / Heartland / Livin' it up / See you on the TV / Louise / On the beach / Don't fool around with love / Working in a parking lot
CD _____ LICD 901202
Line / Jun '92 / CM / Grapevine / ADA / Conifer / Direct.

Hearts & Flowers

NOW IS THE TIME/OF HORSES, KIDS AND FORGOTTEN WOMEN
Now is the time / Save some time / Try for the rain / Rain rain / Now from want 3 / Rock 'n' roll gypsies / Reason to believe / Please / 1-2-3 Rhyme in Carnivour thyme / I'm a lonesome fugitive / Road to nowhere / 10,000 Sunsets / Now is the time for hearts and flowers / Highway in the wind / Second hand sundown queen / She sang hyms out of tune / Ode to a tin angel / When I was a cowboy / Legend of Ol' Tenbrookes / Colour your daytime / Two little boys / Extra extra
CD _____ EDCD 428
Edsel / Jul '95 / Pinnacle / ADA.

Heartsman, Johnny

TOUCH, THE
Serpent's touch / Paint my mailbox blue / You're so fine / Tongue / Attitude / Got to find my baby / Butler did it / Please don't be scared of my love / Oops / Walkin' blues / Let me love you baby / Heartburn / Endless
CD _____ ALCD 4800
Alligator / May '93 / Direct / ADA.

Heat Exchange

ONE STEP AHEAD
You're gonna love this / Shake down / Love is the reason / One step ahead / Check it out / Lost on you
CD _____ C5CD 609
See For Miles/C5 / Feb '94 / Pinnacle.

Heath, Jimmy

LITTLE MAN BIG BAND
CD _____ 5139562
Verve / Apr '92 / PolyGram.

Heath, Ted

FROM MOIRA WITH LOVE
Folks who live on the hill / Melody in F / Clair de Lune / Our love / Liebestraum / Song of india / Look for the silver lining / Procession / Skylark / Retrospect (Not on CD.) / Bill / Nearness of you / Fourth dimension / Thou swell / September song / Memories of you / Birth of the blues (Not on CD.) / Sixteen going on seventeen (Not on CD.) / Hot toddy (Not on CD.) / Georgia on my mind / I'arlem nocturne (Not on CD.) / Someone to watch over me (Not on CD.) / St. Louis blues (Not on CD.) / How high the moon (Not on CD.) / Tonight / Faithful Hussar / Blues for moderns (Not on CD.) / Our waltz / Obsession / Lush slide (Not on CD.) / Eloquence / Rhapsody for drums
CD _____ CDSIV 6106
Horatio Nelson / Jul '95 / THE / BMG / Avid/BMG / Koch.

GOLDEN AGE OF TED HEATH VOL.1, THE
Opus one / Somebody loves me (Not on CD.) / Swinging shepherd blues / My favourite things / Maria / Lullaby of Broadway / Holiday for strings / Flying home / I get a kick out of you / Jumpin' at the woodside / Man I love / Hawaiian war chant / At last / Cherokee / We'll git it / 'S Wonderful / You stepped out of a dream / Sabre dance / Blues in the night / Royal Garden blues (Not on CD.) / Moonlight in Vermont / Apple honey / Fly me to the moon / Listen to my music / Pick yourself up / Hawk talks / And the angels sing / Champ
CD _____ CDSIV 6102
Horatio Nelson / Apr '93 / THE / BMG / Avid/BMG / Koch.

GOLDEN AGE OF TED HEATH VOL.2, THE
9.20 special / East of the sun and west of the moon / Intermission riff / Ad lib frolic / Girl talk / South Rampart street parade / American patrol / That lovely weekend / Swanee river / Artistry in rhythm / Nightingale sang in Berkeley Square / Bakerloo non stop / In the mood / I had the craziest dream / Soon amapola / I can't get started (with you) / Perdido / C jam blues / Sophisticated lady / First jump / Night and day / Poor little rich girl / Swing low, sweet chariot
CD _____ CDSIV 6121
Horatio Nelson / Jul '95 / THE / BMG / Avid/BMG / Koch.

GOLDEN AGE OF TED HEATH VOL.3, THE
Let's dance / Chattanooga choo choo / Swingin' the blues / My guy's come back / Touch of your lips / Chicago / Skyliner / Nightmare / Lush slide / Serenade in blue / At the woodchoppers' ball / I've got a gal in Kalamazoo / On the sunny side of the street / I got bad and that ain't good / Sidewalks of Cuba / After you've gone / Big John special / Oboe / Jersey bounce / Contrasts / Cotton tail / Fascinating rhythm / Snowfall / Headin' north
CD _____ CDSIV 6135
Horatio Nelson / Jul '95 / THE / BMG / Avid/BMG / Koch.

GOLDEN AGE OF TED HEATH VOL.4, THE
CD _____ CDSIV 6137
Horatio Nelson / Jul '95 / THE / BMG / Avid/BMG / Koch.

HEADIN' NORTH
King's Cross climax / Sloppy Joe / Slim Jim / Amothurt / Shish kebab / Ballyhoo / Cruse eleven / Vanessa / Creep / Siboney / Hot toddy / Lullaby of birdland / Cloudburst / Strolling with the blues / Jazzboat / Armen's theme / Maguena / Cool for cats / Swinging shepherd blues / Wigwam / Mairi's wedding / Mah jong / Headin' north / Walking shoes
CD _____ CDMOIR 505
Memoir / Sep '93 / Target/BMG.

SALUTE TO THE BIG BAND (Heath, Ted Band)
Moonlight serenade / I'm getting sentimental over you / Uptown blues / Take the 'A' train / Listen to my music / Let's dance / When it's sleepy time down South / Body and soul / I can't get started (with you) / One o'clock jump / Very thought of you / Skyliner / Nightmare / Blue flame / Artistry in rhythm / Flying home
CD _____ PWKM 4077P
Carlton Home Entertainment / Aug '91 / Carlton Home Entertainment.

TED HEATH AT CARNEGIE HALL
CD _____ 8209502
Deram / Jan '96 / PolyGram.

THANKS FOR THE MEMORY (Heath, Ted & His Music)
Thanks for the memory / Trumpet voluntary / Botch a me / Poor little rich girl / In a little Spanish town / Early Autumn / Don't let the stars get in your eyes / Mademoiselle / Velvet glove / Auld lang syne / Them who has gets / Open the door Richard / Oliver Twist / Narcissus / Gone gone / Old Mother Hubbard / Leave it to love / Get out of the town before sundown / This is the time (to fall in love) / Sixty second get together
CD _____ PLCD 529

President / '90 / Grapevine / Target/BMG / Jazz Music / President.

VERY BEST OF TED HEATH
CD _____ CDSIV 6150
Horatio Nelson / Jul '95 / THE / BMG / Avid/BMG / Koch.

Heathen

BREAKING THE SILENCE
Death by hanging / Goblins blade / Open the grave / Pray for death / Set me free / Breaking the silence / World's end / Save the skull
CD _____ CDMFN 75
Music For Nations / Aug '89 / Pinnacle.

Heather & Kirsten

BETCHA DIDN'T KNOW
CD _____ CD 08717
Arcade / Jan '91 / Sony / Grapevine.

Heatmiser

COP AND SPEEDER
Disappearing ink / Bastard John / Flame / Temper / Why did I decide to stay / Collect to NYC / Hitting on the waiter / Busted lip / Antionio Carlos Jobin / It's not a prop / Something to lose / Sleeping pill / Trap door / Nightcap
CD _____ 310632
Frontier / Apr '95 / Vital.

DEAD AIR
Still / Candyland / Mock-up / Dirt / Bottle rocket / Blackout / Stray / Can't be touched / Cannibal / Don't look down / Sands hotel / Lowlife / Buick / Dead air
CD _____ 310572
Frontier / Jun '93 / Vital.

YELLOW NO.5
Wake / Fortune 500 / Corner seat / Idler / Junior mint / Yellow No.5
CD _____ 31062-2
Frontier / Jul '94 / Vital.

Heaven 17

BEST OF HEAVEN 17
(We don't need this) fascist groove thang / I'm your money / Height of the fighting (he-la-hu) / Play to win / Penthouse and pavement / Sunset now / Flame down / This is mine / Foolish thing to do / Contenders / And that's no lie / Temptation
CD _____ CDVIP 110
Virgin VIP / Dec '93 / Carlton Home Entertainment / THE / EMI.

HIGHER AND HIGHER - THE BEST OF HEAVEN 17
(We don't need this) fascist groove thang (remix) / Let me go / Come live with me / This is mine / I'm your money / Play to win / And that's no lie / Contenders / We live so fast / Sunset now / Trouble / Height of the fighting (He-la-hu) / Penthouse and pavement / Crushed by the wheels of industry / (We don't need this) fascist groove thang / Temptation (Original Version)
CD _____ CDV 2717
Virgin / Mar '93 / EMI.

HOW MEN ARE
Five minutes to midnight / Sunset now / This is mine / Fuse / Shame is on the rocks / Skin I'm in / Flamedown / Reputation / And that's no lie
CD _____ CDV 2273
Virgin / Jul '87 / EMI.

LUXURY GAP
Crushed by the wheels of industry / Who'll stop the rain / Let me go / Key to the world / Temptation / Come live with me / Lady Ice and Mr. Hex / We live so fast / Best kept secret
CD _____ CDV 2253
Virgin / '83 / EMI.

PENTHOUSE AND PAVEMENT
(We don't need this) fascist groove thang / Penthouse and pavement / Soul warfare / Geisha boys and temple girls / Let's all make a bomb / Height of the fighting (he-la-hu) / Song with no name / Play to win / We're going to live for a very long time
CD _____ CDV 2208
Virgin / Jul '87 / EMI.

REMIX COLLECTION, THE
Temptation / Facist groove thang / That's no lie / Crushed by the wheels of industry / Train of love in motion / This is mine / Foolish things to do / Play to win / Let me go / Penthouse and pavement / All come live with me
CD _____ CDVIP 133
Virgin / Apr '95 / EMI.

Heavenly

DECLINE AND FALL OF HEAVENLY, THE
Me and my madness / Modestic / Skylark / Itchy chin / Sacramento / Three star compartment / Sperm meets egg, so what / She and me
CD _____ SARAH 623CD
Sarah / Sep '94 / Vital.

Heavenly Bodies

CELESTIAL
Rains on me / Obsession / Time stands still / Con / Stars collide / Road to Maralinga / Shades of love / Cavatina / Senderoluminoso
CD _____ TMCD 27
Third Mind / Jun '89 / Pinnacle / Third Mind.

Heavenly Music...

CONSCIOUSNESS (Heavenly Music Corporation)
CD _____ SR 9458
Silent / Oct '94 / Plastic Head.

IN A GARDEN OF EDEN (Heavenly Music Corporation)
CD _____ SR 9335
Silent / Mar '94 / Plastic Head.

LUNAR PHASE (Heavenly Music Corporation)
CD _____ SR 9571
Silent / Feb '95 / Plastic Head.

Heaven's Gate

LIVE FOR SALE
CD _____ SPV 07776742
SPV / Apr '94 / Plastic Head.

LIVIN' IN HYSTERIA
CD _____ 0876312
Steamhammer / May '91 / Pinnacle / Plastic Head.

Heavy Load

METAL ANGELS IN LEATHER
CD _____ 15215
Laserlight / Aug '91 / Target/BMG.

Heavy Shift

UNCHAIN YOUR MIND/LIVE...
CD Set _____ WOLCDL 1050
China / Feb '95 / Pinnacle.

Heckman, Thomas

SPECTRAL EMOTIONS
CD _____ DBMLABCD 4
Labworks / Oct '95 / SRD / Disc.

Heckstall-Smith, Dick

BIRD IN WIDNES (Heckstall-Smith, Dick & John Stevens)
CD _____ EFA 084302
Konnex / Jul '95 / SRD.

DICK HECKSTALL-SMITH QUARTET
Venerable Bede / Woza nasu / Moongoose / Baiere
CD _____ CDLR 45028
L&R / May '91 / New Note.

STORY ENDED, A
Future song / Crabs / Moses in the bullrushourses / What the morning was after / Pirate's dream / Same old thing / Moses in the bullrushourses (Live) / Pirates dream (Live) / No amount of loving (Live)
CD _____ NEMCD 641
Sequel / Mar '93 / BMG.

WOZA NASU
CD _____ AUCD 737
Aura / Jan '91 / Cadillac.

Heddix, Travis

WRONG SIDE OUT
Caught in the middle / Nobody wants you when you're old / Old time music / Two people are better than one / Wrong side out / Time to take change / Old cliche / Don't take everything away from me
CD _____ CDICH 1033
Ichiban / Feb '89 / Koch.

Hedgehog

MERCURY RED
CD _____ VOW 37C
Voices Of Wonder / Apr '94 / Plastic Head.

PRIMAL GUTTER
CD _____ VOW 034C
Voices Of Wonder / Dec '93 / Plastic Head.

THORN CHORD WONDER
CD _____ VOW 044C
Voices Of Wonder / Jun '95 / Plastic Head.

Hedges, Chuck

NO GREATER LOVE
There is no greater love / My old flame / Samba dees days / I'll be seeing you / I'm getting sentimental over you / Magnolia rag / I thought about you / Jitterbug waltz / I remember you / I love you / Cheek to cheek
CD _____ ARCD 19121
Arbors Jazz / Nov '94 / Cadillac.

SWINGTET LIVE AT ANDY'S
CD _____ DD 465
Delmark / Aug '94 / Hot Shot / ADA / CM / Direct / Cadillac.

Hedges, Michael

BREAKFAST IN THE FIELD
CD _____ 01934110172
Windham Hill / Jul '93 / Pinnacle / BMG / ADA.

TAPROOT
Naked stalk / Jealous tunnel / About face / Jade stalk / Nomad land / Point A / Chava's song / Ritual dance / Scenes / First cutting / Point B / Song of the spirit farmer / Rootwitch / I carry your heart
CD _____ 1934110932
Windham Hill / Sep '95 / Pinnacle / BMG / ADA.

WATCHING MY LIFE GO BY
Face yourself / I'm coming home / Woman of the world / Watching my life go by / I want you / Streamlined man / Out on the parkway / Holiday / All along the watchtower / Running blind
CD _____ 01934103032
Windham Hill / Jul '93 / Pinnacle / BMG / ADA.

Hedges, Ray

TUBULAR BELLS
CD _____ GRF 216
Tring / Mar '93 / Tring / Prism.

TUBULAR BELLS 2
CD _____ GRF 217
Tring / Mar '93 / Tring / Prism.

Hedningarna

HEDNINGARNA
CD _____ ALICD 009
Alice / Dec '93 / ADA / Cadillac.

KAKSI
CD _____ XOUCD 101
Xource / Oct '93 / ADA / Cadillac.

TRA
CD _____ MWCD 4011
Music & Words / Dec '95 / ADA / Direct.

Hedonist

H.E.A.D.
CD _____ BLUE 16CD
Blue / Oct '95 / Plastic Head.

Heeman, Christopher

AFTERSOLSTICE
CD _____ BAR 012
Staalplaat / Sep '95 / Vital/SAM.

Heffern, Gary

PAINFUL DAYS
CD _____ GRCD 362
Glitterhouse / Jun '95 / Direct / ADA.

Heights Of Abraham

ELECTRIC HUSH
CD _____ PORK 028
Pork / Jan '96 / Kudos.

Heino

SINGLE HITS (1966-68)
CD _____ 16007
Laserlight / Aug '91 / Target/BMG.

Heinz

TRIBUTE TO EDDIE
Tribute to Eddie / Hush-a-bye / I ran all the way home / Country boy / Don't you knock at my door / Summertime blues / Don't keep picking on me / Cut across shorty / Three steps to heaven / Come on and dance / Twenty flight rock / Look for a star / My dreams / I remember / Been invited to a party / Rumble in the night / I get up in the morning / Just like Eddie
CD _____ RCCD 3008
Rollercoaster / Jan '94 / CM / Swift.

Heitor

HEITOR
Ligeirin / Infinity / River of life / Mal da lua / Casa do baiao / Pulsar / Manchester / Unreal / Marcha do tempo / Joao pernambuco / Frevo (pra nitera) / Mara
CD _____ 450994610-2
WEA / Jan '94 / Warner Music.

Helen Love

RADIO HITS
CD _____ DAMGOOD 51CD
Damaged Goods / Oct '94 / SRD.

Helian, Jacques

JACQUES HELIAN & STAN KENTON 1938-54 (Helian, Jacques & Stan Kenton)
CD _____ 8274172
Jazztime / Jan '95 / Discovery / BMG.

Helias, Mark

LOOPIN' THE COOL
Munchkins / Loop the cool / One time only / Sector 51 / Seventh sign / Penta houve /

Thumbs up / Hung over easy / El baz / Pacific rim
CD _____ ENJ 90492
Enja / Feb '96 / New Note / Vital/SAM.

Helicon

HELICON
CD _____ N 0213-2
Noise/Modern Music / Mar '93 / Pinnacle / Plastic Head.

Helicopter

HELICOPTER HAS LANDED
CD _____ ACTIVCD 4
Activ / Jun '95 / Total/BMG.

Helios Creed

BURSTING THROUGH THE VAN ALLAN BELT
CD _____ CLEO 94652
Cleopatra / Jun '94 / Disc.

HELIOS CREED LIVE
CD _____ YCLS 018CD
Your Choice / Jun '94 / Plastic Head.

KISS TO THE BRAIN
CD _____ ARR 223CD
Amphetamine Reptile / Nov '92 / SRD.

PLANET X
CD _____ ARRCD 56353
Amphetamine Reptile / Oct '94 / SRD.

X RATED FAIRYTALES/SUPER CATHOLIC FINGER
CD _____ CLEO 94902
Cleopatra / Sep '94 / Disc.

Helium

DIRT OF LUCK, THE
Pat's trick / Trizie's star / Silver angel / Baby's goin' underground / Medusa / Comet / Skeleton / Superball / Heaven / Oh the wind and rain / Honeycomb / Latin song
CD _____ OLE 1242
Matador / Apr '95 / Vital.

PIRATE PRUDE
Baby vampire made me / Wanna be a vampire too, baby / XXX / OOO / I'll get you, I mean it / Love $$$
CD _____ OLE 078-2
Matador / May '94 / Vital.

Helivator

GASOLINE T SHIRT
CD _____ ORGAN 7 CD
Lungcast / Mar '93 / SRD.

Helix

BACK FOR ANOTHER TASTE
Storm / That's life / Heavy metal cowboys / Back for another taste / Midnight express / Give it to you / Running wild in the 21st century / Breakdown / Wild in the streets / Rockin' rollercoaster / Good to the last drop / Wheels of thunder
CD _____ CLACD 346
Castle / May '94 / BMG.

IT'S BUSINESS DOING PLEASURE
CD _____ CDIRS 986969
Intercord / Aug '93 / Plastic Head.

Hell Bastards

NATURAL ORDER
CD _____ MOSH 022CD
Earache / Jun '90 / Vital.

Hell, Richard

DESTINY STREET (Hell, Richard & The Voidoids)
Kid with the replaceable head / You gotta / Going going gone / Lowest common denominator / Downtown at dawn / Time / I can only give you everything / Ignore that door / Staring in her eyes / Destiny Street
CD _____ DAN 9306CD
Danceteria / Feb '95 / Plastic Head / ADA.

GO NOW
CD _____ CODE 3CD
Overground / Apr '95 / SRD.

Hellberg Duo

IHRE GROBTEN ERFOLGE
CD _____ 16019
Laserlight / Nov '91 / Target/BMG.

Hellbilly's

TORTURE GARDEN
CD _____ RNR 005CD
Ransom Note / Oct '95 / Plastic Head.

Hellborg, Jonas

AXIS
Touch my soul / Definer of out / Roman / Liquid sunshine / What can I say / Money talk / You want me / Tomorrow / No 5 / Trombone
CD _____ DEMCD 006
Day Eight Music / Jun '93 / New Note.

ELEGANT PUNK
Drone / Little wing / Glad to be back from Paris / Rosa / It's the pits, slight return / Cafe ariman / Blue in green / Hm / Reebop / Jan Johansson / Kader, the Algerian / Elegant punk for guitars / Wal / White women / Northpole English
CD _____ DEMCD 004
Day Eight Music / Jun '93 / New Note.

WORD, THE
Akasha / Zat / Saut e sarmad / Two rivers / Be and all became / Poets / Black rite / Cherokee mist / Miklagaard / Path over clouds
CD _____ AXCD 3009
Axiom / Oct '91 / PolyGram / Vital.

Hellcats

HOODOO TRAIN
Where the hell is Memphis / Crazy about you baby / Baby, please don't go / I did my part / When you walk in the room / Black door slam / Wall of death / I don't need / I've been a good thing (for you) / Hoodoo train / Don't fight it / Antartica / Shine / Silly whim / Love is dying / Hard time killin' floor blues / What'cha doing in the woods / Where the sirens cry
CD _____ ROSE 197CD
New Rose / Aug '90 / Direct / ADA.

Heller, Jana

LAUGHING IN CRIME
CD _____ CYCLECD 003
Cycle / Jan '96 / Direct / ADA.

Hellion

BLACK BOOK, THE
CD _____ CDMFN 108
Music For Nations / Oct '90 / Pinnacle.

Hellkrusher

BUILDINGS FOR THE RICH
Buildings for the rich / Third world exploitation / War, who needs it / Full of shit / Path to destruction / Chase is on / Sick / Conform / Dying for who / Smash the trash / Destined to die / System dictates / Threat of war / Burn a rock star / Who's system / War games / Clear the debt / Scared of change / Dead zone / Hellkrusher
CD _____ CASE 004CD
SMR / Feb '93 / Vital.

Hello

NEW YORK GROOVE...THE BEST OF HELLO
CD _____ MCCD 112
Music Club / Jun '93 / Disc / THE / CM.

Helloween

BEST, THE REST, THE RARE, THE (The Collection 1984-1988)
CD _____ N 01762
Noise/Modern Music / Jan '92 / Pinnacle / Plastic Head.

CHAMELEON
First time / When the sinner / I don't wanna cry no more / Crazy cat / Giants / Windmill / Revolution now/San Francisco (Be sure to wear some flowers in your hair) / In the night / Music / Step out of hell / I believe / Longing
CD _____ CDFA 3308
Fame / Nov '94 / EMI.

MASTER OF THE RINGS
Irritation / Sole survivor / Where the rain grows / Why / Mr. Ego / Perfect gentleman / Game is on / Secret alibi / Take me home / In the middle of a heartbeat / Still we go
CD _____ RAWCD 101
Raw Power / Aug '94 / BMG.

Hellwitch

TERRAASYMMETRY
CD _____ LMCD 1111
Lethal / Nov '93 / Plastic Head.

Helmet

BETTY
Wilma's rainbow / I know / Biscuits for smut / Milquestoast / Tic / Rollo / Street crab / Clean / Vaccination / Beautiful love / Speechless / Silver Hawaiian / Overrated / Sam Hell
CD _____ 654492404-2
Interscope / Jun '94 / Warner Music.

BORN ANNOYING
CD _____ ARRCD 60003
Amphetamine Reptile / Apr '95 / SRD.

MEANTIME
In the meantime / Ironhead / Give it / Unsung / Turned out / He feels bad / Better / You borrowed / FBLA II / Role model
CD _____ 7567921622
Interscope / Jun '92 / Warner Music.

STRAP IT ON
Repitition / Rude / Bad mood / Sinatra / FBLA / Blacktop / Distracted / Make room / Murder
CD _____ 756792235-2
Interscope / Jul '93 / Warner Music.

Helms, Bobby

FRAULEIN (His Decca Recordings/2CD Set)
Tennessee rock 'n' roll / I need to know how / I don't owe you nothing / Sowin' teardrops / (Got a) heartsick feeling / Far away heart / Just a little lonesome (1) / Fool such as I / I'm leaving now (long gone daddy) / Tonight's the night / Jingle bell rock / Captain Santa Claus / No other baby / Standing at the end of my world / My shoes keep walking back to you / New river train / Hundred hearts / Hurry baby / Sad eyed baby / Someone was already there / To my sorrow / Lonely River Rhine (2) / Then came you / Just between old sweethearts / I can't take it like you can / My greatest weakness / Yesterday's champagne (1) / One deep love / Once in a lifetime / Fraulein / Most of the time / My special angel / just a little lonesome (2) / Magic song / Sugar moon / Schoolboy crush / If I only knew / Love my lady / Plaything / Jacqueline / Living in the shadows of the past / Forget about him / I guess I'll miss the prom / Miss memory / Soon it can be told / Fool and the angel / Someone for everyone / Yesterday's champagne (2) / Lonely River Rhine (1) / How can you divide a little child / Borrowed dreams / You're no longer mine / My lucky day / Let me be the one / Guess we thought the world would end / Teach me
CD Set _____ BCD 15594
Bear Family / Mar '92 / Rollercoaster / Direct / CM / Swift / ADA.

Helsinki Mandoliners

HELSINKI MANDOLINERS
CD _____ KICD 38
KICD / Nov '95 / ADA.

Helstar

DISTANT THUNDER, A
King is dead / Bitter end / Abandon ship / Tyrannicide / Scorcher / Genius of insanity / Whore of Babylon / Winds of love / He's a woman, she's a man
CD _____ RR 95242
Roadrunner / Aug '88 / Pinnacle.

MULTIPLES IN BLACK
CD _____ MASSCD 053
Massacre / May '95 / Plastic Head.

Heltir

NEUE SACHLICHKEIT
CD _____ DV 024CD
Dark Vinyl / Sep '95 / Plastic Head.

Hemingway, Gerry

DEMON CHASER (Hemingway, Gerry Quintet)
CD _____ ARTCD 6137
Hat Art / Jan '94 / Harmonia Mundi / ADA / Cadillac.

SPECIAL DETAILS (Hemingway, Gerry Quintet)
CD _____ ARTCD 6084
Hat Art / Jul '91 / Harmonia Mundi / ADA / Cadillac.

Hemphill, Julius

FAT MAN & THE HARD BLUES (Hemphill, Julius Sextet)
CD _____ 1201152
Black Saint / Mar '92 / Harmonia Mundi / Cadillac.

FIVE CHORD STUD (Hemphill, Julius Sextet)
CD _____ 120140-2
Black Saint / Oct '94 / Harmonia Mundi / Cadillac.

FLAT OUT JUMP SUITE (Hemphill, Julius Quartet)
CD _____ 120040-2
Black Saint / May '92 / Harmonia Mundi / Cadillac.

LIVE FROM THE NEW MUSIC CAFE (Hemphill, Julius Trio)
CD _____ CD 731
Music & Arts / Sep '92 / Harmonia Mundi / Cadillac.

LIVE IN NEW YORK (Hemphill, Julius & Abdul Wadud)
CD _____ 1231382
Red / Apr '95 / Harmonia Mundi / Jazz Horizons / Cadillac / ADA.

OAKLAND DUETS (Hemphill, Julius & Abdul Wadud)
CD _____ CD 791
Music & Arts / Jan '94 / Harmonia Mundi / Cadillac.

Henderson, Bugs

AT LAST
CD _____ TX 1002CD
Taxim / Jan '94 / ADA.

THAT'S THE TRUTH
CD _____ TX 1013CD
Taxim / Jul '95 / ADA.

YEARS IN THE JUNGLE
CD _____ TX 1011CD
Taxim / Dec '93 / ADA.

Henderson, Chick

BEGIN THE BEGUINE (1937-1940)
(Henderson, Chick & The Joe Loss Band)
While a cigarette was burning / I still love to kiss you goodnight / On a little dream ranch / My prayer / Begin the beguine / By an old pagoda / Girl in the Alice blue gown / I know now / I shall be waiting / I'll remember / It looks like rain in Cherry Blossom Lane / It's a lovely day tomorrow / May I have the next romance with you / Music maestro please / On the sentimental side / Remember me / September in the rain / Seventeen candles
CD _____ CD AJA 5083
Living Era / Apr '91 / Koch.

BLUE ORCHIDS
CD _____ CDMOIR 310
Memoir / May '95 / Target/BMG.

MAN WHO BEGAN THE BEGUINE
CD _____ MWMCDSP 15
Mawson & Wareham / Nov '94 / BMG / THE.

REMEMBER ME
Till the lights of London shine again / Serenade in blue / We'll go smiling along / Somewhere in France with you / My prayer / Black out stroll / Sweet little sweetheart / Shabby old cabby / Wish me luck as you wave me goodbye / Begin the beguine / You can't stop me from dreaming / That old feeling / You're an education / Thanks for everything / Let the curtain come down / Music maestro please / I still love to kiss you goodnight / I know how / Remember me / Small cafe by Notre Dame
CD _____ PAR 2025
Parade / Jul '94 / Koch / Cadillac.

Henderson, Di

BY ANY OTHER NAME
CD _____ DHC 001
Deeaitch / Dec '93 / Friendly Overtures.

Henderson, Duke

GET YOUR KICKS
CD _____ DD 668
Delmark / Dec '94 / Hot Shot / ADA / CM / Direct / Cadillac.

Henderson, Eddie

THINK OF ME (Henderson, Eddie Quintet)
CD _____ SCCD 31264
Steeplechase / Oct '90 / Impetus.

Henderson, Fletcher

1921-1923 VOL.1
CD _____ DOCD 5342
Blues Document / May '95 / Swift / Jazz Music / Hot Shot.

1923-1924 VOL.2
CD _____ DOCD 5343
Blues Document / May '95 / Swift / Jazz Music / Hot Shot.

1924-1938
CD _____ CD 53179
Giants Of Jazz / Nov '95 / Target/BMG / Cadillac.

CLASSICS 1921-23
CD _____ CLASSICS 751
Classics / Jan '95 / Discovery / Jazz Music.

CLASSICS 1923-1924 (Henderson, Fletcher & His Orchestra)
CD _____ CLASSICS 683
Classics / Mar '93 / Discovery / Jazz Music.

CLASSICS 1924
CD _____ CLASSICS 673
Classics / Nov '92 / Discovery / Jazz Music.

CLASSICS 1931-1932
CD _____ CLASSICS 546
Classics / Dec '90 / Discovery / Jazz Music.

CROWN KING OF SWING, THE (Henderson, Fletcher & His Orchestra)
After you've gone / Stardust / Tiger rag / Somebody stole my gal / (I'll be glad when you're dead) you rascal you / Blue rhythm / Sugarfoot stomp / Low down on the bayou / Twelth street rag / Milenberg joys
CD _____ SV 0254
Savoy Jazz / Nov '94 / Conifer / ADA.

FLETCHER HENDERSON (1937-8)
CD _____ TPZ 1004
Topaz Jazz / Jul '94 / Pinnacle / Cadillac.

FLETCHER HENDERSON & HIS ORCHESTRA (Henderson, Fletcher & His Orchestra)
Back in your own backyard / Rose room / Stampede / Chris and his gang / All God's chillun got rhythm / Posin' / Let 'er go / Great Caesar's ghost / If you should ever leave / Worried over you / Rhythm of the

tambourine / Slumming on Park Avenue / It's wearin' me down / Trees / If it's the last thing I do / You're in love with love / Don't let the rhythm go to your head / There's rain in my eyes / Saving myself for you / What do you hear from the mob in Scotland / It's the little things that count / Moten stomp / Stealin' apples / Sing you sinners / What's your story (what's your jive)
CD _____ CDGRF 088
Tring / '93 / Tring / Prism.

FLETCHER HENDERSON 1923 (Henderson, Fletcher & His Orchestra)
CD _____ CLASSICS 697
Classics / Jul '93 / Discovery / Jazz Music.

FLETCHER HENDERSON 1924-25 (Henderson, Fletcher & His Orchestra)
CD _____ CLASSICS 633
Classics / '92 / Discovery / Jazz Music.

FLETCHER HENDERSON 1925-26 (Henderson, Fletcher & His Orchestra)
CD _____ CLASSICS 610
Classics / Feb '92 / Discovery / Jazz Music.

FLETCHER HENDERSON AND HIS ORCHESTRA - 1927 (Henderson, Fletcher & His Orchestra)
CD _____ CLASSICS 580
Classics / Oct '91 / Discovery / Jazz Music.

FLETCHER HENDERSON AND HIS ORCHESTRA - 1936-27 (Henderson, Fletcher & His Orchestra)
CD _____ CD 597
Classic Jazz Masters / Sep '91 / Wellard / Jazz Music / Jazz Music.

FLETCHER HENDERSON AND HIS ORCHESTRA VOL.2 (Henderson, Fletcher & His Orchestra)
CD _____ VILCD 0202
Village Jazz / Sep '92 / Target/BMG / Jazz Music.

FLETCHER HENDERSON SEXTET 1950
CD _____ RST 91537
RST / Mar '95 / Jazz Music / Hot Shot.

INTRODUCTION 1921-41
CD _____ BEST 4019
Best Of Jazz / Mar '95 / Discovery.

JAZZ PORTRAITS
Moten stomp / Sing you sinners / Back in your own backyard / Rhythm of the tambourine / Christopher Columbus / Yeah man / Clarinet marmalade / Wang wang blues / I'm coming Virginia / What'cha call 'em blues / Teapot dome blues / Stampede / Big John special / Singin' the blues / Shanghai shuffle / Chinatown, my Chinatown / New King Porter stomp / Sugarfoot stomp
CD _____ CD 14522
Jazz Portraits / May '94 / Jazz Music.

RARE RECORDINGS (The Golden Age of Jazz)
CD _____ JZCD 366
Suisa / Jun '92 / Jazz Music / THE.

STUDY IN FRUSTRATION, A (The Fletcher Henderson Story/3CD Set)
CD Set _____ C3K 57596
Columbia / Oct '94 / Sony.

UNDER THE HARLEM MOON
Honeysuckle Rose / New King Porter stomp / Underneath the Harlem moon / Queer notions / Night life / Nagasaki / Rhythm crazy now / Ain't cha glad / Hocus pocus / Tidal wave / Christopher Columbus / Blue lou / Stealin' apples / Jangled nerves / Grand Terrace rhythm / Riffin' / Shoe shine boy / Sing, sing, sing / Jimtown blues / Rhythm of the tambourine / Back in your own backyard / Chris and his gang
CD _____ CD AJA 5067
Living Era / Mar '90 / Koch.

WILD PARTY (Henderson, Fletcher & His Orchestra)
Hocus pocus / Phantom fantasie / Harlem madness / Tidal wave / Limehouse blues / Shanghai shuffle / Big John Special / Happy as the day is long / Down South camp meeting / Wrappin' it up / Memphis blues / Wild party / Rug cutters' swing / Hotter than 'Ell / Liza (all the clouds'll roll away)
CD _____ HEPCD 1009
Hep / Aug '94 / Cadillac / Jazz Music / New Note / Wellard.

Henderson, Ingrid

LIGHT OF THE MOUNTAIN (Henderson, Ingrid & Allan)
CD _____ LDL 1204CD
Lochshore / May '93 / ADA / Direct / Duncans.

PERPETUAL HORSESHOE (Henderson, Ingrid & Allan)
CD _____ LDL 1216CD
Lochshore / Jun '94 / ADA / Direct / Duncans.

Henderson, Joe

BARCELONA
Barcelona / Barcelona (contd.) / Mediterranean sun / Y yo la quiero (and I love her)

CD _____ ENJACD 30372
Enja / Jun '93 / New Note / Vital/SAM.

DOUBLE RAINBOW
CD _____ 5272222
Verve / Mar '95 / PolyGram.

FOUR
CD _____ 5236572
Verve / Jan '95 / PolyGram.

KICKER, THE
CD _____ OJCCD 465
Original Jazz Classics / Nov '95 / Wellard / Jazz Music / Cadillac / Complete/Pinnacle.

LUSH LIFE
Isfahan / Johnny come lately / Blood count / Raincheck / Lotus blossom / Flower is a lovesome thing / Take the 'A' train / Drawing room blues / Upper Manhattan medical group (U.M.M.G.) / Lush life
CD _____ 5117792
Verve / Sep '92 / PolyGram.

MIRROR MIRROR (Henderson, Joe & Chick Corea)
CD _____ 5190922
Verve / Apr '93 / PolyGram.

RELAXIN' AT CAMARILLO
CD _____ OJCCD 776
Original Jazz Classics / Sep '93 / Wellard / Jazz Music / Cadillac / Complete/Pinnacle.

SO NEAR, SO FAR
CD _____ 517674-2
Verve / Jan '92 / PolyGram.

STANDARD JOE, THE
CD _____ 123248-2
Red / May '92 / Harmonia Mundi / Jazz Horizons / Cadillac / ADA.

STATE OF THE TENOR, VOLS. 1 & 2
Beatrice / Friday the 13th / happy reunion / Loose change / Ask me now / Isotope / Stella by starlight / Boo Boo's birthday / Cheryl / Y ya la quiero / Soulville / Portrait / Bead game / All the things you are
CD _____ CDP 8288792
Blue Note / May '94 / EMI.

TETRAGON/IN PURSUIT OF BLACKNESS
Invitation / R.J. / Bead game / Tetragon / Waltz for sweetie / First trip / I've got you under my skin / No me esqueca / Shade of jade / Gazelle / Mind over matter
CD _____ CDBGPD 084
BGP / Mar '94 / Pinnacle.

Henderson, Michael

BEST OF MICHAEL HENDERSON
Be my girl / I can't help it / In the night time / To be loved / (We are here) to geek you up / You are my starship / Make me feel better / Let me love you / You haven't made it to the top / Take me i'm yours / Do it all / Wide reciever / Valentine love / Reach out for me / Am I special
CD _____ NEXCD 117
Sequel / May '90 / BMG.

Henderson, Mike

EDGE OF NIGHT
CD _____ DR 0004
Round Tower / Jan '96 / Pinnacle / ADA / Direct / BMG / CM.

Henderson, Scott

DOG PARTY
Hole diggin' / Fence climbin' blues / Dog party / Same as you / Milk bone / Hell bent pup / Too many gittars / Smelly ol' dog blues / Dog walk / Hound dog
CD _____ R2 79073
Mesa / Nov '94 / Total/BMG.

ILLICIT (Henderson, Scott & Tribal Tech)
Big waves / Stoopid / Black cherry / Torque / Slidin into charlisa / Root food / Riot / Paha-sapa / Babylon / Passion dance / Just because
CD _____ R27 91802
Bluemoon / Oct '92 / New Note.

NOMAD (Henderson, Scott & Tribal Tech)
Renegade / Nomad / Robot immigrants / Tunnel vision / Elegy for shoe / Bofat / No, no, no / Self defence / Rituals
CD _____ CDLR 45022
L&R / Aug '90 / New Note.

PRIMAL TRACKS (Henderson, Scott & Gary Willis)
Elvis at the top / Got tuh b / Sub aqua / Nomad / Necessary blonde / Bofat / Wasteland / Mango prom / Self defence / Rain / Ominous / Twilight in Northridge / Dense dance
CD _____ R2 79196
Bluemoon / Nov '94 / New Note.

Henderson, Wayne

RUGBY GUITAR
CD _____ FF 542CD
Flying Fish / '92 / Roots / CM / Direct / ADA.

SKETCHES OF LIFE (Henderson, Wayne & The Next Crusade)
Strange love / We're gonna rock your sock off / Men cry too / I'll take you there / Color of love / Just because its jazz, (Don't mean ya can't dance) / Portrait of a dream / Ancestral chant / For old time's sake / Survival (I can't get started with you / Just because it's jazz (don't mean ya can't dance)
CD _____ CPCD 8125
Charly / Oct '95 / Charly / THE / Cadillac.

Hendon Citadel Band

MARCHING WITH THE SALVATION ARMY
Starlake / Torchbearers / Bravest of the Brave / Wellingtonian / Cairo red shield / Crown of conquest / In the King's service / Roll call / Salute to America / To regions fair / Joyful news / On the news / On the king's highway / Fighting for the Lord / Fount / Victors acclaimed / Southall 100
CD _____ BNA 5041
Bandleader / '91 / Conifer.

Hendricks, Jon

FREDDIE FREELOADER
Jumpin' at the woodside / In Summer / Freddie Freeloader / Stardust / Sugar / Take the 'A' train / Fas' livin' blues / High as a mountain / Trinkle tinkle / Swing that music / Finer things in life / Listen to Monk / Sing, sing, sing
CD _____ CY 76302
Denon / Aug '90 / Conifer.

LOVE (Hendricks, Jon & Co)
Royal Garden blues / Bright moments / Willie's tune / Good ol' lady / Li'l darlin' / I'll die happy / Love (Berkshire blues) / Tell me the truth / Swinging groove merchant(groove merchant) / Angel eyes / In a Harlem airshaft
CD _____ MCD 5258
Muse / Sep '92 / New Note / CM.

Hendricks, Michele

CARRYIN' ON
CD _____ MCD 5336
Muse / Sep '92 / New Note / CM.

KEEPIN' ME SATISFIED
CD _____ MCD 5363
Muse / Sep '92 / New Note / CM.

Hendriks, Karl

BUICK ELECTRA (Hendriks, Karl Trio)
CD _____ GROW 382
Grass / Feb '95 / SRD.

MISERY & WOMEN (Hendriks, Karl Trio)
CD _____ FIRECD 39
Fire / Jun '94 / Disc.

Hendrix, Jimi

ARE YOU EXPERIENCED?
Foxy lady / Manic depression / Red house / Can you see me / Love or confusion / I don't live today / May this be love / Fire / Third stone from the sun / Remember / Are you experienced / Purple haze / Hey Joe / Wind cries Mary
CD _____ 5210362
Polydor / Oct '93 / PolyGram.

AXIS BOLD AS LOVE
Experience / Up from the skies / Spanish castle magic / Wait until tomorrow / Ain't no tellin' / Little wing / If six was nine / You've got me floating / Castles made of sand / She's so fine / One rainy wish / Little Miss Lover / Bold as love
CD _____ 847 243-2
Polydor / Jun '89 / PolyGram.

BAND OF GYPSIES
Who knows / Machine gun / Changes / Power to love / Message of love / We gotta live together / Hear my train a comin' / Foxy lady / Stop
CD _____ 847 237-2
Polydor / Jun '91 / PolyGram.

BLUES
Hear my train a comin' (acoustic & electric versions) / Born under a bad sign / Red house / Catfish blues / Voodoo chile blues / Mannish boy / Once I had a woman / Bleeding heart / Jelly 292 / Electric Church Red house
CD _____ 5210372
Polydor / Apr '94 / PolyGram.

COLLECTION, THE
CD _____ COL 017
Collection / Jan '95 / Target/BMG.

CONCERTS, THE
Fire / I don't live today / Red house / Stone free / Are you experienced / Little wing / Voodoo chile / Bleeding heart / Hey Joe / Wild thing / Hear my train a comin' / Foxy lady
CD _____ CCSCD 235
Castle / Feb '92 / BMG / CM.

CORNERSTONES 1967-1970
Hey Joe / Purple haze / Wind cries Mary / Foxy lady / Crosstown traffic / All along the watchtower / Voodoo chile / Have you ever been (to Electric Ladyland) / Star spangled banner (Studio version) / Stepping stone /

Room full of mirrors / Ezy ryder / Freedom / Drifting / In from the storm / Angel / Fire (Not on LP) / Stone free (Not on LP)
CD _____ 8472312
Polydor / Jan '93 / PolyGram.

CROSSTOWN CONVERSATION
CD P.Disc _____ CBAK 4082
Baktabak / Feb '94 / Baktabak.

EARLY JIMI HENDRIX, THE
CD _____ 3179
Scratch / Mar '95 / BMG.

EARLY YEARS, THE
CD _____ CDCD 1189
Charly / Sep '94 / Charly / THE / Cadillac.

ELECTRIC LADYLAND
And the gods made love / Electric ladyland / Voodoo Chile / Crosstown traffic / Still raining, still dreaming / House burning down / All along the watchtower / Long hot summer night / Little Miss Strange / Come on / Gypsy eyes / Burning of the midnight lamp / Rainy day / 1983 / Moon turn the tides / Gently, gently away
CD _____ 847 233-2
Polydor / Oct '93 / PolyGram.

EXPERIENCE
CD _____ NTRCD 036
Nectar / Mar '95 / Pinnacle.

FOOTPRINTS (Isle Of Wight/Band Of Gypsys/At Winterland/Plays Monterey)
CD Set _____ 8472352
Polydor / Mar '91 / PolyGram.

FREE SPIRIT
Good times / Voices / Suspicious / Whipper / Bessie Mae / Soul food / Voice in the wind / Free spirit
CD _____ CDTB 094
Thunderbolt / Jan '91 / Magnum Music Group.

GOLD COLLECTION, THE
CD _____ D2CD03
Recording Arts / Dec '92 / THE / Disc.

GREATEST HITS: JIMI HENDRIX
CD Set _____ PULS 301
Pulsar / Oct '95 / BMG.

INTERVIEWS
CD _____ 8122707712
WEA / Jul '93 / Warner Music.

INTROSPECTIVE: JIMI HENDRIX
Red house / Wake up this morning and find yourself dead / Interview part one / Bleeding heart / Interview part two
CD _____ CINT 5006
Baktabak / Apr '91 / Baktabak.

JIMI HENDRIX (2CD Set)
CD Set _____ R 2CD4003
Deja Vu / Jan '96 / THE.

JIMI HENDRIX AT THE MONTEREY POP FESTIVAL 1967
CD _____ ITM 960008
ITM / Sep '93 / Tradelink / Koch.

JIMI HENDRIX AT WOODSTOCK
Introduction / Fire / Izabella / Hear my train a comin' / Red house / Jam back at the house (Beginnings) / Voodoo chile / Star spangled banner / Purple haze / Woodstock improvisation / Villanova Junction / Farewell
CD _____ 523384-2
PolyGram / Aug '94 / PolyGram.

JIMI HENDRIX BOX SET
CD Set _____ JH 1
UFO / Oct '92 / Pinnacle.

JIMI HENDRIX COLLECTOR'S EDITION
CD _____ DVBC 9032
Deja Vu / Apr '95 / THE.

JIMI HENDRIX EXPERIENCE IN 1967 (Hendrix, Jimi Experience)
CD Set _____ JH 001
Revolver / Jul '92 / Revolver Music / Sony.

JIMI HENDRIX GOLD (2CD Set)
CD Set _____ D2CD 4003
Deja Vu / Jun '95 / THE.

JIMI PLAYS MONTEREY
Killing floor / Foxy lady / Like a rolling stone / Rock me baby / Hey Joe / Can you see me / Wind cries Mary / Purple Haze / Wild thing
CD _____ 847 244-2
Polydor / Jun '91 / PolyGram.

LAST EXPERIENCE, THE
CD _____ CD 101
Timeless Treasures / Oct '94 / THE.

LAST EXPERIENCE, THE
CD _____ SRCD 115
Strawberry / Jul '95 / Magnum Music Group.

LIVE AT THE ISLE OF WIGHT
Midnight lightning / Foxy lady / Lover man / Freedom / All along the watchtower / In from the storm / Intro (God save the Queen) / Message to love / Voodoo Chile / Machine gun / Dolly dagger / Red house / New rising sun
CD _____ 8472362
Polydor / Jan '93 / PolyGram.

LIVE AT WINTERLAND
Prologue / Fire / Manic depression / Sunshine of your love / Spanish castle magic /

Red house / Killing floor / Tax free / Foxy lady / Hey Joe / Purple haze / Wild thing / Epilogue
CD _____ 847 238-2
Polydor / Jun '91 / PolyGram.

LIVE IN NEW YORK
CD _____ MU 5018
Musketeer / Oct '92 / Koch.

NIGHT LIFE
Good feeling / Hot trigger / Psycho / Come on baby (part 1) / Come on baby (part 2) / Night life / Foxy lady / Woke up this morning / Lime line / Peoples people / Whoa eeh
CD _____ CDTB 075
Thunderbolt / May '95 / Magnum Music Group.

PURPLE HAZE IN WOODSTOCK
CD _____ ITM 960004
ITM / Feb '94 / Tradelink / Koch.

RADIO ONE
Stone free / Radio one theme / Day tripper / Killing floor / Love or confusion / Catfish blues / Drivin' South / Wait until tomorrow / Hear my train a comin' / Hound dog / Fire / Hoochie coochie man / Purple haze / Spanish castle magic / Hey Joe / Foxy lady / Burning of the midnight lamp
CD _____ CCSCD 212
Castle / Feb '89 / BMG.

REVENGE (A Tribute To Jimi Hendrix) (Various Artists)
Foxy lady / Up from the skies / Electric ladyland / Remember / Fire / Purple haze / Burning of the midnight lamp / Voodoo chile / Hey Joe dub / Red house / Angel / Crosstown traffic / Little Miss Lover / Message to love
CD _____ 682550
Gravity / May '95 / New Note.

STONE FREE (A Tribute To Jimi Hendrix) (Various Artists)
Purple haze / Stone free / Spanish castle magic / Red house / Hey Joe / Manic depression / Fire / Bold as love / You got me floatin' / I don't live today / Are you experienced / Crosstown traffic / Third stone from the sun / Hey baby (Land of the new rising sun)
CD _____ 9362454382
WEA / Oct '93 / Warner Music.

SUPERSESSION
Red house / Woke up this morning and found myself dead / Peoples peoples aka bleeding heart / Morrison's lament / Tomorrow never knows / Vranus rock / Outside woman blues / Sunshine of your love / Goodbye Bessie Mae / Soul food
CD _____ CD 8442002
Voice Print / Jul '95 / Voice Print.

ULTIMATE EXPERIENCE, THE
All along the watchtower / Purple haze / Hey Joe / Wind cries Mary / Angel / Voodoo chile / Foxy lady / Burning of the midnight lamp / Highway chile / Crosstown traffic / Castles made of sand / Long hot summer night / Red house / Manic depression / Gypsy eyes / Little wing / Fire / Wait until tomorrow / Star spangled banner / Wild thing
CD _____ 5172352
Polydor / Sep '95 / PolyGram.

VOODOO SOUP
CD _____ 5275202
Polydor / May '95 / PolyGram.

Henley, Don

ACTUAL MILES (Greatest Hits)
Dirty laundry / Boys of summer / All she wants to do is dance / Not enough love in the world / Sunset grill / End of innocence / Last worthless evening / New York minute / I will jot go quietly / Heart of the matter / Garden of Allah / You don't know me at all
CD _____ GED 24834
Geffen / Nov '95 / BMG.

BUILDING THE PERFECT BEAST
Boys of Summer / You can't make love / Man with a mission / You're not drinking enough / Not enough love in the world / Building the perfect beast / All she wants to do is dance / Sunset grill / Drivin' with your eyes closed / Land of the living
CD _____ GFLD 19267
Geffen / Feb '95 / BMG.

END OF THE INNOCENCE, THE
End of the innocence / How bad do you want it / I will not go quietly / Last worthless evening / New York minute / Shangri la / Little tin god / Gimme what you got / If dirt were dollars / Heart of the matter
CD _____ GFLD 19285
Geffen / Oct '95 / BMG.

I CAN'T STAND STILL
I can't stand still / You better hang up / Long way home / Nobody's business / Talking to the moon / Dirty laundry / Johnny can't read / Them and us / La elite / Lilah / Unclouded day
CD _____ K 9600482
WEA / Jun '89 / Warner Music.

Hennessey, Mike

SHADES OF CHAS BURCHELL
Shades / High on you / Blues on my mind / Days of wine and roses / Dreamstepper / Dig it / Gaby / Just friends / Soft shoe / Hanging loose / Westwood walk / Fair weather / You've changed
CD _____ IOR 70252
In & Out / Sep '95 / Vital/SAM.

Hennessy, Christie

LORD OF YOUR EYES
CD _____ 4509975862
WEA / Feb '95 / Warner Music.

YEAR IN THE LIFE, A
Quest / Lonely boy / Remember me / If you were to fall (and I ... / Lost in love with you) / Pain / Norfolk square / Vision / You can go far (if you know where you're going) / Sheila Doran / By bye love
CD _____ 4509919632
WEA / Sep '93 / Warner Music.

Hennessy, Frank

THOUGHTS AND MEMORIES
Brother eagle / Jenkin's history / Keeper / Newfoundland / Valley lights / Old men and children / Mickey's song / Start and end with you / Sun's last rays / Old Camarhten oak / Fading away / Hearts on fire
CD _____ SAIN 8084CD
Sain / Aug '94 / Direct / ADA.

Hennessys

EARLY SONGS, THE
CD _____ SCD 2044
Sain / Feb '95 / Direct / ADA.

Henry & Louis

RUDIMENTS
Youth dub / Dub rebellion / Need some dub / Instilled dub / Tenth dub / Been here dub / Dub nation / Re-dub / Dublight / War and dub / Rainbus (CD only)
CD _____ ZCDKR 003
More Rockers / Oct '95 / 3MV / Sony.

Henry, Clarence

BUT I DO (Henry, Clarence 'Frogman')
Ain't got no home / It won't be long / I found a home / Baby baby please / Never never / Oh Mickey / But I do / Just my baby and me / Live it right / I want to be a movie star / Steady date / Oh why / Little Susie / You always hurt the one you love / I love you, yes I do / Lonely street / Your picture / I wish I could say the same / Standing in the need of love / Little too much / On bended knees / Jealous kind / Dream myself a sweetheart / Lost without you / Takes two to Tango / Long lost and worried / Looking back
CD _____ CPCD 8007
Charly / Feb '94 / Charly / THE / Cadillac.

Henry Cow

IN PRAISE OF LEARNING
Living in the heart of the beast / War / Beginning / Long march / Beautiful as the moon / Terrible as an army with banners / Morning star
CD _____ ESD 80502
ReR Megacorp / Sep '93 / These / ReR Megacorp.

LEGEND
CD _____ ESD 80482
ReR Megacorp / Nov '93 / These / ReR Megacorp.

UNREST
Bitter storm over Ulm / Half asleep / Half awake / Ruins / Solemn music / Linguaphonie / Upon entering the Hotel Adlon / Arcades / Deluge
CD _____ ESD 80492
ReR Megacorp / Sep '93 / These / ReR Megacorp.

VIRGIN YEARS, THE
CD _____ CSB 1
ReR Megacorp / Dec '92 / These / ReR Megacorp.

WESTERN CULTURE
CD _____ BCD 1
ReR Megacorp / Dec '92 / These / ReR Megacorp.

Henry, Joe

KINDNESS OF THE WORLD
One day when the weather is warm / Fireman's wedding / She always goes / This close to you / Kindness of the world / Third reel / Dead to the world / I flew over our house last night / Some champions / Buck-dancer's choice / Who would know
CD _____ MR 057-2
Mammoth / Sep '93 / Vital.

Henry, Vincent

VINCENT
CD _____ CHIP 101
Jive / Jul '90 / BMG.

Henrys

PUERTO ANGEL
CD _____ FIENDCD 769
Demon / Oct '95 / Pinnacle / ADA.

Hensley, Ken

FROM TIME TO TIME
CD _____ RMCCD 0195
Red Steel Music / Jun '94 / Grapevine.

Heptones

20 GOLDEN HITS
CD _____ SONCD 0021
Sonic Sounds / Apr '92 / Jetstar.

BETTER DAYS
CD _____ RRTGCD 7715
Rohit / Jan '89 / Jetstar.

FATTIE FATTIE
Fattie fattie
CD _____ SOCD 9002
Studio One / Mar '95 / Jetstar.

GOOD VIBES
CD _____ CDSGP 048
Prestige / Jun '93 / Total/BMG.

NIGHT FOOD
CD _____ RRCD 19
Reggae Refreshers / Nov '90 / PolyGram / Vital.

OBSERVER STYLE
CD _____ CC 2713
Crocodisc / Sep '94 / THE / Magnum Music Group.

ON TOP
CD _____ SOCD 0016
Studio One / Mar '95 / Jetstar.

PARTY TIME
CD _____ RRCD 14
Reggae Refreshers / Sep '90 / PolyGram / Vital.

PRESSURE
CD _____ RASCD 3164
Ras / Oct '95 / Jetstar / Greensleeves / SRD / Direct.

RAINBOW VALLEY
CD _____ CDSGP 0132
Prestige / Aug '94 / Total/BMG.

VOLUMES 1 & 2
CD _____ CDTRL 357
Trojan / Jul '95 / Jetstar / Total/BMG.

WONDERFUL WORLD
CD _____ RNCD 2045
Rhino / Mar '94 / Jetstar / Magnum Music Group / THE.

Herawi, Aziz

MASTER OF AFGHANI LUTES
CD _____ ARHCD 387
Arhoolie / Apr '95 / ADA / Direct / Cadillac.

Herbaliser

REMEDIES
Intro / Scratchy noise / Blomp / Styles / Interloodle / Bust a nut / Herbalize it / Wrong place / Little groove / Da trax / Up / Get downs / K-doing / Chill / Real killer (Remix) / Repetitive loop (Remix)
CD _____ ZENCD 018
Ninja Tune / Sep '95 / Vital / Kudos.

Herborn, Peter

ACUTE INSIGHT
Free, forward and ahead / All along the sunstream / Beauty is... / Love in tune / Life force / Living yet
CD _____ 8344172
JMT / May '91 / PolyGram.

TRACES OF TRANE
CD _____ 5140022
JMT / Apr '92 / PolyGram.

Herd

FROM THE UNDERWORLD
CD _____ BX 4512
BR Music / Oct '95 / Target/BMG.

Herdman, Priscilla

FOREVER & ALWAYS
CD _____ FF 70637
Flying Fish / Feb '95 / Roots / CM / Direct / ADA.

WATER LILY, THE
CD _____ CDPH 1014
Philo / Aug '95 / Direct / CM / ADA.

Here & Now

I CAN DELIVER
Are you ready / Ten times the power / Here and now sound / I can deliver / Let's start over again / Tastin' love again / Come home / I am that I am / She loves me (not) / Hip-hop-jazz-religion
CD _____ 756792238-2
WEA / Jun '93 / Warner Music.

U.F.OASIS
CD _____ TRUCKCD 022
Terrapin Truckin' / Dec '94 / Total/BMG / Direct / ADA.

Here Kitty Kitty

KISS ME YOU FOOL
CD _____ IT 5CD
Iteration / Nov '94 / SRD.

Heresy

VOICE YOUR OPINION
CD _____ LF 042CD
Lost & Found / Nov '92 / Plastic Head.

Hereticks

GODS AND GANGSTERS
CD _____ CID 9954
Island / Mar '90 / PolyGram.

Heretix

ADVENTURES OF SUPER DEVIL, THE
CD _____ CH 22891-2
Cherrydisc / Oct '94 / Plastic Head.

Heritage

TELL TAE ME
CD _____ COMD 2051
Temple / Feb '94 / CM / Duncans / ADA / Direct.

Heritage Hall Jazz Band

COOKIN'
CD _____ BCD 287
GHB / Jul '93 / Jazz Music.

Herman, Hampton

CALDONIA
CD _____ JTM 6121
Jazztime / Apr '94 / Discovery / BMG.

Herman, Jerry

EVENING WITH JERRY HERMAN, AN
CD _____ CDSL 5173
DRG / Jan '93 / New Note.

Herman, Woody

1981 - CHICAGO (Herman, Woody & His Orchestra)
Four brothers / Come rain or come shine / Theme in search of a movie / Bijou / What are you doing the rest of your life / Sonny boy / Greasy sack blues / After hours / Take the 'A' train / As time goes by / Mood indigo / Blue flame / Woody's whistle
CD _____ STATUSCD 105
Status / Nov '90 / Cadillac.

ANTIBES 1965 (Herman, Woody & His Orchestra)
CD _____ CD 53110
Giants Of Jazz / Jan '95 / Target/BMG / Cadillac.

AT THE WOODCHOPPERS BALL
At the woodchoppers' ball / On the Atchison, Topeka and the Sante Fe / Wild root / Bijou / Caldonia / Put that ring on my finger / There, I've said it again / Who dat up dere / Apple honey / Goosey gander / I'll get by / Walkin' my baby back home / Spruce juice / Kiss goodnight / Noah
CD _____ CDCD 1120
Charly / Jul '93 / Charly / THE / Cadillac.

AT THE WOODCHOPPERS' BALL
At the woodchoppers' ball / Better get off your high horse / Blue flame / Blues downstairs / Blues in the night / Blues upstairs / Boogie woogie bugle boy / Bounce me brother with a solid four / Careless / Deep in a dream / Dr. Jazz / Dream valley / Fine and dandy / Frenesi / G'bye now / I'm thinking tonight of my blue eyes / Rumboogie / Rosetta / Sheikh of araby / Skylark / Sleepy serenade / Someone's rocking my dreamboat / String of pearls / They say / Whistler's mother-in-law
CD _____ CDAJA 5143
Living Era / Nov '94 / Koch.

BEST OF THE BIG BANDS
Caldonia / Laura / Sabre dance / I've got the world on a string / Blue prelude / Blowin' up a storm / P.S. I love you / Atlanta / G.A. / Apple honey / Happiness is a thing called Joe / Put that ring on my finger / Goosey Gander / Everybody knew but me / Everywhere / Northwest passage / I told ya I love ya, now get out / Now get out
CD _____ 4666212
CBS / '91 / Sony.

BEST OF WOODY HERMAN
CD _____ DLCD 4017
Dixie Live / Mar '95 / Magnum Music Group.

BLUE FLAMES
Theme: Blue flame / I say a little prayer / At the woodchoppers' ball
CD _____ CDC 9049
LRC / Nov '92 / New Note / Harmonia Mundi.

CONCORD YEARS, THE
Things ain't what they used to be / Four brothers / Round Midnight / It don't mean a thing if it ain't got that swing / Dolphin / Woody 'n' you / Blues for red / Perdido / Central Parkwest / Lemon drop / What are you doing the rest of your life / Battle royal
CD _____ CCD 4557
Concord Jazz / Jun '93 / New Note.

CREAM OF EARLY WOODY HERMAN, THE
Blues downstairs / Changing world / Herman at the Sherman / Jumpin' blues / East side kick / Big wig in the wigwam / It's a blue world / Paleface / Give a little whistle / Blues upstairs / Big morning / Jukin' / Blue ink / Farewell blues / Blues on parade / Blue prelude / Fan it / Sheikh of Araby / Blue flame / Indian boogie woogie / Dupree blues / At the woodchoppers' ball
CD _____ PASTCD 9780
Flapper / Apr '92 / Pinnacle.

CROWN ROYAL
CD _____ 15775
Laserlight / Aug '93 / Target/BMG.

FIRST HERD, THE
CD _____ LEJAZZCD 53
Le Jazz / Jan '96 / Charly / Cadillac.

GIANT STEPS
CD _____ FCD 6099432
Fantasy / Nov '86 / Pinnacle / Jazz Music / Wellard / Cadillac.

HERD RIDES AGAIN, THE
CD _____ ECD 220102
Evidence / Jul '92 / Harmonia Mundi / ADA / Cadillac.

HERMAN'S HEAT AND PUENTE'S BEAT (Herman, Woody & Tito Puente)
CD _____ ECD 220082
Evidence / Jul '92 / Harmonia Mundi / ADA / Cadillac.

HOLLYWOOD PALLADIUM (Herman, Woody & His Orchestra)
CD _____ RST 91536-2
RST / Jun '93 / Jazz Music / Hot Shot.

JAZZ COLLECTOR EDITION (5CD/MC Set) (Herman, Woody/Duke Ellington/Artie Shaw)
CD Set _____ 15911
Laserlight / Jan '92 / Target/BMG.

JAZZ PORTRAIT
CD _____ CD 14574
Complete / Nov '95 / THE.

LIVE 1957, VOL. 1 (Herman, Woody & Bill Harris)
Stairway to the stars / Wailing in the woodshed / Midnight sun / Pennies from heaven / Barfly blues / At the woodchoppers' ball / Let's talk / Sleepy serenade / Preacher / Comes love / Our love is here to stay / G string strut / Trouble in mind / Pimlico
CD _____ STATUSCD 107
Status / Nov '90 / Cadillac.

LIVE 1957, VOL. 2 (Herman, Woody & Bill Harris)
Would he / Body and soul / Why you / Ronettes / Square circle / Move my way / Four brothers / Stardust
CD _____ STATUSCD 111
Status / Oct '91 / Cadillac.

LIVE AT MONTEREY
CD _____ 7567900442
Atlantic / Jul '93 / Warner Music.

LIVE AT NEWPORT 1966
CD _____ EBCD 81108
JSP / Oct '90 / ADA / Target/BMG / Direct / Cadillac / Complete/Pinnacle.

LIVE IN ANTIBES 1965
CD _____ FCD 117
France's Concert / May '89 / Jazz Music / BMG.

LIVE IN STEREO - 1963 (Herman, Woody & The Fourth Herd)
CD _____ JH 1006
Jazz Hour / Oct '91 / Target/BMG / Jazz Music / Cadillac.

NORTHWEST PASSAGE, VOL. 2 (Herman, Woody & The First Herd)
CD _____ JASSCD 625
Jass / '91 / CM / Jazz Music / ADA / Cadillac / Direct.

PRESENTS A CONCORD JAM, VOL 1
At the woodchoppers' ball / Rose room / Just friends / Nancy with the laughing face / Body and soul / Someday you'll be sorry / My melancholy baby / Apple honey
CD _____ CCD 4142
Concord Jazz / Aug '90 / New Note.

RAVEN SPEAKS, THE
Fat mama / Alone again (naturally) / Watermelon man / It's too late / Raven speaks / Summer of '42 / Reunion at Newport / Bill's blues
CD _____ OJCCD 663-2
Original Jazz Classics / Jun '94 / Wellard / Jazz Music / Cadillac / Complete/Pinnacle.

READY, GET SET, JUMP
CD _____ JHR 73527
Jazz Hour / May '93 / Target/BMG / Jazz Music / Cadillac.

SCENE AND HERD 1952 (Herman, Woody Orchestra)
(I would do) anything for you / Love is here to stay / Last of the sun / Harlem nocturne / Moten swing / Nice work if you can get it / I can't believe that you're in love with me / This is new / Goof and I / Early Autumn / Blues in advance / Woodchopper's ball / Stompin' at the savoy / Comedy sequence / Holiday for strings / Stars fell on Alabama / Jump in the line / Concerto for clarinet / New golden wedding / Closing
CD _____ EBCD 2125
Jazzband / Jun '95 / Jazz Music / Wellard.

THUNDERING HERD 1944, THE
Jass / Feb '91 / CM / Jazz Music / ADA / Cadillac / Direct.
CD _____ JCD 621

THUNDERING HERD 1945, THE
CD _____ JCD 625
Jass / Feb '91 / CM / Jazz Music / ADA / Cadillac / Direct.

V DISC YEARS VOLS.1 & 2, (1944-46) (Herman, Woody & His Orchestra)
Flying home / It must be jelly, 'cause jam don't shake like that / Dancing in the dawn / Happiness is a thing called Joe / Red top / Jones beachead / I can't put my arms around a memory / There are no wings on a foxhole / Apple honey / Time waits for no one / Billy Bauer's tune / Golden wedding / I've got the world on a string / Yeah man (Amen) / He's funny that way (take 1) / Lover man / Your father's moustache / Don't worry 'bout that mule / 125th Street prophet / I can't put my arms around a memory (2) / Somebody loves me / John Hardy's wife / Meshugah / He's funny that way / Secunda / Jones Beachead (2) / Caledonia / Jackson fiddles while Ralph burns / Happiness is a thing called Joe (2) / Mean to me / Blowin' up a storm / C Jam blues / Reprise
CD Set _____ HEPCD 34 & 35
Hep / Nov '92 / Cadillac / Jazz Music / New Note / Wellard.

V DISC YEARS, THE
CD _____ HEPCD 2
Hep / Jun '87 / Cadillac / Jazz Music / New Note / Wellard.

WILDROOT
CD _____ TCD 1009
Rykodisc / Feb '96 / Vital / ADA.

WOODCHOPPER'S BALL
Pillar to post / Sweet Lorraine / Blues on parade / Woodchopper's ball / Early Autumn / Stompin' at the Savoy / Linger in my arms a little longer / Surrender / Mabel Mabel / Steps / Four men on a horse / Igor / Fan it / Nero's conception / Heads up / Wild root / Tito meets Woody / Cha cha chick / Carioca / Summer sequence / Latin flight / New cha cha / Mambo hero / Blue stations
CD _____ CDGRF 069
Tring / '93 / Tring / Prism.

WOODCHOPPERS' BALL
CD _____ JASSCD 621
Jass / Aug '90 / CM / Jazz Music / ADA / Cadillac / Direct.

WOODSHEDDIN' WITH WOODY
Blue ink / Careless / Herman at the Sherman / Get your boots laced Papa / Jukin' / It's a blue world / East side kick / Who's dat up dere / Indian boogie woogie / Woodsheddin' with Woody / Fan it / South / Too late / Four or five times / Fort Worth jail / Blues downstairs / Blues on parade / Golden wedding / Yardbird shuffle / At the woodchoppers' ball
CD _____ RAJCD 838
Empress / Oct '94 / THE.

WOODY AND FRIENDS
Caravan / I got it bad and that ain't good / Count down / Better git it in your soul / Woody 'n' you / What are you doing the rest of your life / Manteca
CD _____ CCD 4170
Concord Jazz / Jan '92 / New Note.

WOODY HERMAN & HIS ORCHESTRA 1 (Herman, Woody & His Orchestra)
CD _____ JH 1014
Jazz Hour / '92 / Target/BMG / Jazz Music / Cadillac.

WOODY HERMAN & HIS ORCHESTRA 2 (Herman, Woody & His Orchestra)
CD _____ JH 1015
Jazz Hour / '92 / Target/BMG / Jazz Music / Cadillac.

WOODY HERMAN & HIS THUNDERING HERD (Herman, Woody & His Herd)
CD _____ 15774
Laserlight / Jul '93 / Target/BMG.

WOODY HERMAN & ORCHESTRA 1937
CD _____ CCD 95
Circle / Apr '94 / Jazz Music / Swift / Wellard.

WOODY HERMAN AND HIS ORCHESTRA 1945-1947 (Herman, Woody & His Orchestra)
CD _____ 11087
Laserlight / '88 / Target/BMG.

WOODY HERMAN PRESENTS A GREAT AMERICAN EVENING
I've got the world on a string / I cover the waterfront / Leopardskin pillbox hat / Avalon / Beautiful friendship / Pennies from Heaven / Wave / Caldonia
CD _____ CCD 4220
Concord Jazz / '83 / New Note.

WOODY'S GOLD STAR (Herman, Woody Big Band)
Battle royal / Woody's gold star / Mambo rockland / Round Midnight / Great escape / Dig / Rose room / In a mellow tone / Watermelon man / Samba song
CD _____ CCD 4330
Concord Jazz / Oct '87 / New Note.

WOODY'S WINNERS
23 red / My funny valentine / Northwest passage / Poor butterfly / Greasy sack blues / Woody's whistle / Red roses for a blue lady / Opus de funk
CD _____ 4776312
Sony Jazz / Jan '95 / Sony.

Herman's Hermits

BEST OF HERMAN'S HERMITS
I'm into something good / Silhouettes / Wonderful world / No milk to day / There's a kind of hush / Sunshine girl / Something is happening / My sentimental friend / Can't you hear my heartbeat / Your hand in mine / I know why / Dream girl / Take love, give love / Smile please / Museum / Man with the cigar / Listen people / For love / My reservations been confirmed / What is wrong - what is right / Gaslite Street / Moonshine man / Just one girl / Sleepy Joe / East West
CD _____ CC 251
Music For Pleasure / Sep '89 / EMI.

BEST OF THE EMI YEARS, THE VOL. 1 (1964-1966)
I'm into something good / I'm Henery the Eighth (I am) / Silhouettes / Show me girl / Can't you hear my heartbeat / Take love, give love / Wonderful world / Mrs. Brown you've got a lovely daughter / Just a little bit better / Must to avoid / You won't be leaving / Listen people / Hold on / This door swings both ways / Leaning on a lamp-post / All the things I do for you / Little boy sad / Dial my number / George and the dragon / East west / Dandy / No milk today
CD _____ CDEMS 1415
EMI / Sep '91 / EMI.

BEST OF THE EMI YEARS, THE VOL. 2 (1967-1971)
There's a kind of hush / Green Street green / Little Miss Sorrow, child of tomorrow / One little packet of cigarettes / Don't go out into the rain (you're going to melt) / Jezebel / Busy line / Museum / Father / I can take or leave your loving / It's nice to be out in the morning / Ooh, she's done it again / Sleepy Joe / Sunshine girl / Most beautiful thing in my life / Something is happening / My sentimental friend / Here comes the star / Years may come years may go / Bet your life I do / Lady Barbara / Oh you pretty thing
CD _____ CDEMS 1416
EMI / Feb '92 / EMI.

EP COLLECTION: HERMAN'S HERMITS
Sea cruise / Mother in law / I understand / Mrs. Brown you've got a lovely daughter / Show me girl / Silhouettes / Wonderful world / Can't you hear my heartbeat / I'm into something good / Must to avoid / I'm Henery the Eighth (I am) / Just a little bit better / Walkin' with my angel / Where were you when I needed you / Hold on / George and the dragon / All the things I do for you / Wild love / Dandy / No milk today / For love
CD _____ SEECD 284
See For Miles/C5 / Jan '90 / Pinnacle.

LEGENDS IN MUSIC - HERMAN'S HERMITS
Wisepack / Nov '94 / THE / Conifer.
CD _____ LECD 103

NO MILK TODAY
CD _____ 15078
Laserlight / Aug '91 / Target/BMG.

YEARS MAY COME....
Years may come, years may go / I can't take or leave your lovin' / This door swings both ways / Mrs. Brown you've got a lovely daughter / Leaning on a lampost / Must to avoid / Sleepy Joe / Something's happening / Sunshine girl / My sentimental friend / Can't you hear my heartbeat / There's a kind of hush / I'm into something good / Silhouettes / No milk today / East west / Oh you pretty things / Meet me on the corner down at Joe's cafe
CD _____ BR 1352
BR Music / Dec '95 / Target/BMG.

Hermans, Ruud

BLUE HORIZON
CD _____ MW 1004CD
Music & Words / Aug '94 / ADA / Direct.

Hermetic

BROTHERHOOD
CD _____ 367 0006.2
Mausoleum / Oct '91 / Grapevine.

Hernon, Marcus

BÉAL A'MHURLAIGH (Hernon, Marcus & P.J.)
CD _____ CEFCD 141
Gael Linn / Jan '94 / Roots / CM / Direct / ADA.

Heroin

SHOWING A LUMINOUS BALL
CD _____ USR 001CD
Cold Spring / Aug '95 / Plastic Head.

Herold, Ted

DIE SINGLES 1958-1960
Ich brauch' keinen ring / Lover doll / So schon ist nur die allererste liebe / Wunderbar wie du heut' wieder kusst / Hula rock / Dixieland rock / Dein kleiner bruder / Texas baby / Ich bin ein mann / Carolin / Hey baby / Kuss mich / Isabell / Crazy boy / Moonlight / 1:0 / Sunshine baby / Hast du funf minuten zeit / Auch du wirst gehn' / Hey little girl / Lonely / Oh so sweet / Nur sie / Wunderland
CD _____ BCD 15404
Bear Family / Jul '87 / Rollercoaster / Direct / CM / Swift / ADA.

DIE SINGLES 1961-62
CD _____ BCD 15592
Bear Family / Apr '92 / Rollercoaster / Direct / CM / Swift / ADA.

Heron

BEST OF HERON
Only a hobo / Lord and master / Sally Goodin / Yellow roses / Little angel / Car crash / Little boy / Goodbye / For you / John Brown / Wanderer / Great dust storm / Minstrel and a king / Winter harlequin / Smiling ladies (CD only) / Love 13 (lone) (CD only) / Big A (CD only) / Miss Kiss (CD only) / Upon reflection (CD only)
CD _____ SEECD 242
See For Miles/C5 / Nov '88 / Pinnacle.

Heron, Mike

SMILING MEN WITH BAD REPUTATIONS
Call me diamond / Flowers of the forest / Audrey / Brindaban / Feast of Stephen / Spirit beautiful / Warm heart pastry / Beautiful stranger / No turning back / Make no mistake / Lady no wonder
CD _____ IMCD 129
Island / Jun '91 / PolyGram.

Herring, Vincent

DAWNBIRD
Sound check / August afternoon / Almost always / Toku do / Dr. Jamie / Who's kidding who / Dark side of dewey
CD _____ LCDI 5332
Landmark / Nov '93 / New Note.

EVIDENCE
Mr. Wizard / Voyage / Stars fell on Alabama / Never forget / I sing a song / Evidence / Soul Leo / Hindsight (CD only.)
CD _____ LCD 15272
Landmark / Aug '93 / New Note.

Herron, Paul

DIFFERENT WORLDS
Voiceless millions / Spanish point / Connemara awakes / Summer sunsets / Lonely at the station / You've got me / Blue skies / In a song / Donegal dreams / Just down the road / Feeling great / When darkness falls / Last chance
CD _____ CDTRAX 055
Greentrax / Aug '92 / Conifer / Duncans / ADA / Direct.

Hersch, Fred

EVANESSENCE
My bells / Turn out the stars / Nardis/Lonely woman / Peri's scope / Wish I knew
CD _____ 66053027
Jazz City / Dec '91 / New Note.

LIVE AT MAYBECK RECITAL HALL, VOL. 31
Embraceable you / Haunted heart / In walked Bud / You don't know what love is / If I loved you / Heartsong / Everything I love / Sarabande / Song is you / Ramblin' / Body and soul
CD _____ CCD 4596
Concord Jazz / May '94 / New Note.

POINT IN TIME
Point in time / You don't know what love is / As long as there's music / Spring is here / Peacocks / Infant eyes / Cat's paws / Too soon / Evidence / Drew's blues
CD _____ ENJ 90352
Enja / Oct '95 / New Note / Vital/SAM.

Hersh, Kristin

HIPS AND MAKERS
Your ghost / Beestung / Teeth / Sundrops / Sparky / Houdini blues / Loon / Velvet days / Close your eyes / Me and my charms / Tuesday night / Letter / Lurch / Cuckoo / Hips and makers

CD _____ CAD 4002CD
4AD / Jan '94 / Disc.

Hertfordshire Chorus

FOLLOW THAT STAR (Hertfordshire Chorus & Roger Sayer)
CD _____ CD 340152
Koch / Nov '93 / Koch.

Hertz

TALES
CD _____ ACVCD 12
ACV / Jan '96 / Plastic Head / SRD.

Herwig, Conrad

NEW YORK HARD BALL (Herwig, Conrad Quartet)
Hardball / Vendetta / Zal / Code blue / I'm getting sentimental over you / Master's image / Hey, new day / Out of darkness, into light
CD _____ 66056002
Ken Music / Jan '92 / New Note.

Hess, Fred

SWEET THUNDER
CD _____ 74032
Capri / Nov '93 / Wellard / Cadillac.

Hess, Nigel

WIND BAND MUSIC, THE
CD _____ FLYCD 105
Fly / Oct '92 / Bucks Music.

Hession, Carl

OLD TIME NEW TIME
CD _____ CEFCD 173
Gael Linn / Aug '95 / Roots / CM / Direct / ADA.

Hester, Carolyn

AT TOWN HALL (THE COMPLETE CONCERT)
Come on back / Come on in / 2.10 train / Captain, my captain / Water is wide / Carry it on / High flying bird / Three young men / Outward bound / Weaving song / Sing hallelujah / That's my song / Summertime / It takes so long / Ain't that rain / Buckeye Jim / Will you send your love / Jute mill song / What's that I hear / Where did my little boy go / Sidewalk city / I saw her / Bad girl / Playboys and playgirls
CD _____ BCD 15520
Bear Family / Jul '90 / Rollercoaster / Direct / CM / Swift / ADA.

DEAR COMPANION (2CD Set)
Swing and turn jubilee / Come back baby / I'll fly away / Dear companion / Los bibilicos / Once I had a sweetheart / Galway shawl / When Jesus lived in Galilee / Dink's song / Pobre de mi / Yarrow / Virgin Mary / My love is a rider / Gregorio cortez / Simple gits / Brave wolfe / Sally free and easy / I found a lass / This life I'm living / Pera Stous / Tumbando cana / Coo-coo / Praties they grow small / East Virginia / Come O my love / I want Jesus / That's my song / Stay not late / Amapola / Ain't that rain / Momma's tough little soldier / Lonesome tears / Everytime / Can't help but wonder where I'm bound / Ten thousand candles / Times I've had / Jute mill song / Flowers of Texas / Earl morning / Don't ask questions / Reason to believe / Blues run the game / I love my dog / Bye bye brown eyes / One in a million sunshine girl / Majhires / Outside the window / Hello you tomorrows / Penny Lane / Blues run the game (2) / Come back baby (2) / Los bibilicos (2) / I'll fly away (2) / Virgin Mary (2) / Lonesome tears (3) / Summertime / I want Jesus (2) / Lonesome tears (3) / Outside the window (2) / Lonesome tears (4)
CD Set _____ BCD 15701 BH
Bear Family / Oct '95 / Rollercoaster / Direct / CM / Swift / ADA.

TEXAS SONGBIRD (Warriors Of The Rainbow/Music Medicine)
CD _____ RGFCD 019
Road Goes On Forever / Aug '94 / Direct.

TRADITIONAL ALBUM, THE
CD _____ RGFCD 021
Road Goes On Forever / Dec '95 / Direct.

Hetsheads

WE HAIL THE POSSESSED
CD _____ RPS 003CD
Repulse / Apr '95 / Plastic Head.

Hewerdine, Boo

BAPTIST HOSPITAL
CD _____ 0630120452
Blanco Y Negro / Jan '96 / Warner Music.

EVIDENCE (Hewerdine, Boo & Darden Smith)
All I want is everything / Reminds me (a little of you) / These chains / Out of this world / Evidence / Who, what, when, where and why / Under the darkest moon / South by South West / First chill of Winter / Love is

a strange hotel / Oil on the water / Town called blue
CD _____ HAVENCD 6
Haven/Backs / Nov '95 / Disc / Pinnacle.

Hewett, Howard

IT'S TIME
Crystal clear / This love is forever / Your body needs healin' / For the love in you / I wanna know you / Say goodbye / How do I know I love you / Love of your own / Just to keep you satisfied / On and on / Call his name
CD _____ EXCDP 9
Expansion / Dec '94 / Pinnacle / Sony / 3MV.

Hex

HEX
Diviner / Hermaphrodite / Ethereal message / Mercury towers / Out of the pink / Fire Island / In the net / Silvermine / Elizabeth Green / Arrangement
CD _____ FIENDCD 156
Demon / Feb '90 / Pinnacle / ADA.

Hexenhaus

AWAKENING
CD _____ CDATV 19
Active / Aug '91 / Pinnacle.

EDGE OF ETERNITY
CD _____ CDATV 13
Active / May '90 / Pinnacle.

Heymann, Ann

HARPERS LAND, THE (Heymann, Ann & Alison Kinnaird)
CD _____ COMD 2012
Temple / Feb '94 / CM / Duncans / ADA / Direct.

QUEEN OF HARPS
CD _____ COMD 2057
Temple / Oct '94 / CM / Duncans / ADA / Direct.

Heyward, Nick

BEST OF NICK HEYWARD AND HAIRCUT 100
Favourite shirts (boy meets girl) / Take that situation / Fantastic day / Laura / Marine boy / Blue hat for a blue day / Whistle down the wind / Love plus one / Warning sign / Baked beans / Love all day / Snow girl / Over the weekend / Nobody's fool
CD _____ 260 366
Ariola / Dec '89 / BMG.

I LOVE YOU AVENUE
You're my world / If that's the way you feel / Traffic in Fleet Street / Lie with you / My kind of wonderful / I love you avenue / Hold on / Tell me why / Pizza tears / This is love / Change of heart / August in the morning
CD _____ 7599257582
WEA / Jan '96 / Warner Music.

TANGLED
Kill another day / Blinded / Backdated / She says she knows / World / Carry on loving / I love the things you know I don't know / Can't explain / Believe in me / Rollerblade / Breadwinner / London / She's another girl / 1961
CD _____ 4811732
Epic / Oct '95 / Sony.

Heywood, Heather

BY YON CASTLE WA'
Sands of the shore / Far over the forth / For a new baby / False, false hae ye been / I hae but son / Wandering piper / Jamie / Wife of Usher's well / Mistress Heywood's fancy / Dowie dens of yarrow / Some people cry / MacCrimmon's sweetheart / Corn-crake among the whinnie knows / Aye wau-kin' o / Young watters / Paul's song / MacCrimmon's lament
CD _____ CDTRAX 054
Greentrax / Dec '92 / Conifer / Duncans / ADA / Direct.

SOME KIND OF LOVE
Sally gardens / Lord Lovat / Song for Ireland / Some kind of love / Let no man steal your thyme / Bonnie laddie ye gang by me / My bonnie moorhen / Cruel mother / Wid ye gang love
CD _____ CDTRAX 010
Greentrax / Oct '94 / Conifer / Duncans / ADA / Direct.

Hi Standard

GROWING UP
CD _____ FAT 534CD
Fat Wreck Chords / Jan '96 / Plastic Head.

Hi-Fi

FEAR CITY (Hi-Fi & Roadrunners)
CD _____ VE 17CD
Victory / Mar '95 / Plastic Head.

Hi-Five

FAITHFUL
CD _____ CHIP 145
Jive / Jan '94 / BMG.

HI FIVE
CD _____ CHIP 108
Jive / Feb '91 / BMG.

HI-FIVE'S GREATEST HITS
CD _____ CHIP 155
Jive / Nov '94 / BMG.

KEEP IT GOIN' ON
CD _____ CHIP 131
Jive / Nov '92 / BMG.

Hi-Lo's

CHERRIES AND OTHER DELIGHTS
CD _____ HCD 603
Hindsight / Mar '94 / Target/BMG / Jazz Music.

Hi-Ryze

SODIUM
CD _____ GPRCD 10
General Production Recordings / Mar '95 / Pinnacle.

Hiatt, John

HIATT COMES ALIVE AT BUDOKAN
Through your hands / Real fine love / Memphis in the meantime / Icy blue heart / Paper thin / Angel eyes / Your Dad did / Have a little faith in me / Drive South / Thing called love / Perfectly good guitar / Feels like rain / Tennessee plates / Lipstick sunset / Slow turning
CD _____ 540284-2
A&M / Nov '94 / PolyGram.

PERFECTLY GOOD GUITAR
Something wild / Straight outta time / Perfectly good guitar / Buffalo river home / Angel / Blue telescope / Cross my finger / Old habits / Wreck of the Barbie Ferrari / When you old me tight / Permanent hurt / Loving a hurricane / I'll never get over you
CD _____ 5401302
A&M / Sep '93 / PolyGram.

SLOW TURNING
Drive south / Trudy and Dave / Tennessee plates / Icy blue heart / Sometime other than now / Georgia Rae / Ride along / Slow turning / It'll come to you / Is anybody there / Paper thin / Feels like rain
CD _____ CDA 5206
A&M / Aug '88 / PolyGram.

SLUG LINE/TWO BIT MONSTERS
CD _____ BGOCD 176
Beat Goes On / Jun '93 / Pinnacle.

STOLEN MOMENTS
Real fine love / Seven little indians / Child in the wild blue yonder / Back of my mind / Stolen moments / Bring back your love to me / Rest of the dream / Thirty years of tears / Rock back Billy / Listening to old voices / Through your hands / One kiss
CD _____ 3953102
A&M / Apr '95 / PolyGram.

WALK ON
Cry love / You must go on / Walk on / Good as she could be / River knows your name / Native son / Dust down a country road / Ethylene / I can't wait / Shredding the document / Wrote it down and burned it / Your love is my rest / Friend of mine / Mile high
CD _____ CDP 8334162
Capitol / Oct '95 / EMI.

Hiatus

FROM RESIGNATION...TO REVOLT
CD _____ POLLUTE 12
Sound Pollution / Mar '94 / Plastic Head.

Hibbler, Al

AFTER THE LIGHTS GO DOWN LOW
CD _____ 7567820442
Atlantic / Jun '95 / Warner Music.

Hicken, David

FINAL TOCATTA, THE
Final toccata / Harbour of passion / Lost caribbean / Quarters / Foreign land / Serenity / Fantasia / Reflections of time / Raindance / Legacy / English rhapsody
CD _____ PRCD 139
President / Jul '91 / Grapevine / Target/BMG / Jazz Music / President.

SHADOW OF YOUTH
CD _____ CDSGP 9022
Prestige / Jun '95 / Total/BMG.

Hickey, Ersel

BLUEBIRDS OVER THE MOUNTAINS
Bluebirds over the mountain (US Version) / Hangin' around / You never can tell / Wedding / Lover's land / Goin' down that road / Love in bloom / Another wasted day / You threw a gate / Shame on me / What do you want / Due time (Incomplete) / Mighty square love affair / Teardrops at dawn / Magical love / I guess you could call it love / Lips of roses / What have I done to me /

Stardust brought me you / Roll on little river (Unknown) / Don't be afraid of love / People gotta talk / I can't love another / Bluebirds over the mountain (Can version)
CD _____ BCD 15676
Bear Family / May '93 / Rollercoaster / Direct / CM / Swift / ADA.

Hickman, John

DON'T MEAN MAYBE
Don't mean maybe / Salt river / Turkey knob / Birmingham fling / Sweet Dixie / Sally Goodin / Train 405 / Banjo signal / Ghost dance / Pike county breakdown / Goin' to town / Dixie breakdown
CD _____ ROUCD 0101
Rounder / Feb '95 / CM / Direct / ADA / Cadillac.

Hickman, Sara

NECESSARY ANGELS
Pursuit of happiness / Shadowboxing / Best of times / Sister and Sam / Time will tell / Eye of the storm / Oh Daddy / Room of one's own / Tiger in a teacup town / Slippery / Joy / Place where the garage used to stand
CD _____ 1046770102
Discovery / Jun '95 / Warner Music.

Hickoids

HICKOID HEAVEN
CD _____ EFA 11340CD
Musical Tragedies / Sep '93 / SRD.

Hicks, Dan

VERY BEST OF DAN HICKS (Hicks, Dan & His Hot Licks)
CD _____ SEECD 65
See For Miles/C5 / Aug '91 / Pinnacle.

Hicks, Joe

SOMETHING SPECIAL (Hicks, Joe & Jimmy Hughes)
Team / Nobody knows you (when you're down and out) / Train of thought / Rock me baby / Could it be love / Rusty old halo / All in / Water water / Ruby Dean / I like everything about you / Let 'em down baby / I'm so glad / Lay it on the line / Sweet things you do / Chains of love / I'm not ashamed to beg or plead / It's all up to you / Lock me up / What side of the door / Peeped around yonder's bend / Just ain't as strong as I used to be / Did you forget
CD _____ CDSXD 098
Stax / Jul '93 / Pinnacle.

Hicks, John

BEYOND EXPECTATIONS
CD _____ RSRCD 130
Reservoir Music / Oct '94 / Cadillac.

CRAZY FOR YOU
CD _____ 4722052
Sony Jazz / Nov '92 / Sony.

FRIENDS OLD AND NEW
Hicks tone / I want to talk about you / Bop scotch / True blue / It don't mean a thing if it ain't got that swing / Nutty / Makin' whoopee / Rosetta
CD _____ 01241631412
Novus / Oct '92 / BMG.

GENTLE RAIN
CD _____ SSCD 8062
Sound Hills / Jan '96 / Harmonia Mundi / Cadillac

IN CONCERT
Some other time/Some other spring / Nica's pal / Pas de trois (Dance for three) / Say it (over and over again) / Soul eyes / Take the coltrane / Oblivion
CD _____ ECD 22048
Evidence / Mar '93 / Harmonia Mundi / ADA / Cadillac.

IN THE MIX
In the mix / Yemenja / Elation / Soul eyes / Motivation / Weaver of dreams / Mind wine / Once in a while
CD _____ LCD 15422
Landmark / Mar '95 / New Note.

LUMINOUS (Hicks, John & Elise Wood)
CD _____ ECD 220332
Evidence / Sep '92 / Harmonia Mundi / ADA / Cadillac.

SOME OTHER TIME
Naima's love song / Mind wine / Peanut butter in the desert / Ghost of yesterday / Some other time / With malice towards none / Dark side, light side / Night journey / After the morning / Epistrophy
CD _____ ECD 220972
Evidence / Jul '94 / Harmonia Mundi / ADA / Cadillac.

STEADFAST
One for John Mixon / Lush life / Pensivita / Sophisticated lady / Hamp's dance / My one and only love / Steadfast / Without a song / Soul eyes
CD _____ 66051010
Strata East / Nov '91 / New Note.

TWO OF A KIND (Hicks, John & Ray Drummond)
I'll be around / Take the Coltrane / Very early / Getting sentimental over you / For Heaven's sake / Come rain or come shine / Rose without a thorn / Without a song
CD _____ ECD 220172
Evidence / Jul '92 / Harmonia Mundi / ADA / Cadillac.

Hidalgo, Giovanni

VILLA HIDALGO
CD _____ MES 158172
Messidor / Nov '92 / Koch / ADA.

WORLDWIDE
It don't mean a thing if it ain't got that swing / Canadian sunset / Think of me / Summertime / Exit seven / Yuliria II / Moonchild / Seven steps to heaven / Blue minor
CD _____ 66058026
RMM / Nov '93 / New Note.

Higbie, Barbara

SIGNS OF LIFE
Waiting song / Evening rain / Signs of life / Wishing well / Safest place / Sunken gold / Love never dies / Open eyes / Lullaby / Someday
CD _____ WD 1090
Windham Hill / Jun '91 / Pinnacle / BMG / ADA.

Higgins, Billy

MR. BILLY HIGGINS
Dance of the clones / John Coltrane / Morning awakening / Humility / East side stomp
CD _____ ECD 220612
Evidence / Nov '93 / Harmonia Mundi / ADA / Cadillac.

SOWETO
CD _____ 123141-2
Red / Apr '94 / Harmonia Mundi / Jazz Horizons / Cadillac / ADA.

Higgins, Chuck

PACHUKO HOP
Pachuko hop / Motor head baby / Blues and mambo / Long long time / Chuck's fever / Iron pipe / Big fat Mama / Real gone hound dog / Boyle heights / Papa Charlie / Rooster / Duck walk / Stormy / Just won't treat me rite
CD _____ CDCHD 394
Ace / Mar '92 / Pinnacle / Cadillac / Complete/Pinnacle.

Higgins, Eddie

BY REQUEST
CD _____ SACD 104
Solo Art / Oct '93 / Jazz Music.

IN CHICAGO
CD _____ SACD 124
Solo Art / Aug '95 / Jazz Music.

PRELUDE TO A KISS
CD _____ PS 010CD
P&S / Sep '95 / Discovery.

THOSE QUIET DAYS
CD _____ SSC 1052D
Sunnyside / Jun '91 / Pinnacle.

Higgs, Joe

FAMILY
CD _____ SHANCD 43053
Shanachie / '88 / Koch / ADA / Greensleeves.

TRIUMPH
CD _____ ALCS 8313
Alligator / Aug '92 / Direct / ADA.

High

HYPE
Better left untold / Healer / Sweet liberty / This is your life / Let nothing come between us / Goodbye girl / Keep on coming / Slowly happens here / Can I be / Lost and found
CD _____ 8283542
London / Jan '93 / PolyGram.

SOMEWHERE SOON
Box set go / Take your time / This is my world / Rather be Marsanne / So I can see / Minor turn / Dream of dinesh / Up and down / P.W.A. / Somewhere soon
CD _____ 828 224 2
London / Oct '90 / PolyGram.

High Back Chairs

CURIOUSITY AND RELIEF
CD _____ DIS 75CD
Dischord / Nov '92 / SRD.

High Llamas

GIDEON GAYE
CD _____ CDWOOL 1
Alpaca Park / Jul '95 / 3MV.

High Noon

GLORY BOUND
Train of misery / Midnight shift / Rickin' wildcat / Glory bound / Too much trouble / Baby let's play house / Hold me baby / All night long / Late train / Mona Lisa / Your new flame / Who was that cat / Crazy fever / Don't have a heart left to break / Rocks me right / Feelin' no pain / Branded outlaw / Hannah Lee / Don't have a heart left to break (alt.take) / Beaumont boogie / Ain't it wrong / Havin' a whole lotta fun
CD _____ CDGR 6039
Sun Jay / Apr '94 / Magnum Music Group / Rollercoaster.

High Tea

NEW St. GEORGE, THE
CD _____ FE 1415
Folk Era / Nov '94 / CM / ADA.

High Tension

LEATHER BEAUTY
CD _____ 15198
Laserlight / Aug '91 / Target/BMG.

High Tide

SEA SHANTIES/HIGH TIDE
Futilist's lament / Death warmed up / Pushed, but not forgotten / Walking down their outlook / Missing out / Nowhere / Blankman cries again / Joke / Saneonymous
CD _____ CZ 530
EMI / Aug '94 / EMI.

Higham, Darrel

MOBILE CORROSION
Like a brand new man / If you can live with it / Long lonely road / Deep in the heart of Texas / I like me just fine / Second hand information / In my heart / No will will grieve / Revenue man / Country Lila Rhue / You were right I was wrong / I've been gone a long time / Don't bug me baby / Amanda's song / Travis pickin' / Life goes on / Rockin' band blues
CD _____ NERCD 082
Nervous / Oct '95 / Nervous / Magnum Music Group.

Higher Heights

TWINKLE IN A POLISH STYLEE
CD _____ NGCD 537
Twinkle / Jan '93 / SRD / Jetstar / Kingdom.

Higher Intelligence...

FREE FLOATER (Higher Intelligence Agency)
Elapse / Hubble / Fleagle / Thirteen / Skank / Tortoise / Ting / Pinkgreen / U.H.I. / Taz
CD _____ RBADCD 13
Beyond / Sep '95 / Kudos / Pinnacle.

Highland Connection

GAINING GROUND
Carn na cailliich / Knockdhu reel / Helsinki harbour / My tocher's the jewel / Mrs. Major L. Stewart of the island / Of java and c / Haud yer tongue Dear Sally / Campbell's roup / Seven seas hornpipe / Losing ground
CD _____ CDTRAX 087
Greentrax / Jan '95 / Conifer / Duncans / ADA / Direct.

Highway 101

101 SQUARED
CD _____ 925742 2
Curb / Sep '88 / PolyGram.

Highway QC's

COUNT YOUR BLESSINGS
CD _____ CPCD 8113
Charly / Jul '95 / Charly / THE / Cadillac.

Highwayman

HICHWAYMAN 2 (Cash, Johnny/W. Jennings/K. Kristofferson/W. Nelson)
Silver saddaro / Born and raised in black and white / Two stories wide / We're all in your corner / American remains / Anthem '84 / Angels love bad men / Songs that make a difference / Living legend / Texas
CD _____ 4666522
CBS / Apr '90 / Sony.

Highwaymen

ROAD GOES ON FOREVER, THE
Devil's right hand / Live forever / Everybody gets crazy / It is what it is / I do believe / End to understanding / True love travels a gravel road / Death and hell / Waiting for a long time / Here comes that rainbow again / Road goes on forever
CD _____ CDEST 2253
Liberty / Apr '95 / EMI.

Highwoods String Band

FEED YOUR BABIES ONIONS
CD _____ ROUCD 11569

Rounder / Feb '95 / CM / Direct / ADA / Cadillac.

Higsons

ATTACK OF THE CANNIBAL ZOMBIE BUSINESS MEN, THE
CD _____ SORT 3 CD
Mixture / Apr '92 / Pinnacle.

CURSE OF THE HIGSONS
CD _____ SORT 2CD
Mixture / Apr '92 / Pinnacle.

Hijack

HORNS OF JERICHO, THE
Intro (Phantom of the opera) / Syndicate outta jail / Daddy rich / Back to Brixton / Airwave hijack / Hijack the terrorist group / Badman is robbin' / I had to serve you / Don't go with strangers / Brother versus brother / Paranoid schizophrenic with homicidal tendencies / Contract
CD _____ 7599263862
WEA / Oct '91 / Warner Music.

Hildebeutel

LOOKING BEYOND
Looking beyond / Follow me / Journey / Prelude (formthe timeless time) / Coming back / Inner peace
CD _____ 450995344-2
Warner Bros. / Mar '94 / Warner Music.

Hildegarde

DARI ING, JE VOUS AIME DEAUCOUP
CD _____ PASTCD 7066
Flapper / Jul '95 / Pinnacle.

DARLING, JE VOUS AIME BEAUCOUP
Darling Je vous aime beaucoup / Honey coloured moon / I believe in miracles / Listen to the german band / For me, for you / Gloomy Sunday / Isn't this a lovely day (to be caught in the rain) / Cheek to cheek / Glory of love / Hildegarde look back (Medley) / Pretty girl is like a melody / Love walked in / It's the natural thing to do / Will you remember / There's a small hotel / This year's kisses / Pennies from heaven / (I love you) for sentimental reasons / Room with a view / my ship / Saga of Jenny Pts. 1 and 2 / Lili Marlene / Goodnight angel
CD _____ CDAJA 5161
ASV / May '95 / Koch.

Hill & Wiltchinsky

ROMANTIC GUITARS
When I fall in love / Gymnopedie / Way we were / Cavatina / Lady in red / Mona Lisa / Ave Maria / Memory / Annie's song / Romanza / Adagio Rodriguez / Music of the night / Barcarolle / I know him so well / Here, there and everywhere / If / Hello / Love story / Greatest love of all / For the love of Annie
CD _____ CDSR 024
Telstar / Sep '93 / BMG.

Hill, Andrew

FACES OF HOPE
CD _____ 121 010 2
Soul Note / Oct '90 / Harmonia Mundi / Wellard / Cadillac.

LIVE AT MONTREUX: ANDREW HILL
Snake hip waltz / Nefertisis / Come Sunday / Relativity
CD _____ FCD 41023
Freedom / Dec '87 / Jazz Music / Swift / Wellard / Cadillac.

SHADES
CD _____ 121113-2
Soul Note / Jan '91 / Harmonia Mundi / Wellard / Cadillac.

SMOKE STACK
Smoke stack / Day after / Wailing wall / Ode to von / Not so / Verne / 30 Pier Avenue
CD _____ CDP 8320972
Blue Note / Aug '95 / EMI.

SPIRAL
Tomorrow / Laverne / Message / Invitation / Today / Spiral / Quiet dawn
CD _____ FCD 41007
Freedom / Sep '87 / Jazz Music / Swift / Wellard / Cadillac.

STRANGER SERENADE (Hill, Andrew Trio)
CD _____ 1210132
Soul Note / Aug '91 / Harmonia Mundi / Wellard / Cadillac.

Hill, Benny

ON TOP WITH....
Gather in the mushrooms / Harvest of love / My garden of love / Pepy's diary / In the papers / Jose's cantina / Flying south / What a world / Andalucian gypsies / Transistor radio / Egg marketing board tango / Lonely boy / Gypsy rock / Wild women / I'll never know / Piccolo song / Bamba 3688 / Old fiddler
CD _____ 550 765-2
Spectrum/Karussell / May '95 / PolyGram / THE.

Hill, Bertha

COMPLETE RECORDED WORKS 1925-29 (Hill, Bertha 'Chippie')
CD _____ DOCD 5330
Blues Document / Mar '95 / Swift / Jazz Music / Hot Shot.

Hill, Buck

CAPITAL HILL
CD _____ MCD 5384
Muse / Sep '92 / New Note / CM.

IMPULSE
Blues in the closet / You taught my heart to sing / Random walk / Impulse / In a sentimental mood / Sweet Georgia Brown / Solitude (in my solitude) / Owwowa bash / How do you keep the music playing / Now's the time
CD _____ MCD 5483
Muse / Apr '95 / New Note / CM.

Hill, Dan

GREATEST HITS AND MORE
CD _____ 341852
Koch International / Nov '95 / Koch.

Hill, Faith

IT MATTERS TO ME
CD _____ 9362458722
Warner Bros. / Aug '95 / Warner Music.

TAKE ME AS I AM
Take me as I am / Wild one / Just about now / Piece of my heart / I've got this friend / Life's too short to love like that / But I will / Just around the eyes / Go the distance / I would be stronger than that
CD _____ 936245389-2
Warner Bros. / Jun '94 / Warner Music.

Hill, Joe

DON'T MOURN - ORGANISE (Songs Of Labour Songwriter Joe Hill) (Various Artists)
CD _____ SFCD 40026
Smithsonian Folkways / Nov '94 / ADA / Direct / Koch / CM / Cadillac.

Hill, Michael

BLOODLINES (Hill, Michael Blues Mob)
CD _____ AL 4821
Alligator / Jul '94 / Direct / ADA.

Hill, Noel

IRISH CONCERTINA, THE
Last night's fun/Trip to Durrow / Boy in the bush / Kiss the maid behind the barrel/ Dublin reel / Laird of Drumblair / Pigeon on the gate/Sean sa cheo / Farewell to Ireland / Old goman's reel / Wind that shakes the barley / Taimse I'm choladh / Wise maid/ Bells of Tipperary / Gold ring/Larks in the morning / Salamanca reel / Over the moor to Maggie / Chicago reel / An draigheann / Thrush in the morning / Drunken sailor / Moving clouds/Devanny's goat/Mc-Dermott's reel
CD _____ CCF 21CD
Claddagh / Oct '88 / ADA / Direct.

NOEL HILL AND TONY LINNANE (Hill, Noel & Tony Linnane)
Humours of Ballyconnell / Drunken landlady / Ryan's reel / Geese in the bog / Joe Cooley's hornpipe / Miss Monaghan / Skylark / Foxhunter / Reevey's reel / Golden keyboard / Killoran's reel / Mountain road / Anderson's reel / Carthy's / Sweeney's reel / Johnny Cope / Scotsman over the border / Tom Billy's jig / Pigeon on the gate / Daniel O'Connell / Home ruler / Kitty's wedding / Lady Ann Montgomery / Cooley's reel
CD _____ TARACD 2006
Tara / Jan '96 / CM / ADA / Direct / Conifer.

Hill Smith, Marilyn

IS IT REALLY ME
CD _____ CDVIR 8314
TER / Sep '91 / Koch.

Hill, Teddy

UPTOWN RHAPSODY
Lookie lookie here comes Cookie / Got me doin' things / When the robin sings her song again / When love knocks on your heart / Uptown rhapsody / At the rug cutter's ball / Blue rhythm fantasy / Passionette / Love bug will bite you / Would you like to buy a dream / Big boy blue / Where is the sun / Harlem, twister / Marie / I know now / Lady who couldn't be kissed / You and me that used to be / Study in brown / Twilight in Turkey / China boy / San Anton / I'm happy darling, dancing with you / Yours and mine / I'm feelin' like a million / King Porter stomp
CD _____ HEPCD 1033
Hep / Mar '92 / Cadillac / Jazz Music / New Note / Welland.

Hill, Tiny

TINY HILL & HIS HILLTOPPERS 1943-44
CD _____ CCD 55
Circle / Jan '94 / Jazz Music / Swift / Welland.

Hill, Tommy

GET READY BABY
Ain't nothing like loving / In the middle of the morning / Can't help / Life begins at four o'clock / Oh get ready, Baby (1) / Love words / Do me a favour / Have a little faith in me / O get ready baby (2) / In the middle of the morning (2)
CD _____ BCD 15709
Bear Family / Mar '93 / Rollercoaster / Direct / CM / Swift / ADA.

Hill, Vince

GREATEST HITS: VINCE HILL (An Hour of Hits)
Take me to your heart again / Importance of your love / Little bluebird / Somewhere my love / Love letters in the sand / Doesn't anybody know my name / Here, there and everywhere / Wives and lovers / Girl talk / Merci cherie / Heartaches / Roses of Picardy / Moonlight and roses / Look around / Love story / Close to you / Danny boy / You're my world / Time for us / Spanish eyes
CD _____ CC 201
Music For Pleasure / May '88 / EMI.

I WILL ALWAYS LOVE YOU
I will always love you / Desperado / Love dies hard / Crying in the wind / Sweet dreams / Pray for love / When you walk through life / I want to know you / Sweet music man / Loving arms / It's not supposed to be that way / Sea of heartbreak / Always on my mind
CD _____ GRCD 24
Grasmere / Feb '89 / Target/BMG / Savoy.

LOVE SONGS
I will always love you / Desperado / Love dies hard / Crying in the wind / Sweet dreams / Pray for love / When you walk through life / I want to know you / Sweet music man / Loving arms / It's not supposed to be that way / Sea of heartbreak / Always on my mind
CD _____ PWKM 4074
Carlton Home Entertainment / Feb '96 / Carlton Home Entertainment.

THAT LOVING FEELING
CD _____ PRCD 142
President / May '93 / Grapevine / Target/ BMG / Jazz Music / President.

Hill, Warren

KISS UNDER THE MOON
Promises / Kiss under the moon / One touch / Take-out dreams / Swept away / Waiting for a love / No disguise / Maybe tomorrow / Thirty days / Too little, too late
CD _____ PD 83117
Novus / Jul '91 / BMG.

Hill, Z.Z.

BRAND NEW Z.Z. HILL, THE
It ain't no use / Ha ha (laughing song) / Second chance / Our love is getting better / Faithful and true / Chockin' kind / Hold back (one man at a time) / Man needs a woman (woman needs a man) / Early in the morning / I think I'd do it / She's all I got / Raining on a sunny day / Sweeter than sweetness / Sidewalks, fences and walls / I did the woman wrong / Yours love / Laid back and easy / You and me together forever / Ain't nothin' in the news (but the blues) / Did I come back to soon (or stay away too long) / Wy whole world has ended (without you) / Cuss the wind
CD _____ CDCHD 532
Ace / Jun '94 / Pinnacle / Cadillac / Complete/Pinnacle.

DOWN HOME SOUL OF Z.Z. HILL, THE
Baby I'm sorry / I need someone (to love me) / Have mercy someone / Kind of love I want / Hey little girl / I found love / No more doggin' / You can't hide a heartache / That's it / Happiness is all I need / Everybody has to cry / Nothing can change this love / Set your sights higher / Steal away / You're gonna need my loving / You're gonna make me cry / Oh darling / If I could do it all over / You don't love me / You won't hurt no more / What more / You got what I need
CD _____ CDKEN 099
Kent / Sep '92 / Pinnacle.

Hillage, Steve

FISH RISING
Fish / Meditation of the snake / Solar musick suite (Sun song/Canterbury sunrise/ Hiram Aftaglid meets the dervish/Sun song - reprise) / Salmon song (Salmon pool/Solomon's Atlantis/Swimming with the salmon/King of the fishes) / Aftaglid (Sun Moon surfing/Great wave and the boat of Hermes/Silver ladder/Astral meadows/Lafta yoga song/Gliding/Golden vibe)
CD _____ CDV 2031
Virgin / Jun '87 / EMI.

FOR TO NEXT - AND NOT OR
These uncharted lands / Kamikaze eyes / Alone / Anthems for the blind / Bright future / Frame by frame / Waiting / Glory
CD _____ CDV 2244
Virgin / Jul '90 / EMI.

GREEN
Sea nature / Ether ships / Musick of the trees / Palm trees (love guitar) / Unidentified (flying being) / U.F.O. over Paris / Leylines to Glassdom / Crystal City / Activation meditation / Glorious OM riff
CD _____ CDV 2098
Virgin / Jun '90 / EMI.

IN CONCERT
CD _____ WINCD 014
Windsong / Mar '92 / Pinnacle.

L
Hurdy gurdy man / Hurdy gurdy glissando / Elecktrick Gypsies / Om nama shivaya / Lunar musick suite / It's all too much
CD _____ CDV 2066
Virgin / Jun '87 / EMI.

LIVE HERALD
Salmon song / Dervish riff / Castle in the clouds / Light in the sky / Searching for the spark / Electric gypsies / Radiom / It's all too much / Talking to the sun / 1988 aktivator / New age synthesis (unzipping the zype) / Healing feeling / Lunar musick suite / Meditation of the dragon / Golden vibe
CD _____ CDVM 3502
Virgin / Jun '90 / EMI.

MOTIVATION RADIO
Hello dawn / Motivation / Light in the sky / Radio / Wait one moment / Saucer surfing / Searching for the spark / Octave doctors and the crystal machine / Not fade away (glide forever)
CD _____ CDV 2777
Virgin / Jun '88 / EMI.

OPEN
Day after day / Getting in tune / Open / Definite activity / Don't dither do it / Fire inside / Earthrise
CD _____ CDV 2135
Virgin / Jun '90 / EMI.

RAINBOW DOME MUSICK
Garden of paradise / Four ever rainbow
CD _____ CDVR 1
Virgin / Jun '88 / EMI.

Hiller, Holger

AS IS
CD _____ CDSTUMM 60
Mute / Sep '91 / Disc.

OBEN IM ECK
CD _____ CDSTUMM 38
Mute / Nov '86 / Disc.

Hilliard Ensemble

CODEX SPECIALNIK
CD _____ 4478072
ECM / Apr '95 / New Note.

PEROTIN
CD _____ 8377512
ECM / Jan '90 / New Note.

Hillier, Paul

PROENSA
CD _____ 8373602
ECM / Apr '89 / New Note.

Hillman, Steve

MATRIX
Overdrive / Matrix pt.1 / Interchange / Ascendant / Sphinx dancer / Into space / Now or never / Sequent 7 / Matrix pt.2 / Dawning light / Into the blue / Tritone
CD _____ CYCL 011
Cyclops / Sep '94 / Pinnacle.

Hillmen

HILLMEN, THE
Brown mountain light / Ranger's command / Sangeree / Blue grass choppere / Barbara Allen / Fair and tender ladies / Goin' up / When the ship comes in / Fare thee well / Winsborough Cotton Mill blues / Prisoner's plea / Back road fever / Rollon muddy river
CD _____ SHCD 3719
Sugarhill / Nov '95 / Roots / CM / ADA / Direct.

Hills, Anne

ANGEL OF LIGHT
CD _____ FF 648CD
Flying Fish / Nov '95 / Roots / CM / Direct / ADA.

DON'T PANIC
CD _____ FF 608CD
Flying Fish / Apr '94 / Roots / CM / Direct / ADA.

NEVER GROW OLD (Hills, Anne & Cindy Mangsen)
CD _____ FF 70638
Flying Fish / Feb '94 / Roots / CM / Direct / ADA.

Hilton, Ronnie

RONNIE HILTON
I still believe / No other love / Veni vidi vici / Around the world / Magic moments / Blossom fell / Stars shine in your eyes / Yellow rose of Texas / Woman in love / Wonderful, wonderful / I may never pass this way again

/ Miracle of love / World outside / Don't let the rain come down / As I love you / One blade of grass (in a meadow) / On the street where you live / She / Marching along to the blues / Her hair was yellow / Day the rains came / Do I love you / Gift / Beautiful bossa nova
CD _____ CC 258
Music For Pleasure / Oct '90 / EMI.

Himber, Richard

RICHARD HIMBER & HIS ORCHESTRA 1938-40
CD _____ CCD 7
Circle / Jan '94 / Jazz Music / Swift / Welland.

Hinchcliffe, Keith

CAROLAN'S DREAM
CD _____ KH 001CD
Ranmoor / Mar '94 / ADA.

Hinds, Justin

SKA UPRISING (Hinds, Justin & The Dominoes)
CD _____ CDTRL 314
Trojan / Mar '94 / Jetstar / Total/BMG.

THIS CARRY GO BRING HOME (Hinds, Justin & The Dominoes)
CD _____ RNCD 2044
Rhino / Feb '94 / Jetstar / Magnum Music Group / THE.

Hindu

READY FOR DEM
CD _____ MAC 4161-2
Mac-D/Divine / Jan '94 / Koch.

Hine, Rupert

RUPERT HINE
CD _____ PERMCD 25
Permanent / Jun '94 / Total/BMG.

Hines, Earl

1928-1932
CD _____ CLASSICS 545
Classics / Dec '90 / Discovery / Jazz Music.

AALBORG, DENMARK 1965
Medley: Monday date/Blues in thirds/You can depend on me / Tea for two / Medley / Shiny stockings / Perdido / Black coffee / Medley #2 / Boogie woogie on St. Louis blues
CD _____ STCD 8222
Storyville / Aug '94 / Jazz Music / Welland / CM / Cadillac.

BACK ON THE STREET (Hines, Earl & Jonah Jones)
CD _____ CRD 118
Chiara Scuro / Nov '95 / Jazz Music / Kudos.

BASIN STREET BLUES
CD _____ CDCH 560
Milan / Feb '91 / BMG / Silva Screen.

BLUES IN THIRDS
CD _____ CDJJ 611
Jazz & Jazz / Jan '92 / Target/BMG.

BLUES SO LOW - 1966
Oh Lady good / It had to be you / Black and blue / Two sleepy people / Ain't misbehavin' / Jitterbug waltz / Squeeze me / Honeysuckle rose / Epinal blues / Birth of the blues / Memphis blues / Basin Street blues / Tin roof blues / Rhapsody in blue / Shiny stockings / Sweet Lorraine / Boogie woogie on St. Louis blues / I wish you love / It's a pity to say goodnight
CD _____ STCD 537
Stash / '91 / Jazz Music / CM / Cadillac / Direct / ADA.

EARL HINES & THE DUKE'S MEN
CD _____ DD 470
Delmark / Dec '94 / Hot Shot / ADA / CM / Direct / Cadillac.

EARL HINES 1932-34 & 1937 (Hines, Earl & His Orchestra)
CD _____ 3801022
Jazz Archives / Jun '92 / Jazz Music / Discovery / Cadillac.

EARL HINES, 1941 (Hines, Earl & His Orchestra)
CD _____ CLASSICS 621
Classics / '92 / Discovery / Jazz Music.

FATHA
CD _____ CD 14556
Jazz Portraits / Jul '94 / Jazz Music.

FATHA
CD _____ TPZ 1006
Topaz Jazz / Aug '94 / Pinnacle / Cadillac.

FATHER STEPS IN
G.T. stomp / Jezebel / Dominick swing / Grand terrace shuffle / Father steps in / Piano man / Father's getaway / Me and Columbus / Please be kind / Goodnight, sweet dreams, goodnight / Tippin' at the terrace / XYZ / Gator swing / Got I've been to you / Mellow bit of rhythm / Ridin' a riff / Solid mama / Jack climbed a beanstalk /

Ridin' and jivin' / (Back home again in) Indiana / Reminiscing at Blue Note / Riff medley
CD _____ CDGRF 092
Tring / '93 / Tring / Prism.

FINE AND DANDY
Snappy rhythm / I never dreamt / Chicago / Night life in Pompeii / Japanese sandman / Rhythm business / Tea for two / Air France stomp / Chicken jump / Honeysuckle rose / Fine and dandy / Sugar / Boogie woogie on St. Louis blues / Singin' for my French brother
CD _____ 74321115082
Vogue / Jul '93 / BMG.

HINE'S TUNE (Paris 1965)
Hine's tune / One I love (belongs to someone else) / Bag's Groove / Blue turning grey over you / Don's blues / Tenderly / Boogie woogie on St. Louis blues / These foolish things / I'm a little brown bird / Que reste t'il de nos amours / Little girl blue / You are the cream in my coffee / I can't get started (with you) / Petite laitue / Cherry / Sweet lorraine / I've got the world on a string / Body and soul / Clopin clopant / C'est si bon
CD _____ FCD 101
Esoldun / '88 / Target/BMG.

HINES '74
CD _____ 233073
Black & Blue / May '87 / Wellard / Koch.

HINES SHINES
CD _____ 17030
Laserlight / May '94 / Target/BMG.

IN PARIS
CD _____ 500502
Musidisc / May '94 / Vital / Harmonia Mundi / ADA / Cadillac / Discovery.

INDISPENSABLE EARL HINES VOLS.5 & 6 (1944-66)
My fate is in your hands / I've got a feeling I'm falling in love / Honeysuckle rose / Squeeze me / Undecided / I've found a new baby / Fatha's blues / Sunday kind of love / Tosca's dance / Jim / Black coffee / You always hurt the one you love / Save it pretty Mama / Bye bye baby / Smoke rings / Shoe shine boy / Stanley steamer / Bernard's tune / Dream of you
CD _____ ND 896182
Jazz Tribune / Jun '94 / BMG.

JUST FRIENDS
CD _____ JHR 73506
Jazz Hour / May '93 / Target/BMG / Jazz Music / Cadillac.

LIVE AT SARALEE'S
CD _____ 15790
Laserlight / Aug '92 / Target/BMG.

MASTER OF PIANO
Earls's pearl / It it's true / Rosetta / Chicago / One night in Trinidad / I know that you know / If I had you / St. Louis blues
CD _____ 722019
Scorpio / Sep '92 / Complete/Pinnacle.

MASTERPIECES # 14 1934-42
CD _____ MASTER 158332
Masterpieces / Mar '95 / BMG.

MASTERS OF JAZZ, VOL. 2
CD _____ STCD 4102
Storyville / '89 / Jazz Music / Wellard / CM / Cadillac.

ONE FOR MY BABY
CD _____ BLCD 760198
Koch / Nov '94 / Koch.

PIANO MAN
Blues in thirds / Boogie woogie on St. Louis blues / Cavernism / Chicago rhythm / Chimes blues / Comin' in home / Earl / Every evening / Father's getaway / Fifty seven varieties / Fireworks / Harlem lament / Honeysuckle rose / Love me tonight / Monday date / Piano man / Ridin' a riff / Rosetta / Save it pretty Mama / Skip the gutter / Smokehouse blues / Solid mama / Stowaway / Two deuces / Weatherbird
CD _____ CDJAA 5131
Living Era / Oct '94 / Koch.

PIANO MAN 1928-1955
CD _____ CD 53118
Giants Of Jazz / Jan '94 / Target/BMG / Cadillac.

PLAYS DUKE ELLINGTON
CD _____ NW 361/362
New World / Aug '92 / Harmonia Mundi / ADA / Cadillac.

PLAYS GEORGE GERSHWIN
CD _____ 500522
Musidisc / May '94 / Vital / Harmonia Mundi / ADA / Cadillac / Discovery.

REUNION IN BRUSSELS
CD _____ 4722072
Sony Jazz / Nov '92 / Sony.

ROSETTA
CD _____ JTM 8118
Jazztime / Apr '94 / Discovery / BMG.

SWINGIN' AWAY
CD _____ BLCD 760210
Black Lion / Nov '95 / Jazz Music / Cadillac / Wellard / Koch.

TOUR DE FORCE
When your lover has gone / Indian Summer / Mack the knife / I never knew (I could love anyone like I'm loving you) / Say it isn't so / Lonesome road
CD _____ BLCD 760140
Black Lion / May '90 / Jazz Music / Cadillac / Wellard / Koch.

TOUR DE FORCE ENCORE
CD _____ BLCD 760157
Black Lion / '91 / Jazz Music / Cadillac / Wellard / Koch.

WAY DOWN YONDER IN NEW ORLEANS
My Monday date / Song of the Islands / There'll be some changes made / Jelly Roll / Tishomingo blues / One I love (belongs to somebody else) / Rosetta / Way down yonder in New Orleans / Do you know what it means to miss New Orleans / Bouncin' for panassie / If I could be with you one hour tonight / Moonglow
CD _____ BCD 108
Biograph / Jul '91 / Wellard / ADA / Hot Shot / Jazz Music / Cadillac / Direct.

WEST SIDE STORY
West Side story medley / Close to you / Why do I love you / In my solitude / Don't get around much anymore
CD _____ BLCD 760186
Black Lion / Jul '93 / Jazz Music / Cadillac / Wellard / Koch.

Hinge

ACCIDENTAL MEETING OF MINDS
Pyramid club / floar / form / Rest / Quirky / Basilisk / Major 7th / Ransom / Rising man
CD _____ CDVEST 34
Bulletproof / Oct '94 / Pinnacle.

Hinnies

DEAD FOUR
CD _____ BGRL 015 CD
Bad Girl / Sep '92 / Pinnacle.

Hino, Mtohiko

IT'S THERE
CD _____ ENJACD 80302
Enja / Sep '95 / New Note / Vital/SAM.

Hino-Kikuchi

TRIPLE HELIX (Hino-Kikuchi & Togashi)
Trial / Dr. U / Twilight south west / Blue monk / Saphire way
CD _____ ENJACD 80562
Enja / Jun '94 / New Note / Vital/SAM.

Hinojosa, Tish

AQUELLA NOCHE
Tu que puedas, vuelvete / Cumbia, pola y mas / Manos, hueso y sangre / Reloj / La llorona / Azul cristal / Aquella noche / Historia de un amor / Una noche mas / Carlos dominguez / Samba san pedro / Malaguena salerosa / Estrellita
CD _____ MRCD 156
Munich / '91 / CM / ADA / Greensleeves / Direct.

CULTURE SWING
By the Rio Grande / Something in the rain / Bandera de Sol/Flag in the sun / Every word / Louisiana road song / Corazon viajero / Drifter's wind / Window / In the real West / Chanate el vaquero (Chanate the vaquero) / San Antonio Romeo / Closer still
CD _____ MRCD 155
Munich / '94 / CM / ADA / Greensleeves / Direct.

DESTINY'S GATE
Destiny's gate / Saying you will / What more can you say in a song / Esperate (wait for me) / Looking for my love in the pouring rain / I'm not through loving you yet / Love of mine / I want to see you again / Noche sin estrellas (night without stars) / Yesterday's paper / Baby believe
CD _____ 936245566-2
Warner Bros. / Jul '94 / Warner Music.

FRONTEJAS
CD _____ ROUCD 3132
Rounder / Apr '95 / CM / Direct / ADA / Cadillac.

MEMORABILIA NAVIDENA
Abolito (little Christmas tree) / Milagro / Building / A la nanita nana / Arbolita (in English) / Cada nino/Every child / Everything you wish / Memorabilia (Honky tonker's christmas)
CD _____ WMCD 1006
Watermelon / Jun '93 / ADA / Direct.

TAOS TO TENNESSEE
Midnight moonlight / Prairie song / According to my heart / Taos to Tennessee / River / Amanecer / Please be with me / Crazy wind and flashing yellows / Highway calls / Who showed you the way to my heart / Let me remember / Always
CD _____ MRCD 164
Munich / '92 / CM / ADA / Greensleeves / Direct.

Hinton, Eddie

LETTERS FROM MISSISSIPPI
My searching is over / Sad and lonesome / Everybody needs love / Letters from Mississippi / Everybody meets Mr.Blue / Uncloudy day / I want a woman / Ting a ling ling / Wet weather man / I will love you / It's all right / I'll come running (back to you)
CD _____ ZNCD 1001
Zane / Oct '95 / Pinnacle.

VERY BLUE HIGHWAY
I love someone / Rock of my soul / Poor Ol' me / Sad Carol / Very blue highway / Call a blues physician / Good love is hard to find / Just don't know / Let it roll / How you goin' to Georgia / Standin' / Hey Justine / Nobody but you
CD _____ ZNCD 1005
Zane / Oct '95 / Pinnacle.

Hinton, Milt

BACK TO BASS-ICS (Hinton, Milt Trio)
CD _____ PCD 7084
Progressive / Jun '93 / Jazz Music.

LAUGHING AT LIFE
Child is born / Sweet Georgia Brown / Laughing at life / How high the moon / Prelude to a kiss / (Back home again in) Indiana / Mona's feeling lonely / Jon John / Old man Harlem / Just friends / Judge and jury
CD _____ 4781782
Sony Jazz / Apr '95 / Sony.

OLD MAN TIME
CD _____ CRD 310
Chiara Scuro / Dec '95 / Jazz Music / Kudos.

Hip Hop Fanatics

STOMPIN' 4 DA '94
CD _____ KIK 4186CD
Kik-Azz / May '94 / Koch.

Hip Young Things

DEFLOWERED
CD _____ GRCD 244
Glitterhouse / Apr '93 / Direct / ADA.

ROOT 'N' VARIES
CD _____ GRCD 281
Glitterhouse / Aug '93 / Direct / ADA.

SHRUG
CD _____ GRCD 347
Glitterhouse / Dec '94 / Direct / ADA.

Hipsway

HIPSWAY
Honey thief / Ask the Lord / Bad thing longing / Upon a thread / Long white car / Broken years / Tinder / Forbidden / Set this day apart
CD _____ 8268212
Mercury / Sep '92 / PolyGram.

Hird Family

HIRD FAMILY IN NEW ORLEANS
CD _____ BCD 332
GHB / Mar '95 / Jazz Music.

Hirota, Joji

RAIN FOREST DREAM
Ubiquity / Purple spring / Celebration of harvest / Malaysian image / Satellite express / Rain forest dream / Demon dance / Pacific samba
CD _____ CDSDL 384
Saydisc / Mar '94 / Harmonia Mundi / ADA / Direct.

Hirst, Clare

TOUGH AND TENDER
Heavy hipsters / Tough and tender / Salsita / Beautiful(ish) / Little steps / Strollin' / Just an emotion / Rudie's blues / Mi cancion / Gallicia
CD _____ 33JAZZ025
33 Jazz / Dec '95 / Cadillac / New Note.

Hirt, Al

OUR MAN IN NEW ORLEANS
Clarinet marmalade / Ol' man river / New Orleans / Panama / Birth of the blues / Ja da / Wolverine blues / Oh dem golden slippers / When the saints go marching in / When it's steamy then down South / Muskrat ramble / Dear old Southland
CD _____ 01241631432
Novus / Oct '92 / BMG.

Hirt, Erhard

GUTE UND SCHLECHTE ZEITEN
CD _____ EMPCD 9003
FMP / Oct '94 / Cadillac.

His Name Is Alive

HOME IS IN YOUR HEAD
CD _____ CADCD 1013
4AD / Sep '91 / Disc.

LIVONIA
CD _____ CAD 0008CD
4AD / Jun '90 / Disc.

MOUTH TO MOUTH
CD _____ CAD 3006CD
4AD / Apr '93 / Disc.

Hislop, Joseph

SONGS OF SCOTLAND, THE
Prelude to the songs of Robert Burns / Bonnie banks ol Loch Lomond / Ye banks and braes o' bonnie Doon / Bonnie Mary of Argyle / Annie Laurie / Afton water / Land of the leal / Ariskay love lift / Island herdsmaid / Lea rig / MacGregor's gathering / Rigs O' Barley / My love is like a red red rose / Bonnie wee thing / Jessie the flower O' Dunblane / My love she's but a lassie yet / O my love's bonnie / Herding song / Island shieling song / Turn ye tae me
CD _____ MIDCD 003
Moidart / Jan '95 / Conifer / ADA.

Hissanol

47TH AND BACK
CD _____ VIRUS 160CD
Alternative Tentacles / Apr '95 / Pinnacle.

History Of Drum And Bass

HARDLEADERS
CD _____ KICKCD 35
Kickin' / Jan '96 / SRD.

Hit Parade

SOUND OF THE HIT PARADE, THE
On the road to Beaconsfield / As I lay dying / Grace darling / Hello Hannah hello / Walk away boy / Farewell my kilo / Fool / House of Saran / She won't come back / Crying / She's lost everything / So this is London
CD _____ SARAH 622CD
Sarah / Jul '94 / Vital.

Hitchcock, Robyn

BLACK SNAKE DIAMOND ROLE
Man who invented himself / Brenda's iron sledge / Lizard / Meat / Do policemen sing / Acid bird / I watch the cars (2 versions) / Out of the picture / City of shame / Love / Dancing on God's thumb / Happy the golden prince / Kingdom of love / It was the night
CD _____ RSACD 819
Sequel / Feb '95 / BMG.

ELEMENT OF LIGHT
If you were a priest / Winchester / Somewhere apart / Ted, Woody and Junior / President / Raymond Chandler evening / Bass / Airscape / Element of light / Never stop bleeding / Lady Waters and the hooded one / Black crow knows / Crawling / Leopard / Tell me about your drugs / Can opener (On CD) / Raymond Chandler evening (demo) (On CD) / President (demo) (On CD) / If you were a priest (demo) (On CD) / Airscape (demo) (On CD) / Leopard (demo) (On CD)
CD _____ RSACD 824
Sequel / Mar '95 / BMG.

EYE
Cynthia Mask / Certainly clickot / Queen Elvis / Flesh cartoons / Chinese water python / Executioner / Linctus house / Sweet ghost of light / College of ice / Transparent lover / Beautiful girl / Raining twilight coast / Clean Steve / Agony of pleasure / Glass hotel / Satellite / Aquarium / Queen Elvis II / Clean Steve (2) / Agony of pleasure (2) / Ghost ship
CD _____ RSACD 826
Sequel / Mar '95 / BMG.

FEGMANIA
Egyptian cream / Another bubble / I'm only you / My wife and my dead wife / Goodnight I say / Man with the lightbulb head / Insect mother / Strawberry mind / Glass / Fly / Heaven / Bells of Rhymney / Dwarfbeat / Somebody / Egyptian cream (demo) (On CD) / Heaven (live) (On CD) / Insect mother (demo) (On CD) / Pit of Souls (parts I-IV) (On CD)
CD _____ RSACD 822
Sequel / Mar '95 / BMG.

GOTTA LET THIS HEN OUT! (Hitchcock, Robyn & The Egyptians)
Listening to the Higsons / Fly / Kingdom of love / Leppo and the fly / Man with the lightbulb head / Cars she used to drive / Sounds great when you're dead / Only the stones remain / America / Heaven / My wife and my dead wife / I often dream of trains / Surgery / Brenda's iron sledge
CD _____ RSACD 823
Sequel / Mar '95 / BMG.

GROOVY DECAY
Night ride to Trinidad / Fifty two stations / Young people scream / Rain / America / How do you work this thing / Cars she used to drive / Grooving on an inner plane / St. Petersburg / When I was a kid / Midnight fish / It was the night / Nightride to Trinidad (disco mix) (Sequel CD only) / Midnight fish (mix) (Sequel CD only)
CD _____ RSACD 820
Sequel / Feb '95 / BMG.

I OFTEN DREAM OF TRAINS
(Hitchcock, Robyn & The Egyptians)
Nocturne / Sometimes I wish I was a pretty girl / Cathedral / Uncorrected personality traits / Sounds great when you're dead / Flavour of night / Sleeping knights of Jesus / Mellow together / Winter love / Bones in the ground / My favourite buildings / I used to say I love you / This could be the day / Trams of old London / Furry green atom bowl / Heart full of leaves / Autumn is your last chance / I often dream of trains /
CD _____ RSACD 821
Sequel / Feb '95 / BMG.

INVISIBLE HITCHCOCK (Hitchcock, Robyn & The Egyptians)
All I wanna do is fall in love / Give me a spanner Ralph / Skull, a suitcase and a long red bottle of wine / It's a mystic trip / My favourite buildings / Falling leaves / Eaten by her own dinner / Pit of souls / Trash / Mr. Deadly / Star of hairs / Messages of dark / Vegetable friends / I got a message for you / Abandoned brain / Point it at Gran / Let there be more darkness / Blues in A
CD _____ RSACD 825
Sequel / Mar '95 / BMG.

KERSHAW SESSIONS
CD _____ ROOTCD 001
Strange Fruit / Jun '94 / Pinnacle.

YOU AND OBLIVION
You've got / Don't you / Bird's head / She reached for a light / Victorian squid / Captain Dry / Mr. Rock 'n' Roll / August hair / Take your knife out of my back / Surgery / Dust / Polly on the shore / Aether / Fiend before the shrine / Nothing / Into it / Stranded in the future / Keeping still / September cones / Ghost ship / You and me / If I could look
CD _____ RSACD 827
Sequel / Mar '95 / BMG.

Hitchin Post

DEATH VALLEY JUNCTION
CD _____ GRCD 313
Glitterhouse / Apr '94 / Direct / ADA.

Hitmen DTK

SURFIN' IN ANOTHER DIRECTION
CD _____ 842618
New Rose / May '94 / Direct / ADA.

Hittman

HITTMAN
CD _____ 857568
Steamhammer / '88 / Pinnacle / Plastic Head.

Hoax

SOUND LIKE THIS
CD _____ 450997964-2
Warner Bros. / Dec '94 / Warner Music.

Hobbs Angel Of Death

HOBBS ANGEL OF DEATH
CD _____ 857525
Steamhammer / '89 / Pinnacle / Plastic Head.

Hobbs, Steve

CULTURAL DIVERSITY
Missing Carolina / On the run / Blame it on my youth / Sea breeze / Bag's groove / Cor-reaaah / Jane / D.A. / Astrud / Bernie's tune
CD _____ CDSJP 375
Timeless Jazz / Mar '92 / New Note.

LOWER EAST SIDE, THE
CD _____ CACD 797042
Candid / Dec '95 / Cadillac / Jazz Music / Wellard / Koch.

Hoch Und Deutschmeister

25 JAHRE ORIGINAL HOCH UND DEUTSCHMEISTER
CD _____ 340012
Koch / Apr '92 / Koch.

Hochman, I.J.

FUN DER KHUPE
CD _____ GVCD 114
Global Village / Mar '95 / ADA / Direct.

Hock, Paul

FRESH FRUIT
Fresh fruit / Barricade / Voir un ami pleurer / Sneaky / Samba for Johan Cruyff / Yvette in wonderland / Missing keys / Estate
CD _____ CDSJP 343
Timeless Jazz / Oct '91 / New Note.

Hodes, Art

ART HODES & THE MAGNOLIA JAZZ BAND - VOLS. 1 & 2
CD _____ BCD 171/172
GHB / Oct '93 / Jazz Music.

FINAL SESSIONS, THE
CD _____ CD 782
Music & Arts / May '94 / Harmonia Mundi / Cadillac.

HODES' ART
CD _____ DD 213
Delmark / Dec '94 / Hot Shot / ADA / CM / Direct / Cadillac.

KEEPIN' OUT OF MISCHIEF NOW
CD _____ CCD 79117
Candid / Nov '95 / Cadillac / Jazz Music / Wellard / Koch.

PAGIN' MR.JELLY
Grandpa's spells / Mamie's blues / High society / Mr. Jelly lord / Buddy Bolden's blues / Pagin' Mr Jelly / Wolverine blues / Ballin' the Jack / Pearls / Gone Jelly blues / Dr. Jazz / Oh didn't he ramble
CD _____ CCD 79037
Candid / Mar '90 / Cadillac / Jazz Music / Wellard / Koch.

SENSATION (Hodes, Art & John Petters Hot Three)
Clarinet marmalade / Lazybones / Mama's gone goodbye / Lonesome blues / Jackass blues / Cake walkin' babies from home / Sensation / Jeep's blues / Ballin' the Jack / Snowball / Dear old Southland / Wolverine blues
CD _____ CMJCD 007
CMJ / Apr '90 / Jazz Music / Wellard.

SESSIONS AT BLUE NOTE
Maple leaf rag / Yellow dog blues / Slow 'em down blues / Dr. Jazz / Shoe shiner's drag / There'll be some changes made / Jug head boogie / Back room blues / Sweet Georgia Brown / Squeeze me / Bugle call rag / Gut bucket blues / Apex blues / Shake that thing / That eccentric rag / KMH drag / Blues 'n' booze / Mr. Jelly Lord / Willie the weeper / Jack Daily blues
CD _____ DMI CDX 04
Dormouse / Dec '91 / Jazz Music / Target/ BMG.

UP IN VOLLY'S ROOM
CD _____ DD 217
Delmark / Jan '93 / Hot Shot / ADA / CM / Direct / Cadillac.

Hodges, Johnny

CLASSIC SOLOS 1928-42
CD _____ TPZ 1008
Topaz Jazz / Oct '94 / Pinnacle / Cadillac.

COMPLETE SMALL GROUP SESSIONS VOL.1 1937-38
CD _____ BMCD 1019
Blue Moon / Sep '95 / Magnum Music Group / Greensleeves / Hot Shot / ADA / Cadillac / Discovery.

COMPLETE SMALL GROUP SESSIONS VOL.2 1939-40
CD _____ BMCD 1020
Blue Moon / Sep '95 / Magnum Music Group / Greensleeves / Hot Shot / ADA / Cadillac / Discovery.

EVERYBODY KNOWS JOHNNY HODGES
Everybody knows / Flower is a lovesome thing / Papa knows / 310 blues / Jeep is jumpin' / Main stem / I let a song go out of my heart / Don't get around much anymore / Open mike / Stompy Jones / Mood indigo / Good Queen Bess / Little brother / Jeep's blues / Do nothin' 'til you hear from me / Ruint / Sassy cue
CD _____ GRP 11162
Impulse Jazz / Jul '92 / BMG / New Note.

HODGE PODGE
CD _____ EK 66972
Sony Jazz / Jan '95 / Sony.

JOHNNY HODGES AND WILD BILL DAVIS, 1965 - 1966 (Hodges, Johnny & Wild Bill Davis)
On the sunny side of the street / On Green Dolphin Street / Li'l darlin' / Con sould and sax / Jeep is jumpin' / I'm beginning to see the light / Sophisticated lady / Drop me off in Harlem / No one / Johnny come lately / It's only a paper moon / Taffy / Good Queen Bess / L.B. blues / In a mellow tone / Rockville / I'll always love you / It don't mean a thing if it ain't got that swing / Belle of the Belmont
CD Set _____ ND 89765
Jazz Tribune / May '94 / BMG.

JOHNNY HODGES PLAYS BILLY STRAYHORN
CD _____ 5218572
Verve / Apr '94 / PolyGram.

MASTERS OF JAZZ VOL.9
Cambridge blue / Brute's roots / Bouncing with Ben / One for the duke / Walkin' the frog / Rabbit day / On the sunny side / Good Queen Bess / Jeep is jumpin' / Things ain't what they used to be
CD _____ STCD 4109
Storyville / May '89 / Jazz Music / Wellard / CM / Cadillac.

PASSION FLOWER
Day dream / Good queen Bess (takes 1 and 2) / That's the blues / Old man / Junior hop / Squaty roo / Passion flower / Thing's ain't / Never no lamet / Blue goose / In a mellow tone / Warm valley / After all / Giddybug gallop / I got it bad and that ain't good / Clementine / Moon mist / Sentimen-
tal lady / Come Sunday / Mood to be wooed / Rock-a-bye river
CD _____ 7863 666162
Bluebird / Aug '95 / BMG.

PASSION FLOWER 1950-60
Giants Of Jazz / Sep '94 / Target/BMG / Cadillac.
CD _____ CD 53171

RARITIES AND PRIVATE RECORDINGS (The Golden Age of Jazz)
CD _____ JZCD 361
Suisa / May '92 / Jazz Music / THE.

Hoenig, Michael

DEPARTURE FROM THE NORTHERN WASTELAND
Departure from the northern wasteland / Hanging garden transfer / Voices of where / Sun and moon
CD _____ CDKUCK 079
Kuckuck / Sep '87 / CM / ADA.

Hoffner, Helen

WILD ABOUT NOTHING
Wild about nothing / Summer of love / Sacrifice / Holy river / Is there anybody out there / Perfect day / Lovers come, lovers go / Whispers in the wind / Papa's car / Say a prayer / This is the last time / Edge of a dream
CD _____ 450992399-2
Magnet / Apr '93 / Warner Music.

Hofmann, Holly

FURTHER ADVENTURE
CD _____ 74022
Capri / Nov '93 / Wellard / Cadillac.

TAKE NOTE
CD _____ 74011
Capri / Nov '93 / Wellard / Cadillac.

Hofner, Adolph

SOUTH TEXAS SWING
CD _____ FL 7029
Folklyric / Apr '95 / Direct / Cadillac.

Hogan, John

HUMBLE MAN
Don't fight the feeling / Still got a crush on you / Walkin' in the sun / She's more to be pitied / Picture / Wreck of old no.9 / China doll / Let it be you / Humble man / I'll be gone / Something's wrong / Down by the river / Follow me / Please don't forget me
CD _____ RITZCD 0062
Ritz / Nov '91 / Pinnacle.

IRISH HARVEST DAY, AN
Irish harvest day / I'll buy her roses
CD _____ RITZCD 248
Ritz / Sep '92 / Pinnacle.

NASHVILLE ALBUM
Till the mountains disappear / Walk through this world with me / Irish harvest day / Cottage in the country / Your cheatin' heart / China doll / My feelings for you / Wreck of old no.9 / Turn back the years / Red river valley / Back home again / My guitar / I'll buy her roses / Brown eyes / Stepping stone / Please don't forget me / Still got a crush on you / Moonlight in Mayo / I know that you know (that I love you) / Battle hymn of love
CD _____ RITZRCD 531
Ritz / Aug '93 / Pinnacle.

TURN BACK THE YEARS
CD _____ KCD 305
Prism / '90 / Prism.

VERY BEST OF JOHN HOGAN, THE
Thank God I'm a country boy / Walk through this world with me / Cottage in the country / Your cheatin' heart / China doll / My feelings for you / Wreck of old no.9 / Turn back the years / Red river valley / Back home again / My guitar / I'll buy her roses / Brown eyes / Stepping stone / Please don't forget me / Still got a crush on you / Moonlight in Mayo / I know that you know (that I love you) / Battle hymn of love
CD _____ RCD 552
Ritz / Jul '95 / Pinnacle.

Hogan, Silas

SO LONG BLUES
I'm gonna quit you pretty baby / Trouble at home blues / You're too late baby / Airport blues / Go on pretty baby / Here they are again / Lonesome la la / Roamin' woman blues / I'm goin' in the valley / Everybody needs somebody / Just give me a chance / Dark clouds rollin' / Early one morning / I'm in love with you baby / More trouble at home / Sittin' here wonderin' / So glad / Every Saturday night / Baby please come back to me / If I ever need you baby / Out and down blues / So long blues
CD _____ CDCHD 523
Ace / May '94 / Pinnacle / Cadillac / Complete/Pinnacle.

Hogg, Smokey

ANGELS IN HARLEM
I want a roller / Nobody treats me right / Evil mind blues / I'm through with you / What's
on your mind / You better watch that jive / Goin' back to Texas / I want my baby for Christmas / Gonna leave town / I ain't gonna put you down / Every mornin' at sunrise / If it hadn't been for you / Boogie all night long / Worryin' my life away / Angels in Harlem / Born on the 13th / Crawdad / Size 4 shoe / Little fine girl / Good mornin' baby / Sure nuff
CD _____ CDCHD 419
Ace / Sep '92 / Pinnacle / Cadillac / Complete/Pinnacle.

Hoggard, Jay

LITTLE TIGER, THE
CD _____ MCD 5410
Muse / Sep '92 / New Note / CM.

LOVE IS THE ANSWER
Harlem air shaft / Good bait / Donna Lee / As quiet as it's kept / Nearness of you / Love is the answer / Celestial prayer / Worship God in spirit, truth and love / Wisdom of the baobab tree / Ring shout
CD _____ MCD 5527
Muse / Dec '94 / New Note / CM.

OVERVIEW
CD _____ MCD 5383
Muse / Sep '92 / New Note / CM.

Hogia'r Wyddfa

GOREUON
Safwn yn y bwlch / Pentre bach llanber / Y gwanwyn / TYlluanod / Ddoi di gyda mi / Titw tomos las / Llanc ifanc o lyn / Teifi / Bysus bach y wlad / Tocyn / Nyth y hud / Olwen / Gwaun cwm brwynog / Hwiangerddi / Hen wr ar bont y bala / Ti a dy ddoniau / Pan fyddo'r nos yn hir / Mae nhwyr y dydd
CD _____ SCD 4094
Sain / Jun '88 / Direct / Cadillac.

Hogman, John

GOOD NIGHT SISTER
CD _____ SITCD 9202
Sittel / Aug '94 / Cadillac / Jazz Music.

Hokum Boys

HOKUM BOYS & BOB ROBINSON 1935-1937 (Hokum Boys & Bob Robinson)
CD _____ DOCD 5237
Blues Document / May '94 / Swift / Jazz Music / Hot Shot.

HOKUM BOYS 1929
CD _____ DOCD 5236
Blues Document / May '94 / Swift / Jazz Music / Hot Shot.

Hold True

FADE
CD _____ LF 144CD
Lost & Found / Jun '95 / Plastic Head.

Holden, Lorenzo

CRY OF THE WOUNDED JUKEBOX
CD _____ SCD 26
Southland / Oct '93 / Jazz Music.

Holderlin Express

HOLDERLIN EXPRESS
CD _____ ADCD 3025
Music Contact/Akku Disc / Jul '94 / ADA.

Holdsworth, Dave

TEN DAY SIMON (Holdsworth, Dave & Liane Carroll)
Skylark / Fever / Maurice the mole / Ten day Simon / It's all right with me / Something / spring can really hang you up the most / Most / Buy and sell
CD _____ SGCD 02
Cadillac / Dec '90 / Cadillac / Wellard.

Hole

LIVE THROUGH THIS
Violet / Miss World / Plump / Asking for it / Jennifers body / Doll parts / Credit in the straight world / Softer, softest / She walks on me / I think that I would die / Gutless / Rock star
CD _____ EFA 49352
City Slang / Apr '94 / Disc.

PRETTY ON THE INSIDE
Baby doll / Garbage man / Sassy / Good sister bad sister / Mrs. Jones / Berry / Loaded / Star belly / Pretty on the inside / Clouds / Teenage whore
CD _____ EFA 040712
City Slang / Aug '95 / Disc.

Hole, Dave

PLUMBER
CD _____ PRD 70462
Provogue / Mar '93 / Pinnacle.

SHORT FUSE BLUES
CD _____ ALCD 4807
Alligator / May '93 / Direct / ADA.

STEEL ON STEEL
CD _____ PRD 70782
Provogue / Jul '95 / Pinnacle.

WORKING OVERTIME
CD _____ PRD 70562
Provogue / May '94 / Pinnacle.

Holi

UNDER THE MONKEY PUZZLE TREE
Under the monkey puzzle tree / Right place / Five years / Meera's sigh / I need you / First impression / Lonely swan / Chandrika / Losin' my head / Green and blue
CD _____ RES 105CD
Resurgence / Nov '94 / Vital.

Holiday, Billie

16 MOST REQUESTED SONGS
Miss Brown to you / If you were mine / These foolish things / Way you look tonight / Pennies from heaven / I can't give you anything but love / I've got my love to keep me warm / Why was I born / Carelessly / Easy living / My man / I'm gonna lock my heart (and throw away the key) / Body and soul / Gloomy Sunday / God bless the child / I'm a fool to want you
CD _____ 474401 2
Columbia / Feb '94 / Sony.

1939-40 (Holiday, Billie & Her Orchestra)
CD _____ CLASSICS 601
Classics / '91 / Discovery / Jazz Music.

1958-59
CD _____ CD 53205
Giants Of Jazz / Jan '95 / Target/BMG / Cadillac.

AS TIME GOES BY
CD _____ CD 53092
Giants Of Jazz / Nov '92 / Target/BMG / Cadillac.

AT CARNEGIE HALL
CD _____ 5277772
Verve / Oct '95 / PolyGram.

AT STORYVILLE
I cover the waterfront / Too marvellous for words / I loves you Porgy / Them there for you / You go to my head / He's funny that way / Willow weep for me / I only have eyes for you / Billie's blues / Miss Brown to you / Lover come back to me / T'ain't nobody's business if I do / You're driving me crazy
CD _____ BLC 760921
Black Lion / Apr '91 / Jazz Music / Cadillac / Wellard / Koch.

BACK TO BACK (Holiday, Billie & Sarah Vaughan)
My man (mon homme) / Lover man / I cover the waterfront / Don't explain / Them there eyes / East of the sun and west of the moon / Signing off / No smoke blues / What more can a woman do / Mean to me
CD _____ TKOCD 023
TKO / May '92 / TKO.

BEST OF BILLIE HOLIDAY
CD _____ 4670292
Sony / Jan '95 / Sony.

BEST OF BILLY HOLIDAY
CD _____ DLCD 4015
Dixie Live / Mar '95 / Magnum Music Group.

BILLIE HOLIDAY
CD _____ MATCD 285
Castle / Mar '94 / BMG.

BILLIE HOLIDAY
CD _____ CD 105
Timeless Treasures / Oct '94 / THE.

BILLIE HOLIDAY
CD _____ DVX 08072
Deja Vu / May '95 / THE.

BILLIE HOLIDAY (2CD Set)
CD Set _____ R2CD 4006
Deja Vu / Jan '96 / THE.

BILLIE HOLIDAY & HER ORCHESTRA
Lover come back to me / You go to my head / East of the sun and west of the moon / Blue moon / Solitude / I only have eyes for you / Autumn in New York / Tenderly / These foolish things / Remember / I can't face the music / I cried for you / Love me or leave me / Please don't talk about me when I'm gone / It had to be you / P.S. I love you
CD _____ CD 53089
Giants Of Jazz / May '92 / Target/BMG / Cadillac.

BILLIE HOLIDAY 1940-1942
CD _____ CLASSICS 680
Classics / Mar '93 / Discovery / Jazz Music.

BILLIE HOLIDAY AND HER ORCHESTRA 1933-37 (Holiday, Billie & Her Orchestra)
CD _____ CLASSICS 582
Classics / Oct '91 / Discovery / Jazz Music.

BILLIE HOLIDAY AND HER ORCHESTRA 1937-39 (Holiday, Billie & Her Orchestra)
CD _____ CD 592
Classic Jazz Masters / Sep '91 / Wellard / Jazz Music / Jazz Music.

BILLIE HOLIDAY AND TONY SCOTT (Holiday, Billie & Tony Scott Orchestra)
CD _____ GOJCD 53074
Giants Of Jazz / Mar '92 / Target/BMG / Cadillac.

BILLIE HOLIDAY GOLD (2CD Set)
CD Set _____ D2CD 4006
Deja Vu / Jun '95 / THE.

BILLIE HOLIDAY WITH BARNEY KESSEL (Holiday, Billie & Orchestra/ Barney Kessel)
CD _____ GOJCD 53038
Giants Of Jazz / Mar '90 / Target/BMG / Cadillac.

BILLIE HOLIDAY/ELLA FITZGERALD ESSENTIALS (Holiday, Billie & Ella Fitzgerald)
CD _____ LECDD 629
Wisepack / Aug '95 / THE / Conifer.

BILLIE'S BEST
CD _____ 5139432
Verve / May '92 / PolyGram.

BILLIE'S BLUES
1-2 Button your shoe / Let's call a heart a heart / Billie's blues / No regrets / I can't give you anything but love / This year's kisses / He ain't rhythm / Let's call the whole thing off / They can't take that away from me / Sentimental and melancholy / Way you look tonight / I'll get by / Summertime / Who wants love / He's funny that way / Now they call it swing / Nice work if you can get it / Things are looking up
CD _____ MUCD 9002
Start / Apr '95 / Koch.

BILLIE, ELLA, LENA AND SARAH (Holiday, Billie, Ella Fitzgerald, Lena Horne & Sarah Vaughan)
Man I love / My melancholy baby / Prisoner of love / Nice work if you can get it / I'll never be the same / East of the sun and west of the moon / What a little moonlight can do / Ain't misbehavin' / Out of nowhere / All my life / I'm gonna lock my heart (and throw away the key) / Goodnight my love
CD _____ 9826002
Pickwick/Sony Collector's Choice / Oct '91 / Carlton Home Entertainment / Pinnacle / Sony.

BROADCAST PERFORMANCES VOL. 1
CD _____ ESP 3002-2
ESP / Jan '93 / Jazz Horizons / Jazz Music.

BROADCAST PERFORMANCES VOL. 2
CD _____ ESP 3003-2
ESP / Jan '93 / Jazz Horizons / Jazz Music.

BROADCAST PERFORMANCES VOL. 3
CD _____ ESP 3005-2
ESP / Jan '93 / Jazz Horizons / Jazz Music.

BROADCAST PERFORMANCES VOL. 4
CD _____ ESP 3006-2
ESP / Jan '93 / Jazz Horizons / Jazz Music.

CLASSICS 1944
CD _____ CLASSICS 806
Classics / Mar '95 / Discovery / Jazz Music.

COLLECTION
CD _____ COL 018
Collection / Apr '95 / Target/BMG.

COLLECTION, THE
CD _____ CCSCD 381
Castle / Oct '93 / BMG.

COMPLETE RECORDINGS 1933-1940, THE (8CD Set)
Your mother's son-in-law / Riffin' the scotch / I wished on the moon / What a little moonlight can do / Miss Brown to you / Sun bonnet blue / What a night / What a moon, what a girl / I'm painting the town red / It's too hot for words / Yankee Doodle never went to town / Eeny meeny miney mo / If you were mine / These 'n' that 'n' those / You let me down / Spreadin' rhythm around / Life begins when you're in love / It's like reaching for the moon / These foolish things / I cried for you / Guess who / Did I remember / No regrets / Summertime / Billie's blues / Fine romance / I can't pretend / 1-2 Button your shoe / Let's call a heart a heart / Easy to love / With thee I swing / Way you look tonight / Who loves you / That's life I guess / I can't give you anything but love / One never knows, does one / I've got my love to keep me warm / If my heart could only talk / Please keep me in your dreams / He ain't got rhythm / This year's kisses / Why was I born / I must have that man / Twenty four hours a day / Mood that I'm in / You showed me the way / Sentimental and melancholy / My last affair / Carelessly / How could you / Moanin' low / Where is the sun / Let's call the whole thing off / They can't take that away from me / Don't know if I'm

coming or going / Sun showers / Yours and mine / I'll get by / Mean to me / Foolin' myself / Easy living / I'll never be the same / Me, myself and I / Sailboat in the moonlight / Born to love / Without your love / Getting some fun out of life / Who wants love / Trav'lin' all alone / He's funny that way / Nice work if you can get it / Things are looking up / My man / Can't help lovin' dat man / My first impression of you / When you're smiling / I can't believe that you're in love with me / If dreams come true / Now they call it swing / On the sentimental side / Back in your own backyard / When a woman loves a man / You go to my head / Man looks down and laughs / If I were you / Forget if you can / Having myself a time / Says my heart / I wish I had you / I'm gonna lock my heart (and throw away the key) / Any old time / Very thought of you / I can't get started (with you) / I've got a date with a dream / You can't be mine and someone else's too) / Everybody's laughing / Here it is tomorrow again / Say it with a kiss / April in my heart / I'll never fail you / They say / You're so desirable / You're gonna see a lot of me / Hello my darling / Let's dream in the moonlight / That's all I ask of you / Dream of life / What shall I say / It's easy to blame the weather / More than you know / Sugar / You're too lovely to last / Under a blue jungle moon / Everything happens for the best / Why did I always depend on you / Long gone blues / Strange fruit / Yesterdays / Fine and mellow / I gotta right to sing the blues / Some other Spring / Night and day / Man I love / You're just a no account / You're a lucky guy / Ghost of yesterdays / Body and soul / What is this thing going to get us / Falling in love again / I'm pulling through / Tell me more / Laughing at life / Time on my hands / I'm all for you / I hear music / It's the same old story / Practice makes perfect / St. Louis blues / Loveless love
CD Set _____ CDAFS 1019-8
Affinity / Jun '93 / Charly / Cadillac / Jazz Music.

COMPLETE STORYVILLE CLUB SESSION, THE
CD _____ FSRCD 151
Fresh Sound / Dec '90 / Jazz Music / Discovery.

COMPLETE VERVE RECORDINGS, THE (10CD Set/1945-1959)
CD Set _____ 5176582
Verve / Jun '93 / PolyGram.

EARLY CLASSICS, THE
Summertime / Sentimental and melancholy / Who loves you / Pennies from heaven / That's life, I guess / Billie's blues / When you're smiling / Carelessly / If dreams come true / Fine romance / Mood that I'm in / Let's call a heart a heart / Where is the sun / Don't know if I'm coming or going / I can't believe that you're in love with me / He's funny that way / Now they call it swing / Miss Brown to you
CD _____ PASTCD 9756
Flapper / Aug '91 / Pinnacle.

ESSENTIAL BILLIE HOLIDAY, THE
St. Louis blues / Solitude / Man I love / Georgia on my mind / I've got my love to keep me warm / My last affair / I'll never be the same / If dreams come true / Summertime / Billie's blues / I cried for you / Mean to me / He's funny that way / My man (mon homme) / Nice work if you can get it / Night and day
CD _____ 467149 2
Columbia / Jul '93 / Sony.

ESSENTIAL RECORDINGS, THE
That old devil called love / Keeps on a rainin' / Porgy / No good man / God bless the child / What is this thing called love / My man (mon homme) / Easy living / Lover man / Good morning heartache / T'ain't nobody's business if I do / You're my thrill / Solitude / There is no greater love / You better go now / Weep no more
CD _____ MCCD 095
Music Club / Mar '93 / Disc / THE / CM.

FINE AND MELLOW (1936-1941)
CD _____ IGOCD 2034
Indigo / Oct '95 / Direct / ADA

FINE AND MELLOW, 1939 & 1944
Strange fruit / Yesterdays / Fine and mellow / I gotta right to sing the blues / How am I to know / My old flame / I'll get by / I cover the waterfront
CD _____ CDSGP 046
Prestige / May '94 / Total/BMG.

GOD BLESS THE CHILD
CD _____ 17013
Laserlight / Jul '94 / Target/BMG.

GOLD COLLECTION, THE
CD _____ D2CD06
Recording Arts / Dec '92 / THE / Disc.

GOLDEN GREATS
CD _____ MCLD 19096
Chess/MCA / Nov '91 / BMG / New Note.

GOOD MORNING HEARTACHE
Good morning heartache / What is this thing called love / God bless the child / This is heaven to me / Solitude / Don't explain / My man (mon homme) / That ole devil called love / Crazy he calls me / You're my thrill /

No good man / You better go now / Weep no more / Lover man
CD _____ PWKS 571
Carlton Home Entertainment / Apr '90 / Carlton Home Entertainment.

GREAT AMERICAN SONGBOOK, THE
CD _____ 523003-2
Verve / Aug '94 / PolyGram.

IMMORTAL LADY IN CONCERT, THE
CD _____ MU 5013
Musketeer / Oct '92 / Koch.

IMMORTAL, THE
Swing brother swing / They can't take that away from me / Do nothin' 'til you hear from me / I'll get by / I love my man / I cover the waterfront / Do you know what it means to miss New Orleans / Don't explain / Keeps on a rainin' / Lover come back to me
CD _____ CDBH 1
CBS / May '87 / Sony.

INTRODUCTION TO BILLIE HOLIDAY 1935-42
CD _____ 4003
Best Of Jazz / Dec '93 / Discovery.

JAZZ MASTERS
CD _____ 519825-2
Verve / Feb '94 / PolyGram.

JAZZ PORTRAITS
Your mother's son-in-law / Sun showers / They can't take that away from me / Say / Sugar / More that you know / I gotta right to sing the blues / Fine and mellow / Strange fruit / Yesterdays / St. Louis blues / Georgia on my mind / All of me / Easy living / It / Romance in the dark / Love me or leave me / I cover the waterfront / It's a sin to tell a lie
CD _____ CD 14512
Jazz Portraits / May '94 / Jazz Music.

LADY DAY AND PREZ 1937-1941 (Holiday, Billie & Lester Young)
This year's kisses / Without your love / All of me / Me, myself and I / I'll get by / Mean to me / Sailboat in the moonlight / I'll never be the same / Getting some fun out of life / Man I love / Trav'lin' all alone / Time on my hands / Laughing at life / Back in your own backyard / Georgia on my mind / Let's do it / Foolin' myself / Easy living / Say it with a kiss / You can't be mine and (someone else's too) / I can't believe that you're in love with me / She's funny that way / Romance in the dark / I must have that man
CD _____ CD 53006
Giants Of Jazz / Mar '92 / Target/BMG / Cadillac.

LADY DAY'S 25 GREATEST HITS 1933-1944
Back in your own backyard / Did I remember / Easy living / Fine and mellow / Ghost of yesterday / He's funny that way / I can't give you anything but love / I love my man / I must have that man / I'll get by / I'll be the same / Long gone blues / You Mother's son in law / You go to my head / What a little moonlight can do / They can't take that away from me / Them there eyes / That ole devil called love / Swing, brother, swing / Strange fruit / Some other spring / No more / My last affair / Moanin' low / Miss Brown to you
CD _____ CDAJA 5181
Living Era / Jan '96 / Koch.

LADY DAY'S IMMORTAL PERFORMANCES 1933-1942
CD Set _____ CDB 1204
Giants Of Jazz / Apr '92 / Target/BMG / Cadillac.

LADY DAY'S IMMORTAL PERFORMANCES 1942-1957
CD Set _____ CDB 1212
Giants Of Jazz / Jun '92 / Target/BMG / Cadillac.

LADY IN SATIN
I'm a fool to want you / For heaven's sake / You don't know what love is / I get along without you very well / For all we know / Violets for your furs / You've changed / Easy to remember / But beautiful / Glad to be unhappy / I'll be around / End of a love affair
CD _____ 4508832
CBS / '91 / Sony.
CD _____ 4804192
Epic / Jun '95 / Sony.

LADY SINGS THE BLUES - VOCAL CLASSICS
Lady sings the blues / Travelin light / I must have that man / Some other Spring / Strange fruit / No good man / God bless the child / Good morning heartache / Love me or leave me / Too marvelous for words / Willow weep for me / I thought about you
CD _____ 833 770-2
Verve / Nov '90 / PolyGram.

LADY SINGS, THE
What a little moonlight can do / Miss Brown to you / These foolish things / Summertime / Fine romance / Way you look tonight / This year's kisses / Let's call the whole thing off / Easy livin' / He's funny that way / Yesterdays / I hear music / Some other Spring / Them there eyes / Night and day / Body and soul

CD _____ CDCD 1005
Charly / Mar '93 / Charly / THE / Cadillac.

LEGACY 1933-58, THE (3CD Set)
Your mother's son-in-law / I wished on the moon / What a little moonlight can do / Miss Brown to you / Saddest tale / If you were mine / These 'n' that 'n' those / You let me down / Life begins when you're in love / It's like reaching for the moon / These foolish things / Summertime / Billie's blues / Fine romance / I can't pretend / 1-2 button your shoe / Let's call a heart a heart / Easy to love / Pennies from Heaven / That's life, I guess / I can't give you anything but love / One never knows does one / I've got my love to keep me warm / Having myself a time / This year's kisses / Why was I born / I must have that man / Mood that I'm in / My last affair / Moaning low / Where is the sun / Let's call the whole thing off / Don't know if I'm coming or going / I'll get by / Foolin' myself / Easy living / I'll never be the same / I wished on / Sailboat in the moonlight / Born to love / Without your love / They can't take that away from me / Swing brother swing / I can't get started (with you) / Who wants love / Trav'lin' all alone / He's funny that way / My man (mon homme) / Who wants love / I can't believe that you're in love with me / When a woman loves a man / You go to my head / Having myself a time / Says my heart / Very thought of you / I cried for you / Jeepers creepers / Long gone blues / Some other Spring / Them there eyes / Night and day / Man I love / Let's do it all / All of me / God bless the child / Gloomy Sunday / Until the real thing comes along / Fine and mellow / You've changed / For all we know
CD Set _____ 4690492
Columbia / Nov '91 / Sony.

LEGEND OF BILLIE HOLIDAY
That ole devil called love / Lover man / Don't explain / Good morning heartache / There is no greater love / Easy living / Solitude / Porgy / My man (mon homme) / Them there eyes / No one never / Ain't nobody's business / Somebody's on my mind / Keeps on a rainin' / You're my thrill / God bless the child
CD _____ MCLD 19216
MCA / Aug '93 / BMG.

LEGEND, UNISSUED AND RARE MASTERS 1935-38
CD _____ JZ-CD305
Suisa / Feb '91 / Jazz Music / THE.

LEGEND, UNISSUED AND RARE MASTERS 1939-52
CD _____ JZ-CD306
Suisa / Feb '91 / Jazz Music / THE.

LEGEND, UNISSUED AND RARE MASTERS 1952-58
CD _____ JZ-CD307
Suisa / Feb '91 / Jazz Music / THE.

LEGENDARY MASTERS, THE (Unissued/ Rare 1935-1958)
CD Set _____ RARECD 01/02/03
Recording Arts / '88 / THE / Disc.

LEGENDARY MASTERS, THE (Unissued/ Rare 1935-38)
What a little moonlight can do / Miss Brown to you / Twenty four hours a day / Yankee Doodle never went to town / If you were mine / These 'n'that 'n'those / Spreadin' rhythm around / Let's call a heart a heart / please keep me in your dreams / I wish I had you / I'll never fail you / You're so desirable / You're gonna see a lot of me / Hello my darling / Let's dream in the moonlight
CD _____ RARECD 01
Recording Arts / '88 / THE / Disc.

LEGENDS IN MUSIC - BILLIE HOLIDAY
CD _____ LECD 071
Wisepack / Jul '94 / THE / Conifer.

LIVE AND RARE 1937-56
CD _____ 11049
Laserlight / '86 / Target/BMG.

LONG GONE BLUES
CD _____ 4741692
Sony Jazz / Jan '95 / Sony.

LOVE FOR SALE
CD _____ CDSGP 0102
Prestige / May '94 / Total/BMG.

MAN I LOVE 1937-39, THE (Holiday, Billie & Lester Young)
This year's kisses / I must have that man / I'll get by / Mean to me / I'll never be the same / Easy living / Foolin' myself / Without your love / Me, myself and I / Sailboat in the moonlight / Trav'lin' all alone / She's funny that way / Getting some fun out of life / I can't believe that you're in love with me / Back in your own backyard / You can't be mine (and someone else's too) / Say it with a kiss / Man I love
CD _____ CD 56008
Jazz Roots / Aug '94 / Target/BMG.

MAN I LOVE, THE (Holiday, Billie & Lester Young)
CD _____ CD 14529
Jazz Portraits / Jan '94 / Jazz Music.

MASTERPIECES 1935-42
CD _____ 158182
Masterpieces / Mar '94 / BMG.

ME MYSELF I
CD _____ 219912
Milan / Mar '95 / BMG / Silva Screen.

MISS BROWN TO YOU
What a little moonlight can do / Miss Brown to you / Twenty four hours a day / Yankee Doodle never went to town / If you were mine / These n'that n'those / Spreadin' rhythm around / Let's call a heart a heart / Please keep me in your dreams / I wish I had you / I'll never fail you / You're so desirable / You're gonna see a lot of more of me / Hello my darling / Let's dream in the moonlight / More than you know / Under a blue jungle moon / Night and day / What is this going to get us / Loveless love / Georgia on my mind / Romance in the dark
CD _____ CDGRF 075
Tring / '93 / Tring / Prism.

MY MAN (Holiday, Billie & Teddy Wilson Orchestra)
CD _____ CD 14536
Jazz Portraits / Jan '94 / Jazz Music.

MY MAN (Holiday, Billie & Teddy Wilson Orchestra)
CD _____ CD 56028
Jazz Roots / Jul '95 / Target/BMG.

NIGHT AND DAY
I'm gonna lock my heart / Very thought of you / I can't get started / You can't be mine / Say it with a kiss / I'll never fail you / They say / That's all I ask of you / Yesterdays / Them there eyes / Night and day / You're just a no account / Body and soul / Falling in love again / I hear music / St Loius blues / When you're smiling / I can't believe that you're in love with me / Now they call it the swing / On the sentimental side / Born to love / Without your love
CD _____ RAJCD 857
Empress / Oct '95 / THE.

PEARLS FROM THE PAST VOL. 2 - BILLIE HOLIDAY
CD _____ KLMCD 021
Scratch / May '94 / BMG.

QUINTESSENTIAL VOL. 1 (1933-1935)
Your mother's son-in-law / Riffin' the scotch / I wished on the moon / What a little moonlight can do / Miss Brown to you / Sun bonnet blue / What a night / What a moon / What a girl / I'm painting the town red / It's too hot for words / Twenty four hours a day / Yankee Doodle never went to town / Eeny meeny miney mo / If you were mine / These 'n' that 'n' those / You let me down / Spreadin' rhythm around
CD _____ 4509872
Sony Jazz / Jan '95 / Sony.

QUINTESSENTIAL VOL. 2 (1935-1936)
Life begins when you're in love / It's like reaching for the moon / These foolish things / I cried for you / Guess who / Did I remember / No regrets / Summertime / Billie's blue / Them there eyes / I can't pretend / 1-2 Button your shoe / Let's call a heart a heart / Easy to love / With these I swing / Way you look tonight
CD _____ 4600602
Sony Jazz / Jan '95 / Sony.

QUINTESSENTIAL VOL. 3 (1936-1937)
Who loves you / Pennies from Heaven / That's life I guess / I can't give you anything but love / One never knows, does one / I've got my love to keep me warm / If my heart could only talk / Please keep me in your dreams / He ain't got rhythm / This year's kisses / Why was I born / I must have that man / Mood that I'm in / You showed me the way / Sentimental and melancholy / My last affair
CD _____ 4608202
Sony Jazz / Jan '95 / Scny.

QUINTESSENTIAL VOL. 4 (1937)
Carelessly / How could you / Moanin' low / Where is the sun / Let's call the whole thing off / They can't take away from me / I don't know If I'm coming or going / Sun showers / Yours and mine / I'll get by / Mean to me / Foolin' myself / Easy living / I'll never be the same / My, myself and I / Sailboat in the moonlight
CD _____ 4633332
Sony Jazz / Jan '95 / Sony.

QUINTESSENTIAL VOL. 5 (1937-1938)
Born to love / Without your love / Getting some fun out of life / Who wants love / Trav'lin all alone / He's funny that way / Nice work if you can get it / Things are looking up / My man (mon homme) / Can't help lovin' dat man / My first impression of you / When you're smiling / I can't believe that you're in love with me / If dreams come true / Now they call it swing / On the sentimental side / Back in your own backyard / When a woman loves a man
CD _____ 4651902
Sony Jazz / Jan '95 / Sony.

QUINTESSENTIAL VOL. 6 (1938)
CD _____ 4663132
Sony Jazz / Jan '95 / Sony.

QUINTESSENTIAL VOL. 7 (1938-1939)
CD _____ 4669662
Sony Jazz / Jan '95 / Sony.

QUINTESSENTIAL VOL. 8 (1939-1940)
CD _____ 4679142
Sony Jazz / Jan '95 / Sony.

QUINTESSENTIAL VOL. 9 (1940-1942)
CD _____ 4679152
Sony Jazz / Jan '95 / Sony.

SILVER COLLECTION, THE
I wished on the moon / Moonlight in Vermont / Say it isn't so / Love is here to stay / Dam that dream / But not for me / Body and soul / Comes love / They can't take that away from me / Let's call the whole thing off / Gee baby ain't I good to you / Embraceable you / All or nothing at all / We'll be together again
CD _____ 8234492
Verve / Mar '92 / PolyGram.

SONGBOOK
Good morning heartache / My man / Billie's blues / Don't explain / Lady sings the blues / Lover man / God bless the child / Fine and mellow / Strange fruit / Stormy blues / Trav-lin light
CD _____ 823 246-2
Verve / Jan '90 / PolyGram.

SPOTLIGHT ON BILLIE HOLIDAY
Lover man / Ain't nobody's business / Billie's blues / Miss Brown to you / Good morning heartache / My man / My man / I cover the waterfront / Lover come back to me / Them there eyes / He's funny that way / You're driving me crazy / Fine and mellow
CD _____ HADCD 114
Javelin / Feb '94 / THE / Henry Hadaway Organisation.

STAY WITH ME
CD _____ 5115232
Verve / Feb '92 / PolyGram.

STRANGE FRUIT
CD _____ CD 53085
Giants Of Jazz / May '93 / Target/BMG / Cadillac.

SUMMERTIME (Holiday, Billie & Her Orchestra)
CD _____ CD 14539
Jazz Portraits / Jan '94 / Jazz Music.

SUMMERTIME 1936-1940
CD _____ CD 56035
Jazz Roots / Nov '94 / Target/BMG.

THINGS ARE LOOKING UP
That's life I guess / I can't give you anything but love / Me, myself and I / Sailboat in the moonlight / Mood that I'm in
CD _____ CDMOIR 305
Memoir / Jul '91 / Target/BMG.

TRAV'LIN LIGHT, TRAV'LIN ALL ALONE
CD _____ CDCD 1202
Charly / Sep '94 / Charly / THE / Cadillac.

TWO ON ONE: BILLIE HOLIDAY & ELLA FITZGERALD (Holiday, Billie & Ella Fitzgerald)
CD _____ CDTT 9
Charly / Apr '94 / Charly / THE / Cadillac.

WITH TEDDY WILSON ORCHESTRA 1935-42 (Holiday, Billie & Teddy Wilson)
CD _____ GOJCD 53055
Giants Of Jazz / Mar '90 / Target/BMG / Cadillac.

DAVE HOLLAND & SAM RIVERS (Holland, Dave & Sam Rivers)
CD _____ 1238432
IAI / Mar '92 / Harmonia Mundi / Cadillac.

DREAM OF THE ELDERS
Winding way / Lazy snake / Claressence / Equality (vocal) / Ebb and flo / Dream of the elders / Second thoughts / Equality (instrumental)
CD _____ 5290842
ECM / Feb '96 / New Note.

EMERALD TEARS
Spheres / Combination / Under Redwoods / Flurries / Emerald tears / B40, RS4W, M236k / Solar / Hooveling
CD _____ 5290872
ECM / Dec '95 / New Note.

EXTENSIONS (Holland, Dave Quartet)
Nemesis / Processional / Black hole / Oracle / 101 fahrenheit (slow meltdown) / Color of mind
CD _____ 8417782
ECM / Oct '90 / New Note.

JUMPIN' IN (Holland, Dave Quintet)
CD _____ 8174372
ECM / '88 / New Note.

LIFE CYCLE (Solo Cello)
CD _____ 8292002
ECM / Oct '86 / New Note.

ONES ALL
Homecoming / Three step dance / Pork pie hat / Jumpin' in / Reminiscence / Mr P C / Little girl I'll miss you / Cashet / Blues for CM / Pass it on / God bless the child
CD _____ VBR 21482
Intuition / Jan '96 / New Note.

RAZOR'S EDGE, THE (Holland, Dave Quintet)
Brother Ty / Vedana / Razor's edge / Blues for C.M. / Vortex / Five four six / Wights waits for weights / Fight time
CD _____ 8330482
ECM / Oct '87 / New Note.

SEEDS OF TIME (Holland, Dave Quintet)
Uhren / Homecoming / Perspicuity / Celebration / World protection blues / Grid lock / Walk away / Good doctor / Double vision
CD _____ 8253222
ECM / Aug '85 / New Note.

TRIPLICATE (Holland, Dave Trio)
CD _____ 8371182
ECM / Sep '88 / New Note.

FIDDLESTICKS COLLECTION, THE (1982-1992)
CD _____ GLCD 1156
Green Linnet / Dec '95 / Roots / CM / Direct / ADA.

A-Z OF PIANO
Brick Lane / Newgates Knocker / Temple Bar / Canary Wharf / Birdcage walk / Seven Dials / Rotten Row Boogie / Wapping Steps / St. Martin In The Fields / St. Andrews by the wardrobe / Between the dilly and the blue gate fields (city) / High street (ken) / Speaker's corner / Soho / Tranquil passage
CD _____ ALTGOCD 001
Alter Ego / Oct '95 / BMG.

BOOGIE WOOGIE PIANO
CD _____ TMPCD 022
Telstar / Oct '95 / BMG.

JAZZ PIANO
CD _____ TMPCD 024
Telstar / Oct '95 / BMG.

LIVE PERFORMANCE
Bumble boogie / Bad luck blues / Skin the cat / Mean old man's world / Dr. Jazz / High street / I saw the light / Should've known better / Able Mable / Maiden's lament / Biggie wiggie / Maybe I need her / I gotta woman / Smoking shuffle / Hop, skip and jump
CD _____ BT 002CD
Beautiful / Nov '94 / Vital.

RAG TIME PIANO
CD _____ TMPCD 023
Telstar / Oct '95 / BMG.

BY HEART
Oxford girl / Rosie / Only dreaming / Smokey's bar / Cathy come home / Catharine of Aragon's song / Rowan tree / May morning dew / Evergreen / Colorado song / Postcards from Scarborough / Tank park salute / Jack Haggerty / Company of strangers / Seven gypsies / Invitation to the blues / Taoist tale
CD _____ RHYD 5008
Rhiannon / Sep '95 / Vital / Direct / ADA.

ACCIDENTAL FORTUNE (Hollander, Rick Quartet)
Accidental fortune / My old flame / Point of the pen / I've grown accustomed to her face / Some lovely dreams / I should care / Big Stacey / Theme for Ernie / Beautiful / Beginning / Pull
CD _____ CCD 4550
Concord Jazz / May '93 / New Note.

ONCE UPON A TIME (The Music Of Hoagy Carmichael)
Skylark / Star dust / Baltimore Oriole / Georgia on my mind (Mixes) / Hong kong blues / Rockin' chair / Ivy / Nearness of you
CD _____ CCD 4666
Concord Jazz / Sep '95 / New Note.

HOLLIDAY WITH MULLIGAN (Holliday, Judy & Gerry Mulligan)
What's the rush / Loving you / Lazy / It must be Christmas / Party's over / It's bad for me / Suppertime / Pass that peace pipe / I've got a night to sing the blues / Summer's over / Blue prelude
CD _____ CDSL 5191
DRG / Mar '87 / New Note.

30TH ANNIVERSARY COLLECTION
Yellow rose of Texas / Gal with the yaller shoes / Love you darlin' / Keep your heart / Story of my life / Stairway of love / My heart is an open book / Palace of love / Life is a circus / For you, for you / I have waited / Steady game / Starry eyed / Dream talk / One finger symphony / Young in love / I wonder who's kissing her now / Miracle of Monday morning / Remember me / Dream boy dream / I don't want you to see me cry / Wishin' on a rainbow / Have I told you lately that I love you / Tears / I just can't win / Laugh and the world laughs with you /

Just to be with you again / Drums / My last date with you
CD _____ CDEMS 1509
EMI / Feb '94 / EMI.

EP COLLECTION: MICHAEL HOLLIDAY
Runaway train / Yaller yaller gold / Darlin' Katie / Marrying for love / I'll be loving you too / Lonesome road / Just a wearyin' for you / Ramblin' man / Kentucky babe / In the good old summertime / Stairway of love / Four feather halls / Happy hearts and friendly faces / Way back home / Show me the way to go home / Side by side / Alexander's ragtime band / Just a prayer away / Careless hands / Dearest between hello and goodbye / Story of my life / I can't give you anything but love (CD only) / Winter wonderland (CD only) / Perfect day (CD only) / Four walls (CD only) / I can't begin to tell you (CD only) / Margie (CD only)
CD _____ SEECD 311
See For Miles/C5 / Feb '91 / Pinnacle.

TOGETHER AGAIN (Holliday, Michael & Edna Savage)
Story of my life / Arrivederci darling / Rooney / Tear fell / Tip toe through the tulips / Once / Girl in the yaller shoes / Long ago and far away / We'll gather lilacs / S wonderful / In the wee small hours of the morning / My house is your house / Let me be loved / Hot diggity (dog ziggity boom) / Tea for two / Catch me a kiss / I promise you / Me head in de barrel / I saw Esau / Never leave me / I'll be seeing you / Why why why / Nothin' to do / Goodnight my love
CD _____ CC 252
Music For Pleasure / May '90 / EMI.

Holliday, Simon

RAGS, BOOGIE AND SWING
Should I reveal / As long as I live / Maple leaf rag / Airmail special / Climax rag / Boogie joys / All the things you are / Way down yonder in New Orleans / Winin' boy blues / Nagasaki
CD _____ CMJCD 009
CMJ / Mar '90 / Jazz Music / Wellard.

Hollies

AIR THAT I BREATHE, THE
CD _____ BR 1302
BR Music / May '94 / Target/BMG.

AIR THAT I BREATHE, THE - THE BEST OF THE HOLLIES
Air that I breathe / Bus stop / Just one look / Yes I will / Look through my window / He ain't heavy, he's my brother / I can't let go / We're through / Searchin' / Stay, I'm alive / If I needed someone / Here I go again / Stop stop stop / On a carousel / Carrie Anne / King Midas in reverse / Jennifer Eccles / Listen to me / Sorry Suzanne / I can't tell the bottom from the top / Gasoline Alley bred / Hey Willy / Long cool woman in a black dress / Baby / Woman I love
CD _____ CDEMTV 74
EMI / Mar '93 / EMI.

ALL THE WORLD IS LOVE
CD _____ BR 1462
BR Music / Nov '94 / Target/BMG.

ANOTHER NIGHT/RUSSIAN ROULETTE/ 5317704/BUDDY HOLLY (4 Hollies Originals/4CD Set)
Another night / 4th Of July, Asbury Park (Sandy) / Lonely hobo lullaby / Second hand hang-ups / Machine jive / I'm down / Look out Johnny (there's a monkey on your back) / Give me time / Too late now / Find me a family (with that look on your eyes) / Lucy / Wiggle that wotsit / Forty eight hour parole / Thanks for the memories / My love / Lady of the night / Russian roulette / Draggin' my heels / Louise / Be with you / Daddy don't mind / Say it ain't so Jo / maybe it's dawn / Song of the sung / Harlequin / When I'm yours / Something to live for / Stormy waters / Boys in the band / Satelite three / It's in every one of us / Peggy Sue / Wishing / Love's made a fool of you / Take your time / Heartbeat / Tell me how / Think it over / Maybe baby / Midnight shifts / I'm gonna love you too / Peggy Sue got married / What to do / That'll be the day / It doesn't matter anymore / Everyday / Medley
CD Set _____ HOLLIES 1
EMI / Feb '95 / EMI.

BUTTERFLY
Dear Eloise / Maker / Would you believe / Postcard / Try it / Step inside / Away away away / Pegasus / Wish you a wish / Charlie and Fred / Elevated observations / Butterfly
CD _____ BGOCD 79
Beat Goes On / '89 / Pinnacle.

CONFESSIONS OF THE MIND
Survival of the fittest / Man without a heart / Little girl / Isn't it nice / Confessions of a mind / Lady please / Frightened lady / Too young to be married / Seperated / I wanna shout
CD _____ BGOCD 96
Beat Goes On / '89 / Pinnacle.

DISTANT LIGHT
CD _____ BGOCD 97
Beat Goes On / Jul '91 / Pinnacle.

EP COLLECTION: HOLLIES
Woodstock / Here I go again / You know he did / What kind of boy / Baby that's all / Look through my window / What kind of love / When I'm not there / Rockin' Robin / Lucille / Memphis / Just one look / I'm alive / Come on back / We're through / I've got a way of my own / So lonely / To you my love / What'cha gonna do about it / Come on home / I can't let you go
CD _____ SEECD 94
See For Miles/C5 / Mar '95 / Pinnacle.

EVOLUTION
Then the heartaches begin / Water on the brain / Have you ever loved somebody / Heading for a fall / Ye olde toffee shoppe / When your lights turned on / Stop right there / Lullaby to Tim / You need love / Rain on the window / Leave me / Games we play
CD _____ BGOCD 80
Beat Goes On / '89 / Pinnacle.

FOR CERTAIN BECAUSE
CD _____ BGOCD 9
Beat Goes On / Dec '89 / Pinnacle.

HOLLIES LIVE
CD _____ BRCD 123
BR Music / Jul '94 / Target/BMG.

HOLLIES SING DYLAN
When the ship comes in / I'll be your baby tonight / I want you / This wheel's on fire / I shall be released / Blowin' in the wind / Quit your low down ways / Just like a woman / Times they are a changin' / All I really want to do / My back pages / Mighty Quinn
CD _____ CZ 520
EMI / Jun '93 / EMI.

HOLLIES, THE
CD _____ BGOCD 25
Beat Goes On / May '91 / Pinnacle.

HOUR OF THE HOLLIES, AN
Stop stop stop / Gasoline Alley bred / Searchin' / Listen to me / What kind of boy / Rockin' robin / Come on back / Memphis, Tennessee / Too young to be married / Dear Eloise / He ain't heavy, he's my brother / Sweet little sixteen / Nobody (Mono) / Hey Willy / Just like me / Sorry Suzanne / Lucille / Keep off that friend of mine (Mono.) / On a carousel / Pay you back with interest / Clown / If I needed someone / Blowin' in the wind
CD _____ CC 216
Music For Pleasure / '91 / EMI.

IN THE HOLLIES STYLE
CD _____ BGOCD 8
Beat Goes On / Oct '88 / Pinnacle.

NOT THE HITS AGAIN
Wings / It's in her kiss (Shoop shoop song) / You'll be mine / Take your time / I am a rock / Honey and wine / Very last day / It's only make believe / That's my desire / So lonely / Now's the time / Hard, hard year / Put yourself in my place / Please don't feel too bad / Nitty gritty-Something's got a hold on me / You better move on / I take what I want / Talkin 'bout you / Candy man / Set me free / Lawdy Miss Clawdy / Sweet little sixteen
CD _____ SEECD 63
See For Miles/C5 / May '89 / Pinnacle.

OTHER SIDE OF THE HOLLIES
'Cos you like to know me / Everything is sunshine / Signs that will never change / Not that way at all / You know he did / Do the best you can / So lonely / I've got a way of my own / Don't run and hide / Come on back / Open up your eyes / All the world is love / Whole world over / Row the boat together / Mad professor Blyth / Dandelion wine / Baby that's all / Nobody / Keep off that friend of mine / Running through the night / Hey what's wrong with me / Blowin' in the wind
CD _____ SEECD 302
See For Miles/C5 / '90 / Pinnacle.

SINGLES A'S AND B'S 1970-1979
I can't tell the bottom from the top / Mad Professor Blyth / Gasoline alley bred / Dandelion wine / Hey Willy / Row the boat together / Long cool woman in a black dress / Cable car / Baby / Oh Granny / Day that Curly Billy shot crazy Sam McGhee / Born a man / Air that I breathe / No more riders / Star / Love is the thing / Hello to romance / Forty eight hour parole / Something to live for / Song of the sun
CD _____ CDMFP 5980
EMI / Apr '93 / EMI.

STAY WITH THE HOLLIES
CD _____ BGOCD 4
Beat Goes On / Oct '88 / Pinnacle.

Hollmer, Lars

12 SIBIRISKA CYKLAR/VILL DU HORA MER
CD _____ RES 512CD
Resource / Dec '94 / ADA.

LOOPING HOME
CD _____ VICTOCD 024
Victo / Oct '94 / These / ReR Megacorp / Cadillac.

SIBERIAN CIRCUS, THE
CD _____ RESCD 502
Resource / Oct '93 / ADA.

Holloway, Laurie

ABOUT TIME
Tricrotism / Teach me tonight / For you / Quinta do lago / Nothing quite like love / Good to know / s'posin' / Gettin' there / Revelation / Love for sale / I should n' ave ever / No greater love / Bye bye blues
CD _____ C6CD 606
See For Miles/C5 / Jan '93 / Pinnacle.

Holloway, Loleatta

LOLEATTA
Hit and run / Is it just a man's way / We're getting stronger / Dreamin' / Ripped off / Worn out broken heart / That's how heartaches are made / What now
CD _____ CPCD 8063
Charly / Nov '94 / Charly / THE / Cadillac.

LOVE SENSATION
Love sensation / Dance wet 'cha wanna / I'll be standing there / I've been loving you too long / Short end of the stick / My way / Long hard climb to love / Two become a crowd
CD _____ CPCD 8095
Charly / Apr '95 / Charly / THE / Cadillac.

Holloway, Red

LOCKSMITH BLUES (Holloway, Red & Clark Terry Sextet)
CD _____ CCD 4390
Concord Jazz / Nov '89 / New Note.

RED HOLLOWAY AND COMPANY
But not for me / Caravan / Passion flower / Blues for Q.M. / Well you needn't / What's new / Summertime / Tokyo express
CD _____ CCD 4322
Concord Jazz / Jul '87 / New Note.

Holloway, Stanley

MANY HAPPY RETURNS
Penny on the drum / Pick up tha' musket / Lion and Albert / Join the Navy / Three ha'pence a foot / Dinder courtship / Old Sam's party / Albert comes back / Jubilee Sovereign / Sometimes I'm happy / Many happy returns / My old Dutch / Sam drummed out / Albert and the 'eadsman / Hand in hand
CD _____ CMSCD 007
Movie Stars / '89 / Conifer.

PICK OOP THA MUSKET
Sam, pick oop tha musket / 'Alt, who goes theer / Marksman Sam / Sam's medal / Sam Small at Westminster / Up'ards / Three ha'pence a foot / 'Ole in the ark / With her head tucked underneath her arm / Lion and Albert / Song of the sea / Beefeater / Many happy returns / Gunner Joe / Beat the retreat / One each a piece all round / Sam Small's party
CD _____ PASTCD 7021
Flapper / Aug '93 / Pinnacle.

Holly, Buddy

20 GOLDEN GREATS: BUDDY HOLLY (Holly, Buddy & The Crickets)
That'll be the day / Peggy Sue / Words of love / Everyday / Not fade away / Oh boy / Maybe baby / Listen to me / Heartbeat / Think it over / It doesn't matter anymore / It's so easy / Well alright / Rave on / Raining in my heart / True love ways / Peggy Sue got married / Bo Diddley / Brown eyed handsome man / Wishing
CD _____ DMCTV 1
MCA / Aug '93 / BMG.

BEST OF BUDDY HOLLY
CD _____ PWKS 595
Carlton Home Entertainment / Sep '93 / Carlton Home Entertainment.

BUDDY HOLLY TRIBUTE (Various Artists)
CD _____ MCD 11260
MCA / Jan '96 / BMG.

BUDDY HOLLY/THAT'LL BE THE DAY
I'm gonna love you too / Peggy Sue / Look at me / Listen to me / Valley of tears / Ready teddy / Everyday / Mailman bring me no more blues / Words of love / Baby I don't care / Rave on / Little baby / You are my one desire / Blue days black nights / Modern Don Juan / Rock around with Ollie Vee / Ting-a-ling / Girl on my mind / That'll be the day / Love me / I'm gonna change all those changes / Don't come back knockin' / Midnight shift / Rock around with Ollie Vee (alternative version)
CD _____ MCLD 19242
MCA / May '94 / BMG.

BUDDY'S BUDDYS (The Buddy Holly Songbook) (Various Artists)
CD _____ VSOPCD 175
Connoisseur / Sep '92 / Pinnacle.

GOLDEN GREATS: BUDDY HOLLY
Peggy Sue / That'll be the day / Listen to me / Everyday / Oh boy / Not fade away / Raining in my heart / Brown eyed handsome man / Maybe baby / Rave on / Think it over / It's so easy / It doesn't matter an-

ymore / True love ways / Peggy Sue got married / Bo Diddley
CD _____ MCLD 19046
MCA / Apr '92 / BMG.

LEGENDARY BUDDY HOLLY, THE
Listen to me / Words of love / You've got to love / Learning the game / Not fade away / What to do / Early in the morning / Wishing / Love's made a fool of you / Love is strange / Baby I don't care / Midnight shift / Reminiscing / Valley of tears
CD _____ PWKS 523
Carlton Home Entertainment / Feb '89 / Carlton Home Entertainment.

LOVE SONGS
CD _____ MCBD 19522
MCA / Jul '95 / BMG.

MOONDREAMS
Moondreams / Because I love you / I guess I was just a fool / Girl on my mind / I'm gonna love you too / You and I are through / Come back baby / You're the one / I gambled my heart / You are my one desire / Door to my heart / Crying, waiting, hoping / Now we're one / Love me / Soft place in my heart / Have you ever been lonely
CD _____ PWKS 560
Carlton Home Entertainment / Mar '90 / Carlton Home Entertainment.

ORIGINAL VOICES OF THE CRICKETS
True loves ways / Every day / Love me / Don't come back knockin' / Baby I don't care / Reminiscing / Peggy Sue / Well alright / Midnight shift / Blue days black nights / That's what they say / Rock-a-bye rock / Heartbeat / Girl on my mind / Ting-a-ling / I'm gonna set my foot down / It's not my fault / Rock around with Ollie Vee / You are my one desire / Because I love you / Modern Don Juan / Words / You've lost that lovin' feelin'
CD _____ CDMF 088
Magnum Force / May '93 / Magnum Music Group.

SPECIAL COLLECTION, A
Listen to me / Words of love / You've got love / Learning the game / Not fade away / What to do / Early in the morning / Wishing / Love's made a fool of you / Love is strange / Baby I don't care / Midnight shift / Reminiscing / Valley of tears / That'll be the day / Maybe baby / Peggy Sue got married / Rave on / True love ways / Bo Diddley / Oh boy / Peggy Sue / Everyday / Think it over / Brown eyed handsome man / Heartbeat / Raining in my heart / It doesn't matter anymore / Moondreams / Because I love you / I guess I was a fool for you / Girl on my mind / I'm gonna love you too / You and I are through / Come back baby / You're the one / Door to my heart / Crying, waiting, hoping / Now we're one / Love me / Soft place in my heart / Have you ever been lonely
CD Set _____ BOXD 26T
Carlton Home Entertainment / Oct '94 / Carlton Home Entertainment.

THAT'LL BE THE DAY
You are my one desire / Blue days black nights / Modern Don Juan / Rock around with Ollie Vee / Ting a ling / Girl on my mind / Love me / I'm changing all those changes / Don't come back knockin' / Midnight shift
CD _____ CLACD 309
Castle / Jan '96 / BMG.

TRUE LOVE WAYS
Raining in my heart / Peggy Sue / That'll be the day / Oh boy / Everyday / True love ways / I'm gonna love you too / Ready Teddy / Wishing / Well alright / Midnight shift / Love's made a fool of you / Reminiscing
CD _____ TCD 2339
Telstar / Feb '89 / BMG.

WORDS OF LOVE - 28 CLASSIC SONGS (Holly, Buddy & The Crickets)
Words of love / That'll be the day / Peggy Sue / Think it over / True loves ways / What to do / Crying, waiting, hoping / Well alright / Love's made a fool of you / Peggy Sue got married / Valley of tears / Wishing / Raining in my heart / Oh boy / Rave on / Brown eyed handsome man / Bo Diddley / It's so easy / It doesn't matter anymore / Maybe baby / Early in the morning / Love is strange / Listen to me / I'm gonna love you too / Learning the game / Baby I don't care / Heartbeat / Everyday
CD _____ 514487-2
PolyGram TV / Feb '93 / PolyGram.

Holly Golightly

GOOD THINGS, THE
CD _____ DAMGOOD 65CD
Damaged Goods / Jun '95 / SRD.

Hollyday, Christopher

AND I'LL SING ONCE MORE
Heroes / Kate the roommate / Sound of music / Storm / Beyond the barren lands / Chant / Nefertiti / Let the moon stand still / Very thought of you
CD _____ PD 90685
Novus / Jul '92 / BMG.

313

CHRISTOPHER HOLLYDAY
Appointment in Ghana / Omega / Bloomdido / This is always / Koko / Little Melonae / Embraceable you / Blues inn / Be bop
CD _____ PD 83055
Novus / Aug '89 / BMG.

NATURAL MOMENT, THE
Scorpio rising / Had to be Brad / All new meaning / Every time we say goodbye / Point of delirium / Johnny Red / Afterglow / Idleism / Natural moment
CD _____ PD 83118
Novus / Jul '91 / BMG.

ON COURSE
No second quartet / Lady Street / Memories of you / West side winds / Hit and run / Skeptical skeptical / In a love affair / Sixth worl!
CD _____ PD 83087
Novus / Jun '90 / BMG.

Hollyfaith

PURRR
Bliss / Who is you / Delicacies / Watching, waiting, turning / Zero / Voodoo doll / Whatsamatta / Whirlwind / Color of blood / Needs
CD _____ CRECD 163
Creation / Aug '93 / 3MV / Vital.

Hollywood Brats

HOLLYWOOD BRATS
Chez maximes / Another schoolday / Nightmare / Empty bottles / Courtesan / Then he kissed me / Tumble with me / Zurich 17 / Southern belles / Drowning sorrows / Sick on you
CD _____ CDMRED 106
Cherry Red / Dec '93 / Pinnacle.

Hollywood Fats Band

ROCK THIS HOUSE
CD _____ BT 1097CD
Black Top / Jan '94 / CM / Direct / ADA.

Hollywood Flames

HOLLYWOOD FLAMES, THE
Wheel of fortune / Later / Tabarin / Wine / My confession / Sound of your voice / Crazy / Buzz buzz buzz / Ooh baby ooh / This heart of mine / Little bird / Give me back my heart / Two little bees / It's love / Your love / Frankenstein's den / Strollin' on the beach / Chains of love / Let's talk it over / Star fell / I'll get by / Just for you / Hollywood Flames / I'll be seeing you / There is something on your mind / So good / Romance in the dark / Much too much
CD _____ CDCHD 420
Ace / Sep '92 / Pinnacle / Cadillac / Complete/Pinnacle.

Holm, Michael

MICHAEL HOLM
CD _____ 16005
Laserlight / Aug '92 / Target/BMG.

Holman, Bill

BILL HOLMAN BAND (Holman, Bill Band)
CD _____ JD 3308
JVC / Sep '88 / New Note.

VIEW FROM THE SIDE, A (Holman, Bill Band)
No joy in mudville / Any dude'll do / But beautiful / Petaluma Lu / I didn't ask / Make my day / Peacock / Tennessee waltz / View from the side
CD _____ JVC 20502
JVC / Aug '95 / New Note.

Holman, Eddie

EDDIE'S MY NAME
This can't be true / You can tell / I surrender / Return to me / Don't stop now / I'll cry 1000 tears / Where I'm not wanted / Hurt / Peace of mind / Never let me go / Been so long / Sexy Ed hare wants a lonely girl / Eddie's my name / Sweet memories / Stay mine for heaven's sake / Free country / You know that I will / Am I a loser / I'm not gonna give up / I'll cry 1000 tears (unreleased version)
CD _____ GSCD 031
Goldmine / Dec '93 / Vital.

I LOVE YOU
CD _____ VSD 5492
Varese Sarabande/Colosseum / Mar '95 / Pinnacle / Silva Screen.

NIGHT TO REMEMBER, A
CD _____ CPCD 8061
Charly / Nov '94 / Charly / THE / Cadillac.

Holmes Brothers

JUBILATION
CD _____ CDRW 21
Realworld / Mar '92 / EMI / Sterns.

SOUL STREET
CD _____ ROU 2124CD
Rounder / Oct '93 / CM / Direct / ADA / Cadillac.

Where It's At

WHERE IT'S AT
That's where it't at / Love is you / You can't hold on to a love that's gone / I've been a loser / Hi-heel sneakers / Worried life blues / Never let me go / Give it up / I've been to the well before / I saw the light / Drown in my own tears
CD _____ ROUCD 2111
Rounder / Jun '95 / CM / Direct / ADA / Cadillac.

Holmes, David

THIS FILM'S CRAP LET'S SLASH THE SEATS
No man's land / Slash the seats / Shake ya brain / Got fucked up along the way / Gone / Atom and you / Minus 61 in Detroit / Inspired by Leyburn / Coming home to the sun
CD _____ 8286312
Go Discs / Jul '95 / PolyGram.

Holmes, Richard

BLUES ALL DAY LONG (Holmes, Richard 'Groove')
CD _____ MCD 5358
Muse / Sep '92 / New Note / CM.

GROOVE'S GROOVE
Grooves groove / California blues / What a wonderful world / Misty / Walking on a tightrope / Slow blues in G / Song for my father / My friend / Lonesome road blues / On say a joy / Danger zone is everywhere / Time has come
CD _____ JHR 73585
Jazz Hour / Apr '95 / Target/BMG / Jazz Music / Cadillac.

GROOVIN' WITH GROOVE (Holmes, Richard 'Groove')
Go away little girl / Young and foolish / It's impossible / You've got it bad / Choo choo / How insensitive / Red onion / No trouble on the mountain / Meditation / Good vibration / It's gonna take some time / Grooves groove
CD _____ CDC 9084
LRC / Apr '95 / New Note / Harmonia Mundi.

GROOVIN' WITH JUG (Holmes, Richard 'Groove' & Gene Ammons)
Happy blues (good vibrations) / Willow weep for me / Juggin' around / Hittin' the jug / Exactly like you / Groovin' with jug / Morris the monor / Hey you what's that
CD _____ CZ 257
Pacific Jazz / Jan '90 / EMI.

SOUL MESSAGE (Holmes, Richard 'Groove')
CD _____ OJCCD 329
Original Jazz Classics / Dec '95 / Wellard / Jazz Music / Cadillac / Complete/Pinnacle.

Holocaust

HYPNOSIS OF BIRDS
Hypnosis of birds / Tower / Book of seasons / Mercier and camier / Small hours / Into Lebanon / Summer tides / Mortal Mother / Cairnpapple hill / In the dark places of the earth / Caledonia
CD _____ TRMCD 010
Taurus Moon / Apr '93 / Taurus Moon.

Holroyd, Bob

FLUIDITY & STRUCTURE
CD _____ BHCD 1001
Holroyd / Jul '94 / Direct.

Holst, Ivan

PA FRI FUD
CD _____ MECCACD 1023
Music Mecca / Nov '94 / Jazz Music / Cadillac / Wellard.

Holt, John

1000 VOLTS OF HOLT
Never, never, never / Morning of my life / Stoned out of my mind / Baby I want you / Help me make it through the night / Mr. Bojangles / I'd love you to want me / Killing me softly / You baby / Too much love / Girl from Ipanema / Which way you going, baby
CD _____ CDTRL 75
Trojan / Mar '94 / Jetstar / Total/BMG.

16 SONGS FOR SOULFUL LOVERS
I'd love you to want me / You'll never find / Too good to be forgotten / Help me make it through the night / Winter world of love / Killing me softly / If I were a carpenter / Rainy night in Georgia / I'll never fall in love again / Just the way you are / Wherever I lay my hat / Touch me in the morning / Love I can feel / Too much love / When I fall in love / I'll be there
CD _____ PLATCD 16
Platinum Music / Jul '89 / Prism / Ross.

20 GOLDEN LOVE SONGS: JOHN HOLT
Never never never / I'd love you to want me / Killing me softly / You will never find another love like mine / When I fall in love / I'll take a melody / Just the way you are / Too good to be forgotten / Dr. Love / Help me make it through the night / Stoned out of my life / Touch me in the morning / I'll be lonely / Too much love / Love so right /

Rainy night in Georgia / If I were a Carpenter / Everybody's talkin' / Baby don't get hooked on me / Last farewell
CD _____ CDTRL 192
Trojan / May '90 / Jetstar / Total/BMG.

20 GREAT HITS
CD _____ CDSGP 067
Prestige / Oct '93 / Total/BMG.

COLLECTION, THE
CD _____ COL 069
Collection / Feb '95 / Target/BMG.

GOLDEN HITS
CD _____ RNCD 2110
Rhino / Jun '95 / Jetstar / Magnum Music Group / THE.

GREATEST HITS OF JOHN HOLT
CD _____ SOCD 1115
Studio One / Mar '95 / Jetstar.

LOVE I CAN FEEL
CD _____ SOCD 9017
Studio One / Mar '95 / Jetstar.

LOVE SONGS VOL.2
CD _____ EPCD 1
Parish / Apr '92 / Jetstar.

PARTY TIME (Holt, John & Dennis Brown)
CD _____ SONCD 0068
Sonic Sounds / Sep '94 / Jetstar.

PEACEMAKER
CD _____ CDSGP 049
Prestige / Jun '93 / Total/BMG.

PLEDGING MY LOVE
CD _____ RNCD 2019
Rhino / Sep '93 / Jetstar / Magnum Music Group / THE.

REGGAE CHRISTMAS ALBUM, THE
CD _____ CDTRL 230
Trojan / Nov '95 / Jetstar / Total/BMG.

TIME IS THE MASTER
Time is the master / Everybody Knows / Riding For A Fall / Looking Back / Love is gone / Stick By Me / Lost Love / It May Sound Silly / Again / Oh Girl
CD _____ RNCD 2002
Rhino / Jun '92 / Jetstar / Magnum Music Group / THE.

TONIGHT AT TREASURE ISLE
CD _____ RNCD 2081
Rhino / Dec '94 / Jetstar / Magnum Music Group / THE.

TREASURE OF LOVE
CD _____ SONCD 0074
Sonic Sounds / Mar '95 / Jetstar.

Holt, Steve

CATWALK (Holt, Steve Jazz Quartet)
CD _____ SKCD 2-2032
Sackville / Feb '94 / Swift / Jazz Music / Jazz Horizons / Cadillac / CM.

JUST DUET (Holt, Steve & Kieran Overs)
CD _____ SKCD 2-2025
Sackville / Jul '93 / Swift / Jazz Music / Jazz Horizons / Cadillac / CM.

Holy Gang

FREE TYSON FREE
Free Tyson free (Mixes) / Get chained / Power is my life / Murder as religion / Tyson Vs Washington (F.T.F.) / Sanity fair / Sanity (Karaoke ambient) / Sanity B.
CD _____ BIAS 270CD
Play It Again Sam / Sep '94 / Vital.

Holy Joy

MANIC, MAGIC AND MAJESTIC (Band Of Holy Joy)
Bride / What the Moon saw / Blessed boy / Baubles, bangles, emotional tangles / Manic, magic, majestic / You're not singing anymore / Route to love
CD _____ ROUGHCD 125
Rough Trade / Jan '89 / Pinnacle.

POSITIVELY SPOOKED (Band Of Holy Joy)
CD _____ ROUGHCD 155
Rough Trade / Mar '90 / Pinnacle.

TRACKSUIT VENDETTA, A
CD _____ EQCD 004
Ecuador / Jun '92 / Vital.

Holy Moses

NO MATTER WHAT'S THE CAUSE
CD _____ SPV 8476862
SPV / Oct '94 / Plastic Head.

WORLD CHAOS
CD _____ 845700
SPV / Jul '90 / Plastic Head.

Holy Terror

MIND WARS
CD _____ CDFLAG 25
Under One Flag / Oct '88 / Pinnacle.

Holzman, Adam

ADAM HOLZMAN
CD _____ LIP 890332
Lipstick / Oct '95 / Vital/SAM.

Hom Bru

ROWIN FAULA DOON
CD _____ CDLDL 1230
Lochshore / Jul '95 / ADA / Direct / Duncans.

Home

ALCHEMIST, THE
School days / Old man dying / Time passes by / Old man calling (save the people) / Disaster / Sun's revenge / Secret to keep / Brass band played / Rejoicing / Disaster return (Devastation) / Death of the alchemist / Alchemist
CD _____ 4809712
Columbia / Aug '95 / Sony.

Home Bru

ROWIN FOULA DOON
CD _____ LDL 1230C
Klub / Jul '95 / CM / Ross / Duncans / ADA / Direct.

Home Service

WILD LIFE
CD _____ FLED 3001
Fledg'ling / Apr '95 / CM / ADA / Direct.

Homesick James

BLUES ON THE SOUTHSIDE
CD _____ OBCCD 529
Original Blues Classics / Nov '92 / Complete/Pinnacle / Wellard / Cadillac.

GOT TO MOVE
Can't afford to do it / Tin pan alley / Mr. Pawnshop man / Crossroad blues / Baby, please set a date / Welfare girl / Hawaiian boogie / Dust my broom / That's all right / Highway / Tennessee woman / Got to move / Bein' with the one you love (lost lover blues) / Homesick's woman / Homesick talking
CD _____ TRIX 3320
Trix / Mar '95 / New Note.

JUANITA
CD _____ AP 097
Appaloosa / Oct '95 / ADA / Magnum Music Group.

Hone, Ged

SMOOTH SAILING
CD _____ LACD 52
Lake / Aug '95 / Target/BMG / Jazz Music / Direct / Cadillac / ADA.

THROWING STONES AT THE SUN (Hone, Ged & New Orleans Boys)
Smile darn you smile / Montmartre / Africa blues / Throwing stones at the sun / Tuxedo rag / Maple leaf rag / Ella Speed / I can't sleep / Streamline train / Sobbin' blues / Japansy / Blue blood blues / West End blues / Smiling the blues away / I've got a feeling I'm falling in love / Ukelele lady / Climax rag
CD _____ LACD 28
Lake / Jun '93 / Target/BMG / Jazz Music / Direct / Cadillac / ADA.

Honey Boy

LOVE YOU TONIGHT
CD _____ RNCD 2123
Rhino / Nov '95 / Jetstar / Magnum Music Group / THE.

Honey Boy Hickling

STRAIGHT FROM THE HARP
CD _____ CMMR 943
Music Masters / Feb '95 / Target/BMG.

Honey Cone

ARE YOU MAN ENOUGH
CD _____ HDHCD 507
HDH / Nov '91 / Pinnacle.

Honey Drippers

HONEY DRIPPERS - VOLUME 1
I get a thrill / Sea of love / I got a woman / Young boy blues / Rockin' at midnight
CD _____ 7567902202
East West / Feb '94 / Warner Music.

Honey Tongue

NUDE NUDES
CD _____ AMUSE 012CD
Playtime / Mar '95 / Pinnacle / Discovery.

Honeybus

AT THEIR BEST
Story / Fresher than the sweetness in water / Ceilings No. 1 / She said yes / I can't let Maggie go / Right to choose / Delighted to see you / Tender are the ashes / She sold Blackpool rock / Black mourning band / He was Columbus / Under the silent tree / I

remember Caroline / Julie in my heart / Do I still figure in your life / Would you believe / How long
CD _____ SEECD 264
See For Miles/C5 / Aug '89 / Pinnacle.

Honeycombs

ALL SYSTEMS GO
CD _____ REP 4121-WZ
Repertoire / Aug '91 / Pinnacle / Cadillac.

HONEYCOMBS
CD _____ REP 4098-WZ
Repertoire / Aug '91 / Pinnacle / Cadillac.

HONEYCOMBS, THE
Have I the right / Can't get through to you / I want to be free / Leslie Anne / Colour slide / This year, Next year / That loving feeling / That's the way / It ain't necessarily so / How the mighty have fallen / I'll cry tomorrow / I'll see you tomorrow / Is it because / She's too way out / Something better beginning / Eyes / Just a face in the crowd / Since while it lasted / It's so hard / I can't stop / Don't love her no more / All systems go / Totem pole (instrumental) / Emptiness / Oooee tram / She ain't coming back / Something I got to tell you / Nobody but me / There's always me / Love in Tokyo
CD _____ CDEMS 1475
EMI / May '87 / EMI.

LIVE IN TOKYO
CD _____ REP 4180-WZ
Repertoire / Aug '91 / Pinnacle / Cadillac.

Hong Kong Philharmonic

COLOURFUL CLOUDS
CD _____ 8.240102
Impetus / '88 / CM / Wellard / Impetus / Cadillac.

EVERLASTING LOVE
CD _____ 8.240171
Impetus / '88 / CM / Wellard / Impetus / Cadillac.

PLAY THE MOST FAMOUS TV THEMES
CD _____ 8.240 149
Impetus / '88 / CM / Wellard / Impetus / Cadillac.

UNDER THE SILVER MOON
CD _____ 8.240279
Impetus / '88 / CM / Wellard / Impetus / Cadillac.

Honky

EGO HAS LANDED, THE
Who am I / Love thy neighbor / Hold it / Chains / Whistler / Supertight love / Honky doodle day / Stormy weather / Eazee street / KKK / Karaoke Joe / Eleven brides of Frankenstein / Wha ga do / Oranges and lemons / Goodnight from him
CD _____ 450995455-2
WEA / Mar '94 / Warner Music.

Honolulu Mountain...

ALOHA SAYONARA (Honolulu Mountain Daffodils)
Avenues and alleyways / Hurricane Marilyn / Electronic alcoholic / Drug dog girl / Rhine women and song / Farenheit 192 / Grungeda / Stigmata non starter / Psychic hitlists victim no.8 / Slaughterhouse blues / Chien d'enfer / Celestial siren / Song of the wind surgeons / Aloha seyonara / Kramer versus Williamson / Bathtime for beelzebub / Free men of mauna loa
CD _____ MISSCD 1991
Mission Discs / Aug '93 / Pinnacle.

GUITARS OF THE OCEANIC UNDERGROWTH/TEQUILA DEMENTIA (Honolulu Mountain Daffodils)
Hanging on the crosses (by the side of the road) / Wolverine / Electrified sons of Randy Alvev / Guitars of the oceanic undergrowth / Sinner's club / Black car drives south / El muerto / Final solution / Disturbo charger (I feel like a) Francis Bacon painting / Mule brain / Collector of souls / Also sprach Scott Thurston / Death bed bimbo / Menace in the front / Tequila dementia
CD _____ MISSCD 1992
Mission Discs / Aug '93 / Pinnacle.

Hood, Robert

NIGHTMARE WORLD VOL.1
CD _____ CHEAPCD 25
Cheap / Oct '95 / Plastic Head.

Hoodlum Priest

BENEATH THE PAVEMENT
Beneath the pavement
CD _____ CPRODCD 25
Concrete Productions / May '94 / Plastic Head.

Hoodoo Gurus

CRANK
Right time / Crossed wires / Quo vadis / Nobody / Form a circle / Fading slow / Gospel train / Less than a feeling / You open my eyes / Hypocrite blues / I see you / Judgement day / Mountain

---

CD _____ LD 9453CD
LD / Sep '94 / Vital.

Hooka Hey

FURY IN THE SLAUGHTERHOUSE
CD _____ 0888402
SPV / May '91 / Plastic Head.

Hooker, Earl

PLAY YOUR GUITAR, MR.HOOKER
CD _____ BT 1093CD
Black Top / Aug '93 / CM / Direct / ADA.

SWEET BLACK ANGEL
CD _____ MCAD 22120
One Way / May '94 / Direct / ADA.

TWO BUGS AND A ROACH
CD _____ ARHCD 324
Arhoolie / Apr '95 / ADA / Direct / Cadillac.

Hooker, John Lee

1948-1949
Morning blues / Boogie awhile / Tuesday evening / Miss Pearl boogie / Good business / Mercy blues / Poor Slim / We gonna make / Low down boogie / Cotton pickin' boogie / Must I make / Roll me baby / I've been down so long / Christmas time blues
CD Set _____ KKCD 05
Krazy Kat / Oct '90 / Hot Shot / CM.

ALONE
CD _____ 269 660 2
Tomato / Mar '90 / Vital.

BEST OF JOHN LEE HOOKER
CD _____ GNPD-10007
GNP Crescendo / Jan '88 / Silva Screen.

BEST OF JOHN LEE HOOKER 1965-1974, THE
CD _____ MCAD 10539
MCA / May '93 / BMG.

BEST OF JOHN LEE HOOKER, THE
I'm in the mood / Boogie chillun / Serves me right to suffer / This is hip / House rent boogie / I'm so excited / I love you honey / Hobo blues / Crawlin' kingsnake / Maudie / Dimples / Boom boom / Louise / Ground hog blues / Ramblin' by myself / Walkin' the boogie / One bourbon, one scotch, one beer / Sugar mama / Peace lovin' man / Leave my wife alone / Blues before sunrise / Time is marching
CD _____ MCCD 020
Music Club / Jun '91 / Disc / THE / CM.

BLUES BEFORE SUNRISE
CD _____ TKOCD 006
TKO / '92 / TKO.

BLUES BROTHER
Boogie chillun / Rollin' blues / I need lovin' / Grinder man / Women in my life / My baby's got something / Momma poppa boogie / Sailing blues / Graveyard blues / Huckle up baby / Alberta / Three long years today / Do my baby think of me / Burnin' hell / Goin' on highway / Sail on little girl, sail on / Alberta No.2 / Find me a woman / Hastings street boogie / Canal street blues / War is over (Goodbye California) / Henry's swing club
CD _____ CDCHD 405
Ace / Nov '93 / Pinnacle / Cadillac / Complete/Pinnacle.

BLUES FOR BIG TOWN (Charly Blues - Masterworks Vol. 38)
Blues before sunrise / Hey boogie / Just me and my telephone / Dreamin' blues / Walkin' the boogie / I don't want your money / Hey baby / Journey / Bluebird / Apologise / Lonely boy boogie / Please don't go / Worried life blues / Blues for big town / Big fine woman / Blues for Christmas
CD _____ CDBM 38
Charly / Jan '93 / Charly / THE / Cadillac.

BOOGIE CHILLUN
Tupelo / Boogie chillun / Dimples / Drug store woman / Boom boom / Frisco blues / No shoe / I'm in the mood / Hobo blues / Baby Lee / Trouble blues / Old time shimmy / Little wheel / Whiskey and wimmen / Process / Dusty road / Send me your pillow / I'm so excited / Onions / Good rockin' mama / Thelma / Keep your hands to yourself / What do you say / Lost a good girl / Let's make it / Hard hearted woman / I'm going upstairs / I'm leaving baby
CD _____ CDGRF 023
Tring / '93 / Tring / Prism.

BOOGIE CHILLUN
Dimples / Every night / Little wheel / You can lead me baby / I love you honey / Maudie / I'm in the mood / Boogie chillun / Hobo blues / Crawlin' kingsnake / Drive me away / Solid sender / No shoes / Want ad blues / Will the circle be unbroken / I'm goin' upstairs / Boom boom / Bottle up and go / This is hip / Big legs, tight skirt / Serves me right to suffer / Your baby ain't sweet like mine
CD _____ CD 52003
Blues Encore / '92 / Target/BMG.

BOOGIE MAN, THE
Boom boom / Dirty groundhog / I'm goin' home / I love you honey / I'm in the mood / Crawling black spider / House rent boogie

---

/ Dimples / Mambo chillun / This is hip / I'm so excited / Hobo blues / Loudella / She shot me down
CD _____ CDINS 5009
Instant / Aug '89 / Charly.

BOOGIE MAN, THE (4CD Set)
CD _____ CDDIG 5
Charly / Feb '95 / Charly / THE / Cadillac.

BOOM BOOM
Boom boom / I'm bad like Jesse James / Same old blues again / Sugar Mama / Trick bag / Boogie at Russian hill / Hittin' the bottle again / Bottle up and go / Thought I heard / I ain't gonna suffer no more / Hobo blues / I want to hug you / House rent boogie / Want ad blues / I'm so excited / Hard headed woman / I wanna walk / Onions / What do you say / She shot me down / Keep your hands to yourself / Dusty road / Send me your pillow / I want to shout / I'm leaving baby
CD _____ VPBCD 7
Pointblank / Oct '92 / EMI.

BOOM BOOM
Boom boom / Proces / Lost a good girl / New leaf / Blues before sunrise / Let's make it / I got a letter this morning / Thelma / House rent boogie / Keep your hands to yourself / What do you say / Big legs, tight skirt / Everybody rockin' / Onions / Wheel and deal / Sadie Mae
CD _____ CDCD 1038
Charly / Mar '93 / Charly / THE / Cadillac.

BOOM BOOM
Prestige / May '93 / Total/BMG.
CD _____ CDSGP 066

BOOM BOOM
CD _____ 12333
Laserlight / May '94 / Target/BMG.

BOOM BOOM
Boom boom / Send me your pillow / Good rockin' Mama / I'm so excited / Dimples / Old time shimmy / Baby Lee / No shoes / Dusty road / Onions
CD _____ 16219CD
Success / Sep '94 / Carlton Home Entertainment.

BOSS, THE
CD _____ MATCD 320
Castle / Oct '94 / BMG.

BURNIN' HELL
Burning hell / Graveyard blues / Baby, please don't go / Jackson, Tennessee / You live your life and I'll live mine / Newstack lightnin' / How can you do it / I don't want no woman if her hair ain't longer than mine / I rolled and turned and cried the whole night long / Blues for my baby / Key to the highway / Natchez fire
CD _____ OBCCD 555
Original Blues Classics / Feb '93 / Complete/Pinnacle / Wellard / Cadillac.

CHILL OUT
Chill out (things gonna change) / Deep blue sea / Kiddio / Medley: Serves me right to suffer/Syndicator / One bourbon, one scotch, one beer / Tupelo / Woman on my mind / Annie Mae / Too young / Talkin' the blues / If you've never been in love / We'll meet again
CD _____ VPBCD 22
Virgin / Feb '95 / EMI.

COLLECTION: JOHN LEE HOOKER (20 Blues Greats)
Dimples / I'm in the mood / Hobo blues / Boogie chillun / Boom boom / Blues before sunrise / Time is marching / Tupelo / Little wheel / Shake, holler and run / Want ad blues / Crawlin' kingsnake / Whisky and wimmen / Tease me baby / Wednesday evenin' blues / My first wife left me / Maudie / No shoes / I love you honey / Rock house boogie
CD _____ CCSCD 410
Castle / Feb '95 / BMG.

COUNTRY BLUES OF JOHN LEE HOOKER
Black snake / How long blues / Wobblin' baby / She's long, she's tall, she weeps like a willow / Pea vine special / Tupelo blues / I'm prison bound / I rowed a little boat / Waterboy / Church bell tone / Bundle up and go / Good morning little school girl / Behind the plow
CD _____ OBCCD 542
Original Blues Classics / Nov '92 / Complete/Pinnacle / Wellard / Cadillac.

CRAWLING KINGSNAKE 1948-52
CD _____ OCD 103
Opal / Nov '95 / ADA.

DETROIT BLUES 1950-1951
House rent boogie / Wandering blues / Making a fool out of me / Questionnaire blues / Real gone gal / Squeeze me baby / Feed her all night / Gangsters blues / Where did you stay last night / My daddy was a jockey / Little boy blue / How long must I be your slave / Grieving blues / Ground hog blues / Mean old train / Catfish
CD _____ FLYCD 23
Flyright / Oct '90 / Hot Shot / Wellard / Jazz Music / CM.

DETROIT LION, THE
House rent boogie / I'm in the mood / Baby how can you do it / Let's talk it over / Yes, baby, baby, baby / I got the key / Four women in my life / Do my baby think of me / I'm gonna git me a woman / It hurts me so / Bluebird, bluebird, take a letter down South / Boogie chillun / Hello baby / This is 19 and 52, babe / Blues for Abraham Lincoln / Hey
CD _____ FIENDCD 154
Demon / Feb '90 / Pinnacle / ADA.

DIMPLES
CD _____ CDCD 1144
Charly / Mar '93 / Charly / THE / Cadillac.

DON'T YOU REMEMBER ME?
Stomp boogie / Blues been jivin' you / Hobo man blues / Poor Joe / Nightmare blues / Late last night / Wandering blues / Don't go baby / Devil's jump / I'm gonna kill that woman / Moaning blues / Numbers / Heart trouble blues / Slim's stomp / Thinking blues / Don't you remember me
CD _____ CDCHARLY 245
Charly / Oct '90 / Charly / THE / Cadillac.

E.P. COLLECTION, THE
Madman blues / You know, I know / Leave my wife alone / Down at the landing / Ground hog blues / High priced woman / Love blues / Union Station blues / Louise / One bourbon, one scotch, and one beer / Just me and my telephone / Apologise / Worried life blues / Journey / I don't want your money / Lonely boy boogie / Ramblin' by myself / Sugar Mama / It's my own fault / Women and money / Walking the boogie / Stella Mae / Let's go out tonight / Baby, please don't go
CD _____ SEECD 402
See For Miles/C5 / Jul '94 / Pinnacle.

ENDLESS BOOGIE
(I got) a good 'un / Pots on, gas on high / Kick hit / I don't need no stream heat / We might as well call it through (I didn't get married) / Sittin' in my dark room / Endless boogie parts 27 and 28
CD _____ BGOCD 70
Beat Goes On / '89 / Pinnacle.

EVERYBODY'S BLUES
Do my baby think of me / Three long years today / Strike blues / Grinder man / Walkin' this highway / Four women in my life / I need lovin' / Find me a woman / I'm mad / I been done so wrong / Boogie rambler / I keep the blues / No more doggin' (aka no more foolin') / Everybody's blues / Anybody's blues / Locked up in jail / Nothin' but trouble (don't take your wife's family in) / I need love so bad / I had a good girl / Odds against me (aka backbiters and syndicators)
CD _____ CDCHD 474
Ace / Jun '93 / Pinnacle / Cadillac / Complete/Pinnacle.

FOLK BLUES OF JOHN LEE HOOKER, THE
Black snake / How long blues / Wobblin' baby / She's long, she's tall, she weeps like a willow / Pea vine special / Tupelo blues / I'm prison bound / I rowed a little boat / Waterboy / Church bell tone / Bundle up and go / Good morning little school girl / Behind the plow
CD _____ CDCH 282
Ace / Nov '93 / Pinnacle / Cadillac / Complete/Pinnacle.

FREE BEER AND CHICKEN
Make it funky / Five long years / 713 blues / 714 blues / One bourbon, one scotch, one beer / Bluebird / Sittin' on top of the world / I'll never amount to anything / If you don't go to) College / I know how to rock / Nothin' but the best / Scratch
CD _____ BGOCD 123
Beat Goes On / Sep '91 / Pinnacle.

GET BACK HOME
CD _____ ECD 260042
Evidence / Jan '92 / Harmonia Mundi / ADA / Cadillac.

GOLD COLLECTION, THE
CD _____ D2CD07
Recording Arts / Dec '92 / THE / Disc.

GRAVEYARD BLUES
War is over (Goodbye California) / Henry's swing club / Alberta / Street boogie / Build myself a cave / Momma poppa boogie / Graveyard blues / Burnin' hell / Sailing blues / Black cat blues / Miss Sadie Mae / Canal street blues / Huckle up baby / Goin' down highway / Sail on little girl, sail on / My baby's got something / Boogie chillun no. 2 / Twenty one boggie / Rollin' blues
CD _____ CDCHD 421
Ace / Sep '92 / Pinnacle / Cadillac / Complete/Pinnacle.

HEALER, THE
Healer / I'm in the mood / Baby Lee / Cuttin' out / Think twice before you go / Sally Mae / That's alright / Rockin' chair / My dream / No substitute
CD _____ ORECD 508
Silvertone / Oct '89 / Pinnacle.

HOOKER SINGS THE BLUES
CD _____ OBCCD 538
Original Blues Classics / Nov '92 / Complete/Pinnacle / Wellard / Cadillac.

I WANNA DANCE ALL NIGHT
CD _____ 500512
Musidisc / Oct '93 / Vital / Harmonia
Mundi / ADA / Cadillac / Discovery.

I'M IN THE MOOD
Baby Lee / Dimples / Blues before sunrise
/ I'm goin' upstairs / Thelma / I'm in the
mood / Let's make it / Whiskey and wimmen / No shoes / Crawlin' kingsnake / Old
time shimmy / Little wheel / Process / Good
rockin' mama / When my first wife left me
CD _____ CDSGP 027
Prestige / May '93 / Total/BMG.

JOHN LEE HOOKER (2CD Set)
CD Set _____ R2CD 4007
Deja Vu / Jan '96 / THE.

JOHN LEE HOOKER BOXSET (3CD Set)
Dusty road / My first wife left me / Maudie
/ Time is marching / Hug and squeeze /
Blue before sunrise / Run on / That's my
story / I wanna walk / Wenesday evening
blues / You're leavin' me baby / I'm a
stranger / Old time shimmy / No more doggin' / Solid sender / Syndicator / Tupelo /
House rent boogie / Mama, you got a
daughter / Tease me baby / Ground hog
blues / Leave me alone / Dimples / Boom
boom / Bottle up and go / Cry before I go
/ Back biter and syndicaters / Think twice
before you go / I'm in the mood / Little
wheel / Want ad blues / Whiskey and winmen / Crawling king snake / Sugar Mama /
Hobo blues / Baby Lee / I love you baby /
Hobo blues / I'm so excited / She left me
on bended knee / Process / Good rockin'
Mama / No shoes / Send me the pillow you
dream on / Onions / Frisco / Drug store
woman / Let your Daddy ride / Don't you
remember me / Boogie chillen
CD Set _____ KBOX 345
Collection / Nov '95 / Target/BMG.

**JOHN LEE HOOKER COLLECTOR'S
EDITION**
CD _____ DVBC 9012
Deja Vu / Apr '95 / THE.

JOHN LEE HOOKER LIVE
CD _____ 269 602 2
Tomato / May '88 / Vital.

LEGENDARY HITS
CD _____ 90151-2
Jazz Archives / Oct '92 / Jazz Music /
Discovery / Cadillac.

**LEGENDARY MODERN RECORDINGS
1948-1954, THE**
Boogie chillun / Sally Mae / Hoogie boogie
/ Hobo blues / Weeping willow boogie /
Drifting from door to door / Crawlin' kings-
nake / Women in my life / Howlin' Wolf /
Playing the races / Let your Daddy ride /
Queen bee / Wednesday evenin' blues / I'm
in the mood / Tease me baby / Turn over a
new leaf / Rock house boogie / Too much
boogie / Need somebody / Gotta boogie /
Jump me up one more time / Down child /
Bad boy / Please take me back
CD _____ CDCHD 315
Ace / Apr '93 / Pinnacle / Cadillac / Com-
plete/Pinnacle.

LIVE AT CAFE AU GO GO
I'm bad like Jesse James / She's long,
she's tall, she weeps like a willow / When
my first wife left me / Heartaches and misery / One bourbon, one scotch, and one
beer / I don't want no trouble / I'll never get
out of these blues alive / Seven days
CD _____ BGOCD 39
Beat Goes On / Oct '88 / Pinnacle.

LIVE AT SUGARHILL VOL 1 & 2
I can't hold on much longer / Key to the
highway / My babe / You been dealin' with
the devil / Money / Run on / Matchbox /
Night time is the right time / Boogie chillun
/ I'm gonna keep on walking / T.B. is killing
me / This world (no man's land) / I like to
see you walk / It's you I love, baby / Driftin'
and driftin' / You're gonna miss me / You're
nice and kind to me Lou Della / I want to
get married
CD _____ CDCHD 938
Ace / Nov '93 / Pinnacle / Cadillac / Com-
plete/Pinnacle.

LONDON SESSIONS 1965
I don't want nobody else / Storming on the
deep blue sea / I'm losing you / Go back to
school, little girl / Don't be messing with my
bread / Mary Lee / I cover the waterfront /
Crazy mixed up world / Seven days / Little
dreamer / Lost everything
CD _____ NEBCD 657
Sequel / Jul '93 / BMG.

**MAMBO CHILLUN (Charly Blues -
Masterworks Vol 19)**
Mambo chillun / Wheel and deal / Unfriendly woman / Time is marching / I'm so
married baby / Baby Lee / Road is so rough
/ Trouble blues / Stop talking / Everybody
rockin' / I'm so excited / I see you when
you're weak / Crawlin' black spider / Little
fine woman / Rosie Mae / You can lead me
baby
CD _____ CDBM 19
Charly / Apr '92 / Charly / THE / Cadillac.

MR. LUCKY
I want to hug you / Mr. Lucky / Backstabbers / This is hip / I cover the waterfront /

Highway 13 / Stripped me naked / Susie /
Crawlin' kingsnake / Father was a jockey
CD _____ ORECD 519
Silvertone / Aug '91 / Pinnacle.

NOTHING BUT THE BLUES
I feel good / Baby baby / Dazie May / Stand
by / Call it the night / Going home / We are
cooking / Lookin' over my day / Roll
and tumble / Bottle of wine / Baby don't do
me wrong
CD _____ CDBM 070
Blue Moon / Apr '91 / Magnum Music
Group / Greensleeves / Hot Shot / ADA /
Cadillac / Discovery.

ORIGINAL FOLK BLUES...PLUS
Boogie chillun / Queen bee / Crawling king
snake / Weeping willow boogie / Whistlin'
and moanin' blues / Sally Mae / I need love
so bad / Let's talk it over / Syndicator / Let
your Daddy ride / Drifting from door to door
/ Baby, I'm gonna miss you / Cold chills /
Cool little car / I wonder little darling / Jump
me one more time / Lookin' for a woman /
Ride till I die
CD _____ CDCHM 530
Ace / Feb '94 / Pinnacle / Cadillac / Com-
plete/Pinnacle.

ORIGINAL MR LUCKY, THE
TB is killing me / Motor city is burning / Tu-
pelo / One of these days
CD _____ CD 52024
Blues Encore / Aug '92 / Target/BMG.

REAL FOLK BLUES
Let's go out tonight / Peace lovin' man /
Stella Mae / I put my trust in you / I'm in
the mood / You know, I know / I'll never
trust your love again / One bourbon, one
scotch, one beer / Waterfront
CD _____ CHLD 19097
Chess/MCA / Nov '91 / BMG / New Note.

RISING SUN COLLECTION
CD _____ RSCD 001
Just A Memory / Apr '94 / Harmonia
Mundi.

SAD AND LONESOME
I bought you a brand new home / I believe
I'll lose my mind / Teasin' me / My cryin'
days are over / Sittin' here thinkin' / Mean
mistreatin' / How long / How many more
years / C.C. rider / Sad and lonesome /
Can't you see what you're doing to me /
When my wife quit me
CD _____ MCD 6009
Muse / Feb '91 / New Note / CM.

**SHAKE IT BABY (Charly Blues -
Masterworks Vol. 45)**
CD _____ CDBM 45
Charly / Jun '93 / Charly / THE / Cadillac.

SIMPLY THE TRUTH
I don't wanna go to Vietnam / I wanna boo-
galoo / Tantalizing with the blues / I'm just
a drifter / Mini skirts / Mean mean woman /
One room country shack
CD _____ MCAD 22136
One Way / Oct '94 / Direct / ADA.

TANTALIZING WITH THE BLUES
Serves me right to suffer / Shake it up baby
/ Bottle up and go / Cry before I go / Back-
biters and syndicators / Think twice before
you go / I don't wanna go to Vietnam / Mini
skirts / Mean mean woman / Tantalizing
with the blues / I'm just a drifter / Kick hit /
I'll never get out of these blues alive
CD _____ MCLD 19033
MCA / Apr '92 / BMG.

THAT'S MY STORY (NYC 1960)
CD _____ CDCH 260
Ace / Nov '93 / Pinnacle / Cadillac /
Complete/Pinnacle.

**THAT'S MY STORY/ FOLK BLUES OF
JOHN LEE HOOKER**
I need some money / I'm wanderin' / Demo-
crat man / I want to talk about you / Gonna
use my rod / Wednesday evenin' blues / No
more doggin' / One of these days / I believe
I'll go back home / You're leavin' me, baby
/ That's my story / Black snake / How long
blues / Wobblin' baby / She's long, she's
tall, she weeps like a willow / Pea vine spe-
cial / Tupelo blues / I rowed a little boat /
Waterbory / Church bell tone / Bundle up
and go
CD _____ CDCH 927
Ace / '90 / Pinnacle / Cadillac / Complete/
Pinnacle.

THAT'S WHERE IT'S AT
CD _____ CDSXE 064
Stax / Jul '92 / Pinnacle.

**THIS IS HIP (Charly Blues -
Masterworks Vol. 7)**
Dimples / Every night / Little wheel / Maudie
/ I'm in the mood / Boogie chillun / Hobo
blues / Crawlin' kingsnake / Solid sender /
Will the circle be unbroken / Boom boom /
This is hip / Big legs, tight skirt / Serves me
right to suffer
CD _____ CD BM 7
Charly / Apr '92 / Charly / THE / Cadillac.

**TWO ON ONE: JOHN LEE HOOKER &
MUDDY WATERS (Hooker, John Lee &
Muddy Waters)**
CD _____ CDTT 3
Charly / Apr '94 / Charly / THE / Cadillac.

URBAN BLUES
Cry before I go / Boom boom / Backbiters
and syndicators / Mr. Lucky / My own blues
/ I can't stand to leave you / Think twice
before you go / I'm standing in line / Hot
spring water (pts 1 & 2) / Motor city is burning / Want ad blues
CD _____ BGOCD 122
Beat Goes On / Sep '91 / Pinnacle.

VEE JAY YEARS 1955-1964 (6CD Set)
Unfriendly woman / Wheel and deal /
Mambo chillun / Time is marching / I'm so
worried baby / Baby Lee / Dimples / Every
night / Road is so rough / Trouble blues /
Stop talking / Everybody rockin' / I'm so ex-
cited / I can see you when you're weak /
Crawlin' black spider / Little find woman /
Rose Mae / You can lead me baby / I love
you honey / You've taken my woman /
Mama / You got a daughter / Nightmare /
House rent boogie / Trying to find a woman
/ Drive me away / I'm goin' home / Love me
all the time / Lou della / Bundle up and go
/ Wrong doin' woman / Maudie / Tennessee
blues / I'm in the mood / Boogie chillun /
Hobo blues / Crawlin' kingsnake / I wanna
talk / Canal street blues / I'll know tonight /
I can't believe / Goin' to California / Whiskey
and winmen / Run on / Solid sender / Sunnyland / Dusty road / I'm a stranger / No
shoes / Five long years / I like to see you
walk / Wednesday evenin' blues / Take me
as I am / My first wife left me / You're looking good to me / You're gonna miss me
when I'm gone / Dirty groundhog / She
loves my best friend / Sally Mae / Moanin'
blues / Hobo / Tupelo / Want ad blues / Will
the circle be unbroken / I'm goin' upstairs /
I left my baby / Hard headed woman / I'm
mad again / Process / Thelma / What do
you say / Boom boom / Blues before sunrise / I lost a good girl / She's mine / I got
a letter this morning / New leaf / Let's make
it / Drug store woman / Old time shimmy /
Onions / You know I love you / Send me
your pillow / Big soul / Frisco blues / She
shot me down / Take a look at yourself /
Good rockin' mama / I love her / No one
told me / Don't look back / One way ticket
/ Half a stranger / Bottle up and go / My
grinding mill / I want to ramble / Sadie Mae
/ This is hip / Poor me / I want to shout /
Love is a burning thing / I want to hug you
/ I'm leaving baby / Birmingham blues / I
can't quit you now blues / Stop talking /
Don't hold me / Bus station blues / Freight
train to my friend / Talk that talk baby /
Sometimes baby you make me feel so bad
/ You've got to walk yourself / Might fine /
Big legs / Tight skirt / Flowers on the hour
/ Serves me right to suffer / It ain't no big
thing / She left me one Wednesday / You
can run / Your baby ain't sweet like mine /
She's long / She's tall / You're the right
CD Set _____ CDREDBOX 6
Charly / Dec '92 / Charly / THE / Cadillac.

VERY BEST OF JOHN LEE HOOKER
Boom boom / Shake it baby / Right time /
Dimples / Boogie chillun / Mambo chillun /
Wheel and deal / I'm so excited / Trouble
blues / Everybody rockin' / Unfriendly
woman / Time is marching / I see you when
you're weak / I'm in the mood / Will the cir-
cle be unbroken / This is hip / Hobo blues
/ Solid sender
CD _____ 500432
Musidisc / May '93 / Vital / Harmonia Mundi
/ ADA / Cadillac / Discovery.

**VERY BEST OF JOHN LEE HOOKER,
THE (& Roots Of The Blues #1
Compilation/3CD Set)**
High priced woman / Leave my wife alone
/ Ramblin' by myself / Walkin' the boogie /
Love blues / Please don't go / Down at the
landing / Mambo chillun / Time is marchin'
/ Dimples / Every night / Crawlin' black spi-
der / I love you honey / House rent boogie
/ Trying to find a woman / Maudie / I'm in
the mood / Boogie Chillun / Hobo blues
crawlin' kingsnake / No shoes / Dirty
ground hog / Hobo blues (AKA the hobo) /
I'm goin' upstairs / I'm mad again / What
do you say / Boom boom / She's mine /
Drug store woman / You know I love you /
Send me your pillow / Don't look back / One
way ticket / Bottle up and go / This is hip /
Big legs / Tight skirt / It serves me right to
suffer / Stella Mae / One bourbon / One
scotch / One beer / Waterfront / Stack
O'Lee blues / 44 Blues / Divin' duck blues /
Gimme a pigfoot / Revenue man blues /
Sagefield woman blues / Old times blues /
Cross road blues / Harmonica blues / Ea-
syrider / Crawling king snake / Can't you
read / Bad acting women / Take a walk with
me / I got a break, baby
CD Set _____ VBCD 301
Charly / Jul '95 / Charly / THE / Cadillac.

WATERFRONT GROUNDHOG
CD _____ 3001072
Scratch / Jul '95 / BMG.

WHISKEY AND WOMEN
CD _____ IMP 301
Iris Music / Jul '95 / Discovery.

Hooker, William

ARMAGEDDON
CD _____ HMS 2232
Homestead / Aug '95 / SRD.

**ENVISIONING (Hooker, William & Lee
Ranaldo)**
CD _____ KFWCD 159
Knitting Factory / Feb '95 / Grapevine.

RADIATION
CD _____ HMS 2162
Homestead / Oct '94 / SRD.

**SHAMBALLA (Hooker, William &
Thurston Moore/Elliott Sharp)**
CD _____ KFWCD 151
Knitting Factory / Feb '95 / Grapevine.

Hooker, Zakiya

**ANOTHER GENERATION OF THE
BLUES**
CD _____ ORECD 526
Silvertone / Apr '93 / Pinnacle.

Hoopsnakes

JUMP IN AND HANG ON
CD _____ MPD 6002
Flying Fish / Nov '94 / Roots / CM / Direct
/ ADA.

Hoosier Hot Shots

ARE YOU READY, HEZZIE?
CD _____ CCD 905
Circle / Jan '94 / Jazz Music / Swift /
Wellard.

Hooters

NERVOUS NIGHT
We danced / Day by day / All you zombies
/ Don't take my car out tonight / Nervous
night / Hanging on a heartbeat / Where do
the children go / South ferry road / She
comes in colours / Blood from a stone
CD _____ 462485 2
Columbia / May '94 / Sony.

ONE WAY HOME
Satellite / Karla with a K / Graveyard waltz
/ Fightin' on the same side / One way home
/ Washington's day / Hard rockin' summer
/ Engine 999 / Johnny B.
CD _____ 4655642
Columbia / Apr '92 / Sony.

Hootie & The Blowfish

CRACKED REAR VIEW MIRROR
CD _____ 7567826132
Atlantic / Feb '95 / Warner Music.

Hope, Bob

BOB HOPE
CD _____ DVGH 7102
Deja Vu / May '95 / THE.

**BOB HOPE AND HIS CHRISTMAS
PARTY 1945**
CD _____ VJC 1031-2
Vintage Jazz Classics / '91 / Direct / ADA
/ CM / Cadillac.

Hope, Elmo

ALL STAR SESSIONS, THE
CD _____ MCD 47037
Milestone / Jun '95 / Jazz Music /
Pinnacle / Wellard / Cadillac.

Hope, Lynn

JUICY (Hope, Lynn & Clifford Scott)
Juicy / Blue and sentimental / Hang out /
Stardust / Oo wee / Tenderly / Shu-ee /
Very thought of you / Shockin' / Rose room
/ Cutie / Ghost of a chance / Little landslide
/ Full moon / Blue lady / Sands of the Sa-
hara / Fros-tee nite / Body and soul
CD _____ CDCHARLY 280
Charly / Oct '91 / Charly / THE / Cadillac.

Hopkin, Mary

EARTH SONG - OCEAN SONG
International / There's got to be more / Sil-
ver birch and weeping willow / How come
the sun / Earth song / Martha / Streets of
London / Wind / Water, paper and clay /
Ocean song
CD _____ CDP 7986952
Apple / Jun '92 / EMI.

POSTCARD
Those were the days / Lord of the reedy
river / Happiness runs (pebble and the man)
/ Love is the sweetest thing / Y blodyn gwyn
/ Honeymoon song / Puppy song / Inchworm / Voyage of the moon / Lullaby of the
leaves / Young love / Someone to watch
over me / Prince en avignon / Game / There's no business like show business / Turn
turn turn (to everything there is a) / Those
were the days (quelli erano giorni) / Those
were the days (en aquellos días)
CD _____ CDP 7975782
Apple / Oct '91 / EMI.

THOSE WERE THE DAYS
Those were the days / Goodbye / Temma
harbour / think about your children / Knock
knock who's there / Whatever will be will be
(Que sera sera) / Lontano degli occhi /
Sparrow / Heritage / Fields of St. Etienne /
Jefferson / Let my name be sorrow / Kew
Gardens / When I am old one day / Silver

birch / Streets of London / Water, paper and clay
CD _____ CDSAPCOR 23
Apple / Apr '95 / EMI.

Hopkins, Claude

CLAUDE HOPKINS 1932-33 & 1940 (Hopkins, Claude & His Orchestra)
CD _____ 3801042
Jazz Archives / Jun '92 / Jazz Music / Discovery / Cadillac.

CLAUDE HOPKINS 1932-34
CD _____ CLASSICS 699
Classics / Jul '93 / Discovery / Jazz Music.

CLAUDE HOPKINS 1934-35
CD _____ CLASSICS 716
Classics / Jul '93 / Discovery / Jazz Music.

CLAUDE HOPKINS 1937-40
CD _____ CLASSICS 733
Classics / Jan '94 / Discovery / Jazz Music.

MONKEY BUSINESS
Three little words / Margie / King Porter stomp / Monkey business / Mandy / Honey / Church Street / Sobbin' blues
CD _____ HEPCD 1031
Hep / Jul '93 / Cadillac / Jazz Music / New Note / Wellard.

SINGIN' IN THE RAIN (Hopkins, Claude & His Orchestra)
CD _____ 3801272
Jazz Archives / Oct '92 / Jazz Music / Discovery / Cadillac.

Hopkins, David

HEAR THE GRASS/ECHOES FROM THE WORLD OF BAMBOO
CD _____ SM 1082-2
Wergo / Jun '91 / Harmonia Mundi / ADA / Cadillac.

Hopkins, Lightnin'

1946-1960
CD _____ SOB 35242CD
Story Of The Blues / Apr '95 / Koch / ADA.

AUTOBIOGRAPHY IN BLUES
CD _____ TCD 1002
Rykodisc / Feb '96 / Vital / ADA.

BLUES IN MY BOTTLE
Buddy Brown's blues / Wine drinkin' spo-dee-o-dee / Sail on little girl, sail on / DC-7 / Death bells / Goin' to Dallas to see my pony run / Jailhouse blues / Blues in the bottle / Beans beans beans / Catfish blues / My grandpa is old too
CD _____ OBCCD 506
Original Blues Classics / Nov '92 / Complete/Pinnacle / Wellard / Cadillac.

BLUES IN MY BOTTLE/WALKIN' THIS ROAD BY MYSELF
Buddy Brown's blues / Wine drinkin' spo-dee-o-dee / Sail on little girl, sail on / D.C. 7 / Goin' to Dallas to see my pony run / Jailhouse blues / Blues in the bottle / Beans beans beans / Catfish blues / My grandpa is old too / Walkin' this road by myself / Black gal / How many more years I got to let you dog me around / Baby don't you tear my clothes / Worried life blues / Happy blues for John Glenn / Good morning little school girl / Devil jumped the black man / Coffee blues / Black Cadillac
CD _____ CDCHD 930
Ace / Mar '90 / Pinnacle / Cadillac / Complete/Pinnacle.

BLUES IS MY BUSINESS
CD _____ EDCD 353
Edsel / Apr '95 / Pinnacle / ADA.

CALIFORNIA MUDSLIDE (AND EARTHQUAKE)
California muslide / Rosie Mae / Los Angeles Blues / Easy on your heels / New Santa Fe / Jesus will you come by here / No education / Antoinette's blues / Change my way of living / Los Angeles boogie / Call on my baby
CD _____ CDCHM 546
Ace / Nov '94 / Pinnacle / Cadillac / Complete/Pinnacle.

COFFEE HOUSE BLUES (Charly Blues - Masterworks Vol.33)
Big car blues / Coffee house blues / Stool pigeon blues / Ball of twine / Mary Lou / Want to come home / Rolling and rolling / Devil is watching you / Please don't quit me / Coon is hard to catch / Heavy snow / Walking round in circles / War is starting again / Got me a Louisiana woman
CD _____ CDBM 33
Charly / Jan '93 / Charly / THE / Cadillac.

COLLECTION, THE
CD _____ COL 068
Collection / Feb '95 / Target/BMG.

COMPLETE PRESTIGE AND BLUESVILLE RECORDINGS, THE (7CD Set)
CD Set _____ 7PCD 4406
Prestige / Nov '91 / Complete/Pinnacle / Cadillac.

COUNTRY BLUES
CD _____ TCD 1003
Rykodisc / Feb '96 / Vital / ADA.

DOUBLE BLUES
Let's go sit on the lawn / I'm taking a devil man / Just a wristwatch on my arm / I woke up this morning / I was standing on 75 highway / I'm going to build me a heaven of my own / My babe / Too many drivers / I'm a crawling black snake / Rocky mountain blues / I mean goodbye / Howling wolf / Black ghost blues / Darling do you remember me / Lonesome graveyard
CD _____ CDCH 354
Ace / Nov '93 / Pinnacle / Cadillac / Complete/Pinnacle.

FOREVER 1981
CD _____ 157792
Blues Collection / Feb '93 / Discovery.

FREE FORM PATTERNS
Mr. Charlie / Give me time to think / Fox chase / Mr. Ditta's grocery store / Open up your door / Baby child / Cooking done / Got her letter this morning / Rain falling / Mini skirt
CD _____ CDCHARLY 294
Charly / Jul '95 / Charly / THE / Cadillac.

GOIN' BACK HOME
CD _____ CDSGP 090
Prestige / Nov '93 / Total/BMG.

GOLD STAR SESSIONS VOL.1
CD _____ ARHCD 330
Arhoolie / Apr '95 / ADA / Direct / Cadillac.

GOLD STAR SESSIONS VOL.2
CD _____ ARHCD 337
Arhoolie / Apr '95 / ADA / Direct / Cadillac.

HOOTIN' THE BLUES
CD _____ OBCCD 571
Original Blues Classics / Jul '95 / Complete/Pinnacle / Wellard / Cadillac.

HOW MANY MORE YEARS I GOT
How many more years I got to let you dog me around / Walkin' this road by myself / Devil jumped the black man / My baby don't start no cheatin' / Black cadillac / You is one black rat / Fox chase / Mojo hand / Mama blues / My black name / Prison farm blues / Ida Mae / I got a leak in this old building / Happy blues for John Glenn / Worried life blues / Sinner's prayer / Angel child / Pneumonia blues / Have you ever been mistreated
CD _____ CDCH 409
Ace / Nov '92 / Pinnacle / Cadillac / Complete/Pinnacle.

IN NEW YORK
CD _____ CCD 79010
Candid / Oct '93 / Cadillac / Jazz Music / Wellard / Koch.

KING OF DOWLING STREET
Mean old twister / L.A. Blues / Little Mama boogie / Woman, woman (change your ways) / Mistreated blues / Liquor drinking woman / Shotgun blues / Rolling blues / Nightmare blues / Lightnin's boogie (Sis boogie) / Morris is rising / Have to let you go / Come back baby / Short haired woman / Big Mama jump / Thinkin' and worryin'
CD _____ BGOCD 103
Beat Goes On / Sep '91 / Pinnacle.

LAST NIGHT BLUES (Hopkins, Lightnin' & Sonny Terry)
CD _____ OBCCD 548
Original Blues Classics / Nov '92 / Complete/Pinnacle / Wellard / Cadillac.

LIGHTNIN'
CD _____ ARHCD 390
Arhoolie / Apr '95 / ADA / Direct / Cadillac.

LIGHTNIN'
CD _____ OBCCD 342
Original Blues Classics / Nov '92 / Complete/Pinnacle / Wellard / Cadillac.

LIGHTNIN' HOPKINS
CD _____ CDSF 40019
Smithsonian Folkways / Aug '94 / ADA / Direct / Koch / CM / Cadillac.

LIGHTNIN' HOPKINS (1946-1960)
CD _____ SOB 35242
Story Of The Blues / Dec '92 / Koch / ADA.

LIGHTNIN' IN NEW YORK
Take it easy / Mighty crazy / Your own fault, baby, to treat me the way you do / I've had my fun / Trouble blues / Lightnin's piano boogie / Wonder why / Mr. Charlie
CD _____ CCD 9010
Candid / Sep '87 / Cadillac / Jazz Music / Wellard / Koch.

LIVE AT THE RISING SUN
CD _____ RS 0009CD
Rising Sun / Jul '95 / ADA.

LONESOME DOG BLUES
Lonesome dog blues / Glory be / Sometimes she will / Shine on moon / Santa / Have you ever loved a woman / Shake that thing / I'm leaving you now / Walk a long time / Bring me my shotgun / Just pickin' / Last night / Mojo hand / Coffee for mama / Awful dreams / Black mare trot
CD _____ CDGRF 060
Tring / '93 / Tring / Prism.

LONESOME LIFE
Rainy days in Houston / You just gotta miss me / Pine gum boogie / Wake up the dead / How does it / Got a letter this morning / Stinking foot / Walking and walking / Good old time religion / Born in the bottoms / Ballin' the Jack / World's in a tangle / Man like me is hard to find
CD _____ CDBM 093
Blue Moon / Jul '92 / Magnum Music Group / Greensleeves / Hot Shot / ADA / Cadillac / Discovery.

MORNING BLUES (Charly Blues - Masterworks Volume 8)
Found my baby crying / Letter to my (back door friend) / Fishing clothes / Morning blues / Gambler's blues / Wig wearing woman / Lonesome dog blues / Last affair / Lovin' arms / Rock me mama / Mr. Charlie (Part 1) / Mr. Charlie (Part 2) / Play with your poodle / You're too fast / Love me this morning / I'm coming home / Ride in your new automobile / Breakfast time
CD _____ CD BM 8
Charly / Apr '92 / Charly / THE / Cadillac.

NOTHIN' BUT THE BLUES
Blues in the bottle / Catfish blues / DC-7 / Death bells / Rock me baby / Shotgun
CD _____ CD 52023
Blues Encore / Aug '92 / Target/BMG.

PO' LIGHTNIN'
CD _____ ARHCD 403
Arhoolie / Apr '95 / ADA / Direct / Cadillac.

SHAKE THAT THING
CD _____ 422173
New Rose / May '94 / Direct / ADA.

SMOKES LIKE LIGHTNING
T model blues / Jackstropper blues / You cook alright / My black name / You never miss your water / Let's do the Susie-Q / Ida Mae / Smokes like lightning / Prison farm blues
CD _____ OBCCD 551
Original Blues Classics / Jan '96 / Complete/Pinnacle / Wellard / Cadillac.

SOUL BLUES
CD _____ OBCCD 540
Original Blues Classics / Nov '92 / Complete/Pinnacle / Wellard / Cadillac.

SWARTHMORE CONCERT
CD _____ OBCCD 563
Original Blues Classics / Jul '94 / Complete/Pinnacle / Wellard / Cadillac.

TEXAS BLUES MAN
Mojo hand / Cotton / Little wail / Hurricane Betsy / Take me back, baby / Really nothin' but the blues / Guitar lightnin' / Woke up this morning / Shake yourself / California showers / Goin' out / Tom Moore blues / I would if I could / At home blues / Watch my fingers / Bud Russell blues / Cut me out baby
CD _____ ARHCD 302
Arhoolie / Apr '95 / ADA / Direct / Cadillac.

TEXAS BLUES MAN
CD _____ CD 52005
Blues Encore / '92 / Target/BMG.

TEXAS COUNTRY BLUES (Hopkins, Lightnin' & Joel/John Henry)
CD _____ ARHCD 340
Arhoolie / Apr '95 / ADA / Direct / Cadillac.

Hopkins, Nicky

REVOLUTIONARY PIANO OF NICKY HOPKINS, THE
Mr. Big / Yesterday / Goldfinger / Don't get around much anymore / Jenni / Acapulco 1922 / You came a long way from St. Louis / Love letters / Unlonely bull / Satisfaction / Paris belles v the llejistry pig
CD _____ 4785022
Columbia / Feb '95 / Sony.

TIN MAN WAS A DREAMER, THE
Sundown in Mexico / Waiting for the band / Edward / Dolly / Speed on / Dreamer / Banana Anna / Lawyer's lament / Shout it out / Pigs boogie
CD _____ 4809692
Columbia / Aug '95 / Sony.

Hopkins, Rich

DIRT TOWN (Hopkins, Rich & Luminarios)
CD _____ OUT 118-2
Brake Out / Nov '94 / Vital.

Hopley, David

SEQUENCE SELECTION
CD _____ SAV 238CD
Savoy / Dec '95 / THE / Savoy.

Hoppe, Michael

QUIET STORMS
CD _____ 710 092
Innovative Communication / Apr '90 / Magnum Music Group.

Hopper, Kev

STOLEN JEWELS
CD _____ GHETTCD 4
Ghetto / May '90 / Sony.

Horde

HELLIG USVART
CD _____ NB 1282
Nuclear Blast / Mar '95 / Plastic Head.

Horiuchi, Glenn

OXNARD BEET
CD _____ 121228-2
Soul Note / Sep '92 / Harmonia Mundi / Wellard / Cadillac.

Horizon 222

3 OF SWANS
CD _____ CHARRMCD 18
Charrm / Mar '94 / Plastic Head.

THROUGH THE ROUND WINDOW
CD _____ HY 39100252
Hyperium / Mar '94 / Plastic Head.

Horlen, Johan

DANCE OF RESISTANCE
CD _____ DRCD 260
Dragon / Oct '95 / Roots / Cadillac / Wellard / CM / ADA.

Horler, John

LOST KEYS
I'm a fool to want you / Mood river / Abstract no.4 / Waltz / Blue in green / This is my lovely day / Lost keys / Re: Person I knew / Abstract no.2 / Mabel/Gentle peace
CD _____ CHECD 00109
Master Mix / Jun '94 / Wellard / Jazz Music / New Note.

QUIET PIECE
CD _____ SPJCD 542
Spotlite / May '93 / Cadillac / Jazz Horizons / Swift.

Horn, Jim

NEON LIGHTS
CD _____ 7599257282
WEA / Jan '96 / Warner Music.

WORK IT OUT
CD _____ 7599259112
WEA / Jan '96 / Warner Music.

Horn, Paul

CHINA
CD _____ CDKUCK 080
Kuckuck / Sep '87 / CM / ADA.

INSIDE THE CATHEDRAL
Song for friendship / Song for peace / Moscow blues / Song for love / Syrinx / Song for understanding / Song for Gagarin / Song for Edward / Song for Marina / Song for Riya / Oche chernouiye / Song for Rimsky / Song for Trane
CD _____ CDKUCK 075
Kuckuck / Feb '87 / CM / ADA.

INSIDE THE GREAT PYRAMID
Prologue / Inside / Mantra 1 / Meditation / Mutaz Mahal / Unity / Agra vibrations / Akasha / Jumma / Shah Jahan / Mantra II / Duality / Ustad Isa / Mantra III
CD Set _____ CDKUCK 060/061
Kuckuck / Feb '87 / CM / ADA.

INSIDE THE TAJ MAHAL
CD _____ CDKUCK 11062
Kuckuck / Nov '89 / CM / ADA.

PEACE ALBUM
CD _____ CDKUCK 11083-2
Kuckuck / Dec '88 / CM / ADA.

Horn, Shirley

HERE'S TO LIFE
Here's to life / Come a little closer / How am I to know / Time for love / Where do you start / You're nearer / Return to paradise / Isn't it a pity / Quietly there / If you love me (really love me) / Summer (Estate)
CD _____ 5118792
Verve / Jan '92 / PolyGram.

I LOVE YOU, PARIS
CD _____ 5234682
Verve / Dec '94 / PolyGram.

LIGHT OUT OF DARKNESS (A Tribute To Ray Charles)
CD _____ 519703-2
Verve / Feb '94 / PolyGram.

SOFTLY
CD Set _____ APCD 224
Audiophile / Apr '89 / Jazz Music / Swift.

YOU WON'T FORGET ME
Music that makes me dance / Come dance with me / Don't let the sun catch you crying / Beautiful love / Come back to me / Too late now / I just found out about love / It had to be you / Soothe me / Foolin myself / If you go / You stepped out of a dream / You won't forget me / All my tomorrows
CD _____ 847 482-2
Verve / May '91 / PolyGram.

Horne, Lena

ESSENTIAL LENA HORNE (Horne, Lena & Gabor Szabor)
CD _____ ATJCD 5958
All That's Jazz / Jun '92 / THE / Jazz Music.

FEELIN' WANNA
On a wonderful day like today / Take the moment / I wanna be around / Feelin' good / Who can I turn to / Less than a second / Willow weep for me / Girl from Ipanema / Softly as I leave you / And I love him / Hello young lovers / Moon river / I love Paris / Never on Sunday / Somewhere / It's a mad mad mad world / What the world needs now is love / Let the little people talk / I get along without you very well / It had better be tonight
CD _____ CDSL 8269
Music For Pleasure / Nov '95 / EMI.

LA SELECTION 1936-41
CD _____ 011
Art Vocal / Sep '93 / Discovery.

LADY IS A TRAMP, THE
CD _____ CDSGP 059
Prestige / Aug '93 / Total/BMG.

LENA
CD _____ CDPC 7900
Prestige / Aug '90 / Complete/Pinnacle / Cadillac.

LENA GOES LATIN
CD _____ CDMRS 510
DRG / '88 / New Note.

LENA GOES LATIN AND SINGS YOUR REQUESTS
CD _____ LDJ 274945
Radio Nights / Sep '92 / Harmonia Mundi / Cadillac.

SONG FOR YOU, A
CD _____ ATJCD 5962
All That's Jazz / Oct '92 / THE / Jazz Music.

SPOTLIGHT ON LENA HORNE
Close enough for love / Ours / Every time we say goodbye / Fine romance / Round about / September song / Joy / Eagle and me / When I fall in love / Look for the rainbow / It could happen to you / Sing my heart / Don't squeeze me / Whispering / Hesitating blues / Beale Street blues
CD _____ HADCD 129
Javelin / Feb '94 / THE / Henry Hadaway Organisation.

STORMY WEATHER
You're my thrill / Good for nothin' Joe / Love me a little little / Don't take your love from me / Stormy weather / What is this thing called love / Ill wind / Man I love / Where or when / I gotta right to sing the blues / Moanin' low / I didn't know about you / One for my baby / As long as I live / I ain't got nothin' but the blues / How long has this been going on / It's love / Let me love you / It's all right with me / People will say we're in love / Just in time / Get out of town
CD _____ CDCD 1084
Charly / Apr '93 / Charly / THE / Cadillac.

STORMY WEATHER
Stormy weather / Good for nothin' Joe / Diga diga doo / I can't give you anything but love / Mad about the boy / As long as I live / Deed I do / Once in a lifetime / Meantime / Silent spring / Slowin' in the wind / Best things in life are free / Lost in the stars / Now / Wouldn't it be lovely / More than you know / At long last love / Nobody knows the trouble I've seen / Blue prelude / Little girl blue / It's a rainy day / Frankie and Johnny / Lady is a tramp
CD _____ CDGRF 062
Tring / '93 / Tring / Prism.

Horne, Marilyn

60TH BIRTHDAY
CD _____ 09026625472
RCA Victor / Oct '94 / BMG.

MEN IN MY LIFE, A
Swinging on a star / Man I love / You're just in love / Blah blah blah/Just in time / Small world / Long before I knew you / Friendship / All the things you are / In the still of the night / Some enchanted evening / I get embarrassed / All through the night / Bewitched, bothered and bewildered / All I ask of you / Little things you do together / Love walked in/Our love is here to stay
CD _____ 09026626472
RCA Victor / Nov '94 / BMG.

Hornsby, Bruce

HARBOR LIGHTS
Harbour lights / Talk of the town / Long tall cool one / China doll / Fields of gray / Rainbow's cadillac / Passing through / Tide will rise / What a time / Pastures of plenty
CD _____ 07863661142
RCA / Mar '93 / BMG.

HOT HOUSE
Spider fingers / White wheeled limosine / Walk in the sun / Changes / Tango king / Big rumble / Country doctor / Longest night / Hot house ball / Swing street / Cruise control
CD _____ 07863665842
RCA / Aug '95 / BMG.

NIGHT ON THE TOWN, A (Hornsby, Bruce & The Range)
Night on the town / Fire on the cross / Across the river / Stander on the mountain / Another day / These arms of mine / Carry the water / Barren ground / Stranded on Easy Street / Lost soul / Special night
CD _____ 74321 16001-2
RCA / Sep '93 / BMG.

SCENES FROM THE SOUTH SIDE (Hornsby, Bruce & The Range)
Look out any window / Valley Road / I will walk with you / Road not taken / Show goes on / Old playground / Defenders of the flag / Jacob's ladder / Till the dreaming's done
CD _____ ND 90492
RCA / Nov '90 / BMG.

WAY IT IS, THE (Hornsby, Bruce & The Range)
On the Western skyline / Every little kiss / Mandolin rain / Long race / Way it is / Down the road tonight / Wild frontier / River runs low / Red plains
CD _____ PD 89901
RCA / Jan '87 / BMG.

Horo, Krachno

TRADITIONAL BULGARIAN
CD _____ Y 225217CD
Silex / Oct '94 / ADA.

Horo, Slobo

ESMA
CD _____ ZENCD 2401
Rockadillo / Apr '95 / Direct / ADA.

Horse

GOD'S HOME MOVIE
Celebrate / Shake this mountain / God's home movie / Years from now / Natural law / Letter to Anne-Marie / Hold me now / Imitation / Sorry my dear / Finer
CD _____ MCD 10935
MCA / Oct '93 / BMG.

Horse Latitudes

HORSE LATITUDES
Oh Caroline / What is more than life / Baby don't go / Harvest days / Thrown away / Building mansions / Northern country lie / I can't stop loving you / Younger generation (On CD only) / Someone (On CD only) / There I go again (On CD only)
CD _____ CDBRED 90
Cherry Red / Sep '90 / Pinnacle.

Horseflies

HUMAN FLY
Human fly / Hush little baby / Jenny on the railroad / Rub alcohol blues / Cornbread / Who throwed lye on my dog / I live where it's gray / Link of chain / Blueman's daughter
CD _____ COOKCD 013
Cooking Vinyl / Aug '88 / Vital.

Horslips

ALIENS
Before the storm / Wrath of the rain / Speed the plough / Sure the boy was green / Come Summer / Stowaway / New York wakes / Exiles / Second Avenue / Ghosts / Lifetime to pay
CD _____ MOOCD 014
Outlet / Jan '95 / ADA / Duncans / CM / Ross / Direct / Koch.

BEST OF HORSLIPS
My Lagan love (downtown) / Dearg doom / Green gravel / Oisin's tune / Birn Istigh ag ol / Johnny's wedding / Daybreak (opening the station) / More than you can chew / King of the fairies / Musical far East / High reel / Flower among them all
CD _____ CMOD 021
Outlet / '89 / ADA / Duncans / CM / Ross / Direct / Koch.

BOOK OF INVASIONS, THE
Daybreak / March into trouble / Trouble with a capital T / Power and the glory / Rocks remain / Dusk / Sword of light / Warm sweet breath of love / Fantasia (my lagan love) / King of morning, Queen of day / Sideways to the sun / Drive the cold winter away / Ride to hell / Dark
CD _____ MOOCD 012
Outlet / Jan '95 / ADA / Duncans / CM / Ross / Direct / Koch.

COLLECTION
CD _____ MOOCD 025
Outlet / Oct '95 / ADA / Duncans / CM / Ross / Direct / Koch.

DANCEHALL SWEETHEARTS
Nightown boy / Blind can't lead the blind / Stars / We bring the Summer with us / Sunburst / Mad Pat / Blind man / King of the fairies / Lonely hearts / Best years of my life
CD _____ MOOCD 007
Outlet / Jan '95 / ADA / Duncans / CM / Ross / Direct / Koch.

DRIVE THE COLD WINTER AWAY
Rug muire mac do dhia / Sir Festus Burke/ Carolan's frolic / Snow that melts the soonest / Piper in the meadow straying / Drive the cold winter away / Thompson's cottage to the grove / Ny kirree fo naghtey / Crabs in the skillet / Dennis O'Connor / Dо'n oiche i mbeithil / Lullaby / Snow and frosts are all over / Paddy Fahey's / When a man's in love
CD _____ MOOCD 009
Outlet / Jan '95 / ADA / Duncans / CM / Ross / Direct / Koch.

GUESTS OF THE NATION
King of the fairies / Flower among them all / Johnny's wedding / Daybreak / Furniture / King of the morning, Queen of the day / Dearg doom / Trouble with a capital T / Man who built America / I'll be waiting / Power and the glory / Speed the plough / Long weekend / Guests of the nation
CD _____ MOOCD 024
Outlet / Jan '95 / ADA / Duncans / CM / Ross / Direct / Koch.

HAPPY TO MEET, SORRY TO PART
Happy to meet / Hall of mirrors / Clergy's lanentation / An bratach ban / Shamrock shore / Flower among them all / Bim istigh ag ol / Furniture / Ace and deuce of pipering / Dance to your daddy / High reel / Scalloway rip off / Musical priest / Sorry to part
CD _____ MOOCD 003
Outlet / Jan '95 / ADA / Duncans / CM / Ross / Direct / Koch.

HORSLIPS LIVE
Mad Pat / Blindman / Silver spear / High reel / Stars / Hall of mirrors / If that's what you want (That's what you get) / Self defence / Everything will be alright / Rakish Paddy / King of the fairies / Furniture / You can't fool the beast / More than you can chew / Dearg doom / Comb your hair and curl it / Johnny's wedding
CD _____ MOOC 010
Outlet / Jan '95 / ADA / Duncans / CM / Ross / Direct / Koch.

HORSLIPS STORY - STRAIGHT FROM THE HORSE'S MOUTH
High reel / Night town boy / Flower among them all / Dearg doom / Faster than the hounds / Best years of my life / Man who built America / Guests of the nation / Daybreak / Everything will be alright / Power and the glory / Sword of light / Warm sweet breath of love / Speed the plough / Trouble with a capital T / Shamrock shore / King of the fairies / High water / An bratach ban / Silver spear
CD _____ DHCD 802
Outlet / Feb '95 / ADA / Duncans / CM / Ross / Direct / Koch.

LIVE IN BELFAST
Trouble with a capital T / Man who built America / Warm sweet breath of love / Power and the glory / Blindman / Shakin' all over / King of the fairies / Guests of the nation / Dearg doom
CD _____ MOOCD 020
Outlet / Jan '95 / ADA / Duncans / CM / Ross / Direct / Koch.

MAN WHO BUILT AMERICA
Man who built America / Tonight / I'll be waiting / If it takes all night / Green star liner / Loneliness / Homesick / Long weekend / Letters from home / Long time ago
CD _____ MOOCD 017
Outlet / Jan '95 / ADA / Duncans / CM / Ross / Direct / Koch.

SHORT STORIES TALL TALES
Guests of the nation / Law on the run / Unapproved road / Ricochet man / Back in my arms / Summer's most wanted girl / Amazing offer / Rescue me / Life you save / Soap opera
CD _____ MOOCD 019
Outlet / Jan '95 / ADA / Duncans / CM / Ross / Direct / Koch.

TAIN, THE
Setanta / Meave's court / Charolais / March / You can't fool the beast / Dearg doom / Ferdia's song / Gae bolga / Cu chulainn's lament / Faster than the hounds / Silver spear / More than you can chew / Morrigan's dream / Time to kill / March #2
CD _____ MOOCD 005
Outlet / Jan '95 / ADA / Duncans / CM / Ross / Direct / Koch.

TRACKS FROM THE VAULTS
Motorway madness / Johnny's wedding / Flower among them all / Green gravel / Fairy king / Dearg doom / High reel / King of the fairies / Phil the fluter's ball / Come back Beatles / Fab four-four / Daybreak / Oisin's tune

CD _____ MOOCD 013
Outlet / Jan '95 / ADA / Duncans / CM / Ross / Direct / Koch.

TRADITIONAL IRISH MUSIC
CD _____ MOOCD 013
Outlet / Feb '95 / ADA / Duncans / CM / Ross / Direct / Koch.

UNFORTUNATE CUP OF TEA
If that's what you want (That's what you get) / Ring-a-rosey / Flirting in the shadows / Self defence / High volume love / Unfortunate cup of tea / Turn your face to the wall / Snakes' farewell to the Emerald Isle / Everything will be alright
CD _____ MOOCD 008
Outlet / Jan '95 / ADA / Duncans / CM / Ross / Direct / Koch.

Horta, Toninho

ONCE I LOVED
CD _____ 5135612
Verve / Apr '92 / PolyGram.

Horton, Big Walter

BIG WALTER HORTON WITH CAREY BELL (Horton, Big Walter & Carey Bell)
CD _____ ALCD 4702
Alligator / May '93 / Direct / ADA.

LITTLE BOY BLUE
CD _____ JSPCD 208
JSP / Jan '88 / ADA / Target/BMG / Direct / Cadillac / Complete/Pinnacle.

MOUTH HARP MAESTRO
Jumpin' blues / Hard hearted woman / Cotton patch hot foot / I'm in love with you baby / What's the matter with you / Black gal / Go 'long woman / Little boy blues / Blues in the morning
CD _____ CDCH 252
Ace / Nov '93 / Pinnacle / Cadillac / Complete/Pinnacle.

Horton, Johnny

1956 - 1960
I'm a one woman / Honky tonk man / I'm ready if you're willing / I got a hole in my pirogue / Take me like I am / Sugar coated baby / I don't like I did / Hooray for that little difference / I'm coming home / Over loving you / She know why / Honky tonk mind (the woman I need) / Tell me baby I love her / Goodbye lonesome, hello baby doll / I'll do it everytime / You're my baby / Let's take the long way home / Lover's rock / Honky tonk hardwood floor / Wild one / Everytime I'm kissing you / Lonesome and heartbroken / Seven come eleven / I can't forget you / Wise to the ways of a woman / Out in New Mexico / Tetched in the head / Just walk a little closer / Don't use my heart for a stepping stone / I love you baby / Counterfeit love / Mr. Moonlight / All grown up / Got the bull by the horns / When it's springtime in Alaska / Whispering pines / Battle of New Orleans / All for the love of a girl / Lost highway / Sam Magee / Cherokee Boogie / Golden Rocket / Joe's been a gittin' there / First train headin' South / Sal's got a sugar lip / Words / Johnny reb / Ole slew foot / They shined up rudolph's nose / Electrified donkey / Same old tale crow told me / Sink the Bismarck / Ole slew foot (CD 3) / Miss Marcy / Sleepy eyed John / Mansion you stole / They'll never take her love from me / Sinking of the Reuben James / Jim Bridger / Battle of Bull Run / Snow shoe thompson / John paul jones / Comanche / Young abe lincoln / O'leary's cow / Johnny freedom / Go north / North to alaska / Rock is / Land line / Hank and joe and me / Sleeping at the foot of the bed / Old blind barnabas / Evil hearted me / Hot in the sugarcane field / You don't move me anymore baby / Gosh darn wheel / Broken hearted gypsy / Church by the side of the road / Vanishing race / Broken hearted gypsy (2) / That boy got the habit / Hot in the sugarcane field (2) / You don't move anymore baby (CD 4) / Church by the side of the road (CD 4) / Take it like a man / Hank and joe and me (CD 4) / Old blind barnabas (CD 4) / Empty bed blues / Rock Island line / Snake, rattle and roll / A Sleeping at the foot of the bed (2) / Old dan tucker / Gosh darn wheel (CD 4) / From memphis to mobile / Back up train / Schottische in texas / My heart stopped, trembled and died / Alley gir ways / How you gonna make it / Witch walking baby / Down that river road / Big wheels rollin' / I got a slow leak in my heart / What will i do without you / Janey / Streets of dodge / Give me back my picture and you can keep the frame
CD Set _____ BCD 15470
Bear Family / May '91 / Rollercoaster / Direct / CM / Swift / ADA.

ROCKIN' ROLLIN' JOHNNY HORTON
Sal's got a sugar lip (Previously unissued) / Honky tonk hardwood floor / Honky tonk man / I'm coming home / Tell my baby I love her / Woman I need / First train headin' South / Lover's rock / All grown up / Electrified donkey / Sugar coated baby / Let's take the long way home / Ole slew foot / Sleepy eyed John / Wild one / I'm ready if you're willing

CD _____ BCD 15543
Bear Family / Oct '90 / Rollercoaster / Direct / CM / Swift / ADA.

Horton, Pug

DON'T GO AWAY
By myself / Sweetheart o'mine / I'll string along with you / Don't go away / Tipperary / Miss my lovin' time / I / Breezin' along / I can dream / Melancholy / Send a little love my way / I found a new baby
CD _____ ACD 224
Audiophile / Apr '94 / Jazz Music / Swift.

Horzu

DIE RITTER DER SCHWARFELRUNDE
CD _____ MOVE 7015CD
Move / Jul '95 / Plastic Head.

Hostility

BRICK
CD _____ CM 77103CD
Century Media / Jan '96 / Plastic Head.

Hot Chocolate

GREATEST HITS: HOT CHOCOLATE
Love is life / You could've been a lady / I believe (in love) / You'll always be a friend / Brother Louie / Rumours / Emma / Cheri babe / Disco queen / Child's prayer / You sexy thing / Don't stop it now / Man to man / Heaven is in the back seat of my cadillac
CD _____ CDMFP 6009
Music For Pleasure / Sep '87 / EMI.

GREATEST HITS: HOT CHOCOLATE #2
So you win again / Put your love in me / Every 1's a winner / I'll put you together again / Mindless boogie / Going through the motions / No doubt about it / Are you getting enough of what makes you happy / Love me to sleep / You'll never be so wrong / Ciri crazy / It started with a kiss / Chances / What kinda boy you looking for (girl) / Tears on the telephone / I gave you my heart (didn't I)
CD _____ CDMFP 6130
Music For Pleasure / Nov '95 / EMI.

REST OF THE BEST OF HOT CHOCOLATE, THE
Heaven is in the back seat of my cadillac / Man to man / You could've been a lady / Rumours / Mary Anne / You'll always be a friend / Mindless boogie / Heartache no.9 (remix) / Cheri babe / Going through the motions / Blue night / Every 1's a winner / You'll never be so wrong / I'm sorry / Chances / Tears on the telephone / Love me to sleep / You sexy thing (remix)
CD _____ CDGO 2060
EMI / Sep '94 / EMI.

THEIR GREATEST HITS
You sexy thing / It started with a kiss / Brother Louie / Girl crazy / So you win again / Put your love in me / Love is life / I'll put you together again / No doubt about it / Every 1's a winner / Emma / I gave you my heart (Didn't I) / You could've been a lady / Don't stop it now / Child's prayer / What kinda boy you looking for (girl) / I believe (in love) / Are you getting enough happiness
CD _____ CDEMTV 73
EMI / Mar '93 / EMI.

Hot Club De Norvege

SWINGIN' WITH JIMMY (Hot Club De Norvege & Jimmy Rosenberg)
CD _____ HCRCD 4
Hot Club / Oct '94 / Cadillac.

Hot Damn

HIGH HEELS SLUT
CD _____ HELLYEAH 031CD
Hell Yeah / Sep '95 / Plastic Head.

Hot Knives

WAY THINGS/BLACK (Hot Knives & Liquidators)
CD _____ PHZCD 82
Unicorn / Sep '94 / Plastic Head.

Hot Pastrami

WITH A LITTLE HORSERADISH ON THE SIDE
CD _____ GV 158CD
Global Village / May '94 / ADA / Direct.

Hot Rize

BLASTS FROM THE PAST (Red Knuckles Trailblazers)
CD _____ SH 3767CD
Sugarhill / '88 / Roots / CM / ADA / Direct.

HOT RIZE (Red Knuckles Trailblazers)
Travellin' blues / Honky tonk man / Slade's theme / Dixie cannonball / I know my baby loves me / Trailblazers theme / Always late / Honky tonk song / Kansas city star / Waldo's discount donuts / Boot hill drag / Window up above / You're gonna change (or I'm gonna leave) / Long gone John from bowling green / Let me love you one more time / Goin' across the sea / My little darlin' / I've been all around this world / I'm gonna

sleep with one eye open / Martha White theme / Sally Goodin / Your light leads me on / Sugarfoot rag / Intro of Red Knuckles and The Trailblazers / Texas hambone blues / Wendell's fly swatters / Oh Mona / Rank stranger / Shady grove
CD _____ FF 70107
Flying Fish / '89 / Roots / CM / Direct / ADA.

TAKE IT HOME
Colleen Malone / Rocky road blues / Voice in the wind / Bending blades / Gone fishing / Think of what you've done / Climb the ladder / Money to burn / Bravest cowboy / Lamplighting time in the valley / Where the wild river rolls / Old rounder / Tenderly calling (Home, come on home)
CD _____ SH 3784CD
Sugarhill / '90 / Roots / CM / ADA / Direct.

TRADITIONAL TIES
Hard pressed / If I should wander back to-night / Walk the way the wind blows / Hear Jerusalem moan / Frank's blues / Lost John / Montana cowboy / Footsteps so near / Leather britches / Working on a building / John Henry / Keep your lamp trimmed and burning
CD _____ SH CD 3748
Sugarhill / Mar '89 / Roots / CM / ADA / Direct.

UNTOLD STORIES
Are you tired of me darling / Untold stories / Just like you / Country blues / Bluegrass / Won't you come and sing for me / Life's too short / You don't have to move the mountain / Shadows in my room / Don't make me believe / Wild ride / Late in the day
CD _____ SH 3756CD
Sugarhill / Mar '89 / Roots / CM / ADA / Direct.

Hot Stuff

CELEBRATING EARLY JAZZ
CD _____ LACD 40
Lake / Feb '95 / Target/BMG / Jazz Music / Direct / Cadillac / ADA.

Hot Tuna

DOUBLE DOSE
Winin' boy blues / Keep your lamp trimmed and burning / Embryonic journey / Killing time in the Crystal City / I wish you would / Genesis / Extrication love song / Talking about you / Funky No. 7 / Serpent of dreams / Bowlegged woman, knock kneed man / I see the light / Watch the north wind rise / Sunrise dance with the Devil / I can't be satisfied
CD _____ EDCD 397
Edsel / Nov '94 / Pinnacle / ADA.

HOT TUNA
CD _____ EDCD 331
Edsel / Jul '91 / Pinnacle / ADA.

TRIMMED & BURNING
CD _____ EDCD 396
Edsel / Aug '94 / Pinnacle / ADA.

Hotel Hunger

AS LONG AS
CD _____ EIGEN 013CD
Pingo / Dec '94 / Plastic Head.

Hotel X

ENGENDERED SPECIES
CD _____ SST 304CD
SST / Jan '95 / Plastic Head.

LADDERS
CD _____ SST 317CD
SST / Nov '95 / Plastic Head.

RESIDENTIAL SUITE
CD _____ SST 301CD
SST / Jul '94 / Plastic Head.

Hothouse Flowers

HOME
Hardstone City / Give it up / Christchurch bells / Sweet Marie / Giving it all away / Shut up and listen / I can see clearly now / Movies / Eyes wide open / Water / Home / Trying to get through (CD only) / Dance to the storm (CD only) / Seoladh na ngamhna
CD _____ 828 197 2
London / Jun '90 / PolyGram.

PEOPLE
I'm sorry / Don't go / Forgiven / It'll be easier in the morning / Hallelujah Jordan / If you go / Older we get / Yes I was / Love don't work this way / Ballad of Katie / Feet on the ground / Lonely lane (CD only) / Saved (CD only)
CD _____ 828 101 2
London / May '88 / PolyGram.

SONGS FROM THE RAIN
This is it (Your soul) / One tongue / Emotional time / Be good / Good for you / Isn't it amazing / Thing of beauty / Your nature / Spirit of the land / Gypsy fair / Stand beside me
CD _____ 828350-2
London / Mar '93 / PolyGram.

Houdini, Wilmouth

POOR BUT AMBITIOUS
CD _____ FL 7010
Folklyric / Apr '95 / Direct / Cadillac.

Houdinis

HYBRID
CD _____ CHR 70004
Challenge / Aug '95 / Direct / Jazz Music / Cadillac / ADA.

PLAY THE BIG FIVE
CD _____ CHR 70027
Challenge / Nov '95 / Direct / Jazz Music / Cadillac / ADA.

Houghton Weavers

BEST OF HOUGHTON WEAVERS, THE
Ballad of Wigan Pier / Where do you go from here / We want to work / Martians have landed in Wigan / Blackpool belle / Maggie / All for me grog / Home boys home / When you were sweet sixteen / Rose of Tralee / Old miner / Mist over the Mersey / Room in the sky / Dutchman / On the banks of the roses / God must love the poor / That stranger is a friend / Will ye go lassie go / Success to the Weavers / Mingulay boat song
CD _____ CDSL 8272
Music For Pleasure / Sep '95 / EMI.

WORK OF THE WEAVERS
CD _____ KFS 040
Sound Waves / Oct '93 / Target/BMG.

Houmark, Karsten

FOUR (Houmark, Karsten Quartet)
Four / Again and again / Rangoon / Little man / Simple song / Blue planet / B flat for Bob / Waltz for Kenny
CD _____ STCD 4197
Storyville / Mar '95 / Jazz Music / Wellard / CM / Cadillac.

Houn, Fred

TOMORROW IS NOW (Houn, Fred & The Afro-Asian Music Ensemble)
CD _____ 121117-2
Soul Note / Nov '93 / Harmonia Mundi / Wellard / Cadillac.

House Band

ANOTHER SETTING
CD _____ GL 1143CD
Green Linnet / Jul '94 / Roots / CM / Direct / ADA.

GROUNDWORK
Trip to amnesia / Diamantina drover / Anti-social worker / For the sake of example / Tornado two-step/The Cooper/The woodpecker / Joy after sorrow / War party / Cobb/Slip jig/The metric fox / Pit stands idle / Here's the tender coming / Four courts/ Fox on the prowl / Major Harrison's fedora
CD _____ GLCD 1132
Green Linnet / Mar '94 / Roots / CM / Direct / ADA.

STONETOWN
Skepper schotish-schotish fra lyo / Lonesome drunkards walk stonetown / Eliz iza / Sunday's best / New tobacco / Rolling waves ryans / Final trawl / Killybegs highland / Charlie O'Neils / Rond De Loudeac / Here come the weak / On the turn / Herons / Phoenix / Geordie / Wals voor polle / Baldazka
CD _____ RAHCD 019
Harbour Town / Nov '91 / Roots / Direct / CM / ADA.

WORD OF MOUTH
CD _____ GLCD 3045
Green Linnet / Oct '93 / Roots / CM / Direct / ADA.

House, James

DAYS GONE BY
This is me missing you / Real good way to wind up lonesome / Until you set me free / Anything for love / Little by little / Only a fool / Silence makes a lonesome sound / Days gone by / Take me away / That's something (you don't see everyday)
CD _____ 4783402
Columbia / Feb '95 / Sony.

House Of Dreams

HOUSE OF DREAMS
CD _____ NAK 6124CD
Naked Language / Jun '94 / Koch.

House Of Freaks

INVISIBLE JEWEL
CD _____ OUT 117-2
Brake Out / Nov '94 / Vital.

TANTILLA
When the hammer came down / Righteous will fall / White folk's blood / Birds of prey / King of kings / Family tree / Sun gone down / Kill the mockingbird / Broken bones / I want answers / Big houses / World of tomorrow

CD _____ 8122708462
WEA / Jul '93 / Warner Music.

House Of Lords

SAHARA
Shoot / Chains of love / Can't find my way home / Heart on the line / Laydown staydown / Sahara / It ain't my love / Remember my name / American Babylon / Kiss of fire
CD _____ PD 82170
RCA / Sep '90 / BMG.

House Of Love

AUDIENCE WITH THE MIND
CD _____ 5148802
Fontana / Jun '93 / PolyGram.

BABE RAINBOW
You don't understand / Crush me / Cruel / High in your face / Fade away / Feel / Girl with the loneliest eyes / Burn down the world / Philly Phile / Yer eyes
CD _____ 5125492
Fontana / Jul '92 / PolyGram.

HOUSE OF LOVE
CD _____ CRELP 034CD
Creation / Jun '88 / 3MV / Vital.

HOUSE OF LOVE.
Hanah / Shine on / Beatles and the Stones / Shake and crawl / Hedonist / I don't know why I love you / Never / Somebody's got to love you / In a room / Blind / 32nd Floor / So dest
CD _____ 8422932
Fontana / Jan '96 / PolyGram.

HOUSE OF LOVE/SPY IN THE HOUSE OF LOVE (2 CDs)
Hanah / Shine on / Beatles and the Stones / Shake and crawl / Hedonist / I don't know why I love you / Never / Somebody's got to love you / In a room / Blind / Thirty second floor / Se Dest / Safe / Marble / D song '89 / Scratched inside / Phone / Cut the fool down / Ray / Love II / Baby teen / Love III / Soft as fire / Love IV / No fire / Love V
CD Set _____ 5286022
Fontana / Aug '95 / PolyGram.

SPY IN THE HOUSE OF LOVE, A
Safe / Marble / D song 89 / Scratched inside / Phone / Cut the fool down / Ray / Love / Baby teen / Love 3 / Soft as fire / Love 4 / No fire / Love 5
CD _____ 8469782
Fontana / Oct '90 / PolyGram.

House Of Pain

HOUSE OF PAIN
CD _____ XLCD 111
XL / Nov '92 / Warner Music.

SAME AS IT EVER WAS
CD _____ XLCD 115
XL / Jun '94 / Warner Music.

House, Simon

YASSASIM
Yassasim / Orion / Northlands / Omedlok rides again / Laithwaite stardrive / Neuroscape / Sherwood / Oldayze
CD _____ EBSSCD 115
Emergency Broadcast System / Jul '95 / Vital.

House, Son

DEATH LETTER
Death letter / Pearline / Louise McGhee / John the revelator / Empire state express / Preachin' blues / Grinnin' in your face / Sundown / Levee camp moan
CD _____ EDCD 167
Edsel / Dec '90 / Pinnacle / ADA.

DELTA BLUES (Congress Sessions From Field Recordings)
Levee camp blues / Government fleet blues / Walkin' blues / Shetland pony blues / Delta blues / Special rider blues / Low down dirty dog blues / Depot blues / American defense / Am I right or wrong / County farm blues / Pony blues / Jinx blues
CD _____ BCD 118
Biograph / Jul '91 / Wellard / ADA / Hot Shot / Jazz Music / Cadillac / Direct.

DELTA BLUES AND SPIRITUAL
Monologue - the B.L.U.E.S. / Between midnight and day / Levee camp moan / This little light of mine / Monologue - thinkin' strong / Death letter / How to treat a man / Grinnin' in your face / John the Revelator
CD _____ CZ 545
Capitol Jazz / Jul '95 / EMI.

FATHER OF THE DELTA BLUES (Complete 1965 Sessions/2CD Set)
Death letter / Pearline / Louise McGhee / John the revelator / Empire state express / Preachin' blues / Levee camp moan / President Kennedy / Down the staff / Motherless children / Yonder comes my mother / Shake it and break it / Pony blues / Downhearted blues
CD Set _____ 4716622
Columbia / Jul '92 / Sony.

319

LIBRARY OF CONGRESS SESSIONS
Levee camp blues / Government fleet blues / Special rider blues / Low down dirty dog blues / Walkin' blues / Depot blues / Camp hollars
CD _____ TMCD 02
Travellin' Man / Apr '90 / Wellard / CM / Jazz Music.

SON HOUSE AND THE GREAT DELTA BLUES SINGERS (1928-1930) (House, Son & The Great Delta Blues Singers)
CD _____ DOCD 5002
Blues Document / Feb '92 / Swift / Jazz Music / Hot Shot.

SON HOUSE IN CONCERT
It's so hard / Judgement day / New York central / True friend is hard to find / Preachin' the blues / Change your mind
CD _____ CDBM 020
Blue Moon / 91 / Magnum Music Group / Greensleeves / Hot Shot / ADA / Cadillac / Discovery.

Household Cavalry Band

BEATING RETREAT
CD _____ BNA 5088
Bandleader / Sep '93 / Conifer.

MUSICAL RIDE
CD _____ MMCD 442
Music Masters / Jun '94 / Target/BMG.

Household Regiment Bands

GUARDS IN CONCERT, THE
Royale / Capital city / La Ronde / Academic festival overture / Arrival of the Queen of Sheba / Phantom of the opera / Intermezzo / Can can for band / Cavalry of the steppes / Entry of the boyards / Les miserables / Slave's chorus / Earl of Oxford's march / Sospan tach / Star of St. Patrick / Great gate of kiev
CD _____ BNA 5042
Bandleader / '91 / Conifer.

MASSED BANDS HOUSE REGIMENT
CD _____ BNA 5086
Bandleader / Oct '91 / Conifer.

Housemartins

LONDON 0 HULL 4
Happy hour / Get up off our knees / Flag day / Anxious / Reverend's revenge / Sitting on a fence / Sheep / Over there / Think for a minute / We're not deep / Lean on me / Freedom / I'll be your shelter (just like a shelter) (Extra track on cassette version only.)
CD _____ 8283472
Go Discs / Jan '95 / PolyGram.

NOW THAT'S WHAT I CALL QUITE GOOD (Greatest Hits)
I smell winter / Bow down / Think for a minute / There is always something there to remind me / Mighty ship / Sheep / I'll be your shelter (just like a shelter) / Five get over excited / Everybody's the same / Build / Step outside / Flag day / Happy hour / You've got a friend / He ain't heavy, he's my brother / Freedom / People who grinned themselves to death / Caravan of love / Light is always green / We're not deep / Me and the farmer / Lean on me
CD _____ 8283442
Go Discs / Jan '95 / PolyGram.

PEOPLE WHO GRINNED THEMSELVES TO DEATH, THE
People who grinned themselves to death / I can't put my finger on it / Light is always green / World's on fire / Pirate aggro / We're not going back / Me and the farmer / Five get over excited / Johannesburg / Bow down / You better be doubtful / Build
CD _____ 8283312
Go Discs / Oct '92 / PolyGram.

Housley, Chris

TIME TO DANCE
CD _____ SAV 184CD
Savoy / May '93 / THE / Savoy.

Housten, Day

MARIE'S HAEDWALTZ
CD _____ WB 1134CD
We Bite / Sep '95 / Plastic Head.

Houston, Cisco

FOLKWAYS 1944-61
CD _____ SFCD 40059
Smithsonian Folkways / Jun '94 / ADA / Direct / Koch / CM / Cadillac.

Houston, Cissy

MIDNIGHT TRAIN TO GEORGIA (The Janus Years)
CD _____ SCL 2102
Ichiban Soul Classics / May '95 / Koch.

Houston, Clint

WATERSHIP DOWN
CD _____ STCD 4150
Storyville / Feb '90 / Jazz Music / Wellard / CM / Cadillac.

Houston, Joe

CORNBREAD & CABBAGE GREENS
Cornbread and cabbage greens / Jay's boogie / Blues after hours / Sentimental journey / Celebrity club drag / Gordon's knot / All night long / Ruth's rock / Flying home / Walkin' home / Lester leaps in / I cover the waterfront / Troubles and worries / Huggy boy radio ad / Rockin' and boppin' / She's gone / Anything / Richie's roll / Thom's tune / Teen-age hop / Well, well my love / Mambo / Shake it up / Coastin' / Midnight
CD _____ CDCHD 395
Ace / Mar '92 / Pinnacle / Cadillac / Complete/Pinnacle.

RETURN OF HONK, THE (Houston, Joe & Otis Grand)
CD _____ JSPCD 251
JSP / Feb '94 / ADA / Target/BMG / Direct / Cadillac / Complete/Pinnacle.

Houston, Penelope

BIRD BOYS
Harry Dean / Talking with you / Voices / Living dolls / Out of my life / Waiting room / Bed of lies / Wild mountain thyme / Putting me in the ground / Full of wonder / Summers of war / Stoli / Rock 'n' roll show / All that crimson
CD _____ NORM 173CD
Normal/Okra / Nov '93 / Direct / ADA.

KARMAL APPLE
CD _____ NORMAL 183CD
Normal/Okra / Dec '94 / Direct / ADA.

SILK PURSE
CD _____ RTS 2CD
Normal/Okra / Mar '94 / Direct / ADA.

WHOLE WORLD, THE
CD _____ NORMAL 153CD
Normal/Okra / Mar '94 / Direct / ADA.

Houston, Thelma

DON'T LEAVE ME THIS WAY
Don't leave me this way / I don't want to go back there again / Don't know why I love you / I can't go on living without your love / Saturday night, Sunday morning / Give me something to believe in / If it's the last thing I do / I've got the devil in me / I need you right now / Come to me / I'm letting go / I ain't that easy to lose / Stormy weather / I can't stand the rain / Don't pity me / I'm here again / Any way you like it
CD _____ 5510702
Spectrum/Karussell / Jul '95 / PolyGram / THE.

Houston, Whitney

I'M YOUR BABY TONIGHT
I'm your baby tonight / My name is not Susan / All the man that I need / Lover for life / Anymore / Miracle / I belong to you / Who do you love / We didn't know / After we make love / I'm knockin'
CD _____ 261039
Arista / Nov '90 / BMG.

WHITNEY
I wanna dance with somebody (who loves me) / Just the lonely talking again / Love will save the day / Didn't we almost have it all / So emotional / Where you are / Love is a contact sport / You're still my man / For the love of you / Where do broken hearts go / I know him so well
CD _____ 258141
Arista / May '87 / BMG.

WHITNEY HOUSTON
How will I know / Take good care of my heart (with Jermaine Jackson) / Greatest love of all / Hold me (with Teddy Pendergrass) / You give good love / Thinking about you / Someone for me / Saving all my love for you / Nobody loves me like you do (with Jermaine Jackson) / All at once
CD _____ 610359
Arista / Aug '86 / BMG.

Hoven Droven

HIA HIA
CD _____ XOU 110
Xource / Dec '94 / ADA / Cadillac.

Howard, Adina

ADINA HOWARD
CD _____ 7567617572
Atlantic / Feb '95 / Warner Music.

Howard, Camille

ROCK ME DADDY
Boogie and the blues / You don't love me / You used to be mine / Unidentified boogie / Has your love grown cold / Mood I'm in / Gotta have a little lovin' / How long can I go on like this / Cry over you / O sole mio boogie / Within this heart of mine / Boogie in G / I'm blue / Rock me Daddy / Broken memories sad and blue / I ain't got the spirit / Shrinking up fast / Easy / Money blues / Schuberts serenade boogie / You lied to me baby / Real gone Daddy
CD _____ CDCHD 511

Ace / Jan '94 / Pinnacle / Cadillac / Complete/Pinnacle.

Howard, Eddy

EDDY HOWARD
CD _____ CCD 029
Circle / Oct '93 / Jazz Music / Swift / Wellard.

Howard, George

ATTITUDE ADJUSTMENT
Watch your back / Best friend / One last time / Diana's blues / Attitude adjustment / Let's unwind / Been thinking / Whole lot of drum in you
CD _____ GRP 98392
GRP / Jan '96 / BMG / New Note.

HOME FAR AWAY, A
Miracle / If you were mine / Doria / Till tomorrow / If you can make the story right / Grover's groove / No ordinary love / Home far away / For our fathers / Renewal
CD _____ GRP 97802
GRP / Jul '94 / BMG / New Note.

Howard, Joe

JAZZ HIGHWAY 20
CD _____ PS 007CD
P&S / Sep '95 / Discovery.

SWINGIN' CLOSE IN
CD _____ PS 005CD
P&S / Sep '95 / Discovery.

Howard, Johnny

BEST OF THE DANSAN YEARS, VOL 6 (Howard, Johnny & His Orchestra)
CD _____ DACD 1006
Dansan / Jul '92 / Savoy / President / Target/BMG.

DANSAN YEARS VOL. 7 (Howard, Johnny & Ray McVay)
CD _____ DACD 7
Dansan / Mar '95 / Savoy / President / Target/BMG.

FOREVER DANCE (Howard, Johnny & His Orchestra)
CD _____ CDTS 2001
Maestro / Nov '93 / Savoy.

Howard, Kid

LAVIDA
CD _____ AMCD 054
American Music / Oct '93 / Jazz Music.

Howard, Miki

FEMME FATALE
Good morning heartache / This better earth / Hope that we can be together soon / Shining through / But I love you / Ain't nobody like you / I've been through it / Release me / Thank you for takin' me to Africa / Cigarette ashes on the floor
CD _____ 07599244522
Giant / Oct '92 / BMG.

Howard, Rosetta

ROSETTA HOWARD 1939-47
CD _____ JPCD 1514
Jazz Perspectives / Dec '94 / Jazz Music / Hot Shot.

Howe, Greg

GREG HOWE
CD _____ RR 9531 2
Roadrunner / Aug '88 / Pinnacle.

Howe, Steve

BEGINNINGS
Doors of sleep / Australia / Nature of the sea / Lost symphony / Beginnings / Will o' the wisp / Ram / Pleasure stole the night / Breakaway from it all
CD _____ 756780319-2
Atlantic / Sep '94 / Warner Music.

EARLY YEARS, THE (Howe, Steve & Bodast)
Do you remember / Beyond winter / Once in a lifetime / Black leather gloves / I want you / Tired towers / Mr. Jones / 1000 years / Nether Street / Nothing to cry for
CD _____ C5CD-528
See For Miles/C5 / May '90 / Pinnacle.

GRAND SCHEME OF THINGS
Grand scheme of things / Desire comes first / Blinded by science / Beautiful ideas / Valley of rocks / At the gates of the new world / Wayward course / Reaching the point / Common goal / Luck of the draw / Fall of civilisation / Passing phase / Georgia's theme / Too much is taken and not enough given / Maiden voyage / Road to one's self
CD _____ RR 90862
Roadrunner / Aug '93 / Pinnacle.

MOTHBALLED SESSIONS 1964-69
Maybellene / True to me / Howlin' for my baby / What to do / Leave me kitten alone / Don't know what to do / On the horizon / Stop, wait a minute / You're on your own / Why must I criticise / I don't mind / Finger

poppin' / Mothballs / You never can stay in one place / Real life permanent dream / Claremont lake / Revolution / Hallucinations / Three jolly little dwarfs / My white bicycle / Kid was a killer / Come over stranger / Beyond winter / Nothing to cry for / Nether street
CD _____ RPM 140
RPM / Oct '94 / Pinnacle.

NOT NECESSARILY ACOUSTIC
CD _____ CSA 104
RPM / Jun '95 / Pinnacle.

STEVE HOWE ALBUM
Pennants / Cactus boogie / All's a chord / Diary of a man who's disappeared / Look over your shoulder / Meadow rag / Continental / Surface tension / Double rondo / Concerto in D 2nd movement
CD _____ 756781559-2
Atlantic / Sep '94 / Warner Music.

Howell, Eddie

MAN FROM MANHATTAN, THE
Happy affair / First day in exile / Miss America / If I knew / Young Lady / Walls / Chicago kid / Man from Manhattan / Can't get over you / Waiting in the wings / Little crocodile / You'll never know / Enough for me / Don't say you love me
CD _____ BUD 001CD
Bud / Nov '94 / Vital.

Howell, Peg Leg

PEG LEG HOWELL - VOL.1 1926-27
Sadie Lee blues / Too tight blues / Moanin' and groanin' blues / Hobo blues / Peg Leg stomp / Doin' wrong / Skin game blues / Coal man blues / Tashomingo blues / New prison blues / Fo'day blues / New jelly roll blues / Beaver slide rag / Papa stobb blues
CD _____ MBCD 2004
Matchbox / Jan '94 / Roots / CM / Jazz Music / Cadillac.

PEG LEG HOWELL - VOL.2 1928-29
Please ma'am / Rock and gravel blues / Low down rounder blues / Fairy blues / Banjo blues / Turkey buzzard blues / Turtle dove blues / Walkin' blues / Broke and hungry / Rolling Mill blues / Ball and chain blues / Monkey man blues / Chittlin' supper / Away from home
CD _____ MBCD 2005
Matchbox / Jan '94 / Roots / CM / Jazz Music / Cadillac.

Howie B

MUSIC FOR BABIES
CD _____ 5294642
Polydor / Jan '96 / PolyGram.

Howlin' Wolf

COMPLETE RECORDINGS 1951-1967 (7CD Set)
Moaning at midnight / How many more years / Wolf is at your door (Howlin' for my baby) / Howlin' Wolf boogie / Getting old and gray / Mr. Highway man / Saddle my pony / Worried all the time / Oh red / My last affair / Baby ride with me (ridin' in the moonlight) / California boogie / Look a here baby / Everybody's in the mood / Color and kind / Bluebird / Sweet woman / Well that's alright / Decoration day / Dorothy Mae / Come back home / Smile at me / California blues / My baby walked off / My troubles and me / Chocolate drop / Drinkin' CV wine / Baby ride with me / I've got a woman / Just my kind / Work for your money / I'm not joking / Mama died and left me / Highway be my friend / Hold to your money / Streamline woman / Stay here 'till my baby comes / Crazy about you baby / All night boogie / I love my baby / No place to go / Neighbors / I'm the wolf / Rockin' daddy / Baby how long / Evil / I'll be around / Forty four / Who will be next / I have a little girl / Come to me baby / Don't mess with me baby / Smokestack lightnin' / You can't be beat / I asked for water (she gave me gasoline) / So glad / Break of day / Natchez burning / Going back home / My life / You ought to know / Who's been talkin' / Tell me / Somebody in my home / Nature / Walk to camp hall / Poor boy / My baby told me / Sittin' on top of the world / Howlin' blues / I better go now / I didn't know / Moaning for my baby / I'm leaving you / Can't put me out / Change my way / Getting late / I've been abused / Howlin' for my darling / My people's gone / Mr. Airplane man / Wang dang doodle / Back door man / Spoonful / Little baby / Down in the bottom / Shake for me / Red rooster / You'll be mine / You need love / I ain't superstitious / Goin' down slow / Mama's baby / Do the do / Tail dragger / Long green stuff / Sugar mama / May I have a talk with you / Hidden charms / 300 pounds of joy / Joy to my soul / Built for comfort / Love me darlin' / Killing floor / My country sugar mama / Louise / I walked from Dallas / Tell me what I've done / Don't laugh at me / Ooh baby / Hold me / Poor wind that never change / New crawlin' king snake / My mind is ramblin' / Commit a crime / Pop it to me / I had a dream / Dust my broom / Mary Sue / Hard luck / Tired of crying / You gonna wreck my life / I'm leavin' you / You

can't put me out / Wolf in the mood / Rollin' and tumblin' / Ain't goin' about that dirt road / Conversation
CD Set _____ CDREDBOX 7
Charly / Jun '93 / Charly / THE / Cadillac.

GENUINE ARTICLE, THE (The Best Of Howlin' Wolf)
Moanin' at midnight / How many more years / I'm the wolf / Baby how long / Evil / Forty four / Smokestack lightnin' / I asked for water (she gave me gasoline) / Natchez burning / Who's been talkin' / Sittin' on top of the world / I've been abused / Howlin' for my baby (darling) / Wang dang doodle / Back door man / Spoonful / Down in the bottom / Red rooster / 300 pounds of joy / Killing floor / Don't my broom / Ain't goin' down that dirt road
CD _____ MCD 11073
MCA / Jun '94 / BMG.

HOWLIN' FOR MY BABY
My baby walked off / Smile at me / Bluebird blues / Everybody's in the mood / Chocolate drop / Come back home / Dorothy Mae / Highwayman / Oh Red / My last affair / Howlin' for my baby / Sweet woman / C.V. wine blues / Look-a-here baby / Decoration day / Well that's alright / California blues / My troubles are / California boogie
CD _____ CDCHARLY 66
Charly / Apr '87 / Charly / THE / Cadillac.

HOWLIN' WOLF COLLECTOR'S EDITION
CD _____ DVBC 9022
Deja Vu / Apr '95 / THE.

I AM THE WOLF
I've got a woman / Just my kind / Work for your money / All night boogie / I love you baby / No place to go / Neighbours / I am the wolf / Rockin' daddy / Baby how long / I'll be around / Who will be next / I have a little girl / You can't be beat / Goin' back home / My life / You ought to know / Tell me / Somebody in my home / Nature / Poor boy / My baby told me / Little baby / I ain't superstitious
CD _____ CDRED 32
Charly / Jan '92 / Charly / THE / Cadillac.

KILLING FLOOR
Little red rooster / Killing floor / Smokestack lightnin' / Moanin' at midnight / Dorothy Mae / Wang dang doodle / Back door man / Built for comfort / How many more years / Goin' down slow / Natchez burnin / Who's been talkin' / I asked for water (she gave me gasoline) / Louise / Bluebird / 300 pounds of joy
CD _____ CDCD 1041
Charly / Mar '93 / Charly / THE / Cadillac.

LEGENDARY MASTERS SERIES, THE
CD _____ COLLECT 3CD
Aim / Oct '95 / Direct / ADA / Jazz Music.

LIVE IN CAMBRIDGE, MASS. 1966
CD _____ 422175
New Rose / May '94 / Direct / ADA.

LONDON REVISITED (Charly Blues - Masterworks Vol. 46)
CD _____ CDBM 46
Charly / Jun '93 / Charly / THE / Cadillac.

MEMPHIS DAYS #1 (Definitive Edition)
Oh red / My last affair / Come back home / California boogie / California blues / Look-a-here baby / Smile at me / My baby walked off / Drinkin' CV wine / My troubles and me / Chocolate drop / Mr. Highwayman / Bluebird blues / Color and kind / Everybody's in the mood / Dorothy Mae / I got a woman / Decoration day / Well that's alright / How many more years / Baby ride with me
CD _____ BCD 15460
Bear Family / Apr '89 / Rollercoaster / Direct / CM / Swift / ADA.

MEMPHIS DAYS #2 (Definitive Edition)
Baby ride with me / How many more years / Moanin' at midnight / Howlin' Wolf boogie / Wolf is at your door (howlin' for my) / Mr. Highwayman / Gettin' old and grey / Worried all the time / Saddle my pony / Oh red / My last affair / Come back home / Dorothy Mae / Oh red (2)
CD _____ BCD 15500
Bear Family / Sep '90 / Rollercoaster / Direct / CM / Swift / ADA.

MOANIN' AND HOWLIN'
Moanin' at midnight / How many more years / Evil / Forty four / Smokestack Lightnin' / I asked for water / Natchez burning / Bluebird / Who's been talkin' / Walk to camp hall / Sittin' on top of the world / Howlin' for my baby / Wang dang doodle / Back door man / Spoonful / Down in the bottom / Shake for me / Red rooster / You'll be mine / Goin' down slow / Tail dragger / 300 pounds of joy / Built for comfort / Killing floor
CD _____ CDRED 3
Charly / Oct '88 / Charly / THE / Cadillac.

MOANIN' FOR MY BABY (Vol. 2)
CD _____ RTS 33038
Roots / May '92 / Direct.

POWER OF THE VOICE, THE
I ain't superstitious / Sittin' on top of the world / Built for comfort / Red rooster / Highway 49 / Cause of it all / Killing floor /

Brown skin woman / Sun is rising / I'm the wolf / House rockin' boogie / Dog me around / Keep what you got / My baby stole off / Crying at day break / Passing by blues / Poor boy / Commit a crime / Wang dang doodle / Do the do / Worried about my baby / Rockin' daddy
CD _____ CD 52002
Blues Encore / '92 / Target/BMG.

REAL FOLK BLUES
Killing floor / Louise / Poor boy / Sittin' on top of the world / Nature / My country sugar mama (aka Sugar Mama) / Tail dragger / 300 pounds of joy / Natchez burning / Built for comfort / Ooh baby, hold me / Tell me what I've done
CD _____ CHLD 19098
Chess/MCA / Nov '92 / BMG / New Note.

RED ROOSTER
CD _____ IMP 302
Iris Music / Jul '95 / Discovery.

RED ROOSTER, THE
Shake for me / Red rooster / You'll be mine / Who's been talkin' / Wang dang doodle / Little baby / Spoonful / Goin' down slow / Down in the bottom / Back door man / Howlin' for my baby / Tell me / My baby walked off / Killing floor / Country sugar mama / My life / Goin' back home / Louise / Highway 49 / Hold onto your money / Built for comfort / Ain't superstitious / My last affair / Dorothy Mae / Commit a crime / Moanin' at midnight
CD _____ CDGRF 026
Tring / '93 / Tring / Prism.

RIDES AGAIN
House rockin' boogie / Crying at daybreak / Keep what you got / Dog me around / Moanin' at midnight / Chocolate drop / My baby stole off / I want your picture / Passing by blues / Worried about my baby / Driving this highway / Sun is rising / Riding in the moonlight / My friends / I'm the Wolf
CD _____ CDCHD 333
Ace / Oct '91 / Pinnacle / Cadillac / Complete/Pinnacle.

SMOKESTACK LIGHTNIN'
CD _____ MCSTD 1960
MCA / May '94 / BMG.

SPOONFUL
Smokestack lightnin' / Back door man / Evil / Tell me / Watergate blues / Tail dragger
CD _____ CDRB 2
Charly / Apr '94 / Charly / THE / Cadillac.

SPOONFUL OF BLUES
Scratch / Jul '95 / BMG.
CD _____ 3001092

VERY BEST OF HOWLIN' WOLF, THE (& Roots Of The Blues #3 Compilation/3CD Set)
Moanin' at midnight / How many more years / Wolf is at your door / Dorothy Mae / Work for your money / All night boogie / Neighbours / I'm the wolf / Baby how long / Evil / Forty four / Who will be next / Smokestack lightnin' / I asked for water (she gave me gasoline) / Natchez burning / Tell me / Sittin' on top of the world / I've been abused / Wang dang doodle / Back door man / Spoonful / Little baby / Down in the bottom / Shake for me / Red rooster / You'll be mine / I ain't superstitious / Goin' down slow / Do the do / Trail dragger / Long green stuff / 300 Pounds of joy / Built for comfort / Killing floor / What a woman / Who's been talkin' / Poor boy / Rockin' Daddy / Life savers blues / Frankie / Big fat Mama blues / Blind Arthur's breakdown / Milk cow blues / Preachin' the blues / Do your duty / Brown skin girls / Back door blues / Evil hearted woman blues / Love in vain / Fox chase / I done got wise / Yancy stomp / Leaving the blues / You gonna miss me when I'm gone
CD Set _____ VBCD 303
Charly / Jul '95 / Charly / THE / Cadillac.

WHO WILL BE NEXT (Charly Blues - Masterworks Vol. 30)
Who will be next / I have a little girl / Come to me baby / Don't mess with me baby / Smokestack lightnin' / You can't be beat / I asked for water (she gave me gasoline) / So glad / Break of the day / Natchez burning / Goin' back home / Bluebird / My life / You ought to know / Who's been talkin' / Nature
CD _____ CDBM 30
Charly / Sep '92 / Charly / THE / Cadillac.

WOLF IS AT YOUR DOOR, THE (Charly Blues - Masterworks Volume 5)
Moanin' at midnight / How many more years / Wolf is at your door (howlin' for my baby) / California blues / California boogie / Look-a-here baby / Howlin' wolf boogie / Smile at me / Getting old and gray / Mr. Highwayman / My baby walked off / Champagen velvet blues (C.V Wine Blues) / My troubles and me / Chocolate drop / Highway man / Everybody in the mood / Bluebird / Saddle my pony
CD _____ CD BM 5
Charly / Apr '92 / Charly / THE / Cadillac.

WOLF IS AT YOUR DOOR, THE (2CD Set)
Somebody's in my home / My mind is ramblin' / I walked from Dallas / Streamline

woman / Cause of it all / Do the do / Worried about you / Poor boy / Shake for me / Red rooster / You'll be mine / Who's been talkin' / Wang dang doodle / Little baby / Spoonful / Goin' down slow / Down in the bottom / Back door man / Howlin' for my baby / Tell me / My baby walked off / Killing floor / My country sugar mama / My life / Goin' back home / Louise / Highway 49 / Hold on to your money / Built for comfort / I ain't superstitious / My last affair / Dorothy Mae / Commit a crime / Moanin' at midnight / Riding in the moonlight / Everybody's in the mood / Wolf is at your door (howlin' for my baby) / I better go now
CD Set _____ 422176
New Rose / May '94 / Direct / ADA.

Hoy, Johnny

TROLLING THE HOOTCHY (Hoy, Johnny & the Bluefish)
CD _____ CDTC 1151
Tonecool / Apr '95 / Direct / ADA.

HP Lovecraft

HP LOVECRAFT LIVE
Wayfaring stranger / Drifter / It's about time / White ship / At the mountains of madness / Bag I'm in / I've never been wrong before / Country boy and Bleeker Street
CD _____ EDCD 345
Edsel / Nov '91 / Pinnacle / ADA.

HR

HUMAN RIGHTS
CD _____ SST 117 CD
SST / Mar '88 / Plastic Head.

ROCK OF ENOCH
CD _____ SST 274 CD
SST / May '93 / Plastic Head.

SINGIN' IN THE HEART
Fool's gold / Rasta time / Singin' in the heart / Treat street / Youthman sufferer / Fools gold (dub) / Don't trust no (shadows) / Youthman sufferer (dub)
CD _____ SST 224 CD
SST / Sep '89 / Plastic Head.

Hradistan

MORAVIAN ECHOES
CD _____ LT 0018
Lotos / Nov '95 / Czech Music Enterprises.

Hsiao-Yueh, Tsai

NAN-KOUAN VOL. 1
CD _____ C 559004
Ocora / Sep '93 / Harmonia Mundi / ADA.

NAN-KOUAN VOL. 2
CD _____ C 560037
Ocora / Sep '93 / Harmonia Mundi / ADA.

NAN-KOUAN VOL. 3
CD _____ C 560038
Ocora / Sep '93 / Harmonia Mundi / ADA.

NAN-KOUAN VOLS 4, 5 & 6
CD Set _____ C 560039/41
Ocora / Sep '93 / Harmonia Mundi / ADA.

Hubbard, Freddie

ALL BLUES
All blues / God bless the child / Bolivia / Dear John
CD _____ JWD 102217
JWD / Apr '95 / Target/BMG.

ARTISTRY OF FREDDIE HUBBARD, THE
Caravan / Bob's place / Happy times / Summertime / Seventh day
CD _____ MVCZ 22
Telstar / Oct '95 / BMG.
CD _____ IMP 11792
Impulse Jazz / Jan '96 / BMG / New Note.

BACKLASH
Backlash / Return of the prodigal son / Little sunflower / On the que tee / Up jumped spring / Echoes of blue
CD _____ 7567904662
Atlantic / Jul '93 / Warner Music.

BORN TO BE BLUE
Gibraltar / True colors / Born to be blue / Joy spring / Up jumped spring
CD _____ OJCCD 7342
Original Jazz Classics / Jun '94 / Wellard / Cadillac / Complete/Pinnacle.

FREDDIE HUBBARD/WOODY SHAW SESSIONS, THE (2 CDs) (Hubbard, Freddie & Woody Shaw)
Sandu / Boperation / Lament for Booker / Hub tones / Desert moonlight / Just a ballad for Woody / Lotus blossom / Down under / Eternal triangle / Moontrane / Calling Miss Khadija / Nostrand and Fulton / Tomorrow's destiny / Sao Paulo / Reets and I
CD Set _____ CDP 8327472
Blue Note / Sep '95 / EMI.

HUB OF HUBBARD, A
Without a song / Just one of those things / Blues for Duane / Things we did last summer / Muses for Richard Davis
CD _____ 825 956-2
Polydor / '88 / PolyGram.

HUB'S NUB

CD _____ CD 53206
Giants Of Jazz / Jan '95 / Target/BMG / Cadillac.

MINOR MISHAP

CD _____ BLCD 760122
Black Lion / Aug '89 / Jazz Music / Cadillac / Wellard / Koch.

NIGHT OF THE COOKERS VOLS. 1 & 2
Pensativa / Walkin' / Jodo / Breaking point
CD _____ CDP 8288822
Blue Note / May '94 / EMI.

OUTPOST
CD _____ ENJACD 309653
Enja / Jan '95 / New Note / Vital/SAM.

READY FOR FREDDIE
Arietis (Mixes) / Weaver of dreams / Marie Antoinette (Mixes) / Birdlike / Crisis
CD _____ CDP 8320942
Blue Note / Aug '95 / EMI.

RIDE LIKE THE WIND
Hubbard's cupboard / This is it / Condition alpha / Ride like the wind / Birdland / Brigitte / Two moods for Freddie
CD _____ 9600292
Elektra / Jul '84 / Warner Music.

Hubbard, Joe

VANISHING POINT
CD _____ CMMR 921
Music Maker / Jun '92 / Grapevine / ADA.

Hucko, Peanuts

SWING THAT MUSIC
CD _____ SLCD 9005
Starline / Feb '94 / Jazz Music.

TRIBUTE TO BENNY GOODMAN (Hucko, Peanuts/Butterfield/Erstrand)
CD _____ CDTTD 513
Timeless Traditional / Jul '94 / New Note.

Huddersfield Choral...

CAROLS ALBUM, THE (Huddersfield Choral Society)
O come all ye faithful (Adeste Fidelis) / Unto us is born a son / I saw three ships / Joy to the world / Away in a manger / God rest ye merry gentlemen / It came upon a midnight clear / Shepherds farewell / Good Christian men rejoice / Good King Wenceslas / Once in Royal David's City / We three kings of Orient are / In the bleak midwinter / O come, o come Emmanuel / While shepherds watched their flocks by night / First Noel / Silent night / Angles from the realms of glory / As with gladness men of old / Hark the herald angels sing / See amid the winter's snow (CD only.)
CD _____ CDMFP 6038
Music For Pleasure / Dec '94 / EMI.

CHRISTMAS FANTASY (Huddersfield Choral Society)
We wish you a Merry Christmas / O come all ye faithful (Adeste Fidelis) / Sussex carol / Ding dong merrily on high / First Noel / In dulci jubilo / Silent night
CD _____ CHAN 8679
Chandos / Nov '88 / Chandos.

Hudson, Dave

NIGHT AND DAY
You make me feel / Now that love has gone / Love and happiness / Translover / Let's get back together / Thin line / Love in the fast lane / Just a feeling / That's what dreams are made of / Night and day
CD _____ WAY 269507-2
Waylo / Apr '92 / Charly.

Hudson, Keith

BRAND
CD _____ CDPS 004
Pressure Sounds / Jul '95 / SRD / Jetstar.

GREATEST HITS PART 1
CD _____ CD 1019
Sky-Hi / Oct '94 / Pinnacle.

STUDIO KINDA CLOUDY (Hudson, Keith & Friends)
CD _____ CDTRL 258
Trojan / Sep '94 / Jetstar / Total/BMG.

Hue & Cry

BEST OF HUE & CRY, THE
Labour of love / Looking for Linda / Under neon / Wide screen / Ordinary angel / Sweet invisibility / Peaceful face / I refuse / She makes a sound / Too shy to say / Mother Glasgow / Stars crash down
CD _____ CDVIP 134
Virgin / Apr '95 / EMI.

LABOURS OF LOVE - THE BEST OF HUE & CRY
Labour of love / I refuse / Sweet invisibility / Looking for Linda / My salt heart / Violently (Your words hit me) / Strength to strength / Ordinary angel / Long term lovers of pain / She makes a sound / Widescreen / Stars crash down / Peaceful face (live) / Man with the child in his eyes / Truth / Labour of love (7" urban edit)

HUE & CRY

CD _____ HACCD 1
Circa / Mar '93 / EMI.

PIANO AND VOCAL
CD _____ PERMCD 39
Permanent / Oct '95 / Total/BMG.

REMOTE
Ordinary angel / Looking for Linda / Guy on the wall / Violently / Dollar William / Under neon (Not on LP) / Only thing (more powerful than the boss) / Where we wish to remain / Sweet invisibility / Three foot blasts of fire / Remote / Family of eyes (Not on LP)
CD _____ CIRCD 6
Circa / Nov '88 / EMI.

REMOTE/BITTER SUITE (Limited Edition 2CD Set)
Mother Glasgow (Live) / Man with the child in his eyes / Shipbuilding / Rollin' home / Peaceful face (live) / Widescreen (live) / O God head hid (live) / Looking for Linda (live) / Remote (live) / It was a very good year (live) / Round midnight / Truth (Mixes) / Ordinary angel / Looking for Linda / Guy on the wall / Violently (your words hit me) / Dollar William / Only thing more powerful than the boss / Where we wish to remain / Sweet invisibility / Three foot blasts of fire / Remote
CD Set _____ CDHUE 6
Circa / '89 / EMI.

SEDUCED AND ABANDONED
Strength to strength / History city / Goodbye to me / Human touch / Labour of love / I refuse / Something warmer (CD only) / Alligator man / Love is the master / Just one word / Truth
CD _____ CIRCD 2
Circa / '87 / EMI.

STARS CRASH DOWN
My salt heart / Life as text / She makes a sound / Making strange / Remembrance and gold / Long term lovers of pain / Stars crash down / Vera drives / Woman in time / Late in the day
CD _____ CIRCD 15
Circa / Jun '91 / EMI.

Hue B

GOOD IN A ME, THE
CD _____ CRCD 31
Charm / Mar '94 / Jetstar.

Huevos Rancheros

DIG IN
CD _____ LOUDEST 7
One Louder / Apr '95 / SRD.

Hufschmidt, Thomas

PEPILA (Hufschmidt, Thomas & Tyron Park)
CD _____ BEST 1034CD
Acoustic Music / Nov '93 / ADA.

Huge Baby

SUPER FRANKENSTEIN
CD _____ PILLMCD 5
Placebo / Aug '94 / Disc.

Huggy Bear

TAKING THE ROUGH WITH THE SMOOCH
Dissthentic penetration / Sizzle meat / Shaved pussy poetry / Pansy twist / Concrete life / Pro no from now / Prayer / Herjazz / Teen tighterns / Derwin / No sleep / Can't kiss
CD _____ BOMB 015CD
Wiiija / Sep '93 / Vital.

WEAPONRY LISTENS TO LOVE
Immature adolescence / Fuck your heart / Face down / Warming rails / On the wolves tip / Erotic bleeding / Sixteen and suicide / Obesity and speed / Insecure offenders / Why am I a lawbreaker / Local arrogance
CD _____ WIJ 037CD
Wiiija / Oct '94 / Vital.

Hughes, Brian

BETWEEN DUSK...AND DREAMING
CD _____ JUST 362
Justin Time / Mar '92 / Harmonia Mundi / Cadillac.

UNDER ONE SKY
CD _____ JUST 49-2
Justin Time / Jan '93 / Harmonia Mundi / Cadillac.

Hughes, David

ACTIVE IN THE PARISH
Millenium song / Active in the parish / Human heart / Everybody's talking about FM / Who's that (the summer of love) / Trace elements / Girls play hockey 1966 / Solid ground / Wasted / Willy Waldergrave story / State of the nation / Modest proposal
CD _____ TFCCD 999
Folk Corporation / Oct '95 / ADA.

CURTAINS
CD _____ HY 200126CD
Hypertension / Feb '95 / Total/BMG / Direct / ADA.

Hughes, Glenn

BLUES
Boy can sing the blues / I'm the man / Here comes the rebel / What can I do for ya / So much love to give / Shake the ground / Hey buddy (you got me wrong) / Have you read the book / Life of misery / Can't take away my pride / Right to live
CD _____ RR 90882
Roadrunner / Jan '93 / Pinnacle.

BURNING JAPAN LIVE
CD _____ SPV 08518202
SPV / Jul '95 / Plastic Head.

FEEL
CD _____ CD 08589762
SPV / Nov '95 / Plastic Head.

FROM NOW ON
CD _____ RR 90072
Roadrunner / Feb '94 / Pinnacle.

PLAY ME OUT
I got it covered / Space high / It's about time / L.A. cut off / Well / Solution / Your love is like a fire / Destiny / I found a woman / Smile / Getting near to you / Fools condition / Take me with you / She knows
CD _____ RPM 149
RPM / Feb '95 / Pinnacle.

Hughes, Howard

CAR GOING OVER A BRIDGE
CD _____ USRCD 3
Ultrasonic / Nov '93 / Pinnacle.

Hughes, Joe

DOWN AND DEPRESSED - DANGEROUS
CD _____ MRNETCD 0044
Munich / Jul '93 / CM / ADA / Greensleeves / Direct.

TEXAS GUITAR MASTER-CRAFTSMAN
CD _____ DTCD 3019
Double Trouble / Aug '88 / CM / Hot Shot.

TEXAS GUITAR SINGER
CD _____ MMBCD 1
Me & My / Oct '95 / Direct.

Hughes, Spike

COMPLETE VOLS 3 & 4
CD _____ KCM 0034
Kings Cross Music / Aug '95 / Cadillac / Harmonia Mundi / Wellard.

HIGH YELLOW
CD _____ 5129
Largo / Mar '95 / Complete/Pinnacle.

HIS DECCA-DENTS, DANCE ORCHESTRA & HIS THREE BLIND MICE 1930
CD _____ KCM 001/002
Kings Cross Music / Mar '95 / Cadillac / Harmonia Mundi / Wellard.

Hugill, Stan

CHANTS PAS MARINS ANGLAIS
CD _____ SCM 021
Diffusion Breizh / May '93 / ADA.

Hula

BEST OF HULA, THE
Fever car / Get the habit / Freeze out (Club mix) / Ghost rattle / Black wall blue / Big heat / Mother courage / Walk on stalks of shattered glass / Tear up / Hard stripes / Poison (Club mix) / Give me money / Cut me loose / Seven sleepers / Junshi
CD _____ CDGRAM 81
Anagram / Jun '94 / Pinnacle.

Hulbaekmo, Tone

KONKYLIE
CD _____ GR 4095CD
Grappa / Apr '95 / ADA.

Hull, Alan

BACK TO BASICS
CD _____ CRESTCD 017
Mooncrest / Jun '94 / Direct / ADA.

PIPEDREAM
Breakfast / Just another sad song / Money game / United states of mind / Country gentleman's wife / Numbers (travelling band) / For the bairns / Drug song / Song for a windmill / Blue murder / I hate to see you cry
CD _____ CASCD 1069
Charisma / Feb '91 / EMI.

Hullabaloo

LUBITORIUM
CD _____ CZ 027CD
C/Z / Sep '91 / Plastic Head.

REGURGITATED
CD _____ EFA 11381CD
Musical Tragedies / Jun '93 / SRD.

Hum Projimo

ALPENGLUH'N: SONGS FROM MURMI
CD _____ EFA 112842
Glasnost / Oct '95 / SRD.

Humair, Daniel

EDGES
CD _____ LBLC 6545
Label Bleu / Jan '92 / New Note.

Human Beinz

NOBODY BUT ME
Nobody but me / Foxey lady / Shamen / Flower grave / Dance on through / Turn on your lights / It's fun to be clean / Black is the colour of my true love's hair / This lonely town / Sueno / Serenade to Sarah
CD _____ SEECD 327
See For Miles/C5 / Jul '91 / Pinnacle.

Human Chains

HUMAN CHAINS
Freely / My Girl / Antonia / Elderberries / La la la / Grinding to the miller men / Hollyhocks / Golden slumbers / Further away / Suguxhama / Jolobe / Ikebana / Bon / Nancy D / Death
CD _____ AHUM 002
Ah-Um / Jun '89 / New Note / Cadillac.

Human League

CRASH
Money / Swang / Human / Jam / Are you ever coming back / I need your lovin' / Party / Love on the run / Real thing / Love is all that matters
CD _____ CDV 2391
Virgin / May '86 / EMI.

DARE
Things that dreams are made of / Open your heart / Sound of the crowd / Darkness / Do or die / Get Carter / I am the law / Seconds / Love action (I believe in love) / Don't you want me
CD _____ CDV 2192
Virgin / Oct '81 / EMI.

GREATEST HITS
Don't you want me / Love action / Mirror man / Tell me when / Stay with me tonight / Open your heart / Keep feeling Fascination / Sound of the crowd / Being boiled / Lebanon / Love is all that matters / Louise / Life on your own / Together in electric dreams / Human / Don't you want me (Snap remix)
CD _____ CDV 2792
Virgin / Oct '95 / EMI.

HYSTERIA
I'm coming back / I love you too much / Rock me again and again and again..... / Louise / Lebanon / Betrayed / Sign / So hurt / Life on your own / Don't you know I want you
CD _____ CDV 2315
Virgin / Jul '87 / EMI.

OCTOPUS
Tell me when / These are the days / One man in my heart / Words / Filling up with heaven / Housefull of nothing / John Cleese; is he funny / Never again / Cruel young lover
CD _____ 4509987502
East West / Jan '95 / Warner Music.

REPRODUCTION
Almost medieval / Circus of death / Path of least resistance / Blind youth / Word before last / Empire state human / Morale...You've lost that loving feeling / Austerity/Girl one (medley) / Zero as a limit
CD _____ CDV 2133
Virgin / '87 / EMI.

TRAVELOGUE
Black hit of space / Only after dark / Life kills / Dreams of leaving / Toyota city / Crow and a baby / Touchables / Gordon's gin / Being boiled / WXJL tonight
CD _____ CDV 2160
Virgin / '87 / EMI.

Humara, Walter Salas

RADAR
CD _____ NORMAL 193CD
Normal/Okra / Jan '96 / Direct / ADA.

Humble Pie

COLLECTION: HUMBLE PIE
Bang / Natural born boogie / I'll go alone / Buttermilk boy / Desperation / Nifty little number like you / Wrist job / Stick shift / Growing closer / As safe as yesterday / Heartbeat / Down home again / Take me back / Only you can see / Silver tongue / Every mother's son / Sad bag of Shaky Jake / Cold lady / Home and away / Light of love
CD _____ CCSCD 104
Castle / Apr '94 / BMG.

EARLY YEARS
Natural born boogie / Wrist job / Stick shift / As safe as yesterday / Alabama 69 / Nifty number like you / What you will / Sad bag

of Shaky Jake / Light of love / Ollie Ollie / Every mother's son / Home and away
CD _____ EARLD 4
BMG / Nov '92 / BMG.

IMMEDIATE YEARS, THE (2CD Set)
Natural born bugie / Wrist job / Desperation / Stick shift / Buttermilk boy / Growing closer / As safe as yesterday is / Bang / Alabama 69 / I'll go alone / Nifty little number like you / What you will / Greg's song / Take me back / Sad bag of shaky Jake / Light of love / Cold lady / Down home again / Ollie Ollie / Every mother's son / Heartbeat / Only you can see / Silver tongue / Home and away
CD Set _____ CDIMMBOX 3
Charly / Aug '95 / Charly / THE / Cadillac.

NATURAL BORN BOOGIE
CD _____ BOJCD 010
Band Of Joy / Feb '95 / ADA.

PIECE OF THE PIE, A
CD _____ 5401792
A&M / Apr '95 / PolyGram.

TOWN AND COUNTRY
Take me back / Sad bag of Shaky Jake / Light of love / Cold lady / Down home again / Ollie Ollie / Every mother's son / Heartbeat / Only you can see / Silver tongue / Home and away
CD _____ CDIMM 020
Charly / Feb '94 / Charly / THE / Cadillac.

Humeniuk, Pawlo

KING OF THE UKRAINIAN FIDDLERS
CD _____ FL 7025
Folklyric / Apr '95 / Direct / Cadillac.

Humes, Helen

HELEN HUMES AND THE MUSE ALL STARS
I'm gonna move to the outskirts of town / These foolish things / Woe is me / I've got a crush on you / Body and soul / My old flame / Loud talking woman / These foolish things (alt.) / I've got a crush on you (alt.)
CD _____ MCD 5473
Muse / Jun '93 / New Note / CM.

NEW YEARS EVE, THE
CD _____ LDJ 274914
Radio Nights / Nov '91 / Harmonia Mundi / Cadillac.

ON THE SUNNY SIDE OF THE STREET
Alright O.K. you win / If I could be with you one hour tonight / Ain't nobody's business / Kansas City / I'm satisfied / Blue because of you / On the sunny side of the street / I got it bad and that ain't good
CD _____ BLCD 760185
Black Lion / Jul '93 / Jazz Music / Cadillac / Wellard / Koch.

Hummel, Mark

FEEL LIKE ROCKIN'
CD _____ FF 70061
Flying Fish / Nov '94 / Roots / CM / Direct / ADA.

Hummon, Marcus

ALL IN GOOD TIME
Hittin' the road / God's country USA / One of these days / Honky tonk Mona Lisa / Next step / I do / Virginia reelin' / Somebody's leaving / Bless the broken road / As the crow flies / Bridges over blue / All in good time
CD _____ 4810282
Columbia / Jan '96 / Sony.

Humperdinck, Engelbert

16 GREATEST LOVE SONGS
Man without love / What now my love / I wish you love / There goes my everything / Dommage dommage / Yours until tomorrow / Gentle on my mind / Am I that easy to forget / Shadow of your smile / Love letters / Way it used to be / Can't take my eyes off you / What a wonderful world / Misty blue / I'm a better man (for having loved you) / This is my song
CD _____ PWKS 528
Carlton Home Entertainment / Jun '89 / Carlton Home Entertainment.

AND I LOVE YOU SO
CD _____ 12567
Laserlight / Oct '95 / Target/BMG.

CLOSE TO YOU
Close to you / My cherie amour / Everybody's talkin' / Killing me softly / Just the way you are / Love me tender / Raindrops keep falling on my head / And I love you so / Another time another place / You are the sunshine of my life / Something / Leaving on a jet plane / What I did for love / Help me make it through the night / Forever and ever (and ever) / Love me with all your heart / Without you / You light up my life
CD _____ CDMFP 5932
Music For Pleasure / Oct '91 / EMI.

ENGELBERT
Love can fly / Love was here before the stars / Don't say no (Again) / Let me into your life / Through the eyes of love / Les

bicyclettes de belsize / Way it used to be /
Marry me / To get to you / You're easy to
love / True / Good thing going / Stay / Come
over here / You love / If I were you / Two
different worlds / Am I that easy to forget
CD _____ 8205762
London / Jan '93 / PolyGram.

ENGELBERT HUMPERDINCK
I'm a better man (for having loved you) /
Gentle on my mind / Love letters / Time for
us / Didn't we / I wish you love / Aquarius
/ All you've got to do is ask / Signs of love
/ Cafe / Let's kiss tomorrow goodbye / Win-
ter world of love / Those were the days /
Can't take my eyes off you / Love was here
before the stars / Stardust
CD _____ 8205772
London / Jan '93 / PolyGram.

**ENGELBERT HUMPERDINCK'S
GREATEST HITS**
Release me / Man without love / Way it
used to be / Quando, quando, quando /
Everybody knows we're through / There's a
kind of hush / There goes my everything /
Les bicyclettes de Belsize / I'm a better
man (for having loved you) / Winter world of
love / My world / Ten guitars / Am I that
easy to forget / Last waltz
CD _____ 8203672
London / Jul '89 / PolyGram.

ENGELBERT IN LOVE
Man without love / Killing me softly / Last
waltz / Help me make it through the night /
There goes my everything / My cherie
amour / Winter world of love / Way it used
to be / Something / Close to you / Am I that
easy to forget / Love me tender / Release
me / Quando, quando, quando (tell me
when) / Most beautiful girl / Spanish eyes /
Just the way you are / First time ever I saw
your face / You are the sunshine of my life
/ And I love you so
CD _____ 9022952
Pickwick/Sony Collector's Choice / Apr '90
/ Carlton Home Entertainment / Pinnacle /
Sony.

EYES OF LOVE
Way it used to be / Can't take my eyes off
you / Gentle on my mind / Everybody
knows / Call on me / Nature boy / Love was
there before the stars / Les bicyclettes de
Belsize / Last waltz / This is my song /
Spanish eyes / Place in the sun / Man with-
out love / Quiet nights / How near is love /
Through the eyes of love
CD _____ PWKS 4026
Carlton Home Entertainment / Sep '90 /
Carlton Home Entertainment.

HIS ROMANTIC HITS
CD _____ CD 3503
Cameo / Aug '94 / Target/BMG.

IN THE STILL OF THE NIGHT
In the still of the night / I'm getting sentimental over you / I'll walk alone / Moonlight
becomes you / You'll never know / I don't
want to walk without you / Stardust /
Embraceable you / Lovely way to spend an
evening / Long ago and far away / Red sails in the sunset
/ Far away places / My foolish heart / Very
thought of you / They say it's wonderful /
Harbour lights / More I see you / Yours / As
time goes by
CD _____ MCCD 055
Music Club / Mar '92 / Disc / THE / CM.

LAST WALTZ, THE
Last waltz / Dance with me / Two different
worlds / If it comes to that / Walk hand in
hand / Place in the sun / Long gone / All
this world and the seven seas / Miss Elaine
E.S. Jones / Everybody knows (we're
through) / To the ends of the earth / That
promise / Three little words / Those were
the days / What now my love
CD _____ 8205752
London / Jul '91 / PolyGram.

LET ME INTO YOUR LIFE
Winter world of love / Wonderland by night
/ By the time I get to phoenix / Don't say
no (again) / All this world and the seven
seas / From here to eternity / Didn't we /
Ten guitars / Quando, quando, quando /
Cafe / Talking love / Funny familiar forgotten
feelings / Let's kiss tomorrow goodbye /
There goes my everything
CD _____ PWKS 4105P
Carlton Home Entertainment / Apr '92 /
Carlton Home Entertainment.

LIVE AND LOVE
Help me make it through the night / Most
beautiful girl / I don't break easily / Maybe
this time / And if I love you so / Girl of mine
/ Medley / Winter wonderland / You don't
love me anymore / Without you / Till I get it
right / Baby me baby / Ladies night / After
the lovin'
CD _____ PWKS 4186
Carlton Home Entertainment / Nov '93 /
Carlton Home Entertainment.

LOVE HAS BEEN A FRIEND OF MINE
CD _____ RLBTC 008
Realisation / Oct '93 / Prism.

LOVE SONGS
CD _____ CD 3028
Scratch / Oct '94 / BMG.

LOVE UNCHAINED
Too young / Secret love / Unchained melody / Answer me / (Sittin' on) the dock of
the bay / No other love / Stranger in paradise / I apologise / Smoke gets in your eyes
/ Such a night / Love me tender / Love is a
many splendoured thing
CD _____ CDEMTV 94
EMI / May '95 / EMI.

MAN WITHOUT LOVE, A
Man without love / Can't take my eyes off
you / From here to eternity / Spanish eyes
/ Man and a woman / Quando, quando,
quando / Up, up and away / Wonderland
by night / What a wonderful world / Call on
me / By the time I get to phoenix / Shadow
of your smile / Stardust / Pretty ribbon /
Dommage dommage / When I say goodnight / Funny familiar forgotten feelings /
There goes my everything
CD _____ 8207682
London / Nov '88 / PolyGram.

MASTERPIECES
CD _____ 12329
Laserlight / May '94 / Target/BMG.

**MERRY CHRISTMAS WITH
ENGELBERT, A**
O come all ye faithful (Adeste Fidelis) / Have
yourself a merry little Christmas / Blue
Christmas / Away in a manger / O little town
of Bethlehem / We three kings of Orient are
/ First Noel / Silent night / Winter wonder-
land / Mary's boy child / God rest ye merry
gentlemen / Lord's prayer
CD _____ PWKS 4033
Carlton Home Entertainment / Sep '93 /
Carlton Home Entertainment.

RELEASE ME
Last waltz / Spanish eyes / This is my song
/ Nature boy / There's a kind of hush /
Everybody knows / How near is love / Walk
hand in hand / Quiet nights / Man and a
woman
CD _____ PWKS 584
Carlton Home Entertainment / May '90 /
Carlton Home Entertainment.

RELEASE ME
CD _____ 8204592
London / Jan '93 / PolyGram.

SIMPLY THE BEST - RELEASE ME
CD _____ WMCD 5694
Disky / May '94 / THE / BMG / Discovery /
Pinnacle.

SINGS THE CLASSICS
CD _____ CCSCD 432
Castle / Mar '95 / BMG.

STARDUST
Stardust / I'll be seeing you / Yours / More
I see you / In the still of the night / I'm get-
ting sentimental over you / Moonlight be-
comes you / But beautiful / I'll be around /
Harbour lights / They say it's wonderful /
Long ago and far away
CD _____ MSCD 21
Music De-Luxe / Jun '95 / Magnum Music
Group.

STEP INTO MY LIFE
Red roses for my lady / You are so beautiful
/ I get lonely / Step into my life / Sentimental
lady / You are my love / Sweet lady Jane /
I wanna rock you / You're my heart my soul
/ Dancing with tears in my eyes
CD _____ CDWM 102
Westmoor / '91 / Target/BMG.

THROUGH THE EYES OF LOVE
There goes my everything / Walk through
the world / Ten guitars / Dommage domm-
age / What now my love / Come over here
/ There's a kind of hush (all over the world)
/ This is my song / Stay / Misty blue / Take
my heart / Funny familiar forgotten feelings
/ When I say goodnight / Release me
CD _____ 5500222
Spectrum/Karussell / May '93 / PolyGram /
THE.

Humpff Family

FATHER'S
That's what I see / Triangle / Magic journey
/ Can of beans / Future imperfect / Skye
Bridge song / Love, death, divorce, prison,
alcohol, rivers and trains / Be there / Joan-
ie's letter / Mary's luck / Rain / Henryetta /
Conduct of pigeons
CD _____ IGCD 208
Iona Gold / Jul '94 / Total/BMG / ADA.

MOTHERS
CD _____ IRCD 019
Iona / Oct '91 / ADA / Direct / Duncans.

Humphrey, Percy

**PERCY HUMPHREY & MARYLAND
JAZZBAND**
CD _____ BCD 318
GHB / Apr '94 / Jazz Music.

Humphrey, Willie

**NEW ORLEANS TRADITIONAL JAZZ
LEGENDS**
CD _____ MG 9002
Mardi Gras / Feb '95 / Jazz Music.

Hungry Chuck

SOUTH IN NEW ORLEANS
Hats off, America / Cruisin' / Old Thomas
Jefferson / Play that country music / Find
the enemy / People do / Watch the trucks
go by / Dixie highway / You better watch it
Ben / Someday you're gonna run out of gas
/ Hoona, spoona / All bowed down / Doin'
the funky lunch box / Cruising / Play Old
thomas jefferson
CD _____ C5CD 590
See For Miles/C5 / Aug '92 / Pinnacle.

Hunks, Beau

**CELEBRATION ON THE PLANET MARS,
A (A Tribute To Raymond Scott) (Hunks,
Beau Sextette)**
CD _____ 379092
Koch International / Nov '95 / Koch.

Hunningale, Peter

MR. GOVERNMENT
Mr. Songbird / Tweet dub / Jump / Babylon
/ War on babylon / Mr. Government / Down-
ing St. dub / One people / One dub / Sensi
sensi
CD _____ ARICD 101
Ariwa Sounds / Apr '94 / Jetstar / SRD.

MR. VIBES
CD _____ ARKCD 102
Arawak / Jan '93 / Jetstar.

NAH GIVE UP
Nah give up / Trust me / Lover's affair /
Thinking about you / Praises / Good and
ready / Hoots and culture / Sorry (Mixes) /
Waiting on your love / Declaration of rights
/ Perfect lady / Baby please
CD _____ DTJCD 001
Down To Jam / Feb '95 / Jetstar / Total/
BMG.

Hunt, Marsha

WALK ON GILDED SPLINTERS
Walk on gilded splinters / Let the sunshine
in / Hot rod pappa / Stacey Grove / No face,
no name, no number / My world is empty
without you / Moan, you moaners / Keep
the customer satisfied / Long black veil /
You ain't goin' nowhere / Woman child /
Desdemona / Wild thing / Hippy Gumbo
CD _____ CSAPCD 116
Connoisseur / Jun '94 / Pinnacle.

Hunt, Steve

HEAD, HEART AND HAND
CD _____ IRR 015CD
Irregular / Dec '93 / Irregular / ADA.

Hunter, Alberta

20'S - 30'S
CD _____ JCD 6
Jass / Jun '87 / CM / Jazz Music / ADA /
Cadillac / Direct.

**CHICAGO-THE LIVING LEGENDS
(Hunter, Alberta & Lovie Austin)**
St. Louis blues / Moanin' low / Down-
hearted blues / How I'm satisfied / Sweet
Georgia Brown / You better change / C jam
blues / Streets paved with gold / Gallion
stomp / I will always be in love with you
CD _____ OBCCD 510
Original Blues Classics / Nov '92 / Com-
plete/Pinnacle / Wellard / Cadillac.

**SONGS WE TAUGHT YOUR MOTHER
(Hunter, Alberta/Victoria Spivey/Lucille
Hegamin)**
I got myself a workin' man / St. Louis blues
/ Black snake blues / I got a mind to ramble
/ You'll want my love / Going blues / You
gotta reap what you sow / Arkansas blues
/ Got the blues so bad / Chirpin' the blues
/ Has anybody seen my Corine / Let him
beat me
CD _____ OBCCD 520
Original Blues Classics / Nov '92 / Com-
plete/Pinnacle / Wellard / Cadillac.

YOUNG AH, THE
CD _____ JASSCD 5
Jass / '88 / CM / Jazz Music / ADA /
Cadillac / Direct.

Hunter, Charlie

BING BING BING (Hunter, Charlie Trio)
Greasy granny / Wornell's Yorkies / Fistful
of haggis / Come as you are / Scrabbling
gor purchase / Bullethead / Bing, bing, bing,
bing / Squiddlesticks / Lazy Susan (with a
client now) / Elbo room
CD _____ CDP 8318092
Blue Note / Jul '95 / EMI.

**CHARLIE HUNTER TRIO (Hunter,
Charlie Trio)**
Fred's life / Live oak / 20 30 40 50 60 dead
/ Funky niblets / Fables of Faubus / Dance
of the jazz fascists / Telephone's a'ringin' /
Rhythm comes in 12 tones / Mule / Faffer
time
CD _____ MR 066-2
Mammoth / Mar '94 / Vital.

Hunter, Chris

SCARBOROUGH FAIR
Scarborough fair / Boplicity / God bless the
child / Prelude by George Gershwin / Bud,
Bird and Gil / Beauty and the beast / Round
Midnight
CD _____ KICJ 5
King/Paddle Wheel / Jul '90 / New Note.

THIS IS CHRIS
Jail blues / Talk of the wild / Chelsea bridge
/ London / Gingerbread boy / Cherokee /
Lover man / Confirmation / Here's that rainy
day
CD _____ K32Y 6261
King/Paddle Wheel / Jun '89 / New Note.

Hunter, Ian

COLLECTION: IAN HUNTER
CD _____ CCSCD 290
Castle / Jul '91 / BMG.

IAN HUNTER
Once bitten twice shy / Who do you love /
Lounge lizard / Boy / 3000 miles from here
/ Truth / Whole truth nothin' but the truth /
It ain't easy when you fall / Shades off / I
get so excited
CD _____ 477359-2
Columbia / Aug '94 / Sony.

**LIVE IN CONCERT (Hunter, Ian & Mick
Ronson)**
Once bitten twice shy / How much more
can I take / Beg a little love / Following in
your footsteps / Irene Wilde / All the way
from Memphis / Your never too old to hit
the big time / Loner / Bastard / Standin' in
my light / (Give me back my) Wings / Sweet
dreamer / Just another night
CD _____ WINCD 078
Windsong / Oct '95 / Pinnacle.

**SHORT BACK 'N' SIDES PLUS LONG
ODDS & OUTTAKES**
Central park 'n' west / Lisa likes rock 'n' roll
/ I need your love / Old records never die /
Noises / Rain / Gun control / Theatre of the
absurd / Leave me alone / Keep on burning
/ Detroit (Rough mix instrumental) / Na na
na / I need your love (Rough mix) / Rain
(Alternative mix) / I believe in you / Listen to
the eight track / You stepped into my
dreams / Venus in a bathtub / Theatre of
the absurd (Wessex mix) / Detroit (Out take
5 - Vocal) / Na na na (Extended mix) / China
(Ronson vocal) / Old records never die (Version 1)
CD Set _____ CDCHR 6074
Chrysalis / May '94 / EMI.

WELCOME TO THE CLUB
F.B.I. / Once bitten twice shy / Angeline /
Laugh at me / All the way from Memphis / I
wish I was your mother / Irene Wilde / Just
another night / Cleveland rocks / Standin'
in my light / Bastard / Walkin' with a mountain / All the young dudes / Slaughter on
10th Avenue / We gotta get out of here /
Silver needles / Man 'o' war / Sons and
daughters
CD Set _____ CDCHR 6075
Chrysalis / May '94 / EMI.

**YOU'RE NEVER ALONE WITH A
SCHIZOPHRENIC**
Just another night / Wild east / Cleveland
rocks / Ships / When the daylight comes /
Life after death / Standin' in my light / Bas-
tard / Outsider
CD _____ CD25CR 03
Chrysalis / Mar '94 / EMI.

Hunter, Ivory Joe

16 GREATEST HITS
Jealous heart / I quit my pretty mama /
Waiting in vain / No money, no luck blues /
Too late / I like it / I have no reason to com-
plain / Lying woman / Guess who / In time
/ Code song / Please don't cry anymore /
Don't fall in love with me / False friend blues
/ It's you just you / Changing blues
CD _____ KCD 605
King/Paddle Wheel / Sep '92 / New Note.

Hunter, Jim

FINGERNAIL MOON
CD _____ COMD 2047
Temple / Feb '94 / CM / Duncans / ADA /
Direct.

UPHILL SLIDE
CD _____ COMD 2040
Temple / Feb '94 / CM / Duncans / ADA /
Direct.

Hunter, Long John

RIDE WITH ME
CD _____ BMCD 9020
Black Magic / Apr '93 / Hot Shot / Swift /
CM / Direct / Cadillac / ADA.

Hunter, Robert

BOX OF RAIN
Box of rain / Scarlet begonias / Franklin's
tower / Jack Straw / Brown eyed women /
Reuben and Cerise / Space / Deal / Prom-
ontory rider / Ripple / Boys in the bar room
/ Stella blue

HUNTER, ROBERT

CD _____ RCD 10214
Rykodisc / Sep '91 / Vital / ADA.

SENTINEL
Pride of bone / Gingerbread man / Idiot's delight (excerpt) / Red dog's decoration day / Trapping a muse / Jazz #3 / Toad in love / Rimbaud at 20 / Rain in a courtyard / Way of the ride / Sentinel / Preserpie / Poets on poets / Like a basket / Yagritz / Cocktails with Hindemith / Blue moon alley / New jungle / Full moon cafe / Tango hit palace / Exploding diamond blues / Rainwater sea / Holiogomena
CD _____ RCD 20265
Rykodisc / Nov '93 / Vital / ADA.

TALES OF THE GREAT RUM RUNNERS
Lady Simplicity / Dry dust road / Rum runners / Maybe she's a playbird / It must have been the roses / Standing at your door / Keys to the rain / That train / I heard you singing / Children's lament / Boys in the bar room / Arizona lightning / Mad
CD _____ GCD 4013
Grateful Dead / May '89 / Pinnacle.

TIGER ROSE
Tiger rose / Rose of Sharon / Dance a hole / Over the hills / Yellow moon / One thing to try / Wild Bill / Cruel white water / Last flash / Ariel
CD _____ GDCD 4010
Grateful Dead / Jul '90 / Pinnacle.

Hunter, Sonya

FAVOURITE SHORT STORIES
CD _____ NORMAL 165
Normal/Okra / Nov '94 / Direct / ADA.

FINDERS KEEPERS
CD _____ RTS 19
Return To Sender / Aug '95 / Direct / ADA.

GEOGRAPHY
Unlikely combinations / Can two worlds collide / Middle of somewhere / Atlases / Just a job / Heart cryin' in the wind / Mama sky / Baby girl / I can't reach you / Get back on that horse / London bridges
CD _____ NORMAL 160CD
Normal/Okra / Mar '94 / Direct / ADA.

PEASANT PIE
CD _____ NORM 190CD
Normal/Okra / Apr '95 / Direct / ADA.

Hunter, Willie

1982
CD _____ CMCD 010
Celtic Music / Apr '94 / CM / Roots.

Hunters & Collectors

DEMON FLOWER
CD _____ TVD 93401
Mushroom / May '94 / BMG / 3MV.

Hunting Lodge

EIGHT BALL
CD Set _____ NORMAL 61/62CD
Normal/Okra / '89 / Direct / ADA.

NECROPOLIS
CD _____ DV 17
Dark Vinyl / Jan '94 / Plastic Head.

WILL
CD _____ DV 10
Dark Vinyl / Mar '94 / Plastic Head.

Hurdy Gurdy

HURDY GURDY
CD _____ HBG 122/11
Background / Apr '94 / Background.

Hurrah

SOUND OF PHILADELPHIA
CD _____ CREV 014CD
Rev-Ola / Sep '93 / 3MV / Vital.

Hurricane

AMERICA'S MOST HARDCORE
(Hurricane & DFL)
Hurra / Can we get along / Elbow room / Pizza man / America's most hardcore / U don't understand / Knucklehead nation / Think about the pit / Smoke bomb / My crazy life
CD _____ WIJ 034CD
Wiiija / Apr '94 / Vital.

Hurst, Robert

PRESENTS: ROBERT HURST
CD _____ 4742952
Sony Jazz / Jan '95 / Sony.

Hurt, Mississippi John

AIN'T NOBODY'S BUSINESS
(Mississippi John)
CD _____ CDSGP 037
Prestige / Jan '93 / Total/BMG.

AVALON BLUES
Stackolee / Coffee blues / Slidin' delta / Corina Corina / Nobody's dirty business / Monday morning blues

---

CD _____ CDROU 1081
Rounder / Feb '92 / CM / Direct / ADA / Cadillac.

IMMORTAL
CD _____ VND 79248
Vanguard / Oct '95 / Complete/Pinnacle / Discovery.

IN CONCERT
Nobody's business but mine / Angels laid him away / Baby what's wrong with you / Casey Jones / Candy man / Lonesome blues / My creole belle / Make me a pallet on the floor / Trouble I had all my days / C-H-I-C-K-E-N blues / Coffee blues / Shake that thing / Monday morning blues / Frankie and Albert / Salty dog / Spike driver's blues
CD _____ CDBM 083
Blue Moon / Apr '91 / Magnum Music Group / Greensleeves / Hot Shot / ADA / Cadillac / Discovery.

MEMORIAL ANTHOLOGY
Slidin' delta / Salty dog / Louis Collins / stagger lee / Monday mornin' blues / Comin' home / Candy man blues / Hot time in the old town tonight / K.C. Jones blues / Make me a pallet on the floor / You can't come in / Joe Turner / Spanish flangdang / Lonesome am I / I shall not be moved / C.C. rider / Trouble blues
CD _____ EDCD 381
Edsel / Feb '94 / Pinnacle / ADA.

MISSISSIPPI JOHN HURT
CD _____ DOCD 5003
Blues Document / Feb '92 / Swift / Jazz Music / Hot Shot.

TODAY
CD _____ VND 79220
Vanguard / Oct '95 / Complete/Pinnacle / Discovery.

WORRIED BLUES
CD _____ CDROU 1082
Rounder / Feb '92 / CM / Direct / ADA / Cadillac.

Hurvitz, Sandy

SANDY'S ALBUM IS HERE AT LAST
CD _____ EDCD 399
Edsel / Nov '94 / Pinnacle / ADA.

Hush

HUMAN
CD _____ SHCD 5704
Shanachie / Oct '95 / Koch / ADA / Greensleeves.

Husik, Lida

RETURN OF RED EMMA, THE
Back in the march / Highgate / AZT No / Sedan / Earthquake blues / Light of the day / Hopi ants / Hemlock / Pyramus and thisbe / Match girl / Boy at the bus stop / Nothing / Happy, happy
CD _____ SHIMMY 061CD
Shimmy Disc / Dec '92 / Vital.

Husker Du

CANDY APPLE GREY
Crystal / Don't want to know if you are lonely / I don't know for sure / Sorry somehow / Too far down / Hardly getting over / Dead set on destruction / Eiffel Tower high / No promise have I made / All this I've done for you
CD _____ 7599253852
WEA / Nov '92 / Warner Music.

CASE CLOSED (A Tribute To Husker Du) (Various Artists)
CD _____ SRC 19
SPV / May '94 / Plastic Head.

EVERYTHING FALLS APART
From the gut / Blah blah blah / Punch drunk / Bricklayer / Afraid of being wrong / Sunshine superman / Signals from above / Everything falls apart / Wheels / Target / Obnoxious / Gravity / In a free land / What do I want / M.I.C. / Statues / Let's go die / Amusement / Do you remember
CD _____ 812271163-2
WEA / Mar '93 / Warner Music.

FLIP YOUR WIG
Flip your wig / Every everything / Makes no sense at all / Hate paper doll / Green eyes / Divide and conquer / Games / Find me / Baby song / Flexible flyer / Private plane / Keep hanging on / Wit and the wisdom / Don't want yet
CD _____ SST 055 CD
SST / May '93 / Plastic Head.

LAND SPEED RECORD
CD _____ SST 195 CD
SST / Nov '88 / Plastic Head.

LIVING FREE, THE
New day rising / Heaven hill / Standing in the rain / Back from somewhere / Ice cold ice / Everytime / Friend you're gonna fail / She floated away / From the gut / Target / It's not funny anymore / Hardly getting over it / Terms of psychic warfare / Powertime / Books about U.F.O.'s / Divide and conquer / Keep hanging on / Celebrated Summer / Now that you know me / Ain't no water in

---

the well / What's goin' on / Data control / In a free land / Sheena is a punk rocker
CD _____ 9362455822
WEA / May '94 / Warner Music.

NEW DAY RISING
CD _____ SST 031 CD
SST / May '93 / Plastic Head.

THERE'S A BOY WHO LIVES ON HEAVEN HILL (A Tribute To Husker Du) (Various Artists)
CD _____ BHR 009
Burning Heart / Nov '94 / Plastic Head.

WAREHOUSE SONGS AND STORIES
These important years / Charity, chastity, prudence and hope / Standing in the rain / Back from somewhere / Ice cold ice / You're a soldier / Could you be the one / Too much spice / Friend, you've got to fall / She floated away / Bed of nails / Tell you why tomorrow / It's not peculiar / Actual condition / No reservations / Turn it around / She's a woman / Up in the air / You can live at home
CD _____ 7599255442
WEA / Oct '92 / Warner Music.

ZEN ARCADE
Something I learned today / Broken home broken heart / Never talking to you again / Chartered trips / Dreams reoccuring / Indecision time / Hare krishna / Beyond the threshold / Pride / I'll never forget you / Biggest lie / What's going on / Masochism world / Standing by the sea / Somewhere / One step at a time / Pink turns to blue / Newest industry / Monday will never be the same / Whatever / Tooth fairy and the princess / Turn on the news / Recurring dream
CD _____ SST 027 CD
SST / May '93 / Plastic Head.

Husky, Ferlin

CAPITOL COLLECTORS SERIES: FERLIN HUSKY
Feel better all over / I'll baby sit with you / Gone / Fallen star / My reason for living / Dragging the river / Wings of a dove / Waltz you saved for me / Somebody save me / I know it was you / Timber, I'm falling / I could sing all night / I hear Little Rock calling / Once / You pushed me too far / Just for you / That's why I love you so much / Every step of the way / Heavenly sunshine / Sweet misery
CD _____ CZ 230
Capitol / Sep '89 / EMI.

SIX DAYS ON THE ROAD
CD _____ PWK 012
Carlton Home Entertainment / '88 / Carlton Home Entertainment.

Hussain, Zakir

MAKING MUSIC (Hussain, Zakir & John McLaughlin)
Making music / Zakir / Water girl / Toni / Anisa / Sunjog / You and me / Sabah
CD _____ 8315442
ECM / Jul '87 / New Note.

VENU
CD _____ RCD 20128
Rykodisc / Nov '91 / Vital / ADA.

ZAKIR HUSSAIN & THE RHYTHM EXPERIENCE (Hussain, Zakir & The Rhythm Experience)
Balinese fantasy / Nines over easy / Lineage / Def and drum / Triveni / Rapanagutan / Ryupak / Rhythm sonata in E major
CD _____ MRCD 1007
Moment / Jun '94 / ADA / Koch.

Hustles Of Culture

MANY STYLES
CD _____ WALLLP 007
Wall Of Sound / Aug '95 / Disc / Soul Trader.

Hutch

CREAM OF HUTCH VOLUME II, THE
CD _____ PASTCD 7036
Flapper / Aug '94 / Pinnacle.

HUTCH
I forgot the little things / Begin the beguine / Don't make me laugh / Broken hearted clown / Night and day / Dusty shoes / I need you / If I should lose you / Good night my beautiful / East of the sun and west of the moon / I couldn't believe my eyes / Turn on the old music box / You made me care / Kiss in the dark / My heart is haunted / Faithful forever / That old feeling / Indian Summer / Body and soul / I've got my eyes on you / I know now / You're just looking for romance
CD _____ PASTCD 9755
Flapper / Aug '91 / Pinnacle.

HUTCH (SINGS COLE PORTER & OTHER SONGS)
Let's do it let's fall in love / I'm a gigolo / Looking at you / What is sthis thing called love / Two little babes in the wood / Night and day / Anything goes / Begin the beguine / Just one of those things / Easy to love / I've got you under my skin / It's delovely / Do I love you / I've got my eyes on you / You'd be so nice to come home to /

Half caste woman / I'll follow my secret heart / I travel alone / Close your eyes / All I do is dream of you / I nearly let love go slipping through my fingers / Says my heart / You go to my head / Cole Porter medley (Parts one and two)
CD _____ CDCHD 213
Happy Days / Mar '94 / Conifer.

SINGING FOR YOU EVERYBODY
Singing for you / These foolish things / Once in a while / September in the rain / Girl in the Alice blue gown / Moon at sea / Carelessly / No regrets / Tomorrow is another day / Your heart and mine / Night and day / Red sails in the sunset / Morning after / There's rain in my eyes / Love is like a cigarette / My heart is haunted by the ghost of your smile
CD _____ CDHD 155
Happy Days / Oct '89 / Conifer.

THAT OLD FEELING
Where are you / September in the rain / Tomorrow is another day / In the chapel in the moonlight / Moon or no moon / Afterglow / In an old cathedral town / That old feeling / Paris is not the same / Singing for you / Stardust on the moon / They can't take that away from me / Way you look tonight / Carelessly / Whispers in the dark / Greatest mistake of my life / Just remember / Goodnight to you all
CD _____ 2 BUR 011
Burlington / Sep '88 / CM.

TREASURED MEMORIES
Begin the beguine / All the things you are / Mist on the rivers / I've got my eyes on you / Violins and violets / Man I love / Among my souvenirs / There's a small hotel / When love comes your way / Try a little tenderness / Don't make me laugh / It's a lovely day tomorrow / Shake down the stars / Should I tell you that I love you / Dusty shoes / It happens every day / Where or when / That's the beginning of the end / Let's fall in love / Cole Porter medley / Small cafe by Notre Dame / Careless / Rosita
CD _____ CDAJA 5084
Living Era / Mar '92 / Koch.

Hutcherson, Bobby

AMBOS MUNDOS (BOTH WORLDS)
Pomponio / Tin tin deo / Both worlds / Street song / Beep d' bop / Poema para ravel / Yelapa / Besame mucho
CD _____ LCD 15222
Landmark / Nov '89 / New Note.

CRUISIN' THE BIRD
CD _____ LCD 15172
Landmark / Oct '88 / New Note.

FAREWELL KEYSTONE
Crescent Moon / Short stuff / Prism / Starting over / Rubber man / Mapenzi
CD _____ ECD 220182
Evidence / Jul '92 / Harmonia Mundi / ADA / Cadillac.

FOUR SEASONS (Hutcherson, Bobby & George Cables)
I mean you / All of you / Spring is here / Star eyes / If I were a bell / Summertime / Autumn leaves
CD _____ CDSJP 210
Timeless Jazz / Jan '87 / New Note.

MIRAGE
Nascimento / Mirage / Beyond the bluebird / Pannonica / Del Valle / I am in love / Zingargo / Ground work / Love letters / Heroes
CD _____ LCD 15292
Landmark / Aug '91 / New Note.

PATTERNS
Patterns / Time to go / Ankara / Effi / Irina / Nocturnal / Patterns (alt. take) (CD only)
CD _____ CDP 8335832
Blue Note / Oct '95 / EMI.

Hutchings, Ashley

ALBION JOURNEY, AN
CD _____ HNCD 4802
Hannibal / May '89 / Vital / ADA.

AS YOU LIKE IT (Hutchings, Ashley All Stars)
CD _____ SPINCD 135
Making Waves / Jan '90 / CM.

ASHLEY HUTCHINGS BIRTHDAY BASH CONCERT
CD _____ HTD 39CD
HTD / Jul '95 / Pinnacle.

GUV'NOR VOL.3, THE
CD _____ HTD 38CD
HTD / Jul '95 / Pinnacle.

GUVNOR
CD _____ HIDCD 23
HTD / Jul '94 / Pinnacle.

GUVNOR VOL 2
CD _____ HTDCD 29
HTD / Mar '95 / Pinnacle.

KICKIN' UP THE SAWDUST
La russe (medley) / Buttered peas / Hullichan jig / Wave of joy / Heel and toe polka (the Belfast polka) / Tavern in the town / Double quadrille / Jumping Joan / Dorset

four hand reel / Hornpipes (medley) / Speed the plough / Cumberland square eight
CD _____ BGOCD 244
Beat Goes On / Oct '94 / Pinnacle.

SON OF MORRIS ON
Winter processional / Monck's mark / Old hog or none / As I was going to Banbury / Happy man / Fieldtown processional/Glorishears / Bob and Joan / Ladies of pleasure / Bring your fiddle / Jockey to the fair/Room for cuckolds / Saturday night / Roasted woman/Rigs of Marlow/Getting upstairs / Ye wild Morris/Wild Morris / Postman's knock / Ring O'bells / Gallant hussar / Bonnets so blue
CD _____ CZ 535
EMI / Jul '94 / EMI.

SWAY WITH ME (Hutchings, Ashley & Judy Dunlop)
CD _____ RGFCD 008
Road Goes On Forever / '92 / Direct.

TWANGIN & A TRADDIN
CD _____ HTDCD 25
HTD / Sep '94 / Pinnacle.

Hutson, Leroy

MAN, THE
Can't say enough about Mom / Gotta move gotta groove / Ella Weez / Give this love a try / Getto '74 / After the fight / Could this be love / Dudley Do-Right
CD _____ CPCD 8128
Charly / Oct '95 / Charly / THE / Cadillac.

Hutto, J.B.

HAWK SQUAT (Hutto, J.B. & His Hawks)
CD _____ DD 617
Delmark / Mar '95 / Hot Shot / ADA / CM / Direct / Cadillac.

MASTERS OF MODERN BLUES SERIES (Hutto, J.B. & His Hawks)
CD _____ TCD 5020
Testament / Apr '95 / Complete/Pinnacle / ADA / Koch.

SLIDESLINGER (Hutto, J.B. & The New Hawks)
CD _____ ECD 260092
Evidence / Jan '92 / Harmonia Mundi / ADA / Cadillac.

Hutton, Betty

SPOTLIGHT ON BETTY HUTTON
It had to be you / Square in the social circle / I wake up in the morning feeling fine / Love is the darndest thing / Stuff like that there / What do you want to make those eyes at me for / Hamlet / His rocking horse ran away / I wish I didn't love you so / Rumble rumble rumble / Blue skies / That's loyalty / Poppa, don't preach to me / Doin' it the hard way / Sewing machine / Now that I need you / Doctor, lawyer, indian chief
CD _____ CDP 7899422
Capitol / Apr '95 / EMI.

Hutton, Joe

NORTHUMBRIAN PIPER
CD _____ EAR 15CD
East Allen / Oct '94 / ADA.

Hutton, Tim

CONSCIOUS KIND, THE
CD _____ SBZCD 005
Somo Bizarro / Dec '91 / Pinnacle.

Huub De Lange

LIFE AND DEATH ON A STREET ORGAN
CD _____ PAN 145CD
Pan / Dec '94 / ADA / Direct / CM.

Huun-Huur-Tu

ORPHANS LAMENT
CD _____ SHAN 64058CD
Shanachie / Apr '95 / Koch / ADA / Greensleeves.

SIXTY HORSES IN MY HERD (Old Songs & Tunes Of Tuva - Throat Singing)
CD _____ SHCD 64050
Shanachie / Mar '94 / Koch / ADA / Greensleeves.

Huxley, George

SWING THAT MUSIC
CD _____ JCD 239
Jazzology / Mar '95 / Swift / Jazz Music.

Huygen, Michel

BARCELONA 1992
Carvalho / Impossible love / Chase / Meeting at the hilton / Loneliness / Barcelona 1992 / Tonight
CD _____ CDTB 056
Thunderbolt / Feb '88 / Magnum Music Group.

INTIMO
Tenderness / Light being / When I stop the time / Remoteness / El mar de la Soledad / Tempestad cerebral / Vital breath / Infinite tenderness
CD _____ CDTB 092
Thunderbolt / Sep '90 / Magnum Music Group.

Hwan, Kang Tae

KANG TAE HWAN & SAINKHO NAMTCHYLAK LIVE (Hwan, Kang Tae & Sainkho Namtchylak)
CD _____ FINCD 9301
Free Improvision Network / Apr '94 / Harmonia Mundi.

Hyatt, Walter

MUSIC TOWN
CD _____ SH 1039CD
Sugarhill / Jan '94 / Roots / CM / ADA / Direct.

Hybernoid

HYBERNOID
CD _____ D 00028CD
Displeased / Jan '95 / Plastic Head.

LAST DAY
CD _____ D 00028CD
Foundation 2000 / Aug '95 / Plastic Head.

Hykes, David

CURRENT CIRCULATION (Hykes, David & The Harmonic Choir)
CD _____ CDCEL 13010
Celestial Harmonies / Nov '92 / ADA / Select.

CURRENT MEETINGS (Hykes, David & The Harmonic Choir)
CD _____ CDCEL 14013
Celestial Harmonies / Nov '92 / ADA / Select.

HARMONIC MEETINGS (Hykes, David & The Harmonic Choir)
CD Set _____ CDCEL 013/14
Celestial Harmonies / Jul '88 / ADA / Select.

Hyla, Lee

IN DOUBLE LIGHT
CD _____ AVAN 015
Avant / Sep '93 / Harmonia Mundi / Cadillac.

Hyland, Brian

VERY BEST OF BRIAN HYLAND
CD _____ MCCD 146
Music Club / Nov '93 / Disc / THE / CM.

Hylton, Jack

CREAM OF JACK HYLTON
Rhythm like this / Trouble in Paradise / Gold diggers song (We're in the money) / I can't remember / Hallelujah, I'm a tramp / Stormy weather / Shadow waltz / Dancing butterfly / With you here, and me here / Honeymoon

hotel / You're an old smoothie / You are too beautiful / You've got me crying again / Close your eyes / (In) a shanty in old Shanty Town / Try a little tenderness / Ride tenderfoot ride / Good morning / Love makes the world go round / What goes on here
CD _____ PASTCD 9775
Flapper / Feb '92 / Pinnacle.

JACK'S BACK (Hylton, Jack & His Orchestra)
Happy days are here again / Speaking of Kentucky days / My bundle of love / I'm looking over a four leaf clover / World's greatest sweetheart is you / Harmonica Harry / Gentlemen prefer blondes / Broadway melody / Happy feet / I wanna go places and do things / Guy that wrote 'The stein' song / Meadow lark / Choo choo / Life is just a bowl of cherries / Da da da / Life is the ukelele tree / Hang on to me / When day is done
CD _____ CD AJA 5018
Living Era / '87 / Koch.

THIS'LL MAKE YOU WHISTLE
Chasing shadows / Nothing lives longer than love / South American Joe / About a quarter to nine / She's a latin from Manhattan / Drop in next time you're passing / Put on an old pair of shoes / Life begins at Oxford Circus / She wore a little jacket of blue / Did I remember / There isn't any limit to my love / I believe in miracles / This'll make you whistle / In the middle of a kiss / Kiss me goodnight / Can't we meet again / Oh my heart beat / You've got me crying again
CD _____ 2 BUR 005
Burlington / Sep '88 / CM.

Hyman, Dick

CONCORD DUO SERIES VOLUME 6 (Hyman, Dick & Ralph Sutton)
I've found a new baby / I'm gonna sit right down and write myself a letter / Always / I'm sorry I made you cry / Everything happens to me / All of me / Sunday / Ol' man river / Spider and the fly / World is waiting for the sunrise / Dinah / Emaline
CD _____ CCD 4603
Concord Jazz / Jul '94 / New Note.

DICK HYMAN PLAYS COLE PORTER: ALL THROUGH THE NIGHT
CD _____ MM 5060
Music Masters / Oct '94 / Nimbus.

DICK HYMAN PLAYS FATS WALLER (Hyman, Dick & His Trio)
CD _____ RR 33CD
Reference Recordings / Sep '91 / May Audio.

FACE THE MUSIC (A Century Of Irving Berlin)
CD _____ MM 5002
Music Masters / Oct '94 / Nimbus.

GERSHWIN SONGBOOK: JAZZ VARIATIONS
CD _____ MM 65094
Music Masters / Oct '94 / Nimbus.

GREAT AMERICAN SONGBOOK, THE
CD _____ 01612651202
Music Masters / Sep '95 / Nimbus.

KINGDOM OF SWING & THE REPUBLIC OF OOP BOP SH'BAM (Jazz In July - Live At The 92nd Street Y)
Lester leaps in / Joshua fit de battle of jericho
CD _____ MM 5016
Music Masters / Oct '94 / Nimbus.

LIVE AT THE 92ND STREET Y (Hyman, Dick Piano Players & Significant Others)
CD _____ MM 5042
Music Masters / Oct '94 / Nimbus.

MANHATTAN JAZZ (Hyman, Dick & Ruby Braff)
Jubilee / You're lucky to me / Man I love / How long has this been going on / He loves and she loves / I'm crazy 'bout my baby / Some day you'll be sorry / Don't worry 'bout me / Jeepers creepers / I'm just wild about Harry / Man that got away / If only I had a brain / Somewhere over the rainbow / Blues for John W.

CD _____ MM 5031
Music Masters / Oct '94 / Nimbus.

THEY GOT RHYTHM (Hyman, Dick & Derek Smith)
CD _____ JCD 635
Jass / Oct '93 / CM / Jazz Music / ADA / Cadillac / Direct.

Hyman, Phyllis

BEST OF PHYLLIS HYMAN (The Buddah Years)
Loving you - losing you / No one can love you more / One thing on my mind / I don't want to lose you / Deliver the love / Night bird gets the love / Beautiful man of mine / Children of the world / Living inside your love / Sweet music / Answer is you / Love is free / Sing a song / Soon come again / Be careful (how you treat my love)
CD _____ NEXCD 138
Sequel / Oct '90 / BMG.

Hype-A-Delics

MO FUNK FOR YOUR ASS
CD _____ EFA 11935-2
Juiceful / Mar '94 / SRD.

Hyperhead

METAPHASIA
CD _____ CDDVN 16
Devotion / Dec '92 / Pinnacle.

Hypersax

STEPDANCE
Stepdance / Run for fun / Sailing around / Greek islands / Princy palace / Long distance education / Update / Song for Contessa / Red Bank N.J. / Solo in the night / Starlight / Rush hour / Rainy days / Pop song / V.I.B.S.A.X.
CD _____ 101 2 7054 2
New Note / Nov '92 / New Note / Cadillac.

Hypnodance

HYPNODANCE
CD _____ CONTE 129CD
Contempo / Nov '89 / Plastic Head.

Hypnolovewheel

ALTERED STATES
You choose / Peace of mind / Watermelon song / Turn you off / I know / Model railroad / Right on / Dysfunctional friend / Electric brown / Nightly grind / Kerosene kiss / Dodge city
CD _____ A 034D
Alias / May '93 / Vital.

ANGEL FOOD
CD _____ A 020D
Alias / Jun '92 / Vital.

SPACE MOUNTAIN
CD _____ A 011D
Alias / Jul '92 / Vital.

Hypnotone

AI
CD _____ CRECD 080
Creation / May '94 / 3MV / Vital.

HYPNOTONE
CD _____ CRECD 067
Creation / May '94 / 3MV / Vital.

Hypocrisy

ABDUCTED
CD _____ NB 133CD
Nuclear Blast / Jan '96 / Plastic Head.

FOURTH DIMENSION, THE
CD _____ NB 112-2
CD _____ NB 112DIGI
Nuclear Blast / Oct '94 / Plastic Head.

INFERIOR DEVOTIES
CD _____ NB 098CD
Nuclear Blast / Mar '94 / Plastic Head.

OBSCULUM OBSCENUM
CD _____ NB 080
Nuclear Blast / Aug '93 / Plastic Head.

PENETRALIA
CD _____ NB 067CD
Nuclear Blast / Nov '92 / Plastic Head.

I

I

TINNED MUSIC
CD _____ PODCD 033
Pod Communication / Feb '95 / Plastic
Head.

I Compani

LUNA TRISTE
CD _____ BVHAASTCD 9012
Bvhaast / Oct '93 / Cadillac.

SOGNI D'ORO
CD _____ BVHAASTCD 9404
Bvhaast / Oct '94 / Cadillac.

I Connection

MAGIC
CD _____ MUSCD 512
MCI / May '95 / Disc / THE.

I Salonisiti

CAFE VICTORIA
Los mareados / Poema valseado / Re-
cuerdo / Coral / Romance de barrio / Uno /
Payadora / Flores negras / Severina / Flor
de lino / Contra bajilismo
CD _____ CDC 169531-2
Harmonia Mundi / Jul '86 / Harmonia Mundi
/ Cadillac.

I Start Counting

FUSED
CD _____ CDSTUMM 50
Mute / Jun '89 / Disc.

MY TRANSLUCENT HANDS
Introduction / My translucent hands / Catch
that look / You and I / Lose him / Keep the
sun away / Cranley Gardens / Which way is
home / Letters to a friend / Still smiling /
Small consolation / (There is always the)
unexpected
CD _____ CDSTUMM 30
Mute / Oct '86 / Disc.

I Suanatori Delle Quatro.

**RACCONTI A COLORI (I Suanatori Delle
Quatro Province)**
CD _____ NT 6720
Robi Droli / Jan '94 / Direct / ADA.

I-Roy

BLACK MAN TIME
CD _____ JMC 200217
Jamaica Gold / Jun '95 / THE / Magnum
Music Group / Jetstar.

CRISUS TIME
Heart of a lion / Casmas Town / Tonight /
Wrap 'n' bap 'n' / Union call / London /
Roots man time / African tak / Crisus time
/ Equality and justice / Hypocrite back out
/ Musical injection / Don't touch I man locks
/ Satta amasa gana (sette messgana) / Af-
rican herbsman / Love your neighbour /
Send us little power oh jah / Moving on
strong
CD _____ CDFL 9015
Frontline / Jul '93 / EMI / Jetstar.

GREAT GODFATHER
CD _____ RNCD 2079
Rhino / Dec '94 / Jetstar / Magnum Music
Group / THE.

**KING TUBBY'S STUDIO (I-Roy &
Dillinger)**
CD _____ LG 2 1116
Lagoon / Oct '95 / Magnum Music Group
/ THE.

I-Shen Sound

KING SIZE DUB
CD _____ HYPOXIA 002CD
Hypoxia / Oct '95 / Plastic Head.

I.Q.

ARE YOU SITTING COMFORTABLY?
War heroes / Drive on / Nostalgia / Falling
apart at the seams / Sold on you / Through
my fingers / Wurensh / Nothing at all
CD _____ GEPCD 1013
Giant Electric Pea / Feb '95 / Pinnacle.

EVER
CD _____ GEPCD 1006
Giant Electric Pea / Aug '94 / Pinnacle.

J'AI POLLETE D'ARNU
CD _____ GEPCD 1001
Giant Electric Pea / Aug '93 / Pinnacle.

LIVING PROOF
CD _____ GEPCD 1004
Giant Electric Pea / Aug '93 / Pinnacle.

NOMZAMO
No love lost / Promises (as the years go by)
/ Nomzamo / Still life / Passing strangers /
Human nature / Screaming / Common
ground
CD _____ GEPCD 1012
Giant Electric Pea / Oct '94 / Pinnacle.

TALES FROM THE LUSH ATTIC
Last human gateway / Awake and nervous
/ Enemy smacks / Just changing hands /
Through the corridors / My baby treats me
right, cause I'm a hard lovin' man all nig
CD _____ GEPCD 1010
Giant Electric Pea / Aug '94 / Pinnacle.

WAKE, THE
Outer limits / Magic roundabout / Widow's
peak / Headlong / Thousand days (demo) /
Wake / Corners / Thousand days / Dans le
Parc du chateau noir / Magic roundabout
(demo)
CD _____ GEPCD 1011
Giant Electric Pea / Aug '94 / Pinnacle.

i0

**90 MINUTES IN THE EYES OF IO (i0 &
Adsr)**
CD _____ CHEAP ONE
Cheap / Apr '95 / Plastic Head.

Ian & Sylvia

GREATEST HITS
Early morning rain / Tomorrow is a long time
/ Little beggar man / Mighty Quinn / Nancy
Whisky / Catfish blues / Come in stranger /
French girl / Renegade / Mary Anne / You
were on my mind / Four strong winds /
Short grass / Southern comfort / Someday
soon / Ella Speed / Circle game / 90 x 90 /
Cutty Wren / Un Canadien errant / Lonely
girls / Spanish is a loving tongue / This
wheel's on fire
CD _____ VCD 5
Vanguard / Jan '90 / Complete/Pinnacle /
Discovery.

Ian, Janis

AFTERTONES
Aftertones / I would like to dance / Love is
blind / Roses / Belle of the blues / Goodbye
to morning / Boy I really tried one on / This
must be wrong / Don't cry / Old man /
Hymn
CD _____ GRACD 304
Grapevine / Jan '96 / Grapevine.

BETWEEN THE LINES
When the party's over / At seventeen / From
me to you / Bright lights and promises / In
the Winter / Water colors / Between the
lines / Come on / Light a tight / Tea and
sympathy / Lover's lullaby
CD _____ GRACD 303
Grapevine / Aug '95 / Grapevine.

BREAKING SILENCE
All roads to the river / Ride me like a wave
/ Tattoo / Guess you had to be there / What
about the love / His hands / Walking on sa-
cred ground / This train / His house / Through
the years / This house / Some people's lives
/ Breaking silence
CD _____ 519614-2
Polydor / Jul '93 / PolyGram.

JANIS IAN
Grand illusion / Some people / Tonight will
last forever / Hotels and one night stands /
Do you wanna dance / Silly habits / Bridge
/ My mama's house / Street life serenaders
/ I need to live alone again / Hopper painting
CD _____ GRACD 306
Grapevine / Jan '96 / Grapevine.

LIVE ON THE TEST
CD _____ WHISCD 008
Windsong / Apr '95 / Pinnacle.

MIRACLE ROW
Party lights / I want to make you love me /
Sunset of your life / Take to the sky /
Candlelight / Let me be lonely / Slow dance
romance / Will you dance / I'll cry tonight /
Miracle row / Maria
CD _____ GRACD 305
Grapevine / Aug '95 / Grapevine.

NIGHT RAINS
Other side of the sun / Fly too high / Mem-
ories / Photographs / Here comes the night
/ Day by day / Have mercy love / Lay low /
Night rains / Jenny
CD _____ GRACD 307
Grapevine / Jan '96 / Grapevine.

PRESENT COMPANY
Seaside / Present company / See my
grammy ride / Here in Spain / On the train
/ He's a rainbow / Weary Lady / Nature's at
peace / See the river / Let it run free / Alabama / Liberty / My land / Hello Jerry / Can
you reach me / Sunlight

CD _____ BGOCD 165
Beat Goes On / Nov '92 / Pinnacle.

RESTLESS EYES
Under the covers / I remember yesterday /
I believe I'm myself again / Restless eyes /
Get ready to roll / Passion play / Down and
away / Bigger than real / Dear Billy / Sugar
mountain
CD _____ GRACD 308
Grapevine / Jan '96 / Grapevine.

REVENGE
CD _____ GRACD 301
Grapevine / May '95 / Grapevine.

SOCIETY CHILD - THE VERVE YEARS
CD _____ 5275912
Verve / Aug '95 / PolyGram.

STARS
Stars / Man you are in me / Sweet sympathy / Page nine / Thank yous / Dance with
me / Without you / You've got me on a
string / Applause
CD _____ GRACD 302
Grapevine / Jan '96 / Grapevine.

UNCLE WONDERFUL
CD _____ GRACD 309
Grapevine / Jan '96 / Grapevine.

Ibis

EARTH CITIZEN
CD _____ 092032
Cobalt / Nov '92 / Grapevine.

Ibrahim, Abdullah

**AFRICAN MARKETPLACE (Brand,
Dollar)**
Whoza mtwana / Homecoming song / Wed-
ding / Moniebah / African marketplace /
Mama / Anthem for the new nations / Ubu
suku
CD _____ 1046710162
Discovery / May '95 / Warner Music.

AFRICAN PIANO (Brand, Dollar)
Bra Joe from Kilimanjaro / Selby that the
eternal spirit / Is the only reality / Moon /
Xaba / Sunset in the blue / Kippy / Jabulani
/ Tintinyana
CD _____ 8350202
ECM / Sep '88 / New Note.

AFRICAN SKETCH BOOK (Brand, Dollar)
CD _____ ENJACD 20262
Enja / Nov '94 / New Note / Vital/SAM.

**AFRICAN SPACE PROGRAMME (Brand,
Dollar)**
CD _____ ENJACD 20322
Enja / Nov '94 / New Note / Vital/SAM.

AFRICAN SUN (Brand, Dollar)
Ishmael / Bra Joe from Kilimanjaro / Rol-
lin' / Memories of you / Sathima / African
herbs / Nobody knows the trouble I've seen
/ Blues for B / Gwidza / Kamalie
CD _____ KAZ CD 102
Kaz / Jul '88 / BMG.

**ANATOMY OF A SOUTH AFRICAN
VILLAGE (Brand, Dollar & Gertze/
Ntshoko)**
CD _____ BLC 760172
Black Lion / Nov '92 / Jazz Music /
Cadillac / Wellard / Koch.

ANCIENT AFRICA
Bra Joe from Kilimanjaro / Mama / Tokai /
Ilanga / Cherry / African sun / Tintinyana /
Xaba / Peace - Salaam air
CD _____ SKCD 2-3049
Sackville / Oct '94 / Swift / Jazz Music /
Jazz Horizons / Cadillac / CM.

**ANTHEM FOR THE NEW NATIONS
(Brand, Dollar)**
Anthem for the new nations / Biral / Libera-
tion dance / Trial / Cape Town / Wedding
suite / Wedding / Lovers / I surrender dear
/ One day when we were young / Thaba
nchu
CD _____ DC 8588
Denon / Sep '91 / Conifer.

BLUES FOR A HIP KING (Brand, Dollar)
Ornette's cornet / All day and all night long
/ Sweet Basil blues / Blue monk / Tsakwe
here comes the postman / Blues for a hip
king / Blues for B / Mysterioso / Just you,
just me / Eclipse at dawn / King Kong / King
Khumbula Jane / Boulevarde East (not on
CD)
CD _____ KAZ CD 104
Kaz / Oct '88 / BMG.

DUKES' MEMORIES (Brand, Dollar)
CD _____ 233853
Black & Blue / '86 / Wellard / Koch.

FATS, DUKE AND THE MONK
CD _____ SKCD2-3048
Sackville / Feb '93 / Swift / Jazz Music /
Jazz Horizons / Cadillac / CM.

**GOOD NEWS FROM AFRICA (Brand,
Dollar Duo)**
CD _____ ENJACD 20482
Enja / Nov '94 / New Note / Vital/SAM.

KNYSNA BLUE
Knysna blue / You can't stop me now /
Peace / Three no.1 / Kofifi / Three no.2 /
Cape Town / Ask me now
CD _____ 8888162
Enja / Jun '94 / New Note / Vital/SAM.

**LIVE AT MONTREUX: DOLLAR BRAND
(Brand, Dollar)**
CD _____ ENJACD 30792
Enja / Nov '94 / New Note / Vital/SAM.

MANTRA MODE
CD _____ 847810-2
New Note / Nov '91 / New Note / Cadillac.

MINDIF (Brand, Dollar)
CD _____ ENJA 5073-50
Enja / Jul '88 / New Note / Vital/SAM.

**MOUNTAIN, THE (Ibrahim, Abdullah &
Ekaya)**
Mountain / Bra timing from Phomolong /
Ekaya / Sotho blue / Tuang Guru / Ntyilo
ntyilo / Nelson Mandela / Wedding / Man-
nenberg / Cape Town
CD _____ KAZCD 7
Kaz / Jun '89 / BMG.

NO FEAR, NO DIE
Calypso minor / Angelica / Meditation #2 /
Nisa / Kata / Meditation / Calypso major
CD _____ TIP 8888152
Tiptoe / Jul '93 / New Note.

REFLECTIONS (Brand, Dollar)
Honeysuckle rose / Resolution / Knight's
night / Mood indigo / Don't get around
much anymore / Take the 'A' train / Monk's
mood / You are too beautiful / Little Niles /
Pye R squared / On the banks of Allen Wa-
ters / Reflections / Which way
CD _____ BLCD 760127
Black Lion / May '90 / Jazz Music / Cadillac
/ Wellard / Koch.

**ROUND MIDNIGHT AT MONTMARTRE
(Brand, Dollar)**
CD _____ BLCD 76011
Black Lion / Feb '89 / Jazz Music /
Cadillac / Wellard / Koch.

TINTINYANA
Soweto is where it's at / Tintinyana / Little
boy / Cherry / Bra Joe from Kilimanjaro /
Shrimp boats / Salaam / Just a song
CD _____ KAZ CD 103
Kaz / Oct '88 / BMG.

VOICE OF AFRICA
Black lightning / Little boy / Black and
brown cherries / Ntyilo, Ntyilo / Mannenberg
/ Pilgrim
CD _____ KAZCD 101
Kaz / Feb '89 / BMG.

WATER FROM AN ANCIENT WELL
Mandela / Song for Fathima / Manenberg
revisited / Tuang Guru / Water from an an-
cient well / Wedding / Mountain / Sameeda
CD _____ 8888122
Tiptoe / Nov '89 / New Note.

YARONA
Nisa / Duke / Cherry / Mannenberg / African
river / Tuang guru / Stardance / African mar-
ketplace / Tintinyana / Barakaat
CD _____ 8888202
Enja / Jul '95 / New Note / Vital/SAM.

ZIMBABWE (Brand, Dollar)
CD _____ ENJA 3112 2
Enja / '88 / New Note / Vital/SAM.

Ice

UNDER THE SKIN
CD _____ PATH 11CD
Trident / Jul '93 / Pinnacle.

Ice Age

LIFE'S A BITCH
CD _____ HMIXD 154
FM / Aug '90 / Sony.

Ice Cold July

THERE WILL COME A DAY
CD _____ SECTOR 10002
Sector 2 / Jul '95 / Direct / ADA.

Ice Cube

AMERIKKKA'S MOST WANTED
Better off dead / Nigga ya love to hate /
What they hittin foe / You can't fade me/
JD's gaffilin / Once upon a time in the projects / Turn off the radio / Endangered
species (Tales from the darkside) / Gangsta's tailpiece / I'm only out for one thang /
Get off my dick and tell yo bitch to come
here / Drive-by / Rollin' wit' tha lench mob

326

/ Who's the mack / Amerikkka's most wanted / It's a man's world / Bomb
CD _____ BRCD 551
4th & Broadway / Jun '90 / PolyGram.

DEATH CERTIFICATE
Funeral / Wrong nigga to fuck wit / My summer vacation / Steady mobbin / Robin Lench / Givin' up the nappy dug out / Look who's burnin / Bird in the hand / Man's best friend / Alive on arrival / Death / Birth / I wanna kill Sam / Horny Lil devil / True to the game / Color blind / Doing dumb shit / Us
CD _____ BRCD 579
4th & Broadway / Oct '91 / PolyGram.

KILL AT WILL
Endangered species (Tales from the darkside) / Jackin' for beats / Get off my dick and tell yo bitch to come here / Product / Dead homiez / J.D. gaffilin #2 / I gotta say what up
CD _____ BRCD 572
4th & Broadway / Mar '91 / PolyGram.

LETHAL INJECTION
Shot / Really doe / Ghetto bird / You know how we do it / Cave bitch / Bop gun (one nation) / What can I do / Lil ass gee / Make it ruff, make it smooth / Down for whatever / Enemy / When I get to heaven
CD _____ BRCD 609
4th & Broadway / Nov '93 / PolyGram.

PREDATOR, THE
First day of school (intro) / When will they shoot / I'm scared (insert) / Wicked / Now I gotta wet 'cha / Predator / It was a good day / We had to tear this MF up / Dirty mack / Don't trust 'em / Gangsta's fairytale 2 / Check yo' self / Who got the camera / Integration (insert) / Say hi to the bad guy
CD _____ BRCD 592
4th & Broadway / Nov '92 / PolyGram.

Ice-T

CLASSIC COLLECTION, THE
Ice-a-mix / Coldest rap / Killers / Ya don't quit / Six in the mornin' / Body rock / Cold wind madness / Dog 'n the wax / Icapella / Ice-o-tek
CD _____ 812271170-2
Street Knowledge / May '93 / Warner Music.

HOME INVASION
Warning / It's on / Ice M/F T / Home invasion / G style / Addicted to danger / Question and answer / Watch the ice break / Race war / That's how I'm livin' / I ain't new ta this / Pimp behind the wheels / Gotta lotta love / Shit hit the fan / Depths of hell / Ninety nine problems / Funky gripsta / Message to the soldier / Ain't a damn thing changed
CD _____ RSYND 1
Rhyme Syndicate / Mar '93 / EMI.

ICEBERG/FREEDOM OF SPEECH
Shut up / Be happy / Iceberg / lethal weopon / You played yourself (aka the boss) / Peel their caps back / Girl tried to kill me / Black 'n' decker / Hit the deck / This one's for me / Hunted child / What ya wanna do (aka do you wanna go party) / Freedom of speach / my word is bond
CD _____ 9260282
Street Knowledge / Oct '89 / Warner Music.

OG - ORIGINAL GANGSTER
First impression / Ziplock / New jack hustler / Bitches 2 / Straight up nigga / O.G. original gangster / House / Evil E - what about sex / Fly by / Fried chicken / Lifestyles of the rich and famous / Body Count / Prepared to die / Escape from the killing fields / Ya shoulda killed me last year / Home of the bodybag (Not on LP) / Mic contract (Not on LP) / Mind over matter (Not on LP) / Ed (Not on LP) / Midnight / M.V.P.S. (Not on LP) / Street killer (Not on LP) / Pulse of the rhyme (Not on LP)
CD _____ 7599264922
Street Knowledge / May '91 / Warner Music.

POWER
Intro / Power / Drama / Heartbeat / I'm your pusher / L.G.B.N.A.F. / Syndicate / Radio suckers / Soul on ice / Outro / High rollers / Personal
CD _____ 925765 2
Street Knowledge / Sep '88 / Warner Music.

RHYME PAYS
Intro / Six 'n the mornin' / Make it funky / Somebody gotta do it / 409 / I love ladies / Sex / Pain / Squeeze the trigger
CD _____ 7599256022
Street Knowledge / Jan '93 / Warner Music.

Iceberg Slim

REFLECTIONS
CD _____ 74321299652
Infinite Zero / Oct '95 / BMG.

Iceburn

POETRY OF LIFE
CD _____ REV 36CD
Revelation / Jun '95 / Plastic Head.

SPLIT E.P. (Iceburn & Engine Kid)
CD _____ REVEL 034CD
Revelation / Oct '94 / Plastic Head.

Iced Earth

BURNT OFFERINGS
CD _____ CM 770932
Century Media / May '95 / Plastic Head.

ICED EARTH
CD _____ 8497142
Century Media / Feb '91 / Plastic Head.

Icho Candy

GLORY AND THE KING (Icho Candy & Jah Shaka)
CD _____ SHAKACD 948
Jah Shaka / Jul '93 / Jetstar / SRD / Greensleeves.

Ichor

NONPLUS
CD _____ EFA 112372
Danse Macabre / May '95 / SRD.

Ichu

ICHU
CD _____ BLR 84 023
L&R / May '91 / New Note.

Icicle Works

BBC LIVE IN CONCERT
Who do you want for your love / Evangeline / Starry blue eyed wonder / Little girl lost / Up here in the North of England / Understanding Jane / When it all comes down
CD _____ WINCD 063
Windsong / Feb '94 / Pinnacle.

BEST OF THE ICICLE WORKS
CD _____ BEGA 124CD
Beggars Banquet / Aug '92 / Warner Music / Disc.

BLIND
Intro / Shit creek / Little Girl Lost / Starry blue eyed wonder / One true love / Blind / Two two three / What do you want me to do / Stood before Saint Peter / Here comes trouble / Kiss off / Walk a while with me
CD _____ IWA 2CD
Beggars Banquet / Apr '88 / Warner Music / Disc.

ICICLE WORKS, THE
Chop the tree / Love is a wonderful colour / As the dragonfly flies / Lover's day / In the cauldron of love / Out of season / Factory in the desert / (Birds fly) Whisper to a scream / Nirvana / Reaping the rich harvest
CD _____ BBL 50CD
Lowdown/Beggars Banquet / Jul '88 / Warner Music / Disc.

IF YOU WANT TO DEFEAT THE ENEMY SING HIS SONG
Hope springs eternal / Travelling chest / Sweet Thursday / Up here in the North of England / Who do you want for your love / When you were mine / Evangeline / Truck driver's lament / Understanding Jane / Walking with a mountain / Please don't let it rain on my parade (Not on LP) / Everybody loves to play the fool (Not on LP) / I never saw my hometown 'till I went around the world (CD only.) / Into the mystic (CD only)
CD _____ BBL 78CD
Lowdown/Beggars Banquet / Feb '90 / Warner Music / Disc.

SEVEN SINGLES DEEP
Hollow horse / Love is a wonderful colour / (Birds fly) Whisper to a scream / All the daughters / When it all comes down / Seven horses / Rapids
CD _____ BBL 71 CD
Lowdown/Beggars Banquet / Sep '88 / Warner Music / Disc.

SMALL PRICE OF A BICYCLE, THE
Hollow horse / Perambulator / Seven horses / Rapids / Windfall / Assumed sundowns / Saint's sojourn / All the daughters / Book of reason / Conscience of Kings
CD _____ BBL 61CD
Lowdown/Beggars Banquet / Jan '89 / Warner Music / Disc.

Icky Joey

POOH
CD _____ CZ 026CD
C/Z / Sep '91 / Plastic Head.

Idaho

THIS WAY OUT
Drop off / Drive it / Weird wood / Fuel / Still / Sweep / Glow / Taken / Crawling out / Zabo / Forever
CD _____ QUIGD 7
Quigley / Jan '95 / EMI.

YEAR AFTER YEAR
God's green earth / Skyscrape / Gone / Here to go / Sundown / Memorial day / One Sunday / Only road / Let's cheat death / Save / Year after year / Endgame
CD _____ QUIGD 4
Quigley / Sep '93 / EMI.

Idee Des Nordens

ELATION, ELEGANCE, EXALTATION
CD _____ EFA 155832
Gymnastic / Apr '95 / SRD.

Ides Of May

FEED BACK
CD _____ TRCD 9908
Tramp / Nov '93 / Direct / ADA / CM.

Idha

MELODYINN
CD _____ CRECD 160
Creation / Jan '94 / 3MV / Vital.

Idol, Billy

BILLY IDOL
Come on come on / White wedding / Hot in the city / Dead on arrival / Nobody's business / Love calling / Hole in the wall / Shooting star / It's so cruel / Congo man
CD _____ ACCD 1377
Chrysalis / Jul '94 / EMI.

CHARMED LIFE
Loveless / Pimping on steel / Prodigal blues / L.A. woman / Trouble with the sweet stuff / Cradle of love / Mark of Caine / Endless sleep / Love unchained / Right way / License to thrill
CD _____ CCD 1735
Chrysalis / Apr '90 / EMI.

CYBERPUNK
Wasteland / Shock to the system / Tomorrow people / Adam in chains / Neuromancer / Power junkie / Love labours on / Heroin / Shangri la / Concrete kingdom / Venus / Then the night comes / Mother Dawn
CD _____ CDCHR 6000
Chrysalis / Jun '93 / EMI.

IDOL SONGS (11 Of The Best)
Rebel yell / Hot in the city / White wedding / Eyes without a face / Catch my fall / Mony mony / To be a lover / Sweet sixteen / Flesh for fantasy / Don't need a gun / Dancing with myself
CD _____ BIL CD 1
Chrysalis / Jun '88 / EMI.

REBEL YELL
Rebel yell / Daytime drama / Eyes without a face / Blue highway / Flesh for fantasy / Catch my fall / Crank call / Stand in the shadows / Dead next door / Do not stand
CD _____ CD25CR 06
Chrysalis / Mar '94 / EMI.

VITAL IDOL
Dancing with myself / White wedding / Flesh for fantasy / Catch my fall / Mony mony / Love calling (dub) / Hot in the city
CD _____ CCD 1502
Chrysalis / '86 / EMI.

Idols

IDOLS WITH SID VICIOUS (Idols & Sid Vicious)
CD _____ 422429
New Rose / May '94 / Direct / ADA.

If

FORGOTTEN ROADS
CD _____ NEMCD 773
Sequel / Oct '95 / BMG.

Ifang Bondi

DABA JA
CD _____ MW 3009CD
Music & Words / Jul '94 / ADA / Direct.

Ifield, Frank

REST OF THE EMI YEARS
Lucky devil / I remember you / She taught me how to yodel / Lovesick blues / Confessin' (that I love you) / Loan me one more chance / Nobody's darlin' but mine / Wayward wind / My blue heaven / Say it isn't so / Don't blame me / You came a long way from St. Louis / Summer is over / Once a jolly swagman (From film: Up Jumped A Swagman) / Botany Bay (From film: Up Jumped A Swagman) / Paradise / Wild rover (From film: Up Jumped A Swagman) / Call her your sweetheart / No one will ever know / Give me your word
CD _____ CDEMS 1402
EMI / May '91 / EMI.

Iggy Pop

AMERICAN CAESAR
Character / Wild America / Mixin' the colors / Jealousy / Hate / It's our love / Plastic and concrete / Fuckin' alone / Highway song / Beside you / Sickness / Boogie boy / Perforation problems / Social life / Louie Louie / Caesar / Girls of N.Y.
CD _____ CDVUS 64
Virgin / Aug '93 / EMI.

BLAH BLAH BLAH
Real wild child / Baby, it can't fall / Shades / Fire girl / Isolation / Cry for love / Blah blah blah / Hideaway / Winners and losers
CD _____ CDMID 159
A&M / Oct '92 / PolyGram.

BRICK BY BRICK
Home / I won't crap out / Butt town / Moonlight lady / Neon forest / Pussy power / Brick by brick / Main Street eyes / Candy / Undefeated / Something wild / Starry night / My baby wants to rock 'n' roll / Livin' on the edge of the night
CD _____ CDVUS 19
Virgin / Apr '92 / EMI.

FUN HOUSE (Iggy & The Stooges)
Down on the street / Loose / T.V. Eye / Dirt / 1970 / Fun house / L.A. Blues
CD _____ 7559606692
Elektra / Oct '93 / Warner Music.

I'M SICK OF YOU/KILL CITY
Kill city / Sell your love / Beyond the law / I got nothing / Johanna / Night theme / Night theme (2) / Consolation prizes / No sense of crime / Lucky moments / Master charge / I'm sick of you / Tight pants / I got a right / Johanna (2) / Consolation prizes (2) / Scene of the crime / Gimme some skin / Jesus loves the Stooges
CD Set _____ LICD 921175
Line / May '92 / CM / Grapevine / ADA / Conifer / Direct.

IDIOT, THE
Sister midnight / Nightclubbing / Fun time / Baby / China girl / Dum dum boys / Tiny girls / Mass production
CD _____ CDOVD 277
Virgin / Apr '90 / EMI.

IGGY AND THE STOOGES (Iggy & The Stooges)
CD _____ 890050
New Rose / May '94 / Direct / ADA.

JESUS LOVES THE STOOGES (Iggy & The Stooges)
CD _____ BCD 114
Bomp / Nov '95 / Pinnacle.

KILL CITY (Iggy Pop & James Williamson)
Kill City / Sell your love / Beyond the law / I got nothing / Johanna / Night theme / Consolation prizes / No sense of crime / Lucky moments / Master charge
CD _____ LICD 900131
Line / Oct '92 / CM / Grapevine / ADA / Conifer / Direct.
CD _____ BCD 4042
Bomp / Jan '93 / Pinnacle.

LIVE 1971 & EARLY LIVE RARITIES (Iggy & The Stooges)
CD _____ 642011
New Rose / Sep '94 / Direct / ADA.

LIVE AT THE WHISKEY A GO GO (Iggy & The Stooges)
CD _____ 895104F 104
Revenge / Nov '94 / Pinnacle.

LIVE: CHANNEL BOSTON M.A. 1988
CD _____ 642005
New Rose / May '94 / Direct / ADA.

LIVE: HIPPODROME, PARIS 1977
CD _____ 893334
New Rose / May '94 / Direct / ADA.

LIVE: NEW YORK RITZ 1986
CD _____ 642044
New Rose / May '94 / Direct / ADA.

LUST FOR LIFE
Lust for life / Sixteen / Some weird sin / Passenger / Tonight / Success / Turn blue / Neighbourhood threat / Fall in love with me
CD _____ CDOVD 278
Virgin / Apr '90 / EMI.

LUST FOR LIFE/THE IDIOT/BRICK BY BRICK (3CD Set)
CD _____ TPAK21
Virgin / Jan '93 / EMI.

METALLIC KO (Iggy & The Stooges)
Raw power / Head on the curb / Gimme danger / Search and destiny / Heavy liquid / I wanna be your dog / Recital / Open up and bleed / I got nothing / Rich bitch / Cock in my pocket / Louie Louie
CD _____ 622322
Skydog / Apr '88 / Discovery.

MY GIRL HATES MY HEROIN (Iggy & The Stooges)
CD _____ 890028
New Rose / Jun '94 / Direct / ADA.

NEW VALUES
Tell me a story / New values / Girls / I'm bored / Don't look down / Endless sea / Five foot one / How do you fix a broken heart / Angel / Curiosity / African man / Billy is a runaway
CD _____ 260997
Arista / Nov '90 / BMG.

NIGHT OF DESTRUCTION (Iggy & The Stooges)
CD _____ 642100
New Rose / Jun '94 / Direct / ADA.

OPEN UP AND BLEED (Iggy & The Stooges)
CD _____ BCD 4051
Bomp / Feb '96 / Pinnacle.

POP SONGS
Loco mosquito / Bang bang / Pumpin' for Jill / Tell me a story / Take care of me / Mr. Dynamite / I'm bored / Sea of love / Play it

safe / Endless sea / Pleasure / Five foot one / Houston is hot tonight / Dog food
CD _____ 262178
Arista / Jan '92 / BMG.

RAW MIXES VOL.1 (Iggy & The Stooges)
CD _____ 895002
New Rose / Sep '94 / Direct / ADA.

RAW MIXES VOL.2 (Iggy & The Stooges)
CD _____ 895003
New Rose / Sep '94 / Direct / ADA.

RAW MIXES VOL.3 - SEARCH & DESTROY (Iggy & The Stooges)
CD _____ 895004
New Rose / Sep '94 / Direct / ADA.

RAW POWER (Iggy & The Stooges)
Search and destroy / Gimme danger / Your pretty face is going to hell / Penetration / Raw power / I need somebody / Shake appeal / Death trip
CD _____ 476610 2
Columbia / Apr '94 / Sony.

ROUGH POWER (Iggy & The Stooges)
CD _____ BCD 4049
Bomp / Feb '95 / Pinnacle.

RUBBER LEGS (Iggy & The Stooges)
CD _____ 422351
New Rose / May '94 / Direct / ADA.

SOLDIER
Loco mosquito / Ambition / Take care of me / Get up and get out / Play it safe / I'm a conservative / Dog food / I need more / Knocking 'em down (in the city) / Mr. Dynamite / I snub you
CD _____ 251160
Arista / Apr '91 / BMG.

STOOGES, THE (Iggy & The Stooges)
1969 / I wanna be your dog / We will fall / No fun / Real cool time / Ann / Not right / Little doll
CD _____ 7559606672
Elektra / Oct '93 / Warner Music.

SUCK ON THIS
CD _____ 642 050
Trident / May '93 / Pinnacle.

TILL THE END OF THE NIGHT (Iggy & The Stooges)
CD _____ 642042
New Rose / Jun '94 / Direct / ADA.

TV EYE (1977 LIVE)
TV eye / Fun time / Sixteen / I got a right / Lust for life / Dirt / Nightclubbing / I wanna be your dog
CD _____ CDOVD 448
Virgin / Jun '94 / EMI.

WILD ANIMAL
CD _____ 642050
New Rose / Oct '94 / Direct / ADA.

Iglesias, Julio

1100 BEL AIR PLACE
All of you (with Diana Ross) / Two lovers / Bambou medley / Air that I breathe / Last time / Moonlight lady / When I fall in love / Me va, me va / To all the girls I've loved before (with Willie Nelson)
CD _____ CD 86308
CBS / Sep '86 / Sony.

AMERICA
Ay ay ay / Aima llanera / Caminito / Recuerdos de ipacarai / Historia de un amor / Obsesion / Sombras / Cancion de orfeo / Guantanamera / Vaya con dios / Moliendo cafe / Recuerdos de ipacarai / Obsession / Cancion de orfeo (Manana de carnaval) / Jurame / Vaya con dios #2 / Alma llanera
CD _____ 982831-2
Pickwick/Sony Collector's Choice / Apr '94 / Carlton Home Entertainment / Pinnacle / Sony.

BEGIN THE BEGUINE
Begin the beguine / Quiereme / Me olvide de vivir / Por un poco de tu amour / Grande, grande, grande / Como tu / Guantanamera / Quiereme mucho / Hey / Un dia ty, un dia yo / Soy un truhan, soy un senor / Candilejas / El amor / 33 anos / Isla en el sol
CD _____ CD 85462
CBS / Aug '87 / Sony.

CALOR
Milonga / Milonga sentimental / Vivo / Lia / Cana v a cafe / La quiero como es / De Domingo a Domingo / Uno / Y anunque te haga calor / Me amo mo / Somos / Esos amores
CD _____ 4716012
Columbia / Jun '92 / Sony.

CALOR/BEGIN THE BEGUINE
CD Set _____ 4716012 D
Columbia / Feb '93 / Sony.

CRAZY
Crazy / Let it be me / Mammy blue / Fragile / Guajira/Oye como va / When you tell me that you love me / I keep telling myself / Pelo amor de uma mulher (Por el amor de una mujer) / Caruso / Song of joy
CD _____ 474738 2
Columbia / May '94 / Sony.

DE NINA A MUJER
De nina a mujer / Volver a empezar / Despues de ti / Que nadie sepa mi sufrir / Isal

en el sol / O me quieres o me dejas / Y pensar..si madam / Grande, grande, grande / Come tu
CD _____ 983323 2
Pickwick/Sony Collector's Choice / Nov '93 / Carlton Home Entertainment / Pinnacle / Sony.
CD _____ 4654502
Columbia / Oct '95 / Sony.

HEY
For Elle / Amantes / Morrinas / Viejas tradiciones / Ron y coco cola / Hey / Sentimental / Paloma blanca / La Nave del Olvido / Pajaro chogui
CD _____ 4510582
Columbia / Apr '94 / Sony.

HEY/JULIO/LIBRA (3CD Set)
CD Set _____ 4688082
Columbia / Jan '95 / Sony.

JULIO
Begin the beguine / Forever and ever / Yours / La paloma / Pensami / D'abord...il puis / Never, never, never / Nathalie / Feelings / Hey, amor / Limelight / Rum and coca cola / Sono lo / Je nais pas change / So close to me
CD _____ 4510772
CBS / Feb '88 / Sony.

LA CARRETERA
La carretera / Cosae de la vida / Baila morena / Derroche el ultimo / Verano / Agua dulce, agua sala / Sin exasas ni rodeos / Mal de amores / Rumbas / Vuela alto
CD _____ 4807042
Columbia / Jul '95 / Sony.

LIBRA
Ni te tengo, ni te olvido / Tu y yo / I've got you under my skin / Dire / Abrail en Portugal / Felicidades / Esto cobardia / Coracao apaixonado / Ni tu gato gris / Ni tu perro fiel / Todo Y nada
CD _____ 982635 2
Pickwick/Sony Collector's Choice / Aug '91 / Carlton Home Entertainment / Pinnacle / Sony.

MOMENTOS/1100 BEL AIR PLACE/DE NINER A MUJER (3CD Set)
CD Set _____ 4741442
Columbia / Jan '95 / Sony.

NON STOP
Love is on our side again / I know it's over / Never, never, never / AE, AO / Words and music / My love (featuring Stevie Wonder) / Everytime we fall in love / Too many women / If I ever needed you (I need you now)
CD _____ 4609902
Columbia / Oct '95 / Sony.

SOY
Vivencias / En una ciudad culaquiera / Soy / Minueto / Mi amor es mas joven que you / Dieciseis anos / Nian / Una layenda / Asi nacemos / Vete ya
CD _____ 982279 2
Pickwick/Sony Collector's Choice / Sep '93 / Carlton Home Entertainment / Pinnacle / Sony.

STARRY NIGHT.
Can't help falling in love / And I love her / Mona Lisa / Crying time / Yesterday when I was young / When I need you / Ninety nine miles from L.A. / Vincent (starry starry night) / If you go away / Love has been a friend to me
CD _____ 4672842
CBS / Nov '90 / Sony.

Ignatzek, Klaus

ANSWER, THE (Ignatzek, Klaus Quintet)
CD _____ CCD 79534
Candid / Feb '94 / Cadillac / Jazz Music / Wellard / Koch.

RETURN VOYAGE (Ignatzek, Klaus Jazztet)
CD _____ CCD 79716
Candid / Nov '95 / Cadillac / Jazz Music / Wellard / Koch.

Ignite

FAMILY
CD _____ LF 192CD
Lost & Found / Jul '95 / Plastic Head.

IN MY TIME
CD _____ LF 124CD
Lost & Found / Feb '95 / Plastic Head.

SCARRED FOR LIFE
CD _____ LF 104CD
Lost & Found / Aug '94 / Plastic Head.

Ignition

COMPLETE SERVICES
CD _____ DIS 88CD
Dischord / Mar '94 / SRD.

Ignorance

CONFIDENT RAT, THE
CD _____ CDZORRO 17
Metal Blade / Feb '91 / Pinnacle.

POSITIVELY SHOCKING
CD _____ CDZORRO 48
Metal Blade / Sep '92 / Pinnacle.

Igus Orchestra

SCOTLAND FOR ME
CD _____ CDKLP 59
Igus / Apr '87 / CM / Ross / Duncans.

TASTE OF SCOTLAND
CD _____ CDKLP 60
Igus / Jun '87 / CM / Ross / Duncans.

Iiuvatar

CHILDREN
CD _____ IOMCD 003
Cyclops / Nov '95 / Pinnacle.

Ijahman Levi

AFRICA
CD _____ CDJMI 400
Jahmani / Dec '95 / Jetstar / Grapevine / THE.

ARE WE A WARRIOR
Are we a warrior / Moulding / Church / Miss Beverly / Two sides of love
CD _____ RRCD 25
Reggae Refreshers / Nov '90 / PolyGram / Vital.
CD _____ CDJMI 200
Jahmani / Dec '95 / Jetstar / Grapevine / THE.

BLACK ROYALITIES
CD _____ CDJMI 1800
Jahmani / Dec '95 / Jetstar / Grapevine / THE.

CULTURE COUNTRY
CD _____ CDJMI 700
Jahmani / Dec '95 / Jetstar / Grapevine / THE.

ENTITLEMENT
CD _____ CDJMI 1600
Jahmani / Dec '95 / Jetstar / Grapevine / THE.

FORWARD RASTAMAN
Waitin' on you / Gambler's blues / Tired of your jive / Night life / Buzz me / Sweet sixteen part 1 / Don't answer the door / Blind love / I know what you're puttin' down / Baby get lost / Gonna keep on loving you / Sweet sixteen part 2
CD _____ CDJMI 800
Jahmani / Dec '95 / Jetstar / Grapevine / THE.

GEMINI MAN
CD _____ JMICD 1500
Jahmani / Dec '95 / Jetstar / Grapevine / THE.

HAILE I HYMN
Jah heavy load / Jah is no secret / Zion hut / Love / Praises in strange places / Marcus hero / Zion train
CD _____ CDJMI 100
Jahmani / Dec '95 / Jetstar / Grapevine / THE.

I DO (Ijahman Levi & Madge Sutherland)
CD _____ CDJMI 600
Jahmani / Dec '95 / Jetstar / Grapevine / THE.

IJAHMAN & FRIENDS
Master ideas / Mellow music / African train / Struggling dub / Extended dub / Master dub / Struggling times / Let him go / Jah is coming
CD _____ CDJMI 900
Jahmani / Dec '95 / Jetstar / Grapevine / THE.

IJAHMAN LEVI & BOB MARLEY IN DUB (Ijahman Levi & Bob Marley)
CD _____ CDJMI 2200
Jahmani / Dec '95 / Jetstar / Grapevine / THE.

INSIDE OUT
CD _____ CDJMI 1100
Jahmani / Dec '95 / Jetstar / Grapevine / THE.

KINGFARI
CD _____ CDJMI 1400
Jahmani / Dec '95 / Jetstar / Grapevine / THE.

LILY OF MY VALLEY
CD _____ CDJMI 500
Jahmani / Dec '95 / Jetstar / Grapevine / THE.

LIVE IN PARIS '94
CD _____ CDJMI 2000
Jahmani / Dec '95 / Jetstar / Grapevine / THE.

LIVE OVER EUROPE
CD _____ CDJMI 1000
Jahmani / Dec '95 / Jetstar / Grapevine / THE.

LOVE SMILES
CD _____ CDJMI 1200
Jahmani / Dec '95 / Jetstar / Grapevine / THE.

ON TRACK
CD _____ CDJMI 1300
Jahmani / Dec '95 / Jetstar / Grapevine / THE.

SINGS BOB MARLEY
CD _____ CDJMI 1900
Jahmani / Dec '95 / Jetstar / Grapevine / THE.

TELL IT TO THE CHILDREN
CD _____ CDJMI 300
Jahmani / Dec '95 / Jetstar / Grapevine / THE.

TWO DOUBLE SIX 701
CD _____ CDJMI 1700
Jahmani / Dec '95 / Jetstar / Grapevine / THE.

Ikeno, Shigeaki

MUSIC TO DREAM BY (Ikeno, Shigeaki & His Naughty Boys)
My funny valentine / Among my souvenirs / Deep purple / One note samba / My foolish heart / Autumn leaves / I can't get started (with you) / Moonlight in Vermont / Summertime / As time goes by / Night and day / Bewitched, bothered and bewildered / Girl from Ipanema / After you've gone / Fly me to the moon
CD _____ DC 8506
Denon / '88 / Conifer.

TOUCH OF SATIN (Ikeno, Shigeaki & His Naughty Boys)
Misty / Day by day / Man I love / Take the 'A' train / Canadian sunset / I left my heart in San Francisco / Yes sir that's my baby / Bye bye blues / Satin doll / Blue skies / Somebody loves me / Lover come back to me / End of the world / Stompin' at the Savoy / Days of wine and roses / Zing went the strings of my heart / Pennies from Heaven
CD _____ DC 8505
Denon / '88 / Conifer.

Ikettes

FINE, FINE, FINE
(He's gonna be) Fine fine fine / Can't sit down / Don't feel sorry for me / Camel walk / Blue on blue / I'm so thankful / You're trying to make me lose my mind / Sally go round the roses / Peaches and cream / Never more will I be lonely for you / Not that I recall / Your love is here / Biggest players / How come / Nobody loves me / It's been so long / Through with you (CD only) / Cheater (CD only) / I'm leaving you (CD only) / You're still my baby (CD only) / Give me a chance (try me) (CD only) / Love of my man (live/CD only) / Living for you (CD only) / I love the way you love (live/CD only)
CD _____ CDKEN 063
Kent / Sep '92 / Pinnacle.

Ikhwani Safaa Musical...

TAARAB MUSIC OF ZANZIBAR VOL.2 (Ikhwani Safaa Musical Club)
Usiji gambe / Nna zama / Pendo la wasikitisha / Nipe pee / Kanilemaza / Uki chungua / Waridi lisilo miba / Hidaya
CD _____ CDORB 033
Globestyle / Oct '88 / Pinnacle.

Ikon

MOMENT IN TIME, A
CD _____ EFA 121672
Apollyon / Nov '95 / SRD.

Ile Axe

BRAZILIAN PERCUSSION
CD _____ PS 65059
Playasound / Nov '90 / Harmonia Mundi / ADA.

Ilg, Dieter

SUMMERHILL
It's getting better / Spring fever / Shadows of the fall / Summerhill / All childrens love song / Somersault / Under the skin of the earth
CD _____ LIP 890062
Lipstick / Feb '95 / Vital/SAM.

Illapu

RAZA BRAVA
CD _____ MCD 71811
Monitor / Jun '93 / CM.

Illdisposed

FOUR DEPRESSIVE SEASONS
CD _____ NB 103
Nuclear Blast / Apr '94 / Plastic Head.

HELVEDE
CD _____ RRS 945CD
Lost & Found / Sep '95 / Plastic Head.

RETURN FROM TOMORROW
CD _____ NB 116
Nuclear Blast / Aug '94 / Plastic Head.

SUBMIT
CD _____ PCD 021
Progress / Nov '95 / Plastic Head.

Illusion

ENCHANTED CARESS
CD _____ PL 92152

Promised Land / Aug '90 / Kingdom / Direct.

OUT OF THE MIST / ILLUSION
Isadora / Roads to freedom / Beautiful country / Solo flight / Everywhere you go / Face of yesterday / Candles are burning / Madonna blues / Never be the same / Louis theme / Wings across the sea / Cruising nowhere / Man of miracles / Revolutionary
CD _____ EDCD 369
Edsel / Mar '94 / Pinnacle / ADA.

Illusion Of Safety

WATER SEEKS IT'S OWN LEVEL
CD _____ SR 9351
Silent / Mar '94 / Plastic Head.

Illustrious

NO NO NO (Illustrious GY)
CD _____ 7432115729-2
RCA / Nov '93 / BMG.

Iluyenkori

CUBAN DRUMS
CD _____ PS 65084
Playasound / Mar '92 / Harmonia Mundi / ADA.

Imagination

VERY BEST OF IMAGINATION, THE
CD _____ BX 4182
BR Music / Apr '95 / Target/BMG.

Imlach, Hamish

SONNY'S DREAM
Cod liver oil and orange juice / Ballad of William Brown / Mary Anne / Reprobate's lament / Salonika / Kisses sweeter than wine / Smoker's song / Sonny's dream / If it wasn't for the union / Parcel o' rogues / I didn't raise my boy to be a soldier / Goodbye booze / D-day dodgers / Seven men of Knoydart
CD _____ LCOM 7006
Lismor / May '95 / Lismor / Direct / Duncans / ADA.

Immaculate Fools

TOY SHOP
Stand down / Heaven down here / Political Wish / Cotillas / Leaving song / Wonder of things / Good times / Through these eyes / Bed of tears / How the west was won
CD _____ 19209-2
Continuum / Oct '92 / Pinnacle.

WOODHOUSE
Rain / Some of us / Ship song / Time to kill / Profit for prophets / Pass the jug / Rudy / Home / Bury my heart / Wish you were here / If you go
CD _____ COOKCD 085
Cooking Vinyl / Apr '95 / Vital.

Immersion

FULL IMMERSION
CD _____ VWM 40
Swim / Jun '95 / SRD / Disc.

OSCILLATING
CD _____ WM 4CD
Swim / Sep '94 / SRD / Disc.

Immolation

DAWN OF POSSESSION
CD _____ RC 93102
RC / Jan '94 / Pinnacle.

HERE IN AFTER
CD _____ 3984102CD
Metal Blade / Jan '96 / Plastic Head.

STEPPING ON ANGELS... BEFORE DAWN
CD _____ RPS 004CD
Repulse / Jan '95 / Plastic Head.

Immortal

BATTLES IN THE NORTH
CD _____ OPCD 027
Osmose / May '95 / Plastic Head.

PURE HOLOCAUST
CD _____ OPCD 19
Osmose / Dec '93 / Plastic Head.

Impaled Nazarene

SUOMI FINLAND
CD _____ OPCD 026
Osmose / Apr '95 / Plastic Head.

TOL CORMPT NORZ NORZ NORZ
CD _____ OPCD 010LTD
Osmose / Nov '95 / Plastic Head.

UGRA KARMA
CD _____ OPCD 018
Osmose / Apr '95 / Plastic Head.

Impatient Youth

ALL FOR FUN
CD _____ LF 76CD
Lost & Found / Nov '94 / Plastic Head.

Imperial Court Ensemble

GAGAKU - ANCIENT JAPANESE COURT & DANCE MUSIC
CD _____ CD 402
Bescol / Aug '94 / CM / Target/BMG.

Implant Code

BIODIGIT
CD _____ MHCD 020
Minus Habens / Mar '94 / Plastic Head.

Impressions

ALL THE BEST (Impressions & Curtis Mayfield)
Gypsy woman / It's all right / People get ready / Talking about my baby / I'm so proud / I've been trying / Amen / You've been cheating / I'm the one who loves you / We're a winner / Keep on pushing / Right on time / Move on up / Freddie's dead / First impressions
CD _____ PWKS 4206
Carlton Home Entertainment / Feb '96 / Carlton Home Entertainment.

DEFINITIVE IMPRESSIONS, THE
Gypsy woman / Grow closer together / Little young lover / Minstrel and queen / I'm the one who loves you / Sad, sad girl and boy / It's all right / Talking about my baby / I'm so proud / Keep on pushing / I've been trying / Girl you don't know me / I made a mistake / You must believe me / Amen / People get ready / Woman's got soul / Meeting over yonder / I need you / Just one kiss from you / You've been cheating / Since I lost the one I love / I can't satisfy / You always hurt me / I can't stay away from you / We're a winner / We're rolling on / I loved and I lost
CD _____ CDKEND 923
Kent / Oct '89 / Pinnacle.

FOR YOUR PRECIOUS LOVE
For your precious love / Sweet was the wine / Come back my love / At the county fair / That you love me / Gift of love / Senorita I love you / Let me know / Don't drive me away / Lover's lane / Believe in me / Young lover / Long time ago / Lovely one
CD _____ CDCD 1105
Charly / Jul '93 / Charly / THE / Cadillac.

IMPRESSIONS/THE NEVER ENDING IMPRESSIONS
It's all right / Gypsy woman / Grow closer together / Little young lover / I love come home / Never let me go / Minstrel and queen / I need your love / I'm the one who loves you / Sad, sad girl and boy / As long as you love me / Twist and limbo / Sister love / Little boy blue / Satin doll / Girl don't you know me / I gotta keep on moving / You always hurt the one you love / That's what love will do / I'm so proud / September song / Lemon tree / Ten to one / Woman who loves me
CD _____ CDKEND 126
Kent / Aug '95 / Pinnacle.

KEEP ON PUSHING/PEOPLE GET READY
CD _____ CDKEND 130
Kent / Feb '96 / Pinnacle.

THIS IS MY COUNTRY/YOUNG MODS FORGOTTEN
CD _____ CDGR 108
Charly / Jan '96 / Charly / THE / Cadillac.

Impromptu

SWEET KAFKA
Hiedeggar's lobster / Sweet Kafka / Avenue / Simply breathing / Fountain / Me and Louise / Med mig sjalv / Ginsberg / What can I say / Ten unicorns / Flay / La petite mort
CD _____ RGM 194CD
Red Gold Music / Dec '94 / Red Gold Music.

Impulse Manslaughter

LOGICAL END
CD _____ NB 013CD
Nuclear Blast / Jun '89 / Plastic Head.

Imru-Ashah, Ras

TRIBUTE TO SELASSIE 1
CD _____ HA 1CD
House Of Ashah / Jul '95 / Jetstar / SRD.

In Cahoots

RECENT DISCOVERIES
Riffy / Trick of the light / Opener / Recent discoveries / Chez gege / Tide / Breadhead
CD _____ CD 003CD
Voice Print / Sep '94 / Voice Print.

In Crowd

NATURAL ROCK 'N' REGGAE
CD _____ RNCD 2003
Greensleeves / Nov '92 / Total/BMG / Jetstar / SRD.

In My Rosary

STRANGE EP
CD _____ SPV 06519042
SPV / Aug '95 / Plastic Head.

In The Nursery

AMBUSH OF GHOSTS, AN (Original Soundtrack)
CD _____ TM 90382
Roadrunner / Oct '93 / Pinnacle.

ANATOMY OF A POET
CD _____ TM 89762
Roadrunner / Oct '94 / Pinnacle.

DUALITY
CD _____ TM 91632
Roadrunner / Jun '92 / Pinnacle.

KODA
CD _____ CORP 008CD
ITN Corporation / Jun '95 / Plastic Head.

L'ESPRIT
CD _____ TMCD 48
Third Mind / Feb '90 / Pinnacle / Third Mind.
CD _____ CORP 010CD
ITN Corporation / Jun '95 / Plastic Head.

PRELUDE
CD _____ CORP 007CD
ITN Corporation / Jun '95 / Plastic Head.

SCATTER
CD _____ CORP 011CD
ITN Corporation / Jun '95 / Plastic Head.

SENSE
CD _____ TM 92/112
Roadrunner / Aug '91 / Pinnacle.

TWINS
CD _____ CORP 009CD
ITN Corporation / Jun '95 / Plastic Head.

In The Woods

HEART OF THE AGES
CD _____ AMAZON 004CD
Misanthropy / May '95 / Plastic Head.

In Your Face

COLLECTIVE WORKS, THE
CD _____ LF 106CD
Lost & Found / Oct '94 / Plastic Head.

Inanna

NOTHING
CD _____ DVLR 08CD
Dark Vinyl / Jun '95 / Plastic Head.

Inbreds

KOMBINATOR
Kombinator / Round 12 / You will know / Any sense of time / Turn my head / Dale says / She's acting / Scratch / Link / Dangerous / Don't try so hard / Cruise control / Last flight / Amelia Earhart
CD _____ 926062
Seed / Jan '96 / Vital.

Incantation

BEST OF INCANTATION
On the wing of a condor / Cutimy / Sacsaywaman / Dance of the flames / Sonccuiman / Noches de luna / Cacharpaya / Papel de plata / Virgins of the sun / Atahuallpa / Dolencias / Festival of Yotala / Los senors de Potasi
CD _____ NAGE 100CD
Art Of Landscape / May '92 / Sony.

INCANTATION
Ganado feroz / Wild / Herd / Brazfest / Reunion / Santa Cruz jit / Doina cestriana / Electric snake charmer / Llaulillay / Dawn at volcabamba / Serenading chango / Little flute player / Remembrance of Mary and Ellen / Cacharpaya shuffle
CD _____ COOKCD 073
Cooking Vinyl / May '95 / Vital.

INCANTATION CHRISTMAS
What is this fragrance / I saw three ships come sailing by / Torches / Our lady / How hard it bloweth / Solis ortus / Cardine / Virgin Mother / Holly and the ivy / In dulci jubilo / Lullay thou tiny little child / Angel Gabriel / Wexford Carol / Virgin most pure / Jesus redemption omnia
CD _____ 30360 00102
Carlton Home Entertainment / Oct '95 / Carlton Home Entertainment.

MEETING, THE
De mis huellas / Antiguos duenos de las flechas / Old thatched cabin / Canto del agua / Scarborough Fair / On earth as it is in heaven (Theme from the mission) / Pinca runas/Waya yay / El amor es una camina / Cuando / Cancion de carnival / Night shadows
CD _____ COOKCD 068
Cooking Vinyl / Jun '94 / Vital.

MORTAL THRONE OF NAZARENE
CD _____ RR 69052
Nuclear Blast / Dec '94 / Plastic Head.

On Gentle Rocks

ON GENTLE ROCKS
CD _____ DMUS 101
Destiny / Aug '92 / Total/BMG.

ONWARD TO GOLGOTHA
CD _____ RR 60372CD
Relapse / Nov '92 / Plastic Head.

PANPIPES OF THE ANDES
Amores hallaras / Cacharpaya / Papel de plata / Friends of the Andes / El pajaro madrugador / Condor dance / Sonccuiman / Dolencias / Winds on the mountain / On the wing of a condor / Sikuriadas / High flying bird
CD _____ NAGE 101CD
Art Of Landscape / Oct '92 / Sony.

SERGEANT EARLY'S DREAM/ GHOST DANCES
May morning dew / Sergeant early's dream / Eighteen years old / Maid of mount / Sisco/Skylark/Richard Dwyers / Geordie / Love will you marry me/Plains of boyle / Black is the colour of my true love's hair / Peggy Gordon / Gospel ship / Barbara Allen / Junior Crehan's / Favourite/Corney is coming / Ojo azules / Huajra / Dolencias / Papel de plata / Mis Llamitas / Sikuriadas / Ojos azules
CD _____ COOKCD 069
Cooking Vinyl / Feb '95 / Vital.

SONGS FOR THE SEASON
CD _____ ACD 501CD
Aeolian / Oct '94 / ADA.

Inch

STRESSER
Linger / No. 48 Vs SI / A / Kermit the hostage / Stresser / I'm the cat / Kane / Icepick / Surprise / Root canal/Manatoba / Oxidizer / Were riding
CD _____ 14252-2
Seed / May '94 / Vital.

Incognito

INSIDE LIFE
Metropolis / Smile / One step to a miracle / Can you feel me / Gypsy / Inside life / Love is the colour / Sketches in the dark / Soho / Always there
CD _____ 8485462
Talkin' Loud / Jul '91 / PolyGram.

ONE HUNDRED DEGREES AND RISING
Where did we go wrong / Good love / Hundred and rising / Roots / Everyday / Too far gone / After the fall (Not on LP) / Spellbound and speechless / I hear your name / Barumba / Millenium / Time has come / Jacob's ladder
CD _____ 5280002
Talkin' Loud / May '95 / PolyGram.

POSITIVITY
Still a friend of mine / Smiling faces / Keep the fire burning / Do right / Positivity / Talkin' loud / Deep waters / Where do we go from here / Giving it up / Thinking about tomorrow
CD _____ 518260-2
Talkin' Loud / Nov '93 / PolyGram.

TRIBES, VIBES AND SCRIBES
Colibri / Change / River in my dreams / Don't you worry about a thing / Magnet ocean / I love what you do for me / Closer to the feeling / L'Arc en ciel de miles / Need to know / Pyramids / Tribal vibes
CD _____ 5123632
Talkin' Loud / Jun '92 / PolyGram.

Incredible String Band

5000 SPIRITS OR THE LAYERS OF THE ONION
Chinese white / No sleep blues / Painting box / Mad hatter's song / Little cloud / Eyes of fate / Blues for the muse / Hedgehog's song / First girl I loved / You know that you could be / My name is death / Gently tender / Way back in the 1960's
CD _____ HNCD 4438
Hannibal / Jun '94 / Vital / ADA.

BIG HUGE, THE
Maya / Greatest friend / Son of Noah's brother / Lordly nightshade / Mountain of God / Cousin caterpillar / Iron stone / Douglas Traherne Harding / Circle is unbroken
CD _____ 7559615482
Elektra / Jul '93 / Warner Music.

CHANGING HORSES
Big Ted / White bird / Dust be diamonds / Sleeper's awake / Mr. and Mrs. / Creation
CD _____ HNCD 4439
Rykodisc / Nov '94 / Vital / ADA.

HANGMAN'S BEAUTIFUL DAUGHTER
Koee / Addi there / Minotaur's song / Witches hat / Very cellular song / Mercy I cry city / Waltz of the new moon / Water song / Three is a green crown / Swift as the wind / Nightfall
CD _____ HNCD 4421
Hannibal / Jun '94 / Vital / ADA.

HARD ROPE AND SILKEN TWINE
Maker of islands / Cold February / Glancing love / Dreams of no return / Dumb Kate / Ithkos
CD _____ EDCD 368
Edsel / Jan '93 / Pinnacle / ADA.

I LOOKED UP
CD _____ HNCD 4440
Rykodisc / Nov '94 / Vital / ADA.

INCREDIBLE STRING BAND
Maybe someday / October song / When the music starts to play / Schaeffer's jig / Womankind / Tree / Whistle tune / Dandelion blues / How happy I am / Empty pocket blues / Smoke shovelling song / Can't keep me here / Good as gone / Footsteps of the heron / Niggertown / Everything's fine right now
CD _____ HNCD 4437
Hannibal / Jun '94 / Vital / ADA.

LIQUID ACROBAT AS REGARDS AIR
Talking of the end / Dear old battlefield / Cosmic boy / Worlds they rise and fall / Evolution rag / Painted chariot / Adam and Eve / Red hair / Here till here is there / Tree / Jigs / Darling belle
CD _____ IMCD 130
Island / Jun '91 / PolyGram.

NO RUINOUS FEUD
CD _____ EDCD 367
Edsel / Nov '92 / Pinnacle / ADA.

ON AIR
Dreams of no return / Jane / Oh did I love a dream / Black jack David / Little girl / Rends-moi demain / Dear old battlefield / Cold days of February / Witches hat / Koeeoaaddi there / Very cellular song
CD _____ BOJCD 004
Band Of Joy / Oct '91 / ADA.

WEE TAM
Job's tears / Puppies / Beyond the sea / Yellow snake / Log cabin in the sky / You get brighter / Half remarkable question / Air / Ducks on a pond
CD _____ HNCD 4802
Rykodisc / Nov '94 / Vital / ADA.

Incredibles

HEART & SOUL
Heart and soul / (I love you) for sentimental reasons / Lost without you / Standing here crying / Black jack David / Little girl / Without a word / All of a sudden / Another dirty deal / There's nothing else to say baby / Fool, fool, fool (version 1) / Try me again / A little bit of soap / Standing here crying (2) / I found another love / Crying heart (version 1) / Without a word (2) / Standing here crying (2) / Miss Treatment (45 version) / I can't get over losing your love / Fool, fool, fool (version 2)
CD _____ GSCD 018
Goldmine / Jul '93 / Vital.

Incubus

BEYOND THE UNKNOWN
CD _____ NB 039CD
Nuclear Blast / Jan '91 / Plastic Head.

Incubus Succubus

BELLADONNA & ACONITE
CD _____ NIGHTCD 003
Contempo / Sep '93 / Plastic Head.

India

DICEN QUE SOY
Nunca voy a olvidarte / Que ganas de no verte mas / Ese hombre / Dicen que soy / O ella o yo / Dejate amar / I just want to hang around you / No me conviene / Vivir lo nuestro
CD _____ 66058065
RMM / Jul '95 / New Note.

Indian Bingo

OVERWROUGHT
CD _____ ROCK 6079-2
Rockville / Mar '93 / SRD.

PICTURE SHOP, THE
CD _____ ROCK 6133-2
Rockville / Jan '94 / SRD.

Indian National Sitar...

TRADITIONAL SONGS/DANCES OF INDIA (Indian National Sitar Ensemble)
CD _____ CD 403
Bescol / Aug '94 / CM / Target/BMG.

Indicate

WHELM
CD _____ TO 25
Touch / Jun '95 / These / Kudos.

Indigo Girls

4.5
Joking / Hammer and a nail / Kid fears / Galileo / Tried to be true / Power of two / Pushing the needle too far / Reunion / Closer to fine / Three hits / Least complicated / Touch me fall / Love's recovery / Land of Canaan / Ghost
CD _____ 4804392
Epic / Jul '95 / Sony.

INDIGO GIRLS
Closer to fine / Secure yourself / Kid fears / Prince of Darkness / Blood and fire / Tried to be true / Love's recovery / Land of Canaan / Center stage / History of us

---

CD _____ 4634912
Epic / Jul '89 / Sony.

RITES OF PASSAGE
Three hits / Galileo / Ghost / Joking / Jonas and Ezekial / Love will come to you / Romeo and Juliet / Virginia Woolf / Chicken man / Airplane / Nashville / Let it be me / Cedar tree
CD _____ 471363 2
Epic / '89 / Sony.

SWAMPOPHELIA
Fugitive / Least complicated / Language of the kiss / Reunion / Power of two / Touch me fall / Wood song / Mystery / Dead man's hill / Fare thee well / This train revised
CD _____ 475931 2
Epic / May '94 / Sony.

Inertia

INFILTRATOR
CD _____ EFA 125292
Celtic Circle / Nov '95 / SRD.

Infectious Grooves

GROOVE FAMILY CYCO
Violent and funky / Boom boom boom / Frustrated again / Rules go out the window / Groove family cyco / Die like a pig / Do what I tell ya / Cousin Randy / Why / Made it
CD _____ 475929 2
Epic / May '94 / Sony.

PLAGUE THAT MAKES YOUR BOOTY MOVE, THE (It's The Infectious Groovers)
Punk it up / Therapy / I look funny / Stop funk'n with my head / I'm gonna be my King / Closed session / Infectious grooves / Infectious blues / Monster skank / Back to the people / Turn your head / You lie...and yo breath stank / Do the sinister / Mandatory love song / Infecto groovalistic / Thanx but no thanx
CD _____ 4687292
Epic / Sep '91 / Sony.

Inferno

PSYCHIC DISTANCE
CD _____ MASSCD 043
Massacre / Jan '95 / Plastic Head.

Infinite Wheel

INFINITE WHEEL, THE
CD _____ BRAINK 41CD
Brainiak / Oct '94 / 3MV / Sony.

Infinity Project

MYSTICAL EXPERIENCES
CD _____ BR 005CD
Blue Room Released / Jan '96 / SRD.

Infor/Mental

MIND DRONE
Mind drone / Wave / Pleasuredance / Dream mode mutation / Mental journey / Frenzy / Trance induction (Poison mix/CD only) / Dream mode mutation (mix) / Insanity (CD only) / Device trigger (CD only) / Ambient one (CD only)
CD _____ LUDDITECD 066
Death Of Vinyl / Oct '93 / Vital.

Ingham, Keith

KEITH INGHAM & MARTY GROSZ/ COSMOPOLITES (Ingham, Keith & Marty Grosz)
CD _____ SOSCD 1285
Stomp Off / Mar '95 / Jazz Music / Wellard.

OUT OF THE PAST
CD _____ SKCD 2-3047
Sackville / '92 / Swift / Jazz Music / Jazz Horizons / Cadillac / CM.

Ingleton Falls

ABSCONDED
CD _____ CHARRMCD 20
Charrm / Mar '95 / Plastic Head.

Ingman, Nick

HOME (Ingman, Nick & Friends)
Home / Homeward bound / Now and then / Just be close / Making tracks / Staying in / Help me make it through the night / Missing you again / Welcome home / By your side / Late night talking / Woman / Sunday morning / Home is where the heart is / On the road / Green green grass of home / When day is done / Cosy / Safe and sound / Here where you are
CD _____ BATCD 10.01
Baton / Jul '89 / RRD.

Ingram, James

ALWAYS YOU
Someone like you / Let me love you this way / Always you / Treat her right / Baby's born / This is the night / You never know what you've got / Too much from this heart / Sing for the children / Any kind of love
CD _____ 9362452275-2
Qwest / May '93 / Warner Music.

IT'S YOUR NIGHT
Party animal / Yah mo be there / She loves me (the best that I can be) / Try your love again / Whatever we imagine / One more rhythm / There's no easy way / It's your night / How do you keep the music playing
CD _____ 923970 2
Qwest / '86 / Warner Music.

POWER OF GREAT MUSIC, THE
Where did my heart go / How do you keep the music playing / Just once / Somewhere out there / I don't have the heart / There's no easy way / Get ready / Baby, come to me / Hundred ways / Yah mo be there / Remember the dream / Whatever we imagine
CD _____ 7599267002
Qwest / Mar '94 / Warner Music.

Ingram, Luther

I LIKE THE FEELING
CD _____ URG 4119CD
Urgent / Feb '94 / Koch.

Ink Spots

20 CLASSICS
CD _____ CDCD 1197
Charly / Sep '94 / Charly / THE / Cadillac.

BEST OF THE INK SPOTS
If I didn't care / Bless you for being an angel / When the swallows come back to Capistrano / Whispering grass / Maybe / Java jive / Do I worry / I don't want to set the world on fire / Every night about this time / Don't get around much anymore / To each his own / Ring, telephone, ring / I'd climb the highest mountain / Puttin' and takin' / Cow cow boogie / Into each life some rain must fall / Your feet's too big / I'll never smile again / It's a sin to tell a lie / Someone's rocking my dreamboat
CD _____ CDMFP 6064
Music For Pleasure / May '89 / EMI.

BLESS YOU
Bless you / If I didn't care / Whispering grass / Stop pretending / When the swallows come back to Capistrano / So sorry / Do I worry / We'll meet again / I'd climb the highest mountain / Ring, telephone, ring / That cat is high / Memories of you / My prayer / Just for a thrill / We three / Someone's rocking my dreamboat / Maybe / I'll never smile again / I'm getting sentimental over you / Coquette / Oh red / When the sun goes down
CD _____ PLCD 535
President / Mar '93 / Grapevine / Target/ BMG / Jazz Music / President.

INK SPOTS, THE
CD _____ CD 110
Timeless Treasures / Oct '94 / THE.

INTO EACH LIFE
CD _____ CDCD 1258
Charly / Jun '95 / Charly / THE / Cadillac.

JAVA JIVE
CD _____ 15430
Laserlight / Jan '93 / Target/BMG.

SENTIMENTAL OVER YOU
CD _____ HADCD 194
Javelin / Nov '95 / THE / Henry Hadaway Organisation.

SWING HIGH, SWING LOW
Keep away from my doorstep / Alabama barbecue / T'ain't nobody's business if I do / That cat is high / Swing gate swing / Slap that bass / Christopher Columbus / Ye suh / Your feet's too big / When the sun goes down / Swingin' on the strings / Stompin' at the Savoy / With plenty of money and you / Let's call the whole thing off / Don't let old age creep up on you / Mama don't allow it / Oh Red / Old Joe's hittin' the jug / Whoa babe / Swing high swing low
CD _____ CDHD 143
Happy Days / Apr '89 / Conifer.

SWING HIGH, SWING LOW (1936-1940)
Bless you / Java jive / When the swallows come back to Capistrano / My prayer / Christopher Columbus / I'll never smile again / Stompin' at the Savoy / Whispering grass / If I didn't care / I'm getting sentimental over you / Keep away from my doorstep / Let's call the whole thing off / Maybe / Oh Red / Slap that bass / Stop pretending / Swing high swing low / That cat is high / When the sun goes down / With plenty of money and you / Yes suh / Your feet's too big
CD _____ CDAJA 5082
Living Era / Apr '91 / Koch.

WHISPERING GRASS
Bless you / Stop pretending / That cat is high / When the swallows come back to Capistrano / Mama don't allow it / My prayer / Whispering grass / We three (my echo, my shadow and me) / I'm getting sentimental over you / Java jive / With plenty of money and you / Keep away from my doorstep / Do I worry / I'll never smile again / Don't let old age creep up on you / Maybe / If I didn't care / Stompin' at the Savoy / Coquette / Swing high swing low / Your feet's too big / When the sun goes down
CD _____ PASTCD 9757
Pearl / Aug '91 / Harmonia Mundi.

Inmates

INMATES
CD _____ 892223
New Rose / May '94 / Direct / ADA.

INSIDE OUT
CD _____ 422178
New Rose / May '94 / Direct / ADA.

WANTED
CD _____ 422460
New Rose / May '94 / Direct / ADA.

Inner Circle

BAD TO THE BONE
Sweat (a la la la la long) / Shock out Jamaican style / Bad to the bone / Rock with you / Long time / Hey love / Slow it down / Living it up / Stuck in the middle / Looking for a better way / Wrapped up in your love / Bad boys / Party party / Sunglasses at nite / Tear down these walls / Down by the river / Hold on to the ridim / Why them a gwan so
CD _____ 903177677-2
Magnet / May '93 / Warner Music.

BEST OF INNER CIRCLE
Rock the boat / Curfew / Duppy gunman / None shall escape the judgement / You make me feel brand new / Some guys have all the luck / Everything I own / T.S.O.P. / Westbound train / Book of rules / Natty dread / I shot the sheriff / Irie feelings / Forward Jah Jah children / Blame it on the sun / Curly locks / Your kiss is sweet / Burial / Roadblock / When will I see you again
CD _____ CDTRL 318
Trojan / Mar '94 / Jetstar / Total/BMG.

BEST OF INNER CIRCLE, THE
CD _____ CID 8007
Island / Jan '94 / PolyGram.

FORWARD JAH JAH PEOPLE
Rastaman / Forward Jah Jah children / Last crusade / Lively up yourself / Funky reggae / One love
CD _____ CPCD 8133
Charly / Oct '95 / Charly / THE / Cadillac.

ONE WAY
One way / Front and centre / Champion / Keep the faith / Love one another / Massive / Bad boys / Life / Stay with me
CD _____ RASCD 3030
Ras / Oct '87 / Jetstar / Greensleeves / SRD / Direct.

REGGAE DANCER
CD _____ 450996116-2
Magnet / May '94 / Warner Music.

REGGAE THINGS
CD _____ NSPCD 510
Connoisseur / Mar '95 / Pinnacle.

Inner City

PARADISE
Inner city theme / Ain't nobody better / Big fun / Good life / And I do / Paradise / Power of passion / Do you love what you feel / Set your body free / Secrets of the mind
CD _____ DIXCD 81
10 / May '89 / EMI.

PARADISE REMIXED
Big fun / Good life / Ain't nobody better / Do you love what you feel / What'cha gonna do with my lovin' / House fever / Paradise megamix (Only on MC and CD.)
CD _____ XIDCD 81
10 / Feb '90 / EMI.

PRAISE
One nation / Praise / Pennies from heaven / Hallelujah / Follow your heart / Slaves of dance / Let it reign / United / Faith / Save the children
CD _____ DIXCD 107
10 / Jun '92 / EMI.

TESTAMENT '93
Good life (CJ's living good club mix) / Pennies from heaven (Kevin's tunnel mix) / Hallelujah (mixes) / Praise (Future Sound Of London concept dub) / Follow your heart (Mixes) / Good life (Unity remix)
CD _____ CDOVD 438
Virgin / May '93 / EMI.

Inner Sanctum

12 A.M.
CD _____ WDR 42101
Rock The Nation / Nov '94 / Plastic Head.

Innersphere

OUTER WORKS
Out of body / Toys in the attic / Let's go to work / Mine drift / Infernal aftershock / Tuberculosis / Necronomicon / Biomechanoid / 3750 Miles / Out of body (Reprise)
CD _____ SBRCD 002
Sabrettes Of Paradise / Oct '94 / Vital.

Innes, Heather

COAINEADH - SONGS FROM THE HEART
CD _____ FE 99CD
Fellside / Jun '94 / Target/BMG / Direct / ADA.

Innes, Neil

RE-CYCLED VINYL BLUES
Recycled vinyl blues / Angelina / Come out into the open / Prologue / Momma Bee / Lie down and be counted / Immortal invisible / Age of desperation / Topless a go-go / Feel no shame / How sweet to be an idiot / Dream on / L'amour perdu / Song for Yvonne / This love of ours / Fluff on the needle / Singing a song is easy / Bandwagon
CD _____ CZ 536
EMI / Aug '94 / EMI.

Innocence

BELIEF
Silent voice / Let's push it / Reflections / Natural thing / Matter of fact / Higher ground / Remember the day / Moving upwards / Come together / Reprise
CD _____ CCD 1797
Cooltempo / Oct '90 / EMI.

BUILD
Family ties / I'll be there / Build / Looking for someone / Solitude / Family ties(Reprise) / One love in my lifetime / Promise of love / Hold on / Respect / No sacrifice / Build (reprise)
CD _____ CTCD 26
Cooltempo / Oct '92 / EMI.

Innocents

COMPLETE INDIGO RECORDINGS
Gee whiz / Please Mr. Sun / Walking along / Once in a while / Pain in my heart / Chiquita / Girl in my dreams / Because I love you / Sleeping beauty / Donna / Kathy / My baby Hully Gullys / Honest I do / Beware / I'm a hog for you / When I become a man / Two young hearts / Dee dee di oh / I believe in you / It was a tear / You got me goin' / Little blue star / I know a valley / Time makes you change / In the beginning
CD _____ CDCHD 374
Ace / Jun '92 / Pinnacle / Cadillac / Complete/Pinnacle.

Insane Jane

EACH FINGER
CD _____ SKY 75041
Sky / Sep '94 / Koch.

GREEN LITTLE PILL
CD _____ SKY 75040CD
Sky / Sep '94 / Koch.

Insanity Sect

MANISOLA
CD _____ RBADCD 15
Beyond / Jan '96 / Kudos / Pinnacle.

Insaurralde, Mirta

DE IGGUAL A IGUAL (Insaurralde, Mirta & Ruben Ferrero)
CD _____ SLAMCD 502
Slam / Oct '94 / Cadillac.

Insekt

DREAMSCAPE
CD _____ KK 074CD
KK / Mar '92 / Plastic Head.

STRESS
CD _____ KK 054 CD
KK / Mar '91 / Plastic Head.

WE CAN TRUST THE INSECT
CD _____ KK 00 00
KK / Jan '90 / Plastic Head.

WE CAN'T TRUST THE INSEKT
CD _____ KK 036CD
KK / Jun '93 / Plastic Head.

Inside Out

SHE LOST HER HEAD
CD _____ COX 032CD
Meantime / Apr '92 / Vital / Cadillac.

Insides

CLEAR SKIN
CD _____ TU 7
4AD / Feb '94 / Disc.

EUPHORIA
CD _____ GU 4CD
Guernica / Oct '93 / Pinnacle.

Inspiral Carpets

BEAST INSIDE, THE
Caravan / Please be cruel / Born yesterday / Sleep well tonight / Grip / Beast inside / Niagara / Mermaid / Further away / Dreams are all we have
CD _____ DUNG 14CD
Cow / May '91 / Pinnacle.

DEVIL HOPPING
CD _____ LDUNG 25CD
Cow / Feb '94 / Pinnacle.

LIFE
CD _____ DUNG 008CD
Cow / Mar '90 / Pinnacle.

REVENGE OF THE GOLDFISH
CD _____ DUNG 19CD
Cow / Oct '92 / Pinnacle.

SINGLES, THE
CD _____ CDMOOTEL 3
Cow / Sep '95 / Pinnacle.

TALKING WITH THE BEAST
CD P.Disc _____ CBAK 4047
Baktabak / Jun '91 / Baktabak.

Inspirational Choir

GOSPEL SONGS
Amazing grace / Rock of ages / He's got the whole world in his hands / Deep river / Every time I feel the spirit / Steal away / I've got a robe / Were you there / Old rugged cross / Old time religion / Abide with me / He's got the whole world in his hands (1)
CD _____ 5501912
Spectrum/Karussell / Sep '94 / PolyGram THE.

SWEET INSPIRATION
Sweet inspiration / People get ready / Up where we belong / One love / Jesus dropped the charges / I've got a feeling / You light up my life / Morning has broken / Amazing grace / What a friend we have in Jesus / When He comes / God is / Abide with me
CD _____ CD 10048
CBS / Jan '86 / Sony.

Inspirations

PIANO REFLECTIONS
CD _____ PMCD 7024
Pure Music / Jan '96 / RMG.

PURE EMOTIONS
CD _____ PMCD 7023
Pure Music / Oct '95 / BMG.

Instant Funk

FUNK IS ON, THE
It's cool / Funk is on / Funk 'n' roll / You want my love / What can I do for you / Everybody / Can you see where I'm coming from / You're not getting older
CD _____ CPCD 8097
Charly / Apr '95 / Charly / THE / Cadillac.

INSTANT FUNK
I got my mind made up (You can get it girl) / Crying / Never let it go away / Don't wanna party / Wide world of sports / Dark vader / You say you want me to stay / I'll be doggone
CD _____ CPCD 8075
Charly / Mar '95 / Charly / THE / Cadillac.

Insult

MUTANT PUZZLE
CD _____ SPI 021CD
Spinefarm / Jun '95 / Plastic Head.

Insult II Injury

POINT OF THIS
CD _____ CM 77086
Century Media / Jan '95 / Plastic Head.

Intastella

WHAT YOU GONNA DO
CD _____ SATURNCD 1
China / Oct '95 / Pinnacle.

Integrated Circuits

PREDO
CD _____ BBMLABCD 0
Labworks / Oct '95 / SRD / Disc.

Integrity

HOOKED LUNG STOLEN BREATH
CD _____ LF 112CD
Lost & Found / Nov '94 / Plastic Head.

SYSTEMS OVERLOAD
CD _____ VE 023CD
Victory / Aug '95 / Plastic Head.

THOSE WHO FEAR TOMORROW
CD _____ DEI 2021-2
Homestead / Mar '93 / SRD.

International Children's.

O HOLY NIGHT (International Children's Choir)
CD _____ 15302
Laserlight / Nov '95 / Target/BMG.

International Dub System

I.D.S.
CD _____ SPVCD 55522
Red Arrow / Sep '95 / SRD / Jetstar.

International People

INTERNATIONAL PEOPLE
CD _____ EMIT 3395
Time Recordings / Oct '95 / Pinnacle.

Inti-Illimani

ANDADAS
CD _____ GL 4009CD

Green Linnet / Oct '93 / Roots / CM / Direct / ADA.

CANTO DE PUEBLOS ANDINOS
CD _____ MCD 71787
Monitor / Jun '93 / CM.

CANTO PARA MATAR UNA CULE
CD _____ MCD 71817
Monitor / Jun '93 / CM.

DE CANTO Y BAILE
Mi chiquita / Dedica toria de un libro / Cantiga de la memoria rota / Bailando / Candidos / El colibri / El vals / La muerte no va conmigo / Danza di cala luna
CD _____ MES 159362
Messidor / Apr '93 / Koch / ADA.

LA NUEVA CANCION CHILENA
CD _____ MCD 71794
Monitor / Jun '93 / CM.

VIVA CHILE
CD _____ MCD 71769
Monitor / Jun '93 / CM.

Inti-Raymi

INCA QUENA
CD _____ TUMICD 047
Tumi / '94 / Sterns / Discovery.

INTI-RAYMI
CD _____ TUMICD 009
Tumi / Dec '90 / Sterns / Discovery.

Intini, Cosmo

MY FAVOURITE ROOTS (Intini, Cosmo & The Jazz Set)
When Sunny gets blue / Powerful warrior / Round Midnight / Fatherly love / My one and only love / Steps
CD _____ CDSJP 339
Timeless Jazz / Apr '90 / New Note.

Into Another

IGNAURUS
CD _____ REVEL 35CD
Revelation / May '94 / Plastic Head.

INTO ANOTHER
CD _____ WB 083CD
We Bite / Jan '92 / Plastic Head.

SEEMLESS
CD _____ 1620082
Hollywood / Feb '96 / PolyGram.

Into Paradise

UNDER THE WATER
Bring me closer / Here with you / Red light / Pleasure is you / Circus came to town / Bring me closer (version) / World won't stop / Hearts and flowers / Blue moon express / Say goodnight / Beautiful day / Going home
CD _____ SETCD 1
Setanta / Feb '90 / Vital.

Into The Abyss

FEATHERED SNAKE, THE
CD _____ EFA 112832
Glasnost / Aug '95 / SRD.

MARTYRIUM
CD _____ SPV 08425232
SPV / Feb '94 / Plastic Head.

Intricate

(VA:1)
CD _____ CM 77061-2
Century Media / Jan '94 / Plastic Head.

Intro

INTRO
Love thang / Let me be the one / Anyhting for you / Why don't you love me / It's all about you / Ribbon in the sky / Come inside / One of a kind love / So many reasons / Ecstasy of love
CD _____ 756782463-2
Atlantic / Apr '93 / Warner Music.

NEW LIFE
CD _____ 7567826622
Atlantic / Nov '95 / Warner Music.

Intruder

PSYCHO SAVANT
CD _____ CDZORRO 25
Metal Blade / Jul '91 / Pinnacle.

Intruders

COWBOYS TO COWGIRLS
Love that's real / Cowboys to girls / Together / (We'll be) United / (Love is like a) Baseball game / Slow drag / Sad girl / Me Tarzan, you Jane / When we get married / Friends no more / (Win, place or show) She's a winner / Mother and child reunion / I'll always love my mama / I wanna know your name / Teardrops / Hang on in there / Nice girl like you / Plain ol' fashioned girl / To be happy is the real thing / Save the children
CD _____ 4809032
Columbia / Jan '96 / Sony.

Intuition

INTUITION
CD _____ FAT 002CD
Fat Cat / Sep '93 / Direct / ADA / CM.

Intveld, James

JAMES INTVELD
Perfect world / Blue baby day / Cryin' over you / I'm to blame / Barely hangin' on / Samantha / Standing on a rock / My heart is achin' for you / Important words / Your lovin' / You say goodnight, I'll say goodbye / I love you
CD _____ BCDAH 15900
Bear Family / Oct '95 / Rollercoaster / Direct / CM / Swift / ADA.

Invocator

DYING TO LIVE
CD _____ PCD 020
Progress / Sep '95 / Plastic Head.

EARLY YEARS, THE
CD _____ RRS 943CD
Pingo / Dec '94 / Plastic Head.

EXCURSION DEMISE
CD _____ 8410582
Black Mark / Jan '92 / Plastic Head.

WEAVE THE APOCALYPSE
CD _____ BMCD 34
Black Mark / Jul '93 / Plastic Head.

INXS

FULL MOON, DIRTY HEARTS
Days of rust / Gift / Make your peace / Time / I'm only looking / Please (You've got that) / Full moon, dirty hearts / Freedom deep / Kill the pain / Cut your roses down / Messenger / Viking juice
CD _____ 5186372
Mercury / Oct '93 / PolyGram.

GREATEST HITS, THE
Mystify / Suicide blonde / Taste it / Strangest party / Need you tonight / Original sin / Heaven sent / Disappear / Never tear us apart / Gift / Devil inside / Beautiful girl / Deliver me / New sensation / What you need / Listen like thieves / Bitter tears / Baby don't cry
CD _____ 5262302
Mercury / Oct '94 / PolyGram.

INXS
On a bus / Doctor / Just keep walking / Learn to smile / Jumping / In vain / Roller skating / Body language / Newsreel babies / Wishy washy
CD _____ 8389252
Mercury / May '90 / PolyGram.

INXS: INTERVIEW PICTURE DISC
CD P.Disc _____ CBAK 4038
Baktabak / Apr '90 / Baktabak.

KICK
Guns in the sky / New sensation / Devil inside / Need you tonight / Mediate / Loved one / Wild life / Never tear us apart / Mystify / Kick / Calling all nations / Tiny daggers
CD _____ 832721 2
Mercury / Nov '87 / PolyGram.

LISTEN LIKE THIEVES
What you need / Listen like thieves / Kiss the dirt / Shine like it does / Good and bad times / Biting bullets / This time / Three sisters / Same direction / One x one / Red red sun
CD _____ 824 957-2
Mercury / Jan '86 / PolyGram.

LIVE BABY LIVE
New sensation / Mystify / Shining star / Mediate / Burn for you / This time / Suicide blonde / Never tear us apart / Guns in the sky / By my side / Need you tonight / One x one / One thing / Stairs / Hear that sound / What you need
CD _____ 510 580 2
Mercury / Nov '91 / PolyGram.

SHABOOH SHOOBAH
CD _____ 8120842
Mercury / Jul '93 / PolyGram.

SWING, THE
Original sin / Melting in the sun / Send a message / Dancing on the jetty / Swing / Johnson's aeroplane / Love is (what I say) / Face the change / Burn for you / All the voices
CD _____ 818 553 2
Mercury / Jul '84 / PolyGram.

UNDERNEATH THE COLOURS
Stay young / Horizon / Big go go / Underneath the colours / Fair weather ahead / Night of rebellion / Follow / Barbarian / What would you do / Just to learn again
CD _____ 8387772
Mercury / Jul '89 / PolyGram.

WELCOME TO WHEREVER YOU ARE
Questions / Heaven sent / Communication / Taste it / Not enough time / All around / Baby don't cry / Beautiful girl / Wishing well / Back on line / Strange desire / Men and women
CD _____ 5125072
Mercury / Aug '92 / PolyGram.

X
Suicide blonde / Disappear / Stairs / Faith in each other / By my side / Lately / Who pays the price / Know the difference / Bitter tears / On my way / Hear that sound
CD _____ 8466682
Mercury / Sep '90 / PolyGram.

Iona & Andy

SPIRIT OF THE NIGHT
CD _____ SCD 2071
Sain / Oct '94 / Direct / ADA.

Iona

BOOK OF KELLS, THE
CD _____ WHAD 1287
What / Apr '95 / Total/BMG.

IONA
CD _____ WHAD 1266
What / May '95 / Total/BMG.

JOURNEY INTO THE MORN
3 Cord / Oct '95 / Total/BMG. _____ ALCD 034

Iowa Beef Experience

PERSONALIEN
Guilt and revenge / Hardcore fan / Cum soaked / Making the monster a snack / Pizenhead / Tools of the trade / Love muscle no.96 / Talented amature / Nonstop nacho / Dope smoking redneck... (from cedar rapids trapped in an alternative reality.)
CD _____ OINK 015 CD
Pigboy / Jan '93 / Vital.

Iqulah

MISSION, THE
CD _____ RICD 1301
Rastar International / Dec '93 / SRD.

Irakere

EN VIVO
Bacalao con pan / Moja el pan / Xiomara mayoral xiomara / Taka taka-ta / La similla / Dile a catalina / Baila mi ritmo / El coco / Aguanile bonko
CD _____ PSCCD 1005
Pure Sounds From Cuba / Feb '95 / Henry Hadaway Organisation / THE.

EXUBERANCIA
Xiomara / El guayo de catalina / Chango / El recuentro / Samba para enrique / El guao / Brown music / Guan tan amera / Brown music (encore)
CD _____ JHCD 009
Ronnie Scott's Jazz House / Feb '94 / Jazz Music / Magnum Music Group / Cadillac.

FELICIDAD
Stella, Pete, Ronnie (CD only) / La maquina del sabor / Contradanza / Anabis / Tributoa peruchin / La pastora (CD only)
CD _____ JHCD 014
Ronnie Scott's Jazz House / Jan '94 / Jazz Music / Magnum Music Group / Cadillac.

HOMENAJE A BENY MORE
CD _____ MES 259042
Messidor / Feb '93 / Koch / ADA.

LEGENDARY - LIVE IN LONDON, THE
Bilando asi / Johana / Estela va a estallar (Stella by starlight) / Las margaritas / Lo que va a pasar / Duke
CD _____ JHCD 005
Ronnie Scott's Jazz House / Jan '94 / Jazz Music / Magnum Music Group / Cadillac.

MISA NEGRA (AFRICAN MASS)
CD _____ MES 159722
Messidor / Dec '92 / Koch / ADA.

Irazu

LA FIESTA DEL TIMBALERO
Timbalero / Laura / Me voy contigo / Salseando / A Puerto padre / El son de Irazu / Si vienes te quwdas / Anoranza / Danzon del corazon / Everything happens to me
CD _____ CDLR 45039
L&R / Jan '92 / New Note.

Irby, Jerry

BOPPIN' HILLBILLY SERIES
Hillbilly boogie / Clickety clack / It's time you started looking / Call for me darling / Texas gal polka / Song of San Antone / One cup of coffee and a cigarette / Uptown swing / Mama don't allow it / Super boogie woogie / Nail in my coffin / First time I saw that gal / Forty nine women / One way blues / I've got the blues for Texas / Answer to Drivin' Nails In My Coffin / Don't count your chickens / You just can't be trusted anymore / Ball and chain / Sugar pie / There's a bright star shining for me / Our darling baby girl / Too many women / I'm so disgusted / My gal for Tennessee / Bottom of the list
CD _____ CDCL 2851
White Label/Bear Family / Apr '94 / Bear Family / Rollercoaster.

Irie, Nolan

WORK SO HARD
People can you hear me / People's dub / Work so hard (Featuring U-Roy) / Dub like nails / Irie feelings / Dub feelings / Because of dub / Turn it up / Dub it up / Never give it up / Just dub it up / Beware, the coming is nigh / Beware, the dub is nigh / Educated dub (Featuring Dego Ranks)
CD _____ ARICD 81
Ariwa Sounds / Nov '93 / Jetstar / SRD.

Irie, Tippa

IS IT REALLY HAPPENING TO ME
Unlucky burglar / It's good to have the feeling you're the best / You're the best (86 remix) / Telephone / Heartbeat / Robotic reggae / Married life / Football hooligan / Complain neighbour / Hello darling / Is it really happening to me
CD _____ TIPCD 1
Greensleeves / Sep '86 / Total/BMG / Jetstar / SRD.

REBEL ON THE ROOTS CORNER
CD _____ ARICD 091
Ariwa Sounds / Dec '93 / Jetstar / SRD.

Irie, Tonto

JAMMY'S POSSE
CD _____ 792052
Greensleeves / Nov '92 / Total/BMG / Jetstar / SRD.

Irigara, Carlos Alberto

NAVIDAD CRIOLLA
CD _____ 262063
Milan / Oct '91 / BMG / Silva Screen.

Irini

DON'T MAKE ME WISH
CD _____ HIICD 023
Here It Is / Jan '96 / Jetstar.

Irish Guards Band

MUSIC FOR REMEMBRANCE
National anthem / March of the Royal British Legion / Heart of oak / Life on the ocean wave / Red, white and blue / Lass who loved a sailor / Great little army / W.R.A.C. march / Grey and scarlet / Old comrades / Ulster defence regiment march / Royal Air Force march past / Holyrood / Princess Royals red cross march / Boys of the old brigade / Sunset / Cwm Rhondda / Abide with me / Last post / Reveille / Eternal father strong to save / Rule Britannia / Minstrel boy / Men of Harlech / Isle of beauty / David of the white rock / Oft in the stilly night / Nimrod / Laid in earth / Solemn melody / Funeral march / O God our help in ages past / March melody / It's a long way to Tipperary / Pack up your troubles / There'll always be an England / Keep the home fires burning / Madamoiselle from Armentieres / Take me back to dear old blighty / Run rabbit run / Kiss me goodnight, Sergeant Major / Hang out the washing on the Siegfried line / Wish me good luck as you wave goodbye / Beer barrel polka / Lili Marlene / Walting Mathilda / Maple leaf forever / Maori battalion marching song
CD _____ BNA 5014
Bandleader / Nov '87 / Conifer.

Irish Tradition

CORNER HOUSE, THE
CD _____ GLCD 1016
Green Linnet / Sep '88 / Roots / CM / Direct / ADA.

TIMES WE'VE HAD, THE
Paddy Fahy's reel / Paddy O'Brien's reel / Shipyard apprentice / Quilty/Sault's hornpipe / Michael O'Connor / Paddy's lamentation / Festus Burke / Yellow tinker/Sally gardens / Lady fair / Happy days / Flight of wild geese / Wild rover / Lad O'Beirne's/ Small hills of Offaly
CD _____ GLCD 1063
Green Linnet / Jun '93 / Roots / CM / Direct / ADA.

Iron Butterfly

HEAVY
CD _____ REP 4128-WZ
Repertoire / Aug '91 / Pinnacle / Cadillac.

IN-A-GADDA-DA-VIDA
Most anything you want / My mirage / Termination / Are you happy / In-a-gadda-da-vida / Flowers and beads
CD _____ 8122721962
Atlantic / Jan '96 / Warner Music.

LIGHT & HEAVY
Iron butterfly / Possession / Unconcious power / You can't win / So lo / In-a-gadda-da-vida / Most anything you want / Flowers and beads / My mirage / Termination / In the time of our lives / Soul experience / Real fright / In the crowds / It must be love / Belda beast / I can't help but deceive you little girl / New day / Stone believer / Soldier in our own town / Easy rider (let the wind pay the way)
CD _____ 8122711662
Rhino / Mar '93 / Warner Music.

SUN AND STEEL
CD _____ EDCD 408
Edsel / Feb '95 / Pinnacle / ADA.

Iron Fist

MOTORSEXLE MANIA
CD _____ FDN 2009-2
Foundation 2000 / Jul '94 / Plastic Head.

Iron Horse

FIVE HANDS HIGH
CD _____ LDL 1214CD
Lochshore / Aug '94 / ADA / Direct / Duncans.

IRON HORSE
CD _____ LDL 1202CD
Klub / Aug '94 / CM / Ross / Duncans / ADA / Direct.

THRO' WATER,EARTH & STONE
CD _____ LDLCD 1206
Lochshore / May '93 / ADA / Direct / Duncans.

VOICE OF THE LAND
CD _____ CDLDL 1232
Lochshore / Sep '95 / ADA / Direct / Duncans.

Iron Maiden

FEAR OF THE DARK
Be quick or be dead / From here to eternity / Afraid to shoot strangers / Fear is the key / Childhood's end / Wasting love / Fugitive / Chains of misery / Apparition / Judas be my guide / Weekend warrior / Fear of the dark / Nodding donkey blues (CDEM 1579) / Space station No. 5 (CDEM 1579) / I can't see my feeling (CDEM 1579) / No prayer for the dying (live/CDEM 1579) / Public enema no.1 (live/CDEM 1579) / Hooks in you (live/ CDEM 1579)
CD _____ CDEM 1579
EMI / Nov '95 / EMI.

IRON MAIDEN
Prowler / Remember tomorrow / Running free / Phantom of the opera / Transylvania / Strange world / Charlotte the harlot / Iron Maiden / Sanctuary (CDEM 1570 only) / Burning ambition (CDEM 1570 only) / Drifter (live/CDEM 1570 only) / I've got the fire (CDEM 1570 only)
CD _____ CDEM 1570
EMI / Nov '95 / EMI.

KILLERS
Ides of March / Wrathchild / Murders in the Rue Morgue / Another life / Genghis Khan / Innocent exile / Killers / Prodigal son / Purgatory / Drifter / Twilight zone (CDEM 1571) / Women in uniform (CDEM 1571) / Invasion (CDEM 1571) / Phantom of the opera (live/ CDEM 1571)
CD _____ CDEM 1571
EMI / Nov '95 / EMI.

LIVE AFTER DEATH
Aces high / Two minutes to midnight / Trooper / Revelations / Flight of Icarus / Rime of the ancient mariner / Powerslave / Number of the beast / Hallowed be thy name / Iron Maiden / Run to the hills / Running free / Wrathchild (Not on CD) / 22 Acacia Avenue (Not on CD) / Children of the damned (Not on CD) / Die with your boots on (Not on CD) / Phantom of the opera (Not on CD) / Losfer words (CDEM 1575) / Sanctuary (CDEM 1575) / Murders in the Rue Morgue (CDEM 1575)
CD _____ CDEM 1575
EMI / Nov '95 / EMI.

NO PRAYER FOR THE DYING
Tailgunner / Holy smoke / No prayer for the dying / Public enema no.1 / Fates warning / Assassin / Run silent run deep / Hooks in you / Bring your daughter... to the slaughter / Mother Russia / All in your mind (CDEM 1578) / Kill me ce soir (CDEM 1578) / I'm a mover (CDEM 1578) / Communication breakdown (CDEM 1578) / Roll over Vic Vella (CDEM 1578)
CD _____ CDEM 1578
EMI / Nov '95 / EMI.

NUMBER OF THE BEAST
Invaders / Children of the damned / Prisoner / 22 Acacia Avenue / Number of the beast / Run to the hills / Gangland / Hallowed be thy name / Total eclipse (CDEM 1572) / Remember tomorrow (live/CDEM 1572)
CD _____ CDEM 1572
EMI / Nov '95 / EMI.

PIECE OF MIND
Where eagles dare / Revelations / Flight of icarus / Die with your boots on / Trooper / Still life / Quest for fire / Sun and steel / To tame a land / I've got the fire (CDEM 1573) / Cross-eyed Mary (CDEM 1573)
CD _____ CDEM 1573
EMI / Nov '95 / EMI.

PLAYING WITH MADNESS
CD P.Disc _____ CBAK 4035
Baktabak / Jan '92 / Baktabak.

Powerslave
Aces high / Two minutes to midnight / Losfer words (big 'Orra) / Flash of the blade / Duellists / Back in the village / Powerslave / Rime of the ancient mariner / Rainbow's gold (CDEM 1574) / Mission from 'Arry (CDEM 1574) / King of twilight (CDEM 1574) / Number of the beast (live/CDEM 1574)
CD _____ CDEM 1574
EMI / Nov '95 / EMI.

REAL DEAD ONE, A
Number of the beast / Trooper / Prowler / Transylvania / Remember tomorrow / Where eagles dare / Sanctuary / Running free / Two minutes to midnight / Iron maiden / Hallowed be thy name
CD _____ CDEMD 1048
EMI / Oct '93 / EMI.

REAL LIVE ONE, A
Be quick or be dead / From here to eternity / Can I play with madness / Wasting love / Tailgunner / Evil that men do / Afraid to shoot strangers / Bring your daughter... to the slaughter / Heaven can wait / Clairvoyant / Fear of the dark
CD _____ CDEMD 1042
EMI / Mar '93 / EMI.

SEVENTH SON OF A SEVENTH SON
Moonchild / Infinite dreams / Can I play with madness / Evil that men do / Seventh son of a seventh son / Prophecy / Clairvoyant / Only the good die young / Black Bart blues (CDEM 1577) / Massacre (CDEM 1577) / Prowler ('88/CDEM 1577) / Charlotte the harlot ('88/CDEM 1577) / Infinite dreams (live) (CDEM 1577) / Clairvoyant (live) (CDEM 1577) / Prisoner (live/CDEM 1577) / Killers (live/CDEM 1577) / Still life (live/ CDEM 1577)
CD _____ CDEM 1577
EMI / Nov '95 / EMI.

SOMEWHERE IN TIME
Caught somewhere in time / Wasted years / Sea of madness / Heaven can wait / Loneliness of the long distance runner / Stranger in a strange land / Deja vu / Alexander the great / Reach out (CDEM 1576) / Juanita (CDEM 1576) / Sheriff of Huddersfield (CDEM 1576) / That girl (CDEM 1576)
CD _____ CDEM 1576
EMI / Nov '95 / EMI.

X FACTOR, THE
Sign of the cross / Lord of the flies / Man on the edge / Fortunes of war / Look for the truth / Aftermath / Judgement of heaven / Blood on the world's hands / Edge of darkness / 2 am / Unbeliever
CD _____ CDEMD 1087
EMI / Oct '95 / EMI.

Iron Man

BLACK NIGHT
CD _____ HELL 022
Hellhound / Jul '93 / Plastic Head.

PASSAGE, THE
Fury / Unjust reform / Gargoyle / Harvest of earth / Passage / Iron warrior / Freedom fighters / Waiting for tomorrow / Time of indecision / Tony stark / End of the world
CD _____ H 00222 CD
Hellhound / Oct '94 / Plastic Head.

Irresistable Force

FLYING HIGH
CD _____ RSNCD 5
Rising High / Nov '92 / Disc.

GLOBAL CHILLAGE
CD _____ RSNCD 24
Rising High / Nov '94 / Disc.

Irvine, Andy

ANDY IRVINE & PAUL BRADY (Irvine, Andy & Paul Brady)
Plains of Kildare / Lough Erne shore / Fred Finn's reel/Sailing into Walpole's marsh / Bonny woodhall / Arthur McBride / Jolly soldier / Blarney pilgrim / Autumn gold / Mary and the Soldier / Streets of Derry / Martinmas time / Little stack of wheat
CD _____ GL 3201CD
Green Linnet / Jul '94 / Roots / CM / Direct / ADA.

EAST WIND (Irvine, Andy & Davy Spillane)
Chetvorno horo / Bear's rock / Dance of suleiman / Illyrian dawn / Two steps to the bar / Pride of Macedonia / Kadana / Hard on the heels
CD _____ TARACD 3027
Tara / Apr '92 / CM / ADA / Direct / Conifer.

RAINY SUNDAYS, WINDY DREAMS
Come to the land of sweet liberty / Farewell to old Ireland / Edward Connors / Longford weaver / Christmas Eve / farewell to Ballymoney / Romanian song / Paidushko horo / King Bore and sandman / Rainy Sundays
CD _____ CDTUT 72141
Wundertüte / '88 / CM / Duncans / ADA.

RUDE AWAKENING
CD _____ GLCD 1114
Green Linnet / Apr '92 / Roots / CM / Direct / ADA.

Isaacs, Barry

REVOLUTIONARY MAN
CD _____ ROTCD 7
Reggae On Top / Sep '95 / Jetstar / SRD.

Isaacs, Gregory

ABSENT
CD _____ GRELCD 190
Greensleeves / Aug '93 / Total/BMG /
Jetstar / SRD.

AT THE MIXING LAB
CD _____ MLCD 005
Mixing Lab / Jul '90 / Jetstar.

**BLOOD BROTHERS (Isaacs, Gregory &
Dennis Brown)**
CD _____ RASCD 3116
Ras / Feb '94 / Jetstar / Greensleeves /
SRD / Direct.

CALL ME COLLECT
CD _____ RASCD 3067
Ras / Nov '90 / Jetstar / Greensleeves /
SRD / Direct.

CLASSIC HITS VOL. 2
CD _____ SONCD 0027
Sonic Sounds / Apr '92 / Jetstar.

COME AGAIN DUB
CD _____ RE 193CD
Reach Out International / Nov '94 /
Jetstar.

COME CLOSER
CD _____ 503382
Declic / Sep '04 / Jetstar.

COOL DOWN
Cool down / Black kill a black / I am alright
/ Good luck and goodbye / Love is all I need
/ Come rain or come shine / Mr. Babylon /
Don't want to be your man / Cross the line
CD _____ CY 78935
Nyam Up / Mar '95 / Conifer.

**COOL RULER - SOON FORWARD -
SELECTION**
Native woman / John Public / Party in the
slum / Uncle Joe / Word of the farmer / One
more time / Let's dance / Created by the
father / Raving tonight / Don't pity me
CD _____ CDFL 9012
Frontline / Sep '90 / EMI / Jetstar.

COOL RULER RIDES AGAIN
CD _____ MCCD 144
Music Club / Nov '93 / Disc / THE / CM.

DANCE HALL DON
CD _____ SHCD 45015
Shanachie / Jun '94 / Koch / ADA /
Greensleeves.

DANCING FLOOR
Dancing floor / Crown and anchor / Give it
all up / Private lesson / Nobody knows /
Dealing / Shower me with love / Opel ride /
Chips is down / Rock me
CD _____ MRCD 148
Munich / Jul '90 / CM / ADA / Greensleeves
/ Direct.

DEM TALK TOO MUCH
CD _____ CDTRL 355
Trojan / Jul '95 / Jetstar / Total/BMG.

DREAMING
CD _____ CDHB 155
Heartbeat / Jul '95 / Greensleeves /
Jetstar / Direct / ADA.

EARLY YEARS, THE
Rock away / Sweeter the victory / Sinner
man / Lonely lover / Loving pauper / Prom-
ised land / Love is overdue / Bad da / Way
of life / Financial endorsement / Give a hand
/ All I have is love
CD _____ CDTRL 196
Trojan / Mar '94 / Jetstar / Total/BMG.

ENCORE
Out Deh / Tune in / Top ten / Private sec-
retary / My only lover / All I have is love /
Love is overdue / Can't give my love / Cool
down the pace / Oh what a feeling / Ad-
dicted to you / Night nurse
CD _____ CD KVL 9030
Kingdom / '88 / Kingdom.

GREGORY ISAACS & FRIENDS
CD _____ SHCD 150
Shanachie / Jun '94 / Koch / ADA /
Greensleeves.

GREGORY ISAACS COLLECTION, THE
CD _____ RNCD 2102
Rhino / Apr '93 / Jetstar / Magnum Music
Group / THE.

**GREGORY ISAACS MEETS
YELLOWMAN (Isaacs, Gregory &
Yellowman)**
CD _____ MM 2537 CD
Mixing Lab / May '93 / Jetstar.

HARDCORE
CD _____ GSCD 70035
Greensleeves / Nov '92 / Total/BMG /
Jetstar / SRD.

HEARTACHE AVENUE
CD _____ WRCD 009
World Enterprise / Oct '94 / Jetstar.

HEARTBREAKER
CD _____ RRTGCD 7788
Rohit / Jul '90 / Jetstar.

I AM GREGORY
CD _____ CRCD 22
Charm / Sep '93 / Jetstar.

I'LL NEVER TRUST YOU
CD _____ LG 21098
Lagoon / May '94 / Magnum Music Group
/ THE.

I.O.U.
CD _____ GRELCD 136
Greensleeves / Aug '89 / Total/BMG /
Jetstar / SRD.

LADY OF YOUR CALIBRE
CD _____ WRCD 13
World / Aug '95 / Jetstar / Total/BMG.

**LEE PERRY PRESENTS GREGORY
ISAACS**
Rhino / Dec '93 / Jetstar / Magnum Music
Group / THE.

LIVE AT THE ACADEMY
My number one / All I ask is love / My only
lover / Love overdue / Storm / Mr. Brown /
Slave master / Oh what a feeling / Soon
forward / Sunday morning / Addicted to you
/ Front door / Border / Can't give my love
(CD only.) / Cool down the pace (CD only.)
CD _____ CD KVL 9027
Kingdom / Jan '87 / Kingdom.

LIVE IN FRANCE
CD _____ SONCD 0060
Sonic Sounds / Mar '94 / Jetstar.

LONELY DAYS
CD _____ JMC 200205
Jamaica Gold / Sep '94 / THE / Magnum
Music Group / Jetstar.

LONELY LOVER
Happy anniversary / Gi me / Tribute to
Waddy / Poor and clean / Poor natty / I am
sorry / Few words / Protection / Hard time
/ Tune in
CD _____ RNCD 2047
Rhino / Mar '94 / Jetstar / Magnum Music
Group / THE.

MAXIMUM RESPECT
CD _____ CDSGP 070
Prestige / Mar '94 / Total/BMG.

MEMORIES
Make love to me / Memories / Say a prayer
/ You keep me waiting / Spend sometime /
Common sense / My apology / Love you
more / Cry over me / Who will see / All in
the game
CD _____ 112082
Musidisc / Aug '95 / Vital / Harmonia Mundi
/ ADA / Cadillac / Discovery.

MIDNIGHT CONFIDENTIAL
Make me prosper / Goodbye love / Hello
stranger / Non stop loving / I could not believe / Don't take your love / Not because I
smile / Let's talk / One good turn / Twelve
tribe dance
CD _____ GRELCD 205
Exterminator / Jul '94 / Jetstar.

MR. COOL
CD _____ RFCD 001
Record Factory / Oct '95 / Jetstar.

MR. ISAACS
CD _____ OH 003
Ossie / Nov '95 / Jetstar.

MR. LOVE
Mr. Brown / Word of the farmer / Black
liberation struggle / Poor and clean / Slave
master / Uncle Joe / Universal tribulation /
Confirm reservation / Protection / Tribute to
Waddy / Let's dance / One more time /
John Public / Native woman / Lonely girl /
If I don't have you / Poor millionaire / My
only lover / Raving tonight / Hush darling /
Soon forward
CD _____ CDFL 9021
Frontline / Jun '95 / EMI / Jetstar.

MY NUMBER ONE
CD _____ CDHB 61
Heartbeat / Mar '90 / Greensleeves /
Jetstar / Direct / ADA.

MY POOR HEART
CD _____ HBCD 167
Heartbeat / Aug '94 / Greensleeves /
Jetstar / Direct / ADA.

NIGHT NURSE
Material man / Not the way / Sad to know
you're leaving / Hot stepper / Cool down
the pace / Night nurse / Stranger in town /
Objection overruled
CD _____ RRCD 9
Reggae Refreshers / Sep '90 / PolyGram /
Vital.

NO INTENTIONS
CD _____ VPCD 1133
RF / Jun '91 / Jetstar.

NO LUCK
CD _____ LG 21049
Lagoon / Nov '92 / Magnum Music Group
/ THE.

NO SURRENDER
CD _____ GVCD 2020
Greensleeves / Nov '92 / Total/BMG /
Jetstar / SRD.

NOT A ONE MAN THING
CD _____ RASCD 3145
Ras / Jul '95 / Jetstar / Greensleeves /
SRD / Direct.

NUMBER ONE
CD _____ CPCD 8026
Charly / Feb '94 / Charly / THE / Cadillac.

ONCE AGO
Tribute to Waddy / Gimme / Poor and clean
/ Poor Natty / I am sorry / Few words / Pro-
tection / Hard time / Hush darling / Confirm
reservation / Front door / Permanent lover /
My only lover / If I don't have you / Substi-
tute / Poor millionaire / Fugitive / Once ago
CD _____ CDFL 9004
Frontline / Jul '90 / EMI / Jetstar.

OUT DEH
Good morning / Private secretary / Yes I do
/ Sheila / Out deh / Star / Dieting / Love me
with feeling
CD _____ RRCD 46
Reggae Refreshers / Jul '94 / PolyGram /
Vital.

OVER THE BRIDGE
Someone con the don / Student of your
class / One one coco full basket / Spot and
beat the banker / Just in case / Over the
bridge / Hide and lick / Stop what you're
doing / Mail box / Dub them mail
CD _____ 111862
Musidisc / Feb '94 / Vital / Harmonia Mundi
/ ADA / Cadillac / Discovery.

OVER THE YEARS
CD _____ AMCD 011
African Museum / Jun '95 / Jetstar.

PARDON ME
CD _____ RASCD 3100
Greensleeves / Sep '93 / Total/BMG /
Jetstar / SRD.

PRIVATE BEACH PARTY
Wish you were mine / Feeling irie / Bits and
pieces / Let off supm / No rushings / Private
beach party / Better plant some loving / Got
to be in tune / Special to me / Promise is a
comfort
CD _____ GRELCD 85
Greensleeves / Jul '95 / Total/BMG / Jetstar
/ SRD.

PRIVATE LESSON
CD _____ DUBID 2CD
Acid Jazz Roots / Sep '95 / SRD.

RED ROSE FOR GREGORY
CD _____ GRELCD 118
Greensleeves / Sep '88 / Total/BMG /
Jetstar / SRD.

**REGGAE GREATS: GREGORY ISAACS
LIVE**
Number one / Tune in / Substitute / Soon
forward / Mr. Brown / Sunday morning / Oh
what a feeling / Love is overdue / Top 10 /
Front door / Border
CD _____ RRCD 42
Reggae Refreshers / Jan '94 / PolyGram /
Vital.

RESERVED FOR GREGORY
CD _____ EXCD 1
Exodus / Nov '95 / Jetstar.

SET ME FREE
CD _____ VYDCD 02
Vine Yard / Sep '95 / Grapevine.

SLUM IN DUB
CD _____ CDTRL 344
Trojan / Jul '94 / Jetstar / Total/BMG.

**SLY & ROBBIE PRESENT GREGORY
ISAACS**
CD _____ RASCD 3206
Ras / Dec '95 / Jetstar / Greensleeves /
SRD / Direct.

**TWO BAD SUPERSTARS (Isaacs,
Gregory & Dennis Brown)**
CD _____ CDTRL 335
Trojan / Mar '94 / Jetstar / Total/BMG.

UNFORGETTABLE
CD _____ RRTGCD 7736
Rohit / '88 / Jetstar.

UNLOCKED
CD _____ GRELCD 193
Greensleeves / Sep '93 / Total/BMG /
Jetstar / SRD.

VICTIM
CD _____ VPCD 1033
VP / Apr '89 / Jetstar.

WATCHMAN OF THE CITY
CD _____ RIFWLCD 9300
Rohit / Mar '88 / Jetstar.

WILLOW TREE
CD _____ JMC 200204
Jamaica Gold / Jun '94 / THE / Magnum
Music Group / Jetstar.

WORK UP A SWEAT
CD _____ AMCD 010
African Museum / Feb '95 / Jetstar.

YOU'RE DIVINE
CD _____ RB 3002
Reggae Best / May '94 / Magnum Music
Group / THE.

Isaak, Chris

FOREVER BLUE
CD _____ 9362458452
Reprise / May '95 / Warner Music.

HEART SHAPED WORLD
Heart shaped world / I'm not waiting / Don't
make me dream about you / Kings of the
highway / Wicked game / Blue spanish sky
/ Wrong to love you / Forever young / Noth-
ing's changed / In the heat of the jungle
CD _____ 925837 2
Reprise / Jun '89 / Warner Music.

SAN FRANCISCO DAYS
San Francisco days / Beautiful homes /
Round and round / Two hearts / Can't do a
thing (to stop me) / Except the new girl /
Waiting / Move along / I want your love /
5.15 / Lonely with a broken heart / Solitary
man
CD _____ 936245116-2
Reprise / Apr '93 / Warner Music.

SILVERTONE
Dancin' / Talk to me / Living for your lover
/ Back on your side / Voodoo / Funeral in
the rain / Lonely one / Unhappiness / Tears
/ Gone ridin' / Pretty girls don't cry /
Western stars
CD _____ 925156 2
Reprise / Dec '87 / Warner Music.

WICKED GAME
Wicked game / You owe me some kind of
love / Blue Spanish sky / Heart shaped
world / Heart full of soul / Funeral in the rain
/ Blue Hotel / Dancin' / Nothings changed /
Voodoo / Lie to me / Wicked game
(instrumental)
CD _____ 7599265132
Reprise / Jan '91 / Warner Music.

Isalonisti

HUMORESQUE
Souvenir / Whispering flowers / Czardas /
Come away to Madrid / My sweet little
friend / On the sea shore / My heart only
calls to you / Humoresque / Slavonic dance
No.6 / Melody in F / Syncopation / Gypsy
Capriccio / Poeme / Little Viennese march
/ Mill in the black forest / Maiden's prayer /
We wander the world / Eight in the night /
When a toreador falls in love
CD _____ CDC 169513-2
Harmonia Mundi / Oct '86 / Harmonia
Mundi / Cadillac.

Isan Slete

FLOWER OF ISAN, THE
Lai lam toei sam jangwa / Hua ngawk yawk
sao / Sutsanaen-noeng mode / Lam phloen
/ Lai pu pa lan / Toei khong / Lam doeng
dong / Lai-yai mode / Lam toei thammada
/ Lai ngua khuen phu / Lam kio / Lai phu
thai / Sutsanaen mode / Kawn lawng la /
Lai an nang-sue / Imae, imae
CD _____ CDORB 051
Globestyle / Oct '89 / Pinnacle.

Isbin, Gilbert

BLUE SOUNDS AND TOUCHES
Quite blue / Sueno / Tell me / In balance /
Leon / Mosca Espagnola / Mar abrierto /
Full moon and little bastion / Nenia / Blue 2
/ Camino verde / Come into my door / A
nice advance / Blue in blue / Ballad in a
cave / HWYL
CD _____ HWYLCD 4
Hwyl / Jun '91 / Hwyl.

Isengard

HOSTMORKE
CD _____ FOG 007CD
Moonfog / Jun '95 / Plastic Head.

Isham, Mark

BLUE SUN
Barcelona / Beautiful sadness / Trapeze /
Lazy afternoon / Blue sun / In more than
love / Miles to go before he sleeps / In a
sentimental mood / Tour de chance
CD _____ 4813042
Sony Jazz / Oct '95 / Sony.

COOL WORLD
CD _____ VSCD 5382
Varese Sarabande/Colosseum / Aug '92 /
Pinnacle / Silva Screen.

SKETCH ARTIST
CD _____ VSCD 53776
Varese Sarabande/Colosseum / Aug '92 /
Pinnacle / Silva Screen.

SONGS MY CHILDREN TAUGHT ME
Steadfast tin soldier / Emperor and the
nightingale / Thumbelina / Emperor's new
clothes
CD _____ WD 1101
Windham Hill / May '91 / Pinnacle / BMG /
ADA.

TIBET
CD _____ 01934110802
Windham Hill / Sep '95 / Pinnacle / BMG / ADA.

VAPOR DRAWINGS
Many Chinas / Sympathy and acknowledgement / On the threshold of liberty / When things dream / Raffles in Rio / Something nice for my dog / Men before the mirror / Mr. Moto's penguin (Who'd be an Eskimo's wife) / In the blue distance
CD _____ 01934110272
Windham Hill / Jul '93 / Pinnacle / BMG / ADA.

Ishii, Ken

INNERELEMENT
Encoding / A.F.I.A.C. / Twist of space / QF / Flurry / Garden of the palm / Pneuma / Sponge / Radiation / Loop / Fragment of yesterday / Kala / Decoding
CD _____ RS 94038CD
R & S / May '94 / Vital.

JELLY TONES
Extra / Cocoa mousse / Stretch / Ethos 9 / Moved by air / Pause in herbs / Frame out / Endless season
CD _____ RS 95065CD
R & S / Oct '95 / Vital.

Isiro

EVERYTHING BUT ANTARCTICA
CD _____ TWI 9142
Les Disques Du Crepuscule / Aug '90 / Discovery / ADA.

Islam, Yusuf

LIFE OF THE LAST PROPHET, THE
Tala'a al-badru' alayna / La iiaha illa allah / Muhammad al mustafa
CD Set _____ MOL 7001CD3
Voice Print / Sep '95 / Voice Print.

Island, Johnny

REGGAE SOUNDS FROM JAMAICA (Island, Johnny Reggae Group)
CD _____ 15287
Laserlight / '91 / Target/BMG.

Islandica

SONGS AND DANCES FROM ICELAND
CD _____ EUCD 1187
ARC / Apr '92 / ARC Music / ADA.

Isley Brothers

BATTLE OF THE GROUPS
CD _____ NEMCD 691
Sequel / Aug '94 / BMG.

BEAUTIFUL BALLADS
Brown eyed girl / Hello it's me / Let's fall in love (parts 1 and 2) / You're the key to my heart / You're beside me / I once had your love (and I can't let go) / Caravan of love / All in my lovers eyes / Don't let me be lonely tonight / Make me say it again girl / Voyage to Atlantis / Choosey lover / Lay lady lay / Don't say goodnight
CD _____ 4805042
Epic / May '95 / Sony.

BEST OF THE ISLEY BROTHERS, THE
CD _____ 12549
Laserlight / May '95 / Target/BMG.

BROTHERS IN SOUL
Twist and shout / Rockin' McDonald / Drag / Don't be jealous / This is the end / Twistin' with Linda / Spanish twist / Let's twist again / Rubber legs twist / Shake it with me baby / Nobody but me / Snake / Hold on baby / Don't you feel / You better come home / I say love / I'm laughing to keep from crying / Time after time / Right now / Never leave me baby / Long tall Sally
CD _____ CDCD 1107
Charly / Jul '93 / Charly / THE / Cadillac.

COMPLETE UA SESSIONS, THE (Legends of Rock & Roll Series)
Surf and shout / Please please please / She's the one / Tango / What'cha gonna do / Stagger Lee / You'll never leave him / Let's go, let's go, let's go / She's gone / Shake it with me baby / Long tall Sally / Do the twist / My little girl / Open up her eyes / Love is a wonderful thing / Footprints in the snow / Who's that lady / Basement / Conch / My little girl (2)
CD _____ CZ 421
EMI / Apr '91 / EMI.

FUNKY FAMILY
Liquid loves / I wanna be with you / Who loves you better / Pride / Take me to the next phase / Hope you feel better / Heat is on / Ain't giving up no love / When you need it again / Climbing up the ladder / Winner takes all / Coolin' me out / Fun and games
CD _____ 4805072
Epic / May '95 / Sony.

LIVE
Here we go again / Between the sheets / Smooth sailin' tonight / Voyage to Atlantis / Take me to the next phase / Choosey lover / Footsteps in the dark / Groove with you / Hello it's me / Don't say goodnight (it's time

for love) / Spend the night / Who's that lady / It's your thing / Shout / For the love / Fight the power / Make me say it again girl
CD _____ 7559615382
Elektra / Sep '93 / Warner Music.

MOTOWN'S GREATEST HITS: ISLEY BROTHERS
This old heart of mine / Just ain't enough love / Put yourself in my place / I guess I'll always love you / There's no love left / It's out of the question / Take some time out for love / Whispers / Nowhere to run / Who could ever doubt my love / Behind a painted smile / That's the way love is / Tell me it's just a rumour baby / Take me in your arms / Got to have you back / Little Miss Sweetness / My love is your love (forever) / Why when the love has gone / All because I love you / I hear a symphony
CD _____ 530053-2
Motown / Jan '92 / PolyGram.

PEARLS FROM THE PAST - ISLEY BROTHERS
CD _____ KLMCD 009
Scratch / Nov '93 / BMG.

SHOUT
Shout (part 1) / Shout (part 2) / Tell me who / How deep is the ocean (1) / Respectable / Say you love me too / Open up your heart / He's got the whole world in his hands / Without a song / Yes indeed / Ring-a-ling-a-ling / That lucky old sun / How deep is the ocean (2) / Respectable #2 / When the saints go marching in / Gypsy love song / St. Louis blues / (We're gonna) Rock around the clock / Turn to me / Not one minute more / I'm gonna knock on your door
CD _____ BCD 15425
Bear Family / Dec '88 / Rollercoaster / Direct / CM / Swift / ADA.

SHOUT AND TWIST WITH RUDOLPH, RONALD AND O'KELLY
Twist and shout / Nobody but me / Crazy love / Snake / Make it easy on yourself / Right now / You better come home / Twistin' with Linda / Never leave me baby / Two stupid feet / Time after time / Let's twist again / Wah watusi / I say love / Rubberleg twist / Hold on baby / I'm laughing to keep from crying / Don't you feel / Spanish twist
CD _____ CDCH 928
Ace / Apr '90 / Pinnacle / Cadillac / Complete/Pinnacle.

SOUL KINGS VOL.1
Twist and shout / Time after time / I say love / Right now / Drag / Don't be jealous / Rockin' McDonald / Let's twist again / Nobody but me / Crazy love / You better come home / Shake it with me baby
CD _____ SMS 056
Carlton Home Entertainment / Oct '92 / Carlton Home Entertainment.

THIS OLD HEART OF MINE (Isley Brothers/Impressions)
CD _____ RMB 75051
Remember / Nov '93 / Total/BMG.

TRACKS OF LIFE
Get my licks in / No axe to grind / Searching for a miracle / Sensitive lover / Bedroom eyes / Lost in your love / Whatever turns you on / Morning love / Dedicate this song / Red hot / Koolin' out / Brazilian wedding song / I'll be there / Turn on the moon
CD _____ 7599266202
WEA / Jun '92 / Warner Music.

Israel Vibration

BEST OF ISRAEL VIBRATION, THE
CD _____ NETCD 1001
Network / Jan '91 / SRD.

DUB THE ROCK
CD _____ RASCD 3190
Ras / Aug '95 / Jetstar / Greensleeves / SRD / Direct.

FOREVER
CD _____ RASCD 3080
Ras / Sep '91 / Jetstar / Greensleeves / SRD / Direct.

ISRAEL VIBRATION IV
CD _____ RASCD 3120
Ras / Aug '93 / Jetstar / Greensleeves / SRD / Direct.

LIVE AT REGGAE SUNSPLASH (Israel Vibration & Gladiators)
CD _____ NETCD 8925
Network / Nov '92 / SRD.

ON THE ROCK
CD _____ RASCD 3175
Ras / Mar '95 / Jetstar / Greensleeves / SRD / Direct.

PERFECT LOVE & UNDERSTANDING
CD _____ NETCD 1006
Network / Jun '93 / SRD.

PRAISES
CD _____ RASCD 3054
Ras / Jul '90 / Jetstar / Greensleeves / SRD / Direct.

RUDEBOY SHUFFLIN'
CD _____ CRCDM 1
Ras / Aug '95 / Jetstar / Greensleeves / SRD / Direct.

SAME SONG, THE
Same song / Weep and mourn / Walk the streets of glory / Ball of fire / I'll go through / Why worry / Lift up your conscience / Prophet has arisen / Jah time has come / Licks and kicks
CD _____ CDPS 003
Pressure Sounds / Jun '95 / SRD / Jetstar.

STRENGTH OF MY LIFE
CD _____ RASCD 3037
Ras / Dec '88 / Jetstar / Greensleeves / SRD / Direct.

SURVIVE
CD _____ LG2 1115
Lagoon / Oct '95 / Magnum Music Group / THE.

UNCONQUERED PEOPLE
CD _____ GRELCD 148
Greensleeves / Jul '90 / Total/BMG / Jetstar / SRD.

VIBES ALIVE
CD _____ RASCD 3091
Ras / Nov '92 / Jetstar / Greensleeves / SRD / Direct.

Israel, Yoron

GIFT FOR YOU, A (Israel, Yoron Connection)
CD _____ FRLCD 024
Freelance / Jan '96 / Harmonia Mundi / Cadillac / Koch.

It

ON TOP OF THE WORLD
CD _____ BCKCD 1
Black Market International / Jul '90 / Soul Trader.

It Bites

BIG LAD IN THE WINDMILL
I got you eating out of my hand / All in red / Whole new world / Screaming on the beaches / Turn me loose / Cold, tired and hungry / Calling all the heroes / You'll never go to heaven / Big lad in the windmill / Wanna shout
CD _____ CDV 2378
Virgin / Jul '86 / EMI.

CALLING ALL THE HEROES (The Best Of It Bites)
Still too young to remember / Calling all the heroes / Strange but true / All in red / Kiss like Judas / Murder of the planet Earth / Midnight / Sister Sarah / Old man and the angel / Underneath your pillow / Screaming on the beaches / Whole new world / Yellow christian / You'll never go to heaven (live)
CD _____ CDOVD 453
Virgin / Feb '95 / EMI.

EAT ME IN ST LOUIS
Positively animal / Underneath your pillow / Let us all go / Still too young to remember / Murder of the planet earth / People of America / Sister Sarah / Leaving without you / Till the end of time (Not on LP) / Ice melts (into water) (Not on LP) / Charlie (CD only) / Having a good day (CDST only) / Reprise (CDST only) / Bullet in the barrel (CDST only)
CD _____ CDV 2591
Virgin / Aug '91 / EMI.

ONCE AROUND THE WORLD
Midnight / Kiss like Judas / Yellow christian / Rose Marie / Old man and the angel / Hunting the whale (CD only) / Plastic dreamer / Once around the world / Black December
CD _____ CDV 2456
Virgin / Aug '91 / EMI.

THANK YOU & GOODNIGHT - THE BEST OF IT BITES
Kiss like Judas / All in red / Underneath your pillow / Murder of the planet earth / Ice melts (into water) / Yellow christian / You'll never go to heaven / Calling all the heroes / Screaming on the beaches / Still too young to remember
CD _____ VGDCD 3516
Virgin / Oct '91 / EMI.

Italian Instabile...

SKIES OF EUROPE (Italian Instabile Orchestra)
Il maestro muratore / Squilli di morte / Corbu / Meru lo snob / L'arte mistica del vasaio / Il maestro muratore (reprise) / Du duchampo / Quand duchamp joue du marteau / Il suono giallo / Mariene e gli ospiti misteriosi / Satie satin / Masse d'urto / Fellini song

CD _____ 5271812
ECM / Mar '95 / New Note.

Itals

BRUTAL OUT DEH
CD _____ NHCD 303
Nighthawk / '89 / Pinnacle / Direct / Hot Shot / ADA.

GIVE ME POWER
CD _____ NHCD 307
Nighthawk / '89 / Pinnacle / Direct / Hot Shot / ADA.

Ithaca

GAME FOR ALL WHO KNOW, A
CD _____ HBG 122/3
Background / Apr '94 / Background.

It's A Beautiful Day

LIVE AT THE CARNEGIE HALL
Give your woman what she wants / Hot summmer day / Angels and animals / Bombay calling / Going to another party / Good lovin' / Grand camel suite / White bird
CD _____ 4809702
Columbia / Aug '95 / Sony.

It's Alive

EARTHQUAKE VISIONS
CD _____ CDMFN 177
Music For Nations / Dec '94 / Pinnacle.

It's Immaterial

SONG
New Brighton / Endless holiday / Ordinary life, An / Heaven knows / In the neighbourhood / Missing / Homecoming / Summer winds / Life on the hill / Your voice
CD _____ CDSRN 27
Siren / Apr '92 / EMI.

Ivers, Eileen

EILEEN IVERS
CD _____ GLCD 1139
Green Linnet / Apr '94 / Roots / CM / Direct / ADA.

TRADITIONAL IRISH MUSIC
CD _____ GL 1139CD
Green Linnet / Jun '94 / Roots / CM / Direct / ADA.

Iversen, Einor

WHO CAN I TURN TO
CD _____ GMCD 73
Gemini / Jan '87 / Cadillac.

Ives, Burl

LITTLE BITTY TEAR, A (5CD Set)
Little bitty tear / Long black veil / Shanghai'd / Almighty dollar bill / Forty hour week / Delia / Oh my side / Lenora, lest your hair hang down / Mocking bird hill / I walk the line / Drink to me only with thine eyes / Mama don't want no peas, no rice, no coconut oil / Empty saddles / Oregon trail / Home on the range / When the bloom is on the sage / My adobe hacienda / Cowboy's dream / Mexicali rose / Last round-up / Oh bury me not on the lone prairie / Jingle jangle jingle / Cool water / Tumbling tumbleweeds / Royal telephone / Holding hands for Joe / Sixteen fathoms deep / What you gonna do Leroy / Brooklyn bridge / Poor little jimmy / Thumbin' Johnny Brown / Funny way of laughing / That's all I can remember / Ninety mine / Call me Mr. In-between / I ain't comin' home tonight / How do you fall out of love / In foggy old London / Mother wouldn't do that / Bring them in / Let the lower lights be burning / Beulah land / Standing on the promises / Fairest Lord Jesus / We're marching to Zion / Sunshine on the everlasting arms / Where he leads me / Will there be any stars / When they ring those golden bells / Same old hurt / Wishin' she was here (instead of me) / Busted / Poor boy in a rich man's town / Mary Ann regrets / Billy Bayou / Moon is high / Green turtle / Bury the bottle with me / Blizzard / It comes and goes / I'm the boss / Same old hurt (remake) / Curry road / Deepening snow / She didn't let the ink dry on the paper / Late movie / Home James / Man about town / She called me baby / My chicken run away to the bush / Baby come home to me / Roses and orchids / Lynching party / Hundred twenty miles from nowhere / Two car garage / I found my best friend in the world / I'll hit it with a stick / Saskatoon, Saskatchewan / Some folks / I'll walk away smiling / There goes another pal of mine / This is your day / This is all I ask / Lower forty / Four initials on a tree / Someone hangin' round you all the time / Beautiful Annabelle Lee / Hobo jungle / Strong as a mountain / Can't you hear me / Cherry blossom song / What I want (I can never have) / Can angels fly over the Rockies / Legend of the T / Kentucky turkey buzzard / Funny little show / Hard luck and misery / Pearly shells / What little tears are made of / Short on love / Who done it / Two of the usual / Tell me / Among my souvenirs / Ga-

ter hollow / I ain't missing nobody / Catfish Bill / Time to bum again / Born for trouble / Unemployment check / Atlantic coastal line / Don't let love die / How deep is the ocean / Okeechobee ocean / My melancholy baby / Jealous / My gal Sal / By the light of the silvery moon / For me and my gal / Red sails in the sunset / Make believe / Oh how I miss you tonight / You know you belong to somebody else / Down in the Okefenokee / (I hear you) Call my name / Mr. Make-up man / River boy / Drifting and dreaming / Beyond the reef / My Isle of golden dreams / Now is the hour / Sweet Leilani / Moon of Manakoora / Song of the Islands / Keep your eyes on the hands / Hawaiian bells / Little brown girl / On the beach of Waikiki / Aloha oe / Thirty thousand feet over Denver / Betsy the cow

CD _____ BCD 15667
Bear Family / Jul '93 / Rollercoaster / Direct / CM / Swift / ADA.

VERY BEST OF BURL IVES
CD _____ SOWCD 708
Sound Waves / May '93 / Target/BMG.

Iveys

MAYBE TOMORROW
See saw, Granpa / Beautiful and blue / Dear Angie / Think about the good times / Yesterday ain't coming back / Fisherman / Maybe tomorrow / Sali bloo / Angelique / I'm in love / They're knocking down our home / I've been waiting / No escaping your love / Mrs. Jones / And her daddy's a millionaire / Looking for my baby

CD _____ CDP 7986922
Apple / Jun '92 / EMI.

Ivorys

BALA
CD _____ WWCD 06
World / Dec '88 / Grapevine.

Ivy League

THIS IS THE IVY LEAGUE
CD _____ REP 4094-WZ
Repertoire / Aug '91 / Pinnacle / Cadillac.

Ivy N.Y.C.

REALISTIC
Get enough / No guarantee / Decay / Fifteen seconds / Everyday / Point of view / Don't believe word / Beautiful / Shallow / In the shadows / Dying star / Over

CD _____ 142532
Seed / Feb '95 / Vital.

Iwan, Dafydd

CANEUON QWERIN
CD _____ SCD 2062
Sain / Feb '95 / Direct / ADA.

DALIGREDU
CD _____ SCD 4053
Sain / Mar '95 / Direct / ADA.

YMA O HYD (Iwan, Dafydd & Ar Log)
Y wen na phyla amser / Cwm ffynnon ddu / Adlais y gog lwydlas / Tra bo hedydd / Laura Llwelyn / Ffidl yn y to / Hoffedd Gwilym/Mynydd yr heliwr/Mans o'r felin / Hoffedd Jac Nurphy / Can Wiliam / Can y medd / Per oslef / Y chwe chant a naw / Yma o hyd

CD _____ SCD 2063
Sain / Feb '95 / Direct / ADA.

Izit

IMAGINARY MAN
Mother of mine / Just a matter of time / Architecture / Undiscovered land / I believe von daniken / Feel like makin' love / Change / Imaginary man / You're losing me / Oasis / This harmony / Elijah's blue

CD _____ TNGCD 007
Tongue 'n' Groove / May '95 / Vital.

WHOLE AFFAIR
Izit everywhere / Sharing our lives / Bird of paradise / Bio white and the 7 chords / One by one / Say yeah / Whole affair (part 1) / Sugar and spice / Don't give up now / Rhyme of the ancient groove / Whole affair (part 2)

CD _____ TNGCD 001
Tongue 'n' Groove / Oct '93 / Vital.

J

J

WE ARE THE MAJORITY
Keep the promise / Beast no one ever tamed / Best thaing / School power / Randy / Born on the wrong side of town / First they came / Nightime / We are the majority / Badge of pride / In the trench / Take a chance / Come over here / Justice of burn / After
CD _____ 517 710-2
A&M / Jan '93 / PolyGram.

J Bad

MAKE WAY FOR THE GRIMREAPER
CD _____ RAP 6007-2
We Bite / May '94 / Plastic Head.

J, David

SONGS FROM ANOTHER SEASON
I'll be your chauffeur / Fingers in the grease / Longer look / Sad side to the sandboy / New woman is an attitude / Sweet anaesthesia / On the outskirts (of a strange dream) / I'll be your chauffeur (original version) / Moon in the man / Little star / Stranded trans-atlantic hotel nearly famous blues / National anthem of nowhere / Nature boy
CD _____ BEGA 112 CD
Beggars Banquet / Jul '90 / Warner Music / Disc.

J To The D

LIVING ON THE EDGE
Detroit / Givin' you that funk / 2 make U dance / Sach chaser / Bay bay kids / Nympho / Caught up in the game / Murder game / Girls with game / Fuck that
CD _____ CDWRA 8104
Wrap / Feb '92 / Koch.

J-Funk Express

GETTIN' BACK TO MY ROOTS
Sing a simple song / Sweety pie / In the middle / Groove with Mr. JB / Nothin' but the soul / Sweet emotion / Humpty Dumpty / Dry spell / Monie in the middle
CD _____ 101 S877080
101 South / Jan '96 / New Note.

J. Church

RECESSION OF SIMULACRA, THE
CD _____ JT 1019CD
Jade Tree / Jul '95 / Plastic Head.

J. Quest

QUEST IS ON, THE
Given it all / Quest is on / It's gonna be alright / Brand new love / Up and down / Anything / Don't stop ya luv / From now on / Come and give it (you know what I want) / On my mind / Behind the scenes / Up and down (original mix)
CD _____ 5285342
Mercury / Sep '95 / PolyGram.

J.B. Horns

FUNKY GOOD TIMES
CD _____ GCD 79485
Gramavision / Sep '95 / Vital/SAM / ADA.

J.F.K.

FOUR DAYS THAT SHOCK THE WORLD
CD _____ RPM 122
RPM / Oct '93 / Pinnacle.

J.S.D. Band

FOR THE RECORD
CD _____ VMCD 001
Village Music / Nov '95 / Direct.

Jach'a Mallku

GRAN CONDOR
CD _____ TUMICD 037
Tumi / Jun '93 / Sterns / Discovery.

Jacinta

AUTRES CHANSONS YIDDISH
CD _____ C 560033
Ocora / May '92 / Harmonia Mundi / ADA.

TANGO, MI CORAZON
CD _____ MES 159112
Messidor / Jun '93 / Koch / ADA.

Jack, Dandy

DANDY JACK AND THE COSMIC TOUSERS
CD _____ RIO 33CD
Rather Interesting / Jan '96 / Plastic Head.

Jack O'Nuts

ON YOU
Hook / Citation / Q / Showcase / Chump change / Feelin' Freddy / Raw candle vote / Starbane
CD _____ RDL 006-2
Radial / May '94 / Vital.

Jack Radics

I'LL BE SWEETER
CD _____ PHCD 23
Penthouse / Sep '93 / Jetstar.

OPEN REBUKE
CD _____ HBST 168CD
Heartbeat / Aug '94 / Greensleeves / Jetstar / Direct / ADA.

RADICAL
CD _____ SHCD 45003
Shanachie / Jun '93 / Koch / ADA / Greensleeves.

SOMETHING
CD _____ TOPCD 1
Top Rank / Nov '92 / Jetstar.

TEQUILA SUNSET
CD _____ SFCD 002
Sprint / Jul '95 / Jetstar / THE.

WHAT ABOUT ME
CD _____ RN 0039
Runn / Nov '94 / Jetstar / SRD.

Jack The Lad

IT'S JACK THE LAD
Boilermaker blues / Back on the road again / Plain dealing / Fast lane driver / Turning into winter / Why I can't be satified / Song without a band / Rosalie / Promised land / Corny pastiche / Black cock of Wickham/ Chief O'Neill's favourite / Golden rivet/ Staten Island/ The cook in the kitchen / Lying in the water / One more dance / Make me happy
CD _____ CASCD 1085
Charisma / Nov '92 / EMI.

ROUGH DIAMONDS
Rocking chair / Smokers coughin' / My friend, the drink / Letter from France / Gentlemen soldier / Gardener of eden / One for the boy / Beachcomber / Ballad of Winston O'Flaherty / Jackie Lusive / Draught genius / Baby let me take you home
CD _____ CASCD 1110
Charisma / Nov '92 / EMI.

Jackie & Roy

SPRING CAN REALLY HANG YOU UP THE MOST
CD _____ BLCD 760904
Black Lion / Jun '88 / Jazz Music / Cadillac / Wellard / Koch.

Jacks

WHY DON'T YOU WRITE ME VOL.2
Why don't you write me / Since my baby's been gone / Heaven help me / Do you wanna rock / Away / How soon / I cry / They turned the party out down at Bessie's house / Dream a little longer / Fine lookin' baby / So wrong / Wiggie waggie woo / I'm confessin' that I love you / Let's make up / If it is wrong / Annie meet Henry / My reckless heart / Why did I fall in love / I want you / You belong to me / Dancin' Dan / This empty heart / So will I / My Darling
CD _____ CDCHD 535
Ace / Apr '95 / Pinnacle / Cadillac / Complete/Pinnacle.

Jackson Five

ANTHOLOGY - JACKSON FIVE (2CD Set/Volumes 1 & 2)
I hear a symphony / Dancing machine / Body language / Got to be there / Rockin' robin / Ben / Daddy's home / ABC / I want you back / I'll be there / Sugar daddy / Maybe tomorrow / Mama's pearl / I am love / Teenage symphony / Skywriter / Hallelujah day / Bogie man / Let's get serious / Let me tickle your fancy / You're supposed to keep your love for me / Love don't want to leave / That's how love goes / Just a little bit of you / We're almost there / I wanna be where you are / Forever came today / All I do is think of you / I was made to love her / Whatever you got, I want / Get it together
CD Set _____ 5301932
Motown / Jan '92 / PolyGram.

CHILDREN OF THE LIGHT
Love you save / Ain't nothing like the real thing / Lookin' through the windows / Don't let your baby catch you / I can only give you love / Little bitty pretty one / Zip-a-dee doo-dah / Ready or not, here I come / E-ne-me-ne-mi-ne-moe (The choice is yours

to pull) / If I have to move a mountain / Don't want to see tomorrow / Children of the light / Doctor my eyes / My cherie amour
CD _____ 5500762
Spectrum/Karussell / May '93 / PolyGram / THE.

CHRISTMAS ALBUM
Have yourself a merry little Christmas / Santa Claus is coming to town / Christmas song / Up on the house top / Frosty the snowman / Little drummer boy / Rudolph the red nosed reindeer / Christmas won't be the same this year / Give love on Christmas Day / Some day at Christmas / I saw Mommy kissing Santa Claus
CD _____ 5501412
Spectrum/Karussell / Nov '94 / PolyGram / THE.

HISTORIC EARLY RECORDINGS
You've changed / We don't have to be over 21 (to fall in love) / Jam session / Big boy / Michael the lover / My girl / Soul jerk / Under the boardwalk / Saturday night at the movies / Tracks of my tears
CD _____ CPCD 8122
Charly / Oct '95 / Charly / THE / Cadillac.

JACKSON FIVE, THE
CD _____ STACD 081
Stardust / Apr '93 / Carlton Home Entertainment.

MAYBE TOMORROW
Maybe tomorrow / She's good / Never can say goodbye / Wall / Petals / Sixteen candles / (We've got) Blue skies / My little baby / It's got to be here / Honey chile / I will find a way
CD _____ 5301612
Motown / Aug '93 / PolyGram.

SKYWRITER
Skywriter / Hallelujah day / Boogie man / Touch / Corner of the sky / I can't quit your love / Uppermost / World of sunshine / Ooh, I'd love to be with you / You made me what I am
CD _____ 5302092
Motown / Aug '93 / PolyGram.

SOULSATION (4CD Set)
CD Set _____ 5304892
Motown / Jul '95 / PolyGram.

THIRD ALBUM
I'll be there / Ready or not, here I come / Oh how happy / Bridge over troubled water / Can I see you in the morning / Goin' back to Indiana / How funky is your chicken / Mama's pearl / Reach in / Love I saw in you was just a mirage / Darling dear
CD _____ 5301602
Motown / Sep '93 / PolyGram.

Jackson Singers

GOSPEL EMOTIONS
Storm is passing / This little light of mine / You've got to move / God has smiled on me / Over my head / Nobody knows the trouble I've seen / Put your trust in Jesus / I've decided to make Jesus my choice / Jesus said if you go / If it had not been for the Lord / Pass me not / Precious Lord
CD _____ CDLR 44016
L&R / May '92 / New Note.

Jackson, Alan

GREATEST HITS COLLECTION
Chattahoochee / Gone country / She's got rhythm / Midnight in Montgomery / Tall, tall trees / Chasin' that neon rainbow / I'll try / Don't rock the jukebox / Livin' on love / Summertime blues / Love's got a hold on you / (Who says) You can't have it all / Home / Wanted / I don't even know your name / Dallas / Here in the real world / Someday / Mercury blues / I'd love you all over again
CD _____ 07822188012
Arista / Oct '95 / BMG.

HERE IN THE REAL WORLD
Ace of hearts / Blue blooded woman / Chasin' that neon rainbow / I'd love you all over again / Home / Here in the real world / Wanted / She don't get the blues / Dog river blues / Short sweet ride
CD _____ 260817
Arista / Jul '90 / BMG.

HONKY TONK CHRISTMAS
Honky tonk christmas / Angels cried / If we make it through December / If you don't wanna see Santa Claus cry / I only want you for christmas / Merry Christmas to me / Holly jolly christmas / There's a new kid in town / Santa's gonna come in a pickup truck / Please daddy (don't get drunk this Christmas)
CD _____ 7822187362
Arista / Nov '95 / BMG.

LOT ABOUT LIVIN', A (And A Little 'Bout Love)
Chattanoochee / She's got the rhythm (I got the blues) / Tonight I climbed the wall / I don't need the booze (To get a buzz on) / (Who says) You can't have it all / Up to my ears in tears / Tropical depression / She likes it too / If it ain't one thing (It's you) / Mercury blues
CD _____ 07822187112
Arista / Jun '94 / BMG.

Jackson, Billy

LONG STEEL RAIL
CD _____ TCD 5014
Testament / Dec '94 / Complete/Pinnacle / ADA / Koch.

MISTY MOUNTAIN (Jackson, Billy & Billy Ross)
Beinn a' cheataich / Landfall / Glen of co-peswood / Lass o'glenshee / Boyne water / Guidnicht and joy be wi' ye a' / Country girl and the hungarian fiddler / Tar the house / Little cascade / Geil mill / First step / Trusdar bodaich, drochaid, luideach / Na'm faighin gille ri cheannach / For our lang bidin' here / Meudail is m'aighear s'mo ghradh
CD _____ IRCD 005
Iona / '88 / ADA / Direct / Duncans.

WELLPARK SUITE, THE (Jackson, Billy & Ossian)
Glasgow 1885 / Dear green place changed life in the city / March of the workers / Molendinar: The spring / Brewing / Fermentation / Glasgow celebration
CD _____ IRCD 008
Iona / Aug '91 / ADA / Direct / Duncans.

Jackson, Bleu

GONE THIS TIME
CD _____ TX 1005CD
Taxim / Jan '94 / ADA.

Jackson, Bull Moose

BAD MAN JACKSON, THAT'S ME
Big ten inch record / Bad man Jackson, that's me / Jammin' and jumpin / We ain't got nothin' but the blues / Bull Moose Jackson blues / Honey dripper / Hold him Joe / I want a bowlegged woman / Oh John / Fare thee well / Nosey Joe / Bearcat blues / Why don't you haul off and love me / Cherokee boogie / Meet me with your black dress on / Hodge podge / Big fat mamas are back in style again / All night long / Bootsie / If you ain't lovin' (you ain't livin') / I wanna hug ya, kiss ya, squeeze ya
CD _____ CDCHARLY 274
Charly / Jan '95 / Charly / THE / Cadillac.

Jackson, Chubby

HAPPY MONSTER, THE (Small Groups 1944-1947)
CD _____ C&BCD 109
Cool 'n Blue / Oct '93 / Jazz Music / Discovery.

Jackson, Chuck

ENCORE/MR. EVERYTHING
Tell him I'm not home / Blue holiday / Tomorrow / Two stupid feet / This broken heart (that you gave me) / Since then / Donna / King of the Mountain / Invisible / Another day / Lonely am I / Go on Yak Yak / Getting ready for the heartbreak / Since I don't have you / I just don't know what to do with myself / I need you / I'm your man / Human / Love is a many splendoured thing / Work song / If I didn't love you / Something you've got / D-5 / Somebody new / Tears of joy
CD _____ CDKEND 110
Kent / Aug '94 / Pinnacle.

GOOD THINGS
Tell him I'm not home / Beg me / I keep forgettin' / Millionaire / Hand it over / Two stupid feet / Make the night a little longer / I wake up crying / I'm your man / Castanets / Who's gonna pick up the pieces / Good things come to those who wait / I don't want to cry / Breaking point / Any other way / Any day now / Since I don't have you / They don't give medals (to yesterday's heroes) / Where do I go from here / These chains of love (are breaking me down) / What's with this loneliness / Forget about me / I just don't know what to do with myself / I can't stand to see you cry
CD _____ CDKEND 935
Kent / Aug '90 / Pinnacle.

I DON'T WANT TO CRY
I didn't want to cry / Tell him I'm not home / I wake up crying / Any day now / Beg me / Millionaire / Hand it over / They don't give medals / Since I don't have you / Breaking point / Any other way

/ These chains of love / I just don't know what to do with myself / Forget about me / I'm your man
CD _____ CDCD 1025
Charly / Mar '93 / Charly / THE / Cadillac.

I DON'T WANT TO CRY/ANY DAY NOW
I don't want to cry / Tears on my pillow / My willow tree / In between tears / Tear of the year / I cried for you / Lonely teardrops / Don't let the sun catch you crying / Salty tears / I wake up crying / Tear / Man ain't supposed to cry / I keep forgettin' / Any day now / Just once / Same old story / What'cha gonna say tomorrow / Make the night a little longer / Who's gonna pick up the pieces / In real life / Angel of angels / Breaking point / Prophet / Everybody needs love
CD _____ CDKEND 107
Kent / Aug '93 / Pinnacle.

Jackson, Cliff

CAROLINA SHOUT
Honeysuckle rose / Ain't misbehavin' / 'S wonderful / Tin roof blues / You took advantage of me / Carolina shout / I'm coming Virginia / Crazy rhythm / Beale Street blues / Someday, sweetheart / Who's sorry now
CD _____ BLC 760194
Black Lion / Mar '94 / Jazz Music / Cadillac / Wellard / Koch.

Jackson, D.D.

PEACE SONG
CD _____ JUST 722
Justin Time / Apr '95 / Harmonia Mundi / Cadillac.

Jackson, Franz

SNAG IT
CD _____ DD 223
Delmark / Nov '93 / Hot Shot / ADA / CM / Direct / Cadillac.

Jackson, Freddie

DON'T LET LOVE SLIP AWAY
Nice 'n' slow / Hey lover / Don't let love slip away / Crazy (for me) / One heart too many / If you don't know me by now / You and I got a thang / Special lady / Yes, I need you / It's gonna take a long, long time
CD _____ CZ 401
Capitol / Mar '91 / EMI.

GREATEST HITS OF FREDDIE JACKSON
Do me again / Rock me tonight / I don't want to lose your love / I could use a little love (right now) / Jam tonight / Nice and slow / You are my lady / Love me down / Have you ever loved somebody / Hey lover / Love is just a touch away / Tasty love / Christmas forever
CD _____ CDEST 2226
Capitol / Feb '94 / EMI.

HERE IT IS
Was it something / Comin' home II u / Here it is / How does it feel / Givin' my love / Paradise / Make love easy / Addictive 2 touch / I love / My family
RCA / Jan '94 / BMG. ___ 7863 66318-2

JUST LIKE THE FIRST TIME
You are my love / Tasty love / Have you ever loved somebody / Look around / Jam tonight / Just like the first time / I can't let you go / I don't want to lose your love / Still waiting / Janay
CD _____ CZ 110
Capitol / Jan '87 / EMI.

ROCK ME TONIGHT
He'll never love you (like I do) / Love is just a touch away / I wanna say I love you / You are my lady / Rock me tonight / Sing a song of love / Calling / Good morning heartache
CD _____ CZ 364
EMI / Oct '90 / EMI.

Jackson, George

CAIRITIONA (Jackson, George & Maggie McInnes)
CD _____ IRCD 006
Iona / '88 / ADA / Direct / Duncans.

Jackson, J.J.

GREAT J.J. JACKSON, THE
But it's alright / Try me / That ain't right / You've got me dizzy / Change is gonna come / I dig girls / Come and see me (I'm your man) / Stones that I throw / Give me back the love / Ain't too proud to beg / Love is a hurtin' thing / Boogaloo baby / Let it out
CD _____ SEECD 281
See For Miles/C5 / Feb '94 / Pinnacle.

Jackson, Jack

THINGS ARE LOOKING UP (Jackson, Jack & His Orchestra)
Things are looking up / Faint harmony / Soon / You turned your head / Kiss me dear / Ache in my heart / Now that we're sweethearts again / Have a little dream on me / Don't you cry when we say goodbye /

Lonely feet / I'm on a see-saw / Dancing with a ghost / Play to me gypsy / Lonely singing fool / What's good for the goose / Because it's love / Ole faithful / What shall I do / I think I can / Goodnight lovely little lady
CD _____ CDSVL 173
Saville / Apr '93 / Conifer.

Jackson, Janet

CONTROL
Control / What have you done for me lately / You can be mine / Pleasure principle / When I think of you / He doesn't know I'm alive / Let's wait awhile / Funny how time flies / Nasty
CD _____ CDMID 178
A&M / Mar '93 / PolyGram.

CONTROL - THE REMIXES
Control / When I think of you / Pleasure principle (2 mixes) / What have you done for me lately / Let's wait awhile / Nasty (Remixes)
CD _____ CDMID 149
A&M / Aug '91 / PolyGram.

DESIGN OF A DECADE 1986-1996
What have you done for me lately / Best things in life are free / Nasty / Control / When I think of you / Pleasure principle / Escapade / Black cat / Miss you much / Rhythm nation / Whoops now / That's the way love goes / Love will never do (without you) / Come back to me / Alright / Let's wait awhile / Runaway / Twenty foreplay
CD _____ 5404002
CD _____ 5404382
CD Set _____ 5404222
A&M / Sep '95 / PolyGram.

JANET
Morning / That's the way love goes / You know... / You want this / A gender love boy / If / Back / This time / Go on Miss Janet / Throb / What'll I do / Lounge / Funky big band / Racism / New agenda / Love pt.2 / Because of love / Wind / Again / Another lover / Where are you now / Hold on baby / Body that loves you / Rain / Anytime anyplace / Are you still up / Sweet dreams / Whoops now
CD _____ CDV 2720
Virgin / May '93 / EMI.

JANET JACKSON
Say you do / You'll never find (a love like mine) / Young love / Love and my best friend / Don't mess up a good thing / Forever yours / Magic is working / Come give your love to me
CD _____ CDMID 114
A&M / Oct '92 / PolyGram.

JANET REMIXED
That's the way love goes (mixes) / If / Because of love (mixes) / And on and on / Throb / You want this (mixes) / Anytime anyplace (mixes) / Where are you now / 70's love groove / What'll I do / One more chance
CD _____ CDVY 2720
Virgin / Mar '95 / EMI.

RHYTHM NATION 1814
Rhythm nation / State of the world / Knowledge / Miss you much / Love will never do (without you) / Livin' in a world (they didn't make) / Alright / Escapade / Black cat / Lonely / Come back to me / Someday is tonight
CD _____ CDA 3920
A&M / Sep '89 / PolyGram.

Jackson, Javon

FOR ONE WHO KNOWS
For one who knows / Etcetera / Angola / Notes in three / Jane's theme / Paradox / Useless landscape / Formosa (gorgeous)
CD _____ CDP 8203442
Blue Note / Jun '95 / EMI.

ME AND MR. JONES (Jackson, Javon Quartet)
CD _____ CRISS 1053CD
Criss Cross / May '92 / Cadillac / Harmonia Mundi.

Jackson, Jerry

SHRIMP BOATS A-COMIN', THERE'S DANCIN' TONIGHT
Hey sugarfoot / Se habla espanol / Tell her Johnny said goodbye / La dee dah / You don't wanna hurt me / They really don't know you / If teardrops were diamonds / I don't play games / You might be there with him / Shrimp boats / It hurts me / Till the end of time / Blowin' in the wind / Blues in the night / Time / If I had only known / Are you glad when we're apart / Always / You're mine (and I love you) / Gone to pieces / Turn back / Wide awake in a dream / Gypsy feet / She lied
CD _____ BCD 15481
Bear Family / May '90 / Rollercoaster / Direct / CM / Swift / ADA.

Jackson, Jim

COMPLETE RECORDED WORKS VOL. 1
CD _____ DOCD 5114
Blues Document / Nov '92 / Swift / Jazz Music / Hot Shot.

Jackson, Joe

COMPLETE RECORDED WORKS VOL. 2
CD _____ DOCD 5115
Blues Document / Nov '92 / Swift / Jazz Music / Hot Shot.

Jackson, Joe

BODY AND SOUL
Verdict / Cha cha loco / Not here, not now / You can't get what you want / Go for it / Loisaida / Happy ending / Be my number two / Heart of ice
CD _____ CDMID 118
A&M / Oct '92 / PolyGram.

CHRONICLES
CD _____ 5404022
A&M / Sep '95 / PolyGram.

I'M THE MAN
On your radio / Geraldine and John / Kinda kute / It's different for girls / I'm the man / Band wore blue shirts / Don't wanna be like that / Amateur hour / Get that girl / Friday
CD _____ CDMID 117
A&M / Oct '92 / PolyGram.

JUMPIN' JIVE
Jumpin' with symphony Sid / Jack you're dead / Is you is or is you ain't my baby / We the cats (shall help ya) / San Francisco fan / Five guys named Moe / Jumpin' jive / You run your mouth, I'll run my business / What's the use of getting sober / You're my meat / Tuxedo junction / How long must I wait for you
CD _____ 5500622
Spectrum/Karussell / May '93 / PolyGram / THE.

LOOK SHARP
One more time / Sunday papers / Is she really going out with him / Happy loving couples / Throw it away / Baby stick around / Look sharp / Fools in love / Do the instant mash / Pretty girls / Got the time
CD _____ CDMID 115
A&M / Oct '92 / PolyGram.

NIGHT AND DAY
Another world / Chinatown / T.V. age / Target / Steppin' out / Breaking us in two / Cancer / Real men / Slow song
CD _____ CDMID 158
A&M / Oct '92 / PolyGram.

NIGHT AND DAY/LOOK SHARP (2CD Set)
CD Set _____ CDA 24121
A&M / Jul '93 / PolyGram.

NIGHT MUSIC
Nocturne no. 1 / Flying / Ever after / Nocturne no. 2 / Man who wrote Danny Boy / Nocturne no. 3 / Lullaby / Only the future / Nocturne no. 4 / Sea of secrets
CD _____ CDVUS 78
Virgin / Oct '94 / EMI.

STEPPIN' OUT (Very Best Of Joe Jackson)
Is she really going out with him / Fools in love / I'm the man / It's different for girls / Beat crazy / Jumpin' jive / Breaking us in two / Steppin' out / Slow song / You can't get what you want / Be my number two / Right and wrong / Home town / Down to London / Nineteen forever
CD _____ 3970522
A&M / Sep '90 / PolyGram.

Jackson, John

DON'T LET YOUR DEAL GO DOWN
CD _____ ARHCD 378
Arhoolie / Apr '95 / ADA / Direct / Cadillac.

Jackson, Latoya

BAD GIRL
Sexual feeling / You and me / He's my brother / Restless heart / Playboy / You can count on me / Somewhere / Bad girl / Be my lover / He's so good to me / Do the salsa / Piano man
CD _____ CDTB 127
Magnum Music / Feb '92 / Magnum Music Group.

SPOTLIGHT ON LATOYA JACKSON
Sexual feeling / You and me / He's my brother / Be my lover / Piano man / Restless heart / Do the salsa / Playboy / He's so good to me / Somewhere / Bad girl / You can count on me
CD _____ HADCD 111
Javelin / Feb '94 / THE / Henry Hadaway Organisation.

Jackson, Lil' Son

BLUES COME TO TEXAS
CD _____ ARHCD 409
Arhoolie / Apr '95 / ADA / Direct / Cadillac.

COMPLETE IMPERIAL RECORDINGS, THE
Ticket agent blues / True love blues / Evening blues / Spending money blues / Tough luck blues / Peace breaking people / Rockin' and rollin' / Two timin' woman / Rocky road / Disgusted / Travelin' alone / New year's resolution / Mr. Blues / Time changes things / Wondering blues / Restless blues / All alone / Everybody's blues /

Travelin' woman / Stop for the red light / Aching heart / Upstairs boogie / All my love / My little girl / Big gun blues / Get high everybody / Let me down easy / My younger day / I wish to go home / Black and brown / Journey back home / Sad letter blues / Rockin' and rollin' # 2 / Lonely blues / Freight train blues / How long / Good ole wagon / Blues by the hour / Pulp wood boogie / Losin' my woman / Trouble don't last always / Movin' to the country / Thrill me baby / Confession / Doctor doctor / Piggly wiggly / Dirty work / Little girl / Big rat / Suagar Mama / Messin' up / Prison bound / Rolling mill / Can't keep a good man down / T-Bone blues
CD Set _____ CDEM 1551
Capitol Jazz / Jul '95 / EMI.

Jackson, Mahalia

BEST OF MAHALIA JACKSON
CD _____ DLCD 4013
Dixie Line / Mar '95 / Magnum Music Group.

GOSPELS, SPIRITUALS AND HYMNS (2CD/MC Set)
CD Set _____ 468663 2
Columbia / May '94 / Sony.

HE'S GOT THE WHOLE WORLD IN HIS HANDS
CD _____ JW 77004
JWD / '90 / Target/BMG.

I'M ON MY WAY
CD _____ CD 12509
Music Of The World / Nov '92 / Target/BMG / ADA.

QUEEN OF GOSPEL
CD _____ MCCD 122
Music Club / Aug '93 / Disc / THE / CM.

QUEEN OF GOSPEL, THE
CD _____ GOJCD 53028
Giants Of Jazz / Mar '92 / Target/BMG / Cadillac.

SILENT NIGHT
Silent night / Go tell it on the mountain / Bless this house (Not on CD) / Sweet little Jesus boy / Star stood still (Song of the nativity) / Hark the herald angels sing / Christmas comes to us all once a year / Joy to the world / O come all ye faithful (adeste fideis) / O little town of Bethlehem / What can I give
CD _____ CK 62130
Columbia / Nov '95 / Sony.

WE SHALL OVERCOME
Rusty bell / If I could help somebody / Didn't it rain / Holding my saviour's hand / This is my faith / Elijah rock / We shall overcome / We have come a mighty long way / How I got over / I would rather have Jesus / Down by the riverside / It's in my heart / Come on children, let us sing
CD _____ CDCD 1129
Charly / Nov '93 / Charly / THE / Cadillac.

WHEN THE SAINTS GO MARCHING IN
CD _____ CD 3554
Cameo / Jul '95 / Target/BMG.

Jackson, Michael

BAD
Bad / Way you make me feel / Speed demon / Liberian girl / Just good friends / Another part of me / Man in the mirror / I just can't stop loving you / Dirty Diana / Smooth criminal / Leave me alone (CD only)
CD _____ 4502902
Epic / Sep '87 / Sony.

BEN
Ben / Greatest show on earth / People make the world go round / We've got a good thing going / Everybody's somebody's fool / My girl / What goes around comes around / In our small way / Shee-be-doo-be-doo-a-day / You can cry on my shoulder
CD _____ 5301632
Motown / Sep '93 / PolyGram.

BIG BOY (Jackson, Michael/Jackson Five)
CD _____ PLD 8122
Charly / Jul '95 / Charly / THE / Cadillac.

DANGEROUS
Jam / Why you wanna trip on me / In the closet / She drives me wild / Remember the time / Can't let her get away / Heal the world / Black or white / Who is it / Give in to me / Will you be there / Keep the faith / Gone too soon / Dangerous
CD _____ 4658022
Epic / Nov '91 / Sony.

GOT TO BE THERE
Ain't no sunshine / I wanna be where you are / Girl don't take your love from me / In our small way / Got to be there / Rockin' robin / Wings of my love / Maria / Love is here and now you're gone / You've got a friend
CD _____ 5301632
Motown / Aug '93 / PolyGram.

HISTORY PAST PRESENT AND FUTURE BOOK 1
Billie Jean / Way you make me feel / Black or white / Rock with you / She's out of my

life / Bad / I just can't stop loving you / Man in the mirror / Thriller / Beat it / Girl is mine / Remember the time / Don't stop till you get enough / Wanna be startin' something / Heal the world / Scream / They don't care about us / Stranger in Moscow / This time around / Earth song / D.S. / Money / Come together / You are not alone / Childhood / Tabloid junkie / 2 Bad / History / Little Susie / Smile
CD Set _____ 4747092
MJJ Music / Jun '95 / Sony.

MOTOWN'S GREATEST HITS: MICHAEL JACKSON
I want you back (PWL mix) / Doctor my eyes / One day in your life / Lookin' through the windows / Got to be there / I'll be there / Love you save / ABC / Rockin' Robin / Happy (love theme from Lady Sings The Blues) / Ben / Never can say goodbye / Farewell my summer love / I want you back (original) / Mama's pearl / Ain't no sunshine / Girl you're so together / Hallelujah day / Skywriter / We're almost there
CD _____ 5300142
Motown / Feb '92 / PolyGram.

MUSIC AND ME
With a child's heart / Up again / All the things you are / Happy / Too young / Doggin' around / Johnny Raven / Euphoria / Morning glow / Music and me / Rockin' Robin
CD _____ 5500782
Spectrum/Karussell / May '93 / PolyGram / THE.

OFF THE WALL
Don't stop till you get enough / Rock with you / Working day and night / Get on the floor / Off the wall / Girlfriend / She's out of my life / I can't help it / It's the falling in love / Burn this disco out
CD _____ CD 83468
Epic / '83 / Sony.

THRILLER
Wanna be startin' something / Baby be mine / Girl is mine / Thriller / Beat it / Billie Jean / Human nature / P.Y.T. (pretty young thing) / Lady in my life
CD _____ CD 85930
Epic / '83 / Sony.

Jackson, Michael Gregory

CLARITY
CD _____ ESP 3028-2
ESP / Jan '93 / Jazz Horizons / Jazz Music.

KARMONIC SUITE
CD _____ 123857-2
IAI / Sep '93 / Harmonia Mundi / Cadillac.

Jackson, Millie

21 OF THE BEST (1971-1983)
Child of God / Ask me what you want / My man, a sweet man / Breakaway / It hurts so good / How do you feel the morning after / (If loving you is wrong) I don't want to be right / Loving arms / Bad risk / You can't turn me off (in the middle of turning me on) / If you're not back in love by Monday / All the way lover / Go out and get some (get it out 'cha system) / Keep the home fire burnin' / Never change lovers in the middle of the night / Kiss you all over / This is it (part 2) / It's gonna take some time this time / Do you wanna make love / Blues don't get tired of me / I feel like walking in the rain
CD _____ CDSEWD 100
Southbound / Sep '94 / Pinnacle.

CAUGHT UP
(If loving you is wrong) I don't want to be right / Rap / All I want is a fighting chance / I'm tired of hiding / It's all over but the shouting / So easy going so hard coming back / I'm through trying to prove my love to you / Summer (first time)
CD _____ CDSEWM 003
Southbound / Jun '89 / Pinnacle.

E.S.P. (Extra Sexual Persuasion)
Sexercise (Parts 1 and 2) / This girl could be dangerous / Slow tongue (Working your way down) / Why me / I feel like walking in the rain / Too easy being easy / Slow tongue / You're working me
CD _____ CDSEWM 093
Southbound / Apr '94 / Pinnacle.

FEELIN' BITCHY
All the way lover / Lovin' your good thing away / Angel in your arms / Little taste of outside love / You created a monster / Cheatin' is / If you're not back in love by Monday / Feeling like a woman
CD _____ CDSEWM 042
Southbound / Oct '91 / Pinnacle.

FOR MEN ONLY
This is where I came in / This is it / If that don't turn you on / I wish that I could hurt that way again / Fool's affair / You must have known I needed love / Despair / Not on your life / Ain't no coming back
CD _____ CDSEWM 070
Southbound / Jun '93 / Pinnacle.

FREE AND IN LOVE
House for sale / I'm free / Tonight I'll shoot the moon / There you are / Do what makes the world go round / Bad risk / I feel like

making love / Solitary love affair / I'm in love again
CD _____ CDSEW 032
Southbound / Aug '90 / Pinnacle.

GET IT OUTCHA SYSTEM
Go out and get some (get it out 'cha system) / Keep the home fire burnin' / Logs and thangs / Put something down on it / Here you come again / Why say you're sorry / He wants to hear the words / I just wanna be with you / Sweet music man
CD _____ CDSEWM 046
Southbound / Mar '92 / Pinnacle.

HARD TIMES
Blufunkes / Special occasion / I don't want to cry / We're gonna make it / Hard times / Blues don't get tired of me / Mess on your hands / Finger rap / Mess on your hands (reprise) / Finger rap (reprise) / Feel love comin' on
CD _____ CDSEWM 090
Southbound / Mar '94 / Pinnacle.

I GOT TO TRY IT ONE TIME
How do you feel the morning after / Get your love right / My love is so fly / Letter full of tears / Watch the one who brings you the news / I got to try it one time / Gospel truth / One night stand / I gotta do something about myself / I'm in the wash
CD _____ CDSEW 023
Southbound / Feb '90 / Pinnacle.

I HAD TO SAY IT
I had to say it / Loving arms / Rap / Stranger / I ain't no glory story / It's gonna take some time this time / Fancy this / Ladies first / Somebody's love died here last night / You owe me that much
CD _____ CDSEWM 086
Southbound / Nov '93 / Pinnacle.

IT HURTS SO GOOD
I cry / Hypocrisy / Two-faced world / It hurts so good / Don't send nobody else / Hypocrisy (reprise) / Good to the very last drop / Help yourself / Love doctor / Now that you got it / Close my eyes / Breakaway (Reprise)
CD _____ CDSEW 019
Southbound / Nov '89 / Pinnacle.

IT'S OVER
CD _____ ICH 15022
Ichiban / Dec '95 / Koch.

JUST A LIL' BIT COUNTRY
I can't stop loving you / Till I get it right / Pick me up on your way down / Loving you / I laughed a lot / Love on the rocks / Standing in your line / Rose coloured glasses / It meant nothing to me / Anybody that don't like Millie Jackson
CD _____ CDSEWM 089
Southbound / Jan '94 / Pinnacle.

LIVE AND UNCENSORED/LIVE AND OUTRAGEOUS (2CD Set)
Keep the home fire burnin' / Logs and thangs / Put something down on it / Da ya think I'm sexy / Just when I needed you most / Phuck u symphony / What am I waiting for / I still love you (you still love me) / All the way lover / Soaps / Hold the line / Be a sweetheart / Didn't I blow your mind this time / Give it up / Moment's pleasure / (If loving you is wrong) I don't want to be right / Rap / Never change lovers in the middle of the night / Sweet music man / It hurts so good / Passion (CD only) / Horse or mule (CD only) / Lovers and girlfriends (CD only) / Don't you ever stop loving me (CD only) / I ugly men (CD only) / Still (CD only) / Ugly men (CD only) / This is it (CD only)
CD Set _____ CDSEW2 038
Southbound / Mar '91 / Pinnacle.

LOVINGLY YOURS
You can't turn me off (in the middle of turning me on) / Something 'bout you / I'll continue to love you / I can't say goodbye / Love of your own / I'll live my love for you / Body movements / From her arms to mine / Help me finish my song / I'll be rolling
CD _____ CDSEWM 037
Southbound / Feb '91 / Pinnacle.

MILLIE JACKSON
If this is love / I ain't giving up / I miss you baby / Child of God / Ask me what you want / My man, a sweet man / You're the joy of my life / I gotta get away from my own self / I just can't stand it / Strange things
CD _____ CDSEW 009
Southbound / Aug '89 / Pinnacle.

MOMENT'S PLEASURE, A
Never change lovers in the middle of the night / Seeing you again / Kiss you all over / Moment's pleasure / What went wrong last night / Rising cost of love / We got to hit it off / Once you've had it
CD _____ CDSEWM 053
Westbound / Sep '92 / Pinnacle.

ROYAL RAPPIN'S (Jackson, Millie & Isaac Hayes)
Sweet music, soft lights and you / Feels like the first time / You never cross my mind / Love changes / I changed my mind / Do you wanna make love / If I had my way / If you had your way / You needed me
CD _____ CDSEW 059
Southbound / Jan '93 / Pinnacle.

STILL CAUGHT UP
Loving arms / Making the best of a bad situation / Memory of a wife / Tell her it's over / Do what makes you satisfied / You can't stand the thought of another me / Leftovers / I still love you (you still love me)
CD _____ CDSEW 027
Southbound / Jul '90 / Pinnacle.

YOUNG MAN, OLDER WOMAN
CD _____ ICH 1159CD
Ichiban / Feb '94 / Koch.

Jackson, Milt

AIN'T BUT A FEW OF US LEFT (Jackson, Milt & Oscar Peterson/Grady Tate/Ray Brown)
Ain't but a few of us left / Time for love / If I should lose you / Stuffy / Body and soul / What am I here for
CD _____ OJCCD 785-2
Original Jazz Classics / Jun '94 / Wellard / Jazz Music / Cadillac / Complete/Pinnacle.

BAGS MEETS WES (Jackson, Milt & Wes Montgomery)
CD _____ OJCCD 234
Original Jazz Classics / Apr '86 / Wellard / Jazz Music / Cadillac / Complete/Pinnacle.

BAGS' BAG
Blues for Roberta / Groovin' / How are you / Slow boat to China / I cover the waterfront / Rev / Tour angel / Blues for Tomi-Oka
CD _____ PACD 23108422
Pablo / Oct '94 / Jazz Music / Cadillac / Complete/Pinnacle.

BEBOP
Au privave / Good bait / Woody 'n' you / Now's the time / Ornithology / Groovin' high / Birk's works / Salt peanuts
CD _____ 7567909912
Atlantic / Jul '93 / Warner Music.

BEST OF MILT JACKSON
Once I loved / If you went away / Yes sir that's my baby / Three thousand miles ago / Ain't misbehavin' / My kind of trouble is / Your soul fusion / Blues for Edith
CD _____ PACD 24054052
Pablo / Jul '94 / Jazz Music / Cadillac / Complete/Pinnacle.

BIG BAGS
CD _____ OJCCD 366
Original Jazz Classics / Nov '95 / Wellard / Jazz Music / Cadillac / Complete/Pinnacle.

BIG THREE, THE (Jackson, Milt & Joe Pass/Ray Brown)
Pink panther / Nuages / Blue bossa / Come Sunday / Wave / Moonglow / You stepped out of a dream / Blues for Sammy
CD _____ OJCCD 805
Original Jazz Classics / Jul '93 / Wellard / Jazz Music / Cadillac / Complete/Pinnacle.

BROTHER JIM (Jackson, Milt & His Gold Medal Winners)
Brother Jim / Ill wind / Rhythm-a-ning / Sudden death / How high the moon / Back to Bologna / Sleeves / Lullaby of the leaves / Weasel
CD _____ PACD 23109162
Pablo / Oct '94 / Jazz Music / Cadillac / Complete/Pinnacle.

FEELINGS
Feelings / Come to me / Trouble is a man / Moody blue / Day it rained / My kind of trouble is you / If you went away / Tears / Blues for Edith / You don't know what love is
CD _____ OJCCD 448
Original Jazz Classics / Jul '93 / Wellard / Jazz Music / Cadillac / Complete/Pinnacle.

FOR SOMEONE I LOVE
CD _____ OJCCD 404
Original Jazz Classics / Jul '93 / Wellard / Jazz Music / Cadillac / Complete/Pinnacle.

HAREM, THE
Blues for Gene / Holy land / Ellington's Strayhorn / Harem / N. P. S. / Old folks / Olinga / All members / Every time we say goodbye
CD _____ MM 5061
Music Masters / Oct '94 / Nimbus.

IN THE BEGINNING (Jackson, Milt & Sonny Stitt)
CD _____ OJCCD 1771
Original Jazz Classics / Oct '94 / Wellard / Jazz Music / Cadillac / Complete/Pinnacle.

INVITATION (Jackson, Milt Sextet)
Invitation / Too close for comfort / Ruby my dear (Take 6) / Ruby my dear (Take 5) / Sealer / Poom-a-loom / Stella by starlight / Ruby / None shall wander (Take 8) / None shall wander (Take 6)
CD _____ OJCCD 260
Original Jazz Classics / Sep '93 / Wellard / Jazz Music / Cadillac / Complete/Pinnacle.

IT DON'T MEAN A THING IF YOU CAN'T TAP YOUR FOOT TO IT (Jackson, Milt Quartet)
Midnight waltz / Ain't that nuthin' / Stress and strain / Used to be Jackson / It don't mean a thing if it ain't got that swing / If I were a bell / Close enough for blood
CD _____ OJCCD 601-2
Original Jazz Classics / Feb '92 / Wellard / Jazz Music / Cadillac / Complete/Pinnacle.

JACKSON
CD _____ CD 20022
Pablo / May '86 / Jazz Music / Cadillac / Complete/Pinnacle.

JACKSON'S VILLE
Now's the time / In a sentimental mood / Mood indigo / Azure / Minor conception / Soul 3/4
CD _____ SV 0175
Savoy Jazz / Apr '93 / Conifer / ADA.

JAZZ SKYLINE
Lover / Can't help lovin' dat man / Lady is a tramp / Angel face / Sometimes I'm happy / What's new
CD _____ CY 78997
Savoy Jazz / Nov '95 / Conifer / ADA.

LIVE AT THE VILLAGE GATE
Bags of blue / Little girl blue / Gemini / Gerri's blues / Time after time / Ignunt oil / Willow weep for me / All members
CD _____ OJCCD 309
Original Jazz Classics / May '93 / Wellard / Jazz Music / Cadillac / Complete/Pinnacle.

LONDON BRIDGE, A
CD _____ CD 2310932
Pablo / '93 / Jazz Music / Cadillac / Complete/Pinnacle.

MEET MILT JACKSON
They can't take that away from me / Soulful / Flamingo / Telefunken blues / I've lost your love / Hearing bells / Junior / Bluesology / Bubu
CD _____ SV 0172
Savoy Jazz / Aug '93 / Conifer / ADA.

MILT JACKSON
Au privave / Why I should care / Stonewall / My funny Valentine / Nearness of you / Moonray
CD _____ OJCCD 001-2
Original Jazz Classics / Mar '92 / Wellard / Jazz Music / Cadillac / Complete/Pinnacle.

MILT JACKSON & COUNT BASIE BIG BAND VOL.1 (Jackson, Milt & Count Basie Big Band)
9.20 special / Moonlight becomes you / Shiny stockings / Blues for me / Every tub / Easy does it / Lena and Lenny / Sunny side of the street / Back to the apple / I'll always be in love with you / Come back / Basie / Corner pocket / Lady in lace / Blues for Joe Turner / Good time blues / Li'l darlin' / Big stuff / Blue and sentimental
CD _____ OJCCD 740
Original Jazz Classics / May '93 / Wellard / Jazz Music / Cadillac / Complete/Pinnacle.

MILT JACKSON & COUNT BASIE BIG BAND VOL.2 (Jackson, Milt & Count Basie)
9/20 special / Moonlight becomes you / Shiny stockings / Blues for me / Every tub / Easy does it / Lena and Lenny / Sunny side of the street / Back to the apple / I'll always be in love with you
CD _____ OJCCD 741
Original Jazz Classics / May '93 / Wellard / Jazz Music / Cadillac / Complete/Pinnacle.

MILT JACKSON AT LONDON BRIDGE
CD _____ PACD 23109322
Pablo / Jul '93 / Jazz Music / Cadillac / Complete/Pinnacle.

MONTREUX '77 (Jackson, Milt & Ray Brown)
Slippery / Beautiful friendship / Mean to me / You are my sunshine / C.M.J. / That's the way it is
CD _____ OJCCD 375
Original Jazz Classics / Apr '93 / Wellard / Jazz Music / Cadillac / Complete/Pinnacle.

MOSTLY DUKE
CD _____ PACD 23109442
Pablo / Jan '93 / Jazz Music / Cadillac / Complete/Pinnacle.

NIGHT MIST
Blues in my heart / Double B / Blues for Clyde / Matter of adjustment / Night mist blues / Other bag blues / D.B. blues
CD _____ OJCCD 827
Original Jazz Classics / Jul '93 / Wellard / Jazz Music / Cadillac / Complete/Pinnacle.

OPUS DE JAZZ
Opus de funk / Opus pocus / You leave me breathless / Opus and interlude
CD _____ SV 0109
Savoy Jazz / Apr '92 / Conifer / ADA.

ROLL 'EM BAGS
Conglomeration / Bruz / You go to my head / Roll 'em Bags / Faultless / Hey, Frenchy / Come rain or come shine / Fred's mood / Wild man
CD _____ SV 0110
Savoy Jazz / Apr '92 / Conifer / ADA.

SOUL FUSION (Jackson, Milt & Monty Alexander)
Parking lot blues / Three thousand miles ago / It's the lovely / Soul fusion / Compassion / Once I loved / Yano / Bossa nova do marilla
CD _____ OJCCD 731
Original Jazz Classics / '93 / Wellard / Jazz Music / Cadillac / Complete/Pinnacle.

SOUL ROUTE (Jackson, Milt Quartet)
Sittin' in the sandtrap / Blues for Gene / How long has this been going on / Dejection blues / Soul route / Afterglow / In a mellow tone / My romance / Chloe
CD _____ PACD 23109002
Pablo / Jul '93 / Jazz Music / Cadillac / Complete/Pinnacle.

VERY TALL (Jackson, Milt & Oscar Peterson)
On Green Dolphin Street / Work song / Heartstrings / John Brown's body / Wonderful guy / Reunion blues
CD _____ 8278212
Verve / Sep '93 / PolyGram.

Jackson, Nicole

SENSUAL LOVING
CD _____ XECD 4
Debut / Jun '95 / Pinnacle / 3MV / Sony.

Jackson, P.J

P.J. JACKSON
CD _____ SP 1178CD
Stony Plain / Oct '93 / ADA / CM / Direct.

Jackson, Papa Charlie

VOLUME 1 - 1924-25
CD _____ DOCD 5087
Blues Document / '92 / Swift / Jazz Music / Hot Shot.

VOLUME 2 - 1924-25
CD _____ DOCD 5088
Blues Document / '92 / Swift / Jazz Music / Hot Shot.

VOLUME 3 - 1924-25
CD _____ DOCD 5089
Blues Document / '92 / Swift / Jazz Music / Hot Shot.

Jackson, Paul

MR. DESTINY
CD _____ SPCD 11
Spindle / Aug '95 / Jetstar / Else.

Jackson, Ron

THINKING OF YOU
If I love again / You'd be so nice to come home to / Thinking of you / With a song in my heart / Caught up in the rapture / Circle / Estate / Santa Lucia / So far away
CD _____ MCD 5515
Muse / Dec '94 / New Note / CM.

Jackson, Ronald Shanon

RAVEN ROC. (Jackson, Ronald Shanon & The Decoding Society)
CD _____ DIW 862
DIW / Sep '92 / Harmonia Mundi / Cadillac.

RED WARRIOR (Jackson, Ronald Shanon & The Decoding Society)
Red warrior / Ashes / Gate to heaven / In every face / Elders / What's not said
CD _____ AXCD 3008
Axiom / Oct '91 / PolyGram / Vital.

Jackson, Wanda

LET'S HAVE A PARTY
Let's have a party / Rock your baby / Mean mean man / There's a party goin' on / Fujiyama mama / Honey bop / Rip it up / Man we had a party / Hot dog that made him mad / You hup me har / Who shot Sam / Tongue tied / Sparklin' brown eyes / Lost weekend / Brown eyed handsome man / Honey don't / It doesn't matter anymore / Whole lotta shakin' goin' on / Long tall Sally / Money honey / Searchin' / Hard headed woman / Slippin' and slidin' / Riot in cell block 9 / I gotta know / Baby loves him / Let me explain / Savin' my love / Just a queen for a day / Cool love / Bye bye baby / Right or wrong
CD _____ CDCD 1022
Charly / Mar '93 / Charly / THE / Cadillac.

RIGHT OR WRONG 1954-1962 (4CD Set)
If you knew what I know / Lovin' country style / Heart / You could have had / Right to love / You can't have my love / If you don't, somebody else will / You'd be the first one to know / It's the same world (Wherever you go) / Tears at the Grand Old Opre / Don't do the things he'd do / Nobody's darlin' but mine / Wasted / I cried / I'd rather have a broken heart / You won't forget about me / Step by step / Half as good a girl / I gotta know / Cryin' thru the night / Baby loves him / Honey bop / Silver threads and golden needles / Hot dog that made him mad / Did you miss me / Cool love / Let me explain / Don'a wan'a / No wedding bells for Joe / Fujiyama Mama / Just queen for a day / Making believe / Just call me lonesome / Happy, happy birthday / Let me go, lover / Let's have a party / Daydreaming / Heartbreak ahead / Here we are again / I wanna waltz / I can't make my dreams understand / Moner Honey / Long tall Sally / Sinful heart / Mean mean man / Rock your baby / Date with Jerry / (Every time they play) our song / You've turned to a stranger / Reaching / I'd

rather have you / Savin' my love / You're the one for me / In the middle of a heartache / Please call today / My destiny / Wrong kind of girl / Kansas City / Fallin' / Sparkling brown eyes / Hard headed woman / Baby, baby, bye bye / It doesn't matter anymore / Lonely weekends / Tweedle dee / Riot in cell block 9 / Little charm bracelet / Right or wrong / Funnel of love / Tongue tied / There's a party goin' on / Lost weekend / Man we had a party / Why I'm walkin / I may never get to heaven / Stupid cupid / Brown eyed handsome man / I cried again (2) / Last letter / Who shot Sam / Slippin' and slidin' / My baby left me / So soon / Window up above / Sticks and stones / I don't wanta go / In the middle of a heartache (2) / Little bitty tear / I'd be ashamed / Seven lonely days / Don't ask me why / I need you now / This should go on forever / Is it wrong / We could / You don't know baby / Before I lose my mind / Tip of my fingers / Let me talk to you / (Let's stop) Kickin' our hearts around / Between the window and the phone / If I cried every time you hurt me / I misunderstood / Let my love walk in / To tell you the truth / Greatest actor / You bug me bad / One teardrop at a time / Funny how time slips away / These empty arms / But I was lying / We haven't a moment to lose / How important can it be / Things I might've been / Little things mean a lot / Have you ever been lonely / Please love me forever / Since I met you baby / May you never be alone / Sympathy / Whirlpool / Pledging my love / What am I living for
CD Set _____ BCD 15629
Bear Family / Mar '93 / Rollercoaster / Direct / CM / Swift / ADA.

SANTA DOMINGO (Her German Recordings)
CD _____ BCD 15582
Bear Family / Apr '92 / Rollercoaster / Direct / CM / Swift / ADA.

WANDA JACKSON: CAPITOL COUNTRY MUSIC CLASSICS
I gotta know / Silver threads and golden needles / Cool love / Don'a wan'a / Fujiyama Mama / Making believe / Let's have a party / Long tall Sally / Mean mean man / Tweedle dee / Little charm bracelet / Right or wrong / There's a party goin' on / I may never get to heaven / Slippin' and slidin' / In the middle of a heartache / This should go on forever / (Let's stop) Kickin' our hearts around / Between the window and the phone / If I cried every time you hurt me / Slippin' / Violet and a rose / Box it came in / Blue yodel No. 6 / Because it's you / Tears will be a chaser for your wine / Both sides of the line / Girl don't have to drink to have fun / My big iron skillet / Woman lives for love / Fancy satin pillows
CD _____ CDEMS 1485
Capitol / Apr '93 / EMI.

Jackson, William

CELTIC SUITE FOR GLASGOW
Bird / Tree / Bell / Fish
CD _____ CDTRAX 041
Greentrax / Dec '90 / Conifer / Duncans / ADA / Direct.

CELTIC TRANQUILITY
Dove across the water / Light on a distant shore / Harvest of the fallen / Glasgow 1885 / Dear green place unchanged / Molendinar: The spring / Fermentation / Paradise valley, angel's ascent / Landfall / Fish
CD _____ IR 016CD
Iona / Jun '93 / ADA / Direct / Duncans.

HEART MUSIC
Lady Amelia Murray's strathspey / Breton march / Wauking o' the fauld's / Port lennox / Strike the young harp / John Maclean of lewis / Paradise alley / Angel's ascent / Threefold flame / Air by fingal / Emigrant peak / St Kilda dance / Fair shoemaker / Rose without rue
CD _____ IRCD 010
Iona / Sep '91 / ADA / Direct / Duncans.

INCHCOLM
CD _____ AKD 037
Linn / Mar '95 / PolyGram.

Jackson, Willis

BAR WARS
CD _____ MCD 6011
Muse / Sep '92 / New Note / CM.

CALL OF THE GATORS
CD _____ DD 460
Delmark / Jul '93 / Hot Shot / ADA / CM / Direct / Cadillac.

PLEASE MR. JACKSON
CD _____ OJCCD 321
Original Jazz Classics / Dec '95 / Wellard / Jazz Music / Cadillac / Complete/Pinnacle.

SINGLE ACTION
Evergreen / Bolita / Makin' whoopee / You are the sunshine of my life / Hittin' the numbers / Single action
CD _____ MCD 5179
Muse / May '95 / New Note / CM.

Jackson, Yvonne

I'M TROUBLE
I'm trouble / Sweet memories / Woman in me / She set you free / No deposit, no return / What I'd do to get your love back / Common, ordinary housewife gone bad / What'cha gonna do about it / If tears are only water / I'm walking out
CD _____ BLU 10162
Blues Beacon / Jun '94 / New Note.

Jacksons

AMERICAN DREAM, AN
CD _____ 5301192
Motown / Jan '94 / PolyGram.

GOIN' PLACES
Music's takin' over / Goin' places / Different kind of lady / Even though you're gone / Jump for joy / Heaven knows I love you, girl / Man of war / Do what you wanna / Find me a girl
CD _____ 982836 2
Pickwick/Sony Collector's Choice / May '94 / Carlton Home Entertainment / Pinnacle / Sony.

JACKSONS, THE
Enjoy yourself / Think happy / Good times / Keep on dancing / Blues away / Show you the way to go / Living together / Strength of one man / Dreamer / Style of life
CD _____ 9827382
Pickwick/Sony Collector's Choice / Jun '94 / Carlton Home Entertainment / Pinnacle / Sony.

ORIGINAL CLASSIC ALBUM
CD _____ 9826402
Pickwick/Sony Collector's Choice / Nov '91 / Carlton Home Entertainment / Pinnacle / Sony.

TRIUMPH
Can you feel it / Lovely one / Your ways / Everybody / This place hotel / Time waits for no one / Walk right now / Give it up / Wondering who
CD _____ 986640 2
Pickwick/Sony Collector's Choice / Mar '94 / Carlton Home Entertainment / Pinnacle / Sony.

VICTORY
Torture / Wait / One more chance / Be not always / State of shock / We can change the world / Hurt / Body
CD _____ 450450-2
Epic / Sep '94 / Sony.

Jacobites

HOWLING GOOD TIMES
CD _____ JANIDA 004
Trident / May '94 / Pinnacle.

JACOBITES (Sudden, Nikki & Dave Kusworth)
CD _____ JANIDA 001
Trident / May '93 / Pinnacle.

OLD SCARLETT
CD _____ GRCD 382
Glitterhouse / Dec '95 / Direct / ADA.

Jacob's Mouse

RUBBER ROOM
CD _____ WIJ 040CD
Wiija / Feb '95 / Vital.

WRYLY SMILERS
Good / Dusty / Group of seven / Palace / Jay bay / Fandango widewheels / B12 / Marmites / Three pound apathy / Keen apple / Lip and cheek
CD _____ JCOB 001CD
Wiija / Feb '94 / Vital.

Jacob's Optical Stairway

JACOB'S OPTICAL STAIRWAY
Fragments of a lost language / Naphosisous wars / Chase the escape / Fusion formula (the meetamophosis) / Majestic 12 / Solar feelings / Jacob's optical illusion / Harsh realities / Engulfing whirlpool / Quatrain 72 (fled horizon) / 20 Degrees of Taurus
CD _____ RS 95079CD
R & S / Jan '96 / Vital.

Jacobs, Peter

PIANO MUSIC OF BILLY MAYERL
CD _____ PRCD 399
Priory / Jul '92 / Priory.

Jacobsen, Pete

EVER ONWARD
CD _____ FMRCD 12
Future / Apr '95 / Harmonia Mundi / ADA.

Jacquet, Illinois

BIG HORN, THE
Lester leaps in / You're my thrill / Canadian sunset / When my dreamboat comes home / Desert winds / Star eyes / Blues for the early bird / On a clear day (you can see forever) / Illinois Jacquet flies again / Robbin's nest / Watermelon man / I want a little girl / Pamela's blues / Jan

CD _____ LEJAZZCD 50
Le Jazz / Oct '95 / Charly / Cadillac.

BLACK VELVET BAND
Jet propulsion / King Jacquet / Try me one more time / Embryo / Riffin' at the 24th Street / Mutton leg / Symphony in Sid / Jacquet for Jack the Belboy / Big foot / Black velvet / B-yot / Adam's alley / Blue satin / My old gal / Slow down baby / Hot rod / You gotta change / Flying home
CD _____ ND 86571
Bluebird / Nov '88 / BMG.

COMEBACK, THE
CD _____ BLCD 760160
Black Lion / Oct '92 / Jazz Music / Cadillac / Wellard / Koch.

FLYING HOME - THE BEST OF THE VERVE YEARS
CD _____ 521644-2
Verve / Jun '94 / PolyGram.

ILLINOIS JACQUET (Jacquet, Illinois & Wild Bill Davis)
CD _____ 233044
Black & Blue / May '87 / Wellard / Koch.

ILLINOIS JACQUET AND ALL STAR NEW YORK BAND
CD _____ JSPCD 212
JSP / Jan '88 / ADA / Target/BMG / Direct / Cadillac / Complete/Pinnacle.

JACQUET'S STREET
CD _____ BLE 591122
Black & Blue / Oct '94 / Wellard / Koch.

LOOT TO BOOT
CD _____ CDC 9034
LRC / Jul '91 / New Note / Harmonia Mundi.

Jade

JADE TO THE MAX
Don't walk away / I wanna love you / I want 'cha baby / That boy / Out with the girls / Hold me close / One woman / Give me what I'm missing / Looking for Mr. Do Right / Don't ask my neighbour / Blessed
CD _____ 759924466-2
WEA / Mar '93 / Warner Music.

MIND, BODY & SONG
When will I see you again / Every day of the week / Hangin' / What's goin' on / 5-4-3-2 (Yo' time is up) / I like the way / Do you want me / If the mood is right / Bedroom / If the lovin' ain't good / Let's get it on / It's on / There's not a man / Everything / Mind body and song
CD _____ 74321226052
Giant / Oct '94 / BMG.

Jade Warrior

BREATHING THE STORM
CD _____ CDR 105
Red Hot / Mar '94 / THE.

DISTANT ECHOES
CD _____ CDR 106
Red Hot / Jan '94 / THE.

FLOATING WORLD
Clouds / Mountain of fruit and flowers / Waterfall / Red lotus / Rainflower / Easty / Monkey chant / Memories of a distant sea / Quba
CD _____ IMCD 99
Island / Feb '90 / PolyGram.

JADE WARRIOR
Traveller / Masai morning / Dragonfly day / Telephonie girl / Slow ride / Prenormal day at Brighton / Windweaver / Petunia / Psychiatric sergeant / Sundial song
CD _____ 900548
Line / Sep '94 / CM / Grapevine / ADA / Conifer / Direct.

WAY OF THE SUN
Sun ra / Sun child / Moontears / Heaven stone / Way of the sun / River song / Carnival / Dance of the sun / Death of Ra
CD _____ IMCD 100
Island / Feb '90 / PolyGram.

Jadis

ACROSS THE WATER
CD _____ GEPCD 1009
Giant Electric Pea / May '94 / Pinnacle.

MORE THAN MEETS THE EYE
Sleepwalk / Hiding in the corner / G 13 / Wonderful world / More than meets the eye / Beginning and the end / Holding your breath
CD _____ GEPCD 1002
Giant Electric Pea / Dec '93 / Pinnacle.

Jaffa, Max

MUSIC FOR A GRAND HOTEL (Jaffa, Max Orchestra)
Roses from the South / Gypsy carnival / Great waltz / Canto amoroso / Fascination / Scarborough fair / Some day I'll find you / Dobra dobra / Gentle maiden / I dream of Jeannie with the light brown hair / Memories of Richard Tauber / Adoration / Annen polka / Victor Herbert medley / Ave Maria
CD _____ VALD 8057
Valentine / Feb '86 / Conifer.

MUSIC FOR A PALM COURT
Serenade / Parlez-moi d'amour / Tristesse / On wings of song / Bittersweet medly / Traumeri / Cradle song / Love will find a way / Waltzes from the operas / Barcarolle / Bonnie Mary of Argyll / Fly home little heart / Romanian carnival / None but the lonely heart / Somewhere my love / Swan / Rosemary / Meditation / Perfect day
CD _____ VALD 8061
Valentine / '91 / Conifer.

Jaffe, Andy

MANHATTON PROJECTIONS
CD _____ STCD 549
Stash / '92 / Jazz Music / CM / Cadillac / Direct / ADA.

Jag Panzer

DISSIDENT AGGRESSOR
CD _____ 62292CD
SPV / Nov '94 / Plastic Head.

Jagger, Chris

ATCHA
CD _____ NEXCD 258
Sequel / Mar '94 / BMG.

Jagger, Mick

PRIMITIVE COOL
Throwaway / Let's work / Radio control / Say you will / Primitive cool / Kowtow / Shoot off your mouth / Peace for the wicked / Party doll / War baby
CD _____ 7567825542
East West / Sep '87 / Warner Music.

SHE'S THE BOSS
Lonely at the top / Half a loaf / Running out of luck / Turn the girl loose / Hard woman / Just another night / Lucky in love / Secrets / She's the boss
CD _____ 7567825532
East West / Apr '92 / Warner Music.

WANDERING SPIRIT
Wired all night / Sweet thing / Out of focus / Don't tear me up / Put me in the trash / Use me / Evening gown / Mother of man / Think / Wandering spirit / Hang on to me tonight / I've been lonely for so long / Angel in my heart / Handsome Molly
CD _____ 7567824362
East West / Feb '93 / Warner Music.

Jagoda, Flory

GRANDMOTHER SINGS, THE (Jagoda, Flory & Family)
CD _____ GV 155CD
Global Village / Nov '93 / ADA / Direct.

Jagwarr, Don

FADED
Intro (live) / Bad boy / What set U from / Whose is it / Steppin' / Who do you fear / My law / Skank wit' U / Cure / R.E.S.P.E.C.T / Roll 'em up / She loves me not / Rewind (live) (Outro)
CD _____ CDPTY 112
Priority/Virgin / Dec '94 / EMI.

Jah Lion

COLOMBIA COLLY
Wisdom / Dread ina Jamdong / Hay fever / Flashing whip / Colombia colly / Fat man / Bad luck Natty / Black lion / Little Sally Dater / Sata / Soldier and police war
CD _____ RRCD 47
Reggae Refreshers / Jul '94 / PolyGram / Vital.

Jah Messengers

REGGAE TIME
CD _____ HBCD 115
Heartbeat / May '93 / Greensleeves / Jetstar / Direct / ADA.

Jah Power Band

LIGHT UP THE CITY - THE DUB ALBUM
CD _____ SPVCD 08455282
Red Arrow / Apr '95 / SRD / Jetstar.

Jah Red

MR. BOGLE
CD _____ JR 220561
Deleeuwauc / Mar '93 / Jetstar.

Jah Shaka

AT ARIWA SOUNDS (Jah Shaka & Mad Professor)
CD _____ ARICD 027
Ariwa/Shaka / Sep '94 / SRD.

COMMANDMENTS OF DUB CHAPTER 1
CD _____ SHAKACD 824
Jah Shaka / Sep '90 / Jetstar / SRD / Greensleeves.

COMMANDMENTS OF DUB CHAPTER 9
CD _____ SHAKACD 872
Jah Shaka / Sep '90 / Jetstar / SRD / Greensleeves.

DISCIPLES, THE
CD _____ SHAKACD 871
Jah Shaka / Sep '90 / Jetstar / SRD / Greensleeves.

DUB SALUTE 1
CD _____ SHAKACD 940
Ariwa Sounds / Jul '94 / Jetstar / SRD.

DUB SALUTE 2
CD _____ SHAKACD 941
Ariwa Sounds / Jul '94 / Jetstar / SRD.

DUB SALUTE 3
CD _____ SHAKACD 942
Ariwa Sounds / Jul '94 / Jetstar / SRD.

DUB SALUTE 4
CD _____ SHAKACD 953
Greensleeves.

DUB SALUTE 5
CD _____ SHAKACD 954
Jah Shaka / Jan '96 / Jetstar / SRD / Greensleeves.

DUB SYMPHONY
Black steel / Dub symphony / Sound clinic dub / True independence / Immortal dub / Dance wicked / Come and get dub / Cryptic dub / Mystic dub / Earth rightful dub
CD _____ CIDM 1044
Mango / Jul '90 / Vital / PolyGram.

FARI SHIP DUB (Jah Shaka & Max Romeo)
CD _____ SHAKACD 989
Jah Shaka / Nov '92 / Jetstar / SRD / Greensleeves.

JAH CHILDREN GATHER ROUND (Jah Shaka & Prince Allah)
CD _____ SHAKACD 952
Jah Shaka / Dec '95 / Jetstar / SRD / Greensleeves.

JAH SHAKA & THE FASIMBAS IN THE GHETTO
CD _____ SHAKACD 935
Jah Shaka / Dec '93 / Jetstar / SRD / Greensleeves.

JAH SHAKA MEETS HORACE ANDY
CD _____ SHAKA CD947
Jah Shaka / Jul '93 / Jetstar / SRD / Greensleeves.

MESSAGE FROM AFRICA (Jah Shaka All Stars)
CD _____ SHAKACD 848
Jah Shaka / Sep '90 / Jetstar / SRD / Greensleeves.

NEW TESTAMENT OF DUB VOL 2
CD _____ SHAKACD 936
Jah Shaka / Dec '93 / Jetstar / SRD / Greensleeves.

OUR RIGHTS (Jah Shaka & Max Romeo)
CD _____ SHAKACD 951
Jah Shaka / Mar '95 / Jetstar / SRD / Greensleeves.

Jah Stitch

LOVE AND HARMONY
CD _____ RNCD 2058
Rhino / May '94 / Jetstar / Magnum Music Group / THE.

Jah Thomas

LYRICS FOR SALE
CD _____ RNCD 2071
Rhino / Jul '94 / Jetstar / Magnum Music Group / THE.

Jah Wobble

HEAVEN AND EARTH
Heaven and earth / Love song / Dying over Europe / Divine Mother / Gone to Croatan / Hit me / Om namah shiva / All life is sacred (part 1) / All life is sacred (part 2)
CD _____ CID 8044
Island / Nov '95 / PolyGram.

PSALMS
CD _____ 18522-2
Southern / Jul '94 / SRD.

RISING ABOVE BEDLAM (Jah Wobble's Invaders Of The Heart)
Visions of you / Relight the flame / Bomba / Ungodly kingdom / Rising above bedlam / Erzulie / Everyman's an island / Soledad / Sweet divinity / Wonderful world
CD _____ 9031754702
East West / Sep '91 / Warner Music.

TAKE ME TO GOD (Jah Wobble's Invaders Of The Heart)
God in the beginning / Becoming more like God / Whisky priests / I'm an Algerian / Amor / Amor dub / Take me to God / Sun does rise / When the storm comes / I love everybody / Yoga of the nightclub / I am the music / Bonds of love / Angels / No chance is sexy / Raga / Forever
CD _____ CID 8017
Island / May '94 / PolyGram.

WITHOUT JUDGEMENT (Jah Wobble's Invaders Of The Heart)
CD _____ KKUK 001CD
KK / '90 / Plastic Head.

Jah Woosh

AT LEGGO SOUND
CD _____ OMCD 31
Original Music / Jan '96 / SRD / Jetstar.

BEST OF JAH WOOSH, THE
CD _____ RNCD 2005
Rhino / May '93 / Jetstar / Magnum Music Group / THE.

DUB PLATE SPECIAL
CD _____ OMCD 024
Original Music / Jan '93 / SRD / Jetstar.

MARIJUANA WORLD TOUR
CD _____ OMCD 17
Original Music / Dec '93 / SRD / Jetstar.

WE CHAT YOU ROC (Jah Woosh & I Roy)
CD _____ CDTRL 296
Trojan / Jul '91 / Jetstar / Total/BMG.

Jahson, David

NATTY CHASE
CD _____ CC 2717
Crocodisc / Apr '95 / THE / Magnum Music Group.

Jaildog

PUNKROCK, HIPHOP AND OTHER OBSCURE STUFF
CD _____ NO 2512
Noise/Modern Music / Jul '95 / Pinnacle / Plastic Head.

Jakko

ARE MY EARS
CD _____ RES 110CD
Resurgence / Dec '95 / Vital.

KINGDOM OF DUST
Hands of Che Guevara / Drowning in my sleep / It's only the moon / Judas kiss
CD _____ RES 101CD
Resurgence / Jun '94 / Vital.

MUSTARD GAS AND ROSES
Just another day / Little town / Devil's dictionary / Damn this town / Borders we traded / Perfect kiss / Saddleworth moor / Learning to cry / Handful of pearls / Then and now / Mustard gas and roses / We'll change the world
CD _____ RES 103CD
Resurgence / Oct '94 / Vital.

Jalal

MANKIND
CD _____ EFACD 0748
On-U Sound / Sep '93 / SRD / Jetstar.

Jam

ALL MOD CONS
All mod cons / To be someone / Mr. Clean / David Watts / English rose / In the crowd / Billy Hunt / It's too bad / Fly / Place I love / Bomb in Wardour Street / Down in the tube station at midnight
CD _____ 823 282-2
Polydor / '89 / PolyGram.

BEAT SURRENDER
Beat surrender / Town called Malice / Pretty green / That's entertainment / Life / Carnaby Street / Batman / In the city / All mod cons / Modern world / When you're young / Funeral pyre / Private hell / In the midnight hour
CD _____ 5500062
Spectrum/Karussell / May '93 / PolyGram / THE.

DIG THE NEW BREED
In the city / All mod cons / To be someone / It's too bad / Start / Big bird / Set the house ablaze / Ghosts / Standards / In the crowd / Going underground / Dreams of children / That's entertainment / Private hell
CD _____ 810 041-2
Polydor / Jun '90 / PolyGram.

EXTRAS
Dreams of the children / Tales from the riverbank / Liza radley / Move on up / Shopping / Smithers Jones / Pop art poem / Boy about town / Solid bond in your heart / No one in the world / And your bird can sing / Burning sky / Thick as thieves / Disguises
CD _____ 5131772
Polydor / Apr '92 / PolyGram.

GIFT, THE
Happy together / Ghosts / Precious / Just who is the five o'clock hero / Trans-Global express / Running on the spot / Circus / Planner's dream goes wrong / Carnation / Town called Malice / Gift
CD _____ 823 285-2
Polydor / Jun '90 / PolyGram.

GREATEST HITS: JAM
In the city / All around the world / News of the world / Modern world / David Watts / Down in the tube station at midnight / Strange town / When you're young / Eton rifles / Going underground / Start / That's entertainment / Funeral pyre / Absolute beginners / Town called malice / Precious / Just who is the five o'clock hero / Bitterest pill (I ever had to swallow) / Beat surrender

IN THE CITY
Art school / I've changed my address / Slow down / I got by in time / Away from the numbers / Batman / In the city / Sounds from the street / Non-stop dancing / Time for truth / Takin' my love / Bricks and mortar
CD _____ 817 124-2
Polydor / Jul '90 / PolyGram.

IN THE CITY/THIS IS THE MODERN WORLD
Art school / I've changed my address / Slow down / I got by in time / Sway from the numbers / Batman / In the city / Sounds from the street / Non-stop dancing (Non stop) / Time for truth / Takin' my love / Bricks and mortar / Modern world / London traffic / Standards / Life from a window / Combine / Don't tell them you're sane / In the street today / London girl / I need you for someone / Here comes the weekend / Tonight at noon / In the midnight hour
CD _____ 847 730-2
Polydor / Jan '91 / PolyGram.

LIVE JAM
Modern world / Billy Hunt / Thick as thieves / Burning sky / Mr. Clean / Smithers Jones / Little boy soldiers / Eton rifles / Away from the numbers / Down in the tube station at midnight / Strange town / When you're young / Bomb in Wardour Street / Pretty green / Boy about town / Man in the corner shop / David Watts / Funeral pyre / Precious / Town called malice / Heatwave
CD _____ 5196672
Polydor / Oct '93 / PolyGram.

SETTING SONS
Burning sky / Eton rifles / Girl on the phone / Heatwave / Little boy soldiers / Private hell / Saturday's kids / Smithers Jones / Thick as thieves / Wasteland
CD _____ 831 314-2
Polydor / May '88 / PolyGram.

SOUND AFFECTS
Pretty green / Monday / But I'm different now / Set the house ablaze / Start / That's entertainment / Dreamtime / Man in the corner shop / Music for the last couple / Boy about town / Scrape away
CD _____ 823 284 2
Polydor / May '88 / PolyGram.

THIS IS THE MODERN WORLD
Modern world / London traffic / Standards / Life from a window / Combine / Don't tell them you're sane / In the street today / London express / I need you for someone / Here comes the weekend / Tonight at noon / In the midnight hour
CD _____ 823 281-2
Polydor / Jul '90 / PolyGram.

WASTELAND
News of the world / Burning sky / Saturday's kids / Art school / In the street today / Non-stop dancing / Wasteland / In the city / Strange town / Standards / Bomb in Wardour street / In the crowd / London girl / David Watts / I got by in time / All around the world
CD _____ PWKS 4129P
Carlton Home Entertainment / Oct '92 / Carlton Home Entertainment.

Jam & Spoon

TRIPOMATIC FAIRYTALES 2001
Heart of Africa / Odyssey to Anyoona / Two spys in the house of love / Stella / Neurotrance adventure / Operating spaceship Earth / Zen flash zen bones / Who opened the door to nowhere / Right in the night / Muffled drums / Path of harmony / Paradise garage / Earth spirit / Stellas cry
CD _____ 474928 2
Epic / Feb '94 / Sony.

TRIPOMATIC FAIRYTALES 2001 SPECIAL EDITION
Heart of Africa / Fine me (odyssey to Anyoona) / Two spys in the house of love / Stella / Neurotrance adventure / Operating spaceship earth / Zen flash zen bones / Who opened the door to nowhere / Right white (fall in love with music) / Muffled drums / Path of harmony / Paradise garage / Earth spirit / Stellas cry
CD _____ 4809632
Epic / Jul '95 / Sony.

TRIPOMATIC FAIRYTALES 2002
Hermaphrodite / N.A.S.A. Nocturnal Audio Sensory Awakening / LSD Nikon / Future is in small hands / Salinas afternoon / V Angel is calling / Words and Dana / Ancient dream / I saw the future / Castaneda future illuminations / Secret kind of love / World of X-T-C
CD _____ 474918 2
Epic / Feb '94 / Sony.

Jam Nation

WAY DOWN BELOW BUFFALO HELL
First time / Sleeping / Awakening / Sunstroke / She moved through the fair / Mekong / Meeting of the people / Harmonix / 454 / Pre-pubescent grand prix / La visite est terminee / Prehistoric (Bone us)

CD _____ CDRW 36
Realworld / Aug '93 / EMI / Sterns.

Jamaaladen, Tacuma

JUKEBOX
Metamorphosis / Rhythm of your mind / In the mood for mood / Naima / Time a place / Jam-all / Jukebox / Zam Zam was such a wonderful.. / Solar system blues
CD _____ 1888032
Gramavision / Dec '88 / Vital/SAM / ADA.

Jamaican Maroon Music

DRUMS OF DEFIANCE
CD _____ SFCD 40412
Sackville / Mar '93 / Swift / Jazz Music / Jazz Horizons / Cadillac / CM.

Jamal, Ahmad

CHICAGO REVISITED - LIVE AT JOE SEGAL'S JAZZ SHOWCASE
CD _____ CD 83327
Telarc / Feb '93 / Conifer / ADA.

CRYSTAL
CD _____ 7567817932
Atlantic / Jul '93 / Warner Music.

DIGITAL WORKS
Poinciana / But not for me / Midnight sun / Footprints / Once upon a time / One / La Costa / Misty / M.A.S.H. (Suicide is painless) / Biencavo / Time for love / Wave
CD _____ 756781258-2
Atlantic / Jun '93 / Warner Music.

I REMEMBER DUKE, HOAGY & STRAYHORN
My flower / I got it bad / In a sentimental mood / Ruby / Don't you know I care (or don't you care to) / Prelude to a kiss / Do nothin' 'til you hear from me / Chelsea bridge / I remember Hoagy / Skylark / Never let me go / Goodbye
CD _____ CD 83339
Telarc / Mar '95 / Conifer / ADA.

LIVE AT THE PERSHING & THE SPOTLIGHT CLUB
CD _____ JHR 73522
Jazz Hour / Sep '93 / Target/BMG / Jazz Music / Cadillac.

MASTERS OF PIANO (Jamal, Ahmed & Teddy Wilson)
Waltz for Debbie / Folks who live on the hill / People / Baia / Good life / In New York / I've never been in love before / Limehouse blues / Sweet Sue, just you
CD _____ 722016
Scorpio / Sep '92 / Complete/Pinnacle.

MONTREAL JAZZ FESTIVAL
CD _____ 756781699-2
Atlantic / Jun '93 / Warner Music.

MY FUNNY VALENTINE
CD _____ ATJCD 5955
All That's Jazz / '92 / THE / Jazz Music.

NIGHT SONG
When you wish upon a star / Deja vu / Need to smile / Bad times / Touch me in the morning / Night song / M.A.S.H. (Suicide is painless) / Something's missing in my life
CD _____ 5303032
Verve / Apr '94 / PolyGram.

ROSSITER ROAD
CD _____ 756781645-2
Atlantic / Jun '93 / Warner Music.

Jamal, Khan

DON'T TAKE NO
CD _____ STCD 20
Stash / Aug '90 / Jazz Music / CM / Cadillac / Direct / ADA.

THINKING OF YOU
CD _____ STCD 4138
Storyville / Feb '89 / Jazz Music / Wellard / CM / Cadillac.

James

GOLD MOTHER
Come home / Government walls / God only knows / How much suffering / Crescento / How was it for you / Hang one / Walking the ghost / Gold mother / Top of the world / Lose control / Sit down
CD _____ 8487312
Fontana / Apr '91 / PolyGram.

LAID
Out to get you / Sometimes / Dream thrum / One of the three / Say something / Five-O / P.S. / Everybody knows / Knuckle too far / Low low low / Laid / Lullaby / Skindiving
CD _____ 5149432
Fontana / Apr '94 / PolyGram.

ONE MAN TALKING
CD P.Disc _____ CBAK 4049
Baktabak / Jun '91 / Baktabak.

SEVEN
Born of frustration / Ring the bells / Sound / Bring a gun / Mother / Don't wait that long / Live a love of life / Next lover (Not on LP format.) / Heavens / Protect me / Seven

---

CD _____ 5109322
Fontana / Feb '92 / PolyGram.

STRIP MINE
What for / Charlie dance / Fairground / Are you ready / Medieval / Not there / Ya ho / Riders / Vulture / Strip mining
CD _____ 9256572
Sire / Feb '95 / Warner Music.

STUTTER
Skullduggery / Scarecrow / So many ways / Just hipper / John Yen / Summer songs / Really hard / Billy's shirts / Why so close / Withdrawn / Black hole
CD _____ 7599254372
Sire / Jul '91 / Warner Music.

James, Bob

COOL (James, Bob & Earl Klugh)
Movin' on / As it happens / So much in common / Fugitive life / Night that love came back / Secret wishes / New York samba / Handara / Sponge / Terpsichore / San Diego stomp / Miniature
CD _____ 759926392
WEA / Sep '92 / Warner Music.

DOUBLE VISION (James, Bob & David Sanborn)
Maputo / More than friends / Moontune / Since I fell for you / It's you / Never enough / You don't know me
CD _____ 925393 2
WEA / Jun '86 / Warner Music.

GRAND PIANO CANYON
Bare bones / Restoration / Wings for Sarah / Svengali / Worlds apart / Stop that / Xraxse / Just listen / Far from turtle
CD _____ 7599262562
WEA / Sep '90 / Warner Music.

RESTLESS
Lotus leaves / Under me / Restless / Kissing cross / Storm warning / Animal dreams / Back to Bali / Into the light / Serenissima / Awaken us to the blue
CD _____ 936245536-2
Warner Bros. / Mar '94 / Warner Music.

James, Boney

BACKBONE
CD _____ 9362456112
Warner Bros. / Feb '95 / Warner Music.

James, Brian

BRIAN JAMES
CD _____ 422181
New Rose / May '94 / Direct / ADA.

James, Carla

SACRIFICE
Sacrifice / Round and round / Love will see us through / My very first lover / Virginia's secret / Something sacred / Oh mother / Things that we all do for love / No one else will do / So what's going on / Actions speak louder
CD _____ 5403782
A&M / Jul '95 / PolyGram.

James, Colin

COLIN JAMES
Five long years / Voodoo thing / Down in the bottom / Chicks 'n' cars / Why'd you lie / Hidden charms / Bad girl / Dream of satin / Three sheets to the wind / Lone wolf
CD _____ CDV 2542
Virgin / Jul '93 / EMI.

COLIN JAMES AND THE LITTLE BIG BAND
Cadillac baby / That's what you do to me / Sit right here / Three hours past midnight / Satellite / Surely (I love you) / Breakin' up the house / No more doggin' / Evening / Train kept a rollin' / Leading me on / Boogie twist (part 2) / Cha shooky doo
CD _____ VPBCD 18
Pointblank / Jan '94 / EMI.

SUDDEN STOP
CD _____ CDVUS 20
Virgin / Oct '90 / EMI.

James, Ellen

RELUCTANTLY WE (James, Ellen Society)
CD _____ DR 01CD
Daemon / Sep '90 / Direct.

James, Elmore

BEST OF THE EARLY YEARS
Dust my broom / I held my baby last night / Baby, what's wrong / I believe / Sinful woman / Early in the morning / Hawaiian boogie / Can't stop lovin' / Make a little love / Strange kinda feeling / Please find my baby / Hand in hand / Make my dreams come true / Sho 'nuff I do / Dark and dreary / Rock my baby night / Sunnyland / Standing at the crossroads / Late hours at midnight / Way you treat me / Happy home / No love in my heart (For you) / Dust my blues / I was a fool / Blues before sunrise / Goodbye baby / Wild about you / Long tall woman
CD _____ CDCHD 583

Ace / Jun '95 / Pinnacle / Cadillac / Complete/Pinnacle.

CLASSIC EARLY RECORDINGS, THE (1951-1956/3CD Set)
Dust my broom / Please find my baby / Hawaiian boogie (take 1) / Hand in hand / Long tall woman / Rock my baby night / One more drink / My baby's gone / Lost woman blues / I believe / I held my baby last night / Baby what's wrong / Sinful woman / Round house boogie / Dumb woman blues / Saxony boogie / Kicking the blues around / I may be wrong, but I think you're wonderful / Sweet little woman / Early in the morning / Can't stop lovin' / Hawaiian boogie / Make a little love / My best friend (take 1) / Make my dreams come true / Strange kinda feeling (takes 1-6) / Dark and dreary (takes 1, 2 & 4) / Quarter past nine / Where can my baby be (takes 1, 8 & 9) / Please come back to me (sho'nuff I do) / Session talk and sho-'nuff I do / Sho'nuff I do (alternate take) / Sho'nuff I do / 1839 blues / I got a strange baby / Canton Mississippi breakdown / Standing at the crossroads / Late hours at midnight / Happy home / Sunnyland / Way you treat me / No love in my heart / Dust my blues / I was a fool / Blues before sunrise / Goodbye baby) / So mean to me (takes 2, 3 & 4) / Wild about you baby / Wild about you / Elmo's shuffle (takes 3, 4 & 5)
CD Set _____ ABOXCD 4
Ace / Oct '93 / Pinnacle / Cadillac / Complete/Pinnacle.

COME GO WITH ME
Baby, please set a date / So unkind / Sunnyland train / Twelve year old boy / My kind of woman / Hand in hand / My baby's gone / Make my dreams come true / Anna Lee / Bobby's rock / Find my kinda woman / Stranger blues / Mean mistreatin' mama / I can't stop loving you / She moved / I'm worried
CD _____ CDCHARLY 180
Charly / May '89 / Charly / THE / Cadillac.

DUST MY BROOM
Coming home / Dust my broom / Hand and hand / I believe / (I) done somebody wrong / It hurts me too / Pickin' the blues / Look on yonder wall / Mean mistreatin' mama / Rollin' and tumblin' / Standing at the crossroads / Sky is crying
CD _____ CDCD 1027
Charly / Mar '93 / Charly / THE / Cadillac.

ELMORE'S CONTRIBUTION TO THE BLUES (The Complete Chess/Chief/Fire Sessions/4CD Set)
I believe my time ain't long (Dust my broom) / Country boogie / I see my baby / She just won't do right / My best friend / Whose muddy shoes / Twelve year old boy / Coming home / It hurts me too / Knocking at your door / Elmore's contribution to jazz / Cry for me baby / Take me where you go / Bobby's rock / Sky is crying / Baby, please set a date / Held my baby last night / Dust my broom / Sun is shining / I can't hold out / Stormy Monday blues / Strange angels / Rollin' and tumblin' / (I) done somebody wrong / Something inside of me / I'm worried / Fine little mama / I need you / She done moved / I can't stop loving you / Early one morning / Stranger blues / Anna Lee / Standing at the crossroads / My bleeding heart / My kind of woman / Got to move / So unkind / Person to person / One way out / Go back home again / Look on yonder wall / Shake your moneymaker / Mean mistreatin' mama / Sunnyland train / You know you're wrong / My baby's gone / Find my kind of woman / Pickin' the blues / Every-day I have the blues / I've got a right to love my baby / She's got to go / I gotta go now / Talk to me baby / Mean mistreatin' mama / Hand in hand / Conversation (Back in Mississippi) / I can't stop lovin' my baby / Up jumped Elmore / I believe
CD Set _____ CDREDBOX 4
Chess/Charly / Nov '92 / Charly.

IMMORTAL ELMORE JAMES, THE (King Of The Bottleneck Blues)
Dust my broom / Everyday I have the blues / Sky is crying / I'm worried / Coming home / Stranger blues / Fine little mama / Make my dreams come true / Early one morning / It hurts me too / Mean mistreatin' mama / Shake your moneymaker / Can't stop loving my baby / My bleeding heart / Look on yonder wall / Hand in hand / (I) done somebody wrong / Rollin' and tumblin' / Standing at the crossroads / I can't stop lovin' you
CD _____ MCCD 083
Music Club / Apr '92 / Disc / THE / CM.

LET'S CUT IT
Dust my blues / Blues before sunrise / No love in my heart / Sho' nuff I do / Standing at the crossroads / I was a fool / Sunnyland / Canton Mississippi breakdown / Happy home / Wild about you baby / Long tall woman / So mean to me / Hawaiian boogie / Mean and evil / Dark and dreary / My best friend / I believe / Goodbye baby
CD _____ CDCH 192
Ace / Nov '93 / Pinnacle / Cadillac / Complete/Pinnacle.

SKY IS CRYING, THE (Charly Blues - Masterworks Volume 12)
Sky is crying / Bobby's rock (Instrumental) / Held my baby last night / Dust my broom / Baby please set a date / Rollin' and tum-

---

blin' / I'm worried / (I) done somebody wrong / Fine little mama / I can't stop lovin' you / Early one morning / I need you (baby) / Strange angels / She done moved (Instrumental) / Something inside of me / Stranger blues
CD _____ CDBM 12
Charly / Apr '92 / Charly / THE / Cadillac.

STANDING AT THE CROSSROADS (Charly BLues - Masterworks Vol. 28)
Anna Lee / Stranger blues / My bleeding heart / Standing at the crossroads / One way out / Person to person / No kind of woman / So unkind / Got to move / Shake your moneymaker / Mean mistreatin' mama (Takes 1-3) / Sunnyland train / My baby's gone / Find my kinda woman
CD _____ CDBM 28
Charly / Apr '92 / Charly / THE / Cadillac.

STREET TALKIN' (James, Elmore & Jimmy Reed)
CD _____ MCD 5087
Muse / Sep '92 / New Note / CM.

James, Ethan

WHAT ROUGH BEAST
CD _____ EFA 121112
Moll / Apr '95 / SRD.

James, Etta

AT LAST
Anything to say you're mine / My dearest darling / Trust in me / Sunday kind of love / Tough Mary / I just want to make love to you / At last / All I could do was cry / Stormy weather / Girl of my dreams
CD _____ CDCD 1053
Charly / Mar '93 / Charly / THE / Cadillac.

BLUES IN THE NIGHT (James, Etta & Eddie 'Cleanhead' Vinson)
Kidney stew / Railroad porter blues / Something's got a hold on me / Medley: at last / Trust in me / Sunday kind of love / I just want to make love to you / Please send me someone to love / Love man / Misty
CD _____ FCD 9647
Fantasy / Apr '94 / Pinnacle / Jazz Music / Wellard / Cadillac.

GOSPEL SOUL OF ETTA JAMES
CD _____ KWEST 5403
Disky / Sep '93 / THE / BMG / Discovery / Pinnacle.

LATE SHOW, THE (James, Etta & Eddie 'Cleanhead' Vinson)
Cleanhead blues / Old maid boogie / Home boy / Cherry red / Baby, what you gonna do / So / Sweet little angel / I'd rather go blind / Teach me tonight / Only women bleed / He's got the whole world in his hands
CD _____ FCD 9655-2
Fantasy / Apr '94 / Pinnacle / Jazz Music / Wellard / Cadillac.

LEGENDARY HITS
CD _____ 90152-2
Jazz Archives / Oct '92 / Jazz Music / Discovery / Cadillac.

LIVE FROM SAN FRANCISCO
CD _____ 1005821252
Private Music / Feb '95 / BMG.

MULTI-CULTURAL CHILDREN'S SONGS
CD _____ SFWCD 45045
Smithsonian Folkways / Nov '95 / ADA / Direct / Koch / CM / Cadillac.

MYSTERY LADY
Don't explain / You've changed / Man I love / Embraceable you / How deep is the ocean / (I'm afraid) The masquerade is over / Body and soul / Very thought of you / Lover man / I'll be seeing you
CD _____ 1005 82114-2
Private Music / Apr '94 / BMG.

R & B DYNAMITE
W.O.M.A.N. / Number one / I'm a fool / Strange things happening / Hey Henry / I hope you're satisfied / Good rockin' daddy / Sunshine of love / That's all / How big a fool / Market place / Tough lover / Do something crazy / Be my lovey dovey / Nobody loves you (like me) / Hickory dickory dock / You know what I mean / Wallflower / Baby, baby, every night / We're in love / Tears of joy (Not on LP) / Pick-up (Not on LP)
CD _____ CDCH 210
Ace / Nov '93 / Pinnacle / Cadillac / Complete/Pinnacle.

RIGHT TIME, THE
I sing the blues / Love and happiness / Evening of love / Wet match / You're taking up another man's place / Give it up / Let it rock / ninety nine and a half (won't do) / You've got me / (Night time) Is the right time / Down home blues
CD _____ 7559613472
WEA / Apr '92 / Warner Music.

SOMETHING'S GOT A HOLD
CD _____ CDRB 3
Charly / Apr '94 / Charly / THE / Cadillac.

SOULFUL MISS PEACHES
Tell Mama / I'd rather go blind / Security / I'm loving you more everyday / Mellow fellow / In the basement (pt 1/Duet with Sugar Pie Desanto) / Love of my man / Same rope

/ I'm gonna take what he's got / Just a little bit / Steal away / I'm waiting for Charlie to come home / You got it / Almost persuaded / I got you babe / Losers weepers / All the way down / Let's burn down the cornfield / Feelin' uneasy / Out on the street again
CD _____ CPCD 8017
Charly / Feb '94 / Charly / THE / Cadillac.

STICKIN' TO MY GUNS
Whatever gets you through the night / Love to burn / Blues don't care / Your good thing is about to end / Get funky / Beware / Out of the rain / Stolen affection / Fool in love / I've got dreams to remember
CD _____ IMCD 191
Island / Jul '94 / PolyGram.

TELL MAMA
If I can't have you / Spoonful / Nobody but you / Next door to the blues / Something's got a hold on me / (You better) do right / I'm loving you more everyday / Breaking point / Mellow fellow / Steal away / Just a little bit / Don't lose your good thing / Watchdog / I'm gonna take what he's got / I'd rather go blind / Love of my man / It hurts me so much / Same rope / I got you babe / I worship the ground you walk on / You got it / Fire / Miss Pitiful
CD _____ CDRED 7
Charly / Oct '88 / Charly / THE / Cadillac.

James Gang

ALL THE BEST (Walsh, Joe & The James Gang)
Rocky mountain way / Turn to stone / Time out / Meadows / Bookends / Help me through the night / Welcome to the club / Walk away / Yadig / Funk No.49 / Ashes the rain and I / Take a look around
CD _____ PWKS 4207
Carlton Home Entertainment / May '94 / Carlton Home Entertainment.

JAMES GANG RIDES AGAIN
CD _____ BGOCD 121
Beat Goes On / Sep '91 / Pinnacle.

LIVE IN CONCERT
CD _____ BGOCD 120
Beat Goes On / Sep '91 / Pinnacle.

THIRDS
CD _____ BGOCD 119
Beat Goes On / Sep '91 / Pinnacle.

TRUE STORY OF THE JAMES GANG ...PLUS
Take a look around / Bluebird / Collage / Wrap city in English / Yadig / Woman / Ashes the rain and I / It's all the same / Things I could be / Live my life again / I'll tell you why / Run run run / Midnight man / My door is open / Everybody needs a hero / Up to yourself / Funk 49
CD _____ SEECD 367
See For Miles/C5 / Feb '93 / Pinnacle.

YER ALBUM
Take a look around / Bluebird / Stone rap / I don't have the time / Fred / Funk / Lost woman / Collage / Wrapcity in English / I Stop
CD _____ BGOCD 60
Beat Goes On / Oct '90 / Pinnacle.

James, Harry

1944-THE D-DAY REMOTES (James, Harry Orchestra)
CD _____ JH 1023
Ronnie Scott's Jazz House / Feb '93 / Jazz Music / Magnum Music Group / Cadillac.

1946-55 (James, Harry Orchestra)
CD _____ CD 53185
Giants Of Jazz / Jan '95 / Target/BMG / Cadillac.

1948 - BROADCASTS (James, Harry Orchestra)
CD _____ JH 1007
Jazz Hour / Oct '91 / Target/BMG / Jazz Music / Cadillac.

1954-1966 (James, Harry Orchestra)
CD _____ CD 53191
Giants Of Jazz / Jan '95 / Target/BMG / Cadillac.

1964 LIVE IN THE HOLIDAY BALLROOM (James, Harry Orchestra)
Ciribiribin / Cubana chant / In a mellow tone / Sultry serenade / I'm getting sentimental over you / Koo koo / Flyin' home / Two o'clock jump / Drum solo by Buddy Rich / Malaguana Saleroso / Blues inside out / Sunday morning / He's gone now / Tuxedo junction / King Porter stomp / Big time / Rainbow kiss
CD _____ JH 1001
Jazz Hour / Apr '90 / Target/BMG / Jazz Music / Cadillac.

ALL OR NOTHING AT ALL (James, Harry & Frank Sinatra)
Ciribiribin / My buddy / Avalon / All or nothing at all / Mean to me / Melancholy mood / I found a new baby / From the bottom of my heart / Sweet Georgia Brown / To you / I poured my heart into a song / Japanese sandman / Here comes the night / Undecided / On a little street in Singapore / Let's disappear / I'm forever blowing bubbles

---

CD _____ HCD 263
Hindsight / Nov '95 / Target/BMG / Jazz Music.

ALL TIME STANDARDS 1938-1954 (James, Harry Orchestra)
CD _____ 11082
Laserlight / '88 / Target/BMG.

BANDSTAND MEMORIES (James, Harry Orchestra)
CD Set _____ HBCD 503
Hindsight / Nov '94 / Target/BMG / Jazz Music.

BEST OF HARRY JAMES
CD _____ DLCD 4002
Dixie Live / Mar '95 / Magnum Music Group.

BEST OF THE BIG BANDS
I've heard that song before / Man with the horn / I had the craziest dream / Sleepy lagoon / I can't begin to tell you / Trumpet blues and cantabile / You made me love you / It's been a long, long time / Ciribiribin / I'll get by (as long as I have you) / I don't want to walk without you / Carnival / Devil sat down and cried / Music makers / I'm beginning to see the light
CD _____ 4669552
CBS / Sep '90 / Sony.

HARRY JAMES
CD _____ 22711
Music / Nov '95 / Target/BMG.

HARRY JAMES & HIS GREAT VOCALISTS
I'll get by / I don't want to walk without you / It's the dreamer in me / One dozen roses / My silent love / I had the craziest dream / I've heard that song before / I'm beginning to see the light / It's been a long, long time / I can't begin to tell you / Who's sorry now / This is always / As long as I'm dreaming / You can do no wrong / What am I gonna do about you / You'll never know
CD _____ CK 66371
Columbia / Jul '95 / Sony.

JUMP SAUCE (James, Harry & His Music Makers)
CD _____ VNG 201
Viper's Nest / Jul '94 / Direct / Cadillac / ADA.

LIVE IN CONCERT (James, Harry & His Music Makers)
Opener / King size blues / Shiny stockings / Harry's delight / Two o'clock jump / Jumpin' at the woodside / One on the house / Rockin' in rhythm / Don't get around much anymore / Tweet tweet
CD _____ DBCD 03
Dance Band Days / Jul '89 / Prism.

LIVE IN LONDON
Don't be that way / Moonglow / Opus #1 / That's all / Charade / HJ blues / Apples / Two o'clock jump / Hits medley
CD _____ JASMCD 2533
Jasmine / Feb '95 / Wellard / Swift / Conifer / Cadillac / Magnum Music Group.

MISTER TRUMPET (James, Harry & His Band)
CD _____ HCD 702
Hindsight / Jul '94 / Target/BMG / Jazz Music.

RARE 1940 VARSITY TITLES (James, Harry & Dick Haymes)
CD _____ FLYCD 943
Flyright / Jun '95 / Hot Shot / Wellard / Jazz Music / CM.

RAZZLE DAZZLE
Carnival of Venice / (Back home again in) Indiana / I've heard that song before / Texas chatter / Eli-Eli / Trumpet blues and cantabile / Song of the wanderer / Back beat boogie / Duke's mixture / Record session / Concerto for trumpet / Flight of the bumble bee / Cherry / Trumpet rhapsody / Little bit of heaven / Let me up / I cried for you / Flat bush Flanagan / Sleepy time gal / memphis blues
CD _____ PASTCD 7044
Flapper / May '94 / Pinnacle.

STOMPIN' AT THE SAVOY (James, Harry Orchestra)
CD _____ 15771
Laserlight / Jul '92 / Target/BMG.

UNFORGETTABLE, THE
CD _____ ENTCD 227
Entertainers / Nov '87 / Target/BMG.

YES INDEED
All or nothing at all / Back beat boogie / Boo-woo / Ciribiribin / Everybody's laughing / Flash / I found a new baby / I had the craziest dream / Jubilee / Just a mood / Life goes to a party / Night special / Nobody knows the trouble I've seen / One o'clock jump / Out of nowhere / Shoe shiner's drag / Spreadin' knowledge around / Sugarfoot stomp / Two o'clock jump / Woo woo / Wrappin' it up / Yes indeed / You made me love you / Zoom, zoom, zoom
CD _____ CDAJA 5120
Living Era / Nov '93 / Koch.

James, Hilary

BURNING SUN (James, Hilary & Simon Mayor)
CD _____ CDACS 016
Acoustics / Aug '93 / Conifer / Direct / ADA.

CHILDREN'S FAVOURITES - MUSICAL MYSTERY TOUR (James, Hilary & Simon Mayor)
Snowman's song / Magpie sitting on a broken chair / Parrot song / Chico the bandit / My bike / Big surprise / Slippery slimy trout / Road to Banbury / Trumpet hornpipe / Fireman's song / Fat fat farmer / Farmyard tango / Gobble gobble gobble gobble gobble / King Wastelot and the Right Royal rubbish dump / Australian Santa Claus / Sally Ann Johnson / Up in a big balloon
CD _____ CDACS 002
Acoustics / Aug '93 / Conifer / Direct / ADA.

James, Jan

COLOR OF THE ROSE
CD _____ PRD 70862
Provogue / Jan '96 / Pinnacle.

LAST TRAIN
CD _____ PRD 70702
Provogue / Feb '95 / Pinnacle.

James, John

SKY IN MY PIE HEAD
CD _____ ESMCD 358
Essential / Jan '96 / Total/BMG.

James, Joni

LET THERE BE LOVE
Let there be love / You're my everything / You're fooling someone / Am I in love / My love, my love / Purple shades / Almost always / I'll be seeing you / When we come of age / These foolish things / It's talk of the town / Too late now / In love in vain / That old feeling / I'm through with love / Little girl blue
CD _____ JASCD 316
Jasmine / Jan '95 / Wellard / Swift / Conifer / Cadillac / Magnum Music Group.

James, Laurence

THEATRE ORGAN, THE (Wurlitzer and Compton Theatre Organs) (James, Laurence & Ronald Curtis)
Whispering / Lullaby of the leaves / Alone / Five foot two, eyes of blue / Autumn concerto / Lover / Only make believe/Who do I love you / Caribbean honeymoon / Nightingale sang in Berkeley Square / Only a rose / Top hot, white tie and tails / Funiculi, funicula / What a perfect combination / Over the rainbow / Falling in love with love / Bye bye blues / I know that you know / It's the talk of the town / Goody goody / Kiss in the dark / Lazy river / I know why / Tuxedo junction / I won't dance / All the things you are / Alley cat / Walkin' my baby back home / After you've gone
CD _____ CDSDL 392
Saydisc / Aug '91 / Harmonia Mundi / ADA / Direct.

James, Paul

ACOUSTIC BLUES
CD _____ SP 1133CD
Stony Plain / Oct '93 / ADA / CM / Direct.

ROCKIN' THE BLUES
CD _____ SP 1135CD
Stony Plain / Oct '93 / ADA / CM / Direct.

James, Rick

GREATEST HITS: RICK JAMES
Super freak / You turn me on / You and I / Mary Jane / Ebony eyes / Give it to me baby / Dance wit' me / Cold blooded / Seventeen
CD _____ 5300982
Motown / Jul '93 / PolyGram.

STREET SONGS
Give it to me baby / Ghetto life / Make love to me / Mr. Policeman / Super freak / Fire and desire / Call me up / Below the funk
CD _____ 5302182
Motown / Sep '93 / PolyGram.

James, Sian

CYSGODION KARMA
Dacw 'nghariad / Marchnad Llangollen / Mynwent eglwys / Ffarwel i ddociau Ierpwl / Hiraeth am feirion / Gosip swnt / Camu nol (wrth gamu 'mlaen) / Merch ifanc o'r ben bore / Sgerbwd ar y bryn / Fy ngeneth fach / Mae'r rhod yn troi / Ev chistr 'ta laou
CD _____ SAIN 4037CD
Sain / Aug '94 / Direct / ADA.

DISTAW
CD _____ SAIN 2025CD
Sain / Aug '94 / Direct / ADA.

James, Skip

COMPLETE 1931 RECORDINGS
CD _____ DOCD 5005

Blues Document / Feb '92 / Swift / Jazz Music / Hot Shot.

COMPLETE EARLY RECORDINGS, THE
CD _____ YAZCD 2009
Yazoo / Oct '94 / CM / ADA / Roots / Koch.

GREATEST OF THE DELTA BLUES SINGERS
CD _____ BCD 122
Biograph / '92 / Wellard / ADA / Hot Shot / Jazz Music / Cadillac / Direct.

SHE LYIN'
CD _____ EDCD 379
Edsel / Nov '93 / Pinnacle / ADA.

TODAY
CD _____ VND 79219
Vanguard / Jan '95 / Complete/Pinnacle / Discovery.

James, Steve

AMERICAN PRIMITIVE
CD _____ ANT 0030CD
Antones / Jul '94 / Hot Shot / Direct / ADA.

TWO TRACK MIND
CD _____ ANTCD 0024
Antones / May '94 / Hot Shot / Direct / ADA.

James, Tommy

CRIMSON & CLOVER/CELLOPHANE SYMPHONY (James, Tommy & The Shondells)
Crimson and clover / Kathleen McArthur / I am a tangerine / Do something for me / Crystal blue persuasion / Sugar on Sunday / Breakaway / Smoky roads / I'm alive / Crimson and clover (Reprise) / Cellophane symphony / Makin' good time / Evergreen / Sweet cherry wine / Papa rolled his own / Changes / Loved one / I know who I am / Love of a woman / On behalf of the entire staff and management
CD _____ NEMCD 647
Sequel / Nov '93 / BMG.

HANKY PANKY/MONY MONY (James, Tommy & The Shondells)
Hanky panky / I'll go crazy / I'm so proud / Lover / Love makes the world go round / Good lovin' / Say I am / Cleo's mood / Don't throw our love away / Shake a tail feather / Soul searchin' baby / Lots of pretty girls / Mony mony / Do unto me / (I'm) Taken / Nightime (I'm a lover) / Run away with me / Somebody cares / Get out now / I can't go back to Denver / Some kind of love / Gingerbread man / 1-2-3 And I fell
CD _____ NEMCD 646
Sequel / Nov '93 / BMG.

Jamieson, Ronnie

AALD NOOST
CD _____ AT 040CD
Attic / Jul '95 / CM / ADA.

Jamiroquai

EMERGENCY ON PLANET EARTH
When you gonna learn / Too young to die / Hooked up / If I like it, I do it / Music of the mind / Emergency on planet Earth / Whatever it is I just can't stop / Blow your mind / Revolution 1993 / Didgin' out
CD _____ 474069 2
Sony Soho2 / Jun '93 / Sony.

RETURN OF THE SPACE COWBOY
Just another story / Stillness in time / Half the man / Light years / Manifest destiny / Kids / Mr. Moon / Scam / Journey to Arnhemland / Morning glory / Space cowboy
CD _____ 477813-2
Sony Soho2 / Oct '94 / Sony.

Jamison, Mac

HOW CAN I EXPLAIN
CD _____ HBC 1218DAAD
Heartbeat City / Aug '94 / Jetstar.

Jams

BASTARDMUSIK
CD _____ TUT 72156
Wundertute / Jan '94 / CM / Duncans / ADA.

Jan & Dean

BEST OF JAN AND DEAN
CD _____ MATCD 329
Castle / Feb '95 / BMG.

DEAD MAN'S CURVE/NEW GIRL IN SCHOOL, THE
Dead man's curve / Three window coupe / Bucket T / Rockin' little roadster / B gas rickshaw / Mighty GTO / New girl in school / Linda / Barons west LA / School days / It's as easy as 1,2,3 / Hey little freshman
CD _____ C5CD-550
See For Miles/C5 / Jun '93 / Pinnacle.

JAN & DEAN STORY, THE
CD _____ RNCD 1010
Rhino / Jun '93 / Jetstar / Magnum Music Group / THE.

LITTLE OLD LADY FORM PASADENA, THE

Little old lady from Pasadena / Memphis / When it's over / Horace the swingin' school bus driver / Old ladies seldom power shift / Sidewalk surfin' / Anaheim, Azusa and Cucamonga sewing circle / Summer means fun / It's as easy as 1 2 3 / Move over little mustang / Skateboarding / One piece top-less bathing suit
CD _____ C5CD 574
See For Miles/C5 / Oct '91 / Pinnacle.

SURF CITY

Surf City / Detroit city / Tallahassee Lassie / Manhattan / I left my heart in San Francisco / Kansas City / Memphis / Soul City / Way down yonder in New Orleans / Philadelphia Pa / Honolulu Lulu / You came a long way from St. Louis
CD _____ C5CD 585
See For Miles/C5 / Apr '92 / Pinnacle.

TAKE LINDA SURFIN'

Linda / Surfin' / Rhythm of the rain / Walk right in / Gypsy cried / When I learn to cry / Walk like a man / Let's turkey trot / Mr. Bass Man / Best friend I ever had / My foolish heart / Surfin' Safari
CD _____ C5CD 584
See For Miles/C5 / Apr '92 / Pinnacle.

Jan, Anne-Marie

PARALLELES

CD _____ KMRSCD 214
Keltia Musique / Dec '94 / ADA / Direct / Discovery.

Jane Pow

LOVE IT, BE IT

Sanitized / It's on its way / Walker / Get by / Sand barrier / Shutdown / 90's / Love it, be it / Track 9 / Playpower / Morningside / Out of it / On hold / Through / Latitude / Take / Jack Boot / Warm room / Bophia Green / Fruity
CD _____ SLUM 025
Slumberland / Jul '93 / Vital.

Jane's Addiction

JANE'S ADDICTION

Trip away / Rock 'n' roll / I would for you / Jane says / Pigs in zen / My time / Whores / Sympathy / Chip away / 1%
CD _____ 7599265992
WEA / Apr '91 / Warner Music.

NOTHING'S SHOCKING

Up the beach / Had a dad / Standing in the shower / Jane Says / Thank you boys / Mountain song / Summertime rolls / Ted, just admit it / Ocean size / Idiots rule / Pigs in Zen
CD _____ K925727-2
WEA / Mar '94 / Warner Music.

RITUAL DE LO HABITUAL

Stop / No one's leaving / Ain't no right / Obvious / Been caught stealing / Three days / Then she did / Of course / Classic girl
CD _____ 7599259932
WEA / Feb '95 / Warner Music.

Jang, Jon

SELF DEFENSE (Jang, Jon & the Pan-Asian Arkestra)

CD _____ 121203-2
Soul Note / Nov '92 / Harmonia Mundi / Wellard / Cadillac.

TIANANMEN (Jang, Jon & the Pan-Asian Arkestra)

CD _____ 121223-2
Soul Note / Nov '92 / Harmonia Mundi / Wellard / Cadillac.

Janis, Conrad

CONRAD JANIS AND HIS TAILGATE JAZZ BAND

CD _____ BCD 71
GHB / Jun '95 / Jazz Music.

Janitor Joe

LUCKY

CD _____ ARRCD 52326
Amphetamine Reptile / May '94 / SRD.

Jankowski, Horst

BEST OF MR. BLACK FOREST

CD _____ ISCD 108
Intersound / Jun '95 / Jazz Music.

PIANO INTERLUDE

CD _____ ISCD 147
Intersound / Jun '95 / Jazz Music.

Jannah, Denise

TAKE IT FROM THE TOP

Pennies from Heaven / Willow weep for me / Fragile / I've got the world on a string / I'm in a minor key today / I get along without you very well / Groovin' high / I'm a fool to want you / Sleepin' bee / My funny valentine
CD _____ CDSJP 308
Timeless Jazz / Jan '92 / New Note.

Jansch, Bert

BBC LIVE IN CONCERT

CD _____ WINCD 039
Windsong / Aug '93 / Pinnacle.

BERT JANSCH/JACK ORION

Smoky river / Oh how your love is so strong / I have no time / Finches / Rambling's gonna be the death / Strolling down the highway / Veronica / Needle of death / Do you hear me now / Alice's wonderland / Running from home / Courting blues / Casbah / Ve-ronica / Nottamun town / Go your way my love / Love is teasin' / I had no time / Ring-a-ding bird / I am lonely
CD _____ TDEM 14
Trandem / Apr '94 / CM / ADA / Pinnacle.

COLLECTION, THE

CD _____ CCSCD 430
Castle / Mar '95 / BMG.

ESSENTIAL COLLECTION #1, THE (Strolling Down The Highway)

Strolling down the highway / Running run-ning from home / Oh how your love is strong / Needle of death / Tinker's blues / Courting blues / As the day grows longer now / Wheel / It don't bother me / Gardener / 900 miles / In this game / Casbah / Ve-ronica / Nottamun town / Go your way my love / Love is teasin' / I had no time / Ring-a-ding bird / I am lonely
CD _____ TRACD 604
Transatlantic / Jul '87 / BMG / Pinnacle / ADA.

ESSENTIAL COLLECTION #2, THE (Black Water Side)

Angie / My lover / Want my daddy now / First time ever I saw your face / Come back baby / Weeping willow blues / Little sweet sunshine / Blackwater side / Dissatisfied blues / Henry Martin / Woman like you / Miss Heather Rosemary Sewell / Birthday blues / Wishing well / Reynardine / Rose-mary lane / Alman / Wayward child / No-body's bar / Peregrinations / Bird song
CD _____ TRACD 607
Transatlantic / Sep '87 / BMG / Pinnacle / ADA.

FROM THE OUTSIDE

CD _____ HYCD 200128
Hypertension / Mar '95 / Total/BMG / Direct / ADA.

GARDENER/ESSENTIAL BERT JANSCH 1965-71

CD _____ TDEM 09
Trandem / Mar '94 / CM / ADA / Pinnacle.

HEARTBREAK

Is it real / Up to the stars / Give me the time / If I were a carpenter / Wild mountain thyme / Heartbreak hotel / Sit down beside me / No rhyme, no reason / Blackwater side / And not a word was said
CD _____ HNCD 1312
Hannibal / Jul '93 / Vital / ADA.

IT DON'T BOTHER ME

CD _____ TDEM 16
Trandem / Apr '94 / CM / ADA / Pinnacle.

LEATHER LAUNDERETTE (Jansch, Bert & Rod Clements)

Strolling down the highway / Sweet Rose / Brafferton / Ain't no more cane / Why me / Sundown station / Knight's move / Browns-ville / Bogie's bonnie belle / Leather laun-derette / Been on the road so long
CD _____ CROCD 218
Black Crow / Mar '88 / Roots / Jazz Music / CM.

MOONSHINE

Yarrow / Brought with the rain / January man / Night time blues / Moonshine / First time ever I saw your face / Ramble away / Twa corbies / Oh my Father
CD _____ BJ 001CD
Jansch / Jul '95 / ADA.

NICOLA/BIRTHDAY BLUES

CD _____ TDEM 17
Demon / Apr '94 / Pinnacle / ADA.

ROSEMARY LANE

Tell me what is true love / Rosemary Lane / M'lady Nancy / Dream, a dream, a dream / Alman / Waychild child / Nobody's bar / Reynardine / Silly woman / Peregrinations / Slyvie / Sarabande / Bird song
CD _____ TACD 900784
Line / Sep '94 / CM / Grapevine / ADA / Conifer / Direct.

SKETCHES

CD _____ COMD 2035
Temple / Feb '94 / CM / Duncans / ADA / Direct.

THREE CHORD TRICK

Fresh as Sunday morning / Chambertin / For Jo / Needle of death / Cluck old hen / Love alone / Lost and gone / Blues run the game / When the teardrops fall / Kingfisher / Daybreak / Doctor doctor / Cur-ragh of Kildare / Looking for a home / Poor mouth / In the bleak midwinter
CD _____ CDVM 9024
Virgin / Jul '93 / EMI.

WHEN THE CIRCUS COMES TO TOWN

Walk quietly by / Open road / Back home / On one around / Step around / Step back / When the circus comes to town / Summer heat / Just a dream / Lady doctor from Ash-ington / Steal the night away / Honey don't you understand / Born with the blues / Morning brings peace of mind / Living in the shadows
CD _____ COOKCD 092
Cooking Vinyl / Aug '95 / Vital.

Jansen, Steve

BEGINNING TO END REMIXES (Jansen, Steve & Richard Barbieri/Mick Karn)

Medium / Aug '94 / Vital.
CD _____ MPCD 002

BEGINNING TO MELT (Medium Series Vol. 1) (Jansen, Steve & Richard Barbieri/Mick Karn)

Beginning to melt / Wilderness / March of the innocents / Human agie / Shipwrecks / Ego dance / Orange asylum
CD _____ MPCD 001
Medium / Mar '94 / Vital.

SEED (Jansen, Steve & Richard Barbieri/Mick Karn)

Beginning to melt / In the black of desire / Insect tribe / Prey
CD _____ MPCD 002
Medium / Oct '94 / Vital.

STONE TO FLESH (Jansen, Steve & Richard Barbieri)

Mother London / Sleeper's awake / Ringing the bell backwards (pt 1 & 2) / Everything ends in darkness / Closer than I / Swim there
CD _____ MPCD 003
Medium / Sep '94 / Vital.

STORIES ACROSS BORDERS (Jansen, Steve & Richard Barbieri)

Long tales, tall shadows / When things dream / Lumen / Insomniac's bed / Night gives birth / Celebration / Nocturnal night-seeing / One more zombie
CD _____ CDVE 908
Virgin / Jul '94 / EMI.

Janson, Claes

ALL OF ME

CD _____ SITCD 9209
Sittel / Mar '94 / Cadillac / Jazz Music.

Janssen, Gus

CLAVECIMBEL

CD _____ GEESTCD 12
Geest Gronden / Aug '87 / Cadillac.

PIANO/KLANKKAST

CD _____ GEESTCD 09
Geest Gronden / Mar '89 / Cadillac.

POK

CD _____ GEESTCD 08
Geest Gronden / Oct '89 / Cadillac.

Jansson, Lars

SADHANA

CD _____ 1264
Caprice / Oct '92 / CM / Complete/ Pinnacle / Cadillac / ADA.

Jansson, Lena

EVERYTHING I LOVE

CD _____ SITCD 9206
Sittel / Jun '94 / Cadillac / Jazz Music.

LENA JANSSON & NILS LINDBERG BIG BAND 1983/1986 (Jansson, Lena & Nils Lindberg)

CD _____ ABCD 3005
Bluebell / Feb '95 / Cadillac / Jazz Music.

Japan

EXORCISING GHOSTS

Methods of dance / Swing / Gentlemen take polaroids / Quiet life / Foreign place / Night porter / My new career / Other side of life / Visions of China / Sons of pioneers / Talking drum / Art of parties / Taking islands in Af-rica / Voices raised in welcome, hands held in prayer / Life without buildings / Ghosts
CD _____ VGDCD 3510
Virgin / Jan '85 / EMI.

GENTLEMEN TAKE POLAROIDS

Gentlemen take polaroids / Swing / Burning bridges / My new career / Methods of dance / Ain't that peculiar / Nightporter / Taking islands in Africa
CD _____ CDV 2180
Virgin / Jun '88 / EMI.

GENTLEMEN TAKE POLAROIDS/TIN DRUM/OIL ON CANVAS (3CD Set)

CD Set _____ TPAK 6
Virgin / Oct '90 / EMI.

OIL ON CANVAS

Sons of pioneers / Cantonese boy / Visions of China / Ghosts / Voices raised in wel-come, hands held in prayer / Nightporter / Still life in mobile homes / Methods of dance / Quiet life / Art of parties / Temple of dawn / Oil on canvas / Gentlemen take polaroids / Canton

CD _____ CDVD 2513
Virgin / Apr '92 / EMI.

SOUVENIR FROM JAPAN, A

I second that emotion / Life in Tokyo / De-viation / Surburban Berlin / Adolescent sex / European son / All tomorrow's parties / Communist China / State line / Rhodesia / Obscure alternatives / Quiet life
CD _____ 260360
Arista / Dec '89 / BMG.

TIN DRUM

Visions of China / Art of parties / Talking drum / Cantonese boy / Canton / Ghosts / Still life in mobile homes / Sons of pioneers
CD _____ CDV 2209
Virgin / Jun '88 / EMI.

Jara, Victor

15 YEARS OF TRADITIONAL PORTUGUESE MUSIC

CD _____ PS 65111
Playasound / Nov '93 / Harmonia Mundi / ADA.

CANTO LIBRE VOL.2

CD _____ MCD 71799
Monitor / Jun '93 / CM.

VIENTOS DEL PUEBLO

CD _____ MCD 71778
Monitor / Jun '93 / CM.

Jarboe

SACRIFICIAL CAKE

Lavender girl / Ode to V / Shimmer 1 / My buried child / Nnt lingual / Spiral staircase / Yum yab / Surgical saviour / Cache toi / Tragic seed / Troll lullaby / Deflowered / Body lover / Shimmer 2 / Act 3 / Troll
CD _____ YGCD 008
Young God / Jun '95 / Vital.

Jarman, Joseph

AS IF IT WERE THE SEASON

CD _____ DD 417
Delmark / Oct '82 / Hot Shot / ADA / CM / Direct / Cadillac.

SONG FOR JOSEPH JARMAN

CD _____ DD 410
Delmark / Jan '89 / Hot Shot / ADA / CM / Direct / Cadillac.

Jarocha, Alma

SONES JAROCHOS (Music Of Mexico Vol. 1) (Jarocha, Conjunto Alma)

CD _____ ARHCD 354
Arhoolie / Apr '95 / ADA / Direct / Cadillac.

Jarre, Jean Michel

CHRONOLOGIE

CD _____ 519 373-2
Polydor / Jan '82 / PolyGram.

CONCERTS IN CHINA

Overture / Arpegiator / Equinoxe part 4 / Fishing junks at sunset / Band in the rain / Equinoxe part 7 / Orient Express / Magnetic fields III / Magnetic fields IV / Laser harp / Night in Shanghai / Last rumba / Magnetic fields II / Souvenir of China
CD Set _____ 811 551-2
Polydor / '83 / PolyGram.

EQUINOXE

Equinoxe part 1 / Equinoxe part 2 / Equi-noxe part 3 / Equinoxe part 4 / Equinoxe part 5 / Equinoxe part 6 / Equinoxe part 7 / Equinoxe part 8
CD _____ 8000252
Polydor / '83 / PolyGram.

IMAGES (The Best Of Jean Michel Jarre)

Oxygene 4 / Equinoxe part 5 / Magnetic fields II / Oxygene 2 / Computer week-end / Equinoxe part 4 / Band in the rain / Ren-dezvous #2 / London kid / Ethnicolor 1 / Orient express / Calypso 1 / Calypso 3 (fin de siecle) / Rendezvous #4 / Moon machine / Eldorado / Globetrotter
CD _____ 5113062
Polydor / Nov '91 / PolyGram.

IN CONCERT LYON/HOUSTON

Oxygene V / Ethnicolour / Magnetic fields I / Souvenir (Of China) / Equinoxe part 5 / Rendezvous #3 / Rendezvous #2 / Ron's place / Rendezvous #4
CD _____ 8331702
Polydor / Jul '87 / PolyGram.

JEAN MICHEL JARRE 10TH ANNIVERSARY SET (8CD Set)

CD Set _____ 8337372
Polydor / Dec '87 / PolyGram.

LIVE: JEAN-MICHEL JARRE

CD _____ 841 258-2
Polydor / Oct '89 / PolyGram.

MAGNETIC FIELDS

Parts 1-5 / Last rumba
CD _____ 800 024-2
Polydor / Dec '81 / PolyGram.

OXYGENE

Oxygene part 1 / Oxygene part 2 / Oxygene part 3 / Oxygene part 4 / Oxygene part 5 / Oxygene part 6

CD _____ 8000152
Polydor / '83 / PolyGram.

RENDEZVOUS
First Rendez-vous / Second rendezvous part 1 / Second rendez-vous part 2 / Second rendezvous part 3 / Third Rendez-vous / Fourth Rendez-vous / Fifth Rendez-vous part 1 / Fifth Rendez-vous part 2 / Fifth Rendez-vous part 3 / Last Rendez-vous / Ron's piece
CD _____ 829 125-2
Polydor / Aug '86 / PolyGram.

REVOLUTIONS
CD _____ 837 098-2
Polydor / Sep '88 / PolyGram.

WAITING FOR COUSTEAU
CD _____ 843 614-2
Polydor / Jun '90 / PolyGram.

ZOOLOOK
Ethnicolour / Diva / Zoolook / Wooloomoo-loo / Zoolookologie / Blah-blah
CD _____ 823 763-2
Polydor / Nov '84 / PolyGram.

Jarreau, Al

AIN'T NO SUNSHINE (A Salute To Bill Withers)
Ain't no sunshine / Lean on me / Use me / Kissing my love / Grandma's hands / You / Lonely town / Lonely street / Same love that made me laugh
CD _____ CDBM 011
Blue Moon / Jun '88 / Magnum Music Group / Greensleeves / Hot Shot / ADA / Cadillac / Discovery.
CD _____ CDCD 1196
Charly / Sep '94 / Charly / THE / Cadillac.

HEAVEN AND EARTH
What you do to me / It's not hard to love you / Blue angel / Heaven and earth / Superfine love / Whenever I hear your name / Love of my life / If I break / Blue in green (tapestry) (parts 1 & 2)
CD _____ 9031774662
Warner Bros. / Jul '92 / Warner Music.

HERE I AM BABY
CD _____ 32512
Scratch / Mar '95 / BMG.

LIVING FOR YOU
Living for you / Call me / Here I am / Let's get married / Let's stay together / You ought to be with me / Love and happiness / Tired of being alone / Look what you done for me / Still in love with you
CD _____ CDBM 107
Blue Moon / Oct '95 / Magnum Music Group / Greensleeves / Hot Shot / ADA / Cadillac / Discovery.

MASQUERADE IS OVER, THE
My favourite things / Stockholm sweetnin' / Sleeping babe / (I'm afraid) the masquerade is over / Sophisticated lady / Joey / Come rain or come shine / One note samba
CD _____ CDBM 079
Blue Moon / Nov '89 / Magnum Music Group / Greensleeves / Hot Shot / ADA / Cadillac / Discovery.

SPOTLIGHT ON AL JARREAU
Ain't no sunshine / Kissing my love / You / Same love that made me laugh / Rainbow in your eyes / Grandma's hands / Lonely town, lonely street / Lean on me / One good turn / We got by / Use me (till you use me up) / Loving you / Letter perfect
CD _____ HADCD 115
Javelin / Feb '94 / THE / Henry Hadaway Organisation.

TENDERNESS
Mas que nada / Try a little tenderness / Your song / My favorite things / She's leaving home / Summertime / We got by / Save your love for me / You don't see me / Wait for the magic / Dinosaur / Go away little girl
CD _____ 450993778-2
Warner Bros. / Jun '94 / Warner Music.

Jarrett, Keith

ARBOUR ZENA
Dunes / Solara march / Mirrors
CD _____ 8255922
ECM / Aug '85 / New Note.

AT THE DEER HEAD INN
Solar / Basin Street blues / Chandra / You don't know what love is / You and the night and the music / Bye bye blackbird / It's easy to remember
CD _____ 5177202
ECM / May '94 / New Note.

BELONGING
Spiral dance / Blossom / Long as you know you're living yours / Belonging / Windup / Solstice
CD _____ 8291152
ECM / Jun '86 / New Note.

BOOK OF WAYS (Solo Clavichord/2CD Set)
CD Set _____ 8313962
ECM / Oct '87 / New Note.

BRIDGE OF LIGHT
Elegy / Adagio / Celebration / Song / Dance / Birth / Bridge of light

CD _____ 4453502
ECM / May '94 / New Note.

BYE BYE BLACKBIRD (Jarrett, Keith & Jack DeJohnette/Gary Peacock)
Bye bye blackbird / You won't forget me / Butch and butch / Summer night / For miles / Straight no chaser / I thought about you / Blackbird bye bye
CD _____ 5130742
ECM / May '93 / New Note.

CELESTIAL HAWK (For Orchestra, Percussion & Piano) (Jarrett, Keith & Syracuse Symphony)
CD _____ 8293702
ECM / Aug '88 / New Note.

CHANGELESS (Jarrett, Keith & Jack DeJohnette/Gary Peacock)
Dancing / Endless / Lifeline / Ecstacy
CD _____ 8396182
ECM / Oct '89 / New Note.

CHANGES (Jarrett, Keith & Jack DeJohnette/Gary Peacock)
Flying / Prism (In digital stereo)
CD _____ 8174362
ECM / Oct '84 / New Note.

COMPLETE BLUE NOTE RECORDINGS, THE (6CD Set)
In your own sweet way / How long has this been going on / While we're young / Partners / No lonely nights / Now's the time / Lament / I'm old fashioned / Everything happens to me / If I were a bell / In the wee small hours of the morning / Oleo / Alone together / Skylark / Things 'ain't what they used to be / Autumn leaves / Days of wine and roses / Bop-be / You don't know what love is Muezzin / When I fall in love / How deep is the ocean / Close your eyes / Imagination / I'll close my eyes / I fall in love to easily / On Green Dolphin Street / My romance / Don't ever leave me / You'd be so nice to come home to / La valse bleue / Straight, no chaser / Time after time / For heaven's sake / Desert sun / How about you
CD Set _____ 5276382
ECM / Oct '95 / New Note.

CONCERTS: BREGENZ
CD _____ 8272862
ECM / Aug '88 / New Note.

CURE, THE (New York Town Hall/April 1990)
Old folks / Body and soul / Woody 'n' you / Things ain't what they used to be
CD _____ 8496502
ECM / Oct '91 / New Note.

DARK INTERVALS
Opening / Hymn / Americana / Entrance / Parallels / Fire dance / Ritual prayer / Recitative
CD _____ 8373422
ECM / Oct '88 / New Note.

EXPECTATIONS
Expectations / Take me back / Circular letter (for J.K.) / Sundance / Bring back the time when (iff) / There is a road (God's River) / Common mama / Magician in you / Roussillon / Nomads
CD _____ 4679022
Columbia / Jan '92 / Sony.

EYES OF THE HEART
Eyes of the heart (1 & 2) / Encore (A-B-C)
CD _____ 8254762
ECM / Oct '85 / New Note.

FACING YOU
In front / Ritooria / Lalene / My lady: my child / Landscape for future earth / Starbright / Vapallia / Semblence
CD _____ 8271322
ECM / Dec '85 / New Note.

FORT YAWUH
If the misfits wear it / Fort Yawuh / De drums / Still life, still life
CD _____ MCAD 33122
Impulse Jazz / Oct '90 / BMG / New Note.

IN THE LIGHT (2CD Set)
CD Set _____ 8350112
ECM / Jul '88 / New Note.

INVOCATIONS: THE MOTH AND THE FLAME (2CD Set)
Invocations (1st to 7th) / Moth and the flame (parts 1-5)
CD Set _____ 8254732
ECM / Oct '85 / New Note.

KOLN CONCERT, THE
CD _____ 8100672
ECM / '83 / New Note.

LUMINESSENCE (Music For String Orchestra & Saxophone) (Jarrett, Keith & Jan Garbarek)
CD _____ 8393072
ECM / Sep '89 / New Note.

MY SONG
Questar / My song / Tabarka / Mandela / Journey home
CD _____ 8214062
ECM / '84 / New Note.

MYSTERIES
Rotation / Everything that lives laments / Flame / Mysteries
CD _____ MCAD 33113
Impulse Jazz / Jan '90 / BMG / New Note.

NUDE ANTS (Live At The Village Vanguard/2CD Set)
Chant of the soil / Innocence / Processional / Oasis / New dance / Sunshine song
CD Set _____ 8291192
ECM / Jun '86 / New Note.

PARIS CONCERT (Solo Piano/October 17th 1988/Salle Pleyel)
October 17, 1988 / Wind / Blues
CD _____ 8391732
ECM / Oct '88 / New Note.

RUTA AND DAITYA
CD _____ 8293882
ECM / Oct '88 / New Note.

SACRED HYMNS OF G.I. GURDJIEFF
Reading of sacred books / Prayer and despair / Religious ceremony / Hymn / Orthodox hymn from Asia minor / Hymn for Good Friday / Hymn for Easter Thursday / Hymn to the endless creator / Hymn from a great temple / Story of the resurrection of Christ / Holy affirming, holy denying, holy reconciling / Easter night procession / Meditation
CD _____ 8291222
ECM / Jun '86 / New Note.

SOLO CONCERTS - BREMEN/LAUSANNE (2CD Set)
CD Set _____ 8277472
ECM / Jul '86 / New Note.

SOMEWHERE BEFORE
My back pages / Pretty ballad / Moving son / Somewhere before / New rag / Moment for tears / Pout's over (and the day's not through) / Dedicated to you / Old rag
CD _____ 756781455-2
WEA / Mar '93 / Warner Music.

SPHERES
Spheres (movements 1, 4, 7 & 9)
CD _____ 8274632
ECM / Jul '86 / New Note.

SPIRITS (2CD Set)
CD Set _____ 8294672
ECM / Oct '86 / New Note.

STAIRCASE (2CD Set)
Staircase (pts 1-3) / Hourglass (pts 1 & 2) / Sundial (pts 1-3) / Sand (pts 1-3)
CD Set _____ 8273372
ECM / Dec '85 / New Note.

STANDARDS #1 (Jarrett, Keith & Jack DeJohnette/Gary Peacock)
Meaning of the blues / All the things you are / It never entered my mind / (I'm afraid) the masquerade is over / God bless the child
CD _____ 8119662
ECM / Aug '88 / New Note.

STANDARDS #2 (Jarrett, Keith & Jack DeJohnette/Gary Peacock)
So near / Moon and sand / In love in vain / Never let me go / If I should lose you / I fall in love too easily
CD _____ 8250152
ECM / May '85 / New Note.

STANDARDS IN NORWAY
All of you / Little girl blue / Just in time / Old folks / Love is a many splendoured thing / Dedicated to you / I hear a rhapsody / How about you
CD _____ 5217172
ECM / Apr '95 / New Note.

STANDARDS LIVE (Jarrett, Keith & Jack DeJohnette/Gary Peacock)
Stella by starlight / Wrong blues / Falling in love with love / Too young to go steady / Way you look tonight / Old country
CD _____ 8278272
ECM / Feb '86 / New Note.

STILL LIVE (Jarrett, Keith & Jack DeJohnette/Gary Peacock)
My funny valentine / Autumn leaves / When I fall in love / Song is you / Come rain or come shine / Late lament / You and the night and the music / Someday my Prince will come / I remember Clifford
CD Set _____ 8350082
ECM / May '88 / New Note.

SUN BEAR CONCERTS (Piano Solo/Kyoto/Osaka/Tokyo/Sapporo November 1976/6CD Set)
Kyoto/November 5th 1976 (Parts 1 & 2) / Osaka/November 8th 1976 (Parts 1 & 2) / Tokyo/November 14th November (Parts 1 & 2) / Sapporo/November 18th 1976 (Parts 1 & 2)
CD Set _____ 8430282
ECM / Oct '90 / New Note.

SURVIVOR'S SUITE
CD _____ 8271372
ECM / Dec '85 / New Note.

TRIBUTE (2CD Set) (Jarrett, Keith & Jack DeJohnette/Gary Peacock)
Lover man / I hear a rhapsody / Little girl blue / Solar / Sun prayer / Just in time / Smoke gets in your eyes / All of you / Ballad of the sad young man / All the things you are / It's easy to remember
CD Set _____ 8471352
ECM / Nov '90 / New Note.

VIENNA CONCERT (Recorded At The Vienna State Opera)
Vienna #1 / Vienna #2
CD _____ 5134372
ECM / Sep '92 / New Note.

WELL TEMPERED CLAVIER BOOK, THE (2CD Set)
CD Set _____ 8352462
ECM / Nov '88 / New Note.

Jarrett, Winston

TOO MANY BOUNDARIES
CD _____ RASCD 3167
Ras / Dec '95 / Jetstar / Greensleeves / SRD / Direct.

TRIBUTE TO BOB MARLEY (Jarret, Winston & The Righteous Flames)
CD _____ OMCD 28
Original Music / Jul '94 / SRD / Jetstar.

WISE MAN
CD _____ TWCD 1001
Tamoki Wambesi / '88 / Jetstar / SRD / Roots Collective / Greensleeves.

Jarvis, Jane

CUT GLASS
CD _____ ACD 258
Audiophile / Apr '93 / Jazz Music / Swift.

JANE JARVIS' L.A. QUARTET
CD _____ ACD 248
Audiophile / '89 / Jazz Music / Swift.

Jasani, Viram

RAGS, MALKAUNS AND MEGH (Jasani, Viram & Gurdev Singh/U.L.A. Khan)
Rag Malkauns / Rag Megh
CD _____ CDSDL 377
Saydisc / Mar '94 / Harmonia Mundi / ADA / Direct.

Jasmine Minks

JASMINE MINKS
CD _____ CRECD 007
Creation / May '94 / 3MV / Vital.

SCRATCH THE SURFACE
CD _____ CRELP 044 CD
Creation / Feb '89 / 3MV / Vital.

SOUL STATION
CD _____ CRECD 112
Creation / Sep '91 / 3MV / Vital.

Jason & The Scorchers

BLAZING GRACE, A
Cry by night operator / 200 Proof lovin' / Country roads / Where bridges never burn / Shadow of night / One more day of weekend / Hell's gate / Why baby why / Somewhere within / American legion party
CD _____ MR 1012
Mammoth / Feb '93 / Vital.

Jason, Sonya

TIGRESS
Tigress / Exotica / Forbidden love / Green eyes / Just take a chance / Tryst (secret lover) / Easy love / Mystery man / Cartoon blues / Touch and go / Escape to dreamland
CD _____ 77002
Discovery / Jun '93 / Warner Music.

Jaspar, Bobby

AT RONNIE SCOTT'S, 1962 (Jaspar, Bobby Quartet)
Be like Bud / Our delight / Darn that dream / Pent-up house / Oleo / Sonnymoon for two (on CD only) / Like someone in love (on CD only) / Stella by starlight (on CD only)
CD _____ MOLECD 11
Mole Jazz / Nov '89 / Jazz Horizons / Jazz Music / Cadillac / Wellard / Impetus.

BOBBY JASPAR
CD _____ OJCCD 1788
Original Jazz Classics / Feb '93 / Wellard / Jazz Music / Cadillac / Complete/Pinnacle.

Jasper & The Prodigal...

EVERYTHING IS EVERYTHING (Jasper & The Prodigal Sons)
Niyabingi / Peace and one love / Word to the Mother / All brothers ain't brothers / Sincerely Jasper / Yesteryear / Give me a tenth / Without you / Freedom / Babylon is falling / Only in the South / Thanks & praise
CD _____ GED 24804
Geffen / Jul '95 / BMG.

Jasraj, Pandit

INVOCATION
CD _____ WLAES 31CD
Waterlilly Acoustics / Nov '95 / ADA.

TABLA (Jasraj, Pandit & Shri Swapan Chaudhuri)
CD _____ WRCD 1009
Koch / Dec '94 / Koch.

Jaume, Andre

ABBAYE DE L'EPAU (Jaume, Andre/ Charlie Haden/Olivier Clerc)
CD _____ CELC C20
CELP / Mar '92 / Harmonia Mundi / Cadillac.

GIACOBAZZI - "AUTOUR DE LA ROUTE" (Jaume, Andre/Barry Altschul)
CD _____ CELPC 25
CELP / Nov '93 / Harmonia Mundi / Cadillac.

PEACE/PACE/PAIX (Jaume, Andre/ Charlie Haden/Olivier Clerc)
CD _____ CELP C19
CELP / Feb '92 / Harmonia Mundi / Cadillac.

Javalins

JAVALINS BEAT
Caroline / Mr. Chang aus Chinatown / Al Capone / Javalin's beat / Sherry / Twisting away / Hey Hey Ha Ha / Joe der Gitarrenman / Hully gully hop / Lass sie reden / Scherben / Tanz doch mit mir Swim / Jenny Jenny / Monkey walk / Be my baby / Loveliest night of the year / Es gibt kein bier aus Hawaii / Ya Ya twist / Footpatter / Git it / Sweet Georgia Brown / Twist and shout
CD _____ BCD 15798
Bear Family / May '94 / Rollercoaster / Direct / CM / Swift / ADA.

Javier

HARD WAY, THE (Javier & The Str8jackers)
Intro / Shoot out / F. I. U. Jay / Other guy / Hammer break / Real deal / Talking shit / Plain ole gangster / Pass me da 40 ounce / Talkin' shit again / Jones / Never heard rappin' / Baddest M. F. out da ATL / Chillin' at da crib / Candy / Players dialoque / Player style / Str8jackin' / Wildest fantasy / Outtro
CD _____ CDICH 1109
Ichiban / Oct '93 / Koch.

Jawara, Jali Musa

DIRECT FROM WEST AFRICA
Fote Mogoban / Haidari / Yeke yeke / Yasimika
CD _____ GGXCD 1
Go Discs / Sep '88 / PolyGram.

SOUBINDOOR
CD _____ WCD 008
World Circuit / '88 / New Note / Direct / Cadillac / ADA.

Jawbox

FOR YOUR OWN SPECIAL SWEETHEART
City Slang / Mar '94 / Disc.
CD _____ EFA 49322

GRIPPE
CD _____ DIS 52CD
Dischord / May '94 / SRD.

NOVELTY
CD _____ DIS 69CD
Dischord / May '94 / SRD.

Jaye Consort

BAWDY ELIZABETHAN EVENING IN MERRY OLD ENGLAND
CD _____ CD 401
Bescol / Aug '94 / CM / Target/BMG.

Jaye, Jerry

MY GIRL JOSEPHINE
My girl Josephine / Long black veil / In the middle of nowhere / Oet my mojo werking / Pipeliner blues / I'm in love again / Sugar bee / I washed my hands in muddy water / Honky tonk women love redneck men / Standing room only / Drinkin' my way back home / When morning comes to Memphis / Hot and still heating / Let your love flow / Forty days
CD _____ HIUKCD 122
Hi / Feb '92 / Pinnacle.

Jayhawks

HOLLYWOOD TOWN HALL
Waiting for the sun / Crowded in the wings / Clouds / Two Angels / Take me with you / Sister cry / Settle down like rain / Witghita / Nevada, California / Martin's song
CD _____ 74321239942
American / Apr '95 / BMG.

TOMORROW THE GREEN GRASS
Blue / I'd run away / Miss Williams' guitar / Two hearts / Real light / Over my shoulder / Bad time / See him on the streets / Nothing left to borrow / Anne Jane / Pray for me / Red's song / Ten little kids
CD _____ 74321236802
American / Feb '95 / BMG.

Jays

UNFORGETTABLE TIMES
CD _____ JJCD 027
Jetstar / Sep '95 / Jetstar.

Jazayer

JAZAYER (Jazayer & Ali Jihad Racy)
CD _____ CDEB 2549
Earthbeat / May '93 / Direct / ADA.

Jazz Artists Guild

JAZZ LIFE, THE
CD _____ CCD 9019
Candid / May '86 / Cadillac / Jazz Music / Wellard / Koch.

Jazz Butcher

BIG PLANET
CD _____ CRELPCD 49
Creation / May '94 / 3MV / Vital.

CONDITION BLUE
CD _____ CRELPCD 110
Creation / Oct '91 / 3MV / Vital.

CULT OF THE BASEMENT
Basement / Pineapple Tuesday / Daycare nation / Mr. Odd / Panic in room 109 / Turtle bait / She's on drugs / Onion field / My Zeppelin / After the euphrates / Girl go / Sister death
CD _____ CRECD 62
Creation / May '94 / 3MV / Vital.

ILLUMINATE (Jazz Butcher Conspiracy)
CD _____ CRECD 182
Creation / Apr '95 / 3MV / Vital.

WAITING FOR THE LOVE BUS
CD _____ CRECD 156
Creation / May '93 / 3MV / Vital.

WESTERN FAMILY
Southern Mark Smith / Shirley Maclaine / Sister death / Still and all / Pineapple Tuesday / Angles / Beautiful snow-white hair / She's on drugs / Girl-go / She's a yoyo / Racheland / Everybody's talkin' / Tugboat Captain / Over the rainbow
CD _____ CRED 148
Creation / Jan '93 / 3MV / Vital.

Jazz Composer's Orchestra

COMMUNICATIONS
CD _____ 8411242
ECM / Nov '89 / New Note.

Jazz Furniture

JAZZ FURNITURE
CD _____ CAP 21449
Caprice / Oct '94 / CM / Complete/ Pinnacle / Cadillac / ADA.

Jazz Grass Ensemble

TICO BANJO
CD _____ PV 758 091
Disques Pierre Verany / Feb '86 / Kingdom.

Jazz Hole

AND THE FEELING GOES AROUND
CD _____ 7567925862
Atlantic / Jan '96 / Warner Music.

JAZZ HOLE
CD _____ PERMCD 24
Permanent / Jun '94 / Total/BMG.

Jazz Hot Ensemble

JAZZ HOT ENSEMBLE
CD _____ JCD 242
Jazzology / Jun '95 / Swift / Jazz Music.

Jazz Jamaica

SKARAVAN
CD _____ SKACD 001
Skazz / Jun '94 / Cadillac.

Jazz Passengers

IMPLEMENT YOURSELF
CD _____ NW 398
New World / Aug '92 / Harmonia Mundi / ADA / Cadillac.

JAZZ PASSENGERS IN LONDON
CD _____ 02902103282
Windham Hill / Mar '95 / Pinnacle / BMG / ADA.

LIVE AT THE KNITTING FACTORY
CD _____ KFWCD 107
Knitting Factory / Nov '94 / Grapevine.

PLAIN OLD JOE
CD _____ KFWCD 139
Knitting Factory / Feb '95 / Grapevine.

Jazz Police

LONG NIGHT COMING, A
CD _____ CDPC 748
Prestige / Oct '90 / Total/BMG.

Jazz Posse

BLUE
Antistrophy / We know who we are / Woody / Gemini / Crescent / Integrate / Skag / Countdown / Juke joint / Horny / Un loco loco / Blue / Metafisico / Frog sauce / Anna
CD _____ FSCD 004
Freak Street / Oct '95 / Vital.

Jazz Trio

S'WONDERFUL JAZZ
'S Wonderful / Cherokee / That old feeling / You are too beautiful / Bali Ha'i / Jitterbug waltz / You've changed
CD _____ WCD 8418
Wilson Audiophile / Sep '91 / Quantum Audio.

Jazz Warriors

OUT OF MANY ONE PEOPLE
Warriors / In reference to our forefathers' fathers' dreams / Minor groove / St. Maurice (of Aragon) / Many pauses
CD _____ IMCD 111
Antilles/New Directions / May '91 / PolyGram.

Jazzsick

JAZZSICK
CD _____ EFA 120702
Hotwire / Apr '95 / SRD.

Jazztet

KILLER JOE
CD _____ LEJAZZCD 15
Le Jazz / Jun '93 / Charly / Cadillac.

MOMENT TO MOMENT
CD _____ SNCD 1066
Soul Note / '86 / Harmonia Mundi / Wellard / Cadillac.

REAL TIME
Whisper not / Sad to say / Are you real / Autumn leaves / Along came Betty
CD _____ CCD 14034
Contemporary / Jan '94 / Jazz Music / Cadillac / Pinnacle / Wellard.

JC 001

RIDE THE BREAK (JC 001 & D.J. D'Zire)
Never again / Favourite breaks / Sea of MC's / Cupid / Build the mutha up / Words within words / Flow / Ride the break / Virtual reality / All my children
CD _____ 450991406-2
Anxious / Apr '93 / Warner Music.

Jeanneau, Francois

MALOYA TRANSIT
CD _____ LBLC 6546
Label Bleu / Jul '92 / New Note.

Jeck, Philip

LOOPHOLES
CD _____ TO 26
Touch / Jun '95 / These / Kudos.

Jedi Knights

NEW SCHOOL SCIENCE
CD _____ EV 0042CD
Universal Language / Feb '96 / Disc.

Jeep Beat Collective

ATTACK OF THE WILD STYLE
CD _____ RUF 008
Ruf / Jan '96 / Pinnacle / ADA.

Jefferson Airplane

BACK2BACK
CD Set _____ 74321291452
RCA / Sep '95 / BMG.

BEST OF JEFFERSON AIRPLANE
Blues from an airplane / White rabbit / Somebody to love / Ballad of you and me and Pooneil / Crown of creation / Plastic fantastic lover / Volunteers / When the earth moves again / Aerie (gang of eagles) / Milk train / Mexico
CD _____ ND 89186
RCA / Jan '92 / BMG.

LIVE AT THE MONTEREY FESTIVAL
Somebody to love / Other side of this life / White rabbit / High flying bird / Today / She has funny cars / Young girl with Sunday blues / Ballad of you and me and Pooneil
CD _____ CDTB 074
Thunderbolt / May '90 / Magnum Music Group.

WHITE RABBIT
CD _____ RMB 75065
Remember / Aug '93 / Total/BMG.

Jefferson Starship

DEEP SPACE
CD _____ ESSCD 300
Essential / Aug '95 / Total/BMG.

GREATEST HITS (TEN YEARS AND CHANGE 1979-1991) (Starship)
Jane / Find your way back / Stranger / No way out / Laying it on the line / Don't lose any sleep / We built this city / Sara / Nothing's gonna stop us now / It's not over 'til it's over) / It's not enough / Good enough
CD _____ 74321289902
RCA / Aug '95 / BMG.

Jefferson, Blind Lemon

BLIND LEMON JEFFERSON
CD _____ DVBC 9072
Deja Vu / May '95 / THE.

BLIND LEMON JEFFERSON (1925-26)
CD _____ DOCD 5017
Blues Document / Aug '91 / Swift / Jazz Music / Hot Shot.

CAT MAN BLUES
CD _____ ALB 1009CD
Aldabra / Mar '94 / CM / Disc.

IN CHRONOLOGICAL ORDER
CD _____ DOCD 5018
Blues Document / Nov '93 / Swift / Jazz Music / Hot Shot.

ONE DIME BLUES
CD _____ ALB 1006CD
Aldabra / Mar '94 / CM / Disc.

Jefferson, Carter

RISE OF ATLANTIS, THE
Why / Rise of Atlantis / Wind chimes / Changing trains / Song for Gwen / Blues for wood
CD _____ CDSJP 126
Timeless Jazz / Mar '91 / New Note.

Jefferson, Eddie

BODY AND SOUL
See if you can get to that / Body and soul / Mercy mercy mercy / So what / There I go, There I go again / Psychedelic Sally
CD _____ OJCCD 396
Original Jazz Classics / Jan '94 / Wellard / Jazz Music / Cadillac / Complete/Pinnacle.

GODFATHER OF VOCALESE
CD _____ MCD 6013
Muse / Sep '92 / New Note / CM.

HIPPER THAN THOU
So what / Moody's mood for love / Sister Sadie / It's only a paper moon / TD's boogie / Now's the time / Body and soul / Workshop / Sherry / Baby girl (These foolish things) / Memphis / Honeysuckle Rose / Preacher / Night train / NJR (I'm gone) / I got the blues / Silly little Cynthia / Red's new dream
CD _____ LDJ 274946
Radio Nights / Sep '92 / Harmonia Mundi / Cadillac.

JAZZ SINGER, THE (Vocal Improvisations On Famous Jazz Solos)
So what / Moody's mood for love / Sister Sadie / Lester's trip to the moon (Paper moon) / T.D.'s boogie woogie / Now's the time / Body and soul / Workshop / Sherry / Baby girl (These foolish things) / Memphis / Honeysuckle rose / Crazy romance / Night train / NJR (I'm gone) / I've got the blues / Silly little Cynthia / Red's new dream
CD _____ ECD 22062
Evidence / Oct '93 / Harmonia Mundi / ADA / Cadillac.

LETTER FROM HOME
CD _____ OJCCD 307
Original Jazz Classics / Jan '94 / Wellard / Jazz Music / Cadillac / Complete/Pinnacle.

Jefferson, Thomas

THOMAS JEFFERSON
CD _____ EDCD 416
Edsel / Mar '95 / Pinnacle / ADA.

Jeffrey's Accordion Band

36 CHRISTMAS CRACKERS
Sleigh ride / Good King Wenceslas / Jingle bells / Rudolph the red nosed reindeer / In dulce jubilo / I saw 3 ships / We three kings / Frosty the snowman / Rockin' around the Christmas tree / I saw Mommy kissing Santa Claus / Santa Claus is coming to town / So this is Christmas / Holly and the ivy / Mistletoe and wine / We wish you a merry Christmas / Deck the halls / While shepherds watched / Dong dong merrily on high / God rest ye merry gentlemen / Have yourself a merry little Christmas / Mary's boy child / Oh little town of Bethlehem / Stop the cavalry / Little donkey / Troika / Once in royal David's city / Hark the herald angels sing / Silent night / First noel / Away in a manger / I wish it could be Christmas everyday / So here it is, merry Christmas / White Christmas / Christmas alphabet / Winter wonderland / Auld lang syne
CD _____ SOW 508
Sound Waves / Nov '91 / Target/BMG.

50 WARTIME MEMORIES VOL. 3
CD _____ SOW 511
Sound Waves / May '94 / Target/BMG.

HOOKED ON VICTORY
CD _____ SOW 121
Sound Waves / May '95 / Target/BMG.

Jegede, Tunde

LAMENTATION
Lamentation / Songs of the eternal / African path / Heat haze / Hill of solitude - valley of festivity / Caravans of gold / Buffalo's tail / Departure / Song of the waterfall / Island of cold

CD _____ TRICD 1001
Triciom / Oct '95 / New Note.

Jellyfish

BELLYBUTTON
Man I used to be / That is why / King is half undressed / I wanna stay home / She still loves him / All I want is everything / Now she knows she's wrong / Bed spring kiss / Baby coming back / Calling Sarah
CD _____ CDCUX 3
Charisma / Feb '92 / EMI.

SPILT MILK
Joining a fan club / Sebrina, Paste and Plato / New mistake / Glutton of sympathy / Ghost at number one / Bye bye bye / All is forgiven / Russian hill / He's my best friend / Too much, too little, too late / Brighter day
CD _____ CDCUS 20
Charisma / May '93 / EMI.

Jellyfish Kiss

ANIMAL RITES
Sinbad / Regular folk / Dead / Overdone / Wave goodbye / Zero tolerance / Screwed up papers / Little red car / Big talk / Underground / Muttonhead
CD _____ SDE 9028
Shimmy Disc / Nov '90 / Vital.

Jenkins, Billy

BLUE MOON IN A FUNCTION ROOM (Jenkins, Billy & The Voice Of God Collective)
Blue of the night / Vision on / Bye bye bluebird / On the street where you live / Take five / Baby elephant walk / Ruby, don't take your love to town / Liebestraum / Pick a bale of cotton / Maria Elena / Georgia / Kalinka / Moon river
CD _____ BDV 9402
Babel / Mar '95 / ADA / Harmonia Mundi / Cadillac / Diverse.

ENTERTAINMENT U.S.A.
CD _____ BDV 9401CD
Babel / Jul '94 / ADA / Harmonia Mundi / Cadillac / Diverse.

FIRST AURAL ART EXHIBITION (Jenkins, Billy & The Voice Of God Collective)
Brilliant / Expensive equipment / Fat people / Blues / Sade's lips / Johnny Cash / Discoboats at two o'clock / Cooking oil / Donkey droppings / Elvis Presley
CD _____ VOCD 921
VOTP / Sep '92 / VOTP / These / Diverse.

IN THE NUDE
Misterioso / Standard blues / Bottle up and go / In a sentimental mood / Don't get around much anymore / Night and day / I mean you / I wish I knew (how it would feel to be free) / Donkey droppings / On Green Dolphin street / Lover man / Isn't she lovely / They can't take that away from me / Well you needn't / O come o come Emmanuel / Swinging shepherd blues
CD _____ WWCD 010
West Wind / Jul '88 / Swift / Charly / CM / ADA.

SCRATCHES OF SPAIN
Monkey men / Cuttlefish / Barcelona / Benidorm motorway services / Bilbao/ St.Columbus day / Cooking oil / McDonalds
CD _____ BDV 9404
Babel / Oct '94 / ADA / Harmonia Mundi / Cadillac / Diverse.

Jenkins, Ella

YOU'LL SING A SONG AND I'LL SING A SONG
CD _____ SF 45010CD
Smithsonian Folkways / Dec '94 / ADA / Direct / Koch / CM / Cadillac.

Jenkins, John

JAZZ EYES (Jenkins, John & Donald Byrd)
Star eyes / Orpheus / Honeylike / Rockaway
CD _____ SV 0230
Savoy Jazz / Oct '93 / Conifer / ADA.

Jenkins, Leroy

LEGEND OF AL GLATSON, THE
Al Glatson / Brax Stone / Albert Ayler / Tuesday child / What goes around comes around
CD _____ 1200222
Black Saint / Nov '90 / Harmonia Mundi / Cadillac.

LIFELONG AMBITIONS (Jenkins, Leroy & Muhal Richard Abrams)
CD _____ 120033-2
Black Saint / Jan '94 / Harmonia Mundi / Cadillac.

LIVE
CD _____ 120122-2
Black Saint / Sep '93 / Harmonia Mundi / Cadillac.

Jenkins, Lillette

LILLETTE JENKINS PLAYS LIL HARDIN
CD _____ CR (D) 302
Chiara Scuro / Jan '93 / Jazz Music / Kudos.

Jenks, Glenn

DUETS OF RAGS (Jenks, Glenn & Dan Gunstead)
CD _____ SOSCD 1292
Stomp Off / Nov '95 / Jazz Music / Wellard.

Jennings, Waylon

ABILENE
CD _____ CDSGP 0129
Prestige / Jan '95 / Total/BMG.

BACK IN THE SADDLE
CD _____ HADCD 181
Javelin / Nov '95 / THE / Henry Hadaway Organisation.

BEST OF WAYLON JENNINGS, THE
CD _____ MU 3010
Start / Oct '94 / Koch.

CLOVIS TO PHOENIX (The Early Years)
My baby walks all over me / Stage / Another blue day / My world / Never again / Jole Blon / When sin stops / Crying / Sally was a good ole girl / Burning memories / Big mambou / Money / Don't think twice, it's alright / Dream baby / It's so easy / Lorena / Love's gonna live here / Abilene / White lightning
CD _____ ZCD 2021
Zu Zazz / Aug '95 / Rollercoaster.

GREATEST HITS: WAYLON JENNINGS
Lonesome, on'ry and mean / Ladies love outlaws / I've always been crazy / I'm a ramblin' man / Only daddy that'll walk the line / Amanda / Honky tonk heroes / Mamas don't let your babies grow up to be cowboys / Good hearted woman / Luckenbach, Texas (Back to the basics of love) / Texas / Are you sure Hank done it this way
CD _____ ND 90304
RCA / '90 / BMG.

MAGIC OF WAYLON JENNINGS, THE
Sally was a good old girl / Big mamou / Don't think twice, it's alright / It's so easy / Love's gonna live here / White lightning / Crying / Burning memories / Dream baby / Abilene / Jolie blon / Money (that's what I want) / Lorena / When sin stops
CD _____ TKOCD 024
TKO / Apr '92 / TKO.

OUTLAWS, THE (Jennings, Waylon & Willie Nelson)
CD _____ CTS 55407
Country Stars / Jan '92 / Target/BMG.

WAYMORE'S BLUES (PART 2)
Endangered species / Waymore's blues (part 2) / This train (Russell's song) / Wild ones / No good for me / Old timer / Up in Arkansas / Nobody knows come back and see me / You don't mess around with me (CD only)
CD _____ 7863664092
RCA / Oct '94 / BMG.

WHITE LIGHTNING
CD _____ CDCD 1111
Charly / Jul '93 / Charly / THE / Cadillac.

WHITE LIGHTNING
CD _____ 15486
Laserlight / Dec '94 / Target/BMG.

WILL THE WOLF SURVIVE
Will the wolf survive / They ain't got em' all / Working without a net / Where does love go / Dog won't hunt / What you'll do when I'm gone / Suddenly single / Shadow of your distant friend / I've got me a woman / Devil's right hand
CD _____ MCAD 5688
MCA / '88 / BMG.

Jensen, Ingrid

VERNAL FIELDS
Marsh blues / Skookum spook / Vernal fields / Every time we say goodbye / I love you / Mingus that I knew / Stuck in the dark / Christiane / Be myself
CD _____ ENJ 90132
Enja / May '95 / New Note / Vital/SAM.

Jentekor, Sandefjord

PA FOLKEMUNNE
CD _____ BD 7023CD
Musikk Distribujson / Apr '95 / ADA.

Jeremy Days

CIRCUSHEAD
Give it a name / Sylvia suddenly / My man / Mr. Judge / Virginia / Room to revolution / Red river / 1987 / History / Sleeping room / Circushead / What the wind's blowin roun / Clouds of maine / Sacrifice
CD _____ 843 998-2
Polydor / Mar '91 / PolyGram.

Jericho

JERICHO
CD _____ REP 4058-WZ
Repertoire / Aug '91 / Pinnacle / Cadillac.

Jericho Jones

JUNKIES, MONKEYS AND DONKEYS
CD _____ REP 4101-WZ
Repertoire / Aug '91 / Pinnacle / Cadillac.

Jerling, Michael

NEW SUIT OF CLOTHES
CD _____ SHCD 8010
Shanachie / Dec '94 / Koch / ADA / Greensleeves.

Jerolamon, Jeff

INTRODUCING
CD _____ CCD 79522
Candid / Nov '93 / Cadillac / Jazz Music / Wellard / Koch.

SWING THING
CD _____ CCD 79538
Candid / Nov '94 / Cadillac / Jazz Music / Wellard / Koch.

Jerry, Clark

FLUTIN' AND FLUGIN'
All That's Jazz / Jun '92 / THE / Jazz Music.
CD _____ ATJCD 5963

Jerry's Kids

KILL, KILL, KILL
CD _____ T 027CD
Taang / Apr '89 / Plastic Head.

Jeru The Damaja

SUN RISES IN THE EAST
Intro (life) / D. Original / Brooklyn took it / Perverted monks in tha house / Mental stamina / Da bichez / You can't stop the prophet / Ain't the devil happy / My mind spray / Come clean / Jungle music / Statik
FFRR / May '94 / PolyGram.
CD _____ 828526-2

Jerusalem Slim

JERUSALEM SLIM
CD _____ 5146802
Phonogram / Jan '93 / PolyGram.

Jesus & Mary Chain

AUTOMATIC
Here come Alice / Coast to coast / Blues from a gun / Between planets / U.V. ray / Her way of praying / Head on / Take it / Halfway to crazy / Gimme hell / Drop / Sunray
CD _____ 2462212
Blanco Y Negro / Oct '89 / Warner Music.

BARBED WIRE KISSES
Kill surf city / Head / Rider / Hit / Don't ever change / Just out of reach / Happy place / Psycho candy / Sidewalking / Who do you love / Surfin' USA / Everything's alright when you're down / Upside down / Taste of Cindy / Swing / On the wall-f hole / Bo Diddley is Jesus (Not on LP) / Here it comes again (Not on LP) / Cracked (Not on LP) / Mushroom (Not on LP)
CD _____ 2423312
Blanco Y Negro / Apr '88 / Warner Music.

DARKLANDS
April skies / Happy when it rains / Down on me / Deep one perfect / Fall / About you / Cherry came too / On the wall / Nine million rainy days
CD _____ K 2421802
Blanco Y Negro / Nov '94 / Warner Music.

HONEY'S DEAD
CD _____ 9031765542
Blanco Y Negro / Apr '92 / Warner Music.

PEEL SESSIONS:JESUS & MARY CHAIN (3 February 1985/25 November 1986)
Inside me / Living end / Just like honey / Fall / Happy place / In the rain (about you)
CD _____ SFMACD 210
Strange Fruit / Aug '91 / Pinnacle.

PSYCHO CANDY
Just like honey / Living end / Taste the floor / Hardest walk / Cut dead / In a hole / Taste of Cindy / Never understand / It's so hard / Inside me / Sowing seeds / My little underground / You trip me up / Something's wrong
CD _____ 2420002
Blanco Y Negro / Oct '86 / Warner Music.

SOUND OF SPEED, THE
Snakedriver / Reverence / Heat / Teenage lust / Why'd you want me / Don't come down / Guitar man / Something I can't have / Sometimes / Write record release blues / Shimmer / Penetration / My girl / Tower of song / Little red rooster / Break me down / Lowlife / Deviant slice / Reverberation (Doubt) / Sidewalking
CD _____ 4509931052
Blanco Y Negro / Jul '93 / Warner Music.

STONED & DE-THRONED
CD _____ 450996717-2
Blanco Y Negro / Aug '94 / Warner Music.

Jesus Jones

DOUBT
Trust me / Who, Where, Why / International bright young thing / I'm burning / Right here, right now / Nothing to hold me / Real real real / Welcome back Victoria / Two and two / Stripped / Blissed
CD _____ FOODCD 5
Food / Feb '94 / EMI.

LIQUIDIZER
Move mountains / Never enough / Real world / All the answers / What's going on / Song 33 / Info freako / Bring it on down / Too much to learn / What would you know / One for the money / Someone to blame
CD _____ FOODCD 3
Food / Oct '89 / EMI.

PERVERSE
Zeroes and ones / Devil you know / Get a good thing / From love to war / Yellow brown / Magazine / Right decision / Your crusade / Don't believe it / Tongue tied / Spiral / Idiot stare
CD _____ FOODCD 8
EMI / Nov '92 / EMI.

Jesus Lizard

DOWN
CD _____ TG 131CD
Touch & Go / Aug '94 / SRD.

GOAT
CD _____ TG 68CD
Touch & Go / Feb '91 / SRD.

HEAD
CD _____ TGCD 54
Touch & Go / Jul '93 / SRD.

LIAR
CD _____ TG 100CD
Touch & Go / Oct '92 / SRD.

Jesus Loves You

MARTYR MANTRAS, THE
Generations of love / One on one / Love's gonna let you get down / After the love / I specialize in loneliness / No clause / Love hurts / Siempre te amare / Too much love / Bow down mister
CD _____ CUMCD 1
More Protein / Mar '91 / Total/BMG.

Jet Red

JET RED
CD _____ CDMFN 94
Music For Nations / Aug '89 / Pinnacle.

Jeter, Reverend Claude

YESTERDAY AND TODAY
CD _____ SHCD 6010
Shanachie / Mar '95 / Koch / ADA / Greensleeves.

Jethro Tull

20 YEARS OF JETHRO TULL
Stormy Monday blues / Love story / New day yesterday / Summer day sands / Coronach / March the mad scientist / Pibroch (pee break) / Black satin / Lick your fingers clean / Overhead / Crossword / Saturation / Jack-a-Lynn / Motoreyes / Part of the machine / Mayhem / Maybe / Kelpie / Under wraps 2 / Wond'ring aloud / Dun ringill / Life's a long song / Nursie grace / Witch's promise / Teacher / Living in the past / Aqualung / Locomotive breath
CD _____ CCD 1655
Chrysalis / Nov '89 / EMI.

25TH ANNIVERSARY BOX SET (4CD Set)
My Sunday feeling (Remix) / Song for Jeffrey (Remix) / Living in the past (Remix) / Teacher (Remix) / Sweet dream (Remix) / Cross-eyed Mary (Remix) / Witch's promise (Remix) / Life is a long song (Remix) / Bungle in the jungle (Remix) / Minstrel in the gallery (Remix) / Cold wind to Valhalla (Remix) / Too old to rock 'n' roll (Remix) / Too young to die (Remix) / Songs from the wood (Remix) / Heavy horses (Remix) / Black Sunday (Remix) / Broadsword (Remix) / My God / With you there to help me / Song for Jeffrey / To cry you a song / Sossity, you're a woman / Reasons for waiting / We used to know / Guitar solo / For a thousand mothers / So much trouble / My Sunday feeling / Someday the sun won't shine for you / Living in the past / Bouree / With you there to help me (2) / Thick as a brick / Cheerio / New day yesterday / Protect and survive / Jack-a-Lynn / Whistler / My God (2) / Aqualung / To be sad is a mad way to be (Live) / Back to the family (Live) / Passion play extract (Live) / Wind-up/Locomotive breath/ Land of Hope and Glory/Wind-up / Seal driver (Live) / Nobody's car (Live) / Pussy willow (Live) / Budapest (Live) / Nothing is easy (Mess) / Kissing Willie (Live) / Still loving you tonight (Live) / Beggar's farm' (Live) / Song Jig (Live) / Song for Jeffrey (Live) / Living in the past (Live)

CD _____ CDCHR 6004
Chrysalis / Apr '93 / EMI.

A
Crossfire / Flyingdale flyer / Working John,
working Joe / Black Sunday / Protect and
survive / Batteries not included / Uniform /
4 WD (low ratio) / Pine martin's jig / And
further on / Bod
CD _____ CCD 1301
Chrysalis / Jan '89 / EMI.

AQUALUNG
Aqualung / Cross-eyed Mary / Cheap day
return / Mother goose / Wond'ring aloud /
Up to me / My God / Hymn 43 / Slipstream
/ Locomotive / Breath / Wind up
CD _____ CD25CR 08
Chrysalis / Mar '94 / EMI.

BENEFIT
With you there to help me / Nothing to say
/ Alive and well and living in / Son for Mi-
chael Collins / Jeffrey and me / To cry you
a song / Time for everything / Inside / Play
in time / Sossity / You're a woman
CD _____ CPCD 1043
Chrysalis / Jun '87 / EMI.

**BEST OF THE ANNIVERSARY
COLLECTION, THE**
Song of Jeffrey / beggar's farm / Christmas
song / New day yesterday / Bouree / Nothing is easy / Living in the past / To cry you
a song / Teacher / Sweet dream / Cross-
eyed Mary / Mother goose / Aqualung / Locomotive breath / Life is a long song / Thick
as a brick (extract) / Passion play / Skating
away on the thin ice of the new day / Bungle in the jungle / Minstrel in the gallery /
Too old to rock and roll / Too young to die
/ Songs from the wood / Jack in the green
/ Whistler / Heavy horses / Dun ringill /
Flyingdale flyer / Jack-a-Lynn / Pussy willow / Broadsword / Under wraps 11 / Steel
monkey / Farm on the freeway / Jump start
/ Kissing Willie / This is not love
CD _____ CDCHR 6001
Chrysalis / May '93 / EMI.

BROADSWORD AND THE BEAST, THE
Beastie / Clasp / Fallen on hard times / Fly-
ing colours / Slow marching / Broadsword
/ Pussy willow / Watching me watching you
/ Seal driver / Cheerio
CD _____ CCD 1380
Chrysalis / Apr '82 / EMI.

CATFISH RISING
This is not love / Occasional demons /
Rocks on the road / Thinking round corners
/ Still loving you tonight / Doctor to my dis-
ease / Like a tall thin girl / Sparrow on the
schoolyard wall / Roll yer own / Gold-tipped
boots, black jacket and tie
CD _____ CCD 1886
Chrysalis / Sep '91 / EMI.

**CLASSIC CASE, A (The Music Of Jethro
Tull Featuring Ian Anderson) (Palmer,
David & The London Symphony
Orchestra)**
Locomotive breath / Thick as a brick / Elegy
/ Bouree / Fly by night / Aqualung / Too old
to rock 'n' roll / Teacher / Bungle in the jun-
gle / Rainbow blues / Living in the past /
War child
CD _____ 09026625102
RCA / Apr '94 / BMG.

CREST OF A KNAVE
Steel monkey / Farm on the freeway / Jump
start / Said she was a dancer / Budapest /
Mountain men / Raising steam / Waking
edge (Not on LP) / Dogs in the midwinter
(Extra on cassette and CD)
CD _____ CCD 1590
Chrysalis / Sep '87 / EMI.

HEAVY HORSES
And the mouse police never sleeps / Acres
wild / No lullaby / Moths / Journeyman /
Rover / One brown mouse / Heavy horses
/ Weathercock
CD _____ CCD 1175
Chrysalis / '86 / EMI.

JETHRO TULL IN CONCERT
CD _____ WINCD 070
Windsong / Apr '95 / Pinnacle.

LITTLE LIGHT MUSIC, A
Some day the sun won't shine for you / Living in the past / Life is a long song / Under
wraps / Rocks on the road / Nursie / Too
old to rock 'n' roll, too young to die / One
white duck / New day yesterday / John Barleycorn / Look into the sun / Christmas
song / From a dead beat to an old greaser
/ Bouree / Pussy willow
CD _____ CCD 1954
Chrysalis / Sep '92 / EMI.

LIVE AT HAMMERSMITH 1984
CD _____ FRSCD 004
Raw Fruit / Dec '90 / Pinnacle.

LIVING IN THE PAST
Witches promise / Song for Jeffrey / Love
story / Christmas song / Living in the past
/ Driving song / Bouree / Sweet dream /
Singing all day / Witch's promise / Inside /
Just trying to be / By kind permission of you
/ Dharma for one / Wondering again / Lo-
comotive breath / Life is a long song / Up
the 'Pool / Dr. Bogenbroom / For later /
Nursie

CD _____ CCD 1575
Chrysalis / Feb '94 / EMI.

MINSTREL IN THE GALLERY
Minstrel in the gallery / Cold wind to Valhalla
/ Black satin dancer / Requiem / One white
duck / O 10 equals nothing at all / Baker St.
muse / Including pig me and the whore /
Nice little tune / Crash barrier waltzer /
Mother England reverie / Grace
CD _____ CCD 1082
Chrysalis / '86 / EMI.

MU - THE BEST OF JETHRO TULL #1
Teacher / Aqualung / Thick as a brick / Bun-
gle in the jungle / Locomotive breath / Fat
man / Living in the past / Passion play /
Skating away on the thin ice of the new day
/ Rainbow blues / Nothing is easy
CD _____ ACCD 1078
Chrysalis / Dec '85 / EMI.

**NIGHT CAP - THE UNRELEASED
MASTERS 1972-1991**
First post / Animelee / Tiger toon / Look at
the animals / Law of the bungle / Law of the
bungle (part II) / Left right / Solitaire / Critique oblique / First post / Scenario / Audition / No rehearsal / Paradise steakhouse /
Sealion II / Piece of cake / Quartet / Silver
river turning / Crew nights / Curse / Rosa
on the factory floor / Small cigar / Man of
principle / Commons brawl / No step / Drive
on the young side of life / I don't want to
be me / Broadford bazaar / Lights out /
Truck stop runner / Hard liner
CD Set _____ CDCHR 6057
Chrysalis / Nov '93 / EMI.

ORIGINAL MASTERS
Living in the past / Aqualung / Too old to
rock 'n' roll, too young to die / Locomotive
breath / Skating away on the thin ice of the
new day / Bungle in the jungle / Sweet
dream / Songs from the wood / Witches
promise / Thick as a brick / Minstrel in the
gallery / Life is a long song
CD _____ CCD 1515
Chrysalis / Apr '86 / EMI.

PASSION PLAY, A
CD _____ CCD 1040
Chrysalis / Jan '89 / EMI.

**REPEAT - THE BEST OF JETHRO TULL
#2**
Minstrel in the gallery / Cross-eyed Mary /
New day yesterday / Bouree / Thick as a
brick / War child / Passion play / To cry you
a song / Too old to rock 'n' roll, too young
to die / Glory row
CD _____ CCD 1135
Chrysalis / Apr '86 / EMI.

ROCK ISLAND
Kissing Willie / Rattlesnake trail / Ears of tin
/ Undressed to kill / Rock Island / Heavy
water / Another Christmas song / Whaler's
dues / Big riff and Mando / Strange avenues
CD _____ CCD 1708
Chrysalis / Aug '89 / EMI.

ROOTS TO BRANCHES
Roots to branches / Rare and precious
chain / Out of the noise / This free will /
Valley / Dangerous veils / Beside myself /
Wounded, old and treacherous / At last for-
ever / Stuck in the August rain / Another
Harry's bar
CD _____ CDCHR 6109
Chrysalis / Sep '95 / EMI.

SONGS FROM THE WOOD
Songs from the wood / Jack in the green /
Cup of wonder / Hunting girl / Ring out, Sol-
stice bells / Velvet green / Whistler / Pibroch
(cap in hand) / Fire at midnight
CD _____ ACCD 1132
Chrysalis / '86 / EMI.

STAND UP
New day yesterday / Jeffrey goes to Leices-
ter Square / Bouree / Back to the family /
Look into the sun / Nothing is easy / Fat
man / We used to know / Reasons for wait-
ing / For a thousand mothers
CD _____ CCD 1042
Chrysalis / Jan '89 / EMI.

STORM WATCH
North Sea oil / Orion / Home / Dark ages /
Warm sporran / Something's on the move /
Old ghosts / Dunringill / Flying Dutchman /
Elegy
CD _____ CCD 1238
Chrysalis / Jan '89 / EMI.

THIS WAS
My Sunday feeling / Someday the sun
won't shine for you / For you / Beggar's
farm / Move on alone / Serenadeto a
cuckoo / Dharma for one / It's breaking me
/ Cat's squirrel / Song for Jeffrey / Round
CD _____ CCD 1041
Chrysalis / '86 / EMI.

TOO OLD TO ROCK AND ROLL
Quizz kid / Crazed institution / Salamander
/ Taxi grab / From a dead beat to an old
greaser / Bad eyed and loveless / Big dipper / Too old to rock 'n' roll; too young to
die / Pied piper / Chequered flag (dead of
alive)
CD _____ CCD 1111
Chrysalis / '86 / EMI.

UNDER WRAPS
Lap of luxury / Under wraps (part 1) / European legacy / Later the same evening /

Saboteur / Radio free Moscow / Nobody's
car / Heat / Under wraps (part 2) / Paparazzi
/ Apologee
CD _____ CCD 1461
Chrysalis / Sep '84 / EMI.

Jets

ALL FIRED UP
CD _____ KRYPCD 202
Krypton / Aug '91 / Magnum Music
Group.

ONE FOR THE ROAD
CD _____ KYPCD 204
Krypton / Apr '95 / Magnum Music Group.

Jetset

BEST OF THE JETSET TOO
CD _____ TANGCD 5
Tangerine / May '93 / Disc.

BEST OF THE JETSET, THE
CD _____ TANGCD 1
Tangerine / Aug '92 / Disc.

Jett, Joan

**NOTORIOUS (Jett, Joan & The
Blackhearts)**
Backlash / Ashes in the wind / Only good
thing (you ever said was goodbye) / Lie to
me / Don't surrender / Goodbye / Ma-
chismo / Treadin' water / I want you / Wait
for me
CD _____ 9070802
Silenz / Jun '92 / BMG.

Jewish Theatre Orchestra

**YIDDISH FOLKSONGS (Spiritual and
traditional music)**
CD _____ 15185
Laserlight / '91 / Target/BMG.

Jezebelle

BAD ATTITUDE
Ain't no lady / Leave me alone / Travel on
gypsy / Other side / Scandal / No mercy /
Satisfaction guaranteed / Boulevard / Burn
CD _____ HMRXD 148
Heavy Metal / May '90 / Sony.

Jhelisa

GALACTICA RUSH
Galactica rush / There's nothing wrong /
Hold my peace / Whirl keeps turning /
Death of a soul diva / Friendly pressure /
Baby god / Sweet dreams (4UIC) / Secret
place
CD _____ DOR 026CD
Dorado / Sep '94 / Disc.

Jigsy King

ASHES TO ASHES
CD _____ VPCD 1427
VP / Sep '95 / Jetstar.

HAVE TO GET YOU
CD _____ CRCD 19
Charm / Jul '93 / Jetstar.

Jim & Jesse

BLUEGRASS AND MORE (5 CDs)
Stormy horizons / Gosh I miss you all the
time / Flame of love / Beautiful moon of
Kentucky / My empty arms / Diesel train /
Voice of my darling / Uncle Will played the
fiddle / Fireball / Heartaches are heartaches /
Sweet little miss blue eyes / Somebody
loves you darlin' / She left me standing on
the mountain / Don't say goodbye if you
love me / Wish you knew / When it's time
for the whippoorwill to sing / Grave in the
valley / Blue bonnet lane / Are you missing
me / Congratulations, anyway / Pickin' and
a-grinnin / Stoney creek / Sixteen hundred
miles from home / South bound train / Ballad of Thunder Road / Uncle Jimmy Lee /
What about you / When my blue moon
turns to gold again / Nine pound hammer /
Little paper boy / I wonder where you are
tonight / Just when I needed you / Las Cas-
sas, Tennessee / Drifting and dreaming of
you / Grass is greener / Violet and the rose
/ Take my ring from your finger / Why not
confess / Better times a-coming / Wild
Georgia boys / Cotton mill man / To the top
of the world / Old time religion / Old camp
meeting days / Old country church / Are
you washed in the blood / It's a lonesome
road / Swing low, sweet chariot / Kneel at
the cross / Rock of ages / Where the roses
never fade / Lord I'm coming home / This
world is not my home / Where the soul
never dies / Ole slew foot / Sleepy eyed
John / Tell her lies and feed her candy / Y'all
come / Company's coming / Stay a little
longer / Rabbit in the log / Salty dog blues
/ Alabama / Good bunch of bisquits / Blue
grass banjo / Don't let nobody tie you down
/ Big hands / Dancing Molly / If you've seen
one you've seen them all / Memphis / Maybellene / Johnny B. Goode / Sweet little sixteen / Roll over Beethoven / Reelin' and
rockin' / Brown eyed handsome man / Too
much monkey business / Bye bye Johnny /
Back in the U.S.A / God moved in / I'll wear
the banner / Weapon of prayer / Angel
mother / Sing unto him a new song / In

God's eyes / Who did, Jesus did / How
much are you worth / He walks on the water
/ River of Jordan / Where the chilly winds
don't blow / All for the love of a girl / Diesel
on my tail / Truck driving man / Six days on
the road / Sam's place / Ballad of Thunder
Road (2) / Lovin' machine / Hot rod race /
Girl on the billboard / Give me forty acres /
Tijuana taxi / Greenwich Village folksongs
salesman / Pretty girls (in mini skirts) / Yonder comes a freight train / Rose City Chimes
/ Wildwood flower / Orange blossom special / Buckaroo / Remington ride / Sugarfoot
rag / Maiden's prayer / Down yonder / Banderilla / We'll build a bridge / When the
snow is on the roses / Then I'll stop goin'
for you / Big job / Are you teasing me / I
don't believe you've met my baby / My baby's gone / Cash on the barrelhead / Childish love / Must you throw dust in my face /
When I stop dreaming / Knoxville girl / I take
the chance / I'm hoping that you're hoping
/ Fire ball mail / Streamlined cannonball /
Tennessee Central 9 / (I heard that) Lonesome whistle / Pan American / Golden
rocket / Freight train in my mind / I like trains
/ Wabash cannonball
CD Set _____ BCD 15716
Bear Family / Sep '94 / Rollercoaster /
Direct / CM / Swift / ADA.

CLASSIC RECORDINGS (1952-1955)
I'll wash your love from my heart / Just
knowing will / Are you missing me / I will
always be waiting for you / Virginia waltz /
Are you lost in sin / Look for me (I'll be
there) / Purple heart / Air mail special / My
little honeysuckle rose / Waiting for a
message / Too many tears / My darling's in
heaven / Two arms to hold me / Is it true /
Memory of you / I'll wear the banner / My
garden of love / Tears of regret / I'll see you
tonight (in my dreams)
CD _____ BCD 15635
Bear Family / Apr '92 / Rollercoaster / Direct
/ CM / Swift / ADA.

Jimenez, Don Santiago

HIS FIRST AND LAST RECORDINGS
CD _____ ARHCD 414
Arhoolie / Apr '95 / ADA / Direct /
Cadillac.

Jimenez, Fernando

LA FIESTA
CD _____ TUMICD 012
Tumi / Apr '90 / Sterns / Discovery.

Jimenez, Flaco

ARIBA EL NORTE
CD _____ NETCD 1008
Munich / Aug '94 / CM / ADA /
Greensleeves / Direct.

AY TE DEJO EN SAN ANTONIO
CD _____ ARHCD 318
Arhoolie / Apr '95 / ADA / Direct /
Cadillac.

ENTRE HUMO Y BOTELLAS
CD _____ NETCD 1007
Munich / Aug '94 / CM / ADA /
Greensleeves / Direct.

**FLACO JIMENZ (14 Tracks Of Border
Music From Texas And Mexico)**
Se me olvido / La tracionera / Celos y sen-
timiento / Los barandeles del puente / Los
recuerdos del troquero / Suena y quereme
/ Deje mis padres / El corride de carascio /
Vualta mia / Vualta mia / Se apago me es-
trella / Amor chiquito / Chuquitata / Fichas
negras / Soy chicano / Como amigos /
Cayo una lagrima
CD _____ 90847-2
PMF / Jul '94 / Kingdom / Cadillac.

FLACO'S AMIGOS
La tumba sera el final / Did I tell you / Jen-
nette / Te quiero mas / Mi primer amor /
Free Mexican air force / Lucerito / Espero
tu regreso / Poquita fe / Feria polka / Para
toda la vida / I'm gonna love you like there
is no tomorrow / Yo quisiera saber /
Atotonilco
CD _____ ARHCD 3027
Arhoolie / Apr '95 / ADA / Direct / Cadillac.

FLACO'S FIRST
CD _____ ARHCD 370
Arhoolie / Apr '95 / ADA / Direct /
Cadillac.

PARTNERS
Change partners / Marina / Carmelita / El
puente roto / Across the borderline / Me
esta matando / Girl from Texas / West
Texas waltz / Las golondrinas / Eres un en-
canto / Don't worry baby
CD _____ 7599268222
WEA / Aug '92 / Warner Music.

SAN ANTONIO SOUL
CD _____ NETCD 1009
Munich / Aug '94 / CM / ADA /
Greensleeves / Direct.

**UN MOJADA SIN LICENCIA (Original
Hits 1955-1967)**
CD _____ ARHCD 396
Arhoolie / Apr '95 / ADA / Direct /
Cadillac.

VIVA SEGUIN

Viva seguin / La botellita / Hasta la vista / Los amores del flaco / Mi duice amor / Horalia / Arriba el norte / Polka town / La piedrera / Viajando en polka marianela / Adios muchachos
CD _____ SCR 42
Strictly Country / Nov '95 / ADA / Direct.

Jimenez, Santiago Jr.

CANCIONES DE MI PADRE

CD _____ WM 1019CD
Watermelon / May '94 / ADA / Direct.

EL MERO, MERO DE SAN ANTONIO

CD _____ ARHCD 317
Arhoolie / Apr '95 / ADA / Direct /
Cadillac.

LIVE IN HOLLAND

CD _____ SCR 38
Strictly Country / Mar '95 / ADA / Direct.

MUSICA DE TIEMPOS PASADOS DEL PRESENTE Y FUTURO

CD _____ WM 1035
Watermelon / Jul '95 / ADA / Direct.

Jinda, George

RELIABLE SOURCES (Jinda, George & World News)

Reliable sources / Behind the scenes / Storyteller / High road / Overleafing a new turn / Code of silence / Serengeti sky / Force of habit / For the rain forest
CD _____ JVC 20232
JVC / Nov '93 / New Note.

Jing, Pang

CLASSICAL CHINESE FOLK MUSIC (Jing, Pang & Ensemble)

CD _____ EUCD 1186
ARC / Apr '92 / ARC Music / ADA.

Jing Ying Soloists

EVENING SONG (Traditional Chinese Music)

Autumn moon / Ducks quacking / Love song of the grassland / Singing the night among fishing boats / Fishing song / Marriage of Chan Xian-Yuen / Moonlight over the spring river / Happy reunion / Bamboo song from the village / Variations on Yang City tune / Meditating on the past / Moon over Quan-Shan
CD _____ CDSDL 368
Saydisc / Mar '94 / Harmonia Mundi / ADA / Direct.

LIKE WAVES AGAINST THE SAND

Flowing streams / Suzhou scenery / Races / Love at the fair / High moon / Night / Chinese martial arts / Flower fair / Shenpadei folksong / Like waves against the sand (CD only) / Bird song / Legend
CD _____ CDSDL 325
Saydisc / Mar '94 / Harmonia Mundi / ADA / Direct.

Jinmo

LIVE AT THE KNITTING FACTORY

CD _____ KFWCD 129
Knitting Factory / Feb '95 / Grapevine.

Jivaros Quartet

NEAR THE NOISE

CD _____ L 8909301
Danceteria / Jan '90 / Plastic Head / ADA.

Jive Bunny

SWING THE MOOD

CD _____ CDSR 062
Telstar / Oct '94 / BMG.

Jive Five

OUR TRUE STORY

My true story / Do you hear wedding bells / Beggin' you please / Rain / Johnny never knew / People from another world / What time is it / When I was single / These golden rings / Girl with the wind in her hair / I don't want to be without you baby / No not again / You know what I would do / Never never / Hully gully callin' time / Hurry back
CD _____ CDCH 76
Ace / Aug '91 / Pinnacle / Cadillac / Complete/Pinnacle.

Jive Turkey

PERFUME EXPERIMENT

CD _____ DANCD 042
Danceteria / Sep '90 / Plastic Head / ADA.

Jo, Via

VIA JO

Fal / N-gai / Sutu kun / Banana / Lee / Mansani / Kumba / Farabi / Fern
CD _____ 3202092
Triloka / Apr '95 / New Note.

Jobim, Antonio Carlos

ANTONIO BRASILIERO

So dance samba / Piano na manguiera / How insensitive / Querida surfboard /

Samba de maria luiza / Forever green / Maracangalha / Maricotinha pato preto / Meu amigo radames / Blue train (trem azul) / Radames y pele / Chora coracao / Trem de ferro
CD _____ 4762812
Sony Jazz / May '95 / Sony.

E CONVIDADOS

CD _____ 826 665-2
Verve / Sep '91 / PolyGram.

GIRL FROM IPANEMA

CD _____ CD 62084
Saludos Amigos / Jan '96 / Targei/BMG.

JAZZ MASTERS

CD _____ 5164092
Verve / Apr '93 / PolyGram.

STONE FLOWER

Brazil / Stone flower / God and the devil in the land of the sun / Sabia / Choro / Andorinha / Amparo / Children's games / Tereza my love
CD _____ 4722382
Sony Jazz / Jan '95 / Sony.

WONDERFUL WORLD OF ANTONIO CARLOS JOBIM, THE

She's a carioca / Agua de Beber / Surfboard / Useless landscape / So tinha de ser com voce / A felicidade / Bonita / Favela / Valsa de Porto das Caixas / Samba do aviao / Por toda a minha vida / Dindi
CD _____ 1046708982
Discovery / Jun '95 / Warner Music.

Jocque, Beau

BEAU JOCQUE BOOGIE (Jocque, Beau & The Zydeco Hi-Rollers)

CD _____ ROUCD 2120
Rounder / Jun '93 / CM / Direct / ADA / Cadillac.

GIT IT BEAU JOCQUE (Jocque, Beau & The Zydeco Hi-Rollers)

CD _____ ROUCD 2134
Rounder / Apr '95 / CM / Direct / ADA / Cadillac.

PICK UP ON THIS (Jocque, Beau & The Zydeco Hi-Rollers)

CD _____ ROU 2129CD
Rounder / Apr '94 / CM / Direct / ADA / Cadillac.

Jodeci

DIARY OF A MAD BAND

My heart belongs to you / Cry for you / Feenin' / What about us / Ride and slide / Alone / You got it / Won't waste you / In the meanwhile / Gimme all you got / Sweaty / Jodecidal hotline / Lately (Not on LP) / Let's go through the motions (Not on LP) / Success (CD only)
CD _____ MCD 11019
MCA / Jan '95 / BMG.

FOREVER MY LADY

CD _____ MCLD 19307
MCA / Oct '95 / BMG.

SHOW, THE AFTER-PARTY, THE HOTEL, THE

Show / Bring on da funk / Room 723 / Fun 2 nite / Room 577 / S-more / After party / Get on up / Room 499 / Can we flo / Zipper / Let's do it all / Pump it back / D.J. Don Jeremy / Freek 'n you / Room 454 (De-Vante's inhermission) / Time and place / Fallin' / Love U 4 life / 4 U / Good luv
CD _____ MCD 11258
MCA / Jul '95 / BMG.

Jodimars

LETS ALL ROCK TOGETHER

CD _____ RSRCD 007
Rockstar / Jan '95 / Rollercoaster / Direct / Magnum Music Group / Nervous.

Joe

EVERYTHING

One for me / I'm in luv / All or nothing / It's alright / (If loving you is wrong) I don't want to be right / What's on your mind / Finally back / Get a little closer / I can do it right / Everything / Baby don't stop / Do me
CD _____ 518807-2
Vertigo / Feb '94 / PolyGram.

Joel, Billy

52ND STREET

Big shot / Honesty / My life / Zanzibar / Stiletto / Rosalinda's eyes / Half a mile away / Until the night / 52nd Street
CD _____ CD 83181
CBS / Nov '87 / Sony.
CD _____ CK 64412
Columbia / Feb '95 / Sony.

BRIDGE, THE

Running on ice / This is the time / Matter of trust / Baby grand / Big man on Mulberry street / Temptation / Code of silence / Getting closer / Modern woman
CD _____ 4655612
CBS / Feb '94 / Sony.

COLD SPRING HARBOUR

She's got a way / You can make me free / Everybody loves you now / Why Judy why

/ Falling of the rain / Turn around / You look so good to me / Tomorrow is today / Nocturne / Got to begin again
CD _____ 982637 2
Pickwick/Sony Collector's Choice / Aug '91 / Carlton Home Entertainment / Pinnacle / Sony.

GLASS HOUSES

You may be right / Sometimes a fantasy / Don't ask me why / It's still rock and roll to me / All for Leyna / I don't want to be alone / Sleeping with the television on / C'etait toi / Close to the borderline / Through the long night
CD _____ 4500872
CBS / Apr '94 / Sony.

GREATEST HITS: BILLY JOEL VOLS. 1 & 2 (2CD/LP/1MC Set)

Piano man / Say goodbye to Hollywood / New York state of mind / Stranger / Just the way you are / Movin' out (Anthony's song) / Only the good die young / She's always a woman / My life / Big shot / Honesty / You may be right / It's still rock and roll to me / Pressure / Allen town / Goodnight Saigon / Tell her about it / Uptown girl / Longest time / You're only human (Second wind) / Night is still young
CD _____ CD 88666
CBS / May '94 / Sony.

INNOCENT MAN, AN

Easy money / Innocent man / Longest time / This night / Tell her about it / Uptown girl / Careless talk / Christie Lee / Leave a tender moment alone / Keeping the faith
CD _____ 4663292
CBS / Aug '90 / Sony.

INNOCENT MAN, AN/52ND STREET/ THE STRANGER (3CD Set)

CD Set _____ 4673822
CBS / Dec '90 / Sony.

INNOCENT MAN, AN/THE STRANGER (2CD Set)

CD Set _____ 4716042
Columbia / Jul '92 / Sony.

KOHUEPT

Odoya / Angry young man / Honesty / Goodnight Saigon / Stiletto / Big man on Mulberry Street / Baby grand / Innocent man / Allentown / Matter of trust / Only the good die young / Sometimes a fantasy / Uptown girl / Big shot / Back in the U.S.S.R / Times they are a changin'
CD _____ 4674482
Columbia / May '92 / Sony.

NYLON CURTAIN

Allentown / Laura / Pressure / Goodnight Saigon / She's right on time / Room of our own / Surprises / Scandinavian skies / Where's the orchestra
CD _____ 4601862
CBS / Mar '88 / Sony.

PIANO MAN

Travellin' prayer / Ain't no crime / You're my home / Ballad of Billy The Kid / Worst comes to worst / Stop in Nevada / If I only had the words (to tell you) / Somewhere along the line / Captain Jack
CD _____ CD 32002
CBS / Apr '89 / Sony.

PIANO MAN/GLASS HOUSES/THE BRIDGE (3CD Set)

CD Set _____ 4683332
Columbia / Jan '93 / Sony.

RIVER OF DREAMS

No man's land / Great wall of China / Blonde over blue / Minor variation / Shades of grey / All about soul / Lullaby (Goodnight, my angel) / River of dreams / Two thousand years / Famous last words
CD _____ 4738722
Columbia / Aug '93 / Sony.

SONGS IN THE ATTIC

Miami 2017 / Summer, highland falls / Street life serenade / Los Angelenos / She's got a way / Everybody loves you now / Say goodbye to Hollywood / Captain Jack / You're my home / Ballad of Billy The Kid / I've loved these days
CD _____ CD 32364
CBS / Jun '89 / Sony.

SOUVENIR - THE ULTIMATE COLLECTION/INTERVIEW WITH BILLY JOEL (5CD Set)

CD Set _____ 4691742
Columbia / Jan '93 / Sony.

STORM FRONT

That's not her style / We didn't start the fire / Downeaster Alexa / I go to extremes / Shameless / Storm front / Leningrad / State of grace / When in Rome / And so it goes
CD _____ 4656582
CBS / Oct '89 / Sony.

STRANGER, THE

Movin' out / Just the way you are / Scenes from an Italian restaurant / Vienna / Stranger / Only the good die young / She's always a woman / Get it right the first time / Everybody has a dream
CD _____ 4509142
CBS / Jun '89 / Sony.

STREETLIFE SERENADE

Los Angelenos / Great suburban showdown / Root beer rag / Roberta / Entertainer / Last

of the big time spenders / Street life serenade / Weekend song / Souvenir / Mexican connection
CD _____ 4766112
Columbia / Apr '94 / Sony.

TURNSTILES

I've loved these days / Miami 2017 / Angry young man / Say goodbye to Hollywood / James / New York State of mind / Prelude / angry young man / Summer / Highland falls / All you wanna do is dance
CD _____ 982197 2
Pickwick/Sony Collector's Choice / Sep '93 / Carlton Home Entertainment / Pinnacle / Sony.

Jog, Pandit V.G.

VIOLIN

CD _____ MR 1003
Moment / Jul '93 / ADA / Koch.

Johansen, Bjorn

DEAR HENRIK

CD _____ GMCD 152
Gemini / Oct '89 / Cadillac.

Johansen, David

BUSTER'S HAPPY HOUR (Poindexter, Buster)

CD _____ RSFCD 818
Sequel / Oct '94 / BMG.

HERE COMES THE NIGHT

She loves strangers / Bohemian love pad / You fool you / My obsession / Marquesa De Sade / Here comes the night / Havin' so much fun / Rollin' job / Heart of gold
CD _____ 477848 2
Columbia / Oct '94 / Sony.

Johansson, Ulf

BIG BAND WULF

I let a song out of my heart / City express / In a mellow tone / I want to be happy / Ankbrand / Nuages / I won't dance / Bye bye blackbird
CD _____ NCD 8820
Phontastic / '93 / Wellard / Jazz Music / Cadillac.

TRACKIN' THE WULF

Leopard shoe / Lover come back to me / China boy / Song of Sarek / Nice work if you can get it / Moose blues / Sweet Lorraine / 2.19 Blues
CD _____ NCD 8809
Phontastic / Dec '94 / Wellard / Jazz Music / Cadillac.

John & Mary

VICTORY GARDENS

Red wooden beads / Azalea festival / Piles of dead leaves / We have nothing / Rags of flowers / I became alive / Open window / July 6th / Pram / Un Canadien errant
CD _____ RCD 10203
Rykodisc / Jul '91 / Vital / ADA.

WEEDKILLERS DAUGHTER, THE

Two worlds parted / Angels of stone / Your return / Clare's scarf / Cemetary ridge / Nightfall / I wanted you / One step backward / Fly me to the north / Clouds of reason / Maid of the mist / Poor murdered woman
CD _____ RCD 10259
Rykodisc / Mar '93 / Vital / ADA.

John Ac Alun

YR WYLAN WEN CHWARELWR

CD _____ SCD 2077
Sain / Dec '94 / Direct / ADA.

John Came

RHYTHMICON

CD _____ CDSTUMM 140
Mute / Jun '95 / Disc.

John, Elton

17.11.70

CD _____ 5281652
Rocket / Oct '95 / PolyGram.

21 AT 33

Changing the crown / Dear God / Give me the love / Little Jeannie / Never gonna fall in love again / Sartorial eloquence / Take me back / Two rooms at the end of the world / White lady white powder
CD _____ 800 055-2
Rocket / '83 / PolyGram.

BLUE MOVES

Your starter tonight / One horse town / Chameleon / Boogie pilgrim / Cage the songbird / Crazy water / Shoulder holster / Sorry seems to be the hardest word / Out of the blue / Between 17 and 20 / Wide-eyed and laughter / Someone's final love song / Where's the shoorah / If there's a God in Heaven (what's he waiting for) / Idol / Non-existent TV series, theme from / Bite your lip (get up and dance)
CD _____ 8228182
Rocket / Jun '89 / PolyGram.

BREAKING HEARTS
Restless / Slow down Georgie / Who wears these shoes / Breaking hearts / Li'l refrigerator / Passengers / In neon / Burning bridges / Did he shoot her / Sad songs
CD _____ 822 088-2
Rocket / Jun '84 / PolyGram.

CAPTAIN FANTASTIC & THE BROWN DIRT COWBOY
Captain Fantastic and the Brown Dirt Cowboy / Tower of Babel / Bitter fingers / Tell me when the whistle blows / Someone saved my life tonight / Gotta get a) meal ticket / Better off dead / Writing / We all fall in love sometimes / Curtains / Lucy in the sky with diamonds ('95 CD only) / One day at a time ('95 CD only) / Philadelphia freedom ('95 CD only)
CD _____ 5281602
Rocket / Jul '95 / PolyGram.

CARIBOU
Bitch is back / Pinky / Dixie Lily / Solar prestige a gammon / Don't let the sun go down on me / Ticking / Grimsby / You're so static / I've seen the saucers / Stinker / Pinball wizard / Sick city / Cold highway / Step into Christmas
CD _____ 5281582
Rocket / May '95 / PolyGram.

CHARTBUSTERS GOES POP
Don't forget to remember / I can't tell the bottom from the top / Young, gifted and black / Signed, sealed, delivered (I'm yours) / Natural sinner / She sold me magic / Cotton fields / Spirit in the sky / Good morning freedom / Travelling band / In the summertime / Yellow river / United we stand / My baby loves lovin' / Love of the common people / Lady D'arbanville / Snake in the grass / Up around the bend
CD _____ RPM 142
RPM / Mar '95 / Pinnacle.

DON'T SHOOT ME I'M ONLY THE PIANO PLAYER
Daniel / Teacher I need you / Elderberry wine / Blues for my baby and me / Midnight creeper / Have mercy on the criminal / I'm gonna be a teenage idol / Texan love song / Crocodile rock / High flying bird / Screw you ('95 reissue only) / Jack Rabbit ('95 reissue only) / Whenever you're ready (we'll go steady again) ('95 reissue only) / Skyline pigeon ('95 reissue only)
CD _____ 5281542
Rocket / May '95 / PolyGram.

DUETS (John, Elton & Various Artists)
Teardrops / When I think about love (I think about you) / Power / Shaky ground / True love / If you were me / Woman's needs / Don't let the sun go down on me / Old friend / Go on and on / Don't go breaking my heart / Ain't nothing like the real thing / I'm your puppet / Love letters / Born to lose / Duet for one
CD _____ 5184782
Rocket / Dec '93 / PolyGram.

ELTON JOHN
Your song / I need you to turn to / Take me to the pilot / No shoe strings on Louise / First episode at Heinton / Sixty years on / Border song / Greatest discovery / Cage / King must die / Bad side of the moon / Grey seal / Rock 'n' roll Madonna
CD _____ 5281562
Rocket / May '95 / PolyGram.

ELTON JOHN COLLECTION, THE
Funeral for a friend (Love lies bleeding) / Sweet painted lady / Elderberry wine / Come down in time / Border song / Crocodile rock / Mona Lisas and mad hatters / Greatest discovery / Country comfort / Blues for my baby and me / Ballad of a well known gun
CD _____ PWKS 551
Carlton Home Entertainment / Oct '89 / Carlton Home Entertainment.

EMPTY SKY
Empty sky / Valhalla / Western Ford gateway / Hymn 2000 / Lady what's tomorrow / Sails / Scaffold / Skyline pigeon / Gulliver/ It's hay chewed/Reprise / Lady Samantha / All across the heavens / It's me that you need / Just like strange rain
CD _____ 5281572
Rocket / May '95 / PolyGram.

FOX, THE
Breaking down barriers / Heart in the right place / Just like Belgium / Fox / Nobody wins / Fascist faces / Carla etude - fanfare / Chloe / Heels of the wind / Elton's song
CD _____ 800 063-2
Rocket / Jun '89 / PolyGram.

GOODBYE YELLOW BRICK ROAD
Funeral for a friend (Love lies bleeding) / Candle in the wind / Benny and the jets / Goodbye yellow brick road / This song has no title / Grey seal / Jamaica jerk off / I've seen that movie too / Sweet painted lady / Ballad of Danny Bailey (1909-1934) / Dirty little girl / All the girls love Alice / Your sister can't twist (But she can rock 'n' roll) / Saturday night's alright for fighting / Roy Rogers / Social disease / Harmony
CD _____ 5281592
Rocket / May '95 / PolyGram.

HERE AND THERE (Live At Royal Festival Hall/Madison Square Gardens 1974)
Skyline pigeon / Border song / Take me to the pilot / Country comfort / Love song / Bad side of the moon / Burn down the mission / Honky cat / Crocodile rock / Candle in the wind / Your song / Saturday night's alright for fighting / Funeral for a friend (Love lies bleeding) / Rocket man / Take me to the pilot #2 / Benny and the jets / Grey seal / Daniel / You're so static / Whatever gets you thru the night / Lucy in the sky with diamonds / I saw her standing there / Don't let the sun go down on me / Your song #2 / Bitch is back
CD Set _____ 5281642
Rocket / Oct '95 / PolyGram.

HONKY CHATEAU
Honky cat / Mellow / I think I'm going to kill myself / Susie (dramas) / Rocket man / Salvation / Slave / Amy / Mona Lisas and mad hatters / Hercules / Slave (alternative version) ('95 CD only)
CD _____ 5281622
Rocket / Jul '95 / PolyGram.

ICE ON FIRE
This town / Cry to heaven / Soul glove / Nikita / Too young / Wrap her up / Satellite / Tell me what the papers say / Candy by the pound / Shoot down the moon
CD _____ 8262132
Rocket / Jan '95 / PolyGram.

JUMP UP
Dear John / Spiteful child / Ball and chain / Legal boys / I am your robot / Blue eyes / Empty garden / Princess / Where have all the good times gone / All quiet on the Western Front
CD _____ 8000372
Rocket / Jan '95 / PolyGram.

LADY SAMANTHA
Rock 'n' roll Madonna / Whenever you're ready / Bad side of the moon / Jack rabbit / Into the old man's shoes / It's me that you need / Ho ho ho (Who'd be a turkey at Christmas) / Screw you / Skyline pigeon / Just like strange rain / Grey seal / Honey roll / Lady Samantha / Friends
CD _____ 8320192
Rocket / Jun '87 / PolyGram.

LEATHER JACKETS
Leather jackets / Hoop of fire / Don't trust that woman / Go it alone / Gypsy heart / Slow rivers / Heartache all over the world / Angeline / Memory of love / Paris I fall apart
CD _____ 830 487-2
Rocket / Nov '86 / PolyGram.

LIVE IN AUSTRALIA
Sixty years on / I need you to turn to / Greatest discovery / Tonight / Sorry seems to be the hardest word / King must die / Take me to the pilot / Tiny dancer / Have mercy on the criminal / Madman across the water / Candle in the wind / Burn down the mission / Your song / Don't let the sun go down on me
CD _____ 832 470-2
Rocket / Feb '87 / PolyGram.

LOVE SONGS
Sacrifice / Candle in the wind / I guess that's why they call it the blues / Don't let the sun go down on me / Sorry seems to be the hardest word / Blue eyes / Daniel / Nikita / Your song / One / Someone saved my life tonight / True love / Can you feel the love tonight / Circle of life / Blessed / Please / Song for Guy
CD _____ 5287882
Rocket / Nov '95 / PolyGram.

MADE IN ENGLAND
Believe / Made in England / House / Cold / Pain / Belfast / Latitude / Please / Man / Lies / Blessed
CD _____ 5261852
Rocket / Mar '95 / PolyGram.

MADMAN ACROSS THE WATER
Levon / Razor face / Madman across the water / Indian sunset / Holiday inn / Rotten peaches / All the nasties / Goodbye / Tiny dancer
CD _____ 5281612
Rocket / Jul '95 / PolyGram.

ONE, THE
Simple life / One / Sweat it out / Whitewash country / North / When a woman doesn't want you / Runaway train / Last song / Understanding women / On dark street / Emily / The one
OD _____ 5123602
Rocket / Jun '92 / PolyGram.

RARE MASTERS
Madman across the water / Into the old man's shoes / Rock me when he's gone / Slave / Skyline pigeon / Jack rabbit / Whenever you're ready (we'll go steady again) / Let me be your car / Screw you / One day at a time / Cold highway / Sick city / Ho ho ho (Who'd be a turkey at Christmas) / Step into Christmas / I saw her standing there / Here's to the next time / Lady Samantha / All across the havens / It's me that you need / Just like strange rain / Bad side of the moon / Rock 'n' roll Madonna / Grey seal / Friends / Michelle's song / Seasons / Variation on Michelle's song / Can I put you on / Honey roll / Reprise seasons / Four

moods / I meant to do my work today (a day in the country) / Variation on friends
CD Set _____ 5143052
Rocket / Jan '93 / PolyGram.

REG STRIKES BACK
Town of plenty / Word in Spanish / Mona Lisas and mad hatters part II / I don't wanna go on with you like that / Goodbye Marlon Brando / Heavy traffic / Poor cow / Camera never lies / Since God invented girls
CD _____ 8347012
Rocket / Jan '95 / PolyGram.

ROCK 'N' ROLL MADONNA
Spectrum/Karussell / Mar '94 / PolyGram / THE.
CD _____ 5502132

ROCK OF THE WESTIES
Yell help / Wednesday night / Ugly / Dan Dare (pilot of the future) / Island girl / Grow some funk of your own / I feel like a bullet (in the gun of Robert Ford) / Street kids / Hard luck story / Feed me / Billy Bones and the white bird / Don't go breaking my heart ('95 CD only)
CD _____ 5281632
Rocket / Jul '95 / PolyGram.

SINGLE MAN, A
Big dipper / Georgia / I don't care / It ain't gonna be easy / Madness / Part time love / Return to Paradise / Reverie / Shine on through / Shooting star / Song for Guy
CD _____ 8268052
Rocket / Sep '89 / PolyGram.

SLEEPING WITH THE PAST
Club at the end of the street / Durban deep / Sacrifice / Blue Avenue / Healing hands / Whispers
CD _____ 8388392
Rocket / Sep '89 / PolyGram.

SOLO PIANO PLAYS THE HITS OF ELTON JOHN (Various Artists)
CD _____ GRF 233
Tring / Aug '93 / Tring / Prism.

SONGBOOK
All quiet on the Western front / Tiny dancer / Where to now St. Peter / Ego / Shooting star / Wrap her up / Texan love song / Nobody wins / Empty garden / Lady what's tomorrow / Who wears these shoes / Just like Belgium / Empty sky / Crazy water / Island girl / Friends
CD _____ PWKS 4126 P
Carlton Home Entertainment / Oct '92 / Carlton Home Entertainment.

SONGBOOK
CD _____ VSOPCD 192
Connoisseur / Oct '93 / Pinnacle.

TO BE CONTINUED....THE VERY BEST OF ELTON JOHN (4CD/MC Set)
Come back baby / Lady Samantha / It's me that you need / Your song / Rock 'n' roll Madonna / Bad side of the moon / Take me to the pilot / Border song / Sixty years on / Country comfort / Gray seal / Friends / Levon / Tiny dancer / Madman across the water / Honky cat / Mona Lisa's and mad hatters / Rocket man / Daniel / Crocodile rock / Benny and the jets / Goodbye yellow brick road / All the girls love Alice / Funeral for a friend (Love lies bleeding) / Love lies / Bleeding / Whenever you're ready (we'll go steady again) / Saturday night's alright for fighting / Jack Rabbit / Harmony / Young man's blues / Step into Christmas / Bitch is back / Pinball wizard / Someone saved my life tonight / Philadelphia freedom / One day at a time / Lucy in the sky with diamonds / I saw her standing there / Island girl / Sorry seems to be the hardest word / Don't go breaking my heart / I feel like a bullet (in the gun of Robert Ford) / Ego / Empty garden (hey hey Johnny) / I guess that's why they call it the blues / I'm still standing / Sad songs (say so much) / Act of war / Nikita / Candle in the wind / Carla etude / Don't let the sun go down on me / I don't want to go on with you like that / Give peace a chance / Sacrifice / Made for me / Easier to walk away / Understanding women / Suit of wolves
CD Set _____ 8482362
Rocket / Nov '91 / PolyGram.

TOO LOW FOR ZERO
Cold as Christmas / I'm still standing / Too low for zero / I guess that's why they call it the blues / Crystal / Kiss the bride / Whipping boy / My baby's a saint / One more arrow
CD _____ 811 052-2
Rocket / '83 / PolyGram.

TUMBLEWEED CONNECTION
Ballad of a well known gun / Come down in time / Country comfort / Son of your father / My father's gun / Where to now St. Peter / Love song / Amoreena / Talking old soldiers / Burn down the mission / Into the old man's shoes ('95 CD/MC only) / Madman across the water ('95 CD/MC only)
CD _____ 5281552
Rocket / May '95 / PolyGram.

TWO ROOMS (A Celebration Of The Songs Of Elton John & Bernie Taupin) (Various Artists)
Border song / Rocket man / Come down in time / Saturday night's alright for fighting / Crocodile rock / Daniel / Sorry seems to be

the hardest word / Levon / Bitch is back / Your song / Philadelphia freedom / Don't let the sun go down on me / Madman across the water / Burn down the mission / Tonight
CD _____ 8457492
Rocket / Oct '91 / PolyGram.

VERY BEST OF ELTON JOHN, THE (2CD/MC/LP Set)
Your song / Rocket man / Crocodile rock / Daniel / Goodbye yellow brick road / Saturday night's alright for fighting / Candle in the wind / Don't let the sun go down on me / Lucy in the sky with diamonds / Philadelphia freedom / Someone saved my life tonight / Pinball wizard / Bitch is back (Additional track on CD and cassette.) / Bitch is back (Additional track on CD and cassette.) / Don't go breaking my heart / Benny and the jets / Sorry seems to be the hardest word for Guy / Part time love / Blue eyes / I guess that's why they call it the blues / I'm still standing / Kiss the bride / Sad songs / Passengers / Nikita / Sacrifice / You gotta love someone / I don't wanna go on with you like that (Additional tracks on CD and cassette.) / Easier to walk away (Additional track on CD and cassette.)
CD Set _____ 846 947 2
Rocket / Oct '95 / PolyGram.

VICTIM OF LOVE
Johnny B. Goode / Warm love in a cold world / Born bad / Thunder in the night / Spotlight / Street boogie / Victim of love
CD _____ 5128812
Rocket / Jan '95 / PolyGram.

John F. Kennedy Memorial.

PLAYING POPULAR IRISH MARCHES (John F. Kennedy Memorial Pipe Band)
CD _____ IRB 1922CD
Outlet / May '95 / ADA / Duncans / CM / Ross / Direct / Kooh.

John, Little Willie

FEVER
Fever / I'm stickin' with you baby / Do something for me / Love, life and money / Suffering with the blues / Dinner date / All around the world / Need your love so bad / Young girl / Letter from my darling / I've got to go cry / My nerves
CD _____ CDCHARLY 246
Charly / Oct '90 / Charly / THE / Cadillac.

MISTER LITTLE WILLIE JOHN
You're a sweetheart / Let's rock while the rockin's good / Look what you've done to me / Home at last / Are you ever coming back / Don't leave me dear / All my love belongs to you / Spasms / Will the sun shine tomorrow / You got to get up early in the morning / Little bit of lovin' / Why don't you haul off and love me
CD _____ KCD 603
King/Paddle Wheel / Mar '90 / New Note.

SURE THINGS
CD _____ KCD 000739
King/Paddle Wheel / Dec '92 / New Note.

John, Mable

STAY OUT OF THE KITCHEN
Stay out of the kitchen / Leftover love / Able Mable / Shouldn't I love him / Catch that man / Ain't giving it up / Running out / Love tornado / Bigger and better / Sweet devil / It's crying / Drop on in / That woman will give it a try / That's what my love can do / I love you more than words can say / Have your cake / Be warm to me / I taught you how / If you rturn up what you got (see what you lost / Don't get caught / Man's too busy / I'm a big girl now / To love what I want, and want what I love / Sorry about that / I need your love so bad
CD _____ CDSXD 048
Stax / Sep '92 / Pinnacle.

Johnboy

CLAIM DEDICATIONS
CD _____ TR27CD
Trance / Aug '94 / SRD.

PISTOL SWING
CD _____ TR 16D
Trance / Jun '93 / SRD.

Johnnie & Jack

JOHNNIE AND JACK AND THE TENNESSEE MOUNTAIN BOYS (Johnnie & Jack & The Tennessee Mountain Boys)
Lord watch over my daddy / There's no housing shortage in heaven / Love in the first degree / Too many blues / This is the end / Paper boy / Sing Tom Kitty / Jolie blon / I'll be listening / This world can't stand long / Old country church / I heard my name on the radio / Turn your radio on / He will set your fields on fire / What about you / For old times sake / Just when I need you / She went with a smile / Trials and tribulations / Burial alive / That was my saviour call / Pray together and we'll stay together / Shout / You better get down on your knees and pray / Too much sinning / Jesus hits like the atom bomb / Too far from God / Jesus remembered me / Poison love / Lonesome / I'm gonna love you one more

349

time / Smile on my lips / Take my ring from your finger / I can't tell my heart that / Cryin' heat blues / Let your conscience be your guide / Hummingbird / How can I believe in you / You tried to ruin my name / Ashes of love / Three ways of knowing / When you want a little loving / You can't fool God / Precious memories / Shake my mothers hand for me / When the saviour reached down for me / Slow poison / But I love you just the same / Just for tonight / Don't show off / Heart trouble / Two loving blues / I've gone and done it again / Don't let the stars get in your eyes / Only one I ever loved I lost / Borrowed diamonds / Private property / S.O.S. / Called from Potter's field / I'll live with God (to die no more) / Angel's rock me to sleep / Eastern gate / Hank Williams will live forever / South in New Orleans / You're my downfall / Winner of your heart / Don't say goodbye if you love me / Pig latin song / Love tags / Cheated out of love / From the manger to the cross / I'm ready to go / God put a rainbow in the cloud / Don't give away your bible / Crazy worried mind / Love's a pleasure not a habit in Mexico / You've got me in your power / Dynamite kisses / I loved you better than you knew / Pick-up date / I get so lonely / You're just what the doctor ordered / I ain't got time / All the time / Goodnight sweetheart, goodnight / Honey, I need you / Kiss crazy baby / Beware of it / Sincerely / Carry on / No one dear but you / We live in two different worlds / So lonely baby / Look out / Don't waste your tears / Weary moments / Dream when you're lonely / Tom cat's kittens / Feet of clay / I want to be loved / You can't divorce my heart / Baby, it's in the making / I wonder why you said goodbye / Love love love / What's the reason I'm not pleasin' you / Love fever / Live and let live / When my blue moon turns to gold again / Why not confess / Banana boat song (Day O) / Mr. Clock / Love me now / If tears would bring you back / That's why I'm leavin' / Oh boy, I love her / Baby I need you / Nothing but sweet lies / Move it on over / No one will ever know / I don't mean to cry / I wonder where you are tonight / Slowly / Wedding bells / I never can come back to you / You are my sunshine / Stop the world (and let me off) / Camel walk stroll / I've seen this movie before / Yeah / Leave our moon alone / Lonely island pearl / That's the way the cookie crumbles / Just when I needed you / With a smile on my lips / What do you know about heartaches / I wonder if you know / It's just the idea / Sailor man / Wild and wicked world / Sweetie pie / Happy, lucky love / Just like you / Dreams come true / She loves me no more / Country music has gone to town / Talkin' eyes / Lonesome night blues / Love problems / I'm always by myself when I'm alone / Smiles and tears / Uncle John's bongos / Let my heart be broken / Sweet baby / The moon is high and so am I / 36-22-36 / What do you think of her now / Bye bye love / Foolin' around / Waterloo / Little bitty tear / I overlooked an orchard / You'll never get a better chance than this
CD Set _____ BCD 15553
Bear Family / Jun '92 / Rollercoaster / Direct / CM / Swift / ADA.

JOHNNY & JACK WITH KITTY WELLS AT KWKH
Raining on the mountain / Intro / Orange blossom special / White dove / Singing waterfall / Sweeping through the gate / Wake up Susan / I heard my mother weeping / My bucket's got a hole in it / This world can't stand / Cheatam country breakdown / Death of little Kathy Fiscus / No letter in the mail today / I saw the light / Mississippi sawyer / Cotton eyed Joe / Little cabin home on the hill / Love or hate / He will set your fields on fire / It's raining on the mountain
CD _____ BCD 15808
Bear Family / Nov '94 / Rollercoaster / Direct / CM / Swift / ADA.

Johnny & The Hurricanes

RED RIVER ROCK
CD _____ RMB 75026
Remember / Nov '93 / Total/BMG.

Johnny & The Roccos

GREAT SCOTS
Crazy baby / Cat talk / Rockabilly / My baby's crazy about Elvis / Don't wake up the kids / Sneaky Pete / Stompin with the wildcats / Blue blue day / Cherokee boogie / Rock 'n' roll record girl / Holocaust boogie / My baby left me / I'm a little mixed up / Honey rush / Flying saucers / Hey little girl / Beat / Feelings of love / Southern guitar boogie / Good rockin' tonight
CD _____ CDMF 091
Magnum Force / Mar '95 / Magnum Music Group.

Johnny Hates Jazz

TURN BACK THE CLOCK
Shattered dreams / Heart of gold / Turn back the clock / Don't say it's love / What other reason / I don't want to be a hero / Listen / Different reasons / Don't let it end this way / Foolish heart / Turn back the clock (extended) (CD only) / Heart of gold

(extended) (CD only) / Shattered dreams (extended) (CD only)
CD _____ CDV 2475
Virgin / '88 / EMI.

VERY BEST OF JOHNNY HATES JAZZ
Shattered dreams / My secret garden / Me and my foolish heart / Living in the past / I don't want to be a hero / Cage / Turn the tide / Heart of gold / Don't say it's love / Let me change your mind tonight / Last to know / Fool's gold / Cracking up / Turn back the clock
CD _____ CDVIP 119
Virgin VIP / Nov '93 / Carlton Home Entertainment / THE / EMI.

Johnny P.

BAD IN A DANCEHALL
CD _____ RRTGCD 7784
Rohit / Jul '90 / Jetstar.

Johnny Was

SUMMER LOVERS
CD _____ CDREP 8013
Candor / Mar '95 / Else.

Johns, Bibi

BELLABIMBA
Night filled with echoes / Someone to love your tears away / Puppy love / Two faced clock / I could never be ashamed of you / I wish I was a puppet on a string / Auf Jamaika schenken abends die Maltrosen / Bella bimba / Ich habe solche Angst / Sehnsucht / Bye bye baby / Little rock / Bimbo / In Barrabana / An jedem finger zehn / Gilly gilly ossenfeffer Katzenellenbogen the sea / Carnavalito / Ro ro ro ro Robinson / Die gipsy band / Papa tanzt mambo / Nach uns die sintflut / Zwei herzen im mai / Ich mocht auf deiner hochzeit tanzen
CD _____ BCD 15649
Bear Family / Mar '92 / Rollercoaster / Direct / CM / Swift / ADA.

John's Black Dirt

PERPETUAL OPTIMISM IS A FORCE MULTIPLIER
CD _____ GROW 202
Grass / Oct '94 / SRD.

John's Children

LEGENDARY ORGASM ALBUM, THE
Smashed blocked / Just what you want - just what you'll get / Killer Ben / Jagged time lapse / Smashed blocked (Live) / You're a nothing / Not the sort of girl / Cold on me / Leave me alone / Let me know / Just what you want -just what you'll get (Live) / Why do you lie / Strange affair / But she's mine
CD _____ CDMRED 31
Cherry Red / May '94 / Pinnacle.

BOMBS AWAY (Johns, Evan & The H-Bombs)
Love is gone / I'm a little mixed up / Done by me / Twister county / Dance, Frannie, Dance / Lessons that burn / Oh! New Orleans / Boudin man / Pain of love / Tired of trash / Still feels good / Poor boy's dream
CD _____ RCD 10117
Rykodisc / Dec '92 / Vital / ADA.

KINSFOLK
CD _____ VIRUS 19CD
Alternative Tentacles / Jun '93 / Pinnacle.

ROLLIN' THRU THE NIGHT (Johns, Evan & The H-Bombs)
CD _____ VIRUS 47CD
Alternative Tentacles / '92 / Pinnacle.

Johns, Evan

Johnson Mountain Boys

BLUE DIAMOND
Duncan and Brady / My better days / It don't bring you back to me / Christine Leroy / See God's ark movin' / Blue diamond mines / Teardrops like raindrops / Our last goodbye / Future remains / You done me wrong / Roll on blues / There goes my love / Only a hobo / Harbor of love
CD _____ CDROU 0293
Rounder / Apr '93 / CM / Direct / ADA / Cadillac.

FAVOURITES
CD _____ CD 11509
Rounder / '88 / CM / Direct / ADA / Cadillac.

LET THE WHOLE WORLD TALK
Let the whole world talk / Maury river blues / Memories cover everything I own / He said if I be lifted up / Goodbye to the blues / Virginia waltz / Maybe you will change your mind / Memories that we shared / Sweeter love than yours / I'll never know / Shouting in the air / Beneath the old Southern skies
CD _____ CD 0225
Rounder / '88 / CM / Direct / ADA / Cadillac.

LIVE AT THE BIRCHMERE
CD _____ ROUCD 0191
Rounder / Oct '94 / CM / Direct / ADA / Cadillac.

Johnson, Anthony

TOGETHERNESS
CD _____ CDSGP 050
Prestige / Aug '93 / Total/BMG.

Johnson, Blind Willie

COMPLETE RECORDINGS, THE (2CD Set)
I know his blood can make me whole / Jesus make up my dying bed / It's nobody's fault but mine / Mother's children have a hard time / Dark was the night / Cold was the ground / If I had my way I'd tear the building down / I'm gonna run to the city of refuge / Jesus is coming soon / Lord I can't just keep from crying / Keep your lamp trimmed and burning / Let your light shine on me / God don't never change / Bye and bye I'm going to see the King / Sweeter as the years roll by / You'll need somebody on your bond / When the war was on / Praise God I'm satisfied / Take your burden to the Lord and leave it / There / Take your stand / God moves on the water / Can't nobody hide from God / If it had not been for Jesus / Rain don't fall on me / Trouble will soon be over / Soul of a man / Everybody ought to treat a stranger right / Church, I'm fully saved today / John the revelator / You're gonna need somebody on your bond
CD Set _____ 4721902
Columbia / May '93 / Sony.

DARK WAS THE NIGHT
CD _____ IGOCD 2024
Indigo / Sep '95 / Direct / ADA.

SWEETER AS THE YEARS GO BY
CD _____ YAZCD 1078
Yazoo / Apr '91 / CM / ADA / Roots / Koch.

Johnson, Bob

KING OF ELFLANDS DAUGHTER, THE (Johnson, Bob & Peter Knight)
Request / Lirazel / Witch / Alveric's journey / Through Elfland / Rune of the elf king / Cooing of the troll / Just another day of searching / Too much magic / Beyond the fields / We know
CD _____ EDCD 342
Edsel / Feb '92 / Pinnacle / ADA.

Johnson, Buddy

AT THE SAVOY BALLROOM 1945-46
CD _____ 3801252
Jazz Archives / Oct '92 / Jazz Music / Discovery / Cadillac.

BUDDY & ELLA JOHNSON 1953-1964 (Johnson, Buddy & Ella Johnson)
CD Set _____ BCD 15479
Bear Family / Mar '92 / Rollercoaster / Direct / CM / Swift / ADA.

COME HOME
Come home / Search / There'll be no one / I lost track of everything / Have a little faith in me / Too many hearts / Whisperers / My lonely heart / Crazy afternoon / Keep a light in the window for me / My one desire / Muddy water
CD _____ KCD 0569
King/Paddle Wheel / Mar '93 / New Note.

Johnson, Bunk

BUNK & LU (Johnson, Bunk & Lu Watters)
CD _____ GTCD 12024
Good Time Jazz / Oct '93 / Jazz Music / Wellard / Pinnacle / Cadillac.

BUNK JOHNSON
Panama / Down by the riverside / Storyville blues / Ballin' the Jack / Make me a pallet on the floor / Weary blues / Moose march / Bunk's blues / Yes Lord I'm crippled / Bunk Johnson talking
CD _____ GTJCD 12048-2
Good Time Jazz / Jul '94 / Jazz Music / Wellard / Pinnacle / Cadillac.

BUNK JOHNSON & LEADBELLY (Johnson, Bunk & Leadbelly)
CD _____ AMCD 11
American Music / Oct '93 / Jazz Music.

BUNK JOHNSON 1944-45
CD _____ AMCD 12
American Music / Apr '94 / Jazz Music.

BUNK JOHNSON AND HIS SUPERIOR JAZZ BAND
Panama / Down by the riverside / Storyville blues / Ballin' the Jack / Make me a pallet on the floor / Yes Lord I'm crippled / Weary blues / Moose march / Bunk's blues / Bunk Johnson talking
CD _____ GTJCD 120482
Good Time Jazz / Jul '94 / Jazz Music / Wellard / Pinnacle / Cadillac.

IN SAN FRANCISCO
CD _____ AMCD 16
American Music / Jan '93 / Jazz Music.

KING OF THE BLUES
CD _____ AMCD 1
American Music / Oct '92 / Jazz Music.

Johnson, Dick

PLAYS ALTO SAX & FLUTE & SOPRANO SAX & CLARINET
All the things you are / I'm old fashioned / Donna Lee / Star crossed lovers / Kelly Green / When the world was young / Who cares / Kelly Blue / In a sentimental mood / Everything I love / Get out of time
CD _____ CCD 4107
Concord Jazz / Mar '92 / New Note.

Johnson, Dink

PIANO PLAYERS, THE (Johnson, Dink & Charlie Thompson)
CD _____ AMCD 11
American Music / Jun '93 / Jazz Music.

Johnson, Don

HEARTBEAT
Heartbeat / Voice on a hotline / Last sound / Coco don't / Heartache away / Love roulette / Star tonight / Gotta get away / Can't take your memory
CD _____ 983290 2
Pickwick/Sony Collector's Choice / Sep '93 / Carlton Home Entertainment / Pinnacle / Sony.

Johnson, Ella

SAY ELLA
CD _____ RBD 604
Jukebox Lil / Apr '91 / Swift / Wellard.

Johnson, Freddy

CLASSICS 1933-39
CD _____ CLASSICS 829
Classics / Sep '95 / Discovery / Jazz Music.

Johnson, General

WHAT GOES AROUND COMES AROUND (Johnson, General & Chairmen Of The Board)
CD _____ SUR 4168
Ichiban / Feb '94 / Koch.

Johnson, Henry

NEW BEGINNINGS
CD _____ 101 S 7138 2
101 South / Jun '93 / New Note.

UNION COUNTY FLASH
Join the army / Who's going home with you / Boogie baby / Rufe's imprmptu rag / My Mother's grave will be found / My baby's house / Be glad when you're dead / Little Sally Jones / John Henry / Crow Jane / My dog's blues / Old home town / Sign of the judgement
CD _____ TRIX 3304
Trix / Jun '94 / New Note.

Johnson, Howard

ARRIVAL (Johnson, Howard's Nubia)
CD _____ 5239852
Verve / May '95 / PolyGram.

Johnson, J.J.

BE-BOP LEGENDS
CD _____ MCD 0722
Moon / Aug '95 / Harmonia Mundi / Cadillac.

J.J. JOHNSON'S JAZZ QUINTETS
Jay bird / Coppin' the bop / Jay jay / Mad be bop / Boneology / Down Vernon's alley / Audobon / Don't blame me / Goof square / Bee jay / Yesterdays / Riffette
CD _____ SV 0151
Savoy Jazz / Apr '92 / Conifer / ADA.

JAY AND KAI (Johnson, J.J. & Kai Winding)
Bernie's tune / Blues for trombones / Major / Yesterdays / Co-op / Reflections / Blues in twos / What is this thing called love / Boy next door / I could write a book / Carioca
CD _____ SV 0163
Savoy Jazz / Apr '93 / Conifer / ADA.

SOUTH PACIFIC JAZZ
Royal garden blues / St. Louis blues / Mood indigo / Perido / Man with the horn / Oh Lady be good / Stormy weather / Stompin' at the Savoy / Body and soul / One o'clock jump / Don't blame me / Harvest time
CD _____ SV 0219
Savoy Jazz / May '93 / Conifer / ADA.

TANGENCE
CD _____ 5265882
Verve / May '95 / PolyGram.

THINGS ARE GETTING BETTER (Johnson, J.J. & Al Gree)
Soft winds / Let me see / Softly as in a morning sunrise / It's only a paper moon / Boy meets horn / Things ain't what they used to be / Things are getting better all the time / Don't cha hear me callin' to ya

Johnson, Bob

Last Testament

CD _____ DD 225
Delmark / Mar '95 / Hot Shot / ADA / CM / Direct / Cadillac.

350

CD _____ OJCCD 745
Original Jazz Classics / May '93 / Wellard /
Jazz Music / Cadillac / Complete/Pinnacle.

TROMBONE MASTER, THE
CD _____ 4633402
Sony Jazz / Jan '95 / Sony.

Johnson, James

JAMES 'STUMP' JOHNSON 1929-1933
(Johnson, James 'Stump')
CD _____ DOCD 5250
Blues Document / May '94 / Swift / Jazz
Music / Hot Shot.

Johnson, James P.

CAROLINA SHOUT
Steeplechase rag / Twilight rag / Carolina
shout / Baltimore buzz / Gypsy blues / Har-
lem strut / Eccentricity / Don't mess with
me / Nervous blues / Ole Miss blues / Isn't
givin' nothin' away / Muscle shoal blues /
Farewell blues / Charleston
CD _____ BCD 105
Biograph / Jul '91 / Wellard / ADA / Hot
Shot / Jazz Music / Cadillac / Direct.

CLASSICS 1928-38
CD _____ CLASSICS 671
Classics / Nov '92 / Discovery / Jazz
Music.

CLASSICS 1943-44
CD _____ CLASSICS 824
Classics / Jul '95 / Discovery / Jazz
Music.

CLASSICS 1944
CD _____ CLASSICS 835
Classics / Sep '95 / Discovery / Jazz
Music.

FEELIN' BLUE
All that I had is gone / Snowy morning blues
/ Chicago blues / Mournful tho'ts / Riffs /
Feelin' blue / Put your mind right on it / Fare
thee honey blues / You don't understand /
You've got to be modernistic / Crying for
the Carolines / What is this thing called love
/ Jingles / Go Harlem / Just a crazy song
CD _____ DHDL 107
Halcyon / May '95 / Jazz Music / Wellard /
Swift / Harmonia Mundi / Cadillac.

JAMES P. JOHNSON 1938-42
CD _____ CLASSICS 711
Classics / Jul '93 / Discovery / Jazz
Music.

**SYMPHONIC JAZZ OF JAMES P
JOHNSON**
CD _____ MMD 60066 A
Music Masters / Jan '89 / Nimbus.

Johnson, Jimmy

BAR ROOM PREACHER
CD _____ ALCD 4744
Alligator / May '93 / Direct / ADA.

JOHNSON'S WHACKS
CD _____ DD 644
Delmark / Dec '89 / Hot Shot / ADA / CM
/ Direct / Cadillac.

Johnson, Johnnie

BLUE HANDED JOHNNIE
CD _____ ECD 26017
Evidence / Feb '93 / Harmonia Mundi /
ADA / Cadillac.

JOHNNIE B. BAD
Tanqueray / Hush oh hush / Johnny B.
Badde / Creek mud / Fault line tremor /
Stepped in what / Can you stand it / Key to
the highway / Blues no. 572 / Baby what's
wrong / Cow cow blues / Movin' out
CD _____ 7559611492
Elektra Nonesuch / Sep '91 / Warner Music.

**ROCKIN' EIGHTY-EIGHTS (Johnson,
Johnnie, Clayton Love & Jimmy Vaughn)**
CD _____ MBCD 1201
Modern Blues / Jun '93 / Direct / ADA.

**THAT'LL WORK (Johnson, Johnnie &
Kentucky Headhunters)**
That'll work / Sunday blues / Johnnie's
breakdown / I'm not runnin' / Burned about
love / Stumblin' / Back to Memphis / Feel /
I know you can / She's got to have it /
Derby day special / Tell me baby
CD _____ 7559614762
Elektra / Aug '93 / Warner Music.

Johnson, L.V.

I GOT THE TOUCH
I got the touch / Take a little time to know
her / Are you serious / I don't want to lose
your love / What do you mean love ain't got
nothing to do / I am missing you / I just
can't get over you / Stroking kind (choking
kind)
CD _____ CDICH 1112
Ichiban / Oct '93 / Koch.

IT'S SO COLD AND MEAN
Get him out of your system / It's so cold
and mean (the drug scene) / One in a million
you / Blues in the north / It's not my time /
Make you mine / Steal away / How can I
live without you

CD _____ CDICH 1050
Ichiban / Oct '93 / Koch.

UNCLASSIFIED
CD _____ ICH 1137CD
Ichiban / May '94 / Koch.

Johnson, Larry

RAILROAD MAN
CD _____ JSPCD 237
JSP / Aug '90 / ADA / Target/BMG /
Direct / Cadillac / Complete/Pinnacle.

Johnson, Laurie

LONDON BIG BAND 2
CD _____ CDSIV 6144
Horatio Nelson / Jul '95 / THE / BMG /
Avid/BMG / Koch.

MUSIC OF LAURIE JOHNSON, THE
CD _____ UKCD 2057
Unicorn-Kanchana / Jul '92 / Harmonia
Mundi.

Johnson, Lil

**COMPLETE RECORDED WORKS VOL. 2
1936-37**
CD _____ DOCD 5308
Blues Document / Dec '94 / Swift / Jazz
Music / Hot Shot.

HOTTEST GAL IN TOWN 1936-1937
CD _____ SOBCD 35132
Story Of The Blues / Mar '92 / Koch /
ADA.

**LIL JOHNSON & BARRELHOUSE ANNIE
1937 (Johnson, Lil & Barrelhouse Annie)**
CD _____ DOCD 5309
Blues Document / Dec '94 / Swift / Jazz
Music / Hot Shot.

LIL JOHNSON VOL. 1 1929-36
CD _____ DOCD 5307
Blues Document / Dec '94 / Swift / Jazz
Music / Hot Shot.

Johnson, Linton Kwesi

BASS CULTURE
Bass culture / Street 66 / Reggae fi peach
/ De black petty booshwah / Inglan is a
bitch / Lorraine / Reggae sounds / Two
sides of silence
CD _____ RRCD 26
Reggae Refreshers / Nov '90 / PolyGram /
Vital.

DREAD BEAT AND BLOOD
Dread beat and blood / Five nights of
bleeding / Doun de road / Song of blood /
It dread inna Inglun (for George Lindo) /
Come wi goh dung deh / Man free (for Dar-
cus Howe) / All wi doin' is defendin'
CD _____ CDFL 9009
Frontline / Sep '90 / EMI / Jetstar.

FORCES OF VICTORY
Want fi goh rave / It noh funny / Sonny's
lettah / Independent intavenshan / Fite dem
back / Reality poem / Forces of vicktry /
Time come
CD _____ RRCD 32
Reggae Refreshers / Sep '91 / PolyGram /
Vital.

**IN CONCERT: LINTON KWESI
JOHNSON**
CD _____ SHANCD 43034/5
Shanachie / '88 / Koch / ADA /
Greensleeves.

LKJ IN CONCERT
CD _____ LKJCD 03
LKJ / Mar '95 / Jetstar / Grapevine.

LKJ IN DUB
Victorious dub / Reality dub / Peach dub /
Shocking dub / Iron bar dub / Bitch dub /
Cultural dub / Brain smashing dub
CD _____ RRCD 34
Reggae Refreshers / Sep '91 / PolyGram /
Vital.

LKJ IN DUB VOL.2
CD _____ LKJCD 02
LKJ / Mar '05 / Jetstar / Grapevine

REGGAE GREATS
Reggae sounds / Independent intavenshan
/ Street 66 / Bass culture / Di great insoh-
reckshan / It noh funny / Sonny's lettah /
Reggae fi radni / Fit dem back / Making
history
CD _____ IMCD 14
Island / '89 / PolyGram.

TINGS AND TIMES
CD _____ LKJCD 013
LKJ / Oct '95 / Jetstar / Grapevine.

Johnson, Lonnie

ANOTHER NIGHT TO CRY
CD _____ OBCCD 550
Original Blues Classics / Nov '92 /
Complete/Pinnacle / Wellard / Cadillac.

**BLUES & BALLADS (Johnson, Lonnie &
Elmer Snowden)**
CD _____ OBCCD 531
Original Blues Classics / Nov '92 /
Complete/Pinnacle / Wellard / Cadillac.

BLUES BY LONNIE JOHNSON
Don't ever love / No love for sale / There's
no love / I don't hurt anymore / She devil /
One-sided love affair / Big legged woman /
There must be a way / Blues 'round my door
/ Blues 'round my door / You don't move me
/ You will need me
CD _____ OBCCD 502
Original Blues Classics / Nov '92 / Com-
plete/Pinnacle / Wellard / Cadillac.

BLUES IN MY FINGERS
CD _____ IGOCD 2009
Indigo / Nov '94 / Direct / AUA.

**BLUES, BALLADS AND JUMPIN' JAZZ
#2 (Johnson, Lonnie & Elmer Snowden)**
CD _____ OBCCD 570
Original Blues Classics / Jul '95 /
Complete/Pinnacle / Wellard / Cadillac.

COMPLETE FOLKWAYS RECORDINGS
CD _____ SFWCD 40067
Smithsonian Folkways / Sep '94 / ADA /
Direct / Koch / CM / Cadillac.

COMPLETE RECORDINGS VOL. 1
CD _____ BDCD 6024
Blues Document / Nov '92 / Swift / Jazz
Music / Hot Shot.

COMPLETE RECORDINGS VOL. 2
CD _____ BDCD 6025
Blues Document / Nov '92 / Swift / Jazz
Music / Hot Shot.

COMPLETE RECORDINGS VOL. 3
CD _____ BDCD 6026
Blues Document / Nov '92 / Swift / Jazz
Music / Hot Shot.

HE'S A JELLY ROLL BAKER
Why women go wrong / Nothing but a rat /
Jersey belle blues / Loveless blues / I'm just
dumb / Get yourself together / Crowing
rooster blues / That's love / Somebody's
got to go / Lazy woman blues / Chicago
blues / I did all i could / In love again / Last
call / Rambler's blues / Baby, remember me
/ He's a Jelly Roll Baker / When you feel
low down / Victim of love / Watch shorty
CD _____ 07863660642
Bluebird / Oct '92 / BMG.

**IDLE HOURS (Johnson, Lonnie &
Victoria Spivey)**
CD _____ OBCCD 518
Original Blues Classics / Nov '92 /
Complete/Pinnacle / Wellard / Cadillac.

LOSING GAME
CD _____ OBCCD 543
Original Blues Classics / Nov '92 /
Complete/Pinnacle / Wellard / Cadillac.

ME AND MY CRAZY SELF
You can't buy love / It was all in vain / Noth-
ing but trouble / Me and my crazy self /
What do you want that I've got / Pretty boy
/ I'm guilty / What a woman / Falling rain
blues / Playing around / It's too late to cry
/ Seven long days / Why should I cry /
Friendless blues / Happy new year darling /
You only want me when you're lonely / Old
fashioned love / My my baby / Just another
day / What a real woman / Can't sleep
anymore
CD _____ CDCHARLY 266
Charly / Mar '91 / Charly / THE / Cadillac.

**ORIGINATOR OF MODERN GUITAR
BLUES**
In love again / Rambler's blues / Keep what
you got / Little rocking chair / Nothin'
clickin' chicken / My mother's eyes / I can't
sleep any more
CD _____ RBD 300
Mr. R&B / Dec '90 / Swift / CM / Wellard.

PLAYING WITH THE STRINGS
CD _____ JSPCD 335
JSP / Dec '94 / ADA / Target/BMG /
Direct / Cadillac / Complete/Pinnacle.

STEPPIN' ON THE BLUES
Mr. Johnson's blues / Sweet potato blues /
Steppin' on the blues / I done told you /
Mean old bedbug blues / Toothache blues
- (part 1) / Toothache blues - (part 2) / Have
to change keys (to play these blues) / Guitar
blues / She's making whoopee in hell tonight / Playing with the strings / No more
women blues / Deep blue sea blues / No
more troubles now / Got the blues for murder only / Untitled / 6-88 glide / Racketeer's
blues / I'm nuts about that gal
CD _____ 4672522
Columbia / May '91 / Sony.

**STOMPIN' AT THE PENNY (Johnson,
Lonnie & Jim McHarg's Metro
Stompers)**
China boy / Mr. Blues walks / Dippermouth
blues / Trouble in mind / Bring it home to
Mam / West End blues / Stompin' at the
Penny / Old rugged cross / Go go swing /
My mother's eyes / Canal street blues /
14th of July / Marines' hymn
CD _____ 4767202
Legacy / May '94 / Sony.

TOMORROW NIGHT
You will need me / I don't hurt anymore /
She's drunk again / Nothing but I trouble /
She devil / Little rocking chair / Trouble ain't
nothing but the blues / Leave me or love
me / Tomorrow night / Blues 'round my
door / Workin' man blues / Jelly roll baker /

End it all / Blues stay away from me / Care-
less love / C.C. rider / Clementine blues /
Backwater blues / Jelly jelly / Love is the
answer / Keep what you got
CD _____ CD 52016
Blues Encore / '92 / Target/BMG.

Johnson, Luther

**GET DOWN TO THE NITTY GRITTY
(Johnson, Luther 'Georgia Snake Boy')**
CD _____ 422182
New Rose / May '94 / Direct / ADA.

**ON THE ROAD AGAIN (Johnson, Luther
'Georgia Snake Boy')**
On the road again / Back door man / Things
I used to do / Catfish blues / Aces blues /
You move me / Rock me baby / She moves
me / You've got me running / Hoochie coo-
chie man / Impressions from France / Mel-
low down easy / Little red rooster
CD _____ ECD 260472
Evidence / Mar '94 / Harmonia Mundi / ADA
/ Cadillac.

Johnson, Luther

**COUNTRY SUGAR PAPA (Johnson,
Luther 'Guitar Junior')**
CD _____ BB 9546CD
Bullseye Blues / May '94 / Direct.

**IT'S GOOD TO BE ME (Johnson, Luther
'Guitar Junior')**
Feel so bad / Come on back to me / Deep
down in Florida / I'm leaving you / If you
love me like you say / Ronettes / Stealin'
chicken / It's good to me / Raise your window / Next door neighbour / That's all you
need / In my younger days
CD _____ CDBB 9516
Bullseye Blues / Nov '92 / Direct.

**LUTHER'S BLUES (Johnson, Luther
'Guitar Junior')**
CD _____ ECD 260102
Evidence / Oct '94 / Harmonia Mundi /
ADA / Cadillac.

Johnson, Luther

**HOUSEROCKIN' DADDY (Johnson,
Luther 'Houserocker')**
I'm Mr. Luck / Bad luck blues / You could
have fooled me / Fool's advice / She wants
to sell my monkey / Rockin' daddy / You
know I love you baby / Something you got
/ Don't say that no more / Things I used to
do
CD _____ ICH 9010 CD
Ichiban / Nov '91 / Koch.

**LONESOME IN MY BEDROOM
(Johnson, Luther 'Houserocker')**
CD _____ ECD 260052
Evidence / Jan '92 / Harmonia Mundi /
ADA / Cadillac.

Johnson, Marc

BASS DESIRES
Samurai hee-haw / Resolution / Black is the
colour of my true love's hair / Bass desires
/ Wishing doll / Mojo highway / Thanks
again
CD _____ 8277432
ECM / Feb '86 / New Note.

**SECOND SIGHT (Johnson, Marc Bass
Desires)**
Crossing the corpus callosum / Small hands
/ Sweet soul / Twister / Thrill seekers /
Player beads / 1061 / 1 j are for her
CD _____ 8330382
ECM / Oct '87 / New Note.

Johnson, Mark

DAYDREAM
On the sky / Blue smoke / When you were
nine / Way you do the things you do / Dim
the lights / Gotta do it good / Daydream /
Island lullaby / You're the one / Long
goodbye
CD _____ JVC 20432
JVC / Apr '95 / New Note.

MARK JOHNSON
Overture / Exit 33 / Gift for the ages / Street
samba / Come on / Mud hut / She's so
funktional / Bad influence / Funky James /
Hipocket / Devotional
CD _____ JVC 20322
JVC / Apr '94 / New Note.

Johnson, Marv

VERY BEST OF MARV JOHNSON, THE
Can't take another day / Paper kisses /
Whole lotta shakin' in my heart / It's magic
between us / Night / Something's burning
deep in my heart / Gonna fix you good (every time
you're bad) / Look it's raining sunshine /
Pull myself together / I'll pick a rose for my
rose / Heart for sale / Better love next time
/ Another chance / Beware there's danger /
Riding for a fall / Nothing can stop me / By
hook or by crook / Come to me
CD _____ 30359 90032
Carlton Home Entertainment / Oct '95 /
Carlton Home Entertainment.

Johnson, Mary

COMPLETE RECORDED WORKS 1929-36
CD _____ DOCD 5305
Blues Document / Dec '94 / Swift / Jazz
Music / Hot Shot.

Johnson, Merline

YAS YAS GIRL VOL. 1 1937-38
CD _____ DOCD 5292
Blues Document / Dec '94 / Swift / Jazz
Music / Hot Shot.

YAS YAS GIRL VOL. 2 1938-39
CD _____ DOCD 5293
Blues Document / Dec '94 / Swift / Jazz
Music / Hot Shot.

YAS YAS GIRL VOL. 3 1939-40
CD _____ DOCD 5294
Blues Document / Dec '94 / Swift / Jazz
Music / Hot Shot.

YAS YAS GIRL VOL. 4 1940-41
CD _____ DOCD 5295
Blues Document / Dec '94 / Swift / Jazz
Music / Hot Shot.

Johnson, Paul

BUMP TALKIN'
Hour glass figure / Fantasise / World / Time
of love / Caught up in your love / Bump
talkin' / Bouncing bed springs / Autobahn
cruise / Tenacious
CD _____ PF 041CD
Peacefrog / Jan '96 / Disc.

Johnson, Pete

CENTRAL AVENUE BOOGIE
CD _____ DDCD 656
Delmark / Aug '93 / Hot Shot / ADA / CM
/ Direct / Cadillac.

CLASSICS 1939-41
CD _____ CLASSICS 665
Classics / Nov '92 / Discovery / Jazz
Music.

KING OF THE BOOGIE
CD _____ CDCH 546
Milan / Oct '91 / BMG / Silva Screen.

PETE'S BLUES
Pete's lonesome blues / Mr. Dram meets Mr
Piano / Mutiny in the dog house / Mr. Clari-
net knocks twice / Page Mr Trumpet / Ben
rides out / J.C. from K.C. / Pete's house
warming blues / Atomic boogie / Back room
blues / 1280 Stomp / I may be wonderful /
Man wanted
CD _____ SV 0196
Savoy Jazz / Nov '92 / Conifer / ADA.

Johnson, Robb

HEART'S DESIRE (Johnson, Robb & Pip Collins)
Weathering the storm / Merrie olde Eng-
lande / Tomorrow will be better / Happy
song / After the rain / End of the day / Glid-
ers for Tim / Eddie outside / Nobody but
yours / Pity and mercy / Heart's desire /
Sunlight on the harbour / Wall came down
/ Die Moorsoldaten / Bells of freedom /
More than enough
CD _____ IRR 014CD
Irregular / Aug '93 / Irregular / ADA.

LACK OF JOLLY PLOUGHBOY (Johnson, Robb & Pip Collins)
Welcome to the warehouse / Wendy and
Michelle / Paper poppies / House with no-
body home / Shame of the nation / Dancing
on a Sunday / Uncle Cyril / Mother and the
motorway / Turning year / James Dean and
Sameena / We rise up / Lack of jolly plough-
boy / Blame the snow for falling
CD _____ IRR 017CD
Irregular / Oct '94 / Irregular / ADA.

ROBB JOHNSON
CD _____ IRR 018CD
Irregular / Aug '95 / Irregular / ADA.

THIS IS THE U.K. TALKING
Amateur dramatics / Rosa's lovely daugh-
ters / I close my eyes / Jolly sailor / Animals
song / Herald of free enterprise / Ever-
green / Like a brother / Another cold Sat-
urday in hell / Sunday morning St.Denis /
Uprising / Justice in Knightsbridge / Wasted
years / Not in my name / 6B go swimming
/ Hounslow boys / U.K. Talking /
Undefeated
CD _____ RHYD 5002
Rhiannon / Jun '94 / Vital / Direct / ADA.

Johnson, Robert

COMPLETE RECORDINGS, THE (All 41 Recordings - 2CD/MC Set)
Kind hearted woman blues / I believe I'll
dust my broom / Sweet home Chicago /
Ramblin' on my mind / When you got a
good friend / Come on in my kitchen / Terraplane blues / Phonograph blues / 32-20
blues / They're red hot / Dead shrimp blues
/ Crossroads blues / Walkin' blues / Last fair
deal gone down / Preachin' blues / If I had
possession over judgement day / Stones in
my passway / I'm a steady rollin' man /
From four till late / Hellhound on my trail /

Little Queen of Spades / Malted milk /
Drunken hearted man / Me and the devil
blues / Stop breakin' down blues / Travel-
ling riverside blues / Honeymoon blues /
Love in vain / Milkcow's calf blues
CD Set _____ CD 46222
Columbia / May '94 / Sony.

CROSSROAD BLUES
CD _____ NTMCD 504
Nectar / Jun '95 / Pinnacle.

DELTA BLUES #1 (Myth & Reality)
Crossroads blues / Terraplane blues /
Come on in my kitchen / Walking blues /
Last fair deal gone down / 32-20 blues /
Kindhearted women blues / If I had pos-
session over judgement day / Preaching
blues / When you got a good friend / Ram-
bling on my mind / Stones in my passway
/ Traveling riverside blues / Milkcow's calf
blues / Me and the devil blues / Hellhound
on my trail
CD _____ ALB 1001CD
Aldabra / Nov '95 / CM / Disc.

DELTA BLUES #2
CD _____ ALB 1002CD
Aldabra / Nov '95 / CM / Disc.

DELTA BLUES #3 (Alternative Takes)
CD _____ ALB 1003CD
Aldabra / Nov '95 / CM / Disc.

DELTA BLUES LEGEND (Charly Blues - Masterworks Vol. 13)
Kind hearted woman blues / I believe I'll
dust my broom / Sweet home Chicago /
Ramblin' on my mind / When you got a
good friend / Come on in my kitchen / Terraplane blues / Phonograph blues / 32-20
blues / They're red hot / Dead shrimp blues
/ Crossroads blues / Walkin' blues / Last fair
deal gone down / Preachin' blues / If I had
possession over judgement day / Stones in
my passway / I'm a steady rollin' man /
From four till late / Hellhound on my trail /
Little queen of spades / Malted milk / Me
and the devil blues
CD _____ CDBM 13
Charly / Apr '92 / Charly / THE / Cadillac.

GOLD COLLECTION, THE
CD _____ D2CD14
Recording Arts / Dec '92 / THE / Disc.

HELLHOUND ON MY TRAIL
CD _____ IGGCD 2017
Indigo / Mar '95 / Direct / ADA.

KING OF THE DELTA BLUES SINGERS
Crossroads blues / Terraplane blues /
Come on in my kitchen / Last fair deal gone
down / 32-20 blues / Kind hearted woman
blues / If I had possession over judgement
day / Preachin' blues / When you got a
good friend / Ramblin' on my mind / Stones
in my passway / Traveling riverside blues /
Milkcow's calf blues / Me and the devil
blues / Hellhound on my trail
CD _____ CK 52944
Legacy / Nov '94 / Sony.

LEGENDARY BLUES SINGER
Kind hearted woman blues / Sweet Chicago
home / Terraplane blues / Phonograph
blues / Crossroads blues / Preachin' blues
/ I'm a steady rollin' man / Little queen of
spades / Drunken hearted man / Me and
the devil blues / Stop breakin' down blues /
Love in vain
CD _____ CDCD 1049
Charly / Mar '93 / Charly / THE / Cadillac.

ROBERT JOHNSON (2CD Set)
CD Set _____ R2CD 4014
Deja Vu / Jan '96 / THE.

ROBERT JOHNSON COLLECTOR'S EDITION
CD _____ DVBC 9052
Deja Vu / Apr '95 / THE.

ROBERT JOHNSON GOLD (2CD Set)
CD Set _____ D2CD 4014
Deja Vu / Jun '95 / THE.

ROOTS OF ROBERT JOHNSON (Various Artists)
CD _____ YAZCD 1073
Yazoo / Apr '91 / CM / ADA / Roots /
Koch.

TRAVELING RIVERSIDE BLUES
Kind hearted woman blues / Sweet home
Chicago / Ramblin' on my mind / I believe
I'll dust my broom / When you got a good
friend / Come on in my kitchen / Terraplane
blues / Phonograph blues / 32-20 blues /
They're red hot / Crossroads blues / Walkin'
blues / Preachin' blues / If I had possession
over Judgement Day / I'm a steady rollin'
man / Little Queen of Spades / Me and the
devil blues / Stop breakin' down blues /
Traveling riverside blues / Love in vain /
Milkcow's calf blues
CD _____ CD 52019
Blues Encore / Aug '92 / Target/BMG.

Johnson, Ronnie

GIVE THEM ENOUGH ROPE
CD _____ BRGCD 1
Music Maker / Jul '94 / Grapevine / ADA.

HOW THE LAND LIES
CD _____ BRGCD 06
Music Maker / Jul '94 / Grapevine / ADA.

Johnson, Ruby

I'LL RUN YOUR HURT AWAY
I'll run your heart away / What more can a
woman do / Won't be long / Love of my
man / Why not give me a chance / It's not
that easy / Don't play that song (You lied) /
Come to me my darling / It's better to give
than to receive / keep on keepin' on / How
strong is my love / Need your love so bad
/ Leftover love / I'd better check on myself
/ I'd rather fight than switch / No no no / If
I ever needed love (I sure do need it now) /
When my love comes down / Weak spot
CD _____ CDSXD 049
Stax / Mar '93 / Pinnacle.

Johnson, Shirley

LOOKING FOR LOVE
CD _____ AP 094CD
Appaloosa / Jul '94 / ADA / Magnum
Music Group.

Johnson, Snuff

WILL THE CIRCLE BE UNBROKEN
CD _____ BMCD 9026
Black Magic / Sep '94 / Hot Shot / Swift /
CM / Direct / Cadillac / ADA.

Johnson, Syl

A SIDES, THE
Love you left behind / I wanna satisfy your
every need / We did it / Back for a taste of
your love / I'm yours / Let yourself go / I
want to take you home (to see mama) /
Take me to the river / I only have love / Star
bright, star light / About to make me leave
home / Fonk you / Stand by me / Mystery
lady
CD _____ HILOCD 06
Hi / Mar '94 / Pinnacle.

BACK FOR A TASTE OF YOUR LOVE
CD _____ HIUKCD 142
Hi / Jun '93 / Pinnacle.

BACK IN THE GAME
CD _____ DE 674
Delmark / Feb '95 / Hot Shot / ADA / CM
/ Direct / Cadillac.

IS IT BECAUSE I'M BLACK
Come on sock it to me / Dresses too short
/ I can take care of business / I'll take those
skinny legs / I resign / Get ready / I feel an
urge / I take care of homework / Is it because I'm black / Concrete reservation / I
walk a mile in my shoes / I'm talkin' 'bout
freedom / Right on / Different strokes (On
CD only) / Going to the shack (On CD only)
/ One way to nowhere (On CD only) / Thank
you baby (On CD only) / One way ticket to
nowhere (On CD only) / Kiss by kiss (On CD
only) / Same kind of thing (On CD only)
CD _____ CPCD 8011
Charly / Feb '94 / Charly / THE / Cadillac.

MUSIC TO MY EARS
CD _____ HIUKCD 117
Hi / Jun '93 / Pinnacle.

TOTAL EXPLOSION & UPTOWN SHAKEDOWN
I only have love / Bustin' up or bustin' out
/ Star bright, star light / Watch what you do
to me / Steppin' out / Take me to the river
/ It ain't easy / About to make me leave
home / That's just my luck / Mystery lady /
Let's dance for love / Gimme little sign /
You're the star of the show / Blue water /
Who's gonna love you / Otis Redding
medley
CD _____ HIUKCD 143
Hi / Jun '93 / Pinnacle.

Johnson, Thomas

HOUSE PARTY
House party / It's alright / Missing love that
I never had / Ain't the river that drowns /
Good thangs come to them that wait / I ain't
gonna hanky panky / Snake pinto beans
CD _____ CDICH 1031
Ichiban / Feb '89 / Koch.

Johnson, Tommy

COMPLETE RECORDINGS 1928-30
CD _____ WSECD 104
Wolf / Jan '94 / Jazz Music / Swift / Hot
Shot.

TOMMY JOHNSON (1928-29)
CD _____ DOCD 5001
Blues Document / Aug '91 / Swift / Jazz
Music / Hot Shot.

Johnson, Wilko

BARBED WIRE BLUES
CD _____ FREUDCD 26
Jungle / Nov '88 / Disc.

ICE ON THE MOTORWAY
Bottle up and go / Cairo blues / Down by
the waterside / Ice on the motorway / Can
you please crawl out of your window /
Leave my woman alone / When I'm gone /
All right / Keep it out of sight / Long tall
texan / Whammy
CD _____ BUTCD 001
Hound Dog / Jan '91 / Street link.

Johnston, Daniel

YIP JUMP MUSIC
CD _____ HMS 142-2
Homestead / Nov '94 / SRD.

Johnson, Freedy

CAN YOU FLY
Trying to tell you I don't know / In the new
sunshine / Tearing down this place / Re-
member me / Wheels / Lucky one / Can you
fly / Responsible / Mortician's daughter /
Sincere / Down in love / California thing /
We will shine
CD _____ 7559615872
Elektra / Sep '93 / Warner Music.

THIS PERFECT WORLD
Bad reputation / Evie's tears / Can't sink
this town / This perfect world / Cold again
/ Two lovers stop / Across the avenue /
Gone like the water / Delores / Evie's gar-
den / Disappointed man / I can hear the
laughs
CD _____ 755961655-2
Elektra / Jul '94 / Warner Music.

TROUBLE TREE, THE
Innocent / Down on the moon no. 1 / No
violins / That's what you get / Fun ride /
Gina / Nauture boy / Bad girl / After my
shocks / Tucumcari / Down on the moon
no. 2 / Little red haired girl
CD _____ FIENDCD 208
Demon / '91 / Pinnacle / ADA.

Johnston, Jan

NAKED BUT FOR LILIES
If heaven callz / Paris / I learned (you blew
me out) / Wild child / Don't be lonely / Don't
make promises / Calling you / Something's
in the house / Alive / Strange day
CD _____ 540242-2
A&M / Aug '94 / PolyGram.

Johnston, Philip

BIG TROUBLE
CD _____ 120152-2
Black Saint / Sep '93 / Harmonia Mundi /
Cadillac.

Johnston, Randy

JUBILATION
Jubilation / One for Detroit / You are too
beautiful / Willow weep for me / Angela /
Come rain or come shine / 9W blues / Baby,
you should know it
CD _____ MCD 5495
Muse / Mar '94 / New Note / CM.

Johnston, Tom

EVERYTHING YOU'VE HEARD IS TRUE
Man on the stage / Show me / Savannah
lights / Down along the river / Reachin' out
for lovin' / Small time talk / You can count on
you / Outlaw
CD _____ 7599267562
WEA / Jan '96 / Warner Music.

STILL FEELS GOOD
CD _____ 7599267572
WEA / Jan '96 / Warner Music.

Johnstone, Arthur

NORTH BY NORTH
North by North / Oil beneath the sea / Tink-
ermans daughter / Christmas 1914 / Mar-
garet and me / Benny Lynch / Doomsday in
the afternoon / Take her in your arms / Rag-
lan Road / Crooked Jack / It's my union /
Ballad of Joe Hill / Bandiera Rosa
CD _____ LCOM 9039
Lismor / Apr '91 / Lismor / Direct / Duncans
/ ADA.

Johnstone, Jim

TRIBUTE TO JIMMY SHAND
CD _____ COMD 2039
Temple / Feb '94 / CM / Duncans / ADA /
Direct.

Johnstons

TRANSATLANTIC YEARS
Fhir a bhata / O'Carolan's concerto / Lark
in the morning / Apprentice song / You keep
going your way / Urge for going / Hey, that's
no way to say goodbye / Both sides now /
Ye Jacobites by name / Coleraine regatta /
Barleycorn / Flower of Northumberland /
Fuigfidh mise'n baile sea / Story of Isaac /
Bitter green / Marcie / Spanish lady / If I
could / Colours of the dawn / If I sang my
song / Continental trailways bus
CD _____ TDEM 13
Trandem / Mar '94 / CM / ADA / Pinnacle.

Joi

JOYSTICK
CD _____ REV 4154CD
Revolution / Apr '94 / Koch.

Joli, France

ESSENTIAL DISCO VOL. 2
CD _____ DGPCD 729
Deep Beats / May '95 / BMG.

Jolliffe, Steve

WARRIOR
CD _____ WVCD 005
Warrior / Oct '92 / Conifer.

Jolly Boys

POP'N'MENTO
Mother and wife / Love in the cemetery / River come down / Ten dollars to two / Banana / Big bamboo / Ben Wood Dick / Touch me tomato / Shaving cream / Watermelon / Back to back / Nightfall
CD _____ COOKCD 040
Cooking Vinyl / Jun '90 / Vital.

Jolly Brothers

CONSCIOUS MAN (LEE PERRY PRESENTS)
CD _____ RRCD 001
Greensleeves / Feb '93 / Total/BMG / Jetstar / SRD.

Jolson, Al

AL JOLSON COLLECTOR'S EDITION
CD _____ DVGH 7042
Deja Vu / Apr '95 / THE.

AL JOLSON VOL.3
CD _____ PASTCD 7045
Flapper / Jan '96 / Pinnacle.

CALIFORNIA HERE I COME
CD _____ CMSCD 008
Movie Stars / Oct '91 / Conifer.

FIRST RECORDINGS, THE
CD _____ STCD 564
Stash / May '93 / Jazz Music / CM / Cadillac / Direct / ADA.

GREAT ORIGINAL PERFORMANCES 1926-32
CD _____ RPCD 300
Moidart / Jul '92 / Conifer / ADA.

GREATEST ENTERTAINER, THE
April showers / Rock-a-bye your baby / I'm sitting on top of the world / There's a rainbow 'round my shoulder / When the red, red robin comes bob, bob, bobbin' along / Tonight's my night with baby / My mammy / Swanee / When the little red roses / Liza (All the clouds'll roll away) / Hallelujah, I'm a bum / California here I come / The one I love / Golden gate / Back in your own backyard / Sonny boy
CD _____ HADCD 157
Javelin / May '94 / THE / Henry Hadaway Organisation.

I LOVE TO SING
CD _____ JASCD 100
Jasmine / Nov '95 / Wellard / Swift / Conifer / Cadillac / Magnum Music Group.

JAZZ SINGER
CD _____ CDMR 1070
Derann Trax / Aug '91 / Pinnacle.

JAZZ SINGER, THE
California here I come / Pasadena / I'm sitting on top of the world / Blue river / Golden gate / Back in your own backyard / My Mammy / Dirty hands, dirty face / There's a rainbow 'round my shoulder / Sonny boy / I'm in seventh heaven / Little pal / Used to you / Why can't you / Liza / Let me sing and I'm happy / April showers / Rock-a-bye your baby with a Dixie melody
CD _____ JZCD 309
Suisa / Feb '91 / Jazz Music / THE.

LET ME SING AND I'M HAPPY
CD _____ RMB 75019
Remember / Nov '93 / Total/BMG.
CD _____ PARCD 004
Parrot / Jan '96 / THE / Wellard / Jazz Music.

SALESMAN OF SONG 1911-1923
That haunting melody / Everybody sang your fingers with me / Revival day / Back to the Carolina you love / I sent my wife to the Thousand Isles / I'm saving up the means to get to New Orleans / Someone else may be there while I'm gone / Don't write me letters / Broken doll / Every little while / Wedding bells / I've got my captain working for me now / You ain't heard nothin' yet / I gave her that / Tell me / Chloe / In sweet September / O-hi-o / Yoo hoo / Angel child / Lost: a wonderful girl / Stella / You've simply got me cuckoo / That big blond mumma / Coal black Mammy of mine
CD _____ PASTCD 9796
Flapper / Jul '92 / Pinnacle.

SINGING FOOL, THE (Jolson, Al & Bing Crosby)
CD _____ ENTCD 276
Entertainers / '88 / Target/BMG.

STAGE HIGHLIGHTS, 1911-25
CD _____ PASTCD 9748
Flapper / Jul '91 / Pinnacle.

VERY BEST OF AL JOLSON (20 greatest hits)
Swanee / Toot toot Tootsie / Mammy / California here I come / Sonny boy / April showers / You made me love you
CD _____ PLATCD 15
Platinum Music / Mar '92 / Prism / Ross.

VERY BEST OF AL JOLSON
There's a rainbow 'round my shoulder / Let me sing and I'm happy / Carolina in the morning / Give my regards to Broadway / About a quarter to nine / April showers / I was wild about Harry / Rock-a-bye your baby / With a Dixie melody / For me and my gal / When the red, red robin comes bob, bob, bob / My mammy / California here I come / De Campton races / Alabamy bound / Swanee / When you were sweet sixteen / I only have eyes for you / Pretty baby / I'm sitting on top of the world / Oh you beautiful doll / Toot toot tootsie goodbye / I want a girl - just like the girl that married dear old Dad / By the light of the silvery moon / Waiting for the Robert E. Lee / Spaniard that blighted my life / Anniversary song
CD _____ MCCD 074
Music Club / Jun '92 / Disc / THE / CM.

YOU AIN'T HEARD NOTHIN' YET
California here I come / Sonny boy / April showers / Pasadena / When the red, red robin comes bob, bob, bobbin' along / You made me love you / I'm ka-razy for you / You ain't heard nothin' yet / Swanee / When the little red roses get the blues for you / Rock-a-bye your baby with a Dixie melody / Blue river / Used to you / Steppin' out / Spaniard that blighted my life / Golden gate / My Mammy / Miami
CD _____ CD AJA 5038
Living Era / Dec '85 / Koch.

YOU MADE ME LOVE YOU
CD _____ PLCD 542
President / Aug '95 / Grapevine / Target / BMG / Jazz Music / President.

Jomanda

NUBIA SOUL
Never / Don't deny / Just a little more time / I like it / I cried the tears / Does the music love you / Life / What you go through for love / Island / Don't fight the feelings / Kiss you / Back to you / Gotta be with you
CD _____ 756780548-2
Atlantic / Dec '93 / Warner Music.

SOMEONE TO LOVE ME
Make my body rock / Someone to love me / Share / Don't you want my love / You know / Boy / Dance / Got a love for you / It ain't no big thing / When love hurts / True meaning of love / What's the deal (Not available on LP) / I will always be there for you (Not available on LP) / Without you (Available on CD only)
CD _____ 7599244142
Sire / Jul '91 / Warner Music.

Jon & Vangelis

BEST OF JON AND VANGELIS
Italian song / I'll find my way home / State of independence / One more time / Play within a play / Friends of Mr. Cairo / Outside of this (inside of that) / He is sailing / I hear you now
CD _____ 821 929-2
Polydor / Aug '84 / PolyGram.

CHRONICLES
I hear you now / He is sailing / Thunder / Beside / Bird song / Play within a play / When the night comes / Deborah / Curious electric / Friends of Mr. Cairo / Back to school / Italian song / Polonaise / Love is
CD _____ 5501962
Spectrum/Karussell / Sep '94 / PolyGram / THE.

FRIENDS OF MR.CAIRO
Friends of Mr. Cairo / Back to school / Outside of this, inside of that / State of independence / Beside / Mayflower
CD _____ 8000212
Polydor / Jun '88 / PolyGram.

PAGE OF LIFE
Wisdom chain / Page of life / Money / Jazzy box / Garden of senses / Is it love / Anyone can light a candle / Be a good friend of mine / Shine for me / Genevieve / Journey to Ixtlan / Little guitar
CD _____ 261373
Arista / Feb '94 / BMG.

PRIVATE COLLECTION
And when the night comes / Deborah / He is sailing / Polonaise / Horizon / King is coming
CD _____ 813 174-2
Polydor / '83 / PolyGram.

Jon B

BONA FIDE
Bona fide / Simple melody / Love is Candi / Mystery 4 two / Someone to love / Time after time / Overflow / Pretty girl / Pants off / Isn't it scary / Burning for you / Gone before light / Love didn't do
CD _____ 4005012
Epic / Nov '95 / Sony.

Jonas Jinx

CASE OF..., A
CD _____ SPV 08445692
SPV / May '95 / Plastic Head.

Jones, Al

WATCH THIS
Three times a fool / Don't change your mind / Ain't that just like a woman / Society woman / Come on home / Please please please / All your love / Feel so bad / Just the blues / Watch this
CD _____ BLU 10242
Blues Beacon / Apr '95 / New Note.

Jones, Aled

ALED JONES WITH THE BBC WELSH CHORUS
Away in a manger / Come unto Him / Sussex carol / O little town of Bethlehem / St. Joseph's carol / Christmas star / Ding dong merrily on high / Deck the halls with boughs of holly / Holy Boy / Jesus Christ the apple tree / Gabriel's message / Rocking / Ave Maria / My heart ever faithful / Good king Wenceslas / Hevaenghard mair / Unto us is born a son
CD _____ CDVIP 104
Virgin VIP / Dec '94 / Carlton Home Entertainment / THE / EMI.

ALL THROUGH THE NIGHT
CD _____ PWKM 646
Carlton Home Entertainment / '91 / Carlton Home Entertainment.

BEST OF CHRISTMAS ALBUM
Holy City / Bridge over troubled water / Ave Maria (Version 1) / O Holy night (Version 1) / Ombra / Bless this house / O for the wings of a dove / How beautiful are the feet / Star of Bethlehem / O Holy night (Version 2) / All through the night / Where e'er you walk / Ave Maria (Version 2) / Yesterday / Little road to Bethlehem
CD _____ PWKM 662
Carlton Home Entertainment / Nov '90 / Carlton Home Entertainment.

PIE JESU
Art thou troubled / If I can help somebody / Zion hears the watchmen's voices / Jesu joy of man's desiring / Lullaby (op.49 no.4) / I'll wake beside you / Crown of roses / I know that my redeemer liveth (From 'Messiah') / Lausanne / God so loved the world / At the end of the day / Pie Jesu / Laudate dominum
CD _____ CDVIP 107
Virgin VIP / Nov '93 / Carlton Home Entertainment / THE / EMI.

VOICES FROM THE HOLY LAND (Jones, Aled & BBC Welsh Chorus)
Let us break bread together / Ave Maria / My Lord, what a morning / Deep river / Holy City / There is a green hill far away / How beautiful are the feet (From Messiah) / Ave Verum Corpus / Easter hymn / Jesu joy of man's desiring / Little road to Bethlehem / Shepherds farewell (From 'Childhood of Christ') / O for a closer walk with God / O for the wings of a dove / Tua Bethlem dref / O Holy Night / Virgin Mary had a baby boy
CD _____ PWKS 651
Carlton Home Entertainment / Aug '90 / Carlton Home Entertainment.

Jones, Barbara

FOR YOUR EARS ONLY
CD _____ JMC 200216
Jamaica Gold / Jun '95 / THE / Magnum Music Group / Jetstar.

Jones, Carlo

CARLO JONES & THE KASEKO BURIIIAM TROUBADOURS
CD _____ MW 3011CD
Music & Words / Jul '95 / ADA / Direct.

Jones, Charles

LIFE BEHIND THE MICROPHONE
CD _____ ISS 003CD
SST / Sep '94 / Plastic Head.

Jones, Chris

BLINDED BY THE ROSE
CD _____ SCR 40
Strictly Country / Sep '95 / ADA / Direct.

Jones, Curtis

CURTIS JONES VOL. 1 1937-38
CD _____ DOCD 5296
Blues Document / Dec '94 / Swift / Jazz Music / Hot Shot.

CURTIS JONES VOL. 2 1938-39
CD _____ DOCD 5297
Blues Document / Dec '94 / Swift / Jazz Music / Hot Shot.

CURTIS JONES VOL. 3 1939-40
CD _____ DOCD 5298
Blues Document / Dec '94 / Swift / Jazz Music / Hot Shot.

CURTIS JONES VOL. 4 1941-53
CD _____ DOCD 5299
Blues Document / Dec '94 / Swift / Jazz Music / Hot Shot.

IN LONDON
Shake it baby / Syl-vous play blues / Young generation boogie / Skid row / Honey drip-

per / Lonesome bedroom blues / Alley bound blues / Curtis Jones boogie / Dust my broom / Red river blues / Good woman blues / Please send me someone to love / You got good business / Roll me over
CD _____ 8206242
Limelight / Jul '91 / PolyGram.

LONESOME BEDROOM BLUES
CD _____ 158312
Blues Collection / Apr '95 / Discovery.

TROUBLE BLUES
Lonesome bedroom blues / Whole lot of talk for you / Suicide blues / Please say yes / Weekend blues / Good woman blues / Trouble blues / Love season / Low down worried blues / Good time special / Fool blues
CD _____ OBCCD 515
Original Blues Classics / Apr '94 / Complete/Pinnacle / Wellard / Cadillac.

Jones, David

BRIDGES
Bridges / I found a honky tonk angel / Let's stop living together, alone / You don't miss what you got / I'm all that I got left / Blues after sundown / Nothing lasts forever / She's got that loved on look / You're no longer mine / Tears out weigh the whiskey
CD _____ ZNCD 1007
Zane / Oct '95 / Pinnacle.

Jones, Duke

THUNDER ISLAND
Little boy blues / No ordinary love / You and I (Thunder Island) / Let's have it all / You don't know what love is / Caribbean Windsor / Thunder (In the sky) / True lovers
CD _____ ESJCD 239
Essential Jazz / Oct '93 / BMG.

Jones, Ed

PIPER'S TALE
So the story goes / Returning / Long days / Piper's tale / Out in the open / Past tense / Kindred spirit
CD _____ ASCCD 2
ASC / Jun '95 / New Note / Cadillac.

Jones, Eddie Lee

YONDER GO THAT OLD BLACK DOG (Jones, Eddie Lee 'Mustright' & Family)
CD _____ TCD 5023
Testament / May '95 / Complete/Pinnacle / ADA / Koch.

Jones, Elvin

HEAVY SOUNDS (Jones, Elvin & Richard Davis)
Raunchy Rita / Shiny stockings / M.E. / Summertime / Elvin's guitar blues / Here's that rainy day
CD _____ MCAD 33114
Impulse Jazz / Jan '90 / BMG / New Note.

IT DON'T MEAN A THING
Green chimneys / Lullaby of Itsugo village / It don't mean a thing if it ain't got that swing / Lush life / Zenzo spirit / Flower is a lovesome thing / Ask me now / Bopsy / Fatima's waltz / Change is gonna come
CD _____ ENJ 80662
Enja / Nov '94 / New Note / Vital/SAM.

LIVE AT THE VILLAGE VANGUARD VOL.1
It's easy to remember / Front line / Tohryanse, tohryanse / George and me / Love supreme
CD _____ LCDI 53423
Landmark / Nov '93 / New Note.

LIVE IN JAPAN 1978 (Jones, Elvin Jazz Machine)
Keiko's birthday march / Bessie's blues / Antigua / E.J. blues / Love supreme
CD _____ KCD 5041
Konnex / Nov '92 / SRD.

LOVE & PEACE
Little rock blues / Hip Jones / Korina / For tomorrow / Sweet and lovely / Origin / House that love built
CD _____ ECD 220872
Evidence / Jun '94 / Harmonia Mundi / ADA / Cadillac.

ON THE MOUNTAIN
One Way / Sep '94 / Direct / ADA.
CD _____ OW 30328

VERY R.A.R.E.
Sweet mama / Passion flower / Zange / Tin tin deo / Pitter pat / Witching hour / E.J.Blues / Love supreme
CD _____ ECD 22053
Evidence / Jul '93 / Harmonia Mundi / ADA / Cadillac.

Jones, Etta

AT LAST
At last / You're a sweetheart / God bless the child / He's my guy / Where are you / Wonder why / I can't get started (with you) / If you were mine / You're driving me crazy / Cottage for sale / Don't take your love / From me

CD _____ MCD 5511
Muse / Jul '95 / New Note / CM.

CHRISTMAS WITH ETTA JONES
CD _____ MCD 5411
Muse / Sep '92 / New Note / CM.

DON'T GO TO STRANGERS
CD _____ OJCCD 298
Original Jazz Classics / Jul '93 / Wellard /
Jazz Music / Cadillac / Complete/Pinnacle.

**FINE & MELLOW/SAVE YOUR LOVE
FOR ME**
CD _____ MCD 6002
Muse / Sep '92 / New Note / CM.

I'LL BE SEEING YOU
CD _____ MCD 5351
Muse / Sep '93 / New Note / CM.

LONELY AND BLUE
CD _____ OJCCD 702
Original Jazz Classics / Jan '94 / Wellard /
Jazz Music / Cadillac / Complete/Pinnacle.

REVERSE THE CHARGES
Ma. He's making eyes at me / Say it isn't
so / Indecided / Someone to watch over me
/ Reverse the charges / P.S. I love you / I
could have danced all night / Perdido
CD _____ MCD 5474
Muse / Nov '92 / New Note / CM.

SOMETHING NICE
CD _____ OJCCD 221
Original Jazz Classics / Jun '95 / Wellard /
Jazz Music / Cadillac / Complete/Pinnacle.

SUGAR
CD _____ MCD 5379
Muse / Sep '92 / New Note / CM.

Jones, Floyd

MASTERS OF MODERN BLUES SERIES
(Jones, Floyd & Eddie Taylor)
CD _____ TCD 5001
Testament / Aug '94 / Complete/Pinnacle /
ADA / Koch.

Jones, George

DON'T STOP THE MUSIC
Into my arms again / Who shot Sam / You
gotta be my baby / Mr. Fool / Time lock /
Candy hearts / What'cha gonna do / Vita-
mins l-o-v-e / Don't stop the music / Accidentally on purpose / All I want to do / Giveaway / Cup of loneliness / Wanderin'
soul / My sweet Imogene / Likes of you /
What am I worth / Boogie woogie Mexican
boy / I'm with the wrong one / With half a
heart / Ship of love / Honky tonk downstairs
CD _____ CDCH 912
Ace / Nov '93 / Pinnacle / Cadillac / Com-
plete/Pinnacle.

EMI COUNTRY MASTERS (2CD Set)
She thinks I still care / Sometimes you just
can't win / Ragged but right / Color of the
blues / We must have been out of our
minds / Open pit mine / Girl I used to love
/ Precious jewel / Lovin' lies / Running bear
/ Big fool of the year / Give my love to Rose
/ Beggar to a King / Wait a little longer,
please Jesus / Not what I had in mind / I
saw me / Take me as I am (Or let me go) /
You comb her hair / Ain't it funny what a
fool will do / Wings of a dove / Seasons of
my heart / Little bitty tear / My tears are
overdue / What's in our heart / Your heart
turned left (And I was on the right) / Race
is on / Something I dreamed / It scares me
half to death / Rose from a bride's bouquet
/ Where does a tear come from / Please be
my love / Gold and silver / Warm red wine
/ We could / Love's gonna live here / Multi-
ply the heartaches / Don't let the stars get
in your eyes / Least of all / Rollin' in my
sweet baby's arms / Book of memories / I'm
gonna change everything / I've been known
to cry / Wrong number / She's mine /
What's money / I'm just blue enough (To do
most anything) / Let's invite them over /
Where did the sunshine go / World's worst
loser / Peace in the valley
CD Set _____ CDEM 1502
EMI / Aug '93 / EMI.

FRIENDS IN HIGH PLACES
Few ole country boys / All fall down / Fiddle
and guitar band / All that we've got left /
Love's gonna live here / If I could bottle this
up / I've been there / You can't do wrong
and get by / It hurts as much in Texas (as
it did in Tennessee) / Travellers prayer
CD _____ 4680992
Epic / Apr '91 / Sony.

**GEORGE AND TAMMY (Jones, George
& Tammy Wynette)**
One / Old love thing / Whatever happend to
us / Will you travel down this road with me
/ (She's just) an old love turned memory / If
God met you / Just look what we've started
again / All I have to offer you is me / They're
playing our song / Solid as a rock
CD _____ MCD 11248
MCA / Aug '95 / BMG.

GEORGE JONES & GENE PITNEY
(Jones, George & Gene Pitney)
Why baby why / Someday you'll want me
to want you / For me this is happy / That's
all it took / I'm gonna listen to me / I'm a
fool to care / She thinks I still care / Big job

/ I'm up to my neck in IOU's / Sweeter than
the flowers / Wreck on the highway / More
I saw of her / Thousand arms (five hundred
arms) / I've got five dollars and it's Saturday
night / Louisiana man / Drinking from the
well of your love / Life to go / One has my
name / Mockin' bird hill / I'd like to see me
stop you / I can't stop loving you / Your old
standby / Won't take long / I've got a new
heartache / My shoes keep walking back to
you / I really don't want to know / As long
as I live / Born to lose / Don't rob another
man's castle / Love bug / Y'all come
CD _____ BCDAH 15790
Bear Family / Feb '95 / Rollercoaster /
Direct / CM / Swift / ADA.

**GREATEST COUNTRY HITS OF THE
60'S**
CD _____ PWKS 4264
Carlton Home Entertainment / Jul '95 /
Carlton Home Entertainment.

HIGH TECH REDNECK
High tech redneck / I've still got some hur-
tin' left to do / Love in your eyes / Visit /
Silent partners / Tear me out of the picture
/ Thousand times a day / Never bit a bullet
like this / Forever's here to stay / Hello
darlin'
CD _____ MCAD 10910
MCA / Mar '94 / BMG.

LEGEND LIVES ON, THE
Good year for the roses / Developing my
pictures / Tender years / Say it's not you /
From here to the door / If my heart had win-
dows / My favourite lies / Accidentally on
purpose / Where grass won't grow / Sweet
dreams / Things have gone to pieces /
White lightning / Four-o-thirty three / Take
me / I'm a people / I'm wasting good paper
/ Old brush abors / Love bug / Walk through
this world with me / Race is on
CD _____ MSCD 24
Music De-Luxe / Oct '95 / Magnum Music
Group.

LIVE AT DANCETOWN USA
White lightning / Something I dreamed /
Achin' breaking heart / Window up above /
Bony Moronie / She thinks I still care / Rag-
ged but right / Poor man's riches / Jolie
blon / Where does a little tear come from /
Big Harlan Taylor / She's lonesome again /
Race is on
CD _____ CDCHM 156
Ace / May '92 / Pinnacle / Cadillac / Com-
plete/Pinnacle.

MR COUNTRY MUSIC
CD _____ CDCD 1139
Charly / Feb '94 / Charly / THE / Cadillac.

MY VERY SPECIAL GUESTS
Night life (With Waylon Jennings) / Bartender's blues (With James Taylor) / Here we
are (With Emmylou Harris) / I've turned you
to stone (With Linda Ronstadt) / It sure was
good (With Tammy Wynette) / I gotta get
drunk (With Willie Nelson) / Proud Mary
(With Johnny Paycheck) / Stranger in the
house (With Elvis Costello) / I still hold her
body (but I think I've lost her mind) (With
Dennis and Ray of Dr.Hook) / Will the circle
be unbroken (With Pop and Mavis Staples)
CD _____ 982655 2
Carlton Home Entertainment / Feb '94 /
Carlton Home Entertainment.

TENDER YEARS
CD _____ 15488
Laserlight / Dec '94 / Target/BMG.

Jones Girls

COMING BACK
CD _____ ARPCD 02
ARP / Oct '92 / Jetstar.

Jones, Glenn

ALL FOR YOU
CD _____ CHIP 74
Jive / May '90 / BMG.

HERE I AM
Here I am / It's gonna be alright / Love song
/ Round and round / Make it up to you /
Coming back to you / Give love a chance /
Everything to me / Since you've been gone
(a house is not a home) / Don't walk away
/ In you
CD _____ 756782513-2
Warner Bros. / Apr '94 / Warner Music.

Jones, Grace

FAME
Do or die / Pride / Fame / Autumn leaves /
All on a summer's night / Am I ever gonna
fall in love in NYC / Below the belt
CD _____ 5501322
Spectrum/Karussell / Oct '93 / PolyGram /
THE.

ISLAND LIFE
Slave to the rhythm / Pull up to the bumper
/ Private life / La vie en rose / I need a man
/ My Jamaican guy / Walking in the rain /
Libertango / Love is the drug / Do or die
CD _____ IMCD 16
Island / Apr '91 / PolyGram.

LIVING MY LIFE
My Jamaican guy / Nipple to the bottle /
Apple stretching / Everybody hold still / Cry

now - laugh later / Inspiration / Unlimited
capacity for love
CD _____ IMCD 18
Island / Jun '89 / PolyGram.

NIGHTCLUBBIN'
Feel up / Walking in the rain / Pull up to the
bumper / Use me / Art groupie / Libertango
/ I've done it again
CD _____ IMCD 17
Island / Jun '89 / PolyGram.

PORTFOLIO
Send in the clowns / What I did for love /
Tomorrow / La vie en rose / Sorry / That's
the trouble / I need a man
CD _____ IMCD 19
Island / Jun '89 / PolyGram.

SLAVE TO THE RHYTHM
Jones the rhythm / Fashion show / Frog and
the princess / Operattack / Slave to the
rhythm / Crossing (ooh the action) / Don't
cry - it's only the rhythm / Ladies and gentlemen: Miss Grace Jones
CD _____ IMCD 65
Island / '89 / PolyGram.

WARM LEATHERETTE
Warm leatherette / Private life / Rollin' stone
/ Love is the drug / Hunter gets captured
by the game / Bullshit / Breakdown / Pars
CD _____ IMCD 15
Island / Jun '89 / PolyGram.

Jones, Hank

ARIGATO
CD _____ PCD 7004
Progressive / Oct '91 / Jazz Music.

HANDFUL OF KEYS
CD _____ 5127372
Verve / May '92 / PolyGram.

HANK
Just squeeze me / In a sentimental mood /
Satin doll / Prelude to a kiss / What am I
here for / Do nothin' 'til you hear from me /
Sophisticated lady / Oh look at me now /
Alone together / Don't blame me / Gone
with the wind / My heart stood still / If I had
you / Very thought of you
CD _____ AAJ 11003
Jazz Alliance / Jan '92 / New Note.

HANK JONES QUARTET
Moonlight becomes you / Relaxin' at Cam-
arillo / Minor contention / Sunday in savan-
nah / Spontaneous combustion
CD _____ SV 0236
Savoy Jazz / Nov '93 / Conifer / ADA.

HANK JONES TRIO (Jones, Hank Trio)
CD _____ STCD 4180
Storyville / Jan '94 / Jazz Music / Wellard
/ CM / Cadillac.

I REMEMBER YOU
CD _____ BLE 233122
Black & Blue / Oct '94 / Wellard / Koch.

**JAZZ TRIO OF HANK JONES, THE
(Jones, Hank & Kenny Clarke/Wendell
Marshall)**
We're all together / Odd number / When
hearts are young / There's a small hotel /
Cyrano / Now's the time / My funny valen-
tine / We could make such beautiful music
CD _____ SV 0184
Savoy Jazz / Oct '92 / Conifer / ADA.

LAZY AFTERNOON
Speak low / Lazy afternoon / Intimidation /
Comin' home baby / Sublime / Peedlum /
Work song / Lament / Passing time / Arrival
CD _____ CCD 4391
Concord Jazz / '89 / New Note.

**LIVE AT MAYBECK RECITAL HALL,
VOL. 16**
I guess I'll have to change my plan / It's the
talk of the town / Very thought of you / Night
we called it a day / Bluesette / Child is born
/ What is this thing called love / Oh what a
beautiful mornin' / Six and four / I cover the
waterfront / Memories of you / Blue monk /
Round Midnight / Oh, look at me now
CD _____ CCD 4502
Concord Jazz / Mar '92 / New Note.

**MEETS LOUIS BELLSON AND IRA
SULLIVAN**
CD _____ STCD 553
Stash / '92 / Jazz Music / CM / Cadillac /
Direct / ADA.

QUARTET - QUINTET
Almost like being in love / Evening at Papa
Joe's / An' then some / Summer's gone /
Don't blame me
CD _____ SV 0147
Savoy Jazz / Apr '93 / Conifer / ADA.

**SPIRIT OF 176, THE (Jones, Hank &
George Shearing)**
CD _____ CCD 4371
Concord Jazz / Apr '89 / New Note.

Jones, Howard

12 INCH ALBUM, THE
Always asking questions / New song (new
version) / What is love / Like to get to know
you well / Pearl in the shell (extended mix)
/ Total conditioning
CD _____ 2405432
WEA / Jul '88 / Warner Music.

BEST OF HOWARD JONES, THE
Look mama / Prisoner / Everlasting love /
Lift me up / Tears to tell / Two souls / I.G.Y.
/ City song / What is love / New song / Pearl
in the shell / Always asking questions /
Things can only get better / Life in one day /
You know I love you don't you / Hide and seek / No
one is to blame
CD _____ 450992701-2
WEA / May '93 / Warner Music.

CROSS THAT LINE
Prisoner / Powerhouse / Cross that line /
Guardians of the breath / Wanders to you /
Everlasting love / Last supper / Out of thin
air / Fresh air waltz / Those who move
clouds
CD _____ 244176 2
WEA / Mar '89 / Warner Music.

DREAM INTO ACTION
Things can only get better / Life in one day
/ Dream into action / No one is to blame /
Look mama / Assault and battery / Auto-
mation / Is there a difference / Elegy / Spe-
cialty / Why look for the key / Hunger for
flesh
CD _____ 240632 2
WEA / Apr '85 / Warner Music.

HUMAN'S LIB
Conditioning / What is love / Pearl in the
shell / Hide and seek / Hunt the self / New
song / Don't always look at the rain / Equality / Natural / Human's lib
CD _____ K 240335 2
WEA / Jun '84 / Warner Music.

IN THE RUNNING
Lift me up / Fallin' away / Show me / Voices
are back / Exodus / Tears to tell / Two souls
/ Gun turned on the world / One last try /
City song
CD _____ 9031763362
WEA / Apr '92 / Warner Music.

ONE TO ONE
You know I love you don't you / Balance of
love / All I want / Where are we going /
Don't want to fight anymore / Step into
these shoes / Will you still be there / Good
luck bad luck / Give me strength / Little bit
of snow
CD _____ 242011 2
WEA / Oct '86 / Warner Music.

WHAT IS LOVE
CD _____ 4509 918872
Carlton Home Entertainment / Jan '93 /
Carlton Home Entertainment.

Jones, Hughie

HUGHIE'S DITTY BAG
Champion of the seas / Marques / Coal,
coal for Manchester / Christmas time odd-
job man / Marco polo / Navvies' way / Fair-
lie duplex engine / Ellen Vannin tragedy /
Stockholm tar / Shortness of sight / Greys-
black stone of ffestinog / Wavertree / New
York girls are pretty
CD _____ FE 081CD
Fellside / '92 / Target/BMG / Direct / ADA.

Jones, Ivan

**MINDBENDER, THE/ MY FIRE (Jones,
Ivan 'Boogaloo Joe')**
Mindbender / There is a mountain / Games
/ Sticks and stones / Blues for Bruce / Beat
goes on / Right now / Call me / Light my
fire / For big Hal / St. James Infirmary / Face
all / Time after time / Ivan the Terrible
CD _____ CDBGPD 067
BGP / Jun '93 / Pinnacle.

**SNAKE RHYTHM ROCK/BLACK WHIP
(Jones, Ivan 'Boogaloo Joe')**
Hoochie coo chickie / Snake rhythm rock /
First time ever I saw your face / He's so fine
/ Big bad midnight roller / Black whip / My
love / Freak off / Daniel / Ballad of mad
dogs and Englishmen / Crank me up
CD _____ CDBGPD 043
BGP / Sep '92 / Pinnacle.

Jones, Jack

BEST OF JACK JONES
CD _____ DSHCD 7003
D-Sharp / Dec '92 / Pinnacle.

BEWITCHED
My kind of town / Along the way / She loves
me / Lollipops and roses / Gypsies, the jugglers and the clowns / From Russia with
love / Canoca / Feeling good / My favourite
things / I don't care much / You'd better
love me / Bewitched / Beautiful friendship /
I must know / Afterthoughts / Mood I'm in
/ Julie / I will wait for you / Far away / I'm
all smiles / Brother, where are you / Wives
and lovers / This is all I ask / Travellin' on
CD _____ 30359 00042
Carlton Home Entertainment / Oct '95 /
Carlton Home Entertainment.

JACK JONES COLLECTOR'S EDITION
CD _____ DVAD 6042
Deja Vu / Apr '95 / THE.

JACK JONES ENTERTAINS
Wives and lovers / Alfie / Lollipops and
roses / You've got your troubles / More /
Yesterday / What now my love / Shadow of
your smile / Dear heart / If you go away /

Girl talk / I believe in you / She loves me / Watch what happens / Impossible dream / What the world needs now is love / Our song (CD only) / Love bug (CD only) / Fly me to the moon (CD only) / Charade (CD only)
CD _____ CDMFP 6054
Music For Pleasure / Mar '89 / EMI.

LIVE AT THE LONDON PALLADIUM
I had a dream / Gypsies, jugglers and clowns / Gershwin medley (Summertime; Embraceable; Man; I got plenty of nothing; Bess you is my woman) / Just one of those things / Child is born / Hopeless romantic / This all I ask / Falling in love / Right here waiting / Music of the night / Wives and lovers / Lady / Call me irresponsible / If / Soliloquy / Imagine / From a distance
CD _____ DSHCD 7009
D-Sharp / Sep '95 / Pinnacle.

LOOK OF LOVE, THE
Look of love / She / Make it with you / If you could read my mind / Without her / God only knows / All cried out / Once in a while / It's too late / Goin' out of my head / What are you doing the rest of your life / Mean to me / You and the night and the music / For all we know
CD _____ 74321339442
Camden / Jan '96 / BMG.

Jones, Jim

TRUST, CONTRAFUSION (Jones, Jim & The Kool Ade Kids)
CD _____ CC 004
Common Cause / Nov '93 / Plastic Head / SRD.

Jones, Jo

JO JONES TRIO (Jones, Jo Trio)
CD _____ FSCD 40
Fresh Sound / Oct '90 / Jazz Music / Discovery.

Jones, Joe

YOU TALK TOO MUCH
You talk too much / Take a little walk / McDonald's daughter / Tisket-a-tasket / One big mouth (two big ears) / Here's what you gotta do / Where is my baby / To prove my love to you / Big mule / I cried for you / Just write / You talk too much (original) / I'm glad for your sake / One big mouth (original) / I love you still / Every night about eight / Tell me what's happening / Please don't talk about me when I'm gone / I need someone / Always picking on me / California sun / Because I love you / I've got a uh-uh wife / Oh gee how I cried / Indian love call / Down by the river
CD _____ NEMCD 672
Sequel / Jun '94 / BMG.

Jones, Jonah

AT THE EMBERS
It's all right with me / From this moment on / Learnin' the blues / Something's gotta give / All of you / Lullaby of Birdland / Basin Street blues / High society / Tin roof blues / Muskrat ramble / At sundown
CD _____ 74321185232
RCA Victor / Oct '94 / BMG.

Jones, Keziah

AFRICAN SPACE CRAFT
African space craft / Million miles from home / Colorful world / Prodigal funk / Splash / Dear Mr. Cooper / Speech / Cubic space division / Funk 'n' circumstance / Man with the scar / Never gonna let you go / If you know
CD _____ CDDLB 14
Delabel / Oct '95 / EMI.

BLUFUNK IS A FACT
CD _____ CDDLB 1
Delabel / Mar '92 / EMI.

Jones, Leroy

MO' CREAM FROM THE CROP
When my dreamboat comes home / Mo' cream from the crop / Sweet Lorraine / How come you do me like you do / Time for love / Bourbon street parade / Tin roof blues / Mosey roun' bring it down / Blues for Z.W. / new Orleans / Carnival's in town / Mood indigo / Bei mir bist du schon
CD _____ 477751-2
Columbia / Oct '94 / Sony.

Jones, Linda

YOUR PRECIOUS LOVE
Your precious love / I do / I love you (I need you) / I've given you the best years of my life / Don't go (I can't stand to be alone) / Not on the outside / Doggin' me around / Let it be me / Hypnotised / If only we had met sooner / Fugitive from love / I'm so glad I found you / Stay with me forever / Things I've been through / When hurt comes back / I can't make it alone / Behold / Dancing in the street
CD _____ NEXCD 167
Sequel / Jul '91 / BMG.

Jones, Lloyd

TROUBLE MONKEY
Can't get you off my mind / I broke my baby's heart / Trouble monkey / Old friends / I'll be laughing (when he makes you cry) / (Just about to) bust up a love / Don't call me today / No more crying / Long, long way to go / Rosemary / When I get back home / Drop down Mama
CD _____ AQCD 1037
Audioquest / Nov '95 / New Note.

Jones, Mazlyn

ANGELS OVER WATER
Eden / Flying / Water and stone / Kelda / Windsmith / First light / Angels over water / Great rock (I) / Sea of glass (II) / Glistening waters (II)
CD _____ BWKD 211
Brainworks / Oct '95 / Pinnacle.

Jones, Michael

AIR BORN
Air born / Summer in Chimo / Lark in the clear air / Voices in the wind
CD _____ ND 61042
Narada / Jul '94 / New Note / ADA.

Jones, Mick

MICK JONES
CD _____ 7567819912
Atlantic / Jan '96 / Warner Music.

Jones, Mose

MOSE NOSE KNOWS
CD _____ 901269
Line / Oct '94 / CM / Grapevine / ADA / Conifer / Direct.

Jones, Nic

PENGUIN EGGS
Canadee-i-o / Drowned lovers / Humpback whale / Little pot stove / Courting is a pleasure / Barrack Street / Planxty Davis / Flandyke Shore / Farewell to the gold
CD _____ TSCD 411
Topic / Nov '90 / Direct / ADA.

Jones, Oliver

CLASS ACT, A
CD _____ JUST 41-2
Justin Time / Sep '91 / Harmonia Mundi / Cadillac.

COOKIN' AT SWEET BASIL
Hymn to a friend / You are too beautiful / Blue mountain / Young and foolish / Take the 'A' train / Pe gros bois blues / Fly me to the moon / Someone to watch over me
CD _____ BRMCD 020
Bold Reprive / Aug '88 / Pinnacle / Bold Reprive / Harmonia Mundi.

FROM LUSH TO LIVELY (Jones, Oliver Big Band)
CD _____ JUST 73-2
Justin Time / Dec '95 / Harmonia Mundi / Cadillac.

JAZZ & RIBS LIVE AT BIDDLE'S (Jones, Oliver Trio & Charles Biddle & Bernard Primeau)
CD _____ JUST 1-2
Justin Time / May '91 / Harmonia Mundi / Cadillac.

NORTHERN SUMMIT (Mones, Oliver)
CD _____ JUST 34-2
Justin Time / Apr '91 / Harmonia Mundi / Cadillac.

REQUESTFULLY YOURS
CD _____ JUST 11-2
Justin Time / May '91 / Harmonia Mundi / Cadillac.

SPEAK LOW SWING HARD
CD _____ BRMCD 019
Bold Reprive / Aug '88 / Pinnacle / Bold Reprive / Harmonia Mundi.

Jones, Paul

AMERICAN GUESTS VOL. 1
CD _____ JSPCD 210
JSP / Oct '92 / ADA / Target/BMG / Direct / Cadillac / Complete/Pinnacle.

CRUCIFIX IN A HORSESHOE
CD _____ REP 4196-WP
Repertoire / Aug '91 / Pinnacle / Cadillac.

I NEED A STORM (Jones, Paul Urbana)
CD _____ FF 606CD
Flying Fish / Feb '93 / Roots / CM / Direct / ADA.

Jones, Peter

WITH TUNNELS
CD _____ OZ 004-2
Ozone / Jan '94 / SRD.

Jones, Philly Joe

FILET DE SOLE
CD _____ 151972
Marge / Nov '92 / Discovery.

Jones, Quincy

BACK ON THE BLOCK
Prologue (2 Q's rap) / Back on the block / I don't go for that / I'll be good to you / Verb: To be / Wee b dooinit / Places you find love / Jazz corner of the world / Birdland (Inst.) / Setembro / One man woman / Tomorrow (a better you, better me) / Prelude to the garden / Secret garden
CD _____ 926020 2
Qwest / Dec '89 / Warner Music.

DUDE, THE
Ai no corrida / Dude / Just one / Betcha wouldn't hurt me / Something special / Razzamatazz / Hundred ways / Valas / Turn on the action
CD _____ CDMID 119
A&M / Oct '92 / PolyGram.

FREE AND EASY (Live In Sweden 1960)
Moanin / Tickle toe / I remember Clifford / Whisper not / Phantom's blues / Birth of a band / Gypsy / Ghana / Walkin' / Big red
CD _____ ANC 95002
Ancha / Aug '94 / Jazz Music / Wellard / Cadillac.

FREE AND EASY - IN SWEDEN 1960
CD _____ ANC 9500
Ancha / Sep '94 / Jazz Music / Wellard / Cadillac.

LISTEN UP - THE LIVES OF QUINCY JONES
Listen up (instrumental version) / Kansas city wrinkles / Killer Joe / Let the good times roll / Air mail special / Perry's theme / Kingfish / Birth of a band / Fly me to the moon / Midnight sun will never set / Rack 'em up / TV medley / Maybe God is tryin' tn tell you somethin' / Walking in space / Pop medley / How do you keep the music playing / Back on the block album medley / Somewhere / Listen up (vocal version)
CD _____ 7599263222
Qwest / Sep '90 / Warner Music.

LIVE LAUSANNE 1960 (Jones, Quincy & His Orchestra)
Cherokee / Chinese checkers / Birth of a band / I remember Clifford / Ghana / Big red / My reverie / Parisian thoroughfare / Moanin' / Soul / Midnight sun will never set / Phantom's blues / Airmail special / Airmail special (Encore)
CD _____ TCB 02012
TCB / Jul '94 / New Note.

Q'S JUKE JOINT
CD _____ 9362458752
Qwest / Nov '95 / Warner Music.

SOUNDS...AND STUFF LIKE THAT
Stuff like that / Love I never had it so good / Superwoman / I'm gonna miss you in the morning / Love me by my name / Takin' it to the streets
CD _____ CDMID 120
A&M / Oct '92 / PolyGram.

WALK ON THE WILD SIDE
CD _____ MSCD 18
Music De-Luxe / Apr '95 / Magnum Music Group.

WALK ON THE WILD SIDE
CD _____ CDCD 1194
Charly / Sep '94 / Charly / THE / Cadillac.

WATERMELON MAN
CD _____ HADCD 182
Javelin / Nov '95 / THE / Henry Hadaway Organisation.

Jones, Richard M.

CLASSICS 1923-27
CD _____ CLASSICS 826
Classics / Sep '95 / Discovery / Jazz Music.

Jones, Rickie Lee

FLYING COWBOYS
CD _____ GEFD 24246
Geffen / Nov '91 / BMG.

MAGAZINE
Prelude to gravity / Gravity / Jukebox fury / It must be love / Magazine / Real end / Deep space / Runaround Rorschachs / Theme for the Pope / Unsigned painting / Weird beast
CD _____ 925117 2
WEA / Mar '86 / Warner Music.

NAKED SONGS
CD _____ 9362459502
WEA / Sep '95 / Warner Music.

PIRATES
We belong together / Living it up / Skeletons / Woody and Dutch on the slow train to Peking / Pirates / Lucky guy / Traces of western slopes / Returns
CD _____ 256816
WEA / Jan '86 / Warner Music.

POP POP
CD _____ GFLD 19293
Geffen / Oct '95 / BMG.

MO' JOE
CD _____ BLC 760154
Black Lion / Apr '91 / Jazz Music / Cadillac / Wellard / Koch.

Jones, Rickie Lee

ON SATURDAY AFTERNOONS IN 1963

[right column entries under Jones, Rickie Lee:]

Rickie Lee Jones
On Saturday afternoons in 1963 / Night train / Young blood / Easy money / Last chance Texaco / Danny's all star joint / Coolsville / Weasel and the white boy's cool / Company / After hours (12 bars past midnight) / Chuck E's in love
CD _____ K2 56628
WEA / '89 / Warner Music.

TRAFFIC FROM PARADISE
Pink flamingoes / Alter boy / Stewart's coat / Beat angels / Tigers / Rebel rebel / Jolie jolie / Running from mercy a stranger's car / Albatross
CD _____ GED 24602
Geffen / Sep '93 / BMG.

Jones, Robin

CHANGO (Jones, Robin & King Salsa)
Elugua / King Salsa theme / Vamonos Pa'l Monte / Sonando / Manteca / Controladora / Viva la vida contento / Mi songo / Mama guela / Mozambique pa'gozar / Bomba de salon / June / Tremendo / Songo for Jo / Dominican dream / Amor verdadero / Olufina / Chango
CD _____ PARCD 502
Parrot / Jul '93 / THE / Wellard / Jazz Music.

Jones, Rodney

ARTICULATION
Articulation / 1978 / Hard New York swing / Interlude 1 / Childville / Blues for Wes / Nereda
CD _____ CDSJP 121
Timeloss Jazz / Jun '91 / New Note.

Jones, Sam

VISITATION
CD _____ SCCD 31097
Steeplechase / Jul '88 / Impetus.

Jones, Shirley

WITH YOU
Gonna get over you / What about me / I've been expecting you / Say / Come closer / Perfect love / Nights over Eygpt / With you / I just can't wait / Dreams do come true / I'm yours tonight / I ain't going nowhere
CD _____ DIVCD 3
Diverse / Jul '94 / Grapevine.

Jones, Spike

AND HIS CITY SLICKERS
CD _____ ENTCD 247
Entertainers / Mar '92 / Target/BMG.

BEST OF SPIKE JONES & HIS CITY SLICKERS, THE (Jones, Spike & His City Slickers)
Cocktails for two / William Tell overture / Chloe / My old flame / Glow worm / None but the lonely heart / Laura / Man on the flying trapeze / You always hurt the one you love / Der Fuhrer's face / Dance of the hours / Hawaiian war chant
CD _____ 74321135762
RCA / May '93 / BMG.

DIRECT OFF THE AIR 1949
CD _____ HQCD 30
Harlequin / Jan '95 / Swift / Jazz Music / Wellard / Hot Shot / Cadillac.

MUSICAL DEPRECIATION (Original Mono Recordings 1941-1945) (Jones, Spike & His City Slickers)
Cocktails for two / Chloe / Behind those two swingin' doors / Red wing / Covered wagon rolled right along / Clink, clink another drink / Little Bo Peep has lost her jeep / Pass the biscuits, Mirandy / Der Fuehre's face / I wanna go back to West Virginia / Hotcha cornia (black eyes) / Leave the dishes in the sink Ma / Serenade to a jerk / Holiday for strings / Blue Danube / You always hurt the one you love / Hawaiian war chant / Liebestraum / That old black magic / Nutcracker suite
CD _____ CDAJA 5189
Living Era / Jan '96 / Koch.

RADIO DAYS (Jones, Spike & His City Slickers)
CD _____ RMB 75017
Remember / Nov '93 / Total/BMG.

RIOT SQUAD (Jones, Spike & His City Slickers)
By the beautiful sea / Liebestraum / Red wing / Der Fuhrer's face / You're a sap Mr. Jap / Never hit your grandma with a shovel / Oh by jingo / I wanna go back to West Virginia
CD _____ HQCD 01
Harlequin / '86 / Swift / Jazz Music / Wellard / Hot Shot / Cadillac.

RIOT SQUAD VOL 2 (1942-1945) (Jones, Spike & His City Slickers)
Blacksmith song / Moo woo woo / Don't give the chair to Buster / Big bad Bill / Red grow the roses / Casey Jones / And the great big saw came nearer / No no Nora
CD _____ HQCD 02
Harlequin / Nov '86 / Swift / Jazz Music / Wellard / Hot Shot / Cadillac.

Jones, Thad

GREAT CONCERT, THE (Jones, Thad & Mel Lewis)
CD _____ COD 017
Jazz View / Jun '92 / Harmonia Mundi.

MAD THAD
CD _____ FSCD 117
Fresh Sound / Jan '91 / Jazz Music / Discovery.

ORCHESTRA, THE (Jones, Thad & Mel Lewis)
CD _____ WWCD 2044
West Wind / Jan '91 / Swift / Charly / CM / ADA.

SWISS RADIO DAYS JAZZ SERIES, VOL.4
Second race / Don't ever leave me / Waltz you swang for me / A - that's freedom / Come Sunday / Don't get sassy / Bible story / Groove merchant
CD _____ TCB 02042
TCB / Jan '95 / New Note.

THAD JONES AND THE DANISH RADIO BIG BAND (Jones, Thad & The Danish Radio Big Band)
CD _____ STCD 4172
Storyville / Feb '90 / Jazz Music / Wellard / CM / Cadillac.

Jones, Tom

13 SMASH HITS
Don't fight it / You keep me hangin' on / Hold on I'm comin' / I wake up crying / Keep on running / Get ready / I'll never fall in love again / I know / I wake up crying / Funny how time slips away / Danny boy / It's a man's man's man's world / Yesterday
CD _____ 8 205242
London / Jan '93 / PolyGram.

A-TOM-IC JONES
Dr. Love / Face of a loser / It's been a long, long time / Coming / In a woman's eyes / More / I'll never let you go / Loser / To make a big man cry / Key to my heart / True love comes only once in a lifetime / Little you / You're so good to me / Where do you belong / These things you don't forget / Stop breaking my heart / Hide and seek / Not responsible / This and that / Promise her anything / Thunderball
CD _____ 8 205562
London / Jan '93 / PolyGram.

ALONG CAME JONES
I've got a heart / It takes a worried man / Skye boat song / Once upon a time / Memphis, Tennessee / What'cha gonna do / I need your loving / It's not unusual / Autumn leaves / Rose / If you need me / Some other guy / Endlessly / It's just a matter of time / Spanish harlem / When the world was beautiful
CD _____ 8440252
London / Jan '93 / PolyGram.

COLLECTION
It's not unusual / Spanish harlem / Detroit city / What's new pussycat / My prayer / Sixteen tons / Nearness of you / Not responsible / Loser / Lucille (live) / Cool water / This and that / I'll never let you go / Dr. Love / More / Ten guitars / If you need me / Green, green grass of home
CD _____ 5515202
Spectrum/Karussell / Aug '95 / PolyGram / THE.

COLLECTION, THE
CD _____ CCSCD 431
Castle / Mar '95 / BMG.

DELILAH
Delilah / Riders in the sky / To wait for love is to waste your life away / Funny familiar forgotten feelings / Get ready / Delilah to my mind / When I fall in love / Danny boy / Begin the beguine / Help yourself / I was made to love her / Hey Jude / If you go away / Yesterday / My foolish heart / Let it be me / What's he got that I ain't got / One day soon / Weeping Annaleah / Make this heart of mine smile again / Lingering on / You can't stop love / My elusive dreams / Just out of reach / Only a fool breaks his own heart / Why can't I cry / Take me
CD _____ 8 204862
London / Jan '93 / PolyGram.

DELILAH
CD _____ 12575
Laserlight / Oct '95 / Target/BMG.

FROM THE HEART
Begin the beguine / You came a long way from St. Louis / My foolish heart / It's magic / Someday (you'll want me to want you) / Georgia on my mind / Kansas city / Hello, young lovers / Taste of honey / Nearness of you / When I fall in love / If ever I would leave you / My prayer / That old black magic / Any day now / I'm coming home / Thing called love / Green green grass of home
CD _____ 8205572
London / Apr '89 / PolyGram.

GOLDEN HITS: TOM JONES
Green green grass of home / I'm coming home / I'll never fall in love again / Not responsible / Help yourself / What's new pussycat / Love me tonight / It's not unu-

sual.. / Funny familiar forgotten feelings / Detroit city / With these hands / Minute of your time / Without love / Delilah
CD _____ 8101922
London / Jan '93 / PolyGram.

GREAT LOVE SONGS, THE
I can't stop loving you / Without you / When I fall in love / With these hands / Little green apples / Once upon a time / I'm coming home / Nearness of you / Funny familiar forgotten feelings / Smile / I believe / Green green grass of home / Wichita lineman / My elusive dreams / If you go away / I'll never fall in love again
CD _____ PWKS 587
Carlton Home Entertainment / Jul '90 / Carlton Home Entertainment.

GREATEST HITS: TOM JONES
It's not unusual / Delilah / Help yourself / Daughter of darkness / I'll never fall in love again / Without love / With these hands / I'm coming home / Funny familiar forgotten feelings / Green green grass of home / Detroit city / Something 'bout you baby I like / I who have nothing / Till
CD _____ TCD 2296
Telstar / Nov '88 / BMG.

GREEN GREEN GRASS OF HOME
Green green grass of home / She's a lady / Funny familiar forgotten feelings / Delilah / Not responsible / Detroit city / Help yourself / Till / Love me tonight / It's not unusual / I'll never fall in love again / Daughter of darkness / What's new pussycat / I'm coming home / Once upon a time / This and that / Riders in the sky / He'll have to go / Sixteen tons / Two brothers / My mother's eyes / Ring of fire / Field of yellow daisies / Wish I could say no to you / All I get from you is heartaches / Mohair Sam / Cool water
CD _____ 8201822
London / Jan '93 / PolyGram.

HELP YOURSELF
Help yourself / I can't break the news to myself / Bed / Isadora / Set me free / I get carried away / This house (the house song) / So afraid / If I promise / If you go away / My girl Maria / All I can say is goodbye / Ten guitars / What a party / Looking out my window / Can't stop loving you / Let there be love / Without love
CD _____ 8 205592
London / Jan '93 / PolyGram.

HITS
CD _____ CD 12331
Laserlight / Apr '94 / Target/BMG.

I'M COMING HOME
I'll never fall in love again / To wait for love (is to waste your life away) / I can't stop loving you / Once there was a time / Untrue / Someday (you'll want me to want you) / To make a big man cry / Won't you give him (one more chance) / He'll have to go / Some other guy / Field of yellow daisies / I wake up crying / Autumn leaves / Funny familiar forgotten feelings
CD _____ 5500202
Spectrum/Karussell / May '93 / PolyGram / THE.

IN NASHVILLE
Darlin' / What in the world's come over you / Lady lay down / But I do / It's for in the morning / Not another heart song / Give her all the roses / I'm an old rock 'n' roller / Don't want to be alone tonight / My last goodbye / I've been rained on too / This time / All the love is on radio / Come home Rhonda Boy / Dime Queen of Nevada / Woman's touch / Touch me (then I'll be your fool once more) / I'll be me / I don't want to be alone tonight
CD _____ 5513402
Spectrum/Karussell / Aug '95 / PolyGram / THE.

IT'S NOT UNUSUAL
It's not unusual / Delilah / Land of 1000 dances (live mix) / With these hands / Kansas City / It's magic / Promise her anything / When I fall in love / Memphis, Tennessee / (Sittin' on) the dock of the bay / If you go away / Green green grass of home / What's new pussycat / I'll never fall in love again / I'm coming home / Hey Jude / Detroit city / Not responsible / My prayer
CD _____ PWKS 529
Carlton Home Entertainment / Jul '89 / Carlton Home Entertainment.

IT'S NOT UNUSUAL - HIS GREATEST HITS
It's not unusual / Green green grass of home / Help yourself / I'll never fall in love again / Not responsible / Love me tonight / Without love / Delilah / What's new pussycat / Detroit city / Once upon a time / Thunderball / Minute of your time / With these hands / Funny familiar forgotten feelings / I'm coming home / You keep me hangin' on (Cassette & CD only.) / Land of 1000 dances
CD _____ 8205442
London / Jul '87 / PolyGram.

KISS
CD _____ EMPRCD 555
Emporio / Mar '95 / THE / Disc / CM.

LEAD AND HOW TO SWING IT, THE
CD _____ 6544924982
ZTT / Nov '94 / Warner Music.

LEGENDARY TOM JONES, THE
CD _____ 8445522
Deram / Jan '96 / PolyGram.

LIVE AT CAESAR'S PALACE
Dance of love / Cabaret / Soul man / I who have nothing / Delilah / Bridge over troubled water / My way / God bless the children / Resurrection shuffle / She's a lady / Till / I'll never fall in love again / Daughter of darkness / Love me tonight / It's not unusual / Hi-heel sneakers / Johnny B. Goode / Bony Moronie / Long tall Sally
CD _____ CDMFP 5931
Music For Pleasure / Oct '91 / EMI.

LIVE IN LAS VEGAS
Turn on your love light / Bright lights and you girl / I can't stop loving you / Hard to handle / Delilah / Danny boy / I'll never fall in love again / Help yourself / Yesterday / Hey Jude / Love me tonight / It's not unusual / Twist and shout
CD _____ 8203182
London / Jan '93 / PolyGram.

LOVE ALBUM, THE (Jones, Tom & Engelbert Humperdinck)
CD _____ DCD 5385
Disky / Jul '94 / THE / BMG / Discovery / Pinnacle.

MINUTE OF YOUR TIME, A
Minute of your time / Not responsible / When I fall in love / Let there be love / Without love / Wichita lineman / He'll have to go / Help yourself / My prayer / My elusive dreams / Taste of honey / It's magic / It takes a worried man / Mohair Sam / This house / Endlessly
CD _____ PWKS 4027P
Carlton Home Entertainment / Sep '90 / Carlton Home Entertainment.

SIMPLY THE BEST - SHE'S A LADY
CD _____ WMCD 5693
Disky / May '94 / THE / BMG / Discovery / Pinnacle.

SOUL OF TOM JONES, THE
(Sittin' on) the dock of the bay / Hold on I'm comin' / It's a man's man's man's world / Hard to handle / I was made to love her / If you need me / Don't fight it / Shake / Get ready / Turn on your love light / You keep me hangin' on / I need your loving / Without love / I wake up crying / Just out of reach / Land of 1000 dances / It's not unusual
CD _____ PWKS 4101P
Carlton Home Entertainment / Mar '92 / Carlton Home Entertainment.

STOP BREAKING MY HEART
Stop breaking my heart / Before / Once in a while / Triple cross / Shake / If I had you / It ain't gonna be that way / How do you say goodbye / Things I wanna do / For the first time in my life / Tupelo Mississippi Flash / Lonely one / Smile / Day by day / Out in the cold again / Unfinished song / Man who knows too much / Minute of your time / With one exception / It's not unusual
CD _____ 8207732
London / Jan '93 / PolyGram.

THIS IS TOM JONES
Fly me to the moon / Little green apples / Wichita lineman / (Sittin' on) the dock of the bay / Dance of love / Hey Jude / Without you / That's all a man can say / That wonderful sound / Only once / I'm a fool to want you / Let it be me
CD _____ 8202342
London / Jan '93 / PolyGram.

TOM JONES LIVE IN LONDON
Star theme (Intro) / Ain't that good news / Hello, young lovers / I can't stop loving you / What's new pussycat / Not responsible / I believe / My yiddishe Momme / Shake / That lucky old sun / Thunderball / That old black magic / Green green grass of home / It's not unusual / Land of 1000 dances
CD _____ 8205582
London / Jan '93 / PolyGram.

VELVET & STEEL/GOLD (2CD Set)
CD Set _____ 8440962
London / Jan '93 / PolyGram.

VOICE, THE
It's not unusual / (Sittin' on) the dock of the bay / What's new pussycat / let it be me / Green green grass of home / It's magic / Memphis, Tennessee / I can't stop loving you / If you go away / Kansas City / Promise her anything / Detroit city / With these hands / I'll never fall in love again / My prayer / Love me tonight / I'm coming home
CD _____ MCCD 057
Music Club / Mar '92 / Disc / THE.

WHAT A PARTY
CD _____ 8440262
London / Jan '93 / PolyGram.

WHAT'S NEW PUSSYCAT
What's new pussycat / Some other guy / I've got a heart / Little by little / Won't you give him (one more chance) / Bama lama bama loo / With these hands / Untrue / To wait for love is to waste your life away / I tell the sea / Rose / Endlessly / Memphis,

Tennessee / Kiss kiss / Once upon a time / What'cha gonna do
CD _____ 8205232
London / Jan '93 / PolyGram.

Jones, Tutu

I'M FOR REAL
Sweet woman / I'm for real / My own fault / Excited / (Do you love) steppin' on me / She's my woman / I still love you / Too blues to be true / Stubborn woman / I'm not your fool / Outstanding
CD _____ JSPCD 252
JSP / Jun '94 / ADA / Target/BMG / Direct / Cadillac / Complete/Pinnacle.

Jones, Vince

COMPLETE, THE
If you're going to the city / Lobster / Detour ahead / Nature boy / My ideal / Big city / Blue / Don't worry about a thing / Nature of power / Since I fell for you / I put a spell on you / Dream / Not much / Budgie / Sensual item / Never let me go
CD _____ INT 30902
Intuition / Nov '93 / New Note.

FUTURE GIRL
CD _____ INT 31092
Intuition / Oct '92 / New Note.

ONE DAY SPENT
Detour ahead / Let's get lost / I wish you love / Since I fell for you / Afterthought / I thought about you / Time after time / Never let me go / Save your love for me / There'll never be another you
CD _____ INT 30872
Intuition / Feb '92 / New Note.

SPELL
CD _____ INT 30672
Intuition / Oct '91 / New Note.

TRUSTWORTHY LITTLE SWEETHEARTS
Big city / Don't worry about a thing / Stricken by a storm / Trustworthy little sweethearts / I'm a fool to want you / Like young / My only friend / That odd feeling / In an attempt to be fascinating / I didn't know what time it was / Not much / Turn around / (I'm afraid) the masquerade is over
CD _____ INT 3046 2
Intuition / Mar '91 / New Note.

WATCH WHAT HAPPENS
CD _____ INT 30702
Intuition / Oct '91 / New Note.

Jones, Vivian

BANK ROBBERY
CD _____ RRCD 013
Roots Collective / May '95 / SRD / Jetstar / Roots Collective.

BEWARE DUB (Yabby You)
CD _____ RE 188CD
Danceteria / Feb '95 / Plastic Head / ADA.

DELIVER ME FROM MY ENEMIES (Yabby You)
CD _____ YVJ 006
Vivian Jones / Apr '92 / Jetstar.

IYAHMAN
CD _____ IHCD 007
Imperial House / Jul '95 / Jetstar / THE.

KING TUBBY'S PROPHECY OF DUB (Yabby You)
CD _____ BAFCD 5
Blood & Fire / Jan '95 / Grapevine / PolyGram.

LOVE IS FOR LOVERS
CD _____ IHCD 006
Imperial House / Jun '95 / Jetstar / THE.

YABBY YOU & MICHAEL PROPHET MEET SCIENTIST (Yabby You & Michael Prophet)
CD _____ YVJ 008
Yabby You / May '95 / Jetstar / THE.

YABBY YOU MEETS MAD PROFESSOR & BLACK STEEL (Yabby You)
CD _____ ARICD 083
Ariwa Sounds / Apr '93 / Jetstar / SRD.

Jones, Wizz

LATE NIGHTS & LONG DAYS (Jones, Wizz & Simeon)
CD _____ FE 091CD
Fellside / Jul '93 / Target/BMG / Direct / ADA.

VILLAGE TAPES
CD _____ TUT 72157
Wundertute / Jan '94 / CM / Duncans / ADA.

Jonny L.

THIS TIME
CD _____ XLEP 118CD
XL / Jan '96 / Warner Music.

Jonsson, Lennart

I THOUGHT ABOUT YOU
CD _____ SITCD 9220
Sittel / Aug '95 / Cadillac / Jazz Music.

Jontef

KLEZMER & YIDDISH
CD _____ EUCD 1303
ARC / Jul '95 / ARC Music / ADA.

Joolz

HEX
Protection / Cat / Facade / Love is (sweet romance) / Stand / Storm / Mummy's boy / Ambition / House of dreams / Requiem / Musket fife and drum (CD only.) / Legend (CD only.) / Mad, bad and dangerous to know (CD only.)
CD _____ CDGRAM 44
Anagram / Apr '90 / Pinnacle.

Joos, Herbert

DAYBREAK - THE DARK SIDE OF TWILIGHT
Why / When were you born / Leicester Court 1440 / Daybreak / Black trees / Fasten your seatbelt / Dark side of twilight
CD _____ 8414792
ECM / Jan '90 / New Note.

Joplin, Janis

18 ESSENTIAL SONGS
Trouble in mind / Down on me / Bye bye baby / Ball and chain / Piece of my heart / I need a man to love / Summertime / Try (just a little bit harder) / One good man / Kozmic blues / Raise your hand / Tell Mama / Move over / Mercedes Benz / Get it while you can / Me and Bobby McGee / Half moon
CD _____ 4785152
Columbia / Apr '95 / Sony.

CHEAP THRILLS/PEARL/KOSMIC BLUES (3CD Set)
CD Set _____ 4673872
Columbia / Dec '90 / Sony.

GREATEST HITS: JANIS JOPLIN
Piece of my heart / Summertime / Try (just a little bit harder) / Cry baby / Me and Bobby McGee / Down on me / Get it while you can / Bye bye baby / Move over / Ball and chain / Everybody loves you now / Why Judy why / Falling of the rain / Turn around / You look so good to me / Tomorrow is today / Nocturne / Got to begin again
CD _____ CD 32190
CBS / May '90 / Sony.

JANIS (3CD Set)
What can drinkin' do / Trouble in mind / Hesitation blues / Easy rider / Coo coo / Down on me / Last time / All is loneliness / Call on me / Women is losers / Intruder / Light is faster than sound / Bye bye baby / Farewell song / Flower in the sun / Misery'n / Roadblock / Ball and chain / Combination of the two / I need a man to love / Piece of my heart / Turtle blues / Oh sweet Mary / Catch me daddy / Summertime / Kozmic blues / Try (just a little bit harder) / One good man / Dear landlord / To love somebody / As good as you've been to this world / Little girl blue / Work me Lord / Raise your hand / Maybe / Me and Bobby McGee / One night stand / Tell mama / Cry baby / Move over / Woman left lonely / Half moon / Happy birthday John (happy trails) / My baby / Mercedes Benz / Trust me / Get it while you can
CD Set _____ CD 48845
Columbia / Jan '94 / Sony.

JANIS JOPLIN: LIVE AT WOODSTOCK 1969
CD _____ ITM 960007
Koch / Sep '93 / Koch.

MAGIC OF LOVE
CD _____ ITM 96001
ITM / Nov '92 / Tradelink / Koch.

PEARL
Move over / Cry baby / Woman left lonely / Half moon / Buried alive in the blues / Me and Bobby McGee / Mercedes Benz / Get it while you can / Trust me / My baby
CD _____ 4804152
Columbia / Jul '95 / Sony.

PEARL/KOSMIC BLUES
Move over / Cry baby / Woman left lonely / Half moon / Buried alive in the blues / My baby / Me and Bobby McGee / Mercedes benz / Trust me / Get it while you can / Try / Maybe / One good man / As good as you've been to this / To love somebody / Kozmic blues / Little girl blue / Work me Lord
CD Set _____ 4610202
Columbia / Jul '92 / Sony.

Joplin, Scott

ELITE SYNCOPATION
Elite syncopations / Country club / Paragon rag / Eugenia / Cleopha / Real slow rag / Scott Joplin's new rag / Leola / Lily Queen / Chrysanthemum / Heliotrope bouquet / Reflection rag / Maple leaf rag (On CD only) / Ole Miss Rag (On CD only) / Magnetic rag (On CD only) / Silver swan rag (On CD only)
CD _____ BCD 102
Biograph / Jul '91 / Wellard / ADA / Hot Shot / Jazz Music / Cadillac / Direct.

ENTERTAINER, THE
Elite syncopations / Chrysanthemum / Scott Joplin's new rag / Eugenia / Paragon rag / Euphonic sounds / Pineapple rag / Entertainer / Maple leaf rag / Sunflower slow drag / Stoptime rag / Reflection rag / Cleopha / Lily Queen / Heliotrope bouquet / Country club / Real slow rag / Leola
CD _____ GOJCD 0220
Giants Of Jazz / '88 / Target/BMG / Cadillac.

ENTERTAINER, THE (Classic Ragtime From Rare Piano Rolls)
Maple leaf rag / Something doing / Weeping willow rag / Entertainer / Easy winners / Pineapple rag / Solace / Gladiolus rag / Ragtime dance / Sugarcane / Crush collision march / Bethena / Combination march / Breeze from Alabama
CD _____ BCD 101
Biograph / Jul '91 / Wellard / ADA / Hot Shot / Jazz Music / Cadillac / Direct.

ENTERTAINER, THE
CD _____ ENTCD 220
Entertainers / Feb '88 / Target/BMG.

ENTERTAINER, THE
CD _____ SHAN 98016
Shanachie / May '93 / Koch / ADA / Greensleeves.

GOLD COLLECTION, THE
CD _____ D2CD13
Recording Arts / Dec '92 / THE / Disc.

HIS GREATEST HITS WITH RICHARD ZIMMERMAN
CD _____ CD 46
Bescol / '87 / CM / Target/BMG.

JAZZ PORTRAITS
Chrisanthemum / Scott Joplin's new rag / Something doing / Original rags / Entertainer / Maple leaf rag / Sunflower slow drag / Elite syncopations / Eugenia / Paragon rag / Euphonic sounds / Pineapple rag / Stoptime rag / Reflection rag / Cleopha / Lily Queen / Heliotrope bouquet / Country club
CD _____ CD 14518
Jazz Portraits / May '94 / Jazz Music.

KING OF JAZZ
Elite syncopations / Chrisanthemum / Scott Joplin new rag / Eugenia / Paragon rag / Euphonic sounds / Pineapple rag / Something doing / Original rags / Entertainer / Maple leaf rag / Sunflower slow drag / Stoptime rag / Reflection rag / Cleopha / Lily Queen / Heliotrope Bouquet / Country club / Areal slow drag / Leola
CD _____ CDGRF 080
Tring / '93 / Tring / Prism.

KING OF RAGTIME
CD _____ CD 53004
Giants Of Jazz / Mar '92 / Target/BMG / Cadillac.

KING OF RAGTIME (3CD Set)
CD Set _____ 55542
Laserlight / Oct '95 / Target/BMG.

KING OF RAGTIME
CD _____ CD 56056
Jazz Roots / Mar '95 / Target/BMG.

KING OF RAGTIME WRITERS
Cascades / Strenuous life / Felicity rag / swipsey cakewalk / Peacherine rag / Something doing / Search light / Rose leaf rag / Fig leaf rag / Maple rag medley no. 6 - pineapple rag / Euphonic sounds / Palm leaf rag / Kismet rag / Wall Street rag / Pleasant moments / Original rags / Sunflower slow drag / Maple leaf rag
CD _____ BCD 110
Biograph / Jul '91 / Wellard / ADA / Hot Shot / Jazz Music / Cadillac / Direct.

MARCHES, WALTZES & RAGS
CD _____ MM 67102
Music Masters / Oct '94 / Nimbus.

PIANO RAGS OF SCOTT JOPLIN
CD _____ EMPRCD 539
Empress / Sep '94 / THE.

PIANO RAGS PLAYED BY THE COMPOSER - 1896-07
CD _____ JZ-CD321
Suisa / Feb '91 / Jazz Music / THE.

PIANO RAGS PLAYED BY THE COMPOSER - 1907-17
CD _____ JZ-CD322
Suisa / Feb '91 / Jazz Music / THE.

PIANO RAGS, THE
CD _____ CDSGP 0118
Prestige / May '94 / Total/BMG.

SCOTT JOPLIN (2CD Set)
CD Set _____ R2CD 4013
Deja Vu / Jan '96 / THE.

SCOTT JOPLIN GOLD (2CD Set)
CD Set _____ D2CD 4013
Deja Vu / Jun '95 / THE.

Jordan, Charley

CHARLEY JORDAN, VOL. 1 (1930-31)
CD _____ DOCD 5097
Blues Document / '92 / Swift / Jazz Music / Hot Shot.

CHARLEY JORDAN, VOL. 2 (1931-34)
CD _____ DOCD 5098
Blues Document / '92 / Swift / Jazz Music / Hot Shot.

CHARLEY JORDAN, VOL. 3 (1935-37)
CD _____ DOCD 5099
Blues Document / '92 / Swift / Jazz Music / Hot Shot.

Jordan, Chris

TWILIGHT OF THE GODS
Pilgrims / Evening star / Grail / Dance for dead lovers / Prize / Rhinegold / Valkyrie's dream / Bride's lament
CD _____ NAGE 14 CD
Art Of Landscape / Jan '87 / Sony.

Jordan, Clifford

CLIFFORD JORDAN (Featuring Junior Cook) (Jordan, Clifford Quartet)
Criss Cross / Nov '90 / Cadillac / Harmonia Mundi.
CD _____ CRISS 1011CD

GLASS BEAD GAMES 2
Shoulders / Bridgework / Maimoun / Alias Buster Henry / One for Amos
CD _____ 66051023
Strata East / Nov '93 / New Note.

ROYAL BALLADS (Jordan, Clifford Quartet)
Criss Cross / Nov '91 / Cadillac / Harmonia Mundi.
CD _____ CRISS 1025CD

Jordan, Duke

DO IT YOURSELF JAZZ VOLS. 1 & 2
Sometimes I'm happy / Embraceable you / Jordu / Oh yeah! / Pennies from heaven / Yesterdays / It's only a paper moon / You'd be so nice to come home to
CD _____ SV 0130
Savoy Jazz / Apr '93 / Conifer / ADA.

DUKE'S ARTISTRY (Jordan, Duke Quartet)
CD _____ SCCD 31033
Steeplechase / Jul '88 / Impetus.

FLIGHT TO DENMARK (Jordan, Duke Trio)
CD _____ SCCD 31011
Steeplechase / Oct '90 / Impetus.

FLIGHT TO JORDAN
Flight to Jordan / Starbrite / Squawkin' / Deacon Joe / Split quick / Si Joya / Diamond stud / I should care
CD _____ VGCD 650118
Vogue / Oct '93 / BMG.

JORDU
CD _____ VGCD 655010
Vogue / Oct '93 / BMG.

ONE FOR THE LIBRARY
CD _____ STCD 4194
Storyville / Aug '94 / Jazz Music / Wellard / CM / Cadillac.

OSAKA CONCERT VOLUME 1 (Jordan, Duke Trio)
CD _____ SCCD 31271
Steeplechase / Nov '90 / Impetus.

TIME ON MY HANDS (Jordan, Duke Trio)
CD _____ SCCD 31232
Steeplechase / Jul '88 / Impetus.

TRIO & QUINTET
Forecast / Sultry eve / They can't take that away from me / Night in Tunisia / Summertime / Flight to Jordan / Two lovers / Cula / Yesterdays / Scotch blues
CD _____ SV 0149
Savoy Jazz / Apr '93 / Conifer / ADA.

Jordan, Lorraine

CRAZY GUESSING GAMES
CD _____ LDL 1212CD
Lochshore / Mar '94 / ADA / Direct / Duncans.

INSPIRATION
CD _____ LDL 1205CD
Lochshore / May '93 / ADA / Direct / Duncans.

Jordan, Louis

AT THE SWING CATS' BALL, 1937-39
Gee but you're swell / Honey in the bee ball / Keep a knockin' / Doug the jitterbug / You're my meat
CD _____ JSPCD 330
JSP / Oct '91 / ADA / Target/BMG / Direct / Cadillac / Complete/Pinnacle.

CLASSIC RECORDINGS
CD Set _____ BCD 15557
Bear Family / Apr '92 / Rollercoaster / Direct / CM / Swift / ADA.

COMPLETE ALADDIN SESSIONS (Jordan, Louis & His Tympany Five)
Yeah yeah baby / Louis blues / I've seen what you've done / Fat back and corn liquor / Put some money in the pot boy cause the juice is running low / Gotta go / Dipper / Time's a passin' / Whiskey do your stuff /

Gal you need a whippin' / It's hard to be good / Dollar down / Dad gum ya hide, boy / Till we two are one / Ooo wee / Private property (no trespassing) / For you / Messy Bessy / I'll die happy / If I had any sense, I'd go back home / Hurry home
CD _____ CZ 426
EMI / May '91 / EMI.

FIVE GUYS NAMED MOE
CD _____ MCLD 19048
MCA / Apr '92 / BMG.

FIVE GUYS NAMED MOE (The V Discs)
CD _____ CDCD 1085
Charly / Jun '93 / Charly / THE / Cadillac.

FIVE GUYS NAMED MOE - RADIO RARITIES
CD _____ VJC 1037-2
Vintage Jazz Classics / Oct '92 / Direct / ADA / CM / Cadillac.

G.I. JIVE (1940 - 1947) (Jordan, Louis & His Tympany Five)
Pompton turnpike / T-Bone blues / Deacon Jones / G.I. Jive / You're much too fat / Chicky Mo craney Crow / We can't agree / Friendship
CD _____ RBD 602
Jukebox Lil / Apr '91 / Swift / Wellard.

G.I. JIVE (Jordan, Louis & His Tympany Five)
CD _____ CDCD 1236
Charly / Jun '95 / Charly / THE / Cadillac.

GOOD TIMES
Let the good times roll / Five guys named Moe / Daddy-O / Texas and the Pacific
CD _____ BSTCD 9103
Best Compact Discs / May '92 / Complete/Pinnacle.

I BELIEVE IN MUSIC
CD _____ ECD 260062
Evidence / Jan '92 / Harmonia Mundi / ADA / Cadillac.

JUMP OVER JORDAN
Five guys named Moe / Choo choo ch' boogie / Mop mop / If you're so smart how come you ain't rich / Barnyard boogie / Fat Sam from Birmingham / Ain't nobody here but us chickens / Saturday night fish fry / Is you is or is you ain't my baby / Open the door Richard / What's the use of getting sober / Run Joe / Chartreuse / Tamburitza boogie / Hog wash / School days
CD _____ MCCD 085
Music Club / Dec '92 / Disc / THE / CM.

LIVE JIVE (Jordan, Louis & His Tympany Five)
Five guys named Moe / Buzz me / Knock me a kiss / Let the good times roll / I like 'em fat like that / Choo choo ch' boogie / On the sunny side of the street / All for the love of Lil / Safe, sane and single / Broke but happy / Texas and Pacific / Drippy drippers / Don't let the sun catch you crying / How long must I wait for you / Daddy-O / Jumping at the Jubilee / Baby that's alright for you
CD _____ DATOM 4
A Touch Of Magic / Jul '89 / Harmonia Mundi.

LOUIS JORDAN & TYMPANY FIVE 1939-1944
CD _____ 158372
Jazz Archives / Jul '95 / Jazz Music / Discovery / Cadillac.

LOUIS JORDAN 1941-43
CD _____ CLASSICS 741
Classics / Feb '94 / Discovery / Jazz Music.

LOUIS JORDAN AND CHRIS BARBER (Jordan, Louis & Chris Barber)
CD _____ BLCD 760156
Black Lion / '91 / Jazz Music / Cadillac / Wellard / Koch.

NO MOE - GREATEST HITS
CD _____ 5125232
Verve / Apr '92 / PolyGram.

ROCK 'N' ROLL CALL
It's been said / Whatever Lola wants (Lola gets) / Slo' smooth and easy / Bananas / Baby let's do it up / Chicken back / Baby you're just too much / Where can I go / Rock 'n' roll call / Man ain't a man / Texas stew / Hard head
CD _____ 07863 66145-2
Bluebird / Apr '93 / BMG.

Jordan, Marc

BLUE DESERT
CD _____ 7599262332
WEA / Jan '96 / Warner Music.

MANNEQUINN
CD _____ 7599262322
WEA / Jan '96 / Warner Music.

Jordan, Marlon

UNDAUNTED, THE
CD _____ 4730562
Sony Jazz / Jan '95 / Sony.

Jordan, Montell

THIS IS HOW WE DO IT
My Mommy intro / Somethin' 4 da honeyz / This is how we do it / Payback / I'll do anything / Don't keep me waiting / Comin' home / Introducing shaunta / It's over / Midnight interlude / I wanna / Down on my knees / Gotta get my roll on / Close the door / Daddy's home
CD _____ 5271272
Def Jam / May '95 / PolyGram.

Jordan, Ronny

ANTIDOTE, THE
Get to grips / Blues grinder / After hours / See the new / So what / Nite spice / Summer smile
CD _____ CID 9988
Island / Feb '92 / PolyGram.

BAD BROTHERS (Jordan, Ronny & DJ Krush)
Jackal / Shit goes down / Love I never had it so good / So what / Season for a change / Bad brother
CD _____ IMCD 8024
Island / Aug '94 / PolyGram.

QUIET REVOLUTION, THE
Season for change / In full swing / Slam in a jam / Mr. Walker / Jackal / Come with me / Morning after / Under your spell / Tinseltown / Vanston place (00 am)
CD _____ CID 8009
Island / Sep '93 / PolyGram.

Jordan, Sass

RACINE
Make you a believer / If you're gonna love me / You don't have to remind me / Who do you think you are / Windin' me up / I want to believe / Goin' back again / Do what you want / Cry baby / Where there's a will / Time flies
CD _____ CDP 7450082
EMI / Aug '94 / EMI.

RATS
Damaged / Slave / Pissin' down / High road easy / Sun's gonna rise / Head / Ugly / I'm not / Honey / Wish / Breakin' / Give
CD _____ CDEMC 3675
EMI / Apr '94 / EMI.

TELL SOMEBODY
CD _____ REV XD 193
FM / Nov '92 / Sony.

Jordan, Sheila

HEART STRINGS
Haunted heart / Out to sea (sail away) / Japanese dream / If I had you / Heart's desire / Inchworm / Caterpillar song / Comes love / Look for the silver lining / What'll I do
CD _____ MCD 5468
Muse / Dec '94 / New Note / CM.

LOST & FOUND
CD _____ MCD 5390
Muse / Sep '92 / New Note / CM.

OLD TIME FEELING (Jordan, Sheila & Harvie Swartz)
CD _____ MCD 5366
Muse / Sep '92 / New Note / CM.

ONE FOR JUNIOR (Jordan, Sheila & Mark Murphy)
Where you at / Round about / One for junior / Trust in me / Bird / Aria 18 / Best thing for you / Eastern ballad / Don't like goodbyes
CD _____ MCD 5489
Muse / Nov '93 / New Note / CM.

PORTRAIT OF SHEILA JORDAN
Falling in love with love / If you could see me now / Am I blue / Dat dere / When the world was young / Let's face the music and dance / Laugh clown laugh / Who can I turn to now / Baltimore Oriole / I'm a fool to want you / Hum drum blues / Willow weep for me
CD _____ BNZ 230
Blue Note / Jan '90 / EMI.

Jordan, Stanley

BEST OF STANLEY JORDAN, THE
Jumpin' Jack / Eleanor Rigby / Lady in my life / All the children / Impressions / My favourtie things / Georgia on my mind / Stairway to heaven / Flying home / Still got the blues / Over the rainbow
CD _____ CDP 8315022
Blue Note / Apr '95 / EMI.

BOLERO
Bolero Parts 1-6 / Always and forever / Cheleon / Betcha by golly wow / Drifting / Plato's blues / Always and forever (solo)
CD _____ 07822187032
Arista / Feb '94 / BMG.

STANDARDS, VOL 1
Sound of silence / Sunny / Georgia on my mind / Send one your love / Moon River / Guitar man / One bell less to answer / Because / My favourite things / Silent night
CD _____ BNZ 56
Blue Note / Apr '87 / EMI.

Jordan, Steve

HERE COMES MR. JORDAN
CD _____ ACD 114
Audiophile / Oct '93 / Jazz Music / Swift.

MANY SOUNDS OF STEVE 'ESTEBAN' JORDAN, THE (Jordan, Esteban)
Arhoolie / Apr '95 / ADA / Direct / Cadillac.
_____ ARHCD 319

RETURN OF EL PARCHE, THE
CD _____ CD 6019
Rounder / '88 / CM / Direct / ADA / Cadillac.

Jordanaires

SING ELVIS'S FAVOURITE SPIRITUALS
Didn't it rain / Peace in the valley / Joshua fit de battle of Jericho / Search me lord / Dig a little deeper / You better run / Let us break bread together / Wonderful time up there / How great thou art / I'm a rollin' / Dip your fingers in some water / Roll Jordan roll / Onward christian soldiers
CD _____ PWKS 4216
Carlton Home Entertainment / Oct '94 / Carlton Home Entertainment.

SONGS WE SANG WITH ELVIS
CD _____ WMCD 5691
Disky / Apr '94 / THE / BMG / Discovery / Pinnacle.

TRIBUTE TO ELVIS
Return to sender / That's alright mama / Jailhouse rock / All shook up / Good luck charm / Got a lot of lovin' to do / Can't help falling in love / It's now or never / Love me tender / Are you lonesome tonight / Teddy bear / Don't be cruel / You're the devil in disguise / Wear my ring around your neck / Heartbreak hotel / Always on my mind
CD _____ 5501282
Spectrum/Karussell / Oct '93 / PolyGram / THE.

Jorgensen, Knud

JAZZ TRIO
CD _____ OP 8401CD
Opus 3 / Sep '91 / May Audio / Pentacone.

Jory, Sarah

20 CLASSIC SONGS (THE EARLY YEARS)
Walk the way the wind blows / Somewhere between / I'll leave this world loving you / Just out of reach / Why me Lord / Beyond the point of no return / Let me be there / Dear God / Always have, always will / How great thou art / Jones on the jukebox / Before I'm over you / Just because I'm a woman / Faded love / It is no secret / No time at all / Funny face / Yesterday just passed my way again / Beneath still waters / Old rugged cross
CD _____ RITZSCD 429
Ritz / Apr '93 / Pinnacle.

20 STEEL GUITAR FAVOURITES
Sticky fingers / Deep in the heart of Texas / Orange blossom special / Jealous heart / Under the boardwalk / Careless hands / Steel line / Way to survive / San Antonio stroll / She believes in me / Oklahoma stomp / Highway 40 blues / Rose coloured glasses / Blue jade / Cold cold heart / Three of us / In the garden / City lights / Once upon a time in the West / Remington ride
CD _____ RITZSCD 428
Ritz / Apr '93 / Pinnacle.

LOVE WITH ATTITUDE
CD _____ RITZCD 0076
Ritz / Oct '95 / Pinnacle.

NEW HORIZONS
Never had it so good / Look at us / Take your memory with you / Strings that tie you down / Darlin' / Wind beneath my wings / Do / Till each tear becomes a rose / You'll never get to heaven (if you break my heart) / Take a love off my mind / Heartaches by the number / Sarah's dream
CD _____ RITZCD 0067
Ritz / May '92 / Pinnacle.

WEB OF LOVE
Before I call it love / Even then / Candle burning / If I love you / Every time / Binding me like a chain / Web of love / When you walk in the room / Over you / Even a fool / Two sparrows in a hurricane / Who's crying now / On the way to a dream / Real slow / Stop playing with my heart (Features on CD only.)
CD _____ CD 0073
Ritz / Jul '94 / Pinnacle.

Jose, Don

FIESTA
Bamboleo / Amor / Welcome to my heart / Annabel / Ave Mario, no morro / Djobi djoba / Lola from Barcelona / A mi manera (Comme d'habitude) / El porompompero / Cuando calienta el sol / Costa brava / Munira, munira, munira / Me va, me va / San Jose / Tu quieras volver / Quantanamera / Maria Isabel

Joseph, David

BRITISH HUSTLE - THE BEST OF DAVID JOSEPH & HI-TENSION (Joseph, David & Hi-tension)
You can't hide (Your love from me) / Hi tension / Joys of love / Funktified / British hustle / There's a reason / Let's live it up (Nite people) / Latin inspiration / You're my girl / Discover / Expansions '86 / Power and lighting / Peace on earth
CD _____ IMCD 157
Island / Jul '93 / PolyGram.

Joseph, Julian

LANGUAGE OF TRUTH, THE
Miss Simmons / Language of truth / Don't chisel the shisel / Art of the calm / Wash house / Other side of town / High priestess / Magical one / Brothers of the bottom row / Tyrannosaurus Rex / Ode to the time our memories forgot
CD _____ 9031751222
East West / Aug '91 / Warner Music.

LIVE AT THE WIGMORE HALL
CD _____ 0630113702
East West / Aug '95 / Warner Music.

REALITY
Bridge to the south / Body and soul / Easy for you to say / Look out for love / Dance in a perfect world / Swingstone / Empty dream / Reality / Jean-ee-t / Creation constellation / Whispering dome / My desire
CD _____ 450993024-2
East West / Jul '93 / Warner Music.

Joseph, Margie

ATLANTIC SESSION, THE (The Best Of Margie Joseph)
CD _____ SLC 2503
Ichiban / Apr '95 / Koch.

MAKES A NEW IMPRESSION/ PHASE II
Women talk / Stop in the name of love / Punish me / Medicine bend / Come tomorrow / Sweeter tomorrow / Same thing / How beautiful the rain / I'm fed up / Make me believe you'll stay / Temptation's about to take your love / That other woman got my man and gone / My world is empty without you / I'll always love you / Strung out / Please don't stop loving me / I love you too much to say goodbye / Didn't have to tell me / Takin' all the love I can
CD _____ CDSXD 097
Stax / Jul '93 / Pinnacle.

Joseph, Martyn

MARTYN JOSEPH
Change your world / Gift to me / Between the raindrops / Talk about it in the morning / Everything in heaven comes apart / Home to you / If I should fall / If heaven's waiting / Condition of my heart / Cardiff bay / Carried in sunlight
CD _____ 4806572
Epic / Jul '95 / Sony.

Joshi, Pandit Bhimsen

VOCAL
CD _____ MR 1002
Moment / Apr '95 / ADA / Koch.

Josi, Christian

I WALKS WITH MY FEET OFF THE GROUND
Just in time / Whenever I take my sugar to tea / This time the dreams on me / Let's get lost / Sleepin' bee / Watch what happens / You've met your match / Azure te / Nightingale sang in Berkley square / Whenever that gal comes around / Gotta be this or that / Girl of my dreams / I concentrate on you / Forgetful / Birth of the blues / Party's over
CD _____ CHECD 00111
Master Mix / Aug '94 / Wellard / Jazz Music / New Note.

Jouissance

INFERNAL NEBULA
CD _____ MHCD 019
Minus Habens / Jul '94 / Plastic Head.

Journey

ESCAPE
Don't stop believin' / Stone in love / Who's crying now / Keep on running / Still they ride / Escape / Lay it down / Dead or alive / Mother, Father / Open arms
CD _____ 4602852
CBS / Apr '89 / Sony.

GREATEST HITS: JOURNEY
Only the young / Don't stop believin' / Wheel in the sky / Faithfully / I'll be alright without you / Anyway you want it / (Ask) the lonely / Who's crying now / Separate ways / Lights / Lovin' touchin' squeezin' / Open arms / Girl can't help it / Send her my love / Be good to yourself

CD _____ 4631492
CBS / Dec '88 / Sony.

INFINITY
Lights / Feeling that way / Anytime / La do da / Patiently / Wheel in the sky / Somethin' to hide / Winds of March / Can do / Open the door
CD _____ CK 57207
Mastersound / Nov '94 / Sony.

JOURNEY
Of a lifetime / In the morning day / Kohoutek / To play some music / Topaz / In my lonely feeling/conversations
CD _____ 477854 2
Columbia / Oct '94 / Sony.

RAISED ON RADIO
Girl can't help it / Positive touch / Suzanne / Be good to yourself / Once you love somebody / Happy to give / Raised on radio / I'll be alright without you / It could have been you / Eyes of a woman / Why can't this night go on forever
CD _____ 4679922
Columbia / Apr '91 / Sony.

Journeyman

NEW IDOL SON
New idol son
CD _____ RED 005
Redemption / Jun '93 / SRD.

Journeymen

WANDERLUST
CD _____ CDLDL 1235
Lochshore / Nov '95 / ADA / Direct / Duncans.

Joy Division

COMPLETE PEEL SESSIONS: JOY DIVISION
Exercise one / Insight / She's lost control / Transmission / Love will tear us apart / Twenty four hours / Colony / Sound of music
CD _____ SFRCD 111
Strange Fruit / Jul '90 / Pinnacle.

MEANS TO AN END, A (The Music Of Joy Division) (Various Artists)
She's lost control / Day of Lords / New dawn fades / Transmission / Atmosphere / Insight / Love will tear us apart / Isolation / Heart and soul / Twenty four hours / Warsaw / They walked in line / Interzone / As you said
CD _____ CDHUT 29
Hut / Oct '95 / EMI.

PERMANENT
Love will tear us apart / Transmission / She's lost control / Shadow play / Day of the lords / Isolation / Passover / Heart and soul / Twenty four hours / These days / Novelty / Dead souls / Only mistake / Something must break / Atmosphere
CD _____ 8286242
London / Jun '95 / PolyGram.

SUBSTANCE (1977 - 1980)
She's lost control / Dead souls / Atmosphere / Love will tear us apart / Warsaw / Leaders of men / Digital / Transmission / Autosuggestion
CD _____ 520014-2
London / Jul '93 / PolyGram.

Joy Of Life

ENJOY
CD _____ HY 39100292
Hyperium / Nov '92 / Plastic Head.

Joya

JOYA
Intro / I like what you're doing to me / Takin' care of business / Love u all over / Here I am / Gettin' off on you / Do it like this, do it like that / Willing and waiting / I just can't help myself / Shouldn't be hard to tell / Outro
CD _____ 5403302
Polydor / Aug '95 / PolyGram.

Joykiller

JOYKILLER
CD _____ 864521
Epitaph / Apr '95 / Plastic Head / Pinnacle.

Joyland

SUN
CD _____ NBX 014
Noisebox / Jul '95 / Disc.

Joyner, Bruce

HOT GEORGIA NIGHTS
CD _____ ROSE 129CD
New Rose / Dec '87 / Direct / ADA.

OUTTAKES COLLECTION, 78/88
CD _____ FC 045CD
Fan Club / Aug '88 / Direct.

JPP

KAUSTINEN RHAPSODY
CD _____ OMCD 53
Olarin Musiiki Oy / Dec '94 / ADA / Direct.

JPS Experience

BLEEDING STAR
CD _____ FNCD 246
Flying Nun / Sep '93 / Disc.

Jr. Gone Wild

PULL THE GOALIE
CD _____ TX 2011CD
Taxim / Jan '94 / ADA.

TOO DUMB TO QUIT
CD _____ SP 1160CD
Stony Plain / Oct '93 / ADA / CM / Direct.

Jr. Medlow

THRILL FOR THRILL
CD _____ LIZARD 80006
Lizard / Aug '95 / Direct / Disc.

Juana, Harold

HIGHER
CD _____ RUNECD 001
Mystic Stones / Aug '92 / Vital.

Jubelklaenge

200 YEARS OF THE BAD BLEIBERG BRASS BAND
CD _____ 322766
Koch / Oct '92 / Koch.

Jubilee Hummingbirds

GUILTY OF SERVING GOD (Jubilee Hummingbirds & James Carr)
God is worthy to be praised / Guilty of serving God / My soul is satisfied / He'll be there / Jesus changed me / Doin' the best I can / In the name of Jesus / Where Jesus is / Jordan river
CD _____ CDCHM 611
Ace / Jul '95 / Pinnacle / Cadillac / Complete/Pinnacle.

Jubilees

REGGAE CARNIVAL
CD _____ BRMCD 027
Bold Reprive / Oct '88 / Pinnacle / Bold Reprive / Harmonia Mundi.

Judas Priest

COLLECTION: JUDAS PRIEST
One for the road / Rocka rolla / Winter / Deep freeze / Winter retreat / Cheater / Never satisfied / Run of the mill / Dying to meet you / Victim of changes / Ripper / Dream deceiver / Prelude / Tyrant / Genocide / Epitaph / Island of domination
CD _____ CCSCD 213
Castle / Apr '89 / BMG.

HERO HERO
Dreamer deceiver / Deceiver / Winter / Deep freeze / Winter retreat / Cheater / Diamonds and rust / Run of the mill / Genocide / Caviar and meths / Prelude / Tyrant / Rocka rolla / One for the road / Victim of changes / Dying to meet you / Never satisfied
CD _____ CSAPCD 119
Connoisseur / Jul '95 / Pinnacle.

METAL WORKS 1973-1993 (LOB/M8 Set)
Hellion / Electric eye / Victim of changes / Painkiller / Eat me alive / Devil's child / Dissident aggressor / Delivering the goods / Exciter / Breaking the law / Hell bent for leather / Blood red skies / Metal gods / Before the dawn / Turbo lover / Ram it down / Metal meltdown / Screaming for vengeance / You've got another thing comin' / Beyond the realms of death / Solar angels / Bloodstone / Desert plains / Wild nights, Hot and Crazy Days / Heading out to the highway / Living after midnight / Touch of Evil / Rage / Night comes down / Sinner / Freewheel burning / Night crawler
CD Set _____ 4730502
Columbia / Oct '93 / Sony.

SIN AFTER SIN
Sinner / Diamonds and rust / Starbreaker / Last rose of summer / Let us prey / Call for the priest / Raw deal / Here come the tears / Dissident aggressor
CD _____ 983286 2
Pickwick/Sony Collector's Choice / Nov '93 / Carlton Home Entertainment / Pinnacle / Sony.

UNLEASHED IN THE EAST
Exciter / Running wild / Sinner / Ripper / Green manalishi / Diamonds and rust / Victim of changes / Genocide / Tyrant
CD _____ 4686042
Columbia / Apr '94 / Sony.

Judd, Wynonna

WYNONNA
What it takes / She is his only need / I saw the light / My strongest weakness / When I reach the place I'm goin' / No one else on

Earth / It's never easy to say goodbye / Little bit of love (goes a long long way) / All of that love from here / Live with Jesus
CD _____ 4716712
Curb / May '92 / PolyGram.

Judds

LOVE CAN BUILD A BRIDGE
This country's rockin' / Calling in the wind / In my dreams / Rompin' stompin' blues / Love can build a bridge / Born to be blue / 102 / John Deere tractor / Talk about love / Are the roses not blooming
CD _____ PD 90531
RCA / Sep '90 / BMG.

Judge

NO APOLOGIES/CHUNG
CD _____ LF 033CD
Lost & Found / Apr '92 / Plastic Head.

WHAT WE SAID
CD _____ LF 217CD
Lost & Found / Nov '95 / Plastic Head.

Judge Dread

40 BIG ONES
Lover's rock / This little piece of dinkle / Banana throat song / Confessions of a bouncer / Y'viva suspenders / Six wives of Dread / Donkey dick / Fatty dread / Oh she is a big girl now / Big 7 / Dread rock / My ding a ling / Rasta chat / Big 6 / Come outside / One eyed lodger / Belle of Snodland Town / Workers lament / Big 5 / Up with the cock / Big punk / Look a pussy / Dr. Kitch / Winkle man / Jamaica jerk off / Grandad's flannelette nightshirt / Move over darling / Will I what / Big 1 / Rudeness train / Bring back the skins / Take off your clothes / Christmas in Dreadland / Rhyme in time / What kung fu dat / Big 10 / Je t'aime / Dread's law / Trenchtown Billy / Big everything
CD _____ RNCD 2001
Rhino / Jun '92 / Jetstar / Magnum Music Group / THE.

40 BIG ONES 2
CD _____ RNCD 2121
Rhino / Sep '95 / Jetstar / Magnum Music Group / THE.

BEDTIME STORIES
CD _____ RNCD 2013
Rhino / Jun '93 / Jetstar / Magnum Music Group / THE.

BIG TWENTY FOUR, THE
CD _____ CDTRL 333
Trojan / Feb '94 / Jetstar / Total/BMG.

JUDGE DREAD VOL. 1 & 2
CD _____ LOMACD 19
Loma / Aug '94 / BMG.

LAST OF THE SKINHEAD
CD _____ RNCD 2023
Rhino / Oct '93 / Jetstar / Magnum Music Group / THE.

VERY BEST OF JUDGE DREAD, THE
Big 6 / Big 7 / Big 8 / Je t'aime / Big 9 / Big 10 / Come outside / Bring back the skins / Winkle man / Y viva suspenders / Will I what / Jamaica jerkoff / Up with the cock / Lover's rock / Dread rock / Big 1
CD _____ MCCD 040
Music Club / Sep '91 / Disc / THE / CM.

Judge Smith, Chris

DEMOCRAZY
CD _____ THEBES 001
Oedipus / Jun '92 / Plastic Head.

DOME OF DISCOVERY
CD _____ THEBES 03CD
Oedipus / Apr '94 / Plastic Head.

Judybats

DOWN IN THE SHACKS WHERE THE SATELLITE DISHES GROW
Our story / She's sad she said / How it is / Down in the shacks where the satellite dishes grow / Margot known as missy / Witch's night / Is anything / Poor bruised world / Animal farm / Saturday / Lullaby / Weren't we wild / When things get slow round here
CD _____ 7599268012
Sire / Oct '92 / Warner Music.

Juggernaut

BLACK PAGODA
Shedding / Bitter / Decide / Difference / Green lightening / I.O. / Reality easel / Whisper / Make it so hard / Machine / Cry for a better high
CD _____ N 0215-2
Noise/Modern Music / Sep '94 / Pinnacle / Plastic Head.

Jughead's Revenge

13 KIDDIE FAVOURITES
CD _____ EFA 127222
Do It / May '95 / SRD.

ELIMINATION

CD _____ EFA 118722
Do It / Mar '94 / SRD.

Juice With Soul

BODY ARMOR
Gang lingo / To the uumhm / It's on / Just because you're black / Kill or get killed / Money ain't shit when you're dead / Body armor / Like father, like son / Born suspect / Nickel plated funk / No bizness in show bizness / System / Juice with soul
CD _____ 756782468-2
Atlantic / Jul '93 / Warner Music.

Juiceful Jazz

BETWEEN THE CHAPTERS
CD _____ EFA 127572
Juiceful / Jul '95 / SRD.

STREETZ OF DESIRE
CD _____ EFA 126012
Juiceful / Aug '95 / SRD.

Juicemen

META LUNA
CD _____ MASSCD 029
Massacre / Apr '94 / Plastic Head.

Juicy Lucy

BEST OF JUICY LUCY
Who do you love / Midnight rider / Pretty woman / That woman's got something / Jessica / Willie the pimp/Lie back and enjoy it / Changed my mind, changed my sign / Just one time / I'm a thief / Built for comfort / Mr. Skin / Mr. A. Jones / Future days (CD only.) / Chicago north western (CD only.) / Hello LA, bye bye Birmingham (CD only.) / Thinking of my life (CD only.)
CD _____ NEXCD 105
Sequel / Mar '90 / BMG.

HERE SHE COMES AGAIN
Pretty woman / Try my love / Who do you love / Voodoo child / Saturday night / Up to the tracks / Talk to me / Drug squad
CD _____ HTDCD 28
HTD / Jan '95 / Pinnacle.

JUICY LUCY/LIE BACK AND ENJOY IT
Mississippi woman / Who do you love / She's mine / She's yours / Just one time / Chicago North Western / Train / Nadine / Are you satisfied / Thinking of my life / Built for comfort / Pretty woman / Whiskey in my jar / Hello LA, bye bye Birmingham / Changed my mind / That woman's got something / Willie the pimp / Lie back and enjoy it
CD _____ BGOCD 279
Beat Goes On / Jun '95 / Pinnacle.

PRETTY WOMAN
Who do you love / Pretty woman / Jessica / Built for comfort / Mississippi woman / Thinking of my life / Willie the pimp/Lie back and enjoy it / Midnight rider / Changed my mind, changed my sign / Hello LA, bye bye Birmingham / Are you satisfied / I'm a thief / Just one time / Chicago North Western / That woman got something
CD _____ 5507662
Spectrum/Karussell / Mar '95 / PolyGram / THE.

Julian, Don

HEAVEN AND PARADISE (Julian, Don & The Meadowlarks)
Heaven and paradise / Love only you / I got tore up / Untrue / Oop boopy oop / Devil or angel / Boogie woogie teenage / Blue moon / Please (say you love me) / Mine all mine / This must be paradise / Real pretty Mama / I am a believer / Big Mama wants to rock / Please love a fool / Thrill me night and day / L.F.M.S.T. Blues / Embarrasing moments / Always and always / Doin' the cha cha / Pass the gin
CD _____ CDCHD 552
Ace / Aug '95 / Pinnacle / Cadillac / Complete/Pinnacle.

Julian's Treatment

TIME BEFORE THIS, A
First oracle / Coming of the mule / Phantom city / Black tower / Alda, dark lady of the outer worlds / Altarra, princess of the blue women / Second oracle / Twin suns of Centauri / Alkon, planet of Centauri / Terran / Fourth from the sun / Strange things / Time before this / Child of the night (1 and 2) (Available on CD only) / Stranger (Available on CD only) / Death of Alda (Available on CD only) / Cycles (Available on CD only) / Soldiers of time (Available on CD only)
CD _____ SEECD 288
See For Miles/C5 / Jan '90 / Pinnacle.

Julie Dolphin

LIT
CD _____ TIMBCD 602
Timbuktu / Mar '94 / Pinnacle.

Julinho

ACCORDEON DO BRASIL
CD _____ BPE 107
Kardum / Nov '92 / Discovery.

Juluka

SCATTERLINGS OF JULUKA
CD _____ SHAKACD 2
Safari / Sep '91 / Pinnacle.

Juma, Issa

SIGLAME 2 (Juma, Issa & Les Wanyika)
Siglame 2 / Money / Pole pole / Rafki uangu / Ateka / Sarah
CD _____ AFRIZZ 008
Disc Afrique / May '90 / Roots / CM.

Jumble Lane

JUMBLE LANE
CD _____ HBG 123/3
Background / Apr '94 / Background.

Jump

MYTH OF INDEPENDENCE, THE
Tower of babel / Princess of the people / On the wheel / Heaven and earth / Runaway / Keep the blues / Blind birds / Drivetime / Valediction / On my side / Shallow man
CD _____ CYCL 027
Cyclops / Sep '95 / Pinnacle.

Jumpin' The Gunn

SHADES OF BLUE
Cryin' blues / Green all over / Turtle blues / Crossed wires / More and more / Tired of tryin' / Shades of blue / Mind reader / Sweet Jesus / All I say to you
CD _____ VPBCD 14
Pointblank / Apr '93 / EMI.

Junaro, Emma

SI DE AMOR SE TRATA
CD _____ TUMICD 015
Tumi / '92 / Sterns / Discovery.

Juncosa, Sylvia

NATURE
CD _____ SST 146 CD
SST / Jun '93 / Plastic Head.

Junction

SWINSSET
CD _____ RED 014CD
Redemption / Jan '94 / SRD.

June Brides

1983 TO 1986
CD _____ OVER 40CD
Overground / Jan '95 / SRD.

June Of 44

ENGINE TAKES TO THE WATER
CD _____ QS 32CD
Quarter Stick / Jun '95 / SRD.

Jung, Robert

DIE SCHONSTEN LIEDER VON
CD _____ 15359
Laserlight / Nov '91 / Target/BMG.

Jungle Band

JUNGLE GROOVE
Dancing in the street - part one / Jungle groove / You got to make it funky / Full speed ahead / Under the control of love / South fights back / Marvellous (red clay mix) / Dancing in the street - part two
CD _____ CDCHARLY 134
Charly / Aug '88 / Charly / THE / Cadillac.

Jungle Brothers

DONE BY THE FORCES OF NATURE
Beyond this world / Feelin' alright / Sunshine / What U waitin' 4 / U make me sweat / Acknowledge your own history / Belly dancin' Dina / Good newz comin' / Done by the forces of nature / Beeds on a string / Tribe vibes / J. Beez comin' through / Black woman / In dayz 2 come / Doin' our own dang / Kool accordin' 2 a Jungle Brother
CD _____ 7599263642
Warner Bros. / Aug '90 / Warner Music.

J.BEEZ WIT THE REMEDY
Forty below trooper / Book of rhyme pages / My Jimmy weighs a ton / Good ole hype shit / Blahbludifly / Spark a new flame / I'm in love with Indica / Simple as that / All I think about is you / Good lookin' out / J. Beez comin' through / Spittin wicked randomness / For the headz at company Z / Man made material
CD _____ 759926679-2
Warner Bros. / Jun '93 / Warner Music.

Jungr & Parker

CANADA
CD _____ HARCD 023

Harbour Town / Oct '93 / Roots / Direct / CM / ADA.

OFF THE PEG
CD _____ UTIL 003 CD
Utility / Jun '90 / Grapevine.

Junior M.A.F.I.A.
JUNIOR MAFIA
CD _____ 7567926142
Atlantic / Sep '95 / Warner Music.

Junk Head
ADDICTION
CD _____ JUNKCD 001
Punk / Nov '95 / Plastic Head.

Junk Monkeys
BLISS
CD _____ CDZORRO 51
Metal Blade / Aug '92 / Pinnacle.

Juno Reactor
BEYOND THE INFINITE
CD _____ BR 009CD
Blue Room Released / Oct '95 / SRD.

LUCIANA
CD _____ INTA 002CD
Intermodo / Jul '94 / Disc.

TRANSMISSIONS
CD _____ NOMU 24CD
Mute / Sep '93 / Disc.

Jupp, Mickey
AS THE YEARS GO BY
CD _____ 901026
Line / Oct '94 / CM / Grapevine / ADA / Conifer / Direct.

JUPPANESE/LONG DISTANCE ROMANCER
Making friends / Short list / Old rock 'n' roller / School / If only mother / Down in old New Orleans / You'll never get me up in one of those / Pilot / S.P.Y. / Ballad of Billy Bonney / Partir c'est mourir un peu / Brother doctor, sister nurse / You made a fool out of me / Chevrolet / Barbara / You know what I mean / True love / Politics / Hard times / Switchboard Susan / I'm in control / Make it fly
CD Set _____ LICD 921188
Line / May '92 / CM / Grapevine / ADA / Conifer / Direct.

SOME PEOPLE CAN'T DANCE
Modern music / Taxi driver / Superman / Jogging / Virginia weed / Maybe baby / Feel free / Some people can't dance / So that's what it is / Gospel song
CD _____ 900069
Line / Jul '95 / CM / Grapevine / ADA / Conifer / Direct.

Jurie, Renat
ENTRE LA RIVIERA ET LA MER
CD _____ Y225025
Silex / Jun '93 / ADA.

Juris, Vic
NIGHT TRIPPER
CD _____ SCCD 31353
Steeplechase / Sep '95 / Impetus.

Just A Groove
SELECTED DISCO MUSIC
CD _____ RESO 052
Resolution / Oct '95 / Pinnacle.

Just, Andy
DON'T CRY
CD _____ CCD 11044
Crosscut / Nov '94 / ADA / CM / Direct.

Juster
REMEMBER THAT NIGHT
CD _____ CDVEST 48
Bulletproof / Apr '95 / Pinnacle.

WHAT I SEE WHAT I THINK
Boom boom boom / What I see / Buck your head / Blow the shack up / Common thief / I remember that night / For the mobiles /

No room / Officer Murphy / Don't ask me why
CD _____ CDVEST 54
Bulletproof / Aug '95 / Pinnacle.

Justice League Of Zion
DISCOVERERS
CD _____ CEND 1900
Century / Oct '94 / Total/BMG / Jetstar.

Justice, Jimmy
WHEN MY LITTLE GIRL IS SMILING/ BEST OF JIMMY JUSTICE
I understand / Bloodshot eyes / When love has left you / Teacher / Little bit of soap / Little lonely one / When my little girl is smiling / If I lost your love / Ain't that funny / One / My one sin / Spanish harlem / Write me a letter / Dawning / Too long will be too late / Early in the morning / Hallelujah, I love her so / World of lonely people / I wake up crying / Little cracked bell / Guitar player / Don't let the stars get in your eyes / Night has a thousand eyes / Save the last dance for me / Tell her / Folk singer / Can't get used to losing you / Up on the roof / You're gonna need my loving / Since you've been gone / Only heartbreaks for me / Everything in the garden
CD _____ NEXCD 241
Sequel / Jun '93 / BMG.

K

K, Paul

BIG NOWHERE, THE
Poor man's eyes / Robespierre / Flood the market / Too many yakking passengers / Superhighway / Post office pinup / Nashville, Tennessee / Midtown motel / One more joke / Needle park / Already in the ground / Arzon biz / Thousand dollar wedding / Herbert Hunke says
CD _____ 2695762
Silenz / Jun '92 / BMG.

GARDEN OF THE FORKING PATHS (K, Paul & The Weathermen)
CD _____ 907 096 2
MMS / Apr '94 / BMG.

KILLER IN THE RAIN, THE (K, Paul & The Weathermen)
CD _____ 907 087 2
MMS / Apr '94 / BMG.

K-Klass

UNIVERSAL
1-2-3 / Rhythm is a mystery / Let me show you / Don't stop / Underground express / What you're missing / Taking me over / La cassa / Share your love / I can take some more (Available on CD only)
CD _____ CDPCSD 149
EMI / Dec '93 / EMI.

K-Passa

AFTER THE HEADRUSH
CD _____ QP 6651CD
Que-P / Sep '94 / Direct / ADA.

K.A.O.S.

INTERNATIONAL DOPE DEALERS
CD _____ EFA 61003-2
Blitzvinyl / May '94 / SRD.

K.C. & The Sunshine Band

BEST OF KC AND THE SUNSHINE BAND
Sound your funky horn / Get down tonight / I'm your boogie man / (Shake shake shake) Your booty / Queen of clubs / That's the way (I like it) / Keep it comin' love / Please don't go / Boogie shoes / Let's go rock and roll / Give it up / Do you wanna go party (CD only.) / I like to do it (CD only.) / Shotgun shuffle (CD only.) / Wrap your arms around me (CD only.) / All I want
CD _____ CDROU 5007
Roulette / Jul '90 / EMI.

BEST OF KC AND THE SUNSHINE BAND
CD _____ 112011-2
Scratch / Oct '94 / BMG.

K.C. & THE SUNSHINE BAND
CD _____ MUSCD 504
MCI / Sep '94 / Disc / THE.

K.C.M. INC.

BOIN' IT FUNKY SMOOTH
Peachtume party jam / Is it worth it / Love stepped / That love thang / Let me groove you / All 'n' all / It's all about lovin' you / Real love / Do you / Emotion
CD _____ PEA 4110CD
Haven/Backs / Sep '91 / Disc / Pinnacle.

K.Hand

ON A JOURNEY
CD _____ K 7R001CD
Studio K7 / Feb '96 / Disc.

K.M.D.

MR. HOOD
Mr. Hood at Piocalles jewelry/crackpot, who me / Boogie man / Mr. Hood meets onyx / Subroc's mission / Humrush / Figure of speech / Bananapeel blues / Nitty gritty / Trial 'n error / Hard wit no hoe / Mr. Hood gets a haircut / 808 man / Boy who cried wolf / Peach fuzz / Preacher porkchop / Soulflexin'
CD _____ 7559609772
WEA / Aug '91 / Warner Music.

K.M.F.D.M.

ANGST
CD _____ RR 89872
Roadrunner / Jul '94 / Pinnacle.

WHAT DO YOU KNOW DEUTSCHLAND
CD _____ CDSAW 004
Skysaw / Feb '88 / Pinnacle.

WORLD VAIOE
CD _____ SBR 032 CD
Strike Back / May '89 / Vital / Grapevine.

Ka-Spel, Edward

CHINA DOLL
CD _____ STCD 090
Staalplaat / Sep '95 / Vital/SAM.

TANITH AND THE LION TREE
CD _____ TM 92671
Roadrunner / Oct '91 / Pinnacle.

Kaaos

TOTAL CHAOS
CD _____ LF 130
Lost & Found / Mar '95 / Plastic Head.

Kaas, Patricia

TOUR DE CHARME
Y'avait tant d'etoiles (There were so many stars) / Hotel Normandy / Je retiens mon souffle (Holding my breath) / Ceux qui n'ont rien (Those who have nothing) / Space in my heart / Il me dit que je suis belle (He tells me I'm beautiful) / La vie en rose / Je te dis vous / Out of the rain / Fatiguee d'attendre (Weary of waiting) / Saint Lunaire / It's a man's man's man's world / Reste sur moi (Rest on me) / Entrer dans la lumiere (Coming into the light)
CD _____ 474229 2
Columbia / Feb '94 / Sony.

Kaasa, Anne Karin

SOLEFALLSTIME
CD _____ FXCD 117
Kirkelig Kultuverksted / Jul '93 / ADA.

SVALANDE VIND
CD _____ FXCD 103
Kirkelig Kultuverksted / Jul '93 / ADA.

Kaasinen, Sari

JOUKU JOULUN ALKKAA SAA (Kaasinen, Sari & Mari)
CD _____ MIPU 205CD
Mipu / Dec '93 / ADA / Direct.

Kabaya, Tsuruhiko

SOUND OF AFRICA, THE
CD _____ CG 1005
Denon / Jan '89 / Conifer.

Kada, Cheb

FROM ORAN TO PARIS
CD _____ CHCD 64029
Shanachie / Jul '91 / Koch / ADA / Greensleeves.

MEGOUANI
Alech Tadi / Meguoani / Kirani Nedmene / El hob / Adbouk / Chkoune Li Bik / Anna / Changhalato / Allah Ghaleb / Halek
CD _____ VA 018
Voix D'Afrique / Aug '94 / New Note.

Kadison, Joshua

PAINTED DESERT SERENADE
Jessie / Painted desert serenade / Beau's all night radio love line / Invisible man / Mama's arms / Beautiful in my eyes / Picture postcards from L.A. / When a woman cries / Georgia rain
CD _____ SBKCD 22
SBK / May '95 / EMI.

Kaempfert, Bert

BERT KAEMPFERT COLLECTION
Bye bye blues / Remember when / When you're smiling / Tahitian sunset / Once in a while / Steady does it / It makes no difference / You stepped out of a dream / Wiederseh n / I'm beginning to see the light / Melina / Out of nowhere / Take the 'A' train / Sunny side of life / My melancholy baby / Time to dream / What is this thing called love / Love is wonderland / Wheeling free / Good life / Bert's bossa No.2 / Skyliner / Manhattan merengue / Honeysuckle rose
CD Set _____ 843 710-2
Polydor / May '91 / PolyGram.

MAGIC MUSIC OF BERT KAEMPFERT, THE
Strangers in the night / Afrikaan beat / Bass walks / Bye bye blues / Maltese melody / Red roses for a blue lady / Spanish eyes / Remember when / Swingin' safari / Love / Danke schon / Wonderland by night
CD _____ 843 986-2
Polydor / May '91 / PolyGram.

RED ROSES
Red roses for a blue lady / Almost there / Blue midnight / Sentimental journey / Stardust / Dream / Wonderland by night / Moonglow / Three O'clock in the morning / Happy trumpeter / Swingin' safari / Winoweh / Afrikaan beat / Zambesi
CD _____ 5500962

Spectrum/Karussell / Oct '93 / PolyGram / THE.

Kahamba, Shaka

NAWEYI
CD _____ S 1830CD
Paris - Tropical / Nov '90 / Triple Earth.

Kahn, Brenda

EPIPHANY IN BROOKLYN
I don't sleep, I drink coffee instead / Mojave winters / She's in love / Anesthesia / Mint juleps and needles / My lover / Sleepwalking / Lost / Great divide / Madagascar / Losing time / In Indiana
CD _____ SHED 004CD
Creation / Aug '93 / 3MV / Vital.

Kahn, Si

GOOD TIMES & BED TIMES
CD _____ ROU 8027CD
Rounder / Dec '93 / CM / Direct / ADA / Cadillac.

I HAVE SEEN FREEDOM
CD _____ FF 70578
Flying Fish / Jul '92 / Roots / CM / Direct / ADA.

I'LL BE THERE
CD _____ FF 70509
Flying Fish / Oct '89 / Roots / CM / Direct / ADA.

IN MY HEART
CD _____ PH 1169CD
Philo / May '94 / Direct / CM / ADA.

Kahr, Jim

BACK TO CHICAGO
CD _____ BEST 1027CD
Acoustic Music / Nov '93 / ADA.

Kaiser & Kuriokhin

POPULAR SCIENCE
CD _____ RCD 20118
Rykodisc / Nov '91 / Vital / ADA.

Kaiser, Henry

ACOUSTICS
CD _____ VICTOCD 025
Victo / Oct '94 / These / ReR Megacorp / Cadillac.

ALTERNATIVE VERSIONS
CD _____ SST 237 CD
SST / Mar '89 / Plastic Head.

DEVIL IN THE DRAIN
Sugagaki for conlon / King of the wild frontier / Dark memory / Smokestack lightnin' / Roadside picnic / Free to choose / I hope horizons / Devil in the drain / If this goes on...
CD _____ SST 118 CD
SST / May '93 / Plastic Head.

ETERNITY BLUE
CD _____ SHCD 6018
Shanachie / Dec '95 / Koch / ADA / Greensleeves.

LEMON FRESH TWEEZER
CD _____ RUNE 45
Cuneiform / Dec '89 / ReR Megacorp.

RE-MARRYING FOR MONEY
CD _____ SST 222 CD
SST / May '93 / Plastic Head.

SWEET SUNNY NORTH (Kaiser, Henry & David Lindley)
CD _____ SH 64057
Koch / Nov '94 / Koch.

TOMORROW KNOWS WHERE YOU LIVE (Kaiser, Henry & Jim O'Rourke)
CD _____ VICTOCD 014
Victo / Nov '94 / These / ReR Megacorp / Cadillac.

WIREWORKS (Kaiser, Henry & Derek Bailey)
CD _____ SHAN 5011CD
Shanachie / Apr '95 / Koch / ADA / Greensleeves.

WORLD OUT OF TIME, A (Kaiser, Henry & David Lindley)
CD _____ SHAN 64041CD
Shanachie / '92 / Koch / ADA / Greensleeves.

WORLD OUT OF TIME, A - VOL.2 (Kaiser, Henry & David Lindley)
CD _____ SHAN 64048CD
Shanachie / Aug '93 / Koch / ADA / Greensleeves.

Kaisers

BEAT IT UP
CD _____ NOHITCD 017
No Hit / Jul '95 / SRD.

Kajagoogoo

TOO SHY - THE SINGLES...AND MORE
Too shy / Ooh to be ah / Hang on now / Big apple / Lion's mouth / Turn your back on me / Shouldn't I do that / Only for love / Too much trouble / Never ending story / Love in your eyes / Inside to outside / Too shy (midnight mix) / Hang on now (extended version) / Turn your back on me (extended mix) / Never ending story (club mix)
CD _____ CZ 524
EMI / Sep '93 / EMI.

Kalamas Quartette

EARLY HAWAIIAN CLASSICS
CD _____ FL 7028
Folklyric / Apr '95 / Direct / Cadillac.

Kalaschjan

RURAL & URBAN TRADITIONAL MUSIC FROM ARMENIA
CD _____ SM 1505-2
Wergo / Jan '93 / Harmonia Mundi / ADA / Cadillac.

Kaleidoscope

BLUES FROM BAGDAD
Egyptian gardens / If the night / Please / Keep your mind open / Pulsating dream / Oh death / Why try / Rampe rampe / I found out / Life will pass you by / Greenwood side / Beacon from Mars / Lie to me / Petite fleur / Banjo / Nobody / Elevator man / Hello trouble / Cuckoo / Sweet ate sweet
CD _____ EDCD 375
Edsel / Aug '93 / Pinnacle / ADA.

INCREDIBLE
Lie to me / Let the good love flow / Killing floor / Petite fleur / Banjo / Cuckoo / Seven ate sweet
CD _____ EDCD 292
Edsel / Feb '91 / Pinnacle / ADA.

SIDE TRIPS
Egyptian gardens / If the night / Please / Keep your mind open / Pulsating dream / Oh death / Come on in / Why try / Minnie the moocher
CD _____ ED CD 284
Edsel / Aug '88 / Pinnacle / ADA.

Kalin Twins

WHEN
Sweet sweet sugar lips / Chicken chief / Oh my goodness / Jumpin' Jack / Clickety clack / Three o'clock thrill / Spider and the fly / No money can buy / When / Forget me not / Picture of you / Zing went the strings of my heart / Walkin' to school / Momma poppa / It's only the beginning / You mean the world to me
CD _____ BCD 15597
Bear Family / Feb '92 / Rollercoaster / Direct / CM / Swift / ADA.

Kaliphz

SEVEN DEADLY SINS
Blood in blood out / Wass the deal / Bang bang boogie / Why im ez / Knockout position / Kloud 9 / Open up your mind / Rokk on shokk on / Sx horra vylence / Citi neva sleepz / Police n thievez / Eat the world / Kashflows / Props 2 tha thru skool
CD _____ 8286752
Payday / Oct '95 / PolyGram / Vital.

Kalis

ROCK AROUND
CD _____ SYN CD 151
Topic / Apr '93 / Direct / ADA.

Kalle, Pepe

GIGANTAFRIQUE
Tiembe raid pa moli / Ce chale carnaval / Marche commun / Bilala lala / Pron moun paka bouge / Ndaka ya zeke
CD _____ CDORB 062
Globestyle / Jul '90 / Pinnacle.

L'ARGENT NE FAIT LE BONHEUR
CD _____ KLCD 032
Gefraco / Nov '90 / Triple Earth.

Kallick, Kathy

MATTERS OF THE HEART
CD _____ SH 3820CD
Sugarhill / Jan '94 / Roots / CM / ADA / Direct.

USE A NAPKIN NOT YOUR MUM
CD _____ SHCD 3833
Sugarhill / May '95 / Roots / CM / ADA /
Direct.

Kalte Farben

TRUST
CD _____ EFA 112352
Danse Macabre / Dec '94 / SRD.

Kalyna Krasnaya

AT NARODA
CD _____ SYN 189CD
Syncoop / Nov '95 / ADA / Direct.

Kam

KAM
CD _____ 7567617542
Street Knowledge / Mar '95 / Warner
Music.

NEVA AGAIN
Intro / Peace treaty / Stereotype / Still got
love 4 'um / Hang 'um high / Drama / Neva
again / Y'all don't hear me dough / Ain't that
a bitch / Holiday madness / Watts riot /
Outro
CD _____ 756792208-2
Street Knowledge / Mar '93 / Warner Music.

Kamal

DANCE (Kamal & The Brothers)
CD _____ NI 4022
Natasha / Nov '93 / Jazz Music / ADA /
CM / Direct / Cadillac.

Kamen, Michael

**CONCERTO FOR SAXOPHONE (Kamen,
Michael & David Sanborn)**
Concerto for saxophone / Helen-Claire /
Sasha / Zoe / Sandra / Waiting for daddy
CD _____ 7599261572
WEA / Nov '90 / Warner Music.

Kamen, Nick

EACH TIME YOU BREAK MY HEART
CD _____ 4509 918882
Carlton Home Entertainment / Jan '93 /
Carlton Home Entertainment.

Kamikaze Ground Crew

**MADAME MARIE'S TEMPLE OF
KNOWLEDGE**
CD _____ 804382
New World / Sep '93 / Harmonia Mundi /
ADA / Cadillac.

SCENIC ROUTE, THE
CD _____ NW 400
New World / Aug '92 / Harmonia Mundi /
ADA / Cadillac.

Kamoze, Ini

HERE COMES THE HOTSTEPPER
Call the police / Rough / Here comes the
hotstepper / Gunshot / World-a-music /
Trouble you trouble me / General / Pull up
the cork / Pirate / Babylon, Babylon, I want
Ital / Burnin'
CD _____ 4785362
Columbia / May '95 / Sony.

ORIGINAL HOT STEPPER
CD _____ RRCD 49
Reggae Refreshers / Jan '95 / PolyGram /
Vital.

SHOCKING OUT
Cool it off / Clown talking / Cone now / Boss
/ We run the country / Shocking out / Rev-
olution / Girl E / Hole in the pumpkin /
Spread out
CD _____ GRELCD 115
Greensleeves / Jan '95 / Total/BMG / Jets-
tar / SRD.

Kamuca, Richie

JAZZ EROTICA
CD _____ FSCD 500
Fresh Sound / Feb '88 / Jazz Music /
Discovery.

Kanchay

MACHU PICCHU
CD _____ TUMICD 011
Tumi / Apr '90 / Sterns / Discovery.

Kanda Bongo Man

AMOUR YOU
CD _____ HNCD 1337
Hannibal / Jan '89 / Vital / ADA.

KWASSA-KWASSA
CD _____ HNCD 1343
Hannibal / May '89 / Vital / ADA.

NON STOP NON STOP
Iyole / Ida / Djessy / Amina / Mazina
CD _____ CDORB 005
Globestyle / Mar '90 / Pinnacle.

SOUKOUS IN CENTRAL PARK
Liza / Bedy / Yesu Christu / J.T. / Wallow /
Luta / Sai / Lela lela

CD _____ HNCD 1374
Hannibal / Mar '93 / Vital / ADA.

ZING ZONG
Zing zong / Isambe / Mosali / Wallow /
Monie / Yonde love me / Yesu Christu /
Freres soki / Kadhi
CD _____ HNCD 1366
Hannibal / Jul '91 / Vital / ADA.

Kane, Candye

HOME COOKIN'
CD _____ ANT 0033CD
Antones / Sep '94 / Hot Shot / Direct /
ADA.

Kane, Chet

TEARS FOR COLUMBIA
CD _____ GRCD 315
Glitterhouse / Sep '94 / Direct / ADA.

Kane, Eden

HITS ALBUM, THE
CD _____ MOGCD 005
Moggie / Dec '94 / Else.

WELL I ASK YOU
CD _____ 8209662
Deram / Jan '96 / PolyGram.

Kane Gang

MOTORTOWN
Motortown / Amusement park / Smalltown
creed / Brother brother / Mighty day /
Crease in his hat / Giving up / Don't look
any further / Finer place / Respect yourself
/ What time is it / Spend / It's a gift / King
Street rain
CD _____ 5501952
Spectrum/Karussell / Mar '94 / PolyGram /
THE.

Kane, Helen

**GREAT ORIGINAL PERFORMANCES
1928-1930**
Get out and get under the moon / That's
my weakness now / I wanna be loved by
you / Is there anything wrong in that / Don't
be like that / Me and the main in the moon
/ Button up your overcoat / I want to be bad
/ Do something / That's why I'm happy / I'd
do anything for you / He's so unusual / Ain't
cha / I have to have you / I'd go barefoot
all winter long / Dangerous Nan McGrew /
Thank your Father / I owe you / Readin',
ritin' and rhythm / I've got it (But it don't do
me no good) / My man is on the make / If I
knew you better
CD _____ RPCD 323
Robert Parker Jazz / Aug '94 / Conifer.

Kane, Kieran

DEAD RECKONING
CD _____ DR 001
Dead Reckoning / Aug '95 / Direct.

Kangaroo Moon

BAGPIPES ON THE BEACH
CD _____ MS 117CD
Kangaroo / Apr '94 / ADA.

BELONGIL
CD _____ KM 02CD
Kangaroo Moon / Jan '96 / ADA.

Kansas

FREAKS OF NATURE
CD _____ ESSCD 299
Essential / Aug '95 / Total/BMG.

KANSAS
Can I tell you / Bringing it back / Lonely
wind / Belexes / Journey from Mariabronn /
Pilgrimage / Apercu / Death of Mother Na-
ture suite
CD _____ 9827332
Pickwick/Sony Collector's Choice / Apr '92
/ Carlton Home Entertainment / Pinnacle /
Sony.

KANSAS BOXED SET, THE
Can I tell you / Death of mother nature suite
/ Journey from Mariabronn / Song for America / Devil game / Incomudro-hymm to the
atman / Child of innocence / Icarus / Borne
on wings of steel / Mysteries and mayhem
/ Pinnacle / Carry on wayward son / Wall /
What's on my mind / Opus insert / Magnum
opus / Father Padilla meets the perfect gnat
/ Howling at the moon / Industry on parade
/ Release the beavers / Gnat attack / Point
of no return / Portrait (He Knew) / Dust in
the wind / Closet chronicles / People of the
south wind / On the other side / Glimpse of
home / Relentless / Loner / Hold on /
Wheels
CD Set _____ CD 47364
Legacy / Jul '94 / Sony.

LEFTOVERTURE
Carry on wayward son / Wall / What's on
my mind / Miracles out of nowhere / Opus
insert / Questions of my childhood / Cheyenne anthem / Magnum opus / Father Padilla meets the perfect gnat / Howling at the
moon / Man overboard / Industry on parade
/ Release the beavers / Gnat attack

CD _____ 982837 2
Carlton Home Entertainment / Nov '92 /
Carlton Home Entertainment.

Kansas City Stompers

40-ARS JUBILEAUM
CD _____ MECCACD 1018
Music Mecca / Nov '94 / Jazz Music /
Cadillac / Wellard.

HAPPY JAZZ
CD _____ MECCACD 1041
Music Mecca / Nov '94 / Jazz Music /
Cadillac / Wellard.

Kanta, Kiri

CONTRAT ABENI
Contrat abeni / M'banakwa / Dounyan / A
Sinde / Sembe / Tankpika / Akoumanderi /
Salifou
CD _____ VA 016
Voix D'Afrique / Feb '95 / New Note.

Kante, Mory

AKWABA BEACH
Yeke yeke / Deni / Inch Allah / Tama / Africa
2000 / Dia / Nanfoulen / Akwaba beach
CD _____ 833 119 2
London / Apr '91 / PolyGram.

Kanu Nan

CHIMBALOMA
CD _____ TUMICD 027
Tumi / '91 / Sterns / Discovery.

Kanyakumari, A

**VADYA LAHARI (Kanyakumari, A &
South Indian Music Ensemble)**
CD _____ CDT 125
Topic / Apr '93 / Direct / ADA.

Kapel, Jons Jazz

LAZY 'SIPPI STEAMER
CD _____ MECCACD 1019
Music Mecca / Nov '94 / Jazz Music /
Cadillac / Wellard.

Kapelye

**KAPELYE: ON THE AIR (Old-Time
Jewish American Radio)**
CD _____ SHCD 67005
Shanachie / Mar '95 / Koch / ADA /
Greensleeves.

Kaplansky, Lucy

TIDE, THE
CD _____ RHRCD 65
Red House / May '95 / Koch / ADA.

Kapoor, Mahendra

FROM BIRMINGHAM TO SOUTHALL
CD _____ DMUT 1069
Multitone / Apr '89 / BMG.

Kapstad, Egil

CHEROKEE
CD _____ GMCD 161
Gemini / Oct '90 / Cadillac.

Karaindrou, Eleni

MUSIC FOR FILMS
Farwell theme / Elegy for rosa / Fairytale /
Parade / Return / Wandering in Alexandria
/ Voyage / Scream / Adagio / Rosa's song
/ Improvisation on farewell and waltz theme
/ Song / Waltz and farewell theme
CD _____ 8476092
ECM / May '91 / New Note.

**SUSPENDED STEP OF THE STORK,
THE**
Refugee's theme / Search - refugee's
theme variation A / Suspended step / Train-
car neighbourhood variation A / River / Re-
fugee's theme symphonic variation No. 1 /
Train-car neighbourhood variation B / Re-
fugee's theme symphonic variation No. 2 /
Hassaposerviko / Search - refugee's theme
variation B / Waltz for the bride / Final
CD _____ 5115142
ECM / Mar '94 / New Note.

Karayorgis, Pandelis

**IN TIME (Karayorgis, Pandelis & Mat
Maneri)**
CD _____ LABCD 002
Leo / Oct '94 / Wellard / Cadillac /
Impetus.

Karen

BETWEEN ME AND YOU
CD _____ JJCD 1017
Beechwood / Jan '92 / Ross / Duncans.

Karizma

(FOREVER IN THE ARMS) OF LOVE
CD _____ MAXCD 2039
Maxus / Nov '92 / Harmonia Mundi.

Karklins, Ingrid

ANIMA MUNDI
CD _____ GLCD 1141
Green Linnet / May '94 / Roots / CM /
Direct / ADA.

DARKER PASSION, A
Leatherwing bat / Big one/Little one / Es ap-
kalu ozolinu/Oceans apart / Hiro/Smitten /
Time/Incredible march of the spiny lobsters
/ Kupla, kupla liepa auga / Crack the slab /
Visas manas sikus dziesmas / Ar vilcinu riga
braucu / Metenitis
CD _____ GLCD 1118
Green Linnet / Mar '92 / Roots / CM / Direct
/ ADA.

Karlsson, Stefan

BELOW ZERO
CD _____ JR 07032
Justice / Mar '94 / Koch.

ROOM 292
CD _____ JR 007012
Justice / Oct '92 / Koch.

Karn, Mick

BESTIAL CLUSTER
Bestial cluster / Back in the beginning /
Beard in the letterbox / Drowning dream /
Sad velvet breath of summer and winter /
Saday, Maday / Liver and lungs / Bones of
mud
CD _____ CMP CD 1002
CMP / Jun '93 / Vital/SAM.

**DREAMS OF REASON PRODUCE
MONSTERS**
First impression / Language of ritual / Buoy
/ Land / Three fates / When love walks in /
Dream of reason / Answer
CD _____ CDV 2389
Virgin / '87 / EMI.

TITLES
Tribal dawn / Lost affections in a room /
Passion in moisture / Weather the windmill
/ Saviour are you with me / Trust me /
Sensitive / Piper blue
CD _____ CDV 2249
Virgin / Oct '90 / EMI.

TOOTH MOTHER, THE
Thundergirl mutation / Plaster the magic
tongue / Lodge of skins / Gossip's cup /
Feta funk / Tooth Mother / Little less hope
/ There was not anything but nothing
CD _____ CMPCD 1008
CMP / May '95 / Vital/SAM.

Karolinka

SONGS AND DANCES FROM POLAND
CD _____ EUCD 1124
ARC / '91 / ARC Music / ADA.

Karozi, Michael

DELUGE
CD _____ SPOONCD 16
Spoon / Mar '95 / CM / Disc.

Karp

SUPLEX
CD _____ KLP 48 CD
K / Oct '95 / SRD.

Karrie, Peter

THEATRICALLY YOURS
CD _____ FG 012
Fog & Gas Co / Jan '96 / Total/BMG.

Karukas, Gregg

SUMMERHOUSE
Summerhouse / My best friend / Moonlit
breeze / Desert dancing / First love / Whale
watching / Spinning dreams / Thanks for
the reason / Autobahn / I dream of you
CD _____ 101S 8770672
101 South / Apr '95 / New Note.

Kashif

BEST OF KASHIF
I just gotta have you (lover turn me on) /
Baby don't break your baby's heart / Are
you the woman / Reservations for two /
Love changes / Fifty ways (to fall in love) /
Stay the night / Love me all over / Help
yourself to my love / Dancing in the dark
CD _____ 262817
Arista / Jun '92 / BMG.

Kashmir

TRAVELOGUE
Story of Jamie fame flame / Art of me / Rose
/ Leather crane / Don't look back it's prob-
ably hypochondriac Jack / Vicious passion
CD _____ 4807632
Epic / Jul '95 / Sony.

Kastrierte Philosophen

LEIPZIG D.C.
CD _____ NORMAL 124 CD
Normal/Okra / Dec '90 / Direct / ADA.

Kataklysm

MYSTICAL GATE OF REINCARNATION
CD _____ NB 093-2
Nuclear Blast / Feb '94 / Plastic Head.

SORCERY
CD _____ NB 1082
Nuclear Blast / Mar '95 / Plastic Head.

Katatonia

DANCE OF THE DECEMBER SOULS
CD _____ NFR 005
No Fashion / Oct '94 / Plastic Head.

Katch 22

NON CONFORMIST RITUALS
CD _____ KSCD 340
Kold Sweat / Jul '94 / 3MV.

Kater, Peter

COLLECTION 1983-90
CD _____ SD 605
Silver Wave / Sep '92 / New Note /
Jazzizit Organisation.

FOOL & THE HUMMINGBIRD, THE
CD _____ SD 502
Silver Wave / Jan '93 / New Note / Jazzizit
Organisation.

FOR CHRISTMAS
CD _____ SD 503
Silver Wave / Jan '93 / New Note / Jazzizit
Organisation.

GATEWAY
CD _____ SD 161
Silver Wave / Jan '93 / New Note / Jazzizit
Organisation.

HOMAGE
CD _____ 139017-2
Gaia / May '89 / New Note.

MOMENTS, DREAMS & VISIONS
CD _____ SD 509
Silver Wave / Jan '93 / New Note / Jazzizit
Organisation.

NATIVES
CD _____ SD 601
Silver Wave / Jan '93 / New Note / Jazzizit
Organisation.

ROOFTOPS
CD _____ SD 608
Silver Wave / Sep '92 / New Note /
Jazzizit Organisation.

SEASON, THE
CD _____ SD 702
Silver Wave / Jan '93 / New Note / Jazzizit
Organisation.

Katmandu

CASE FOR THE BLUES, A
CD _____ SARCD 007
Saraja / Apr '94 / THE.

KATMANDU
Creation / Welcome to California / Price of
darkness / Alvin Aspel-nervous actor /
Nineteen guitars / Julie's zoo / Paris, Texas:
Waikiki, venus / Lusitania / Seabesift
CD _____ LEBCD 035
Handlebar / Feb '95 / Vital.

Kato, Ano

CHTES TA KANAME
CD _____ CDPAN 144
Pan / Apr '93 / ADA / Direct / CM.

Katon, Michael

GET ON THE BOOGIE TRAIN
CD _____ PRD 70492
Provogue / Apr '93 / Pinnacle.

PROUD TO BE LOUD
CD _____ PRD 70532
Provogue / Sep '93 / Pinnacle.

RIP IT HARD
CD _____ PRD 70642
Provogue / May '94 / Pinnacle.

Katz, Bruce

TRANSFORMATION
Chicago transformation / Boppin' out of the
abyss / Sweeper / What might have been /
Larry the spinning poodle / Circular notion
/ Deep pockets / Crime novel / Window of
soul / But now I see
CD _____ AQCD 1026
Audioquest / Jul '95 / New Note.

Katz, Dick

3 WAY PLAY
CD _____ RSRCD 127
Reservoir Music / Nov '94 / Cadillac.

Katze, Nav

NEVER MIND THE DISTORTION
CD _____ SSR 154
SSR / Oct '95 / Grapevine.

Kaufmann, Anna Maria

ANNA MARIA KAUFMANN
CD _____ MSPCD 9502
Mabley St. / Sep '95 / Grapevine.

Kauriga Balalaika...

**RUSSIAN DANCES (Kauriga Balalaika
Ensemble)**
CD _____ MCD 71789
Monitor / Jun '93 / CM.

Kava Kava

YOU CAN LIVE HERE
Headset / Sync / Gil / Revenge of the
pseuds / Tat tvam asi / Swivel / Beat their
chests / Loudest lebenstraum / In transits
destined / For Uranus (CD only) / Hippy bollocks (CD only) / Silliness (CD only)
CD _____ DELECCD 024
Delerium / Apr '95 / Vital.

Kavana, Ron

GALWAY TO GRACELAND
CD _____ CDARK 002
Alias / Oct '95 / Vital.

Kavanagh, Niamh

FLYING BLIND
When there's time for love / Romeo's twin
/ White city of lights / Let's make trouble /
Miles away / I can't make you love me /
Whatever it takes / Don't stop now / Flying
blind / Red roses for me
CD _____ 74321255412
Arista / Oct '95 / BMG.

Kawaguchi, George

**JAZZ BATTLE (Kawaguchi, George &
Art Blakey)**
EJ's blues / Third plane / Moanin' / Man I
love / George's boogie
CD _____ KICJ 40
King/Paddle Wheel / May '91 / New Note.

Kay, Arthur

RARE 'N' TASTY
CD _____ LOMACD 33
Loma / Aug '94 / BMG.

Kay, Fiede

VOLKSSANGER AUS DEM NORDEN
CD _____ EUCD 1118
ARC / '91 / ARC Music / ADA.

Kay Gees

**ESSENTIAL DANCEFLOOR ARTISTS
VOL. 5**
You've got to / Keep on bumpin' / Get
down / Masterplan / Hustle wit every
muscle / Waiting at the bus stop / Cheek to
cheek / I believe in music / Tango hustle /
Killowatt / Killowatt/Invasion / Who's the
man (with the master plan)
CD _____ DGPCD 707
Deep Beats / Sep '94 / BMG.

Kay, Janet

CAPRICORN WOMAN
CD _____ ARKCD 3
Pressure / Sep '89 / Jetstar / Black
Marketing.

DUB DEM JILL?
CD _____ ARKCD 105
Arawak / Dec '93 / Jetstar.

I'LL ALWAYS LOVE YOU
CD _____ JFRCD 001
Joe Frazier / Dec '93 / Jetstar.

IMMACULATE COLLECTION
So amazing / Look what love can do / Almaz / Loving you / Moving away / Kiss
away / Bad, bad girl / Chariots of fire / I'd
rather go blind / Closer I get to you / For
the good times / Music man / Dreams of
emotion / Have you ever loved somebody /
Since I fell for you / One day I'll fly away /
He reminds me / Trade winds / Show me
the way / So good, so right / Imagine /
Computer love / I want to be the one / Love
won't let me wait
CD _____ JANETCD 2
New Name / Nov '93 / Jetstar.

ORCHESTRAL DUB COLLECTION
CD _____ JANETCD 3
Body Music / Jul '94 / Jetstar.

SILLY GAMES
Silly games / Imagine that / Feel no way /
Rock the rhythm / Closer to you / Do you
love me / Can't give it up / That night / Cap-
ricorn woman
CD _____ CECD 1001
Jetstar / Aug '90 / Jetstar.

SO AMAZING
CD _____ JANETCD 01
Body Music / Apr '94 / Jetstar.

SWEET SURRENDER
CD _____ JANCD 05
Body Music / Jul '89 / Jetstar.

ULTIMATE COLLECTION, THE
CD _____ ARKCD 106
Arawak / Oct '95 / Jetstar.

Kay, Sammy

22 ORIGINAL BIG BAND RECORDINGS
CD _____ HCD 402
Hindsight / Oct '92 / Target/BMG / Jazz
Music.

Kay Yn't Seil

T'MALLE SCHIP
CD _____ SYNCD 164
Syncoop / Jun '94 / ADA / Direct.

Kaye, Danny

SINGS YOUR FAVOURITE SONGS
CD _____ CD 340
Entertainers / Aug '94 / Target/BMG.

**VERY BEST OF DANNY KAYE (20
golden greats)**
I'm Hans Christian Andersen / Inchworm /
King's new clothes / Thumbelina / Ugly
duckling / Wonderful Copenhagen / Tubby
the tuba (parts 1 and 2) / Woody Woodpecker song / Popo the puppet / I taut I taw
a puddy tat / Ballin' the Jack / Tchaikovsky
/ Civilization / Molly Malone / Oh by jingo,
oh by gee / Candy kisses / St. Louis blues
/ Manic depressive parents lobby number
part I and part II
CD _____ MCLD 19049
MCA / Aug '94 / BMG.

Kaye, Sammy

**SAMMY KAYE 1944/LES ELGART 1946
(Kaye, Sammy & Les Elgart)**
CD _____ CCD 93
Circle / Aug '94 / Jazz Music / Swift /
Wellard.

Kayirebwa, Cecile

RWANDA
Rwanamiza / Tarihinda / Kana / Inkindi /
Mundeke mbaririmbire / Urusamaza / Ru-
byiruko / Umulisa / Cyusa / Ndare /
Umunezero
CD _____ CDORBD 083
Globestyle / Aug '94 / Pinnacle.

Kazazian, Georges

SABIL
CD _____ ED 13034CD
L'Empreiente Digitale / Jul '95 / Harmonia
Mundi / ADA.

Kazda

NEW STRATEGIES OF RIDING
CD _____ ITM 1492
ITM / Oct '95 / Tradelink / Koch.

Kazjurol

DANCE TARANTELLA
CD _____ CDATV 12
Active / Sep '90 / Pinnacle.

KBZ 200

EXOTIC TRILOGY, THE
CD _____ KBZ 200
Staalplaat / Dec '95 / Vital/SAM.

Keane, Brian

**BEYOND THE SKY (Keane, Brian &
Omar Faruk Tekbilek)**
Beyond the sky / Imaginary traveller / Ko-
laymi / Bridge / Chargah Sorti / Your love
Is My Cure / Selemet / Strange Little Corner
/ Sisler / Sweet Trouble / Al Fatiha (#)
CD _____ CDCEL 13047
Celestial Harmonies / Jul '92 / ADA / Select.

SNOWFALLS
CD _____ FFK 70452
Flying Fish / Oct '89 / Roots / CM / Direct
/ ADA.

Keane, Conor

COOLEY'S HOUSE
CD _____ CKCD 01CD
Conor Keane / Oct '95 / ADA.

Keane, Dolores

**FAREWELL TO EIREANN (Keane,
Dolores & John Faulkner/Eamonn
Curran)**
CD _____ CDTUT 724004
Wundertute / Oct '89 / CM / Duncans /
ADA.

LION IN A CAGE
I feel it in my bones / Lion in a cage / Room
/ Moorlough shore / Across the bridge /
Walking on seashells / One golden rule /
Island / Hold me
CD _____ RTMCD 7
Round Tower / Jan '94 / Pinnacle / ADA /
Direct / BMG / CM.

**SAIL ÓG RUA (Keane, Dolores & John
Faulkner)**
CD _____ CEFCD 101
Gael Linn / Jan '94 / Roots / CM / Direct /
ADA.

SOLID GROUND
CD _____ SHCD 8007
Shanachie / Mar '93 / Koch / ADA /
Greensleeves.
CD _____ DARACD 065
Dara / Mar '95 / Roots / CM / Direct /
ADA / Koch.

THERE WAS A MAID
Generous lover / Bantry girl's lament / My
match is made / Lord Gordon's reel / Laurel
bush / Johnny and Molly / Shaskeen reel /
Lament for Owen Roe O'Neill / Seven yellow gypsies / Tommy Coen's reel / There
was a maid in her father's garden / Carraroe
jig / Whelan's jig / Bonnie bunch of roses
CD _____ CC 23CD
Claddagh / Nov '90 / ADA / Direct.

Keane, James

ROLL AWAY THE REEL WORLD
Crossing the Shannon / Blooming mead-
ows / Maud Miller's reels/The sailor's return
CD _____ GLCD 1026
Green Linnet / '92 / Roots / CM / Direct /
ADA.

THAT'S THE SPIRIT
CD _____ GLCD 1138
Green Linnet / Jan '95 / Roots / CM /
Direct / ADA.

Keane, Sean

**FIRE AFLAME, THE (Keane, Sean &
Matt Molloy & Liam O'Flynn)**
Wheels of the world / Pinch of snuff/Micho
Russell's reel / Bellharbour hornpipe/Old ru-
ined cottage in the Glen / Geese in the bog/
Little fair cannavans/Whelan's old sow /
Maid of Ballingarry/Stack of barley / J.B.
Reel/Lads of Laois/Rambling thatcher /
Drunken sailor / Night fishing 30th January
1972/Rights of man / Johnny 'Watt' Henry's
reel/Jerry McMahon's reel / Pat Ward's jig/
Dusty Miller / Ask my Father/Connaught
heifer / Casadh na nGeanna / Ace and
deuce of pipering / Eire / Sean Ryan's reel
/Grand spey
CD _____ CCF 30CD
Claddagh / Feb '93 / ADA / Direct.

GUSTY'S FROLICS
CD _____ CC 17CD
Claddagh / Nov '95 / ADA / Direct.

JIG IT IN STYLE
Baker/Miss Mary Walkr/The hawk/Marquis
of Huntley / O'Farrel's welcome to Limerick/
Kitty come down from Limerick / Kiss the
Maid behind the barrel / Dark Lochnagar /
McLean of Pennycross/Maggie Cameron/
Duntroon Castle / Maiden that jigs it in
style/Girl in the big house/Alasdruim / Ten-
nessee stud/Arkansas traveller/Miss Susan
Cooper / Bereton's reel/Bucks of Oranmore
/ Heartbreak hotel/Cliffs of Moher / Golden
eagle/Tommy Hill's favourite / Willie's sin-
gle/Glen road to Carrick / Blue angel/Strike
the gay harp / Willie's fling / Atlantic roar /
Margaret Jackson/Reavy's reel
CD _____ CCF 25CD
Claddagh / '90 / ADA / Direct.

Keane, Sean

21 IRISH ACCORDION FAVOURITES
CD _____ WMCD 2001
Westmoor / Sep '94 / Target/BMG.

ALL HEART, NO ROSES
CD _____ CBM 007CD
Cross Border Media / Nov '93 / Direct /
ADA.

Keane, Tommy

PIPERS APRON, THE
CD _____ CLUNCD 052
Mulligan / Aug '86 / CM / ADA.

WIND AMONG THE REEDS, THE
CD _____ MMCCD 51
Maree Music / Oct '95 / Direct / ADA.

Keating, Matt

SCARYAREA
Boxed inn / McHappiness / (I thought I
heard my) Head exploding / Way to go / Pull
some strings / Wrong God / Opportunist /
Never fit in / Later October / You other face
/ All the rest / Naggin' feelin'
CD _____ A 069D
Alias / Oct '94 / Vital.

TELL IT TO YOURSELF
Sanity in the asylum / Don't suffer in silence
/ When you don't have to work / Little talk
/ Lonely blue / Arrangements / Show me
how / Nostalgia / So near, so far / '92 / Lost
again / Hard place to be
CD _____ A 035D
Alias / Jun '93 / Vital.

Keatons

BEIGE ALBUM, THE
CD _____ FSHH 7
Dogfish / Oct '94 / Plastic Head / SRD.

Keb Mo'

KEB MO'
Am I wrong / Come on in my kitchen / Dirty low down and bad / Don't try to explain / Kind hearted woman blues / City boy / Every morning / Tell everybody I know / Love blues / Victims of comfort / Angelina / Anybody seen my girl / She just wants to dance
CD _____ 4781732
Epic / Jul '95 / Sony.

Kebnekajse

ELECTRIC MOUNTAIN
CD
Resource / Oct '93 / ADA.

Kee, John

COLOUR BLIND
CD _____ VTYCD 001
Verity / Jun '94 / BMG.

Keel

LARGER THAN LIFE
CD _____ SPV 08512102
SPV / Aug '95 / Plastic Head.

Keel, Howard

BEST OF HOWARD KEEL, THE
CD _____ EMPRCD 559
Emporio / Mar '95 / THE / Disc / CM.

CLOSE TO MY HEART
There's no business like show business / O what a beautiful morning / Secret love / Surrey with the fringe on top / If I loved you / Bless your beautiful hide / Wind beneath my wings / So in love / Make believe / Love changes everything / Bring him home / Prelude into music of the night / Colours of my life / Rose Marie (video only)
CD _____ CDKEEL 1
Premier/MFP / Apr '91 / EMI.

COLLECTION: HOWARD KEEL
Some enchanted evening / This nearly was mine / I won't send roses / If ever I would leave you / You needed me / Love story / Come in from the rain / MacArthur Park / Send in the clowns / You were always on my mind / I've never been to me
CD _____ CLACD 367
Castle / Aug '93 / BMG.

ENCHANTED EVENING WITH HOWARD KEEL, A
Oklahoma medley / Some enchanted evening / This nearly was mine / I won't send roses / If ever I would leave you / La Mancha medley / You needed me / Love story / Come in from the rain / Yesterday / Something / Once upon a time / What are you doing for the rest of your life / Wave / MacArthur Park / Send in the clowns / You were always on my mind / I've never been to me / Annie get your gun medley
CD _____ MCCD 006
Music Club / Feb '91 / Disc / THE / CM.

FILM AND MUSICAL FAVOURITES
CD _____ 15093
Laserlight / May '94 / Target/BMG.

GREAT SONGS, THE
CD _____ MU 5024
Musketeer / Oct '92 / Koch.

Keelaghan, James

MY SKIES
CD _____ GLCD 2112
Green Linnet / Jun '93 / Roots / CM / Direct / ADA.

RECENT FUTURE, A
CD _____ GLCD 2120
Green Linnet / Aug '95 / Roots / CM / Direct / ADA.

Keen, Robert Earl

BIGGER PIECE OF SKY, A
So I can take my rest / Whenever kindness fail / Amarillo highway / Night night for love / Jesse with the long hair...Blow you away / Here in Arkansas / Daddy had a buick / Corpus Christie / Crazy cowboy dream / Paint the town beige
CD _____ SPDCD 1048
Special Delivery / May '93 / ADA / CM / Direct.

GRINGO HONEYMOON
CD _____ SPDCD 1051
Special Delivery / Oct '94 / ADA / CM / Direct.

LIVE ALBUM, THE
I wanna know / Torch song / Goin' down in style / It were King / Copenhagen / I would change my life / Stewball / I'll go on downtown / Bluegrass widow / Who'll be lookin' out for me
CD _____ SHCD 1024
Sugarhill / '88 / Roots / CM / ADA / Direct.

NO KINDA DANCER

No kinda dancer / Front porch song / Between hello and goodbye / Swervin' in my lane / Christabel / Willie / Young lovers waltz / Death of tail Fitzsimmons / Rolling by / Armadillo jackal / Lu Ann / Coldest day of Winter
CD _____ SHCD 1049
Sugarhill / Apr '95 / Roots / CM / ADA / Direct.

Keenan, Paddy

POIRT AN PHÍOBAIRE
CD _____ CEFCD 099
Gael Linn / Jan '94 / Roots / CM / Direct / ADA.

Keene, Steven

NO ALTERNATIVE
CD _____ 2351
Moo / Jan '96 / Total/BMG.

Keene, Tommy

DRIVING INTO THE SUN
Places that are gone / Nothing happened yesterday / Baby face / Back to zero / When the truth is found / Hey little child / Something got a hold of me / Real underground / Misunderstood / That you do / Mr. Roland / Back again / Safe in the light / People with fast cars drive fast / Love is the only thing that matters / Dull afternoon / Tattoo / Don't sleep in the daytime / Hey man / Andrea / Something to rave about / Sleeping on a rollercoaster
CD _____ A 059D
Alias / Apr '94 / Vital.

TEN YEARS AFTER
Going out again / Turning on blue / Today and tomorrow / If your heart beats alone / If you're getting married tonight / On the runway / We started over again / Good thing going / Compromise / You can't wait for time / Before the lights go down / It's now true
CD _____ OLE 1772
Matador / Feb '96 / Vital.

Keepers

LOOKING FOR A SIGN
CD _____ LIZARD 80003
Lizard / Mar '95 / Direct / Disc.

Keezer, Geoff

OTHER SPHERES
CD _____ DIW 871
DIW / Jul '93 / Harmonia Mundi / Cadillac.

WORLD MUSIC (Keezer, Geoff Trio)
CD _____ 4728112
Sony Jazz / Jan '95 / Sony.

Keiji, Haino

ALLEGORICAL MISUNDERSTANDING
CD _____ AVAN 015
Avant / Sep '93 / Harmonia Mundi / Cadillac.

Keineg, Katell

O SEASONS O CASTLES
Hestia / Partisan / Cut bop / Burden / Franklin / Conch shell / Coolea / Destiny's Darling / Waiting for you to smile / Paris / O seasons / O lesu mawr / Gulf of Araby
CD _____ 755961657-2
Warner Bros. / Sep '94 / Warner Music.

Keita, Salif

AMEN
CD _____ CIDM 1073
Mango / Apr '91 / Vital / PolyGram.

FOLON
Tekere / Mandiou / Africa / Nyanyama / Mandela / Sumun / Seydou / Dakan-fe / Folon
CD _____ CIDM 1108
Mango / Oct '95 / Vital / PolyGram.

KO-YAN
Lyada / Nou pas bouger / Ko-yan / Fe-so / Primpin / Tenin / Sabou
CD _____ CIDM 1002
Mango / Apr '89 / Vital / PolyGram.

MANSA OF MALI, THE
Sina / Mandjou / Nyanafin / Ignadjidje / Nou pas bouger / Djembe / Souarebe / Tenin / Sanni Kegniba / Dalimansa
CD _____ CIDM 1107
Mango / Jun '95 / Vital / PolyGram.

SORO
Wamba / Soro / Souareba / Sina / Cono / Sanni Kegniba
CD _____ STCD 1020
Sterns / Mar '89 / Sterns / CM.

Keith, Ben

SEVEN GATES - A CHRISTMAS ALBUM
CD _____ 936245773-2
Warner Bros. / Nov '94 / Warner Music.

Keith, Bill

BEATING AROUND THE BUSH
Beating around the bush / Don't let your deal go down / Cherokee shuffle / Liebestraum / Bay state bounce / Step lively / Drop in the bucket / Little old log cabin / Old hickory / Ready for the times / Bending the strings / Hornswoggled / Crab waltz
CD _____ GLCD 2107
Green Linnet / Feb '93 / Roots / CM / Direct / ADA.

Kellaway, Roger

ALONE TOGETHER (Kellaway, Roger & Red Mitchell)
Alone together / Just friends / I should care / I surrender dear / Blue blues / It's a wonderful world / Dear old Stockholm / Emily
CD _____ DRCD 168
Dragon / Apr '89 / Roots / Cadillac / Wellard / CM / ADA.

FIFTY FIFTY (Kellaway, Roger & Red Mitchell)
CD _____ CDNI 4014
Natasha / Apr '93 / Jazz Music / ADA / CM / Direct / Cadillac.

LIFE'S A TAKE (Kellaway, Roger & Red Mitchell)
If I were a bell / Mean to me / I have the feeling I've been here before / Life's a mistake / Lover man / It's a wonderful world / Take the 'A' train / Have you met Miss Jones
CD _____ CCD 4551
Concord Jazz / May '93 / New Note.

LIVE AT MAYBECK RECITAL HALL, VOL. 11
How deep is the ocean / I'm still in love with you / Love of my life / Close your eyes / New Orleans / My one and only love / Creole love call / I'm getting sentimental over you
CD _____ CCD 4470
Concord Jazz / Jul '91 / New Note.

PORTRAIT OF ROGER KELLAWAY
CD _____ FSRCD 147
Fresh Sound / Dec '90 / Jazz Music / Discovery.

Kellso, Jon Erik

CHAPTER 1
CD _____ ARCD 9125
Arbors Jazz / Nov '94 / Cadillac.

Kelly, Dave

BEST OF THE 80'S
CD _____ RPM 118
RPM / Oct '93 / Pinnacle.

DAVE KELLY BAND LIVE
CD _____ APCD 033
Appaloosa / '92 / ADA / Magnum Music Group.

MAKING WHOOPEE 1979-1982 (Kelly, Dave Band)
makin' whoopee / Hey baby / Ungrateful / Return to sender / Put your money where your mouth is / I'm into something good / Best part of breaking up / It feels right / Dawn surprise / You're gonna make me lonesome when you go / Two more bottles of wine / Red red wine / House lights / Don't cha hang up the phone / Can't win 'em all / Time after time / When I'm dead and gone / That's why / My heart in your hands / Worried man / Lights out
CD _____ RPM 118
RPM / Oct '93 / Pinnacle.

STANDING AT THE CROSSROADS (Kelly, Dave Band)
CD _____ INAK 8807
In Akustik / May '95 / Magnum Music Group.

WHEN THE BLUES COMES TO CALL
CD _____ HY 141CD
Hypertension / Jul '94 / Total/BMG / Direct / ADA.

Kelly, Ed

ED KELLY & PHAROAH SANDERS (Kelly, Ed & Pharoah Sanders)
Rainbow song / Newborn / You send me / Pippin / Answer me my love / You've got to have freedom / Song for the street people / West Oakland strutt / Lift every voice / Just the two of us / Well you needn't
CD _____ ECD 22056
Evidence / Jul '93 / Harmonia Mundi / ADA / Cadillac.

Kelly Family

OVER THE HUMP
Why why why / Father's nose / First time / Baby smile / Cover the road / She's crazy / Ares qui / Key to my heart / Roses of red / Once in a while / Break free / Angel / Wolf / Santa Maria
CD _____ CDEMC 3713
EMI / Jun '95 / EMI.

WOW
CD _____ CD 93909
Scratch / Apr '94 / BMG.

Kelly, Gene

GENE KELLY
CD _____ DVGH 7082
Deja Vu / May '95 / THE.

Kelly, Jack

1933-1939 (Kelly, Jack & His South Memphis Jug Band)
CD _____ BDCD 6005
Blues Document / '91 / Swift / Jazz Music / Hot Shot.

Kelly, James

TRADITIONAL MUSIC OF IRELAND
CD _____ SH 34014
Shanachie / Apr '95 / Koch / ADA / Greensleeves.

Kelly, Jane

PARTICULAR PEOPLE
CD _____ TWICD 851
Les Disques Du Crepuscule / Sep '88 / Discovery / ADA.

SOULS ON DELAY
CD _____ TWI 9012
Les Disques Du Crepuscule / '90 / Discovery / ADA.

Kelly, Jo Ann

WOMEN IN (E)MOTION FESTIVAL
CD _____ T&M 110
Tradition & Moderne / Dec '95 / Direct / ADA.

Kelly, John

IN THE UNIQUE WEST CLARE STYLE (Kelly, John & James)
CD _____ PTICD 1041
Outlet / Oct '95 / ADA / Duncans / CM / Ross / Direct / Koch.

IRISH TRADITIONAL FIDDLE MUSIC (Kelly, John & James)
CD _____ PTICD 1041
Pure Traditional Irish / Jul '95 / ADA.

Kelly, Kirk

GO MAN GO
CD _____ SST 223 CD
SST / Jan '89 / Plastic Head.

Kelly, Luke

COLLECTION, THE
CD _____ CHCD 1041
Chyme / Aug '94 / CM / ADA / Direct.

IRISH FAVOURITES VOL.1 (Kelly, Luke & Dubliners)
Raglan Road / Whiskey in the jar / Donegal Danny / Old triangle / Spancil Hill / Black velvet band / Town I loved so well / Dirty old town / McAlpine's fusiliers / Song for Ireland / All for me grog / Molly Malone
CD _____ CHCD 1033
Chyme / Apr '93 / CM / ADA / Direct.

IRISH FAVOURITES VOL.2 (Kelly, Luke & Dubliners)
Rare ould times / Fiddlers green / Biddy Mulligan / Avondale / Wild rover / Seven drunken nights / Finnegan's wake / Weila weila weila / Foggy dew / Lord of the dance / Johnston's motorcar / Farewell to Ireland
CD Set _____ CHCD 1034
Chyme / Apr '93 / CM / ADA / Direct.

LUKE KELLY ALBUM, THE (Kelly, Luke & Dubliners)
Button pusher / Scorn not his simplicity / Sun is burning / Blantyre explosion / For what died the sons of Roisin / Town I loved so well / Rare ould times / Dirty old town / Foggy dew / Farewell to Carlingford / Parcel o' rogues / Bunclody / dainty Davie / Unquiet grave
CD _____ CHCD 1016
Chyme / Jul '93 / CM / ADA / Direct.

LUKE'S LEGACY (Kelly, Luke & Dubliners)
Song for Ireland / Wild rover / School days over / Monto / Joe Hill / Auld triangle / Whiskey in the jar / Raglan road / Hand me down me bible / Free the people / Peat bog soldiers / Lifeboat Mona / Springhill disaster / Gartan mothers lullaby
CD _____ CHCD 1031
Chyme / May '89 / CM / ADA / Direct.

Kelly, Pat

BUTTERFLIES
CD _____ SONCD 0076
Sonic Sounds / May '95 / Jetstar.

CLASSIC HITS
CD _____ RNCD 2113
Rhino / Apr '95 / Jetstar / Magnum Music Group / THE.

PORTRAIT OF A LEGEND
CD _____ ANGCD 21
Angela / Oct '93 / Jetstar.

Kelly, Pat

HIGH HEELS
Jam box / Peaceful / Midnight Cafe / High heels / Senor si / Cappuccino chat / Be here with me tonight / Continuum / True spirit / Eye of the beholder
CD _____ CY 73764
Denon / Nov '89 / Conifer.

Kelly, Paul

COMEDY
CD _____ TVD 93343
Mushroom / Jan '95 / BMG / 3MV.

DEEPER WATER
CD _____ TVD 93340
Mushroom / Oct '95 / BMG / 3MV.

GONNA STICK & STAY
CD _____ BB 9523CD
Bullseye Blues / May '93 / Direct.

HIDDEN THINGS
CD _____ D 30748
Mushroom / Mar '95 / BMG / 3MV.

LIVE
CD _____ D 16061
Mushroom / Feb '95 / BMG / 3MV.

LOST
CD _____ D 19467
Mushroom / Mar '95 / BMG / 3MV.

WANTED MAN
Summer rain / God's hotel / She's rare / Just like animals / Love never runs out on time / Song from the 16th floor / Maybe this time for sure / Ball and chain / Still picking the same sore / Everybody wants to touch me / We've started a fire / Lately / Nuhkanya
CD _____ FIENDCD 758
Demon / Aug '94 / Pinnacle / ADA.

Kelly, Sandy

MUSICAL TRIBUTE TO PATSY CLINE, A
CD _____ KCD 347
K-Tel / Mar '94 / K-Tel.

Kelly, Sean

50 SCOTTISH CELILDH ACCORDION FAVOURITIES
CD _____ CDSCOT 050
Outlet / Oct '95 / ADA / Duncans / CM / Ross / Direct / Koch.

CELTIC TRANQUILITY (Kelly, Sean Ensemble)
CD _____ CHCD 1043
Chyme / Jan '95 / CM / ADA / Direct.

Kelly, Wynton

LAST TRIO SESSION
CD _____ DD 441
Delmark / Aug '94 / Hot Shot / ADA / CM / Direct / Cadillac.

TAKIN' CHARGE
CD _____ LEJAZZCD 16
Le Jazz / Jun '93 / Charly / Cadillac.

Kelsall, Phil

ALL I ASK OF YOU
Clarinet polka / All I ask of you (Taken from The Phantom Of The Opera.) / Waltzing in the clouds / Two hearts in waltz time / I just called to say I love you / Circus Renz / Embraceable you / I got plenty o' nuttin' / Llun? Banna / Queen? / They began / Music of the night / Rouge et noir / Come to Fiona's wedding / If I can help somebody / I only have eyes for you / My melancholy baby / Poor butterfly / Romeo / Don't say goodbye / Your eyes / Love is a many splendoured thing / I'm in the mood for love / I'll see you in my dreams
CD _____ GRACC 23
Grasmere / May '94 / Target/BMG / Savoy.

BENEATH THE LIGHTS OF HOME (At the Wurlitzer Organ Tower Ballroom, Blackpool)
Folies Bergere / Wedding of the painted doll / Stella by starlight / Nancy with the laughing face / Laura / In a party mood / Everything I have is yours / How are things in Glocca Morra / On a clear day / Black and white rag / Pennsylvania polka / Catari, catari / Come back to Sorrento / Santa Lucia / O Maria Mari / Funiculi, funicula / Let's face the music and dance / Top hat, white tie and tails / You were never lovelier / Cheek to cheek / Wistful waltz / Dicky bird hop / Ave Maria / Canadian capers / Ain't we got fun / Good morning / Everything's in rhythm with my heart / Roses of Picardy / Beneath the lights of home / Whispering grass / Trolley song
CD _____ PWK 109
Carlton Home Entertainment / May '89 / Carlton Home Entertainment.

BLACKPOOL MAGIC
Entry of the gladiators / Sanctuary of the heart / Chattanooga choo choo / You'll never know / September in the rain / Jeepers creepers / Shadows on the Seine / Russian flag / For you alone / Shuffle off to Buffalo / About a quarter to nine / Shadow waltz / Dames, young and healthy / Lullaby of Broadway / 42nd Street / Coronation scot / Dubarry waltz / Dardanella / Pied Piper / Chanson d'amour / Old fashioned way / Can't smile without you / Bless this house / Rag doll / Paradise for two / My gal's a yorkshire gal / In the twi-twi-twilight / In the shade of the old apple tree / Wonderful guy / My favourite things / Wonderful, wonderful day
CD _____ GRCD 43
Grasmere / '91 / Target/BMG / Savoy.

BLUE VELVET
Delicado / I dreamed a dream / Doll dance / Drigo's seranade / Chihuahua / Wind beneath my wings / Easy winners / Bluebells polka / Voices of spring / Flea market / Music from across the way / In the shadows / Meditation from Thais / Tambourin / Blue velvet / Barcarolle / I'm getting sentimental over you / I don't want to walk without you / Goodnight sweetheart / Masquerade
CD _____ GRCD 47
Grasmere / '92 / Target/BMG / Savoy.

CENTENARY SPECIAL
CD _____ SOW 517
Sound Waves / Jul '94 / Target/BMG.

COME DANCING AT THE TOWER BALLROOM
You're driving me crazy / I wonder where my baby is tonight / Lulu's back in town / Doin' the raccoon / Anniversary waltz / When I grow too old to dream / Tammy / Charmaine / Am I blue / September song / Blue moon / Sweet and lovely / Whatever Lola wants (Lola gets) / Adios muchachos / Tower ballroom tango / Should I / Sweet and gentle / Kiss me honey, honey kiss me / Greey eyes / Sway / More than ever / Magic is the moonlight / Pierrette / Mademoiselle from Armentieres / Man who broke the bank at Monte Carlo / Wot'cher (Knocked 'em in the Old Kent Road) / Constantinople / I'm Henery the Eighth (I am) / Down forget-me-not Lane / I leave my heart in an english garden / Try a little tenderness / Moonlight bay / Chalk farm to Camberwell Green / Are we to part like this, Bill / Let me call you sweetheart / Bird in a gilded cage / Kind regards / Tiddley on pom / Morning promenade / Cindy swing / Dear hearts and gentle people / Back in your own backyard / Nice people / What can I say after I say I'm sorry / Linger awhile
CD _____ GRCD 50
Grasmere / '92 / Target/BMG / Savoy.

CONGRATULATIONS
CD _____ GRCD 62
Grasmere / Mar '94 / Target/BMG / Savoy.

I DO LIKE TO BE BESIDE THE SEASIDE
Oh I do like to be beside the seaside / Darling buds of May / Nights of gladness / Amazing grace / South Rampart street parade / At last / Goodbye blues / He loves and she loves / How long has this been going on / Love is here to stay / Bye bye blues / Farewell blues / Soon / They all laughed / Liza / Blackpool belle / Friends for life (Amigos para siempre) / Crystal chandeliers / Crazy / Blanket on the ground / Colonel Bogey / Sprinkling tam / Parade of the tin soldiers / Holy city / Dance of comedians
CD _____ GRCD 58
Grasmere / Jun '93 / Target/BMG / Savoy.

LOVE CHANGES EVERYTHING
Heyken's first serenade / Morgens um sieben / Happy talk / I enjoy being a girl / Hello, young lovers / Love changes everything / Roses from the South / True love / Let's do it / Wunderbar / Just one of those things / Choo rinon samba / Triplle / Petite waltz / Plink plank plunk / Tango in D (Albeniz) / Exactly like you / Way down yonder in New Orleans / T'aint what you do / Braes of Strathnaver / Two sleepy people / For all we know / World is waiting for the sunrise / Romeo (CD only.) / Don't say goodbye (CD only.) / Your eyes (CD only.) / Rouge et noir (CD only.)
CD _____ GRCD 36
Grasmere / Sep '89 / Target/BMG / Savoy.

MEMORIES ARE MADE OF THIS
CD _____ GRCD 67
Grasmere / Apr '95 / Target/BMG / Savoy.

PHIL KELSALL AT THE YAMAHA FX20
hors d'oeuvres / I won't dance / Stepping out with my baby / Love's last word is spoken / Shadow waltz / Emmeline / Innamorata / If I didn't care / Body and soul / Unchained melody / Romance in A minor / Perhaps, perhaps, perhaps / Garden in Granada / More I see you / Amor / Cocktails for two / Tangerine / Carioca / South American way / It had better be tonight / Boogie woogie bugle boy from Company B / Dolores / Every little while / I don't want to set the world on fire / J'Attendrai / Chapel in the moonlight / Soldiers in the park / Soldiers of the Queen / Take me back to dear old blighty / Hold your hand out, naughty boy / Blame it on the Bossa Nova / Meditation / I was never kissed before / Someday my Prince will come / Say you will not forget / Love's dream after the ball / Tell me I'm forgiven / Cafe in Vienna / Whispering tango / Birth of the blues / Back home in Tennessee / Nevertheless / Music maestro please / We're gonna hang out the washing on the Siegfried Line / I've got sixpence / Five minutes more / Rolling around the world / Walking the floor / Please don't talk about me when I'm gone
CD _____ GRCD 60
Grasmere / Oct '93 / Target/BMG / Savoy.

PHIL KELSALL SELECTION
Shuffle off to Buffalo / About a Quarter to Nine / Shadow waltz / Dames / Coronation Scot / Catani, catari / Come back to Sorrento / Santa Lucia / Oh Maria Mari, Funiculi, Funicula / Pretty little black eyed Susie / Singin' the blues / Chicka boom / Dance of the comedians / You're driving me crazy / I wonder where my baby is tonight / Pink Lady / Paradise / Wyoming lullaby / Put me amongst the girls / Jolly good company beside the sea / When the guards are on parade / Tower Ballroom tango / Dancing with tears in my eyes / Diane / I love the moon / Garden in the rain / Rose of Washington Square / I'll string along with you / Stars fell on Alabama / Make mine love / There's no other love / El choclo / Oh Rosalita / La cumparsita / Circus Renz / My song of love / Two hearts in waltz time / Waltzing in the clouds / Choo choo samba / Braes of Strathnaver / Flea market / I dreamed a dream / Phantom of the Opera
CD _____ GROSCD 1
Grasmere / Oct '93 / Target/BMG / Savoy.

SEQUENCE OF DANCING FAVOURITES
I can't give you anything but love / Chicago / Hello Dolly / After you've gone / Dancing with tears in my eyes / Diane / I love the moon / Memories of you / Stars fell on Alabama / Make mine love / There's no other love / El choclo / Oh Rosalita / How wonderful to know / Always in my heart / Indian summer / A-you're adorable / One / Frenesi / Take the 'A' train / You're sixteen / Tower ballroom jive / That's my weekness now / Moonstruck / If I had a talking picture of you / Put me amongst the girls / Jolly good company beside the sea / When the guards are on parade / P.s. I love you / Louise / Polka dots and moonbeams / Meet me tonight in Dreamland / Three o'clock in the morning / Eton boating song / If I had my way / Glad rag doll / Broken doll / Goodbye-ee / In the good old summertime / Tulips from Amsterdam / By the side of the Zuyder Zee / Mother Machree / Keep young and beautiful / Varsity drag / Black bottom / Charleston
CD _____ GRCD 39
Grasmere / May '90 / Target/BMG / Savoy.

SOME ENCHANTED EVENING
Phantom of the opera / Some enchanted evening / Thoroughly modern Millie / No no Nanette / Hey there / Can't help lovin' dat man / And this is my beloved / I've got the sun in the morning and the moon at night / I whistle a happy tune / Best of times / I don't know how to love him / March of the siamese children / Out of my dreams / Girl that I marry / Waltz at Maxim's / If I loved you / Wouldn't it be loverly / Spring, spring, spring / Mame / My dream will do / Leap year waltz / Highwayman love / Fold your wings / One flower grows alone in your garden / One alone / Indian love call / Wonderful day like today / There is nothin' like a dame / Do re mi / I could have danced all night / Oklahoma
CD _____ GRCD 54
Grasmere / Oct '92 / Target/BMG / Savoy.

SWINGING SLEIGH BELLS
CD _____ GRCD 70
Grasmere / Oct '93 / Target/BMG / Savoy.

THANK YOU FOR THE MUSIC
Waterloo / Hasta Manana / Money, money, money / Cavatina / As time goes by / Thanks for the memory / S-H-I-N-E / God bless our love / Floral dance / Isn't it a pity? / Somewhere my love / Bridge too far / All creatures great and small / Pass me by / Stein song / Hey look me over / Around the world / Kiss me again / Dream lover / Whispering / Change partners / Five foot two, eyes of blue / Who pays the ferryman / Enemy at the door / Here, there and everywhere / When I'm sixty four / All my loving / Sailing / Casatschok / Rasputin / Midnight in Moscow / Devil's gallop / World of sport march / Out of the blue / Match of the day / Agadoo / Under the linden tree / Out of nowhere / Only you / When the day is done / Cha Cha Cha / In a little Spanish town / Want to be happy, I / Orange coloured sky / Home (when shadows fall) / She's funny that way / By a waterfall / Irish lullaby / How can you buy Killarney / Believe me, if all those endearing young charms / Everything stops for tea / Underneath the arches / Ragtime cowboy Joe / Crazy people / Sweet Sue, just you / If you knew Susie like I know Susie / Ma, he's making eyes at me / Scotch broth / Hundred pipers / Campbells are coming / Fernando / Dancing queen / Thank you for the music
CD Set _____ CDDL 1206
Music For Pleasure / May '91 / EMI.

TIME FOR DANCING
Mr. Sandman / Avalon / Crazy rhythm / Dancing with tears in my eyes / Diane / Love the moon / Memories of you / Stars fell on Alabama / Make mine love / Bewitched, bothered and bewildered / Love in bloom / Someone to watch over me / Here's that rainy day / La golondrina / Cherry pink and apple blossom white / Por favor / Skater's waltz / Spanish gypsy dance / Nagasaki / Little red monkey / One the prom prom promenade / Consider yourself / Garden in the rain / Rose of Washington Square / I'll string along with you / Girl form Ipanema / Destination love / There's no other love / El choclo / Oh Rosalita / La cumparsita / Pink Lady / Paradise / Wyoming lullaby / Little white lies / Happy feet / It's just the time for dancing / If I had my way / Glad rag doll / Broken doll / Goodbye-ee / Blees'em all / Band played on / Ash grove / Daisy bell / Tip toe through the tulips / Don't know why (I just do) / My Mammy / Scotch mist
CD _____ PWKS 4210
Carlton Home Entertainment / Aug '94 / Carlton Home Entertainment.

Keltz

PRINCE OF PEACE
Gate / Siyah Chal / Mountains of Sulaymaniyyih / Exile / Garden of Ridvan / Reel of revelation / Release jig / Ascension
CD _____ IRCD 024
Iona / Jan '94 / ADA / Direct / Duncans.

Kelvynator

REFUNKANATION
CD _____ EMY 1302
Enemy / Mar '92 / Grapevine.

Kemp, Gary

LITTLE BRUISES
Standing in love (the still point) / Brother heart / Inexperienced man / Wasted / Little bruises / Ophelia drowning / She said / Shadowman / These are the days (born under twins) / My lady soul
CD _____ 4795702
Columbia / Oct '95 / Sony.

Kemp, Hal

HAL KEMP & ORCHESTRA 1934-36
CD _____ CCD 25
Circle / Apr '94 / Jazz Music / Swift / Wellard.

Kemp, Tara

TARA KEMP
Prologue / Hold you tight / Be my lover / Too much / One love / Tara by the way / Piece of my heart / Together / Way you make me feel / Something to groove to / Monday love / Epilogue
CD _____ 7599244082
WEA / May '91 / Warner Music.

Kemperle, Bagad

KEJADENN
CD _____ Y225023
Silex / Jun '93 / ADA.

Kendrick, Graham

IS ANYONE THIRSTY
Is anyone thirsty / Psalm 126 / Wake up o sleeper / How good and how pleasant / I was made for this / Knowing you / For this I have Jesus / Let me fill the room / Day of his power / Declare his glory
CD _____ ALD 035
Alliance Music / Sep '95 / EMI.

LAMB OF GOD
Great is the Lord / Rejoice / Let praise arise / Sing for joy in the Lord / His love endures forever / Lord have mercy / Lamb of God / My heart overflows / Think about His love / Lord thy God / Steadfast love of the Lord / Thou art worthy / Song for the nations
CD _____ HMD 000
Nelson Word / Jan '88 / Nelson Word.

Kendrick, Matt

COMPOSITE
CD _____ ICH 1166CD
Ichiban / May '94 / Koch.

Kendrick, Rodney

DANCE, WORLD, DANCE
CD _____ 521937-2
Verve / Oct '94 / PolyGram.

SECRETS OF RODNEY KENDRICK, THE
CD _____ 517558-2
Verve / Jul '93 / PolyGram.

Kenia

KENIA
Introducing the Band / E hora / Distant horizon / Good morning heartache / Estamos aj / What are you looking for / Girl from Ipanema / Aqui oh and e (it is) / Over the rainbow
CD _____ 66050006
Bellaphon / Jul '93 / New Note.

LOVE LIVES ON
CD _____ CY 77400
Denon / Jun '91 / Conifer.

WHAT YOU'RE LOOKING FOR
Once I was / Flor de lis / Answer is on the road / Gaboo / What you're looking for / If not today / Over the rainbow / Brazillian touch / I know / Let me dance for you / Fruta boa

CD _____ **CY 76363**
Denon / Sep '90 / Conifer.

Kenkulian, Hrant

UDI HRANT KENKILIAN
CD _____ **CD 4265**
Traditional Crossroads / Dec '94 / CM /
Direct.

Kennedy, Charlie

**CRAZY RHYTHMS (Kennedy, Charlie &
Charlie Ventura)**
I'll see you in my dreams / Whispering /
Crazy rhythm / I can't give you anything but
love / I can't get started (with you) / Dark
eyes / Charlie comes on / Ever so thought-
ful / Big deal / Jackpot
CD _____ **SV 0195**
Savoy Jazz / Nov '92 / Conifer / ADA.

Kennedy, Fiona

MAIDEN IN HEAVEN
CD _____ **CD 001**
Colin Campbell / Nov '95 / Duncans.

Kennedy, Frankie

ALTAN (Kennedy, Frankie & Mairead)
Highlandman / An Seanchaileach Gallda /
Ta mo Chleamhnas a Dheanamh / Cat that
ate the candle / Ceol A'Phiobaire / Tommy
Peoploe's loch Altan / Danny Meehan's /
Rogha an Ghabha / Sunset / Thug me
Ruide / Humours of whiskey / Jimmy Lyon's
Les / Citi na cumann / Con Cassidy's high-
land reel
CD _____ **GLCD 1078**
Green Linnet / Apr '93 / Roots / CM / Direct
/ ADA.

Kennedy, Joan

CANDLE IN THE WIND
CD _____ **322543**
Koch International / Dec '95 / Koch.

HIGHER GROUND
CD _____ **341072**
Koch International / Dec '95 / Koch.

Kennedy, Pete

**RIVER OF FALLEN STARS (Kennedy,
Pete & Maura)**
CD _____ **GLCD 2116**
Green Linnet / Feb '95 / Roots / CM /
Direct / ADA.

Kennedy, Ray

IRISH BALLADS LIVE
CD _____ **KVCD 003**
Irish / Oct '95 / Target/BMG.

IRISH SING-A-LONG LIVE, AN
CD _____ **KVCD 001**
Irish / Oct '95 / Target/BMG.

Kennedy, Ronnie

THOSE WERE THE DAYS
Those were the days / Dingle regatta / Irish
medley / Whistling Rufus / Alpine slopes/
Jacqueline waltz / Country favourites med-
ley / Looking for a partner / Lara's theme /
Scottish medley / Birdie song / Cuckoo
waltz / Bluebell polka / Edelweiss
CD _____ **RITZCD 514**
Ritz / '91 / Pinnacle.

Kennedy, Ross

**TWISTED SINGERS (Kennedy, Ross &
Archie McAllister)**
CD _____ **CDLDL 1218**
Lochshore / Oct '94 / ADA / Direct /
Duncans.

Kennel, Hans

MYTHA
CD _____ **ARTCD 6110**
Hat Art / Aug '92 / Harmonia Mundi / ADA
/ Cadillac.

MYTHAHORNS 2
CD _____ **ARTCD 6151**
Hat Art / Apr '95 / Harmonia Mundi / ADA
/ Cadillac.

Kenney, Beverly

COME SWING WITH ME
CD _____ **FSCD 560**
Fresh Sound / Feb '88 / Jazz Music /
Discovery.

Kenny & The Kasuals

**THINGS GETTING BETTER/NOTHING
BETTER TO DO**
CD _____ **EVA 642390B39**
EVA / Nov '94 / Direct / ADA.

Kenny G.

BREATHLESS
Joy of life / Forever in love / In the rain /
Sentimental / By the time this night is over
(With Peabo Bryson.) / End on the night /
Morning / Even if my heart would break

(With Aaron Neville.) / G bop / Sister Rose
/ Year ago / Homeland / Natural ride / Wed-
ding song / Alone
CD _____ **07822186462**
Arista / Mar '93 / BMG.

G FORCE
Hi, how ya doin' / I've been missing you /
Tribeca / G force / Do me right / I wanna
be yours / Sunset at noon / Help yourself
to my love
CD _____ **259059**
Arista / May '88 / BMG.

GRAVITY
Love on the rise / One man's poison (an-
other man's sweetness) / Where do we take
it (from here) / One night stand / Japan /
Sax attack / Virgin island / Gravity / Last
night of the year
CD _____ **7432116164-2**
Arista / Feb '94 / BMG.

KENNY G.
Mercy mercy mercy / Here we are / Stop
and go / I can't tell you why / Shuffle / Tell
me / Find a way / Crystal mountain / Come
close
CD _____ **259337**
Arista / Sep '95 / BMG.

MIRACLES - THE HOLIDAY ALBUM
Winter wonderland / White christmas / Have
yourself a merry little christmas / Christmas
song / Silent night / Brahms lullaby / Greensleeves / Miracles / Away in a manger /
Chanukah song / Little drummer boy / Silver
bells / Spring breeze
CD _____ **07822187672**
Arista / Oct '95 / BMG.

MONTAGE
Songbird / I can't tell you why / Tribeca /
Virgin island / I've been missing you / Uncle
Al / What does it take (to win your love) /
Silhouette / Midnight motion / Against doc-
tor's orders / Hi, how ya doin' / Sade / Go-
ing home / We've saved the best for last
CD _____ **260621**
Arista / Apr '90 / BMG.

Kenny, Gerard

EVENING WITH GERARD KENNY, AN
CD _____ **ACLCD 1005**
Westmoor / Jun '95 / Target/BMG.

**PLAY ME SOME PORTER PLEASE
(Kenny, Gerard & Royal Philharmonic
Orchestra)**
Play me some Porter please / Anything
goes / Night and day / Miss Otis regrets /
True love / Begin the beguine / From this
moment on / Every time we say goodbye /
So in love / I've got you under my skin
CD _____ **CDWM 106**
Westmoor / May '92 / Target/BMG.

Kenso

KENSO
CD _____ **ARC 1003**
Arc / Jan '96 / Harmonia Mundi.

Kent, Willie

AIN'T IT NICE
CD _____ **DD 653**
Delmark / Jun '89 / Hot Shot / ADA / CM /
Direct / Cadillac.

TOO HURT TO CRY
CD _____ **DD 667**
Delmark / May '94 / Hot Shot / ADA / CM
/ Direct / Cadillac.

Kenton, Stan

18 ORIGINAL BIG BAND RECORDINGS
CD _____ **HCD 407**
Hindsight / Sep '92 / Target/BMG / Jazz
Music.

**1952 - 1956 INTERMISSION RIFF
(Kenton, Stan Orchestra)**
CD _____ **CD 53109**
Giants Of Jazz / Jun '92 / Target/BMG /
Cadillac.

**7.5 ON THE RICHTER SCALE (Kenton,
Stan Orchestra)**
Live and let die / Body and soul / Down and
dirty / Country cousin / Two thousand /
2000 - Zarathustrevisited / It's not easy
bein' green / Speak softly love
CD _____ **STD 1070**
GNP Crescendo / May '93 / Silva Screen.

ARTISTRY IN RHYTHM
CD _____ **JHR 73540**
Jazz Hour / May '93 / Target/BMG / Jazz
Music / Cadillac.

AT FOUNTAIN STREET CHURCH VOL.1
CD _____ **DSTS 1014**
Status / Oct '95 / Jazz Music / Wellard /
Harmonia Mundi.

AT FOUNTAIN STREET CHURCH VOL.2
CD _____ **DSTS 1016**
Status / Oct '95 / Jazz Music / Wellard /
Harmonia Mundi.

**AT MARCH FIELD AIR FORCE BASE,
CALIFORNIA DECEMBER 1959
(Previously Unissued Recordings)
(Kenton, Stan Orchestra)**
Street of dreams / I'm glad there is you /
Young and foolish / Where or when / How
deep is the ocean / My heart stood still / All
of you / Early Autumn / Chocolate caliente
/ Night we called it a day / You better go
now / They didn't believe me / Twilight riff
/ Take the 'A' train / September song/Star-
dust / Eager beaver/Dynaflow/Jump for
Joe/Artistry in rhythm
CD _____ **DSTS 1011**
Status / May '95 / Jazz Music / Wellard /
Harmonia Mundi.

AT THE RENDEZVOUS VOL. 1
My old flame / Out of this world / Time on
my hands / Tequila / I hear music / Cuban
mumble / Artistry in rhythm / Jump for Joe
/ Kingfish / Eager beaver / Glad to be
unhappy
CD _____ **STATUSCD 102**
Status / Mar '90 / Cadillac.

AT THE RENDEZVOUS VOL.2
Beyond the blue horizon / I concentrate on
you / Begin the beguine / Everything hap-
pens to me / Get out of town / Nice work if
you can get it / Old devil moon / Take the
'A' train / I get along without you very well
/ When Sunny gets blue / Nightingale / They
didn't believe me / Street of dreams / Wind
/ I should care / I remember you
CD _____ **STATUSCD 108**
Status / Nov '90 / Cadillac.

BEST OF STAN KENTON
Dixie Live / Mar '95 / Magnum Music
Group.
CD _____ **DLCD 4012**

BEST OF STAN KENTON, THE
Artistry in rhythm / Eager beaver / Artistry
jumps / Painted rhythm / Intermission riff /
Collaboration / Lover / Unison riff / Peanut
vendor / Interlude / Love for sale / Laura /
Twelve degrees north / Invention for guitar
and trumpet / Stompin' at the Savoy / La
suerte de los tontos (fortune of fools) / Waltz
of prophets / Malageuna
CD _____ **CDP 8315042**
Capitol Jazz / Apr '95 / EMI.

**BIRTHDAY IN BRITAIN (Kenton, Stan
Orchestra)**
Happy birthday to you / Daily dance / Street
of dreams / Of space and time / For better
and for Worseter / No harmful side effects
/ Ambivalence / Blues between and betwixt
CD _____ **STD 1065**
GNP Crescendo / May '93 / Silva Screen.

**BROADCAST TRANSCRIPTIONS 1941-
45**
Music & Arts / Sep '95 / Harmonia Mundi
/ Cadillac.
CD _____ **CD 883**

CLASSICS 1940-44
Classics / Nov '95 / Discovery / Jazz
Music.
CD _____ **CLASSICS 848**

**CONCERT IN MINIATURE ENCORES
1952-53**
Natasha / Oct '93 / Jazz Music / ADA /
CM / Direct / Cadillac.
CD _____ **N 14017**

EARLY CONCEPTS
Le Jazz / Jan '96 / Charly / Cadillac.
CD _____ **LEJAZZCD 54**

**FESTIVAL OF MODERN AMERICAN
JAZZ**
Opening / Theme of four valves / Saxonia /
Sam meets the Mambo / Cuba jazz /
Sweets / That old black magic / Pennies
from heaven / Improvisation / Fearless
Finlay
CD _____ **STATUSCD 101**
Status / Mar '90 / Cadillac.

**FIRE, FURY AND FUN (Kenton, Stan
Orchestra & The Four Freshmen)**
CD _____ **STD 1073**
GNP Crescendo / May '93 / Silva Screen.

FOUR FRESHMEN, THE
CD _____ **STD 1059**
GNP Crescendo / May '93 / Silva Screen.

JOURNEY INTO CAPRICORN
CD _____ **STD 1077**
GNP Crescendo / May '93 / Silva Screen.

KENTON '76
Time for a change / Send in the clowns /
Tiburon / My funny valentine / Decoupage /
Smith named Greg / Samba de naps
CD _____ **STD 1076**
GNP Crescendo / May '93 / Silva Screen.

**LIVE AT BARSTOW 1960 (Kenton, Stan
Orchestra)**
CD _____ **DSTS 1001**
Status / May '94 / Jazz Music / Wellard /
Harmonia Mundi.

LIVE AT BRIGHAM UNIVERSITY
CD _____ **STD 1039**
GNP Crescendo / May '93 / Silva Screen.

**LIVE AT BUTLER UNIVERSITY (Kenton,
Stan Orchestra & The Four Freshmen)**
CD _____ **STD 1058**
GNP Crescendo / May '93 / Silva Screen.

**LIVE AT CARTHAGE COLLEGE VOL.1
(Kenton, Stan Orchestra)**
CD _____ **DAWE 69**
Magic / May '94 / Jazz Music / Swift /
Wellard / Cadillac / Harmonia Mundi.

**LIVE AT CARTHAGE COLLEGE VOL.2
(Kenton, Stan Orchestra)**
Here's that rainy day / 2002 - Zarathustrev-
isited / Macarthur park / Peanut vendor /
Street of dreams / Malaguena / Artistry in
rhythm / Happy birthday to you / Take the
'A' train
CD _____ **DAWE 70**
Magic / Jun '94 / Jazz Music / Swift / Wel-
lard / Cadillac / Harmonia Mundi.

LIVE AT PALO ALTO 1955
CD _____ **STATUSCD 112**
Status / '92 / Cadillac.

LIVE AT REDLANDS UNIVERSITY
Here's that rainy day / MacArthur Park / Mi-
nor booze / Didn't we / Terry talk / Tico-tico
/ Granada / Chia-pas / More peanut vendor
/ Artistry in rhythm / Bon homme Richard /
Tiare / Hey Jude
CD _____ **STD 1015**
GNP Crescendo / May '93 / Silva Screen.

LIVE AT THE LONDON HILTON 1973
CD _____ **DSTS 1003**
Status / '94 / Jazz Music / Wellard /
Harmonia Mundi.

**LIVE AT THE MACUMBA CLUB - PART
2**
El Congo Valiente / Fuego Cubano / Big
chase / My funny valentine / Opener / I concentrate on you / I remember you / Harlem
nocturne / Between the Devil and the deep
blue sea / Swing house / Love for sale /
Royal blue / Artistry in rhythm
CD _____ **DAWE 53**
Magic / Nov '91 / Jazz Music / Swift / Wellard / Cadillac / Harmonia Mundi.

**LIVE AT THE MACUMBA CLUB - SAN
FRANCISCO 1956**
Walking shoes / Autumn nocturne / Artistry
in rhythm / Winter in Madrid / My old flame
/ La suerte de los tontos (Fortune of fools)
/ I concentrate on you / Theme on variations
/ Young blood / Collaboration / Stella by
starlight / Cherokee / Intermission riff /
Laura / Stompin' at the Savoy / Out of
nowhere
CD _____ **DAWE 50**
Magic / '91 / Jazz Music / Swift / Wellard /
Cadillac / Harmonia Mundi.

**LIVE AT THE SUNSET RIDGE CLUB
1976**
CD _____ **DAWE 59**
Magic / Jazz Music / Swift / Wellard /
Cadillac / Harmonia Mundi.

**LIVE AT THE SUNSET RIDGE CLUB
1976 - PART 2**
CD _____ **DAWE 61**
Magic / Jazz Music / Swift / Wellard /
Wellard / Cadillac / Harmonia Mundi.

LIVE IN 1951
CD _____ **EBCD 21052**
Flyright / Feb '94 / Hot Shot / Wellard /
Jazz Music / CM.

LIVE IN COLOGNE 1976, VOL. 1
CD _____ **DAWE 64**
Magic / Jul '93 / Jazz Music / Swift /
Wellard / Cadillac / Harmonia Mundi.

LIVE IN COLOGNE 1976, VOL. 2
CD _____ **DAWE 65**
Magic / Jul '93 / Jazz Music / Swift /
Wellard / Cadillac / Harmonia Mundi.

LIVE IN LONDON: STAN KENTON (1972)
CD _____ **8204662**
London / Aug '87 / PolyGram.

LIVE, SALT LAKE CITY VOL. 1
CD _____ **DAWE 56**
Magic / Feb '94 / Jazz Music / Swift /
Wellard / Cadillac / Harmonia Mundi.

LIVE, SALT LAKE CITY VOL. 2
CD _____ **DAWE 57**
Magic / Nov '92 / Jazz Music / Swift /
Wellard / Cadillac / Harmonia Mundi.

LIVE, SALT LAKE CITY VOL. 3
CD _____ **DAWE 58**
Magic / Nov '92 / Jazz Music / Swift /
Wellard / Cadillac / Harmonia Mundi.

LONDON HILTON 1973 VOL. 2
CD _____ **DSTS 1005**
Status / Dec '94 / Jazz Music / Wellard /
Harmonia Mundi.

**MELLOPHONIUM MAGIC 1962 (Kenton,
Stan Orchestra & The Four Freshmen)**
All the things you are / Suddenly it's Spring
/ Reuben's blues / Tuxedo blues / Tenderly
/ Foggy day / East of the sun and west of
the moon / You stepped out of a dream /
Take me in your arms / Saga of the blues
CD _____ **STATUSCD 103**
Status / Mar '90 / Cadillac.

MELLOPHONIUM MOODS 1962
Lullaby of Birdland / Reuben's blues / Like
someone in love / Cha cha sombrero / Misty
/ Easy to love / Caress the sea / Exit stage
left / Blues story / Angel eyes / Blue oint-

ment / How long has this been going on / Dragonwyck / Night at the gold nugget / Fitz
CD _____ **STATUSCD 106**
Status / Nov '90 / Cadillac.

MORE MELLOPHONIUM MOODS
Fly me to the moon / Foggy day / Misty / You stepped out of a dream / Reuben's blues / Magic moment / Blues story / Easy to love / Warm blue stream / Lot of lovin 'to do / My one and only love / Maria / Time after time / Love walked in / Like someone in love / Lazer beaver/Opus in chartreuse/ Dynaflow/Jump for Joe / Java junction/Tea for two / Artistry in rhythm
CD _____ **DSTS 1010**
Status / Apr '95 / Jazz Music / Wellard / Harmonia Mundi.

NEW CONCEPTS OF ARTISTRY IN RHYTHM (Kenton, Stan Orchestra)
Twenty three degrees north - eighty two degrees west / Portrait of a count / Invention for guitar and trumpet / My lady / Young blood / Frank speaking / Prologue (this is an orchestra) / Improvisation / Taboo (CD only.) / Lonesome train (CD only.) / Swing house (CD only.) / You go to my head (CD only.)
CD _____ **CZ 299**
Pacific Jazz / Apr '90 / EMI.

ONE NIGHT STAND (Kenton, Stan Orchestra)
CD _____ **DAWE 66**
Magic / Dec '93 / Jazz Music / Swift / Wellard / Cadillac / Harmonia Mundi.

OPUS IN PASTELS
CD _____ **CD 56023**
Jazz Roots / Aug '94 / Target/BMG.

PLAYS BOB GRAETTINGER CITY OF GLASS
Thermopylae / Everything happens to me / Incident in jazz / House of strings / Horn / City of glass (first movements part 1 to 4) / Orchestra / Trumpet / You got to my head / Cello / Modern opus / Reflections / Dance before the mirror / Entrance into the city
CD _____ **CDP 8320842**
Capitol Jazz / Aug '95 / EMI.

RARE RECORDINGS
CD _____ **15725**
Laserlight / Sep '92 / Target/BMG.

RED HILL INN PENNSAUKEN NEW JERSEY (1959)
Home journey / Laura / Frenesi / Mexican jumping bean / Lazy afternoon / Street scene / Bernie's tune / Lush life / Night in Tunisia / Thrill is gone / Obu / Opus in pastels
CD _____ **STATUSCD 104**
Status / Mar '90 / Cadillac.

RENDEZVOUS OF STANDARDS AND CLASSICS (A Collection Of Five Albums 2CD/MC Set)
Artistry in rhythm / Eager beaver / Collaboration / Peanut vendor / Intermission riff / Concerto to end all concertos / Artistry jumps / Sophisticated lady / Begin the beguine / Lover man / Pennies from heaven / Over the rainbow / Fascinating rhythm / There's a small hotel / Shadow waltz / Tampico / Artistry in boogie / Southern scandal / Machito / Her tears flowed like wine / Minor riff / Across the valley from the Alamo / Unison riff / April in Paris / How high the moon / Crazy rhythm / I got it bad and that ain't good / You and the night and the music / Under a blanket of blue / I've got you under my skin / Autumn in New York / With the wind and rain in your hair / Memories of you / These things you left me / Two shades of autumn / They didn't believe me / Walkin' by the river / High on a windy hill / Love letters / I get along without you very well / Desiderata / This is no laughing matters / I see your face before me
CD Set _____ **CDDL 1293**
Music For Pleasure / Jun '95 / EMI.

STAN KENTON
CD _____ **22714**
Music / Jul '95 / Target/BMG.

STAN KENTON & HIS INNOVATIONS ORCHESTRA (Kenton, Stan Orchestra)
Spirals / Ennui / In Veradero / Shelly Manne / Conte Candoli / Art Pepper / Improvisation / Love for sale / Bob Cooper / Reflections
CD _____ **15770**
Laserlight / May '94 / Target/BMG.

STAN KENTON AND HIS ORCHESTRA (Kenton, Stan Orchestra)
CD _____ **90 108 2**
Jazz Archives / Aug '91 / Jazz Music / Discovery / Cadillac.

STAN KENTON AND ORCHESTRA LIVE IN BILOXI (Kenton, Stan Orchestra & The Four Freshmen)
Lasuerte de los tontos / I concentrate on you / Lullaby of Broadway / Nearness of you / Kingfish / Early Autumn / Love for sale / My old flame / Yesterdays / Out of nowhere / Night we called it a day / Everything happens to me / There will never be another you / So in love / With the wind and rain in your hair / Big chase
CD _____ **DAWE 32**
Magic / Apr '89 / Jazz Music / Swift / Wellard / Cadillac / Harmonia Mundi.

STAN KENTON IN HI FI
Artistry jumps / Interlude / Intermission riff / Minor riff / Collaboration / Painted rhythm / Southern scandal / Peanut vendor / Eager Beaver / Concerto to end all concertos / Artistry in boogie / Lover / Unison riff / Opus in pastels (CD only) / Machito (CD only) / Artistry in rhythm (CD only) / Minor riff (alt. take)
CD _____ **CZ 511**
Capitol / Jul '92 / EMI.

STAN KENTON LIVE
CD _____ **NI 4017**
Natasha / May '93 / Jazz Music / ADA / CM / Direct / Cadillac.

STAN KENTON PLAYS CHICAGO (Kenton, Stan Orchestra & The Four Freshmen)
CD _____ **STD 1072**
GNP Crescendo / May '93 / Silva Screen.

STREET OF DREAMS (Kenton, Stan Orchestra & The Four Freshmen)
Send in the clowns / Rhapsody in blue / Street of dreams / Body and soul / Tiare / Too shy to say / My funny valentine
CD _____ **STD 1079**
GNP Crescendo / Jun '95 / Silva Screen.

UKIAH, 1959
How deep is the ocean / Walking shoes / Nearness of you / Lullaby of Broadway / Where or when / End of a love affair / Artistry in rhythm / Jump for Joe / Tenderley
CD _____ **STATUSCD 109**
Status / Jan '91 / Cadillac.

UNCOLLECTED 1941 VOLUME.2, THE
Congo clambako / Arkansas traveller / Shuffling the chords / Take sixteen / Opus in pastels / Reed rapture / Etude for saxophones / Tribute to flatted fifth / Quit your show / Underneath the stars / Let her go / Too soon / Hold back the dawn / Low bridge / Popocatepeil / Blue falre
CD _____ **HCD 124**
Hindsight / Apr '95 / Target/BMG / Jazz Music.

WEST SIDE STORY (Kenton, Stan Orchestra)
Prologue / Something's coming / Maria / America / Tonight / Cool / I feel pretty / Gee officer Krupke / Taunting scene / Somewhere (finale)
CD _____ **CDP 8299142**
Capitol Jazz / Nov '94 / EMI.

APPALACHIAN SWING
Clinch mountain backstep / Nine pound hammer / Listen to the mockingbird / Wild Bill Jones / Billy in the lowground / Lee Highway blues / I am a pilgrim / Prisoner's song / Sally Goodin / Faded love / John Henry / Flat fork
CD _____ **ROUSS 31CD**
Rounder / Aug '93 / CM / Direct / ADA / Cadillac.

LONG JOURNEY HOME
CD _____ **VCD 77004**
Vanguard / Oct '95 / Complete/Pinnacle / Discovery.

ROOTS, AFRICAN DRUMS (Kenyan National Percussion Team)
CD _____ **DC 8559**
Denon / '88 / Conifer.

KENYATTA
Touch me / Turn me on / Baby can I hold you / Good vibes / Love again / I wanna do something freaky to you / Keep me comin' / R U ready / Feels so nice / Thank you (for loving me like you do) / I wanna do something freaky to you (ragga mix) / Love again (Mix)
CD _____ **BRCDX 568**
4th & Broadway / Apr '92 / PolyGram.

GHOST STORIES
CD _____ **ITM 970060**
ITM / Apr '91 / Tradelink / Koch.

ROBIN KENYATTA'S FREE STATE BAND
CD _____ **500572**
Musidisc / May '94 / Vital / Harmonia Mundi / ADA / Cadillac / Discovery.

TAKE THE HEAT OFF ME
CD _____ **ITMP 970069**
ITM / Mar '92 / Tradelink / Koch.

JOURNEYS BY DJ'S INTERNATIONAL
CD _____ **JDJIL 5020-2**
Journeys By DJ International / Aug '94 / 3MV / Sony.

SKIN
CD _____ **QS 33CD**
Quarter Stick / Sep '95 / SRD.

UGLY DANCE
CD _____ **QS 27CD**
Quarter Stick / Aug '94 / SRD.

COMPLETE FREDDIE KEPPARD 1923-27
CD _____ **KJ 111FS**
King Jazz / Oct '93 / Jazz Music / Cadillac / Discovery.

NEW ORLEANS GIANTS VOL. 2 1922-28 (Keppard, Freddie & Ory/Dodds/carey)
CD _____ **152222**
Hot 'n' Sweet / Dec '93 / Discovery.

BLACK HERITAGE
Black heritage / I wanna go back to Hollywood / Hello fellas / Chances / Soul food / Fall / Heaven / Bu bu gree gree / Front line II parts 1 and 2 / Fatou rama / Odeylo (Live) / Don't touch my friend (live)
CD _____ **BW 062**
B&W / Apr '95 / New Note.

TOTALLY SWITCHED
End of green / Dry riser / Dead anyway / Cleaver / Earthworks / Dummy crusher / Inseminator / Clock / Schism / Scram
CD _____ **518866-2**
Vertigo / Apr '94 / PolyGram.

SITTING PRETTY
CD _____ **803872**
New World / Aug '92 / Harmonia Mundi / ADA / Cadillac.

ARRHYTHMIA
Spring / Everybody's icon / Worthless / Excess / Shame / Come alive / My friends / Everything / Mercy / So plain / Joanne / Feeling within
CD _____ **936245279-2**
WEA / Oct '93 / Warner Music.

BE THOU MY VISION
Be thou my vision / Who would true valour see / I vow to thee my country / Holy holy holy / Teach me, my God and King / O thou carnest from above / By cool Siloam's shady rill / Stand up, stand up for Jesus / Dear Lord and Father of mankind / Immortal, invisible, God only wise / Forty days and forty nights / Breathe on me, breath of God / Alleluia, sing to Jesus / Jerusalem
CD _____ **CFTMCD 01**
Tangmere / Mar '95 / Conifer.

BRAVEST HEART
Bravest heart / Corryvreckan / She moved through the fair / Only a woman's heart / Island in the mist / Queens Four Marys / Fear a bhata / For justice and honour (Rob Roy) / Safely ashore / Long black veil / House carpenter / Highlanders
CD _____ **CDMAYK 09**
Mayker / Oct '95 / Conifer.

GLENCOE + THE GLEN OF WEEPING
CD _____ **MAYK 001CD**
Mayker / Jan '95 / Conifer.

GLENCOE THE GLEN OF WEEPING
Closer to heaven / This child / Oban bay / Loch Lomond hills / Three months of the year / Glen of weeping / Glean bhaile chaoil / When I dream / Courtyard of Kildare / Isle of Innisfree / Arran, the island i love / You'll be there / Glen of weeping (instrumental)
CD _____ **CDMAYK 1**
Mayker / Nov '94 / Conifer.

MACIAIN OF GLENCOE
Maciain of Glencoe / Dark island / Charles Edward Stuart / Skye boat song / Island of Tiree / Always Argyll / I once loved a lad / Ca' the yowes / Mingulay boat song / Farewell to Tarwathie / Loch Lomond / Sense of belonging
CD _____ **MOICD 003**
Moidart / Apr '92 / Conifer / ADA.

WHERE EAGLES FLY
Banquo's Walk / Right line / Mountaineer's reel / Where eagles fly / Greatest stack of Handa / Sands of time / MacCrimmon's lament / You take me higher / Swans on the Dee / Everlasting visions / Paradise for two / Skye high / Cuillin
CD _____ **MOICD 004**
Moidart / Apr '92 / Conifer / ADA.

CAJUN GREATS
CD _____ **12474**
Laserlight / Jun '95 / Target/BMG.

HOT DIGGITY DOUG
Cajun baby / Louisiana / Jambalaya / I wanna hold you / Callin' Baton rouge / My toot toot / Boogie queen / Just like you / Louisiana man / Mansion in Spain / Cajun stripper / Fiddlin' man
CD _____ **CDSD 066**
Sundown / Oct '89 / Magnum Music Group.

COLLECTION: NIK KERSHAW
CD _____ **MCLD 19309**
MCA / Oct '95 / BMG.

WOULDN'T IT BE GOOD
Wouldn't it be good / Running scared / Radio Musicola / Wild horses / When a heart beats / L.A.B.A.T.Y.D. / Dancing girls / Nobody knows / Human racing / Violet to blue / Faces / Save the whale / Drum talk
CD _____ **PWKS 4177**
Carlton Home Entertainment / Oct '93 / Carlton Home Entertainment.

LOUISIANA MAN (Kershaw, Rusty & Doug)
Louisiana man / Diggy liggy lo / Cheated too / Cajun Joe / We'll do it anyway / Jolie blon / So lovely baby / Look around / Mr. Love / Going down the road / Never love again / Kaw-liga
CD _____ **CDSD 022**
Sundown / Mar '92 / Magnum Music Group.

FEELIN' GOOD TRAIN
CD _____ **5221252**
Mercury / Jan '95 / PolyGram.

ARTISTRY OF BARNEY KESSEL, THE
CD _____ **FCD 60021**
Fantasy / Oct '93 / Pinnacle / Jazz Music / Wellard / Cadillac.

AUTUMN LEAVES
CD _____ **BLCD 760112**
Black Lion / Jun '88 / Jazz Music / Cadillac / Wellard / Koch.

GREAT GUITARS AT CHARLIE'S, GEORGETOWN (Kessel, Barney/ Charlie Byrd/ Herb Ellis)
Where or when / New Orleans / When the saints go marching in / Change partners / Opus one / Old folks / Get happy / Trouble in mind
CD _____ **CCD 4209**
Concord Jazz / May '94 / New Note.

IT'S A BLUE WORLD
CD _____ **JHR 73526**
Jazz Hour / May '93 / Target/BMG / Jazz Music / Cadillac.

LIMEHOUSE BLUES (Kessel, Barney & Stephane Grappelli)
It don't mean a thing if it ain't got that swing / Out of nowhere / Tea for two / Limehouse blues / How high the moon / Willow weep for me / Little star / Undecided
CD _____ **BLCD 760158**
Black Lion / Oct '92 / Jazz Music / Cadillac / Wellard / Koch.

LIVE AT SOMETIME
CD _____ **STCD 4157**
Storyville / Feb '90 / Jazz Music / Wellard / CM / Cadillac.

PLAYS "CARMEN"
CD _____ **OJCCD 269-2**
Original Jazz Classics / Feb '92 / Wellard / Jazz Music / Cadillac / Complete/Pinnacle.

POLL WINNERS RIDE AGAIN, THE
CD _____ **OJCCD 6072**
Original Jazz Classics / Feb '92 / Wellard / Jazz Music / Cadillac / Complete/Pinnacle.

POLL WINNERS, THE (Kessel, Barney/ Ray Brown/Shelly Manne)
Jordu / Satin doll / It could happen to you / Mean to me / Don't worry 'bout me / On green dolphin street / You go to my head / Minor mood / Nagasaki
CD _____ **OJCCD 156**
Original Jazz Classics / Sep '93 / Wellard / Jazz Music / Cadillac / Complete/Pinnacle.

POOR BUTTERFLY (Kessel, Barney & Herb Ellis)
Dearly beloved / Monsieur Armand / Poor butterfly / Make someone happy / Early autumn / Hello / Blueberry Hill / I'm a lover / Brigitte
CD _____ **CCD 4034**
Concord Jazz / Aug '95 / New Note.

RED, HOT AND BLUES
CD _____ **CCD 14044**
Contemporary / Mar '95 / Jazz Music / Cadillac / Pinnacle / Wellard.

SOARING
You go to my head / Get out of town / Seagull / Like someone in love / You're the one for me / Beautiful love / Star eyes / I love you

CD _____ CCD 6033
Concord Jazz / Feb '92 / New Note.

TO SWING OR NOT TO SWING
Begin the blues / Louisiana / Happy feeling / Embraceable you / Wail Street / (Back home again in) Indiana / Moten swing / Midnight sun / Contemporary blues / Don't blame me / Twelfth St. rag
CD _____ OJCCD 3172
Original Jazz Classics / '93 / Wellard / Jazz Music / Cadillac / Complete/Pinnacle.

YESTERDAY (Recorded Live At The Montreux Festival 1973)
CD _____ BLCD 760183
Black Lion / Apr '93 / Jazz Music / Cadillac / Wellard / Koch.

Ketama

KETAMA
Sueno Ipossible / Luna, Quedate commigo / Ketama / Me lilama / Slo para dos / Domo arigato / No se si vivo o sueno / Vacio / Galuchi / Cuando salga la luna / Chupendi / Canasteros
CD _____ HNCD 1336
Hannibal / May '89 / Vital / ADA.

Ketchum, Hal

PAST THE POINT OF NO RETURN
CD _____ CURCD 004
Curb / Mar '94 / PolyGram.

SURE LOVE
CD _____ CURCD 7
Curb / Apr '94 / PolyGram.

Ketting, Otto

LIGHT OF THE SUN
CD _____ BVHAASTCD 9105
Bvhaast / Oct '93 / Cadillac.

Ketty, Rina

CHANSOPHONE 1936-39
CD _____ 701292
Chansophone / Jun '93 / Discovery.

Keun

KEUN
CD _____ GWP 008CD
Diffusion Breizh / Aug '91 / ADA.

Key Of Life

IMPRESSIONS FROM THE TOP OF THE WORLD
CD _____ 341122
Koch / Apr '94 / Koch.

VISIONS
CD _____ 341112
Koch / Apr '94 / Koch.

Key, Tara

BOURBON COUNTY
CD _____ HMS 210-2
Homestead / Jan '94 / SRD.

Keyes, Colin

KEYES ON KEYS
Remember the carpenters / Windmill of your mind / I'll never fall in love again / Entertainer / Tribute to Nat King Cole / Golden touch / Manhattan / Memory / Passing strangers
CD _____ CDWM 101
Westmoor / '91 / Target/BMG.

Khaled, Cheb

KUTCHE (Khaled, Cheb & Safy Boutella)
CD _____ STCD 1024
Sterns / Mar '89 / Sterns / CM.

N'ISSI N'ISSI
Serbi serbi / Hebou / Adieu / Chebba / Les ailes / Alech tadi / Bahhta / N'issi n'issi / Zine a zine / Abdel hader / El marsem
CD _____ CIDM 1111
Mango / May '94 / Vital / PolyGram.

Khan, Ali Akbar

DUET
CD _____ RSMCD 103
Ravi Shankar Music Circle / Apr '94 / Conifer.

GARDEN OF DREAMS
Two lovers / India blue / Garden of dreams / Blessings of the heart / Emperor / Power of joy / Mother goddess / Water lady
CD _____ 3201992
Triloka / Nov '93 / New Note.

JOURNEY
Come back my love / Fantasy / Lullaby / Anticipation / Farewell / Journey / Carnival of Mother Kali / Temple music / Morning meditation
CD _____ 3201842
Triloka / May '92 / New Note.

Khan, Chaka

CHAKA
I'm every woman / Love has fallen on me / Roll me through the rushes / Sleep on it /

Life is a dance / We got the love / Some love / Woman in a man's world / Message in the middle of the bottom / I was made to love him
CD _____ 7599258662
WEA / Jan '96 / Warner Music.

CK
Signed, sealed, delivered (I'm yours) / Soul talkin' / It's my party / Eternity / Sticky wicked / End of a love affair / Baby me / Make it last / Where are you tonight / I'll be around
CD _____ WX 124CD
WEA / Nov '88 / Warner Music.

I FEEL FOR YOU
This is my night / Stronger than before / My love is alive / Eye to eye / La flamme / I feel for you / Hold her / Through the fire / Caught in the act / Chinatown
CD _____ 925162 2
WEA / Oct '84 / Warner Music.

LIFE IS A DANCE (The Remix Project)
Life is a dance / This is my night / Slow dancing / I'm every woman / Ain't nobody / I feel for you / I know you, I live you / Eye to eye / Fate / Million kisses / Clouds / Clouds (classic trax version)
CD _____ 925946 2
WEA / May '89 / Warner Music.

WHATCHA GONNA DO FOR ME
We can work it out / What'cha gonna do for me / I know you, I live you / Any old Sunday / We got each other / Night in Tunisia / Night moods / Heed the warning / Father he said / Fate / I know you, I live you (reprise)
CD _____ 7599258672
WEA / Jan '96 / Warner Music.

WOMAN I AM, THE
Everything changes / Give me all / Telephone / Keep givin' me lovin' / Facts of love / Love you all my lifetime / I want / You can make the story right / Be my eyes / This time / Woman I am / Don't look at me that way
CD _____ 7599262962
WEA / Apr '92 / Warner Music.

Khan, Imrat

INDIAN MUSIC FOR SITAR AND SURBAHAR (Khan, Imrat & Sons)
CD _____ LYRCD 7376
Lyrichord / '91 / Roots / ADA / CM.

RAG DARBARI/RAG CHANDRA KANHRA
CD _____ NI 5118
Nimbus / Sep '94 / Nimbus.

RAG JHINJOTI/RAG PILU
CD _____ NI 5195
Nimbus / Sep '94 / Nimbus.

RAG MADHUR RANJANI
CD _____ CDT 123
Topic / Apr '93 / Direct / ADA.

RAG MIYA KI TODI/RAG BILASKHANI TODI
CD _____ NI 5153
Nimbus / Sep '94 / Nimbus.

RAGA MARWA
CD _____ NI 5356
Nimbus / Sep '94 / Nimbus.

Khan, Nishat

RAG BHIMPALASI/RAG TILAK KAMOD (Khan, Nishat & Irshad)
CD _____ NI 5233
Nimbus / Sep '94 / Nimbus.

Khan, Nusrat Fateh Ali

BACK TO QAWWALI
CD _____ 122083CD
Long Distance / Apr '95 / ADA / Discovery.

DEVOTIONAL SONGS
Allah hoo allah hoo / Yaad-e-nabi gushan mehka / Haq ali ali haq / Ali maula ali maula ali dam dam / Mast nazroon se allah bach-hae / Ni main jogi de naal
CD _____ RWMCD 2
Realworld / Nov '92 / EMI / Sterns.

IN CONCERT IN PARIS (VOL 1)
CD _____ C558 658
Ocora / '88 / Harmonia Mundi / ADA.

IN CONCERT IN PARIS (VOL 2)
CD _____ C558 659
Ocora / '88 / Harmonia Mundi / ADA.

LAST PROPHET, THE
Mani madni / Sahib teri bandi / Ganj-e-shakar / Sochan dongian
CD _____ CDRW 44
Realworld / Apr '94 / EMI / Sterns.

LOVE SONGS
Woh hata rahe hain pardah / Yeh jo halka saroor hae / Biba sada dil morr de / Yaadan vichre sajan dian aiyan / Sanson ki mala / Un ke dar pen pohchne to payen
CD _____ RWMCD 3
Realworld / Nov '92 / EMI / Sterns.

MUSTT MUSTT
CD _____ CDRW 15
Realworld / Nov '90 / EMI / Sterns.

SANSON KI MALA
Sanson ki mala / Aag damna mein lag jai
CD _____ JARO 41812
Jaro / Dec '94 / New Note.

SHAHBAAZ
Beh haadh ramza dhasdha / Shahbaaz qalandar / Dhyahar eh isqmeh / Jewleh lal
CD _____ CDRW 16
Realworld / '91 / EMI / Sterns.

VOLUME 3
Star / Aug '90 / Pinnacle / Sterns.
CD _____ CDSR 003

VOLUME 5
Star / Aug '90 / Pinnacle / Sterns.
CD _____ CDSR 017

Khan, Praga

SPOONFUL OF MIRACLE, A (Khan, Praga & Jade 4 U)
Injected with a poison ('93 remix) / Phantasia forever / I feel good / Give me your lovin' / Rave alert / Moonday / Travel through time / God of Abraham / Flesh and blood / Love me baby / I will survive / Love peace freedom
CD _____ FILECD 439
Profile / May '93 / Pinnacle.

Khan, Rashid

RAGA TODI/BHAIR
CD _____ DSAV 1028
Multitone / Dec '95 / BMG.

Khan, Salamat Ali

RAGAS GUNKALI
CD _____ NI 5307
Nimbus / Sep '94 / Nimbus.

Khan, Si

NEW WOOD
CD _____ PHCD 1168
Philo / Oct '94 / Direct / CM / ADA.

Khan, Steve

LOCAL COLOUR (Khan, Steve & Rob Mounsey)
Tafiya / Blue rose / I see a long journey / Gondolas / Intruder the hunt / Mahana
CD _____ CY 1840
Denon / '91 / Conifer.

Khan, Ustad Imrat

AJMER
CD _____ WLAES 17CD
Waterlilly Acoustics / Nov '95 / ADA.

LALITA
CD _____ WLAES 26CD
Waterlilly Acoustics / Nov '95 / ADA.

Khan, Ustad Sabri

INDIAN SARANGI AND TABLA RECITAL (Khan, Ustad Sabri & Sawar Sabri)
CD _____ EUCD 1172
ARC / '91 / ARC Music / ADA.

Khan, Ustad Salamat Ali

BREATH OF THE ROSE
CD _____ WLAES 18CD
Waterlilly Acoustics / Nov '95 / ADA.

Khan, Ustad Sultan

SARANGI INDIA
CD _____ RCD 10104
Rykodisc / Nov '91 / Vital / ADA.

Khanyile, Noise

ART OF NOISE, THE
Igobondela / Izulu seliyaduma / Viva Scotch land / Mapantsula jive / Jika jika jive / Ugabuzela / Kwazamazama / U.S.A. special / Dlamini / Baba wami / Umamemeza / London Ave. / Marimba jive / Groovin' jive (no. 1)
CD _____ CDORB 045
Globestyle / Jun '89 / Pinnacle.

Kiani, Madjid

TRADITION CLASSIQUE DE L'IRAN - VOL. 3 (Le Santour) (Kiani, Madjid & Djamchid Chemirani)
CD _____ HMA 190395
Musique D'Abord / Nov '93 / Harmonia Mundi.

Kicklighter, Richy

IN THE NIGHT
Night after night / Without you / Under another sky / Between the worlds / Lucky / Time will tell / Tamiami / Angel
CD _____ CDICH 1051
Ichiban / Oct '93 / Koch.

JUST FOR KICKS
Jungle Song / in the wind / Change love / Till then / Wind in the curtains / After You're Gone / Phantoms / Now and then
CD _____ CDICH 1019
Ichiban / Oct '93 / Koch.

Kid Creole

BEST OF KID CREOLE & THE COCONUTS (Kid Creole & The Coconuts)
Lifeboat party / Gina Gina / Me no pop I / Off the coast of me / Don't take my coconuts / Maladie d'amour / There's something wrong in paradise / Stool pigeon / Annie I'm not your daddy / Latin music / I'm a wonderful thing, baby / Imitation / Dear Addy / Back in the field again
CD _____ IMCD 216
Island / Mar '96 / PolyGram.

FRESH FRUIT/ TROPICAL GANGSTERS (Kid Creole & The Coconuts)
CD Set _____ ITSCD 7
Island / Nov '92 / PolyGram.

STOOL PIGEON (Kid Creole & The Coconuts)
CD _____ ST 5002
Star Collection / Nov '93 / BMG.

TROPICAL GANGSTERS (Kid Creole & The Coconuts)
Annie (I'm not your daddy) / I'm a wonderful thing, baby / Imitation / I'm corrupt / Loving you made a fool out of me / Stool pigeon / Love wo name / No fish today
CD _____ IMCD 6
Island / '89 / PolyGram.

Kid 'N' Play

FACE THE NATION
It's alright y'all / Back on wax / Got a good thing going on / Next question / Face the nation / Foreplay / Slippin' / Ain't gonna hurt nobody / Give it here / Bill's at the door / Toe to toe
CD _____ 3368612062
WEA / Oct '91 / Warner Music.

Kid Rock

POLYFUZE METHOD
CD _____ CDCTUM 2
Continuum / Sep '93 / Pinnacle.

Kidd, Carol

ALL MY TOMORROWS
Don't worry 'bout me / I'm all smiles / Autumn in New York / My funny valentine / Round Midnight / Dat dere / Angel eyes / When I dream / I thought about you / Folks who live on the hill / Haven't we met / All my tomorrows
CD _____ AKHCD 005
Linn / Aug '90 / PolyGram.

CAROL KIDD
Then I'll be tired of you / We'll be together / You go to my head / It isn't so good it couldn't be better / More I see you / I've grown accustomed to your face / Yes, I know when I've had it / Waltz for Debbie / Never let me go / I'm shadowing you / Spring can really hang you up the most / I like to recognise the tune
CD _____ AKHCD 003
Linn / Aug '90 / PolyGram.

CRAZY FOR GERSHWIN
CD _____ AKD 026

I'M GLAD WE MET
Lean baby / Don't go to strangers / Bad, bad Leroy Brown / I guess I'll hang my tears out to dry / Georgia on my mind / You're cheating yourself / I wish I'd met you / You're awful / Don't take your love from me / I'm a fool to want you / Please don't talk about me when I'm gone / Sometimes (not often)
CD _____ AKD 017
Linn / Nov '91 / PolyGram.

NICE WORK (If You Can Get It)
Nice work if you can get it / Havin' myself a time / Isn't it a pity / Bidin' my time / Sing for your supper / Daydream / I'll take romance / New York on Sunday / What is there to say / Mean to me / I guess I'll have to change my plan / Starting tomorrow / Confessions
CD _____ AKHCD 006
Linn / Aug '90 / PolyGram.

NIGHT WE CALLED IT A DAY, THE
How little it matters, how little we know / Where or when / I fall in love too easily / I loved him / Night we called it a day / Where are you / Glory of you / I could have told you so / I think it's going to rain today / Gloomy Sunday
CD _____ AKHCD 007
Linn / Sep '90 / PolyGram.

THAT'S ME
You don't bring me flowers / Send in the clowns / When the world was young / Round midnight / I can't get started / I'm always chasing rainbows / Let me sing and I'm happy / This bitter earth / Somewhere over the rainbow / Trolley song / That's me
CD _____ AKD 044
Linn / Sep '95 / PolyGram.

Kidd, Johnny

CLASSIC AND RARE (Kidd, Johnny & The Pirates)

I want that / So what / Feeling / Please don't touch / Restless / Let's talk about us / Birds and the bees / It's got to be you / Some other guy / Shakin' all over / I'll never get over you / Send me some lovin' / Fool / Hungry for love / Your cheatin' heart / My babe / Casting my spell / Big blon' baby
CD _____ SEECD 287
See For Miles/C5 / Jun '93 / Pinnacle.

COMPLETE JOHNNY KIDD (Best Of The EMI Years/2CD Set) (Kidd, Johnny & The Pirates)
Please don't touch / Growl / Yes sir that's my baby / Steady date / Feelin' / If you were the only girl in the world / You got what it takes / Longin' lips / Shakin' all over / Restless / Magic of love / Linda Lou / Let's talk about us / Big blon' baby / More of the same / My baby / More of the same / I just want to make love to you / Please don't bring me down (version 2) / So what / Please don't bring me down / Hurry on back to love / I want that / I can tell / Shot of rhythm and blues / Some other guy / Then I got everything / Ecstacy / Hungry for love / Casting my spell / My babe / Dr. Feelgood / Always and ever / Whole lotta woman / Your cheatin' heart / Let's talk about us (alt. version) / Little bit of soap / Fool (version 2) / Oh boy / Send me some lovin' / Big blon' baby (#2) / Please don't touch (version 2) / Right string baby, but the wrong yo-yo / Shop around / I know / Jealous girl / Where are you / Don't make the same mistake as I did / Birds and the bees / Can't turn you loose / Gotta travel on / Bad case of love / You can have her / I hate getting up in the morning / This golden ring / It's got to be you / I hate getting up in the morning (version 2) / Send for that girl / Fool / Send for that girl (2)
CD Set _____ CDKIDD 11
EMI / Aug '92 / EMI.

RARITIES (Kidd, Johnny & The Pirates)
I Know / Where are you / Little bit of soap / Oh boy / Steady date / More of the same / I just want to make love to you / This golden ring / Right string baby, but the wrong yo-yo / Can't turn you loose / Shakin' all over 65 / I hate getting up in the morning / Send for that girl / Hurry on back to love / You got what it takes / Fool / Ecstacy / Shop around / Weep no more / Whole lotta woman
CD _____ SEECD 120
See For Miles/C5 / Jun '93 / Pinnacle.

VERY BEST OF JOHNNY KIDD & THE PIRATES, THE (Kidd, Johnny & The Pirates)
Please don't touch / If you were the only girl in the world / Feelin' / You got what it takes / Shakin' all over / Yes sir that's my baby / Restless / Hurry on back to love / Shot of rhythm and blues / I'll never get over you / Hungry for love / Always and ever / Dr. Feelgood / Whole lotta woman / Your cheatin' heart / Gotta travel on / Fool / Birds and the bees / Send me some lovin' / Some other guy
CD _____ CDSL 8256
EMI / Jul '95 / EMI.

Kidjo, Angelique

AYE
Agolo / Adouma / Azan nkp ke / Tatchedogbe / Djan djan / Lon lon vadjro / Houngbati / Idje idje / Yemandja / Tombo
CD _____ 518432-2
Mango / Dec '93 / Vital / PolyGram.

FIFA
CD _____ CIDM 1112
Mango / Mar '96 / Vital / PolyGram.

LOGOZO
CD _____ CIDM 1091
Mango / Oct '91 / Vital / PolyGram.

PARA KOU
CD _____ 8482192
Mango / Apr '91 / Vital / PolyGram.

WOMBO LOMBO
CD _____ CIDM 830
Mango / Jan '96 / Vital / PolyGram.

Kiem

YOU SHOULD TRY
CD _____ CD 029
Torso / Jul '87 / SRD.

Kiermyer, Franklin

SOLOMON'S DAUGHTER
Three jewels / Akdemus / Peace on earth / Solomon's daughter / Birds of the Nile / If I die before I wake
CD _____ ECD 220832
Evidence / May '94 / Harmonia Mundi / ADA / Cadillac.

Kiernan, Ken

ERINSAGA (Kiernan, Ken & Ger MacDonald)
I am Tuan / Vision / Belgatan (our will is strong) / Tailitu's lament / Crom cruach / Dream of nuada / Battle-frenzy / My love is yours / Last battle / Erinsaga
CD _____ ERCD 1

Round Tower / Nov '89 / Pinnacle / ADA / Direct / BMG / CM.

Kiesewetter, Knut

HIS BEST SONGS
CD _____ EUCD 1182
ARC / Apr '92 / ARC Music / ADA.

WENN WIEHNACHTEN KUMMT (Kiesewetter, Knut & Fiede Kay)
CD _____ EUCD 1130
ARC / '91 / ARC Music / ADA.

WO GEIHST DU HEN
CD _____ EUCD 1117
ARC / '91 / ARC Music / ADA.

Kihn, Greg

MUTINY
Blood red roses / Mutiny / Sittin' on top of the world / Anniversary of my broken heart / Joshua gone Barbados / Anastasia / I wish it would rain / Not fade away Mona / Femme fatale / Shot in the dark / Subterranean homesick blues / Love of the land / Been on the job too long / Gwabi
CD _____ FIENDCD 755
Demon / Aug '94 / Pinnacle / ADA.

Kikoski, Dave

DAVE KIKOSKI
E / B flat nung / Giant steps / Long ago and far away / Chant / Shadow / 7/4 ballad / Spacing
CD _____ 4781742
Epicure / Feb '95 / Sony.

PERSISTENT DREAMS
CD _____ 3201912
Triloka / Jul '92 / New Note.

PRESAGE
CD _____ FRLCD 011
Freelance / Oct '92 / Harmonia Mundi / Cadillac / Koch.

Kikuchi, Masabumi

TETHERED MOON
You're my everything / Misterioso / So in love / Moniker / P.S. / Moor / Tethered moon
CD _____ ECD 220712
Evidence / Nov '93 / Harmonia Mundi / ADA / Cadillac.

Kikuchi, Teiko

TRADITIONAL MUSIC OF JAPAN
CD _____ 824612
Buda / Nov '90 / Discovery / ADA.

Kila

MIND THE GAP
CD _____ KR 004CD
Kila / Jul '95 / ADA.

Kilbey, Steve

UNEARTHED
CD _____ 3297 2
Enigma / Oct '87 / EMI.

Kilbride, Pat

LOOSE CANNON
CD _____ GLCD 1148
Green Linnet / Feb '95 / Roots / CM / Direct / ADA.

NOOR AND MORE ROSES
CD _____ COMD 2011
Temple / Feb '94 / CM / Duncans / ADA / Direct.

UNDOCUMENTED DANCING
Live bait / Aires de Pontevedra / All the leaves / Hunter's house / Milestones and memories / Patrick / Unfinished revolution / Munster bacon and the jig of slurs / Wearing of the breeches / Blind Mary / Flower of Magherally / Piccadilly / Cittern jig
CD _____ GLCD 1120
Green Linnet / Feb '91 / Roots / CM / Direct / ADA.

Kilduff, Vinnie

BOYS FROM BLUE HILL
CD _____ LUNCD 050
Mulligan / Jan '95 / CM / ADA.

Kilgore, Merle

TEENAGER'S HOLIDAY
Ride Jesse ride / Hang doll / Everybody needs a little lovin' / Ernie / Start all over again / Tom Dooley Jr. / More and more / It can't rain all the time / Seein' double, feelin' single / What makes me love you / Funny feeling / Now that you are leavin' / That's when my blues began / Teenager's holiday / Please please please / I feel guilty / Trying to find (someone like you) / Goodbye / Forty two in Chicago / Wicked city / I'll take Ginger and run away / Girl named Liz / Ain't nothin' but a man / Somethin' goin' on that I can't see / There's no food in this house / Lover's hell / Back street affair / Trouble at the tower / Love bug / I'll shake your hand

CD _____ BCD 15544
Bear Family / May '91 / Rollercoaster / Direct / CM / Swift / ADA.

Kilgour, David

SUGAR MOUTH
CD _____ FNCD 282
Flying Nun / Oct '94 / Disc.

Kill City Dragons

KILL CITY DRAGONS
CD _____ WBRCD 002
Wideboy / Jan '91 / Vital.

Kill Creek

St. VALENTINE'S GARAGE
Cosmetic surgery / Busted / Stretch / Mother's friends / Gett on / Kelly's dead / 7-11 / Killing / Fruit pie / Million / Harass / Wuss cliff / Die young / Funeral
CD _____ MR 091-2
Mammoth / Oct '94 / Vital.

Killa Instinct

ESCAPISM
CD _____ MOVE 70132
Move / Mar '95 / Plastic Head.

Killarney Singers

50 FAVOURITE IRISH PUB SONGS
CD _____ CDIRISH 001
Outlet / Jan '95 / ADA / Duncans / CM / Ross / Direct / Koch.

Killdozer

GOD HEARS PLEAS OF THE INNOCENT
CD _____ TG 139CD
Touch & Go / Feb '95 / SRD.

WAR ON ART
CD _____ TG 82CD
Touch & Go / '94 / SRD.

Killer

FATAL ATTRACTION
CD _____ 367 0001.2
Mausoleum / Oct '91 / Grapevine.

MURDER ONE
Impaler / Beast arises / Children of the revolution / S and M / Takin' no prisoners / Marshall Lokjaw / Protector / Dream keeper / Awakening / Remember tomorrow
CD _____ PD 90643
RCA / May '92 / BMG.

Killer Bee

CRACKED UP
CD _____ FRCD 9501
Mauve / May '95 / Pinnacle.

Killer Bees

LIVE IN BERLIN
CD _____ DANCD 053
Reach Out International / Nov '94 / Jetstar.

Killer Dwarfs

DIRTY WEAPONS
Dirty weapons / Nothin' gets nothin' / All that we dream / Doesn't matter / Last laugh / Comin' through / One way out / Appeal / Not foolin' / Want it bad
CD _____ 4659082
Epic / Apr '90 / Sony.

Killer Shrews

KILLER SHREWS
CD _____ EMY 141-2/1
Enemy / Nov '94 / Grapevine.

Killers

MENACE TO SOCIETY
CD _____ CDBLEED 11
Bleeding Hearts / Oct '94 / Pinnacle.

Killing Floor

KILLING FLOOR
CD _____ SYC 006CD
BGR / May '95 / Plastic Head.

Killing Joke

BBC RADIO 1 LIVE IN CONCERT
Twilight of the mortals / Chessboards / Kings and queens / Darkness before dawn / Love like blood / Sanity / Love of the masses / Requiem / Complications / Wardance / Tabazan / Tension / Psyche
CD _____ WINCD 068
Windsong / Oct '95 / Pinnacle.

BRIGHTER THAN A 1000 SUNS
Adorations / Sanity / Chessboards / Twilight of the moral / Love of the masses / Southern sky / Winter gardens / Rubicon / Goodbye to the village (CD & cassette only) / Victory (CD & cassette only) / Exile
CD _____ EGCD 66
EG / Nov '86 / EMI.

Kilpatrick, Tom

EXTREMITIES, DIRT AND VARIOUS REPRESSED EMOTIONS
Money is not our God / Age of greed / Beautiful dead / Extremities / Intravenous / Inside the termite mound / Solitude / North of the border / Slipstream / Kaliyuga / Struggle
CD _____ AGR 0544
Noise/Modern Music / Nov '90 / Pinnacle / Plastic Head.

FIRE DANCES
Gathering / Fun and games / Rejuvenation / Frenzy / Harlequin / Feast of blaze / Song and dance / Dominator / Let's all go (to the fire dances) / Lust almighty
CD _____ EGCD 60
EG / '87 / EMI.

KILLING JOKE
Requiem / War dance / Tomorrow's World / Bloodsport / Wait / Complications / S.O. 36 / Primitive
CD _____ EGCD 57
EG / '87 / EMI.

LAUGH I NEARLY BOUGHT ONE!
Turn to red / Pssyche / Requiem / Wardance / Follow the leaders / Unspeakable / Butcher / Exit / Hum / Empire song / Chop chop / Sun goes down / Eighties / Darkness before dawn / Love like blood / WIntergardens / Age of greed
CD _____ CDV 2693
EG / Oct '92 / EMI.

NIGHT TIME
Night Time / Darkness before dawn / Love like blood / Kings and Queens / Tabazan / Multitudes / Europe / Eighties
CD _____ EGCD 61
EG / Jan '88 / EMI.

OUTSIDE THE GATE
America / My love of this land / Stay one jump ahead (Mixes) / Unto the ends of the earth / Calling / Obsession / Tiahuanaco / Outside the gate / America (mix) (CD only)
CD _____ EGCD 73
EG / May '88 / EMI.

PANDEMONIUM
Pandemonium / Exorcism / Millennium / Communion / Black moon / Labyrinth / Jana / Whiteout / Pleasures of the flesh / Mathematics of chaos
CD _____ BFLCD 09
Big Life / Jul '94 / Pinnacle.

WHAT'S THIS FOR
Fall of because / Tension / Unspeakable / Butcher / Who told you how / Follow the leader / Madness / Exit
CD _____ EGCD 58
EG / '87 / EMI.

WILFUL DAYS
Are you receiving / Follow the leaders / Sun goes down / Dominator / Me or you / Wilful days / Eighties / New day / Love like blood / Madding crowd / Ecstasy / America / Change
CD _____ CDOVD 440
Virgin / May '95 / EMI.

Killing Time

BRIGHTSIDE
CD _____ LF 157CD
Lost & Found / Jul '95 / Plastic Head.

Killjoys

MILLION SONGS, A
CD _____ D 30930
Mushroom / Oct '93 / BMG / 3MV.

Killrays

SPACE GIANT
CD _____ LF 203CD
Lost & Found / Nov '95 / Plastic Head.

Kilmarnock Edition

FROM FAR HORIZONS
CD _____ MANU 1501CD
Manu / Nov '95 / Discovery / ADA.

Kilo

BLUNTLY SPEAKING
CD _____ WRA 8118CD
Wrap / May '94 / Koch.

GET THIS PARTY STARTED
CD _____ WRA 8147
Wrap / Aug '95 / Koch.

GIT WIT DA PROGRAM
CD _____ WRA 8123CD
Wrap / Feb '94 / Koch.

Kilpatrick, Tom

FIFTY SHADES OF GREEN
CD _____ CDITV 538
Scotdisc / Jul '91 / Duncans / Ross / Conifer.

SHADES OF GREEN
CD _____ PLATCD 3922
Prism / May '94 / Prism.

SHAMROCK STRAND, THE
CD _____ CDITV 560
Scotdisc / Sep '92 / Duncans / Ross / Conifer.

Kimball, Bobby

CLASSIC TOTO HITS (Kimball, Bobby & Frankfurt Rock Orchestra)
Child's anthem / Out of love / Rosanna / I won't hold you back / Hold the line / I'll be over you / Africa / Holyanna / Anna / Isolation / One day at a time / Cool change
CD _____ 903 001 2
MMS / Apr '94 / BMG.

RISE UP
CD _____ 9041012
Mausoleum / Jun '95 / Grapevine.

Kimbrough, Junior

ALL NIGHT LONG
CD _____ FIENDCD 742
Demon / Nov '93 / Pinnacle / ADA.

Kimmel, Tom

5 TO 1
That's freedom / Shake / Tryin to dance / A to Z / True love / Heroes / On the defensive / Violet eyes / No tech / Five to one
CD _____ 832 248-2
Vertigo / Nov '87 / PolyGram.

Kin Of Tears

SHIT HAPPENS
CD _____ LF 198CD
Lost & Found / Jan '96 / Plastic Head.

Kina, Shoukichi

ASIA CLASSICS 2 - THE BEST OF SHOUKICHI PEPPERMINT TEA HOUSE
CD _____ 936245159-2
Luaka Bop / Jul '94 / Warner Music.

Kinder Der Erde

KINDER DER ERDE
CD _____ EFA 119722
High Society / Apr '95 / SRD.

Kindness Of Strangers

HOPE
Kindness of strangers / Across the border / Tomorrow / Memory takes my hand / Walk away / On my America / Live in the world / Sunday / Day that I found love / Shelter for love / Desire / Kindness of strangers (reprise)
CD _____ 654492241-2
East West / Feb '94 / Warner Music.

Kindred

SO YOU SAY
CD _____ CDSGP 022
Prestige / Jan '94 / Total/BMG.

Kinesthesia

EMPATHY BOX
CD _____ CAT 022CDR
CD _____ CAT 022CD
Rephlex / Jan '96 / Disc.

King, Albert

AS YEARS GO BY
CD _____ CDSXD 045
Stax / Apr '92 / Pinnacle.

BEST OF ALBERT KING, THE (I'll Play the Blues For You)
Born under a bad sign / Answer to The Laundromatt Blues / You threw your love on me too strong / Crosscut saw / I'll play the blues for you (pt 1) / Angel of mercy / Heart fixing business / Killing floor / Sky is crying / Going back to luka / Drowning on dry land #2 / That's what the blues is all about / Left hand woman (get right with me) / Drivin' wheel / Firing line (Available on CD only) / Don't burn the bridge (cause you might wanna come back... (Available on CD only) / Can't you see what you're doing to me (Available on CD only)
CD _____ CDSX 007
Stax / Jan '90 / Pinnacle.

BIG BLUES, THE
CD _____ KCD 000852
King/Paddle Wheel / Sep '92 / New Note.

BLUES AT SUNRISE
CD _____ CD 52034
Blues Encore / May '94 / Target/BMG.

BLUES DON'T CHANGE, THE
Blues don't change / I'm doing fine / Nice to be nice / Oh pretty woman / King of kings / Feel the need / Firing line / Pinch paid off (Part I) / Pinch paid off (Part II) / I can't stand the rain / Ain't it beautiful
CD _____ CDSXE 085
Stax / Feb '93 / Pinnacle.

BLUES FOR YOU (The Best Of Albert King)
Born under a bad sign / Killing floor / Breaking up somebody's home / Can't you see what you're doing to me / Going back to luka / Answer to the laundromat blues /

That's what the blues is all about / Phone booth / I'll play the blues for you (Parts 1 & 2) / Left hand woman (Get right with me) / Flat tire / Drowning on dry land / Pinch paid off / Sky is crying / Driving wheel / Everybody wants to go to heaven / Angel of mercy / Wrapped up in love again / Blues power / Crosscut saw
CD _____ CDSXD 120
Stax / Sep '95 / Pinnacle.

CHICAGO 1978
CD _____ CDBL 754
Charly / Nov '94 / Charly / THE / Cadillac.

CROSSCUT SAW
Crosscut saw / Down don't bother me / Honey bee / Ask me no questions / I'm gonna move to the outskirts of town / They made the Queen welcome / Floodin' in California / I found love in the food stamp line / Matchbox blues / Why you so mean to me
CD _____ CDSXE 076
Stax / Oct '92 / Pinnacle.

GREAT KING ALBERT
CD _____ 2696032
Tomato / May '88 / Vital.

I WANNA GET FUNKY
I wanna get funky / Playing on me / Walking the back streets and crying / Till my back ain't got no bone / Flat tire / I can't hear nothing but the blues / Travelin' man / Crosscut saw / That's what the blues is all about
CD _____ CDSXE 081
Stax / Jul '93 / Pinnacle.

I'M IN A PHONE BOOTH BABY
Phone booth / Dust my broom / Sky is crying / Brother go ahead and take her / Your bread ain't done / Firing line / Game goes on / Truck load of lovin / You gotta sacrifice
CD _____ CDSXE 083
Stax / Jul '93 / Pinnacle.

JUST PICKIN'
CD _____ MBCD 721
Modern Blues / Jun '93 / Direct / ADA.

KING ALBERT
Love shock / You upset me baby / Chump chance / Let me rock you easy / Boot lace / Love mechanic / Call my job / Good time Charlie
CD _____ CDCRB 1191
Charly / Jul '88 / Charly / THE / Cadillac.

KING DOES THE KING'S THINGS (Blues For Elvis)
Hound dog / That's all right / All shook up / Jailhouse rock / Heartbreak hotel / Don't be cruel / One night / Blue suede shoes / Love me tender
CD _____ CDSXE 073
Stax / Sep '92 / Pinnacle.

KING OF THE BLUES GUITAR
Cold feet / You're gonna need me / Born under a bad sign / I love Luzy / Crosscut saw / You sure drive a hard bargain / Oh pretty woman / Overall junction / Funk-shun / Laundromat blues / Personal manager
CD _____ 756782017-2
Atlantic / Mar '93 / Warner Music.

LET'S HAVE A NATURAL BALL
CD _____ MBCD 723
Modern Blues / Jun '93 / Direct / ADA.

LIVE
Watermelon man / Don't burn down the bridge / Blues at sunrise / That's what the blues is all about / Stormy Monday / Kansas City / I'm gonna call you as soon as the sun goes down / Matchbox blues / my clothes (Not on reissue) / Jam in a flat (Not on reissue) / As the years go passing by / Overall junction / I'll play the blues for you
CD _____ CDBM 18
Charly / Apr '92 / Charly / THE / Cadillac.

LIVE IN CANADA
King's groove / King's jump / Watermelon man / I'm gonna move to the outskirts of town / Kansas city / Someday baby / Truckers blues / As the years go by / Rainin' in California / I'll play the blues for you / Sky is crying
CD _____ CDCBL 755
Charly / Oct '95 / Charly / THE / Cadillac.

LIVE WIRE/BLUES POWER (VOLUME 1)
Watermelon man / Blues power / Night stomp / Blues at sunrise / Please love me / Lookout
CD _____ CDSXE 022
Stax / Nov '89 / Pinnacle.

LOST SESSION, THE
She won't gimme no lovin' / Cold in hand / Stop lying / All the way down / Tell me what true love is / Down the road I go / Money lovin' women / Sun gone down / Brand new razor / Sun gone down (take 2)
CD _____ CDSXE 066
Stax / Nov '92 / Pinnacle.

NEW ORLEANS HEAT
Get out of my life woman / Born under a bad sign / Feeling / We all wanna boogie / Very thought of you / I got the blues / I get evil / Angel of Mercy / Flat tire
CD _____ CDCHARLY 49
Charly / Jan '87 / Charly / THE / Cadillac.

RED HOUSE
Stop / Bluesman / Don't let me be lonely / When you walk out the door / Problems / Our love is going to win / Trouble / If you got it / Red house
CD _____ ESMCD 147
Essential / May '95 / Total/BMG.

SO MANY ROADS (Charly Blues - Masterworks Volume 2) (King, Albert & Otis Rush)
Bad luck blues / Be on your merry way / Murder / Searching for a woman / California blues / Wild woman / Won't be hangin' around no more / Howlin' for my darling / So many roads, so many trains / I'm satisfied / So close / All your love / You know my love / I can't stop baby
CD _____ CD BM 2
Charly / Apr '92 / Charly / THE / Cadillac.

THURSDAY NIGHT IN SAN FRANCISCO
San-Ho-Zay / You upset me baby / Stormy Monday blues / Everyday I have the blues / Driftin' blues / I've made nights by myself / Crosscut saw / I'm gonna move to the outskirts of town / Ooh-ee baby
CD _____ CDSXE 032
Stax / Oct '90 / Pinnacle.

TRUCKLOAD OF LOVIN'
Cold women with warm hearts / Gonna make it somehow / Sensation, communication, together / I'm your mate / Truckload of lovin' / Hold hands with one another / Cadillac assembly line / Nobody wants a loser
CD _____ CDCHARLY 112
Charly / Apr '88 / Charly / THE / Cadillac.

VINTAGE BLUES (King, Albert & Otis Rush)
Be on your merry way / Bad luck blues / Murder / Searchin' for a woman / California blues / Wild woman / Won't be hangin' around / Howlin' for my darling / So many roads, so many trains / I'm satisfied / So close / All your love / You know my love / I can't stop baby / If I must have been the devil / Five spot / I'm leaving you / I'm in love with you baby / Ice cream man / Rattlesnake / Be careful / Tough times / You got me
CD _____ CDRED 7
Charly / May '89 / Charly / THE / Cadillac.

WEDNESDAY NIGHT IN SAN FRANCISCO
CD _____ CDSXE 031
Stax / Sep '90 / Pinnacle.

King, B.B.

BEST OF B.B. KING
Hummingbird / Cook County jail introduction / How blue can you get / Sweet sixteen / Ain't nobody home / Why I sing the blues / Thrill is gone / Nobody loves me but my mother / Caldonia
CD _____ MCLD 19099
Chess/MCA / Nov '90 / BMG / New Note.

BEST OF B.B. KING
CD _____ DLCD 4026
Dixie Live / Mar '95 / Magnum Music Group.

BEST OF B.B. KING VOL 1
You upset me baby / Everyday / Five long years / Sweet little angel / Beautician blues / Dust my broom / Three o'clock blues / Ain't that just like a woman / I'm King / Sweet sixteen / Whole lot of love / Mean ol' Frisco / Please accept my love / Going down slow / Blues for me / You don't know / Early every morning / Blues at sunrise / Please love me
CD _____ CDCH 908
Ace / '89 / Pinnacle / Cadillac / Complete/Pinnacle.

BLUES IS KING
Waitin' on you / Gambler's blues / Tired of your jive / Night life / Buzz me / Sweet sixteen part 1 / Don't answer the door / Blind love / I know what you're puttin' down / Baby get lost / Gonna keep on loving you / Sweet sixteen part 2
CD _____ SEECD 216
See For Miles/C5 / Apr '92 / Pinnacle.

BLUES ON TOP OF BLUES
Heartbreaker / Losing faith in you / Dance with me / That's wrong little mama / Having my say / I'm not wanted anymore / Worried dream / Paying the cost to be the boss / Until I found you / I'm gonna do what they do to me / Raining in my heart / Now that you've lost me
CD _____ BGOCD 69
Beat Goes On / '89 / Pinnacle.

BLUES SUMMIT
Playin' with my friends / Since I met you / Something you got / There's something on your mind / Call it stormy Monday / You're the boss / I gotta move out of this neighbourhood / Nobody loves me but my mother / Little by little / Everybody's had the blues
CD _____ MCD 10710
MCA / Jun '93 / BMG.

COLLECTION, THE
CD _____ COL 022
Collection / Feb '95 / Target/BMG.

COLLECTION: B.B. KING (20 Blues Greats)
Help the poor / Everyday I have the blues / Woke up this morning / Worry worry / Sweet little angel / How blue can you get / You upset me baby / It's my own fault / Please love me / She don't love me no more / Three o'clock blues / Fine looking woman / Blind love / You know I love you / Ten long years / Mistreated woman / Shake it up and go / Sweet sixteen / You done lost your good thing now / Outside help
CD _____ CCSCD 412
Castle / Feb '95 / BMG.

DO THE BOOGIE (B.B.King's Early 50's Classics)
Boogie woogie woman / Past day / I gotta find my baby / Woke up this morning (my baby's gone) / Please love me / Blind love / When my heart beats like a hammer / Whole lotta love / That ain't the way to do it / Everyday I have the blues / Let's do the boogie / Dark is the night (Part 1) / Dark is the night (Part 2) / Why I sing the blues / Everything I do is wrong / Woman I love / Jump with you baby / Troubles, troubles, troubles / Crying won't help you
CD _____ CDCHD 916
Ace / '89 / Pinnacle / Cadillac / Complete / Pinnacle.

EARLY BLUES BOY YEARS VOL.1
CD _____ OCD 101
Opal / Nov '95 / ADA.

EARLY BLUES BOY YEARS VOL.2
CD _____ OCD 102
Opal / Nov '95 / ADA.

FABULOUS B.B. KING, THE
Three o'clock blues / You know I love you / Please love me / You upset me baby / Bad luck / On my word of honor / Everyday I have the blues / Woke up this morning (my baby's gone) / When my heart beats like a hammer / Sweet little angel / Ten long years / Whole lotta love
CD _____ CDFAB 004
Ace / Aug '91 / Pinnacle / Cadillac / Complete/Pinnacle.

FRIENDS
Friends / I got them blues / Baby, I'm yours / Philadelphia / When everything else is gone / My song
CD _____ BGOCD 125
Beat Goes On / Sep '91 / Pinnacle.

GREATEST HITS 1951-1960
Three o'clock blues / You know I love you / Boogie woogie woman / Woke up this morning / Please love me / You upset me baby / Whole lotta love / Sneaking around / Every day I have the blues / Crying won't help you / Sweet little angel / Bad luck / I want to get married / Troubles, troubles,troubles / Please accept my love / Sweet sixteen part 1 / Sweet sixteen part 2 / (I've) Got a right to love my baby / My fault / You done lost your good thing now / Now
CD _____ CSAPCD 117
Connoisseur / Aug '94 / Pinnacle.

GUESS WHO
Summer in the city / Just can't please you / Any other you / You don't know nothin' about love / Found what I need / Neighborhood affair / It takes a young girl / Better lovin' man / Guess who / Shoudn't have left me / Five long years
CD _____ BGOCD 71
Beat Goes On / May '90 / Pinnacle.

HEART & SOUL (A Collection Of Blues Ballads)
Lonely and blue / Sneakin' around / You can't fool my heart / Story from my heart and soul / Don't get around much anymore / You know I love you / I'm lonely / Lonely lover's plea / My heart belongs to only you / Don't cry anymore / Please accept my love / Peace of mind / I was blind / On my word of honour / I'll survive / If I lost you / My reward / I am / I love you so / Key to my kingdom
CD _____ CDCH 376
Ace / Oct '92 / Pinnacle / Cadillac / Complete/Pinnacle.

HIS BEST - THE ELECTRIC KING
Tired of your jive / B.B. Jones / Paying the cost to be the boss / I done got wise / Sweet sixteen / I don't want you cuttin' your hair / Don't answer the door / All over again / Think it over / Meet my happiness / You put it on me
CD _____ BGOCD 37
Beat Goes On / Oct '88 / Pinnacle.

HOW BLUE CAN YOU GET
Rock me baby / Blues at midnight / How blue can you get / You upset me baby / I done got wise / Lucille / Thrill is gone / Please accept my love / Ask me no questions / Five long years / To know you is to love you / Don't make me pay for his mistakes / Everyday I have the blues / Mother fuyer / Midnight believer / Better not look down / There must be a better world somewhere / Six silver strings / I'm movin' on
CD _____ NTRCD 013
Nectar / Feb '94 / Pinnacle.

IN LONDON
Caldonia / Blue shadows / Alexis' boogie / We can't agree / Ghetto woman / Wet hay-

shark / Part time love / Power of the blues / Ain't nobody home
CD _____ BGOCD 42
Beat Goes On / Oct '88 / Pinnacle.

INDIANOLA MISSISSIPPI SEEDS
Nobody loves me but my mother / You're still my woman / Ask me no questions / Until I'm dead and cold / King's special / Ain't gonna worry my life anymore / Chains and things / Go underground / Hummingbird
CD _____ BGOCD 237
Beat Goes On / Mar '95 / Pinnacle.

INTRODUCING B. B. KING
Into the night / Better not look down / My Lucille / Caldonia / Sell my monkey / In the midnight hour / Thrill is gone / Broken heart / Victim / Sweet sixteen / Rock me baby
CD _____ MCLD 19036
MCA / Apr '92 / BMG.

KANSAS CITY 1972
CD _____ CDCBL 752
Charly / Jan '94 / Charly / THE / Cadillac.

KING OF THE BLUES
(You've become a) Habit to me / Drowning in the sea of love / Can't get enough / Standing on the edge of love / On Let's staighten it out / Change in your lovin' / Undercover man / Lay another log on the fire / Business with my baby tonight
CD _____ MCLD 19214
MCA / Aug '93 / BMG.

KING OF THE BLUES
Early every morning / Sweet little angel / Dark is the night (part 1) / It just like a woman / Dark is the night (part 1) / Dark is the night (part 2) / Rock me baby / I've got a right to love my baby / Bad luck soul / Did you ever love a woman / King of guitar / You upset me baby / Get out of here / Troubles, troubles, troubles / Sweet sixteen part 1 / Sweet sixteen Part 2 / That ain't the way to do it / Ten long years / Powerhouse / Going down slow
CD _____ PWKS 4211
Carlton Home Entertainment / Aug '94 / Carlton Home Entertainment.

KING OF THE BLUES (4CD Set)
Miss Martha King / She's dynamite / Three O'clock in the morning / Ain't that just me baby / Everyday I have the blues / Rock me baby / Recession blues / Don't get around much anymore / I'm gonna sit in til you give in / Blues at midnight / Sneakin' around / My baby's coming home / Slowly losing my mind / How blue can you get / Rockin' awhile / Help the poor / Stop leadin' me on / Never trust a woman / Sweet little angel (live) / All over again / Sloppy drunk / Don't answer the door / I done got wise / Think it over / Gambler's blues (live) / Goin' down slow (live) / Tired of your jive (live) / Sweet sixteen (live) / I'm gonna do what they do to me / Lucille / Watch yourself / You put it on me / Get myself somebody / I want you so bad / Why I sing the blues / Get off my back woman / Please accept my love (live) / Fools get wise / No good / So exited / Thrill is gone / Confessin' the blues / Nobody loves me but my mother / Hummingbird / Ask me no questions / Chains and things / Eyesight to the blind / Niji baby (live) / Blue shadows / Ghetto woman / Ain't nobody home / I got some help I don't need (7" version) / Five long years / To know you is to love you / I like to live the love / Don't make me pay for his mistakes / Let the good times roll (Live with Bobby Bland) / Pauu jiu ti lu mo / Mother fiiver / Never make a move too soon / When it all comes down (I'll still be around) / Better not look down / Caldonia (live) / There must be a better world somewhere / Play with your poodle (solo) / Darlin' you know I love you / Inflation blues / Make love to me / Into the night / Six silver strings / When love comes to town (7" version with U2.) / Right time, wrong place (With Bonnie Raitt.) / Many miles travelled / I'm movin' on / Since I met you baby (With Gary Moore.)
CD Set _____ MCAD 410677
MCA / Oct '92 / BMG.

LIVE & WELL
Don't answer the door / Just a little love / My mood / Sweet little angel / Please accept my love / I want you so bad / Friends / Get off my back woman / Let's get down to business / Why I sing the blues
CD _____ BGOCD 233
Beat Goes On / Jun '94 / Pinnacle.

LIVE AT SAN QUENTIN
Intro / Let the good times roll / Everyday I have the blues / Whole lotta lovin' / Sweet little angel / Never make a move too soon / Into the night / ain't nobody's business / Thrill is gone / Peace to the world / Nobody loves me but my mother / Sweet sixteen / Rock me baby
CD _____ MCLD 19253
MCA / Nov '94 / BMG.

LIVE AT THE APOLLO
When love comes to town / Sweet sixteen / Thrill is gone / Ain't nobody's business / All over again / Nightlife / Since I met you baby / Guess who / Peace to the world
CD _____ MCD 9637
MCA / Jan '93 / BMG.

LIVE AT THE REGAL
Everyday I have the blues / Sweet little angel / It's my own fault / How blue can you get / Please love me / You upset me baby / Worry worry / Woke up this morning / You done lost your good thing now / Help the poor
CD _____ BGOCD 235
Beat Goes On / Oct '94 / Pinnacle.

LUCILLE
Lucille / You move me so / Country girl / No money no luck / I need your love / Rainin' all the time / I'm with you / Stop putting the hurt on me / Watch yourself
CD _____ BGOCD 36
Beat Goes On / Feb '89 / Pinnacle.

LUCILLE AND FRIENDS
When love comes to town / Playin' with my friends / To know you is to love you / Caught a touch of your love / All you ever give me is the blues / You shook me / Spirit in the dark / Can't get enough / Since I met you baby / B.B.'s blues / Better not look down / Frosty / Hummingbird / Ghetto woman / Let the good times roll
CD _____ MCD 30038
MCA / Jul '95 / BMG.

MY SWEET LITTLE ANGEL
My sweet little angel / Crying won't help you / Ten long years / Quit my baby / Don't look now but I've got the blues / You know I go for you / Why do everything happen to me / Worry worry / Shake yours / Please accept my love / Treat me right / Going down slow / Just like a woman / Time to say goodbye / Early every morning / You've been an angel
CD _____ CDCHD 300
Ace / Mar '92 / Pinnacle / Cadillac / Complete/Pinnacle.

SINGIN' THE BLUES AND THE BLUES
Please love me / You upset me baby / Everyday I have the blues / Bad luck / Three o'clock blues / Blind love / Woke up this morning (my baby's gone) / Sweet little angel / Ten long years / Did you ever love a woman / Crying won't help you / Why do everything happen to me / Ruby Lee / When my heart beats like a hammer / Past day / Boogie woogie woman / Early every morning / I want to get married / That ain't the way to do it / Troubles, troubles / Don't you want a man like me / You know I go for you / What can I do
CD _____ CDCHD 320
Ace / Apr '91 / Pinnacle / Cadillac / Complete/Pinnacle.

SPOTLIGHT ON LUCILLE
Six silver strings / Big boss man / In the midnight hour / Into the night / My Lucille / Memory blues / My guitar sings the blues / Double trouble / Memory lane
CD _____ CDCH 187
Ace / Sep '86 / Pinnacle / Cadillac / Complete/Pinnacle.

THERE IS ALWAYS ONE MORE TIME
CD _____ MCAD 10295
MCA / Aug '91 / BMG.

THERE MUST BE A BETTER WORLD SOMEWHERE
Victim / More, more, more / You're going with me / Life ain't nothing but a party / Born again human / There must be a better world somewhere
CD _____ BGOCD 124
Beat Goes On / Sep '91 / Pinnacle.

TOGETHER FOR THE FIRST TIME (King, B.B. & Bobby Bland)
CD _____ BGOCD 161
Beat Goes On / Jun '94 / Pinnacle.

King, Ben E.

ANTHOLOGY (2CD Set)
There goes my baby / Dance with me / This magic moment / Lonely winds / Save the last dance for me / I count the tears / Brace yourself / Show me the way / Spanish harlem / First taste of love / Young boy blues / Stand by me / On the horizon / Here comes the night / Amor / Ecstasy / Yes / Walking in the footstesps of a fool / Don't play that song (You lied) / Ecstasy / Gypsy / I who have nothing / What now my love / Groovin' / That's when it hurts / Let the water run down / It's all over / River of tears / Seven letters / Record (Baby I love you) / She's gone again / Cry no more / Goodnight my love / Pleasant dreams / So much love / I swear by stars above / What is soul / Man without a dream / Tears, tears, tears / We got a thing going on / Don't take your love from me / It's amazing / Till I can't take it anymore / It ain't fair / Hey little one / Supernatural thing / Do it in the name of love / I had a love / Get it up for love / Star in the ghetto / Music trance
CD Set _____ 8122712152
Atlantic / Oct '93 / Warner Music.

BEN E. KING
CD _____ KLMCD 033
Scratch / Nov '94 / BMG.

BROTHERS IN SOUL (The Best Of Ben E. King & The Drifters) (King, Ben E. & The Drifters)
Stand by me / Up on the roof / Dance with me / Don't play that song (You lied) / On broadway / This magic moment / I who have nothing / Spanish Harlem / Saturday night at the movies / Please stay / There goes my baby / Supernatural thing (Part 1) / Under the boardwalk / Save the last dance for me / You send me / Unchained melody
CD _____ ECD 3044
K-Tel / Jan '95 / K-Tel.

COLLECTION, THE
CD _____ COL 055
Collection / Jan '95 / Target/BMG.

GREATEST HITS: BEN E KING
CD _____ CDSGP 045
Prestige / Apr '93 / Total/BMG.

LEGENDARY BEN E. KING
CD _____ HADCD 180
Javelin / Nov '95 / THE / Henry Hadaway Organisation.

SOUL KINGS VOL.3
Stand by me / Spanish harlem / I who have nothing / Don't play that song (You lied) / Supernatural thing / Take me to the pilot / Travellin woman / Love is / Into the mystic / Poison in my mind / She does it right / Beginning of it all / All your tomorrows
CD _____ SMS 058
Carlton Home Entertainment / Oct '92 / Carlton Home Entertainment.

STAND BY ME (THE ULTIMATE COLLECTION)
Stand by me / Save the last dance for me / I who have nothing / That's when it hurts / I could have danced all night / First taste of love / Dream lover / Moon river / Spanish harlem / Amor / I count the tears / Don't play that song (You lied) / This magic moment / Young boy blues / It's all in the game / Supernatural thing (part 1)
CD _____ 7802132
Atlantic / Feb '87 / Warner Music.

WHAT'S IMPORTANT TO ME
CD _____ ICH 1133CD
Ichiban / Jan '94 / Koch.

King, Bill

MAGNOLIA NIGHTS
CD _____ 139023-2
Gaia / May '89 / New Note.

King, Bob

BOB KING AND THE COUNTRY KINGS
Laurel Lee / Give my love to Rose / Hey mommy / Waltz of two broken hearts / Going back to an old love affair / Why don't you leave me / My petite Marie / If the things they say are true / Be careful of stones are throw / She went without saying goodbye / Pray for me mother of mine / Let's take a fair trade / Nothing ventured nothing gained / Lonely city park / That's what's on my mind / All Canadian boy / My home by the fraser / My son calls another man daddy / Rose of ol' pawnee / I dreamed about mom last night / No parking here / Just call on me / Boy with a future / I've been dreaming / Between our hearts / It's goodbye and so long to you
CD _____ BCD 15719
Bear Family / Aug '93 / Rollercoaster / Direct / CM / Swift / ADA.

JUST ME AND MY GUITAR
You and my old guitar / Little shirt my mother made for me / Patanio, the pride of the plains / Mommy please stay home with me / I'm just here to get my baby out of jail / French song / On the banks of the old pontchartrain / When the work's all done this fall / Old dog cabin for sale / Girlfriend on the river / Strawberry roan / Rockin' alone in an old rocking chair / I've been down that road before / Ballad of the chapeau boys / Mary Ann regrets / Memories of you / Rescue from the moose river gold mine / When it's lamplighting time in the valley / Cat came back / Ballad of Jed Clampett / Bluest man in the town / Cowboy / Jimmie Brown / Newboy / Little Tom / Train of memories / French Canadian girl / Road paved with heartaches / It breaks a mother's heart / Once more / Coconut Joe
CD _____ BCD 15718
Bear Family / Aug '93 / Rollercoaster / Direct / CM / Swift / ADA.

King, Bobby

LIVE AND LET LIVE (King, Bobby & Terry Evans)
CD _____ SPCD 1016
Special Delivery / Apr '94 / ADA / CM / Direct.

RHYTHM, BLUES, SOUL AND GROOVES (King, Bobby & Terry Evans)
CD _____ ROUCD 2101
Rounder / Dec '94 / CM / Direct / ADA / Cadillac.

King, Carole

FANTASY
Fantasy (beginning) / You've been around too long / Being at war with each other / Directions / That's how things go down / Weekends / Haywood / Quiet place to live / Welfare symphony / You light up my life / Corazch / Believe in humanity / Fantasy end

CD _____ 983307 2
Pickwick/Sony Collector's Choice / Oct '93 / Carlton Home Entertainment / Pinnacle / Sony.

HER GREATEST HITS
Jazzman / So far away / Sweet seasons / I feel the earth move / Brother brother / Only love is real / It's too late / Nightingale / Smackwater Jack / Been to Caanan / Corazon / Believe in humility
CD _____ CD 32345
CBS / Mar '91 / Sony.

IN CONCERT - THE GREATEST HITS LIVE
CD _____ CKINGCD 01
Quality / Feb '94 / Pinnacle.

MUSIC
Brother brother / It's going to take some time / Sweet seasons / Some kind of wonderful / Surely / Carry your load / Music / Song of long ago / Brighter / Growing away from me / Too much rain / Back to California
CD _____ 9825952
Pickwick/Sony Collector's Choice / Jun '94 / Carlton Home Entertainment / Pinnacle / Sony.

NATURAL WOMAN: THE ODE COLLECTION 1968-1976 (2CD Set)
Now that everything's been said / Hi de ho / Up on the roof / Child of mine / I feel the earth move / So far away / It's too late / I'm going again / Beautiful / Way over yonder / Where you lead / Will you still love me tomorrow / Smackwater Jack / Tapestry / (You make me feel like) A natural woman / You've got a friend / Music / Brother brother / It's going to take some time / Sweet seasons / Bitter with the sweet / Goodbye don't mean I'm gone / Been to Canaan / Corazon / Believe in humanity (live at Carnegie Hall) / Jazzman / Wrap around joy / Nightingale / Really Rosie / Alligators all around / There's a space between us / Only love is real / Ties that bind / You've got a friend (live) / Pocket money / This time in my life
CD Set _____ E2K 48833
Legacy / Oct '94 / Sony.

PEARLS/TIME GOES BY
CD _____ VSOPCD 199
Connoisseur / Jun '94 / Pinnacle.

REALLY ROSIE
Really Rosie / One was Johnny / Alligators all round / Pierre / Screaming and yelling / Ballad of chicken soup / Chicken soup with rice / Avenue P / My simple humble neighourhood / Awful truth / Such sufferin' / Chicken soup with rice (Repeat) / Really Rosie (reprise)
CD _____ 983257 2
Pickwick/Sony Collector's Choice / Aug '93 / Carlton Home Entertainment / Pinnacle / Sony.

SPEEDING TIME
Computer eyes / Small voice / Crying in the rain / Sacred of heart stone / Speeding time / Standin' on the borderline / So ready for love / Chalice borealis / Dancing / Alabastor lady
CD _____ 7567801182
Atlantic / Jan '96 / Warner Music.

TAPESTRY
I feel the earth move / So far away / Beautiful / You've got a friend / Where you lead / Will you still love me tomorrow / Smack water Jack / Tapestry / It's too late / Home again / Way over yonder / (You make me feel like) a natural woman
CD _____ CD 32110
Epic / Jun '89 / Sony.
CD _____ 4804222
Epic / Jun '89 / Sony.

WRAP AROUND JOY
Nightingale / Change in mind, change in heart / Jazzman / You go your way, I'll go mine / You're something new / We are all in this together / Wrap around joy / You gentle me / My lovin' eyes / Sweet Adonis / Night this side of dying / Best is yet to come
CD _____ CDTB 137
Thunderbolt / Mar '92 / Magnum Music Group.

King, Charlie

FOOD, PHONE, GAS & LODGING
CD _____ FF 536CD
Flying Fish / '92 / Roots / CM / Direct / ADA.

King, Claude

MORE THAN CLIMBING THAT MOUNTAIN, WOLVERTON MOUNTAIN THAT IS (5CD Set)
Flying saucers / I want to be loved / Million mistakes / Why should I / Beers and pinballs / Fifty one beers / She knows why / She's my baby / Take it like a man / So close to me / Got the world by the tail / Slow thinking heart / I think of you and me / Now that I love you / My future life will be my past / Over again / Run baby run / Not sure of you / Big river, big man / Sweet loving / Comancheros / I can't get over the way you got over me / Give me your love

and I'll give you mine / Pistol packin' papa / You're breaking my heart / I'm here to get my baby out of jail / Little bitty heart / Would you care / I backed out / Wolverton mountain / This land of yours and mine / Sheepskin valley / Burning of Atlanta / Don't that moon look lonesome / I'll go for the world by the tail / Culpepper community / Building a bridge / What will I do / Scarlet O'Hara / Hey Lucille / Where the red red roses grow / Sixteen tons / Lace mantilla and a rose of red / That's what makes the world go around / Sam Hill / Big ole shoulder / Whirl-pool (of your love) / When you gotta go (you gotta go) / Tiger woman / Great big tears / I won't belong in your town / Hold that tiger (tiger rag) / That's the way the wind blows / Little buddy / Come on home / Ancient history / There ain't gonna be no more / It's good to have my baby back home / Catch a little raindrop / Anna / Right place at the right time / Little things that every girl should know / Juggler / Watchman / Laura / Goodbye my love / Green green grass of home / Ruby, don't take your love to town / Almost persuaded / Ninety nine years / Parchman farm blues / Birmingham bus station / Yellow haired woman / Power of your sweet love / Beertops and teardrops / Sweet love on your mind / Green mountain / Four roses / I remember Johnny / Honky tonk man / First train headin' South / Ole slewfoot / North to Alaska / Battle of New Orleans / Sink the bismarck / All for the love of a girl / Whispering pines / When it's springtime in Alaska / House of the rising sun / Friend, lover, woman, wife / When you're twenty-one / I'll be your baby tonight / Turn it around in your mind / Mary's vineyard / Heart / Johnny Valentine / Highway lonely / Chip 'n' Dale's place / Help me make it through the night / Lady of our town / Just as soon as I get over loving you / Sweet Mary Ann / (Darlin' raise the shade) let the sun shine in / I know it's not been easy lovin' me / I know it's not been easy lovin' me (with strings) / This time I'm through / He ain't country / If my heart could stop / Don't do me bad / It's such a perfect day for making love / Sometimes you lose, sometimes you win / Cotton Dan / I'll spend a lifetime loving you / Night I cried / Cry yourself a river / Sugar baby candy girl / How long would it take / Just a bum husband / Best mistake I ever made / Bucks worth of change / I wonder who she missed me with today / I sat down on a beartrap (just this morning) / It starts off good (and keeps gettin' better) / Times and things keep changing / Last days of love
CD Set _____ **BCD 15619 EI**
Bear Family / Sep '94 / Rollercoaster / Direct / CM / Swift / ADA.

King Crimson

B BOOM OFFICIAL LIVE IN ARGENTINA
Vroom / Frame by frame / Sex, sleep, eat, drink, dream / Red / One time / B'boom / Thrak / Two sticks / Elephant talk / Indiscipline / Vroom vroom / Matte kudasai / Talking drum / Lark's tongues in aspic (part 2) / Heartbeat / Sleepless / People / B'boom (Reprise)
CD _____ **DGM 9503**
Discipline / Jul '95 / Pinnacle.

BEAT
Neal and Jack and Me / Heartbeat / Sartori in Tangier / Waiting man / Neurotica / Two Hands / Howler / Requiem
CD _____ **EGCD 51**
EG / Jan '87 / EMI.

COMPACT COLLECTION
CD _____ **TPAK 28**
Virgin / Nov '93 / EMI.

COMPACT KING CRIMSON, THE
Discipline / Thel hun ginjeet / Matte Kudasai / Three of a perfect pair / Frame by frame / Sleepless / Heartbeat / Elephant talk / 21st century schizoid man / I talk to the wind / Epitaph / March for no reason (part of Epitaph) / Tomorrow and tomorrow (part of Epitaph) / Red (LP & cassette only) / Cat food (LP & cassette only) / Court of the crimson king / Return of the fire witch / Dance of the puppets
CD _____ **EGCD 68**
EG / Jan '86 / EMI.

CONCISE KING CRIMSON, THE
21st Century schizoid man / Epitaph / In the court of the Crimson King (abridged) / Cat food / Ladies in the road / Starless (abridged) / Red / Fallen angel / Elephant talk / Frame by frame / Matte kudesai / Heartbeat / Three of a perfect pair / Sleepless
CD _____ **CDV 2721**
Virgin / Oct '93 / EMI.

DISCIPLINE
Elephant talk / Frame by frame / Matte Kudasai / Indiscipline / Thel hun ginjeet / Sheltering sky / Discipline
CD _____ **EGCD 49**
EG / Jun '88 / EMI.

FRAME BY FRAME - THE ESSENTIAL KING CRIMSON
21st Century schizoid man / I talk to the wind / Epitaph / Moonchild / In the court of the crimson King / Peace - a theme / Cat food / Groon / Cadence and cascade / La-

dies of the road / Sailor's tale / Bolero / Larks' tongues in aspic / Night watch / Great deceiver / Fracture / Starless / Red / Fallen angel / One more red nightmare / Elephant talk / Frame by frame / Matte Kudesai / Thela Hun Gingeet / Heartbeat / Waiting man / Neurotica / Requiem / Three of a perfect pair / Sleepless / Sheltering sky / Discipline / King Crimson barbershop / Get thy bearings and variations / Travel weary Capricorn / Mars / Talking drum / 21st Century schizoid man (2) / Asbury Park / Larks' tongues in aspic part 3 / Sartori in Tangiers / Indiscipline
CD Set _____ **KCBOX 1**
Virgin / Jul '95 / EMI.

GREAT DECEIVER, THE
CD Set _____ **KCDIS 1**
Virgin / Nov '92 / EMI.

IN THE COURT OF THE CRIMSON KING
21st century schizoid man / I talk to the wind / Epitaph / Tomorrow and tomorrow (part of Epitaph) / Moonchild / Illusion (Part of Moonchild.) / Court of the Crimson King / Return Of The fire witch / Dance of the puppets / March for no reason (part of Epitaph) / Dream
CD _____ **EGCD 1**
EG / Jan '87 / EMI.

IN THE WAKE OF POSEIDON
Peace - a beginning / Pictures of a city / Cadence and cascade / In the wake of Poseidon / Peace - a theme / Cat food / Devil's triangle / Merday Morn (part 1 of the Devil's Triangle) / Hand of Sceiron (Part 2 of the Devil's Triangle) / Garden of worm (part 3 of the Devil's triangle) / Peace - an end
CD _____ **EGCD 2**
EG / Jul '92 / EMI.

LARKS' TONGUES IN ASPIC
Lark's tongues in aspic (part 1) / Book of Saturday / Exiles / Easy Money / Talking drum / Lark's tongues in aspic (part 2)
CD _____ **EGCD 7**
EG / Jul '92 / EMI.

LIZARD
Cirkus / Indoor games / Happy family / Lady of the dancing water / Lizard / Prince Rupert awakes (part 1 of Lizard) / Bolero (The peacocks tale) / Battle of glass tears / Dawn song (part a of battle of glass tears) / Last skirmish (part b of Battle of Glass Tears) / Prince Rupert's lament (Part C of Battle of Glass Tears) / Big top
CD _____ **EGCD 4**
EG / '88 / EMI.

RED
Red / Fallen angel / One more red nightmare / Providence / Starless
CD _____ **EGCD 15**
EG / Jan '87 / EMI.

STARLESS AND BIBLE BLACK
Great deceiver / Lament / We'll let you know / Night watch / Trio / Mincer / Starless / Bible black / Fracture
CD _____ **EGCD 12**
EG / '87 / EMI.

THRAK
Vroom / Coda: marine 475 / Dinosaur / Walking on air / B'boom / Thrak / Inner garden / People / Radio I / One time / Radio II / Inner garden II / Sex, sleep, eat, drink, dream / Vroom vroom / Vroom vroom coda
CD _____ **KCCDY 1**
CD _____ **KCCDX 1**
Virgin / Apr '95 / EMI.

THREE OF A PERFECT PAIR
Model man / Sleepless / Man with an open heart / Nuages (that which passes, passes like clouds) / Dig me / No warning / Lark's tongues in aspic (part 3) (In digital stereo) / Three of a perfect pair / Industry
CD _____ **EGCD 55**
EG / Jan '87 / EMI.

VROOOM
Vroom / Sex, sleep, eat, drink, dream / Cage / Thrack / When I say stop, continue / One time
CD _____ **DGM 0004**
Discipline / Oct '94 / Pinnacle.

King Curtis

BLUES AT MONTREUX (King Curtis & Champion Jack Dupree)
Junker's blues / Sneaky Pete / Everything's gonna be alright / Get with it / Poor boy blues / I'm having fun
CD _____ **7567813892**
Atlantic / Jan '96 / Warner Music.

CAPITOL YEARS: KING CURTIS (1962-1965)
Turn 'em on / Beach party / Beautiful brown eyes / Your cheatin' heart / Tennessee waltz / Wagon wheels / High noon / Anytime / Home on the range / Night train to Memphis / I'm movin' on / Raunchy / Tumbling tumbleweeds / Walking the floor over you / Slow drag / New dance / Frisky / Alexander's ragtime band / Amorosa (Bossa Nova) / Strollin' home / Mess around / Sukiyaki / Summer dream / Do the monkey / Feel all right / Turn 'em on (Mono) / Theme from Lillies Of The Field (Amen) (pts 1 & 2) / More soul / Soul serenade / Honky tonk / Watermelon man / Memphis / Soul twist / Night train / Tequila / Wiggle wobble / One mint

julep / Can't sit down / Swingin' shepherd blues / My last date / Hideaway / Harlem Nocturne / Java / Stranger on the shore / Melancholy serenade / Summer dream (2) / Tanya / Hung over / Soul twine (Stereo) / Hungover / Soul twine (Mono) / Moon river / Girl from Ipanema / Sister Sadie / Something you've got / Take these chains from my heart / Let it be me / Hung over (Remake) / Misty (Re-make) / Bill Bailey, Won't you please come home / Peter Gunn / Shake / Ain't that good news / Twistin' the night away / Good times / Send me home / Bring it on home to me / Change is gonna come / You send me / Cupid / Having a party / Chain gang / Prance / Something you've got (Overdub)
CD Set _____ **BCD 15670**
Bear Family / Mar '93 / Rollercoaster / Direct / CM / Swift / ADA.

HONKERS AND BAR WALKERS VOL.2 (King Curtis/C. Ferguson)
CD _____ **DD 452**
Delmark / Oct '86 / Hot Shot / ADA / CM / Direct / Cadillac.

IT'S PARTY TIME
Free for all / Easy like / Hot saxes / I'll wait for you / Party time twist / Low down / Keep movin' / (Let's do) the hully gully twist / Slow motion / Firefly / Something frantic
CD _____ **CDCH 262**
Ace / Nov '93 / Pinnacle / Cadillac / Complete/Pinnacle.

OLD GOLD/DOING THE DIXIE TWIST
Fever / Honky tonk / So rare / Tippin' in / You came a long way from St. Louis / Tuxedo junction / Hucklebuck / Lean baby / Harlem nocturne / Night train / Soft / Sweet Georgia Brown / Alexander's ragtime band / (In) a shanty in old Shanty Town / St. Louis blues / Royal garden blues / When the saints go marching in / Basin Street blues / Muskrat ramble / Up a lazy river / St. James infirmary
CD _____ **CDCHD 614**
Ace / Jul '95 / Pinnacle / Cadillac / Complete/Pinnacle.

TROUBLE IN MIND
Trouble in mind / Jivin' time / Nobody wants you when you're down and out / Bad bad whiskey / I have to worry / Woke up this morning / But that's alright / Ain't nobody's business / Don't deceive me / Deep fry
CD _____ **CDCHD 545**
Ace / Jul '94 / Pinnacle / Cadillac / Complete/Pinnacle.

King Diamond

ABIGAIL
CD _____ **RR 349622**
Roadrunner / Jun '87 / Pinnacle.

CONSPIRACY
At the graves / Lies / Wedding dream / Something weird / Let it be done / Sleepless nights / Visit from the dead / Amon belongs to them / Victimised / Cremation
CD _____ **RR 9461-2**
Roadrunner / Aug '89 / Pinnacle.

DARK SIDES, THE
Halloween / Tem / No presents for Christmas / Shrine / Lake / Phone call
CD _____ **RR 24552**
Roadrunner / Oct '88 / Pinnacle.

EYE, THE
CD _____ **RR 93462**
Roadrunner / Nov '90 / Pinnacle.

FATAL PORTRAIT
CD _____ **RR 349721**
Roadrunner / '87 / Pinnacle.

IN CONCERT 1987
CD _____ **RR 92872**
Roadrunner / Dec '91 / Pinnacle.

SPIDERS LULLABY, THE
CD _____ **MASSCD 062**
Massacre / Jun '95 / Plastic Head.

THEM
CD _____ **RR 95502**
Roadrunner / Jul '88 / Pinnacle.

King, Diana

TOUGHER THAN LOVE
Love me thru the night / Shy guy / Love triangle / Ain't nobody / Tougher than love / Can't do without you / Slow rush / Treat me like a lady / Black roses / Tumble down
CD _____ **47777562**
Columbia / Jul '95 / Sony.

King, Earl

GLAZED (King, Earl & Roomful Of Blues)
It all went down the drain / Your love was never there / Everybody's gotta cry something / Love rent / Iron cupid / Somebody's got a tail / I met a stranger / Mardi gras in the city / Those lonely lonely nights / One step beyond love
CD _____ **CD 1035**
Black Top / '88 / CM / Direct / ADA.

HARD RIVER TO CROSS
CD _____ **BT 1090CD**
Black Top / Jun '93 / CM / Direct / ADA.

SEXUAL TELEPATHY
Old Mr. Bad Luck / I'll take you back home / Weary silent night / Time for the sun to rise / No one more for the road / Going public / Love is the way of life / Sexual telepathy / Happy little nobody's waggy tail dog / Always a first time / Make a better world
CD _____ **FIEND CD 168**
Demon / Aug '90 / Pinnacle / ADA.

King, Evelyn

BEST OF EVELYN 'CHAMPAGNE' KING, THE (King, Evelyn 'Champagne')
Shame / I'm in love / If you want my lovin' / Just for the night / Betcha she don't love you / I'm so romantic / Back to love (Only on cassette and CD.) / I don't know if it's right / Love come down / Action / High horse / Get loose / Music box / Shake down / I can't stand it / Your personal touch
CD _____ **ND 74538**
RCA / Apr '90 / BMG.

I'LL KEEP A LIGHT ON (King, Evelyn 'Champagne')
CD _____ **XECD 1**
Expansion / Jul '95 / Pinnacle / Sony / 3MV.

King Felix

OWL PLANE CRASH
CD _____ **SR 9450**
Silent / May '94 / Plastic Head.

King Ferus

MACEDONIAN WEDDING SOUL COOKING
Revisko oro / Romaniada / Kumov cocek / Olimpijski cocek / Bassal ferus / Staro cunovo oro / Turska igra / Romska gajda / Stipski cocek / Romska riznica / Bugarsko K4 oro / Dada sali / Dikman / Stipski sa sa / Tikino sa sa / Kocovo oro
CD _____ **CDORBD 089**
Globestyle / May '95 / Pinnacle.

King, Freddie

BLUES GUITAR HERO: THE INFLUENTIAL EARLY SESSIONS
Hideaway / Lonesome whistle blues / San-Ho-Zay / I'm tore down / See see baby / Christmas tears / You've got to love her with a feeling / Have you ever loved a woman / You know that you love me / I love the woman / It's too bad things are going so tough / Sen-sa-shun / Takin' care of business / Stumble / Sittin' on the boat dock / Side tracked / What about love / Come on / Just pickin' / I'm on my way to Atlanta / In the open / (The welfare) turns its back on you / She put the whamee on me
CD _____ **CDCHD 454**
Ace / Aug '93 / Pinnacle / Cadillac / Complete/Pinnacle.

BURGLAR
Pack it up / My credit didn't go through / I got the same old blues / Only getting second best / Texas flyer / Pulp wood / She's a burglar / Sugar sweet / I had a dream / Come on (let the good times roll)
CD _____ **BGOCD 137**
Beat Goes On / Apr '92 / Pinnacle.

FREDDIE KING
CD _____ **DVBC 9062**
Deja Vu / May '95 / THE.

FREDDIE KING LIVE
Big legged woman / Woman across the river / Look on yonder wall / Ain't no sunshine / Red light / Green light / We're gonna boogie / Have you ever loved a woman / Let the good times roll / Going down (encore)
CD _____ **CDCBL 759**
Charly / May '95 / Charly / THE / Cadillac.

FREDDIE KING SINGS
CD _____ **MBCD 722**
Modern Blues / Jun '93 / Direct / ADA.

HIDE AWAY DANCE AWAY
CD _____ **KCD 000773**
King/Paddle Wheel / Sep '92 / New Note.

KING OF THE BLUES
Same old blues / Dust my broom / Worried life blues / Five long years / Key to the highway / Going down / Living on the highway / Walking by myself / Tore down / Palace of the king / Lowdown in Lodi / Reconsider baby / Big legged woman / Me and my guitar / I'd rather be blind / Can't trust your neighbour / You was wrong / How many more years / Ain't no sunshine / Sky is crying / That's all right / Woman across the river / Hoochie coochie man / Danger zone / Boogie man / Leave my woman alone / Just a little bit / Yonder wall / Help me through the day / I'm ready / Trouble in my mind / You don't have to go / Please send me someone to love / Gimme some lovin' / Love her with a feeling / Boogie fuck / It hurts me too / Something you got / Ain't no big deal on you / I just want to make love to you / Hide away
CD _____ **CDEM 1580**
Premier / Nov '95 / EMI.

LIVE AT THE LIBERTY HALL
Hey baby / Feeling alright / Ain't no sunshine / Going down / Have you ever loved

a woman / My feeling for the blues / I love you so / Let the good times roll / Kansas City
CD _____ CDBM 097
Blue Moon / Jul '95 / Magnum Music Group / Greensleeves / Hot Shot / ADA / Cadillac / Discovery.

LIVE IN ANTIBES 1974
Going down the Highway / Woman across the river / T'ain't nobody's business if I do / Let the good times roll / Big legged woman / Have you ever loved a woman / Hideaway
CD _____ FCD 111
France's Concert / Jun '88 / Jazz Music / BMG.

LIVE IN NANCY 1975 VOL.1
CD _____ FCD 126
France's Concert / Jun '89 / Jazz Music / BMG.

MY FEELING FOR THE BLUES
CD _____ REP 4170-WZ
Repertoire / Aug '91 / Pinnacle / Cadillac.

PALACE OF THE KING
Living in the palace of the king / Please accept my love / Shake your booty baby / Mojo boogie / Big legged man / Hey baby / Look on yonder wall / Woman across the river / Have you ever loved a woman / Rock me baby
CD _____ CDBM 089
Blue Moon / Feb '92 / Magnum Music Group / Greensleeves / Hot Shot / ADA / Cadillac / Discovery.

TEXAS CANNONBALL
Freddie Kings with the Buggs Henderson band / Spoken introduction / Your move / Ain't gonna worry anymore / Hideaway / Guitar blues / Meet me in the morning / Boogie on down / Sweet home Chicago
CD _____ CDBM 062
Blue Moon / Nov '90 / Magnum Music Group / Greensleeves / Hot Shot / ADA / Cadillac / Discovery.

TEXAS SENSATION
You've got to love her with a feeling / Hideaway / Have you ever loved a woman / Sensa-shun / Look ma, I'm cryin' / San-Ho-Zay / I'm too down / Driving sideways / Takin' care of business / Someday after a while / Side tracked / You know that you love me / Teardrops on your letter / Stumble / She's put the whammy on me / Lonesome whistle blues / High rise / It's too bad (things are going so tough) / Welfare (turns its back on you) / Double eyed whammy
CD _____ CDCHARLY 247
Charly / Oct '90 / Charly / THE / Cadillac.

THIS IS THE BLUES
CD _____ IMP 701
Iris Music / Nov '95 / Discovery.

King Galliard

ROCKY ROAD TO DUBLIN
CD _____ 15370
Laserlight / '91 / Target/BMG.

King Hash

HUMDINGER
Hard as I try / I'm the one / Jessie May / Hey now / All I ever wanted was you / She's on the move / Deliver me from evil / What can I do / Leave a light on / Jack fell down / Jessie May (Reprise)
CD _____ IGCD 201
Iona / Jan '94 / ABA / Direct / Duncans

King Jammy

COMPUTER STYLE
CD _____ 792022
Ras / Nov '92 / Jetstar / Greensleeves / SRD / Direct.

HITS STYLE
CD _____ 792032
Ras / Nov '92 / Jetstar / Greensleeves / SRD / Direct.

ROOTS & HARMONY STYLE
CD _____ 792012
Ras / Nov '92 / Jetstar / Greensleeves / SRD / Direct.

King, James

LONESOME AND THEN SOME
CD _____ ROUCD 0350
Rounder / Oct '95 / CM / Direct / ADA / Cadillac.

THESE OLD PICTURES
CD _____ ROU 305CD
Rounder / Jan '94 / CM / Direct / ADA / Cadillac.

King, Jonathan

ANTICLONING
CD _____ REVVC 1
Sounds Of Revolution / Dec '92 / Grapevine.

MANY FACES OF JONATHAN KING
CD _____ MCCD 108
MCI / May '93 / Disc / THE.

King, Jonny

IN FROM THE COLD
CD _____ CRISS 1093CD
Criss Cross / Sep '95 / Cadillac / Harmonia Mundi.

King Krab

KICKING ROSE
CD _____ EAR 1-2
Earthling / Mar '93 / SRD.

King Kurt

DESTINATION DEMOLAND
67 Heaven / Slick black cadillac / Stomp / Jungle feet / Bye bye baby / Momma kurt / Zulu Joe / New club / Humpin' in the backseat / Martian Momma / Loud and dirty
CD _____ LINKCD 133
Street Link / Jul '90 / BMG.

LIVE AND ROCKIN'
CD _____ LOMACD 18
Loma / Aug '94 / BMG.

OOH WALLAH WALLAH
Zulu beat / Destination zululand / Bo Diddley goes east / King Kurt's hound dog / Wreck a party rock / Ghost riders in the sky / Gather your limbs / Rockin' Kurt / Lonesome train / Mack the knife / Oedipus rex / Do the rat / She's as hairy / Mack the knife (Remix) / Wreck a party rock (Extended version) / Banana banana banana / Scraming abdabs / Ape hour
CD _____ DOJOCD 91
Dojo / Dec '92 / BMG.

POOR MAN'S DREAM
CD _____ FIENDCD 761
Demon / Nov '94 / Pinnacle / ADA.

King L

GREAT DAY FOR GRAVITY
Tragedy girl / Dumbest story / Tom Driver / Greedy / All hail the alien Queen / Back to loving arms / Life after you / That's how it works / Hoping they'll be open / First man on the sun / Two cars collide / Don't believe in Hollywood / Lost and found and lost again / My last cigarette
CD _____ CIRCD 32
Circa / Oct '95 / EMI.

King, Lana

KING AND COUNTRY
Blue bayou / I will always love you / Stand by your man / Carolina moon / He'll have to go / Desperado / Don't it make my brown eyes blue / Take these chains / Will you still love me tomorrow / Make it through the night / Rose / Amazing grace
CD _____ SOV 001CD
Sovereign / Jul '92 / Target/BMG.

King, Little Jimmy

SOMETHING INSIDE OF ME
CD _____ BB 9537
Bullseye Blues / Apr '94 / Direct.

King Loser

YOU CANNOT KILL WHAT DOES NOT LIVE
CD _____ FNCD 309
Flying Nun / Oct '95 / Disc.

King Missile

HAPPY HOUR
Sink / Martin Scorsese / (Why are we) Trapped / It's Saturday / Vulvavoid / Metanoia / Detachable penis / Take me home / Ed / Anywhere / Evil children / Glass / And / King Murdock / I'm sorry / Heaven / Happy hour
CD _____ 7567824592
WEA / Feb '93 / Warner Music.

KING MISSILE
Love is / What if / Let's have sex / Pigs will fly / These people / Open up / Wind up toys / Delores / Tongue / Dishwasher / Socks / Bloodletting / Lien / Commercial / King David's dirge / Psalm / Happy note
CD _____ 756782589-2
WEA / Jun '94 / Warner Music.

King, Morgana

ANOTHER TIME, ANOTHER SPACE
CD _____ MCD 5339
Muse / Sep '92 / New Note / CM.

EVERYTHING MUST CHANGE
CD _____ MCD 5190
Muse / Feb '86 / New Note / CM.

FOR YOU, FOR ME
CD _____ 5140772
Verve / May '93 / PolyGram.

I JUST CAN'T STOP LOVING YOU
Drive / Song for you / Human nature / Love of my love / How about you / Sleepin' bee / It only happens when I dance with you / Summer me, winter me / They all laughed / I just can't stop loving you
CD _____ MCD 5408
Muse / Nov '94 / New Note / CM.

LOOKING THROUGH THE EYES OF LOVE
Through the eyes of love / Gentlemen friend / Time after time / I wished on the moon / Love is sweeping the country / Who's you / I'm born again / Imagination / I'm old fashioned / Dearly beloved / Lilac wine
CD _____ MCD 5257
Muse / Dec '95 / New Note / CM.

SIMPLY ELOQUENT
CD _____ MCD 5326
Muse / Sep '92 / New Note / CM.

TASTE OF HONEY, A
Taste of honey / Fascinating rhythm / Prelude to a kiss / Easy living / All blues / Bluesette / Easy to love / Night has a thousand eyes / Lady is a tramp / Try to remember / Imitation / I'll follow you / Sometimes I feel like a motherless child
CD _____ 4744132
Sony Jazz / Dec '93 / Sony.

THIS IS ALWAYS
This is always / They can't take that away from me / Let's get away from it all / It's you or no one / On a slow boat to China / Just friends / Best things in life are free / Things we did last summer / Can't believe that you're in love with me
CD _____ MCD 5493
Muse / Mar '94 / New Note / CM.

King, Nancy

CLIFF DANCE (King, Nancy & Glen Moore)
CD _____ JR 08032
Justice / Jun '94 / Koch.

POTATO RADIO (King, Nancy & Glen Moore)
CD _____ JR 008022
Justice / Oct '92 / Koch.

King Of The Slums

BLOWZY WEIRDOS
Gone all weirdo / Smile so big / Casin' the joint / Hot pot shebeen / Keepin' it all sweet / Clubland gangs / Joy / Rimo / Mard arse / Mood on / Blowzy luv of life
CD _____ CDBRED93
Cherry Red / Jul '91 / Pinnacle.

King, Paul

BEEN IN THE PEN TOO LONG/ TROUBLE AT MILL (King, Paul/King Earl Boogie Band)
Grey eyed Athena / Jean Harlow / Sugarcane / Three dog night / Whoa Buck / Clockwork machine / Candy man / I've changed my face / One legged man in a goldfish bowl / Bad storm coming / Take me back / Live your own life / Bovver blues / Plastic Jesus / If the Lord don't got you / Goin' the German / Keep your hands off my woman / Go down you murderer
CD _____ SEECD 429
See For Miles/C5 / Jul '95 / Pinnacle.

King, Pee Wee

PEE WEE KING & THE GOLDEN WEST COWBOYS (7 CDs) (King, Pee Wee & The Golden West Cowboys)
That cheap look in your eye / You were the cause of it all / Texas Toni Lee / Tennessee central / Southland polka / Steel guitar rag / Hear you honeych / Keep them cold icy fingers off of me / Don't feel sorry for me / Arkansas traveller / Out of my mind / Ten gallon boogie / Kentucky waltz / Don't forget / Jukebox blues / Chattanooga Bess / Say good mornin' Nellie / Forty nine women / Ghost and honest Joe / New York to New Orleans / I'm satisfied with you / Quit honkin' that horn / Oh Monah / Bull fiddle boogie / Tennessee waltz / Rootie tootie / Gotta climb those golden stairs / Every time I feel the spirit / Gospel boogie / Singin' as I go / Waltz of the Alamo / Whisper waltz / I lost my love (the color song) / Bonaparte's retreat / Blue grass waltz / Alabama moon / Tennessee tears / Get together polka / Nashville waltz / Waltz of regret / Lonesome steel guitar / Cornbread, lasses and sassafras tea / Fire on the mountain / Shocking rye straw / Billy in the lowground / Devil's dream / Fisher's hornpipe / Sally Goodin / Whistling Rufus / Going back to L.A. / You call everybody darlin' / Battle hymn of the Republic / Black eyed Susie / When they played that old Missouri waltz / Blame it all on Nashville / Kissing dance / Rag mop / What, where and when / Birmingham bounce / We're gonna go fishin' (next Saturday night) / Cincinnati dancing pig / River road two step / Mop rag boogie / No one but you / Within my heart (la golondrina) / Helegged hilegged / You drifted / Strange little girl / Chew tabacco rag / Slow poke / You won't need my love anymore / Two roads / Railroad boogie / Makin' like a train / Crying steel guitar waltz / Ragtime Annie Lee / Slow bloke / Slow coach / Silver and gold / If and when / Busybody / I don't mind / Two-faced clock / Mighty pretty waltz / Tennessee tango / Crazy waltz / Varsoviana / San Antonio rose / My adobe hacienda / One rose (that's left in my heart) / Under the double eagle / Spanish two step / Over the waves / Screwball / Last night on the back porch / Till I waltz again with you / Gone /

I'll go on alone / That's me without you / Your kisses aren't kisses anymore / Here lies my heart / Ricochet / Ricochet / Dragnet / Deck of cards / Huggin' my pillow / Changin partners / Bimbo / Backward, turn backward / In a garden of roses / Red deck of cards / Keep your eye on my darling / Indian giver / Why don't you all go home / How long / Peek-a-boo waltz / Peaches and cream / I can't tell a waltz from a tango / Flying home / Woodchopper's ball / Seven come eleven / Farewell blues / Tippin' in / Melody of love / You can't hardly get them no more / Tweedle Dee / Plantation boogie / Jim, Johnny and Jonas / Nevermind / Beauty as as beauty does / Half a dozen boogie / Blue suede shoes / Tennessee dancin' doll / Ballroom baby / Catty town / Absolutely, positively / Hoot scoot / I'll be walking alone in a crowd / Sugar beet / (I tasted) tears on your lips / Catchy tune / My darlin' (we're not too young to know) / Do you remember / Congratulations Joe / Prelude to a broken heart / Unbreakable heart / Janie / Little bit about myself (a phonobiography)
CD Set _____ BCDFI 15727
Bear Family / Feb '85 / Rollercoaster / Direct / CM / Swift / ADA.

King, Peter

SPEED TRAP
CD _____ JHCD 041
Ronnie Scott's Jazz House / Jan '96 / Jazz Music / Magnum Music Group / Cadillac.

TAMBURELLO
Dido's lament / You taught my heart how to sing / Boxer's demise / Leona / Bess, oh where's my Bess / My man's gone now / Yes or no / Imola / Ayrton / Tamburello / Theme from bartok's violin concert No.2 / Please don't ever leave me
CD _____ MMCD 083
Miles Music / Jul '95 / Wellard / New Note / Cadillac.

King Pin

GOD OF LOVE
CD _____ ARICD 072
Ariwa Sounds / Apr '92 / Jetstar / SRD.

LETTER FROM JAIL
CD _____ ARICD 059
Ariwa Sounds / Sep '90 / Jetstar / SRD.

King Pleasure

BETTER BEWARE (King Pleasure & The Biscuit Boys)
CD _____ ESSCD 259
Essential / Feb '95 / Total/BMG.

BLUES & RHYTHM VOL.1
CD _____ ESSCD 270
Essential / Jul '95 / Total/BMG.

LIVE AT RONNIE SCOTT'S
CD _____ ESSCD 261
Essential / Nov '94 / Total/BMG.

THIS IS IT (King Pleasure & The Biscuit Boys)
CD _____ ESSCD 247
Essential / Feb '95 / Total/BMG.

King Pleasure

KING PLEASURE & ANNIE ROSS SING (King Pleasure & Annie Ross)
Red top / Sometimes I'm happy / What can I say after I say I'm sorry / Parker's mood / Twisted / Time was right / Jumpin' with symphony sid / This is always / Don't get scared / I'm gone / Farmer's market / Annie's lament
CD _____ OJCCD 217
Original Jazz Classics / Nov '95 / Wellard / Jazz Music / Cadillac / Complete/Pinnacle.

King Rosa

CHEATING ON ME (King Rosa & Upside Down)
CD _____ BL 013
Bloomdido / Oct '93 / Cadillac.

King, Sandra

CONCERT OF VERNON DUKE, A (King, Sandra & Pat Smythe)
CD _____ ACD 197
Audiophile / Mar '95 / Jazz Music / Swift.

SANDRA KING & FRIENDS
CD _____ ACD 222
Audiophile / Aug '94 / Jazz Music / Swift.

SONGS OF VERNON DUKE
CD _____ ACD 187
Audiophile / Oct '93 / Jazz Music / Swift.

King, Shirley

JUMP THROUGH MY KEYHOLE
CD _____ GBW 007
GBW / Nov '94 / Harmonia Mundi.

King, Sid

GONNA SHAKE THIS SHACK TONIGHT (King, Sid & The Five Strings)

Good rockin' baby / Put something in the pot boy / Drinkin' wine spoli-oli / When my baby left me / Gonna shake this shack to-night / It's true, I'm blue / Crazy little heart / Mama I want you / I like it / But I don't care / Warmed over kisses (Previously unissued) / What have ya got to lose / I've got the blues / Ooby dooby / Booger eed / Twenty one (Previously unissued) / Sag, drag and fall / Blue suede shoes / Let 'er roll / Purr, kitty, purr
CD _____ BCD 15535
Bear Family / Mar '92 / Rollercoaster / Direct / CM / Swift / ADA.

King Sisters

GREAT LADIES OF SONG, THE
Memories of you / Don't take your love from me / But beautiful / What's new / I hadn't anyone till you / Early autumn / How long has this been going on / Imagination / There is no greater love / Deep purple / Spring is here / Four brothers / Nearness of you / That old feeling / Imposible / Take the 'A' train / That's all / Aloha oe
CD _____ CDP 8312032
Capitol Jazz / Aug '95 / EMI.

King Sounds

I SHALL SING
CD _____ VZA 002 CD
Viza / Jan '94 / Jetstar.

King, Tempo

TEMPO KING 1936-1937
Bojangles of Harlem / I'll sing you a thousand love songs / Organ grinder swing / Papa tree top tall / William Tell / (I would do) anything for you / High hat, a piccolo and a cane / We can cuddle at home / You're giving me a song and a dance / Alabama barbecue / That's what you mean to me / Sweet Adeline / You've got something there / Through the courtesy of love / I was saying to the moon / One hour for lunch / To Mary, with love / Swingin' the jinx away / Keepin' out of mischief now / You turned the tables on me / Swing high swing low / Floating on a bubble / Gee but you're swell
CD _____ CBC 1002
Timeless Historical / Jan '92 / New Note / Pinnacle.

King Tubby

CREATION DUB
CD _____ LG2 1111
Lagoon / Jul '95 / Magnum Music Group / THE.

CROSSFIRE
CD _____ LG 21050
Lagoon / Nov '92 / Magnum Music Group / THE.

DUB GONE CRAZY (The Evolution Of Dub At King Tubby's 1975-79) (King Tubby & Friends)
Champion version / Satta dread dub / Real gone crazy dub / Exalted dub / Dreada version / No love version / Peace and love in the dub / Wreck up a version / Hold them in dub / Jah love rockers dub / Step it up in dub / Dub with a view / Dub to the rescue / Dub fi gwan
CD _____ BAFCD 2
Blood & Fire / May '94 / Grapevine / PolyGram.

FIRST PROPHET OR DUB
CD _____ TWCD 1012
Tamoki Wambesi / Dec '95 / Jetstar / SRD / Roots Collective / Greensleeves.

HOUSE OF DUB (Channel One & King Tubby)
CD _____ GR 006CD
Sprint / May '95 / Jetstar / THE.

I AM THE KING
CD _____ SFCD 003
Sprint / Jul '95 / Jetstar / THE.

I AM THE KING VOL.2
CD _____ SFCD 4
Sprint / May '95 / Jetstar / THE.

KING TUBBY MEETS VIVIAN JACKSON (King Tubby & Vivian Jackson)
CD _____ YYJ 002CD
Yabby You / May '95 / Jetstar / THE.

KING TUBBY ON THE MIX 2 (Various Artists)
CD _____ OMCD 023
Original Music / Jul '93 / SRD / Jetstar.

KING TUBBY'S SOUNDCLASH VOLUMES 1 & 2
CD _____ SONCD 0012
Sonic Sounds / Jan '91 / Jetstar.

KING TUBBY'S SPECIAL 1973 - 1976
CD _____ CDTRD 409
Trojan / Mar '94 / Jetstar / Total/BMG.

MEMORIAL DUB
CD _____ RNCD 2060
Rhino / Sep '94 / Jetstar / Magnum Music Group / THE.

PSALM OF THE TIME DUB
CD _____ TWCD 1024
Tamoki Wambesi / Aug '95 / Jetstar / SRD / Roots Collective / Greensleeves.

ROOTS & SOCIETY
CD _____ RB 3003
Reggae Best / May '94 / Magnum Music Group / THE.

SENSI DUB VOLUME 3 (King Tubby & Prince Jammy)
Black up (dub) / Sensi dub (part 3) / Free herb (Dub) / Ministers (dub) / No bush (dub) / Meditation / Court house (dub) / Heavy metal (dub)
CD _____ OMCD 16
Original Music / '92 / SRD / Jetstar.

SHALOM DUB (King Tubby & the Aggrovators)
CD _____ RNCD 2107
Rhino / Jun '95 / Jetstar / Magnum Music Group / THE.

STUDIO V VS. CHANNEL 1
CD _____ RNCD 2126
Rhino / Nov '95 / Jetstar / Magnum Music Group / THE.

SURROUNDED BY THE DREADS AT THE NATIONAL ARENA
CD _____ STCD 003
Studio 16 / May '93 / Jetstar.

UNLEASHED DUB VOL 1
CD _____ FMCD 003
Fatman / Nov '94 / SRD / Jetstar / THE.

UPSET THE UPSETTERS
CD _____ RNCD 2037
Rhino / Nov '93 / Jetstar / Magnum Music Group / THE.

WATER DUB
CD _____ LG 21055
Lagoon / Feb '93 / Magnum Music Group / THE.

King Ubu Orchestra

BINAURALITY
CD _____ FMPCD 49
FMP / Sep '87 / Cadillac.

Kingdom Come

BAD IMAGE
Passion departed / You're the one / Fake believer / Friends / Mad queen / Pardon the difference (but I like it) / Little wild thing / Can't resist / Talked too much / Glove of stone / Outsider
CD _____ 450993148-2
WEA / Feb '94 / Warner Music.

JAM
CD _____ VP 163CD
Voice Print / Feb '95 / Voice Print.

Kingmaker

EAT YOURSELF WHOLE
Revelation / Really scrape the sky / Two headed, yellow bellied hide digger / When Lucy's down / Wave / Lady Shakespear's bomb / Everything in life / High as a kite
CD _____ CCD 1878
Chrysalis / Oct '91 / EMI.

IN THE BEST POSSIBLE TASTE
In the best possible taste (pt 2) / You and I will never see things eye to eye / Hey, birdman / Frustrated gangster / Story of my life / Sometimes I think she takes along just for the ride / One false move / Side by side / Fool like you / End of the line / In the best possible taste (pt 1)
CD _____ CDCHR 6098
Chrysalis / Apr '95 / EMI.

SLEEPWALKING
Playground brutality / Armchair anarchist / Queen Jane / Sad to see you go / Help yourself / Tomorrow's world / Ten years asleep / Honesty kills / Sequinned thug / Sleepwalking in the five o'clock shadow / Stay free / Pyromaniacs anonymous
CD _____ CDCHR 6014
Chrysalis / May '93 / EMI.

TO HELL WITH HUMDRUM
Saturday's not what it used to be / Never too high to fall / Lies before kisses / Loose lips sink ships / Ten years asleep / Honesty kills / Sleepwalking in the five o'clock shadow / Queen Jane
CD _____ CDCHR 6055
Chrysalis / Nov '94 / EMI.

King's College Choir

CHRISTMAS MUSIC FROM KINGS
CD _____ CDM 7641302
EMI Classics / Oct '91 / EMI.

SOUND OF KING'S, THE
On Christmas night / Hodie Christus natus est / For unto us a child (Messiah.) / Allegri / Miserere mei, Deus / Nunc dimittis / Funeral music for Queen Mary / Thou knowest, Lord / Dixit dominus (Psalm 109) / Nationibus / Pie Jesu (Requiem.) / Ave verum corpus (K 618) / Psalm 84 / O how amiable / No. 5 Antiphon / Gloria (Missa Brevis.) / Ceremony of carols (There is no rose.) / Ag-

nus dei (Requiem Op. 9.) / In paradisum (Requiem.)
CD _____ CDKCC 1
EMI / Oct '89 / EMI.

King's Own Royal Border..

BATTLE HONOURS (King's Own Royal Border Regiment)
CD _____ BNA 5075
Bandleader / Feb '93 / Conifer.

King's Singers

BEATLES CONNECTION
Penny Lane / Mother nature's son / Ob la di ob la da / Help / Yesterday / Hard day's night / Girl / Got to get you into my life / Back in the U.S.S.R / Eleanor Rigby / Blackbird / Lady Madonna / I'll follow the sun / Honey pie / Can't buy me love / Michelle / You've got to hide your love away / I want to hold your hand
CD _____ CDC 7495562
EMI / May '88 / EMI.

CHANSONS D'AMOUR
CD _____ 9026614272
WEA / Apr '93 / Warner Music.

DECK THE HALL (Songs For Christmas)
CD _____ CDM 7641332
EMI Classics / Oct '91 / EMI.

HERE'S A HOWDY DO
CD _____ 09026618852
RCA / Dec '93 / BMG.

MADRIGAL HISTORY TOUR
Amore vittorioso / Lirum bililirum / Il bianco e dolce cigno / La bella Franceschina / Ultimi miei sospiri / Alla cazza / Or si rallegri il cielo / Fine knacks for ladies / Who made thee, Hob, forsake the plough / Of all the birds that I do know / Too much I once lamented / Fair Phyllis I saw / Silver swan / Now is the month of maying / La Guerre / La la la je ne l'ose dire / Bon jour, et puis, quelles nouvelles / Mignonne, allons voir si la rose / Il est bel et bon / Margot labourez les vignes / Un gentil amoureux / Faulte d'argent / La tricota / Triste estaba el rey David / Cucu, cucu / Fatal la parte / Tres morillas m'enamoran / La bomba / Tanzen und Springen / Ach weh des Leiden / Vitrum nostrum gloriosum / Ach Elslein / Das g'laut zu Speyer / Herzliebstes bild
CD _____ CDM 769 837 2
EMI / Jul '89 / EMI.

POPS ALBUM
CD _____ 902660938-2
WEA / Apr '93 / Warner Music.

RENAISSANCE DESPREZ
CD _____ 09026618142
RCA / Dec '93 / BMG.

Kings X

DOGMAN
Dogman / Shoes / Pretend / Flies and blue skies / Black the sky / Fool you / Don't care / Sunshine rain / Complain / Human behaviour / Cigarettes / Go to hell / Pillow / Manic depression
CD _____ 756782558-2
Atlantic / Jan '94 / Warner Music.

GRETCHEN GOES TO NEBRASKA
Out of the silent planet / Over my head / Summer land / Everybody knows a little bit of something / Difference (in the garden of St. Anne's-on-the-hill) / I'll never be the same / Mission / Fall on me / Pleiades / Don't believe it (It's easier said than done) / Send a message / Burning down
CD _____ 781 997-2
Atlantic / Jan '89 / Warner Music.

KINGS X
World around me / Prisoner / Big picture / Lost in Germany / Chariot song / Ooh song / Junior's gone wild / Now just for the dead / What I know about love / Black flag / Dream in my life / Silent wind
CD _____ 7567805062
Atlantic / Mar '94 / Warner Music.

Kingsmen

JERK & TWINE TIME
You really got me / All day and all of the night / Money / Jolly green giant / Twine time / Land of 1000 dances / In crowd / Jerk / Jerktown / She's not there / Downtown / Limbo rock / In the misty moonlight / Beau and John interview
CD _____ CDSC 6010
Sundazed / Jan '94 / Rollercoaster.

KINGSMEN VOL. 1 (Louie, Louie)
Louie Louie / Waiting / Mojo workout / Fever / Money / Bent scepter / Long tall Texan / You can't sit down / Twist and shout / J.A.J. / Night train / Mashed potatoes / Haunted castle / Krunch / (You got) The gamma coochee
CD _____ CDSC 6004
Sundazed / Jan '94 / Rollercoaster.

KINGSMEN VOL. 2
Kingsmen introduction / Little latin lupe lu / Long green / Do you love me / New Orleans / Walking the dog / David's mood / Something's got a hold on me / Let the good times roll / Ooh poo pah doo / Great balls

of fire / Linda Lou / Death of an angel / And you believed him / Give her lovin'
CD _____ CDSC 6005
Sundazed / Feb '94 / Rollercoaster.

KINGSMEN VOL. 3
Over you / That's cool, that's trash / Jolly green giant / Don't you just know it / La do dada / Long green / Mother in law / Shout / Searchin' for love / Tall cool one / Comin' home baby / Since you been gone / It's only the dog / Wolf of Manhattan / I'll go crazy
CD _____ CDSC 6006
Sundazed / Jan '94 / Rollercoaster.

LIES
Lies / I can do it better / Can't you see I'm trying / Please don't fight it / Just one girl / I believe in her / Wishful thinking / You'll never walk alone / Your kind of lovin' / Harlem nocturne / It's not unusual / Turn to me / Just out of reach / Beau and John Charles interview
CD _____ CDSC 6011
Sundazed / Jan '94 / Rollercoaster.

LOUIE LOUIE
CD _____ CPCD 8160
Charly / Nov '95 / Charly / THE / Cadillac.

ON CAMPUS
Annie Fanny / Rosalie / Hard day's night / I like it like that / Stand by me / Little green thing / Climb / Sticks and stones / Peter Gunn / Sometimes / Shotgun / Genevieve / Get out of my life woman / Don't say no / My wife can't cook (mono)
CD _____ CDSC 6014
Sundazed / Jan '94 / Rollercoaster.

UP AND AWAY
Trouble / If I needed someone / Grass is green / Tossin' and turnin' / Under my thumb / Wild thing / (I have found) another girl / Daytime shadows / Shake a tail feather / Children's caretaker / Land of 1000 dances / Mustang Sally / Little Sally tease / Hush-a-bye / Killer Joe
CD _____ CDSC 6015
Sundazed / Jan '94 / Rollercoaster.

Kingston Trio

CAPITOL COLLECTORS SERIES; KINGSTON TRIO
Scarlet ribbons (From CBS TV presentation 'Playhouse 90'.) / Tom Dooley / Raspberries, strawberries / Tijuana trail / M.T.A. / Worried man / Coo coo-u / El matador / Bad man's blunder / Everglades / Where have all the flowers gone / Scotch and soda / Jane Jane Jane / One more town / Greenback dollar / Reverend Mr. Black / Desert Pete / Ally ally oxen free / Patriot game / Seasons in the sun
CD _____ CZ 384
Capitol / Jan '91 / EMI.

LIVE AT NEWPORT 1959
CD _____ VCD 77009
Vanguard / Oct '95 / Complete/Pinnacle / Discovery.

NICK, BOB & JOHN
CD _____ FE 5271
Folk Era / Dec '94 / CM / ADA.

ON STAGE
Tom Dooley / Greenback Dollar / Tijuana Jail / Where have all the flowers gone / Scotch and soda / Lion sleeps tonight / Early morning rain / Baby you've been on my mind / Shape of things / Hard ain't it hard / I'm goin' home / Colours / Hard travellin' / Tomorrow is a long time / Roving gambler / One too many mornings / Goodnight Irene / M.T.A. / Get away John / When the saints go marching in / Mood Indigo
CD _____ STOCD 103
Start / Oct '94 / Koch.

SPOTLIGHT ON KINGSTON TRIO
Tom Dooley / Lion sleeps tonight / Greenback dollar / Baby, you've been on my mind / Goodnight Irene / I'm goin' home / Roving gambler / Tijuana jail / Where have all the flowers gone / Colours / M.T.A. / Early morning rain / Shape of things to come / Tomorrow is a long time / When the saints go marching in
CD _____ HADCD 106
Javelin / Feb '94 / THE / Henry Hadaway Organisation.

STAY AWHILE
CD _____ FE 5435
Folk Era / Dec '94 / CM / ADA.

Kingstonians

SUFFERER
CD _____ CDAT 114
Attack / Jun '94 / Jetstar / Total/BMG.

Kinks

ARTHUR OR THE DECLINE AND FALL OF THE BRITISH EMPIRE
Victoria / Yes Sir, no Sir / Some mother's son / Drivin' / Brainwashed / Australia / Shangri la / Mr. Churchill says / She bought a hat like Princess Marina / Young and innocent days / Nothing to say / Arthur
CD _____ CLACD 162
Castle / Dec '89 / BMG.

BEST OF THE BALLADS, THE
Days / Waterloo sunset / Wonder boy / Ring the bells / Sunny afternoon / Two sisters / God's children / Death of a clown / Stopping you sobbing (Live) / Rock 'n' roll fantasy / Misfits / Heart of gold / Full moon / Don't forget to dance / Missing persons / Lonely hearts / Better things / Living on a thin line / Good day / Celluloid heroes (Live)
CD _____ 74321136872
Arista / May '93 / BMG.

BEST OF THE KINKS 1966-67, THE
Sunny afternoon / Afternoon tea / Rainy day in June / Mr. Pleasant / Most exclusive residence for sale / World keeps going round / Big black smoke / Dedicated follower of fashion / Dead end street / Love me till the sun shines / Autumn almanac / David Watts / Act nice and gentle / Dandy / I'm not like everybody else / Waterloo sunset
CD _____ PWKS 4075
Carlton Home Entertainment / Aug '91 / Carlton Home Entertainment.

BEST OF THE KINKS, THE
You really got me / All day and all of the night / Come on now / Set me free / Till the end of the day / Where have all the good times gone / Well respected man / Tired of waiting for you / See my friends / It's all right / Long tall Sally / Who'll be next in line / You still want me / I've got that feeling / I gotta move / Everybody's gonna be happy
CD _____ PWKS 527
Carlton Home Entertainment / May '89 / Carlton Home Entertainment.

COLLECTION, THE
Come dancing / Rock 'n' roll fantasy / Misfits / Superman / Lola (Live) / Low budget / Don't forget to dance / Good day / Living on a thin line / Heart of gold / Celluloid heroes (Live) / Full moon / Better things / You really got me (Live)
CD _____ 262794
Arista / Jun '92 / BMG.

DEFINITIVE COLLECTION, THE
You really got me / All day and all of the night / Stop your sobbing / Tired of waiting for you / Everybody's gonna be happy / Set me free / See my friends / Till the end of the day / Where have all the good times gone / Well respected man / Dedicated follower of fashion / Sunny afternoon / Dead end street / Waterloo sunset / Death of a clown / Autumn almanac / Suzannah's still alive / David Watts / Wonder boy / Days / Plastic man / Victoria / Lola / Apeman / Come dancing / Don't forget to dance
CD _____ 516465-2
PolyGram TV / Sep '93 / PolyGram.

EARLY YEARS, THE
CD _____ EARLD 15
Castle / Nov '94 / BMG.

EP COLLECTION: KINKS
See my friends / I gotta move / I've got that feeling / Don't you fret / Things are getting better / Set me free / Wait till the summer comes along / Such a shame / David Watts / Lazy old sun / Death of a clown / Funny face / All day and all of the night / Louie Louie / Well respected man / It's all right / I gotta go now / You really got me / Till the end of the day / Dedicated follower of fashion / Two sisters / Situation vacant / Love me till the sun shines / Suzannah's still alive
CD _____ SEECD 295
See For Miles/C5 / Aug '90 / Pinnacle.

FAB FORTY (The Kinks' Singles Collection 1964-1970/2CD Set)
I took my baby home / Long tall Sally / You really got me / All day and all of the night / I gotta move / Tired of waiting for you / Come on now / Everybody's gonna be happy / Who'll be next in line / I need you / Set me free / See my friends / Never met a girl like you before / Till the end of the day / Where have all the good times gone / Sunny afternoon / I'm not like everybody else / Dead end street / Big black smoke / Waterloo sunset / Act nice and gentle / Autumn almanac / Mr. Pleasant / Polly / Wonder boy / Days / She's got everything / King kong / Plastic man / This man he weeps tonight / Shangri la / Victoria / Mr. Churchill says / Lola / Berkeley mews / Rats / Apeman
CD Set _____ CDLIK 74
Decal / Jan '91 / Charly / Swift.

FACE TO FACE
Party line / Rosy won't you please come home / Dandy / Too much on my mind / Session man / Rainy day in June / House in the country / Holiday in Waikiki / Most exclusive residence for sale / Fancy / Little Miss Queen of Darkness / You're looking fine / Sunny afternoon / I'll remember
CD _____ CLACD 158
Castle / Dec '89 / BMG.

GIVE THE PEOPLE WHAT THEY WANT
Around the dial / Give the people what they want / Killer's eyes / Predictable / Add it up / Destroyer / Yo yo / Back to front / Art lover / Little bit of abuse / Better things
CD _____ 253 943
Arista / Sep '93 / BMG.

GREATEST HITS: THE KINKS
CD _____ BRCD 15
BR Music / May '94 / Target/BMG.

INTROSPECTIVE: KINKS
Waterloo sunset / Lola / Apeman / Interview part one / Where have all the good times gone / Dedicated follower of fashion / You really got me / Interview part two
CD _____ CINT 5005
Baktabak / Apr '91 / Baktabak.

KINDA KINKS
Look for me baby / Got my feet on the ground / Nothin' in the world can stop me worryin' 'bout that girl / Something better beginning / Naggin' woman / Wonder where my baby is tonight / Tired of waiting for you / Dancing in the street / So long / Don't ever change / Come on now / You shouldn't be sad
CD _____ CLACD 156
Castle / Dec '89 / BMG.

KINK KONTROVERSY, THE
Milk cow blues / Gotta get the first plane home / I am free / When I see that girl of mine / Till the end of the day / World keeps going round / I'm on an island / Where have all the good times gone / It's too late / What's in store for my life / You can't win / Ring the bells
CD _____ CLACD 157
Castle / Dec '89 / BMG.

KINKS
Beautiful Delilah / So mystifying / Just can't go to sleep / Long tall shorty / I took my baby home / I'm a lover not a fighter / You really got me / Cadillac / Bald headed woman / Revenge / Too much monkey business / I've been driving on bald mountain / Stop your sobbing / Got love if you want it
CD _____ CLACD 155
Castle / Dec '89 / BMG.

KINKS, THE
You really got me / Tired of waiting for you / Sunny afternoon / Autumn almanac / Lola / Days / Plastic man / Waterloo sunset / Dedicated follower of fashion / All day and all of the night / Victoria / See my friends / Death of a clown / Where have all the good times gone / Big black smoke / Powerman / I'm not like everybody else / Shangri la / Sittin' on my sofa / Top of the pops
CD _____ CDMFP 5921
Music For Pleasure / Oct '91 / EMI.

LIVE AT KELVIN HALL
All day and all of the night / Well respected man / You're looking fine / Sunny afternoon / Dandy / I'm on an island / Come on now / You really got me / Milk cow blues / Tired of waiting for you / Batman
CD _____ CLACD 160
Castle / Dec '89 / BMG.

LOLA
Lola / Tired of waiting for you / Victoria / So long / Got my feet on the ground / Dancing in the street / Nothing to say / Just friends / Got to be free / Dedicated follower of fashion / Village Green Preservation Society / Tin soldier man / Don't ever change / Dead End Street / Starstruck / Holiday in Waikiki / Milk cow blues / Dandy
CD _____ 5507232
Spectrum/Karussell / Jul '95 / PolyGram / THE.

LOLA VS POWERMAN AND THE MONEY-GO-ROUND
Contenders / Strangers / Denmark Street / Get back in line / Lola / Top of the pops / Money-go-round / This time tomorrow / Long way from home / Rats / Apeman / Powerman / Got to be free
CD _____ CLACD 163
Castle / Dec '89 / BMG.

LOW BUDGET
Attitude / Catch me now I'm falling / Pressure / National health / Superman / Low budget / In a space / Little bit of emotion / Gallon of gas / Misery / Moving pictures
CD _____ 251 146
Arista / Sep '93 / BMG.

MISFITS
Misfits / Hayfever / Black messiah / Rock 'n' roll fantasy / In a foreign land / Permanent waves / Live life / Out of the wardrobe / Trust your heart / Get up
CD _____ 260 173
Arista / Sep '93 / BMG.

PHOBIA
Opening / Wall of fire / Drift away / Still searching / Phobia / Only a dream / Don't / Babies / Over the edge / Surviving / It's alright (Don't think about it) / Informer / Hatred (A duet) / Somebody stole my car / Close to the wire / Scattered / Did ya
CD _____ 472489 2
Columbia / Mar '93 / Sony.

REMASTERED
CD _____ ESBCD 268
Castle / Mar '95 / BMG.

SHANGRI LA (A Tribute To The Kinks) (Various Artists)
CD _____ ILLCD 300
Imaginary / Apr '89 / Vital.

SOMETHING ELSE BY THE KINKS
David Watts / Death of a clown / Two sisters / No return / Harry rag / Tin soldier man / Situation vacant / Love me till the sun shines / Lazy old sun / Afternoon tea / Funny face / End of the season / Waterloo sunset
CD _____ CLACD 159
Castle / Dec '89 / BMG.

STATE OF CONFUSION
Definite maybe / State of confusion / Property / Labour of love / Come dancing / Don't forget to dance / Young Conservatives / Heart of gold / Once a thief / Bernadette
CD _____ 255 275
Arista / Sep '93 / BMG.

TO THE BONE
CD _____ KNKCD 1
Konk / Oct '94 / Grapevine.

VILLAGE GREEN PRESERVATION SOCIETY, THE
Village Green Preservation Society / Do you remember Walter / Picture book / Johnny Thunder / Last of the steam powered trains / Big sky / Sitting by the riverside / Animal farm / Starstruck / Phenomenal cat / All of my friends were there / Monica / People take pictures of each other / Wicked Annabella / Village green
CD _____ CLACD 161
Castle / Jan '88 / BMG.

YOU REALLY GOT ME
You really got me / I need you / Till the end of the day / Come on now / Long tall Sally / Cadillac / Beautiful Delilah / Everybody's gonna be happy / Things are getting better / All day and all of the night / Everybody / Don't ever change / David Watts / You still want me / Wonder where my baby is tonight / Don't you fret / Just can't go to sleep / Well respected man / I'm not like everybody else / Tired of waiting for you
CD _____ 5507222
Spectrum/Karussell / Aug '94 / PolyGram / THE.

Kinky Machine

BENT
CD _____ MCD 11085
MCA / Oct '94 / BMG.

Kinlochard Ceilidh Band

SLAINTE
CD _____ CDITV 601
Scotdisc / Mar '95 / Duncans / Ross / Conifer.

Kinnaird, Alison

MUSIC IN TRUST (Kinnaird, Alison & The Battlefield Band)
CD _____ COMD 2010
Temple / Feb '94 / CM / Duncans / ADA / Direct.

MUSIC IN TRUST, VOL.2 (Kinnaird, Alison & The Battlefield Band)
CD _____ COMD 2004
Temple / Feb '94 / CM / Duncans / ADA / Direct.

QUIET TRADITION, THE (Kinnaird, Alison & Christine Primrose)
CD _____ COMD 2041
Temple / Feb '94 / CM / Duncans / ADA / Direct.

SCOTTISH HARP, THE
CD _____ COMD 2005
Temple / Feb '94 / CM / Duncans / ADA / Direct.

Kinney, Fern

CHEMISTRY (The Best Of Fern Kinney)
Groove me / If tomorrow never comes / Together we are beautiful / Easy lovin' / Under fire / Nothing takes the place of you / Boogie box / Don't make me wait / Angel on the ground / I'm ready for your love / Sweet music man / Beautiful love song / Most girls / Sun, moon, rain / Baby let me kiss you / Pipin' hot / Pillow talk
CD _____ MCCD 167
MCI / Jul '94 / Disc / THE.

Kinney, Kevin

DOWN & OUT LAW
Down and out law / Save for me / Midwestern blues / Eye of the hurricane / Shindig with the lord / Bird / Tell him something for me / Chattahoochie coochie man / So take a look at me now / Mountain top / Never far behind / Epilogue / Beatnik Knight Street Kerouacian rip off in E
CD _____ MR 073-2
Mammoth / Jan '94 / Vital.

Kinsey, Big Daddy

CAN'T LET GO (Kinsey, Big Daddy & Sons)
CD _____ CDBP 73489
Blind Pig / May '94 / Hot Shot / Swift / CM / Roots / Direct / ADA.

Kinsey Report

CROSSING BRIDGES
Too early to tell / I take what I want / She's gone / Midnight drive / Strange things / Release yourself / Five women / Chicken heads / One too many / Key to your heart / Love is real / My kind of woman / Dancin' with the beast / I take what I want (version 2)
CD _____ VPBCD 9
Pointblank / Mar '93 / EMI.

EDGE OF THE CITY
Poor man's relief / I can't let you go / Got to play someday / Answering machine / Give me what I want / Full moon on Main Street / Lucky charm / Back door man / Over & love / Come to me
CD _____ ALCD 4758
Alligator / May '93 / Direct / ADA.

MIDNIGHT DRIVE
CD _____ ALCD 4775
Alligator / May '93 / Direct / ADA.

Kipper, Sid

LIKE A RHINESTONE PLOUGHBOY
CD _____ LER 2115CD
Leader / Mar '94 / Roots / Ross / Duncans / CM.

Kips Bay Ceili Band

DIGGING IN
You / Battle of New Orleans / Suite for Hillary / Affligem night / Talk to me / Place I am bound / Broken promises / Big dig / Boozoo goes to heaven / Crab song
CD _____ GLCD 1130
Green Linnet / Jul '93 / Roots / CM / Direct / ADA.

Kirby, John
1941-44
CD _____ TAX 37142
Tax / Aug '94 / Jazz Music / Wellard / Cadillac.

BIGGEST LITTLE BAND IN THE LAND, THE (2CD Set) (Kirby, John Sextet)
It feels so good / Effervescent blues / Turf / Dawn on the desert / Anitra's dance / When the eyes / Minute waltz / Front and center / Royal garden blues / Opus 5 / Fantasy impromptu / Blue skies / Rose room / I may be wrong, but I think you're wonderful / Little brown jug / Nocturne / One alone / Humoresque / Serenade / Jumpin' in the pump room / Milumbu / You go your way / Twentieth century closet / St. Louis blues / Hour of parting / Temptation / Blues petite / On a little street in Singapore / Chloe / Andiology / Let's be friends / Then I'll be happy / I love you truly / Frasquita serenade / Sextet from 'Lucia' / Coquette / Zooming at the zombie / If I had a ribbon bow / Who is Sylvia / Molly Malone / Barbara Allen / Bounce of the sugar plum fairy / Beethoven riffs on / Double talk / Cutting the capers
CD _____ 4776352
Sony Jazz / Jan '95 / Sony.

CLASSICS 1938-39
CD _____ CLASSICS 750
Classics / Aug '94 / Discovery / Jazz Music.

CLASSICS 1939-41
CD _____ CLASSICS 770
Classics / Aug '94 / Discovery / Jazz Music.

CLASSICS 1941-43
CD _____ CLASSICS 792
Classics / Jan '95 / Discovery / Jazz Music.

JOHN KIRBY 1941-44
CD _____ CD 37142
Tax / '92 / Jazz Music / Wellard / Cadillac.

Kirby, Kathy

BEST OF THE EMI YEARS, THE
My way / My Yiddishe Momme / Time / Come back here with my man / Wheel of fortune / So here I go / Turn around / In all the world / Yes I've got is that all there is / Little song for you / Oh pleasure man / Do you really have a heart / Please help me, I'm falling / Here, there and everywhere / Golden days / Little green apples / I'll catch the sun / Let the music start / My thanks to you
CD _____ CDEMS 1452
EMI / Jun '92 / EMI.

Kirchen, Bill

TOMBSTONE EVERY MILE
CD _____ BT 1109CD
Black Top / Oct '94 / CM / Direct / ADA.

Kirk

MAKIN' MOVES
CD _____ 7467826012
East West / May '94 / Warner Music.

375

Kirk, Andy

12 CLOUDS OF JOY, THE (Kirk, Andy & Mary Lou Williams)
Bearcat shuffle / Big Jim Blues / Close to five / Corky stomp / Dunkin' a doughnut / Floyd's guitar blues / Froggy Bottom / Gettin' off a mess / In the groove / Jump Jack jump / Little Joe from Chicago / Loose ankles / Lotta sax appeal / Margie / Mary's idea / Mellow bit of rhythm / Mess-a-stomp / Moten swing / Puddin' head serenade / Steppin' pretty / Toadie toddle / Twinklin' / Walkin' and swingin' / Wednesday night hop / Wham
CD _____ CDAJA 5108
Living Era / Apr '93 / Koch.

ANDY KIRK & HIS 12 CLOUDS OF JOY 1937-1938
CD _____ CLASSICS 581
Classics / Oct '91 / Discovery / Jazz Music.

ANDY KIRK & HIS 12 CLOUDS OF JOY 1940-1942 (Kirk, Andy & His Clouds Of Joy)
CD _____ CLASSICS 681
Classics / Mar '93 / Discovery / Jazz Music.

KANSAS CITY BOUNCE (Kirk, Andy & His Twelve Clouds of Joy)
CD _____ BLE 592402
Black & Blue / Dec '92 / Wellard / Koch.

MELLOW BIT OF RHYTHM, A (Kirk, Andy & His Orchestra)
Mellow bit of rhythm / Little Joe from Chicago / McGhee special / Hey lawdy mama / Cloudy / Froggy bottom / Wednesday night hop / Walkin' and swingin' / Scratchin' in the gravel / Toadie toddle / Take it and git / Boogie woogie cocktail
CD _____ 74321 13028-2
RCA / Sep '93 / BMG.

Kirk, Rahsaan Roland

CASE OF THE THREE SIDED DREAM IN AUDIO COLOR, THE
CD _____ 7567813962
Atlantic / Apr '95 / Warner Music.

DOES YOUR HOUSE HAVE LIONS (Rahsaan Roland Kirk Anthology)
Wham bam thank you ma'am / Bye bye blackbird / If I loved you / Old rugged cross / Ain't no sunshine / Volunteered slavery / Seasons / Going home / Black and crazy blues / I say a little prayer / This love of mine / Roots / Inflated tear / Blacknuss / I love you yes I do / Portrait of those beautiful ladies / Water for Robeson and Williams / Laugh for Rory / Entertainer (same in the style of blues) / Black root / Carney and bedgard dance / Anysha / Making love after hours / Freaks for the festival / Bye bye blackbird (2) / Three for the festival / Bright moments
CD _____ 812271406-2
Atlantic / Feb '94 / Warner Music.

INFLATED TEAR, THE
Black and crazy blues / Laugh for Rory / Many blessings / Fingers in the wind / Inflated tear / Creole love call / Handful of fives / Fly by night / Lovelieveliloqui
CD _____ 7567900462
Atlantic / Jul '93 / Warner Music.

JAZZ MASTERS
CD _____ 5220622
Verve / Feb '94 / PolyGram.

KIRK'S WORK
Three for Dizzy / Makin' Whoopee / Funk underneath / Kirk's work / Doin' the sixtyeight / Too Late Now / Skater's waltz
CD _____ OJCCD 459
Original Jazz Classics / '93 / Wellard / Jazz Music / Cadillac / Complete/Pinnacle.

LIVE IN PARIS 1970 VOL 2
Sweet fire / Make me a pallet on the floor / Charlie Parker medley / Volunteer slavery / You did it, you did it / Satin doll
CD _____ FCD 115
France's Concert / Jun '88 / Jazz Music / BMG.

RAHSAAN - THE COMPLETE MERCURY RECORDINGS 1961-1965 (11CD Set)
CD Set _____ 8466302
Mercury / Feb '91 / PolyGram.

RIP, RIG AND PANIC/NOW PLEASE DON'T CRY, BEAUTIFUL EDITH
CD _____ 8321642
Emarcy / Jul '90 / PolyGram.

SIMMER, REDUCE, GARNISH & SERVE
CD _____ 9362458112
Warner Bros. / May '95 / Warner Music.

SOUL STATION
Call / Soul station / Our waltz / Our love is here to stay / Spirit girl / Jack the ripper
CD _____ LEJAZZ 35
Le Jazz / Sep '94 / Charly / Cadillac.

SWEET FIRE
CD _____ JHR 73579
Jazz Hour / Jun '94 / Target/BMG / Jazz Music / Cadillac.

THREE FOR THE FESTIVAL
CD _____ LEJAZZCD 6
Le Jazz / Mar '93 / Charly / Cadillac.

WE FREE KINGS
Three for the festival / Moon song / Sackful of soul / Haunted melody / Blues for Alice / We free kings / You did it, you did it / Some kind of love / My delight
CD _____ 8264552
Mercury / Nov '86 / PolyGram.

Kirk, Richard H.

BLACK JESUS VOICE
CD _____ KIRKCD 3
Grey Area / Feb '95 / Pinnacle.

ELECTRONIC EYE
CD Set _____ RBADCD 8
Beyond / Aug '94 / Kudos / Pinnacle.

HIGH TIME FICTION
CD _____ KIRK 2CD
Grey Area / Oct '94 / Pinnacle.

NUMBER OF MAGIC, THE
CD _____ WARPCD 32
Warp / Jul '95 / Disc.

UGLY SPIRIT
Emperor / Confession / Infantile / Frankie machine (I) / Hollywood babylon / Thai / Voodoo / Frankie machine (II)
CD _____ KIRKCD 4
Grey Area / Feb '95 / Pinnacle.

VIRTUAL STATE
CD _____ WARPCD 19
Warp / Feb '94 / Disc.

Kirkintilloch Band

BRASS O' SCOTLAND
CD _____ BNA 5078
Bandleader / Mar '93 / Conifer.

Kirkland, Eddie

ALL AROUND THE WORLD
Shake it up / All I've got to offer / Live with it / Forty days and forty nights / Pick up the pieces / All around the world / Love don't love nobody / Country boy / There's gonna be some blues / Big city behind the sun / Someone to stand by me
CD _____ DELCD 3001
Deluge / Jan '96 / Koch.

DEVIL & OTHER BLUES DEMONS, THE
Devil / Rollin' stone man / Got to love my baby / I'm going to wait for you / Snake in the grass / Pity on me / Monther-in-law / Georgia woman / Hard to raise a family today / Burnin' love / Spank the butterfly / Tell me, baby / Mink hollow slide
CD _____ TRIX 3308
Trix / Nov '93 / New Note.

FRONT AND CENTRE
When I first started hoboing / I tried to be a friend / Eddie's boogie chillen / Nora / I need a love, not just a friend / I walked twelve miles / I've got an evil woman / Goin' back to Mississippi / Lonesome talking blues / Detroit rock island / Jerdine / Have you seen that lonesometrain / Going to the river, see can I look across
CD _____ TRIX 3301
Trix / Nov '95 / New Note.

HAVE MERCY
CD _____ ECD 26018
Evidence / Feb '93 / Harmonia Mundi / ADA / Cadillac.

IT'S THE BLUES MAN
Down on my knees / Don't take my heart / Daddy please don't cry / Have mercy on me / Saturday night stomp / I'm gonna forget you / I tried / Man of stone / I'm goin' to keep loving you / Train done gone / Something's gone wrong in my life / Baby you know it's true
CD _____ OBCCD 513
Original Blues Classics / Apr '94 / Complete/Pinnacle / Wellard / Cadillac.

SOME LIKE IT RAW
CD _____ DELD 3007
Deluge / Dec '95 / Direct / ADA.

WHERE YOU GET YOUR SUGAR
CD _____ DELD 3012
Deluge / Dec '95 / Direct / ADA.

Kirkpatrick, John

EARTHLING
CD _____ MW 4006CD
Music & Words / Jul '94 / ADA / Direct.

PLAIN CAPERS
Glorishears / Hammersmith flyover / Old Molly Oxford / Black Jack/Old Black Joe / Blue eyed stranger/Willow tree / Brighton camp/March past / Bobby and Joan / Monk's march/Fieldtown professional / Sweet Jenny Jones/Sherbourne jig / Lumps of plum pudding / Highland Mary / Wheatley processional / Maid of the mill/Cuckoo's nest/William and Nancy / Buffoon/Fool's jig / Constant Billy
CD _____ TSCD 458
Topic / Aug '92 / Direct / ADA.

SHEEPSKINS
Last night with Archie / Three jolly black sheepskins / Mad moll - the lively jig / Over the moon / Ronnets so blue / There's no doubt about it / Beating the oak / Dick the Welshman / Todley Tome / Blue eyed stranger / Watterdldy Lane / Tun dish / Maiden's prayer / Turn again Martha / Churning butter / Abram circle dance / Raddled tup / Hunting the squirrel / Zot for Joe / Four lane end / Cocking the chafer / Threepenny ha'penny treacle / Martha's comet or the evening star / Three hand reel / Green and yellow handkerchief dance / Prince of Wales / Morning star / Half a farthing candle / Hindley circle dance
CD _____ MWCD 4002
Music & Words / Jun '93 / ADA / Direct.

SHORT HISTORY OF JOHN KIRKPATRICK, A
CD _____ TSCD 473
Topic / Aug '94 / Direct / ADA.

STOLEN GROUND (Kirkpatrick, John & Sue Harris)
CD _____ TSCD 453
Topic / Aug '89 / Direct / ADA.

TRANS EUROPE DIATONIQUE (Kirkpatrick, J. & R. Tessi)
CD _____ Y225026
Silex / Jun '93 / ADA.

Kirtley, Peter

PETER KIRTLEY
CD _____ HY 200119CD
Hypertension / Feb '95 / Total/BMG / Direct / ADA.

Kirwan, Dominic

EVERGREEN
Hold me just one more time / Only couple on the floor / My happiness / Picture of you / If you've ever in my arms again / I really don't want to know / Evergreen / Absent friends / Release me / One bouquet of roses / Way love's supposed to be / Hello Mary Lou / Bless this house
CD _____ CD 0065
Ritz / Nov '91 / Pinnacle.

IRISH FAVOURITES
Through the eyes of an Irishman / Tipperary on my mind / Irish eyes / Star of the Country Down / If we had only had Ireland over here / Sprig of Irish heather / Medley / Village of Astee / Limerick you're a lady / My Galway queen / My mother's home / Rose of Tralee / My own Donegal / Song for Ireland / Medley #2 / Cavan girl
CD _____ RITZRCD 539
Ritz / Aug '94 / Pinnacle.

LOVE WITHOUT END
Like father, like son / Almost persuaded / Love letters in the sand / Straight and narrow / Just for old times sake / Stranger things have happened / Say you'll stay until tomorrow / When the girl in your arms (is the girl in your heart) / Love without end, amen / There's always me / Hand that rocks the cradle / Fool's pardon / Life is what you make it / Noreen Bawn
CD _____ RITZRCD 527
Ritz / Apr '93 / Pinnacle.

ON THE WAY TO A DREAM
Where does love go when it dies / Tonight we just might fall in love again / Hands across the ocean / Northern lights are shining for me / On the way to a dream / Answer to everything / Our love / Someone in your eyes / We'll be together from now on / My love is like a red red rose / I won't forget you / In my sleepless nights / What am I gonna do with all this love / Thank you for being a friend
CD _____ CD 0074
Ritz / Mar '95 / Pinnacle.

TODAY
CD _____ RITZCD 0071
Ritz / Oct '93 / Pinnacle.

TRY A LITTLE KINDNESS
Oh lonesome me / I'll leave this world loving my prince will come / Funkallero / Stella by starlight / Only trust your heart / You make me feel brand new / Lafite '82 / Gone / With a little song
CD _____ RITZCD 504
Ritz / '91 / Pinnacle.

Kishino, Yoshiko

FAIRY TALE
Beautiful love / Fairy tale / Island / Someday my prince will come / Funkallero / Stella by starlight / Only trust your heart / You make me feel brand new / Lafite '82 / Gone / With a little song
CD _____ GRP 98362
GRP / Jan '95 / BMG / New Note.

Kisor, Ryan

ON THE ONE
CD _____ 4737682
Sony Jazz / Jan '95 / Sony.

Kiss

CRAZY NIGHTS
Crazy crazy nights / Hell to hold you / Bang bang you / No no no / Hell or high water / My way / When your walls come down / Reason to live / Good girl gone bad / Turn on the night / Thief in the night
CD _____ 8326262
Casablanca / Feb '91 / PolyGram.

DESTROYER
Detroit rock city / King of the night time world / God of thunder / Great expectations / Flaming youth / Sweet pain / Shout it out loud / Beth / Do you love me
CD _____ 824 149-2
Casablanca / Apr '87 / PolyGram.

DOUBLE PLATINUM
Strutter ('78) / Do you love me / Hard luck woman / Calling Dr. Love / Let me go Rock 'n' Roll / Love gun / God of thunder / Firehouse / Hotter than hell / I want you / Deuce / 100,000 Years / Detroit rock city / She / Rock 'n' Roll all nite / Beth / Making love / C'mon and love me / Cold gin / Black diamond
CD _____ 8241552
Casablanca / Apr '87 / PolyGram.

FIFTEEN YEARS ON (The Interview)
CD P.Disc _____ CBAK 4002
Baktabak / Apr '88 / Baktabak.

HOT IN THE SHADE
Rise to it / Betrayed / Hide your heart / Prisoners of love / Read my body / Love's a slap in the face / Forever / Silver spoon / Cadillac dreams / King of hearts / Street Giveth and the Street Taketh Away / You love me to hate you / Somewhere between heaven and hell / Little Caesar / Boomerang
CD _____ 8389132
Casablanca / Oct '93 / PolyGram.

KISS ALIVE II (2CD Set)
Detroit rock city / King of the night time world / Ladies room / Making love / Love gun / Calling Dr. Love / Christine sixteen / Shock me / Hard luck woman / Tomorrow and tonight / I stole your love / Beth / God of thunder / I want you / Shout it out loud / All American man / Rockin' in the USA / Larger than life / Rocket ride / Anyway you want it
CD Set _____ 8227812
Casablanca / May '89 / PolyGram.

KISS ALIVE III
Creatures of the night / Deuce / I just wanna / Unholy / Heaven's on fire / Watchin' you / Domino / I was made for lovin' you / I still love you / Rock 'n' roll all nite / Lick it up / Forever / Take it off / I love it loud / Detroit rock city / God gave rock 'n' roll to you II / Star spangled banner
CD _____ 5148272
Vertigo / May '93 / PolyGram.

SMASHES, TRASHES AND HITS
Let's put the X in sex / Crazy crazy nights / (You make me) rock hard / Love gun / Detroit rock city / I love it loud / Deuce / Lick it up / Heaven's on fire / Strutter / Beth (feat. Eric Carr) / Tears are falling / I was made for lovin' you / Rock 'n' roll all nite / Shout it out loud
CD _____ 836 427-2
Vertigo / Nov '88 / PolyGram.

Kiss My Poodle's Donkey

NEW HOPE FOR THE DEAD
Sacred cow / Truck / Bad hair day / Psychoman / Mood B / Gett off / See my eye / Lizard
CD _____ HOT 1048CD
Hot / Feb '94 / Vital.

Kiss Of Life

REACHING FOR THE SUN
Love has put a spell on me / Fiction in my mind / As long as we're together / Only a fool / Pushing in / Love connection / Heaven is waiting / Holding on to a dream / Reaching for the sun / Be strong
CD _____ CIRCD 26
Circa / Oct '93 / EMI.

Kissoon, Mac & Katie

STAR COLLECTION
CD _____ STCD 1003
Disky / Jun '93 / THE / BMG / Discovery / Pinnacle.

SWINGING SOUL OF MAC AND KATIE KISSOON
Hey you love / Pidgeon / Chirpy chirpy cheep cheep / It's a hang up world / Change it all / (I found my) freedom / True love forgives / It's all over now / Love will keep us together / Vow / Love grows (Where my Rosemary grows) / Bless me / Don't make me cry / Swinging on a star / Black skinned blue eyed boys / Sing along / Love me baby / Show me / Hey diddle diddle
CD _____ C5CD-538
See For Miles/C5 / '89 / Pinnacle.

Kitaro

BEST OF KITARO
Morning prayer / Eternal springs / Oasis / Westbound / Silver moon / Four changes / Tunhuang / Sacred journey II / Revelation / Silk road fantasy / Shimmering light / Everlasting road
CD _____ CDKUCK 073
Kuckuck / Feb '87 / CM / ADA.

BEST SELECTION
CD _____ P 3012
Kuckuck / Jan '86 / CM / ADA.

DREAM
Symphony of the forest / Mysterious island / Lady of dreams / Drop of silence / Passage of life / Agreement / Dream of chant / Magical wave / Symphony of dreams / Island of life
CD _____ GEFD 24477
Geffen / Jul '92 / BMG.

IN PERSON/DIGITAL
CD _____ CDKUCK 054
Kuckuck / Jan '87 / CM / ADA.

KI
Revelations / Stream of being / Kaleidoscope / Oasis / Sun / Endless water / Tree / Cloud
CD _____ CDKUCK 057
Kuckuck / May '87 / CM / ADA.

LIVE IN AMERICA
CD _____ GEFD 24323
Geffen / Aug '91 / BMG.

OASIS
Rising sun / Moro-rism / New wave / Cosmic energy / Aqua / Moonlight / Shimmering horizon / Fragrance of nature / Innocent people / Oasis
CD _____ CDKUCK 053
Kuckuck / Jun '87 / CM / ADA.

TUNHAUNG
CD _____ CDKUCK 058
Kuckuck / May '87 / CM / ADA.

Kitchen Radio

VIRGIN SMILE
CD _____ GRCD 339
Glitterhouse / Dec '94 / Direct / ADA.

Kitchens Of Distinction

COWBOYS & ALIENS
Sand on fire / Get over yourself / Thought he had everything / Cowboys and aliens / Come on now / Remember me / One of those sometimes is now / Here comes the swans / Now it's time to say goodbye / Pierced / Prince of Mars
CD _____ TPLP 53CD
One Little Indian / Aug '94 / Pinnacle.

DEATH OF COOL
CD _____ TPCD 39
One Little Indian / Jul '92 / Pinnacle.

LOVE IS HELL
CD _____ TPCD 9
One Little Indian / May '89 / Pinnacle.

STRANGE FREE WORLD
CD _____ TPCD 19
One Little Indian / Apr '91 / Pinnacle.

Kitt, Eartha

BACK IN BUSINESS
Back in business / Let's misbehave / Solitude / Why can't I / Ain't misbehavin' / Usamore ot you / Glone enough for love / Brother can you spare a dime / Angelitos negros / Moon river / Speak low / Here's to life
CD _____ DRGCD 91431
DRG / Nov '94 / New Note.

BEST OF THE FABULOUS EARTHA KITT
CD _____ MCLD 19120
MCA / Oct '92 / BMG.

EARTHA KITT
CD _____ DVAD 6092
Deja Vu / May '95 / THE.

EARTHA KITT IN PERSON AT PLAZA
CD _____ GNPD 2008
GNP Crescendo / '88 / Silva Screen.

EARTHA-QUAKE
Annie doesn't live here any more / Lilac wine / I want to be evil / C'est si bon / Two lovers / Mountain high, valley low / Angelitos negros / Uska Dara / Avril au Portugal / African lullaby / Senor / Santa baby / Under the bridges of Paris / Oh John (please don't kiss me) / Let's do it / Salamgadou / Sandy's tune / Smoke gets in your eyes / Blues / My heart belongs to Daddy / Lovin' spree / Somebody bad stole the wedding bell / Looking for a boy / Lonely girl / Easy does it / I wantcha round / Apres moi / Mink shmink / This year's Santa baby / Hey Jacques / Strangers in the starlight / Do you remember / Day that the circus left town / Heel / Mambo de Paree / I've got that lovin' bug itch / Dinner for one please James / My heart's delight / Freddy / Sweet and gentle / Sho-ji-jo / Nobody taught me / Nothin' for Christmas / Je cherche un homme / If I can't take it with me / Just an old fashioned

girl / Mademoiselle Kitt / Oggere / No importa si menti / Lazy afternoon / There is no cure for l'amore / Lisbon Antigua / Lullaby of Birdland / Jonny / Fascinating man / Thursday's child / Le danseur de Charleston / Honolulu rock and roll / Vid kajen / Rosenkyssar / Put more wood on the fire / I'm a funny dame / Woman wouldn't be a woman / Toujour Gai / Waydown blues / Proceed with caution / Yomme, yomme / Take my love, take my love / Careless love / Beale Street blues / Hesitating blues / Memphis blues / Friendless blues / Yellow dog blues / Chantez les bas / St. Louis blues / Long gone / Steal away / Hist the window, Noah / Shango / Sholem / Torah dance / Tierra va temblar / Mack the knife / I'd rather be burned as a witch / Independent / Love is a gamble / Yellow bird / Jambo hippopotami / In the evening (when the sun goes down) / Lamplight / Let's do it again / April in Portugal / Johnny with the gentle hands / Johnny with the gentle hands (2) / Monotonus / Love is a simple thing / Bal petit bal / Overture / Dialogue : Mrs. Patterson / Mrs. Patterson / Devil scene / I was a boy / Fantasy / I wish I was a bumble-bee / Card game scene / Be good, be good, be good / Tea party scene / Tea in Chicago / My Daddy is a dandy / Finale / I can't give you anything but love / Solitude / Since I fell for you / What is this thing called love / Callete (caliente)
CD Set _____ BCD 15639
Bear Family / Oct '93 / Rollercoaster / Direct / CM / Swift / ADA.

LIVE IN LONDON
CD _____ JHD 083
Tring / Mar '93 / Tring / Prism

LIVE ON BROADWAY
CD _____ LDJ 274930
Radio Nights / Nov '91 / Harmonia Mundi / Cadillac.

SENTIMENTAL EARTHA
It is love (por amor) / Wear your love like heaven / I remember the rhymes / Paint me black angels (angelitos negros) / Catch me the wind / My sentimental friend / Once we loved / Way you are (asi eres tu) / Geneis / Hurdy gurdy man
CD _____ C5LCD 628
See For Miles/C5 / Sep '95 / Pinnacle.

STANDARDS
CD _____ ITM 1484
Hightone / Jul '94 / ADA / Koch.

THAT SEDUCTIVE EARTHA
Uska dara – a Turkish tale / Cest si bon / I want to be evil / Santa baby / Somebody bad stole de wedding bell / Lovin' spree / Under the bridges of Paris / If I love ya then I need ya if I need ya then I want you aro / Let's do it / Smoke gets in your eyes / Lookin' for a boy / Fascinating man / Mademoiselle Kitt / Just an old fashioned girl / I wantcha around
CD _____ 74321339472
Camden / Jan '96 / BMG.

Kix

SHOW BUSINESS
CD _____ CDMFN 159
Music For Nations / Mar '95 / Pinnacle.

K'Jarkas

CANTO A LA MUJER DE MI PUEBLO
CD _____ TUMICD 010
Tumi / Feb '90 / Sterns / Discovery.

EL AMUM I LA LIBENTAB
CD _____ TUMICD 013
Tumi / Apr '90 / Sterns / Discovery.

Klange

TIME 2/TIME 3 (Time Cubed In Time Square)
CD _____ MHCD 024
Minus Habens / Jan '95 / Plastic Head.

Klearview Harmonix

HAPPY MEMORIES VOLS 1 & 2
CD _____ DTCD 07
Discotex / Jul '92 / Jetstar.

THOSE WERE THE DAYS VOL.1
CD _____ DTCD 21
Discotex / May '94 / Jetstar.

Klein Healy, Eloise

ARTENIS IN ECHO PARK
CD _____ NAR 103 CD
SST / Jan '94 / Plastic Head.

Kleinow, Pete

LEGEND AND THE LEGACY, THE
CD _____ CDSD 076
Sundown / May '94 / Magnum Music Group.

Kleive, Iver

KYRIE
CD _____ FXCD 142
Musikk Distribusjon / Jan '95 / ADA.

Klemmer, John

MOSAIC (The Best Of Of John Klemmer)
Touch / Talking hands / Free fall love / Watrefall II / My love has butterfly wings / Barefoot ballet / Whisper to the wind / Body pulse / Walk with my love and dream / Tone row weaver / Quite afternoon
CD _____ GRP 98382
GRP / Jan '96 / BMG / New Note.

Klezmer Conservatory Band

JUMPIN' NIGHT IN THE GARDEN OF EDEN, A
CD _____ CD 3105
Rounder / '88 / CM / Direct / ADA / Cadillac.

KLEZMER CONSERVATORY BAND LIVE
CD _____ ROU 3125CD
Rounder / Jan '94 / CM / Direct / ADA / Cadillac.

OY CHANUKAH
CD _____ CD 3102
Rounder / Oct '88 / CM / Direct / ADA / Cadillac.

Klezmer Groove

TOO LOUD FOR DINNER
CD _____ OOMCD 1
Oom-Cha / Jan '95 / ADA.
CD _____ MSPCD 9503
Mabley St. / Sep '95 / Grapevine.

Klezmer Orchestra

KLEZMER SUITE
CD _____ SHCD 21005
Shanachie / May '95 / Koch / ADA / Greensleeves.

Klezmorim

FIRST RECORDINGS 1976-78
CD _____ ARHCD 309
Arhoolie / Apr '95 / ADA / Direct / Cadillac.

IS GEWIJN A FOLK
CD _____ EUCD 1059
ARC / '89 / ARC Music / ADA.

SHALOM
CD _____ EUCD 1060
ARC / '89 / ARC Music / ADA.

Klinghagen, Goran

TIME AGIN
CD _____ DRCD 247
Dragon / Oct '94 / Roots / Cadillac / Wellard CM / ADA.

Klingonz

BOLLOX
CD _____ FCD 3030
Fury / Apr '95 / Magnum Music Group / Nervous.

FLANGE
CD _____ FCD 3017
Fury / Apr '95 / Magnum Music Group / Nervous.

GHASTLY THINGS
CD _____ RUMBCD 013
Rumble / Aug '92 / Nervous.

Klugh, Earl

BALLADS
This time / Waltz for Debbie / If you're still in love with me / April fools / Rayna / Natural thing / Waiting for Cathy / Julie / Nature boy / Dream come true / Shadow of your smile / Christina
CD _____ CDP 8273262
Capitol / Feb '94 / EMI.

BEST OF EARL KLUGH
Tropical legs (Wishful thinking) / Amazon (Dream come true) / Magic in your eyes / Calypso getaway / Dr. Macumba / Long ago and far away / Angelina / Heart string / I vin' inside your love / Christina (Love ride) / Wishful thinking / I don't want to leave you alone anymore
CD _____ BNZ 264
Blue Note / Mar '91 / EMI.

BEST OF EARL KLUGH - VOL.2
Crazy for you / Night drive / Goodtime Charlie's got the blues / Cabo frio / Back in Central Park / Natural thing / Jolanta / Rainmaker / Captain Caribe / Cast your fate to the wind / I'll see you again / Right from the street
CD _____ BNZ 307
Blue Note / Feb '93 / EMI.

FINGER PAINTING
Dr. Macumba / Long ago and far away / Cabo frio / Keep your eye on the sparrow / Catherine / Dance with me / Jolanta / Summer song / This time
CD _____ CDP 7483862
Blue Note / '95 / EMI.

MOVE
Across the sand / Move / Far from home / Tiptoein' / Nightwalk / Face in the wind /

Big turtle river / Highway song / Winter rain / Doin' it / Across the sand part II
CD _____ 936245596-2
Warner Bros. / May '94 / Warner Music.

TWO OF A KIND (Klugh, Earl & Bob James)
Falcon / Whiplash / Sandstorm / Where I wander / Ingenue / Wes
CD _____ CDP 7991912
Capitol / Feb '94 / EMI.

Kluner, Kerry

LIVE AT WEST END CULTURAL CENTRE (Kluner, Kerry Big Band)
CD _____ JTR 84362
Justin Time / Jul '92 / Harmonia Mundi / Cadillac.

KMFDM

NIHIL
CD _____ IRS 993603CD
Intercord / Jan '96 / Plastic Head.

Knack

GET THE KNACK/BUT THE LITTLE GIRLS UNDERSTAND
Let me out / Your number or your name / Oh Tara / (She's so) selfish / Maybe tonight / Good girls don't / My Sharona / Heartbeat / Siamese twins / Lucinda / That's what the little girls do / Frustrated / Baby talks dirty / I want ya / Tell me you're mine / Mr. Handleman / Can't put a price on love / Hold on tight and don't let go / Hard way / It's you / End of the game / Feeling I get / (Havin' a) Rave up / How can love hurt so much
CD _____ BGOCD 248
Beat Goes On / Dec '94 / Pinnacle.

Knapsack

SILVER SWEEPSTAKES
Cellophane / Trainwrecker / Effortless / Fortunate and holding / Silver sweepstakes / Addressee / True to form / Symmetry / Centennial / Makeshift / Casanova
CD _____ A 075D
Alias / May '95 / Vital.

Knauber, Carol

NOW YOU'RE TALKIN'
Away with words / Bubbles, giggles and chuckles / Swinging banana shuffle / Half time / P.C.L. / Dangerous dreams / New day / No 1 funk / Casey's samba / Are you still thinking (Intro) / Now you're talkin'
CD _____ 101S 70592
101 South / Nov '93 / New Note.

Knepper, Jimmy

CUNNINGBIRD
CD _____ SCCD 31061
Steeplechase / Jul '88 / Impetus.

DREAM DANCING (Knepper, Jimmy Quintet)
CD _____ CRISS 1024CD
Criss Cross / May '92 / Cadillac / Harmonia Mundi.

I DREAM TOO MUCH (Knepper, Jimmy Sextet)
CD _____ SNCD 1092
Soul Note / '86 / Harmonia Mundi / Wellard / Cadillac.

SPECIAL RELATIONSHIP
John's bunch / Stella by starlight / Just friends / Intied John / Hoedwary of Jnm Lafitte / Sophisticated lady / Lester leaps / Primrose path / What is there to say / Gnome on the range / Round Midnight / Latterday saint
CD _____ HEPCD 2012
Hep / Mar '94 / Cadillac / Jazz Music / New Note / Wellard.

Knickerbockers

DRIVING RHYTHM GUITARS, WILD SOLOS...
Lies / One track mind / I can do it better / Just one girl / I must be doing something right / Chuck Berry medley / High on love / Stick with me / Love is a bird / I love / They ran for their lives / My feet are off the ground / She said goodbye / You're bad / Rumours, the places that make you / Rumours, gossip, words untrue / Comin' generation / Can't you see I'm trying / Sweet green fields / Give a little bit / Guaranteed satisfaction / Little children
CD _____ CDWIKD 122
Big Beat / Jan '94 / Pinnacle.

Knight, Beverley

B FUNK, THE
CD _____ DOMECD 6
Dome / Oct '95 / 3MV / Sony.

Knight, Brian

BLUE EYED SLIDE (Featuring Laurence Scott)
CD _____ LMCD 022
Lost Moment / Dec '94 / Else.

FILE UNDER BLUES
CD _____ CDEC 3
Blooze / Dec '94 / Else.

Knight, Curtis

LIVE IN EUROPE
CD _____ 858817
SPV / '90 / Plastic Head.

Knight, Frederick

I'VE BEEN LONELY FOR SO LONG
I've been lonely for so long / This is my song of love to you / Take me on home with-cha / Friend / I let my chance go by / Your love's all over me / Pick 'um up, put 'um down / Now that I've found you / Lean on me / Trouble / Someday we'll be together
CD _____ CDSXE 099
Stax / Nov '93 / Pinnacle.

Knight, Gladys

17 GREATEST HITS: GLADYS KNIGHT
CD _____ 530043-2
Motown / Jan '92 / PolyGram.

ANTHOLOGY - GLADYS KNIGHT
(Volumes 1 and 2) (Knight, Gladys & The Pips)
Every beat of my heart / Letter full of tears / Giving up / Just a little, honey / You don't love me no more / Take me in your arms and love me / Everybody needs love / I heard it through the grapevine / End of our road / I know better / Don't let her take your love from me / It should have been me / I wish it would rain / Valley of the dolls / Didn't you know (you'd have to cry some-time) / Got myself a good man / All I could do was cry / Friendship train / Tracks of my tears / You need love like I do / Every little bit hurts / If I were your woman / I don't want to do wrong / One less bell to answer / Is there a place (in his heart for me) / Master of my mind / For once in my life / Make the woman that you come home to / Help me make it through the night / Neither one of us / Daddy could swear, I declare / All I need is time / Don't tell me I'm crazy / Oh what a love I have found / Only time you love me is when you're losing me / Between her goodbye and my hello
CD _____ 530187-2
Motown / Jan '92 / PolyGram.

BEST OF GLADYS KNIGHT & THE PIPS (Knight, Gladys & The Pips)
Taste of bitter love / Ain't no greater love / I will fight / Save the overtime for me / When you're far away / You're number one (in my book) / Landlord / Hero / Friend of mine / My time
CD _____ 9827352
Pickwick/Sony Collector's Choice / Apr '92 / Carlton Home Entertainment / Pinnacle / Sony.

BEST OF GLADYS KNIGHT & THE PIPS (Knight, Gladys & The Pips)
CD _____ MATCD 205
Castle / Dec '92 / BMG.

BEST OF GLADYS KNIGHT & THE PIPS, THE (1980 - 1985) (Knight, Gladys & The Pips)
Licence to kill / Taste of bitter love / Bourgie bourgie / Love overboard / I will fight / My time / Landlord / Baby don't change your mind / Come back and finish what you started / Nobody but you / Part time love / One and only / Midnight train to Georgia / Wind beneath my wings / Try to remember (the way we were) / Best thing that ever happened to me
CD _____ 472038 2
Sony Music / '93 / Sony.

CLAUDINE/STILL TOGETHER (Knight, Gladys & The Pips)
Mr. Welfare man / To be invisible / On and on / Makings of you / Claudine theme (in-strumental) / Hold on / Make yours a happy home / Love is always on your mind / Home is where the heart is / Little bit of love / Baby don't change your mind / Walk softly / I love to feel that feeling / To make a long story short / You put a new life in my body
CD _____ NEXCD 206
Sequel / Jun '92 / BMG.

COLLECTION, THE (Knight, Gladys & The Pips)
CD _____ COL 058
Collection / Feb '95 / Target/BMG.

COLLECTION: GLADYS KNIGHT & THE PIPS (Knight, Gladys & The Pips)
Make yours a happy home / Best thing that ever happened to me / I feel a song (in my heart) / Georgia on my mind / Midnight train to Georgia / On and on / Where peaceful waters flow / I've got to use my imagination / I can see clearly now / Try to remember / One and only / Come back and finish what you started / It's a better than good time / Be yourself / So sad the song / Nobody but you / Pipe dreams / Baby don't change your mind / Part time lover / Way we were
CD _____ CCSCD 206
Castle / Oct '88 / BMG.

EVERY BEAT OF MY HEART (Knight, Gladys & The Pips)
CD _____ CDCD 1055
Charly / Mar '93 / Charly / THE / Cadillac.

EVERY BEAT OF MY HEART (Knight, Gladys & The Pips)
CD _____ CDSGP 0130
Prestige / Nov '95 / Total/BMG.

GLADYS KNIGHT
CD _____ LECD 048
Dynamite / May '94 / THE.

GLADYS KNIGHT & THE PIPS - 2ND ANNIVERSARY / PIPE DREAMS (Knight, Gladys & The Pips)
Money / Street brother / Part time love / At every end there's a beginning / Georgia on my mind / You and me against the world / Where do I put his memory / Summer sun / Feel like makin' love / So sad the song / Alaskan pipeline / Pot of Jazz / I'll miss you / Nobody but you / Pipe dreams / Every-body's got to find a way / I will follow my dream
CD _____ NEXCD 236
Sequel / Mar '93 / BMG.

HIT SINGLE COLLECTABLES (Knight, Gladys & The Pips)
CD _____ DISK 4506
Disky / Apr '94 / THE / BMG / Discovery / Pinnacle.

IMAGINATION/I FEEL A SONG (Knight, Gladys & The Pips)
Midnight train to Georgia / I've got to use my imagination / Storms of troubled times / Best thing that ever happened to me / Once in a lifetime thing / Where peaceful waters flow / I can see clearly now / Perfect love / Window raisin' Granny / I feel a song (in my heart) / Love finds it's own way / Seconds / Going ups and coming downs / Way we were / Try to remember / Better go your own way / Don't burn down the bridge / Need to be / Tenderness is his way
CD _____ NEXCD 192
Sequel / Feb '92 / BMG.

MIDNIGHT TRAIN TO GEORGIA
Baby don't change your mind / One and only / Georgia on my mind / Best thing that ever happened to me / Perfect love / On and on / Come back and finish what you started / Better you go your way / Home is where the heart is / Midnight train to Geor-gia / Nobody but you / Feel like making love / I'm coming home again / I feel a song (in my heart) / Where peaceful waters flow / Part time love / Sorry doesn't always make it right / I can see clearly now
CD _____ 5507352
Spectrum/Karussell / Sep '94 / PolyGram / THE.

ONE AND ONLY/MISS GLADY'S KNIGHT (Knight, Gladys & The Pips)
One and only / What if I should ever need you / Sorry doesn't always make it right / Don't say no to me tonight / Butterfly / Sail away/Freedom for the stallion / It's better than a good time (Disco) / Way it was / With you in mind / Be yourself / All the time / Come back and finish what you started / It's up to you (Do what you do) / I'm coming home again / You can't catch up with you / We don't make each other laugh anymore / I'll take a melody / Love gives you the power
CD _____ NEMCD 645
Sequel / Apr '94 / BMG.

SINGLES ALBUM - GLADYS KNIGHT & THE PIPS (Knight, Gladys & The Pips)
Licence to kill / Help me make it through the night / Best thing that ever happened to me / Baby don't change your mind / Bour-gie bourgie / Taste of bitter love / One and only / Just walk in my shoes / Midnight train to Georgia / Try to remember / Look of love / Part time love / Come back and finish what you started / So sad the song / Take me in your arms and love me / Love over-board / Lovin' on next to nothin' / Neither one of us
CD _____ 842 003 2
PolyGram TV / Oct '89 / PolyGram.

SOUL QUEENS VOL.2
Every beat of my heart / Room in your heart / Runnin' around / Trust in you / Letter full of tears / You broke your promise / Operator / Come see about me / Morning, noon and night / Guess who / What shall I do
CD _____ SMS 060
Carlton Home Entertainment / Oct '92 / Carlton Home Entertainment.

VERY BEST OF GLADYS KNIGHT, THE
CD _____ TRTCD 132
TrueTrax / Feb '96 / THE.

VISIONS (Knight, Gladys & The Pips)
When you're far away / Just be my lover / Save the overtime for me / Heaven sent / Don't make me run away / Ain't no greater love / Seconds / You're number one (in my book) / Oh la de da / Hero
CD _____ 902119-2
Carlton Home Entertainment / Jul '89 / Carl-ton Home Entertainment.

WAY WE WERE, THE (Knight, Gladys & The Pips)
Midnight train to Georgia / So sad the song / Baby don't change your mind / Home is where the heart is / Nobody but you / I feel a song (in my heart) / Feel like makin' love / Hold on / Little bit of love / Try to remem-ber (the way we were) / Come back and finish what you started / Part time love / It's a better than good time / Georgia on my mind / Make yours a happy home / Best thing that ever happened to me / We don't make each other laugh anymore / Sorry doesn't always make it right
CD _____ MCCD 005
Music Club / Feb '91 / Disc / THE / CM.

YOU'VE LOST THAT LOVIN' FEELIN' (Knight, Gladys & The Pips)
Every beat of my heart / Groovin' / Every little bit hurts / Nitty gritty / Your old standby / Valley of the Dolls (theme) / Look of love / Just walk in my shoes / Don't let her take your love from me / I wish it would rain / Tracks of my tears / It's summer / You've lost that lovin' feelin' / Yesterday
CD _____ 5500742
Spectrum/Karussell / May '93 / PolyGram / THE.

Knight, Jean

MR BIG STUFF
Mr. Big Stuff / Little bit of something / Don't talk about Jody / Think it over / Take him (you can have my man) / You city slicker / Why I keep living these memories / Call me your fool if you want to / One way ticket to nowhere (It's the end of the ride) / You six-bit change / Do me / Helping man / Carry on / Save the last kiss for me / Pick up the pieces / You think you're hot stuff
CD _____ CDSX 003
Stax / Apr '90 / Pinnacle.

Knight, Peter

NUMBER ONE (Knight, Peter & Danny Thompson)
CD _____ RES 108CD
Resurgence / Aug '95 / Vital.

Knights Of The...

KNEES UP MOTHER EARTH (Knights Of The Occasional Table)
CD _____ FUCD 1
Middle Earth / Mar '95 / Disc.

PLANET SWEET, THE (Knights Of The Occasional Table)
CD _____ MIDDL 2CD
Middle Earth / Jul '95 / Disc.

Knochengirl

KNOCHEN = GIRL
CD _____ EFA 127232
Fidel Bastro / Apr '95 / SRD.

Knock Down Ginger

SNOWMANS LAND
CD _____ ZULU 017CD
Zulu / Oct '95 / Plastic Head.

Knopfler, David

GIVER, THE
CD _____ PERMCD 26
Permanent / Jul '94 / Total/BMG.

Knopfler, Mark

GOLDEN HEART
Darling pretty / Imelda / Golden heart / No can do / Vic and Ray / Don't you get it / Night in summer long ago / Cannibals / I'm the fool / Je suis desole / Ridiger / Nobo-dy's got the gun / Done with Bonaparte / Are we in trouble now
CD _____ 514 732 2
Mercury / Mar '96 / PolyGram.

Know How

REALITY
CD _____ 558442
P1 / '89 / Plastic Head.

Knowledge

STUMBLING BLOCK
Tamoki Wambesi / Feb '95 / Jetstar / SRD _____ TWCD 1034
/ Roots Collective / Greensleeves.

Knowles, Chris

FRAME OF HARMONY
CD _____ FH 0010CD
Brenin / Apr '95 / ADA.

Knox, Buddy

PARTY DOLL
CD _____ RSRCD 004
Rockstar / Apr '94 / Rollercoaster / Direct / Magnum Music Group / Nervous.

Knox, Chris

SONGS OF YOU AND ME
CD _____ FN 313
Flying Nun / Mar '95 / Disc.

Knuckles, Frankie

WELCOME TO THE REAL WORLD (Knuckles, Frankie & Adeva)
Fanfare / Welcome to the real world / Too many fish / Love can change it / Keep it real / You're number one (in my book) / Passion and pain / What am I missin' / Whadda U want (from me) / Tell me why / Walkin' / Tribute / Reprise
CD _____ CDVUS 82
Virgin / May '95 / EMI.

Knudsen, Kenneth

COMPACKED
CD _____ MECCACD 1008
Music Mecca / Nov '94 / Jazz Music / Cadillac / Wellard.

I ME HIM
CD _____ MECCACD 1007
Music Mecca / Nov '94 / Jazz Music / Cadillac / Wellard.

Knuttson, Jones

VIEWS
CD _____ 1426
Caprice / Jan '89 / CM / Complete / Pinnacle / Cadillac / ADA.

Kobat

PIECES FOR PREPARED PIANO
Bindu / Ghafla / Naib / Akarso / Quanat / Varota / Semuta / Harq-al-ada / Ix / Urosh-nor / Ilm / Caladan / Burseg
CD _____ 950220CD
Source / Aug '95 / Vital.

Koch, Hans

CHOCKSHUT
CD _____ INTAKTCD 031
Intakt / Oct '94 / Cadillac / SRD.

Kode IV

INSANE
CD _____ KK 078CD
KK / Jun '92 / Plastic Head.

POSSESSED
CD _____ KK 052 CD
KK / Sep '90 / Plastic Head.

SILICON CIVILISATION
CD _____ KK 109CD
KK / Feb '95 / Plastic Head.

Koenig, Brian

WAKE UP (Koenig, Brian & The Standback Blues Band)
CD _____ BLUELOONCD 027
Blue Loon / Jul '95 / Hot Shot.

Koenig, Michael

ACOUSMATRIX 1/2
CD Set _____ BHVAASTCD 9001/2
Bvhaast / Jan '92 / Cadillac.

Koerner, John

BLUES, RAGS AND HOLLERS (Koerner, Ray & Glover)
CD _____ RHR 76CD
Red House / Jul '95 / Koch / ADA.

RAISED BY HUMANS
CD _____ RHRCD 44
Red House / Oct '95 / Koch / ADA.

Kofi

FRIDAY'S CHILD
CD _____ ARICD 064
Ariwa Sounds / Dec '94 / Jetstar / SRD.

VERY REGGAE CHRISTMAS, A
CD _____ 7567827132
WEA / Nov '94 / Warner Music.

WISHING WELL
CD _____ ARICD 092
Ariwa Sounds / Jan '95 / Jetstar / SRD.

Koga, Miyuki

DREAMIN'
My buddy / Do do do / I surrender dear / I don't know why / Blues serenade/Serenade in blue / Isn't it a lovely day / Put the blame on mame / When my sugar walks down the street / You made me love you / My mel-ancholy baby / S'posin' / I know that you know / Let me sing and I'm happy
CD _____ CCD 4588
Concord Jazz / Feb '94 / New Note.

Koglmann, Franz

ABOUT YESTERDAY'S EZZTHETICS
CD _____ ARTCD 6003
Hat Art / Jul '88 / Harmonia Mundi / ADA / Cadillac.

CANTOS I-IV
CD _____ ARTCD 6123
Hat Art / Jan '94 / Harmonia Mundi / ADA / Cadillac.

L'HEURE BLEUE
CD _____ ARTCD 6093
Hat Art / Jan '92 / Harmonia Mundi / Cadillac.

SCHLAF SCHLEMMER, SCHLAF MAGRITTE
CD _____ ARTCD 0100
Hat Art / Sep '92 / Harmonia Mundi / Cadillac.

Koinonia

PILGRIMS PROGRESSION - THE BEST OF KOINONIA
CD _____ MAXCD 1019
Maxus / Oct '92 / Harmonia Mundi.

Koken, Walt

BANJONIQUE
CD _____ ROUCD 0337
Rounder / Oct '94 / CM / Direct / ADA / Cadillac.

HEI-WA HOEDOWN
CD _____ ROUCD 0367
Rounder / Nov '95 / CM / Direct / ADA / Cadillac.

Koko

BALFONS & AFRICAN DRUMS VOL.2 (Music From Bakino Faeo)
CD _____ PS 65101
Playasound / Apr '93 / Harmonia Mundi / ADA.

Kokubu, Hiroko

MORE THAN YOU KNOW
CD _____ JD 3312
JVC / Oct '88 / New Note.

PURE HEART
Barefoot steppin' / Luck in the rain / Smooth struttin' / Vitamina / Once and forever / Mrs. Robinson / Annabella / Weekend / It's cool / Happiest for you (for your wedding)
CD _____ JVC 20422
JVC / Mar '95 / New Note.

Kol Aviv

CHANTS ET DANSES D'ISRAEL
Meh'ol halahat / Et dodim kala / Suite yemenite / Ai dididdai / Bein n'har prat ounh'ar h'idekal / Hine ma tov / Chibolet basade / Suite h'assidique / Chnei h'alilim / Ke chochana / El ginat egoz / Debka rafiah / Leorh'i oukhekh / Rikoud harabbi / Debka druze / Debka kafrit / Chir Hanokdim / Im houpalnou-chevat ne'ourim
CD _____ ARN 64033
Arion / '88 / Discovery / ADA.

Kolinda

IL JU HARAMIA
CD _____ 199722
Hexagone / Oct '93 / Roots / ADA / Discovery.

Koloc, Bonnie

WITH YOU ON MY SIDE
CD _____ FF 70437
Flying Fish / Nov '94 / Roots / CM / Direct / ADA.

Kolyma

SONGS OF NATURE AND ANIMALS
CD _____ 925662
Buda / Aug '93 / Discovery / ADA.

Komariah, Euis

JAIPONGAN JAVA (Komariah, Euis & Jugala Orchestra)
Engalkeun / Bulan sapasi / Bardin / Toka toka / Seunggah / Teuteup abdi / Sinden beken / Daun pulus (Available on CD format only)
CD _____ CDORB 057
Globestyle / Apr '90 / Pinnacle.

SOUND OF SUNDA, THE (Komariah, Euis & Yus Wiradiredja)
Sorban palid / Salam sono / Asa tos tepang / Bulan sapasi / Campaka kambar / Duh leung / Ramalan asih / Pengkolan / Balingding asih
CD _____ CDORB 060
Globestyle / Jul '90 / Pinnacle.

Kommunity FK

VISION AND THE VOICE
CD _____ CLEO 94152
Cleopatra / Nov '94 / Disc.

Kondo, Toshinori

BRAIN WAR (Kondo, Toshinori & Ima)
Brain war / Blue stone / Fly, Jack / Invisible man / Fire makes darkness / Bone man / Marginal moon / Space radio / Ice city

CD _____ JARO 41612
Jaro / Sep '92 / New Note.

Kondole

PSYCHIC
CD _____ TOPY 046CD
Temple / Dec '89 / Pinnacle / Plastic Head.

Kone, Aicha

MANDINGO LIVE FROM COTE D'IVOIRE
CD _____ SM 1514-2
Wergo / Sep '93 / Harmonia Mundi / ADA / Cadillac.

Koner, Thomas

PERMAFROST
CD _____ BAR 9
Barooni / Jul '93 / SRD.

Kong

MULTIPOETVOCALISER
CD _____ CDKTB 1
Dreamtime / Aug '95 / Kudos / Pinnacle.

PUSH COMES TO SHOVE
CD _____ CDKTB 17
Dreamtime / Feb '95 / Kudos / Pinnacle.

Kongos, John

TOKOLOSHE MAN...PLUS
Jubilee cloud / Gold / Lift me from the ground / Tomorrow I'll go / Can someone please direct me back to Earth / Try to touch just one / Weekend lady / I would have had a good time / Come on down Jesus / Sometimes it's not enough / He's gonna step on you again / Great white lady (Only on CD.) / Higher than God's hat (Only on CD.) / Ride the lightning (Only on CD.) / Tokoloshe man
CD _____ SEECD 221
See For Miles/C5 / May '90 / Pinnacle.

Konig, Klaus

TIME FRAGMENTS
Waltzin' over t'yours / Once upon a time / Call that gong, call that on / Mean wile / Does time go by / Later that night that knight laid her / Fine Nelly in fin alley
CD _____ ENJ 80762
Enja / Nov '94 / New Note / Vital/SAM.

Konitz, Lee

12 GERSHWIN IN 12 KEYS (Konitz, Lee & D'Andrea, Franco)
CD _____ W 312-2
Philology / Aug '92 / Harmonia Mundi / Cadillac.

ANTI HEROES (Konitz, Lee & Gil Evans)
CD _____ 5116222
Verve / Mar '92 / PolyGram.

CHICAGO 'N' ALL THAT JAZZ
My own best friend / Razzle dazzle / Loopin' the loop / Funny honey / Class / Me and my baby / Roxie / Ten per cent
CD _____ CDC 7971
LRC / Nov '90 / New Note / Harmonia Mundi.

FIGURE AND SPIRIT (Konitz, Lee Quintet)
CD _____ PCD 7003
Progressive / Oct '91 / Jazz Music.

FREE WITH LEE
CD _____ W 62-2
Philology / Dec '95 / Harmonia Mundi / Cadillac.

FRIENDS
CD _____ DRCD 240
Dragon / Feb '94 / Roots / Cadillac / Wellard / CM / ADA.

FROM NEWPORT TO NICE
CD _____ CD 214 W65-2
Philology / May '92 / Harmonia Mundi / Cadillac.

HEROES (Konitz, Lee & Gil Evans)
CD _____ 5116212
Verve / Mar '92 / PolyGram.

I CONCENTRATE ON YOU
CD _____ SCCD 31018
Steeplechase / Jul '88 / Impetus.

IDEAL SCENE
CD _____ 121119-2
Soul Note / Harmonia Mundi / Wellard / Cadillac.

JAZZ AT STORYVILLE
CD _____ BLCD 760901
Black Lion / Jun '88 / Jazz Music / Cadillac / Wellard / Koch.

JAZZ NOCTURNE
You'd be so nice to come home to / Everything happens to me / Alone together / Misty / Body and soul / My funny valentine / In a sentimental mood
CD _____ ECD 220852
Evidence / Jun '94 / Harmonia Mundi / ADA / Cadillac.

Konitz

Bop goes the leesel / Easy livin' / Mean to me / I'll remember April / Skylark / Nursery rhyme / Limehouse blues
CD _____ BL 760922
Black Lion / Oct '93 / Jazz Music / Cadillac / Wellard / Koch.

KONITZ MEETS MULLIGAN (Konitz, Lee & Gerry Mulligan)
Too marvellous for words / Lover man / I'll remember April / These foolish things / All the things you are / Bernie's tune / Almost like being in love / Sextet / Broadway / I can't believe that you're in love with me / Lady be good / Lady be good (alt. take)
CD _____ CDP 7851082
Blue Note / Mar '95 / EMI.

LIVE AT LAREN
April / Who you / Without a song / Moon dreams / Times lie / Matrix
CD _____ SNCD 1069
Soul Note / '86 / Harmonia Mundi / Wellard / Cadillac.

LIVE AT THE HALF NOTE
CD _____ 521659-2
Verve / Nov '94 / PolyGram.

LIVE IN EUROPE
CD _____ COD 031
Jazz View / Jul '92 / Harmonia Mundi.

LULLABY OF BIRDLAND (Konitz, Lee Quartet)
CD _____ CCD 79709
Candid / '95 / Cadillac / Jazz Music / Wellard / Koch.

LUNA3EA (Konitz, Lee & Peggy Stern)
CD _____ 121249-2
Soul Note / Sep '92 / Harmonia Mundi / Wellard / Cadillac.

ONCE UPON A LINE (Konitz, Lee & Harold Danko)
CD _____ 500162
Musidisc / Nov '93 / Vital / Harmonia Mundi / ADA / Cadillac / Discovery.

PALO ALTO 1949-1960
CD _____ CD 53182
Giants Of Jazz / Sep '94 / Target/BMG / Cadillac.

QUINTETS (Konitz, Lee & Bob Brookmeyer)
I'll remember April / Lost Henri / You're so nice to come home to / All the things you are / These foolish things / 9.20 Special / I never knew / Steeplechase loverman
CD _____ 74321115032
Vogue / Jul '93 / BMG.

RHAPSODY
I hear a rhapsody / Kokomo and frizz / Aerie / Trio no.1 / All the things you are / Exposition / Flyin' mumbles and jumbles
CD _____ KICJ 174
King/Paddle Wheel / Feb '94 / New Note.

RHAPSODY 2
Body and soul / Short cut #1 / Another view / Lover man / Short cut #2 / Kary's trance / Trio #2 / Indiana Jones / You don't know what love is / Variation #1 / Variation #2 / Some blues / Short cut #3 / Indiana Jones #2 / Round and round and round / Sittin' in / Indiana Jones #3 / Body and soul (Finale)
CD _____ KICJ 210
King/Paddle Wheel / Aug '94 / New Note.

ROUND AND ROUND
Round and round and round / Someday my Prince will come / Luv / Nancy / Boo doo / Valse hot / I over man / Bluesette / Giant steps
CD _____ CIJD 60167M
Music Masters / '89 / Nimbus.

SPEAKIN' LOW (Konitz, Lee & R. Sellani)
CD _____ W 71-2CD
Philology / Jul '94 / Harmonia Mundi / Cadillac.

SUBCONSCIOUS LEE
CD _____ OJCCD 186
Original Jazz Classics / Nov '95 / Wellard / Jazz Music / Cadillac / Complete/Pinnacle.

SWISS KISS
Boom Lee boggie / Friends / Moonlight promenade / Mr. Dream / Cafezinho / Days of wine and roses / Philtre d'amour / Game, set and match / Zizipanan / Joyeux universe sert / Living in your eyes / Sambalain / Le lecon des choses / I lov you
CD _____ TCB 33072
TCB / Jun '94 / New Note.

VENEZIA, A (Konitz, Lee & Il Suono Improvviso)
CD _____ W 53-2
Philology / Nov '93 / Harmonia Mundi / Cadillac.

ZOUNDS (Konitz, Lee Quartet)
CD _____ 1212192
Soul Note / Mar '92 / Harmonia Mundi / Wellard / Cadillac.

Konkhra

SEXUAL AFFECTIVE DISORDER
CD _____ NB 105CD
Nuclear Blast / Mar '94 / Plastic Head.

SPIT OR SWALLOW
CD _____ PCD 019
Lost & Found / Sep '95 / Plastic Head.

STRANDED
CD _____ CD 7913002
Progress Red / Jun '93 / Plastic Head.

Konte, Dembo

JALI ROLL (Konte, Dembo & Kausu Kuyateh)
CD _____ FMSD 5020
Rogue / Feb '90 / Sterns.

JALIOLOGY (Konte, Dembo & Kausu Kuyateh)
CD _____ XENO 4036CD
Xenophile / Jun '95 / Direct / ADA.

SIMBOMBA (Konte, Dembo & Kausu Kuyateh)
CD _____ FMSD 5011
Rogue / Nov '87 / Sterns.

Kool & The Gang

ANTHOLOGY
Kool and the gang / Let the music take your weight (part 1) / Love the life you live (part 1) / Country junkie / Funky stuff / Jungle boogie / Hollywood swinging / Rhyme tyme people / Spirit of the boogie / Open sesame (part 1) / Jones Vs. Jones / Take my heart (you can have it if you want it) / Big fun / Tonight / Fresh / Victory / Stone love / Celebration (1988 remix)
CD _____ VSOPCD 168
Connoisseur / Nov '91 / Pinnacle.

BEST OF KOOL & THE GANG 1969-1976, THE
CD _____ 514 822-2
Mercury / Jun '93 / PolyGram.

DANCE COLLECTION
Celebration / Get down on it / Let's go dancin' (ooh la la la) / Big fun / Ladies night / Take my heart (you can have it if you want it) / In the heart / Straight ahead / Hi de hi, hi de ho / Steppin' out / Good time tonight / Fresh / Peacemaker / Emergency / Victory
CD _____ 8425202
Mercury / Aug '92 / PolyGram.

GREAT AND REMIXED '91
CD _____ 848 604-2
Mercury / Jul '91 / PolyGram.

GREATEST HITS LIVE
Victory / Ladies night / Fresh / Take my heart (You can have it if you want it) / Hollywood swinging / Too hot / Joanna / Cherish / Ooh la la la (Let's go dancin') / Get down on it / Celebration / Tonight / Emergency
CD _____ 16225 CD
Success / Sep '94 / Carlton Home Entertainment.

IN CONCERT
CD _____ HP 93472
Start / Nov '94 / Koch.

KOOL AND THE GANG
CD _____ 0143561
Arcade / May '90 / Sony / Grapevine.

KOOL AND THE GANG
CD _____ 12607
Laserlight / Oct '95 / Target/BMG.

LIVE ON STAGE
Victory / Ladies night / Fresh / Take my heart / Hollywood / Too hot / Joanna / Cherish / Ooh la la la (let's go dancin') / Get down / Celebration / Tonight / Emergency
CD _____ MSCD 7
Music De-Luxe / Nov '94 / Magnum Music Group.

NIGHT PEOPLE
Get down on it / Stand up and sing / Hangin' out / Morning star / Love and understanding / My lady / Caribbean festival / Emergency (remix) / Never give up / Good time tonight / Home is where the heart is / All she really wants to do is dance / September love / Night people
CD _____ 5501982
Spectrum/Karussell / Aug '94 / PolyGram / THE.

NYC COOL
(Jump up on the) Rhythm and ride / I think I love you / Love come down / Pretty little sexy Miss / Better late than never / Heart / My search is over / Summer / Brown / Give right now to you / Weight / Show us the way to love / Unite / God will find you
CD _____ MDCD 4
Magnum Music / Jan '94 / Magnum Music Group.

SINGLES COLLECTION, THE
Celebration / Ladies night / Too hot / Get down on it / Joanna / Jones vs. Jones / Straight ahead / Fresh / Ooh la la la (let's go dancin') / Big fun / Cherish / In the heart / Hi de hi, hi de ho / Take it to the top / Victory / Steppin' out
CD _____ 8366362
Polystar / Oct '88 / PolyGram.

STEPPIN OUT
Steppin' out / Funky stuff / Hollywood swinging / Peace maker / Victory / Rags to

riches / Hangin' out / Big fun / Cherish / Too hot / Just friends / Good time tonight / Emergency / Stone love / Strong / Let's go dancin' (ooh la la la)
CD _____ **PWKS 4109 P**
Carlton Home Entertainment / Sep '92 / Carlton Home Entertainment.

UNITE
(Jump up on the) Rhythm and ride / I think I love you / Love comes down / Sexy Miss / Better late than never / Heart / My search is over / Summer / Brown / Give right now / Weight / Show us the way / Unite / God will find you
CD _____ **CDUNITE 1**
Charly / Oct '93 / Charly / THE / Cadillac.

UNITE
CD _____ **ST 5010**
Star Collection / Apr '95 / BMG.

VERY BEST OF KOOL & THE GANG
CD _____ **01440062**
Arcade / Sep '90 / Sony / Grapevine.

Kool Ace

MACKATHERMASTATICZXONE
CD _____ **MRR 4212**
Ichiban / Aug '95 / Koch.

Kool G Rap

4, 5, 6
Blowin' up in the wind / Fast life / Ghetto knows / It's a shame / Money on my brain / Intro / 4, 5, 6 / It's a shame (2) / Take 'em to war / Executioner style / For da brothaz
CD _____ **4814722**
Epic / Oct '95 / Sony.

Kool Moe Dee

GREATEST HITS: KOOL MOE DEE
Do you know what time it is / Bad mutha / Dumb dick / Turn it up / Gotta rock / Downbeat / Heartbeat / At the party / Body rock / Action / Christmas rap
CD _____ **NEMCD 623**
Sequel / May '92 / BMG.

Kooper, Al

SUPERSESSION (Kooper, Al/Mike Bloomfield/Stephen Stills)
Alberts shuffle / Stop / Man's temptation / His holy modal majesty / Really / It takes a lot to laugh, it takes a train to cry / Season of the witch / You don't love me / Harvey's tune
CD _____ **CK 64608**
Columbia / Jul '95 / Sony.

Koral, Rob

WAS IT SOMETHING YOU SAID (Koral, Rob & Sue Hawker)
Yesterday's / Polka dots and moonbeams / Dance with me / Little piece of heaven / 500 Miles high / Her ways / Remember this / Horizons / I could write a book / Stay away / Crazy Sunday / Waiting for Norman / Lies / He's funny that way / I need your love so bad / Just the way things are / Was it something you said / Perdido
CD _____ **CHECD 00112**
Master Mix / Jul '95 / Wellard / Jazz Music / New Note.

Korn

KORN
Blind / Ball tongue / Need to / Clown / Divine / Faget / Shoots and ladders / Predictable / Fake / Lies / Helmet in the bush / Daddy
CD _____ **4780802**
Epic / Nov '95 / Sony.

Korn, Paddy

BACK BEAT INSPIRED (Korn, Paddy & White Bread)
CD _____ **CDST 2**
Stumble / Nov '95 / Direct.

Korner, Alexis

ALEXIS KORNER - CD BOX SET
CD Set _____ **CLA BX 914**
Castle / Feb '92 / BMG.

BLUES INCORPORATED
CD _____ **TACD 9006340**
Line / Jun '94 / CM / Grapevine / ADA / Conifer / Direct.

BOOTLEG HIM
She fooled me / Hoochie coochie man / Yellow dog blues / I wonder who / Dee / Oh Lord don't let them drop that atomic bomb on me / Rockin' honesty / I got a woman / Might mighty spade and whitey / Corine Corina / Operator / Love you save / Jesus is just alright / That's all / Evil hearted woman / Clay House Inn / Love is gonna go / Sunrise / Hellhound on my trail
CD _____ **CLACD 291**
Castle / Feb '93 / BMG.

COLLECTION: ALEXIS KORNER
Gospel ship / Captain America / Thief / Robert Johnson / Get off my cloud / Honky tonk woman / Spoonful / Daytime song / Lend me some time / Hey pretty mama /

Stump blues / I got my mojo working / Geneva / Wreck of ol' 97 / Casey Jones / Hiheel sneakers / King BB / Juvenile delinquent
CD _____ **CCSCD 192**
Castle / Sep '88 / BMG.

COLLECTION: ALEXIS KORNER 1961-72
She fooled me / Hoochie coochie man / Oh Lord don't let them drop that atom bomb on me / I got a woman / Corine Corina / Everyday I have the blues / Operator / Rosie / Polly put the kettle on / I see it / You don't miss your water / Mighty mighty spade and whitey / Lo and behold / Louisiana blues / Ooh wee baby / Rock me baby / Sweet sympathy / Country shoes
CD _____ **CCSCD 150**
Castle / Apr '94 / BMG.

GET OFF MY CLOUD
I got cha number / Wasp (Texas radio) / Robert Johnson / Tree top fever / You are my sunshine / Strange 'n' deranged / Slow down / Song for Jim / Ain't the peculiar / Get off my cloud
CD _____ **NEXCD 134**
Sequel / Sep '90 / BMG.

I WONDER WHO
Watermelon man / Streamline train / Rock me / Come back / Going down slow / 2.19 blues / River's invitation / I wonder who / Chicken shack back home / County jail blues / Roll 'em Pete / Betty and Dupree / C.C. rider
CD _____ **BGOCD 136**
Beat Goes On / Aug '95 / Pinnacle.

LIVE IN PARIS (Korner, Alexis & Colin Hodgkinson)
Blue Monday / Key to the highway / Catcoke rag / Phonograph blues / Little bitty gal blues / Sweet home Chicago / Cherry red / I got my mojo working / Gospel ship / Geneva / Working in a coalmine / Flocking with you
CD _____ **CDTB 109**
Thunderbolt / '91 / Magnum Music Group.

LOST ALBUM, THE
CD _____ **CDTB 162**
Thunderbolt / Nov '94 / Magnum Music Group.

ME
Honky tonk woman / Louise / Hammer and nails / Santa Fe blues / How long blues / Robert / Precious lord / Honour the young man / And again / East St. Louis blues
CD _____ **CLACD 292**
Castle / Feb '93 / BMG.

NEW GENERATION OF BLUES, A
Mary open the door / Little bitty girl / Baby don't you love me / Go down sunshine / Same for you / I'm tore down / In the evening / Somethin' you got / New worried blues / What's that sound I hear / Flower
CD _____ **BGOCD 102**
Beat Goes On / Jul '91 / Pinnacle.

PARTY ALBUM
Things ain't what they used to be / Captain's tiger / Skipping / Spoonful / Finkless cafe / Dooji wooji / Whole mess of blues / Lining the track / Robert Johnson
CD _____ **CLACD 290**
Castle / Feb '93 / BMG.

SKY HIGH (Korner, Alexis & Blues Inc)
CD _____ **IGOCD 2012**
Indigo / Dec '94 / Direct / ADA.

TESTAMENT (Korner, Alexis & Colin Hodgkinson)
One scotch, one bourbon, one beer / Stump blues / Streamline train / My babe / 32-20 blues / Hi-heel sneakers / Will the circle be unbroken / Mary open the door
CD _____ **CDTB 2.026**
Thunderbolt / '86 / Magnum Music Group.

Kornog

ON SEVEN WINDS
Gavotten ar menez / Sir Aldingar / Toniou Bale / Ronds de St. Vincent / Helen of Kirkconnel / Trip to Flagstaff / Shuttle rins / Dans plinn / Gavotten / Varbishka ratchenitza
CD _____ **GLCD 1062**
Green Linnet / Feb '92 / Roots / CM / Direct / ADA.

PREMIERE
CD _____ **GLCD 1055**
Green Linnet / Feb '90 / Roots / CM / Direct / ADA.

Korpse

PULL THE FLOOD
CD _____ **CANDLE 005**
Candlelight / May '94 / Plastic Head.

Korriganed

RU HA DU
CD _____ **KEL 003CD**
Diffusion Breizh / Aug '95 / ADA.

Kosmic Twins

PSYCHO CONNECTION
CD _____ **DIS 009CD**
Disturbance / Mar '94 / Plastic Head.

Kosmik Kommando

FREQUENSEIZE
CD Set _____ **CAT 010CD**
Rephlex / May '94 / Disc.

Kossoff, Paul

BACK STREET CRAWLER
I'm ready / Time away / Molton gold / Backstreet crawler / Tuesday morning
CD _____ **IMCD 84**
Island / Feb '90 / PolyGram.

BLUE SOUL
Over the green hills (Part 1) / Worry / Moonshine / Trouble on double time / Crossroads / Oh I wept / We got time / Oh how we danced / Stealer / Hold on / Catch a train / Come together in the morning / Molten gold / I know why the sun don't shine / Tricky Dicky rides again / I'm ready / Blue soul
CD _____ **IMCD 144**
Island / Jul '92 / PolyGram.

KOSSOFF, KIRKE, TETSU, RABBIT (Kossoff/Kirke/Tetsu/Rabbit)
Bluegrass / Sammy's alright / Anna / Just for the box / Hold on / Fool's life / Yellow house / Dying fire / I'm on the run / Colours
CD _____ **IMCD 139**
Island / Aug '91 / PolyGram.

Kostadinos

GUITAR GYPSY THE NEXT STEP
CD _____ **CDSGP 023**
Prestige / Jan '94 / Total/BMG.

Kostia

SUITE ST. PETERSBURG
First touch / Secret garden / Winter ride / Reflections / Sunrise / Face to face / Warm stones / Building bridges / Farewell
CD _____ **ND 61040**
Narada / May '94 / New Note / ADA.

Kottke, Leo

BALANCE
Tell Mary / I don't know why / Embryonic journey / Disguise / Whine / Losing everything / Drowning / Dolores / Half acre of garlic / Learning the game
CD _____ **BGOCD 263**
Beat Goes On / Aug '95 / Pinnacle.

BEST, THE
Machine no.11 / Cripple creek / Bourree / When shrimps learn to whistle / Bill Cheatham / Song of the swamp / Last stream engine train / Bean time / Spanish entomologist / Short stories / Hole in the day / Mona Roy / Venezuela, there you go / Monkey lust / Busted bicycle / June bug / Eggtooth / Stealing / Living in the country / Medley: Crow river waltz/Jesu joy of man's desiring/Jack Fig / Standing in my shoes / Bumble bee / Eight miles high / Tilt billilngs and the student prince / Pamela Brown / Standing on the outside / Power failure
CD _____ **BGOCD 277**
Beat Goes On / Jun '95 / Pinnacle.

BURNT LIPS
Endless sleep / Cool water / Frank forgets / Sonora's death row / Quiet man / Everybody lies / I called back / Low thud / Orange room / Credits / Out takes from Terry's movie / Voluntary target / Burnt lips / Sand street / Train and the gate / From Terry's movie
CD _____ **BGOCD 259**
Beat Goes On / Dec '94 / Pinnacle.

CHEWING PINE
Standing on the outside / Power failure / Venezuela, there you go / Don't you think / Regards from Chuck Pink / Monkey money / Scarlatti rip-off / Wheels / Grim to the bone / Rebecca / Trombone / Can't quite put it into words
CD _____ **BGOCD 148**
Beat Goes On / Mar '93 / Pinnacle.

DREAMS & ALL THAT STUFF
CD _____ **BGOCD 132**
Beat Goes On / Nov '92 / Pinnacle.

GREENHOUSE
CD _____ **BGOCD 90**
Beat Goes On / Oct '90 / Pinnacle.

GUITAR MUSIC
Part 2 / Available space / Side one suite / Some birds / Slang / My double / Three walls and bars / Some birds (reprise) / Perforated sleep / Strange / Little shoes / Jib's hat / Tumbling tumbleweeds / Agile / Song for the night of the hunter / All I have to do is dream / Sleepwalk
CD _____ **BGOCD 250**
Beat Goes On / May '95 / Pinnacle.

ICE WATER
CD _____ **BGOCD 146**
Beat Goes On / Jul '92 / Pinnacle.

LEO KOTTKE
Buckaroo / White ape / Haysee suede / Rio Leo / Range / Airproofing / Maroon / Waltz / Death by reputation / Up tempo / Shadowland
CD _____ **BGOCD 257**
Beat Goes On / Oct '94 / Pinnacle.

LIVE IN EUROPE
Train and the gate / Open country joy: Theme and adhesions / Airproofing / Toll Mary / Wheels / Up tempo / Palms blvd / Shadowland / Eggtooth / Pamela Brown / Range
CD _____ **BGOCD 265**
Beat Goes On / Aug '95 / Pinnacle.

MUDLARK
CD _____ **BGOCD 101**
Beat Goes On / Apr '91 / Pinnacle.

MY FEET ARE SMILING
CD _____ **BGOCD 134**
Beat Goes On / Feb '92 / Pinnacle.

PECULIAROSO
Peg leg / Poor boy / Parade / Wonderland by night / World made to order / Room service / Turning into Randolph Scott (Humid child) / Porky and pale arms of Mary / Room at the stop of the stairs / Big situation / Twilight time
CD _____ **1005 82111-29**
Private Music / Apr '94 / BMG.

TIME STEP
Running all night long / Bungle party / Rings / Mr. Fonebone / Julie's house / Memories are made of this / Saginaw Michigan / I'll break out again / Wrong track / Starving / Here comes that rain again
CD _____ **BGOCD 255**
Beat Goes On / Apr '95 / Pinnacle.

Kouyate, Famoro

ASSUSU (Kouyate, Famoro & Kike)
CD _____ **OA 204**
PAM / Feb '94 / Direct / ADA.

Kouyate, Ousmane

DOMBA (Kouyate, Ousmane Band)
Djougouya / Domba / Kounady / Miriya / An' fananta lele / N'nafanta
CD _____ **STCD 1030**
Sterns / May '90 / Sterns / CM.

Kouyate, Tata Bambo

JATIGUI
Hommage a baba cissoko / Mama batchily / Goundo tandja / Ainana bale / Ahourou bocoum / Amadou traore
CD _____ **CDORB 042**
Globestyle / Jun '89 / Pinnacle.

Kovac, Boris

FROM RITUAL NOVA I & II
CD _____ **BKCD 1**
ReR Megacorp / Feb '94 / These / ReR Megacorp.

Koverhult, Tommy

JAZZ IN SWEDEN 1983
CD _____ **1289**
Caprice / Jan '83 / CM / Complete/ Pinnacle / Cadillac / ADA.

Kovriga Balalaika...

RUSSIAN FAVOURITES (Kovriga Balalaika Orchestra)
CD _____ **MCD 71793**
Monitor / Jun '93 / CM.

Kowald, Peter

DUOS USA JAPAN
CD _____ **FMPCD 21**
FMP / Sep '87 / Cadillac.

Kox Box

FOREVER AFTER
CD _____ **HHCD 12**
Harthouse / Jun '95 / Disc / Warner Music.

Koyake, Tamami

ASK ME NOW (I REMEMBER THOSE DAYS)
Out of nowhere / Goodbye pork pie hat / Another dream / Seven steps to heaven / Old country / Monk's dream / Ask me now / Comin' home baby
CD _____ **KICJ 85**
King/Paddle Wheel / Feb '94 / New Note.

Kpiaye, John

RED GOLD & BLUE
CD _____ **LJKCD 012**
LKJ / Jun '94 / Jetstar / Grapevine.

Kraftwerk

AUTOBAHN
Autobahn / Kometenmelodie 1 / Kometenmelodie 2 / Mitternacht / Morgenspaziergang
CD _____ **CDP 7461532**
EMI / Aug '95 / EMI.

COMPUTER WORLD
Pocket calculator / Numbers / Computer world / Computer love / It's more fun to compute / Home computer
CD _____ **CDEMS 1547**
Capitol / Apr '95 / EMI.

ELECTRIC CAFE
Boing boom tschak / Techno pop / Musique non stop / Telephone call / Sex object / Electric cafe
CD _____ CDEMS 1546
EMI / Aug '95 / EMI.

MAN MACHINE
Robots / Spacelab / Metropolis / Model / Neon lights / Man machine
CD _____ CDEMS 1520
Capitol / Apr '95 / EMI.

MIX, THE
Robots / Computer love / Pocket calculator / Dentaku / Autobahn / Radioactivity / Trans Europe express / Abzug / Metal on metal / Homecomputer / Musique non stop
CD _____ CDEM 1408
EMI / May '95 / EMI.

RADIO ACTIVITY
Geiger counter / Radioactivity / Radioland / Airwaves / Intermission / News / Voice of energy / Antenna / Radio stars / Uranium / Transistir / Ohm sweet ohm
CD _____ CDEMS 1524
Capitol / Apr '95 / EMI.

TRANS - EUROPE EXPRESS
Europe endless / Hall of mirrors / Showroom dummies / Trans - Europe express / Metal on metal / Franz Schubert / Endless endless
CD _____ CDP 7464732
EMI / Aug '95 / EMI.

Krakatau

MATINALE
Matinale / Unseen sea scene / Jai ping / Rural / For Bernard Moore / Sarajevo / Shuka / Raging thirst
CD _____ 5232932
ECM / Nov '94 / New Note.

VOLITION
Brujo / Volition / Nai / Changgo / Little big horn / Dalens ande
CD _____ 5119832
ECM / May '94 / New Note.

Kral, Ivan

NATIVE
CD _____ ZS 124
Special Delivery / Jul '92 / ADA / CM / Direct.

Krall, Diana

ONLY TRUST YOUR HEART
Is you is or is you ain't my baby / Only trust your heart / I love being here with you / Broadway / Folks who live on the hill / I've got the world on a string / Sqeeze me / All night long / C.R.S. Craft
CD _____ GRP 98102
GRP / Mar '95 / BMG / New Note.

Kramer, Billy J.

BEST OF THE EMI YEARS: BILLY J. KRAMER (Kramer, Billy J. & The Dakotas)
Do you want to know a secret / Bad to me / I call your name / I'll keep you satisfied / I know / I'll be on my way / Cruel sea / Little children / Second to none / They remind me of you / From a window / Sneakin' around / I'll be doggone / Neon city / Take my hand / Trains and boats and planes / That's the way I feel / It's gotta last forever / We're doing fine / Forgive me / Going going gone / I Do Can't live on memories
CD _____ CDEMS 1392
EMI / May '91 / EMI.

EP COLLECTION, THE (Kramer, Billy J. & The Dakotas)
I call your name / Bad to me / Do you want to know a secret / I'll be on my way / I'll keep you satisfied / Dance with me / It's up to you / I know / Little children / They remind me of you / Beautiful reminder / From a window / Second to none / Twelfth of never / Sugar babe / Tennessee waltz / Irresistible you / Twilight time / Cruel sea / Millionaire / Magic carpet / Humdinger / Trains and boats and planes
CD _____ SEECD 422
See For Miles/C5 / May '95 / Pinnacle.

Kramer, Wayne

DEATH TONGUE
CD _____ ITEM CD2
Progress / Jul '92 / Vital.

HARDSTUFF, THE
CD _____ E 864472
Epitaph / Jan '95 / Plastic Head / Pinnacle.

Krantz, Wayne

2 DRINK MINIMUM
Whippersnapper / Dove Gloria / Shirts off / Dream called love / AFKap / Isabelle / Alliance / Secrets / Lynxpaw
CD _____ ENJ 90432
Enja / Jul '95 / New Note / Vital/SAM.

LONG TO BE LOOSE
These instrumental pieces were / Not conciously written about / Specific people,

places, things or ideas / Although one began / From a little croaking sound / Friend's DAT machine makes / What they were written about / Is something I don't understand yet / But I know it when I see it / And, hopefully, so will you
CD _____ ENJ 70992
Enja / Jul '93 / New Note / Vital/SAM.

SIGNALS
CD _____ 60482
Enja / Nov '90 / New Note / Vital/SAM.

Krashman

BLACK CIRCLE
Got you faded / Something for the player to roll on / It be's like that / Caught up / Gitten mine / Making of a madman / Booty mack / Sister Suzie / Down in the ghetto / Four 40's / Black circle / Watch yo bitch / Nuthin' but a party
CD _____ BRCD 601
4th & Broadway / Sep '93 / PolyGram.

Kraus, Peter

DIE SINGLES 1958-1960
Sugar baby / Ich denk'an dich / Honey baby (du passt so gut zu mir) / Come on and swing / Kitty kat / Havanna love / Wunderbar wie du / Hey du bist okay / Tiger / Ich bin ja so alien / Wenn / Oh Veronika / Die jungen Jahre / Wenn du heute ausgehst / Das ist prima / OK / Cowboy Billy / Sensationell / Auf wiederseh'n und lass dir's gut ergehen / Genau wie du / Ten o'clock rock / Keine nacht kann ich schlafen / Dream face / Nohody else/Du gehorst mir
CD _____ BCD 15453
Bear Family / Apr '89 / Rollercoaster / Direct / CM / Swift / ADA.

DIE SINGLES 1960
Susi sagt es Gabi / Doll doll dolly / Alle Madchen wollen kussen / Wenn sie dich allein lasst / Va Bene / Sag mir was du denkst / Honeymoon / Mondschein und Liebe / Ein rendezvous mit dir / Rote rosen / Ein haus in Tennessee / Blue river / Cherie, cherie / Cowboy Jenny / Rose Marie / Alles ist anders / Ausgerechnet ich / Come on and swing (live) / Basin Street blues / When the saints go marching in / Get happy / Love me or leave me / Alright O.K. you win / Nobody else
CD _____ BCD 15457
Bear Family / Apr '89 / Rollercoaster / Direct / CM / Swift / ADA.

DIE SINGLES 1961-62
CD _____ BCD 15527
Bear Family / Apr '92 / Rollercoaster / Direct / CM / Swift / ADA.

DIE SINGLES 1962-63
CD _____ BCD 15528
Bear Family / Apr '92 / Rollercoaster / Direct / CM / Swift / ADA.

HERZLICHST IHR PETER KRAUS
CD _____ BCD 15478
Bear Family / '88 / Rollercoaster / Direct / CM / Swift / ADA.

Krause, Bernie

GORILLAS IN THE MIX
CD _____ RCD 10119
Rykodisc / Dec '92 / Vital / ADA.

Krause, Dagmar

SUPPLY AND DEMAND (Songs by Brecht, Weill & Eisler)
CD _____ HNCD 1317
Hannibal / Mar '86 / Vital / ADA.

TANK BATTLES: SONGS OF HANNS EISLER, THE
Song of the whitewash / You have to pay / Ballad of the sack slingers / Perhaps song / Mankind / Song of a German mother / Bankenlied / Und endlich stirbt / Mother's hands / Genvieve: Ostern ist ball sur Seine / Trenches / (I read about) tank battles / Chanson allemande / Mother Beimlein / Rat men - the nightmare / Bettellied / Change the world - it needs it / Failure in loving / Ballad of (Bourgeois) welfare / Benin 1919 / Homecoming / To a little radio
CD _____ VP 138CD
Voice Print / Apr '94 / Voice Print.

Krauss, Alison

EVERYTIME YOU SAY GOODBYE
Everytime you say goodbye / Another night / Last love letter / Cluck old hen / You can blame you / It work this time / Heartstrings / I don't know why / Cloudy days / New fool / Shield of faith / Lose again / Another day another dollar / Jesus help me stand
CD _____ ROUCD 0285
Rounder / '92 / CM / Direct / ADA / Cadillac.

I KNOW WHO HOLDS THE FUTURE (Krauss, Alison & The Cox Family)
CD _____ ROU 307CD
Rounder / Mar '94 / CM / Direct / ADA / Cadillac.

I'VE GOT THAT OLD FEELING
I've got that old feeling / Dark skies / Wish I still had you / Endless highway / Winter of a broken heart / It's over / Will you be leav-

ing / Steel rails / Tonight I'll be lonely too / One good reason / That makes two of us / Longest highway
CD _____ CD 0275
Rounder / '90 / CM / Direct / ADA / Cadillac.

NOW THAT I'VE FOUND YOU
CD _____ ROUCD 0325
Rounder / Feb '95 / CM / Direct / ADA / Cadillac.

TOO LATE TO CRY (Krauss, Alison & Various Artists)
Too late to cry / Foolish heart / Song for life / Dusty Miller / If I give my heart / In your eyes / Don't follow me / Gentle river / On the borderline / Forgotten pictures / Sleep on
CD _____ CD 0235
Rounder / Aug '88 / CM / Direct / ADA / Cadillac.

TWO HIGHWAYS (Krauss, Alison & Union Station)
Two highways / I'm alone again / Wild Bill Jones / Beaumont rag / Heaven's bright shore / Love you in vain / Here comes goodbye / As lovely as you / Windy City rag / Lord don't you forsake me / Teardrops will kiss the morning dew / Midnight rider
CD _____ CD 0257
Rounder / '89 / CM / Direct / ADA / Cadillac.

WHEN YOU SAY NOTHING AT ALL
CD _____ CRCDS 7
Rounder / Nov '95 / CM / Direct / ADA / Cadillac.

Kravitz, Lenny

ARE YOU GONNA GO MY WAY
Are you gonna go my way / Believe / Come on and love me / Heaven help / Just be a woman / Is there any love in your heart / Black girl / My love / Sugar / Sister / Eleutheria
CD _____ CDVUS 60
Virgin / Mar '93 / EMI.

CIRCUS
Rock and roll is dead / Circus / Beyond the 7th sky / Tunnel vision / Can't get you off my mind / Magdalene / God is love / Thin ice / Don't go and put a bullet in your head / In my life today / Resurrection
CD _____ CDVUS 86
Virgin / Sep '95 / EMI.

LET LOVE RULE
Sittin' on top of the world / Let love rule / Freedom train / My precious love / I build this garden for us / Fear / Does anybody out there even care / Mr. Cabdriver / Rosemary / Be / Blues for sister someone (Only on CD and MC.) / Empty hands (Only on CD and MC.) / Flower child (Only on CD and MC.)
CD _____ CDVUS 10
Virgin / May '90 / EMI.

MAMA SAID
Fields of joy / Always on the run / Stand by my woman / It ain't over 'til it's over / More than anything in this world / What goes around comes around / Difference is why / Stop draggin' around / Flowers for Zoe / Fields of joy (reprise) / All I ever wanted / When the morning turns to night / What the fuck are we saying / Butterfly
CD _____ CDVUS 31
Virgin / Apr '91 / EMI.

Kreator

OUT OF THE DARK
CD _____ N 02002
Noise/Modern Music / Sep '92 / Pinnacle / Plastic Head.

RENEWAL
CD _____ NO 1932
Noise/Modern Music / Oct '92 / Pinnacle / Plastic Head.

Kreitzer, Scott

NEW YORK STATE OF MIND
New York state of mind / Way you look tonight / Smoke gets in your eyes / Pivotal epicentre / Internalized / Chief crazy horse / Runaway / All the things you are / So be it
CD _____ 66053022
Jazz City / Jun '91 / New Note.

Krekel, Tim

OUT OF THE CORNER
CD _____ AP 083CD
Appaloosa / Jun '92 / ADA / Magnum Music Group.

Kreusch, Cornelius C.

BLACK MUD SOUND
CD _____ ENJACD 90872
Enja / Sep '95 / New Note / Vital/SAM.

Kreuz

KREUZ KONTROL
CD _____ DESCD 1
Diesel / Mar '95 / Jetstar.

NEW GENERATION
Interlude / When you smile / Baby come back / Crush on you / Hush-hush / U.K. Swing / Do you right / That jazz feeling (Mixes) / Hangin' on / I never knew / Interlude (sunshine) / Deja vu / Don't take it off / New generation / 101% / Sunshine / You are the one
CD _____ 530203-2
Motown / Apr '93 / PolyGram.

Krewmen

FINAL ADVENTURES PT.1
CD _____ LMCD 023
Lost Moment / Apr '92 / Else.

PLAGUE OF THE DEAD
CD _____ LMCD 020
Lost Moment / Oct '88 / Else.

POWER
CD _____ LMCD 021
Lost Moment / Sep '90 / Else.

SINGLED OUT
CD _____ LMCD 024
Lost Moment / Oct '94 / Else.

Krimsky, Katrina

STELLA MALU (Krimsky, Katrina & Trevor Watts)
CD _____ 8335162
ECM / Jul '88 / New Note.

Krishan, Gopal

NORTHERN INDIA - THE ART OF THE VICHITRA VEENA
CD Set _____ C 560048/49
Ocora / Jan '94 / Harmonia Mundi / ADA.

Krishnan, Ramnad

SONGS OF THE CARNATIC TRADITION OF SOUTH INDIA
CD _____ 7559720232
Elektra Nonesuch / Jan '95 / Warner Music.

Krispy Three

CAN'T MELT THE WAX
CD _____ KSCD 6
Kold Sweat / Jun '93 / 3MV.

HERD OUT DA GATE
CD _____ KSMCD 302
Kold Sweat / May '94 / 3MV.

Kriss Kross

DA BOMB
Intro / Da bomb / Sound of my hood / It don't stop (hip hop classic) / D.J. Nabs break / Alright / I'm real / 2 Da beat ch'yall / Freak da funk / Lot 2 live 4 / Take um out / Alright (extended remix)
CD _____ 474212 2
Columbia / Sep '93 / Sony.

Kristina, Sonja

HARMONICS OF LOVE
CD _____ HTDCD 34
HTD / Apr '95 / Pinnacle.

Kristofferson, Kris

LEGENDARY YEARS, THE
Me and Bobby McGee / Josie / Lover please / Jesus was a Capricorn / Magdalena / Living legend / Help me make it through the night / Silver tongued devil / When she's wrong / I my smoke too much / Easter Island / It's never gonna be the same again / Golden Idol / I'd rather be sorry / Bigger the fool / Shake hands with the Devil / Nobody loves anybody anymore / Broken freedom song / Here comes that rainbow again / Epitaph (black and blue)
CD _____ KKVSOPCD 141
Connoisseur / Apr '90 / Pinnacle.

MOMENT OF FOREVER, A
CD _____ TRACD 220
Transatlantic / Nov '95 / BMG / Pinnacle / ADA.

NATURAL ACT (Kristofferson, Kris & Rita Coolidge)
Blue as I do / Not everyone knows / I fought the law / Number one / You're gonna love yourself in the morning / Loving her was easier (than anything I'll ever do again) / Back in my baby's arms / Please don't tell me how the story ends / Hoola hoop / Love to live here anymore / Silver mantis
CD _____ 5507702
Spectrum/Karussell / Aug '94 / PolyGram / THE.

Krokus

TO ROCK OR NOT TO BE
CD _____ SPV 08543872
SPV / Aug '95 / Plastic Head.

Kronos Quartet

BOXSET 2
CD _____ 7559793122

Elektra Nonesuch / Jul '94 / Warner Music.

IN FORMATION
CD _____ RR 9CD
Reference Recordings / Sep '91 / May Audio.

KRONOS QUARTET (Music Of Sculthorpe/Hendrix/Sallinen/Glass & Nancarrow)
CD _____ 7559791112
Elektra Nonesuch / Jan '87 / Warner Music.

MONK SUITE
Well you needn't / Rhythm-a-ning / Crepuscule with Nellie / Off moinor/Spistrophy / Round Midnight / Misterioso / It don't mean a thing it it ain't got that swing / Black and tan fantasy / Brilliant corners
CD _____ LCD 15052
Landmark / Aug '93 / New Note.

MUSIC OF BILL EVANS
Waltz for Debbie / Very early / Nardis / RE: Person I knew / Time remembered / Walling up / Turn out the stars / Five / Peace piece
CD _____ LCD 15102
Landmark / Aug '93 / New Note.

PIECES OF AFRICA
CD _____ 7559792752
Elektra Nonesuch / Jan '92 / Warner Music.

SHORT STORIES
CD _____ 7559793102
Elektra Nonesuch / Jan '95 / Warner Music.

WHITE MAN SLEEPS (Music Of Volans/Ives/Hassell/Coleman/Lee/Johnston & Bartok)
White man sleeps no 1 / White man sleeps no 3 / White man sleeps no 5 / Scherzo holding your own / Pano da costa (Cloth from the coast) / Lonely woman / Amazing grace
CD _____ 7559791632
Elektra Nonesuch / Jul '88 / Warner Music.

WINTER WAS HARD (Sallinen/Riley/Part/Zorn/Webern/Piazzolla/Schnittke/Barber)
Winter was hard / Fratres / Bella by barlight / Door is ajar / Half wolf dances mad in moonlight / Forbidden fruit / Quartet No 3
CD _____ 7559791812
Elektra Nonesuch / '88 / Warner Music.

KRS 1

KRS 1
CD _____ CHIP 165
Jive / Oct '95 / BMG.

Krunchjam

KRUNCHJAM
CD _____ OME 4148CD
Ichiban / Feb '94 / Koch.

Krupa, Gene

CLASSICS 1935-38
CD _____ CLASSICS 754
Classics / May '94 / Discovery / Jazz Music.

CLASSICS 1938
CD _____ CLASSICS 767
Classics / Aug '94 / Discovery / Jazz Music.

CLASSICS 1939-40
CD _____ CLASSICS 834
Classics / Sep '95 / Discovery / Jazz Music.

DRUM BOOGIE
CD _____ 473659 2
Columbia / Aug '93 / Sony.

DRUMMER, THE
Drum boogie / Ta-ra-ra-boom-der-e (ta-ra-ra-boom-de-ay) / Rhythm jam / Moonlight serenade / Big do / Jam on toast / Meet the beat of my heart / My own / You're as pretty as a picture / I'm gonna clap my hands / I hope Gabriel likes my music / My old Kentucky home / You and your love / Jazz me blues / Tutti frutti / Wire brush stomp / Old black Joe / Drumboogie / Apurskody / Tropical magic / Last round-up / Blues of Israel
CD _____ PASTCD 7008
Flapper / Mar '93 / Pinnacle.

DRUMMIN' MAN
CD _____ CD 56080
Jazz Roots / Mar '95 / Target/BMG.

GENE KRUPA & HIS ORCHESTRA 1939
CD _____ CLASSICS 799
Classics / Mar '95 / Discovery / Jazz Music.

GENE KRUPA LIVE 1946 (Krupa, Gene & His Orchestra)
CD _____ JH 1039
Jazz Hour / Feb '95 / Target/BMG / Jazz Music / Cadillac.

IT'S UP TO YOU (1946 Vol. 2)
Blue Lou / Summertime / Hodge podge / Boogie blues / Bugle call rag / Ain't nowhere / Man I love / 10 Ritchie Drive / It's

up to you / Yesterdays / Margie / Night and day / By the river Sainte Marie / These foolish things / Medley: Mood indigo/Prelude to a kiss/Solitude / Medley: In a sentimental mood/Sophisticated Lady / I hear you screaming / Baby, won't you please come home / How high the moon / Dear Old Southland
CD _____ HEPCD 46
Hep / May '95 / Cadillac / Jazz Music / New Note / Wellard.

LEAVE US LEAP (Krupa, Gene & His Orchestra)
CD _____ VJC 1047
Vintage Jazz Classics / Jul '93 / Direct / ADA / CM / Cadillac.

MASTERPIECES # 13 1936-42
CD _____ 158302
Masterpieces / Mar '95 / BMG.

PERDIDO
CD _____ SWH 21
Swing House / Oct '92 / Harmonia Mundi.

WHAT'S THIS (1946-1947) (Krupa, Gene & His Orchestra)
(Back home again) in Indiana / My old flame / Up and atom / Wings on my shoes / Calling Dr. Gillespie / They didn't believe me / Stompin' at the Savoy / What's this / Begin the beguine / My ideal / Love's in my heart / Tea for two / Bolero at the Savoy / Leave us leap / Star dust / King Porter stomp / I'll never be the same / Wire brush stomp / Otto make that riff staccato / You go to my head / Lyonaisse potatoes and some pork chops / Lover
CD _____ HEPCD 26
Hep / Aug '93 / Cadillac / Jazz Music / New Note / Wellard.

Kruth, John

BANSHEE MANDOLIN
CD _____ FF 602CD
Flying Fish / May '93 / Roots / CM / Direct / ADA.

Kubek, Smokin' Joe

CHAIN SMOKIN' TEXAS STYLE (Kubek, Smokin' Joe Band)
CD _____ BBCD 9524
Bullseye Blues / Jan '93 / Direct.

CRYIN' FOR THE MOON
CD _____ CDBB 9560
Bullseye Blues / May '95 / Direct.

TEXAS CADILLAC (Kubek, Smokin' Joe Band)
CD _____ BB 9543CD
Bullseye Blues / Feb '94 / Direct.

Kubis, Tom

TOM KUBIS BIG BAND (Kubis, Tom Big Band)
CD _____ CDSB 109
Sea Breeze / '88 / Jazz Music.

Kuepper, Ed

BLACK TICKET
CD _____ HOT 1040CD
Hot / Jul '95 / Vital.

BUTTERFLY NET, THE
Not a soul around / At times, so emotional / Nothing changes in my house / Sometimes / Everything's fine / Also sprach / Ghost of an ideal wife / New bully in the town / Sea air / Electrical storm / What you don't know / Black ticket day / Way I made you feel / Real wild life / Always the woman pays / It's lunacy / Honey steel's gold / Everything I've got
CD _____ HOT 1045CD
Hot / Mar '95 / Vital.

CHARACTER ASSASSINATION
By the way / Little fiddle (And the ghost of Xmas past) / Cockfighter / My best interests at heart / Take it by the hand / La di doh / I'm with you / Ill wind / So close to certainty / Good soundtrack / Ring of fire / If I had a ticket
CD Set _____ HOT 1049CD
Hot / Aug '94 / Vital.

ELECTRICAL STORM
CD _____ HOT 1020CD
Hot / Jul '95 / Vital.

EVERYBODY'S GOT TO
Everybody's got to / Too many clues / When there's this party / Standing in the cold, in the rain / Lonely paradise / Burned my fingers / Not a soul around / Nothing changes in my house / Spartan spirituals / No skin off your nose
CD _____ HOT 1044CD
Hot / Jul '95 / Vital.

HONEY STEEL'S GOLD
King of vice / Everything I've got belongs to you / Friday's blue cheer/Libertines of Oxley / Honey Steel's gold / Way I made you feel / Not too soon / Closer (but disguised) / Summer field
CD _____ HOT 1036CD
Hot / Mar '95 / Vital.

KING IN THE KINDNESS ROOM, THE
Confessions of a window cleaner / Pissed off / Highway to hell / Messin' part II / They call me Mr Sexy / Sundown / Space pirate / Diving board
CD _____ HOT 1052CD
Hot / Jul '95 / Vital.

LEGENDARY BULLY, THE
CD _____ CCSCD 384
Castle / Sep '93 / BMG.

ROOMS OF THE MAGNIFICENT
Rooms of the magnificent / Also sprach the king of Euro-Disco / Sea air / Sixteen days / Without your mirror / No point in working / I am your prince / Spend five years / Show pony / Nothing you can do
CD _____ HOT 1027CD
Hot / Jul '95 / Vital.

SERENE MACHINE
When she's done / Sleepy head (serene machine) / Who's been talkin' / It's happening before / I wish you were here / Maria peripatetica / Sounds like mysterious wind / Reasons / This hideous place / (You) don't know what to steal / You can't please everybody / Married to my lazy life
CD _____ HOT 1042CD
Hot / Mar '95 / Vital.

TODAY WONDER
Horse under water / Always the woman pays / Everything I've got belongs to you / What you don't know / I'd rather be the devil / There's nothing natural / Medley / Pretty Mary / Eternally yours / If I were a carpenter
CD _____ HOT 1032CD
Hot / Mar '95 / Vital.

Kuhn, Josie

PARADISE
CD _____ RTMCD 41
Round Tower / Nov '92 / Pinnacle / ADA / Direct / BMG / CM.

WALKS WITH LIONS
CD _____ RTMCD 68
Round Tower / Oct '95 / Pinnacle / ADA / Direct / BMG / CM.

Kuhn, Judy

JUST IN TIME
CD _____ VSD 5472
Varese Sarabande/Colosseum / Feb '95 / Pinnacle / Silva Screen.

Kuhn, Steve

LIVE AT MAYBECK RECITAL HALL, VOL. 13
Old folks / Solar / I remember you / Autumn in New York / Meaning of the blues
CD _____ CCD 4484
Concord Jazz / Oct '91 / New Note.

LOOKING BACK (Kuhn, Steve Trio)
Looking back / Duke / How insensitive / Stella by starlight / Alone together / Gee baby ain't I good to you / Bangles, bangles and beads / Zingaro / Will you still be mine / Emmanuel
CD _____ CCD 4446
Concord Jazz / Feb '91 / New Note.

MOSTLY BALLADS
Yesterdays gardenias / Tennessee waltz / Danny boy / Don't explain / Body and soul / Emily / Airegin / How high the moon
CD _____ NW 351
New World / May '87 / Harmonia Mundi / ADA / Cadillac.

YEARS LATER
Gloria's theme / Upper Manhattan medical group / Years later / In a sentimental mood / Ladies in Mercedes / Good bait / Sometime ago / Silver's serenade / Born to be blue / Soul eyes
CD _____ CCD 4554
Concord Jazz / Jun '93 / New Note.

Kukuruza

CROSSING BORDERS
CD _____ SH 3814CD
Sugarhill / Mar '94 / Roots / CM / ADA / Direct.

Kullman, Charles

SERENADE
CD _____ CDMOIR 429
Memoir / Aug '95 / Target/BMG.

Kumar, Pramod

INDIA RAGA ROUTE
CD _____ ARN 64277
Arion / Oct '94 / Discovery / ADA.

Kumara

CONFLUENCE
White spring / Red spring / Influence / Confluence
CD _____ KU 9471
CDS / Feb '95 / Pinnacle.

Kuni Kids

CONGO SQUARE
CD _____ MWCD 3003
Music & Words / Jun '93 / ADA / Direct.

Kunz, Charlie

CHARLIE KUNZ - THE MEDLEY KING
CD _____ PASTCD 9783
Flapper / Jun '92 / Pinnacle.

CLAP HANDS, HERE COMES CHARLIE KUNZ
Clap hands, here comes Charlie / Feller that played the pianner / Solo medley / Juggler / Solo medley (r15) / He was a handsome young soldier / Solo medley of Astaire/Rogers hits / Solo medley (s15) / Life begins when you're in love / Solo medley (r22) / St. James's Park / Solo medley (r1) / Star fell out of heaven / Medley: Piccadilly pickle / I was in the mood for love / Solo medley (r18) / Intro (March winds and April showers)
CD _____ PASTCD 9730
Flapper / Jan '91 / Pinnacle.

MUSIC GOES ROUND, THE
When Irish eyes are smiling / Comin' thro' the rye / Oh you beautiful doll / Yip-I-addy-I-ay / On Treasure Island / Thanks a million / Music goes round and around / I can't give you anything but love / Ain't she sweet / Auf wiedersehen my dear / Lost / Glory of love / Is it true what they say about dixie / I ain't got nobody / If I had you / Time on my hands / I'll see you again / Desert song / My hero / Can't we talk it over / Dinah / Annie Laurie / Loch Lomond / Auld lang syne / She shall have music / Alone at a table for two / Pink elephants / Merry widow waltz / Love will find a way / Blue Danube / Some of these days / With a song in my heart / Night and day / What'll I do / Always / When you and I were seventeen / You are my lucky star / I've got a feelin' you're foolin' / She's funny that way / Shoe shine boy / When I'm with you / Somebody stole my gal / Poor butterfly / After you've gone / Whispering / Some other time / Little bit independent / Goodnight sweetheart
CD _____ CDHD 162
Happy Days / Oct '89 / Conifer.

PRETTY GIRL IS LIKE A MELODY, A
Crying my heart out for you / Till tomorrow / Would you / Pretty girl is like a melody / Love is a dancing thing / Cheek to cheek / Misty islands of the highlands / Look up and laugh / Boo-hoo / All alone in Vienna / When my dreamboat comes home / Learn to croon / Lazybones / Did my heart beat, did I fall in love / Dear stranger / Life is empty without love / Moonstruck / Unless
CD _____ 2 BUR 010
Burlington / Sep '88 / CM.

THERE GOES THAT SONG AGAIN
CD _____ PASTCD 7037
Flapper / Apr '94 / Pinnacle.

Kunzel, Erich

AMEN
CD _____ CD 80315
Telarc / Aug '93 / Conifer / ADA.

BOND AND BEYOND
CD _____ CD 80251
Telarc / Apr '91 / Conifer / ADA.

MANCINI'S GREATEST HITS (Kunzel, Erich & The Cincinnati Pops Orchestra)
CD _____ CD 80183
Telarc / Aug '90 / Conifer / ADA.

POMP AND PIZAZZ (Kunzel, Erich & The Cincinnati Pops Orchestra)
CD _____ CD 80122
Telarc / '88 / Conifer / ADA.

ROUND UP
Sounds of the west / Gioacchino Rossini / Magnificent seven / Furies suite / Round up / How the west was won / Gunfight at the O.K. Corral / Pops Hoedown / Big country / High noon / Western medley / Silverado
CD _____ CD 80141
Telarc / Apr '87 / Conifer / ADA.

SAILING (Kunzel, Erich & The Cincinnati Pops Orchestra)
Sailing / Great Whales (theme) / Dove / Love came for me / Wave / Under the sea / New Hampshire hornpipe / Ebb tide / Sea shanties / Beyond the sea / Lonely looking sky / Die / Dear Father / Banana boat song (Day O) / Sleepy lagoon / (Sittin' on) the dock of the bay / Sleepy shores / Margaritaville / Calypso
CD _____ CD 80292
Telarc / Jul '92 / Conifer / ADA.

STAR TRACKS II (Kunzel, Erich & The Cincinnati Pops Orchestra)
CD _____ CD 80146
Telarc / '88 / Conifer / ADA.

VERY BEST OF ERICH KUNZEL
Round up / Star Trek (theme) / Sing, sing, sing / Tara's theme (Gone with the wind) / Unchained melody / Nessun dorma / Little fugue in G minor / Star Wars / Batman / Grand Canyon suite / From Russia with love / Olympic fanfare / Opening sequence from Chiller / Overture to the Phantom Of The Opera / Godfather (theme) / Pink Panther (theme) / O mio babbino caro / Non-stop

fast polka / Op 112 / Honor, honor, do lord / Cybergenesis / Terminator / Jurassic lunch
CD _____ CD 80401
Telarc / Sep '94 / Conifer / ADA.

YOUNG AT HEART (Kunzel, Erich & The Cincinnati Pops Orchestra)
CD _____ 80245
Telarc / Oct '92 / Conifer / ADA.

Kupper, Eric

FROM THE DEEP
Intro / K-Scope theme / Katerpillar / Warble / Purple daizies / Midtro / Peace / Stonk / Organism / Planet K / Outro
CD _____ TRIUK 009CD
Tribal UK / Oct '95 / Vital.

Kuriya, Makoto

X-BASED MUSIC
Thousand days in motion / Watch out / Shake up the orient / Body and soul / Tokyo bay living struggle / Madame blonde / Peace
CD _____ KICJ 171
King/Paddle Wheel / Feb '94 / New Note.

Kurnia, Detty

COYOR PANON
CD _____ FLTRCD 519
Flame Tree / Sep '93 / Pinnacle.

DARI SUNDA
Sorban palid / Dar der dor / Emansipasi / Bandondari / Si kabayan / Bengawan solo / Asih kuring / Duriran / Mamanis / Sunayama / Hana
CD _____ TUGCD 1011
Riverboat / Oct '95 / New Note / Sterns.

Kursaal Flyers

CHOCS AWAY/ THE GREAT ARTISTE
CD _____ FOAMCD 3
On The Beach / Jan '94 / Pinnacle / Direct.

FORMER TOUR DE FORCE IS FORCED TO TOUR
CD _____ WF 044CD
Waterfront / Aug '88 / Jazz Music / ADA / CM.

Kustbandet

IN SWEDEN
CD _____ CK 83401
Kenneth / Jun '94 / Wellard / Cadillac / Jazz Music.

OSREGN (Kustbandet In Sweden)
F and B flat 7 / Heavenly music / Stackars VI / Snofall / Hon ar en skon juvel / En liten sang om dig / Honeymooning / Osregn / Rhythm in blue / Sla dig los och ta semester / Tillie / Archipelago / Drommen / Karlek ar karlek / Regntunga skyar
CD _____ CKS 3401
Kenneth / Jun '94 / Wellard / Cadillac / Jazz Music.

Kustomized

BATTLE FOR SPACE, THE
Day I had some fun / Throw your voice / Puff piece / Fifth / Gorgeous / 33 1/3 / Place where people meet / Phantasmagoria, now / La guene / Air freshner
CD _____ OLE 1132
Matador / Feb '95 / Vital.

Kusworth, Dave

WIVES, WEDDINGS AND ROSES (Kusworth, Dave & The Bounty Hunters)
CD _____ CRECD 092
Creation / Apr '91 / 3MV / Vital.

Kut Klose

SURRENDER
CD _____ 7559616682
Warner Bros. / Mar '95 / Warner Music.

Kutbay, Aka Gunduz

PLAYS THE TURKISH NEY
CD _____ PS 65078
Playasound / Aug / Harmonia Mundi / ADA.

Kuti, Fela

2000 BLACKS (Kuti, Fela & Roy Ayers)
CD _____ 760230
Justin / Nov '90 / Triple Earth.

AFRO BEAT
CD _____ MPG 74024
Movieplay Gold / Jan '94 / Target/BMG.

BUY AMERICA (Kuti, Fela Anikulapo)
CD _____ MAUCD 631
Mau Mau / Dec '92 / Pinnacle.

FELA'S LONDON SCENE
CD _____ STCD 3007
Sterns / Oct '94 / Sterns / CM.

MUSIC IS THE WEAPON 75-78
CD _____ 760443
Justin / Nov '90 / Triple Earth.

MUSIC IS THE WEAPON 81-84
CD _____ 760444
Justin / Nov '90 / Triple Earth.

MUSIC IS THE WEAPON 85-86
CD _____ 760445
Justin / Nov '90 / Triple Earth.

UNDERGROUND SYSTEM
CD _____ STCD 1043
Sterns / Nov '92 / Sterns / CM.

KWS

ALBUM
CD _____ KWSCD 1
Network / Dec '92 / Sony / 3MV.

Kydd, Christine

HEADING HOME
CD _____ FE 93CD
Dara / Oct '93 / Roots / CM / Direct / ADA / Koch.

Kynard, Charles

REELIN' WITH THE FEELIN'/WA-TU-WA-ZUI
Reelin' with the feelin' / Soul reggae / Slow burn / Boogaloogin' / Be my love / Stomp / Wa-tu-wa-zui / Winter's child / Zebra walk / Something / Change up

CD _____ CDBGPD 055
BGP / Aug '93 / Pinnacle.

Kyoma

RIGHT HERE WAITING
CD _____ CCD 7
Music / Apr '95 / Jetstar.

Kyoto Nohgaku Kai

JAPANESE NOH MUSIC
CD _____ LYRCD 7137
Lyrichord / Feb '94 / Roots / ADA / CM.

Kyoto Temple Monks

BUDDHIST BELLS, DRUMS & CHANTS
CD _____ LYRCD 7200
Lyrichord / Dec '94 / Roots / ADA / CM.

Kyser, Kay

SONGS OF WORLD WAR II VOL.2 (Kyser, Kay Orchestra)
CD _____ VJC 1042
Vintage Jazz Classics / Feb '93 / Direct / ADA / CM / Cadillac.

Kyuss

AND THE CIRCUS LEAVES TOWN
CD _____ 7559618112
Warner Bros. / Jun '95 / Warner Music.

BLUES FOR THE RED SUN
Thumb / Green machine / Molten universe / Fifty Million year trip (Downside up) / Thong song / Apothecarie's weight / Caterpillar march / Freedom run / 800 / Writhe / Capsized
CD _____ 370561340-2
Warner Bros. / Feb '93 / Warner Music.

WELCOME TO SKY VALLEY
Gardenia / Asteroid / Supa scoopa and mighty scoop / 100 Degrees / Space cadet / Demon cleaner / Odyssey / Conan troutman / N.O. / Whitewater
CD _____ 755961571-2
Warner Bros. / Jun '94 / Warner Music.

L

L Big Band

LIVE WITH BLUE BIRD
CD _____ LBBCD 6
Ad Lib / Oct '94 / Cadillac.

L Kage

BRAZILLIANT
CD _____ TPLP 26 CD
One Little Indian / Jun '93 / Pinnacle.

L.A. 4

EXECUTIVE SUITE
Blues wellington / Amazonia / You and I / Simple invention / Entr'Acte / My funny valentine / Chega de Saudade
CD _____ CCD 4215
Concord Jazz / Nov '95 / New Note.

L.A. FOUR
Dindi / Rainbows / Rondo es pressivo / Manteca / St. Thomas / Concierto de Aranjuez
CD _____ CCD 4018
Concord Jazz / Sep '86 / New Note.

L.A. FOUR SCORES
CD _____ CCD 6008
Concord Jazz / Jul '88 / New Note.

MONTAGE
Madame butterball / Syrinx / Samba for Ray / Teach me tonight / Rado's got the blues / My romance / Bachianas brasilerias No.5 / Squatty roo
CD _____ CCD 4156
Concord Jazz / Jan '95 / New Note.

ZACA
Zaca / You can't go home again / Child is born / O barquinho / Close ecounter for love / Pavanne op.50 / Secret love
CD _____ CCD 4130
Concord Jazz / Feb '94 / New Note.

L.A. Blues Authority

CREAM OF THE CROP
CD _____ RR 89662
Roadrunner / Nov '94 / Pinnacle.

FIT FOR A KING
CD _____ RR 90492
Roadrunner / Aug '93 / Pinnacle.

HATS OFF TO STEVIE RAY
CD _____ RR 90502
Roadrunner / Aug '93 / Pinnacle.

L.A. Guns

VICIOUS CIRCLE
Face down / No crime / Long time dead / Killing machine / Fade away / Tarantula / Crystal eyes / Nothing better to do / Chasing the dragon / Kill that girl / I'd love to change the world / Who's in control (Let 'em roll) / I'm the one / WHy ain't I bleeding / Kiss of death
CD _____ 5231582
Polydor / Apr '95 / PolyGram.

L.A. Jazz Quintet

LA JAZZ QUINTET
CD _____ K32Y 6116
King/Paddle Wheel / Apr '87 / New Note.

L.A. Mix

ON THE SIDE
Get loose / You are the one / Breathe deep / Don't turn away / Love together / Just waiting / Mellow mellow / Don't stop / Check this out
CD _____ CDA 9009
A&M / Sep '89 / PolyGram.

L.A. Star

POETESS
Wonderous dream / N.P.T. posse / Do you still love me / Swing to the beat / It's like that / Fade to black / My tale / It takes a real woman / Once upon a time / If you don't wanna party / N.P.T. posse (UK remix)
CD _____ FILECD 290
Profile / Jul '91 / Pinnacle.

L.A. Transit

DE NOVO
Mas que nada / Wave / Zazuiera / How insensitive / Muito mais / Agua de Beber / Pretty world / Anything can happen / Summer without you / Tristeza
CD _____ CY 1004
Denon / '88 / Conifer.

L.A. Workshop

NORWEGIAN WOOD
Overture / Norwegian wood / And I love her / Fool on the hill / Nowhere man / Blackbird / Yesterday / Michelle / When I'm sixty four / Penny Lane / Hey Jude
CD _____ CA 72725
Denon / Oct '90 / Conifer.

NORWEGIAN WOOD II
Julia / Sergeant Pepper's lonely hearts club band / Eleanor Rigby / Anna / Something / Norwegian Wood / This boy / Roll over Beethoven / If I fell / Long and winding road
CD _____ CA 73412
Denon / Nov '90 / Conifer.

L.A.P.D.

WHO'S LAUGHING
CD _____ TX 93152
Roadrunner / May '91 / Pinnacle.

L.I.L.T.

FOR THE CHILDREN
CD _____ ETCD 191
Alias / Nov '90 / Grapevine.

L.L. Cool J

14 SHOTS TO THE DOME
How I'm comin' / Buckin' em down / Stand by your man / Little somethin' / Pink cookies in a plastic bag getting crushed by buildings / Straight from Queens / Funkadelic relic / All we got left is the beat (NFA) / No frontin' allowed / Back seat / Soul survivor / Ain't no stoppin' this / Diggy down / Crossroads
CD _____ 5234882
Def Jam / Jan '96 / PolyGram.

BIGGER AND DEFFER
I'm bad / Get down / Bristol Hotel / My rhyme ain't done / 357 - Break it on down / Go cut creator go / Breakthrough / I need love / Ahh, let's get ill / Doo wop / On the ill tip
CD _____ 5273532
Def Jam / Jul '95 / PolyGram.

MAMA SAID KNOCK YOU OUT
Boomin' system / Around the way girl / Eat 'em up L. Chill / Mr. Good Bar / Murdergram (live at Rapmania) / Cheesy rat blues / Farmers boulevard (our anthem) / Mama said knock you out / Milky cereal / Jingling baby / To da break of dawn / Six minutes of pleasure / Illegal search / Power of God
CD _____ 5234772
Def Jam / Jul '95 / PolyGram.

MR. SMITH
Make it hot / Hip hop / Hey lover / Doin it / Life as / I shot ya / Mr. Smith / No aeplay / Loungin / Hollis to Hollywood / God bless / Get the drop on em
CD _____ 5297242
Def Jam / Nov '95 / PolyGram.

RADIO
I can't live without my radio / You can't dance / Dear Yvette / I can give you more / Dangerous / Rock the bells / I need a beat / You'll rock / I want you
CD _____ 5273522
Def Jam / Jul '95 / PolyGram.

WALKING WITH A PANTHER
Droppin' em / Smokin', doipin' / Fast peg / Clap your hands / Nitro / You're my heart / I'm that type of guy / Why do you think they call it dope / It gets no rougher / Big ole butt / One shot at love / 1-900 LL Cool J / Two different worlds / Jealous / Jingling baby / Def Jam in the motherland / Going back to Cali (Not on LP) / Crime stories (MC only) / Change your ways (MC only) / Jack the ripper (MC only)
CD _____ 5273552
Def Jam / Jul '95 / PolyGram.

L.S.G.

RENDEZVOUS IN OUTER SPACE
Wrong time wrong place / Lonely casseopaya / My time is yours / Can you see the yellow turtles / Miss Understanding / Sweet gravity / Sweet g (#2) / Hidden sun of Venus / Lunar orbit / Everything is / Ebter - paradise / Fontana / Reprise
CD _____ SUPER 2038CD
Superstition / Jun '95 / Vital / SRD.

L.S.O.

SERENITY, TRANQUILITY & PEACE
CD _____ TASTE 061CD
Taste / Aug '95 / Plastic Head.

L7

BRICKS ARE HEAVY
Wargasm / Scrap / Pretend we're dead / Diet pill / Everglade / Slide / One more thing / Mr. Integrity / Monster / Shitlist / This ain't pleasure
CD _____ 8283072
Slash / May '92 / PolyGram.

HUNGRY FOR STINK

Andres / Baggage / Can I run / Bomb / Questioning my sanity / Riding with a movie star / Stuck here again / Fuel my fire / Freak magnet / She has eyes / Shirley / Talk box
CD _____ 828531-2
Slash / Jul '94 / PolyGram.

LA 1919

TO PLAY (Jour Speilen)
Drumming ralk / Red wire / Un mondo invisible / Donne kamikaze / Qua qua que singing ducks / Storie del dormiveglia / Fate fagotto / Sheffield Wednesday / Hanna seppellito l'uomo sbagliato
CD _____ MASOCD 90063
Materiali Sonori / May '94 / New Note.

La Argentinita

DUENDE Y FIGURA
CD _____ 20062CD
Sonifolk / Nov '95 / ADA / CM.

La Beef, Sleepy

NOTHIN' BUT THE TRUTH
Tore up over you / How do you talk to a baby / Milk cow blues / Just pickin' / Gunslinger / Ring of fire / Boogie at the Wayside Lounge / Worried man blues / Let's talk about us / My toot toot / Jambalaya / Whole lot of shakin'
CD _____ CD 3072
Rounder / Jul '91 / CM / Direct / ADA / Cadillac.

STRANGE THINGS HAPPENING
CD _____ ROU 3129CD
Rounder / Apr '94 / CM / Direct / ADA / Cadillac.

La Belle Epoque

MEXICAN LANDSCAPES VOL. 6
CD _____ PS 65906
Playasound / Feb '93 / Harmonia Mundi / ADA.

La Bolduc

SONGS OF QUEBEC 1929-39
CD _____ Y225108CD
Silex / Oct '94 / ADA.

La Bradford

LA BRADFORD
CD _____ FNCD 329
Flying Nun / Jun '95 / Disc.

La Costa Rasa

AUTOPILOT
CD _____ 11316832
Merciful Release / Jul '94 / Warner Music.

La Cucina

CHUCHERIA
CD _____ LAC 123CD
La Cucina / Mar '94 / CM / Direct.
CD _____ OSMOCD 002
Osmosys / '95 / Direct / ADA.

NABUMLA
Embers / Buddhas (are we) / Light shine through / Heart again / Runner / Guy Debord is sleeping / L'Americana / Villa laterno / Struggle / Question / Naked in the sunshine
CD _____ OSMO CD007
Osmosys / Jan '96 / Direct / ADA.

La Flamme, David

WHITE BIRD/INSIDE OUT
White bird / Hot summer day / Swept away / Easy woman / This man / Baby be wise / Spirit of America / Who's gonna love me / My life / Night song / Forever and a day / Somewhere down the road / Where flamingos fly / Day you went away / Need something / Can't wait until tomorrow
CD _____ EDCD 419
Edsel / Aug '95 / Pinnacle / ADA.

La Floa Maldita

DEDICATION SEPERATION
CD _____ EEFA 127522
Kodex / Nov '95 / SRD.

La Gran Manzana

ME GUSTA MERENGUE
CD _____ INT 31192
Intuition / Jun '93 / New Note.

La Grand Rouge

TRAVERSER DU PAYS
CD _____ 199732

La Grande Bande Des...

FAUT QU' CA BRILLE (La Grande Bande Des Cornemuses)
CD _____ B 6743CD
Auvidis/Ethnic / Jul '94 / Harmonia Mundi.

La Lann, Eric

NEW YORK
CD _____ OMCD 053
OMD / Sep '92 / Koch.

La Marienne

UN BAL EN VENDEE
CD _____ MRV 797CD
MRV / Nov '95 / ADA.

La Mirlitanouille

1975-1980
CD _____ IG 7779CD
Diffusion Breizh / Aug '95 / ADA.

La Misma Gente

EL LOCO
CD _____ TUMICD 030
Tumi / '92 / Sterns / Discovery.

La Moposina, Toto

LA CANDELA VIVA
Dos de febrero / Adios fulana / El pescador / La sombra negra / Dame la mano juancho / Malanga / Mapale / Curura / Chi chi mani / La candela viva / La acabacion
CD _____ CDRW 31
Realworld / Jun '93 / EMI / Sterns.

La Morte De La Maison

ARROND RED
CD _____ SPV 08419592
SPV / May '95 / Plastic Head.

La Muerte

RAW
Speed, steel and gasoline / Serial killer / Black God, white devil / Hate love / Power / Wild fucker / Cravacher / Burst my soul / I would die faster / Lucifer Sam / KKK / Couteau dans l'eau / Blood on the moon / Ecoute cette priere / Mannish boy / Shoot in your back / Kung fu fighting / Wild thing
CD _____ BIAS 266CD
Play It Again Sam / May '94 / Vital.

La Musgana

EL DIABLO COJUELO
CD _____ H 028CD
Sonifolk / Jun '94 / ADA / CM.

LAS SEIS TENTACIONS
CD _____ XENO 4030
Xenophile / Apr '95 / Direct / ADA.

LUBICAN
CD _____ GL 4010CD
Green Linnet / Jan '94 / Roots / CM / Direct / ADA.

La Negra Graciana

SON JAROCHO
CD _____ COCD 109
Corason / Oct '94 / CM / Direct / ADA.

La Nina De Los Peines

ART OF FLAMENCO VOL. 7, THE
CD _____ MAN 4856
Mandala / Oct '95 / Mandala / Harmonia Mundi.

La Piva Del Carner

LA PEGRA A LA MATEINE
CD _____ NT 6735CD
Robi Droli / Apr '95 / Direct / ADA.

La Roca, Pete

BASRA
Malaguena / Candu / Tears come down from heaven / Basra / Lazy afternoon / Eiderdown
CD _____ CDP 8320912
Blue Note / May '95 / EMI.

Sonora Matan

ESTE CHA CHA CHA
CD _____ CD 62012
Saludos Amigos / Apr '94 / Target/BMG.

La Souris Deglinguee

LA SOURIS DEGLINGUEE
CD _____ ROSE 6CD
New Rose / '88 / Direct / ADA.

La Touche

CAJUN DANCE PARTY
CD _____ PLATCD 3938
Prism / Mar '95 / Prism.

La Verne, Andy

TIME WELL SPENT
Common knowledge / There is no greater
love / Cantaloupe island / On a misty night
/ Time well spent / I should care / Lover man
/ Singel petal of a rose / Fall / Blue interlude
/ Rhythm and blues
CD _____ CCD 4680
Concord Jazz / Feb '96 / New Note.

La Vienta

JAZZMENCO
CD _____ CD 83353
Telarc / Aug '93 / Conifer / ADA.

NIGHT DANCE
Journey / Love for Isabel / Ariana / Tranquilo
/ El gato negro / Ojo caliente carnival / Be-
to's turn / Goodbye tomorrow / En la cueva
/ Promise of St Matthew / Samba loco
CD _____ CD 83359
Telarc / Jun '94 / Conifer / ADA.

Lab Report

FIGURE X-71
CD _____ CDDVN 27
Under One Flag / Dec '93 / Pinnacle.

UNHEALTHY
CD _____ CDDVN 31
Devotion / Jun '94 / Pinnacle.

Labanda

NO TODO ES SEDA
CD _____ 21065CD
Sonifolk / Nov '95 / ADA / CM.

LaBarbera, Joe

JMOG
Game's afoot / Elvin's share / Dark ocean /
Sierra Nevada / Elk the moochie / Another
rainy day / Night/Morning
CD _____ SKCD 2-2031
Sackville / Jun '93 / Swift / Jazz Music /
Jazz Horizons / Cadillac / CM.

Labelle, Patti

**EARLY YEARS, THE (Labelle, Patti &
The Bluebells)**
Sold my heart to the junkman / One phone
call / Have I sinned / Academy award / Go
on (This is goodbye) / Island of unbroken
hearts / Impossible / Decatur street / Where
are you / Down the aisle / Tear after tear /
What kind of heart / Danny boy / Please
hurry home / I believe / I walked right in /
Itty bitty twist / When Johnny comes
marching home / You'll never walk alone /
Joke's on you / You will fill my eyes no more
/ Love me just a little / Cool water / My bridal gown / I sold my heart to the junkman
(outtake)
CD _____ CDCHD 441
Ace / Feb '93 / Pinnacle / Cadillac / Com-
plete/Pinnacle.

I SOLD MY HEART TO THE JUNKMAN
CD _____ HADCD 179
Javelin / Nov '95 / THE / Henry Hadaway
Organisation.

**LADY MARMALADE (The Best Of Patti
Labelle)**
Lady Marmalade / What can I do for you /
Are you lonely / You turn me on / Messin
with my mind / Take the night off / Get you
someone new / Isn't it a shame / Joy to
have your love / I think about you / You are
my friend / Teach me tonight (me gusta tu
baile) / Quiet time / It's all right with me /
Don't make your angel cry / Come what
may
CD _____ 4805102
Epic / May '95 / Sony.

NIGHTBIRDS
Lady Marmalade / Somebody somewhere /
Are you lonely / It took a long time / Don't
bring me down / What can I do for you /
Nightbird / Space children / All girl band /
You turn me on
CD _____ 983382 2
Carlton Home Entertainment / Feb '94 /
Carlton Home Entertainment.

**OVER THE RAINBOW (The Atlantic
Sessions)**
CD _____ SLC 2501
Ichiban / Apr '95 / Koch.

Labeque, Katia

LITTLE GIRL BLUE
We will meet again / My funny valentine /
On fire / Besame mucho / Prologue / Little
girl blue / Quizas quizas quizas / Volcano
for hire / Turn out the stars / Summertime /
La comparsa

CD _____ FDM 361862
Dreyfus / Oct '95 / ADA / Direct / New Note.

Laboriel, Abraham

DEAR FRIENDS
Quote, unquote / And I do / Holidays / Look
at me / Goyo / Dear friends / Samba 7 / My
joy is you / Simple self / Arroyo
CD _____ 101 S 7166 2
101 South / Jun '93 / New Note.

GUIDUM
Wassup / Exchange / Slippin' and slidin' /
You can't hide / Let my people / Guidum /
Out from darkness / Vamos a gozar / An-
other day / Bass sweet / Final degree / Be
bop drive / Breakfast at Tiffany's
CD _____ 101S 8770562
101 South / Oct '94 / New Note.

Labradford

PRAZISION
CD _____ FNCD 342
Flying Nun / Feb '96 / Disc.

Lacen, Anthony

**ANTHONY 'TUBA FATS' LACEN/RUE
CONTI JAZZBAND/D.KELLIN**
CD _____ BCD 344
GHB / Jun '95 / Jazz Music.

Lacrimosa

INFERNO
CD _____ DW 088CD
Deathwish / Jun '95 / Plastic Head.

Lacy, Steve

AXIEME
CD _____ 123120-2
Red / Apr '93 / Harmonia Mundi / Jazz
Horizons / Cadillac / ADA.

CHIRPS (Lacy, Steve & Evan Parker)
CD _____ FMPCD 29
FMP / Mar '87 / Cadillac.

CLANGS (Lacy, Steve Double Sextet)
CD _____ ARTCD 6116
Hat Art / Jan '94 / Harmonia Mundi / ADA
/ Cadillac.

FLAME, THE
CD _____ 1210352
Soul Note / Nov '90 / Harmonia Mundi /
Wellard / Cadillac.

FLIM-FLAM (Lacy, Steve & Steve Potts)
CD _____ ARTCD 6087
Hat Art / Nov '91 / Harmonia Mundi / ADA
/ Cadillac.

FOREST AND THE ZOO, THE
CD _____ ESP 1060-2
ESP / Jan '93 / Jazz Horizons / Jazz
Music.

**HOT HOUSE (Lacy, Steve & Mal
Waldron)**
House party starting / Hot house / I'll keep
loving you / Friday the 13th / Mistral breeze
/ Mooche / Petite fleur / Snake out / Retreat
CD _____ PD 83098
Novus / Apr '91 / BMG.

**IMAGE (DUO PERFORMANCES) (Lacy,
Steve & Steve Arguelles)**
Ah-Um / Apr '89 / New Note / Cadillac.
CD _____ AHUM 001

**LIVE AT SWEET BASIL (Lacy, Steve
Sextet)**
Prospectus / Bath / Morning joy / Wane /
Blinks
CD _____ PD 90647
Novus / May '92 / BMG.

**LIVE IN BUDAPEST (Lacy, Steve &
Steve Potts)**
Prospectus / Gleam / Morning joy / Crust
stands / Stand / Cliches
CD _____ WWCD 011
West Wind / Dec '88 / Swift / Charly / CM
/ ADA.

MOMENTUM
Bath / Momentum / Song
CD _____ PD 83021
Novus / Dec '88 / BMG.

MORE MONK
CD _____ 121210-2
Soul Note / Apr '91 / Harmonia Mundi /
Wellard / Cadillac.

**PACKET (Lacy, Steve & Irene Aebi/
Frederic Rzewski)**
CD _____ NA 080
New Albion / Dec '95 / Harmonia Mundi /
Cadillac.

**REFLECTIONS: PLAYS THELONIUS
MONK**
Four in one / Reflections / Hornin' in / Bye-
ya / Let's call this / Ask me now / Skippy
CD _____ OJCCD 063
Original Jazz Classics / Sep '93 / Wellard /
Jazz Music / Cadillac / Complete/Pinnacle.

REMAINS
CD _____ ARTCD 6102
Hat Art / May '92 / Harmonia Mundi / ADA
/ Cadillac.

**SCHOOL DAYS (Lacy, Steve & Roswell
Rudd Quartet)**
CD _____ ARTCD 6140
Hat Art / Apr '94 / Harmonia Mundi / ADA
/ Cadillac.

**SIDELINES (Lacy, Steve & Michael
Smith)**
CD _____ 123847-2
IAI / Sep '92 / Harmonia Mundi / Cadillac.

SOPRANO SAX
CD _____ OJCCD 130
Original Jazz Classics / Nov '95 / Wellard /
Jazz Music / Cadillac / Complete/Pinnacle.

**SPIRIT OF MINGUS (Lacy, Steve & Eric
Watson)**
CD _____ FRLCD 016
Freelance / Oct '92 / Harmonia Mundi /
Cadillac / Koch.

STEVE LACY
Easy to love / Day dream / Let's cool one /
Rockin in rhythm / Something to live for /
Alone together / Work / Skippy / Monk's
wood / Bye-ya
CD _____ CD 53260
Giants Of Jazz / Jan '96 / Target/BMG /
Cadillac.

STRAIGHT HORN OF STEVE LACY, THE
CD _____ CCD 9007
Candid / Jul '87 / Cadillac / Jazz Music /
Wellard / Koch.

TRICKLES
CD _____ 1200082
Black Saint / Oct '90 / Harmonia Mundi /
Cadillac.

VESPERS (Lacy, Steve Octet)
CD _____ 121260-2
Soul Note / Nov '93 / Harmonia Mundi /
Wellard / Cadillac.

WE SEE
CD _____ ARTCD 6127
Hat Art / Sep '93 / Harmonia Mundi / ADA
/ Cadillac.

WEAL AND WOE
CD _____ EM 4004
Emanem / Dec '95 / Cadillac / Harmonia
Mundi.

WINDOW, THE (Lacy, Steve Trio)
CD _____ 121185-2
Soul Note / Oct '90 / Harmonia Mundi /
Wellard / Cadillac.

Ladonnas

LADONNALAND
CD _____ IFACD 015
IFA / Nov '95 / Plastic Head.

Lady G

GOD DAUGHTER
CD _____ VPCD 1436
VP / Oct '95 / Jetstar.

Lady June

LADY JUNE'S LINGUISTIC LEPROSY
Some day silly twenty three / Reflections /
Am I / Everythingnothing / Tunion / Tourist
/ Bars / Letter / Mangel/Wurzel / To whom
it may not concern / Optimism / Touch-
downer
CD _____ SEECD 350
See For Miles/C5 / Jun '92 / Pinnacle.

Ladysmith Black Mambazo

**BEST OF LADYSMITH BLACK
MAMBAZO**
CD _____ SHCD 43098
Shanachie / Jul '92 / Koch / ADA /
Greensleeves.

CLASSIC TRACKS
CD _____ SHANCD 43074
Shanachie / Oct '90 / Koch / ADA /
Greensleeves.

INALA
Buya uz'ekhaya / That's why I choose you
/ Wahlala emnyango / Ngothandaza njalo /
Kulomhlaba (thula) / Udla nge'nduku za
banye / Pauline / Isala kutshelwa / Kwash-
intsh's isthothobala / Uthando oluphelayo
CD _____ SHANCD 43040
Shanachie / Mar '89 / Koch / ADA /
Greensleeves.

INDUKU ZETHU
Mangosuthu / Induku selhu / Vukani / Kubi
ukungalaeli / Ithemba lethu / Umzali
sentombi / Ingwe idla ngamabla / Umzal-
wane / Ifa lobukhosana / Wayabimba mfana
/ Watatazela / Bakhuphuka izwe lande
CD _____ SHANCD 43021
Shanachie / '88 / Koch / ADA /
Greensleeves.

INKANYEZI NEZAZI
CD _____ FLTRCD 502
Timbuktu / Dec '92 / Pinnacle.

JOURNEY OF DREAMS
Umusa kankulunkulu / Lindelani / Ukhalan-
gami / Bhasobha / Hamba dompasi / Un-
gayoni into enhle / Amaphiko okundiza /
Wayibambezeka / Ungakhowlwa rain /
Amazing grace

CD _____ 925753 2
WEA / Aug '88 / Warner Music.

LIPH'IQINISO
CD _____ FLTRCD 522
Timbuktu / Feb '94 / Pinnacle.

SHAKA ZULU
Unomathemba / Hello my baby / At Gol-
gotha / King of kings / Earth is never sat-
isfied / How long / Home of the heroes /
These are the guys / Rain rain beautiful rain
/ Who were you talking to
CD _____ K 9255822
WEA / Mar '94 / Warner Music.

STAR & THE WISE MAN, THE
CD _____ 669112
Melodie / Nov '92 / Triple Earth /
Discovery / ADA / Jetstar.

TWO WORLDS ONE HEART
Township jive / Ofana naye (nobody like
him) / Bala ubhale (count and write) / Love
your neighbor / Leaning on the everlasting
arms / Rejoice / Hayi ngalesiskhathi (not
right now) / Emhlabeni (in this world) / Isi-
hathi siyimal (time is money) / Ngomnyango
(by the door)
CD _____ 7599261252
WEA / May '90 / Warner Music.

UMTHOMBO WAMANZI
CD _____ SHANCD 43055
Shanachie / Aug '88 / Koch / ADA /
Greensleeves.

LaFarge, Peter

**ON THE WARPATH/AS LONG AS THE
GRASS SHALL GROW**
Look again to the wind / Senecas / Damn
redskins / Tecumseh / Take back your atom
bomb / Vision of a past warrior / Coyote /
My little brother / Alaska / Custer trail of
tears / Hey Mr. President / Touriste / Last
words / Ballad of Ira Hayes / Johnny half
breed / Radioactive Eskimo / Crimson par-
son / Move over, grap a 'holt / Gather round
/ If I could not be an Indian / Drums / White
girl / I'm an Indian, I'm an alien / Stampede
/ Please come back, Abe-War Whoop
Father
CD _____ BCD 15626
Bear Family / Jun '92 / Rollercoaster / Direct
/ CM / Swift.

**SONGS OF THE COWBOYS/IRON
MOUNTAIN SONGS**
Whoopee ti yi yo / Chisholm trail / Sirey
peaks / Lavendar cowboy / I've got no use
for the women / I ride old paint / Cowboy's
lament / Yavipii Pete / When the work's all
done this fall / Cowboy's dream / Black
walkin' / John Strawberry Roan / Rodeo
hand / Cattle calls / Stumbling / Pop Reed
/ Pony called Nell / Marijuana blues / Snow
bird blues / Hungry blues / Avril blues /
Santa Fe / Alaska 49th State / Iron mountain / Falling stars / Abraham Lincoln / Cisco
Houston
CD _____ BCD 15627
Bear Family / Jun '92 / Rollercoaster / Direct
/ CM / Swift / ADA.

LaFave, Jimmy

AUSTIN SKYLINE
CD _____ BBEAT 8004
Bohemia Beat / Jan '94 / Direct / CM /
ADA.

HIGHWAY TRANCE
CD _____ LDCD 80002
Lizard / Sep '94 / Direct / Disc.

Laffy, Gerry

MUSIC AND THE MAGIC
CD _____ WKFMXD 152
FM / Jul '90 / Sony.

Lafitte, Guy

**LOTUS BLOSSOM (Lafitte, Guy & Wild
Bill Davis)**
CD _____ BLE 591882
Black & Blue / Apr '91 / Wellard / Koch.

THINGS WE DID LAST SUMMER, THE
CD _____ BLE 591922
Black & Blue / Apr '91 / Wellard / Koch.

Lag Wagon

HOSS
CD _____ FAT 532CD
Fat Wreck Chords / Nov '95 / Plastic
Head.

TRASHED
CD _____ FAT 513-2
Fat Wreck Chords / Feb '94 / Plastic
Head.

Lagaretta, Felix

PUPY Y SU CHARANGA
CD _____ TUMICD 033
Tumi / '93 / Sterns / Discovery.

Lagonia

ETC, ETC
CD _____ HBG 122/12
Background / Apr '94 / Background.

Lagowski

WIRE SCIENCE
CD _____ TEQM 93002
TEQ / May '95 / Plastic Head.

Lagrave, Jean-Francois

ZOUK MALOYA
CD _____ PS 65077
Playasound / Aug '91 / Harmonia Mundi / ADA.

Lagrene, Birelli

ACOUSTIC MOMENTS
Made in France / Rhythm things / Claire Marie / All the things you are / Three views of a secret / Impressions / Stretch / Acoustic moments / Bass ballad / Metal earthquake
CD _____ CDP 795 263 2
Blue Note / Nov '90 / EMI.

BIRELLI LAGRENE WITH LARRY CORYELL & MIROSLAV VITOUS
CD _____ INAK 8610
In Akustik / Jun '95 / Magnum Music Group.

LIVE
CD _____ INAK 865 CD
In Akustik / '88 / Magnum Music Group.

LIVE AT CARNEGIE HALL - A TRIBUTE TO DJANGO REINHARDT
CD _____ CDJP 1040
Jazz Point / May '94 / Harmonia Mundi / Cadillac.

LIVE IN MARCIAC
Softly as in a morning sunrise / Days of wine and roses / Donna Lee / Smile / Autumn leaves / Nuages / C'est si bon / Blues walk / Stella by starlight / I got rhythm
CD _____ FDM 365672
Dreyfus / Jul '94 / ADA / Direct / New Note.

MY FAVOURITE DJANGO
Daphne / Moppin' the bride / Babik / Melodie au creuscule / Place de brouckere / Nuages / Blues for Ike / Nuits de saint germaine des pres / Clair de lune / Troublant bolero / Solo
CD _____ FDM 365742
Dreyfus / Oct '95 / ADA / Direct / New Note.

Lahiri, Bappi

HEARTRAVE
CD _____ FLTRCD 515
Flame Tree / Sep '93 / Pinnacle.

Laibach

BAPTISM, A
CD _____ SUB 3306779 CD
Sub Rosa / Dec '90 / Vital / These / Discovery.

KAPITAL
CD _____ CDSTUMM 82
Mute / Apr '92 / Disc.

KRST POD TRIGLAVOM BAPTISM
CD _____ CD 0019
Sub Rosa / Aug '88 / Vital / These / Discovery.

LAIBACH
CD _____ EFA 131322
Nika / Aug '95 / SRD.

LET IT BE
Get back / Dig a pony / Across the universe / Dig it / I've got a feeling / Long and winding road / One after 909 / Maggie Mae / For you blue
CD _____ CDSTUMM 58
Mute / Oct '88 / Disc.

LJUBLJANA, ZAGREB, BEOGRAD
CD _____ NSK 1CD
Grey Area / May '93 / Pinnacle.

MACBETH
Preludium / Agnus dei / Wutach schlucht / Die Zeit / Ohne geld / U.S.A. / 10th May 1941 / Expectans exprectavus / Coincidentia oppositorum / Wolf
CD _____ STUMM 70 CD
Mute / Jan '90 / Disc.

NATO
CD _____ CDSTUMM 121
Mute / Oct '94 / Disc.

NOVA AKROPOLA
Four personen / Nova akropola / Krvava fruda-plodna zemja / Vojna poema / Ti ki izzivas
CD _____ CDMRED 67
Cherry Red / Mar '95 / Pinnacle.

OPUS DEI
Great seal / How the west was won / Transnational / Opus dei / Leben-tod / F I A T / Geburt einer nation / Leben heist leben
CD _____ CDSTUMM 44
Mute / Apr '87 / Disc.

SLOVENSKA ARKOPOLA
CD _____ EFA 200252
Nika / Aug '95 / SRD.

Laika

INSTRUMENTS OF TERROR (Laika & The Cosmonauts)
CD _____ UPSTART 005
Upstart / Apr '94 / Direct / ADA.

SILVER APPLES OF THE MOON
CD _____ PURECD 042
Too Pure / Oct '94 / Vital.

Laika & The Cosmonauts

AMAZING COLOSSAL BAND, THE
CD _____ UPSTART 10
Upstart / Mar '95 / Direct / ADA.

Laine, Cleo

BEAUTIFUL THING, A
All in love is fair / Skip a long Sam / Send in the clowns / Least you can do is the best you can / They needed each other / I loves you Porgy / Until it's time for you to go / Life is a wheel / Summer knows / Beautiful thing
CD _____ 09026616642
RCA / Oct '94 / BMG.

BLUE AND SENTIMENTAL
Lies of handsome men / I've got a crush on you / Blue and sentimental / Afterglow / Not you again / Primrose colour blue / What'll I do / Love me (if it takes you all night long) / Creole love call
CD _____ 09026614192
RCA / Sep '94 / BMG.

CLEO AT CARNEGIE
Any place (Medley.) / I'm shadowing you / Crazy rhythm / Primrose colour blue / We are the music makers / You spotted snakes / Methuselah / When I was one and twenty / Sing me no song / Triboro' fair / You've got to do what you've got to do / He was beautiful / Turkish delight / Never let me go / I want to be happy
CD _____ CDXP 2101
DRG / Apr '87 / New Note.

I AM A SONG
I'm gonna sit right down and write myself a letter / Early Autumn / Friendly persuasion / There is a time / Day when the world comes alive / I am a song / It might as well be Spring / Music / But not for me / Two part invention / Talk to me baby / Thieving boy / Hi-heel sneakers
CD _____ 09026616702
RCA / Oct '94 / BMG.

JAZZ
Just a sittin' and a rockin' / My one and only love / Walking shoes / Told you so / It don't mean a thing if it ain't got that swing / Won't you tell me why / Bluesette / Midnight sun / Lady be good / St. Louis blues / I'm born / You can always count on me
CD _____ RD 60548
RCA / Oct '91 / BMG.

SOLITUDE (Laine, Cleo & John Dankworth/Duke Ellington Orchestra)
Don't get around much anymore / Sophisticated lady / I'm beginning to see the light / All too soon / Take all my loves / I got it bad and that ain't good / Love call / Don't you know I care (Or don't you care to) / Solitude / Reflections / We're rockin' in rhythm / Come Sunday / September rain / Cleo's 'A' train
CD _____ 09026681242
RCA Victor / Jul '95 / BMG.

SOMETIMES WHEN WE TOUCH (Laine, Cleo & James Galway)
Drifting dreaming / Title track / Play it again sam / Skylark / How, where, when / Fluter's ball / Consuelo's love theme / Keep loving me / Anyone can whistle / Still was the night / Lo here the gentle lark / Like a sad song
CD _____ RD 83628
RCA / Jan '87 / BMG.

WORD SONGS
All the world's a stage / If music be the food of love / You spotted snakes / Winter, when icicles hang by the wall / Fear no more the heat o' the sun / It was a lover and his lass / Sigh no more ladies / Dunsinane blues / When that I was a little boy / Shall I compare thee to a summer's day / Blow, blow thou winter wind / O mistress mine, where you are roaming / Take all my loves / My love is as a fever / Who is Sylvia / Compleat works / Our revels now are ended / Lines to Ralph Hodgson Esquire / Goe, and catche a falling starre / Bread and butter / Dr. David Mantle / Advice to a girl / O tell me the truth about love / In Tenebris 1 / Sun and fun / song / English teeth / Viva sweet love / Mungojerrie and rumpelteazer / Thieving boy / Sing me no song
CD _____ 8304612
Philips / Feb '94 / PolyGram.

Laine, Denny

BEST OF DENNY LAINE, THE
CD _____ WCPCD 1008
West Coast / Jun '94 / BMG.

BLUE NIGHTS
Wings on my feet / Japanese tears / Go now / Say you don't mind / Hometown girls / Weep for love / Send me the heart / Caribbean sun / If I tried / Money talks / Stay away / Roll the dice / Land of peace / Blue nights / Blushing bride
CD _____ PCOM 1132
President / Feb '94 / Grapevine / Target/ BMG / Jazz Music / President.

MASTER SUITE
Loving touch / Blue musician / Rory's theme / La Manzanera / Campfire / Read the cards / Thin air / Mountain pass / Highlands / Moors and Christmas / Old man loving / Diego
CD _____ CDTB 058
Thunderbolt / '88 / Magnum Music Group.

Laine, Frankie

1947: FRANKIE LAINE (Laine, Frankie & the Carl Fischer Orchestra)
CD _____ HCD 198
Hindsight / Jun '94 / Target/BMG / Jazz Music.

20 GREAT TRACKS (Laine, Frankie & Friends)
CD _____ PRCDSP 301
Prestige / Aug '93 / Total/BMG.

ALL TIME HITS
High noon / I believe / Answer me / Granada / Jealousy / Rain rain rain / Cool water / Strange lady in town / Hummingbird / Sixteen tons / Woman in love / Moonlight gambler / Cry of the wild goose / Mule train / Jezebel / Wheel of fortune / Rose rose I love you / Rawhide / Don't fence me in (CD only) / There must be a reason (CD only)
CD _____ CDMFP 5907
Music For Pleasure / Apr '91 / EMI.

BEST OF FRANKIE LAINE
I believe / Mule train / Jezebel / High noon / Answer me
CD _____ MU 3011
Musketeer / Oct '92 / Koch.

COLLECTION
CD _____ COL 039
Collection / Apr '95 / Target/BMG.

DEUCES WILD/CALL OF THE WILD
Hard way / Camptown races / Luck be a lady / Get rich quick / Horses and women / Moonlight gambler / Ace in the hole / Man who broke the bank at Monte Carlo / Dead man's hand / Roving gambler / Deuces wild / Gamblin' woman / Song of the open road / North to Alaska / Swamp girl / Beyond the blue horizon / Call of the wild / On the trail / Wayfaring stranger / Tumbling tumble weeds / High road / Rollin' stone / New frontier / Girl in the wood
CD _____ 4810172
Columbia / Aug '95 / Sony.

FRANKIE LAINE
CD _____ CD 108
Timeless Treasures / Oct '94 / THE.

GOIN' LIKE WILDFIRE (Laine, Frankie & Jo Stafford)
Pretty eyed baby / That's the one for me / That's good, that's bad / In the cool, cool, cool of the evening / Cambella / Hey good lookin' / Ham bone / Let's have a party / Settin' the woods on fire / Piece a puddin' / Christmas roses / Chow willy / Bushel and a peck / Floatin' down to cotton town / Way down yonder in New Orleans / Basin Street blues / High society / Back where I belong
CD _____ BCD 15620
Bear Family / Nov '93 / Rollercoaster / Direct / CM / Swift / ADA.

GREATEST HITS: FRANKIE LAINE
Rawhide / Moonlight gambler / I believe / Hummingbird / Don't fence me in / Strange lady in town / Red rose I love you / There must be a reason / Answer me / Jezebel / High noon / Mule train / Jealousy / Sixteen tons / Cool water / Wheel of fortune / Rain rain rain / Woman in love / Granada / Cry of the wild goose
CD _____ CDGRF 044
Tring / Feb '93 / Tring / Prism.

HIGH NOON
CD _____ CDCD 1023
Charly / Mar '93 / Charly / THE / Cadillac.

MEMORIES IN GOLD (20 great hits)
Memories in gold / Jealousy / High noon / On the sunny side of the street / Mule train / Cool water / Kid's last flight / Woman in love / Georgia on my mind / Moonlight gambler / You gave me a mountain / Jezebel / That's my desire / Cry of the wild goose / I believe / Your cheatin' heart / Rawhide / That lucky old sun / Shine / We'll be together again
CD _____ CDPC 5004
Prestige / Mar '92 / Total/BMG.

ON THE TRAIL
High noon / Cool water / 3.10 to Yuma / Gunfight at the O.K. Corral / Wanted man / Bowie knife / Mule train / Hanging tree / Along the Navajo trail / City boy / Cry of the wild goose / Rawhide / Gunslinger / Green leaves of Summer / On the trail / North to Alaska / Call of the wild / Tumbling tumbleweeds / Ghost riders in the sky / Prairie bell / Lonely man
CD _____ BCD 15480
Bear Family / Aug '90 / Rollercoaster / Direct / CM / Swift / ADA.

ON THE TRAIL AGAIN
Strange lady in town / Ramblin' man / Rawhide / Champion the wonderhorse / Black gold / Where the wind blows / I let her go / Drill ya tarriers drill / El diablo / Ride through the night / Ghost riders in the sky / Beyond the blue horizon / Swamp girl / Song of the open road / My journey's end / Wagon wheels / 3.10 to Yuma / Cool water / Gunfight at the O.K. Corral / High noon / New frontier / Deuces wild / Moonlight gambler / Wheel of fortune / Dead man's hand / Hard way / Wayfaring stranger / Roving gambler / El diablo 2
CD _____ BCD 15632
Bear Family / Jun '92 / Rollercoaster / Direct / CM / Swift / ADA.

PORTRAIT OF A SONG STYLIST
Blue moon / Side by side / Body and soul / Too marvellous for words / Try a little tenderness / Cottage of sale / Answer me / I get along without you very well / I cover the waterfront / Woman in love / We just couldn't say goodbye / Lover come back to me / I'm gonna live till I die / September in the rain / Second honeymoon / Touch of your lips / On the road to Mandalay
CD _____ HARCD 102
Masterpiece / Apr '89 / Meg.

RETURN OF MR RHYTHM
CD _____ HCD 256
Hindsight / May '95 / Target/BMG / Jazz Music.

SOMETHIN' OLD, SOMETHIN' NEW
CD _____ PRCDSP 300
Prestige / Jun '92 / Total/BMG.

VERY BEST OF FRANKIE LAINE, THE
I believe / Hey Joe / Answer me / Woman in love / Where the wind blows / Blowing / Cool water / Kids / Cry of the wild goose / Tell me a story / Strange lady in town / Rawhide / High noon / Hawkeye / Sugarbush / Rain rain rain
CD _____ PWKS 4167
Carlton Home Entertainment / Sep '93 / Carlton Home Entertainment.

Laing, Robin

WALKING IN TIME
Soldier maid / Kilbowie hill / Summer of '45 / Punters / Unquiet grave / Lass O'Patie's mill / El punado de centeno / Jamie Foyers / Billy Taylor / Forth Bridge song / Loose noose / Deacon Brodie / When two hearts combine / Neil Gow lament / Calypso's Island
CD _____ CDTRAX 072
Greentrax / Apr '94 / Conifer / Duncans / ADA / Direct.

Lakatos, Roby

IN GYPSY STYLE
CD _____ MW 4010CD
Music & Words / Jul '95 / ADA / Direct.

Lakatos, Sandor

GYPSY VIOLINS (Lakatos, Sandor & His Gypsy Band)
CD _____ HMP 3903027
HM Plus/Quintana / Oct '94 / Harmonia Mundi.

HUNGARIAN GYPSY MUSIC (Lakatos, Sandor & His Gypsy Band)
CD _____ QUI 903009
Quintana / Mar '91 / Harmonia Mundi.

HUNGARY - MUSIC TZIGANE
CD _____ HMP 393009
Musique D'Abord / Oct '94 / Harmonia Mundi.

MUSIC FROM HUNGARY (Lakatos, Sandor & His Gypsy Band)
CD _____ 15187
Laserlight / '91 / Target/BMG.

Lakatos, Tony

NEWS, THE
CD _____ JL 111402
Lipstick / May '95 / Vital/SAM.

Lake, Kirk

SO YOU GOT ANYTHING ELSE
CD _____ CHE 27CD
Che / Apr '95 / SRD.

Lake Of Tears

GREATER ART
CD _____ BMCD 49
Black Mark / May '94 / Plastic Head.

HEADSTONES
CD _____ BMCD 072
Black Mark / Sep '95 / Plastic Head.

Lake, Oliver

BOSTON DUETS (Lake, Oliver & Donal Leonellis Fox)
CD _____ CD 732
Music & Arts / Sep '92 / Harmonia Mundi / Cadillac.

COMPILATION
CD _____ R 279458
Gramavision / Aug '94 / Vital/SAM / ADA.

EDGE-ING
CD _____ 121014-2
Black Saint / Oct '94 / Harmonia Mundi / Cadillac.

HOLDING TOGETHER
CD _____ 1200092
Black Saint / Nov '90 / Harmonia Mundi / Cadillac.

OTHERSIDE
CD _____ 188901 2
Gramavision / Feb '89 / Vital/SAM / ADA.

ZAKI (Lake, Oliver Trio)
CD _____ ARTCD 6113
Hat Art / Aug '92 / Harmonia Mundi / ADA / Cadillac.

Lakeland, Christine

RECKONING
Black cat / Always something / To my man / Who knows / Good faith / Listening to my heart / On the house / Hard day / I must be / Storm comin' on / Ain't love funny / On a good day
CD _____ 882712
Sky Ranch / Oct '93 / New Note.

Lakeman Brothers

THREE PIECE SUITE
CD _____ CRM 01CD
Crapstone / Jun '94 / ADA.

Lakeside

BEST OF LAKESIDE
Shot of love / One minute after midnight / Given in love / It's all the way live / Rough rider / If you like our music (Get on up and move) / Fantastic voyage / Your love is on the one / We want you (On the floor) / Say yes / Ever ready man / I want to hold your hand / Raid / Outrageous / Bulls eye
CD _____ NEMCD 681
Sequel / Aug '94 / BMG.

Lalama, Ralph

FEELIN' AND DEALIN' (Lalama, Ralph & His Manhattan All Stars)
CD _____ CRISS 1046CD
Criss Cross / May '91 / Cadillac / Harmonia Mundi.

MOMENTUM (Lalama, Ralph Quartet)
CD _____ CRISS 1063CD
Criss Cross / Oct '92 / Cadillac / Harmonia Mundi.

YOU KNOW WHAT I MEAN
CD _____ CRISS 1097
Criss Cross / Apr '95 / Cadillac / Harmonia Mundi.

Lally, Michael

WHAT YOU FIND THERE
CD _____ NAR 102CD
SST / Jul '94 / Plastic Head.

Lam, Kine

PRAISE
CD _____ SHCD 64062
Shanachie / Jan '96 / Koch / ADA / Greensleeves.

Lamb, Andrew

PORTRAIT IN THE MIST
CD _____ DE 479
Delmark / Aug '95 / Hot Shot / ADA / CM / Direct / Cadillac.

Lamb, Barbara

FIDDLE FATALE
Sally Gooden / Panhandle rag / Good woman's love / Paddy on the turnpike/gone again / Montana glide / Herman's hornpipe / So what / Foster's reel / Old French reel / I'll never be free / Katy Hill / Princess Angeline / Ducks on the Millpond (ducks with bongas)
CD _____ SH 3810CD
Sugarhill / May '93 / Roots / CM / ADA / Direct.

Lamb, Natalie

I'M A WOMAN (Lamb, Natalie & The Perune Jazz Band)
CD _____ BCD 329
GHB / Aug '94 / Jazz Music.

Lamb, Paul

FINE CONDITION (Lamb, Paul & The King Snakes)
CD _____ IGOCD 2019
Indigo / Mar '95 / Direct / ADA.

Lambchop

HOW I QUIT SMOKING
CD _____ EFA 049692
City Slang / Jan '96 / Disc.

I HOPE YOU'RE SITTING DOWN
CD _____ EFA 049532
City Slang / Mar '95 / Disc.

Lambert, Franz

FOR YOU
Right here waiting / Morgenstimmung / 1492 Conquest of paradise / Almeria / Only love / Mowe Jonathan / Exodus / Pomp and circumstance / Nights in white satin / Don't cry for me argentina / When a man loves a woman / For you / Dornenvogel-rhapsodie / Atlantis / Fifa - Hymne
CD _____ 29001054
Bellaphon / Sep '95 / New Note.

Lambert, Gary

GUITAR PICKIN' RARITIES (Lambert, Gary & Eddie Cochran)
CD _____ SJCD 594
Sun Jay / Mar '92 / Magnum Music Group / Rollercoaster.

Lambert, Hendricks & Ross

WITH GUESTS
CD _____ CD 53127
Giants Of Jazz / Jan '95 / Target/BMG / Cadillac.

Lambeth Community Youth..

BEST OF CARIBBEAN STEEL DRUMS (Lambeth Community Youth Steel Orchestra)
CD _____ EUCD 1140
ARC / '91 / ARC Music / ADA.

STEEL DRUMS PARTY (Lambeth Community Youth Steel Orchestra)
CD _____ EUCD 1325
ARC / Nov '95 / ARC Music / ADA.

Lambrettas

BEAT BOYS IN THE JET AGE
Da-a-ance / Cortina Mk.II / London calling / Poison ivy / Leap before you look / Beat boys in the jet age / Page three / Living for today / Watch out I'm back / Don't push me / Runaround / Face to face
CD _____ DOJOCD 187
Dojo / Nov '94 / BMG.

BEST OF THE LAMBRETTAS
CD _____ DOJOCD 195
Dojo / May '95 / BMG.

Lament

LEVITATE
CD _____ TOODAMNHY 82
Too Damn Hype / Jan '95 / SRD.

Lammas

BROKEN ROAD, THE
CD _____ EFZ 1015
EFZ / Jan '96 / Vital/SAM.

THIS MORNING
CD _____ EFZ 1008
EFZ / Nov '94 / New Note.

Lamond, Mary Jane

BHO THIR NAN CRAOBH
CD _____ BR 001CD
Macmeanma / Aug '95 / Duncans / CM / ADA.

FROM THE LAND OF THE TREES
CD _____ BRCD 0001
Macmeanma / May '95 / Duncans / CM / ADA.

Lampi, Jim

TV WEATHER
CD _____ ZCD 001
Zok / Mar '94 / Grapevine / PolyGram / Pinnacle / Koch.

Lan Doky, Niels

DAYBREAK
All or nothing at all / Why / Final decision / Jet lag / Natural / Daybreak
CD _____ STCD 4160
Storyville / '88 / Jazz Music / Wellard / CM / Cadillac.

DREAMS
CD _____ MCD 9178
Milestone / Oct '93 / Jazz Music / Pinnacle / Wellard / Cadillac.

FRIENDSHIP
Real mccoy / Endless vision / Christmas song / Confidence / K.S. / Point of no return / Friendship / To the limit / Center of gravity
CD _____ MCD 9183
Milestone / Oct '93 / Jazz Music / Pinnacle / Wellard / Cadillac.

HERE OR THERE (Lan Doky, Niels Trio)
CD _____ STCD 4117
Storyville / Feb '89 / Jazz Music / Wellard / CM / Cadillac.

TARGET, THE (Lan Doky, Niels Trio)
CD _____ STCD 4140
Storyville / Feb '89 / Jazz Music / Wellard / CM / Cadillac.

TRUTH, THE (Live at Montmartre) (Lan Doky, Niels Trio)
CD _____ STCD 4144
Storyville / Feb '89 / Jazz Music / Wellard / CM / Cadillac.

Lancaster, Alan

LIFE AFTER QUO
CD _____ JVOCD 1001
JVO / Feb '95 / Pinnacle.

Lancaster, Ernie

ERNESTLY
Jelly box / Ivory towers / Ernestly / Lucky punch / Gatorslapped / Nightclubbing / Roy boy / Neckin' / Blues for Betty / Hooked
CD _____ ICH 9011 CD
Ichiban / Nov '91 / Koch.

Land

LAND
CD _____ XCD 032
Extreme / May '95 / Vital/SAM.

Land, Harold

MAPENZI (Land, Harold & Blue Mitchell Quintet)
CD _____ CCD 4044
Concord Jazz / Dec '90 / New Note.

XOCIA'S DANCE
CD _____ MCD 5272
Muse / Sep '92 / New Note / CM.

Landgren, Nils

FOLLOW YOUR HEART
CD _____ 21393
Caprice / Mar '89 / CM / Complete/ Pinnacle / Cadillac / ADA.

LIVE IN STOCKHOLM
Traci / Soundcheck / Impressions / Cheyenne / Simple life / Chicken / Ain't nobody / So what / Mr. M / Red horn / Yo yo
CD _____ 92232
Act / Jul '95 / New Note.

Landreth, Sonny

OUTWARD BOUND
Soldier of fortune / Back to Bayou Teche / When you're away / Sacred ground / New landlord / Speak of the devil / Yokamoma / Planet cannonball / Common law love / Bad weather / Outward bound
CD _____ 72445110322
Zoo Entertainment / Jul '92 / BMG.

SOUTH OF 1-10
Shooting for the moon / Creole angel / Native stepson / Orphans of the motherland / Congo square / Turning wheel / South of 1-10 / Cajun waltz / Mojo boogie / C'est chaud / Great gull wind
CD _____ 72445110702
Zoo Entertainment / Mar '95 / BMG.

Lands End

PACIFIC COAST HIGHWAY
Conspicuously empty / Neptunes last tear part 1 / Pacific coast highway / Requiem of the sea / Persistent memories / At lands end / Last word
CD _____ LECD 2
Cyclops / Sep '95 / Pinnacle.

Landsborough, Charlie

SONGS FROM THE HEART
I dreamed I was in heaven / Sill blue / Things that my ears can do / Walking on my memories / Song of my heart / All over but crying / One more time / You and me / Constantly I cried / You're not the only one / Fireside dreaming / Summer country skies / Close your eyes / lily of the valley / still blue
CD _____ RITZRCD 521
Ritz / Jun '92 / Pinnacle.

WHAT COLOUR IS THE WIND
Million ways to fall / Forever friend / Dream or two / When you're not a dream / What colour is the wind / Once bitten twice shy / Throw me away / When the counting's done / Funny way to say goodbye / Song of the ocean / Dance with me / White lies and windows
CD _____ RCD 542
Ritz / Sep '94 / Pinnacle.

Landscape

FROM THE TEA ROOMS OF MARS... (To the Hell Holes of Uranus)
European man / Shake the West awake / Computer person / Alpine tragedy / Sisters / Face of the 80's / New religion / Einstein a go go / Norman Bates / Doll's house / From the tea rooms of Mars / Beguine / Mambo / Tango
CD _____ MAUCD 618
Mau Mau / Jul '92 / Pinnacle.

Landstrumm, Neal

BROWN BY AUGUST
Shuttlecock / DX Serve / Index revisited / Sibling rivalry / Shake the hog / Custard tracks / Finnish deception / Home delivery / Squeeze / She-ra extra speaker
CD _____ PF 040CD
Peacefrog / Nov '95 / Disc.

Lane, Anita

PEARL & DIRTY
CD _____ CDSTUMM 81
Mute / Sep '93 / Disc.

Lane, Frankie

DÓBRÓ
CD _____ CEFCD 159
Gael Linn / Jan '94 / Roots / CM / Direct / ADA.

Lane, Ronnie

ANYMORE FOR ANYMORE...PLUS (Lane, Ronnie & Slim Chance)
CD _____ SEECD 338
See For Miles/C5 / Apr '92 / Pinnacle.

Lane, Steve

EASY COME - EASY GO (Lane, Steve & Red Hot Peppers)
Sing baby sing / London blues / Weatherbird rag / Easy come, easy go / Roy 'n' Audrey's stomp / Hindu blues / I'd love to take orders from you / Just too bad / Shakin' the blues away / I guess it wasn't meant to be / I can't believe that you're in love with me / Gotcha / Lazybones / Them there eyes / Jazz me blues / Cabinet shuffle / You're getting to be a habit with me
CD _____ AZCD 14
Azure / Nov '92 / Jazz Music / Swift / Wellard / Azure / Cadillac.

Lanegan, Mark

WHISKEY FOR THE HOLY GHOST
CD _____ SPCD 78249
Sub Pop / Jan '94 / Disc.

WINDING SHEET
CD _____ GR 095CD
Sub Pop / Mar '94 / Disc.

Lang, Eddie

HANDFUL OF RIFFS, A
Eddie's twister / April kisses / Prelude / Melody man's dream / Perfect / Rainbow / Add a little wiggle / Jeannine / I'll never be the same / Church Street sobbin' blues / There'll be some changes made / Two tone stomp / Jet black blues / Blue blood blues / Bullfrog moan / Handful of riffs / Bugle call rag / Freeze and melt / Hot heels / Walking the dog / March of the hoodlums
CD _____ CD AJA 5061
Living Era / May '89 / Koch.

JAZZ GUITAR RARITIES
Recording Arts / Jun '93 / THE / Disc.

TROUBLES, TROUBLES (Lang, Eddie/ Edgar Blanchard & The Gondoliers)
CD _____ CD 2080
Rounder / '88 / CM / Direct / ADA / Cadillac.

Lang, k.d.

ABSOLUTE TORCH AND TWANG (Lang, k.d. & The Reclines)
Luck in my eyes / Trail of broken hearts / Didn't I / Full moon full of love / Big big love / Walkin' in and out of your arms / Three days / Big boned gal / Wallflower waltz / Pullin' back the reins / It's me / Nowhere to stand
CD _____ K 9258772
Sire / Mar '94 / Warner Music.

ALL YOU CAN EAT
CD _____ 9362460342
Warner Bros. / Oct '95 / Warner Music.

ANGEL WITH A LARIAT (Lang, k.d. & The Reclines)
Turn me round / High time for a detour / Diet of strange places / Got the bull by the horns / Watch your step polka / Rose garden / Tune into my wave / Angel with a lariat / Pay dirt / Three cigarettes in an ashtray
CD _____ 7599254412
Sire / Aug '88 / Warner Music.

EVEN COWGIRLS GET THE BLUES
Just keep me moving / Much finer place / Or was I / Hush sweet lover / Myth / Apogee / Virtual vortex / Lifted by love / Overture / Kundalini yoga night / In perfect dreams / Curious soul astray / Ride of bonanza jellybean / Don't be a lemming polka / Sweet little Cherokee / Cowgirl pride
CD _____ 9362454332
WEA / Oct '93 / Warner Music.

INGENUE
Save me / Mind of love / Miss Chatelaine / Wash me clean / So it shall be / Still thrives this love / Seasons of hollow soul / Outside myself / Tear of love's recall / Constant craving

CD _____ 7599268402
Sire / Mar '92 / Warner Music.

SHADOWLAND (The Owen Bradley Sessions) (Lang, k.d. & The Reclines)
Western stars / Lock, stock and teardrops / Sugar moon / I wish I didn't love you to / Once again around the dance floor / Black coffee / Shadowland / Don't let the stars get in your eyes / Tears don't care who cry them / I'm down to my last cigarette / Too busy being blue / Honky tonk angel's medley
CD _____ 925724 2
WEA / Apr '88 / Warner Music.

Lang, Thiery

BLUE PEACH
Blue peach / Vendredi 18 / La riviere tranquille / Body and soul / Valse / My funny valentine / My foolish heart / Three lines
CD _____ TCB 95302
TCB / Sep '95 / New Note.

Lang, Thomas

LOST LETTER Z, THE
CD _____ DRYC 10012
Dry Communications / Sep '91 / Total/ BMG.

OUTSIDE OVER THERE
CD _____ DRYCCD 15
Dry Communications / Nov '92 / Total/ BMG.

Langa-Langa, Zaiko

GRAND SUCESS DE LANGA
CD _____ FLTRCD 521
Timbuktu / Dec '93 / Pinnacle.

Langeleik, Levande

LEVANDE LANGELEIK
CD _____ HCD 7106
Helio / Nov '95 / ADA.

Langford, Frances

GETTIN' SENTIMENTAL
I'm in the mood for love / Once in a while / Sweet someone / Is it true what they say about Dixie / Silhouetted in the moonlight / I don't want to make history / Everything you said came true / Deep shadows / I've got you under my skin / Harbour lights / You are my lucky star / Let's call a heart a heart / So do I / Speaking confidentially / Melody from the sky / Can't teach my old heart new tricks / If it's the last thing I do / So many memories / Rap tap on wood / Sweet heartache / I'm gettin' sentimental over you
CD _____ CMSCD 002
Movie Stars / Feb '93 / Conifer.

SOMEONE TO WATCH OVER ME
You hi-de-hi-ing me / Stormy weather / I feel a song coming on / Easy to love / Swingin' the jinx away / When did you leave Heaven / Farewell my love / My cabin of dreams / I'm falling in love with someone (with Bing Crosby) / At long last love / It's all yours / Gypsy love song (with Bing Crosby) / This is it / I'm in love with the honourable Mr. So and so / Someone to watch over me / Between the Devil and the deep blue sea / Boulevard of broken dreams / Am I blue / Mama I love / Fool for love / Say it (over and over again) / Love lies / Blue moon / Who am I / In the cool, cool, cool of the evening / And so do I / In Waikiki
CD _____ CDHD 204
Happy Days / Sep '93 / Conifer.

Lanin, Lester

THIS IS SOCIETY DANCE MUSIC
Just one of those things / Cheek to cheek / Lady is a tramp / Dancing on the ceiling / Muskrat ramble / Waltz from 'Der Rosenkavalier' / Steppin' in society / I've got a crush on you / Riding high / I love Paris / C'est manefique / It's all right with me / Mine / From this moment on / Mountain greenery / Dancing in the dark / Continental / When the saints go marching in / Acceleration waltz / Mississippi mud / Toot toot Tootsie goodbye / If you knew Susie like I know Susie / Sweet Georgia Brown
CD _____ 473656 2
Epic / Sep '93 / Sony.

Lanois, Daniel

ACADIE
Still water / Maker / O Marie / Jolie Louise / Fisherman's daughter / White mustang II / Under a stormy sky / Where the knowledge kills / Silium's hill / Ice / St. Ann's gold / Amazing grace
CD _____ K 925969 2
WEA / Sep '89 / Warner Music.

FOR THE BEAUTY OF WYONNA
Messenger / Brother La.. / Still learning how to crawl / Beatrice / Waiting / Collection of Marie Claire / Death of a train / Unbreakable chain / Lotta love to give / Sleeping in the devil's bed / For the beauty of Wyonna / Rocky world / Indian red
CD _____ 936245030-2
Warner Bros. / Mar '93 / Warner Music.

Lanphere, Don

DON LANPHERE AND LARRY CORYELL (Lanphere, Don & Larry Coryell)
Dragon gate / Very early / Ascending truth / Imagination / Green tutu / Spring can really hang you up the most / Sunset blues / My ideal / Beach at Nerja / Here they come, there they go / Peace
CD _____ HEPCD 2048
Hep / Dec '90 / Cadillac / Jazz Music / New Note / Wellard.

DON LOVES MIDGE (Lanphere, Don Quintet)
And the angels sing / Easy living / I remember Clifford / Try a little tenderness / Poor butterfly / I'll never be the same again / Once in a while / Old cape cod / Good bless the child / Gone with the wind / Polka dots and moonbeams / Everything I have is yours / Put your dreams away / Soon / My foolish heart / There's a sweet spirit...
CD _____ HEPCD 2027
Hep / Sep '93 / Cadillac / Jazz Music / New Note / Wellard.

GO AGAIN (Lanphere, Don Sextet)
Which / Go again / Darn that dream / Shangri la / I love you / Midges late valentine / What are you doing for the rest of your life / Maddie's dance / Music that makes me dance / Darkness on the Delta / Maestro
CD _____ HEPCD 2040
Hep / Jul '90 / Cadillac / Jazz Music / New Note / Wellard.

LOPIN' (Lanphere, Don & Bud Shank & Denny Goodhew)
I really didn't think that / Love's question / Lighten up / Time for love / Lope of a doll / Have you met Miss Jones / Fall / El balie de la munecas (Dance of the dolls) / M.K. and M.K.
CD _____ HEPCD 2058
Hep / Sep '94 / Cadillac / Jazz Music / New Note / Wellard.

Lanz, David

BELOVED
Beloved / Leaves on the seine / Madree de la tierra / Madrona / Return to the heart / First light / Courage of the wind / Summer's child / Before the last leaf falls / Reverie / Angel of hope / Cristofori's dream / Variations on a theme from pachebel's canon in D major
CD _____ ND 64009
Narada / Oct '95 / New Note / ADA.

BRIDGE OF DREAMS (Lanz, David & Paul Speer)
Day in the life / Into the dream / And the world falls away / Whispered in signs / Bridge of dreams / She stands on the mountain, still / Veil of fears / Reverie / Ode to a dark star / Song of the east (in this dream)
CD _____ ND 63024
Narada / Oct '93 / New Note / ADA.

CHRISTMAS EVE
CD _____ ND 61046
Narada / Oct '94 / New Note / ADA.

DESERT VISION (Lanz, David & Paul Speer)
Eagle's path / Seguaro / Desert rain / Sculptures / Canyon lands / Carlsbad / White sands / Stormlight / Tawtoma
CD _____ CD 3003
Narada / Aug '92 / New Note / ADA.

NATURAL STATES (Lanz, David & Paul Speer)
Miranova / Faces of the forest (part 1) / Faces of the forest (part 2) / Behind the waterfall / Mountain / Allegro 1985 / Lento 1984 / Rainforest / First light
CD _____ CD 3001
Narada / Aug '92 / New Note / ADA.

RETURN TO THE HEART
Return to the heart / Near the still waters of Amsterdam / Madre de la Tierra / Sounds from Koepel / Heartsounds / Manana, mi amor / Cori, Rio, Corre / Behind the waterfall/Desert rain / White shade of pale / Heart of the night / Dream of the forgotten child / Out of the darkness / Cristofori's dream / Gli uccelli di carpi / Variations on a theme / Return to the heart (reprise)
CD _____ CD 4005
Narada / Jun '92 / New Note / ADA.

SKYLINE FIREDANCE
CD Set _____ CD 4001
Narada / Aug '94 / New Note / ADA.

Lanza, Mario

BE MY LOVE
Be my love / Temptation / Wanting you / I'll be seeing you / With a song in my heart / Without a song / Danny boy / My wild Irish rose / And this is my beloved / Because / Only a rose / Funiculi, funicula / Come back to Sorrento / Maria Maria / O sole mio / Neapolitan love song / Arrivederci Roma / Ah sweet mystery of life / Look for the silver lining / Memories / Song is you / Ave Maria / You'll never walk alone / Serenade
CD _____ GD 60720
RCA / Mar '91 / BMG.

CHRISTMAS WITH MARIO LANZA
CD _____ GD 86427
RCA Victor / Nov '93 / BMG.

COLLECTION
CD _____ COL 061
Collection / Jun '95 / Target/BMG.

DON'T FORGET ME
CD _____ 09026614202
RCA / Jun '93 / BMG.

ESSENTIAL COLLECTION, THE
Serenade / More than you know / Torna a surriento / Vogliatemi bene / Mamma mia che vo'sape / Because you're mine / Donkey serenade / Softly as in a morning sunrise / Song of songs / Loveliest night of the year / I love thee / Ave Maria / Without a song / Catari, catari / Cosi, costa / Parig, O'Cara / Un di all azziro spazio / Une furtiva lagrima / O soave fanciulla / E lucevan le stelle / Parlami d'amore, mariu / Temptation / La donna e mobile / Kiss
CD _____ PWKS 4230
Carlton Home Entertainment / Nov '94 / Carlton Home Entertainment.

FOR THE FIRST TIME/ THAT MIDNIGHT KISS
Come prima / Tarantella / O sole mio / Neapolitan dance / Hofbrauhaus song / O mon amour / Mazurka / Pineapple pickers / Pagliacci - vesta la giubba / Otello - finale / Aida - grand finale / Ich liebe dich / Ave Maria / La Boheme / Che gelida manina / Mamma mia che vo'sape / I know, I know, I know / They didn't believe me / Core 'ngrato / Aida - celeste Aida
CD _____ GD 60516
RCA / Mar '91 / BMG.

LIVE IN LONDON
CD _____ 09026618842
RCA Victor / Nov '94 / BMG.

LOVELIEST NIGHT OF THE YEAR, THE
CD _____ MU 5049
Musketeer / Oct '92 / Koch.

MARIO LANZA
CD _____ ENTCD 245
Entertainers / Mar '92 / Target/BMG.

MARIO LANZA
CD _____ MATCD 287
Castle / Mar '94 / BMG.

MARIO LANZA - LIVE
Funiculi, funicula / My song, my love / Granada / Diane / Thine alone / Vesti la giubba / Vuchella / Toselli's serenade / Because you're mine / Loveliest night of the year / O paradiso / Marechiare / Rosary / Lolita / If / Mattinata / They didn't believe me / Lord's prayer / Be my love
CD _____ DATOM 2
A Touch Of Magic / Apr '94 / Harmonia Mundi.

MARIO LANZA COLLECTION, THE
Be my love / I'll never love you / Because you're mine / Song angels sing / Drink, drink, drink / Serenade / Loveliest night of the year / Great / La donna e mobile / Because / For you alone / Golden days / Deep in my heart / I loved you / One night of love / Beloved / Beautiful love / With a song in my heart / You are my love / Call me fool / All the things you are / My song, my love / Love is the sweetest thing / Will you remember / Granada / Lolita / Temptation / Lygia / Lady of Spain / This land / Lee ah loo / Tina-lina / Boom biddy boom boom / Bayou lullaby / Lord's prayer / And here you are / Song of songs / Somewhere a voice is calling / I never knew / Ciribiribin / Wonder why / Come dance with me / O sole mio / Younger than springtime / For the first time / Never till now / Arrivederci / If you were mine / Behold / Night to remember / Love in a home / Do you wonder / Softly as in a morning sunrise / One alone / Celeste aida / Flower song / Brindisi - libiamo, libiamo / Questa o quella / Vesti la giubba / Addio all madre
CD Set _____ GD 60889
RCA / Mar '92 / BMG.

MARIO LANZA ON RADIO (CBS Radio Show From The Fifties)
CD _____ CDMR 1121
Radiola / Oct '90 / Pinnacle.

ULTIMATE COLLECTION, THE
Be my love / Drink, drink, drink / La donna e mobile / Danny Boy / Granada / Because you're mine / Ave Maria / Valencia / Loveliest night of the year / Song of India / Because / O sole mio / Donkey serenade / Vesti la giubba / Serenade / Funiculi, funicula / Golden days / Arrivederci Roma / You'll never walk alone / Beloved / Come prima / E lucevan le stelle / Santa Lucia / I'll walk with God
CD _____ 74321185742
RCA Victor / Jan '94 / BMG.

WITHOUT A SONG
Cose cosa / Donkey serenade / Parliamo d'amore Maria / Kiss / Recondito armante / Softly as in a morning sunrise / Una furtiva lagrima / Song of songs / Mamma mia che vo'sape / Come back to sorrento / Without a song / O sole mio / Ave maria / Perigi o cara / Voglidemi bene, un pese piccolino

/ O souve funchilla / More than you know / La spagnola
CD _____ MUCD 9019
Start / Apr '95 / Koch.

YOU'LL NEVER WALK ALONE
I'll walk with God / Trembling of a leaf / Lord's prayer / Love in a home / Somebody bigger than you and I / Through the years / Ave Maria / Without a song / Hills of home / I love thee / Rosary / Look for the silver lining / None but the lonely heart / My buddy / Guardian angels / Somewhere a voice is calling / Trees / Ave Maria (2) / Because / Roses of Picardy / For you alone / You'll never walk alone
CD _____ 09026680732
RCA Victor / Jun '95 / BMG.

Lao, Molam

MUSIC FROM SOUTHERN LAOS
CD _____ NI 5401CD
Nimbus / Jun '94 / Nimbus.

Lara, Catherine

LA ROCKEUSE DE DIAMANTS
CD _____ 710 15A E880
Ariola / '88 / BMG.

Laraaji

DAYS OF RADIANCE
Dance no. 1 / Dance no. 2 / Dance no. 3 / Meditation / Meditation no.2
CD _____ EEGCD 19
EG / '87 / EMI.

FLOW GOES THE UNIVERSE
CD _____ ASCD 10
All Saints / Jun '92 / Vital / Discovery.

Larguinho, Mathilde

BEST OF FADO PORTUGUESE
CD _____ EUCD 1174
ARC / '91 / ARC Music / ADA.

Laritz, Jamie

JAMIE LARITZ
Creativity / Possibilities / Piece of mind / Eau de funk / Lonely nights blues / Hot off the frets (licks from hell) / Dreaming in colour
CD _____ STA 4028 CD
Star Track / Jul '90 / Koch.

Lark

0002K
CD _____ 2100053
Indisc / Jun '93 / Pinnacle.

Larkin, Kenny

METAPHOR
Intro / Metaphor / Nocturnal / Loop 1 / Java / Groove / Loop 1.5 (LP only) / Catatonic part 2 (LP only) / Catatonic (first state) (CD only) / Loop 2 / Soul man / Sympthy / Butterflies / Amethyst
CD _____ RS 95954CD
R & S / Feb '95 / Vital.

Larkin, Patty

ANGELS RUNNING
Who holds your hand / Do not disturb / Banish misfortune / Open hand / Might as well dance / Ain't that as good / Helen / I told him that my dog wouldn't run / Pundits and poets / Booth of glass / Winter wind
CD _____ 72902103182
Windham Hill / Nov '93 / Pinnacle / BMG / ADA.

I'M FINE
Rescue me / Justine / Window / Dangerous / I'm fine / Pucker up / Lately / On the run / Don't want to give it up / Island of time / If I were made of metal / Caffeine / Valentine / Day to day
CD _____ CDPH 1115
Philo / Oct '88 / Direct / CM / ADA.

STEP INTO THE LIGHT
CD _____ PH 1103CD
Philo / Apr '94 / Direct / CM / ADA.

Larkins, Ellis

LIVE AT MAYBECK RECITAL HALL, VOL. 22
How'd ya like to love me / Perfume and rain / Lady be good / I don't want to cry anymore / Blue skies / No more/God bless' The Child / I let a song go out of my heart / Spring will be a little late this year / Leave me alone / Things ain't what they used to be / When a woman loves a man/For through with love
CD _____ CCD 4533
Concord Jazz / Nov '92 / New Note.

SMOOTH ONE, A
CD _____ BLE 591232
Black & Blue / Oct '94 / Wellard / Koch.

Larrissey, Brendan

FLICK OF THE WRIST
CD _____ CBM 016CD

Cross Border Media / Jul '95 / Direct / ADA.

Larsen, Grey

ORANGE TREE, THE (Larsen, Grey & Andre Marchand)
CD _____ SH 1136CD
Sugarhill / Apr '94 / Roots / CM / ADA / Direct.

Larsen-Feiten Band

FULL MOON
CD _____ 7599262732
WEA / Jan '96 / Warner Music.

LARSEN-FEITEN BAND
CD _____ 7599262772
WEA / Jan '96 / Warner Music.

Larson, Nicolette

ALL DRESSED UP
CD _____ 7599266032
WEA / Jan '96 / Warner Music.

IN THE NICK OF TIME
Dancing Jones / In the nick of time / Let me go, lover / Rio De Janeiro blue / Breaking too many hearts / Back in my arms again / Fallen / Daddy / Isn't it always love / Trouble
CD _____ 7599266012
WEA / Jan '96 / Warner Music.

NICOLETTE
Lotta love / Rumba girl / You send me / Can't get away from you / Mexican divorce / Baby, don't you do it / Give a little / Angels / Rejoiced / French waltz / Come early mornin' last in love
CD _____ 7599273662
WEA / Jan '96 / Warner Music.

RADIOLAND
Radioland / Ooo-eee / How can we go on / When you come around / Tears, tears and more tears / Straight from the heart / Been gone too long / Fool for love / Long distance love
CD _____ 7599266022
WEA / Jan '96 / Warner Music.

SLEEP, BABY SLEEP
Welcome to the world / Oh bear / Starlight, starbright / Irish lullaby / Barefoot floors / Appalachian lullaby / I bid you goodnight / Moon and me / Moment I saw you
CD _____ LK 57672
Sony Wonder / Apr '95 / Sony.

La's

LA'S
Son of a gun / I can't sleep / Timeless melody / Liberty ship / There she goes / Doledrum / Feelin' / Way out / Freedom song / Failure / I.O.U. / Looking glass
CD _____ 828202 2
Go Discs / Nov '90 / PolyGram.

Las Hermanas Mendoza

JUANITA Y MARIA
CD _____ ARHCD 430
Arhoolie / Jun '95 / ADA / Direct / Cadillac.

Lasalle, Denise

HEHE I AM AGAIN
Here I am again / Married, but not to each other / Share your man with me / I wanna do what's on your mind / Trying to forget / My brand on you / Stay with me awhile / Anytime is the right time / Don't nobody live here (by the name of fool) / Hit and run / We've got love / Get up off my mind / Who's the fool / Best thing I ever had
CD _____ CDSEW 066
Westbound / Sep '93 / Pinnacle.

TRAPPED BY A THING CALLED LOVE/ ON THE LOOSE
Man size job / What it takes to get a good woman / Harper Valley PTA / What am I doing wrong / Breaking up somebody's home / There ain't enough hate around / Your man and your best friend / Lean on me / Making a good thing better / I'm over you / I'm satisfied / Trapped by a thing called love / Now run and tell that / Heartbreaker of the year / Goody goody getter / Catch me if you can / Hung up, strung out / Do me right / Deeper I go (better it gets) / You'll lose a good thing / Keeping it coming / It's too late
CD Set _____ CDSEWD 018
Westbound / Feb '92 / Pinnacle.

Lashout

DARKEST HOUR, THE
CD _____ SSR 001
Stormstrike / Nov '94 / Plastic Head.

Lask, Ulrich

INDEAN POA
CD _____ CMPCD 62
CMP / Sep '95 / Vital/SAM.

Lasser, Max Ark

DIFFERENT KIND OF BLUE, A
Wehoma / Naturtrueb / Different kind of blue / Little China / Simple thoughts / Spring again / Mountain magic / Oceana / Rough cut / Sad walk / Mid Eastern dawn / Evening star / Ry's blues
CD _____ BW 018
B&W / Sep '93 / New Note.

Lassigue Bendthaus

MATTER
CD _____ KK 113
KK / Jan '94 / Plastic Head.

RENDER
CD _____ KK 115CD
KK / May '94 / Plastic Head.

Last

AWAKENING
CD _____ SST 230 CD
SST / Jul '89 / Plastic Head.

Last Dance

TRAGEDY
CD _____ EFA 12169-2
Apollyon / Jan '96 / SRD.

Last, David

INTRODUCING DAVID LAST
Nocturne in eb / Skye boat song/Scottish soldier / Bewitched, bothered and bewildered / C'est si bon/I love Paris / Don't cry for me Argentina / Sometimes when we touch/Shenandoah / My boy lollipop / Swingin' safari / Lass of Richmond Hill / Farmer and the cowman/Alias Smith and Jones / Only you / Feelings/Music of the night / Tritsch tratsch polka / Eye level/Windmill in old Amsterdam / Unforgettable/When I fall in love / Minuet in G/Pathetique sonata
CD _____ CDTS 035
Maestro / Aug '93 / Savoy.

MELODIES FOR YOU
CD _____ CDTS 038
Maestro / Sep '93 / Savoy.

Last Delay

JAIL
CD _____ EFA 125332
Celtic Circle / Oct '95 / SRD.

Last Exit

BEST OF LIVE
CD _____ EMCD 110
Enemy / Feb '90 / Grapevine.

IRON PATH
Prayer / Iron path / Black bat / Marked for death / Fire drum / Detonator / Sand dancer / Cut and run / Eye for an eye / Devil's rain
CD _____ CDVE 38
Venture / Feb '89 / EMI.

LAST EXIT
CD _____ EMY 101-2
Enemy / Nov '94 / Grapevine.

NOISE OF TROUBLE
CD _____ EMY 103-2
Enemy / Oct '92 / Grapevine.

Last Great Dreamers

RETROSEXUAL
CD _____ CDBLEED 10
Bleeding Hearts / Oct '94 / Pinnacle.

Last Illusion

IN A ROOTSMAN STYLE
CD _____ JMF 001CD
Jah Mountain Fountain / Feb '95 / SRD.

Last, James

AT ST. PATRICK'S CATHEDRAL, DUBLIN
In the cathedral / Ave Maria / Conversation / An caoineadh / Scherzo / Away in a manger / Intermezzo of Notre Dame / Darkest midnight / Cavalleria rusticana / Holly and the ivy / Coulin / Seinn ailliu / Abide with me
CD _____ 823 669-2
Polydor / Dec '84 / PolyGram.

BEST FROM 150 GOLD, THE
Starparade / Hora staccato / Charmaine / Morgens um sieben (morning's at seven) / Don't cry for me Argentina / Happy music / La entrada del bilbao / Knock on wood / Ballade pour Adeline / Hppy heart / Der seinsamer hirte (the lonely shepherd) / Liechtensteiner polka / Romance for violin and orchestra / Anvil polka / Salome / Petersburger schlittenfahrt
CD _____ 835 562-2
Polydor / Oct '90 / PolyGram.

BLUEBIRD
Morning at Cornwall / Proud as a peacock / Love bird / Sandpiper / Quiberon / Bird of paradise / Alassio / Night owl / Over valley and mountain / Bill MaGee / Kingfisher / Roter Milan
CD _____ 811 517-2
Polydor / '88 / PolyGram.

BY REQUEST
Mornings at 7 / Elvira Madigan / Air that I breathe / Adagio from the New World Symphony / Lonely shepherd / Roses of the south / Sabre dance / Lonely bull / Tulips from Amsterdam / Seduction / Zip a dee doo dah / Spanish eyes / Valencia / That's life
CD _____ 831 786-2
Polydor / Apr '87 / PolyGram.

CHRISTMAS ALBUM
Ave verum corpus / Winter (Largo) / Here I stand at your cradle / Largo (From The Christmas Concerto) / For unto us a child is born / Adagio / Largo (From Opera Xerxes) / Christmas concerto / Thus loved God the world
CD _____ 5506412
Spectrum/Karussell / Nov '94 / PolyGram / THE.

CLASSIC TOUCH
Overture marriage of Figaro / Traumerei / Eine kleine nachtmusik / Intermezzo from cavalleria rusticana / Chanson triste / Rodrigo's guitar concerto de Aranjuez / Barcarolle / In the hall of the mountain king / Adagio from the sonata pathetique no.8 / Libestraum / Elvira Madigan / Hungarian dance No. 5 / Ballet music / Bolero
CD _____ 5500982
Spectrum/Karussell / Oct '93 / PolyGram / THE.

CLASSICS
Mascagni's cavalleria / Schumann's symphony no.2 / Bach's double violin concerto / Hayden's trumpet concerto / Symphonie fantastique / Mozart's symphony no.39 / Beethoven's romance no.I / Gieg's incidental music to Peer Gynt / Brahms symphony no.3
CD _____ 800 017-2
Polydor / Sep '88 / PolyGram.

CLASSICS BY MOONLIGHT
Bolero / Romeo and Juliet / Swan lake / New World symphony / Spring from 'The four seasons' / Rhapsody in blue / Morning / Blue danube / Rhapsody on a theme of Paganini / Nabucco
CD _____ 843 218-2
Polydor / Mar '90 / PolyGram.

DANCE DANCE DANCE
You win again / Frankie / Reet petite / Love will save the day / Saving all my love for you / Power of love / You keep me hangin' on / Heaven is a place on earth / Respect yourself / Don't leave me this way / Everybody have fun tonight / Chain reaction / Gimme hope Jo'anna / Easy lover / Rhythm is gonna get you / Doctorin' the tardis / So macho / Always on my mind / Nothing's gonna stop us now / La Bamba / My toot toot
CD _____ 837 453-2
Polydor / Nov '88 / PolyGram.

FANFARE
Happy music / Begin the beguine / Skokiaan / Always / Donkey serenade / Hava Nagila / Caravan / Carmen 68 / La mer / Un poco rio / La golondrina / Down by the riverside
CD _____ PWKS 4081P
Carlton Home Entertainment / Oct '91 / Carlton Home Entertainment.

GAMES THAT LOVERS PLAY
Lara's theme / Man and a woman / Games that lovers play / This is my song / What now my love / Close your eyes / I left my heart in San Francisco / Fly me to the moon / Now I know / Elizabethan serenade / Never on Sunday / Sandy's theme
CD _____ 821 610-2
Polydor / PolyGram.

HAPPY HEART
Happy heart / Amboss polka / Happy Luxemburg / Games that lovers play / Music from across the way / Mornings at seven / Fool / I left my heart in San Francisco / Happy music / Root beer rag / Lonely shepherd
CD _____ 839 613-2
Polydor / Aug '89 / PolyGram.

IN IRELAND
CD _____ 829 027 2
Polydor / '88 / PolyGram.

INSTRUMENTALS FOREVER
CD _____ 815 250-2
Polydor / '89 / PolyGram.

JAMES LAST IN SCOTLAND
Skye boat song / My love is like a red red rose / I love a lassie / Roamin' in the gloamin' / Scottish soldier / Will ye no' come back again / I belong to Glasgow / Flower of Scotland / Auld lang syne / Ye banks and braes o' bonnie Doon / Days of auld lang syne / Keel row / Barren rocks of Aden / Loch Lomond / My bonnie Mary of Argyle / Annie laurie
CD _____ 823 743-2
Polydor / Jun '85 / PolyGram.

JAMES LAST LIVE IN LONDON
Intro '78 / Tiger feet / Radar love / Jesus loves you / Bridge over troubled water / I've got you under my skin / Was ich dir sagen will / Jog dig das / Rum and coca cola / Quando, quando, quando / South America take it away / Lonely shepherd / Larry

O'Gaff / Fire on the mountain / Center amigos / Schwarze estrella / Ay ay ay / Costa brava / Eso es el amor / Star Wars / Amek Side story / Silly love songs / With one more look at you / Watch closely now / Love me tender / Rip it up / Don't be cruel / Jailhouse rock / Hound dog / Chicken reel / Turkey in the straw / Orange blossom special / Cockles and mussels / Daisy Daisy / Abide with me / Yes sir, I can boogie / Sorry I'm a lady / Don't leave me this way / Don't cry for me Argentina / Games that lovers play
CD _____ 843 809-2
Polydor / Nov '90 / PolyGram.

JAMES LAST PLAYS ANDREW LLOYD WEBBER
With one look / Jesus Christ Superstar / Memory / I don't know how to love him / Music of the night / Any dream will do / Love changes everything / Don't cry for me Argentina / Tell me on a Sunday / Take that look off your face / Phantom of the opera / Point of no return
CD _____ 519 910-2
Polydor / Nov '93 / PolyGram.

LEAVE THE BEST TO LAST
Tell her about it / Karma chameleon / Wake me up before you go go / Heartbreaker / Take a chance on me / You can't hurry love / Uptown girl / Caribbean queen (no more love on the run) / That was yesterday / Ghostbusters / Hooray hooray it's a holi holiday / Agadoo / I just called to say I love you / Wanderer / Easy lover / Every breath you take / You're my heart you're my soul / Super trouper / Half a minute / Do the conga / Hello / One more night / Red red wine / Live is life / Imagine
CD _____ 827 393-2
Polydor / Sep '85 / PolyGram.

MAKE THE PARTY LAST
Cracklin' Rosie / Rose garden / Knock three times / Banks of the Ohio / Song sung blue / Tie a yellow ribbon round the ole oak tree / Summer knows / Close to you / Soley soley / Is this the way to Amarillo / You are the sunshine of my life / Never can say goodbye / La bamba / Hava nagila / Pushbike song / What have they done to my song Ma / Joy to the world / What now my love / I don't know how to love him / In the summertime / Goodbye Sam, hello Samantha / I hear you knocking / (We're gonna) Rock around the clock / See you later alligator / Hound dog
CD _____ 5500332
Spectrum/Karussell / May '93 / PolyGram / THE.

NON STOP EVERGREEN
Deep in the heart of Texas / Manana / Sugarbush / Exodus song / Who's sorry now / La Bamba / Love is a many splendoured thing / My happiness / Rum and coca cola / Quando, quando, quando / South America take it away / Goody goody / Ain't she sweet / Bei mir bist du schon / Blacksmith blues / Sixteen tons / Don't fence me in / Night and day / In the mood / How high the moon / Happy days are here again / Yearning / La Bostella
CD _____ PWKS 4020 P
Carlton Home Entertainment / Sep '90 / Carlton Home Entertainment.

PEACE
CD _____ 5176392
Polydor / Jan '93 / PolyGram.

PIANO A GO GO
Java / My Bonnie / Maria / Lingering on / Mack the knife / Everybody loves a lover / Happy days are here again / My guy's come back / Mambo Italiano / Dream / Bei mir bist du schon / America
CD _____ PWKS 4015
Carlton Home Entertainment / Sep '90 / Carlton Home Entertainment.

PLAYS MOZART
CD _____ 839 043-2
Polydor / Mar '89 / PolyGram.

POP SYMPHONIES (Last, James Orchestra)
Lady in red / Nights in white satin / Power of love / Another day in love / Hotel California / Living years / Sorry seems to be the hardest word / Broken wings / Africa / One more night / Hard to say i'm sorry / Angelia
CD _____ 849 429-2
Polydor / Jun '91 / PolyGram.

ROSE OF TRALEE AND OTHER IRISH FAVOURITES
Maggie / Irish stew / Coulin / Come back to Erin / Rii mhor bhaile an chalaidh / An erskay love lilt / On the banks of my own lovely Lee / Summer in Dublin / When Irish eyes are smiling / Rose of Tralee / Londonderry air / Sweepstake / Cockles and mussels / I.R.E.L.A.N.D.
CD _____ 815 984-2
Polydor / '88 / PolyGram.

ROSES FROM THE SOUTH (James Last Plays Johann Strauss)
Roses from the South / Leichtes blut / Tales from the Vienna Woods / Annen polka / Voices of spring / Waltz / Thunder and lightning / Emperor waltz / Eljen a magyar / Radetzky march
CD _____ 823 738-2
Polydor / Aug '88 / PolyGram.

389

SPECIAL COLLECTION, A
Java / Maria / Mack the knife / Happy days are here again / Mexico City / Bei mir bist du schon / My Bonnie / Lingering on / Everybody loves a lover / My guy's come back / Poeme / America / Air that I breathe / Don't let the sun go down on me / Hey Jude / Let it be / Whiter shade of pale / Was ich dir sagen will / Sound of silence / Unchained melody / You make me feel brand new / Violins in love / Deep in the heart of Texas / Sugarbush / Who's sorry now / Love / Manana / Exodus song / La Bamba / Love is a many splendoured thing / My happiness / Rum and coca cola / Quando, quando, quando / South America take it away / Goody goody / Ain't she sweet / Bei mir bist du schoen / Blacksmith blues / Sixteen tons / Don't fence me in / Night and day / In the mood / How high the moon / Yearning / La bostella
CD Set _____ BOXD 18P
Carlton Home Entertainment / Nov '91 / Carlton Home Entertainment.

VERY BEST OF JAMES LAST
CD _____ 5295562
Polydor / Oct '95 / PolyGram.

VIOLINS IN LOVE
Air that I breathe / Was ich dir sagen will / don't let the sun go down on me / Sound of silence / Hey Jude / Unchained melody / Let it be / You make me feel brand new / Whiter shade of pale / Violins in love
CD _____ PWKS 4016 P
Carlton Home Entertainment / Sep '90 / Carlton Home Entertainment.

Last Poets

BEST OF THE PRIME TIME RHYME, THE
On the subway / True blues / Mean machine / Tribute at Obabi / Bird's world / Blessed are those who struggle / Sport / Jones comin' down / Mean machine chant / O.D. / Jazzoetry / It's a trip / Delights of the garden / Spoon
CD _____ SPOA 22
On The One / Apr '95 / New Note.

BEST OF VOL.II
El pluribus unum / Tranquility / African slave / Beyonder / Oh my people / What will you do / Enough emotion / Unholy alliance
CD _____ SP 21CD
On The One / Nov '95 / New Note.

HOLY TERROR
Invocation / Homesick / Black rage / Mentality / Last rite / Talk show / Illusion of self / If only we knew / Funk / Phelhourinho
CD _____ RCD 10319
Rykodisc / May '95 / Vital / ADA.

THIS IS MADNESS
CD _____ CPCD 8154
Celluloid / Nov '95 / Charly.

Last Real Texas Blues...

LAST REAL TEXAS BLUES BAND (Last Real Texas Blues Band)
CD _____ ANT 0036
Antones / May '95 / Hot Shot / Direct / ADA.

Laswell, Bill

AXIOM AMBIENT - LOST IN THE TRANSLATION
Eternal drift / Peace (CD only) / Aum / Cosmic Trigger (CD only) / Dharmapala / Flash of panic (CD only) / Holy mountain / Ruins (CD only) / Eternal drift (Techno mix) (LP only) / Aum (Drift mix) (LP only)
CD Set _____ 5240532
Axiom / Nov '94 / PolyGram / Vital.

DIVINATION - LIGHT IN EXTENSION
Divination / Seven heavens / Erratta / Delta / Tian zhen / Agrippa / Godspeed / Ain soph aour / Najaran alim / Dead slow / Baraka / Silent fields / Evil eye / Dream light / Journeys / Last words of hassan I sabbath
CD Set _____ SHCD 001
Stoned Healers / Jun '94 / PolyGram / Vital.

FUNKRONMICON
Order within the universe / Under the influence / If six was nine / Orbitron attack / Cosmic slop / Free bass / Tell the world / Pray my soul / Hideous mutant freekz / Sax machine / Animal behaviour / Trumpets and violins, violins / Telling time / Jungle free bass / Blackout / Sacred to the pain
CD Set _____ 5240772
Axiom / Aug '95 / PolyGram / Vital.

HEAR NO EVIL
Lost roads / Bullet hole memory / Illinois central / Assassin / Stations of the cross / Kingdom come
CD _____ CDVE 12
Venture / Mar '88 / EMI.

Lateef, Yusef

AFRICAN-AMERICAN EPIC SUITE
CD _____ 892142
Act / Jun '94 / New Note.

BLUE YUSUF LATEEF, THE
CD _____ 756782290-2
WEA / Mar '93 / Warner Music.

EASTERN SOUNDS
CD _____ OJCCD 612-2
Original Jazz Classics / Feb '92 / Wellard / Jazz Music / Cadillac / Complete/Pinnacle.

JAZZ MOODS
Metaphor / Yusef's mood / Beginning / Morning / Blues in space
CD _____ SV 0237
Savoy Jazz / Nov '93 / Conifer / ADA.

NOCTURNES
CD _____ 7567819772
Atlantic / Jul '93 / Warner Music.

PRAYER TO THE EAST
Night in Tunisia / Endura / Prayer to the East / Love dance / Lover man
CD _____ SV 0210
Savoy Jazz / Apr '93 / Conifer / ADA.

Latimer

LATIMER
Neolida / Kiss / Stabs the reason / Carolida / Chicken the goon / Cold front killer / Dirgesque / Hold down / Auto-redeemer / Stringbender / Poseur / Rek O Kut
CD _____ WDOM 016CD
World Domination / May '95 / Pinnacle.

Latimore

SWEET VIBRATIONS
Stormy Monday / Ain't nothin' you can do / Snap your fingers / Let's straighten it out / Keep the home fire burnin' / There's a redneck in the sould band / Qualified man / It ain't where you been / Something 'bout you / Sweet vibrations / I get lifted / Dig a little deeper / Long distance love
CD _____ NEXCD 166
Sequel / May '91 / BMG.

Latin Jazz Quintet

LATIN JAZZ QUINTET
CD _____ FCD 24129
Fantasy / Oct '93 / Pinnacle / Jazz Music / Wellard / Cadillac.

Latin Playboys

LATIN PLAYBOYS
Viva la raza / Ten believers / Chinese surprise / Mira / Manifold de amour / New zandu / Rudy's party / If / Same brown earth / Lagoon / Gone / Crayon sun / Pink steps / Forever nightshade Mary
CD _____ 828 222-2
London / May '94 / PolyGram.

Latin Quarter

LONG PIG
Long pig / Better helter skelter / King for a day / Bitter to the south / Phil Ochs / More than a trace / Desert rose / Contention city / Hoopoe / Church on fire / Coming down to pray / Like a miracle / Faith and reason
CD _____ CLD 91082
Cloud Nine / Jun '95 / Conifer / Silva Screen.

Latin Touch

FIESTA
La senorita / Loco / Misunderstood / Fiesta / Conchita / Adios amigo / Ti me cuando / My love / Viva / Soul mate / Without you / Please tell me (illusions)
CD _____ 74321 18324-2
Ariola Express / Feb '94 / BMG.

Lattau, Kevin

KEVIN LETTAU
CD _____ NOVA 9135
Nova / Jan '93 / New Note.

Lauder, Sir Harry

I LOVE A LASSIE
I love a lassie / Roamin' in the gloamin' / Wedding of Sandy McNab / Waggle o' the kilt / O sing to me the auld Scotch songs / When I get back to bonnie Scotland / Keep right on to the end of the road / It's just like being at home / Bonnie Leezie Lindsay / I'm looking for a bonnie lass tae love me / She makes the world a merry go round / She is my daisy / Wee Deoch an' Doris / I think I'll get wed in the summer / I like my old home town / I'm the boss of the hoose / I've loved her ever since she was a baby / Soosie MacLean
CD _____ PASTCD 9719
Flapper / Oct '90 / Pinnacle.

SIR HARRY LAUDER (Britain's First Knight Of The Music Hall)
Overture - The Harry Lauder medley / I love a lassie / Will you stop your tickling jock / Breakfast in bed / Roamin' in the gloamin' / Waggle o' the kilt / Soosie Maclean / There's a wee hoose' mang the heather / I've just got off the chain / Just a wee deoch an' Doris / We parted on the shore / Keep right on to the end of the road
CD _____ LCOM 5232
Lismor / May '94 / Lismor / Direct / Duncans / ADA.

Lauderdale, Jim

PLANET OF LOVE
Heaven's flame / Maybe / Wake up screaming / I wasn't fooling around / Bless her heart / Where the sidewalk ends / Planet of love / King of broken hearts / What you don't know / My last request
CD _____ 7599265562
Reprise / May '92 / Warner Music.

Laudet, Francois

MY DRUMMER IS RICH... (Laudet, Francois Big Band)
CD _____ BBRC 9312
Big Blue / Jan '94 / Harmonia Mundi.

Laughing Clowns

GHOSTS OF AN IDEAL WIFE
Crystal clear / Diabolic creature / No words of honour / Winter's way / Ghosts of an ideal wife / Only one that knows / New bully in town / It gets so sentimental / Flypaper
CD _____ HOT 1013CD
Hot / Nov '93 / Vital.

GOLDEN DAYS WHEN GIANTS WALKED THE EARTH
Eternally yours / Theme from Mad flies, mad flies / Winter's way / Mr. Uddich-Smuddich / Holy Joe / I don't know what I want / Possessions / Eulogy / Flypaper / Every dog has it's day
CD _____ HOT 1055CD
Hot / Aug '95 / Vital.

HISTORY OF ROCK 'N' ROLL VOLUME 1, THE
CD _____ HOT 1010CD
Hot / Mar '93 / Vital.

Laughing Hyenas

CRAWL
CD _____ TG 102CD
Touch & Go / Oct '92 / SRD.

HARD TIMES
CD _____ TG 136CD
Touch & Go / Feb '95 / SRD.

MERRY GO ROUND
CD _____ TG 25CD
Touch & Go / Sep '95 / SRD.

Laughlin, Tim

NEW ORLEANS RHYTHM
CD _____ JCD 235
Jazzology / Apr '94 / Swift / Jazz Music.

NEW ORLEANS SWING
CD _____ JCD 265
Jazzology / Dec '95 / Swift / Jazz Music.

SWING THAT MUSIC (Laughlin, Tim & Jack Maheu)
CD _____ JCD 245
Jazzology / Jun '95 / Swift / Jazz Music.

Laughner, Peter

TAKE THE GUITAR PLAYER FOR A RIDE
Baudelaire / Rock it down / Sylvia Plath / Pledging my time (LP only) / Lullaby / In the bar / Cinderella backstreet / Only love can break your heart / Visions of Johanna (LP only) / Amphetamine / Life stinks / What love is (LP only) / Ain't it fun / Dear Richard / Calvary cross / Take your love away / Baby's on fire / Me and the devil blues
CD _____ TK 92CD045
T/K / Aug '94 / Pinnacle.

Laula, Carol

STILL
Bad case of you / Child of mine / It's true / Gonna b.u. / Home to sister / Stay with me angel / Restless / Old brick wall / By the minute / White dress / Stars with my coffee
CD _____ IRCD 020
Iona / '93 / ADA / Direct / Duncans.

Laundry

BLACK TONGUE
Windsheild / Blizzard face / Blacktongue / Monarch man / Canvas / Monkey's wrench / Misery alarm / Hole / Moss covered rocks / Skin / Stitch / Bloodclot / Laundry / Nineteen
CD _____ MR 0982
Mammoth / Feb '95 / Vital.

Lauper, Cyndi

HAT FULL OF STARS
That's what I think / Product of misery / Who let in the rain / Lies / Broken glass / Sally's pigeons / Feels like Christmas / Dear John / Like I used to / Someone like me / Part hate / Hat full of stars
CD _____ 473054 2
Epic / Nov '93 / Sony.

NIGHT TO REMEMBER, A
Intro / I drove all night / Primitive / My first night without you / Like a cat / Heading West / Night to remember / Unconditional love / Insecurious / Dancing with a stranger / I don't want to be your friend / Kindred spirit

---

CD _____ 4624992
Epic / Apr '92 / Sony.

NIGHT TO REMEMBER/SHE'S SO UNUSUAL/TRUE COLOURS
I drove all night / Primitive / My first night without you / Like a cat / Heading west / Night to remember / Unconditional love / Insecurious / Dancing with a stranger / I don't want to be your friend / Kindred spirit / Money changes everything / Girls just wanna have fun / When you were mine / Time after time / She bop / All through the night / Witness / I'll kiss you / She's so unusual / Yeah yeah / Change of heart / Maybe he'll know / Boy blue / True colors / Calm inside the storm / What's going on / Iko iko / Faraway nearby / 911 / One track mind
CD Set _____ 471622 2
Epic / Oct '94 / Sony.

SHE'S SO UNUSUAL
Money changes everything / Girls just wanna have fun / When you were mine / Time after time / She bop / All through the night / Witness / I'll kiss you / He's so unusual / Yeah yeah
CD _____ 4633622
Epic / Feb '89 / Sony.

SHE'S SO UNUSUAL/A NIGHT TO REMEMBER
Money changes everything / Girls just wanna have fun / When you were mine / Time after time / She bop / All through the night / Witness / I'll kiss you / He's so unusual / Yeah yeah / Intro / I drove all night / My first night without you / Like a cat / Heading West / Night to remember / Unconditional love / Insecurious / Dancing with a stranger / I don't want to be your friend / Kindred spirit
CD Set _____ 4784832
Epic / Mar '95 / Sony.

TRUE COLORS
Change of heart / Maybe he'll know / Boy blue / True colors / Calm inside the storm / What's going on / Iko iko / Faraway nearby / 911 / One track mind
CD _____ 462 493 2
Portrait / Aug '90 / Sony.

TWELVE DEADLY CYNS - AND THEN SOME
I'm gonna be strong / Girls just wanna have fun / Money changes everything / Time after time / She bop / All through the night / Change of heart / True colors / What's going on / I drove all night / World is stone / Who let in the rain / That's what I think / Sally's pigeons / Hey now (girls just wanna have fun) / Come on home
CD _____ 477363-2
Epic / Aug '94 / Sony.

Laurel Canyon Ramblers

RAMBLER'S BLUES
CD _____ SHCD 3834
Sugarhill / May '95 / Roots / CM / ADA / Direct.

Lauren, Jessica

SIREN SONG
Leo rises / Fire monkey / Siren song / When you call my name / Serengeti / Just a dream / Dance for Lotte / Dangerous curves / Freefall
CD _____ SJRCD 020
Soul Jazz / Sep '94 / New Note / Vital.

Laurence, Zack

SING-A-LONG PIANO
Beatles medley / U.S.A. medley / Italian medley / Irving Berlin medley / Jolson medley / European medley / Roaring twenties / Waltz medley / Soft shoe medley / Oriental medley / Fats Waller medley / Spanish medley / Vaudeville medley / Ragtime medley / London medley / Girls medley
CD _____ PWK 132
Carlton Home Entertainment / May '90 / Carlton Home Entertainment.

Lauria, Nando

POINTS OF VIEW
Back home / After dawn / Take two / If I fell / Cry and the smile / Saudade (longing) / Que xote (what a rhythm) / Northeast tide / Episode: Prelude / Episode
CD _____ ND 63026
Narada / Apr '94 / New Note / ADA.

Laurie Accordian...

SPIRIT OF SCOTLAND (Laurie Accordian Orchestra)
CD _____ CDLOC 1087
Lochshore / Jun '95 / ADA / Direct / Duncans.

Laury, Booker T.

BOOKER IN PARIS 1980
CD _____ 157912
Blues Collection / Jun '93 / Discovery.

NOTHIN' BUT THE BLUES
CD _____ BB 9542CD
Bullseye Blues / Feb '94 / Direct.

Laury, Steve

KEEPIN' THE FAITH
Keepin' the faith / Close your eyes / Street of gold / Steppin' in / Ocyober / There's one way / Revelation / Tears in the rain / Astoria
CD _____ CY 75283
Denon / Feb '93 / Conifer.

PASSION
All the way / In my dreams / Getaway / I need you so / I like that / Come back to me / No kidding / Passion / Jeananne
CD _____ CY 79043
Denon / '90 / Conifer.

STEPPING OUT
Stepping out / All because of you / Kiss me goodbye / Soulful eyes / Just like an angel / Walk your talk / Manyana / Shake down / Day she went away
CD _____ CY 76870
Denon / '91 / Conifer.

Lauth, Wolfgang

LAUTHER
Ice nenne alle frauen baby / Est ist nur die leibe / Durch dich wird diesse welt erst schon / Bei dir war es immer so schon / Mein herz hat heut premiere / Warum bist du fortegangen / Ich werede jede nacht von ihnen traumen / Kauf dir einen bunten luftballon / Lauther / Donald / Johnnie Walker / Cool cave / I only have eyes for you / Pastels / Lauthentic / Jeb / These foolish things / Indian summer / Goofy / French fries / Can't help lovin' dat man / Chicken feet / Date on wax
CD _____ BCD 15717
Dear Family / May '03 / Rollorcoastor / Direct / CM / Swift / ADA.

Lava Love

WHOLE LAVA LOVE
CD _____ SKY 72003CD
Sky / Sep '94 / Koch.

Lavelle, Caroline

SPIRIT
CD _____ 4509981372
Warner Bros. / Mar '95 / Warner Music.

Laverne, Andy

FIRST TANGO IN NEW YORK
CD _____ 500472
Musidisc / Nov '93 / Vital / Harmonia Mundi / ADA / Cadillac / Discovery.

LIVE AT MAYBECK RECITAL HALL, VOL. 28
Yesterdays / I loves you Porgy / Sweet and lovely / Star eyes / My melancholy baby / When you wish upon a star / Beautiful love / Turn out the stars / Moonlight in Vermont / Impression for piano / Stan Getz in Chappaqua
CD _____ CCD 4577
Concord Jazz / Oct '93 / New Note.

NATURAL COLORS (Laverne, Andy & John Abercrombie)
CD _____ 500092
Musidisc / Nov '93 / Vital / Harmonia Mundi / ADA / Cadillac / Discovery.

TRUE COLORS
True colors / Maximum density / Song is you / Cubic zirconia / Night and day / Once I loved / I hear a rhapsody / Pannonica / If I were a bell / In your own sweet way
CD _____ 66053015
Jazz City / Feb '91 / New Note.

Lavette, Bettye

NEARER TO YOU
CD _____ CDCHARLY 276
Charly / Jan '91 / Charly / THE / Cadillac.

Lavin, Christine

ATTAINABLE LOVE
Attainable love / Castlemaine / Yonder blue / Sensitive new age guys / Victim/volunteer / Kind of love you never recover from / Fly on a plane / Venus kissed the moon / Moving target / Shopping cart of love: The play
CD _____ CDPH 1132
Philo / Jul '90 / Direct / CM / ADA.

BEAU WOES AND OTHER PROBLEMS
CD _____ CDPH 1107
Philo / Oct '88 / Direct / CM / ADA.

FUTURE FOSSILS
CD _____ CDPH 1104
Philo / '86 / Direct / CM / ADA.

GOOD THING HE CAN'T READ MY MIND
Good thing he can't read my mind / Bumble bees / Santa Monica Pier / Waltzing with him / Mysterious woman / Realities / Downtown / Never go back / Eighty five degrees / Somebody's baby / Ain't love grand
CD _____ CDPH 1121
Philo / '88 / Direct / CM / ADA.

LIVE AT THE CACTUS CAFE - WHAT WAS I THINKING
CD _____ PH 1159CD
Philo / Jan '94 / Direct / CM / ADA.

ON A WINTER'S NIGHT
CD _____ PH 1167CD
Philo / Feb '94 / Direct / CM / ADA.

PLEASE DON'T MAKE ME TOO HAPPY
CD _____ SHAN 8016CD
Shanachie / Apr '95 / Koch / ADA / Greensleeves.

Lavitz, T

MOODSWING
CD _____ NOVA 9134
Nova / Jan '93 / New Note.

Law

LAW, THE
For a little ride / Miss you in a heartbeat / Stone cold / Come save me (Julianne) / Laying down the law / Nature of the beast / Stone / Anything for you / Best of my love / Tough love / Missing you bad girl
CD _____ 7567821952
East West / Apr '91 / Warner Music.

Law, Johnny

JOHNNY LAW
CD _____ CDZORRO 18
Music For Nations / Apr '91 / Pinnacle.

Lawal, Gasper

KADARA
Kadara / Iregbogbo / Irin ajo / Oyeye / Ase / Omo araye / Ola / Awo
CD _____ CDORB 071
Globestyle / Apr '91 / Pinnacle.

Lawley, Linda

LINDA LAWLEY
CD _____ 900800
Line / Feb '95 / CM / Grapevine / ADA / Conifer / Direct.

Lawndale

SASQUATCH ROCK
CD _____ SST 125 CD
SST / May '93 / Plastic Head.

Lawnmower Deth

BELLY
Somebody call me a taxi / Billy / I need to be my main / Squeeze / Do you wanna be a chuffed core / Buddy Holly never wrote a song called we're too punk / Up the junction / If it was grey you'd say it's black / Kids in America / March of the dweebs / Funny thing about it is / Purple haze
CD _____ MOSH 098CD
Earache / Oct '93 / Vital.

OOH CRIKEY IT'S...
CD _____ MOSH 025CD
Earache / Sep '90 / Vital.

Lawrence, Denise

LET IT SHINE
Papa de da da / Seven golden daffodils / Way you do the things you do / Saturday night function / Mardi Gras in New Orleans / Shady green pastures / Down in Honky Tonk Town / Wasted life blues / Let your light from the lighthouse shine on me / Around the clock / New Orleans wiggle / Nice feeling
CD _____ LACD 37
Lake / Feb '95 / Target/BMG / Jazz Music / Direct / Cadillac / ADA.

Lawrence, Steve

STEVE LAWRENCE
CD _____ KCD 593
King/Paddle Wheel / May '93 / New Note.

WE'LL TAKE ROMANCE (Lawrence, Steve & Eydie Gorme)
CD _____ MCCD 168
MCI / Jul '94 / Disc / THE.

Lawrence, Syd

BIG SOUND OF SYD LAWRENCE AND HIS ORCHESTRA (Lawrence, Syd Orchestra)
CD _____ PWK 102
Carlton Home Entertainment / '89 / Carlton Home Entertainment.

PLAYS GLENN MILLER (Lawrence, Syd Orchestra)
In the mood / St. Louis blues / At last / Tuxedo junction / Chattanooga choo choo / String of pearls / Little brown jug / Anchors aweigh / American patrol / Stardust / I know why / Pennsylvania 6-5000 / Frenesi / Humpty Dumpty heart / Adios / Moonlight serenade
CD _____ CDGM 1
Premier/MFP / Jul '92 / EMI.

REMEMBER GLENN MILLER (Lawrence, Syd Orchestra)
Moonlight serenade / Little brown jug / Anchors aweigh / String of pearls / At last / I've got a gal in Kalamazoo / American patrol / Pennsylvania 6-5000 / Slow freight / Elmer's tune / St. Louis blues / In the mood / Stardust / I dreamt I dwelt in Harlem / Serenade in blue / Pennsylvania 6-5000 / Caribbean clipper / Tuxedo Junction / Story of a starry night / Chattanooga choo choo / Frenesi / Falling leaves / Adios
CD _____ PWK 094
Carlton Home Entertainment / Mar '89 / Carlton Home Entertainment.

REMEMBERS GLENN MILLER
In the mood / Pennsylvania 6-5000 / American patrol / Tuxedo junction / Serenade in blue / Perfidia / Stardust / Moonlight serenade / I've got a gal in Kalamazoo / Little brown jug / St. Louis blues / Chattanooga choo choo / Falling leaves / Frenesi
CD _____ 5501872
Spectrum/Karussell / Mar '94 / PolyGram / THE.

Lawrence, Tracy

ALIBIS
I threw the rest away / Can't break it to my heart / We don't love here anymore / Crying ain't dying / Alibis / My second home / Don't talk to me that way / It only takes one bar (to make a prison) / Back to back / If the good die young
CD _____ 756782483-2
Atlantic / Jul '93 / Warner Music.

I SEE IT NOW
CD _____ 756782656-2
Warner Bros. / Oct '94 / Warner Music.

Laws, Hubert

LAWS OF JAZZ/FLUTE BY-LAWS, THE
Miss thing / All soul / Black eyes peas and rice / Bessie's blues / Don't you forget it / Bimbo blue / Capers / Bloodshot / Miedo / Mean lene / No you'd better not / Let me go / Strange girl / Baila cinderella
CD _____ 812271636-2
Atlantic / May '94 / Warner Music.

Laws, Ronnie

BEST OF RONNIE LAWS
Always there / Night breeze / Let's keep it together / Karmen / Friends and strangers / New day / Just love / Flame / Solid ground / Just as you are / Living love / Love is here / Saturday evening
CD _____ BNZ 287
Blue Note / Feb '92 / EMI.

BROTHERHOOD
Still in the band / I feel fine / See the day / Night thing / Handyman / Brotherhood / Tidal wave / Distant lover / My river / When I fall in love
CD _____ 101S 71492
101 South / Aug '94 / New Note.

DEEP SOUL
CD _____ 101S 8771252
101 South / Aug '94 / New Note.

IDENTITY
CD _____ 101S 70892
101 South / Aug '94 / New Note.

PRESSURE SENSITIVE (Laws, Ronnie & Pressure)
Always there / Momma / Never be the same / Tell me something good / Nothing to lose / Tidal wave / Why do you laugh at me / Mis' Mary's place
CD _____ CDP 7465542
EMI / Jun '95 / EMI.

TRUE SPIRIT
Gotta say goodbye / Love this way again / Virgin winds / From a glance / Song for Hiram / Heart station / Favorite love / Imo
CD _____ CPCD 8126
Charly / Oct '95 / Charly / THE / Cadillac.

Lawson, Doyle

HEAVEN'S JOY AWAITS (Lawson, Doyle & Quicksilver)
CD _____ SH 3760CD
Sugarhill / Dec '87 / Roots / CM / ADA / Direct.

HEAVENLY TREASURES (Lawson, Doyle & Quicksilver)
CD _____ SH 3735CD
Sugarhill / Oct '94 / Roots / CM / ADA / Direct.

I HEARD THE ANGELS SINGING (Lawson, Doyle & Quicksilver)
Holy city / Stormy weather / Little mountain church house / In the shelter of his arms / I heard the angels singing / He's my guide / Little white church / City where's comes no strife / Rock of ages / I won't have to cross Jordan alone / That new Jerusalem / That home far away
CD _____ SH 3774CD
Sugarhill / '89 / Roots / CM / ADA / Direct.

I'LL WANDER BACK SOMEDAY (Lawson, Doyle & Quicksilver)
CD _____ SH 3769CD
Sugarhill / '88 / Roots / CM / ADA / Direct.

MY HEART IS YOURS (Lawson, Doyle & Quicksilver)
All in my love for you / Still got a crush on you / Move to the top of the mountain / I don't care / My heart is yours / Dreaming of you / Look for me (I'll be there) / Between us / I'm satisfied with you / We were made for each other
CD _____ SH 3782CD
Sugarhill / '90 / Roots / CM / ADA / Direct.

NEVER WALK AWAY (Lawson, Doyle & Quicksilver)
CD _____ SHCD 3842
Sugarhill / Oct '95 / Roots / CM / ADA / Direct.

Lawson, Yank

SOMETHING OLD, SOMETHING NEW, SOMETHING BORROWED, SOMETHING (Lawson, Yank Jazzband)
CD _____ APCD 240
Audiophile / Apr '89 / Jazz Music / Swift.

WITH A SOUTHERN ACCENT (Lawson-Haggart Jazz Band)
CD _____ JCD 203
Jazzology / Feb '93 / Swift / Jazz Music.

YANK LAWSON & BOB HAGGART (Lawson, Yank & Bob Haggart)
CD _____ JCD 183
Jazzology / Jul '92 / Swift / Jazz Music.

Lay Quiet Awhile

DELICATE WIRE
CD _____ 185172
Southern / Jun '94 / SRD.

Lay, Sam Band

LIVE
CD _____ AP 115
Appaloosa / Oct '95 / ADA / Magnum Music Group.

Layhe, Edgerton

ROUGH AND TUMBLE
Buffalo blues / Eleanor / Why would she go / Billy can / Everybody needs something nobody knows / Teardrop whisky / Dancing down at the crossroads/The convenience reel / All the tears in Liverpool / Lonely as Los Angeles, restless as New York / I'm on your side / Six thousand shoes
CD _____ FE 096CD
Fellside / Jan '94 / Target/BMG / Direct / ADA.

Layton & Johnstone

ALABAMY BOUND
Anytime anywhere / Up with the lark / Wedding of the painted doll / Alabamy bound / New kind of girl with a new kind of love form / Weary river / Paddlin' Madelin' home / Turner Layton piano medley / Birth of the blues / Coquette / Hillo, 'tucky / Don't put the blame on me / Hard hearted Hannah / It all depends on you / At dawning / Medley of Layton and Johnstone successes
CD _____ PASTCD 9712
Flapper / '90 / Pinnacle.

GETTING SENTIMENTAL OVER YOU
Auf wiedersehen my dear / Deep purple / Don't you ever cry / Home on the range / I wanna sing about you / I'm getting sentimental over you / It was so beautiful / I've got a feeling I'm falling in love / Coquette / Bye bye blackbird/Always/My blue heaven/It ain't gonna rain no more) / Medley #2 (Who/Tea for two/Lover come back to me/I want to be happy/Wild flower/Bambalina) / Miracles sometimes happen / More than you know / Night and day / Nightfall / Nightingale sang in Berkeley Square / The ra'n min in my aiee / I hnnn foolish things / To be in love espesh'lly with you / We just couldn't say goodbye / We three / Where or when / Wind and the rain / Without a song
CD _____ CDAJA 5111
Living Era / Jun '93 / Koch.

Layton, Turner

THANKS FOR THE MEMORY
These foolish things / Cool river / I get along without you very well / Stormy weather / Just let me look at you / Smoke gets in your eyes / Trees / Remember me / Thanks for the memory / Deep purple / Never in a million years miracles sometimes happen / I fall in love with you every day / You stepped out of a dream / This is no laughing matter / Dinner for one please james / East of the sun and west of the moon / If I didn't care / Transatlantic lullaby / Something to remember you by / Au revoir / Heaven can wait / Two sleepy people / Music maestro please / nightingale sang in berkeley square
CD _____ CDHD 202
Happy Days / Jun '93 / Conifer.

Lazarus, Ken

SINGS REGGAE OF THE 70'S
CD _____ PKCD 61094
K&K / Sep '94 / Jetstar.

Lazonby

YOUR HUMBLE SERVANT
CD _____ BRAINK 44CD
Brainiak / Mar '95 / 3MV / Sony.

Lazure, Gabrielle

OUT OF THE BLUE
CD _____ TWI 8812
Les Disques Du Crepuscule / '90 /
Discovery / ADA.

Lazy Cowgirls

RAGGED SOUL
CD _____ EFA 115912
Crypt / Jul '95 / SRD.

Lazy Lester

HARP AND SOUL
I done got over it / I'm a man / Dark end of
the street / Bye bye baby / Alligator shuffle
/ Take me in your arms / Patrol wagon /
Raining in my heart / Bloodstains on the
wall / Five long years
CD _____ ALCD 4768
Alligator / May '93 / Direct / ADA.

I'M A LOVER NOT A FIGHTER
I'm a lover not a fighter / Sugar coated love
/ Lester's stomp / I told my little woman /
Tell me pretty baby / Whoa now / I hear you
knocking / Through the goodness of my
heart / I love you, I need you / Late in the
evening / Real combination for love / Bloodstains on the wall / You got me where you
want me / I'm so tired / Patrol blues / I'm
so glad / Sad city blues / If you think I've
lost you / I made up my mind / Lonesome
highway blues / You're gonna ruin me baby
/ Same thing could happen to you / Take
me in your arms / You better listen to what
I said
CD _____ CDCHD 518
Ace / Apr '94 / Pinnacle / Cadillac / Com-
plete/Pinnacle.

Le Gop

LE GOP
CD _____ Y 225030CD
Silex / Dec '93 / ADA.

Le Grand Blues Band

LE GRAND BLUES
CD _____ 422430
New Rose / May '94 / Direct / ADA.

Le June, Iry

CAJUN'S GREATEST
Grande nuit especial / Grande bosco / Dur-
aldo waltz / I went to the dance / La valse
de bayou cheme / I made a big mistake /
Come and get me / Donnes moi mon chapeau / Waltz of the mulberry limb / Church
point breakdown / La valse du grande
chemin / Jolie catin / La fitte la vovar / Bayou
pon pon special / La valse de cajun / Don't
get married / Convict waltz / It happened to
me / Parting waltz / Evangeline special /
Love bridge waltz / Te mone special / Calcasieu waltz / Te mone / Lacassine special
CD _____ CDCHD 428
Ace / Oct '92 / Pinnacle / Cadillac / Com-
plete/Pinnacle.

Le Maistre, Malcolm

1968 SARAJEVO EP
CD _____ 12032CD
Unique Gravity / Jul '95 / Pinnacle / ADA.

NOTHING STRANGE
CD _____ UGCD 5401
Unique Gravity / Jun '94 / Pinnacle / ADA.

Le Meut, Jean

PE YUVANKIZ KUHET
CD _____ KM 44
Keltia Musique / Sep '94 / ADA / Direct /
Discovery.

Le Mystere Des Voix...

**CATHEDRAL CONCERT, A (Le Mystere
Des Voix Bulgares)**
CD _____ JARO 41382
Jaro / Jul '91 / New Note.

**LE MYSTERE DES VOIX BULGARES (Le
Mystere Des Voix Bulgares)**
CD _____ CAD 603 CD
4AD / May '87 / Disc.

**LE MYSTERE DES VOIX BULGARES
VOL.2 (Le Mystere Des Voix Bulgares)**
CD _____ CAD 801CD
4AD / Nov '88 / Disc.

Le, Nguyen

MILLION WAVES
Mille vagues / Trilogy / Be good / Mango
blues / Butterflies and zebras / Little wing /
El saola / Sledge / Moonshine / I feel good
CD _____ 92212
Act / May '95 / New Note.

MIRACLES
CD _____ 500102
Musidisc / Nov '93 / Vital / Harmonia
Mundi / ADA / Cadillac / Discovery.

ZANZIBAR

CD _____ 500352
Musidisc / Nov '93 / Vital / Harmonia
Mundi / ADA / Cadillac / Discovery.

Le Quintette De...

**MENAGERIE (Le Quintette De
Cornemuses)**
CD _____ B 6795CD
Auvidis/Ethnic / Jul '94 / Harmonia Mundi.

Le Rue

SWAMP RAT BOOGIE
CD _____ MW 2003CD
Munich / Jul '92 / CM / ADA /
Greensleeves / Direct.

Le Rue, Pierre

IN TWO WORLDS
CD _____ GWCD 005
Weaving / Nov '95 / Koch / Direct / ADA.

Le Thugs

LABF
CD _____ VIRUS 93CD
Alternative Tentacles / '92 / Pinnacle.

Lea, Barbara

**ATLANTA JAZZ PARTY (Lea, Barbara &
Ed Polcer)**
CD _____ JCD 218
Jazzology / Jul '93 / Swift / Jazz Music.

DO IT AGAIN
CD _____ ACD 175
Audiophile / Jun '95 / Jazz Music / Swift.

**HOAGY'S CHILDREN (Lea, Barbara/Bob
Dorough/Dick Sudhalter)**
CD _____ ACD 291
Audiophile / Apr '94 / Jazz Music / Swift.

HOAGY'S CHILDREN VOL. 2
CD _____ ACD 292
Audiophile / Apr '94 / Jazz Music / Swift.

**SONGS FROM 'POUSSE CAFE' (Lea,
Barbara & Ellis Larkin)**
CD _____ ACD 263
Audiophile / Apr '93 / Jazz Music / Swift.

Lead Into Gold

AGE OF REASON
CD _____ CDDVN 7
Devotion / Mar '92 / Pinnacle.

Leadbelly

ALABAMA BOUND
Pick a bale of cotton / Whoa Buck / Mid-
night special / Alabamy bound / Good
morning blues / Red Cross store blues / Al-
berta / You can't lose-a me cholly / Gray
goose / Stewball / Can't you line 'em / Rock
Island line / Easy rider / New York City /
Roberta / On my last go round
CD _____ ND 90321
Bluebird / Oct '94 / BMG.

CONGRESS BLUES
CD _____ ALB 1007CD
Aldabra / Mar '94 / CM / Disc.

CONVICT BLUES
CD _____ ALB 1004CD
Aldabra / Mar '94 / CM / Disc.

**GO DOWN OLD HANNAH (Library Of
Congress Recordings Vol. 6)**
CD _____ ROU 1099CD
Rounder / Apr '94 / CM / Direct / ADA /
Cadillac.

**GOOD BLUES TONIGHT (Leadbelly/
Robert Johnson)**
CD _____ CDMOIR 503
Memoir / Aug '93 / Target/BMG.

GOOD MORNING BLUES
CD _____ IGOCD 2007
Indigo / Nov '94 / Direct / ADA.

GOOD MORNING BLUES
CD _____ TPZ 1029
Topaz Jazz / Oct '95 / Pinnacle / Cadillac.

GOODNIGHT IRENE
CD _____ TCD 1006
Rykodisc / Feb '96 / Vital / ADA.

**GWINE DIG A HOLE TO PUT THE DEVIL
IN**
CD _____ CDROU 1045
Rounder / Feb '92 / CM / Direct / ADA /
Cadillac.

IRENE GOODNIGHT
CD _____ CD 52028
Blues Encore / Nov '93 / Target/BMG.

KING OF THE TWELVE STRING GUITAR
Packin' trunk / Becky Deem, she was gamblin' girl / Honey, I'm all out and down / Four
day worry blues / Roberta part 1 / Roberta
part 2 / Death letter #1 / Death letter #2 /
Kansas city papa / Wort Worth and Dallas
blues / Daddy I'm coming back to you /
Shorty George / Yellow jacket / TB woman
blues

CD _____ 4678932

Columbia / Nov '91 / Sony.

LAST SESSIONS
CD Set _____ SFWCD 40068
Smithsonian Folkways / Oct '94 / ADA /
Direct / Koch / CM / Cadillac.

LEADBELLY 1939-40
CD _____ DOCD 5226
Blues Document / Apr '94 / Swift / Jazz
Music / Hot Shot.

LEADBELLY 1940-43
CD _____ DOCD 5227
Blues Document / Apr '94 / Swift / Jazz
Music / Hot Shot.

LEADBELLY 1943-44
CD _____ DOCD 5228
Blues Document / Apr '94 / Swift / Jazz
Music / Hot Shot.

LEADBELLY 1944
CD _____ DOCD 5310
Blues Document / Dec '94 / Swift / Jazz
Music / Hot Shot.

LEADBELLY 1944-46
CD _____ DOCD 5311
Blues Document / Dec '94 / Swift / Jazz
Music / Hot Shot.

LEGENDARY MASTERS SERIES, THE
CD _____ COLLECT 4CD
Aim / Oct '95 / Direct / ADA / Jazz Music.

LET IT SHINE ON ME
CD _____ CDROU 1046
Rounder / Mar '92 / CM / Direct / ADA /
Cadillac.

MIDNIGHT SPECIAL
CD _____ CDROU 1044
Rounder / Feb '92 / CM / Direct / ADA /
Cadillac.

**NOBODY KNOWS THE TROUBLE I'VE
SEEN (Library Of Congress Recordings
Vol. 5)**
CD _____ ROUCD 1098
Rounder / May '94 / CM / Direct / ADA /
Cadillac.

SINGS FOLK SONGS
CD _____ SFWCD 40010
Smithsonian Folkways / Aug '95 / ADA /
Direct / Koch / CM / Cadillac.

**TITANIC, THE (Library Of Congress
Recordings Vol. 4)**
CD _____ ROU 1097CD
Rounder / Apr '94 / CM / Direct / ADA /
Cadillac.

VERY BEST OF LEADBELLY, THE
CD _____ MCCD 102
MCI / May '93 / Disc / THE.

Leaders Of The New School

T.I.M.E
Eternal / Understanding the inner mind's
eye / Syntax era / Classical material / Daily
reminder / Quarter to cutthroat / Connections / What's next / Time will tell / Bass is
loaded / Spontaneous / Noisy medication /
End is near / Zearocks / Difference / Final
solution
CD _____ 755961382-2
WEA / Oct '93 / Warner Music.

Leaf, Ann

**MIGHTY WURLITZER, THE (Leaf, Ann &
Gaylord Carter)**
Great day / Strike up the band / You do
something to me / Son of the Sheik / You
were meant for me / Orphans of the storm
/ Jeannine / For heaven's sake / My ro-
mance / Charmaine / Intolerance / Phantom
of the opera
CD _____ NW 227
New World / Aug '92 / Harmonia Mundi /
ADA / Cadillac.

Leafhound

GROWERS OF MUSHROOM
Freelance fiend / Sad road to the sea /
Drowned my life in fear / Work my body /
Stray / With a minute to go / Growers of
mushroom / Stagnant pool / Sawdust Cae-
sar / It's going to get better
CD _____ SEECD 403
See For Miles/C5 / Jul '94 / Pinnacle.

Leandre, Joelle

**PALIMPSESTE (Leandre, Joelle & Eric
Watson)**
CD _____ ARTCD 6103
Hat Art / May '92 / Harmonia Mundi / ADA
/ Cadillac.

Leary, Timothy

**YOU CAN BE ANYONE THIS TIME
AROUND**
CD _____ BFTPCD 006
UFO / Oct '91 / Pinnacle.

Leather Nun

FORCE OF HABIT
CD _____ WRCD 008
Wire / Nov '87 / Pinnacle.

INTERNATIONAL HEROES
CD _____ WIRE CD 011
Wire / Aug '90 / Pinnacle.

Leather Strip

SERENADE FOR THE DEAD
CD _____ CDZOT 114
Music Research / Oct '94 / Plastic Head.

Leatherface

LAST, THE
CD _____ WIGCD 10
Domino / Mar '94 / Pinnacle.

MINX
CD _____ NECKCD 011
Roughneck / May '93 / Disc.

MUSH
CD _____ NECKCD 005
Roughneck / Sep '91 / Disc.

Leaves

1966
CD _____ 422194
New Rose / May '94 / Direct / ADA.

Leaving Trains

BIG JINX
CD _____ SST 293CD
SST / Jul '94 / Plastic Head.

KILL TUNES
CD _____ SST 071 CD
SST / May '93 / Plastic Head.

LOSER ILLUSION PART 0
CD _____ SST 284 CD
SST / May '93 / Plastic Head.

LUMP IN MY FOREHEAD
CD _____ SST 288 CD
SST / May '93 / Plastic Head.

ROCK'N'ROLL MURDER
CD _____ SST 283 CD
SST / May '93 / Plastic Head.

SLEEPING UNDERWATER SURVIVORS
CD _____ SST 271 CD
SST / May '93 / Plastic Head.

TRANSPORTATIONAL D. VICES
CD _____ SST 221 CD
SST / Feb '89 / Plastic Head.

Lebombo

KHWELA JAZZ
CD _____ BVHAASTCD 9220
Bvhaast / Jan '93 / Cadillac.

Lebrijano, Juan Pena

ENCUENTROS
Vivir un cuento de hadas / Dame la libertad
/ Las mil y una noches / Desafinado / El
anillo (chibuli) / Pensamientos / Amigo mio,
no / Esos ojos asesinos
CD _____ CDORB 024
Globestyle / Jan '89 / Pinnacle.

L'Echo Desluthes

MUSIQUE DE HAUTE BRETAGNE
CD _____ BUR 822CD
Escalibur / '88 / Roots / ADA / Discovery.

Lecuona Cuban Boys

CONGAS AND RUMBAS
CD _____ CD 62014
Saludos Amigos / Apr '94 / Target/BMG.

HISTORIC RECORDINGS
Cafunga conga / Panama / Tabou / Hindou
/ Amapola / La conga / Canto indio / La
cucaracha
CD _____ CAL 50586
Calig / Apr '91 / Priory.

IN VENEZUELA 1940
CD _____ HQCD 54
Harlequin / Jun '95 / Swift / Jazz Music /
Wellard / Hot Shot / Cadillac.

LECUONA CUBAN BOYS 1934-44
CD _____ HQCD 07
Harlequin / Oct '91 / Swift / Jazz Music /
Wellard / Hot Shot / Cadillac.

LECUONA CUBAN BOYS, VOL. 1
CD _____ HQCD 11
Harlequin / '91 / Swift / Jazz Music /
Wellard / Hot Shot / Cadillac.

LECUONA CUBAN BOYS, VOL. 5
CD _____ HQCD 35
Harlequin / Feb '94 / Swift / Jazz Music /
Wellard / Hot Shot / Cadillac.

Led Zeppelin

4 SYMBOLS
Black dog / Rock and roll / Battle of Evermore / Stairway to heaven / Misty mountain
hop / Four sticks / Going to California /
When the levee breaks

CD _____ 756782638-2
Atlantic / Jun '94 / Warner Music.

CODA
We're gonna groove / Poor Tom / I can't quit you baby / Walter's walk / Darlene / Ozone baby / Wearing and tearing / Bonzo's Montreux
CD _____ 756792444-2
Atlantic / Aug '94 / Warner Music.

COMPLETE STUDIO RECORDINGS, THE
Good times, bad times / Babe I'm gonna leave you / You shook me / Dazed and confused / Your time is gonna come / Black mountain side / Communication breakdown / I can't quit you baby / How many more times / Whole lotta love / What is and what should never be / Thank you / Heartbreaker / Livin' lovin' maid (she's just a woman) / Ramble on / Moby Dick / Bring it on home / Immigrant song / Friends / Celebration day / Since I've been loving you / Out on the tiles / Gallows pole / Tangerine / That's the way / Bron-y-aur stomp / Hats off to (Roy) Harper / Black dog / Rock and roll / Battle of Evermore / Stairway to heaven / Misty mountain hop / Four sticks / Going to California / When the levee breaks / Song remains the same / Rain song / Over the hills and far away / Crunge / Dancing days / D'yer mak'er / No quarter / Ocean / Achille's last stand / For your life / Royal Orleans / Nobody's fault but mine / Candy store rock / Hots on for nowhere / Tea for one / Custard pie / Rover / In my time of dying / Houses of the holy / Trampled underfoot / Kashmir / In the light / Bron-y-aur / Down by the seaside / Ten years gone / Night flight / Wanton song / Boogie with Stu / Black country woman / Sick again / In the evening / South bound saurez / Fool in the rain / Hot dog / Carouselambra / All my love / I'm gonna crawl / We're gonna groove / Poor Tom / Walter's walk / Ozone baby / Darlene / Bonzo's Montreux / Wearing and tearing / Baby, hey what can I do
CD Set _____ 756782526-2
Atlantic / Apr '94 / Warner Music.

ENCOMIUM - A TRIBUTE TO LED ZEPPELIN (Various Artists)
CD _____ 7567827312
Warner Bros. / Apr '95 / Warner Music.

HOUSES OF THE HOLY
Song remains the same / Rain song / Over the hills and far away / Crunge / Dancing days / D'yer mak'er / No quarter / Ocean
CD _____ 756782639-2
Atlantic / Jul '94 / Warner Music.

IN THROUGH THE OUT DOOR
In the evening / South bound saurez / Fool in the rain / Hot dog / Carouselambra / All my love / I'm gonna crawl
CD _____ 756792443-2
Atlantic / Aug '94 / Warner Music.

LED ZEPPELIN
Good times, bad times / Babe I'm gonna leave you / You shook me / Dazed and confused / Your time is gonna come / Black mountain side / Communication breakdown / I can't quit you baby / How many more times
CD _____ 756782632-2
Atlantic / Jun '94 / Warner Music.

LED ZEPPELIN (BOX SET)
Whole lotta love / Heartbreaker / Communication breakdown / Babe I'm gonna leave you / Dazed and confused / Thank you / Your time is gonna come / What is and what should never be / Thank you / I can't quit you baby / Friends / Celebration day / Travelling riverside blues / Hey hey what can I do / White summer/Black mountain side / Black dog / Over the hills and far away / Immigrant song / Battle of Evermore / California / Since I've been loving you / D'yer mak'er / Gallows pole / Custard pie / Misty mountain hop / Rock and roll / Rain song / Stairway to heaven / Kashmir / Trampled underfoot / For your life / No quarter / Dancing days / When the levee breaks / Song remains the same / Achille's last stand / Ten years gone / Candy store rock / Moby Dick / In the evening / Ocean / Ozone baby / Houses of the holy / Wearing and tearing / Poor Tom / Nobody's fault but mine / Fool in the rain / In the light / Wanton song / I'm gonna crawl / All my love
CD Set _____ 7567 821 44 2
Atlantic / Oct '90 / Warner Music.

LED ZEPPELIN 2
Whole lotta love / What is and what should never be / Lemon song / Thank you / Heartbreaker / Livin' lovin' maid (she's a woman) / Ramble on / Moby Dick / Bring it on home
CD _____ 756782633-2
Atlantic / Jun '94 / Warner Music.

LED ZEPPELIN 3
Immigrant song / Friends / Celebration day / Since I've been loving you / Out on the tiles / Gallows pole / Tangerine / That's the way / Bron-y-aur stomp / Hats off to (Roy) Harper

CD _____ 756782678-2
Atlantic / Aug '94 / Warner Music.

LED ZEPPELIN BOXED SET 2
Good times, bad times / We're gonna groove / Night flight / That's the way / Baby, come on home / Lemon song / You shook me / Boogie with Stu / Bron-y-aur stomp / Down by the seaside / Out on the tiles / Black mountain side / Moby Dick / Sick again / Hot dog / Carouselambra / South bound saurez / Walter's walk / Darlene / Black country woman / How many more times / Rover / Four sticks / Hats off to (Roy) Harper / I can't quit you baby / Hots on for nowhere / Livin' lovin' maid (She's just a woman) / Royal Orleans / Bonzo's Montreux / Crunge / Bring it on home / Tea for one
CD Set _____ 7567824772
Atlantic / Sep '93 / Warner Music.

LED ZEPPELIN: INTERVIEW PICTURE DISC
CD P.Disc _____ CBAK 4042
Baktabak / Apr '90 / Baktabak.

PHYSICAL GRAFFITI
Houses of the holy / Trampled underfoot / Kashmir / Custard pie / Rover / In my time of dying / In the light / Bron-y-aur stomp / Down by the seaside / Ten years gone / Night flight / Wanton song / Boogie with Stu / Black country woman / Sick again
CD _____ 756792442-2
Atlantic / Aug '94 / Warner Music.

PRESENCE
Achille's last stand / For your life / Royal Orleans / Nobody's fault but mine / Candy store rock / Hots on for nowhere / Tea for one
CD _____ 756792439-2
Atlantic / Aug '94 / Warner Music.

REMASTERS
Communication breakdown / Babe I'm gonna leave you / Good times, bad times / Dazed and confused / White lotta love / Heartbreaker / Ramble on / Immigrant song / Celebration day / Since I've been loving you / Black dog / Rock and roll / Battle of Evermore / Misty mountain hop / Stairway to heaven / Song remains the same / Rain song / D'yer mak'er / No quarter / Houses of the holy / Kashmir / Trampled underfoot / Achille's last stand / All my love / In the evening
CD Set _____ 7567 80415 2
Atlantic / Oct '90 / Warner Music.

SONG REMAINS THE SAME, THE
Rock and roll / Celebration day / Song remains the same / Rain song / Dazed and confused / No quarter / Stairway to heaven / Moby Dick / Whole lotta love
CD Set _____ SK 289402
Swansong / Feb '87 / Warner Music.

Leda Trio

AIRS FOR THE SEASONS
CD _____ SPRCD 1036
Springthyme / May '94 / Direct / Roots / CM / Duncans / ADA.

Ledernacken

BOOGALOO AND OTHER NATTY DANCERS
Strike Back / Oct '87 / Vital / Grapevine. SBR 14CD

L
CD _____ E 11930-2
Derriere / Dec '93 / SRD.

SEX METAL
CD _____ SBR 16 CD
Strike Back / Jan '89 / Vital / Grapevine.

Ledgerwood, Leeann

YOU WISH
Robbin's row / Taisho pond / Miss Perfect / Chance / Nardis / Afterglow / You wish / Smash and grab / Terribillis / I want to talk about you
CD _____ 3201872
Triloka / May '92 / New Note.

LeDonne, Mike

COMMON GROUND (LeDonne, Mike Trio)
CD _____ CRISS 1058CD
Criss Cross / May '92 / Cadillac / Harmonia Mundi.

SOULMATES (LeDonne, Mike Sextet)
CD _____ CRISS 1074CD
Criss Cross / Nov '93 / Cadillac / Harmonia Mundi.

LeDoux, Chris

HAYWIRE
Honky tonk world / Tougher than the rest / Big love / Love needs a fool / Slow down / Sons of the pioneers / Billy the Kid / Hairtrigger colts .44 / Light of the world
CD _____ CDP 8287702
Liberty / Sep '94 / EMI.

Lee, Albert

ALBERT LEE & HOGAN'S HEROES - IN FULL FLIGHT
CD _____ RTMCD 60
Round Tower / Jan '94 / Pinnacle / ADA / Direct / BMG / CM.

BLACK CLAW AND COUNTRY FEVER
CD _____ 9010570
Line / Jun '94 / CM / Grapevine / ADA / Conifer / Direct.

HIDING
Country boy / Billy Tyler / Are you wasting my time / Now and then it's gonna rain / O a real good night / Setting me up / Ain't living long like this / Hiding / Hotel love / Come up and see me anytime
CD _____ CDMID 121
A&M / Oct '92 / PolyGram.

Lee, Alvin

LIVE IN VIENNA
CD _____ CDTB 171
Thunderbolt / Oct '95 / Magnum Music Group.

NINETEEN NINETY FOUR
Keep on rockin' / Long legs / I hear you knocking / I want you (she's so heavy) / I don't give a damn / Give me your love / Play it like it used to be / Take it easy / My baby's come back to me / Boogie all day / Bluest blues / Ain't nobody's business
CD _____ CDTB 150
Thunderbolt / Mar '95 / Magnum Music Group.

PURE BLUES
Don't want you woman / Bluest blues / I woke up this morning / Real life blues / Stomp / Slow blues in C / Wake up Mama / Talk don't bother me / Every blues you've ever heard / I get all shook up / Lost in love / Help me baby / Outside my window
CD _____ CDCHR 6102
Chrysalis / Jul '95 / EMI.

RETROSPECTIVE
Johnny B. Goode / Help me / Good morning little school girl / Slow blues in C / Love until I die / Love like a man / One more chance / You told me / I'm going home / Jenny Jenny / Little bit of love / Truckin' down the other way
CD _____ MMGV 064
Magnum Music / Mar '95 / Magnum Music Group.

Lee, Arthur

ARTHUR LEE & LOVE (Lee, Arthur & Love)
CD _____ 422214
New Rose / May '94 / Direct / ADA.

Lee, Bonnie

SWEETHEART OF THE BLUES
CD _____ DE 676
Delmark / Aug '95 / Hot Shot / ADA / CM / Direct / Cadillac.

Lee, Brenda

BEST OF BRENDA LEE
Sweet nothin's / I'm sorry / Emotions / Dum dum / Fool number one / You always hurt the one you love / Will you still love me tomorrow / When I fall in love / I'll be seeing you / Speak to me pretty / Here comes that feeling / It started all over again / My colouring book / Someday you'll want me to want you / End of the world / All alone am I / Losing you / Rockin' around the Christmas tree / Sweet impossible you / As usual / Is it true / Think / Love letters / Too many rivers / Make the world go away / Crying time / Sweet dreams / Yesterday / Always on my mind / For the good times / Feelings
CD _____ MCBD 19518
MCA / Apr '95 / BMG.

BEST OF BRENDA LEE, THE
CD _____ TCD 2738
Telstar / Oct '94 / BMG.

BEST OF BRENDA LEE, THE
CD _____ MCCD 213
Music Club / Oct '95 / Disc / THE / CM.

BRENDA LEE
Wiedersehn ist wunderschon / Kansas City / Ohne dich / Drei rote rosen bluh'n / Ich will immer auf dich warten / No my boy / Geh am gluck nicht vorbei / Am strand von Hawaii / Darling bye bye / In meinen traumen / Wo und wann fangt die liebe an / Darling was ist los mit dir / La premiere fool / Pourqui jamais moi / Sono sciocca / Nulla di me
CD _____ BCD 15644
Bear Family / Jun '92 / Rollercoaster / Direct / CM / Swift / ADA.

COMING ON STRONG
CD _____ MU 5037
CD _____ MU 4037
Musketeer / Oct '92 / Koch.

CRYING GAME, THE
Crying game / Can't help falling in love / September in the rain / When I fall in love / Will you still love me tomorrow / Close to you / Fools rush in / You always hurt the

one you love / Words / If you go away / Let it be me / Our day will come / This girl's in love with you / You don't have to say you love me / If I don't care / I'll be seeing you / Lover come back to me / Softly as I leave you / What kind of fool am I / End of the world
CD _____ MCLD 19241
MCA / May '94 / BMG.

EP COLLECTION, THE
Rock the bop / Weep no more baby / (If I'm dreaming) Just let me dream / Crazy talk / Speak to me pretty / Here comes that feeling / Ring-a-my-phone / Love you till I die / Rock-a-bye baby blues / Thanks a lot / All alone am I / If you love me (really love me) / I'm sorry / Georgia on my mind / I left my heart in San Francisco / Your used to be / She'll never know / Coming on strong / That's all you gotta do / Let's jump the broomstick / Stroll / Kansas City / Bigelow 6200 / Sweet nothin's / Rockin' around the Christmas tree
CD _____ SEECD 425
See For Miles/C5 / May '95 / Pinnacle.

FAVOURITES
Coming on strong / Silver threads and golden needles / Johnny one time / You're the one that I want / You don't have to say you love me / Jambalaya / Is it true / My whole world / Sweet nothin's / End of the world / All alone am I / Fool no.1 / Too many rivers / How much love / That's all you gotta do / I'm sorry / Ramble / Dance / God ole acapella (soul to soul) / Old landmarks / I'll flyaway some glad morning / Operator / Up above my head / Saved / When you're smiling / You ought to be in pictures / Put on a happy face / Smile / Baby face
CD _____ MUCD 9001
Start / Apr '95 / Koch.

GREATEST HITS
Coming on strong / Silver threads and golden needles / Johnny one time / You're the one that I want / You don't have to say you love me / Jambalaya / Is it true / My whole world is falling down / Sweet nothin's / End of the world / All alone am I / How much love / All you gotta do / You mama don't dance / I'm sorry / When you're smiling / You ought to be in pictures / Put on a happy face / Smile / Baby face / Soul to soul / Old landmarks / Some glad morning / Operator / Up above my head / Saved / Dum dum / Fool number one / Too mnay rivers
CD _____ PLATCD 362
Prism / '91 / Prism.

I'M SORRY
CD _____ WMCD 5570
Disky / Oct '94 / THE / BMG / Discovery / Pinnacle.

LEGENDS IN MUSIC - BRENDA LEE
CD _____ LECD 058
Wisepack / Jul '94 / THE / Conifer.

LITTLE MISS DYNAMITE (4 CD)
Jambalaya (on the bayou) / Bigelow 6-200 / Bigelow 6-200 (2) / Some people / Your cheatin' heart / Doodle bug rag / Christy Christmas / I'm jeanna lasso Santa Claus / Fairyland / One step at a time / Dynamite / Ain't that love / Love you till I die / One teenager to another / Rock a baby blues / Rock the bop / Ring-a-my-phone / Golden key / Little Jonah (rock on your steel guitar) / My baby likes Western guys / Papa Noel / Rockin' around the Christmas tree / Bill Bailey, won't you please come home / Heading home / Let's jump the broomstick / Hummin' the blues over you / Stroll / Rock-a-bye your baby with a dixie melody / Pretty baby / St. Louis blues / Nmmies from heaven / Baby face / Ballin' the jack / Just because / Side by side / Good man is hard to find / Some of these days / Back in your own backyard / Toot toot tootsie goodbye / Sweet nothin's / (If I'm dreaming) Just let me dream / Weep no more my baby / That's all you gotta do / I want to be wanted (per tutta la vita) / Just a little / Build a big fence / Be my love again / I'm sorry / Dynamite (2) / Love and learn / Wee Wee Willie / Jambalaya (on the bayou) (2) / No I worry (yes I do) / Emotions / I want to be wanted (per tutta la vita) (2) / No one / Crazy talk / Big chance / It's never too late / I'm learning about love / Careless, that's all / We three (my echo, my shadow and me) / If I didn't care / When my dreamboat comes home / Walkin' to New Orleans / Hallelujah I love him so / I'm in the mood for love / Svanee river rock / Pretend / If I didn't care (2) / If you love me (really love me) / Teach me tonight / Blueberry Hill / Around the world / Fools rush in (where angels fear to tread) / Someone to love (The prisoner's song) / Zing went the strings of my heart / Georgia on my mind / Just another lie / When I fall in love / Cry / Will you love me tomorrow / You can depend on me / Careless, that's all (2) / Love, come back to me / Kansas City / On the sunny side of the street / All the way / How deep is the ocean (how high is the sky) / Tragedy / Talkin' 'bout you / Tables are turning / Funny feelin' / Eventually / Dum dum / Let me be the one / Speak to me pretty / Time is not enough / Here comes that feeling / Just forget / Break it to me gently / Fool no.1 / Anybody but me / So deep / Only you (and you alone)

/ You've got me crying again / It's the talk of the town / You always hurt the one you love / I miss you so / I'll be seeing you / Lazy river / Send me some lovin' / Hold me / I'll always be in love with you / Organ grinder's swing / Let the four winds blow / Everybody loves me but you / Heart in hand / She'll never know / Why me / It takes one to know one / Sweet lovin'

CD Set _____ **BCD 15772 DK**
Bear Family / Oct '95 / Rollercoaster / Direct / CM / Swift / ADA.

ROCKIN' AROUND WITH BRENDA LEE
(If I'm dreaming) Just let me dream / Ain't that love / Bigelow 6200 / Bill Bailey, won't you please come home / Dum dum / Dynamite / Jambalaya / Let's jump the broomstick / Little Jonah (Rock on your little guitar) / Love and learn / My baby likes western guys / One step at a time / Ring-a-myphone / Rock the bop / Rock-a-bye baby blues / Rockin' around the Christmas tree / Sweet nothin's / That's all you gotta do / Wee wee Willie's / Weep no more my baby

CD _____ **PWKS 4232**
Carlton Home Entertainment / Nov '94 / Carlton Home Entertainment.

SINGS HER MOST BEAUTIFUL SONGS
CD _____ **CD 3501**
Cameo / Aug '94 / Target/BMG.

Lee, Bryan

BLUES IS..., THE (Lee, Bryan & Jump Five Street)
Circles / Think / Waiting on ice / Let me down easy / It's your move / Gelle / There it is / You done me wrong / So low down / Pretty Jeanine / I worry / Blues is...

CD _____ **BLU 10122**
Blues Beacon / Feb '92 / New Note.

MEMPHIS BOUND
CD _____ **JUST 52-2**
Justin Time / Sep '93 / Harmonia Mundi / Cadillac.

Lee, Byron

BEST OF SKA (Lee, Byron & The Dragonaires)
CD _____ **JMC 200104**
Jamaica Gold / Dec '92 / THE / Magnum Music Group / Jetstar.

BEST OF SKA VOL. 2
CD _____ **JMC 200105**
Jamaica Gold / Feb '93 / THE / Magnum Music Group / Jetstar.

BEST OF SKA VOL. 3
CD _____ **JMC 200106**
Jamaica Gold / Feb '93 / THE / Magnum Music Group / Jetstar.

ORIGINAL BYRON LEE, THE (Lee, Byron & The Dragonaires)
CD _____ **KENTONE 106**
Kentone / Jul '93 / Jetstar.

PEOPLE GET READY (Lee, Byron & The Dragonaires)
CD _____ **JMC 200113**
Jamaica Gold / Jun '94 / THE / Magnum Music Group / Jetstar.

PLAY DYNAMITE SKA (Lee, Byron & The Dragonaires)
CD _____ **JMC 200276**
Jamaica Gold / Feb '93 / THE / Magnum Music Group / Jetstar.

REGGAE BLAST OFF (Lee, Byron & The Dragonaires)
Monkey man / Elizabethan reggae / Love at first sight / Birth control
CD _____ **JMC 200108**
Jamaica Gold / Jul '94 / THE / Magnum Music Group / Jetstar.

REGGAE EYES
CD _____ **JMC 200107**
Jamaica Gold / Jul '94 / THE / Magnum Music Group / Jetstar.

SOFT LEE (Lee, Byron & The Dragonaires)
CD _____ **DYCD 3423**
Dynamic / Oct '95 / Jetstar.

SOFT LEE VOL.2 (Lee, Byron & The Dragonaires)
CD _____ **DYCD 3456**
Dynamic / Sep '95 / Jetstar.

SOFT LEE VOL.3 (Lee, Byron & The Dragonaires)
CD _____ **DYCD 3460**
Dynamic / Sep '95 / Jetstar.

SOFT LEE VOL.5 (Lee, Byron & The Dragonaires)
CD _____ **DYCD 3489**
Dynamic / Jan '94 / Jetstar.

WINE DOWN (Lee, Byron & The Dragonaires)
CD _____ **DY 3479**
Dynamic / May '92 / Jetstar.

Lee, Darrell

DARRELL LEE
Slow dance / Just a little bit / Girl, I'm alone / Sexy / She made me / Lisa / Big city life / Lock these people up

---

CD _____ **CDGEM 4005**
Gemc / Jul '89 / Disc.

Lee, Dee C.

SHRINE
Shrine / Hey what'd ya say / That's when something special starts / He's gone / Come hell or waters high / What about me / Still the children cry / Just my type / Hold on / See the day

CD _____ **982999 2**
Pickwick/Sony Collector's Choice / Aug '93 / Carlton Home Entertainment / Pinnacle / Sony.

THINGS WILL BE SWEETER
CD _____ **CTNCD 001**
Cleartone / Oct '95 / Pinnacle.

Lee, Dino

NEW LAS VEGAN, THE
CD _____ **ROSE 127CD**
New Rose / Oct '87 / Direct / ADA.

Lee, Frankie

GOING BACK HOME
CD _____ **BPCD 5013**
Blind Pig / Dec '94 / Hot Shot / Swift / CM / Roots / Direct / ADA.

SOONER OR LATER (Lee, Frankie & the Bluzblasters)
CD _____ **FF 595CD**
Flying Fish / Feb '93 / Roots / CM / Direct / ADA.

Lee Harvey Oswald Band

TASTE OF PRISON
CD _____ **TGCD 84**
Touch & Go / Feb '94 / SRD.

Lee, Jackie

DUCK, THE
CD _____ **GSCD 011**
Goldmine / Feb '93 / Vital.

Lee, Jeanne

NATURAL AFFINITIES
CD _____ **260702**
Owl / Nov '92 / Harmonia Mundi (USA).

Lee, John

BAMBOO MADNESS (Lee, John & Gerry Brown)
Infinite Jones / Deliverance / Jua / Absitively posolutely / Rise on / Who can see the shadow of the moon / Bamboo madness
CD _____ **FCD 0001**
Limetree / Nov '95 / New Note.

Lee, Julia

KANSAS CITY STAR
Down home syncopated / Merritt stomp / If I could be with you one hour tonight / Paseo Street / Ruff scufflin' / St. James Infirmary / He's tall, dark and handsome / Won't you come over to my house / Come over to my house / Trouble in mind / It it's good / Missouri blues / Lotus blossom / Charmaine / Lucky blues / We baby blues / I've got a crush on the fuller brush man / Two loves have I / Some of these days / St. Louis blues / Shake that thing shake it and break it / Julia's blues / Lies gotta gimme what you got / When a woman loves a man / Oh Marie / I'll get along somehow / Porter's love song / Have you ever been lonely / Since I've been with you / Out in the cold again / Young girl's blues / On my way out there / Snatch and grab it / If you hadn't gone away / Nobody knows you when you're down / Curse of an aching heart bleeding hearted blues / Living backstreet for you / You're a wise guy / Mama don't allow it / Doubtful blues / Ain't it a crime knock me a kiss / Cold hearted Daddy / My sin / When you're smiling / I was wrong / Pagan love song / All I ever do is worry / Take it or leave it / That's what I like / King size papa blues for somebody / I'm forever blowing bubbles / Breeze (blow my baby back to me) / Spinach song / Crazy world / Tell me Daddy / Christmas spirits / Until the real thing comes along / Charmaine / Lotus blossom marijuana / Sit down and drink it over / Away from you / Glory of love / Tonight's the night / My man stands out / Do you want it / It comes in like a lion / Don't come to soon / Ugly Papa / Don't save it too long / After hours waltz / You ain't got it no more / When your lover has gone / Oh chuck it (in a bucket) / Woman blues / Draggin' my heart around / It won't be long / You're gonna miss it / Can't get enough of that stuff / When a man has two women / Scream in the night / I know it's wrong / Music maestro please / Pipe dreams / When Jenny does that low down dance / I didn't care / Lazy river / All this beef and big red tomatoes / Can't get you off my mind / I got news for you / Goin' to Chicago blues / Last call for alcohol kansas city boogie / Love in bloom / Keep 'em barefoot and busy baby / I'm through / Scat you cats / I can't see how / King size Papa / Bop and rock lullaby

---

CD Set _____ **BCD 15770**
Bear Family / Mar '95 / Rollercoaster / Direct / CM / Swift / ADA.

UGLY PAPA (Lee, Julia & Boyfriends)
CD _____ **RBD 603**
Mr. R&B / Oct '91 / Swift / CM / Wellard.

Lee, Laura

THAT'S HOW IT IS
Wanted: Lover no experience necessary / Up tight good man / Another man's woman / He will break your heart / Dirty man / Hang it up / Man with some backbone / It ain't what you do / Meet love halfway
CD _____ **CDRED 27**
Charly / Sep '91 / Charly / THE / Cadillac.

Lee, Michael

FIRKINS
Laughing stacks / Runaway train / Deja blues / Rain in the tunnel / Sargasso sea / 24 Grand Avenue / Cactus cruz / Space crickets / Hula hoops
CD _____ **RR 93992**
Roadrunner / Aug '90 / Pinnacle.

Lee, Peggy

BASIN STREET PROUDLY PRESENT
Day in day out / Moments like this / Fever / Second time around / One kiss / My romance / Vagabond king waltz / I got a man / Peggy Lee Bow music / Ball me darling / I love being here with you / But beautiful / Them there eyes / Tribute to Ray Charles / Just for a thrill / Yes indeed
CD _____ **CDP 8327442**
Capitol / Aug '95 / EMI.

BEST OF PEGGY LEE, THE
CD _____ **MCCD 157**
Music Club / May '94 / Disc / THE / CM.

BEST OF PEGGY LEE, THE
CD _____ **MATCD 316**
Castle / Dec '94 / BMG.

CHRISTMAS ALBUM, THE
I like a sleighride (Jingle bells) / Christmas song / Don't forget to feed the reindeer / Star carol / Christmas list / Christmas carousel / Santa Claus is coming to town / Christmas waltz / Christmas riddle / Tree / Deck the halls with boughs of holly / White Christmas / Winter wonderland / Little drummer boy / Happy holiday / Christmas spell / Toys for tots
CD _____ **CDMFP 6149**
Music For Pleasure / Oct '94 / EMI.

CLOSE ENOUGH FOR LOVE
CD _____ **CDSL 5190**
DRG / '88 / New Note.

FEVER
CD _____ **PRS 23012**
Personality / Aug '93 / Target/BMG.

GREAT VOCALIST, THE
CD _____ **CDSR 051**
Telstar / Nov '94 / BMG.

I'VE GOT A CRUSH ON YOU
Wonderful guy / I've got a crush on my head / Just one of those things / Trouble is a man / Golden earrings / Just squeeze me / Happiness is a thing called Joe / It takes a long, long train with a red caboose / So dear to my heart / Louisa from Lake Louise / When you speak with your eyes / Lover / You and the night and the music / It's lovin' time / Then I'll be happy / Linger in my arms a little longer / Orange coloured sky / I've got a crush on you / I'm sweet, shy Ophelia / Dream is a wish your heart makes / Bali Ha'i / Speaking of angels / What is this thing called love / When is sometime / For just the chance to love you
CD _____ **AVC 549**
Avid / Jun '95 / Avid/BMG / Koch.

IF I COULD BE WITH YOU
If I could be with you one hour tonight / Too young / Clarinade / Shangai / Guy is a guy / Lady is a tramp / Dorsey medley / These foolish things / Just one more chance / Make the man love me
CD _____ **JASMCD 2534**
Jasmine / Jan '95 / Wellard / Swift / Conifer / Cadillac / Magnum Music Group.

IT'S A GOOD DAY (Lee, Peggy & Bing Crosby)
It's a good day / Everything's movin' too fast / Baby you can count on me / Best man / I still suits me / You came a long way from... / Exactly like you / I got rhythm / Little bird told me / On a slow boat to China / Cuanta La Gusta / What is thing thing called love / He's just my kind / Linger in my arms / What more can a woman do / I love you) for sentimental reasons / It's all over now / Nightingale can sing the blues / I'll close my eyes / It takes a long, long train with a red caboose / Just an old love of mine / Golden earrings / Love your magic spell is everywhere / Top hat, white tie and tails / Isn't this a lovely day (to be caught in the rain) / They can't take that away from me / Dearly beloved / Catalogue / Then I'll be happy / Maybe you'll be there / Cheek to cheek / Fine romance / Smoke gets in your eyes / White Christmas / Kahehameha day / I got lucky in the rain

---

CD _____ **PARCD 001**
Parrot / Jan '96 / THE / Wellard / Jazz Music.

LEGENDS IN MUSIC - PEGGY LEE
CD _____ **LECD 092**
Wisepack / Nov '94 / THE / Conifer.

LET THERE BE LOVE
I've got a right to sing the blues / Let there be love / If I could be with you one hour tonight / These foolish things / Shanghai / Make the man love me / Lady is a tramp / It's all over now / It takes a long, long train with a red caboose / Golden earrings / I got lucky in the rain / He's just my kind / What is this thing called love / (I love you) for sentimental reasons / My last affair / Just one more chance / Love is just around the corner / Love your magic spell is everywhere / OH what a beautiful morning / Linger in my arms a little longer
CD _____ **TRTCD 153**
TrueTrax / Dec '94 / THE.

LIVE 1947-52
CD _____ **EBCD 2115-2**
Jazzband / Jul '93 / Jazz Music / Wellard.

MISS PEGGY LEE SINGS THE BLUES
C.C. rider / Basin Street blues / Squeeze me / You don't know / Fine and mellow / Baby please come home / Kansas City / Birmingham jail / Love me / Beale Street blues / T'ain't nobody's business if I do / God bless the child
CD _____ **8208092**
Limelight / Nov '89 / PolyGram.

SINGS FOR YOU
CD _____ **AVC 514**
Avid / Dec '92 / Avid/BMG / Koch.

SPOTLIGHT ON PEGGY LEE
I've got the world on a string / When a woman loves a man / I'm beginning to see the light / There is no greater love / Too close for comfort / Unforgettable / Close your eyes / If I should lose you / I'm just wild about Harry / Deep purple / It's been a long, long time / Man I love / Best is yet to come / Come rain or come shine / Fever / I wanna be around / I hear music / That's all
CD _____ **CDP 8285332**
Capitol / Jul '95 / EMI.

THERE'LL BE ANOTHER SPRING
Circle in sky / He's a tramp / Johnny guitar / I'll give it all to you / Where can I go without you / Things are swingin' / Singing sea / I just want to dance all night / There'll be another Spring / Fever / Sans souci / Boomerang (I'll come back to you) / Over the wheel
CD _____ **8208212**
Limelight / Jul '90 / PolyGram.

UNCOLLECTED 1948, THE
CD _____ **HCD 220**
Hindsight / Jul '94 / Target/BMG / Jazz Music.

YOU GIVE ME FEVER
Misty / What I did for love / Every little movement / Mr. Wonderful (Live) / Is that all there is (live) / Folks that live on the hill (Live) / Love for sale (Live) / Fever / Mack the knife (live) / Sing a rainbow / I'm not in love / Hungry years / Lover / Star sounds
CD _____ **5500882**
Spectrum/Karussell / Oct '93 / PolyGram / THE.

Lee, Phil

TWICE UPON A TIME (Lee, Phil & Jeff Clyne)
Blue Serge / Eiderdown / Soiree / Everything I love / P.S. for Scott / Mar descancado / Peau douce / So tender / They say its wonderful
CD _____ **SGCCD 1018**
Cadillac / '87 / Cadillac / Wellard.

Lee, Philip John

FIVE SWORDS
Alegrias / London lilacs / Bulerias 1 / Travellers lament / Rumba / Five words / Fall of the leaf / Bulerias 2 / E Sacramonte / Lullaby for a baby toad / Verdiales
CD _____ **RRACD 002**
Run River / Nov '90 / Direct / ADA / CM.

Lee, Ranee

LIVE AT LE BIJOU
CD _____ **JUST 2-2**
Justin Time / Sep '93 / Harmonia Mundi / Cadillac.

MUSICALS, THE (Jazz on Broadway)
CD _____ **JUST 42-2**
Justin Time / Jun '92 / Harmonia Mundi / Cadillac.

Lee, Soren

SOREN LEE QUARTET
New York subway waltz / Dr. Jekyll / My funny valentine / Darn that dream / Blues in the closet / Secret love / Lee meets Ray / St. Thomas / Blues for Philly Joe
CD _____ **CDLR 45073**
L&R / Sep '93 / New Note.

Lee, Will

OH
CD _____ GOJ 60172
Go Jazz / Dec '95 / Vital/SAM.

Leeman, Mark

MEMORIAL ALBUM (Leeman, Mark Five)
CD _____ SEECD 317
See For Miles/C5 / Jun '91 / Pinnacle.

Leer, Thomas

BRIDGE
CD _____ BRIDGE 1CD
Grey Area / Jun '92 / Pinnacle.

CONTRADICTIONS
Hear what I say / Mr. Nobody / Contradictions / Looks that kill / Soul gypsy / Choices / Gulf stream / Private plane / International / Kings of sham / Dry land / Don't / Letter from America / Tight as a drum / West End / All about you
CD _____ CDBRED 105
Cherry Red / Dec '93 / Pinnacle.

Leeway

ADULT CRASH
Simple life / You / Make a move / Three wishes / Withering heights / Ten years / Silver tongue / Grip / Roulaison / Clueless
CD _____ CDVEST 4
Bulletproof / Mar '94 / Pinnacle.

OPEN MOUTH KISS
Foot the bill / Compromise / I believe / Hornet's nest / Manufabricate / Comes back / Product / State / Novena / Jock hop show / Old man of sorrow
CD _____ CDVEST 64
Bulletproof / Oct '95 / Pinnacle.

Lefebvre, Patrick

ACCORDEAN GAVOTTE
CD _____ CD 431
Diffusion Breizh / Apr '95 / ADA.

Lefevre, Raymond

DEMONSTRATION
CD _____ 819 921 2
Bar / '88 / Pinnacle.

Left Banke

WALK AWAY RENEE
CD _____ LNCD 951166
Line / Sep '92 / CM / Grapevine / ADA / Conifer / Direct.

Left Hand Freddy

BLUE TONIGHT (Left Hand Freddy & The Aces)
CD _____ MWCD 2010
Music & Words / Dec '95 / ADA / Direct.

Leftfield

BACKLOG
CD _____ OUTERCD 1
Outer Rhythm / Dec '92 / Vital.

LEFTISM
Release the pressure / Pressure / Afro left / Melt / Song of life / Original black flute / Space shanty / Inspection (check one) / Storm 3000 / Half fast dub / Open up / 21st Century poem
CD _____ HANDCD 2
Columbia / Jan '95 / Sony.

Lefty Dizz

AIN'T IT NICE TO BE LOVED
Cloudy weather / That's alright in the dark / I feel like jumping / Bad avenue / Ain't it nice to be loved / look on yonder wall / Too late / Sadie / Where the hell were you when I got home
CD _____ JSPCD 259
JSP / Mar '95 / ADA / Target/BMG / Direct / Cadillac / Complete/Pinnacle.

Legacy, Doug

KING CAKE PARTY (Legacy, Doug & Zydeco Party Band)
CD _____ FIENDCD 206
Demon / Jan '91 / Pinnacle / ADA.

Legal Weapon

TAKE OUT THE TRASH
CD _____ TX 92772
Roadrunner / Sep '91 / Pinnacle.

Legend

RED BOOT ALBUM
CD _____ REP 4061-WP
Repertoire / Aug '91 / Pinnacle / Cadillac.

Legend

LEGEND
Friendly fire / Don't believe it / Angela / After the fall / Carry me / Set this place on fire / Colours / They that wait / Lead me back / Always and forever

CD _____ 70193002637
Nelson Word / Apr '92 / Nelson Word.

Legend

AD 1980
Legend / My heart is there / Forgotten self / Heaven sent / Advantages / Way love's meant to be / Fantasy / Behind locked doors / Inside out / Silent world / Wooden sword / A.M. static / Favour
CD _____ ETHEL 4
Vinyl Tap / Dec '94 / Vinyl Tap.

Legendary Blues Band

KEEPING THE BLUES ALIVE
I don't wanna know / Stuck in the bottom / I love my woman / Cook me / Open your eyes / Nobody knows / Without her / What's wrong / Shake it for me / Reach way back / Steady worried man
CD _____ CDICH 1052
Ichiban / Oct '93 / Koch.

LIFE OF EASE
CD _____ ROUCD 2029
Rounder / Oct '94 / CM / Direct / ADA / Cadillac.

MONEY TALKS
CD _____ DOG 9107CD
Ichiban / May '94 / Koch.

RED HOT 'N' BLUE
CD _____ ROUCD 2035
Rounder / Oct '94 / CM / Direct / ADA / Cadillac.

U B DA JUDGE
Got love if you want it / Things could be worse / Eye to eye / In the rain / Watch your enemies / Don't say that no more / I don't trust you / Man / No one to love me / When the blues come around / Who's been talkin'
CD _____ ICH 9001 CD
Ichiban / Apr '91 / Koch.

WOKE UP WITH THE BLUES
Another mule / I woke up with the blues / Your daughter looks good to me / Honey bee / I need you so bad / Don't throw your love on me so strong / I'd like to have a girl like you / I've got to be with you tonight / You're looking good again tonight / Having a hard time
CD _____ CDICH 1039
Ichiban / Oct '93 / Koch.

Legendary Pink Dots

9 LIVES TO WONDER
Madame Guillotine / On another shore / Softly, softly / Crumbs on the carpet / Hotel Z / Oasis malade / Crack in melancholy time / Siren / Angel trail / Nine shades to the circle / Terra firma welcome
CD _____ BIAS 280CD
Play It Again Sam / Feb '94 / Vital.

ANY DAY NOW
Casting the runes / Strychnine kiss / Laguna beach / Gallery / Neon mariners / True love / Peculiar funfair / Waiting for the cloud / Cloud zero
CD _____ CDBIAS 080
Play It Again Sam / Nov '87 / Vital.

ASYLUM
CD _____ CDBIAS 012
Play It Again Sam / Mar '88 / Vital.

BRIGHTER NOW
CD _____ TK 001 CD
Terminal Kaleidoscope / Aug '88 / Vital.

CURSE
CD _____ TK 002 CD
Terminal Kaleidoscope / Aug '88 / Vital.

FACES IN THE FIRE
CD _____ CDBIAS 001
Play It Again Sam / Aug '88 / Vital.

FROM HERE YOU'LL WATCH THE WORLD GO BY
CD _____ STCD 099
Staalplaat / Sep '95 / Vital/SAM.

GOLDEN AGE, THE
CD _____ CDBIAS 103
Play It Again Sam / Jul '89 / Vital.

ISLAND OF JEWELS
CD _____ CDBIAS 041
Play It Again Sam / '88 / Vital.

MARIA DIMENSION, THE
CD _____ BIAS 184 CD
Play It Again Sam / Jan '91 / Vital.

SHADOW WEAVER
Zero zero / Guilty man / Ghosts of unborn children / City of needles / Stitching time / Twilight hour / Key to heaven / Laughing guest / Prague spring / Leper colony
CD _____ BIAS 225CD
Play It Again Sam / Aug '92 / Vital.

SHADOW WEAVER PT 2: MALACHAI
Joey the canary / Kingdom of the flies / Encore une fois / Wildlife estate / Pavanne / Window on the world / On the boards / We bring the day / Paris 4am
CD _____ BIAS 236CD
Play It Again Sam / Mar '93 / Vital.

Storm Circles

STORM CIRCLES
Love puppets / Black zone / Golden dawn / Curious day / Hanging gardens / Fifteen flies / Our lady in darkness / Apocalypse / Gladiators version
CD _____ BIAS CD 1001
Play It Again Sam / Apr '89 / Vital.

TOWER, THE
CD _____ TK 003 CD
Terminal Kaleidoscope / Aug '88 / Vital.

Legg, Adrian

MRS CROWE'S BLUES WALTZ
Kinvarra's child / Frank the part-time clown / Mrs. Crowe's Blues waltz / Gebrauchmusik II / Brooklyn blossom / Sour grapes / Norah Handley's waltz / Kiss-curl / Lunch time at Rosie's / Paddy goes to Nashville / Green ballet II / Last track
CD _____ CDRR 9085 2
Roadrunner / Mar '93 / Pinnacle.

WINE, WOMEN & WALTZ
CD _____ RR 90242
Roadrunner / Nov '93 / Pinnacle.

Legion

DIE DATENSCHLEUDER
CD _____ HY 39100982
Hyperium / Apr '94 / Plastic Head.

Legrand, Michel

COLUMBIA ALBUM OF COLE PORTER, THE
CD _____ 4692892
Sony Jazz / Jan '95 / Sony.

Legs Diamond

CAPTURED LIVE
CD _____ CDMFN 137
Music For Nations / Jun '92 / Pinnacle.

TOWN BAD GIRL
CD _____ CDZORRO 16
Metal Blade / Nov '90 / Pinnacle.

WISH
CD _____ CDMFN 154
Under One Flag / Oct '93 / Pinnacle.

Leich, Peter

EXHILARATION
CD _____ RSRCD 118
Reservoir Music / Nov '94 / Cadillac.

Leigh, Carol

CAROL LEIGH & THE DUMDUSTIER STOMPERS
CD _____ BCD 341
GHB / Jun '95 / Jazz Music.

Leighton, Jo

OCEANS OF LOVE
CD _____ LJCD 001
Scratch / Aug '94 / BMG.

Leimgruber, Urs

L'ENIGMATIQUE (Leimgruber, Urs & Fritz Hauser)
CD _____ ARTCD 6091
Hat Art / Jun '92 / Harmonia Mundi / ADA / Cadillac.

Leiner, Robert

VISIONS OF THE PAST
Out of control / Visions of the past / Interval / To places you've never been / Aqua viva / Full moon ritual / Zenit / Dream or reality / From beyond and back / Northern dark
CD _____ AMB 3925CD
Apollo / Jan '94 / Vital.

Leitch, Peter

ON A MISTY NIGHT
CD _____ CRISS 1026CD
Criss Cross / May '94 / Cadillac / Harmonia Mundi.

RED ZONE
CD _____ RSRCD 103
Reservoir Music / Oct '89 / Cadillac.

SPECIAL RAPPORT, A
CD _____ RSRCD 129
Reservoir Music / Nov '94 / Cadillac.

Leixapren

GAITROPOS
CD _____ J 1024CD
Sonifolk / Jun '94 / ADA / CM.

LeJeune, Eddie

CAJUN SOUL
Le two-step a pop / Grand bosco / La valse de Samedi au soir / Don't cry my children / Le branche de murrier / Lascassine special / J'ai ete au bal / Mistake I made / Little broken heart / Love bridge waltz / Cher'ti monde / Saturday night special
CD _____ HNCD 1353
Hannibal / Feb '90 / Vital / ADA.

It's In The Blood

IT'S IN THE BLOOD
Le l'ai rencontree / Duralde waltz / Boire mon whiskey / Happy hop / Valse criminelle / Madeleine / Les conseils j'ai ecoutes / Je serais ta apres t'espere / J'ai quitte ma famille dans les miseres / Teche / Fille a 'n oncle Hilaire / Reve du saoulard / Donnez moi la / J'aimerais tu viens me chercher
CD _____ HNCD 1364
Hannibal / Jul '91 / Vital / ADA.

Lellis, Tom

TAKEN TO HEART
Mountain flight / Taken to heart / I'm late/ Alice in wonderland/You can fly / Milton's moment / Nobody does it better / Love is / My one and only love / Dukedom / It never entered my mind / It's not where you think it is / Wistful thinking
CD _____ CCD 4574
Concord Jazz / Nov '93 / New Note.

Lema, Ray

EURO AFRICAN SUITE (Lema, Ray & Joachim Kuhn)
CD _____ 925492
Buda / Nov '92 / Discovery / ADA.

GAIA
CD _____ CIDM 1055
Mango / Nov '90 / Vital / PolyGram.

NANGADEF
Kamulang / H.A.I. 99 / Moni mambo / Boyele / Afcoeur / Nangadef / Pongi / What we need / Orchestra of the forest
CD _____ CIDM 1000
Mango / Apr '89 / Vital / PolyGram.

Lemer, Peter

LOCAL COLOUR
CD _____ ESP 1057-2
ESP / Jan '93 / Jazz Horizons / Jazz Music.

Lemon, Brian

BEAUTIFUL FRIENDSHIP, A
Them there eyes / Fine and dandy / Nobody else but me / What's new / This love of mine / Comes love / Makin whoopee / One morning in May / Just friends / As time goes by / Moten swing / Up with the lark / Skylark / Beautiful friendship
CD _____ ZECD 4
Zephyr / Nov '95 / New Note.

BUT BEAUTIFUL
Ill wind / Old folks / Exactly like you / I thought about you / It's you or no one / But beautiful / In a sentimental mood / This can't be love / That old feeling / Gee baby ain't I good to you / I'm putting all my eggs in one basket / Blues for Suzanne / St. Thomas / My one and only love
CD _____ ZECD 1
Zephyr / Oct '95 / New Note.

OVER THE RAINBOW
Over the rainbow / What is this thing called love / Ghost of a chance / Have you met Miss Jones / When lights are low / Dearly beloved / Secret love / Emily / Star eyes / Straight no chaser / Alone together / You don't know what love is
CD _____ ZECD 2
Zephyr / Oct '95 / New Note.

Lemon Pipers

GREEN TAMBOURINE
CD _____ REP 4016-WZ
Repertoire / Aug '91 / Pinnacle / Cadillac.

LEMON PIPERS, THE
CD _____ NEXCD 131
Sequel / Jul '90 / BMG.

Lemon Sol

ENVIRONMENTAL ARCHITECTURE
Sun flash / Memorandum / Natural ratio / Polymorph / Red drift / Powers of invasion / Fuse / Universal / Environmental architecture
CD _____ GRCD 014
Guerilla / Jul '94 / Pinnacle.

Lemongrowers

SEGMENTS
CD _____ NBX 011
Noisebox / Apr '95 / Disc.

Lemonheads

COME ON FEEL THE LEMONHEADS
Great big no / Into your arms / It's about time / Down about it / Paid to smile / Big gay heart / Style / Rest assured / Dawn can't decide / I'll do it anyway / Rick james style / Being around / Favorite T / You can take it with you / Jello fund
CD _____ 756782537-2
Atlantic / Oct '93 / Warner Music.

CREATOR
CD _____ TAANG 23CD
Taang / Aug '93 / Plastic Head.

HATE YOUR FRIENDS
CD _____ TAANG 15CD
Taang / Nov '92 / Plastic Head.

IT'S A SHAME ABOUT RAY
Rockin' stroll / Confetti / It's a shame about Ray / Rudderless / Buddy / Turnpike down / Bit part / Alisons starting to happen / Hannah and Gabi / Kitchen / Ceiling fan in my spoon / Frank Mills / Mrs. Robinson (Features on CD only.)
CD _____ 7567823972
Atlantic / Feb '95 / Warner Music.

LICK
Mallo cup / Glad I don't know / Seven Powers / Circle of one / Cazzo di Ferro / Anyway / Luka / Come back D.A. / I am a rabbit / Sad girl / Ever / Strange / Mad
CD _____ T 032CD
Taang / Nov '92 / Plastic Head.

LOVEY
Ballarat / Half the time / Year of the cat / Ride with me / Li'l seed / Stove / Come downstairs / Left for dead / Brass buttons / Door
CD _____ 7567821372
Atlantic / Feb '93 / Warner Music.

Lemos, Paul

MUSIC FOR STOLEN ICONS VOL.2
CD _____ EFA 11939-2
Artware / Jan '94 / Vital.

Lennon Family

DANCE OF THE HONEY BEES
CD _____ CEFCD 167
Gael Linn / Dec '95 / Roots / CM / Direct / ADA.

Lennon, John

DOUBLE FANTASY (Lennon, John & Yoko Ono)
(Just like) starting over / Kiss kiss kiss / Clean up time / Give me something / I'm losing you / I'm movin' on / Beautiful boy / Watching the wheels / I'm your angel / Woman / Dear Yoko / Every man has a woman who loves him / Hard times are over
CD _____ CDP 791 425 2
Capitol / Jan '89 / EMI.

IMAGINE
Imagine / Crippled inside / Jealous guy / It's so hard / I don't want to be a soldier / Gimme some truth / Oh my love / How do you sleep / Oh Yoko
CD _____ CDP 746 641 2
EMI / May '87 / EMI.

IMAGINE (John Lennon Forever) (Various Artists)
CD _____ CA 10515
Denon / Mar '93 / Conifer.

IMAGINE - THE MOVIE
Real love / Twist and shout / Help / In my life / Strawberry fields forever / Day in the life / Revolution / Ballad of John and Yoko / Julia / Don't let me down / Give me a chance / How / Imagine / God / Mother / Stand by me / Jealous guy / Woman / Beautiful boy / (Just like) starting over
CD _____ CDPCSP 722
Parlophone / Oct '88 / EMI.

JOHN LENNON COLLECTION (The)
Give peace a chance / Instant karma / Power to the people / Whatever gets you through the night / Number 9 dream / Mind games / Love / Happy Christmas (war is over) / Imagine / Jealous guy / Stand by me / (Just like) starting over / Woman / I'm losing you / Beautiful boy / Watching the wheels / Dear Yoko / Move over Ms. L. (CD only.) / Cold turkey (CD only.)
CD _____ CDEMTV 37
Parlophone / Oct '89 / EMI.

JOHN LENNON/PLASTIC ONO BAND
Mother / Hold on / I found out / Working class hero / Isolation / Remember / Love / Well well well / Look at me / God / My mummy's dead
CD _____ CDFA 3310
Fame / Nov '94 / EMI.

LENNON
Give peace a chance / Blue suede shoes / Money (that's what I want) / Dizzy Miss Lizzy / Yer blues / Cold turkey / Instant karma / Mother / Hold on / I found out / Working class hero / Isolation / Remember / Love / Well well well / Look at me / God / My mummy's dead / Power to the people / Well (baby please don't go) / Imagine / Crippled inside / Jealous guy / It's so hard / Give me some truth / Oh my love / How do you sleep / How / Oh Yoko / Happy Christmas (war is over) / Woman is the nigger of the world / New York City / John Sinclair / Come together / Hound dog / Mind games / Aisumasen (I'm sorry) / One day (at a time) / Intuition / Out the blue / Whatever gets you through the night / Going down on love / Old dirt road / Bless you / Scared / Number 9 dream / Surprise surprise (sweet bird of paradox) / Steel and glass / Nobody loves you (when you're down and out) / Stand by me / Ain't that a shame / Do you want to dance / Sweet little sixteen / Slippin' and slidin' / Angel baby / Just because / Whatever gets you through the night (live) / Lucy in the sky with diamonds / I saw her standing there / (Just like) starting over / Cleanup time / I'm losing you / Beautiful boy / Watching the wheels / Woman / Dear

Yoko / I'm stepping out / I don't wanna face it / Nobody told me / Borrowed time / (Forgive me) my little flower princess / Every man has a woman who loves him / Boys and girls / Grow old with me
CD Set _____ LENNON 1
Parlophone / Oct '90 / EMI.

LIVE IN NEW YORK CITY
New York City / It's so hard / Woman is the nigger of the world / Well, well, well / Instant Karma / Mother / Come together / Imagine / Cold turkey (With Frank Zappa and The Mothers of Invention.) / Hound dog / Give peace a chance
CD _____ CDP 746 196 2
Parlophone / May '86 / EMI.

LIVE JAM (Plastic Ono Band)
Cold turkey / Don't worry Kyoko / Well (baby please don't go) / Jamrag / Scumbag / AU
CD _____ CDP 746 783 2
Parlophone / Aug '87 / EMI.

LOVE (John Lennon Forever) (Various Artists)
Ballad of John and Yoko / Love / Jealous guy / Help / Stand by me / (Just like) starting over / Don't let me down / Eleanor Rigby / Come together / Imagine
CD _____ CA 79371
Denon / Mar '92 / Conifer.

MENLOVE AVE
Here we go again / Rock 'n' roll people / Angel baby / My baby left me / To know her is to love her / Steel and glass / Scared / Old dirt road / Nobody loves you (when you're down and out) / Bless you
CD _____ CDPCS 7308
Parlophone / Apr '87 / EMI.

MIND GAMES
Mind games / Tight as / Aisumasen (I'm sorry) / One day (at a time) / Bring on the Lucie / Nutopian international anthem / Intuition / Out of the blue / Only people / I know (I know) / You are here / Meat city
CD _____ CDP 746 769 2
Parlophone / Aug '87 / EMI.

ROCK 'N' ROLL
Be bop a lula / Stand by me / Rip it up / You can't catch me / Ain't that a shame / Do you wanna dance / Sweet little sixteen / Slippin' and slidin' / Peggy Sue / Bring it on home to me / Bony Moronie / Ya ya / Just because / Ready teddy
CD _____ CDP 746 707 2
Parlophone / May '87 / EMI.

SHAVED FISH
Give peace a chance / Cold turkey / Instant karma / Power to the people / Mother / Woman is the nigger of the world / Imagine / Whatever gets you through the night / Mind games / No. 9 dream / Happy Christmas (war is over) / Give peace a chance (reprise)
CD _____ CDP 746 642 2
EMI / May '87 / EMI.

TESTIMONY
CD _____ CDTB 095
Thunderbolt / Apr '91 / Magnum Music Group.

WALLS AND BRIDGES
Going down on love / Whatever gets you through the night / Old dirt road / What you got / Bless you / Scared / No. 9 dream / Surprise surprise (sweet bird of paradox) / Steel and glass / Beef jerky / Nobody loves you (when you're down and out) / Ya ya
CD _____ CDP 746 768 2
Parlophone / Jul '87 / EMI.

WORKING CLASS HERO (A Tribute To John Lennon) (Various Artists)
I found out / I don't want to be a soldier / Steel and glass / Imagine / Working class hero / Power to the people / How do you sleep / Nobody told you / Well well well / Cold turkey / Isolation / Jealous guy / Instant karma / Grow old with me / Mind games
CD _____ 6201152
Hollywood / Oct '95 / PolyGram.

WORKING CLASS HERO: A TRIBUTE TO JOHN LENNON (Various Artists)
CD _____ 1620152
Polydor / Sep '95 / PolyGram.

Lennon, Julian

SECRET VALUE OF DAYDREAMING, THE
Stick around / You get what you want / Let me tell you / I've seen your face / Coward till the end / This is my day / You didn't have to tell me / Everyday / Always think twice / I want your body
CD _____ CASCD 1171
Charisma / Jul '87 / EMI.

VALOTTE
Valotte / OK for you / On the phone / Space / Well I don't know / Too late for goodbyes / Lonely / Say your wrong / Jesse / Let me be
CD _____ JLCD 1
Charisma / Oct '84 / EMI.

Lennox, Annie

DIVA
Why / Walking on broken glass / Precious / Legend in my living room / Cold / Money can't buy it / Little bird / Primitive / Stay by me / Gift / Keep young and beautiful (CD only)
CD _____ PD 75326
RCA / Aug '95 / BMG.

MEDUSA
No more I love you's / Take me to the river / Whiter shade of pale / Don't let it bring you down / Train in vain / I can't get next to you / Downtown lights / Thin line between love and hate / Waiting in vain / Something so right
CD _____ 74321257172
RCA / Mar '95 / BMG.

MEDUSA (inc. Live in Central Park)
CD Set _____ 74321331632
RCA / Nov '95 / BMG.

Lennox CF

PICNICS & HOLIDAYS
CD _____ BRAM 198905-2
Brambus / Nov '93 / ADA / Direct.

Lenoir, J.B.

ALABAMA BLUES
Alabama blues / Mojo boogie / God's word / Whale has swallowed me / Move this rope / I feel so good / Alabama march / Talk to your daughter / Mississippi road / Good advice / Vietnam / I want to go / Down in Mississippi / If I get lucky / Born dead / Feeling good
CD _____ CDLR 42001
L&R / Feb '91 / New Note.

MAMA, WATCH YOUR DAUGHTER (Charly Blues - Masterworks Vol. 47)
CD _____ CDBM 47
Charly / Jun '93 / Charly / THE / Cadillac.

TROPICAL BLUESMAN, THE (From Korea to Vietnam)
Natural man / When I'm drinking / Back door / Lou Ella / Mojo Boogie / Low down dirty shame / I don't care what nobody say / Move to Kansas City / I been down so long / Man watch your woman / Mama talk to your daughter / Alabama blues / Eisenhower blues / I'm in Korea / Carrie Lee / Korea blues / Sittin' down thinkin' / Let's roll / J.B.'s rock / I'll die trying / How much more / Don touch my head / Voodoo boogie / Everybody crying about Vietnam
CD _____ CD 52017
Blues Encore / '92 / Target/BMG.

Lens Cleaner

WITH VOICE INSTRUMENTS
CD _____ SAB 002CD
Sabotage / Nov '95 / Plastic Head.

Leonard, Deke

ICEBERG/KAMIKAZE
Razor blade and rattlesnake / I just can't win / Lisa / Nothing is happening / Looking for a man / Hard way to live / Broken ovation / Jesse / Ten thousand takers / Ghost of musket flat / Crosby (Second class citizen blues) / 7171 551 / Cool summer rain / Jayhawk special / Sharpended claws / Taking the easy way out / Black gates of death / Stacia / Broken glass and limejuice / April the third / Louisiana hoedown / In search of Sarah and twenty six horses / Devil's gloves
CD _____ BGOCD 288
Beat Goes On / Aug '95 / Pinnacle.

Leonard, Harlan

CLASSICS 1940 (Leonard, Harlan & His Rockets)
CD _____ CLASSICS 670
Classics / Nov '92 / Discovery / Jazz Music.

Leonhart, Jay

FOUR DUKE (Leonhart, Jay & Gary Burton)
In a mellow tone / Rockin' in rhythm / C jam blues / Love you madly / Azure / Cotton tail / Creole love song / Take the 'A' train / Squeeze me / Caravan / Ishfanhan / Satin doll
CD _____ CDC 9089
LRC / Aug '95 / New Note / Harmonia Mundi.

LIVE AT FAT TUESDAY'S (Leonhart, Jay & Friends)
Smile / Let the flower grow / Robert Frost / Lonely rider / Strangest thing / They're coming to get me / Unhappy / Momma don't you think we ought to be going / Impossible to sing and play the bass / Kentucky wild flower / Me and Lenny
CD _____ 8439
DRG / Nov '93 / New Note.

Leroi Brothers

CHECK THIS ACTION
Are you with me baby / I can't be satisfied / Ain't I'm a dog / Big time operator / Steady with Betty / Check this action / Chicken and

honey / Rockin' Daddy / Cotton pickin' / Crazy crazy lovin' / Ballad of a juvenile delinquent / Till it's too late / Arms race / Damage / Little Miss Understanding / Straight jacket / Mad about the wrong boy / Motorworld / On the third stroke / Slow patience / La la la la la loved you / Single girl / Lonesome little town / Taste of poison / High rise housewife / Talk about me / Sad about girls / Camera camera / I feel like breaking up somebody's home / Why do I / Laughin' and clownin' / If I ever had a good thing / Scarred knees / From the heart / Your love is so doggone good / We don't see eye to eye / Roadblock / Teach me to forget
CD _____ ROUCD 9034
Rounder / Nov '94 / CM / Direct / ADA / Cadillac.

Les Aborigenes

SONGS AND DANCES FROM NORTH AUSTRALIA
CD _____ ARN 64056
Arion / Apr '91 / Discovery / ADA.

Les Ballets Africains

HERITAGE
CD _____ 926342CD
Euda / Nov '95 / ADA.

Les Calamites

COMPILATION
CD _____ FC 041CD
Fan Club / '88 / Direct.

Les Calchakis

FLUTES DE PAN DES ANDES
Recuerdo azul / Lima morena / Presencia lejana / Coplas de marzo / El colibri / Linda cambita / Jesusana / Cuculi / Blanca palomita / Aires de mi tierra / Sol nocturno / Amankay / Tiempo de paz / Requiem para un afilador / Uskil / Kena y siku / Sikus del titicaca / Triste tondero / Urpillay / Acuarela de sikus
CD _____ ARN 64005
Arion / '88 / Discovery / ADA.

FLUTES DES TERRES INCAS
La pastora / El centinela et anata morena / Lejana purmamarca / La maya / Reservista purajhey / Soplo del oriente / El pastor / Sol de vilcabamba / La bocina / El sacha puma / Kacharpari / Crepusculo costeno / Tuntuneando / Kurikinga / Casi me quisiste / Himno al sol / Sanjuanero / Sonkoy / Selvas y valles / Kapullay
CD _____ ARN 64002
Arion / '88 / Discovery / ADA.

HARPE, MARIMBA ET GUITARS LATINO-AMERICAINES
Cambai / El toro rabon / Carta a Buenos Aires / Bailecito triple / Isla saca / Nieve viento y sol / La escala / Campanas a M. Nunez / Angata / La rielera / Imagenes Argentinas / Cuerdita / Joropeando / Poncho verde / Bailecito Calchaki / Concierto en la llanura / La zandunga / Lunarcito / Madrecita / Bachue
CD _____ ARN 64032
Arion / '88 / Discovery / ADA.

PRESTIGE DE LA MUSIQUE LATINO-AMERICAINE
Quiero contarte / Hilanderita / Tema boliviano / Cotopaxi / Sube a nacer conmigo / Rasguido de la paz / Chimborazo / Papel de plata / El aguaceral / Kalahuayo yuyay / Si tu me olvidas / Cullaguada / Alejandra / Del otro lado del mar
CD _____ ARN 64025
Arion / '88 / Discovery / ADA.

Les Freres Guillemain

BERRY BOURBONNAIS
CD _____ Y 225105CD
Silex / Oct '93 / ADA.

HISTORICAL BAGPIPE/HURDY GURDY
CD _____ Y 225105
Silex / Oct '93 / ADA.

Les Hommes Qui Wear...

KAIRO (Les Hommes Qui Wear Espadrillos)
CD _____ EFA 127922
Blu Noise / Dec '95 / SRD.

Les Jumeaux

FEATHERCUT
CD _____ CORP 013CD
ITN Corporation / Jan '96 / Plastic Head.

Les Maniacs

LIVE AT BUDOKAN
CD _____ STOP 09CD
Danceteria / Feb '90 / Plastic Head / ADA.

Les Negresses Vertes

10 REMIXES 87-93
Face a la mer / Hou Mamma mia (Ethnik extended) / Sous le soleil de bodega / 200 Ans d'hypocrisie / Orane (Hypnotik edit) / Voila l'ete / Dun de nuit / Famille heureuse / Les yeux de ton pere (I'll kill you edit)

Zobi la mouche / Sous le soleil de bogeda
(Di moko) / Hou Mamma Mia (House mix)
CD _____ CDDLB 9
Delabel / Jun '93 / EMI.

FAMILLE HEUREUSE
CD _____ CDDLB 2
Delabel / Feb '92 / EMI.

MLAH
La valse / Zobi la mouche / C'est pas la mer
a boire / Voila l'ete / Orane / La faim des
haricots / Les yeux de ton pere / Il /
L'homme des marais / Les rablablas les
roubliblis / Marcelle Ratafia / La danse des
negresses vertes / Hey Maria / Le pere
Magloire
CD _____ CDDLB 5
Delabel / Apr '92 / EMI.

ZIG-ZAGUE
Fanfaron / Tous des ouvriers / Apres la pluie
/ La main verte / Mambo show / Comme
toujours / A quoi bon / Enfer et paradis /
Bourre d'allegresse / Iza mellino/mellino /
Le poete / Ivresse / Footballer du Dimanche
/ Tu m'as saoule
CD _____ CDDLB 12
Virgin / Feb '95 / EMI.

Les Tambours Du Bronx

MONOSTRESS 225L
La Valse des Nuls / Tchi tchi ou la valse /
Metropolis / Heya / Cadence 22 / Le cre-
puscle des Crapules / Locomotive / Mon-
ostress 225L
CD _____ 592048
FNAC / Nov '93 / Discovery.

Les Thugs

AS HAPPY AS POSSIBLE
CD _____ SOL 39CD
Vinyl Solution / Oct '93 / Disc.

Lesh, Lagen

SEASTONES
CD _____ RCD 40193
Rykodisc / Dec '92 / Vital / ADA.

Leslie, Chris

GIFT, THE
Tenpence coloured / Shaker music / Sa-
muel's shoes/Imogen's reel / Sir John Fen-
wick's/John's fairy dance / No tune for the
wicked / Red haired man's wife / Eighteenth
century English dances / Gow rediscovered
/ I wandered by a brookside / Linda's tune
/ Of all the ways the wind can blow / Cape
Breton set / She once loved me / Buffoon/
Black joke / Highland medley
CD _____ BEJOCD 5
Beautiful Jo / Jun '94 / ADA.

L'Esprit

FAR JOURNEY
Complete / Turning of the tide / Trust / That
special place / Far journey / Release / Bali
sure / Highlands
CD _____ KCD 002
Ki-Productions / May '92 / Ki-Productions.

LANGUAGE OF TOUCH
Kaira / Sea of change / Ripples / Shoji /
Taiga / Language of touch / Verandah
CD _____ KCD 001
Ki-Productions / May '92 / Ki-Productions.

Lester Bangs

JOOK SAVAGES ON THE BRAZOS
(Lester Bangs & The Delinquents)
CD _____ EFA 121662
Moll / Mar '95 / SRD.

Lester, Van

EN TRANSICION
A mi fiesta / De una manera especial / Dime
de que presumes / Como dice el refran /
Dime la verdad / Mi mejor momento / Quis-
iera sonarte / Sigue queriendome asi
CD _____ 6605807
RMM / Nov '95 / New Note.

Let Loose

LET LOOSE
Crazy for you / Seventeen / One night stand
/ Way I wanna be / I love your smile / Card-
board city / Shame / Super sexy real thing /
Best in me / Devotion / I believe / Love
like there's no tomorrow
CD _____ 5260182
A&M / Nov '94 / PolyGram.

Let Me Dream

MY DEAR
CD _____ CDAR 027
Adipocre / Jun '95 / Plastic Head.

Lethal

PROGRAMMED
Fire in your skin / Programmed / Plan of
peace / Another day / Arrival / What they've
done / Obscure the sky / Immune / Pray for
me / Killing machine
CD _____ CDZORRO 15
Metal Blade / Nov '90 / Pinnacle.

YOUR FAVOURITE GOD
CD _____ CDMVEST 44
Bulletproof / Mar '95 / Pinnacle.

Lettau, Kevyn

ANOTHER SEASON
Another season / Summer dreams / Morning kisses / Foundation of humanity / I've
got a crush on you / Ella / You don't love
me like you used to / Father, Mother / Colors of joy / Inside your love / Retrato em
branco e petro / Shower the people
CD _____ JVC 20302
JVC / Mar '94 / New Note.

UNIVERSAL LANGUAGE
Tribute to you / Secretly begin / Universal
language / Underneath / Seeing for the very
first time / Our lasting love / Beatriz / Gentle
flower / Three little words / Love is unconditional / Dein ist mein ganzes herz / Only
trust your heart
CD _____ JVC 20482
JVC / May '95 / New Note.

Letters To Cleo

AURORA GORY ALICE
CD _____ WOLCD 1057
China / Apr '95 / Pinnacle.

Leukemia

SUCK MY HEAVEN
Into the morgue / I nearly forgot / Uncarved
miseria / Wandering / Sick inside / You as
of ey / Everything falls apart / Memorized /
Different but same
CD _____ BMCD 029
Black Mark / Mar '93 / Plastic Head.

Levallet, Didier

GENERATIONS (Levallet, Didier Tentet)
CD _____ EVCD 212
Evidence / Feb '94 / Harmonia Mundi /
ADA / Cadillac.

Levanders, Jan

MUSAIK (Levanders, Jan Octet)
CD _____ DRCD 232
Dragon / Oct '94 / Roots / Cadillac /
Wellard / CM / ADA.

Levant, Oscar

OSCAR LEVANT PLAYS GERSHWIN
Rhapsody in blue / Second rhapsody for pi-
ano and orchestra / I got rhythm (variations)
/ Preludes for piano / Piano concerto in F
CD _____ CD 47681
Sony Classical / Jan '92 / Sony.

PLAYS LEVANT & GERSHWIN
Gershwin: A portrait by Levant / Liza / My
cousin in Milwaukee / Foggy day / Half of it
dearie blues / But not for me / Rhapsody in
blue / Concerto in F (third movement) / Then
farewell / King and country call / Ah romantic love dream / First movement: Con ritmo
/ Second movement: Andantion poco
mosso / Third movement: Allegro deciso /
Piano concerto / Young in heart
CD _____ DRGCD 13113
DRG / Oct '94 / New Note.

Level 42

FOREVER NOW
Forever now / Model friend / Tired of waiting
/ All over you / Love in a peaceful world /
Romance / Billy's anne / One in a million /
Sunbed song / Talking in your sleep / Don't
bother me
CD _____ 74321 18996-2
RCA / Mar '94 / BMG.

LEVEL 42
Turn it on / Forty three / Why are you leav-
ing / Almost there / Heathrow / Love games
/ Dune tune / Starchild
CD _____ 821 935-2
Polydor / Jul '84 / PolyGram.

LEVEL BEST
Running in the family / Sun goes down (Living it up) / Something about you / Tracie /
Starchild / It's over / Hot water / Take care
of yourself / Heaven in my hands / Children
say / Love games / Chinese way / Leaving
me now / Lessons in love / Micro kid (Not
on LP) / Take a look (Not on LP) / To be
with you again (Not on LP) / Chant has begun (Not on LP)
CD _____ 841 399-2
Polydor / Nov '89 / PolyGram.

ON A LEVEL
Running in the family / Physical presence /
Take care of yourself / Love games / Two
hearts collide / Love meeting love / True be-
lievers / Children say / Two solitudes / Turn
it on / Chinese way / Almost there / Wings
of love / Coup d'etat
CD _____ 5500102
Spectrum/Karussell / May '93 / PolyGram /
THE.

PHYSICAL PRESENCE, A
Almost there / Turn it on / Mr. Pink / Eyes
waterfalling / Kansas city milkman / Follow
me / Foundation and empire / Chant has
begun / Chinese way / Sun goes down (liv-

---

ing it up) / Hot water / Love games / 88
(Available on LP and cassette only)
CD _____ 825 677-2
Polydor / Jun '85 / PolyGram.

PURSUIT OF ACCIDENTS, THE
Weave your spell / Pursuit of accidents /
Last chance / Are you hearing (what I hear)
/ You can't blame Louis / Eyes waterfalling
/ Shapeshifter / Chinese way / Chinese way
(extended) (CD only) / You can't blame
Louis (extended) (CD only)
CD _____ 810 015-2
Polydor / Jun '90 / PolyGram.

RUNNING IN THE FAMILY
Lessons in love / Children say / Running in
the family / It's over / To be with you again
/ Two solitudes / Fashion fever / Sleepwalk-
ers / Freedom someday
CD _____ 831 593-2
Polydor / Mar '87 / PolyGram.

STANDING AT THE LIGHT
Micro-kid / Sun goes down (living it up) /
Out of sight out of mind / Dance on heavy
weather / Pharaoh's dream of endless time
/ Standing in the light / I want eyes / People
/ Machine stops
CD _____ 813 865-2
Polydor / Jun '90 / PolyGram.

STARING AT THE SUN
Heaven in my hands / I don't know why /
Take a look / Over there / Silence / Tracie /
Staring at the sun / Two hearts collide / Man
/ Gresham blues
CD _____ 837 247-2
Polydor / Sep '88 / PolyGram.

TRUE COLOURS
Chant has begun / Kansas City milkman /
Seven days / Hot water / Floating life / True
believers / Kouyate / Hours by the window
CD _____ 823 545-2
Polydor / '88 / PolyGram.

WORLD MACHINE
World machine / Physical presence / Something about you / Leaving me now / I sleep
on my heart / It's not the same for us /
Good man in a storm / Coup d'etat / Lying
still / Dream crazy / Love games (Extra track
on limited cassette) / Hot water (12" mix/
Ltd MC only) / Sun goes down (living it up)
(Mix) (Ltd ed MC only) / Chinese way (US
mix) (Ltd ed MC only) / I sleep on my heart
(remix) (Ltd ed MC only) / Something about
you (2)
CD _____ 827 487-2
Polydor / Oct '85 / PolyGram.

Levellers

LEVELLERS
CD _____ WOLCD 1034
China / Aug '93 / Pinnacle.

LEVELLING THE LAND
One way / Game / Boatman / Liberty song
/ Far from home / Sell out / Another man's
cause / Road / Riverflow / Battle of the
beanfield
CD _____ WOLCD 1022
China / Sep '91 / Pinnacle.

WEAPON CALLED THE WORD, A
CD _____ 105572
Musidisc / May '90 / Vital / Harmonia
Mundi / ADA / Cadillac / Discovery.

ZEITGEIST
CD _____ WOLCD 1064
China / Sep '95 / Pinnacle.

Levellers 5

SPRINGTIME
CD _____ PROBE 26 CD
Probe Plus / Jul '90 / Vital.

Leven, Jackie

**FORBIDDEN SONGS OF THE DYING
WEST**
Young male suicide blessed by invisible
woman / Some ancient misty morning /
Working alone/A blessing / Leven's lament
/ Marble city bar / Wanderer / Exultation /
Men in prison / Birds leave shadows / Stor-
noway girl / Silver roof / Lammermuir hills /
Come back early or never of come / By the
sign of the shettered star / Scene that
haunts my memory / My lord what a
morning
CD _____ COOKCD 090
Cooking Vinyl / Sep '95 / Vital.

**MYSTERY OF LOVE IS GREATER THAN
THE MYSTERY OF DEATH**
Clay jug / Shadow in my eyes / Old Chance
a lonely field / Crazy song / Farm boy / Gar-
den / Snow in Central Park / Looking for
love / Heartsick land / Gylen Gylen / I say
a little prayer / Bars of Dundee / Donna
Karan (LP only) / Ballad of a simple heart
(LP only) / Stranger on the square (LP only)
/ Horseshoe and jug (LP only) / Mary Jones'
dog (LP only) / So my soul can sing (LP
only)
CD _____ COOKCD 064
Cooking Vinyl / Jul '94 / Vital.

Levene, Keith

VIOLENT OPPOSITION
CD _____ RCD 10049
Rykodisc / Mar '92 / Vital / ADA.

Levert

BIG THROWDOWN, THE
Casanova / Good stuff / Don't u think it's
time / My forever love / Love the way U love
/ Sweet sensation / In 'n' out / Temp-
tation / Throwdown
CD _____ 781 773-2
Atlantic / Sep '87 / Warner Music.

FOR REAL THO'
Me 'n' you / Clap your hands / Tribute song
/ Good ol' days / She's all that (I've been
looking for) / For real tho' / Quiet storm / Do
the thangs / My place (your place) / Say you
will / ABC 123
CD _____ 756782462-2
East West / Mar '93 / Warner Music.

ROPE A DOPE STYLE
Now you know / Rope a dope style /
Absolutely positive / All season / Rain / No-
body does it better / I've been waiting /
Baby I'm ready / Hey girl / Give a little love
CD _____ 7567821642
East West / Nov '90 / Warner Music.

Levert, Gerald

GROOVE ON
Groove on / Rock me (all night long) / Let
the juices flow / I'd give anything / Answering service / Someone / How many times /
Can't help myself / Have mercy / Same
place, same time / Nice and wet / Love
street
CD _____ 756792416-2
Warner Bros. / Sep '94 / Warner Music.

Leverton, Jim

**FOLLOW YOUR HEART (Leverton, Jim
& Geoffrey Richardson)**
CD _____ MSECD 008
Mouse / May '95 / Grapevine.

Leviathan

DEEPEST SECRETS BENEATH
CD _____ RTN 41201
Rock The Nation / Nov '94 / Plastic Head.

Leviev, Milcho

**BLUES FOR THE FISHERMAN (Leviev,
Milcho Quartet & Art Pepper)**
CD _____ MOLECD 1
Mole Jazz / May '87 / Jazz Horizons /
Jazz Music / Cadillac / Wellard / Impetus.

**ORACLE, THE (Live at Suntory Hall)
(Leviev, Milcho & Dave Holland)**
Oracle / Everybody's song but my own /
Thracian flamenco / New one / Andante
tranquillo / You, I love / Samba Deborah /
First snow / Shoobee doobee / Warm valley
CD _____ PMC 1112
Pan Music / May '94 / Harmonia Mundi.

Levin, Pete

MASTERS IN THIS HALL
CD _____ GV 794262
Gramavision / Dec '90 / Vital/SAM / ADA.

PARTY IN THE BASEMENT
Bells / For a place to sleep / Party in the
basement / Gone / Ragtime: Saturday night
at the Last Chance / Subway / Something I
said / Hunter / Complaint department / One
day in the schoolyard
CD _____ GV 794562
Gramavision / Apr '90 / Vital/SAM / ADA.

SOLITARY MAN
Abraham / Solitary man / Gil sings with the
angels / Either or end up down / Sad truth
/ Street band / Best pasta in jamaica /
Through rose glasses / Colossus
CD _____ GCD 79457
Gramavision / Sep '95 / Vital/SAM / ADA.

Levin, Tony

WORLD DIARY
CD _____ DGM 9601
Discipline / Jan '96 / Pinnacle.

Levine, Duke

COUNTRY SOUL GUITAR
CD _____ DARING 3011CD
Daring / Nov '94 / Direct / CM / ADA.

NOBODY'S HOME
CD _____ DRCD 3005
Daring / Jan '93 / Direct / CM / ADA.

Levine, Mike

SMILEY AND ME
Our delight / When your heart's on fire
smoke gets in your eyes / Stablemates /
Daydream / Stompin' at the Savoy / My little
brown book / Social call / Now
CD _____ CCD 4352
Concord Jazz / Feb '95 / New Note.

Levitation

COTTERIE
CD _____ TOPPCD 001
Ultimate / Jul '94 / 3MV / Vital.

NEED FOR NOT
CD _____ R 3862
Rough Trade / May '92 / Pinnacle.

Levy, Barrington

20 VINTAGE HITS
CD _____ SONCD 0025
Sonic Sounds / Apr '92 / Jetstar.

COLLECTION: BARRINGTON LEVY
CD _____ CORCD 06
Time / Jul '91 / Jetstar / Pinnacle.

D.J. COUNTERACTION
CD _____ GRECD 216
Greensleeves / Jun '95 / Total/BMG /
Jetstar / SRD.

DIVINE
CD _____ CIDM 1077
Mango / Apr '91 / Vital / PolyGram.
CD _____ RASCD 3124
Ras / '95 / Jetstar / Greensleeves / SRD /
Direct.

LOVE THE LIFE YOU LIVE
Love the life you live / Girl, I like your style
/ Too experienced / Why you do it / Long
time friction / I've caught you / My woman
/ Come on little girl, come on / Two sounds
/ She's mine
CD _____ TORCD 100
Time / '89 / Jetstar / Pinnacle.

REGGAE VIBES
CD _____ RGCD 022
Rocky One / Nov '94 / Jetstar.

Levy, Lou

LUNARCY
CD _____ 5124362
Verve / May '92 / PolyGram.

YA KNOW
CD _____ 519700-2
Verve / Jun '94 / PolyGram.

Levy, Ron

**B-3 BLUES & GROOVES (Levy, Ron Wild
Kingdom)**
CD _____ BB 9532CD
Bullseye / May '93 / Bullseye / ADA.

**RON LEVY'S WILD KINGDOM (Levy,
Ron Wild Kingdom)**
I know you know I know / Chicken fried
snake / So many roads / Why you stay out
so late / Party in Nogales / Big town playboy
/ My heart's in trouble / It's hot in here /
Knee squeeze / Must have missed a turn
somewhere
CD _____ CD 1034
Black Top / '88 / CM / Direct / ADA.

**SAFARI TO NEW ORLEANS (Levy, Ron
Wild Kingdom)**
CD _____ CD 1040
Black Top / '88 / CM / Direct / ADA.

**WILD KINGDOM/GLAZED (Levy, Ron &
Earl King)**
CD _____ FIENDCD 712
Demon / Feb '92 / Pinnacle / ADA.

Lew, Benjamin

**NEBKA (Lew, Benjamin & Steven
Brown)**
CD _____ MTM 17CD
Made To Measure / Sep '88 / Grapevine.

Lewie, Jona

HEART SKIPS BEAT
I think I'll get my hair cut / Cream Jacque-
line strawberry / Stop the cavalry / Abra-
cadabra / Louise / Seed that always dies /
Heart skips beat / What have I done / You
go / Guessing games / Rearranging the
deckchairs on the Titanic
CD _____ STIFFCD 09
Disky / Jan '94 / THE / BMG / Discovery /
Pinnacle.

ON THE OTHER HAND THERE'S A FIST
Kitchen at parties / Baby she's on the street
/ Big shot - momentarily / Bit higher / Feel-
ing stupid / Vous et moi / God bless who-
ever made you / Hallelujah Europa / On the
road / I'll get by in Pittsburgh
CD _____ REP 4222-WY
Repertoire / Aug '91 / Pinnacle / Cadillac.

Lewin, Hakan

**HAKAN LEWIN & ALDO MERISTO
(Lewin, Hakan & Aldo Meristo)**
CD _____ SITCD 9211
Sittel / Jun '94 / Cadillac / Jazz Music.

Lewis, Barbara

**HELLO STRANGER (The Best Of
Barbara Lewis)**
My heart went do dat da / My Mama told
me / Puppy love / Hello stranger / Think a
little sugar / Straighten up your heart / Snap
your fingers / How can I say goodbye /
Spend a little time / Someday we're gonna
love again / Pushin' a good thing too far /
Baby, I'm yours / Make me your baby /
Don't forget about me / Make me belong to
you / Baby, what you want me to do / I
remember the feeling / I'll make him love me
/ Thankful for what I got / Sho' nuff (it's got
to be your love)
CD _____ 8122716192
Atlantic / Feb '92 / Warner Music.

**MANY GROOVES OF BARBARA LEWIS,
THE**
Baby that's a no no / Windmills of your
mind / Slip away / How can I tell / I can't
break away (from your love) / Oh be my love
/ Just the way you are today / Anyway / But
you know I love you / You made me a
woman / Stars / Do I deserve it baby / Ask
the lonely (Not on LP) / Why did it take you
so long (Not on LP) / That's the way I like it
(Not on LP)
CD _____ CDSXE 077
Stax / Jul '93 / Pinnacle.

Lewis, C.J.

DOLLARS
Everything is alright (Uptight) / Chill 'n' cool
/ Dollars / Best of my love / Cloud 9 /
Sweets for my sweet / Use me / Bad bwoy
/ Maximum respect / Two timer / Human
nature / Cloud 9 (Ambient mix)
CD _____ MCD 11131
MCA / Aug '94 / BMG.

Lewis, David

NO STRAIGHT LINE
CD _____ DJD 3215
Dejadisc / Aug '95 / Direct / ADA.

Lewis, Furry

IN HIS PRIME (1927-29)
CD _____ YAZCD 12050
Yazoo / Jun '91 / CM / ADA / Roots /
Koch.

SHAKE 'EM ON DOWN
John Henry / When my baby left me / Shake
'em on down / Big chief blues / Old blue /
I'm going to Brownsville / Back on my feet
again / White lightning / Roberta / St. Louis
blues / Baby you don't want me / Done
changed my mind / Goin' to Kansas city /
Judge boushay blues / Casey Jones / This
time tomorrow / I will turn your money green
/ Frankie and Johnny / Longing blues / Long
tall gal blues
CD _____ CDCH 486
Ace / Nov '93 / Pinnacle / Cadillac / Com-
plete/Pinnacle.

Lewis, George

AT HERBERT OTTO'S PARTY
CD _____ AMCD 74
American Music / Apr '94 / Jazz Music.

CLASSIC NEW ORLEANS JAZZ VOL. 1
CD _____ BCD 127
Biograph / Oct '93 / Wellard / ADA / Hot
Shot / Jazz Music / Cadillac / Direct.

**GEORGE LEWIS & BARRY MARTYN
BAND**
CD _____ BCD 37
GHB / Jan '94 / Jazz Music.

**GEORGE LEWIS & KID SHOTS (Lewis,
George & Kid Shots)**
CD _____ AMCD 2
American Music / Oct '92 / Jazz Music.

**GEORGE LEWIS & PAPA BUES VIKING
JAZZ BAND**
CD _____ STCD 6018
Storyville / Aug '94 / Jazz Music / Wellard
/ CM / Cadillac.

**GEORGE LEWIS BANDS/TRIOS/
QUINTETS**
CD _____ AMCD 83
American Music / Aug '95 / Jazz Music.

**GEORGE LEWIS WITH KEN COLYER'S
JAZZMEN 1957 VOL.1**
CD _____ 504CD 50
504 / Jun '95 / Wellard / Jazz Music /
Target/BMG / Cadillac.

**GEORGE LEWIS WITH KEN COLYER'S
JAZZMEN 1957 VOL.2**
CD _____ 504CD 51
504 / Jun '95 / Wellard / Jazz Music /
Target/BMG / Cadillac.

**GEORGE LEWIS WITH KEN COLYER'S
JAZZMEN 1966 (Lewis, George & Ken
Colyer's Jazzmen)**
My old Kentucky home / Just a closer walk
with thee / Melancholy blues / Ice cream /
Martha / Tishomingo blues / Old rugged
cross / St. Phillip's Street breakdown / Cor-
ine Corina / Climax rag / Home sweet home
CD _____ LACD 27
Lake / Feb '95 / Target/BMG / Jazz Music
/ Direct / Cadillac / ADA.

IN STOCKHOLM
CD _____ DRAGONCD 221
Dragon / Sep '89 / Roots / Cadillac /
Wellard / CM / ADA.

JAZZ AT VESPERS

CD _____ OJCCD 1721
Original Jazz Classics / Jun '94 / Wellard /
Jazz Music / Cadillac / Complete/Pinnacle.

**JAZZ BAND BALL (Lewis, George & His
New Orleans Band)**
Yaaka hula hickey dula / Burgundy St.
Blues / Willie the weeper / Mama don't al-
low / Shake that thing / Brother Lowdown /
Kansas city blues / Yellow dog blues / St.
Louis blues / Blues for Jimmy Noone / Ory's
boogie / Clarinet marmalade / Yelping
hound blues / Jazz man strut
CD _____ GTCD 12005
Good Time Jazz / Oct '93 / Jazz Music /
Wellard / Pinnacle / Cadillac.

**JAZZ IN THE CLASSIC NEW ORLEANS
TRADITION**
St. Phillip's street breakdown / Salty dog /
Old rugged cross / Red wing / Lou-easy-
an-i-a / Careless love / Weary blues / Bill
Bailey, won't you please come home / Tin
roof blues / Dippermouth blues / It's a long
way to Tipperary / Bugle call rag
CD _____ OJCCD 1736
Original Jazz Classics / Mar '94 / Wellard /
Jazz Music / Cadillac / Complete/Pinnacle.

**OXFORD SERIES VOL 1 (Lewis, George
& His Ragtime Band)**
CD _____ AMCD 21
American Music / Oct '92 / Jazz Music.

OXFORD SERIES VOL 2
CD _____ AMCD 22
American Music / Oct '92 / Jazz Music.

**OXFORD SERIES VOL 5 (Concert 1st
half)**
CD _____ AMCD 25
American Music / Apr '93 / Jazz Music.

**OXFORD SERIES VOL 6 (Concert 2nd
half)**
CD _____ AMCD 26
American Music / Apr '93 / Jazz Music.

OXFORD SERIES VOL 7
CD _____ AMCD 27
American Music / Jun '93 / Jazz Music.

OXFORD SERIES VOL 8
CD _____ AMCD 28
American Music / Jun '93 / Jazz Music.

OXFORD SERIES VOL 9
CD _____ AMCD 029
American Music / Oct '93 / Jazz Music.

OXFORD SERIES VOL. 10
CD _____ AMCD 30
American Music / Jan '94 / Jazz Music.

OXFORD SERIES VOL. 11
CD _____ AMCD 31
American Music / May '95 / Jazz Music.

OXFORD SERIES VOL. 12
CD _____ AMCD 32
American Music / May '95 / Jazz Music.

PORTRAIT OF GEORGE LEWIS, A
CD _____ LACD 50
Lake / Aug '95 / Target/BMG / Jazz Music
/ Direct / Cadillac / ADA.

**SPIRIT OF NEW ORLEANS (Lewis,
George & His Ragtime Band)**
CD _____ MECCACD 1014
Music Mecca / Jul '93 / Jazz Music /
Cadillac / Wellard.

TRIOS & BANDS
CD _____ AMCD 4
American Music / Jan '93 / Jazz Music.

Lewis, George

CHANGING WITH THE TIMES
CD _____ 804242
New World / Nov '93 / Harmonia Mundi /
ADA / Cadillac.

**HOMAGE TO CHARLES PARKER
(Lewis, George & Anthony Davis)**
CD _____ 120029-2
Black Saint / May '92 / Harmonia Mundi /
Cadillac.

MONADS/TRIPLE SLOW MIX
CD _____ 120016
Black Saint / Apr '94 / Harmonia Mundi /
Cadillac.

VOYAGER
CD _____ AVANT 014
Avant / Nov '93 / Harmonia Mundi /
Cadillac.

Lewis, Gov

DUB RISE (Lewis, Gov & Jimmy Ranks)
CD _____ SRDCD 003
Roots Collective / Sep '95 / SRD / Jetstar
/ Roots Collective.

Lewis, Hopeton

GROOVING OUT OF LIFE
CD _____ JMC 200109
Jamaica Gold / Sep '93 / THE / Magnum
Music Group / Jetstar.

Lewis, Huey & The News

FORE!
Jacob's ladder / Stuck with you / Whole
lotta lovin' / Hip to be square / I know what
I like / I never walk alone / Power of love /
Naturally / Simple as that / Doin' it all for my
baby
CD _____ CCD 1534
Chrysalis / Jul '94 / EMI.

**FOUR CHORDS & SEVERAL YEARS
AGO**
Shake, rattle and roll / Blue Monday /
Searching for my love / Some kind of wonderful / But it's alright / If you gotta make a
fool of somebody / Mother in law / Little
bitty pretty one / Good morning little school
girl / Stagger lee / She shot a hole in my
soul / Surely I love you / You left the water
running / Your cash ain't nothin' but trash /
Function at the junction / Better to have and
not need / Going down slow
CD _____ 755961500-2
Warner Bros. / May '94 / Warner Music.

HARD AT PLAY
Build me up / It hit me like a hammer / At-
titude / He don't know / Couple days off /
That's not me / We should be making love
/ Best of me / Do you love me, or what /
Don't look back / Time ain't money
CD _____ CCD 1847
Chrysalis / Feb '94 / EMI.

**HEART OF ROCK AND ROLL, THE (The
Best Of Huey Lewis And The News)**
Power of love / Hip to be square / Do you
believe in love / If this is it / Some of my lies
are true / Workin' for a livin' (live) / Bad is
bad / I want a new drug / Heart of rock and
roll / Heart and soul / Jacob's ladder / Stuck
with you / Trouble in paradise / Walking on
a thin line / Perfect world / Small world (part
one) / Back in time
CD _____ CDCHR 1934
Chrysalis / Oct '92 / EMI.

**HUEY LEWIS & THE NEWS/PICTURE
THIS/SPORTS (3 CDs)**
Some of my lies are true (sooner or later) /
Don't make me do it / Stop trying / Now
here's you / I want you / Don't ever tell me
that you love me / Hearts / Trouble in para-
dise / Who cares / If you really love me
you'll let me / Change of heart / Tell me a
little lie / Tattoo (giving it all up for love) /
Hope you love me like you say you do /
Workin' for a livin' / Do you believe in love
/ Is it me / Whatever happened to true love
/ Only one / Buzz buzz buzz / Heart of ro-
ck'n'roll / Heart and soul / Bad is bad / I
want a new drug / Walking on a thin line /
Finally found a home / If this is it / You crack
me up / Honky tonk blues
CD Set _____ CDMB 010
Chrysalis / Oct '95 / EMI.

SPORTS
Heart of rock and roll / Heart and soul / Bad
is bad / I want a new drug / Walking on a
thin line / Finally found a home / If this is it
/ You crack me up / Honky tonk blues
CD _____ CD25CR 20
Chrysalis / Mar '94 / EMI.

Lewis, Jerry Lee

BEST OF JERRY LEE LEWIS
CD _____ MCCD 081
Music Club / May '92 / Disc / THE / CM.

CHANTILLY LACE
Me and Bobby McGee / There must be
more to love than this / What made Milwaukee famous (has made a loser out of
me) / I'm so lonesome I could cry / Heartaches by the number / I'm left, you're right,
she's gone / Cold cold heart / Chantilly lace
/ Would you take another chance on me /
He'll have to go / I love you because / For
the good times / Oh lonesome me / I can't
stop loving you
CD _____ 5501802
Spectrum/Karussel / Mar '94 / PolyGram /
THE.

COLLECTION : JERRY LEE LEWIS
Be bop a lula / Dixie / Goodnight Irene /
Great balls of fire / High school confidential
/ Lewis boogie / Matchbox / Money / Sixty
minute man / Ubangi stomp / Whol lotta
shakin' goin' on / Wine drinkin' spo-dee-o-
dee / C.C. rider / Good golly Miss Molly /
Good rockin' tonight / Hang up my rock 'n'
roll shoes / Johnny B. Goode / Long gone
lonesome blues / Mean woman blues /
Pumpin' piano rock / Sweet little sixteen /
What'd I say / Will the circle be unbroken /
Let the good times roll
CD _____ CCSCD 143
Castle / Dec '90 / BMG.

**COMPLETE SUN RECORDINGS (8-CD
Box Set)**
Crazy arms / End of the road / You're the
only star in my blue heaven / Born to lose /
Silver threads among the gold / I'm throwing rice (at the girl I love) / I love you so
much it hurts / Deep Elem blues / Goodnight Irene / Goodnight Irene (undubbed
master) / Honey hush / Crawdad song /
Dixie / Marines' hymn / That lucky old sun
/ Hand me down my walking cane / You're
the only star in my blue heaven (Lewis boogie) / I love you because / I can't help it /
Cold cold heart / Shame on you / I'll keep

on loving you / You are my sunshine / Tomorrow night / Sixty minute man / It all depends (who will buy the wine) / I don't love nobody / Whole lotta shakin' goin' on / It'll be me (alt.) / It'll be me (alt.2) / Whole lotta shakin' goin' on (master) / False start and It'll be me / Ole pal of yesterday / You win again / Love letters in the sand / Little green valley (unissued) / Lewis boogie (master) / Pumpin' piano rock / It'll be me (LP & single masters) / All night long / Old time religion / When the saints go marching in (undubbed master) / My Carolina sunshine girl / Long gone lonesome blues / Drinkin' wine spo-dee-o-dee / Singin' the blues / Keep your hands off it / Matchbox (undubbed master) / Matchbox / Ubangi stomp / Rock 'n' roll Ruby / So long I'm gone / Ooby dooby / I forgot to remember to forget (unissued) / You win again (undubbed master) / I'm feeling sorry (4 takes) / Mean woman blues / Turn around / Great balls of fire (movie cut) / Chatter/Great balls of fire / Why should I cry over you / Religious discussion / Great balls of fire (master) / You win again (overdubbed master) / Down the line (unissued) / Down the line (false start) / I'm sorry I'm not sorry / Down the line (master) / Sexy ways (false start) / Cool cool ways / Milkshake madamoiselle / Breathless (unissued) / Milkshake madamoiselle (false starts) / Breathless (master) / High school confidential (false start) / High school confidential (unissued) / High school confidential / Put me down (unissued) / Good rockin' tonight / Pink pedal pushers / Jailhouse rock / Hound dog / Don't be cruel / Someday / Jambalaya / Friday nights / Big legged woman / Hello hello baby / Frankie and Johnny / Your cheatin' heart / Lovesick blues / Goodnight Irene (overdubbed master) / When the saints go marching in (overdubbed master) / Matchbox (overdubbed master) / Put me down / Fools like me (undubbed master) / Carrying on (sexy ways) / Crazy heart (false start) / High school confidential (master) / Slippin' around / I'll see you in my dreams / Real wild child / Let the good times roll / Fools like me (overdubbed master) / Settin' the woods on fire (unissued) / Memory of you / Come what may / Break up / Crazy heart / Live and let live / I'll make it all up to you (false start) / Johnny B. Goode / Settin' the woods on fire (false start) / Return of Jerry Lee / Break up (unissued) / I'll make it all up to us (unissued) / Break up (master) / I'll make it all up to you / I'll sail my ship alone / It hurt me so (chatter) / You're the only star in my blue heaven (unissued) / It hurt me so / Lovin' up a storm (unissued) / Big blon' baby / Lovin' up a storm / Sick and tired / Shanty town / Frankie and Johnny / C.C. rider / When my blue moon turns to gold again (unissued) / *gold again (unissued)* / *(stereo)* / When my blue moon turns to gold again (stereo) / When I get paid / Love made a fool of me (stereo) / No more than I get (stereo) / Livin' lovin' wreck / Cold cold heart (stereo) / I forgot to remember to forget / It won't happen with me / I love you because (stereo) / Save the last dance for me / Hello Josephine (My girl Josephine) / High powered woman / My blue heaven 1 (stereo) / My blue heaven 2 (stereo) / Sweet little sixteen / Ramblin' rose (master extended) / Money (stereo) / Rockin' the boat of love / Ramblin' rose / I've been twistin' / Whole lotta twistin' goin' on / I've been twistin' (stereo) / I know what it means / Sweet little sixteen #2 / My girl Josephine (stereo) / Set my mind at ease / Waiting for a train 1 (stereo) / Waiting for a train 2 (stereo) / How's my ex treating you (stereo and unissued) / Good rockin' tonight (stereo) / Be bop a lula (stereo) / My girl Josephine (stereo and unissued) / How's my ex treating you / Good golly Miss Molly (unissued) / I can't trust me (in your arms anymore) / My pretty quadroon (stereo) / Waiting for a train (unissued) / Teenage letter (stereo) / Seasons of my heart / Your lovin' ways / Just who is to blame / Just who is to blame (unissued) / Hong Kong blues / Love on Broadway / One minute past eternity (stereo) / Invitation to your party (false start and unissued) / Invitation to your party (stereo) / I can't seem to say goodbye / Carry me back to old Virginia (unissued) / Carry me back to old Virginia (stereo)

CD Set _____ **BCD 15420**
Bear Family / Aug '89 / Rollercoaster / Direct / CM / Swift / ADA.

COMPLETE SUN YEARS, THE (12CD Set)
CD Set _____ **CDSUNBOX 4**
Sun / Feb '93 / Charly.

COUNTRY CLASSICS
You win again / What made Milwaukee famous (has made a loser out of me) / I can't stop loving you / Your cheatin' heart / Middle aged crazy / Mexicali rose / Bootles and barstools / Cold cold heart / Another place another time / I'll find it where I can / Careless hands / There must be more to love than this / Touching home / You are my sunshine / Thirty nine and holding / Hey good lookin' / She even woke me up to say goodbye / Will the circle be unbroken
CD _____ **MUCD 9018**
Start / Apr '95 / Koch.

COUNTRY SOUND OF, THE
CD _____ **PWK 015**
Carlton Home Entertainment / '88 / Carlton Home Entertainment.

E.P. COLLECTION PLUS, THE
Ballad of Billie Joe / Let's talk about us / Little Queenie / I could never be ashamed of you / It won't happen with me / Cold cold heart / Baby, baby, bye bye / Old black Joe / It hurt me so / I'll sail my ship alone / Ramblin' Rose / As long as I live / When I get paid / Mean woman blues / Down the line / Breathless / I'm feeling sorry / Matchbox / Ubangi stomp / Break up / I'll make it all up to you / Big blon' baby / High school confidential / Whole lotta shakin' goin' on / Hound dog / Good rockin' tonight / Drinkin' wine spo-dee-o-dee / Great balls of fire
CD _____ **SEECD 397**
See For Miles/C5 / Mar '94 / Pinnacle.

EP COLLECTION: JERRY LEE LEWIS
CD _____ **SEECD 307**
See For Miles/C5 / Dec '90 / Pinnacle.

ESSENTIAL COLLECTION
CD Set _____ **LECD 610**
Wisepack / Apr '95 / THE / Conifer.

FERRIDAY FIREBALL
Lewis boogie / It'll be me / High school confidential / Whole lotta shakin' goin' on / Good rockin' tonight / Big legged woman / Great balls of fire / Drinkin' wine spo-dee-o-dee / Matchbox / You win again / Will the circle be unbroken / Crazy arms / Break up / Memory of you / Johnny B. Goode / Little Queenie / Milkshake mademoiselle / Big blon' baby / Breathless / Mean woman blues / Down the line / When the saints go marching in / End of the road / What'd I say
CD _____ **CDCHARLY 1**
Charly / Mar '86 / Charly / THE / Cadillac.

GOOD ROCKIN' TONITE
Whole lotta shakin' goin' on / Don't be cruel / Down the line / Let the good times roll / Jambalaya / High school confidential / Jailhouse rock / Hound dog / What'd I say / Lovin' up a storm / Wild one / Good rockin' tonight / It'll be me / End of the road / Sixty minute man / Lewis boogie
CD _____ **CDCD 1016**
Charly / Mar '93 / Charly / THE / Cadillac.

GREAT BALLS OF FIRE
Great balls of fire / Breathless / Sweet little sixteen / Big blon' baby / It'll be me / Crazy arms / Your cheatin' heart / Good golly Miss Molly / What'd I say / Whole lotta shakin' goin' on / High school confidential / Little Queenie / You win again / That lucky old sun / Frankie and Johnny / Big legged woman / Let the good times roll / Release me / Lovin' up a storm / Wild one
CD _____ **PWKS 501**
Carlton Home Entertainment / Dec '89 / Carlton Home Entertainment.

GREAT BALLS OF FIRE
CD _____ **CD 12332**
Laserlight / Apr '94 / Target/BMG.

GREAT BALLS OF FIRE
Whole lotta shakin' goin' on / It'll be me / Lewis boogie / Drinkin' wine spo-dee-o-dee / Rock 'n' roll Ruby / Matchbox / Ubangi stomp / Great balls of fire / You win again / Mean woman blues / Milkshake mademoiselle / Breathless / Down the line / Good rockin' tonight / Pink pedal pushers / Don't be cruel / Johnny B. Goode / Break up / Big blon' baby / Lovin' up a storm / Little queenie / In the mood / What'd I say / Sweet little sixteen / Good golly Miss Molly / Be bop a lula / Teenage letter / Carry me back to old Virginia
CD _____ **CD CHARLY 185**
Charly / Jul '89 / Charly / THE / Cadillac.

GREATEST HITS, VOL 2: JERRY LEE LEWIS
CD _____ **PWK 025**
Carlton Home Entertainment / '91 / Carlton Home Entertainment.

GREATEST LIVE SHOWS ON EARTH, THE
Jenny Jenny / Who will the next fool be / Memphis, Tennessee / Hound dog / Mean woman blues / Hi-heel sneakers / No particular place to go / Together again / Long tall Sally / Whole lotta shakin' goin' on / Little queenie / How's my ex treating you / Johnny B. Goode / Green green grass of

home / What'd I say (part 2) / You win again / I'll sail my ship alone / Crying time / Money / Roll over Beethoven
CD _____ **CD 15608**
Bear Family / Nov '91 / Rollercoaster / Direct / CM / Swift / ADA.

HEARTBREAK
What made Milwaukee famous (has made a loser out of me) / Careless hands / Who will the next fool be / Touching home / More to love than this / Cold cold heart / You win again / Your cheatin' heart / I can't stop lovin' you / Another place another time / Thirty nine and holding / She even woke me up / I wish I was eighteen again / Who is going to play this ole piano
CD _____ **598 0067 29**
Tomato / Aug '93 / Vital.

HONKY TONK ROCK'N'ROLL PIANO MAN
My fingers do the talkin' / Why you been gone so long / Daughters of Dixie / Teenage Queen / I'm looking over a four leaf clover / I am what I am / Better not look down / Only you / Honky tonk rock 'n' roll piano man / Circumstantial evidence / I'm lookin' under a skirt / Rock 'n' roll money / Forever forgiving (alternative take no.1) / Why you been gone so long (alt. take no.3) / Get out your big roll daddy
CD _____ **CDCH 332**
Ace / Oct '91 / Pinnacle / Cadillac / Complete/Pinnacle.

I AM WHAT I AM
Whole lotta shakin' goin' on / Great balls of fire / Big legged woman / Breathless / High school confidential / I'm throwing rice (at the girl I love) / Crazy arms / That lucky ole sun / What'd I say / Sweet little sixteen / Good rockin' tonight / Big legged / Wild one / Jailhouse rock / Be bop a lula
CD _____ **CDINS 5008**
Instant / Aug '89 / Charly.

IN CONCERT
CD _____ **CDSGP 0163**
Prestige / Oct '95 / Total/BMG.

JERRY LEE LEWIS/ROY ORBISON ESSENTIALS (Lewis, Jerry Lee & Roy Orbison)
CD _____ **LECDD 631**
Wisepack / Aug '95 / THE / Conifer.

LEGENDS IN MUSIC - JERRY LEE LEWIS
CD _____ **LECD 079**
Wisepack / Jul '94 / THE / Conifer.

LIVE AT THE STAR CLUB, HAMBURG
Mean woman blues / High school confidential / Money / Matchbox / What'd I say / Great balls of fire / Good golly Miss Molly / Lewis boogie / Your cheatin' heart / Hound dog / Long tall Sally / Whole lotta shakin' goin' on / Down the line
CD _____ **BCD 15467**
Bear Family / Jul '89 / Rollercoaster / Direct / CM / Swift / ADA.

LIVE AT THE VAPORS CLUB
Don't put no headstone on my grave / Chantilly lace / I'll find it where I can / Drinkin' wine spo-dee-o-dee / Sweet little sixteen / Boogie woogie country man / Me and Bobby McGee / Rockin' my life away / Whole lotta shakin' goin' on / You can have her / Hey good lookin' / Will the circle be unbroken
CD _____ **CDCH 326**
Ace / May '91 / Pinnacle / Cadillac / Complete/Pinnacle.

LIVE IN ITALY
Rollin' in my sweet baby's arms / High school confidential / Me and Bobby McGee / Jackson / There must be more to love than this / Great balls of fire / What'd I say / Jerry Lee's rock and roll revival show / I am what I am / Whole lotta shakin' goin' on / You win again / Mona Lisa / One of those things we all go through / Hang up my rock 'n' roll shoes
CD _____ **CDMF 071**
Magnum Force / Jun '89 / Magnum Music Group.

LOCUST YEARS/RETURN TO THE PROMISED LAND (9 CDs)
Whole lotta shakin' goin' on / Crazy arms / Great balls of fire / High school confidential / I'll make it all up to you / Break up / Down the line / Hit the road Jack (version 1) / End of the road / Your cheatin' heart / Wedding bells / Just because / Breathless / He took it like a man / Drinkin' wine spo-dee-o-dee / Johnny B. Goode / Hallelujah, I love her so / You went back on your word / Pen and paper / Hole se said he'd dig for me / You win again / Fools like me / Hit the road Jack / I'm on fire / She was my baby (he was my friend) / Bread and butter man / I bet you're gonna like it / Got you on my mind / Mathilda / Corine Corina / Sexy ways / Wild side / Flip flop and fly / Don't let go / Raylettone / Roll over Beethoven / Just in time / I believe in you / Herman the hermit / Baby, hold me close / Skid row / This must be the place / Rockin' pneumonia and the boogie woogie flu / Seasons of my heart / Big boss man / Too young / Danny boy / City lights / Funny how time slips away / North to Alaska / Walk right in / Wolverton mountain / King of the road / Detroit city / Ring of fire

/ Baby, you got what it takes / Green green grass of home / Sticks and stones / What a heck of a mess / Lincoln limousine / Rockin' Jerry Lee / Memphis beat / Urge / Whenever you're ready / She thinks I still care / Twenty four hours a day / Swinging doors / If I had it all to do over / Just dropped in / It's a hang up / Holdin' on / Hey baby / Dream baby / Treat her right / Turn on your love light / Shotgun man / All the good is gone / Another place another time / Walking the floor over you / I'm a lonesome fugitive / Break my mind / Play me a song I can cry to / Before the next teardrop falls / All night long / We live in two different worlds / What made Milwaukee famous (has made a loser out of me) / On the back row / Slippin' around / Ahe still comes around / Today I started loving you again / Louisiana man / There stands the glass / I can't have a merry Christmas, Mary / Out of my mind / I can't get over you / Listen they're playing my song / Echoes / Release me / Let's talk about us / To make love sweeter for you / Don't let me cross over / Born to lose / You belong to me / Oh lonesome me / Sweet dreams / Cold cold heart / Fraulein / Why don't you love me like you used to do / Four walls / It makes no difference now / I love you because / I'm so lonesome I could cry / Jambalaya / More and more / One has my name (the other has my heart) / Burning memories / Mom and Dad's last waltz / Pick me up on your way down / I heartaches by the number / I can't stop loving you / My blue heaven / I wonder where you are tonight / Jackson / Sweet thang / He'll have to go / You've still got a place in my heart / I get the blues when it rains / Gotta travel on / Milwaukee here I come / Crying time / Secret places / Don't take it out on me / Earth up above / Waiting for a train / Love for all seasons / She even woke me up to say goodbye / When the grass grows over me / Wine me up / Since I met you baby / Workin' man blues / Once more with feeling / In loving memories / You went out of your way (to walk on me) / My only claim to fame / Brown eyed handsome man
CD Set _____ **BCD 15783**
Bear Family / Nov '94 / Rollercoaster / Direct / CM / Swift / ADA.

PEARLS FROM THE PAST VOL. 2 - JERRY LEE LEWIS
CD _____ **KLMCD 012**
Scratch / Apr '94 / BMG.

PRETTY MUCH COUNTRY
Honky tonk heaven / She never said goodbye / That was the way it was then / Candy kisses / I am what I am / Come as you were / She sang amazing grace / Have I got a song for you / Daughters of Dixie / Send me the pillow that you dream on / She sure makes leavin' look easy / My fingers do the talkin' / Honky tonk heart / Careless hands / Honky tonk rock 'n' roll piano man / Forever forgiving
CD _____ **CDCH 348**
Ace / Feb '92 / Pinnacle / Cadillac / Complete/Pinnacle.

RARE AND ROCKIN'
It won't happen with me / Teenage letter / Pink pedal pushers / Hillbilly music / Deep Elem blues / You win again / I'm feeling sorry / I'm the guilty one / It hurt me so / I love you because / Cold cold heart / Whole lotta shakin' goin' on / In the mood / Great balls of fire / I forgot to remember to forget / Turn around / It all depends (who will buy the wine) / It'll be me (fast & slow versions) / Sixty minute man / Lovin' up a storm / Rockin' with red / Honey hush / Hound dog / Hang up my rock 'n' roll shoes
CD _____ **CDCHARLY 70**
Charly / Apr '87 / Charly / THE / Cadillac.

ROCKET
Meat man / Jailhouse rock / House of blue lights / Rock 'n' roll funeral / Don't touch me / Changing mountains / Beautiful dreamer / I'm alone because I love you / Lucille / Seventeen / Mathilda / Wake up little Susie
CD _____ **CDINS 5023**
Instant / Feb '90 / Charly.

ROCKIN' ALL NIGHT LONG
CD _____ **QSCD 6001**
Quality (Charly) / Oct '91 / Charly.

ROCKIN' MY LIFE AWAY
CD _____ **269661-2**
Tomato / Apr '90 / Vital.

ROLL OVER BEETHOVEN
CD _____ **15100**
Laserlight / Aug '91 / Target/BMG.

SESSION, THE
Johnny B. Goode / Trouble in mind / Early morning rain / No headstone on my grave / Pledging my love / Memphis / Drinkin' wine spo-dee-o-dee / Music to the man / Bad moon rising / Sea cruise / Sixty minute man / Movin' on down the line / What'd I say
CD _____ **822 751-2**
Mercury / May '85 / PolyGram.

SPOTLIGHT ON JERRY LEE LEWIS
Hey baby / Roll over Beethoven / Boogie woogie country man/Rockin' / Sweet Georgia Brown / Just because / You win again / Sweet little sixteen / I'll find it where I can /

No headstone on my grave / Whole lotta shakin' goin' on / Hadacol boogie / Middle aged crazy / Who will the next fool be / Down the line
CD _____ HADCD 124
Javelin / Feb '94 / THE / Henry Hadaway Organisation.

SUN CLASSICS (4CD Box Set)
Whole lotta shakin' goin' on / Great balls of fire / High school confidential / Be bop a lula / Good golly Miss Molly / Down the line / Lovin' up a storm / Wild one / Ooby dooby / End of the road / Pumping piano rock / Put me down / Don't be cruel / I'm feeling sorry / Home / Wild side of life / When my blue moon turns to gold again / I love you because / Born to lose / Jambalaya / You win again / Crazy heart / Long gone lonesome blues / Cold cold heart / I can't help it (if I'm still in love with you) / Your cheatin' heart / Big blon' baby / Rock 'n' roll Ruby / Breathless / I'm sorry I'm not sorry / Ubangi stomp / It'll be me / Milkshake Madamoiselle / Baby, baby, bye bye / Break up / It won't happen with me / Bonnie B / Livin' lovin' wreck / Your lovin' ways / Crazy arms / I'll make it all up to you / Let's talk about us / It hurt me so / As long as I live / How's my ex treating you / I can't seem to say goodbye / I'll sail my ship alone / Someday (you'll want me to want you) / Set my mind at ease / Seasons of my heart / It all depends (on who'll buy the wine) / Slippin' around / Night train to Memphis / Big legged woman / Rockin' with Red / Sixty minute man / I've been twistin' / Teenage letter / Mean woman blues / Drinkin' wine spo-dee-o-dee / Keep your hands off it (Birthday cake) / Money / Hound dog / Cool cool ways / Hello hello baby / I know what it means / It'll be me (alt.) / Hillbilly music / Turn around / Fools like me / I forgot to remember to forget / I can't trust me (In your arms anymore) / I'm the guilty one / Hand me down my walking cane / Crawdad song / Don't drop it / Memory of you / Crazy arms (Remake) / What I'd say / Honey hush / Tomorrow night / Carrying on (sexy ways) / Good rockin' tonight / Come what may / Hello Josephine / Little Queenie / Johnny B. Goode / Hang up my rock 'n' roll shoes / Sweet little sixteen / Matchbox / C.C. rider / Lewis boogie / My pretty quadroon / That lucky old sun / Goodnight Irene / Will the circle be unbroken / Great speckled bird / John Henry / Frankie and Johnny / You're the only star in my blue heaven / Waiting for a train / Deep Elem blues / You are my sunshine / Carry me back to Old Virginia
CD Set _____ CDDIG 8
Charly / Feb '95 / Charly / THE / Cadillac.

THAT BREATHLESS CAT
Ragtime doodle / Meat man / Lovin' up a storm / Ubangi stomp / Rock 'n' roll ruby / Piano doodle / House of blue lights / My life would make a damn good country song / Beautiful dreamer / Autumn leaves / Pilot baby / Room full of roses / Keep a knockin' / Silver threads among the gold / Alabama jubilee / Lazy river / Mama this song's for you / Breathless / Whole lotta shakin' goin' on
CD _____ STCD 2
Stomper Time / Feb '93 / Magnum Music Group.

TWO ON ONE: JERRY LEE LEWIS & CARL PERKINS (Lewis, Jerry Lee & Carl Perkins)
CD _____ CDTT 5
Charly / Apr '94 / Charly / THE / Cadillac.

UP THROUGH THE YEARS 1956-63
End of the road / Crazy arms / It'll be me / Whole lotta shakin' goin' on / You win again / Mean woman blues / Great balls of fire / Down the line / Breathless / Put me down / Put me down / I'll make it up to you / I'll sail my ship alone / Lovin' up a storm / Big blon' baby / Night train to Memphis / Little Queenie / John Henry / Livin' lovin' wreck / What'd I say / Cold cold heart / Sweet little sixteen / Carry me back to old Virginia
CD _____ BCD 15408
Bear Family / Dec '87 / Rollercoaster / Direct / CM / Swift / ADA.

WHOLE LOTTA HITS
CD _____ CPCD 8121
Charly / Aug '95 / Charly / THE / Cadillac.

WHOLE LOTTA SHAKIN'
Whole lotta shakin' / Don't be cruel / Down the line / Let the good times roll / Jambalaya / High school confidential / Jailhouse rock / Lewis boogie / Hound dog / What's I say / Lovin' up / Storm / Wild one / Great balls of fire / Singing the blues / Little Queenie / Mean woman blues / Sixty minute man / Lovesick blues / Breathless / It'll be me
CD _____ QSCD 6010
Charly / Aug '93 / Charly / THE / Cadillac.

YOUNG BLOOD
CD _____ 7559617952
Warner Bros. / Jun '95 / Warner Music.

Lewis, John

AMERICAN JAZZ ORCHESTRA PLAYS ELLINGTON

CD _____ 7567914232
Atlantic / Apr '95 / Warner Music.

WONDERFUL WORLD OF JAZZ
CD _____ 7567909792
Atlantic / Apr '95 / Warner Music.

Lewis, Laurie

LOVE CHOOSES YOU
Old friend / Hills of home / Point of no return / I don't know why / I'd be lost without you / When the nightbird sings / Women of Ireland / Ryestraw / Light / Texas bluebonnets / Love chooses you
CD _____ FF 70487
Flying Fish / Oct '89 / Roots / CM / Direct / ADA.

OAK AND THE LAUREL, THE (Lewis, Laurie & Tom Rozum)
CD _____ ROUCD 0340
Rounder / Jul '95 / CM / Direct / ADA / Cadillac.

SINGIN' MY TROUBLES AWAY (Lewis, Laurie & Grant Street)
CD _____ FF 515CD
Flying Fish / '92 / Roots / CM / Direct / ADA.

TOGETHER (Lewis, Laurie & Kathy Kallick)
Going up the mountain / Just like the rain / Is the blue moon still shining / Don't you see the train / Hideaway / Touch of the master's hand / Lost John / Maverick / That dawn the day you left me / Count your blessings / Little Annie / Don't leave your little girl all alone / Gonna lay down my old guitar
CD _____ ROUCD 0318
Rounder / Feb '95 / CM / Direct / ADA / Cadillac.

TRUE STORIES
CD _____ ROU 0309
Rounder / Sep '93 / CM / Direct / ADA / Cadillac.

Lewis, Lew

SAVE THE WAIL (Lewis, Lew Reformer)
CD _____ REP 4216-WY
Repertoire / Aug '91 / Pinnacle / Cadillac.

Lewis, Linda

SECOND NATURE
CD _____ TPN 3CD
Turpin / Nov '95 / Pinnacle.

Lewis, Margaret

LONESOME BLUEBIRD
Shake a leg / One day, another tomorrow / Goin' to St Louie / From the cradle to the blues / Roll over Beethoven / Love is a fortune / Birmingham valley blues / You can't break my heart no more / No no never / Cheater's can't win / That's why I cry / Raggedy Ann and the player piano / There was no / Bow wow puppy love / Dust my blues / Those lonely lonely nights / Reconsider me / You ought to see my baby / It's alright (you can go) / John De Lee (I love you) / Full grown man / Emmitt Lee / Lover's land / Baby please forgive me / Every time you turn me down / My blue eyed boy / Look what you're doing to me
CD _____ CDCHARLY 268
Charly / Jun '91 / Charly / THE / Cadillac.

Lewis, Meade Lux

1936-41 (Lewis, Meade Lux/Albert Ammons & Pete Johnson)
CD _____ BDCD 6046
Blues Document / Jun '95 / Swift / Jazz Music / Hot Shot.

1939-54
CD _____ SOB 35062CD
Story Of The Blues / Apr '95 / Koch / ADA.

BARRELHOUSE PIANO
Six wheel chaser / How long blues / Someday sweetheart / Bugle call rag / I ain't gonna give nobody none o' this jelly roll / Mike / Darktown strutter's ball / Birth of the blues / Tidal boogie / Mardi Gras drag / Tishomingo blues / Jada / Basin Street blues / Fast 'A' blues / 12th Street blues / St. Louis blues
CD _____ JASMCD 2536
Jasmine / Mar '95 / Wellard / Swift / Conifer / Cadillac / Magnum Music Group.

CLASSICS 1927-39
CD _____ OJCCD 722
Original Jazz Classics / Dec '93 / Wellard / Jazz Music / Cadillac / Complete/Pinnacle.

CLASSICS 1941-44
CD _____ CLASSICS 841
Classics / Nov '95 / Discovery / Jazz Music.

MEADE LUX LEWIS 1927-1939
CD _____ CLASSICS 722
Classics / Dec '93 / Discovery / Jazz Music.

MEADE LUX LEWIS 1939-41
CD _____ CLASSICS 743
Classics / Feb '94 / Discovery / Jazz Music.

Lewis, Mel

DEFINITIVE THAD JONES VOL. 1 (Live From Village Vanguard) (Lewis, Mel Jazz Orchestra)
Low down / Quietude / Three in one / Walkin' about / Little pixie
CD _____ MM 5024
Music Masters / Oct '94 / Nimbus.

DEFINITIVE THAD JONES VOL. 2 (Live At The Village Vanguard) (Lewis, Mel Jazz Orchestra)
CD _____ MM 5046
Music Masters / Oct '94 / Nimbus.

MELLIFLUOUS
Blue note / Giving away / Audrey / I'm old fashioned / Warm valley / John's abbey / Blue note (alt. take)
CD _____ LCD 15432
Landmark / Mar '95 / New Note.

SOFT LIGHTS AND HOT MUSIC (Lewis, Mel & The Jazz Orchestra)
Soft lights and sweet music / Compensation / Lester left town / It could happen to you / Off the cuff / Love is here to stay / Little man you've had a busy day / How long has this been going on / Touch of your lips
CD _____ MM 5012
Music Masters / Dec '94 / Nimbus.

SOFT LIGHTS AND SWEET MUSIC (Lewis, Mel & The Jazz Orchestra)
CD _____ 50122C
Music Masters / Dec '94 / Nimbus.

TO YOU
Paper spoons / Five and a half weeks / Nightingale sang in Berkeley Square / Nocturne / ABC blues / Bob Brookmeyer / To you
CD _____ 820 832-2
Deram / Aug '90 / PolyGram.

Lewis, Pete

SCRATCHIN' (Lewis, Pete/Jimmy Nolen/ Cal Green)
Strollin' with Nolen / Louisiana hop / How fine can you be / Scratchin' / You've been goofing / Crying with the rising sun / Way you do / Big push / Raggedy blues / I can't stand you no more / After hours / Harmonica boogie / Don't leave me no more / Chocolate pork chop man / Wipe your tears / Green's blues / It hurts me too / Blast / Strawberry jam / Ooh midnight / Movin' on down the line
CD _____ CDCHARLY 268
Charly / Jun '91 / Charly / THE / Cadillac.

Lewis, Peter

PETER LEWIS
CD _____ TX 2008CD
Taxim / Jul '95 / ADA.

Lewis, Ramsey

16 GREATEST HITS
16 / May '94 / BMG.

COLLECTION: RAMSEY LEWIS
Wade in the water / Something you got / Hard day's night / Hang on Sloopy / Ain't that peculiar / Blues for the night owl / Hi-heel sneakers / Function at the junction / Uptight (everything's alright) / Lonely avenue / Day tripper / 1-2-3 / Felicidade / Les fleurs / Caves / Since I fell for you / All my love belongs to you / He's a real gone guy / Soul man / In crowd
CD _____ MOCD 3012
More Music / Feb '95 / Sound & Media.

IN CONCERT - 1965 (Lewis, Ramsey Trio)
Satin doll / And I love her / Come Sunday / Hard day's night / In crowd
CD _____ CD 53108
Giants Of Jazz / May '92 / Target/BMG / Cadillac.

IN CROWD, THE - GREATEST HITS
Hang on sloopy / In crowd / Dancing in the street / Hi-heel sneakers / Something you got / Soul man / 1-2-3 / Since I fell for you / Wade in the water / Hard day's night / Uptight / You been talking 'bout me baby / Since you've been gone / Les fleurs / Tennessee waltz / Felicidade / Spartacus love theme / Come Sunday
CD _____ CDCD 1103
Charly / Jul '93 / Charly / THE / Cadillac.

INSTRUMENTAL SOUL HITS (Lewis, Ramsey & King Curtis)
CD _____ RMB 75047
Remember / Nov '93 / Total/BMG.

IVORY PYRAMID
Bazilica / People make the world go round / Ivory pyramid / Sarah Jane / Tequila mockingbird / Night in Bahia / Malachi / Pavanne / Love's gotta hold / Jackson park
CD _____ GRP 96882
GRP / Nov '92 / BMG / New Note.

LIVE (Lewis, Ramsey Trio)
CD _____ JHR 73524
Jazz Hour / May '93 / Target/BMG / Jazz Music / Cadillac.

SKY ISLANDS
Julia / Aprez vous / Who are you / Suavecito / Tonight / Sky islands / Song for you / Medley / Love will find a way / Come back to me / Tonight (instrumental version)
CD _____ GRP 97452
GRP / Oct '93 / BMG / New Note.

Lewis, Smiley

SHAME, SHAME, SHAME
Turn on your volume, baby / Here comes Smiley / Tee-nah-nah / Lowdown / Slide me down / Growing old / If you ever loved a woman / Dirty people / Where were you / My baby / Sad life / Bee's boogie / Don't jive me / My baby was right / Bells are ringing / Lillie Mae / You're gonna miss me / Gypsy blues / You're not the one / Gumbo blues / Ain't gonna do it / It's so peaceful / Calsonia's party / Lonesome highway / Standing on the corner / Oh baby / Big mamou / Play girl (I love you) for sentimental reasons / Lying woman / Little Fernandez / It's music / Show me the way / Down the road / One night / Blue Monday / Rocks / Nothing but the blues / That certain door / Nobody knows / She's got me hook, line and sinker / Can't stop loving you / Baby please / Ooh la la / By the water / Too many drivers / Rootin' and tootin' / Lost weekend / Jailbird / Please listen to me / Farewell / No, no / Real gone lover / Bumpity bump / Someday you'll want me / I can't believe it / I hear you knocking / Hey girl / Down yonder we go ballin' / Come on / Queen of hearts / No letter today / Li'l Liza Jane / I shall not be moved / Mama don't like / Ain't goin there no more / Shame, shame, shame / Oh Red / Last night / I want to be with her / Shame, shame, shame (2) / Tell me who / Stormy Monday blues / These bones / Goin' down the road / Sweeter words (have never been told) / Tore up / When did you leave Heaven / You are my sunshine / I'm coming down with the blues / I wake up screamin' / Tomorrow night / Go on fool / To the river / How long / Ronettes / Sometimes / Lookin' for my woman / Goin' to jump and shout / One night of sin / Sheikh of araby / Back luck blues / Bells are ringing (2) / Jump (instrumental) / School days are back again / My love is gone / Walkin' the girl (instrumental) / Oh Red (2) / Ain't goin there no more (2)
CD Set _____ BCD 15745
Bear Family / Nov '93 / Rollercoaster / Direct / CM / Swift / ADA.

SMILEY LEWIS VOL 1
Lillie Mae / Gypsy blues / My baby was right / Blue Monday / Playgirl / Oh baby / Gumbo blues / No no / Oh Red, don't jive me / Big mamou
CD _____ KCCD 01
KC / Apr '90 / CM / Wellard / Cadillac.

SMILEY LEWIS VOL 2
Down the road / Rocks
CD _____ KCCD 02
KC / Apr '90 / CM / Wellard / Cadillac.

Lewis, Ted

CLASSIC SIDES 1928-29
I'm the medicine man for the blues / Maybe - who knows / In the land of jazz / Lewisada blues / Farewell blues / Wabash blues / Limehouse blues / Glad rag doll / I ain't got nobody / Jungle blues / She's not funny that way
CD _____ JSPCD 326
JSP / Oct '91 / ADA / Target/BMG / Direct / Cadillac / Complete/Pinnacle.

Lewis, Vic

PLAY BILL HOLMAN (Lewis, Vic West Coast All Stars)
Oleo / Yesterdays / Sizzler before lunch / When I fall in love / Easter parade / As we speak / Sizzler after lunch
CD _____ CDMOLE 14
Mole Jazz / Jan '90 / Jazz Horizons / Jazz Music / Cadillac / Wellard / Impetus.

SHAKE DOWN THE STARS (The Music of Jimmy Van Heusen) (Lewis, Vic West Coast All Stars)
CD _____ CCD 79526
Candid / Mar '93 / Cadillac / Jazz Music / Wellard / Koch.

WEST COAST ALL STARS
CD _____ CCD 79535
Candid / Mar '94 / Cadillac / Jazz Music / Wellard / Koch.

Lewis, Willie

CLASSICS 1932-36
CD _____ CLASSICS 822
Classics / Jul '95 / Discovery / Jazz Music.

CLASSICS 1936-38
CD _____ CLASSICS 847
Classics / Nov '95 / Discovery / Jazz Music.

Lex Talionis

INTO THE SHADE
CD _____ EFA 084652
Dossier / Dec '94 / SRD.

Ley, Tabu

BABETI SOUKOUS
Presentation / Kinshasa / Soroza / Linga ngai / Moto akokufa / Nairobi / Seli ja / I need you / Amour nala / Tu as dit que / Sentimenta / Pitie / Mosola
CD _____ RWCD 5
Virgin / Jun '89 / EMI.

MUZINA
CD _____ ROUCD 5059
Rounder / Nov '94 / CM / Direct / ADA / Cadillac.

Leyland DAF Band

ROMANCE IN BRASS
Love changes everything / Spring / Summer night / Song of the seashore / All I ask of you / Elvira Madigan (Theme) / Drink to me only with thine eyes / Can't take my eyes off you / Romance from 'The Gadfly' / Anything but lonely / Romance from 'Fair Maid of Perth' / Someone to watch over me / Serenata / Flower duet / Forgotten dreams / Fanfare, romance and finale
CD _____ QPRL 043D
Polyphonic / Jun '90 / Conifer.

Leyli

SPIRITUAL BELLY DANCE
CD _____ EUCD 1251
ARC / Mar '94 / ARC Music / ADA.

Leyton, Johnny

BEST OF JOHN LEYTON
Johnny remember me / Wild wind / Six white horses / Son this is she / Lone rider / Lonely city / I think I'm falling in love / Lonely Johnny / Oh lover / I don't care if the sun don't shine / (I love you) for sentimental reasons / That's how to make love / I'll cut your tail off / Land of love / Cupboard love / How will it end / It would be easy / Beautiful dreamer / Another man / Make love to me / You took my love for granted (CD only) / I guess you are always on my mind (CD only) / Funny man (CD only) / Man is not supposed to cry (CD only) / Girl on the floor above (CD only) / Tell Laura I love her (CD only) / On Lovers Hill (CD only) / Too many late nights (CD only) / Lover's lane (CD only) / I'm gonna let my hair down (CD only) / Don't let her go away (CD only) / All I want is you (CD only) / I want a love I can see (CD only)
CD _____ SEECD 201
See For Miles/C5 / Sep '87 / Pinnacle.

EP COLLECTION: JOHNNY LEYTON
Son this is she / That's a woman / Fabulous / Voodoo woman / Wild wind / Six white horses / Thunder and lightning / Goodbye to teenage love / You took my love for granted / I don't care if the sun don't shine / Down the River Nile / Terry Brown's in love with Mary Dee / Walk with me my angel / There must be / Cupboard love / I'll cut your tail off / Beautiful dreamer / Another man / Oh lover / Lone rider / Lonely city / Lonely Johnny / On Lovers Hill / (I love you) For sentimental reasons / That's how to make love / Johnny remember me / Make love to me
CD _____ SEECD 401
See For Miles/C6 / Mar '94 / Pinnacle.

LFO

ADVANCE
CD _____ WARPCD 39
Warp / Jan '96 / Disc.

FREQUENCIES
CD _____ WARPCD 3
Warp / Aug '91 / Disc.

Li Calzi, Giorgio

GIORGIO LI CALZI
CD _____ PHIL 67-2
Philology / Oct '94 / Harmonia Mundi / Cadillac.

Li He

CHINESE CLASSICAL FOLK MUSIC
CD _____ EUCD 1155
ARC / '91 / ARC Music / ADA.

Liangxing, Tang

HIGH MOUNTAIN, FLOWING WATER
CD _____ SHAN 65012CD
Shanachie / Oct '93 / Koch / ADA / Greensleeves.

Libana

BORDERLAND
CD _____ SHCD 67003
Shanachie / Mar '94 / Koch / ADA / Greensleeves.

Liberation Through...

LIBERATION THROUGH HEARING (Liberation Through Hearing)
CD _____ DELECCD 023
Delerium / Aug '94 / Vital.

Libertine, Eve

SKATING
CD _____ RH 2CD
Red Herring / Nov '92 / SRD.

Libertines

LIBERTINES, THE
Love wears a white stetson / Big indian / Throw your arms around me / Watching the big sea / Don't be a stranger / Gotta dash / Chasing your love / Mean old you / Reality and rumour / Safety zone / St. Patrick's day / Long distance love
CD _____ GAIS 001CD
Gai Saber / May '95 / Vital.

Liberty

LIBERTY
CD _____ BLIPCD 101
Urban London / Mar '94 / Jetstar.

Liberty Cage

SLEEP OF THE JUST
Everything's different now / Fires below / Throwing stones at the sea / On her majesty's service / Swimming against the tide / One for the road / Judgement day / You make my mind stand still / Mercy of the guarde / Cat and mouse affair / Murder in cell no.9
CD _____ LICD 901293
Linecheck / Sep '94 / ADA / Direct.

Libido Boyz

OPGU
CD _____ CDZORRO 42
Metal Blade / Jul '90 / Pinnacle.

Library Of Congress...

MUSIC FOR THE GODS (Library Of Congress Endangered Music Project)
CD _____ RCD 10315
Rykodisc / Feb '95 / Vital / ADA.

Lick

BREECH
CD _____ INV 046CD
Invisible / Jan '96 / Plastic Head.

Licursi, Silvana

FAR FROM THE LAND OF EAGLE
CD _____ LYRCD 7413
Lyrichord / '91 / Roots / ADA / CM.

LIDJ Incorporated

BLACK LIBERATION
CD _____ YOCD 1
LIDJ Inc. / Dec '95 / SRD.

DUB LIBERATION
CD _____ YOCD 002
LIDJ Inc. / Dec '95 / SRD.

Liebman, David

IF ONLY THEY KNEW (Liebman, David Quintet)
If only they knew / Canistrano / Moontide / Reunion / Autumn in New York / Move on some
CD _____ CDSJP 151
Timeless Jazz / Feb '91 / New Note.

JOY - THE MUSIC OF JOHN COLTRANE
CD _____ CCD 79553 1
Candid / Nov '93 / Cadillac / Jazz Music / Wellard / Koch.

PLAY THE MUSIC OF COLE PORTER (Liebman, David, Steve Gilmore & Bill Goodwin)
CD _____ 123236-2
Red / Apr '91 / Harmonia Mundi / Jazz Horizons / Cadillac / ADA.

SONGS FOR MY DAUGHTERS
CD _____ 1212952
Soul Note / Sep '95 / Harmonia Mundi / Wellard / Cadillac.

TREE, THE
CD _____ 1211952
Soul Note / Nov '91 / Harmonia Mundi / Wellard / Cadillac.

Liebzeit, Jaki

NOWHERE
CD _____ SPOONCD 17
Spoon / Feb '95 / CM / Disc.

Liedes, Anna-Kaisa

KUUTTAREN KORET
CD _____ OMCD 44
Olarin Musiiki Oy / Dec '93 / ADA / Direct.

OI MIKSI

CD _____ TUG 1099CD
Tugboat / Feb '95 / ADA.

Liege Lord

MASTER CONTROL
CD _____ 1995412
Metal Blade / Jan '89 / Pinnacle.

Lien, Annbjorg

ANNBJORG LIEN
CD _____ FXCD 88
Kirkelig Kulturverksted / Jul '93 / ADA.

FELEFEBER
CD _____ GR 4081CD
Grappa / Dec '94 / ADA.

Liers In Wait

SPIRITUALY UNCONTROLLED ART
CD _____ DOL 007CD
Dolores / Nov '92 / Plastic Head.

Lieutenant Stitchie

BANGARANG
CD _____ SHCD 45023
Shanachie / Aug '95 / Koch / ADA / Greensleeves.

GHETTO SOLDIER
CD _____ GRELCD 213
Greensleeves / Dec '94 / Total/BMG / Jetstar / SRD.

LIEUTENANT STITCHIE BEENIE MAN & COBRA & FRIENDS (Lieutenant Stitchie & Beenie Man & Cobra)
CD _____ RNCD 2070
Rhino / Jul '94 / Jetstar / Magnum Music Group / THE.

RUDE BOY
Jamaican addiction / Cab / Can U read my mind / Prescription / Mr. Good stuff / Twenty one governor salute / Rude boy chat / Ton load a fat / Rough rider / Nurse me / (I need) sexual healing / Tug of war / Bad like yaws
CD _____ 756782479-2
Warner Bros. / May '93 / Warner Music.

Life Of Agony

RIVER RUNS RED
CD _____ RR 90432
Roadrunner / Oct '93 / Pinnacle.

UGLY
CD _____ RR 89242
CD _____ RR 89249
Roadrunner / Oct '95 / Pinnacle.

Life Sex & Death

SILENT MAJORITY, THE
Blue velvet/we're here now / Jawohl asshole / School's for fools / Telephone call / Farm song / Fuckin' shit ass / Hey buddy / Careful love / Homecoming blues / Baby I can't forget you / Don't put me down / Nite life boogie / Mississippi boogie / Come back baby / Answer to Teardrop Blues / That song is gone / Saturday night boogie woogie man / Shuffle shock / Washboard special / That's what's knockin' me out / Hep cat boogie / I want my baby for Christmas / Train blues / Baby's boogie / Drunk / Going away / Come back home
CD _____ 7599269582
WEA / Aug '92 / Warner Music.

Lifeson, Alex

VICTOR
CD _____ 7567828522
Warner Bros. / Jan '96 / Warner Music.

Liggins, Jimmy

JIMMY LIGGINS AND HIS DROPS OF JOY (Liggins, Jimmy & His Drops Of Joy)
I can't stop it / Troubles goodbye / Teardrop blues / Cadillac boogie / Move out baby / Careful love / Homecoming blues / Baby I can't forget you / Don't put me down / Nite life boogie / Mississippi boogie / Come back baby / Answer to Teardrop Blues / That song is gone / Saturday night boogie woogie man / Shuffle shock / Washboard special / That's what's knockin' me out / Hep cat boogie / I want my baby for Christmas / Train blues / Baby's boogie / Drunk / Going away / Come back home
CD _____ CDCHD 306
Ace / Oct '90 / Pinnacle / Cadillac / Complete/Pinnacle.

ROUGH WEATHER BLUES VOL.2 (Liggins, Jimmy & His Drops Of Joy)
Bye bye baby goodbye / Lookin' for my baby / Rough weather blues / Misery blues / Give up little girl / Lonely nights blues / Saturday night boogie woogie man / Lover's prayer / Now's the time / Sincere lover's blues / Down and out blues / Unidentified instrumental / Blues for love / Brown skin baby / Stolen love / Jumpin' and stompin' / Low down blues / Cloudy day blues / Goin' down with the sun / Dark hour blues / Pleading my cause / I'll never let you go / Railroad blues / Drunk / I'll always love you
CD _____ CDCHD 437
Ace / Jan '93 / Pinnacle / Cadillac / Complete/Pinnacle.

Liggins, Joe

JOE LIGGINS AND THE HONEYDRIPPERS (Liggins, Joe & His Honey Drippers)
Pink champagne / Ramblin' blues / Rag mop / Rhythm in the barnyard / Going back to New Orleans / I've got a right to cry / Honeydripper / I just can't help myself / Don't miss that train / Frankie Lee / Brand new deal in mobile / Little Joe's boogie / One sweet letter / Whiskey, gin and wine / Louisiana woman / Trying to lose the blues / Shuffle boogie blues / Rain rain rain / Flying Dutchman / Tanya / Blues for Tanya / Freight train blues / Whiskey, women and loaded dice / Big dipper / Do you love me pretty baby
CD _____ CDCHD 307
Ace / Oct '90 / Pinnacle / Cadillac / Complete/Pinnacle.

Light Division

HORSE GUARDS PARADE (Massed Bands Of The Light Division)
Bugle calls / Light Division assembly / Advance / Sambre et meuse / Les clarions anglais / Mechanised infantry / Quick silver / Slave's chorus / Silver bugles / St. Mary / Run runaway / Light Cavalry / Keel row / Road to the Isles / Five to one / Three to one / Bugle boy / Secunderabad / Horse Guards echoes / Cat gate of Kiev / Fanfare Sir John Moore / Sunset / National Anthem / Light Infantry regimental march / Royal Green Jackets / No more parades today / High on a hill
CD _____ BNA 5021
Bandleader / Jul '88 / Conifor.

Light Of The World

BEST OF LIGHT OF THE WORLD, THE
CD _____ MCCD 189
Music Club / Nov '94 / Disc / THE / CM.

VERY BEST OF LIGHT OF THE WORLD, THE
Somebody help me out (mixes) / Swingin' / Save the dream alive / I'm so happy / Midnight groovin' / Expansions / Parisienne girl / London town / Pete's crusade / Time / I shot the sheriff / Got to get your own
CD _____ MOCD 3007
More Music / Feb '95 / Sound & Media.

Lightfoot, Gordon

DID SHE MENTION MY NAME/BACK HERE ON EARTH PLUS SPIN, SPIN
Did she mention my name / Wherefor and why / Last time I saw her / Black day in July / May I / Magnificent outpourings / Does your mother know / Affair on 8th Avenue / Mama / Pussy willows, cat tails / I want to hear from you / Something very special / Boss man / Long way back home / Unsettled ways / Long thin dawn / Bitter green / Circle is small / Marie Christine / Cold hands from New York / Affair on 8th Avenue / Don't beat me down / Gypsy / If I could / Spin, spin (New Yok remake version)
CD _____ BGOCD 167
Beat Goes On / Mar '93 / Pinnacle.

EARLY LIGHTFOOT/SUNDAY CONCERT
Rich man's spiritual / Long river / Way I feel / For lovin' me / First time / Changes / Early morning rain / Steel rail blues / Sixteen miles / I'm not saying / Pride of man / Ribbon of darkness / Oh Linda / Peaceful waters / In a windowpane / Lost children / Leaves of grass / Medley: I'm not sayin'; Ribbon of darkness / Apology / Bitter green / Ballad of Yarmouth Castle / Softly / Boss man / Pussy willows, cat tails / Canadian road trilogy
CD _____ BGOCD 166
Beat Goes On / Apr '93 / Pinnacle.

IF YOU COULD READ MY MIND
Minstrel of the dawn / Me and Bobby McGee / Approaching lavender / Saturday clothes / Cobwebs and dust / Poor little Allison / Sit down young stranger / If you could read my mind / Baby it's alright / Your love's return (song for Stephen Foster) / Pony man
CD _____ 7599274512
WEA / Feb '92 / Warner Music.

LIGHTFOOT
If you got it / Softly / Crossroads / Minor ballad / Go go round / Rosanna / Home from the forest / I'll be alright / Song for a winter's night / Canadian railroad trilogy / Way I feel / Rich man's spiritual / Long river / For lovin' me / First time / Changes / Early morning rain / Steel rail blues / Sixteen miles / I'm not saying / Pride of man / Ribbon of darkness / Oh Linda / Peaceful waters
CD _____ BCD 15576
Bear Family / Apr '92 / Rollercoaster / Direct / CM / Swift / ADA.

SUNDAY CONCERT PLUS EXTRA STUDIO CUTS
In a windowpane / Lost children / Leaves of grass / I'm not sayin and ribbon of darkness / Apology / Bitter green / Ballad of Yarmouth Castle / Softly / Boss man / Pussy willows, cat tails / Canadian railroad trilogy / Just like Tom Thumb's blues / Movin' / I'll

be alright / Spin, spin (Nashville version, Tk 8) / Movin' (2)
CD _____ BCD 15691
Bear Family / Mar '93 / Rollercoaster / Direct / CM / Swift / ADA.

SUNDOWN
Somewhere USA / High and dry / Seven Island suite / Circle of steel / Is there anyone home / Watchman's gone / Sundown / Carefree highway / List / Too late for pryin'
CD _____ 7599272112
WEA / Feb '92 / Warner Music.

WAY I FEEL, THE
Walls / If you got it / Softly / Crossroads / A-minor ballad / Go go round / Rosanna / Home from the forest / I'll be alright / Song for a winter's night / Canadian railroad trilogy / Way I feel
CD _____ BGOCD 296
Beat Goes On / Nov '95 / Pinnacle.

Lightfoot, Papa George

GOIN BACK TO THE NATCHEZ TRACE
My woman is tired of me lyin / New mean old train / Love my baby / Goin' down that muddy road / Ah come on honey / I heard somebody crying / Take it witcha / Nighttime / Early in the morning / Walkin' / Goin' back to Natchez / Baby, please don't go / Train tune / Papa George - Talkin' about it
CD _____ CDCHD 548
Ace / Nov '94 / Pinnacle / Cadillac / Complete/Pinnacle.

Lightfoot, Terry

AT THE JAZZBAND BALL (Lightfoot, Terry & His Band)
CD _____ BRMCD 028
Bold Reprive / Oct '88 / Pinnacle / Bold Reprive / Harmonia Mundi.

DOWN ON BOURBON STREET (Lightfoot, Terry & His Jazzmen)
Bourbon street parade / Do you know what it means to miss New Orleans / De Luxe / When we danced at the Mardi Gras / Grandpa's spells / Closer walk with thee / Petite fleur / Chimes blues / Solace / Ole man moose / Hiawatha rag / Trouble in mind / Ice cream / Lonesome / Maryland / Ragtime music
CD _____ CDTTD 581
Timeless Jazz / Mar '94 / New Note.

LIVE IN LEIPZIG
CD _____ BLCD 760513
Black Lion / Nov '95 / Jazz Music / Cadillac / Wellard / Koch.

SPECIAL MAGIC OF LOUIS ARMSTRONG, THE (Lightfoot, Terry & His Band)
Jeepers creepers / Muskrat ramble / Give me a kiss to build a dream on / You'll never walk alone / Mack the knife / Wonderful world / Hello Dolly / Tin roof blues / Dardanella / Now you has jazz / All the time in the world / Mame / Dippermouth blues / Lazy river / Faithful hussar / Cabaret / Sleepy time down south / Westherbird rag / Blueberry hill / Indiana
CD _____ STOCD 104
Start / Sep '95 / Koch.

STARDUST (Lightfoot, Terry & His Band)
At the woodchoppers' ball / Just a gigolo / Fish seller / Stardust / Bad, Bad Leroy Brown / Undecided / Gone fishin' / Jumpin' at the woodside / Frim fram sauce / Ragtime music / Black and Tan fantasy / Big noise from Winnetka / Bye and bye / Drum boogie
CD _____ URCD 104
Upbeat / Dec '90 / Target/BMG / Cadillac.

Lighthouse

BEST OF LIGHTHOUSE - SUNNY DAYS AGAIN
One fine morning / Hats off to a stranger / Little kind words / 1849 / Sunny days / Sweet lullaby / Take it slow / Broken down guitar blues / I just wanna be you friend / You girl / Silver bird / Lonely places / Pretty lady / Can you feel it / Magic's in the dancing / Good day
CD _____ CAN 9002
Marquis / Oct '93 / Kingdom.

LIGHTHOUSE LIVE
Just wanna be your friend / Take it slow / Old man / Rockin' chair / You and me / Sweet lullaby / 1849 / Eight miles high / One fine morning / Insane
CD _____ CAN 9010
Marquis / Oct '93 / Kingdom.

Lighthouse Family

OCEAN DRIVE
Lifted / Heavenly / Loving every minute / Ocean drive / Way you are / Keep remembering / Sweetest operator / What could be better / Beautiful night / Goodbye heartbreak
CD _____ 5237872
Wild Card / Feb '96 / PolyGram.

Lightnin' Slim

BLUE LIGHTNING
Mama talk to your daughter / My baby left me this morning / It's mighty crazy / Caress me baby / I love you baby / Sky is crying / G.I. Slim / Help me spend my gold / My little angel child / Too close blues / I want you to love me / Bedbug blues / I'm tired waitin' baby / Ah'w baby
CD _____ IGOCD 2002
Indigo / Jul '95 / Direct / ADA.

HIGH AND LOW DOWN/OVER EASY (Lightnin' Slim & Whispering Smith)
Rooster blues / Things I used to do / Bad luck blues / My baby / G.I. blues / Oh baby / That's all right / Can't hold out much longer / Good morning heartaches / Hoodoo blues / I man in the world's come over me / Mojo hand / Way you treat me / I don't know woman / Everybody needs love / I know I've got a sure thing (Smith's jam) / Why am I treated so bad / Rock me baby / Married man / I know you don't love me / It's all over / You want to do it again
CD _____ CDCHD 578
Ace / Jul '95 / Pinnacle / Cadillac / Complete/Pinnacle.

IT'S MIGHTY CRAZY
Rock me Mama / Bad luck / West Texas / What evil have I done / Lightnin' blues / I can't be successful / I'm him / I can't understand / Just made twenty one / Sugar plum / Goin' home / Wonderin' and goin' / Bad luck and trouble / Have you way / I'm grown / Mean old lonesome train / Rocky mountain blues / Love me Mama / I'm a rollin' stone / Hoodoo blues / It's mighty crazy / Bedbug blues / Tom Cat blues / Flaming blues
CD _____ CDCHD 587
Ace / Apr '95 / Pinnacle / Cadillac / Complete/Pinnacle.

ROOSTER BLUES
Rooster blues / Long leanie Mama / My starter won't work / G.I. Slim / Lightnin's troubles / Bedbug blues / Hoodoo blues / It's mighty crazy / Sweet little woman / Tom cat blues / Feelin' awful blues / I'm leavin' you baby / Lightnin' blues / I can't be successful / Sugar plum / Just made twenty one / Goin' home / Wonderin' and goin'
CD _____ ELDIABLO 8038
El Diablo / Mar '94 / Vital.

ROOSTER BLUES/LIGHTNIN' SLIM/ BELL RINGER
Rooster blues / Long Leanie Mama / My starter won't work / G.I. Slim / Lightnin' troubles / Bedbug blues / Hoodoo blues / It's mighty crazy / Sweet little woman / Tom cat blues / Feelin' awful blues / I'm leavin' you baby / Love me Mama / She's my crazy little baby / Have mercy on me baby / Winter time blues / If you ever need me / Mean old lonesome train / Baby please come back / Love is just a gamble / Somebody knockin' / You give me the blues / Don't start me talkin' / You move me baby
CD _____ CDCHD 517
Ace / Feb '94 / Pinnacle / Cadillac / Complete/Pinnacle.

Lightning Seeds

CLOUD CUCKOO LAND
All I want / Bound in a nutshell / Pure / Sweet dreams / Nearly man / Joy / Love explosion / Don't let go / Control the flame / Price / Good help them
CD _____ CDOVD 436
Virgin / May '92 / EMI.

JOLLIFICATION
Perfect / Lucky you / Open goals / Change / Why why why / Marvellous / Feeling lazy / My best day / Punch and Judy / Telling tales
CD _____ 477237-2
Columbia / Sep '94 / Sony.

SENSE
Sense / Life of Riley / Blowing bubbles / Cool place / Where flowers fade / Small slice of heaven / Tingle tangle / Happy / Marooned / Thinking up, looking down
CD _____ CDV 2690
Virgin / Apr '92 / EMI.

Lights In A Fat City

SOMEWHERE
CD _____ THESE 003CD
These Records/Recommended / Feb '89 / These / SRD.

Lightsey, Kirk

EVERYTHING HAPPENS TO ME (Lightsey, Kirk Trio)
CD _____ CDSJP 176
Timeless Jazz / Nov '90 / New Note.

FROM KIRK TO NAT (Lightsey, Kirk Trio)
CD _____ CRISS 1050CD
Criss Cross / Nov '91 / Cadillac / Harmonia Mundi.

TEMPTATION (Lightsey, Kirk Trio)
Society red / Brigette / Evidence / Temptation / Love is a many splendoured thing / Gibraltar

CD _____ CDSJP 257
Timeless Jazz / Aug '90 / New Note.

L'il Brian

FRESH (L'il Brian & The Zydeco Travellers)
CD _____ ROUCD 2136
Rounder / Apr '95 / CM / Direct / ADA / Cadillac.

Lil' Ed

CHICKEN, GRAVY AND BISCUITS (Lil' Ed & The Blues Imperials)
CD _____ ALCD 4772
Alligator / Oct '93 / Direct / ADA.

ROUGHHOUSIN' (Lil' Ed & The Blues Imperials)
CD _____ ALCD 4749
Alligator / May '93 / Direct / ADA.

WHAT YOU SEE IS WHAT YOU GET (Lil' Ed & The Blues Imperials)
Life is like gambling / Find my baby / Older woman / Please help / Toothache / Living for today / Travellin' life / Out of the house / Upset man / Long long way from home / What you see is what you get / Bluesmobile / What am I gonna do / Packin' up
CD _____ ALCD 4808
Alligator / May '93 / Direct / ADA.

Lil' Mac

MAKIN' LOVE TO MONEY (Lil' Mac & D.J. Trick)
CD _____ WRA 8149
Wrap / Jan '96 / Koch.

Lilac Time

AND LOVE FOR ALL
Fields / All for love and love for all / Let our land be the one / I went to the dance / Wait and see / Honest to God / Laundry / Paper boat / Skabasikiblio / It'll end in tears (I won't cry) / Trinity / And on we go
CD _____ 8461902
Fontana / Jan '96 / PolyGram.

ASTRONAUTS
CD _____ CRECD 098
Creation / May '94 / 3MV / Vital.

LILAC TIME, THE
Black velvet / Rockland / Return to yesterday / You've got to love / Love becomes a savage / Together / Road to happiness / Too sooner late than better / Trumpets from Montparnasse
CD _____ 8348352
Fontana / Jan '96 / PolyGram.

PARADISE CIRCUS
American eyes / Lost girl in the midnight sun / Beauty in your body / If the stars shine tonight / Days of the week / She still loves you / Paradise circus / Girl who waves at trains / Last to know / Father mother wife and child / Rollercoaster song / Work for the weekend / Twilight beer hall
CD _____ 8386412
Fontana / Jan '96 / PolyGram.

Lilier

BACK TO THE ROOTS (Lilier & Doc Houlind)
CD _____ MECCACD 1020
Music Mecca / Nov '94 / Jazz Music / Cadillac / Wellard.

Lillian Axe

POETIC JUSTICE
CD _____ CDMFN 131
Music For Nations / Jul '92 / Pinnacle.

PSYCHOSCHIZOPHRENIA
Crucified / Deep freeze / Moonlight in your blood / Stop the hate / Sign of the times / Needle and your pain / Those who prey / Voices in my walls / Now you know / Deep blue shadows / Day that I met you / Psychoschizophrenia
CD _____ CDMFN 151
Music For Nations / Sep '93 / Pinnacle.

Lillie, Beatrice

UNIQUE, THE INCOMPARABLE BEA LILLIE, THE
There are fairies at the bottom of our garden / I'm a campfire girl / He was a gentleman / Nicodemus / Paree / Mad about the boy / Baby doesn't know / Marvellous party / I hate spring / Trains
CD _____ PASTCD 7054
Flapper / Nov '94 / Pinnacle.

Lilly, John C.

E.C.C.O.
CD _____ SR 9452
Silent / Mar '94 / Plastic Head.

Limerick, Alison

AND STILL I RISE
Make it on my own / Getting it right / Where love lives / Hear my call / Trouble / Come back (for real love) / Tell me what you mean / Let's make a memory / You and I / Difference is you

CD _____ 262365
Arista / Apr '92 / BMG.

WITH A TWIST
Time of our lives / Love come down / Twisted / No way out / Crime to be that cool / So long / Sentimental / Buck the system / Take it back / Let's just pretend / Build your love / Unique / Come home
CD _____ 74321193202
Arista / Mar '94 / BMG.

Lince, Louis

AT THE DOT (Lince, Louis Jelly Roll Kings)
CD _____ BCD 336
GHB / Aug '95 / Jazz Music.

Lincoln Centre Jazz...

FIRE OF THE FUNDAMENTALS (Lincoln Centre Jazz Orchestra)
CD _____ 4743482
Sony Jazz / Jan '95 / Sony.

PORTRAITS OF ELLINGTON (Lincoln Centre Jazz Orchestra)
Portrait of Louis Armstrong / Thanks for the beautiful land on the delta / Portrait of Bert Williams / Bojangles / Self portrait of the bean / Second line / Total jazz / Liberian suite / Like the sunrise / Dance 1 / Dance 2 / Dance 3 / Dance 4 / Dance 5
CD _____ 472814 2
Columbia / May '93 / Sony.

THEY CAME TO SWING (Lincoln Centre Jazz Orchestra)
CD _____ 4772842
Sony Jazz / Jan '95 / Sony.

Lincoln, Abbey

ABBEY IS BLUE
CD _____ OJCCD 069
Original Jazz Classics / Oct '92 / Wellard / Jazz Music / Cadillac / Complete/Pinnacle.

DEVIL GOT YOUR TONGUE
CD _____ 5135742
Verve / Apr '92 / PolyGram.

GOTTA PAY THE BAND
CD _____ 5111102
Verve / Apr '91 / PolyGram.

IT'S MAGIC
CD _____ OJCCD 205-2
Original Jazz Classics / Feb '92 / Wellard / Jazz Music / Cadillac / Complete/Pinnacle.

PEOPLE IN ME (Lincoln, Abbey & Dave Liebman)
CD _____ 514626-2
Verve / Mar '94 / PolyGram.

STRAIGHT AHEAD
Straight ahead / When Malindy sings / In the red / Blue monk / Left alone / African lady / Retribution
CD _____ CCD 9015
Candid / Sep '88 / Cadillac / Jazz Music / Wellard / Koch.

THAT'S HIM
Strong man / Happiness is a thing called Joe / My man (mon homme) / Tender as a rose / That's him / Porgy / When a woman loves a man / Don't explain
CD _____ OJCCD 085
Original Jazz Classics / Oct '92 / Wellard / Jazz Music / Cadillac / Complete/Pinnacle.

TURTLE'S DREAM, A
CD _____ 5273822
Verve / May '95 / PolyGram.

WHEN THERE IS LOVE (Lincoln, Abbey & Hank Jones)
CD _____ 519697-2
Verve / Mar '94 / PolyGram.

Lind, Ove

GERSHWIN - EVERGREEN
'S wonderful / Summertime / Swanee / Embraceable you / Bidin' my time / Our love is here to stay / But not for me / Changing my tune / Of thee I sing / Somebody loves me / Someone to watch over me / Oh lady be good / Aren't you kind of glad we did / I got plenty o' nuttin' / They can't take that away from me / Strike up the band / Man I love / Nice work if you can get it / Who cares / Love is sweeping the country / I've got a crush on you / Love walked in / Foggy day / My one and only / I was doing all right / They all laughed / How long has this been going on / Let's call the whole thing off
CD _____ PHONTCD 7410
Phontastic / Aug '94 / Wellard / Jazz Music / Cadillac.

ONE MORNING IN MAY (Lind, Ove Quartet)
Just friends / Tangerine / Sky fell down / So would I / Cheek to cheek / I thought about you / Down by the old mill stream / Baby won't you please / I've got a feeling I'm falling in love / Stay as sweet as you are / I've got my eyes on you / True / One morning in May
CD _____ PHONTCD 7501
Phontastic / Aug '94 / Wellard / Jazz Music / Cadillac.

ORCHESTRA SWEDISH EVERGREENS WITH CHARLIE PARKER
CD _____ PHONTCD 7408/9
Phontastic / Aug '94 / Wellard / Jazz Music / Cadillac.

SUMMER NIGHT
Summer night / You leave me breathless / Say my heart / Changing my tune / Ill wind / You're a lucky guy / Lady be good / My cabin of dreams / You're the cream in my coffee / This heart of mine / Louise / Swinging on a star
CD _____ PHONTCD 7503
Phontastic / Aug '94 / Wellard / Jazz Music / Cadillac.

Lindberg, John

DODGING BULLETS (Lindberg, John & Albert Mangelsdorff & Eric Watson)
CD _____ 12010502
Black Saint / Jan '93 / Harmonia Mundi / Cadillac.

PARIS PERFORMANCES
CD _____ WWCD 014
West Wind / Oct '88 / Swift / Charly / CM / ADA.

Lindberg, Nils

SAX APPEAL & TRISECTION
CD _____ DRAGONCD 220
Dragon / Jan '89 / Roots / Cadillac / Wellard / CM / ADA.

SAXES & BRASS GALORE
CD _____ ABCD 3004
Bluebell / Jun '94 / Cadillac / Jazz Music.

Lindbloom, Rolf

GERSHWIN
CD _____ PRCD 9001
Prestige / Aug '94 / Complete/Pinnacle / Cadillac.

Lindemann, David

ANCIENT EVENINGS, DISTANT MUSIC
CD _____ CDSGP 9025
Prestige / Jun '95 / Total/BMG.

ETERNAL BOUNDARIES
CD _____ CDSGP 9002
Prestige / Apr '95 / Total/BMG.

Lindemann, Francois

SOLO
La fee verte / Occirient / L'ami chilien / Le centaure / Blue cage / La betise / A l'ancienrt / Candi / Selemat siang / Le voyage
CD _____ TCB 01022
TCB / Feb '95 / New Note.

Lindgren, Kurt

LADY M
CD _____ DRCD 189
Dragon / Oct '88 / Roots / Cadillac / Wellard / CM / ADA.

Lindgren, Lasse

TO MY FRIENDS
CD _____ DRCD 227
Dragon / Dec '88 / Roots / Cadillac / Wellard / CM / ADA.

Lindisfarne

AMIGOS
9hi i nlnl / Everything changes / Working for the man / Roll on that day / You're the one / Wish you were here / Do it like this / Anyway the wind blows / Strange affair
CD _____ CLACD 384
Castle / May '93 / BMG.

BARREL FULL OF HIT, A
CD _____ ESSCD 214
Essential / Sep '94 / Total/BMG.

BEST OF LINDISFARNE
Meet me on the corner / Lady Eleanor / All fall down / We can swing together / Fog on the Tyne / Road to Kingdom Come / Scarecrow song / Winter song / Clear white light / January song / Down / Walk up little sister / Together forever / Alright on the night / Go back / Don't ask me
CD _____ CDVIP 103
Virgin VIP / Dec '93 / Carlton Home Entertainment / THE / EMI.

BURIED TREASURES VOL 1
Buried treasures vol.1 / Red square dance / Finest hour / Together forever (Live) / Together crack - spoken word / Happy or sad / Way behind you / Behind crack - spoken word / Old peculiar feeling / True love / Love crack - spoken word / City song / Rock 'n' roll town / Swiss maid (live) / Sporting life blues (Demo) / Karen Marie (live) / From my window / Window crack - spoken word / Run Jimmy run / Malvinas melody (live) / Let's dance (live)
CD _____ CDVM 9012
Virgin / Nov '92 / EMI.

BURIED TREASURES VOL 2
Save our ales / Ale crack (Spoken) / Golden apples / Try giving everything / Nothing's

gonna break us now / January song (Live) / Living on the baseline / On my own I built a bridge / Bridge crack (Spoken) / Roll on that day (Live) / Loving around the clock / Reunion / Reunion (2) (Spoken) / Friday girl / Tomorrow if I'm hungry / Hungry crack (Spoken) / Fog on the Tyne (Pudding mix) / Winning the games / Peter Gunn theme (Live) / Run for home (Live)
CD _____ CDVM 9013
Virgin / Nov '92 / EMI.

DANCE YOUR LIFE AWAY
Shine on / Love on the run / Heroes / All in the same boat / Dance your life away / Beautiful day / Broken doll / Hundred miles to Liverpool
CD _____ CLACD 383
Castle / Apr '93 / BMG.

ELVIS LIVES ON THE MOON
CD _____ ESSCD 197
Castle / Jun '93 / BMG.

FOG ON THE TYNE
Meet me on the corner / Alright on the night / Uncle Sam / Together forever / January song / Peter Brophy don't care / City song / Passing ghosts / Train in G major / Fog on the Tyne / Scotch mist (CD only) / No time to lose (CD only)
CD _____ CASCD 1050
Charisma / '88 / EMI.

NICELY OUT OF TUNE
Lady Eleanor / Road to Kingdom come / Winter song / Turn a deaf ear / Clear white light part 2 / We can swing together / Alan in the river with flowers / Down / Things I should have said / Jackhammer blues / Scarecrow song / Knackers yard blues (CD only) / Nothing but the marvellous is beautiful (CD only)
CD _____ CASCD 1025
Charisma / '88 / EMI.

SLEEPLESS NIGHTS
Nights / Start again / Cruising to disaster / Same way down / Winning the game / About you / Sunderland boys / Love is a pain / Do what I want / Never miss the water
CD _____ CLACD 382
Castle / Mar '93 / BMG.

Lindley, David

VERY GREASY (Lindley, David & El Rayo X)
CD _____ 7559607682
Carlton Home Entertainment / Oct '94 / Carlton Home Entertainment.

WIN THIS RECORD (Lindley, David & El Rayo X)
Talk to the lawyer / Look so good / Something's got a hold on me / Ram a lamb a man / Premature / Rock it with I / Brother John / Make it on / Turning point / Spodie
CD _____ 7559601782
WEA / Feb '92 / Warner Music.

Lindo, Kashief

KASHIEF SINGS CHRISTMAS
CD _____ CRCD 37
Charm / Dec '94 / Jetstar.

SOUL & INSPIRATION
CD _____ CRCD 45
Charm / Jan '96 / Jetstar.

Lindsay, Arto

ARTO LINDSAY
CD _____ KFWCD 164
Knitting Factory / Feb '95 / Grapevine.

Lindsay, Erica

DREAMER
Daydream / First movement / Walking together / Dreamer / At the last moment / Gratitude
CD _____ CCD 79040
Candid / Mar '90 / Cadillac / Jazz Music / Wellard / Koch.

Lindsay, Reg

REASONS TO RISE
CD _____ LARRCD 300
Larrikin / Nov '94 / Roots / Direct / ADA / CM.

Lindup, Mike

CHANGES
Changes / Lovely day / Fallen angel / Spirit is free / Desire / West coast man / Judgement day / Life will never be the same / Paixao (Passion)
CD _____ LV 101CD
Voice Print / Sep '94 / Voice Print.

Lingomania

LINGOMANIA
Camminando / Rain squash / Terra / Sale for love / Backwards / Vision of the master
CD _____ CDSGP 041
Prestige / Jan '94 / Total/BMG.

Linhart, Peter

BLUE NIGHTS
CD _____ EFA 120652
Hotwire / Dec '94 / SRD.

Linka, Rudy

CZECH IT OUT
Old and new / Just on time / Uptown express / How deep is the ocean / Traveler / Welcome to the club / Folk song / At this point / Love letters
CD _____ ENJ 90012
Enja / Dec '94 / New Note / Vital/SAM.

LIVE IT UP
Waltz for Stephanie / Swing tune / I wish I knew / Live it up / To be named later / Outside the city / Someday my prince will come / Live it up II / Somewhere, someday / Beautiful friendship / Very last
CD _____ CDSJP 407
Timeless Jazz / Apr '94 / New Note.

Linkchain, Hip

AIRBUSTERS
House cat blues / I had a dream / Blow wind blow / Bedbug blues / On my way / Keep on searching / Gambler's blues / I'll overcome / Strain on my heart / Take out your false teeth / Bad news / Airbusters / Fugitive / Diggin' my potatoes
CD _____ ECD 260382
Evidence / Sep '93 / Harmonia Mundi / ADA / Cadillac.

Linsky, Jeff

ANGEL'S SERENADE
Later / Black sand / Angel's serenade / Bop bop / In out heart / Leo / Over the rainbow / Can't dance / Beautiful love / Speak low
CD _____ CCD 4611
Concord Picante / Sep '94 / New Note.

UP LATE
Armony / Besame mucho / Berimbau / Carlos / Hermosa / I didn't know what time it was / Lanikai / Monterrey / Up late / Wave (Only on CD.)
CD _____ CCD 4363
Concord Jazz / Nov '88 / New Note.

Linton, Steffan

UNFINISHED AFFAIR
CD _____ DRCD 193
Dragon / Aug '88 / Roots / Cadillac / Wellard / CM / ADA.

Linus

YOUGLI
CD _____ ELM 19CD
Elemental / Apr '94 / Disc.

Lions Den

ON LINE
CD _____ RTCD 001
RT / Apr '95 / SRD.

Lionsheart

LIONSHEART
CD _____ CDMFN 139
Music For Nations / Jul '92 / Pinnacle.

PRIDE IN FACT
CD _____ CDMFN 167
Music For Nations / Nov '94 / Pinnacle.

Lipovsky, Shura

MOMENTS OF JEWISH LIFE
CD _____ SYNCD 153
Syncoop / Jun '93 / ADA / Direct.

Lipscomb, Mance

TEXAS BLUES GUITAR
CD _____ ARHCD 001
Arhoolie / Apr '95 / ADA / Direct / Cadillac.

TEXAS SONGSTER
CD _____ ARHCD 306
Arhoolie / Apr '95 / ADA / Direct / Cadillac.

YOU GOT TO REAP WHAT YOU SOW
CD _____ ARHCD 398
Arhoolie / Apr '95 / ADA / Direct / Cadillac.

Liquid

LIQUID CULTURE
CD _____ XLCD 113
XL / Jul '95 / Warner Music.

Liquid Hips

FOOL INJECTION
CD _____ EMY 138-2
Enemy / Nov '94 / Grapevine.

STATIC
CD _____ EMY 142-2
Enemy / Nov '94 / Grapevine.

Liquid Z

AMPHIBIC
CD _____ GAMMA 002CD
Gamma / Oct '95 / Plastic Head.

Liquor Bike

NEON HOOP RIDE
CD _____ GROW 352
Grass / Feb '95 / SRD.

Liquorice

LISTENING CAP
Trump suite / Team player / Keeping the weekend free / Drive around / Cheap cuts / Trump suit edit / Jill of all trades / No excuses / Breaking the ice / Blew it
CD _____ CAD 5008CD
4AD / Jul '95 / Disc.

Lir

MAGICO MAGICO
CD _____ VELO 2003CD
Cross Border Media / Jan '94 / Direct / ADA.

Listening Pool

STILL LIFE
CD _____ TLGCD 002
Telegraph / Feb '95 / BMG.

Lister, Anne

SPREADING WINGS
CD _____ HFCD 02
Heartfire / May '93 / ADA.

Lister, Ayako

JAPANESE KOTO, THE
CD _____ EUCD 1105
ARC / '91 / ARC Music / ADA.

Litherland, James

4TH ESTATE
CD _____ CMMR 942
Music Maker / Nov '94 / Grapevine / ADA.

Litter

$100 FINE
CD _____ TX 2004CD
Taxim / Jan '94 / ADA.

DISTORTIONS
CD _____ TX 2003CD
Taxim / Jan '94 / ADA.

DISTORTIONS + $100 FINE
CD _____ 842077
EVA / May '94 / Direct / ADA.

Little Angels

DON'T PREY FOR ME
Do you wanna riot / Kick hard / Big bad world / Kicking up dust / Don't prey for me / Broken wings of an angel / Bitter and twisted / Promises / When I get out of here / No solution / Passage pyre
CD _____ 8412542
Polydor / Jun '90 / PolyGram.

JAM
Way that I live / Too much too young / Spotlight isolation / Soap box / S.T.W. / Don't n-t-re you-rb .trp. / W-+++-kl-. / Eyes wide open / Colour of love / I was not wrong / Sail away / Tired of waiting for you (So tired) / Reprise/S.T.W. / She's a little angel (live) (Limited edition double-sets only) / Product of the working class (Grooved and jammed) (Ltd ed only) / I ain't gonna cry (Ltd ed only) / Boneyard 1993 (Ltd ed-only) / Don't prey for me (Extended) (Ltd ed only) / Won't get fooled again (Ltd ed only)
CD _____ 5176762
Polydor / Jun '93 / PolyGram.

LITTLE OF THE PAST
She's a little angel / Too much too young / Hadical your lover / Womankind / Boneyard / Kicking up dust / I ain't gonna cry / Sail away / Young Gods / Ninety in the shade / Product of the working class / Soapbox / First cut is the deepest / Ten miles high / I wanna be loved by you / Don't pray for me
CD _____ 521936-2
Polydor / Apr '94 / PolyGram.

TOO POSH TO MOSH
CD _____ ESSCD 213
Essential / Jun '94 / Total/BMG.

Little Annie

SHORT AND SWEET
CD _____ ONUCD 16
On-U Sound / Jun '93 / SRD / Jetstar.

Little Anthony

DON'T WAIT ON ME (Little Anthony & The Locomotives)
CD _____ DELCD 3013
Deluge / Jan '96 / Koch.

Little Bob

RENDEZVOUS IN ANGEL CITY
Isn't it enough / There'll never be another
you / I can't wait / True love / Gimme you /
Midnight crisis / As the lights go out / Keep
on running / When the night falls / Never
cry about the past
CD _____ 104 182
Musidisc / Mar '90 / Vital / Harmonia Mundi
/ ADA / Cadillac / Discovery.

Little Buster

**RIGHT ON TIME (Little Buster & The
Soul Brothers)**
CD _____ CDBB 9562
Bullseye Blues / Oct '95 / Direct.

Little, Booker

**FIRE WALTZ (Little, Booker & Eric
Dolphy)**
Number eight / Fire waltz / Bee vamp
CD _____ ECD 220742
Evidence / Nov '93 / Harmonia Mundi / ADA
/ Cadillac.

**LIVE - THE COMPLETE CONCERT
(Little, Booker & Teddy Charles Group)**
CD _____ COD 032
Jazz View / Jul '92 / Harmonia Mundi.

OUT FRONT
We speak / Strength and sanity / Calm,
please / Moods in free time / Man of words
/ Hazy hues / New day
CD _____ CCD 9027
Candid / Jul '87 / Cadillac / Jazz Music / Wel-
lard / Koch.

**REMEMBERED LIVE AT SWEET BASIL
(Little, Booker & Eric Dolphy)**
Prophet / Aggression / Booker's waltz
CD _____ ECD 220732
Evidence / Nov '93 / Harmonia Mundi / ADA
/ Cadillac.

Little Caesar

LITTLE CAESAR
CD _____ DGLD 19128
Geffen / May '92 / BMG.

Little Charlie

**ALL THE WAY CRAZY (Little Charlie &
The Nightcats)**
T.V. crazy / Right around the corner /
Clothes line / Living hand to mouth / Suicide
blues / Poor Tarzan / When girls do it / Eyes
like a cat / I'll take you back / Short skirts
CD _____ ALCD 4753
Alligator / May '93 / Direct / ADA.

**BIG BREAK, THE (Little Charlie & The
Nightcats)**
CD _____ ALCD 4776
Alligator / May '93 / Direct / ADA.

**CAPTURED LIVE (Little Charlie & The
Nightcats)**
Tomorrow night / Run me down / Rain /
Dump that chump / Ten years ago / Think-
ing with the wrong head / Wildcattin' /
Crawlin' kingsnake / Smart like Einstein /
Eyes like a cat
CD _____ ALCD 4794
Alligator / Oct '93 / Direct / ADA.

**DISTURBING THE PEACE (Little Charlie
& The Nightcats)**
That's my girl / Nervous / My money's
green / If this is love / I ain't lyin' / She's
talking / My last meal / Booty song / Don't
boss me / VB Ford blues / I feel good /
Run me down
CD _____ ALCD 4761
Alligator / Apr '93 / Direct / ADA.

**NIGHT VISION (Little Charlie & The
Nightcats)**
CD _____ ALCD 4812
Alligator / May '93 / Direct / ADA.

**STRAIGHT UP (Little Charlie & The
Nightcats)**
CD _____ ALCD 4829
Alligator / Apr '95 / Direct / ADA.

Little Chief

SPIRIT
CD _____ FGUTCD 001
Futgut / Jan '94 / CM.

Little Feat

AIN'T HAD ENOUGH FUN
Drivin' blind / Blue jean blues / Cadillac hotel
/ Romance without finance / Big band the-
ory / Cajun rage / Heaven's where you find
it / Borderline blues / All that you can stand
/ Rock 'n' roll every night / Shaketown /
Ain't had enough fun / That's a pretty good
love
CD _____ 72445110972
Zoo Entertainment / Jun '95 / BMG.

**AS TIME GOES BY - THE VERY BEST
OF LITTLE FEAT**
Dixie chicken / Willin' / Rock 'n' roll doctor
/ Two trains / Truck stop girl / Fat man in
the bath tub / Trouble / Sailin' shoes /
Spanish moon / Feats don't fail me now /
Oh Atlanta / All that you dream / Long dis-

tance love / Mercenary territory / Rocket in
my pocket / Texas twister / Let it roll / Hate
to lose your lovin' / Old folks boogie /
Twenty million things
CD _____ 954832247-2
WEA / Aug '93 / Warner Music.

DIXIE CHICKEN
Dixie chicken / Two Trains / Roll um easy /
On Your Way Down / Kiss it off / Fool your-
self / Walkin' all night / Fat man in the bath-
tub / Juliet / Lafayette Railroad
CD _____ K 246 200
WEA / Jul '88 / Warner Music.

DOWN ON THE FARM
Down on the farm / Six feet of snow / Per-
fect imperfection / Kokomo / Be one now /
Straight from the heart / Front page news /
Wake up dreaming / Feel the groove
CD _____ K2 56667
WEA / Jul '88 / Warner Music.

FEATS DON'T FAIL ME NOW
Rock 'n' roll doctor / Cold cold cold / Tripe
face boogie / Fan / Oh Atlanta / Skin it back
/ Down The Road / Spanish Moon / Feats
Don't Fail Me Now
CD _____ 256030
WEA / Jul '88 / Warner Music.

LAST RECORD ALBUM, THE
Romance Dance / All that you dream / Long
Distance Love / Day or Night / One Love /
Down below the borderline / Somebody's
leavin' / Mercenary Territory
CD _____ K 256156
WEA / May '88 / Warner Music.

LET IT ROLL
Hate to lose your lovin' / One clear moment
/ Cajun girl / Hangin' on to the good times
/ Listen to your heart / Let it roll / Long time
till I get over you / Business as usual /
Change in luck / Voices on the wind
CD _____ 925750 2
WEA / Aug '88 / Warner Music.

LITTLE FEAT
Snakes on everything / Strawberry flats /
Truck stop girl / Brides of Jesus / Willin' /
Hamburger midnight / Forty four blues /
How many more years / Crack in your door
/ I've been the one / Takin' my time / Crazy
captain Gunboat Willie
CD _____ 7599271892
WEA / Feb '92 / Warner Music.

REPRESENTING THE MAMBO
Texas twister / Daily grind / Representing
the mambo / Woman in love / Rad gumbo
/ Teenage warrior / That's her / She's mine
/ Feeling's all gone / Those feat'll steer ya
wrong sometimes / Ingenue / Silver screen
CD _____ 7599261632
WEA / Apr '90 / Warner Music.

SAILIN' SHOES
Easy to slip / Cold cold cold / Trouble /
Tripe face boogie / Willin' / Apolitical blues /
Sailin' Shoes / Teenage nervous break-
down / Got no shadows / Cat fever / Texas
Rose Cafe
CD _____ 246156
WEA / '88 / Warner Music.

TIME LOVES A HERO
Time loves a hero / Hi roller / New Delph
freight train / Old folks boogie / Red stream-
liner / Keeping up with the Joneses / Rocket
in my pocket / Missin' you / Day at the
races
CD _____ 256349
WEA / Jul '89 / Warner Music.

WAITING FOR COLUMBUS
Join the band / Fat man in the bathtub / All
that you dream / Oh Atlanta / Old folks'
boogie / Time loves a hero / Day or night /
Mercenary territory / Spanish moon / Dixie
chicken / Tripe face boogie / Rocket in my
pocket / Willin' / Don't Bogart that joint /
Political blues / Sailin' shoes / Feats don't
fail me now
CD _____ 7599273442
WEA / Feb '92 / Warner Music.

Little Hatch

**WE'RE ALL RIGHT (Little Hatch & The
Houserockers)**
CD _____ MB 1204
Modern Blues / Feb '94 / Direct / ADA.

Little Lenny

ALL THE GIRLS
CD _____ GVCD 1700
Ras / Dec '95 / Jetstar / Greensleeves /
SRD / Direct.

LITTLE LENNY IS MY NAME
CD _____ VPCD 1172
Steely & Cleevie / Nov '92 / Jetstar.

Little Mike & The...

**FLYNN'S PLACE (Little Mike & The
Tornados)**
CD _____ FF 641CD
Flying Fish / Jul '95 / Roots / CM / Direct /
ADA.

Little Milton

**BLUES 'N' SOUL/WAITING FOR LITTLE
MILTON**

It's amazing / Who can handle me is you /
Woman, you don't have to be so cold / Thrill
is gone / Monologue 1 / That's how strong
my love is / What it is / Little bluebird /
Woman across the river / Behind closed
doors / Sweet woman of mine / Worried
dream / How could you do it to me / You're
no good / T'ain't nobody's business if I do
/ Hard luck blues
CD _____ CDSXD 052
Stax / Jun '92 / Pinnacle.

BLUES IS ALRIGHT, THE
Blues is alright / How could you do it to me
/ Bad luck is falling / Chains and things /
Walking the back streets and crying / I'd
rather drink muddy water / I'm digging you
/ Things have got to change
CD _____ ECD 260262
Evidence / Feb '93 / Harmonia Mundi / ADA
/ Cadillac.

COMPLETE STAX SINGLES, THE
If that ain't a reason (for your woman to
leave you) / Mr. Mailman (I Don't want no
letter) / I'm living off the love you give /
That's what love will make you do / Before
the honeymoon / Walking the back streets
and crying / I'm gonna cry a river / What it
is / Rainy day / Lovin' stick / Who can handle me is you / Tin pan alley / Sweet woman
of mine / Behind closed doors (hey you) I
win / Let me back in / Let your loss be your
lesson / If you talk in your sleep / How could
you do it to me / Packed up and took my
mind
CD _____ CDSXD 106
Stax / Jan '95 / Pinnacle.

LIVE AT WESTVILLE PRISON
CD _____ DE 681
Delmark / Dec '95 / Hot Shot / ADA / CM
/ Direct / Cadillac.

**TENDING HIS ROOTS (Charly R&B
Masters Vol. 17)**
Feel so bad / If walls could talk / Life is like
that / Sweet sixteen / I can't quit you baby
/ I'm mighty grateful / Don't talk back / Reconsider baby / Losing hand / We're gonna
make it / Stormy Monday / Blind man / I'm
gonna move to the outskirts of town / Blues
in the night / Did you ever love a woman /
Who's cheating who / Blues get off my
shoulder / Things I used to do / Don't deceive me / Grits ain't groceries
CD _____ CDRB 17
Charly / Mar '95 / Charly / THE / Cadillac.

TK SESSIONS
CD _____ NEXCD 168
Sequel / May '91 / BMG.

Little Richard

20 CLASSIC CUTS
Long tall Sally / Ready Teddy / Girl can't
help it / Rip it up / Miss Ann / She's got it
/ Lucille / Keep a knockin' / Good golly Miss
Molly / Send me some lovin' / Tutti frutti /
Heebie jeebies / Baby face / Jenny Jenny / By the
light of the silvery moon / True fine mama /
Bama lama bama loo / I'll
never let you go (CD & MC only) / Can't
believe you wanna leave (CD & MC only)
CD _____ CDCH 195
Ace / Jul '90 / Pinnacle / Cadillac / Com-
plete/Pinnacle.

22 GREATEST HITS
CD _____ 830 834-2
Polydor / '89 / PolyGram.

BEST OF LITTLE RICHARD, THE
CD _____ CDSGP 085
Prestige / Nov '93 / Total/BMG.

BOY CAN'T HELP IT, THE
CD _____ QSCD 6008
Charly / Jan '94 / Charly / THE / Cadillac.

COLLECTION: LITTLE RICHARD
CD _____ CCSCD 227
Castle / Jul '89 / BMG.

E.P. COLLECTION, THE
Send me some lovin' / I'm just a lonely guy
/ Miss Ann / Oh why / Can't believe you
wanna leave / She's got it / Girl can't help
it / Jenny Jenny / Heebie jeebies / Slippin'
and slidin' / Baby / Baby face / By the light
of the silvery moon / She knows how to
rock / Early one morning / keep a knockin'
/ Good golly Miss Molly / All around the
world / True fine mama / Shake a hand /
Shake a hand / Chicken little baby / Whole
lotta shakin' goin' on / Rip it up / Tutti frutti
/ Ready teddy / Long tall Sally
CD _____ SEECD 366
See For Miles/C5 / Feb '93 / Pinnacle.

ESSENTIAL COLLECTION
CD Set _____ LECD 609
Wisepack / Apr '95 / THE / Conifer.

FABULOUS LITTLE RICHARD, THE
Tutti frutti / Long tall Sally / Slippin' and sli-
din' / Rip it up / Ready Teddy / She's got it
/ Jenny Jenny / Girl can't help it / Lucille /
Baby face / Keep a knockin' / Good golly
Miss Molly
CD _____ CDFAB 001
Ace / Aug '91 / Pinnacle / Cadillac / Com-
plete/Pinnacle.

FORMATIVE YEARS, THE (1951-1953)
Get rich quick / Why did you leave me / Taxi
blues / Every hour / I brought it all on myself
/ Ain't nothing happening / Thinking 'bout
my mother / Please have mercy on me /
Little Richard's boogie / Directly from my
heart / I love my baby / Maybe I'm right /
Ain't that good news / Rice, red beans and
turnip greens / Always
CD _____ BCD 15448
Bear Family / Jul '89 / Rollercoaster / Direct
/ CM / Swift / ADA.

GREATEST HITS: LITTLE RICHARD
CD _____ PWK 003
Carlton Home Entertainment / '88 /
Carlton Home Entertainment.

**HERE'S LITTLE RICHARD/VOLUME 2/
FABULOUS LITTLE RICHARD (His 3
Original Specialty Albums/3CD Set)**
Tutti frutti / True fine mama / Can't believe
you wanna leave / Ready Teddy / Baby /
Slippin' and slidin' / Long tall Sally / Miss
Ann / Oh why / Rip it up / Jenny Jenny /
She's got it / Keep a knockin' / By the light
of the silvery moon / Send me some lovin'
/ I'll never let you go / Good golly Miss Molly
/ Baby face / Hey hey hey / Ooh my soul /
Girl can't help it / Lucille / Shake a hand /
Chicken little baby / All night long / Heat I
can offer / Lonesome and blue / Wonderin'
/ She knows how to rock / Kansas City /
Directly from my heart / Maybe I'm right /
Early one morning / I'm just a lonely guy /
Whole lotta shakin' goin' on
CD Set _____ ABOXCD 2
Ace / Oct '90 / Pinnacle / Cadillac / Com-
plete/Pinnacle.

HIS GREATEST RECORDINGS
Ready Teddy / Rip it up / Girl can't help it
/ I'll never let you go / Miss Ann / Good golly
Miss Molly / Lucille / Keep a knockin' /
Can't believe you wanna leave / Tutti frutti
/ Heebie jeebies / Send me some lovin' /
Chicken little baby / Hey hey hey / She's
got it / Long tall Sally
CD _____ CDCH 109
Ace / Jul '90 / Pinnacle / Cadillac / Com-
plete/Pinnacle.

KINGS OF BEAT (STAR-CLUB)
CD _____ REP 4159-WZ
Repertoire / Aug '91 / Pinnacle / Cadillac.

LITTLE RICHARD
Whole lotta shakin' goin' on / Rip it up /
Baby face / Send me some lovin' / Girl can't
help it / Lucille / Oh my soul / Jenny Jenny
/ Good golly Miss Molly / Tutti frutti / Long
tall Sally / Keep a knockin' / Hey honey /
Hound dog / Groovy little Suzie / Dancing
all around the world / Slippin' and slidin' /
Lawdy Miss Clawdy / Short fat Fanny /
She's got it
CD _____ LECD 036
Dynamite / May '94 / THE.

LITTLE RICHARD
CD _____ CD 106
Timeless Treasures / Oct '94 / THE.

**LITTLE RICHARD & JIMI HENDRIX
(Little Richard & Jimi Hendrix)**
CD _____ CDCD 1108
Charly / Jul '93 / Charly / THE / Cadillac.

LITTLE RICHARD COLLECTION
CD _____ COL 005
Collection / Jun '95 / Target/BMG.

LITTLE RICHARD VOL.2
Keep a knockin' / Send me some lovin' / I'll
never let you go / All around the world / By
the light of the silvery moon / Good golly
Miss Molly / Baby face / Hey hey hey / Ooh
my soul / Lucille / Girl can't help it
CD _____ CDCHM 131
Ace / Jul '89 / Pinnacle / Cadillac / Com-
plete/Pinnacle.

LUCILLE
Lucille / Long tall Sally / Baby face / Good
golly Miss Molly / Tutti frutti (end s1) / Whole
lotta shakin' goin' on / Money, honey / Girl
can't help it / Jenny Jenny / Hound dog
CD _____ 15080
Laserlight / Aug '91 / Target/BMG.

NOW
CD _____ RNCD 1007
Rhino / Jun '93 / Jetstar / Magnum Music
Group / THE.

**PEARLS FROM THE PAST - LITTLE
RICHARD**
CD _____ KLMCD 004
Scratch / Nov '93 / BMG.

**RIP IT UP - THE LITTLE RICHARD
MEGAMIX**
Tutti frutti / Jenny Jenny / Keep a knockin'
/ Girl can't help it / Long tall Sally / Good
golly Miss Molly / Lucille / Ooh my Sally /
Ready Teddy / Can't believe you wanna
leave / Baby face / She's got it / Rip it up /
Slippin' and slidin' / By the light of the sil-
very moon / True fine Mama / All around the
world / Bama lama bama loo / Miss Ann /
Send me some lovin'
CD _____ ECD 3070
K-Tel / Jan '95 / K-Tel.

SPECIALTY SESSIONS, THE (6CD/8LP Set)
CD Set _____ ABOXCD 1
Ace / Jan '92 / Pinnacle / Cadillac / Complete/Pinnacle.

SPOTLIGHT ON LITTLE RICHARD
Babyface / Tutti frutti / Long tall Sally / Keep a knockin' / Groovy little Suzie / Cherry red / Good golly miss Molly / Girl can't help it / Without love / (Sittin' on) the dock of the bay / Rip it up / Money honey / Short fat fanny / Slippin' and slidin' / Talkin' 'bout soul / She's got it
CD _____ HADCD 117
Javelin / Feb '94 / THE / Henry Hadaway Organisation.

WILD AND WONDERFUL
CD _____ QSCD 6002
Charly / Oct '91 / Charly / THE / Cadillac.

WILDEST, THE
Tutti frutti / Long tall Sally / Slippin' and slidin' / Rip it up / Girl can't help it / Lucille / Send me some lovin' / Jenny Jenny / Keep a knockin' / Good golly Miss Molly / Ooh my soul / Baby face / Ready teddy / She's got it / Miss Ann
CD _____ CDCD 1014
Charly / Mar '93 / Charly / THE / Cadillac.

Little Roy

COLUMBUS SHIP
CD _____ COPCD 001
Copasetic / Oct '93 / Jetstar / Pinnacle / Grapevine.

Little Sonny

BLACK & BLUE
Hung up / Sonny's fever / You got a good thing / Woman named trouble / Honest I do / Wade in the water (instrumental) / Paying through the nose / Memphis B-K (instrumental) / Going home (where women got meat on their bones) / I found love / They want money
CD _____ CDSXE 057
Stax / Jul '93 / Pinnacle.

NEW KING OF THE BLUES HARMONICA/HARD GOIN' UP
Baby, what you want me to do / Eli's pork chop / Hey little girl / Hot potato / Don't ask me no questions / Tomorrow's blues today / Back down yonder / Sad funk / Creeper returns / It's hard going up (but twice as hard coming down) / My woman is good to me / You're spreading yourself a little too thin / Day you left me / You can be replaced / Do it right now / You made me strong / Sure is good / I want you
CD _____ CDSXD 968
Stax / Jul '91 / Pinnacle.

NEW ORLEANS RHYTHM & BLUES
CD _____ BM 9023
Black Magic / Feb '94 / Hot Shot / Swift / CM / Direct / Cadillac / ADA.

SONNY SIDE UP
Sonny side up / Positive mind / I got to find my baby / Let me love you / Ready set go / Best of the best / I'm with you all the way / Tough times never last / Next dance with you
CD _____ NEXCD 276
Sequel / Jun '95 / BMG.

Little Steven

FREEDOM NO COMPROMISE
Freedom / Trail of broken treaties / Pretoria / Bitter fruit / No more party's / Can't you feel the fire / Native American / Sanctuary
CD _____ NSPCD 511
Connoisseur / Apr '95 / Pinnacle.

MEN WITHOUT WOMEN (Little Steven & The Disciples Of Soul)
CD _____ NSPCD 508
Connoisseur / Mar '95 / Pinnacle.

REVOLUTION
Where do we go from here / Education / Love and forgiveness / Sexy / Liberation theology / Revolution / Balance / Newspeak / Leonard Peltier / Discipline
CD _____ 7432115901-2
RCA / Feb '94 / BMG.

VOICE OF AMERICA
Voice of America / Justice / Checkpoint Charlie / Solidarity / Out of the darkness / Los desaparecido (The disappeared ones) / Fear / I am not a patriot (and the river opens for the righteous) / Among the believers / Undefeated (everybody goes home)
CD _____ NSPCD 512
Connoisseur / Apr '95 / Pinnacle.

Little Texas

FIRST TIME FOR EVERYTHING
Some guys have all the luck / First time for everything / Down in the valley / You and forever and me / What you were thinkin' / Dance / Better way / I'd rather miss you / Just one more night / Cry on
CD _____ 7599268202
Warner Bros. / May '92 / Warner Music.

KICK A LITTLE
CD _____ 9362457392
Warner Bros. / Nov '94 / Warner Music.

Little Village

LITTLE VILLAGE
CD _____ 7599267132
Reprise / Feb '95 / Warner Music.

Little Walter

BLUES WITH A FEELING
CD _____ CDBM 23
Charly / Apr '92 / Charly / THE / Cadillac.

BLUES WORLD OF LITTLE WALTER
CD _____ DD 640
Delmark / Nov '93 / Hot Shot / ADA / CM / Direct / Cadillac.

BOSS BLUES HARMONICA
Juke / Can't hold out much longer / Mean old world / Sad hours / Tell me mama / Off the wall / Blues with a feeling / Too late / You're so fine / Last night / You better watch yourself / Blue light / My babe / Thunderbird / I got to go / Boom boom out go the lights / Flying saucer / Last night / Teenage beat / Just a feeling / Shake dancer / Ah'w baby / Back track / Just your fool
CD _____ CDRED 4
Charly / Aug '88 / Charly / THE / Cadillac.

CHESS YEARS 1952-1963, THE (4CD Set)
Juke / Can't hold out much longer / Blue midnight / Boogie / Mean old world / Sad hours / Don't have to hurt no more / Crazy legs / Tonight with a fool / Off the wall / Tell me mama / Quarter to twelve / Blues with a feeling / Lights out / Fast large one / You're so fine / Come back baby / Rocker / Oh baby / I got to find my baby / Big leg mama / Mercy babe / Last night / You'd better watch yourself / Blue eight / Mellow down easy / Thunderbird / My babe / Rollercoaster / I got to go / Little girl / Crazy for my baby / Can't stop loving you / Hate to see you go / One more chance with you / Who / Boom boom (out go the lights) / It ain't right / Flying saucer / It's too late brother / Teenage beat / Take me back / Just a feeling / Nobody but you / Temperature / Shake dancer / Everybody needs somebody / Ah'w baby / I had my fun / Toddle / Confessin' the blues / Key to the highway / Rock bottom / You gonna be sorry / Baby / My baby's sweeter / Crazy mixed up world / Worried life / Everything's gonna be alright / Mean ol' Frisco / Back track / One of these mornings / Blue and lonesome / Me and Piney Brown / Break it up / Goin' down slow / I don't play / As long as I have you / You don't know / Just your fool / Up the line / I'm a business man / Dead presidents / Southern feeling / My kind of baby / I love you so / Instrumental / Walkin' on
CD Set _____ CDREDBOX 5
Chess/Charly / Dec '92 / Charly.

ELECTRIC HARMONICA GENIUS, THE
Juke / Can't hold out much longer / Blue midnight / Mean old world / Sad hours / Quarter to twelve / Blues with a feeling / Last night / Mellow down easy / My babe / Hate to see you / Going down slow / It's too late brother / Everybody needs somebody / Confessin' the blues / Key to the highway / Walkin' on / Everything's gonna be alright / Blue and lonesome / I don't play / Peppers thing / Off the wall / You're so fine / Rocker
CD _____ CD 52011
Blues Encore / '92 / Target/BMG.

WINDY CITY BLUES (Little Walter & Otis Rush)
It's hard for me to believe baby / May be the last time / I feel good / Otis blues / Going down slow / Walter's blues / Lovin' you
CD _____ CDBM 028
Blue Moon / May '91 / Magnum Music Group / Greensleeves / Hot Shot / ADA / Cadillac / Discovery.

Little Whitt

MOODY SWAMP BLUES (Little Whitt & Big Bo)
CD _____ ABP 1001
Alabama Blues Project / Apr '95 / Direct / ADA.

Little Wolf Band

DREAM SONG
Prayer song / Oweegon / Coyote dance / Song for the journey / Moonlight / Jaguar / Night chant / Buffalo nation / Raven / Twisted hair
CD _____ 3202122
Triloka / Sep '95 / New Note.

Littlefield, Willie

GOING BACK TO KAY CEE (Littlefield, Little Willie)
Turn the lamp down low / Last laugh blues / Monday morning blues / Striking on you baby / Blood is redder than wine / K.C. lovin' / Pleading at midnight / Kansas City / Midnight hour was shining / Rock-a-bye baby / Miss K.C.'s fine / Sitting on the curbstone / Jim Wilson's boogie / My best wishes and regards / Please dont go-o-o-

oh / Falling tears / Goofy dust blues / Don't take my heart little girl
CD _____ CDCHD 503
Ace / Jan '95 / Pinnacle / Cadillac / Complete/Pinnacle.

I'M IN THE MOOD (Littlefield, Little Willie)
CD _____ OLCD 7002
Oldie Blues / Oct '93 / Direct / CM.

YELLOW BOOGIE'N'BLUES (Littlefield, Little Willie)
CD _____ OLCD 7006
Oldie Blues / Dec '94 / Direct / CM.

Littlejohn, Johnny

CHICAGO BLUES STARS
CD _____ ARHCD 1043
Arhoolie / Apr '95 / ADA / Direct / Cadillac.

WHEN YOUR BEST FRIEND TURNS THEIR BACK ON YOU
CD _____ JSPCD 246
JSP / Feb '93 / ADA / Target/BMG / Direct / Cadillac / Complete/Pinnacle.

Litton, Martin

MARTIN LITTON
CD _____ SACD 114
Solo Art / Aug '94 / Jazz Music.

Live

MENTAL JEWELRY
Pain lies on the riverside / Operation spirit (the tyranny of tradition) / Beauty of gray / Brothers unaware / Tired of me / Mirror song / Waterboy / Take my anthem / You / Mother earth is a vicious crowd / 10,000 years (peace is now)
CD _____ RARD 10346
Radioactive / Apr '92 / Vital / BMG.

THROWING COPPER
CD _____ RAD 10997
Radioactive / Oct '94 / Vital / BMG.

Live Action Pussy Show

MONSTER LOVE
CD _____ EFA 12292
Musical Tragedies / Aug '95 / SRD.

Live Skull

POSITRACTION
CD _____ GOES ON 29CD
What Goes On / Mar '89 / SRD.

Live Wire

WIRED
CD _____ CDROU 281
Rounder / Dec '90 / CM / Direct / ADA / Cadillac.

Lively Ones

SURF RIDER/SURF DRUMS
Surfbeat / Let's go trippin' / Misirlou / Guitar man / Caterpillar crawl / Walkin' the board / Paradise cove / Goofy foot / Surf rider / Happy gremmie / Hotdoggen / Surfer's lament / Tuff surf / Rik-a-tik / Wild weekend / Bustin' surfboards / Stoked / Surfer boogie / Surf drums / Shootin' the pier / Mr. Moto / Rumble / Forty miles of bad road / Hillbilly surf
CD _____ CDCHD 957
Ace / May '93 / Pinnacle / Cadillac / Complete/Pinnacle.

Livengood, John

CYBORG SALLY
CD _____ AMPCD 025
AMP / Apr '95 / Cadillac / Magnum Music Group.

Liverpool Cathedral Choir

CAROLS FROM LIVERPOOL
Maiden most gentle / Lulling her child / Gaudete, Christus natus est / On this day earth shall ring / Echo carol / Holly and the ivy / Away in a manger / Ding dong merrily on high / Little baby born at dark midnight / Christ is the flower / World's desire / Tomorrow shall be my dancing day / Spotless rose / Lamb lay-ly-bounden / In dulci jubilo / Noble stem of Jesse / Blessed song of God / Tyrley, tyrlow / Alleluia, a new work / Hark the herald angels sing / O come, all ye faithful / Once in royal David's City
CD _____ CDPS 386
Alpha / Nov '91 / Abbey Recording.

YOUR FAVOURITE HYMNS
CD _____ VC 7912092
Virgin Classics / Mar '92 / EMI.

Lives & Times

GREAT SAD HAPPY ENDING, THE
Begin and end / Strange world / Sweet / Wired to the moon / Oversized / You roll through me / One step forward / Quiet afternoon / Sick of ordinary / Good day / Procession

CD _____ SIMPLY 57
SI / Jan '95 / No Image.

THERE AND BACK AGAIN LANE
Why do I watch / Trust me I'm your doctor / Darker / Ten boats on the river / Show me an answer / Lizard baby / Long gone / This years drift
CD _____ CYCL 029
Cyclops / Sep '95 / Pinnacle.

WAITING FOR THE PARADE
Immortal / Corners / Conformity song / Dirty oooroto / I don't want to know today / Deadline / Divide / Hopes of yesterday / Ascent
CD _____ SIMPLY 43
SI / Jan '94 / No Image.

Livin' Blues

HELL'S SESSION
CD _____ REP 4138-WZ
Repertoire / Aug '91 / Pinnacle / Cadillac.

WANG DANG DOODLE
CD _____ REP 4111-WZ
Repertoire / Aug '91 / Pinnacle / Cadillac.

Living Colour

GREATEST HITS
Pride / Sacred ground / Visions / Love rears it's ugly head / These are happy times / Release the pressure / Memories can't wait / Cult of personality / Funny vibe / WTFF / Glamour boys / Open letter to a landlord / Solace of you / Nothingness / Type / Time's up / What's your favourite colour
CD _____ 4810212
Epic / Nov '05 / Sony.

TIME'S UP
Time's up / History lesson / Pride / Love rears its ugly head / New Jack theme / Someone like you / Elvis is dead / Type / Information overload / Under cover of darkness / Ology 1 / Fight the fight / Tag team partners / Solace of you / This is the life
CD _____ 4669202
Epic / Mar '91 / Sony.

Living Proof

LIVING PROOF
Hold on to your dreams / Something I like / Stay forever / Fell in love too late / Where did I go wrong / Apple of my eye / Special invitation / I'll always know
CD _____ CDGEM 4002
Gemc / Jul '89 / Disc.

Livingston, Carlton

EMOTIONS
CD _____ GVDCD 2025
Grapevine / Jun '94 / Grapevine.

Livingstone, Bill

WORLD'S GREATEST PIPERS VOL. 9 (Livingstone, Pipe Major Bill)
CD _____ LCOM 9045
Lismor / Jul '91 / Lismor / Direct / Duncans / ADA.

Lizard Music

FASHIONABLY LAME
Esquire / Kill for a sprinkle / She's a very, very fat fat weirdo / Costume jewelry / Soft focus a.m. / Goin' back to Orangeland / Routine / Jacko's book / Water / Deep in the heart of Texas / Howard's machinery / I see France / Frugal lame
CD _____ WDOM 017CD
World Domination / Jul '95 / Pinnacle.

Lizzy Borden

BEST OF LIZZY BORDEN
CD _____ CDMZORRO 72
Metal Blade / May '94 / Pinnacle.

MASTER OF DISGUISE
Master of disguise / One false move / Love is a crime / Sins of the flesh / Phantoms never too young / Be one of us / Psychodrama / Waiting in the wings / Roll over and play dead / Under the nose / We got the power
CD _____ RR 9454-2
Roadrunner / Aug '89 / Pinnacle.

VISUAL LIES
CD _____ RR 349592
Roadrunner / Sep '87 / Pinnacle.

Llan De Cubel

DEVA
CD _____ FA 8701CD
Fono Astur / Jul '95 / ADA.

L'OTRU DE LA MAR
CD _____ FA 8734CD
Fono Astur / Jul '95 / ADA.

Lloyd, A.L.

BALLADS ET SHANTIES (Lloyd, A.L. & Friends)
CD _____ SCM 030CD
Diffusion Breizh / Aug '94 / ADA.

CLASSIC A.L. LLOYD
CD _____ FECD 098
Fellside / Jul '94 / Target/BMG / Direct /
ADA.

Lloyd, Charles

ALL MY RELATIONS
Piercing the veil / Little peace / Thelonious
theonlyus / Cape to Cairo suite / Evanstide,
where lotus bloom / All my relations /
Hymme to the Mother / Milarepa
CD _____ 5273442
ECM / May '95 / New Note.

CALL, THE (Lloyd, Charles Quartet)
Nocturne / Song / Dwija / Glimpse / Imke /
Amarma / Figure in blue, memories of Duke
/ Blessing / Brother on the rooftop
CD _____ 5177192
ECM / Oct '93 / New Note.

FISH OUT OF WATER (Lloyd, Charles Quartet)
Fish out of water / Haghia Sophia / Dirge /
Bharti / Eyes of love / Mirror
CD _____ 8410882
ECM / Jan '90 / New Note.

NOTES FROM BIG SUR
Requim / Sister / Pilgrimage to the mountain / Sam song / Takur / Monk in Paris /
When Miss Jessye sings / Pilgrimage to the
mountain - part 2 surrender
CD _____ 5119992
ECM / May '92 / New Note.

Lloyd, David

CYFOL 1 (1940-41)
CD _____ SCD 2076
Sain / Aug '95 / Direct / ADA.

Lloyd, Floyd

MEET LAUREL AITKEN (Lloyd, Floyd & Potato Five)
CD _____ GAZCD 001
Gaz's Rockin' Records / '89 / Pinnacle.

Lloyd, John

SYZGY (Lloyd, John Quartet)
CD _____ CDLR 173
Leo / '90 / Wellard / Cadillac / Impetus.

Lloyd-Langton, Huw

RIVER RUN (Lloyd-Langton, Huw Group)
CD _____ LLG 6CD
Allegro / Dec '94 / Plastic Head.

Lloyd-Tucker, Colin

SKYSCAPING
CD _____ BAH 8
Humbug / Jul '93 / Pinnacle.

Lo, Ismael

DIAWAR
CD _____ STCD 1027
Sterns / Nov '89 / Sterns / CM.

ISMAEL LO
CD _____ CIDM 1093
Mango / Mar '92 / Vital / PolyGram.

ISO
Dibi dibi rek / Nafanta / La femme sans
haine / Rero / Senegambie / Baol Baol / Nabou / Nassarane / Wassalia / Setsinala /
Khar / Samayaye
CD _____ 522362-2
Mango / Jun '94 / Vital / PolyGram.

Lo-Key

BACK 2 DA HOUSE
Welcome / Back 2 da howse / 26c / Don't
trip on me / Getcha girlfriend / Li'l shumpin',
shumpin' / Tasty / Play with me / Good ole
fashion love / Turn around / Call my name
/ Interlude / My desire / We ain't right /
Come on in
CD _____ 5490102
Perspective / Dec '94 / PolyGram.

Lobban, David

101 SINGALONG WURLITZER FAVOURITES
CD _____ SOW 506
Sound Waves / Jul '93 / Target/BMG.

STEP BY STEP VOLUME 1
CD _____ SEQCD 001
Sound Waves / Jan '94 / Target/BMG.

STEP BY STEP VOLUME 2
CD _____ SEQCD 002
Sound Waves / Jan '94 / Target/BMG.

STEP BY STEP VOLUME 3
CD _____ SEQCD 003
Sound Waves / Jan '94 / Target/BMG.

STEP BY STEP VOLUME 4
CD _____ SEQCD 004
Sound Waves / Jan '94 / Target/BMG.

STEP BY STEP VOLUME 5
CD _____ SEQCD 005
Sound Waves / Jan '94 / Target/BMG.

STEP BY STEP VOLUME 6
CD _____ SEQCD 006
Sound Waves / Jul '94 / Target/BMG.

STEP BY STEP VOLUME 7
CD _____ SEQCD 007
Sound Waves / Jul '94 / Target/BMG.

WURLITZER FAVOURITES
CD _____ SOW 514
Sound Waves / Jul '94 / Target/BMG.

Lobo

VERY BEST OF LOBO, THE
CD _____ 8122712542
Rhino / Mar '95 / Warner Music.

Lobotomy

LOBOTOMY
CD _____ CHAOSCD 004
Chaos / Jan '96 / Plastic Head.

Locke, Jimmy

DANCETIME AT THE ORGAN VOL. 3
CD _____ SAV 236CD
Savoy / Dec '95 / THE / Savoy.

IT'S DANCE TIME
CD _____ SAV 188CD
Savoy / May '93 / THE / Savoy.

JIMMY LOCKE PLAYS MUSIC MUSIC MUSIC
Heartaches / Amy / I'm a dreamer (aren't
we all) / Little girl / I wonder who's kissing
her now / True love / My mothers pearls /
Memories / Foolishly yours / Yesterdays
dreams / I apologise / How soon / Too
young / Only you / Just loving you / Be
careful it's my heart / Till / Petticoats of Portugal / From here to eternity / Return to me
/ In the spirit of the moment / I talk to the
trees / Amapola / Strangers in the night /
Oh Donna CLara / You were meant for me
/ Pretty baby / Heart of my heart / Breezin'
along with the breeze / Someday (you'll
want me to want you) / C'est magnifique /
Rose of Washington Square / Whispering /
Broadway melody / Is it true what they say
in love with you / Under the lidden tree the
one rose / When your old wedding ring was
new / Pal of my cradle days / Kiss me again
/ Cry / If I could only make you care / Sierra
Sue / Nevertheless / You were only fooling
/ There must be a way
CD _____ SAV 171CD
Savoy / Mar '92 / THE / Savoy.

JIMMY'S MAGIC MELODIES
If your face wants to laugh/Follow the swallow / Three little words/Everything in rhythm
with my heart / Silver wedding waltz/Last
waltz of the evening / Kiss in your eyes/
Memories live longer than dreams / Look for
the silver lining/When did you leave heaven
/ My gypsy dream girl/If I didn't care / Glory
of love / Rock-a-bye your baby/Have you
ever been lonely / It's magic/Don't take your
love from me / Love is all / Fools rush in /
Cherry pink and apple blossom white/Love
me tender / Mr. Sandman/Five foot two,
eyes of blue / Wait till the sun shines Nellie/
I'm nobody's baby / Please/Shine through
my dreams / Once in a while/Portrait of
love / Your lips are red / Isle of Capri/Echo
of a serenade / Maybe/Shepherd of the
hills/Home / It had to be you/Love letters in
the sand
CD _____ SAV 175CD
Savoy / Jul '92 / THE / Savoy.

Locke, Joe

RESTLESS DREAMS (Locke, Joe-Phil Markowitz Quartet)
Restless dreams / My foolish heart / Kahalid
the warrior / May moon (Phil Markowitz) /
You and I / Calypso nouveau
CD _____ CHIEFCD 1
Chief / Mar '89 / Cadillac.

Locke, Josef

HEAR MY SONG
Hear my song Violetta / Soldier's dream /
March of the Grenadiers / Blaze away /
Goodbye you / At the end of the day / Mother
Machree / Love's last word is spoken / Cara
mia / O maiden, my maiden / If I could hear
again Kathleen / Holy City / Drinking song /
Santa Lucia / When you were sweet sixteen
/ Count your blessings / My heart and I /
Goodbye (from the The White Horse Inn) /
Galway Bay / Macushla / Rose of Tralee /
Bard of Armagh / When it's moonlight in
Mayo / How can you buy Killarney / Dear
old Donegal / Isle of Innisfree / Maire my girl
/ Shades of Old Blarney / Shawl of Galway
grey
CD Set _____ CDDL 1033
EMI / Nov '92 / EMI.

HEAR MY SONG - THE BEST OF JOSEF LOCKE
Hear my song Violetta / I'll take you home
again Kathleen / Blaze away / Count your
blessings / Oh maiden, my maiden / Drinking song / Love's last word is spoken /
Charmaine / You are my heart's delight / If

I can help somebody / Cara mia / Come
back to Sorrento / It is no secret / When
you were sweet sixteen / Rose of Slievenamon / You'll never forget about Ireland /
Eileen O'Grady / I'll walk beside you / At the
end of the day / My heart and I / How can
you buy Killarney / When you talk about old
Ireland / If I were a blackbird / Garden
where the praties grow / Goodbye
CD _____ CDGO 2034
EMI / Feb '92 / EMI.

HYMNS WE ALL LOVE
All people that on earth do dwell / When the
roll is called up yonder / Old rugged cross
/ Lead kindly light / One love everlasting /
There's a great new prospect in the sky /
Onward Christian soldiers / It is no secret /
Nearer my God to thee / Shall we gather at
the river / Abide with me / God be with you
till we meet again
CD _____ DOCD 2027
Koch / Nov '93 / Koch.

LET THERE BE PEACE - COLLECTED SONGS
CD _____ ARANCD 601
Aran / Nov '95 / CM / Koch.

SINGALONG
In the shade of the old apple tree / My bonnie lies over the ocean / Daisy Daisy / East
side, west side / Sweet Rosie O'Grady /
She's only a bird in a gilded cage / In this
good old summertime / If those lips could
only speak / Clementine / Michael, row the
boat ashore / He's got the whole world in
his hands / John Brown's body / Red river
valley / On top of old smokey / Beautiful
brown eyes / Old faithful / Roll along covered wagon / South of the border / Let him
go, let him tarry / Ma goes Dixie / Rose of
Tralee / Slaney Valley / Where the Blarney
roses grow / Heaven street / Saints / Down
by the Severnside / Loch Lomond / Annie
Laurie / Will ye no' come back again / Oh
Susanna / Beautiful dreamer / Camptown
races / Quartermaster's stores / Old soldiers never die
CD _____ DOCD 2026
Koch / Nov '93 / Koch.

SONGS I LOVED SO WELL, THE
CD _____ HMCD 5
Outlet / Jan '95 / ADA / Duncans / CM /
Ross / Direct / Koch.

TAKE A PAIR OF SPARKLING EYES
It's a grand life in the army / Take a pair of
sparkling eyes / Macushla / Dear old Donegal / St. Lucia / Galway Bay / While the
Angelus was ringing / Old bog road / Wonderful Copenhagen / Soldier's dream /
Mother Machree / Maire my girl / Soldiers
of the Queen / Shades of old Blarney / Rose
of Tralee / When it's moonlight in Mayo /
Toselli's serenade / Bless this house / Bard
of Armagh / March of the grenadiers /
Shawl of Galway grey / Tobermory bay / Isle
of Innisfree / Ireland must be heaven / Ave
Maria
CD _____ CDP 7996402
EMI / Jun '92 / EMI.

TEAR, A KISS, A SMILE, A
Melba waltz (dream time) / Tonight beloved
(Ritorna amore) / Holy city / In the chapel in
the moonlight / People like us / Brown bird
singing / Bonnie Mary of Argyle / My miss-daughter of Rose of Tralee / Beneath
thy window (O solo mio) / When you're in
love / Love me and the world is mine /
Strange music / Song of songs / When you
hear Big Ben / (It happened at the) festival
of roses / We all have a song in our hearts
/ Tear, a kiss, a smile / Keys to heaven /
Hush-a-bye Rose of Killarney / You're just
a flower from an old bouquet / Love me little, love me long / Teddy bears' picnic / Silent night / O come all ye faithful (Adeste
fidelis)
CD _____ CDGO 2042
EMI / Aug '92 / EMI.

Lockheart, Mark

MATHERAN (Lockheart, Mark & John Parricelli)
CD _____ IS 02CD
Isis / Apr '94 / ADA / Direct.

Locklin, Hank

MAGIC OF HANK LOCKLIN, THE
Please help me, I'm falling / Geisha girl /
Happy birthday to me / Happy journey /
Send me the pillow that you dream on / Let
me be the one / It's a little more like heaven
/ Flying South / From here to there to you /
I was coming home to you / We're gonna
go fishin' / Queen of hearts / Mysteries of
life / I'm lonely darling / Come share the
sunshine with me / Your sweet love / To whom
it may concern / Tell me you love me / Who
you think you're foolin' / I could call you
darling
CD _____ TKOCD 025
TKO / May '92 / TKO.

PLEASE HELP ME I'M FALLING
Please help me, I'm falling / Geisha girl /
Send me the pillow that you dream on / It's
a little more like heaven / Let me be the one
/ Happy Birthday to me / Happy journey /
Down on my knees / Night life queen / Daytime love affair / There never was a time /
Baby I need you

CD _____ CDCD 1062
Charly / Mar '93 / Charly / THE / Cadillac.

PLEASE HELP ME I'M FALLING (4CD Set)
CD _____ BCD 15730
Bear Family / Jun '95 / Rollercoaster /
Direct / CM / Swift / ADA.

Locks, Fred

BLACK STAR LINER
CD _____ STCD 001
Starlight / Nov '94 / Jetstar.
CD _____ VPCD 2037
VP / Sep '95 / Jetstar.

LOVE & ONLY LOVE
CD _____ TMCD 2
Tribesman / Nov '94 / Jetstar / SRD.

Lockwood, Didier

NEW YORK RENDEZ-VOUS
Juggling in Central Park / Waltzy / Cousin
William / Anbatole blues / Gordon / Reminiscence / Don't drive so fast / Eastern
dance / Tom Thumb
CD _____ JMS 186692
JMS / May '95 / BMG / New Note.

Lockwood, Robert Jnr.

CONTRASTS
Little blue boy / Hold everything / Come day
go day / Dust my broom / Annie's boogie /
Majors, minors and ninths / Drivin' wheel /
Forever on my mind / Funny, but true / I am
to blame / Mr. Downchild / Howdy dowdy /
Lonely man / Empty life
CD _____ TRIX 3307
Trix / Nov '93 / New Note.

PLAYS ROBERT JOHNSON
CD _____ BLE 597402
Black & Blue / Sep '92 / Wellard / Koch.

STEADY ROLLIN' MAN
CD _____ DD 630
Delmark / Jan '93 / Hot Shot / ADA / CM /
Direct / Cadillac.

Locust

TRUTH IS BORN OF ARGUMENTS
Truth is born of arguments / Penetration / I
feel cold inside because of the things you
say / Saturated love / When we coincide / I
believe in a love I may never know / Optimist / I became overwhelmed / I am afraid
of who I am / Inside I am crying / Love you
cruelly gave me would not last
CD _____ AMB 5940CD
R & S / Jan '95 / Vital.

WEATHERED WELL
Prospero / Moist moss / Xenophobe /
Weathered gate / Tamed / Still / Music
about love / Lust / Fawn
CD _____ AMB 3929CD
Apollo / Mar '94 / Vital.

Locust Fudge

ROYAL FLUSH
CD _____ GRCD 370
Glitterhouse / Jun '95 / Direct / ADA.

Lodge, J.C.

I BELIEVE IN YOU
I believe in you / I found love / Let me down
easy / Too good to be true / Night work /
Cool mover / Given up / You don't want my
love / Together we will stay / Happy now
sorry later
CD _____ RRTGCD 7712
Rohit / '88 / Jetstar.

SELFISH LOVER
Love's gonna break your heart / Conversations / Way up / I am in love / Sweet
dreams / Cautious / Operator / Hardcore
loving / Selfish love / Telephone love / Love
me baby / Lonely nights / Since you came
into my life
CD _____ GRELCD 143
Greensleeves / Apr '90 / Total/BMG / Jetstar / SRD.

SPECIAL REQUEST
CD _____ RASCD 3168
Ras / Jun '95 / Jetstar / Greensleeves /
SRD / Direct.

TO THE MAX
CD _____ RASCD 3128
Ras / Nov '94 / Jetstar / Greensleeves /
SRD / Direct.

Lodge, June

SOMEONE LOVES YOU HONEY
CD _____ RGCD 6053
Rocky One / Mar '94 / Jetstar.

Loeb, Chuck

MY SHINING HOUR
Chant / Asi sera / My shining hour / If I were
a bell / Maxine / Let all notes ring / Tarde
(Milton Nascimento) / I just can't stop loving
you / Burnet / My funny valentine
CD _____ 66053009
Jazz City / Feb '91 / New Note.

Loeb, Lisa

TAILS (Loeb, Lisa & Nine Stories)
It's over / Snow day / Taffy / When all the stars are falling / Do you sleep / Hurricane / Rose-colored times / Sandalwood / Alone waiting for Wednesday / Lisa listen / Garden of delights / Stay
CD _____ GED 24734
Geffen / Sep '95 / BMG.

Lofgren, Nils

BEST OF NILS LOFGREN, THE
CD _____ CDMID 160
A&M / Oct '92 / PolyGram.

CHRONICLES
CD Set _____ 5404112
A&M / Oct '92 / PolyGram.

CODE OF THE ROAD
Secrets in the street / Across the tracks / Delivery night / Cry tough / Dreams die hard / Believe / Sun hasn't set on this boy yet / Code of the road / Moontears / Back it up / Like rain
CD _____ CLACD 311
Castle / '92 / BMG.

CRY TOUGH
Cry tough / It's not a crime / Incidentally... it's over / It's over / For your love / Share a little / Mud in your eye / Can't get closer / You lit a fire / Jailbait
CD _____ CDMID 122
A&M / Oct '92 / PolyGram.

DAMAGED GOODS
CD _____ ESSCD 337
Essential / Oct '95 / Total/BMG.

DON'T WALK ROCK (The Best Of Nils Lofgren)
Moontears (Live) / Back it up / Keith don't go / Sun hasn't set on this boy yet / Goin' back / Cry tough / Jailbait / Can't get closer / Mud in your eye / I came to dance / To be a dreamer / No mercy / Steal away / Baltimore / Shine silently / Secrets in the street / Flip ya flip / Delivery night / Anytime at all (Live)
CD _____ VSOPCD 152
Connoisseur / Jun '90 / Pinnacle.

EVERY BREATH
CD _____ PERMCD 28
Permanent / Oct '94 / Total/BMG.

FLIP
Flip ya flip / Secrets in the street / From the heart / Delivery night / King of the rock / Sweet midnight / New holes in old shoes / Dreams die hard / Big tears fall / Beauty and the beast
CD _____ CLACD 312
Castle / Nov '92 / BMG.

LIVE ON THE TEST
CD _____ WHISCD 001
Windsong / May '94 / Pinnacle.

SHINE SILENTLY
Secrets in the street / Flip ya flip / King of the rock / Delivery night / New holes in old shoes / Keith don't go (live) / Like rain (live) / Shine silently (live) / I came to dance (live) / Anytime at all (live) / Beauty and the beast / Dreams die hard / From the heart / Sweet midnight
CD _____ 5507502
Spectrum/Karussell / Jan '95 / PolyGram THE.

SOFT FUN TOUGH TEARS 1971-1979
CD _____ RVCD 44
Raven / Jun '95 / Direct / ADA.

Luft

ONCE AROUND THE FAIR
CD _____ CRECD 047
Creation / Jun '89 / 3MV / Vital.

Loft Line

NINE STEPS
CD _____ BEST 1041CD
Acoustic Music / Nov '93 / ADA.

Loftus, Caroline

SUGAR
CD _____ LRF 268
Larrikin / Oct '93 / Roots / Direct / ADA / CM.

Logan, Giuseppi

MORE GIUSEPPI LOGAN
CD _____ ESP 1013
ESP / Feb '93 / Jazz Horizons / Jazz Music.

Logan, Jack

BULK
Fuck everything / Shrunken head / Love not lunch / Female Jesus / Escape clause / Underneath your bed / Just go away / Lazy girl blues / New used car and a plate of Bar-B-Que / Opposite direction / Fifteen years in Indiana / Heart attack on the prairie / Optimist / Voodoo doll / Chloroform / Vegetable belt / Aloha-ha / Sweetest fruit / Lovely / Sometimes it's you / Monday night / Giant city, tiny town / Graves are fun to dig /

Floating cowboy / Peace o' mind / Ship-building blues / Parishioners / Would I be happy then / Farsighted / On the beach / Yes I can / Grey steel train / Drunken arms / Good times, bad memories / Shit for brains / Heaven on earth / Idiot's waltz / Terminal gate / Weathermen / Tex / Cartoons / Town crier
CD Set _____ 89261-2
Medium Cool / Jul '94 / Vital.

MOOD ELEVATOR
Teach me the rules / Unscathed / Chinese Lorraine / When it all comes down / My new town / Ladies and gentlemen / Just babies / Sky won't fall / No offense / Another life / Estranged / Neon tombstone / What's tickling you / What was burned / Vintage man / Suicide doors / Bleed
CD _____ 892902
Restless / Jan '96 / Vital.

Logan, Johnny

LIVING FOR LOVING
Living for loving / I don't want to fall in love / In London / Man with the accordion / Hey kid / Sad little woman / Carneval do Brazil / Honesty / Lonely tonight / Please please please
CD _____ PZA 002CD
Plaza / Feb '94 / Pinnacle.

Logan, Michael

NIGHT OUT
Unit 7 / Cry me a river / Recado bossa nova / Night out / Newark / Hello / Blue vibration / Dat dere / Blues on the spot
CD _____ MCD 5458
Muse / Feb '95 / New Note / CM.

Logg

LOGG
You've got that something / Dancing into the stars / Something else / I know you will / Lay it on the line / Sweet to me
CD _____ CPCD 8076
Charly / Mar '95 / Charly / THE / Cadillac.

Loggins, Kenny

NIGHTWATCH
CD _____ 9829652
Pickwick/Sony Collector's Choice / Jun '93 / Carlton Home Entertainment / Pinnacle / Sony.

OUTSIDE: FROM THE REDWOODS
Conviction of the heart / What a fool believes / Your mama don't dance / I would do anything / Now and then / Angry eyes / If you believe / Celebrate me home / Love will follow / Leap of faith / This is it / Footloose / I'm alright
CD _____ 474347 2
Columbia / Oct '93 / Sony.

Logsdon, Jimmy

I GOT A ROCKET IN MY POCKET
Hank Williams sings the blues no more / Death of Hank Williams / It's all over but the shouting / I can't make up my mind / No longer / I'm gonna back to Tennessee / Midnight boogie / My sweet French baby / Good deal Lucille / Pa-paya Mama / I got a rocket in my pocket / You're gone baby / Where the Rio de Rosa flows / You ain't nothing but the blues / Love you gave to me / One way ticket to nowhere / Let's have a happy time / As long as we're together / In the Mission of St. Augustine / Where the old red river flows / That's when I'll love you the best / Midnight blues / Cold, cold rain / I'll never know / These lonesome blues / I wanna be Mama'd / (We've reached the) Beginning of the end / Road of regret
CD _____ BCD 15650
Bear Family / Oct '93 / Rollercoaster / Direct / CM / Swift / ADA.

Lohan, Sinead

WHO DO YOU THINK I AM
CD _____ DARA 186CD
Dara / Apr '95 / Roots / CM / Direct / ADA / Koch.
CD _____ GRACD 207
Grapevine / Aug '95 / Grapevine.

Lois

BET THE SKY
CD _____ KLP 36 CD
K / Nov '95 / SRD.

BUTTERFLY KISS
Davey / Narcissus / Press play and record / Staring at the sun / Valentine / Stroll always / Spray / Never last / Bonds in seconds / Sorara / Look who's sorry
CD _____ KLP 15 CD
K / Nov '95 / SRD.

STRUMPET
CD _____ KLP 21 CD
K / Nov '95 / SRD.

Loitima

LOITIMA
CD _____ KICD 106
KICD / Nov '95 / ADA.

Loketo

EXTRA BALL
CD _____ SHCD 64028
Shanachie / Jul '91 / Koch / ADA / Greensleeves.

Lol Interceps

MUSIC FOR MOVIES
CD _____ MHCD 023
Minus Habens / Nov '94 / Plastic Head.

Lolitas

FUSEE D'AMOUR
CD _____ ROSE 170CD
New Rose / Apr '89 / Direct / ADA.

Lombardi, Carlos

TANGO ARGENTINA
CD _____ SOW 90111
Sounds Of The World / Sep '93 / Target/BMG.

Lombardo, Guy

I'LL SEE YOU IN MY DREAMS
(Lombardo, Guy & His Royal Canadians)
Deep purple / Boom / Faithful forever / Start the day right / Nearness of you / When the swallows come back to Capistrano / Scatterbrain / It's a hap-hap-happy day / I don't want to set the world on fire / Rainbow valley / Concerto in the park / Blues in the night / Along the Sante fe trail / Tea for two / Hawaiian war chant / Who / Three little fishes / Cancel the flowers / Take it easy / I'll see you in my dreams / It's love love love / Goodnight sweetheart
CD _____ RAJCD 851
Empress / May '95 / THE.

LIVE AT THE WALDORF
Horatio Nelson / Jul '95 / THE / BMG / Avid/BMG / Koch.
CD _____ CDSIV 1141

UNCOLLECTED 1950, THE (Lombardo, Guy & His Royal Canadians)
CD _____ HCD 187
Hindsight / Jan '95 / Target/BMG / Jazz Music.

London Adventist Choral

DEEP RIVER
CD _____ PDSM 1
Paradisum / Aug '95 / Grapevine.

London All Stars Steel...

LATIN AMERICAN HITS (London All Stars Steel Orchestra)
CD _____ EUCD 1161
ARC / '91 / ARC Music / ADA.

London Beat

HARMONY
You bring the sun / Lover you send me colours / That's how I feel about you / Some lucky guy / Secret garden / Give a gift to yourself / Harmony / All born equal / Rainbow ride / Keeping the memories alive / Sea of tranquility
CD _____ 74321 11060-2
RCA / Apr '94 / BMG.

London Community Gospel..

GOSPEL GREATS (London Community Gospel Choir)
Swing low, sweet chariot / Precious Lord, amazing grace / Nobody knows the trouble I've seen / What a friend we have in Jesus / Kumbaya / Count your blessings / Love lifted me / When the saints go marching in / There is a great host far away / Oh happy day / Old rugged cross
CD _____ CDMFP 5731
Music For Pleasure / Apr '91 / EMI.

London Festival Orchestra

SILENT NIGHT
CD _____ CNCD 5933
Hermanex / Nov '92 / THE.

London Funk Allstars

LONDON FUNK VOL.1
Sure shot / Coolin' out / Booyakka / Six million dollar man / Listen to the beat / So good / Fetch / What's in the basket / Represent / Funky sweater / Chicago / Everybody get funky / Chun Li vs. Wah Wah Man / Wikki's revenge / Good life / Body rock / Can ya understand (On CD only) / Bang boogie boogie (On CD only)
CD _____ ZENCD 016
Ninja Tune / May '95 / Vital / Kudos.

London Gabrieli Brass...

UNDER THE INFLUENCE OF JAZZ (London Gabrieli Brass Ensemble)
CD _____ CDTTD 569
Timeless Traditional / Mar '92 / New Note.

London, Julie

ALL THROUGH THE NIGHT (Songs Of Cole Porter)
I've got you under my skin / You do something to me / Get out of town / All through the night / So in love / At long last love / Easy to love / My heart belongs to daddy / Every time we say goodbye / In the still of the night
CD _____ JASCD 308
Jasmine / May '94 / Wellard / Swift / Conifer / Cadillac / Magnum Music Group.

CRY ME A RIVER
Cry me a river / Boy on a dolphin / Saddle the wind / Must be catchin' / Come on-a my house / Broken hearted melody / Love letters / Besame mucho / Vaya con dios / I'm coming back to you / When snowflakes fall in the Summer / Say wonderful things / End of the world / Fascination / Second time around / More / Girl talk / I left my heart in San Francisco / Good life / Our day will come
CD _____ CDSL 8267
Music For Pleasure / Nov '95 / EMI.

JULIE IS HER NAME VOLS. 1 & 2
CD _____ CDP 7998042
Liberty / Oct '92 / EMI.

London Philharmonic...

TORVILL & DEAN'S FIRE AND ICE (London Philharmonic Orchestra)
Fire and ice / Prelude/ Fire world / Ice world / Meeting / Ice court / Mask dance / Ice warriors / Skating lesson / Fire and ice(love duet) / Ambush / Lament/war dance / Melting/battle / After the war / Dance of hope
CD _____ CASTCD 7
First Night / Nov '86 / Pinnacle.

London Ragtime Orchestra

EASY WINNERS
Easy winners / Bright star blues / Mr. Jelly Lord / Pleasant moments / Do doodle oom / Ory's creole trombone / Magnetic rag / Louisiana swing / Solace / Black bottom stomp / Sunflower slow drag / Silver leaf rag / Wolverines / Kiss me sweet / Cornet chop suey / Heliotrope bouquet / Grant
CD _____ LRHOCD 501
LRO / Jan '93 / Jazz Music / Cadillac.

London Studio Orchestra

MUSIC OF MORRICONE
CD _____ ENTCD 269
Entertainers / Jul '88 / Target/BMG.

London Symphony Orchestra

CLASSIC ROCK - THE LIVING YEARS
I want it all / External flame / Against all odds / I still haven't found what I'm looking for / Sailing / Eloise / Smooth criminal / Clouds over aysgarth/In the air tonight / Prelude in motion/The first time / Groovy kind of love / One moment in time / Living years
CD _____ 4660502
Epic / May '91 / Sony.

CLASSIC ROCK 2 (The Second Movement)
Eve of the war / Pinball wizard / Hey Joe / Day in the life / Question / Space oddity / God only knows / River deep, mountain high / American trilogy / Don't cry for me Argentina
CD _____ TCD 6002
Telstar / Dec '88 / BMG.

CLASSIC ROCK 3 (Rhapsody In Black)
Fanfare intro-rhapsody in black / Reach out, I'll be there / You keep me hangin' on / First time ever I saw your face / Superstition / Standing in the shadows of love / Don't leave me this way / Tears of a clown / Rasputin / I heard it through the grapevine / Ain't no mountain high enough
CD _____ TCD 6003
Telstar / Nov '86 / BMG.

CLASSIC ROCK 4 (Rock Classics)
Get back / Layla / Stairway to heaven / Baker Street / Another brick in the wall pt 2 / Jet / Ruby Tuesday / I don't like Mondays / Bright eyes / Hey Jude
CD _____ TCD 6004
Telstar / Dec '88 / BMG.

CLASSIC ROCK 5 (Rock Symphonies)
Born to run / For your love / Chariots of fire / House of the rising sun / You really got me / MacArthur park / Eye of the tiger / Vienna / She's out of my life / Pictures of Lily / Since you've been gone / Gloria
CD _____ TCD 6005
Telstar / Dec '88 / BMG.

CLASSIC ROCK COUNTDOWN
Final countdown / Take my breath away / You can call me Al / Lady in red / Separate lives / We don't need another hero / It's a sin / Sex won't give up / You're the voice / Abbey road medley / Golden slumbers / Carry that weight / End
CD _____ 4604822
CBS / Mar '90 / Sony.

407

POWER OF CLASSIC ROCK (London Symphony Orchestra & London Choral Society)
Two tribes, relax / I want to know what love is / Drive / Purple rain / Time after time / Born in the USA / Power of love / Thriller / Total eclipse of the heart / Hello / Modern Girl / Dancing in the dark
CD _____ 4634022
Epic / Feb '89 / Sony.

POWER OF CLASSIC ROCK/LIVING YEARS/COUNTDOWN (3CD Set)
Two tribes/Relax / Drive / Purple rain / Time after time / I want to know what love is / Born in the USA/Dancing in the dark / Power of love / Thriller / Total eclipse of the heart / Hello / Modern girl / I want it all / Eternal flame / Against all odds / I still haven't found what I'm looking for / Sailing / Eloise / Smooth criminal / Clouds over aysgarth/In the air tonight / Prelude in motion/The first time / Groovy kind of love / One moment in time / Living years / Final countdown / Take my breath away / You can call me Al / Lady in red / Separate lives / It's a sin / She's not there / Don't give up / You're the voice / Golden slumbers / Carry that weight / End
CD Set _____ 4775172
Columbia / Oct '94 / Sony.

London Welsh Male Voice..

IN BRIGHT ARRAY ASSEMBLE (1000 Welsh Voices) (London Welsh Male Voice Choir)
Roman war song / Soldier's farewell / Pilgrims / O Gymru / Myfanwy / Crimond / Tydi a roddaist / Rhythm of life / Rose / Love changes everything / Casatschok / Dry bones / Y nefoedd / Timeless moment / Y dref wen / Where shall I be / An American triology / Finlandia / Bryn myrddin / Cwm rhondda
CD _____ QPRZ 015D
Polyphonic / Jan '95 / Conifer.

Lone Justice

BBC LIVE IN CONCERT
CD _____ WINCD 048
Windsong / Oct '93 / Pinnacle.

SHELTER
I found love / Shelter / Reflected / Beacon / Wheels / Belfry / Dreams come true / Gift / Inspiration / Dixie storms
CD _____ GFLD 19059
Geffen / Feb '94 / BMG.

Lone Star

LONE STAR
She said / Lonely soldier / Flying in the reel / Spaceships / New day / Million stars / Illusions
CD _____ BGOCD 183
Beat Goes On / Apr '93 / Pinnacle.

Lonely, Roy

ACTION SHOTS
CD _____ USMCD 1024
Marilyn / Sep '93 / Direct.

Lonesome Pine Fiddlers

WINDY MOUNTAIN
Pain in my heart / Lonesome sad and blue / Don't forget me / Will I meet Mother in Heaven / You broke your promise / I'm left alone / Nobody cares (not even you) / Twenty one years / My brown eyed darling / You left me to cry / That's why you left me so blue / I'll never make you blue / Honky tonk blues / You're so good / I'll never change my mind / Dirty dishes blues / Lonesome pine breakin' / Free string rag / Baby you're cheatin' / I'm feeling for you (but I can't reach you) / Some kinda sorry / Windy mountain / No curb service / New set of blues / There's just one you
CD _____ ECD 501
Rollercoaster / Apr '92 / CM / Swift.

Lonesome River Band

OLD COUNTRY TOWN
CD _____ SH 3818CD
Sugarhill / Mar '94 / Roots / CM / ADA / Direct.

Lonesome Standard Time

LONESOME AS IT GETS
CD _____ SHCD 3839
Sugarhill / Oct '95 / Roots / CM / ADA / Direct.

MIGHTY LONESOME
CD _____ SH 3816CD
Sugarhill / Mar '94 / Roots / CM / ADA / Direct.

Lonesome Strangers

LONESOME STRANGERS
CD _____ HCD 8016
Hightone / Sep '94 / ADA / Koch.

Lonesome Sundown

BEEN GONE TOO LONG
They call me sundown / One more night / Louisiana lover man / Dealin' from the bottom / Midnight blues again / Just got to know / Black cat bone / I betcha / You don't miss your water / If you ain't been to Houston
CD _____ HCD 8031
Hightone / Jun '94 / ADA / Koch.

I'M A MOJO MAN
Gonna stick to you baby / I'm a mojo man / I stood by / Don't go / Lonely, lonely me / You know I love you / Learn to treat me better / Lonesome lonely blues / I'm glad she's mine / Sundown blues / My home ain't there / What you wanna do it for / I woke up crying (oh what a dream) / When I had, I didn't need (now I need, don't have a dime) / I'm a samplin' man / It's easy when you know how / I got a broken heart / Don't say a word / Lost without love / Leave my money alone / My home is a prison / Lonesome whistler
CD _____ CDCHD 556
Ace / Feb '95 / Pinnacle / Cadillac / Complete/Pinnacle.

Loney, Roy

SCIENTIFIC BOMBS AWAY, THE (Loney, Roy & Phantom Movers)
CD _____ AIM 1025CD
Aim / Oct '93 / Direct / ADA / Jazz Music.

Long, Barbara

SOUL
Trolley song / Gee baby / Largo to Oscar / When you are smiling / Call me darling / Where is lonesome / Green dolphin street / You don't know what / Love is / Serenade / Squeeze me / Swan lake / It's heaven
CD _____ SV 0216
Savoy Jazz / Jun '93 / Conifer / ADA.

Long Fin Killie

HOUDINI
Man Ray / How I blew it with Houdini / Homo Erectus / Heads of dead surfers / Montgomery / Love smothers allergy / Hollywood gem / Lamberton lamplighter / Corngold / Idiot hormone / Rockethead on mandatory surveillance / Flower carrier / Unconscious gangs of men
CD _____ PURECD 047
Too Pure / Jun '95 / Vital.

Long, Larry

IT TAKES A LOT OF PEOPLE (A Tribute To Woody Guthrie)
CD _____ FF 70508
Flying Fish / Oct '89 / Roots / CM / Direct / ADA.

Long Ryders

BBC RADIO 1 IN CONCERT
CD _____ WINCD 058
Windsong / Jan '96 / Pinnacle.

METALLIC B.O
CD _____ SID 001
Prima / Apr '95 / Direct.

STATE OF OUR UNION
Looking for Lewis and Clarke / Lights of downtown / WDIA / Mason-Dixon line / Here comes that train again / Years long ago / Good times tomorrow, hard times today / Two kinds of love / You just can't ride the box cars anymore / Capturing the flag / State of my union
CD _____ SID 003
Prima / Mar '95 / Direct.

Long Tall Texans

ACES AND EIGHTS
Notice me / Nothing left but bone / Sister / I wish / Lip service / Everyday / Bloody / (Don't go back to) Rockville / Border radio / Tomorrow today / Innocent look / Piece of your love
CD _____ CDMGRAM 77
Anagram / May '94 / Pinnacle.

IN WITHOUT KNOCKING
Poison / Rockin' Crazy / Mad About You / Saints and sinners / Gotta Go / Texas Beat / Right First Time / Rock 'n' Roll (Part 2)/ Endless Sleep / My Babe / Texas Boogie / Wreckin' me / Who's Sorry Now / Your Own Way / Get Back Wet Back / Long tall Texan / Get Up And Go / Paradise / My Idea Of Heaven / Indians / Off My Mind / Bloody / Dance Of The Headhunters / Should I stay or should I go
CD _____ RAGECD 109
Rage / Aug '92 / Nervous / Magnum Music Group.

SINGING TO THE MOON
Singing to the moon / Rock Bottom Blues / Klub Foot Shuffle / Suicide At The Seaside / Winding me up / Reactor / Witch Hunting / Singing To The Moon (2) / Axe To Grind / Smiling eyes / Alcohol / Indian Reservation / Nine Days Wonder / Senses six and seven / Alabama Song
CD _____ RAGECD 108

Rage / Apr '91 / Nervous / Magnum Music Group.

Longaria, Valerio

CABALLO VIEJO
CD _____ ARHCD 336
Arhoolie / Apr '95 / ADA / Direct / Cadillac.

TEXAS CONJUNTO PIONEER
CD _____ ARHCD 358
Arhoolie / Apr '95 / ADA / Direct / Cadillac.

Longthorne, Joe

ESPECIALLY FOR YOU
CD _____ CDSR 064
Telstar / May '95 / BMG.

I WISH YOU LOVE
Young girl / Lady blue / So deep is the night / If I only had time / Mary in the morning / Say it with flowers / Where are you now / Runaway / Over and over / True love / My funny valentine / Never say never / Walk in the room / I wish you love
CD _____ CEDMC 3662
EMI / Oct '93 / EMI.

JOE LONGTHORNE SONGBOOK, THE
You're my world / My prayer / Always on my mind / My mother's eyes / Just loving / I've loved before / End of the world / It was almost like a song / I don't laugh at me / When your old wedding ring was new
CD _____ CDSR 059
Telstar / Aug '94 / BMG.

LIVE AT THE ROYAL ALBERT HALL
Passing strangers / Mary in the morning / If I only had time / What's going on / Unchained melody / It's not unusual / To all the girls I've loved before / Daniel / I just called to say I love you / Stand by me / This is my life / Life on Mars / Lady is a tramp / Perfect love / You're the first, my last, my everything / Wind beneath my wings / Born free / Portrait of my life / If I never sing another song / Somewhere
CD _____ CDDPR 134
Music For Pleasure / Dec '94 / EMI.

Look People

BOOGASM
CD _____ OUT 112-2
Brake Out / Nov '94 / Vital.

Looker, Sally

PARTY PARTY
Party party / No man's land / She don't mean a thing / I would have loved to have loved you / Days of Summer / Friday on my mind / Who's gonna pick up the pieces / Concrete and clay / Thinking about you / In the night / Don't talk to strangers / Frightened by the night
CD _____ PCOM 1119
President / Nov '91 / Grapevine / Target/ BMG / Jazz Music / President.

Loomis, Hamilton

HAMILTON BLUES
CD _____ HAMBONECD 301
Ham Bone / Jul '95 / Hot Shot.

Loop

DUAL
Collision / Crawling / Thief of fire / Thief (Motherfucker) / Black sun / Circle grave / Mother sky / Got to get it over (live)
CD _____ REACTORCD 5
Reactor / Mar '94 / Vital.

FADE OUT
Black sun / This is where you end / Fever knife / Torched / Fade out / Pulse / Vision stain / Got to get it over / Collision / Crawling heart / Thief of fire / Thief (motherfucker) / Mother sky
CD _____ REACTORCD 4
Reactor / Mar '94 / Vital.

GILDED ETERNITY, A
Vapour / Afterglow / Nail with burn / Blood / Breathe into me / From centre to wave / Be here now / Shot with a diamond / Nail with burn (burn out) / Arc-lite (sonar)
CD _____ BBL 27CD
Beggars Banquet / Sep '95 / Warner Music / Disc.

WOLF FLOW - JOHN PEEL SESSIONS 1987-90
Soundhead / Straight to you / Rocket U.S.A. / Pulse / This is where you end / Collision / From centre to wave / Afterglow / Sunburst
CD _____ REACTORCD 3
Reactor / Mar '94 / Vital.

WORLD IN YOUR EYES, THE
Sixteen dreams / Head on / Burning world / Rocket U.S.A. / Spinning / Deep hit / I'll take you there / Brittle head girl / Burning prisma / Spinning spun out

CD _____ REACTORCD 2
Reactor / Mar '94 / Vital.

Loop Guru

AMRITA
CD _____ GURU 200CD
North South / Sep '95 / Pinnacle.

DUN-YA
CD _____ NATCD 31
Nation / Apr '94 / Disc.

Loopuyt, Marc

ORIENTS OF THE LUTE, THE
CD _____ 925572
Buda / Jun '93 / Discovery / ADA.

Loos

FUNDAMENTAL
CD _____ GEESTCD 10
Geest Gronden / Oct '87 / Cadillac.

Loos, Charles

CHARLES LOOS AND ALI RYERSON (Loos, Charles & Ali Ryerson)
CD _____ EMD 89012
Candid / May '89 / Cadillac / Jazz Music / Wellard / Koch.

Loose

ESPECIALLY FOR YOU
CD _____ LAZEYE 209CD
Lazy Eye / Oct '95 / Plastic Head.

Loose Diamonds

BURNING DAYLIGHT
CD _____ DOSCD 7001
Dos / May '93 / CM / Direct / ADA.

NEW LOCATION
CD _____ DOS 7010
Dos / Oct '95 / CM / Direct / ADA.

Loose Ends

LOOK HOW LONG
Look how long / Don't you ever (try to change me) / Time is ticking / Love's got me / Don't be a fool / Cheap talk / Love controversy / Try my love / Hold tight / I don't need to know / Symptons of love
CD _____ DIXCD 94
10 / Sep '90 / EMI.

REAL CHUCKEEBOO, THE
Watching you / (There's no) gratitude / Real chuckeeboo (1)Tomorrow 2)Mr. Bachelor) / You've just got to have it all / Life / What goes around / Easier said than done / Hungry / Is it ever too late / Remote control / Too much (Not on LP) / Johnny broadhead (Not on LP)
CD _____ CDV 2528
10 / Jun '88 / EMI.

SO WHERE ARE YOU
Magic touch / New horizon / If my lovin' makes you hot / So where are you / Golden years / Hangin' on a string / Give it all you got / Sweetest pain / You can't stop the rain / Silent talking
CD _____ CDV 2340
10 / Feb '87 / EMI.

TIGHTEN UP VOL. 1
Magic touch / Gonna make you mine / Hangin' on a string / Choose me (rescue me) / Little spice / Slow down / Don't worry / Love's got me / Don't be a fool / Watching you / Tell me what you want / Ooh you make me feel / Hangin' on a string (original)
CD _____ DIXCD 112
10 / Jul '94 / EMI.

ZAGORA
Stay a while child / Be thankful (Mama's song) / Slow down / Ooh you make me feel / Just a minute / Who are you / I can't wait / Nights of pleasure / Let's get back to love / Rainbow / Take the 'A' train
CD _____ CDV 2384
10 / Jun '86 / EMI.

Lopato, David

INSIDE OUTSIDE
CD _____ EMY 1322
Enemy / Sep '92 / Grapevine.

Lopez, Isidro

EL INDIO
CD _____ ARHCD 363
Arhoolie / Apr '95 / ADA / Direct / Cadillac.

Lopez, Juan

EL REY DE LA REDOVA
CD _____ ARHCD 407
Arhoolie / Apr '95 / ADA / Direct / Cadillac.

Lopez, Trini

INFECTIOUS
CD _____ STFCD 3
Start / Dec '89 / Koch.

LA BAMBA
CD _____ 15056
Laserlight / Aug '91 / Target/BMG.

LA BAMBA - TWENTY EIGHT GREATEST HITS
CD _____ ENTCD 279
Entertainers / Oct '88 / Target/BMG.

LEGENDS IN MUSIC - TRINI LOPEZ
CD _____ LECD 098
Wisepack / Sep '94 / THE / Conifer.

TRINI LOPEZ
CD _____ GRF 189
Tring / Jan '93 / Tring / Prism.

TRINI LOPEZ LIVE
America / If I had a hammer / Bye bye blackbird / Cielito Lindo / This land is your land / What'd I say / La Bamba / Granada / Bye bye Blondie / Nie meir ohne (German) / Lebewohl daisy girl / Long ago / Folk medley / Unchain my heart
CD _____ BCD 15427
Bear Family / May '89 / Rollercoaster / Direct / CM / Swift / ADA.

VERY BEST OF TRINI LOPEZ
CD _____ WMCD 5647
Woodford Music / Aug '92 / THE.

Lopretti, Jose

CANDOMBE
CD _____ CHR 70013
Challenge / Apr '95 / Direct / Jazz Music / Cadillac / ADA.

Lorca, Federico Garcia

CANCIONES POPULARES ESPANOLAS
CD _____ J 105CD
Sonifolk / Jun '94 / ADA / CM.

POETRY PUT TO SONG
CD _____ 7996502
Hispavox / Jan '95 / ADA.

Lord Belial

KISS THE GOAT
CD _____ NFR 010CD
No Fashion / May '95 / Plastic Head.

Lord, Jon

BEFORE I FORGET
Chance on a feeling / Tender babes / Hollywood rock and roll / Bach onto this / Before I forget / Say it's alright / Burntwood / Where are you / Lady / For a friend / Pavanne / Going home
CD _____ RPM 126
RPM / Mar '94 / Pinnacle.

SARABANDE
CD _____ LICD 900124
Line / Sep '94 / CM / Grapevine / ADA / Conifer / Direct.

Lord Kitchener

STILL ESCALATING
CD _____ JW 055CD
Soca / Feb '94 / Jetstar.

Lord, Mary Lou

MARY LOU LORD
Lights are changing / Helsinki / That kind of girl / He'd be a diamond / Bridge / I'm talking to you / His indie world / Speeding motorcycle
CD _____ KRNB 00000
Kill Rock Stars / Jan '95 / Vital.

Lord Tanamo

IN THE MOOD FOR SKA
CD _____ CDTRL 313
Trojan / Mar '94 / Jetstar / Total/BMG.

Lords Of The Underground

HERE COME THE LORDS
Here come the Lords / From da bricks / Funky child / Keep it underground / Check it (remix) / Grave digga / Lords prayer / Flow on (new symphony) / Madd skillz / Psycho / Chief rocka / Sleep for dinner (remix) / L.O.T.U.G. (Lords Of The Underground) / Lord Jazz hit me one time (make it funky) / What's goin' on
CD _____ CTCD 41
Cooltempo / May '94 / EMI.

KEEPERS OF THE FUNK
Intro / Ready or not / Tic toc / Keepers of the funk / Steam from da knot / What I'm after / Faith / Neva faded / No pain / Frustrated / Yes y'all / What U see / Outro
CD _____ CDCHR 6088
Cooltempo / Oct '94 / EMI.

Lords, Traci

1000 FIRES
Control / Fallen angel / Good 'n' evil / Fly / Distant land / Outlaw lover / I want you / Say something / Father's field / Okey dokey
CD _____ RAD 11211
Radioactive / Apr '95 / Vital / BMG.

Lorelei

HEADSTRONG
CD _____ LDL 1213CD
Lochshore / Jun '94 / ADA / Direct / Duncans.

PROGRESSION
CD _____ CDLDL 1236
Lochshore / Nov '95 / ADA / Direct / Duncans.

Lorenz, Trey

TREY LORENZ
Someone to hold / Photograph of Mary / Just to be to you / Run back to me / Always in love / Wipe all my tears away / Baby I'm in heaven / It only hurts when it's love / How can I say goodbye / Find a way / When troubles come
CD _____ 472172-2
Epic / Dec '92 / Sony.

Los Alfa 8

LA SALSA LLEGO
CD _____ TUMICD 029
Tumi / '92 / Sterns / Discovery.

Los Alhama

FLAMENCO
CD _____ EUCD 1026
ARC / '89 / ARC Music / ADA.

Los Amigos

SOUTH AMERICAN HOLIDAY
CD _____ CNCD 5962
Disky / Jul '93 / THE / BMG / Discovery / Pinnacle.

Los Angeles

FALL AND RISE
CD _____ NO 2572
Noise/Modern Music / Jul '95 / Pinnacle / Plastic Head.

Los Boleros

LOS BOLEROS
CD _____ 12462
Laserlight / Mar '95 / Target/BMG.

Los Caimanes

MUSIC OF MEXICO VOL.3: LA HUASTECA (Los Caimanes & Los Caporales)
CD _____ ARHCD 431
Arhoolie / Jan '96 / ADA / Direct / Cadillac.

Los Camperos De Valles

MUSE
CD _____ CORA 124
Corason / Nov '95 / CM / Direct / ADA.

Los Cenzontles

CO SU PERMISO, SENORES
CD _____ ARHCD 435
Arhoolie / Jan '96 / ADA / Direct / Cadillac.

Los Chumps

PRETTY GIRLS EVERYWHERE
CD _____ TX 2103CD
Taxim / Jul '95 / ADA.

Los Comperos De Valles

EL TRUNFO
CD _____ MT 007
Corason / Jan '94 / CM / Direct / ADA.

Los Gitanillos De Cadiz

FLAMENCO
CD _____ 401982
Musidisc / Aug '90 / Vital / Harmonia Mundi / ADA / Cadillac / Discovery.

Los Hermanos Moreno

TOGETHER
Quimbombo / Hazme el amor / Sin ti no puedo vivir / Mas alla de todo / Quien como tu / Homenaje a mis colegas / Reunited / Por alguien como tu / Te quiero porqe te quiero / Maria Tomasa
CD _____ 66058007
RMM / Sep '93 / New Note.

Los Huertas

YO QUIERO MUSICA
CD _____ 322788
Koch / Oct '92 / Koch.

Los Incas

ALGERIA
CD _____ 824132
Buda / Nov '90 / Discovery / ADA.

EL CONDOR PASA
CD _____ 824122
Buda / Nov '90 / Discovery / ADA.

Los Latinos

BEST OF SALSA
CD _____ EUCD 1125
ARC / '91 / ARC Music / ADA.

Los Lobos

HOW WILL THE WOLF SURVIVE
Don't worry baby / Matter of time / Corrida No.1 / Our last night / Breakdown / I got loaded / Sere nata nortena / Evangeline / I got to let you know / Li'l king of everything / Will the wolf survive
CD _____ 8201842
Slash / Apr '89 / PolyGram.

JUST ANOTHER BAND FROM EAST LA (2CD Set)
CD Set _____ 8284002
Slash / Jan '94 / PolyGram.

KIKO
CD _____ 8282982
Slash / Jun '92 / PolyGram.

NEIGHBORHOOD, THE
Down on the riverbed / Emily / I walk alone / Angel dance / Little John of God / Deep dark hole / Georgia slop / I can't understand / Giving tree / Take my hand / Jenny's got a pony / Be still / Neighborhood
CD _____ 828 190 2
Slash / Sep '90 / PolyGram.

PAPA'S BREATH (Los Lobos & Lalo Guerrero)
CD _____ 942562
Music For Little People / Mar '95 / Direct.

Los Lobotomys

LOS LOBOTOMYS
CD _____ MAXCD 2049
Maxus / Nov '92 / Harmonia Mundi.

Los Machado

JIMENEZ - POETRY PUT TO SONG
CD _____ 7996502
Hispavox / Jan '95 / ADA.

Los Machucambos

LA BAMBA
La Bamba / Mas que nada / Cuando calienta el sol / Pepito / Eso es el amor / Granada / Brazil / Con amor / Esperanza / Fio maravilha / Garota de Ipanema / Amor amor / Tres palabras / El condor pasa / Quiereme / Guantanamera / La cucaracha / Tristeza / Perfidia / Corcovado / La mama / Maria Elena / Tico-tico / Frenesie / El manisero
CD _____ 300052
Musidisc / Aug '90 / Vital / Harmonia Mundi / ADA / Cadillac / Discovery.

Los Malaguenos

FLAMENCO
CD _____ HMA 190965CD
Musique D'Abord / Oct '94 / Harmonia Mundi.

Los Munequitos De...

CANTAR MARAVILLOSO (Los Munequitos De Matanzas)
Oyelos de nuevo / Lo que dice el abakua / Fundamento dilanga / El mariano / Mi arer / Cantar maravilloso / Arague / A los embales
CD _____ CDORB 053
Globestyle / Feb '90 / Pinnacle.

Los Donoheo

ME VOY PA L PUEBLO
CD _____ CD 82026
Saludos Amigos / Apr '94 / Target/BMG.

Los Paraguayos

MALAGUENA
CD _____ CD 62005
Saludos Amigos / Oct '93 / Target/BMG.

MUSIC FROM THE ANDES
CD _____ CD 12517
Music Of The World / Jun '94 / Target/BMG / ADA.

Los Pavros Reales

EARLY HITS
CD _____ ARHCD 410
Arhoolie / Apr '95 / ADA / Direct / Cadillac.

Los Pinguinos Del Norte

CONJUNTOS NORTENOS (Los Pinguinos Del Norte & Conjunto Trio San Antonio)
CD _____ ARHCD 311
Arhoolie / Apr '95 / ADA / Direct / Cadillac.

Los Pinkys

SEGURO QUE SIL
CD _____ ROUCD 6061
Rounder / Dec '94 / CM / Direct / ADA / Cadillac.

Los Reyes

GIPSY FAMILY VOL. 2, THE
CD _____ CD 15493
Laserlight / Aug '93 / Target/BMG.

GIPSY KINGS OF MUSIC, THE
CD _____ EMPRCD 504
Emporio / Apr '94 / THE / Disc / CM.

Los Rupay

FOLKLORE DE BOLIVIA
CD _____ EUCD 1001
ARC / '91 / ARC Music / ADA.

Los Straitjackets

LOS STRAITJACKETS
CD _____ UPSTARTCD 015
Upstart / Apr '95 / Direct / ADA.

Los Timidos

DAME UN BESITO
CD _____ TUMICD 018
Tumi / '91 / Sterns / Discovery.

Los Tres Paraguayos

CELITO LINDO
CD _____ CD 3511
Cameo / Nov '95 / Target/BMG.

GUANTANAMERA & LATIN HITS
CD _____ MCD 71490
Monitor / Jun '93 / CM.

Los Van Van

AZUCAR
CD _____ GLCD 4025
Green Linnet / Nov '94 / Roots / CM / Direct / ADA.

DE CUBA LOS VAN VAN WITH SALSA FORMELL
Nosotros los del Caribe / La Havana si / Si muere la tia / Por encima del nivel / Que pista / Que palo es ese / Canto la ceiba / Baila la palma real / Eso que anda
CD _____ PSCCD 1003
Pure Sounds From Cuba / Feb '95 / Henry Hadaway Organisation / THE.

Loss, Joe

50 GREAT YEARS
I'll be faithful / Red sails in the sunset / Begin the beguine / Goodnight children everywhere / Thrill of a new romance / My prayer / Breeze and I / St. Mary's in the twilight / Stage coach / Tell me Marianne / Gal in calico / Oasis / No orchids for my lady / Put 'em in a box / Sabre dance / Ain't nobody here but us chickens / When it's evening / When you're in love / Enliloro / Flying saucer / With these hands / I wish I knew / Trumpet improptu parts 1 and 2 / Evermore / Crazy otto rag / Why don't you believe me / Be anything / This is heaven / My heart belongs to only you / I'll always love you / My darling, my darling / Luna rossa / Got you on my mind / Wake the town and tell the people / Take care of yourself / Wishing ring / Stardust / March of the mods / Wheels / Caribbean clipper / In the mood / Love story / At the woodchoppers' ball / Sugar blues / So tired / Brazil
CD _____ CDDL 1281
EMI / Nov '94 / EMI.

EARLY YEARS, THE
My heart belongs to daddy / In the mood / Begin the beguine / Boo hoo / Toy trumpet / Little rendezvous in Honolulu / Red sails in the sunset / Happy ending / Over my shoulder / I double dare you / Ooooo-oh boom / Let's dance at the make believe ballroom / Scene changes / South of the border / I've got my eyes on you / You must have been a beautifel baby
CD _____ CDGRF 101
Tring / '93 / Tring / Prism.

HOUR OF SWING, AN (Loss, Joe & His Orchestra)
At the woodchoppers' ball / I'm getting sentimental over you / Stompin' at the Savoy / You made me love you / One o'clock jump / Take the 'A' train / Skylmer / Solitude / Don't be that way / Song of India / Begin the beguine / Trumpet blues and cantabile / Girl from Ipanema / Desafinado / Killing me softly / Sheikh of Araby / Five foot two, eyes of blue / It had to be you / Anvil chorus / Perfidia
CD _____ CC 249
Music For Pleasure / Sep '89 / EMI.

IN THE MOOD
In the mood / Honky tonk train blues / I hear bluebirds / Dreaming / If I didn't care / This can't be love / At the woodchoppers' ball / There goes my dream / Caravan / Blues upstairs and downstairs / Swingin' on the moon / Au revoir
CD _____ SMS 48
Carlton Home Entertainment / Apr '92 / Carlton Home Entertainment.

IT'S PARTY TIME WITH JOE LOSS (Loss, Joe & His Orchestra)
March of the mods / Zorba's dance / Finnjenka dance / Hey Jude / Entertainer / Charleston / This guy's in love with you /

Twistin' in the mood / Celebration / Lily the pink / I came, I saw, I conga'd / (We're gonna) rock around the clock / Shake, rattle and roll / Tea for two / Hokey cokey / This is the life / Stripper / Simon says / Ob la di ob la da / Y viva Espana / Last waltz
CD _____ CDMFP 5904
Music For Pleasure / Oct '90 / EMI.

JOE LOSS AND HIS BAND (Loss, Joe & His Band)
In the mood / Just a little cottage / I hear a rhapsody / Ridin' home in the buggy / Oasis / Down Forget-Me-Not Lane / Hey little hen / Honky tonk train blues / Home sweet home again / Shepherd's serenade / Blues upstairs and downstairs / Put that down in writing / Running wild / I'm nobody's baby / For all that I care / Down every street / Five o'clock whistle / Honeysuckle rose / Russian rose / You say the sweetest things / It's always you / First lullaby
CD _____ PASTCD 9782
Flapper / Jun '92 / Pinnacle.

OVER MY SHOULDER
I've got my love to keep me warm / Head over heels in love / Caravan / I know now / Raindrops / Everything you do / Boo hoo / For you Madonna / At the balalaika / Over my shoulder / September in the rain / Toy trumpet / May I have the next romance with you / What will I tell my heart / When the poppies bloom again / When you've got a little springtime / Love bug will bite you / This year's kisses
CD _____ 2 BUR 004
Burlington / Sep '88 / CM.

WHAT MORE CAN I SAY (Loss, Joe & His Band)
Sioux Sue / Deep in the heart of Texas / You again / That lovely weekend / How green was my valley / Oasis / What more can I say / Razzy lazy lane / Concerto for two / Fur trappers ball / Baby mine / Soft shoe shuffle / When I see an elephant fly / Daddy / You say the sweetest things / I don't want to set the world on fire / There's a land of begin again / Johnny Peddler / Cornsilk / Bounce me brother with a solid four / Rancho pillow / Don't cry Cherie
CD _____ RAJCD 812
Empress / Nov '93 / THE.

WORLD CHAMPIONSHIP BALLROOM DANCES (Loss, Joe & His Orchestra)
Dream / I only have eyes for you / Jealousy / Singin' in the rain / We make music / Toreando / Fascination / Can't help falling in love / Brazil / Something tells me / Mamma mia / Music to watch girls by / Cavatina / Forever and ever / Waltz is for dancing / Save your kisses for me / Don't it make my brown eyes blue / Till / Don't cry for me Argentina / Sunrise sunset / Mull of Kintyre / Spanish gypsy dance / Fernando / Tea for two / Copacabana / Rivers of Babylon / Guantanamera / Is this the way to Amarillo / What's happened to Broadway / I'd like to teach the world to sing / My resistance is low / How deep is your love
CD Set _____ CDDL 1146
Music For Pleasure / May '91 / EMI.

Loss Of Centre

HUMANS LOSING HUMANITY
CD _____ EFA 112862
Glasnost / Jan '96 / SRD.

Lost & Found

FOREVER LASTING PLASTIC WORDS
CD _____ 642420 B42
EVA / Jan '95 / Direct / ADA.

Lost Breed

EVIL IN YOU AND ME, THE
CD _____ HELL 023CD
Invisible / Jul '93 / Plastic Head.

SAVE YOURSELF
Circles / B.A.C. (What you fear) / Gears / Going strong / 472 C.I. of death / Lease on life / Chop / Dragon of chaos / You don't need to live / Tonga slut / Simulator / Up the hill
CD _____ H 0033-2
Hellhound / Aug '94 / Plastic Head.

Lost Soul Band

FRIDAY THE 13TH AND EVERYTHING'S ROSIE
Country boy / When you're gone / Leaving / Last train / H / I don't fear (I'm not alone) / Castration song / Jane / Last time I saw you / Jeanie / Strung out sister / Half the time / If this is love it's not enough / When the dirt comes falling down / Almost here / I love you
CD _____ ORECD 529
Silvertone / Mar '93 / Pinnacle.

LAND OF DO AS YOU PLEASE
CD _____ ORECD 524
Silvertone / Oct '93 / Pinnacle.

Lost Souls

NEVER PROMISED YOU A ROSEGARDEN
CD _____ SPV 08436192
SPV / Oct '94 / Plastic Head.

Lost Tribe

LOST TRIBE
Mythology / Dick Tracy / Procession / Letter to the editor / Eargasm / Rhinoceros / Mofungo / Space / Four directions / Fool for thought / T.A.the W. (Tender as the wind) / Cause and effect
CD _____ 01934101432
Windham Hill / Nov '94 / Pinnacle / BMG / ADA.

SOULFISH
Walkabout / Whodunit / It's not what it is / Daze of ol' / Room of life / Steel orchards / La fontaine (the fountain) / Second story / Planet rock / Fuzzy logic
CD _____ 02902103272
Windham Hill / Nov '94 / Pinnacle / BMG / ADA.

Lost Weekend

LOST WEEKEND
CD _____ LAST/VINTAP 1
Vinyl Tap / Jan '96 / Vinyl Tap.

Lothar

PRESENTING (Lothar & The Hand People)
CD _____ OW S2117960
One Way / Sep '94 / Direct / ADA.

THIS IS IT , MACHINES (Lothar & The Hand People)
Machines / Today is only yesterday's tomorrow / That's another story / Sister lonely / Sex and violence / You won't be lonely / It comes on anyhow / Wedding night for those who love / Yes, I love you / This is it / This may be goodbye / Midnight ranger / Ha (ho) / Sdrawkcab / Space hymn
CD _____ SEECD 75
See For Miles/C5 / May '91 / Pinnacle.

Lotion

NOBODY'S COOL
CD _____ ABB 89CD
Big Cat / Jun '95 / SRD / Pinnacle.

Louchie Lou

FREE 2 LIVE (Louchie Lou & Michie One)
CD _____ WOLCD 1058
China / Aug '95 / Pinnacle.

Loud

D GENERATION
CD _____ WOLCD 1003
China / May '91 / Pinnacle.

PSYCHE 21
CD _____ WOLCD 1026
China / Jun '92 / Pinnacle.

Loud Family

PLANTS AND BIRDS AND ROCKS AND THINGS
He do the police in different voices / Sword swallower / Aerodeliria / Self righteous boy reduced to tears / Jimmy still comes round / Take me down (Too halloo) / Don't thank me all at onece / Idiot son / Some grand vision of motives and irony / Spot the setup / Inverness / Rosy overdrive / Slit my wrists / Isaac's law / Second grade applauds / Last honest face / Even you / Ballad of how you can all shut up / Give in world
CD _____ A033D
Alias / Feb '93 / Vital.

SLOUCHING TOWARDS LIVERPOOL
Take me down / Come on / Back of a car / Slit my wrists / Aerodeliria / Erica's world
CD _____ A 055D
Alias / Oct '93 / Vital.

TAPE OF ONLY LINDA, THE
Soul drain / My superior / Marcia and Etrusca / Hyde street virgins / Baby hard-to-be-around / It just wouldn't be Christmas / Better nature / Still it's own reward / For beginners only / Ballet hetro
CD _____ A 060D
Alias / Jan '95 / Vital.

Loudblast

CROSS THE THRESHOLD
CD _____ NO 2232
Noise/Modern Music / Nov '93 / Pinnacle / Plastic Head.

Loudermilk, John D.

BLUE TRAIN - 1961/1962
Blue train / Mr. Jones / Language of love / Jimmie's song / Angela Jones / Bully of the beach / Rhythm and blues / What would you take for me / Great snowman / Everybody knows / Google eye / Darling Jane / Song of the lonely teen / All of this for Sally / Roadhog / He's just a scientist (that's all) / Rocks of Reno / Big daddy / Callin' Dr Casey / You just reap what you sow / Little wind-up doll / Two strangers in love / Th'wife / Bad news / Run on home baby brother / Oh how sad
CD _____ BCD 15421

Bear Family / Jun '89 / Rollercoaster / Direct / CM / Swift / ADA.

IT'S MY TIME
It's my time / No playing in the snow today / Little grave / I'm looking for a world / What is it / Bubble please break / Ma Baker's little acre / Mary's no future home / To hell with love / Talkin' silver cloud blues / Joey stays with me / Lament of the Cherokee reservation / Jones' / You're the guilty one / Where have they gone / Little bird / Brown girl / Givin' you all my love / I chose you / Honey / That ain't all / Interstate forty / Do you / Tobacco Road
CD _____ BCD 15422
Bear Family / Jun '89 / Rollercoaster / Direct / CM / Swift / ADA.

SITTIN' IN THE BALCONY
Sittin' on the balcony / A-plus in love / It's gotta be you / Teenage queen / 1000c Concrete block / In my simple way / That's all I've got / Asiatic flu / Somebody sweet / They were right / Yearbook / Susie's house / Yo yo / Lover's lane / Goin' away to school / This cold war with you / Please don't play No.9 / Angel of flight 509 / Midnight bus / Red headed stranger / Tobacco road / Happy wonderer / March of the minute men
CD _____ BCDAH 15875
Bear Family / Jun '95 / Rollercoaster / Direct / CM / Swift / ADA.

Loudon, Dorothy

BROADWAY BABY
Broadway baby / It all depends on you / After you / It all belongs to me / Bobo's / Pack up your sins and go to the devil / Any place I hang my hat is home / I got lost in his arms / They say it's wonderful / Do it again / He was too good to me / I had myself a true love / Ten cents a dance
CD _____ CDSL 5203
DRG / Apr '87 / New Note.

Louis, Big Joe

BIG 16
CD _____ CDCHD 622
Ace / Feb '96 / Pinnacle / Cadillac / Complete/Pinnacle.

Louis, Joe Hill

BE BOP BOY, THE
When I am gone / Dorothy Mae / She may be yours / Keep your arms around me / Got me a new woman / I'm a poor boy / In the mood / West winds are blowin' / Little Walter's boogie / Grandmother got Grandfather told / We all gotta go sometime / Walter's boogie / Come see me / Worry you off my mind / Reap what you sow / Walter's instrumental / Hydramatic / Woman tiger / Man keep your arms around me / She may be yours (take 3) / All gotta go sometime / Shine boy
CD _____ BCD 15524
Bear Family / Jun '92 / Rollercoaster / Direct / CM / Swift / ADA.

Louise, Tina

IT'S TIME FOR TINA
Tonight is the night / Hand across the table / Snuggled on your shoulder / Embraceable you / I'm in the mood for love / Baby, won't you say you love me / It's been a long, long time / Hold me / I wanna be loved / Let's do it / How long has this been going on / Goodnight my love
CD Set _____ DIW 322
DIW / Apr '90 / Harmonia Mundi / Cadillac.

Louisiana Playboys

SATURDAY NIGHT SPECIAL
Lafayette / Why don't we do it in the road / Cajun blues / Saturday night special / Maggie Thatcher, won't you give me a hand / Louisiana playboy's theme / Memphis / Jolie blon / Mathilda / Te petite and te meon / Accordion waltz
CD _____ JSPCD 225
JSP / Apr '89 / ADA / Target/BMG / Direct / Cadillac / Complete/Pinnacle.

Louisiana Radio

MAMA ROUX
CD _____ MW 2011CD
Music & Words / Aug '94 / ADA / Direct.

WULF
CD _____ MWCD 2013
Music & Words / Dec '95 / ADA / Direct.

Louisiana Red

ALWAYS PLAYED THE BLUES
CD _____ JSPCD 240
JSP / Oct '91 / ADA / Target/BMG / Direct / Cadillac / Complete/Pinnacle.

BLUES FOR IDA B.
CD _____ JSPCD 209
JSP / Jan '88 / ADA / Target/BMG / Direct / Cadillac / Complete/Pinnacle.

LOWDOWN BACK PORCH BLUES
Ride on Red, ride on / I wonder who (alternate) / Red's dream / Workin' man blues / I'm Louisiana Red / Sweet Alesse / Keep

your hands off my woman / I'm a roaming stranger / Red on red, ride on / I wonder who / Seventh son / Sad news / Two fifty three / Don't cry / Sugar hips / I'm too poor to die / Don't cry (alternate)
CD _____ NEX CD 213
Sequel / Jul '92 / BMG.

MIDNIGHT RAMBLER
CD _____ 269 607 2
Tomato / May '88 / Vital.

RISING SUN
CD _____ RS 0006
Just A Memory / Oct '94 / Harmonia Mundi.

Louisiana Repertory Jazz

HOT AND SWEET SOUNDS OF LOST NEW ORLEANS (Louisiana Repertory Jazz Ensemble)
CD _____ SOSCD 1140
Stomp Off / Jan '88 / Jazz Music / Wellard.

LOUISIANA REPERTORY JAZZ ENSEMBLE (Louisiana Repertory Jazz Ensemble)
CD _____ SOSCD 1055
Stomp Off / May '93 / Jazz Music / Wellard.

LOUISIANA REPERTORY JAZZ ENSEMBLE VOL. 4 (Louisiana Repertory Jazz Ensemble)
CD _____ SOSCD 1197
Stomp Off / Dec '94 / Jazz Music / Wellard.

Louiss, Eddie

EDDIE LOUISS TRIO
Nardis / Blue tempo / Hot house / No smoking / You've changed / Don't want nothin'
CD _____ FDM 365012
Dreyfus / May '94 / ADA / Direct / New Note.

PRESSE DE CONFERENCE (Louiss, Eddy & Michel Petrucciani)
Les grelots / Jean Philippe Herbien / All the things you are / I wrote you a song / So what / These foolish things / Amesha / Simply bop
CD _____ FDM 365682
Dreyfus / Nov '94 / ADA / Direct / New Note.

Louiss, Pierre

CREOLE SWING
CD _____ FA 042
Fremeaux / Nov '95 / Discovery / ADA.

Lounge Lizards

LIVE 1979-1981
CD _____ RE 136CD
Reach Out International / Nov '94 / Jetstar.

LIVE IN BERLIN
CD _____ VBR 20442
Vera Bra / Sep '91 / Pinnacle / New Note.

LIVE IN BERLIN VOL.II
Remember / Evan's drive to Mombasa / King precious / Mr. Stinky's blues / Welcome her Lazaro / What else is in there
CD _____ VBR 20862
Vera Bra / Nov '92 / Pinnacle / New Note.

LOUNGE LIZARDS
Incident on South Street / Harlem nocturne / Do the wrong thing / Au contraire arto / Well you needn't / Ballad / Wangling / Conquest of Rah / Demented / I remember Coney Island / Fatty walks / Epistrophy / You haunt me
CD _____ EEGCD 8
EG / Sep '90 / EMI.

VOICE OF CHUNK
Bob the bob / Voice of chunk / One big yes / Hanging / Uncle Jerry / Paper bag and the Sun / Tarantella / Sharks / Travel
CD _____ VBR 20252
Vera Bra / Aug '94 / Pinnacle / New Note.

Loussier, Jacques

BACH TO BACH
CD _____ SMCD 19
Start / Nov '89 / Koch.

BACH TO THE FUTURE
CD _____ SCD 8
Start / Nov '86 / Koch.

BEST OF BACH, THE
CD _____ MCCD 113
Music Club / Jun '93 / Disc / THE / CM.

BEST OF PLAYS BACH (Volume 1 And 2)
Air on a g string / Invention for two voices no. 8 / Siciliano in G minor / Toccata and Fugue in D minor / Prelude no.1 / Prelude no.2 / Chorale - Jesu, joy of man's desiring / Italian concerto (pts 1-3) / Chorale no.1 / Chromatic fantasy / D minor concerto (pts 1-3)
CD _____ SCD 1
Start / Sep '94 / Koch.

JACQUES LOISSIER PLAYS BACH
CD _____ 556604
Accord / Dec '89 / Discovery / Harmonia
Mundi / Cadillac.

PLAY BACH 2000
CD _____ KAZCD 222
Kaz / Mar '95 / BMG.

Louvin Brothers

CAPITOL COUNTRY MUSIC CLASSICS
Broadminded / Family who prays (Shall
never part) / When I stop dreaming / Alabama / I don't believe you've met my baby
/ Hoping that you're hoping / Kentucky /
Katy dear / Knoxville girl / Don't laugh /
You're running wild / Cash on the barrelhead / Plenty of everything but you / Little
light of mine / Tennessee waltz / Are you
teasing me / My baby's gone / If I could
only win your love / Satan is real / Christian
life / Blues stay away from me / I love you
best of all / How's the world treating you /
Great atomic power / Must you throw dirt
in my face / Stuck up blues / Thank God for
my Christian home / What would you give
me in exchange for my soul
CD _____ CDEMS 1492
Capitol / Apr '93 / EMI.

CLOSE HARMONY (8CD Set)
Alabama Alabama / Seven year blues / My
love song for you / Get acquainted waltz /
They've got the church outnumbered / Do
you live what you preach / You'll be re-
warded over there / I'll live with God (to die
no more) / Rove of white / Great atomic
power / Insured beyond the grave / Gospel
way / Sons and daughters of God / Broadminded / Family who prays (shall never part)
/ I know what you're talking about / Let us
travel on / I love God's way of living / Born
again / Preach the gospel / From mother's
arms to Korea / If we forget God / Satan
and the Saint / Satan lied to me / God bless
her ('cause she's my mother) / Last chance
to pray / No one to sing for me / Swing low,
sweet chariot / Nearer my God to thee /
Make him a soldier / I can't say no / Just
rehearsing / Love thy neighbour as thyself /
Where will you build / Pray for me / When I
stop dreaming / Pitfall / Alabama / Memories and tears / Don't laugh / I don't believe
you've met my baby / Childish love / In the
middle of nowhere / Hoping that you're
hoping / First one to love you / I cried after
you left / That's all he's asking of me / I'll
be all smiles tonight / In the pines / What is
home without love / Mary of the wild moor
/ Knoxville girl / Kentucky / Katy dear / My
brother's wife / Take the news to mother /
Let her go God bless her / Tiny broken heart
/ Plenty of everything but you / Cash on the
barrelhead / You're running wild / New partner waltz / I won't have to cross Jordan
alone / Praying / Wait a little longer, please
Jesus / This little light of mine / Steal away
and pray / There's no excuse / Are you
washed in the blood / Lord I'm coming
home / Thankful / Take me back into your
heart / Here today and gone tomorrow / We
could / Tennessee waltz / Too late / Are you
teasing me / Nobody's darling but mine /
Don't let your sweet love die / I wonder
where you are tonight / Why not confess /
Making believe / Have I stayed away too
long / Call me / I wish you knew / Dog sled
/ When I loved you / My baby's gone / She
didn't even know I was gone / My baby
came back / Are you wasting my time / My
curly headed baby / Lorene / I wish it had
been a dream / While you're cheatin' on me
/ If I could only win your love / You've learn-
inn / Blue from now on / Today / My heart
was trampled on the street / Send me the
pillow that you dream on / On my way to
the show / Red hen hop / She'll get lonesome / I wonder if you know / Blue / Angels
rejoiced last night / Dying from home and
lost / Satan's jewelled crown / River of Jordan / I'm ready to go home / Kneeling
drunkards plea / Satan is real / Christian life
/ Are you afraid to die / He can be found /
There's is a higher power / Drunkard's
doom / I see a bridge / Just suppose / Stagger / Nellie moved to town / What a change
one day / Ruby's song / Last old shovel /
Midnight special / Brown's ferry blues /
Southern moon / Sand mountain blues /
Nashville blues / Blues stay away from me
/ When it's time for the whippoorwill to sing
/ Put me on the train to Carolina / Freight
train blues / Lonesome blues / Gonna lay
down my old guitar / It's Christmas time /
Santa's big parade / Love is a lonely street
/ If you love me stay away / I ain't gonna
work tomorrow / I love you best of all / I
can't keep you in love with me / Scared of
the blues / I have found the way / He set
me free / Kneel at the cross / Leaning on
the everlasting arms / O why not tonight /
You can't find the Lord too soon / Keep
your eyes on Jesus / Almost persuaded / I
feel better now / O who shall be able to
stand / If today was the day / You'll meet
him in the clouds / You'll meet him in the
clouds (alt. take) / Away in a manger /
Friendly beasts / Hark the herald angels
sing / Good christian men rejoice / While
shepherds watched their flocks by night /
First Noel / It came upon a midnight clear /
O come all ye faithful (Adeste Fidelis) / O
little town of Bethlehem / Silent night / Deck
the halls with boughs of holly / Joy to the

world / It hurts me more the second time
around / How's the world treating you /
Every time you leave / Time goes slow / I
died for the red, white and blue / Searching
for a soldier's grave / At mail call today /
Soldier's last letter / There's a star spangled
banner waving somewhere / There's a
grave in the wave of the ocean / Mother I
thank you for the bible you gave / Seaman's
girl / Robe of white / Weapon of prayer /
Broken engagement / First time in life / There's no easy way / Love turned to hate /
Must you throw dirt in my face / Great
speckled bird / Wabash cannonball / Lonely
mound of clay / Wreck on the highway /
Wait for the light to shine / Low and lonely
/ We live in two different worlds / I weep /
jewel / Great judgement morning / Branded
wherever I go / Not a word from home /
Stuck up blues / Don't let them take the
bible out of our school / I'm glad that I'm
not him / Message to your heart / Thank
God for my christian home / I'll never die /
Price on the bottle / I've known a lady / He
included me / Keep watching the sky / Now
Lord, what can I do for you / Way up on a
mountain / Gonna shake hands with mother
over there / He was waiting at the altar / Oh
Lord, my God / What would you take in
exchange for my soul
CD Set _____ BCD 15561
Bear Family / Jun '92 / Rollercoaster / Direct
/ CM / Swift / ADA.

RADIO FAVOURITES 1951-57
CD _____ CMFCD 009
Country Music Foundation / Jul '93 /
Direct / ADA.

RUNNING WILD
When I stop dreaming / I don't believe
you've met my baby / Hoping that you're
hoping / You're running wild / Cash on the
barrelhead / My baby's gone / Knoxville girl
/ I love you best of all / How's the world
treating you / Must you throw dirt in my face
/ if I could only win your love
CD _____ CDSD 044
Sundown / Jul '92 / Magnum Music Group.

Louvin, Charlie

LIVE IN HOLLAND
CD _____ SCR 34
Strictly Country / Jul '95 / ADA / Direct.

Lovano, Joe

RUSH HOUR
Prelude to a kiss / Peggy's blue skylight /
Wildcat / Angel eyes / Rush hour on 23rd
Street / Crepuscule with Nellie / Lament for
M / Topsy turvy / Love I long for / Juniper's
garden / Kathline Gray / Headin' out, movin'
in / Chelsea bridge
CD _____ CDP 8292692
Blue Note / Feb '95 / EMI.

SOUNDS OF JOY
Sounds of joy / Strength and courage / I'll
wait and prey / Cedar Avenue blues / Bass
and space / Ettenro / Until the moment was
now / This one's for Lacy / 23rd Street
theme
CD _____ ENJACD 70132
Enja / Mar '92 / New Note / Vital/SAM.

Love

COMES IN COLOURS
My little red book / Can't explain / Message
to pretty / Softly to me / Hey Joe / Signed
D.C. / And more / Seven and seven is / No
14 / Stephanie knows who / Orange skies /
Que vida / Castle / She comes in colours /
Alone again or / And more again / Old man /
House is not a motel / Daily planet / Live
and let live / Laughing stock / Your mind
and we belong together / August / Arthur
Lee interview
CD _____ RVCD 29
Raven / Jan '93 / Direct / ADA.

DA CAPO
Stephinie knows who / Orange skies / Que
vida / Seven and seven is / She comes in
colours / Revelation / Castle
CD _____ 9740052
Elektra / '89 / Warner Music.

FALSE START
CD _____ MCAD 22029
One Way / Apr '94 / Direct / ADA.

FOREVER CHANGES
Alone again or / House is not a motel / And
more again / Daily planet / Old man / Red
telephone / Maybe the people would be the
times / Live and let live / Good humour man
he sees everything like this / Bummer in the
summer / You set the scene
CD _____ 9606562
Elektra / '89 / Warner Music.

FOUR SAIL
August / Friends of mine / I'm with you /
Good times / Singing cowboy / Dream /
Robert Montgomery / Nothin' / Talking in
my sleep / Always see your face
CD _____ CDTB 047
Thunderbolt / Jun '88 / Magnum Music
Group.

LOVE
My little red book / Can't explain / Message
to pretty / My flash on you / Softly to me /
No matter what you do / Emotions / You I'll

be following / Gazing / Hey Joe / Signed
D.C. / Coloured balls falling / Mushroom
clouds / And more
CD _____ 755974001-2
Elektra / Dec '93 / Warner Music.

OUT HERE
CD _____ MCAD 22030
One Way / Apr '94 / Direct / ADA.

OUT THERE
I'll pray for you / Love is coming / Signed
D.C. / I still wonder / Listen to my song /
Doggone / Nice to be / Stand out / Ever-
lasting first / Gimmi a little break / Willow
willow / You are something / Love is more
than words / Gather round
CD _____ CDWIKD 69
Big Beat / Jul '90 / Pinnacle.

STUDIO/LIVE
CD _____ MCAD 22036
One Way / Apr '94 / Direct / ADA.

**WE'RE ALL NORMAL AND WE WANT
OUR FREEDOM (A Tribute To Arthur
Lee & Love) (Various Artists)**
Emotions / Robert Montgomery / Message
to pretty / Which witch is which / Keep on
shining / She comes in colours / Car lights
on in the daytime / Signed D.C. / I'm down
/ Between Clark and Hilldale / You are
something / Willow willow / Dream / Alone
again or / Que Vidal / Softly to me / No matter what you do / My flash on you / Bummer
in the summer / Stand out / Can't explain
CD _____ A 058D
Alias / Jul '94 / Vital.

Love & Money

LITTLEDEATH
Littledeath (reprise) / Last ship on the river
/ I'll catch you when you fall / Keep looking
for the light / Pray for love / Don't be afraid
of the dark / Ugly as sin / Love is like a wave
/ Bitches breach / Kiss of life / Sweet black
luger / What time is the last train /
Littledeath
CD _____ IGCD 206
Iona Gold / Apr '94 / Total/BMG / ADA.

Love & Rockets

EARTH, SUN, MOON
Mirror people / Light / Welcome tomorrow /
No new tale to tell / Here on earth / Lazy /
Waiting for the flood / Rainbird / Telephone
is empty / Everybody wants to go to heaven
/ Sun / Youth
CD _____ BEGA 84CD
Beggars Banquet / Sep '87 / Warner Music
/ Disc.

EXPRESS
It could be sunshine / Kundalini Express /
All in my mind / Life in Laralay / Yin and
Yang (the flower pot men) / Love me / All in
my mind (acoustic version) / American
dream
CD _____ BBL 74CD
Beggars Banquet / Feb '90 / Warner Music
/ Disc.

HOT TRIP TO HEAVEN
CD _____ BBQCD 145
Beggars Banquet / Sep '94 / Warner
Music / Disc.

LOVE AND ROCKETS
No big deal / Purest blue / Motorcycle / I
feel speed / Bound for hell / Teardrop col-
lector / So alive / Rock 'n' roll Babylon / No
words no more
CD _____ BEGA 99CD
Beggars Banquet / Aug '89 / Warner Music
/ Disc.

**SEVENTH DREAM OF TEENAGE
HEAVEN**
If there's a heaven above / Private future /
Dog end of a day gone by / Game / Seventh
dream of teenage heaven / Haunted when
the minutes drag / Saudade
CD _____ BBL 66 CD
Lowdown/Beggars Banquet / Jan '89 /
Warner Music / Disc.

Love 666

AMERICAN REVOLUTION
CD _____ AMREP 035CD
Amphetamine Reptile / Feb '95 / SRD.

Love, Charlie

**CHARLIE LOVE WITH GEORGE LEWIS
& LOUIS NELSON 1962 (Love, Charlie &
George Lewis & Louis Nelson)**
CD _____ AMCD 60
American Music / Aug '94 / Jazz Music.

Love Coates, Dorothy

GET ON BOARD
Peace, be still / Glory to his name / I'm
sealed / Get away Jordan / Rest for the
weary / Deliver me / Oh my Lord / Lead me
holy father / Old gospel train (the next stop
is mine) / Get on board / Railroad / Plenty
good room / Sometime / No hiding place /
Waiting for me / Wade in the water / I
wouldn't mind dying / I'll be with thee / He's
calling me / Untitled instrumental / Thank
you Lord for using me / These are they / 99
1/2 / That's enough

CD _____ CDCHD 412
Ace / Nov '93 / Pinnacle / Cadillac / Com-
plete/Pinnacle.

VOLUME 1 AND 2
He's calling you / One morning soon / You
better run / No hiding place / When I reach
my heavenly home on high / Get away Jordan / I'm sealed / That's enough / Ninety
nine and a half (won't do) / Where shall I be
/ Jesus laid his hand on me / You can't
hurry God / Jesus knows it all / You must
be born again / These are they / Why not /
I shall know him / Every day will be Sunday
by and by / I wouldn't mind dying / Lord
don't forget about me / There's a God
somewhere / Just to behold his face / Am I
a soldier / Heaven
CD _____ CDCHD 343
Ace / Nov '93 / Pinnacle / Cadillac / Com-
plete/Pinnacle.

Love Corporation

INTELLIGENTSIA
CD _____ CREDCD 116
Creation / May '94 / 3MV / Vital.

LOVERS
CD _____ CRECD 068
Creation / May '94 / 3MV / Vital.

TONES
CD _____ CRECD 56
Creation / May '94 / 3MV / Vital.

Love, Geoff

**BIG WAR MOVIE THEMES (Love, Geoff
& His Orchestra)**
Colonel Bogey / Lawrence of Arabia / Guns
of Navarone / Battle of Britain / Longest Day
/ Where eagles dare / 633 Squadron / Dam-
busters march / Great escape / Green be-
rets / Cavatina (From The Deer Hunter.) /
Winds of war / Victory at sea extracts / We'll
meet again / Is Paris burning / Reach for
the Sky
CD _____ CC 211
Music For Pleasure / May '88 / EMI.

**GOING LATIN (Love, Geoff & His
Orchestra)**
La Bamba / Spanish harlem / Guantana-
mera / Sucu sucu / Girl from Ipanema / One
note Samba (Samba de uma nota so) /
South of the border / Maria Elena / Spanish
eyes / Desafinado / Breeze and I / Mexican
hat dance / Temptation / La Cumparsita /
Blue tango / Spider of the night / Serenta /
La Paloma / Jealousy / Adios muchachos /
Ecstasy
CD _____ CC 270
Music For Pleasure / Aug '91 / EMI.

**IN THE MOOD - FOR LOVE (Love, Geoff
& His Orchestra)**
Cavatina (Solo Violin: William Armon.) / Annie's song / Chi Mai (From The Life & Times
of David Lloyd George) / Misty / Tara's
theme (From Gone With The Wind.) / Begin
the beguine / Time for us (From Romeo &
Juliet.) / We'll meet again / Summer knows
(Theme from Summer of 42.) / Godfather
love theme / Summer place / Man and a
woman / Secret love / When I fall in love /
Love letters / Raindrops keep falling on my
head / Falling in love with love / Where do
I begin (Theme from Love Story.) / Somewhere my love (From Dr. Zhivago) / Spartacus love theme (The Onedin Line.) /
Love walked in (CD only.) / I wish you love
(CD only.) / True love (CD only.) / I will wait
for you (From The Umbrellas of Cherbourg.
CD only.)
CD _____ CC 245
Music For Pleasure / Sep '89 / EMI.

**IN THE MOOD FOR WALTZING (Love,
Geoff & His Orchestra)**
Falling in love with love / Ramona / Anni-
versary song / Always / Beautiful dreamer /
I'll see you again / Fascination / My won-
derful one / Charmaine / Love's last word is
spoken / Love's roundabout / Now is the
hour / Desert song / Around the world /
When I grow too old to dream / Vaya con
dios / One night of love / Lover / Edelweiss
/ Song / Try to remember / Ask me why I
love you / Waltz of my heart / Last waltz
CD _____ CC 261
Music For Pleasure / Oct '90 / EMI.

**MELODIES THAT LIVE FOREVER (In
concert with) (Love, Geoff & His
Orchestra)**
Skater's waltz / Minute waltz / Destiny / In-
vitation to the dance / Morning: Peer Gynt
/ Elizabethan serenade / Largo / Moonlight
sonata / Blue Danube / Sleeping beauty /
Merry widow / Tales from the Vienna
Woods / Dusk / Marriage of Figaro (over-
ture) / Enigma variations: Nimrod / Air on a
G string / Clair de Lune / Jesu joy of man's
desiring / Ave Maria
CD Set _____ CDDL 1098
EMI / Nov '92 / EMI.

**OPERA WITHOUT WORDS (Love, Geoff
Concert Orchestra)**
One furtive tear / Stars were shining / None
shall sleep / What is life without thee / Bella
figlia dell'amore / Oh my beloved father /
Love duet act 1 / Chorus of the Hebrew
slaves / Softly awakes my heart / Musetta's
waltz song / One fine day / Celeste Aida /
Your tiny hand is frozen / Love and music

CD _____ CDP 746 931 2
EMI / Feb '90 / EMI.

SONGS THAT WON THE WAR (Love, Geoff Banjos)
Colonel Bogey / Sentimental journey / Lili Marlene / Good morning / You'll never know / Yours / Let the people sing / That lovely weekend / This is the army Mister Jones / Arm in arm / I'll be with you in apple blossom time / I don't want to set the world on fire
CD _____ CDMFP 5887
Music For Pleasure / Feb '95 / EMI.

WHEN I FALL IN LOVE (Love, Geoff Singers)
Imagine / What are you doing the rest of your life / Moon river / If / I'm stone in love with you (CD only) / When I fall in love / More I see you (CD only) / I only have eyes for you / It's impossible / Annie's song / Without you / My eyes adored you / First time ever I saw your face / My cherie amour / Love story / Something / Don't cry for me Argentina / Vincent / Killing me softly / Snowbird / Send in the clowns (CD only) / For once in my life (CD only) / Michelle / You make me feel brand new (CD only) / Just the way you are / Evergreen
CD Set _____ CDDL 1102
Music For Pleasure / May '92 / EMI.

Love Groove

GLOBAL WARMING
CD _____ MILL 011-2
Millenium / Mar '95 / Plastic Head.

Love Interest

BEDAZZLED
CD _____ INVCD 025
Invisible / Feb '94 / Plastic Head.

Love Is Colder Than Death

OXEIA
CD _____ HY 39100952
Hyperium / Apr '94 / Plastic Head.

Love Like Blood

ECSTASY
CD _____ DW 20625CD
Deathwish / Jan '92 / Plastic Head.

EXPOSURE
CD _____ 08545752
SPV / Jan '96 / Plastic Head.

FLAGS OF REVOLUTION
CD _____ DW 21033CD
Deathwish / Jan '92 / Plastic Head.

ODYSSEE
CD _____ SPV 084-45552
SPV / Apr '94 / Plastic Head.

Love, Mary

THEN AND NOW
I'm in your hands / Let me know / Because of you / I woke up / Hey stoney face / Lay this burden down / Satisfied feeling / I can't wait / Come out of the sandbox / Price / Baby I'll come / Move a little closer / More than enough love / Grace / I've gotta get you back / Talkin' about my man / Mr. Man / B Baby / Caught up / You turned my bitter into sweet / (I'm so glad) He uses me
CD _____ CDKEND 109
Kent / May '94 / Pinnacle.

Love Nut

BASTARDS OF MELODY
She won't do me / Star / I'm a loser / Green tambourine / Images / Into battle / Jane / Touch / Please / Black cat
CD _____ OF 001CD
One Fifteen / Nov '95 / Vital.

Love on Ice

NUDE
Don't leave me / Leave me alone / Goodbye / Ugly / Mine / Bone dance / Foot in the grave / Gone away / Country boy / Backyard / Self in blue / Can o' worms
CD _____ 7567918292
Interscope / Aug '92 / Warner Music.

Love Parade

LOVE IS THE MESSAGE
CD _____ K 7037CD
Studio K7 / Jul '95 / Disc.

Love Republic

IS NOTHING SACRED
CD _____ ARCHO 1666
TEQ / May '95 / Plastic Head.

Love Times Three

LOVE TIMES THREE
CD _____ TRI 4144CD
Ichiban / Feb '94 / Koch.

Love Unlimited Orchestra

BEST OF LOVE UNLIMITED ORCHESTRA, THE

CD _____ 5269452
Mercury / Sep '95 / PolyGram.

FROM A GIRLS POINT OF VIEW
CD _____ VSD 5490
Varese Sarabande/Colosseum / Jan '95 / Pinnacle / Silva Screen.

HE'S ALL I'VE GOT
I did it for love / Never, never say goodbye / Whisper you love me / He's mine (No you can't have him) / I guess I'm just another girl in love / He's all I got
CD _____ CDSEWM 077
Southbound / Feb '94 / Pinnacle.

LET 'EM DANCE
Bayou / Jamaican girl / I wanna boogie and woogie with you / Vieni qua bella mi / Freeway flyer / I'm in the mood / Young America
CD _____ CDSEWM 079
Southbound / Feb '94 / Pinnacle.

LOVE IS BACK
I'm so glad that I'm a woman / High steppin', hip dressin' fella (You got it together) / When I'm in your arms, everything's okay / If you want me say it / I'm giving you a love (every man is searching for) / Gotta be where you are / I'm his woman
CD _____ CDSEWM 078
Southbound / Aug '93 / Pinnacle.

RISE
Take a good look (and what do you see) / My laboratory (Is ready for you) / After five / Do it to the music / In Brazil / Anna Lisa / Goodbye concerto
CD _____ CDSEWM 080
Southbound / Feb '94 / Pinnacle.

Love/Hate

I'M NOT HAPPY
CD _____ 08518222
SPV / Dec '95 / Plastic Head.

LET'S RUMBLE
Let's rumble / Spinning wheel / Boozer / Wrong side of the grape / Devil's squaw / Beer money / Here's to you / Sexical / Miracles / Flower
CD _____ 7432115311-2
RCA / Jul '93 / BMG.

Loved Ones

BETTER DO RIGHT
CD _____ HCD 8057
Hightone / Oct '94 / ADA / Koch.

Loveland

WONDER OF LOVE, THE
CD _____ HF 45CD
PWL / Jun '95 / Warner Music / 3MV.

Loveless, Patty

WHEN ANGELS FLY
Handful of dust / Halfway down / When the fallen angels fly / You don't even know who I am / Feelin' good about feelin' bad / Here I am / I try to think about Elvis / Ships / Old weakness (coming on strong) / Over my shoulder
CD _____ 477183 2
Columbia / Nov '94 / Sony.

Lover Speaks

LOVER SPEAKS,THE
Every lover's sign / No more "I love you's" / Never to forget you / Face me and smile / Absent one / Love is: "I gave you everything" / This can't go on / Still faking this art of love / Tremble dancing / Of tears
CD _____ 3951272
A&M / Apr '95 / PolyGram.

Loves Ugly Children

CAKEHOLE
CD _____ FNCD 324
Flying Nun / Nov '95 / Disc.

Loveslug

CIRCLE OF VALUES
CD _____ GRCD KH
Glitterhouse / May '93 / Direct / ADA.

Lovetrick

LOVETRICK
CD _____ 367 0003.2
Mausoleum / Oct '91 / Grapevine.

Lovett, Eddie

BEST OF REGGAE HITS OF EDDIE LOVETT VOL. 1, THE
CD _____ PKL 514912
K&K / Jul '93 / Jetstar.

LET'S TRY AGAIN
CD _____ PKCD 33193
K&K / Jul '93 / Jetstar.

Lovett, Lyle

I LOVE EVERYBODY
Skinny legs / Fat babies / I think you know what I mean / Hello Grandma / Creeps like me / Sonja / They don't like me / Record lady / Ain't it somethin' / Penguins / Fat girl

/ La to the left / Old friend / Just the morning / Moon on my shoulder / I've got the blues / Goodbye to Carolina / I love everybody
CD _____ MCD 10808
MCA / Sep '94 / BMG.

JOSHUA JUDGES RUTH
CD _____ MCAD 10475
MCA / Mar '92 / BMG.

LYLE LOVETT
CD _____ MCLD 19134
MCA / Oct '90 / BMG.

LYLE LOVETT AND HIS LARGE BAND
Here I am / I know you know / I married her just because she looks / Once is enough / Stand by your man / Crying shame / What do you do / Nobody knows me / Which way does that old pony run / If you were to wake up
CD _____ DMCG 6037
MCA / Feb '89 / BMG.

Lovette, Eddie

BEST REGGAE HITS OF... VOL. 11
CD _____ PKCD 33094
K&K / Sep '94 / Jetstar.

Lovich, Lena

FLEX
CD _____ STIFFCD 21
Disky / May '94 / THE / BMG / Discovery / Pinnacle.

MARCH
Life / Wonderland / Nightshift / Hold on to love / Rage / Natural beauty / Make believe / Sharman / Vertigo / Shadow walk
CD _____ ECD 280012
Evidence / Oct '95 / Harmonia Mundi / ADA / Cadillac.

NO MAN'S LAND
It's you only you (mein schmerz) / Blue hotel / Faces / Walking low / Special star / Sister video / Maria / Savages / Rocky road
CD _____ STIFFCD 22
Line / May '94 / CM / Grapevine / ADA / Conifer / Direct.

STATELESS
Line / Oct '94 / CM / Grapevine / ADA / Conifer / Direct.
CD _____ LICD 901066

STIFF YEARS, THE
CD _____ HRCD 8035
Disky / Jan '94 / THE / BMG / Discovery / Pinnacle.

Lovie, Robert

NORTH EAST SHORE, THE
North east shore / Guise o'tough / Banks o'red roses / Poem / Boggyclairts / Alex Green / Auld meal mill / Butter on the bow / I aince lo'ed a lass / Alford cattle show / Prince and Jean / Band selection / Silver darlings / McGinty's meal and ale / Parting song
CD _____ CDR 003
Donside / Jan '87 / Ross.

Lovin' Spoonful

COLLECTION: LOVIN' SPOONFUL
Do you believe in magic / Did you ever have to make up your mind / Younger girl / Jug band music / Didn't want to have to do it / Daydream / You're a big boy now / Wash her away / Girl beautiful girl (Barbara's theme) / Respoken / Darling be home soon / Lookin' to spy / You didn't have to be so nice / Sittin' here lovin' you / Darling companion / Rain on the roof / Coconut grove / Nashville cats / Summer in the city / She is still a mystery / Boredom / Six o'clock / Younger generation / Till I run with you / Never goin' back
CD _____ CCSCD 187
Castle / Aug '88 / BMG.

DAYDREAM
Daydream / There she is / It's not time now / Warm baby / Day blues / Let the boy rock 'n' roll / Jug band music / Didn't want to have to do it / You didn't have to be so nice / Bald headed Lena
CD _____ CLACD 194
Castle / Aug '90 / BMG.

EP COLLECTION: LOVIN' SPOONFUL
Did you ever.. / Day blues / Blues in the bottle / There she is / Younger girl / Other side of this life / Sporting life / Fishin' blues / Jug band music / Loving you / Let the boy rock 'n' roll / Eyes / You baby / Butchie's tune / Wild about my lovin' / Voodoo in my basement / It's not time now / Don't want to have to do it / Coconut grove / Do you believe in music
CD _____ SEECD 229
See For Miles/C5 / May '88 / Pinnacle.

HIT SINGLE COLLECTABLES
CD _____ DISK 4503
Disky / Apr '94 / THE / BMG / Discovery / Pinnacle.

HUMS OF THE LOVIN' SPOONFUL
Sittin' here lovin' you / Bes' friends / Voodoo in my basement / Darling companion / Henry Thomas / Full measure / Rain on the

roof / Coconut grove / Nashville cats / Four eyes
CD _____ REP 4018WZ
Repertoire / Aug '91 / Pinnacle / Cadillac.

SPOONFUL OF SOUNDTRAKCS, A
CD _____ REP 4115-WZ
Repertoire / Aug '91 / Pinnacle / Cadillac.

SUMMER IN THE CITY
Daydream / Nashville cats / She is still a mystery / Didn't have to have to do it / Coconut grove / You didn't have to be so nice / Rain on the roof / Darling be home soon / Sittin' here lovin' you / On the road again / Do you believe in magic / Close your eyes / Jug band music / Summer in the city / Money / Warm baby / Night owl blues / Never going back (to Nashville)
CD _____ 5507352
Spectrum/Karussell / Jan '95 / PolyGram / THE.

Low

I COULD LIVE IN HOPE
Words / Fear / Cut / Slide / Lazy / Lullaby / Sea / Down / Drag / Rope / Sunshine
CD _____ QUIGD 5
Quigley / Aug '94 / EMI.

Low 948

PACCARISCA
CD _____ KICKCD 20
Kickin' / Jul '95 / SRD.

Low, Bruce

12 UHR MITTAGS
CD _____ BCD 15511
Bear Family / Aug '90 / Rollercoaster / Direct / CM / Swift / ADA.

Low Flying Aircraft

LOW FLYING AIRCRAFT
Sybilization / Fourth dimension / Baptism by fire / Poolside / Abstract blue / Moronathon / Amnesia / Reflection / What did you do / Radically conservative
CD _____ CDR 101
Red Hot / Mar '94 / THE.

Low Gods

MENAGERIE
CD _____ TCCD 9.00614J
Trance / Nov '88 / SRD.

Low Pop Suicide

DEATH OF EXCELLENCE, THE
Bless my body / Almost said / Suicide ego / Zombie / Life and death / No genius / Humbled / More than this / Philo's snag / Sheep's clothing / Face to face / Tell them I was here
CD _____ WDOM 012CD
World Domination / Jan '95 / Pinnacle.

ON THE CROSS OF COMMERCE
Here we go / Kiss your lips / My way / Disengaged / It's easy / Your God can't feel my pain / Crush / Ride / Imagine my love / All in death is sweet
CD _____ WDOM 007CD
World Domination / May '94 / Pinnacle.

Lowe, Allen

DARK WAS THE NIGHT - COLD ON THE GROUND (Lowe, Allen & The American Song Project)
CD _____ CD 811
Music & Arts / May '94 / Harmonia Mundi / Cadillac.

WOYZECK'S DEATH (Lowe, Allen & Roswell Rudd)
Cold as ice / Sun on her bones / Voices in the fiddles / Misery / Beautiful sins / Hard gray sky / On thine after another / Good and beautiful murder / Woyzeck's death / Bonehead / Concentration suite
CD _____ ENJ 90052
Enja / May '95 / New Note / Vital/SAM.

Lowe, Amanda

SPIRAL DANCE
CD _____ GRIN 941CD
Grinnigogs / Jan '95 / ADA / Harmonia Mundi.

Lowe, Frank

LIVE FROM SOUNDSCAPE (Lowe, Frank Quintet)
CD _____ DIW 399CD
DIW / Jul '94 / Harmonia Mundi / Cadillac.

Lowe, Jez

BACK SHIFT
CD _____ FECD 089
Fellside / Nov '95 / Target/BMG / Direct / ADA.

BAD PENNY
Another man's wife / Small coal song / Midnight mail / Dandelion clocks / Land of the living / Nearer to Nettles / Father Mallory's dance / Yankee boots / New town incident
CD _____ FECD 70

Fellside / Dec '95 / Target/BMG / Direct / ADA.

BEDE WEEPS (Lowe, Jez & The Bad Pennies)
Call for the North country / These coal town days / Kid Canute / Scotty Moore's reel / Just like Moses / She'll always be freedom / Greek lightning / Dover / Delaware / Teardrop twostep / Too up and too down / Bulldog breed / Last of the widows / Mike Neville said it / Bede weeps
CD _____ FECD 94
Fellside / Nov '93 / Target/BMG / Direct / ADA.

BRIEFLY ON THE STREET (Lowe, Jez & The Bad Pennies)
You can't take it with you / Famous working man / One man bound / Old hammer-head / Boonas / Soda man / Davis and Golightly / Jordan/ The begging bowl / Alice / Fun without fools / Swiss reel / New moon's arms
CD _____ FE 079CD
Fellside / Feb '88 / Target/BMG / Direct / ADA.

TENTERHOOKS (Lowe, Jez & The Bad Pennies)
CD _____ GLCD 1161
Green Linnet / Jan '96 / Roots / CM / Direct / ADA.

Lowe, Nick

16 ALL-TIME LOWES
American squirm / Big kick, plain scrap / Born fighter / Cruel to be kind / Heart of the city / I love the sound of breaking glass / Little Hitler / Marie Provost / Nutted by reality / Skin deep so it goes / Switchboard Susan / They called it rock / When I write the book / Without love
CD _____ DIAB 801
Diabolo / Oct '93 / Pinnacle.

ABOMINABLE SHOWMAN
Wish you were here / Paid the price / Saint beneath the paint / Time wounds all heals / Tanque-Rae / Around with love / Cool reaction / Chicken and feathers / We want action / Ragin' eyes / How do you talk to an angel / Man or a fall
CD _____ FIENDCD 184
Demon / Apr '90 / Pinnacle / ADA.

BASHER: THE BEST OF NICK LOWE
So it goes / Heart of the city / I love the sound of breaking glass / Little Hitler / No reason / Thirty six inches high / Marie Provost / Nutted by reality / American squirm / Peace, love and understanding / Cracking up / Big kick, plain scrap / Born fighter / Switchboard Susan / Without love / Love so fine / Cruel to be kind / When I write the book / Heart / Stick it where the sun don't shine / Ragin' eyes / Time wounds all heels / Tanque-rae / Maureen / Half a boy and half a man / Breakaway / She don't love nobody / Seven nights to rock / Long walk back / Rose of England / I knew the bride / Lover's jamboree
CD _____ FIENDCD 142
Demon / Aug '89 / Pinnacle / ADA.

BOXED - 4CD SET (Jesus Of Cool/Rose Of England/Cowboy Outfit/Pinker &...)
CD Set _____ NICK 1
Demon / Jan '94 / Pinnacle / ADA.

IMPOSSIBLE BIRD
CD _____ FIENDCD 757
Demon / Oct '94 / Pinnacle / ADA.

JESUS OF COOL
Music for money / I love the sound of breaking glass / Little Hitler / Shake and pop / Tonight / So it goes / No reason / Thirty six inches high / Marie Provost / Nutted by reality / Heart of the city
CD _____ FIENDCD 131
Demon / Oct '88 / Pinnacle / ADA.

LABOUR OF LUST
Cruel to be kind / Cracking up / Big kick, plain scrap / Born fighter / You make me / Skin deep / Switchboard Susan / Endless grey ribbon / Without love / Dose of you / Love so fine
CD _____ FIENDCD 182
Demon / Apr '90 / Pinnacle / ADA.

NICK LOWE AND HIS COWBOY OUTFIT
Half a boy and half a man / You'll never get me up (in one of those) / Maureen / God's gift to women / Gee and the rick and the race card trick / Hey big mouth stand up and stay that / Awesome / Breakaway / Love like a glove / Live fast love hard / L.A.F.S.
CD _____ FIENDCD 185
Demon / May '90 / Pinnacle / ADA.

NICK THE KNIFE
Burning / Heart / Stick it where the sun don't shine / Queen of Sheba / My heart hurts / Couldn't love you / Let me kiss ya / Too many teardrops / Ba doom / Raining / One's too many / Zulu kiss
CD _____ FIENDCD 183
Demon / Apr '90 / Pinnacle / ADA.

PARTY OF ONE PLUS
CD _____ FIENDCD 767
Demon / Jul '95 / Pinnacle / ADA.

PINKER & PROUDER THAN PREVIOUS
(You're my) wildest dream / Crying in my sleep / Big hair / Love gets strange / Black Lincoln Continental / Cry it out / Lover's jamboree / Geisha girl / Wishing well / Big big love
CD _____ FIENDCD 99
Demon / Mar '88 / Pinnacle / ADA.

ROSE OF ENGLAND
I knew the bride / Indoor fireworks / I'm right / I can be the one you love / Everyone / Bob Skaddidle daddle / Darlin' angel eyes / She don't love nobody / Seven nights to rock / Long walk back / Rose of England / Lucky dog
CD _____ FIENDCD 73
Demon / Oct '88 / Pinnacle / ADA.

WILDERNESS YEARS, THE
CD _____ FIENDCD 203
Demon / Oct '90 / Pinnacle / ADA.

Lowery, Ian

KING BLANK NO.. (Lowery, Ian Group)
Need / Sick little minds / Beach fire / One last blast / Kind of loathing / You're gonna pay / Party / Driver's arrived
CD _____ SITL 24CD
Situation 2 / Nov '91 / Pinnacle.

Lowland Band & Pipers Of.

EDINBURGH CASTLE (Lowland Band & Pipers Of The Scottish Division)
Scotland the brave / Scottish black isle / Holyrood / Will ye no come back again / Pentland hills / Festoso / Edinburgh castle / Pipe set 3/4 marches / Hebrides suite / Ye banks and braes / Misty morn / Dunedin / Pipes set 6-8 marches / Garb of the old gaul / Dumbarton's drums / Regimental quick marches / Whistle o'er the lave / Blue bonnest o'er the border / Within a mile o'Edinboro' town
CD _____ BNA 5115
Bandleader / Oct '95 / Conifer.

Lowlife

FROM A SCREAM TO A WHISPER
CD _____ LOLIF 7CD
Nightshift / Feb '90 / Vital.

GODHEAD
CD _____ LOLIF 8CD
Nightshift / May '90 / Vital.

SAN ANTONIUM
CD _____ LOLIF 9CD
Nightshift / Sep '91 / Vital.

Lowman, Annette

ANNETTE LOWMAN
CD _____ MM 801050
Minor Music / Dec '95 / Vital/SAM.

Loxam, Arnold

BLACKPOOL MAGIC
Beside the seaside / Blackpool walk / Blackpool bounce / So blue / Carolina moon / Wyoming lullaby / Tammy / As time goes by / I'll string along with you / Angels never leave heaven / When my dreamboat comes home / Whispering / Shepherd of the hills / Let a smile be your umbrella / If you knew Susie like I know Susie / Bye bye blackbird / Ik hou van Holland / Sing something simple / Strollin' / Love letters in the sand / Bewitched, bothered and bewildered / Neighbours / One of those songs / Cabaret / Mr. Sandman / It's party time again / Sloth song / O.D. junior club song / Dellah / Cruising down the river / Forever and ever / I just called to say I love you / Bunch of thyme / Love changes everything / Strangers in the night / I'm confessin' that I love you / In a little Spanish town / For me and my girl / Underneath the arches / Morningtown ride / Arm in arm / White cliffs of Dover / Blackpool lights / Last mile home / Who's taking you home / Goodnight (dear goodnight) / Now is the hour / It's a pity to say goodnight / It's a lovely day today / Here's to the next time / Wish me luck as you wave me goodbye
CD _____ CDGRS 1215
Grosvenor / '91 / Target/BMG.

STRANGER ON THE SHORE
CD _____ CDGRS1240
Grosvenor / Feb '93 / Target/BMG.

TOWER WORLD DANCETIME
Dear hearts and gentle people/There's always room at our hou (Music music music) / Limehouse blues/Japanese sandman/Dinah / Tear, a kiss, a smile, A/Lucky line / Family Christmas / Days of wine and roses/ Too young/On a slowboat to China / Bye bye love/Bugloah/Sugartime / Morecambe Bay / Tower world waltz / Just a closer walk with thee/Beyond the sunset / Misty Islands of the Highlands/All ashore/ Hello my baby / Hear my song Violetta/O solo mio / Tower ballroom tango / Los amigos / Friends for life / I just want to dance with you/Moving South / Crystal chandeliers/Sleepy time gal/Home is really where the / One of those songs/I'll see you in my dreams/Goodnight sweet / Old romance/ The birthday waltz/Good luck, good health / Come back to Sorrento/Auld lang syne /

Near you/I love you because/Any dream will do (CD only) / Should I/Don't sit under the apple tree/The world is waiting (CD only) / Powder your face with sunshine/I'm sitting on top of the wor (CD only) / Hello Dolly/ Mame/Chinatown, My Chinatown (CD only) / Serenade (CD only) / Lulu's back in town/Don't bring Lulu/Gal in Calico (CD only)
CD _____ CDGRS 1260
Grosvenor / Feb '95 / Target/BMG.

WURLITZER SEASONS
Windermere march / Sunset over Morcambe bay / My darling Clementine / Grasshoppers dance / Perfect year / Dicky bird hop / Windmills of the Zuider Zee / Wear a smile / Londonderry air / End of the pier / To a wild rose / Wishing you were somehow here again / Four seasons in music / Roses of Picardy / Wurlitzer march / Narcissus / 12th Street rag / Kleine melody / Rock gospel melody
CD _____ OS 212
Valentine / Jun '95 / Conifer.

Loy, Myrna

I PRESS MY LIPS
CD _____ NORMAL 108 CD
Normal/Okra / Aug '90 / Direct / ADA.

Lozano & Morgan

SUR
CD _____ 33JAZZ 010CD
33 Jazz / Jun '93 / Cadillac / New Note.

LTG Exchange

LTG EXCHANGE
CD _____ DGPCD 725
Deep Beats / May '95 / BMG.

L'Trimm

GRAB IT
Grab it / Better yet / l'trimm / We can rock that beat / Sexy / Cutie pie / He's a mutt / Don't come to my house / Cars with the boom
CD _____ K 781 925 2
Atlantic / Jan '89 / Warner Music.

Lubricated Goat

FORCES YOU DON'T UNDERSTAND
You remain anonymous / Next world / Crave the hedonists / Half life / Psychic detective / Lost time / Soul remains the pain / Twentieth century rake / Day in rock
CD _____ PCP 012-2
Matador / Aug '94 / Vital.

PADDOCK OF LOVE
CD _____ BLACKCD 6
Black Eye / Nov '94 / Direct.

PSYCHEDELICATESSEN
CD _____ BLACKCD 11
Normal/Okra / Mar '94 / Direct / ADA.

SCHADENFREUDE
CD _____ BLACKCD 3
Normal/Okra / Mar '94 / Direct / ADA.

Lucas

LUCACENTRIC
CD _____ 450996925-2
Warner Bros. / Aug '94 / Warner Music.

Lucas, Gary

BAD BOYS OF THE ARCTIC
CD _____ EMY 146-2
Enemy / Mar '91 / Grapevine.

GODS AND MONSTERS
CD _____ EMY 1332
Enemy / Sep '92 / Grapevine.

SKELETON AT THE FEAST
CD _____ EMY 1262
Enemy / Mar '92 / Grapevine.

Lucas, Robert

BUILT FOR COMFORT
Built for comfort / Walkin' blues / Ringing that lonesome bell / Just a kid / Blues man from LA / Hawaiian boogie / My home is a burning / Change, change / Sleeping by myself / I miss you baby / Talk to me / Come on in my kitchen
CD _____ AQCD 1011
Audioquest / Sep '95 / New Note.

LAYAWAY
CD _____ AQ 1021
Audioquest / May '95 / New Note.

LUKE AND THE LOCOMOTIVE
Good morning little school girl / Big man mambo / Slide on back home / Worried about it baby / Shed a tear / Feel like going home / Don't your peaches look mellow / Meet me in the bottom / Stranger / I'm so tired / Goodbye baby
CD _____ AQCD 1004
Audioquest / Jul '95 / New Note.

USIN' MAN BLUES
Usin' man / Ramblin' on my mind / What happend to my shoes / If I had possession over judgement day / If you see that woman / Moonshine 1 / I'm in jail again / Dancin' with Mr. Jones / Keep your business to

---

yourself / Me and the devil / Jinx around my bed / Motherless children / It's Christmas time baby / New View / Moonshine 2
CD _____ AQCD 1001
Audioquest / Jul '95 / New Note.

Luciano

BACK TO AFRICA
CD _____ EXTCD 3
Exterminator / Sep '94 / Jetstar.

DON'T GET CRAZY
CD _____ CRCD 36
Charm / Dec '94 / Jetstar.

MOVING UP
CD _____ RASCD 3129
Ras / Jan '94 / Jetstar / Greensleeves / SRD / Direct.

ONE WAY TICKET
CD _____ VPCD 1386
VP / Jan '95 / Jetstar.
CD _____ CRCD 41
Charm / Jul '95 / Jetstar.

SHAKE IT UP TONIGHT
CD _____ BSCD 3
Black Scorpio / Feb '94 / Jetstar.

Lucie Cries

RES NON VERRA
CD _____ AJE 09
Alea Jacta Est / Jun '94 / Plastic Head.

Luciferon

DEMONICATION (THE MANIFEST)
CD _____ POSH 007CD
Osmose / Jun '95 / Plastic Head.

Lucifer's Friend

LUCIFER'S FRIEND
CD _____ REP 4059-WP
Repertoire / Aug '91 / Pinnacle / Cadillac.

SUMOGRIP
CD _____ ESSCD 227
Essential / Jan '95 / Total/BMG.

WHERE THE GROUPIES KILLED THE BLUES
CD _____ REP 4143-WP
Repertoire / Aug '91 / Pinnacle / Cadillac.

Lucky Dube

CAPTURED LIVE
CD _____ SHCD 43090
Shanachie / Apr '93 / Koch / ADA / Greensleeves.

TRINITY
CD _____ 5504792
Tabu / Apr '95 / Jetstar.

VICTIMS
CD _____ FLTRCD 512
Flame Tree / Jul '93 / Pinnacle.

Lucky Seven

ONE WAY TRACK
CD _____ DEL 3008
Deluge / Dec '95 / Direct / ADA.

Lucky Strikers

SLIP SLIDE AND HOPE
CD _____ SPV 08498812
SPV / May '95 / Plastic Head.

Ludichrist

IMMACULATE DECEPTION
CD _____ WB 3034-2
We Bite / Sep '93 / Plastic Head.

POWERTRIP
CD _____ WEBITE 35CD
We Bite / Oct '88 / Plastic Head.

Luecking, Juliana

BIG BROAD
Oh / Fancy your hat / Gonna love a woman / 17-18-19 Grrrls / Pull the scam / Head and mouth / Come to Phoenix / Married in mid-air / Beefheart / Thanks for holding / Shiny blade / Rosita and Marita / 28 and 82 / Willy, Thelma and Kitty / Living legend / Stink / You the best / Margaret and Regina / Pretty girl / Esperanza dreams / Hide and seek / Growth spurt / Big broad / H-heart / Stick shift / Bed bath / Rescue squad / Leaf diving / To be touched / Catch
CD _____ KRS 228CD
Kill Rock Stars / Sep '94 / Vital.

Lujan, Tony

MAGIC CIRCLE
CD _____ 74023
Capri / Nov '93 / Wellard / Cadillac.

Lukather, Steve

CANDYMAN
Hero with 1,000 eyes / Freedom / Extinction blues / Born yesterday / Never walk alone / Party in Simon's pants / Borrowed time / Never let them see you cry / Froth / Bomber / Song for Jeff
CD _____ 475964 2
Columbia / Apr '94 / Sony.

Luke, Robin

SUSIE DARLIN'
Well oh well oh (don't you know) / Everlovin' / Five minutes more / You can't stop me from dreaming / Who's gonna hold your hand / Susie darlin' / Part of a fool / Poor little rich boy / So alone / All because of you / Make me a dreamer / Walkin' in the moonlight / My girl / Chicka chicka honey / School bus love affair / Strollin' blues
CD _____ BCD 15547
Bear Family / Aug '93 / Rollercoaster / Direct / CM / Swift / ADA.

Lukie D

CENTRE OF ATTRACTION
CD _____ VPCD 1451
VP / Jan '96 / Jetstar.

Lul

HAIL THE FRISIANS FREE
CD _____ SCH 9013CD
Schemer / Sep '91 / Vital.

Lull

COLD SUMMER
CD _____ SNTX 490
Sentrax Corporation / Sep '94 / Plastic Head.

Lulu

INDEPENDENCE
Independence / There has got to be a way / Restless moods / I'm back for more / How 'bout us / Until I get over you / Let me wake up in your arms / You left me lonely / Rhythm of romance / I'm walking away / Place to fall / Let me wake up in your arms (Romantic reprise) (Not on LP)
CD _____ DOMECD 1
Parlophone / Feb '93 / EMI.

MAN WHO SOLD THE WORLD
CD _____ CHELD 1004
Start / Jun '89 / Koch.

VERY BEST OF LULU
CD _____ BRCD 1003
BR Music / Jan '95 / Target/BMG.

Luman, Bob

LORETTA
Loretta / It's a sin / If you don't love me / Love worked a miracle / Poor boy blues / Sentimental / You're welcome / Running scared / Freedom of living / Tears from out of nowhere / It's all over / Best years of my wife / Bigger man than I / Too hot to dance / I like your kind of love / Hardly anymore
CD _____ CDSD 068
Sundown / Nov '89 / Magnum Music Group.

Lumiere, Jean

ETOILES DE LA CHANSON
CD _____ 882502
Music Memoria / Aug '93 / Discovery / ADA.

Lumukanda

ARAGLIN
CD _____ NZCD 004
Nova Zembla / Feb '94 / Plastic Head.

Luna

BEWITCHED
California (all the way) / Tiger Lily / Friendly advice / Bewitched / This time around / Great Jones Street / Going home / Into the fold / I know you tried / Sleeping pill
CD _____ 755961617-2
WEA / Mar '94 / Warner Music.

LUNAPARK
Slide / Anesthesia / Slash your tyres / Crazy people / Time / Smile / I can't wait / Hey sister / I want everything / Time to quit / Goodbye / We're both confused
CD _____ 7559613602
WEA / Aug '92 / Warner Music.

PENTHOUSE
CD _____ BBQCD 178
Beggars Banquet / Jul '95 / Warner Music / Disc.

Lunachicks

BABYSITTERS ON ACID
CD _____ BFFP 52CD
Blast First / Nov '89 / Disc.

Lunceford, Jimmie

BABY WON'T YOU PLEASE COME HOME
Lonesome road / You set me on fire / Baby, won't you please come home / I've only myself to blame / You're just a dream / Easter parade / Blue blazes / Mixup / What is this thing called swing / Shoemaker's holiday / Ain't she sweet / Mandy / White heat / Well alright then / I love you / Oh why oh why / Who did you meet last night / You let me down / Sassin' the boss / I want the waiter (with the water) / You can fool some of the people (some of the time) / Think of me, little daddy / Liza (all the clouds'll roll away) / Belgium stomp / You let me down (2) / I used to love you (but it's all over now)
CD _____ CDGRF 086
Tring / '93 / Tring / Prism.

BLUES IN THE NIGHT (Lunceford, Jimmie & Orchestra)
T'ain't what you do (it's the way that you do it) / Blues in the night / Organ grinder swing / Margie / Le jazz hot / Uptown blues / Baby, won't you please come home / Twenty four robbers / I'm gonna move to the outskirts of town / For dancers only / Well alright then / Lonesome road / Cheatin' on me / Ain't she sweet / Mandy / Back door stuff / Harlem shout / Four or five times
CD _____ CD 56013
Jazz Roots / Sep '94 / Target/BMG.

FOR DANCERS ONLY (Lunceford, Jimmie & Orchestra)
Close out / Margie / Sit back and relax / Jimmie's / Four or five times / Call the police / Water faucet / Cement mixer / Them who has gets / Shut out / Jay Gee / I need a lift / Just once too often / One o'clock jump
CD _____ CDCD 1118
Charly / Jul '93 / Charly / THE / Cadillac.

INTRODUCTION TO JIMMIE LUNCEFORD 1934-42
CD _____ 4002
Best Of Jazz / Dec '93 / Discovery.

JIMMIE LUNCEFORD
CD _____ HEPCD 1017
Hep / Jan '91 / Cadillac / Jazz Music / New Note / Wellard.

JIMMIE LUNCEFORD & HIS ORCHESTRA (1934-35) (Lunceford, Jimmie & Orchestra)
CD _____ 11088
Laserlight / '88 / Target/BMG.

JIMMIE LUNCEFORD & ORCHESTRA (1934-1939) (Lunceford, Jimmie & Orchestra)
CD _____ BLE 592412
Black & Blue / Dec '92 / Wellard / Koch.

JIMMIE LUNCEFORD & ORCHESTRA 1934-42
CD _____ TPZ 1005
Topaz Jazz / Aug '94 / Pinnacle / Cadillac.

JIMMIE LUNCEFORD - 1940-41 (Lunceford, Jimmie & Orchestra)
CD _____ CLASSICS 622
Classics / '92 / Discovery / Jazz Music.

POLISHED PERFECTION
CD _____ TOPAZ 1005
Topaz/ADA / Mar '95 / ADA.

POWERHOUSE SWING
Well alright / You let me down / I want the waiter (with the water) / I used to love you (but it's all over now) / Belgian stomp / Think of me little Daddy / Liza (all the clouds'll roll away) / Rock it for me / I'm in an awful mood / Uptown blues / Lunceford special / Bugs parade / Blues in the groove / I got it / Chopins prelude No.7 / Swingin' in C / Let's try again / Monotony in four plats / Barefoot blues / Minnie the moocher is dead
CD _____ PAR 2012
Parade / Apr '94 / Koch / Cadillac.

RHYTHM IS OUR BUSINESS
Rhythm is our business / Stratosphere / Un-sophisticated Sue / Four or five times / Bird of paradise / I'll take the South / Hittin' the bottle / Oh boy / Best things in life are free / Muddy water / Hell's bells / He ain't got rhythm / Slumming on Park Avenue / For dancers only / Posin' / Margie / Frisco fog / What is this thing called Swing / Ain't she sweet / Life is fine
CD _____ PPCD 78111
Past Perfect / Feb '95 / THE.

RHYTHM IS OUR BUSINESS
Baby, won't you please come home / Barefoot blues / Belgium stomp / Black and tan fantasy / Flaming reeds and screaming brass / For dancers only / Four or five times / Hittin' the bottle / I'm alone with you / Le jazz hot / Margie / My blue heaven / Organ grinder swing / Pigeon walk / Rhythm is our business / Shake your head / Since my best gal turned me down / Sleepy time gal / Sophisticated lady / T'aint what you do / Ti-me's a wastin' / Uptown blues / What's your story Morning Glory / While love lasts

CD _____ CDAJA 5091
Living Era / May '92 / Koch.

UNCOLLECTED 1944 - LIVE AT JAFFERSON BARRACKS, MISSOURI (Lunceford, Jimmie & His Harlem Express)
CD _____ HCD 221
Hindsight / Sep '94 / Target/BMG / Jazz Music.

Lunch, Lydia

13:13
Stares to nowhere / Three times three / This side of nowhere / Snakepit breakdown / Dance of the dead children / Suicide ocean / Lock your door / Afraid of your company
CD _____ LICD 900096
Line / Oct '94 / CM / Grapevine / ADA / Conifer / Direct.

CRIMES AGAINST NATURE
CD _____ 511572
Trident / May '93 / Pinnacle.

HONEYMOON IN RED
Done dun / Still burning / Fields of fire / Dead in the head / Come fall / So your heart / Dead river / Three kings
CD _____ WSP 12 CD
Widowspeak / Jul '89 / Pinnacle.

HYSTERIE
CD _____ WSPCD 008
Widowspeak / Jun '92 / Pinnacle.

QUEEN OF SIAM (UNCENSORED)
CD _____ WSP 1 CD
Widowspeak / Jul '91 / Pinnacle.

RUDE HIEROGLYPHICS (Lunch, Lydia & Excene Cervenka)
CD _____ RCD 10326
Rykodisc / Oct '95 / Vital / ADA.

SHOTGUN WEDDING
CD _____ WSP 002CD
UFO / Oct '91 / Pinnacle.

STINKFIST/CRUMB
CD _____ WSP 020 CD
Widowspeak / Jul '89 / Pinnacle.

TRANCE MUTATION/SHOTGUN WEDDING
CD Set _____ TWIST 2
Trident / Jul '94 / Pinnacle.

UNCENSORED ORAL FIXATION, THE
CD _____ WSP 016 CD
Widowspeak / '89 / Pinnacle.

Lundeng, Susanne

DRAG
CD _____ FX 140CD
Kirkelig Kulturverksted / Dec '94 / ADA.

Lundy, Carmen

SELF PORTRAIT
Spring can really hang you up the most / Better days / My favourite things / Firefly / Forgive me / These things you are to me / Triste without you / I don't want to love without you / Old friend / My ship / Round Midnight
CD _____ JVC 2047
JVC / Apr '95 / New Note.

Lung

CACTII
CD _____ YELLOWBIKE 003
Plastic Head / Jul '92 / Plastic Head.

Lungfish

PASS AND STOW
CD _____ DIS 92CD
Dischord / Sep '94 / SRD.

RAINBOWS FROM ATOMS
CD _____ DIS 78 D
Dischord / Jun '93 / SRD.

Lunny, Donal

DONAL LUNNY
CD _____ CEFCD 133
Gael Linn / Jan '94 / Roots / CM / Direct / ADA.

Lupone, Patti

LUPONE LIVE
CD Set _____ 09026617972
RCA / Jul '93 / BMG.

LUPONE LIVE (Highlights)
CD _____ 09026618342
RCA / Jul '93 / BMG.

Lurie, Evan

HAPPY? HERE? NOW?
CD _____ TWI 5742
Les Disques Du Crepuscule / Aug '90 / Discovery / ADA.

PIECES OF BANDONEON
CD _____ TWI 8712
Les Disques Du Crepuscule / Jul '89 / Discovery / ADA.

Lurkers

GREATEST HITS LIVE
Ain't got a clue / I don't need to tell her / Unfinished business / Pills / Barbara blue / Rubber room / Just thirteen / Uptown of downtown / Going monkee again (hey hey hey) / Jenny / Shadow / New guitar in town / Miss world / I'm on heat / Freak show / Take me back to babylon / Then I kissed her / Drag you out / Cyanide
CD _____ STR CD 009
Street Link / Oct '92 / BMG.

LAST WILL AND TESTAMENT
I'm on heat / Cyanide / Shadow / Wine drinker me / Out in the dark / Freak show / Jenny / Self destruct / Ain't got a clue / Take me back to Babylon / New guitar in town / Love story / Then I kicked her / Just thirteen / New guitar in town / She knows
CD _____ BBL 2CD
Lowdown/Beggars Banquet / Jul '88 / Warner Music / Disc.

NON STOP NITROPOP
CD _____ WLO 24602
Weser / Oct '94 / Plastic Head.

POWERJIVE/KING OF THE MOUNTAIN
Powerjive / Lipstick and shampoo / Solitaire / Waiting for you / Things will never be the same / World of Jenny Brown / Walk like a superstar (talk like a zombie) / Go go girl / Strange desire (burn, burn, burn) / Raven's wing / I close my eyes / Lullaby / Barbara blue / Never had a beach head / Unfinished business / Going monkee again (hey hey hey) / King of the mountain (part 1) / Lucky John / King of the mountain (part 2)
CD _____ CDPUNK 69
Anagram / Nov '95 / Pinnacle.

WILD TIMES AGAIN
CD _____ WLO 24332
Weser / Oct '94 / Plastic Head.

Luscious Jackson

IN SEARCH OF MANNY
Let yourself get down / Life of leisure / Daughters of the kaos / Keep on rockin' it / She be wantin' it more / Bam-Bam / Satellite
CD _____ ABB 46XCD
Big Cat / Aug '95 / SRD / Pinnacle.

NATURAL INGREDIENTS
City song / Deep slag / Angel / Strongman / Energy sucker / Here / Find your mind / Pele Merengue / Rock freak / Rollin' / Surprise / LP Retreat
CD _____ CDEST 2234
Capitol / Aug '94 / EMI.

Lush

SCAR
CD _____ JADCD 911
4AD / Oct '89 / Disc.

SPLIT
CD _____ CAD 4011CD
4AD / Jun '94 / Disc.

SPOOKY
CD _____ CADC 2002CD
4AD / Feb '92 / Disc.

Lusher, Don

JUST GOOD FRIENDS (Lusher, Don & Maurice Murphy/The Hammonds Sauce Works Band)
CD _____ DOYCD 020
Doyen / Feb '93 / Conifer.

TRIBUTE TO THE GREAT BANDS VOL. 1 (Lusher, Don Big Band)
Peanut vendor / Take the 'A' train / I'll never smile again / Don't be that way / I've got my love to keep me warm / Kid from Red Bank / Opus one / Adios / I get a kick out of you / Early Autumn / Caravan / Two o'clock jump
CD _____ CDSIV 110
Horatio Nelson / Jul '95 / THE / BMG / Avid/ BMG / Koch.

TRIBUTE TO THE GREAT BANDS VOL. 2 (Lusher, Don Big Band)
Trumpet blues and cantabile / Pennsylvania 6-5000 / That lovely weekend / That's right / Westlake / D.L. blues / Sing, sing, sing / April in Paris / I'm getting sentimental over you / Don't get around much anymore / Concerto to end all concertos
CD _____ CDSIV 1114
Horatio Nelson / Jul '95 / THE / BMG / Avid/ BMG / Koch.

TRIBUTE TO THE GREAT BANDS VOL. 3 (Lusher, Don Big Band)
Carnival / Benny rides again / Song of India / Cute / Wales '87 / Moonlight serenade / At the woodchoppers' ball / Boogie woogie / Love for sale / High and mighty / Cotton tail / Tea for two
CD _____ CDSIV 1125
Horatio Nelson / Jul '95 / THE / BMG / Avid/ BMG / Koch.

TRIBUTE TO THE GREAT BANDS VOL. 4 (Lusher, Don Big Band)
Mr. Anthony's boogie / Sunny side of the street / Continental / Isafahan / Mission to Moscow / Night in Tunisia / Apple honey /

Wave / Shiny stockings / Liebestraum / String of pearls / One o'clock jump
CD _____ CDSIV 1133
Horatio Nelson / Jul '95 / THE / BMG / Avid/ BMG / Koch.

Lussia

FLEUR DE MANDRAGORE
CD _____ 422471
New Rose / May '94 / Direct / ADA.

Lussier, Rene

LE TRESOR DE LA LANGUE
CD _____ AM 015CD
ReR Megacorp / Apr '91 / These / ReR Megacorp.

Lustmord

LUSTMORD
CD _____ DV 04
Dark Vinyl / Jan '94 / Plastic Head.

PLACE WHERE THE BLACK STARS HANG, THE
CD _____ DFX 16CD
Dark Vinyl / Jan '95 / Plastic Head.

Lutcher, Nellie

BEST OF NELLIE LUTCHER, THE
Hurry on down / One I love belongs to somebody else / You better watch yourself / Bub / My mother's eyes / He's a real gone guy / Let me love you tonight / Chi-Chi-Chi Chicago / Fine and mellow / I thought about you / Kinda blue and low / Song is ended (but the melody lingers on) / Lake Charles boogie / Fine brown frame / My man (mon homme) / Chicken ain't nothing but a bird / He sends me / My new Papa's got to have everything / Come and get it / Honey / That will just about knock me out, baby / What's your alibi / Pa's not home
CD _____ CDP 8350392
Capitol Jazz / Nov '95 / EMI.

DITTO FROM ME TO YOU
Ditto from me to you / I took a trip on the train / One I love (belongs to somebody else) / Humoresque / Pig latin song / Imagine you having eyes for me / Princess Poo-Poo-Ly has plenty papya / Say a little prayer for me / Baby please stop and think about me / Only you / I really couldn't love you / He sends me / That's how it goes / Mean to me / If I didn't love you like I do / St. Louis blues
CD _____ RBD 1103
Mr. R&B / Oct '90 / Swift / CM / Wellard.

Luter, Claude

RED HOT REEDS
CD _____ BCD 219
GHB / Jul '93 / Jazz Music.

Luxon, Benjamin

I LOVE MY LOVE (A Collection Of British Folk Songs) (Luxon, Benjamin & David Willison)
Jolly miller / Drink to me only with thine eyes / Foggy foggy dew / Isle of Cloy / Trees they grow so high / Died for love / Lovely Mollie / I love my love / Shooting of his dear / Down by the Sally Gardens / Old turf fire / Banks and braes / Barb'ra (H)ellen / Barbara Allen / She moved through the fair / Star of the County Down / Sweet nightingale / Blow the wind southerly / British waterside / Press gang / Little Sir William / Sir Dukes went-a-fishin' / Sweet Polly Oliver / Bold William Taylor / Charlie is my darling / O Waly, Waly
CD _____ CHAN 8946
Chandos / Jun '92 / Chandos.

TWO GENTLEMEN FOLK (Luxon, Benjamin & Friends)
CD _____ CD 84401
Telarc / '88 / Conifer / ADA.

Luxuria

BEAST BOX
Beast box is dreaming / Stupid blood / Against the past / Our curious leader / We keep on getting there / Ticket / Animal in the mirror / Dirty beating heart / Smoking mirror / I've been expecting you / Karezza / Beast box / Jezebel
CD _____ BEGA 106 CD
Beggars Banquet / May '90 / Warner Music / Disc.

UNANSWERABLE LUST
Redneck / Flesh / Public highway / Pound / Lady 21 / Celebrity / Rubbish / Mile / Luxuria
CD _____ BEGA 90CD
Beggars Banquet / '88 / Warner Music / Disc.

Luzzaschi, Luzzasco

SECRET MUSIC OF LUZZASCO LUZZASCHI
CD _____ CDSAR 58
Saydisc / Oct '92 / Harmonia Mundi / ADA / Direct.

Lycia

DAY IN THE STARK CORNER, A
CD _____ HY 39100762CD
Hyperium / Oct '93 / Plastic Head.

Lyman, Arthur

PEARLY SHELLS
Poinciana / Stranger in paradise / Te manu pukarua / Shangri-la / Now is the hour / Vini vini / South sea island magic / Pearly shells / Off shore / Baubles, bangles and beads / Song of India / Pu pu hino hino / Song of Delilah / Cast your fate to the wind / Waltz latino / Simulau / Aloha oe
CD _____ GNPD 606
GNP Crescendo / Oct '95 / Silva Screen.

Lymon, Frankie

BEST OF FRANKIE LYMON AND THE TEENAGERS
Why do fools fall in love / I want you to be my girl / I'm not a know it all / Who can exlain / I promise to remember / ABC's of love / Share / I'm not a juvenile delinquent / Baby baby / Paper castles / Teenage love / Out in the cold again / Goody goody / Creation of love / Please be mine (CD only) / Love is a clown (CD only) / Am I fooling myself again (CD only) / Thumb thumb (CD only) / Portable on my shoulder (CD only) / Little bitty pretty one (CD only)
CD _____ CZ 241
Roulette / Nov '89 / EMI.

COMPLETE RECORDINGS (Lymon, Frankie & The Teenagers)
Why do fools fall in love / Please be mine / Love is a clown / Am I fooling myself again / I'm not a know it all / Who can explain / I promise to remember / ABC's of love (version 2) / Share / I'm not a juvenile delinquent / Baby baby / Paper castles / Teenage love / Together / You / It would be so nice / Out in the cold again / Little white lies / Begin the beguine / Love is a clown (Alt) / I want you to be my girl (3 versions) / I'm not a know it all (Alt) / Who can explain (Alt) / ABC's of love (Version 1) / Promise to remember (Alt) / Share (Alt) / Fortunate fellow / Love put me out of my head / Lost without your love / I'll walk alone (Without love) / Everything to me / Flip flop / Good love / Flop hop / Mama wanna rock / My broken heart / Crying / Tonight's the night / Can you tell me why / Little wiser now / What's on your mind / Love me long / He's no lover / I hear the angels cry / Wild female / Jean of the ville / Draw / Goody goody / It's Christmas once again / Only way to love / Miracle in the rain / Yours / Glow worm / Good good (Version 1) / Love is the thing / You can't be true / Fools rush in / Too young / Over the rainbow / As time goes by / Don't take your love / Ghost of a chance / Goody goody (Version 2) / Creation of love / Blue moon / These foolish things / You were only fooling / Guilty / So goes my love / My girl / My baby just cares for me / Somebody loves me / Silent night / Little girl / Let's fall in love / Thumb thumb / Portable on my shoulder / Footsteps / That's the way love goes / Wake up little Susie / Short fat fannie / Waitin' in school / Next time you see me / Jailhouse rock / Send for me / Buzz buzz buzz / Searchin' / Silouettes / It hurts to be in love / Diana / Diana (Alt) / Little bitty pretty one / Mama don't allow it / Girls were made for boys / Campus queen / No matter what you've done / Melinda / Ain't she sweet / Almost out of my mind / Rockin' tambourine / Danny Boy / Up jumped the rabbit / Before I fall asleep / Prince or pauper / That's my desire / What a night / Deed I do / Since the beginning of time / Pardon me please / Magic song / Kiss from your lips / Joke (Version 1) / Rainbow / Joke (Version 2) / Goody good girl / Blessed are they / I'm not to young to dream / Almost out of my mind (Version 2) / Is you is or is you ain't my baby / Lover come back to me / Change partners / So young / I put the bomp / To each his own / Teacher, teacher / Roll off / Push and pull / Sweet and lovely / Somewhere / Somewhere (Stereo) / I'm sorry / Seabreeze
CD Set _____ BCDEI 15782
Bear Family / Jun '94 / Rollercoaster / Direct / CM / Swift / ADA.

WHY DO FOOLS FALL IN LOVE
CD _____ RMB 75034
Remember / Nov '93 / Total/BMG.

Lynam, Ray

VERY BEST OF RAY LYNAM, THE
If we're not back in love by Monday / What a lie / He stopped loving her today / You put the blue in me / You win again / Gambler / Moon is still over her shoulder / Beautiful woman / To be lovers / Mona Lisa has lost her smile / Girls, women, and ladies / Hold her in your hand / Speak softly (you're talking to my heart) / I'll never get over you / Rainy days stormy nights / I don't want to see another town
CD _____ RITZCD 513
Ritz / Dec '91 / Pinnacle.

Lynch, Brian

IN PROCESS
Four flights up / Flamingo / On process / D.T.M.Y.M. (Do that make you mad) / After dark / New arrival / I should care / So in love / Brydflight
CD _____ 66056011
Ken Music / Aug '92 / New Note.

PEER PRESSURE (Lynch, Brian Sextet)
Thomasville / Park Avenue petite / Peer pressure / Outlaw / Change of plan / Nother never
CD _____ CRISS 1029CD
Criss Cross / Nov '91 / Cadillac / Harmonia Mundi.

Lynch, Claire

MOONLIGHTER
CD _____ ROUCD 0355
Rounder / Jun '95 / CM / Direct / ADA / Cadillac.

Lynch, George

SACRED GROOVE
Memory Jack / Love power from the Mama head / Flesh and blood / We don't own this world / I will remember / Beast part 1 / Beast part 2 / Not necessary evil / Cry of the brave / Tierra del fuego
CD _____ 755961422-2
Elektra / Aug '93 / Warner Music.

Lynch, Kenny

AFTER DARK
CD _____ FRCD 100
Welfare / Jul '93 / Total/BMG.

Lynch Mob

LYNCH MOB
Jungle of love / Tangled in the web / No good / Dream until tomorrow / Cold is the heart / Tie your mother down / Heaven is waiting / I want it / When darkness calls / Secret
CD _____ 75596132212
Elektra / May '92 / Warner Music.

WICKED SENSATION
Wicked sensation / River of love / Sweet sister mercy / All I want / Hell child / She's evil but she's mine / Dance of the dogs / Rain / No bed of roses / Through these eyes / For a million years / Street fighting man
CD _____ 7559609542
Elektra / Oct '90 / Warner Music.

Lynch, Ray

NO BLUE THING
No blue thing / Clouds below your knees / Here and never found / Drifted in a deeper land / Homeward at last / Evenings, yes / True spirit of mom and dad
CD _____ 01934111192
Windham Hill / Jan '94 / Pinnacle / BMG / ADA.

NOTHING ABOVE MY SHOULDERS BUT THE EVENING
Over easy / Her knees deep in your mind / Passion song / Ivory / Mesquite / Only an enjoyment / Vanishing gardens of Cordoba
CD _____ 01934111332
Windham Hill / Nov '93 / Pinnacle / BMG / ADA.

Lynch, Tomas

CRUX OF THE CATALOGUE, THE
CD _____ LE 11005
Linecheck / Apr '94 / ADA / Direct.

Lynn, Barbara

ATLANTIC SESSION, THE (The Best Of Barbara Lynn)
CD _____ SLC 2505
Ichiban / Apr '95 / Koch.

SO GOOD
CD _____ BB 9540CD
Bullseye Blues / Feb '94 / Direct.

Lynn, Loretta

CLASSIC COUNTRY
CD _____ CDSR 069
Telstar / May '95 / BMG.

COAL MINERS DAUGHTER
CD _____ WMCD 5667
Disky / Oct '94 / THE / BMG / Discovery / Pinnacle.

EVENING WITH LORETTA LYNN, AN
CD _____ MU 5069
Musketeer / Oct '92 / Koch.

GOLDEN GREATS: LORETTA LYNN
Before I'm over you / Wine, women and song / Happy birthday / Blue Kentucky girl / You ain't woman enough to take my man / Don't come home a drinkin' / Fist city / Woman of the world / Coalminer's daughter / One's on the way / Love is the foundation / Hey Loretta / Trouble in paradise / Somebody, somewhere / You're got / Out of my head and back in my bed
CD _____ MCLD 19040
MCA / Apr '92 / BMG.

GREATEST HITS
Hey Loretta / You're looking at country / Let your love flow / We've come a long way baby / Spring fever / Your squaw is on the warpath / Fist city / I fall to pieces / Walkin' after midnight / Crazy / Back in baby's arms / She's got you / Me and Bobby McGee / Somebody, somewhere / Out of my head and back in my bed / Coal miner's daugher / They don't make 'em like my daddy / One's on the way / Pill / Y'all come / You ain't woman enough to take my man
CD _____ PLATCD 363
Prism / '91 / Prism.

HER COUNTRY HITS SHOW
CD _____ CD 3502
Cameo / Aug '94 / Target/BMG.

LEGENDS IN MUSIC - LORETTA LYNN
CD _____ LECD 059
Wisepack / Jul '94 / THE / Conifer.

VERY BEST OF LORETTA LYNN
Coal miner's daughter / You're looking at country / Blue Kentucky girl / Wine, women and song / She's got you / One's on the way / Happy birthday / Before I'm over you / Out of my head and back in my bed / Woman of the world / Trouble in paradise / Hey Loretta / You ain't woman enough to take my man / Fist city / Somebody, somewhere / Don't come a drinkin'
CD _____ PLATCD 308
Platinum Music / Dec '88 / Prism / Ross.

WOMAN OF THE WORLD - BEST OF
CD _____ MCCD 142
Music Club / Nov '93 / Disc / THE / CM.

Lynn, Trudy

24 HOUR WOMAN
CD _____ ICH 1172CD
Ichiban / Jun '94 / Koch.

COME TO MAMA
Right back in the water / When something is wrong with my baby / Come to Mama / When you took your love from me / One woman man / Woman's gotta have it / Do I need you (too) / Fish girl blues / Making love to me
CD _____ CDICH 1063
Ichiban / Oct '93 / Koch.

TRUDY SINGS THE BLUES
Sittin' and drinkin' / Just a little bit / I can tell / Trudy sings the blues / Dr. Feelgood / Do I need you / Bring the beef home to me / Ball and chain
CD _____ CDICH 1043
Ichiban / Oct '93 / Koch.

WOMAN IN ME, THE
Woman in me / My baby can / Speak now or forever hold your peace / You owe it to yourself / Can't nothin' keep me from you / Still on my mind / I've been thinkin' / Feel you, feel me / Spare the rod (love the child)
CD _____ CDICH 1125
Ichiban / Oct '93 / Koch.

Lynn, Vera

48 GOLDEN GREATS
CD _____ DBG 53039
Double Gold / Jan '95 / Target/BMG.

CLOSE TO YOU
I'm yours sincerely / I had the craziest dream / Close to you / Really and truly / Little King without a crown / First lullaby / Little rain must fall / Concerto for two / That autumn in old London town / White cliffs of Dover / I'll be with you in apple blossom time / We three / Who am I / Woodpecker song / I don't never know / Who's taking you home tonight / Goodnight and God bless you / With all my heart / All the world sings a lullaby / You're breaking my heart all over again
CD _____ RAJCD 820
Empress / Mar '94 / THE.

COLLECTION
CD _____ COL 053
Collection / Jun '95 / Target/BMG.

GREATEST HITS: VERA LYNN VOL 1
White cliffs of Dover / Anniversary waltz / Yours / Travellin' home / Don't cry for my love / Goodnare / When I grow too old to dream / My son, my son / It's a sin to tell a lie / Glory of love / Harbour lights / As time goes by
CD _____ FWKS 555
Carlton Home Entertainment / Oct '89 / Carlton Home Entertainment.

HARBOUR LIGHTS
CD _____ WMCD 5690
Disky / May '94 / THE / BMG / Discovery / Pinnacle.

HOW LUCKY YOU ARE
How lucky you are / That lovely weekend / I'll keep you in my heart / Little bit of Heaven / So this is love / It can't be wrong / Outside of Heaven / When your hair has turned to silver / Maybe / Goodnight children everywhere (end s1) / Welcome home / My son, my son / Trying / I lived when I met you / Show me the way / Lambeth walk / I'll meet, the robin / Speak a word of love (I wish, I wish) / Wond'ring and wishing / Doonaree
CD _____ PLCD 530

President / Oct '89 / Grapevine / Target / BMG / Jazz Music / President.

IT'S A LOVELY DAY TOMORROW - A TRIBUTE VOL. 2
White cliffs of Dover / Be like the kettle and sing / Goodnight children everywhere / It's a lovely day tomorrow / Only forever / There'll come another day / Anniversary waltz / London I love / Something to remember you by / Over the hill / Harbour lights / That lovely weekend / Cinderella / Mexicali rose / Jealousy / When the lights go on again / Nightingale sang in Berkeley Square / Bells of St. Mary's / It's a sin to tell a lie / I'm in the mood for love / Love bug will bite you / Heart and soul
CD _____ PASTCD 7030
Flapper / Jan '94 / Pinnacle.

LET'S MEET AGAIN
We'll meet again / Wishing (will make it so) / Mexicali rose / I paid for the lie that I told you / I shall be waiting / Who's taking you home tonight / My own / Goodnight children everywhere / Little boy that Santa Claus forgot / Little Sir Echo / Bell's of St Mary's / Harbour lights / It's a sin to tell a lie / Lonely sweetheart / Memory of a rose / It's a lovely day tomorrow / I'll pray for you / Nightingale sang in Berkeley Square / Medley: I hear a dream / Medley: So rare/ You're here you're there, you're everywhere
CD _____ PAR 2010
Parade / Feb '95 / Koch / Cadillac.

SINCERELY YOURS - A TRIBUTE VOL. 1
Wish me luck as you wave me goodbye / Who's taking you home tonight / I'll pray for you / Garden in Granada / Now it can be told / First quarrel / When Mother Nature sings her lullaby / We'll meet again / Love makes the world go round / I won't tell a soul (that I love you) / Over the rainbow / I hear a dream (come again) / It always rains before a rainbow / I'll walk beside you / Wishing (will make it so) / We both told a lie / I'll think of you / I'll remember / Yours / Goodnight wherever you are / I shall be waiting / Maybe
CD _____ PASTCD 9778
Flapper / Mar '94 / Pinnacle.

SOMETHING TO REMEMBER - WARTIME MEMORIES
Something to remember you by / Yours / Wish me luck as you wave me goodbye / I'll pray for you / White cliffs of Dover / I shall be waiting / Over the hill / That lovely weekend / You'll never know / Who's taking you home tonight / Nightingale sang in Berkeley Square / It's a lovely day tomorrow / London I love / When they sound the last All Clear / Wishing (Will make it so) / It's a sin to tell a lie / Be like the kettle and sing / There'll come another day / Only forever / Anniversary waltz / When the lights go on again / We'll meet again
CD _____ JASMCD 2541
Jasmine / May '95 / Wellard / Swift / Conifer / Cadillac / Magnum Music Group.

THANK YOU FOR THE MUSIC
CD _____ MATCD 223
Castle / Dec '92 / BMG.

THERE'S A LAND OF BEGIN AGAIN
CD _____ PASTCD 7064
Flapper / May '95 / Pinnacle.

VERA LYNN REMEMBERS
White cliffs of Dover / Red sails in the sunset / It's a sin to tell a lie / Roll out the barrel / You'll never know / Nightingale sang in Berkeley Square / Sailing / Harbour lights / Auf wiedersehen / Yours / From the time you say goodbye / My mother's eyes / That lovely weekend / Land of hope and glory / Coming in on a wing and a prayer / We'll meet again / Be like the kettle and sing
CD _____ CDSIV 1120
Horatio Nelson / May '95 / THE / BMG / Avid/BMG / Koch.

VERA LYNN REMEMBERS (The Songs That Won World War 2)
Yours / Medley (Who's taking you home tonight/Wishing/With me luck.) / Somewhere in France with you / Medley #2 (The last time I saw Paris/Arm in Arm/I'll be with you in apple blossom time.) / Medley #3 (A pair of silver wings/Silver wings in the moonlight/Comin' in on a wing and a prayer.) / London pride / Nightingale sang in Berkeley Square / White cliffs of Dover / Medley #4 (If I only had wings/The badge from your coat/Roll out the barrel.) / I'll be seeing you / You'd be so nice to come home to / Room five-hundred-and-four / That lovely weekend / Besame mucho / There'll always be an England / You'll never know / It had to be you / Lili Marlene / Medley #5 (Be like the kettle and sing/There's a new world over the skyline/As time goes by.) / Medley #6 (When the lights go on again/I'll pray for you/We'll meet again.) / Land of hope and glory
CD _____ CDEMS 1515
EMI / May '94 / EMI.

VERA LYNN REMEMBERS VOL.2
CD _____ CDSIV 1140
Horatio Nelson / Apr '93 / THE / BMG / Avid/BMG / Koch.

WE'LL MEET AGAIN (The early years)
Be careful it's my heart / Careless / Cinderella / Goodnight and God bless you / I had the craziest dream / I paid for the lie that I told you / I'll be with you in apple blossom time / I'll never smile again / It's a sin to tell a lie / Rosalie / Roses in December / Smilin' through / Someone's rocking my dreamboat / Something to remember you by / There'll come another day / We'll meet again / When they sound the last All Clear / When you wish upon a star / Where in the world / White cliffs of Dover / Wishing / You made me care / You'll never know / Yours
CD _____ CDAJA 5145
Living Era / Oct '94 / Koch.

WE'LL MEET AGAIN
We'll meet again / Bells of St. Mary's / Wish me luck as you wave me goodbye / Love makes the world go round / Over the rainbow / I'll walk beside you / London I love / Up the wooden hill to Bedfordshire / Cinderella / Really and truly / I had the craziest dream / Two sleepy people / You'll never know / That lovely weekend / Over the hill / After a while / Coming home / When they sound the last All Clear
CD _____ MUCD 9020
Start / Apr '95 / Koch.

WE'LL MEET AGAIN
CD _____ CDCD 1250
Charly / Jun '95 / Charly / THE / Cadillac.

WHAT I DID FOR LOVE
Colours of my life / What I did for love / Harbour lights / One voice / Thank you for the music / Rainbow connection / Ronettes / Room 504 / Weekend in New England / Until it's time for you to go / One day I'll fly away / I sing the songs / It's easy to remember / Caravan song / Are you lonesome tonight / You and me against the world / That old feeling / Daybreak / My friend / Sunshine on my shoulders
CD _____ 5507672
Spectrum/Karussell / Mar '95 / PolyGram THE.

WISH ME LUCK
CD _____ MU 5023
Musketeer / Oct '92 / Koch.

YOURS
Yours / Harbour lights / Jealousy / Be like the kettle and sing / When swallows say goodbye / Faraway places / We'll meet again / Windsor waltz / As time goes by / If you love me (I won't care) / Nightingale sang in Berkeley Square / Who's taking you home tonight / When you hear Big Ben / Auf wiedersehen sweetheart
CD _____ 5500162
Spectrum/Karussell / May '93 / PolyGram / THE.

YOURS
Yours / Be like the kettle and sing / Jealousy / I'll pray for you / It's a sin to tell a lie / Up the wooden hill to Befordshire / Who's taking you home tonight / Cinderella (stay in my arms) / It's a lovely day tomorrow / When the lights go on again / White Cliffs Of Dover / Harbour lights / Over the hill / With all my heart / Goodnight children everywhere
CD _____ PWKS 4250
Carlton Home Entertainment / Feb '96 / Carlton Home Entertainment.

Lynne, Bjorn

DREAMSTATE
Universe of the mind (All life is one pt I/Time and growth/Emptiness/The cycle/Mania) / Material matters (Digital phoenix/Mesmerized/Dark star/Sequences/Progress/All life is one pt II) / Now what (medley)
CD _____ CENCD 009
Centaur / Mar '95 / Complete/Pinnacle.

Lynne, Gloria

MISS GLORIA LYNNE
CD _____ ECD 220092
Evidence / Jul '92 / Harmonia Mundi / ADA / Cadillac.

TIME FOR LOVE, A
CD _____ MCD 5381
Muse / Sep '92 / New Note / CM.

Lynott, Phil

SOLO IN SOHO
Solo in Soho / King's call / Child lullaby / Tattoo / Dear Miss Lonely Hearts / Yellow pearl / Girls / Ode to a black man / Jamaican rum / Talk in 79 / So what / Turn the hands of time
CD _____ 8425632
Vertigo / Jul '90 / PolyGram.

Lynwood Slim

LOST IN AMERICA
CD _____ BMCD 9017
Black Magic / Nov '93 / Hot Shot / Swift / CM / Direct / Cadillac / ADA.

Lynyrd Skynyrd

DEFINITIVE LYNYRD SKYNYRD, THE (3CD Set)

CD _____ MCAD 310390
MCA / Feb '92 / BMG.

FREEBIRD
Saturday night special / Whiskey rock'n'roller / Working for MCA / I ain't the one / Sweet home Alabama / Ballad of Curtis Loew / Call me the breeze / Needle and spoon / Swamp music / Gimme 3 steps / Tuesday's gone / Freebird / Gimme back my bullets / What's your name / That smell / You got that right
CD _____ NTRCD 015
Nectar / Feb '94 / Pinnacle.

LAST REBEL, THE
Good lovin's hard to find / One thing / Can't take that away / Best things in life / Last rebel / Outta hell in my dodge / Kiss your freedom goodbye / South of heaven / Love don't always come easy / Born to run
CD _____ 756782447-2
WEA / Feb '93 / Warner Music.

LYNYRD SKYNYRD 1991
Smokestack lightnin' / Keeping the faith / Southern women / Pure and simple / I've seen enough / Backstreet crawler / Good thing / Money man / It's a killer / Mama (afraid to say goodbye) / End of the road
CD _____ 7567822582
East West / Jun '91 / Warner Music.

NUTHIN' FANCY
Made in the shade / Saturday night special / Cheatin' woman / Railroad song / I'm a country boy / On the hunt / Am I losin' / Whiskey rock'n'roller
CD _____ MCLD 19074
MCA / Nov '92 / BMG.

ONE MORE FOR THE ROAD
Workin' for MCA / I ain't the one / Searching / Tuesdays gone / Saturday night special / Travellin' man / Whiskey rock'n'roller / Sweet home Alabama / Gimme three steps / Call me the breeze / T for Texas / Needle and spoon / Crossroads / Freebird
CD Set _____ MCLDD 19139
MCA / Dec '92 / BMG.

PRONOUNCED LEH-NERD SKIN-NERD
I ain't the one / Tuesday's gone / Gimme three steps / Simple man / Things goin' on / Mississippi kid / Poison whiskey / Freebird
CD _____ MCLD 19072
MCA / Nov '91 / BMG.

SECOND HELPING
Sweet home Alabama / I need you / Don't ask me no questions / Workin' for MCA / Ballad of Curtis Loew / Swamp music / Needle and spoon / Call me the breeze
CD _____ MCLD 19073
MCA / Nov '92 / BMG.

SKYNYRD FRYNDS (Various Artists)
CD _____ MCD 11097
MCA / '95 / BMG.

SKYNYRDS INNYRDS
CD _____ DMCG 6046
MCA / Apr '89 / BMG.

SOUTHERN BY THE GRACE OF GOD
Swamp music / Call me the breeze / Dixie / Freebird / Workin' for MCA / That smell / I know a little / Comin' home / You got that right / What's your name / Gimme back my bullets / Sweet home Alabama
CD _____ MCLD 19010
MCA / Apr '92 / BMG.

STREET SURVIVORS
What's your name / That smell / One more time / I know a little / You got that right / I never dreamt / Honky tonk night time man / Ain't no good life
CD _____ MCLD 19248
MCA / Oct '94 / BMG.

VERY BEST OF LYNYRD SKYNYRD
CD _____ MCLD 19140
MCA / Jul '92 / BMG.

Lyons, Jimmy

BURNT OFFERING (Lyons, Jimmy & Andrew Cyrille)
CD _____ 120130-2
Black Saint / Jun '91 / Harmonia Mundi / Cadillac.

GIVE IT UP (Lyons, Jimmy Quintet)
CD _____ BSR 0087
Black Saint / '86 / Harmonia Mundi / Cadillac.

JUMP UP
CD _____ ART 6139CD
Hat Art / Apr '94 / Harmonia Mundi / ADA / Cadillac.

Lyres

LYRES, LYERS
CD _____ ROSE 103CD
New Rose / Nov '86 / Direct / ADA.

NOBODY BUT ME
CD _____ TAANG 058CD
Taang / Jan '93 / Plastic Head.

ON FYRE
CD _____ ROSE 35CD
New Rose / Jul '84 / Direct / ADA.

PROMISE IS A PROMISE, A
Promise is a promise / Here's a heart on fyre / Every man for himself / Feel good / I'll try you anyway / Worried about nothing / Touch / Running through the night / She's got eyes that tell lie / Jagged time lapse / Knock my socks off / Sick and tired / Trying just to please / Witch
CD _____ ROSE 153CD
New Rose / Aug '88 / Direct / ADA.

SOME LYRES
CD _____ TAANG 82
Taang / Aug '94 / Plastic Head.

Lytle, Cecil

READING OF A SACRED BOOK
CD Set _____ CDCEL 028/29
Celestial Harmonies / Feb '89 / ADA / Select.

SEEKERS OF THE TRUTH
CD Set _____ CDCEL 020/21
Celestial Harmonies / Oct '88 / ADA / Select.

Lytle, Johnny

LOOP/NEW & GROOVY
Loop / More I see you / Man / Time after time / Big Bill / Possum grease / Cristo redentor / Shyster / My romance / Hot sauce / Snapper / Summertime / Selim / Shadow of your smile / Come and get it / Pulpit / Too close for comfort / Chanukah / Screamin' loud / El marcel
CD _____ CDBGPD 961
BGP / Oct '90 / Pinnacle.

MOONCHILD
Meet Benny Bailey / Caravan / Here's that rainy day / Watch what happens / Moonchild / I don't want to leave you / Well you needn't
CD _____ MCD 5431
Muse / Nov '92 / New Note / CM.

POSSUM GREASE
Possum grease / Should I love you / Angel eyes / Milestones / Stormy weather / Love for sale / Adoration / September song / Honeysuckle rose
CD _____ MCD 5482
Muse / Apr '95 / New Note / CM.

Lyttelton, Humphrey

BEANO BOOGIE (Lyttelton, Humphrey & His Band)
Say forward I'll march / Ficklefanny strikes again / Apple honey / Do you call that a buddy / Sixth form / Beano boogie / Little king / Echoes of the jungle / Gnasher and me / Strange Mr. Peter Charles/Cop out / In swinger (On CD only) / Yorkville (On CD only)
CD _____ CLGCD 021
Calligraph / Jun '92 / Cadillac / Wellard / Jazz Music.

ECHOES OF THE DUKE (Lyttelton, Humphrey & His Band & Helen Shapiro)
Take the 'A' train / I got it bad and that ain't good / Caravan / Just squeeze me / Drop me off in Harlem / Solitude/Mood indigo / Echoes of The Duke / I ain't got nothin' but the blues / 'Cross a busy street / I let a song go out of my heart / Don't get around much anymore / It don't mean a thing if it ain't got that swing / Do nothin' 'til you hear from me / Pritti Nitti / Just a sittin' and a rockin'
CD _____ CLGCD 002
Calligraph / Jun '92 / Cadillac / Wellard / Jazz Music.

GIGS (Lyttelton, Humphrey & His Band)
Stanley steams in / Black butterfly / Ah mersey / Golden gumboot / Grey turning blue / Barnes bridge
CD _____ CLGCD 015
Calligraph / Nov '87 / Cadillac / Wellard / Jazz Music.

HEAR ME TALKIN' TO YA (Lyttelton, Humphrey & His Band)
Hear me talkin' to ya / Someone to watch over me / Madly / Blues for Zoe / Serenade to Sweden / Lord is listenin' to ya, hallelujah / Good buzz (take it from the top) / One for Al / Swinging scorpio / Beale Street blues / Moten swing / St. James infirmary / Mezzrow / I got rhythm
CD _____ CLGCD 029
Calligraph / Jun '92 / Cadillac / Wellard / Jazz Music.

HUMPH 'N' HELEN (I Can't Get Started) (Lyttelton, Humphrey & Helen Shapiro)
Perdido / It might as well rain until September / I can't get started (with you) / Eventide / Music goes round and round / Make the man love me / Elmer's tune / Bye bye blackbird / Indian Summer / Brazil / I'll never smile again / After you've gone / Crazy he calls me / Why don't you do right / Choo choo ch' boogie / Flying home
CD _____ CLGCD 025
Calligraph / Jun '92 / Cadillac / Wellard / Jazz Music.

JAZZ AT THE ROYAL FESTIVAL HALL
Onions / Old grey mare / New Orleans stomp / Canal Street blues / Big cat little cat / Randolph Turpin
CD _____ DM 22 CD

Dormouse / Aug '91 / Jazz Music / Target/ BMG.

MORE HUMPH & ACKER (Lyttelton, Humphrey & Acker Bilk)
Senora / Sugar / Maybe / I'd climb the highest mountain / Ludo / I told you once, I told you twice / Tiz-dum, tiz-dum / Mound bayou / Bessie couldn't help it / How long has this been going on / Russian lullaby / Blues and sentimental / Maritiniquen song / Three in the morning / Last smile blues / Easter parade

CD _____ CLGCD 030
Calligraph / Feb '95 / Cadillac / Wellard / Jazz Music.

MOVIN' AND GROOVIN'
CD _____ BLCD 760504
Black Lion / Oct '90 / Jazz Music / Cadillac / Wellard / Koch.

PARLOPHONE YEARS, THE
Memphis blues / Snake rag / Bad penny blues / Lady in red / Lightly and politely /

Blues excursion / London blues / Onions / Dallas blues / Dormouse
CD _____ DM 21 CD
Dormouse / Feb '89 / Jazz Music / Target/ BMG.

ROCK ME GENTLY
Rock me gently / Top 'n' tail / Jack the bear / My funny valentine / Frankie and Johnny / Sea-lion's siesta / Lester and Herschel / Heads or tails / Royal flush / Sidney my man / Tribal dance / If we never meet again / Lady of the lavender mist / St. Louis blues

CD _____ CLGCD 026
Calligraph / Sep '91 / Cadillac / Wellard / Jazz Music.

TROGLADYTES (Lyttelton, Humphrey & Wally Fawkes)
CD _____ SOSCD 1238
Stomp Off / May '93 / Jazz Music / Wellard.

M People

BIZARRE FRUIT
Sight for sore eyes / Search for the hero / Open up your heart / Love rendez-vous / Precious pearl / Sugar town / Walk away / Drive time / Padlock / And finally
CD _____ 74321 24081 2
De-Construction / Nov '94 / BMG.

BIZARRE FRUIT II
Sight for sore eyes / Search for the hero / Open your heart (Mixes) / Love rendezvous / Sugar town (Mixes) / Walk away (Mixes) / Drive time (Mixes) / Padlock (Mixes) / Someday (Mixes) / Colour my life (Mixes) / Moving on up (Mixes)
CD Set _____ 74321328172
De-Construction / Nov '95 / BMG.

ELEGANT SLUMMING
One night in heaven / Moving on up / Renaissance / You just have to be there / Love is in my soul / Don't look any further / Natural thing / Little packet / La vida loca / Melody of life
CD _____ 74321 16678-2
De-Construction / Nov '93 / BMG.

NORTHERN SOUL
Colour my life / How can I love you more / Inner city cruise / It's your world / Someday / Sexual freedom / Kiss it better / Tumbling down / Colour my life (original mix) / Kiss it better (guitar mix) / Platini / Excited (reissues only) / Man Smart (reissues only) / Colour my life (pt 2) (reissues only) / Excited (Judge Jules remix) (reissues only)
CD _____ 74321117772
De-Construction / Aug '95 / BMG.

M-3

M-3
CD _____ NAR 057 CD
New Alliance / Dec '93 / Pinnacle.

M-Base Collective

ANATOMY OF A GROOVE
CD _____ 4729742
Sony Jazz / Jan '95 / Sony.

M. Age

UNDER A CUBIC SKY
CD _____ RSNCD 29
Rising High / Jan '95 / Disc.

M.C. 900ft Jesus

HELL WITH THE LID OFF
Greater God / U.F.O.'s are real / I'm going straight to heaven / Talking to the spirits / Place of lonliness / Real black angel / Shut up / Spaceman / Too bad
CD _____ NETCD 015
Nettwerk / Feb '90 / Vital / Pinnacle.

ONE STEP AHEAD OF THE SPIDER
New moon / But if you go / If I only had a brain / Stare and stare / Buried at sea / Tiptoe through the inferno / Garacias pepe / New Year's eve / Bill's dream / Rhubarb
CD _____ 74321242312
American / Mar '94 / BMG.

WELCOME TO MY DREAM
CD _____ NET 035CD
Nettwerk / Oct '91 / Vital / Pinnacle.

M.C. Breed

BEST OF MC BREED, THE
CD _____ WRA 8150
Wrap / Nov '95 / Koch.

FUNKAFIED
CD _____ RAP 60132
Rapture / Sep '94 / Plastic Head.

NEW BREED, THE
CD _____ WRA 81202CD
Wrap / Jan '94 / Koch.

M.C. Duke

ORGANISED RHYME
Organised rhyme / We go to work / Free / Throw your hands in the air / I'm riffin' / Miracles / For the girls / Gotta get your own / Running man / Alternative argument
CD _____ DUKE 1CD
Music Of Life / Nov '89 / Grapevine.

M.C. Hammer

FUNKY HEADHUNTER, THE
Oaktown / It's all good / Somethin' for the O.G.'s / Don't stop / Pumps and a bump / One mo time / Clap yo' hands / Break 'em off somethin' propa / Don't fight the feeling / Goldie in me / Sleepin' on a master plan / That's what / Funky headhunter / Pumps and a bump reprise (bump Teddy bump) / Help

---

Lord (won't you come) / Do it like this (CD only) / Heartbreaka (is what they call me) (CD only)
CD _____ 74321 18862-2
RCA / Mar '94 / BMG.

LET'S GET IT STARTED
Intro (Turn this mutha out) / Let's get it started (radio edit) / Ring 'em / Cold go MC Hammer / You're being served / Turn this mutha out (edit) / It's gone / They put me in the mix (edit) / Son of the king / That's what I said / Feel my power / Pump it up (here's the news) (radio edit)
CD _____ CDEST 2140
Capitol / Apr '91 / EMI.

M.C. Lyte

AIN'T NO OTHER
Intro / Brooklyn / Ruffneck / What's my name yo / Li'l Paul / Ain't no other / Hard copy / Fuck that motherfucking bullshit / Intro (2) / I go on / One nine nine three / Never heard nothin' like this / Can I get some dap / Let me adem / Steady fucking / Who's Jack (CD only) / I cram to understand U (CD only)
CD _____ 756792230-2
Elektra / Jul '93 / Warner Music.

M.C. Shy D

COMEBACK, THE
CD _____ WRA 8124-2
Wrap / Apr '94 / Koch.

M.C. Solaar

PROSE COMBAT
Aurade / Obsolette / Nouveau Western / A la claire fontaine / Superstarr / La concubine de l'hemoglobine / Devotion / Temps mort / L'nmiaccd htck72kpdp / Sequelles / Dieu ait son ame / A dix de mes disciples / La paim justifie les moyene / Relations humaines / Prose combat
CD _____ 5212892
Talkin' Loud / Apr '94 / PolyGram.

M.I.R.V.

COSMODROME
Nightmare premonition / Walk back home / Drunk lad / Learning pipeline / Club owner / On the prowl / Surfin' Soviet / Cantina / Seductress / Jumpin' bones / Whips and chains / Hocus pocus ding dong / Annoying phone call / Souvlaki / Nuclear family / Mutants and manholes / Jerky beef / Zuort / Pipe wrench / Shave my face off / Loading into the cosmodrome / Performance / Final theme
CD _____ MR 065-2
Mammoth / Mar '94 / Vital.

M.K.B.

FRENCHIE'S BAD INDIANS
CD _____ ODE 003
Odessa / Mar '94 / Plastic Head.

M.L.

I'LL BE THERE FOR YOU
CD _____ KIK 4176CD
Ichiban / Feb '94 / Koch.

M.L.O. Poductions

I.O.
CD _____ RSNCD 16
Rising High / Apr '94 / Disc.

M.O.D.

DEVOLUTION
CD _____ CDMFN 163
Music For Nations / Jun '94 / Pinnacle.

LOVED BY THOUSANDS HATED BY MILLIONS
Noize / Aren't you hungry / Spandex enormity / Aids / Hate tank / Goldfish / Surfin USA / Surfs up / Mr Oofus / No glove no love / True colours / Livin in the city / Get up and dance / Rhymestein / Irresponsible / Rally (NYC) / Ballad of Dio / Bubble butt / Short but sweet / Ode to Harry / Vents / Theme song / Bonanza / Buckshot blues / Clubbin seals / US Dreams / He's dead Jim / Get the boot
CD _____ CDVEST 66
Bulletproof / Oct '95 / Pinnacle.

M.T.A.

BY THE BULLET OR THE BALLOT
CD _____ MIA 002CD
MIA / Sep '94 / Plastic Head.

Maal, Baaba

BAAYA
CD _____ CIDM 1061
Mango / Apr '91 / Vital / PolyGram.

DJAM LEELII (Maal, Baaba & Mansour Seck)
Rogue / Mar '89 / Sterns.

FIRIN' IN FOUTA
Sidiki / African woman / Swing Yela / Mbaye / Njilou / Gorel / Sama Duniya / Salimoun (funky Kora) / Ba / Tiedo (Not on LP) / Toure (LP only) / Ca et la (LP only) / Yoni (LP only)
CD _____ CIDM 1109
Mango / Jul '94 / Vital / PolyGram.

LAM TORO
CD _____ CIDM 1080
Mango / Aug '92 / Vital / PolyGram.

Maar, Doe

4 US
CD _____ CDM 183
Sky / '88 / Koch.

Mabern, Harold

LEADING MAN, THE
Look at the bright side / Save the best for last / Full house / Alone together / It's a lonesome old town / Yes and no / Moments notice / Au privave / B and B / Mercury retro
CD _____ 4772882
Sony Music / Apr '95 / Sony.

LOOKIN' ON THE BRIGHT SIDE (Mabern, Harold Trio)
CD _____ DIW 614
DIW / Nov '93 / Harmonia Mundi / Cadillac.

PHILADELPHIA BOUND
CD _____ SKCD 2-3051
Sackville / Oct '94 / Swift / Jazz Music / Jazz Horizons / Cadillac / CM.

STRAIGHT STREET (Mabern, Harold Trio)
CD _____ DIW 608
DIW / Sep '91 / Harmonia Mundi / Cadillac.

Mabon, Willie

SEVENTH SON, THE (Charly Blues - Masterworks Vol. 44)
CD _____ CDBM 44
Charly / Jun '93 / Charly / THE / Cadillac.

Mabsant

HUMOUR & SONG WITH MABSANT & EIRY PALFREY
CD _____ SAIN 2029CD
Sain / Aug '94 / Direct / ADA.

MABSANT (MABSANT & GYDA EIRY PALFREY)
Carol y blwch / Diary / Suai'r gwynt / Child's Christmas / Ar gyfer hiddiw'r bore / Red cock / Curlews / Dear John / Y wasael / Maggie fach / Holiday memory / Ar kan y mor / Local boy/Sell out / Gwennyn / Mrs. Evans/Meanwhile Dai / Y deryn du / Blodeuwedd / Moliannwn
CD _____ SCD 2029
Sain / Oct '87 / Direct / ADA.

Mabuses

MABUSERS
CD _____ R 2272
Rough Trade / Oct '91 / Pinnacle.

MELBOURNE METHOD, THE
My brilliant way / Glass of bourbon / Tongues / Keeler joins the joyce gang / Whose party is this / Rooms / Paper plane / Lynched / Picnic at the red house / Fetch the hammer / Oscar / Narc fears / She went wild
CD _____ R 3132
Rough Trade / Apr '94 / Pinnacle.

Mac-Talia

MAIRIDH GAOL IS CEOL
Boys be happy / Old hunting song / Beloved Gregor / Mouth music / Talla story / Barcelona / Brown haired Alan / Mrs. Jamieson's favourite / Mouth music (2) / Beautiful girl / Setting a course for Lewis / Uig Brae
CD _____ COMD 2054
Temple / Feb '94 / CM / Duncans / ADA / Direct.

Macabre

SINISTER SLAUGHTER
CD _____ NB 070CD
Nuclear Blast / Jun '93 / Plastic Head.

Macaire, Mack

SOUCI Y A LA VIE
CD _____ JIP 064
JIP / Jan '96 / Jetstar.

McAlmont

MCALMONT
Either / Not wiser / Unworthy (edit) / Misunderstood / Is it raining / Conversation / He loves you / From away / It's always this way / My grey boy / They hide / Through the door / Placed aside / Unworthy / As if I'd known
CD _____ CDHUT 12
Hut / Jan '95 / EMI.

McAlmont & Butler

SOUND OF MCALMONT AND BUTLER, THE
Yes / What's the excuse this time / Right thing / Although / Don't call it soul / Disappointment / Debitor / How about you / Tonight / You'll lose a good thing / You do
CD _____ CDHUT 32
Hut / Nov '95 / EMI.

MacAlpine, Tony

EDGE OF INSANITY
CD _____ RR 349706
Roadrunner / '89 / Pinnacle.

EVOLUTION
Sage / Overseas evolution / Eccentrist / Time table / Seville / Futurism / Etude no 5 opus 10 F / Powerfield / Plastic people / Sinfonia / Asturias kv 467
CD _____ CDRR 89012
Roadrunner / Oct '95 / Pinnacle.

PREMONITION
CD _____ RR 89652
Roadrunner / Sep '94 / Pinnacle.

McAnuff, Winston

ONE LOVE
CD _____ CC 2716
Crocodisc / Apr '95 / THE / Magnum Music Group.

McAulay, Jacki

JACKIE MCAULEY...PLUS
CD _____ SEECD 315
See For Miles/C5 / Apr '91 / Pinnacle.

McBride, Christian

GETTIN' TO IT
CD _____ 5239892
Verve / Mar '95 / PolyGram.

McBride, Joe

GIFT FOR TOMORROW, A
Evening in Dallas / Secrets / Never be lonely / Walking in rhythm / Gift for tomorrow / Messenger / Deja vu / World to me / Everybody needs love / Reunion / You've got a friend
CD _____ 101S8770502
101 South / Jul '94 / New Note.

GRACE
CD _____ 101S 8771282
101 South / Aug '94 / New Note.

McBride, Martina

WAY THAT I AM, THE
Heart trouble / My baby loves me / That wasn't me / Independence day / Where I used to have a heart / Goin' to work / She ain't seen nothing yet / Life / Strangers / Ashes
CD _____ 74321 19229-2
RCA / Mar '94 / BMG.

WILD ANGELS
Wild angels / Phones are ringin' all over town / Great disguise / Swingin' doors / All the things we've never done / Two more bottles of wine / Cry on the shoulder of the road / You've been driving all the time / Born to give my love to you / Beyond the blue / Safe in the arms of love
CD _____ 07863665092
RCA / Oct '95 / BMG.

McBride, Owen

LAWEESH ROCK AND OTHER SONGS
CD _____ CIC 072CD
Clo Iar-Chonnachta / Nov '93 / CM.

McBroom, Amanda

LIVE FROM RAINBOW & STARS, NEW YORK
September song / No fear / I love this day / Everybody wants to be Sondheim / Days of wine and roses / Time after time / I love

---

men / Ship in a bottle / Here and now / Portrait / Rose / Carousel / Errol Flynn / Dieter's prayer / Baltimore Oriole / Breathing / My foolish heart / I can't make you love me
CD _____ DRGCD 91432
DRG / Feb '95 / New Note.

Macc Lads

BEER NECESSITIES, THE
Alcohol / Germans / Fallatio Nell, son / Desperate Dan / Grease song / Apprentice dentist / Man in the boat / Newcy Brown / Macavity / Chester Zoo / Naughty boy / Mr. Methane / More tea vicar / Two stroke Eddie / Animal testing / Don't fear the sweeper / Poodles
CD _____ DOJOCD 158
Dojo / May '94 / BMG.

BEER, SEX, CHIPS AND GRAVY
Lads from Macc / Beer, sex and chips 'n' gravy / Boddies / Sweaty Betty / England's glory / Blackpool / Miss Macclesfield / God's gift to women / Get weavin' / Now he's a poof / Nagasaki sauce / Saturday night / Buenos aires / Charlotte / Failure with girls / Do you love me / Dan's underpants / Twenty pints / Macc Lads party
CD _____ DOJOCD 154
Dojo / Nov '93 / BMG.

BITTER, FIT CRACK
Barrel's round / Guess me weight / Uncle Knobby / Maid of ale / Dan's big log / Got to be Gordon's / Bitter fit crack / Julie the schooly / Doctor doctor / Torremolinos / Al o'peesha
CD _____ DOJOCD 155
Dojo / Nov '93 / BMG.

FROM BEER TO ETERNITY
Alton Towers / Geordie girl / No sheep 'til Buxton / All day drinking / Tab after tab / Lucy Lastic / My pub / Dead cat / Lady Muck / Gordon's revenge / Pie taster / Dans round yer landbag / Ben Nevis / Fluffy pup / Stoppyback / Ugly women
CD _____ DOJOCD 157
Dojo / May '94 / BMG.

LIVE AT LEEDS (The Who?)
Sweaty Betty / Ben Nevis / Bloink / Do you love me / God's gift to women / Charlotte / Blackpool / Lads from Macc / Now he's a poof / Doctor doctor / Julie the schooly / Guess me weight / Miss Macclesfield / Fat bastard / Get weavin / Barrels' round / Dan's underpants
CD _____ DOJOCD 161
Dojo / Mar '94 / BMG.

ORIFICE AND A GENITAL, AN (Outtakes 1986-1991)
Eh up lets sup / Fat bastard / Baggy Anne / Head kicked in / Knutsford / No sheep 'til buxton / Pie taster / Love Macc / Made of ale / Knock knock / Brevil brevil / Manfred Macc / Buenos aires '90 / Fellatio Nell, son / Two stroke Eddie / Even uglier women
CD _____ DOJOCD 141
Dojo / Feb '94 / BMG.

TWENTY GOLDEN CRATES
No sheep 'til Buxton / Sweaty Betty / Buenos aires 91 / Beer + sex + chips 'n' gravey / Guess me weight / Made of ale / Ben Nevis / Blackpool / Dan's underpants / Knock knock / Gordon's revenge / My pub / Charlotte / Dead cat / Boddies / Fluffy pup / Julie the schooly / Macc muck / Miss Macclesfield / Nagasaki sauce / Barrels round / Twenty pints (CD only) / Saturday night (CD only)
CD _____ DOJOCD 115
Dojo / May '94 / BMG.

McCafferty, Dan

DAN MCCAFFERTY
Honky Tonk downstairs / Cinnamon girl / Great pretender / Boots of Spanish leather / What'cha gonna do about it / Out of time / You can't lie to a liar / Trouble / You got me hummin' / Stay with me baby / Nightingale
CD _____ NEMCD 640
Sequel / Jun '94 / BMG.

McCaffrey, Frank

PLACE IN MY HEART, A
Clock in the tower / Place in my heart / Day the world stood still / Drive safely darlin' / I'd rather be sorry / Annie's story / Blackboard of my heart / All alone in New York City / It's our anniversary / Give a lonely heart a home / Rose / Always Mayo
CD _____ RITZCD 512
Ritz / '91 / Pinnacle.

TODAY
Today / Things I wish I'd said / Silver medals and sweet memories / I wish it was me / You make me feel like a man / Forever lovers / In dreams / Wedding song / Broken wings / Lady from Glenfarn / Memories of Mayo / Sarah's smile
CD _____ RITZCD 0063
Ritz / Apr '91 / Pinnacle.

VERY BEST OF FRANK MCCAFFREY
It's our anniversary / Blackboard of my heart / I'll take you home again Kathleen / Ring your mother wore / Silver medals and sweet memories / Little grey home in the west / I wish it was me / Daisy a day / Place

in my heart / Memories of Mayo / More than yesterday / If we only had old Ireland over here / Clock in the tower / Give a lonely heart a home / Moonlight in Mayo / My lady from Glenfarne / Things I wish I'd said / Broken wings / Day the world stood still / Wedding song
CD _____ RITZCD 532
Ritz / Apr '93 / Pinnacle.

YOUR SPECIAL DAY
Here's my native country / Midnight to midnight / I'm a fool / Always on my mind (forever in my heart) / Nobody's Darlin' but mine / Emigrant eyes / When your old wedding ring was new / You special day / Forty shades of green / Cr oce di oro / You're a friend of mine / Less of me / Our Lady of knock / Heart that beats in Ireland
CD _____ RCD 548
Ritz / May '95 / Pinnacle.

McCain, Jerry

BLUES 'N' STUFF
Messin' with me baby / Three wives / Brand new mojo / Spoiled rotten (to the bone) / Love makin' showdown / Rose for my lady / My baby's got it / Goin' to the dogs
CD _____ CDICH 1047
Ichiban / Dec '89 / Koch.

LOVE DESPERADO
Blues tribute / Burn the crackhouse down / I need to do something / Love desperado / World's on fire / Lovin' school / I used to have it / Mercy mercy mercy / Non-stop lovin'
CD _____ ICH 9008CD
Ichiban / Aug '91 / Koch.

STRANGE KIND OF FEELIN' (McCain, Jerry 'Boogie' & Tiny Kennedy, Clayton Love)
CD _____ ALCD 2701
Alligator / Oct '93 / Direct / ADA.

McCalla

HOT FROM THE SMOKE
Cause and effect / Family affair / Count all your blessings / Simmer down / Fly like an eagle / Lay you low / Ain't no sunshine / Your happiness / Let's go deeper / International music
CD _____ SEA 41622
Uplands / Oct '95 / Total/BMG.

McCallister, Don Jr.

DON MCCALLISTER JR. & HIS COWBOY JAZZ REVUE
Dejadisc / May '94 / Direct / ADA. DJD 3206

McCallum

BIG BIGG MARKET
CD _____ BIGCD 1
Mawson & Wareham / Dec '94 / BMG / THE.

McCallum, Craig

IN A DIFFERENT LIGHT (McCallum, Craig Scottish Dance Band)
Gay Gordons / Dumbarton's drums / Pride of Erin Waltz / Canadian Barn dance / Pipe medley / Eva three step / Wild geese / Military two step / Irish reels / Highland Schottische / Circle waltz / Strip the willow / Party polka / Dashing white sergeant
CD _____ CDTRAX 037
Greentrax / Oct '90 / Conifer / Duncans / ADA / Direct.

McCallum, William

HAILEY'S SONG
CD _____ COMD 2060
Temple / Oct '95 / CM / Duncans / ADA / Direct.

PIPERS OF DISTINCTION
CD _____ CDMON 801
Monarch / Dec '89 / CM / ADA / Duncans / Direct.

McCalmans

FESTIVAL LIGHTS
Don't call me early in the morning / Pills / Far down the line / Highland road / Some hae meat / Tearing our industry down / Golden arches / Shanties / Bonnie barque the bergen / Barnyards of Delgaty / Goodnight sweetheart / Festival lights
CD _____ CDTRAX 097
Greentrax / Oct '95 / Conifer / Duncans / ADA / Direct.

FLAMES ON THE WATER
Ah'm a man at muffed it / Isle of Eigg / Devolution anthem / Farewell tae the haven / Sounding / Hawks and eagles / Siege / Who pays the piper / Festival lights / Shian Road / Men o' worth / Curtain call
CD _____ CDTRAX 036
Greentrax / Jul '90 / Conifer / Duncans / ADA / Direct.

HONEST POVERTY
Man's a man for a' that / Single handed sailor / Your daughters and your ons / Neil Gow's apprentice / Children are running

away / Kelvingrove/Paddy's leather britches/Behind the haystack / War outside/ The white collar holler / I feel like Buddy Holly / Parade / Portnahaven / 8-2-0 / Wha'll be King but Charlie / Father Mallory's dance / New Year's Eve song / Harmless
CD _____ CDTRAX 067
Greentrax / Sep '93 / Conifer / Duncans / ADA / Direct.

IN HARMONY - 30TH ANNIVERSARY COMPILATION ALBUM
Pace egging song / Sun rises bright in / France / Broom / Windmills / My Johnny is a shoemaker / Smuggler / Ye Jacobites by name / Farewell to Sicily / Burn the witch / Ladies evening song / Kelty clippie / Bonnie maid of fire / Scotland / Bonnie lass o'Gala water / Mothers, daughters, wives / Rambling rover / Farewell tae the haven / Last session / Man's a man for a' that / Bound to go
CD _____ CDTRAX 086
Greentrax / Jan '95 / Conifer / Duncans / ADA / Direct.

LISTEN TO THE HEAT - LIVE
I have seen the Highlands / Town of Kiandra / Mount and go / Sister Josephine / 23rd June / Prisoner's song / Song song / Rambling Rover / Rory Murphy / First Christmas / Lakewood (instr.) / Thriepmuir hornpipe (instr.) / Royal Belfast (instr.) / President's men / Air fa la la la lo / Sickening thank you song
CD _____ CDTRAX 019
Greentrax / Aug '88 / Conifer / Duncans / ADA / Direct.

PEACE AND PLENTY
Tullochgorum / Bells of the town / Song of the plough / Colliery gate / No you won't get me down in your mines / Black bear / Drover's lad / Top house / South Australia / Esikibo river / Blood red roses / Little Sally Rackett / Up and rin awa' Geordie / Mothers, daughters, wives / Highland road / Barratt's privateers / Men of the sea / Song for Europe / Tae the weavers gin ye gang / Leave her Johnny
CD _____ CDTRAX 002
Greentrax / Feb '89 / Conifer / Duncans / ADA / Direct.

SONGS FROM SCOTLAND
Boys that broke the ground / Tiree love song / Highland laddie / Roll the woodpile down / Hundred years ago / Westering home / Last session / All the tunes in the world / Most amazing thing of all / I will go / Widow MacKay / April waltz / Up and awa' wi' the Laverock / Scarce o'tatties / Lark in the morning / Anster Harbour / Twa recruitin' / Sergeants / Rollin' home
CD _____ CDTRAX 045
Greentrax / Jul '91 / Conifer / Duncans / ADA / Direct.

McCann, Eamon

EVERYTHING THAT I AM
Love is blind / Small town saturday night / Hey good lookin' / Past the point of rescue / It's all over now / Don't call me, I'll call you / Everything that I am / I promised you the world / When you come to land / Can't break it to my heart / Life after you / Gift of love / Bunch of bright red roses / Mother nature's son / I'm no stranger to the rain / Only when I laugh
CD _____ RCD 544
Ritz / Oct '94 / Pinnacle.

McCann, Phillip

ALL OF THE WORLD'S MOST BEAUTIFUL MELODIES (5CD Set)
CD Set _____ CHAN 4536
Chandos / Sep '95 / Chandos.

WORLD'S MOST BEAUTIFUL MELODIES VOL. 5, THE (McCann, Phillip & Sellers Engineering Band)
Meditation from Thais / Salut d'amour / Suo gan / Beau soir / La calinda / Pavanne / I'll walk beside you / Clair de Lune / Exotica / On wings of song / Largo / Eriskay love lilt / Vissi d'arte / To a wild rose / Sheep may safely graze / Adagio from Symphony No. 2 / Czardas
CD _____ CHAN 4532
Chandos / Aug '94 / Chandos.

McCann, Susan

COUNTRY LOVE AFFAIR
Never ending love affair / Johnny lovely Johnny / Blue velvet / Forever and ever Amen / Little ole wine drinker me / Travellin' light / Let the rest of the world go by / Two broken hearts / Someone is looking for someone like you / Irish eyes / Boy in your arms / Wind in the willows / Mother's love's a blessing / Patches in heaven / How great thou art / When the sun says goodbye to the mountain
CD _____ IHCD 482
Irish Music Heritage / Nov '90 / Prism.

DIAMONDS AND DREAMS
Love me one more time / When I hear the music / Have you ever been lonely / String of diamonds / Always / You're never too old to love / He never will be mine / Loving you / I vow to thee my country / Yellow roses / Sonny's dream / Broken speed of the

sound of the loneliness / Rose of my heart / Hillbilly girl with the blues / Everything is beautiful / Give me more time
CD _____ IHCD 371
Irish Music Heritage / Oct '91 / Prism.

MEMORIES
Softly, softly / String of diamonds / Whatever happened to old fashioned love / Irish memories (medley) / Dreaming of a little island / Help me make it through the night / Bus To L.A. / Penny arcade / If the whole world stopped loving / Once A Day / Love Has Joined Us Together / Since Johnny went away / Darlin' / Angels, Roses And Rain
CD _____ IHCD 592
Irish Music Heritage / Nov '92 / Prism.

SUSAN MCCANN'S IRELAND
CD _____ TSCD 220
Outlet / Jan '95 / ADA / Duncans / CM / Ross / Direct / Koch.

McCarthy, Cormac

PICTURE GALLERY BLUES
CD _____ GLCD 2122
Green Linnet / Aug '95 / Roots / CM / Direct / ADA.

McCarthy, Jimmy

SONG OF THE SINGING HORSEMAN, THE
On my enchanted sight / Hard man to follow / Mystic lipstick / Missing you / Ride on / No frontiers / Mad lady and me / Grip of parallel / Bright blue rose / Ancient rain / Song of the singing horseman
CD _____ LUNCD 053
Mulligan / Jan '91 / CM / ADA.

McCartney, Mike

MCGEAR
Sea breezes / Norton / Have you got problems / Casket / Rainbow lady / Givin' grease a ride / What do we really want to know / Leave it / Dance the do / Sweet baby / Simply love you / Man who found God in the moon
CD _____ SEECD 339
See For Miles/C5 / Jun '94 / Pinnacle.

McCartney, Paul

ALL THE BEST
Coming up / Ebony and ivory / Listen to what the man said / No more lonely nights / Silly love songs / Let 'em in / C mon / Pipes of peace / Live and let die / Another day / Maybe I'm amazed / Goodnight tonight / Once upon a long ago / Say say say / With a little luck / My love / We all stand together / Mull of Kintyre / Jet / Band on the run
CD _____ CDPMTV 1
Parlophone / Nov '87 / EMI.

CHOBA B CCCP
Kansas City / Twenty flight rock / I'm in love again / Lawdy Miss Clawdy / Bring it on home to me / Lucille / Don't get around much anymore / I'm gonna be a wheel someday / That's all right mama / Summertime / Ain't that a shame / Crackin' up / Just because / Midnight special
CD _____ CDPCSD 117
Parlophone / Aug '91 / EMI.

FLOWERS IN THE DIRT
My brave face / Rough ride / You want her too / Distractions / We got married / We got there / Figure of eight / This one / Don't be careless love / That day is done / How many people / Motor of love / Ou est le soleil (Not on album.)
CD _____ CDPMCOL 16
Parlophone / Jun '93 / EMI.

LIVERPOOL ORATORIO (Various Artists)
CD _____ CDPAUL 1
EMI Classics / Oct '91 / EMI.

LIVERPOOL ORATORIO (HIGHLIGHTS) (Various Artists)
CD _____ CDC 7546422
EMI Classics / Oct '92 / EMI.

MCCARTNEY
Lovely Linda / That would be something / Valentine's day / Every night / Hot as sun / glasses / Junk / Man we was lonely / Oo you / Momma Miss America / Teddy boy / Singalong junk / Maybe I'm amazed / Kree nakoorie
CD _____ CDPMCOL 1
Parlophone / Apr '93 / EMI.

MCCARTNEY II
Coming up / Temporary secretary / On the way / Waterfalls / Nobody knows / Front parlour / Summer's day song / Frozen jap / Bogey music / Dark room / One of these days / Check my machine / Secret friend
CD _____ CDPMCOL 11
Parlophone / Jun '93 / EMI.

OFF THE GROUND
Off the ground / Looking for changes / Hope of deliverance / Mistress and maid / I owe it all to you / Biker like an icon / Peace in the neighbourhood / Golden earth girl / Lovers that never were / Get out of my way / Winedark open sea / C'mon people

CD _____ CDPCSD 125
Parlophone / Nov '92 / EMI.

PAUL IS LIVE
Drive my car / Let me roll it / Looking for changes / Peace in the neighbourhood / All my loving / Robbie's bit / Good rockin' tonight / We can work it out / Hope of deliverance / Michelle / Biker like an icon / Here, there and everywhere / My love / Magical mystery tour / C'mon people / Lady Madonna / Paperback writer / Penny Lane / Live and let die / Kansas City / Welcome to soundcheck / Hotel in Benidorm / I wanna be your man / Fine day
CD _____ CDPCSD 147
Parlophone / Nov '93 / EMI.

PIPES OF PEACE
Pipes of peace / Say say say / Other me / Keep under cover / So bad / Man / Sweetest little show / Average person / Hey hey / Tug of peace / Through our love
CD _____ CDPMCOL 13
Parlophone / Jun '93 / EMI.

PRESS TO PLAY
Strangehold / Good times coming / Talk more talk / Footprints / Only love remains / Press / Pretty little head / Move over busker / Angry / However absurd / Write away (CD only) / It's not true (CD only) / Tough on a tightrope (CD only) / Feel the sun / Once upon a long ago (long version) / Spies like us
CD _____ CDPMCOL 15
Parlophone / Jun '93 / EMI.

RAM (McCartney, Paul & Linda)
Too many people / Three legs / Ram on / Dear boy / Uncle Albert / Smile away / Heart of the country / Monkberry moon delight / Eat at home / Long haired lady / Backseat of my car
CD _____ CDPMCOL 2
Parlophone / Apr '93 / EMI.

RED ROSE SPEEDWAY (McCartney, Paul & Wings)
Big barn bed / My love / Get on the right thing / One more kiss / Little lamb dragonfly / Single pigeon / When the night / Loup (1st indian on the moon) / Hold me tight / Lazy dynamite / Hands of love / Power cut / Mony mony (instrumental version)
CD _____ CDPMCOL 4
Parlophone / Apr '93 / EMI.

THRILLINGTON (Thrillington, Percy 'Thrills')
Too many people / Three legs / Ram on / Dear boy / Uncle Albert / Admiral Halsey / Smile away / Heart of the country / Back seat of my car / Long haired lady / Eat at home / Monkberry moon delight
CD _____ CZ 543
Parlophone / May '95 / EMI.

TRIPPING THE LIVE FANTASTIC
Showtime / Figure of eight / Jet / Rough ride / Got to get you into my life / Band on the run / Birthday / Ebony and ivory / We got married / Inner city madness / Maybe I'm amazed / Long and winding road / Crackin' up / Fool on the hill / Sergeant Pepper's lonely hearts club band / Can't buy me love / Matchbox / Put it there / Together / Things we said today / Eleanor Rigby / This one / My brave face / Back in the U.S.S.R / I saw her standing there / Twenty flight rock / Coming up / Sally / Let it be / Ain't that a shame / Live and let die / If I were not upon the stage / Hey Jude / Yesterday / Get back / Golden slumbers / Don't let the sun catch you crying
CD Set _____ CDPCST 73461
Parlophone / Nov '90 / EMI.

TRIPPING THE LIVE FANTASTIC - HIGHLIGHTS
Got to get you into my life (Not on LP.) / Birthday / We got married (Not on LP.) / Long and winding road / Sergeant Pepper's lonely hearts club band / Can't buy me love / All my trials / Things we said today (Not on LP.) / Eleanor Rigby / My brave face / Back in the U.S.S.R (Not on LP.) / I saw her standing there / Coming up / Let it be / Hey Jude / Get back / Golden slumbers (Not on LP.) / Carry that weight
CD _____ CDPCSD 114
Parlophone / Nov '90 / EMI.

TUG OF WAR
Tug of war / Take it away / Always somebody who cares / What's that you're doing / Here today / Ballroom dancing / Pound is sinking / Wanderlust / Get it / Be what you see / Dress me up as a robber / Ebony and ivory
CD _____ CDPMCOL 12
Parlophone / Jun '93 / EMI.

UNPLUGGED (The Official Bootleg)
Be bop a lula / I lost my little girl / Here, there and everywhere / Blue moon of Kentucky / We can work it out / San Francisco Bay blues / I've just seen a face / Every night / She's a woman / Hi-heel sneakers / And I love her / That would be something / Blackbird / Ain't no sunshine / Good rockin' tonight / Singin' the blues / Junk
CD _____ CDPCSD 116
Parlophone / May '91 / EMI.

McCarty, K.

DEAD DOG'S EYEBALL - SONGS OF DANIEL JOHNSTON
Intro / Walking the cow / Rocket ship / Living life / I had a dream / I am a baby (in my universe) / Hey Joe / Like a monkey in a zoo / Sorry entertainer / Desperate man blues / Oh no / Hate song / Golly gee / Going down / Museum of love / Wild West Virginia / Running water / Grievances / Creature
CD _____ JUSCD 002
Justine / Jul '95 / Vital.

MacCaskill, Ishbel

SIODA
CD _____ SKYECD 006
Sky / Jan '95 / Koch.

McCaslin, Mary

BEST OF MARY MCCASLIN
Things we said today / Northfield / Wayward wind / Prairie in the sky / San Bernardino waltz / Dealers / Ghost riders in the sky / Cole Younger / Living without you / Circle of friends / Blackbird / Bramble and the rose / Last cannonball / Way out west / My world is empty without you / Young Westerly / Back to Salinas / Old friends
CD _____ PHCD 1149
Philo / '92 / Direct / CM / ADA.

BROKEN PROMISES
CD _____ PH 1160CD
Philo / May '94 / Direct / CM / ADA.

PRAIRIE IN THE SKY
Pass me by / Priscilla Drive / Ballad of Weaverville / Back to Silas / Ghost riders in the sky / Last cannonball / It's my time / Cornerstone cowboy / Prairie in the sky / Cole Younger / Dealers / My love
CD _____ CDPH 1024
Philo / Nov '95 / Direct / CM / ADA.

McCavity's Cat

GENEVER CONVENTION, THE
CD _____ CDMW 1003
Music & Words / Apr '93 / ADA / Direct.

SCRATCH
CD _____ MW 1006CD
Music & Words / Dec '95 / ADA / Direct.

McClain, Sam

GIVE IT UP TO LOVE
Give it up to love / Too proud / What you want me to do / Here I go falling in love again / Got to have your love / Child of the mighty mighty / I'm tired of these blues / I feel good / Love me if you want to / Don't turn back now / Lonesome road
CD _____ AQCD 1015
Audioquest / Jul '95 / New Note.

KEEP ON MOVIN'
CD _____ AQ 1031
Audioquest / May '95 / New Note.

McClatchy, Debby

LIGHT YEARS AWAY
CD _____ PLCD 084
Plant Life / Jan '93 / Soundalive / ADA / Symposium.

McClennan, Tommy

TRAVELLIN' HIGHWAY MAN - 1939-1942
You can mistreat me here / New shake 'em on down / Bottle it up and go / Baby please don't go / Cross cut saw blues / I'm a guitar king / Mr. So and so blues / I love my baby / It's hard to be lonesome / Blue as I can be / Roll me baby / New highway 51
CD _____ TMCD 06
Travellin' Man / Oct '90 / Wellard / CM / Jazz Music.

McClinton, Delbert

DELBERT MCCLINTON
CD _____ CURBCD 008
Curb / Mar '94 / PolyGram.

LIVE FROM AUSTIN
CD _____ ALCD 4773
Alligator / May '93 / Direct / ADA.

NEVER BEEN ROCKED ENOUGH
Every time I roll the dice / I used to worry / Miss you fever / Why me / Have a little faith in me / Never been rocked enough / Blues as blues can get / Can I change my mind / Cease and desist / Stir it up / Good man, good woman
CD _____ CURBCD 005
Curb / Mar '94 / PolyGram.

McClure, Bobby

BOBBY MCCLURE & WILLIE CLAYTON (McClure, Bobby & Willie Clayton)
CD _____ HIUKCD 134
Hi / Aug '92 / Pinnacle.

McClure, Ron

YESTERDAY'S TOMORROW (McClure, Ron/John Abercrombie/Aldo Romano)

CD _____ EPC 884
European Music Production / Feb '92 / Harmonia Mundi.

McCluskey Brothers

AWARE OF ALL
CD _____ ASKCD 13
Vinyl Japan / Jul '92 / Vital.

FAVOURITE COLOURS
Perfect afternoon / Lonely satelite / Favourite colours / She said to the driver / 1000 Years / Better days / Cinder street / When the loving comes / Slip away / Passport
CD _____ KF 001 CD
Kingfisher / Jan '93 / Vital.

MacColl, Ewan

BLACK AND WHITE (The Definitive Ewan MacColl Collection)
Ballad of accounting / Driver's song / My old man / Dirty old town / Black and white / Brother did you weep / Press gang / Shoals of herring / Sheath and knife / Highland muster roll / Cam ye o'er frae France / Maid gaed tae the mill / Nobody knew she was there / Looking for a job / Kilroy was here / First time ever I saw your face / Foggy dew / Joy of living
CD _____ COOKCD 038
Cooking Vinyl / Feb '95 / Vital.

BOTHY BALLADS
CD _____ OSS 101CD
Ossian / Apr '94 / ADA / Direct / CM.

JACOBITE REBELLIONS, THE
Ye Jacobites by name / Such a parcel of rogues in a nation / Will ye go to Sherriffmuir / Wae's me for Prince Charlie / Charlie is my darling / Haughs o' Cromdale / Bonnie moorhen / Johnny Cope / Lewie or frae France / There's three brave loyal fellows / This is no my ain house / Piper o'Dundee / Donald MacGillavry / MacLean's welcome / Will ye no' come back again
CD _____ OSS 103CD
Ossian / Apr '94 / ADA / Direct / CM.

LEGEND OF EWAN MACCOLL
CD _____ NTMCD 502
Nectar / Jun '95 / Pinnacle.

NAMING OF NAMES (MacColl, Ewan & Peggy Seeger)
Economic miracle / Just the tax for me / Grocer / Not going to give it back / Sellafield child / Bring the Summer home / Maggie went green / Nuclear means jobs / Nose hunting blues / Dracumag / Rogue's gallery / Island / We remember (naming of names)
CD _____ COOKCD 036
Cooking Vinyl / May '90 / Vital.

REAL MACCOLL, THE
Ye Jacobites by name / Johnny Cope / Cam ye o'er frae France / Haughs o' Cromdale / Such a parcel of rogues in a nation / Farewell to Sicily / Derek Bentley / Johnny O'Breadislee / Go down ye murderers / Van Diemen's land / Minorie / Sheep crook and black dog / Bramble briar / One night as I lay on my bed / Grey cock / Blantyre explosion / Gresford disaster / Four loom weaver / Song of the iron road / Dirty old town
CD _____ TSCD 463
Topic / May '93 / Direct / ADA.

SCOTTISH POPULAR SONGS
CD _____ OSS 105CD
Ossian / Apr '94 / ADA / Direct / CM.

SONGS OF ROBERT BURNS
CD _____ OSS 102CD
Ossian / Apr '94 / ADA / Direct / CM.

TRADITIONAL SONGS & BALLADS
CD _____ OSS 104CD
Ossian / Apr '94 / ADA / Direct / CM.

MacColl, Kirsty

ELECTRIC LANDLADY
Walking down Madison / All I ever need / Children of the revolution / Halloween / My affair / Lying down / He never mentioned love / We'll never pass this way again / Hardest word / Maybe it's imaginary / My way home / One and only
CD _____ CDV 2663
Virgin / Jul '91 / EMI.

GALORE (The Best Of Kirsty MacColl)
They don't know / There's a guy works down the chip shop swears he's Elvis / New England / He's on the beach / Fairytale of New York / Miss Otis regrets / Free world / Innocence / You just haven't earned it yet baby / Days / Don't come the cowboy with me Sonny Jim / Walking down Madison / My affair / Angel / Titanic days / Can't stop killing you / Caroline / Perfect day
CD _____ CDV 2763
Virgin / Mar '95 / EMI.

KITE
Innocence / Mother's ruin / No victims / Don't come the cowboy with me Sonny Jim / What do pretty girls do / End of a perfect day / Free world / Days / Fifteen minutes / Tread lightly / Dancing in limbo / You and me baby / You just haven't earned it yet baby (CD only) / La foret de mimosas (CD only) / Complainte pour ste. Catherine (CD only)

CD _____ CDKM 1
Virgin / Apr '89 / EMI.

TITANIC DAYS
You know it's you / Soho sqaure / Angel / Last day of summer / Bad / Can't stop killing you / Titanic days / Don't go home / Big boy on a Saturday night / Just woke up / Tomorrow never comes
CD _____ 450994711-2
WEA / Feb '94 / Warner Music.

McColl, Billy

CREATIVE FIRE
CD _____ RBCD 2001
Total / Sep '95 / Total/BMG.

McComb, Dave

LOVE OF WILL
CD _____ D 31071
Mushroom / Mar '94 / BMG / 3MV.

McComiskey, Billy

MAKIN' THE ROUNDS
CD _____ GLCD 1034
Green Linnet / '92 / Roots / CM / Direct / ADA.

McConnell, Cathal

FOR THE SAKE OF OLD DECENCY (McConnell, Cathal & Len Graham)
CD _____ SA 22012CD
Sage Arts / Jan '94 / ADA.

McConnell, Rob

BRASS IS BACK, THE (McConnell, Rob & The Boss Brass)
Strollin' (Only on CD) / All the things you are / Love of my life / Who asked / Slow grind (Only on CD) / Winter in Winnipeg / Days gone by / Them there eyes
CD _____ CCD 4458
Concord Jazz / May '91 / New Note.

BRASSY AND SASSY (McConnell, Rob & The Boss Band)
Strike up the band / Hey / Very early / Things ain't what they used to be / Scrapple from the apple / Embraceable you/Why did I choose you / Blue serge suit(e) (CD only) / Club Sirocco / Samnamblues / Blues unblue
CD _____ CCD 4508
Concord Jazz / Jun '92 / New Note.

DON'T GET AROUND MUCH ANYMORE (McConnell, Rob & The Boss Brass)
Don't get around much anymore / Waltz you knew was blue / Once I loved / If you never came to me / Crazy rhythm / Gee baby ain't I good to you / (Back home again in) Indiana / Donna Lee / Bad and the beautiful / Robin / Back beat / Rockin' in rhythm
CD _____ CCD 4661
Concord Jazz / Aug '95 / New Note.

LIVE IN DIGITAL (McConnell, Rob & The Boss Brass)
CD _____ CDSB 106
Sea Breeze / Nov '88 / Jazz Music.

OUR 25TH YEAR (McConnell, Rob & The Boss Brass)
4 BC / Imagination / What am I here for / Just tell me yes or no / Riffs I have known / T.Q.2 / Nightfall / Broadway / My bells / Flying home
CD _____ CCD 4559
Bellaphon / Jun '93 / New Note.

OVERTIME (McConnell, Rob & The Boss Brass)
Overtime / Touch of your lips / Stella by starlight / Hawg jawz / After you / Alone together / This may be your lucky day / Wait and see
CD _____ CCD 4618
Concord Jazz / Nov '94 / New Note.

TRIO SKETCHES (McConnell, Rob & Ed Bickert, Neil Swanson)
Snow White / My ideal / I have dreamed / Can't we be friends / Baubles, bangles and beads / This is love of mine, this is always / Long ago and far away / I'm gonna sit right down and write myself a letter / Ornithardy / Deed I do
CD _____ CCD 4591
Concord Jazz / Mar '94 / New Note.

McConville, Tom

CROSS THE RIVER
Hurleys / Homes of Donegal / Tone Rowe's/ Smithy's baccy lin / Caliope house / How can my poor heart / Frenchie's reel / President Garfield's reel / Johnny miner / Gold ring / Cross the river / Lark in the morning / Goodnight waltz / Overgate / Calum Donaldson/Mick Johnson's parrot/Da grocer / Wish the wars were all over / Ben's foot/Birmingham fling
CD _____ OBM 01CD
Old Bridge / '92 / ADA.

FIDDLER'S FANCY
Quayside / Champion hornpipe / Cliff / Hill's no. 8 / Gateshead hornpipe / Pear tree / Cage / High level hornpipe / Flight of fancy / Hawk polka / Barber's pole / Beeswing /

Lads like beer/Marquis of Waterford / Hawk / Proudlock's fancy / Fiddler's fancy / Bottle bank / Blaydon fairs / Earl Grey
CD _____ OBMCD 04
Old Bridge / Jan '94 / ADA.

McCook, Tommy

DOWN ON BOND STREET
Inez / Yellow basket, The (a tisket a tasket) / Down on Bond Street / Wall Street shuffle / Moody ska / Real cool / Tommy's rock-steady / Soul serenade / Persian cat (in a Persian market) / Saboo / Shadow of your smile / Music is my occupation / Our man Flint / Mad mad mad / Ode to billy joe / Heatwave / World needs love / Flying home / Mary Poppins / Second fiddle
CD _____ CDTRL 326
Trojan / Mar '94 / Jetstar / Total/BMG.

McCorkle, Susannah

FROM BESSIE TO BRAZIL
Love / People that you never get to love / Thief in the night / Waters of March / Accentuate the positive / How deep is the ocean / Lady is a tramp / Quality time / My sweetie went away / Still crazy after all these years / Adeus America / That old devil called love / Hit the road to dreamland / You go to my head
CD _____ CCD 4547
Concord Jazz / May '93 / New Note.

FROM BROADWAY TO BEBOP
Guys and dolls / Once you've been in love / Chica chica boom chic / My buddy / It's easy to remember / Don't fence me in / One of the good guys / I don't think I'll end it all today (CD only) / Moody's mood / He loves me (CD only) / Friend like me (CD only) / I remember Bill
CD _____ CCD 4615
Concord Jazz / Oct '94 / New Note.

I'LL TAKE ROMANCE
Beautiful friendship / My foolish heart / I'll take romance / Get out of town / It never entered my mind / Let's get lost / Spring is here / Taking a chance on love / I concentrate on you / Lover man / That old feeling (CD only) / Zing went the strings of my heart / Where do you start (CD only) / I thought about you
CD _____ CCD 4491
Concord Jazz / Jan '92 / New Note.

NO MORE BLUES
CD _____ CCD 4370
Concord Jazz / Apr '89 / New Note.

SABIA
Tristeza (sadness, please go away) / Estate / Dilemma / Vivo sohando (CD only) / Sabia / So many stars (CD only) / So dance samba / Manda de carnaval / P'ra machucar meu coracao / Travessia (CD only) / A felicidade
CD _____ CCD 4418
Concord Jazz / Oct '90 / New Note.

McCormack, John

CHRISTIAN CELEBRATION, A (Favourite hymns, carols and sacred music)
CD _____ GEMM CD 9990
Gemm / Nov '92 / Pinnacle.

COUNT JOHN MCCORMACK, VOLUME VII
Snowy breasted pearl / Meeting of the waters / When shall the day break in Erin / Molly Bawn / Irish emigrant / Avourneen / Killarney / Green Isle of Erin / Love thee dearest, love thee / Believe me, if all those endearing young charms / Norah the pride of Kildare / Come back to Erin / Eileen Alannah, Augus Asthore / Minstrel boy / Foggy dew / Kathleen Mavoureen / Dear little shamrock / Lily of Killarney / Once again / Wearing of the green / God save Ireland / Boys of Wexford / Nation once again / Croppy boy / Home to Athlone
CD Set _____ OPAL CDS9847
Opal / Aug '91 / Harmonia Mundi.

GREAT VOICES OF THE CENTURY
CD _____ CDMOIR 418
Memoir / Dec '92 / Target/BMG.

JOHN MCCORMACK IN AMERICAN SONG
CD _____ GEMM CD 9971
Gemm / Oct '92 / Pinnacle.

KERRY DANCE (And Other Fine Irish Ballads)
Come back to Erin / She is far from the land / Irish emigrant / Low backed car / My lagan loce / Kathleen Mavoureen / Killarney / Macushla / Molly Brannigan / Eileen Alannah / Mother Machree
CD _____ CDCH 207
Happy Days / Jun '93 / Conifer.

POPULAR SONGS & IRISH BALLADS
Garden where the praties grow / Believe me, if all those endearing young charms #2 / Star of the county down / Bless this house / Terence's farewell to Kathleen / I'll walk beside you / Believe me, if all those endearing young charms / Drink to me only with thine eyes / Green isle of Erin / Jeanie with the light brown hair / Kerry dance / O Mary dear / Linden lea / Little silver ring / Old house / She is far from the land / Oft in

the stilly night / Meeting of the waters / Bard of Armagh / Down by the Sally gardens / She moved through the fair / Green bushes / Off to Philadelphia / Bantry Bay / I hear you calling me / I know of two bright eyes / Sweetly she sleeps / Kashmiri song / Passing by
CD _____ CDH 769 788 2
HMV / May '93 / EMI.

SCOTTISH & IRISH SONGS
Trottin' to the fair / Bonnie wee thing / My lagan love / Bonnie Mary of Argyle / Snowy breasted pearl / Turn ye to me / Wearing of the green / When the dew is falling / Low backed car / Annie Laurie / When you and I were young Maggie / Auld Scotch sangs / Irish emigrant / Maiden of morven / She moved through the fair / Ye banks and braes o' bonnie Doon / Green bushes / Song to the seals / Maureen / Star O' the country down
CD _____ MIDCD 005
Moidart / Apr '95 / Conifer / ADA.

SONGS OF JOHN MCCORMACK
CD _____ CDIRISH 014
Outlet / Oct '95 / ADA / Duncans / CM / Ross / Direct / Koch.

WHEN IRISH EYES ARE SMILING
Angels guard thee / Bard of Armagh / Believe me, if all those endearing young charms / Brown bird singing / Come into the garden Maud / Dear old pal of mine / Dream once again / Flirtation / Garden where the praties grow / I hear you calling me / I'll sing thee songs of Araby / Irish emigrant / Jeanie with the light brown hair / Kerry dance / Macushla / She moved through the fair / Since you went away / South winds / Star of the County Down / Sunshine of your smile / Turn ye to me / Venetian song / Waiting for you / When Irish eyes are smiling / When you and I were young Maggie
CD _____ CDAJA 5119
Living Era / Mar '94 / Koch.

WHERE THE RIVER SHANNON FLOWS
Londonderry air / When Irish eyes are smiling / Garden where the praties grow / Eileen Alannah / Mother in Ireland / Ballynore ballad / Harp that once through Tara's halls / Kathleen Mavoureen / Padraic the fiddler / Mother Machree / Bard of Armagh / My Irish song of songs / Norah O'Neale / By the short cut of the Rosses / Irish Emigrant / Snowy breasted pearl / My dark Rosaleen / Love's old sweet song / Macushla / Low back'd car / Where the River Shannon flows / Foggy dew / Rose of Tralee / Kitty my love / Star of the County Down
CD _____ PASTCD 7022
Flapper / Mar '94 / Pinnacle.

McCormick, John

MERCURY'S WELL
CD _____ PH 009CD
Phantom / Jul '95 / ADA.

McCoury Brothers

MCCOURY BROTHERS
CD _____ ROUCD 0230
Rounder / Apr '95 / CM / Direct / ADA / Cadillac.

RONNIE & ROB MCCOURY
CD _____ ROUCD 0353
Rounder / Oct '95 / CM / Direct / ADA / Cadillac.

McCoury, Del

BLUE SIDE OF TOWN, THE
Beauty of my dreams / Queen Anne's Lace / If you need a fool / Old memories mean nothing to me / Try me one more time / Before the fire comes down / Blue side of town / Seasons in my heart / That's alright mama / Make room for the blues / High on the mountain / I believe
CD _____ CD 0292
Rounder / '92 / CM / Direct / ADA / Cadillac.

DEEPER SHADE OF BLUE, A
CD _____ ROU 303CD
Rounder / Jan '94 / CM / Direct / ADA / Cadillac.

HIGH ON A MOUNTAIN (McCoury, Del & The Dixie Pals)
CD _____ ROUCD 0019
Rounder / Sep '95 / CM / Direct / ADA / Cadillac.

I WONDER WHERE YOU ARE TONIGHT
CD _____ ARHCD 5006
Arhoolie / Apr '95 / ADA / Direct / Cadillac.

McCowan, Andrew

FLING TIME
CD _____ CDMON 823
Monarch / May '95 / CM / ADA / Duncans / Direct.

FLING TIME 2
CD _____ CDMON 824
Monarch / May '95 / CM / ADA / Duncans / Direct.

McCoy, Charlie

GREATEST HITS: CHARLIE MCCOY
CD _____ 4658622
Monument / Aug '90 / Sony.

McCoy, Hank

MOHAWK STREET (McCoy, Hank & The Dead Ringers)
CD _____ OK 33026CD
Normal/Okra / Feb '95 / Direct / ADA.

McCoys

HANG ON SLOOPY (The Best Of The McCoys)
Meet the McCoys / Hang on sloopy / I can't explain / Fever / Sorrow / Up and down / If you tell a lie / Come on let's go / Little people / Smoky Joe's cafe / Mr. Summer / Everyday I have to cry / (You make me feel) So good / Runaway / Gaitor tails and monkey ribs / Koko / Bald headed Lena / Say those magic words / Don't worry Mother (Your son's heart is pure) / I got to go back (And watch that little girl dance) / Dynamite / Beat the clock
CD _____ ZK 47074
Columbia / Jul '95 / Sony.

McCracklin, Jimmy

HIGH ON THE BLUES
CD _____ CDSXE 072
Stax / Jul '93 / Pinnacle.

MERCURY RECORDINGS, THE
Wobble / Georgia slop / Hitched / No one to love me (I'll be glad when you're dead) you rascal you / By myself / Doomed lover / With your love / Let's do it / Bridge / What's that (part 1) / What's that (part 2) / Folsom prison blues
CD _____ BCD 15558
Bear Family / Mar '92 / Rollercoaster / Direct / CM / Swift / ADA.

TASTE OF THE BLUES, A
CD _____ BB 9535CD
Bullseye Blues / Aug '94 / Direct.

McCrae, George

LOVE'S BEEN GOOD TO ME
Love's been good to me / Every time you say goodbye / If it wasn't for you / Now that I have you / One step closer to love) / Listen to your heart / Just another fool / Let's dance / I never forgot your eyes / Own the night / I'm still believing / Fire in the night / Out of nowhere (into my life) / It was always you / Never too late / Own the night (12" dance mix)
CD _____ PCOM 1135
President / May '94 / Grapevine / Target/ BMG / Jazz Music / President.

ROCK YOUR BABY
Ooh baby / Rock your baby / You go to my head / Don't you feel my love / Let your love / You can have it all / Let's dance / Kiss me / Look at you / I can't leave you alone
CD _____ MUSCD 503
MCI / Sep '94 / Disc / THE.

McCray, Larry

DELTA HURRICANE
Delta hurricane / Adding up / Last four nickels / Soul shine / Not that much / Last hand of the night / Witchin' moon / Blue river / Hole in my heart / Three straight days of rain / Blues in the city
CD _____ VPBCD 10
Pointblank / May '93 / EMI.

McCue, Bill

COUNT YOUR BLESSINGS
Count your blessings / Softly and tenderly Jesus is calling / Where's he'll never grow old / What a friend we have in Jesus / Lord's prayer / If I can help somebody / Going home / Beautiful Isle of somewhere / Shall we gather at the river / Bless this house / Whispering hope / Little drummer boy / Blessed assurance / Amazing grace
CD _____ CDITV 467
Scotdisc / Dec '88 / Duncans / Ross / Conifer.

HEART OF SCOTLAND, THE (McCue, Bill & Kinlochard Ceilidh Band)
Broadsword of Scotland / Irish reels / Ye banks and braes o' bonnie Doon / Waltz for Elizabeth / Ca' the Yowes / Military two step / Slow air / Hiking song / Jimmy Shand

hornpipes / Bonnie Strathyre / Margaret's waltz / Rob Roy MacGregor / Loch Ard / Strip the willow / Christine McRichie / Whispering Hope / Amazing grace
CD _____ CDITV 552
Scotdisc / Apr '94 / Duncans / Ross / Conifer.

LUCKY WHITE HEATHER
CD _____ CDITV 484
Scotdisc / Jul '89 / Duncans / Ross / Conifer.

SCOTLAND'S ROYAL HIGHLAND SHOW
CD _____ CDITV 594
Scotdisc / Jun '95 / Duncans / Ross / Conifer.

MacCuish, Alasdair

BLACK ROSE
CD _____ CDLOC 1086
Lochshore / May '95 / ADA / Direct / Duncans.

McCulloch, Danny

BEOWULF (McCulloch, Danny & Friends)
Hallowed ground / Cat house / Mary Jane / Waitin' for a dream / Mama sure could swing a deal / Headin' out East / Love me / Praise the Lord and pass the soup / You're the one to blame / Mind your business
CD _____ EDCD 423
Edsel / Oct '93 / Pinnacle / ADA.

McCulloch, Ian

CANDLELAND
Flickering wall / White hotel / Proud to fall / Cape / Candleland / Horse's head / Faith and healing / I know you well / In boom / Start again
CD _____ K 2462252
WEA / Sep '89 / Warner Music.

MYSTERIO
Magical world / Close your eyes / Dug for love / Honey drip / Damnation / Lover lover lover / Webbed / Pmegranate / Vibor blue / Heaven's gate / In my head
CD _____ 9031762642
WEA / Mar '92 / Warner Music.

McCulloch, Jimmy

COMPLETE (McCulloch, Jimmy & White Line)
CD _____ MSCD 004
Mouse / Feb '95 / Grapevine.

McCulloch, Keff

PURPLE REIGN (The synth plays Prince)
Take me with U / Paisley Park / Arms of Orion / Raspberry beret / Kiss / Nothing compares 2 U / Girls and boys / 1999 / Little red corvette / I wish U heaven / I feel for you / Thieves in the temple / Trust / Sign o' the times / When doves cry / Purple rain
CD _____ PWKS 4055
Carlton Home Entertainment / May '91 / Carlton Home Entertainment.

McCusker, John

JOHN MCCUSKER
CD _____ COMD 2059
Temple / Apr '95 / CM / Duncans / ADA / Direct.

McCutcheon, John

BETWEEN THE ECLIPSE
CD _____ ROUCD 0336
Rounder / Oct '94 / CM / Direct / ADA / Cadillac.

FAMILY GARDEN
CD _____ ROU 8026CD
Rounder / Feb '93 / CM / Direct / ADA / Cadillac.

FINE TIMES AT OUR HOUSE
CD _____ GR 70710
Greenhays / Dec '94 / Roots / Jazz Music / Duncans / CM / ADA.

GONNA RISE AGAIN
CD _____ CD 0222
Rounder / Aug '88 / CM / Direct / ADA / Cadillac.

HOWJADOO
CD _____ CD 8009
Rounder / '88 / CM / Direct / ADA / Cadillac.

NOTHING TO LOSE
CD _____ ROUCD 0358
Rounder / Oct '95 / CM / Direct / ADA / Cadillac.

SIGNS OF THE TIMES (McCutcheon, John & Si Kahn)
CD _____ ROU 4017CD
Rounder / Aug '94 / CM / Direct / ADA / Cadillac.

STEP BY STEP
CD _____ CD 0216
Rounder / Aug '88 / CM / Direct / ADA / Cadillac.

SUMMERSONGS
CD _____ ROUCD 8036
Rounder / Apr '95 / CM / Direct / ADA /
Cadillac.

WINTER SOLSTICE
CD _____ CD 0192
Rounder / Dec '86 / CM / Direct / ADA /
Cadillac.

McDaniel, Floyd

**LET YOUR HAIR DOWN (McDaniel,
Floyd & Blues Swingers)**
CD _____ DE 671
Delmark / Feb '95 / Hot Shot / ADA / CM
/ Direct / Cadillac.

McDermott's Two Hours

ENEMY WITHIN, THE
CD _____ HAGCD 2
Hag / Aug '94 / Pinnacle.

McDermott, John

DANNY BOY
Green fields of France / By yon bonnie
banks / Danny boy / Last rose of summer /
And the band played waltzing Matilda / Old
house / Faded coat of blue / Rose of Tralee
/ Sun is burning / Christmas in the trenches
/ Minstrel boy / Auld lang syne / Danny boy
(acapella)
CD _____ CDEMC 3666
EMI / Nov '93 / EMI.

OLD FRIENDS
Ye banks and braes o' bonnie Doon / One
last cold kiss / She moved through the fair
/ Bard of Armagh / Meeting of the waters /
Old man / Mother Machree / Amazing
Grace / Farewell to Tarwathie / Skye boat
song / Lachin y gair (Dark Loch Nagar) / My
love is a red, red rose / Massacre of Glen-
coe / Dutchman / Parting glass
CD _____ CDEMC 3697
EMI / Mar '95 / EMI.

McDermott, Josie

**DARBY'S FAREWELL (Traditional Songs
Played On Flute & Whistle)**
CD _____ OSS 20CD
Ossian / Mar '94 / ADA / Direct / CM.

McDermott, Kevin

**LAST SUPPER, THE (McDermott, Kevin
Orchestra)**
CD _____ IGCDM 207
Iona Gold / Jun '94 / Total/BMG / ADA.

**MOTHER NATURE'S KITCHEN
(McDermott, Kevin Orchestra)**
Wheels of wonder / Slow boat to something
better / King of nothing / Diamond / Mother
nature's kitchen / Line to the blue / Where we
were meant to be / Statue to a stone / What
comes to pass / Suffocation blues / Angel
/ Healing at the harbour
CD _____ CID 9920
Island / Jul '91 / PolyGram.

McDevitt, Chas

**FREIGHT TRAIN (McDevitt, Chas &
Nancy Whisky)**
Freight train / Badman Stackolee / County
jail / I'm satisfied / She moved through the
fair / My old man / Poor Howard / Greenback dollar / Sing, sing, sing / BB Blues /
Deep down / Born to be with you / I want
a little girl / Across the bridge / Come all ye
fair and tender maidens / Sportin' life / Trottin' to the fair / Everyday of the week / Face
in the rain / Goin' home / Tom Hark / It
makes no difference now / Good mornin'
blues / Real love / Pop pourri / Everyday I
have the blues / I dig you baby / Ace in the
hole / Tom Hark (2)
CD Set _____ RCCD 3007
Rollercoaster / Nov '93 / CM / Swift.

MacDhonnagain, Tadhg

RAIFTEIRI SAN UNDERGROUND
CD _____ CICD 094
Clo Iar-Chonnachta / Jan '94 / CM.

MacDonald, Catriona

OPUS BLUE
CD _____ ARADCD 103
Acoustic Radio / May '94 / CM.

MacDonald, Fergie

AGUS NA MUIDEARTAICH
Ceili music / Hebridean reels / Bothan bal-
lads (Fergie's Gaelic waltz) / Hooligan's jig
/ Moidart reels / Benbecula barn dance /
Real fergie jigs / Tribute to Bobby Macleod
/ Jig Runrig / Button box schottische / Ian
MacFarlane "On the fiddle" / Jigs / Talla
a'bhaile reels / Ceilidh on the croft / Isle of
Skye reels / Ceol eirainn
CD _____ LCOM 5222
Lismor / Oct '93 / Lismor / Direct / Duncans
/ ADA.

MacDonald, Jeanette

**TOGETHER AGAIN 1948 (MacDonald,
Jeanette & Nelson Eddy)**

CD _____ CDSH 2101
Derann Trax / Nov '91 / Pinnacle.

**VERY BEST OF JEANETTE
MACDONALD, THE**
CD _____ SWNCD 005
Sound Waves / Oct '95 / Target/BMG.

**WHEN I'M CALLING YOU (MacDonald,
Jeanette & Nelson Eddy)**
Ah sweet mystery of life / At the Balalaika /
Beyond the blue horizon / Dear when I met
you / Farewell to dreams / I'm falling in love
with someone / Indian love call / Isn't it romantic / Lover come back to me / March of
the grenadiers / Mounties / One kiss / One
hour with you / Rose Marie / Smilin' through
/ Softly as in a morning sunrise / Sun up to
sundown / Toreador's song / Tramp, tramp,
tramp along the highway / Vilia / Waltz aria
/ Will you remember
CD _____ CDAJA 5124
Living Era / Mar '94 / Koch.

MacDonald, Kenneth

**SOUND OF KINTAIL FEATURING
KENNETH MACDONALD**
John MacColl's march to Kilbowie cottage
/ Col. David Murray's welcome to Kintail /
Tulloch Castle / Piobaireacho, Donald
Gruanach's / Gregory Blend and Roddy
MacDonald / Boys of Glendale / I'm going
home to Kintail
CD _____ CDITV 460
Scotdisc / Oct '88 / Duncans / Ross /
Conifer.

MacDonald, Rod

BRING ON THE LIONS
CD _____ BRAM 198908-2
Brambus / Nov '93 / ADA / Direct.

MAN ON THE LEDGE, THE
CD _____ SHCD 8011
Shanachie / Dec '94 / Koch / ADA /
Greensleeves.

WHITE BUFFALO
CD _____ BRAM 199129-2
Brambus / Nov '93 / ADA / Direct.

MacDonald, Alastair

SONGS GRETNA TO GLENCOE
CD _____ CDITV 547
Scotdisc / Sep '91 / Duncans / Ross /
Conifer.

VELVET & STEEL
Jamie Foyers / Bruce / Bonnie Earl O'Moray
/ Harlaw / Seer / Lock the door / Haughs o'
Cromdale / Killiecrankie / My bonnie Mary /
Blue bonnets / Flodden/Flooers o' the for-
est / Culloden's harvest / Fyvie / Sheep and
stag remain
CD _____ CDTRAX 078
Greentrax / Mar '95 / Conifer / Duncans /
ADA / Direct.

McDonald, Angus

A' SIREADH SPORS
CD _____ COMD 2043
Temple / Feb '94 / CM / Duncans / ADA /
Direct.

WORLD'S GREATEST PIPERS, THE
6/8 Marches / Strathspeys and reels / 6/8
Jigs / Gaelic air and 2/4 marches / 3/4 Retreat marches / Hornpipes / Flowers of the
forest / Hornpipes and jigs / 2/4 Competition marches / Lament for the children
CD _____ LCOM 5143
Lismor / Jun '93 / Lismor / Direct / Duncans
/ ADA.

McDonald, Country Joe

CARRY ON
Picks and lasers / Lady with the lamp /
Joe's blues / Hold on to each other / Stolen
heart blues / Trilogy / Going home / Carry
on / My last song
CD _____ 901302
Line / Feb '95 / CM / Grapevine / ADA /
Conifer / Direct.

CLASSICS
CD _____ CDWIK 108
Big Beat / Jul '92 / Pinnacle.

**COLLECTORS ITEMS (The First Three
EPs) (Country Joe & The Fish)**
I feel like I'm fixin' to die rag (takes 1 & 2) /
Super bird / (Thing called) love / Bass
strings / Section 43 / Fire in the city / John-
ny's gone in the war / Kiss my ass / Tricky
dicky / Free some day
CD _____ RBCD 901201
Line / Jun '92 / CM / Grapevine / ADA /
Conifer / Direct.
CD _____ NEXCD 228
Sequel / Nov '92 / BMG.

**ELECTRIC MUSIC FOR THE MIND AND
BODY (Country Joe & The Fish)**
Flying high / Not so sweet Martha Lorraine
/ Death sound blues / Porpoise mouth /
Section 43 / Super bird / Sad and lonely
times / Love / Bass strings / Masked ma-
rauder / Grace
CD _____ VMCD 79244
Vanguard / Oct '95 / Complete/Pinnacle /
Discovery.

**I FEEL LIKE I'M FIXIN' TO DIE (Country
Joe & The Fish)**
Fish cheer and I feel like I'm fixing to die rag
/ Who am I / Pat's song / Rock coast blues
/ Magoo / Though dream / Thursday /
Eastern jam / Colors for Susan
CD _____ VND 79266
Vanguard / Oct '95 / Complete/Pinnacle /
Discovery.

TOGETHER (Country Joe & The Fish)
CD _____ VND 79277
Vanguard / '95 / Complete/Pinnacle /
Discovery.

McDonald, Kathi

SAVE YOUR BREATH
CD _____ HYCD 200142
Hypertension / Jan '95 / Total/BMG /
Direct / ADA.

McDonald, Michael

BLINK OF AN EYE
I stand for you / East of Eden / More to us
than that / I want you / No more prayin' /
Matters of the heart / Hey girl / What makes
a man hold on / Blink of an eye / Everlasting
/ For a child
CD _____ 9362452932
WEA / Aug '93 / Warner Music.

IF THAT'S WHAT IT TAKES
Playin' by the rules / I keep forgettin' / Love
lies / Gotta try / I can let go now / That's
why / If that's what it takes / No such luck
/ Losin' end / Believe in it
CD _____ 9237032
WEA / Jul '88 / Warner Music.

NO LOOKIN' BACK
No looking back / By heart / Bad times / (I'll
be your) Angel / Any foolish thing / Our love
/ (I hang) On your every word / Lost in the
parade / Don't let me down
CD _____ 7599252912
WEA / Feb '87 / Warner Music.

**SWEET FREEDOM: BEST OF MICHAEL
MCDONALD**
Sweet freedom / I'll be your angel / Yah mo
be there / I gotta try / I keep forgettin' / Any
love / On my own / No lookin back / Any
foolish thing / That's why / What a fool believes / I can let go now
CD _____ 2410492
WEA / Nov '86 / Warner Music.

TAKE IT TO HEART
All we got / Get the word started / Love can
break your heart / Take it to heart / Tear it
up / Lonely talk / Searchin' for understanding / Homeboy / No amount of reason / One
step away / You show me
CD _____ 7599259792
WEA / May '90 / Warner Music.

McDonald, Skip

**WOLF THAT HOUSE BUILT, THE (Little
Axe)**
CD _____ WIRED 27
Wired / Jan '95 / 3MV / Sony.

MacDonnchadha, Johnny...

**CONTAE MHUIGHEO (MacDonnchadha,
Johnny Mhairtin Learai)**
CD _____ CICD 013
Clo Iar-Chonnachta / Dec '93 / CM.

McDougall, Ian

WARMTH OF THE HORN, THE
Warm / You go to my head / Like someone
in love / Blue Daniel / Sixth sense / Lament
/ I remember you / How long has this been
going on / Centerpiece / Blue skies / Mc not
Mac and two L's
CD _____ CCD 4652
Concord Jazz / Jul '95 / New Note.

MacDowell, Al

MESSIAH (MacDowell, Al & Timepiece)
Messiah / Powerful one / Playing in the
sand / Close to the edge / Jamming in the
pyramids / Offset / Second calling / Let the
music sing / Latin lady / Here we come
again
CD _____ GV 794512
Gramavision / May '91 / Vital/SAM / ADA.

TIME PEACE
Fantastic voyage / St. Alban's tango / Nina's line of no return / Somewhere / Fantasia / Maybe / Peng shui / Ode bra / View
from a window / Come see tomorrow / Blue
age
CD _____ GCD 79450
Gramavision / Sep '95 / Vital/SAM / ADA.

MacDowell, Lenny

MAGIC FLUTE
CD _____ BLR 84 027
L&R / May '91 / New Note.

McDowell, Fred

AMAZING GRACE
CD _____ TCD 5004
Testament / Aug '94 / Complete/Pinnacle /
ADA / Koch.

GOOD MORNING LITTLE SCHOOLGIRL
CD _____ ARHCD 424
Arhoolie / Apr '95 / ADA / Direct /
Cadillac.

LONG WAY FROM HOME
CD _____ OBCCD 535
Original Blues Classics / Nov '92 /
Complete/Pinnacle / Wellard / Cadillac.

MISSISSIPPI BLUES
CD _____ BLCD 760179
Black Lion / Mar '93 / Jazz Music /
Cadillac / Wellard / Koch.

**MISSISSIPPI FRED MCDOWELL
(McDowell, Mississippi Fred)**
CD _____ ROUCD 2138
Rounder / Sep '95 / CM / Direct / ADA /
Cadillac.

**MY HOME IS IN THE DELTA BLUES &
SPIRITUALS (McDowell, Fred & Annie
Mae)**
CD _____ TCD 5019
Testament / Apr '95 / Complete/Pinnacle /
ADA / Koch.

**SHAKE 'EM ON DOWN (McDowell,
Mississippi Fred)**
CD _____ 269 373 2
Tomato / Mar '90 / Vital.

**THIS AIN'T NO ROCK 'N' ROLL
(McDowell, Mississippi Fred)**
CD _____ ARHCD 441
Arhoolie / Sep '95 / ADA / Direct /
Cadillac.

**WHEN I LAY MY BURDEN DOWN
(McDowell, Fred & Furry Lewis)**
If you see my baby / John Henry / Louise /
61 highway blues / Big fat mama / When I
lay my burden down / Dankin farm / Casey
Jones / Harry furry blues / Everyday in the
week / Grieve my mind / Beale Street blues
CD _____ BCD 130
Biograph / Jun '94 / Wellard / ADA / Hot
Shot / Jazz Music / Cadillac / Direct.

**YOU GOT TO MOVE (McDowell,
'Mississippi' Fred)**
Some day baby / Milk cow blues / Train I
ride / Over the hill / Goin' down to the river
/ I wished I were in heaven sittin' down /
Louise
CD _____ ARHCD 304
Arhoolie / Apr '95 / ADA / Direct / Cadillac.

McDuff, Jack

ANOTHER REAL GOOD 'UN
Another real good 'un / Summertime / Off
the beaten path / Long day blues / Rock
candy / I can't get started (with you) / I
cover the waterfront
CD _____ MCD 5374
Muse / Sep '92 / New Note / CM.

BRONX TALE (McDuff, Jack & Friends)
C Jam blues / Streets of the Bronx / Time
after time / Pepper and salt / Cry me a river
/ Ice candy / Old folks / Martino / Lover man
CD _____ KICJ 204
King/Paddle Wheel / Aug '94 / New Note.

**COLOUR ME BLUE (McDuff, Jack &
Friends)**
CD _____ CCD 4516
Concord Jazz / Aug '92 / New Note.

HEATIN' SYSTEM, THE
601 1/2 No. Poplar / Put on a happy face /
Sundown / Mr. T / Jimmy Smith / In a sentimental mood / Fly away / Pink Panther
(theme) / Playoff
CD _____ CCD 4644
Concord Jazz / Jun '95 / New Note.

HONEYDRIPPER, THE
CD _____ OJCCD 222
Original Jazz Classics / Dec '95 / Wellard /
Jazz Music / Cadillac / Complete/Pinnacle.

HOT BARBEQUE (McDuff, Brother Jack)
Hot barbeque / Party's over / Briar patch /
Hippy dip / 601 1/2 no. Poplar / Cry me a
river / Three day thang
CD _____ CDBGP 053
BGP / May '93 / Pinnacle.

**HOT BARBEQUE/LIVE (AT THE FRONT
ROOM) (McDuff, Brother Jack)**
Hot barbeque / Party's over / Briar patch /
Hippy dip / 601 1/2 No. poplar / Cry me a
river / Three day thang / Rock candy / It's
ain't necessarily so / Sanctified samba /
Whistle while you work / Real good'n /
Undecided
CD _____ CDBGPD 053
BGP / Apr '93 / Pinnacle.

WRITE ON CAP'N
Spec-tator / From the pulpit / Killer Joe /
Room / Night in Tunisia / Captain's quarters
/ Billyjack / Out of my head / Goin' to the
wall / Havin' a good time
CD _____ CCD 4568
Concord Jazz / Sep '93 / New Note.

McDuff, Larry

RE-ENTRY, THE
CD _____ MCD 5361
Muse / Sep '92 / New Note / CM.

McEachern, Malcolm

MALCOLM MC EACHERN
Oh ruddier than the cherry / Lord is a man of war / Honour and arms / Arm, arm ye brave / Lord God of Abraham / Revenge, Timotheus cries / I am a roamer / O tu palermo / Le veau d'or / Sperate, O Figli...d'egitto la sui lidi / Mighty deep / On the road to Mandalay / Australian bush songs / Excelsior / Blow, blow thou winter wind / Danny Deever / Song of the Volga boatmen / Hundred pipers / Drinking / Gendarmes duet
CD _____ GEMM CD 9455
Pearl / '90 / Harmonia Mundi.

McEntire, Reba

FOR MY BROKEN HEART
CD _____ MCAD 10400
MCA / Oct '91 / BMG.

GREATEST HITS: REBA MCENTIRE
Just a little love / He broke your memory last night / How blue / Somebody should leave / Have I got a deal for you / Only in my mind / Whoever's in New England / Little rock / What am I gonna do about you / One promise too late
CD _____ MCLD 19177
MCA / Mar '94 / BMG.

GREATEST HITS: REBA MCENTIRE #2
Does he love you / You lie / Fancy / For my broken heart / Love will find it's way to you / They asked about you / Is there life out there / Rumour has it / Walk on / Greatest man I never knew
CD _____ MCD 10906
MCA / Oct '93 / BMG.

IT'S YOUR CALL
It's your call / Straight from you / Take it back / Baby's gone blues / Heart won't lie / One last good hand / He wants to get married / For herself / Will he ever go away / Lighter shade of blue
CD _____ MCD 10673
MCA / Jan '93 / BMG.

READ MY MIND
Everything that you want / Read my mind / I won't stand in line / I wish that I could tell you / She think's his name was John / Why haven't I heard from you / Still / Heart is a lonely hunter / I wouldn't want to be you / Till you love me
CD _____ MCD 10994
MCA / Jun '94 / BMG.

STARTING OVER
Talking in your sleep / Please come to Boston / On my own / I won't mention it again / You're no good / Ring on her finger, time on her hands / 500 miles away from home / Starting over again / You keep me hangin' on / By the time I get to Phoenix
CD _____ MCD 11264
MCA / Oct '95 / BMG.

Maceration

SERENADE OF AGONY, A
CD _____ CD 7913004
Progress Red / Jun '93 / Plastic Head.

Macero, Teo

BEST OF TEO MACERO
CD _____ STCD 527
Stash / Aug '90 / Jazz Music / CM / Cadillac / Direct / ADA.

McEvoy, Johnny

SONGS OF IRELAND
Home boys home / Red is the rose / Black velvet band / Maggie / Good ship Kangaroo / Wild mountain thyme / I wish I had someone to love me / Town of ballybay / Molly,my Irish Molly / Rare ould times / Streets of New York / Travelling people / shores of americaky / Bunch of thyme / Irish soldier laddie / Song for Ireland
CD _____ MCBD 19520
MCA / Apr '95 / BMG.

MacEwan, Sydney

FOLK SONGS AND BALLADS
Bonnie Earl O'Moray / Lark in the clear air / She moved thro the fair / O men from the fields / Dawning of the day / Mowing the barley / Silent O'Moyle / Duna / Since first I saw your face / In summertime in Bredon / Foggy dew / Pleading / Coronach / Green bushes / Banks of Allan Water / Jeanie with the light brown hair / Macishia / As I sit here / Maiden of Morven
CD _____ MIDCD 007
Moidart / May '95 / Conifer / ADA.

GREAT SCOTTISH TENOR, THE
(MacEwan, Father Sydney)
Turn ye to me / Duna / Mowing the barley / Annie Laurie / Mother of mercy / Foggy dew / Maiden of Morven
CD _____ GEMMCD 9107
Pearl / May '94 / Harmonia Mundi.

ROAD TO THE ISLES 1934-6, THE
(MacEwan, Father Sydney)
Road to the isles / Lark in the clear air / Macushla / Turn ye to me / Loch Lomond / Island moon / Mnhathan a ghlinne so / Bon-

---

nie Earl O'Moray / O men from the fields / Bonnie Mary of Argyle / Lewis bridal song / Ye banks and braes o' bonnie Doon / Peat fire flame / Tog orm mo phiob / She moved through the fair / Annie Laurie / As I sit here / Maiden of Morven / Maighdeanan na h-airidh / Will ye no' come back again
CD _____ CDHD 148
Happy Days / Feb '89 / Conifer.

SONGS OF SCOTLAND, THE
Road to the isles / Peat fire flame / Maighdeanan na h-airidh / Island moon / Morag bheag / Bonnie banks of Loch Lomond / Ye banks and braes o' bonnie Doon / Togorm mo phiob / When the kye come home / Rowan tree / An eriskay love lilt / Herding song / Mnhathan a ghlinne
CD _____ MIDCD 002
Moidart / Jan '95 / Conifer / ADA.

MacEwan, William

WILLIAM MCEWAN (The Original Glasgow Street Singer-Evangelist)
Sunrise / Pull for the shore / Throw out the lifeline / I would be like Jesus / Merrily sing / Sweetest song I know / Pardoning grace / Not now but in the coming years / When the roll is called up yonder / We will talk it o'er together by and by / Old rugged cross / God be with you till we meet again / Will the circle be unbroken / My mothers hand is on my brow / Sinking sands (In loving kindness Jesus came) / He died of a broken heart / God will take care of you / I know my heavenly father knows / Someday / My ain countrie
CD _____ LCOM 5235
Lismor / May '94 / Lismor / Direct / Duncans / ADA.

McFadden & Whitehead

AIN'T NO STOPPING US NOW
CD _____ KWEST 5406
Disky / May '93 / THE / BMG / Discovery / Pinnacle.

McFadden, Charlie

CHARLIE 'SPECKS' MCFADDEN 1929-1940 (McFadden, Charlie 'Specks')
CD _____ BDCD 6041
Blues Document / May '93 / Swift / Jazz Music / Hot Shot.

McFadden, Gerry

IRISH TRADITIONAL UILLEANN PIPES
CD _____ PTICD 1031
Outlet / Oct '95 / ADA / Duncans / CM / Ross / Direct / Koch.

UILLEANN PIPES
CD _____ PTI 1031CD
Pure Traditional Irish / Jul '95 / ADA.

MacFayden, Iain

WORLD'S GREATEST PIPERS VOL. 7
March, strathspey and reel / 6/8 marches / Gaelic air and hornpipes / Jigs / 9/8 marches / Piobaireachd / 6/8 march and jig / 2/4 marches / 6/8 marches (2) / Strathspeys and reels / Piobaireachd (2)
CD _____ LCOM 5180
Lismor / Mar '95 / Lismor / Direct / Duncans / ADA.

McFerrin, Bobby

BANG ZOOM
Bang zoom / Remembrance / Friends / Selim / Freedom is a voice / Heaven's design / My better half / Kid's toys / Mere words
CD _____ CDP 8316772
Blue Note / Jan '96 / EMI.

MacGabhann, Antoin

AR AON BHUILE
CD _____ CICD 105
CICD / Jan '95 / ADA.

McGann, Andy

ANDY MCGANN & PADDY REYNOLDS FIDDLE (McGann, Andy & Paddy Reynolds)
CD _____ SHANCD 34008
Shanachie / Jan '95 / Koch / ADA / Greensleeves.

IT'S A HARD ROAD TO TRAVEL
CD _____ SHCD 34011
Shanachie / Jul '95 / Koch / ADA / Greensleeves.

TRADITIONAL MUSIC OF IRELAND (McGann, Andy & Paul Brady)
CD _____ SHAN 34011CD
Shanachie / Apr '95 / Koch / ADA / Greensleeves.

TRADITIONAL MUSIC OF IRELAND SERIES (McGann, Andy & Paul Brady)
CD _____ SH 34011
Shanachie / Apr '95 / Koch / ADA / Greensleeves.

McGann, John

UPSIDE
CD _____ GLCD 2118
Green Linnet / Mar '95 / Roots / CM / Direct / ADA.

McGarrigle, Kate

DANCER WITH BRUISED KNEES (McGarrigle, Kate & Anna)
Dancer with bruised knees / Southern boys / Biscuit song / First born / Blanche comme la neige / Perrine etait servante / Be my baby / Walking song / Naufragee du tendre / Hommage a grungie / Kitty come home / Come a long way / No biscuit blues
CD _____ 759925958-2
Warner Bros. / Jun '94 / Warner Music.

FRENCH RECORD (McGarrigle, Kate & Anna)
CD _____ HNCD 1302
Rykodisc / Oct '92 / Vital / ADA.

HEARTBEATS ACCELERATING (McGarrigle, Kate & Anna)
Heartbeats accelerating / I eat dinner / Rainbow ride / Mother, mother / Love is / D.J. serenade / I'm losing you / Hit and run love / Leave me be / St. James Hospital
CD _____ 261.142
Private Music / Nov '90 / BMG.

KATE & ANNA MCGARRIGLE (McGarrigle, Kate & Anna)
Kiss and say goodbye / My town / Blues in D / Heart like a wheel / Foolish you / Talk to me of Mendocino / Complainte pour Ste. Catherine / Tell my sister / Swimming song / Jigsaw puzzle of Life / Go leave / Travelling on for Jesus
CD _____ 936245677-2
Warner Bros. / Jun '94 / Warner Music.

McGee, Dennis

COMPLETE EARLY RECORDINGS, THE (Early American Cajun Classics)
CD _____ YAZCD 2012
Yazoo / Dec '94 / CM / ADA / Roots / Koch.

McGhee, Brownie

AT THE 2ND FRET (McGhee, Brownie & Sonny Terry)
CD _____ OBCCD 561
Original Blues Classics / Jan '94 / Complete/Pinnacle / Wellard / Cadillac.

BROWNIE MCGHEE - 1944-1955
Watch out / Dissatisfied woman / Rum cola papa / My baby likes to shuffle / Daybreak / Doggin' blues / I'm gonna rock / Evil but kindhearted / Drinkin' wine spo-dee-o-dee
CD _____ TMCD 04
Travellin' Man / Oct '94 / Wellard / CM / Jazz Music.

BROWNIE'S BLUES
CD _____ OBCCD 505
Original Blues Classics / Nov '92 / Complete/Pinnacle / Wellard / Cadillac.

CLIMBIN' UP (McGhee, Brownie & Sonny Terry)
Gone baby gone / Tell me baby / Sittin' pretty / Bottom blues / Dissatisfied blues / Diamond ring / Way I feel / So much trouble / When It's love time / I'd love to love you / Love's a disease / My fault
CD _____ SV 0256
Savoy Jazz / Nov '94 / Conifer / ADA.

COMPLETE BROWNIE MCGHEE, THE (2CD Set)
Picking my tomatoes / Me and my dog / Blues / Born for bad luck / I'm callin Daisy / Step it up and go / My barkin' bulldog blues / Let me tell you 'bout my baby / Prison woman blues / Back door stranger / Be good to me / Not guilty blues / Coal miner's blues / Step it up and go 2 / Money spending woman / Death of blind boy fuller / Good to find my little woman / I'm a black woman's man / Dealing with the devil / Double trouble / Woman I'm done / Key to my door / Million lonesome woman / Ain't no tellin' / Try me one more time / I want to see Joeus / Dono what my Lord said / I want King Jesus / What will I do (Without the Lord) / Key to the highway / I don't believe in love / So much trouble / Goodbye now / Jealous of my woman / Unfair blues / Barbecue any old time / Workin' man blues / Sinful disposition woman / Back home blues / Deep sea diver / It must be love / Studio chatter / Swing soldier swing
CD Set _____ 475700 2
Columbia / May '94 / Sony.

McGhee, Howard

DIAL MASTERS, THE
Intersection / Lifestream / Mop mop / Stardust / You / Stop time blues / Sleepwalker boogie / Surrender / Turnip blood / Night music / Coolie-rini / Night mist / Dorothy / High wind in Hollywood / Up in Dodo's room / Midnight at Mintons / Dialated pupils / Therodynamics / Trumpet at Tempo
CD _____ SPJCD 131
Spotlite / Jul '95 / Cadillac / Jazz Horizons / Swift.

McGhee, Howard & Milt Jackson

HOWARD MCGHEE & MILT JACKSON (McGhee, Howard & Milt Jackson)
Double or nothing / Tale of the town / Bass C Jam / Flip lip / Belle from Bunnycock / Down home / Sweet and lovely / Fiesta / I'm in the mood for love / Man I love / Last word
CD _____ SV 0167
Savoy Jazz / Apr '93 / Conifer / ADA.

MAGGIE
Merry Lee / Short life / Talk of the town / Bass C Jam / Down home / Sweet and lovely / Fiesta / I'm in the mood for love / Belle from Bunnycock / Lip flip / Man I love / Last word / Royal Garden blues / Mood indigo / St. Louis blues / One o'clock jump / Stormy weather / Man with a horn / Stompin' at the Savoy / Lady be good / Stardust / How high the moon / Don't blame me / Body and soul / Harvest time
CD _____ SV 0269
Savoy Jazz / Sep '95 / Conifer / ADA.

SHARP EDGE
CD _____ BLCD 760110
Black Lion / Dec '88 / Jazz Music / Cadillac / Wellard / Koch.

SUNSET SWING (McGhee, Howard & Previn/Edison/Thompson)
CD _____ BLCD 760171
Black Lion / Mar '93 / Jazz Music / Cadillac / Wellard / Koch.

McGhee, Stick

NEW YORK BLUES (McGhee, Stick & His Spo-Dee-O-Dee Buddies)
Real good feeling / Hoartacho blues / Heart breakin' woman / Watchin' my stuff / Gonna hop on down the line / Do right / Why'd you do it / Door bell blues / I'm doin' all this time (and you put me down) / Wiggle waggie woo / Dealin' from the bottom / Whiskey, women and loaded dice / Little things we used to do / Blues in my heart and tears in my eyes / Head happy with wine / Jungle juice / Sad, bad, glad / Six to eight / Get your mind out of the gutter / Double crossin' liquor
CD _____ CDCHD 502
Ace / Jan '95 / Pinnacle / Cadillac / Complete/Pinnacle.

McGhee, Wes

BORDER GUITARS
CD _____ RGFCD 018
Road Goes On Forever / Jul '94 / Direct.

McGillivray, James

WORLD'S GREATEST PIPERS VOL. 10
CD _____ LCOM 5216
Lismor / Oct '90 / Lismor / Direct / Duncans / ADA.

McGlynn, Arty

MCGLYNN'S FANCY
Carolan's draught / Floating crowbar / I wish my love was a red, red rose / Peter Byrne's fancy / Blackbird / Creeping Docken / Charles O'Connor / Arthur Darley / Hills above Drumquin / Sally gardens
CD _____ BERCD 011
Emerald / Nov '94 / Direct.

MacGowan, Geraldine

RECONCILIATION
CD _____ CMBOD 011
Cross Border Media / Jan '95 / Direct / ADA.

MacGowan, Shane

SNAKE, THE (MacGowan, Shane & The Popes)
CD _____ 0630104022
ZTT / Jun '95 / Warner Music.

McGrattan, Paul

FROST IS ALL OVER, THE
Speed the plough / Abbey reel/Primrose lass / Hare in the corn/Grainne's welcome / Sailor's return/Chattering magpie/House on the hill / Slan le Maigh/Tailor's twist/Mayo reels / Stone in the field/John Egan's reel/Dublin porter / Up and away/Mountain pathway/Egan's polkas / Skylark/Jenny Dang the weaver / Frost is all over/Coleman's jig/Rambling pitchfork / Johnny O'Leary's/Padraig O'Keeffe's slide / Byrne's hornpipes / Gehan's reel/Crosses of Annagh/An untitled reel / Tracey's jig/Rose in the heather/Blackthorn stick / Hardiman the fiddler/Taim in arrears / Christmas eve/Old bush/The scholar reel / Tommy People's reel
CD _____ CC 58CD
Claddagh / Jan '93 / ADA / Direct.

McGraw, Tim

ALL I WANT
CD _____ CURCD 16
Curb / Sep '95 / PolyGram.

McGregor, Chris

COUNTRY COOKING
Country cookin' / Bakwetha / Sweet as honey / You and me / Big G / Maxine / Dakar / Thunder in the mountains (Cassette only)
CD _____ CDVE 17
Venture / May '88 / EMI.

GRANDMOTHER'S TEACHING
CD _____ ITM 1428
ITM / Jan '91 / Tradelink / Koch.

IN MEMORIUM (McGregor, Chris & Brotherhood Of Breath)
CD _____ ITMP 970086
ITM / Oct '95 / Tradelink / Koch.

McGregor, Freddie

ALL IN THE SAME BOAT
All in the same boat / Hungry belly pickney / Push comes to shove / Jah a the don / I'm coming home / Glad you're here with me / I don't want to see you cry / Somewhere / Mama Mama / Peace in the valley
CD _____ RASCD 3014
Ras / May '87 / Jetstar / Greensleeves / SRD / Direct.

CARRY GO BRING COME
CD _____ GRELCD 197
Greensleeves / Dec '93 / Total/BMG / Jetstar / SRD.

COME ON OVER
Shirley come on over / Apple of my eye / Go away pretty woman / Stand up and fight / Shortman / Are you crazy / Reggae feeling / Rhythm so nice / Natty dread / Brother man
CD _____ RASCD 3002
Ras / Apr '92 / Jetstar / Greensleeves / SRD / Direct.

COMPILATION
CD _____ RNCD 2131
Rhino / Nov '95 / Jetstar / Magnum Music Group / THE.

FOREVER MY LOVE
CD _____ RASCD 3160
Ras / Aug '95 / Jetstar / Greensleeves / SRD / Direct.

JAMAICAN CLASSICS VOL 2
CD _____ BSCD 2
Big Ship / Nov '92 / Jetstar.

LEGIT (McGregor, Freddie, Cocoa T & Dennis Brown)
CD _____ GRELCD 189
Greensleeves / Aug '93 / Total/BMG / Jetstar / SRD.

LIVE IN LONDON 1991
CD _____ CPCD 8027
Charly / Feb '94 / Charly / THE / Cadillac.

MAGIC IN THE AIR
CD _____ BSCD 5
Big Ship / Aug '95 / Jetstar.

NOW
CD _____ VPCD 1163
Steely & Cleevie / Jun '91 / Jetstar.

PUSH ON
CD _____ BSCD 4
Big Ship / Apr '94 / Jetstar.

REGGAE ROCKERS
CD _____ RRTGCD 7714
Rohit / '89 / Jetstar.

SINGS JAMAICAN CLASSICS
CD _____ BSCD 1
Jetstar / Oct '91 / Jetstar.

ZION CHANT
CD _____ HB 138CD
Heartbeat / Sep '94 / Greensleeves / Jetstar / Direct / ADA.

McGriff, Jimmy

GEORGIA ON MY MIND
Let's stay together / Shaft / What's going on / Georgia on my mind / April in Paris / Everyday I have the blues / Yardbird suite / It's you I adore / Lonesome road / Mack the knife / There will never be another you / Canadian sunset / Mr. Lucky / Moonglow / Red sails in the sunset / Secret love
CD _____ CDC-8513
LRC / Nov '90 / New Note / Harmonia Mundi.

JIMMY MCGRIFF FEATURING HANK CRAWFORD (McGriff, Jimmy & Hank Crawford)
CD _____ CDC 9001
LRC / Oct '90 / New Note / Harmonia Mundi.

PULLIN' OUT THE STOPS - BEST OF JIMMY MCGRIFF
All about my girl / I've got a woman / Discotheque / Kiko / See see rider / Cash box / Gospel time / Where it's at / Last minute / Blue juice / Step one / Chris cross / South Wes / Black pearl / Worm / Ain't it funky now / Fat cakes
CD _____ CDP 8307242
Blue Note / Sep '94 / EMI.

RED BEANS
Red beans and rice / Big booty bounce / Space cadet / Alive and well / Sweet love / Love is my life / It's been so long now / Overweight shark bait
CD _____ CDC 9083
LRC / Apr '95 / New Note / Harmonia Mundi.

SONNY LESTER COLLECTION
CD _____ CDC 9070
LRC / Nov '93 / New Note / Harmonia Mundi.

TRIBUTE TO BASIE (McGriff, Jimmy Big Band)
CD _____ CDC 9027
LRC / Mar '91 / New Note / Harmonia Mundi.

McGuinn, Roger

RETURN FLIGHT VOL.2 (McGuinn, Roger & Gene Clark & Chris Hillman)
Little mama / Stopping traffic / Feelin' higher / Release me girl / Bye bye baby / One more chance / Won't let you down / Street talk / Deeper in / Painted fire / Mean streets / Entertainment / Soul shoes / Love me tonight / Secret side of you / Ain't no money / Making movies
CD _____ EDCD 373
Edsel / Jun '93 / Pinnacle / ADA.

RETURN FLYTE (McGuinn & Clark)
CD _____ EDCD 358
Edsel / Dec '92 / Pinnacle / ADA.

McGuire, Sean

BROTHERS TOGETHER (McGuire, Sean & Jim)
CD _____ PTICD 1055
Pure Traditional Irish / Apr '94 / ADA.

TWO CHAMPIONS (McGuire, Sean & Joe Burke)
CD _____ PTICD 1014
Outlet / Feb '95 / ADA / Duncans / CM / Ross / Direct / Koch.

McGuire, Séamus

CAROUSEL (McGuire, Séamus & Manus Mcguire, Daithi Sproule)
CD _____ CEFCD 105
Gael Linn / Jan '94 / Roots / CM / Direct / ADA.

MISSING REEL, THE (McGuire, Séamus & John Lee)
CD _____ CEFCD 146
Gael Linn / Jan '94 / Roots / CM / Direct / ADA.

WISHING TREE, THE
CD _____ GL 1151CD
Green Linnet / Jul '95 / Roots / CM / Direct / ADA.

MacGuish, Alasdair

ALASDAIR MACGUISH & THE BLACK ROSE CEILIDH BAND
CD _____ LOC 1086CD
Lochshore / Jul '95 / ADA / Direct / Duncans.

McHael, Allan

NEW RIVER TRAIN
CD _____ FE 1408
Folk Era / Nov '94 / CM / ADA.

OLD COUNTRY RADIO SONGS (McHael, Allan & Old Time Radio Gang)
CD _____ FE 2062CD
Folk Era / Dec '94 / CM / ADA.

McHaile, Tom

PURE TRADITIONAL TIN WHISTLE
CD _____ PTICD 1001
Pure Traditional Irish / Apr '94 / ADA.

McHargue, Rosy

OH HOW HE CAN SING
CD _____ SOSCD 1253
Stomp Off / Jul '93 / Jazz Music / Wellard.

Machete Ensemble

MACHETE ENSEMBLE, THE
CD _____ CDEB 2501
Earthbeat / May '93 / Direct / ADA.

Machine Head

BURN MY EYES
Davidian / Old / Thousand eyes / None but my own / Rage to overcome / Death church / I'm your God now / Blood for blood / Nation on fire / Real eyes, realize, real lies / Block
CD _____ RR 9016S
CD _____ RR 9016?
Roadrunner / May '95 / Pinnacle.

Machine In The Garden

VEILS AND SHADOWS EP
CD _____ ISOL 80022
Isol / Feb '95 / Plastic Head.

Machines Of Loving Grace

CONCENTRATION
CD _____ 4509968522
WEA / Nov '94 / Warner Music.

MACHINES OF LOVING GRACE
CD _____ MR 00292
Mammoth / Feb '92 / Vital.

Machito

AFRO CUBAN JAZZ (Machito/Charlie Parker/Stan Kenton)
CD _____ CD 53170
Giants of Jazz / Aug '95 / Target/BMG / Cadillac.

BONGO FIESTA
Adios / Holiday mambo / Bongo fiesta / Mambo mucho mambo / Ay que mate / Mambo inn / Zambia / Blem blem blem / Beerebee cum bee / Tremendo cumban / Hay que recordar / Freezelandia / Oboe mambo / Donde estabas tu / Mambo a la savoy
CD _____ CD 62070
Saludos Amigos / Apr '95 / Target/BMG.

MACHITO & HIS ORCHESTRA (Machito & His Orchestra)
CD _____ CD 62045
Saludos Amigos / Nov '93 / Target/BMG.

MACHITO AT THE CRESCENDO
CD _____ GNPD 58
GNP Crescendo / '88 / Silva Screen.

MAMBO IN JAZZ
CD _____ CD 62015
Saludos Amigos / Jan '93 / Target/BMG.

SALSA BIG BAND 1982 (Machito & His Salsa Big Band)
Elas de la rumba / Quimbobo / Piniero tenia razon / Caso perdido / Manicero / Sambia
CD _____ CDSJP 161
Timeless Jazz / '89 / New Note.

Machlis, Paul

BRIGHT FIELD, THE (Machlis, Paul & Alasdair Fraser)
CD _____ CULD 107
Culburnie / Jun '95 / Ross / ADA.

McIlwaine, Ellen

LOOKING FOR TROUBLE
CD _____ SPCD 1110
Stony Plain / Apr '94 / ADA / CM / Direct.

MacInnes, Mairi

CAUSEWAY
Clachan uaine (The green village) / Mendocino / Puirt a beul (mouth music) / Eala bhan (The white swan) / Eilidh / Cuachag nana craobh (The tree cuckoo) / Morag's na horo ghealliadh (walking song) / Mairead og / Soraidh le eilean a'cheo / Back home again in) Indiana / Tuireadh mhic criomain (MacCrimmon's lament) / Mo chridhe trom's duilich leam / Everlasting gun
CD _____ LCOM 9018
Lismor / Oct '92 / Lismor / Duncans / ADA.

THIS FEELING INSIDE
Puert a beul / Follow the light / Cum ar'naire / Come back to me / Neamhnaid gheal dochais / Sit at my table / Fraoch a ronaidh / Far from home / Fear a'bhata / Precious days / Mile marphaisg air a ghaol / Eilean m'araich / Puirt a beul / This feeling inside
CD _____ CDTRAX 092
Greentrax / Jul '95 / Conifer / Duncans / ADA / Direct.

McIntyre, Ken

INTRODUCING THE VIBRATIONS (McIntyre, Ken Sextet)
CD _____ SCCD 31065
Steeplechase / Dec '95 / Impetus.

Mack, Bobby

HONEYTRAP
CD _____ PRD 70542
Provogue / Sep '93 / Pinnacle.

RED HOT & HUMID
Black Jack / In the open / Maudie / Look watcha done / She's so fine / Phillip West / Ain't nobody's business / Change my mind / All night long / Take it home
CD _____ PRD 70692
Provogue / Aug '94 / Pinnacle.

SAY WHAT
CD _____ PRD 70502
Provogue / Apr '93 / Pinnacle.

Mack, Craig

PROJECT: FUNK DA WORLD
Project: Funk da world / Get down / Making moves with puff / That y'all / Flava in ya ear / Funk wid da style / Judgement day / Real raw / Mainline / When God comes / Welcome to 1994
CD _____ 78612 73001-2
Arista / Oct '94 / BMG.

Mack, Lonnie

ATTACK OF THE KILLER V (Lonnie Mack Live)
CD _____ ALCD 4786
Alligator / May '93 / Direct / ADA.

HOME AT LAST
CD _____ OW S2117963
One Way / Sep '94 / Direct / ADA.

LONNIE MACK & PISMO
CD _____ OW S2117964
One Way / Sep '94 / Direct / ADA.

LONNIE ON THE MOVE
I found a love / Soul express / I've had it / Wildwood flower / Snow on the mountain / I washed my hands in muddy water / Shotgun / Sticks and stones / Jam and butter / One mint julep / Florence of Arabia / Lonnie on the move / Sa-ba-hoola / Money (that's what I want) / Dorothy on my mind / Men at play / Oh boy / Stand by me / Don't make my baby blue
CD _____ CDCH 352
Ace / Feb '92 / Pinnacle / Cadillac / Complete/Pinnacle.

SECOND SIGHT
Me and my car / Rock 'n' roll bones / Tough on me tough on you / Camp Washington Chili / Cincinnati / Rock people / Buffalo woman / Ain't nobody / Back on the road again / Song I haven't sung
CD _____ ALCD 4750
Alligator / Oct '93 / Direct / ADA.

STRIKE LIKE LIGHTNING
Hound dog man / Satisfy Susie / Stop / Long way from Memphis / Double whammy / Strike like lightning / Falling back in love with you / If you have to know / You ain't got me / Oreo cookie blues
CD _____ ALCD 4739
Alligator / May '93 / Direct / ADA.

Macka B

BUPPIE CULTURE
CD _____ ARICD 48
Ariwa Sounds / Jan '91 / Jetstar / SRD.

DISCRIMINATION
CD _____ ARICD 098
Ariwa Sounds / Jun '94 / Jetstar / SRD.

HERE COMES TROUBLE
Promises / Here comes trouble / Do the butterfly / Getting blacker / Don't worry / Thank you Father / Squeeze me / Reggae on the rampage / Crackpot / Rottweiler
CD _____ ARICD 088
Ariwa Sounds / Oct '93 / Jetstar / SRD.

HOLD ON TO YOUR CULTURE
Bob / Legalize the herb / Beautiful eyes / Greetings / Hold on to your culture / Give the workers / Woman / Put down the gun / Tribute to Garnett Silk
CD _____ ARICD 108
Ariwa Sounds / Oct '95 / Jetstar / SRD.

JAMAICA, NO PROBLEM
CD _____ ARICD 078
Ariwa Sounds / May '92 / Jetstar / SRD.

PEACE CUP
CD _____ ARICD 068
Ariwa Sounds / Jul '91 / Jetstar / SRD.

ROOTS RAGGA
Roots Ragga / (Get up I feel like being a) sex machine / Drink too much / Revelation time / Big mack / Devil dance / Rodney King medley / One man, one vote / Unemployment blues / Proud to be black / Back off / Buppie / Respect to the mother (CD only) / Apartheid (CD only)
CD _____ ARICD 082
Ariwa Sounds / Nov '92 / Jetstar / SRD.

SIGN OF THE TIMES
CD _____ ARICD 028
Ariwa Sounds / Feb '89 / SRD.

McKagan, Duff

BELIEVE IN ME
Believe in me / Man in the meadow / (Fucked up) Beyond belief / Could it be U / Just not there / Punk rock song / Majority / Ten years / Swamp song / Trouble / Fuck you / Lonely tonite
CD _____ GED 24605
Geffen / May '93 / BMG.

McKay, Iain

SEOLADH
CD _____ SKYECD 07
Macmeanma / Sep '95 / Duncans / CM / ADA.

McKee, Maria

MARIA MCKEE
I've forgotten what it was in you / To miss someone / Am I the only one (who ever felt this way) / Nobody's child / Panic beach / Can't pull the wool down (over the lamb's eyes) / More than a heart on hold / This property is condemned / Breathe / Has he got a friend for me
CD _____ GFLD 19200
Geffen / Mar '93 / BMG.

YOU GOTTA SIN TO GET SAVED
I'm gonna soothe you / My lonely sad eyes / My girlhood among the outlaws / Only once / I forgive you / I can't make it alone / Precious time / Way young lovers do / Why wasn't I more grateful (when life was so sweet) / You gotta sin to get saved
CD _____ GFLD 19290
Geffen / Oct '95 / BMG.

McKellar, Kenneth

LAND OF HEART'S DESIRE
Think on me / Old turf fire / Fairy lullaby / Ho ro my nut brown maiden / David of the White Rock / MacPherson's farewell / Land of heart's desire / Star of the county down / Ellan Vannin / Bonnie Earl O'Moray / Wee Cooper o' Fife / Old house o' O'er ye slee-pin' Maggie / She moved through the fair / Durisdeer / Next market day / Watching the wheat / Twa corbies / My Irish jaunting car / O' a the airts / Wee Hughie / Gortnamona
CD _____ LCOM 9044
Lismor / Aug '91 / Lismor / Direct / Duncans / ADA.

LAUGHTER AND THE TEARS, THE
(Songs Of The Jacobite Risings - Vol. 2)
Wah widna' fecht for Charlie / Charlie is my darling / Hey Johnny Cope / Our ain coun-trie / Your welcome Charlie Stuart / Ken-more's up and awa' / Come o'er the stream Charlie / Highland laddie / There'll never be peace till Jamie comes hame / Wi' a hun-dred pipers / Twa bonnie maidens / Women are a' gane wud / Highland widows lament / Campbells are coming / Sound the pi-broch / We will take the good old way / Loch Lomond
CD _____ LCOM 6036
Lismor / Dec '93 / Lismor / Direct / Duncans / ADA.

MIST COVERED MOUNTAINS OF HOME, THE
Mist covered mountains of home / Bonnie Strathyre / Nicky Tams / Oor ain fireside / O gin I were whar' gadie rins / To peopie who have gardens / Amazing grace / Kelvin Grove / Corn rigs / Bonnie lass o' Fyvie / O gin I were a baron's heir / Wee cock sparra / Iona boat song / Pan drap song / Flowers of the forest / Scotland the brave
CD _____ LCOM 6043
Lismor / Nov '95 / Lismor / Direct / Duncans / ADA.

SCOTLAND THE BRAVE
Scotland the brave / Rowan tree / Song of the Clyde / Kismuil's galley / Highlands and lowlands / Northern lights of old Aberdeen / Loch Lomond / My love she's but a lassie yet / Bluebells of Scotland / Will ye no' come back again / Roamin' in the gloamin' / Annie Laurie / Gordon for me / Eriskay love lilt / Lewis bridal song / Marching through the heather / My heart's in the heather / Proud peaks of Scotland / Keep right on to the end of the road / Auld Lang syne
CD _____ PWK 115
Carlton Home Entertainment / Jun '89 / Carlton Home Entertainment.

SCOTTISH JOURNEY, A
CD _____ LISMOR 6037
Lismor / Jan '95 / Lismor / Direct / Duncans / ADA.

TODAY
Island of Tiree / Flower of Scotland / Braes o'Balquhidder / Old ballad (the farmer's daughter) / Northern lights of old Aberdeen / Rovan tree / Glencoe (the massacre of) / Wee place in the Highlands / Jean / Scot-land again / Thou Bonnie Wood O Craigielea / I Mingulay boat song / O' de muirly / Otar O' rabbie burns / Mull of the cool pens (Only on CD) / Eriskay love lilt (only on CD) / Ye banks and braes o' bonnie Doon (Only on CD)
CD _____ LCOM 9011
Lismor / Aug '91 / Lismor / Direct / Duncans / ADA.

McKenna, Dave

CELEBRATION OF HOAGY CARMICHAEL
Stardust / Riverboat shuffle / One morning in May / Moon country / Two sleepy people / Come easy, go easy love / Nearness of you / Lazybones / Sky lark / Georgia / Lazy river
CD _____ CCD 4227
Concord Jazz / May '94 / New Note.

**CONCORD DUO SERIES, VOL 2
(McKenna, Dave & Gray Sargent)**
Sheikh of Araby / Girl of my dreams / Red woods in the sunset / I'm gonna sit right down and write myself a letter / Blue and sentimental / I Deed I do / Time after time / time on my hands / Exactly like you
CD _____ CCD 4552
Concord Jazz / May '93 / New Note.

EASY STREET
Broadway / Basin Street blues / Street of dreams / Don't forget 127th street / Easy street / On Green Dolphin Street / On the street where you live / Cat's cradle / My honey's lovin' arms / When your lover is gone / Now that you're gone / After you've gone / Gone with the wind / Theodore the thumper

GIANT STRIDES
If dreams come true / Yardbird suite / Wind-song / Dave's blues / I've got the world on a string / Love letter / Cherry / Lulu's back in town / Walkin' my baby back home / Un-derdog / I've found a new baby
CD _____ CCD 4099
Concord Jazz / Feb '95 / New Note.

HANDFUL OF STARS, A
Estrela, estrela / Stella by starlight / Star eyes / Star kissed / Handful of stars / Star-dust / Song from the stars / Swinging in the stars / When you wish upon a star / Lost in the stars / I've told every little star / Stars fell on Alabama / Estrela, estrela (reprise)
CD _____ CCD 4580
Concord Jazz / Nov '93 / New Note.

HANGIN' OUT
Have you met Miss Jones / Just as though you were here / (Back home again in) Indi-ana / Splendid splinter / I'll be seeing you / Wrap your troubles in dreams (and dream your troubles away) / Easy living / Mixed emotions / When day is done / Thanks for the memories
CD _____ CCD 4123
Concord Jazz / Feb '92 / New Note.

MY FRIEND THE PIANO
Margie / Only trust your heart / Mean to me / Slowly / You're driving me crazy / Summer medley: guess I'll go back home this su / Indian Summer / Baby, baby, all the time / Always medley: It's always you / Always / This is always
CD _____ CCD 4313
Concord Jazz / Jul '87 / New Note.

NO BASS HIT
But not for me / If dreams come true / Long ago and far away / Drum boogie / I love you, samaritan / I'm gonna sit right down and write myself a letter / Easy to love / Get happy
CD _____ CCD 4097
Concord Jazz / Oct '91 / New Note.

NO MORE OUZO FOR PUZO (McKenna, Dave Quartet)
Look for the silver lining / Smile / For you, for me, for evermore / You and I / You brought a new kind of love to me / Talk of the town / Shake down the stars / Lone-some me / No more ouzo for Puzo / Keep going back to Joe's / Talk to me / Please don't talk about me when I'm gone
CD _____ CCD 365
Concord Jazz / Jan '89 / New Note.

SOLO PIANO
Chiara Scuro / Feb '95 / Jazz Music / Kudos.
CD _____ CRD 119

McKenna, Joe

AT HOME (McKenna, Joe & Antoinette)
CD _____ GRACC 27
Grasmere / May '94 / Target/BMG / Savoy.

HIS ORIGINAL RECORDINGS
CD _____ JMCK 1
John McKenna Society / Nov '94 / Direct.

MAGENTA MUSIC (McKenna, Joe & Antoinette)
CD _____ SHCD 79076
Shanachie / Jun '91 / Koch / ADA / Greensleeves.

McKenna, Mae

MIRAGE & REALITY
CD _____ HY 200121CD
Hypertension / Sep '93 / Total/BMG / Direct / ADA.

McKenna, Terence

**DREAM MATRIX TELEMETRY
(McKenna, Terence & Zuvuya)**
CD _____ DELECCD 2012
Delerium / Nov '93 / Vital.

McKennitt, Loreena

ELEMENTAL
CD _____ QRCD 101
Quinlan Road / Oct '94 / ADA / Direct.

MASK & THE MIRROR, THE
Mystic's dream / Bonny swans / Dark night of the soul / Marrakesh night market / Full circle / Santiago / Ce he mise le ulaingt / Two trees / Prospero's speech
CD _____ 450995296-2
WEA / May '95 / Warner Music.

PARALLEL DREAMS
CD _____ QRCD 103
Quinlan Road / Oct '94 / ADA / Direct.

TO DRIVE THE COLD WINTER AWAY
CD _____ QRCD 102
Quinlan Road / Dec '95 / ADA / Direct.

VISIT, THE
All souls night / Bonny Portmore / Between the shadows / Lady of Shalott / Green-

sleeves / Tango to evora / Courtyard lullaby / Old ways / Cymbeline
CD _____ 9031751512
WEA / Apr '95 / Warner Music.

WINTER GARDEN, A
CD _____ 0630122902
Quinlan Road / Dec '95 / ADA / Direct.

MacKenzie, Eilidh

RAIMENT OF THE TALE, THE
CD _____ COMD 2048
Temple / Feb '94 / CM / Duncans / ADA / Direct.

MacKenzie, Kate

LET THEM TALK
CD _____ RHRCD 66
Red House / May '95 / Koch / ADA.

Mackenzie, Malcolm M.

**MACKENZIES PIPES AND BANJO
(Mackenzie, Pipe Major Malcolm M.)**
CD _____ CDLOC 1059
Lochshore / Dec '90 / ADA / Direct / Duncans.

**MACKENZIES PIPES AND STRINGS
(Mackenzie, Pipe Major Malcolm M.)**
Maggie / Bunch of thyme / Silver threads among the gold / Canon in D / Annie Laurie / Rose of Tralee / Penhalonga piper / Way old friends do / MacKenzies tune / Danny boy / Scotland the brave / Isle of Arran / Mull of Kintyre / Will ye no' come back again / Amazing grace / Flower of Scotland / Bright eyes
CD _____ CDLOC 1033
Lochshore / Jun '87 / ADA / Direct / Duncans.

MacKenzie, Talitha

SOLAS
CD _____ TUGCD 1007
Riverboat / Mar '94 / New Note / Sterns.

McKenzie, Red

1935-37
Murder in the moonlight (it's love in the first degree) / Let's swing it / Double trouble / That's what you think / Georgia rockin' chair / Monday in Manhattan / Every now and then / Wouldn't it be a wonder / Sing me an old fashioned song / I'm building up to an awful let-down / Don't count your kisses (before you're kissed) / When love has gone / I don't know your name (but you're beauti-ful) / Moon rose / I can't get started (with you) / I can pull a rabbit out of my hat / Sweet Lorraine / Wanted / I cried for you / Trouble with me is you / Farewell my love / You're out of this world / Sail along silv'ry moon / Georgianna
CD _____ CBC 1019
Timeless Historical / Aug '94 / New Note / Pinnacle.

McKeown, Susan

BONES (McKeown, Susan & Chanting House)
CD _____ SNG 701CD
Sheila-Na-Gig / Nov '95 / ADA.

Mackie Ranks

LICK OUT
CD _____ HCD 7001
Hightone / Aug '94 / ADA / Koch.

McKillop, Jim

TRADITIONAL IRISH FIDDLE AND PIANO (McKillop, Jim & Josephine Keegan)
CD _____ PTICD 1045CD
Pure Traditional Irish / Jul '95 / ADA.

McKinley, Ray

**BACK TO THE MILLER SOUND
(McKinley, Ray & New Glenn Miller Orchestra)**
Jeep Jockey jump / On the street where you live / Am I blue / Howdy friends / Laura / Here we go again / I'm thrilled
CD _____ DAWE 46
Magic / Nov '93 / Jazz Music / Swift / Wel-lard / Cadillac / Harmonia Mundi.

BORDERLINE (McKinley, Ray & His Orchestra)
Sand storm / Tumble bug / Hangover Square / Comin' out / I've got a right to sing the blues / Mint julep / Borderline / How by friends / Atomic era / Chief / Over the rain-bow / Jiminy Crickets
CD _____ SV 0203
Savoy Jazz / Apr '93 / Conifer / ADA.

CLASS OF '49, THE
It's only a paper moon / Blue moon / Stom-pin' at the savoy / Stardust / Laura / How high the moon / Lullabye in rhythm / Harlem nocturne / I gotta right to sing the blues / Don't be that way
CD _____ HEPCD 4
Hep / Dec '95 / Cadillac / Jazz Music / New Note / Wellard.

JAZZ PORTRAIT
CD _____ CD 14586
Complete / Nov '95 / THE.

McKinney's Cotton Pickers

1928-29
CD _____ CLASSICS 609
Classics / Oct '92 / Discovery / Jazz Music.

MCKINNEY'S COTTON PICKERS - 1929-30
CD _____ CLASSICS 625
Classics / '92 / Discovery / Jazz Music.

MacKintosh, Iain

RISKS AND ROSES
If I had a boat / Remember when the music / I wish I was in Glasgow / Cheeky young lad / Rats are winning / King of Rome / Flowers are red / My home town / Roses from the wrong man / Acceptable risks / Dill pickle rag / Annie McKelvie / Kilkelly / Hug song
CD _____ CDTRAX 043
Greentrax / Feb '91 / Conifer / Duncans / ADA / Direct.

STAGE BY STAGE (MacKintosh, Iain & Brian McNeil)
Plainstanes / Glasgow magistrate / Wind and rain / Sea maiden / Balkan hills / Bonny wee lassie who never said no / Holyrood house / Generations of change / Dallas do-mestic / Smoky mokes / Beautiful dreamer / Traveller's moon / Summer of love / Re-cruited collier / Tank / Cronin's / Fisher-man's lilt / What do you do with what you've got / Black swan / Roslin Castle / You can't take it with you when you go
CD _____ CDTRAX 101
Greentrax / Nov '95 / Conifer / Duncans / ADA / Direct.

MacKintosh, Ken

BLUES SKIES
CD _____ DLD 1014
Dance & Listen / '92 / Savoy.

McKnight, Brian

I REMEMBER YOU
CD _____ 5284302
Talkin' Loud / Aug '95 / PolyGram.

McKoy

FULL CIRCLE
CD _____ TUMCD 1
Right Track / Apr '94 / Jetstar.

McKuen, Rod

FRENCH CONNECTION, A
CD _____ 12444
Laserlight / Mar '95 / Target/BMG.

GREATEST HITS: ROD MCKUEN
CD _____ BX 408-2
BR Music / Mar '94 / Target/BMG.

ROD MCKUEN SINGS JACQUES BREL
CD _____ BX 4072
BR Music / Mar '94 / Target/BMG.

McKusick, Hal

EAST COAST JAZZ (McKusick, Hal Quartet)
CD _____ FSCD 41
Fresh Sound / Oct '90 / Jazz Music / Discovery.

McLachlan, Sarah

FUMBLING TOWARDS ECSTASY
Possession / Wait / Plenty / Good enough / Mary / Elsewhere / Circle / Ice / Hold on / Ice cream / Fear / Fumbling towards ecstasy
CD _____ 74321190322
Arista / Oct '94 / BMG.

SOLACE
Drawn to the rhythm / Into the fire / Path of thorns / I will not forget you / Lost / Back door man / Shelter / Black / Home / Mercy / Wear your love like heaven
CD _____ 261.955
Arista / Mar '92 / BMG.

McLain, Raymond W.

PLACE OF MY OWN, A
CD _____ FF 587CD
Flying Fish / Feb '93 / Roots / CM / Direct / ADA.

McLain, Tommy

SWEET DREAMS
Sweet dreams / Before I grow too old / Think it over / Faithfully yours / There's no more / Try to find another man / When a man loves a woman / After loving you / Trib-ute to Fats Domino / Going home / Poor me / Going to the river / Just because / Legend in my time / Together again / I thought I'd never fall in love again / So sad (to watch good love go bad) / Sticks and stones / Mu heart remembers
CD _____ CDCH 285

Ace / Jan '90 / Pinnacle / Cadillac / Complete/Pinnacle.

McLaren, Malcolm

DUCK ROCK
Obatala / Buffalo gals / Merengue / Punk it up / Legba / Jive my baby / Song for Chango / Soweto / World's famous / Duck for the oyster / Double Dutch
CD _____ MMCD 1
Charisma / Apr '88 / EMI.

PARIS
CD _____ NOMC 100
No / Aug '94 / 3MV / Sony.

ROUND THE OUTSIDE (McLaren, Malcolm & World Famous Supreme Team)
CD _____ CDV 2646
Virgin / Apr '92 / EMI.

WALTZ DARLING
House of the blue Danube / Waltz darling / Deep in vogue / Algernon's simply awfully good at ... / Something's jumping in your shirt / Shall we dance / Call a wave / I like you in velvet
CD _____ 4607362
Epic / Jul '89 / Sony.

McLaughlin, John

AFTER THE RAIN
CD _____ 5274672
Verve / Jun '95 / PolyGram.

APOCALYPSE (Mahavishnu Orchestra)
CD _____ 4670922
Sony Jazz / Jan '95 / Sony.

BEST OF SHAKTI, THE (McLaughlin, John/Shankar & Zakir Hussain)
CD _____ MRCD 1010
Koch / Jan '95 / Koch.

BEST OF THE MAHAVISHNU ORCHESTRA (Mahavishnu Orchestra)
Birds of fire / Open country joy / Wings of Karma / Sister Andrea / Dance of Maya / Meeting of the spirits / Lila's dance / Be happy
CD _____ 4682262
Sony Jazz / Jan '94 / Sony.

BETWEEN NOTHING AND ETERNITY LIVE (Mahavishnu Orchestra)
CD _____ BGOCD 31
Beat Goes On / Dec '88 / Pinnacle.

BIRDS OF FIRE (McLaughlin, John & Mahavishnu Orchestra)
Birds of fire / Miles beyond / Celestial terrestrial commuters / Sapphire bullets of pure love / Thousand Island park / Hope / One word / Sanctuary / Open country / Resolution
CD _____ 4682242
Columbia / Jan '92 / Sony.

COLLECTION: JOHN McLAUGHLIN
CD _____ CCSCD 305
Castle / Oct '91 / BMG.

ELECTRIC DREAMS (McLaughlin, John & The One Truth Band)
Guardian angels / Miles Davis / Electric dreams / Electric sighs / Love and understanding / Desire and the comforter / Singing earth / Dark prince / Unknown dissident
CD _____ 4722102
Sony Jazz / Jan '95 / Sony.

ELECTRIC GUITARIST
New York on my mind / Friendship / Every tear from every eye / Do you hear the voices you left behind / Are you the one / Pehnomenon / Compulsion / My foolish heart
CD _____ 4670932
Columbia / Jan '95 / Sony.

EXTRAPOLATION
Extrapolation / It's funny / Arjen's bag / Pete the poet / This is for us to share / Spectrum / Blinky's beam / Really you know / Two for two / Peace piece
CD _____ 841598-2
Polydor / Oct '90 / PolyGram.

INNER WORLDS
CD _____ 4769052
Sony Jazz / Jan '95 / Sony.

LIVE AT THE ROYAL FESTIVAL HALL
CD _____ 834 436 2
Mercury / Apr '90 / PolyGram.

MY GOAL'S BEYOND (McLaughlin, John & Mahavishnu Orchestra)
CD _____ RCD 10051
Rykodisc / May '92 / Vital / ADA.

PASSION GRACE AND FIRE (McLaughlin, John/Al Di Meola/Paco De Lucia)
Aspen / Orient blues / Chiquito / Sichia / David / Passion, grace and fire
CD _____ 811 334 2
Mercury / Jun '83 / PolyGram.

SHAKTI & JOHN McLAUGHLIN (McLaughlin, John & Shakti)
CD _____ 4679052
Sony Jazz / Jan '95 / Sony.

TIME REMEMBERED
CD _____ 591861-2
Verve / Feb '94 / PolyGram.

TOKYO LIVE
CD _____ 521870-2
Verve / May '94 / PolyGram.

VISIONS OF THE EMERALD BEYOND (Mahavishnu Orchestra)
CD _____ 4679042
Sony Jazz / Jan '95 / Sony.

WHERE FORTUNE SMILES
Glancing backwards (For junior) / Earth bound hearts / Where fortune smiles / New place, old place / Hope
CD _____ BGOCD 191
Beat Goes On / Jun '93 / Pinnacle.

McLaughlin, Pat

GET OUT AND STAY OUT
CD _____ DOS 7012
Dos / Oct '95 / CM / Direct / ADA.

UNGLUED
CD _____ DOSCD 7005
Dos / Apr '94 / CM / Direct / ADA.

MacLean, Dougie

CRAIGIE DHU
Gin I were a baron's heir / Read for the storm / It was a' for our rightful king (Patsy Seddon: clarsach.) / High flying seagull / Edmonton airbus / Craigie Dhu / Bonnie Bessie Logan / Seanair's song / It fascinates me / Tullochgorum / Caledonia
CD _____ DUNCD 001
Dunkeld / Feb '90 / Direct / ADA / CM.

DOUGIE MACLEAN'S CALEDONIA (The Plant Life Years)
CD _____ OSMOCD 004
Osmosys / Oct '95 / Direct / ADA.

FIDDLE
Osprey / Bob MacIntosh Atholl Arms kurring-gai chase / Farewell to Craigie Dhu / Tattie ball / When are you coming over / Mr. and Mrs. MacLean of Snaigow / Roy Ashby's buckny burn / One summer's morning / Ferry / Spoutwells riechip leduckie / Centre / Gin I were a baron's heir
CD _____ DUNCD 002
Dunkeld / Oct '93 / Direct / ADA / CM.

INDIGENOUS
CD _____ DUNCD 015
Dunkeld / Feb '89 / Direct / ADA / CM.

MARCHING MYSTERY
CD _____ DUN 019CD
Dunkeld / Jul '94 / Direct / ADA / CM.

REAL ESTATE
CD _____ DUNCD 008
Dunkeld / Nov '92 / Direct / ADA / CM.

SEARCH, THE
CD _____ DUNCD 011
Dunkeld / Nov '*? / Direct / ADA / CM.

SINGING LAND
Singing land / Desperate man / This love will carry / Kelphope glen / Another story / Bonnie woods o'Hatton / Other side / Tumbling down / Guillotine release / Goodnight and joy
CD _____ DUNCD 004
Dunkeld / Oct '93 / Direct / ADA / CM.

SUNSET SONG
CD _____ DUNCD 17
Dunkeld / Oct '93 / Direct / ADA / CM.

TRIBUTE
CD _____ DUNCD 020
Dunkeld / Nov '95 / Direct / ADA / CM.

WHITEWASH
CD _____ DUNCD 010
Dunkeld / Jul '90 / Direct / ADA / CM.

McLean, Andy

ANDY'S THEME
Two hearts / Funny / Saliya / Take 5 and 6 / Please stay / Andy's theme / Is this for real / Make it last / Summer song / Early bird
CD _____ CALLCD 001
Callisto / Sep '94 / Timewarp.

McLean, Bitty

NATURAL HIGH
CD _____ BRILCD 2
Brilliant / Jul '95 / 3MV.

McLean, Don

AMERICAN PIE
American pie / Till tomorrow / Vincent / Crossroads / Winterwood / Empty chairs / Everybody loves me / Fatima / Grave / Babylon
CD _____ CDFA 3023
Fame / May '88 / EMI.

BEST OF DON McLEAN
American pie / Castles in the air (1981 version) / Dreidel / Winterwood / Everyday / Sister Fatima / Empty chairs / Birthday song / Wonderful baby / La la I love you / Vincent / Crossroads / And I love you so / Fools paradise / If we try / Mountains of Mourne / Grave / Respectable / Going for the gold / Crying
CD _____ CDMTL 1065
EMI Manhattan / Dec '91 / EMI.

DON McLEAN
If we try / Narcissima / Dreidel / Bronco Bill's lament / Birthday song / Pride parade / More you pay (The more it's worth) / Falling through time / On the Amazon / Oh my what a shame
CD _____ BGOCD 246
Beat Goes On / Mar '95 / Pinnacle.

HOMELESS BROTHER
Winter has me in its grip / La la means I love you / Homeless brother / Sunshine life for me / Legend of Andrew McCrew / Wonderful baby / You have lived / Great big man / Tangled / Crying in the chapel / Did you know
CD _____ BGOCD 247
Beat Goes On / Oct '94 / Pinnacle.

PLAYIN' FAVORITES
Mule skinner blues / Bill Cheatham = Old Joe Clark / Love O love / Fool's paradise / Mountain's O'Mourne / Lovesick blues / Sitting on top the world / Ancient history / Everyday / Over the mountains / Living with the blues / Happy trails
CD _____ BGOCD 21
Beat Goes On / Apr '95 / Pinnacle.

RIVER OF LOVE, THE
CD _____ CURCD 19
Curb / Nov '95 / PolyGram.

SOLO
Magdalene lane / Masters of war / Wonderful baby / Where were you baby / Empty chairs / Geordie's lost his penker / Babylon / I love you so / Mactavish is dead / Cripple creek/Muleskinner blues / Great big man / Bronco Bill's lament / Happy trails / Circus song / Birthday song / On the Amazon / American pie / Over the waterfall/Arkansas traveller / Homeless brother / Castles in the air / Three flights up / Lovesick blues / Winter has me in it's grip / Legend of Andrew McCrew / Dreidel / Vincent / Till tomorrow
CD _____ BGOCD 300
Beat Goes On / Sep '95 / Pinnacle.

TAPESTRY
Castles in the air / General store / Magdalene Lane / Tapestry / Respectable / Orphans of wealth / Three flights up / I love you so / Bad girl / Circus song / No reason for your dreams
CD _____ BGOCD 232
Beat Goes On / Jun '94 / Pinnacle.

McLean, Jackie

DESTINATION OUT
Love and hate / Esoteric / Kahlil the prophet / Riff raff
CD _____ CDP 8320872
Blue Note / May '95 / EMI.

DR. JACKIE (McLean, Jackie Quartet)
CD _____ SCCD 36005
Steeplechase / Oct '90 / Impetus.

LET FREEDOM RING
Melody for Melonae / I'll keep loving you / Rene / Omega
CD _____ BNZ 58
Blue Note / May '87 / EMI.

NEW YORK CALLING
CD _____ SCCD 31023
Steeplechase / Jul '88 / Impetus.

RHYTHM OF THE EARTH
CD _____ 5139162
Verve / Apr '92 / PolyGram.

McLean, John

MEN ARE LOVERS TOO
Life after you / Can't hold on / Time for love / Playboy / Love at first sight / Spreading rumours / Proud to be your lover / Never risk / We both belong to someone else / Dedication of love
CD _____ ARICD 104
Ariwa Sounds / Oct '94 / Jetstar / SRD.

MacLellan, Colin

WORLD'S GREATEST PIPERS VOL. 11
2/4 Marches / Strathspeys and reels #2 / Retreat marches / 6/8 Marches / Slow air and jigs / March, strathspey and reel / Hornpipes / Slow air / Strathspeys and reels / Piobaireachd
CD _____ LCOM 5219
Lismor / Jan '93 / Lismor / Direct / Duncans / ADA.

MacLellan, John A.

SCOTTISH BAGPIPES (MacLellan, Pipe Major John A.)
CD _____ OSS 113CD
Ossian / Apr '94 / ADA / Direct / CM.

McLennan, Grant

FIREBOY
CD _____ BBQCD 127
Beggars Banquet / Mar '93 / Warner Music / Disc.

HORSEBREAKER STAR
CD _____ BEGA 162CD
Beggars Banquet / Sep '95 / Warner Music / Disc.

SIMONE & PERRY
CD _____ BBQ 57CD
Beggars Banquet / Jun '95 / Warner Music / Disc.

WATERSHED
When word gets around
Haven't I been a fool / Haunted house / Stones for you / Easy come, easy go / Black mule / Putting the wheel back on / You can't have everything / Sally's revolution / Broadway bride / Just get that straight / Dream about tomorrow
CD _____ BEGACD 118
Beggars Banquet / Jun '91 / Warner Music / Disc.

MacLeod, Doug

54TH AND VERMONT
CD _____ 900817
Line / Feb '95 / CM / Grapevine / ADA / Conifer / Direct.

AIN'T THE BLUES EVIL
CD _____ VCD 3409
Volt / Apr '92 / Pinnacle.

COME TO FIND
CD _____ AQ 1027
Audioquest / May '95 / New Note.

NO ROAD BACK HOME
CD _____ HCD 8002
Hightone / Jun '94 / ADA / Koch.

WOMAN IN THE STREET
Smoke gets a / Workin' man blues / Highway they called the blues / I might bend (but I won't break) / I think you're foolin' me / King Freddie / Still some smoke / Splain it to me / Send the soul on home / Woman in the street / One good women / Church street Serenade
CD _____ 900444
Line / May '95 / CM / Grapevine / ADA / Conifer / Direct.

MacLeod, Jim

CEILIDH
CD _____ CDITV 604
Scotdisc / Oct '95 / Duncans / Ross / Conifer.

JIM MACLEOD'S DANCE PARTY FAVOURITES
Bluebell polka / Will you save the last dance just for me / Just for old times sake / Come by the hills / Dashing white sergeant / Dashing white sergeant (encore) / Do you think you could love me again / Amazing grace / Pittenweem Jo / Shetland reels / Cruising down the river / Loch Lomond / After all these years / Gay Gordons / Gay Gordons (encore) / Leaving Dundee / Shufflin' Sammy
CD _____ CD ITV 422
Scotdisc / Dec '86 / Duncans / Ross / Conifer.

JIM MACLEOD'S HOGMANAY PARTY
Auld lang syne / Gay Gordons / Waltz / Strip the willow / Whistle and I'll dance / Bonnie lass o'Bon Accord / St. Bernard's waltz / Dashing white sergeant / My love is like a red red rose / Pipe selection / Barn dance / Crooked bawbee / Military two step
CD _____ CD ITV 444
Scotdisc / Dec '87 / Duncans / Ross / Conifer.

LAND OF MACLEOD, THE (MacLeod, Jim & His Band)
CD _____ CDITV 548
Scotdisc / Aug '91 / Duncans / Ross / Conifer.

PLAY SELECTED SCOTTISH COUNTRY DANCES (MacLeod, Jim & His Band)
CD _____ CDITV 491
Scotdisc / Oct '89 / Duncans / Ross / Conifer.

ROAD AND MILES, THE (MacLeod, Jim & His Band)
CD _____ CDITV 583
Scotdisc / Nov '94 / Duncans / Ross / Conifer.

SCOTTISH TOUR, A (MacLeod, Jim & His Band)
CD _____ CDITV 565
Scotdisc / Aug '93 / Duncans / Ross / Conifer.

WELCOME TO MY WORLD
CD _____ CDITV 461
Scotdisc / Nov '89 / Duncans / Ross / Conifer.

MacLeod, John

MACLEOD OF DUNVEGAN
Scots wha hae / Ae fond kiss / Birlinn ghoraidh chro'bhain / Barbara Allen / Bonnie Strathyre / Mo nighean chiuin donn / Ca' the yowes / Bonnie Earl O'Moray / Ho ro mo nighean donn bhoid heach / Maw neil / Maiden of Morven / Cha tillmaccrimmon / O my love is like a red red rose / Mo run geal dileas / O'er the moor / Loch Lomond / Soinidh / Skye boat song / Tog orm mo phiob
CD _____ LCOM 5206

Lismor / Mar '92 / Lismor / Direct / Duncans / ADA.

McLeod, Enos Genius

ENOS IN DUB
CD _____ CEND 2004
Century / Feb '96 / Total/BMG / Jetstar.

GOODIES BEST
CD _____ CEND 2003
Century / Feb '96 / Total/BMG / Jetstar.

McLeod, Rory

ANGRY LOVE
Farewell welfare / Shirley's her name / Stop the apartheid fascists / Pauline's song / Wind is getting stronger / Angry love / Walking towards each other / Passing the pain down / Criminals of hunger
CD _____ COOKCD 051
Cooking Vinyl / Feb '95 / Vital.

FOOTSTEPS AND HEARTBEATS
Love like a rock (in a stormy sea) / Till I don't know who I am / Collectorman / Moments shared / Wandering fool / Take me home / Singing copper / Kind of loneliness / Mariachis love song
CD _____ COOKCD 018
Cooking Vinyl / Feb '95 / Vital.

KICKING THE SAWDUST
Baksheesh dance / Huge sky / Rip Van Winkle / Kicking the sawdust / Dad's dance song / Sssh baby / Interrogations and confessions / Dance of measureless love / Hug you like a mountain / In the ghetto of our love / When children starve in peacetime / Harmonikikas dreams / Last tree / Divorcee blues / Old brigades song / Commentator cried / Hymn for her
CD _____ COOKCD 067
Cooking Vinyl / Mar '94 / Vital.

TRAVELLING HOME
CD _____ COOKCD 048
Cooking Vinyl / Feb '95 / Vital.

McLeod, Zan

RING SESSIONS, THE (McLeod, Zan & James Kelly)
CD _____ SPIN 99CD
Spin / Jan '96 / Direct / ADA.

McLoughlin, Noel

20 BEST OF IRELAND
CD _____ EUCD 1079
ARC / '89 / ARC Music / ADA.

20 BEST OF SCOTLAND
CD _____ EUCD 1080
ARC / '89 / ARC Music / ADA.

BEST OF IRELAND
CD _____ EUCD 1111
ARC / '91 / ARC Music / ADA.

CHRISTMAS AND WINTER SONGS FROM IRELAND
CD _____ EUCD 1086
ARC / '91 / ARC Music / ADA.

MacLure, Pinkie

FAVOURITE
CD _____ PILLCD 7
Placebo / May '95 / Disc.

THIS DIRTY LIFE
CD _____ BND 5 CD
One Little Indian / Feb '90 / Pinnacle.

MacMahon, Tony

I GCNOC NA GRÁII (MacMahon, Tony & Noel Hill)
CD _____ CEFCD 114
Gael Linn / Jan '94 / Roots / CM / Direct / ADA.

TONY MACMAHON
CD _____ SHCD 34006
Claddagh / May '93 / ADA / Direct.

TRADITIONAL IRISH ACCORDION
CD _____ CEFCD 033
Gael Linn / Jan '94 / Roots / CM / Direct / ADA.

McManus, Tony

TONY MCMANUS
Doherty's / Return to Milltown / Tommy Peoples / Sweetness of Mary / Piper's bonnet / Emigrant's farewell / Flanagan Brothers jig / Dermot Byrnes / Miss Sarah Mcfadyen / Jackie Coleman's / Millner's daughter / Rakish Paddy / Connor Dunn's / Breizh / Duck / Seagull / Humours of Barrack Street / Letterkenny blacksmith / Ar bhruach na laoi / Snowy path / Harper's chair / Gavotte de marcel / Dans fisel / Hector the hero / Girls at Martinfield / Shannon reel / What a wonderful world / Charlie Hunter's / Humours of Tulla
CD _____ CDTRAX 096
Greentrax / Dec '95 / Conifer / Duncans / ADA / Direct.

MacMaster, Natalie

FIT AS A FIDDLE
CD _____ NMAS 1972CD
CBC Maritimes / Jul '95 / ADA.

MacMathúna, Pádraic

HIVES OF HONEYED SOUND
CD _____ CEFCD 157
Gael Linn / Jan '94 / Roots / CM / Direct / ADA.

McMeen, El

IRISH GUITAR ENCORES
CD _____ SHCD 97017
Shanachie / Apr '92 / Koch / ADA / Greensleeves.

OF SOUL AND SPIRIT
CD _____ SHCD 97012
Shanachie / Jun '91 / Koch / ADA / Greensleeves.

McMurdo, Dave

LIVE AT MONTREAL BISTRO (McMurdo, Dave Jazz Orchestra)
CD _____ SKCD 2-2029
Sackville / Jun '93 / Swift / Jazz Music / Jazz Horizons / Cadillac / CM.

McNabb, Ian

HEAD LIKE A ROCK
Fire inside my soul / You must be prepared to dream / Child inside a father / Still got the fever / Potency / Go into the light / As a life goes by / Sad strange solitary catholic mystic / This time is forever / May you always
CD _____ 5222982
This Way Up / May '94 / PolyGram / SRD.

TRUTH AND BEAUTY
(I go) My own way / These are the days / Great dreams of heaven / Truth and beauty / I'm game / If love was like guitars / Story of my life / That's why I believe / Trip with me / Make love to you / Presence of the one
CD _____ 5143782
Phonogram / Jan '93 / PolyGram.

McNally, John

EVERGREENS
CD _____ EMPRCD 561
Emporio / Mar '95 / THE / Disc / CM.

McNally, Larry John

VIBROLUX
CD _____ DIGIT 5679152
Dig It / Dec '95 / Direct.

MacNamara, Mary

TRADITIONAL MUSIC FROM EAST CLARE
Cailleach an airgid / Kerfunten jig / Rolling in the barrel / Tap room / Earl's chair / Humours of Tullycrine / Mikey Callaghan's / Pigeon on the gate / Lad O'Beirne's / John Naughton's / Reel with the birl / Paddy Lynn's delight / Connie Hogan's / Kitty goes milking / Killavil jig / Have a drink with me / Toss the feathers / Boys of Ballisodare / Fisherman's lilt / My love is in America / Rooms of Doogh / Walls of Liscarroll / Caoilte mountains / Green gowned lass / John Naughton's jigs / McGreevy's favourite / Miss McGuinness / Sweetheart reel / Maghera mountain / Fluomours of Castlefin / Glen of Ahelow / Killarney boys of pleasure
CD _____ CC 60CD
Claddagh / Oct '94 / ADA / Direct.

MacNamara, Paddy

IRISH PARTY
CD _____ SOW 90124
Sounds Of The World / Apr '94 / Target/BMG.

MacNamara, Pat

TWO SIDES OF PAT MAC, THE
CD _____ GTDCD 006
GTD / Jan '95 / Else / ADA.

McNeely, Big Jay

BIG 'J' IN 3-D
Goof / Ice water / Big Jay shuffle / Rock candy / Whipped cream / Hot cinders / 3-D / Hardtack / Nervous man / Mule milk / Let's work / Beachcomber
CD _____ KCD 650
King/Paddle Wheel / Mar '90 / New Note.

BLUES AT DAYBREAK (McNeel, Big Jay & C. Rannenberg)
CD _____ BEST 1018CD
Acoustic Music / Nov '93 / ADA.

McNeely, James

LIVE AT MAYBECK RECITAL HALL, VOL. 20
There will never be another you / Zingaro / Bye ya / Round Midnight / Touch / All the

things you are / Body and soul / Breaking up breaking out
CD _____ CCD 4522
Concord Jazz / Sep '92 / New Note.

PLOT THICKENS, THE
CD _____ MCD 5378
Muse / Sep '92 / New Note / CM.

MacNeil, Flora

CRAOBH NAN UBHAL
CD _____ COMD 1002
Temple / Jan '94 / CM / Duncans / ADA / Direct.

McNeil, Rita

FLYING ON YOUR OWN
Flying on your own / Neon city / She's called Nova Scotia / Baby baby / Leave her memory / Fast train to Tokyo / Everybody / Used to you / Loser (when it comes to love) / Realised your dreams
CD _____ 8434232
Polydor / Jul '92 / PolyGram.

HOME I'LL BE
CD _____ 5112772
Polydor / Jul '92 / PolyGram.

REASON TO BELIEVE
Walk on through / Two steps from broken / City child / Doors of the cemetary / Reason to believe / When the loving is through / Causing the fall / Music's going round again / Sound your own horn / Working man / Good friends
CD Set _____ D 5177793
LPO / Oct '94 / Total/BMG.

WORKING MAN (The Best Of Rita MacNeil)
CD _____ 5178612
Polydor / Sep '90 / PolyGram.

McNeil, John

EMBARKATION (McNeil, John Quintet)
CD _____ SCCD 31099
Steeplechase / Oct '95 / Impetus.

THINGS WE DID LAST SUMMER
CD _____ SCCD 31231
Steeplechase / Jan '88 / Impetus.

McNeill, Brian

BACK O' THE NORTH WIND, THE (Tales Of The Scots In America)
Back o' the North wind / Entail / Strong women rule us with their tears / Rock and the tide / Destitution road / Muir and the master builder / Atlantic reels / Best o' the barley / Ewen and the gold / Drive the golden spike / Lang Johnnie More / Steel man / Bridal boat
CD _____ CDTRAX 047
Greentrax / Sep '91 / Conifer / Duncans / ADA / Direct.

BUSKER AND THE DEVIL'S ONLY DAUGHTER, THE
CD _____ COMD 2042
Temple / Feb '94 / CM / Duncans / ADA / Direct.

HORSES FOR COURSES
CD _____ CDTRAX 054
Greentrax / Mar '94 / Conifer / Duncans / ADA / Direct.

MONKSGATF
CD _____ CDTRAX 062
Greentrax / May '93 / Conifer / Duncans / ADA / Direct.

NO GODS
No gods and precious few heroes / Miss Michison regrets / Any Mick'll do / Drover's road / Breton wedding march / Trains and my grandfather / Tommy Sheridan's / Annie Lawson / Jocky's treble tops / Assynt crofters / Montrose / Inside the whale / Princess Augusta / Fighter / Alison Hargreaves / Veillon's / Young master Haigh / Steady as she goes / Bring back the wolf
CD _____ CDTRAX 098
Greentrax / Dec '95 / Conifer / Duncans / ADA / Direct.

McNeir, Ronnie

LOVE SUSPECT
Love suspect / Lately / Summertime medley / Sexy Mama / Everybody's in a hurry / I'll be loving you / Follow your heart / Tying to keep my heart / Please come and be with me
CD _____ EXCDP 1
Debut / Jun '93 / Pinnacle /3MV / Sony.

RARE MCNEIR
Baby I know / Different kind of love / Lonely superstar / Southern pearl / Ain't no woman like my baby / This is my prayer / I want to thank you / Strong for each other / Good side of your love / Your best friend and me / I'll come running back / Remember baby / I got someone
CD _____ ATCD 024
About Time / Aug '95 / Target/BMG.

McPartland, Jimmy

THAT HAPPY DIXIELAND (McPartland, Jimmy & his Dixielanders)
High society / That's a plenty / Way down yonder in New Orleans / Muskrat ramble / When the saints go marching in / Darktown strutter's ball / Original Dixieland one-step / Fidgety feet / South Rampart Street parade / Farewell blues
CD _____ 74321 18518-2
RCA / Jul '94 / BMG.

McPartland, Marian

AMBIANCE
What is this thing called love / Aspen / Sounds like seven / Ambiance / Rime / Three little words / Hide and seek with the bombay bicycle club / Afterglow / Lost one / Wisdom of the heart / Glimpse
CD _____ TJA 10029
Jazz Alliance / Feb '96 / New Note.

AT THE FESTIVAL
I love you / Willow weep for me / Windows / In the days of our love / Cotton tail / Here's that rainy day / On green dolphin street / Oleo
CD _____ CCD 4118
Concord Jazz / Oct '94 / New Note.

AT THE HICKORY HOUSE
I hear music / Tickle toe / Street of dreams / How long has this been going on / Let's call the whole thing off / Lush life / Mad about the boy / Love you madly / Skylark / Ja da / I've told every little star / Moon song
CD _____ JASCD 312
Jasmine / Aug '95 / Wellard / Swift / Conifer / Cadillac / Magnum Music Group.

FROM THIS MOMENT ON
From this moment on / Emily / Sweet and lovely / Ambiance / You and the night and the music / If you could see me now / Lullaby of the leaves / No greater love / Polka dots and moonbeams
CD _____ CCD 4086
Concord Jazz / Aug '91 / New Note.

GREAT BRITAINS (McPartland, Marian & George Shearing)
It might as well be Spring / Gypsy in my soul / Strike up the band / Love is here to stay / Love for sale / Yesterdays / All the things you are / Sweet and lovely / When darkness falls / So rare / Bop's your uncle / Sophisticated lady / Buccaneer's bounce / Cozy's bop / Have you met Miss Jones
CD _____ SV 0160
Savoy Jazz / Apr '92 / Conifer / ADA.

IN MY LIFE
CD _____ CCD 4561
Concord Jazz / May '94 / New Note.

LOOKING FOR A BOY (McPartland, Marian & Barbara Carroll/Adelaide Robbins)
Great day / Everything but you / Gentleman is a dope / Looking for a boy / You stepped out of a dream / Dancing on the ceiling / Liza / September song / Laura / Embraceable you / Barbara's Carroll / Puppet that dances be-bop
CD _____ SV 0226
Savoy Jazz / Oct '93 / Conifer / ADA.

MARIAN MCPARTLAND IN CONCERT
Gypsy in my soul / These foolish things / Get happy / Strike up the band / Foggy day / Lady is a tramp / I've got the world on a string / Manhattan / Aunt Hagar's blues / Four brothers / Once in a while
CD _____ SV 0202
Savoy Jazz / Apr '92 / Conifer / ADA.

MARIAN MCPARTLAND PLAYS THE MUSIC OF ALEC WILDER
Jazz waltz for a friend / Why / While we're young / Lullaby for a lady / Inner circle / I'll be around / Trouble is a man / Homework / Where are the good companions / It's so peaceful in the country
CD _____ TJA 10016
Jazz Alliance / Oct '92 / New Note.

PERSONAL CHOICE
I hear a rhapsody / Meditation / In your own sweet way / Sleeping bee / I'm old fashioned / Whon the sun comes out / Tricrotism / Melancholy mood
CD _____ CCD 4202
Concord Jazz / Mar '87 / New Note.

PIANO JAZZ
Snapper / Come Sunday / There'll be other times / Mumbles / Simple waltz / Michelle / Memories of you / Wham
CD _____ TJA 12009
Jazz Alliance / Aug '94 / New Note.

PIANO JAZZ (McPartland, Marian & Stanley Cowell)
Top of your head blues / Stella by starlight / Round Midnight / Juan Valdez / Watergate blues / Equipoise / You took advantage of me / God bless the child / Cherokee
CD _____ TJA 12013
Jazz Alliance / Feb '95 / New Note.

PIANO JAZZ (McPartland, Marian & Mercer Ellington)
C Jam blues / Kinda dukish / Caravan / Prelude to a kiss / Chelsea bridge / Moon mist / Thing's ain't waht they used to be / Portrait of Mercer Ellington / Solitude

CD _____ TJA 12014
Jazz Alliance / Feb '95 / New Note.

PIANO JAZZ (MacPartland, Marian & Benny Carter)
Easy money / Faraway / Blues in my heart / Lonely woman / Only trust your heart / Evening star / Kiss from you / Key largo / Summer serenade / When lights are low
CD _____ TJA 12015
Jazz Alliance / Feb '95 / New Note.

PIANO JAZZ (McPartland, Marian & Jack DeJohnette)
Freddie freeloader / I loves you Porgy / It could happen to you / Alice in wonderland / Ambiance / Blue in green / Silver hollow / Mr. PC
CD _____ TJA 12018
Jazz Alliance / May '95 / New Note.

PIANO JAZZ (McPartland, Marian & Jess Stacy)
Dancing fool / Lover man / Oh baby / Keepin' out of mischief now / Improv in A minor / Autumn of New York / I would do most anything for you / Moon mist / Heavy hearted blues / St. Louis blues
CD _____ TJA 12017
Jazz Alliance / May '95 / New Note.

PIANO JAZZ (McPartland, Marian & Mary Lou Williams)
Space playing blues / Baby man / What's your story Morning Glory / Scratchin' in the gravel / Medi no 2 / Rosa Mae / Caravan / I can't get started (with you) / Jeep is jumpin' / Exit playing
CD _____ TJA 12019
Jazz Alliance / Jul '95 / New Note.

PIANO JAZZ (McPartland, Marian & Kenny Burrell)
Listen to the dawn / Round midnight / I'm old fashioned / All too soon / Don't worry 'bout me / Spring can really hang you up the most / I'm just a lucky so and so / Raincheck
CD _____ TJA 12021
Jazz Alliance / Aug '95 / New Note.

PIANO JAZZ (McPartland, Marian & Amina Claudine)
B I / Mood indigo / Windows / So what / Call him / Do you wanna be saved / Free impro / Have mercy upon us / Portrait of Amina / Sonnymoon for two
CD _____ TJA 12022
Jazz Alliance / Oct '95 / New Note.

PIANO JAZZ (McPartland, Marian & Dave McKenna)
Cat's cradle / Theodore the thumper / Just the way you are / I'm a fool to want you / Let's get away from it all / My cherie amour / All in love is fair / Isn't she lovely / I'll never be the same / Struttin' with some barbeque
CD _____ TJA 12023
Jazz Alliance / Nov '95 / New Note.

PIANO JAZZ (McPartland, Marian & Henry Mancini)
Two for the road / Meggie's theme / Pink Panther / Mr Lucky / Dreamsville / Charade / Baby elephant walk / Moon river / Days of wine and roses
CD _____ TJA 12024
Jazz Alliance / Dec '95 / New Note.

PIANO JAZZ (McPartland, Marian & Roy Eldridge)
Fast boogie / Ball of fire / Une petite laitue / Rockin' chair / I want a little girl / Indian summer / M & R Blues
CD _____ TJA 12025
Jazz Alliance / Feb '96 / New Note.

PIANO JAZZ (McPartland, Marian & Lee Konitz)
I'm gettin' sentimental over you / All the things you are / Stella by starlight / In your own sweet way / Body and soul / Tactile talk / Little girl blue / Naima / Like someone in love
CD _____ TJA 12026
Jazz Alliance / Feb '96 / New Note.

PIANO JAZZ WITH BARBARA CARROLL
Too soon / My man's gone now / This time the dream's on me / Imagination / Old friends / Marbara / There will never be another you
CD _____ TJA 12008
Jazz Alliance / Jun '94 / New Note.

PIANO JAZZ WITH BOBBY SHORT
Mood indigo / Nobody's heart / Experiment / Round Midnight / I guess I'll have to change my plan / Just one of those things / Reflections in D / My shining hour / It don't mean a thing if it ain't got that swing
CD _____ TJA 12010
Jazz Alliance / Sep '94 / New Note.

PIANO JAZZ WITH DICK HYMAN
Carousel memories / Relax / Handful of keys / Gone with the wind / Body and soul / Flower is a lovesome thing / This time the dream's on me / Delicate balance / Skylark / Lover come back to me
CD _____ TJA 12012
Jazz Alliance / Nov '94 / New Note.

PIANO JAZZ WITH DICK WELLSTOOD
Ain't misbehavin' / Medley / Lulu's back in town / Deed I do / See baby ain't I good to you / Detour ahead / Fine and dandy
CD _____ TJA 12007
Jazz Alliance / May '94 / New Note.

PIANO JAZZ WITH DIZZY GILLESPIE
Con alma / In a mellow tone / On the alamo / Manteca / For Dizzy / Lullaby of the leaves / Round Midnight / Portrait of Diz / Night in Tunisia
CD _____ TJA 12005
Jazz Alliance / Feb '94 / New Note.

PIANO JAZZ WITH EUBIE BLAKE
Betty Washboard rag / Valse Marion / Song for Marian (Margaret) / You're lucky to me / Charlston rag / Dream rag / For the last time call me sweetheart / Stars and stripes forever / Falling in love with someone / Kiss me again / St. Louis blues / I'm just wild about Harry / Little gypsy sweetheart
CD _____ TJA 12006
Jazz Alliance / Mar '94 / New Note.

PIANO JAZZ WITH GUEST DAVE BRUBECK
St. Louis blues / Thank you / Duke / In your own sweet way / One moment worth years / Summer song / Free piece / Polytonal blues / Take five
CD _____ TJA 12001
Bellaphon / Jun '93 / New Note.

PIANO JAZZ WITH GUEST TEDDY WILSON
CD _____ TJA 12002
Jazz Alliance / Jul '93 / New Note.

PIANO JAZZ WITH MILT HINTON
Milt's rap (MH solo) / All the things you are / My one and only love (Duet) / Joshua / Willow weep for me / Old man time (duet) / These foolish things (remind me of you) / Stranger in a dream / How high the moon
CD _____ TJA 12016
Jazz Alliance / Apr '95 / New Note.

PIANO JAZZ WITH RED RICHARDS
Have you met Miss Jones / What a wonderful world / Tangerine / Hundred years from today / Keepin' out of mischief now / Echoes of spring / Someday you'll be sorry / Talk of the town / Running wild
CD _____ TJA 12011
Jazz Alliance / Oct '94 / New Note.

PLAYS THE BENNY CARTER SONG BOOK
When lights are low / I'm in the mood for swing / Kiss from you (Only on CD.) / Key largo / Another time another place / Summer serenade / Doozy / Lonely woman / Only trust your heart / Evening star (Only on CD.) / Easy money
CD _____ CCD 4412
Concord Jazz / Jun '90 / New Note.

PLAYS THE MUSIC OF BILLY STRAYHORN
Intimacy of the blues / Isfahan / Lotus blossom / Raincheck / Lush life / U.M.M.G. / Flower is a lovesome thing / Take the 'A' train / Daydream / After all
CD _____ CCD 4326
Concord Jazz / Oct '87 / New Note.

PLAYS THE MUSIC OF MARY LOU WILLIAMS
Scratchin' the gravel / Lonely moments / What's your story Morning Glory / Easy blues / Threnody (a lament) / It's a grand night for swingin' / In the land of Oo-Bla-Dee / Dirge blues / Koolbonga / Walkin' and swingin' / Cloudy / My blue heaven / Mary's waltz / St. Martin de Porres
CD _____ CCD 4605
Concord Jazz / Jul '94 / New Note.

PORTRAIT OF MARIAN MCPARTLAND
CD _____ CCD 4101
Concord Jazz / Oct '91 / New Note.

SENTIMENTAL JOURNEY, A (McPartland, Marian & Jimmy)
Royal garden blues / Sentimental journey / Blue prelude / Dinah / Basin Street blues / When you wish upon a star / Avalon / Perdido / Willow weep for me / I'm gonna sit right down and write myself a letter / Polka dots and moonbeams / Wolverine blues
CD _____ TJA 10025
Jazz Alliance / Oct '94 / New Note.

McPhatter, Clyde

BEST OF CLYDE MCPHATTER, THE
CD _____ RSACD 812
Sequel / Oct '94 / BMG.

MacPhee, Catherine-Anne

CANAN NAN GAIDHEAL
Hi ri rio ra ill o / Nighean nan geug taladh / Puirt a buel / Soiridh leis a' bhreacan ur / lomair thusa, choinnich chridhe / Ca' nan gaidheal / 'S fliuch an oidhche / Onan an Iolaire / Cearcall a' chuain / Ataireach ard
CD _____ CDTRAX 009
Greentrax / May '93 / Conifer / Duncans / ADA / Direct.

CHI MI'N GEAMHRADH (I SEE WINTER)
Chi mi'n geamhradh / Chaidh mo dhunnchadh dha'n bheinn / Oh hi ri nan / Bidh clann ulaidh / Mile marbhphaisg air a' ghaol / Seathan bu deonach leam tilleadh / 'S muladach mi 's mi air m'aineol / Bothan airigh am braigh raineach / Tha na h-uain air an tulaich / Na libh o ho I
CD _____ CDTRAX 038
Greentrax / Apr '91 / Conifer / Duncans / ADA / Direct.

SINGS MAIRI MHOR
Nuair bha mu og / Coinneamh nan croiteran / Eilean a cheo / Soraidh leis an nollaig uir / Soraidh le eilean a'cheo / Oran beinn / Camanachd glaschu / Oran sarachaidh / Clach caidheil
CD _____ CDTRAX 070
Greentrax / Jun '94 / Conifer / Duncans / ADA / Direct.

McPhee, Joe

IMPRESSIONS OF JIMMY GIUFFRE (McPhee, Joe Trio)
CD _____ CELPC 21
CELP / Jan '93 / Harmonia Mundi / Cadillac.

LINEAR B (McPhee, Joe PO Music)
CD _____ ARTCD 6057
Hat Art / Dec '91 / Harmonia Mundi / ADA / Cadillac.

OLD EYES AND MYSTERIES (McPhee, Joe PO Music)
CD _____ ARTCD 6047
Hat Art / Apr '92 / Harmonia Mundi / ADA / Cadillac.

SWEET FREEDOM - NOW WHAT
CD _____ ARTCD 6162
Hat Art / Sep '95 / Harmonia Mundi / ADA / Cadillac.

McPhee, Tony

FOOLISH PRIDE
CD _____ HTDCD 10
HTD / Nov '92 / Pinnacle.

SLIDE, T.S. SLIDE
CD _____ HTDCD 26
HTD / Nov '94 / Pinnacle.

TWO SIDES OF TONY MCPHEE
Three times seven / All my money, alimony / Morning's eyes / Dog me bitch / Take it out / Hunt
CD _____ CLACD 267
Castle / Jun '92 / BMG.

MacPherson, Donald

MASTER PIPER, THE
CD _____ LCDM 9013
Lismor / '90 / Lismor / Direct / Duncans / ADA.

MacPherson, Fraser

ENCORE (MacPherson, Fraser Quartet)
CD _____ JTR 8420-2
Justin Time / Jan '94 / Harmonia Mundi / Cadillac.

HONEY AND SPICE (MacPherson, Fraser Quartet)
CD _____ JUST 23-2
Justin Time / Jan '94 / Harmonia Mundi / Cadillac.

IN THE TRADITION (MacPherson, Fraser Quintet)
Louisiana / Why am I blue / Struttin' with some barbecue / Hundred years from today / Constantly / When it's sleepy time down South / Desolation blues / You're lucky to me / If you could see me now / Dream of you / Ol' Bill's blues
CD _____ CCD 4506
Concord Jazz / May '92 / New Note.

McPherson, Charles

CHARLES MCPHERSON
CD _____ PCD 24135
Prestige / Nov '95 / Complete/Pinnacle / Cadillac.

COME PLAY WITH ME
Get happy / Lonely little chimes / Mario-nette / Pretty girl blues / Darn that dream / Bloomdido / Jumping Jacks / Fun house / Blues for Camille
CD _____ AJ 0117
Arabesque / Oct '95 / New Note.

FIRST FLIGHT OUT
Lynn grins / Lizabeth / Blues for Chuck / Nostalgia in Times Square / Well you needn't / Seventh Dimension / Goodbye pork pie hat / Deep night / Portrait / Karen / My funny valentine / First flight out
CD _____ AJ 0113
Arabesque / Jan '95 / New Note.

McRae, Carmen

ANY OLD TIME
Tulip or turnip / Old devil moon / Have you met Miss Jones / Love me tender / I hear music / This is always / Body and soul / Prelude to a kiss / Mean to me / Any old time / It could happen to you / I'm glad there is you / Billie's blues
CD _____ CY 1216
Denon / Oct '88 / Silver Note.

BEST OF CARMEN MCRAE, THE
Like a lover / I have the feeling I've been here before / Man I love / Would you believe / Child is born / Star eyes / Miss Otis regrets / Too close for comfort / Old folks / Dindi / T'ain't nobody's bizness if I do

---

CD _____ CDP 8335782
Capitol Jazz / Nov '95 / EMI.

BLACK MAGIC 'LIVE'
CD _____ JHR 73558
Jazz Hour / Oct '92 / Target/BMG / Jazz Music / Cadillac.

CARMEN MCRAE LIVE
CD _____ CDGATE 7001
Kingdom Jazz / Sep '88 / Kingdom.

EVERYTHING HAPPENS TO ME
CD _____ JHR 73582
Jazz Hour / Dec '94 / Target/BMG / Jazz Music / Cadillac.

FOR LADY DAY VOL. 1
Intro / Miss Brown to you / Good morning heartache / I'm gonna lock my heart (and throw away the key) / Fine and mellow / Them there eyes / Lover man / I cried for you (Now it's your turn to cry over me) / God bless the child / I hear music / I'm pulling through / Don't explain / What a little moonlight can do
CD _____ 01241631632
Novus / Jun '95 / BMG.

GREAT AMERICAN SONGBOOK, THE
Satin doll / At long last love / If the moon turns green / Day by day / What are you doing the rest of your life / I only have eyes for you / Easy living / Days of wine and roses / It's impossible / Sunday / Song for you / I cried for you / Behind the face / Ballad of Thelonious Monk / There's no such thing as love / Close to you / Three little words / Mr. Ugly / It's like reaching for the moon / I thought about you
CD _____ 756781323-2
Atlantic / Jun '93 / Warner Music.

I'LL BE SEEING YOU (2CD Set)
Something to live for / Speak low / But beautiful / Midnight sun / Good morning heartache / Ghost of a chance / We'll be together again / Star eyes / Whatever Lola wants (Lola gets) / Lush life / Until the real thing comes along / You don't know me / Skyliner / Party's over / East of the sun and west of the moon / Dream of life / Perdido / Exactly like you / I'm through with love / I'll see you again / Invitation / Bye bye blackbird / Flamingo / Oh yes, I remember Clifford / If I were a belt / Any old time / Please be kind / Thrill is gone / My myself / Do you know why / More I see you / When your lover has gone / If I could be with you one hour tonight / I only have eyes for you / I'm glad there is you / Ain't misbehavin' / I'll be seeing you
CD _____ GRP 2647
GRP / Aug '95 / BMG / New Note.

SARAH - DEDICATED TO YOU
Poor butterfly / I've got the world on a string / Misty / Wonder why / Send in the clowns / Black coffee / Tenderly / Best is yet to come / I will say goodbye / Lamp is low / It's magic / Dedicated to you / I'll be seeing you / Sarah
CD _____ PD 90546
Novus / Apr '91 / BMG.

ULTIMATE CARMEN MCRAE, THE
Life is just a bowl of cherries / Who can I turn to / Music that makes me dance / Gentleman friend / Alfie / It shouldn't happen to a dream / Love is a night time thing / Because you're mine / Cloudy morning / Limehouse blues / Blame it on my youth / Sweet Georgia Brown / Don't leave me / Fooling myself
CD _____ 4744122
Sony Jazz / Jan '95 / Sony.

VELVET SOUL
Nice work if you can get it / It takes a whole lot of human feeling / I fall in love too easily / Hey John / Where are the words / Straighten up and fly right / Inside a silent tear / Imagination / Right to love / All the things you are / You're mine you / You and I / How could I settle for less / Good life / Sunshine of my life / Exactly like you / There will come a time / (I'm afraid) the masquerade is over
CD _____ CDC 7970
LRC / Nov '90 / New Note / Harmonia Mundi.

YOU'RE LOOKING AT ME
I'm an errand girl for rhythm / Beautiful moons ago / Frim fram sauce / Come in and out of the rain / How does it feel / If I had you / I can't see for lookin' / Sweet Lorraine / You're lookin' at me / Just you, just me
CD _____ CCD 4235
Concord Jazz / Sep '86 / New Note.

MacRae, Gordon

BEST OF GORDON MACRAE, THE
Dear hearts and gentle people / Mule train / Sunshine of your smile / Younger than Springtime / Lover's waltz (with Gisele Mackenzie) / On Rosary Hill (with Gisele Mackenzie) / My Buick, my love and I (with Gisele Mackenzie) / If someone had told me / How do you speak to an angel / Face to face / Be my little baby bumble bee (with June Hutton) / By the light of the silvery moon (with June Hutton) / Beela notte / Who are we / People will say we're in love

(with Ray Anthony) / Surrey with the fringe on top (with Ray Anthony) / Woman in love / I've grown accustomed to her face / Sound of music / If ever I would leave you
CD _____ CDSL 8275
Music For Pleasure / Nov '95 / EMI.

CAPITOL YEARS: GORDON MACRAE
Stranger in paradise / June in January / My funny valentine / It might as well be Spring / So in love / Spring is here / I'll remember April / Where or when / That's for me / All the things you are / Begin the beguine / Indian Summer / September song / Autumn leaves / And this is my beloved / Without a song
CD _____ CDEMS 1352
Capitol / Feb '90 / EMI.

McShane, Ian

FROM BOTH SIDES NOW
Avalon / Fool (if you think it's over) / This guy's in love with you / I'd really love to see you tonight / From both sides now / I don't mind / I'm not in love / I could have been a sailor / Drive / Every breath you take / Reason to believe / Little in love / Shadow of your smile
CD _____ 517 619-2
PolyGram TV / Nov '92 / PolyGram.

McShane, Joe

PLACES, THOUGHTS AND FEELINGS
Places, thoughts and feelings
CD _____ JMSCD 001
Prism / May '91 / Prism.

McShann, Jay

1941-43
CD _____ CLASSICS 740
Classics / Feb '94 / Discovery / Jazz Music.

AIRMAIL SPECIAL
CD _____ SKCD 2-3040
Sackville / '88 / Swift / Jazz Music / Jazz Horizons / Cadillac / CM.

AT CAFE DES COPAINS
CD _____ SKCD 2-2024
Sackville / Jun '93 / Swift / Jazz Music / Jazz Horizons / Cadillac / CM.

GOING TO KANSAS CITY (McShann, Jay & The All Stars)
CD _____ NW 358
New World / '88 / Harmonia Mundi / ADA / Cadillac.

MISSOURI CONNECTION, THE (McShann, Jay & John Hicks)
CD _____ RSRCD 124
Reservoir Music / Nov '94 / Cadillac.

PARIS ALL-STAR BLUES: A TRIBUTE TO CHARLIE PARKER
CD _____ MM 5052
Music Masters / Oct '94 / Nimbus.

PIANO SOLOS
CD _____ SWAGGIECD 401
Swaggie / Jul '93 / Jazz Music.

SWINGMATISM (McShann, Jay/Don Thompson/Archie Alleyne)
CD _____ SKCD 2-3046
Sackville / Jun '93 / Swift / Jazz Music / Jazz Horizons / Cadillac / CM.

VINE STREET BOOGIE
My chile / Hootie blues / Satin doll / I'm beginning to see the light / Vine Street boogie / Confessin' the blues / Yardbird waltz / Hootie's ignorant oil
CD _____ BLCD 760187
Black Lion / Jul '93 / Jazz Music / Cadillac / Wellard / Koch.

McShee, Jacqui

ABOUT THYME
Jabalpur / Lovely Joan / Thyme / Factory girl / Would you / Little voices (Leah's song) / Sandalwood down to Kyle / Indiscretion / Don't turn on the light / Wife of Usher's well
CD _____ GJSCD 012
GJS / Jul '95 / Pinnacle.

McTell, Blind Willie

1927 - 1935
CD _____ YAZCD 1037
Yazoo / Apr '91 / CM / ADA / Roots / Koch.

BLIND WILLIE MCTELL, VOL. 1 (1927 - 1931)
CD _____ DOCD 5006
Blues Document / Feb '92 / Swift / Jazz Music / Hot Shot.

BLIND WILLIE MCTELL, VOL. 2 (1931 - 1933)
CD _____ DOCD 5007
Blues Document / Feb '92 / Swift / Jazz Music / Hot Shot.

COMPLETE BLIND WILLIE MCTELL, THE (2CD Set)
Alanta strut / Travellin' blues / Come on round to my house Mama / Kind Mama / Talking to myself / Razor ball / Southern can is mine / Broke down engine blues / Stomp down rider / Scary day blues / Rough alley

blues / Experience blues / Painful blues / Low riders blues / Georgia rag / Low down blues / Warm it up to me / It's your time to worry / It's a good little thing / You was born to die / Dirty mistreater / Lord have mercy if you please / Don't you see how this world made a change / Savannah Mama / Broke engine No.2 / My baby's gone / Love makin' Mama / Death room blues / Death room blues (2) / Death cells blues / Lord send me an angel (1) / Lord send me an angel (2) / B and O Blues No.2 / B and O BLues No.2 (2) / Weary hearted blues / Bell St. lightening / Southern can Mama / Runnin' me crazy / East Saint Louis blues (Fare you well)
CD Set _____ 475701 2
Columbia / May '94 / Sony.

LAST SESSION
CD _____ OBCCD 517
Original Blues Classics / Nov '92 / Complete/Pinnacle / Wellard / Cadillac.

LIBRARY OF CONGRESS RECORDINGS - 1940
CD _____ BDCD 6001
Blues Document / '91 / Swift / Jazz Music / Hot Shot.

PIG 'N' WHISTLE RED
CD _____ BCD 126
Biograph / May '93 / Wellard / ADA / Hot Shot / Jazz Music / Cadillac / Direct.

STATESBORO BLUES
CD _____ IGOCD 2015
Indigo / Feb '95 / Direct / ADA.

McTell, Ralph

BEST OF RALPH MCTELL, THE
CD _____ MATCD 214
Castle / May '93 / BMG.

BLUE SKIES, BLACK HEROES
CD _____ TPGCD 10
Leola / Dec '94 / Direct / ADA.

BOY WITH A NOTE, THE
CD _____ TPGCD 11
Leola / Dec '94 / Direct / ADA.

COMPLETE ALPHABET ZOO, THE
CD _____ RGFCD 016
Road Goes On Forever / Jan '94 / Direct.

RALPH MCTELL GREATEST HITS
CD _____ CD 845008
Bluebird / Jan '94 / BMG.

SAND IN MY SHOES
CD _____ TRACD 119
Transatlantic / Oct '95 / BMG / Pinnacle / ADA.

SILVER CELEBRATION
CD _____ 08431822
CTE / Dec '95 / Koch.

SLIDE AWAY THE SCREEN
Love grows (Where my Rosemary grows) / One heart / Gold in california / Van nuys, cruise night / London apprentice / Traces / Heroes and villains / Harry / Autumn / Promises / White dress / Save the last dance for me
CD _____ RGF 021CD
Road Goes On Forever / Sep '94 / Direct.

STEALIN' BACK
I'm going to Germany / Sugar babe / Prison wall blues / Hesitation blues / Weeping willow / When you've got a good friend / Candy man / When did you leave Heaven / Stealin' / That ll do babe / Black girl / Sweet Petulie / Nobody knows you (when you're down and out) / Lovin' I crave / Dyin' crap-shooters blues / This'll bring you back
CD _____ ESMCD 137
Essential / May '95 / Total/BMG.

STREETS
Streets of London / You make me feel good / Grande affaire / Seeds of Heaven / El progresso / Red apple juice (trad) / Heron song / Pity the boy / Interest on the loan / Jenny Taylor - Je n'tais la / Lunar lullaby
CD _____ TPGCD 12
Leola / Apr '96 / Diroot / ADA.

STREETS OF LONDON
CD _____ TACD 900556
Line / Sep '94 / CM / Grapevine / ADA / Conifer / Direct.

VERY BEST OF RALPH MCTELL
CD _____ SCD 17
Start / Jun '88 / Koch.

McTells

WHAT HAPPENS NEXT
Expecting Joe / Trash can man / Everytime / Uncle Joe / All the time / Villiers Street / Buffalo / Jesse Rae / That / Sweetly breathing / Never look down / Francis said / Fridge freezer / This afternoon / Shadders / Secret wish / Everything heaven sent you / Theme / Back of my hand / Of only if / It happens / Side by side / Snowy white / Right way round / Rotten / Take the car / Virginia MC / Sometimes
CD _____ ASKCD 040
Vinyl Japan / Jun '94 / Vital.

McVea, Jack

TWO TIMIN' BABY (McVea, Jack & His Door Openers)
New worried life / Houseparty boogie / Listen baby blues / Silver symphony / Frantic boogie / Lonesome blues / Richard gets hitched / Bulgin' eyes / Jam boogie / Slowly goin' crazy blues / Groove juice / Blues with a feeling / Swing man / Fighting mama blues
CD _____ RBD 612
Jukebox Lil / Apr '91 / Swift / Wellard.

McVie, Christine

CHRISTINE MCVIE
Love will show us now / Challenge / So excited / One in a million / Ask anybody / Got a hold on me / Who's dreaming this dream / I'm the one / Keeping secrets / Smile I live for
CD _____ 7599250592
WEA / Jan '96 / Warner Music.

McWilliams, Brigette

TAKE ADVANTAGE OF ME
Set up / Cherish this love / Baby don't play me / Take advantage of me / No groove sweating (A funky space reincarnation) / Gotta be down / It's on / I get the job done / That's on me / Blankets of playboys / You got someth'n I want / (Don't let me catch you) slippin' / I'm ready
CD _____ CDVUS 77
Virgin / Jul '94 / EMI.

Mad Cobra

GOLDMINE
CD _____ RASCD 3110
Greensleeves / Apr '93 / Total/BMG / Jetstar / SRD.

MAD COBRA (Cobra)
CD _____ CSCD 001
Graylan / Oct '92 / Jetstar / Grapevine / THE.

SHOOT TO KILL
CD _____ RNCD 2020
Rhino / Aug '93 / Jetstar / Magnum Music Group / THE.

VENOM
Platinum / Mark 10 / Mr. Pleasure / Wife and darling / R.I.P. / Length and bend / Hotness / To the max / Gal a model / Heartless / Fat and buff / Mate no ready
CD _____ GRELCD 202
Greensleeves / Mar '94 / Total/BMG / Jetstar / SRD.

YOUR WISH (Cobra)
CD _____ LG2 1059
Lagoon / Nov '92 / Magnum Music Group / THE.

Mad Cow Disease

TANTRIC SEX DISCO
My death squad / Craw / As good a place as any / Goatsucker / Exit / White dove / Annie Leiboritz version / Keep smiling / Elevator (going down) / Unicycle / Plague song / Epic departure
CD _____ 118052
CD Set _____ 118042
Musidisc / Sep '95 / Vital / Harmonia Mundi / ADA / Cadillac / Discovery.

Mad Jocks

TAKE JOCK AND PARTY
CD _____ CDSKM 1
Skratch / Nov '95 / Sony / 3MV.

Mad Lads

MAD, MAD, MAD, MAD, MAD LADS, THE/NEW BEGINNING, A
So nice / Cry baby / I just can't forget / These old memories / By the time I get to Phoenix / No strings attached / It's lovin' time / Love is here today and gone tomorrow / Make this young lady mine / I've never found a girl / Monkey time / Patch my heart / No so glad I fell in love with you / Seeing is believing / I'll still be loving you / Gone, the promises of yesterday / I forgot to be your lover / I'm afraid (of losing you) / Destination / Make room
CD _____ CDSXD 958
Stax / Oct '90 / Pinnacle.

Mad Lion

REAL LOVER
CD _____ VPCD 1402
VP / Mar '95 / Jetstar.

Mad Monster Party

WANDERING
CD _____ BNVCD 09
Black & Noir / Jan '92 / Plastic Head.

Mad Parade

THIS IS LIFE
CD _____ LF 166CD
Lost & Found / Aug '95 / Plastic Head.

Mad Professor

ADVENTURES OF A DUB SAMPLER, THE
CD _____ ARICD 033
Ariwa Sounds / Oct '92 / Jetstar / SRD.

ANTI-RACIST DUB BROADCAST (Black Liberation Dub Chapter 2)
Anti-racist dub broadcast / Dangerous escapades of dub / King Jimmy's dub / Basking in colonialism / Petty bourgeois dub / Pandora's box / Battle of Ciskei / Buthelezi trump card / Lion's domain / Rough rough dub / Legacy of Mussolini / Ethnic cleansing dub
CD _____ ARICD 100
Ariwa Sounds / Sep '94 / Jetstar / SRD.

AT CHECKPOINT CHARLIE
CD _____ DANCD 089
Danceteria / Nov '94 / Plastic Head / ADA.

BEYOND THE REALMS OF DUB
CD _____ AFRICD 003
Ariwa Sounds / Jan '91 / Jetstar / SRD.

BLACK LIBERATION DUB
Psychological warfare / Black liberation dub / Riot in Capetown / Slavery 21st century / Freedom must be taken / Chip on the slave master shoulder / When revolution comes / Black skin white minds / Tribal dub / Dub in D minor / Medicine doctor / Colonial mentality
CD _____ ARICD 095
Ariwa Sounds / Mar '94 / Jetstar / SRD.

DUB ME CRAZY #1
CD _____ ARICD 015
Ariwa Sounds / Feb '89 / Jetstar / SRD.

DUB ME CRAZY #12 (Dub Maniacs On The Rampage)
CD _____ ARICD 075
Ariwa Sounds / Oct '92 / Jetstar / SRD.

DUB ME CRAZY #3 (The African Connection)
CD _____ ARICD 005
Ariwa Sounds / Aug '94 / Jetstar / SRD.

DUB ME CRAZY #9 (Science & The Witchdoctor)
Anansi skank / Blue ball fire / Cry of thee old higue / Coming of the obeahe man / Witch's brew / Mistaken identity / Natural react / Jumbie umbrella / Bacoo in the bottle / Bohra seed / Holokoko dub
CD _____ ARICD 045
Ariwa Sounds / May '89 / Jetstar / SRD.

FEAST OF YELLOW DUB, A
CD _____ RAS 3069CD
Ras / Feb '91 / Jetstar / Greensleeves / SRD.

IN A RUB A DUB STYLE
Dubbing Jah / Bad man dubbing / Lighting dub / Cruel dub / Classic dub / True skank / Wicked skank / Skanking girl / Wolf skank / Skanking princess
CD _____ CDBM 105
Blue Moon / Jun '95 / Magnum Music Group / Greensleeves / Hot Shot / ADA / Cadillac / Discovery.

IT'S A MAD MAD MAD MAD PROFESSOR
CD _____ CRMCD 1
CRS / Jun '95 / Direct / ADA.

JAH SHAKA MEETS MAD PROFESSOR AT ARIWA SOUNDS (Mad Professor & Jah Shaka)
CD _____ ARICD 020
Ariwa Sounds / Sep '94 / Jetstar / SRD.

LOST SCROLLS OF MOSES, THE
African Hebrew chant / African Hebrew dub / Land of Canaan / Moses in the bullrushes / Jordan crossing / Fire on Mount Sinai / Dub on Mount Sinai / Amorites dub / Dead Sea scrolls / Subversive literature / Bogle soca / Los Lomas
CD _____ ARICD 080
Ariwa Sounds / Jul '93 / Jetstar / SRD.

MAD PROFESSOR CAPTURES PATO BANTON (Mad Professor & Pato Banton)
CD _____ ARICD 023
Ariwa Sounds / Oct '94 / Jetstar / SRD.

PSYCHEDELIC DUB
CD _____ ARICD 057
Ariwa Sounds / Sep '90 / Jetstar / SRD.

TRUE BORN AFRICAN DUB
CD _____ ARICD 073
Ariwa Sounds / May '92 / Jetstar / SRD.

WHO KNOWS THE SECRET OF THE MASTER TAPE
CD _____ ARICD 021
Ariwa Sounds / Aug '94 / Jetstar / SRD.

Mad River

MAD RIVER
Merciful monks / High all the time / Amphetamine gazelle / Eastern light / Wind chimes / War goes on / Julian Hush
CD _____ EDCD 140
Edsel / Mar '85 / Pinnacle / ADA.

PARADISE BAR AND GRILL
Harfy magnum / Paradise bar and grill / Love's not the way to treat a friend / Leave

me stay / Copper plates / Equinoxe / They
bought sadness / Revolution's in my
pockets / Academy cemetry / Cherokee
queen
CD _____ ED CD 188
Edsel / May '86 / Pinnacle / ADA.

Mad Season

MAD SEASON
Wake up / X-ray mind / River of deceit / I'm
above / Artificial red / Lifeless dead / I don't
know anything / Long gone day / November
hotel / All alone
CD _____ 4785072
Columbia / Mar '95 / Sony.

Mad Skillz

FROM WHERE
CD _____ 7567926232
Atlantic / Feb '96 / Warner Music.

Madame Christine

REAL EXPERIENCE
CD _____ SUNCD 006
Sunvibe / May '93 / Jetstar / EWM.

Madball

SET IT OFF
Set it off / Lockdown / New York City /
Never had it / It's time / C.T.Y.C. / Across
your face / Down by law / Spit on your
grave / Face to face / Smell the bacon / Get
out / World is mine / Friend or foe
CD _____ RR 89912
Roadrunner / Aug '94 / Pinnacle.

Madden, Glyn

CHRISTMAS WISHES
Winter wonderland / Silver bells / Fist Noel
/ I'm walking in the air / In the bleak midwinter / God rest ye merry gentlemen / Rudolph the red nosed reindeer / I saw
Mommy kissing Santa Claus / Ave Maria /
O little town of Bethlehem / Silent night /
Frosty the snowman / Once in Royal David's city / Christmas tree with its candles
gleaming / Dance of the snowmen / Sleigh
ride / Have yourself a merry little Christmas
/ Christmas song / Ding dong merrily on
high / White Christmas / O come all ye faithful (Adeste fidelis) / Jingle bells / Here we
come a-wassailing / I heard the bells on
Christmas day / O little one sweet / We wish
you a Merry Christmas
CD _____ CDGRS 1221
Grosvenor / '91 / Target/BMG.

ON TOUR
CD _____ CDGRS 1272
Grosvenor / Feb '95 / Target/BMG.

TICO TICO
CD _____ CDGRS1234
Grosvenor / Feb '93 / Target/BMG.

**ZWEI NACHTS IN EINER GROSSEN
STADT**
CD _____ CDGRS1250
Grosvenor / Feb '93 / Target/BMG.

Madden, Joanie

WHISTLE ON THE WIND
CD _____ GL 1142CD
Green Linnet / Aug '94 / Roots / CM /
Direct / ADA.

Madder Rose

BRING IT DOWN
Beautiful John / While away / Bring it down
/ Twenty foot red / Swim / Lay down low /
Altar boy / Lights go down / (Living a) day-
dream / Sugarsweet / Razor pilot / Waiting
for engines / Pocket fulla medicine
CD _____ 142292
Seed / Jun '93 / Vital.

PANIC ON
CD _____ 756782581-2
WEA / Mar '94 / Warner Music.

Madding Crowd

I HATE FLIES
CD _____ FETMC 1
Fuller's Earth / Mar '95 / Else.

Maddox Brothers

**AMERICA'S MOST COLOURFUL
HILLBILLY BAND (Maddox Brothers &
Rose Maddox)**
CD _____ ARHCD 391
Arhoolie / Apr '95 / ADA / Direct /
Cadillac.

**AMERICA'S MOST COLOURFUL
HILLBILLY BAND VOL. 2 (Maddox
Brothers & Rose Maddox)**
CD _____ ARHCD 437
Arhoolie / Sep '95 / ADA / Direct /
Cadillac.

**STANDARD SACRED SONGS (Maddox
Brothers & Rose Maddox)**
CD _____ KCD 000669
King/Paddle Wheel / Dec '92 / New Note.

Maddox, Rose

$35 & A DREAM
CD _____ ARHCD 428
Arhoolie / Apr '95 / ADA / Direct /
Cadillac.

ONE ROSE, THE (4CD Set)
What makes me hang around / Bill Cline /
Gambler's love / Lies and alibis / Custer's
last stand / I lost today / Live and let live /
My little baby / Philadelphia lawyer / Tramp
on the street / Gathering flowers for the
master's bouquet / I'm happy every day I
live / Sally let your bangs hang down /
Whoa sailor / On the banks of the old Ponchartrain / Honky tonkin' / At the first fall of
snow / Why don't you haul off and love me
/ Chocolate ice cream cone / Move it on
over / Shining silver, gleaming gold / Down
down down / Please help me, I'm falling /
Johnny's last kiss / Philadelphia lawyer (2)
/ Johnny's last kiss (2) / Wait a little longer,
please Jesus / Empty mansions / Great
speckled bird / This world is not my home
/ That glory bound train / Drifting too far
from the shore / When I take my vacation
in heaven / How beautiful heaven must be
/ I'll reap my harvest in heaven / Smoke, fire
and brimstone / Will the circle be unbroken
/ Kneel at the cross / There's better times
a comin' / I want to live again / Kissing my
pillow / Dime a dozen / Loose talk / Mental
cruelty / Conscience I'm guilty / Read my
letter once again / Tall men / Early in the
morning / There ain't no love / What am I
living for / Stop the world (and let me off) /
Jim Dandy / North to Alaska / Lonely Street
/ Gotta travel on / Just one more time /
Don't tell me your troubles / There ain't no
love (2) / Your kind of lovin' won't do / Take
me back again / Fool me again / Long journey home / From a beggar to a Queen /
Let's pretend we're strangers / If you see
my baby / Let those brown eyes smile at
me / When the sun goes down / Alone with
you / My life has been a pleasure / Curly
Joe / Here we go again / Long black limousine / White lightning / Uncle Pen / Footprints in the snow / Blue moon of Kentucky
/ My rose of old Kentucky / Molly and Tenbrooks / Rollin' in my sweet baby's arms /
Cotton fields / Each season changes you /
Old crossroad is waitin' / I'll meet you in
church Sunday morning / Down down
down #2 / Lonely teardrops / Sing a little
song of heartache / Tie a ribbon in the apple
tree / George Carter / Let me kiss you for
old times / I don't hear you / Down to the
river / Somebody told somebody / Sweethearts in heaven / We're the talk of the town
/ Back street affair / No fool like an old fool
/ I won't come in while he's there / Silver
threads and golden needles / Bluebird let
me tag along / That's a mighty long way to
fall / Stand up fool / Silver threads and
golden needles (2) / Great pretender / Tia
Lisa Lynn / Lonely one / Big Ball in Cowtown / Wabash cannonball / I'll always be
loving you / Mad at the world / Big big day
tomorrow / Cotton wood road / Down to the
river (live)
CD Set _____ BCD 15743
Bear Family / Oct '93 / Rollercoaster / Direct
/ CM / Swift / ADA.

ROSE OF THE WEST COUNTRY
CD _____ ARHCD 314
Arhoolie / Apr '95 / ADA / Direct /
Cadillac.

Maderna, Bruno

OBOE CONCERTOS
CD _____ BVHAASTCD 9302
Bvhaast / Oct '94 / Cadillac.

Madison, Art

LET IT FLOW
CD _____ 7567820042
Atlantic / Apr '90 / Warner Music.

Madkatt Courtship

BY DAWN'S EARLY LIGHT
Wet Wednesday / By dawn's early light /
Tha' mental blowout / Panic 60466 / Lov-
etraxx 1990 / Who tha' critics / Revelation
/ Da mindfuck / Phuzon
CD _____ SLIKCD 001
Deep Distraxion/Profile / Oct '95 / Pinnacle.

Madness

7
Cardiac arrest / Shut up / Sign of the times
/ Missing you / Mrs. Hutchinson / Tomorrows dream / Grey day / Pac-a-mac / Promises, promises / Benny bullfrog / When
dawn arrives / Opium eaters / Day on the
town
CD _____ CDOVD 135
Virgin / Nov '89 / EMI.

ABSOLUTELY
Baggy trousers / Embarrassment /
E.R.N.I.E. / Close escape / Not home today
/ On the beat Pete / Solid gone / Take it or
leave it / Shadow of fear / Disappear / Over-
done / In the rain / You said / Return of the
Los Palmas 7
CD _____ CDOVD 134
Virgin / Nov '89 / EMI.

**BUSINESS, THE (The Definitive Singles
Collection/3CD Set)**
Prince / Madness / One step beyond / Mistakes / Nutty theme / My girl / Stepping into
line / In the rain / Night boat to Cairo / Deceives the eye / Young and the old / Don't
quote me on that / Baggy trousers / Business / Embarrassment / Crying shame / Return of the Los Palmas 7 / That's the way
you do it (aka odd jobman) / My girl (demo
version) / Swan lake / Grey day / Memories
/ Shut up / Town wih no name / Never ask
twice (aka airplane) / It must be love /
Shadow on the house / Cardiac arrest / In
the city / House of fun / Don't look back /
Driving in my car / Terry Wogan jingle / Annual farm / Riding on my bike / Walking with
Mr. Wheeze / Our house (stretch mix) / Tomorrow's just another day / Madness #2 /
Wings of a dove / Behind the eight ball /
Calling cards / Second thoughtlessness /
Sun and the rain / Fireball XL5 / Wish to
Dracstein castle / Michael Caine / If you
think there's something / One better day /
Guns / Victoria gardens / Sarah / Yester-
day's men / All I knew / It must be love (live)
/ Uncle Sam / David Hamilton jingle / Inanity
over Christmas / Please don't go / Sweetest
girl / Jen-nie / Tears you can't hide / Call me
/ Waiting for the ghost train / One step
beyond (Italian version) / Maybe in another
life / Seven year scratch / Release me / Carols
on 45 / Na-tional anthem
CD Set _____ MADBOX 1
Virgin / Dec '93 / EMI.

COMPLETE MADNESS
Embarrassment / Shut up / My girl / Baggy
trousers / It must be love / Prince / Bed and
breakfast man / Night boat to Cairo / House
of fun / One step beyond / Cardiac arrest /
Grey day / Take it or leave it / In the city /
Madness / Return of the Los Palmas 7
CD _____ HITCD 1
Virgin / Jul '86 / EMI.

DIVINE MADNESS
Prince / One step beyond / My girl / Night
boat to Cairo / Baggy trousers / Embarrassment / Return of the Los Palmas 7 /
Grey day / Shut up / It must be love / Cardiac arrest / House of fun / Driving in my
car / Our house / Tomorrow's just another
day / Wings of a dove / Sun and the rain /
Michael Caine / One better day / Yesterday's men / Uncle Sam / Waiting for the
ghost train
CD _____ CDV 2692
Virgin / Feb '92 / EMI.

IT'S MADNESS
House of fun / Don't look back / Wings of
a dove / Young and the old / My girl / Stepping into line / Baggy trousers / Business /
Embarrassment / One's second thoughtlessness / Grey day / Memories / It must be
love / Deceives the eye / Driving in my car
/ Animal farm
CD _____ CDVIP 105
Virgin VIP / Mar '94 / Carlton Home Entertainment / THE / EMI.

IT'S MADNESS TOO
Prince / Madness / One step beyond / Mistakes / Return of the Los Palmas 7 / Night
boat to Cairo / Shut up / Town with no
name / Cardiac arrest / In the city / Our
house / Walking with Mr. Wheeze / Tomorrow's just another day / Victoria Gardens /
Sun and the rain / Michael Caine
CD _____ CDVIP 117
Virgin / Jun '94 / EMI.

KEEP MOVING
Keep moving / Michael Caine / Turning blue
/ One better day / March of the gherkins /
Waltz into mischief / Brand new beat / Vic-
toria gardens / Samantha / Time for tea /
Prospects / Give me a reason
CD _____ CDOVD 191
Virgin / Nov '89 / EMI.

MAD NOT MAD
I'll remember / Yesterday's men / Uncle Sam
/ White heat / Mad not mad / Sweetest girl
/ Burning the boats / Tears you can't hide /
Time / Coldest day
CD _____ JZCD 1
Zarjazz / Jul '87 / EMI.

MADNESS, THE
Nail down the days / What's that / I pro-
nounce you / Oh / In wonder / Song in red
/ Nightmare nightmare / Thunder and light-
ning / Beat the bride / Gabriel's horn / Elev-
enth hour (CD only) / Be good boy (CD only)
/ Flashings (CD only) / 4BF (CD only)
CD _____ CDV 2507
Virgin / Aug '91 / EMI.

MADSTOCK
One step beyond / Prince / Embarrassment
/ My girl / Sun and the rain / Grey day / It
must be love / Shut up / Driving in my car
/ Bed and breakfast man / Close escape /
Wings of a dove / Our house / Night boat
to Cairo / Madness / House of fun / Baggy
trousers / Harder they come
CD _____ 8283672
Go Discs / Nov '92 / PolyGram.

ONE STEP BEYOND
One step beyond / My girl / Night boat to
Cairo / Believe me / Land of hope and glory
/ Prince / Tarzan's nuts / In the middle of
the night / Bed and breakfast man / Razor

blade alley / Swan lake / Rockin' in AB /
Mummy's boy / Chipmunks are go
CD _____ CDOVD 133
Virgin / Apr '90 / EMI.

**ONE STEP BEYOND/ABSOLUTELY/RISE
AND FALL (3CD Set)**
CD Set _____ TPAK 8
Virgin / Oct '90 / EMI.

RISE AND FALL
Rise and fall / Tomorrow's just another day
/ Blue skinned beast / Primrose hill / Mr.
Speaker gets the word / Sunday morning /
Our house / Tiptoes / New Delhi / That face
/ Calling cards / Are you coming (with me)
/ Madness
CD _____ CDOVD 190
Virgin / Nov '89 / EMI.

UTTER MADNESS
Our house / Driving in my car / Michael
Caine / Wings of a dove / Yesterday's men
/ Tomorrow's just another day / I'll compete
/ Waiting for the ghost train / Uncle Sam /
Sun and the rain / Sweetest girl / One better
day / Victoria gardens
CD _____ JZCD 2
Zarjazz / Nov '86 / EMI.

Madonna

BEDTIME STORIES
Survival / Secret / I'd rather be your lover /
Don't stop / Inside of me / Human nature /
Forbidden love / Love tried to welcome me
/ Sanctuary / Bedtime story / Take a bow
CD _____ 9362454767-2
Maverick / Oct '94 / Warner Music.

EROTICA
Erotica / Fever / Bye bye baby / Deeper and
deeper / Where life begins / Bad girl / Waiting / Thief of hearts / Words / Rain / Why's
it so hard / In this life / Did you do it / Secret
garden
CD _____ 9362450312
Sire / Oct '92 / Warner Music.

FIRST ALBUM, THE
Lucky star / Borderline / Burning up / I know
it / Holiday / Think of me / Physical attrac-
tion / Everybody
CD _____ 9238672
Sire / Oct '84 / Warner Music.

I'M BREATHLESS
He's a man / Sooner or later / Hanky panky
/ I'm going bananas / Cry baby / Something
to remember / Back in business / More /
What can you lose / Now I'm following you
(pts 1 & 2) / Vogue
CD _____ 7599262092
Sire / May '90 / Warner Music.

**IMMACULATE COLLECTION (Best of
Madonna)**
Holiday / Lucky star / Borderline / Like a
virgin / Material girl / Crazy for you / Into the
groove / Live to tell / Papa don't preach /
Open your heart / La Isla Bonita / Like a
prayer / Express yourself / Cherish / Vogue
/ Justify my love / Rescue me
CD _____ 7599264402
Sire / Nov '90 / Warner Music.

**IN THE BEGINNING (Madonna & Otto
Van Wernherr)**
CD _____ CDKNOB 1
Receiver / Jul '93 / Grapevine.

**INTERVIEW COMPACT DISC:
MADONNA**
CD P.Disc _____ CBAK 4019
Baktabak / Nov '89 / Baktabak.

LIKE A PRAYER
Like a prayer / Love song / Promise to try /
Dear Jessie / Keep it together / Act of con-
trition / Express yourself / Till death do us
part / Cherish / Oh Father / Spanish eyes
CD _____ K 925844 2
Sire / Mar '94 / Warner Music.

SOMETHING TO REMEMBER
I want you / I'll remember / Take a bow /
You'll see / Crazy for you / This used to be
my playground / Live to tell / Love don't live
here anymore (remix) / Something to remember / Forbidden love / One more
chance / Rain / Oh father / I want you
(orchestral)
CD _____ 9362461002
Maverick / Nov '95 / Warner Music.

TRUE BLUE
Papa don't preach / Open your heart / Love
makes the world go round / Jimmy Jimmy
/ La Isla Bonita / True blue / Where's the
party / Live to tell / White heat
CD _____ K 9254422
Sire / Mar '94 / Warner Music.

**WHO'S THAT GIRL (Music Of Madonna
- 16 Instrumental Hits) (Various Artists)**
CD _____ 5708574338066
Carlton Home Entertainment / Sep '94 /
Carlton Home Entertainment.

**WILD DANCING (Madonna & Otto Van
Wernherr)**
CD _____ CDCD 1224
Charly / Jun '95 / Charly / THE / Cadillac.

YOU CAN DANCE
Spotlight (Mixes) / Holiday / Everybody /
Physical attraction / Over and over / Into the
groove / Where's the party / Holiday (dub)
/ Into the groove (dub) / Over and over (dub)

CD _____ 9255352
Sire / Feb '95 / Warner Music.

Madsen, Peter

THREE OF A KIND (Madsen, Peter/ Dwayne Dolphin/Bruce Cox)
Paul's pal / I'm old fashioned / Makin' whoopee / My buddy / Take the six train / Every time we say goodbye / On a misty night / Three of a kind / Between the devil and the deep blue sea / Danni
CD _____ MM 801039
Minor Music / May '94 / Vital/SAM.

Madura

MUSIQUE SAVANTE (Music From Indonesia)
CD _____ C 560083
Ocora / Dec '95 / Harmonia Mundi / ADA.

Mady, Kasse

FODE
CD _____ STCD 1025
Sterns / Mar '89 / Sterns / CM.

Maes, Christian

TILTED HOUSE (Maes, Christian & Sandi Miller)
CD _____ KM 43CD
Keltia Musique / Feb '94 / ADA / Direct / Discovery.

Magadini, Pete

BONES BLUES (Magadini, Pete Quartet)
Old devil moon / Freddie freeloader / Poor butterfly / Solar / I remember Clifford / What a time we had / Bones blues / Freddie freeloader no. 2
CD _____ SKCD 2-4004
Sackville / Jun '93 / Swift / Jazz Music / Jazz Horizons / Cadillac / CM.

NIGHT DREAMS (Magadini, Pete Quintet)
Friendly imposition / Exchanging love / Sunny side / Giant steps / Carolyn / Shutterbug / In a sentimental mood / Stablemates
CD _____ CDSJP 317
Timeless Jazz / Aug '91 / New Note.

Magazine

BBC LIVE IN CONCERT
Definitive gaze / Great beautician in the sky / Give me everything / My Tulpa / Back to nature / Shot by both sides
CD _____ WINCD 040
Windsong / Jul '93 / Pinnacle.

CORRECT USE OF SOAP, THE
Because you're frightened / Model worker / I'm a party / You never knew me / Philadelphia / I want to burn again / Thank you (faletimme be mice elf agin) / Sweetheart contract / Stuck / Song from under the floorboards
CD _____ CDV 2156
Virgin / '88 / EMI.

MAGIC, MURDER AND THE WEATHER
About the weather / So lucky / Honeymoon killers / Vigilance / Come alive / Great man's secrets / This poison / Naked eye / Suburban Rhonda / Garden
CD _____ CDV 2200
Virgin / '88 / EMI.

PLAY
Give me everything / Song from under the floorboards / Permafrost / Light pours out of me / Model worker / Parade / Thank you (faletimme be mice elf agin) / Because you're frightened / Twenty years ago / Definitive gaze
CD _____ CDV 2184
Virgin / '88 / EMI.

RAYS AND HAIL 1978-1981 (The Best Of Magazine)
Shot by both sides / Definitive gaze / Motorcade / Light pours out of me / Feed the enemy / Rhythm of cruelty / Back to nature / Permafrost / Because you're frightened / You never knew me / Song from under the floorboards / I want to burn again / About the weather / Parade
CD _____ CDVM 9020
Virgin / Jul '94 / EMI.

REAL LIFE
Definitive gaze / My tulpa / Shot by both sides / Recoil / Burst / Motorcade / Great beautician in the sky / Light pours out of me / Parade
CD _____ CDV 2100
Virgin / '88 / EMI.

SCREE (Rarities 1976-1981)
My mind ain't so open / Touch and go / Goldfinger / Give me everything / I love you big dummy / Rhythm of cruelty / TV baby / Book / Light pours out of me / Feed the enemy (Live) / Twenty years ago (Mixes) / Shot by both sides / In the dark / Operative
CD _____ CDOVD 312
Virgin / Jul '90 / EMI.

SECONDHAND DAYLIGHT
Feed the enemy / Rhythm of cruelty / Cut out shapes / Talk to the body / I wanted

your heart / Thin air / Back to nature / Believe that I understand / Permafrost
CD _____ CDV 2121
Virgin / '88 / EMI.

Magdallan

BIG BANG
CD _____ FLD 9098
Frontline / Apr '92 / EMI / Jetstar.

Magellan

IMPENDING ASCENSION
Estadium Nacional / Waterfront weirdos / Songsmith / Virtual reality / No time for words / Storms and mutiny / Under the wire
CD _____ RR 90572
Roadrunner / Jun '93 / Pinnacle.

Magic Affair

OMEN - THE STORY CONTINUES
Communication / Omen III / In the middle of the night / Homicidal / Fire / Water of sin / Under the sea / Carry on / Make your mind up / Give me all your love / Wonderland / Thin line
CD _____ CDEMC 3686
EMI / Aug '94 / EMI.

Magic Carpet

MAGIC CARPET
CD _____ ESS 1005CD
Eclectic / Apr '94 / Pinnacle.

Magic Dick

BLUESTIME (Magic Dick & Jay Geils)
Rounder / Oct '94 / CM / Direct / ADA / Cadillac.

Magic Hour

NO EXCESS IS ABSURB
CD _____ CHE 20CD
Che / Oct '94 / SRD.

WILL THEY TURN YOU ON OR WILL THEY TURN ON YOU
CD _____ CHE 30CD
Che / Jun '95 / SRD.

Magic Mushroom Band

FRESHLY PICKED
CD _____ EYECD 7
Magick Eye / Feb '93 / SRD.

SPACED OUT
CD _____ EYECDLP 6
Magick Eye / Aug '94 / SRD.

Magic Sam

BLACK MAGIC (Magic Sam Blues Band)
CD _____ DD 620
Delmark / Mar '95 / Hot Shot / ADA / CM / Direct / Cadillac.

GIVE ME TIME
CD _____ DD 654
Delmark / Sep '91 / Hot Shot / ADA / CM / Direct / Cadillac.

MAGIC TOUCH
CD _____ BT 1085CD
Black Top / May '93 / CM / Direct / ADA.

WEST SIDE SOUL (Charly Blues - Masterworks Vol. 29)
All your love / Love me with a feeling / Everything gonna be alright / Look watcha done / All night long / All my whole life / Easy baby / Twenty one days in jail / Love me this way / Magic rocker / Roll your moneymaker / Call me if you need me / Every black magic this time / Blue light boogie / Out of bad luck / She belongs to me
CD _____ CDBM 29
Charly / Apr '92 / Charly / THE / Cadillac.

Magic Slim

GRAVEL ROAD
CD _____ CCD 11027
Crosscut / '92 / ADA / CM / Direct.

HIGHWAY IS MY HOME
CD _____ ECD 260122
Evidence / Jan '92 / Harmonia Mundi / ADA / Cadillac.

RAW MAGIC (Magic Slim & The Teardrops)
CD _____ ALCD 4726
Alligator / May '93 / Direct / ADA.

Magical Strings

BELL OFF THE LEDGE
CD _____ FF 70631CD
Flying Fish / Apr '94 / Roots / CM / Direct / ADA.

CROSSING TO SKELLIG
CD _____ FF 531CD
Flying Fish / '92 / Roots / CM / Direct / ADA.

Magick Heads

BEFORE WE GO UNDER
CD _____ FNCD 290
Flying Nun / Apr '95 / Disc.

Magid, Yakov

LEKHAYM YIDN
CD _____ MU 3101762
Multisonic / Dec '93 / Priory / Koch.

Magma

1001 CENTIGRADES
CD _____ REX 6
Rex / Apr '91 / Pinnacle.

ATTAHK
Last seven minutes (1970-71, phase II) / Spiritual (negro song) / Rinde (Eastern song) / Lirik necronomicus kant / Maahnt / Dondai (to an eternal love) / Nono
CD _____ REX 13
Seventh / Mar '93 / Harmonia Mundi / Cadillac.

BOBINO 1981
CD _____ AKT V
AKT / Aug '95 / Harmonia Mundi / Cadillac.

LES VOIX - CONCERT 1992
CD _____ AKT 1
AKT / Nov '92 / Harmonia Mundi / Cadillac.

MAGMA
CD Set _____ REX 4/5
Seventh / Mar '93 / Harmonia Mundi / Cadillac.

MYTHS & LEGENDS (1969-1972)
CD _____ REX 14
Seventh / Mar '93 / Harmonia Mundi / Cadillac.

RETROSPEKTIW 3
CD _____ REX 15
Seventh / Mar '93 / Harmonia Mundi / Cadillac.

UDU WUDU
Udu wudu / Weidorje / Troller tanz (ghost dance) / Soleil d'ork / Zombies / De futura
CD _____ REX 12
Seventh / Mar '93 / Harmonia Mundi / Cadillac.

Magna Carta

HEARTLAND
CD _____ HYCD 200145
Hypertension / Jan '95 / Total/BMG / Direct / ADA.

LORD OF THE AGES
CD _____ 8464482
Vertigo / Jul '90 / PolyGram.

SEASONS
Airport song / Autumn song / Elizabethan / Epilogue / Give me no goodbye / Goin' my way / Road song / Prologue / Ring of stones / Scarecrow / Spring poem / Spring song / Winter song
CD _____ 8464472
Vertigo / May '90 / PolyGram.

STATE OF THE ART
CD _____ HYCD 200144
Hypertension / Apr '95 / Total/BMG / Direct / ADA.

Magnapop

HOT BOXING
Slowly slowly / Texas / Lay it down / Here it comes / Piece of cake / Free mud / Leo / Crush / Ride / In the way / Idiot song / Get it right / Emergency / Skinburns
CD _____ BIAS 251CD
Play It Again Sam / Feb '94 / Vital.

MAGNAPOP
Garden / Guess / Ear / Thirteen / Spill it / Chemical / Favourite writer / Complicated / Merry
CD _____ BIAS 220CD
Play It Again Sam / Jul '92 / Vital.

Magnarelli, Joe

WHY NOT
CD _____ CRISS 1104
Criss Cross / Oct '95 / Cadillac / Harmonia Mundi.

Magnetic Fields

CHARM OF THE HIGHWAY STRIP, THE
Lonely highway / Long vermont roads / Born on a train / I have the moon / Two characters in search of a country song / Crowd of drifters / Fear of trains / When the open road in closing in / Sunset city / Dustbowl
CD _____ SETCD 021
Setanta / Aug '95 / Vital.

DISTANT PLASTIC TREES
Railroad boy / Smoke signals / You love to fail / Kings / Babies falling / Living in an abandoned firehouse with you / Tarheel boy / Falling in love with the wolfboy / Josephine / 100,000 fireflies / Plant white roses

CD _____ RFCD 3
Red Flame / Feb '91 / Pinnacle.

Magnificent

HIT AND RUN
CD _____ AHOY 30
Captain Oi / Dec '94 / Plastic Head.

Magnificent VII

LIVE AT THE HILTON
CD _____ ARCD 19123
Arbors Jazz / Nov '94 / Cadillac.

Magnolia Jazz Band

MAGNOLIA ANYTIME
CD _____ BCD 220
GHB / Aug '95 / Jazz Music.

Magnolias

OFF THE HOOK
CD _____ A 024D
Alias / Jun '92 / Vital.

Magnum

ARCHIVE
CD _____ JETCD 1005
Jet / Apr '93 / Total/BMG.

CHASE THE DRAGON
Lights burned out / We all play the game / Teacher / Spirit / Soldier of the line / On the edge of the world / Walking the straight line / Sacred hour
CD _____ CLACD 222
Castle / '91 / BMG

COLLECTION: MAGNUM
CD _____ CCSCD 272
Castle / Oct '90 / BMG.

ELEVENTH HOUR, THE
Prize / Great disaster / Vicious companions / One night of passion / Word / Road to paradise / Breakdown / So far away / Hit and run / Young and precious souls
CD _____ CLACD 223
Castle / '91 / BMG.

FIREBIRD
Back to earth / Prize / So far away / Hit and run / Lights burned out / Soldier of the line / Changes / Foolish heart / All of my life / Great adventure / Invasion / Kingdom of madness / Universe / Firebird
CD _____ 5507372
Spectrum/Karussell / Jun '95 / PolyGram / THE.

GOODNIGHT L.A.
Rockin' chair / Only a memory / Matter of survival / Heartbroke and busted / No way out / Born to be king / Mama / Reckless man / What kind of love is this / Shoot / Cry for you
CD _____ 843 568-2
Polydor / Jul '90 / PolyGram.

INVASION-MAGNUM LIVE
CD _____ RRCD 113
Receiver / Jul '93 / Grapevine.

KEEPING THE NITE LITE BURNING
CD _____ JETCD 1006
Jet / Nov '93 / Total/BMG.

KINGDOM OF MADNESS
In the beginning / Baby rock me / Universe / Kingdom of madness / All that is real / Bringer / Invasion / Lords of chaos / All come together
CD _____ CLACD 126
Castle / '86 / BMG.

MAGNUM II
Great adventure / Changes / Battle / If I could live forever / Reborn / So cold the night / Foolish heart / Stayin' alive / Firebird
CD _____ CLACD 125
Castle / Mar '87 / BMG.

ON A STORYTELLER'S NIGHT
How far Jerusalem / Just like an arrow / Before first light / On a storytellers night / Les morts dansant / Endless love / Two hearts / Steal your heart / All England / Last dance
CD _____ JETCD 1007
Jet / Jul '93 / Total/BMG.

ROCK ART
We all need to be loved / Hard hearted woman / Back in your arms again / Rock heavy / Tall ships / Tell tale eyes / Love's a stranger / Hush-a-bye baby / Just this side of heaven / I will decide myself / On Christmas Day
CD _____ CDEMD 1066
EMI / Jun '94 / EMI.

SLEEP WALKING
CD _____ CDMFN 143
Music For Nations / Oct '92 / Pinnacle.

UNCORKED - THE BEST OF MAGNUM
CD _____ JETCD 1008
Jet / Jun '94 / Total/BMG.

VINTAGE MAGNUM
Back to earth / Hold back your love / Long days black nights / Lonesome star / Everybody needs / Changes / All of my life / Kingdom of madness / Invasion / Great adventure

CD _____ EMPRCD 596
Emporio / Oct '95 / THE / Disc / CM.

Magpie Lane

OXFORD RAMBLE, THE
Magpie Lane / As I walked through the meadows / First of May / Oxford city / Oxfordshire Damosel / John Barleycorn / Johnny so long/Eynsham poaching song / Old Molly Oxford / Boar's head carol / Oxford scholar / Great Tom is cast / Old Tom of Oxford/Bonny Christ church bells / Astley's ride / Oxford ramble / Trunkles / Near Woodstock town / Double lead through / Princess Royal / Husbandman and servingman / Banbury Bill/As I was going to Banbury / Adderbury medley / May Day carol
CD _____ BEJOCD 3
Beautiful Jo / Jun '94 / ADA.

SPEED THE PLOUGH
Carter's health / Regent's fete/Sir Roger de Coverley / Green bushes / Highwayman outwitted / Jockey to the fair / Bonny at Morn / Davy, Davy, knick-knack / Poor old horse / Kempshott hunt/Death of the fox / Swaggering Boney / Painful plough / Fool's jig / Mistress's health / Girl with the blue dress on/Swiss boy / Bushes and briars / Reading summer dance / Beverly maid and the tinker / Turtle dove/Bobbing Joe / Shepherd's song / Shooter's hornpipe / Bill Brown / Streets of Oxford / We're all jolly fellows that follow the plough / Speed the plough
CD _____ BEJOCD 4
Beautiful Jo / Jun '94 / ADA.

Maguire, Sean

SEAN MAGUIRE
Someone to love / Love by candlelight / Take this time / My heart won't let you go / No choice in the matter / Suddenly / As soon as you know / Sun shines from you / Devotion / It's always Christmas time
CD _____ CDPCSD 164
Parlophone / Nov '94 / EMI.

Mahaleo

MAHALEO (Music From Madagascar)
CD _____ PS 65157
Playasound / Oct '95 / Harmonia Mundi / ADA.

Maher, Big Joe

GOOD ROCKIN' DADDY
Good rockin' Daddy / Cat scratchin' / Let's go jumpin' / Hook, line and sinker / No good woman blues / Okeshemokeshepop / Handclappin' / You know yeah / Don't send me no flowers / Blow man blow / Dynaflow
CD _____ POW 4102 CD
Power House / Apr '91 / Direct.

Maher, Tony

IRISH TRANQUILITY
CD _____ HCD 009
GTD / Apr '95 / Else / ADA.

Mahlathini

BEST OF MAHLATHINI & THE MAHOTELLA QUEENS
Madlamini / Lilileza millileza / I'm in love with a rastaman / Makhomabaji / Gxreka / Marabi-yo / Thokozilie / Won't you please sing along / Melodi yalla / Sengikala Ngiyabaleka / Reya dumedisa / Jive motella / Thutswane basadi / Music of our soul
CD _____ KAZCD 27
Kaz / Nov '92 / BMG.

KING OF THE GROANERS
Umkhovu / Intombi emnyama / Nomacala / Wavutha umlilo / Woza zoxolisa / Isitha ihliziyo / Mtaka mama / Umona / Isikhonyane / We-somhlolo / Ithemba alibulali / Ngizothi mamakubani / Mbaka aka / Umama ithembalmi / Guluva / Izandie jive / Selimathunzi / Normalanga / Inkosi yomkulo / Umkhenyana
CD _____ CDEWV 29
Earthworks / Mar '93 / EMI / Sterns.

LION OF SOWETO
Baba-ye / Bayasazi / Kudala besifuna / Kwa mfazi onge mama / Bhula mngoma / Kumnyama endlini / Kumnandi Emgababa / Amagoduka / Mahlalela / Abake ba bonana / Bayasimenmeza / Ngibuzindela
CD _____ CDEWV 4
Earthworks / '87 / EMI / Sterns.

LION ROARS, THE (Mahlathini & The Mahotella Queens)
Lion roars
CD _____ SHCD 43081
Shanachie / Jun '91 / Koch / ADA / Greensleeves.

MBAQANGA (Mahlathini & The Mahotella Queens)
Mbaqanga / Yuya / Bayeza / Umashihlalisane / Jive motella / Thonthodi / Hayi kabi / Stop crying / Bon jour / Josefa / Noluthando / Kwa makhutha
CD _____ KAZ CD 901
Kaz / Oct '91 / BMG.

THOKOZILE (Mahlathini & The Mahotella Queens)
Thokozilie / Lilieza millileza / Sibuyile / Nina Majuba / I wanna dance / Uyavutha umlilo / Sengikala Ngiyabaleka / Izulu liyaduduma
CD _____ CDEWV 6
Earthworks / Feb '88 / EMI / Sterns.

Mahogany Hall Stompers

MAHOGANY HALL STOMPERS
CD _____ SOSCD 1221
Stomp Off / Oct '92 / Jazz Music / Wellard.

Mahogany Rush

CHILD OF THE NOVELTY
CD _____ REP 4029-WZ
Repertoire / Aug '91 / Pinnacle / Cadillac.

DOUBLE LIVE
CD _____ 874 614
Maze / May '89 / Plastic Head.

LEGENDARY MAHOGANY RUSH, THE (Child Of The Novelty/Maxoom/Strange Universe)
Look outside / Thru the milky way / Talking 'bout a feelin' / Child of the novelty / Makin' my wave / New rock and roll / Changing / Plastic man / Guit war / Chains of (s)pace / Maxoom / Buddy / Magic man / Funky woman / Madness / All in your mind / Blues / Boardwalk lady / Back on home / New beginning / Tales of the Spanish warrior / King who stole (The universe) / Satisfy your soul / Land of 1000 nights / Moonlight lady / Dancing lady / Once again / Tryin' anyway / Dear music / Strange universe
CD _____ CDWKM2 149
Big Beat / Jul '95 / Pinnacle.

STRANGE UNIVERSE
CD _____ REP 4028-WZ
Repertoire / Aug '91 / Pinnacle / Cadillac.

Mahogany, Kevin

DOUBLE RAINBOW
All blues / Confirmation / Save that time / Double rainbow / Our love remains / Dat dere / Little butterfly (Pannonica) / My dungeon shook / Since I fell for you / Three little words / Duke Ellington's sound of love / No one knows what love holds in store (two degrees east, thr / Bring it on home
CD _____ ENJ 70972
Enja / Jul '93 / New Note / Vital/SAM.

SONGS AND MOMENTS
Coaster / West coast blues / City lights / Night flight / Next time you see me / Songs and moments / Caravan / My foolish heart / Red top / Jim's ballad / Take the 'A' train / When I fall in love
CD _____ ENJ 80722
Enja / Oct '94 / New Note / Vital/SAM.

YOU GOT WHAT IT TAKES
Baby you got what it takes / Stockholm sweetnin' / Just in time / Sophisticated lady / Route 66 / Here's the rainy day / Yardbird suite / My funny valentine / Old times sake / BG's groove / God bless the children / Little Sherri / Please send me someone to love
CD _____ ENJ 90392
Enja / Oct '95 / New Note / Vital/SAM.

Mahotella Queens

PUTTING ON THE LIGHT (Mahotella Queens, Mahlathini & others)
Umthakathi / Uyagiyaumahlathini / Umoya / Imbodlomane / Izulungelami / Duduzile / Sithunyiwe / Ukohhliwe / Dolly swidilami / Thina siyakhanyisa / Gabi gabi / Bantwanyana
CD _____ HNCD 4415
Hannibal / Jul '93 / Vital / ADA.

WOMEN OF THE WORLD
CD _____ FLTRCD 510
Timbuktu / Jun '93 / Pinnacle.

Maids Of Gravity

STRANGE CHANNEL
Your ground / Slave and rule / Moonspiders / Taste / In other words
CD _____ CDVUSM 85
Virgin / Apr '95 / EMI.

Mailhes, Rene

GOPALINE (Mailhes, Rene Trio)
CD _____ IMP 922
Iris Music / Nov '95 / Discovery.

Main

CORONA
CD _____ HERTZ 1
Beggars Banquet / Jun '95 / Warner Music / Disc.

FIRMAMENT II
CD _____ BBQCD 168
Beggars Banquet / Nov '94 / Warner Music / Disc.

HERTS SERIES, THE
CD _____ HERT 16CD
Beggars Banquet / Jan '96 / Warner Music / Disc.

HYDRA/CALM
CD _____ SITL 39CD
Situation 2 / Jun '92 / Pinnacle.

MAIN
CD _____ HSRTZ 3
Beggars Banquet / Aug '95 / Warner Music / Disc.

MOTION POOL
CD _____ BBQCD 148
Beggars Banquet / Apr '94 / Warner Music / Disc.

NEPER
CD _____ HERT 26
Beggars Banquet / Nov '95 / Warner Music / Disc.

Main Ingredient

I JUST WANNA LOVE YOU
CD _____ 841 249-2
Polydor / Mar '90 / PolyGram.

Main Source

FUCK WHAT YOU THINK
Diary of a hit man / Only the real survive / What you need / Merrick Boulevard / Down low / Intermission / Where we're coming from / Hellavision / Fuck what you think / Set it off / Scrach and kut
CD _____ CDPITCH 002
Wild Pitch / Mar '94 / EMI.

Mainesthal

OUT TO LUNCH
CD _____ CDZOT 117
Zoth Ommog / Aug '94 / Plastic Head.

Mainieri, Mike

AMERICAN DIARY, AN
Somewhere / King Kong / Piano sonata (vivace) / Piano sonato No 1 / Town meeting / Overture to the school for scandal / Hudson river valley / Sometimes I feel like a motherless child / Song of my people / In the gloaming / Out of the cage / In the universe of Ives
CD _____ NYC 60152
NYC / Jul '95 / New Note.

COME TOGETHER
Come together / She's leaving home / Here, there and everywhere / And I love her / Michelle / Something / Eleanor Rigby / Norwegian wood / Blackbird / Within you without you / Yesterday
CD _____ NYC 60042
NYC / Jun '93 / New Note.

MAN BEHIND BARS
ESP / Trinary motion / Push-pull / Equinox / Satyr dance / Momento No 1 / Nearness of you / Momento No 2 / All the things you are / Binary motion
CD _____ NYC 60192
NYC / Dec '95 / New Note.

WANDERLUST
Bullet train / Sara's touch / Crossed wires / Flying colours / L'image / Bamboo / Wanderlust
CD _____ NYC 60022
NYC / Oct '92 / New Note.

WHITE ELEPHANT
Peace of mind / Jones / Battle royal / Look in his eyes / White elephant / Easy on / Animal fat / Monkey
CD _____ NYC 60082
NYC / Jun '93 / New Note.

WHITE ELEPHANT VOL II
More to love / Broadway Joe / Dreamsong / Gunfighter / Right back / Sunshine clean / Save the water / Auld lang syne / Field song / Battle royal
CD _____ NYC 60112
NYC / Feb '96 / New Note.

Maipu

MUSIC FROM THE ANDES
CD _____ 15496
Laserlight / Jan '94 / Target/BMG.

Maitra, Kamalesh

TABLA TARANG - RAGAS ON DRUMS
CD _____ SM 1602-2
Wergo / Nov '93 / Harmonia Mundi / ADA / Cadillac.

Majella

EVERY BEND IN THE ROAD
CD _____ CDKLP 68
Igus / Dec '89 / CM / Ross / Duncans.

MAGIC OF MAJELLA
CD _____ CDKLP 66
Igus / Nov '88 / CM / Ross / Duncans.

REQUESTS
CD _____ CDKLP 70
Igus / Dec '90 / CM / Ross / Duncans.

Majestic

NO WORDS, NO MISUNDERSTANDINGS
CD _____ EFA 125172
Celtic Circle / Sep '95 / SRD.

Major Worries

BABYLON BOOPS
CD _____ 792082
Jammy's / Apr '93 / Jetstar.

Makeba, Miriam

AFRICA
Mbube / Nomeva / Olilili / Suliram / Retreat song / Click song / Saduva / Iya guduza / Lakutshon ilanga / Umhome / Amanpondo / Dubula / Kwendini / Umhome (2) / Pole mze / Le fleuve / Qhude / Mayibuye / Maduna / Kilimanjaro / Kwazulu (in the land of the Zulus) / Nonggonggq (To those we love) / Khawuleza / Ndodemnyama (Beware, Verwoerd)
CD _____ ND 83155
Novus / Jan '92 / BMG.

BEST OF MIRIAM MAKEBA & THE SKYLARKS
Uthando luyaphela / Table mountain / Miriam and spokes phatha phatha / Mtshakasi / Ndimsbone dluca / Makoti / Ndidliwe zintaba / Inkomo zodwa / Sindiza ngecadillacs / Nomalungelo / Kutheni sithandwa / Vula amasango / Owakho / Baya ndi memeza / Yini madoda / Ekoneni / Uyadela
CD _____ KAZCD 26
Kaz / Nov '92 / BMG.

FOLK SONGS FROM AFRICA
CD _____ CD 12514
Music Of The World / Jun '94 / Target/BMG / ADA.

Makem, Tommy

CLASSIC GOLD (Makem, Tommy & Liam Clancy)
CD _____ TF 1010
Third Floor / Oct '94 / Total/BMG / ADA / Direct.

COLLECTION (Makem, Tommy & Liam Clancy)
CD _____ TFCB 1009CD
Third Floor / Oct '94 / Total/BMG / ADA / Direct.

DUTCHMAN, THE (Makem, Tommy & Liam Clancy)
CD _____ SHCD 52005
Shanachie / May '93 / Koch / ADA / Greensleeves.

FROM THE ARCHIVES
CD _____ SHCD 52040
Shanachie / Mar '95 / Koch / ADA / Greensleeves.

IN CONCERT (Makem, Tommy & Liam Clancy)
CD _____ TF 1002
Third Floor / Oct '94 / Total/BMG / ADA / Direct.

LARK IN THE MORNING, THE (Makem, Tommy & Liam Clancy)
CD _____ TCD 1001
Rykodisc / Feb '96 / Vital / ADA.

REUNION (Makem, Tommy & The Clancy Brothers)
CD _____ TF 5009
Third Floor / Oct '94 / Total/BMG / ADA / Direct.

Makowicz, Adam

CLASSIC JAZZ DUETS (Makowicz, Adam & George Mraz)
CD _____ NI 4021
Natasha / Feb '94 / Jazz Music / ADA / CM / Direct / Cadillac.

CONCORD DUO SERIES VOLUME 5 (Makowicz, Adam & George Mraz)
Don't ever leave me / 400 West d-flat / Where is love / Anything goes / Mito / Say it isn't so / Culebra / Concordance / I loves you Porgy / Cherokee
CD _____ CCD 4597
Concord Jazz / Jun '94 / New Note.

MUSIC OF JEROME KERN, THE (Makowicz, Adam Trio)
All the things you are / Way you look tonight / Who / Song is you / I won't dance / Ol' man river / Long ago and far away / Smoke gets in your eyes / Yesterdays / Dearly beloved / I'm old fashioned
CD _____ CCD 4575
Concord Jazz / Nov '93 / New Note.

MY FAVOURITE THINGS (The Music Of Richard Rodgers)
Where or when / I didn't know what time it was / Surrey with the fringe on top / My favourite things / Lady is a tramp / This can't be love / My funny valentine / My romance / Lover / It might as well be spring / Have you met Miss Jones
CD _____ CCD 4631
Concord Jazz / Feb '95 / New Note.

Makwerhu

SOMANDALA
Somandla / Zulu beat / Nhongane / Mahayeng / Mabadi / Mazala / Shifaki / Ahivi / Rito / Khale wa khaleni
CD _____ ADR 00012
African Dance / Oct '95 / EWM.

Malach, Bob

SEARCHER, THE
CD _____ GOJ 60152
Go Jazz / Sep '95 / Vital/SAM.

Malaria

REVISITED
CD _____ DANCD 083
Danceteria / Nov '94 / Plastic Head / ADA.

Malasek, Jiri

ROMANTIC PIANO OF JIRI MALASEK, THE
CD _____ CDSGP 051
Prestige / Sep '93 / Total/BMG.

Malcahy, Mick

MICK MULCAHY AND FRIENDS
CD _____ CEFCD 143
Gael Linn / Jan '94 / Roots / CM / Direct / ADA.

Malcolm, James

SCONEWARD
Scotch blues / Neptune / Losin' auld reeki / Wild geese / Scotlandshire / Achiltibuie / Lochs of the Tay / Wisest fool / Noran water / Barrenlands / Grandfathers / Party / Flowers of Edinburgh
CD _____ CDTRAX 083
Greentrax / Mar '95 / Conifer / Duncans / ADA / Direct.

Malfunkshun

RETURN TO OLYMPUS
Enter landrew / My only pan / Mr. Liberty (with morals) / Jezebel woman / Shotgun wedding / Wang dang sweet footang / San Diego beach / I wanna be yo Daddy / Winter bites / Make sweet love / Region / Luxury bed (the rocketship chair) / Enit landrew
CD _____ 4784242
Epic / Jul '95 / Sony.

Mali Rain

WE SHALL RETURN TO THE SEA
Basking / Arp-aht / Statikat / Simms / Tranquility bass / Canopy / Callow Hill 508 AM / Peyostasia / Octane / Koan
CD _____ STONE 017CD
3rd Stone / Aug '95 / Vital / Plastic Head.

Malicious Onslaught

BRUTAL CORE
CD _____ USR 007CD
Unisound / Jan '96 / Plastic Head.

REBELLIOUS MAYHEM
CD _____ BROO 1CD
Brain Crusher / Nov '92 / Plastic Head.

Malicorne

LEGENDE: DEUXIEME EPOQUE
Le Prince D'Orange / Le ballet des coqs / Compagnons qui roulez en provence / La mule la conduite / Pierre De Grenoble / Vive la lune / La danse des dames / La Chasse Gallery / La nuit des sorcieres / Dormeur / L'ecolier assassin / Beau charpentier / Quand le cypes
CD _____ HNCD 1360
Hannibal / Jul '91 / Vital / ADA.

Malie

DANCE MUSIC FROM TONGA
■■ _____ PANCD 2011
Pan / May '93 / ADA / Direct / CM.

Malik, Anu

EYES
CD _____ MCD 450
Melody / Jan '96 / Total/BMG.

Malik, Raphe

21ST CENTURY TEXTS
CD _____ FMPCD 43
FMP / Sep '89 / Cadillac.

Malinga, Joe

ITHI GQI (Malinga, Joe Group)
CD _____ BRAM 199011-2
Brambus / Nov '93 / ADA / Direct.

Malka Spiget

ROSH BALLATA
CD _____ WM 1
Swim / Mar '94 / SRD / Disc.

Mallan, Peter

SCOTLAND IN SONG
CD _____ CDLOC 1088
Lochshore / Jul '95 / ADA / Direct / Duncans.

Mallett, David

FOR A LIFETIME
For a lifetime / Sweet Tennessee / My old man / Some peace will come / Night on the

town / Hometown girls / This city life / Lost in a memory of you / Light at the end of the tunnel / Summer of my dreams
CD _____ FF 70497
Flying Fish / Jul '89 / Roots / CM / Direct / ADA.

OPEN DOORS AND WINDOWS
CD _____ FF 70291
Flying Fish / Feb '95 / Roots / CM / Direct / ADA.

Mallku De Los Andes

ON THE WINGS OF THE CONDOR
CD _____ TUMICD 004
Tumi / '86 / Sterns / Discovery.

Malmkvist, Siw

HARLEKIN
CD _____ BCD 15661
Bear Family / Oct '93 / Rollercoaster / Direct / CM / Swift / ADA.

LIEBESKUMMER 1961-1968
CD _____ BCD 15660
Bear Family / Oct '93 / Rollercoaster / Direct / CM / Swift / ADA.

Malmsteen, Yngwie

COLLECTION
CD _____ 8492712
Polydor / Jul '94 / PolyGram.

FIRE AND ICE
CD _____ 7559611372
Elektra / Feb '92 / Warner Music.

MAGNUM OPUS
Vengeance / No love lost / Tomorrows gone / Only one / Die without you / Overture 1622 / Voodoo / Cross the line / Time will tell / Fire in the sky / Amber dawn / Cantabile
CD _____ CDMFN 188
Music For Nations / Jul '95 / Pinnacle.

MARCHING OUT (Malmsteen, Yngwie & Rising Force)
Prelude / I'll see the light tonight / Don't let it end / Disciples of hell / I'm a viking / Overture 1383 / Anguish and fear / On the run again / Soldier without faith / Caught in the middle / Marching out
CD _____ 825 733-2
Polydor / Aug '85 / PolyGram.

ODYSSEY (Malmsteen, Yngwie & Rising Force)
Rising force / Hold on / Heaven tonight / Dreaming (tell me) / Bite the bullet / Riot in the dungeons / Deja vu / Crystal ball / Now is the time / Faster than the speed of light / Krakatau / Memories
CD _____ 8354512
Polydor / Jul '91 / PolyGram.

RISING FORCE
Black star / Far beyond the sun / Now your ships are burned / Evil eye / Icarus' dream suite / As above so below / Little savage / Farewell
CD _____ 825 324-2
Polydor / May '88 / PolyGram.

SEVENTH SIGN
Never die / I don't know / Meant to be / Forever one / Hairtrigger / Brothers / Seventh sign / Bad blood / Prisoner of your love / Pyramid of cheops / Crash and burn / Sorrow
CD _____ CDMFN 158
Music For Nations / Mar '94 / Pinnacle.

Malo

BEST OF MALO
CD _____ GNPD 1
GNP Crescendo / Jan '92 / Silva Screen.

Malone, Debbie

GOOD LIFE
CD _____ PULSECD 6
Pulse / Nov '92 / BMG.

Malone, Michelle

NEW EXPERIENCE
CD _____ SKY 75025CD
Sky / Sep '94 / Koch.

Malone, Russell

BLACK BUTTERFLY
Jingles / With Kenny in mind / Dee's song / Cedar tree / After her bath / I say a little prayer (for you) / Black butterfly / All through the night / Other man's grass / Gaslight / Sno' peas
CD _____ 474805 2
Columbia / Oct '93 / Sony.

RUSSELL MALONE
CD _____ 4722612
Sony Jazz / Jan '95 / Sony.

Maloney, Bunny

SINGS OLDIES IN A REGGAE
CD _____ HM 501172
Mudies / Sep '95 / Jetstar.

Malta

HIGH PRESSURE
CD _____ JD 3303
JVC / Jul '88 / New Note.

MY BALLADS
CD _____ JD 3315
JVC / May '89 / New Note.

OBSESSION
CD _____ JD 3310
JVC / Oct '88 / New Note.

Maltese

COUNT YOUR BLESSINGS
CD _____ CDATV 21
Active / Jul '92 / Pinnacle.

Mama Sana

MUSIC FROM MADAGASCAR
CD _____ SHCD 65010
Shanachie / May '95 / Koch / ADA / Greensleeves.

Mamas & Papas

20 GREATEST HITS: MAMAS & PAPAS
California dreamin' / I saw her again / I call your name / Twist and shout / Sing for your supper / Look through my window / Do you wanna dance / Dancing in the street / You baby / Dedicated to the one I love / Monday, Monday / Words of love / Glad to be unhappy / Go where you wanna go / Safe in my garden / Spanish Harlem / Trip, stumble and fall / My girl / Creeque Alley / Dream a little dream of me
CD _____ CDMFP 50493
Music For Pleasure / Dec '92 / EMI.

BEST OF THE MAMAS & PAPAS
CD _____ MCBD 19519
MCA / Apr '95 / BMG.

CALIFORNIA DREAMIN' - THE BEST OF THE MAMAS & PAPAS
California dreamin' / Dedicated to the one I love / Monday Monday / Dream a little dream of me / Creeque Alley / I saw her again / It's getting better / Words of love / In crowd / Dancing in the street / Spanish Harlem / Twist and shout / Do you wanna dance / Go where you wanna go / Look through my window / You baby / For the love of Ivy / Make your own kind of music / Twelve thirty (Young girls are coming to the canyon) / I call your name / My girl / California earthquake / Straight shooter / Glad to be unhappy
CD _____ 5239732
PolyGram / Jan '95 / PolyGram.

CREEQUE ALLEY
CD _____ MCLD 19124
MCA / Sep '94 / BMG.

ELLIOTT, PHILLIPS, GILLIAM, DOCHERTY
California dreamin' / Dedicated to the one I love / Even if I could / Once there was a time I thought / You baby / In crowd / I saw her again / Did you ever want to cry / John's music box / Too late / Go where you wanna go / Midnight voyage / Creeque alley / Strange young girls / Spanish harlem / No salt on her tail / My cart stood still / Dream a little dream of me / California earthquake / Somebody groovy / Sing for your supper / Free advice / String man / I can't wait
CD _____ VSOPCD 119
Connoisseur / Jul '88 / Pinnacle.

EP COLLECTION, THE
California dreamin' / Somebody groovy / Monday, Monday / In crowd / I saw her again / Go where you wanna go / Look through my window / Trip, stumble and fall / Dedicated to the one I love / Free advice / Straight shooter / Get a feeling / Hey girl / You baby / Even if I could / I call your name / Words of love / Dancing in the street / I can't wait / That kind of girl
CD _____ SEECD 333
See For Miles/C5 / Feb '92 / Pinnacle.

GOLDEN GREATS: MAMAS & PAPAS
Dedicated to the one I love / Monday, Monday / Look through my window / California dreamin' / I call your name / My girl / Dream a little dream of me / Go where you wanna go / Got a feelin' / I saw her again / Words of love / There's no other / Dancing in the street / Glad to be unhappy / Creeque alley / Midnight voyage / Spanish Harlem / You baby / Do you wanna dance / Twist and shout / Safe in my garden / California earthquake
CD _____ MCLD 19125
MCA / Jul '92 / BMG.

HITS OF GOLD
California dreamin' / Dedicated to the one I love / Monday, Monday / I saw her again / Creeque alley
CD _____ MCLD 19050
MCA / Apr '92 / BMG.

VERY BEST OF MAMAS & PAPAS
Monday, Monday / California dreamin' / Dedicated to the one I love / Creeque alley / It's getting better / Straight shooter / Spanish Harlem / Twelve thirty / Go where you wanna go / I saw her again / People like us / My girl / California earthquake / For the love of ivy / Got a feelin'

CD _____ PLATCD 302
Platinum Music / Dec '88 / Prism / Ross.

VERY BEST OF THE MAMAS & PAPAS
California dreamin' / Dream a little dream of me / Monday, Monday / Dedicated to the one I love / Make your own kind of music / Do you wanna dance / Dancing in the street / Spanish Harlem / I call your name / Words of love / It's getting better / In crowd / Go where you wanna go / Creeque Alley / My heart stood still / I saw her again
CD _____ PWKS 500
Carlton Home Entertainment / Nov '94 / Carlton Home Entertainment.

Mama's Boys

LIVE TONITE
CD _____ CDMFN 114
Music For Nations / Apr '91 / Pinnacle.

Mambo

MAMBOS QUE HICIERON HISTORIA
CD _____ 995202
EPM / Aug '93 / Discovery / ADA.

Mambo Macoco

MAMBO MACOCO WITH TITO PUENTE AND HIS ORCHESTRA (Mambo Macoco & Tito Puente Orchestra)
CD _____ TCD 018
Fresh Sound / Dec '92 / Jazz Music / Discovery.

Mamduko

MUNDIALISTAS
CD _____ TUMICD 020
Tumi / '92 / Sterns / Discovery.

Mamu

TOWNSHIP BOY
What a lie / Soweto so where to / Mpoho / We don't buy from town / Love / Township boy / Today someone died / Prologue/monologue / Don't bother me / War is declared
CD _____ KAZ CD 9
Kaz / Nov '89 / BMG.

Man

2OZ OF PLASTIC WITH A HOLE IN THE MIDDLE
Prelude / Storm / It is as it must be / Spunk box / My name is Jesus Smith / Parchment and candles / Brother Arnold's red and white striped tent
CD _____ SEECD 273
See For Miles/C5 / Nov '89 / Pinnacle.

BACK INTO THE FUTURE
CD _____ BGOCD 211
Beat Goes On / Nov '93 / Pinnacle.

BE GOOD TO YOURSELF AT LEAST ONCE A DAY
C'mon / Keep on crinting / Bananas / Life on the road
CD _____ BGOCD 14
Beat Goes On / '89 / Pinnacle.

CALL DOWN THE MOON
CD _____ HYCD 200154
Hypertension / May '95 / Total/BMG / Direct / ADA.

MAXIMUM DARKNESS
CD _____ BGOCD 43
Beat Goes On / Nov '91 / Pinnacle.

REVELATION
And in the beginning / Sudden life / Empty room / Puella, puella (woman, woman) / Love / Erotica / Blind man / And castles rise in children's eyes / Don't just stand there (come out of the rain) / Missing pieces / Future hides its face
CD _____ REP 4024WZ
Repertoire / Aug '91 / Pinnacle / Cadillac.

RHINOS, WINOS AND LUNATICS
CD _____ BGOCD 208
Beat Goes On / Oct '93 / Pinnacle.

SLOW MOTION
CD _____ BGOCD 209
Beat Goes On / Oct '93 / Pinnacle.

Man + Mouse

HEROIC COUPLET
Fuck the lottery / I don't care what you say, think or do / Hex / Spin / Towards tomorrow / Testify / Rejecting the authority of Vedas / England's glory, my shame / Blownole / No extra track / You're going down with the Mackems
CD _____ HOVE 1CD
Stereophonic Hovesound / Dec '94 / Hovesound.

Man Called Adam

APPLE
CD _____ BLRCD 7
Big Life / Oct '91 / Pinnacle.

Man Or Astro Man

DESTROY ALL ASTRO MEN
CD _____ ESD 1215
Estrus / Jul '95 / Plastic Head.

INTRAVENOUS TELEVISION CONTINUUM
CD _____ LOUDEST 8
One Louder / Jul '95 / SRD.

IS IT
CD _____ ESD 129
Estrus / Jul '95 / Plastic Head.

LIVE TRANSMISSIONS FROM URANUS
CD _____ LOUDEST 4
One Louder / Mar '95 / SRD.

PROJECT INFINITY
CD _____ ES 1221CD
Estrus / Jul '95 / Plastic Head.

YOUR WEIGHT ON THE MOON
CD _____ LOUDEST 4
One Louder / Aug '94 / SRD.

Man With No Name

MOMENT OF TRUTH
CD _____ DICCD 125
Beggars Banquet / Feb '96 / Warner Music / Disc.

Manahedji, Behnam

MASTER OF THE PERSIAN SANTOOR
CD _____ SM 1508-2
Wergo / Feb '94 / Harmonia Mundi / ADA / Cadillac.

Mance, Junior

AT THE TOWN HALL
CD _____ ENJACD 90852
Enja / Dec '95 / New Note / Vital/SAM.

JUNIOR MANCE QUARTET PLAY THE MUSIC OF DIZZY GILLESPIE (Mance, Junior Quintet)
CD _____ SKCD2-3050
Sackville / Feb '93 / Swift / Jazz Music / Jazz Horizons / Cadillac / CM.

JUNIOR MANCE SPECIAL
CD _____ SKCD 2-3043
Sackville / Oct '92 / Swift / Jazz Music / Jazz Horizons / Cadillac / CM.

SMOKEY BLUES (Mance, Junior Trio)
CD _____ JSPCD 219
JSP / Jul '88 / ADA / Target/BMG / Direct / Cadillac / Complete/Pinnacle.

SOFTLY AS IN A MORNING (Mance, Junior Trio)
CD _____ ENJACD 80802
Enja / Jan '95 / New Note / Vital/SAM.

Mancini, Henry

BLUES AND THE BEAT, THE
Blues / Smoke rings / Misty / Blue flame / After hours / Mood indigo / Beat / Big noise from Winnetka / Alright O.K. you win / Tippin' in / How could you do a thing like that to me / Sing, sing, sing / House of the rising sun / C jam blues / Green onions / Night train
CD _____ 74321260472
RCA / Jun '95 / BMG.

IN THE PINK
Pink Panther theme / Moon river / Days of wine and roses / Baby elephant walk / Theme from Hatari / Charade / Thorn birds theme / Blue satin / Two for the road / My lucky / Theme from the Molly Maguires / Moment to moment / As time goes by / Shot in the dark / Misty / Theme from love story / Pennywistle jig / Everything I do (I do it for you) / Moonlight sonata / Tender is the night / Theme from Mommie Dearest / Raindrops keep falling on my head / Crazy world / Mona Lisa / Peter Gunn / Unchained melody / Summer knows / Experiment in terror / Windmills of your mind / Til there was you / Speedy gonzales / Sweetheart tree / Love theme from Romeo and Juliet / Dream a little dream of me / Lonesome / Pie in the face polka / Love is a many splendoured thing / By the time I get tp Phoenix / Dear heart / Charade (opening titles) / Shadow of your smile / One for my baby / Breakfast at Tiffany's / That old black magic / Evergreen / Midnight cowboy
CD _____ 74321244832
RCA / Nov '95 / BMG.

MANCINI ROCKS THE POPS (Mancini, Henry & The Royal Philharmonic Pops Orchestra)
Walk like an Egyptian / In the air tonight / Thriller / Every breath you take / Material girl / With or without you / Sweet dreams (are made of this) / La Bamba / On the turning away / It's a sin / Imagine / Good old rock 'n' roll / (We're gonna) Rock around the clock / Bye bye love / Bad, Bad Leroy Brown / Blue suede shoes / Shake, rattle and roll / Peggy Sue
CD _____ CO 73078
Denon / Apr '89 / Conifer.

MERRY MANCINI CHRISTMAS, A
Little drummer boy / Jingle bells / Sleigh ride / Christmas song / Winter wonderland / Silver bells / Frosty the snowman / Rudolph the red nosed reindeer / White Christmas / Carol for another Christmas / Silent night / O holy night / O little town of Bethlehem / God rest ye merry gentlemen / Deck the halls with boughs of holly / Hark the herald angels sing / We three kings of Orient are / O come all ye faithful (Adeste Fidelis) / Joy to the world / It came upon a midnight clear / Away in a manger / First Noel
CD _____ ND 81928
Arista / Oct '94 / BMG.

PETER GUNN
CD _____ 15412
Laserlight / Jan '93 / Target/BMG.

PREMIER POPS (Mancini, Henry & The Royal Philharmonic Pops Orchestra)
Overture to a pop concert / Thorn Birds Suite / Hong Kong fireworks / Sunflower / Inspector Clouseau theme / Charade / Glass menagerie / Sons of Italy / Ohio riverboat / Great mouse detective / Moon river
CD _____ CO 2320
Denon / Aug '88 / Conifer.

ROMANTIC MOMENTS
CD _____ VSD 5530
Varese Sarabande/Colosseum / Nov '94 / Pinnacle / Silva Screen.

Mandalaband

EYE OF WENDOR, THE
Eye of Wendor / Florians song / Ride to the city / Almar's tower / Like the wind / Tempest / Dawn of a new day / Departure from Carthillas Elsethea / Witch of Waldow wood / Silesandre / Aenord's lament / Funeral of the king / Coronation of Damien
CD _____ RPM 105
RPM / Jul '93 / Pinnacle.

MANDALABAND
Om mani padme hum (in four movements) / Determination / Song for a king / Roof of the world / Looking in
CD _____ EDCD 343
Edsel / Feb '92 / Pinnacle / ADA.

Mandators

POWER OF THE PEOPLE
CD _____ CDBH 156
Heartbeat / Apr '94 / Greensleeves / Jetstar / Direct / ADA.

Mandel, Harvey

BABY BATTER
Baby batter / One way street / Freedom ball / Hank the ripper / Midnight sun / Morton grove Mama / El stinger
CD _____ BGOCD 252
Beat Goes On / Feb '95 / Pinnacle.

Mandingo

LO MEJER DE LA SALSA VENEZOLANA
CD _____ EUCD 1258
ARC / Mar '94 / ARC Music / ADA.

NEW WORLD POWER
CD _____ AXCD 3004
Axiom / Sep '90 / PolyGram Vital.

WATTO SITTA
CD _____ CPCD 8153
Celluloid / Nov '95 / Charly.

Mandolin Allstars

MANDOLIN ALLSTARS
CD _____ ACS 27CD
Acoustics / Aug '95 / Conifer / Direct / ADA.

Mandragora

EARTHDANCE
Sometimes / Earthdance / Xylem / Zarg / Great rubbings of parts / Factory in the jungle / Around the world (Live)
CD _____ RUNECD 013
Mystic Stones / Mar '93 / Vital.

TEMPLE BALL
Temple ball / Dr. Temple's abduction / Zarg / Talking to God (Part IV) / This is... / Jazz message from the mothership / Inside the crystal circle / Null gravity generator / Rainbow warrior
CD _____ RUNECD 014
Mystic Stones / Jun '94 / Vital.

Mandukhai Ensemble

MANDUKHAI ENSEMBLE OF MONGOLIA
CD _____ PS 65115
Playasound / Nov '93 / Harmonia Mundi / ADA.

Manfila, Kante

KANKAN BLUES (Manfila, Kante & Balla Kalia)
CD _____ OA 201
PAM / Feb '94 / Direct / ADA.

N'NA NIWALE: KANKAN BLUES CHAPTER 2
CD _____ PAM 402CD
PAM / Mar '94 / Direct / ADA.

Manfred Mann

20 YEARS OF MANFRED MANN'S EARTHBAND (Manfred Mann's Earthband)
Blinded by the light / Joybringer / Somewhere in Africa / You angel you / Questions / For you / California / Tribal statistics / Davy's on the road again / Runner / Mighty quinn / Angels at the gate
CD _____ BOMME 1CD
Cohesion / Nov '90 / Grapevine.

AGES OF MANN
5-4-3-2-1 / Pretty flamingo / Do wah diddy diddy / Sha la la / If you gotta go, go now / Oh no not my baby / Come tomorrow / My name is Jack / One in the middle / I put a spell on you / Just like a woman / Poison Ivy / Mighty quinn / Semi-detached suburban Mr. James / Ha ha said the clown / Raggamuffin man / Hubble bubble toil and trouble / There's no living without your love / You gave me somebody to love / Got my mojo working / With God on our side / Fox on the run
CD _____ 5143262
PolyGram TV / Sep '95 / PolyGram.

ANGEL STATION (Manfred Mann's Earthband)
Don't kill it Carol / You angel you / Hollywood town / Belle of the earth / Platform end / Angels at the gate / You are / I am / Waiting for the rain / Resurrection
CD _____ COMMECD 4
Cohesion / Nov '90 / Grapevine.

BEST OF 1964-1966
Do wah diddy diddy / 5-4-3-2-1 / Sha la la / Hubble bubble toil and trouble / If you gotta go, go now / Oh no not my baby / Bare hugg / Got my mojo working / Hoochie coochie man / Smokestack lightnin' / Pretty flamingo / You gave me somebody to love / Don't ask me what I say / I'm your kingpin / It's gonna work out fine / Hi lili hi lo / Stormy Monday blues / Abominable snowman / Since I don't have you / Come tomorrow
CD _____ CDMFP 5994
Music For Pleasure / Dec '93 / EMI.

BEST OF THE EMI YEARS 1963-1965, THE
Do wah diddy diddy / Cock-a-hoop / I've got my mojo working / Sticks and stones / 5-4-3-2-1 / Why should we not / I'm your kingpin / Without you / I put a spell on you / Hubble bubble toil and trouble / Dashing away with a smoothing iron / Sha la la / Hi lili hi lo / I can't believe what you say / One in the middle / Watermelon man / With God on our side / Come tomorrow / I think it's gonna work out fine / She / Oh not my baby / My little red book / Come home baby / Pretty flamingo / If you gotta go, go now / Tired of trying, bored with lying, scared of dying / There's no living without your loving / You gave me somebody to love / Do wah diddy diddy (Unedited)
CD _____ CDEMS 1500
EMI / May '93 / EMI.

CHANCE (Manfred Mann's Earthband)
Lies (through the 80's) / One the run / For you / Adolescent dream / Fritz the blank / Stranded / This is your heart / No guarantee / Heart on the street
CD _____ COMMECD 9
Cohesion / Nov '90 / Grapevine.

CRIMINAL TANGO (Manfred Mann's Earthband)
Going underground / Who are the mystery kids / Banquet / Killer on the loose / Do anything you wanna do / Rescue / You got me right through the heart / Hey bulldog / Crossfire
CD _____ DIXCD 35
10 / Jul '86 / EMI.

EP COLLECTION: MANFRED MANN
5-4-3-2-1 / Cock-a-hoop / Without you / Groovin' / Do wah diddy diddy / Can't believe it / One in the middle / Watermelon man / What am I to do / With God on our side / There's no living without your loving / Tired trying, bored of lying, scared of dying / Machines / She needs company / Tenessee waltz / When will I be loved / I got you babe
CD _____ SEECD 252
See For Miles/C5 / Oct '94 / Pinnacle.

GLORIFIED MAGNIFIED (Manfred Mann's Earthband)
Meat / Look around / One way glass / I'm gonna have you all / Down home / Our friend George / Ashes to the wind / Wind / It's all over now / Baby blue / Glorified magnified

---

CD _____ MFMCD 11
Cohesion / Nov '93 / Grapevine.

GOOD EARTH, THE (Manfred Mann's Earthband)
Give me the good earth / Launching place / I'll be gone / Earth hymn (parts 1 and 2) / Sky high / Be not too hard
CD _____ MFMCD 12
Cohesion / Nov '93 / Grapevine.

LIVE IN BUDAPEST (Manfred Mann's Earthband)
Spirits in the night / For you / Lies (through the 80's) / Redemption song / Demolition man / Davy's on the road again / Blinded by the light / Mighty Quinn
CD _____ COMMECD 10
Cohesion / Nov '90 / Grapevine.

MANFRED MANN CHAPTER THREE VOL. 1 (Manfred Mann Chapter 3)
CD _____ MFMCD 14
Cohesion / Feb '94 / Grapevine.

MANFRED MANN CHAPTER THREE VOL. 2 (Manfred Mann Chapter 3)
CD _____ MFMCD 15
Cohesion / Feb '94 / Grapevine.

MANFRED MANN'S EARTHBAND (Manfred Mann's Earthband)
California coastline / Captain Bobby Stout / Sloth / Living without you / Tribute / Please Mrs. Henry / Jump sturdy / Prayer / Part time man / Up and leaving
CD _____ COMMECD 6
Cohesion / Nov '90 / Grapevine.

MASQUE (Manfred Mann's Earthband)
Joybringer / Billie's orno bounce / What you give is what you get / Rivers run dry / Planets schmanets / Geronimo's cadillac / Sister Billie's bounce / Telegram to Monica / Couple of mates, A (from Mars and Jupiter) / Neptune (icebringer) / Hymn (from Jupiter) / We're going wrong
CD _____ DIXCD 69
10 / Apr '92 / EMI.

MESSIN' (Manfred Mann's Earthband)
Messin' / Buckland / Cloudy eyes / Get your rocks off / Sad joy / Black and blue / Mardi Gras day
CD _____ COMMECD 7
Cohesion / Nov '90 / Grapevine.

NIGHTINGALES AND BOMBERS (Manfred Mann's Earthband)
Spirits in the night / Countdown / Time is right / Cross fade / Visionary mountains / Nightingales and bombers / Fat Nelly / As above so below
CD _____ COMMECD 8
Cohesion / Nov '90 / Grapevine.

ROARING SILENCE, THE (Manfred Mann's Earthband)
Blinded by the light / Singing the dolphin through / Waiter, there's a yawn in my ear / Road to Babylon / This side of paradise / Starbird / Questions
CD _____ COMMECD 3
Cohesion / Nov '90 / Grapevine.

SOLAR FIRE (Manfred Mann's Earthband)
CD _____ COMMECD 1
Cohesion / Nov '90 / Grapevine.

SOMEWHERE IN AFRICA (Manfred Mann's Earthband)
Tribal statistics / Eyes of Nostradamus / Third world service / Demolition man / Brothers and sisters / To Bantustan (Africa suite) / Koze koberini / Laiela, redemption song (no kwazulu) / Somewhere in Africa
CD _____ COMMECD 5
Cohesion / '90 / Grapevine.

SPOTLIGHT (Manfred Mann's Earthband)
CD _____ MFMCD 013
PolyGram TV / Sep '92 / PolyGram.

VERY BEST OF MANFRED MANN'S EARTHBAND, THE
CD _____ ARC 3100162
Arcade / Aug '94 / Sony / Grapevine.

WATCH (Manfred Mann's Earthband)
CD _____ COMMECD 3
Cohesion / Nov '90 / Grapevine.

Mangas, Yiorgos

YIORGOS MANGAS
Tsifteteli rok / Roumaniko / Autoschediasmos / Ibori / Chorepste / Ta chrysa dactyla / Yia tous anthropous pou agapao / Skaros / To diko mou
CD _____ CDORB 021
Globestyle / Jul '90 / Pinnacle.

Manhattan Jazz Quintet

AUTUMN LEAVES
Jordu / Recado bossa nova / Confirmation / Autumn leaves / Mood piece
CD _____ 240 E 6805
King/Paddle Wheel / Jul '90 / New Note.

CARAVAN
Caravan / Cloudy / Five spot after dark / Night in Tunisia / Broadway stroll / You and the night and the music / For Duke
CD _____ 292 E 6002
King/Paddle Wheel / Feb '91 / New Note.

FUNKY STRUT
Swing street / Hot grits / Mercy mercy mercy / Sister Sadie / Song for my father / Funky strut / Foxy little thang
CD _____ 66055006
Sweet Basil / Oct '91 / New Note.

LIVE AT PIT INN VOL 1
So this / Angel eyes / Round Midnight / Misticzd
CD _____ K32Y 61011
King/Paddle Wheel / Jul '90 / New Note.

LIVE AT PIT INN VOL 2
Recado bossa nova / S.V. blues / Autumn leaves / Rosario
CD _____ K32Y 61012
King/Paddle Wheel / Jul '90 / New Note.

MANHATTAN JAZZ QUINTET
Summertime / Rosario / Milestones / My favourite things / Airegin / Summer waltz
CD _____ 240E 6804
King/Paddle Wheel / Jul '90 / New Note.

MY FAVOURITE THINGS
CD _____ K32Y 6210
Electric Bird / Sep '88 / New Note.

MY FUNNY VALENTINE
Mr. P.C. / Round Midnight / On a clear day / New York state of mind / U blues
CD _____ K32Y 6070
King/Paddle Wheel / Oct '87 / New Note.

PLAYS BLUE NOTE
Cleopatra's dream / Cool struttin' / Sweet love of mine / Dear old Stockholm / Wolf pack / Cheesecake / For Alfred / Moanin'
CD _____ K32Y 6230
King/Paddle Wheel / Jun '89 / New Note.

Manhattan New Music...

MOOD SWING (Manhattan New Music Project)
CD _____ 121207-2
Soul Note / Apr '93 / Harmonia Mundi / Wellard / Cadillac.

Manhattan Project

DREAMBOAT
Dreamboat / Cape Town ambush / Misty / Depth / I remember / Sacrifice / Someday my Prince will come / I didn't know what time it was / Alluding to
CD _____ CDSJP 327
Timeless Jazz / Aug '90 / New Note.

Manhattan Transfer

BEST OF MANHATTAN TRANSFER
Tuxedo junction / Boy from New York City / Twilight zone / Body and soul / Candy / Four brothers / Birdland / Gloria / Trickle trickle / Operator / Java jive / Nightingale sang in Berkeley Square
CD _____ 2508412
WEA / Aug '84 / Warner Music.

BODIES AND SOULS
Spice of life / This independence / Mystery / American pop / Code of ethics / Malaise en malaise / Down South camp meeting / Why not / Goodbye love / Night that Monk returned to heaven
CD _____ 756780104-2
WEA / Mar '93 / Warner Music.

BOP DOO WOP
Unchained melody / Route 66 / My cat fell in the well / Duke of Dubuque / How high the moon / Baby come back to me / Safronia B / Heart's desire / That's the way it goes
CD _____ 756781233-2
WEA / Mar '93 / Warner Music.

BRASIL
Soul food to go / Zoo blues / So you say / Capim / Metropolis / Hear the voices / Agua / Jungle pioneer / Notes from the underground
CD _____ 756781803-2
WEA / Mar '93 / Warner Music.

COMING OUT
Don't let go / Zindy Lou / Chanson d'amour / Helpless / Scotch and soda / Speak up mambo / Cuentame / Poinciana / S.O.S. / Popsicle toes / It wouldn't have made any difference / Thought of loving you
CD _____ 756781502-2
WEA / Mar '93 / Warner Music.

DOWN IN BIRDLAND
Trickle trickle / Gloria / Operator / Helpless / Ray's rockhouse / Heart's desire / Zindy Lou / Mystery / Baby come back to me (morse code of love) / Route 66 / Java jive / Chanson d'amour / Foreign affairs / Smile again / Spice of life / Speak up Mambo / Soul food to go (Sina) / So you say (Esquinas) / Boy from New York City / Twilight zone / Twilight zone / Four brothers / Bee blop blues / Candy / Gal in Calico / Love for sale / On a little street in Singapore / Tuxedo junction / That cat is high / Body and soul / Meet Benny Bailey / Sing joy spring / To you / Down south camp meeting / Until I met you / Why not / Another night in Tunisia / Capim / Nightingale sang in Berkley Square / Birdland (Vocal)
CD _____ 812271053-2
WEA / Jan '94 / Warner Music.

EXTENSIONS
Birdland / Wacky dust / Nothin' you can do about it / Coo coo-u / Body and soul (Eddie and the bean) / Twilight zone (part 1) / Twilight zone (part 2) / Trickle trickle / Shaker song / Foreign affair
CD _____ 756781565-2
WEA / Mar '93 / Warner Music.

LIVE: MANHATTAN TRANSFER
Four brothers / Rambo / Meet Benny Bailey / Airegin II / To you / Sing joy Spring / Move / That's killer Joe / Duke of Dubuque / Gloria / On the boulevard / Shaker song / Ray's rockhouse
CD _____ 7567817232
WEA / Oct '87 / Warner Music.

MANHATTAN TRANSFER
Tuxedo Junction / Sweet talking guy / Operator / Candy / Gloria / Clap your hands / That cat is high / You can depend on me / Blue champagne / Occapella / Heart's desire
CD _____ 7567814932
WEA / '87 / Warner Music.

MECCA FOR MODERNS
On the Boulevard / Boy from New York City / Smile again / Wanted dead or alive / Spies in the night / Corner pocket / Confirmation / Kafka / Nightingale sang in Berkeley Square
CD _____ 756781482-2
WEA / Mar '93 / Warner Music.

PASTICHE
Four brothers / Gal in Calico / Love for sale / Je voulais (te dire que t'attends) / On a little street in Singapore / In a mellow tone / Walk in love / Who, what, when, where and why / It's not the spotlight / Pieces of dreams / Where did our love go
CD _____ 8122718092
WEA / Jun '95 / Warner Music.

TONIN'
CD _____ 7567826612
WEA / Jun '95 / Warner Music.

Manhattans

BEST OF THE MANHATTANS, THE
I'll never find another / Shining star / Hurt / We never danced to a love song / Reasons / Am I losing you / Fever / There's no me without you / Kiss and say goodbye / Don't take your love from me / Soul train / Summertime in the city / It's you / Crazy / I kinda miss you / It feels good to be loved so bad
CD _____ 9827282
Pickwick/Sony Collector's Choice / Apr '92 / Carlton Home Entertainment / Pinnacle / Sony.

DEDICATED TO YOU/ FOR YOU AND YOURS
Follow your heart / That new girl / Can I / Boston monkey / I've got everything but you / Manhattan stomp / Searchin' for my baby / Our love will never die / I'm the one love forgot / What's it gonna be / Teach me the Philly dog) / Baby I need you / I call it love / I betcha / Sweet little girl / Every beat of my heart / Alone on New Year's Eve / All I need is your love / I wanna be / When we're made as one / Call somebody please / For the very first time / It's that time of year / Baby I'm sorry
CD _____ CDKEND 103
Kent / Jun '93 / Pinnacle.

KISS AND SAY GOODBYE
I'm not a run around / You'd better believe it / Falling apart at the seams / We'll have forever to love / Take it or leave it / Hurt / If you're ever gonna love me / Shining star / Crazy / I'll never find another / Where did we go wrong / Am I losing you / Way we were/Memories / Here comes the hurt again / How can anything so good be so bad for you / Kiss and say goodbye
CD _____ PWKS 4172
Carlton Home Entertainment / Sep '93 / Carlton Home Entertainment.

KISS AND SAY GOODBYE
Kiss and say goodbye / Don't take your love / There's no me without you / Wish that you were mine / Day the robin sang to me / That's how much I love you / Hurt / La la la wish upon a star / I kinda miss you / It feels good to be loved so bad / Am I losing you / Everybody has a dream / Shining star / I'll never find another (find another like you) / Just one moment away / I was made for you / Just the lonely talking again / You send me / Goodbye is the saddest word
CD _____ 4808992
Columbia / Jan '96 / Sony.

Manic Eden

MANIC EDEN
CD _____ NTHEN 15
Now & Then / Sep '95 / Plastic Head.

Manic P

GOD'S TEARS
CD _____ HY 39100742CD
Hyperium / Oct '93 / Plastic Head.

Manic Street Preachers

GENERATION TERRORISTS
Slash 'n' burn / Nat West-Barclays-Midland-Lloyds / Born to end / Motorcycle emptiness / You love us / Love's sweet exile / Little baby nothing / Repeat (stars and stripes) / Tennessee / Another invented disease / Stay beautiful / So dead / Repeat (UK) / Spectators of suicide / Damn dog / Crucifix kiss / Methadone pretty / Condemned to rock 'n' roll
CD _____ 4710602
Columbia / Jun '92 / Sony.

GOLD AGAINST THE SOUL
Sleepflower / From despair to where / La tristesse durera (scream to a sigh) / Yourself / Life becoming a landslide / Drug drug druggy / Roses in the hospital / Nostalgic pushead / Symphony of tourette / Gold against the soul
CD _____ 4740642
Columbia / Jun '93 / Sony.

HOLY BIBLE
Yes / Ifwhiteamericatoldthetruthforoneday-itsworldwouldfallapart / Of walking abortion / She is suffering / Archives of pain / Revol / 4st 7lb / Faster / This is yesterday / Die in the summertime / Intense humming of evil / PCP / Mausoleum
CD _____ 4774212
Columbia / Aug '94 / Sony.

Manilla Road

CIRCUS MAXIMUS
CD _____ BDCD 53
Black Dragon / Oct '92 / Elco.

Manilow, Barry

BARRY - LIVE IN BRITAIN
It's a miracle / Old songs medley (Tracks include The Old Songs, Don't wanna walk without you, Let's hang o) / Stay / Beautiful music / I made it through the rain / Bermuda Triangle / Break down the door / Who's been sleeping in my bed / Copacabana / Could it be magic / Mandy / London - we'll meet again / One voice
CD _____ 261320
Arista / Apr '91 / BMG.

BECAUSE IT'S CHRISTMAS
Christmas song / Jingle bells / Silent night / I guess there ain't no Santa Claus / First Noel / When the meadow was bloomin' / For unto us a child is born / Because it's Christmas (for all children) / Baby, it's cold outside / White Christmas / Carol of the bells / Bells of Christmas / Joy to the world / Have yourself a merry little Christmas / We wish you a Merry Christmas / It's just another New Year's Eve
CD _____ 262 484
Arista / Oct '94 / BMG.

EVEN NOW
Copacabana / Somewhere in the night / Linda song / Can't smile without you / Leavin' in the morning / Where do I go from here / Even now / I was a fool (to let you go) / Losing touch / I just want to be the one in your life / Starting again / Sunrise
CD _____ 251125
Arista / Oct '88 / BMG.

GREATEST HITS: BARRY MANILOW
Ships / Some kind of friend / I made it through the rain / Put a quarter in the jukebox / One voice / Old songs / Let's hang on / Memory / You're looking hot tonight
CD _____ 258552
Arista / May '88 / BMG.

IF I SHOULD LOVE AGAIN/ONE VOICE/ BARRY (3CD Set)
CD Set _____ 354296
Arista / Feb '93 / BMG.

LIVE ON BROADWAY
Sweet life / It's a long way up / Brooklyn blues / Memory / Upfront / God bless the other 99 / Mandy / It's a miracle / Some good things never last / If you remember me / Do like I do / Best seat in the house / Gonzo hits medley / It's all can dream
CD _____ 353785
Arista / Feb '90 / BMG.

MANILOW
At the dance / If you were here with me tonight / Sweet heaven / Ain't nothing like the real thing / It's a long way up / I'm your man / It's all behind us now / In search of love / He doesn't care (but I do) / Some sweet day
CD _____ PD 87044
Arista / Feb '86 / BMG.

REFLECTIONS
It's a miracle / Could it be magic / Looks like we made it
CD _____ PWKS 514
Carlton Home Entertainment / Sep '88 / Carlton Home Entertainment.

SHOWSTOPPERS
Give my regards to Broadway / Overture of overtures / All I need is the girl / Real live girl / Where or when / Look to the rainbow / Once in love with Amy / Dancing in the dark / You can have the TV / I'll be seeing you / Fugue for tinhorns / Old friends /

Never met a man I didn't like / Bring him home / If we only have love
CD _____ 262 091
Arista / Oct '91 / BMG.

SINGING WITH THE BIG BANDS
Sentimental journey (featuring Les Brown & his Band of Renown) / And the angels sing / Green eyes (featuring The Jimmy Dorsey Orchestra with Rosemary Clooney) / I should care / On the sunny side of the street (featuring The Jimmy Dorsey Orchestra) / All or nothing at all (featuring The Harry James Orchestra) / I'm getting sentimental over you / I'll never smile again (featuring The Tommy Dorsey Orchestra) / Don't get around much anymore (featuring The Duke Ellington Orchestra) / I can't get started (with you) / Chattanooga choo choo (featuring The Glenn Miller Orchestra) / Moonlight serenade / Don't sit under the apple tree (featuring The Glenn Miller Orchestra with Debra Byrd) / I'll be with you in apple blossom time / Where does the time go
CD _____ 07822187712
Arista / Oct '94 / BMG.

SONGS 1975-1990, THE
I write the songs / One voice / Old songs / Don't want to walk without you / Some good things never last / Somewhere down the road / When I wanted you / Stay / Even now / Read 'em and weep / Somewhere in the night / I made it through the rain / Daybreak (live) / Please don't be scared / Looks like we made it / Mandy / If I should love again (live) / All the time / Copacabana / Keep each other warm / Weekend in New England / Lonely together / Can't smile without you / Trying to get the feeling again / Could it be magic / Brooklyn blues / Who needs to dream / Ready to take a chance again / If I can dream
CD _____ 353868
Arista / Jun '90 / BMG.

SONGS TO MAKE THE WHOLE WORLD SING
Please don't be scared / One that got away / Keep each other warm / Once and for all / When the good times come again / In another world / My moonlight memories of love / Little travelling music please / Some good things never last / You begin again / Anyone can do the heartbreak
CD _____ 259927
Arista / May '89 / BMG.

Manly, Gill

DETOUR HEAD
CD _____ PARCD 505
Parrot / Dec '94 / THE / Wellard / Jazz Music.

Mann, Aimee

I'M WITH STUPID
Long shot / Choice in the matter / Sugarcoated / You could make a killing / Superball / Amateur / All over now / Par for the course / You're with stupid now / That's just what you are / Frankenstein / Ray / It's not safe
CD _____ GED 24951
Geffen / Oct '95 / BMG.

Mann, Carl

MONA LISA (4CD Set)
Gonna rock and roll tonight / Rockin' love / Mona Lisa (master) / Foolish one / Rockin' love (master) / Pretend / I can't forget you (master) / Some enchanted evening / I'm coming home / Quality of the border (master) / Ain't got no home / If I ever needed you / Island of love / Walkin' and thinkin' / Baby I don't care / I'm bluer than anyone can be / Wayward wind / Born to be bad / If I could change you / When I grow too old to dream / Mountain dew / Mona Lisa (alt.) / Look at that moon / Rockin' love (alt.) / Too young / Take these chains from my heart / I can't forget you (undubbed) / South of the border (alt.) / Kansas city / Today is Christmas / Crazy fool / Blueberry Hill / I'll always love you darlin' / Ain't you got no lovin' for me / Then I turned and walked slowly away / Serenade of the bells / It really doesn't matter now / Sentimental journey / Born to be bad (undubbed) / I love you, I adore you / Are you teasing me / Stop the world (and let me off) / I don't care / I'm walking the dog / Ubangi stomp / Don't let the stars get in your eyes / Long black veil / Canadian sunset / Even tho' / Chinatown, my China-town / Because of you / Till the end of forever / Mexicali rose / Hey doll baby / Vanished / Down to my last forgive you / Blue river / Yesterday is gone / Burnin' holes in the eyes of Abraham Lincoln / German town / She was young / Paying for the crimes / Hear in Alaska / Funny way of gettin' over someone else / When the leaves turn brown / Everyday grows sweet with the wine / More to life / Going to church with mama / It really matters / Toast to a fool / I'm married friend / My favorite bunch of roses / Ballad of Johnny Clyde / Cheatin' time / Keep feeding her the wine / Let's turn back the pages / If I ever love again / Make a man want to / Neon lights / I'm just about out of my mind / It's not the coffee that's keeping me awake / No easy way to say goodbye / Back lovin' / Annie over time /

I've got feelings too / Twilight time / Eighteen yellow roses / Belly rubbin' country soul / Tennemonk, Georgia / She loves to love for the feeling / Love died a long time ago / Darling of Atlanta / Country was the song / Second guessing / One last goodbye / On the back streets of Dallas / Tripping on teardrops / I love you too much
CD Set _____ BCD 15713
Bear Family / Aug '93 / Rollercoaster / Direct / CM / Swift / ADA.

Mann, Dany

SEXIE HEXY
CD _____ BCD 15483
Bear Family / '88 / Rollercoaster / Direct / CM / Swift / ADA.

Mann, Geoff

IN ONE ERA
Piccadilly square / I wouldn't lie to you / Kingdom come / Afterwards / For God's sake / Green paper snow / My soul / Slow one / Creation / Dance / Gethsemane / Waves / Flowers
CD _____ CYCL 004
Cyclops / Mar '94 / Pinnacle.

LOUD SYMBOLS
CD _____ CDGRUB 15
Food For Thought / Jul '91 / Pinnacle.

MINISTRY OF THE INTERIOR (Mann, Geoff Band)
CD _____ CDGRUB 21
Food For Thought / Sep '91 / Pinnacle.

Mann, Herbie

AT THE VILLAGE GATE
Comin' home baby / Summertime / It ain't necessarily so
CD _____ 756781350-2
Atlantic / Mar '93 / Warner Music.

BEST OF HERBIE MANN, THE
Comin' home baby / Memphis underground / Philly dog / Man and a woman / This little girl of mine
CD _____ 756781369-2
Atlantic / Mar '93 / Warner Music.

COPACABANA
CD _____ CD 62059
Saludos Amigos / May '94 / Target/BMG.

DEEP POCKET
Down in the corner / Knock on wood / Moanin' / When something is wrong with my baby / Papa was a rollin' stone / Sunny / Mercy mercy mercy / Go home / Amazing grace
CD _____ KOKO 1296
Kokopelli / Sep '94 / New Note.

EVOLUTION OF MANN, THE (2CD Set/ The Herbie Mann Anthology)
Baghdad/Asia minor / Sawa sawa de / This little girl of mine / Comin' home baby / One note samba (samba de uma nota so) / Blues walk / Gymnopedie / I love you / Soul guajira / Mushi mushi / Feeling good / Philly dog / Memphis underground / Claudia one / Muscle shoals nitty gritty / Yesterday's kisses / Push push / Hold on I'm comin' / In memory of Elizabeth Reed / Mellow yellow / Hijack / Lugar comun (Common place) / Draw your breaks / Cricket dance / Birdwalk / Aria / Dona primeira / Amazing grace
CD Set _____ 812271634-2
Atlantic / May '94 / Warner Music.

FLUTE SOUFFLE (Mann, Herbie & Bobby Jaspar)
Tel aviv / Somewhere else / Let's march / Chasin' the Bird
CD _____ OJCCD 760
Original Jazz Classics / Apr '93 / Wellard / Jazz Music / Cadillac / Complete/Pinnacle.

JAZZ WE HEARD LAST SUMMER, THE
S.M.T.W.T.F.S. blues / Rockaway / Things we did last summer / Green stamp monsta / World wide boots
CD _____ SV 0228
Savoy Jazz / Oct '93 / Conifer / ADA.

MEMPHIS UNDERGROUND
Memphis underground / New Orleans / Hold on I'm comin' / Chain of fools / Battle hymn of the Republic
CD _____ K781 364 2
Atlantic / '88 / Warner Music.

NIRVANA (Mann, Herbie & Bill Evans)
Nirvana / Gymnopedie / I love you / Willow weep for me / Lover man / Cashmere
CD _____ 7567901412
Atlantic / Jun '95 / Warner Music.

OPALESCENCE
Dona Palermeira / Comin' home baby / Song for Lea / Bahia de tadas as contas / Dry land / Two rivers / Do oiapoque ao chui) / Sir Charles Duke / Number fifty-five / Calling you
CD _____ KOKO 1298
Kokopelli / Sep '94 / New Note.

PEACE PIECES
Peri's scope / Funkallero / Interplay / Turn out the stars / We will meet again / Blue in green / Waltz for Debbie / Very early / Peace piece

CD _____ KOKO 1306
Kokopelli / Feb '96 / New Note.

PUSH, PUSH
CD _____ 7567903062
Atlantic / Jul '93 / Warner Music.

YARDBIRD SUITE
Yardbird suite / Here's that man / One for Tubby / Squire's parlor / Who knew / Opicana
CD _____ SV 0193
Savoy Jazz / Nov '92 / Conifer / ADA.

Mann, John

ALL TIME FAVOURITES JUST FOR YOU
CD _____ CDGRS 1281
Grosvenor / Aug '95 / Target/BMG.

ASPECTS OF MUSIC
All the world's a stage / My heart and I / Annen polka / Kiss me / Romantica / Lost chord / Me and my girl / Love makes the world go round / Leaning on a lamp-post / Lambeth walk / Sun has got his hat on / Music in May / Czardas / Non, je ne regrette rien / L'accordeoniste / Hymne a l'amour / Funicula, funicula / Melody of love / My blue heaven / Happy days and lonely nights / Bells are ringing / Ave Maria / Mistakes / Where is your heart (Moulin Rouge) / Gigi / Waltz at Maxim's / Night they invented champagne / Thank heavens for little girls / I remember it well / Parisians, I'll be seeing you
CD _____ CDGRS 1232
Grosvenor / '91 / Target/BMG.

EVERGREENS
Medley: Our Gracie Fields / Medley: De Sylva Brown and Henderson / Medley: Rodgers and Hammerstein / Intermezzo from Cavalleria Rusticana / Thunder and lightning polka / Dolores / Song of paradise / Blue tango / Brown bird singing / Post horn gallop / Medley: Off to the sea / Medley: Minstrel magic (Available on CD only)
CD _____ CDGRS 1263
Grosvenor / Mar '95 / Target/BMG.

MOONLIGHT AND ROSES
Theme from the last rhapsody / Varsity drag / Doin' the raccoon / Don't bring Lulu / Charleston / Barney Google / Nagaski / Minuet from Berenice / Maiden's prayer / Cavatina / Delicado / Irving Berlin's popular waltzes / Sheep may safely graze / Love is the sweetest thing / Makin' whoopee / You made me love you / Meditation / Moonlight and roses / Serenade / Camelot / If ever I would leave you / Thank heavens for little girls / Rain in Spain / Wouldn't it be lovely / Wandering star / I talk to the trees / Parisians / Lovely way to spend an evening / Nola (On CD only) / Send in the clowns (On CD only)
CD _____ CDGRS 1266
Grosvenor / Feb '95 / Target/BMG.

THAT'S ENTERTAINMENT
And all that jazz / Dreaming ballerina / La cumparsita / Marigold / My curly headed baby / Nicola / Summer in Venice / My foolish heart / Amor amor / Narcissus / It had to be you / Hello Dolly / Walking my baby back home / Any dream will do / Vienna / Neapolitan serenade / Flirtation waltz / Temptation rag / Grasshoppers dance / Catari, catari / Roses of Picardy / Windows of Paris / Bye bye blues
CD _____ PLATCD 3918
Prism / Apr '93 / Prism.

VIENNA CITY OF MY DREAMS
CD _____ CDGRS1254
Grosvenor / Feb '93 / Target/BMG.

Mann, Woody

STAIRWELL SERENADE
Acoustic Music / Aug '95 / ADA.
CD _____ BEST 1072CD

STORIES
CD _____ GR 70724
Greenhays / Nov '94 / Roots / Jazz Music / Duncans / CM / ADA.

Manna

MANNA
From heaven / Secret life of bass / Mr. Echo (go to hell) / Eat it, weave it and wear it / Kelham's island / Transport of delight / Lonely tones
CD _____ AMB 5937CD
Apollo / Jan '95 / Vital.

Manne, Shelly

ALIVE IN LONDON
Three on a match / Once again / Big oak basin / Illusion / Don't know
CD _____ OJCCD 773-2
Original Jazz Classics / Jan '94 / Wellard / Jazz Music / Cadillac / Complete/Pinnacle.

AT THE BLACK HAWK VOL.1 (Manne, Shelly & His Men)
Summertime / Our delight / Poinciana / Blue Daniel / Blue Daniel (alternate version) (Pniously Unissued) / Theme: A gem from Tiffany
CD _____ OJCCD 6562
Original Jazz Classics / Apr '93 / Wellard / Jazz Music / Cadillac / Complete/Pinnacle.

AT THE BLACK HAWK VOL.2 (Manne, Shelly & His Men)
CD _____ OJCCD 657
Original Jazz Classics / Mar '93 / Wellard / Jazz Music / Cadillac / Complete/Pinnacle.

AT THE BLACK HAWK VOL.3 (Manne, Shelly & His Men)
CD _____ OJCCD 658
Original Jazz Classics / Mar '93 / Wellard / Jazz Music / Cadillac / Complete/Pinnacle.

AT THE BLACK HAWK VOL.4 (Manne, Shelly & His Men)
CD _____ OJCCD 659
Original Jazz Classics / Mar '93 / Wellard / Jazz Music / Cadillac / Complete/Pinnacle.

AT THE BLACK HAWK VOL.5 (Manne, Shelly & His Men)
CD _____ OJCCD 660
Original Jazz Classics / Mar '93 / Wellard / Jazz Music / Cadillac / Complete/Pinnacle.

DEEP PEOPLE (Manne, Shelly & Bill Russo)
Pooch McGooch / Count on Rush Street / All of me / It don't mean a thing if it ain't got that swing / Deep purple / Princess of evil / Slightly brightly / Ennui / Gloomy Sunday / Vignette / Esthete on Clarke Street / S'posin' / Cathy / Cookie / Strange fruit
CD _____ SV 0186
Savoy Jazz / Oct '92 / Conifer / ADA.

MY FAIR LADY (Manne, Shelly/Andre Previn/Leroy Vinnegar)
Get me to the church on time / I've grown accustomed to her face / Ascot gavotte / With a little bit of luck / On the street where you live / Wouldn't it be lovely / Show me / I could have danced all night
CD _____ OJCCD 3362
Original Jazz Classics / Jan '92 / Wellard / Jazz Music / Cadillac / Complete/Pinnacle.

PERK UP
Perk up / I married an angel / Seer / Come back / Yesterdays / Drinking and driving / Bleep / Bird of paradise
CD _____ CCD 4021
Concord Jazz / Aug '95 / New Note.

SHELLY MANNE & HIS FRIENDS (Manne, Shelly & His Friends)
Tea for two / How high the moon / When we're alone / On the sunny side of the street / Time on my hands / Moonglow / Them there eyes / Sarcastic lady / Night and day / Flamingo / Steps steps up / Steps steps down
CD _____ OJCCD 240
Original Jazz Classics / Oct '92 / Wellard / Jazz Music / Cadillac / Complete/Pinnacle.

WEST COAST SOUND VOL.1, THE (Manne, Shelly & His Men)
CD _____ OJCCD 152
Original Jazz Classics / Feb '93 / Wellard / Jazz Music / Cadillac / Complete/Pinnacle.

Mannheim Steamroller

CHRISTMAS
Deck the halls with boughs of holly / We three kings / Bring a torch, Jeannette, Isabella / Coventry carol / Good king Wenceslas / Wassail, wassail / Carol of the birds / I saw three ships / God rest ye merry Gentlemen / Stille nacht
CD _____ AGCD 1984
American Gramophone / Nov '94 / New Note.

FRESH AIRE CHRISTMAS, A
Hark the herald trumpets sing / Hark the herald angels sing / Holly and the ivy / Little drummer boy / Still, still, still / Lo how a rose e'er blooming / In dulci jubilo / Greensleeves / Carol of the bells / Traditions of Christmas / Cantique de noel (o holy night)
CD _____ AGCD 1988
American Gramophone / Nov '94 / New Note.

FRESH AIRE I
CD _____ AGCD 359
American Gramophone / Dec '88 / New Note.

FRESH AIRE II
CD _____ AGCD 359
American Gramophone / Dec '88 / New Note.

FRESH AIRE III
CD _____ AGCD 365
American Gramophone / Dec '88 / New Note.

FRESH AIRE IV
CD _____ AGCD 370
American Gramophone / Dec '88 / New Note.

FRESH AIRE V
CD _____ AGCD 385
American Gramophone / Dec '88 / New Note.

FRESH AIRE VI
CD _____ AGCD 386
American Gramophone / Dec '88 / New Note.

Manning, Anthony

CHROMIUM NEBULAE
CD _____ 56IRDAEV3CD
Irdial / Nov '95 / Disc.

Manning, Barbara

ONE PERFECT GREEN BLANKET
CD _____ NORMAL 138CD
Normal/Okra / Mar '94 / Direct / ADA.

Manning, Bob

SPOTLIGHT ON BOB MANNING
These foolish things / I had the craziest dream / That old feeling / When your lover has gone / P.S. I love you / It's easy to remember / You've changed / I'm through with love / You made me love you (I didn't want to do it) / Alone together / Very thought of you / Love letter / I hadn't anyone till you / It's all right with me / My ideal / Nearness of you / My love song to you / Goodbye
CD _____ CDP 7899402
Capitol / Apr '95 / EMI.

Manning, Lynn

CLARITY OF VISION
CD _____ NAR 093CD
SST / Sep '94 / Plastic Head.

Manning, Roger

ROGER MANNING
Busy body blues (E.5th Street blues) / Take back the night / No. 19 blues (pearly blues no.3) / Hitchhiker's blues no.2 (pearly blues no.3) / Traitors / Radical blues / Speaker phone / Persia blues / Unrequited / Waterloo blues / Subway blues / Waterloo calling/ Parade account / Pacifica blues / Dallas blues / Serious blues (no.18 blues) / Tompkins Square blues (no.99) / Gallows pole / Sub folk
CD _____ EFA 121102
Moll / Mar '95 / SRD.

Mano Negra

KING OF BONGO
Bring the fire / King of bongo / Don't want you no more / Le bruit du frigo / Letter to the censors / El jako / It's my heart / Madman's dead / Out of time man / Madame Oscar / Welcome in occident / Furious fiesta / Fool / Paris la nuit
CD _____ CDVIR 5
Virgin / Jul '91 / EMI.

PUTA'S FEVER
Man negra / Rock 'n' roll band / King kong five / Soledad / Sidi hbibi / Rebel spell / Peligro / Pas assez de toi / Magic dice / Mad house / Guayaquil City / Voodoo / Patchanka / La rancon du succes / Devil's call / Roger Cageot / El sur / Patchuko hop
CD _____ CDV 2608
Virgin / Jan '90 / EMI.

Manone, Wingy

CLASSICS 1927-34
CD _____ CLASSICS 774
Classics / Aug '94 / Discovery / Jazz Music.

CLASSICS 1935-36
CD _____ CLASSICS 828
Classics / Sep '95 / Discovery / Jazz Music.

CLASSICS 1936
CD _____ CLASSICS 849
Classics / Nov '95 / Discovery / Jazz Music.

COLLECTION VOL 1
CD _____ COCD 03
Collector's Classics / Jan '89 / Cadillac / Complete/Pinnacle.

WINGY MANONE & HIS ORCHESTRA 1934-35
CD _____ CLASSICS 798
Classics / Mar '95 / Discovery / Jazz Music.

WINGY MANONE COLLECTION VOLUME 4, 1935-36, THE
Every little moment / Black coffee / Sweet and slow / Lulu's back in town / Let's swing it / Little door, little lock, little key / Love and kisses / Rhythm is our business / From the top of your head / Takes two to make a bargain / Smile will go a long, long way / I'm gonna sit right down and write myself a letter / Every now and then / I've got a feelin' you're foolin' / You're my lucky star / I've got a note / I've got a note (1) / I'm shooting high / Music goes round and around / You let me down / I've got my fingers crossed / Rhythm in my nursery rhymes / Old man mose / Broken record / Please believe me
CD _____ COCD 20
Collector's Classics / Nov '94 / Cadillac / Complete/Pinnacle.

Manouri, Olivier

CUMPARSITA - TANGOS (Manouri, Olivier & E. Pascualia)

CD _____ Y225212
Silex / Jun '93 / ADA.

Manowar

HAIL TO ENGLAND
Blood of my enemies / Each dawn I die / Kill with power / Hail to England / Army of the immortals / Black arrows / Bridge of death
CD _____ GED 24539
Geffen / Nov '93 / BMG.

HELL OF STEEL, THE (The Best Of Manowar)
Fighting the world / Kings of metal / Demon's whip / Warriors prayer / Defender / Crown and the ring / Blow your speakers / Metal warriors / Black wind, fire and steel / Hail and kill / Power of thy sword / Herz aus stahl / Kingdom come / Master of the wind
CD _____ 7567805782
Atlantic / Feb '92 / Warner Music.

INTO GLORY RIDE
Warlord / Secret of steel / Gloves of metal / Gates of Valhalla / Hatred / Revelation (death's angel) / March for revenge / By the soldiers of death
CD _____ GED 24538
Geffen / Nov '93 / BMG.

TRIUMPH OF STEEL
Achilles, agony and ecstacy in eight parts / Metal warriors / Ride the dragon / Spirit of the cherokee / Burning / Power of sword / Demon's whip / Master of the wind
CD _____ 7567824232
Atlantic / Oct '92 / Warner Music.

Manring, Michael

DRASTIC MEASURE
Spirits in the material world / Hopefull / Red right returning / Gizmo / Oyasumi nasai / Purple haze / Doja voodoo / Watson and Crick / Wide asleep / 500 miles high / When we last spoke
CD _____ WD 1102
Windham Hill / May '91 / Pinnacle / BMG / ADA.

THONK
Big fungus / Snakes got legs / Monkey businessman / Disturbed / On a day of many angels / My three moons / Cruel and unusual / Bad hair day / Adhan / You offered only parabolas / Enormous room
CD _____ 7290210322-2
Windham Hill / Feb '94 / Pinnacle / BMG / ADA.

Manson, Marilyn

PORTRAIT OF AN AMERICAN FAMILY
CD _____ 654492344-2
Warner Bros. / Sep '94 / Warner Music.

Mantaray

SOME POP
CD _____ GOODCD 3
Dead Dead Good / Oct '94 / Pinnacle.

Mantas

WINDS OF CHANGE
Hurricane / Desperado / Sionara / Nowhere to hide / Deceiver / Let it rock / King of the rings / Western days / Winds of change
CD _____ NEATCD 1042
Neat / Jan '96 / Plastic Head.

Manteca

LATER IS NOW!
CD _____ JTR 8438-2
Justin Time / Oct '92 / Harmonia Mundi / Cadillac.

Mantilla, Ray

HANDS OF FIRE (Mantilla, Ray Space Station)
CD _____ 123174-2
Red / Apr '93 / Harmonia Mundi / Jazz Horizons / Cadillac / ADA.

SYNERGY (Mantilla, Ray Space Station)
CD _____ 123198-2
Red / Apr '93 / Harmonia Mundi / Jazz Horizons / Cadillac / ADA.

Mantler, Karen

GET THE FLU (Mantler, Karen & Her Cat Arnold)
Flu / I love Christmas / Let's have a baby / My organ / Au lait / Waiting / Call a doctor / Good luck / I'm not such a bad guy / Mean to me
CD _____ 8471362
ECM / Nov '90 / New Note.

MY CAT ARNOLD
CD _____ 839 093 2
ECM / Jun '89 / New Note.

Mantler, Michael

ALIEN
Alien (Pts 1-4)
CD _____ 8276392
ECM / Dec '85 / New Note.

HAPLESS CHILD, THE
CD _____ 8318282
ECM / Jul '87 / New Note.

I SEARCH FOR AN INNOCENT LAND
CD _____ 5270922
ECM / Jul '95 / New Note.

LIVE: MICHAEL MANTLER
Preview - no answer / Slow orchestra piece no.3 (Prisonniers) / For instance / Slow orchestra piece no.8 (A l'abattoir) / When I run / Remembered visit / Slow orchestra piece no.6 / Hapless child / Doubtful guest
CD _____ 8333842
ECM / Oct '87 / New Note.

MANY HAVE NO SPEECH
CD _____ 8355802
ECM / Jul '88 / New Note.

SOMETHING THERE
CD _____ 8318292
ECM / Jul '87 / New Note.

Mantovani

ALL TIME FAVOURITES (Mantovani & His Orchestra)
CD _____ MU 5010
Musketeer / Oct '92 / Koch.

ALL TIME HITS
CD _____ MATCD 298
Castle / Apr '94 / BMG.

AND I LOVE YOU SO
CD _____ 8441852
Decca / '88 / PolyGram.

CHRISTMAS CAROL SELECTION
CD _____ KLMCD 042
Scratch / Dec '94 / BMG.

CHRISTMAS GREETINGS
First nowell / Good King Wenceslas / O holy night / God rest ye merry gentlemen / Nazareth / Holly and the ivy / Midnight waltz / O little town of Bethlehem / White Christmas / O tannenbaum / Toy waltz / O come all ye faithful (Adeste fidelis) / Mary's boy child / O thou that tellest good tidings / Skaters / Silent night
CD _____ 5501432
Spectrum/Karussell / Nov '94 / PolyGram / THE.

CHRISTMAS WITH MANTOVANI
CD _____ 15150
Laserlight / Nov '95 / Target/BMG.

CLASSICAL LOVE THEMES
CD Set _____ MBSCD 430
Castle / Nov '93 / BMG.

ESSENTIAL MANTOVANI
CD Set _____ TFP 023
Tring / Nov '92 / Tring / Prism.

FROM ROME TO VIENNA
CD Set _____ 24027
Laserlight / Sep '92 / Target/BMG.

GOLDEN AGE OF MANTOVANI, THE
Siboney / Woman in love / Amazing grace / Candy man / Nessun Dorma / Italian Medley / I'll get By / Zorba the Greek / Ben Hur / Tara's Theme / Ay ay ay / Tie A Yellow Ribbon / People / Cara mia / Elizabethan serenade / For All We Know / Green Cockatoo / Big Country / Legend Of The Glass Mountain / Yellow rose of Texas / Sweetest sounds / Dream of Olwen / Trolley Song (Cassette Only)
CD _____ CDSIV 6128
Horatio Nelson / Jul '95 / THE / BMG / Avid/ BMG / Koch.

GOLDEN HITS: MANTOVANI
Charmaine / Moon river / Moulin Rouge / Summertime in Venice / Diane / Exodus / Greensleeves / True love / La vie en rose / Around the world / Some enchanted evening / Swedish Rhapsody
CD _____ 8000852
Decca / '88 / PolyGram.

GREAT MANTOVANI, THE
Story of three loves / Dream of Olwen / Around the world / Waltz from Swan Lake / Song of India / Moulin Rouge / Blue Danube / Stranger in Paradise / Charmaine / Lonely ballerina / Gigi / Tenderly / With these hands / Tonight
CD _____ PLCD 520
President / Jan '87 / Grapevine / Target/ BMG / Jazz Music / President.

INTERNATIONAL HITS (Mantovani & His Orchestra)
CD _____ PWK 079
Carlton Home Entertainment / Jan '89 / Carlton Home Entertainment.

LATINO CONNECTION
CD _____ 12307
Music Of The World / Apr '94 / Target/ BMG / ADA.

LOVE ALBUM - 20 ROMANTIC FAVOURITES, THE
Some enchanted evening / Very thought of you / I can't stop loving you / April love / It's impossible / My cherie amour / Shadow of your smile / Lovely way to spend an evening / Love is all / Charmaine / Hello, young lovers / Man and a woman / Dear heart / For all we know / She / I will wait for you /

And I love you so / What are you doing the rest of your life / Spanish eyes / More
CD _____ PLATCD 14
Platinum Music / Dec '88 / Prism / Ross.

LOVE THEMES, THE
Charmaine / Love story / For once in my life / Shadow of your smile / If I loved you / Love letters / Stardust / Long ago and far away / Some enchanted evening / Embraceable you / Moon river / Tenderly / When I fall in love / Most beautiful girl / And I love you so / Till there was you (Not on CD.) / Way you look tonight / Love me with all your heart / Nearness of you / You are beautiful (Not on CD.) / Tea for two / Lover / Till / I have dreamed / September song / I wish you love / My prayer (Not on CD.) / Very thought of you (Not on CD.)
CD _____ CDSIV 6101
Horatio Nelson / Jul '95 / THE / BMG / Avid/ BMG / Koch.

MAGIC OF MANTOVANI
CD _____ DCD 5301
Disky / Dec '93 / THE / BMG / Discovery / Pinnacle.

MANHATTAN
Give my regards to Broadway / Autumn in New York / Bowery / Harlem nocturne / Slaughter on 10th Avenue / Manhattan serenade / Take the 'A' train / Manhattan lullaby / Maria / Somewhere / Belle of New York / Tenement symphony
CD _____ 8204752
London / Jun '87 / PolyGram.

MANTOVANI MAGIC 2
Love is a many splendoured thing / Charmaine / Send in the clowns / Cavatina / Flizabethan serenade / Three coins in the fountain / Summertime in Venice / Merry widow waltz / Entertainer / Sound of music / Italian fantasy / Autumn leaves / What are you doing for the rest of your life / Some enchanted evening / Big country / Swedish Rhapsody
CD _____ TCD 2237
Telstar / Jul '87 / BMG.

ROMANTIC MELODIES (Mantovani & His Orchestra)
CD _____ DCD 5392 LM/VM
Disky / Apr '94 / THE / BMG / Discovery / Pinnacle.

SERENADE
Around the world / Elizabethan serenade / Stardust / Old fashioned way / As time goes by / Anniversary waltz / And I love you so / Blue Danube / Very thought of you / Walk in the Black Forest / Stranger in paradise / Londonderry air / Spanish eyes / Swedish rhapsody
CD _____ 5500172
Spectrum/Karussell / May '93 / PolyGram / THE.

TENDERLY (Mantovani & His Orchestra)
Flamingo / Midnight cowboy / La mer / Begin the beguine / Send in the clowns / Song of Skye / Autumn leaves / Some enchanted evening / Love is a many splendoured thing / Deep purple / Swedish rhapsody / What are you doing for the rest of your life / Tenderly / Colours of my life / Three coins in the fountain / Charmaine
CD _____ PWK 031
Carlton Home Entertainment / '88 / Carlton Home Entertainment.

VINTAGE MANTOVANI (Mantovani & His Tipica Orchestra)
Raggamuffin / Fete in Santa Lucia / Have you forgotten so soon / Madame, you're lovely / You're laughing at me / Snirler of the night / No more you / In a German beergarden / September in the rain / Aromas mendocinas / Marcay / Eto nutche / Traumerei / Romany / Speak to me of love / Smoke gets in your eyes / Her name is Mary / Rose dreams / Nothing lives longer than love / Serenade / Ten pretty girls
CD _____ PASTCD 9724
Flapper / Nov '90 / Pinnacle.

Mantra, Michael

SONIC ALTAR
CD _____ SR 9449
Silent / Mar '94 / Plastic Head.

Manu Lann Huel

CADOU
CD _____ RS 209CD
Keltia Musique / May '94 / ADA / Direct / Discovery.

Manuel

INSTRUMENTAL LOVE SONGS (3CD Set) (Manuel & Geoff Love)
Moon river / Begin the beguine / Very thought of you / Smoke gets in your eyes / All the things you are / Moonlight serenade / Clair de Lune / What are you doing the rest of your life / Chanson d'amour / And I love you so / How deep is your love / Romeo and Juliet / Amor amor / Somewhere my love / You'll never find another love like mine / Twelfth of never / You make me feel brand new / You are the sunshine of my life / Feelings / Fernando / Way we were / As time goes by / Forever and ever / Misty /

Dream lover / When I fall in love / I wish you love / Girl from Ipanema / Tara's theme (Gone with the wind) / Stranger on the shore / Chi Mai / Annie's song / Cavatina / In the mood / Summer place / Love is blue / Falling in love with love / Love Story / Secret love / Love letters / Portrait of my love / Love is here to stay / Plaisir d'amour / You made me love you / True love / Love walked in
CD Set _____ CDTRBOX 116
Trio / Oct '94 / EMI.

MAGIC OF MANUEL AND THE MUSIC OF THE MOUNTAINS
Somewhere my love / Sunrise sunset / Love story / Shadow of your smile / Spanish Harlem / Strangers in the night / If / Bali Ha'i / El condor pasa / Cuando calienta el sol / Spartacus love theme / Moonlight serenade / Sun, sea and the sky / Do you know the way to San Jose / Cavatina / Autumn leaves / Ebb tide / Moon river / Begin the beguine / Stranger on the shore / Misty / What are you doing the rest of your life / And I love you so / Killing me softly
CD Set _____ CDDL 1086
Music For Pleasure / Nov '91 / EMI.

MANUEL WITH LOVE
Windmills of your mind (Theme from The Thomas Crown Affair.) / As time goes by / Very thought of you / La vie en rose / Strangers in the night / I wish you love / Evergreen / When I need you / If / How near am I to love / How deep is your love / Way we were / You light up my life / And this is my beloved / Yesterday / Moonlight serenade / All the things you are / You like these (From the Italian Job.) / One and only / Somewhere my love
CD _____ CC 289
Music For Pleasure / Dec '92 / EMI.

MOUNTAIN FIESTA (Manuel & The Music Of The Mountains)
Moonlight fiesta / Windmills of your mind / Stranger in Paradise / On days like these / Girl from Impanema / Bossa de Cial / Ladies' theme / Little sparrow of Paris / La golondrina / Wandering star / You and the night and the music / Time for love is anytime / Umbrellas of Cherbourg / Stella by starlight / Malaguena / Singer not the song / Carnival / Gardens in Ibiza / Al di la / Boa noite
CD _____ CC 253
Music For Pleasure / May '90 / EMI.

Manuel, Manny

REY DE CORAZONES
Mi problema / Estrellita / Distanciado / Los hombres no debenllorar / Por que necesidad / Se acabo lo que de daba / Si una vez / Rey de corsazones / Maniqui / Illusionado
CD _____ 66058055
RMM / Sep '95 / New Note.

Manusardi, Guido

COLORED PASSAGES (Manusardi, Guido & Garzone/Lockwood/Gullotti)
CD _____ RMCD 4504
Ram / Nov '93 / Harmonia Mundi / Cadillac.

TOGETHER AGAIN (Manusardi, Guido & Red Mitchell)
CD _____ 1211812
Soul Note / Nov '91 / Harmonia Mundi / Wellard / Cadillac.

Manzanera, Phil

801 LIVE
Lagrima / TNK (Tomorrow never knows) / East of Asteroid / Rongwrong / Sombre reptiles / Baby's on fire / Diamond head / Miss Shapiro / You really got me / Third uncle
CD _____ EGCD 26
EG / '87 / EMI.

GUITARISSIMO
La Escena (1)K-scope 2)Frontera 3)TNK) / Criollo / Diamond head / You are here / Rude awakening / Listen now / Big dome (part 2) / Caracas / Lagrima / Europe 70-1 / Island (pt 3 of La Tristeza) / That falling feeling / Big dome (part 1) (Not on LP) / City of light (Not on LP) / Initial speed (Not on LP)
CD _____ EGCD 69
EG / '87 / EMI.

MANZANERA & MACKAY (Manzanera, Phil & Andy Mackay)
Black gang chine / Free yourself / Built for speed / Many are the ways / I can be tender / Dreams of the East / Sacrosanct / Every king of stone / Men with extraordinary / Safe in the arms of love / Forgotten man
CD _____ EXPCD 4
Expression / Nov '90 / Pinnacle.

MANZANERA COLLECTION, THE (2CD Set)
Tomorrow never knows / Over you / Out of the blue / Fat lady of Limbourg / Impossible guitar / Charlie / Take a chance with me / Frontera / Diamond head / Needle in a camel's eye / Miss Shapiro / End / Gun / Europe 70-1 / Leyenda / Frontera 91 / Southern cross / Sphinx / Amazona / Million reasons why / Fifth wheel / It's just love / Talk to me / Suzanne / Blackgang Chine /

Lorelei / Criollo / Mama hue / Corazon Corazon / Flor de azalea / Espiritu
CD _____ CDVDM 9033
Virgin / May '95 / EMI.

SOUTHERN CROSS
CD _____ EXPCD 1
Expression / Oct '90 / Pinnacle.

Manzarek, Ray

LOVE LION (Manzarek, Ray & M. McClure)
CD _____ SHAN 5006CD
Shanachie / Oct '93 / Koch / ADA / Greensleeves.

Mao Tse Tung Experience

ARMOURER
CD _____ RTD 19519092
Our Choice / Nov '94 / Pinnacle.

Mapfumo, Thomas

CHIMURENGA FOREVER (The Best Of Thomas Mapfumo)
Serevende / Mhondoro / Vanhu vetama / Nyoka musango / Hanzvadzi / Nyarara mukadzi wangu / Zvenyika / Hondo / Ndave kuende / Shumba / Zvandivringa / Hwa hwa
CD _____ CDEMC 3722
Hemisphere / Oct '95 / EMI.

Mar-Keys

BACK TO BACK (Mar-Keys/Booker T. & MG's)
Introduction / Green onions / Red beans and rice / Tic-tac toe / Hip hug-her / Philly dog / Grab this thing / Last night / Gimme some lovin' / Booker-loo / Outrage
CD _____ 7567903072
Atlantic / Feb '93 / Warner Music.

DAMIFIKNOW/MEMPHIS EXPERIENCE (2 Albums on 1 CD)
Mustang Sally / Knock on wood / Double or nothing / Black / Soul man / I never loved a man (the way I love you) / Daydream / Coffee cup / One with sugar / Heads or tails / Cloud 9 / After the affair / Reach out, I'll be there / Angel dust / Hummingbird / Let it be / Creeper's funkatrations / Jive man
CD _____ CDSXD 959
Stax / Oct '90 / Pinnacle.

GREAT MEMPHIS SOUND, THE
Honey pot / Plantation Inn / I've been loving you too long / Cleo's back / Grab this thing / Philly dog / Walking with the Duke / Girl from Ipanema / In the mood / Dear James
CD _____ 7567823392
Atlantic / Jul '93 / Warner Music.

Mara

DON'T EVEN THINK
CD _____ SSMCD 042
Sandstock / May '94 / CM / ADA / Direct.

POETRY & MOTION
CD _____ CDVEST 11
Bulletproof / May '94 / Pinnacle.

Marachi Sol

MEXICO LINDO
CD _____ EUCD 1249
ARC / Mar '94 / ARC Music / ADA.

Maraire, Dumisani

CHAMINUKA
CD _____ CDC 208
Music Of The World / Jun '93 / Target/ BMG / ADA.

Maralung, Alan

BUNGGRIDJ-BUNGGRIDJ: WANGGA SONGS FROM NORTHERN AUSTRALIA
CD _____ SFCD 40430
Smithsonian Folkways / Jan '94 / ADA / Direct / Koch / CM / Cadillac.

Marano, Nancy

DOUBLE STANDARDS (Marano, Nancy & Eddie Monteiro)
All or nothing at all / I've got the world on a string / I guess I'll have my tears out to dry / Make this city ours tonight (Cancao do Sal) / Joy spring / If you could see me now / Up jumped a bird / Water or march / You are there / Whisper not / Bridges / I'm getting sentimental over you / Speak low
CD _____ CY 78901
Denon / '94 / Conifer.

PERFECT MATCH, A (Marano, Nancy & Eddie Monteiro)
This happy madness / Love dance / Passarim / I have the feeling I've been here before / Autumn nocturne / Cinnamon and clove / I hear the shadows dancing / Skylark / One note samba / I told you so / Sleepin' bee / That's all
CD _____ CY 79407
Denon / '91 / Conifer.

Marbele, Aurulus

SEBENE DANCE
CD _____ JIP 51
JIP / Jan '96 / Jetstar.

Marce Et Tumpak

ZOUK CHOUV
Gren-n Ianmou / Chien cho / Zouk chouv / Lans difou / Lese woule
CD _____ CDORB 035
Globestyle / May '89 / Pinnacle.

Marcello, Melis

FREE TO DANCE
CD _____ 120023-2
Black Saint / Oct '94 / Harmonia Mundi / Cadillac.

Marcels

MARCELS COMPLETE COLPIX SESSIONS, THE
Blue moon / Goodbye to love / Loved her the whole week through / Peace of mind / I'll be forever loving you / Most of all / Sunday kind of people / Two people in the world / Sweet was the wine / Fallen tear / Over the rainbow / Crazy bells / Tetter totter love / Hold on / Footprints in the sand / You are my sunshine / Find another fool / Summertime / Flower pot / Heartaches / Allright, okay, you win / My love for you / Don't cry for me this xmas / Merry twistmas / Twistin' fever / My melancholy baby / Really need your love / Don't turn your back on me / That old black magic / Give me back your love / Tell them about it / Baby where y'been / I wanna be the leader / Friendly loans / Blue heartaches / Lollipop baby / One last kiss / Honestly sincere
CD _____ NEDCD 264
Sequel / Nov '93 / BMG.

March, Peggy

MEMORIES OF HEIDELBERG
Memories in Heidelberg / Antwort weiss ganz allein der wind / Tausend steine / Lass mich nie allein / Romeo und Julia / Fallt der regen in das meer / Spar dir deine dollar / Mississippi shuffle boat / Ender der zwanziger jahre / Es war hochste eisenbahn / Bahama lullaby / Telegramm aus Tennessee / Das ist musik for mich / Ein zigeuner ohne geige / Wedding in my dreams / Du, du, du gehst mir ein kopf herum / Die sonne kommt ja wieder / Hey (das ist musik fur dich) / Ich frage die zigeunerin / Weil die liebe zaubern kann / Der mond scheint schon / Mr. Giacomo Puccini / 1969 (weil es so schon war) / Male nicht den teufel an die wand / Yesterday waltz / Canale grande / Wiedersehn
CD _____ BCD 15602
Bear Family / Nov '91 / Rollercoaster / Direct / CM / Swift / ADA.

MIT SIBZEHN HAT MAN NOCH TRAUME
CD _____ BCD 15536
Bear Family / Mar '91 / Rollercoaster / Direct / CM / Swift / ADA.

March Violets

BOTANIC VERSES
CD _____ FREUDCD 42
Jungle / Sep '93 / Disc.

Marchand, Erik

ERIK MARCHAND
CD _____ Y 225043CD
Silex / Oct '94 / ADA.

Marcotulli, Rita

NIGHT CALLER
CD _____ LBLC 6551
Label Bleu / Jan '93 / New Note.

Marcus, Michael

UNDER THE WIRE
CD _____ 6064-2
Enja / Apr '91 / New Note / Vital/SAM.

Marcus, Steve

201
CD _____ 4722082
Sony Jazz / Nov '92 / Sony.

Marden Hill

BLOWN AWAY
Come on / Hijack / Bombed on heavy / Thelonius / Up in smoke / Into the future / Get some in / Uptown theme / End
CD _____ DST 010CD
On Delancey Street / Oct '94 / Vital.

Marduk

DARK ENDLESS
CD _____ NFR 003
No Fashion / Oct '94 / Plastic Head.

OPUS NOCTURNE
CD _____ OPCD 028
Osmose / Jan '95 / Plastic Head.

Margitza, Rick

HANDS OF TIME
CD _____ CHR 70021
Challenge / Sep '95 / Direct / Jazz Music / Cadillac / ADA.

Margo

IRELAND ON MY MIND
I would like to see you again / Poverty / Tribute to Packie Bonner / Tipperary far away / Born in Ireland / Consider the children / Little town on the Shannon / Man from the glen / Rented room / Little white house / Ireland on my mind / How far is heaven
CD _____ RITZRCD 516
Ritz / Apr '92 / Pinnacle.

NEW BEGINNINGS
You'll remember me / Eyes of a child / Back in baby's arms / Irish harvest day / Home is where the heart is / Infamous angel / Memories of Mayo / I'll forgive and I'll try to forget / Pick me up on your way down / Paper mansions / If I kiss you / To my children I'm Irish / Sitting alone / Friends
CD _____ RITZCD 540
Ritz / Aug '94 / Pinnacle.

Margolin, Bob

DOWN IN THE ALLEY
CD _____ ALCD 4816
Alligator / Nov '93 / Direct / ADA.

MY BLUES AND MY GUITAR
CD _____ ALCD 4835
Alligator / Nov '95 / Direct / ADA.

Margolis, Kitty

EVOLUTION
CD _____ MKCD 1004
Mad Kat / Feb '95 / Vital/SAM.

Margy, Lina

ETOILES DE LA CHANSON
CD _____ 882402
Music Memoria / Aug '93 / Discovery / ADA.

Maria, Tania

BEST OF TANIA MARIE
I don't go / Made in New York / I do / love you / Valeu / Bronx / Tanoca Vignette / Chuleta / Please don't stay / O bom e / Ca c'est bon / Marguerita / 210 West
CD _____ CDP 7986342
World Pacific / Jun '93 / EMI.

COME WITH ME
Sangria / Embraceable you / Lost in Amazonia / Come with me / Sementes, graines and seeds / Nega / Euzinha / It's all over now
CD _____ CCD 4200
Concord Picante / Jul '95 / New Note.

LOVE EXPLOSION
Funky tambourine / It's all in my hands / You've got me feeling your love / Love explosion / Bela la bela / Rainbow of your love / Deep cove view / Pour toi
CD _____ CCD 4230
Concord Jazz / Dec '86 / New Note.

NO COMMENT
Pelham melody / Liqued groove / Keep in mind / Desire / Marvin my love / Who knows / Jack Hammer / Gotcha / Fanatic / Bali / Something for now
CD _____ TKM 50012
TKM / May '95 / New Note.

OUTRAGEOUS
Dear Dee Vee / Confusion / She's outrageous / Bom bom bom / Happiness / Amei demais / Ta tudo certo / I can do it / Minha Moe / Happiness (2) / Granada
CD _____ CCD 4563
Concord Picante / Aug '93 / New Note.

PIQUANT
CD _____ CCD 4151
Concord Jazz / Jul '88 / New Note.

REAL TANIA MARIA-WILD, THE
Yatra - ta / A cama na varanda / Vem pra roda / Come with me / Funy tambourine / 2 a.m. / Sangria
CD _____ CCD 4264
Concord Jazz / Nov '86 / New Note.

TAURUS
CD _____ CCD 4175
Concord Picante / Oct '87 / New Note.

Maria-Jose

ETOILES DE LA CHANSON
CD _____ 882412
Music Memoria / Aug '93 / Discovery / ADA.

Mariachi Azteca

BEST OF MARIACHI AZTECA, THE
CD _____ EUCD 1119
ARC / '91 / ARC Music / ADA.

Mariachi Cobre

MARIACHI COBRE
CD _____ CDKUCK 11095
Kuckuck / Jun '92 / CM / ADA.

Mariachi Reyes Del...

SONES FROM JALISCO (Mariachi Reyes Del Aserradero)
CD _____ CO 108
Corason / Feb '94 / CM / Direct / ADA.

Mariachi Sol

CU CU RRU CU CU PALOMA
CD _____ EUCD 1246
ARC / Nov '93 / ARC Music / ADA.

Mariano, Charlie

70 (Mariano, Charlie & Friends)
Il Piacere / Everybody's song / Deep river / Rabou abou kabou / Crystal bells / Seva la murga
CD _____ VBR 21492
Vera Bra / Feb '94 / Pinnacle / New Note.

BOSTON DAYS 1954 (Mariano, Charlie Quintet)
CD _____ FSRCD 207
Fresh Sound / Nov '94 / Jazz Music / Discovery.

FRIENDS (Mariano, Charlie & Stephen Diez)
CD _____ ISCD 121
Intersound / '91 / Jazz Music.

FROM ME TO YOU
CD _____ ISCD 148
Intersound / Jun '95 / Jazz Music.

JYOTHI
Voice   solo   (Ramamani,R.A.-Tamboura.Mani,T.A.S.-Mridangam.Rajagopal,R.A.-ghatam,morsi) / Vandanam / Varshini / Saptarshi / Kartik / Bhajan
CD _____ 8115482
ECM / Aug '86 / New Note.

WARUM BIST DU TRAURIG (Mariano, Charlie, Quartet)
Mobile / Leaves adventures / Warum bist du traurig / Echo / Choral / Running / Meeting / Search und suche / Tanzen
CD _____ BW 019
B&W / Sep '93 / New Note.

Mariano, Torcuato

LAST LOOK
Africa / Everything I couldn't say with words / Last look / In the rhythm of my heart / Very special place / Secrets / Ocean way / Walking on clouds / Rio stomp / Dindi
CD _____ 01934111672
Windham Hill / Oct '95 / Pinnacle / BMG / ADA.

PARADISE STATION
Train to Uberaba / Upon the sea / Just for you / I can't help it / Other side / On a summer night / Xufle / Sincere lies / Eastern winds / Paradise station / Mariana and Paula good night
CD _____ 01934111372
Windham Hill / Feb '94 / Pinnacle / BMG / ADA.

Marias, Gerard

EST.
CD _____ HOP 200001
Label Hopi / May '94 / Harmonia Mundi.

Marie, Teena

STAR CHILD
Lovergirl / Help youngblood get to the freaky party / Out on a limb / Alibi / Jammin' / Star child / We've got to stop (meeting like this) / My Dear Mr.Gaye / Light
CD _____ 7464 39528-2
Epic / Feb '85 / Sony.

Marienthal, Eric

ONE TOUCH
No doubt about it / That's the way / One for James / Walk through the fire / Ouch / Westland / Village / Tanto amor / Backtalk / Where are you
CD _____ GRP 96912
GRP / May '93 / BMG / New Note.

STREET DANCE
Street dance / Kids stuff / Moment of silence / Shake it loose / Fafaru / Legenda / Nothin' but everything / Where you belong / Yosemite / Hold on to my heart / Forces of nature / Have I told you lately that I love you
CD _____ GRP 97992
GRP / Nov '94 / BMG / New Note.

Marillion

AFRAID OF SUNLIGHT
Gazpacho / Cannibal surf babe / Beautiful / Afraid of sunrise / Out of this world / Afraid of sunlight / Beyond you / King
CD _____ CDEMD 1079
EMI / Jun '95 / EMI.

B'SIDES THEMSELVES

Grendel / Charting the single / Market square heroes / Three boats down from the Candy / Cinderella search / Lady Nina / Freaks / Tux on / Margaret
CD _____ CZ 39
EMI / Jul '88 / EMI.

BRAVE

Bridge / Living with the big lie / Runaway / Goodbye to all that / Wave / Mad / Opium den / Slide / Standing in the swing / Hard as love / Hollow man / Alone again in the lap of luxury / Now wash your hand / Paper lies / Brave / Great escape / Last of you / Falling from the moon / Made again
CD _____ CDEMD 1054
EMI / Feb '94 / EMI.

CLUTCHING AT STRAWS

Hotel hobbies / Warm wet circles / That time of the night / Going under / Just for the record / White Russian / Incommunicado / Torch song / Slainte Mhath / Sugar mice / Last straw
CD _____ CZ 214
EMI / '89 / EMI.

FUGAZI

Assassing / Punch and Judy / Jigsaw / Emerald lies / She chameleon / Incubus / Fugazi
CD _____ CDEMC 3682
EMI / May '94 / EMI.

HOLIDAYS IN EDEN

Splintering heart / Cover my eyes (pain and heaven) / Party / No one can / Holidays in Eden / Dry land / Waiting to happen / This town / Rakes progress / 100 nights
CD _____ CDEMD 1022
EMI / Jun '91 / EMI.

MISPLACED CHILDHOOD

Pseudo-silk kimono / Kayleigh / Lavender / Bitter suite / Heart of Lothian / Waterhole / Lords of the backstage / Blind curve / Childhood's end / White feather
CD _____ CDEMC 3684
EMI / May '94 / EMI.

SCRIPT FOR A JESTER'S TEAR

He knows you know / Web / Garden party / Chelsea Monday / Forgotten sons
CD _____ CDEMC 3683
EMI / May '94 / EMI.

SCRIPT FOR A JESTER'S TEAR/ FUGAZI/MISPLACED CHILDHOOD (3CD Set)

Script for a jester's tear / He knows you know / Web / Garden party / Chelsea Monday / Forgotten sons / Punch and Judy / Jigsaw / Emerald lies / She chameleon / Incubus / Fugazi / Pseudo silk kimono / Kayleigh / Lavender / Bitter suite / Heart of Lothian / Waterhole (Expresso Bongo) / Lords of the backstage / Blind curve / Childhood's end / White feather
CD Set _____ CDOMB 015
EMI / Oct '95 / EMI.

SEASONS END

King of Sunset town / Easter / Uninvited guest / Season's end / Holloway girl / Berlin / After me (MC/CD only) / Hooks in you / Space
CD _____ CDEMD 1011
EMI / Aug '89 / EMI.

SINGLES COLLECTION 1982-1992, A

Cover my eyes (pain and heaven) / Kayleigh / Easter / Warm wet circles / Uninvited guest / Assassing / Hooks in you / Garden party / No one can / Incommunicado / Dry land / Lavender / I will walk on water / Sympathy
CD _____ CDEMD 1033
EMI / May '92 / EMI.

THIEVING MAGPIE, THE (La Gazza Ladra)

La gazza ladra / Slainte Mhath / He knows you know / Chelsea Monday / Freaks (Not on LP) / Jigsaw / Punch and Judy / Sugar mice / Incommunicado / White Russian / Pseudo-silk kimono / Kayleigh / Lavender / Bitter suite / Heart of Lothian / Waterhole / Lords of the backstage / Blind curve / Childhood's end / White feather
CD Set _____ CDMARIL 1
EMI / Nov '88 / EMI.

Marilyn Decade

MARILYN DECADE CD, THE
CD _____ FRR 015
Freek / Dec '95 / SRD.

Marine Girls

LAZY WAYS/BEACH PARTY
CD _____ CDMRED 44
Cherry Red / Aug '88 / Pinnacle.

Marino

BLUES FOR LOVERS
CD _____ WKFMXD 167
FM / Mar '91 / Sony.

Marion

THIS WORLD AND BODY
CD _____ 8286952
London / Feb '96 / PolyGram.

Marionettes

MEPHISTO'S MOB
CD _____ Z 910062
Jungle / May '93 / Disc.

RISE
CD _____ BACCYCD 005
Diversity / Oct '95 / 3MV / Vital.

Mariteragi, Marie

TUAMOTU AND BORA BORA ISLANDS
CD _____ S 65817CD
Manuiti / Apr '95 / Harmonia Mundi.

Marjane, Leo

CHANSOPHONE 1937-42
CD _____ 701282
Chansophone / Jun '93 / Discovery.

Mark F.

RESULT OF RANDOM
CD _____ ZETD 04
Zeitgeist / Jun '94 / Plastic Head.

Mark, Jon

ALHAMBRA
CD _____ CDKUCK 11100
Kuckuck / Nov '92 / CM / ADA.

CELTIC STORY, A
CD _____ WCL 11002
White Cloud / May '94 / Select.

HOT NIGHT
Hot night / City of dreams / Burning / Isa / Island / Oh babe / Still of the night / Black bird on a white sky
CD _____ LICD 901129
Line / Apr '92 / CM / Grapevine / ADA / Conifer / Direct.

LADY & THE ARTIST, THE
China dolls / Anybody home / Song for the big man / Stay / Lady and the artist / City of runaways / Look at you now / You / When we were young / Love shines
CD _____ LICD 900063
Line / Apr '92 / CM / Grapevine / ADA / Conifer / Direct.

LAND OF MERLIN
Land of Merlin / Tintagel / Birth of Arthur / Child grows / Merlin and the unicorn / Dream of Arthur / Perilous and mystical journey / King, Queen and castle
CD _____ CDKUCK 11094
Kuckuck / Apr '92 / CM / ADA.

SONGS FOR A FRIEND
Signal hill / Joey / Ballad of the careless man / Someday I'll build a boat / Bay / Liars of love / Alone with my shadow / Old people's home / Carousel
CD _____ LICD 900598
Line / Sep '94 / CM / Grapevine / ADA / Conifer / Direct.

STANDING STONES OF CALLANDISH
CD _____ CDKUCK 11082-2
Kuckuck / Dec '88 / CM / ADA.

SUNDAY IN AUTUMN, A
CD _____ WCL 110032
White Cloud / May '95 / Select.

TUESDAY IN NEW YORK (Mark, Jon & Marc Almond)
Safe harbour / Tuesday in New York / In between / Lady of independent means / Once I loved a girl / I love you / Carousel
CD _____ LICD 900056
Line / Oct '94 / CM / Grapevine / ADA / Conifer / Direct.

Mark T.

GARDEN OF LOVE, THE
CD _____ FSCD 20
Folksound / '92 / Roots / CM.

Mark-Almond Band

LAST AND LIVE, THE
Then I have you / You look just like a girl / London / Lonely girl / Other people's rooms / New York state of mind / City - part 1 / City - part 2 / Girl on table four
CD _____ 900415
Line / Oct '94 / CM / Grapevine / ADA / Conifer / Direct.

MARK-ALMOND I & II
Ghetto / City / Tramp and the young girl / Love / Song for you / Sausalito Bay suite / Bridge / Bay / Solitude / Friends / Journey through New England / Sunset / Ballad of a man
CD Set _____ LICD 921186
Line / Mar '92 / CM / Grapevine / ADA / Conifer / Direct.

Marketts

BATMAN THEME
CD _____ EVA 642360B36
EVA / Nov '94 / Direct / ADA.

Marks, Kenny

MAKE IT RIGHT
CD _____ DAYCD 4151
Dayspring / Nov '87 / Nelson Word.

Marky Mark

MUSIC FOR THE PEOPLE (Marky Mark & The Funky Bunch)
Music for the people / Good vibrations / Wildside / 'Bout time I funk you / Peace / So what'cha saying / Marky Mark is here / On the house tip / Make me say ooh / I need money / Last song on side B
CD _____ 7567917372
Interscope / Oct '91 / Warner Music.

YOU GOTTA BELIEVE
Intro (The crisis) / You gotta believe / Gonna have a good time / Loungin' / Don't ya sleep / I want you / American dream / M / Get up / Super cool mack daddy / I run rhymes / Ain't no stoppin the funky bunch / Last song on side B / Solution
CD _____ 7567922032
Interscope / Nov '92 / Warner Music.

Marley, Bob

AFRICAN HERBSMAN
Lively up yourself / Small axe / Keep on moving / Duppy conqueror / Trench town rock / African herbsman / Fussing and fighting / All in one / Stand alone / Don't rock the boat / Put it on / Sun is shining / Kaya / 400 years / Riding high / Brain washing
CD _____ CDTRL 62
Trojan / Mar '94 / Jetstar / Total/BMG.

ALL THE HITS
CD _____ RRTGCD 7757
Rohit / Apr '91 / Jetstar.

AUDIO ARCHIVE
CD _____ CDAA 047
Tring / Jun '92 / Tring / Prism.

BABYLON BY BUS (Marley, Bob & The Wailers)
Positive vibration / Funky reggae party / Exodus / Rat race / Lively up yourself / Rebel music / War / No more trouble / Stir it up / Concrete jungle / Kinky reggae / Is this love / Heathen / Jamming
CD _____ TGDCD 1
Tuff Gong / Jan '94 / Jetstar / PolyGram.

BEST OF BOB MARLEY (1968-1972)
Trench town rock / Don't rock the boat / Kaya / Soul shakedown party / Cheer up / Keep on moving / Try me / Lively up yourself / All in one / Soul rebel / Duppy conqueror / Keep on skanking / Caution / Mr. Brown
CD _____ CSAPCD 107
Connoisseur / Jun '90 / Pinnacle.

BEST, THE
CD _____ 15499
Laserlight / Nov '92 / Target/BMG.

BIRTH OF A LEGEND, THE
I made a mistake / One love / Let me go / Love and affection / Simmer down / Maga dog / I am going home / Donna / Nobody knows / Lonesome feeling
CD _____ 9825882
Pickwick/Sony Collector's Choice / May '94 / Carlton Home Entertainment / Pinnacle / Sony.

BOB MARLEY
CD _____ 24090
Laserlight / Apr '94 / Target/BMG.

BOB MARLEY AND THE WAILERS (Upsetter Record Shop Pt.1) (Marley, Bob & The Wailers)
CD _____ LG 21040
Rhino / Aug '92 / Jetstar / Magnum Music Group / THE.

BOB MARLEY AND THE WAILERS (Upsetter Record Shop Pt.2) (Marley, Bob & The Wailers)
CD _____ LG 21044
Rhino / Aug '92 / Jetstar / Magnum Music Group / THE.

BOB MARLEY COLLECTION, THE
Don't rock my boat / Soul shakedown party / There she goes / Stop the train / Mellow mood / Caution / Treat you right / Soul almighty / Sun is shining / Chances are / Kaya / Back out / Hammer / Lively up yourself / Cheer up / Mr. Brown / Reaction / Riding high / Rainbow country / Small axe / Soul captives / Kinky reggae / Can't you see / Natural mystic / Soon come / Trench town rock / No sympathy / Put it on / Fussing and fighting / Corner stone / African herbsman / No water / Stand alone / Brain washing / Rebel's hop / Go tell it to the mountains / All in one / 400 years / Duppy conqueror / Soul rebel / You can't do that to me / Touch me / Try me / How many times / Memphis / It's alright
CD Set _____ TFP 010
Tring / Nov '92 / Tring / Prism.

BOB MARLEY VOL. 2
CD _____ KLMCD 038
Scratch / Nov '94 / BMG.

BURNIN' (Marley, Bob & The Wailers)
Get up stand up / Hallelujah time / I shot the sheriff / Burnin' and lootin' / Put it on / Small axe / Pass it on / Duppy conqueror / One foundation / Rastaman chant
CD _____ TGLCD 2
Tuff Gong / Jan '94 / Jetstar / PolyGram.

CATCH A FIRE
Concrete jungle / 400 years / Stop the train / Baby we got a date / Rock it baby / Kinky reggae / No more trouble / Midnight ravers
CD _____ TGLCD 1
Tuff Gong / Jan '94 / Jetstar / PolyGram.

COLLECTION
CD _____ COL 024
Collection / Apr '95 / Target/BMG.

CONFRONTATION (Marley, Bob & The Wailers)
Chant down Babylon / Buffalo soldier / Jump Nyabinghi / Mix up, mix up / Give thanks and praises / Blackman redemption / Trench town / I know / Stiff necked fools / Rastaman live up
CD _____ TGLCD 10
Tuff Gong / Jan '94 / Jetstar / PolyGram.

EARLY COLLECTION (Marley, Bob & The Wailers)
Wings of a dove / Do you remember / Love and affection / Donna / It hurts to be alone / Do you feel the same way / Dancing shoes / I'm still waiting / I made a mistake / One love / Maga dog / Nobody knows / Lonesome feeling / Let him go / Lonesome track / I'm going home
CD _____ 4679542
Columbia / Oct '95 / Sony.

EXODUS (Marley, Bob & The Wailers)
Natural mystic / So much things to say / Guiltiness / Heathen / Exodus / Jamming / Waiting in vain / Turn your lights down low / Three little birds / One love - people get ready
CD _____ TGLCD 6
Tuff Gong / Jan '94 / Jetstar / PolyGram.

GREAT VOL.2, THE
Gold / Apr '95 / Magnum Music Group.
CD _____ GLD 63185

HIS 24 GREATEST HITS
CD _____ ENTCD 282
Entertainers / Mar '92 / Target/BMG.

IN MEMORIAM (3CD Set)
CD Set _____ CDTAL 400
Trojan / Mar '94 / Jetstar / Total/BMG.

IN THE BEGINNING
Soul shakedown party / Adam and Eve / Brand new secondhand / Cheer up / This train / Jah is mighty / Caution / Thank you Lord / Keep on skanking / Wisdom / Stop the train / Mr. Chatterbox / Turn me loose
CD _____ CDTRL 221
Trojan / Mar '94 / Jetstar / Total/BMG.

JAMAICAN DUB VERSIONS VOL.2
CD _____ 60022
Declic / Nov '95 / Jetstar.

JAMAICAN SINGLES VOL.1
CD _____ 60012
Declic / Nov '95 / Jetstar.

JAMAICAN SINGLES VOL.2
CD _____ CB 6002
Caribbean / Jan '96 / Magnum Music Group.

KAYA (Marley, Bob & The Wailers)
Easy skanking / Is this love / Sun is shining / Satisfy my soul / She's gone / Misty morning / Crisis / Kaya / Running away / Time will tell
CD _____ TGLCD 7
Tuff Gong / Jan '94 / Jetstar / PolyGram.

LEE PERRY SESSIONS, THE
Lively up yourself / Small axe / Trench town rock / Sun is shining / Kaya / African herbsman / Brainwashing / Mr. Brown / Try me / No sympathy / Duppy conqueror / Stand alone / Fussing and fighting / Rebel's hop / Soul almighty / It's alright / Don't rock the boat / Put it on / All in one / Keep on moving
CD _____ CPCD 8009
Charly / Oct '93 / Charly / THE / Cadillac.

LEGEND (Marley, Bob & The Wailers)
Is this love / Jamming / No woman, no cry / Stir it up / Get up and stand up / Satisfy my soul / I shot the sheriff / One love / Buffalo soldier / Exodus / Redemption song / Could you be loved / Want more
CD _____ BMWCDX 1
Tuff Gong / May '91 / Jetstar / PolyGram.

LEGEND IN SAX
CD _____ AACD 88
A & A Productions / Jun '95 / Jetstar.

LIVE AT THE LYCEUM (Marley, Bob & The Wailers)
Trench town rock / Burnin' and lootin' / Them belly full (But we hungry) / Lively up yourself / No woman, no cry / I shot the sheriff / Get up stand up
CD _____ TGLCD 4
Tuff Gong / Jan '94 / Jetstar / PolyGram.

LIVELY UP YOURSELF
Soul shakedown party / Lively up yourself / Riding high / It's alright / Reaction / My cup / Can't you see / No water / Trenchtown rock / No sympathy / Stop the train

CD _____ CDSGP 056
Prestige / May '93 / Total/BMG.

MARLEY FAMILY ALBUM (Various Artists)
CD _____ HBCD 160
Heartbeat / Feb '95 / Greensleeves / Jetstar / Direct / ADA.

NATTY DREAD (Marley, Bob & The Wailers)
Lively up yourself / No woman, no cry / Them belly full (But we hungry) / Rebel music / So yah say / Natty dread / Bend down low / Talkin' blues / Revolution
CD _____ TGLCD 3
Tuff Gong / Jan '94 / Jetstar / PolyGram.

NATURAL MYSTIC
CD _____ AVC 506
Avid / Dec '92 / Avid/BMG / Koch.

NATURAL MYSTIC - THE LEGEND LIVES ON
Natural mystic / Easy skanking / Iron Lion Zion / Crazy baldheads / So much trouble in the world / War / Africa unite / Trenchtown rock (live) / Keep on moving / Sun is shining / Who the cap fits / One drop / Roots, rock, reggae / Pimpers paradise / Time will tell
CD _____ BMWCD 2
Tuff Gong / May '95 / Jetstar / PolyGram.

ONE LOVE/ROOTS VOL. 2
CD _____ CDBM 052
Blue Moon / Mar '95 / Magnum Music Group / Greensleeves / Hot Shot / ADA / Cadillac / Discovery.

PEARLS FROM THE PAST - BOB MARLEY
CD _____ KLMCD 003
Scratch / Nov '93 / BMG.

RAINBOW COUNTRY
Kaya / Rainbow country / Put it on / Fussing and fighting / Duppy conqueror / Memphis / Small axe / Soul rebel / Try me / Stand alone / Sun is shining / Brain washing
CD _____ CDCD 1152
Charly / Feb '94 / Charly / THE / Cadillac.

RASTAMAN (2CD Set)
Soul shakedown party / Caution / Do it twice / Back out / Try me / Corner stone / No water / Soul almighty / I made a mistake / Let him go / I'm going home / Nobody knows / Wings of a dove / Soul captive / Don't rock my boat / Stand alone / Love and affection / One love / Mega dog / Donna / Lonesome feeling / It hurts to be alone / Who feels it / Dancing shoes / Lonesome talk / Ten commandments of love / Chances are
CD Set _____ CDBM 501
Blue Moon / Sep '95 / Magnum Music Group / Greensleeves / Hot Shot / ADA / Cadillac / Discovery.

RASTAMAN VIBRATION (Marley, Bob & The Wailers)
Positive vibration / Roots, rock, reggae / Johnny was / Cry to me / Want more / Crazy baldheads / Who the cap fits / Night shift / War / Rat race
CD _____ TGLCD 1
Tuff Gong / Jan '94 / Jetstar / PolyGram.

REACTION
Reaction / I gotta keep on moving / Put it on / Go tell it on the mountain / Can't you see / Cheer up - good times are comin' / Don't rock the boat / Fussing and fighting / Memphis / African herbsman / Stand alone / Sun is shining / Brain washing / Mr. Brown / All in one / Soul rebel / Try me / Caution / No sympathy / It's alright
CD _____ PWK 072
Carlton Home Entertainment / Sep '88 / Carlton Home Entertainment.

REBEL MUSIC (Marley, Bob & The Wailers)
Rebel music / So much trouble in the world / Them belly full (But we hungry) / Rat race / War / Roots / Slave driver / Ride natty ride / Crazy baldheads / Get up stand up / No more trouble
CD _____ TGLCD 11
Tuff Gong / Jan '94 / Jetstar / PolyGram.

RIDING HIGH (Marley, Bob & The Wailers)
CD _____ CPCD 8029
Charly / Feb '94 / Charly / THE / Cadillac.

ROOTS
I made a mistake / Let him go / I'm going home / Nobody knows / Wings of a dove / Soul captives / Don't rock my boat / Stand alone / Soul shakedown party / Caution / Do it twice / Back out / Try me / Corner stone / No water / Soul almighty
CD _____ CDBM 032
Blue Moon / Mar '95 / Magnum Music Group / Greensleeves / Hot Shot / ADA / Cadillac / Discovery.

ROOTS VOL 2: ONE LOVE
One love / Love and affection / Mega dog / Donna / Lonesome feeling / It hurts to be alone / Who feels it / Dancing shoes / Lonesome talk / Ten commandments of men / Soul rebel / Chances are
CD _____ CDBM 1052

Blue Moon / '89 / Magnum Music Group / Greensleeves / Hot Shot / ADA / Cadillac / Discovery.

SIMMER DOWN AT STUDIO ONE (Marley, Bob & The Wailers)
CD _____ CDHB 171
Heartbeat / May '95 / Greensleeves / Jetstar / Direct / ADA.

SONGS OF FREEDOM (3CD Set)
Judge not / One cup of coffee / Simmer down / I'm still waiting / One love / Put it on / Bus dem shut (pyaka) / Mellow mood / Bend down low / Hypocrites / Stir it up / Nice time / Thank you Lord / Hammer / Caution / Back out / Soul shakedown party / Do it twice / Soul rebel / Sun is shining / Don't rock the boat / Small axe / Duppy conqueror / Mr. Brown / Screwface / Lick samba / Trenchtown rock / Craven choke puppy / Guava jelly / Acoustic medley (Guava jelly/This train/Cornerstone/Comma comma/Dewdrops/Stir it up/I'm hurting inside) / High tide or low tide / Slave driver / No more trouble / Concrete jungle / Get up stand up / Rastaman chant / Burnin' and lootin' / Iron lion zion / Lively up yourself / Natty dread / I shot the sheriff / No woman, no cry / Who the cap fits / Jah live / Crazy baldheads / War / Johnny was / Rat race / Jammin' / Waiting in vain / Exodus / Natural mystic / Three little birds / Running away / Keep on moving / Easy skanking / Is this love / Smile Jamaica / Time will tell / Africa unite / Survival / One drop / One dub / Zimbabwe / So much trouble in the world / Ride natty ride / Babylon system / Coming in from the cold / Real situation / Bad card / Could you be loved / Forever loving Jah / Rastaman live up / Give thanks and praise / One love/People get ready (12" mix) / Why should I / Redemption song
CD Set _____ TGCBX 1
Tuff Gong / Sep '92 / Jetstar / PolyGram.

SOUL ALMIGHTY (Natural Mystic II)
Try me / Touch me / Soul almighty / Do it twice / Back out / Cheer up / Put it on / Kaya / Fussin' and fightin' / Corner stone / African herbman / No water / Stand alone / Rebels hop / All in one / Duppy conqueror / 400 years / You can't do that to me / How many times
CD _____ AVC 563
Avid / Dec '95 / Avid/BMG / Koch.

SOUL CAPTIVE (Marley, Bob & The Wailers)
CD _____ RB 3010
Reggae Best / Nov '94 / Magnum Music Group / THE.

SOUL REVOLUTION I & II (2CD Set) (Marley, Bob & The Wailers)
Keep on moving / Don't rock my boat / Fussing and fighting / Put it on / Memphis / Soul rebel / Riding high / Kaya / Stand alone / African herbsman / Brain washing / Mr. Brown
CD Set _____ CDTRD 406
Trojan / Mar '94 / Jetstar / Total/BMG.

STIR IT UP
Stir it up / Trenchtown rock / Soul captive / Riding high / Soul shakedown party / Lively up yourself / Rebel's hop / Small axe / Back out / Do it twice / 400 Years / Stop the train
CD _____ SMS 04
Carlton Home Entertainment / Oct '92 / Carlton Home Entertainment.

SURVIVAL (Marley, Bob & The Wailers)
So much trouble / Africa unite / Babylon system / Ride Natty ride / One prop / Fighting against ism and skism / Top ranking / Wake up and live / Survival / Zimbabwe
CD _____ TGLCD 8
Tuff Gong / Jan '94 / Jetstar / PolyGram.

TALKIN' BLUES (Marley, Bob & The Wailers)
Talkin' blues / Burnin' and lootin' / Kinky reggae / Get up, stand up / Slave driver / Walk the proud land / You can't blame the youth / Rastaman chant / Am-a-do / Bend down low / I shot the sheriff
CD _____ TGLCD 12
Tuff Gong / Feb '91 / Jetstar / PolyGram.

TREAT ME RIGHT (Marley, Bob & The Wailers)
CD _____ CDCD 1036
Charly / Mar '93 / Charly / THE / Cadillac.

TRIBUTE TO BOB MARLEY (Various Artists)
CD _____ CDTRL 332
Trojan / Mar '94 / Jetstar / Total/BMG.

TRIBUTE TO BOB MARLEY (Various Artists)
CD _____ CC 2709
Crocodisc / Apr '94 / THE / Magnum Music Group.

TRIBUTE TO BOB MARLEY (Various Artists)
CD _____ RNCD 2089
Rhino / Feb '95 / Jetstar / Magnum Music Group / THE.

TRIBUTE TO BOB MARLEY VOL. 2 (Various Artists)
CD _____ RNCD 2117
Rhino / Sep '95 / Jetstar / Magnum Music Group / THE.

UPRISING (Marley, Bob & The Wailers)
Coming in from the cold / Real situation / Bad card / We and them / Work / Zion train / Pimpers paradise / Could you be loved / Forever living Jah / Redemption song
CD _____ TGLCD 9
Tuff Gong / Jan '94 / Jetstar / PolyGram.

VERY BEST OF THE EARLY YEARS (Marley, Bob & The Wailers)
Trenchtown rock / Lively up yourself / Soul almighty / Wisdom / Caution / Cheer up / Thank you lord / Stop the train / This train / Small axe / More axe / Don't rock my boat / Keep on moving / Brand new secondhand / Kaya / Turn me loose / Sun is shining / Keep on skanking
CD _____ MCCD 033
Music Club / Sep '91 / Disc / THE / CM.

WAILING WAILERS AT STUDIO ONE (Marley, Bob & The Wailers)
CD _____ CDHB 172
Heartbeat / May '95 / Greensleeves / Jetstar / Direct / ADA.

Marley, Rita

HARAMBE
CD _____ SHANCD 43010
Shanachie / Nov '87 / Koch / ADA / Greensleeves.

WE MUST CARRY ON
CD _____ SHCD 43082
Shanachie / Jun '91 / Koch / ADA / Greensleeves.

WHO FEELS IT KNOWS IT
CD _____ SHANCD 43003
Shanachie / '87 / Koch / ADA / Greensleeves.

Marley, Ziggy

CONSCIOUS PARTY
Conscious party / Tumblin' down / Who a say / Have you ever been to hell / Lee and Molly / Tomorrow people / We propose / What's true / Dreams of home / We a guh some weh (CD only) / New love
CD _____ CDV 2506
Virgin / Mar '88 / EMI.

CONSCIOUS PARTY/JAHMEKYA/ONE BRIGHT DAY (3CD Set) (Marley, Ziggy & The Melody Makers)
CD _____ TPAK 31
Virgin / Nov '93 / EMI.

FREE LIKE WE WANT TO BE
CD _____ 7559617022
Warner Bros. / Jun '95 / Warner Music.

JAHMEKYA (Marley, Ziggy & The Melody Makers)
Raw riddin' / Kozmik / Rainbow country / Drastic / Good time / What conquers defeat / First night / Wrong right wrong / Herbs an' spices / Problem with my woman / Jah is true and perfect / Small people / So good, so right / Namibia / New time and age / Generation
CD _____ CDVUS 35
Virgin / Apr '92 / EMI.

JOY AND BLUES (Marley, Ziggy & The Melody Makers)
CD _____ CDVUS 65
Virgin / Jul '93 / EMI.

ONE BRIGHT DAY
Black my story (not history) / One bright day / Who will be there / When the lights gone out / Problems / All love / Look who's dancing / Justice / Love is the only law / Pains of life / Ur-ban music / Give it all you got / When the light's gone out (Jamaican style)
CD _____ CDVUS 5
Virgin / Aug '91 / EMI.

TIME HAS COME - THE BEST OF ZIGGY MARLEY & MELODY MAKERS (Marley, Ziggy & The Melody Makers)
Give a little love / Get up jah children / Freedom road / Children playing in the streets / Lyin' in bed / Aiding and abetting / Say people / Natty dread rampage / Naah leggo / Met her on a rainy day / Reggae revolution / Reggae is now
CD _____ CDFA 3221
Fame / Mar '91 / EMI.

Marley/Booker/Cedella

AWAKE ZION
CD _____ DANCD 067
Danceteria / Nov '94 / Plastic Head / ADA.

Marlo, Clair

BEHAVIOUR SELF
CD _____ WLD 9208
Varese Sarabande/Colosseum / Apr '95 / Pinnacle / Silva Screen.

Marmalade

ALL THE HITS OF MARMALADE
CD _____ KLMCD 046
Scratch / Nov '94 / BMG.

FALLING APART AT THE SEAMS... PLUS
CD _____ C5CD 578
See For Miles/C5 / Mar '92 / Pinnacle.

HITS
CD _____ 12275
Laserlight / Apr '94 / Target/BMG.

REFLECTIONS OF THE MARMALADE
Super clean Jean / Carolina in my mind / I'll be home (in a day or so) / And it was / Is a piece of mine / Some other guy / Kaleidoscope / Dear John / Right say the mighty / Reflections of my life / Life is / Rainbow / Ballad of Cherry Flavar / My little one / Sarah / Just one woman / Cousin Norman / Back on the road / Radancer
CD _____ 8205624
London / Jan '93 / PolyGram.

Marmoj, Cirilo

MEXICO'S PIONEER MARIACHIS VOL.1
CD _____ FL 7011
Folklyric / Apr '95 / Direct / Cadillac.

Marmolejo, Jose

MEXICO'S PIONEER MARIACHIS VOL.2
CD _____ FL 7012
Folklyric / Apr '95 / Direct / Cadillac.

Maroa

ASTIMETRIX : NEW DIRECTIONS IN JAZZ
CD _____ DIS 80018
Dorian Discovery / Jan '94 / Conifer.

Marocana

TESTAMENT
Testament / Arab zenith / First light / Blue town / Evocation / Marooned / Desert uprising / Memories / Betrayal / 1000 years / New dawn / Slaves of time / Crucifixion
CD _____ MDMCD 004
Moidart / Nov '95 / Conifer / ADA.

Marohnic, Chuck

PAGES OF STONE (Marohnic, Chuck, David Friesen & Joe Labarbera)
CD _____ ITMP 970064
ITM / Apr '92 / Tradelink / Koch.

Maroon Town

ONE WORLD
Every little step / Prince of peace / Fix the future / Return of the django / Chameleon / Pound to the dollar / Streets of San Francisco / One world / Swing easy / Nostalgia / Vision of hope
CD _____ INT 30922
Intuition / Feb '94 / New Note.

Maros

FOLK MUSIC FROM EASTERN EUROPE (Maros & Szarvady Gyula)
Piron kancso / Piros bor / Harom csango nepdal csillagok / Rupulj madar
CD _____ 15283
Laserlight / Apr '94 / Target/BMG.

Marqua Y Su Combo

SABOR TROPICAL
CD _____ TUMICD 016
Tumi / '91 / Sterns / Discovery.

Marquet, Alain

CLARINET JOY (Marquet, Alain & Reimer von Essen)
CD _____ SOSCD 1259
Stomp Off / Jul '93 / Jazz Music / Wellard.

HOP SCOT BLUES
CD _____ SOSCD 1229
Stomp Off / Nov '92 / Jazz Music / Wellard.

Marr, Hank

GREASY SPOON
Ram-bunk-shush / Greasy spoon / Push / Mellow thing / Let's cut one / Tonk game / Number two / Wild shindig / Foggy night / Hank's idea / Molasses / Late freight / Silver spoon / Sabotage / Headache (donkey walk) / Travelin' heavy / Squash / Jim Dawg / Mexican vodca (bossa nova sandman) / Black slop
CD _____ CDCHARLY 271
Charly / Jun '91 / Charly / THE / Cadillac.

Marra, Michael

CANDY PHILOSOPHY
Land of golden slippers / Don't look at me / Johnny Hallyday (Je vous salue) / True love (something no one should ever be without) / Violin lesson / To beat the drum / Painters painting paint / King Kong's visit to Glasgow / Guernsey kitchen porter / Australia instead of stars / O fellow man / This evergreen bough
CD _____ ECLCD 9309
Eclectic / Jan '96 / Pinnacle.

GAELS BLUE
Mincing wi' Chairlhi / Racing from Newburgh / Angus man's welcome to Mary Stuart / King George III's return to sanity / General Grant's visit to Dundee / Black babies / Monkey hair / Altar boys / Gael's blue / Happed in mist

CD _____ ECLCD 9206
Eclectic / Jan '96 / Pinnacle.

ON STOLEN STATIONERY
Margaret Reilly's arrival at Craiglockhart / Wise old men of Mount Florida / Under the ullapool moon / Rats / Hamish / Harmless / Neil Gow's apprentice / Humphrey Kate's song / Like another rolling stone / Here come the weak / Bawbee birlin' / O penitence
CD _____ ECLCD 9104
Eclectic / Jan '96 / Pinnacle.

Marriott, Beryl

WEAVE THE MIRROR
Big strong lad herding the goats/High road to Linton / Phantasy in fives/Searching for lambs/Bold fisherman / Cam ye by athol/ Laird O'Drumblair/Glengarry's march / Whelan's jig/Morrison's jig/McFadden's favourite/Smokey hous / Jenny Nettles/Give me your hand/March of the King of Louise / Dance of the kings of man/Gillie Callum / Y deryn pur / Brigadier cruise/Carolan's cup / Kid on the mountain / Lochaber no more / Carolan's welcome / Black nag/Nonsuch
CD _____ WRCD 016
Woodworm / Jan '92 / Pinnacle.

Marriott, Steve

30 SECONDS TO MIDNIGHT
Knocking on your door / All or nothing / One more heartache / Um um um um um song / Superlungs my supergirl / Get up stand up / Rascal you / Life during wartime / Phone call away / Clapping song / Shakin' all over / Gypsy woman
CD _____ CLACD 386
Castle / Mar '93 / BMG.

DINGWALLS, 6.7.84
CD _____ MAUCD 609
Mau Mau / Sep '91 / Pinnacle.

Mars

MARS LIVE
CD _____ CDSA 54025
Semantic / Feb '94 / Plastic Head.

Mars, Johnny

KING OF THE BLUES HARP
Horses and places / Rocket 88 / Johnny's groove / Desert island / I'll go crazy / Imagination / Mighty Mars / Cash ain't nothing / If I had a woman
CD _____ JSPCD 217
JSP / Jul '88 / ADA / Target/BMG / Direct / Cadillac / Complete/Pinnacle.

LIFE ON MARS
Born under a bad sign / Don't start me talkin' / Back door man / Steal away / Standing in line / Hot lips boogie / I can't take a jealous woman / Get on up / Desert island / Keep on swinging
CD _____ BGOCD 159
Beat Goes On / Oct '93 / Pinnacle.

Marsala, Joe

CLASSICS 1936-42
CD _____ CLASSICS 763
Classics / Jun '94 / Discovery / Jazz Music.

Marsalis, Branford

BEAUTYFUL ONES ARE NOT YET BORN, THE
Roused about / Beautyful ones are not yet born / Xavier's lair / Gillinan's Isle / Cain and Abel / Citizen Tain / Dewey baby / Beat's remark
CD _____ 4668962
Columbia / Jan '95 / Sony.

BLOOMINGTON
CD _____ 4737712
Sony Jazz / Jan '95 / Sony.

CRAZY PEOPLE MUSIC
Spartacus / Dark knight / Wolverine / Mr. Steepee / Rose petals / Ransom abstract (diddle it) / Ballad of Chet Kincald (hikky burr)
CD _____ 4668702
Columbia / Jan '95 / Sony.

I HEARD YOU TWICE THE FIRST TIME
Brother trying to catch a cab / (On the East side) blues / B.B's blues / Rib tip Johnson / Mabel / Sidney in da haus / Berta Berta / Stretto from the ghetto / Dance of the Hei Gui / Road you choose / Simi valley blues
CD _____ 472169-2
Columbia / Jul '93 / Sony.

RANDOM ABSTRACT
Yes and no / Crescent city / Broadway fools / Lonjellis / I thought about you / Lonely woman / Steep's theme
CD _____ 4687072
Sony Jazz / Jan '95 / Sony.

ROYAL GARDEN BLUES
Swingin' at the haven / Dienda / Strike up the band / Emanon / Royal garden blues / Shadows / Wrath of Tain
CD _____ 4687042
Sony Jazz / Jan '95 / Sony.

SCENES IN THE CITY
No backstage pass / Scenes in the city / Solstice / Waiting for Tain / No sidestepping / Parable
CD _____ 4684582
Sony Jazz / Jan '95 / Sony.

TRIO GP
Housed from Edward / Three little words / UMMG / Doxy / Stardust / Random abstract (Tain's rampage) / Nearness of you / Makin' whoopee / Gut bucket steepy / Makin' whoopee (reprise) / Peace
CD _____ 4651342
Sony Jazz / Jan '95 / Sony.

Marsalis, Delfeayo

PONTIUS PILATE'S DECISION
Pontius Pilate's decision / Adam's ecstasy / Eve's delight / Barabbas / Weary ways of Mary Magdalene / Nicodemus / Son of the Virgin Mary / Reverend Judas Escariot / Simon's journey / Last supper / Crucifixion
CD _____ PD 90669
Novus / Jun '92 / BMG.

Marsalis, Ellis

CLASSIC MARSALIS, THE
Monkey puzzle / Whistle stop / After / Dee Wee / Twelve's it / Yesterdays / Magnolia triangle / Little joy / Swinging at the Haven / Round Midnight / Night in Tunisia
CD _____ CDBOP 016
Boplicity / Apr '93 / Pinnacle / Cadillac.

NIGHT AT SNUG HARBOR, NEW ORLEANS, A
Introduction / Nothin' but the blues / Call / After / Some monk funk / I can't get started / Jitterbug / Very thought of you / Night in Tunisia
CD _____ ECD 221292
Evidence / Sep '95 / Harmonia Mundi / ADA / Cadillac.

PIANO IN E - SOLO PIANO
Hallucinations / Django / Jitterbug waltz / Nica's dream / So in love / Fourth autumn / Zee blues
CD _____ CD 2100
Rounder / May '91 / CM / Direct / ADA / Cadillac.

WHISTLE STOP
Whistle stop / Dee wee / Moment alone / Magnolia triangle / Mozartin' / Cry again / Cochise / Li'l boy man / Monkey puzzle / After / Beautiful old ladies / Little joy / When we first met
CD _____ 474555 2
Columbia / Apr '94 / Sony.

Marsalis, Wynton

AMERICAN HERO, AN
One by one / My funny valentine / Round Midnight / ETA / Time will tell / Blakey's theme
CD _____ CDGATE 7018
Kingdom Jazz / Nov '86 / Kingdom.

BLACK CODES (From The Underground)
Black codes / For wee folks / Delfeayo's dilemma / Phryzzian march / Aural oasis / Chambers of Tain / Blues
CD _____ 468711 2
Columbia / Feb '94 / Sony.

BLAKEY'S THEME (Marsalis, Wynton & Art Blakey's Jazz Messengers)
CD _____ WW 2045
West Wind / Mar '93 / Swift / Charly / CM / ADA.

BLUE INTERLUDE
CD _____ 4716352
Sony Jazz / Jan '95 / Sony.

CARNAVAL (With Eastman Wind Ensemble)
Variations on Le Carnaval de Venise / Grand Russian fantasia / Debutante / Believe me, if all those endearing young charms / Moto perpetuo / 'Tis the last rose of Summer / Flight of the bumble bee / Napoli / Variations on a Neapolitan song / Fantasie brillante / Sometimes I feel like a motherless child / Valse brillante
CD _____ MK 42137
CBS / Apr '87 / Sony.

CITI MOVEMENT (Griot New York) (Marsalis, Wynton Septet)
CD _____ 4730552
Sony Jazz / Jan '95 / Sony.

CRESCENT CITY CHRISTMAS CARD
Carol of the bells / Silent night / Hark the herald angels sing / Little drummer boy / We three kings of Orient are / Oh tannenbaum / Sleigh ride / Let it snow, let it snow, let it snow / God rest ye merry gentlemen / Winter wonderland / Jingle bells / O come all ye faithful (Adeste Fidelis) / 'Twas the night before Christmas
CD _____ 4658792
CBS / Dec '89 / Sony.

FIRST RECORDINGS WITH ART BLAKEY
Angel eyes / Bitter dose / Wheel within a wheel / Gypsy / Jody
CD _____ CDGATE 7013
Kingdom Jazz / Oct '87 / Kingdom.

HOT HOUSE FLOWERS
Stardust / Lazy afternoon / For all we know / When you wish upon a star / Django / Melancholia / Hot house flowers / Confession
CD _____ 468710 2
Columbia / Feb '94 / Sony.

IN THIS HOUSE, ON THIS MORNING (2CD Set) (Marsalis, Wynton Septet)
CD Set _____ 474552 2
Columbia / Apr '94 / Sony.

J MOOD
J mood / Presence that lament brings / Insane asylum / Skain's domain / Melodique / After / Much later
CD _____ 4687122
Sony Jazz / Jan '95 / Sony.

JOE COOL'S BLUES (Marsalis, Wynton & Ellis)
Linus and Lucy / Buggy ride / Peppermint Patty / On Peanuts playground / Oh good grief / Wright Brothers rag / Charlie Brown / Little Red Haired Girl / Pebble Beach / Snoopy and Woodstock / Little birdie / Why Charlie Brown / Joe Cool's blues
CD _____ 4782502
Sony Jazz / Jan '95 / Sony.

LEVEE LOW MOAN SOUL GESTURES IN SOUTHERN BLUE #3
CD _____ 4686582
Sony Jazz / Jan '95 / Sony.

LIVE AT BUBBA'S 1980 (Marsalis, Wynton & Art Blakey's Jazz Messengers)
CD Set _____ JWD 102311
JWD / Oct '94 / Target/BMG.

MAJESTY OF THE BLUES, THE
Majesty of the blues (Puheeman strut) / Hickory dickory dock / New Orleans function / Death of jazz / Premature autopsies (sermon) / Oh, but on the third day (happy feet blues)
CD _____ 4651292
Sony Jazz / Jan '95 / Sony.

MARSALIS STANDARD TIME
Caravan / April in Paris / Cherokee / Goodbye / New Orleans / Soon all will know / Foggy day / Song is you / Memories of you / In the afterglow / Autumn leaves
CD _____ 4510392
CBS / Oct '87 / Sony.

MASTER OF TRUMPET
One by one / My funny valentine / Round Midnight / ETA / Time will tell / Blakey's theme / Jody
CD _____ 722008
Scorpio / Sep '92 / Complete/Pinnacle.

MY FUNNY VALENTINE
Jody / Wheel within a wheel / Gypsy / One by one / My funny valentine / Round Midnight / ETA / Time will tell / Blakey's theme
CD _____ AAOHP 93372
Start / Dec '94 / Koch.

MY IDEAL
CD _____ JHR 73562
Jazz Hour / Oct '92 / Target/BMG / Jazz Music / Cadillac.

SOUL GESTURES IN SOUTHERN BLUE #1 (Thick In The South)
CD _____ 4686592
Sony Jazz / Jan '95 / Sony.

SOUL GESTURES IN SOUTHERN BLUE #2 (Uptown Ruler)
CD _____ 4686602
Columbia / Jul '94 / Sony.

THINK OF ONE
Think of one / Knozz-Moe-King / Fuschia / My ideal / What is happening here (now) / Bell ringer / Later / Melancholia
CD _____ 468709 2
Columbia / Feb '94 / Sony.

TIME WILL TELL
CD _____ JHR 73561
Jazz Hour / Oct '92 / Target/BMG / Jazz Music / Cadillac.

WYNTON MARSALIS
Father time / I'll be there when the time is right / R.J. / Hesitation / Sister Cheryl / Who can I turn to / Twilight / Knozz-Moe-King / Just friends / Knozz-moe-king (Interlude) / Juan / Cherokee / Delfeayo's dream / Chambers of Tain / Au privave / Do you know what it means to miss New Orleans / Juan (Skip Mustaad) / Autumn leaves / Skain's domain / Much later
CD _____ 468708 2
Columbia / Nov '93 / Sony.

WYNTON MARSALIS QUARTET LIVE AT BLUES ALLEY, THE (2CD Set) (Marsalis, Wynton Quartet)
Knozz-Moe-King / Just friends / Juan / Cherokee / Delfeayo's dilemma / Chambers of Tain / Au privave / Do you know what it means to miss New Orleans / Skain's domain / Much later
CD Set _____ 4611092
Sony Jazz / Jan '95 / Sony.

WYNTON MARSALIS STANDARD TIME #1
CD _____ 4687132
Sony Jazz / Jan '95 / Sony.

WYNTON MARSALIS STANDARD TIME #2 (Intimacy Calling)
CD _____ 4682732
Sony Jazz / Jan '95 / Sony.

WYNTON MARSALIS STANDARD TIME #3 (The Resolution Of Romance)
CD _____ 4668712
Sony Jazz / Jan '95 / Sony.

Marscape

MARSCAPE
CD _____ EFA 132412
Ozone / Jan '94 / SRD.

Marsden, Bernie

AND ABOUT TIME TOO
You're the one / Song for Fran / Love made a fool of me / Here we go again / Still the same / Sad clown / Brief encounter / Are you ready / Head the ball
CD _____ RPM 152
RPM / Oct '95 / Pinnacle.

FRIDAY ROCK SHOW/LIVE AT READING '82, THE
CD _____ FRSCD 007
Raw Fruit / May '92 / Pinnacle.

GREEN AND BLUES
CD _____ ESSCD 324
Essential / Nov '95 / Total/BMG.

LOOK AT ME NOW
Look at me now / So far away / Who's foolin' who / Always love you so / Behind your dark eyes / Byblos shack / Thunder and lightning / Can you do it / After all the madness
CD _____ RPM 153
RPM / Oct '95 / Pinnacle.

Marsh, Hugh

BEAR WALKS, THE
CD _____ VBR 20112
Vera Bra / Dec '90 / Pinnacle / New Note.

Marsh, Warne

DUO - LIVE AT THE SWEET BASIL 1980 (Marsh, Warne & Red Mitchell)
CD _____ FSCD 1038
Fresh Sound / Nov '94 / Jazz Music / Discovery.

NEWLY WARNE
CD _____ STCD 4162
Storyville / Feb '90 / Jazz Music / Wellard / CM / Cadillac.

TWO DAYS IN THE LIFE OF....
CD _____ STCD 4165
Storyville / Feb '90 / Jazz Music / Wellard / CM / Cadillac.

Marshall, Evan

IS THE LONE ARRANGER
CD _____ ROUNCD 0338
Rounder / May '95 / CM / Direct / ADA / Cadillac.

Marshall, Julian

CELEBRATION
CD _____ C5CD-561
See For Miles/C5 / Jul '91 / Pinnacle.

Marshall, Larry

I ADMIRE YOU
CD _____ IJD99 IT
Greensleeves / Dec '92 / Total/BMG / Jetstar / SRD.

THROW MI CORN
CD _____ OMCD 29
Original Music / Sep '94 / SRD / Jetstar.

Marshall, Mike

GATOR STRUT
CD _____ CD 0208
Rounder / Aug '88 / CM / Direct / ADA / Cadillac.

Marshall, Peter

CHANNEL ONE REVISITED
CD _____ TBXCD 002
Top Beat / Oct '95 / Jetstar / SRD.

Marshall, Wayne

90 DEGREES AND RISING
CD _____ SOULCD 31
Soultown / Jun '94 / Pinnacle / Jetstar.

BLESSED IS THE CHILD
CD _____ EWCD 003
Teams / May '95 / Jetstar.

CENSORED
CD _____ SOULCD 34
Soultown / Dec '94 / Pinnacle / Jetstar.

Martains

LOW BUDGET STUNT KING
CD _____ ALLIED 057CD
Allied / Nov '95 / Plastic Head.

441

Martell, Lena

BEST OF LENA MARTELL
CD _____ MATCD 220
Castle / Dec '92 / BMG.

FEELINGS
Help me make it through the night / One day at a time / You've got a friend / Feelings / Take me home country roads / First time ever I saw your face / Hello misty morning / Bridge over troubled water / I can see clearly now / Old rugged cross / With pen in hand / You'll never walk alone
CD _____ PWKM 4069
Carlton Home Entertainment / Jul '91 / Carlton Home Entertainment.

FEELINGS - BEST OF LENA MARTELL
One day at a time / Don't cry for me Argentina / Nevertheless (I'm in love with you) / Let me try again / Old fashioned way / Running bear / Call collect / Old rugged cross / Danny come home / Six weeks every summer / Movin' on / Until it's time for you to go / Pledging my love / Love letters / Why did I choose you / Make the world go away / Everybody get together / Feelings / Call / Four and twenty hours / Forever in blue jeans
CD _____ TRTCD 131
TrueTrax / Oct '94 / THE.

Martha & The Muffins

FARAWAY IN TIME
Echo beach / Paint by number heart / Saigon / Indecision / Terminal twilight / Hide and seek / Monotone / Sinking land / Revenge (against the world) / Cheesies and gum / Insect love / About insomnia / Motor bikin' / Suburban dream / Was ezo / Women around the world at work / This is the ice age
CD _____ COMCD 12
Virgin / May '88 / EMI.

Martika

12" TAPE: MARTIKA
More than you know (House mix part 1) / Toy soldiers (Special version) / Martika's kitchen (mix) / Coloured kisses / I feel the earth move
CD _____ 4730402
Columbia / Mar '93 / Sony.

MARTIKA
If you're Tarzan, I'm Jane / Cross my heart / More than you know / Toy soldiers / You got me into this / I feel the earth move / Water / It's not what you're doing / See if I care / Alibis
CD _____ 4633552
Columbia / Oct '91 / Sony.

MARTIKA'S KITCHEN
Martika's kitchen / Spirit / Love... thy will be done / Magical place / Coloured kisses / Safe in the arms of love / Pride and prejudice / Take me forever / Temptation / Don't say U love me / Broken heart / Mi tierra
CD _____ 4671892
Columbia / Apr '94 / Sony.

Martin, Billie Ray

DEADLINE FOR MY MEMORIES
CD _____ 0630121802
Magnet / Jan '96 / Warner Music.

Martin, Carl

MARTIN, BOGAN & ARMSTRONG/ OLD GANG OF MINE (Martin, Carl & Ted Bogan/Howard Armstrong)
CD _____ FF 003CD
Flying Fish / Feb '93 / Roots / CM / Direct / ADA.

Martin, Carl

CARL MARTIN 1930-6/WILLIE BLACKWELL 1941 (Martin, Carl & Willie Blackwell)
CD _____ DOCD 5229
Blues Document / Apr '94 / Swift / Jazz Music / Hot Shot.

Martin, Claire

DEVIL MAY CARE
Devil may care / Victim of circumstance / If love were all / Devil's gonna git you / By myself / Close enough for love / Cant's give enough / Sun was falling from the sky / October thoughts / On thin ice / Save your love for me
CD _____ AKD 021
Linn / Apr '93 / PolyGram.

OFFBEAT
Offbeat / Buy and sell / Come back to me / I'll close my eyes / Monk's new tune / I do it for your love / Worth the wait / Wishful thinking / Comes love / Would you believe / Lost in his arms / Something real / Make sure you're sure / Some other time
CD _____ AKD 046
Linn / Nov '95 / PolyGram.

OLD BOYFRIENDS
When the sun comes out / Close as pages in a book / Partners in crime / Chased out / Moon ray / Old boyfriends / Out of my

---

continental mind / I've got news for you / Wheelers and dealers / I was telling him about you / Gentleman friend / Killing time
CD _____ AKD 028
Linn / Sep '94 / PolyGram.

WAITING GAME, THE
You hit the spot / Be cool / This funny world / Better than anything / If you could see me now / Some cats / Four AM / People that you never get to love / Tight / Everything happens to me / Key to your Ferrari
CD _____ AKD 018
Linn / Mar '92 / PolyGram.

Martin, Dean

ALL THE HITS 1948-63
CD _____ PRS 23015
Personality / Jan '94 / Target/BMG.

ALL THE HITS 1948-69
CD Set _____ DBP 102005
Double Platinum / Jan '94 / Target/BMG.

ALL THE HITS 1964-69
CD _____ PRS 23016
Personality / Jan '94 / Target/BMG.

BEST OF DEAN MARTIN (The Capitol Years)
That's amore / Kiss / Memories are made of this / Sway / Money burns a hole in my pocket / Hey brother pour the wine / Naughty lady of Shady Lane / Man who plays the mandolino / Mambo Italiano / Innamorata / Volare / Relax-ay-voo / All in a nights work / Return to me / Cha cha cha d'amour / Just in time
CD _____ CDEMS 1297
Capitol / Jan '89 / EMI.

BEST OF DEAN MARTIN
CD _____ CPCD 8150
Charly / Nov '95 / Charly / THE / Cadillac.

BEST OF DEAN MARTIN, THE
CD _____ CDGR 106
Charly / Jan '96 / Charly / THE / Cadillac.

COLLECTION: DEAN MARTIN
Everybody loves somebody / My heart cries for you / I'll hold you in my heart / In the chapel in the moonlight / Release me / Born to lose / Somewhere there's a someone / Green green grass of home / You've still got a place in my heart / You'll always be the one I love / Door is still open / Welcome to my world / In the misty moonlight / Room full of roses / I wonder who's kissing her now / Crying time / One I love (belongs to somebody else) / I'm so lonesome I could cry / Take these chains from my heart / I can't help it (if I'm still in love with you)
CD _____ CCSCD 207
Castle / Nov '88 / BMG.

DEAN MARTIN
That's amore / Innamorata / Buona sera / I'm yours / Memories are made of this / Return to me / Volare / Write to me from Naples / One I love / Release me / Sway / My heart cries for you / Everybody loves somebody / Crying time / When you're smiling / Take these chains from my heart / Rio Bravo / Lullaby / Basin Street blues / Angel baby / Rain / Wrap your troubles in dreams (and dream your troubles away) / Canadian sunset / Born to lose / Somewhere there's a someone / Baby, it's cold outside
CD _____ CD 0224
Entertainers / Apr '90 / Target/BMG.

DEAN MARTIN
CD _____ DVGH 7092
Deja Vu / May '95 / THE.

GREAT GENTLEMEN OF SONG, THE
All I do is dream of you / Please don't talk about me when I'm gone / Things we did last summer / Mean to me / Wrap your troubles in dreams (and dream your troubles away) / Imagination / Sleepy time gal / You're nobody til' somebody loves you / Dream / Someday (you'll want me to want you) / June in January / I can't believe that you're in love with me / Dream a little dream of me / Just in time / Cuddle up a little closer / Lovely mine / Until the real thing comes along / Hit the road to dreamland / Goodnight sweetheart
CD _____ CDP 8320982
Capitol / Aug '95 / EMI.

MEMORIES ARE MADE OF THIS
CD Set _____ HP 93522
Start / Nov '94 / Koch.

SINGLES, THE
You was (With P. Lee) / That lucky old sun / Night train to Memphis / In the cool, cool, cool of the evening / Kiss / There's my lover / When you're smiling / Pretty as a picture / How do you speak to an angel / Every street's a boulevard / Long long ago / Let me go, lover / Under the bridges of Paris / Two sleepy people / Young and foolish / Just one more chance / Standing on the corner / Me 'n' you 'n' the moon / You can't love 'em all / I wish you love
CD _____ CDMFP 6129
Music For Pleasure / Sep '94 / EMI.

VERY BEST OF DEAN MARTIN, THE
Return to me / Angel baby / Rio bravo / I've got my love to keep me warm / Baby, it's cold outside / Buona sera / That's amore / Goodnight sweetheart / Volare / Write to me

---

from Naples / Memories are made of this / June in January / Come back to Sorrento / Hey brother pour the wine / Cha cha cha d'amour / I have but one heart
CD _____ CDMFP 6032
Music For Pleasure / Sep '88 / EMI.

Martin, Emile

EMILE MARTIN
CD _____ BCD 317
GHB / Oct '93 / Jazz Music.

Martin, George

BEATLES TO BOND AND BACH
CD _____ REP 4142-WZ
Repertoire / Aug '91 / Pinnacle / Cadillac.

Martin, Janis

FEMALE ELVIS, THE
Drug store rock 'n' roll / Will you Willyum / Love and kisses / My boy Elvis / Crackerjack / Bang bang / Ooby dooby / Barefoot baby / Good love / Little bit / Two long years / All right baby / Billy boy my Billy boy / Let's elope baby / Love me love / Love me to pieces / William / Here today and gone tomorrow / Teen street / Hard times ahead / Cry guitar / Just squeeze me / One more year to go / Blues keep calling / Please be my love / I don't hurt anymore / Half loved / My confession / I'll never be free
CD _____ BCD 15406
Bear Family / Jul '87 / Rollercoaster / Direct / CM / Swift / ADA.

Martin, Jimmy

JIMMY MARTIN & THE SUNNY MOUNTAIN BOYS (Martin, Jimmy & The Sunny Mountain Boys)
Save it save it / Chalk up another one / I pulled a boo boo / They didn't know the difference (but I did) / 20/20 Vision / That's how I count on you / Before the sun goes down / Skip, hop and wobble / You'll be a lost ball / Hitparade of love / Grand ole opry song / I'm the boss (of this here house) / Dog bite your hide / I'll drink no more wine / Ocean of diamonds / Sophronie / I'll never take no for an answer / Rock hearts / I like to hear 'em preach it / Voice of my saviour / Night / It's not like your hearts / Cripple creek / In foggy old London / Joke's on you / Wooden shoes / Home run man / Who'll sing for me / God is always the same / All the good times are past and gone / You don't know my mind / Old fashioned christmas / He-de diddle / Don't cry to me / My walking shoes / Hold to God's unchanging hand / Undo what's been done / Deep river / What was I supposed to do / I can, I will, I can believe / There was a love / Poor little bull frogs / Steppin' stones / There ain't nobody gonna miss me / Little angels in heaven / Pretending I don't care / Leavin' town / Don't give your heart to a rambler / God guide our leader's hand / Train 45 / Mr. Engineer / This world is not my home / Drink up and go home / Lord I'm coming home / Goodbye / Pray the clouds away / Give me the roses now / Prayer bell of heaven / Moonshine hollow / Give me your hand / Stormy waters / What would you give in exchange / Shut in's prayer / Beautiful life / Little white church / Old man's drunk again / Hey lonesome / Tennessee / Widow maker / I'm thinking tonight of my blue eyes / Red river valley / John Henry / Truck driving man / There's more pretty girls than one / Six days on the road / Truck driver's queen / I'd rather have America / Little Robin / There's better times a coming / Guitar picking president / It takes one to know one / Sunny side of the mountain / Snow white grave / Poor Ellen Smith / Shenandoah waltz / Coming back but I don't know when / In the pines / Last song / Sweet Dixie / Wild indian / Run boy run / Theme time / Orange blossom special / I can't quit cigarettes / Lost highway / Good things out weigh the bad / Summer's come and gone / Fraulein / You're gonna change (or I'm gonna leave) / Tennessee waltz / Little Maggie, she's so sweet / Big country / Red rooster / Crow on the banjo / You are my sunshine / Going up dry branch / Living like a fool / Union county / Uptown blues / Goin' ape (over you) / Steal away somewhere and die / Freeborn man / Losing you / Just and old standby / Slowly / Lonesome prison blues / Shackles and chains / Doin' my time / Milwaukee here I come / Arab bounce (I've got my) Future on ice / Midnight rambler / Between fire and water / Singing all day / Lift your eyes to Jesus / Shake hands with Mother again / When the saviour reached down for me / Help thy brother / My Lord keeps a record / I'd like to be sixteen again / I cried again / Chattanooga dog / Mary Ann / I buried my future / Just plain yellow / Fly me to Frisco / Grave upon the green hillside / Lost to a stranger / Beautiful brown eyes
CD Set _____ BCDEI 15705
Bear Family / Sep '94 / Rollercoaster / CM / Swift / ADA.

YOU DON'T KNOW MY MIND
CD _____ CDROU 5521
Rounder / Dec '90 / CM / Direct / ADA / Cadillac.

Martin, Juan

ANDALUCIAN SUITES, THE
CD _____ CD FV 01
Flamencovision / Jun '91 / Pinnacle.

LUNA NEGRA
CD _____ CDFV 02
Flamencovision / May '93 / Pinnacle.

PICASSO PORTRAITS
Harlequin / Desire caught by the tail / Three musicians / Sleeping girl / Self portrait / Aficionado / Girls of Algiers / Weeping woman / Piccador
CD _____ CDFV 03
Flamencovision / Apr '94 / Pinnacle.

Martin, Marilyn

MARILYN MARTIN
Body and the beat / Night moves / Too much too soon / Turn it on / Thank you (Available on Album and cassette) / One step closer to you / Beauty or the beast / Move closer / Dream is always the same / Here is the news
CD _____ 7567802112
Atlantic / Jan '96 / Warner Music.

THIS IS SERIOUS
Possessive love / This is serious / Best is yet to come / Quiet desperation / Lay me down / Love takes no prisoners / Try me / Wait is over / Homeless / Pretender
CD _____ 7567818142
Atlantic / Jan '96 / Warner Music.

Martin, Mary

DECCA YEARS 1938-1946, THE
CD _____ 379062
Koch International / Nov '95 / Koch.

Martin, Mel

PLAYS BENNY CARTER
Kiss from you / Hello / Zanzibar / When lights are low / Summer serenade / Souvenir / Another time, another place / Wonderland / Only trust your heart
CD _____ ENJ 90412
Enja / Jul '95 / New Note / Vital/SAM.

Martin, Moon

SHOTS FROM A COLD NIGHTMARE/ ESCAPE FROM DOMINATION
Hot nite in Dallas / Victim of romance / Nite thoughts / Paid killer / Cadillac walk / Bad case of lovin' you / Hands down / All I've got to do / You don't care about me / She's a pretender / I've got a reason / She made a fool of you / Dreamer / Gun shy / Hot house baby / Feeling's right / Rolene / No chance / Dangerous / Bootleg woman
CD _____ EDCD 432
Edsel / Jul '95 / Pinnacle / ADA.

STREET FEVER/MYSTERY TICKET
CD _____ EDCD 433
Edsel / Oct '95 / Pinnacle / ADA.

Martin, Nicholas

HAPPY DAYS ARE HERE AGAIN (At the Wurlitzer Organ)
CD _____ GRCD 49
Grasmere / '92 / Target/BMG / Savoy.

Martin, Sallie

PRECIOUS LORD (Martin, Sallie Singers)
Precious Lord / That's what he done for me / Old ship of Zion / Own me as a child / Search my heart / God is moving / Let me cross over / There's not a friend / No one ever cared / God is here / I need him / Nothing but the grace of God / He's in my heart / Seeking for me / Let Jesus come into my heart / I need you / Keep me Jesus / Closer to Jesus / I was glad when they said to me / Jesus I love you
CD _____ CPCD 8116
Charly / Jul '95 / Charly / THE / Cadillac.

THROW OUT THE LIFELINE (Martin, Sallie Singers & Cora Martin)
God is a battle axe / Didn't it rain / I'll make it somehow / Oh yes, he set me free / He's able to carry me through / Oh what a time / Throw out the lifeline / Eyes hath not seen / Good old way / Jesus is waiting / Great day / I know it's well with my soul / Jesus said / I called the Lord and got an answer / There is a fountain filled with blood / It's a long, long way / I'm bound for the promised land / Hold to God's unchanging hand / Ain't that good news (There is no sorrow) that heaven cannot heal / I'm getting nearer to my lord / Every once in a while / One of these mornings / Thy servant's prayer / On the other side / He put his trust in me / I know that he cares for me / Lord I need you every day of my life
CD _____ CDCHD 481
Ace / Jul '93 / Pinnacle / Cadillac / Complete/Pinnacle.

Martin, Tony

SOMETHING IN THE AIR
Rainbow on the river / Star fell out of heaven / It's love i'm after / Where the lazy river goes by / Afraid to dream / By a wish-

ing well / My sweetheart / That week in
Paris / When did you leave Heaven / Love-
liness of you / Sweetheart let's grow old to-
gether / There's something in the air / Mist
is over the moon / You're slightly terrific /
Song of old Hawaii / This may be the night
/ So do I / World is mine tonight
CD _____ CMSCD 004
Movie Stars / '88 / Conifer.

THIS MAY BE THE NIGHT
By a wishing well / Cancel the flowers /
Donkey serenade / Dream valley / Flamingo
/ I hadn't anyone till you / Island of Maui
Hula / Just let me look at you / Last time I
saw Paris / Marching along with time / My
sweetheart / Now it can be told / One love
affair / Rhythm of the waves / Song of old
Hawaii / That week in Paris / This may be
the night / 'Tis Autumn / Too beautiful to
last / Where in the world / You couldn't be
cuter / You stepped out of a dream
CD _____ CD AJA 5099
Living Era / Dec '92 / Koch.

Martinez, Narciso

**FATHER OF TEX MEX CONJUNTO -
1948-1960**
CD _____ ARHCD 361
Arhoolie / Apr '95 / ADA / Direct /
Cadillac.

Martino, Al

AL MARTINO
Spanish eyes / Red roses for a blue lady /
My way / Hey Mama / Sweet Caroline / Ev-
erybody's talkin'
CD _____ 16114
Laserlight / May '94 / Target/BMG.

AL MARTINO IN CONCERT
CD _____ CDPT 841
Prestige / Feb '91 / Total/BMG.

ALL OR NOTHING AT ALL
CD _____ CDCD 1266
Charly / Oct '95 / Charly / THE / Cadillac.

GREATEST HITS
Song is you / I have but one love / Cuando
cuando cuando / Feelings / More I see you
/ Somewhere my love / Mary in the morning
/ Spanish eyes / Strangers in the night / As
long as you're with me / Lonely is a man
without love / I love you because / I love
you more and more every day / Wild and
lovely rose / Speak softly love / End of the
line / Come into my life / I've got to be me
/ Can't help falling in love / Volare
CD _____ PLATCD 364
Prism / '91 / Prism.

HITS OF AL MARTINO, THE
Here in my heart / Spanish eyes / Granada
/ Wanted / Story of Tina / Now (before an-
other day goes by) / Mary in the morning /
White rose of Athens / Man from Laramie /
Volare / Painted tainted rose / To the door
of the sun / Rachel / I won't last a day with-
out you / Take my heart / I love you
because
CD _____ CDMFP 6030
Music For Pleasure / Jul '88 / EMI.

QUANDO QUANDO QUANDO
CD _____ WMCD 5695
Disky / Oct '94 / THE / BMG / Discovery /
Pinnacle.

SPANISH EYES
CD _____ MU 5063
Musketeer / Oct '92 / Koch.

SPANISH EYES
Now / Say you'll wait for me / Way paesano
/ There'll be no teardrops tonight / Wanted
/ Give me something to go with the wine /
No one can change destiny / I still believe /
No one but you / Not as a stranger / Don't
go to strangers / Snowy, snowy mountains
/ To please my lady / Small talk / Somebody
else is taking my place / What now my love
/ Melody of love / Spanish eyes / My love
forgive me / You belong to me
CD _____ CDMFP 6176
Music For Pleasure / Nov '95 / EMI.

Martino, Pat

CONSCIOUSNESS
Impressions / Consciousness / Passata on
guitar / Along came Betty / On the stairs /
Willow / Both sides now
CD _____ MCD 5039
Muse / Sep '92 / New Note / CM.

DESPERADO
Blackjack / Dearborn walk / Oleo / Deper-
ado / Portrait of Diana / Express
CD _____ OJCCD 397
Original Jazz Classics / Apr '93 / Wellard /
Jazz Music / Cadillac / Complete/Pinnacle.

EXIT
CD _____ MCD 5075
Muse / Sep '93 / New Note / CM.

INTERCHANGE
Catch / Black glass / Interchange / Just for
then / Blue in green / Recollection
CD _____ MCD 5529
Muse / Sep '94 / New Note / CM.

PAT MARTINO LIVE
CD _____ MCD 5026
Muse / Sep '92 / New Note / CM.

RETURN, THE
CD _____ MCD 5328
Muse / Sep '92 / New Note / CM.

Martland, Steve

MARTLAND - FACTORY MASTERS
Babi Yar / Drill / Crossing the border / Prin-
cipia / American invention / Re-mix / Shoul-
der to shoulder
CD _____ 09026683982
Catalyst / Nov '95 / BMG.

PATROL
CD _____ 09026626702
Catalyst / Sep '94 / BMG.

Martyn, Barry

BARRY MARTYN
CD _____ SKCD 2-3056
Sackville / Jun '94 / Swift / Jazz Music /
Jazz Horizons / Cadillac / CM.

ON TOUR
CD _____ BCD 255
GHB / Aug '94 / Jazz Music.

Martyn, Jean

REFLECTIONS
CD _____ CDGRS 1276
Grosvenor / Mar '95 / Target/BMG.

Martyn, John

APPRENTICE, THE
Live on love / Look at that gun / Send me
one line / Hold me / Apprentice / River /
Income town / Deny this love / UPO / Pat-
terns in the rain
CD _____ HY 2001101CD
Hypertension / Sep '93 / Total/BMG / Direct
/ ADA.

BBC LIVE IN CONCERT
CD _____ WINCD 012
Windsong / Feb '92 / Pinnacle.

BLESS THE WEATHER
Go easy / Bless the weather / Sugar lump
/ Walk to the water / Just now / Head and
heart / Let the good things come / Back
down the river / Glistening Glyndebourne /
Singin' in the rain
CD _____ IMCD 135
Island / Jul '91 / PolyGram.

COOL TIDE
CD _____ HY 200116CD
Hypertension / Sep '93 / Total/BMG /
Direct / ADA.

**COULDN'T LOVE YOU MORE - BEST
OF JOHN MARTYN**
CD _____ PERMCD 9
Permanent / Aug '92 / Total/BMG.

ELECTRIC JOHN MARTYN, THE
Johnny too bad / Certain surprise / Sweet
little mystery / Dancing
CD _____ IMCD 66
Island / '89 / PolyGram.

FOUNDATIONS
Mad dog days / Angeline / Apprentice / May
you never / Deny this love / Send me one
line / John Wayne / Johnny too bad / Over
the rainbow
CD _____ IMCD 179
Island / Mar '94 / PolyGram.

GRACE AND DANGER
Some people are crazy / Grace and danger
/ Lookin' on / Johnny too bad / Sweet little
mystery / Hurt in your heart / Baby please
come home / Save some for me / Our love
CD _____ IMCD 67
Island / '90 / PolyGram.

INSIDE OUT
Fine lines / Eibi gheal chiuin ni chearbhaill /
Ain't no saint / Outside in / Glory of love /
Look in / Beverley / Make no mistake /
Ways to cry / So much in love with you
CD _____ IMCD 172
Island / Mar '94 / PolyGram.

JOHN MARTYN LIVE (2CD Set)
CD Set _____ PERMCD 33
Permanent / Jun '95 / Total/BMG.

LIVE AT LEEDS
Outside in / Solid air / Make no mistake /
Bless the weather / Man in the station / I'd
rather be the devil
CD _____ HYCD 200114
Hypertension / Jul '95 / Total/BMG / Direct
/ ADA.

LONDON CONVERSATION
Fairytale lullaby / Sandy Grey / London conversation / Ballad of an elder woman / Cocaine / Run honey run / Back to stay / Rollin' home / Who's grown up now / Golden
girl / This time / Don't think twice, it's alright
CD _____ IMCD 134
Island / Jun '91 / PolyGram.

ONE WORLD
Dealer / One world / Smiling stranger / Big
muff / Couldn't love you anymore / Certain
surprise / Dancing / Small hours

CD _____ IMCD 86
Island / Feb '90 / PolyGram.

PIECE BY PIECE
Nightline / Lonely lover / Angeline / One
step too far / Piece by piece / Serendipity /
Who believes in angels / Love of mine /
John Wayne
CD _____ IMCD 68
Island / Nov '89 / PolyGram.

**ROAD TO RUIN, THE (Martyn, John &
Beverley)**
Primrose Hill / Parcels / Auntie Aviator /
New day / Give us a ring / Sorry to be so
long / Tree green / Say what you can / Road
to ruin
CD _____ IMCD 165
Island / Mar '93 / PolyGram.

SAPPHIRE
Over the rainbow / You know / Watching
her eyes / Acid rain / Sapphire / Fisherman's dream / Mad dog days / Climb the
walls / Coming in on time / Rope souled
CD _____ IMCD 164
Island / Mar '93 / PolyGram.

SOLID AIR
Over the hill / Don't want to know / I'd rather
be the devil / Go down easy / Dreams by
the sea / May you never / Man in the station
/ Easy blues / Solid air
CD _____ IMCD 85
Island / Feb '90 / PolyGram.

**STORMBRINGER (Martyn, John &
Beverley)**
Go out and get it / Can't get the one I want
/ Stormbringer / Sweet honesty / Wood-
stock / John the baptist / Ocean / Traffic
light lady / Tomorrow time / Would you be-
lieve me
CD _____ IMCD 131
Island / Jun '91 / PolyGram.

SUNDAY'S CHILD
One day without you / Lay it all down / Root
love / My baby girl / Sunday's child / Spencer the rover / Clutches / Message / Satisfied mind / You can discover / Call me crazy
CD _____ IMCD 163
Island / Mar '93 / PolyGram.

**SWEET LITTLE MYSTERIES - ISLAND
ANTHOLOGY (2CD Set)**
Bless the weather / Head and heart /
Glistening Glyndebourne / Solid air / Over
the hill / Don't want to know / I'd rather be
the devil / May you never / Fine lines / Make
no mistake / One day without you / Lay it
all down / Root love / Sunday's child /
Spencer the rover / You can discover / Call
me crazy / Couldn't you love me more /
Certain surprise / Dancing / Small hours /
Dealer / One world / Some people are crazy
/ Lookin' on / Johnny too bad / Sweet little
mystery / Hurt in your heart / Baby please
come home / Sapphire / Fisherman's dream
/ Angeline / Send me one line / eibhli ghail
chuin ni chearbaill
CD Set _____ CRNCD 4
Island / Jun '94 / PolyGram.

TUMBLER, THE
Sing a song of summer / River / Goin' down
to Memphis / Gardener / Day at the sea /
Fishin' blues / Dusty / Holto train / Winding
boy / Fly on home / Kuckledy crunch and
slipledge slee song / Seven black roses
CD _____ IMCD 173
Island / Mar '94 / PolyGram.

Martyr Whore

ROULIDOLVEI BALLET
CD _____ EFA 121612
Apollyon / Aug '95 / SRD.

Martyrium

MARTYRIUM
CD _____ MRCD 002
Modern Invasion / Jul '95 / Plastic Head.

Marusia, Sergei

RUSSIAN GYPSY SONGS
CD _____ MCD 71565
Monitor / Jun '93 / CM.

Marvelettes

**VERY BEST OF THE MARVELETTES,
THE**
Make it right / Blame it on yourself / Ride
the storm / Secret love affair / Right away /
For the rest of my life / Just in the nick of
time / Bad case of nerves / My wheel of
fortune / When you're young and in love /
Pushing too hard / Time has a new meaning
/ Holding on with both hands / We're gonna
stay in love / You're my remedy / All things
abide / Special feeling / Universal love
CD _____ 30359 90022
Carlton Home Entertainment / Oct '95 /
Carlton Home Entertainment.

Marvellous Caine

GUN TALK
CD _____ SUBBASE CD3
Suburban Base / Nov '95 / SRD.

Marvin & Johnny

CHERRY PIE
Cherry pie / Tick tock / Forever / Kiss me /
Sugar / Dear one / Honey girl / Little honey
/ Vip vop / Kokomo / Sometimes I wonder
/ Baby, won't you marry me / I love you,
yes I do / Butter ball / Sugar Mama / Oh me
oh my / Sweet dreams / Will you love me /
I wanna / Let me know / Ain't that right /
Sweet potato / Wonderful, wonderful one /
Yes I do / Tell me darling / Have mercy Miss
Percy / Have mercy Miss Percy (Take 1)
CD _____ CDCHD 509
Ace / Feb '94 / Pinnacle / Cadillac / Com-
plete/Pinnacle.

FLIPPED OUT
Wine woogie / Old man's blues / Dream girl
/ As long as you're satisfied / My baby
won't let me in / Sun was shining / Baby
doll / I'm not a fool / Jo Jo / Honey / How
long time been gone / If I should lose you /
Boy loves girl / School of love / I want lovin'
/ Day in, day out / What's the matter / Flip
/ Hunter Hancock radio ad / Mamo mamo /
Ding dong baby / Tell me darling / Yak yak
woman / Pretty one / Bye bye my baby
CD _____ CDCHD 385
Ace / May '92 / Pinnacle / Cadillac / Com-
plete/Pinnacle.

Marvin, Greg

I'LL GET BY
Ding dong the witch is dead / Our angel /
Devil's dream / I'll get by (as long as I have
you) / Over the rainbow / How deep is the
ocean / Old faithful / 317 East 32nd / Tues-
day / Yesterdays / I'm with you
CD _____ CDSJP 347
Timeless Traditional / Oct '91 / New Note.

Marvin, Hank

ALL ALONE WITH FRIENDS
Just another heartbreak / Hawk and the
dove / Invisible man / Lelia (Danny's got a
song) / Where do you go when you dream
/ Don't answer / Stardom / Rainy day good-
bye / Ninety nine days / All alone with
friends
CD _____ PWKS 4070
Carlton Home Entertainment / Aug '91 /
Carlton Home Entertainment.

**HANK MARVIN AND JOHN FARRAR
(Marvin, Hank & John Farrar)**
CD _____ SEECD 322
See For Miles/C5 / Jul '91 / Pinnacle.

HANK MARVIN GUITAR SYNDICATE
New Earth / Have you never been mellow /
St. Louis blues / I've got you under my skin
/ Syndicated / Ebb tide / Bird of beauty /
Thunder thumbs and lightnin' licks /
Flamingo / Silvery rain / You are everything
CD _____ SEECD 289
See For Miles/C5 / Apr '93 / Pinnacle.

HANK PLAYS CLIFF
CD _____ 5294262
PolyGram / Oct '95 / PolyGram.

HEARTBEAT
CD _____ 521322-2
PolyGram TV / Nov '93 / PolyGram.

INTO THE LIGHT
We are the champions (Featuring Brian
May.) / Pipeline (Featuring Duane Eddy.) /
Sylvia / Jessica / Another day in paradise /
Everybody wants to rule the world / Don't
know much / Road train / Sumiko / Into the
light / Everything I do (I do it for you) / Rikki
don't lose that number / Scirocco / Moon-
talk / Tailspin / Steel wheel
CD _____ 517 148-2
Polydor / Oct '94 / PolyGram.

**MARVIN, WELCH & FARRAR (Marvin,
Welch & Farrar)**
CD _____ SEECD 324
See For Miles/C5 / Jul '91 / Pinnacle.

**SECOND OPINION (Marvin, Welch &
Farrar)**
CD _____ SEECD 289
See For Miles/C5 / Jul '91 / Pinnacle.

WORDS AND MUSIC
Don't call / Slow down / Bad cop / Tahlia
take your time / Chinatown / Captain Zlogg
/ Trouble with me is you / Oh Suzie / Night
nurse / Go Jimmy / Then I found love /
Lifeline
CD _____ PWKS 4040
Carlton Home Entertainment / Feb '91 /
Carlton Home Entertainment.

WOULD YOU BELIEVE IT... PLUS
Aquarius / Born free / This guy's in love with
you / Tokyo guitar / Chameleon / Lara's
theme / Big Country / Love and occasional
rain / Georgia on my mind / Windmills of
your mind / Sacha / High sierra / Evening
comes / Wahine / Morning star / Sunday for
seven days / Boogatoo / Would you believe
it / Midnight cowboy / Goodnight Dick
CD _____ SEECD 210
See For Miles/C5 / May '89 / Pinnacle.

Marx, Richard

PAID VACATION
Way she loves me / One more try / Silent
scream / Nothing to hide / Whole world to

save / Soul motion / Now and forever / Goodbye / Hollywood / Heaven's waiting / Nothing left behind us / What you want / One man / Miami 2017 / Baby blues
CD _____ CDESTU 2208
EMI / Feb '94 / EMI.

REPEAT OFFENDER
Nothin' you can do about it / Satisfied / Angelia / Too late to say goodbye / Right here waiting / Heart on the line / Living in the real world / That was Lulu / Wait for the sunrise / Children of the night
CD _____ CDEST 2153
Capitol / Oct '91 / EMI.

RICHARD MARX
Should've known better / Don't mean nothing / Endless Summer nights / Lonely heart / Hold on to the nights / Have mercy / Remember Manhattan / Flame of love / Rhythm of life / Heaven only knows
CD _____ CDEST 2152
Capitol / Oct '91 / EMI.

RUSH STREET
Playing with fire / Love unemotional / Keep coming back / Take this heart / Hazard / Hands in your pocket / Calling you / Superstar / Street of pain / I get no sleep / Big boy now / Chains around my heart / Your world
CD _____ CDESTU 2158
Capitol / Nov '91 / EMI.

Marxer, Marcy

JUMP CHILDREN
CD _____ CD 8012
Rounder / '88 / CM / Direct / ADA / Cadillac.

Marxman

33 REVOLUTIONS PER MINUTE
Theme from Marxman / All about Eve / Father like son / Ship ahoy / Do you crave mystique / Sad affair / Droppin' elocution / Dark are the days / Drifting / Demented / Spot on my nose (CD only) / Sad affair (2) (CD only)
CD _____ 514 538 2
Talkin' Loud / Apr '93 / PolyGram.

Mary Beats Jane

MARY BEATS JANE
CD _____ MCD 11135
MCA / Oct '94 / BMG.

Mary My Hope

MONSTER IS BIGGER THAN THE MAN
CD _____ MMHCD 1
Silvertone / Feb '90 / Pinnacle.

MUSEUM
Wildman childman / Suicide king / Communion / Heads and tales / Death of me / It's about time / Untitled / I'm not singing / I'm not alone
CD _____ ORECD 504
Silvertone / Mar '94 / Pinnacle.

Mary's Danish

CIRCA
CD _____ 5117862
Morgan Creek / Jun '92 / PolyGram.

Mas Optica

CHOOSE TO SEE MORE
CD _____ IRS 972234
Rising Sun / Jun '94 / Plastic Head.

Masakowski, Steve

DIRECT AXECESS
Paladia / Burgundy / Voluntary simplicity / Monk's mood / Kayak / Headed West / Emily / Lush life / For Django / St. John / Visit / New Orleans
CD _____ CDP 6311082
Blue Note / Jun '95 / EMI.

Masaray

COSMIC TRANCER
CD _____ PSY 017CD
PSY Harmonics / Oct '95 / Plastic Head.

Maschinenzimmer 412

NACHT DURCH STIMME
CD _____ DVLR 7CD
Soleilmoon Recordings / Mar '95 / Plastic Head.

Masekela, Hugh

AFRICAN BREEZE
Don't go lose it baby / African breeze / Rainmaker (Motla le pula) / It's raining / Grazing in the grass / Wimoweh / Lady / Politician / Joke of life / Ritual dancer / Zulu wedding / Run no more (A vuo mo)
CD _____ MOCD 3013
More Music / Feb '95 / Sound & Media.

BEATIN' AROUND DE BUSH
Steppin' out / Ngena-ngena (instrumental) / Ngena (acapella) / Batsumi (mayibuye i Afrika) / Rock with you / Polina / Languta /

Sekunjalo / U-mama / Beatin' aroun' de bush
CD _____ PD 90686
Novus / Jul '92 / BMG.

HOPE
Abangoma / Uptownship / Mandela (Bring him back home) / Grazin in the grass / Lady / Until when / Languta / Nomali / Market place / Ntyilo ntyilo (The love bird) / Ha le se (The dowry song) / Stimela (coaltrain)
CD _____ 3202032
Triloka / Feb '94 / New Note.

STIMELA
Languta / Child of the earth / Ha lese le di khanna / Coincidence / Bajabula bonke (the healing song) / Grazing in the grass / If there's anybody out there / Mace and grenades / Felicidade / African secret society / Such a long time / Stimela (coaltrain)
CD _____ VSOPCD 200
Connoisseur / Jun '94 / Pinnacle.

Masi

VERTICAL INVADER
Instant army / Rhythm workers / Silver memories / Dance of floda / Trapped in a warm feeling / Rock of changes / Finn (she's so pink) / Quick escape / Tribute to T.B. / Xperimental
CD _____ CDZORRO 9
Metal Blade / Jul '90 / Pinnacle.

Maslak, Keshavan

EXCUSE ME MR. SATIE (Maslak, Keshavan & Katsuyuki Itakura)
CD _____ CDLR 199
Leo / Oct '94 / Wellard / Cadillac / Impetus.

MOTHER RUSSIA
CD _____ CDLR 177
Leo / '90 / Wellard / Cadillac / Impetus.

NOT TO BE A STAR (Maslak, Keshavan & Paul Bley)
CD _____ 120149-2
Black Saint / Sep '93 / Harmonia Mundi / Cadillac.

Masochistic Religion

AND FROM THIS BROKEN CROSS
CD _____ EL 111
Electrip / Sep '94 / Plastic Head.

SONIC REVOLUTION
CD _____ EL 102
Electrip / Nov '92 / Plastic Head.

Mason, Barbara

PHILADELPHIA'S LADY LOVE (Best of Barbara Mason)
Give me your love / Bed and board / Shackin' up / Caught in the middle / 1-2-3 / There's one man between us / You can be with the one you don't love / So he's yours now / Yes I'm ready / From his woman to you / Me and Mrs. Jones / Your old flame / What am I gonna do / Let me in your life / (He wants) the two of us / I miss you Gordon
CD _____ NEXCD 115
Sequel / May '90 / BMG.

Mason, Dave

LONG LOST FRIEND (The Best Of Dave Mason)
Baby please / Misty morning stranger / It's like you never left / Show me some affection / Every woman / Bring it on home to me / You can't take it when you go / Spilt coconut / You can lose it / Long lost friend / We just disagree / So high (rock me baby and roll me away) / Let it go let it flow / Will you still love me tomorrow / Don't it make you wonder / Save me, feelin' alright (live) / You know and I know (Live) / All along the watchtower
CD _____ CK 57165
Columbia / Jul '95 / Sony.

SHOW ME SOME AFFECTION
I'm missing you / Save me / Tryin' to get back to you / Let it go let it flow / Show me some affection / Will you still love me tomorrow / Every woman / Only you know and I know / Spend your life with me / Searchin' (for a feeling) / Warm and tender love / So good to be home / Look at you, look at me / Gimme some lovin' / Take it to the limit / Sad and deep as you
CD _____ ELITE 010 CD
Elite/Old Gold / Aug '93 / Carlton Home Entertainment.

Mason, Ian

AT FARNHAM MALTINGS (Mason, Ian & Rod Mason)
CD _____ BCD 335
GHB / Aug '95 / Jazz Music.

Mason, Phil

HERE'S TO YOU (Mason, Phil New Orleans All-Stars)
CD _____ LACD 41
Lake / Mar '95 / Target/BMG / Jazz Music / Direct / Cadillac / ADA.

PHIL MASON & NEW ORLEANS ALL STARS
CD _____ BCD 315
GHB / Apr '94 / Jazz Music.

YOU DO SOMETHING TO ME (With The New Orleans Allstars & Christine Tyrrell)
I wish I were in Dixie / Jersey lightning / My curly headed baby / You do something to me / Bugle call rag / Gulf coast blues / Dreaming the hours away / Mahogany Hall stomp / That teasin' rag / When I grow too old to dream / Sheikh of Araby / My silent love / In the mood / Fair and square / Squeeze me / High society
CD _____ LACD 33
Lake / Jan '95 / Target/BMG / Jazz Music / Direct / Cadillac / ADA.

Mason, Rod

ROD MASON'S HOT FIVE (Featuring Angela Brown) (Mason, Rod Hot Five)
Drop that sack / Am I blue / Droppin' shucks / Take me for a buggy ride / At the Jazz band ball / Lonesomest girl in town / St. Louis blues / Tuxedo rag / Who's it / I wish I could shimmy like my sister kate / Two nineteen blues / Georgia bo bo / Atlanta blues / Weary blues / Wild turkey / Struttin' with some barbecue / Savoy blues / What a wonderful world
CD _____ CDTTD 563
Timeless Traditional / Jan '92 / New Note.

STRUTTIN' WITH SOME BARBECUE
Black Lion / Jun '94 / Jazz Music /
CD _____ BLCD 760511
Cadillac / Wellard / Koch.

Masqualero

RE-ENTER
Re-enter / Li'l Lisa / Heimo gardsjenta / Gaia / Little song / This is no jungle in Baltimore / Find another animal / Stykkevis og delt
CD _____ 8479392
ECM / May '91 / New Note.

Mass Psychosis

FACE
CD _____ 341912
No Bull / Nov '95 / Koch.

Massacre

ENJOY THE VIOLENCE
CD _____ SHARK 018 CD
Shark / Mar '91 / Plastic Head.

FINAL HOLOCAUST
CD _____ SHARK 014 CD
Shark / Apr '90 / Plastic Head.

FROM BEYOND
CD _____ MOSH 027CD
Earache / Jul '91 / Vital.

KILLING TIME
CD _____ RECDEC 906
Rec Rec / Nov '93 / Plastic Head / SRD / Cadillac.

Massed Bands Of HM Forces

MILITARY PAGEANT, A
CD _____ TRTCD 201
TrueTrax / Jun '95 / THE.

Massed Pipes & Drums

MARIE CURIE FIELDS OF HOPE
CD _____ LCOM 5247
Lismor / May '95 / Lismor / Direct / Duncans / ADA.

Massengill, David

COMING UP FOR AIR
CD _____ FF 590CD
Flying Fish / Apr '94 / Roots / CM / Direct / ADA.

Massey, Cal

BLUES TO COLTRANE
CD _____ CCD 9029
Candid / Dec '87 / Cadillac / Jazz Music / Wellard / Koch.

Massey, Zane

BRASS KNUCKLES
CD _____ DD 464
Delmark / Aug '94 / Hot Shot / ADA / CM / Direct / Cadillac.

Massive Attack

BLUE LINES
Safe from harm / One love / Blue lines / Be thankful for what you've got / Five man army / Unfinished sympathy / Daydreaming / Lately / Hymn of the big wheel
CD _____ WBRCD 1
Wild Bunch / Jun '91 / EMI.

NO PROTECTION (Massive Attack Vs. The Mad Professor)
Radiation ruling the nation (Protection) / Bumper ball dub (Karmacoma) / Trinity dub (Three) / Cool monsoon (Weather storm) / Eternal feedback (Sly) / Moving dub (Better

things) / I spy (Spying glass) / Backward sucking (Heat miser)
CD _____ WBRCD 3
Wild Bunch / Feb '95 / EMI.

PROTECTION
Protection / Karmacoma / Three / Weather storm / Spying glass / Better things / Euro child / Sly / Heat miser / Light my fire (live)
CD _____ WBRCD 2
Wild Bunch / Sep '94 / EMI.

Masso, George

JUST FOR A THRILL
Summer night / Child is born / You brought a new kind of love to me / Soft lights and sweet music / Just for a thrill / Love walked in / Touch of your lips / I remember you / That old feeling / Half of it dearie blues / Sleepin' bee / Fred
CD _____ SKCD 2-2022
Sackville / Jan '93 / Swift / Jazz Music / Jazz Horizons / Cadillac / CM.

LET'S BE BUDDIES (Masso, George & Dan Barrett)
CD _____ ARCD 19127
Arbors Jazz / Nov '94 / Cadillac.

Master

MASTER
CD _____ NB 040
Nuclear Blast / Jan '91 / Plastic Head.

ON THE 7TH DAY GOD CREATED MASTER
CD _____ NB 054CD
Nuclear Blast / Feb '92 / Plastic Head.

Master Ace

SLAUGHTAHOUSE
Walk through the valley / Slaughtahouse / Late model sedan / Jeep ass niguh / Big east / Jack B. Nimble / Boom bashin' / Mad wunz / Style wars / Who you jackin' / Rollin' wit' um dada / Ain't u da masta / Crazy drunken style / Don't fuck around outro / Saturday nite live
CD _____ BRCD 602
4th & Broadway / Aug '93 / PolyGram.

Master Hammers

RITUAL
CD _____ OPCD 031
Osmose / Feb '95 / Plastic Head.

Master Musicians Of...

JOUJOUKA BLACK EYES (Master Musicians Of Jajouka)
CD _____ SR 87
Le Coeur Du Monde / Jan '96 / Direct.

Mastermind

TRAGIC SYMPHONY
Tiger tiger / Power and the passion / All the king's horses / Tragic symphony / Sea of tears / Nothing left to say / Into the void
CD _____ CYCL 026
Cyclops / Jul '95 / Pinnacle.

Masters Of Reality

SUNRISE ON SUFFERBUS
She got me (when she got her dress on) / J.B. Witchdance / Jody sings / Rolling green / Ants in the kitchen / V.H.V. / Bicycle / 100 years (of tears on the wind) / T.U.S.A. / Tilt-a-whirl / Rabbit one / Madonna / Gimme water / Moon in your pocket
CD _____ 514947-2
American / Jun '93 / BMG.

Masters, Frank

FRANKIE MASTERS
CD _____ CCD 048
Circle / Oct '93 / Jazz Music / Swift / Wellard.

Masters, Mark

PRIESTESS (Masters, Mark Jazz Composers Orchestra)
CD _____ 74031
Capri / Nov '93 / Wellard / Cadillac.

Masters, Paul

JAZZ MASTERS
CD _____ SPOOKCD 02
Scratch / Nov '93 / BMG.

Masterson, Declan

END OF THE HARVEST
CD _____ CEFCD 148
Gael Linn / Jun '94 / Roots / CM / Direct / ADA.

TROPICAL TRAD
Tropical trad / Down the back lane/Kit O'Mahony's / Ravelled Hank of Yarn/Picking the spuds/London jig / Kildare fancy/Jimmy Reilly's / Young Tom Ennis/King of the pipers / Aisling gheal / Mistress/John Kelly's / When you go home/Caterpillar / Jack Rowe's/The goosebery bush / Lady Gethin / Munster bank/The mile bush / Hazel woods / Boys of the town/James Kel-

ly's/Bernie Cunnion's jig / Conor Tully's/ Chattering magpie / Hibernian/Contentment is wealth/Katie's fancy / Cambar lassies/ Crowley's/James Kelly / Full moon/Trail of tears/Keep her going
CD _____ SCD 1093
Starc / Jan '94 / ADA / Direct.

Mastroianni, John

COOKIN ON
CD _____ ST-CD 24
Stash / Nov '90 / Jazz Music / CM / Cadillac / Direct / ADA.

Masuda, Mikio

SMOKIN' NIGHT
CD _____ JD 3313
JVC / Oct '88 / New Note.

Masuka, Dorothy

PATA PATA
CD _____ CIDM 1074
Mango / Jul '91 / Vital / PolyGram.

Matata

FEELIN' FUNKY
Wanna do my thing / Return to you / Good good understanding / Gettin' together / I believed her / Good samaritan / I feel funky / I don't have to worry / Something in mind / I want you / Love is the only way / Gimme some lovin / Talkin' talkin
CD _____ PCOM 1134
President / Mar '94 / Grapevine / Target/ BMG / Jazz Music / President.

WILD RIVER
Wild river / Beautiful burra / Mayo mayo / Jungle warrior / Wowo wowo / I need somebody / Vuana Africa / Pigha yako / Mosala tokosalaka / You've gotta find me / Maendeleo yakenya / Ulimwengu
CD _____ PCOM 1133
President / Mar '94 / Grapevine / Target/ BMG / Jazz Music / President.

Matchbox

MATCHBOX LIVE
CD _____ PEPCD 102
Pollytone / Jan '95 / Pollytone.

ROCKABILLY REBEL
CD _____ 4509 91882
Carlton Home Entertainment / Jan '93 / Carlton Home Entertainment.

SHADES OF GENE
Dance in the street / In my dreams / Got my eyes on you / Summertime / Everybody's talkin' 'bout Gene / Wedding bells / Ain't misbehavin' / Right here on Earth / Woman love / Be bop a lula / Lonesome fugitive / Git it / Sure fire way / Rocky road blues
CD _____ PEPCD 108
Pollytone / Mar '94 / Pollytone.

Matching Mole

BBC RADIO 1 LIVE IN CONCERT
Instant pussy / Litheing and graceing / Marchides / Part of the dance / Brandy as benge
CD _____ WINCD 063
Windsong / Jun '94 / Pinnacle.

LITTLE RED RECORD
Gloria Gloom / God song / Flora Fidgit / Smoke signal / Starting in the middle of the day we can drink our politics a / Marchides / Nan True's hole / Righteous rhumba / Brandy as in Benj
CD _____ BGOCD 174
Beat Goes On / Jun '93 / Pinnacle.

MATCHING MOLE
O Caroline / Instant pussy / Signed curtain / Part of the dance / Instant karma / Dedicated to you but you weren't listening / Beer as in braindeer / Immediate curtain
CD _____ BGOCD 175
Beat Goes On / Mar '93 / Pinnacle.

Material

HALLUCINATION ENGINE
Black light / Mantra / Ruins / Eternal drift / Words of advice / Cucumber slumber / Hidden garden: naima
CD _____ 5183512
Axiom / Dec '93 / PolyGram / Vital.

LIVE FROM SOUNDSCAPE
CD _____ DIW 389
DIW / Feb '94 / Harmonia Mundi / Cadillac.

SECRET LIFE (1979-81)
CD _____ FREUDCD 011
Jungle / Aug '91 / Disc.

Mateu, Jaque

DE VILLAVICENCIO
CD _____ 21044CD
Sonifolk / Jun '94 / ADA / CM.

Matheson, William

SCOTTISH TRADITION VOL.16 (Gaelic Bards & Minstrels)
CD _____ CDTRAX 9016

Greentrax / Feb '94 / Conifer / Duncans / ADA / Direct.

Mathews, Ronnie

SHADES OF MONK
CD _____ SSCD 8064
Sound Hills / Jan '96 / Harmonia Mundi / Cadillac.

SONG FOR LESLIE
CD _____ RED 1231622
Red / Aug '95 / Harmonia Mundi / Jazz Horizons / Cadillac / ADA.

Mathieson, Greg

FOR MY FRIENDS
I don't know / Song for my Grandfather / For my friends / All blues / Savada / Goe / Twenty bar blues / Slow glide / LMNOP
CD _____ 101 S877069
101 South / Jun '95 / New Note.

Mathieson, Robert

EBB-TIDE (Mathieson, Pipe Major Robert)
CD _____ LCOM 9038
Lismor / Oct '90 / Lismor / Direct / Duncans / ADA.

GRACE NOTES (Mathieson, Pipe Major Robert)
Hornpipes / Air and jigs / March, strathspey and reel / Galician dance / Irish reels and hornpipe / Mazurka / Air and jigs (2) / Dance and jig / Hornpipes (2) / Slip jig and Viennese waltz / Jigs / Airs and reels
CD _____ LCOM 5171
Lismor / Oct '92 / Lismor / Direct / Duncans / ADA.

Mathis, Johnny

16 MOST REQUESTED SONGS
Chances are / It's not for me to say / Misty / Wild is the wind / Wonderful, wonderful / Maria / Twelfth day of never / Small world / Evergreen / Time for us (Theme from Romeo and Juliet) / What will my Mary say / When Sunny gets blue / Certain smile / Love story / Didn't we / Gina
CD _____ CD 57059
CBS / '91 / Sony.

99 MILES FROM LA
You light up my life / When I need you / I write the songs
CD _____ PWKS 537
Carlton Home Entertainment / '89 / Carlton Home Entertainment.

CELEBRATION - THE ANNIVERSARY ALBUM
You saved my life / Wonderful, wonderful / It's not for me to say / Chances are / When a child is born / Too much, too little, too late / Last time I felt like this / Stop, look, listen (to your heart) / With you I'm born again / Three times a lady / She believes in me / I will survive / Evergreen / When I need you / Sweet surrender / How deep is your love / We're all alone / Misty / I'd rather be here with you / If it's magic
CD _____ 4674522
CBS / Oct '90 / Sony.

CELEBRATION/TEARS & LAUGHTER/ UNFORGETTABLE (3CD Set)
CD Set _____ 474142 2
Columbia / Jul '93 / Sony.

COLLECTION: JOHNNY MATHIS
CD _____ CCSCD 343
Castle / Jun '92 / BMG.

HITS OF JOHNNY MATHIS, THE
Misty / Love story / Time for us / Twelfth of never / Look of love / This guy's in love with you / When will I see you again / I'm stone in love with you / Killing me softly / Me and Mrs. Jones / First time ever I saw your face / Do you know where you're going to / Moon river / Feelings / How deep is your love / When a child is born
CD _____ 4679532
Columbia / Oct '95 / Sony.

HOW DO YOU KEEP THE MUSIC PLAYING
How do you keep the music playing (Intro) / Summer knows / Something new in my life / What are you doing the rest of your life / Way she makes me feel / I was born in love with you / On my way to you / After the rain / Windmills of your mind / Summer me, Winter me / How do you keep the music playing
CD _____ 473601-2
Columbia / Jun '93 / Sony.

I'M STONE IN LOVE WITH YOU
Life is a song worth singing / I'm coming home / I'd rather be here with you / And I think that's what I'll do / I'm stone in love with you / Stop, look, listen (to your heart) / Foolish / I just want to be me / Sweet child / Baby's born
CD _____ PWKS 531
Carlton Home Entertainment / Jul '89 / Carlton Home Entertainment.

JOHNNY MATHIS SINGS DUKE ELLINGTON
Overture - a musical tribute to Duke Ellington / Lush life / Don't you know I care (or

don't you care to) / I didn't know about you / Things ain't what they used to be (instrumental) / In a sentimental mood / What am I here for / I got it bad and that ain't good / Something to live for / Solitude / Perdido (instrument) / Prelude to a kiss / In a mellow tone / Don't get around much anymore / Satin doll (instrumental) / Come Sunday / Do nothin' 'til you hear from me / Caravan (piano interlude) / Daydream
CD _____ 4671302
Columbia / Mar '91 / Sony.

MERRY CHRISTMAS
Winter wonderland / Christmas song / Sleigh ride / Blue Christmas / I'll be home for christmas / White Christmas / O holy night / What child is this / First Noel / Silver bells / It came upon a midnight clear / Silent night
CD _____ 4814382
Columbia / Nov '95 / Sony.

MISTY
What'll I do / More than you know / Strangers in the night / Baby, baby, baby / Danke schon / Stranger in paradise / Misty / By myself / Spanish eyes / There goes my heart / L.O.V.E. / That's all
CD _____ PWKS 526
Carlton Home Entertainment / May '89 / Carlton Home Entertainment.

NIGHT AND DAY
Night and day / Would you like to spend the night with me / Help me make it through the night / Midnight blue / Stardust / Last night I didn't get to sleep at all / Midnight cowboy / Come Saturday morning / You are the sunshine of my life / Yesterday when I was young / Those were the days / Aquarius / Let the sunshine in / Yellow days / One day in your life / Good morning heartache / On a clear day
CD _____ 982592 2
Pickwick/Sony Collector's Choice / Aug '91 / Carlton Home Entertainment / Pinnacle / Sony.

OPEN FIRE, TWO GUITARS
Open fire / Bye bye blackbird / In the still of the night / Embraceable you / I'll be seeing you / When I fall in love / Tenderly / I concentrate on you / Please be kind / You'll never know / I'm just a boy in love / My funny valentine
CD _____ CK 64199
Legacy / Nov '94 / Sony.

PERSONAL COLLECTION, A (2CD Set)
CD Set _____ CD 48932
Legacy / May '94 / Sony.

RAINDROPS KEEP FALLING ON MY HEAD/LOVE STORY (2CD Set)
Man and a woman / Odds and ends / Jean / Everybody's talkin' / Bridge over troubled water / Raindrops keep falling on my head / Honey come back / Watch what happens / Something / Alfie / Midnight cowboy / Love story / Rose garden / Ten times forever more / It's impossible / I was there / What are you doing the rest of your life / We've only just begun / Traces / For the good times / My sweet lord / Loss of love
CD Set _____ 477594 2
Columbia / Oct '94 / Sony.

THAT'S WHAT FRIENDS ARE FOR (Mathis, Johnny & Deniece Williams)
You're all I need to get by / Until you come back to me / You're a special part of my life / Ready or not / Me for you, you for me / Your precious love / Just the way you are / That's what friends are for / I just can't get over you / Touching me with love
CD _____ 903114 0
Carlton Home Entertainment / Jul '89 / Carlton Home Entertainment.

WHEN A CHILD IS BORN
When a child is born / Silent night / White Christmas / Little drummer boy
CD _____ PWKS 596
Carlton Home Entertainment / Sep '93 / Carlton Home Entertainment.

Matire

MATIRE
CD _____ DOMCD 015
Dominator / Apr '95 / Plastic Head.

Matt Bianco

BEST OF MATT BIANCO
Don't blame it on that girl / Yeh yeh / Sneaking out the back door / Half a minute / Dancing in the street / Fire in the blood / Wap bam boogie / Good times / More than can bear / Get out of your lazy bed / Matt's mood / Just can't stand it (LP only) / Whose side are you on (Not on LP) / Say it's not too late (Not on LP) / Nervous (Not on LP) / We've got the mood (Not on LP)
CD _____ 9031725902
WEA / Oct '90 / Warner Music.

WHOSE SIDE ARE YOU ON
More than I can bear / No no never / Half a minute / Matt's mood / Get out of your lazy bed / It's getting late / Sneaking out the back door / Riding with the wind / Matt's mood II / Whose side are you on / Big Rosie (MC only) / Other side (MC only)
CD _____ 2404722
WEA / Aug '84 / Warner Music.

Yeah Yeah

YEAH YEAH
CD _____ 4509 918842
Carlton Home Entertainment / Jan '93 / Carlton Home Entertainment.

Mattea, Kathy

READY FOR THE STORM (Favourite Cuts)
Rock me on the water / Last night I dreamed of loving you / Nobody's gonna rain on our parade / Ready for the storm / I will / Untasted honey / Mary did you know / Asking us to dance / Few good things remain / Summer of my dreams / Late in the day
CD _____ 5280062
Mercury / Apr '95 / PolyGram.

WALKING AWAY A WINNER
CD _____ 5188522
Mercury / Mar '94 / PolyGram.

Matthew's Southern...

LATER THAT SAME YEAR (Matthew's Southern Comfort)
CD _____ LCCD 901264
Line / Sep '94 / CM / Grapevine / ADA / Conifer / Direct.

SCION (Matthew's Southern Comfort)
Touch her if you can / Yankee lady / Belle / Later that same year / I believe in you / Sylvie / And when she smiles / And me / Old Rud / Jinkson Johnson / Something in the way she moves / Ballad of Obray Ramsey / Touch her if you can (no.2)
CD _____ BOJCD 007
Strange Fruit / Apr '94 / Pinnacle.

Matthews, David

AMERICAN PIE (Matthews, David Trio & Gary Burton)
American pie / Mr. Tambourine man / My back pages / Sound of silence / Sunny / Como en Vietnam / Taste of honey / Moonlight melody
CD _____ 66055005
Sweet Basil / Jul '91 / New Note.

AND THEN IT HAPPENED (Matthews, David & New Satelite)
Endless dream / Thinking 'bout you / And then it happened / Dance tune / Why did you go / Forever didn't last so long / I'm flying / I'll meet you halfway there
CD _____ 292 E 6040
King/Paddle Wheel / Mar '90 / New Note.

BILLY BOY (Matthews, David Trio)
CD _____ K32Y 6108
King/Paddle Wheel / Oct '87 / New Note.

SPEED DEMON (Matthews, David Orchestra)
CD _____ K32Y 6056
King/Paddle Wheel / '88 / New Note.

TENNESSEE WALTZ (Matthews, David Trio)
Tennessee waltz / Something / Soul to soul / I got rhythm / Child is born / Dolphin dance / Autumn sunset
CD _____ 292 E 6050
King/Paddle Wheel / Mar '90 / New Note.

UNKNOWN STANDARDS (Matthews, David Trio)
CD _____ K32Y 6269
King/Paddle Wheel / Apr '89 / New Note.

Matthews, David

UNDER THE TABLE AND DREAMING
Best of what's around / What would you say / Satellite / Rhyme and reason / Typical situation / Dancing nannies / Ants marching / Lover lay down / Jimi thing / Warehouse / Pay for what you get / No 34
CD _____ 07863664492
RCA / Mar '95 / BMG.

Matthews, Eric

IT'S HEAVY IN HERE
CD _____ SPCD 312
Sub Pop / Mar '96 / Disc.

Matthews, Iain

DARK SIDE, THE
CD _____ WM 1025
Watermelon / Oct '94 / ADA / Direct.

JOURNEYS FROM GOSPEL OAK
Things you gave me / Tribute to Hank Williams / Met her on a plane / Do right woman, do right man / Knowing the game / Polly / Mobile blue / Bride 1945 / Franklin Avenue / Sing me back home
CD _____ CRESTCD 004
Mooncrest / Mar '91 / Direct / ADA.

NIGHT IN MANHATTAN
CD _____ TX 2001CD
Taxim / Dec '93 / ADA.

ORPHANS & OUTCASTS
CD _____ CDL 102
Dirty Linen / Jun '94 / Direct / ADA.

PURE AND CROOKED
Like dominoes / Mercy Street / Hardly innocent mind / Rains of '62 / New shirt /

445

MATTHEWS, IAIN

Bridge of Cherokee / Busby's babes / Say no more / Perfect timing / Out of my range / This town's no lady
CD _____ WMCD 1029
Watermelon / Dec '94 / ADA / Direct.

SKELETON KEYS
Cover girl / Jumping Off The Roof / Compass and chart / God's empty chair / True location of the heart / Back of the bus / Cross to bear / Ties we break / Timing / Get it back / Every crushing blow / Living in reverse
CD _____ LICD 901182
Line / Oct '92 / CM / Grapevine / ADA / Conifer / Direct.

SOUL OF MANY PLACES (THE ELEKTRA YEARS, 1972-74), THE
Old 55 / For the second time / Keep on sailing / Old man at the mill / Wailing goodbye / Shady lies / I'll fly away / True story of Amelia Earhart / Seven Bridges Road / Biloxi / Propinquity / Fault / Even the guiding light / I don't want to talk about it / Louse / These days / Call the tune / Poor ditching boy / You fell through my mind
CD _____ 755961457-2
Elektra / Dec '92 / Warner Music.

STEALIN' HOME
CD _____ LICD 900740
Line / Nov '92 / CM / Grapevine / ADA / Conifer / Direct.

STEALIN' HOME/SIAMESE FRIENDS
CD Set _____ LICD 921193
Line / Mar '92 / CM / Grapevine / ADA / Conifer / Direct.

Matthews, Jessie

DANCING ON THE CEILING
Dancing on the ceiling / When you've got a little springtime in your heart / It's love again / Gangway / Everything's in rhythm with my heart / Your heart skips a beat / One little kiss from you / When you gotta sing you gotta sing / Tony's in town / By the fireside / Head over heels in love / Lord and Lady Whoozis / One more kiss and then goodnight / Let me give my happiness to you / Tinkle tinkle tinkle / Just by your example / I'll stay with you / Three wishes / May I have the next romance with you / Looking around corners for you / Souvenir of love / My river
CD _____ CD AJA 5063
Living Era / Jul '89 / Koch.

MY HEART STOOD STILL
CD _____ PASTCD 9746
Flapper / Aug '91 / Pinnacle.

Matthews, Ronnie

AT CAFE DES COPAINS
CD _____ SKCD 2-2026
Sackville / Jun '93 / Swift / Jazz Music / Jazz Horizons / Cadillac / CM.

DARK BEFORE THE DAWN
CD _____ DIW 604
DIW / Jun '91 / Harmonia Mundi / Cadillac.

LAMENT FOR LOVE
CD _____ DIW 612
DIW / Jan '93 / Harmonia Mundi / Cadillac.

SELENA'S DANCES
In a sentimental mood / My funny valentine / Stella by starlight / Selena's dance / Body and soul / There is no greater love / Blue bossa / Fee fi fo fum
CD _____ CDSJP 304
Timeless Jazz / Aug '90 / New Note.

Matthews, Wendy

LILY
Friday's child / Walk away / T.K.O. / Mother can't do / Quiet art / Day you went away / If only I could / Homecoming song / Face of Appalachia / Naming names / Inexorably yours
CD _____ 450990547-2
East West / Mar '93 / Warner Music.

Matto Congrio

MATTO CONGRIO
CD _____ F 1031CD
Sonifolk / Jun '94 / ADA / CM.

Mauger, Jacques

SHOWCASE FOR TROMBONE
CD _____ DOYCD 027
Doyen / Nov '93 / Conifer.

Maulidi & Musical Party

MOMBASA WEDDING SPECIAL
Mkufu / Hukomi mpelelezi / Shuga dedi / Mume ni moshi wa koko / Fadhila kama kukopa / Vinshido vya mashua / Ukiondoka mpenzi / Hasidi
CD _____ CDORBD 058
Globestyle / May '90 / Pinnacle.

Maurinier, Charles

ZOUK POWER
CD _____ MCD 51349
Sonodisc / '91 / Sterns.

Mauro, Turk

JAZZ PARTY
CD _____ BL 011
Bloomdido / Oct '93 / Cadillac.

LIVE IN PARIS
CD _____ BL 006
Bloomdido / Oct '93 / Cadillac.

PLAYS LOVE SONGS
CD _____ BL 009
Bloomdido / Oct '93 / Cadillac.

Mavericks

MAVERICKS, THE
CD _____ MCAD 10544
MCA / Mar '94 / BMG.

SONGS FOR ALL OCCASIONS
Foolish heart / One step away / Here comes the rain / Missing you / All you ever do is bring me down / My secret flame / Writing on the wall / Loving you / If you only knew / I'm not gonna cry for you / Something stupid / Blue moon (On CD)
CD _____ MCAD 11344
MCA / Oct '95 / BMG.

WHAT A CRYING SHAME
There goes my heart / What a crying shame / Pretend / I should have been true / Things you said to me / Just a memory / All that heaven will allow / Neon blue / O what a thrill / Ain't found nobody / Losing side of me
CD _____ MCD 10961
MCA / Aug '94 / BMG.

Maxeen

DIARY, THE
CD _____ SOULCD 35
Soultown / Jan '96 / Pinnacle / Jetstar.

Maximalist

WHAT THE BODY DOESN'T REMEMBER
CD _____ SUBCD 008-26
Sub Rosa / '89 / Vital / These / Discovery.

Maxx

TO THE MAXIMUM
CD _____ PULSE 15CD
Pulse 8 / Jul '94 / Pinnacle / 3MV.

May, Billy

CAPITOL YEARS: BILLY MAY
Mad about the boy / When your lover has gone / Perfidia / Top hat, white tie and tails / You're driving me crazy / If I had you / Lulu's back in town / Rose Marie / Show me the way to go home / Say it isn't so / Star eyes / March of the toys / If I were a bell / Till there was you / Brassmens holiday / Pawn ticket / Rhythm is our business / Blues in the night (Parts 1 & 2) / In the mood cha cha / Autumn leaves / No strings / Loads of love / Late late show
CD _____ CDEMS 1472
Capitol / Mar '93 / EMI.

May, Brian

BACK TO THE LIGHT
Dark / Back to the light / Love token / Resurrection / Too much love will kill you / Driven by you / Nothin' but blue / I'm scared / Last horizon / Let your heart rule your head / Just one life / Rollin' over
CD _____ CDPCSD 123
Parlophone / Oct '92 / EMI.

LIVE AT THE BRIXTON ACADEMY
Back to the light / Driven by you / Tie your mother down / Love token / Headlong / Love of my life / Let your heart rule your head / Too much love will kill you / Since you've been gone / Now I'm here / Guitar extravaganza / Resurrection / Last horizon / We will rock you / Hammer to fall
CD _____ CDPCSD 150
Parlophone / Jan '94 / EMI.

THEMES AND DREAMS AND LOVE SONGS
CD _____ HADCD 190
Javelin / Nov '95 / THE / Henry Hadaway Organisation.

May, Brother Joe

LIVE 1952-1955
God leads his children along / I'm a child of the king / Move on up a little higher / He's waiting for me / Old ship of Zion / Vacation in heaven / Jesus is real to me / All of my burdens (don't that good news) / He's the one / I want Jesus on the road I travel / How I got over / Hold to God's unchanging hand / By and by when I get home / Speak, Lord Jesus / He'll understand and say well done
CD _____ CDCHD 565
Ace / Mar '94 / Pinnacle / Cadillac / Complete/Pinnacle

THUNDERBOLT OF THE MIDDLE WEST
Old ship of zion (live) / WDIA plug / Search me lord / How much more of life's burden can we bear / In that day / I'm gonna live the life I sing about in my songs / Day is past and gone / Do you know him / I just can't keep from cryin' sometime / I want Jesus on the road I travel / Precious Lord / What do you know about Jesus / Our father / I'll make it somehow / Your sins will find you out / Remember me / I claim Jesus first / It's a long, long way / Don't forget the name of the lord / He'll understand and say Well Done / I'm happy working for the Lord / Grow closer / Jesus knows / Vacation in heaven / Going home
CD _____ CDCHD 466
Ace / Mar '93 / Pinnacle / Cadillac / Complete/Pinnacle.

May Linn

MAY LINN
Soldier / Joey don't care / In the shelter of the night / Breakout / Dangerous games / Backstreet life / Fit for fight / Long way from home
CD _____ SHARK 007CD
Shark / Jun '88 / Plastic Head.

May, Simon

NEW VINTAGE
CD _____ CDART 102
ARC / Oct '94 / ARC Music / ADA.

May, Tina

FUN (May, Tina Quartet)
CD _____ 33JAZZ 013CD
33 Jazz / Jun '93 / Cadillac / New Note.

IT AIN'T NECESSARILY SO
It ain't necessarily so / Maestro / Rosy glow / Chelsea bridge / They can't take that away from me / Wanting to be home / Les feuilles mortes / Solitude / Writers block
CD _____ 33JAZZ 017
33 Jazz / May '95 / Cadillac / New Note.

NEVER LET ME GO (May, Tina Quartet)
CD _____ 33JAZZ 005CD
33 Jazz / Jun '93 / Cadillac / New Note.

May, Tom

RIVER AND THE ROAD
CD _____ FE 1420
Folk Era / Dec '94 / CM / ADA.

Maya

CROSS OF SILENCE
CD _____ MAYACD 1
Maya / May '95 / Complete/Pinnacle / Direct / Cadillac.

Mayall, John

1982 REUNION CONCERT, THE
CD _____ OW 30008
One Way / Apr '94 / Direct / ADA.

BANQUET IN BLUES, A
CD _____ MCAD 22075
One Way / Apr '94 / Direct / ADA.

BARE WIRES (Mayall, John & The Bluesbreakers)
Bare wires suite / Where did I belong / Start walking / Open a new door / Fire / I know now / Look in the mirror / I'm a stranger / No reply / Hartley quits / Killing time / She's too young / Sandy
CD _____ 8205382
London / Jun '88 / PolyGram.

BEHIND THE IRON CURTAIN
Somebody's acting like a child / Rolling with the blues / Laws must change / Parchman farm / Have you heard / Fly tomorrow / Steppin' out
CD _____ GNPD 2184
GNP Crescendo / Nov '95 / Silva Screen.

BLUES ALONE, THE
Brand new start / Please don't tell / Down the line / Sonny boy blow / Marsha's mood / No more tears / Catch that train / Cancelling out / Harp man / Brown sugar / Broken wings / Don't kick me
CD _____ 8205352
London / Jun '88 / PolyGram.

BLUES FROM LAUREL CANYON
Vacation / Walking on sunset / Laurel Canyon home / 2401 / Ready to ride / Medicine man / Somebody's acting like a child / Bear / Miss James / First time alone / Long gone midnight / Fly tomorrow
CD _____ 8205392
Deram / Jan '88 / PolyGram.

CROSS COUNTRY BLUES
CD _____ OW 30009
One Way / Apr '94 / Direct / ADA.

CRUSADE (Mayall, John & The Bluesbreakers)
Oh pretty woman / Stand back baby / My time after awhile / Snowy wood / Man of stone / Tears in my eyes / Driving sideways / Death of J.B. Lenoir / I can't quit you baby / Streamline / Me and my woman / Checkin' up on my baby
CD _____ 8205372
Deram / Jun '88 / PolyGram.

DIARY OF A BAND VOL 2 (Mayall, John & The Bluesbreakers)
CD _____ 8440302
Deram / '92 / PolyGram.

HARD CORE PACKAGE, A
CD _____ MCAD 22071
One Way / Apr '94 / Direct / ADA.

HARD ROAD, A (Mayall, John & The Bluesbreakers)
Hard road / It's over / You don't love me / Stumble / Another kinda love / Hit the highway / Leaping Christine / Dust my blues / There's always work / Same way / Supernatural / Top of the hill / Some day after a while (you'll be sorry) / Living alone
CD _____ 8204742
London / Jul '89 / PolyGram.

JOHN LEE BOOGIE
CD _____ CDCD 1278
Charly / Nov '95 / Charly / THE / Cadillac.

LAST OF THE BRITISH BLUES, THE
Tucson lady / Parchman farm / There's only now / Teaser / Hideaway / Bear / Lonely birthday / Lowdown blues / It must be there
CD _____ MCAD 22074
One Way / Apr '94 / Direct / ADA.

LIFE IN THE JUNGLE (Charly Blues - Masterworks Vol. 4)
Ridin' on the L and M / Help me / All your love / I ain't got you / One life to live / Last time / Fascinating lover / Life in the jungle
CD _____ CDBM 4
Charly / Apr '92 / Charly / THE / Cadillac.

LOOKING BACK (Mayall, John & The Bluesbreakers)
Mr. James / Blues city shake down / They call it stormy Monday / So many roads / Looking back / Sitting in the rain / It hurts me too / Double trouble / Suspicions (part 2) / Jenny / Picture on the wall
CD _____ 8203312
Deram / Jan '89 / PolyGram.

LOTS OF PEOPLE (Live In L.A. 1976)
CD _____ MCAD 22073
One Way / Apr '94 / Direct / ADA.

NEW YEAR, NEW BAND, NEW COUNTRY (Live In L.A. 1976)
CD _____ MCAD 22072
One Way / Apr '94 / Direct / ADA.

NOTICE TO APPEAR
CD _____ MCAD 22070
One Way / Apr '94 / Direct / ADA.

PRIMAL SOLOS
Intro (Maudie) / It hurts to be in love / Have you ever loved a woman / Bye bye bird / Hoochie coochie man / Intro (Look at the girl) / Wish you were mine / Start walking
CD _____ 8203202
Deram / Nov '88 / PolyGram.

RETURN OF THE BLUESBREAKERS
CD _____ AIM 1004CD
Aim / Oct '93 / Direct / ADA / Jazz Music.

ROADSHOW BLUES
Why worry / Road show / Mama talk to your daughter / Big man / Lost and gone / Mexico City / John Lee Boogie / Reaching for a mountain / Baby, what you want me to do
CD _____ CDTB 060
Thunderbolt / Oct '88 / Magnum Music Group.

SENSE OF PLACE, A (Mayall, John & The Bluesbreakers)
I want to go / Send me down to Vicksburg / Sensitive kid / Let's work together / Black cat moan / All my life / Congo square / Without her / Jacksborn highway / I can't complain / Sugarcane
CD _____ IMCD 167
Island / Mar '93 / PolyGram.

SPINNING COIN
CD _____ ORECD 537
Silvertone / Feb '95 / Pinnacle.

STORMY MONDAY
Oh pretty woman / Sitting in the rain / Long gone midnight / No reply / Hartley quits / Jenny / Room to move / They call it Stormy Monday / Don't pick a flower / Thinking of my woman / Don't waste my time / Plan your revolution / Took the car / Time's moving on
CD _____ 5507172
Spectrum/Karussell / Sep '94 / PolyGram / THE.

THRU THE YEARS
Crocodile walk / My baby is sweeter / Crawling up a hill / Mama talk to your daughter / Alabama blues / Out of reach / Greeny / Curly / Missing you / Please don't tell / Your funeral and my trial / Suspicions (part 1) / Knockers step forward / Hide and seek
CD _____ 8440302
Deram / Jan '91 / PolyGram.

TURNING POINT
Laws must change / Saw Mill Gulch Road / I'm gonna fight for you J.B. / So hard to share / California / Thoughts about Roxanne / Room to move
CD _____ BGOCD 145
Beat Goes On / Jun '92 / Pinnacle.

WAITING FOR THE RIGHT TIME
Hideaway / Steppin' out / They call it stormy Monday / Hard road / Laurel Canyon home / Ramblin' on my mind / Man of stone / Don't waste my time / Waiting for the right time / Red sky / Crying / R 'n' B time / Another kinda love / Another man / Picture on the wall / No reply / It hurts me too / Crawling up a hill / Ready to ride
CD _____ ELITE 001 PCD
Elite/Old Gold / May '91 / Carlton Home Entertainment.

WAKE UP CALL
CD _____ ORECD 527
Silvertone / Apr '93 / Pinnacle.

Mayerl, Billy

BILLY MAYERL
CD _____ PASTCD 7053
Flapper / Oct '94 / Pinnacle.

BILLY MAYERL FAVOURITES
In my garden / Hop-o-my thumb / Four aces suite / Ten cents a dance / Jasmine / Mignonette / Limehouse blues / Eskimo shivers / All-of-a-twist / Sing you sinners / Millionaire kid medley / Chopsticks / Puppets suite no 3 / Nimble fingered gentleman / Ace of spades / Balloons / Aquarium suite / Desert song medley (Available on CD only) / Anytime's the time to fall in love (Available on CD only) / Match parade (Available on CD only)
CD _____ CDGRS 1265
Grosvenor / Jun '93 / Target/BMG.

VERSATILITY OF BILLY MAYERL
Golliwog / Judy / Punch / Honky tonk - A rhythmical absurdity / Sweet nothin's / Wistaria / Personal course in modern syncopation / Rag doll / Sennen Cove / Wedding of the painted doll / Old fashioned girls / He loves and she loves / It don't do nothing but rain / Drink to me only with thine eyes / Rainbow / Chopsticks / Masculine women, feminine men / Lay me down to sleep in Carolina / I ain't got nobody / Toodle-oo-sai / Hire purchase system / When lights are low in Cairo / More we are together
CD _____ PASTCD 9708
Flapper / '90 / Pinnacle.

Mayes, Sally

OUR PRIVATE WORLD
CD _____ VSD 5529
Varese Sarabande/Colosseum / Mar '95 / Pinnacle / Silva Screen.

Mayfield, Curtis

BACK TO THE WORLD
Back to the world / Future shock / Right on for the darkness / Future song (love a good woman, love a good man) / If I were a child again / Can't say nothin' / Keep on trippin'
CD _____ MPG 74029
Movieplay Gold / Jan '94 / Target/BMG.
CD _____ CPCD 8040
Charly / Jun '94 / Charly / THE / Cadillac.

BBC RADIO 1 LIVE IN CONCERT
Superfly / It's all right / I'm so proud / Billy Jack / Freddie's dead / People get ready / We've gotta have peace / Homeless / Move on up / Invisible / (Don't worry) If there's a hell below, we're all gonna go
CD _____ WINDCD 052
Windsong / Jan '94 / Pinnacle.

CURTIS
(Don't worry) If there's a hell below, we're all gonna go / Other side of town / Wild and free / Makings of you / Miss Black America / Move on up / We the people who are darker than blue / Give it up
CD _____ MPG 74026
Movieplay Gold / Jan '94 / Target/BMG.
CD _____ CPCD 8036
Charly / Jun '94 / Charly / THE / Cadillac.

CURTIS IN CHICAGO
Superfly / For your precious love / I'm so proud / Preacher man / If I were a child again / Duke of Earl / Love oh love / Amen
CD _____ CPCD 8046
Charly / Sep '94 / Charly / THE / Cadillac.

CURTIS LIVE (2CD Set)
Mighty mighty / I plan to stay a believer / We've only just begun / People get ready / Star and snare / Check out your mind / Gypsy woman / Makings of you / We the people who are darker than blue / (Don't worry) If there's a hell below, we're all gonna go / Stone junkie / We're a winner
CD _____ CPCD 8038
Charly / Jun '94 / Charly / THE / Cadillac.
CD Set _____ MPG 74176
Movieplay Gold / Mar '94 / Target/BMG.

CURTIS MAYFIELD
Move on up / Soul music / In your arms again (shake it) / Do do wap is strong in here / Hard times / So in love / Now you are / Pusherman / Never stop loving me / Tripping out / Ain't no love lust / Superfly / Freddie's dead / This year / Give me your love / (Don't worry) If there's a hell below, we're all gonna go
CD _____ 12364
Laserlight / May '94 / Target/BMG.

CURTIS MAYFIELD'S CHICAGO SOUL
(Various Artists)
You can't hurt me no more / What would you do / I'm the one who loves you / I can't work no longer / Good times (Gonna be good times) / Monkey time / Patty cake (I've got a feeling) You're gonna be sorry / Think nothing about it / Nevertheless (I love you) / It's all over / Found true love / You'll want me back / That's what mama say / Gotta get away / Funny (not much) / You're gonna be sorry / Gonna get married
CD _____ 4810292
Columbia / Jan '96 / Sony.

DO IT ALL NIGHT
Do it all night / No goodbyes / Party party / Keeps me loving you / In love, in love, in love / You are, you are
CD _____ CPCD 8050
Charly / Sep '94 / Charly / THE / Cadillac.

GET DOWN TO THE FUNKY GROOVE
Get down / Superfly / Freddie's dead / Move on up / Wild and free / (Don't worry) If there's a hell below, we're all gonna go / Little child runnin' wild / Pusherman / If I were only a child again / Beautiful brother of mine / Now you're gone / Keep on trippin' / Right on for the darkness
CD Set _____ CPCD 8034
Charly / Feb '95 / Charly / THE / Cadillac.

GIVE GET TAKE AND HAVE
CD _____ CPCD 8070
Charly / Jun '94 / Charly / THE / Cadillac.

GOT TO FIND A WAY
Love me (right in the pocket) / So you don't love me / Prayer / Mother's son / Cannot find a way / Ain't no love lost
CD _____ CPCD 8048
Charly / Sep '94 / Charly / THE / Cadillac.

GROOVE ON UP
CD _____ CPCD 8043
Charly / Jun '94 / Charly / THE / Cadillac.

HEARTBEAT
Tell me, tell me / What is my woman for / Between you baby and me / Victory / Over the hump / You better stop / You're so good to me / Heartbeat
CD _____ CPCD 8071
Charly / Jun '94 / Charly / THE / Cadillac.

MAN LIKE CURTIS, A
Move on up / Superfly / (Don't worry) If there's a hell below, we're all gonna go / You are, you are / Give me your love / Never stop loving me / Tripping out / Soul music / This year / Ain't no love lost / Pusherman / Freddie's dead / Do do wap is strong in here / Hard times / In your arms again (Shake it) / So in love
CD _____ MUSCD 007
MCI / Nov '92 / Disc / THE.

NEVER SAY YOU CAN'T SURVIVE
Show me / Just want to be with you / When we're alone / Never say you can't survive / I'm gonna win your love / All night long / When you used to be mine / Sparkle
CD _____ CPCD 8049
Charly / Sep '94 / Charly / THE / Cadillac.

PEOPLE GET READY (Live At Ronnie Scott's)
Little child runnin' wild / It's all right / People get ready / Freddie's dead / Pusherman / i'm so proud / We've gotta have peace / Billy Jack / Move on up / To be invisible
CD _____ CLACD 329
Castle / '93 / BMG.

POWER FOR THE PEOPLE
CD _____ CDCD 1211
Charly / Jun '94 / Charly / THE / Cadillac.

ROOTS
Get down / Keep on keeping on / Underground / We got to have peace / Beautiful brother of mine / Now you're gone / Love to keep you in mind
CD _____ MPG 74027
Movieplay Gold / Jan '94 / Target/BMG.
CD _____ CPCD 8037
Charly / Jun '94 / Charly / THE / Cadillac.

SOMETHING TO BELIEVE IN
Love me love me now / Never let me go / Tripping out / People never give up / It's all right / Something to believe in / Never stop loving me
CD _____ CPCD 8073
Charly / Jun '94 / Charly / THE / Cadillac.

SUPERFLY
CD _____ CPCD 8039
Charly / Jun '94 / Charly / THE / Cadillac.

SWEET EXORCIST
Ain't got time / Sweet exorcist / To be invisible / Power to the people / Kung fu / Suffer / Make me believe in you
CD _____ CPCD 8047
Charly / Sep '94 / Charly / THE / Cadillac.

THERE'S NO PLACE LIKE AMERICA TODAY
Billy Jack / When seasons change / So in love / Jesus / Blue monday people / Hard times / Love to the people
CD _____ CPCD 8069
Charly / Jun '94 / Charly / THE / Cadillac.

TRIBUTE TO CURTIS MAYFIELD, A
(Various Artists)
Choice of colors / It's all right / Let's do it again / Billy Jack / Look into your heart / Gypsy woman / You must believe me / I'm so proud / Fool for you / Keep on pushing / Making of you / Woman's got soul / People get ready / (Don't worry) If there's a hell below, we're all gonna go / I've been trying / I'm the one who loves you / Amen
CD _____ 9362455002
WEA / Feb '94 / Warner Music.

TRIPPING OUT
CD _____ CPCD 8065
Charly / Nov '94 / Charly / THE / Cadillac.

Mayfield, Percy

MEMORY PAIN
Please send me someone to love / Strange things happen / Two hearts are greater than one / Big question / My blues / Nightless lover / How deep is the well / Ruthie Mae / My heart / Lonesome highway / Lonely one / I ain't gonna cry no more / Memory pain / You are my future / Kiss tomorrow goodbye / Advice (For men only) / I need love so bad / Does anyone care for me / It's good to see you baby / Sugar mama - Peachy papa / You were lyin' to me / Voice within / Please believe me / Diggin' the moonglow / Hit the road Jack
CD _____ CDCHD 438
Ace / Jan '93 / Pinnacle / Cadillac / Complete/Pinnacle.

POET OF THE BLUES
Please send me someone to love / Prayin' for your return / Strange things happening / Life is suicide / What a fool I was / Lost love / Nightless lover / Advice (for men only) / Cry baby / Lost mind / I dare you baby / Hopeless / Hunt is on / River's invitation / Big question / Wasted dream / Louisiana / Bachelor blues / Get way back / Memory pain / Loose ups / You don't exist anymore / Nightmare / Baby, you're rich / My heart is cryin'
CD _____ CDCHD 283
Ace / Oct '90 / Pinnacle / Cadillac / Complete/Pinnacle.

Mayhem

DE MYSTERIIS DOM SATHANAS
CD _____ ANTI-MOSH 006CD
Deathlike Silence / Mar '94 / Plastic Head.

LIVE IN LEIPZIG
CD _____ CDAV 004
Obscure Plasma / Apr '94 / Plastic Head.

Mayor, Simon

ENGLISH MANDOLIN, THE
CD _____ ACS 025CD
Acoustics / Jul '95 / Conifer / Direct / ADA.

MANDOLIN ALBUM, THE
CD _____ CDACS 012
Acoustics / Aug '95 / Conifer / Direct / ADA.

SECOND MANDOLIN ALBUM
Hungarian dance no. 1 / Buttermere waltz / Huppings / Finale spirituoso / Three part invention / Pipped at the post / Two days in Tuscany / Great bear / Concerto for two mandolins / Old man of the mountain / Sonata / Hornpipe / Dead sea dances
CD _____ CDACS 014
Acoustics / Aug '95 / Conifer / Direct / ADA.

WINTER WITH MANDOLINS
CD _____ CDACS 015
Acoustics / Aug '95 / Conifer / Direct / ADA.

Mays, Bill

CONCORD DUO SERIES VOLUME 7
(Mays, Bill & Ed Bickert)
Sometime ago / Taking a chance on love / Gee baby ain't I good to you / On the trail / Quietly / Do nothin' 'til you hear from me / Crazy she calls me / Bick's bag
CD _____ CCD 4626
Concord Jazz / Nov '94 / New Note.

ELLINGTON AFFAIR, AN
I'm just a lucky so and so / Satin doll / Something to live for / My azure / Don't get around much anymore / In a sentimental mood / Dancers in love / Single petal of a rose / Passion flower / Little African flower / Wig wise / Daydream / I let a song go out of my heart
CD _____ CCD 4651
Concord Jazz / Jul '95 / New Note.

GONE WITH THE WIND (Mays, Bill & Keith Copeland/Martin Wind)
Gone with the wind / I remember you / Lagrimo agradecida (A thankful tear) / Black Jack / Najul / Someone to watch over me / Born to be blue / High street / Sevillo / I should care / Sad story / Midnight song for Thalia / Gone with the wind (Bass solo)
CD _____ CD 5116
September / Feb '94 / Kingdom / Cadillac.

LIVE AT MAYBECK RECITAL HALL, VOL. 26
Nightingale sang in Berkeley Square / I wish I knew / Stompin' at the Savoy / Boardwalk

blues / Lush life / I'm confessin' that I love you / Guess I'll hang my tears out to dry / Jitterbug waltz / Thanksgiving prayer / Why did I choose you / Never let me go / Grandpa's spells
CD _____ CCD 4567
Concord Jazz / Aug '93 / New Note.

Mays, Lyle

LYLE MAYS
Highland aire / Teiko / Slink / Mirror of the heart / Alaskan suite: Northern Lights invocation ascent / Close to home
CD _____ GFLD 19193
Geffen / Mar '93 / BMG.

SWEET DREAMS
Feet first / August / Chorinho / Possible straight / Hangtime / Before you go / Newborn / Sweet dreams
CD _____ GFLD 19194
Geffen / Mar '93 / BMG.

Maysa

MAYSA
Prelude / What about our love / Black heaven / Sexy / More than you know / Can we change the world / Goodbye Manhattan / J.F.S. / Let it go / Alone at last / Raindrops / Peace of mind / Goodbye / All or nothing at all
CD _____ BTR 70052
Blue Thumb / Oct '95 / BMG / New Note.

Mayte

CHILD OF THE SUN
CD _____ 0061622 NPG
Edel / Jan '96 / Pinnacle.

Maytones

BROWN GIRL IN THE RING
CD _____ CDTRL 363
Trojan / Oct '95 / Jetstar / Total/BMG.

FUNNY MAN
CD _____ JMC 200206
Jamaica Gold / Nov '93 / THE / Magnum Music Group / Jetstar.

Mayweather, George

WHUP IT, WHUP IT (Mayweather, George 'Earring')
CD _____ TONECOOLCD 1147
Tonecool / May '94 / Direct / ADA.

Maze

BACK TO BASICS
Nobody knows what you feel inside / Love is / Morning after / Laid back girl / What goes up / In time / All night long / Don't wanna lose your love / Twilight
CD _____ 9362452972
Warner Bros. / Sep '93 / Warner Music.

CAN'T STOP THE LOVE (Maze & Frankie Beverly)
Back in stride / Can't stop the love / Reaching down inside / Too many games / I want to feel I'm wanted / Magic / Place in my heart
CD _____ MUSCD 502
MCI / Sep '94 / Disc / THE.

LIFELINES VOL. 1 (Maze & Frankie Beverly)
Joy and pain (Featuring Kurtis Blow.) / golden time of day / Happy feelin's / Back in stride / Before I let go (Featuring Woody Wood.) / Running away / while I'm alone / Southern girl / Joy and pain (original LP version) / Before I let go #2
CD _____ CDEST 2111
Capitol / Nov '89 / EMI.

MAZE LIVE IN NEW ORLEANS
CD _____ CUTLEGCD 4
Beechwood / Jul '95 / BMG / Pinnacle.

SILKY SOUL
Silky soul / Can't get over you / Just us / Somebody else's arms / Love's on the run / Change our ways / Songs of love / Mandela / Midnight / Africa
CD _____ K 9258022
WEA / Mar '94 / Warner Music.

Mazeltones

LATKES & LATTES
CD _____ GV 159CD
Global Village / May '94 / ADA / Direct.

Mazetier, Louis

ECHOES OF CAROLINA (Mazetier, Louis & Francois Rilhac)
CD _____ SOSCD 1218
Stomp Off / Oct '92 / Jazz Music / Wellard.

IF DREAMS COME TRUE (Mazetier, Louis & Neville Dickie)
CD _____ SOSCD 1289
Stomp Off / Nov '95 / Jazz Music / Wellard.

Mazey Fade

SECRET WATCHERS BUILT THE WORLD

447

CD _____ WIGCD 9
Domino / Apr '94 / Pinnacle.

Mazuo, Yoshiaki

SUBTLE ONE, A
Opus de funk / You're my everything / No more dreams / Nightingale sang in Berkeley Square / Reminiscence / Subtle one / My friend Jim / Anohini Keritai
CD _____ 66053030
Jazz City / Feb '92 / New Note.

Mazur, Marilyn

CIRCULAR CHANT (Mazur, Marilyn & Pulse Unit)
Circular chant / Celldance / Louise / Pulsens sang / Gong piece 1 / Reeds duo / Amulu / Chordal piece / Gong piece 2 / Green bones / Balophone tune / Circular chant (2)
CD _____ STCD 4200
Storyville / Mar '95 / Jazz Music / Wellard / CM / Cadillac.

FUTURE SONG
First dream / Saturn song / When I go to the mountain / Urstro / Rainbow birds #2 / Aina's travels / Rainbow birds #3 / Well of clouds / Rainbow birds / Seventh dream
CD _____ VBR 21052
Vera Bra / Aug '92 / Pinnacle / New Note.

Mazurek, Robert

BADLANDS (Mazurek, Robert/Eric Anderson)
Arthur's seat / Angel eyes / Badlands / Deep purple / Kay's birthday / Everytime we say goodbye / Edinburgh nights / Stranger in paradise / I fall in love to easily / Nomad
CD _____ HEPCD 2065
Hep / Jun '95 / Cadillac / Jazz Music / New Note / Wellard.

MAN FACING EAST
Manaus / Pretty blue butterfly / Flora's house / Tenderly / Man facing east / Roselis / Freddies blues / I wish I knew / Dragoon blue
CD _____ HEPCD 2059
Hep / Sep '94 / Cadillac / Jazz Music / New Note / Wellard.

Mazzy Star

SHE HANGS BRIGHTLY
Halah / Blue flower / She hangs brightly / I'm sailing / Give you my lovin / Be my angel / Taste of blood / Ghost highway / Free / Before I sleep
CD _____ CDEST 2196
Capitol / May '93 / EMI.

SO TONIGHT THAT I MIGHT SEE
Fade into you / Bells ring / Mary of silence / Five string serenade / Blue light / She's my baby / Unreflected / Wasted / Into dust / So tonight that I might see
CD _____ CDEST 2206
Capitol / Nov '93 / EMI.

Mbango, Charlotte

CHARLOTTE MBANGO, VOL. 3
CD _____ CD 54681
Sonodisc / '91 / Sterns.

Mbarga, Prince Nico

AKI SPECIAL
CD _____ CD 11545
Rounder / May '88 / CM / Direct / ADA / Cadillac.

M'boom

COLLAGE
Circles / It's time / Jamaican sun / Street dance / Mr. Seven / Quiet place
CD _____ SNCD 1059
Soul Note / '86 / Harmonia Mundi / Wellard / Cadillac.

Mbuli, Mzwakhe

CHANGE IS PAIN
Many years ago / Behind the bars / Drumbeats / Now is the time / Change is pain / Day shall dawn / Ignorant / Triple M / What a shame / I have travelled / Spear has fallen / Last struggle / Ngizwa ubgina bguzwa usajako / Sisi bayasinyanyisa
CD _____ PIR 3 CD
World Circuit / Sep '88 / New Note / Direct / Cadillac / ADA.

MC5

AMERICAN RUSE, THE
CD _____ NERCD 2001
Alive / Feb '95 / Disc.

BABES IN ARMS
Shakin' street / American ruse / Skunk (sonically speaking) / Tutti frutti / Poison / Gotta keep movin' / Tonite / Kick out the jams / Sister / Future now / Gold / I can only give you everything / One of the guys / I just don't know / Looking at you
CD _____ RE 122CD
Reach Out International / Nov '94 / Jetstar.

BACK IN THE USA
Tutti frutti / Tonight / Teenage lust / Let me try / Looking at you / High school / Call me animal / American ruse / Shakin' street / Human being lawnmower / Back in the U.S.A
CD _____ 812271033-2
Atlantic / Mar '93 / Warner Music.

BLACK TO COMM
CD _____ RRCD 185
Receiver / May '94 / Grapevine.

HIGH TIME
Sister Anne / Baby won't ya / Miss X / Gotta keep movin' / Future/now / Poison / Over and over / Skunk (sonically speaking)
CD _____ 812271034-2
WEA / Mar '93 / Warner Music.

KICK OUT THE JAMS
Ramblin' rose / Kick out the jams / Come together / Rocket reducer No.62 / Borderline / Motor city is burning / I want you right now / Starship
CD _____ 7559740402
Elektra / Jan '93 / Warner Music.

LIVE DETROIT 68/69
Intro / Come together / I want you right now / I believe / Come on down (High rise) / It's a man's man's man's world / Looking at you / Fire of love
CD _____ 895050
New Rose / Nov '94 / Direct / ADA.

POWER TRIP
CD _____ ALIVE 005CD
Alive / Oct '94 / Disc.

M'Carver, Kimberly

BREATHE THE MOONLIGHT
Silver wheeled pony / Whistle down the wind / Cryin' wolf / Borrowed time / Only in my dreams / Jose's lullaby / Springtime friends / My way back home to you / Carnival man / Serious doubt / Texas home
CD _____ CDPH 1129
Philo / '90 / Direct / CM / ADA.

INHERITED ROAD
CD _____ CDPH 1179
Philo / Dec '94 / Direct / CM / ADA.

MCM

IT'S WHAT YOU GOTTA GO THRU (MCM & Hype Crew)
CD _____ DRC 4183CD
Ichiban / Mar '94 / Koch.

MDC

HEY COP, IF I HAD A FACE LIKE YOURS
CD _____ MDC 812
R Radical / Mar '92 / SRD.

METAL DEVIL COKES
CD _____ WB3 110-2
We Bite / Apr '94 / Plastic Head.

MILLIONS OF DAMN CHRISTIANS
CD _____ WB 3022-2
We Bite / Sep '93 / Plastic Head.

MILLIONS OF DEAD COPS
CD _____ WB 31092
We Bite / Apr '94 / Plastic Head.

MORE DEAD COPS
CD _____ WB 3033-2
We Bite / Sep '93 / Plastic Head.

SHADES OF BROWN
CD _____ WB3 112-2
We Bite / Apr '94 / Plastic Head.

Me

FECUND HAUNTS
Selfish gene / Our love is real / Green Antarctica society / And human small / Hubble / Comet cometh / Hiding from the sun / Lost it / Oono moon / Billy Liar / Since we haven't been together / Wide awake and dancing in a beautiful field / Fecund with Ballacks / World peace now / It isn't you / Tipsy turvy / Clocks unwind / Awake forever
CD _____ PGCD 037
Pop God / Jun '95 / Vital.

HARMONISE OR DIE
Together alone / We must be / Funny thing / Here comes everybody / Dreambleeding / To the stars / Yousong / Water / Where do you think / Guilty feet fall foul / Quester / Paul / Happy place / Threticular grussock (CD only) / Can't stop (CD only) / Sweepin dust (CD only) / Upsmile down (CD only) / Don't paint me in your colours (CD only) / Pygmy songs (CD only)
CD _____ PGCD 026
Pop God / Jun '93 / Vital.

Me Phi Me

ONE
Intro (A call to arms) / Credo / Sad new day / Poetic moment I: The dream / Dream of you / Not my brotha / Keep it goin' / Poetic moment II: The streets / Black sunshine / And I believe / Pu' sho hands 2getha / Poetic moment III: The light / Road to life / It ain't the way it was / (Think...) / Where are you going / Return to arms: In closing

CD _____ 74321124372
RCA / Apr '93 / BMG.

Mead, Steven

WORLD OF THE EUPHONIUM, THE
Sonata in F / Partita Op. 89 / Vocalise / Soliloquy IX / Fantasy for euphonium / Variations for ophicleide / Sonata euphonica / Apres un reve / Weber's last waltz / Heart to heart / Barcarolle / New carnival of Venice
CD _____ QPRZ 014D
Polyphonic / Jul '92 / Conifer.

WORLD OF THE EUPHONIUM, THE #2
Concert gallop / Solo de Concurse / Fantasia / Swan / Fantasie contertante / Song for Ina / Ransomed / Libesfreud / Largo eiegaico / Panache / Two Faure duets / Ball of fire / Horo staccato
CD _____ QPRZ 017D
Polyphonic / Nov '95 / Conifer.

Meadows, Marion

BODY RHYTHM
My cherie amour / Be with you / South beach / Later on / Get involved / One more chance / Kool / Marion's theme / Wanna be loved by you / Body rhythm / Deep waters / Summer's over / Lift
CD _____ 07863666232
Novus / Aug '95 / BMG.

FORBIDDEN FRUIT, THE
Red lights / Always on my mind / Asha / Forbidden fruit / Whenever your heart wants to song / You will never know what you're missing / Back2back / Save the best for last / Somewhere island / Comin' home to you / Nocturnal serenade
CD _____ 01241631672
Novus / Mar '94 / BMG.

Mean Cat Daddies

GHOST OF YOUR LOVE
Sally-Ann / Just a memory / Sign of the times / Why do I cry / Drivin' all night / I can tell / Decision time / Tell me / Am I the one / Ghost of your love / Midnight cruise / Losing game / Waiting for you / This is the end
CD _____ NERCD 079
Nervous / Oct '94 / Nervous / Magnum Music Group.

Mean Red Spiders

DARK HOURS
Love in a bottle / Live and let live / Arms open wide / Just can't stop / Feel so bad / Drunken fool / Dangerous game / Heaven above / Teacher / Happy on my own / Murder my baby / Love won't save you now / Sure can't hide / Lie and cheat you blind / No more work song / Coming back for more / Call me long distance
CD _____ GBCD 1
Gray Brothers / Sep '95 / Pinnacle.

Meanies

GANGRENOUS
Vince Lombard / Mar '94 / SRD.
CD _____ EFA 12301-2

Meanstreak

ROADKILL
Roadkill / Nostradamus / Lost stranger / Congregation / Searching forever / It seems to me / Warning
CD _____ CDMFN 89
Music For Nations / Oct '88 / Pinnacle.

Meantime

WELCOME: MOTHER EARTH
CD _____ JUST 80-2
Justin Time / Dec '95 / Harmonia Mundi / Cadillac.

Meantime

UNSOPHISTICATED
CD _____ SPV 08056822
Wolverine / Sep '94 / Plastic Head.

Meanwhile

REMAINING RIGHT
CD _____ RAD 001CD
Nuclear Blast / Jun '95 / Plastic Head.

Mears, Pat

HARD CHOICES
Ready to pay / When she comes back / Hard candy / Take that chance / Tell me a story / Raised on the wrong track / Oh darlin' / Big city girl / Drownin' man / Find another town / Houston on the line / I got a feelin' / My friends know how to travel / Billy's gal
CD _____ 9070852
Silenz / Sep '92 / BMG.

THERE GOES THE RAINBOW
There goes the rainbow / Just experience / I try and try / Look for you / Can you spare it baby / Bird in hand / Someone is crying for you / Making up for lost time / When the time is right / Baby's blues / River road

CD _____ 2695612
Silenz / Jun '92 / BMG.

Meat Beat Manifesto

99%
CD _____ BIAS 180 CD
Play It Again Sam / May '90 / Vital.

PEEL SESSIONS
CD _____ SFPSCD 088
Strange Fruit / Nov '93 / Pinnacle.

SATYRICON
Postsounds / Mindstream / Drop / Original control (version 1) / Your mind belongs to the state (CD only) / Circles / Sphere / Brainwashed this way/Zombie/That shirt (CD only) / Original control (version 2) (CD only) / Euthanasia / Edge of no control (part 1) / Edge of no control (part 2) / Untold stories / Son of Sam (CD only) / Track 15 (CD only) / Placebo
CD _____ BIAS 202CD
Play It Again Sam / Aug '92 / Vital.

VERSION GALORE
CD _____ BIAS 192CD
Play It Again Sam / Feb '91 / Vital.

Meat Loaf

12" MIXES - MEAT LOAF
Bat out of hell / Dead ringer for love / Read 'em and weep / If you really want to / Razor's edge
CD _____ 4501032
Epic / Mar '93 / Sony.

ALIVE IN HELL
CD _____ PMCD 7002
Pure Music / Oct '94 / BMG.

BAD ATTITUDE
Bad attitude / Modern girl / Nowhere fast / Surf's up / Piece of the action / Jumping the gun / Cheatin' in your dreams / Don't leave your mark on me / Sailor to a siren
CD _____ 259049
Arista / Dec '93 / BMG.

BAT OUT OF HELL
You took the words right out of my mouth / Heaven can wait / All revved up and no place to go / Two out of three ain't bad / Bat out of hell / For cryin' out loud / Paradise by the dashboard light / Praying for the end of time / Man and woman / Dead ringer for love
CD _____ 4804112
Epic / Jul '95 / Sony.

BAT OUT OF HELL II: BACK INTO HELL
I'd do anything for love (But I won't do that) / Life is a lemon and I want my money back / Rock 'n' roll dreams come through / It just won't quit / Out of the frying pan (and into the fire) / Objects in the rear view mirror may appear closer than they / Wasted youth / Everything louder than everything else / Good girls go to heaven (bad girls go everywhere) / Back into hell / Lost boys and golden girls
CD _____ CDV 2710
Virgin / Aug '93 / EMI.

BLIND BEFORE I STOP
Execution day / Rock 'n' roll mercenaries / Getting away with murder / One more kiss (night of the soft parade) / Blind before I stop / Burning down / Standing on the outside / Masculine / Man and a woman / Special girl / Rock 'n' roll here
CD _____ 257741
Arista / Dec '93 / BMG.

BLIND BEFORE I STOP/BAD ATTITUDE
Execution day / Rock 'n' roll mercenaries / Getting away with murder / One more kiss (night of the soft parade) / Blind before I stop / Burning down / Standing on the outside / Masculine man and woman / Special girl / Rock 'n' roll here / Bad attitude / Modern girl (Live) / Special girl / Standing on the outside / Cheatin' in your dreams / Masculine / Rock 'n' roll mercenaries
CD Set _____ 74321259572
Arista / Mar '95 / BMG.

COLLECTION, THE
Bat out of hell / Bad attitude / One more kiss (Night of the soft parade) / Execution day / Jumpin' the gun / Sailor to a siren / Modern girl (Live) / Special girl / Standing on the outside / Cheatin' in your dreams / Masculine / Rock 'n' roll mercenaries
CD _____ 74321 15218-2
Ariola Express / Sep '93 / BMG.

DEAD RINGER
Peel out / I'm gonna love her for both of us / More than you deserve / I'll kill you if you don't come back / Read 'em and weep / Nocturnal pleasure / Dead ringer for love / Everything is permitted
CD _____ CD 83645
Epic / Nov '87 / Sony.

DEAD RINGER/MIDNIGHT AT THE LOST AND FOUND (2CD Set)
Peel out / I'm gonna love her for both of us / More than you deserve / I'll kill you if you don't come back / Read 'em and weep / Nocturnal pleasure / Dead ringer for love / Everything is permitted / Razor's edge / Midnight at the lost and found / Wolf at your door / Keep driving / Promised land / You

never can be too sure about the girl / Priscilla / Don't you look at me like that / If you really want to / Fallen angel
CD Set _____ 4784862
Epic / Mar '95 / Sony.

HITS OUT OF HELL
Bat out of hell / Read 'em and weep / Midnight at the lost and found / To out of three ain't bad / Dead ringer for love / Modern girl / I'm gonna love her for both of us / You took the words right out of my mouth (Hot Summer night) / Razor's edge / Paradise by the dashboard light
CD _____ 4504472
Epic / Mar '91 / Sony.

LIVE AND KICKING
Bat out of hell / Two out of three ain't bad / Modern live / Blind before I stop / Piece of the action / Rock 'n' roll mercenaries / Paradise by the dashboard light / Masculine / Took the words / Midnight at the lost and found / Bad attitude / Medley: Johnny B. Goode:Slow down:Jailhouse rock:Blue suede s
CD _____ 74321339422
Camden / Jan '96 / BMG.

LIVE AT WEMBLEY
Blind before I stop / Rock 'n' roll mercenaries / Took the words / Midnight at the lost and found / Modern girl / Paradise by the dashboard light / Two out of three ain't bad / Bat out of hell / Masculine (CD/MC only) / Johnny B. Goode/Slow down/Jailhouse rock/Blue suede shoes (CD/MC only)
CD _____ 258599
Arista / Oct '87 / BMG.

MEAT LOAF & FRIENDS
Paradise by the dashboard light / Holding out for a hero / You took the words right out of my mouth / We belong to the night / Bad for good / What's the matter baby / Two out of three ain't bad / Faster than the speed of night / Dead ringer for love / Night out / Total eclipse of the heart / Left in the dark
CD _____ 472419 2
Epic / Oct '94 / Sony.

MIDNIGHT AT THE LOST AND FOUND
Razor's edge / Midnight at the Lost and found / Wolf at your door / Keep driving / Promised land / You never can be too sure about the girl / Priscilla / Don't you look at me like that / If you really want to / Fallen angel
CD _____ 4503602
Epic / Jan '94 / Sony.

PRIMECUTS
Modern girl / Getting away with murder / Bat out of hell / Surf's up / Blind before I stop / Bad attitude / Jumpin' the gun / Two out of three ain't bad (Live) / Paradise by the dashboard light (live) / Rock 'n' roll mercenaries
CD _____ 260.363
Arista / Dec '89 / BMG.

ROCK 'N' ROLL HERO
Modern girl / Rock 'n' roll mercenaries / Midnight at the lost and found (Live) / Paradise by the dashboard light (live) / You took the words right out of my mouth (live) / Bat out of hell / Surf's up / Nowhere fast / Bad attitude / Rock 'n' roll hero / Piece of the action / Getting away with murder
CD _____ PWKS 4121
Carlton Home Entertainment / Apr '94 / Carlton Home Entertainment.

WELCOME TO THE NEIGHBOURHOOD
When the rubber meets the road / I'd lie for you (and that's the truth) / Original sin / 45 seconds of ecstasy / Runnin' for the red light (I gotta life) / Fiesta de Las Almas Perdidas / Left in the dark / Not a dry eye in the house / Amnesty is granted / If this is the last kiss (let's make it last all night) / Martha / Where angels sing
CD _____ CDV 2799
Virgin / Oct '95 / EMI.

Meat Puppets

1
CD _____ SST 009 CD
SST / May '93 / Plastic Head.

HUEVOS
CD _____ SST 150 CD
SST / May '93 / Plastic Head.

II
CD _____ SST 019 CD
SST / May '93 / Plastic Head.

MIRAGE
CD _____ SST 100 CD
SST / Jul '87 / Plastic Head.

MONSTERS
CD _____ SST 253 CD
SST / Oct '89 / Plastic Head.

NO JOKE
Scum / Nothing / Head / Taste of the sun / Vampires / Predator / Poison arrow / Eyeball / For free / Cobbler / Inflatable / Swet ammonia / Chemical garden
CD _____ 8286652
London / Oct '95 / PolyGram.

NO STRINGS ATTACHED
CD _____ SST 265 CD
SST / May '93 / Plastic Head.

OUT MY WAY
CD _____ SST 049 CD
SST / Sep '87 / Plastic Head.

TOO HIGH TO DIE
Violet eyes / Never to be found / We don't exist / Severed Goddess head / Flaming heart / Shine / Backwater / Roof with a hole / Station / Things / Why / Evil love / Comin' down / Lake of fire
CD _____ 828484-2
London / Feb '94 / PolyGram.

UP ON THE SUN
CD _____ SST 039 CD
SST / Aug '87 / Plastic Head.

Meatfly

FATNESS
CD _____ DISC 1CD
Vinyl Japan / '92 / Vital.

Meathook Seed

EMBEDDED
Famine sector / Furned grave / My infinity / Day of conceiving / Cling to an image / Wilted remnant / Forgive / Focal point blur / Embedded / Visible shallow self / Sea of tranquility
CD _____ MOSH 088CD
Earache / Mar '93 / Vital.

Meatlocker

TRIANGLE OF PAIN
CD _____ PRLCD 7913011
Progress Red / Apr '95 / Plastic Head.

Meatmen

CRIPPLED CHILDREN SUCK
CD _____ TG 59 CD
Touch & Go / Feb '91 / SRD.

Mecano

AIDALAI
El fallo positivo / El uno, el dos, el tres / Bilando salsa / El 7 Septiembre / Naturaleza muerta / 1917 / Una rosa es una rosa / El lago artificial / Tu / Dalai Lama / El peon del rey de negras / J.C. Sentia
CD _____ 261.786
Ariola / Nov '91 / BMG.

Mecca Normal

SITTING ON SNAPS
Vacant night sky / Something to be said / Crimson dragnet / Frozen rain / Only heat trapped / Inside your heart / Alibi / Pamela makes waves / Bepo's room / Cyclone / Gravity believes
CD _____ OLE 1122
Matador / Feb '95 / Vital.

Mecolodians

JOE BAIZA/RALPH GORODETZSKY/ TONY CICERO
CD _____ EMY 147-2
Enemy / Nov '94 / Grapevine.

Medalark 11

MEDALARK 11
Cute / Smoke / Coffee / Throw down a rope / Metalark / Snake / Socket / Call your name / Diving / Querelcia / Big sharp
CD _____ CRECD 145
Creation / Dec '93 / 3MV / Vital.

Medardo Y Su Orquesta

LA BODA
CD _____ TUMICD 032
Tumi / '92 / Sterns / Discovery.

Medeski, John

FRIDAY AFTERNOON IN THE UNIVERSE (Medeski, John & Billy Martin/Chris Wood)
Lover / Paper bass / House mop / Last chance to dance trance (perhaps) / Baby clams / We're so happy / Shack / Tea / Chinoiserie / Between two limbs / Sequel / Friday afternoon in the universe / Billy's tool box / Chubb sub / Khob khun krub
CD _____ GCD 79503
Gramavision / Mar '95 / Vital/SAM / ADA.

IT'S A JUNGLE IN HERE (Medeski, John & Billy Martin)
Beeah / Where's sly / Shuck it up / Sand / Worms / bemsha swing / Moti mo / It's a jungle in here / Syeeda's song flute / Wiggles way
CD _____ GCD 79495
Gramavision / Sep '95 / Vital/SAM / ADA.

Media Form

BEAUTY REPORTS
CD _____ SOHO 18CD
Suburbs Of Hell / Nov '94 / Pinnacle / Plastic Head / Kudos.

Medicine

BURIED LIFE
CD _____ ARBCD 5
Beggars Banquet / Oct '93 / Warner Music / Disc.

HER HIGHNESS
All good things / Wash me out / Candy Candy / Feel nothing at all / Fractured smile / Farther down / Aarhus / Seen the light alone / Heads
CD _____ 74321287572
American / Nov '95 / BMG.

SHOT FORTH SELF LIVING
One More / Aruca / Defective / Short happy life / 5ive / Sweet Explosion / Queen of tension / Miss Drugstore / Christmas Song
CD _____ CRECD 142
Creation / Oct '92 / 3MV / Vital.

Medicine Head

NEW BOTTLES OLD MEDICINE
When night falls / Ooee baby / Next time the sun comes round / This love of old / Home's odyssey / Oh my heart to peace / Do it now / Be it as we are / Fire under the mountain / Two men now / Crazy about you baby / Goin' home / His guiding hand / Walkin' blues / Pictures in the sky / Natural sight / Just like Tom Thumb's blues / Blue suede shoes / To train time
CD _____ SEECD 411
Repertoire / Oct '94 / Pinnacle / Cadillac.

TIMEPEACE (BOOM, HOWL AND MOAN)
CD _____ RMOCD 0201
Red Steel Music / Sep '95 / Grapevine.

Meditation Dub

MEDITATION DUB
CD _____ WRCD 15
Techniques / Oct '92 / Jetstar.

Meditation Singers

GOOD NEWS
My soul looks back and wonders / Ain't that good news / You don't know how blessed you are / He's alright with me / Remember me / One river to cross / Know the day is over / Make a sing in the right direction / Day is past and gone / I'm saying yes / I'm determined to run this race / Do you know Jesus / Promise to meet me there / Until I reach my heavenly home / He made it all right / Jesus is always there / Too close to heaven / God is good to me / WDIA plug / My soul looks back in wonders
CD _____ CDCHD 465
Ace / Mar '93 / Pinnacle / Cadillac / Complete/Pinnacle.

Meditations

DEEPER ROOTS
Heartbeat / Jun '94 / Greensleeves / Jetstar / Direct / ADA.
CD _____ HBCD 158

FOR THE GOOD OF MAN
Mr. Vulture man / Roots man party / Tin sardin / Wallah up / For the good of man / Bourgeois game / Dem a fight / Man no better than woman / Woman woman / Rocking in America
CD _____ GRELCD 114
Greensleeves / Aug '88 / Total/BMG / Jetstar / SRD.

NO MORE FRIEND
No more friend / Forcing me / Jack on top / Mother love / Book of history / Carpenter rebuild / Fuss and fight / Slick chick / Talk of the town / Big city
CD _____ GRELCD 52
Greensleeves / Aug '95 / Total/BMG / Jetstar / SRD.

RETURN OF THE MEDITATIONS
CD _____ HBCD 130
Heartbeat / Nov '92 / Greensleeves / Jetstar / Direct / ADA.

Medium Cool

IMAGINATION
How long has this been going on / That old feeling / I fall in love too easily / Look for the silver lining / My foolish heart / Like someone in love / Let's get lost / My buddy / Imagination / Little girl blue
CD _____ COOKCD 055
Cooking Vinyl / Apr '93 / Vital.

Mednick, Lisa

ARTIFACTS OF LOVE
CD _____ DJD 3209
Dejadisc / May '94 / Direct / ADA.

Meek, Gary

TIME ONE
Time one / Misturada / Eva Marie / Bosporous blues / Sierra highway / For a long time / On the road / New day / Sun is out / Free
CD _____ BW 057
B&W / Mar '95 / New Note.

Meek, Joe

I HEAR A NEW WORLD (Meek, Joe & The Blue Men)
Love dance of the Saroos / Glob waterfall / Magnetic field / Valley of the Saroos
CD _____ RPM 103
RPM / Jan '92 / Pinnacle.

JOE MEEK STORY VOL.1, THE (Various Artists)
Just too late / Friendship / Magic wheel / Happy Valley / Let's go see Gran'ma / Believe me / With this kiss / Don't tell me not to love you / Entry of the Globbots / Valley of the Saroo's / Magnetic field / Orbit around the moon / Green jeans / You are my sunshine / Chick a'roo / Don't pick on me / Heart of a teenage girl / I'm always chasing rainbows / Angela Jones / Don't want to know
CD _____ 901081
Line / Jul '95 / CM / Grapevine / ADA / Conifer / Direct.

JOE MEEK STORY VOL.2, THE (1960-1961) (Various Artists)
Tell Laura I love her / Sunday date / Make way baby / Paradise garden / Along came Caroline / Early in the morning / Can't you hear my heart / Time will tell / I'm waiting for tomorrow / No more tomorrows / My baby doll / Teenage love / Swinging low / My baby's gone away / You got what I like / Ambush / I'm in love with you / Lone rider / Sweet little sixteen / Johnny remember me
CD _____ 901082
Line / May '95 / CM / Grapevine / ADA / Conifer / Direct.

WORK IN PROGRESS
CD _____ RPM 121
RPM / Oct '93 / Pinnacle.

Meeting

UPDATE
CD _____ HIBD 8008
Hip Bop / Sep '95 / Conifer / Total/BMG / Silva Screen.

Mega City Four

INSPIRINGLY TITLED - THE LIVE ALBUM
Thanx / Shivering sand / Props / Messenger / Stop / Revolution / Words that say / Callous / Lipscar / Peripheral / Clown / Open / What you've got / Don't want to know if you are lonely / Who cares / Finish
CD _____ MEGCD 2
Big Life / Nov '92 / Pinnacle.

MAGIC BULLETS
Perfect circle / Drown / Rain man / Toys / Iron sky / So / Enemy skies / Wallflower / President / Shadow / Underdog / Greener / Speck
CD _____ MEGCD 003
Big Life / May '93 / Pinnacle.

PEEL SESSIONS
Strange Fruit / Oct '93 / Pinnacle.
CD _____ SFRCD 124

SEBASTOPOL RD
Ticket collector / Scared of cats / Callous / Peripheral / Anne Bancroft / Prague / Clown / Props / What's up / Vague / Stop / Wasting my breath
CD _____ MEGCD 1
Big Life / Feb '92 / Pinnacle.

TERRIBLY SORRY BOB
Miles apart / Running in darkness / Distant relatives / Clear blue sky / Less than sensefree / Dancing days are over / Awkward kid / Cradle / Finish / Severance / Thanx / Square through a circle
CD _____ DYL 024 CD
Decoy / Jun '92 / Vital.

TRANZOPHOBIA
Start / Pride and prejudice / Severe attack of the truth / Paper tiger / January / Twenty one again / On another planet / Things I never said / New Year's day / Occupation / Alternative arrangements / Promise / What you've got / Stupid way to die
CD _____ DYL 003 CD
Decoy / Jun '92 / Vital.

WHO CARES WINS
Who cares / Static interference / Rose coloured / Grudge / Me not you / Messenger / Violet / Rail / Mistook / Open / Revolution / No such place as home / Storms to come / Balance
CD _____ DYL 020 CD
Decoy / Jun '92 / Vital.

Mega Mosh

DIFFERENT KIND OF MEAT, A
CD _____ PROPH 4CD
Prophecy / Nov '92 / Plastic Head.

Mega, Tom

FOR YOU ONLY
CD _____ ITM 001485
ITM / Dec '93 / Tradelink / Koch.

Megabyte

GO FOR IT
CD _____ 710 106

Innovative Communication / Aug '90 / Magnum Music Group.

POWERPLAY
Glow energy / My father was a teacher / Skyline sculptures / Powerplay / Hello, Ralph here / Secret destination
CD _____ CDTB 2.049
Thunderbolt / Jan '88 / Magnum Music Group.

Megadeth

COUNTDOWN TO EXTINCTION
Skin o' my teeth / Symphony of destruction / Architecture of aggression / Foreclosure of a dream / Sweating bullets / This was my life / Countdown to extinction / High speed dirt / Psychotron / Captive honour / Ashes in your mouth
CD _____ CDESTU 2175
Capitol / Jun '92 / EMI.

KILLING IS MY BUSINESS AND BUSINESS IS GOOD
Last rites / Skin beneath the skin / These boots were made for walking / Rattle head / Looking down the cross / Mechanix
CD _____ CDMFN 46
Music For Nations / Aug '87 / Pinnacle.

PEACE SELLS....BUT WHO'S BUYING
Wake up dead / Conjuring / Peace sells / Devil's Island / Good morning / Bad omen / I ain't superstitious / My last words / Black Friday
CD _____ CDEST 2022
Capitol / Jul '94 / EMI.

RUST IN PEACE
Holy wars... the punishment due / Hangar 18 / Take no prisoners / Five magics / Poison was the cure / Lucretia / Tornado of souls / Dawn patrol / Rust in peace...Polaris
CD _____ CDEST 2132
Capitol / Sep '90 / EMI.

SO FAR SO GOOD SO WHAT
Into the lungs of hell / Set the world afire / Anarchy in the U.K. / Mary Jane / 502 / In my darkest hour / Liar / Hook in mouth
CD _____ CDEST 2053
Capitol / Mar '88 / EMI.

YOUTHANASIA
Reckoning day / Train of consequences / Addicted to chaos / Tout le monde / Elysian fields / Killing road / Blood of heroes / Family tree / Youthanasia / I thought I knew it all / Black curtains / Victory / No more Mr. Nice Guy (2CD only) / Breakpoint (2CD only) / Go to hell (2CD only) / Angry again (2CD only) / Ninety nine ways to die (2CD only) / Paranoid (2CD only) / Diadems (2CD only) / Problems (2CD only)
CD _____ CDEST 2244
Capitol / Oct '94 / EMI.

Megakronkel

MEGAKRONKEL
CD _____ K 148D
Konkurrel / Mar '93 / SRD.

Megalon

PANDORA'S BOX
CD _____ PLKCD 002
Plink Plonk / Oct '94 / Plink Plonk.

Megora

WAITING
CD _____ SPV 08496742
SPV / Dec '94 / Plastic Head.

Mehegan, John

PAIR OF PIANOS, A (Mehegan, John & E. Costa)
I'll remember April / Laura / All of you / Easy living / Intermission blues / Cheek to cheek / Mambo inn / Blues for a set
CD _____ SV 0206
Savoy Jazz / Apr '93 / Conifer / ADA.

REFLECTIONS
Lullaby of Birdland / Every time we say goodbye / Blue skies / Those little white lies / My heart stood still / Nice work if you can get it / At long last love / Song is you / Round Midnight / Night and day
CD _____ SV 0204
Savoy Jazz / Apr '93 / Conifer / ADA.

Meices

GREATEST BIBLE STORIES EVER TOLD
CD _____ EFA 11382 2
Empty / Sep '94 / Plastic Head / SRD.

TASTES LIKE CHICKEN
That good one / Good one / Daddy's gone to California / All time high / Light 'em up / Slide / Until the weekend / Lettuce is far out / Big shitburger / Untruly / Hopin' for a ride / Now / That other good one / Don't let the soap run out (CD only) / Alex put something in his pocket (CD only) / Pissin' in the sink (CD only) / Number one (CD only)
CD _____ BLUFF 013CD
Deceptive / Feb '95 / Vital.

Mekon

WELCOME TO TACKLETOWN
CD _____ WALLCD 006
Wall Of Sound / Feb '96 / Disc / Soul Trader.

Mekong Delta

VISIONS FUGITIVES
CD _____ CDVEST 19
Bulletproof / Jul '94 / Pinnacle.

Mekons

MEKONS
Snow / St. Patrick's day / D.P. Miller / Institution / I'm so happy / Chopper squad / Business / Trimden grange explosion / Karen / Corporal chalkie / John Barry / Another one
CD _____ CDMGRAM 76
Cherry Red / Feb '94 / Pinnacle.

RETREAT FROM MEMPHIS
CD _____ QS 26CD
Quarter Stick / Jun '94 / SRD.

ROCK 'N' ROLL
Memphis, Egypt / Club Mekon / Only darkness has the power / Ring o'roses / Learning to live on your own / Cocaine Lil / Empire of the senseless / Someone / Amnesia / I am crazy / Heaven and back / Blow your tuneless trumpet / Echo / When darkness fails
CD _____ BFFP 40CD
Blast First / '89 / Disc.

Mel & Tim

STARTING ALL OVER AGAIN
Don't you mess with my money, my honey or my woman / Starting all over again / I may not be what you want / Carry me / Free for all / Heaven knows / Wrap it up / What's your name / I'm your puppet / Too much wheelin' and dealin' / Forever and a day / It's those little things that count / Same folks / Yes we can-can
CD _____ CDSXE 078
Stax / Jan '93 / Pinnacle.

Melanie

BEST OF MELANIE
CD _____ MATCD 276
Castle / Sep '93 / BMG.

BEST OF MELANIE, THE
Ruby Tuesday / Brand new key / Animal crackers / Mr. Tambourine man / Baby day / Beautiful people / Save the night / Lay down (candles in the rain) / Close it all / What have they done to my song Ma / Lay lady lay / Some day I'll be a farmer / Good book / Peace will come / Gardens in the city / Nickel song / Pebbles in the sand / Tell me why
CD _____ MCCD 011
Music Club / Feb '91 / Disc / THE / CM.

BORN TO BE
In the hour / Bo Bo's party / Momma momma / Animal crackers / Close to it all / I'm back in town / Mr. Tambourine man / Really loved Harold / Christopher Robin / Merry Christmas
CD _____ C5CD 582
See For Miles/C5 / Apr '92 / Pinnacle.

COLLECTION: MELANIE
Somebody loves me / Beautiful people / In the hour / I really loved Harold / Johnny boy / Any guy / I'm back in town / What have they done to my song Ma / Lay down (candles in the rain) / Peace will come / Good book / Nickle song / Babe rainbow (reprise) / Carolina on my mind / Ruby Tuesday / Sign in the window / Lay lady lay / Christopher Robin / Animal crackers / I don't eat animals / Psychotherapy / Leftover wine
CD _____ CCSCD 195
Castle / Jun '88 / BMG.

GOOD BOOK, THE
Good book / Babe rainbow / Sign on the window / Saddest thing / Nickel song / Isn't it a pity / My father / Chords of fame / You can go fishin / Birthday of the sun / Prize
CD _____ C5CD 597
See For Miles/C5 / Feb '93 / Pinnacle.

HIT SINGLE COLLECTABLES
CD _____ DISK 4505
Disky / Apr '94 / THE / BMG / Discovery / Pinnacle.

RUBY TUESDAY
Mr. Tambourine man / Beautiful people / Carolina in my mind / Lay lady lay / Kansas / My bonny lies over the ocean / Someday I'll be a farmer / Nickel song / Happy birthday / Ruby Tuesday / What have they done to my song Ma / Somebody loves me / Tell me why / Candles in the rain / Leftover wine / Brand new key / Stop, I don't wanna hear it anymore / Peace will come
CD _____ 5507512
Spectrum/Karussell / Jan '95 / PolyGram / THE.

SILENCE IS KING
CD _____ HY 200130CD
Hypertension / Feb '95 / Total/BMG / Direct / ADA.

SILVER ANNIVERSARY
CD Set _____ HYCD 200136
Hypertension / Mar '95 / Total/BMG / Direct / ADA.

Meldonian, Dick

SWING ALTERNATE (Meldonian, Dick & Orchestra)
CD _____ CLCD 150
Circle / Mar '90 / Jazz Music / Swift / Wellard.

SWING OF ARR. OF GENEROLA (Meldonian, Dick & Orchestra)
CD _____ CCD 150
Circle / Oct '91 / Jazz Music / Swift / Wellard.

YOU'VE CHANGED (Meldonian, Dick Quartet)
CD _____ PCD 7052
Progressive / Jun '93 / Jazz Music.

Melford, Myra

ALIVE IN THE HOUSE OF SAINTS (Melford, Myra Trio)
Hat Art / Nov '93 / Harmonia Mundi / ADA / Cadillac.
CD _____ ARTCD 6136

JUMP
CD _____ EMY 115-2
Enemy / Nov '94 / Grapevine.

NOW & NOW (Melford, Myra Trio)
CD _____ EMY 1312
Enemy / Oct '92 / Grapevine.

Mellencamp, John

AMERICAN FOOL (Mellencamp, John Cougar)
Can you take it / Hurts so good / Jack and Diane / Hand to hold on to / Danger list / Can you take it / Thundering hearts / China girl / Close enough / Weakest moments
CD _____ 8149932
Mercury / '88 / PolyGram.

BIG DADDY (Mellencamp, John Cougar)
Big daddy of them all / To live / Martha say / Theo and weird Henry / Jackie Brown / Pop singer / Void in my heart / Mansions in heaven / Sometimes a great notion / Country gentleman / J.M.'s question
CD _____ 8382202
Mercury / May '89 / PolyGram.

COLLECTION: JOHN COUGAR MELLENCAMP
American dream / Oh pretty woman / Jailhouse rock / Dream killin' town / Supergirl / Chestnut Street revisited / Kid inside / Take what you want / Cheap shot / Sidewalks and street lights / R. gang / Good girls / Do you believe in magic / Twentieth Century Fox / Sad lady / Gearhead / Young genocides / Too young to live / Survive
CD _____ CCSCD 124
Castle / Apr '86 / BMG.

DANCE NAKED
CD _____ 5224282
Mercury / Jun '94 / PolyGram.

HUMAN WHEELS
CD _____ 518008-2
Mercury / Sep '93 / PolyGram.

JOHN COUGAR
Little night dancin' / Miami / Do you think that's fair / Welcome to Chinatown / Pray for me / Small paradise / Great midwest / I need a lover / Sugar Marie / Taxi dancer
CD _____ 8149952
Mercury / Jan '86 / PolyGram.

KID INSIDE, THE (Mellencamp, John Cougar)
Kid inside / Take what you want / Cheap shot / Sidewalks and streetlights / R. Gang / American son / Gearhead / Young genocides / Too young to live / Survive
CD _____ CLACD 112
Castle / Nov '86 / BMG.

LONESOME JUBILEE, THE
Paper in fire / Down and out in paradise / Check it out / Real life / Cherry bomb / We are the people / Empty hands / Hard times for an honest man / Hot dogs and hamburgers / Rooty toot toot
CD _____ 8324652
Mercury / Jul '92 / PolyGram.

SCARECROW
Rain on the scarecrow / Grandmas's theme / Small town / Minutes to memories / Lonely ol' night / Face of the nation / Justice and independence '85 / Between a laugh and a tear / Rumbleseat / You've got to stand for something / R.O.C.K. in the U.S.A. / Kind of fella I am
CD _____ 8248652
Mercury / Nov '85 / PolyGram.

UH-HUH
Crumblin' down / Pink houses / Authority song / Hurts so good / Thundering hearts / Warmer place to sleep
CD _____ 8144502
Mercury / Oct '91 / PolyGram.

WHENEVER WE WANTED
Love and happiness / Now more than ever / I ain't never satisfied / Get a leg up / Crazy

ones / Last chance / They're so tough / Melting pot / Whenever we wanted / Again tonight
CD _____ 5101512
Mercury / Oct '91 / PolyGram.

Mellow Candle

SWADDLING SONGS
Heaven Heath / Sheep season / Silversong / Poet and the witch / Messenger birds / Dan the wing / Reverend Sisters / Break your token / Buy or beware / Vile excesses / Lonely man / Boulders on my grave
CD _____ SEECD 404
See For Miles/C5 / Jul '94 / Pinnacle.

Mellow Fellows

STREET PARTY
I've got to find a way / Street party / I've got a feeling / Feels like rain / Drivin' wheel / We'll be friends / Don't turn your heater down / Since I fell for you / Last night / Me and my woman / Broad daylight
CD _____ ALCD 4793
Alligator / May '93 / Direct / ADA.

Mellstock Band

CAROLS & DANCES OF HARDY'S WESSEX
CD _____ CDSDL 360
Saydisc / Oct '92 / Harmonia Mundi / ADA / Direct.

SONGS OF THOMAS HARDY'S WESSEX (With Sally Dexter/Julie Murphy/Ian Giles/Andy Turner)
Foggy dew / Jockey to the fair/Dame Durden / Mistletoe bough / Cupid's garden / Queen Eleanor's confession / Spotted cow / Seeds of love / Barley mow / Prentice boy / I have parks, I have hounds / Break o'the day / Sheepshearing song / Tailor's breeches / Downhills of life / I wish I wish / Joan's ale / Outlandish knight / Such a beauty I did grow / Banks of Allan Water / King Arthur had three sons / Light of the moon
CD _____ CDSDL 410
Saydisc / Mar '95 / Harmonia Mundi / ADA / Direct.

Melly, George

BEST OF GEORGE MELLY
CD _____ KAZCD 22
Kaz / Jul '92 / BMG.

BEST OF GEORGE MELLY, THE
Anything goes / Oh Chubby, stay the way you are / House of the rising sun / Porter's love song / Nobody knows you when you're down and out / Hard hearted Hannah / Puttin' on the ritz / I ain't got nobody / Someday sweetheart / Route 66 / September song / Maybe not at all / It had to be you / Wrap your troubles in dreams (and dream your troubles away) / Chicago (That toddling town) / I hate a man like you / Sundown mamma / I don't want to set the world on fire
CD _____ TRTCD 160
TrueTrax / Dec '94 / THE.

BEST OF LIVE
CD _____ LCD 7019
D-Sharp / Jul '95 / Pinnacle.

FRANKIE & JOHNNY
CD _____ DSHCD 7001
D-Sharp / Dec '92 / Pinnacle.

Melodian, Dick

DICK MELODIAN TRIO (Melodian, Dick Trio)
CD _____ JCD 164
Jazzology / Aug '94 / Swift / Jazz Music.

Melodians

SWING & DINE
CD _____ HBCD 129
Heartbeat / Nov '92 / Greensleeves / Jetstar / Direct / ADA.

Melodie E Canzoni

ERIK SATIE
CD _____ NT 6717
Robi Droli / Jan '94 / Direct / ADA.

Melody, Courtney

COURTNEY MELODY CLASH WITH SANCHEZ (Melody, Courtney & Sanchez)
CD _____ RNCD 2072
Rhino / Jul '94 / Jetstar / Magnum Music Group / THE.

Melonz Bustin'

WATCH YOUR SEEDS POP OUT
CD _____ CDCTUM 9
Continuum / Sep '94 / Pinnacle.

Melvin, Brian

NIGHT FOOD
Ain't nothin' but a party / Don't forget the bass / Night food / Zen turtles / For Max /

Polly wanna rhythm / Primalass / Warrior / Continuum
CD _____ CDSJP 214
Timeless Jazz / '88 / New Note.

NIGHT FOOD (FEATURING JACO PASTORIUS) (Melvin, Brian's Nightfood)
Sexual healing / Fever / CIA / Dania / Did you hear that Monie / Mercy mercy mercy / Bahama Mama / J.P.'s shuffle / Milers mode
CD _____ 66052003
Global Pacific / Feb '91 / Pinnacle.

OLD VOICES (Melvin, Brian Trio)
Hackensack / I thought about you / Over the rainbow / Black Narcissus / Segment / Joe / Shiny stockings / I want to talk about / Giant steps / Naima / Blues for Al
CD _____ CDSJP 396
Timeless Jazz / Aug '94 / New Note.

STANDARDS ZONE (Melvin, Brian Trio & Jaco Pastorius)
Morning star / Days of wine and roses / Wedding waltz / Moon and sand / So what / Fire water / If you could see me now / Out of the night / Tokyo blues / Village blues
CD _____ 66052008
Global Pacific / May '91 / Pinnacle.

Melvin, Harold

IF YOU DON'T KNOW ME BY NOW (The Best Of Cabaret) (Melvin, Harold & The Bluenotes)
Cabaret / Love I lost / If you don't know me by now / Don't leave me this way / I'm weak for you / Everybody's talkin' / Hope that we can be together soon / Keep on lovin' you / Tell the world how I feel about cha baby / I miss you / Satisfaction guaranteed / Yesterday I had the blues / Yesterday / Wake up everybody / Where are all my friends / Bad luck
CD _____ 4805092
Epic / May '95 / Sony.

SATISFACTION GUARANTEED (The Best Of Harold Melvin & The Blue Notes) (Melvin, Harold & The Bluenotes)
Don't leave me this way / Satisfaction guaranteed / Love I lost / Wake up everybody / Hope that we can be together soon / You know how to make me feel so good / Be for real / Nobody could take your place / Bad luck / Where are all my friends / Keep on loving you / Tell the world about how I feel about cha baby / To be true / I'm searching for a love / To be free to be who we are / If you don't know me by now
CD _____ 4720392
Epic / Jul '92 / Sony.

Melvins

HOUDINI
Hooch / Night goat / Lizzy / Goin' blind / Honey bucket / Hag me / Set me straight / Sky pup / Joan of arc / Teet / Copache / Pearl bomb / Spread eagle beagle
CD _____ 7567825322
Atlantic / Sep '93 / Warner Music.

LYSOL
CD _____ TUP 422
Tupelo / Nov '92 / Disc.

MELVINS: LIVE
CD _____ YCR 012CD
Your Choice / '92 / Plastic Head.

PRICK
CD _____ ARRCD53 333
Amphetamine Reptile / Sep '94 / SRD.

STONER WITCH
CD _____ 7567827042
WEA / Nov '94 / Warner Music.

Members

SOUND OF THE SUBURBS (A Collection Of The Members' Finest)
Handling the big jets / Sally / G.L.C. / Offshore banking business/Pennies in the pound / Solo a go-go / Muzak machine / Phone-in show / Brian was / Killing time / Clean men / Romance / Flying again / Solitary confinement / Chelsea nightclub / Gang war / Police car
CD _____ CDOVD 455
Virgin / Feb '95 / EMI.

Members Only

MEMBERS ONLY WITH NELSON RANGELL (Members Only & Nelson Rangell)
CD _____ MCD 5332
Muse / Sep '92 / New Note / CM.

TOO
CD _____ MCD 5348
Muse / Sep '92 / New Note / CM.

Membranes

TO SLAY THE ROCK PIG
CD _____ SUK 9CD
Vinyl Drip / Nov '89 / Disc.

WRONG PLACE AT THE WRONG TIME
CD _____ CCON 001CD
Constrictor Classics / Jul '93 / SRD.

Memento Mori

LIFE, DEATH AND OTHER MORBID TALES
CD _____ BM 051CD
Black Mark / Aug '94 / Plastic Head.

Memphis Horns

MEMPHIS HORNS
Take me to the river / Fa fa fa fa fa (Sad song) / I've been loving you too long / Somebody have mercy / Break the chain / Holding on to love / I'm just another soldier / Rumours / Rollercoaster / You don't miss your water / Desire in your eyes
CD _____ CD 83344
Telarc / Jul '95 / Conifer / ADA.

Memphis Jug Band

1932-34
CD _____ BCD 6002
Blues Document / '91 / Swift / Jazz Music / Hot Shot.

MEMPHIS JUG BAND
CD _____ YAZCD 1067
Yazoo / Apr '91 / CM / ADA / Roots / Koch.

MEMPHIS JUG BAND VOL.1
CD _____ JSPCD 606
JSP / Oct '93 / ADA / Target/BMG / Direct / Cadillac / Complete/Pinnacle.

MEMPHIS JUG BAND VOL.2
CD _____ DOCD 5022
Blues Document / Nov '93 / Swift / Jazz Music / Hot Shot.

MEMPHIS JUG BAND VOL.3
CD _____ JSPCD 608
JSP / Feb '93 / ADA / Target/BMG / Direct / Cadillac / Complete/Pinnacle.

Memphis Minnie

ANTHOLOGY 1929-44
CD _____ EN 520
Encyclopaedia / Sep '95 / Discovery.

CITY BLUES
CD _____ ALB 1008CD
Aldabra / Mar '94 / CM / Disc.

IN MY GIRLISH DAYS
CD _____ CD 52036
Blues Encore / May '94 / Target/BMG.

MEMPHIS MINNIE & KANSAS JOE (Memphis Minnie & Kansas Joe)
CD _____ DOCD 5031
Blues Document / Nov '93 / Swift / Jazz Music / Hot Shot.

TRAVELLING BLUES
CD _____ ALB 1005CD
Aldabra / Mar '94 / CM / Disc.

Memphis Slim

4.00 BLUES
4.00 Blues / Trouble in mind / Worried life blues / Cow cow blues / Lonesome in my bedroom / Diggin' my potatoes / In the evening (when the sun goes down) / Blue and disgusted / Miss Ida Bea / I'll take her to Chicago / Lonesome / Cold blooded woman / One man's mad / Let the good times roll creole / What is the mare rack / Pigalle love / Four walls / It's been too long / Big Bertha / I'm lost without you / I'll just keep on singing the blues / True love
CD _____ CDGRF 059
Tring / '93 / Tring / Prism.

ALL KINDS OF BLUES
Blues is trouble / Grinder man blues / Three in one boogie / Letter home / Churnin' man blues / Two of a kind / Blacks / If you see Kay / Frankie and Johnny Boogie / Mother earth
CD _____ OBCCD 507
Original Blues Classics / Nov '92 / Complete/Pinnacle / Wellard / Cadillac.

BLUE THIS EVENING
CD _____ BLCD 760155
Black Lion / '91 / Jazz Music / Cadillac / Wellard / Koch.

BLUES BEFORE SUNRISE
CD _____ TKOCD 017
TKO / '92 / TKO.

COMPLETE RECORDINGS 1940-41
CD _____ 158032
Blues Collection / Jun '93 / Discovery.

DIALOGUE IN BOOGIE (Memphis Slim & Philippe Lejeune)
Rockin' / E.E.C. boogie / C'est normal, c'est normal / Jefferson country blues / Fourth and beale / This is the way I feel / Three, two, one boogie / Midnite tempo / Cooky boogie / C and L boogie
CD _____ 157112
Blues Collection / Feb '93 / Discovery.

I AM THE BLUES
CD _____ CDSGP 080
Prestige / Jan '95 / Total/BMG.

LIFE IS LIKE THAT
Life is like that / Nobody loves me / Sometimes I feel like a motherless child / Pacemaker boogie / Harlem bound / Darling / I

miss you so / Lend me your love / Cheatin' around / Letter home / Now I got the blues / Grinder man blues / Don't ration my love / Slim's boogie / Little Mary / Mistake in life / Messin' around with the blues / Midnight jump
CD _____ CDCHARLY 249
Charly / Oct '90 / Charly / THE / Cadillac.

LONDON SESSIONS, THE
Help me some / Fattenin' frogs for snakes / I feel so good / Every day / One more time / I feel so good (Take 2) / Every day (Take 1) / Blues in London (Parts 1 & 2) / Ain't nobody's business (Take 1 & 2) / Ain't nobody's business (Take 1) / Fattenin' frogs for snakes (Take 1)
CD _____ NEXCD 252
Sequel / Sep '93 / BMG.

MEMPHIS BLUES - PARIS SESSIONS
CD _____ STCD 11
Stash / Aug '89 / Jazz Music / CM / Cadillac / Direct / ADA.

MEMPHIS SLIM
CD _____ DVBC 9082
Deja Vu / May '95 / THE.

MEMPHIS SLIM & CANNED HEAT (Memphis Slim & Canned Heat)
CD _____ 5197252
Verve / Feb '94 / PolyGram.

MEMPHIS SLIM USA
Born with the blues / Just let it be me / Red haired boogie / Blue and disgusted / New key to the highway / I'd take her to Chicago / Harlem bound / El capitan / I just landed in your town / John Henry / I believe I'll settle down / Bad luck and trouble / Late afternoon blues / Memphis Slim U.S.A
CD _____ CCD 9024
Candid / Apr '87 / Cadillac / Jazz Music / Wellard / Koch.

MOTHER EARTH
CD _____ OW 30007
One Way / Jul '94 / Direct / ADA.

RAINING THE BLUES
Beer drinking woman / Teasing the blues / I.C. Blues / Baby doll / Just blues / Blue and disgusted / Blue brew / Rack 'em back Jack / Motherless child / Brenda / When your dough roller is gone / Hey slim / Darling I miss you so / Lonesome traveller / No strain / Don't think you're smart / Raining the blues / You're gonna need my help one day / Angel child / Fast and free / My baby left me / Lucille / Nice stuff
CD _____ CDCH 485
Ace / Nov '93 / Pinnacle / Cadillac / Complete/Pinnacle.

ROCKIN' THE BLUES
Gotta find my baby / Come back / Messin' around / Sassy Mae / Lend me your love / Guitar cha cha / Stroll on little girl / Rockin' the house / Wish me well / Blue and lonesome / My gal keeps me crying / Slim's blues / Steppin' out / Mother Earth / What's the matter / This time I'm through
CD _____ CDBM 21
Charly / Apr '92 / Charly / THE / Cadillac.

STEADY ROLLIN' BLUES
CD _____ OBCCD 523
Original Blues Classics / Nov '92 / Complete/Pinnacle / Wellard / Cadillac.

STEPPIN' OUT (Live at Ronnie Scott's)
Health shaking / Mother earth / Rock this house / Tribute to Gaillard / Four hundred years / Steppin' out / Baby please come home / Where do I go from here / Didn't we / Christina / Animal / Beer drinking woman / What is this world coming to / Bye bye blues
CD _____ CLACD 334
Castle / '93 / BMG.

TRAVELLING WITH THE BLUES
Memphis boogie / St. Louis blues / Santa Fe blues / Chicago new home of the blues / Chicago house / Rent party blues / Arkansas road house blues / Midnight jump / Goodbye blues / Reminiscin' with the blues / Good rockin' blues / Blues confession / Boogie woogie / Blues made up / Worries all the time
CD _____ STCD 8021
Storyville / Mar '95 / Jazz Music / Wellard / CM / Cadillac.

TRIBUTE TO BIG BILL BROONZY
CD _____ CCD 79023
Candid / Jul '93 / Cadillac / Jazz Music / Wellard / Koch.

YOU GOT TO HELP ME SOME
Pinetop's blues / Rock me baby / Rack em back Jack / Motherless child / Teasing the blues / Letter home / Sassy Mae / Blacks / Joggie boogie / Little peace of mind / Blues / Blue and lonesome / Two of a kind / Mother earth / Slim was just kiddin' / Having fun / Jive time bounce / Beer drinking woman / You got to help me some / Empty room blues / Slim's blues
CD _____ CD 52013
Blues Encore / Nov '92 / Target/BMG.

Memphis Willie B

HARD WORKING MAN BLUES
CD _____ OBCCD 578
Original Blues Classics / Jan '96 / Complete/Pinnacle / Wellard / Cadillac.

Men At Large

ONE SIZE FITS ALL
CD _____ 756792459-2
Warner Bros. / Oct '94 / Warner Music.

Men At Work

BUSINESS AS USUAL
Who can it be now / I can see it in your eyes / Down under / Underground / Helpless automaton / People just love to play with words / Be good Johnny / Touching the untouchables / Catch a star / Down by the sea
CD _____ 4508872
Epic / Apr '94 / Sony.

CARGO
Dr. Heckyll and Mr. Jive / Overkill / Settle down my boy / Upstairs in my house / No sign of yesterday / It's a mistake / Highwire / Blue for you / I like to / No restrictions
CD _____ 983287 2
Pickwick/Sony Collector's Choice / Nov '93 / Carlton Home Entertainment / Pinnacle / Sony.

CARGO/BUSINESS AS USUAL
Dr. Heckyll and Mr. Jive / Overkill / Settle down my boy / Upstairs in my house / No sign of yesterday / It's a mistake / Highwire / Blue for you / I like to / No restrictions / Who can it be now / I can see it in your eyes / Down under / Underground / Helpless automaton / People just love to play with words / Be good Johnny / Touching the untouchables / Catch a star / Down by the sea
CD Set _____ 4610232
Columbia / Jul '92 / Sony.

Men They Couldn't Hang

FIVE GLORIOUS YEARS
CD _____ ORECD 509
Silvertone / Nov '89 / Pinnacle.

HOW GREEN IS THE VALLEY
Gold strike / Ghosts of Cable Street / Bells / Shirt of blue / Tiny soldiers / Parted from you / Gold rush / Dancing on the pier / Going back to Coventry / Rabid underdog / Parade
CD _____ MCLD 19075
MCA / Nov '92 / BMG.

NIGHT OF A THOUSAND CANDLES
Day after / Jack Dandy / Night to remember / Johnny come home / Green fields of France / Iron masters / Hush little baby / Walkin' talkin' / Kingdom come / Scarlet ribbons
CD _____ FIENDCD 50
Demon / '88 / Pinnacle / ADA.

WAITING FOR BONAPARTE
Crest / Smugglers / Dover lights / Bounty hunter / Island in the rain / Colours / Midnight train / Father's wrong / Life of a small fry / Mary's present / Silver dagger (Not on LP) / Restless highway (Not on LP) / Country song (Not on LP) / Crest #2 (CD only)
CD _____ 242 380 2
Magnet / Mar '88 / Warner Music.

WELL HUNG
CD _____ CDAFTER 10
Fun After All / Mar '91 / Pinnacle.

Menace

GLC - R.I.P
CD _____ AHOY 17
Captain Oi / Nov '94 / Plastic Head.

Menace To Society

LIFE OF A REAL ONE
CD _____ CUS 41602CD
Ichiban / May '94 / Koch.

Menano, Antonio

ARQUIVOS DO FADO
CD _____ HTCD 31
Heritage / Jun '95 / Swift / Roots / Wellard / Direct / Hot Shot / Jazz Music / ADA.

Menard, D.L

NO MATTER WHERE YOU AT, THERE YOU ARE
Wildwood flower / I passed in front of your door / Let's gallop to Mamou / Convict waltz / Big Texas / Heart of the city / I went to tha dance last night / Little black eyes / Water pump / Every night / Lafayette two-step / No christmas for the poor
CD _____ HNCD 1352
Hannibal / Feb '90 / Vital / ADA.

SWALLOW RECORDINGS, THE (Menard, D.L. & Austin Pitre)
Louisiana aces special / Back door / I can't forget you / She didn't know I was married / Bachelor's life / Valse de Jolly Rodgers / Miller's cave / Water pump / It's too late you're divorced / Riches of a musician / Vail

and the crown / I can live a better life / Rebecca Ann / Two step de bayou teche / Opelousas waltz / Two step a tante adele / Rainbow waltz / Rene's special / Grand mamou blues / Flumes d'enfer / Chinaball blues / Le pauvre hobo / Pretty rosie cheeks / Don't shake my tree / La valse d'amour / Jungle club waltz / J'ai coiner a ta porte / Chataigner waltz
CD _____ CDCHD 327
Ace / Jul '91 / Pinnacle / Cadillac / Complete/Pinnacle.

Mendes, Sergio

BRASILEIRO
Fanfarra / Magalenha / Indiado / What is this / Lua soberana / Sambadouro / Senhoras do amazonas / Kalimba / Barabare / Esconjuros / Pipoca / Magano / Chorado
CD _____ 7559613152
Elektra / May '92 / Warner Music.

GREATEST HITS: SERGIO MENDES
Mas que nada / Scarborough Fair / With a little help from my friends / Like a lover / Look of love / Night and day / Masquerade / Fool on the hill / Goin' out of my head / Look around / So many stars / Day tripper / Pretty world / What the world needs now is love
CD _____ CDMID 123
A&M / Oct '92 / PolyGram.

Mendoza, Celesta

LA REINA DEL GUAGUANCO
Papa ogun / Estas acabando / Recordare / Mi rumba echando candela / Yo le llamo vivir / A ti na ma / Que me castigue dios / Muere la luz / carinto ven / Lo que vale mi querer / Si yo fuera / En la cumbre
CD _____ PSCCD 1009
Pure Sounds From Cuba / Feb '95 / Henry Hadaway Organisation / THE.

Mendoza, Lydia

LA GLORIA DE TEXAS
CD _____ ARHCD 3012
Arhoolie / Apr '95 / ADA / Direct / Cadillac.

MAL HOMBRE
CD _____ FL 7002
Folklyric / Apr '95 / Direct / Cadillac.

Mendoza, Victor

IF ONLY YOU KNEW
Para gozar un poquinto / If only you knew / Siempre caliente / Terri by the sea / Snow samba / At the tortilla factory / Cancao da noite / Santa Fe
CD _____ CDLR 45019
L&R / Nov '90 / New Note.

Mendoza, Vince

JAZZ PANA (Mendoza, Vince & Arif Mardin)
El vito cante / Tangos / Entre tinieblas / Tanguillo / Soy gitano / Bulena / Suite fraternidad / El vito en gran tamano
CD _____ 92122
Act / Apr '94 / New Note.

SKETCHES
CD _____ 892152
Act / Jul '94 / New Note.

Mengelberg, Misha

DUTCH MASTERS (Mengelberg, Misha/Steve Lacy/George Lewis)
CD _____ 1211542
Soul Note / Mar '92 / Harmonia Mundi / Wellard / Cadillac.

IMPROMPTUS
CD _____ FMPCD 07
FMP / May '86 / Cadillac.

WHO'S BRIDGE
CD _____ DIW 036
DIW / May '95 / Harmonia Mundi / Cadillac.

Menhaden Countrymen

WON'T YOU HELP ME TO RAISE 'EM
CD _____ GV 220CD
Global Village / Nov '93 / ADA / Direct.

Menswear

NUISANCE
125 West 3rd Street / I'll manage somehow / Sleeping in / Little Miss Pin Point Eyes / Daydreamer / Hollywood girl / Being brave / Around you again / One / Stardust / Piece of me / Stardust (Reprise)
CD _____ 8286762
Laurel / Oct '95 / Pinnacle / PolyGram.

Mental Hippie Blood

MENTAL HIPPIE BLOOD
CD _____ SPV 08476752
SPV / Oct '94 / Plastic Head.

Mental Overdrive

PLUGGED
CD _____ LDO 001CD

Love Od Communications / Jan '96 / Plastic Head.

Mentallo & The Fixer

NO REST FOR THE WICKED
CD _____ BIOCD 02
Messerschmitt / Mar '94 / Plastic Head.

WHERE ANGELS FEAR TO TREAD
CD _____ CDZOT 108
Zoth Ommog / Mar '94 / Plastic Head.

Mentally Damaged

PUNK GRUNK
CD _____ SPV 08456802
Wolverine / Oct '94 / Plastic Head.

Menuhin, Yehudi

MENUHIN & GRAPPELLI PLAY BERLIN/KERN/PORTER (Menuhin, Yehudi & Stephane Grappelli)
Cheek to cheek / Isn't this a lovely day to be caught in the rain) / Piccolino / Change partners / Top hat, white tie and tails / I've got my love to keep me warm / Heatwave / Way you look tonight / Pick yourself up / Fine romance / All the things you are / Why do I love you / I get a kick out of you / Night and day / Looking at you / Just one of those things / My funny valentine / Thou swell / Lady is a tramp / Blue room
CD _____ CDM 769 219 2
EMI / Feb '88 / EMI.

MENUHIN AND GRAPPELLI PLAY 'JEALOUSY' (and Other Great Standards) (Menuhin, Yehudi & Stephane Grappelli)
Jealousy / Tea for two / Limehouse blues / These foolish things / Continental / Nightingale sang in Berkeley Square / Sweet Sue, just you / Skylark / Laura / Sweet Georgia Brown / I'll remember April / April in Paris / Things we did last summer / September in the rain / Autumn leaves / Autumn in New York / Button up your overcoat
CD _____ CDM 769 220 2
EMI / Mar '88 / EMI.

MENUHIN AND GRAPPELLI PLAY GERSHWIN (Menuhin, Yehudi & Stephane Grappelli)
Fascinating rhythm / Summertime / Nice work if you can get it / Foggy day / 'S wonderful / Man I love / I got rhythm / They all laughed / Funny face / Lady be good
CD _____ CDM 769 218 2
Angel / Mar '88 / EMI.

STRICTLY FOR THE BIRDS (Menuhin, Yehudi & Stephane Grappelli)
Nightingale sang in Berkeley Square / Lullaby of Birdland / When the red, red robin comes bob, bob, bobbin' along / Skylark / Bye bye blackbird / Coucou / Flamingo / Dinah / Rosetta / Sweet Sue, just you / Once in love with Amy / Laura / La route du roi / Sweet Georgia Brown
CD _____ CDCFP 4549
Classics For Pleasure / Mar '89 / EMI.

Mephisto

SUBTERRANEAN SOUND, THE
CD _____ SSR 162CD
Crammed Discs / Feb '96 / Grapevine / New Note.

Mephisto Waltz

CROCOSMIA
CD _____ EFA 15564
Gymnastic / Apr '93 / SRD.

ETERNAL DEEP, THE
CD _____ CLEO 63082
Cleopatra / Apr '94 / Disc.

TERROR REGINA
CD _____ CLEO 9259-2
Cleopatra / Mar '94 / Disc.

THALIA
CD _____ CLEO 95112
Cleopatra / Aug '95 / Disc.

Mera

HUNGARIAN FOLK MUSIC FROM TRANSYLVANIA
CD _____ SYN 188
Syncoop / Nov '95 / ADA / Direct.

Merauder

MASTER KILLER
CD _____ CM 77104CD
Century Media / Nov '95 / Plastic Head.

Mercedes

LIVING FOR THE MOMENT
Living for the moment
CD _____ STORM 82CD
Vinyl Solution / May '94 / Disc.

Mercer, Johnny

PARDON MY SOUTHERN ACCENT
CD _____ CDHD 203
Happy Days / Aug '93 / Conifer.

SWEET GEORGIA BROWN
CD _____ HCD 152
Hindsight / Nov '95 / Target/BMG / Jazz Music.

Mercey, Larry

FULL SPEED AHEAD
CD _____ 322544
Koch / Jul '91 / Koch.

Merchant, Natalie

TIGERLILY
CD _____ 7559617452
Elektra / Jun '95 / Warner Music.

Merciless

TREASURES WITHIN, THE
CD _____ CDATV 26
Active / Jun '92 / Pinnacle.

UNBOUND
CD _____ NFR 007
No Fashion / Oct '94 / Plastic Head.

Merciless

LEN OUT MI MERCY
CD _____ ANXCD 1
Annex / Jun '95 / Jetstar.

Mercury Rev

BOCES
CD _____ BBQCD 140
Beggars Banquet / May '93 / Warner Music / Disc.

YERSELF IS STEAM
CD _____ MINTCD 4
Mint / Dec '90 / Direct.

YERSELF IS STEAM/LEGO IS MY EGO
CD _____ BBQCD 125
Beggars Banquet / Nov '92 / Warner Music / Disc.

Mercury, Freddie

BARCELONA (Mercury, Freddie & Montserrat Caballe)
Barcelona / Fallen priest / Golden boy / Guide me home / Overture piccante / La japonaise / Ensueno / Guid me home / How can I go on
CD _____ 837 277-2
Polydor / Oct '88 / PolyGram.

FREDDIE MERCURY ALBUM, THE
Great pretender / Foolin' around / Time / Your kind of lover / Exercises in free love / In my defence / Mr. Bad Guy / Let's turn it on / Living on my own / Love kills / Barcelona
CD _____ CDPCSD 124
Parlophone / Nov '92 / EMI.

MAN FROM MANHATTAN, THE (Mercury, Freddie & Brian May & Eddie Howell)
CD _____ BUD 002CD
Voice Print / Feb '95 / Voice Print.

Mercy

WITCHBURNER
CD _____ ERCD 921
Now & Then / Jul '92 / Plastic Head.

Merciful Fate

BEGINNING, THE
CD _____ RR 349603
Roadrunner / Nov '87 / Pinnacle.

BELLWITCH
CD _____ CDMZORRO 78
Metal Blade / Jun '94 / Pinnacle.

DON'T BREAK THE OATH
CD _____ RR 349835
Roadrunner / '89 / Pinnacle.

IN THE SHADOWS
Egypt / Bell Witch / Shadows / Gruesome time / Thirteen invitations / Room of golden air / Legend of the Headless river / Is that you Melissa / Return of the vampire
CD _____ CDZORRO 61
Metal Blade / Jun '93 / Pinnacle.

MELISSA
CD _____ RR 349898
Roadrunner / '89 / Pinnacle.

RETURN OF THE VAMPIRE
CD _____ RR 91842
Roadrunner / May '92 / Pinnacle.

TIME
CD _____ CDZORRO 80
Metal Blade / Oct '94 / Pinnacle.

Mercyland

SPILLAGE
Minutes and parts / Who hangs behind your eyes / Mr. Right / Service economy / Uncle / Eula Geary is dead / Like a whore / Waiting for the garbage can / John D. White / Freight truck / Touch ass twelve / Do you know what I mean / Tears towards heaven / Guessing time is gone / Fall of the city / Imperial vision / Black on black on black / Ciderhead / Amerigod / Burning bath

CD _____ RCD 10314
Rykodisc / Oct '94 / Vital / ADA.

Mercyless

ABJECT OFFERINGS
CD _____ FT 05035
Flametrader / Apr '94 / Plastic Head.

COLOURED FUNERAL
CD _____ CM 77054-2
Century Media / Nov '93 / Plastic Head.

Mergener, Peter

BEAM SCAPE (Mergener, Peter & Michael Weisser)
CD _____ 710 046
Innovative Communication / Apr '90 / Magnum Music Group.

Meridian Arts Ensemble

ZAPPA/BEEFHEART/BABBIT
CD _____ CCS 8195
Channel Classics / Dec '95 / Vital/SAM / Select.

ZAPPA/HENDRIX/NUROCK
CD _____ CCS 4192
Channel Classics / Dec '95 / Vital/SAM / Select.

Merino Brothers

VALLENTINO DYNAMOS
De mi vida una ilusion / Acompaname a sufrir / Mal procedimiento / La democracia / Riquezas de la vida / Minutos felices / Ese soy yo / Maria Elena / Noches de desvelos / Mi padre el campesino
CD _____ CDORB 049
Globestyle / Nov '89 / Pinnacle.

Merlons Of Nehemiah

CANTONEY
CD _____ EFA 11395-2
Musical Tragedies / Jan '94 / SRD.

ROMANOIR
CD _____ EFA 122222
Musical Tragedies / Apr '95 / SRD.

Merman, Ethel

EARFUL OF MERMAN, AN
I got rhythm / Sam and Delilah / Shake well / Eadie was a lady / Animal in me / Spanish custom / He reminds me of you / Earful of music / Shake it off with rhythm / You're the top / Shanghai-de-ho / Riding high / It's delovely / Hot and happy / You are the music to the words in my heart / Heatwave / Marching along with time / This is it / I'll pay the check / Friendship / Make it another old-fashioned please / Let's be buddies
CD _____ CMSCD 015
Movie Stars / May '94 / Conifer.

I GET A KICK OUT OF YOU
CD _____ PASTCD 7056
Flapper / Jan '95 / Pinnacle.

MERMAN SINGS MERMAN
You're the top / I got rhythm / You're just in love / Alexander's ragtime band / I got lost in his arms / Eadie was a lady / There's no business like show business / They say it's wonderful / It's de-lovely / I get a kick out of you / Everything's coming up roses / Blow Gabriel blow
CD _____ 8440862
Deram / Aug '92 / PolyGram.

Merricks

IN SCHWIERIGKEITEN
CD _____ EFA 155462
Sub Up / Apr '95 / SRD.

Merrill, Helen

BROWNIE
CD _____ 5223632
Verve / Dec '94 / PolyGram.

CLEAR OUT OF THIS WORLD
Out of this world / Not like this / I'm all smiles / When I grow too old to dream / Some of these days / Maybe / Tender thing is love / Soon it's gonna rain / Willow weep for me
CD _____ 510 691-2
Emarcy / Jun '92 / PolyGram.

DREAM OF YOU
CD _____ 5140742
Verve / Feb '93 / PolyGram.

HELEN MERRILL WITH CLIFFORD BROWN (Merrill, Helen & Clifford Brown)
CD _____ 8382922
Emarcy / Jan '93 / PolyGram.

IN ITALY
CD _____ IRS 0063/5
Liuto / Aug '91 / Harmonia Mundi / Cadillac.

OUT OF THIS WORLD
CD _____ 5106912
Philips / Feb '92 / PolyGram.

Mertens, Henri

UNDER THE LINDEN
CD _____ TWI 8182
Les Disques Du Crepuscule / Jun '90 /
Discovery / ADA.

Mertens, Wim

AT HOME-NOT AT HOME
At home / Not at home
CD _____ TWI 047CD
Les Disques Du Crepuscule / Jul '88 / Dis-
covery / ADA.

FOR AMUSEMENT ONLY
Insert coin / Deluxe / 8 ball / Mystik / Fireball
/ Invader / Dog in / Gorf
CD _____ TWI 048CD
Les Disques Du Crepuscule / Jul '88 / Dis-
covery / ADA.

STRUGGLING FOR PLEASURE
Tavtour / Struggle for pleasure / Salernes /
Close cover / Bresque / Gentleman of
leisure
CD _____ TWI 189CD
Les Disques Du Crepuscule / Jul '88 / Dis-
covery / ADA.

VERGESSEN
Inergys / Circular breathing / Mildly sheem-
ing / Four mains / Multiple 12 / Inergys
(reprise)
CD _____ TWI 092CD
Les Disques Du Crepuscule / Jul '88 / Discovery / ADA.

WHISPER ME
CD _____ 01934111412
Windham Hill / Sep '05 / Pinnacle / DMQ /
ADA.

Merton, Johnny

**PARTY HITS NON-STOP (Merton,
Johnny Party Sound)**
Let's twist again / Roll over Beethoven /
Rock 'n' roll music / Hound dog / Twist and
shout / Baby come back / Black is black /
Hippy hippy shake / Bend me shape me /
Back in the USSR / Massachussetts / San
Francisco / Air that I breathe / All I have to
do is dream / California dreaming / Keep on
running / Hey tonight / Girls, girls, girls / Fox
on the run / Whiskey in the jar / Relax / Like
a virgin / Super trouper / Final countdown /
Mr. Vain / Sing hallelujah / Don't talk just
kiss / Rhythm is dancer / It's my life
CD _____ 333304
Music / Dec '95 / Target/BMG.

Merzbow

VENEREOLOGY
CD _____ RR 69102
Soliemloon Recordings / Mar '95 / Plastic
Head.

Merzy

MERZY
CD _____ MMT 3303CD
Shark / May '90 / Plastic Head.

Meshuggah

CONTRADICTIONS COLLAPSE
CD _____ NB 049CD
Nuclear Blast / Jun '95 / Plastic Head.

DESTROY ERASE
CD _____ NB 121DCD
Nuclear Blast / May '95 / Plastic Head.

NONE
CD _____ NB 102CD
Nuclear Blast / Jun '95 / Plastic Head.

Message

ART OF BLAKEY, THE
Mosaic / Eternal messenger / Blue moon /
Ping pong / Back in the day / Moanin' / Afro
soul / Great wall / Red, black and green / A
la mode
CD _____ KICJ 162
King/Paddle Wheel / Oct '93 / New Note.

Messaoud, Bellemou

LE PERE DU RAI
CD _____ WCD 011
World Circuit / May '89 / New Note /
Direct / Cadillac / ADA.

Messer, Michael

MOONBEAT
CD _____ AP 123
Appaloosa / Nov '95 / ADA / Magnum
Music Group.

Messiah

21ST CENTURY JESUS
Age of the machine / Beyond good and evil
/ Defiance / There is no law / Temple of
dreams / Creator / Peace and tranquility /
Thunderdome / Destroyer / I feel love /
20,000 hardcore members / Desire
CD _____ 450994393-2
WEA / Dec '93 / Warner Music.

Messiah

PSYCHOMORPHIA
CD _____ N 0180-3
Noise/Modern Music / '91 / Pinnacle /
Plastic Head.

ROTTEN PERISH
CD _____ NO 1952
Noise/Modern Music / Jul '92 / Pinnacle /
Plastic Head.

UNDERGROUND
CD _____ N 0244-2
Noise/Modern Music / Jun '94 / Pinnacle /
Plastic Head.

Messiah Force

LAST DAY, THE
Sequel / Watch out / White night / Hero's
saga / Third one / Call from the night / Spirit
killer / Silent tyrant / Last day
CD _____ BRMCD 022
Bold Reprive / Oct '88 / Pinnacle / Bold Reprive / Harmonia Mundi.

Meta

SONGS AND DANCES FROM HUNGARY
CD _____ EUCD 1068
ARC / '89 / ARC Music / ADA.

**WINTER AND CHRISTMAS SONGS
FROM HUNGARY**
CD _____ EUCD 1085
ARC / '91 / ARC Music / ADA.

Metal Church

HANGING IN THE BALANCE
CD _____ SPV 085-62170
SPV / May '94 / Plastic Head.

Metal Sound

METAL SOUND
CD _____ 503412
Declic / Apr '95 / Jetstar.

Metal Urbaine

L'AGE D'OR
CD _____ FC 011CD
Fan Club / Direct.

Metallica

AND JUSTICE FOR ALL
Blackened / Eye of the beholder / Shortest
straw / Frayed ends of sanity / Dyes eve /
And justice for all / One / Harvester of sor-
row / To live is to die
CD _____ 836 062-2
Vertigo / Oct '88 / PolyGram.

KILL 'EM ALL
Hit the lights / Four horsemen / Motorbreath
/ Jump in the fire / Pulling teeth (Anasthesia)
/ Whiplash / Phantom lord / No remorse /
Seek and destroy / Metal militia
CD _____ 8381422
Vertigo / May '89 / PolyGram.

MASTER OF PUPPETS
Battery / Master of puppets / Thing that
should not be / Welcome home (Sanitarium)
/ Disposable heroes / Leper messiah / Orion
/ Damage Inc.
CD _____ 8381412
Vertigo / May '89 / PolyGram.

**METAL MILITIA (A Tribute To Metallica)
(Various Artists)**
Disposable heroes / Leper messiah / For
whom the bell tolls / Fight fire with fire /
Battery / Escape / Motorbreath / Thing that
should not be / Damage Inc. / Eye of the
beholder / Fade to black
CD _____ BS 01CD
Dolores / Feb '95 / Plastic Head.

METALLICA
Enter sandman / Sad but true / Holier than
thou / Unforgiven / Wherever I may roam /
Don't tread on me / Through the never /
Nothing else matters / Of wolf and man /
God that failed / My friend of misery / Strug-
gle within
CD _____ 5100222
Vertigo / Aug '91 / PolyGram.

**METALLICA: INTERVIEW COMPACT
DISC**
CD P.Disc _____ CBAK 4016
Baktabak / Nov '89 / Baktabak.

**METALLICA: INTERVIEW COMPACT
DISC II**
CD P.Disc _____ CBAK 4053
Baktabak / Apr '92 / Baktabak.

RIDE THE LIGHTNING
Fight fire with fire / Ride the lightning / For
whom the bell tolls / Fade to black /
Trapped under ice / Escape / Creeping
death / Call of Ktulu
CD _____ 8384102
Vertigo / May '89 / PolyGram.

Metamora

DALGLISH-LARSEN-SUTHERLAND
CD _____ SHCD 1131
Sugarhill / May '95 / Roots / CM / ADA /
Direct.

Meteors

BEST OF THE METEORS, THE
Voodoo rhythm / Graveyard stomp /
Wreckin' crew / Mutant rock / Hills have
eyes / Johnny remember me / When a
stranger calls / I don't worry about it / I'm
just a dog / Stampede / Fire, fire / Hogs and
cuties / Bad moon rising / Rhythm of the
bell / Surf city / Go Buddy go / Don't touch
the bang bang fruit / Swamp thing / Rawhide / Surfin' on the planet zorch / Somebody put something in my drink / Please
don't touch / Chainsaw boogie / Madman
roll / Who do you love
CD _____ CDMGRAM 66
Anagram / Sep '93 / Pinnacle.

**GRAVEYARD STOMP (Best Of The
Meteors 1981-1988)**
Voodoo rhythm / Graveyard stomp /
Wreckin' crew / Sick things / Blue sunshine
/ Mutant rock / Hills have ears / Michael My-
ers / Bad moon rising / Fire fire / Power of
steel / Eat the baby / Rhythm of the bell /
Surf city / Go Buddy go / Somebody put
something in my drink / Don't touch the
bang bang fruit / Corpse grinder
CD _____ NTMCD 508
Nectar / Sep '95 / Pinnacle.

LIVE, LEARY AND FUCKING LOUD
Wipeout / Maniac rockers from hell / Lonesome train / I ain't ready / Ain't gonna bring
me down / Sick things / Crazy lovin' / When
a stranger calls / Rawhide / I don't worry
about it / Voodoo rhythm / You crack me
up / Mutant rock / Graveyard stomp /
Wreckin' crew / Long blonde hair
CD _____ DOJOCD 213
Dojo / Jun '06 / BMG.

LIVES OF THE SICK AND SHAMELESS
Ex man boogie / Wipeout / Rattlesnakin'
daddy / Mutant rock / Maniac / Blue sunshine / Mind over matter / These boots are
made for walking / Little Red Riding Hood /
Hills have eyes / Wild thing / I go to bed
with the undead / Voodoo rhythm / I ain't
ready / Wreckin' crew / Lonesome train (CD
only) / Rock bop (CD only) / Ain't gonna
bring me down (CD only) / Graveyard stomp
(CD only)
CD _____ CDGRAM 45
Anagram / May '90 / Pinnacle.

**MUTANT MONKEY AND THE SURFERS
FROM ZORCH**
Swamp thing / Electro II (the revenge) / Side
walk psycho / I'm invisible man / She's my
baby again / Surfin' on the planet Zorch /
Spine bender / Dance crazy baby / Rawhide
/ Oxygen dog / Zombie stomp / Meet me in
the morgue
CD _____ CDGRAM 37
Anagram / Jul '89 / Pinnacle.

**ONLY THE METEORS ARE PURE
PSYCHOBILLY**
Voodoo rhythm / Graveyard stomp /
Wreckin' crew / Sick things / Blue sunshine
/ Mutant rock / Hills have eyes / Fire, fire /
Power of steel / Eat the baby / Rhythm of
the bell / Sure city / Go buddy go / Some-
body put something in my drink
CD _____ CDMGRAM 33
Anagram / Mar '88 / Pinnacle.

SEWERTIME BLUES
Ain't taking a chance / So sad / Here's
Johnny / Mind over matter / Acid and
psyam / Sewertime blues / Return of Ethel
Merman / Deep dark jungle / Never get
away / I bury the living / Vibrate / Surf city
/ Go Buddy go / Midnight people / Low livin'
daddy / Your worst nightmare / Wildkat
wave / Reno man / Don't touch the bang
bang fruit / Crack me up / Shaky shaky /
Psycho kat / Let's go / Revenge of the el
trio los bastados
CD _____ CDMPSYCHO 3
Anagram / Apr '91 / Pinnacle.

STAMPEDE/MONKEY BREATH
Ex man boogie / Power of steel / Hoover
rock / Kit boy / Maybe tomorrow / Electro /
Stampede / Just a dog / In too deep / Cecil
drives a combine harvester / Michael Myers
/ Only a fury in my heart / Hogs and cuties
/ Alligator man / Rhythm of the bell / You're
out of time / Ain't gonna bring me down /
Night uf the werewulf / Take a ride / Just
the three of us / Meat is meat / Jobba's
revenge
CD _____ CDMPSYCHO 9
Anagram / Oct '95 / Pinnacle.

TEENAGERS FROM OUTER SPACE
Voodoo rhythm / Maniac rockers from hell
/ My daddy is a vampire / You can't keep
a good man down / Graveyard stomp /
Radioactive kid / Leave me alone / Dog eat
robot / Walter Mitty blues / Just the three
of us / Blue sunshine / Insight / Attack of
the zorch men / Jupiter stroll / Another half
hour till sunrise (CD only) / Island of lost
souls (CD only) / Napoleon solo (CD only) /
Get me to the world on time (CD only)
CD _____ CDWIK 47
Big Beat / May '86 / Pinnacle.

**UNDEAD, UNFRIENDLY AND
UNSTOPPABLE**
Razor back / Disneyland / My kind of rockin'
/ Lonesome train / Johnny God / I go to bed
with the undead / Out of the attic / Brains
as well / Charlie Johnny Rawhead and me

/ Lies in wait / Surf mad pig / Please don't
touch
CD _____ CDMPSYCHO 2
Cherry Red / Apr '95 / Pinnacle.

WRECKIN' CREW
Wreckin' crew / Scream of the mutants /
Hills have eyes / Mutant rock / I don't worry
about it / Zombie noise / Rattlesnakin'
Daddy / When a stranger calls / Blue sun-
shine / Sick things / Wild things / I'm not
giving up my cloud / Insane / I ain't ready
/ Johnny remember me
CD _____ DOJOCD 121
Dojo / Apr '93 / BMG.

Meters

**CRESCENT CITY GROOVE
MERCHANTS**
CD _____ CPCD 8066
Charly / Nov '94 / Charly / THE / Cadillac.

FUNDAMENTALLY FUNKY
CD _____ CPCD 8044
Charly / Jun '94 / Charly / THE / Cadillac.

FUNKY MIRACLE
CD _____ CDNEV 2
Charly / Mar '91 / Charly / THE / Cadillac.

GOOD OLD FUNKY MUSIC
Look-ka-py-py / Seahorn's farm / Art / Ease
back / Cissy strut / Message from the Meters / Thinking / Good old funky music / Live
wire / Stretch your rubber band / Doodle-
opp / Tippi toes / Rigor mortis / Nine to five
/ Sophisticated Cissy / Chicken strut / Here
come the metermen / Darling darling / Dry
spell / Ride your pony
CD _____ ROUCD 2104
Rounder / Dec '94 / CM / Direct / ADA /
Cadillac.

**SECOND HELPING (Meters & J.B.
Horns)**
CD _____ LAKE 2026
Lakeside / Aug '95 / Magnum Music
Group.

**UPTOWN RULERS (Live On The Queen
Mary 1975)**
Fire on the bayou / Africa / It ain't no use /
Make it with you / Cissy strut / Cardova /
It's your thing / Love the one you're with /
Rockin' pneumonia and the boogie woogie
flu / I know / Everybody loves a lover / Liar
/ Mardi gras mambo / Hey pocky away
CD _____ NEXCD 220
Sequel / Sep '92 / BMG.

Metheny, Pat

80-81 (2CD Set)
Goin' ahead / Two folk songs / Bat / Turn
around / Open / Pretty scattered / Everyday
I thank you
CD Set _____ 843 169 2
ECM / Oct '90 / New Note.

AMERICAN GARAGE
(Cross the) Heartland / Airstream / Search /
American garage / Epic
CD _____ 8271342
ECM / Dec '85 / New Note.

**AS FALLS WICHITA, SO FALLS
WICHITA FALLS (Metheny, Pat & Lyle
Mays)**
As falls Wichita, so falls Wichita Falls / Sep-
tember 15th / It's for you / Estupenda graca
CD _____ 8214162
ECM / Jul '85 / New Note.

BRIGHT SIZE LIFE
Bright size life / Sirabhorn / Unity village /
Missouri uncompromised / Midwestern
nights dream / Unquity road / Omaha cel-
ebration / Round trip-Broadway blues
CD _____ 8271332
ECM / Dec '86 / New Note.

FIRST CIRCLE (Metheny, Pat Group)
Forward march / Yolanda / You learn / First
circle / If I could / Tell it all / End of the game
/ Mas alla (beyond) / Praise
CD _____ 8233422
ECM / Nov '84 / New Note.

NEW CHAUTAUQUA
New chautauqua / Country poem / Long
ago (child) / Fallen star / Hermitage / Sueno
con Mexico / Daybreak
CD _____ 8254712
ECM / Aug '85 / New Note.

OFFRAMP
Barcarolle / Are you going with me / Au lait
/ Eighteen / Offramp / James / Bat (part 2)
CD _____ 8171382
ECM / Sep '84 / New Note.

**PAT METHENY GROUP (Metheny, Pat
Group)**
San Lorenzo / Phase dance / Jaco / April-
wind / April joy / Lone jack
CD _____ 8255932
ECM / Aug '88 / New Note.

**QUESTION AND ANSWER (Metheny,
Pat/Dave Holland/Roy Haynes)**
Solar / Question and answer / H and H /
Never too far away / Law years / Change of
heart / All the things you are / Old folks /
Three flights up
CD _____ GFLD 19197
Geffen / Mar '93 / BMG.

REJOICING
Lonely woman / Tears inside / Humpty dumpty / Blues for Pat / Rejoicing / Story from a stranger / Calling / Waiting for an answer
CD _____ 8177952
ECM / Jun '84 / New Note.

ROAD TO YOU, THE
Have you heard / First circle / Road to you / Half life of absolution / Last train home / Better days ahead / Naked moon / Beat 70 / Letter from home / Third wind / Solo from More travels
CD _____ GED 24601
Geffen / Jul '93 / BMG.

SECRET STORY
Above the treetops / Facing west / Cathedral in a suitcase / Finding and believing / Longest summer / Sunlight / Rain river / Always and forever / See the world / As a flower blossoms (I am running to you) / Antonia / Truth will always be / Tell her you saw me / Not to be forgotten (our final our)
CD _____ GEFD 24468
Geffen / Jul '92 / BMG.

STILL LIFE TALKING (Metheny, Pat Group)
Minuano / So may it secretly begin / Last train home / It's just talk / Third wind / Distance / In her family
CD _____ GFLD 19196
Geffen / Mar '93 / BMG.

TRAVELS (2CD Set) (Metheny, Pat Group)
Are you going with me / Freeway, the sky / Goodbye / Phase dance / Straight on red / Farmer's trust / Extradition / Goin' ahead / As falls Wichita, so falls Wichita Falls / Travels / Song for Bilbao / San Lorenzo
CD Set _____ 8106222
ECM / Aug '86 / New Note.

WATERCOLORS
Watercolors / Icefire / Lakes / River Quay / Florida Greeting song / Legend of the fountain / Sea song
CD _____ 8274092
ECM / Feb '86 / New Note.

WE LIVE HERE
Here to stay / And then I knew / Girls next door / To the end of the world / We live here / Episode d'azur / Something to remind you / Red sky / Stranger in town
CD _____ GED 24729
Geffen / Jan '95 / BMG.

ZERO TOLERANCE FOR SILENCE
CD _____ GED 24626
Geffen / Apr '94 / BMG.

Method Man

TICAL
CD _____ 5238392
Def Jam / Dec '94 / PolyGram.

Methodist Central Hall...

20 FAVOURITE HYMNS OF CHARLES WESLEY (Methodist Central Hall Choir)
O for a thousand tongues to sing / Lo he comes with clouds descending / Father of everlasting grace / Forth in thy name, O lord, I go / Charge to keep I have / Captain of Israel's host / Happy the man that finds the grace / All praise to our redeeming lord / Jesu lover of my soul / Ye servants of God / Come sinners to the gospel feast / Christ, whose glory fills the skies / Jesus the first and last / Thou God of truth and love / Earth rejoice, our lord is king / What shall I do my lord to love / O thou who camest from above / Let earth and heaven agree / Come thou long expected Jesus / And can it be that I should gain
CD _____ CDMVP 828
SCS Music / Apr '94 / Conifer.

Metri

METRI
CD _____ SAHK 0006
Sahko / Apr '94 / Plastic Head.

Metro

TREE PEOPLE
CD _____ LIP 890312
Lipstick / Sep '95 / Vital/SAM.

Metura, Philip

SENTIMENTAL LOVE
CD _____ LM 6073-2
Melodie / '91 / Triple Earth / Discovery / ADA / Jetstar.

Metz, Henrik

HENRIK METZ, FREDRIK LUNDIN & NIELS PEDERSON (Metz, Henrik & Fredrik Lundin/Niels Pederson)
CD _____ MECCACD 1024
Music Mecca / Oct '93 / Jazz Music / Cadillac / Wellard.

Meurkens, Hendrik

CLEAR OF CLOUDS
Samba for Claudio / Clear of clouds / Seu acalento / Mambo inn / Estate / Chega de

sudada/To Brenda with love / Hesitation / Beauty and the priest / You go to my head / Joe's donut / Allan's theme
CD _____ CCD 4531
Concord Picante / Nov '92 / New Note.

OCTOBER COLORS
October colors / Who did it / In motion / Night in the afternoon / Brigas, nunca mais / Footprints / Chorinho no 1 / Summer in San Francisco / Tranchan / High tide
CD _____ CCD 4670
Concord Jazz / Nov '95 / New Note.

SLIDIN'
Come rain or come shine / Have you met Miss Jones / Slidin' / Cottage / Bolero para paquito / All of you / Stolen moments / Fortuna / Tribute / Voyage / Once was / Talking trout
CD _____ CCD 4628
Concord Jazz / Jan '95 / New Note.

VIEW FROM MANHATTAN, A
Meet any after dark / Whisper not / Park Avenue South / Speak low / Naima / Prague in March / Monster and the flower / Body and soul / Madison Square / Moment's notice / Child is born
CD _____ CCD 4585
Concord Jazz / Dec '93 / New Note.

Mexican Mariachi Band

MARIACHI FROM MEXICO
CD _____ 15284
Laserlight / '91 / Target/BMG.

Mexico 70

DUST HAS COME TO STAY, THE
Wonderful lie / Just like we never came down / What's in your mind / Sacred heart / I feel fine / Drug is the love / All day long / Find someone else to play Misty / For you / Always by your side / Queen of swords / You make it worse / Make it right / Kenton's lane
CD _____ CDBRED 101
Cherry Red / Jun '92 / Pinnacle.

Mey, Reinhard

DIE GROSSEN ERFOLGE
CD _____ INT. 860 191
Interchord / '88 / CM.

DIE ZWOLFTE
CD _____ INT 865 001
Interchord / '88 / CM.

Meyer, Liz

WOMANLY ARTS
CD _____ SCR 37
Strictly Country / Dec '94 / ADA / Direct.

Meyer, Richard

LETTER FROM THE OPEN SKY, A
CD _____ SHCD 8012
Shanachie / Dec '94 / Koch / ADA / Greensleeves.

Meyers, Augie

WHITE BOY
CD _____ MWCD 2019
Music & Words / Dec '95 / ADA / Direct.

Meza, Lisandro

AMOR LINDO
CD _____ TUMICD 017
Tumi / '91 / Sterns / Discovery.

CUMBIAS COLOMBIANAS
CD _____ TUMICD 046
Tumi / '94 / Sterns / Discovery.

Mezcla

FRONTERAS DE SUENOS
La Guagua / Fronteras de Suenos / La mulata de Caramelo / Ikiri adda / Rio quibu / Vivir para ver / Como una campana de cristal / Muros transparentes / Ando buscando uno amor
CD _____ INT 30472
Intuition / Feb '91 / New Note.

Mezzrow, Mezz

KING JAZZ VOL 1 (Mezzrow-Bechet Quintet & Septet)
CD _____ KJ 101FS
King Jazz / Oct '93 / Jazz Music / Cadillac / Discovery.

KING JAZZ VOL 2 (Mezzrow-Bechet Quintet & Septet)
CD _____ KJ 102FS
King Jazz / Oct '93 / Jazz Music / Cadillac / Discovery.

KING JAZZ VOL 3 (Mezzrow-Bechet Quintet & Septet)
CD _____ KJ 103FS
King Jazz / Oct '93 / Jazz Music / Cadillac / Discovery.

KING JAZZ VOL 4 (Mezzrow-Bechet Quintet & Septet)
CD _____ KJ 104FS
King Jazz / Oct '93 / Jazz Music / Cadillac / Discovery.

MAKIN' FRIENDS
CD _____ 158042
Jazz Archives / Sep '93 / Jazz Music / Discovery / Cadillac.

MEZZ MEZZROW 1928-36
CD _____ CLASSICS 713
Classics / Jul '93 / Discovery / Jazz Music.

MEZZ MEZZROW 1936-1939
CD _____ CLASSICS 694
Classic Jazz Masters / May '93 / Wellard / Jazz Music / Jazz Music.

MEZZROW/BECHET QUINTET/SEPTET (Mezzrow-Bechet Quintet & Septet)
CD _____ STCD 8212
Storyville / May '93 / Jazz Music / Wellard / CM / Cadillac.

MEZZROW/BECHET QUINTET/SEPTET VOL.2 (Mezzrow-Bechet Quintet & Septet)
CD _____ STCD 8213
Storyville / May '93 / Jazz Music / Wellard / CM / Cadillac.

MEZZROW/BECHET QUINTET/SEPTET VOL.3
CD _____ STCD 8214
Storyville / May '93 / Jazz Music / Wellard / CM / Cadillac.

MEZZROW/BECHET QUINTET/SEPTET VOL.4
CD _____ STCD 8215
Storyville / May '93 / Jazz Music / Wellard / CM / Cadillac.

MFSB

LOVE IS THE MESSAGE
Interlude / Love is the message / Poinciana / Freddie's dead / My one and only love / Sexy / Something for nothing / Zack's fanfare (I hear music) / Back Stabbers / Bitter sweet / TSOP (The sound of Philadelphia) / Cheaper to keep her / My mood / T.L.C. (Tender lovin' care) / Philadelphia freedom / Smile happy
CD _____ 4809042
Columbia / Jan '96 / Sony.

Mhlongo, Busi

BABHEMU
Izinziswa / Ting-tingu (Cash dispenser) / Unomkhubulwane (African angel) / Umenthisi (Matches) / Shosholoza (Keep going) / Mfazonga phesheva (Woman from abroad) / Ujantshi (Rails) / Ntandane (Orphan)
CD _____ STCD 1053
Sterns / Mar '94 / Sterns / CM.

Mhoireach, Anna

OUT OF THE BLUE
CD _____ CDLDL 1219
Lochshore / Nov '94 / ADA / Direct / Duncans.

Miah, Shahjahan

MYSTICAL BAUL SONGS OF BANGLADESH
CD _____ AUW 260039
Auvidis/Ethnic / Feb '93 / Harmonia Mundi.

Miasma 1195

EMIT 1195
CD _____ EMIT 1195
Time Recordings / Mar '95 / Pinnacle.

Mic Force

IT AIN'T OVER
CD _____ MOVE 7009-2
We Bite / Apr '94 / Plastic Head.

Michael Learns To Rock

MICHAEL LEARNS TO ROCK
My blue angel / Looking at love / Kiss in the rain / Actor / Messages / I still carry on / Crazy dream / African Queen / Come on and dance / Let's build a room
CD _____ CDEMC 3625
Impact/EMI / Aug '92 / EMI.

Michael, George

FAITH
Faith / Father figure / I want your sex (pts 1 & 2) / One more try / Hard day / Hand to mouth / Look at your hands / Monkey / Kissing a fool / Last request (I want your sex, pt 3) (Not on LP)
CD _____ 4600002
Epic / Nov '87 / Sony.

LISTEN WITHOUT PREJUDICE VOLUME 1
Praying for time / Freedom 90 / They won't go when I go / Something to save / Cowboys and angels / Waiting for that day / Mothers pride / Heal the pain / Soul free / Waiting (Reprise)
CD _____ 4672952
Epic / Sep '90 / Sony.

Michael, Walt

MUSIC FOR HAMMERED DULCIMER
CD _____ EP 101
Eastwick Productions / Mar '94 / Inform.

STEP STONE
CD _____ FF 70480
Flying Fish / Apr '94 / Roots / CM / Direct / ADA.

Michaels, Lee

COLLECTION
CD _____ 8122703742
WEA / Jul '93 / Warner Music.

Michel, Matthieu

ESTATE
Leaving / Never let me go / Moon princess / It could be worse / Estate / Round trip / Sail away / Caruso / On the spot / Moment to moment
CD _____ TCB 95802
TCB / Dec '95 / New Note.

Michelle Baresi

BERLIN & POGO
CD _____ EFA 800402
Twah / Sep '95 / SRD.

Michigan & Smiley

DOWNPRESSION (Michigan, Papa & General Smiley)
Downpression / Natty heng on in deh / Come when Jah call you / Ghetto man / Jah army / Diseases / Living in a babylon / Jah know / Arise / Come on black people
CD _____ GRELCD 42
Greensleeves / Aug '95 / Total/BMG / Jetstar / SRD.

RUB A DUB STYLE
CD _____ HBCD 3512
Heartbeat / May '92 / Greensleeves / Jetstar / Direct / CM.

SUGAR DADDY
CD _____ RASCD 3004
Ras / Nov '92 / Jetstar / Greensleeves / SRD / Direct.

Michigan State University

TRIBUTE (featuring Steven Mead)
Original fantasie / Night in June / From the shores of the mighty Pacific / Rhapsody / Beautiful Colorado / Concertino / Fanrasia di concerto / Estrellita / Atlantic Zephyrs / Believe me, if all those endearing young charms / Flower Song / Auld lang syne
CD _____ QPRM 118D
Polyphonic / Aug '92 / Conifer.

Mickey & Ludella

BEDLAM A GO-GO
That look that you gave to me / I believed your lies / Stop and listen / Ain't nobody's friend / I'm afraid they're all talkin about me / Tell me / Surfin' snow matador / Bedlam a go-go / Bring it back / Do I expect to much / Standing next to the railway track / We're gonna get married / I'm on the way down / She's drunk / Well now
CD _____ ASKCD 052
Vinyl Japan / Jan '96 / Vital.

Mickey & Sylvia

LOVE IS STRANGE (2CD Set)
Forever and a day / Se de boom run dun / I'm so glad / Rise Sally rise / Seems like just yesterday / Peace of mind / No good lover / Love is strange / Walkin' in the rain / Two shadows on your window / Who knows why / In my heart / I'm gonna home / Two shadows on your window (with chorus) / There oughta be a law / Dearest / Where is my honey / Too much weight / Let's have a picnic / New sides on love / Say the word / Love will make you fall in school / I gotta be home by ten / Love is a treasure / Loving you darling / I'm working at the five and dime / Shake it up / There'll be no backin' out / Summertime / Rock and stroll room (take 1) / Rock and stroll room (take 12) / It's you love / True, true, love / Bewildered (Take 2) / Oh yeah! Uh huh / To the valley / Mommy out de light / Gonna work out fine / What would I do / Sweeter as the days goes by / I'm glad for your sake / I hear you knocking / Love lesson / This is my story / Baby you're so fine / Love is the only thing / Dearsest / From the beginning of time / Fallin' in love / Gypsy / Yours / Let's shake some more
CD Set _____ BCD 15438
Bear Family / May '90 / Rollercoaster / Direct / CM / Swift / ADA.

WILLOW SESSIONS
Love is strange / He gave me everything / Love drops / Hucklebuck / Baby you're so fine / Mickey's blues / Anytime / Darling (I miss you so) / Walking in the rain / I'm guilty / Loving you darling / Sylvia's blues / Since I fell for you / Love is the only thing / I can't help it / Our name (alternative take) / Because you do it to me / Soulin' with Mickey and Sylvia

CD _____ **NEM 763**
Sequel / Jan '96 / BMG.

Microdisney

BIG SLEEPING HOUSE (A Collection Of Choice Cuts)
Horse overboard / Loftholdingswood / Singer's Hampstead home / She only gave in to her anger / Gale force wind / I can't say no / Angels / Mrs. Simpson / Armadillo man / And he descended into hell / Rack / Big sleeping house / Back to the old town / Send Herman home / Town to town / Begging bowl
CD _____ **CDOVD 452**
Virgin / Feb '95 / EMI.

PEEL SESSIONS: MICRODISNEY
Sun / Moon / Everybody is dead / Friend with a big mouth / Teddy dogs / Before famine / 7 464 / Loftholdingswood / Horse overboard / Town to town / Bullwhip road / Begging bowl
CD _____ **SFRCD 105**
Strange Fruit / Nov '94 / Pinnacle.

Microscopic 7

BEAUTY BASED ON SCIENCE
CD _____ **STCD 8**
Stash / May '89 / Jazz Music / CM / Cadillac / Direct / ADA.

Microstoria

INIT DING
CD _____ **EFA 006672**
Mille Plateau / Oct '95 / SRD.

Micus, Stephan

ATHOS
CD _____ **5232922**
ECM / Sep '94 / New Note.

DARKNESS AND LIGHT
CD _____ **8472722**
ECM / Dec '90 / New Note.

EAST OF THE NIGHT
East of the night / For Nobuko
CD _____ **8256552**
ECM / Mar '88 / New Note.

LISTEN TO THE RAIN
For Abai and Togshan / Dancing with the morning / Listen to the rain / White paint on silver wood
CD _____ **8156142**
ECM / '88 / New Note.

OCEAN
Part 1 / Part II / Part III / Part IV
CD _____ **8292792**
ECM / Jun '86 / New Note.

TILL THE END OF TIME
CD _____ **5137862**
ECM / '88 / New Note.

TO THE EVENING CHILD
Nomad song / Yuko's eyes / Young moon / To the evening child / Morgenstern / Equinox / Desert poem
CD _____ **5137802**
ECM / Sep '92 / New Note.

TWILIGHT FIELDS
CD _____ **8350852**
ECM / Feb '88 / New Note.

WINGS OVER WATER
CD _____ **8310582**
ECM / Aug '88 / New Note.

Middle Of The Road

MIDDLE OF THE ROAD
CD _____ **295594**
Ariola / Dec '92 / BMG.

Middleton, Arthur

HARMONICA FAVOURITES
CD _____ **CDR 012**
Donside / Oct '89 / Ross.

Middleton-Pollock,...

DOLL'S HOUSE, A (Middleton-Pollock, Marilyn)
CD _____ **FE 006CD**
Fellside / Feb '87 / Target/BMG / Direct / ADA.

MARILYN MIDDLETON POLLOCK & LAKE RECORDS ALL STAR JAZZ BAND (Middleton-Pollock, Marilyn)
CD _____ **LACD 35**
Lake / Oct '94 / Target/BMG / Jazz Music / Direct / Cadillac / ADA.

RED HOT AND BLUE (Middleton-Pollock, Marilyn)
CD _____ **LACD 42**
Lake / Jan '95 / Target/BMG / Jazz Music / Direct / Cadillac / ADA.

THOSE WOMEN OF THE VAUDEVILLE BLUES (Middleton-Pollock, Marilyn)
Miss Jenny's blues / Aggravatin' papa / Handyman / Barrelhouse blues / It's just like that / Moanin' the blues / Mighty tight woman / Trouble in mind / Hot time in the old town / Last journey blues / Wild women don't get the blues / Dark man / I got a mind

to ramble / St. Louis blues / Women don't need no mens / Nobody knows you (when you're down and out) / Some of these days
CD _____ **LACD 18**
Lake / Feb '91 / Target/BMG / Jazz Music / Direct / Cadillac / ADA.

Midi Rain

ONE
CD _____ **STEAM 56CD**
Vinyl Solution / Jul '94 / Disc.

Midler, Bette

BETTE OF ROSES
CD _____ **7567828232**
Atlantic / Nov '95 / Warner Music.

BROKEN BLOSSOM
Empty bed blues / Dream is a wish your heart makes / Paradise / Yellow umbrella / La vie en rose / Make yourself comfortable / You don't know me / Say goodbye to Hollywood / I never talk to strangers / Storybook children / Red
CD _____ **756780410-2**
Atlantic / Dec '93 / Warner Music.

EXPERIENCE THE DIVINE BETTE MIDLER (The Greatest Hits Of Bette Midler)
Hello in there / Do you want to dance / From a distance / Chapel of love / Only in Miami / When a man loves a woman / Rose / Miss Otis regrets / Shiver me timbers / Wind beneath my wings / Boogie woogie bugle boy / One for my baby (and one more for the road) / Friends / In my life
CD _____ **756782497-2**
Atlantic / Oct '93 / Warner Music.

LIVE AT LAST
Hospital: friends / Oh my my / Bang you're dead / Birds / Comic relief / In the mood / Hurry on down / Shiver me timbers / Vicki Eydie show around the world / Istanbul / Fiesta in Rio / South seas scene / Hawaiian war chant / Lullaby of Broadway / Intermission / Delta town / Long John blues / Those wonderful Sophie Tucker jokes / Story of Nanette / Nanette / Alabama song / Drinking again / Mr. Rockefeller / Boogie to begin again / Do you wanna dance / Hello in there / Up the ladder to the roof / Boogie woogie bugle boy / Friends
CD _____ **756781461-2**
Atlantic / Dec '93 / Warner Music.

SOME PEOPLES LIVES
One more round / Some people's lives / Miss Otis regrets / Spring can really hang you up the most / Night and day / Girl is on to you / From a distance / Moonlight dancing / He was too good to me/Since you stayed here / All of a sudden / Gift of love
CD _____ **8567821292**
Atlantic / Sep '90 / Warner Music.

Midnight Configuration

GOTHTEC
CD _____ **NIGHTMCD 001**
Nightbreed / Mar '94 / Plastic Head.

SPECTARAL DANCE
CD _____ **NIGHTMAXICD 003**
Nightbreed / Nov '94 / Plastic Head.

Midnight Oil

10,9,8,7,6,5,4,3,2,1
Outside world / Only the strong / Short memory / Read about it / Scream in blue / U.S. Forces / Power and the passion / Maralinga / Tinlegs and tin mines / Somebody's trying to tell me something
CD _____ **4624862**
CBS / '91 / Sony.

BLUE SKY MINING
Blue sky mining / Stars of Warburton / Bedlam bridge / Forgotten years / Mountains of Burma / King of the mountain / River runs red / Shakers and movers / One country / Antarctica
CD _____ **465653 2**
Columbia / Sep '93 / Sony.

DIESEL AND DUST
Beds are burning / Put down that weapon / Dreamworld / Arctic world / Warakuma / Dead heart / Woah / Bullroarer / Sell my soul / Sometimes
CD _____ **4600052**
CBS / May '88 / Sony.

DIESEL AND DUST/HEAD INJURIES/MIDNIGHT OIL (3CD Set)
Beds are burning / Put down that weapon / Dreamworld / Artic world / Warakuma / Dead heart / Whoah / Bullroarer / Sell my soul / Sometimes / Cold cold change / Section 5 (bus to Bondi) / Naked flame / Back on the borderline / Koala sprint / No reaction / Stand in line / Profiteers / Is it now / Powderworks / Head over heels / Dust used and abused / Surfing with a spoon / Run by night / Nothing lost, nothing gained
CD Set _____ **477520 2**
Columbia / Oct '94 / Sony.

EARTH AND SUN AND MOON
Feeding frenzy / My country / Renaissance man / Earth and sun and moon / Truganini / Bush fire / Drums of heaven / Outbreak of

love / In the valley / Tell me the truth / Now or never land
CD _____ **473605 2**
Columbia / Apr '93 / Sony.

MIDNIGHT OIL
Powderworks / Head over heels / Dust used and abused / Surfing with a spoon / Run by night / Nothing lost, nothing gained
CD _____ **4509022**
CBS / May '94 / Sony.

RED SAILS.../PLACE WITHOUT A POSTCARD/10,9,8,7,6,5,4,3,2,1 (3CD Set)
CD Set _____ **4673922**
CBS / Dec '90 / Sony.

SCREAM IN BLUE
Scream in blue / Read about it / Dreamworld / Brave faces / Only the strong / Stars of Warburton / Progress / Beds are burning / Sell my soul / Sometimes / Hercules / Powderworks / Burnie
CD _____ **41714532**
Columbia / May '92 / Sony.

Midnight Star

BEST OF MIDNIGHT STAR, THE
I've been watching you / Hot spot / Feels so good / Playmates / Scientific love / Headlines / Don't rock the boat / I won't let you be lonely / Wet my whistle / Curious / Let's celebrate / Operator / Midas touch
CD _____ **NEMCD 682**
Sequel / Nov '94 / BMG.

VERY BEST OF MIDNIGHT STAR, THE
Headlines / Midas touch / Freakazoid / Operator / Engine No. 9 / Electricity / No parking on the dancefloor / Make it last / Slow jam / Luv u up / Wet my whistle / Victory / Money can't buy you love / Work it out / Snake in the grass / Heartbeat
CD _____ **CCSCD 805**
Renaissance Collector Series / Sep '95 / BMG.

WORK IT OUT
Do it (one more time) / Work it out / All I want / Money can't buy you love / Love of my life / Luv-u-up / Red roses / One life to live / If walls could talk / Take your shoes off
CD _____ **983252 2**
Pickwick/Sony Collector's Choice / Aug '93 / Carlton Home Entertainment / Pinnacle / Sony.

Midway Still

DIAL SQUARE
CD _____ **NECKCD 008**
Roughneck / Apr '92 / Disc.

LIFE'S TOO LONG
CD _____ **NECKCD 12**
Roughneck / Jun '93 / Disc.

Miel, Melinda

KISS ON A TEAR, A
CD _____ **NORM 161CD**
Normal/Okra / Mar '94 / Direct / ADA.

LAW OF THE DREAM, THE
CD _____ **NORMAL 113CD**
Normal/Okra / Mar '94 / Direct / ADA.

Migenes Johnson, Julia

JULIA MIGENES JOHNSON (Greatest hits)
I could have danced all night / Oh mein papa / Tonight / Chim chim cheree / Johnny Guitar / So in love / La Paloma / Someone's waiting for you / Man I love / Embraceable you / Someone to watch over me / Summertime
CD _____ **610 232**
Eurodisc / Oct '91 / BMG.

LIVE AT OLYMPIA
CD _____ **CDCH 503**
Milan / Mar '90 / BMG / Silva Screen.

MY FAVOURITE SONGS
CD _____ **8478842**
Polydor / Jul '93 / PolyGram.

Mighty Baby

MIGHTY BABY
Egyptian tomb / Friend you know but never see / I've been down so long / Same way from the sun / House without windows / Trials of a city / I'm from the country / At a point between fate and destiny / Only dreaming / Dustbin full of rubish / Understanding love / My favourite day / Saying for today
CD _____ **CDWIKD 120**
Big Beat / Feb '94 / Pinnacle.

Mighty Clouds Of Joy

POWER
In God's will / Have you told him lately / We will stand / He saw me / I'm ready / I've been in the storm to long / What a wonderful God / Hold on / Nearer my God to thee / Hour of the holy ghost
CD _____ **CDK 9147**
Alliance Music / Aug '95 / EMI.

Mighty Diamonds

BEST OF MIGHTY DIAMONDS
CD _____ **MDRP 001CD**
Hitbound / May '95 / Jetstar / THE.

GET READY
Schoolmate / Another day another raid / Tonight I'm gonna take it easy / Idlers' corner / Cannot say you didn't know / Sensimilla / My baby / Get ready / Up front / Modeller
CD _____ **GRELCD 112**
Greensleeves / Jun '88 / Total/BMG / Jetstar / SRD.

GO SEEK YOUR RIGHTS
Right time / Why me black brother why / Have mercy / Shame and pride / Gnashing of teeth / Them never love poor Marcus / One brother short / Masterplan / I need a roof / Go seek your rights / Bodyguard / Natural Natty / Africa / Sweet lady / Got to get away / Let the answer be yes
CD _____ **CDFL 9002**
Frontline / Jul '90 / EMI / Jetstar.

IF YOU'RE LOOKING FOR TROUBLE
Peace pipe / Where is Garvey / Fight, fight, fight / Make up your mind / Accept me / That's the life / Cartoon living / African rootsman / If you looking for trouble / Love love come get me tonight
CD _____ **LLCD 22**
Live & Love / Sep '86 / Jetstar.

LIVE IN EUROPE
Party time / Country living / Mr. Botha / Have mercy / I need a roof / My baby / Puttin' on the Ritz / Real enemy / I don't mind / Right time / Africa / Keep on moving / Heavy load
CD _____ **GRELCD 124**
Greensleeves / Feb '89 / Total/BMG / Jetstar / SRD.

MIGHTY DIAMONDS MEETS DON CARLOS & GOLD AT CHANNEL 1 STUDIO (Mighty Diamonds & Don Carlos)
CD _____ **JJ 084085**
Jetstar / Jun '94 / Jetstar.

MOMENT OF TRUTH
CD _____ **CIDM 1098**
Mango / Dec '92 / Vital / PolyGram.

NEVER GET WEARY
CD _____ **LLCD 29**
Live & Love / Aug '88 / Jetstar.

PAINT IT RED
CD _____ **RASCD 3114**
Greensleeves / Jun '93 / Total/BMG / Jetstar / SRD.

REGGAE STREET
CD _____ **SHANCD 43004**
Shanachie / May '90 / Koch / ADA / Greensleeves.

RIGHT TIME
Right time / Why me black brother why / Shame and pride / Gnashing of teeth / Them never love poor Marcus / I need a roof / Go seek your rights / Have mercy / Natural natty / Africa
CD _____ **SHANCD 43014**
Shanachie / Jan '84 / Koch / ADA / Greensleeves.

Mighty Sparrow

SALVATION WITH SOCA BALLADS
CD _____ **BLSCD 1017**
Soca / Feb '94 / Jetstar.

Mighty Truth

FROM THE CITY TO THE SEA
Rebirth / Is it a wizard or a blizzard / Don't you ever learn / Connexion / Blowing for the 6th sign / Hear the voice / End of an era / Heavy knowledge / Miro / City to the sea / Wandering world / Pure as the driven
CD _____ **TNGCD 006**
Tongue 'n' Groove / May '95 / Vital.

Mike & The Mechanics

BEGGAR ON A BEACH OF GOLD
Beggar on a beach of gold / Another cup of coffee / You've really got a hold on me / Mea Culpa / Over my shoulder / Someone always hates someone / Ghost of sex and you / Web of lies / Plain and simple / Something to believe in / House of many rooms / I believe (when I fall in love it will be forever) / Going, going... home
CD _____ **CDV 2772**
Virgin / Mar '95 / EMI.

LIVING YEARS, THE
Nobody's perfect / Seeing is believing / Nobody knows / Poor boy down / Blame / Don't / Black and blue / Beautiful day / Why me / Living years
CD _____ **256004 2**
WEA / Oct '88 / Warner Music.

MIKE AND THE MECHANICS
Silent running / All I need is a miracle / Par avion / Hanging by a thread / I get the feeling / Take the reins / You are the one / Call to arms / Taken in
CD _____ **252496 2**
WEA / Jul '86 / Warner Music.

WORD OF MOUTH
Get up / Word of mouth / Time and place / Yesterday, today, tomorrow / Way you look at me / Everybody gets a second chance / Stop baby / My crime of passion / Let's pretend it didn't happen / Before (the next heartache falls)
CD _____ CDV 2662
Virgin / May '91 / EMI.

Miki & Griff

LITTLE BITTY TEAR
CD _____ SSLCD 203
Savanna / Jun '95 / THE.

MIKI & GRIFF
CD _____ MATCD 259
Castle / Apr '93 / BMG.

VERY BEST OF MIKI & GRIFF, THE
CD _____ SOW 702
Sound Waves / May '94 / Target/BMG.

Mila Et Loma

TAHITI: BELLE EPOQUE 2
CD _____ S 65809
Manuiti / Jul '92 / Harmonia Mundi.

Milder, Joakim

STILL IN MOTION
CD _____ DRCD 188
Dragon / Jan '88 / Roots / Cadillac / Wellard / CM / ADA.

WAYS
CD _____ DRCD 231
Dragon / Jan '89 / Roots / Cadillac / Wellard / CM / ADA.

Miles, Buddy

HELL AND BACK (Miles, Buddy Express)
Born under a bad sign / Change / All along the watchtower / Let it be me / Come back home / Be kind to your girlfriend / Decision / Nothing left to lose
CD _____ RCD 10305
Black Arc / Jun '94 / Vital.

MIGHTY RHYTHM TRIBE
CD _____ LAKE 2020
Lakeside / Aug '95 / Magnum Music Group.

THEM CHANGES
CD _____ LMCD 951170
Line / Sep '92 / CM / Grapevine / ADA / Conifer / Direct.

Miles, Butch

LIVE (Miles, Butch & Kansas City Big Band)
CD _____ MECCACD 1013
Music Mecca / Nov '94 / Jazz Music / Cadillac / Wellard.

Miles, Floyd

GOIN' BACK TO DAYTONA
Same thing / Goin' back to Daytona / Mean heartbreaker / No life at all / Oh, Mary / Two against them all / All the love I can / Samson and Delilah / That's why I'm here tonight / Love on the rocks
CD _____ FCD 752
Demon / Jun '94 / Pinnacle / ADA.

Miles, John

ANTHOLOGY
Remember yesterday / Music / High fly / When you lose someone so young / Slow down / Man behind the guitar / Stranger in the city / Time / Manhattan skyline / Zaragon / Can't keep a good man down / Sweet Lorraine / Jose / Come away Melinda / Why don't you love me / Sterotomy / La sagrada familia
CD _____ VSOPCD 191
Connoisseur / Oct '93 / Pinnacle.

JOHN MILES LIVE IN CONCERT
CD _____ WINCD 021
Windsong / Nov '92 / Pinnacle.

REBEL
Music / Everybody wants some more / High fly / You have it all / Rebel / When you lose someone so young / Lady of my life / Pull the damn thing down / Music (reprise)
CD _____ 8200802
London / Mar '87 / PolyGram.

Miles, Lizzie

LIZZIE MILES
CD _____ AMCD 73
American Music / Feb '95 / Jazz Music.

Miles, Ron

WITNESS
CD _____ 740142
Capri / '90 / Wellard / Cadillac.

Milk

NEVER DATED EP
Intro / Get off my log / Laid and paid II / Spam / Rude and cocky / Go 2 hell / Ask me how thick
CD _____ 74321260332
American / Oct '95 / BMG.

TANTRUM
CD _____ CDEVER 007
Eve / Oct '91 / Grapevine.

Milk & Honey Band

ROUND THE SUN
Tin cans / Not heaven / Another perfect day / Out of nowhere / Tea / Round the sun / Pier view / Puerto / Off my hands / Light / Raining / Bird song
CD _____ R 3572
Rough Trade / Oct '94 / Pinnacle.

Milkshakes

107 TAPES (Early Demos & Live Recordings)
Pretty baby / Ruhrge beat / Well well / I want you / Flat foot / I say you lie / Shed country 81 / Don't love another / Mumble the peg / You did her wrong / Red monkey / Let's stomp / Eaten more honey / Tell me where's that girl / Girl called mine / Little Queenie / Jaguar / Cadillac / Black sails (In the moonlight) / Sit right down and cry / She tells me she loves me / Soldiers of love / Monkey business / Let me love you / El Salvador / Boys
CD _____ ASK 8CD
Vinyl Japan / '91 / Vital.

19TH NERVOUS SHAKEDOWN
It's you / Please don't tell my baby / Shed country / Pretty baby / Don't love another / Another midnight / Seven days / Black sails (In the moonlight) / Caldonia / You did her wrong / Shimmy shake / Hide and scatter / El Salvador / Jaguar / General Belgrano / Klansmen kometh / Brand new Cadillac / Love can lose / Little Bettina / I'm the one for you / Let me love you / Quiet lives / Wounded knee / I'm needing you / Red monkey / Ambassador of love / Can't seem to love that girl / Cassandra / Green hornet / Out of control
CD _____ CDWIKD 939
Big Beat / Jul '90 / Pinnacle.

20 ROCK'N'ROLL HITS OF THE 50'S & 60'S
Hippy hippy shake / Rip it up / I'm gonna sit right down and cry over you / Say mama / Peggy Sue / Jaguar and the thunderbirds / Comanche / I'm talking about you / Sweet little sixteen / Money (that's what I want) / Carol / Boys / Something else / Some other guy / Who do you love / Jezebel / Hidden charms / Little Queenie / Ya ya twist / I wanna be your man
CD _____ CDWIKM 20
Big Beat / Mar '91 / Pinnacle.

KNIGHTS OF TRASHE
CD _____ SCRAG 5CD
Hangman's Daughter / Oct '95 / SRD.

MILKSHAKES REVENGE, THE
Let me love you / I want you / If I saw you / Graveyard words / Boys / Little girl be good / Pipeline / She tells me loves me / Little girl (mumble the peg) / Every girl I meet / One I get / Baby what's wrong
CD _____ HOG1
Hangman's Daughter / Sep '94 / SRD.

STILL TALKIN' BOUT
CD _____ ASK 10CD
Vinyl Japan / Nov '92 / Vital.

TALKING 'BOUT - MILKSHAKES
She'll be mine / Pretty baby / For she / I want'cha for my little girl / Ruhrge beat / After midnight / Bull's nose / Shed country / Don't love another / Tell me where's that girl / Can'tcha see / Love you the whole night through / Nothing you can say or do / I say you lie
CD _____ SCRAG 4CD
Hangman's Daughter / Jul '95 / SRD.

Milky Way

MILKY WAY
CD _____ CDLR 45012
L&R / Jun '89 / New Note.

Milla

DIVINE COMEDY, THE
Alien song (For those who listen) / Gentlemen who fell / It's your life / Reaching from nowhere / Charlie / Ruby Lane / Bang your head / Clock / Don't fade away / You did it all before / In a glade
CD _____ SBKCD 28
SBK / Jun '94 / EMI.

Milladoiro

GALICIA NO TEMPO
CD _____ GLCD 3073
Green Linnet / Feb '93 / Roots / CM / Direct / ADA.

Millencoln

LIFE ON A PLATE
CD _____ BHR 033CD
Burning Heart / Oct '95 / Plastic Head.

SKAUCH
CD _____ BHR 016
Burning Heart / Oct '94 / Plastic Head.

STORY OF MY LIFE
CD _____ BHR 032CDS
Burning Heart / Feb '95 / Plastic Head.

TINY TUNES
CD _____ BHR 019
Burning Heart / Feb '95 / Plastic Head.

Miller, Al

COMPLETE RECORDED WORKS 1927-36
CD _____ DOCD 5306
Blues Document / Dec '94 / Swift / Jazz Music / Hot Shot.

WILD CARDS
CD _____ DE 675
Delmark / Aug '95 / Hot Shot / ADA / CM / Direct / Cadillac.

Miller, Buddy

YOUR LOVE AND OTHER LIES
CD _____ HCD 8063
Hightone / Aug '95 / ADA / Koch.

Miller, Byron

GIT WIT ME
CD _____ NOVA 9029
Nova / Jan '93 / New Note.

Miller, Cercie

DEDICATION
CD _____ ST 580
Stash / Jun '94 / Jazz Music / CM / Cadillac / Direct / ADA.

Miller, Ed

AT HOME WITH THE EXILES
Pittenween Jo / Darling Allie / John McLean march / Blood upon the grass / Bottle o'the best / Mistress / Yellow on the broom / Jute Mill song / Crooked Jack / Broom o'the cowdenknowes / Generations of change / Man's man / At home with the exiles / Tak a dram
CD _____ CDTRAX 089
Greentrax / Jul '95 / Conifer / Duncans / ADA / Direct.

Miller, Frankie

BBC LIVE IN CONCERT
Free and safe on the road / Play something sweet (Brickyard blues) / It takes a lot to laugh, it takes a train to cry / With you in mind / Rock / Be good to yourself / Fool in love / Jealous guy / I can't break away / Double heart trouble / Stubborn kind of fellow / Falling in love / Goodnight sweetheart / Woman to love / When I'm away from you / When something is wrong with my baby / Darlin' / Ain't got no money
CD _____ WINDCD 054
Windsong / Feb '94 / Pinnacle.

BEST OF FRANKIE MILLER, THE
Darlin' / When I'm away from you / Be good to yourself / I can't change it / Highlife / Brickyard blues / Fool in love / Have you seen me lately Joan / Love letters / Caledonia / Stubborn kind of fellow / Devil gun / Hard on the levee / Tears / I'm ready / Shoo-rah shoo-rah / Double heart trouble / So young, so young
CD _____ CDCHR 1981
Chrysalis / Feb '94 / EMI.

HIGH LIFE
High life / Brickyard blues / Trouble / Fool / Little angel / Devil gun / I'll take a melody / Just a song / Shoo rah, shoo rah / I'm falling in love again / With you in mind
CD _____ CD25CR 04
Chrysalis / Mar '94 / EMI.

Miller, Glenn

1938-42 BROADCAST VERSIONS (Miller, Glenn Orchestra)
CD _____ JH 1004
Jazz Hour / Feb '91 / Target/BMG / Jazz Music / Cadillac.

1941 SUNSET SERENADE-CAFE ROUGE
CD _____ JH 1021
Jazz Hour / Feb '93 / Target/BMG / Jazz Music / Cadillac.

1942 CHESTERFIELD SHOWS (Miller, Glenn Orchestra)
CD _____ JH 1028
Jazz Hour / Feb '93 / Target/BMG / Jazz Music / Cadillac.

20 GREATEST HITS: GLENN MILLER
CD _____ ENTCD 201
Entertainers / '88 / Target/BMG.

Air Force Orchestra - 1944

CD _____ CDCD 1267
Charly / Oct '95 / Charly / THE / Cadillac.

AMERICAN PATROL VOL.2 (Miller, Glenn Orchestra)
CD _____ DAWE 55
Magic / Nov '93 / Jazz Music / Swift / Wellard / Cadillac / Harmonia Mundi.

ARMY AIR FORCE BAND 1943-44, THE
St. Louis blues march / Peggy, the pin-up girl / Speak low / Tail-end Charlie / Anvil chorus / Oh what a beautiful morning / There are Yanks / Everybody loves my baby / Enlisted mens mess / I'll be around / There'll be air hot time in the town of Berlin / People will say we're in love / Pearls on velvet / Poinciana / It must be jelly, 'cause jam don't shake like that / Jeep jockey jump / Victory polka
CD _____ ND 86360
Bluebird / Jun '88 / BMG.

AT MEADOWBROOK 1939 (Miller, Glenn Orchestra)
Moonlight serenade (theme) / Little brown jug / Blue rain / Oh johnny oh johnny oh / In an old Dutch garden / Tiger rag / Love with a capital you / Bugle call rag / Blue moonlight / Indian Summer / Why couldn't it last last night / This chungled world / I just got a letter / On a little street in Singapore / Faithful to you / Farewell blues / Moonlight serenade (theme and fadeout)
CD _____ DAWE 34
Magic / Sep '89 / Jazz Music / Swift / Wellard / Cadillac / Harmonia Mundi.

BEST OF GLENN MILLER
CD _____ DCD 5333
Disky / Dec '93 / THE / BMG / Discovery / Pinnacle.

BEST OF GLENN MILLER
CD _____ DLCD 4006
Dixie Live / Mar '95 / Magnum Music Group.

BEST OF GLENN MILLER, THE (2CD Set)
CD Set _____ MOVCDD 1
Backs / Nov '95 / Disc.

BEST OF THE BIG BANDS
Blues serenade / Moonlight on the Ganges / I got rhythm / Sleepy time gal / Community swing / Time on my hands / My fine feathered friend / Humoresque / Don' the jive / Silhouetted in the moonlight / Every day's a holiday / Sweet stranger / Don't wake up my heart / Why'd ya make me fall in love / Sold American / Dippermouth blues
CD _____ 4716562
Columbia / Jun '92 / Sony.

BIG BAND BASH
Moonlight serenade / Pennsylvania 6-5000 / American patrol / Tuxedo junction / I've got a gal in Kalamazoo / String of pearls / Song of the Volga boatmen / Perfidia / In the mood / Chattanooga choo choo / St. Louis blues march / Anvil chorus / Serenade in blue / Jumpin' jive / Farewell blues / Little brown jug / Hallelujah / Under a blanket of blue
CD _____ GOJCD 53024
Giants Of Jazz / Mar '90 / Target/BMG / Cadillac.

CHATTANOOGA CHOO CHOO (The #1 Hits)
Wishing (will make it so) / Stairway to the stars / Moon love / Over the rainbow / Man with the mandolin / Blue orchids / In the mood / Careless / Tuxedo junction / When you wish upon a star / Woodpecker / Imagination / Fools rush in / Blueberry Hill / Song of the Volga boatmen / You and I / Chattanooga choo choo / Elmer's tune / String of pearls / Moonlight cocktail / Don't sit under the apple tree / I've got a gal in Kalamazoo / That old black magic
CD _____ ND 90584
Bluebird / Oct '91 / BMG.

CLASSIC YEARS, THE (Miller, Glenn Orchestra)
CD _____ CDSGP 092
Prestige / Oct '93 / Total/BMG.

COLLECTION
CD _____ COL 025
Collection / Apr '95 / Target/BMG.

COMMEMORATION 1944-1994
CD _____ OVCCD 002
Satellite Music / May '94 / THE.

COMPLETE GLENN MILLER, THE (1938-1942) (13CD Set) (Miller, Glenn Orchestra)
My reverie / By the waters of Minnetonka / King Porter stomp / Shut eye / How I'd like to be with you in Bermuda / Cuckoo in the clock / Romance runs in the family / Chestnut tree / And the angels sing / Moonlight serenade / Lady's in love with you / Wishing (will make it so) / Three little fishes (itty bitty poo) / Sunrise serenade / Little brown jug / My last goodbye / But I don't mean a thing / Pavanne / Running wild / To you / Stairway to the stars / Blue evening / Lamp is low / Rendezvous time in Paris / We can live on love / Cinderella / Moon love / Guess I'll go back home / I'm sorry for myself / Back to back / Sliphorn jive / Oh you crazy

moon / Ain't cha comin' out / Day we meet again / Wanna hat with cherries / Solid American / Pagan love song / Ding dong the witch is dead / Over the rainbow / Little man who wasn't there / Man with the mandolin / Starlit hour / Blue orchids / Glen Island special / Love with a capital you / Baby me / In the mood / Wah (re-bop-boom-bam) / Angel in a furnished room / Twilight interlude / I want to be happy / Farewell blues / Who's sorry now / My isle of golden dreams / My prayer / Blue moonlight / Basket weaver man / Melancholy baby / (Why couldn't it last) last night / Out of space / So many times / Blue rain / Can I help it / I just got a letter / Bless you / Bluebirds in the moonlight (silly idea) / Faithful forever / Speaking of Heaven / Indian Summer / It was written in the stars / Johnson rag / Ciribiribin / Careless / Oh Johnny oh Johnny oh Johnny oh / In an old Dutch garden (by an old Dutch mill) / This changing world / On a little street in Singapore / Vagabond dreams / I beg your pardon / Faithful to you / Gaucho serenade / Sky fell down / When you wish upon a star / Give a little whistle / Missouri waltz / Beautiful Ohio / What's the matter with me / Say si si / Fhumba jumps / Star dust / My melancholy baby / Let's all sing together / Rug cutter's swing / Woodpecker song / Sweet potato piper / Too romantic / Tuxedo junction / Danny boy / Imagination / Shake down the stars / I'll never smile again / Starlight and music / Polka dots and moonbeams / My my / Say it / Moments in the moonlight / Hear my song Violetta / Sierra Sue / Boog it / Yours is my heart alone / I'm stepping out with a memory tonight / Alice blue gown / Wonderful one / Devil may care / April played the fiddle / Fools rush in / I haven't time to be a millionaire / Slow freight / Pennsylvania 6-5000 / Bugle call rag / Nearness of you / Mr. Meadowlark / My blue heaven / When the swallows come back to Capistrano / Million dreams ago / Chattanooga choo choo / I know why / You and I / Adios / Elmer's tune / String of pearls / White cliffs of Dover / Moonlight cocktail / Skylark / Always in my heart / Don't sit under the apple tree / American patrol / I've got a gal in Kalamazoo / Serenade in blue / At last / Old black magic / Jukebox Saturday night

CD _____ 07863766520
Bluebird / Apr '95 / BMG.

ESSENTIAL V-DISCS, THE
CD _____ JZ CD302
Suisa / Feb '91 / Jazz Music / THE.

FRESH AS A DAISY (Miller, Glenn Orchestra)
Cabana in Havana / Fresh as a daisy / Stardust / Sweeter than the sweetest / Don't cry cherie / Blue moonlight / Farewell blues / Who's sorry now / I dreamt I dwelt in Harlem / Let's have another cup of coffee / It was written in the stars / My melancholy lullaby / All I do is dream of you / Blue orchids / Blue rain / Wonderful one / Twilight interlude / Pagan love song / Running wild / Ciribiribin / My isle of golden dreams / In the mood
CD _____ RAJCD 841
Empress / Feb '95 / THE.

GENIUS OF GLENN MILLER, THE
Moonlight serenade / Little brown jug / I got rhythm / Blue skies / Sliphorn jive / String of pearls / Don't sit under the apple tree / Song of the Volga boatmen / Elmer's tune / My blue Heaven / American patrol / Sun Valley jump / Anvil chorus / King Porter stomp / Jukebox Saturday night / Farewell blues
CD _____ ND 90090
RCA / Apr '88 / BMG.

GLENN MILLER
CD _____ 295045
Ariola / Apr '83 / BMG.

GLENN MILLER
Sun valley jump / Oh, what a beautiful morning / Jeep jocky jump / Rhapsody in blue / Moonlight sonata / Tchaikovsky's piano concerto / In a sentimental mood / Serenade in blue / Lamplighter's serenade / Little brown jug / Woodpecker song / American patrol / String of pearls / Tuxedo junction / In the mood / Stardust / Moonlight serenade / At last
CD _____ 24037
Laserlight / Dec '95 / Target/BMG.

GLENN MILLER
CD _____ 22702
Music / Jul '95 / Target/BMG.

GLENN MILLER (2CD/MC Set)
CD Set _____ R 2CD4001
Deja Vu / Jan '96 / THE.

GLENN MILLER & HIS AMERICAN BAND 1945
CD _____ DAWE 72
Magic / Dec '94 / Jazz Music / Swift / Wellard / Cadillac / Harmonia Mundi.

GLENN MILLER & HIS ARMY AIR FORCE ORCHESTRA (1944)
CD _____ DAWE 62
Magic / Jul '93 / Jazz Music / Swift / Wellard / Cadillac / Harmonia Mundi.

GLENN MILLER 1943-1944
CD _____ PHONTCD 9307
Phontastic / Aug '94 / Wellard / Jazz Music / Cadillac.

DANCE TIME U.S.A. (1939-40) (Miller, Glenn Orchestra)
Slumber song / Song of the Volga boatmen / You walk by / There I go / Oh so good / Stone's throw from Heaven / I dreamt I dwelt in Harlem / Moonlight serenade / Beer barrel polka / Cinderella / Back to back / Pagan love song / Dippermouth blues / Moon love / Guess I'll go back home / Moon is a silver dollar / Heaven can wait / Bugle call rag / Sometime
CD _____ DAWE 51
Magic / Nov '93 / Jazz Music / Swift / Wellard / Cadillac / Harmonia Mundi.

DECEMBER 25TH 1943 (Miller, Glenn & The Army Airforce Orchestra)
CD _____ JH 1041
Jazz Hour / Feb '95 / Target/BMG / Jazz Music / Cadillac.

ESSENTIAL GLENN MILLER ORCHESTRA, THE
CD _____ 4715582
Sony Jazz / Jan '95 / Sony.

ESSENTIAL GLENN MILLER, THE
Moonlight serenade / Wishing (Will make it so) / Sunrise serenade / Little brown jug / Running wild / Stairway to the stars / Moon love / Over the rainbow / My isle of golden dreams / In the mood / Indian summer / It's a blue world / Gaucho serenade / When you wish upon a star / Say si si (Para vigo me voy) / Star dust / Tuxedo junction / Danny Boy / Imagination / Fools rush in / Pennsylvania 6-5000 / Nearness of you / When the swallows come back to Capistrano / Million dreams ago / Nightingale sang in Berkley Square / Along the Santa Fe trail / Yes my darling daughter / Anvil chorus / Song of the Volga boatmen / Perfidia / Chattanooga choo choo / I know why / You and I / Adios / Elmer's tune / String of pearls / White cliffs of Dover / Moonlight cocktail / Skylark / Always in my heart / Don't sit under the apple tree / American patrol / I've got a gal in Kalamazoo / Serenade in blue / At last / Old black magic / Jukebox Saturday night

---

GLENN MILLER AND HIS ORCHESTRA (1938-40) (Miller, Glenn Orchestra)
CD _____ VJC 1014-2
Vintage Jazz Classics / Oct '92 / Direct / ADA / CM / Cadillac.

GLENN MILLER AND HIS ORCHESTRA (1939-40) (Miller, Glenn Orchestra)
CD _____ 90 508 2
Jazz Archives / Aug '91 / Jazz Music / Discovery / Cadillac.

GLENN MILLER ARMY AIR FORCE BAND(1943-1944),THE
Anvil chorus / Stormy weather / Jukebox Saturday night / Jeep jockey jump / All the things you are / Song of the Volga boatmen / With my head in the clouds / I hear you screaming / Long ago and far away / Cherokee / Peggy and the pin-up girl / In the mood / Holiday for strings / String of pearls / Don't be that way
CD _____ ND 89767
Jazz Tribune / Jun '94 / BMG.

GLENN MILLER COLLECTOR'S EDITION
CD _____ DVX 8022
Deja Vu / Apr '95 / THE.

GLENN MILLER GOLD (2CD Set)
CD Set _____ D2CD 4001
Deja Vu / Jun '95 / THE.

GLENN MILLER ORCHESTRA
Moonlight serenade / Sunrise serenade / Don't sit under the apple tree / Bugle call rag / Anvil chorus / Moonlight cocktail / Indian summer / Sun Valley jump / Farewell blues / Under a blanket of blue / Penfida / Stardust / At last / St. Louis blues march / Adios / Little brown jug / American patrol / Tuxedo junction / Slumber song / My blue heaven / Blues in my heart / Begin the beguine / Everybody loves my baby / Over there / Song of the Volga boatmen / Enlisted mens blues / It must be jelly, 'cause jam don't shake like that / Rainbow rhapsody / Londonderry air / I've got a gal in Kalamazoo / Pennsylvania 6-5000 / String of pearls / April in Paris / Little man who wasn't there / Georgia on my mind / Baby me / Chestnut tree / Kings march / I dreamt I dwelt in Harlem / Starlit hour / Glenn Island line / That old black magic / In the mood / Serenade in blue / Pin ball Paul / Chatanooga choo choo / String of pearls (2) / Blue champagne / When Johnny comes marching home / Jeanie with the light brown hair / Serenade in blue (2) / In a sentimental mood / Elmer's tune / Seven-o-five / Falling leaves / Caribbean clipper / My love for you / Lover (2) / Woodpecker song / Hallelujah
CD Set _____ TFP 017
Tring / Nov '92 / Tring / Prism.

GLENN MILLER ORCHESTRA
CD _____ KLMCD 047
Scratch / Jan '95 / BMG.

GLENN MILLER REUNION IN CONCERT
CD _____ GNPD 76
GNP Crescendo / '88 / Silva Screen.

GLENN MILLER'S MEN IN PARIS (Various Artists)
CD _____ STD 1
Starlite / Nov '95 / Wellard / Jazz Music.

GLENN MILLER/DUKE ELLINGTON/ BENNY GOODMAN (Miller, Glenn & Duke Ellington/Benny Goodman)
CD Set _____ MAK 104
Avid / Nov '94 / Avid/BMG / Koch.

GLENN MILLER: LIVE 1940
CD _____ TAXCD 3704
Tax / Feb '89 / Jazz Music / Wellard / Cadillac.

GO TO WAR (Radio Broadcasts From The 1940's) (Miller, Glenn Orchestra)
CD _____ CDMR 1160
Radiola / Nov '90 / Pinnacle.

GOLD COLLECTION, THE
CD _____ D2CD01
Recording Arts / Dec '92 / THE / Disc.

GOLDEN GREATS (Miller, Glenn & Dorsey Brothers)
CD _____ ATJCD 5956
All That's Jazz / '92 / THE / Jazz Music.

GREAT BRITISH DANCE BANDS SALUTE GLENN MILLER (2CD Set) (Various Artists)
I've got a gal in Kalamazoo / You'll never know / Don't sit under the apple tree / Take the 'A' train / Always in my heart / Shoo shoo baby / Deep in the heart of Texas / Lamplighter's serenade / I'm old fashioned / Sweet Eloise / Blues in the night / This is no laughing matter / Perfect beloved / Elmer's tune / My devotion / Yes my darling / I'd know you anywhere / American patrol / Chattanooga choo choo / I'll never smile again / Is my baby blue tonight / I know why / In the mood / String of pearls / Moonlight cocktail / Little brown jug / Five o' clock whistle / St. Louis blues / Serenade in blue / Pennsylvania 6-5000 / Beat me Daddy, eight to the bar / I guess I'll have to dream the rest / I don't want to set the world on fire / Miss you / Humpty dumpty heart / Sierra Sue / Bugle call rag / Falling leaves / April played the fiddle / Farewell blues / Sleep song / Sunrise serenade / Johnson

---

rag / I haven't time to be a millionaire / Tuxedo junction / Stardust / Moonlight serenade
CD Set _____ CDDL 1251
Music For Pleasure / Dec '93 / EMI.

GREATEST HITS
In the mood / String of pearls / Pennsylvania 6-500 / Chattanooga choo choo / Tuxedo junction / Little brown jug / (I've got a gal in) Kalamazoo / American patrol / Moonlight serenade / Don't sit under the apple tree (with anyone else but me) / Serenade in blue / Song of the Volga boatmen
CD _____ 74321339352
Camden / Jan '96 / BMG.

GREATEST HITS LIVE 1940-42 (Miller, Glenn Orchestra)
CD _____ DLWE 1
Magic / Nov '93 / Jazz Music / Swift / Wellard / Cadillac / Harmonia Mundi.

GREATEST HITS, THE (Miller, Glenn Orchestra)
Wishing / Stairway to the stars / Moon love / Over the rainbow / In the mood / Careless / Tuxedo junction / When you wish upon a star / Imagination / Fools rush in (where angels fear to tread) / Song of the Volga boatmen / You and I / Chattanooga choo choo / Elmer's tune / String of pearls / Moonlight cocktail
CD _____ CDCD 1006
Charly / Mar '93 / Charly / THE / Cadillac.

HANDFUL OF STARS 1940, A
CD _____ DAWE 71
Magic / '94 / Jazz Music / Swift / Wellard / Cadillac / Harmonia Mundi.

I SUSTAIN THE WINGS VOL. 2 (U.S.A. 1943) (Miller, Glenn & The Army Airforce Orchestra)
CD _____ DAWE 67
Magic / Jan '94 / Jazz Music / Swift / Wellard / Cadillac / Harmonia Mundi.

IN REAL HI-FI STEREO 1941 (Miller, Glenn Orchestra)
CD _____ JH 1042
Jazz Hour / Feb '95 / Target/BMG / Jazz Music / Cadillac.

IN THE CHRISTMAS MOOD (Miller, Glenn Orchestra)
CD _____ 15418
Laserlight / Nov '95 / Target/BMG.

IN THE MOOD (1939-40)
Blueberry Hill / Bugle call rag / Careless / Danny Boy / Imagination / In the mood / Indian summer / It's a blue world / Moonlight serenade / My My / Nearness of you / Out of space / Pennsylvania 6-5000 / Rug cutters' swing / Say it / Slow freight / Stairway to the stars / Stardust / Sunrise serenade / Tuxedo junction / Wishing / Woodpecker song
CD _____ CD AJA 5078
Living Era / Apr '91 / Koch.

IN THE MOOD
CD _____ QSCD 6003
Charly / Oct '91 / Charly / THE / Cadillac.

IN THE MOOD
In the mood / Pennsylvania 6-5000 / Moonlight becomes you / Sunrise serenade / Serenade in blue / Elmer's tune / Jukebox Saturday night / Tuxedo junction / Chattanooga choo choo / Caribbean clipper / Moonlight cocktail / American patrol / I got a gal in Kalamazoo / Danny Boy / Serenade in blue / String of pearls / At last / Going home / I know why / Don't sit under the apple tree
CD _____ MVCD 9010
Start / Apr '95 / Koch.

IN THE MOOD - GLENN MILLER AND HIS ORCHESTRA 1939-1944
In the mood / Pennsylvania 6-5000 / Moonlight serenade / American patrol / Sunrise serenade / Jumpin' jive / Tuxedo junction / Chattanooga choo choo / Johnson rag / String of pearls / St. Louis blues march / I've got a gal in Kalamazoo / Song of the Volga boatmen / Perfidia / Little brown jug / My melancholy baby / Serenade in blue
CD _____ CD 56006
Jazz Roots / Aug '94 / Target/BMG.

IN THE MOOD - THE BEST OF GLENN MILLER
CD _____ TRTCD 192
TrueTrax / Jun '95 / THE.

JAZZ PORTRAITS (Miller, Glenn Orchestra)
In the mood / Pennsylvania 6-5000 / Moonlight serenade / American patrol / Sunrise serenade / Jumpin' jive / Tuxedo junction / Anvil chorus / Chattanooga choo choo / Johnson rag / String of pearls / St. Louis blues march / I've got a gal in Kalamazoo / Song of the Volga boatmen / Perfidia / Little brown jug / My melancholy baby / Serenade in blue
CD _____ CD 14502
Jazz Portraits / May '94 / Jazz Music.

LEGEND
Jeep jockey jump / Symphony / Rhapsody in blue / Seven-o-five / Killarney / I've got a heart filled with love / Wabash blues / Everybody loves my baby / In the mood /

There'll be a hot time in the town of Berlin / Speak low / Keep 'em flying / Moonlight serenade / Why dream / Here we go again / Fellow on a furlough / Passage interdit / Little brown jug / Deep purple / Jukebox Saturday night / Now I know / Bubble bath / Closing time
CD _____ DBCD 01
Dance Band Days / Oct '87 / Prism.

LEGENDARY PERFORMER, A
Moonlight serenade / Sunrise serenade / Little brown jug / Danny boy / Tuxedo junction / My melancholy baby / Pennsylvania / So you're the one / Sentimental me / Song of the Volga boatmen / Jack and Jill / String of pearls / Star dust / Everything I love / Jingle bells / In the mood / Chattanooga choo choo / At last / Moonlight cocktail / Saturday night
CD _____ ND 90586
Bluebird / Oct '91 / BMG.

LIFE STORY AND MUSIC OF GLENN MILLER
Moonlight serenade / King Porter stomp / Little brown jug / In the mood / Tuxedo junction / American patrol / Don't sit under the apple tree / Chattanooga choo choo / Elmer's tune / String of pearls / Pennsylvania
CD _____ VLF 5
Talking Volumes / Apr '95 / BMG.

LITTLE BROWN JUG
CD _____ VJC 1038-2
Vintage Jazz Classics / Oct '92 / Direct / ADA / CM / Cadillac.

LIVE 1938/39 PARADISE RESTAURANT NEW YORK (Miller, Glenn Orchestra)
Lovelight in the starlight / How'd ya like to love me / You leave me breathless / Please come out of your dream / What have you got that get's me / Room with a view / Wait until
CD _____ DAWE 42
Magic / '89 / Jazz Music / Swift / Wellard / Cadillac / Harmonia Mundi.

LIVE 1940
CD _____ TAX 37042
Tax / Aug '94 / Jazz Music / Wellard / Cadillac.

LIVE AT CAFE ROUGE 1940 (Miller, Glenn Orchestra)
CD _____ JH 1037
Jazz Hour / Feb '95 / Target/BMG / Jazz Music / Cadillac.

LIVE AT THE HOLLYWOOD PALLADIUM 1946
CD _____ CD 53200
Giants Of Jazz / Aug '95 / Target/BMG / Cadillac.

LIVE IN HI-FI, GLEN ISLAND 1939 (Miller, Glenn Orchestra)
CD _____ JH 1012
Jazz Hour / '91 / Target/BMG / Jazz Music / Cadillac.

LOST RECORDINGS, THE
In the mood / Stardust / Song of the Volga boatmen / Long ago and far away / Is you is or is you ain't my baby / Great day / Summertime / Tuxedo junction / Begin the beguine / Anvil chorus / Poinciana / American patrol / Here we go again / My heart tells me / String of pearls / Stormy weather / Little brown jug / Where or when / Cow cow boogie / Holiday for strings / All I do is dream of you / Farewell blues / I've got a heart filled with love / Dear / Caribbean clipper / Smoke gets in your eyes / Tail end Charlie / Everybody loves my baby / Jeep jockey jump / All the things you are / Swing low, sweet chariot / Body and soul / Beat me Daddy, eight to the bar / Eight to the bar / Get happy / Moonlight serenade
CD Set _____ CDHD 4012
Happy Days / Feb '95 / Conifer.

MAGIC OF GLENN MILLER (4 CD Box Set)
CD _____ CDDIG 14
Charly / Apr '95 / Charly / THE / Cadillac.

MAJOR GLENN MILLER ARMY AIRFORCE OVERSEAS ORCHESTRA (Miller, Glenn Orchestra)
Flying home / Long ago and far away / Moonlight serenade / I can't give you anything but love / Symphony / Cherokee / Laura
CD _____ DAWE 47
Magic / Nov '93 / Jazz Music / Swift / Wellard / Cadillac / Harmonia Mundi.

MEMORIAL FOR GLENN MILLER VOL.2
King's march / Tuxedo Junction / All the things you are / April in Paris / American patrol / Song of the Volga boatmen / Night and day / Baby me / Georgia on my mind / Dream / Over the rainbow / Running wild / Stormy weather / Man I love / Lady is a tramp / Adios / Tisket-a-tasket
CD _____ 139 005
Accord / Dec '86 / Discovery / Harmonia Mundi / Cadillac.

MEMORIAL FOR GLENN MILLER VOL.3
CD _____ 139 218
Accord / Dec '86 / Discovery / Harmonia Mundi / Cadillac.

MISSING CHAPTERS #1 - AMERICAN PATROL
Sun valley jump / Pearls on velvet / With my head in the clouds / Speak low / Here we go again / Rhapsody in blue / Dipsy doodle / String of pearls / Cherokee / Music stopped / It must be jelly / Songs my Mother taught me / Stompin' at the Savoy / Poinciana / Tail-end Charlie / Summertime / Song of the Volga boatmen / Oh what a beautiful morning / Suddenly it's Spring / Honeysuckle rose / Star dust / Anvil chorus
CD _____ AMSC 556
Silver City / Dec '95 / BMG / Koch.

MISSING CHAPTERS #2 - KEEP 'EM FLYING
Bubble bath / Blue Danube / Everybody loves my baby / Blues in the night / In the mood / In the gloaming / Over there / Stormy weather / Victory polka / Tuxedo junction / I love you / Holiday for strings / Jeanie with the light brown hair / Enlisted men's mess / Now I know / Guns in the sky / Don't be that way / All through the night / Put your arms around me / Moondreams / Keep 'em flying / All the things you are / Music makers / Squadron song
CD _____ AMSC 557
Silver City / Dec '95 / BMG / Koch.

MISSING CHAPTERS #3 - ALL'S WELL MADEMOISELLE
Moonlight serenade / 705 / Sweet Lorraine / Tuxedo junction / Jeannie with the light brown hair / Begin the beguine / Blue rain / Down the road apiece / Great day / Jerry's Aachen back / Anchors aweigh / Song of the Volga boatmen / Little brown jug / Parachute jump / Wham / Mission to Moscow / Git along song / What is this thing called love / Time alone will tell / All's well Mademoiselle / Hog snortin' romp / I sustain the wings / I'll see you again / Londonderry air / Way you look tonight / I'll be seeing you / I sustain the wings #2
CD _____ AMSC 558
Silver City / Dec '95 / BMG / Koch.

MISSING CHAPTERS #4 - THE RED CAVALRY MARCH
Moonlight serenade / Song of the Volga boatmen / Laura / Get happy / Drink to me with thine eyes / There goes that song again / Music makers / Farewell blues / Red cavalry march / I've got sixpence / String of pearls / Trolley song / Shoo shoo baby / Time alone will tell / My guy's come back / Everybody loves my baby / Moonlight serenade #2 / Here we go again / I'll be seeing you / Swing low sweet chariot / Poinciana / Moonlight serenade #3
CD _____ AMSC 559
Silver City / Dec '95 / BMG / Koch.

MISSING CHAPTERS #5 - THE COMPLETE ABBEY ROAD RECORDINGS
Moonlight serenade / In the mood / Stardust / Song of the Volga boatmen / Long ago and far away / Is you is or is you ain't my baby / Great day / Moonlight serenade #2 / American patrol / Summertime / Tuxedo junction / Now I know / Begin the beguine / Anvil chorus / Moonlight serenade #3 / Here we go again / My heart tells me / String of pearls / Stormy weather / Poinciana / Moonlight serenade #4
CD _____ AMSC 560
Silver City / Dec '95 / BMG / Koch.

MISSING CHAPTERS #6 - BLUE CHAMPAGNE
Army Air Corps/I sustain the wings / Sun valley jump / Suddenly it's Spring / All through the night / I love you / Take it easy / Blue Hawaii / Juke box Saturday night / Pearls on velvet / There are Yanks / I sustain the wings #2 / My ideal / Holiday for strings / Goin' home / Dipsy doodle / Stormy weather / It must be jelly / Annie Laurie / In the mood / In an 18th century drawing room / Guns in the sky / Deep purple / Oh what a beautiful morning / Now I know / Put your arms around me honey / Blue champagne / Snafu jump / Army Air Corps song
CD _____ AMSC 561
Silver City / Dec '95 / BMG / Koch.

MOONLIGHT COCKTAIL (Miller, Glenn & Ray Eberle)
Too romantic / Imagination / Danny boy / Say it / Hear my song violetta / Pennsylvania 6-5000 / Sierra Sue / Devil may care / Bugle call rag / Nearness of you / Moonlight cocktail / Story of a starry night / Indian summer / Serenade in blue / At last / Beethoven's moonlight sonata / Who's sorry now / Out of space / One I love / Brahms cradle song / Slow freight / Blue orchids
CD _____ CDMOIR 309
Memoir / Apr '95 / Target/BMG.

MOONLIGHT SERENADE
Moonlight serenade / King Porter stomp / Little brown jug / In the mood / Tuxedo junction / Pennsylvania 6-5000 / String of pearls / Elmer's tune / Chattanooga choo choo / Don't sit under the apple tree / American patrol
CD _____ ND 90626
Bluebird / Apr '92 / BMG.

MOONLIGHT SERENADE
Moonlight serenade / Wham / Sunrise serenade / Ciribiribin / Bluebirds in the moonlight / My prayer / Little brown jug / Near-ness of you / Fresh as a daisy / Blueberry Hill / Boogie wooglie piggy / When the swallows come back to Capistrano / Boulder buff / Handful of stars / Kiss polka / I know why / Chattanooga choo choo / It happened in Sun Valley / Let's have another cup of coffee / Story of a starry night / Don't sit under the apple tree / Jukebox Saturday night / Adios
CD _____ CDHD 210
Happy Days / May '93 / Conifer.

MOONLIGHT SERENADE
CD _____ AVC 508
Avid / Dec '92 / Avid/BMG / Koch.

MOONLIGHT SERENADE
Moonlight / Little brown jug / Sunrise serenade / Pin ball paul / Indian summer / Woodpecker song / Pennsylvania 6-5000 / Slumber song / Chatanooga choo choo / String of pearls / Don't sit under the apple tree / My blue heaven / In the wood / Sun valley jump / Farewell blues / Tuxedo junction / Blues in my heart / Begin the beguine / Anvil chorus / St. Louis blues march / Everybody loves my baby / Over there / Song of the Volga boatmen / Enlisted mens mess / It must be jelly, 'cause jam don't shake like that
CD _____ CDGRF 076
Tring / '93 / Tring / Prism.

MOONLIGHT SERENADE
CD _____ CDCD 1091
Charly / Apr '93 / Charly / THE / Cadillac.

MOONLIGHT SERENADE
Moonlight serenade / Pennsylvania 6-5000 / Johnson rag / Blue orchids / American patrol / Moonlight cocktail / Little brown jug / Frenesi / Elmer's tune / Slip horn jive / Don't sit under the apple tree / String of pearls / Chattanooga choo choo / Take the 'A' train / Perfidia / Tuxedo Junction / Nightingale sang in Berkeley Square / Boulder buff / Story of a starry night / At last / Serenade in blue / I've got a gal in Kalamazoo / In the mood
CD _____ PPCD 78116
Past Perfect / Feb '95 / THE.

MOOR MILLER MUSIC (Miller, Glenn Orchestra)
CD _____ CDCD 1179
Charly / Apr '94 / Charly / THE / Cadillac.

ON THE AIR
Pennsylvania 6-5000 / My isle of golden dreams / Booglie wooglie piggy / Tuxedo junction / People like you and me / Bless you / Fresh as a daisy / Limehouse blues / Woodpecker song / Sweet and lovely/Sierra Sue/Very thought of you/Blue evening / Keep 'em flying / Jingle bells / Introduction to a waltz / Five o'clock whistle / Here we go again / St. Louis blues / I've got no strings / Handful of stars / Baby me / Blueberry hill / Chattanooga choo choo / Song of the Volga boatmen / Everybody loves my baby / Rumba jumps
CD _____ AVC 550
Avid / Jun '95 / Avid/BMG / Koch.

ON THE RADIO (1939-41) (Miller, Glenn Orchestra)
CD _____ DAWE 63
Magic / Sep '93 / Jazz Music / Swift / Wellard / Cadillac / Harmonia Mundi.

ORIGINAL GLENN MILLER & HIS ORCHESTRA, THE (Miller, Glenn Orchestra)
When Johnny comes marching home / man with the mandolin / American patrol / Sweet Eloise / Chip off the old block / My blue heaven / Sweet potato piper / Wishing / My, my / Let's have another cup of coffee / Over the rainbow / Boog it / Chattanooga choo choo / Alice blue gown / Wonderful one / Day we meet again / Boulder buff / Frenesi / Booglie wooglie piggy / I know why / Anvil chorus
CD _____ PASTCD 7011
Flapper / Apr '93 / Pinnacle.

RARITIES 1938-40
CD _____ JZCD 337
Suisa / Jan '93 / Jazz Music / THE.

RETURN TO THE CAFE ROUGE
CD _____ DAWE 38
Magic / '89 / Jazz Music / Swift / Wellard / Cadillac / Harmonia Mundi.

RHAPSODY (Miller, Glenn & The Army Airforce Orchestra)
CD _____ SWS 11
Swing World / Oct '92 / Wellard / Swift / CM / Submarine / Charly.

SING-ALONG PARTY
String of pearls / Song of the Volga boatmen / Chatanooga choo choo / Pennsylvania 6-5000 / Don't sit under the apple tree / American patrol / Sun valley jump / Little brown jug / In the mood / Tuxedo junction / St. Louis blues / My blue heaven / Anvil chorus / Over there / Indian summer / Moonlight serenade / Miller's megamix (Incl: Little brown jug, In the mood, American patrol & Don't sit under the apple tree,) / Swingalong megamix (Incl: Chattanooga choo choo, Pensylvania 6-5000 & String of pearls,)
CD _____ CDGRF 152
Tring / '93 / Tring / Prism.

SPIRIT IS WILLING 1939-1942, THE
King Porter stomp / Slip horn jive / Pagan love song / Glen island special / I want to be happy / Farewell blues / Johnson rag / Rug cutter's swing / Slow freight / Bugle call rag / My blue heaven / I dreamt I dwelt in Harlem / Sun valley jump / Spirit is willing / Boulder buff / take the 'a' train / Long tall Mama / Keep 'em flying / Caribbean clipper / Here we go again / Rainbow rhapsody / Rhapsody in blue
CD _____ 7863665292
Bluebird / Apr '95 / BMG.

SPOTLIGHT ON GLENN MILLER & THE DORSEY BROTHERS (Miller, Glenn & Dorsey Brothers)
Boogie woogie / Moonlight serenade / String of pearls / Amapola / Little brown jug / Chattanooga choo choo / Green eyes / In the mood / Serenade in blue / I'm getting sentimental over you / Over the rainbow / Song of India / So rare / I've got a gal in Kalamazoo / Sunrise serenade
CD _____ HADCD 128
Javelin / Feb '94 / THE / Henry Hadaway Organisation.

STORY OF A MAN AND HIS MUSIC, THE
CD _____ 11017
Laserlight / '86 / Target/BMG.

STRING OF PEARLS
Little brown jug / Sunrise serenade / In the mood / I'm sitting on top of the world / Jumpin' jive / Moonlight Bay / String of pearls
CD _____ BSTCD 9107
Best Compact Discs / May '92 / Complete/ Pinnacle.

STRING OF PEARLS
Always in my heart / American patrol / At last / Chip off the old block / Don't sit under the apple tree / Elmer's tune / Humpty Dumpty heart / I guess I'll have to dream the rest / It must be jelly, 'cause jam don't shake like that / I've got a gal in Kalamazoo / Jukebox Saturday night / Lamplighter's serenade / Let's have another cup of coffee / Moonlight cocktail / Moonlight becomes you / Serenade in blue / Skylark / Story of a starry night / String of pearls / Sweet Eloise / Take the 'A' train / That old black magic / This is no laughing matter / When Johnny comes marching home
CD _____ CDAJA 5109
Living Era / Jun '93 / Koch.

SUN VALLEY SERENADE/ORCHESTRA WIVES
Blue Moon / Jan '95 / Magnum Music Group / Greensleeves / Hot Shot / ADA / Cadillac / Discovery.
CD _____ BMCD 7001

SUNSET SERENADE BROADCAST 22 NOV 1941 (Miller, Glenn Orchestra)
Intro / Tuxedo junction / Dreamsville Ohio / Chattanooga choo choo / I know why / It happened in Sun Valley / Everything I love / V Hop / In a sentimental mood / I guess I'll have to dream the rest / Do you care / Tschaikovsky's piano concerto / Till reveille / I don't want to set the world on fire / Papa Niccolini / In the mood / Close
CD Set _____ JH 1002
Jazz Hour / Apr '90 / Target/BMG / Jazz Music / Cadillac.

SUSTAINING REMOTE BROADCASTING, VOL. 2 (Miller, Glenn Orchestra)
CD _____ VJC 1022-2
Vintage Jazz Classics / '91 / Direct / ADA / CM / Cadillac.

SWINGING MR. MILLER
It happened in Sun Valley / When Johnny comes marching home / American patrol / I got a gal in Kalamazoo / Ida, sweet as apple cider / Song of the Volga boatmen / Sun valley jump / Frenesi / Five o'clock whistle / Beat me Daddy, eight to the bar / Yes my darling daughter / Pennsylvania 6-5000 / My blue heaven / Caribbean clipper / Old black magic / Jukebox Saturday night / It must be jelly, 'cause jam don't shake like that / Pagan love song / Glen island special / Take the 'A' train / Tuxedo junction / Wonderful one
CD _____ 74321155222
Jazz Tribune / Jun '94 / BMG.

TWO ON ONE: GLENN MILLER & BENNY GOODMAN (Miller, Glenn & Benny Goodman)
CD _____ CDTT 10
Charly / Apr '94 / Charly / THE / Cadillac.

ULTIMATE GLENN MILLER, THE
In the mood / Little brown jug / Sliphorn jive / My prayer / Tuxedo junction / Fools rush in / Pennsylvania 6-5000 / Blueberry Hill / Song of the Volga boatmen / Perfidia / Chattanooga choo choo / I know why / Adios / String of pearls / Skylark / Don't sit under the apple tree / American patrol / Serenade in blue / I've got a gal in Kalamazoo / St. Louis blues march / At last / Moonlight serenade
CD _____ 74321131372
RCA / Feb '93 / BMG.

UNFORGETTABLE GLENN MILLER, THE
CD _____ PD 89260
RCA / Apr '84 / BMG.

WE'RE STILL IN LOVE

Caribbean clipper / April in Paris / Take the 'A' train / Elmer's tune / Moonlight cocktail / Slumber song / When you wish upon a star / Under a blanket of blue / Blueberry hill / I've got a gal in Kalamazoo / You and I / Moon love / I know why / Stairway to the stars / Careless / Over the rainbow / Ciri-biribin / Danny boy / American patrol / Wishing (Will make it so) / Imagination / Johnson rag / Running wild / Serenade in blue / Adios

CD _____ AVC 547
Avid / Dec '95 / Avid/BMG / Koch.

Miller, Herb

BACK TO BACK (Miller, Herb & His Orchestra)

String of pearls / That old devil called love / Pennsylvania 6-5000 / Serenade in blue / Jeep jockey jump / Five o'clock whistle / Song of the Volga boatmen / St. Louis blues march / Stardust / Elmer's tune / Back to back / Poinciana / Don't sit under the apple tree / Swing low, sweet chariot

CD _____ CDSGP 018
Prestige / Jan '94 / Total/BMG.

OTHER BROTHER, THE (Miller, Herb & His Orchestra)

Herbie's jive / Tuxedo junction / At last / Lover / Little brown jug / I got rhythm / I got a gal in Kalamazoo / Sunrise serenade / Tail end Charlie

CD _____ CDSGP 016
Prestige / Jan '94 / Total/BMG.

REMEMBER GLENN MILLER (Miller, Herb & His Orchestra)

Sun Valley jump / I'm thrilled / Johnson rag / Angel divino / Bugle call rag / Quiet nights of quiet stars / Long tall mama / Slumber song / Caribbean clipper / Remember Glenn Miller / Anchors aweigh / Days of wine and roses / Here we go again / Skylark / I dreamt I dwelt in Harlem

CD _____ CDPT 504
Prestige / Jan '94 / Total/BMG.

Miller, Jacob

I'M JUST A DREAD
CD _____ RGCD 6016
Rocky One / Mar '94 / Jetstar.

JACOB MILLER MEETS FATMAN RIDDIM SECTION
CD _____ CC 2715
Crocodisc / Apr '95 / THE / Magnum Music Group.

MIXED UP ROOTS
CD _____ CC 2707
Crocodisc / Jan '94 / THE / Magnum Music Group.

NATTY CHRISTMAS
CD _____ RASCD 3103
Ras / Nov '92 / Jetstar / Greensleeves / SRD / Direct.

REGGAE GREATS
Shaky girl / Tenement yard / Suzy Wong / Sinners / Healing of the nation / 80,000 careless Ethiopians / I've got the handle / Tired fe lickweed in a bush / Roman soldiers of Babylon / Standing firm / All night 'til daylight / Forward Jah Jah children
CD _____ CIDRG 11
Mango / '88 / Vital / PolyGram.

WHO SAY JAH NO DREAD
CD _____ GRELCD 166
Greensleeves / Nov '92 / Total/BMG / Jetstar / SRD.

WITH THE INNER CIRCLE BAND & AUGUSTUS PABLO
CD _____ LG2 1053
Rhino / Nov '92 / Jetstar / Magnum Music Group / THE.

Miller, Julie

INVISIBLE GIRL
CD _____ SPARK 7037CD
Spark / Feb '95 / ADA.

MEET JULIE MILLER
CD _____ MYRRH 5610CD
Myrrh / Feb '95 / Nelson Word.

ORPHANS & ANGELS
CD _____ MYRRH 7616CD
Myrrh / Jan '95 / Nelson Word.

Miller, Luella

LUELLA MILLER & LONNIE JOHNSON
CD _____ DOCD 5183
Blues Document / Oct '93 / Swift / Jazz Music / Hot Shot.

Miller, Marcus

SUN DON'T LIE, THE
Panther / Steveland / Rampage / Sun don't lie / Scoop / Mr. Pastorius / Funny (all she needs is love) / Moons / Teen town / Ju Ju / King is gone (for miles)
CD _____ FDM 365602
Dreyfus / Aug '93 / ADA / Direct / New Note.

TALES
Blues / Tales / Eric / True geminis / Rush over / Running through my dreams / Erhio-

pia / Strange fruit / Visions / Brazilian rhyme / Forevermore / Infatuation / Tales (reprise) / Come together
CD _____ FDM 365712
Dreyfus / Apr '95 / ADA / Direct / New Note.

Miller, Max

CHEEKY CHAPPIE (Holborn Empire and Finsbury Park 1936-39)
Max with the band / Max on stage - Holborn Empire #1 / Max on stage - Holborn Empire #2 / Max on stage - Finsbury Park Empire
CD _____ PASTCD 0714
Flapper / '90 / Pinnacle.

CHEEKY CHAPPIE ENTERTAINS, THE (3CD Set)
Lulu / She said she wouldn't / Doing all the nice things / With a bit of luck / Influence / Mother Brown Story / There's always someone worse / Mary from the dairy (introduction) / Passing the time away / Hearts and flowers / Be sincere / Girls I like / Fan dancer (oh, Dear what can the matter be) / Mary Anne (the five year plan) / Josephine / Twin sisters / On the banks of the Nile / Hiking / Tit bits / Market song / When we go on our holiday / Cheeky chappie tells a few / I thought we came here to pick some flowers / All because I rolled my eyes / Girls who work where I work / Every Sunday afternoon / New kind of old fashioned girl / Cheeky chappie picks from the white book and blue book / Is there no end to his cleverness / What ju-ju wants ju-ju must have / Stringing along with you / Sitting in the old armchair / Jean Carr asks some questions but Max knows all the answers / Max gives Jean some chocolates / Hiking song / Do re mi / No, no, no / Cheeky chappie tells some / Cheeky Chappie chats about etiquette and manners / Down where the rambling roses grow / I don't like the girls / All good stuff lady / Mary Anne
CD Set _____ MAGPIE 4
See For Miles/C5 / Sep '95 / Pinnacle.

CHEEKY CHAPPIE, THE
That's the way to fall in love / When you're feeling lonely / She'll never be the same again / My favourite lodger
CD _____ CDHD 209
Happy Days / May '93 / Conifer.

CHEEKY CHAPPIE...PLUS
Lulu / Lulu (Reprise) / She said she wouldn't / Doing all the nice things / With a little bit of luck / Influence / Mother Brown story / There's always someone worse off than you
CD _____ C5LCD 613
See For Miles/C5 / Sep '94 / Pinnacle.

MAX AT THE MET/THAT'S NICE MAXIE
Mary from the dairy / Hearts and flowers / Be sincere (Introduction) / Fan dancer (Oh dear what can the matter be) / Mary Ann (The five year plan) / Twin sister / Tit bits / Passing the time away / Be sincere / Girls I like / Hikin / Josephine / On the banks of The Nile / Market song
CD _____ C5LCD 598
See For Miles/C5 / Sep '94 / Pinnacle.

MAX MILLER VOL 2 (The Pure Gold of Music Hall)
Julietta / Love bug will bite you / Max with the forces / Confessions of a cheeky chappy / Woman improver / Weeping willow / You can't blame me for that / Backscratcher / Impshe / Max the auctioneer / Girl next door / How the so-and-so can I be happy / Do re mi / Everything happens to me / At the bathing parade / No, no, no
CD _____ PASTCD 9736
Flapper / Feb '91 / Pinnacle.

Miller, Mulgrew

COUNTDOWN, THE
CD _____ LCD 15192
Landmark / Apr '89 / New Note.

FROM DAY TO DAY
CD _____ LCD 15252
Landmark / Nov '90 / New Note.

GETTING TO KNOW YOU
CD _____ 1241631882
RCA / Jan '96 / BMG.

HAND IN HAND
CD _____ 01241631532
Novus / Jul '93 / BMG.

TIME AND AGAIN
Tongue twister / Broad Street / You and the night and the music / Woeful blues / Lord in the morning thou shalt hear / Who can I turn to / I'll keep loving you / My minute / If ain't one thing it's two / Song of today
CD _____ LCD 15322
Landmark / Aug '93 / New Note.

WINGSPAN
CD _____ LCD 15152
Landmark / Jul '88 / New Note.

WITH OUR OWN EYES
Somewhere else / Carousel / Small portion / Dreamin' / Body and soul / New wheels / Words / When I get there / Summer me, Winter me / Another type thang
CD _____ 1241 63171-2
RCA / Jul '94 / BMG.

Miller, Ned

FROM A JACK TO A KING
From a jack to a king / Parade of broken hearts / Turn around / Lights in the street / Old mother nature and old father time / Roll o' rollin' stone / One among the many / Man behind the gun / Another fool like me / Magic moon / Sunday morning tears / Big love / Old restless ocean / Invisible tears / Do what you do oh well / Dusty guitar / Just before dawn / Go on back you fool / Dark moon / Cold grey bars / My heart waits at the door / Big lie / Heart without a heartache / Billy Carino / Cry of the wild goose / Long shadow / Mona Lisa / Stage coach / You belong to my heart / King of fools / Girl across the table
CD _____ BCD 15496
Bear Family / Feb '91 / Rollercoaster / Direct / CM / Swift / ADA.

Miller, Phil

CUTTING BOTH WAYS
Green and purple extract / Hic haec hoc / Simple man / Eastern region / Hard shoulder / Figures of speech / Green and purple
CD _____ RUNE 11
Cuneiform / Dec '89 / ReR Megacorp.

DIGGING IN
CD _____ RUNE 34
Cuneiform / Oct '90 / ReR Megacorp.

IN CAHOOTS - LIVE IN JAPAN
No holds barred / Bass motives / Speaking to Lydia / Truly yours / Second sight / Green and purple extract / Digging in extract
CD _____ CD 2CD
Crescent Discs / Jun '93 / Vital.

Miller, Punch

ICON
CD _____ AMCD 52
American Music / May '95 / Jazz Music.

LARRY BORENSTEIN VOL. 5
CD _____ 504CD 34
504 / Oct '94 / Wellard / Jazz Music / Target/BMG / Cadillac.

PUNCH MILLER
CD _____ 504CD 40
504 / Dec '95 / Wellard / Jazz Music / Target/BMG / Cadillac.

PUNCH MILLER 1925-30
CD _____ JPCD 1517
Jazz Perspectives / May '95 / Jazz Music / Hot Shot.

Miller, Rodney

GREASY COAT
CD _____ SA 1301CD
Sage Arts / Apr '94 / ADA.

Miller, Roger

BEST OF ROGER MILLER, THE
CD _____ MATCD 327
Castle / Feb '95 / BMG.

DANG ME - GREATEST HITS
CD _____ 15479
Laserlight / Aug '94 / Target/BMG.

KING OF THE ROAD
You're part of me / Fair Swiss maiden / Every which a way / It happened just that way / I get up early in the morning / I catch myself crying / I'll be somewhere / Little green apples / I know who it is (and I'm gonna tell on him) / Don't I love you mister / I you want me too / Burma shave / You don't want my love / Sorry Willie / You can't do me that way / When two worlds collide / Lock, stock and teardrops / Trouble on the turnpike / Rey little star / Footprints in the snow / Hitch hiker / Dang me / King of the road / Chug-a-lug / Engine no.9 / Kansas City star / England swings / Do wacka do / One dyin' and a buryin'
CD _____ BCD 15477
Bear Family / Feb '90 / Rollercoaster / Direct / CM / Swift / ADA.

KING OF THE ROAD
CD _____ 15478
Laserlight / Jun '93 / Target/BMG.

KING OF THE ROAD
CD _____ WMCD 5658
Woodford Music / Jul '92 / THE.

LEGENDS IN MUSIC - ROGER MILLER
CD _____ LECD 083
Wisepack / Jul '94 / THE / Conifer.

Miller, Roger

ELEMENTAL GUITAR
CD _____ SST 318CD
SST / Aug '95 / Plastic Head.

OH
We grind open (in) / Meltdown man / Chinatown samba / Firetruck / Cosmic battle / You son of a bitch / War bolts / Fun world reductions / Space is the place / Forest / Kalgastak
CD _____ NAR 097
New Alliance / Mar '94 / Pinnacle.

UNFOLD (Miller, Roger Exquisite Corpse)
CD _____ SST 307CD
SST / Sep '94 / Plastic Head.

Miller, Sing

BLUES, BALLADS & SPIRITUALS
CD _____ MG 9006
Mardi Gras / Feb '95 / Jazz Music.

Miller, Steve

ABHACADABRA (Miller, Steve Band)
Keeps me wondering why / Something special / Give it up / Never say no / Things I told you / Young girl's heart / Goodbye love / Abracadabra / Cool magic / While I'm waiting
CD _____ ARC 947402
Arcade / Jun '92 / Sony / Grapevine.

BEST OF THE STEVE MILLER BAND 1968-1973, THE (Miller, Steve Band)
Joker / livin' in the USA / My dark hour / Going to the country / Shu ba da du ma ma / Going to Mexico / Come on into the kitchen / Evil / Song for our ancestors / Your saving grace / Quicksilver girl / Seasons / Space cowboy / Gangster of love / Kow kow calculator / Little girl (CD only.) / Don't let nobody turn you around (CD only.) / Jackson-Kent blues / Sugar babe
CD _____ CDEST 2133
Capitol / Oct '90 / EMI.

BOOK OF DREAMS (Miller, Steve Band)
Threshold / Jet airliner / Winter time / Swingtown / True fine love / Wish upon a star / Jungle love / Electro lux imbroglio / Sacrifice / Stake / My own space / Babes in the wood
CD _____ ARC 947202
Arcade / Jun '92 / Sony / Grapevine.

CIRCLE OF LOVE (Miller, Steve Band)
Heart like a wheel / Get on home / Circle of love / Baby wanna dance / Macho city
CD _____ ARC 947302
Arcade / Jun '92 / Sony / Grapevine.

FLY LIKE AN EAGLE (Miller, Steve Band)
Blue odyssey / Dance, dance, dance / Fly like an eagle / Mercury blues / Rock 'n' me / Serenade / 2001 / Sweet Marie / Take the money and run / Wild mountain honey / Window / You send me
CD _____ ARC 947102
Arcade / Jun '92 / Sony / Grapevine.

GREATEST HITS: STEVE MILLER (Decade of American Music 76-86) (Miller, Steve Band)
Space intro / Fly like an eagle / Bongo bongo / Rock 'n' me / Jet airliner / Take the money and run / Mercury blues / Swing town / Shangri la / Abracadabra / Italian x rays / Out of the night / Who do you love / Harmony of the spheres
CD _____ 830978-2
Mercury / May '87 / PolyGram.

ITALIAN X RAYS (Miller, Steve Band)
Radio 1 and 2 / Italian X Rays / Daybreak / Shangri la / Who do you love / Harmony of the spheres / Bongo bongo / Out of the night / Golden opportunity / Hollywood dream / One in a million
CD _____ ARC 947502
Arcade / Jun '92 / Sony / Grapevine.

JOKER, THE (Miller, Steve Band)
Sugar babe / Mary Lou / Shu ba da du ma ma / Your cash ain't nothin' but trash / Joker / Lovin' cup / Come on in my kitchen / Evil / Something to believe in
CD _____ CDFA 3250
Fame / Oct '90 / EMI.

SAILOR (Miller, Steve Band)
Song for our ancestors / Dear Mary / My friend / Living in the U.S.A. / Quicksilver girl / Lucky man / Gangster of love / You're so fine / Overdrive / Dime-a-dance romance
CD _____ CDFA 3254
Fame / Apr '91 / EMI.

STEVE MILLER BAND LIVE (Miller, Steve Band)
Gangster of love / Rock 'n' me / livin' in the USA / Fly like an eagle / Jungle love / Joker / Mercury blues / Take the money and run / Abracadabra / Jet airliner
CD _____ ARC 947602
Arcade / Jun '92 / Sony / Grapevine.

WIDE RIVER (Miller, Steve Band)
Wide river / Midnight train / Blue eyes / Lost in your eyes / Perfect world / Horse and rider / Circle of fire / Conversation / Cry cry cry / Stranger blues / Walks like a lady / All your love (I miss loving)
CD _____ 519441-2
Polydor / Jul '93 / PolyGram.

Millinder, Lucky

LUCKY MILLINDER 1941-42
CD _____ CLASSICS 712
Classics / Jul '93 / Discovery / Jazz Music.

RAM-BUNK-SHUSH
Ram-bunk-shush / Oh babe / Please open your heart / Silent George / I'm waiting just for you / No one else could be / It's been a

459

long, long time / Please be careful / Loaded with love / When I gave you my love / Heavy sugar / Old spice / I'm here love / It's a sad, sad feeling / Owl / Goody good love
CD _____ CDCHARLY 288
Charly / Sep '91 / Charly / THE / Cadillac.

Million Dollar Quartet

COMPLETE MILLION DOLLAR QUARTET
You belong to my heart / When God dips his love in my heart / Just a little talk with Jesus / Walk that lonesome valley / I shall not be moved / Peace in the valley / Down by the riverside / I'm in the crowd but no so alone / Farther along / Blessed Jesus hold my hand / As we travel along the Jericho road / I just can't make it by myself / Little cabin home on the hill / Summertime is passed and gone / I hear a sweet voice calling / Sweetheart you done me wrong / Keeper of the key / Crazy arms / Don't forbid me / Brown eyed handsome man / Out of sight out of mind / Brown eyed handsome man (take 2) / Don't be cruel / Don't be cruel (take 2) / Paralysed / Don't be cruel (take 3) / There's no place like home / When the saints go marching in / Softly and tenderly / Is it so strange / That's when the heartaches begin / Brown eyed handsome man (take 3) / Rip it up / I'm gonna bid my blues goodbye / Crazy arms (take 2) / That's my desire / End of the road / Jerry's boogie / You're the only star in my blue heaven / Elvis, farewell
CD _____ CDCHARLY 102
Charly / Jan '88 / Charly / THE / Cadillac.

Millns, Paul

AGAINST THE TIDE
CD _____ HYCD 200138
Hypertension / Jan '95 / Total/BMG / Direct / ADA.

SIMPLY BLUE
CD _____ HYCD 200131
Hypertension / Jan '95 / Total/BMG / Direct / ADA.

Mills Blue Rhythm Band

BLUE RHYTHM
CD _____ HEPCD 1008
New Note / Aug '92 / New Note / Cadillac.

KEEP THE RHYTHM GOING (1935-36)
CD _____ 3801102
Jazz Archives / Feb '93 / Jazz Music / Discovery / Cadillac.

MILLS BLUE RHYTHM BAND 1934-36
CD _____ CLASSICS 710
Classics / Jul '93 / Discovery / Jazz Music.

MILLS BLUE RHYTHM BAND 1936-37
CD _____ CLASSICS 731
Classics / Jan '94 / Discovery / Jazz Music.

RHYTHMS SPASM
Cabin in the cotton / Minnie the moocher's wedding day / Growl / Might sweet / Rhythm spasm / Swanee lullaby / White lightning / Wild waves / Sentimental gentlemen from Georgia / You gave me everything but love / Ol' yazoo / Reefer man / Jazz cocktail / Smoke rings / Ridin' in rhythm / Weary traveller / Buddy's Wednesday outing / Harlem after midnight / Jazz martini / Feelin' gay / Break it down / Kokey Joe / Love's serenade
CD _____ HEPCD 1015
Hep / Jun '93 / Cadillac / Jazz Music / New Note / Wellard.

Mills Brothers

CHRONOLOGICAL, VOLUME 1
CD _____ JSPCD 301
JSP / Oct '88 / ADA / Target/BMG / Direct / Cadillac / Complete/Pinnacle.

CHRONOLOGICAL, VOLUME 2
CD _____ JSPCD 302
JSP / Apr '89 / ADA / Target/BMG / Direct / Cadillac / Complete/Pinnacle.

CHRONOLOGICAL, VOLUME 3
CD _____ JSPCD 303
JSP / Apr '89 / ADA / Target/BMG / Direct / Cadillac / Complete/Pinnacle.

CHRONOLOGICAL, VOLUME 4
CD _____ JSPCD 304
JSP / Oct '88 / ADA / Target/BMG / Direct / Cadillac / Complete/Pinnacle.

CHRONOLOGICAL, VOLUME 5
Organ grinder swing / Elder Eatmore's sermon on throwing stones / Shuffle your feet / Bandana babies / Flat foot floogie / My walking stick / Caravan / Asleep in the deep
CD _____ JSPCD 320
JSP / Apr '91 / ADA / Target/BMG / Direct / Cadillac / Complete/Pinnacle.

CHRONOLOGICAL, VOLUME 6
CD _____ JSPCD 345
JSP / Jul '93 / ADA / Target/BMG / Direct / Cadillac / Complete/Pinnacle.

DARLING NELLY GRAY 1936-1940
CD _____ CD 56072
Jazz Roots / Jul '95 / Target/BMG.

FOUR BOYS AND A GUITAR
CD _____ CDSH 2063
Derann Trax / Aug '91 / Pinnacle.

I'VE FOUND A NEW BABY 1932-34
CD _____ CD 56057
Jazz Roots / Jul '95 / Target/BMG.

JAZZ PORTRAIT 1
CD _____ CD 14584
Complete / Nov '95 / THE.

JAZZ PORTRAIT 2
CD _____ CD 14587
Complete / Nov '95 / THE.

JAZZ PORTRAIT 3
CD _____ CD 14577
Complete / Nov '95 / THE.

LA SELECTION 1931-38
CD _____ 012
Art Vocal / Sep '93 / Discovery.

MILLS BROTHERS 1931-1934, THE
CD _____ CD 53086
Giants Of Jazz / May '92 / Target/BMG / Cadillac.

MILLS BROTHERS, THE
Swing is the thing / Star dust / Shoe-shine boy / Nagasaki / Flat foot floogie / Window washing man / How did she look / Boog it / When you were sweet sixteen / (I'll be glad when you're dead) you rascal you / It don't mean a thing if it ain't got that swing / Caravan / Georgia / Jeepers creepers / Organ grinder swing / Lazy bones / F.D.R. Jones / My Gal Sal / Sleepy time gal / Shine / Smoke rings / London rhythm
CD _____ PASTCD 7049
Flapper / May '94 / Pinnacle.

SWEETER THAN SUGAR
Tiger rag / Old-fashioned love / Fiddlin' Joe / Smoke rings / I've found a new baby / Chinatown, my Chinatown / Lazybones / Diga diga doo / Nagasaki / Sweeter than sugar / Miss Otis regrets / Ida, sweet as apple cider / Rockin' chair / Some of these days / Sweet Georgia Brown / Nobody's sweetheart
CD _____ CD AJA 5032
Living Era / Feb '87 / Koch.

TIGER RAG (1931-1932)
CD _____ CD 56050
Jazz Roots / Nov '94 / Target/BMG.

Mills, Jeff

WAVEFORM TRANSMISSION 1
CD _____ EFA 0174226
Tresor / Feb '93 / SRD.

Mills, Stephanie

BEST OF STEPHANIE MILLS, THE
CD _____ 5267202
Mercury / Sep '95 / PolyGram.

PERSONAL INSPIRATIONS
I had a talk with God / Sweepin' through the city / He cares / In the morning time / Everything you touch / Everybody ought to know / Power of God / People get ready / He cares (reprise) / I'm gonna make you proud
CD _____ GCD 2123
Alliance Music / Jul '95 / EMI.

Milltown Brothers

VALVE
When it comes / Turn off / Killing all the good men, Jimmy / Pictures (Round my room) / Turn me over / Trees / Sleepwalking / Falling straight down / Crawl with me / Someday / It's all over now baby blue / Cool breeze
CD _____ 540132-2
A&M / Apr '94 / PolyGram.

Milteau, J.J.

LIVE : J J MILTEAU
CD _____ 192007
Saphir / Sep '95 / New Note.

Milton, Richie

STRAIGHT AHEAD, NO STOPPIN' (Milton, Richie & The Lowdown)
CD _____ RTCD 017
Right Track / Jul '95 / Hot Shot.

Milton, Roy

BLOWIN' WITH ROY VOL.3 (Milton, Roy & His Solid Senders)
Coquette / Song is ended (but the melody lingers on) / Them there eyes / When I grow too old to dream / What's the use / Train blues / L.A. Hop / Blue skies / If you don't know / Along the navajo trail / You mean so much to me / My new year's resolution / I've had my moments / Old man river / Everything I do is wrong / There is something missing / My sweetheart / Believe me baby / Blowin' with Roy / Thelma Lou / Sad feeling / Practice what you preach / If you love me baby / Blues ain't news / Cool down
CD _____ CDCHD 575

Ace / Jul '94 / Pinnacle / Cadillac / Complete/Pinnacle.

GROOVY BLUES VOLUME 2 (Milton, Roy & His Solid Senders)
Groovy blues / Rhythm cocktail / On the sunny side of the street / Little boy blue / Pack your sack Jack / Roy rides / Cryin' and singin' the blues / Unidentified shuffle blues / I want a little girl / My blue heaven / T ain't me / Junior jumps / Sympathetic blues / Oh Marie / Waking up baby / Playboy blues / Bye bye baby blues / Don't you remember baby / One O'clock jump / Marie / Unidentified novelty song No.1 / That's the one for me / Cold blooded woman / Short, sweet and snappy / I stood by
CD _____ CDCHD 435
Ace / Jan '93 / Pinnacle / Cadillac / Complete/Pinnacle.

ROY MILTON AND HIS SOLID SENDERS (Milton, Roy & His Solid Senders)
Milton's boogie / R.M. blues / True blues / Camille's boogie / Thrill me / Big fat mama / Keep a dollar in your pocket / Everything I do is wrong / Hop, skip and jump / Porter's love song to a chamber maid / Hucklebuck / Information blues / Where there is no love / Junior jives / Bartender's boogie / Oh babe / Christmas time blues / It's later than you think / Numbers blues / I have news for you / T town twist / Best wishes / So tired / Night and day I miss you / Blue turning grey over you
CD _____ CDCHD 308
Ace / Oct '90 / Pinnacle / Cadillac / Complete/Pinnacle.

Milwaukee Slim

LEMON AVENUE
CD _____ BLUELOONCD 016
Blue Loon / Jul '95 / Hot Shot.

Mimani Park Orchestra

SUNGI
CD _____ PAM 403
PAM / Dec '94 / Direct / ADA.

Mimms, Garnet

CRY BABY/WARM AND SOULFUL
For your precious love / Cry to me / Nobody but you / Until you were gone / Baby don't you weep / Anytime you need me / Runaway lover / Cry baby / Don't change your heart / Quiet place / So close / Wanting you / I'll take good care of you / Looking for you / It won't hurt / Thinkin' / Prove it to me / More than a miracle / As long as I have you / One girl / There goes my baby / It's just a matter of time / Little bit of soap / Look away / I'll make it up to you
CD _____ BGOCD 268
Beat Goes On / Apr '95 / Pinnacle.

Minafra, Pina

NOCI ... STRANI FRUTTI (Minafra, Pina & Reijseger/Bennik)
CD _____ CDLR 176
Leo / '90 / Wellard / Cadillac / Impetus.

Mind Funk

PEOPLE WHO FELL FROM THE SKY
CD _____ CDMFN 182
Music For Nations / Mar '95 / Pinnacle.

Mind Over 4

HALF WAY DOWN
Introduction (Charged) / Honor / Barriers and passages / Cycle of experience / Unknown peers / Faith / My name is nothing / Struggle / Conscience of nation / Then and now / Funny pocket / Coffee
CD _____ CDRR 9072 2
Roadrunner / Apr '93 / Pinnacle.

Mind Over Matter

COLOURS OF LIFE, THE
La vie (the dance of life) / Bali sunrise / Ganga (The river of life) / Mountains of karma
CD _____ 710076
Innovative Communication / Aug '88 / Magnum Music Group.

TRANCE 'N' DANCE
CD _____ 710 090
Innovative Communication / Apr '90 / Magnum Music Group.

Mind Over Matter

SECURITY
CD _____ WAR 015-2CD
Wreckage / Aug '94 / Plastic Head.

Mind Riot

PEAK
CD _____ GOD 012CD
Godhead / May '95 / Plastic Head.

Mindbomb

TRIPPIN' THRU THE MINEFIELD VOL.1
CD _____ RUF 009CD
Ruf / Jan '96 / Pinnacle / ADA.

Mindjive

MINDJIVE
CD _____ BHR 020
Burning Heart / Feb '95 / Plastic Head.

Mindrot

DAWNING
CD _____ NB 138CD
Nuclear Blast / Nov '95 / Plastic Head.

Mindstorm

LOVE GOES BLIND
CD _____ PRS 10292
Provogue / Sep '91 / Pinnacle.

Minger, Pete

LOOK TO THE SKY
(I'm afraid) the masquerade is over / Night has a thousand eyes / Make someone happy / Falling in love with love / Soon / Moose the mooche / Like someone in love / Blue 'n' boogie / I hear a rhapsody / Look to the sky
CD _____ CCD 4555
Concord Jazz / Jun '93 / New Note.

Mingus Big Band

GUNSLINGING BIRDS
Gunslinging birds / Reincarnation of a lovebird / O P / Please don't come back from the moon / Fables of Faubus / Jump monk / Noon night / Hog callin' blues / Started melody
CD _____ FDM 365752
Dreyfus / Jul '95 / ADA / Direct / New Note.

NOSTALGIA IN TIMES SQUARE (Mingus Big Band '93)
Nostalgia in Times Square / Moanin' / Self portrait in three colours / Don't be afraid... / Duke Ellington's Sound of love / Mingus fingers / Weird nightmare / Open letter to Duke / Invisible lady / Ecclusiastics
CD _____ FDM 365592
Dreyfus / Aug '93 / ADA / Direct / New Note.

Mingus, Charles

BETTER GIT IT IN YOUR SOUL
Better git it in your soul / Wednesday night prayer meeting Part 1 / Wednesday night prayer meeting Part 2 / Folk forms No.2
CD _____ CDCD 1013
Charly / Mar '93 / Charly / THE / Cadillac.

BLACK SAINT AND THE SINNER LADY, THE
Solo dancer / Group and solo dancers / Single solos and group dance / Trio and group dancers / Group dancers freewoman / Duet solo dancers / Stop, look and listen / Sinner Jim Whitney / Heart's beat and shades in physical embraces / Stop, look and sing songs of revolutions / Saint and sinner join in merriment on battle front / Group and solo dance of love / Pain and passioned revolt then / Farewell my beloved
CD _____ IMP 11742
Impulse Jazz / Nov '95 / BMG / New Note.

BLUES AND ROOTS
Wednesday night prayer meeting / Cryin' blues / Moanin' / Tension / My Jelly Roll soul / E's flat ah's flat too
CD _____ 756781336-2
Atlantic / Mar '93 / Warner Music.

CHARLES MINGUS
Better git it in your soul / Wednesday night prayer meeting / Prayer for passive resistance / I'll remember April / What love / Folk forms
CD _____ GOJCD 0236
Giants Of Jazz / '89 / Target/BMG / Cadillac.

CHARLES MINGUS AT CARNEGIE HALL
CD _____ 7567813952
Atlantic / Jun '95 / Warner Music.

CHARLES MINGUS WITH ORCHESTRA
Man who never sleeps / O.P / Portrait
CD _____ DC 8565
Denon / Aug '90 / Conifer.

COLLECTION
CD _____ CCSCD 382
Castle / Nov '93 / BMG.

COMPLETE DEBUT RECORDINGS (12CD Set)
CD Set _____ 12DCD 4402
Debut / Sep '93 / Complete/Pinnacle / Cadillac.

COMPLETE TOWN HALL CONCERT, THE
Freedom (pts 1 & 2) / Osmotin / Epitaph (pt 1) / Peggy's blue skylight / Epitaph (pt 2) / My search / Portrait / Duke's choice (Don't come back) / Please don't come back from the moon / In a mellow tone (finale) / Epitaph (pt 1 alt. take)
CD _____ CDP 8283532
Blue Note / Jul '94 / EMI.

CONCERTGEBOUW AMSTERDAM APRIL 1964 VOL.1
CD _____ 087112
Ulysse / Sep '95 / Discovery.

CONCERTGEBOUW AMSTERDAM APRIL 1964 VOL.2
CD _____ 087122
Ulysse / Sep '95 / Discovery.

CUMBIA & JAZZ FUSION
CD _____ 812271785-2
Atlantic / Sep '94 / Warner Music.

DEBUT RARITIES #1 (Mingus, Charles Octet/Jimmy Knepper Quintet)
CD _____ OJCCD 1807
Original Jazz Classics / Apr '93 / Wellard / Jazz Music / Cadillac / Complete/Pinnacle.

DEBUT RARITIES #2
What is this thing called love / Blue moon / Blue tide / Jeepers creepers / Daydream / Rhapsody in blue
CD _____ OJCCD 1810
Original Jazz Classics / Apr '93 / Wellard / Jazz Music / Cadillac / Complete/Pinnacle.

DEBUT RARITIES #3
CD _____ OJCCD 1821
Original Jazz Classics / Apr '93 / Wellard / Jazz Music / Cadillac / Complete/Pinnacle.

DEBUT RARITIES #4
CD _____ OJCCD 1829
Original Jazz Classics / Apr '93 / Wellard / Jazz Music / Cadillac / Complete/Pinnacle.

EPITAPH (2CD Set)
Main score (part 1) / Percussion discussion / Main score (part 2) / Started melody / Better git it in your soul / Moods in mambo / Self portrait in three colours / Chill of death / P.O. / Please don't come back from the moon
CD Set _____ 4666312
Sony Jazz / Jan '95 / Sony.

FABLES OF FAUBUS
CD _____ CD 53161
Giants Of Jazz / May '95 / Target/BMG / Cadillac.

GOODBYE PORK PIE HAT
CD _____ JHR 73516
Jazz Hour / '91 / Target/BMG / Jazz Music / Cadillac.

GREAT CONCERT - PARIS 1964
CD _____ 500072
Musidisc / Nov '93 / Vital / Harmonia Mundi / ADA / Cadillac / Discovery.

HIS FINAL WORK
Just for laughs / Peggy's blue skylight / Caroline Keikki Mingus / Fables of Faubus / Duke Ellington's sound of love / Farewell farewell / So long Eric / Slop (CD only.) / It might as well be spring (CD only.)
CD _____ CDGATE 7016
Kingdom Jazz / Oct '87 / Kingdom.

IMMORTAL CONCERTS (Antibes Jazz Festival 13th July 1960) (Mingus, Charles & Eric Dolphy)
Better git it in your soul / Wednesday night prayer meeting / Prayer for passive resistance / I'll remember April / What love / Folk forms 1
CD _____ GOJCD 53013
Giants Of Jazz / Mar '90 / Target/BMG / Cadillac.

IN A SOULFUL MOOD
CD _____ MCCD 201
Music Club / May '95 / Disc / THE / CM.

IN EUROPE
CD _____ ENJACD 30492
Enja / Nov '94 / New Note / Vital/SAM.

JAZZ COMPOSER'S WORKSHOP
Purple heart / Gregorian chant / Eulogy for Rudy Williams / Tea for two / Smog L.A. / Level seven / Transeason / Rose Geranium / Getting together
CD _____ SV 0171
Savoy Jazz / Apr '93 / Conifer / ADA.

JAZZ WORKSHOP
CD _____ VGCD 650132
Vogue / Oct '93 / DMG.

JAZZICAL MOODS (Mingus, Charles & John LaPorta)
CD _____ OJCCD 1857
Original Jazz Classics / Apr '93 / Wellard / Jazz Music / Cadillac / Complete/Pinnacle.

LET MY CHILDREN HEAR MUSIC
Shoes of the fisherman's wife are some jive ass slippers / Adagio ma non troppo / Don't be afraid / Clown's afraid too / Hobo ho / Chill of death / I of Hurricane Sue / Taurus in the arena of life
CD _____ 4712472
Sony Jazz / Jan '95 / Sony.

LIVE AT BIRDLAND 1962
CD _____ COD 028
Jazz View / Mar '92 / Harmonia Mundi.

LIVE IN CHATEAUVALLON 1972
CD _____ FCD 135
France's Concert / '89 / Jazz Music / BMG.

LIVE IN COPENHAGEN
CD _____ LS 2905
Landscape / Nov '92 / THE.

LIVE IN OSLO 1964
Fables of Faubus / Ow / Orange was the colour of her dress / Take the 'A' train
CD _____ LS 2913
Landscape / Feb '93 / THE.

LIVE IN PARIS 1964 VOL 2
CD _____ FCD 110
France's Concert / Jun '88 / Jazz Music / BMG.

MASTER OF BASS
Peggy's blue skylight / Fables of Faubus / Slop / Caroline Keikki Mingus / So long Eric / Farewell farewell / Just for laughs / It might as well be spring / Duke Ellington's sound of love
CD _____ 722014
Scorpio / Sep '92 / Complete/Pinnacle.

MEDITATION
Peggy's blue skylight / Orange was the colour of her dress / Meditation for integration / Fables of Faubus
CD _____ FCD 102
Esoldun / Jan '88 / Target/BMG.

MINGUS
CD _____ CCD 79021
Candid / Nov '93 / Cadillac / Jazz Music / Wellard / Koch.

MINGUS AH UM
Better git it in your soul / Goodbye pork pie hat / Boogie stop shuffle / Self portrait in three colours / Open letter to Duke / Bird calls / Fables of Faubus / Pussy cat dues / Jelly roll
CD _____ 4504362
Columbia / Oct '93 / Sony.

MINGUS AT ANTIBES
Wednesday night prayer meeting / Prayer for passive resistance / What love / I'll remember April / Folk forms 1 / Better git it in your soul
CD _____ 756790532-2
Atlantic / Mar '93 / Warner Music.

MINGUS AT THE BOHEMIA
CD _____ OJCCD 045
Original Jazz Classics / Oct '92 / Wellard / Jazz Music / Cadillac / Complete/Pinnacle.

MINGUS DYNASTY
Slop / Diane / Song with orange / Gunslinging birds / Things ain't the way they used to be / Far wells / Mill valley / New now, know how / Mood indigo / Put me in that dungeon
CD _____ 472995 2
Columbia / Feb '94 / Sony.

MINGUS PLAYS PIANO
Myself when I am real / I can't get started (with you) / Body and soul / Roland Kirk's message / Memories of you / She's just Miss Popular hybrid / Orange was the colour of her dress, then silk blues / Meditations for Moses / Old portrait / I'm getting sentimental over you / Compositional theme story (Medley's, Anthems and Folklore.)
CD _____ MVCZ 83
Telstar / Oct '95 / BMG.

MINGUS, MINGUS, MINGUS, MINGUS, MINGUS
II B.S. / I x love / Celia / Mood indigo / Better git it in your soul / Theme for Lester Young / Hora decubitus
CD _____ MCAD 39119
Impulse Jazz / Jun '89 / BMG / New Note.

MINION INTRUSION
CD _____ CDSGP 0103
Prestige / May '94 / Total/BMG.

MYSTERIOUS BLUES
Mysterious blues / Wrap your troubles in dreams (and dream your troubles away) / Body and soul / Vassarlean / Reincarnation of a love bird / Me and you blues / Melody for the drums
CD _____ CCD 79042
Candid / May '90 / Cadillac / Jazz Music / Wellard / Koch.

NEW TIJUANA MOODS
Dizzy moods (2 takes) / Ysabel's table dance (2 takes) / Los mariachis (the street musicians) (2 takes) / Flamingo (2 takes) / Tijuana gift shop (2 takes)
CD _____ ND 85644
Bluebird / Jun '88 / BMG.

NEWPORT REBELS (Mingus, Charles/ Eric Dolphy/Roy Eldridge/Max Roach/Jo Jones)
Mysterious blues / Cliff walk / Wrap your troubles in dreams (and dream your troubles away) / T'aint nobody's business if I do / Me and you
CD _____ CCD 9022
Candid / Apr '87 / Cadillac / Jazz Music / Wellard / Koch.

OH YEAH
Hog callin' blues / Devil woman / Wham bam thank you ma'am / Ecclusiastics / Oh Lord don't let them drop that atomic bomb on me / Eat that chicken / Passion of a man
CD _____ 756790667-2
Atlantic / Mar '93 / Warner Music.

ORANGE
CD _____ MCD 078
Moon / Dec '95 / Harmonia Mundi / Cadillac.

ORIGINAL FAUBUS FABLES
CD _____ ATJCD 5965
All That's Jazz / Jul '92 / THE / Jazz Music.

PARIS 1964
CD _____ LEJAZZCD 19
Le Jazz / Jun '93 / Charly / Cadillac.

PARIS 1967 VOL. 2 (Mingus, Charles & Sonny Stitt)
So long Eric / Parkeriana
CD _____ LEJAZZCD 38
Le Jazz / May '95 / Charly / Cadillac.

PARIS TNP OCTOBER 1970
CD _____ 087312
Ulysse / Sep '95 / Discovery.

PARIS, 1947
CD _____ CD 56047
Jazz Roots / Nov '94 / Target/BMG.

PITHYCANTHROPUS ERECTUS
CD _____ 556562
Accord / Nov '93 / Discovery / Harmonia Mundi / Cadillac.

PLUS MAX ROACH (Mingus, Charles & Max Roach)
Drums / Haitian fight song / Ladybird / I'll remember April / Love chant
CD _____ OJCCD 440
Original Jazz Classics / Sep '93 / Wellard / Jazz Music / Cadillac / Complete/Pinnacle.

PRESENTS CHARLES MINGUS
CD _____ CCD 9005
Candid / Nov '87 / Cadillac / Jazz Music / Wellard / Koch.

REINCARNATION OF A LOVEBIRD
Reincarnation of a lovebird / Wrap your troubles in dreams (and dream your troubles away) / R 'n' R / Body and soul / Bugs
CD _____ CCD 9026
Candid / Jun '88 / Cadillac / Jazz Music / Wellard / Koch.

RIGHT NOW: LIVE AT THE JAZZ WORKSHOP
New fables / Meditation
CD _____ OJCCD 237
Original Jazz Classics / Sep '93 / Wellard / Jazz Music / Cadillac / Complete/Pinnacle.

SHOES OF THE FISHERMAN'S WIFE
Slop / Song with orange / Gunslinging birds / Things ain't what they used to be / Shoes of the fisherman's wife are some jive ass slippers / Far wells, mill valley / Mood indigo
CD _____ 4608222
Sony Jazz / Jan '95 / Sony.

THREE OR FOUR SHADES OF BLUE
Better git it in your soul / Goodbye pork pie hat (instr.) / Noddin ya head blues / Three or four shade of blues / Nobody knows
CD _____ 756781403-2
Atlantic / Mar '93 / Warner Music.

TOWN HALL CONCERT
So long Eric / Praying with Eric
CD _____ OJCCD 042
Original Jazz Classics / Sep '93 / Wellard / Jazz Music / Cadillac / Complete/Pinnacle.

WEIRD NIGHTMARE (Meditations On Mingus) (Various Artists)
CD _____ 4724672
Sony Jazz / Jan '95 / Sony.

WONDERLAND
Nostalgia in Times Square / I can't get started (with you) / No private income blues / Alice's wonderland
CD _____ CDP 8273252
Blue Note / Feb '94 / EMI.

Mingus Dynasty Band

LIVE AT THE VILLAGE VANGUARD
CD _____ STCD 4124
Storyville / Feb '90 / Jazz Music / Wellard / CM / Cadillac.

REINCARNATION
CD _____ SNCD 1042
Soul Note / '86 / Harmonia Mundi / Wellard / Cadillac.

Minh Doky, Christian

APPRECIATION
CD _____ STCD 4169
Storyville / Feb '90 / Jazz Music / Wellard / CM / Cadillac.

SEQUEL,THE
Fall / Certified / Message / Alone / Sequel / Falling in love with love / Brother / Let's pretend
CD _____ STCD 4175
Storyville / Feb '90 / Jazz Music / Wellard / CM / Cadillac.

Minhinnet, Ray

DON'T GET MAD GET EVEN
CD _____ SPRAYCD 107
Making Waves / Oct '93 / CM.

Minimal Compact

DEADLY WEAPONS/NEXT ONE IS REAL
CD _____ CRAM 3032CD
Crammed Discs / Nov '88 / Grapevine / New Note.

FIGURE ONE CUTS
CD _____ CRAM 055CD
Crammed Discs / Oct '87 / Grapevine / New Note.

LOWLANDS FLIGHT
CD _____ MTM 10CD
Made To Measure / '88 / Grapevine.

MINIMAL COMPACT LIVE
CD _____ CRAM 061CD
Crammed Discs / Nov '88 / Grapevine / New Note.

ONE PLUS ONE BY ONE
CD _____ CRAM 1521CD
Crammed Discs / Nov '88 / Grapevine / New Note.

RAGING SOULS
CD _____ CRAM 042CD
Crammed Discs / '88 / Grapevine / New Note.

Minimal Man

HUNGER IN ALL SHE'S EVER KNOWN/ MOCK HONEYMOON
CD _____ BIAS 071CD
Play It Again Sam / '90 / Vital.

Ministry

FILTH PIG
Reload / Filth pig / Crumbs / Useless / Lava / Dead guy / Face / Brick windows / Game show / Lay lady lay / Reload (edit)
CD _____ 9362458382
WEA / Jan '96 / Warner Music.

LAND OF RAPE AND HONEY
Stigmata / Missing / Deity / Golden dawn / Destruction / Land of rape and honey / You know what you are / Flashback / Abortive / Hizbollah (CD only) / I prefer (CD only)
CD _____ 7599257992
WEA / Nov '92 / Warner Music.

LIVE - IN CASE YOU DIDN'T FEEL LIKE SHOWING UP
Missing / Deity / So what / Burning inside / Thieves / Stigmata
CD _____ 7599262662
WEA / Nov '92 / Warner Music.

MIND IS A TERRIBLE THING, THE
Thieves / Never believe / Breathe / Burning inside / Cannibal song / So what / Test / Dream song / Faith collapsing
CD _____ 7599260042
WEA / Mar '94 / Warner Music.

PSALM 69
N.W.O. / Just one fix / TV II / Hero / Jesus built my hotrod / Scarecrow / Psalm 69 / Corrosion / Grace
CD _____ 7599 26727-2
WEA / Jun '90 / Warner Music.

Ministry Of Terror

FALL OF LIFE
CD _____ FDN 2011CD
Foundation 2000 / Jun '95 / Plastic Head.

Mink Deville

CABRIETTA/RETURN TO MAGENTA/LE CHAT BLEU (3CD Set)
Venus of Avenue D / Little girl / One way street / Mixed up / Shook up girl / Gunslinger / Can't do without it / Cadillac Walk / Spanish stroll / She's so tough / Party girl / Guardian angel / Soul twist / A-train lady / Rolene / Desperate days / Just your friends / Steady drivin' man / Easy slider / I broke that promise / Confidence to kill / This must be the night / Savoire faire / That world outside / Slow drain / You just keep holding on / Lipstick traces / Just to walk that little girl home / Turn you every way but loose / Bad boy / Heaven stood still
CD Set _____ CDOMB 013
EMI / Oct '95 / EMI.

LE CHAT BLEU
This must be the night / Savoir faire / That world outside / Slow drain / You just keep holding on / Lipstick traces / Bad boy / Mazurka / Just to walk that little girl home / Heaven stood still
CD _____ WM 339002
WMD / Jun '93 / BMG.

RETURN TO MAGENTA
Just your friends / Soul twist / A train lady / Rolene / Desperate days / Guardian angel / Steady drivin' man / Easy slider / I broke that promise / Confidence to kill
CD _____ WM 339003
WMD / Jun '93 / BMG.

SPANISH STROLL
CD _____ RVCD 32
Raven / Jun '93 / Direct / ADA.

Mink Stole

EATS HEAD
CD _____ SPV 077-45582
SPV / Jul '94 / Plastic Head.

Minnelli, Liza

COLLECTION, THE
Cabaret (live) / Look of love / On a slow boat to China / Man I love / Stormy weather / Leavin' on a jet plane / Liza (with a Z) (live) / Everybody's talkin'/Good morning star-shine (live) / Come rain or come shine / Love story / Love for sale / Can't help lovin' that man of mine / I will wait for you (live) / Nevertheless (I'm in love with) / For no-one / Macarthur Park / Lazy bones / God bless the child / Maybe this time / How long has this been goin' on
CD _____ 5518152
Spectrum/Karussell / Nov '95 / PolyGram / THE.

LIVE AT CARNEGIE HALL
CD _____ CD 85502
Telarc / '88 / Conifer / ADA.

LIZA MINNELLI LIVE FROM RADIO CITY MUSIC HALL
Overture/Stepping out/Liza with a Z/New York New York / Teach me tonight / Old friends / Live alone and like it / Sorry I asked / So what / Sara Lee / Some people / See-ing things / I wanna get into the act / Men's Medley / Imagine / Here I'll stay/Our love is here to stay / There's no business like show business / Stepping out (Reprise) / New York, New York
CD _____ 472500 2
Columbia / Nov '92 / Sony.

RESULTS
I want you now / Losing my mind / If there was love / So sorry, I said / Don't drop bombs / Twist in my sobriety / Rent / Love pains / Tonight is forever / I can't say goodnight
CD _____ 4655112
Epic / Oct '89 / Sony.

SINGER, THE
I believe in music / Use me / I'd love you to want me / Oh babe / You're a star / Where is the love / Singer / Don't let me be lonely tonight / Dancing in the moonlight / You are the sunshine of my life / Baby don't get hooked on me
CD _____ 9825932
Pickwick/Sony Collector's Choice / Oct '91 / Carlton Home Entertainment / Pinnacle / Sony.

Minogue, Kylie

CELEBRATION - GREATEST HITS
CD _____ HFCD 25
PWL / Aug '92 / Warner Music / 3MV.

ENJOY YOURSELF
Hand on your heart / Wouldn't change a thing / Enjoy yourself / Tell tale signs / Tears on my pillow / Never too late / Nothing to lose / Heaven and earth / I'm over dreaming (over you) / My secret heart
CD _____ HFCD 9
PWL / Oct '89 / Warner Music / 3MV.

INTERVIEW COMPACT DISC: KYLIE & JASON (Minogue, Kylie & Jason Donovan)
CD P.Disc _____ CBAK 4026
Baktabak / Nov '89 / Baktabak.

KYLIE - THE ALBUM
I should be so lucky / Locomotion / Je ne sais pas pourquoi / It's no secret / Got to be certain / Turn it into love / I miss you / I'll still be loving you / Look my way / Love at first sight
CD _____ HFCD 3
PWL / Jul '88 / Warner Music / 3MV.

KYLIE MINOGUE
Confide in me / If I was your lover / Where is the feeling / Put yourself in my place / Dangerous game / Automatic love / Where has the love gone / Falling / Time will pass you by
CD _____ 74321 22749-2
De-Construction / Sep '94 / BMG.

LET'S GET TO IT
CD _____ HFCD 21
PWL / Oct '91 / Warner Music / 3MV.

RHYTHM OF LOVE
CD _____ HFCD 18
PWL / Nov '90 / Warner Music / 3MV.

Minor Threat

COMPLETE DISCOGRAPHY
CD _____ DISCHORD 40
Dischord / Mar '90 / SRD.

Minott, Sugar

20 SUPER HITS
CD _____ SONCD 0009
Sonic Sounds / Oct '90 / Jetstar.

AFRICAN SOLDIER
CD _____ HBCD 49
Heartbeat / '88 / Greensleeves / Jetstar / Direct / ADA.

BLACK ROOTS
Mankind / Hard time pressure / River Jordan / Jailhouse / I'm gonna hold on / Oppressors oppression / Two time loser / Black roots / Clean runnings / Mr. Babylon man
CD _____ RRCD 39
Reggae Refreshers / Jul '92 / PolyGram / Vital.

BOSS IS BACK, THE
CD _____ RASCD 3039
Ras / May '89 / Jetstar / Greensleeves / SRD / Direct.

GOOD THING GOING
Good thing going / High up above / Never my love / House on a hill / My sister / Jasmine / Life without money / Lonely days / Walk on by / Family affair
CD _____ HBCD 13
Heartbeat / Aug '88 / Greensleeves / Jetstar / Direct / ADA.

GOOD THING GOING
CD _____ CDSGP 0146
Prestige / Jul '95 / Total/BMG.

INNA REGGAE DANCE HALL
CD _____ HBCD 29
Heartbeat / Jul '88 / Greensleeves / Jetstar / Direct / ADA.

INTERNATIONAL
Ras / Jan '96 / Jetstar / Greensleeves / SRD / Direct.
CD _____ RASCD 3197

SHOWDOWN (Minott, Sugar & Frankie Paul)
CD _____ 78249700160
Channel One / Apr '95 / Jetstar.

SLICE OF THE CAKE
CD _____ HBCD 24
Heartbeat / '88 / Greensleeves / Jetstar / Direct / ADA.

TOUCH OF CLASS, A
CD _____ JMCD 001
Jammy's / Mar '91 / Jetstar.

WITH LOTS OF EXTRA
CD _____ 78249700120
Channel One / Apr '95 / Jetstar.

Minstrels Of Annie Street

ORIGINAL TUXEDO RAG
CD _____ SOSCD 1272
Stomp Off / Apr '94 / Jazz Music / Wellard.

Mint Juleps

ONE TIME
CD _____ STIFFCD 15
Disky / Jan '94 / THE / BMG / Discovery / Pinnacle.

WOMEN IN (E)MOTION FESTIVAL
CD _____ T&M 104
Tradition & Moderne / Nov '94 / Direct / ADA.

Minucci, Chieli

JEWELS
Courageous cats / Phat city / Only you / Sitting in limbo / Hideaway / Dig the dirt / Mountains / Realm of the senses / Moment of love / Jewels
CD _____ JVC 20442
JVC / May '95 / New Note.

Minus 5

OLD LIQUIDATOR
CD _____ GRCD 350
Glitterhouse / Dec '94 / Direct / ADA.

Minus, Rich

BORDERLINE BLUES
CD _____ 422432
New Rose / May '94 / Direct / ADA.

COLLECTION
CD _____ 422231
New Rose / May '94 / Direct / ADA.

RICH MINUS 3
CD _____ 422497
New Rose / May '94 / Direct / ADA.

Minutemen

3 WAY TIE (FOR LAST)
CD _____ SST 058 CD
SST / Feb '86 / Plastic Head.

BALLOT RESULT
CD _____ SST 068 CD
SST / May '93 / Plastic Head.

BUZZ OR HOWL UNDER THE INFLUENCE OF HEAT
CD _____ SST 016 CD
SST / May '93 / Plastic Head.

DOUBLE NICKELS ON THE DIME
CD _____ SST 028 CD
SST / Oct '87 / Plastic Head.

FAT
CD _____ SST 214 CD
SST / Nov '88 / Plastic Head.

POLITICS OF TIME
CD _____ SST 277 CD
SST / May '93 / Plastic Head.

POST-MERSH, VOL.1
CD _____ SST 138 CD
SST / May '93 / Plastic Head.

POST-MERSH, VOL.2
CD _____ SST 139 CD
SST / May '93 / Plastic Head.

POST-MERSH, VOL.3
CD _____ SST 165 CD
SST / May '93 / Plastic Head.

PROJECT MERSH
CD _____ SST 034 CD
SST / May '93 / Plastic Head.

PUNCH LINE, THE
CD _____ SST 004 CD
SST / May '93 / Plastic Head.

WHAT MAKES A MAN START FIRES
CD _____ SST 014 CD
SST / May '93 / Plastic Head.

Minxus

PABULUM
Minxus / Silk purse / I know you want to stop / Pabulum / Falcon contract / Vultura / Wonderful paradise / Get / I live on sand / Monkey theme / Liberty bodice / Fecund girls / Sunshine / X Y Zoom / Ever since forever
CD _____ PURECD 043
Too Pure / Jan '95 / Vital.

Mioritza

SONGS AND DANCES FROM ROMANIA
CD _____ EUCD 1070
ARC / '89 / ARC Music / ADA.

Miracle Legion

ME AND MR RAY
CD _____ ROUGHCD 136
Rough Trade / Jan '89 / Pinnacle.

Miracle Workers

INSIDE OUT
CD _____ VOXXCD 2031
Voxx / '94 / Else / Disc.

ROLL OUT THE RED CARPET
CD _____ TX 93162
Roadrunner / Apr '91 / Pinnacle.

Miranda Sex Garden

FAIRYTALES OF SLAVERY
CD _____ CDSTUMM 120
Mute / May '94 / Disc.

IRIS
Lovely Joan / Falling / Fear / Blue light / Iris
CD _____ CDSTUMM 97
Mute / May '92 / Disc.

Miranda, Carmen

BRAZILIAN BOMBSHELL, THE
CD _____ LEGEND CD 6005
Fresh Sound / Dec '92 / Jazz Music / Discovery.

CARMEN MIRANDA
CD _____ HQCD 33
Harlequin / Oct '93 / Swift / Jazz Music / Wellard / Hot Shot / Cadillac.

SOUTH AMERICAN WAY
South American way / Mama eu tuero (I want my mama) / I yi yi yi yi (I like you very much) / Chica chica boom chic / Weekend in Havana / When I love / Love / Chatta-nooga choo choo / Manuelo / O passo du kanguru / Bambu bambu / Cae cae / Tur-adas em madrid / Tic tac do meu coracao / Co co co co ro / Cuanto Lagusta / Wedding samba
CD _____ JASCD 317
Jasmine / Nov '93 / Wellard / Swift / Conifer / Cadillac / Magnum Music Group.

Mirrors Over Kiev

NORTHERN SONGS
Jane's farewell / Midnight sky / Rolling in the hay / By your side / Arrows in your eyes / All his women / My cheatin' heart / Scars are healing / Northern song / Dance you through / Hang down your head
CD _____ RRACD 014
Run River / Sep '91 / Direct / ADA / CM.

Mirwais

MIRWAIS
CD _____ ROSE 235 CD
New Rose / Feb '91 / Direct / ADA.

Misanthrope

6666 THEATRE BIZARRE
CD _____ HOLY 016CD
Holy / Nov '95 / Plastic Head.

MIRACLES TOTEM TABOO
CD _____ HOLY 06CD
Holy / Jul '94 / Plastic Head.

VARIATION ON INDUCTIVE THEORIES
CD _____ HOLY 2CD
Holy / May '94 / Plastic Head.

Misery Loves Co

MISERY LOVES CO
My mind still speaks / Kiss your boots / Need another one / Sonic attack / This is my dream / Happy / Scared / I swallow / Private hell / Only way / Two seconds
CD _____ MOSH 133CD
Earache / Apr '95 / Vital.
CD Set _____ MOSH 133CDB
Earache / Aug '95 / Vital.

Misfits

EVIL/EARTH/WOLFS
CD _____ AGO 572
Noise/Modern Music / Jul '91 / Pinnacle / Plastic Head.

MISFITS
Bullet / Horror business / Teenager's from Mars / Night of the living / Where eagles dare / Vampira / Skulls / I turned into a martian / Eyes / Violent world / London dungeon / Ghoul's night out / Halloween / Die die my darling / Mommy, can I go out and kill tonight
CD _____ PL 9CD1
Plan 9 / May '88 / Pinnacle.

Misiani, Daniel Owino

PINY OSE MER/THE WORLD UPSIDE DOWN (Misiani, Daniel Owino & Shirati Band)
Isabella Muga / Rose Akoth / Margret Odero / Piny Ose Mer / Makuru bor / Otieno anyango / Wuoth iye tek / Dora Mamy
CD _____ CDORB 046
Globestyle / Jul '89 / Pinnacle.

Miss Lou

YES M'DEAR
CD _____ SONCD 0079
Sonic Sounds / Nov '95 / Jetstar.

Miss Murgatroid

METHYL ETHYL KEY TONES
CD _____ WOE 24
Worrybird / Nov '93 / SRD.

Miss World

MISS WORLD
First female serial killer / Nine steps to no-where / Watch that man weep / Blow / What a wonderful world / British pharmaceuticals / Highway of dead roads / Mother Mary / Speak / Troubled blood / Love is the whole of the law / Thief inside / Dead flowers
CD _____ 4509903522
Anxious / Nov '92 / Warner Music.

Mission

CARVED IN SAND
Amelia / Into the blue / Butterfly on a wheel / Sea of love / Deliverance / Grapes of wrath / Belief / Paradise (will shine like the moon) / Hungry as the hunter / Lovely
CD _____ 8422512
Mercury / Jan '90 / PolyGram.

CHILDREN
Beyond the pale / Wing and a prayer / Heaven on earth / Tower of strength / Kingdom come / Breathe / Shamera Kye / Black mountain mist / Heat / Hymn (for America)
CD _____ 834 263-2
Mercury / Feb '88 / PolyGram.

CHILDREN/CARVED IN SAND (2CD Set)
Amelia / Into the blue / Butterfly on a wheel / Sea of love / Deliverance / Grapes of wrath / Breathe / Child's play / Shamera Kye / Black mountain mist / Dream on / Heat / Hymn for America / Beyond the pale / Wing and a prayer / Fabienne / Heaven on earth / Tower of strength / Kingdom come / Belief / Paradise (will shine like the moon) / Hungry as the hunter / Lovely
CD Set _____ 5286002
Mercury / Aug '95 / PolyGram.

FIRST CHAPTER, THE
Over the hills and far away / Serpent's kiss / Crystal ocean / Dancing barefoot / Like a hurricane / Naked and savage / Garden of delight / Wake / Tomorrow never knows (Only on UK edition.) / Wishing well (Only on UK edition.)
CD _____ 832 527 2
Mercury / May '88 / PolyGram.

GRAINS OF SAND
Hands across the ocean / Grip of disease / Divided we fall / Mercenary / Mr. Pleasant / Kingdom come / Heaven sends you / Sweet smile of mystery / Love / Bird of passage
CD _____ 846 937 2
Mercury / Oct '90 / PolyGram.

MASQUE
Never again / Shades of green (part II) / Even my own shadow / Trail of scarlet / Spider and the fly / She conjures me wings / Sticks and stones / Like a child again / Who will love me tomorrow / You make me breathe / From one Jesus to another / Until there's another sunrise

CD _____ 5121212
Mercury / Jun '92 / PolyGram.

MISSION, THE - BBC LIVE IN CONCERT
Amelia / Wasteland / Serpent's kiss / Belief / Severina / Butterfly on a wheel / Into the blue / Kingdom come / Tower of strength / Crystal ocean / Deliverance
CD _____ WINCD 035
Windsong / Jul '93 / Pinnacle.

NEVERLAND
Raising cain / Sway / Lose myself in you / Swoon / Afterglow (reprise) / Stars don't shine without you / Celebration / Cry like a baby / Heaven knows / Swim with the dolphins / Neverland (vocal) / Daddy's going to heaven now
CD _____ SMEECD 001
Equator / Feb '95 / Pinnacle.

SALAD DAZE
Like a hurricane / Severina / Sacrilege / Dance goes on / Wasteland / Tomorrow never knows / Wishing well / Shelter from the storm / Deliverance / Grip of disease / Belief / Kingdom come / Butterfly on a wheel / Bird of passage
CD _____ CDNT 005
Strange Fruit / Jun '94 / Pinnacle.

SUM AND SUBSTANCE (The Best Of The Mission)
CD _____ 518447-2
Mercury / Jan '94 / PolyGram.

Mission Of Burma

FORGET
CD _____ TAANG 24CD
Taang / Nov '92 / Plastic Head.

MISSION OF BURMA
CD _____ RCD 40072
Rykodisc / Jun '92 / Vital / ADA.

Mississippi Sheiks

MISSISSIPPI SHEIKS, VOL. 1 (1930)
CD _____ DOCD 5083
Blues Document / '92 / Swift / Jazz Music / Hot Shot.

MISSISSIPPI SHEIKS, VOL. 2 (1930-31)
CD _____ DOCD 5084
Blues Document / '92 / Swift / Jazz Music / Hot Shot.

MISSISSIPPI SHEIKS, VOL. 3 (1931-34)
CD _____ DOCD 5085
Blues Document / '92 / Swift / Jazz Music / Hot Shot.

MISSISSIPPI SHEIKS/CHAPMAN BROTHERS, VOL. 4 (1934-36)
CD _____ DOCD 5086
Blues Document / '92 / Swift / Jazz Music / Hot Shot.

Missourians

MISSOURIANS AND THE CAB CALLOWAY ORCHESTRA (1929 and 1930) (Missourians & Cab Calloway Orchestra)
Market street stomp / Ozark mountain blues / You'll cry for me but I'll be gone / Missouri moan / I've got someone / 400 hop / Vine street drag / Scotty blues / Two hundred squabble / Swingin' dem cats / Stoppin' the traffic / Prohibition blues / Gotta darn good reason now / St. Louis blues / Sweet Jenny Lee / Happy feet / Yaller / Viper's drag / Is that religion / Some of these days
CD _____ JSPCD 328
JSP / Apr '91 / ADA / Target/BMG / Direct / Cadillac / Complete/Pinnacle.

Mistinguett

1926-31
CD _____ 124
Chansophone / Nov '92 / Discovery.

Misty In Roots

CHRONICLES: THE BEST OF MISTY IN ROOTS
CD _____ KAZCD 903
Kaz / Jun '94 / BMG.

EARTH
CD _____ KAZCD 601
Kaz / Aug '95 / BMG.

FORWARD
Fiesta / Midas touch / Hawks on the street / Save a thought / Forward / Jah see Jah know / Envy us / Look before you leap / Feelings / Sinner
CD _____ KAZ CD 900
Kaz / Aug '91 / BMG.

LIVE AT THE COUNTER EUROVISION
Introduction / Mankind / Ghetto of the city / How long Jah / Oh wicked man / Judas Iscariot / See them a-come / Sodom and Gomorrah
CD _____ KAZCD 12
Kaz / Jun '90 / BMG.

MUSI O TUNYA
CD _____ KAZCD 602
Kaz / Aug '95 / BMG.

PEEL SESSIONS
CD _____ SFRCD 132
Strange Fruit / May '95 / Pinnacle.

WISE AND FOOLISH
CD _____ KAZCD 603
Kaz / Aug '95 / BMG.

Misunderstood

BEFORE THE DREAM FADED
Children of the sun / My mind / Who do you love / Unseen / Find a hidden door / I can take you to the sun / I'm not talking / Who's been talkin' / I need your love / You don't have to go / I cried my eyes out / Like I do / Crying over love
CD _____ CDBRED 32
Cherry Red / Oct '94 / Pinnacle.

Mitchell, Blue

BIG SIX
CD _____ OJCCD 615
Original Jazz Classics / Nov '95 / Wellard / Jazz Music / Cadillac / Complete/Pinnacle.

BLUE SOUL
Minor vamp / Head / Way you look tonight / Park avenue petite / Top shelf / Waverley street / Blue soul / Polka dots and moonbeams / Nica's dream
CD _____ OJCCD 765
Original Jazz Classics / Jun '94 / Wellard / Jazz Music / Cadillac / Complete/Pinnacle.

GRAFFITI BLUES
Graffiti blues / Yeah ya right / Express / Asso kam / Dorado / Alone again (naturally) / Where it's at / Funky walk / Blue funk
CD _____ 4744142
Sony Jazz / Dec '93 / Sony.

OUT OF THE BLUE
CD _____ OJCCD 667
Original Jazz Classics / Nov '95 / Wellard / Jazz Music / Cadillac / Complete/Pinnacle.

Mitchell, Chad

VIRGO MOON
CD _____ SCD 91590
Folk Era / Dec '94 / CM / ADA.

Mitchell, George

DOWN MEMORY LANE (3CD Set) (Mitchell, George Minstrels)
Ring up the curtain / Ring ring the banjo / When the saints go marching in / Chicago / You made me love you / Mr. Gallagher and Mr. Shean / Put your arms around me honey / Down where the Swanee river flows / While strolling through the park one day / In the good old summertime / Sweet Rosie O'Grady / I'll be your sweetheart / Little Annie Rooney / And the band played on / Alabamy bound / Swanee / Is it true what they say about Dixie / Carolina / Toot Toot Tootsie goodbye / Old ark's a moverin / Along the Navajo trail / In ol' Oklahoma / Old Dan Tucker / Country Style / Skip to my Lou / Buffalo gal / Singin' in the rain / Together / No two people / My blue Heaven / Falling in love with love / Maria from Bahia / I yi yi yi yi (I like you very much) / When I love I love / Bandit / Cielito lindo / Cuonto le Gusta / I'll si si ya in Bahia / Hard times come again no more / Gentle Annie / Way down upon the Swanee river / Tell me pretty maiden / Put on your tata, little girlie / Hello hello, who's your lady friend / I was a good girl until I met you / In the twi-twi-twilight / Two little girls in blue / North and south / You're in Kentucky sure as you're born / Yellow rose of Texas / Swingin on a star / Stars fell on Alabama / I'm going back to old Nebraska / Dixieland / Carry me back to old Virginny / Lady is a tramp / (In) a shanty in old Shanty Town / Got sum fun / I'm sittin' high on a hill top / Big rock candy mountain / Side by side / Widdicombe fair / Home on the range / Back in those old Kentucky days / I went down to Virginia / Sonny boy / Goin' to the county fair / Dicky bird hop / Cuckoo waltz / She was one of the early birds / When the red, red robin comes bob, bob, bobbin' along / Too-Whit Too-Whoo / Chee Chee oo Chee / Let's all take the birdies sing / Load of hay / 1-2 Button your shoe / You are my sunshine / Bei mir bist du schon / Memories are made of this / Sing a song of sunbeams / South of the border / Where or when / Frog and the mouse / Long long ago / Roamin' in the gloamin' / Let me call you sweetheart / Meet me tonight in dreamland / Pack up your troubles in your old kit bag / Till we meet again / Roses of Picardy
CD Set _____ CDDL 1096
Music For Pleasure / Nov '91 / EMI.

Mitchell, Grover

GROVER MITCHELL & HIS ORCHESTRA (Mitchell, Grover & His Orchestra)
CD _____ STCD 9
Stash / '88 / Jazz Music / CM / Cadillac / Direct / ADA.

Mitchell, Guy

16 MOST REQUESTED SONGS
My heart cries for you / Pittsburgh, Pennsylvania / Roving kind / Knee deep in the blues / Belle belle, my liberty belle / Pretty little black eyed Susie / There's always room at our house / Chicka boom / Sparrow in the tree top / Christopher Columbus / My truly truly fair / She wears red feathers / Feet up pat him on the po po / Day of jubilo / Crazy with love / Singin' the blues
CD _____ 4720482
Columbia / Jul '92 / Sony.

ALL TIME HITS
She wears red feathers / Pretty little black eyed Susie / Feet up / Chicka boom / Cloud lucky seven / Cuff of my shirt / Sippin' soda / Side by side / My heart cries for you / Singin' the blues / Knee deep in the blues / Rockabilly / Call Rosie on the 'phone / Heartaches by the number / Pittsburgh, Pennsylvania / Music music music / Sparrow in the tree top / My truly, truly fair / My shoes keep walking back to you (CD only) / Roving kind (CD only.)
CD _____ CDMFP 5908
Music For Pleasure / Apr '91 / EMI.

GUY MITCHELL
CD _____ GRF 237
Tring / Aug '93 / Tring / Prism.

HEARTACHES BY THE NUMBER
Heartaches by the number / Miracle of love / Rockabilly / Singin' the blues / Notify the FBI / Same old me / Sunshine guitar / My shoes keep walking back to you / Sweet stuff / Knee deep in the blues / Take me back baby / Because I love you / Pittsburgh, Pennsylvania / Roving kind / My heart cries for you / Dime and a dollar / My truly, truly fair / House of the swinging bamboo / Sparrow on the tree top / Christopher Columbus / Belle belle, my liberty belle / Ninety nine years / Pretty little black eyed Susie / Unless
CD _____ BCD 15454
Bear Family / May '90 / Rollercoaster / Direct / CM / Swift / ADA.

HIS GREATEST HITS
CD _____ WMCD 5671
Woodford Music / Feb '93 / THE.

PORTRAIT OF A SONG STYLIST
My heart cries for you / Pennies from Heaven / Pittsburgh, Pennsylvania / My dreams are getting better all the time / Heartaches by the number / Under a blanket of blue / She wears red feathers / Everybody loves a lover / Roving kind / Singin' the blues / My truly, truly fair / I've got a pocketful of dreams / East of the sun and west of the moon / Zip a dee doo dah / Symphony of spring / Allegheny moon / East side of heaven / Was it rain
CD _____ HARCD 106
Masterpiece / Apr '89 / BMG.

Mitchell, Joni

BLUE
All I want / My old man / Little green / Carey / Blue / California / This flight tonight / River / Case of you / Last time I saw Richard
CD _____ K 244 128
Reprise / Jan '87 / Warner Music.

CHALK MARK IN A RAINSTORM
My secret place / Number one / Lakota / Tea leaf prophecy / Dancing clown / Cool water / Beat of black wings / Snakes and ladders / Recurring dream / Bird that whistle
CD _____ GFLD 19199
Geffen / Aug '93 / BMG.

CLOUDS
Tin angel / Chelsea morning / I don't know where I stand / That song about the Midway / Roses blue / Gallery / I think I understand / Songs to aging children come / Fiddle and the drum / Both sides now
CD _____ K2 44070
Reprise / Jan '88 / Warner Music.

COURT AND SPARK
Court and spark / Help me / Free man in Paris / People's parties / Same situation / Car on a hill / Down to you / Just like this train / Raised on robbery / Trouble child / Twisted
CD _____ 253 002-2
Asylum / May '83 / Warner Music.

DOG EAT DOG
Good friends / Fiction / Three great stimulants / Tax free / Smokin' / Dog eat dog / Shiny toys / Ethiopia / Impossible dreamer / Lucky girl
CD _____ GFLD 19198
Geffen / Mar '93 / BMG.

FOR THE ROSES
Banquet / Cold blue steel and sweet fire / Barangrill / Lesson in survival / Let the wind carry me / For the roses / You see some-time / Electricity / You turn me on, I'm a radio / Blonde in the bleachers / Woman of heart and mind / Judgement of the moon and stars
CD _____ 253007
Asylum / Dec '87 / Warner Music.

HEJIRA
Coyote / Amelia / Furry sings the blues / Strange boy / Hejira / Song for Sharon / Black crow / Blue motel room / Refuge of the roads
CD _____ 253053 2
Asylum / Oct '87 / Warner Music.

HISSING OF SUMMER LAWNS, THE
In France they kiss on Main Street / Jungle line / Edith and the kingpin / Don't interrupt the sorrow / Shades of scarlet conquering / Hissing of summer lawns / Boho dance / Harry's house / Sweet bird / Shadows and light
CD _____ 253018
Asylum / Dec '87 / Warner Music.

JONI MITCHELL
I had a king / Michael from the mountains / Night in the city / Marcie / Nathan La Franeer / Sisotowbell Lane / Dawntreader / Pirate of penance / Song to a seagull / Cactus tree
CD _____ 244051
Reprise / '87 / Warner Music.

LADIES OF THE CANYON
Morning Morgantown / For free / Conversation / Ladies of the canyon / Willy / Arrangement / Rainy night house / Priest / Blue boy / Big yellow taxi / Woodstock / Circle game
CD _____ K 244085
Reprise / Jul '88 / Warner Music.

MINGUS
Happy birthday / God must be a boogie man / Funeral / Chair in the sky / Wolf that lives in Lindsey / Is a muggin' / Dry cleaner from Des Moines / Lucky / Goodbye pork pie hat / Sweet sucker dance / Coin in the pocket
CD _____ 253091
Asylum / '88 / Warner Music.

NIGHT RIDE HOME
Night ride home / Passion play (When all the slaves are free) / Cherokee Louise / Windfall (Everything for nothing) / Slouching towards Bethlehem / Come in from the cold / Nothing can be done / Only joy in town / Ray's dad's Cadillac / Two grey rooms
CD _____ GEFD 24302
Geffen / Feb '91 / BMG.

TURBULENT INDIGO
Sunny Sunday / Sex kills / How do you stop / Turbulent indigo / Last chance lost / Magdalene laundries / Not to blame / Borderline / Yvette in English / Sire of sorrow (Job's sad song)
CD _____ 936245786-2
Asylum / Oct '94 / Warner Music.

WILD THINGS RUN FAST
Chinese cafe / Unchained melody / Wild things run fast / Ladies man / Moon at the window / Solid love / Be cool / Baby I don't care / You dream flat tires / Man to man / Underneath the streetlight / Love
CD _____ GFLD 19129
Geffen / Jul '92 / BMG.

Mitchell, Prince Phillip

LONER
While the cat's away / Starting from scratch / Come to bed / Can't nobody love you better than me / Never let her down / Nothing hurts like love / You did what you had to do / Loner / She's a party animal
CD _____ CDICH 1110
Ichiban / Oct '93 / Koch.

Mitchell, Red

ALONE TOGETHER
CD _____ DRAGONCD 168
Dragon / Jan '88 / Roots / Cadillac / Wellard / CM / ADA.

EVOLUTION
CD _____ DRCD 191
Dragon / Jan '89 / Roots / Cadillac / Wellard / CM / ADA.

MITCHELL/KELLAWAY/MILDER (Mitchell, Red & Roger Kellaway/Joakim Milder)
CD _____ DRCD 219
Dragon / Oct '94 / Roots / Cadillac / Wellard / CM / ADA.

TALKING
CD _____ 74016
Capri / Nov '93 / Wellard / Cadillac.

VERY THOUGHT OF YOU, THE
CD _____ DRAGONCD 161
Dragon / Jan '89 / Roots / Cadillac / Wellard / CM / ADA.

Mitchell, Roscoe

3 X 4 EYE
CD _____ 120050
Black Saint / Apr '94 / Harmonia Mundi / Cadillac.

HEY DONALD
CD _____ DE 475
Delmark / Oct '95 / Hot Shot / ADA / CM / Direct / Cadillac.

L.R.G./ THE MAZE/ S II EXAMPLES
CD _____ CHIEFCD 4
Chief / Jun '94 / Cadillac.

LIVE AT THE KNITTING FACTORY (Mitchell, Roscoe & The Sound Ensemble)
CD _____ 120120-2
Black Saint / May '92 / Harmonia Mundi / Cadillac.

463

SONGS IN THE WIND
CD _____ VICTOCD 011
Victo / Nov '94 / These / ReR Megacorp /
Cadillac.

THIS DANCE IS FOR STEVE MCCALL (Mitchell, Roscoe & The Note Factory)
CD _____ 120150-2
Black Saint / Nov '93 / Harmonia Mundi /
Cadillac.

Mitchell, Ross

ALL NIGHT LONG (Mitchell, Ross & His Band & Singers)
CD _____ DLD 1037
Dance & Listen / May '93 / Savoy.

BAM-BOOM
CD _____ DLD 1023
Dance & Listen / '92 / Savoy.

BEST OF THE DANSAN YEARS, VOL 2 (Mitchell, Ross Band & Singers)
CD _____ DACD 1002
Dansan / Jul '92 / Savoy / President /
Target/BMG.

BEST OF THE DANSAN YEARS, VOL 3 (Mitchell, Ross Band & Singers)
CD _____ DACD 1003
Dansan / Jul '92 / Savoy / President /
Target/BMG.

C.F.D. #6
CD _____ DLD 1062
Dance & Listen / Dec '95 / Savoy.

DON'T STOP
CD _____ DLD 1016
Dance & Listen / '92 / Savoy.

GO DANCING
CD _____ DLD 1028
Dance & Listen / Jul '92 / Savoy.

MERRY CHRISTMAS (Mitchell, Ross & His Band & Singers)
CD _____ DLD 1006
Dance & Listen / Jul '92 / Savoy.

OPENING NIGHT (Mitchell, Ross & His Band & Singers)
CD _____ DLD 1031
Dance & Listen / May '93 / Savoy.

RAINBOW COLLECTION, THE
CD _____ DLD 1004
Dance & Listen / Jul '92 / Savoy.

ROSS MITCHELL PRESENTS C.F.D.
CD _____ DLD 1027
Dance & Listen / May '92 / Savoy.

STANDARD AND LATIN DANCES
CD _____ DLD 1042
Dance & Listen / Nov '93 / Savoy.

STAR REQUESTS (Mitchell, Ross & His Band & Singers)
I won't dance / Tap your troubles away /
Desert song / Kisses in the dark / Fasci-
nation / Wish upon a star / Jealousy / Star
/ Tea for two / Brazil / Shall we dance / All
I ask of you / I won't send roses / Wake up
little Susie
CD _____ DLD 1003
Dance & Listen / Oct '88 / Savoy.

ZING '90
CD _____ DLD 1010
Dance & Listen / '92 / Savoy.

ZING II (Mitchell, Ross & His Band & Singers)
Baubles, bangles and beads / Dancing in
the dark / London by night / Where is your
heart (from 'Moulin Rouge') / Swingin'
down the lane / One / Rain in Spain / Wrap
your troubles in dreams (and dream your
troubles away) / Sway / Zambesi / Quand
tu chantes / If I loved you / With a song in
my heart / Trickle trickle
CD _____ DLD 1002
Dance & Listen / Apr '88 / Savoy.

Mitchell, Willie

OOH BABY YOU TURN ME ON/LIVE AT THE ROYAL
CD _____ HIUKCD 132
Hi / Jun '93 / Pinnacle.

SOLID SOUL
Prayer meetin' / Grazing in the grass /
Windy / Sunrise serenade / Horse / Groovin'
/ San-Ho-Zay / Uphard / Monkey jump /
Strawberry soul / Hideaway / Willie-wam
CD _____ HIUKCD 120
Hi / Jul '91 / Pinnacle.

SPARKLE
Sparkle / Reaching out / Honey bear / Mid-
night rhapsody / Give the world more love
/ Sugar candy / Expressions / Happy hour
CD _____ C5CD-517
See For Miles/C5 / Jun '88 / Pinnacle.

WALKIN' WITH WILLIE
CD _____ RCCD 3009
Rollercoaster / Jun '94 / CM / Swift.

Mitchum, Robert

CALYPSO
Jean and Dinah / From a logical point of
view / Not me / What is this generation
coming to / Tic tic tic / Beauty is only skin
deep / I learn a merengue, mama / Take me

down to lover's row / Mama look a boo boo
/ Coconut water / Matilda Matilda / They
dance all night
CD _____ CREV 037CD
Rev-Ola / Jul '95 / 3MV / Vital.

THAT MAN
You deserve each other / Walker's woods /
Wheels (it's rollin' time again) / In my place
/ Ballad of Thunder Road / That man right
there / Little ole wine drinker me / Ricardo's
mountain / Sunny / They dance all night /
Matilda Matilda / Coconut water / Boo Boo
(shut your mouth go away) / Mama look /
Take me down to lovers row / Meremgue,
Mama / I learn A / Beauty is only skin deep
/ Tic, tic, tic (lost watch) / What is this
generation coming to / Not me / From a log-
ical point of view / Jean and dinah / Gotta
travel on / Whip-poor-will / Little white lies
CD _____ BCD 15890
Bear Family / Jun '95 / Rollercoaster / Direct
/ CM / Swift / ADA.

Mittoo, Jackie

EVENING TIME
CD _____ SOCD 8014
Studio One / Mar '95 / Jetstar.

KEYBOARD LEGEND
CD _____ SONCD 0073
Sonic Sounds / Apr '95 / Jetstar.

SHOWCASE VOL. 3
CD _____ JIMCD 4957
A & A Productions / Jun '95 / Jetstar.

TRIBUTE TO JACKIE MITTOO
CD _____ CDHB 189190
Heartbeat / Aug '95 / Greensleeves /
Jetstar / Direct / ADA.

Mixman

EARLY DUB TAPES, THE
CD _____ BLKMCD 011
Blakamix / Oct '94 / Jetstar / SRD.

NEW DIMENSIONS DUB
CD _____ BLKCD 002
Blakamix / Sep '92 / Jetstar / SRD.

SEEK AND YOU WILL FIND - THE DUB PIECES
CD _____ BLKCD 16
Blakamix / Nov '95 / Jetstar / SRD.

Mixmaster Morris

DREAMFISH 2 (Mixmaster Morris & Pete Namlock)
CD _____ PW 16
Fax / Nov '95 / Plastic Head.

Mixon, Donovan

LOOK MA, NO HANDS
CD _____ W 112-2
Philogy / Sep '93 / Harmonia Mundi /
Cadillac.

Miyati, Kohachiro

SHAKUHACHI, THE JAPANESE FLUTE
CD _____ 7559720762
Elektra Nonesuch / Jan '95 / Warner
Music.

Mizarolli, John

MESSAGE FROM THE 5TH STONE
No magic love / Granny did it / Ain't nobody
gonna bring me down / Message from the
5th stone / Lost your love my love / Wake
up and live / Is mamma the president /
Menopause / Mama never told you
CD _____ INAK 867 CD
In Akustik / '88 / Magnum Music Group.

MK

SURRENDER (MK & Alana)
CD _____ ACTIVCD 2
Activ / Jun '95 / Total/BMG.

MK Ultra

THIS IS THIS
CD _____ 13318162
Merciful Release / Jul '94 / Warner Music.

MN8

TO THE NEXT LEVEL
I've got a little something for you / If you
only let me in / Happy / Pathway to the
moon / Lonely / Baby, it's you / Black pearl
/ I'll be gone / Holding hands / I will be there
/ Touch the sky
CD _____ 4802802
Columbia / May '95 / Sony.

Mo Boma

MYTHS OF THE NEAR FUTURE
CD _____ XCD 025
Extreme / Feb '95 / Vital/SAM.

Mob

MOB, THE
Maybe I'll find a way / Once a man, twice
a child / (I'd like to see) more of you / Lost
/ Give it to me / For a little while / Goodtime

baby / I dig everything about you / Love's
got a hold on me / Back on the road again
/ Savin' my love for you / Everyday people/
Love power / Make me yours / All I need /
I feel the earth move / Money (that's what I
want) / Where you lead / Two and two to-
gether / Uh-uh-uh-uh-uh-uh
CD _____ NEMCD 724
Sequel / May '95 / BMG.

Mob

LET THE TRIBE INCREASE
Youth / Crying again / Witch hunt / Shuffling
souls / No doves fly here / I hear you laughing / Mirror breaks / Stay / Another day, another death / Cry of the morning / Dance on
(you fool) / Raised in a prison / Slayed / Our
life, our world / Gates of hell / I wish / Never
understood / Roger
CD _____ SEEP 012
CD _____ SEEP 012CD
Rugger Bugger / Oct '95 / Vital.

Mob 47

GARANTEART MANGEL
CD _____ DISTCD 022
Distortion / Nov '95 / Plastic Head.

Mobb Deep

INFAMOUS MOBB DEEP, THE
Infamous
CD _____ 07863664802
RCA / Apr '95 / BMG.

Mobley, Hank

JAZZ MESSAGE VOL. 1
There'll be another you / Cattin' / Madeline
/ When I fall in love / Budo / I married an
angel / Jazz message (With freedom for all)
CD _____ SV 0133
Savoy Jazz / Apr '92 / Conifer / ADA.

JAZZ MESSAGE VOL. 2
Thad's blues / Doug's minor B, OK / B for
B.B. / Blues no. 2 / Space flight
CD _____ SV 0158
Savoy Jazz / Apr '92 / Conifer / ADA.

SLICE OF THE TOP, A
Hawk's other bag / There's a lull in my life
/ Cute 'n' pretty / Touch of blue / Slice of
the top (CD only)
CD _____ CDP 8335822
Blue Note / Oct '95 / EMI.

WORKOUT
Workout / Uh huh / Smokin' / Best things
in life are free / Greasin' easy / Three coins
in the fountain
CD _____ CDP 7840802
Blue Note / Mar '95 / EMI.

Moby

AMBIENT
CD _____ ATLASCD 002
Arctic / Oct '93 / Pinnacle.

EVERYTHING IS WRONG (2CD/MC Set)
CD _____ LCDSTUMM 130
CD _____ CDSTUMM 130
Mute / Mar '95 / Disc.
CD Set _____ XLCDSTUMM 130
Mute / Jan '96 / Disc.

HYMN
CD _____ CDMUTE 161
Mute / May '94 / Disc.

STORY SO FAR
CD _____ ATLASCD 001
Equator / Jul '93 / Pinnacle.

Moby Grape

VINTAGE - THE VERY BEST OF MOBY GRAPE
Hey grandma / Mr. Blues / Fall on you / 8.05
/ Come in the morning / Omaha / Naked, if
I want to / Rounder / Someday / Ain't no
use / Sitting by the window / Changes /
Lazy me / Indifference / Looper / Sweet ride
/ blues / Big / Skip's song / You can do an-
ything / Murder in my heart / For the judge
/ Can't be so bad / Just like Gene Autry /
Foxtrot / He / Motorcycle Irene / Funky tunk
/ Rose coloured eyes / If you can't learn
from your mistakes / Ooh mama ooh / Ain't
that a shame / Trucking man / Captain
Nemo / What's to choose / Going nowhere
/ I am not willing / It's a beautiful day today
/ Right before my eyes / Truly fine citizen /
Hoochie / Soul stew / Seeing
CD Set _____ CD 53041
Legacy / Nov '93 / Sony.

Mock Turtles

MOCK TURTLES 1987-1990
CD _____ ILLCD 019
Imaginary / Apr '91 / Vital.

TURTLE SOUP
CD _____ ILLCD 012
Imaginary / Jul '90 / Vital.

Moco, Maio

PORTUGAL NOVO
CD _____ PS 65071

Playasound / May '91 / Harmonia Mundi /
ADA.

Model 500

CLASSICS
No U.F.O.'s / Chase / Off to battle / Night
drive / Electric entourage / Electronic /
Ocean to ocean / Techno music / Sound of
stereo
CD _____ RS 931CD
R & S / Jul '93 / Vital.

DEEP SPACE
Milky Way / Orbit / Flow / Warning / Astral-
werks / Starlight / Last transport to (Alpha
Centauri) / I wanna be there / Lightspeed
CD _____ RS 95066CD
R & S / May '95 / Vital.

Modern English

AFTER THE SNOW
I melt with you / Tables turning / Carry me
down
CD _____ CAD 206CD
4AD / Nov '92 / Disc.

MESH AND LACE
Sixteen days / Just a thought / Move in light
/ Grief / Token man / Viable commercial /
Black houses / Dance of devotion (love
song)
CD _____ CAD 105CD
4AD / Nov '92 / Disc.

RICOCHET DAYS
CD _____ CAD 402CD
4AD / Nov '92 / Disc.

Modern Folk Quartet

AT CHRISTMAS
CD _____ FE 1404
Folk Era / Nov '94 / CM / ADA.

Modern Jazz Quartet

2 DEGREES EAST 3 DEGREES WEST
CD _____ VN 161
Viper's Nest / May '95 / Direct / Cadillac /
ADA.

40TH ANNIVERSARY CELEBRATION
Bag's groove / All the things you are / Cher-
okee / (Back home again in) Indiana / Come
rain or come shine / Willow weep for me /
Memories of you / Blues for Juanita / There
will never be another you / Easy living /
Django / Darn that dream / Billie's bounce
CD _____ 7567825382
Atlantic / Feb '93 / Warner Music.

ARTISTRY OF THE MODERN JAZZ QUARTET
Fantasy / Oct '93 / Pinnacle / Jazz Music /
Wellard / Cadillac.
CD _____ FCD 60016

BEST OF MODERN JAZZ QUARTET, THE
Valeria / Le cannet / Nature boy / Watergate
blues / Connie's blues / Reunion blues /
Echoes
CD _____ PACD 24054232
Pablo / Apr '94 / Jazz Music / Cadillac /
Complete/Pinnacle.

BLUES ON BACH
Regret / Blues in B flat / Rise up in the
morning / Blues in A minor / Precious joy /
Blues in C minor / Don't stop this train blues
in H / Tears from the children
CD _____ 756781393-2
Atlantic / Mar '93 / Warner Music.

DJANGO
CD _____ OJCCD 057-2
Original Jazz Classics / Feb '92 / Wellard /
Jazz Music / Cadillac / Complete/Pinnacle.

ECHOES/TOGETHER AGAIN
CD _____ CD 2312142
Pablo / Oct '92 / Jazz Music / Cadillac /
Complete/Pinnacle.

FIRST RECORDINGS
CD _____ JW 77014
JWD / May '93 / Target/BMG.

FONTESSA
CD _____ CD 53219
Giants Of Jazz / Nov '95 / Target/BMG /
Cadillac.

IMMORTAL CONCERTS (Scandinavia, April 1960)
Django / Bluesology / La ronde / I remember Clifford / Vendome / Odds against tomorrow / Pyramid / It don't mean a thing if
it ain't got that swing / Round Midnight /
Bag's Groove / I'll remember April / Skating
in Central Park / I should care / Festival
sketch
CD _____ GOJCD 53012
Giants Of Jazz / Mar '90 / Target/BMG /
Cadillac.

LAST CONCERT, THE
Softly as in a morning sunrise / Cylinder /
Summertime / Trav'lin blues in a minor /
One never knows / Bag's groove / Con-
firmation / Round Midnight / Night in Tunisia
/ Golden striker / Skating in Central Park /
Django / What's new
CD _____ 7567819762
Atlantic / Apr '95 / Warner Music.

LEGENDARY PERFORMANCES, THE
Suisa / Jan '93 / Jazz Music / THE.
CD _____ JZCD 340

LONGING FOR THE CONTINENT
Animal dance / Django / England's carol / Bluesology / Bag's groove / Sketch 3 / Ambiquite / Midsummer
CD _____ CDC 7678
LRC / Nov '90 / New Note / Harmonia Mundi.

MJQ BOX, THE (3CD Set)
Prestige / Oct '93 / Complete/Pinnacle / Cadillac.
CD Set _____ 3PRCD 7711

MJQ FOR ELLINGTON
Atlantic / Mar '93 / Warner Music.
CD _____ 756790926-2

MODERN JAZZ QUARTET (Modern Jazz Quartet & Milt Jackson Quintet)
Original Jazz Classics / May '93 / Wellard / Jazz Music / Cadillac / Complete/ Pinnacle.
CD _____ OJCCD 125

MODERN JAZZ QUARTET
Savoy Jazz / Nov '95 / Conifer / ADA.
CD _____ CY 78986CD

MODERN JAZZ QUARTET LIVE 1956
Jazz Anthology / Oct '89 / Harmonia Mundi / Cadillac.
CD _____ 550062

QUARTET, THE
Softly as in a morning sunrise / Love me pretty baby / Autumn breeze / Milt meets Sid / Moving nicely / D and E blues / Heart and soul / True blues / Bluesology / Yesterdays / Round Midnight / Between the devil and the deep blue sea
CD _____ CY 78986
Savoy Jazz / Nov '95 / Conifer / ADA.

TOGETHER AGAIN (Live At The Montreux Jazz Festival 1982)
Django / Cylinder / Martyr / Really true blues / Odds against tomorrow / Jasmine tree / Monterey mist / Bag's new groove / Woody 'n' you
CD _____ CD 2308244
Pablo / Jun '93 / Jazz Music / Cadillac / Complete/Pinnacle.

TOPSY THIS ONE'S FOR BASIE
Reunion blues / Nature boy / Topsy / D and E blues / Valeria / Milano / Le cannet
CD _____ CD 2310917
Pablo / Apr '94 / Jazz Music / Cadillac / Complete/Pinnacle.

UNDER THE JASMINE TREE
Blue necklace / Three little feelings (parts 1, 2 and 3) / Exposure / Jasmine tree
CD _____ CDP 7975802
Apple / Oct '91 / EMI.

Modern Klezmer Quartet

HORA AND BLUE
Global Village / May '94 / ADA / Direct.
CD _____ GV 156CD

Modernaires Orchestra

TRIBUTE TO GLENN MILLER VOL. 1
Ross / Feb '89 / Ross / Duncans.
CD _____ ROSSCD 6621-2

TRIBUTE TO GLENN MILLER VOL. 2
Ross / Feb '89 / Ross / Duncans.
CD _____ ROSSCD 6622-2

TRIBUTE TO GLENN MILLER VOL. 3
Ross / Feb '89 / Ross / Duncans.
CD _____ ROSSCD 6615-2

Modernettes

GET IT STRAIGHT
Zulu / Oct '95 / Plastic Head.
CD _____ ZULU 013CD

Modest Proposal

CONTRAST
Barooni / Mar '93 / SRD.
CD _____ BAR 999D

Modulations

ROUGH OUT HERE
Rough out here / Head on collision with heartbreak / Love at last / I'll always love you / I'm hopelessly in love / I can't fight your love / Worth your weight in gold / Those were the best days of my life / Share what you got, keep what you need / What good am I / Your love has me locked up
CD _____ NEMCD 628
Sequel / Nov '92 / BMG.

Moebius

DOUBLE CUT (Moebius & Beerbohm)
Sky / May '95 / Koch.
CD _____ SKYCD 3091

EN ROUTE (Moebius & Plank)
No CD / Dec '95 / Vital/SAM.
CD _____ CDNO 011

RASTAKRAUT PASTA/MATERIAL (Moebius & Plank)
Sky / Feb '95 / Koch.
CD _____ SKYCD 32

TONSPUREN
Sky / Feb '95 / Koch.
CD _____ SKYCD 3083

ZERO SET (Moebius, Plank & Neumer)
Sky / Feb '95 / Koch.
CD _____ SKYCD 3085

Moffatt, Hugh

DANCE ME OUTSIDE (Moffatt, Hugh & Katy)
It's been decided / We'll sweep out the ashes in the morning / On the borderline / I don't believe you've met my baby / Dance me outside / Right over me / La Luna / Making new / Walking on the moon / Dark end of the street
CD _____ PH 1144CD
Philo / '92 / Direct / CM / ADA.

LIVE AND ALONE
Brambus / Nov '93 / ADA / Direct.
CD _____ BRAM 199118-2

LOVING YOU
When you held me in your arms / Mama Rita / Old flames can't hold a candle to you / Words at twenty paces / Slow movin' freight train / No stranger to the blues / Loving you / Tomorrow is a long time / Carolina star / Jack and Lucy / Roll with weather
CD _____ PH 1111CD
Philo / '88 / Direct / CM / ADA.

TROUBADOUR
Way love is / Rose of my heart / I'll leave the rest to you / Somewhere in Kansas / How could I love her so much / Roses, love and promises / Hard times come again no more / Praise the Lord and send the money / Devil took the rest / Old songs / For Mary
CD _____ BD 500CD
Breakdown / Feb '90 / SRD.

WOGNUM SESSIONS, THE (Moffatt, Hugh Trio)
Strictly Country / Dec '94 / ADA / Direct.
CD _____ SCR 32

Moffatt, Katy

CHILD BRIDE
Child bride / In a moment / Lonely avenue / Look out it must be love / Playin' fool / We ran / You better move on / Anna / Settin' the woods on fire
CD _____ PH 1133CD
Philo / '90 / Direct / CM / ADA.

GREATEST SHOW ON EARTH
Round Tower / Feb '93 / Pinnacle / ADA / Direct / BMG / CM.
CD _____ RTMCD 50

HEARTS GONE WILD
Hearts gone wild
CD _____ RTMCD 69
Round Tower / Sep '94 / Pinnacle / ADA / Direct / BMG / CM.

WALKIN' ON THE MOON
Walkin' on the moon / I'm sorry darlin' / If anything comes to mind / Papacita (Mama Rita) / Mr. Banker / Borderline / Fire in your eyes / I'll take the blame / Hard time on Easy street / I know the difference now
CD _____ RTM 59CD
Round Tower / Oct '94 / Pinnacle / ADA / Direct / BMG / CM.

Moffett, Charles

GIFT, THE
Avant garde got soul too / Adnerb / Gift / Blues strikes again / Yelrihs
CD _____ SV 0217
Savoy Jazz / Jun '93 / Conifer / ADA.

Moffett, Cody

EVIDENCE
Telarc / Oct '93 / Conifer / ADA.
CD _____ CD 83343

Moffs

LABYRINTH
Citadel / Jun '89 / ADA.
CD _____ CGAS 811 CD

Mofungo

BUGGED
SST / May '93 / Plastic Head.
CD _____ SST 191 CD

Mohead, John

LULA CITY LIMITS
Okra-Tone / Aug '95 / Direct / ADA.
CD _____ OKRATONE 4961

Moher

OUT ON THE OCEAN
Cross Border Media / Jan '95 / Direct / ADA.
CD _____ CBMCD 013

Mohiuddin, Dagar Zia

RAGA YAMAN
Nimbus / Sep '94 / Nimbus.
CD _____ NI 5276

Moholos, Louis

VIVA LA BLACK
Ogun / Sep '94 / Cadillac / Jazz Music / Charly.
CD _____ OGCD 006

Moiseyev Dance Co. ·

RUSSIAN FOLK DANCES
Monitor / Jun '93 / CM.
CD _____ MCD 71310

Moist

SILVER
Push / Believe me / Kill for you / Silver / Freaky be beautiful / Break her down / Into everything / Picture Elvis / Machine punch through / This shrieking love / Low low low
CD _____ CDCHR 6080
Chrysalis / Sep '94 / EMI.

Moist Fist

MOIST FIST
Rise / Jul '93 / Pinnacle.
CD _____ RR 121-2

Mojave 3

ASK ME TOMORROW
Love songs on the radio / Sarah / Tomorrow's taken / Candle song 3 / You're beautiful / Where is the love / After all / Pictures / Mercy
CD _____ BAD 5013CD
4AD / Oct '95 / Disc.

Mojos

EVERYTHING'S ALRIGHT
London / Jan '90 / PolyGram.
CD _____ 8209622

Mokave

AFRIQUE
Sun bone / Africa 3/2 / Fragements/Whispers / Parable / Gloria's step / Bugle Ann / Afrique / Mr. Moore's neighbourhood / Country
CD _____ AQCD 1024
Audioquest / Sep '95 / New Note.

Mokenstef

AZZ IZZ
Sex in the rain / Just be gentle / Azz izz / He's mine / Don't go there / Stop callin' me / It happens / Laid back / Let him know / It goes on / I got him all the time (he's mine remix)
CD _____ 5273642
Def Jam / Sep '95 / PolyGram.

Mokhali, Johnny

SOUND OF FREEDOM, THE
O wa mpelaetsa - I doubt you / Luki / Mafoka a bofelo - Last words / Tsa lerato - Love matters / Ke na le Jesu - I've got Jesus / Setlhare ke sefe - What is the remedy / Rre o kae / Ba tlogeleng - Leave them / Sesa feleng - That doesn't end / Go siame - it is alright / Mosala gae - You remain at home / Ngwanaka - my child / Go sa itse - Not to know
CD _____ ELITE 011 CD
Elite/Old Gold / Apr '91 / Carlton Home Entertainment.

Moland, Joey

PILGRIM, THE
Rykodisc / Jun '92 / Vital / ADA.
CD _____ RCD 10212

Molard, Patrick

ER BOLOM KOH (Molard, Patrick & Y. Le Bihan)
Diffusion Breizh / Jul '95 / ADA.
CD _____ GWP 007CD

PIOBAIREACHD
Gwerz Productions / Aug '93 / ADA.
CD _____ GWP 003CD

Molelekwa, Moses

FINDING ONE'S SELF
Nomkhosi / Nobohle / Finding one's self / Melancholy thoughts / Hwalo / Bo molelekwa / Mountain shade / Marabi a aremogolo / Ntate moholo (grandfather)
CD _____ BW 053
B&W / Mar '95 / New Note.

Moleque De Rua

STREET KIDS OF BRAZIL
Pregoes do Rio / Rap do moleque / Louco e triste / Zumbi / Nao vou pagar pra se boiada / Dor de dente / Herodes / O sosia

/ Filosofia do bom malandro / Assaltar papai noel / Ze do brazil / Ensaio geral
CD _____ MOL 91002
Crammed Discs / Nov '95 / Grapevine / New Note.

Molest

MILKFISH
Progress / Nov '95 / Plastic Head.
CD _____ PCD 023

Moller, Ale

VIND
Xource / Oct '94 / ADA / Cadillac.
CD _____ XOU 106CD

Molloy, Matt

CONTENTMENT IS WEALTH (Molloy, Matt & Sean Keane)
Green Linnet / Jun '93 / Roots / CM / Direct / ADA.
CD _____ GLCD 1058

HEATHERY BREEZE
Shanachie / Aug '93 / Koch / ADA / Greensleeves.
CD _____ SHAN 79064CD

MATT MOLLOY
Mulligan / Aug '94 / CM / ADA.
CD _____ LUNCD 004

STONY STEPS
McFadden's favourite / Boys of the town / City of Savannah / Primrose lass mullinger races / Parting of friends / Stony steps/Mi chael Dwyers's favourite / Mrs. Kenny's barndance / Paddy Murphy's wife / Jig of slurs / O Rathaille's grave / Miss Mcguiness' reel of mullinavat / Frank Roche's favourite / Johnny 'Watt' Henry's favourite / Gravel walk / Slip jig
CD _____ CCF 18 CD
Claddagh / May '88 / ADA / Direct.

Molly Half Head

DUNCE
Breaking the ice / Nature's slice / Aisle 8 / Shine / Dunce / Caprio / Heaton's bliss / What will come / Seat on teak / Meccano / Who buys
CD _____ 4783142
Columbia / Jul '95 / Sony.

SULK
Vivid whitsun / Spectacle clear / Promote / Just / Arty breakfast / Bone idol / Barny / Taste of you / Hopscotch / Inkwell / Writing time / Ginger Pat's avenue / Toe to sand
CD _____ AMUSE 00CD
Playtime / Nov '95 / Pinnacle / Discovery.

Moloko

DO YOU LIKE MY TIGHT SWEATER
Echo / Oct '95 / Pinnacle / EMI.
CD _____ ECHCD 7

Moloney, Mick

3 WAY STREET (Moloney, Mick & Eugene O'Donnell & Seamus Egan)
Green Linnet / Jul '93 / Roots / CM / Direct / ADA.
CD _____ GLCD 1129

MICK MOLONEY WITH EUGENE O'DONNELL (Moloney, Mick & Eugene O'Donnell)
Joseph Baker / John Dwyer's reel/Lasses of Castlebar / Killin's fairy hill / Limerick rake / Clar hornpipe/Pride of Moyvane/Humours of Newcastle West / Blackthorn stick/Poet Carney / Bantry girl's lament / Fairie's hornpipe / Winnie Greene's reel/Boston boys / John of dreams / Kilkenny races / Sean Reid's reel/Toss the feathers / Paddy O'Brien's jig/King of the pipers / Irish maid
CD _____ GLCD 1010
Green Linnet / Oct '88 / Roots / CM / Direct / ADA.

STRINGS ATTACHED
My love is in America/Lisdoonvarna reel / Arthur Darley's reel/Over the hills to Rumbush / Munster grass/Peacock's feathers / Gooseberry bush/Charlie Mulvihill's reels / Loftus Jones / Dunmore lassies/McFadden's handsome daughter / Off to Puck Fair / Ricky's white fence/Top of the stairs / Bush on the hill / Bellharbour reel / Miss Lyon's fancy / Tom of the hill / Jackson's morning brush/Paddy Reynold's dream / Coyle's piano reels
CD _____ CDGL 1027
Green Linnet / Oct '88 / Roots / CM / Direct / ADA.

THERE WERE ROSES
Ballad of Jack Dolan / Allastromm's/Julia Clifford's / Drimin Donn Dilis (Dear brown cow) / Redican's mother/Gan ainm/Blast of wind / Almost every circumstance / I will leave this town / There were roses / Fair haired cassidy/Paddy Gavin/Priest's boots / Commodore/Charleston reel / Harvey Street hornpipe/Birds/O'Connor's frolics / Here I am from Donegal
CD _____ GLCD 1057
Green Linnet / Oct '88 / Roots / CM / Direct / ADA.

UNCOMMON BONDS (Moloney, Mick & Eugene O'Donnell)
St. Brendan's fair Isle / Road to Dunmore / Bow legged tailor/Galway jig/April fool/ O'Lochlainn's / Miss Fogarty's christmas cake / Sean McGlynn's mazurka / Bonny blue-eyed Nancy / O'Hara, Hughes, Mc-Creesh and Sands / Blackbird and hen/ Keane's farewell to Nova Scotia / Mary in the morning / Farewell my gentle harp / Muldoon the solid man / Curlew's reel/Derry reel/Hanly's / Bay of Biscay
CD _____ GLCD 1053
Green Linnet / Oct '88 / Roots / CM / Direct / ADA.

Molton, Flora

UNITED STATES - GOSPEL (Molton, Flora & Eleanor Ellis)
CD _____ C 580053
Ocora / May '94 / Harmonia Mundi / ADA.

Moments

GREATEST HITS: MOMENTS
Lovely way she loves / My thing / If I didn't care / Nine times / To you with love / Girls / Jack in the box / Gotta find a way / All I have / Sexy Mama / Love on a two way street / With you / Life and breath / I do / Not on the outside / Lucky me / What's your name / Dolly my love / Look at me (I'm in love) / Girls (french lyrics)
CD _____ NEMCD 614
Sequel / May '91 / BMG.

LATE NIGHT SOUL
Best thing for me / This ole house / Don't let it get you down / Mama I miss you / Where / Girl I'm gonna miss you / Girl don't go / Baby I'm a want you / Look what you've done / How can I love you / Meeting you was no mistake / Patty / Look at me (I'm in love) / I feel so good again / Beautiful woman / I could have loved you / I'll be around / Just because he wants to make love
CD _____ NEMCD 626
Sequel / Jun '92 / BMG.

Momus

CIRCUS MAXIMUS
Lucky like St. Sebastian / Lesson of Sodom / John the baptist Jones / King Solomon's song and mine / Little Lord Obedience / Day the circus came to town / Rape of Lucretia / Paper wraps rock / Rules of the game of quoits
CD _____ ACME 2 CD
El / Jul '89 / Pinnacle.

HIPPOPOTAMOMUS
CD _____ CRECD 097
Creation / May '94 / 3MV / Vital.

HOLD BACK THE NIGHT
CD _____ CRECD 52
Creation / Nov '89 / 3MV / Vital.

LIVE WHILST OUT OF FASHION
Sinister themes / Last of the window cleaners / Ladies understand / Cape and stick gang / Ultraconformist / Mother-in-law / La catrina / Cheques in the past / Spy on the moon / Forests
CD _____ MONDE 3CD
Richmond / Apr '94 / Pinnacle.

MONSTERS OF LOVE
CD _____ CRECD 059
Creation / May '94 / 3MV / Vital.

PHILOSOPHY OF MOMUS
Toothbrushead / Madness of Lee Scratch Perry / It's important to be trendy / Quark and Charm, the robot twins / Girlish boy / Yokohama Chinatown / Withinity / K's diary / Virtual Valerie / Red pyjamas / Cabinet of Kuniyoshi Kaneko / Slide projector lie detector / Microworlds / Complicated / I had a girl / Philosophy of Momus / Loneliness of lift music / Paranoid acoustic seduction machine / Sadness of things
CD _____ CDBRED 119
Cherry Red / May '95 / Pinnacle.

POISON BOYFRIEND
CD _____ CRELP 021CD
Creation / Apr '88 / 3MV / Vital.

SLENDER SHERBERT (READINGS OF MY EARLY YEARS)
Complete history of sexual jealousy / Guitar lesson / Closer to you / Homosexual / Charm of innocence / Lucky like St Sebastian / I was a maoist intellectual / Lifestyles of the rich and famous / Angels are voyeurs / Hotel Marquis De Sade / Gatecrasher / Hairstyle of the devil / Bi shonen / Angels reprise
CD _____ CDBRED 123
Cherry Red / Oct '95 / Pinnacle.

TENDER PERVERT
CD _____ CRELP 036CD
Creation / Nov '88 / 3MV / Vital.

TIMELORDS
CD _____ CRECD 151
Creation / Oct '93 / 3MV / Vital.

VOYAGER
CD _____ CRECD 113
Creation / Jun '92 / 3MV / Vital.

Mona Lisa

PARTNERS IN PLEASURE
CD _____ CDL 151642
Dino / Jul '92 / Pinnacle / 3MV.

Monastery

SPLIT ALBUM (Monastery & Anarchus)
CD _____ SLAP 152
Slap A Ham / Mar '93 / Plastic Head.

Monastyr

NEVER DREAMING
CD _____ MN 03CD
Nuclear Blast / Jan '95 / Plastic Head.

Moncada Manzanera

LIVE AT THE KARL MARX THEATRE
CD _____ EXCD 2
Expression / Oct '92 / Pinnacle.

Moncur, Grachan III

SOME OTHER STUFF
Gnostic / Thandiwa / Twins / Normadic
CD _____ CDP 8320922
Blue Note / May '95 / EMI.

Mondschein Trio

AUF GEHT'S BEIM
CD _____ 15251
Laserlight / Nov '91 / Target/BMG.

Money Mark

MARK'S KEYBOARD REPAIR
Pretty pain / No fighting / Ba ba ba boom / Have clav will travel / Don't miss the boat / Sunday garden Blvd / Insects are all around us / Scenes from / Poet's walk / Spooky / Cry / Flute / Hand in your head / That's for sure / Stevie / Time lapse / Sly / Sometimes / Latin
CD _____ MW 034CD
Mo Wax / Aug '95 / Vital.

Monger, Eileen

LILTING BANSHEE, THE (Airs & Dances For Celtic Harp)
King of the fairies / Lilting banshee / O South wind / Great high wind / Wild geese / Bonnie Portmore / Morning dew / Ivy leaf / Limerick's lamentation / Give me your hand / Neil Gow's lament / Farewell to Craigie Dhu / Fingal's cave
CD _____ CDSDL 348
Saydisc / Mar '94 / Harmonia Mundi / ADA / Direct.

Moniars

Y GORAU O DDAU FYD
CD _____ CRAICD 045
Crai / Dec '94 / ADA / Direct.

Monica

MISS THANG
Miss Thang / Don't take it personal (just one of dem days) / Like this and like that / Get down / With you / Skate / Angel / Woman in me / Tell me if you still care / Let's straighten it out / Before you walk out of my life / Now I'm gone / Why I love you so much / Never can say goodbye / Forever always
CD _____ 75444370062
Rowdy / Sep '95 / BMG.

Monk, Meredith

BOOK OF DAYS
Early morning melody / Dawn / Traveller 4 / Churchyard entertainment / Afternoon melodies / Field/Clouds / Dusk / Eva's song / Evening / Travellers / Jewish storyteller/ Dance/Dream / Plague / Madwoman's vision / Cave song
CD _____ 8396241
ECM / Apr '90 / New Note.

DO YOU BE
Scared song / I don't know / Window in 7's / Double fiesta / Do you be / Panda chant / 1 Memory song / Panda chant 11 / Quarry lullaby / Shadow song / Astronaut anthem / Wheel
CD _____ 8317822
ECM / Jul '87 / New Note.

DOLMEN MUSIC
Gotham lullaby / Travelling / Biography / Tale / Dolmen music
CD _____ 8254592
ECM / Oct '85 / New Note.

Monk, Thelonious

5 BY MONK BY 5
CD _____ OJCCD 362-2
Original Jazz Classics / Feb '92 / Wellard / Jazz Music / Cadillac / Complete/Pinnacle.

ALONE IN SAN FRANCISCO
CD _____ OJCCD 231-2
Original Jazz Classics / Feb '92 / Wellard / Jazz Music / Cadillac / Complete/Pinnacle.

ALWAYS KNOW (2CD Set)
CD Set _____ 4691852
Sony Jazz / Jan '95 / Sony.

AND THE JAZZ GIANTS
Bemsha swing / Crepuscule with Nellie / Nutty / I mean you / Pea eye / In walked Bud / Little Rootie Tootie / Played twice / San Francisco holiday
CD _____ FCD 60018
Fantasy / Apr '94 / Pinnacle / Jazz Music / Wellard / Cadillac.

AT THE BLACKHAWK
CD _____ OJCCD 305-2
Original Jazz Classics / Feb '92 / Wellard / Jazz Music / Cadillac / Complete/Pinnacle.

AT TOWN HALL
CD _____ OJCCD 135-2
Original Jazz Classics / Feb '92 / Wellard / Jazz Music / Cadillac / Complete/Pinnacle.

BEMSHA SWING
CD _____ ATJCD 5966
All That's Jazz / Jul '92 / THE / Jazz Music.

BEST OF THELONIOUS MONK, THE
Thelonious / Ruby my dear / Well you needn't / April in Paris / Monk's mood / In walked Bud / Round Midnight / Evidence / Misterioso / Epistrophy / I mean you / Four in one / Criss cross / Straight no chaser / Ask me now / Skippy
CD _____ BNZ 261
Blue Note / Mar '91 / EMI.

BIG BAND AND QUARTET IN CONCERT (2CD Set)
Bye-ya / I mean you / Evidence / Epistrophy / When it's darkness on the delta / Played twice / Misterioso / Light blue / Oskat / Four in one
CD Set _____ 476898-2
Columbia / Aug '94 / Sony.

BIG BAND AND QUARTET IN CONCERT
CD _____ 4684082
Columbia / Jan '95 / Sony.

BLUE MONK
CD _____ JHR 73501
Jazz Hour / Sep '93 / Target/BMG / Jazz Music / Cadillac.

BRILLIANT CORNERS (Monk, Thelonious & Sonny Rollins)
CD _____ OJCCD 026-2
Original Jazz Classics / Feb '92 / Wellard / Jazz Music / Cadillac / Complete/Pinnacle.

COMPLETE BLUE NOTE RECORDINGS, THE (4CD Set)
Humph / Evonce (alt. take) / Evonce / Suburban eyes / Suburban eyes (alt. take) / Thelonious / Nice work if you can get it (alt. take) / Nice work if you can get it / Ruby my dear (alt. take) / Ruby my dear / Well you needn't / Well you needn't (alt. take) / April in Paris (alt. take) / April in Paris / Off minor / Introspection / In walked Bud / Monk's mood / Who knows / Round Midnight / Who knows (alt. take) / All the things you are / I should care (alt. take) / I should care / Evidence / Misterioso / Misterioso (alt. take) / Epistrophy / I mean you / Four in one (Mixes) / Criss cross (alt. take) / Eronel / Straight no chaser / Ask me now / Ask me now (alt. take) / Willow weep for me / Skippy / Skippy (alt. take) / Hornin' in (alt. take) / Hornin' in / Sixteen (first take) / Sixteen (second take) / Carolina moon / Let's cool one / I'll follow you / Reflections / Crepuscule with Nellie / Trinkle tinkle
CD Set _____ CDP 8303632
Blue Note / Oct '94 / EMI.

COMPLETE RIVERSIDE RECORDINGS, THE (15CD Set)
CD Set _____ RCD 022-2
Riverside / Nov '92 / Jazz Music / Pinnacle / Cadillac.

COMPOSER, THE
Round Midnight / Bemsha swing / Rhythm-a-ning / Reflections / Straight no chaser / Brilliant corners / Ruby my dear / Well you needn't / Blue monk / Criss cross / Crepuscule with Nellie
CD _____ 4633382
Sony Jazz / Jan '95 / Sony.

CRISS CROSS
Hackensack / Tea for two / Criss cross / Eronel / Rhythm-a-ning / Don't blame me / Think of one / Crepuscule with Nellie / Pannonica
CD _____ 4729912
Columbia / May '93 / Sony.

EPISTROPHY
CD _____ JHR 73546
Jazz Hour / Sep '93 / Target/BMG / Jazz Music / Cadillac.

ESSENTIAL THELONIOUS MONK, THE
CD _____ 4685712
Sony Jazz / Jan '95 / Sony.

EUROPEAN TOUR (Monk, Thelonious & Max Roach)
Blue moon / Light blue / Evidence / To Lady / Stop motion
CD _____ DC 8536
Denon / Apr '89 / Conifer.

EVIDENCE
Rhythm-a-ning / Ruby my dear / Bright Mississippi / Round Midnight / Evidence / Jackie-ing / Stuffy / Blue monk
CD _____ FCD 105
Esoldun / Jan '88 / Target/BMG.

FIRST EUROPEAN CONCERT '61, THE
CD _____ MRCD 120
Magnetic / Sep '91 / Magnum Music Group.

GENIUS OF MODERN MUSIC VOL.1
Round Midnight / Off minor / Ruby my dear / I mean you (Not on CD.) / April in Paris / In walked Bud / Thelonious / Epistrophy / Misterioso (Not on CD.) / Well you needn't / Introspection / Humph / Evonce (CD only) / Evonce (alt. take) (CD only) / Suburban eyes (alt. take) (CD only) / Nice work if you can get it (CD only) / Nice work if you can get it (alt. take) (CD only) / Well you needn't (alt. take) (CD only) / April in Paris (alt. take) (CD only) / Monk's mood (CD only) / Who knows (CD only) / Who knows (alt. take) (CD only)
CD _____ BNZ 244
Blue Note / Sep '92 / EMI.

GENIUS OF MODERN MUSIC VOL.2
Carolina moon / Hornin' in / Skippy / Let's cool one / Suburban eyes (Not on CD.) / Evonce (Not on CD.) / Straight no chaser / Nice work if you can get it (Not on CD.) / Monk's mood (Not on CD.) / Who knows (Not on CD.) / Ask me now / Four in one (CD only. Mixes) / Criss cross (alt. take) (CD only.) / Eronel (CD only.) / Ask me now (alt. take) (CD only.) / Willow weep for me (CD only.) / Skippy (alt. take) (CD only.) / Hornin' in (alt. take) (CD only.) / Sixteen (first take) (CD only.) / Sixteen (second take) (CD only.) / I'll follow you (CD only.)
CD _____ CDP 7815112
Blue Note / Mar '95 / EMI.

IN ACTION (Monk, Thelonious Quartet)
CD _____ OJCCD 103-2
Original Jazz Classics / Feb '92 / Wellard / Jazz Music / Cadillac / Complete/Pinnacle.

IN ITALY
Jackie-ing / Epistrophy / Body and soul / Straight no chaser / Beshma swing / San Francisco holiday / Crepuscule with Nellie / Rhythm-a-ning
CD _____ OJCCD 488
Original Jazz Classics / Apr '93 / Wellard / Jazz Music / Cadillac / Complete/Pinnacle.

IN JAPAN 1963 (Monk, Thelonious Quartet)
Evidence / Blue monk / Just a gigolo / Bolivar blues / Epistrophy
CD _____ PRCDSP 202
Prestige / Aug '93 / Total/BMG.

IT'S MONK'S TIME
Lulu's back in town / Memories of you / Stuffy turkey / Brake's sake / Nice work if you can get it / Shuffle boil
CD _____ 4684082
Sony Jazz / Jan '95 / Sony.

JAZZ PORTRAITS
Round Midnight / Thelonious / Off minor / Well you needn't / Ruby my dear / Epistrophy / Evidence / Mysterioso / Ask me now / Criss cross / Straight no chaser / Hornin' in / Let's cool one / Little rootie tootie / Monk's dream / Bemesha swing / Reflections / Let's call this
CD _____ CD 14510
Jazz Portraits / May '94 / Jazz Music.

LIVE AND RARE IN EUROPE - 1967
CD _____ JZCD 356
Suisa / Feb '92 / Jazz Music / THE.

LIVE AT THE IT CLUB
Blue monk / Well you needn't / Round Midnight / Rhythm-a-ning / Blues five spot / Bemsha swing
CD _____ 4691862
Sony Jazz / Jan '95 / Sony.

LIVE AT THE JAZZ WORKSHOP (2CD Set)
CD _____ 4691832
Sony Jazz / Jan '95 / Sony.

LIVE IN PARIS 1967
Presentation A. Francis / Ruby my dear / We see / Epistrophy / Oska T / Evidence / Blue monk / Epistrophy (reprise)
CD _____ FCD 113
France's Concert / Jun '88 / Jazz Music / BMG.

LIVE IN PARIS, 1964 VOL.1
CD _____ FCD 132
France's Concert / '89 / Jazz Music / BMG.

LONDON COLLECTION, VOLUME 1
Trinkle tinkle / Crepuscule with Nellie / Darn that dream / Little rootie tootie / Meet me tonight in dreamland / Nice work if you can get it / My melancholy baby / Jackie-ing / Lover man / Blue sphere
CD _____ BLCD 760101
Black Lion / Jun '88 / Jazz Music / Cadillac / Wellard / Koch.

LONDON COLLECTION, VOLUME 2
CD _____ BLC 760116
Black Lion / Oct '94 / Jazz Music / Cadillac / Wellard / Koch.

LONDON COLLECTION, VOLUME 3
CD _____ BLCD 760142
Black Lion / Oct '90 / Jazz Music /
Cadillac / Wellard / Koch.

MEMORIAL ALBUM
CD _____ MCD 47064
Milestone / Oct '93 / Jazz Music /
Pinnacle / Wellard / Cadillac.

MISTERIOSO
CD _____ 4684062
Sony Jazz / Jan '95 / Sony.

MONK
CD _____ 4684072
Sony Jazz / Jan '95 / Sony.

MONK AND ROLLINS (Monk, Thelonious & Sonny Rollins)
CD _____ OJCCD 059-2
Original Jazz Classics / Feb '92 / Wellard /
Jazz Music / Cadillac / Complete/Pinnacle.

MONK IN FRANCE
CD _____ OJCCD 670
Original Jazz Classics / '93 / Wellard /
Jazz Music / Cadillac / Complete/Pinnacle.

MONK ON TOUR IN EUROPE
Oska T / Epistrophy / Evidence / Blue monk
/ Monk's mood / We see / Hackensack /
Lulu's back in town / I mean you / Round
Midnight
CD _____ CDCHARLY 122
Charly / Jun '88 / Charly / THE / Cadillac.

MONK QUINTET
CD _____ OJCCD 016-2
Original Jazz Classics / Feb '92 / Wellard /
Jazz Music / Cadillac / Complete/Pinnacle.

MONK'S BLUES
Let's cool one / Reflections / Rootie tootie
/ Just a glance at love / Brilliant corners /
Consecutive seconds / Monk's point / Trin-
kle tinkle / Straight no chaser / Blue Monk
/ Round Midnight
CD _____ 4756982
Columbia / Feb '94 / Sony.

MONK'S DREAM (1952-1956) (Monk, Thelonious Quartet)
Monk's dream / Body and soul / Bright Mis-
sissippi / Five spot blues / Bolivar blues /
Just a gigolo / Bye ya / Sweet and lonely
CD _____ 4600652
Sony Jazz / Jan '95 / Sony.

MONK'S MOOD #1 (Live in Paris 1967) (Monk, Thelonious & Charlie Rouse)
CD _____ CDJJ 622
Jazz & Jazz / Jan '92 / Target/BMG.

MONK'S MOOD #2 (Live in Paris 1967)
CD _____ CDJJ 623
Jazz & Jazz / Jan '92 / Target/BMG.

MONK'S MUSIC
Abide with me / Well you needn't / Ruby my
dear / Epistrophy / Crepuscule with Nellie
CD _____ OJCCD 084-2
Original Jazz Classics / Feb '92 / Wellard /
Jazz Music / Cadillac / Complete/Pinnacle.

MULLIGAN MEETS MONK (Monk, Thelonious & Gerry Mulligan)
Round Midnight / Rhythm-a-ning / Sweet
and lonely / Decidedly / Straight no chaser
/ I mean you
CD _____ OJCCD 301
Original Jazz Classics / Oct '92 / Wellard /
Jazz Music / Cadillac / Complete/Pinnacle.

NEW YORK 1958 (Monk, Thelonious & Johnny Griffin)
CD _____ CD 53112
Giants Of Jazz / Nov '92 / Target/BMG /
Cadillac.

NONET LIVE, THE
Le Jazz / Mar '93 / Charly / Cadillac.
_____ LEJAZZCD 7

ROUND MIDNIGHT
Round Midnight / Off minor / Mysterioso /
Criss cross / Hornin' in well / You needn't /
Ruby my dear / Let's cool one / Straight no
chaser / Ask me now / Thelonious / Evi-
dence / Epistrophy / Monk's dream / Little
rootie tootie / Reflections / Blue monk /
Let's call this / Bemesha swing / Rhythm-
a-ning
CD _____ CD 56022
Jazz Roots / Aug '94 / Target/BMG.

SAN FRANCISCO HOLIDAY
CD _____ MCD 9199
Milestone / Oct '93 / Jazz Music /
Pinnacle / Wellard / Cadillac.

SOLO 1954
Round Midnight / Evidence / Smoke gets in
your eyes / Well you needn't / Reflections /
Wee see / Eronel / Off minor / Hackensack
CD _____ 74321 115022
RCA / Jul '93 / BMG.

SOLO MONK
CD _____ 4712482
Sony Jazz / Jan '95 / Sony.

STANDARDS
CD _____ 4656812
Sony Jazz / Jan '95 / Sony.

SWEET AND LOVELY
CD _____ MCD 079
Moon / Dec '95 / Harmonia Mundi /
Cadillac.

THELONIOUS HIMSELF
April in paris / Ghost of a chance / Func-
tional / I'm getting sentimental over you / I
should care / All alone / Monk's mood /
Round Midnight
CD _____ OJCCD 254-2
Original Jazz Classics / Feb '92 / Wellard /
Jazz Music / Cadillac / Complete/Pinnacle.

THELONIOUS MONK TRIO (Monk, Thelonious Trio)
CD _____ OJCCD 010-2
Original Jazz Classics / Feb '92 / Wellard /
Jazz Music / Cadillac / Complete/Pinnacle.

THELONIUS MONK & JOHN COLTRANE (Monk, Thelonious & John Coltrane)
CD _____ OJCCD 039-2
Original Jazz Classics / Feb '92 / Wellard /
Jazz Music / Cadillac / Complete/Pinnacle.

TRIO AND BLUE MONK VOL. 2
CD _____ CDJZD 009
Prestige / Nov '91 / Complete/Pinnacle /
Cadillac.

UNDERGROUND
CD _____ 4600662
Sony Jazz / Jan '95 / Sony.

UNIQUE, THE
CD _____ OJCCD 064-2
Original Jazz Classics / Feb '92 / Wellard /
Jazz Music / Cadillac / Complete/Pinnacle.

Monkees

BIRDS, BEES & THE MONKEES
CD _____ 4509976562
Warner Bros. / Dec '94 / Warner Music.

CHANGES
CD _____ 4509976572
Warner Bros. / Dec '94 / Warner Music.

GREATEST HITS
CD _____ MPV 5544
Movieola / Apr '94 / Disc.

HEADQUARTERS
CD _____ 4509976622
Warner Bros. / Jan '95 / Warner Music.

INSTANT REPLAY
CD _____ 4509976612
Warner Bros. / Jan '95 / Warner Music.

MONKEES PRESENT..., THE
CD _____ 4509976602
Warner Bros. / Jan '95 / Warner Music.

MONKEES' GREATEST HITS, THE
CD _____ PLATCD 05
Platinum Music / '88 / Prism / Ross.

MONKEES, THE
CD _____ 4509976552
Warner Bros. / Dec '94 / Warner Music.

MORE OF THE MONKEES
She / When love comes knockin' / Mary
Mary / Hold on girl / Your Auntie Grizelda /
Look out (here comes tomorrow) / Kind of
girl I could love / Day we fell in love / Some-
time in the morning / Laugh / I'm a believer
CD _____ 4509976582
Warner Bros. / Dec '94 / Warner Music.

PISCES, AQUARIUS, CAPRICORN & JONES LTD.
CD _____ 4509976632
Warner Bros. / Jan '95 / Warner Music.

POOL IT
Heart and soul / I'd go the whole wide world
/ Long way home / Secret heart / Gettin' in
/ I'll love you forever / Every step of the way
/ Don't bring me down / Midnight / She's
movin' in with Rico / Since you went away
/ Counting on you
CD _____ 8122721542
Rhino / Nov '95 / Warner Music.

Monkey Beat

SHAKE
CD _____ LUCKY 79207
Lucky Seven / Mar '95 / Direct / CM /
ADA.

Monkey Business

IN A TIME LIKE THIS
Much too much / Bad Daddy B / Money /
Conga bop / Let your body go / No time /
Love your neighbour / Tea for two / In a time
like this
CD _____ ME 000292
Soulciety/Bassism / Oct '95 / EWM.

Monkhouse

CAKEY PIG
CD _____ DAMGOOD 55CD
Damaged Goods / Apr '95 / SRD.

Mono Junk

MIND WONDER
CD _____ DUM 017CD
Dum / Jul '95 / Plastic Head.

Mono Men

LIVE AT TOM'S
CD _____ ES 108CD
Estrus / Jun '95 / Plastic Head.

STOP DRAGGIN' ME DOWN
CD _____ ESCD 1R
Estrus / Sep '94 / Plastic Head.

WRECKAGE
CD _____ ESD 123
Estrus / Sep '94 / Plastic Head.

Monochrome Set

BLACK & WHITE MINSTRELS 1975-1979
CD _____ CDMRED 118
Cherry Red / Jan '95 / Pinnacle.

CHARADE
Overture / Forevever young / Clover / Snow
girl / My white garden / Her pain / Little
noises / Crystal chamber / Girl / Angie /
Talking about you / (I've got) No time (for
girls) / Christine / Tilt
CD _____ CDBRED 102
Cherry Red / Jan '95 / Pinnacle.

DANTE'S CASINO
CD _____ ASK 4CD
Vinyl Japan / '92 / Vital.

ELIGIBLE BACHELORS
Jet set junta / I'll cry instead / On the 13th
day / Cloud 10 / Mating game / March of
the eligible bachelors / Devil rides out / Fun
for all the family / Midas touch / Ruling class
/ Great barrier riff
CD _____ CDBRED 34
Cherry Red / Mar '91 / Pinnacle

GOOD LIFE, THE
He's Frank / Martians go home / Straits of
Malacca / Sugar plum / B-I-D spells bid /
Alphaville / Heaven can wait / Goodbye Joe
/ Strange boutique / Strange boutique (re-
prise) / Jacob's ladder / Wallflower / Apo-
calypso / Mr. Bizarro / I'll cry instead / Es-
presso / 405 lines / Eine symphonie des
grauns / Monochrome Set
CD _____ MONDE 8CD
Richmond / Oct '92 / Pinnacle.

MISERE
Milk and honey / Pauper / Dr. Robinson /
Achilles / Leather jacket / Someone has
been sleeping / Handsome boy / Ethereal
one / U.F.O. 10 / Integrate me / Twang 'em
high
CD _____ CDBRED 114
Cherry Red / May '94 / Pinnacle.

TOMORROW WILL BE TOO LONG
Monochrome Set (I presume) / Lighter side
of dating / Expresso / Puerto Rican fence
climber / Tomorrow will be too long / March
of the eligible bachelors / Jet set junta /
Ici les enfants / Etcetera stroll / Goodbye
Joe / Strange boutique / Love zombies / O
come all ye faithful (Adeste fideles) / 405
lines / B-I-D spells bid / R.S.V.P. / Apoca-
lypso / Karma suture / Man with the black
moustache / Weird, wild, wonderful world of
Tony Potts / In love, Cancer
CD _____ CDOVD 458
Virgin / Feb '95 / EMI.

TRINITY ROAD
Flame dials / All over / April dance affair /
Bliss / Bar Madiera / Hob's end / Golden
apples of the sun / Worst is yet to come /
Two fits / Albert bridge / Hula honey /
Snake-fingers / Mousetrap / Kissy kissy / I
love Lambeth
CD _____ CDBRED 122
Cherry Red / Sep '95 / Pinnacle.

VOLUME, CONTRAST, BRILLIANCE...
Eine symphonie des grauns / Jet set junta
/ Love zombies / Silicon carne / Ruling class
/ Viva death row / Man with the black mous-
tache / He's Frank / Fun for all the family /
Lester leaps in / Ici les enfants / Fat fun /
Alphaville / Avanti
CD _____ CDBRED 47
Cherry Red / May '93 / Pinnacle.

WESTMINSTER AFFAIR
Jet set junta / Cast a long shadow / Ruling
class / Lester leaps in / Mating game / On
the 13th day / March of the eligible bachelors / Devil rides out / Fun for all the family
/ Andiamo / Cowboy country /
J.D.H.A.N.E.Y. / Noise / Eine symphonie
des grauns / Viva death row (Extra track,
available on CD only.) / Jacob's ladder (Extra track, available on CD only.) / Ici les enfants (Extra track, available on CD only.) /
Avanti
CD _____ ACME 17 CD
El / Aug '88 / Pinnacle.

Monolith

TALES OF THE MACABRE
Morbid curiosity / Sleep with the dead /
Misery / Undead burial / Devoured from
within / Locked in horror / Catalogue of car-
nage / Maceration
CD _____ SOL 036CD
Vinyl Solution / Mar '93 / Disc.

Monomorph

ALTERNATIVE FLUID
CD _____ DIS 016CD
Disturbance / Sep '94 / Plastic Head.

Monro, Matt

CAPITOL YEARS: MATT MONRO
Put on a happy face / I'm glad there's you
/ Laura / Real live girl / Born free / Wednes-
day's child / I'll take romance / If she
walked into my life / Strangers in the night
/ In the arms of love / Here's to my lady /
When Joanna loved me / You've got pos-
sibilities / People / Sunrise sunset / Man
and a woman / And we were lovers /
Georgy girl / On days like these / Come
back to me
CD _____ CZ 354
Capitol / Nov '90 / EMI.

EMI YEARS, CAPITOL YEARS & THROUGH THE YEARS (2CD Set)
My kind of girl / Portrait of my love / From
Russia with love / Who can I turn to / Let's
face the music and dance / Jeannie / April
fool / Cheek to cheek / Softly as I leave you
/ Here and now / Love is a many splendoured thing / How little it matters, how little we
know / Stardust / Small fry / Skylark / One
morning in May / I get along without you
very well (except sometimes) / Memphis in
June / Blue orchids / I have dreamed / Put
on a happy face / I'm glad there is you /
Laura / Real live girl / Born free / Wednesday's child / I'll take romance / If she
walked into my life / Strangers in the night
/ In the arms of love / Here's to my lady /
When Joanna loved me / You've got possibilities / People / Sunrise sunset / Man
and a woman / We were lovers / Georgy girl
/ On days like these / Come back to me /
As long as I am singing / Fools rush in /
Ethel baby / Ebb tide / Hava nagila / Fly me
to the moon / Good life / Autumn leaves /
Did it happen / Maria / Let me sing a happy
song / Spring is here / Spanish eyes / If you
go away (no me dejes) / Come sta / Roses
and roses / You made me so very happy /
My way / This is all I ask / Party's over
CD Set _____ MONRO 1
EMI / Feb '95 / EMI.

EMI YEARS: MATT MONRO
My kind of girl / Portrait of my love / From
Russia with love / Who can I turn to / Let's
face the music and dance / Jeannie / April
fool / Cheek to cheek / Softly as I leave you
/ Here and now / Love is a many splendoured thing / How little it matters, how little we
know / Stardust / Small fry / Skylark / One
morning in May / I get along without you
very well / Memphis in June / Blue orchids
/ I have dreamed
CD _____ CZ 355
EMI / Nov '90 / EMI.

GREAT GENTLEMEN OF SONG, THE
My kind of girl / I'm glad there is you / I get
along without you very well / I'll take
roamnce / When I fall in love / Laura / Time
after time / Real live girl / Autumn leaves /
Ebb tide / When Sunny gets blue / From
Russia with love / Sweet Lorraine / Stardust
/ When Joanna loved me / This is all I ask
/ Good life / September song
CD _____ CDP 8293942
Capitol / Aug '95 / EMI.

HOLLYWOOD AND BROADWAY
Look for small pleasures / Stranger in para-
dise / Impossible dream / Apple tree / I'll
only miss her when I think of her / Come
back to me / Hello Dolly / Sunrise sunset /
Walking happy / If she walked into my life /
Put on a happy face / Till the end of time /
Charade / Green leaves of summer / Sec-
ond time around / Everybody's talkin' /
Shadow of your smile / I've grown accus-
tomed to her face / Chattanooga choo choo
/ Pretty Polly
CD _____ CDMFP 6137
Music For Pleasure / Oct '94 / EMI.

MATT MONRO SINGS
I have dreamed / When can I turn to / My
friend, my friend / Love is a many splendoured thing / It's a breeze / Without the
one you love / Once in every long and lonely
while / All my loving / If this should be a
dream / How soon? / Exodus / Here and now
/ Friendly persuasion / Start living / Stardust
/ Small fry / How little it matters, how little
we know / Nearness of you / Georgia on my
mind / Skylark / One morning in May / I get
along without you very well / Memphis in
June / I guess it was you all the time / Blue
orchids / Rockin' chair / You're sensational
(CD set only) / Love walked in (CD set only)
/ Yesterday (CD set only) / Alfie (CD set
only) / Hello, young lovers (CD set only) /
Michelle (CD set only) / Softly as I leave you
(CD set only) / Here, there and everywhere
(CD set only) / Somewhere (CD set only) /
From Russia with love (CD set only)
CD Set _____ CDDL 1072
Music For Pleasure / May '91 / EMI.

MATT SINGS MONRO (Monro, Matt Jnr & Matt Monro Snr)
We're gonna change the world / Did it happen / More / You and me against the world
/ You've made me so very happy / All you
know / He ain't heavy, he's my brother / If
I never sing another song / Emotions / Winding road / On days like these / I'll never fall
in love again / I close my eyes and count to
ten / Jean / Didn't we
CD _____ CDEMTV 92
EMI / May '95 / EMI.

SOFTLY AS I LEAVE YOU
Born free / On days like these / Walk away / Softly as I leave you / Michelle / Who can I turn to / Love is a many splendoured thing / From Russia with love / One morning in / May / For all we know / I have dreamed / All my loving / Stardust / Portrait of my love / Nearness of you / Unchained melody / Hello, young lovers / Alfie / September song
CD _____ CDMFP 6003
Music For Pleasure / Oct '87 / EMI.

THIS IS
Portrait of my love / Walk away / Time after time / Cheek to cheek / On a wonderful day like today / For once in my life / Laura / Girl I love / Choose / On days like these / Born free / Why not now / Moment to moment / Singin' in the rain / When Sunny gets blue / This is the life / You're gonna hear from me / Party's over / From Russia with love / My kind of girl / Days of wine and roses / Precious moments / Ten out of ten / As long as she needs me / One day / Happy / Sweet Lorraine / Can this be love / Yesterday / Michelle / If she should come to you / You and me against the world / I'm glad I'm not young anymore / This way Mary / Happening / What to do / My love and devotion / Speak softly love
CD _____ CDDL 1257
Music For Pleasure / Jan '94 / EMI.

THROUGH THE YEARS
As long as I am singing / Fools rush in / Ethel baby / Ebb tide / Hava nagila / Fly me to the moon / Good life / Autumn leaves / Did it happen / Maria / Let me sing a happy song / Spring is here / Spanish eyes / If you go away (no me dejes) / Come sta / Roses and roses / You've made me so very happy / My way / This is all I ask / Party's over
CD _____ CDEMS 1544
EMI / Feb '95 / EMI.

TIME FOR LOVE, A
Portrait of my love / Softly as I leave you / Why not now / Can this be love / My kind of girl / When love comes along / Without you / Speak softly love (Love theme from 'The Godfather'.) / Wednesday's child / I will wait for you / Time after time / Love walked in / And we were lovers (Theme from 'The Sand Pebbles'.) / Time for love / With these hands / Answer me / Til then my love / Man and a woman / On days like these (CD only.) / Didn't we (CD only.) / Alguien Canto (The music played) (CD only.) / Be my love (CD only.) / In the arms of love (CD only.) / You light up my life (CD only.)
CD _____ CDMFP 6070
Music For Pleasure / Aug '89 / EMI.

VERY BEST OF MATT MONRO, THE
Born free / Softly as I leave you / From Russia with love / On days like these / Walk away / Around the world / My love and devotion / Michelle / On a clear day / Somewhere / Impossible dream / Gonna build a mountain / Who can I turn to / Portrait of my love / Speak softly love / My kind of girl / For mama / Yesterday / This time / We're gonna change the world
CD _____ CDMFP 5568
Music For Pleasure / Feb '92 / EMI.

Monroe, Bill

BLUEGRASS 1950-1958 (4CD Set)
Blue grass ramble / New muleskinner blues / My little Georgia rose / Memories of you / I'm on my way to the old home / Alabama waltz / I'm blue, I'm lonesome / I'll meet you in church Sunday morning / Boat of love / Old fiddler / Uncle Pen / When the golden leaves begin to fall / Lord protect my soul / River of death / Letter from my darling / On the old Kentucky shore / Rawhide / Poison love / Kentucky waltz / Prisoner's song / Swing low, sweet chariot / Angels rock me to sleep / Brakeman's blues / When the cactus is in bloom / Sailors plea / My Carolina sunshine girl / Ben Dewberry's final run / Peach pickin' time in Georgia / Those gamblers blues / Highway of sorrow / Rotation blues / Lonesome truck driver's blues / Sugar coated love / You're drifting away / Cabin of love / Get down on your knees and pray / Christmas time's a coming / First whippoorwill / In the pines / Footprints in the snow / Walking in Jerusalem / Memories of Mother and Dad / Little girl and the dreadful snake / Country waltz / Don't put it off till tomorrow / My dying bed / Mighty pretty waltz / Pike County breakdown / Get up John / Sittin' alone in the moonlight / Plant some flowers by my grave / Changing partners / Y'all come / On and on / I believed in you darling / New John Henry blues / White House blues / Happy on my way / I'm working on a building / Voice from on high / He will set your fields on fire / Close by / Blue moon of Kentucky / Wheel hoss / Cheyenne / You'll find her name written there / Roanoke / Wait a little longer, please Jesus / Let the light shine down on me / Used to be / Tall timbers / Brown County breakdown / Fallen star / Four walls / Good woman's love / Cry cry darlin' / I'm sitting on top of the world / Out in the cold world / Roane Country prison / Goodbye old pal / In despair / Molly and tenbrooks / Come back to me in my dreams / Sally Jo / Brand new shoes / Lonesome road I saw the light / Lord build me a cabin / Lord lead me on / Precious jewel / I'll meet you in the morning / Life's railway to heaven / I've found a hiding place / Jesus hold my hand / I am a pilgrim / Wayfaring stranger / Beautiful life / House of gold / Panhandle country / Scotland / Gotta travel on / No one but my darlin' / Big mon / Monroe's hornpipe
CD Set _____ BCD 15423
Bear Family / Jul '89 / Rollercoaster / Direct / CM / Swift / ADA.

BLUEGRASS 1959-1969 (4CD Set)
When the phone rang / Tomorrow I'll be gone / Dark as the night, blue as the day / Stoney lonesome / Lonesome wind blues / Thinking about you / Come go with me / Sold down the river / Linda Lou / You live in a world all your own / Little Joe / Put my rubber doll away / Seven year blues / Time changes everything / Lonesome road blues / Big river / Flowers of love / It's mighty dark to travel / Bluegrass / Little Maggie / I'm going back to old Kentucky / Toy heart / Shady grove / Nine pound hammer / Live and let live / Danny boy / Cotton fields / Journey's end / John Hardy / Bugle call rag / Old Joe Clark / There was nothing we could do / I was left on the street / Cheap love affair / When the bees are in the hive / Big ball in Brooklyn / Columbus / Stockade blues / Blue Ridge mountain blues / How will I explain about you / Foggy river / Old country Baptising / I found the way / This world is not my home / Way down deep in my soul / Drifting too far from the shore / Going home / On the Jericho road / We'll understand it better / Somebody touched me / Careless love / I'm so lonesome I could cry / Jimmie brown the newsboy / Pass me not / Gloryland, way / Farther along / Big Sandy river / Baker's breakdown / Darling Corey / Cindy / Master builder / Let me rest at the end of the day / Salt Creek / Devil's dream / Sailor's hornpipe / Were you there / Pike county breakdown / Shenandoah breakdown / Santa Claus / I'll meet you in church Sunday morning / Mary at the home place / Flophouse of sorrow / One of God's sheep / Roll on Buddy roll on / Legend of the Blue Ridge mountains / Last old dollar / Rich Raymond / Louisville breakdown / Never again / Just over in the Gloryland / Fire on the mountain / Long black veil / I live in the past / There's an old old house / When my blue moon turns to gold again / I wonder where you are tonight / Turkey in the straw / Pretty fair maiden in the garden / Log cabin in the lane / Paddy at the turnpike / That's all right / It makes no difference now / Dusty Miller / Midnight on the stormy deep / All the good times are past and gone / Soldier's joy / Blue night / Grey eagle / Gold rush / Sally Goodin / Virginia darlin' / Is the blue moon still shining / Train 45 / Kentucky mandolin / I want to go with you / Crossing the Cumberlands / Walls of time / I haven't seen Mary in years / Fireball male / Dead march / Cripple creek / What about you / With body and soul / Methodist preacher / Walk softly on my heart / Tall pines / Candy gal / Going up Caney / Lee wedding tune / Bonnie / Sweet Mary and the miles between
CD Set _____ BCD 15529
Bear Family / Feb '91 / Rollercoaster / Direct / CM / Swift / ADA.

BLUEGRASS 1970-1979 (4CD Set)
McKinley's march (Instrumental) / Texas gallop (Instrumental) / Road of life / It's me again Lord / Beyond the gate / I will sing for the glory of God / Kentucky waltz / Girl in the blue velvet band / Lonesome moonlight waltz (Instrumental) / Tallahassee (Instrumental) / Summertime is past and gone / Rocky road blues / Muleskinner blues / Katy hill / Poor white folks / Old grey mare come tearing out / Kiss me waltz (Instrumental) / Jenny Lynn (Instrumental) / Heel and toe polka (Instrumental) / Milenburg joys (Instrumental) / Sweetheart you done me wrong / Banks of the Ohio / Tall pines / Mother's only sleeping / Foggy mountain top / Love please come home / What would you give in exchange / When the golden leaves begin to fall / Walls of time / My old Kentucky and you / Mule skinner blues / You won't be satified that way / Uncle pen / Blue moon of Kentucky / Ole slewfoot / Sweet little miss blue eyes / Please be my love / I wish you knew / Train 45 (Instrumental) / Bonny / When my blue moon turns ot gold again / Hit parade of love / Mary Ann / Sunny side of the mountain / Freedom man / Tennessee / Rollin' in my sweet baby's arms / Feudin' banjos (Instrumental) / Ballad of Jed Clampett / I wonder where you are tonight / Orange blossom special (Instrumental) / Fiddler roll call (Instrumental) / Down under (Instrumental) / Soldier's joy (Instrumental) / Grey eagle (Instrumental) / Swing low, sweet chariot / Clinging to a saving hand / Show me the way / Jerusalem ridge (Instrumental) / Ashland breakdown (Instrumental) / Mary Jane, won't you be mine / Old old house / Watson's blues (Instrumental) / Thank God for Kentucky / Reasons why / Weary traveller / My cabin in Caroline / No place to pillow my head / My sweet blue eyed darling / Monroe's blues (Instrumental) / First whippoorwill / Lucky lady (Instrumental) / My Louisiana love / Christmas time's a coming / Texas

blue-bonnet (Instrumental) / Sunset trail / My sweet memory / She's young and I'm growing old / Blue goose (Instrumental) / My Florida sunshine / Wabash cannonball / Hard times have been here (but they've gone) / Six feet under the ground / Who's gonna shoe your pretty little feet / Jake Satterfield / Muddy waters / Corine Corina / Have a feast here tonight / Golden river / I'm going back to Old Kentucky / Those memories of you / Intro (Watermelon hangin) / John Henry / Dog house blues / Old mountaineer (Instrumental) / Little cabin home on the hill / Orange blossom special / Molly and the Tenbrooks medley: Little Maggie, Train 45 / Little girl and the dreadful snake / In despair / Y'all come
CD Set _____ BCD 15606
Bear Family / Apr '94 / Rollercoaster / Direct / CM / Swift / ADA.

LIVE DUET RECORDINGS 1963-80 (Monroe, Bill & Doc Watson)
CD _____ SF 40064CD
Smithsonian Folkways / Jan '94 / ADA / Direct / Koch / CM / Cadillac.

LIVE RECORDINGS 1956-69 (Monroe, Bill & His Blue Grass Boys)
CD _____ SF 40063CD
Smithsonian Folkways / Nov '94 / ADA / Direct / Koch / CM / Cadillac.

OFF THE RECORD VOLUME 2 (Live Duets from 1963-1980) (Monroe, Bill & Doc Watson)
CD _____ SFWCD 40064
Smithsonian Folkways / Aug '95 / ADA / Direct / Koch / CM / Cadillac.

Monroe, Marilyn

COLLECTION
CD _____ COL 042
Collection / Mar '95 / Target/BMG.

DIAMOND COLLECTION, THE
CD _____ WWRCD 6002
Wienerworld / Jun '95 / Disc.

DIAMONDS ARE A GIRL'S BEST FRIEND
CD _____ WMCD 5675
Woodford Music / Feb '93 / THE.

ESSENTIAL COLLECTION
CD Set _____ LECD 621
Wisepack / Apr '95 / THE / Conifer.

ESSENTIAL RECORDINGS, THE
I wanna be loved by you / Diamonds are a girl's best friend / Some like it hot / I'm gonna file my claim / You'd be surprised / She acts like a woman should / Fine romance / Bye bye baby / Do it again / Running wild / When love goes wrong / Lazy / I'm through with love / River of no return / Heatwave / Kiss / My heart belongs to daddy / Little girl from Little Rock / Happy birthday Mr. President
CD _____ MCCD 062
Music Club / '92 / Disc / THE / CM.

HAPPY BIRTHDAY MR PRESIDENT
CD _____ 189072
Milan / May '94 / BMG / Silva Screen.

LEGENDS IN MUSIC - MARILYN MONROE
CD _____ LECD 067
Wisepack / Jul '94 / THE / Conifer.

MARILYN MONROE
CD _____ 15443
Laserlight / Jan '93 / Target/BMG.

MARILYN MONROE
CD _____ DVGH 7072
Deja Vu / May '95 / THE.

MARILYN MONROE ESSENTIALS
CD _____ LECDD 621A
Wisepack / Aug '95 / THE / Conifer.

MARILYN SINGS
CD _____ CDCD 1195
Charly / Sep '94 / Charly / THE / Cadillac.

PORTRAIT: MARILYN MONROE
I wanna be loved by you / Diamonds are a girl's best friend / Little girl from Little Rock / When love goes wrong / Bye bye baby / My heart belongs to Daddy / I'm gonna file my claim / River of no return / Do it again / Kiss / You'd be surprised / This is a fine romance / I'm through with love / Heatwave / Running wild / Lazy / Happy birthday Mr. President
CD _____ PLATCD 3905
Platinum Music / Dec '88 / Prism / Ross.

SOME LIKE IT HOT
Diamonds are a girl's best friend / Man chases a girl / Every baby needs a da da daddy / Happy birthday Mr. President / Incurably romantic / Down in the meadow / Some like it hot / I found a dream / Anyone can see I love you / Specialization / Heatwave / Ladies of the chorus / When I fall in love / Let's make love / Bye bye baby / Fine romance / One silver dollar / That old black magic / There's no business like show business / I wanna be loved by you
CD _____ HADCD 153
Javelin / May '94 / THE / Henry Hadaway Organisation.

Monsoon

THIRD EYE
Wings of the dawn / Tomorrow never knows / Third eye and Tikka TV / Eyes / Shauti / Ever so lonely / You can't take me with you / And I you / Kashmir / Watchers of the night
CD _____ PIPCD 001
Great Expectations / Jun '89 / BMG.

Monster Magnet

DOPES TO INFINITY
Dopes to Infinity / Negasonic teenage warhead / Look to your orb for warning / All friends and kingdom come / Ego, the living planet / Blow 'em off / Third alternative / I control, I fly / King of Mars / Dead Christmas / Theme from Masterburner / Vertigo / Forbidden planet (On vinyl only)
CD _____ 5403152
A&M / Feb '95 / PolyGram.

SPINE OF GOD
CD _____ GR 0172
Glitterhouse / Jun '92 / Direct / ADA.

Monster Zero

WRECK
CD _____ EVRCD 13
Eve / Nov '92 / Grapevine.

Monsterland

AT ONE WITH TIME
At one with time / Jane Wiedlin used to be a Go-Go / Your touch is uncomfortable to me / Chewbacca / Blank / Girlfriend on drugs
CD _____ 95928-2
Seed / Mar '94 / Vital.

DESTROY WHAT YOU LOVE
Insulation / Rid of you / Lobsterhead / Nobody loves you / Car on fire / Twice at the end / At one with time / Fish eye / Crashing teenage crush / Angel scraper / Bursitis
CD _____ 14236-2
Seed / Nov '93 / Vital.

Monstertruckfive

COLUMBUS OHIO
CD _____ SFTRI 367CD
Sympathy For The Record Industry / Aug '95 / Plastic Head.

Monstrosity

IMPERIAL DOOM
CD _____ NB 055CD
Nuclear Blast / Feb '92 / Plastic Head.

Montanablue

CHAINED TO AN ELEPHANT
CD _____ 57291144
Pinpoint / '90 / SRD.

Montand, Yves

SINGER (Original Recordings 1948-1955)
Le gamin de Paris / C'est si bon / Clopin clopant / Quand un soldat / La goualante du pauvre Jean / Le tete a l'ombre / Grands boulevards / La galerien / Les feuilles mortes / Le musicien / Actualites / Rue lepic / Le roi renaud de guerre revient / La complainte de madrin / J'avions recu commandment / Aux marches du palais / Le roi a fait battre tambour / Chanson du capitaine (Je me suis t'engage) / Le soldat mecontent / Les canuts / Le temps de cerises / La butte rouge / Giroflle, girofla / Le chant de la liberation (Le chant des partisans)
CD _____ CDEMS 1486
EMI / May '93 / EMI.

SONGS OF PARIS
CD _____ MCD 61535
Monitor / Jun '93 / CM.

Monte, Marisa

ROSE AND CHARCOAL
Maria de Verdade / Na Estrada / Ao meu redor / Seque o seco / Pale blue eyes / Danca da Solidao / De Mais / Ninguem / Alta noite / O Ceu / Bem leve / Balanca pema / Enquanto isso / Esta melodia
CD _____ CDP 8300802
Blue Note / Oct '94 / EMI.

Montego Joe

MONTEGO JOE
CD _____ PRCD 24139
Prestige / Jul '93 / Complete/Pinnacle / Cadillac.

Montero, Germaine

GERMAINE MONTERO: SINGS
CD Set _____ LDX 274959/60
La Chant Du Monde / Mar '93 / Harmonia Mundi / ADA.

Monterose, J.R.

LITTLE PLEASURE, A (Monterose, J.R. & Tommy Flanagan)
CD _____ RSRCD 109
Reservoir Music / Dec '94 / Cadillac.

Montez, Chris

LET'S DANCE (The Monogram Sides)
Let's dance / Mona Lisa / You're so fine / Yesterday I heard the rain / Heart and soul / Dolores Dolores / Au no Digas / Little bit of soap / When your heart is full of love / Somebody loves you / Come on let's dance
CD _____ CDCH 369
Ace / Mar '92 / Pinnacle / Cadillac / Complete/Pinnacle.

LET'S DANCE
Let's dance / You're the one / It takes two / Tell me (it's not over) / No no no / Monkey fever / I feel like dancing / Rock 'n' blues / Chiquita mia / He's been leading you on / In an English town / Say you'll marry me / Shoot that curl / Let's do the limbo / All you had to do (was tell me) / It's not puppy love / My baby loves to dance / Love me / Love / Some kinda fun
CD _____ MOCD 3008
More Music / Feb '95 / Sound & Media.

LET'S DANCE AND HAVE SOME KINDA FUN
CD _____ REP 4152-WZ
Repertoire / Aug '91 / Pinnacle / Cadillac.

Montez, Manuelo

STRICTLY DANCING: PASODOBLES (Montez, Manuelo Orchestra)
CD _____ 15334
Laserlight / May '94 / Target/BMG.

Montgomery Brothers

GROOVE YARD
CD _____ OJCCD 139
Original Jazz Classics / Nov '95 / Wellard / Jazz Music / Cadillac / Complete/Pinnacle.

Montgomery, Buddy

LIVE AT MAYBECK RECITAL HALL, VOL. 15
Since I fell for you / Man I love / Cottage for sale / Who cares / Night has a thousand eyes / How to handle a woman / What'll I do / You've changed / Money blues / By myself / This time I'll by sweeter / Soft winds / My lord and master/Something wonderful
CD _____ CCD 4494
Concord Jazz / Jan '92 / New Note.

SO WHY NOT?
CD _____ LCD 15182
Landmark / Apr '89 / New Note.

TIES OF LOVE
CD _____ LCD 1512
PolyGram TV / Aug '88 / PolyGram.

Montgomery, James

OVEN IS ON, THE (Montgomery, James Band)
CD _____ TONECOOLCD 1145
Tonecool / May '94 / Direct / ADA.

Montgomery, John Michael

JOHN MICHAEL MONTGOMERY
CD _____ 7567827282
Warner Bros. / Apr '95 / Warner Music.

KICKIN' IT UP
Be my baby tonight / Full time love / I swear / She don't need a band to dance / ALI in my heart / Friday at five / Rope the moon / If you've got skin / Oh how she shines / Kick it up
CD _____ 7567822592
Warner Bros. / Feb '92 / Warner Music.

Montgomery, Little...

1930-36 (Montgomery, Little Brother)
CD _____ DOCD 5109
Blues Document / Nov '92 / Swift / Jazz Music / Hot Shot.

BAJEZ COPPER STATION (Montgomery, Little Brother)
CD _____ BLU 10022
Blues Beacon / Jun '03 / New Note.

CHICAGO - THE LIVING LEGENDS (Montgomery, Little Brother)
Home again blues / Up the country blues / Saturday night function / Michigan water blues / Sweet daddy (your mam's done gone mad) / Prescription for the blues / 44 Vicksburg / Trouble in mind / Riverside boogie / Oh daddy blues / Somethin' keep worryin' me
CD _____ OBCCD 525
Original Blues Classics / Apr '94 / Complete/Pinnacle / Wellard / Cadillac.

GOODBYE MISTER BLUES (Montgomery, Little Brother)
CD _____ DD 663
Delmark / May '94 / Hot Shot / ADA / CM / Direct / Cadillac.

LITTLE BROTHER MONTGOMERY 1930-54 (Montgomery, Little Brother)
CD _____ BDCD 6034
Blues Document / Apr '93 / Swift / Jazz Music / Hot Shot.

Montgomery, Marian

I GOTTA RIGHT TO SING
In the dark / Deed I do / Love dance / People will say we're in love / That old black magic / You came a long way from St. Louis / Mean to me / Ol' man river / Georgia on my mind / Yesterday's wine / I gotta right to sing the blues / He's my guy / Lady is a tramp
CD _____ JHCD 003
Ronnie Scott's Jazz House / Jan '94 / Jazz Music / Magnum Music Group / Cadillac.

MAKIN' WHOOPEE (Montgomery, Marian & Mart Rodgers Manchester Jazz)
Way down yonder in New Orleans / You took advantage of me / Mean to me / Shake it and break it / Kansas City Man I love / If I ever cease to love / I get the blues when it rains / Sobbin' blues / Dinah / After you've gone / Then it changed / Canal Street blues / My melancholy baby / You're a sweetheart / I'm crazy 'bout my baby / Makin' whoopee / Froggie Moore / Love me or leave me / Riverboat shuffle
CD _____ OWSCD 2602
Bowstone / May '93 / Wellard / Cadillac.

MELLOW
Where or when / Dancing in the dark / I've got you under my skin / Long ago and far away / I thought of you last night / Never let me go / When the world was young / Speak low / It's not over / Skylark / Ill wind / Secret love / Why can't you behave / I guess I'll hang my tears out to dry / Remind me / I got lost in his arms / Why did I choose you
CD _____ C5HCD 594
See For Miles/C5 / Jan '93 / Pinnacle.

NICE AND EASY (Montgomery, Marian & Richard Rodney Bennett)
Ain't no sunshine / It amazes me / Man I love / Loads of love / I wonder what became of me / Partners in crime / In the wee small hours of the morning / Summertime / Nice work if you can get it/Easy to love / Not for me / Blues in the night / If you can't keep the one you love / Bye bye blackbird
CD _____ JHCD 011
Ronnie Scott's Jazz House / Jun '94 / Jazz Music / Magnum Music Group / Cadillac.

SOMETIMES IN THE NIGHT
Man I love / Somebody loves me / Just in time / People that you never get to love / My foolish heart / Maybe (if he knew me) / Tell me softly / You're the best love in / I don't want to walk without you / But love (that's another game) / Very thought of you / You've come a long way from St Louis / Not funny / Tender trap / You are my lucky star / Sometimes in the night
CD _____ C5CD-532
See For Miles/C5 / May '89 / Pinnacle.

Montgomery, Monty

MASSIVE, ARE YOU READY
CD _____ NAK 6111-2
Naked Language / Feb '94 / Koch.

Montgomery, Wes

ALTERNATIVE, THE
Born to be blue / Come rain or come shine / Fried pies / Besame mucho / Way you look tonight / Stairway to the stars / Jingles / Back to back / Movin' along / Body and soul / Tune up
CD _____ MCD 47065
Milestone / Jul '94 / Jazz Music / Pinnacle / Wellard / Cadillac.

ARTISTRY OF WES MONTGOMERY, THE
CD _____ FCD 60019
Fantasy / Oct '93 / Pinnacle / Jazz Music / Wellard / Cadillac.

BOSS GUITAR
Besame mucho / Dearly beloved / Days of wine and roses / Trick bag / Canadian sunset / Fried pies / Breeze and I / For Heaven's sake
CD _____ OJCCD 261-2
Original Jazz Classics / Feb '92 / Wellard / Jazz Music / Cadillac / Complete/Pinnacle.

COMPLETE RIVERSIDE RECORDINGS, THE (12CD Set)
CD Set _____ 12RCD 4408-2
Fantasy / May '93 / Pinnacle / Jazz Music / Wellard / Cadillac.

FULL HOUSE (Montgomery, Wes & Johnny Griffin)
CD _____ OJCCD 106-2
Original Jazz Classics / Feb '92 / Wellard / Jazz Music / Cadillac / Complete/Pinnacle.

FULL HOUSE
CD _____ LEJAZZCD 13
Le Jazz / Jun '93 / Charly / Cadillac.

Montoliu, Tete

MAN FROM BARCELONA, THE (Montoliu, Tete Trio)
Concierto de Aranjuez / Stella by starlight / Easy living / Autumn leaves / For you my love / Tune up / I fall in love too easily / Django / When lights are low / Please, I like to be gentle / Night in Tunisia
CD _____ CDSJP 368
Timeless Jazz / Feb '92 / New Note.

MUSIC I LIKE TO PLAY VOL. 3
CD _____ 1212302
Soul Note / Jan '92 / Harmonia Mundi / Wellard / Cadillac.

MUSIC I LIKE TO PLAY VOL. 4 (Soul Eyes)
CD _____ 1212502
Soul Note / Jan '92 / Harmonia Mundi / Wellard / Cadillac.

TETE!
CD _____ SCCD 31029
Steeplechase / Jul '88 / Impetus.

TOOTIE'S TEMPO
CD _____ SCCD 31108
Steeplechase / Jul '88 / Impetus.

Montoya, Carlos

AIRES FLAMENCOS
CD _____ CD 12510
Music Of The World / Nov '92 / Target/ BMG / ADA.

FLAMENCO
CD _____ TCD 1008
Rykodisc / Feb '96 / Vital / ADA.

Montoya, Ramon

ART OF FLAMENCO VOL. 4, THE
CD _____ MAN 4840CD
Mandala / Apr '95 / Mandala / Harmonia Mundi.

Montreal Jubilation...

CAPPELLA, A (Montreal Jubilation Gospel Choir)
Lord I know I've been changed / There is a balm in Gilead / Ezekiel saw de wheel / Deep river / In that great gettin' up morning / Swing low, sweet chariot / Soon ah will be done

---

CD _____ BLU 10142
Blues Beacon / Nov '92 / New Note.

GLORY TRAIN (Montreal Jubilation Gospel Choir)
CD _____ 1008-2
Blues Beacon / Mar '91 / New Note.

JUBILATION II (Montreal Jubilation Gospel Choir)
CD _____ 1006-2
Blues Beacon / Mar '91 / New Note.

JUBILATION V-JOY TO THE WORLD (Montreal Jubilation Gospel Choir)
CD _____ JUST 54-2
Justin Time / Feb '94 / Harmonia Mundi / Cadillac.

Montreux Band

SIGN LANGUAGE
Skywriting / Sign language / Sweet intentions / Jacob Do Bandolim / In the shadow of the blimp / To be / Grant wood / Circular birds / Just walking
CD _____ 01934110582
Windham Hill / Jul '93 / Pinnacle / BMG / ADA.

Montrose, J.R.

MESSAGE, THE
CD _____ FSRCD 201
Fresh Sound / Dec '92 / Jazz Music / Discovery.

Montrose, Jack

HORN'S FULL, THE (Montrose, Jack Quintet)
Rosanne / Polka dots and moonbeams / Little house / Dark angel / Solid citizen / Goody goody / Do nothin' 'til you hear from me / True blue / Horn's full / Crazy she calls me / Headline
CD _____ 74321 18521-2
RCA / Jul '94 / BMG.

Montrose, Ronnie

DIVA STATION, A
Sorcerer / Weirding way / Choke Canyon / Stay with me / High and dry / Diva station / New kid in town / Little demon / Quid pro quo / Solitaire
CD _____ RR 9400 2
Roadrunner / Apr '90 / Pinnacle.

OPEN FIRE
Openers / Open fire / Mandolinia / Town without pity / Leo rising / Headsup / Rocky road / My little mystery / No beginning, no end
CD _____ 7599263732
WEA / Jan '96 / Warner Music.

WARNER BROS PRESENT MONTROSE (Montrose)
Matriarch / All I need / Twenty flight back / Whaler / Dancin' feet / O lucky man / One and a half / Clown woman / Black train
CD _____ 7599272982
WEA / Jan '96 / Warner Music.

Monty

TYPICAL SCORPIO, A
Mr. Inconsistent / I'm Spartacus / Will I ever learn / Understanding Alfie / Ah Voodoo / Baby octopus / Moving the goalposts / Signorina / Come into my parlour / Can you do the mashed potato / Marianne / Say the word / Apple for the teacher / Bitten by the lovebug
CD _____ BAH 6
Humbug / Oct '93 / Pinnacle.

Monumentum

IN ABSENTIA CHRISTI
CD _____ AMAZON 007CD
Misanthropy / Oct '95 / Plastic Head.

Mooch

3001
CD _____ TASTE 44CD
Taste / Nov '94 / Plastic Head.

POST VORTA
CD _____ TASTE 48
Taste / Jan '95 / Plastic Head.

STARHENGE
CD _____ TASTE 057CD
Taste / Aug '95 / Plastic Head.

Moodie

EARLY YEARS, THE
CD _____ MMCD 1052
Moodie / Jul '94 / Jetstar / SRD.

Moodswings

LIVE AT LEEDS
CD _____ 74321186312
Arista / Feb '94 / BMG.

Moody Blues

COLLECTION: MOODY BLUES
Go now / Steal your heart away / Lose your money / Don't mind / Let me go / I'll go crazy / Time is on my side / It's easy child

---

Montgomery, Marian

[continued — see above]

MOODY BLUES

/ Something you got / I've got a dream / From the bottom of my heart / Can't nobody love you / Come back / Stop / Bye bye bird / It ain't necessarily so / True story / And my baby's gone
CD _____ CCSCD 105
Castle / '86 / BMG.

DAYS OF FUTURE PASSED (Moody Blues/London Festival Orchestra/Peter Knight)
Day begins / Dawn - dawn is a feeling / Morning / Another morning / Lunch break / Peak hour / Afternoon / Forever afternoon (Tuesday?) / Time to get away / Evening / Sunset / Twilight time / Night / Nights in white satin
CD _____ 8200062
London / May '86 / PolyGram.

EVERY GOOD BOY DESERVES FAVOURS
Procession / Story in your eyes / Our guessing game / Emily's song / After you came / One more to live / Nice to be here / You can never go home / My song
CD _____ 8201602
London / '86 / PolyGram.

GO NOW
CD _____ CD 12209
Laserlight / Aug '93 / Target/BMG.

GREATEST HITS: MOODY BLUES
Your wildest dreams / Voice / Gemini dream / Story in your eyes / Tuesday afternoon (Forever Afternoon) / Isn't life strange / Nights in white satin / I know you're out there somewhere / Ride my see-saw / I'm just a singer (in a rock 'n' roll band) / Question
CD _____ 840 659-2
Polydor / Jan '90 / PolyGram.

IN SEARCH OF THE LOST CHORD
Departure / Ride my see-saw / Dr. Livingstone, I presume / House of four doors / Legend of a mind / House of four doors (part 2) / Voices in the sky / Best way to travel / Visions of paradise / Actor / Word / Om
CD _____ 8201682
London / '86 / PolyGram.

KEYS OF THE KINGDOM
Say it with love / Bless the wings (That bring you back) / Is this heaven / Say what you mean (pts 1 & 2) / Lean on me (Tonight) / Hope and pray / Shadows on the wall / Celtic sonant / Magic / Never blame the rainbows for the rain
CD _____ 849 433-2
Polydor / Jul '91 / PolyGram.

LIVE AT RED ROCKS
Overture with excerpts / Late lament / Tuesday afternoon (Forever afternoon) / For my lady / Lean on me (Tonight) / Lovely to see you / I know you're out there somewhere / Voice / Your wildest dreams / Isn't life strange / Other side of life / I'm just a singer (in a rock'n'roll band) / Nights in white satin / Question / Ride me see-saw
CD _____ 517 977-2
Polydor / Nov '93 / PolyGram.

LONG DISTANCE VOYAGER
Voice / Talking out of turn / Gemini dream / In my world / Meanwhile / 22,000 days / Nervous / Painted smile / Reflective smile / Veteran cosmic rocker
CD _____ 8201052
London / '86 / PolyGram.

ON THE THRESHOLD OF A DREAM
In the beginning / lovely to see you / Dear diary / Send me no wine / To share our love / So deep within you / Never comes the day / Lazy day / Are you sitting comfortably / Dream / Have you heard (part 1) / Voyage / Have you heard (part 2)
CD _____ 8201702
London / '86 / PolyGram.

OTHER SIDE OF LIFE
Your wildest dreams / Talkin talkin / Rock 'n' roll over you / I just don't care / Running out of love / Other side of life / Spirit / Slings and arrows / It may be a fire
CD _____ 829 179-2
Polydor / Jan '90 / PolyGram.

PRESENT, THE
Blue world / Meet me halfway / Sitting at the wheel / Going nowhere / Hole in the world / Under my feet / It's cold outside of your heart / Running water / I am / Sorry
CD _____ 8101192
London / Apr '91 / PolyGram.

QUESTION OF BALANCE, A
Question / How is it (we are here) / And the tide rushes in / Don't you feel small / Tortoise and the hare / It's up to you / Minstrel's song / Dawning is the day / Melancholy man / Balance
CD _____ 8202112
London / Jul '92 / PolyGram.

SEVENTH SOJOURN
Lost in a lost world / New horizons / For my lady / Isn't life strange / You and me / Land of make believe / When you're a free man / I'm just a singer (in a rock 'n' roll band)
CD _____ 8201592
London / Sep '86 / PolyGram.

SUR LA MER
I know you're out there somewhere / Want to be with you / River of endless love / No more lies / Here comes the weekend / Vintage wine / Breaking point / Miracle / Love is on the run / Deep
CD _____ 835 756-2
Polydor / Jun '88 / PolyGram.

TIME TRAVELLER
CD Set _____ 516436-2
PolyGram / Sep '94 / PolyGram.

TO OUR CHILDREN'S, CHILDREN'S, CHILDREN
Higher and higher / Eyes of a child / Floating / Eyes of a child II / I never thought I'd live to be a hundred / Beyond / Out and in / Gypsy / Eternity road / Candle of life / Sun is still shining / I never thought I'd live to be a million / Watching and waiting
CD _____ 8203642
London / Aug '86 / PolyGram.

VOICES IN THE SKY
Ride my see-saw / Talking out of question / Driftwood / Never comes the day / I'm just a singer (in a rock 'n' roll band) / Gemini dream / Voice / After you came / Question / Veteran cosmic rocker / Isn't life strange / Nights in white satin
CD _____ 8201552
London / Apr '91 / PolyGram.

Moody Boyz

PRODUCT OF THE ENVIRONMENT
Shango / Pigmy song / Fight back / Head in the sky / Elite presents this / Just out of Africa / July / Glich / Shango (Black dog) / Ogdon / Elite dubs the snooze the sequel / Funny thing happened to me on Wednesday
CD _____ GRCD 013
Guerilla / Jul '94 / Pinnacle.

RECYCLED E.P.
CD _____ GREP 006CD
Guerilla / Jun '94 / Pinnacle.

Moody Brothers

CARLTON MOODY & THE MOODY BROTHERS
Shame on me / I tried at first not to / You turned the light on / Aunt Bea's breakdown / I'll know you're gonna cheat on me / You / You left the water running / Dreaming / Showboat gambler / Little country county fair / Start with the talking / Drive over the mountain
CD _____ LR 10157
Sundown / Dec '87 / Magnum Music Group.

COTTON EYED JOE
Midnight flyer / My mind's already home / Let me dance with you / Redneck girl / It's my turn to sing with ol' Willie / Southern railroad / Brown eyed girl / When she tells you goodbye / Line dancing / Our love / Cotton eyed Joe
CD _____ LRCD 10116-2
Sundown / '89 / Magnum Music Group.

Moody, James

FEELIN' IT TOGETHER
Anthropology / Dreams / Autumn leaves / Wave / Morning glory / Kriss kross
CD _____ MCD 5020
Muse / May '95 / New Note / CM.

MOODY'S PARTY
Birthday tribute / Groovin' high / It might as well be spring / Parker's mood / Eternal triangle / Polka dots and moonbeams / Benny's from heaven / Bebop
CD _____ CD 83382
Telarc / Oct '95 / Conifer / ADA.

SAX TALK (Moody, James & Frank Foster)
Bootsie; I cover the waterfront / Deep purple / Lover come back to me / That's my desire / More than you know / Moody's mode / This is always / Les feuilles mortes / Chanter pour toi / Bedelia / Aimer pour comme je t'aime / Escale / September serenade / My heart stood still / Fat shoes / I'll take romance / Escale e Victoria / Things we did last summer / Just 40 bars
CD _____ 74321134102
Vogue / Jul '93 / BMG.

Moody, Lloyd

BLACKSLATE MEETS SOUL SYNDICATE
CD _____ MMCD 95
Moody Music / Sep '94 / Jazz Music / Else.

Moody Marsden Band

TIME IS RIGHT, THE
CD _____ ESDCD 225
Essential / Sep '94 / Total/BMG.

Moom

TOOT
Prelude / Sally / Astronaught / Void is clear / Babbashagga / Higher the sun / Crocodillian suite / Waiting for the sphere eye / I can't remember the sixties

CD _____ DELECD 035
Delerium / Jul '95 / Vital.

Moon Doc

MOON 'DOC
CD _____ 342052
No Bull / Oct '95 / Koch.

Moon Of Sorrow

CRYSTAL EMOTION
CD _____ IGN-1M
Ignition / Nov '93 / Plastic Head.

NEW DAWN, A
CD _____ IGN 4M
Ignition / Jun '95 / Plastic Head.

Moondog

MOONDOG
Caribea / Lullaby / Tree trail / Death when you come to me / Big cat / Frog bog / To a sea horse / Dance rehearsal / Surf session / Tree against the sky / Tap dance / Oo debut / Drum suite / Street scene
CD _____ OJCCD 1741
Original Jazz Classics / May '93 / Wellard / Jazz Music / Cadillac / Complete/Pinnacle.

MORE
CD _____ OJCCD 1781
Original Jazz Classics / Jun '93 / Wellard / Jazz Music / Cadillac / Complete/Pinnacle.

MORE MOONDOG/THE STORY OF MOONDOG
CD Set _____ CDJZD 006
Fantasy / Sep '91 / Pinnacle / Jazz Music / Wellard / Cadillac.

Moondog Junior

EVERYDAY I WEAR A GREASY BLACK FEATHER
Love 609 / Moondance / Jintro and the great luna / Moondog / Canto hondo / Cachita / Waiting till you're gone / T.V. song / Jo's wine song / Shall I let this good man in / Canto hondo 2 / Love is a heavy brick / Bombo / Blues for Sammy / Ricochet / Ice guitars / Francis
CD _____ CID 8040
Island / Oct '95 / PolyGram.

Mooney, Claire

DRAWING BREATH SKETCHING DREAMS
CD _____ RED 002CD
Red / Apr '95 / Harmonia Mundi / Jazz Horizons / Cadillac / ADA.

Mooney, Gordon

OVER THE BORDER
CD _____ COMD 2031
Temple / Feb '94 / CM / Duncans / ADA / Direct.

Mooney, John

TELEPHONE KING
Wibble whim she when she walk / What'cha gonna do / Telephone king / Let me go / Please baby please / Oh Louise / Rainin' down on my broken heart / Junior / Coal stove Mama / Please please please
CD _____ POW 4101 CD
Power House / Apr '91 / Direct.

TRAVELLIN' ON (Mooney, John & Bluesiana)
CD _____ CCD 10032
Crosscut / May '93 / ADA / CM / Direct.

Moonflowers

FROM WHALES TO JUPITER...
There we will find the sun / Conitations / Summer song / Goldmine / UG / Come by ours, love / Smile in the face of evil and dance / Planet dodo / Serpents of the deep / Share your food / Jupiter / Dream lovers
CD _____ PGCD 025
Pop God / Jun '93 / Vital.

WE COULD FLY AWAY NEVER LOOK BACK AND LEAVE
Future alien / What is going to happen / Nopar King / World leaves the world / Shake it together / Revolution / Path of the free / Whitebird / Sun and moon / Winkstress / I have a friend / Too much love / Colours and sounds / Keepers of the fire / World's most famous unknown people
CD _____ PGCD 034
Pop God / May '95 / Vital.

Moonlight Moods Orchestra

LOVE THEMES
What are you doing the rest of your life / If / You don't bring me flowers / Lullaby in ragtime / September morn / Imagine / After the lovin' / Bright eyes / When a man loves a woman / What I did for love / I won't last a day without you / To that to me one more time / All in love is fair / Greatest love of all / He ain't heavy, he's my brother / I honestly love you / I know him so well / Sometimes when we touch / Reunited / She's out of my life

CD _____ PWKM 4108
Carlton Home Entertainment / Jun '92 / Carlton Home Entertainment.

MOODS
CD _____ PWK 073
Carlton Home Entertainment / Sep '88 / Carlton Home Entertainment.

REFLECTIONS
For once in my life / More / Where or when / Stranger on the shore / On a clear day / Exodus / Softly as I leave you / Shadow of your smile / Love letters / I wish you love / Very thought of you / I'll be seeing you / I have dreamed / Impossible dream / Man and a woman / Long ago and far away
CD _____ PWK 001
Carlton Home Entertainment / '88 / Carlton Home Entertainment.

THEMES AND DREAMS
Deer hunter / Fantasy / Bright eyes / North star / Xanadu / Angel of the morning / Save us shelter / Chariots of fire / M.A.S.H. (Suicide is painless) (theme) / Chi mai / Waterfalls / Bermuda triangle / I made it through the rain / Imagine / To love the Lord / Riders in the sky / For your eyes only / Sukiyaki / Sailing / Magic
CD _____ PWK 006
Carlton Home Entertainment / '90 / Carlton Home Entertainment.

THEMES AND DREAMS, VOL.2
Heartbreaker / One day I'll fly away / Total eclipse of the heart
CD _____ PWK 013
Carlton Home Entertainment / '88 / Carlton Home Entertainment.

Moonlight Serenaders

STARDUST MEMORIES (Hits Of The 1930's/1940's)
Change partners / Night and day / Cheek to cheek / Let's face the music and dance / May you look tonight / You're the top / Ding went the strings of my heart / Nice work if you can get it / We're in the money / I've got a gal in Kalamazoo / In the mood / Chattanooga choo choo / Moonlight serenade / Boogie woogie bugle boy / Don't sit under the apple tree / White cliffs of Dover / Easter parade / Trolley song
CD _____ PWKM 4038
Carlton Home Entertainment / Feb '96 / Carlton Home Entertainment.

Moonlighters

RUSH HOUR
This livin' ain't lovin / Wait in line / I'm gonna put a bar in the back of my car / Coming up on happiness / All tore up / Soul cruisin' / World to lose / Big noise in the neighbourhood / Here she comes / I feel like a motor / Seven nights to rock / Workman on the nightshift
CD _____ DIAB 806
Diabolo / Feb '94 / Pinnacle.

Moonloonies

DETONATOR
Energy temple / Autowave / Oort cloud / Epsilon / Cloned / Isostasis / Crispy cosmic luggage / Hear / Mass transfer / Skullduggery / Skyways / Orbital / Detonator / Celtic tree
CD _____ RUNECD 016
Mystic Stones / Jan '95 / Vital.

Moonshake

BIG GOOD ANGEL
Two trains / Capital letters / Girly loop / Secnce / Flow / Helping hands
CD _____ PURECD 022
Too Pure / May '93 / Vital.

EVA LUNA
Wanderlust / Tar Baby / Seen and not heard / Bleach and salt water / Little Thing / City Poison / Sweetheart / Spaceship Earth / Beautiful Pigeon / Mugshot Heroine
CD _____ PURECD 016
Too Pure / Sep '92 / Vital.

SOUND YOUR EYES SHOULD FOLLOW
CD _____ PURECD 033
Too Pure / Apr '94 / Vital.

Moonspell

UNDER THE MOONSPELL
CD _____ CDAR 021
Adipocre / Jan '96 / Plastic Head.

WOLFHEART
CD _____ CM 77112CD
Century Media / Jan '96 / Plastic Head.

Moorcock, Michael

NEW WORLD FAIR, THE
CD _____ DOJOCD 88
Dojo / May '95 / BMG.

Moore, Abra

SING
CD _____ BBEA 4
Bohemia Beat / Aug '95 / Direct / CM / ADA.

Moore, Alex

FROM NORTH DALLAS TO THE EAST SIDE (Moore, Alex 'Whistling')
CD _____ ARHCD 408
Arhoolie / Apr '95 / ADA / Direct / Cadillac.

WHISTLIN' ALEX MOORE - 1929-1951 (Moore, Whistlin' Alex)
CD _____ DOCD 5178
Blues Document / Oct '93 / Swift / Jazz Music / Hot Shot.

WIGGLE TAIL
CD _____ CD 11559
Rounder / '88 / CM / Direct / ADA / Cadillac.

Moore, Anthony

FLYING DOESN'T HELP
Judy get down / Ready ready / Useless moments / Lucia / Caught being in love / Timeless strange / Girl it's your time / War / Just us / Twilight, Uxbridge Rd
CD _____ VP 177CD
Voice Print / Oct '94 / Voice Print.

Moore, Brew

SVINGET 14
CD _____ BLCD 760164
Black Lion / Oct '93 / Jazz Music / Cadillac / Welland / Koch.

Moore, Chante

LOVE SUPREME
Intro / Searchin' / This time / My special perfect one / I'm what you need / Your love's supreme / Old school lovin' / Free/Sail on without your love / I want to thank you / Mood / Thank you for loving me (CD & MC only) / Soul dance (CD & MC only) / Am I losing you (CD & MC only.) / Thou shalt not (CD & MC only.)
CD _____ MCD 11197
MCA / Nov '94 / BMG.

Moore, Christy

AT THE POINT - LIVE
CD _____ GRACD 203
Grapevine / Jan '95 / Grapevine.

CHRISTY MOORE - COLLECTION 1981-91, THE
Ordinary man / Mystic lipstick / Lakes of Pontchartrain / City of Chicago / Faithful departed / Don't forget your shovel / Delirium tremens / Knock song / Messenger boy / Lisdoonvarna / Voyage / Missing you / Night visit / Biko drum / Time has come / Easter snow / Bright blue rose / Reel in the flickering light / Nancy Spain / Ride on
CD _____ 903173512
WEA / Sep '91 / Warner Music.

IRON BEHIND THE VELVET (Moore, Christy & Friends)
Patrick was a gentleman / Sun is burning / Morrissey and the Russian sailor / Foxy devil / Three reels / Trip to Jerusalem / Three reels (2) / Patrick's arrival / Gabriel McKeon's / Dunlavin Green / Joe McCann
CD _____ TARACD 2002
Tara / Apr '95 / CM / ADA / Direct / Conifer.

KING PUCK
Before the deluge / Two Conneeleys / Lawless / Yellow furze woman / Guiseppe / Sodom and Begorra / Johnny Connors / King Puck / Away ye broken heart / Me and the rose
CD _____ ATLASCD 003
Equator / Oct '93 / Pinnacle.

LIVE IN DUBLIN (Moore, Christy/Donal Lunny/Jimmy Faulkner)
Hey Sandy / Boys of Barr Na Sraide / Little mother / Clyde's bonnie banks / Pretty boy Floyd / Bogey's bonnie banks / Crack was ninety in the Isle of Man / Black is the colour of my true love's hair / One last cold kiss
CD _____ TARACD 2005
Tara / Feb '95 / CM / ADA / Direct / Conifer.

PROSPEROUS
Raggle taggle Gipsies / Tabhair dom do lamh / Dark eyed sailor / I wish I was in England / Lock hospital / James Connolly / Hackler from Grouse Hall / Tribute to Woody / Ludlow massacre / Letter to Syracuse / Spancilhill / Cliffs of Dooneen / Rambling Robin
CD _____ TARACD 2008
Tara / Feb '95 / CM / ADA / Direct / Conifer.

RIDE ON
City of Chicago / Vive la quinte brigada / Song of wandering aengus / Mcilhatton / Lisdoonvarna / Wicklow hills / Sonny's dream / Dying soldier / El Salvador / Back home in Derry / Least we can do
CD _____ 2292404072
WEA / Jul '95 / Warner Music.

SMOKE AND STRONG WHISKEY
CD _____ CM 00022
Newberry / May '91 / Pinnacle.

UNFINISHED REVOLUTION
Biko drum / Natives / Metropolitan Avenue / Unfinished revolution / Other side / Messenger boy / On the bridge / Suffocate / Derby day / Dr. Vibes / Pair of brown eyes

CD _____ 2292421342
WEA / Jul '95 / Warner Music.

VOYAGE
Mystic lipstick / Voyage / Mad lady and me / Deportees club / Night visit / All for the roses / Missing you / Bright blue rose / Farewell to pripchat / Muscha God help her / First time ever I saw your face / Middle of the island
CD _____ 2292461562
WEA / Jul '95 / Warner Music.

Moore, Dudley

SMILIN' THROUGH (Moore, Dudley & Cleo Laine)
Smilin' through / Love me or leave me / I don't know why / When I take my sugar to tea / I'll be around / Strictly for the birds / Before love went out of style / Brown soft shoe / I can't give you anything but love / It's easy to remember / Play it again Sam / Be a child
CD _____ RD 61177
RCA / Jun '92 / BMG.

Moore, Gary

AFTER HOURS
Cold day in hell / Don't you lie to me / Story of the blues / Since I met you baby / Separate ways / Only fool in town / Key to love / Jumpin' at shadows / Blues is alright / Hurt inside / Nothing's the same
CD _____ CDV 2684
Virgin / Mar '92 / EMI.

AFTER THE WAR
After the war / Speak for yourself / Livin' on dreams / Led clones / Running from the storm / This thing called love / Ready for love / Blood of emeralds / Messiah will come again (Not on LP) / Dunluce (pts 1 and 2) (CD only) / Dunluce (MC only)
CD _____ CDV 2575
Virgin / Dec '88 / EMI.

AFTER THE WAR/RUN FOR COVER/ WILD FRONTIER (3CD Set)
CD Set _____ TPAK 18
Virgin / Nov '91 / EMI.

BALLADS AND BLUES (1982-1994)
Always gonna love you / Still got the blues / Empty rooms / Parisienne walkways (live) / One day / Separate ways / Story of the blues / Crying in the shadows / With love (remember) / Midnight blues / Falling in love with you / Jumpin' at shadows / Blues for Narada / Johnny boy
CD _____ CDV 2738
Virgin / Nov '94 / EMI.

BLUES ALIVE
Cold day in hell / Walking by myself / Story of the blues / Oh pretty woman / Separate ways / Too tired / Still got the blues / Since I met you baby / Sky is crying / Further on up the road / King of the blues / Parisienne walkways / Jumpin' at shadows
CD _____ CDVX 2716
Virgin / May '93 / EMI.

BLUES FOR GREENY
If you be my baby / Long grey mare / Merry go round / I loved another woman / I need your love so bad / Same way / Supernatural / Driftin' / Showbiz blues / Love that burns / Looking for somebody
CD _____ CDV 2784
Virgin / May '95 / EMI.

CORRIDORS OF POWER
Don't take me for a loser / Always gonna love you / Wishing well / Gonna break my heart again / Falling in love with you / End of the world / Rockin' every night / Cold hearted / I can't wait until tomorrow
CD _____ CDV 2245
Virgin / Jul '85 / EMI.

DIRTY FINGERS
Hiroshima / Dirty fingers / Bad news / Don't let me be misunderstood / Run to your Mama / Nuclear attack / Kidnapped / Really gonna rock / Lonely nights / Rest in peace
CD _____ CLACD 131
Castle / Apr '87 / BMG.

G-FORCE (G-Force (1))
You / White knuckles / Rockin' and rollin' / She's got you / I look at you / Because of your love / You kissed me sweetly / Hot gossip / Woman's in love / Dancin'
CD _____ CLACD 212
Castle / Feb '91 / BMG.

LIVE AT THE MARQUEE
Back on the streets / Run to your mama / Dancin' / She's got you / Parisienne walkways / You / Nuclear attack / Dallas warhead
CD _____ CLACD 211
Castle / Feb '91 / BMG.

PARISIENNE WALKWAYS
Back on the streets / Fanatical fascists / Don't believe a word / Spanish guitar / Parisienne walkways / Put it this way / Desperado / Castles / Fighting talk / Scorch
CD _____ MCLD 19076
MCA / Jun '92 / BMG.

ROCKIN' EVERY NIGHT (Live In Japan)
Rockin' every night / Wishing well / I can't wait until tomorrow / Nuclear attack / White

knuckles / Rockin' and rollin' / Back on the streets / Sunset
CD _____ XIDCD 1
10 / Jun '88 / EMI.

RUN FOR COVER
Out in the fields / Reach for the sky / Run for cover / Military man / Empty rooms / Nothing to lose / Once in a lifetime / All messed up / Listen to your heartbeat / Out of my system (CD only)
CD _____ DIXCD 16
10 / Feb '86 / EMI.

STILL GOT THE BLUES
Moving on / Oh pretty woman / Walking by myself / Still got the blues / Texas strut / All your love / Too tired / King of the blues / As the years go passing by / Midnight blues / That kind of woman / Stop messin' around
CD _____ CDV 2612
Virgin / Mar '90 / EMI.

VICTIMS OF THE FUTURE
Murder in the skies / All I want / Hold on to love / Law of the jungle / Victims of the future / Teenage idol / Shape of things to come / Empty rooms
CD _____ DIXCD 2
10 / Jun '88 / EMI.

WALKWAYS
Don't let me be misunderstood / Hot gossip / Really gonna rock tonight / Back on the streets / Dallas warhead / Parisienne walkways / Nuclear attack / Run to your Mama / Woman's in love / Kidnapped / Dirty fingers / Dancin' / White knuckles/Rockin' and rollin' / Hiroshima
CD _____ 5507382
Spectrum/Karussell / Sep '94 / PolyGram / THE.

WE WANT MOORE
Murder in the skies / Shape of things to come / Victims of the future / Cold hearted / End of the world / Back on the streets / So far away / Empty rooms / Don't take me for a loser / Rockin' and rollin'
CD Set _____ GMDLD 1
10 / Apr '92 / EMI.

WILD FRONTIER
Over the hills and far away / Wild frontier / Take a little time / Loner / Friday on my mind / Strangers in the darkness / Thunder rising / Johnny boy / Wild frontier (2) (CD only) / Over the hills and far away (12" version) (CD only) / Crying in the shadows (CD only)
CD _____ DIXCD 56
10 / Feb '87 / EMI.

Moore, Glen

DRAGONETTI'S DREAM
Oxeye / Beautiful swan lady / If you can't beat em, beat em / Red and black / Dragonetti's dream / Jade visions / Walcott's pendulum / Enter the king / Vertebra / Travels with my foot / Put in a quarter / Burning fingers / Fat horse / Four queasy pieces / Appalachian dance
CD _____ VBR 21542
Vera Bra / Feb '96 / Pinnacle / New Note.

Moore, Grace

ONE NIGHT OF LOVE
CD _____ CDMOIR 424
Memoir / Sep '94 / Target/BMG.

Moore, Hamish

BEES KNEES, THE (Moore, Hamish & Dick Lee)
Thunderhead / Easy club reel / Rumblin' brig / Boatman Bill / Ian McGhee's Romanian boots / Birnam triangle / Nigheann dubh alainn / Teapot jig / Rock and Wee Pickle tow / Thura a nall ailean thugan / Jenny's chickens / Jenny dang the weaver / Maggie's reel / Slippit bar / Paddy in the sauna / Slow hare / Mongoose in the Byre / bee's knees / Staten island / Trip to Pakistan / Anne's tune / Buccleuch Street / Famous ballymoate
CD _____ HARCD 014
Harbour Town / '90 / Roots / Direct / CM / ADA.

FAREWELL TO DECORUM (Moore, Hamish & Dick Lee)
Third movement of a concerto for bagpipes and jazz orchestra / Autumn returns / Galician jigs / Cat's pyjamas, The / The Mental blockade / Farewell to Nigg / Resolution No. 9 / Te banks and braes/Malts on the optics/ Farewell to decorum / Round dawn / Forest lodge/Primrose lass/Miss Girdle / Monster / 12.12.92 (A march for democracy) / Freedom come all ye
CD _____ CDTRAX 063
Greentrax / Sep '93 / Conifer / Duncans / ADA / Direct.

STEPPING ON THE BRIDGE
King George IV strathspey / King's reel / Blue bonnets / Margaret MacLachlan / Back of the change house / Lucy Campbell / Go immediately / High road to Linton / Father John MacMillian of Barra / Sprig of ivy / St Josephs / Mrs. Gregor's search / Cameron's strathspey / Crippled boy / Helen Black of Inveran / Dal nahas ag / Sparks rant / Drose and butter / Stumpie

CD _____ CDTRAX 073
Greentrax / Jul '94 / Conifer / Duncans / ADA / Direct.

Moore, Ian

IAN MOORE
Nothing / Revelation / Satisfied / Blue sky / Not in vain / Harlem / How does it feel / Deliver me / How long / Please God / Carry on
CD _____ 4771692
Epic / Dec '94 / Sony.

MODERN DAY FOLKLORE
Muddy Jesus / Society / Today / Daggers / Bar line 99 / Dandelion / Lie / Train tracks / Monday afternoon / You'll be gone / Stain / Morning song / Home
CD _____ 4807062
Epic / Sep '95 / Sony.

Moore, Junia

LOVE ME LIKE YESTERDAY
Love me today like yesterday / Stay / If I knew / Woman / Love is a disease / To hell I love you / On your patio / Put your head on my shoulder / Bring it back to me / Hello good looking
CD _____ CY 78938
Nyam Up / Apr '95 / Conifer.

Moore, Kid Prince

KID PRINCE MOORE
CD _____ DOCD 5180
Blues Document / Oct '93 / Swift / Jazz Music / Hot Shot.

Moore, Merrill E.

BOOGIE MY BLUES AWAY (2CD Set)
Rock rock ola / House of blue lights / Big bug boogie / Saddle boogie / Corine Corina / Red light / Bartender's blues / Hard top race / Nola boogie / Bell bottom boogie / Doggie house boogie / Sweet Jenny Lee / Fly right boogie / It's a one-way door / Snatchin' and grabbin' / I think I love you too / Ten ten am / Yes indeed / Five foot two, eyes of blue / Cow cow boogie / Boogie my blues away / Rock Island line / King Porter stomp / Cooing to the wrong pigeon / She's gone / Down the road apiece / Gotta gimme whatcha got / Nursery rhyme blues / Buttermilk baby / Barrel house Bessie / Tuck me to sleep in my old Kentucky home / Music music music / Sun Valley walk / Lazy river / (Back home again in) Indiana / South / (In a shanty in old) Shanty Town / Sweet Georgia Brown / Nobody's sweetheart / Jumpin' at the woodside / Somebody stole my gal / Moore blues / Sentimental journey
CD Set _____ BCD 15505
Bear Family / Sep '90 / Rollercoaster / Direct / CM / Swift / ADA.

Moore, Michael

CHICOUTIMI
CD _____ RAMBOY 06
Bvhaast / Oct '94 / Cadillac.

CONCORD DUO SERIES VOL.9
I remember you / Just me, just me / If I loved you / Limehouse blues / Come Sunday / Ain't she sweet / I should care / Zoot's suite / All the things you are / Old new waltz / Seven, come eleven / Liebst du um schonheit / Cottontail / Deep summer music
CD _____ CCD 4678
Concord Jazz / Dec '95 / New Note.

PLAYS GERSHWIN
Summertime / Love walked in / Shall we dance / Embraceable you / He loves, she loves / But not for me / 'S Wonderful / Foggy day / They all laughed / I've got a crush on you / Someone to watch over me / Who cares
CD _____ CHECD 00110
Master Mix / Mar '95 / Wellard / Jazz Music / Direct.

Moore, Monette

1923-1924 VOL.1
CD _____ DOCD 5338
Blues Document / May '95 / Swift / Jazz Music / Hot Shot.

1924-1932 VOL.2
CD _____ DOCD 5339
Blues Document / May '95 / Swift / Jazz Music / Hot Shot.

Moore, Ralph

FURTHERMORE
CD _____ LCD 15262
Landmark / Nov '90 / New Note.

IMAGES: RALPH MOORE
Freeway / Episode from a village dance / This I dig of you / Punjab / Enigma / Morning star / Blues for John / One second please
CD _____ LCD 15202
Landmark / Jun '89 / New Note.

ROUND TRIP
CD _____ RSRCD 104
Reservoir Music / Oct '89 / Cadillac.

MOORE, RALPH

WHO IT IS YOU ARE (Moore, Ralph Quartet)
Skylark / Recado bossa nova / But beautiful / Testifyin' / Sunday in New York / Yeah you / After your call / Some other time / Esmerelda / Delightful deggy / Since I fell for you
CD _____ CY 75778
Savoy Jazz / Mar '94 / Conifer / ADA.

Moore, Rebecca

REBECCA MOORE
CD _____ KFWCD 162
Knitting Factory / Feb '95 / Grapevine.

Moore, Rudy Ray

GOOD OLE BIG ONES
Fast black / Silent George / Good ole big ones / He can give it / Hell of a blow job / Period / Black topping / White beans / Sack of nookie and others / Dirty dozens, Hercules / Grow nine some nuts / Grow by the minute / St. Peter & Bro. rap
CD _____ CDPS 002
Pulsar / Nov '95 / Magnum Music Group.

Moore, Scotty

GUITAR THAT CHANGED THE WORLD, THE
Hound dog / Loving you / Money honey / My baby left me / Heartbreak hotel / That's all right / Milk cow blues / Don't / Mystery train / Don't be cruel / Love me tender / Mean woman blues
CD _____ 4809662
Epic / Aug '95 / Sony.

Moore, Seamus

WINNING DREAM, THE
CD _____ HRCD 1030
Hazel / Apr '94 / BMG.

Moore, Thomas

DREAMER IN RUSSIA
Molenie o Iybuvi (Prayer for love) / Michael Michael / Lake of Ponchartrain / Schlar / Fog in Monterey / No clouds / Sonya and Amy in Grey / Crooked road / Believe me Sligo
CD _____ SUNCD 2
Sound / '90 / Direct / ADA.

GORGEOUS & BRIGHT
CD _____ SCD 1294
Starc / Feb '95 / ADA / Direct.

Moore, Thurston

PSYCHIC HEARTS
Queen bee and her pals / Ono soul / Psychic hearts / Pretty bad / Patti Smith math scratch / Blues from beyond the grave / See through playmate / Hang out / Feathers / Tranquilizer / Staring statues / Cindy (Rotten Tanx) / Cherry's blues / Female cop / Elegy for all the dead rock stars
CD _____ GED 24810
Geffen / May '95 / BMG.

Moore, Vinnie

MIND'S EYE
In control / Saved by a miracle / Lifeforce / Mind's eye / Journey / Daydream / Hero without honour / N.N.Y. / Shadows of yesterday
CD _____ RR 349635
Roadrunner / Feb '87 / Pinnacle.

Moose

HONEY BEE
Uptown invisible / Meringue / Mondo cane / You don't listen / Joe courtesy / Asleep at the wheel / I wanted to see you to see if I wanted you / Around the warm bend / Stop laughing / Dress you the same / Hold on
CD _____ BIAS 260CD
Play It Again Sam / Oct '93 / Vital.

LIVE A LITTLE, LOVE A LOT
Play God / Man who hanged himself / First balloon to Nice / Rubdown / Poor man / Eve in a dream / Old man time / Love on the dole / So much love so little time / Last of the good old days / Regulo 7
CD _____ BIAS 320CD
Play It Again Sam / Feb '96 / Vital.

SONNY AND SAM
CD _____ HUT 011CD
Hut / Feb '92 / EMI.

XYZ
Soon is never soon enough / I'll See You In My Dreams / High Flying Bird / Screaming / Friends / XYZ / Slip and slide / Little Bird / Don't Bring Me Down / Polly / Whistling Song / Everybody's talkin' / River is nearly dry / Live At The Happy Moustache / Early Morning Rain / Moon Is Blue
CD _____ CDHUT 005
Hut / Aug '92 / EMI.

Moped, Johnny

BASICALLY (Studio Recordings/Live At The Roundhouse 19th Feb '78)
No one / V.D. boiler / Panic button / Little Queenie / Maniac / Darling, let's have another baby / Groovy Ruby / 3D time / Wee / Make trouble / Wild breed / Hell razor / Incendiary device / Somethin' else / Groovy Ruby (Live) / V.D. boiler (Live) / Little Queenie (Live) / Wee wee (Live) / Panic button (Live) / Make trouble (Live) / Somethin' else (Live) / Incendiary device (Live) / Hard lovin' man (Live) / Wild breed (Live) / Hell razor (Live) / Starting a moped / Groovy Ruby #2 / It really digs / Mystery track
CD _____ CDWIKD 144
Chiswick / Sep '95 / Pinnacle.

Moraba, Kori

VICTIMS OF THE SYSTEM
Victims of the system / Kgutlang / Thatohatse / Tsoang tsoang tsoang (trad. wedding song) / Oanqaka / Hope / Batho ke ho to thusana / Ke binela wena / Maditaba / O rata mang / Thsepha thapelo / Don't drive drink / Coming or going / Lenyalo ke kabelo
CD _____ ELITE 016CD
Elite/Old Gold / Jul '91 / Carlton Home Entertainment.

Moradi, Shahmirza

MUSIC OF LORESTAN
CD _____ NI 5397
Nimbus / Sep '94 / Nimbus.

Moraes, Angela

NEW YORK IN THE MIX VOL.1
CD _____ SUB 5D
Subversive / Nov '95 / 3MV / SRD.

Moraito

MORAO Y ORO - FLAMENCO VIVO
CD _____ AUB 6772
Auvidis/Ethnic / Feb '93 / Harmonia Mundi.

Moral Crusade

ACT OF VIOLENCE, AN
CD _____ CMFTCD 5
CMFT / Jul '90 / Plastic Head.

Morath, Max

LIVING A RAGTIME LIFE
CD _____ SACD 110
Solo Art / Jul '93 / Jazz Music.

REAL AMERICAN FOLK SONGS
CD _____ SACD 120
Solo Art / Mar '95 / Jazz Music.

Moravenka Band

MUSIC FOR PLEASURE
CD _____ VA 0039
Musicvars / Nov '95 / Czech Music Enterprises.

Moraz, Patrick

OUT IN THE SUN
Out in the sun / Rana batucada / Nervous breakdown / Silver screen / Tentacles / Kabala / Love hate sun rain you / Time for a change
CD _____ CDOVD 445
Virgin / May '94 / EMI.

STORY OF I, THE
Impact / Warmer hands / Storm / Cachaca / Intermezzo / Indoors / Best years of our lives / Descent / Incantation (procession) / Dancing now / Starting a moped / Impressions (the dream) / Like a child in disguise / Rise and fall / Symphony in the space
CD _____ CDOVD 446
Virgin / May '94 / EMI.

Morbid Angel

ABOMINATIONS
CD _____ MOSH 048CD
Earache / Jan '93 / Vital.

ALTARS OF MADNESS
Visions from the darkside / Chapel of ghouls / Maze of torment / Damnation / Bleed for the devil
CD _____ MOSH 011CD
Earache / Sep '89 / Vital.

BLESSED ARE THE SICK
CD _____ MOSH 031CD
Earache / May '91 / Vital.

COVENANT
Rapture / Pain divine / World of shit / Vengeance is mine / Lion's den / Blood on my hands / Angel of disease / Sworn to black / Nar mattaru / God of emptiness
CD _____ MOSH 081CD
Earache / Jun '93 / Vital.

DOMINATION
Dominate / Where the slime live / Eyes to see, ears to hear / Melting / Nothing to fear / Dawn of the angry / This means war / Caesar's Palace / Dreaming / Inquisition (burn with me) / Hatework
CD _____ MOSH 134CD
Earache / May '95 / Vital.

CD _____ MOSH 123CDSL
Earache / Sep '95 / Vital.

Morbid Saint

SPECTRUM OF DEATH
CD _____ GCI 89803
Plastic Head / Jun '92 / Plastic Head.

Morbius

ALIENCHRIST
CD _____ CYBERCD 16
Cyber / May '95 / Plastic Head.

Mordred

FOOLS GAME
CD _____ CDNUK 135
Noise/Modern Music / May '89 / Pinnacle / Plastic Head.

IN THIS LIFE
Esse quam videri / Downtown / Progress / Killing time / Larger than life / High potence / Falling away / Window / In this life / Strain
CD _____ NO 159-2
Noise/Modern Music / Feb '91 / Pinnacle / Plastic Head.

NEXT ROOM, THE
CD _____ N 0211-2
Noise/Modern Music / Aug '94 / Pinnacle / Plastic Head.

More, Benny

CARICIAS CUBANA
CD _____ SON 035
Iris Music / Jul '95 / Discovery.

EL BARBARO DEL RITMO
Te quedaras / Encatidando de la vida / En el tiempo de la colonia / Oh vida / Locas por el mambo / Mi chiquita / Barbaro del ritmo / A media noche / Cinturita / Corazon rebelde / El bobo de la yuca / Me voy pa'el / Pueblo
CD _____ PSCCD 004
Pure Sounds From Cuba / Feb '95 / Henry Hadaway Organisation / THE.

More Fiends

TOAD LICKIN'
CD _____ SR 330290CD
Semaphore / Dec '90 / Plastic Head.

More, Keith

GUITAR STORIES
CD _____ VGCD 002
Verglas Music / Oct '95 / Pinnacle.

More Rockers

DUB PLATE SELECTION VOL. 1
CD _____ ZCDKR 1
More Rockers / Feb '95 / 3MV / Sony.

Moreira, Airto

COLOURS OF LIFE, THE (Moreira, Airto & Flora Purim)
CD _____ IORCD 001
In & Out / Sep '88 / Vital/SAM.

FORTH WORLD (Moreira, Airto & Forth World)
Ronnie Scott's Jazz House / Sep '92 / Jazz Music / Magnum Music Group / Cadillac.
CD _____ JHRCD 026

KILLER BEES (Moreira, Airto & The Gods Of Jazz)
Banana jam / Be there / Killer bees / City sushi / See ya later / Never mind / Communion / Nasty moves / Chicken in the mind
CD _____ BW 041
B&W / Dec '93 / New Note.

OTHER SIDE OF THIS, THE
CD _____ RCD 10207
Rykodisc / Jun '92 / Vital / ADA.

Morel Inc

NYC JAM SESSION
CD _____ SR 320CD
Strictly Rhythm / Jun '95 / SRD / Vital.

Moreland, Ace

I'M A DAMN GOOD TIME
CD _____ ICH 9014CD
Ichiban / Jun '94 / Koch.

Moreton, Ivor

NIMBLE FINGERS (Moreton, Ivor & Dave Kay)
Aurora / It always rains before a rainbow / Ridin' home on the buggy / That lovely weekend / Sand in my shoes / Do you care / Wrap yourself in cotton wool / Shepherd serenade / Elmer's tune / Sailor with the navy blue eyes / Baby mine / When I love I love / Deep in the heart of Texas / Tica ti tica ta / Tomorrow's sunrise / I don't want to walk without you / Flamingo / Someone's rocking my dreamboat / Arm in arm / Time was / In an old dutch garden / Lamplighter's serenade/Sometimes/Somebody else is taking my / Where in the world/Always in my heart/Soft shoe shuffle / Jersey bounce / Three little sisters / Tell me teacher / Only you / Idaho / It costs so little / Mean to me / Time on my hands / If I had you / Be careful it's my heart / Love is a song/Here you are / Love is a song / Here you are / This is worth fighting for / You walked by / Lovenest / Whispering grass / Three dreams/ There's a harbour of dreamboats / Where's me and/All our tomorrows/There a / Hit the road to dreamland/I spy/Let's get lost / I can't hear you anymore / I haven't time to be a millionaire / We'll go smiling along / All over the place/Maybe/Where was I / All the things you are/Blueberry Hill/Sierra Sue / In the blue hills of Maine / Zoot suit / When your old wedding ring was new
CD _____ RAJCD 822
Empress / Mar '94 / THE.

Moretti, Dan

SAXUAL
Waiting for the call / Hot summer night / Just a matter of time / Midnight layer cake / First love / Cru-cre corroro / Keepin' up the magic / Serenade / Tune for Tina / Be my guest
CD _____ PAR 2019CD
PAR / Apr '94 / Charly / Wellard.

Morgan, Derrick

21 HITS SALUTE
CD _____ SONCD 0077
Sonic Sounds / May '95 / Jetstar.

BLAZING FIRE
CD _____ PHZCD 80
Unicorn / Nov '93 / Plastic Head.

I AM THE RULER
Teach my baby / Hop / Forward march / Housewives' choice / Gypsy woman / Blazing fire / No raise no praise / Look before you leap / I found a Queen / Don't you worry / It's alright / Got you on my mind / You never miss your water / I am the ruler / I want to go home / Conquering ruler / Gimme back / Tears on my pillow
CD _____ CDTRL 300
Trojan / Mar '94 / Jetstar / Total/BMG.

ROCKSTEADY
CD _____ RNCD 2103
Rhino / Apr '95 / Jetstar / Magnum Music Group / THE.

SKA MAN CLASSICS
CD _____ CDBH 170
Heartbeat / Nov '95 / Greensleeves / Jetstar / Direct / ADA.

Morgan, Frank

BEBOP LIVES (Morgan, Frank Quintet)
What is this thing called love / Parker's mood / Well you needn't / Little Melonae / Come Sunday / All the things you are / Night in Tunisia
CD _____ CCD 14026
Contemporary / Apr '94 / Jazz Music / Cadillac / Pinnacle / Wellard.

DOUBLE IMAGE (Morgan, Frank & George Cables)
All the things you are / Virgo / Blues for Rosalinda / After you've gone / Helen's song / Love dance / Love story / I told you so / Blue in green
CD _____ CCD 14035
Contemporary / Apr '94 / Jazz Music / Cadillac / Pinnacle / Wellard.

FRANK MORGAN
CD _____ GNPD 9041
GNP Crescendo / Jul '94 / Silva Screen.

LISTEN TO THE DAWN
CD _____ 518979-2
Antilles/New Directions / Aug '94 / PolyGram.

LOVE, LOST AND FOUND
Nearness of you / Last night when you were young / What is this thing called love / Skylark / Once I loved / I can't get started with you / It's only a paper moon / My one and only love / Someday my prince will come / All
CD _____ CD 83374
Telarc / Oct '95 / Conifer / ADA.

YARDBIRD SUITE (Morgan, Frank Quartet)
Yardbird suite / Night in Tunisia / Billie's bounce / Star eyes / Scrapple from the apple / Skylark / Cheryl
CD _____ CCD 14045
Contemporary / Apr '94 / Jazz Music / Cadillac / Pinnacle / Wellard.

Morgan, Kevin

VIRTUOSO TUBA
CD _____ WILL 2098
White Line / Jan '96 / Koch.

Morgan, Lee

AT THE LIGHTHOUSE 70 (Morgan, Lee Quintet)
CD _____ FSRCD 140
Fresh Sound / Dec '90 / Jazz Music / Discovery.

BEST OF LEE MORGAN (Blue Note Years)
Ceora / Speedball / Night in Tunisia / Since I fell for you / Rumproller / I remember Clifford (CD only.) / Mr. Kenyatta (CD only.) / Cornbread (CD only.) / Sidewinder
CD _____ BNZ 144
Blue Note / Dec '88 / EMI.

EXPOOBIDENT
Expoobident / Easy living / Triple threat / Fire / Just in time / Hearing / Lost and found / Terrible 'T' / Mogie / I'm a fool to want you / Running brook / Off spring / Bess
CD _____ LEJAZZCD 39
Le Jazz / May '95 / Charly / Cadillac.

INTRODUCING LEE MORGAN
Hank's shout / Nostalgia / Bet / Softly as in a morning sunrise / P.S. I love you / Easy living / That's all
CD _____ CY 78985
Savoy Jazz / Nov '95 / Conifer / ADA.

LEEWAY
These are soulful days / Lion and the wolf / Midtown blues / Nakatini suite
CD _____ CDP 8320892
Blue Note / May '95 / EMI.

MINOR STRAIN (Morgan, Lee & Thad Jones)
Suspended sentence / Minor strain / Bid for Sid / Subtle rebuttal / Tip toe / H and T blues / Friday the 13th
CD _____ CDROU 1015
Roulette / Jun '90 / EMI.

PROCRASTINATOR, THE
Procrastinator / Party time / Dear Sir / Stopstart / Rio / Soft touch
CD _____ CDP 8335792
Blue Note / Oct '95 / EMI.

SIDEWINDER
Sidewinder / Totem pole / Gary's notebook / Boy what a night / Hocus pocus
CD _____ CDP 7841572
Blue Note / Mar '95 / EMI.

TAKE TWELVE (Morgan, Lee Quintet)
Raggedy Ann / Waltz for Fran / Lee sure time / Little spain / Take twelve / Second's best (takes 5 & 1)
CD _____ OJCCD 310-2
Original Jazz Classics / Apr '93 / Wellard / Jazz Music / Cadillac / Complete/Pinnacle.

TRIBUTE TO LEE MORGAN (Various Artists)
Lion and the wolf / Sidewinder / Ceora / Speedball / You don't know what love is / Kozo's waltz / Yama / Ca-lee-so / Search for the new land
CD _____ NYC 601062
NYC / Jul '95 / New Note.

WE REMEMBER YOU
CD _____ FSCD 1024
Fresh Sound / Oct '93 / Jazz Music / Discovery.

Morgan, Lorrie

GREATEST HITS
CD _____ 7863665082
RCA / Jul '95 / BMG.

Morgan, Meli'sa

STILL IN LOVE WITH YOU
Still in love with you / Bring you joy / Never had a love like this / Can't wait / Through the tears / I'm gonna be your lover (tonight) / Let's be real / Release me / Now I have someone / What change have you made lately
CD _____ 3360612732
Oasltempo / May '92 / EMI.

Morgan, Mike

AIN'T WORRIED NO MORE (Morgan, Mike & The Crawl)
CD _____ BT 1102CD
Black Top / Apr '94 / CM / Direct / ADA.

LET THE DOGS RUN (Morgan, Mike & Jim Suhler)
CD _____ BT 1106CD
Black Top / Oct '94 / CM / Direct / ADA.

Morgan, Russ

22 ORIGINAL BIG BAND RECORDINGS (Morgan, Russ & His Orchestra)
CD _____ HCD 404
Hindsight / Oct '92 / Target/BMG / Jazz Music.

Morgan, Sonny

COCO DE MER (Morgan, Sonny & Seychellois)
Reggae creole / L'echo des isles / A la creole / Island way of life / Koz mwan / Femme napa marie / Coco de mer / La digue / Gros Claire / Aroa / Libre pou choisir / Tropical girls / Mahe island
CD _____ MISSCD 1990
See For Miles/C5 / Aug '93 / Pinnacle.

Morgan, Tudur

BRANWEN
O Eire/Llongau ddaeth/Efnisien/Wedi'r wledd / Ffarwel i'r marian / Hiraeth am Fei-

rion / Cefnfor Erin / Bryniau Iwerddon / Damhsa tara / Ar Iannau Llinnon / Gwern / Drudwy Branwen/Hiraeth / Cenad Aber Menai / Bendigeidfran a brwydrau Erin / Ffarwel Erin / Alaw'r Alaw / Llongau aeth / Hedd i ti Branwen / Cyn delwyf i Gymru'n ol / Yr eneth glaf / Titrwm tatrwm / Suo gan / Bryniau Wicklow / Mil harddach wyt / Mae 'nghariad i'n fenws
CD _____ SCD 4074
Sain / Feb '95 / Direct / ADA.

Morgana Lefay

PAST, PRESENT, FUTURE
CD _____ BMCD 084
Black Mark / Nov '95 / Plastic Head.

SANCTIFIED
CD _____ BMCD 063
Black Mark / Mar '95 / Plastic Head.

SECRET DOCTRINE, THE
CD _____ BMCD 42
Black Mark / May '94 / Plastic Head.

Morgane

BLUES AND CHANSONS OF DANIELLE MESSIA
CD _____ KM 47CD
Keltia Musique / Jan '95 / ADA / Direct / Discovery.

Morganelli, Mark

SPEAK LOW
CD _____ CCD 79054
Candid / May '91 / Cadillac / Jazz Music / Wellard / Koch.

Morganistic

FLUIDS AMNIOTIC
CD _____ INMCD 1
General Production Recordings / Nov '94 / Pinnacle.

Morgen

MORGEN
CD _____ EVA 842144B19
EVA / Nov '94 / Direct / ADA.

Morgoth

CURSED
CD _____ CM 97192
Century Media / Sep '94 / Plastic Head.

ETERNAL FALL
Burnt identity / White gallery / Eternal sanctify / Female infanticide / Pits of utumno
CD _____ 8497082
Century Media / Aug '90 / Plastic Head.

ETERNAL FALL & RESURRECTION ABSURD
CD _____ CM 97082
Century Media / Sep '94 / Plastic Head.

ODIUM
CD _____ 8497492
Century Media / Jun '93 / Plastic Head.

Moria Falls

LONG GOODBYE
Waking up screaming / Traveller / Out of darkness / Still raining / Mists / Frost / Perfect world / Long goodbye
CD _____ VRCDMF 003
Cyclops / Nov '95 / Pinnacle.

Morin, Christian

ESQUISSE
CD _____ 3052
Deesse / Nov '92 / Discovery.

Morissette, Alanis

JAGGED LITTLE PILL
CD _____ 9362459012
Maverick / Jun '95 / Warner Music.

Moritz, Christoph

YELLOW SIX
Green country / Yellow six / Spin / Welcome / Listen from behind / Blue world / Skyline / Brainland / Il conte / Song for Alex / Stop thinking / Half moon
CD _____ 101 S 7053 2
New Note / Nov '92 / New Note / Cadillac.

Mork Gryning

TUSEN AR HAR GATT
CD _____ NFR 012CD
No Fashion / Jan '96 / Plastic Head.

Morning Glories

FULLY LOADED
CD _____ SCANCD 06
Radar / Oct '95 / Pinnacle.

Morph

STORMWATCH
CD _____ ELEC 11CD
New Electronica / Sep '94 / Pinnacle / Plastic Head.

Morphine

BUENA
CD _____ RCD 51035
Rykodisc / Mar '94 / Vital / ADA.

CURE FOR PAIN
Dawna / Buena / I'm free now / All wrong / Candy / Head with wings / In spite of me / Thursday / Cure for pain / Mary won't you call my name / Let's take a trip together / Sheila / Miles Davis' funeral
CD _____ RCD 10262
Rykodisc / Oct '93 / Vital / ADA.

GOOD
Good / Saddest song / Claire / Have a lucky day / You speak my language / You look like rain / Do not go quietly unto your grave / Lisa / Only one / Test tube baby/Shoot'm down / Other side / I know you (pts 1 & 2)
CD _____ RCD 10263
Rykodisc / Jul '93 / Vital / ADA.

THURSDAY
CD _____ RCD 1036
Rykodisc / May '94 / Vital / ADA.

YES
Honey white / Scratch / Radar / Whisper / Yes / All your way / Super sex / I had my chance / Jury / Sharks / Free love / Gone for good
CD _____ RCD 10320
Rykodisc / Apr '95 / Vital / ADA.

Morris, Butch

DUST TO DUST
CD _____ 804082
New World / Jun '91 / Harmonia Mundi / ADA / Cadillac.

TESTAMENT: A CONDUCTION COLLECTION (10CD Set)
CD Set _____ 80478-2
New World / Dec '95 / Harmonia Mundi / ADA / Cadillac.

Morris, Joe

SYMBOLIC GESTURE
CD _____ SN 121204-2
Soul Note / Oct '94 / Harmonia Mundi / Wellard / Cadillac.

Morris, Lynn

BRAMBLE AND THE ROSE (Morris, Lynn Band)
Blue skies and teardrops / Coat of many colours / Engineers don't wave from trains anymore / Why tell me why / Love grows cold / Bramble and the rose / I'll pretend it's raining / Hey porter / New patches / My younger days / Red line too Shady Grove / Heartstrings
CD _____ CDROU 0288
Rounder / Feb '92 / CM / Direct / ADA / Cadillac.

LYNN MORRIS BAND (Morris, Lynn Band)
My heart skips a beat / You'll get no more me / Adams county breakdown / Black pony / Come early morning / Help me climb that mountain / Kisses don't die / Handyman / What was I supposed to do / If lonely was the wind / Don't tell me stories / Valley of peace
CD _____ ROUNDER 0276CD
Rounder / '90 / CM / Direct / ADA / Cadillac.

MAMA'S HAND
CD _____ ROUCD 0328
Rounder / Oct '93 / CM / Direct / ADA / Cadillac.

Morris On

MORRIS ON
CD _____ HNCD 4406
Hannibal / Nov '89 / Vital / ADA.

Morris, Sarah Jane

BLUE VALENTINE
CD _____ JHCD 038
Ronnie Scott's Jazz House / Apr '95 / Jazz Music / Magnum Music Group / Cadillac.

Morris, Sonny

SONNY SIDE UP (Morris, Sonny & The Delta Jazz Band)
CD _____ PARJ 501
Parrot / May '93 / THE / Wellard / Jazz Music.

SPIRIT LIVES ON, THE (Morris, Sonny & The Delta Jazz Band)
Yaaka hula hickey dula / Hesitation blues / While we danced at the Mardi Gras / Canal street blues / Dusty rag / If I had my life to live over / When you and I were young Maggie / I can't escape from you / Barefoot boy / Sometimes my burden is so hard to bear / Mandy, make up your mind / Give me a june night / Wabash blues / Looks like a big time tonight
CD _____ LACD 46
Lake / Apr '95 / Target/BMG / Jazz Music / Direct / Cadillac / ADA.

Morris, Thomas

CLASSICS 1923-27
CD _____ CLASSICS 823
Classics / Jul '95 / Discovery / Jazz Music.

WHEN A 'GATOR HOLLERS (Thomas Morris 1926)
Lazy drag / Jackass blues (Takes 1 & 3) / Charleston stampede / Georgia grind / Ham gravy (Takes 2 & 3) / Who's dis heah stranger / When a 'gator hollers, folks say it's a sign of rain (Takes 1 & 2) / My baby doesn't squawk (Takes 1 & 2) / King of the Zulus (Takes 1 & 2) / South Rampart Street blues (Takes 1 & 2) / Blues for the Everglades (Takes 1, 2 & 3) / PDQ blues (Takes 1, 2 & 3) / Mess / Chinch (Takes 1 & 2)
CD _____ DGF 1
Frog / May '95 / Jazz Music / Cadillac / Wellard.

Morrisey, Louise

WHEN I WAS YOURS
I couldn't leave you if I tried / He thinks I still care / Old flames / Blue eyes cryin' in the rain / Oh what a love / I still love you / Night Daniel O'Donnell came to town / When I was yours / Tipperary on my mind / Rose of Allendale / Hills of Killinaule / Green willow / Slievenamon / Roses and violets / Amazing grace
CD _____ RITZCD 508
Ritz / '91 / Pinnacle.

YOU'LL REMEMBER ME
Just in case / Out of sight out of mind / Waltzing with you / There's no way to my heart / Come back Paddy Reilly to Ballyjamesduff / Precious memories / Don't say goodbye / You'll remember me / I'd live my life over you / You make me feel like a woman / I'll bet my heart on you / Getting over getting over you / Heaven I call home / Hills I used to roam
CD _____ RITZRCD 546
Ritz / Nov '94 / Pinnacle.

Morrison, Alexander

SCOTTISH MEMORIES
CD _____ CDLOC 1089
Lochshore / Jun '95 / ADA / Direct / Duncans.

Morrison, Fred

BROKEN CHANTER, THE
Reels / Strathspeys and reels / Jigs / Hornpipes / Malcolm Ferguson / Irish reels / Polkas / 2/4 Marches / Jigs (2) / Hector the hero / Strathspeys and reels #2 / Piobaireachd
CD _____ LCOM 5223
Lismor / Sep '93 / Lismor / Direct / Duncans / ADA.

Morrison, Junie

WESTBOUND YEARS
Junie / Tightrope / Walt's first trip / Place / When we do / Johnny Carson samba / Loving arms / Junie II / Not as good as you should / Cookies will get you / Freeze / Super J / Granny's funky rolls royce / Junie III / Surrender / Suzie / Super groupie / Suzy Thundertussy / Spirit / Junie's ultimate departure
CD _____ CDSEWD 064
Westbound / Apr '94 / Pinnacle.

Morrison, Van

ASTRAL WEEKS
Astral weeks / Beside you / Sweet thing / Cyprus Avenue / Young lovers do / Madame George / Ballerina / Slim slow rider
CD _____ 7599271762
Warner Bros. / Jan '87 / Warner Music.

AVALON SUNSET
Whenever God shines his light / Contacting my angel / I'd love to write another song / Have I told you lately that I love you / Coney island / I'm tired Joey Boy / When will I ever learn to live in God / Orangefield / Daring night / These are the days
CD _____ 839 262-2
Polydor / May '89 / PolyGram.

BANG MASTERS
Brown eyed girl / Spanish rose / Goodbye baby (baby goodbye) / Ro ro Rosy / Chicka boom / It's all right / Send your mind / Smile you smile / Back room / Midnight special / TB sheets / He ain't give you none (alternate takes) / Who drove the red sports car / Beside you / Joe Harper saturday morning / Madame George / Brown eyed girl (alternate take) / I love you (the smile you smile)
CD _____ 4683092
Legacy / Mar '92 / Sony.

BEST OF VAN MORRISON, THE
Whenever God shines his light / Jackie Wilson said (I'm in heaven when you smile) / Brown eyed girl / Brown side of the road / Have I told you lately that I love you / Moondance / Here comes the night / Domino / Gloria / Baby, please don't go / And it stoned me / Sweet thing / Warm love / Wild night / Cleaning windows / Did ye get healed / Dweller on the threshold (Only on CD.) / Queen of the slipstream (Only on CD.)

/ Wonderful remark (Only on cassette and CD.) / Full force gale (Only on cassette and CD.)
CD _____ 841 970-2
Polydor / Feb '90 / PolyGram.

BEST OF VAN MORRISON, THE #2
Real real gone / When will I ever learn to live in God / Sometimes I feel like a motherless child / In the garden / Sense of wonder / Carrickfergus / Coney island / Enlightenment / Rave on, John Donne / Look back / It's all over now baby blue / One Irish rover / Mystery / Hymns to the silence / Evening meditation
CD _____ 5177602
Polydor / Jan '93 / PolyGram.

BLOWIN' YOUR MIND
Brown eyed girl / He ain't give you none / T.B. Sheets / Spanish rose / Goodbye baby (baby goodbye) / Ro ro Rosy / Who drove the red sports car / Midnight special
CD _____ 4804212
Columbia / Jun '95 / Sony.

DAYS LIKE THIS
Perfect fit / Russian roulette / Raincheck / You don't know me / No religion / Underlying depression / Songwriter / Days like this / I'll never be free / Melancholia / Ancient highway / In the afternoon
CD _____ 5273072
Polydor / Jun '95 / PolyGram.

ENLIGHTENMENT
Real real gone / Enlightenment / So quiet in here / Avalon of the heart / See me through / Youth of 1,000 summers / In the days before rock 'n' roll / Start all over again / She's a baby / Memories
CD _____ 847 100-2
Polydor / Oct '90 / PolyGram.

HIS BAND & STREET CHOIR
Domino / Crazy face / Give me a kiss / I've been working / Call me up in Dreamland / I'll be your lover too / Blue money / Virgo clowns / Gypsy queen / Sweet Jannie / if I ever needed someone / Street choir
CD _____ 7599271482
Warner Bros. / Oct '93 / Warner Music.

HOW LONG HAS THIS BEEN GOING ON
CD _____ 5291362
Verve / Dec '95 / PolyGram.

HYMNS OF THE SILENCE (2CD Set)
CD _____ 849 026-2
Polydor / Sep '91 / PolyGram.

INARTICULATE SPEECH OF THE HEART
Higher than the world / Connswater / River of time / Celtic swing / Rave on, John Donne / Inarticulate speech of the heart / Irish heartbeat / Street only knew your name / Cry for home / Inarticulate speech of the heart no.2 / September night
CD _____ 839604-2
Polydor / Feb '94 / PolyGram.

INTO THE MUSIC
Bright side of the road / Full force gale / And the healing has begun / Steppin' out queen / Troubadors / Rolling hills / You make me feel so free / Angelou / It's all in the game / You know what they're writing about
CD _____ 839603-2
Polydor / Feb '94 / PolyGram.

IRISH HEARTBEAT (Morrison, Van & The Chieftains)
Star of the County Down / Irish heartbeat / Ta mo chleamhnas deanta / Raglan Road / She moved through the fair / I'll tell me ma / Carrickfergus / Celtic ray / My lagan love / Marie's wedding
CD _____ 834 496-2
Mercury / Jun '88 / PolyGram.

IT'S TOO LATE TO STOP NOW
Ain't nothin' you can do / Warm love / Into the mystic / These dreams of you / I believe in my soul / I've been working / Help me / Wild children / Domino / I just want to make love to you / Bring it on home to me / St. Dominic's preview / Take your hand out of my pocket / Listen to the lion / Here comes the night / Gloria / Caravan / Cyprus Avenue
CD Set _____ 839 166-2
Polydor / '88 / PolyGram.

LOST TAPES VOL.1, THE
Spanish rose / Chicka boom / Smile you smile / It's all right / T.B.Sheets / Beside you / I love you / Send your mind / Brown eyed girl / Twist and shake / Shake and roll / Stomp and scream / Scream and holler / Jump and thump / Drivin' wheel / Just ball / Shake it Mable / Hold on George / Big royalty check / Ring worm / Savoy Hollywood / Freaky if you got this far / Up your mind / Thirty two / All the bits
CD _____ MPG 74012
Movieplay Gold / Oct '94 / Target/BMG.

LOST TAPES VOL.2, THE
Brown eyed girl / Goodbye baby (baby goodbye) / Ro ro Rosy / Back room / Midnight special / He ain't give you none / Who drove the red sports car / Joe Harper Saturday morning / Madame George / You say France and I whistle / Blow in your nose / Nose in your blow / La mambo / Go for yourself / Want a Danish / Here comes dumb George / Chickee coo / Do it / Hang on groovy / Goodbye George / Dum dum

George / Walk and talk / Wobble / Wobble and ball
CD _____ MPG 74013
Movieplay Gold / Oct '94 / Target/BMG.

MOONDANCE
Stoned me / Moondance / Crazy love / Caravan / Into the mystic / Come running / These dreams of you / Brand new day / Everyone / Glad tidings
CD _____ 246040
Warner Bros. / Jan '86 / Warner Music.

NIGHT IN SAN FRANCISCO, A (2CD Set)
Did ye get healed / It's all in the game/Make it real one more time / I've been working / I forgot that love existed / Vanlose stairway/Trans-Euro train/Fool for you / You make me feel so free / Beautiful vision / See me through/Soldier of fortune/Thankyou taletinmebemicei / Ain't that lovin' you baby / Stormy Monday/Have you ever loved a woman/No rollin' blues / Help me / Good morning little school girl / Tupelo honey / Moondance/My funny valentine / Jumpin' with symphony Sid / It fills you up / I'll take care of you/It's a man's man's man's world / Lonely avenue/4 o' clock in the morning / So quiet in here/That's where it's at / In the garden/You send me/Allegheny / Have I told you lately that I love you / Shakin' all over/Gloria
CD Set _____ 521290-2
Polydor / Apr '94 / PolyGram.

NO GURU, NO METHOD, NO TEACHER
Got to go back / Oh the warm feeling / Foreign window / Town called Paradise / In the garden / Tir na nog / Here comes the knight / Thanks for the information / One Irish rover / Ivory tower
CD _____ 849619-2
Polydor / Feb '94 / PolyGram.

NO PRIMA DONNA (A Tribute To Van Morrison) (Various Artists)
You make me feel so free / Queen of the slipstream / Coney Island / Crazy love / Bright side of the road / Irish heartbeat / Full force gale / Tupelo honey / Madame George / Friday's child
CD _____ 5233682
Polydor / Jul '94 / PolyGram.

PAYIN' DUES
Brown eyed girl / He ain't give you none / T.B. Sheets / Spanish rose / Goodbye baby (Baby goodbye) / Ro ro Rosy / Who drove the red sports car / Midnight special / Beside you / It's all right / Madame George / Send your mind / Smile you smile / Back room / Joe Harper Saturday morning / Chicka boom / I love you (The smile you smile) / Brown eyed girl (2) / Twist and shake / Shake and roll / Stomp and scream / Scream and holler / Jump and thump / Drivin' wheel / Just ball / Shake it Mable / Hold on George / Big royalty check / Ring worm / Savoy Hollywood / Freaky if you got this far / Up your mind / Thirty two / All the bits / You say France and I whistle / Blow in your nose / Nose in your blow / La mambo / Go for yourself / Want a Danish / Here comes dumb George / Chickee coo / Do it / Hang on groovy / Goodbye George / Dum dum George / Walk and talk / Wobble / Wobble and ball
CD Set _____ CPCD 8035-2
Charly / Feb '95 / Charly / THE / Cadillac.

PERIOD OF TRANSITION, A
You gotta make it through the world / It fills you up / Eternal Kansas City / Joyous sound / Flamingoes fly (heavy connection) / Cold wind in August
CD _____ 839 165-2
Polydor / '88 / PolyGram.

POETIC CHAMPIONS COMPOSE
Spanish Steps / Mystery / Queen of the slipstream / I forgot that love existed / Sometimes I feel like a motherless child / Celtic excavation / Someone like you / Alan Watts Blues / Give me my rapture / Did ye get healed / Allow me
CD _____ 832 585 2
Polydor / Sep '87 / PolyGram.

TB SHEETS
He ain't give you none / Beside you / It's all right/For sentimental reasons (medley) / Madame George / T.B. Sheets / Who drove the red sports car / Ro Ro Rosy / Brown eyed girl
CD _____ 467827-2
Columbia / May '91 / Sony.

TOO LONG IN EXILE
Too long in exile / Big time operators / Lonely avenue / Ball and chain / In the forest / Till we get the healing done / Gloria / Good morning little school girl / Wasted years / Lonesome road / Moody's mood for love / Close enough for jazz / Before the world was made / Medley: I'll take care of you
CD _____ 519219-2
Polydor / Jun '93 / PolyGram.

TUPELO HONEY
Wild night / Straight to your heart like a cannonball / Old old Woodstock / Starting a new life / You're my woman / Tupelo honey / I wanna hoo you / When that evening sun goes down / Moonshine whisky
CD _____ 839161-2
Polydor / Feb '94 / PolyGram.

WAVELENGTH
Kingdom Hall / Checking it out / Natalia / Venice U.S.A. / Lifetimes / Wavelength / Santa Fe: Beautiful obsession / Hungry for your love / Take it where you find it
CD _____ 839169-2
Polydor / Feb '94 / PolyGram.

Morrison, William

PIPERS OF DISTINCTION
CD _____ MON 821CD
Monarch / Oct '94 / CM / ADA / Duncans / Direct.

Morrissey

BEETHOVEN WAS DEAF
You're the one for me fatty / Certain people I know / National front disco / November spawned a monster / Seasick, yet still docked / Loop / Sister I'm a poet / Jack the ripper / Such a little thing makes such a big difference / I know it's gonna happen someday / We'll let you know / Suedehead / He knows I'd love to see him / You're gonna need someone on your side / Glamorous glue / We hate it when our friends become successful
CD _____ CDCSD 3791
HMV / May '93 / EMI.

BONA DRAG
Piccadilly palare / Interesting drug / November spawned a monster / Will never marry / Such a little thing makes such a big difference / Last of the famous international playboys / Ouija board, ouija board / Hairdresser on fire / Everyday is like Sunday / He knows I'd love to see him / Yes, I am blind / Luckylisp / Suedehead / Disappointed
CD _____ CDCLP 3788
HMV / Mar '94 / EMI.

KILL UNCLE
Our Frank / Asian rut / Sing your life / Mute witness / King Lear / Found found found / Driving your girlfriend home / Harsh truth of the camera eye / (I'm) the end of the family line / There's a place in hell for me and my friends
CD _____ CDCSD 3789
HMV / Feb '91 / EMI.

SOUTHPAW GRAMMAR
Teachers are afraid of the pupils / Reader meet author / Boy racer / Operation / Dagenham Dave / Do your best and don't worry / Best friend on the payroll / Southpaw
RCA / Aug '95 / BMG. _____ 74321 299532

VAUXHALL AND I
Now my heart is full / Spring heeled Jim / Billy Budd / Hold on to your friends / More you ignore me, the closer I get / Why don't you find out for yourself / I am hated for loving / Lifeguard sleeping, girl drowning / Used to be a sweet boy / Lazy sunbathers / Speedway
CD _____ CDPCSD 148
HMV / Mar '94 / EMI.

VIVA HATE
Alsatian cousin / Little man, what now / Everyday is like Sunday / Bengali in platforms / Angel, angel, down we go together / Late night, Maudlin Street / Suedehead / Break up the family / Ordinary boys / I don't mind if you forget me / Dial a cliche / Margaret on the guillotine
CD _____ CDCSD 3787
HMV / Mar '94 / EMI.

WORLD OF MORRISSEY, THE
Whatever happens I love you / Billy Budd / Jack the ripper / Have-a-go merchant / Loop / Sister I'm a poet / You're the one for me fatty (live) / Boxers / Moonriver (extended) / My love life / Certain people I know / Last of the famous international playboys / We'll let you know / Spring heeled Jim
CD _____ CDPCSD 163
HMV / Feb '95 / EMI.

YOUR ARSENAL
You're gonna need someone on your side / Glamorous glue / We'll let you know / National front disco / Certain people I know / We hate it when our friends become successful / You're the one for me fatty / Seasick, yet still docked / I know it's gonna happen someday / Tomorrow
CD _____ CDCSD 3790
HMV / Jul '92 / EMI.

Morrissey, Bill

FRIEND OF MINE (Morrissey, Bill & Greg Brown)
CD _____ PH 1151CD
Philo / May '93 / Direct / CM / ADA.

NIGHT TRAIN
CD _____ PH 1154CD
Philo / Jan '94 / Direct / CM / ADA.

Morriston Orpheus Choir

60 YEARS OF SONG
Rhyfelgrch gwyr Harlech (march of the men of Harlech) / Way you look tonight / Morte Criste (When I survey the wondrous cross) / Memory / How great thou art / Bugeilio'r gwenith gwyn / Did those feet in ancient

time (Jerusalem) / Speed your journey (va pensiero from Nabucco) / Old rugged cross / In my Father's house / Drinking song (from the Student Prince) / You'll never walk alone / Gwahoddiad / Amazing grace / Llanfair / Myfanwy
CD _____ CDPR 133
Premier/MFP / Feb '95 / EMI.

ALWAYS ON MY MIND
Morte christie (When I survey the wonderous cross) / Always on my mind / Just a closer walk with thee / Non nobis, domine / Y nefoedd / Nidaros / Rhythm of life / Give me Jesus / When I fall in love / Where could I go but to the Lord / Sound an alarm / There is a balm in gilead / My wish for you / Cwm rhondda
CD _____ GRCD 59
Grasmere / Jun '93 / Target/BMG / Savoy.

CHRISTMAS FROM THE LAND OF SONG
Have yourself a merry little Christmas / Joy to the world / When a child is born / Ding dong merrily on high / Silent night / God rest ye merry gentlemen / Do they know it's Christmas / Saviour's day / Amahl and wine / Happy Christmas (war is over) / Hark the herald angels sing / Winter wonderland / Holly and the ivy / Deck the halls with boughs of holly / See amid the winter's snow / Child this day is born / Little town of Bethlehem / Good King Wenceslas / Away in a manger / We three Kings / I saw three ships / O come all ye faithful (Adeste Fidelis) / White Christmas
CD _____ CDXMAS 1
Premier/MFP / Dec '94 / EMI.

LAND OF MY FATHERS
Land of my fathers (Hen wlad fy nhadau) / It's now or never / Moonlight and memory / Funiculi, funicula / gloria / Be still my soul / Where shall I be / By babylon's wave / Aberystwyth / Calon lan / Onward, ye peoples / Sanctus / Arwelfa / Do you hear the people sing / I dramed a dream / Master of the house / On my own / Drink with me / Empty chairs at empty tables
CD _____ GRCD 40
Grasmere / Sep '90 / Target/BMG / Savoy.

MYFANWY
Myfanwy / With a voice of singing / Kula serenade / High on a hill / Ave verum corpus / Come back to Sorrento / Old rugged cross / Love could I only tell thee / Roll Jordan roll / Scarborough fair / My little Welsh home / We'll gather lilacs / How soon / Gloria in excelsis / Amazing grace / Eli Jenkin's prayer / Speed your journey / Battle hymn of the Republic / Little drummer boy
CD _____ CDMFP 6027
Music For Pleasure / Jul '88 / EMI.

YOU'LL NEVER WALK ALONE
Dies irae / Let it be me / Anvil chorus / Miserere / Rise up shepherd and follow / You'll never walk alone / Cymru fach / Creation's hymn / Old folks at home / Li'l Liza Jane / My hero / Martyrs of the arena
CD _____ GRACC 7
Grasmere / May '94 / Target/BMG / Savoy.

Morro, Henry J.

SOMOZAS TEETH
CD _____ NAR 112CD
SST / Nov '94 / Plastic Head.

Morse, Steve

INTRODUCTION, THE (Morse, Steve Band)
Cruise missile / General lee / Introduction / V.H.F. / On the pipe / Whistle / Mountain waltz / Huron river blues
CD _____ 7559603692
Asylum / Jan '96 / Warner Music.

Morta Skuld

DYING REMAINS/AS HUMANITY FADES
CD _____ CDVILE 60
Peaceville / May '95 / Pinnacle.

FOR ALL ETERNITY
Bitter / For all eternity / Vicious circle / Justify / Tears / Germ farm / Second thought / Bleeding heart / Crawl inside / Burning daylight
CD _____ CDVILE 57
Peaceville / Oct '95 / Pinnacle.

Mortal Constraint

LEGEND OF DEFORMATION, THE
CD _____ GLA 11269-2
Glasnost / Apr '94 / SRD.

Mortal Memories

STONE AND THE GRAIL, THE
CD _____ FREQCD 005
Hyperium / Jul '93 / Plastic Head.

Mortal Sin

EVERY DOG HAS ITS DAY
CD _____ CDFLAG 61
Music For Nations / Sep '91 / Pinnacle.

Mortification

BLOOD WORLD
CD _____ NB 1182
Nuclear Blast / May '95 / Plastic Head.

MORTIFACTION
CD _____ NB 101CD
Nuclear Blast / Mar '94 / Plastic Head.

POST MOMENTARY AFFLICTION
CD _____ NB 082
Nuclear Blast / Nov '93 / Plastic Head.

PRIMITIVE RHYTHM MACHINE
CD _____ NB 134CD
Nuclear Blast / Aug '95 / Plastic Head.

Mortiis

FOOD TIL A HERSKE
CD _____ MA 003CD
Malicious / Oct '95 / Plastic Head.

Mortimer, Harry

KING OF BRASS (Various Artists)
Mikado / Lost chord / Hallelujah chorus / Solemn melody / Colonel Bogey on parade / William Tell overture - finale / Onward christian soldiers / Grand march from Aida / Nimrod / Finlandia / Hunting medley / Semper sousa / When the saints go marching in / Gallop / Londonderry air / Hailstorm / Waltzing trumpets / Parade of the tin soldiers / March: Kenilworth suite
CD _____ CC 283
Music For Pleasure / Jul '92 / EMI.

TRIBUTE IN MUSIC, A
Cossack / Yeoman of the guard / Three jolly sailormen / Shipbuilders / Trumpet voluntary / Relaxation / Force of destiny / Medallion / Grandfather's clock / Jesu joy of man's desiring / Alla hornpipe / All in the April evening / Life divine / Praise my soul
CD _____ QPRL 050D
Polyphonic / Jun '92 / Conifer.

Morton, Jelly Roll

ANTHOLOGY 1926-39
CD _____ EN 515
Encyclopaedia / Sep '95 / Discovery.

BEST OF JELLY ROLL MORTON 1926-1939
CD _____ 158012
Jazz Archives / Jun '93 / Jazz Music / Discovery / Cadillac.

BLUES AND STOMPS FROM RARE PIANO ROLLS
Jelly Roll blues / Mr. Jelly Lord / London blues / Sweet man / Grandpa's spells / Stratford hunch / Shreveport stomp / Tom cat blues / King Porter stomp / Midnight mama / Tin roof blues / Dead man blues / Pep / Naked dance
CD _____ BCD 111
Biograph / Jul '91 / Wellard / ADA / Hot Shot / Jazz Music / Cadillac / Direct.

CLASSICS 1923-24
CD _____ CLASSICS 584
Classics / Oct '91 / Discovery / Jazz Music.

CLASSICS 1926-28
CD _____ CLASSICS 612
Classics / Feb '92 / Discovery / Jazz Music.

CLASSICS 1928-29
CD _____ CLASSICS 627
Classics / '92 / Discovery / Jazz Music.

CLASSICS 1939-40
CD _____ CLASSICS 668
Classics / Nov '92 / Discovery / Jazz Music.

COMPLETE JELLY ROLL MORTON'S RED HOT PEPPERS
CD _____ MM 30380
Music Memoria / Apr '91 / Discovery / ADA.

DOCTOR JAZZ
CD _____ JHR 73521
Jazz Hour / '91 / Target/BMG / Jazz Music / Cadillac.

DOCTOR JAZZ (His Greatest Recordings)
Ballin' the Jack / Black bottom stomp / Burnin' the iceberg / Chant / Deep Creek / Dirty, dirty, dirty / Dr. Jazz / Don't you leave me here / Freakish / Grandpa's spells / King Porter stomp / Low gravy / Mama Nita / Mamie's blues / Michigan water blues / Mint Julep / Mournful serenade / Pearls / Ponchatrain blues / Seattle hunch / Shreveport stomp / Tia Juana / Turtle twist / Winin' boy blues / Wolverine blues
CD _____ CDAJA 5125
Living Era / Mar '94 / Koch.

INTRODUCTION TO JELLY ROLL MORTON 1926-39
CD _____ 4008
Best Of Jazz / May '94 / Discovery.

JELLY ROLL MORTON
CD _____ RTR 79002
Retrieval / Nov '95 / Retrieval / Wellard / Swift / Cadillac / Jazz Music.

JELLY ROLL MORTON - THE CHICAGO YEARS 1926-1928 (Robert Parker's Jazz Classics In Digital Stereo)
Black bottom stomp / Smokehouse blues / Chant / Sidewalk blues / Dead man blues / Steamboat stomp / Someday sweetheart / Grandpa's spells / Original Jelly Roll blues / Dr. Jazz / Cannonball blues / Hyena stomp / Billy goat stomp / Wild man blues / Jungle blues / Beale Street blues / Pearls / Wolverine blues / Midnight Mama / Mr. Jelly Lord
CD _____ RPCD 623
Robert Parker Jazz / Apr '94 / Conifer.

JELLY ROLL MORTON 1923/24
King Porter stomp / New Orleans joys / Grandpa's spells / Kansas city stomp / Wolverine blues / Pearls / Tia Juana / Shreveport stomp / Froggie Moore rag / Mamanita / Jelly roll blues / Big foot ham blues / My gal / Muddy water blues / Steady roll / Fish tail blues / High society / Weary blues / Tiger rag
CD _____ MCD 47018
Milestone / Jun '93 / Jazz Music / Pinnacle / Wellard / Cadillac.

JELLY ROLL MORTON 1924-26
CD _____ CD 599
Classic Jazz Masters / Sep '91 / Wellard / Jazz Music / Jazz Music.

JELLY ROLL MORTON VOL. 1
CD _____ KJ 105FS
King Jazz / Oct '93 / Jazz Music / Cadillac / Discovery.

JELLY ROLL MORTON VOL. 2
CD _____ KJ 106FS
King Jazz / Oct '93 / Jazz Music / Cadillac / Discovery.

JELLY ROLL MORTON VOL.4 - 1928-29
CD _____ 152132
Hot 'n' Sweet / Oct '93 / Discovery.

JELLY ROLL MORTON'S JAMS (Various Artists)
CD _____ 5177772
Verve / Jan '93 / PolyGram.

LIBRARY OF CONGRESS RECORDINGS (3CD Set)
CD _____ CDAFS 1010-3
Affinity / Oct '92 / Charly / Cadillac / Jazz Music.

LIBRARY OF CONGRESS RECORDINGS 1938 - VOL. 1 (Kansas City Stomp)
CD _____ ROU 1091CD
Rounder / Jan '94 / CM / Direct / ADA / Cadillac.

LIBRARY OF CONGRESS RECORDINGS 1938 - VOL. 2 (Anamule Dance)
CD _____ ROU 1092CD
Rounder / Jan '94 / CM / Direct / ADA / Cadillac.

LIBRARY OF CONGRESS RECORDINGS 1938 - VOL. 3 (The Pearls)
CD _____ ROU 1093CD
Rounder / Jan '94 / CM / Direct / ADA / Cadillac.

LIBRARY OF CONGRESS RECORDINGS 1938 - VOL. 4 (Winin' Boy Blues)
CD _____ ROU 1094CD
Rounder / Jan '94 / CM / Direct / ADA / Cadillac.

LIBRARY OF CONGRESS RECORDINGS VOL. 1
CD _____ SACD 11
Solo Art / Jul '93 / Jazz Music.

MR. JELLY LORD
Dr. Jazz / Original Jelly Roll blues / Mr. Jelly Lord / Beale Street blues / Oh, didn't he ramble / High society / I thought I heard Buddy Bolden say / Kansas city stomp / Shoe shiner's drag / Shreveport stomp / Turtle twist / Georgia swing / Wild man blues / Black bottom stomp / Cannonball blues / Wolverine blues / Boogaboo / Grandpa's spell
CD _____ CD 56017
Jazz Roots / Aug '94 / Target/BMG.

OH DIDN'T HE RAMBLE
CD _____ CDSGP 065
Prestige / Aug '93 / Total/BMG.

PEARLS, THE
Black bottom stomp / Smokehouse blues / Chant / Sidewalk blues / Dead man blues / Steamboat stomp / Grandpa's spells / Original Jelly Roll blues / Dr. Jazz / Cannonball blues / Pearls / Wolverine blues / Mr. Jelly Lord / Georgia swing / Kansas City stomp / Shreveport stomp / Mournful serenade / Red hot pepper stomp / Deep creek / Freakish / Tank town bump / I thought I heard Buddy Bolden say / Winin' boy blues
CD _____ ND 86588
Bluebird / Nov '88 / BMG.

PIANO BLUES AND RAG 1924/25
CD _____ 550122
Jazz Anthology / Jan '94 / Harmonia Mundi / Cadillac.

RARITIES AND ALTERNATIVE 1923-1940
CD _____ JZCD 358
Suisa / Feb '91 / Jazz Music / THE.

RED HOT PEPPERS, NEW ORLEANS JAZZMEN & TRIOS
Oh, didn't he ramble / West End blues / High society / I thought I heard Buddy Bolden say / Kansas city stomp / Shoe shiner's drag / Deep creek / Chant / Original Jelly Roll blues / Mr. Jelly Lord / Shreveport stomp / Turtle twist / Beale Street blues / Georgia swing / Wild man blues / Black bottom stomp / Grandpa's spells / Dr. Jazz / Cannonball blues / Wolverine blues / Boogaboo / Winin' boy blues / Ballin' the Jack
CD _____ GOJCD 53018
Giants Of Jazz / Jun '88 / Target/BMG / Cadillac.

SWEET & HOT
CD _____ TPZ 1003
Topaz Jazz / Jul '94 / Pinnacle / Cadillac.

VOLUME 1
Black bottom stomp / Smoke house / Chant / Sidewalk blues / Dead man's blues / Steamboat stomp / Someday sweetheart / Grandpa's spells / Original Jelly Roll blues / Mr. Jelly lord / Wolverine blues / Wild man blues
CD _____ JSPCD 321
JSP / Oct '90 / ADA / Target/BMG / Direct / Cadillac / Complete/Pinnacle.

VOLUME 2 (1928-1929)
CD _____ JSPCD 322
JSP / Apr '94 / ADA / Target/BMG / Direct / Cadillac / Complete/Pinnacle.

VOLUME 3 (1928-1929)
CD _____ JSPCD 323
JSP / '89 / ADA / Target/BMG / Direct / Cadillac / Complete/Pinnacle.

VOLUME 4 (Alternative takes)
Chant / Sidewalk blues / Dead man blues / Someday sweetheart / Grandpa's spells / Original Jelly Roll blues / Mournful serenade / Pearls / Georgia swing
CD _____ JSPCD 324
JSP / Apr '91 / ADA / Target/BMG / Direct / Cadillac / Complete/Pinnacle.

VOLUME 5
CD _____ JSPCD 325
JSP / Feb '92 / ADA / Target/BMG / Direct / Cadillac / Complete/Pinnacle.

Morton, Mandy

MAGIC LADY (Morton, Mandy & Spriguns)
CD _____ ENG 1011
English Garden / Apr '94 / Background.

Morton, Pete

COURAGE LOVE & GRACE
CD _____ HARDCD 029
Harbour Town / May '95 / Roots / Direct / CM / ADA.

COURAGE, LOVE AND GRACE
CD _____ HAROCD 29
Harbour Town / Apr '95 / Roots / Direct / CM / ADA.

MAD WORLD BLUES
CD _____ HARCD 018
Harbour Town / Oct '93 / Roots / Direct / CM / ADA.

ONE BIG JOKE
Prisoner / Simple love / Water from the houses of our fathers / First day / Little boy's room / Another train / Love / Old grey moon / One big joke / Girls like you / River of love / Somewhere in love / Live your life
CD _____ HARCD 001
Harbour Town / Oct '93 / Roots / Direct / CM / ADA.

Mortuary

BLACKENED IMAGES
CD _____ BR 003CD
Brain Crusher / Nov '92 / Plastic Head.

Mosalini, Juan Jose

BORDONEO Y 900
Bordoneo Y 900 / Lo que vendra / Alma de bohemio / Don goyo / Al maestro con nostagias / Retrato a julio ahumada / De contrapunto / Ojos negros / Danzarin / Adios nonino / Fuego lento / Bien al mango / Dominguera / La bordona / Tres Y dos / Cabulero
CD _____ LBLC 2507
Indigo / Nov '95 / New Note.

LA BORDONA (Mosalini, Juan Jose/Gustavo Beytelmann/Patrice Caratini)
La bordona / El choclo / Cardo y malvon / Nocturna / La cumparsita / Inspiracion / Palomita blanca / Contrajeando la cumparsita / Inspiracion (2) / Palomita blanca (2)
CD _____ LBLC 6548
Label Bleu / Jan '92 / New Note.

Moses, Bob

EAST SIDE (Moses, Bob & Billy Martin)
CD _____ ITM 1415
ITM / '89 / Tradelink / Koch.

STORY OF MOSES
CD _____ 188703-2
Gaia / May '89 / New Note.

Moses, Pablo

BEST OF PABLO MOSES
I am a rastaman / Life he lives / Play, play, play / Tension / Spirit of Jah / Bomb the nation / Freedom for the africans / Live to love / Reggae warrior / Ready, aim, fire / Fight back / Don't force me / I want to be with you / Whats the problem / What is it
CD _____ 198842
Musidisc / Jan '93 / Vital / Harmonia Mundi / ADA / Cadillac / Discovery.

CONFESSION OF A RASTAMAN, THE
Confession of a rastaman / Rastaman / Give up / Lynch mob / What we need / Laugh clowns / is black / African children / Woo-oo / Life is a big shot / Nowadays / Comfort you / Try to know / Everytime / I need a break / Dis reggae
CD _____ 109622
Musidisc / Feb '94 / Vital / Harmonia Mundi / ADA / Cadillac / Discovery.

MISSION
Will power / Brain wash / He was bad / Tick tock / One shot / Too much / Never seen / You got a spell / Stand off back off / These are the days / Live up woman / Mission
CD _____ RASCD 3158
Ras / Jul '95 / Jetstar / Greensleeves / SRD / Direct.

REVOLUTIONARY DREAM
I love i boing / Be not a dread / Give I fe I name / Come mek we run / Revolutionary dream / Where am I / I man a grasshopper / Corrupted man / Blood money / Lonely singer
CD _____ 198832
Musidisc / Feb '94 / Vital / Harmonia Mundi / ADA / Cadillac / Discovery.

Mosole, Gianluca

MAGAZINE
CD _____ CDSGP 0123
Prestige / Jul '95 / Total/BMG.

Moss, Anne Marie

TWO FOR THE ROAD (Moss, Anne Marie & Vivian Lord)
CD _____ STCD 554
Stash / '92 / Jazz Music / CM / Cadillac / Direct / ADA.

Moss, Buddy

BUDDY MOSS 1930-41
I'm on my way down home / Diddle da diddle / She looks so good / She's coming back some cold rainy day / Bye bye mama / Unfinished business / I'm sittin' here tonight / Joy rag / You need a woman / Who stole de lock / Tampa strut / Jealous hearted man / Mistreated boy
CD _____ TMCD 05
Travellin' Man / Oct '90 / Wellard / CM / Jazz Music.

BUDDY MOSS VOL. 1 (1933)
CD _____ DOCD 5123
Blues Document / Oct '92 / Swift / Jazz Music / Hot Shot.

BUDDY MOSS VOL. 3 (1935-41)
CD _____ DOCD 5125
Blues Document / Oct '92 / Swift / Jazz Music / Hot Shot.

Moss, Danny

THA GOOD (Moss, Danny & Jack Jacobs)
CD _____ PCD 7018
Progressive / Aug '94 / Jazz Music.

Moss, David

MY FAVOURITE THINGS
CD _____ CD 022
Intakt / Mar '92 / Cadillac / SRD.

TEXTURE TIME
CD _____ INTAKTCD 034
Intakt / Oct '94 / Cadillac / SRD.

Mossman, Mike

GRANULAT (Mossman, Mike & Daniel Schnyder)

Time Stood Still

TIME STOOD STILL
Prelude: Simul-Circular loopology in A minor / Felonious thunk / Time stood still - Africa and back in a day / Jaco / Gregarious chants / Elegant blue ghosts - Dance like clouds over mean street U.S / Lost in your eyes / Word from the RA / Mbira Tanzania / Black east blues / Deusa do amour / Once in a blue moon / Prayer
CD _____ GCD 79493
Gramavision / Sep '95 / Vital/SAM / ADA.

WHEN ELEPHANTS DREAM OF MUSIC
Trevor / Piccolo and Lulu / Everybody knows when you're up and in / La flava / Happy to be here today / For miles / Black orchid / Disappearing blues / Blame it on the egg / River / Embraceable Jew (CD only) / Bugs Bunny (CD only) / Ripped van Twinkle (CD only)
CD _____ GCD 79491
Gramavision / Sep '95 / Vital/SAM / ADA.

CD _____ 1232402
Red / Nov '91 / Harmonia Mundi / Jazz
Horizons / Cadillac / ADA.

Motaung, Audrey

LIGHT
Imagine / Peace / Amazing grace / God
loves you / Glory of his love / Let the whole
world / Child is born / I believe / Who is pure
and perfect / Jerusalem / Ya-me-mesa
CD _____ MOU 41792
Mountain/EWM / Oct '95 / EWM.

Moten, Bennie

**1923-1927 (Moten, Bennie Kansas City
Orchestra)**
CD _____ CLASSICS 549
Classics / Dec '90 / Discovery / Jazz
Music.

**1930-1932 (Moten, Bennie Kansas City
Orchestra)**
CD _____ CD 591
Classic Jazz Masters / Sep '91 / Wellard /
Jazz Music / Jazz Music.

**INTRODUCTION TO BENNIE MOTEN
1923-32, AN**
CD _____ 4027
Best Of Jazz / Nov '95 / Discovery.

Moten, Wendy

WENDY MOTEN
Matter of fact / Nobody but you / Step by
step / So close to love / Forever yours /
Whatever it takes / Come in out of the rain
/ Make this love last / Magic touch / Won-
derin' / Once upon a time
CD _____ CDMTL 1073
EMI / Mar '94 / EMI.

Moth Macabre

MOTH MACABRE
All great architects are dead / Amazing /
Elizabeth / Pale / Blow / Two days / Malibu
/ Glass eye / Screwdriver girl / Lemuria /
A.E.I.O.U.
CD _____ 756792237-2
WEA / Jun '93 / Warner Music.

Mother Carey's Chickens

I'LL TELL ME MA
CD _____ MCC 010694CD
MCC Music / Aug '94 / Direct.

Mother Earth

PEOPLE TREE
Institution man / Jesse / Stardust bubble-
gum / Mr. Freedom / Warlocks of the mind
/ Dragster / Find it / People tree / Apple
green / Time of the future / Saturation 70 /
Illusions / Trip down brain lane
CD _____ JAZIDCD 083
Acid Jazz / Feb '94 / Pinnacle.

STONED WOMAN
CD _____ JAZIDCD 048
Acid Jazz / May '92 / Pinnacle.

YOU HAVE BEEN WATCHING
CD _____ FOCUSCD 11
Focus / Oct '95 / Pinnacle.

Mother Hen

MOTHER HEN
Sing evermore / My granny's face / Goodbye old razzle dazzle / Lookout Charlie /
Man from Aberdeen / America the san-
dlord's dream / Naked king / He's alive and
remembers / Old before your time / Passage back
CD _____ EDCD 349
Edsel / Jun '92 / Pinnacle / ADA.

Mother Hips

BACK TO THE GROTTO
Hey Emille / Portrero Road / Run around me
/ Chum / Back to the grotto / This is a man
/ Precious opal / Two young queens / Ste-
phanie's for LA / Figure 11 / Hot lunch /
Turtle bones
CD _____ 74321254512
American / Jul '95 / BMG.

Mother Love Bone

STARDOG CHAMPION
CD _____ 5141772
Polydor / Jul '92 / PolyGram.

Mother May I

SPLITSVILLE
Poison dart / Teenage Jesus / Painted on /
Something better / Birthday wish / Disk and
Jane / Meet you there / In a box / Never
ending riddle / In between / Bastard / All
the way in
CD _____ 4782032
Columbia / Nov '95 / Sony.

Mother Station

BRAND NEW BAG
CD _____ 756792366-2
Warner Bros. / Oct '94 / Warner Music.

Mother Tongue

MOTHER TONGUE
Broken / Mad world / Burn baby / Vesper /
Sheila's song / Seed / Damage / Fear of
night / So afraid / Venus beach / Entity /
Using your guns
CD _____ 477366-2
Epic / Dec '94 / Sony.

Motherhips

PART TIMER GOES FULL
Shut the door / Stoned up the road / Mona
Lisa / Poison / Afternoon after afternoon /
Magazine / Are you breathing / Petfoot /
Sunshine feel / Tehachapi / Beat carousel /
Bad Marie / Been lost once / Trunk box
CD _____ 74321289772
American / Nov '95 / BMG.

Mothers

FIRST BORN
Miracle man / Sponge / Even if we lose /
Kingfisher rock / Lady leave the pain / Oasis
/ Drag racer / Make no mistakes / Pond /
Night is my day / Truly
CD _____ 7559610222
Elektra / Apr '91 / Warner Music.

Motian, Paul

CONCEPTION VESSEL
Georgian bay / Ch'l energie / Rebica / Conception vessel / American Indian:Song of
sitting bull / Inspiration from a Vietnamese
lullaby
CD _____ 519279-2
ECM / Jun '93 / New Note.

DANCE
CD _____ 5192822
ECM / Jul '94 / New Note.

ELECTRIC BEBOP BAND
CD _____ 5140042
JMT / Jan '93 / PolyGram.

**IT SHOULD'VE HAPPENED A LONG
TIME AGO (Motian, Paul Trio)**
CD _____ 8236412
ECM / Apr '85 / New Note.

JACK OF CLUBS (Motian, Paul Quintet)
CD _____ SN 1124
Soul Note / '86 / Harmonia Mundi /
Wellard / Cadillac.

LE VOYAGE
Folk song for Rosie / Abacus / Cabla/Drum
music / Sunflower / Le voyage
CD _____ 5192832
ECM / Mar '94 / New Note.

PAUL MOTIAN PLAYS BILL EVANS
Show type tune / Turn out the stars /
Walkin' up / Very early / Five / Time remem-
bered / 34 skidoo / Re: person I knew / Chil-
dren's play song
CD _____ 8344452
JMT / May '91 / PolyGram.

PSALM (Motian, Paul Band)
Psalm / White magic / Boomerang / Fan-
tasm / Mandeville / Second hand / Etude /
Yahllah
CD _____ 8473302
ECM / Mar '92 / New Note.

REINCARNATION OF A LOVEBIRD
CD _____ 5140162
JMT / Mar '95 / PolyGram.

TRIBUTE
Victoria / Tuesdays ends Saturdays / War
orphans / Sod house / Song for Che
CD _____ 5192812-2
ECM / Nov '93 / New Note.

TRIOISM (Motian, Paul Trio)
CD _____ 514012-2
JMT / Jun '93 / PolyGram.

Motley Crue

DECADE OF DECADENCE '81-'91
Live wire / Piece of your action / Shout at
the devil / Looks that kill / Home sweet
home / Smokin' in the boys room / Girls,
girls, girls / Wild side / Dr. Feelgood / Kick-
start my heart / Teaser / Rock 'n' roll junkie
/ Primal scream / Angela / Anarchy in the
U.K.
CD _____ 7559612042
Elektra / Oct '91 / Warner Music.

DECADENT DISCUSSION
CD P.Disc _____ CBAK 4031
Baktabak / Mar '92 / Baktabak.

DOCTOR FEELGOOD
Same old situation / Slice of your pie /
Rattlesnake shake / Kickstart my heart /
Without you / Don't go away mad / She
goes down / Sticky sweet / Time for a
change / T'n'T (Terror 'n Tinseltown) / Dr.
Feelgood
CD _____ 9608292
Elektra / Sep '89 / Warner Music.

GIRLS, GIRLS, GIRLS
Wild side / Girls, girls, girls / Dancin' on
glass / Bad boy boogie / Nona / Five years
dead / All in the name of rock / Somethin'
for nuthin' / All I need / Jailhouse rock (live)
CD _____ 9607252
Elektra / Jun '87 / Warner Music.

Motley Crue

MOTLEY CRUE
Power to the music / Uncle Jack / Hooli-
gan's holiday / Misunderstood / Loveshine
/ Poison apples / Hammered / Till death do
us part / Welcome to the numb / Smoke the
sky / Droppin' like flies / Drift away
CD _____ 755961534-2
Elektra / Mar '94 / Warner Music.

SHOUT AT THE DEVIL
In the beginning / Shout at the devil / Looks
that kill / Bastard / Knock 'em dead kid /
Danger / Too young to fall in love / Helter
skelter / Red hot / Ten seconds to love /
God bless the children of the beast
CD _____ 9602892
Elektra / Jan '86 / Warner Music.

THEATRE OF PAIN
City boy blues / Fight for your rights / Use
it or lose it / Smokin' in the boys room /
Louder than hell / Keep your eye on the
money / Home sweet home / Tonight (we
need a lover) / Save our souls / Raise your
hands to rock
CD _____ 9604182
Elektra / Jul '86 / Warner Music.

TOO FAST FOR LOVE
Live wire / Come on and dance / Public en-
emy No.1 / Merry go round / Take me to
the top / Piece of your action / Starry eyes
/ Too fast for love / On with the show
CD _____ 7559601742
Elektra / Jul '93 / Warner Music.

Motocaster

STAY LOADED
CD _____ BBQCD 165
Beggars Banquet / Oct '94 / Warner
Music / Disc.

Motor Psycho

TIMOTHY'S MONSTER
CD _____ PSYCHOBABBLE 002B
Blue Rose / Nov '95 / 3MV.

Motorcycle Boy

SCARLET
CD _____ CCD 1689
Chrysalis / Sep '89 / EMI.

Motorhead

ACE OF SPADES
Ace of spades / Bite the bullet / Chase is
better than the catch / Dance / Fast and
loose / Fire, fire / Hammer / Jailbait / Live
to win / Love me like a reptile / We are the
road crew / Shoot you in the back
CD _____ CLACD 240
Castle / Sep '91 / BMG.

ALL THE ACES
CD _____ CCSCD 427
Castle / May '95 / BMG.

ANOTHER PERFECT DAY
Back at the funny farm / Shine / Dancing on
your grave / Rock it / One track mind / Another perfect day / Marching off to war / I
got mine / Tales of glory / Die you bastard
CD _____ CLACD 225
Castle / Feb '91 / BMG.

BLITZKREIG ON BIRMINGHAM
CD _____ RRCD 120
Receiver / Oct '89 / Grapevine.

BOMBER
Dead men tell no tales / Lawman / Sweet
revenge / Sharp shooter / Poison / Stone
dead forever / All the aces / Step down /
Talking head / Bomber
CD _____ CLACD 227
Castle / Apr '91 / BMG.

COLLECTION: MOTORHEAD (Bear Trap)
Motorhead / Overkill / Talking head / Rock
it / Iron fist / I got mine / Steal your face /
We are the road crew / Swaggletooth / Stay
clean / Iron horse / One track mind / Speed-
freak / Loser / (Don't need) religion / Stone
dead forever / Sweet revenge / Capricorn /
Love me like a reptile / Ace of spades
CD _____ CCSCD 237
Castle / Mar '90 / BMG.

FROM THE VAULTS
CD _____ NEXCD 136
Sequel / Nov '90 / BMG.

IRON FIST
Iron fist / Heart of stone / I'm the doctor /
Go to hell / Loser / Sex and outrage / Amer-
ica / Shut it down / Speed freak / Don't let
them grind ya down / (Don't need) religion
/ Bang to rights
CD _____ CLACD 123
Castle / Mar '87 / BMG.

IRON FIST/HORDES FROM HELL
CD _____ CLEO 94132
Cleopatra / Dec '94 / Disc.

LEMMY STORY (Lemmy)
CD _____ VSOPCD 206
Connoisseur / Oct '94 / Pinnacle.

LIVE
CD _____ JHD 081
Tring / Mar '93 / Tring / Prism.

LIVE 1983
Back to the funny farm / Tales of glory /
Shoot you in the back / Marching off to war
/ Iron horse / Another perfect day / (Don't
need) Religion / One track mind / Go to hell
/ America / Shine / Dancing on your grave
/ Rock it / I've got mine / Bite the bullet /
Chase is better than the catch
CD _____ DOJOCD 108
Dojo / Feb '94 / BMG.

LIVE JAILBAIT
CD Set _____ RRDCD 005
Receiver / Jul '93 / Grapevine.

**LOCK UP YOUR DAUGHTERS (Live In
St. Albans)**
Motorhead / Leavin' here / Watcher / Louie
Louie / Iron horse / Instrumental / I'll be your
sister / Lost Johnny / Keep us on the road
/ Tear ya down / White line fever
CD _____ RRCD 130
Receiver / Jul '93 / Grapevine.

MELTDOWN
CD _____ ESBCD 146
Essential / May '91 / Total/BMG.

MOTORHEAD
Motorhead / Vibrator / Lost Johnny / Iron
horse / Born to lose / White line fever / Keep
us on the road / Watcher / Train kept a rollin' / City kids / Beer drinkers and hell raisers / On parole / Intro / I'm your witch
doctor
CD _____ CDWIK 2
Chiswick / Jun '88 / Pinnacle.

MOTORHEAD LIVE AND LOUD
CD _____ EMPRCD 575
Emporio / Jul '95 / THE / Disc / CM.

MOTORHEAD VOL.1 - ACES HIGH
Stone dead forever / All the aces / Poison /
Ace of spades / live to win / America / Jail-
bait / Please don't touch / Iron fist / Go to
hell / Don't let 'em grind ya down / Dance
/ Heart of stone / I got mine / Tales of glory
CD _____ 5507242
Spectrum/Karussell / Aug '94 / PolyGram /
THE.

**MOTORHEAD VOL.2 - ULTIMATE
METAL**
Bomber / Louie Louie / Dead men tell no
tales / Metropolis / Stay clean / Back at the
funny farm / Shoot you in the back / Hoo-
chie coochie man (live) / Motorhead (live) /
Killed by death / Turn you round again / Like
a nightmare / Hammer / Over the top / Tear
ya down / Too late, too late
CD _____ 5507252
Spectrum/Karussell / Mar '95 / PolyGram /
THE.

NO REMORSE
Ace of spades / Motorhead / Jailbait / Stay
clean / Too late, too late / Killed by death /
Bomber / Iron fist / Shine / Dancing on your
grave / Metropolis / Snaggletooth / Overkill
/ Please don't touch / Stone dead forever /
Like a nightmare / Emergency / Steal your
face / Louie Louie / No class / Iron horse /
We are the road crew / Leaving here /
Locomotive
CD _____ CLACD 121
Castle / '88 / BMG.

NO SLEEP 'TIL HAMMERSMITH
Ace of spades / Stay clean / Metropolis /
Hammer / Iron horse / No class / Overkill /
We are the road crew / Capricorn / Bomber
/ Motorhead
CD _____ CLACD 179
Castle / Feb '90 / BMG.

NO SLEEP AT ALL
Dr. Rock / Dogs / Built for speed / Deaf forever / Killed by death / Traitor / Ace of
spades / Eat the rich / Just coz you got the
power / Overkill
CD _____ CLACD 285
Castle / Mar '92 / BMG.

ON PAROLE
Motorhead / On parole / Vibrator / Iron
horse / Born to lose / City kids / Fools /
Watcher / Leaving here / Lost Johnny
CD _____ CDFA 3251
Fame / Oct '90 / EMI.

ORGASMATRON
Deaf forever / Nothing up my sleeve / Ain't
my crime / Claw / Mean machine / Built for
speed / Ridin' with the driver / Dr. Rock /
Orgasmatron
CD _____ CLACD 283
Castle / Apr '92 / BMG.

OVERKILL
Overkill / Stay clean / (I won't) Pay your
price / I'll be your sister / Capricorn / No
class / Damage case / Tear ya down / Metropolis / Limb from limb
CD _____ CLACD 178
Castle / Feb '91 / BMG.

ROCK 'N' ROLL
Rock 'n' roll / Eat the rich / Black heart /
Stone deaf in the USA / Wolf / Traitor / Dogs
/ All for you / Boogeyman
CD _____ CLACD 284
Castle / Mar '93 / BMG.

SACRIFICE
CD _____ SPV 08576942
SPV / Mar '95 / Plastic Head.

Motorpsycho

8 SOOTHING SONGS FOR RUT
CD _____ VOW 027C
Voices Of Wonder / Jan '94 / Plastic Head.

DEMON BOX
CD _____ VOW 030CD
Voices Of Wonder / Jun '93 / Plastic Head.

LOBOTOMIZER
CD _____ VOW 026C
Voices Of Wonder / Jan '94 / Plastic Head.

Motors

AIRPORT - THE MOTORS' GREATEST HITS
Dancing the night away / Sensation / Airport / Metropolis / Love and loneliness / Forget about you / Emergency / Tenement steps / Today / Freeze / That's what John said / You beat the hell outta me / Soul redeemer / Cold love / Time for make up / Love round the corner / Here comes the hustler
CD _____ CDVM 9032
Virgin / Jan '95 / EMI.

APPROVED BY
Airport / Mama rock 'n' roller / Forget about you / Do you mind / You beat the hell outta me / Breathless / Soul redeemer / Dreaming your life away / Sensation / Today
CD _____ CDV 2101
Virgin / Oct '90 / EMI.

Mott The Hoople

BALLAD OF MOTT, THE (A Retrospective/2CD Set)
Rock 'n' roll Queen / Walkin' with a mountain / Waterlow / Sweet Angeline / All the young dudes / Momma's little jewel / One of the boys / Sucker / Sweet Jane / Sea diver / Reach for love/After lights / Ballad of Mott The Hoople / Drivin' sister / Violence / Rose / I wish I was your mother / Honaloo-chie boogie / All the way from Memphis / Whizz kid / Hymn for the dudes / Golden age of rock 'n' roll / Rest in peace / Mari-onette / Crash street kids / Born late '58 / Roll away the stone / Where do you all come from / Henry and the H-bomb / Foxy foxy / Saturday gigs / Lounge lizard / Through the looking glass / American pie
CD Set _____ CD 46973
Legacy / Nov '93 / Sony.

GREATEST HITS: MOTT THE HOOPLE
All the way from Memphis / Honaloochie boogie / Hymn for the dudes / Born late '58 / All the young dudes / Roll away the stone / Ballad of Mott the Hoople / Golden age of rock 'n' roll / Foxy foxy / Saturday gigs
CD _____ CD 32007
CBS / Apr '89 / Sony.

MOTT
All the way from Memphis / Whizz kid / Hymn for the dudes / Honaloochie boogie / Violence / Drivin' sister / Ballad of Mott The Hoople / I'm a Cadillac / El camino dolo roso / I wish I was your mother
CD _____ 4674022
Columbia / Mar '95 / Sony.

MOTT THE HOOPLE
Dear louise / Hot footin' / World cruise / Brother soul / 1-2-3-4 Kickalong blues / Wild in the streets
CD _____ SEACD 7
See For Miles/C5 / May '93 / Pinnacle.

MOTT THE HOOPLE/MAD SHADOWS
You really got me / At the crossroads / Laugh at me / Backsliding fearlessly / Rock 'n' roll Queen / Rabbit food and Toby time / Half moon bay / Wrath and roll / Thunderbuck ram / No wheels to ride / You are one of us / Walkin' with a mountain / I can feel / Threads of iron / When my minds gone
CD _____ EDCD 361
Edsel / Jan '93 / Pinnacle / ADA.

WALKING WITH A MOUNTAIN (The Best Of Mott The Hoople 1969-1972)
Rock 'n' roll queen / At the crossroads / Thunderbuck ram / Whiskey woman / Waterlow / Moon upstairs / Second love / Road to Birmingham / Black scorpio (momma's little jewel) / You really got me / Walkin' with a mountain / No wheels to ride / Keep a knockin' / Midnight lady / Death may be your Santa Claus / Darkness darkness / Growing man blues / Black hills
CD _____ IMCD 87
Island / Jun '90 / PolyGram.

Mould, Bob

BLACK SHEETS OF RAIN
Black sheets of rain / One good reason / Hanging tree / Hear me calling / Disappointed / It's too late / Stop your crying / Last night / Out of your life / Sacrifice / Let there be peace
CD _____ CDVUS 21
Virgin / Apr '92 / EMI.

POISON YEARS
Black sheets of rain / It's too late / Stop your crying / Out of your life / Hanging tree / Sacrifice / Wishing well / See a little light

/ All those people know / Compositions for the young and old (Live) / If you're true (Live) / Poison years (Live) / Brasilia crossed with Trenton (Live) / Shoot out the lights (Live)
CD _____ CDVM 9030
Virgin / May '94 / EMI.

WORKBOOK
Sunspots / Wishing well / Heartbreak a stranger / See a little light / Poison years / Sinners and their repentances / Brasilia crossed with Trenton / Compositions for the young and old / Lonely afternoon / Dreaming, I am whichever way the wind blows
CD _____ CDVUS 2
Virgin / Jul '89 / EMI.

Mound City Blues Blowers

1935-36
What's the reason I'm not pleasin' you / She's a Latin from Manhattan / You've been taking lessons in love (from somebody new) / (Back home again in) Indiana / Red sails in the sunset / I'm sittin' high on a hilltop / On Treasure Island / Thanks a million / Eeny meeny miney Mo / Little bit independent / I'm shootin' high / I've got my fingers crossed / High Society / Muskrat ramble / Broken record / Music goes round and around / I'm gonna sit right down and write myself a letter / Mama don't allow it / Rhythm in my nursery rhymes / I hope Gabriel likes my music / You hit the spot / Spreadin' rhythm around / Saddle your blues to a wild mustang / Wah-hoo / I'm gonna clap my hands
CD _____ CBC 1018
Timeless Historical / Aug '94 / New Note / Pinnacle.

Mounsey, Paul

NAHOO
Passing away / Alba / Journeyman / Balmore / Stranger in a strange land / As terras baixas da / Hollanda / From ebb to flood / I will go / My faithful fond one / Illusion
CD _____ IRCD 029
Iona / Jan '95 / ADA / Direct / Duncans.

Mount Shasta

PUT THE CREEP ON
CD _____ GR 013CD
Skingraft / Apr '94 / SRD.

WHO'S THE HOTTIE
CD _____ GR 31CD
Skingraft / May '95 / SRD.

Mountain

BEST OF MOUNTAIN
Never in my life / Taunta (Sammy's tune) / Nantucket sleighride / Roll over Beethoven / For Yasgur's farm / Animal trainer and the toad / Mississippi Queen / Kings Chorale / Boys in the band / Don't look around / Crossroader
CD _____ 4663352
CBS / Aug '90 / Sony.

CLIMBING
Mississippi queen / Theme for an imaginary western / Never in my life / Silver paper / For Yasgur's farm / To my friend / Laird / Sittin' on a rainbow / Boys in the band
CD _____ 4721802
Columbia / Feb '95 / Sony.

FLOWERS OF EVIL
CD _____ BGOCD 113
Beat Goes On / Aug '91 / Pinnacle.

NANTUCKET SLEIGHRIDE (The Best Of Mountain)
Don't look around / You can't get away / Tired angels / My lady / Great train robbery / Taunta (Sammy's tune) / Nantucket sleighride / Animal trainer and the toad / Travellin' in the dark
CD _____ BGOCD 32
Beat Goes On / Mar '89 / Pinnacle.

ROAD GOES ON FOREVER, THE (Mountain Live)
CD _____ BGOCD 111
Beat Goes On / Aug '91 / Pinnacle.

Mountain Ash Band

HERMIT, THE
CD _____ DORIS 2
Vinyl Tap / Jan '96 / Vinyl Tap.

Mountain Bus

SUNDANCE
CD _____ EVA 852121B32
EVA / Nov '94 / Direct / ADA.

Mountain Goats

NINE BLACK POPPIES
CD _____ EJ 02CD
Emperor Jones / Nov '95 / SRD.

Moura, Paulo

RIO NOCTURNES
Guadeloupe / Capricornio / Rio nocturne / Baleias / Jumento elegante / Barbara's vatapa / Sereia do leblon / Mulatas / Tumba-

iele / Concierto brasitalian / Tarde de chuva / Casamento em xaxei
CD _____ 158162
Messidor / Aug '92 / Koch / ADA.

Mourn

MOURN
CD _____ RISE 10CD
Rise Above / Jun '95 / Vital / Plastic Head.

Mourning

GREETINGS FROM HELL
CD _____ FDN 2005
Foundation 2000 / Jul '93 / Plastic Head.

Mourning Sign

ALIENOR
CD _____ GOD 015CD
Godhead / Jun '95 / Plastic Head.

MOURNING SIGN
CD _____ GOD 016CD
Godhead / Oct '95 / Plastic Head.

Mouse & The Traps

PUBLIC EXECUTION
CD _____ 842088
EVA / May '94 / Direct / ADA.

Mouse On Mars

IAORA TAHITI
Stereomission / Kompod / Staurday night world / Cup fieher / Schunkel / Gooard / Kanu / Bib / Schlecktron / Preprise / Pap Antoine / Omnibuzz / Hallo / Die innere orange
CD _____ PURECD 048
Too Pure / Aug '95 / Vital.

VULVA LAND
CD _____ PURECD 036
Too Pure / Jun '94 / Vital.

Mousetrap

CEREBRAL REVOLVER
Cerebral revolver
CD _____ GROW 003-2
Grass / Jul '93 / SRD.

LOVER
CD _____ GROW 023-2
Grass / Jun '94 / SRD.

Mouskouri, Nana

MAGIC OF NANA MOUSKOURI
Only love / White rose of Athens / Never on a Sunday / Yesterday / Amazing grace / Try to remember / Power of love / Bridge over troubled water / Only time will tell / Morning has broken / And I love you so / Ave Maria / Love me tender / Nights in white satin / Song for liberty / Lonely shepherd
CD _____ 8307642
Polystar / Jul '93 / PolyGram.

NANA
Johnny / Half a crown / Just a ribbon / If you love me / Love we never knew / I love my man / Ballinderry / I gave my love a cherry / He didn't know me / Tiny sparrow / My kind of man
CD _____ 810 055-2
Mercury / Sep '84 / PolyGram.

PASSPORT
Amazing grace / And I love you so / Bridge over troubled water / Cu-cu-rru-cu-cu-paloma / Day is done / Enas mithos / Four and twenty hours / I have a dream / If you love me / Last rose of Summer / Loving song / Milisse Mou / My friend the sea / Never on Sunday / Odos oniron / Over and over / Plaisir d'amour / Seasons in the sun / Try to remember / Turn on the Sun / White rose of Athens
CD _____ 8307642
Philips / '88 / PolyGram.

Mouth Music

MODI
CD _____ TRECD 111
Triple Earth / Feb '95 / Sterns / Grapevine.

MOUTH MUSIC
Bratach bana / Mor a' cheannaich / Chi mi na morbheana / Mile marbh'aisg a'ghaol / Froach a ronaigh / Co ni mire rium / Martin Martin / I bhi a da / Air fair a lail o
CD _____ TERRACD 109
Triple Earth / Aug '90 / Sterns / Grapevine.

SHORELIFE
CD _____ TRECD 113
Triple Earth / Oct '94 / Sterns / Grapevine.

Mouzon, Alphonse

MIND TRANSPLANT
Mind transplant / Snowbound / Carbon dioxide / Ascorbic acid / Happiness is loving you / Some of the things people do / Golden rainbows / Nitroglycerin / Real thing
CD _____ RPM 116
RPM / Sep '93 / Pinnacle.

Move

BBC SESSION
CD _____ BOJCD 011
Band Of Joy / Mar '95 / ADA.

BEST OF THE MOVE
Blackberry Way / Curly / Yellow rainbow / I can hear the grass grow / Fire brigade / Hey Grandma / Kilroy was here / Night of fear / Feel too good / Brontosaurus / Flowers in the rain / Walk upon the water / Stephanie knows who / Turkish tram conductor blues / Useless information / Weekend / Cherry blossom clinic revisited / So you want to be a rock 'n' roll star
CD _____ MCCD 009
Music Club / Feb '91 / Disc / THE / CM.

COLLECTION: MOVE
Night of fear / I can hear the grass grow / Wave your flag and stop the train / Flowers in the rain / Fire brigade / Wild tiger woman / Blackberry way / Curly / Brontosaurus / So you want to be a rock 'n' roll star / Something else / I'll be me / Sunshine help me / When Alice comes back to the farm / Zing went the strings of my heart / Cherry blossom clinic revisited / Hello Susie / Kilroy was here / Last thing on my mind / Here we go round the lemon tree / Field's of people / Don't make my baby blue / Yellow rainbow / Walk upon the water
CD _____ CCSCD 135
Castle / '86 / BMG.

EARLY YEARS, THE
Night of fear / Disturbance / I can hear the grass grow / Flowers in the rain / Here we go round the lemon tree / Fire brigade / Girl outside / Mist on a Monday morning / Cherry blossom clinic / Wild tiger woman / Ominibus / Blackberry way / Something / Curly / This time tomorrow / Beautiful daughter / Brontosaurus / Lightning never strikes twice / When Alice comes back to the farm / What
CD _____ EARLD 7
Castle / Nov '92 / BMG.

MESSAGE FROM THE COUNTRY
Message from the country / Ella James / No time / Don't mess up / Until your Mama's gone / It wasn't my idea to dance / Minister / Ben Crawley steel company / Words of Aaron / My Marge
CD _____ BGOCD 238
Beat Goes On / Jun '94 / Pinnacle.

MOVE, THE
CD _____ CUCD 15
Disky / Oct '94 / THE / BMG / Discovery / Pinnacle.

Move D

KUNSTOFF
Eastman / Soap bubbles / Sandman / In/ Out (initial mix) / Hood / Tribute to Mr Fingers / 77 Sunset strip / Beyond the machine / Nimm 2 / Amazing discoveries / Trist / Xing the Jordan/Seven
CD _____ 940917CD
Source / Apr '95 / Vital.

Mover, Bob

YOU GO TO MY HEAD
You stepped out of a dream / You go to my head / Star eyes / Off minor / I fall in love too easily / Gallop's gallop / Concerto for Albert / Blues for the road / Theme for Ernie / Just one of those / Emily
CD _____ 66053013
Jazz City / Feb '91 / New Note.

Movietone

MOVIETONE
CD _____ PUNK 10CD
Planet / Nov '95 / SRD.

Moving Cloud

MOVING CLOUD
CD _____ GLCD 1150
Green Linnet / Feb '95 / Roots / CM / Direct / ADA.

Moving Hearts

DARK END OF THE STREET
CD _____ 229250144
WEA / May '95 / Warner Music.

LIVE HEARTS
CD _____ 2292402302
WEA / May '95 / Warner Music.

STORM, THE
Lark / Storm / Tribute to Peardar O Donnell / Titanic / Finore / May morning dew
CD _____ BUACD 892
Son / Feb '89 / Total/BMG.

Moving Targets

BRAVE NOISE
CD _____ TAANG 030CD
Taang / Jan '93 / Plastic Head.

FALL
CD _____ TG 93042
Roadrunner / May '91 / Pinnacle.

TAKE THIS RIDE
CD _____ TAANG 73CD
Taang / Jun '93 / Plastic Head.

Mowatt, Judy

BLACK WOMAN
Strength to go through / Concrete jungle / Slave queen / Put it on / Zion chant / Black woman / Down in the valley / Joseph / Many are called / Sisters chant
CD _____ GRELCD 111
Greensleeves / Jul '88 / Total/BMG / Jetstar / SRD.

LOVE IS OVERDUE
Sing our own song / Love is overdue / Try a little tenderness / Long long time / Rock dem jah / One more time / Who is he
CD _____ GRELCD 103
Greensleeves / Jul '87 / Total/BMG / Jetstar / SRD.

ONLY A WOMAN
CD _____ SHANCD 43007
Shanachie / '88 / Koch / ADA / Greensleeves.

WORKING WONDERS
CD _____ SHANCD 43028
Shanachie / Aug '85 / Koch / ADA / Greensleeves.

Mowrey, Dude

DUDE MOWREY
CD _____ 07822186782
Arista / Jul '94 / BMG.

Moxham, Stuart

CARS IN THE GRASS (Moxham, Stuart & The Original Artists)
My criteria / Hello world / Return to work / Tug of love / Night by night / Soft eject / Against creating war / God knows / Appropriate response / Cars in the grass / Drifting west
CD _____ ASKCD 035
Vinyl Japan / Mar '95 / Vital.

SIGNAL PATH (Moxham, Stuart & The Original Artists)
Over the sea / Between edits / Her shoes (are right) / Knives (always fall) / Broken heart blues / It says here / No one road / That's my love / I wonder why / Remember / It took you / Mutual gaze / Yeah x 3 / Unit of desire
CD _____ FGAO 015
Feel Good All Over / Mar '93 / Vital.

Moxy Fruvous

BARGAINVILLE
CD _____ 450993134-2
WEA / Apr '94 / Warner Music.

WOOD
CD _____ 0630106162
WEA / Feb '96 / Warner Music.

Moyet, Alison

ALF
Love resurrection / Honey for the bees / For you only / Invisible / Steal me blind / All cried out / Money mile / Twisting the knife / Where hides sleep
CD _____ CD 26229
Columbia / Aug '94 / Sony.

ESSEX
Falling / Whispering your name / Getting into something / Dorothy / So am I / And I know / Ode to boy / Satellite / Another living day / Boys own / Take of me / Ode to boy II / Whispering your name (mix)
CD _____ 475955 2
Columbia / Mar '94 / Sony.

HOODOO
Footsteps / It won't be long / This house / Rise / Wishing you were here / (Meeting my man) main man / Hoodoo / Back where I belong / My night A.R.M. / Never too late / Find me
CD _____ 4682722
Columbia / Apr '91 / Sony.

RAINDANCING
Weak in the presence of beauty / Ordinary girl / You got me wrong / Without you / Sleep like breathing / Is this love / Blow wind blow / Glorious love / When I say (no giveaway) / Stay
CD _____ 4501522
Columbia / Mar '90 / Sony.

SINGLES
First time I ever saw your face / Only you / Nobody's diary / Situation / Love resurrection / All cried out / Invisible / That ole devil called love / Is this love / Weak in the presence of beauty / Ordinary girl / Love letters / It won't be long / Wishing you were here / This house / Falling / Whispering your name / Solid wood / Getting into something / Ode to boy
CD _____ 4806632
Columbia / May '95 / Sony.

Mr. B

SHINING THE PEARLS
CD _____ BP 71886
Blind Pig / Dec '95 / Hot Shot / Swift / CM / Roots / Direct / ADA.

Mr. Big

BUMP AHEAD
Colorado bulldog / Price you gotta pay / Promise her the moon / What's it gonna be / Wild world / Mr. Gone / Whole world's gonna know / Nothing but love / Temperamental / Ain't seen love like that / Mr. Big
CD _____ 7567824952
Atlantic / Sep '93 / Warner Music.

LEAN INTO IT
Daddy / Brother / Lover / Little boy / Alive and kickin' / Green tinted sixties mind / CDFF-Lucky this time / Voodoo kiss / Never say never / Just take my heart / My kinda woman / Little loo loose / Road to ruin / To be with you
CD _____ 7567822092
Atlantic / Apr '91 / Warner Music.

LIVE - MR BIG
Daddy, brother, lover, little boy (the electric drill song) / Alive and kickin' / Green tinted sixties mind / Just take my heart / Road to ruin / Lucky this time / Addicted to that rush / To be with you / Thirty days in the hole / Shy baby / Baba O'Riley
CD _____ 7567805232
Atlantic / Nov '92 / Warner Music.

MR BIG
Addicted to that rush / Wind me up / Merciless / Had enough / Blame it on my youth / Take a walk / Big love / How can you do what you do / Anything for you / Rock 'n' roll over
CD _____ 781 990-2
Atlantic / Jul '89 / Warner Music.

Mr. Blobby

MR. BLOBBY - THE ALBUM
CD _____ DMUSCD 106
Destiny / Nov '95 / Total/BMG.

Mr. Bungle

DISCO VOLANTE
CD _____ 8286942
Slash / Jan '96 / PolyGram.

MR BUNGLE
Quote, unquote / Slowy growing deaf / Squeeze me macaroni / Carousel / Egg / Stubb (a dub) / My ass is on fire / Girls of porn / Love is a fist / Dead goon
CD _____ 8282762
Slash / Sep '91 / PolyGram.

Mr. Doo

PRESENTS THE DOO EXPERIENCE
CD _____ FILERCD 418
Profile / Nov '91 / Pinnacle.

Mr. Electric Triangle

KOSMOSIS OF THE HEART
CD _____ TKCD 20
2 Kool / Oct '95 / SRD.

Mr. President

UP 'N' AWAY
CD _____ 4509997002
East West / Jun '95 / Warner Music.

Mr. Review

MR. REVIEW/SPY EYE (Mr. Review/Spy Eye)
CD _____ PHZCD 81
Unicorn / Nov '94 / Plastic Head.

Mr. So & So

COMPENDIUM
Closet skeletons / Missionary / Bolton-eeny-noo / Tick a box / Primrose days / Sixes and sevens / Hobson the traveller
CD _____ CYCL 014
Cyclops / Feb '95 / Pinnacle.

Mr. Spats

DREAM PATROL
CD _____ NOVA 8913
Nova / Jan '93 / New Note.

Mr. T Experience

ALTERNATIVE IS HERE TO STAY
CD _____ LOOKOUT 126CD
Lookout / Sep '95 / SRD.

EVERYONE'S ENTITLED TO THEIR OWN OPINION
CD _____ LOOKOUT 039CD
Lookout / Jul '95 / SRD.

LOVE IS DEAD
CD _____ LKCD 134
Lookout / Jan '96 / SRD.

OUR BODIES
CD _____ LOOKOUT 80CD
Lookout / Jul '95 / SRD.

Mrs. Mills

EP COLLECTION: MRS MILLS
CD _____ SEECD 332
See For Miles/C5 / Sep '91 / Pinnacle.

PIANO FAVOURITES
Put your arms around me honey / I'm in the mood for love / Yes sir that's my baby / Moonlight and roses / Oh Johnny oh Johnny oh / Give me the moonlight, give me the girl / Winchester Cathedral / Green green grass of home / I'm nobody's baby / In the good old Summertime / Tiptoe through the tulips / You are my sunshine / April showers / Down at the Old Bull and Bush / Cruising down the river / Shine on harvest moon / I do like to be beside the seaside / Out of town / Let's all sing like the birdies sing / Good morning / Me and my shadow / My melancholy baby / Second hand rose / There's a blue ridge 'round my heart / Virginia / Let him go, let him tarry / I belong to Glasgow / Over the rainbow / Get out and get under the moon
CD _____ CC 269
Music For Pleasure / Aug '91 / EMI.

Mseleku, Bheki

CELEBRATION
CD _____ WCD 028
World Circuit / Apr '92 / New Note / Direct / Cadillac / ADA.

MEDITATIONS
CD _____ 5213372
Verve / Jan '95 / PolyGram.

TIMELESSNESS
CD _____ 521306-2
Verve / Feb '94 / PolyGram.

Mtume

YOU, ME AND HE
C.O.D. (I'll deliver) / You are my sunshine / You, me and he / I simply like / Prime time / Tie me up / Sweet for you and me / To be or not to bop
CD _____ 983302 2
Pickwick/Sony Collector's Choice / Oct '93 / Carlton Home Entertainment / Pinnacle / Sony.

Mucky Pup

ACT OF FAITH
CD _____ CM 9731 CD
Century Media / Jul '92 / Plastic Head.

ALIVE AND WELL
CD _____ SPV 08489222
SPV / Jan '95 / Plastic Head.

CAN'T YOU TAKE A JOKE
CD _____ RR 95532
Roadrunner / Feb '93 / Pinnacle.

FIVE GUYS IN A REALLY HOT GARAGE
CD _____ SPV 08544022
SPV / Jan '96 / Plastic Head.

LEMONADE
CD _____ CM 77058
Century Media / Jan '94 / Plastic Head.

NOW
Hippies hate water / Three dead gophers / Jimmy's / Baby / She Quieffed / Feeling sick / Headbangers balls and 120 minutes / My hands, your neck / Face / Hotel Penitentiary / Mucky pumpin' beat / I know nobody / Walkin' with the devil / Yesterdays / To be lonely
CD _____ RO 93402
Roadrunner / Feb '93 / Pinnacle.

Mud

DYNAMITE
CD _____ BX 421-2
BR Music / Jul '94 / Target/BMG.

GREATEST HITS (Mud & The Glitter Band)
CD _____ CDCD 1148
Charly / Feb '94 / Charly / THE / Cadillac.

L-L-LUCY
L-L-Lucy / Dream lover / Careless love / Lean on me / Walk right back / Shake it down / So fine / Drift away / Grecian lament / Why do fools fall in love / Book of love / Just try (a little tenderness) / Show me you're a woman / Cut across shorty / 43792 (I'm bustin' you) / Beating around the bush / Under the moon of love / Who you gonna love / Nite on the tiles
CD _____ 5507522
Spectrum/Karussell / Jan '95 / PolyGram / THE.

Mudane

SEED
CD _____ BMCD 075
Raw Energy / Jun '95 / Plastic Head.

Mudboy

NEGRO STREETS AT DAWN (Mudboy & The Neutrons)
CD _____ 422469
New Rose / May '94 / Direct / ADA.

THEY WALK AMONG US (Mudboy & The Neutrons)
CD _____ 379132
Koch International / Nov '95 / Koch.

Muddle

MUDDLE
CD _____ SST 310CD
SST / Jul '95 / Plastic Head.

Mudhoney

FIVE DOLLAR BOB'S MOCK COOTER STEW
In the blood / No song II / Between me and you kid / Six two one / Make it now again / Thirteen floor opening / Youth body expression explosion / I'm spun / Take me there / Living wreck / Let me let you down / Ritzville / Acetone
CD _____ 936245439-2
WEA / Oct '93 / Warner Music.

MY BROTHER, THE COW
CD _____ 9362458402
WEA / Mar '95 / Warner Music.

PIECE OF CAKE
No end in sight / Make it now / When in Rome / Suck you dry / Blinding sun / Thirteenth floor opening / Youth body expression explosion / I'm spun / Take me there / Living wreck / Let me let you down / Ritzville / Acetone
CD _____ 4509900732
WEA / Oct '92 / Warner Music.

Mudshark

MUDSHARK
Wall of fame / Showtime / Cut on the grain / Cold moon rain / Natural / Gangway / Broadway bound / Put out the word / Out of my hands / It won't shine
CD _____ PONYLPCD 001
Pony / Sep '95 / Vital.

Muffin Men

MULM
CD _____ EFA 034082
Muffin / Jul '94 / SRD.

SAY CHEESE AND THANKYOU
CD _____ EFA 034022
Muffin / Jan '94 / SRD.

Muffs

BLONDER AND BLONDER
CD _____ 9362458522
Warner Bros. / Apr '95 / Warner Music.

MUFFS, THE
Lucky guy / Saying goodbye / Everywhere I go / Better than me / From your girl / Not like me / Baby go round / North pole / Big mouth / Every single thing / Don't waste another day / Stupid jerk / Another day / Eye to eye / I need you / All for nothing
CD _____ 936245251-2
Warner Bros. / Aug '93 / Warner Music.

Mugam Ensemble

AZERBAIJAN - LAND OF FLAMES (Mugam Ensemble Jabbar Karyagdy)
CD _____ PANCD 2012
Pan / Oct '93 / ADA / Direct / CM.

Muhammad, Abu Al-Ila

ABU AL-ILA MUHAMMAD
CD _____ AAA 114
Club Du Disque Arabe / Oct '95 / Harmonia Mundi / ADA.

Muhammad, Idris

BLACK RHYTHM REVOLUTION/PEACE AND RHYTHM
Express yourself / Soulful drums / Super bad / Wander / By the red sea / Peace / Rhythm / Brother you know you're doing wrong / Don't knock my love / I'm a believer
CD _____ CDBPGD 046
BGP / Oct '92 / Pinnacle.

KABSHA
Kabsha / I want to talk to you / Little feet / GCCCG Blues / Soulful drums / St. M / Kabsha (Alternate take) / GCCG Blues
CD _____ ECD 220962
Evidence / Jul '94 / Harmonia Mundi / ADA / Cadillac.

MY TURN
Piece o' cake / Free / There is a girl / Dark road / Dracula / This love / Happenstance / Stranger / Where did we go wrong
CD _____ LIP 890022
Lipstick / Feb '95 / Vital/SAM.

Mujician

JOURNEY, THE
CD _____ RUNE 42
Cuneiform / Dec '87 / ReR Megacorp.

Mujuru, Ephat

RHYTHMS OF LIFE
CD _____ LYRCD 7407
Lyrichord / '91 / Roots / ADA / CM.

Mukherjee, Budhaditya

RAG BAGESRI/RAG DES
CD _____ NI 5268
Nimbus / Sep '94 / Nimbus.

RAG RAMKALI/RAG JHINJOTI
CD _____ NI 5221
Nimbus / Sep '94 / Nimbus.

Muldaur, Geoff

IS HAVING A WONDERFUL TIME
CD _____ 7599262872
Reprise / Jan '96 / Warner Music.

MOTION
CD _____ 7599262882
Reprise / Jan '96 / Warner Music.

POTTERY PIE (Muldaur, Geoff & Maria)
CD _____ 7599262852
Reprise / Jan '96 / Warner Music.

SWEET POTATOES (Muldaur, Geoff & Maria)
CD _____ 7599262862
Reprise / Jan '96 / Warner Music.

Muldaur, Maria

JAZZABELLE
CD _____ HYCD 200139
Hypertension / Jan '95 / Total/BMG / Direct / ADA.

MARIA MULDAUR
Any old time / Midnight at the oasis / My Tennessee mountain home / I never did sing you a love song / Work song / Don't you feel my leg / Walking one and only / Long hard climb / Three dollar bill / Vaudeville man / Mad mad mad
CD _____ 7599272082
Reprise / Sep '93 / Warner Music.

MEET ME AT MIDNIGHT
CD _____ BT 1107CD
Black Top / Oct '94 / CM / Direct / ADA.

OPEN YOUR EYES
Fall in love again / Finally made love to a man / Birds fly South (when Winter comes) / Heart of fire / Lover man / Open your eyes / (No more) dancin' in the street / Eleona / Clean up woman / Love is everything
CD _____ 7599262842
Reprise / Jan '96 / Warner Music.

SOUTHERN WINDS
I got a man / Here is where your love belongs / That's the way love is / My sisters and brothers / I can't say no / I'll keep my light in my window / Cajun moon / Joyful noise / Say you will / Make love to the music
CD _____ 7599262832
Reprise / Jan '96 / Warner Music.

SWEET & SLOW
Stony Plain / Oct '93 / ADA / CM / Direct.
CD _____ SP 1183CD

SWEET HARMONY
CD _____ 7599262822
Reprise / Jan '96 / Warner Music.

WAITRESS IN A DONUT SHOP
Squeeze me / Gringo en Mexico / Cool river / I'm a woman / Sweetheart / Honey babe blues / If you haven't any hay get on down the road / Oh papa / It ain't the meat / Backyard blues / Travellin' shoes
CD _____ 7599262812
Reprise / Sep '93 / Warner Music.

Muldrow, Ronald

DIASPORA
CD _____ ENJACD 80862
Enja / May '95 / New Note / Vital/SAM.

GNOWING YOU (Muldrow, Ronald Trio)
Quasimodal / Deaceleration / Soleshia / Georgia Ann / Gnowing you / Polka dots and moonbeams / Little Wes
CD _____ CDLR 45047
L&R / Feb '92 / New Note.

Mule

IF I DON'T SIX
CD _____ QS 29CD
Quarter Stick / Sep '94 / SRD.

MULE
CD _____ QS 15 CD
Quarter Stick / Feb '93 / SRD.

Mullen, Jim

RULE OF THUMB
CD _____ EFZ 1012
EFZ / May '95 / New Note.

Mullican, Moon

HIS ALL TIME GREATEST HITS
I'll wash my ship alone / Honolulu rock-a-roll-a / Leaves mustn't fall / Mona Lisa / Sugar beet / New Jole Blon / Sweeter than the flowers / Pipeliner blues / I was sorta won-derin' / Cherokee boogie / You don't have to be a baby to cry / Foggy river
CD _____ KCD 555
King/Paddle Wheel / Mar '90 / New Note.

MOON'S ROCK
Moon's rock / Jenny Lee / Pipeliner blues / Sweet rockin' music / That's me / Cush cush ky yay / Writing on the wall / Wedding of the bugs / Nobody knows but my pillow / My love / I'm waiting for the ships that never come in / You don't have to be a baby to cry / I'll sail my ship alone / I was sorta wonderin' / Every which a way / I don't know why (I just do) / Sweeter than the flowers / Leaves mustn't fall / Anything that's part of you / Early morning blues / My baby's gone / Colinda / Make friends / Cajun coffee song / Quarter mile rows / Just to be with you / I'll pour the wine / Fools like me / Big big city / Mr. Tears / She once lived here / This glass I hold
CD _____ BCD 15607
Bear Family / Apr '92 / Rollercoaster / Direct / CM / Swift / ADA.

MOONSHINE JAMBOREE
Hey Mr. Cotton Picker / Leaving you with a worried mind / What's the matter with the mill / Pipeliner blues / Triffin' woman blues / Nine tenths of the Tennessee River / Cherokee boogie / All I need is you / I'll sail my ship alone / Good deal Lucille / Moonshine blues / Rocket to the moon / Downstream / I done it / Goodnight Irene / Rheumatism boogie / Well oh well / Don't ever take my picture down / Lonesome hearted blues / It's a sin to love you like I do / I'm gonna move home and bye and bye / I left my heart in Texas / I'll take your hat right off my rack
CD _____ CDCHD 458
Ace / Sep '93 / Pinnacle / Complete/Pinnacle.

OLD TEXAN, THE
CD _____ KCD 628
King/Paddle Wheel / Mar '90 / New Note.

SINGS HIS ALL TIME HITS
CD _____ KCD 00555
King/Paddle Wheel / Feb '93 / New Note.

Mulligan, Gerry

AT BIRDLAND NEW YORK 1960
CD _____ 550072
Jazz Anthology / Jan '94 / Harmonia Mundi.

BEST OF GERRY MULLIGAN
CD _____ DLCD 4018
Dixie Live / Mar '95 / Magnum Music Group.

BEST OF GERRY MULLIGAN WITH CHET BAKER
Bernie's tune / Nights at the turntable / Freeway / Soft shoe / Walkin' shoes / Ma-whooppee / Carson city stage / My old flame / Love me or leave me / Swing house / Jeru / Darn that dream / I'm beginning to see the light / My funny valentine / Festive minor
CD _____ CZ 416
Pacific Jazz / Sep '92 / EMI.

DREAM A LITTLE DREAM
Nobody else but me / Home (when shadows fall) / Dream a little dream / I'll be around / They say it's wonderful / Real thing / Here's that rainy day / Georgia on my mind / My funny valentine / As close as pages in a book / My shining hour / Walking shoes / Song for Strayhorn
CD _____ CD 83364
Telarc / Nov '94 / Conifer / ADA.

GERRY MEETS HAMP (Mulligan, Gerry & Lionel Hampton)
CD _____ JHR 73555
Jazz Hour / Jan '93 / Target/BMG / Jazz Music / Cadillac.

GERRY MULLIGAN & CONCERT JAZZ BAND
CD _____ 5233422
Verve / Apr '94 / PolyGram.

GERRY MULLIGAN MEETS BEN WEBSTER (Mulligan, Gerry & Ben Webster)
Chelsea Bridge / Cat walk / Sunday / Who's got rhythm / Tell me when / Go home
CD _____ 8416612
Verve / Aug '90 / PolyGram.

GERRY MULLIGAN QUARTET WITH CHET BAKER (Mulligan, Gerry & Chet Baker)
CD _____ GOJCD 53027
Giants Of Jazz / Aug '88 / Target/BMG / Cadillac.

GERRY MULLIGAN SEXTET: 1955-56
CD _____ CD 53141
Giants Of Jazz / Nov '92 / Target/BMG / Cadillac.

GERRY MULLIGAN/ASTOR PIAZZOLLA 1974 (Mulligan, Gerry & Astor Piazzolla)
CD _____ 556642CD
Accord / Aug '94 / Discovery / Harmonia Mundi / Cadillac.

GERRY MULLIGAN/PAUL DESMOND QUARTET (Mulligan, Gerry & Paul Desmond)
CD _____ 519850-2
Verve / Mar '94 / PolyGram.

IMMORTAL CONCERTS
I may be wrong, but I think you're wonderful / Gold rush / Makin' whoopee / Laura / Soft shoe / Nearness of you / Love me or leave me / Bernie's tune / Walking shoes / Five brothers / Lullaby of the leaves / Limelight / Come out wherever you are / Moonlight in Vermont / Lady is a tramp / Bark for Barksdale
CD _____ GOJCD 53020
Giants Of Jazz / Jun '88 / Target/BMG / Cadillac.

IN CONCERT (6.10.62) (Mulligan, Gerry Quartet)
CD _____ RTE 760463
RTE / May '95 / ADA / Koch.

JAM SESSION - 1952-55
CD _____ CDJJ 625
Jazz & Jazz / Jan '92 / Target/BMG.

JERU
Get out of town / Here I'll stay / Inside impromptu / Blue boy / You've come home / Lonely town / Capricious
CD _____ 473685 2
Columbia / Nov '93 / Sony.

LIVE IN STOCKHOLM 1957
Come out wherever you are / Birth of the blues / Moonlight in Velmont / Lullaby of the leaves / Open country / I can't get started (with you) / Frenesi / Baubles, bangles and beads / Yardbird suite / Walkin' shoes / My funny valentine / Blues at the roots / Introduction / Bernie's tune
CD _____ MCD 0462
Moon / Nov '93 / Harmonia Mundi / Cadillac.

MASTER OF SAX
Apple core / Song for Johnny Hodges / Blight of the fumble bee / Gerry meets hamp / Blues for Gerry / Line for Lyons
CD _____ 722018
Scorpio / Sep '92 / Complete/Pinnacle.

MULLIGAN
Jeru / Festive minor / Rose room / North Atlantic run / Taurus moon / Out back of the barn
CD _____ CDC 7682
LRC / Sep '93 / New Note / Harmonia Mundi.

MULLIGAN SONGBOOK, THE
Four and one more / Crazy day / Turnstile / Sextet / Disc jockey jump / Venus de Milo / Revelation / May-reh / Preacher / Good bait / Bags' groove
CD _____ CDP 8335752
Pacific Jazz / Jan '96 / EMI.

NEWS FROM BLUEPORT (Mulligan, Gerry & Art Farmer)
CD _____ JHR 73577
Jazz Hour / May '94 / Target/BMG / Jazz Music / Cadillac.

PARAISO (Mulligan, Gerry & Jane Duboc)
CD _____ CD 83361
Telarc / Oct '93 / Conifer / ADA.

PARIS 1954/L.A. 1953 (Mulligan, Gerry Quartet)
Soft shoes / Five brothers / Lullaby of the leaves / Limelight / Come out wherever you are / Motel / My funny valentine / Turnstile / Speak low / Ladybird / Love me or leave me / Swing house / Varsity drag / Half Nelson
CD _____ VG 655616
Voque / Nov '92 / BMG.

PLEYEL CONCERTS 1954 - VOL.1
Bernie's tune / Presentation of the musicians / Walkin' shoes / Nearness of you / Motel/utter chaos / Love me or leave me / Soft shoe / Bark for Barksdale / My funny valentine / Turnstile/utter chaos / I may be wrong, but I think you're wonderful / Five brothers / Gold rush / Makin' whoopee
CD _____ 74321134112
Vogue / Jul '93 / BMG.

PLEYEL CONCERTS 1954 - VOL.2
Lady is a tramp / Laura / Soft shoe/utter chaos / Five brothers / Lullaby of the leaves / Nearness of you / Limelight / Come out come out / Makin' whoopee / Love me or leave me / Line for Lyons / Moonlight in Vermont / Motel/utter chaos
CD _____ 74321134122
Vogue / Jul '93 / BMG.

SHADOW OF YOUR SMILE (Mulligan, Gerry Quartet)
CD _____ MCD 003
Moon / Sep '89 / Harmonia Mundi / Cadillac.

SOFT LIGHTS AND SWEET MUSIC (Mulligan, Gerry & Scott Hamilton)
Soft lights and sweet music / Gone / Do you know what I see / I've just seen her / Nobiesse / Ghosts / Port of Baltimore blues
CD _____ CCD 4300
Concord Jazz / Jan '87 / New Note.

STOCKHOLM 1959 (Mulligan, Gerry Quartet)
CD _____ TAXCD 3711
Tax / Jan '93 / Jazz Music / Wellard / Cadillac.

TWO TIMES FOUR PLUS SIX
CD _____ EBCD 2127
Jazzband / Dec '95 / Jazz Music / Wellard.

WALKING SHOES 1959/NEW YORK 1977
CD Set _____ JWD 102310
JWD / Oct '94 / Target/BMG.

WHAT IS THERE TO SAY (Mulligan, Gerry Quartet)
What is there to say / Just in time / News from blueport / Festive minor / My funny valentine / As catch can / Blueport / Utter chaos
CD _____ 475699 2
Columbia / Feb '94 / Sony.

Mullins, Rob

5TH GEAR
CD _____ NOVA 8810
Nova / Jan '93 / New Note.

JAZZ JAZZ
CD _____ NOVA 8918
Nova / Jan '93 / New Note.

ONE NIGHT IN HOUSTON
Polka dot dress / Very blue / Quick call the note police / Jazz man / One night in Houston / Plus three / Quiet fire / Holiday / Too cold
CD _____ AQCD 1020
Audioquest / Sep '95 / New Note.

TOKIO NIGHTS
CD _____ NOVA 9026
Nova / Jan '93 / New Note.

Mulo, Alman

AFRODIZIAC DREAMTIME (Mulo, Alman Band)
CD _____ TASTE 41CD
Southern / Nov '93 / SRD.

DIAMONDS AND TOADS (Mulo, Alman Band)
CD _____ TASTE 46
Taste / Jan '95 / Plastic Head.

ORISHA (Mulo, Alman Band)
CD _____ TASTE 37
Taste / Jan '95 / Plastic Head.

Mulqueen, Ann

MO GHRASA THALL NA DEISE (Memorable Songs In The Munster Tradition)
CD _____ CIC 080CD
Clo Iar-Chonnachta / Jan '93 / CM.

Mulvihill, Brendan

FLAX IN BLOOM, THE
Flax in bloom/Honeymoon / Crabs in the skillet / Concertina/The circus / Lament for O'Donnell / John Grady's downfall/The hogging reel / Pigeon on the gate/Miss Monahan's reel / Dr. O'Neill's reel / Home ruler / Brigade / Fermoy lassies/Bunker hill / Hardiman's fancy/Billy Rush's own / First house in Connaught/Dairy maid
CD _____ GLCD 1020
Green Linnet / Feb '93 / Roots / CM / Direct / ADA.

MORNING DEW, THE (Mulvihill, Brendan & Donna Long)
Morning dew/Grants / Brian Maguire/Thomas Judge/The broken pledge/Mc-Glinchey's/Th / Rathlin Island / Shandon bells/Days of the turn/Rakes of Glenheel / Girls of the / Festus Burke/John Drury / An ceileabrad caoine / Morgan Magan/Greig's pipes / Mrs. Judge / Down the broom/Joseph Bars / Kean and Colonel O'Hara/Flaggon reel/Dublin lasses
CD _____ GLCD 1128
Green Linnet / Jul '93 / Roots / CM / Direct / ADA.

Mumbleskinny

HEAD ABOVE WATER
CD _____ SECTOR2 10011
Sector 2 / Jul '96 / Direct / ADA.

Munarriz, Valeria

TANGO
CD _____ MES 159172
Messidor / Feb '93 / Koch / ADA.

Munde, Alan

BLUE RIDGE EXPRESS
CD _____ ROU 0301CD
Rounder / Apr '94 / CM / Direct / ADA / Cadillac.

FESTIVAL FAVOURITES REVISITED
CD _____ CDROU 0311
Rounder / Apr '93 / CM / Direct / Cadillac.

Mundell, Hugh

AFRICA MUST BE FREE BY 1983
Let's all unite / My mind / Africa must be free by 1983 / Why do blackmen fuss and fight / Book of life / Run revolution come / Day of judgement / Jah will provide / Ital sip

CD _____ GRELCD 94
Greensleeves / May '90 / Total/BMG / Jetstar / SRD.

BLACK MAN FOUNDATION
CD _____ SHANCD 43012
Shanachie / Jun '85 / Koch / ADA / Greensleeves.

MUNDELL
Jacqueline / Rasta have the handle / Going places / Red, gold and green / Tell I a lie / Twenty four hours a day / Jah music / Your face is familiar
CD _____ GRELCD 36
Greensleeves / '89 / Total/BMG / Jetstar / SRD.

Mungo Jerry

ALL THE HITS PLUS MORE
CD _____ CDPT 002
Prestige / Jun '92 / Total/BMG.

BEST OF MUNGO JERRY, THE
Lana / It's a secret / Hello Nadine / Let's get started / Forgotten land / Drum song / Somebody stole my wife / Alright, alright / Long legged woman / Sugar Mama / That's my baby / Angel Mama / I'm gonna bop till I drop / Rockin' on the road / Baby jump / You don't have to be in the army to fight the war / Open up / Wild love
CD _____ 4776449
Columbia / Aug '95 / Sony.

ELECTRONICALLY TESTED
She rowed / I just want to make love to you / In the summertime / Somebody stole my wife / Baby jump / Follow me down / Memoirs of a stockbroker / You better leave that whisky alone / Coming back to you
CD _____ REP 4179-WZ
Repertoire / Aug '91 / Pinnacle / Cadillac.

IN THE SUMMERTIME
In the Summertime / Wild love / Summer's gone / Alright alright alright / Hey Rosalyn / Long legged woman / Dressed in black / Baby jump / On a Sunday / Open up / Lady Rose / Going down the dusty road / You don't have to be in the army to fight the war
CD _____ REP 4177-WZ
Repertoire / Aug '91 / Pinnacle / Cadillac.

MUNGO JERRY/ELECTRONICALLY TESTED
Baby let's play house / Johnny B. Badde / San Francisco Bay blues / Sad eyed Joe / Maggie / Peace in the country / See me / Movin' on / My friend / Mother tucker boogie / Tramp / Daddie's brew / She rowed / I just want to make love to you / In the summertime / Somebody stole my wife / Baby jump / Follow me down / Memoirs of a stockbroker / You better leave that whiskey alone / Coming back to you
CD _____ BGOCD 286
Beat Goes On / Aug '95 / Pinnacle.

MUNGO JERRY: THE EARLY YEARS
Maggie / Sad eyed Joe / Peace in the country / In the summertime / Midnight special (Live) / Mighty man (Live) / Baby jump / Man behind the piano / Somebody stole my wife / Have a whiff on me / Lady Rose / You don't have to be in the army to fight the war / Open up / Going back home / Alright alright alright / Wild love / Long legged woman in black
CD _____ EARLD 3
Dojo / Mar '92 / BMG.

SUMMERTIME
In the summertime / Baby jump / Lady Rose / Alright alright alright / Wild love / My girl and me / Maggie / Johnny B. Badde / Don't stop / Long legged woman dressed in black / All dressed up and no place to go / I don't wanna go back to school / Baby let's play house / Gonna bop till I drop / Brand new car / Somebody stole my wife / Sweet Mary Jane / Too fast to live, too young to die
CD _____ 5507492
Spectrum/Karussell / Jan '95 / PolyGram / THE.

YOU DON'T HAVE TO BE IN THE ARMY/BOOT POWER
You don't have to be in the army to fight the war / Ella speed / Pideon stew / Take me back / Give me love / Hey Rosalyn / Northcote arms / There's a man going round taking names / Simple things / Keep your hands off her / On a sunday / That old dust storm / Open up / She's gone / Lookin' for my girl / See you again / Demon / My girl and me / Sweet Mary Jane / Lady Rose / Dusty road / Brand new car / 46 an' on
CD _____ BGOCD 292
Beat Goes On / Nov '95 / Pinnacle.

Munyon, David

CODE NAME: JUMPER
CD _____ GRCD 307
Glitterhouse / Oct '94 / Direct / ADA.

Munzer, Fritz

STRAIGHT OFF (Munzer, Fritz Sound Express)
CD _____ ISCD 112
Intersound / Oct '91 / Jazz Music.

Muppets

CHRISTMAS TOGETHER, A (Denver, John & Muppets)
CD _____ MCCDX 007
Music Club / Nov '94 / Disc / THE / CM.

KERMIT UNPIGGED (Various Artists)
CD _____ 7432123338-2
BMG Kidz / Oct '94 / BMG.

Mur, Mona

WARSZAW
CD _____ SPLCD 1
Solid Pleasure / Jul '92 / Pinnacle.

Murder Inc.

MURDER INC
CD _____ INVCD 013
Invisible / Feb '94 / Plastic Head.

MURDER INC.
Supergrass / Murder Inc. / Mania / Hole in the wall / Uninvited guest / Gambit / Red black / Last of the urgents / Mrs. Whiskey name
CD _____ CDDVN 9
Devotion / May '92 / Pinnacle.

Murmur

DERAILER
CD _____ 7567925022
Warner Bros. / Aug '95 / Warner Music.

SEXPOWDER 2000 VOLTS
CD _____ RAIN 013CD
Cloudland / Apr '95 / Plastic Head / SRD.

Murphy, Dennis

MUSIC FROM SLIABHRA LUCHRA
CD _____ RTE 183CD
RTE / Jan '95 / ADA / Koch.

Murphy, Elliott James

12
CD _____ 422244
New Rose / May '94 / Direct / ADA.

AFFAIRS ETC.
CD _____ 422237
New Rose / May '94 / Direct / ADA.

APRES LE DELUGE
CD _____ FC 034CD
Fan Club / Mar '88 / Direct.

CHANGE WILL COME
CD _____ 422239
New Rose / May '94 / Direct / ADA.

IF POETS WERE KING
CD _____ 422240
New Rose / May '94 / Direct / ADA.

LIVE HOT POINT
CD _____ 422241
New Rose / May '94 / Direct / ADA.

MILWAUKEE
CD _____ ROSE 99CD
New Rose / Nov '86 / Direct / ADA.

MURPH THE SMURF
CD _____ FC 057CD
Fan Club / Aug '89 / Direct.

PARIS-NEW YORK
CD _____ 422401
New Rose / May '94 / Direct / ADA.

PARTY GIRLS/BROKEN POETS
CD _____ DJD 3201
Dejadisc / May '94 / Direct / ADA.

Murphy, Jimmy

SIXTEEN TONS ROCK'N'ROLL
Sixteen tons rock'n'roll / My gal Dottie / Grandpaw's cat / Baboon boogie / I'm looking for a mustard patch / Put some meat on them bones / Here Kitty Kitty / Sweet sweet lips (unissued) / Electricity / Big mama blues / That first guitar of mine / Love that satisfies / Educated fool / Rambling heart / We live a long, long time / Mother where is your daughter
CD _____ BCD 15451
Bear Family / Sep '90 / Rollercoaster / Direct / CM / Swift / ADA.

Murphy, Mark

BEAUTY AND THE BEAST
CD _____ VGCD 600606
Vogue / Jan '93 / BMG.

BOP FOR KEROUAC
Be Bop lives (Boplicity) / Goodbye pork pie hat / Parker's mood / You better go now / You've proven your point (bongo beep) / Bad and the beautiful / Down St. Thomas way / Ballad of the sad young man
CD _____ MCD 5253
Muse / '88 / New Note / CM.

I'LL CLOSE MY EYES
I'll close my eyes / If / Happyin' / Miss you Mr. Mercer / Small world / There is no reason why / Time is on my hands / Ugly woman / Not like this
CD _____ MCD 5436
Muse / Feb '95 / New Note / CM.

KEROUAC, THEN & NOW
CD _____ MCD 5359
Muse / Sep '92 / New Note / CM.

MARK MURPHY SINGS
On the red clay / Naima / Body and soul / Young and foolish / Empty faces / Maiden voyage / How are you dreaming / Canteloupe Island
CD _____ MCD 5078
Muse / Dec '95 / New Note / CM.

NIGHT MOODS (The Music of Ivan Lins)
CD _____ MCD 9145
Milestone / Jan '92 / Jazz Music / Pinnacle / Wellard / Cadillac.

RAH
CD _____ OJCCD 141
Original Jazz Classics / Jun '95 / Wellard / Jazz Music / Cadillac / Complete/Pinnacle.

SINGS NAT'S CHOICE VOLS 1 & 2
Nature boy / Love letters / Oh you crazy moon / 'Tis Autumn / I keep going back to Joe's / Tangerine / Lush life / Never let me go / These foolish things / Portrait of Jenny Ruby / For all we know / Maybe you'll be there / Blue gardenia / Don't let your eyes go shopping / More than you know / Look out for love / End of a love affair / Calypso blues / Serenata
CD _____ MCD 6001
Muse / Feb '87 / New Note / CM.

STOLEN MOMENTS
CD _____ MCD 5102
Muse / Sep '92 / New Note / CM.

WHAT A WAY TO GO
CD _____ MCD 5419
Muse / Sep '92 / New Note / CM.

Murphy, Matt

WAY DOWN SOUTH
Way down South / Big 6 / Gonna be some changes made / Big city takedown / Buck's boogie / Thump tyme / Matt's guitar boogie / Low down and dirty / Gimme somma dat / Blue walls
CD _____ ANTCD 0013
Antones / Mar '91 / Hot Shot / Direct / ADA.

Murphy, Maurice

LIGHTER SIDE OF MAURICE MURPHY
CD _____ DOYCD 007
Doyen / Oct '91 / Conifer.

STARS IN BRASS (Murphy, Maurice/Guy Barker/Derek Watkins)
Trumpet blues and cantabile / Charivari / Anyone can whistle / Carnival of Venice / Softly as I leave you / Stardust / Our one is here to stay / Maiaguena / Li'l darlin' / Street scene / Here comes that rainy day / Bess, you is my woman now / We've only just begun / Three kings swing
CD _____ DOYCD 035
Doyen / Oct '94 / Conifer.

Murphy, Peter

CASCADE
CD _____ BBQCD 175
Beggars Banquet / Apr '95 / Warner Music / Disc.

DEEP
Deep ocean vast sea / Crystal wrists / Seven veils / Cuts you up / Roll call / Shy / Marlene Dietrich's favourite poem / Line between the devil's teeth / Strange kind of love (version one) / Roll call (reprise)
CD _____ BEGA 107CD
Beggars Banquet / '88 / Warner Music / Disc.

LOVE HYSTERIA
All night long / His circle and hers meet / Dragnet drag / Socrates the python / Indigo eyes / Time has nothing to do with it / Blind sublime / My last two years / Fun time
CD _____ BEGA 92 CD
Beggars Banquet / Mar '88 / Warner Music / Disc.

SHOULD THE WORLD FAIL TO FALL APART
Light pours out of me / Confessions / Should the world fail to fall apart / Never man / God sends / Blue heart / Answer is clear / Final solution / Jemal
CD _____ BBL 69CD
Lowdown/Beggars Banquet / Jul '88 / Warner Music / Disc.

Murphy, Phil

TRIP TO CULLENSTOWN, THE (Murphy, Phil, John & Pip)
Flogging reel/Kathy jones/The honeymoon / Shores of Lough Gowna/Humours of Kesh / Wexford and Bannow Bay hornpipes / Pete's polka/The happy polka / Micky the moulder/Tatter Jack Welsh / Shepherd's love dream / Kitty come over/The mug of brown ale / Ballygow reel / Trip to Cullenstown / Congress/The heather breeze/Earl's chair / Lakes of Kincora/Cronin's hornpipe / Mummer's jigs / Pete Bate's hornpipe/Joe Kearne's favourite / Ballygow polka / Wistful lover / Kerry hills / King of Clans/Castlekelly / Listowel polka

CD _____ CC 55CD
Claddagh / Nov '92 / ADA / Direct.

Murphy, Rose

LIVE IN CONCERT 1982
CD _____ EQCD 7002
Equinox / Jan '95 / Discovery.

Murphy, Turk

BEST OF TURK MURPHY, THE
CD _____ MMRC-CD 2
Merry Makers / Jul '93 / Jazz Music.

ITALIAN VILLAGE 1952-53 (Murphy, Turk Jazz Band)
CD _____ MMRCD 11
Merry Makers / Aug '95 / Jazz Music.

SAN FRANCISCO JAZZ (Murphy, Turk Jazz Band)
CD _____ MMRC-CD 3
Merry Makers / Jun '88 / Jazz Music.

SAN FRANCISCO JAZZ VOL.2 (Murphy, Turk Jazz Band)
CD _____ C-MMRC 115
Merry Makers / Jun '88 / Jazz Music.

TURK MURPHY AND HIS SAN FRANCISCO JAZZ BAND (Murphy, Turk & His San Francisco Jazz Band)
CD _____ BCD 91
GHB / Oct '93 / Jazz Music.

TURK MURPHY AND HIS SAN FRANCISCO JAZZ BAND VOL. 2
CD _____ BCD 92
GHB / Jan '93 / Jazz Music.

Murphy's Law

BACK WITH A BONG
Murphy's law / California pipeline / Sit home and rot / Fun / Beer / Wahoo day / Crucial bar-b-q / Day in the life / Care bear / Isla / Skinhead rebel / I've got a right / Intro / Panty raid / Yahoo / Attack of the killer beers / Cavity creeps / Ska song / Quest for herb / America rules / Rage / Wall of death / Secret agent S.K.I.N. / Push comes to shove / Bong
CD _____ AP 6002-2
Another Planet / Sep '94 / Vital.

Murrain

FAMINE, THE
CD _____ MAB 003CD
MAB / Jul '93 / Plastic Head.

Murray

INDELICACY
CD _____ WWCD 005
West Wind / Jul '88 / Swift / Charly / CM / ADA.

Murray, Anne

BEST OF ANNE MURRAY SO FAR, THE
Snowbird / Now and forever (you and me) / Danny's song / Nobody loves me like you do / Love song / Time don't run out on me / You won't see me / Just another woman in love / You needed me / Just another woman in love / I just fall in love again / Somebody's always saying goodbye / Broken hearted me / Could I have this dance / Daydream believer / Another sleepless night / Shadows in the moonlight / Blessed are the believers / Make love to me / Over you
CD _____ CDP 8311582
EMI / Jul '95 / EMI.

CROONIN'
Old cape cod / Wayward wind / Secret love / Fever / When I fall in love / Allegheny moon / You belong to me / Born to be with you / True love / Teach me tonight / Cry me a river / Make love to me / Hey there / It only hurts for a little while / I'm confessin' / I'm a fool to care / Wanted / I really don't want to know / Moments to remember
CD _____ CDEMC 3672
EMI / Mar '94 / EMI.

NOW AND FOREVER (3CD Set)
Little bit of soap / Last thing on my mind / What about me / Just bidin' my time / Snowbird / Rain / Put your hand in the hand / It takes time / Sing high, sing low / Stranger in my place / Talk it over in the morning / Cotton Jenny / Canadian sunset / Robbie's song for Jesus / Drown me / Danny's song / He thinks I still care / Love song / Another pot o' tea / Please don't sell Nova Scotia / Call / You won't see me / Snowbird (alt. version) / Million more / Stars are the window of heaven / Walk right back / You needed me / I still wish the very best for you / Shadows in the moonlight / You've got what it takes / Tuscan Cafe / I just fall in love again / Daydream believer / Broken hearted (Spanish version) / Wintery feeling / Moon over Brooklyn / Nevertheless (I'm in love with you) / Could I have this dance / Blessed are the believers / Another sleepless night / Bigger they are, harder they fall / We don't have to hold out / Somebody's always saying goodbye / Song of the Mira / Unchained melody / Heaven is here (alt. version) / Lonely but only for you / Little good news / Just another woman in love / Sentimental favourite / Time don't run out

on me / Nobody loves me like you do / Now and forever (you and me) / Are you still in love with me / Flying on your own / If I ever fall in love again / Wrong end of the rainbow / Feed this fire / I can see Arkansas / Si jamais je te revois (If I ever see you again) / You sure know how to make a memory / Allegheny moon / Hey there / Moments to remember
CD Set _____ CDS 8311592
EMI / Jul '95 / EMI.

SPECIAL COLLECTION
Snowbird / Destiny / Danny's song / Love song / You won't see me / He thinks I still care / You needed me / I just fall in love again / Shadows in the moonlight / Broken hearted me / Daydream believer / Time don't run out on me / Just another woman in love / Now and forever (you and me) / I'd fall in love tonight / If I ever fall in love again / Little good news / When I fall / Another sleepless night / Blessed are the believers / Nobody loves me like you do
CD _____ CDEST 2112
Capitol / Feb '90 / EMI.

THERE GOES MY EVERYTHING
CD _____ HADCD 183
Javelin / Nov '95 / THE / Henry Hadaway Organisation.

Murray, David

ACOUSTIC OCTFUNK
CD _____ SSCD 8051
Sound Hills / Apr '94 / Harmonia Mundi / Cadillac.

BALLADS FOR BASS CLARINET (Murray, David Quartet)
CD _____ DIW 880
DIW / Jan '94 / Harmonia Mundi / Cadillac.

BLACK & BLACK
CD _____ 4715772
Sony Jazz / Nov '92 / Sony.

BODY AND SOUL (Murray, David Quartet)
CD _____ 120155-2
Black Saint / Nov '93 / Harmonia Mundi / Cadillac.

CHILDREN
CD _____ BSR 0089
Black Saint / '86 / Harmonia Mundi / Cadillac.

DAVID MURRAY BIG BAND
CD _____ DIW 851
DIW / Nov '91 / Harmonia Mundi / Cadillac.

DEATH OF A SIDEMAN (Murray, David Quintet)
CD _____ DIW 866
DIW / Feb '93 / Harmonia Mundi / Cadillac.

FAST LIFE (Murray, David Quartet)
CD _____ 4747112
Sony Jazz / Jan '95 / Sony.

FOR AUNT LOUISE
CD _____ DIW 901
DIW / Dec '95 / Harmonia Mundi / Cadillac.

HEALERS, THE (Murray, David & Randy Weston)
CD _____ 120118-2
Black Saint / Harmonia Mundi / Cadillac.

HOME (Murray, David Quartet)
Home / Santa Barbara and Crenshaw / Follies / Choctaw blues / Last of the hipmen / 3-D family
CD _____ BSRCD 055
Black Saint / Sep '85 / Harmonia Mundi / Cadillac.

HOPE SCOPE (Murray, David Octet)
CD _____ 120139-2
Black Saint / Apr '91 / Harmonia Mundi / Cadillac.

I WANT TO TALK ABOUT YOU (Murray, David Quartet)
CD _____ 120105-2
Black Saint / Sep '89 / Harmonia Mundi / Cadillac.

INTERBOOGIEOLOGY
CD _____ 1200182
Black Saint / Nov '90 / Harmonia Mundi / Cadillac.

JAZZOSAURUS REX
CD _____ 4749832
Sony Jazz / May '94 / Sony.

JAZZPAR PRIZE, THE (Murray, David & Pierre Dorge's New Jungle Orchestra)
Do green ants dream / David in wonderland / Gospel medley / In a sentimental mood / Shakil warriors / Songs for Doni
CD _____ ENJACD 70312
Enja / May '92 / New Note / Vital/SAM.

LIVE AT SWEET BASIL, VOL 1 (Murray, David Big Band)
Lovers / Bechet's bounce / Silence / Duet for big band
CD _____ BSRCD 085
Black Saint / '86 / Harmonia Mundi / Cadillac.

LIVE AT SWEET BASIL, VOL 2 (Murray, David Big Band)
CD _____ BSRCD 0095
Black Saint / '86 / Harmonia Mundi / Cadillac.

MING (Murray, David Octet)
Fast life / Hill / Ming / Jasvan / Dewey's circle
CD _____ BSRCD 045
Black Saint / Sep '85 / Harmonia Mundi / Cadillac.

MODERN PORTRAIT OF LOUIS ARMSTRONG, A (Murray, David, Doc Cheatham, Loren Schoenburg, Allen Lowe)
CD _____ STCD 563
Stash / May '93 / Jazz Music / CM / Cadillac / Direct / ADA.

MORNING SONG (Murray, David Octet)
Morning song / Body and soul / Light blue / Jitterbug waltz / Off season / Duet
CD _____ BSRCD 075
Black Saint / Sep '85 / Harmonia Mundi / Cadillac.

MURRAY'S STEPS (Murray, David Octet)
CD _____ BSR 0065
Black Saint / '86 / Harmonia Mundi / Cadillac.

PICASSO (Murray, David Octet)
CD _____ DIW 879
DIW / Jan '94 / Harmonia Mundi / Cadillac.

REAL DEAL (Murray, David & Milford Graves)
CD _____ DIW 867
DIW / Jan '93 / Harmonia Mundi / Cadillac.

REMEMBRANCES (Murray, David Quintet)
CD _____ DIW 849
DIW / Nov '91 / Harmonia Mundi / Cadillac.

SANCTUARY WITHIN, A
CD _____ 120145-2
Black Saint / Nov '92 / Harmonia Mundi / Cadillac.

SHAKILL'S 2
CD _____ DIW 884
DIW / Oct '94 / Harmonia Mundi / Cadillac.

SHAKILL'S WARRIOR (Murray, David Quartet)
CD _____ DIW 850
DIW / Nov '91 / Harmonia Mundi / Cadillac.

SPECIAL QUARTET
CD _____ 4728122
Sony Jazz / Jan '95 / Sony.

TENORS (Murray, David Quartet)
CD _____ DIW 881
DIW / Jan '94 / Harmonia Mundi / Cadillac.

TIP, THE
CD _____ DIW 891
DIW / Mar '95 / Harmonia Mundi / Cadillac.

Murray, Diedre

FIRESTORM (Murray, Diedre & Fred Hopkins)
CD _____ VICTOCD 020
Victo / Nov '94 / These / ReR Megacorp /

STRINGOLOGY (Murray, Diedre & Fred Hopkins)
CD _____ 120143-2
Black Saint / May '94 / Harmonia Mundi / Cadillac.

Murray, Keith

MOST BEAUTIFULLEST THING IN THE WORLD, THE
CD _____ CHIP 159
Jive / Dec '94 / BMG.

Murray, Pauline

PAULINE MURRAY & THE INVISIBLE GIRLS (Murray, Pauline & The Invisible Girls)
CD _____ PSTRCD 01
Trident / Jun '93 / Pinnacle.

Murray, Ruby

HOUR OF RUBY MURRAY, AN
Softly, softly / Happy days and lonely nights / I'll come when you call / When Irish eyes are smiling / If anyone finds this, I love you / Heartbeat / Mr. Wonderful / Danny boy / You are my sunshine / Smile / When I grow too old to dream / Trottin' to the fair / Let me go, lover / Let him go, let him tarry / Evermore / Real love / Get well soon / You are my first love / Goodbye Jimmy goodbye / Cockles and mussels / Button up your overcoat / Pennies from Heaven / Now is the hour

CD _____ CC 219
Music For Pleasure / May '88 / EMI.

Murray, Sunny

13 STEPS ON GLASS
CD _____ ENJACD 80942
Enja / Sep '95 / New Note / Vital/SAM.

Musci, Oberto

MESSAGES & PORTRAITS (Musci, Oberto & Giovanni Venosta)
CD _____ MVCD 1
RER / Jan '93 / Grapevine.

WATER MESSAGES ON DESERT SAND/ URBAN AND TRIBAL (Musci, Oberto & Giovanni Venosta)
Technowaltz / Water music / Empty boulevard / Mechanic soul versus Pathetic ambient / Nexus on the beach / Vientiana / Malangaan / Digital ketjak / Old time religion / Lilongwa / Tamatave / Dialogue between / Dreamer and others / Batida de coca / Rackrailway to / Ups and cowns of chewing gum / El lamento de los Ayatollah / Starfishes and kangaroos / Lullabies, Mother sings, Father plays
CD _____ RERMVCD
ReR Megacorp / '91 / These / ReR Megacorp.

Music De Madrid

LA FOILE DE LA SPAGNA
CD _____ HM 90 1050
Harmonia Mundi / Oct '88 / Harmonia Mundi / Cadillac.

Music Inc. & Big Band

MUSIC INC. & BIG BAND
CD _____ 66051009
Strata East / Nov '91 / New Note.

Music Machine

TURN ON
CD _____ REP 4154-WZ
Repertoire / Aug '91 / Pinnacle / Cadillac.

Music Revelation Ensemble

IN THE NAME OF
CD _____ DIW 885
DIW / Oct '94 / Harmonia Mundi / Cadillac.

Musica De La Tierra

INSTRUMENTAL & VOCAL MUSIC VOL.II
CD _____ CDC 207
Music Of The World / Jun '93 / Target/ BMG / ADA.

Musikklag,...

KING'S MESSENGER (Musikklag, Eikanger-Bjorsvik)
Songs for B.L / King messenger / Frogs of aristophanes / River dance / Arctic funk / Intrada / Concertino for trombone / Alle fugler / American dream
CD _____ DOYCD 047
Doyen / Oct '95 / Conifer.

Musillami, Michael

GLASS ART
Glass art / Shoeshine / Mars bars / Out of balance / Cousin Jim / Haberdasher blues / I wait for the summertime / Grey Cypress
CD _____ ECD 220602
Evidence / Nov '93 / Harmonia Mundi / ADA / Cadillac.

YOUNG CHILD, THE
CD _____ STCD 556
Stash / Jan '93 / Jazz Music / CM / Cadillac / Direct / ADA.

Muslimgauze

CITADEL
CD _____ XCD 026
Extreme / Feb '95 / Vital/SAM.

INFIDEL
CD _____ XEP 021
Extreme / Feb '95 / Vital/SAM.

INTIFAXA
CD _____ XCD 002
Extreme / May '95 / Vital/SAM.

MAROON
CD _____ STCD 084
Staalplaat / Sep '95 / Vital/SAM.

Musselwhite, Charlie

ACE OF HARPS
Blues overtook me / She may be your woman / River hip mama / Leaving your town / Hello pretty baby / Mean ol' Frisco / Kiddio / Yesterdays / Hangin' on / My road lies in darkness
CD _____ ALCD 4781
Alligator / May '93 / Direct / ADA.

HARMONICA ACCORDING TO CHARLIE MUSSELWHITE, THE
CD _____ BPCD 5016
Blind Pig / Dec '94 / Hot Shot / Swift / Roots / Direct / ADA.

IN MY TIME
CD _____ ALCD 4818
Alligator / Mar '94 / Direct / ADA.

MELLOW DEE
Hey Miss Bessie / Need my baby / I'll get a break / Peach orchard mama / Ask me nice / Come back baby / Comin' home baby / Baby, please don't go / Lotsa poppa / Steady on your trail / Can't you see what you're doing to / Christo redemptor
CD _____ CCD 11013
Crosscut / Nov '88 / ADA / CM / Direct.

MEMPHIS CHARLIE
CD _____ ARHCD 303
Arhoolie / Apr '95 / ADA / Direct / Cadillac.

SIGNATURE
Make my getaway / Blues got me again / Mama long legs / 38 special / It's gettin' warm in here / What's new again / Hey Miss Bessie / Me and my baby and the blues / Catwalk / Cheatin' on me
CD _____ ALCD 4801
Alligator / May '93 / Direct / ADA.

STAND BACK
CD _____ VND 79232
Vanguard / Oct '95 / Complete/Pinnacle / Discovery.

STAND BACK, HERE COMES CHARLIE MUSSELWHITE
CD _____ 662218
Vanguard / Jan '94 / Complete/Pinnacle / Discovery.

STONE BLUES
CD _____ VND 79287
Vanguard / Oct '95 / Complete/Pinnacle / Discovery.

TAKING CARE OF BUSINESS
Louisiana fog / Takin' care of business / Big legged woman / Riffin' / Leavin' / Just a little bit / Fell on my knees / Directly from my heart / Fat city
CD _____ CDTB 172
Thunderbolt / Nov '95 / Magnum Music Group.

Musso, Vido

LOADED (Musso, Vido & Stan Getz)
Moose in a caboose / Moose on the loose / My Jo-Ann / Vido in a jam / Bassology / Spellbound / Lem mego / Jam session at Savoy / Sweet Miss / Loaded / Grab your axe Max / Always
CD _____ SV 0227
Savoy Jazz / Oct '93 / Conifer / ADA.

Mussolini Headkick

BLOOD ON THE FLAG
CD _____ WD 6663CD
World Domination / Oct '90 / Pinnacle.

Mustang Lightning

MUSTANG LIGHTNING
CD _____ 422499
New Rose / May '94 / Direct / ADA.

Musto & Bones

FUTURE IS OURS, THE
CD _____ CBCD 5
City Beat / Apr '90 / Warner Music.

Muta Baruka

BLAKK WI BLAK..K..K
CD _____ 322574
Koch / Oct '91 / Koch.

CHECK IT
CD _____ ALCD 8306
Alligator / Aug '92 / Direct / ADA.

MYSTERY UNFOLDS,THE
Leaders speak / Dub poem / Revolutionary words / My great shun / Old cut bruk / Bun dung Babylon / Mustery unfolds / Dis poem / Famine injection / Eyes of liberty / Walkin' on gravel / Voice
CD _____ SHANCD 43037
Shanachie / Aug '87 / Koch / ADA / Greensleeves.

OUT CRY
CD _____ SHANCD 43023
Shanachie / Nov '87 / Koch / ADA / Greensleeves.

Mutabaruka

MELANIN MAN
CD _____ SHCD 45013
Shanachie / Apr '94 / Koch / ADA / Greensleeves.

Mute Drivers

EVERYONE
CD _____ BND 4CD
One Little Indian / Feb '90 / Pinnacle.

Mutilation

AGGRESSION IN EFFECT
CD Set _____ BR 002CD
Brain Crusher / Nov '92 / Plastic Head.

Mutter

HAUPTSACHE MUSIK
CD _____ EFA 047032
DEG / Jul '94 / SRD.

ICH SCHANE MICH GEDANKEN ZU HAB
CD _____ EFA 047012
DEG / Jul '94 / SRD.

Mutton Birds

NATURE
Nature / Dominion Road / Anchor me / Heater / Giant friend / Your window / White valient / In my room / Thing well made / Queen's English / There's a limit / Too close to the sun
CD _____ CDVIR 39
Virgin / Sep '95 / EMI.

Mutton Gun

AMPLEXUS
Aimless / Thanks, but no thanks / Don't talk to your mother like that / Cutfleisch / Sound track / Kansas / Ruby / Das lied fur dong / Aldgate / Poor unfortunate lovers
CD _____ MINTCD 1
Mint Sauce / Jul '90 / Jetstar.

INTO THE HOGGER
CD _____ MINTCD 3
Mint Sauce / Dec '90 / Jetstar.

MUTTONGUN 111
Rain rain / Turkey / Better / Demon honey / End of it all / Bullet for a guide / Good dog bad dog / Turquoise blue / Chucky bear / Young / Thought for the day / Enter the hogger / Summer in the city
CD _____ KOKOPOP 005CD
Kokopop / Feb '94 / Vital.

Muzsikas

BLUES FOR TRANSYLVANIA
CD _____ HNCD 1350
Hannibal / Feb '90 / Vital / ADA.

KETTO
CD _____ MRCD 175
Munich / Sep '95 / CM / ADA / Greensleeves / Direct.

MARAMAROS (The Lost Jewish Music of Transylvania)
Hasid wedding dances / Rooster is crowning / Dance from maramures / Lamenting song / Anne Maamini / I have just come from gyula / Farewell to Saturday evening / Jewish dance from Szaszregan / Hat ein jid ein wejbele / Jewish csardas series from szek / Hassid dance / Greeting of the bride / Haneros halelu / Farewell to the guests
CD _____ HNCD 1373
Hannibal / Mar '93 / Vital / ADA.

PRISONER'S SONG, THE (Muzsikas/ Marta Sebestyen)
CD _____ HNCD 1341
Hannibal / Jan '89 / Vital / ADA.

Mwenda, Jean Bosco

MWENDA WA BAYEKE
Pension / Bombalaka / Bayeke / Tambala moja / Mbele ya kuina / Safari ya mupenzi / Kuimba ni mawazo / Pole ploe ya kuina / Watoto wawili / Masanga
CD _____ MOU 00762
Mountain/EWM / Sep '95 / EWM.

My Bloody Valentine

ISN'T ANYTHING
Soft as snow / Lose my breath / Cupid come / You're still in a dream / No more sorry / All I need / Feed me with your kiss / Sueisfine / Several girls galore / You never should / Nothing much to lose / I can see it
CD _____ CRELP 040 CD
Creation / Nov '88 / 3MV / Vital.

LOVELESS
Only shallow / Loomer / Touched / To here knows when / When you sleep / I only said / Come in alone / Sometimes / Blown a wish / What you want / Soon

---

CD _____ CRECD 060
Creation / Nov '91 / 3MV / Vital.

My Cat Dances

YOU WILL NEVER WORK AGAIN
Harbourtown / Mound / Something about the rain / My cat dances / Big / Delightful incompetent / Sweet talking bastard / Hoping to fly / Tony / Nowheresville
CD _____ SCRUMMY 3CD
Scrummy / May '95 / Scrummy.

My Dad Is Dead

FOR RICHER, FOR POORER
CD _____ EJ 01CD
Emperor Jones / Nov '95 / SRD.

LET'S SKIP THE DETAILS
CD _____ HMS 109CD
Homestead / Jul '88 / SRD.

My Dying Bride

ANGEL AND THE DARK RIVER
CD _____ CDVILE 50
CD _____ CDXVILE 50
Peaceville / May '95 / Pinnacle.

AS THE FLOWER WITHERS
CD _____ VILE 032CD
Peaceville / Apr '95 / Pinnacle.

STORIES, THE
Symphonaire infernus et spera empyrium / God is alone / De sade soliloquay / Thrash of naked limbs / Le cerf malade / Gather me up forever / I am the bloody earth / Transcending (Into the exquisite) / Crown of sympathy
CD Set _____ VILE 045CD
Peaceville / Oct '94 / Pinnacle.

TRINITY
Symphonaire infernus / Thrash of naked limbs / I am the bloody earth / God is alone / Le cerf malade / Sexuality of bereavement / De sade soliloquy / Gather me up forever / Crown of sympathy
CD _____ CDVILE 46
Peaceville / Sep '95 / Pinnacle.

TURN LOOSE THE SWANS
Sear me MCMXC111 / Songless bird / Snow in my hand / Crown of sympathy / Turn loose the swans / Black God
CD _____ CDVILE 39
Peaceville / Mar '95 / Pinnacle.

My Friend The Chocolate..

BROOD (My Friend The Chocolate Cake)
CD _____ D 31136
Mushroom / Mar '95 / BMG / 3MV.

My Life Story

MORNINGTON CRESENT
CD _____ MOTHERCD 1
Mother Tongue / Jan '95 / Disc.

My Name

MEGACRUSH
CD _____ CZ 046CD
C/Z / Aug '92 / Plastic Head.

My Own Victim

BURNING INSIDE
CD _____ CM 77105CD
Century Media / Jan '96 / Plastic Head.

MY OWN VICTIM
CD _____ CM 770822
Century Media / Mar '95 / Plastic Head.

My Sister's Machine

DIVA
Hands and feet / Pain / I hate you / Wasting time / Love at high speed / I'm sorry / Walk all over you / Sunday / Monster box / Diva
CD _____ CARCD 18
Caroline / Apr '92 / EMI.

WALL FLOWERS
Inside of me / Broken land / This is fear / Steamy swamp thang / Feed / Empty room / Sixteen ways to go / Enemy / I slip away / Burn / Mockingbird / Cracking new ground
CD _____ 3705615122
WEA / Jul '93 / Warner Music.

Myers, Amina Claudine

COUNTRY GIRL
CD _____ MMCD 801012
Minor Music / Apr '90 / Vital/SAM.

SALUTES BESSIE SMITH
CD _____ CDLR 103
Leo / Feb '89 / Wellard / Cadillac / Impetus.

WOMEN IN (E)MOTION FESTIVAL
CD _____ T&M 102
Tradition & Moderne / Nov '94 / Direct / ADA.

Myers, Fraser

FRASER MYERS BIG BAND
CD _____ VCTMD 1
Vocal Cords / Nov '93 / Grapevine.

Myers, Louis

I'M A SOUTHERN MAN
CD _____ TCD 5026
Testament / Aug '95 / Complete/Pinnacle / ADA / Koch.

Myles, Alannah

ALANNAH MYLES
Still got this thing / Black velvet / Lover of mine / If you want to / Who loves you / Love is / Rock this joint / Kickstart my heart / Just one kiss / Make love
CD _____ 781 956-2
Atlantic / Nov '89 / Warner Music.

ROCKING HORSE
Our world our times / Make me happy / Sonny say you will / Tumbleweed / Livin' on a memory / Song instead of a kiss / Love in the big town / Last time I saw William / Lies and rumours / Rocking horse
CD _____ 7567824022
WEA / Nov '92 / Warner Music.

Myles, Heather

JUST LIKE OLD TIMES
Love lyin' down / Why I'm walkin' / Changes / Rum and rodeo / Make a fool out of me / Other side of town / Just like old times / Stay out of my arms / I love you, goodbye / Lovin' the bottle / One good reason why / Playin' in the dirt
CD _____ FIENDCD 717
Demon / Apr '92 / Pinnacle / ADA.

UNTAMED
CD _____ FIENDCD 763
Demon / Jan '95 / Pinnacle / ADA.

Mylett, Peter

SOMETHING OLD, SOMETHING NEW
CD _____ FRCD 030
Foam / Oct '94 / CM.

Mynediad Am Ddim

MYNEDIAD AM DDIM 1974-92
Wa MacSpredar / P-Pendyffryn / Arica / Beti Wyn / Fi / Llwch y glo / Padi / Mi ganaf gan / Ceidwad y goleudy / Ynys Llanddwyn / Mynd yn bell i ffwrdd / y gwrthodedig / Yn y dre / Hi yw fy ffrind / Mae'r byd yn wag / Cofio dy wyneb / Pappagio's / Gwaed i'r llwch / Can y cap / Wini / Casa eroti / Y storu wir
CD _____ SCD 2003
Sain / Feb '95 / Direct / ADA.

Mynox Layh

TERMINUS CLARITATAS
CD _____ HY 39100962
Hy-Ritual / Jun '94 / Plastic Head.

Mynta

NANDOS DANCE
CD _____ XOU 107
Xource / Dec '94 / ADA / Cadillac.

Myrna Loy

IMMERSCHON
CD _____ NORM 158CD
Normal/Okra / Nov '93 / Direct / ADA.

Myster-Me

LET ME EXPLAIN (Myster-Me & DJ 20)
What's the word / Can't fuck with the record / If ever / Playtime's over / Unsolved mysterme / Myster Master / Call me Myster / Happy like death / Whatever whatever / Peepin' the wreck / Hoodie down / Under the influence
CD _____ GEECD 15
Gee Street / Jul '94 / PolyGram.

Mysteries Of Science

EROTIC NATURE OF AUTOMATED UNIVERSE, THE
CD _____ IAE 005CD
Instinct Ambient Europe / Jul '95 / Plastic Head.

Mystery Machine

10 SPEED
CD _____ W 230098
Nettwerk / Oct '95 / Vital / Pinnacle.

GLAZED
Shaky ground / Everyone's alright / Valley song / Ride / Stay high / Hooked / Floored / Hi-test / Invitation / Salty / Underground / Broken / Slack / Stain master
CD _____ NET 043CD
Nettwerk / Mar '93 / Vital / Pinnacle.

Mystery Slang

RIVER TOWNS
Off them metal walls / Stranded man / Cooler girl (blues) / You're a fury / Shakers inn / Bears run / Last call / Calling shelter / Lonesome pride
CD _____ 527500620
Solid / May '93 / Vital.

Mystic Astrologic

FLOWERS NEVER CRY
CD _____ DOCD 1993
Drop Out / Jul '91 / Pinnacle.

Mystic Charm

SHADOWS OF THE UNKNOWN
CD _____ SHR 008CD
Shiver / Aug '95 / Plastic Head.

Mystic Forces

ETERNAL QUEST
CD _____ IRS 972030
Rising Sun / Dec '93 / Vital.

TAKE COMMAND
CD _____ CMFTCD 7
CMFT / Nov '90 / Plastic Head.

Mystic, Mickey

WARZONE
CD _____ RRCD 10
Roots Collective / Sep '94 / SRD / Jetstar / Roots Collective.

Mystic Revealers

JAH WORKS
CD _____ RASCD 3123
Greensleeves / Sep '93 / Total/BMG / Jetstar / SRD.

SPACE AND TIME
CD _____ RASCD 3170
Ras / Aug '95 / Jetstar / Greensleeves / SRD / Direct.

Mystifier

GOETIA
CD _____ OPCD 16
Osmose / Nov '93 / Plastic Head.

Mystik

PERPETUAL BEING
CD _____ MASSCD 028
Massacre / Apr '94 / Plastic Head.

Mythos

PAIN AMPLIFIER
CD _____ EOR 0002
Evil Omen / Feb '95 / Plastic Head.

N 2 Deep

BACK TO THE HOTEL
CD _____ FILERCD 427
Profile / May '92 / Pinnacle.

N-Joi

INSIDE OUT
Set smart / Trauma / Never let you go / Ease yourself / Papillon 2 / Chaser / Zeus / Bad things / Games / Papillon (original) / On the move / Anthem
CD _____ 74321256872
De-Construction / Jul '95 / BMG.

N-Trance

ELECTRONIC PLEASURE
CD _____ GLOBECD 2
All Around The World / Jun '95 / Total/
BMG.

N.E.U.K.

STATE OF MIND
CD _____ BRC 101CD
Black Mail / Jul '95 / Plastic Head.

N.R.A.

SURF CITY AMSTERDAM
CD _____ IGN 2H
Ignition / Mar '94 / Plastic Head.

N.W.A.

EFIL4ZAGGIN
Real niggaz don't die / Niggaz 4 life / Protest / Appetite for destruction / Don't drink that wine / Alwayz into something / To kill a hooker / One less bitch / Findum fuckum and flee / Automobile / She swallowed it / I'd rather fuck you / Approach to danger / 1-900 2 Compton / Dayz of wayback
CD _____ BRCD 562
4th & Broadway / Apr '91 / PolyGram.

STRAIGHT OUTTA COMPTON
Straight outta Compton / Fuck the police / Gangsta gangsta / If it ain't ruff / Parental discretion iz advised / Express yourself / I ain't tha 1 / Dopeman / Compton's 'n the house / 8 ball (remix) / Something like that / Quiet on the set / Something 2 dance 2
CD _____ BRCD 534
4th & Broadway / Aug '89 / PolyGram.

N.Y. Hardbop Quintet

CLINCHER, THE
New jazz world order / How little we know / Leroy street / Poor little birdie / Goodbye / Cape fearsome / Clincher / Blues from the griddle / You and the night and the music
CD _____ TCB 95202
TCB / Sep '95 / New Note.

N.Y.J.O.

BIG BAND CHRISTMAS (National Youth Jazz Orchestra)
Deck the halls with boughs of holly / Silent night / Christians awake / Manxland my Christmas tree / In the bleak midwinter / At Christmas / I saw six ships / My dancing day / Wenceslas squared / Away in a manger / Thirst, The - No ale / O come all ye faithful (Adeste Fidelis) / Christmas blues / Take five kings / I left my heart in Royal David's City / Holly and the ivy / Hark the herald angels sing
CD _____ NYJCD 009
NYJO / Aug '94 / New Note / Magnum Music Group.

COOKIN' WITH GAS (National Youth Jazz Orchestra)
Beyond the Hatfield Tunnel / Hot gospel / Step on the gas / Mr. B.G. / Be gentle / Behind the gasworks / Cookin' with gas / 'S Wonderful / We care for you / Big girl now / Gasanova / Afterburner / Water babies / Heat of the moment
CD _____ NYJCD 010
NYJO / Apr '95 / New Note / Magnum Music Group.

COTTONING ON (National Youth Jazz Orchestra)
Sea island samba / Miss Malfatti, I presume / Cottoning on / Lady can tell / One for Oscar / Tenor each way / Blues for Duke / Be gentle / Night is a pup / Night slide / Gasbag blues
CD _____ NYJCD 016
NYJO / Dec '95 / New Note / Magnum Music Group.

GIANTS OF, THE (National Youth Jazz Orchestra)
CD _____ NYJVC 901
NYJO / Apr '95 / New Note / Magnum Music Group.

HALLMARK (National Youth Jazz Orchestra)
Hallmark / I have been here before / Blood orange / Adeus Tristeza / Samba for Cheryl / Have you seen them cakes / U-Turn / Suits me / While the cat's away / Reepicheep / Tara's Tuesday / Castle's in Spain
CD _____ NYJCD 015
NYJO / Apr '95 / New Note / Magnum Music Group.

IN CONTROL (National Youth Jazz Orchestra)
CD _____ JHCD 037
Ronnie Scott's Jazz House / Mar '95 / Jazz Music / Magnum Music Group / Cadillac.

LOOKING FORWARD, LOOKING BACK (National Youth Jazz Orchestra)
CD _____ NYJCD 012
NYJO / Apr '95 / New Note / Magnum Music Group.

MALTESE CROSS (National Youth Jazz Orchestra)
CD _____ NYJCD 008
NYJO / Apr '95 / New Note / Magnum Music Group.

MERRY CHRISTMAS & A HAPPY NEW YEAR, A (National Youth Jazz Orchestra)
We wish you a Merry Christmas / O come, o come / Bethlehem lift off / While shepherds watched their flocks by night / Midnight clear / My gift to you / Noel nouvelet / OLTOB / Christmas song / Angels from the second storey / Childsotnes / Winter snow / It's Christmas / Twelve bars of Christmas / Auld land syne
CD _____ NYJCD 014
NYJO / Aug '94 / New Note / Magnum Music Group.

PORTRAITS (National Youth Jazz Orchestra)
Blues at the bull / Woody / Basie / Dizzy / Duke / Bird / Quincy / Monk / Duke II / Kenton / Point of no return / Come on the blues / Royal flush / Southern horizons
CD _____ HHCD 007
Hot House / May '95 / Cadillac / Wellard / Harmonia Mundi.

REMEMBRANCE (National Youth Jazz Orchestra)
Remembrance (for Jim) / Remembrance (for Chrish and Eamonn) / Remembrance (for Kenny and Charlie) / Remembrance (for Valery) / I'll never forget / Half steps / Snakes and ladders / Long hot summer / Rodeo / Yessica / Take the CandA train / Almost there / Give up
CD _____ NYJCD 011
NYJO / Apr '95 / New Note / Magnum Music Group.

THESE ARE THE JOKES (National Youth Jazz Orchestra)
Still doing the trick with the horse, Madam / First time I've seen dead people smoke (Smokey eyes) / Keep looking young-hang around with old people / Chef's rash has stained up nicely / Much too much / No hall just a red head / Are we keeping you up like yer / Roxy beaujolais / Audient was on its foot / Watching the traffic lights change / Don't go to her
CD _____ JHCD 024
Ronnie Scott's Jazz House / Jan '95 / Jazz Music / Magnum Music Group / Cadillac.

VIEW FROM THE HILL, A (National Youth Jazz Orchestra)
CD _____ JHCD 044
Ronnie Scott's Jazz House / Jan '96 / Jazz Music / Magnum Music Group / Cadillac.

WITH AN OPEN MIND (National Youth Jazz Orchestra)
Cheese'n'Carrots / Revenge of the Amoebae / With an open mind / Remembrance for Jim / Aardvark / Syrup of Phiggs / Fly to me / Midnight oil / Going Dutch
CD _____ NYJCD 007
NYJO / Apr '95 / New Note / Magnum Music Group.

Na Casaidigh

1691
CD _____ CEFCD 154
Gael Linn / Jan '94 / Roots / CM / Direct / ADA.

Na Fili

PURE TRADITIONAL MUSIC OF IRELAND
CD _____ PTICD 1010
Pure Traditional Irish / Apr '94 / ADA.

Na Firéin

NA FIRÉIN
CD _____ CEFCD 162
Gael Linn / Jan '94 / Roots / CM / Direct / ADA.

Na Lua

CONTRADANZAS
CD _____ GCDF 1002CD
Sons Galiza / Apr '95 / ADA.

PELIQUEIRO
CD _____ SGF 1021CD
Sons Galiza / Apr '95 / ADA.

Naam, Fong

NANG HONG SUITE
CD _____ NI 5332
Nimbus / Sep '94 / Nimbus.

SLEEPING ANGEL, THE
CD _____ NI 5319
Nimbus / Sep '94 / Nimbus.

Nada

CELMETRA
CD _____ CC 006CD
Common Cause / Oct '94 / Plastic Head / SRD.

Nail, Jimmy

BIG RIVER
CD _____ 0630128232
East West / Nov '95 / Warner Music.

CROCODILE SHOES
CD _____ 4509985562
East West / Nov '94 / Warner Music.

GROWING UP IN PUBLIC
Ain't no doubt / Reach out / Laura / Waiting for the sunshine / Real love / Only love (can bring us home) / Wicked world / Beautiful / I believed / Absent friends
CD _____ 4509901442
East West / Dec '94 / Warner Music.

TAKE IT OR LEAVE IT
That's the way love is / Airwaves / Walk away / Your decision today / Ladies and gentlemen of South Africa / Rain burns / Same again / Further on / One more day / Love don't live here anymore
CD _____ CDVIP 111
Virgin VIP / Nov '93 / Carlton Home Entertainment / THE / EMI.

Nailbomb

POINT BLANK
CD _____ RR 90552
Roadrunner / Jul '95 / Pinnacle.

Najma

ATISH
CD _____ TRECD 108
Triple Earth / Nov '93 / Sterns / Grapevine.

QAREEB
Neend koyi / Hár sitani aap ka / Zikar hai apna mehfil mehfil / Karcon na yad magar / Jane kis tarjha / Dil laga ya tha
CD _____ TRECD 103
Triple Earth / Nov '93 / Sterns / Grapevine.

Nakagawa, Masami

PRELUDE FOR AUTUMN
CD _____ JD 3304
JVC / Jul '88 / New Note.

TOUCH OF SPRING
CD _____ JD 3311
JVC / Oct '88 / New Note.

Nakai, R.Carlos

SUNDANCE SEASON
CD _____ CDCEL 024
Celestial Harmonies / Feb '89 / ADA / Select.

Naked City

ABSINTHE
CD _____ AVAN 004
Avant / Jan '94 / Harmonia Mundi / Cadillac.

GRAND GUIGNOL
CD _____ AVANT 002
Avant / Jan '93 / Harmonia Mundi / Cadillac.

HERETIC - JEUX DES DAMES CRUELLES
CD _____ AVANT 001
Avant / Aug '92 / Harmonia Mundi / Cadillac.

Radio

CD _____ AVAN 003
Avant / Jan '94 / Harmonia Mundi / Cadillac.

Naked Ear

ACOUSTIC GUITAR DUOLOG
CD _____ BEST 1022CD
Acoustic Music / Nov '93 / ADA.

Naked Ray Gun

ALL RISE
CD _____ HMS 045CD
Homestead / Jul '88 / SRD.

THROB THROB
CD _____ HMS 008CD
Homestead / Jul '88 / SRD.

Naked Rhythm

FATBOX
CD _____ MASSCD 038
Massacre / Nov '94 / Plastic Head.

Namlock, Pete

KOOLFANG 2 (Namlock, Pete & David Monfang)
CD _____ PK 08106CD
Fax / Jan '96 / Plastic Head.

NAMLOOK ATOM
CD _____ PK 08107CD
Fax / Jan '96 / Plastic Head.

PSYCHONAVIGATION 2 (Namlock, Pete & Bill Laswell)
CD _____ PW 024CD
Fax / Nov '95 / Plastic Head.

Namtchylak, Sainkho

LOST RIVERS
CD _____ FMPCD 42
FMP / Mar '87 / Cadillac.

Namyslowski, Zbigniew

KUJAVIACK GOES FUNKY
CD _____ PBR 33859
Power Bros. / Aug '95 / Harmonia Mundi.

ZBIGNIEW NAMYSLOWSKI QUARTET
CD _____ PBR 33861
Power Bros. / Oct '95 / Harmonia Mundi.

Nancy Boy

PROMOSEXUAL
CD _____ BENDCD 001
Equator / Oct '95 / Pinnacle.

Nannini, Gianna

LATIN LOVER
CD _____ 811 669 2
Ricordi / '88 / Discovery.

PUZZLE
CD _____ 813 387 2
Ricordi / '88 / Discovery.

Napalm

CRUEL TRANQUILITY
Mind melt / A.O.A. / Shake it off / Gag of steel / Devastation / Combat zone / Immoral society / Attack on America / Reanimate / Act of betrayal / Nightmare administrator / Practice what you preach / Kranked up and out
CD _____ 85-7565
Steamhammer / Jun '89 / Pinnacle / Plastic Head.

ZERO TO BLACK
CD _____ 847622
Steamhammer / Nov '90 / Pinnacle / Plastic Head.

Napalm Death

DEATH BY MANIPULATION
CD _____ MOSH 051CD
Earache / Sep '94 / Vital.

DIATRIBES
Greed killing / Glimpse into genocide / Ripe for the breaking / Cursed to crawl / Cold forgiveness / My own worst enemy / Just rewards / Dogma / Take the strain / Corrosive elements / Placate, sedate, eradicate / Diatribes / Take the stain
CD _____ MOSH 141CDD
CD _____ MOSH 141CD
Earache / Jan '96 / Vital.

FEAR, EMPTINESS, DESPAIR
Twist the knife (slowly) / Hung / Remain nameless / Plague rages / More than meets the eye / Primed time / State of mind / Armageddon X 7 / Retching on the dirt / Fasting on deception / Throwaway

CD _____ MOSH 109CD
Earache / Mar '94 / Vital.

**FROM ENSLAVEMENT TO
OBLITERATION**
Evolved as one / It's a M.A.N.'s world / Lucid fairytale / Private death / Unchallenged hate / Uncertainty blurs / Vision / Retreat to nowhere / Display to me / From enslavement / Blind to the truth / Emotional suffocation / Practice what you preach / Mentally murdered / Worlds apart
CD _____ MOSH 008CD
Earache / Sep '94 / Vital.

HARMONY OF CORRUPTION
CD _____ MOSH 019CD
Earache / Sep '94 / Vital.

PEEL SESSIONS
CD _____ SFRCD 120
Strange Fruit / Oct '93 / Pinnacle.

**PEEL SESSIONS: NAPALM DEATH
(13.9.87 - 8.3.88)**
Kill / Prison without walls / Dead part 1 / Deceiver / Lucid fairytale / In extremis / Extremis / Blind to the truth / Negative approach / Common enem6y / Obstinate direction / Life / You suffer pt. 2 / Multinational cooporations / Instinct of survival / Stigatised / Parasites / Moral crusade / Worlds apart / M.A.D. / Divine death / C. 9 / Control / Walls / Raging in hell / Conform or die / S.O.B.
CD _____ SFPMCD 201
Strange Fruit / '89 / Pinnacle.

UTOPIA BANISHED
CD _____ MOSH 053CD
Earache / Sep '94 / Vital.

MY FAVOURITE THINGS
Yume / 93 Degrees / My favourite things / Luvell / My romance / Remember / Kagero / Anti-pasta / How long has this been going on
CD _____ 66053021
Jazz City / Feb '92 / New Note.

Narayan, Aruna

SARANGI
CD _____ NI 5447
Nimbus / Nov '95 / Nimbus.

Narayan, Brij

**RAGA LALIT/RAGA BAIRAGI BHAIRAV
(Narayan, Brij & Zakir Hussain)**
CD _____ NI 5263
Nimbus / Sep '94 / Nimbus.

Narayan, Pandit Ram

RAG BHUPAL TORI/RAG BATDIP
CD _____ NI 5119
Nimbus / Jul '94 / Nimbus.

RAG LALIT
CD _____ NI 5183
Nimbus / Sep '94 / Nimbus.

RAG SHANKARA/RAG MALA IN JOGIA
CD _____ NI 5245
Nimbus / Sep '94 / Nimbus.

Narcotica

DRUG FREE AMERICA
Narcotica / Shores of paradise / Fear and adrenalin / Baby doll / Ransacking the earthnet / Soap opera and Brown / Drop zone / Baby doll (Reprise)
CD _____ CDKTB 21
Dreamtime / Jul '95 / Kudos / Pinnacle.

Nardini, Peter

SCREAMS & KISSES
Don't know / Light up the sky / Wid became an astronaut / And I will fly / She said, O, is that right / Kiss from Wishaw cross / Another star / Zak Anderson / Double take / You're like a rock / Don't shut the door ma / River without you
CD _____ ECLCD 9307
Eclectic / Jan '96 / Pinnacle.

Nardo Ranks

COOL & HUMBLE
CD _____ CDHB 183
Heartbeat / Aug '95 / Greensleeves / Jetstar / Direct / ADA.

ROUGH NARDO RANKING
CD _____ PCD 1417
Profile / Jun '95 / Pinnacle.

Narell, Andy

DOWN THE ROAD
CD _____ 01934101392
Windham Hill / Sep '95 / Pinnacle / BMG / ADA.

HAMMER, THE
CD _____ WD 0107
Windham Hill Jazz / Mar '92 / New Note.

LIGHT IN YOUR EYES
CD _____ WD 0103
Windham Hill Jazz / Mar '92 / New Note.

LITTLE SECRETS
CD _____ WD 0120
Windham Hill Jazz / Mar '92 / New Note.

LONG TIME BAND, THE
Bacchanal / Jenny's rooms / De long time band / You the man / Play one for Keith / Groove town / Dance class / Canboulay / De long time band (conclusion)
CD _____ 01934111722
Windham Hill / Oct '95 / Pinnacle / BMG / ADA.

SLOW MOTION
CD _____ WD 0105
Windham Hill Jazz / Mar '92 / New Note.

STICKMAN
CD _____ WD 0101
Windham Hill Jazz / Mar '92 / New Note.

Narita

NARITA
CD _____ SHARK 022
Shark / Oct '92 / Plastic Head.

Narvalo

LIBRE
CD _____ CDSGP 0135
Prestige / Apr '95 / Total/BMG.

Nas

ILLMATIC
Genesis / N.Y. State of mind / Life's a bitch / World is yours / Half time / Memory lane (sittin' in da park) / One love / One time 4 your mind / Represent / It ain't hard to tell
CD _____ 475959 2
Columbia / Apr '94 / Sony.

Nascimento, Milton

ANGELUS
Seis horas da tarde / Estrelada / De um modo geral / Angelus / Coisas de minas / Hello goodbye / Sofro calado / Clube da Esquina No.2 / Meu veneno / Only a dream in Rio / Qualquer coisa a haver com o paraiso / Vera cruz / Novena / Amor amigo
CD _____ 936245499-2
Warner Bros. / Jul '94 / Warner Music.

CLUBE DA ESQUINA
Tudo que voce podia ser / Cais / O trem azul - part esp: Lo borges / Saidas e bandeiras no.1 - part esp: Beto guedes / Nuvem cigana / Cravo e canela / Dos cruces / Um girassol da cor de seu cabelo - part esp: Lo borges / San Vincente / Estralas - part esp: Lo Borges / Clube da Esquina no. 2 / Paisagem da Janela - part esp: Lo Borges / Me deixz em pas - part esp:: Alaide Costa / Os povos / Saidas e bandeiras no.2 - part esp: Beto guedes / Um gosto de sol / Pelo amor de deus / Lilia / Trem de doido - part esp: Lo Borges / Nada sera como antes - part esp: Beto Guedes / Ao que vai nascer
CD _____ CDEMC 3702
EMI / Mar '95 / EMI.

CLUBE DA ESQUINA 2
Credo / Nascente / Ruas da cidade / Paiuxao e fe / Casmiento de Negros / Olho d'agua / Canoa, canoa / O que foi feito devera (De Vera) (part esp: Elois Regina Gentilmente Cedida Pela Polygram do Brasil) / Misterios / Paco e agua / E dai (A Queda) / Cancao Amiga / Cancion por la unidad Latinoamericana (part esp: Chico Buarque de Hollanda) / Tanto / Dona Olimpia / Testamento / A sede do peixe (Para o que nao tem solucao) / Leo / Maria Maria / Meu Menino / Toshiro / Reis e rainhas do Maracatu / Que bom, amigo
CD Set _____ CDEM 1550
EMI / Mar '95 / EMI.

Nash, Johnny

I CAN SEE CLEARLY NOW
I can see clearly now / Let's be friends / Cream puff / Reggae on Broadway / Wonderful world / Ooh what a feeling / Birds of a feather / Cupid / Tears on my pillow / Guava jelly / That woman / Dream lover / There are more questions than answers / All I have to do is dream / Nice time / You got soul / My merry go round / Halfway to paradise / Stir it up
CD _____ 4653062
Epic / May '89 / Sony.

Nash, Lewis

RHYTHM IS MY BUSINESS
Let me try / 106 Nix / Sing me a song everlasting / My shining hour / Sabuku / Omlette / When you return / Monk's dream / Danuelle's waltz / Pranayama
CD _____ ECD 22041
Evidence / Mar '93 / Harmonia Mundi / ADA / Cadillac.

Nashville All-Stars...

**AFTER THE RIOT IN NEWPORT
(Nashville All-Stars Country Band)**
Relaxin' / Nashville to Newport / Opus de funk / Wonderful / Round Midnight / Frankie and Johnny / Riot-chorus
CD _____ BCD 15447

Bear Family / Jun '89 / Rollercoaster / Direct / CM / Swift / ADA.

Nashville Bluegrass Band

BOYS ARE BACK IN TOWN, THE
Get a transfer to home / Long time singer / Big river / Hard times / Connie and Buster / Don't let our love die / I'm rollin' through this unfriendly world / Rock bottom blues / Diamonds and pearls / Ghost of Eli Renfro / Weary blues from waiting / Big cow in Carlisle / Dark as the night, blue as the day / Boys are back in town
CD _____ SH 3778CD
Sugarhill / '90 / Roots / CM / ADA / Direct.

IDLE TIME
Idle time / Old devil's dream / Two wings / I closed my heart's door / All I want is you / Angeline the baker / Little Maggie / Last night I dreamed of loving you / No one but my darling / My Lord heard Jerusalem when she moaned / Old timey risin' damp / Train carryin' Jimmie Rodgers home
CD _____ CD 0232
Rounder / Aug '88 / CM / Direct / ADA / Cadillac.

MY NATIVE HOME
CD _____ ROUCD 0212
Rounder / Jul '93 / CM / Direct / ADA / Cadillac.

TO BE HIS CHILD
Goodnight the Lord's coming / Every humble knee must bow / No hiding place / You're drifting away / Hold fast to the right / Child enters life / To be his child / Gospel plow / Are you afraid to die / I'll be rested / Old Satan / New born soul
CD _____ CD 0242
Rounder / Aug '88 / CM / Direct / ADA / Cadillac.

UNLEASHED
CD _____ SHCD 3843
Sugarhill / Oct '95 / Roots / CM / ADA / Direct.

WAITIN' FOR THE HARD TIMES TO GO
Back trackin' / Waitin' for the hard times to go / Kansas City railroad line / Open pit mine / Train of yesterday / Father I stretch my arms to thee / When I get where I'm goin' / Waltzing's for dreamers / I ain't goin' down / We decided to make Jesus our choice / On again off again / Soppin' the gravy
CD _____ SH 3809CD
Sugarhill / May '93 / Roots / CM / ADA / Direct.

Nashville Teens

BEST OF THE NASHVILLE TEENS 1964-1969
Tobacco Road / Mona (I need you baby) / TNT / Parchman Farm / Need you / La Bamba / Bread and butter man / Google eye / hoochie coochie man / How deep is the ocean / Find my woman home / Devil-in-law / Too much / Hurtin' inside / I like it like that / Searching / Soon forgotten / This little bird / I'm coming home / Hard way / Words / That's my woman / Lament of the Cherokee reservation Indian / Looking for you
CD _____ CDEMS 1474
EMI / Apr '93 / EMI.

Nashville Voices

NEW COUNTRY HITS
CD _____ 12504
Laserlight / Jun '95 / Target/BMG.

Nasty Idols

CRUEL INTENTION
Way ya walk / Cool way of living / American nights / Don't tear it down / Alive 'n' kickin' / House of rock and roll / B.I.T.C.H. / Can't get ya off my mind / Devil in disguise / Westcoast city rockers / Trashed and dirty / Can't get ya off my mind (2) (CD only)
CD _____ BMCD 022
Black Mark / Apr '92 / Plastic Head.

Nasty Savage

INDULGENCE/ABSTRACT REALITY
CD _____ RR 9566 2
Roadrunner / '89 / Pinnacle.

Nathan & Zydeco Cha Cha's

CREOLE CROSSROADS
CD _____ ROUCD 2127
Rounder / Oct '95 / CM / Direct / ADA / Cadillac.

FOLLOW ME CHICKEN
CD _____ ROU 2122CD
Rounder / Aug '93 / CM / Direct / ADA / Cadillac.

Nathanson, Roy

**COMING GREAT MILLENNIUM, THE
(Nathanson, Roy & Anthony Coleman)**
CD _____ KFWCD 119
Knitting Factory / Oct '92 / Grapevine.

**DERANGED AND DECOMPOSED
(Nathanson, Roy & Curtis Fowlkes &
The Jazz Passengers)**
CD _____ TWI 0462
Les Disques Du Crepuscule / '89 / Discovery / ADA.

**LOBSTER & FRIEND (Nathanson, Roy &
Anthony Coleman)**
CD _____ KFWCD 147
Knitting Factory / Feb '95 / Grapevine.

Nation Of Ulysses

PLAYS PRETTY FOR BABY
CD _____ DIS 71VCD
Dischord / Oct '92 / SRD.

National Gallery

KEEP IT CLEAN
Lost lover blues / Trouble in mind / Keep it clean / Weeping willow blues / When I lay my burden down / Wini' boy blues / From four till late / Sundown / Worried life / Come back baby / Drunken hearted man / Big road blues / Special rider blues / Sittin' on top of the world / Electric chair blues / Police dog blues / Ballad of Fulton Allen / Travellin' light
CD _____ RHYD 5007
Rhiannon / May '95 / Vital / Direct / ADA.

National Health

NATIONAL HEALTH
Tenko breakdown / Brujo / Borogobes (except from 2) / Borogobes (part 1) / Elephants
CD _____ CDLIK 66
Decal / Jul '90 / Charly / Swift.

Native Colours

ONE WORLD
Pumpkin's delight / Freedom / Girlie's world / Highest mountain / Reflections in D / One world / Nature boy / I'm glad there is you / Orion's belt / Time was
CD _____ CCD 4646
Concord Jazz / Jun '95 / New Note.

Natural Four

NATURAL FOUR
Can this be real / You bring out the best inme / Try love again / You can't keep running away / This is what's happening now / Love that really counts / Try to smile / Love's society / Things will be better tomorrow
CD _____ CPCD 8127
Charly / Oct '95 / Charly / THE / Cadillac.

Naturists

FRIENDLY ISLANDS
Shaving cream / Boogie 2 shoes / Green green grass of home / Mavis Riley / Mission impossible / Lost in Tonga
CD _____ ACTIVE 001CD
Interactive / Jan '94 / 3MV / Sony.

Naughty By Nature

POVERTY'S PARADISE
CD _____ BLRCD 28
Big Life / May '95 / Pinnacle.

Naundorf, Frank

FRANK NAUNDORF & BAND
CD _____ BCD 316
GHB / Apr '94 / Jazz Music.

Nauseef, Mark

**SNAKE MUSIC, THE (Nauseef, Mark &
Miroslav Tadic)**
Lizard on a hot rock / Wind cries Mary / Peacock on a hot rock / Rope ladder to the moon / Armacord / Who are the brain police / Hamburg 2 / All souls day / Trio / Walls of the vortex / Fourths
CD _____ CMPCD 60
CMP / Jul '94 / Vital/SAM.

Navarro, Fats

**AT THE ROYAL ROOST (Navarro, Fats &
Tadd Dameron)**
CD _____ COD 010
Jazz View / Mar '92 / Harmonia Mundi.

**AT THE ROYAL ROOST VOL.2 (Navarro,
Fats & Tadd Dameron)**
CD _____ COD 025
Jazz View / Jun '92 / Harmonia Mundi.

**COMPLETE BLUE NOTE & CAPITOL
RECORDINGS, THE (2CD Set) (Navarro,
Fats & Tadd Dameron)**
Chase / Chase (2) / Squirrel / Squirrel (2) / Our delight / Our delight (2) / Dameronia / Dameronia (2) / Jahbero / Jahbero (2) / Lady Bird / Lady Bird (2) / Symphonette / Symphonette (2) / I think I'll go away / Sid's delight / Casbah / John's delight / What's new / Heaven's doors are wide open / Focus / Skunk / Boperation / Boperation (2) / Skunk (2) / Double talk / Double talk (2) / Bouncing with Bud / Dancing with Bud / Bouncing with Bud (2) / Wall / Dance of the infidels / Dance of the Infidels (2) / 52nd Street / Steekin' apples
CD Set _____ CDP 8333732
Blue Note / Oct '95 / EMI.

FATS NAVARRO 1946-49
Giants Of Jazz / Mar '92 / Target/BMG /
CD _____ GOJCD 53076
Cadillac.

IN THE BEGINNING....BE-BOP
Mr. Dues / Saxon / O-Go-Mo / Oh Kai / Blue
brew / Brew blue / More brew / No more
brew / Spinal / Red pepper / Just a mystery
/ Maternity
CD _____ SV 0169
Savoy Jazz / Jul '93 / Conifer / ADA.

MEMORIAL
Serenade to a square / Good kick / Seven
up / Blues in be-bop / Boppin' a riff / Fat
boy / Everything's cool / Webb City / Be
bop carol / Tadd walk / Gone with the wind
/ That someone must be you
CD _____ SV 0181
Savoy Jazz / Jul '92 / Conifer / ADA.

NOSTALGIA
Nostalgia / Barry's bop / Be bop romp /
Fats' blows / Dextivity / Dextrose / Dexter's
mood / Index / Stealing trash / Hollerin' and
screamin' / Fracture / Calling Dr. Jazz
CD _____ SV 0123
Savoy Jazz / Apr '93 / Conifer / ADA.

Nazareth

2 X S
Love leads to madness / Boys in the band
/ You love another / Gatecrash / Games /
Back to the trenches / Dream on / Lonely
in the night / Preservation / Take the rap /
Mexico
CD _____ CLACD 217
Castle / Feb '91 / BMG.

ANTHOLOGY - NAZARETH
Telegram (part 1) / On your way (part 2) /
So you want to be a rock 'n' roll star /
Sound check (part 4) / Here we go again /
Kentucky fried blues / Somebody to roll /
Revenge is sweet / beggar's day / Expect
no mercy / No mean city (parts 1 and 2) /
Silver dollar forger / Cocaine / Tush (live) /
A-shapes of things B-Space safari / Turn on
your receiver / Teenage nervous breakdown
/ Big boy / Go down fighting / Razamanaz
/ Vigilante man / Hair for the dog / Broken
down angel / I want to do everything for you
CD _____ ESBCD 967
Essential / Oct '91 / Total/BMG.

CLOSE ENOUGH FOR ROCK 'N' ROLL
Telegram (On your way/So you want to be
a rock 'n' roll star/Sound check/Here we are
again) / Vicki / Homesick again / Vancouver
shakedown
CD _____ CLACD 182
Castle / Aug '90 / BMG.

EARLY YEARS, THE
Witchdoctor woman / Morning dew / King
is dead / Called her name / Sad song /
Woke up this morning / Broken down angel
/ Razamanaz / Bad bad boy / This flight to-
night / Not faking it / Miss Misery / Chang-
ing times / Jet lag / Shanghai'd in Shanghai
/ Shapes of things / Space safari
CD _____ EARL D2
Castle / Aug '92 / BMG.

EXERCISES
I will not be led / Cat's eye, apple pie / In
my time / Woke up this morning / Called her
name / Fool about you / Love now you're
gone / Madelaine / Sad song / 1692 (Glencoe massacre)
CD _____ CLACD 220
Castle / Feb '91 / BMG.

EXPECT NO MERCY
This flight tonight / Dressed to kill / Love
hurts / Whisky drinkin' woman / Razamanaz
/ I want to do everything for you) / Free
wheeler / Broken down angel / Shanghai'D
in Shanghai / Night woman / Hair of the dog
/ Alcatraz / Sold my soul / Shapes of things
/ Loved and lost / Expect no mercy
CD _____ ELITE 022 CD
Carlton Home Entertainment / Aug '93 /
Carlton Home Entertainment.

EXPECT NO MERCY
All the king's horses / Expect no mercy /
Gimme what's mine / Gone dead train /
Kentucky fried blues / New York broken toy
/ Place in your heart / Revenge is sweet /
Shot me down / Busted
CD _____ CLACD 187
Castle / Aug '90 / BMG.

FOOL CIRCLE, THE
Dressed to kill / Another year / Moonlight
eyes / Pop the silo / Let me be your leader
/ We are the people / Every young man's
dream / Little part of you / Cocaine (live) /
Victoria
CD _____ CLACD 214
Castle / Dec '90 / BMG.

FROM THE VAULTS
Friends / If you see my baby / Hard living /
Spinning top / Love hurts / Down / My white
bicycle / Holy roller / Railroad boy / You're
the violin / Good love / Greens / Desolation
road / Heart's grown cold (live) / Razamanaz (live) / Hair of the dog (live) / Talkin'
to one of the boys (live) / Morning dew /
Juicy Lucy / On the run
CD _____ NEMCD 639
Sequel / Mar '93 / BMG.

GREATEST HITS: NAZARETH
Razamanaz / Holy roller / shanghai'd in
Shanghai / Love hurts / Turn on your re-
ceiver / Bad bad boy / This flight tonight /
Broken down angel / Hair of the dog / Sun-
shine / My white bicycle / Woke up this
morning
CD _____ CLACD 149
Castle / Apr '89 / BMG.

GREATEST HITS: NAZARETH
CD _____ BRCD 1392
BR Music / Jun '94 / Target/BMG.

HAIR OF THE DOG
Hair of the dog / Miss Misery / Guilty /
Changing times / beggar's day / Rose in the
heather / Whisky drinkin' woman / Please
don't Judas me
CD _____ CLACD 241
Castle / '92 / BMG.

LOUD 'N' PROUD
Go down fighting / Not faking it / Turn on
your receiver / Teenage nervous breakdown
/ Free wheeler / This flight tonight / Child in
the sun / Ballad of Hollis Brown
CD _____ CLACD 174
Castle / Dec '89 / BMG.

MALICE IN WONDERLAND
Holiday / Showdown at the border / Talkin'
to one of the boys / Heart's grown cold /
Fast cars / Big boy / Talkin' 'bout love /
Fallen angel / Ship of dreams / Turning a
new leaf
CD _____ CLACD 181
Castle / Aug '90 / BMG.

NAZARETH
Witchdoctor woman / Dear John / Empty
arms, empty heart / I had a dream / Red
light lady / Fat man / Country girl / Morning
dew / King is dead
CD _____ CLACD 286
Castle / Jun '92 / BMG.

NAZARETH (BBC Live in Concert)
CD _____ WINCD 005
Windsong / Nov '91 / Pinnacle.

NAZARETH: THE EARLY YEARS
CD _____ EARLCD 2
Dojo / Mar '92 / BMG.

NO JIVE
CD _____ 36700102
Silenz / Jul '92 / BMG.

NO MEAN CITY
Claim to fame / Just to get into it / May the
sunshine / No mean city / Simple solution /
Star / Whatever you want babe / What's in
it for me
CD _____ CLACD 213
Castle / Dec '90 / BMG.

PLAY 'N' THE GAME
Somebody to roll / Down home girl / Flying
/ Waiting for the man / Born to love / I want
to do everything for you / I don't want to go
on without you / Wild honey / L.A. girls
CD _____ CLACD 219
Castle / Feb '91 / BMG.

RAMPANT
Silver dollar forger / Glad when you're gone
/ Loved and lost / Shanghai'd in Shanghai
/ Jet lag / Light my way / Sunshine / Shapes
of things / Space safari
CD _____ CLACD 242
Castle / Jun '92 / BMG.

RAZAMANAZ
Razamanaz / Alcatraz / Vigilante man /
Woke up this morning / Night woman / Bad
bad boy / Sold my soul / Too bad, too sad
/ Broken down angel
CD _____ CLACD 173
Castle / Dec '89 / BMG.

SINGLES COLLECTION, THE
Broken down angel / Bad bad boy / This
flight tonight / My white bicycle / Out of time
/ Shanghai'd in Shanghai / Love hurts / Hair
of the dog / Holy roller / Carry out feelings
/ You're the violin / Somebody to roll / I
don't want to go on without you / Gone
dead train / Place in your heart / May the
sunshine / Star / Dressed to kill / Morning
dew / Games / Love leads to madness
CD _____ CCSCD 280
Castle / Dec '90 / BMG.

SNAZ
Telegram / Razamanaz / I want to do every-
thing for you / This flight tonight / Beggar's
day / Every young man's dream / Heart's
grown cold / Java blues / Cocaine / Big boy
/ So you want to be a rock 'n' roll star /
Holiday / Let me be your leader / Dressed
to kill / Hair of the dog / Expect no mercy /
Shapes of things / Love hurts / Morning
dew / Juicy Lucy / On your way
CD _____ CLACD 130
Castle / Jul '87 / BMG.

SOUND ELIXIR
All nite radio / Milk and honey / Whipping
boy / Rain on the window / Back room boy
/ Why don't you read the book / I ran / Rags
to riches / Local still / Where are you now
CD _____ CLACD 218
Castle / Feb '91 / BMG.

Nazgul

TOTEM
Vampire / Jan '96 / Plastic Head.
CD _____ VAMP 7495CD

Nazia & Zoher

CAMERA
Timbuktu / Sep '92 / Pinnacle.
CD _____ TIMBCD 500

NCE Engine

GRAVITY WELL
Interfere Chrome / Nov '95 / Plastic Head.
CD _____ SH 1872203

Ndegeocello, Me'shell

PLANTATION LULLABIES
Plantation lullabies / I'm diggin' you (like an
old soul record) / If that's your boyfriend (he
wasn't last night) / Shoot'n up and gett'n
high / Dred loc / Untitled / Step into the
projects / Soul on ice / Call me / Outside
your door / Picture show / Sweet love / Two
lonely hearts (on the subway)
CD _____ 936245754-2
Maverick / Jul '94 / Warner Music.

Ndere Troupe

KIKWABANGA
Pan / Oct '93 / ADA / Direct / CM.
CD _____ PAN 2016CD

N'Dour, Youssou

BEST OF YOUSSOU N'DOUR
Set / Shakin' the tree / Sinebar / Medina /
Lion - Gaiende / Toxiques / Fenene / Mi-
yoko / Bamako / Fakastalu / Bes / Hey you
/ Macoy / Immigres bitim rew / Xale rewmi
/ Kocc barma
CD _____ CDV 2773
Virgin / Oct '94 / EMI.

EYES OPEN
New Africa / Live television / No more /
Country boy / Hope / Africa remembers /
Coupl's choice / Yo le le (Fulani groove) /
Survie / Am am / Marie-Madeleine La
Sainte-Louisiennee / Useless weapons /
Same / Things unspoken
CD _____ 4711862
Columbia / Jun '92 / Sony.

GUIDE (WOMMAT)
Leaving / Old man / Without a smile / Mame
bamba / Seven seconds / How are you /
Generations / Tourista / Undecided / Love
one another / Life / My people / Oh boy /
Silence / Chimes of freedom
CD _____ 476508 2
Columbia / Jun '94 / Sony.

**HEY YOU - THE BEST OF YOUSSOU
N'DOUR**
Music Club / Mar '92 / Disc / THE / CM.
CD _____ MCCD 134

LION, THE
Lion / Gaiende / Shakin' the tree / Kocc
barma / Bamako / Truth / Old tucson /
Macdy / My daughter (sama doom) / Bes
CD _____ CDV 2584
Virgin / Jun '89 / EMI.

SET
Set / Alboury / Sabar / Toxiques / Sinebar
/ Medina / Miyoko / Xale rewmi / Fenene /
Fakastalu / Hey you / Oneday / Ay chono
la
CD _____ CDV 2634
Virgin / Sep '90 / EMI.

Neal & Leandra

HEARTS AND HAMMERS
Red House / Jul '95 / Koch / ADA.
CD _____ RHR 62CD

Neal, Kenny

BAYOU BLOOD
Alligator / May '93 / Direct / ADA.
CD _____ ALCD 4809

BIG NEWS FROM BATON ROUGE
Alligator / Apr '93 / Direct / ADA.
CD _____ ALCD 4764

DEVIL CHILD
Alligator / May '93 / Direct / ADA.
CD _____ ALCD 4774

HOODOO MOON
Alligator / Nov '94 / Direct / ADA.
CD _____ ALCD 4825

WALKING ON FIRE
Look but don't touch / Truth hurts / I put
my trust in you / Blues stew / Morning after
/ I.O.U. / My only good thing / I been miss-
ing you too / Caught in the jaws of a vice /
Things to get better / Walking on fire / Bad
luck card
CD _____ ALCD 4795
Alligator / May '93 / Direct / ADA.

Neal, Raful

I BEEN MISTREATED
I been mistreated / Down in Louisiana /
Hard times / I miss you baby / Man watch
your woman / Spill it on me / Starlight dia-

mond / I have eyes for you / Little red
rooster / Still in love with you
CD _____ ICH 9004CD
Ichiban / Jul '91 / Koch.

LOUISIANA LEGEND
Alligator / May '93 / Direct / ADA.
CD _____ ALCD 4783

Neanders Jazzband

OH DIDN'T HE RAMBLE
Music Mecca / Nov '94 / Jazz Music /
Cadillac / Wellard.
CD _____ MECCACD 1027

Neary, Paddy

MUSICAL GEMS
Scotdisc / Oct '90 / Duncans / Ross /
Conifer.
CD _____ CDITV 512

Necromantia

CROSSING THE FIERY PATH
Osmose / Feb '94 / Plastic Head.
CD _____ OPCD 021

SCARLET EVIL WITCHING BLACK
Osmose / Nov '96 / Plastic Head.
CD _____ OPCD 036

Necronomicon

DEVILS TONGUE, THE
Laserlight / Aug '91 / Target/BMG.
CD _____ 15197

Necrony

NECRONYCISM
Poserslaughter / Jun '94 / Plastic Head.
CD _____ SPV 065-57722

Necrophobic

NOCTURNAL SILENCE
Black Mark / Aug '93 / Plastic Head.
CD _____ BMCD 40

Necrosanct

INCARNATE
Ritual acts / Inevitable demise / Undeath
dead dying / Abhorrence / Incarnate / Necronomicon / Exiternity / Restless dead / Solace / Ominous despair / Oblivion seed
CD _____ BMCD 021
Black Mark / Apr '92 / Plastic Head.

Necrosis

ACTA SANCTORUM
Black Mark / Jun '95 / Plastic Head.
CD _____ BMCD 045

Nectarine

STERLING BEAT
Grass / May '95 / SRD.
CD _____ GROW 0342

Nectarine No.9

GUITAR THIEVES
Strange Fruit / Mar '94 / Pinnacle.
CD _____ CDNT 004

SAINT JACK
Saint Jack / Curdled fragments / Fading
memory babe / Can't scratch out / This ar-
sehole's been burned too many time before
/ It's not my baby putting me at risk / I'm
trapped lightening / Just another fucked up
little druggy on the scene / Couldn't phone
potatoes / Dead horse arum / Firecrackers
/ Un-loaded for you / Clipped wings and
power stings / Tape your gead on
CD _____ DUBH 951CD
Postcard / Jun '95 / Vital.

SEA WITH THREE STARS, A
Pop's love thing / She's a nicer word to sing
/ Holes of corpus christi / Beautiful car /
Twenty two blue / Peanut brain / Smith's
new automatic / Sea with three stars / No,
you mean / Don't worry babe, you're not
the only one awake / Trace nine / Chocolate
swastika
CD _____ DUBH 931CD
Postcard / Feb '93 / Vital.

Ned's Atomic Dustbin

05.22
Saturday night / Scrawl / Aim / Bite / Face-
less / I've never been to me / Cut up (Tartan Shoulders mix) / Kill
your remix / Winey / Flexible head / Sen-
tence / Prostrate / Terminally groove / NAD
V. NDX equals Intact / Twenty three hour
toothache / Titch / Plug me in / That's nice
/ NAD V. NDX equals NSA / Perfectly
rounded / Forty five second blunder
CD _____ 477984 2
Furtive / Nov '94 / Sony.

BITE
Chapter 22 / Sep '91 / Vital.
CD _____ CHAPCD 058

BRAIN BLOOD VOLUME
All I ask of myself is that I hold together /
Floote / Premonition / Talk me down / Bore-

hole / Your only joke / Stuck to be right / I want it over / Traffic / Song eleven could take over
CD _____ 4783302
Furtive / Jul '95 / Sony.

GOD FODDER
Kill your television / Less than useful / Selfish / Grey cell green / Cut up throwing things / Capital letters / Happy / Your complex / Nothing like until you find out / You / What gives my son
CD _____ 4681122
Furtive / Apr '95 / Sony.

Neel, Johnny

COMIN' ATCHA LIVE
CD _____ BIGMO 10272
Big Mo / Aug '95 / Direct / ADA.

Neely, Don

DON NEELY AND HIS ROYAL SOCIETY JAZZ ORCHESTRA
Merry Makers / Feb '94 / Jazz Music.

DON'T BRING... (Neely, Don & His Royal Society Jazz Orchestra)
CD _____ SOSCD 1250
Stomp Off / May '93 / Jazz Music / Wellard.

ROLL UP (Neely, Don & His Royal Society Jazz Orchestra)
CD _____ CCD 147
Circle / Aug '95 / Jazz Music / Swift / Wellard.

Nefertiti

FROM 18TH DYNASTY
CD _____ FILERCD 421
Profile / Nov '91 / Pinnacle.

Negativland

ESCAPE FROM NOISE
CD _____ SST 133CD
SST / May '93 / Plastic Head.

FREE
CD _____ SEELAND 009
Seeland / Jun '93 / SRD.

GUNS
CD _____ SST 291 CD
SST / May '93 / Plastic Head.

HELTER STUPID
CD _____ SST 252 CD
SST / May '93 / Plastic Head.

HELTER STUPID, THE PERFECT CUT
CD _____ RECDEC 29
Rec Rec / Jul '93 / Plastic Head / SRD / Cadillac.

LETTER U & THE NUMBER 2, THE
CD _____ RECDEC 51
Rec Rec / Jul '93 / Plastic Head / SRD / Cadillac.

NEGATIVE CONCERT LAND
CD Set _____ CD 1806
ReR Megacorp / Jan '94 / These / ReR Megacorp.

Negazione

BEHIND THE DOOR
CD _____ 856101
We Bite / '90 / Plastic Head.

LITTLE DREAMER
CD _____ 851277
We Bite / '89 / Plastic Head.

LO SPIRITO CONTINUA
CD _____ TVOR 04CD
Plastic Head / Jan '92 / Plastic Head.

WILD BUNCH
CD _____ 846113
SPV / Aug '90 / Plastic Head.

Neglect

END IT
CD _____ WB 2113
We Bite / Oct '94 / Plastic Head.

Negra, Pata

BLUES DE FRONTORA
CD _____ HNCD 1309
Hannibal / May '89 / Vital / ADA.

Negro, Gato

BLACK CAT DUB
CD _____ RE 203CD
Reach Out International / Nov '94 / Jetstar.

VITAL FORCE DUB
CD _____ RUSCD 8210
Roir USA / Jul '95 / Plastic Head.

Negro, Joey

DISCO HOUSE (Mixed By Joey Negro) (Various Artists)
CD _____ JAPECD 105
Escapade / Jul '95 / 3MV / Sony.

Neil

NEIL'S HEAVY CONCEPT ALBUM
Hello vegetables / Hole in my shoe / Heavy potato encounter / My white bicycle / Neil the barbarian / Lentil nightmare / Computer alarm / Wayne / Gnome / Cosmic jam / Golf girl / Bad karma in UK / Our tune / Ken / End of the world cabaret / God save the Queen / Floating / Hurdy gurdy man / Paranoid mix / Amoeba song
CD _____ 450994852-2
WEA / Jan '94 / Warner Music.

Neil, Alan

STEPPING OUT NO 2
CD _____ DLD 1032
Dance & Listen / Mar '93 / Savoy.

STEPPING OUT, NO. 1
CD _____ DLD 1025
Dance & Listen / '92 / Savoy.

Neil, Fred

EVERYBODY'S TALKIN'
CD _____ CREV 021CD
Rev-Ola / Jan '94 / 3MV / Vital.

Neil, Vince

CARVED IN STONE
CD _____ 9362458772
Warner Bros. / Jul '95 / Warner Music.

EXPOSED
Look in her eyes / Sister of pain / Can't have your cake / Edge / Can't change me / Fine, fine wine / Living is a luxury / You're invited but your friend can't come / Gettin' hard / Forever
CD _____ 936245260-2
Warner Bros. / Apr '93 / Warner Music.

Neither Neither World

MADDENING
CD _____ DVLR 010CD
Dark Vinyl / Nov '95 / Vital.

Nekromantix

CURSE THE COFFIN
CD _____ NERCD 063
Nervous / '91 / Nervous / Magnum Music Group.

HELLBOUND
CD _____ TBCD 2001
Nervous / Mar '93 / Nervous / Magnum Music Group.

Nell, Bob

WHY I LIKE COFFEE
CD _____ 804192
New World / Sep '92 / Harmonia Mundi / ADA / Cadillac.

Nelson

BECAUSE THEY CAN
CD _____ GED 24525
Geffen / Jul '95 / BMG.

Nelson Brothers

HOMETOWN
CD _____ RTMCD 58
Round Tower / Jan '94 / Pinnacle / ADA / Direct / BMG / CM.

Nelson, Bill

BLUE MOONS AND LAUGHING GUITARS
Ancient guitars / Girl from another planet / Spinnin' around / Shaker / God man slain / Dead we wade with the upstairs drum / New moon rising / Glory days / Wishes / Angel in my system / Wings and everything / Boat to forever / Invisible man and the unforgettable girl / So it goes / Fires in the sky / Dream ships set sail
CD _____ CDVE 912
Venture / Aug '92 / EMI.

CRIMSWORTH
CD _____ RES 104CD
Resurgence / Feb '95 / Vital.

PRACTICALLY WIRED
Roses and rocketships / Spinning planet / Thousand fountain island / Piano 45 / Pink buddha blues / Kid with cowboy tie / Royal ghosts and great fires / Her presence in flowers / Big noise in Twanagton / Tiny little thing / Wild blues sky / Every moment infinite / Friends from heaven / Eternal for a-ton / Soapland
CD _____ ASCD 022
All Saints / Mar '95 / Vital / Discovery.

QUIT DREAMING/LOVE THAT WHIRLS/ CHIMERA/SAVAGE GESTURES (4CD Set)
Banal / Living in my limousine / Vertical games / Disposable / False alarms / Decline and fall / White sound / Life runs out like sand / Kind of loving / Do you dream in colour / U.H.F. / Youth of nation on fire / Quit dreaming and get on the beam / Real adventure / Acceleration / Everyday feels like another new drug / Tender is the night /

Glow world / Another day another ray of hope / Man in the rexine suit / Watching my dreamboat go down in flames / Meat room / Narcosis / Another happy thought (carved forever in your cortex) / Portrait of Jan with moon and stars / Empire of the senses / Hope for the heartbeat / Waiting for voices / Private view / Eros arriving / Bride of Christ in Autumn / Flesh / He and sleep were brothers / When your dream of perfect beauty comes true / Flaming desire / Portrait of Jan with flowers / Crystal escalator in the palace of God / Echo in her eyes / Department store / October man
CD Set _____ RES 111CD
Resurgence / Nov '95 / Vital.

Nelson, Oliver

AFRO AMERICAN SKETCHES (Nelson, Oliver Orchestra)
CD _____ OJCCD 1819
Original Jazz Classics / Nov '95 / Wellard / Jazz Music / Cadillac / Complete/Pinnacle.

BLUES AND THE ABSTRACT TRUTH
Stolen moments / Hoedown / Cascades / Yearnin' / Butch and butch / Teenie's blues
CD _____ MCAD 5659
Impulse Jazz / Nov '91 / BMG / New Note.

MEET OLIVER NELSON
CD _____ OJCCD 227
Original Jazz Classics / Nov '95 / Wellard / Jazz Music / Cadillac / Complete/Pinnacle.

SCREAMIN' THE BLUES
Screamin' the blues / March on, march on / Drive / Meetin' / Three seconds / Alto-itis
CD _____ OJCCD 080
Original Jazz Classics / Nov '95 / Wellard / Jazz Music / Cadillac / Complete/Pinnacle.

STRAIGHT AHEAD (Nelson, Oliver & Eric Dolphy)
CD _____ OJCCD 099
Original Jazz Classics / Nov '95 / Wellard / Jazz Music / Cadillac / Complete/Pinnacle.

Nelson, Ozzie

HEAD OVER HEELS IN LOVE
CD _____ HCD 259
Hindsight / Oct '95 / Target/BMG / Jazz Music.

OZZIE NELSON
CD _____ CCD 027
Circle / Oct '93 / Jazz Music / Swift / Wellard.

Nelson, Portia

LET ME LOVE YOU (The Songs Of Bart Howard)
Beautiful woman / On the first warm day / Thank you for the lovely summer / One love affair / Fly me to the moon (in other words) / Be my all / Let me love you / Never kiss / If you leave Paris / It was worth it / Year after year / Music for lovers
CD _____ DRGCD 91442
DRG / Dec '95 / New Note.

Nelson, Red

RED NELSON 1935-1947
CD _____ OTCD 6
Old Tramp / Jul '95 / Swift / Hot Shot.

Nelson, Rick

ALL MY BEST
Travellin' man / Hello Mary lou / Poor little fool / Stood up / You are the only one / It's late / You know what I mean / Young world / Lonesome town / I got a feeling / Just a little too much / Believe what you say / It's up to you / Waitin' in school / Never be anyone else but you / Don't leave me this way / Fools rush in / Teenage idol / I'm walkin' / Mighty good / Sweeter than you / Garden party
CD _____ CDMF 081
Magnum Force / Mar '92 / Magnum Music Group.

BEST OF RICKY NELSON, THE
CD _____ MATCD 328
Castle / Feb '95 / BMG.

COUNTRY MUSIC
CD _____ CD 336
Entertainers / Aug '94 / Target/BMG.

GARDEN PARTY
Let it bring you along / Garden party / So long Mama / I wanna be with you / Are you really real / I'm talking about you / Nightime lady / Flower opens gently by / Don't let your goodbye stand / Palace guard
CD _____ WMCD 5696
Disky / Oct '94 / THE / BMG / Discovery / Pinnacle.

GREATEST HITS
CD _____ MU 5019
Musketeer / Oct '92 / Koch.

IN CONCERT (From Chicago To LA)
Stood up / Waitin' in school / It's up to you / Travellin' man / Hello Mary Lou / Garden party / You know what I mean / That's alright mama / Believe what you say / Milk cow blues boogie / Never be anyone else but you / Fools rush in / It's up to you / Poor

little fool / It's late / Honky tonk woman / My bucket's got a hole in it / Boppin' the blues / Lonesome town
CD _____ CDMF 083
Magnum Force / Jan '92 / Magnum Music Group.

LIVE
CD _____ 15178
Laserlight / Aug '91 / Target/BMG.

LIVE AT THE ALADDIN
Garden party / Poor little fool / My buckets got a hole in it / Last time around / Milkcow blues / She belongs to me / Lonesome town / Travelling man / Hello Mary Lou / It's late / Merry Christmas baby / Mystery train
CD _____ CDMF 078
Magnum Force / Feb '91 / Magnum Music Group.

RICK NELSON & THE STONE BAND
CD _____ EDCD 417
Edsel / Mar '95 / Pinnacle / ADA.

ROCKIN' WITH RICK
Travellin' man / Hello Mary Lou / Poor little fool / Garden party / Young world / Don't leave me this way / I'm walkin' / Lonesome town / Just a little too much / You are the only one / Stood up / Waitin' in school / I got a feeling / You know what I mean / That's alright mama / Believe what you say / Milk cow blues / It's late / Boopin' the blues / Fools rush in
CD _____ CPCD 8004
Charly / Oct '93 / Charly / THE / Cadillac.

Nelson, Sandy

KING OF DRUMS (His Greatest Hits)
Teen beat / There were drums / In beat / Cool operator / Ooh poo pah doo / Freak beat / Big noise from the jungle / You name it / Blues theme / Let there be drums / Mr. John Lee (parts 1 and 2) / Swamp beat / Quite a beat / Drum stuff / Let there be drums and brass / Drums are my beat / Teen beat '65 / Gimme some skin / Drum stomp / Drums a go go / Drummin' up a storm / Soul drums / Live it up / Kitty's theme
CD _____ SEECD 423
See For Miles/C5 / Jul '95 / Pinnacle.

ROCK 'N' ROLL DRUM BEAT
Day train / Slippin' and slidin' / Willie and the hand jive / All night long / My girl Josephine / All shook up / Sandy / Alexis / Let's go / City / Linda Lu / Bullfrog / Bony Moronie / Tough beat / Yakety yak / La bamba bossa nova / Jivin' around / Don't be cruel (to a heart that's true) / Flip / Bebop baby / Live it up / Dumplin's / Wiggle wobble / Limbo rock / School day / In the mood / Charlie Brown / My wife can't cook / I'm gonna be a wheel someday / Let there be drums
CD _____ CDCHD 586
Ace / Oct '95 / Pinnacle / Cadillac / Complete/Pinnacle.

Nelson, Shara

FRIENDLY FIRE
Rough with the smooth / Movin' on / Poetry / I fell (so you could catch me) / Footprint / Between the lines / After you / Exit 1 / Friendly fire / Keeping out the cold / Segabeats
CD _____ CTCD 48
Cooltempo / Sep '95 / EMI.

WHAT SILENCE KNOWS
Nobody / Pain revisited / One goodbye is ten / Inside out / Chance / Uptight / Down that road / Thoughts of you / How close / What silence knows
CD _____ CTCD 35
Cooltempo / Sep '93 / EMI.

Nelson, Steve

COMMUNICATIONS (Nelson, Steve Quartet)
CD _____ CRISS 1034CD
Criss Cross / Nov '90 / Cadillac / Harmonia Mundi.

Nelson, Tracy

I FEEL SO GOOD
CD _____ ROUCD 3133
Rounder / Feb '95 / CM / Direct / ADA / Cadillac.

IN THE HERE & NOW
CD _____ ROUCD 3123
Rounder / Jun '93 / CM / Direct / ADA / Cadillac.

Nelson, Willie

20 OF THE BEST: WILLIE NELSON
Funny how time slips away / Night life / My own peculiar way / Hello walls / Mr. Record man / Hello walls / Make a long story short (she's gone) / Good times / She's still gone / Little things / Pretty paper / Bloody Mary morning / What can you do to me now / December days / Yesterday's wine / Me and Paul / Goodhearted woman / She's not for you / It should be easier now / Phases and stages / Circles, cycles and scenes
CD _____ ND 89137
RCA / Mar '91 / BMG.

ACROSS THE BORDERLINE
American tune / Getting over you / Most un-original sin / Don't give up / Heartland / Across the borderline / Graceland / Farther down the line / Valentine / What was it you wanted / I live the life I live, I live the life I love / If I were the man you wanted / She's not for you / Still is still moving to me
CD _____ 472942 2
Columbia / May '93 / Sony.

AUGUSTA (Nelson, Willie & Don Cherry)
CD _____ CDSD 080
Sundown / Oct '95 / Magnum Music Group.

CITY OF NEW ORLEANS
City of New Orleans / Just out of reach / Good time Charlie's got the blues / Why are you picking on me / She's out of my life / Cry / Please come to Boston / It turns me inside out / Wind beneath my wings / Until it's time for you to go
CD _____ 983309 2
Pickwick/Sony Collector's Choice / Oct '93 / Carlton Home Entertainment / Pinnacle / Sony.

CLASSIC AND UNRELEASED COLLECTION, A
CD _____ 8122714622
WEA / Jan '96 / Warner Music.

COLLECTION
CD _____ COL 026
Collection / Oct '95 / Target/BMG.

COLLECTION: WILLIE NELSON
On the road again / To all the girls I've loved before / Golden earrings / Always on my mind / City of New Orleans / Seven Spanish angels / Georgia on my mind / Highwayman / Over the rainbow / Let it be me
CD _____ 4609302
CBS / Mar '88 / Sony.

COMPLETE LIBERTY RECORDINGS 1962-1964
Roly poly / Lonely little mansion / Am I blue / Willingly / Second fiddle / Let me talk to you / Our chain of love / How long is forever / Things that might have been / Way you see me / There's gonna be love at my house tonight / You dream about me / You took my happy away / Is this my destiny / Hello walls / River boy / Darkness on the face of the Earth / Mr. Record man / I'll walk alone / Take me as I am (Or let me go) / There goes a man / Funny how time slips away / Country Willie / Crazy / Colour of the blues / Wake me when it's over / Right or wrong / Last letter / Night life / Part where I cry / Undo the right / Home Motel / Seasons of my heart / Opportunity to cry / Three days / Where my house lives / Columbus Stockade blues / Half a man / One step beyond / Take my word / Feed it memory / There'll be no teardrops tonight / Tomorrow night / I hope so / Touch me
CD Set _____ CDEM 1505
EMI / Aug '93 / EMI.

COUNTRY'S BEST (3CD Set/Love Songs/20 Years Of Hits/20 Foot-Tappin' Greats) (Nelson, Willie/Tammy Wynette/ Johnny Cash)
To all the girls I've loved before / Blue skies / Let it be me / Tenderly / harbour lights / Mona Lisa / To each his own / Over the rainbow / Seven Spanish angels / Georgia on my mind / Bridge over troubled water / Without a song / Unchained melody / That lucky old sun / In my mother's eyes / Always on my mind / Alive and well / Apartment no. 9 / Your good girl's gonna go bad / I don't wanna play house / D.I.V.O.R.C.E. / Singing my song / Run women run / We sure can love each other / Good lovin' / Bedtime story / Till I get it right / Kids say the darndest things / Another lovely song / We're gonna hold on / Woman to woman / Till I can make it on my own / Golden ring / You and me / One of a kind / Two story house / Folsom prison blues / I walk the line / Ring of fire / Forty shades of green / I still miss someone / There ain't no good chain gang / Busted / Twenty five minutes to go / Orange blossom special / It ain't me babe / Boy named Sue / San Quentin / Don't take your guns to town / One on the right is on the left / Jackson / Hey porter / Daddy sang bass / I got stripes / Thing called love
CD Set _____ 4775222
Epic / Oct '94 / Sony.

ESSENTIAL COLLECTION
CD Set _____ LECD 617
Wisepack / Apr '95 / THE / Conifer.

FACE OF A FIGHTER
CD _____ MU 5067
Musketeer / Oct '92 / Koch.

GREAT WILLIE NELSON, THE
CD _____ CDSR 016
Telstar / Jun '93 / BMG.

HEALING HANDS OF TIME
Funny how time slips away / Crazy / Night life / Healing hands of time / (How will I know) I'm falling in love again / All the things you are / Oh what is seemed to be / If I had my way / I'll be seeing you / There are worse things that being alone
CD _____ CDEMC 3695
EMI / Oct '94 / EMI.

HEARTACHES
CD _____ CDSGP 052
Prestige / Apr '93 / Total/BMG.

IN CONCERT
CD _____ CDCD 1261
Charly / Oct '95 / Charly / THE / Cadillac.

IS THERE SOMETHING ON YOUR MIND
Ghost / Let's pretend / I'm gonna lose a lot of teardrops / Wastin' time / Go away / No tomorrow in sight / New way to cry / Broken promises / I let my mind wander / December days / I can't find the time / I didn't sleep a wink / You wouldn't cross the street to say goodbye / Suffering in silence / I feel sorry for him / You'll always have someone / I just don't understand / Building heartaches / Pages / Is there something on your mind / Face of a fighter / I hope so / Everything but you / Moment isn't very long / Some other time / Shelter of my arms / Blame it on the times / End of an understanding / One step beyond
CD _____ CDGRF 032
Tring / Feb '93 / Tring / Prism.

JUST ONE LOVE
CD _____ TRACD 221
Transatlantic / Nov '95 / BMG / Pinnacle / ADA.

KING OF THE OUTLAWS
CD _____ CDCD 1088
Charly / Jun '93 / Charly / THE / Cadillac.

LEGEND BEGINS, THE
Some other time / I hope so / Will you remember mine / Is there something on your mind / Everything but you / Moment isn't very long / Blame it on the times / Face of a fighter / Shelter of my arms / End of understanding
CD _____ CDMF 086
Magnum Force / Nov '92 / Magnum Music Group.

MOONLIGHT BECOMES YOU
December days / Moonlight becomes you / Afraid / Heart of a clown / Please don't talk about me when I'm gone / Everywhere you go / Have I stayed away too long / Sentimental journey / World is waiting for the sunrise / You'll never know / I'll keep on loving you / You just can't play a sad song on a banjo / You always hurt the one you love / Someday (you'll want me to want you) / In God's eyes
CD _____ 475945 2
Columbia / Mar '94 / Sony.

NIGHTLIFE
CD _____ 15485
Laserlight / May '94 / Target/BMG.

OLD FRIENDS (Nelson, Willie & Waylon Jennings)
We had it all / Why do I have to choose / Blackjack county chains / Till I gain control again / Why baby why / Old friends / Take it to the limit / Would you lay with me (in a field of stone) / No love at all / Homeward bound
CD _____ PWKS 4041
Carlton Home Entertainment / Feb '91 / Carlton Home Entertainment.

OLD TIME RELIGION (Nelson, Willie & Bobby Nelson)
CD _____ 12114
Laserlight / May '93 / Target/BMG.

ONE STEP BEYOND
I let my mind wander / December days / I can't find the time / I didn't sleep a wink / You wouldn't cross the street to say goodbye / Suffering in silence / I feel sorry for him / You'll always have someone / I just don't understand / Pages / Amy old annis won't do / Slow down old world / Healing hands of time / And so will you my love / Things to remember / One step beyond / Undo the wrong / Home is where you're happy / Why are you picking on me / I hope so
CD _____ CDSGP 096
Prestige / Jun '94 / Total/BMG.

OUTLAW REUNION (Nelson, Willie & Waylon Jennings)
Crying / Ghost / Sally was a good old girl / Let's pretend / Abilene / I'm gonna lose a lot of teardrops / It's so easy / Wasting time / Love's gonna live here / Go away / Don't think twice, it's alright / No tomorrow in sight / Dream baby / New way to cry / Lorena / Broken promises / Burning memories / I let my mind wander / Big mamou / I can't find the time / Money / I feel sorry for him
CD _____ CDGRF 058
Tring / Jun '93 / Tring / Prism.

PEACE IN THE VALLEY (Nelson, Willie & Willie Nelson Jr.)
CD _____ PLMCD 052158
Promised Land / Nov '94 / Koch/Prism / Direct.

RED HEADED STRANGER
Time of the preacher / I couldn't believe it was true / Blue rock Montana / Blue eyes cryin' in the rain / Red headed stranger / Just as I am / Denver / O'er the waves / Down yonder / Can I sleep in your arms / Remember me when the candlelights are gleaming / Hands on the wheel / Bandera

CD _____ 902123-2
Carlton Home Entertainment / Jul '89 / Carlton Home Entertainment.

REVOLUTIONS OF TIME - THE JOURNEY 1975-1993 (3CD Set)
Time of the preacher / Blue eyes crying in the rain / If you've got the money I've got the time / Uncloudy day / Always late with your kisses / Georgia on my mind / Blue skies / Whiskey river / Stay a little longer / Mr. Record Man / Loving her was easier / Mammas don't let you babies grow up to be cowboys / It's not supposed to be that way / On the road again / Angel flying too close to the ground / Mona Lisa always on my mind / Last thing I needed the first thing this morning / Party's over / Summertime / Faded love / Pancho and lefty / Old friends / In the jailhouse again / Everything's beautiful (in it's own way) / Take it to the limit / To all the girls I loved before / How do you feel about foolin' around / Seven Spanish angels / Hello walls / I'm movin' on / Highwayman / Slow movin' outlaw / Are there any more real cowboys / They all went to Mexico / Half a man / Texas on a Saturday night / Heartland / Nobody slides my friend / Little old fashioned karma / Harbour lights / Without a song / Good time Charlie's got the blues / City of New Orleans / Who'll buy my memories / Write your own songs / Forgiving you was easy / Me and Paul / When I dream / My own peculiar way / Living in the promiseland / There is no easy way (but there is a way) / Buttermilk sky / Horse called music / Nothing I can do about it now / Is the better part over / Ain't necessarily so / Still is still moving to me
CD Set _____ C3K 64796
Columbia / Nov '05 / Sony.

SHOTGUN WILLIE
Shotgun Willie / Whiskey river / Sad songs and waltzes / Local memory / Slow down old world / Stay all night (stay a little longer) / Devil in a sleepin' bag / She's not for you / Bubbles in my beer / You look like the devil / So much to do / Song for you
CD _____ 756781426-2
WEA / Mar '93 / Warner Music.

SIX HOURS AT PEDERNALES
Nothings changed / Chase the moon / Are you sure / Party's over / We're not talking anymore / Turn me loose / Once your past the blues / It won't be easy / Stray cats, cowboys and girls of the night / Best worst thing / It should be easier now / My own peculiar way
CD _____ SORCD 0084
D-Sharp / Oct '94 / Pinnacle.

SONG FOR YOU, A
Song for you / Just as I am / For the good times / Amazing grace / Stormy weather / Blue eyes cryin' in the rain / Help me make it through the night / Thanks again / One for my baby / Loving her was easier (than anything I'll ever do again) / Moonlight in Vermont / That lucky old sun / Do right woman, do right man / Always on my mind / White shade of pale / Let it be me / Staring each other down / Bridge over troubled water / Old fords and a natural stone / Permanently lonely / Last thing I needed first thing this morning / Party's over
CD _____ PWKS 578
Carlton Home Entertainment / May '90 / Carlton Home Entertainment.

SOUND IN YOUR MIND
That lucky old sun / If you've got the money, I've got the time / Penny for your thoughts / Healing hands of time / Thanks again / I'll have to be crazy / Amazing grace / Sound in your mind / Funny how time slips away / Crazy / Night life
CD _____ 983260 2
Pickwick/Sony Collector's Choice / Aug '93 / Carlton Home Entertainment / Pinnacle / Sony.

SPOTLIGHT ON WILLIE NELSON
I just don't understand / I didn't sleep a wink / Blame it on the times / I let my mind wander / Shelter of my arms / And so will you my love / Home is where you're happy / I feel sorry for him / Slow down old world / Why are you picking on me / Any old arms won't do / Broken promises / I can't find the time / Things to remember / You always have someone / One step beyond
CD _____ HADCD 122
Javelin / Feb '94 / THE / Henry Hadaway Organisation.

STARDUST
Stardust / Georgia on my mind / Blue skies / All of me / Unchained melody / September song / On the sunny side of the street / Moonlight in Vermont / Don't get around much anymore / Someone to watch over me
CD _____ CK 57206
Columbia / Nov '95 / Sony.

THINGS TO REMEMBER
CD _____ CTS 55401
Country Stars / Jan '92 / Target/BMG.

VERY BEST OF WILLIE NELSON, THE
Country Willie / Night life / There'll be no teardrops tonight / Funny how time slips away / Hello walls / Crazy / Touch me / Wake me when it's over / Seasons of my heart / Columbus Stockade blues / San An-

tonio blues / Heartaches by the number / Wabash cannonball / Family bible / Good-hearted woman / Home in San Antone / Have I told you lately that I love you / Help me make it through the night / I love you because / Mr. Record man
CD _____ CDMFP 6110
Music For Pleasure / Dec '93 / EMI.

WILLIE NELSON
CD _____ 295047
Ariola / Oct '94 / BMG.

WILLIE NELSON COLLECTION, THE
Shelter of my arms / Face of a fighter / Things to remember / Moment isn't very long / Blame it on the times / Building heartaches / Undo the right / Will you remember mine / Any old arms won't do / Slow down old world / And so will you my love / Why are you picking on me / I hope so / Everything but you / Healing hands of time / No tomorrow in sight / One step beyond / Go away
K-Tel / Jan '95 / K-Tel. _____ ECD 3073

WILLIE NELSON SINGS KRISTOFFERSON
Me and Bobby McGee / Help me make it through the night / Pilgrim chapter 33 / Why me / For the good times / You show me yours (and I'll show you mine) / Loving her was easier (than anything I'll ever do again) / Sunday morning coming down / Please don't tell me how the story ends
CD _____ 9827262
Pickwick/Sony Collector's Choice / Apr '92 / Carlton Home Entertainment / Pinnacle / Sony.

WILLIE NELSON'S GREATEST HITS (And Some That Will Be)
Railroad lady / Heartaches of a fool / Blue eyes cryin' in the rain / Whiskey river / Good hearted woman / Georgia on my mind / If you've got the money, I've got the time / Look what thoughts will do / Uncloudy day / Mamas / Don't let your babies grow up to be cowboys / My heroes have always been cowboys / Help me make it through the night / Angel flying too close to the ground / I'd have to be crazy / Faded love / On the road again / Heartbreak hotel / (If you could touch her at all / Till I gain control again / Stay a little longer
CD _____ 4714122
Columbia / '92 / Sony.

Nembrionic Hammerdeath
NEMBRIONIC HAMMERDEATH/ CONSOLATION SPLIT ALBUM (Nembrionic Hammerdeath & Consolation)
CD _____ D 00027
Displeased / Mar '94 / Plastic Head.

Nemesis
MUNCHIES FOR YOUR BASS
CD _____ FILERCD 411
Profile / Jul '91 / Pinnacle.

PEOPLE WANT BASS
CD _____ FILECD 461
Profile / May '95 / Pinnacle.

TEMPLE OF BOOM
Temple of boom / Nemesis on the premises / Deep up on it / Cantfiguritout / Big, the bad, the bass / Get ya flow on / Str8jackin' / Hard from birth / Parkin' lot on Dixon / Go Ron C / Brand new / Till I / Bleed it
CD _____ FILECD 441
Profile / Jun '93 / Pinnacle.

Nemeth, Yoska
GYPSY KINGS (Nemeth, Yoska & Paul Toscano)
Les deus guitares / Je vous ai aimee / Cocher vite chez yar / Czardas / Le chant de l'alouette / Fascination / Le temps de cerises / Suite hongroise / Cocher, ralentis tes chevaux / Romance et czardas hongroises / Airs populaires roumains / Confidences de roses rouges / Joue jusqu'au matin / Beltz scha stil / Reviens / Souika hora / Petites clochettes monotones / L'ame des violons / Romance et danse caucasiennes
CD _____ 300062
Musidisc / Aug '90 / Vital / Harmonia Mundi / ADA / Cadillac. Discovery.

Neolithic
PERSONAL FRAGMENT
CD _____ CDAR 028
Adipocre / Jun '95 / Plastic Head.

Neon Judgement
ALASKA HIGHWAY
CD _____ BIAS 167 CD
Play It Again Sam / Jun '90 / Vital.

FIRST JUDGEMENTS
CD _____ CDBIAS 070
Play It Again Sam / Sep '87 / Vital.

Neptune Towers

CARAVANS TO EMPIRE ALGOL
CD _____ FOG 002
Panorama / Dec '94 / Plastic Head.

Neptune, John Kaizan

CIRCLE, THE
Circle / Soul of the deep / Tokyo pace / Ryukyu / India indigo / Mountain mist / Spring breeze / Spirit lift / North of noplace / Musashi
CD _____ C 387770
Denon / '88 / Conifer.

JAZZEN (Jazz + Zen)
Five directions / Waters edge / On a raft / Bamboo born / Can you feel the beat / Essence / Skip it / Todi / Foot notes / Zen forest
CD _____ CY 1570
Denon / '88 / Conifer.

TOKYOSPHERE
CD _____ JD 3316
JVC / May '89 / New Note.

Nerem, Bjarne

BJARNE NAREM & AL GREY
CD _____ GMCD 162
Gemini / Oct '88 / Cadillac.

EVERYTHING HAPPENS TO ME
CD _____ GMCD 71
Gemini / Jan '89 / Cadillac.

HOW LONG HAS THIS BEEN GOING ON
CD _____ GMCD 72
Gemini / Jan '90 / Cadillac.

MOOD INDIGO
CD _____ GMCD 159
Gemini / Jan '90 / Cadillac.

MORE THAN YOU KNOW
When your lover has gone / Everything I have is yours / Easy to love / Autumn nocturne / Miss Mopay / More than you know / Gone with the wind / Cabin in the sky / Emaline
CD _____ GMCD 156
Gemini / Jan '88 / Cadillac.

THIS IS ALWAYS
CD _____ GMCD 147
Gemini / Mar '89 / Cadillac.

Nergal

WIZARD OF NERATH, THE
CD _____ USR 016CD
Unisound / Jan '96 / Plastic Head.

Nerious Joseph

GUIDANCE
CD _____ FADCD 023
Fashion / Nov '92 / Jetstar / Grapevine.

Nerney, Declan

PART OF THE JOURNEY
Part of the journey / With this ring / In your arms / I really don't want to know / Anna from Fernangh / You in the morning / Lovely derry on the banks of the foyle / Honky tonk girl / Blue side of lonesome / Born to hang / Half as much / Cottage on the borderline / Tonight we just might fall in love again / Love me
CD _____ RCD 549
Ritz / Jul '95 / Pinnacle.

WALKIN' ON NEW GRASS
Walkin' on new grass / Among the Wicklow hills / I found my girl in the USA / Give an Irish girl to me / North to Alaska / Your call me lonesome from now on / Stand at your window / Crazy dreams / Tipperary on my mind / Never again will I knock on your door / I still miss someone / I'd rather love and lose you / World of our own / Molly Bawn
CD _____ RITZRCD 526
Ritz / Apr '93 / Pinnacle.

Nero Circus

HUMAN PIGS
CD _____ GOD 018CD
Godhead / Jul '95 / Plastic Head.

Nerve

CANCER OF CHOICE
Coins / Fragments / Oil / Rage / Closedown / Water / Seed / Dedalus / Trust / Waters / Thirties
CD _____ BIAS 261CD
Play It Again Sam / Oct '93 / Vital.

Nervous Fellas

BORN TO BE WILD
CD _____ NERCD 055
Nervous / '90 / Nervous / Magnum Music Group.

Nesmith, Michael

AND THE HITS JUST KEEP ON COMING (Nesmith, Michael & Countryside Band)
CD _____ AWCD 1027
Awareness / Nov '91 / ADA.

INFINITE RIDER
CD _____ AWCD 1031
Awareness / Mar '92 / ADA.

LOOSE SALUTE (Nesmith, Michael & The First National Band)
Silver moon / I fall to pieces / Thanx for the ride / Dedicated friend / Conversations / Tengo amore / Listen to the band / Bye bye bye / Lady of the valley / Hello lady
CD _____ AWCD 1024
Awareness / Mar '91 / ADA.

MAGNETIC SOUTH (Nesmith, Michael & The First National Band)
Calico girlfriend / Nine times blue / Little red rider / Crippled lion / Joanne / First national rag / Mama Nantucket / Keys to the car / Hollywood / One rose / Beyond the blue horizon
CD _____ AWCD 1023
Awareness / Mar '91 / ADA.

NEVADA FIGHTER (Nesmith, Michael & The First National Band)
Grand ennui / Propinquity (I've begun to care) / Here I am / Only bound / Nevada fighter / Texas morning / Tumbling tumbleweeds / I looked away / Rainmaker / Rene
CD _____ AWCD 1025
Awareness / Mar '91 / ADA.

NEWER STUFF, THE
CD _____ AWCD 1014
Awareness / Apr '89 / ADA.

OLDER STUFF, THE
CD _____ AWCD 1032
Awareness / Mar '92 / ADA.

TANTAMOUNT TO TREASON
Mama Rocker / Lazy lady / You are my one / In the afternoon / Highway 99 with Melange / Wax minute / Bonaparte's retreat / Talking to the wall / She thinks I still care
CD _____ AWCD 1026
Awareness / Sep '91 / ADA.

Nestico, Sammy

NIGHT FLIGHT (Nestico, Sammy Big Band)
CD _____ CDSB 103
Sea Breeze / Nov '88 / Jazz Music.

Neto, Jose

NETO
Sorriso do pablo / Release / Arrow / Maria Christina / Flower child / Zingaro / U-boot / Fish 'n' chips / House release / Reunion / Waiting for Zakir
CD _____ BW 037
B&W / Feb '94 / New Note.

Network

INTELLIGENT COMPILATION, AN
CD _____ K 7035CD
Studio K7 / May '95 / Disc.

Network 2

VARIOUS
CD _____ K 7040CD
Studio K7 / Jan '96 / Disc.

Netzer, Effi

HAVA NAGILA
CD _____ EUCD 1052
ARC / '89 / ARC Music / ADA.

Neumann, Roger

RATHER LARGE BAND
CD _____ CDSB 102
Sea Breeze / Nov '88 / Jazz Music.

Neural Network

KINESTHETICS
CD _____ BIOCD 06
Messerschmitt / Jun '94 / Plastic Head.

Neuro

ELECTRIC MOTHERS OF INVENTION
CD _____ 3BTTCD 2
3 Beat / Nov '93 / PolyGram.

Neuronium

ABSENCE OF REALITY
CD _____ TUXCD 5016
Tuxedo Moon / May '95 / Magnum Music Group.

CHROMIUM ECHOES
Prelude / Chromium echoes / Neutron age
CD _____ CDTB 057
Thunderbolt / Jul '89 / Magnum Music Group.

ELIXIR
CD _____ HCCD 001
Magnum Music / Feb '89 / Magnum Music Group.

FROM MADRID TO HEAVEN
Intro / Part 1 / Part 2 / Part 3 / Part 4
CD _____ CDTB 2.064
Thunderbolt / '89 / Magnum Music Group.

HERITAGE
CD _____ TUXCD 5009
Tuxedo Moon / May '95 / Magnum Music Group.

INVISIBLE VIEWS
CD _____ TUXCD 5017
Tuxedo Moon / May '95 / Magnum Music Group.

NEW DIGITAL DREAM
CD _____ TUXCD 5013
Tuxedo Moon / May '95 / Magnum Music Group.

NUMERICA
500 years / Deep illness of love / Promenade / Power of your smile / Numerica / Maze extreme limits / Au revoir
CD _____ CDTB 082
Thunderbolt / Apr '90 / Magnum Music Group.

OLIM
CD _____ TUXCD 5018
Tuxedo Moon / May '95 / Magnum Music Group.

SUPRANATURAL
When the goblins invade Madrid / Digitron / Priorite absolue / Europe is Europe / Sundown at Tanah Lot
CD _____ CDTB 055
Thunderbolt / Mar '88 / Magnum Music Group.

Neuropolitique

ARE YOU OR HAVE YOU EVER BEEN
CD _____ ELEC 22CD
New Electronica / '95 / Pinnacle / Plastic Head.

MENAGE A TROIS
CD _____ IRDMAT 004CD
Irdia / May '94 / Vital.

Neurosis

ENEMY OF THE SUN
CD _____ VIRUS 134CD
Alternative Tentacles / Oct '93 / Pinnacle.

PAIN OF MIND
CD _____ VIRUS 146CD
Alternative Tentacles / May '94 / Pinnacle.

Neutron 9000

LADY BURNING SKY
CD _____ RSNCD 233
Rising High / Sep '94 / Disc.

WALRUS
CD _____ FILERCD 407
Profile / May '91 / Pinnacle.

Nevada Beach

ZERO DAY
CD _____ CDZORRO 13
Metal Blade / Sep '90 / Pinnacle.

Never The Bride

NEVER THE BRIDE
CD _____ 7567827682
Atlantic / Sep '95 / Warner Music.

Nevermore

NEVERMORE
CD _____ CM 77091CD
Century Media / Apr '95 / Plastic Head.

Nevil, Robbie

C'EST LA VIE
Just a little closer / Dominoes / Limousines / Back to you / C'est la vie / Wot's it to ya / Walk your talk / Simple life / Neighbours / Look who's alone tonight
CD _____ NSPCD 513
Connoisseur / Apr '95 / Pinnacle.

Neville Brothers

BROTHERS KEEPER
Brother blood / Steer me right / Sons and daughters / Jah love / Witness / Sons and daughters (reprise) / Bird on the wine / Brother Jake / Fearless / Fallin' rain / River of life / My brother's keeper / Mystery train
CD _____ 395 3122
A&M / Aug '90 / PolyGram.

FAMILY GROOVE
Fly like an eagle / One more day / I can see it in your eyes / Day to day thing / Line of fire / Take me to heart / It takes more / Family groove / True love / On the other side of paradise / Let my people go / Saxafunk / Maori chant / Good song
CD _____ 3971802
A&M / Apr '92 / PolyGram.

FIYO ON THE BAYOU
Hey pocky away / Sweet honey dripper / Fire on the Bayou / Ten commandments / Sitting in limbo / Brother John / Iko iko / Mona lisa / Run Joe
CD _____ CDMID 187
A&M / Jan '94 / PolyGram.

Neville, Aaron

LEGACY (A History Of The Nevilles/2CD Set)
Mardi Gras mambo / Over you / Funky miracle / Little girl from the candy store / Show me the way / Sophisticated Cissy / I'm waiting at the station / My baby don't love me anymore / 6v6 LA / Ride your pony / Wrong number / Cardova / I need someone / How could I help but love you / Cissy strut / Humdinger / That rock'n'roll beat / Chicken strut / Don't cry / All these things / Britches / Even though (reality) / Get out of my life / Darling don't leave me this way / Live wire / House on the hill (rock 'n' roll hootenanny) / Tippi toes / Hook, line and sinker / For every boy there's a girl / Art / Same old thing / You won't do right / Everyday / Sweet little mama / Pains in my heart / Joog / Tell it like it is / Hercules / I'm gonna put some hurt on you / Make me strong / Look ka py py / Ease back / Bo Diddley / Speak to me / Cry me a river / Heartaches / Been so wrong / Message from the Meters / Going home
CD Set _____ CDNEV 1
Charly / Apr '90 / Charly / THE / Cadillac.

LIVE AT TIPITINA'S VOL.2
Wishin' / Rock 'n' roll medley / All over again / Everybody's got to wake up / Dance your blues away / Little Liza Jane / Wildflower / My girl / Riverside / Saib's groove / Pocky way / Doo wop medley / Rockin' pneumonia and the boogie woogie flu / Something you got / I know / Everybody loves a lover
CD _____ CLACD 347
Castle / Jun '94 / BMG.

LIVE ON PLANET EARTH
Shake your tambourine / Voodoo / Dealer / Junk man / Brother Jake / Sister Rosa / Yellow moon / Her African eyes / Sands of time / Congo Square / Love the one you're with / You can't always get what you want / Let my people go/Get up stand up / Amazing Grace / One love/People get ready/Sermon
CD _____ 5402252
A&M / Apr '95 / PolyGram.

NEVILLE-IZATION
Fever / Woman's gotta have it / Mojo Hannah / Tell it like it is / Why you wanna hurt my heart / Fear, hate, envy, jealousy / Caravan / Big chief / Africa
CD _____ FIENDCD 31
Demon / Nov '86 / Pinnacle / ADA.

TELL IT LIKE IT IS
Tell it like it is / Over you / That rock 'n' roll beat / For every boy there's a girl / I'm waiting at the station / House on the hill (rock 'n' roll hootenanny) / How many times / How could I help but love you / All these things / Cry me a river / Speak to me / Hook, line and sinker / Mardi Gras mambo / Cardova / Funky miracle / Ride your pony / Struttin' on Sunday / Make me strong / Heartaches / Show me the way / Wrong number / You won't do right / Get out of my life / Hercules
CD _____ MCCD 022
Music Club / May '91 / Disc / THE / CM.

UPTOWN
Whatever it takes / Forever...for tonight / You're the one / Money back guarantee (my love is guaranteed) / Drift away / Shek-a-na-na / Old habits die hard / I never need no one / Midnight key / Spirits of the world
CD _____ CDFA 3255
Fame / Apr '91 / EMI.

YELLOW MOON
My blood / Yellow moon / Fire and brimstone / Change is gonna come / Sister Rosa / With God on our side / Wake up / Voodoo / Ballad of Hollis Brown / Will the circle be unbroken / Healing chant / Wild injuns
CD _____ 3952402
A&M / Apr '95 / PolyGram.

Neville, Aaron

AARON NEVILLE'S SOULFUL CHRISTMAS
CD _____ 5401272
A&M / Nov '93 / PolyGram.

GRAND TOUR
CD _____ 5401002
A&M / Jan '94 / PolyGram.

HERCULES
Over you / Show me the way / How could I help but love you / Get out of my life / Wrong number / I'm waiting at the station / I found another love / How many times / Hey little Alice / Let's live / Tell it like it is / Struttin' on Sunday / Make me strong / Hercules / Been so wrong / Cry me a river / Greatest love / One fine day / All these things / Performance
CD _____ CPCD 8016
Charly / Feb '94 / Charly / THE / Cadillac.

MAKE ME STRONG
Struttin' on Sunday / Hercules / Make me strong / All these things / Baby I'm a want you / Performance / Mojo Hannah / Greatest love / One fine day / Tell it like it is / Cry me a river / Been so wrong / Speak to me / Wild flower / Feelings / Nadie / For the good times / She's on my mind
CD _____ CDCHARLY 64
Charly / Feb '87 / Charly / THE / Cadillac.

ORCHIDS IN THE STORM
CD _____ 8122709562
Rhino / May '95 / Warner Music.

SHOW ME THE WAY
How could I help but love you / Over you / Even though (reality) / Humdinger / Show me the way / I found another love / How many times / Everyday / Hey little Alice / Sweet little mama / Don't cry / Ticks of the clock / For every boy there's a girl / I'm waiting at the station / Wrong number / I've done it again / Let's live / Get out of my life
CD _____ CDCHARLY 162
Charly / Aug '89 / Charly / THE / Cadillac.

TATTOOED HEART
Can't stop my heart from loving you (The rain song) / Show some emotion / Everyday of my life / Down into muddy water / Some days are made for rain / Try (a little harder) / Beautiful night / My precious star / Why should I fall in love / Use me / For the good times / In your eyes / Little thing called life / Crying in the chapel
_____ 5403492
A&M / May '95 / PolyGram.

WARM YOUR HEART
Louisiana 1927 / Everybody plays the fool / It feels like rain / Somewhere, somebody / Don't go please stay / With you in mind / That's the ways she loves / Angola bound / Close your eyes / La vie dansante / Warm your heart / I bid you goodnight / Ave Maria / House on a hill
CD _____ 3971482
A&M / Jul '91 / PolyGram.

Neville, Art

HIS SPECIALTY RECORDINGS 1956-58
Please believe me / Standing on the highway / Please don't go / When my baby went away / Please listen to my song / Lover's song / Oooh-baby / Whiffenpoof song / Oooh-wee baby / Let's rock / Back home to me / Zing zing / Cha dooky-doo / That old time Rock 'N' Roll / Arabian love call / Rockin' pneumonia and the boogie woogie flu / What's going on / Belle amie / Dummy / I'm a fool to care
CD _____ CDCHD 434
Ace / Jan '93 / Pinnacle / Cadillac / Complete/Pinnacle.

KEYS TO THE CRESCENT (Neville, Art, Eddie Bo, Charles Brown & Willie Tee)
CD _____ CDROU 2087
Rounder / Sep '91 / CM / Direct / ADA / Cadillac.

MARDI GRAS ROCK 'N' ROLL
Zing zing / Oooh-wee baby / Bella Mae / I'm a fool to care / Cha dooky-doo / Back home to me / What's going on / Old time rock 'n' roll / Rockin' pneumonia and the boogie woogie flu / Bring it on home to me / Dummy / Let's rock / Arabian love call / Please listen to my song / Whiffenpoof song
CD _____ CDCHD 188
Ace / Oct '90 / Pinnacle / Cadillac / Complete/Pinnacle.

Neville, Charmaine

IT'S ABOUT TIME
Playing on the front porch / Rocket V / Barbecue Bess / Two to mars / Dance / Softly as in a morning sunrise / Staurday night fish fry / Don't stop the carnival / Right key but the wrong keyhole
CD _____ ME 000392
Soulciety/Bassism / Oct '95 / EWM.

New & Used

2ND
CD _____ KFWCD 163
Knitting Factory / Feb '95 / Grapevine.

NEW AND USED
CD _____ KFWCD 125
Knitting Factory / Nov '92 / Grapevine.

New Age Radio

SURVIVAL SHOW
CD _____ MANCD 1999
Kill City / Nov '95 / Pinnacle.

New Age Steppers

MASSIVE HITS VOL.1
CD _____ ONUCD 10
On-U Sound / May '94 / SRD / Jetstar.

New Atlantic

GLOBAL
CD _____ 3 BTTCD 3
3 Beat / Jul '95 / PolyGram.

New Bomb Turks

DESTROY OH BOY
CD _____ E 11560D
Crypt / Apr '93 / SRD.

INFORMATION HIGHWAY REVISITED
CD _____ EFACD 115852
Crypt / Oct '94 / SRD.

PISSING OUT THE POISON
CD _____ EFA 115982
Crypt / Oct '95 / SRD.

New Bushberry Mountain...

BUSHBERRY MOUNTAIN (New Bushberry Mountain Daredevils)
CD _____ MM 010CD
Mountain Music / Oct '94 / ADA.

New Celeste

CELTIC CONNECTION, THE
Music for a found harmonium / I once loved a lass / Wiggly jig / When a man's in love / Don't think about me / Celtic connection suite / Julie / Fare thee well sweet Mally
CD _____ LCOM 9036
Lismor / Oct '90 / Lismor / Direct / Duncans / ADA.

New Christs

DISTEMPER
CD _____ CGAS 810 CD
Citadel / Jun '89 / ADA.

New Departures Quintet

NEW DEPARTURES QUINTET, THE
CD _____ HHCD 1010
Hot House / Mar '95 / Cadillac / Wellard / Harmonia Mundi.

New Dylans

AMERICAN WAY, THE
CD _____ RHRCD 75
Red House / Jul '95 / Koch / ADA.

WARREN PIECE
CD _____ RHRCD 61
Red House / Oct '95 / Koch / ADA.

New England

YOU CAN'T KEEP LIVING THIS WAY
Suicide / Real live mind / Money / Nine / Communication breakdown / We R 4 U2 / No zone / War / Love
CD _____ STRCD 014
Street Link / Oct '92 / BMG.

New F.A.D.S.

LOVE IT ALL
These foolish things / Life is an accident / Left right / Every once in a while / Why waste your love / Monday it is / Saxophone / What I feel / PSV / Kill my instincts / Souvenir
CD _____ BIAS 285CD
Play It Again Sam / Jan '95 / Vital.

PIGEONHOLE
CD _____ BIAS 185CD
Play It Again Sam / Nov '90 / Vital.

New Grass Revival

WHEN THE STORM IS OVER
CD _____ FF 032CD
Flying Fish / Jul '92 / Roots / CM / Direct / ADA.

New Idol Son

REACH
CD _____ CDVEST 38
Bulletproof / Nov '94 / Pinnacle.

New Islanders

CARIBBEAN DREAMS
CD _____ CNCD 5956
Disky / Jul '93 / THE / BMG / Discovery / Pinnacle.

New Jazz Wizards

GOOD STUFF
CD _____ SOSCD 1244
Stomp Off / May '93 / Jazz Music / Wellard.

New Jersey Kings

PARTY TO THE BUS STOP
CD _____ JAZIDCD 033
Acid Jazz / Jul '92 / Pinnacle.

STRATOSPHERE BREAKDOWN
CD _____ JAZIDCD 123
Acid Jazz / Nov '95 / Pinnacle.

New Kingdom

HEAVY LOAD
Good times / Headhunter / Frontman / Mad mad world / Mama and Papa / Cheap thrills / Mars / Are you alive / Half seas over / Mother nature / Calico cats / Mighty maverick / Lazy smoke
CD _____ GEECD 13
Gee Street / Nov '93 / PolyGram.

New London Consort

MUSIC FROM THE TIME
CD _____ CKHD 007
Linn / Aug '92 / PolyGram.

New London School Of...

DEEPEST CUT (New London School Of Electronics)

CD Set _____ RSNCD 19
Rising High / Jul '94 / Disc.

New Lost City Ramblers

EARLY YEARS, 1958-62, THE
Colored aristocracy / Hopalong Peter / Don't let your deal go down / When first into this country / Sales tax on the women / Rabbit chase / Leaving home / How can a poor man stand such times and live / Franklyn D. Roosevelt's back again / I truly understand you love another man / Old fish song / Battleship of Maine / No depression in heaven / Dallas rag / Bill Morgan and his gal / Fly around my pretty little Miss / Lady from Carlisle / Brown's ferry blues / No long journey home / Talking hard luck / Teetotals / Sal got a meatskin / Railroad blues / On some foggy mountain top / My sweet farm girl / Crow black chicken
CD _____ SFCD 40036
Smithsonian Folkways / '91 / ADA / Direct / Koch / CM / Cadillac.

NEW LOST CITY RAMBLERS VOL.11 (1963-1973)
John Brown's dream / Riding on that train / Titanic / Don't get trouble in your mind / Cowboy waltz / Shut up in the mines of coal creek / Private John Q / Old Johnny Brooker won't do / I've always been a rambler / Automobile trip through Alabama / Who killed poor Robin / My wife died on Saturday night / Little satchel / Black bottom strut / Cat's got the measles / Dog's got the whooping cough / Dear Okie / Smoketown strut / Little girl and the dreadful snake / Fishing creek blues / 31 depression blues / Black Jack daisy / Victory rag / Little carpenter / On our turpentine farm / Parlez - nous a' boire / Valse du bamboucheur / Old Joe bone
CD _____ SFCD 440040
Smithsonian Folkways / '92 / ADA / Direct / Koch / CM / Cadillac.

OLD TIME MUSIC
CD _____ VCD 77018
Vanguard / Oct '95 / Complete/Pinnacle / Discovery.

OUT STANDING IN THE FIELD
CD _____ SF 40040CD
Smithsonian Folkways / Aug '93 / ADA / Direct / Koch / CM / Cadillac.

New Mind

FRACTURED
CD _____ MA 44-2
Machinery / Nov '93 / Plastic Head.

New Model Army

B SIDES AND ABANDONED TRACKS
Heroin (12" mix) / Adrenalin / Nosense / Trust / Brave new world (Gregovich mix) / R.I.P. / Brave new world II / Ten commandments / Courage / Lights go out (US remix) / Prison / Curse / Ghost of your father / Modern times / Drummy B / Marry the sea / Sleepwalking / Heroin (mix)
CD _____ CDEMC 3688
EMI / Sep '94 / EMI.

BBC LIVE IN CONCERT
CD _____ WINCD 051
Windsong / Nov '93 / Pinnacle.

GHOST OF CAIN, THE
Hunt / Lights go out / Fifty first State / All of this / Poison Street / Western dream / Love songs / Heroes / Ballad / Master race
CD _____ CDFA 3237
Fame / '94 / FMI.

HISTORY
No rest / Better than them / Brave new world / Fifty first state / Poison street / White coats / Stupid questions / Vagabonds / Green and grey / Get me out / Purity / Space / Far better thing (free 12" single only.) / Higher wall (Free 12" single only.) / Adrenalin (Free 12" single only.) / Lurstaap (Free 12" single only.)
CD _____ CDEMC 3622
EMI / Apr '92 / EMI.

IMPURITY
Get me out / Space / Innocence / Purity / Whirlwind / Marrakesh (Not on album.) / Lust for power / Bury the hatchet / Eleven years / Lurhstap / Before I get old / Vanity
CD _____ CDFA 3273
Fame / Oct '92 / EMI.

NO REST FOR THE WICKED
Frightened / Ambition / Grandmother's footsteps / Better than them / My country / No greater love / No rest / Young, gifted and skint / Drag it down / Shot 18 / Attack
CD _____ CDFA 3198
Fame / Jul '89 / EMI.

RAW MELODY MEN
Whirlwind / Charge / Space / Purity / White coats / Vagabonds / Get me out / Life / Better than them / Innocence / Love songs / lurhstap / Archway towers / Smalltown England / Green and grey / World
CD _____ CDFA 3296
Fame / May '93 / EMI.

THUNDER AND CONSOLATION
I love the world / Stupid questions / 225 / Inheritance / Green and grey / Ballad of

---

Bodmin Pill / Family life / Vagabonds / 125 mph / Archway towers / Charge (CD only.) / Chinese whispers (CD only.) / Nothing touches (CD only.) / White coats (CD only.)
CD _____ CDFA 3257
Fame / Aug '91 / EMI.

New Musik

FROM A TO B
Straight lines / Sanctuary / Map of you / Science / On islands / This world of water / Living by numbers / Dead fish (don't swim home) / Adventures / Safe side
CD _____ 477353-2
GT / Aug '94 / Sony.

New Noakes

THROUGH GREEN AND PLEASANT LANDS
Second season / First season / Through green and pleasant lands / Easter ballad / Fourth season / Pax latinus / Anti-clockwise / Autumn (A piece for Charlotte)
CD _____ 33JAZZ 004CD
33 Jazz / May '95 / Cadillac / New Note.

UP TO HERE
Creatures of comfort / Landscapes / Distant view / Et voila mon pote / Shine through / First light / Gazeley / Glowing embers / Mumbo Jumbo / May '95 / New Note.
CD _____ MJM 11184

New Order

BBC RADIO 1 LIVE IN CONCERT
CD _____ WINCD 011
Windsong / Feb '92 / Pinnacle.

BEST OF NEW ORDER, THE
True faith '94 / Bizarre love triangle / 1963 / Regret / Fine time / Perfect kiss / Shellshock / Thieves like us / Vanishing point / Run / Round and round / World (price of love) / Ruined in a day / Touched by the hand of God / Blue Monday '88 / World in motion
CD _____ 8285802
Factory / Aug '95 / PolyGram.

COMPLETE PEEL SESSIONS: NEW ORDER
Truth / Senses / I.C.B. / Dreams never end / Turn the heater on / We all stand / Toolate / 5-8-6
CD _____ SFRCD 110
Strange Fruit / Jul '90 / Pinnacle.

REST OF NEW ORDER, THE
World / Blue Monday / True faith / Confusion / Touched by the hand of God / Bizarre love triangle / Everythings gone green / Ruined in a day / Regret / Temptation / Age of consent
CD _____ 8286612
CD _____ 8286572
Factory / Aug '95 / PolyGram.

SUBSTANCE 1987 (2CD Set)
CD Set _____ 520008-2
Factory / Jul '93 / PolyGram.

New Orleans Blue...

NEW ORLEANS BLUE SERENADERS (New Orleans Blue Serenaders)
CD _____ BCD 221
GHB / Jan '93 / Jazz Music.

New Orleans Classic Jazz.

BLOWIN' OFF STEAM (New Orleans Classic Jazz Orchestra)
CD _____ SOSCD 1223
Stomp Off / Oct '92 / Jazz Music / Wellard.

New Orleans Ragtime...

CREOLE BELLES (New Orleans Ragtime Orchestra)
Creole belles / Black and white rag / Purple rose of Cairo / War cloud / Maple leaf rag / High society / Entertainer / Ragtime dance / New Orleans hop scop blues / My Maryland / Chrysanthemum / Panama / Wall Street rag / Love will find a way / Rubber plant rag / You can have it, I don't want it / Tickled to death / Junk man rag / Winin' boy blues / St. Louis tickle / Hindustan / Ethiopia / Red pepper / Pickles and peppers
CD _____ ARHCD 420
Arhoolie / Apr '95 / ADA / Direct / Cadillac.

New Orleans Rhythm Kings

NEW ORLEANS RHYTHM KINGS AND JELLY ROLL MORTON (New Orleans Rhythm Kings & Jelly Roll Morton)
Eccentric / Farewell blues / Discontented blues / Bugle call rag / Panama / Tiger rag / Livery stable blues / Oriental / Sweet lovin' man / That's a plenty / Shimmeshawabbie / Weary blues / That Da DA strain / Wolverine blues / Maple leaf rag / Tin roof blues / Sobbin' blues / Marguerite / Angry / Clarinet / Marmalade / Mr. Jelly Lord / London blues / Milenberg joys / Mad
CD _____ MCD 47020
Milestone / Jan '93 / Jazz Music / Pinnacle / Wellard / Cadillac.

NEW ORLEANS RHYTHM KINGS VOL. 1 - 1922-23
CD _____ KJ 109FS
King Jazz / Oct '93 / Jazz Music / Cadillac / Discovery.

NEW ORLEANS RHYTHM KINGS VOL. 2
CD _____ VILCD 0132
Village Jazz / Aug '92 / Target/BMG / Jazz Music.

NEW ORLEANS RHYTHM KINGS VOL. 2 - 1923-24 (New Orleans Rhythm Kings & Bix Beiderbecke)
CD _____ KJ 110FS
King Jazz / Oct '93 / Jazz Music / Cadillac / Discovery.

RARE RECORDINGS (The Golden Age of Jazz)
CD _____ JZCD 370
Suisa / Jun '92 / Jazz Music / THE.

New Orleans Saxophone...

NEW NEW ORLEANS MUSIC, VOL. 2 (New Orleans Saxophone Ensemble & Improvising Arts Quintet)
CD _____ CD 2066
Rounder / '88 / CM / Direct / ADA / Cadillac.

New Power Generation

EXODUS
CD _____ NPG 61032
New Power Generation / Mar '95 / Grapevine / THE.

New Rhythm & Blues...

GOD BLESS US ALL (New Rhythm & Blues Quintet)
CD _____ CD 3108
Rounder / '88 / CM / Direct / ADA / Cadillac.

GROOVES IN ORBIT (New Rhythm & Blues Quintet)
Smackaroo / When things was cheap / Rain at the drive-in / How can I make you love me / Girl like that / Twelve bar blues / I like that girl / My girlfriend's pretty / Get rhythm / Daddy-O / Hit the hay
CD _____ C5CD 589
See For Miles/C5 / Aug '92 / Pinnacle.

HONEST DOLLAR (New Rhythm & Blues Quintet)
CD _____ RCD 10240
Rykodisc / Jul '92 / Vital / ADA.

UNCOMMON DENOMINATORS (New Rhythm & Blues Quintet)
CD _____ CD 11506
Rounder / '88 / CM / Direct / ADA / Cadillac.

WILD WEEKEND (New Rhythm & Blues Quintet)
It's a wild weekend / Little floater / Fire works / Boy's life / If I don't have you / Boo-zoo / Tha's who / Poppin' circumstance / One and only / Immortal for a while / Fraction of action / This love is true / Like a locomotive
CD _____ VUSCD 12
Virgin / Feb '90 / EMI.

New Riders Of The Purple.

MARIN COUNTY LINE (New Riders Of The Purple Sage)
Till I met you / Llywelyn / Knights and queens / Green eyes a flashing / Oh what a night / Good woman likes to drink with the boys / Turkeys in a straw / Jasper / Echoes / Twenty good men / Little Miss Bad / Take a red
CD _____ MCAD 22107
One Way / Apr '94 / Direct / ADA.

NEW RIDERS OF THE PURPLE SAGE (New Riders Of The Purple Sage)
I don't know you / What'cha gonna do / Portland woman / Henry / Dirty business / Glendale train / Garden of Eden / All I ever wanted / Last lonely eagle / Louisiana lady
CD _____ MCAD 22108
One Way / Apr '94 / Direct / ADA.

WASTED TASTERS 1971-75 (New Riders Of The Purple Sage)
CD _____ RVCD 36
Raven / May '94 / Direct / ADA.

WHO ARE THOSE GUYS (New Riders Of The Purple Sage)
CD _____ MCAD 22109
One Way / Apr '94 / Direct / ADA.

New Seekers

COLLECTION
CD _____ COL 037
Collection / Mar '95 / Target/BMG.

GREATEST HITS: NEW SEEKERS
I'd like to teach the world to sing / Come softly to me / You won't find another fool like me / Morning has broken / What have they done to my song Ma / Circles / I get a little sentimental over you / Your song / Beg, steal or borrow / Nevertheless (I'm in love with you) / Day by day / Georgy girl / Just an old fashioned love song / Goodbye is just another word / Pinball wizard / See

me, feel me / Goin' back / Never ending song of love
CD _____ 845 398-2
Polydor / May '91 / PolyGram.

PERFECT HARMONY
I'd like to teach the world to sing / Beg, steal or borrow / Never ending song of love / Blowin' in the wind / Here, there and everywhere / Circles / Medley: Pinball wizard/See me feel me / You won't find another fool like me / Gentle on my mind / I get a little sentimental over you / Come softly to me / Your song / Unwithered rose / Sing hallelujah
CD _____ 5500842
Spectrum/Karussell / Oct '93 / PolyGram / THE.

New Shtetl Band

JEWISH & BALKAN MUSIC
CD _____ GVM 121CD
Global Village / Jul '95 / ADA / Direct.

New Tradition

AR CAHAINS AR CEDL
CD _____ CDLOC 1090
Lochshore / Jun '95 / ADA / Direct / Duncans.

New Wet Kojak

NEW WET KOJAK
CD _____ TG 144CD
Touch & Go / Oct '95 / SRD.

New Winds

DIGGING IT HARDER FROM AFAR
CD _____ VICTOCD 028
Victo / Nov '94 / These / ReR Megacorp / Cadillac.

New World

CHANGING TIMES
CD _____ RTN 41208
Rock The Nation / Feb '95 / Plastic Head.

New York Band

GRANDES EXITOS
Si tu no estas / Maria / Y tu no estas / Ay Mama / El cibaeno / Dame Vida / Chim pun callao / Corazon de azucar / Que no me adivina / Mambo mix / Que beuno bvaila usted / Ponte el sombrero / Muevelo / El lloron / Pelotero / El caravine / Jala jala / Dancing mood / Nadie como tu
CD _____ 66058069
RMM / Sep '95 / New Note.

New York City

BEST OF NEW YORK CITY
Hang your head in shame / Make me twice the man / Sanity / Set the record straight / Quick, fast, in a hurry / Uncle James / Ain't it so / I'm doing fine now / Reach out / Happiness is / Only you / Darling take me back / Can't survive without my sweets / Got to get you back in my life / Do you remember yesterday / I've had enough / Take my hand / Can't go on without you / Love is what you make it
CD _____ NEMCD 701
Sequel / Nov '94 / BMG.

New York Composers...

FIRST PROGRAM IN STANDARD TIME (New York Composers Orchestra)
CD _____ 804182
New World / Sep '92 / Harmonia Mundi / ADA / Cadillac.

MUSIC BY EHRLICH, HOLCOMB, HOROVITZ & WIESELMAN (New York Composers Orchestra)
CD _____ NW 397
New World / Aug '92 / Harmonia Mundi / ADA / Cadillac.

New York Dolls

AFTER THE STORM (New York Dolls & The Original Pistols)
CD _____ RRCD 102
Receiver / Jul '93 / Grapevine.

LIPSTICK KILLERS
Bad girl / Looking for a kiss / Don't start me talkin' / Don't mess with cupid / Human being / Personality crisis / Pills / Jet boy / Frankenstein
CD _____ RE 104CD
Reach Out International / Nov '94 / Jetstar.

NEW YORK DOLLS, THE
Babylon / Bad detective / Bad girl / Chatterbox / Don't start me talkin' / Frankenstein / Human being / It's too late / Jet boy / Lonely planet boy / Looking for a kiss / Personality crisis / Pills / Private world / Puss 'n' boots / Showdown / Stranded in the jungle / Subway train / Trash / Vietnamese baby / Who are the mystery girls
CD _____ 522129-2
Mercury / Oct '94 / PolyGram.

RED PATENT LEATHER
Girls / Downtown / Pirate love / Personality crisis / Pills / Something else / Daddy rollin' stone / Dizzy Miss Lizzy
CD _____ 422253
New Rose / May '94 / Direct / ADA.

SEVEN DAY WEEKEND
Seven day weekend / Frankenstein / Mystery girls / Showdown / Back in the U.S.A / Endless party / Jet boy / It's too late / Bad detective / Lonely planet boy / Subway train / Private world / Trash / Human being / Don't start me talkin' / Hoochie coochie man / Great big kiss / Vietnamese baby / Babylon
CD _____ RRCD 163
Receiver / Jul '93 / Grapevine.

TOO MUCH TOO SOON
CD _____ 8342302
Mercury / Jan '94 / PolyGram.

New York Saxophone...

NEW YORK SAXOPHONE QUARTET (New York Saxophone Quartet)
Three improvisations / Chant d'amour / Chantefleur / Bach's fireworks music / Three jays and a bee / OT / La blues
CD _____ STCD 15
Stash / Aug '89 / Jazz Music / CM / Cadillac / Direct / ADA.

New York School

NEW YORK SCHOOL, THE
CD _____ ARTCD 6101
Hat Art / Sep '92 / Harmonia Mundi / ADA / Cadillac.

New York Swing

PLAYS JEROME KERN
Song is you / I dream too much / Why do I love you / Smoke gets in your eyes / Can't help lovin' dat man / Sure thing / Pick yourself up / Bill / Yesterdays / Why was I born / I'm old fashioned / All the things you are / Remind me / Nobody else but me
CD _____ CDC 9082
LRC / Apr '95 / New Note / Harmonia Mundi.

New York Unit

TRIBUTE TO THE GREAT TENORS
St. Thomas / Softly as in a morning sunrise / Shadow of your smile / Fee-fi-fo-fum / Dear old Stockholm / Child is born / Impressions / My one and only love
CD _____ KICJ 68
King/Paddle Wheel / Feb '92 / New Note.

Newbeats

BEST OF THE NEWBEATS
Bread and butter / Everything's alright / Break away (from that boy) / (The bees are for the birds) The birds are for the bees / Poison pen / Little child / Patent on love / Run baby run / Shake hands (and come out crying) / Short on love / Evil Ena / Don't turn me loose / Top secret / Swinger / Hide the moon / Michelle de ann / Girls and the boys / I'm a teardrop / Love gets sweeter / In the middle of the night / With tears in my eyes / It's happening again / Stickin' up for my baby / His girl / Laura / Way you do the things you do / Does your body need lovin
CD _____ NEXCD 231
Sequel / Oct '92 / BMG.

Newborn, Phineas Jr.

SOLO
Stompin' at the Savoy / Easy living / How high the moon / Breeze and I / Nature boy / Days of wine and roses / Confirmation / Might as well be Spring / Love me or leave me / Temptation
CD _____ CDLR 45020
L&R / Feb '91 / New Note.

WHILE MY LADY SLEEPS
While my lady sleeps / It's easy to remember / Bali Ha'i / If I should lose you / Moonlight in Vermont / Don't you know I care (or don't you care to) / Lazy mood / I'm old fashioned / Black is the colour of my true love's hair / What's new / No moon at all / Back home / I'll remember April
CD _____ 74321101552
Bluebird / Jul '92 / BMG.

WORLD OF PIANO, A
CD _____ OJCCD 175
Original Jazz Classics / Nov '95 / Wellard / Jazz Music / Cadillac / Complete/Pinnacle.

Newcomer, Carrie

ANGEL AT MY SHOULDER, AN
CD _____ PH 1163CD
Philo / Apr '94 / Direct / CM / ADA.

BIRD OR THE WING, THE
CD _____ CDPH 1183
Philo / May '95 / Direct / CM / ADA.

VISIONS AND DREAMS
CD _____ CDPH 1193
Philo / Nov '95 / Direct / CM / ADA.

Newman, Colin

A - Z
I've waited for ages / And jury / Alone / Order for order / Image / Life on deck / Troisieme / S-S-S Star eyes / Seconds to last / Inventory / But no / B
CD _____ BBL 20 CD
Lowdown/Beggars Banquet / Sep '88 / Warner Music / Disc.

COMMERCIAL SUICIDE
CD _____ CRAM 045 CD
Crammed Discs / Oct '86 / Grapevine / New Note.

IT SEEMS
CD _____ CRAM 058CD
Crammed Discs / May '88 / Grapevine / New Note.

PROVISIONALLY ENTITLED THE SINGING FISH/NOT TO
CD _____ CAD 108/201CD
4AD / Apr '88 / Disc.

Newman, David

BLUE HEAD (Newman, David 'Fathead')
CD _____ CCD 79041
Candid / Oct '90 / Cadillac / Jazz Music / Wellard / Koch.

MR. GENTLE, MR COOL
Don't get around much anymore / Prelude to a kiss / Mr. Gentle and Mr.Cool / Almost cried / I let a song go out of my heart / Azure / What am I here for / Happy reunion / Come Sunday / Creole love call / Jeep's blues
CD _____ KOKO 1300
Kokopelli / Oct '94 / New Note.

RETURN TO THE WIDE (Newman, David 'Fathead')
Buster's tune / Hard times / Thirteenth floor / Thing's ain't what they used to be / Two foolish things / Two bones and a pick / City lights / Lush life / Night in Tunisia
CD _____ CDMT 023
Magnum Music / Mar '93 / Magnum Music Group.

STILL HARD TIMES (Newman, David 'Fathead')
Shana / One for my baby / To love again / Still hard times / Please send me someone to love
CD _____ MCD 5283
Muse / Sep '92 / New Note / CM.

Newman, Denny

NOAH'S GREAT RAINBOW
CD _____ NM 002
New Blue / Jul '95 / Hot Shot.

Newman, Jackie

COMPLETE RECORDED WORKS
CD _____ DOCD 5351
Blues Document / Jun '95 / Swift / Jazz Music / Hot Shot.

Newman, Jimmy C.

BOP A HULA/DIGGY LIGGY LO (2Cd Set)
You didn't have to go / Cry cry darlin' / Can I be right / Your true and faithful one / What will I do / I'll always love you darlin' / Once again / Let me stay in your arms / Night time is cry time / Diggy liggy lo / You don't want me to know / Do you feel like I feel about you / Daydreaming / Dream why do you hurt me so / Crying for a pastime / Angel wave mercy / Blue darlin' / Let me stay in your arms (2) / I thought I'd never fall in love again / God was so good / Let's stay together / What will I do (unissued) / I've got you on my mind / Seasons of my heart / Come back to me / I wanta tell all the world / Yesterday's dreams / Let the whole world talk / Honky tonk tears / Last night / No use to cry / Way you're living is breaking my heart / What a fool I was to fall for you / Fallen star / I can't go on this way / Need me (unissued) / Sweet kind of love / Need me / Cry cry darlin' #2 / You're the idol of my dreams / Step aside shallow water / Bop a hula / Carry on / With tears in my eyes
CD Set _____ BCD 15469
Bear Family / Sep '90 / Rollercoaster / Direct / CM / Swift / ADA.

CAJUN COUNTRY CLASSICS
Alligator man / Thibodeaux and his cajun band / Jambalaya / Jolie blon / Boo-dan / Diggy liggy lo / Big mamou / Louisiana Saturday night / Cajun man can / Big Bayou / Colinda / Basile Waltz / Daydreaming / Lache pas la Patate / Happy Cajun / Sugar bee
CD _____ CDCD 1068
Charly / Mar '93 / Charly / THE / Cadillac.

Newman, Joe

AT THE ATLANTIC
Summertime / Air mail special / I can't get started (with you) / When you're smiling / Caravan / Liza / Stardust
CD _____ NCD 8810
Phontastic / '93 / Wellard / Jazz Music / Cadillac.

GOOD 'N' GROOVY (Newman, Joe Quintet)
CD _____ OJCCD 185
Original Jazz Classics / Nov '95 / Wellard / Jazz Music / Cadillac / Complete/Pinnacle.

GRAND NIGHT FOR SWINGING, A
CD _____ NI 4012
Natasha / Jan '93 / Jazz Music / ADA / CM / Direct / Cadillac.

HANGIN' OUT (Newman, Joe & Joe Wilder)
Midgets / Here's that rainy day / Duet / Battle hymn of the Republic / Secret love / You've changed / Lypso mania / He was too good to me
CD _____ CCD 4262
Concord Jazz / Feb '92 / New Note.

I FEEL LIKE A NEWMAN
CD _____ BLCD 760905
Black Lion / Jun '88 / Jazz Music / Cadillac / Wellard / Koch.

Newman, Randy

BEST OF RANDY NEWMAN (Lonely at the top)
Love story / Living without you / I think it's going to rain today / Mama told me not to come / Sail away / Simon Smith and the amazing dancing bear / Political science / God's song (that's why I love mankind) / Rednecks / Birmingham / Louisiana 1927 / Marie / Baltimore / Jolly coppers of parade / Rider in the rain / Short people / I love L.A. / Lonely at the top / My life is good (Extra track on cassette and C.D.) / In Germany before the war (Extra track on cassette and C.D.) / Christmas in Capetown (Extra track on cassette and C.D.) / My old Kentucky home (Extra track on cassette and C.D.)
CD _____ 241126 2
WEA / Jun '87 / Warner Music.

BORN AGAIN
It's the money that I love / Story of a rock and roll band / Pretty boy / Mr. Sheep / Ghosts / They just got married / Girls in my life / Half a man / William Brown / Pants
CD _____ 7599259172
WEA / Jul '94 / Warner Music.

FAUST
CD _____ 9362456722
Warner Bros. / Sep '95 / Warner Music.

GOOD OLE BOYS
Rednecks / Marie / Guilty / Every man a king / Naked man / Back on my feet again / Birmingham / Mr. President (have a pity on the working man) / Louisiana 1927 / Kingfish / Wedding in Cherokee county / Rollin'
CD _____ 9272142
WEA / Sep '89 / Warner Music.

LITTLE CRIMINALS
Baltimore / I'll be home / In Germany before the war / Jolly coppers on parade / Kathleen / Old man on the farm / Rider in the rain / Short people / Sigmund Freud's impersonation of Albert Einstein In America / Texas girl at the funeral of her father / You can't fool the fat man
CD _____ K 256404
WEA / Jan '88 / Warner Music.

LIVE
CD _____ 7599267062
WEA / May '95 / Warner Music.

RANDY NEWMAN
CD _____ 7599267052
WEA / May '95 / Warner Music.

SAIL AWAY
Sail away / It's lonely at the top / He gives us all his love / Last night I had a dream / Simon Smith and the amazing dancing bear / Old man / Burn on big river / Memo to my son / Dayton, Ohio, 1903 / You can leave your hat on / God's song (that's why I love mankind) / Political science
CD _____ 9272032
WEA / Sep '89 / Warner Music.

TWELVE SONGS
Have you seen my baby / Let's burn down the cornfield / Mama told me not to come / Suzanne / Lover's prayer / Lucinda / Underneath the Harlem moon / Yellow man / Old Kentucky home / Rosemary / If you need oil / Uncle Bob's midnight blues
CD _____ 9274492
WEA / '89 / Warner Music.

Newman, Tom

ASPECTS
CD _____ NAGE 7CD
Art Of Landscape / '86 / Sony.

BAYOU MOON
CD _____ NAGE 2CD
Art Of Landscape / Feb '86 / Sony.

LIVE AT THE ARGONAUT
CD _____ VP 168CD
Voice Print / Feb '95 / Voice Print.

Newport Jazz Festival...

BERN CONCERT '89 (Newport Jazz Festival All Stars)

I want to be happy / Jeep's blues / Just a gigolo (CD only.) / I'm just a lucky so and so / Johnny come lately / Blue and sentimental / In a sentimental mood (CD only.) / Jumpin' at the woodside
CD _____ CCD 4401
Concord Jazz / Jan '90 / New Note.

EUROPEAN TOUR (Newport Jazz Festival All Stars)
Tickle toe / Mood indigo / Love me or leave me / These foolish things / Take the 'A' train / Things ain't what they used to be / Through for the night
CD _____ CCD 4343
Concord Jazz / May '88 / New Note.

Newport Rebels

JAZZ ARTISTS GUILD
Mysterious blues / Cliff walk / Wrap your troubles in dreams (and dream your troubles away) / T'ain't nobody's business if I do / Me and you
CD _____ CCD 79022
Candid / Jul '91 / Cadillac / Jazz Music / Wellard / Koch.

News From Babel

WORK RESUMED ON THE TOWER/ LETTERS HOME
CD _____ RERNFBCD
Recommended / '90 / These / ReR Megacorp.

Newsome, Sam

SAM I AM (Newsome, Sam Quintet)
Criss Cross / May '92 / Cadillac / Harmonia Mundi. _____ CHISS 1056CD

Newton, Anney

NEW HORIZONS (Newton, Anney & The Relics)
CD _____ REL 001CD
Relic / Jul '95 / ADA.

Newton, David

EYE WITNESS
Ol' blues eyes / Bedroom eyes / Angel eyes / Eye witness / Soul eyes / Stars in my eyes / Eye of the hurricane / My mother's eyes
CD _____ AKD 015
Linn / Nov '91 / PolyGram.

IN GOOD COMPANY (Newton, David Trio)
CD _____ CCD 79714
Candid / Nov '95 / Cadillac / Jazz Music / Wellard / Koch.

RETURN JOURNEY
CD _____ AKD 025
Linn / Apr '94 / PolyGram.

Newton, Frankie

EMPEROR JONES
CD _____ 3801092
Jazz Archives / Feb '93 / Jazz Music / Discovery / Cadillac.

Newton, James

ECHO CANYON
CD _____ CDCEL 012
Celestial Harmonies / May '87 / ADA / Select.

IN VENICE
CD Set _____ CDCEL 030/31
Celestial Harmonies / Sep '88 / ADA / Select.

ROMANCE AND REVOLUTION
Forever Charles / Meditation for integration / Peace / Evening leans towards you / Tenderly
CD _____ BNZ 70
Blue Note / Sep '87 / EMI.

SUITE FOR FRIDA KAHLO
Verdict / Price of everything / Elliptical / Frida / Broken column / Las dos Fidas / Love embrace of the universe
CD _____ AQCD 1023
Audioquest / Jul '95 / New Note.

Newton, Wayne

BEST OF WAYNE NEWTON LIVE
CD _____ CHELD 1006
Start / May '89 / Koch.

Newton-John, Olivia

BACK TO BASICS (The Essential Collection 1971-1992)
If not for you / Banks of the Ohio / What is life / Take me home country roads / I honestly love you / Have you never been mellow / Sam / You're the one that I want / Hopelessly devoted to you / Summer nights / Little more love / Xanadu / Magic / Suddenly / Physical / Rumour / Not gonna be the one / I need love / I want to be wanted / Deeper than a river
CD _____ 5126412
Mercury / Jul '92 / PolyGram.

EMI COUNTRY MASTERS (2CD Set)
Love song / Banks of the Ohio / Me and Bobby McGee / If not for you / Help me make it through the night / If you could read my mind / In a station / Where are you going to my love / Lullaby / No regrets / If I gotta leave / Would you follow me / If / It's so hard to say goodbye / Winterwood / What is life / Changes / Everything I own / I'm a small and lonely light / Just a little too much / Living in harmony / Why don't you write me / Angel of the morning / Mary Skeffington / If we only have love / My old man's got a gun / Maybe then I'll think of you / Amoureuse / Take me home country roads / I love you, I honestly love you / Music makes my day / Heartbreaker / Leaving / You ain't got the right / Feeling best / Rose water / Being on the losing end / If we try / Let me be there / Country girl / Loving you ain't easy / Have love will travel / Hands across the sea / Please Mr. please / Air that I breathe / Loving arms / If you love me (Let me know) / Have you never been mellow
CD Set _____ CDEM 1503
EMI / Aug '93 / EMI.

GAIA (One Woman's Journey)
CD _____ DSHCD 7017
D-Sharp / Feb '95 / Pinnacle.

RUMOUR, THE
Rumour / Can't we talk it over in bed / Get out / Walk through the fire / Love and let live / It's not heaven / Big and strong / Tutta la vita
CD _____ 834957-2
Mercury / Oct '88 / PolyGram.

Newtown Neurotics

45 REVOLUTIONS PER MINUTE
CD _____ FREUDCD 31
Jungle / Feb '94 / Disc.

Nganasan

SHAMANIC SONGS OF SIBERIAN ARCTIC
CD _____ 925642
Buda / Jun '93 / Discovery / ADA.

Ni Bheaglaoich, Eilín

MILE DATH/A CLOAK OF MANY COLOURS
Clo Iar-Chonnachta / Jan '92 / CM. _____ CIC 079CD

Ni Bheaglaoich,...

UNDER THE SUN (Ni Bheaglaoich, Seosaimhin)
Gael Linn / Dec '95 / Roots / CM / Direct / ADA. _____ CEFCD 170

Ní Bhrolcháin, Deirbhile

SMAOINTE
CD _____ CEFCD 147
Gael Linn / Jan '94 / Roots / CM / Direct / ADA.

Ni Chathasaigh, Máire

CAROLAN ALBUMS: THE MUSIC OF TURLOUGH O'CAROLAN (Ni Chathasaigh, Máire & Chris Newman)
Carolan's draught / John O'Connor / Colonel John Irwin (Planxty Irwin) / Hewlwtt / Maire Dhall / Lord Inchiquin / Morgan Magan / Si beag si mor / Princess Royal / John Drury (Planxty Drury) / Fanny Power / Carolan's concerto / Maurice O'Connor / Carolan's concerto / Robert Jordan / Bridget Cruise / Frank Palmer / Grace Nugent / George Brabazon / Kean O'Hara / Madam Judge / Eleanor Plunkett / Baptist Johnston
CD _____ OBMCD 06
Old Bridge / Apr '94 / ADA.

LIVE IN THE HIGHLANDS (Ni Chathasaigh, Máire & Chris Newman)
Turkey in the straw / Gander in the pratie hole/Donnybrook boy/Queen of the rushes / Thugamar fein an Samhradh linn (We brought the Summer in) / Unknown title/ Wellington's reel / Eleanor Plunkett / Acrobat/Bonnie banchory/Millbrae / Roisin dubh / Humours of Ballyloughin / A shaighdiuirin a chroi (Dear soldier of my heart)/Blackbird / Salt creek / Tairnse im' Chodladh / Sore point / Stroll on
CD _____ OBMCD 08
Old Bridge / Jul '94 / ADA.

LIVING WOOD, THE (Ni Chathasaigh, Máire & Chris Newman)
Caitlin ni aeotha/The sport of the chase / Lady Dillon / Fiddler's dream/Whiskey before breakfast / Fare thee well lovely Mary / Walsh's hornpipe/The peacock's feather / Flax in bloom/Lough Allen/McAuliffe's / Beating around the bush / An paistin fionn/ La valse d'Hasperren / Charlie Hunter's/ Peggy's leg/Fogarty's jig / Cuach mo londubh bui/The Virginia / Mairead's mazurka / McQuillan's/Sonny Brogan's / Moynihan's polkas
CD _____ OBMCD 07
Old Bridge / '95 / ADA.

OUT OF COURT (Ni Chathasaigh, Máire & Chris Newman)
Out of court / Harper's chair / Cherry blossom / Will you meet me tonight on the shore / Frieze breeches / Lady Gethin / Sore point / Graf spee / Tuirne mhaire / Eclipse/Hurricane / Old bridge / Wild geese / Lakes of Champlain / Stroll on
CD _____ OBMCD 03
Old Bridge / '91 / ADA.

Ni Dhomhnaill, Caitlin

SEAL MO CHUARTA
CD _____ CIC 070CD
Clo Iar-Chonnachta / Nov '93 / CM.

Ni Dhomhnaill, Maighréad

NO DOWRY
CD _____ CEFCD 152
Gael Linn / Jan '94 / Roots / CM / Direct / ADA.

Ní Dhomhnaill, Tríona

TRÍONA
CD _____ CEFCD 043
Gael Linn / Jan '92 / Roots / CM / Direct / ADA.

Ni Mhaonaigh, Mairéad

CEOL ADUAIDH (Ni Mhaonaigh, Mairéad & Frankie Kennedy)
CD _____ CEFCD 102
Gael Linn / Jan '94 / Roots / CM / Direct / ADA.

Ní Riain, Nóirín

CAOINEADH NA MAIGHDINE
CD _____ CEFCD 084
Gael Linn / Jan '94 / Roots / CM / Direct / ADA.

STOR AMHRAN
CD _____ OSS 7CD
Ossian / Mar '95 / ADA / Direct / CM.

VOX DE NUBE
CD _____ CEFCD 144
Gael Linn / Jan '94 / Roots / CM / Direct / ADA.

Niadem's Ghost

IN SHELTERED WINDS
CD _____ GEPCD 1003
Giant Electric Pea / Aug '94 / Pinnacle.

Nice

AMERICA
CD _____ CD 12334
Laserlight / Apr '94 / Target/BMG.

ARS LONGA VITA BREVIS
Daddy, where did I come from / Little Arabella / Happy Freuds / Intermezzo from Karelia suite / Don Edito el Gruva / Ars longa vita brevis (Awakening/Realisation/3rd movement/Denial/Extension to the big note)
CD _____ CLACD 120
Castle / '86 / BMG.

BEST OF THE NICE - AMERICA, THE
CD _____ CSL 6032
Immediate / Nov '93 / Charly / Target/ BMG.

COLLECTION: NICE
America / Happy Freuds / Cry of Eugene / Thoughts of Emerlist Davjak / Rondo / Daddy, where do I come from / Little Arabella / Intermezzo from Karelia Suite / Hang on to a dream / Diamond hard blue apples of the moon / Angel of death / Ars longa vita brevis
CD _____ CCSCD 106
Castle / Jan '93 / BMG.

ELEGY
Third movement / America / Hang on to a dream / My back pages
CD _____ CASCD 1030
Charisma / Feb '91 / EMI.

FIVE BRIDGES SUITE
Fantasia (1st bridge, 2nd bridge) / Chorale (3rd bridge) / High level fugue (4th bridge) / Finale / Intermezzo from Karelia suite / Pathetique (symphony no.6 3rd movement) / Country pie/Brandenburg concerto No. 6 / One of those people
CD _____ CASCD 1014
Charisma / Feb '91 / EMI.

IMMEDIATE YEARS, THE (3CD Set)
Flower kings of flies (Mixes) / Thoughts of Emmerlist Davjack (Mixes) / Bonnie K / Rondo / War and peace / Tantalising Maggie (Mixes) / Dawn (Mixes) / Cry of Eugene / America (Mixes) / Diamond hard blue apples of the moon / Daddy / Where did I come from / Azrael (Mixes) / America 2nd ammendment / Little Arabella / Happy freuds / Intermezzo / Brandenburger (Demo) / Don Edito El Gruva / First movement / Third movement (acceptance brandenburger) / Fourth movement (denial) / Coda / Extension to the big note / Azrael revisited / Hang on to a dream / Diary of an empty day / For example / Rondo (69) / She belongs to me / First movement (awakening) / Second movement (realization)

CD Set _____ **CDIMMBOX 2**
Charly / Aug '95 / Charly / THE / Cadillac.

THOUGHTS OF EMERLIST DAVJACK
Flower kings of flies / Thoughts of Emerlist Davjack / Bonnie K / Rondo / War and peace / Tantalising Maggie / Dawn / Cry of Eugene
CD _____ **CDIMM 010**
Charly / Feb '94 / Charly / THE / Cadillac.

Nice & Easy

NICE AND EASY
CD _____ **TCD 2815**
Telstar / Jan '96 / BMG.

Nice & Smooth

AIN'T A DAMN THING CHANGED
CD _____ **5234782**
Def Jam / Jan '96 / PolyGram.

JEWEL OF THE NILE
Return of the hip hop freaks / Sky's the limit / Let's all get down / Doin' our own thang / Do whatcha gotta / Old to the new / Blunts / Get fucked up / Save the children / Cheri
CD _____ **5233362**
Island / Nov '94 / PolyGram.

Nicholas, John

THRILL ON THE HILL
CD _____ **ANTCD 0032**
Antones / Dec '94 / Hot Shot / Direct / ADA.

Nicholas, Martin

STRICT TEMPO WURLITZER
CD _____ **OS 207**
Valentine / Jul '94 / Conifer.

Nicholas, Paul

COLOURS OF MY LIFE, THE
Sandy / Singin' in the rain / Colours of my life / Greased lightning / Hair / Let the sunshine in / Just good friends / Mr. Mistoffelees / My favourite occupation / High flying adored / All I ask of you / Close every door / Music of the night / Gethsemane / Could we start again please
CD _____ **CASTCD 43**
First Night / Aug '94 / Pinnacle.

THAT'S ENTERTAINMENT
Reggae like it used to be / Shufflin' shoes / Dancing with the captain / Sway / Sunday / If you were the only girl in the world / Grandma's party / Heaven on the 7th floor / Flat foot floyd / Doing it / Only for a minute / When you walk in the room / Mr. Mistoffelees / Old deuteronomy
CD _____ **5500132**
Spectrum/Karussell / May '93 / PolyGram / THE.

Nicholls, Billy

UNDER ONE BANNER
CD _____ **EXPCD 3**
Expression / Nov '90 / Pinnacle.

Nicholls, Gillie

SPIRIT TALK
CD _____ **SPINCD 152**
Spindrift / Jul '94 / CM / Roots.

Nichols, Keith

SYNCOPATED JAMBOREE
CD _____ **SOSCD 1234**
Stomp Off / Oct '92 / Jazz Music / Wellard.

Nichols, Red

1929 RECORDINGS (Nichols, Red & Jack Teagarden)
Dinah / On the Alamo / Somebody to love me / Get happy / Smiles / They didn't believe / Rose of Washington Square / That da da strain / Sally won't you come back / New Yorkers
CD _____ **TAXCD S 5-2**
Tax / Apr '91 / Jazz Music / Wellard / Cadillac.

FIVE PENNIES, THE
CD _____ **CD 56071**
Jazz Roots / Mar '95 / Target/BMG.

RED NICHOLS - ORIGINAL RECORDINGS 1929
CD _____ **TAXS 52**
Tax / '91 / Jazz Music / Wellard / Cadillac.

RED NICHOLS 1936/WILL OSBORNE 1934 (Nichols, Red & Will Osborne)
CD _____ **CCD 110**
Circle / Apr '94 / Jazz Music / Swift / Wellard.

RED NICHOLS AND MIFF MOLE (Nichols, Red & Miff Mole)
CD _____ **VILCD 0152**
Village Jazz / Aug '92 / Target/BMG / Jazz Music.

RHYTHM OF THE DAY (Nichols, Red & His Five Pennies)
Rhythm of the day / Buddy's habit / Boneyard shuffle / Alexander's ragtime band /

Alabama stomp / Hurricane / Cornfed / Mean dog blues / Riverboat shuffle / Eccentric / Feeling no pain / Original Dixieland one-step / Honolulu blues / There'll come a time / Harlem twist / Alice blue gown / Corine Corina / Oh Peter, you're so nice / Waiting for the evening mail / Sweet Sue, just you
CD _____ **CD AJA 5025**
Living Era / Feb '87 / Koch.

Nicholson, Gimmer

CHRISTOPHER IDYLLS
CD _____ **CD 9204**
Lucky Seven / Dec '94 / Direct / CM / ADA.

Nicks, Stevie

BELLA DONNA
Belladonna / Kind of woman / Stop draggin' my heart around / Think about it / After the glitter fades / Edge of seventeen / How still my love / Leather and lace / Highwayman / Outside the rain
CD _____ **CZ 398**
EMI / Mar '91 / EMI.

OTHER SIDE OF THE MIRROR
Rooms on fire / Long way to go / Two kinds of love / Oh my love / Ghosts / Whole lotta trouble / Fire burning / Cry wolf / Alice / Juliet / Doing the best I can (Escape from Berlin) / I still miss someone
CD _____ **CDEMD 1016**
EMI / Feb '94 / EMI.

STREET ANGEL
Blue denim / Greta / Street angel / Docklands / Listen to the rain / Destiny / Unconditional love / Love is like a river / Rose garden / Maybe love / Just like a woman / Kick it / Jane
CD _____ **CDEMC 3671**
EMI / May '94 / EMI.

TIMESPACE - THE BEST OF STEVIE NICKS
Sometimes it's a bitch / Stop draggin' my heart around / Whole lotta trouble / Talk to me / Stand back / Beauty and the beast / If anyone falls / Rooms on fire / Love's a hard game to play / Edge of seventeen / Leather and lace / I can't wait / Has anyone ever written anything for you / Desert angel
CD _____ **CDEMD 1024**
EMI / Aug '91 / EMI.

Nico

CAMERA OBSCURA
Camera obscura / Tanaore / Win a few / My funny valentine / Das lied von einsamen madchens / Fearfully in danger / My heart is empty / Into the arena / Konig
CD _____ **BEG 63CD**
Beggars Banquet / Nov '88 / Warner Music / Disc.

CHELSEA GIRL
Fairest of the seasons / These days / Little sister / Winter song / It was a pleasure then / Chelsea girl / I'll keep it with mine / Somewhere there's a feather / Wrap your troubles in dreams (and dream your troubles away) / Eulogy to Lenny Bruce
CD _____ **835209-2**
Polydor / Apr '94 / PolyGram.

CHELSEA GIRL LIVE
CD _____ **CLEO 6108-2**
Cleopatra / May '94 / Disc.

DESERTSHORE
CD _____ **7599258702**
WEA / Apr '91 / Warner Music.

DO OR DIE
CD _____ **RE 117CD**
Reach Out International / Nov '94 / Jetstar.

END, THE
It has not taken long / Secret side / You forgot to answer / Innocent and vain / Valley of the kings / We've got the gold / End / Das lied der Deutschen
CD _____ **IMCD 174**
Island / Mar '94 / PolyGram.

HEROINE
My heart is empty / Procession / All tomorrow's parties / Valley of the kings / Sphinx / We've got the gold / Mutterlein / Afraid / Innocent and vain / Frozen warnings / Fearfully in danger / Tananore / Femme fatale
CD _____ **CDMGRAM 85**
Anagram / Aug '94 / Pinnacle.

LIVE IN TOKYO
My heart is empty / Purple lips / Tananore / Janitor of lunacy / You forget to answer / 60-40 / My funny valentine / Sad lied von einsannen madchens / All tomorrow's parties / Femme fatale / End
CD _____ **DOJOCD 115**
Dojo / May '95 / BMG.

MARBLE INDEX
Prelude / Lawns of dawns / No one is there / Ari's song / Facing the wind / Julius Caesar (memento hodie) / Frozen warnings / Evening of light / Roses in the snow / Nibelungen
CD _____ **7559610982**
WEA / Apr '91 / Warner Music.

Nicol, Ken

LIVING IN A SPANISH TOWN
CD _____ **EP 0074CD**
Ess'ntial Productions / Jun '94 / ADA.

Nicol, Simon

BEFORE YOUR TIME
Over the Lancashire hills / Caught a whisper / Deserter / Insult to injury / From a distance / Live not where I love / Before your time / Merry Sherwood rangers / Rosemary's sister
CD _____ **TRUCKCD 017**
Terrapin Truckin' / Aug '94 / Total/BMG / Direct / ADA.

Nicolette

NOW IS EARLY
CD _____ **SUADCD 1**
Shut Up & Dance / Apr '92 / SRD.

Nicols, Nichelle

OUT OF THIS WORLD
CD _____ **GNPD 2209**
GNP Crescendo / May '92 / Silva Screen.

Niebla, Eduardo

POEMA (Niebla, Eduardo & Antonio Forcione)
CD _____ **CDJP 1035**
Jazz Point / Sep '93 / Harmonia Mundi / Cadillac.

Niehaus, Lennie

PATTERNS
CD _____ **FSCD 100**
Fresh Sound / Oct '90 / Jazz Music / Discovery.

Niekku

NIEKKU
CD _____ **OMCD 11**
Olarin Musiiki Oy / Dec '93 / ADA / Direct.

Nielson Chapman, Beth

YOU HOLD THE KEY
I don't know / You hold the key / Dance with me slow / Say it to me now / When I feel this way / Rage on rage / Only so many tears / In the time it takes / You say you will / Moment you were mine / Faithful heart / Dancer to the drum
CD _____ **9362452334-2**
Reprise / Sep '93 / Warner Music.

Niemack, Judy

BLUE BOP
CD _____ **FRLCD 009**
Freelance / Oct '92 / Harmonia Mundi / Cadillac / Koch.

HEARTS DESIRE (Niemack, Judy & Kenny Barron)
CD _____ **STCD 548**
Stash / '92 / Jazz Music / CM / Cadillac / Direct / ADA.

LONG AS YOU'RE LIVING
CD _____ **FRLCD 014**
Freelance / Oct '92 / Harmonia Mundi / Cadillac / Koch.

MINGUS, MONK & MAL (Niemack, Judy & Mal Waldron)
CD _____ **FRLCD 021**
Freelance / May '95 / Harmonia Mundi / Cadillac / Koch.

STRAIGHT UP
CD _____ **FRLCD 0018**
Freelance / Apr '93 / Harmonia Mundi / Cadillac / Koch.

Nieve, Steve

KEYBOARD JUNGLE ....PLUS
Ethnic hooligan / Hooligans and hula girls / Al Green / Spanish guitar / Man with a musical lighter / Outline of a hairdo / End of side one / Liquid looks / Thought of being Dad / Pink flamingoes on coffee pot boulevard / Mystery and majesty (of a banyan tree) / Couch potato rag / Page one of a dead girl's diary / End of an era / Pictures from a confiscated camera / Once upon a time in South America / Sword fight / Ghost town / Walk in Monet's back garden / Shadows of Paris / Loveboat / El rey de sol / 9/4 Rag / hands of Oriac / Birdcage walk / Divided heart
CD _____ **DIAB 814**
Diabolo / May '95 / Pinnacle.

Nieves, Tito

ROMPECABEZA THE PUZZLE
Amores como tu / Vuelveme a querer / Desde que lo tengo a ti / You bring me joy / Manias / Lo prometido es deuda / Con you stop the rain / Lo que son las cosa / Mi vida de ayer / Que no fracase este amor / Voy a arrancarte de mi / Mi corazon esta ocupado
CD _____ **66058027**
RMM / Nov '93 / New Note.

UN TIPO COMUN

No me queda mas / Un tipo comun / Te lo pido por favor / Imperdonable / Voy a hacerte feliz / Que me hiciste tu / No me vuelvo a enamorar / Mi primer amor
CD _____ **66058081**
RMM / Nov '95 / New Note.

Night Trains

CHECKMATE
Blow out / Takin' a stroll / Release the chain / Miles away / Take the cash / Hang on to that cove / On your toes / Hot and cool / Bongo breakdown / In the crowd / Checkmate / Street chase
CD _____ **CDBGP 1033**
BGP / Feb '91 / Pinnacle.

LOADED
CD _____ **JAZIDCD 018**
Acid Jazz / Jun '92 / Pinnacle.

SLEAZEBALL
Sure can't go to the moon / Hold on for the truth / Lonely road / On my own / Love is the teacher / Move on out together / What good is love / Smoky's clown / International way / Lovesick / Sleazeball
CD _____ **JAZIDCD 098**
Acid Jazz / Apr '94 / Pinnacle.

Nightblooms

24 DAYS AT CATASTROPHE CAFE
CD _____ **FIRECD 34**
Fire / Sep '93 / Disc.

NIGHTBLOOMS
CD _____ **FRIGHT 58CD**
Fierce / Mar '92 / Disc.

Nightcrawlers

LET'S PUSH IT
Push the feeling on / Surrender your love / Don't let the feeling go / Should never (fall in love) / Just like before / Lift me up / World turns / Let's push it / I like it / All over the world
CD _____ **74321309702**
Arista / Sep '95 / BMG.

Nightfall

ATHENIAN ECHOES
CD _____ **HOLY 014CD**
Holy / Oct '95 / Plastic Head.

EONS AURA
CD _____ **HOLY 09CD**
Holy / Mar '95 / Plastic Head.

MACABRE SUNSETS
CD _____ **HOLY 04CD**
Holy / Jun '94 / Plastic Head.

PARADE INTO CENTURIES
CD _____ **HOLY 01CD**
Holy / Feb '95 / Plastic Head.

Nighthawk, Robert

BLACK ANGEL BLUES
Down the line / Handsome lover / My sweet lovin' woman / Sweet black angel / Anna Lee blues / Return mail blues / Sugar papa / She knows how to love a man / Good news / Six three O / Prison bound / Jackson town gal / Sorry my angel / Someday
CD _____ **CDRED 29**
Charly / Sep '91 / Charly / THE / Cadillac.

MASTERS OF MODERN BLUES SERIES (Nighthawk, Robert & Houston Stackhouse)
CD _____ **TCD 5010**
Testament / Dec '94 / Complete/Pinnacle / ADA / Koch.

RARE CHICAGO BLUES RECORDINGS (From the Collection of Norman Dayron) (Nighthawk, Robert & His Flames Of Rhythm)
CD _____ **CDROU 2022**
Rounder / Sep '91 / CM / Direct / ADA / Cadillac.

Nighthawks

BACKTRACK
CD _____ **CDVR 036**
Varrick / '88 / Roots / CM / Direct / ADA.

HARD LIVING
CD _____ **CDVR 022**
Varrick / '88 / Roots / CM / Direct / ADA.

LIVE IN EUROPE
CD _____ **CCD 11014**
Crosscut / Nov '88 / ADA / CM / Direct.

ROCK THIS HOUSE
CD _____ **BIGMO 1023**
Big Mo / Jul '94 / Direct / ADA.

TROUBLE
Blind love / Ninety nine pounds / T-R-O-U-B-L-E / Hard hearted woman / Why why baby / I wouldn't treat a dog (the way you treated me) / One rock at a time / Get in trouble / Chicken and the hawk / You go your way / Ride and roll / Tryin' to get you
CD _____ **POW 4107CD**
Power House / Aug '91 / Direct.

Nightingale

BREATHING SHADOW
CD _____ BMCD 66
Black Mark / May '95 / Plastic Head.

Nightingales

WHAT A SCREAM (1980-86)
Bristol road leads to Dachau / Hark my love / Nowhere to run / Blisters / Idiot strength / Seconds / Return journey / Crunch / Hedonists sigh / My brilliant career / Use your loaf / Which Hi-Fi / Paraffin brain / Only my opinion / Urban ospreys / This / Surplus and scarcity / Crafty fag / It's a cracker / Here we go now / Heroin / What a carry on / Faithful lump / At the end of the day
CD _____ MAUCD 607
Mau Mau / '91 / Pinnacle.

Nightmare Lodge

NEGATIVE PLANET
CD _____ MHCD 022
Minus Habens / Jun '94 / Plastic Head.

Nightmares On Wax

SMOKERS DELIGHT
CD _____ WARPCD 36
Warp / Sep '95 / Disc.

Nightnoise

DIFFERENT SHORE, A
Call of the child / For Eamonn / Falling apples / Buokor on the beach / Morning in Madrid / Another wee niece / Different shore / Mind the dresser / Clouds go by / Shuan
CD _____ 01934111662
Windham Hill / Aug '95 / Pinnacle / BMG / ADA.

PARTING TIDE, THE
Blue / Irish carol / Jig of sorts / Through the castle garden / Island of hope and tears / Kid in the cot / Tryst / Snow is lightly falling / Abbot
CD _____ WD 1097
Windham Hill / May '91 / Pinnacle / BMG / ADA.

SHADOW OF TIME
One little nephew / March air / Shadow of time / Silky flanks / Water falls / Fionnghuala (mouth music) / Nigh in that land / This just in / For you / Sauvie island / Rose of Tralee / Three little nieces
CD _____ 01934111302
Windham Hill / Nov '93 / Pinnacle / BMG / ADA.

SOMETHING OF TIME
CD _____ 01934110572
Windham Hill / Jul '93 / Pinnacle / BMG / ADA.

WINDHAM HILL RETROSPECTIVE, A
19A / Toys not ties / Timewinds / Hugh / Cricket's wicker / Kid in the cot / Something of time / Swan / Bleu / At the races / Hourglass / End of the evening / Nollaig / Bridges / Bring me back a song
CD _____ 111112
Windham Hill / Mar '92 / Pinnacle / BMG / ADA.

Nightshade

DEAD OF NIGHT
CD _____ CDMFN 122
Music For Nations / Sep '90 / Pinnacle.

Nigra Nebula

LIFE AFTER LIFE
CD _____ EFA 125222
Celtic Circle / Sep '95 / SRD.

Nihilist

HERMIT
CD _____ AFTERCD 6
After 6am / Nov '95 / Plastic Head.

SIBYL AND HERP
CD _____ AFTERCD 5
After 6am / Jan '95 / Plastic Head.

Nihon No Oto Ensemble

TRADITIONAL JAPANESE
CD _____ B 6784
Auvidis/Ethnic / Oct '94 / Harmonia Mundi.

Nika

STATE OF GRACE
CD _____ 110242
Musidisc / Nov '93 / Vital / Harmonia Mundi / ADA / Cadillac / Discovery.

Nikola

BALKAN TRADITIONAL (Nikola & Friends)
CD _____ HMA 1903007CD
Musique D'Abord / Aug '94 / Harmonia Mundi.

Nil 8

HAL LE LUJAH
CD _____ BOOK 2CD
Worrybird / Nov '93 / SRD.

Nilsson, Harry

ALL THE BEST
Without you / Everybody's talkin' / Mother nature's son / It's been so long / Good old desk / Without her / Mournin' glory story / Mr. Richland's favourite song / Mr. Bojangles / She's leaving home / Lullaby in ragtime / Makin' whoopee / Cuddly toy / River deep, mountain high / Little cowboy / As time goes by
CD _____ MCCD 129
Music Club / Sep '93 / Disc / THE / CM.

BEST OF NILSSON, THE
CD _____ 7432122315-2
RCA / Aug '94 / BMG.

LITTLE TOUCH OF SCHMILSSON IN THE NIGHT
For me and my gal / It had to be you / Lazy moon / Always / Makin' whoopee / You made me love you / Lullaby in ragtime / I wonder who's kissing her now / What'll I do / Nevertheless / This is all I ask / As time goes by
CD _____ ND 90582
RCA / Aug '91 / BMG.

PUSSY CATS
Many rivers to cross / Subterranean homesick blues / Don't forget me / All my life / Old forgotten soldier / Save the last dance for me / Mucho mucho/Mt. Elga / Loop de loop / Black sails (in the moonlight) / (We're gonna) Rock around the clock
CD _____ EDCD 337
Edsel / Mar '94 / Pinnacle / ADA.

SIMPLY THE BEST
CD _____ WMCD 5706
Disky / Oct '94 / THE / BMG / Discovery / Pinnacle.

TOUCH MORE SCHMILSSON IN THE NIGHT, A
Intro / I'm always chasing rainbows / Make believe / You made me love you / Trust in me / Lullaby in ragtime / All I think about is you / Perfect day / Always / It's only a paper moon / It had to be you / Thanks for the memory / Outro / Over the rainbow
CD _____ PD 90251
RCA / Feb '94 / BMG.

VERY BEST OF NILSSON #1 (Without Her, Without You)
Over the rainbow / Without her / Cuddly toy / Wailing of the willow / Everybody's talkin' / I guess the Lord must be in New York City / Mother Nature's son / Puppy song / Mournin' glory story / Daddy's song / Maybe / Down to the valley / Life line / River deep, mountain high / Moonbeam song / Without you / Mucho mungo / Mount Elga / Subterranean homesick blues
CD _____ ND 90520
RCA / Nov '90 / BMG.

VERY BEST OF NILSSON #2 (Lullaby In Ragtime)
Jesus Christ you're tall / Lullaby in ragtime / Something true / 1941 / Don't leave me / One / Sister Marie / Together / I will take you there / Think about your troubles / Me and my arrow / Buy my album / Cowboy / You can't do that / Remember (Christmas) / Daybreak / All I think about is you / Nevertheless (I'm in love with you) / Pretty soon there will be nothing left for everybody / Jesus Christ you're tall (2)
CD _____ ND 90659
RCA / Jan '94 / BMG.

Nimoy, Leonard

HIGHLY ILLOGICAL
CD _____ CREV 017CD
Rev-Ola / Sep '93 / 3MV / Vital.

Nimsgern, Frank

FRANK NIMSGERN (Nimsgern, Frank & Chaka Khan/Billy Cobham)
Last Summer / Just another way out / Catch the time / Take me away / Pretty secrets / Don't you think it's alright / Latin jokes / Pat's prelude / On the trip / Spring
CD _____ 890012
Lipstick / Feb '91 / Vital/SAM.

TRUST
CD _____ INAK 9031
In Akustik / Nov '96 / Magnum Music Group.

Nine

NINE LIVEZ
CD _____ FILECD 460
Profile / Mar '95 / Pinnacle.

Nine Below Zero

BACK TO THE FUTURE
Soft touch / Bad town / Down in the dirt again / On the road again / Sweet little contessa / Mama talk to your daughter / Jump back baby / Another kinda love / One way street / Ain't coming back / Three times enough / Don't point your finger / Eleven plus eleven / Egg on my face / Sugar beet / Wipe away your kiss / Can't say yes, can't say no
CD _____ WOLCD 1040
China / Feb '94 / Pinnacle.

ICE STATION ZEBRO
CD _____ 5404302
A&M / Jan '96 / PolyGram.

LIVE IN LONDON
CD _____ IGOCD 2023
Indigo / Jun '95 / Direct / ADA.

OFF THE HOOK
CD _____ WOLCD 1028
China / Sep '92 / Pinnacle.

ON THE ROAD AGAIN
CD _____ WOLCD 1014
China / Apr '91 / Pinnacle.

WORKSHY
CD _____ WOKCD 2027
China / Sep '92 / Pinnacle.

Nine Inch Nails

BROKEN
Pinion / Wish / Last / Help me I am in hell / Happiness in slavery / Gave up / Physical / Suck
CD _____ IMCD 8004
Island / Oct '92 / PolyGram.

DOWNWARD SPIRAL, THE
Mr. Self destruct / Piggy / Heresy / March of the pigs / Closer / Ruiner / Becoming / I do not want this / Big man with a gun / Warm place / Eraser / Reptile / Downward spiral / Hurt
CD _____ CID 8012
Island / Mar '94 / PolyGram.

FIXED
Gave up / Wish / Happiness in slavery / Throw this away / First fuck / Screaming slave
CD _____ IMCD 8005
Island / Dec '92 / PolyGram.

FURTHER DOWN THE SPIRAL
Piggy (Nothing can stop me now) / Art of destruction (part 1) / Self destruction / Heresy / Downward spiral / Hurt (Live) / At the heart of it all / Ruiner / Eraser (Denial, realization) / Self destruction, final
CD _____ IMCD 8041
Island / May '95 / PolyGram.

PRETTY HATE MACHINE
Head like a hole / Terrible lie / Down in it / Sanctified / Something I can never have / Kinda I want to / Sin / That's what I get / Only time / Ringfinger
CD _____ CID 9973
Island / Sep '91 / PolyGram.

Nine Pound Hammer

HAYSEED TIMEBOMB
CD _____ EFA 11583 2
Crypt / Sep '94 / SRD.

Niney The Observer

FREAKS
CD _____ HBGD 99
Heartbeat / Mar '95 / Greensleeves / Jetstar / Direct / ADA.

INTRODUCING
CD _____ CB 6003
Caribbean / Jan '96 / Magnum Music Group.

OBSERVER ATTACK DUB
CD _____ RUSCD 8209
Roir USA / Jul '95 / Plastic Head.

TURBO CHARGE
CD _____ CDHB 85
Rounder / May '91 / CM / Direct / ADA / Cadillac.

Ninja Man

DON BAD MAN, THE
CD _____ SONCD 0040
Sonic Sounds / Feb '93 / Jetstar.

HOLD ME (LIKE A M16)
Discipline child / Lou Lou / One black rat / Donkey mile / Lead me home / Walk that road / Vintage memories / Coming to that / Kecke and kotch / On the road again
CD _____ 113622
Musidisc / Jul '95 / Vital / Harmonia Mundi / ADA / Cadillac / Discovery.

NOBODY'S BUSINESS BUT MY OWN
CD _____ SHCD 45007
Shanachie / May '93 / Koch / ADA / Greensleeves.

RUN COME TEST
CD _____ RASCD 3118
Greensleeves / Sep '93 / Total/BMG / Jetstar / SRD.

Nipa

GHANA A CAPELLA
CD _____ 925692
Buda / Jun '93 / Discovery / ADA.

Nirvana

BLEACH
Blew / Floyd the barber / About a girl / School / Love Buzz / Paper cuts / Negative creep / Scoff / Swap meet / Mr. Moustache / Sifting / Big cheese (Not on LP) / Downer (CD only)
CD _____ GFLD 19291
Geffen / Oct '95 / BMG.

IN UTERO
Serve the servants / Scentless apprentice / Heart shaped box / Rape me / Frances Farmer will have her revenge on Seattle / Dumb / Very ape / Milk it / Pennyroyal tea / Radio friendly unit shifter / Tourrets / All apologies / Gallons of rubbing alcohol flow through the strip (CD only)
CD _____ GED 24536
Geffen / Sep '93 / BMG.

INCESTICIDE
Dive / Sliver / Been a son / Turnaround / Molly's lips / Son of a gun / (New wave) Polly / Beeswax / Downer / Mexican seafood / Hairspray queen / Aero Zeppelin / Big long now / Aneurysm
CD _____ GED 24504
Geffen / Dec '92 / BMG.

NEVERMIND
Smells like teen spirit / In bloom / Come as you are / Breed / Lithium / Polly / Territorial pissings / Drain you / Lounge act / Stay away / On a plain / Something in the way
CD _____ DGCD 244258
Geffen / Aug '91 / BMG.

SINGLE BOX SET (6CD Singles Set)
Smells like teen spirit / Drain you / Even in his youth / Aneurysm / Come as you are / Endless nameless / School (live) / Drain you (live) / Lithium / Been a son (live) / Curmudgeon / D7 / In bloom / Sliver (live) / Polly (live) / Heart shaped box / Milk it / Marigold / All apologies / Rape me / Moist vagina
CD Set _____ GED 24901
Geffen / Nov '95 / BMG.

UNPLUGGED IN NEW YORK
About a girl / Come as you are / Jesus doesn't want me for a sunbeam / Man who sold the world / Pennyroyal tea / Dumb / Polly / On a plain / Something in the way / Plateau / Oh me / Lake of fire / All apologies / Where did you sleep last night
CD _____ GED 24727
Geffen / Oct '94 / BMG.

Nirvana

BLACK FLOWER
Black flower / I believe in magic / It happened two Sundays ago / Life ain't easy / Pentecost Hotel / World is cold without you / We can make it through / Satellite jockey / Excerpt from The blind and the beautiful / June / Tiny goddess / Illinois / Tres tres bien / Love suite
CD _____ EDCD 378
Edsel / Oct '93 / Pinnacle / ADA.

LOCAL ANAESTHETIC
CD _____ REP 4109-WP
Repertoire / Aug '91 / Pinnacle / Cadillac.

SECRET THEATRE
CD _____ EDCD 407
Edsel / Jan '95 / Pinnacle / ADA.

TRAVELLING ON A CLOUD
Rainbow chaser / Pentecost hotel / Tiny Goddess / Girl in the park / Melanie blue / You can try it / Trapeze / Satellite jockey / Wings of love / Show must go on / Touchables (All of us) / We can help you / Oh what a performance / Darling darlane
CD _____ 510 974-2
Island / Jul '92 / PolyGram.

Nishizaki, Takako

BUTTERFLY LOVERS, THE
CD _____ 8.240233
Impetus / '88 / CM / Wellard / Impetus / Cadillac.

HUNG HU
CD _____ 8.240276
Impetus / '88 / CM / Wellard / Impetus / Cadillac.

Nite Life

AS THE NIGHT MOVES THE SINGING J
CD _____ SUNCD 005
Sunvibe / May '93 / Jetstar / EWM.

Nitty Gritty

JAH IN THE FAMILY
CD _____ BCD 005
Greensleeves / Nov '92 / Total/BMG / Jetstar / SRD.

TRIALS AND CROSSES (Tribute To Nitty Gritty) (Various Artists)
CD _____ VPCD 1304
VP / Aug '93 / Jetstar.

Nitty Gritty Dirt Band

ACOUSTIC
How long / Cupid's got a gun / Sarah in the Summer / Let it roll / Hello, I am your heart / Love will find a way / Tryin' times / This train keeps rolling along / One sure honest line / Broken road
CD _____ CDP 8281692
Liberty / Jun '94 / EMI.

ALIVE/RARE JUNK
Crazy words crazy tune / Buy for me the rain / Candy man / Foggy mountain breakdown / Rock me baby / Fat boys (can make it in Santa Monica) / Alligator man / Crazy words, crazy tune (2) / Goodnight my love pleasant dreams / Reason to believe / End of your line / Willie the weeper / Hesitation blues / Sadie Green the vamp of New Orleans / Collegiana / Dr. Heckle and Mr. Jibe / Cornbread and lasses / Number and a name / Mournin' blues / These days
CD _____ BGOCD 245
Beat Goes On / Mar '95 / Pinnacle.

ALL THE GOOD TIMES
Sixteen tracks / Fish song / Jambalaya / Down in Texas / Creepin' round your back door / Daisy / Slim Carter / Hoping to say / Baltimore / Jamaica say you will / Do you feel it to / Civil war trilogy / Diggy liggy lo
CD _____ BGOCD 93
Beat Goes On / Dec '90 / Pinnacle.

HOLD ON
Fishin' in the dark / Joe knows how to live / Keepin' the road hot / Blue Ridge Mountain girl / Angelyne / Baby's got a hold on me / Dancing to the beat of a broken heart / Oh what a love / Oleanna / Tennessee
CD _____ 7599255732
Pickwick/Warner / Feb '95 / Pinnacle / Warner Music / Carlton Home Entertainment.

PURE DIRT
Buy for me the rain / It's raining here in long beach / Dismal swamp / Tide of love / Holding / Call again / You're gonna' get it in the end / Shadow dream song / Song to Jutta / Teddy bears picnic / Truly night / Put a bar in my car / Candy man / I'll search the sky
CD _____ BGOCD 243
Beat Goes On / Sep '94 / Pinnacle.

RICOCHET
CD _____ BGOCD 284
Beat Goes On / Oct '95 / Pinnacle.

STARS AND STRIPES FOREVER
Jambalaya / Dirt band interview / Cosmic cowboy Part 1 / Aluminium record award / Fish song / Mr. Bojangles / Vassar Clements interview / Listen to the mockingbird / Sheikh of Araby / Resign yourself to me / Dixie hoedown / Cripple creek / Mountain whippoorwill / Honky tonkin' / House at Pooh corner / Buy for me the rain / Oh boy / Teardrops in my eyes / Glocoat blues / Stars and stripes forever / Battle of New Orleans / It came from the 50's / My true story / Diggy liggy lo
CD _____ BGOCD 128
Beat Goes On / Jul '90 / Pinnacle.

UNCLE CHARLIE AND HIS DOG TEDDY
Some of Shelly's blues / Rave on / Living without you / Uncle Charlie / Mr. Bojangles / Clinch mountain / Back step / Propinquity / Cure / Opus 36 / Clementi / Chicken reel / Travellin' mood / Billy in the lowground / Swanee river / Randy Lynn rag / Santa Rosa / Prodigal's return / Yukon railroad / House at Pooh Corner
CD _____ BGOCD 22
Beat Goes On / Apr '90 / Pinnacle.

Nitzer Ebb

BELIEF, THE
CD _____ CDSTUMM 61
Mute / Oct '88 / Disc.

BIG HIT
CD _____ CDSTUMM 118
City Slang / Mar '95 / Disc.

EBBHEAD
CD _____ CDTUMM 88
Mute / Sep '91 / Disc.

SHOWTIME
CD _____ CDSTUMM 72
Mute / Feb '90 / Disc.

THAT TOTAL AGE
Fitness to purpose / Violent playground / Murderous / Smear body / Let your body learn / Let beauty loose / Into the large air / Join in the chant / Alarm / Join in the chant (metal mix) (CD only.) / Fitness to purpose (CD only. Mixes) / Murderous (instrumental) (CD only.)
CD _____ CDSTUMM 45
Mute / May '87 / Disc.

Nivens

SHAKE
CD _____ DANCD 022
Danceteria / Jan '90 / Plastic Head / ADA.

Nix, Bern

ALARMS AND EXCURSIONS (Nix, Bern Trio)
CD _____ 804372

New World / Sep '93 / Harmonia Mundi / ADA / Cadillac.

Nix, Don

GONE TOO LONG/SKYRIDER
Goin' thru another change / Feel a whole lot better / Gone too long / Backstreet girl / rollin' in my dreams / Yazoo city jail / Harpoon Arkansas turnaround / Forgotten town / Demain / Skyrider / Nobody else / Maverick woman blues / Do it again / Long tall Sally / I'll be in your dreams / On the town again / All for the love of a woman
CD _____ DIAB 805
Diabolo / Feb '94 / Pinnacle.

Nix, Rev. A.W.

REV. A.W. NIX VOL. 1 1927-28
CD _____ DOCD 5328
Blues Document / Mar '95 / Swift / Jazz Music / Hot Shot.

Nixon, Mojo

HORNY HOLIDAYS (Nixon, Mojo & The Toadliquors)
CD _____ 422427
New Rose / May '94 / Direct / ADA.

WHEREABOUTS UNKOWN
CD _____ 422052
Last Call / May '95 / Direct.

No Comment

EYES
CD _____ SPV 07784712
SPV / Jul '94 / Plastic Head.

No Fraud

NO FRAUD
CD _____ MIND 003CD
Nuclear Blast / Jul '91 / Plastic Head.

No Fun At All

NO STRAIGHT ANGLES
CD _____ BHR 011
Burning Heart / Aug '95 / Plastic Head.

OUT OF BOUNDS
CD _____ BHR 013CD
Burning Heart / Oct '95 / Plastic Head.

STRANDED
CD _____ BHR 023CD
Burning Heart / Aug '95 / Plastic Head.

VISIONS
CD _____ BHR 003
Burning Heart / Aug '95 / Plastic Head.

No Man

DAMAGE THE ENEMY
CD _____ NAR 043 CD
New Alliance / May '93 / Pinnacle.

HOW THE WEST WAS WON
CD _____ SST 281 CD
SST / May '93 / Plastic Head.

WHAMON EXPRESS
CD _____ SST 267 CD
SST / Sep '90 / Plastic Head.

No Man

FLOWERMIX
Angeldust / Faith in you / All I see / Natural neck / Heal the madness / You grow more / Beautiful (version) / Sample / Why the noise / Born simple
CD _____ HIART 002
Hidden Art / Oct '95 / Vital.

FLOWERMOUTH
Angel gets caught in the beauty trap / You grow more beautiful / Animal ghost / Soft shoulders / Shell of a fighter / Teardrop fall / Watching over me / Simple / Things change
CD _____ TPLP 67CD
One Little Indian / Jun '94 / Pinnacle.

HEAVEN TASTE
Long day full / Babyship blue / Bleed / Road / Heaven taste
CD _____ HIART 001
Hidden Art / Sep '95 / Vital.

LOVEBLOWS LOVECRIES
CD _____ TPLP 57CD
One Little Indian / May '93 / Pinnacle.

No Man Is Roger Miller

WIN INSTANTLY
CD _____ SST 243 CD
SST / Jul '89 / Plastic Head.

No Means No

0+2 = 1
CD _____ VIRUS 98CD
Alternative Tentacles / Oct '91 / Pinnacle.

DAY EVERYTHING BECAME ISOLATED AND DESTROYED, THE
CD Set _____ VIRUS 62/63CD
Alternative Tentacles / Jan '89 / Pinnacle.

LIVE AND CUDDLY
CD Set _____ VIRUS 97CD
Alternative Tentacles / '92 / Pinnacle.

MAMA
CD _____ WRONG 001CD
Wrong / Nov '92 / SRD.

NO MEANS NO PRESENTS: MR WRIGHT & MR WRONG
CD _____ WRONG 13
Wrong / Oct '94 / SRD.

SEX MAD
Sex mad / Dad / Obsessed / No fucking / She beast / Dead Bob / Long days / Metronome / Revenge / Self pity
CD _____ VIRUS 56CD
Alternative Tentacles / Nov '94 / Pinnacle.

SMALL PARTS ISOLATED AND DESTROYED
CD _____ VIRUS 63CD
Alternative Tentacles / '88 / Pinnacle.

WHY DO THEY CALL ME MR. HAPPY
CD _____ VIRUS 123CD
Alternative Tentacles / May '93 / Pinnacle.

WORLDHOOD OF THE WORLD AS SUCH
CD _____ VIRUS 171CD
Alternative Tentacles / Nov '95 / Pinnacle.

WRONG
CD _____ VIRUS 77CD
Alternative Tentacles / Oct '89 / Pinnacle.

No No Diet Bang

RAZZIA
CD _____ 199125-2
Brambus / Nov '93 / ADA / Direct.

No One Is Innocent

NO ONE IS INNOCENT
CD _____ 5240112
Island / Jan '96 / PolyGram.

No Quarter

SURVIVORS (The Best Of No Quarter)
Seek 'til I find / No stopping it now / Illusions / Stand for glory / Fooled by your love / Ice cold / Now / Rise to the call / Surrender / Somewhere / What's going on / Survivors / Time and space / Racing for home
CD _____ ETHEL 3
Vinyl Tap / Dec '94 / Vinyl Tap.

No Safety

LIVE AT THE KNITTING FACTORY
CD _____ KFWCD 149
Knitting Factory / Feb '95 / Grapevine.

SPILL
CD _____ KFWCD 127
Knitting Factory / Nov '94 / Grapevine.

No Security

WHEN THE GIST
CD _____ LF 063CD
Lost & Found / Aug '93 / Plastic Head.

No Sports

KING SKA
CD _____ PHZCD 49
Unicorn / Jul '90 / Plastic Head.

No Sweat

NO SWEAT
Heart and soul / Shake / Stay / On the edge / Waters Flow / Tear down the walls / Generation / Lean on me / Stranger / Mover
CD _____ 828 206 2
London / May '92 / PolyGram.

No Use For A Name

DAILY GRIND, THE
CD _____ FATCD 507
Fat Wreck Chords / Sep '93 / Plastic Head.

LECHE CON CARNE
CD _____ FAT 522
Fat Wreck Chords / Mar '95 / Plastic Head.

Noakes, Rab

STANDING UP
I've hardly started / I wish I was in England / What do you want the girl to do / Solid gone / Love is a gamble / Downtown lights / Gently does it / Blue dream / Psycho killer / Deep water / Open all night / Niel gow's apprentice / Goodbye to all that / Lenny Bruce / When this bloody war is over / Remember my name / Absolutely sweet Marie
CD _____ MDMCD 003
Moidart / Oct '94 / Conifer / ADA.

Noble, Liam

CLOSE YOUR EYES
CD _____ FMRCD 25
Future / Oct '95 / Harmonia Mundi / ADA.

Noble, Ray

RAY NOBLE 1941 (Noble, Ray & His Orchestra)
CD _____ CCD 126
Circle / Aug '94 / Jazz Music / Swift / Wellard.

RAY NOBLE LIVE 1935 (Noble, Ray & His American Dance Orchestra)
CD _____ 3801222
Jazz Archives / Jun '92 / Jazz Music / Discovery / Cadillac.

TRANSCRIPTIONS - 1935-36 (Noble, Ray & His American Dance Orchestra)
CD _____ EBCD 21122
Jazzband / Dec '89 / Jazz Music / Wellard.

VERY THOUGHT OF YOU, THE (Noble, Ray & Al Bowlly)
After all, you're all I'm after / Bugle call rag / By the fireside / Close your eyes / Dinah / Don't say goodbye / Double trouble / Down by the river / Goodnight sweetheart / I'll string along with you / Lazy day / Love is the sweetest thing / Love looked out / Mad about the boy / Maybe I love you too much / Oceans of time / Soon / Time on my hands / Very thought of you / When your down yonder in New Orleans / We've got the moon and sixpence / When you've got a little springtime in your heart / Where am I / You ought to see Sally on Sunday / You're more than all the world to me
CD _____ CDAJA 5115
Living Era / May '94 / Koch.

VERY THOUGHT OF YOU, THE
Very thought of you / Love is the sweetest thing / Spanish eyes / Dreaming a dream / Slumming on Park Avenue / By the fireside / Top hat, white tie and tails / I used to be colour blind / Medley / That's what life is made of / Let yourself go / Basin Street blues / Oh you nasty man / Change partners / Love locked out / Goodnight sweetheart / Medley #2 / Medley #3
CD _____ PAR 2032
Parade / Oct '94 / Koch / Cadillac.

Noble Rot

REAL LUST FOR LIFE
CD _____ BMCD 52
Black Mark / May '94 / Plastic Head.

Nock, Mike

IN OUT AND AROUND (Nock, Mike Quartet)
Break time / Dark light / Shadows of forgotten / Gift / Hadrian's wall / In, out and around
CD _____ CDSJP 119
Timeless Jazz / Jun '91 / New Note.

ONDAS
Forgotten love / Ondas / Visionary / Land of the long white cloud / Doors
CD _____ 8291612
ECM / Aug '86 / New Note.

Nocturnal Emissions

BEFEHLSNOTSTAND
CD _____ DV 22
Dark Vinyl / Nov '93 / Plastic Head.

DROWNING IN A SEA OF BLISS
CD _____ TO 4
Touch / Oct '95 / These / Kudos.

MAGNETIZED LIGHT
CD _____ EEE 16CD
Audioglobe / Nov '94 / Plastic Head.

SONGS OF LOVE AND REVOLUTION
CD _____ DVO 19CD
Dark Vinyl / May '95 / Plastic Head.

VIRAL SHREDDING
CD _____ DV 011CD
Dark Vinyl / Nov '94 / Plastic Head.

Nocturne, Johnny

SHAKE 'EM UP (Nocturne, Johnny Band)
CD _____ BBCD 9553
Bullseye Blues / Nov '94 / Direct.

WAILIN' DADDY (Nocturne, Johnny Band)
CD _____ BBCD 9526
Bullseye Blues / Jan '93 / Direct.

Nocturnus

KEY, THE
CD _____ MOSH 023CD
Earache / Sep '90 / Vital.

THRESHOLDS
CD _____ MOSH 055CD
Earache / Apr '92 / Vital.

Node

NODE
Clock / Olivine / Slapback / Levy / Propane
CD _____ DVNT 005CD
Deviant / Oct '95 / Vital.

NOFX

I HEARD THEY SUCK...LIVE
CD _____ FATCD 528
Fat Wreck Chords / Sep '95 / Plastic Head.

LIBERAL ANIMATION
CD _____ E 864172
Epitaph / Nov '92 / Plastic Head / Pinnacle.

LONGEST LINE
CD _____ FAT 503CD
Fat Wreck Chords / Nov '92 / Plastic Head.

MAXIMUM ROCK 'N' ROLL
CD _____ MYSTICCD 180
Mystic / Oct '94 / Plastic Head.

PUNK IN DRUBLIC
CD _____ E 864352
Epitaph / Jun '94 / Plastic Head / Pinnacle.

RIBBED
CD _____ E 864102
Epitaph / Nov '92 / Plastic Head / Pinnacle.

S & M AIRLINES
CD _____ E 86405CD
Epitaph / Nov '92 / Plastic Head / Pinnacle.

WHITE TRASH
CD _____ E 864182
Epitaph / Jun '93 / Plastic Head / Pinnacle.

Nogueras, Jose

TIEMPO NUEVO
CD _____ 66058077
RMM / Dec '95 / New Note.

Noirin Ni Riain

SOUNDINGS
CD _____ OSSCD 88
Ossian / Dec '94 / ADA / Direct / CM.

Noise Annoys

FIRST STEP
CD _____ EFA 11841CD
Vince Lombard / Jul '93 / SRD.

Noise Unit

DECODER
CD _____ EFA 084662
Dossier / May '95 / SRD.

STRATEGY OF VIOLENCE
CD _____ CLEO 94752
Cleopatra / Aug '95 / Disc.

Noiseaddict

YOUNG AND JADED
I wish I was him / My sarong / Meat / Pop queen / Back in your life / Don't leave
CD _____ WIJ 035CD
Wiiija / Apr '94 / Vital.

Noisebox

MONKEY ASS
CD _____ SPV 08422202
SPV / Jun '95 / Plastic Head.

Noitarega

NOITAREGA
CD _____ 40040CD
Sonifolk / Jun '94 / ADA / CM.

Noland, Terry

HYPNOTIZED
Hypnotized / Ten little women / Come marry me / Oh baby look at me / Don't do me this way / Oh Judy / Sugar drop / Guess I'm gonna fall / There was a fungus among us / Everyone but one / One sweet kiss / Crazy dream / Let me be your hero / Puppy love / Patty baby / Teenage teardrops / For ever loving you / You and I / Leave me alone / My teenage heart / She's gone (master) / Ten little women (1) / Hypnotized (1) / World's a rockin' / Heartless woman / She's gone / That ain't right / Hound dog
CD _____ BCD 15428
Bear Family / Feb '90 / Rollercoaster / Direct / CM / Swift / ADA.

Nolet, Jim

WITH YOU
CD _____ KFWCD 150
Knitting Factory / Feb '95 / Grapevine.

Nomad, Naz

GIVE DADDY THE KNIFE, CINDY
(Nomad, Naz & The Nightmares)
Nobody but me / Action woman / Wind blows your hair / Kicks / Cold turkey / She lied / I had too much to dream last night / Trip / I can only give you everything / I can't stand this love, goodbye / Do you know I know / Just call me Sky

CD _____ CDWIKM 21
Big Beat / Jun '88 / Pinnacle.

Nomadix

ROLLING PAPERS (THE REMIXES)
CD _____ NDXCD 001
Roar / Jun '94 / Jetstar / Roots Collective.

Nomads

POWERSTRIP
(I'm) out of it / Bad vibes / Better off dead / I don't know / I don't care / Sacred / Just lost / Kinda crime / Dig up the hatchet / Robert Johnsong / In the doghouse / Glad to be in your past / Blind spot
CD _____ RTD 1578082
World Service / Jun '95 / Vital.

Nomi, Klaus

COLLECTION, THE
Cold song / Can't help falling in love / Der nussbaum / Just one look / Twist / Total eclipse / Three wishes / Icurok / Wasting my times / Rubber band laser / Ding dong / Nomi chant / Death / Wayward sisters / From beyond / Falling in love again
CD _____ ND 75004
RCA / Jan '95 / BMG.

Nomicon

NOMICON/SARNATH (Split CD)
(Nomicon/Sarnath)
CD _____ SHR 011CD
Shiver / Aug '95 / Plastic Head.

Nomos

I WON'T BE AFRAID ANYMORE
CD _____ GRACD 205
Grapevine / Apr '95 / Grapevine.

Non

BLOOD AND FAME
CD _____ CDSTUMM 32
Mute / Jan '87 / Disc.

IN THE SHADOW OF THE SWORD
CD _____ CDSTUMM 113
Mute / Oct '92 / Disc.

MIGHTI
CD _____ CDSTUMM 139
Mute / Oct '95 / Disc.

Non-Fiction

IT'S A WONDERFUL LIE
CD _____ 085518242
SPV / Jan '96 / Plastic Head.

Nonce

WORLD ULTIMATE
CD _____ 74321254522
RCA / Oct '95 / BMG.

Nonet, Arnaud

KAMALA (Nonet, Arnaud Mattei)
CD _____ CDLLL 147
La Lichere / Aug '93 / Discovery / ADA.

Nonoyesno

DEPSHIT ARKANSAS
CD _____ NB 094-2
Nuclear Blast / Feb '94 / Plastic Head.

Nookie

SOUND OF MUSIC, THE
CD _____ RIVETCD 5
Reinforced / Mar '95 / SRD.

Noonan, Carol

ABSOLUTION
CD _____ CDPH 1176
Philo / Sep '95 / Direct / CM / Roots.

Noone, Jimmie

COLLECTION VOL 1
CD _____ COCD 06
Collector's Classics / Nov '92 / Cadillac / Complete/Pinnacle.

COMPLETE RECORDINGS VOL. 1 (3CD Set)
Lonesome and sorry / Baby o' mine / My blue heaven / Miss Annabelle Lee / I know that you know / Sweet Sue, just you / Four or five times / Every evening I miss you / Ready for the river / Forevermore / Oh sister ain't that hold / I ain't got nobody / Apex blues / Monday date / Blues my naughty sweetie gives to me / King Joe / Sweet Lorraine / Some rainy day / It's tight like that / Let's sow a wild oat / She's funny that way / St. Louis blues / Chicago rhythm / I got a misery / Wake up chill'un, wake up / Love me or leave me / Anything you want / Birmingham Bertha / Am I blue / My daddy's rock me / Ain't misbehavin' / That rhythm man / Off time / S'posin' / True blue / Through / Satisfied / I'm doin' what I'm doin' for love / He's a good man to have around / My melancholy baby / After you've gone / Love / El rado scuffle / Deep trouble / Crying for the Carolines / Have a little faith in me / Should I / I'm following you / When you're smiling / I lost my gal from Memphis / On revival day / I'm drifting back to dreamland / Virginia Lee / So sweet / San
CD Set _____ CDAFS 1027-3
Affinity / Oct '92 / Charly / Cadillac / Jazz Music.

JIMMIE NOONE
CD _____ VILCD 0212
Village Jazz / Sep '92 / Target/BMG / Jazz Music.

JIMMIE NOONE - 1930-1935 (Noone, Jimmie & His Apex Club Orchestra)
CD _____ SWAGGIECD 505
Swaggie / Jun '93 / Jazz Music.

JIMMIE NOONE 1923-1928
CD _____ CLASSICS 604
Classics / '91 / Discovery / Jazz Music.

JIMMIE NOONE 1928-1929 (Noone, Jimmie & Friends)
CD _____ CLASSICS 611
Classics / Feb '92 / Discovery / Jazz Music.

JIMMIE NOONE 1929-1930
CD _____ CLASSICS 632
Classics / '92 / Discovery / Jazz Music.

Noone, Peter

I'M INTO SOMETHING GOOD
CD _____ WMCD 5630
Disky / Oct '94 / THE / BMG / Discovery / Pinnacle.

PETER NOONE SINGS HITS OF HERMAN'S HERMITS
CD _____ MU 5021
Musketeer / Oct '92 / Koch.

Nooten, Pieter

SLEEPS WITH THE FISHES (Nooten, Pieter & Michael Brook)
CD _____ CAD 710 CD
4AD / Oct '87 / Disc.

Nora

NORA
CD _____ HABITCD 002
Habit / Oct '95 / Plastic Head.

Norby, Caecilie

CAECILIE NORBY
Wild is the wind / Brand new life / Girl talk / I've been to town / Summertime / By the time I get to Phoenix / All you could ever want / Gentle is my love / Feather in the wind / Night road / Man's got soul / So it is
CD _____ CDP 8322222
Blue Note / Nov '95 / EMI.

Nordenstam, Stina

AND SHE CLOSED HER EYES
CD _____ 450993898-2
East West / Apr '94 / Warner Music.

MEMORIES OF A COLOR
Memories of a color / Return of Alan Bean / Another story girl / His song / He watches her from behind / I'll be cryin' for you / Alone at night / Soon after Christmas / Walk in the dark
CD _____ 4509907672
East West / Oct '92 / Warner Music.

Nordes

CRUZ DE PEDRA
CD _____ 20054CD
Sonifolk / Dec '94 / ADA / CM.

Nordic All Women Big Band

SOMEWHERE IN TIME
CD _____ MECCACD 1048
Music Mecca / Nov '94 / Jazz Music / Cadillac / Wellard.

Nordine, Ken

DEVOUT CATALYST
CD _____ GDCD 4017
Grateful Dead / Feb '92 / Pinnacle.

Noren, Fredrik

JAZZ IN SWEDEN 1980
CD _____ 1211
Caprice / Feb '87 / CM / Complete/ Pinnacle / Cadillac / ADA.

Noris, Gunter

HOLIDAY DANCING (Noris, Gunter & His Gala Big Band)
CD _____ EDL 29172
Savoy / Dec '95 / THE / Savoy.

TANZE MIT MIR IN DEN MORGEN (Noris, Gunter & His Gala Big Band)
CD _____ EDL 29142
Savoy / Dec '95 / THE / Savoy.

WE PLAY REQUESTS
CD _____ WRCD 5001
WRD / Oct '95 / Target/BMG.

WE PLAY REQUESTS 2
CD _____ WRCD 5002
WRD / Oct '95 / Target/BMG.

Norman, Charlie

PAPA PIANO
CD _____ NCD 8830
Phontastic / Jun '94 / Wellard / Jazz Music / Cadillac.

Norman, Chris

MIDNIGHT LADY (16 Original Hits)
CD _____ 12211
Laserlight / Nov '93 / Target/BMG.

SCREAMING LOVE
CD _____ DIMCD 001
Scratch / Nov '94 / BMG.

Normand, Carla

JUST YOU (Normand, Carla & The New Deal Jazz Band)
CD _____ ACD 244
Audiophile / Apr '93 / Jazz Music / Swift.

Normansell, Amanda

PATSY CLINE REVIEW, THE
CD _____ ITSMUSCD 2
It's Music / Oct '95 / Total/BMG.

Norris, Walter

HUES OF BLUES
Fontessa / Serenata / Hues of blues / I want to be happy / I can't get started / Backbone mode / Have you met Miss Jones / Spider web / Orchids in green / Afterthoughts
CD _____ CCD 4671
Concord Jazz / Nov '95 / New Note.

LIVE AT MAYBECK RECITAL HALL 4
Song is you / Round Midnight / Waltz for Wait / Best thing for you / Darn that dream (Only on CD) / Scrambled / Modus vivendi (Only on CD) / It's always Spring / Body and soul
CD _____ CCD 4425
Concord Jazz / Aug '94 / New Note.

SUNBURST (Norris, Walter Quartet)
Sunburst / What's new / Naima / Stella by starlight / Never should it ever end / So in love
CD _____ CCD 4486
Concord Jazz / Nov '91 / New Note.

Norrlatar

RAVN
CD _____ XOU 105CD
Xource / Jun '94 / ADA / Cadillac.

SIGN OF THE RAVEN
CD _____ RESCD 506
Resource / Oct '94 / ADA.

Norte, Marisela

NORTE/WORD
CD _____ NAR 062 CD
New Alliance / May '93 / Pinnacle.

North, Emmet Jnr.

IN THE ZONE
CD _____ CUTUPCD 011
Jump Cut / Sep '95 / Total/BMG / Vital/ SAM.

North Sea Gas

CALEDONIAN CONNECTION
CD _____ CDITV 483
Scotdisc / Jul '89 / Duncans / Ross / Conifer.

KELTIC HERITAGE
CD _____ CDITV 541
Scotdisc / Sep '91 / Duncans / Ross / Conifer.

POWER OF SCOTLAND, THE
CD _____ CDITV 607
Scotdisc / Oct '95 / Duncans / Ross / Conifer.

Northeast Winds

IRELAND BY SAIL
CD _____ FE 2054
Folk Era / Dec '94 / CM / ADA.

NORTHEAST WINDS ON TOUR
CD _____ FE 1403
Folk Era / Nov '94 / CM / ADA.

Northern Jazz Orchestra

GOOD NEWS
CD _____ LACD 38
Lake / Sep '94 / Target/BMG / Jazz Music / Direct / Cadillac / ADA.

Northern Lights

WRONG HIGHWAY BLUES
CD _____ FF 70632CD
Flying Fish / Apr '94 / Roots / CM / Direct / ADA.

Northern Picture Library

ALASKA
Untitled / Into the ether / Catholic Easter colours / Glitter spheres / Insecure / Dreams and stars and sleep / Lucky / L.S.D. icing / Truly madly deeply / Isn't it time you faced the truth / Untitled (2) / Skylight / Of traffic and the ticking / Lucky (reprise) / Monotone
CD _____ ASKCD 023
Vinyl Japan / Oct '93 / Vital.

Northrop, Kate

ROOTS & WINGS
CD _____ BRAM 199234-2
Brambus / Nov '93 / ADA / Direct.

Northup, Harry E.

HOMES
CD _____ NAR 120CD
New Alliance / Nov '95 / Plastic Head.

Norvo, Red

DANCE OF THE OCTOPUS
Knockin' on wood / Honeysuckle rose / Blues in E flat / Gramercy square / Music goes round and round / I got rhythm / Oh Lady be good
CD _____ HEPCD 1044
Hep / Aug '95 / Cadillac / Jazz Music / New Note / Wellard.

FORWARD LOOK, THE (Norvo, Red Quintet)
Rhee waahnee / Forward look / Between the Devil and the deep blue sea / Room 608 / For Lena and Lennie / Cookin' at the Continental
CD _____ RR 8CD
Reference Recordings / Sep '91 / May Audio.

JIVIN' THE JEEP
CD _____ HEPCD 1019
Hep / Dec '87 / Cadillac / Jazz Music / New Note / Wellard.

LIVE FROM THE BLUE GARDENS: JANUARY 1942 (Norvo, Red & His Orchestra)
CD _____ MM 65090
Music Masters / Oct '94 / Nimbus.

MOVE
Move / I can't believe that you're in love with me / I'll remember April / September song / Zing went the strings of my heart / I've got you under my skin / I get a kick out of you / If I had you / Godchild / This can't be love / Cheek to cheek / Swedish pastry
CD _____ SV 0168
Savoy Jazz / Apr '93 / Conifer / ADA.

ON DIAL
Hallelujah / Get happy / Slam slam blues / Congo blues
CD _____ SPJCD 127
Spotlite / Apr '95 / Cadillac / Jazz Horizons / Swift.

RED NORVO WITH TAL FARLOW & CHARLES MINGUS (Norvo, Red/Tal Farlow/Charles Mingus)
I can't believe that you're in love with me / Time and tide / Little white lies / Prelude to a kiss / Know / September song / I'm yours / I get a kick out of you / Zing went the strings of my heart / Cheek to cheek / Night and day / Godchild / Mood indigo / If I had you / Deed I do / I'll remember April / This can't be love / I've got you under my skin / Swedish pastry / Have you met Miss Jones
CD _____ SV 0267
Savoy Jazz / Sep '95 / Conifer / ADA.

RED NORVO WITH TAL FARLOW & CHARLES MINGUS #2 (Norvo, Red/Tal Farlow/Charles Mingus)
CD _____ VJC 1008-2
Vintage Jazz Classics / Oct '92 / Direct / ADA / CM / Cadillac.

RED NORVO'S FABULOUS JAM SESSION
Hallelujah / Congo blues / Slam slam blues
CD _____ STB 2514
Stash / Sep '95 / Jazz Music / CM / Cadillac / Direct / ADA.

RED NORVO, VOL. 1
CD _____ VJC 1005-2
Victorious Discs / Feb '91 / Jazz Music.

RED PLAYS THE BLUES
Britt's blues / Night is blue / Shed no tears / Easy on the eye / Just a wood / I sing the blues / Sunrise blues
CD _____ 74321 13034-2
RCA / Sep '93 / BMG.

ROCK IT FOR ME
Tears in my heart / Worried over you / Clap hands, here comes Charlie / Russian lullaby / Always and always / I was doing all right / 'S Wonderful / Love is here to stay / Serenade to the stars / More than ever / Weekend of a private secretary / Please be kind / Jeannie, I dream of lilac time / Tea time / How can you forget / There's a boy in Harlem / Says my heart / Moonshine over Kentucky / Rock it for me / After dinner speech / If you were in my place (What would you do)

CD _____ HEPCD 1040
Hep / Sep '94 / Cadillac / Jazz Music / New Note / Wellard.

Nosferatu

LEGEND
CD _____ CLEO 1016-2
Cleopatra / Mar '94 / Disc.

PROPHECY, THE
Requiem / Farewell my little earth / Fever / Keeper's call / Thrill killer / Time of legends / Shadow maker / Savage kiss / Grave desires / Soul trader / Enchanted tower
CD _____ POSSCD 008
Possession / Oct '94 / Vital.

RISE
Gathering / Rise / Dark angel / Her heaven / Lucy is red / Lament (CD only) / Alone / Vampyres cry / Crysania (CD only) / Siren / Away / Close
CD _____ POSSCD 006
Possession / May '93 / Vital.

Not Sensibles

INSTANT PUNK CLASSICS
(I'm in love with) Margaret Thatcher / Little boxes / Garry Bushell's band of the week / Death to disco / Coronation Street hustle / Lying on the sofa / Instant classic / Girl with scruffy hair / Freedom / King Arthur / Ploppy / I am a clone / Sick of being normal / (Love is like) Banging my head against a brick wall / Because I'm mine / Wrong love / Blackpool rock / Daddy won't let me love you song / Don't wanna work anymore / I thought you were dead / I make a balls of everything I do / Teenage revolution / I am the bishop / Telephone rings again
CD _____ CDPUNK 38
Anagram / Aug '94 / Pinnacle.

Notes, Freddie

MONTEGO BAY (Notes, Freddie & The Rudies)
CD _____ CDTRL 349
Trojan / Sep '95 / Jetstar / Total/BMG.

Nothing Painted Blue

FUTURE OF COMMUNICATIONS, THE
Sorely tempted / Shaky start / Vengeful as hell / Lapped / I'm a haunted house / Future of communications
CD _____ SCT 0472
Scat / Sep '95 / Vital.

PLACEHOLDERS
Couldn't be simpler / Weak / Drinking game / Career day / Spread your poison / In May / Masonic eye / Ballwalker / Travel well / Rightful heir / Houseguest / Kissing booth / Can't f(x)
CD _____ SCT 037-2
Scat / Oct '94 / Vital.

POWER TRIPS DOWN LOVERS' LANE
White bicycles / Peace dividend / Block Colors / Officer Angel / Campaign song / Register / Storefronts / Unscheduled Train / Epistemophelia / Smothered / Scapegoat / Few / Rock 'n' roll friend / Undeserving
CD _____ KOKOPOP 001CD
Kokopop / Aug '93 / Vital.

Notorious B.I.G.

READY TO DIE
Intro / Things done changed / Gimmie the loot / Machine gun funk / Warning / Ready to die / One more change / Me (interlude) / What / Juicy / Everyday struggle / Me and my / Big poppa / Respect / Friend of mine / Unbelievable / Suicidal thoughts
CD _____ 78612 73000-2
Arista / Oct '94 / BMG.

Notting Hillbillies

MISSING...PRESUMED HAVING A GOOD TIME
Railroad worksong / Bewildered / Your own sweet way / Run me down / One way gal / Blues stay away from me / Will you miss me / Please baby / Weapon of prayer / That's where I belong / I feel like going home
CD _____ 842 671 2
Vertigo / Mar '90 / PolyGram.

Notwist

LIVE
CD _____ YCLS 021
Your Choice / Aug '94 / Plastic Head.

Nouvelles Lectures...

SPIRITUS REX (Nouvelles Lectures Cosmopolites)
CD _____ ETCD 12
Semantic / Apr '94 / Plastic Head.

Nova, Heather

BLOW
Sugar / Maybe an angel / Blessed / Mother tongue / Talking to strangers / Shaking the doll
CD _____ BFLCD 8
Big Life / Jul '95 / Pinnacle.

GLOW STAR
CD _____ BFLCD 2
Big Life / Jul '95 / Pinnacle.

OYSTER
CD _____ BFLCD 12
Big Life / Oct '94 / Pinnacle.

Nova Mob

LAST DAYS OF POMPEII, THE
CD _____ CDR 261
Rough Trade / Apr '91 / Pinnacle.

NOVA MOB
Shoot your way to freedom / Puzzles / Buddy / See and feel and know / Little Miss Information / I won't be there anymore / Please don't ask / Sins of their sons / Beyond a reasonable doubt / If I was afraid/ Coda
CD _____ RTD 15717442
World Service / Apr '94 / Vital.

November's Doom

AMID ITS HALLOWED MIRTH
CD _____ CDAV 010
Avant Garde / Feb '95 / Plastic Head.

Novembre

WISH IT WOULD
CD _____ POLYPH 001CD
Nosferatu / Jun '95 / Plastic Head.

Novick, Billy

REMEMBERING YOU
CD _____ DARINGCD 3018
Daring / Oct '95 / Direct / CM / ADA.

Nowomowa

WASTED LANDS, THE
CD _____ NAGE 20 CD
Art Of Landscape / '88 / Sony.

Nu Civilisation

NU CIVILISATION
CD _____ STEAM 77CD
Vinyl Solution / Feb '94 / Disc.

Nu Philly Groove

NU PHILLY GROOVE, THE
CD _____ ITM 1494
ITM / Oct '95 / Tradelink / Koch.

Nua, Sean

OPEN DOOR, THE
CD _____ SHAN 79082CD
Shanachie / May '93 / Koch / ADA / Greensleeves.

Nuclear Assault

GAME OVER
LSD / Cold steel / Betrayal / Radiation sickness / Hang the Pope / After the holocaust / Mr. Softee theme / Stranded in Hell / Nuclear war / My America / Vengeance / Brain death
CD _____ CDFLAG 5
Under One Flag / Aug '87 / Pinnacle.

OUT OF ORDER
CD _____ CDFLAG 64
Music For Nations / Sep '91 / Pinnacle.

SOMETHING WICKED
Something wicked / Another violent end / Behind glass walls / Chaos / Forge / No time / To serve man / Madness descends / Poetic justice / Art / Other end
CD _____ ALTGOCD 003
Alter Ego / Apr '93 / Vital.

SURVIVE
Brainwashed / Great depression / Equal rights / Good times, bad times / Survive / Wired / Technology
CD _____ CDFLAG 21
Under One Flag / Jul '88 / Pinnacle.

Nucleus

ELASTIC ROCK/WE'LL TALK ABOUT IT LATER
Elastic rock / Striation / Taranaki / Twisted track / Crude blues / Crude blues part two / 1916 (Battle of boogaloo) / Torrid zone / Stonescape / Earth mother / Speaking for myself, personally / Persephones jive / Song for the bearded lady / Sun child / Lullaby for a lonely child / We'll talk about it later / Oasis / Ballad of Joe Pimp / Easter 1916
CD _____ BGOCD 47
Beat Goes On / Mar '94 / Pinnacle.

Nuerosis

SOULS AT ZERO
CD _____ VIRUS 109CD
Alternative Tentacles / Jun '92 / Pinnacle.

Nuff Ruffness

NUFF RUFFNESS
CD _____ WRA 81222CD
Wrap / May '94 / Koch.

Nugent, Ted

CALL OF THE WILD
Call of the wild / Sweet revenge / Pony express / Ain't it the truth / Renegade / Rot gut / Below the belt / cannonballs
CD _____ EDCD 278
Edsel / Oct '89 / Pinnacle / ADA.

ON THE EDGE
Dr. Slingshot / Night time / You talk sunshine, I breathe fire / Scottish tea / Good natured Emma / Prodigal man / Missionary Mary / St. Philip's friend / Journey to the centre of the mind / Flight of the byrd / Baby, please don't go / Inside the outside / Loaded for bear / On the edge
CD _____ CDTB 097
Thunderbolt / '91 / Magnum Music Group.

OUT OF CONTROL
CD Set _____ CD 47039
Epic / May '94 / Sony.

OVER THE TOP
Down on Philips escalator / Surrender to your kings / Gimme love / For his namesake / I'll prove I'm right / Conclusion/Journey / To the centre of the mind / Migration / Lovely lady / Mississippi murderer / Let's go get stoned / It's not true / Ivory castles / Colours / Over the top
CD _____ CDTB 120
Thunderbolt / May '91 / Magnum Music Group.

TOOTH FANG AND CLAW
Lady luck / Living in the woods / Hibernation / Free flight / Maybellene / Great white buffalo / Sasha / No holds barred
CD _____ EDCD 295
Edsel / Oct '89 / Pinnacle / ADA.

Numan, Gary

BERSERKER
CD _____ NUMACD 1001
Numa / Dec '95 / Pinnacle.

BEST OF 1978-83
CD _____ BEGA 150CD
Beggars Banquet / Sep '93 / Warner Music / Disc.

COLLECTION: GARY NUMAN
Cars / Tracks / Down in the park / This wreckage / Random / My shadow in vain / She's got claws / Music for chameleons / Remind me to smile / Stories / Game called echo / Complex / On Broadway (live) / Aircrash bureau / M.E. / Are friends electric / Photograph / We are glass
CD _____ CCSCD 409
Castle / Nov '94 / BMG.

DANCE
Slow car to China / Night talk / Subway called you / Cry the clock said / She's got claws / Crash / Boys like me / Stories / My brother's time / You are, you are / Moral
CD _____ BBL 28CD
Lowdown/Beggars Banquet / '88 / Warner Music / Disc.

DARK LIGHT
CD Set _____ NUMACD 1012
Numa / Jun '95 / Pinnacle.

DREAM CORROSION
CD Set _____ NUMACD 1010
Numa / Aug '94 / Pinnacle.

EXHIBITION
Me, I disconnect from you / That's too bad / My love is a liquid / Music for chameleons / We are glass / Bombers / Sister surprise / Are friends electric / I dream of wires / Complex / Noise noise / Warriors / Everyday I die / Cars / We take mystery to bed / I'm an agent / My centurion / Metal / You are in my vision / I die, you die / She's got claws / This wreckage / My shadow in vain / Down in the dark / Iceman comes
CD Set _____ BEGA 88 CD
Beggars Banquet / Sep '87 / Warner Music / Disc.

FURY, THE
Call out the dogs / This disease / Your fascination / Miracles / Pleasure skin / Creatures / Tricks / God only knows / I still remember
CD _____ CDNUMA 1003
Numa / '86 / Pinnacle.

GARY NUMAN
CD _____ CSAPCD 113
Connoisseur / Oct '92 / Pinnacle.

GHOST
CD _____ NUMACD 1007
Numa / Oct '92 / Pinnacle.

GREATEST HITS (Numan, Gary & Tubeway Army)
CD _____ 5311492
PolyGram TV / Feb '96 / PolyGram.

HUMAN
CD _____ NUMACD 1013
Numa / Oct '95 / Pinnacle.

ISOLATE
CD _____ NUMACD 1008
Numa / Mar '92 / Pinnacle.

MACHINE AND SOUL
CD _____ NUMACD 1009
Numa / Aug '92 / Pinnacle.

MACHINE AND SOUL - REMIXED
CD _____ NUMAXCD 1009
Numa / Sep '93 / Pinnacle.

**PEEL SESSIONS: GARY NUMAN/
TUBEWAY ARMY (29th May 1979)
(Numan, Gary & Tubeway Army)**
Cars / Airlane / Films / Conversation / Me,
I disconnect from you / Down in the park /
I nearly married a human
CD _____ SFPMCD 202
Strange Fruit / '89 / Pinnacle.

PLEASURE PRINCIPLE/WARRIORS
CD Set _____ BEGA 10CD
Beggars Banquet / Dec '87 / Warner
Music / Disc.

REPLICAS (Tubeway Army)
CD _____ MUSCD 509
MCI / May '95 / Disc / THE.

REPLICAS/THE PLAN
Me, I disconnect from you / Are friends
electric / Mach man / Praying to the aliens
/ Down in the park / You are in my vision /
Replicas / It must have been years / When
machines rock / I nearly married a human /
This is my life / Critics / Monday troop /
Mean street / Thoughts of No.2 / Basic J /
Ice / Crime of passion / Check it / Out of
sight
CD Set _____ BEGA 7CD
Beggars Banquet / Dec '87 / Warner Music
/ Disc.

SACRIFICE
CD _____ NUMACD 1011
Numa / Oct '94 / Pinnacle.

SACRIFICE - REMIXED
CD _____ NUMACDX 1011
Numa / Mar '95 / Pinnacle.

SELECTION
CD _____ BBP 5CD
Beggars Banquet / Nov '89 / Warner
Music / Disc.

STRANGE CHARM
CD _____ CDNUMA 1005
Numa / '86 / Pinnacle.

TELEKON/I ASSASSIN
This wreckage / Aircrash bureau / Telekon
/ Sleep by windows / I'm an agent / Remember I was vapour / Please push no
more / Joy circuit / Wars songs / Dream of
siam / Music for chameleons / This is my

house / I, assassin / 1930's rust / We take
mystery to bed
CD _____ BEGA 19CD
Beggars Banquet / '88 / Warner Music /
Disc.

TUBEWAY ARMY/DANCE
Listen to the sirens / Life machines / Friends
/ Something's in the house / Everyday I die
/ Steel and you / Are you real / Dream police
/ Zero bars / Slowcar to China / Night talk
/ Subway called you / She's got claws /
Crash / Boys like me / Stories / My brothers
time / You are, you are
CD _____ BEGA 4CD
Beggars Banquet / Dec '87 / Warner Music
/ Disc.

WHITE NOISE
CD _____ NUMACD 1002
Numa / May '93 / Pinnacle.

Numb

FIXATE
CD _____ KK 094
KK / Feb '94 / Plastic Head.

WASTED SKY
CD _____ KK 126CD
KK / Nov '94 / Plastic Head.

Number One Cup

POSSUM TROT PLAN
CD _____ FLY 012
Flydaddy / Nov '95 / SRD.

Nuncira, Chuco

LA FUERZA MAYOR
CD _____ TUMICD 019
Tumi / '92 / Sterns / Discovery.

Nuns

FOUR DAYS IN A HOTEL ROOM
CD _____ EFA 12201-2
Musical Tragedies / Feb '94 / SRD.

Nuttin' Nyce

DOWN FOR WHATEVER
CD _____ CHIP 160
Jive / Aug '95 / BMG.

Nuyorican Symphony

**NUYORICAN SYMPHONY LIVE AT THE
KNITTING FACTORY**
CD _____ KFWCD 138
Knitting Factory / Feb '95 / Grapevine.

Nyah Fearties

GRANPA CREW
CD _____ NYAH 942
Danceteria / Feb '95 / Plastic Head / ADA.

Nygaard

NO HURRY
CD _____ CDROU 267
Rounder / Dec '90 / CM / Direct / ADA /
Cadillac.

Nyhus, Sven

BERGROSA
CD _____ MASTER 702CD
Master / Jul '93 / ADA.

Nylons

HAPPY TOGETHER
Happy together / Dance of love / Crazy in
love / Touch of your hand / Kiss him goodbye / It's what they call magic / This island
earth / Grown men cry / Chain gang / Face
in the crowd
CD _____ RR 249623
Roadrunner / '89 / Pinnacle.

NYLONS, THE
CD _____ RR 349843
Roadrunner / '89 / Pinnacle.

ONE SIZE FITS ALL
CD _____ RR 349926
Roadrunner / '88 / Pinnacle.

ROCKAPELLA
CD _____ RR 9473 2
Roadrunner / '88 / Pinnacle.

SEAMLESS
CD _____ RR 349856
Roadrunner / '89 / Pinnacle.

Nyman, Michael

ESSENTIAL (Nyman, Michael Band)
CD _____ 4368202
Decca / Jan '93 / PolyGram.

KISS AND OTHER MOVEMENTS, THE
Kiss / Nose list song / Tano between the
lines / Images were introduced / Water
dances (making a splash)-1. Stroking / Wa-
ter dances (making a splash)-2. Gliding /
Water dances (making a splash)-3.
Synchronising
CD _____ EEGCD 40
EG / Jan '87 / EMI.

LIVE
In Re Don Giovanni / Bird list / Queen of the
night / Water dances - dipping / Water
dances - stroking / Upside down violin -
Slow/Faster/Faster still / Piano - concert
suite
CD _____ CDVE 924
Virgin / Oct '94 / EMI.

TIME WILL PRONOUNCE
Self-laudatory hymn of Inanna and her om-
nipotence / Time will pronounce / Convert-
ability of lute strings / For John cage
CD _____ 440282 2
Decca / Jun '93 / PolyGram.

Nyro, Laura

CLASSICS
Wedding bell blues / Stoned soul picnic /
And when I die / Save the country / New
York tendaberry / You've really got a hold
on me / Gibson Street / It's gonna take a
miracle / I never meant to hurt you / Jimmy
Mack / Eli's coming / Time and love / No-
where to run / Lazy Susan / Blackpath /
Monkey time : Dancing in the street / Flim
flam man / Spanish Harlem / Stoney end
CD _____ ELITE 015CD
Elite/Old Gold / Aug '93 / Carlton Home
Entertainment.

GONNA TAKE A MIRACLE
CD _____ BGOCD 27
Beat Goes On / Jul '91 / Pinnacle.

MOTHER'S SPIRITUAL
To a child / Right to vote / Wilderness / Mel-
ody in the sky / Late for love / Free thinker
/ Man in the moon / Talk to a green tree /
Trees of the ages / Brighter song / Road-
notes / Sophia / Mother's spiritual / Refrain
CD _____ CLCD 900924
Line / Oct '94 / CM / Grapevine / ADA /
Conifer / Direct.

O Level

DAY IN THE LIFE OF GILBERT & GEORGE, A
There's a cloud over Liverpool / I helped Patrick McGoohan escape / Odd man out / Apologise / We're not sorry / Sometimes good guys don't follow trends / Storybook beginnings / Sun never sets / Dressing up for the cameras / He's a professional / John Peel march / East Sheen revisited / Pseudo punk / O Level / We love Malcolm / Leave me / Everybody's on revolver tonight / Stairway to boredom / Many unhappy returns / I love to clean my polaris missile / Don't play God with my life / East Sheen
CD _____ CREV 005CD
Rev-Ola / Nov '92 / 3MV / Vital.

O Lieb

CONSTELLATION
Dimension X / Secret visitors / Spice diving / Subsonic interferences
CD _____ 450995345-2
Warner Bros. / Mar '94 / Warner Music.

O, Tony

TOP OF THE BLUES (O, Tony Blues Band)
CD _____ DELCD 3014
Deluge / Jan '96 / Koch.

O Yuki Conjugate

EQUATOR
CD _____ STCD 088
Staalplaat / May '95 / Vital/SAM.

O.B.E.

TUNNEL VISION
CD _____ HOSCD 005
Heidi Of Switzerland / Mar '95 / Pinnacle.

O.G. Funk

OUT OF THE DARK
Me and my folks / Funk is in the house / Funkadelic groupie / Music for my brother / I've been alone / I wanna know / Don't take your love from me / Outta the dark / Angie
CD _____ RCD 10303
Black Arc / Jun '94 / Vital.

O.L.D.

FORMULA
Last look / Break (you) / Devolve / Under glass / Thug / Rid / Amoeba
CD _____ MOSH 131CD
Earache / Oct '95 / Vital.

LO FLUX TUBE
CD _____ MOSH 041CD
Earache / Oct '91 / Vital.

O.M.D.

ARCHITECTURE AND MORALITY
New Stone Age / She's leaving / Souvenir / Sealand / Joan of Arc / Architecture and morality / Georgia / Beginning and the end
CD _____ CDIDX 22
Virgin / Jan '95 / EMI.

BEST OF OMD
Electricity / Messages / Enola Gay / Souvenir / Joan Of Arc / Maid of Orleans / Talking loud and clear / Tesla girls / Locomotion / So in love / Secret / If you leave / (Forever) live and die / Dreaming / Telegraph (CD only) / We love you (CD only) / La femme accident (12" version/CD only) / Genetic engineering (CD only)
CD _____ CDOMD 1
Virgin / Feb '88 / EMI.

CRUSH
So in love / Secret / Bloc bloc bloc / Women 111 / Crush / Eighty eight seconds in Greensboro' / Native daughters of the Golden West / La femme accident / Hold you / Lights are going out
CD _____ CDV 2349
Virgin / Jun '93 / EMI.

DAZZLE SHIPS
Radio Prague / Genetic engineering / ABC auto indistry / Telegraph / This is Helena / International / Romance of the telescope / Silent running / Radio waves / Time zones / Of all the things we've made / Dazzle ships
CD _____ CDV 2261
Virgin / Jun '93 / EMI.

JUNK CULTURE
Junk culture / Tesla girls / Locomotion / Apollo / Never turn away / Love and violence / Hard day / All wrapped up / White trash / Talking loud and clear
CD _____ CDV 2310
Virgin / '86 / EMI.

LIBERATOR

Stand above me / Everyday / King of stone / Dollar girl / Dream of me / Sunday morning / Agnus dei / Love and hate you / Heaven is / Best years of our lives / Christine / Only tears
CD _____ CDV 2715
Virgin / Jun '93 / EMI.

O.M.D. CD BOX SET
CD Set _____ TPAK 7
Virgin / Oct '90 / EMI.

ORCHESTRAL MANOEUVRES IN THE DARK
Bunker soldiers / Almost / Mysterreality / Electricity / Messerschmit twins / Messages / Julia's song / Red frame/White light / Dancing / Pretending to see the future
CD _____ DIDCD 2
Virgin / '87 / EMI.

ORGANISATION
Enola Gay / Second thought / V.C.L. X1 / Motion and heart / Statues / Misunderstanding / More I see you / Promise / Stanlow
CD _____ DIDCD 6
Virgin / Jul '87 / EMI.

PACIFIC AGE
Stay (The black rose and the universal wheel / (Forever) live and die / Pacific age / Dead girls / Shame / Southern / Flame of hope / Goddess of love / We love you / Watch us fall
CD _____ CDV 2398
Virgin / Jun '93 / EMI.

SUGAR TAX
Sailing on the seven seas / Pandora's box / Then you turn away / Speed of light / Was it something I said / Big town / Call my name / Apollo XI / Walking on air / Walk tall / Neon lights / All that matters
CD _____ CDV 2648
Virgin / Apr '91 / EMI.

Oakenfold, Paul

ALL STAR BREAKBEATS VOL. 2 (Bust A Groove)
CD _____ MOLCD 34
Music Of Life / Jun '94 / Grapevine.

Oakey, Philip

PHIL OAKEY/GIORGIO MORODER (Oakey, Philip & Giorgio Moroder)
Why must the show go on / In transit (instrumental) / Goodbye bad times / Brand new love (take a chance) / Valerie / Now / Together in electric dreams (From the soundtrack of 'Electric Dreams') / Be my lover now / Shake it up
CD _____ CDV 2351
Virgin / Jun '88 / EMI.

Oakley, Pete

GHOST IN THE CITY
CD _____ FECD 103
Fellside / Mar '95 / Target/BMG / Direct / ADA.

Oasis

(WHAT'S THE STORY) MORNING GLORY
Hello / Roll with it / Wonderwall / Don't look back in anger / Hey now / Some might say / Cast no shadow / She's electric / Morning glory / Champagne supernova
CD _____ CRECD 189
Creation / Oct '95 / 3MV / Vital.

DEFINITELY MAYBE
Rock 'n' roll star / Shakermaker / Live forever / Up in the sky / Columbia / Supersonic / Bring it on down / Cigarettes and alcohol / Digsy's dinner / Slide away / Married with children
CD _____ CRECD 169
Creation / Aug '94 / 3MV / Vital.

Ob Jay Da

CIRCUS TIME FOR HEARTS
CD _____ OJDCD 6
Burning Ice / Nov '90 / BMG.

PETRIFYING WELL
CD _____ OJDCD 9
Burning Ice / Oct '94 / BMG.

Obadia, Hakki

IRAQI JEWISH/IRAQI MUSIC
CD _____ GV 147CD
Global Village / May '94 / ADA / Direct.

Ó Baoill, Seán

CEOLTA GAEL
CD _____ OSS 2CD
Ossian / Nov '90 / ADA / Direct / CM.

Oberlin, Russell

ENGLISH MEDIEVAL SONGS
CD _____ LEMS 8005
Lyrichord / Aug '94 / Roots / ADA / CM.

ENGLISH POLYPHONY
CD _____ LEMS 8004
Lyrichord / Aug '94 / Roots / ADA / CM.

FRENCH ARS ANTIQUA, THE
CD _____ LEMS 8007
Lyrichord / Aug '94 / Roots / ADA / CM.

LAS CANTIGAS
CD _____ LEMS 8003
Lyrichord / Aug '94 / Roots / ADA / CM.

NOTRE DAME ORGANA
CD _____ LEMS 8002
Lyrichord / Aug '94 / Roots / ADA / CM.

TROUBADOUR/TROUVERE SONGS
CD _____ LEMS 8001
Lyrichord / Aug '94 / Roots / ADA / CM.

Obermayer, Gilles

CONTRACTION
CD Set _____ G 004CD
Musikk Distribusjon / Apr '95 / ADA.

Obey, Ebenezer

GET YOUR JUJUS OUT
CD _____ RCD 20111
Rykodisc / Aug '91 / Vital / ADA.

Obiedo, Ray

IGUANA
Boomerang / Terrible beauty / Werewolf / Iguana / Samba Alegre / Mysterious ways / Small talk / At first glance / Emergency exit
CD _____ WD 0128
Windham Hill / May '91 / Pinnacle / BMG / ADA.

PERFECT CRIME
CD _____ WD 0115
Windham Hill Jazz / Mar '92 / New Note.

ZULAYA
Flamingo / Castile / Zulaya / Midnight taboo / Santa Lucia intro / Aquinas / La samba / Another place / Forever / Santa Lucia
CD _____ 01934111622
Windham Hill / Apr '95 / Pinnacle / BMG / ADA.

Obituary

END COMPLETE, THE
CD _____ RC 92012
Roadrunner / Apr '92 / Pinnacle.

WORLD DEMISE
CD _____ RR 89952
Roadrunner / Sep '94 / Pinnacle.

Oblivions

SOUL FOOD
CD _____ EFA 115892
Crypt / Feb '95 / SRD.

Obmana, Victor

SPIRITUAL BONDING
CD _____ XCD 027
Extreme / Feb '95 / Vital/SAM.

Ó Briain, Garry

SONGS FOR ALL AGES (Ó Briain, Garry & Pádraigín Ní Uallacháin)
CD _____ CEFCD 166
Gael Linn / Jan '95 / Roots / CM / Direct / ADA.

O'Brien, Hod

OPALESSENCE
Opalessence / Touchstone / Bits and pieces / Joy road / Handful of dust / Blues walk / Detour ahead / Joy road (take 1)
CD _____ CRISS 1012CD
Criss Cross / Apr '92 / Cadillac / Harmonia Mundi.

RIDIN' HIGH
CD _____ RSRCD 116
Reservoir Music / Nov '94 / Cadillac.

O'Brien, Kelly

TRADITIONAL MUSIC OF IRELAND (O'Brien, Kelly & Sproule)
CD _____ SHAN 34014CD
Shanachie / Apr '95 / Koch / ADA / Greensleeves.

O'Brien, Michael

BEST OF MICHAEL O'BRIEN
My beautiful green fields / Love at first sight / Ave Maria Moralis / My own native land / My own perculiar way / Foolin' around / Gene Autry is my hero / You never do wrong / Veil of white lace / Walking talking dolly / Country I belong to you / Bed of roses / Shores of Lake McNean / Happy times / Same old fool I used to be / Tears of the bridal bouquet / Birthplace Donegal / Veil of white lace (part 2)
CD _____ KCD 311
Prism / Feb '93 / Prism.

O'Brien, Paddy

BANKS OF THE SHANNON (O'Brien, Paddy & Seamus Connolly)
CD _____ GLCD 3082
Green Linnet / Dec '93 / Roots / CM / Direct / ADA.

STRANGER AT THE GATE
CD _____ GLCD 1091
Green Linnet / Feb '90 / Roots / CM / Direct / ADA.

SUNNYSIDE
Keep on the sunny side / Loreena / Close to you / Little town on the Shannon / My wedding band is a halo of gold) / My lovely Leitrim Shore / Devil woman / Will you think of you / Knock at my window love / She's mine / They gave my everything / Truck driving man / Everybody's reaching out for someone / Sweethearts in heaven / New attraction / She taught me how to yodel
CD _____ HM 051CD
Harmac / Mar '90 / I&B.

O'Brien, Tim

ODD MAN IN
Fell in love (and I can't get out) / One way street / Circles around you / Handsome Molly / Lonely at the bottom too / Like I used to do / Lone tree standing / Love on hold / Flora, lily of the west / Hold to a dream / That's what I like about you / Every tear has a reason why / Hungry eyes / Romance is a slow dance
CD _____ SHCD 3790
Sugarhill / '91 / Roots / CM / ADA / Direct.

OH BOY OH BOY (O'Brien, Tim & The O'Boys)
Church steeple / When I paint my masterpiece / Heartbreak game / Time to learn / Perfect place to hide / Run mountain / Good woman bad / Few are chosen / Shadows to light / Farmer's cused wife / Johnny don't get drunk/Rye straw / He had a long chain on
CD _____ SH 3808CD
Sugarhill / May '93 / Roots / CM / ADA / Direct.

OUT ON THE MOUNTAIN (O'Brien, Tim & Mollie)
CD _____ SH 3825CD
Sugarhill / Oct '94 / Roots / CM / ADA / Direct.

REMEMBER ME (O'Brien, Tim & Mollie)
Looking for the stone / If I had my way / Floods of south Dakota / Shut de do / Stagger lee / Remember me / Somebody the blues / Do right to me baby / That's the way to treat your woman / Motherless children / Pilgrim of sorrow / Hush while the little ones sleep / Out in the country
CD _____ SH CD 3804
Sugarhill / '92 / Roots / CM / ADA / Direct.

ROCK IN MY SHOE
CD _____ SHCD 3835
Sugarhill / Jul '95 / Roots / CM / ADA / Direct.

TAKE ME BACK (O'Brien, Tim & Mollie)
Leave that liar alone / Sweet sunny South / I loved you a thousand ways / Just someone I used to know / Down to the valley to pray / Wave the ocean, wave the sea / Your long journey / When the roses bloom in Dixieland / Unwed fathers / Nobody's fault but mine / Papa's on the housetop / Dream of the miner's child / Christ was born in Bethlehem
CD _____ SH 3766CD
Sugarhill / Mar '89 / Roots / CM / ADA / Direct.

O'Bryant, Jimmy

JIMMY O'BRYANT VOL. 1 (1924-25)
CD _____ JPCD 1518
Jazz Perspectives / May '95 / Jazz Music / Hot Shot.

JIMMY O'BRYANT VOL. 2 (1923-31)
(O'Bryant, Jimmy & Vance Dixon)
CD _____ JPCD 1519
Jazz Perspectives / May '95 / Jazz Music
/ Hot Shot.

Obscur, Clair

PLAY
CD _____ EFAO 15542
Apocalyptic Vision / Apr '95 / Plastic Head
/ SRD.

Obsessed

CHURCH WITHIN, THE
To protect and to serve / Field of hours /
Streamlined / Blind lightning / Neatz brigade
/ World apart / Skybone / Street side / Cli-
mate of despair / Mourning / Touch of
everything / Decimation / Living rain
CD _____ 476504 2
Columbia / Apr '94 / Sony.

LUNAR WOMB
CD _____ H 0015-2
Hellhound / Jan '92 / Plastic Head.

O'Canainn, Thomas

UILEANN PIPES AND SONG
CD _____ PTICD 1035
Outlet / Oct '95 / ADA / Duncans / CM /
Ross / Direct / Koch.

Ocarina

SONG OF OCARINA
CD _____ DSHLCD 7020
D-Sharp / Aug '95 / Pinnacle.

Ocasek, Ric

NEGATIVE THEATER
I still believe / Come alive / Quick change
world / Ride with duce / What's on TV /
Shake a little nervous / Hopped up / Take
me silver / Telephone again / Race to nowhere / Help me find America / Who do I
pay / Wait for fate / America is time / Fade
away
CD _____ 936245248-2
WEA / Mar '93 / Warner Music.

Ó Cathain, Darach

DARACH O CATHAIN
CD _____ SHCD 34005
Claddagh / May '93 / ADA / Direct.

**TRADITIONAL IRISH UNACCOMPANIED
SINGING**
CD _____ CEFCD 040
Gael Linn / Jan '94 / Roots / CM / Direct /
ADA.

Occasional Word

**YEAR OF THE GREAT LEAP SIDEWAYS,
THE**
Open the box / Eternal truth, man /
Thoroughly British affair / Clock clock / I'm
so glad / Barnyard suite / Girl behind me /
Missed my times / Evil venus tree / Eine
steine knack muzak / Trixie's song / Train
set / Sweet tea song / Nuts and bolts / Internal truth, woman / Playground that
fought back / Skin diver / Mrs. Jones / For-
tensia / Close the box
CD _____ SEECD 420
See For Miles/C5 / May '95 / Pinnacle.

Occasionals

**FOOTNOTES: THE COMPLETE
SCOTTISH CEILIDH DANCE**
Gay gordons / Eva three step / St. Bernard's waltz / Gigha white sergeant / Military two step / Canadian barn dance / Pride
of Erin waltz / Strip the willow / Britannia
two step / Waltz country dance / Cumberland square eight / Highland schottische /
Swedish masquerade / Virginia reel / Foula
reel / Veleta waltz / Eightsome reel / Last
waltz
CD _____ IRCD 021
Lismor / Jan '93 / Lismor / Direct / Duncans
/ ADA.

Occult

PREPARE TO MEET THY DOOM
CD _____ FDN 2010
Foundation 2000 / Jun '94 / Plastic Head.

Ocean

SILVER
CD _____ DHR 1
Doll's House / Mar '94 / Pinnacle.

Ocean, Billy

LOVER BOY
Loverboy / Let's get back together / Promise me / Without you / Long and winding
road / It's never too late to try / Here's to
you / Caribbean queen (no more love on the
run) / Stand and deliver / Colour of love /
There'll be sad songs (To make you cry) / If
I should lose you / Showdown / Because of
you
CD _____ 5501182

Spectrum/Karussell / Oct '93 / PolyGram /
THE.

**PEARLS FROM THE PAST - BILLY
OCEAN**
CD _____ KLMCD 001
Scratch / Nov '93 / BMG.

Ocean Blue

BENEATH THE RHYTHM AND SOUND
Peace of mind / Sublime / Listen it's gone
/ Either or / Bliss is unaware / Ice skating at
night / Don't believe everything you hear /
Crash / Cathedral bells / Relatives / Emo-
tions ring
CD _____ 9362453692
Sire / Sep '93 / Warner Music.

Ocean Colour Scene

OCEAN COLOUR SCENE
Talk on / How about you / Giving it all away
/ Justine / Do yourself a favour / Third
shade of green / Sway / Penny pinching
rainy heaven days / One of those days / Is
she coming home / Blue deep ocean /
Reprise
CD _____ 5122692
Fontana / Jan '96 / PolyGram.

Oceanic

THAT ALBUM BY OCEANIC
Is this the end / Insanity / Heavenly feel /
Wicked love / Ignorance / Controlling me /
Strut / Using me / Give this love some
meaning / Moments in time / Insanity (2)
(Not on album) / Wicked love (2) (Not on
album)
CD _____ GOODCD 1
Dead Dead Good / May '92 / Pinnacle.

Ochoa, Calixto

**SALSA, CUMBIA & VALLENATO (Ochoa,
Calixto & Las Vibraciones)**
CD _____ TUMICD 036
Tumi / '94 / Sterns / Discovery.

Ochoa, Rafael

**HARPS OF VENUZUELA (Ochoa, Rafael
& Rafael Aponte)**
CD _____ PS 65083
Playasound / Mar '92 / Harmonia Mundi /
ADA.

Ochs, Phil

ALL THE NEWS THATS FIT TO SING
One more parade / Thresher / Talking Vi-
etnam / Lou Marsh / Power and the glory /
Celia / Bells / Automation song / Ballad of
William Worthy / Knock on the door / Talk-
ing Cuban crisis / Bound for glory / Too
many martyrs / What's that I hear
CD _____ HNCD 4427
Hannibal / Apr '94 / Vital / ADA.

BROADSIDE TAPES PART 1, THE
CD _____ SFWCD 40008
Smithsonian Folkways / Mar '95 / ADA /
Direct / Koch / CM / Cadillac.

GREATEST HITS: PHIL OCHS
One way ticket home / Jim Dean of Indiana
/ My kingdom for a car / Boy in Ohio / Gas
station women / Chords of fame / Ten cents
a coup / Bach, Beethoven, Mozart and me
/ Basket in the pool / No more songs
CD _____ EDCD 201
Edsel / Jul '90 / Pinnacle / ADA.

I AIN'T MARCHING ANYMORE
I ain't marching anymore / In the heat of the
summer / Draft dodger rag / That's what I
want to hear / That was The President / Iron
lady / Highway man / Links on the chain /
Hills of West Virginia / Men behind the guns
/ Talking Birmingham jam / Ballad of the
carpenter / Days of decision / Here's to the
state of Mississippi
CD _____ HNCD 4422
Hannibal / Apr '94 / Vital / ADA.

TOAST TO THOSE WHO ARE GONE, A
Do what I have to do / Ballad of Billie Sol /
Coloured town / AMA Song / William Moore
/ Paul Crump / Going down to Mississippi /
I'll be there / Ballad of Oxford / No Christ-
mas in Kentucky / Toast to those who are
gone / I'm tired
CD _____ DIAB 813
Diabolo / Oct '94 / Pinnacle.

O'Connell, Bill

LOST VOICES
Lost voices / Yellowtail / Good enough /
Chega de saudade (no more blues) / Cosat
verde / Sidestep / Sand stones / Sophie
rose / In time
CD _____ ESJCD 235
Essential Jazz / Oct '94 / BMG.

LOVE FOR SALE
Ping pong / Have you met Miss Jones /
Love dance / Well you needn't / Slow mo-
tion / Casaba / Love for sale / Old folks /
Sweet love / Like someone in love
CD _____ 66053019
Jazz City / Mar '91 / New Note.

O'Connell, Helen

SWEETEST SOUNDS, THE
CD _____ HCD 251
Hindsight / Aug '94 / Target/BMG / Jazz
Music.

O'Connell, Maura

ALWAYS
CD _____ TFCB 5011CD
Third Floor / Oct '94 / Total/BMG / ADA /
Direct.

BLUE IS THE COLOUR OF HOPE
WEA / Jan '95 / Warner Music.
CD _____ 9362450632

JUST IN TIME
Scholar / If you love me / Feet of a dancer
/ Isle of Malachy / New Orleans / Water is
wide / Leaving Neidin / Crazy dreams / Lo-
ve's old sweet song / Another morning / I
will / Just in time
CD _____ CDPH 1124
Philo / '90 / Direct / CM / ADA.

MAURA O'CONNELL
Living in these troubled times / God only
knows / Send this whisper / Lovers at last
/ Till the right one comes along / I don't
know how you do it / Saw you running / All
of me / Love is on a roll / Spend the night
with you / My Lagan love
CD _____ TFCB 5007CD
Third Floor / Oct '94 / Total/BMG / ADA /
Direct.

STORIES
Blue chalk / Hit the ground running / Love
divine / Poetic justice / Stories / Half moon
bay / This town can't get over you / Rainmaker / Shotgun down the avalanche / An
ordinary day / If I fell / Wall around you heart
CD _____ HNCD 1389
Hannibal / Oct '95 / Vital / ADA.

O'Connell, Moloney

**KILKELLY (O'Connell, Moloney &
Keane)**
CD _____ GLCD 1072
Green Linnet / Feb '92 / Roots / CM /
Direct / ADA.

O'Connell, Robbie

CLOSE TO THE BONE
Gay old hag / William Hollander / Week before Easter / Earl of Murray / Waterford
waltz / With Kitty I'll go for a waltz / Torn
petticoat/The rambling pitchfork / I know
where I'm going / Bobby's britches / Sliabh
na mBan / Ferrybank piper / Ham Sunday
CD _____ GLCD 1038
Green Linnet / Oct '88 / Roots / CM / Direct
/ ADA.

LOVE OF THE LAND, THE
Love of the land / Keg of brandy / Early riser
/ Full moon over Managua / Land of Liberty
/ Road to Dunmore / Two nations / Last of
the Gleemen / You're not Irish
CD _____ GLCD 1097
Green Linnet / Nov '92 / Roots / CM / Direct
/ ADA.

NEVER LEARNED TO DANCE
Love knows no bounds / American lives /
Galileo / Winning side / Turning of the tide
/ Hard to say goodbye / Man from Conne-
mara / When the moon is full / Old man of
the mountain / Mistress / So near / Singer
CD _____ GLCD 1124
Green Linnet / May '93 / Roots / CM / Direct
/ ADA.

O'Connor, Cavan

SMILIN' THROUGH
Rose of tralee / One alone / Danny boy / In
the still of the night / Vagabond song / Hear
my song Violetta / Could you be true to
eyes of blue / God will remember / Little
village green / Marie / My heart is always
calling you / Put a little springtime / Shannon river / Smilin' through / Star and the
rose / Star of the County Down / Take me
back to dear old Ireland / There's something in your eyes / When it's springtime in
old Ireland / Without you / Would you take
me back again / You, me and love
CD _____ CD AJA 5085
Living Era / Apr '92 / Koch.

VAGABOND OF SONG, THE
CD _____ PLATCD 35
Prism / Mar '95 / Prism.

**VERY BEST OF THE SINGING
VAGABOND, THE**
CD _____ SWNCD 001
Sound Waves / May '95 / Target/BMG.

O'Connor, Charles

ANGEL ON THE MANTLEPIECE
CD _____ ALZO 1CD
Ritual / Jul '95 / ADA.

O'Connor, Gerry

**LA LUGH (O'Connor, Gerry & Eithne Ni
Uallachain)**
Mal bhan ni Chilleannain/Destitution / Ster-
ling Tom/Tommy Bhetty's hornmmpipe /

One morning in May / Wedding jig/Aunt Lizzie's jig / Liostail me le Sairsint / Shetland
bus / Donellan set / Road to Clady / Mummer's march/The Water Ouzel / Rosebuds
in summer / Launching the boat / Draw near
my wayward Darling / On Brigid's eve / Boy
in his pants/Big John's jig / Emigrant's farewell / Drogheda lassies/The Donegal trav-
eller/Lisa Ornstein's reel
CD _____ CCF 29CD
Claddagh / Jun '93 / ADA / Direct.

TIME TO TIME
CD _____ CLUNCD 051
Mulligan / Sep '86 / CM / ADA.

O'Connor, Hazel

COVER PLUS
We're all grown up / Hanging around / Ee-
i-adio / Not for you / Hold on / So you're
born / Dawn chorus / Animal farm / Runaway / What do you gotta do / Men of good
fortune / That's life
CD _____ MSCD 23
Music De-Luxe / Jul '95 / Magnum Music
Group.

SEE THE WRITING ON THE WALL
CD _____ 901291
Line / Oct '94 / CM / Grapevine / ADA /
Conifer / Direct.

O'Connor, Mark

CHAMPIONSHIP YEARS '75-'84, THE
Grey eagle / Clarinet polka / Dusty Miller / I
don't love nobody / Wednesday night waltz
/ Herman's rag / Sally Goodin / Sally Johnson / Yellow rose waltz / Tom and Jerry /
Billy in the lowground / Herman's rag (2) /
Allentown polka / Brilliancy / Black and
white rag / Tom and Jerry (2) / Clarinet
polka (2) / Dill pickle rag / Grey eagle (2) /
Leather britches / Don't let the deal go
down / Golden eagle hornpipe / I don't love
nobody (2) / Brilliancy (2) / Tug boat / Grey
eagle (3) / Beaumont rag / Hell among the
yearlings / Bill Cheatham / Sally Goodin (2)
/ Herman's rag (3) / Choctaw / Westphalia
waltz / Black and white rag #2 / Herman's
hornpipe / Dill pickle rag (2) / Sally Ann /
Clarinet polka (3) / Arkansas traveller /
Jesse polka
CD _____ CMFCD 015
Country Music Foundation / Jan '93 / Direct
/ ADA.

HEROES
CD _____ 936245257-2
WEA / Feb '94 / Warner Music.

MARKOLOGY
Dixie breakdown / Markology / Kit's waltz /
Fluid drive / Blackberry blossom / Pickin'
the wind / Banks of the Ohio / Berserkeley
/ On top of the world
CD _____ ROU 009CD
Rounder / Aug '93 / CM / Direct / ADA /
Cadillac.

NEW NASHVILLE CATS, THE
Bowtie / Restless / Nashville shuffle boogie
/ Pick it apart / Traveller's ridge / Granny
White special / Cat in the bag / Ballad of
Sally Anne / Swang / Dance of the ol'
swamp rat / Bowl of bula / Lime rock /
Sweet Suzanne / Orange blossom special /
Now it belongs to you
CD _____ 7599265092
Warner Bros. / Jun '92 / Warner Music.

RETROSPECTIVE
CD _____ CD 11507
Rounder / '88 / CM / Direct / ADA /
Cadillac.

SOPPIN' THE GRAVY
Soppin' the gravy / Misty moonlight waltz /
College hornpipe / Calgary polka / Morning
star waltz / Tennessee Wagoner / Yellow
rose waltz / Medley (Speed the plow/The
maid behind the bar (Judy's reel)/Atottler's
reel) / Jesse polka / Dawn waltz / Wild fiddler's rag / Over the rainbow
CD _____ CDROU 0137
Rounder / '92 / CM / Direct / ADA / Cadillac.

O'Connor, Martin

CHATTERBOX
CD _____ DARACD 052
Dara / Oct '93 / Roots / CM / Direct / ADA
/ Koch.

CONNACHTMAN'S RAMBLES
CD _____ LUNCD 027
Mulligan / Feb '95 / CM / ADA.

PERPETUAL MOTION
Fandango / Rags to rock'n'roll / Happy
hours / Carnival of Venice / Perpetual mo-
tion / Ebra polka / Emerald blues / Cajun
medley / Beau St. Waltzes / Bulgarian jig /
Sophie for Sofia / Midnight on the water /
Hound dog
CD _____ CCF 26CD
Claddagh / '90 / ADA / Direct.

O'Connor, Sinead

AM I NOT YOUR GIRL?
Why don't you do right / Bewitched, bothered and bewildered / Secret love / Black
coffee / Success has made a failure of our
home / Don't cry for me Argentina / I wanna

be loved by you / Gloomy Sunday / Love Letters / How insensitive / Don't cry for me Argentina (Inst)
CD _____ CCD 1952
Ensign / Sep '92 / EMI.

I DO NOT WANT WHAT I HAVEN'T GOT
Feel so different / I am stretched on your grave / Three babies / Emperor's new clothes / Black boys on mopeds / Nothing compares 2 U / Jump in the river / You cause as much sorrow / Last day of our acquaintance / I do not want what I haven't got
CD _____ CCD 1759
Ensign / Mar '90 / EMI.

LION AND THE COBRA, THE
Jackie / Mandinka / Jerusalem / Just like u said it would b / Never get old / Troy / I want your (hands on me) / Drink before the war / Just call me Joe
CD _____ CCD 1612
Ensign / Oct '87 / EMI.

UNIVERSAL MOTHER
Speech extract / Fire on Babylon / John I love you / My darling child / Am I a human / Red football / All apologies / Perfect Indian / Scorn not his simplicity / All babies / In this heart / Tiny grief song / Famine / Thank you for hearing me
CD _____ CDCHEN 34
Ensign / Sep '94 / EMI.

Octagon Man

EXCITING WORLD OF...
CD _____ TRONCD 5X
Electron Industries / Nov '95 / Disc.

October Faction

OCTOBER FACTION
CD _____ SST 036 CD
SST / May '93 / Plastic Head.

SECOND FACTIONALISATION
CD _____ SST 056 CD
SST / May '93 / Plastic Head.

October Project

OCTOBER PROJECT
Bury my lovely / Ariel / Where you are / Lonely voice / Eyes of mercy / Return to me / Wall of silence / Take me as I am / Now I lay me down / Always / Paths of desire / Be my hero
CD _____ 474258 2
Epic / Jun '94 / Sony.

October, Gene

LIFE AND STRUGGLE
CD _____ RRCD 196
Receiver / Mar '95 / Grapevine.

O'Day, Anita

ANITA O'DAY & HER QUARTET LIVE
CD _____ SLCD 9004
Starline / Feb '94 / Jazz Music.

ANITA O'DAY 1975
CD _____ STCD 4147
Storyville / Feb '90 / Jazz Music / Wellard / CM / Cadillac.

HIGH STANDARDS
CD _____ CDSL 5209
DRG / Jan '89 / New Note.

I GET A KICK OUT OF YOU
Song for you / Undecided / What are you doing the rest of your life / Exactly like you / When Sunny gets blue / It had to be you / Opus one / Gone with the wind
CD _____ ECD 22054
Evidence / Jul '93 / Harmonia Mundi / ADA / Cadillac.

MEETS THE BIG BANDS
CD _____ MCD 0472
Moon / Nov '93 / Harmonia Mundi / Cadillac.

ONCE UPON A SUMMERTIME
Sweet Georgia Brown / Love for sale / 'S Wonderful / Tea for two / Once upon a summertime / Night and day / Anita's blues / They can't take that away from me / Boogie blues / Girl from Ipanema / Is you is or is you ain't my baby / Nightingale sang in Berkeley Square
CD _____ JASMCD 2531
Jasmine / Feb '95 / Wellard / Swift / Conifer / Cadillac / Magnum Music Group.

PICK YOURSELF UP
Don't be that way / Let's face the music and dance / I never had a chance / Stompin' at the Savoy / Pick yourself up / Stars fell on Alabama / Man with a horn / I used to be colour blind / There's a lull in my life / Let's begin
CD _____ 5173292
Verve / Jun '93 / PolyGram.

RULES OF THE ROAD
Rules of the road / Black coffee / Detour ahead / Shaking the blues away / Music that makes me dance / As long as there's music / Sooner or later / What is a man / Here's that rainy day / It's you or no one / I told ya I love ya, now get out

CD _____ CD 2310950
Pablo / Apr '94 / Jazz Music / Cadillac / Complete/Pinnacle.

WAVE (Live at Ronnie Scott's)
Wave / You'd be so nice to come home to / On Green Dolphin street / I can't get started (with you) / It don't mean a thing if it ain't got that swing / Street of dreams / 'S wonderful / They can't take that away from me / Is you is or is you ain't my baby / My funny valentine / I cried for you / Four brothers
CD _____ CLACD 330
Castle / '93 / BMG.

O'Day, Molly

MOLLY O'DAY AND THE CUMBERLAND MOUNTAIN FOLKS
Tramp on the street / When God comes and gathers his jewels / Black sheep returned to the fold / Put my rubber doll away / Drunken driver / Tear stained letter / Lonely mound of clay / Six more miles / Singing waterfall / At the first fall of snow / Matthew twenty four / I don't care if tomorrow never comes / Hero's death / I'll never see sunshine again / Too late, too late / Why do you weep dear willow / Don't forget the family prayer / I heard my mother weeping / Mother's gone but not forgotten / Evening train / This is the end / Fifteen years ago / Teardrops falling in the snow / With you on my mind / If you see my saviour / Heaven's radio / When my time comes to go / Don't sell Daddy anymore whiskey / Higher in my prayers / Travelling the highway home / It's different now / When the angels rolled the stone away / It's all coming true / When we see our Redeemer's face
CD _____ BCD 15565
Bear Family / Jun '92 / Rollercoaster / Direct / CM / Swift / ADA.

Oden, Jimmy

1932-1948
CD _____ SOB 35082CD
Story Of The Blues / Apr '95 / Koch / ADA.

St. LOUIS JIMMY ODEN VOL. 1 1932-1944
CD _____ DOCD 5234
Blues Document / May '94 / Swift / Jazz Music / Hot Shot.

St. LOUIS JIMMY ODEN VOL. 2 1944-1955
CD _____ DOCD 5235
Blues Document / May '94 / Swift / Jazz Music / Hot Shot.

Odessa Balalaikas

ART OF THE BALALAIKA, THE
CD _____ 7559790342
Elektra Nonesuch / Jan '95 / Warner Music.

Odessa Express

BABEL
CD _____ SYNCD 159
Syncoop / Jun '94 / ADA / Direct.

Odetta

ESSENTIAL, THE
CD Set _____ CDVCD 43/44
Start / Sep '89 / Koch.

ODETTA AND THE BLUES
Hard, oh Lord / Believe I'll go / Oh papa / How long blues / Hogan's alley / Learnin' this morning / Oh, my babe / Yonder come the blues / Make me a pallet on the floor / Weeping willow blues / Go down sunshine / Nobody knows you (when you're down and out)
CD _____ OBCCD 509
Original Blues Classics / Nov '92 / Complete/Pinnacle / Wellard / Cadillac.

ODETTA AT THE TOWN HALL
CD _____ VMD 2109
Vanguard / Jan '96 / Complete/Pinnacle / Discovery.

SINGS BALLADS AND BLUES
CD _____ TCD 1004
Rykodisc / Feb '96 / Vital / ADA.

TIN ANGEL (Odetta & Larry Mohr)
CD _____ OBCCD 565
Original Blues Classics / Jul '94 / Complete/Pinnacle / Wellard / Cadillac.

WOMEN IN (E)MOTION FESTIVAL
CD _____ T&M 101
Tradition & Moderne / Nov '94 / Direct / ADA.

Odom, Andrew

FEEL SO GOOD (Odom, Andrew 'Big Voice' & Magic Slim/Lucky Peterson)
Feel so good / I made up my mind / Mother-in-law blues / Woke up this morning / Memo blues / Bad feeling / You say that you love me baby / Reconsider baby
CD _____ ECD 260272
Evidence / Feb '93 / Harmonia Mundi / ADA / Cadillac.

O'Donnell, Daniel

BOY FROM DONEGAL, THE
Donegal shore / Old rustic bridge / Galway bay / Forty shades of green / My side of the road / 5000 miles from Sligo / Old bog road / Slievenamon / Noreen Bawn / Ballyhoe
CD _____ IHCD 04
Irish Music Heritage / Oct '89 / Prism.

CHRISTMAS WITH DANIEL
Silent night / Memory of an old Christmas card / Silver bells / C-H-R-I-S-T-M-A-S / White Christmas / When a child is born / Rockin' around the Christmas tree / Christmas song / Christmas long ago / Gift / Christmas time in Inisfree / Snowflake / I saw Mommy kissing Santa Claus / Pretty paper
CD _____ BCD 704
Ritz / Nov '94 / Pinnacle.

CLASSIC COLLECTION
CD _____ RITZBCD 705
Ritz / Oct '95 / Pinnacle.

DATE WITH DANIEL O'DONNELL - LIVE, A
I just wanna dance with you / Whatever happened to old fashioned love / Somewhere between / Follow your dream / You're the reason / Love in your eyes / Minute you're gone / Little things / My Irish country home / Isle of Innisfree / I need you / Never ending song of love / Wedding song / My Donegal shore / Stand beside me / Old rugged cross / How great thou art / Pretty little girl from Omagh / My shoes keep walking back to you / Rose of Tralee / Our house are red/Moonlight and roses
CD _____ RITZBCD 702
Ritz / Oct '93 / Pinnacle.

DON'T FORGET TO REMEMBER
I don't care / Old loves never die / I wonder where you are tonight / Don't be angry / Roses are red / Before I'm over you / Take good care of her / Pretty little girl from Omagh / Green willow / Don't let me cross over / Good old days / Pat Murphy's meadow / I just can't make it on my own
CD _____ RITZCD 105
Ritz / Dec '87 / Pinnacle.

ESPECIALLY FOR YOU
Singin' the blues / Lover's chain / You're the first thing I think of / Someday / There'll never be anyone else / Travelling light / Old broken hearts / Leaving is easy / She goes walking through my mind / Come back paddy reilly to Ballyjamesduff / Sweet forget me not / Silver threads among the gold / It comes and goes / Guilty / Happy years
CD _____ BCD 703
Ritz / Oct '94 / Pinnacle.

FAVOURITES
Bed of roses / Excuse me / Geisha girl / Home sweet home / Home is where the heart is / Forever you'll be mine / Streets of Baltimore / Bringing Mary home / Banks of my own lovely Lee / Green hills of Sligo
CD _____ RITZCD 0052
Ritz / Apr '90 / Pinnacle.

FOLLOW YOUR DREAM
I need you (intro) / Stand Beside Me / Eileen / Pretty Little Girl From Omagh / Destination Donegal / Medley / Medley #2 / Wedding song (Ave Maria) / Irish country home / Ramblin' Rose / I just want to dance with you / Medley #3 / Medley #4 / White River stomp / Our House Is A Home / Never Ending Song Of Love / Rockin' alone in an old rocking chair / Standing Room Only / Welcome home / Love in your eyes / You send me your love / Turkey In The Straw / I Need You / Medley #5 / Reprise / How Great Thou Art
CD _____ RITZBCD 701
Ritz / Nov '92 / Pinnacle.

FROM THE HEART
Minute you're gone / Mary from Dungloe / Wasting my time / Things / It doesn't matter anymore / Bye bye love / Kelly / Old rugged cross / Act naturally / Honey / Wooden heart / It keeps right on a-hurtin' / My bonnie Maureen / I know that you know / Old Dungarvan oak / Danny boy
CD _____ RITZCD 0068
Ritz / Oct '92 / Pinnacle.

I NEED YOU
Sing me an old Irish song / I need you / From a jack to a king / Lovely rose of Clare / Stand beside me / Irish eyes / Dear old Galway town / Three leaf shamrock / Veil of white lace / Kickin' each others hearts around / Medals for mothers / Wedding bells / Snowflake / Your friendly Irish way / Lough Melvin's rocky shore / I love you because
CD _____ RITZCD 104
Ritz / Jun '87 / Pinnacle.

LAST WALTZ, THE
Here I am in love again / We could / Last waltz of the evening / When only the sky was blue / Heaven with you / You know I still love you / Talk back trembling lips / Shelter of your eyes / When we get together / Ring of gold / Fool such as I / Memory number one / Look both ways / Little patch of blue / Marianne (Only on CD.)
CD _____ RITZCD 0058
Ritz / Oct '90 / Pinnacle.

THOUGHTS OF HOME
My shoes keep walking back to you / Mountains of Mourne / London leaves / Blue eyes cryin' in the rain / Old days remembered / Send me the pillow that you dream on / Moonlight and roses / Little piece of Heaven / Far far from home / Isle of Innisfree / My heart skips / I know one / I'll take you home again Kathleen / Second fiddle / My favourite memory / Forty shades of green
CD _____ TCD 2372
Telstar / Oct '89 / BMG.

TWO SIDES OF DANIEL O'DONNELL, THE
Green glens of Antrim / Blue hills of Breffni / Any Tipperary town / Latchyco / Home town on the Foyle / These are my mountains / My Donegal shore / Crying my heart out over you / My old pal / Our house is a home / Your old love letters / Twenty one years / Highway 40 blues / I wouldn't change you if I could
CD _____ RITZCD 500
Ritz / '91 / Pinnacle.

VERY BEST OF DANIEL O'DONNELL, THE
I need you / Never ending song of love / Don't forget to remember / Country boy like me / She's no angel / Stand beside me / Eileen / Pretty little girl from Omagh / Danny boy / Wedding song / My Donegal shore / Our house is a home / Loved ones goodbye / Home is where the heart is / Old rugged cross / You send me your love / Take good care of her / Standing room only
CD _____ RITZBCD 700
Ritz / Oct '91 / Pinnacle.

O'Donnell, Eugene

FOGGY DEW, THE (O'Donnell, Eugene & James MacCafferty)
CD _____ GLCD 1084
Green Linnet / Feb '91 / Roots / CM / Direct / ADA.

SLOW AIRS & SET DANCES
Downfall of Paris / Scotsman over the border / Lodge Road / Da auld resting chair / Derry hornpipe / Barney Brallaghan/Ride a mile / Celtic lament / Planxty O'Donnell / Jockey to the fair / Hunt / I won't see you anymore, my dear / Three sea captains / Bonny lass o'Bon Accord / Hurry the jug / Humours of Bandon/Planxty Maggie Brown / Planxty Drury
CD _____ GLCD 1015
Green Linnet / Oct '88 / Roots / CM / Direct / ADA.

O'Donnell, Peter

SHAKESPEARE BLUES
CD _____ QMCD 001
Bareface / Jun '94 / Sony.

O'Dowda, Brendan

IRISH FAVOURITES OF PERCY FRENCH
Phil the fluter's ball / Mountains of Mourne / Whistlin' Phil McHugh / Wait for a while now Mary / Drum colliner / Sweet Marie / Eileen oge / Come back Paddy Reilly / Carmody's Mare / Fortunes of Finnegan / Slattery's mounted foot / Gortnamona / Are you right there Michael / Emigrant's letter / Donegans daughter / Irish mother / That's why we're burying him / Mary Anne McHugh / Inishmeela / Father O'Callaghan
CD _____ CC 267
Classics For Pleasure / May '91 / EMI.

O'Duffy, Michael

SONG FOR IRELAND, A
CD _____ MATCD 267
Castle / Apr '93 / BMG.

Odyssey

GREATEST HITS
Going back to my roots / Inside out / Magic touch / Oh no not my baby / Weekend lover / Don't tell me, tell her / Use it up and wear it out / Hang together / It will be alright / Follow me (play follow the leader) / Easy come, easy go / When you love somebody / If you're looking for a way out / Native New Yorker (Mixes)
CD _____ ND 90436
RCA / Mar '90 / BMG.

ROOTS
Use it up and wear it out / Going back to my roots / Easy come, easy go / Hang together / It will be alright / Lucky star / Magic touch / Don't tell me / Oh no not my baby / Happy together / You keep me dancin' / Comin' back for more / Ever had it all / I can't keep holding back my love / Down boy / Happy people
CD _____ PWKS 4123
Carlton Home Entertainment / Nov '92 / Carlton Home Entertainment.

Oedipussy.

DIVAN
CD _____ HANCD 1
Hansome / Mar '95 / Pinnacle.

O'Farrell, Sean

ALWAYS
Way love ought to be / Eighteen yellow roses / She's good at loving me / I'd love you to want me / Those brown eyes / Soldier's tale / Every road leads back to you / Judy / Champion of 403 Mulberry Drive / Baby don't you know / Always / Do you know how much I love you / Longing to hold you again / Still
CD _____ RCD 535
Ritz / Oct '93 / Pinnacle.

SONGS JUST FOR YOU
When the girl in your arms (is the girl in your heart) / This song is just for you / Love without end, Amen / Galway shawl / Walk on by / Nobody's child / Wanted / Billy can't read / Two loves / Straight and narrow / You would do the same for me / Hey pretty lady / Crystal chandeliers / Missing him
CD _____ RCD 541
Ritz / Jun '94 / Pinnacle.

Offer, Cullen

FEATHER MERCHANT
CD _____ PCD 7091
Progressive / Jun '93 / Jazz Music.

SWINGIN' TEXAS TENOR, THE
CD _____ PCD 7086
Progressive / Jun '93 / Jazz Music.

Offermans, Wil

DAILY SENSIBILITIES
CD _____ BVHAASTCD 9206
Bvhaast / Oct '87 / Cadillac.

Offspring

IGNITION
CD _____ E 864242
Epitaph / Nov '94 / Plastic Head / Pinnacle.

NITRO
CD _____ 158032
Epitaph / Oct '95 / Plastic Head / Pinnacle.

OFFSPRING
Jennifer lost the war / Elders / Out on patrol / Crossroads / Demons / Beheaded / Tehran / Thousand days / Blackball / I'll be waiting / Kill the president
CD _____ 86460-2
Epitaph / Nov '95 / Plastic Head / Pinnacle.

SMASH
CD _____ E 86432CD
Epitaph / May '94 / Plastic Head / Pinnacle.

Oficina De Cordas

PERNAMBUCO'S MUSIC
CD _____ NI 5398
Nimbus / Oct '94 / Nimbus.

Ó Flaharta, John Beag

AN LOCHAN
CD _____ CIC 084CD
Clo Iar-Chonnachta / Nov '93 / CM.

AN TANCAIRE - FICHE AMHRAN 1980-90
CD _____ CIC 025CD
Clo Iar-Chonnachta / Jan '91 / CM.

TÁ AN WORKHOUSE LAN
CD _____ CICD 093
Clo Iar-Chonnachta / Dec '93 / CM.

WINDS OF FREEDOM
CD _____ CICD 106
CICD / Jan '95 / ADA.

O'Flynn, Liam

BRENDAN VOYAGE (O'Flynn, Liam & Orchestra)
CD _____ TARACD 3006
Tara / Oct '89 / CM / ADA / Direct / Conifer.

GIVEN NOTE, THE
O'Farrell's welcome to Limerick / O'Rourke's/The Merry sisters/Colonel Fraser / Come with me over the mountain / Smile in the dark / Farewell to Govan / Joyce's tune / Green island/Spellan the fiddler / Foliada de Elvina / Ag taisteal na Blarnan / Rambler / Aherlow jig / Smith's a gallant fireman / Romeo's exile / Rocks of Bawn / Cailin na gruage doinne / Teno un amor na / Alborada - Unha noite no Santo Cristo
CD _____ TARACD 3034
Tara / Oct '95 / CM / ADA / Direct / Conifer.

OUT TO ANOTHER SIDE
Foxchase / Wild geese / Dean's pamphlet / Gynt at the gate / Winter's end / After Aughrim's great disaster / Blackwells / Ar Bhruach na Iaoi / Lady Dillon / Dollards and the Harlequin hornpipes / Sean O Duibhir a Ghleanna
CD _____ TARACD 3031
Tara / Aug '93 / CM / ADA / Direct / Conifer.

Ogada, Ayub

EM MANA KUOYO
Obiero / Dala / Wa Winjigo Ero / Thum Nyatiti / Kronkrohino / 10% / Ondiek / Kothbiro / En Mana Kuoyo
CD _____ CDRW 42
Realworld / May '93 / EMI / Sterns.

Ogden, Nigel

MUSIC FOR ALL
When the saints go marching in / Border ballad / Mulligan musketeers / Tritsch tratsch polka / Sweet and low / Kalinka / Liberty bell / Going home / Dam busters march / Bobby Shaftoe / Sailing / Storm at sea / Strawberry fair / Bells of St. Mary's / Tydi a roddiast / Jerusalem / Finlandia / Morte criste
CD _____ OS 211
Valentine / Jan '95 / Conifer.

SENTIMENTAL JOURNEY/TRIBUTE TO REGINALD DIXON
Royal Air Force march past / I'll string along with you / You'll never know / Polly / Smile smile smile / Certain smile / Morning, Noon and night / I can't tell a waltz from a tango / Val suzon / Under the linden tree / I kiss your hand, Madame / Spitfire prelude / Cole Porter classics / Sentimental journey / Somebody stole my gal / Why did she fall for the leader of the band / Solitude / Saddle your blues to a wild mustang / Rosalie / I double dare you / Oh ma mai / I love to whistle / You're an education / I won't dance / Lovely to look at / Smoke gets in your eyes / Little girl / As time goes by / When I take my sugar to tea / Happy feet / Manhattan / Boo hoo / Marching with the organ
CD _____ OS 214
Bandleader / Aug '95 / Conifer.

WURLITZER CELEBRATION
Beyond the blue horizon / Valse romantique / Pizzicato polka / Celebration march / How are things in Glocca Morra / Art deco / Three piece suite / Duo / In a clock store / Shadow waltz / At the sign of the swingin' cymbal / Love everlasting / Minuet / Paean / Whistler and his dog / Dusk / Waterloo march / Tell me I'm forgiven / Gymnopedie / Eric coates fantasia
CD _____ OS 206
Valentine / Mar '94 / Conifer.

Ogermann, Claus

CITYSCAPE (Ogermann, Claus & Michael Brecker)
CD _____ 7599236982
Warner Bros. / May '95 / Warner Music.

Ó Gráda, Conal

TOP OF COOM, THE
CD _____ CCF 27CD
Claddagh / Jan '91 / ADA / Direct.

O'Hagan, Sean

HIGH LLAMAS
Perry Como / Edge of the sun / Pretty boy / Hoping you would change your mind / C'mon let's go / Paint and pets / Doggy / Half face cat / Trees / Have you heard the latest news
CD _____ FIENDCD 192
Demon / Jul '95 / Pinnacle / ADA.

O'Hara, Mary

BEAUTIFUL MUSIC OF MARY O'HARA, THE
Lord of the dance (live) / Danny boy / Last rose of summer / In an english country garden (live) / Bunch of thyme / My lagan (live) / Going home / Perhaps love (live) / She moved through the fair / Messenger / One day at a time / Willie's gane to Melville castle (live) / Roisin dubh / Scent of the roses / Scarborough Fair / Never saw the roses / Memory / Quiet land of Erin
CD _____ MCCD 070
Music Club / Jun '92 / Disc / THE / CM.

COLLECTION
CD _____ COL 072
Collection / Mar '95 / Target/BMG.

INSTRUMENTAL COLLECTION, THE
Way we were / Londonderry air / Skye boat song / Pamela Brown / Bunch of thyme / Scarborough Fair / For the good times / Bright eyes / Walking in the air / Three times a lady / Going home / Greensleeves / In an English country garden / Memory / Annie's song / One day at a time
CD _____ VALD 8059
Valentine / Jul '88 / Conifer.

IRISH - SCOTTISH RECITAL VOCALS & HARP
An crann ubhall (the apple tree) / She lived beside the anner / Cucuin a chuauchin / Kitty of Coleraine / Roisin dubh / Down by the Sally gardens / Luibin o luth / I will walk with my love / Seothin seo / Parting / Is ar eirinn ni-n eosfhainn ce h-i / Last rose of summer / Sean sa bhriste leathair (John and his leather breecbes) / Young Brigd O'Malley / Deus Meus (my God) / I know my love (with another) / Varee is love / Sleep talk / Sliabh geal gcua / Trotting to the fair / Willie's gane to Melville castle / Song of the

waterhouse / Annie Laurie / Laird of cockpen / Cro cheann t saile / Shetland lullaby / Fhideag airgid (silver whistle) / Elfin knight / Shetland spinning song / Bonnie Earl O'Moray / Iarla narn bratcha bana (earl fo the white banners) / Willie's drowned in yarrow / Afton water / Hebridean waulking song / TWA Corbies / Lord Randal / Lark in the clear air / Ae fond kiss / Oaken ashes / Pedlar's song / Una bhan (fair una) / Eros / Face to face / Lord of the dance / Among silence / Prayer of the butterfly / New year carol / Come lord
CD _____ MAGPIE 6
See For Miles/C5 / Sep '95 / Pinnacle.

LIVE AT CARNEGIE HALL
Rainy day people / Spanish lady / Ulst castle croon / Chanson pour les petits enfants / Perhaps love / Kitty of Coleraine / Oaken ashes / Judas and Mary / In an English country garden / Rose / Song of Glendun / Willie's gane to Melville castle / Scent of roses / Riddle song / Face to face / Snail / Say that I'll be sure to find you / 'Tis a gift (to be simple) / Lord of the dance / Greensleeves
CD _____ VALD 8056
Valentine / Nov '88 / Conifer.

RECITAL
Lark in the clear air / Oaken ashes / Una bhan (fair una) / Among silence / New year carol / Ae fond kiss / Pedlar's song / Eros / Face to face / Prayer of the butterfly / Come Lord
CD _____ C5MCD 583
See For Miles/C5 / Apr '92 / Pinnacle.

SONG FOR IRELAND, A
My Lagan love / Kitty of Coleraine / Soft day / Danny boy / Spanish lady / She moved through the fair / Gartan mothers lullaby / Down by the Sally gardens / Song of Glendun / Quiet land of Erin
CD _____ VALD 8053
Valentine / '91 / Conifer.

O'Hara, Mary Margaret

MISS AMERICA
To cry about / Year in song / Body's in trouble / Dear darling / New day / When you know why you're happy / My friends have / Help me lift you up / Keeping you in mind / Not be alright / You will be loved again
CD _____ CDV 2559
Virgin / Apr '92 / EMI.

O'Hearn, Patrick

BETWEEN TWO WORLDS
Rainmaker / Sky juice / Cape perpetual / Gentle was the night / Fire ritual / Eighty seven dreams of a lifetime / Dimension D / Forever the optimist / Journey to Yoroba / Between two worlds
CD _____ 259.963
Private Music / Nov '87 / BMG.

ELDORADO
Amazon waltz / Nepalese tango / Black Delilah / Chattahoochee field day / Illusionist / One eyed jacks / Hear our prayer / Delicate / Eldorado / There's always tomorrow
CD _____ 260102
Private Music / Nov '89 / BMG.

TRUST
CD _____ DCR 10012
CDS / Nov '95 / Pinnacle.

O'Higgins, Dave

BEATS WORKING FOR A LIVING
●● _____ EFZ 1009
EFZ / Nov '94 / Vital/SAM.

Ohio Express

OHIO EXPRESS
CD _____ REP 4017-WZ
Repertoire / Aug '91 / Pinnacle / Cadillac.

YUMMY YUMMY
Yummy yummy yummy / Ooh la la / Lucky / Turn to straw / Chewy chewy / Zig zag / Peanuts / It's a sad day / Night time / Down at Lulu's / Sweeter than sugar / First grade reader / Winter skies / Sausalito (is the place to go) / Pinch me (baby convince me) / Mercy / She's not comin' home / Down in Tennessee
CD _____ 5507532
Spectrum/Karussell / Jan '95 / PolyGram / THE.

Ohio Players

ECSTASY
Ecstasy / You and me / (Not so) sad and lonely / (I wanna know) do you feel it / Black cat / Food stamps y'all / Spinning / Sleep talk / Silly Billy / Short change
CD _____ CDSEW 026
Westbound / Feb '90 / Pinnacle.

FUNK ON FIRE (2CD Set)
CD Set _____ 5281022
Mercury / Sep '95 / PolyGram.

ORGASM
Pain / Pleasure / Ecstasy / Climax / Funky worm / Player's balling (players doin' their own thing) / Varee is love / Sleep talk / Walt's first trip / Laid it / What's going on /

Singing in the morning / Food stamps y'all / I want to hear / ain't that lovin' you
CD _____ CDSEWD 062
Southbound / Jun '93 / Pinnacle.

Ohlman, Christine

HARD WAY, THE (Ohlman, Christine & Rebel Montez)
CD _____ DELD 3011
Deluge / Dec '95 / Direct / ADA.

Ohman, Kjell

HAMMOND CONNECTION, THE (Ohman, Kjell & Arne Domnerus)
CD _____ OPUS3CD 19402
Opus 3 / Nov '95 / May Audio / Pentacone.

Oi Polloi

TOTAL ANARCHOI
CD _____ REM 017
Released Emotions / Apr '92 / Pinnacle.

Oige

LIVE
CD _____ LDLCD 1225
Lochshore / Jan '95 / ADA / Direct / Duncans.

Oil Seed Rape

SIX STEPS TO WOMANHOOD
CD _____ JAKCD 2
Jackass / Aug '93 / Pinnacle.

Oisin

BEALOIDEAS
CD _____ OSS 38CD
Ossian / Jul '95 / ADA / Direct / CM.

CELTIC DREAM
CD _____ OSS 85CD
Ossian / Aug '94 / ADA / Direct / CM.

JEANNIE C., THE
CD _____ EUCD 1215
ARC / Sep '93 / ARC Music / ADA.

OISIN
CD _____ OSS 37CD
Ossian / Jul '94 / ADA / Direct / CM.

OVER THE MOOR TO MAGGIE
CD _____ OSS 39CD
Ossian / Jul '95 / ADA / Direct / CM.

WINDS OF CHANGE
CD _____ EUCD 1069
ARC / '91 / ARC Music / ADA.

Oja-Dunaway, Don

RIGHT HERE IN THIS ROOM
Halloween in Marblehead / Dance with me Julie Anne / Enoch Ludford / Second chance / Ballad of Ruby and Jim / Sam's place / Micah's song / Augury / No easy rider / Right here in this room
CD _____ STWCD 7003
Stillwater / Dec '95 / Stillwater.

O'Jays

GIVE THE PEOPLE WHAT THEY WANT
Give the people what they want / Ship ahoy / This is a breather / Don't call me brother / Who am I / Mr. Lucky / Rich get richer / Shiftless, shady, jealous kind of people / When the world's a peace / Unity / How time flies
CD _____ 4805112
Epic / May '95 / Sony.

LOVE TRAIN (Best Of The O'Jays)
Love train / Back stabbers / 992 Arguments / Survival / For the love of money / Put your hands together / Time to get down / Sunshine / Living for the weekend / I love music
CD _____ 4805052
Epic / May '95 / Sony.

Okafor, Ben

GENERATION
She said / Shadows / Love train / Sanctify my soul / Call me / Living in a suitcase / Generation / Go see / Be my brother / Susan / Sweet lady / Hear this voice
CD _____ PCDN 137
Plankton / Aug '92 / Plankton.

Okay Teniz

GREEN WAVE
CD _____ FLTRCD 513
Timbuktu / Aug '93 / Pinnacle.

O'Keefe, Danny

BREEZY STORIES
CD _____ 7567814272
Atlantic / Jan '96 / Warner Music.

O'Keeffe, Máire

HOUSE PARTY
CD _____ CEFCD 165
Gael Linn / Oct '94 / Roots / CM / Direct / ADA.

O'Keeffe, Padraig

KERRY FIDDLES (O'Keeffe, Padraig & Denis Murphy/Julia Clifford)
CD _____ TSCD 309
Topic / May '94 / Direct / ADA.

SLIABH LUACHRA FIDDLE MASTER
CD _____ RTECD 174
RTE / Dec '93 / ADA / Koch.

Okin, Earl

MANGO & OTHER DELIGHTS
CD _____ RGF 014CD
Road Goes On Forever / Oct '93 / Direct.

Okoshi, Tiger

ECHOES OF A NOTE
Hello Dolly / Basin Street blues / I get ideas / St. James infirmary / Rockin' chair / St. Louis blues / Sleepo time down south / Sunny side of the street / When the saints go marching in / What a wonderful world
CD _____ JVC 20222
JVC / Oct '93 / New Note.

FACE TO FACE
Face to face / Summertime / When the moon goes deep / Sentimental journey / Bubble dance / Fisherman's song / One note samba / Man with 20 faces / Don't tell me now / Who can I turn to / Eyes / Over the rainbow
CD _____ JD 3318
JVC / Sep '89 / New Note.

TWO SIDES TO EVERY STORY
Green dolphin street / What it was / Wiz or wizout / Monday blues / Yuki no furu machi wo / Yesterdays / Finders, keepers / My old Kentucky home, goodnight / In your bones / Two sides to every story
CD _____ JVC 20392
JVC / Oct '94 / New Note.

Okossun, Sonny

AFRICAN SOLDIERS
CD _____ FILERCD 414
Profile / Jul '91 / Pinnacle.

Okoudjava, Boulat

LE SOLDAT EN PAPIER
CD _____ LDX 274743
La Chant Du Monde / Jan '94 / Harmonia Mundi / ADA.

Okuta Percussion

OKUTA PERCUSSION
CD _____ SM 1504-2
Wergo / Aug '92 / Harmonia Mundi / ADA / Cadillac.

Ol' Dirty Bastard

RETURN TO THE 36 CHAMBERS
CD _____ 7559616592
Warner Bros. / Mar '95 / Warner Music.

Olatunji, Baba

DROP THE BEAT
CD _____ RCD 10107
Rykodisc / Nov '91 / Vital / ADA.

DRUMS OF PASSION (The Beat)
Menu de ge ogbener / Odun de (Happy new year) / Odun de odun de (Happy new year) / Kiyakiya (Why do you run away) / Jin-go-lo-ba / Oyin momo ado (Sweet as honey bee) / Oya (Primitive fire) / Shango (Chant to the God of thunder) / akiwowo / Baba jinde (Filtration dance) / Jolly mensah / Philistine / Masque dance / Ajua / Zungo / Menu dieyh (Remake) / Gelewenwe / Jolly Mensah (Remake) / Escum buku wa-ya / Jolly Mensah (New version) / Lumumba / Abana / African spiritual world without end / Eye she-she / Uhuru (Freedom) / Hail the king / Adofo / Hail the king (Remake) / Mystery of love / Saturday night limbo / Lady Kennedy / Eyo-Sesel / Ashafa / Ojo Davis / Bo-su-aye / Someday / African waltz / Totofioko / Dye ko dide / Ayinde / Omo pupa / Bethelehemu / Alose / Ire dodo ye / Frekoba / Wasalu / Mbira
CD _____ BCDDI 15747
Bear Family / Jun '94 / Rollercoaster / Direct / CM / Swift / ADA.

Old

HOLD ON TO YOUR FACE
What's the point / Two of me / Scrape remix 1 / Glitch / Scrape remix 2 / To ebb is to drift / Outlive tape edit / Total hag turntable action
CD _____ MOSH 105CD
Earache / Nov '93 / Vital.

MUSICAL DIMENSION OF SLEAKSTAK, THE
Beginning / Two of me / Freak now / Peri cynthion / Happy tantrum / Creyap'nilla / Glitch / Ebb / Backwards through the greedo compressor
CD _____ MOSH 086CD
Earache / Apr '93 / Vital.

Old & In The Way

OLD AND IN THE WAY
Pig in the pen / Old and in the way / Hobo song / Wild horses / White dove / Midnight moonlight / Knockin' on your door / Panama red / Kissimmee kid / Land of the Navajo
CD _____ GDCD 4014
Grateful Dead / May '89 / Pinnacle.

Old & New Dreams

PLAYING
Happy house / Mopti / New dream / Rush hour / Broken shadows / Playing
CD _____ 8291232
ECM / Jun '86 / New Note.

Old Blind Dogs

CLOSE TO THE BONE
CD _____ LDLCD 1209
Lochshore / Oct '93 / ADA / Direct / Duncans.

LEGACY
CD _____ CDLDL 1233
Lochshore / Oct '95 / ADA / Direct / Duncans.

NEW TRICKS
CD _____ LOC 1068CD
Klub / Jul '94 / CM / Ross / Duncans / Direct.

TALL TAILS
CD _____ CDLDL 1220
Klub / Oct '94 / CM / Ross / Duncans / ADA / Direct.

Old Hat Band

OLD HAT DANCE BAND
CD _____ VT/OH 2CD
Veteran Tapes / Jun '93 / Direct / ADA.

Old Swan Band

STILL SWANNING
CD _____ FRCD 31
Free Reed / Aug '95 / Direct / ADA.

STILL SWANNING AFTER ALL THESE YEARS
CD _____ FR 31CD
Free Reed / Jul '95 / Direct / ADA.

Older Than Dirt

NO MORE EXCUSES
CD _____ FNGCD 02
FNG / Sep '94 / Plastic Head.

Oldfield, Mike

AMAROK
CD _____ CDV 2640
Virgin / Jun '90 / EMI.

COMPLETE MIKE OLDFIELD (Best Of Compilation)
Arrival / In dulci jubilo / Portsmouth / Jungle gardenia / Guilty / Blue Peter / Waldberg (the peak) / Etude / Wonderful land / Moonlight shadow / Family man / Mistake / Five miles out / Crime of passion / To France / Shadow on the wall / Excerpt from Tubular bells / Sheba / Mirage / Platinum / Mount Teide / Excerpt from Ommadawn / Excerpt from Hergest Ridge / Excerpt from Incantations / Excerpt from The killing fields
CD _____ CDMOC 1
Virgin / Oct '85 / EMI.

CRISES
Crises / Moonlight shadow / In high places / Foreign affair / Taurus three / Shadow on the wall
CD _____ CDV 2262
Virgin / Mar '94 / EMI.
CD _____ CDVIP 118
Virgin VIP / Mar '94 / Carlton Home Entertainment / THE / EMI.

DISCOVERY
To France / Poison arrows / Crystal gazing / Tricks of the light / Discovery / Talk about your life / Saved by a bell / Lake
CD _____ CDV 2308
Virgin / Apr '92 / EMI.

EARTH MOVING
Holy / Far country / Runaway son / Earth moving / Nothing but / Hostage / Innocent / See the light / Blue night / Bridge to paradise
CD _____ CDV 2610
Virgin / Apr '92 / EMI.

ELEMENTS (The Best Of Mike Oldfield)
Tubular bells / Family man / Moonlight shadow / Heaven's open / Five miles out / To France / Foreign affair / In Dulci jubilo / Shadow on the wall / Islands / Etude / Sentinel / Ommadawn (excerpt) / Incantations / Amarok / Portsmouth
CD _____ VTCD 18
Virgin / Aug '93 / EMI.

ELEMENTS (1973-1991) (4CD Set)
Tubular bells (part one) / Tubular bells (part two) / Hergest ridge (excerpt) / In dulci jubilo / Portsmouth / Vivaldi concerto in C / Ommadawn (part one) / On horseback / William Tell overture / Argiers / First excursion / Sailor's hornpipe / Incantations (pt 2) / I'm

guilty / Path / Blue Peter / Woodhenge / Punkadiddle (live) / Polka (live) / Platinum 3 and 4 / Arrival / Taurus 1 / QE2 / Wonderful land / Sheba / Five miles out / Taurus II / Family man / Mount Teidi / Peak / Crises / Moonlight shadow / Foreign affair / Shadow on the wall / Taurus III / Crime of passion / Jungle gardenia / To France / Afghan / Tricks of the light (instrumental) / Etude / Evacuation / Legend / Islands / Wind chimes / Flying start / Magic touch / Earth moving / Far country / Holy / Amarok / Heaven's open
CD Set _____ CDBOX 2
Virgin / Oct '93 / EMI.

EXPOSED
Incantations (pts 1-4) / Tubular bells (pts 1 & 2) / Guilty
CD Set _____ CDVD 2511
Virgin / Jul '86 / EMI.

FIVE MILES OUT
Taurus II / Family man / Orabidoo / Mount Teidi / Five miles out
CD _____ CDV 2222
Virgin / Apr '94 / EMI.
CD _____ CDVIP 114
Virgin / Jun '94 / EMI.

HEAVEN'S OPEN
Make make / No dream / Mr. Shame / Gimme back / Heaven's open / Music from the balcony
CD _____ CDV 2653
Virgin / Apr '92 / EMI.

HERGEST RIDGE
Hergest ridge (pts 1 & 2)
CD _____ CDV 2013
Virgin / Apr '86 / EMI.

INCANTATIONS
Incantations (pts 1 & 4) / Guilty
CD _____ CDVDT 101
Virgin / Apr '92 / EMI.

ISLANDS
Wind chimes (part 1) / Wind chimes / Islands / Flying start / Northpoint / Magic touch / Time has come / When the night's on fire (CD only)
CD _____ CDV 2466
Virgin / Apr '92 / EMI.

OMMADAWN
Ommadawn (parts 1 and 2)
CD _____ CDV 2043
Virgin / '86 / EMI.

ORCHESTRAL TUBULAR BELLS
CD _____ CDVIP 101
Virgin VIP / Nov '93 / Carlton Home Entertainment / THE / EMI.
CD _____ CDV 2026
Virgin / Apr '94 / EMI.

ORCHESTRAL TUBULAR BELLS/ OMMADAWN/HERGEST RIDGE (3CD Set/Compact Collection #1)
CD Set _____ TPAK 15
Virgin / Oct '90 / EMI.

QE2
Q.E.2. / Taurus / Sheba / Conflict / Arrival / Wonderful land / Mirage / Celt / Molly / Q.E.2. Finale
CD _____ CDV 2181
Virgin / Oct '83 / EMI.

QE2/PLATINUM/FIVE MILES OUT (3CD Set/Compact Collection #2)
CD Set _____ TPAK 16
Virgin / Oct '90 / EMI.

SONGS OF THE DISTANT EARTH
CD _____ 450998581-2
WEA / Nov '94 / Warner Music.

TUBULAR BELLS
Tubular Bells (Part 1) / Tubular Bells (Part 2)
CD _____ CDV 2001
Virgin / '83 / EMI.

TUBULAR BELLS II
Sentinel / Dark star / Clear light / Blue saloon / Sunjammer / Red dawn / Bell / Weightless / Great plain / Sunset door / Tattoo / Altered state / Maya gold / Moonshine
CD _____ 4509906182
WEA / Aug '92 / Warner Music.

TUBULAR BELLS/HERGEST RIDGE/ OMMADAWN (Remixes/3CD Set)
Tubular bells (pts 1 & 2) / Hergest ridge (pts 1 & 2) / Ommadawn (pts 1 & 2) / Phaeacian games / Star's end (extract) / Rio Grande / First excursion / Algiers / Portsmouth / In dulci jubilo / Speak (tho you only say farewell)
CD _____ CDBOX 1
Virgin / Dec '89 / EMI.

Oldfield, Sally

CELEBRATION
Mandela / Morning of my life / Woman of the night / Celebration / Blue water / My damsel heart / Love is everywhere
CD _____ CLACD 103
Castle / Apr '86 / BMG.

EASY
Sun is in my eyes / You set my gypsy blood free / Answering you / Boulevard song / Easy / Sons of the free / Hide and seek / First born of the earth / Man of storm
CD _____ CLACD 102
Castle / Apr '86 / BMG.

Mirrors

MIRRORS
Mirrors / Mandala / Water bearer / Boulevard song / You set my gypsy blood free / Sun in my eyes / Easy / Morning of my life / Love is everywhere / Love of a lifetime / Broken Mona Lisa / Path with a heart / Let it all go / She talk's like a lady / Man child / Never knew love could get so strong
CD _____ 5507262
Spectrum/Karussell / Jan '95 / PolyGram / THE.

PLAYING IN THE FLAME
Playing in the flame / Love of a lifetime / River of my childhood / Let it all go / Song of the lamp / Rare lightning / Manchild / It's your song / Song of the being
CD _____ CLACD 215
Castle / Feb '91 / BMG.

STRANGE DAY IN BERLIN
Path with a heart / Million light years away from home / She talks like a lady / Meet me in Verona / Strange day in Berlin / Never knew love could get so strong / This could be a lover / There's a miracle going on
CD _____ CLACD 216
Castle / Feb '91 / BMG.

WATER BEARER
Water bearer / Songs of the quendi (Night theme/Wampum song/Nenya/Land of the sun) / Weaver / Mirrors / Night of the hunter's moon / Child of Allah / Song of the healer bow / Fire and honey / Song of the healer
CD _____ CLACD 101
Castle / Apr '90 / BMG.

Oldfield, Terry

SPIRAL WAVES
CD _____ VP 117CD
Voice Print / Mar '93 / Voice Print.

Oldham, Andrew

RARITIES (Oldham, Andrew Loog Orchestra & Chorus)
Da doo ron ron / Memphis, Tennessee / I wanna be your man / La Bamba / Funky and fleopatra / 365 rolling stones / Maggie Maggie May (parts 1 and 2) / Oh I do like to be on the B side / There are but five rolling stones / Rise of the Brighton surf / You better move on / Theme for a rolling stone / Tell 'em (you're coming back) / Last time / Needles and pins / Want to hold your hand / Right of way / Satisfaction / Carry on
CD _____ SEECD 394
See For Miles/C5 / Oct '93 / Pinnacle.

Oldland, Misty

SUPERNATURAL
I wrote you a song / Fair affair (Je T'Aime) / Got me a feeling / Imprison me / Why do I trust you (Only on cassette and cd.) / Caroline / Kissing the planet / One world / You are the one / Like I need / I often wonder / Groove eternity
CD _____ 4759588 2
Columbia / Apr '94 / Sony.

O'Leary, Diarmuid

CLASSIC IRISH BALLADS (O'Leary, Diarmuid & The Bards)
Isle of Innisfree / Come back Paddy Reilly / Spancil hill / Green fields of France / Follow me up to carlow / Fields of Athenry / Ferryman / Curragh of Kildare / Dublin in the rare old times / Down by the Sally gardens / Nancy spain / Band played waltzing Matilda / Cliffs of Dooneen / Whiskey in the jar / Bunch of thyme
CD _____ TARACD 3018
Tara / Nov '94 / CM / ADA / Direct / Conifer.

O'Leary, Johnny

TROOPER, THE
CD _____ CEFCD 132
Gael Linn / Jan '94 / Roots / CM / Direct / ADA.

Oliva, Sandro

WHO THE FUCK IS SANDRO OLIVA
CD _____ EFA 034092
Muffin / Nov '94 / SRD.

Oliver, King

1928-30 (Oliver, King Orchestra)
CD _____ CLASSICS 607
Classics / Oct '92 / Discovery / Jazz Music.

COMPLETE VOCALION & BRUNSWICK RECORDINGS (2CD Set)
Too bad / Snag it / Georgia man / Deep henderson / Jackass blues / Home town blues / Sorrow valley blues / Sugarfoot stomp / Wa wa wa / Tack Annie / Someday sweetheart / Dead man blues / New wangwang blues / Dr. Jazz / Showboat shuffle / Every tub / Willie the weeper / Black snake blues / Farewell blues / Sobbin' blues / Tin roof blues / West End blues / Sweet Emmalina / Lazy mama / Got everything / Four or five times / Speakeasy blues / Aunt Hagar's blues / I'm watching the clock / Slow and steady / Papa de da da / Who's blue / Stop crying / Sugar blues / I'm crazy 'bout

my baby / Loveless love / One more time /
When I take my sugar to tea
CD _____ CDAFS 1025-2
Affinity / Oct '92 / Charly / Cadillac / Jazz
Music.

KING OF NEW ORLEANS, THE
CD _____ CD 14547
Jazz Portraits / Jan '94 / Jazz Music.

KING OLIVER & HIS ORCHESTRA 1929-30
West End blues / I've got that thing / Call
of the freaks / Trumpet's prayer / Freakish
light blues / Can I tell you / My good man
Sam / What you want me to do / Sweet like
this / Too late / I'm lonesome, sweetheart /
I want you just myself / I can't stop loving
you / Everybody does it in Hawaii / Frankie
and Johnny / New Orleans shout / St.
James Infirmary / I must have it / Rhythm
club stomp / You're just my type / Zulu /
Boogie woogie / Mule face blues / Struggle
buggy / Don't you think I love you / Oiga /
Shake it and break it / Stingaree blues /
What's the use of living without you / You
were only passing time with me / Nelson
stomp / Stealing
CD Set _____ ND 89770
Jazz Tribune / May '94 / BMG.

**KING OLIVER - 1926-28 (Oliver, King &
His Dixie Syncopators)**
CD _____ CLASSICS 618
Classics / '92 / Discovery / Jazz Music.

KING OLIVER 1927-31
CD _____ TPZ 1009
Topaz Jazz / Oct '94 / Pinnacle / Cadillac.

KING OLIVER 1928-29
CD _____ VILCD 0052
Village Jazz / Sep '92 / Target/BMG / Jazz
Music.

KING OLIVER VOL. 3 - 1926-28
CD _____ KJ 135FS
King Jazz / Oct '93 / Jazz Music / Cadillac
/ Discovery.

KING OLIVER VOL. 4 - 1928
CD _____ KJ 136FS
King Jazz / Oct '93 / Jazz Music / Cadillac
/ Discovery.

KING OLIVER VOL. 5 - 1928-29
CD _____ KJ 137FS
King Jazz / Oct '93 / Jazz Music / Cadillac
/ Discovery.

KING OLIVER VOL. 6 - 1929-31
CD _____ KJ 138FS
King Jazz / Oct '93 / Jazz Music / Cadillac
/ Discovery.

OLIVER KING 1929-1930 VOL.2
CD _____ JSPCD 348
JSP / Aug '92 / ADA / Target/BMG /
Direct / Cadillac / Complete/Pinnacle.

**RARE RECORDINGS AND ALTERNATES
(The Golden Age Of Jazz)**
CD _____ JZCD 367
Suisa / Jun '92 / Jazz Music / THE.

SHAKE IT AND BREAK IT
CD _____ JHR 73536
Jazz Hour / May '93 / Target/BMG / Jazz
Music / Cadillac.

Ollie & The Nightingales

OLLIE & THE NIGHTINGALES
You'll never do wrong / Don't make the
good suffer / Don't do what I did / I've got
a feeling / You're leaving me / Broke in two
/ ABCD / Mellow way you treat your man /
Girl you make my heart long / I've never
found a girl / Showered with love
CD _____ CDSXE 068
Stax / Nov '92 / Pinnacle.

Olney, David

BORDER CROSSING
CD _____ 9070642
Silenz / Aug '92 / BMG.

DEEPER ME
CD _____ CDPH 1117
Philo / Feb '95 / Direct / CM / ADA.

EYE OF THE STORM
CD _____ CD 3099
Rounder / '88 / CM / Direct / ADA /
Cadillac.

LIVE IN HOLLAND
CD _____ SCR 35
Strictly Country / Dec '94 / ADA / Direct.

TOP TO BOTTOM
CD _____ APCD 080
Appaloosa / '92 / ADA / Magnum Music
Group.

Olomide, Koffi

TCHA TCHO
Tcha tcho du sorcier / Elle et moi / V.I.P. /
Mannequin / Henriquet / Mal aime / Experi-
ence / La ruta
CD _____ STCD 1031
Sterns / Jul '90 / Sterns / CM.

Olsen, Kristina

HURRY ON HOME
CD _____ CDPH 1175
Philo / Aug '95 / Direct / CM / ADA.

LOVE, KRISTINA
CD _____ PH 1157CD
Philo / Oct '93 / Direct / CM / ADA.

Olympics

DOIN' THE HULLY GULLY
Big boy Pete / Little Pedro / Stay away from
Joe / Big Chief, Little Puss / Stay where you
are / What'd I say / Private eye / Baby it's
hot / Dooley / Baby hully gully / Dodge City
/ I'll never fall in love again / Working hard
this / Too late / I'm lonesome, sweetheart /
CD _____ CDCHD 324
Ace / Jul '91 / Pinnacle / Cadillac / Com-
plete/Pinnacle.

O'Malley, Tony

NAKED FLAME, THE
Good times / Love of mine / I can under-
stand it / My Buddy / For the children / Tell
me why / Mr. Operator / Still crazy after all
these years / Naked flame / Moody's mood
/ I'm in trouble
CD _____ JHCD 040
Ronnie Scott's Jazz House / May '95 / Jazz
Music / Magnum Music Group / Cadillac.

Omar

FOR PLEASURE
My baby says / I'm still standing / Saturday
/ Keep steppin' / Magical mystery interlude
/ Outside / Little boy / Need you bad / Can't
get nowhere / Confection / Magic mystical
way / Making sense of it / Pleasure
CD _____ 7432120853-2
RCA / Jun '94 / BMG.

MUSIC
Music / You've got to move / Get to know
you better / Tomorrow / Tasty morsel / Winner / Your loss, my gain / Don't sell yourself
short / Who chooses the seasons / Last request / Walk in the park / In the midst of it
CD _____ 5124012
Talkin' Loud / Nov '92 / PolyGram.

THERE'S NOTHING LIKE THIS
There's nothing like this / Don't mean a
thing / You and me / Positive / I'm in love /
Meaning of life / Stop messing around / Se-
rious style / I don't mind the waiting / Fine
(acapella)
CD _____ 5100212
Talkin' Loud / Jul '91 / PolyGram.

Omar & The Howlers

BLUES BAG
CD _____ PRLD 70281
Provogue / Aug '91 / Pinnacle.

COURTS OF LULU
CD _____ PRD 70452
Provogue / Mar '93 / Pinnacle.

I TOLD YOU SO
Border girl / Give me a chance / Shake for
me / Magic man / Rocket to nowhere / I told
you so / Ice cold woman / I'm wish to you
baby / East side blues
CD _____ DFG 8417 CD
Dixie Frog / Oct '93 / Magnum Music
Group.

LIVE AT PARADISO
CD _____ PRD 70352
Provogue / Apr '93 / Pinnacle.

LIVE AT THE PARADISO
CD _____ BB 9529CD
Bullseye Blues / May '93 / Direct.

MONKEY LAND
Monkey land / Big town shakedown / Night
shadows / She's a woman / Dirty people /
Next big thing / Tonight I think of you / Fire
in the jungle / Modern man / Loud mouth
woman / Ding dong clock
CD _____ ANTCD 0011
Antones / Jan '93 / Hot Shot / Direct / ADA.

O'Mara, Peter

STAIRWAY
Abertura / Stairway / Round and round /
Crescent / Mr. Lucky / For Emily / Weather
or not / Change of wind / Continuity / Irish
CD _____ ENJACD 70772
Enja / Jun '93 / New Note / Vital/SAM.

Omen

ESCAPE TO NOWHERE
It's not easy / Radar love / Escape to no-
where / Cry for the morning / Thorn in your
flesh / Poisoned / Nomads / King of the hill
/ No way out
CD _____ RR 95442
Roadrunner / Nov '88 / Pinnacle.

Omlo Vent

MILD LANDING
CD _____ CHILLUM 000
Chill Um / Jan '96 / Plastic Head.

Omni Trio

DEEPEST CUT
CD _____ ASHADOW 1CD
Moving Shadow / Feb '95 / SRD.

Omnia Opera

OMNIA OPERA
Space bastard / Disbelief / Awakening /
Floating settee / Each day / Brighter the sun
/ Bright sun (CD only) / Freeze out (CD only)
CD _____ DELECCD 011
Delerium / May '93 / Vital.

Omnicron

**GENERATION AND MOTION OF A
PULSE, THE**
CD _____ IAE 003CD
Instinct Ambient Europe / May '95 /
Plastic Head.

Omnivore

ONE GIANT LEAP
CD _____ ACTV 5D
Interactive / Sep '94 / 3MV / Sony.

ONE SMALL STEP
Omnivorous / On the tip of my tongue /
Munchies / Ethereal music / 9/10ths sub-
merged / At elegant memorial
CD _____ ACTIVE 002CD
Interactive / Feb '94 / 3MV / Sony.

Omoumi, Hossein

PERSIAN CLASSICAL MUSIC
CD _____ NI 5359
Nimbus / Sep '94 / Nimbus.

On Thorns I Lay

SOUNDS OF BEAUTIFUL EXPERIENCE
CD _____ HOLY 012CD
Holy / Jun '95 / Plastic Head.

One & One

HOW LOW CAN I GO
CD _____ PFP 42042
Ichiban / Apr '95 / Koch.

One Hit Wonder

WHERE'S THE WORLD
CD _____ CDGRUBM 31
Food For Thought / Jan '95 / Pinnacle.

One Jump Ahead

ONE JUMP AHEAD
One jump ahead / Gimme that wine / Blueberry Hill / Three handed woman / I missed
my turning / Hot licks, cold liquor and warm
hearted women / Bald headed blues / But I
was cool / Carnival / She's so green / When
I was in France with Frances / It should've
been me / Margarita / Who drank my beer
while I was in the rear / Bitten by the
jitterbug
CD _____ PCOM 1124
President / Nov '92 / Grapevine / Target/
BMG / Jazz Music / President.

One Style MDV

RIGHT TO SAY
CD _____ CRAICD 034
Crai / Oct '93 / ADA / Direct.

One Way System

BEST OF ONE WAY SYSTEM
Stab the judge / Give us a future / Just an-
other hero / Jerusalem / Jackie was a junkie
/ Ain't no answers / No return / One way
system / Gutter boy / Forgotten generation
/ Cum on feel the noize / Breakin' in / This
is the age / Into the fires / Corrupted world
/ No peace soon / Reason why / Children of
the night / Shine again
CD _____ CDPUNK 50
Anagram / Mar '95 / Pinnacle.

WRITING ON THE WALL
Corrupted world / This is the age / One day
soon / Nightmare / Neurotix / Reason why
/ Into the fires / Days are numbered / On
the line / Life on the outside
CD _____ AHOY 21
Captain Oi / Nov '94 / Plastic Head.

O'Neal, Alexander

HEARSAY/ALL MIXED UP (2CD Set)
(What can I say) to make you love me /
Hearsay / Lovers / Fake / Criticize / Never
knew love like this / Crying overtime / When
the party's over / Fake '88 (house mix) /
(What can I say) to make you love me (re-
mix) / Never knew love like this (extended)
/ Criticize (Mix) / Lovers (extended) / Criti-
cize (remix)
CD Set _____ 4661232
Tabu / Dec '89 / Sony.

LOVE MAKES NO SENSE
In the middle / If you let it / Aphrodisia /
Love makes no sense / Home is where the
heart is / Change of heart / Lady / All that
matters to me / Since I've been loving you
/ What a wonderful world

CD _____ 549502
A&M / Feb '93 / PolyGram.

O'Neal, Shaq

RETURN, THE
CD _____ CHIP 154
Jive / Jan '95 / BMG.

SHAQ DIESEL
CD _____ CHIP 146
Jive / Jan '94 / BMG.

O'Neill, Sean

**50 IRISH SINGALONG FAVOURITES
(O'Neill, Sean Band)**
CD _____ ECD 3136
K-Tel / Jan '95 / K-Tel.

SEAN O'NEIL BAND (O'Neil, Sean Band)
CD _____ EMPRCD 553
Emporio / Nov '94 / THE / Disc / CM.

Ongala, Remmy

KERSHAW SESSIONS
CD _____ ROOTCD 004
Strange Fruit / Mar '95 / Pinnacle.

**REMMY ONGALA & ORCHESTRE
SUPER MATIMLIA (Ongala, Remmy &
Orchestra)**
Dodoma / One world / I want to go home /
Inchi yetu (our country) / What can I say?
(niseme nini) / No money, no life / Living
together (tupendane) / Mrema / Kidogo ki-
dogo (little by little)
CD _____ CDRW 22
Realworld / Mar '92 / EMI / Sterns.

**SONGS FOR THE POOR MAN (Ongala,
Remmy & Orchestra)**
Nasikitka / Karola / Kependa roho / Sauti ya
mnyonge / Usingizi / Pamella / Muziki asili
yake wapi / Mariam wangu / Kifo (Only on
CD and MC.) / Muziki asili yake wapi (ver-
sion) (Only on CD and MC.)
CD _____ CDRW 6
Realworld / '90 / EMI / Sterns.

Only Living Witnesses

PRONE MORTAL FORM
CD _____ CM 770722
Century Media / Jun '94 / Plastic Head.

Only Ones

BIG SLEEP
CD _____ FREUDCD 045
Jungle / Dec '93 / Disc.

EVEN SERPENTS SHINE
From here to eternity / Flaming torch /
You've got to pay / No solution / In be-
tweens / Out there in the night / Curtains
for you / Programme / Someone who cares
/ Miles from nowhere / Instrumental
CD _____ 4785032
Columbia / Feb '95 / Sony.

IMMORTAL STORY, THE
Lovers of today / Peter and the pets / Whole
of the law / Another girl another planet /
Special view (aka telescopic love) / Beast /
It's the truth / No peace for the wicked /
Immortal story / From here to eternity / In
betweens / No solution / Curtains for you /
Someone who cares / Miles from nowhere
/ Your chosen life / Baby's got a gun / Why
don't you kill yourself / Oh Lucinda (love be-
comes a habit) / Big sleep
CD _____ 4712672
Columbia / Feb '92 / Sony.

IN CONCERT
Immortal story / Lovers / Someone / Girl /
Flowers die / She says / Beast / No peace
for the wicked / No solution / In betwens /
Programme
CD _____ WINCD 080
Windsong / Dec '95 / Pinnacle.

ONLY ONES LIVE, THE
Trouble in the world / Beast / Lovers of today / Why don't you kill yourself / As my
wife says / Big sleep / City of fun / Programme / Happy pilgrim (Available on CD
only) / Strange mouth (Available on CD only)
/ No peace for the wicked / Miles from nowhere / Another girl another planet / Me and
my shadow
CD _____ MAUCD 603
Mau Mau / Jul '89 / Pinnacle.

ONLY ONES, THE
Whole of the law / Another girl another
planet / Breaking down / City of fun / Beast
/ Creature of doom / It's the truth /
Language problem / No place for the
wicked / Immortal story
CD _____ 477379-2
Columbia / Aug '94 / Sony.

PEEL SESSIONS: ONLY ONES
Oh Lucinda / No peace for the wicked /
Beast / In betweens / No / No / Prisoners /
From here to eternity / Why don't you kill
yourself / Miles from nowhere / Telescopic
love / Another girl another planet /
Language problem / Happy pilgrim / Big
sleep
CD _____ SFRCD 102
Strange Fruit / Jul '94 / Pinnacle.

REMAINS
Prisoner / Watch you drown / Flowers die / Devon song / My rejection / Baby's got a gun / Hope valley blues / Counterfeit woman / River of no return / I only wanna be your friend / Oh no / Don't hold your breath / Silent night / Don't feel too good
CD _____ CDMGRAM 67
Anagram / Sep '93 / Pinnacle.

Ono, Seigen
NEKONOTOPIA NEKONOMANIA
CD _____ MTMCD 29
Made To Measure / Nov '93 / Grapevine.

Ono, Yoko
ONOBOX (6CD Set)
CD Set _____ RCD 1022429
Rykodisc / Mar '92 / Vital / ADA.

RISING
Warzone / Wouldnit / Ask the dragon / New York woman / Talking to the universe / Turn the corner / I'm dying / Where do we go from here / Kurushi / Will I / Rising / Goodbye my love / Revelations
CD _____ CDEST 2276
Capitol / Jan '96 / EMI.

WALKING ON THIN ICE
CD _____ RCD 20230
Rykodisc / Mar '92 / Vital / ADA.

Onset
POOL OF LIFE REVISITED, THE
Rakin' em down / Taker (2nd take) / Cowboy and his wife / Precious love / Talkin' space travel blues / Too proud to start / Trees and plants / Glad rag (instrumental) / Mansion on the hill / Pool of life (instrumental) / For you / Two times forgotten man / Poor and lonely girl / Starlight tuneful 9 / Another man's crime / Let's go home
CD _____ PROBE 040CD
Probe Plus / Oct '94 / Vital.

Onyx
ALL WE GOT IZ US
Life or death / Last dayz / All we got iz us (Evil streets) / Purse snatchaz / Shout / I murder u / Betta off dead / Live niguz / Funkmotherfukaz / Most def / Act up / Getto mentalitee / Wrongs / Maintain / Walk in New York
CD _____ 5292652
Def Jam / Oct '95 / PolyGram.

BACDAFUCUP
CD _____ 5234472
Def Jam / Jan '96 / PolyGram.

Oomph
FOOLS NEVER FAIL
CD _____ DY 152
Dynamica / Jun '95 / Pinnacle.

SPERM
Suck-taste-spit / Sex / War / Dickhead / Schisma / Feiert das kreuz / Love / Das ist freiheit / Kismet / Bresathtaker / Ich bin der weg / U-said (live)
CD _____ DY 6-2
Dynamica / Apr '94 / Pinnacle.

Oomph
BETWEEN TWO WORLDS
CD _____ GV 135CD
Global Village / May '94 / ADA / Direct.

Oosh
VIEW, THE
Chat up / Missing lover / Spliff culture / Yard has no dandelion / Cloud / View / Charlie / No soul / I got this / Storm
CD _____ 450996286-2
Magnet / Sep '94 / Warner Music.

Opal
HAPPY NIGHTMARE BABY
CD _____ SST 103 CD
SST / May '93 / Plastic Head.

Opaz
BACK FROM THE RAGGEDY EDGE (Opaz/Ray Hayden)
CD _____ OPH 003CD
Opaz / Aug '95 / Pinnacle.

Open House
SECOND STORY
CD _____ GLCD 1144
Green Linnet / Oct '94 / Roots / CM / Direct / ADA.

Open Mind
SPIRITUAL LOVERS
CD _____ RUNECD 009
Mystic Stones / Sep '92 / Vital.

Opera 1X
CALL OF THE WILD
CD _____ MS 005CD
Nosferatu / Apr '95 / Plastic Head.

Operating Strategies
DIFFICULTY OF BEING
CD _____ EFA 11214
Danse Macabre / Apr '93 / SRD.

Operation Ivy
OPERATION IVY
CD _____ LOOKOUT 10CD
Lookout / Oct '94 / SRD.

Opeth
ORCHID
CD _____ CANDLE 010CD
Candlelight / Sep '95 / Plastic Head.

Ophthalamia
JOURNEY INTO DARKNESS, A
CD _____ CDAV 003
Avant Garde / May '94 / Plastic Head.

VIA DOLOROSA
CD _____ AV 013CD
Avant Garde / Jul '95 / Plastic Head.

Opie, Alan
IN PRAISE OF GOD
CD _____ DIONO 01
Revelation / Oct '92 / Plastic Head.

Opik
OPIK
CD _____ HARDCD 4
Concrete / Jun '95 / Disc / BMG.

Opium Den
DIARY OF A DRUNKEN SUN
CD _____ 001AF-2
Southern / Jun '93 / SRD.

Oppermann, Rüdiger
SAME SUN SAME MOON
CD _____ SHAM 017CD
Shamrock / Feb '93 / Wellard / ADA.

Oppressed
BEST OF THE OPPRESSED, THE
CD _____ DOJOCD 227
Dojo / Jan '96 / BMG.

OI OI MUSIC
CD _____ AHOYCD 5
Captain Oi / Jul '93 / Plastic Head.

Optic Eye
LIGHT SIDE OF THE SUN
Sunburst (extended mix) / Brain of Morbius / Listening (Aural sculpture) / Chain reaction / Wobbling in space / Guitar man / Slaves of the crystal brain / On the other side / Far out race / Acid drops
CD _____ CDTOT 17
Jumpin' & Pumpin' / Oct '94 / 3MV / Sony.

TRANCE
CD _____ RUNECD 003
Mystic Stones / Feb '93 / Vital.

Optica
ALL THE COLOURS OF THE RAINBOW
CD _____ KINXCD 2
Kinetix / Apr '95 / Pinnacle.

Optimum Wound Profile
ASPHYXIA
CD _____ WB 11202
We Bite / May '95 / Plastic Head.

Opus III
GURU MOTHER
CD _____ HFCD 33
PWL / Sep '94 / Warner Music / 3MV.

MIND FRUIT
CD _____ HFCD 24
PWL / Jul '92 / Warner Music / 3MV.

Ora
ORA
CD _____ HBG 122/14
Background / Apr '94 / Background.

Oracle
TREE
CD _____ WM 2CD
Swim / Jun '94 / SRD / Disc.

Orang
HERD OF INSTINCT
CD _____ ECHCD 2
Echo / Jul '94 / Pinnacle / EMI.

Orange 9mm
DRIVER NOT INCLUDED
CD _____ 7567617462
Warner Bros. / May '95 / Warner Music.

Orange Deluxe
NECKING
CD _____ GOODCD 4
Dead Dead Good / Mar '95 / Pinnacle.

Orange Juice
HEATHER'S ON FIRE, THE
Falling and laughing / Moscow / Moscow olympics / Blue boy / Lovesick / Simply thrilled honey / Breakfast time / Poor old soul / Poor old soul Pt.2 / Felicity / Upwards and onwards / Dying day / Holiday hymn
CD _____ DUBH 955CD
Postcard / Oct '95 / Vital.

ORANGE JUICE/YOU CAN'T HIDE YOUR LOVE FOREVER
Lean period / I guess I'm just a little bit too sensitive / Burning desire / Scaremonger / Artisans / What presence / Out for the count / Get while the gettings good / All that ever mattered / Salmon fishing in New York / Falling and laughing / Untitled melody / Wan light / Tender objects / Dying day / L.O.V.E. Love / Intuition told me (pt 1) / Upwards and onwards / Satellite city / Three cheers for our side / Consolation prize / Felicity / In a nutshell
CD _____ 847 727-2
Polydor / Jan '91 / PolyGram.

OSTRICH CHURCHYARD
Louise Louise / Three cheers for our side / (To Put It In A) Nutshell / Satellite city / Consolation Prize / Holiday Hymn / Intuition told me (pts 1 & 2) / Wan Light / Dying Day / Texas Fever / Tender Object / Falling And Laughing (Extra track on CD and MC.) / Lovesick (Extra track on CD and MC.) / Poor Old Soul (Extra track on CD and MC.) / You Old Eccentric (Extra track on CD and MC.)
CD _____ DUBH 954CD
Postcard / Oct '95 / Vital.

RIP IT UP
Rip it up / Mud in your eye / Breakfast time / Flesh of my flesh / Hokoyo / Million pleading faces / Turn away / I can't help myself / Louise Louise / Tenterhook
CD _____ 8397682
Polydor / Apr '92 / PolyGram.

VERY BEST OF ORANGE JUICE, THE
Falling and laughing / Consolation prize / You old eccentric / L.O.V.E. love / Felicity / In a nutshell / Rip it up / I can't help myself / Flesh of my flesh / Tenterhooks / Bridge / Day I went down to Texas / Punch drunk / Place in my heart / Sad lament / Lean period / I guess I'm just a little too sensitive / Scaremonger / Artisans / Salmon fishing in New York / What presence / Out for the count
CD _____ 5316182
Polydor / Apr '92 / PolyGram.

Orange Sector
FAITH
CD _____ ZOTCD 18
Talitha / Aug '93 / Plastic Head.

KIDS IN AMERICA
CD _____ CDZOT 126
Zoth Ommog / Nov '94 / Plastic Head.

Orb
ADVENTURES BEYOND THE ULTRAWORLD
Little fluffy clouds / Earth (gala) / Supernova at the end of the universe / Back side of the moon / Spanish castles in space / Perpetual dawn / Into the fourth dimension / Outlands / Star 6 and 7 8 9 / Huge ever growing pulsating brain that rules from the centre (of the ultraworld)
CD _____ CIDD 8032
Island / Oct '94 / PolyGram.

LIVE '93
Huge ever growing pulsating brain that rules from the centre (of the ultraworld) / Plateau / O.O.B.E. / Little fluffy clouds / Star 6 and 7 8 9 / Towers of dub / Blue room / Valley / Perpetual dawn / Assassin / Outlands / Spanish castles in space
CD Set _____ CIDD 8022
Island / Nov '93 / PolyGram.

ORBUS TERRARUM
Valley / Plateau / Oxbow Lakes / Montagne D'Or / Orbus terrarum / Occidental / Slug dub
CD _____ CID 8037
CD _____ CIDX 8037
Island / Mar '95 / PolyGram.

PEEL SESSIONS: ORB
Huge ever growing pulsating brain that rules from the centre (of the ultraworld) / Back side of the moon (Tranquility lunar orbit) / Into the fourth dimension (Essenes in starlight)
CD _____ SFRCD 118
Strange Fruit / Oct '91 / Pinnacle.

U.F.ORB
O.O.B.E. / U.F. Orb / Blue room (LP version) / Towers of dub / Close encounters / Majestic / Sticky end
CD _____ IMCD 219
Island / Mar '96 / PolyGram.

Orbestra
TRANSDANUBIAN SWINEHERDS
CD _____ HNCD 1367
Hannibal / Apr '92 / Vital / ADA.

Orbison, Roy
ALL TIME GREATEST HITS
Only the lonely / Leah / In dreams / Uptown / It's over / Crying / Dream baby / Blue angel / Working for the man / Candy man / Running scared / Falling / Claudette / Ooby dooby / I'm hurtin' / Mean woman blues / Lana / Blue bayou / Oh pretty woman
CD _____ CD 67290
Monument / Jan '89 / Sony.

BIG O, THE
Rock house / It's too late / You're gonna cry / Ooby dooby / You're my baby / Mean little Mama / Fools hall of fame / Cause of it all / True love goodbye / Lovestruck / Clown / One more time / Problem child / Chicken hearted / I like love / Domino
CD _____ CDCD 1051
Charly / Mar '93 / Charly / THE / Cadillac.

BLACK & WHITE NIGHT (Orbison, Roy & Friends)
Oh pretty woman / Only the lonely / In dreams / Dream baby / Leah / Move on down the line / Crying / Mean woman blues / Running scared / Blue bayou / Candy man / Uptown / Ooby dooby / Comedians / (All I can do is) Dream of you / It's over
CD _____ CDV 2601
Virgin / Aug '91 / EMI.

COLLECTION
CD _____ COL 027
Collection / Mar '95 / Target/BMG.

COLLECTION: ROY ORBISON
Trying to get to you / Ooby dooby / Go go go / You're my baby / Domino / Sweet and easy to love / Devil doll / Cause of it all / Fools hall of fame / True love goodbye / Chicken hearted / I like love / Mean little mama / Problem child / This kind of love / It's too late / I never knew / You're gonna cry / One more time (Demo) / Lovestruck (Demo) / Clown / Claudette
CD _____ CCSCD 147
Castle / Feb '93 / BMG.

DEFINITIVE COLLECTION, THE
Only the lonely / Blue angel / Running scared / Cryin' / Dream baby / Crowd / Workin' for the man / In dreams / Falling / Blue bayou / Mean woman blues / It's over / Oh pretty woman / Good night / Ride away / Crawlin' back / Breakin' up is breakin' my heart / Twinkle toes / Lana / Too soon too know / There won't be many coming home / Penny arcade / You got it / She's a mystery to me / I drove all night / Crying / Ooby dooby / Uptown / Love in time / After the love has gone / Let the good times roll / I'm hurtin' / Claudette / Leah / Candy man / California blue / Handle with care / Not alone anymore / Pretty woman / That lovin' feeling again / Pretty paper / Scarlet ribbons / My friend / Unchained melody
CD _____ VISCD 20
Vision / Oct '95 / Pinnacle.

GOLDEN DAYS
Oh pretty woman / Running scared / Falling / Love hurts / Mean woman blues / I can't stop loving you / Crowd / Blue bayou / Borne on the wind / Lana / Only the lonely (know the way I feel) / It's over / Crying / Pretty paper / All I have to do is dream / Dream baby / Blue angel / Working for the man / Candy man / In dreams
CD _____ 4715552
Monument / Apr '92 / Sony.

GOLDEN DECADE 1960-69, THE
Only the lonely / Bye bye love / I'm hurtin' / Love hurts / Here comes that song again / Double date / Legend in my time / Uptown / I can't stop loving you / Candy man / Darkness / Today's teardrops / Twenty two days / Cry / Blue angel / Running scared / Lana / Party heart / Dance / Crying / Dream baby / Beautiful dreamer / Crowd / Leah / Love star / Workin' for the man / Distant drums / Mama / Falling / In dreams / Blue bayou / She wears my ring / How are things in paradise / (They call you) Gigolette / Almost / San Fernando / Mean woman blues / Pretty paper / Borne on the wind / It's over / Oh pretty woman / Let the good times roll / (Say) you're my girl / Yes / Goodnight Claudette / Breakin' up is breakin' my heart / Ride away / Crawling back / Communication breakdown / There won't be many coming home / Too soon to know / Twinkle toes / So good / Cry softly lonely one / Lonesome number one / Walk on / Heartache / My friend / Penny arcade
CD _____ NXTCD 246
Sequel / May '93 / BMG.

HITS #1
Only the lonely (know the way I feel) / Candy man / You're my girl / Working for the man / Bye bye love / In dreams / Dream baby / Crowd / Great pretender / Blue Avenue / Party heart / Blue bayou
CD _____ PWKS 576
Carlton Home Entertainment / Mar '90 / Carlton Home Entertainment.

HITS #1-#3 (3CD Set)
Only the lonely / Candy man / You're my girl / Working for the man / Bye bye love / In dreams / Dream baby / Crowd / Great pretender / Blue avenue / Party heart / Blue bayou / Oh pretty woman / My prayer / She wears my ring / All I have to do is dream / Uptown / Borne on the wind / Running scared / Blue angel / Mean woman blues / Loneliness / Lana / Pretty paper / It's over / Love hurts / I'm hurtin' / Dream House without windows / Goodnight / Crying / Distand drums / Leah / Raindrops / Here comes that song again / Falling
CD Set _____ **BOXD 23**
Carlton Home Entertainment / Oct '94 /
Carlton Home Entertainment.

HITS #2
Running scared / Blue angel / Mean woman blues / Loneliness / Lana / Pretty paper / It's over / Love hurts / I'm hurtin' / Dream / House without windows / Goodnight
CD _____ **PWKS 582**
Carlton Home Entertainment / May '90 /
Carlton Home Entertainment.

HITS #3
Oh pretty woman / My prayer / She wears my ring / All I have to do is dream / Uptown / Born on the wind / Crying / Distant drums / Leah / Raindrops / Here comes that song again / Falling
CD _____ **PWKS 4024**
Carlton Home Entertainment / Oct '90 /
Carlton Home Entertainment.

IN DREAMS/ORBISONGS
In dreams / Lonely wine / Shahdaroba / No one will ever know / Sunset / House without windows / Dream / Blue bayou / (They call you) Gigolette / All I have to do is dream / Beautiful dreamer / My prayer / Oh pretty / Goodnight / Nightlife / Let the good times roll / (I get so) Sentimental / Yo te amo Maria / Wedding day / Sleepy hollow / Twenty two Days / Legend in my time
CD _____ **474957 2**
Monument / Feb '94 / Sony.

KING OF HEARTS
You're the one / Heartbreak radio / We'll take the night / Crying (& k.d. Lang) / After the love has gone / Love in time / I drove all night / Wild hearts run out of time / Coming home / Careless heart
CD _____ **CDVUS 58**
Virgin / Nov '92 / EMI.

LAMINAR FLOW
Easy way out / Love is a cold wind / Lay it down / I care / We're into something good / Movin' / Poor baby / Warm spot hot / Tears / Friday night / Hound dog man
CD _____ **7559608792**
WEA / Jul '94 / Warner Music.

LEGEND IN HIS TIME
Lonesome number one / Oh such a stranger / Legend in my time / I'm a Southern man / Belinda / Under suspicion / No chain at all / Can't wait / I'm hurtin' / Same street / Blue blue day / Too soon to know / I don't really want you / Old love song / Born to love you / Big hearted me / What about me
CD _____ **CDMF 079**
Magnum Force / '91 / Magnum Music Group.

LEGENDS IN MUSIC - ROY ORBISON
CD _____ **LECD 069**
Wisepack / Jul '94 / THE / Conifer.

LONELY & BLUE/CRYING
Only the lonely (Know the way I feel) / Bye bye love / Cry / Blue avenue / I can't stop loving you / Come back to me my love / Blue angel / Raindrops / Lead it my love / I'm hurtin' / Twenty two days / I'll say it's my fault / Crying / Great pretender / Love hurts / She wears my ring / Wedding day / Summer song / Dance / Lana / Loneliness / Let's make a memory / Nite life / Running scared
CD _____ **474956 2**
Monument / Feb '94 / Sony.

MYSTERY GIRL
You got it / Real world / Dream you / Love so beautiful / California blue / She's a mystery to me / Comedians / Windsurfer / Careless heart
CD _____ **CDV 2576**
Virgin / Apr '92 / EMI.

ONLY THE LONELY
Only the lonely / In dreams / Crying / Dream baby / Working for the man / Candy man / Running scared / I'm hurtin' / Oh pretty woman / Ooby dooby / Lana / Blue bayou
CD _____ **CDVIP 113**
Virgin VIP / Nov '93 / Carlton Home Entertainment / THE / EMI.

RARE ORBISON #1
Actress / Paper boy / With the bug / Today's teardrops / Here comes that song again / Only with you / Pretty one / No chain at all / Blues in my mind / Drifting away / Wings of glory / Belinda
CD _____ **9825982**
Pickwick/Sony Collector's Choice / Jul '91 / Carlton Home Entertainment / Pinnacle / Sony.

RARE ORBISON #2
Party heart / How are things in paradise / Darkness / Yes / Double date / Mama / San Fernando / Zig zag / Tired old country song / Mother / Boogie baby / Indian Summer
CD _____ **9825982**
Pickwick/Sony Collector's Choice / Jul '91 / Carlton Home Entertainment / Pinnacle / Sony.

RCA SESSIONS, THE (Orbison, Roy & Sonny James)
Almost eighteen / Bug / I'll never tell / Jolie / Paper boy / Sweet and innocent / Seems to me / Apache / Magnetism / Young love / Lana / Legend of the brown mountain light / Listen to my heart / Hey little ducky / Innocent angel / Broken wings / Day's not over yet / Dance her by me (one more time) / Time's running backwards for me
CD _____ **BCD 15407**
Bear Family / Jul '87 / Rollercoaster / Direct / CM / Swift / ADA.

ROY ORBISON
CD _____ **12330**
Laserlight / May '94 / Target/BMG.

ROY ORBISON
CD Set _____ **KBOX 344**
Collection / Oct '95 / Target/BMG.

ROY ORBISON SONGBOOK (Various Artists)
Oh pretty woman / Dream baby / Oh pretty woman / It's over / Crying / Only the lonely / Down the line / Blue Bayou / Claudette / Best friend
CD _____ **VSOPCD 215**
Connoisseur / Apr '95 / Pinnacle.

SUN YEARS, THE
Ooby dooby / Trying to get to you / Go go go / You're my baby / Rock house / Domino / Sweet and easy / Devil doll / Cause of it all / Fools' hall of fame / True love goodbye / Chicken hearted / I like love / Mean little mama / Problem child / I was a fool / This kind of love / It's too late / I never knew / You're gonna cry / You tell me / I give up / One more time / Lovestruck / Clown / Claudette / Jenny / Find my baby for me
CD _____ **BCD 15461**
Bear Family / Apr '89 / Rollercoaster / Direct / CM / Swift / ADA.

Orbit, William

STRANGE CARGO I (Hinterland)
CD _____ **4509992952**
N-Gram / Feb '95 / Warner Music.

STRANGE CARGO III
Water from a vine leaf / Into the paradise / Time to get wize / Harry flowers / Touch of the night / Story of light / Gringatcho demento / Hazy shade of random / Best friend paranoia / Monkey king / Deus ex machina / Water babies
CD _____ **CDV 2707**
Virgin / Mar '93 / EMI.

Orbital

ORBITAL
Moebius / Speed freak / Oolaa / Desert storm / Fahrenheit 303 / Steel cube idolatory / High rise / Chime / Midnight / Belfast / Untitled (MC) / Macro head (LP)
CD _____ **8282482**
Internal / Aug '95 / PolyGram / Pinnacle.

ORBITAL II
CD _____ **TRUCD 2**
Internal / Aug '93 / PolyGram / Pinnacle.

SNIVILISATION
Forever / I wish I had duck feet / Sad but true / Crash and carry / Science friction / Philosophy by numbers / Quality seconds / Are we here / Kein trink wasser / Attached
CD _____ **TRUCD 5**
Internal / Aug '95 / PolyGram / Pinnacle.

Orchestra

NOT AS SOFTLY AS
CD _____ **MECCACD 1043**
Music Mecca / Nov '94 / Jazz Music / Cadillac / Wellard.

Orchestra Baobab

PIRATE'S CHOICE
CD _____ **WCD 014**
World Circuit / May '90 / New Note / Direct / Cadillac / ADA.

Orchestra Jazz Siciliana

PLAYS THE MUSIC OF CARLA BLEY
440 / Lone arranger / Dreams so real / Baby baby / Joyful noise / Egyptian / Blunt object
CD _____ **843 207 2**
ECM / Nov '90 / New Note.

Orchestra Marrabenta

INDEPENDENCE
CD _____ **CD PIR 12**
World Circuit / Apr '89 / New Note / Direct / Cadillac / ADA.

Orchestra Super Mazembe

MALOBA D'AMOR
Kassongo / Shauri yako / Salima (parts 1 and 2) / Mwana nyiau (parts 1 and 2) / Nabinakate / Maloba d'amor / Samba (parts 1 and 2)
CD _____ **AFRIZZ 007**
Disc Afrique / May '90 / Roots / CM.

Orchestre Contrebasses

BASS, BASS, BASS, BASS, BASS & BASS
CD _____ **86232**
Melodie / Oct '93 / Triple Earth / Discovery / ADA / Jetstar.

Orchestre National

A PLUS TARD (Orchestre National De Jazz)
CD _____ **LBLC 6554**
Label Bleu / Nov '92 / New Note.

Orchid Airburst

SIXTY CYCLE STORIES
CD _____ **ORCH 1202**
Guitar Tree / Oct '95 / Plastic Head.

Orchidee

TRADITIONAL CHINESE ZHENG AND QIN MUSIC
CD _____ **SM 1603-2**
Wergo / Jan '93 / Harmonia Mundi / ADA / Cadillac.

Orchids

EPICUREAN: A SOUNDTRACK
CD _____ **SARAH 611CD**
Sarah / Mar '95 / Vital.

STRIVING FOR THE LAZY PERFECTION
Obsession no.1 / Striving for the lazy perfection / Searching / Welcome to my curious heart / Avignon / Living Ken and Barbie / Beautiful liar / Kind of Eden / Prayers to St. Jude / Lovechild / Give a little honey / I've got to wake up / Perfect reprise
CD _____ **SARAH 617CD**
Sarah / Jan '94 / Vital.

UNHOLY SOUL
CD _____ **SARAH 605CD**
Sarah / Mar '95 / Vital.

Order From Chaos

DAWN BRINGER
CD _____ **SR 9507CD**
Shiadarshana / Sep '95 / Plastic Head.

STILLBIRTH MACHINE
Decapitated / Apr '94 / Plastic Head.
CD _____ **DEC 006**

Ordinaires

ONE
CD _____ **BND 7CD**
One Little Indian / May '90 / Pinnacle.

Ordo Equitum Solis

HECATE
CD _____ **EFA 112822**
Glasnost / May '95 / SRD.

OES
CD _____ **EEE 015**
Musica Maxima Magnetica / Nov '93 / Plastic Head.

PARASKENIA
CD _____ **EEE 18**
Musica Maxima Magnetica / Aug '94 / Plastic Head.

SOLSTITII TEMPORIS SENSUS
CD _____ **EEE 07**
Zoth Ommog / Nov '93 / Plastic Head.

O'Reagan, Brendan

WIND OF CHANGE, A
CD _____ **CLUNCD 056**
Mulligan / Jun '89 / CM / ADA.

Orealis

NIGHT VISIONS
CD _____ **GL 1152CD**
Green Linnet / Nov '95 / Roots / CM / Direct / ADA.

OREALIS
CD _____ **GLCD 1106**
Green Linnet / Nov '92 / Roots / CM / Direct / ADA.

Orefiche, Armando

ARMANDO OREFICHE & HIS HAVANA CUBAN BOYS
CD _____ **HQCD 59**
Harlequin / Dec '95 / Swift / Jazz Music / Wellard / Hot Shot / Cadillac.

Oregon

45TH PARALLEL
CD _____ **VBR 20482**
Vera Bra / Dec '90 / Pinnacle / New Note.

ALWAYS, NEVER AND FOREVER
CD _____ **VBR 20732**
Vera Bra / Sep '91 / Pinnacle / New Note.

CROSSING
Queen of Sydney / Pepe Linque / Alpenbridge / Travel by day / Kronach waltz / Glidj / Amaryllis / Looking glass / Crossing
CD _____ **8253232**
ECM / New Note.

ECOTOPIA
Twice around the sun / Innocente / WBAI / Zephyr / Ecotopia / Leather cats / Redial / Song of the morrow
CD _____ **8331202**
ECM / Oct '87 / New Note.

OREGON
Rapids / Beacon / Toast / Beside a brook / Ariana / There was no Moon that night / Skyline / Impending bloom
CD _____ **8117112**
ECM / Oct '83 / New Note.

TROIKA
Charlotte's tangle / Gekko / Prelude / Mariella / Spanish stairs / Arctic turn/Land rover / Mexico for sure / Pale sun / I said OK / Tower / Minaret / Celeste
CD _____ **VBR 20782**
Vera Bra / Feb '95 / Pinnacle / New Note.

O'Reilly, Marie

IRISH TREASURES AND ORIGINALS 2
CD _____ **CIC 083CD**
Clo Iar-Chonnachta / Nov '93 / CM.

O'Reilly, Melanie

TIR NA MARA
CD _____ **CBM 015CD**
Cross Border Media / Jul '95 / Direct / ADA.

Organisation

FREE BURNING
CD _____ **CDVEST 23**
Bulletproof / Jul '94 / Pinnacle.

SAVOR THE FLAVOR
CD _____ **CDVEST 50**
Bulletproof / May '95 / Pinnacle.

Orgy Of Pigs

WHERE FEELINGS DIE
CD _____ **DOMCD 016**
Dominator / Apr '95 / Plastic Head.

Ó Riada, Seán

MISE ÉIRE
CD _____ **CEFCD 080**
Gael Linn / Jan '94 / Roots / CM / Direct / ADA.

PLAYBOY OF THE WESTERN WORLD, THE
CD _____ **CEFCD 012**
Gael Linn / Jan '91 / Roots / CM / Direct / ADA.

Ó RIADA
CD _____ **CEFCD 032**
Gael Linn / Jan '94 / Roots / CM / Direct / ADA.

Ó RIADA SA GAIETY
CD _____ **CEFCD 027**
Gael Linn / Jan '94 / Roots / CM / Direct / ADA.

Orient Express

BALKANISTICA
CD _____ **RESCD 510**
Resource / Oct '93 / ADA.

KARA TEN
CD _____ **PAN 143CD**
Pan / Jan '94 / ADA / Direct / CM.

Original Dixieland Jazz..

75TH ANNIVERSARY, THE (Original Dixieland Jazz Band)
Livery stable blues / Dixieland jazz band one-step / At the jazz band ball / Ostrich walk / Skeleton jangle / Tiger rag / Bluin' the blues / Fidgety feet / Sensation rag / Mourning blues / Clarinet marmalade / Lazy daddy / Margie Palesteena / Broadway rose / Sweet mama / Home again blues / Crazy blues / Jazz me blues / St. Louis blues / Royal garden blues / Dangerous blues / Bow wow blues
CD _____ **ND 90650**
Bluebird / May '92 / BMG.

COMPLETE ORIGINAL DIXIELAND JAZZ BAND, THE (Original Dixieland Jazz Band)
Livery stable blues / Dixie jass band one-step / At the Jazz Band Ball / Ostrich / Skeleton jangle / Tiger rag / Bluin' the blues / Fidgety feet / Sensation rag / Mournin' blues / Clarinet marmalade / Lazy daddy / Margie / Palesteena / Broadway rose /

Sweet Mama / Home again blues / Crazy blues / Jazz me blues / St. Louis blues / Royal Garden blues / Dangerous blues / Bow wow blues (My Mama treats me like a dog) / Skeeton jangle / Clarinet marmalade (2) / Bluin' the blues (2) / Tiger rag #2 / Barn yard blues / Original Dixieland one-step / Bluin' the blues (3) / Tiger rag #3 / Ostrich walk / Original Dixieland one-step #2 / Satanic blues / Toddlin' blues / Who loves you / Fidgety feet (War cloud)
CD _____ ND 90026
Jazz Tribune / Jun '94 / BMG.

DIXIELAND (Original Dixieland Stompers)
CD _____ 11012
Laserlight / '86 / Target/BMG.

FIRST JAZZ BAND, THE (The Golden Age of Jazz) (Original Dixieland Jazz Band)
CD _____ JZCD 369
Suisa / Jun '92 / Jazz Music / THE.

FIRST JAZZ RECORDINGS 1917-23 (Original Dixieland Jazz Band)
CD _____ 158492
Jazz Archives / Nov '95 / Jazz Music / Discovery / Cadillac.

SENSATION (Original Dixieland Jazz Band)
Livery stable blues / Original Dixie jass band one-step / That teasin' rag / Tiger rag / Bluein' the blues / Fidgety feet / Clarinet marmalade / Lazy daddy / At the Jazz Band Ball / Look at 'em doing it now / Ostrich walk / Satanic blues / Lasses candy / Tell me / I've got a captain working for me now / Mammy o'mine / I've lost my heart in Dixieland / Margie / Singin' the blues
CD _____ CD AJA 5023
Living Era / Oct '88 / Koch.

Original Gospel...

LOVE LIFTED ME (Original Gospel Harmonettes)
Is you all on the altar / I won't let go / Righteous on the march / Step by step / After a while / Camp meeting / Count your blessings / Healer / This will / He's so real to me / In my heart / Love lifted me / He died / Heaven is a beautiful place / You've been good to me / I must tell Jesus / Don't forget about me / Now I'm ready / Royal telephone / Hymn
CD _____ CPCD 8115
Charly / Jul '95 / Charly / THE / Cadillac.

Original Killing Floor

ROCK THE BLUES
Woman you need love / Come home baby / Sunday morning / My mind can ride easy / Keep on walking / Lou's blues / Nobody by my side / Bedtime blues / Try to understand / Wet / Forget it / People change your mind
CD _____ SEECD 355
See For Miles/C5 / Sep '92 / Pinnacle.

Original Rockers

ROCKERS TO ROCKERS
CD _____ CDG 001
Different Drummer / Oct '93 / Pinnacle.

Original Salt City Six

PLAY THE CLASSICS
CD _____ JCD 78
Jazzology / Jul '93 / Swift / Jazz Music.

Original Salty Dogs

JOY JOY JOY
CD _____ SOSCD 1233
Stomp Off / May '93 / Jazz Music / Wellard.

Originals

ANOTHER TIME, ANOTHER PLACE/ COME AWAY WITH ME
Fantasy interlude / Don't put me on / I've loved, I've lost, I've learned / Temporarily out of order / Ladies (we need you) / Take this love / It's alright / Jezebel / J.E.A.L.O.U.S. means I love you / While the cat's away / Come away with me / Stay with me / Blue moon / Thanks for your love (Happiness is you)
CD _____ CDSEWD 084
Southbound / Jul '93 / Pinnacle.

Orioles

JUBILEE RECORDINGS, THE (6CD Set)
At night / Barbara Lee / It's too soon to know / Tell me so (Version 1) / I cover the waterfront / To be you / It seems so long ago / Lonely Christmas / Deacon Jones / Please give my heart a break / Tell me so (Version 2) / Dare to dream / Moonlight / Every dog-gone time / You're gone / Donkey serenade / It's a cold summer / Is my heart wasting time / I challenge your kiss / Kiss and a rose / So much / Forgive and forget / What are you doing New Year's Eve / Would you still be the one in my heart / Would you still be the one in my heart (2) / You are my first love / If it's to be / I wonder / Everything they said came true / I'd

rather have you under the moon / We're supposed to be through / I need you so / Goodnight Irene / I cross my fingers / I cross my fingers (2) / I can't seem to laugh anymore / Walking by the river / I miss you so / Lord's prayer / Oh holy night / I had to leave town / My prayer / I never knew / Pal of mine / Pal of mine (2) / Happy go lucky local blues / Would I love you (Love you, love you) / Would I love you (Love you, love you)(2) / When you're a long way from home / I'm just a fool in love / Barfly / Hold me squeeze me / Baby, please don't go / Don't tell her what happened to me / I may be wrong, but I think you're wonderful / Fool's world / You never cared for me / For all we know / Blame it on yourself / How blind can you be / When you're not around / Waiting / My loved one / Shrimp boats / Trust in me / Scandal / It's over because we're through / It ain't gonna be like that / Gettin' tired, tired / Pretty, pretty rain / Why did you go / This I'll do my darling / Proud of you / No other love / Night has come / Don't stop / I promise you / My baby's gonna get it / Baby, I love you so / Once upon a time / I beginning to think you care for me / Yes indeed / Don't keep it to yourself / I only have eyes for you / Once in a while / Good / Piccadilly / That's how I feel without you / Love birds / Don't cry baby / C.C. rider / Till then #2 / Till then / Feeling Lo / Good looking baby / Along about sundown / You be long to me / Hold me, thrill me, kiss me / Teardrops on my pillow / Congratulations to someone / (Danger) Soft shoulders / I have you heard / Lonely wine / bad little girl / Dem days (Are gone forever) / One more time / Crying in the chapel / Crying in the chapel #2 / Don't you think I out to know / Maybe you'll be there / Drowning every hope I ever had / In the Mission of St. Augustine (versions 1 & 2) / (Please) Write and tell me why (Version 1) / (Please) Write and tell me why (Version 2) / Robe of Cavalry / There's no one but you / Don't go to strangers / Secret love / In the chapel in the moonlight / Thank the Lord, Thank the lord / Longing / If you believe / That's when the good Lord will smile / That's when the good Lord will smile (2) / runaround / Count your blessings / Fair exchange / I love you / Please sing my blues tonight / Cigareetos / Sitting here / Bring the money home / Angel / Don't cry / Sure fire / Danger / Crying in the chapel #3 / Tell me so / At night (2) / Forgive and forget (2) / Come on home / First of summer / Panama Joe / Night and day / Shimmy time / So long
CD Set _____ BCD 15682
Bear Family / Mar '93 / Rollercoaster / Direct / CM / Swift / ADA.

Orion

SOME THINK HE MIGHT BE KING ELVIS
That's all right / Blue moon of Kentucky / Rockabilly rebel / See you later alligator / Suzie Q / I'm gonna be a wheel someday / Rockin' little angel / Crazy little thing called love / Long tall Sally / Memphis sun / Peggy Sue / Matchbox / There's no easy way / Baby please say yes / Born / If I can't have you / Ain't no good / Some you win, some you lose / Look me up (and lay it one me) / Old Mexico / Rainbow maker / Anybody out there / Midnight rendevous / Maybe tomorrow / She hates to be wrong / What now my love / Me and Bobby McGee
CD _____ BCD 15548
Bear Family / May '91 / Rollercoaster / Direct / CM / Swift / ADA.

Orion

BLUE ROOM
CD _____ KMRS 207CD
Keltia Musique / Feb '94 / ADA / Direct / Discovery.

Orlando, Tony

KNOCK THREE TIMES (20 Greatest Hits)
Candida / Knock three times / I play and sing / Summer sand / What are you doing Sunday / Runaway / Happy together / Vaya con dios / You're a lady / Tie a yellow ribbon round the ole oak tree / Say, has anybody seen my sweet gypsy rose / Who's in the strawberry patch with Sally / Steppin' out (gonna boogie tonight) / Look in my eyes pretty woman / Love in your eyes / Up on the roof / Country / Look at / You say the sweetest things / Cupid / He don't love you (like I love you)
CD _____ RMB 75085
Remember / Jan '96 / Total/BMG.

Ornberg, Tomas

THOMAS ORNBERG'S BLUE FIVE (Ornbergs, Tomas Blue Five)
Opus 3 / Sep '91 / May Audio / Pentacone.

Ornicar Big Band

JAZZ CARTOON
CD _____ BBRC 8902
Big Blue / Jun '92 / Harmonia Mundi.

L'INCROYABLE HUCK
CD _____ BBRC 9106
Big Blue / Nov '92 / Harmonia Mundi.

MAIS OU EST DONC ORNICAR?
CD _____ BBRC 9208
Big Blue / Nov '92 / Harmonia Mundi.

Orphan Newsboys

LIVE AT L.A
CD _____ JCD 250
Jazzology / Oct '93 / Swift / Jazz Music.

Orphaned Land

SAHARA
CD _____ HOLY 7CD
Holy / Nov '94 / Plastic Head.

Orphange

ORPHANAGE
CD _____ DFSA 1001CD
Mascot / Jan '96 / Plastic Head.

Orpheus

BEST OF ORPHEUS, THE
Congress alley / Anatomy of I've never seen love like this / I've never seen love like this / Door knob / Can't find time to tell you / Can't find the time / Music machine / I'll stay with you / Never in my life / Dream / I'll fly / Just got back / Mine's yours / So far away in love / Borneo / She's not there / Love over there / Just a little bit / Walk away Renee / Roses / Magic air / Lovin' you / May I look at you / Brown arms in Houston / Me about you / I can make the sun rise / To touch our love again / By the size of my shoes / As they all fall / Joyful / Of enlightenment / I'll be there / Tomorrow man
CD _____ CDWIK 2
Big Beat / Aug '95 / Pinnacle.

Orpheus Boys Choir

FAVOURITE CHRISTMAS
CD Set _____ DCDCD 221
Castle / Nov '95 / BMG.

Orquesta Aragon

LA INSUPERABLE
caserita villarena / Guajira con tumbao / Charlas del momento / Para bailar lo mismo me da / Baila carola / Si sabes bailar mi son / Pare cochero / Muy junto al corazon / Que tenga sabor / Un real de hielo / Busca los lentes / Aprende muchacho
CD _____ PSCCD 1001
Pure Sounds From Cuba / Feb '95 / Henry Hadaway Organisation / THE.

Orquesta Casino De La...

ORQUESTA CASINO DE LA PLAYA (Orquesta Casino De La Playa)
CD _____ HQCD 51
Harlequin / Aug '95 / Swift / Jazz Music / Wellard / Hot Shot / Cadillac.

Orquesta Guayacan

MARCANDO LA DIFERENCIA
Pau pau / Cuanto te quiero / Medellin, medellin / Senora mia / Si tu no estas / Por un beso / Veces / Tu me haces feliz / Recordando todo / Mi billete / Almendra
CD _____ 66058060
RMM / Jul '95 / New Note.

Orquesta Reve

LA EXPLOSION DEL MOMENTO
Rundera (son) / La gente no se puede aguantar (changui son) / De mayo / Changui clave / Mas viejo que ayer, mas joven que manana / El palo de anon / Que te importa a ti / Espero que pase el tiempo / You no quiero que seas celosa / El ron pa despue / Que cuento es ese / Que lastima me da contigo mi amor
CD _____ RWCD 4
Realworld / Jun '89 / EMI / Sterns.

Orta, Paulo

GOOD NIGHT, BUENO NOCHE, BONNE NUIT
CD _____ 422493
New Rose / Nov '94 / Direct / ADA.

Ortega, Anthony

ANTHONY ORTEGA ON EVIDENCE
CD _____ EVCD 213
Evidence / Jan '94 / Harmonia Mundi / ADA / Cadillac.

Ory, Kid

1944-46
CD _____ AMCD 19
American Music / Jan '93 / Jazz Music.

CREOLE JAZZ BAND
Savoy blues / Good man is hard to find / Closer walk with thee / Shake that thing / Copenhagen / Royal garden blues / Mississippi mud / Roof blues / Indianaj
CD _____ GTCD 12008

Good Time Jazz / Oct '93 / Jazz Music / Wellard / Pinnacle / Cadillac.

ECHOES FROM NEW ORLEANS (Ory, Kid & His Creole Jazz Band)
CD _____ GOJCD 53037
Giants Of Jazz / Sep '88 / Target/BMG / Cadillac.

ESSENTIAL NEW ORLEANS JAZZ, THE (Ory, Kid & Sidney Bechet)
CD _____ 4715572
Sony Jazz / Jan '94 / Sony.

FIDGETY FEET (Ory, Kid & His New Orleans Jazz Band)
CD _____ CDJJ 628
Jazz & Jazz / Jan '92 / Target/BMG.

INTRODUCTION TO KID ORY 1922-1944
CD _____ 4023
Best Of Jazz / Sep '95 / Discovery.

KID ORY FAVOURITES
CD _____ FCD 60009
Fantasy / May '95 / Pinnacle / Jazz Music / Wellard / Cadillac.

KID ORY'S CREOLE JAZZ BAND 1944-45
Creole song / Get out of here / Blue for Jimmie Noone / South / Panama / Under the bamboo tree / Careless love / Do what Ory say / Maryland my Maryland / Down home rag / 1919 Rag / Oh didn't he ramble / Ory's creole trombone / Weary blues / Maple leaf rag / Original Dixieland one-step
CD _____ GTCD 12022
Good Time Jazz / Jul '94 / Jazz Music / Wellard / Pinnacle / Cadillac.

LEGENDARY KID, THE
CD _____ GTCD 12016
Good Time Jazz / Oct '93 / Jazz Music / Wellard / Pinnacle / Cadillac.

RARE RECORDINGS (The Golden Age of Jazz)
CD _____ JZCD 368
Suisa / Jun '92 / Jazz Music / THE.

SNAG IT
CD _____ CDJJ 618
Jazz & Jazz / Jan '92 / Target/BMG.

THIS KID'S THE GREATEST (Ory, Kid & His Creole Jazz Band)
South Rampart street parade / Girls go crazy / How come you do me like you do / Four or five times / St. James infirmary / Bill Bailey, won't you please come home / Milneberg joys / Creole song / Bucket's got a hole in it / Creole love call / Ballin' the Jack / Aunt Hagar's blues
CD _____ GTCD 12045
Good Time Jazz / Oct '93 / Jazz Music / Wellard / Pinnacle / Cadillac.

O'Ryan

SOMETHING STRONG
CD _____ CDPAR 001
Parachute Music / Nov '95 / THE.

Oryema, Geoffrey

BEAT THE BORDER
River / Kel kweyo / Market day / Lapwony / Limoja / Gang deyo / Hard labour / Payira wind / Lajok / Nomad
CD _____ CDRW 37
Realworld / Oct '93 / EMI / Sterns.

EXILE
Piny runa woko / Land of Anaka / Piri wango iya / Ye ye ye / Lacan woto kumu / Makambo / Jok omako nyako / Solitude / Lubanga / Exile
CD _____ CDRW 14
Realworld / Sep '90 / EMI / Sterns.

Os Ingenuos

CHOROS FROM BRAZIL
CD _____ NI 5338
Nimbus / Sep '94 / Nimbus.

Osborne Brothers

BLUEGRASS 1956-1968 (4CD Set)
Who done it / Ruby are you mad / My aching heart / Teardrops in my eyes / Wild mountain honey / Down in the willow garden / Ho, honey ho / Della Mae / She's no angel (is this) / My destiny once more / Two lonely hearts / Lost highway / Love pains / It hurts to know / If you don't, somebody else will / Give this message to your heart / You'll never know / I love you only / It's just the idea / Lonely, lonely me / Sweethearts again / Blame me / There's a woman behind every man / Fair and tender ladies / Each season changes you / Black sheep returned to the fold / First fall of snow / Old hickory / Old Joe Clark / Big Ben / Billy in the lowground / John Henry / Banjo boy chimes / Walking cane / Red wing / Seeing Nellie home / Jesse James / Cumberland gap / Lost indian / Poor old cora / Five days of heaven / Ain't gonna rain no mo / Banjo boys / Send me the pillow that you dream / Worried man blues / May you never be alone / New partner / How's the world treating you / Night train to Memphis / Mule skinner blues / White lightning / Bluegrass music's really gone to town / Lovey told me goodbye / Ballad of Jed Clampett / Mem-

ories never die / Mule train / Are you mad / Sourwood mountain / Sweet thing / Take this hammer / Don't even look at me / Cuckoo bird / Bluegrass express / Me and my old banjo / Pathway of teardrops / Gotta travel on / Salty dog blues / Kentucky / Bugle on the banjo (bugle call rag) / Cotton fields / Faded love / This heart of mine (can never say goodbye) / Charlie Cotton / I'll be alright tomorrow / Cut the cornbread / Hey hey bartender / Lonesome day / Big spike hammer / Memories / I know what it means to be lonesome / Up this hill and down the pines / One tear / Making plans / Yesterday's gone / Footprints in the snow / Sure fire / Lonesome feeling / World of unwanted / Hard times / I'm leavin' / Kind of woman I got / One kiss away from loneliness / Let's say goodbye / Like we said hello / Someone before me / Walking the floor over you / Roll Muddy river / My favourite memory / Gal, you got a job to do / Rudy are you mad / Rocky top / When you wind down / Foggy mountain breakdown / Sisters (Billie Jean and Bonnie) / A-model / Lonesome road blues / Jessie James / Maiden's prayer / John Hardy / Little Willie / Hand me down my walking cane
CD Set _____ BCD 15598
Bear Family / Mar '95 / Rollercoaster / Direct / CM / Swift / ADA.

BLUEGRASS 1968-1974 (4CD Set)
I'll never love another / I'll go steppin' too / Will you be lovin' another man / I'll never shed another tear / My little girl in Tennesee / Molly and Tenbrokks / Drivin' nails in my coffin / World of forgotten people / Cut the cornbread, mama / If I could count on you / I bowed on my knees and cried holy / Steal away and pray / Will you meet me over yonder / Where we'll never grow old / Medals for mother / Hide me O blest rock of ages / I pray my way out of trouble / How great thou art / What a friend we have in Jesus / Jesus sure changed me / Light at the river / That was yesterday / Working man / Banjo ringing Saturday night / Thanks for all the yesterdays / Midnight angel / Son of a sawmill man / No good sun of a gun / There'll be teardrops tonight / You win again / Blue moon of Kentucky / Where does the good times go / Put it off until tomorrow / Flyin' south / Will you visit me on Sundays / Nine pound hammer / When the grass grows over me / Tennessee hound dog / Somebody's back in town / Beneath still waters / Ruby are you mad / Siempre / Searching for yesterday / Listening to the rain / Georgia piney woods / Fightin' side of me / Let me be the first to know / Windy city / Kawliga / My sweet love ain't around / You're running wild / My old Kentucky home / Tennesse stud / My heart would know / Muddy bottom / Colour me lonely / Take me home country roads / Tears are no strangers / Oh, the pain of loving you / Unfaithful one / Ballad of forty dollars / Tomorrow never comes / Sometimes you just can't win / Shelly's winter love / I wonder why you said goodbye / Tunnel of your mind / Eight more miles to Louisville / Love lifted me / Stand beside me, behind me / Miss you Mississippi / Teardrops will kiss the morning dew / Long lankly woman / Knoxville girl / Wash my face in the morning dew / Love's gonna live here / Today I started loving you again / Arkansas / Fireball mail / Midnight flyer / How long does it take (to be a stranger) / Blue heartache / Wabash cannonball / Try me one more time / Back to the country roads / Condition of Samuel Wilder's well / Tears / You're heavy on my mind / Checkin' her over / Lizzie Lou / Side saddle / High on a hill top / Sleep wife / I'll lail... / My life last days / I'll of December / Fastest grass alive / Bluegrass melodies / We're holding on (to what we used to be) / Heartache looking for a home / M.A. special / I'm not that good at goodbye / Grandpa John / Little trouble / Born ramblin' man / Here today and gone tomorrow / El randa / In case you ever change your mind / Don't let the smokey mountains smoke get in / Summertime is past and gone / Highway headin' south
CD Set _____ BCD 15748 DI
Bear Family / Nov '95 / Rollercoaster / Direct / CM / Swift / ADA.

Osborne, Jeffrey

JEFFREY OSBORNE
New love / Eeny meeny / I really don't need no light / On the wings of love / Ready for your love / Who you talkin' to / You were made to love / Ain't nothin' missin' baby / Congratulations
CD _____ CDMID 125
A&M / Oct '92 / PolyGram.

Osborne, Mary

MEMORIAL, A
CD _____ STCD 550
Stash / '92 / Jazz Music / CM / Cadillac / Direct / ADA.

Osborne, Mike

CASE FOR THE BLUES, A
CD _____ CCD 11037
Crosscut / Jul '93 / ADA / CM / Direct.

OUTBACK

CD _____ FMR 07
Future / Oct '94 / Harmonia Mundi / ADA.

SHAPES
CD _____ FMRCD 10
Future / Mar '95 / Harmonia Mundi / ADA.

Osbourne, Joan

RELISH
CD _____ 5266922
Mercury / Jan '96 / PolyGram.

Osbourne, Johnny

BAD MAMA JAMA
CD _____ RNCD 2059
Rhino / Jun '94 / Jetstar / Magnum Music Group / THE.

DANCING TIME
CD _____ LG 21099
Lagoon / May '94 / Magnum Music Group / THE.

MR BUDY BYE
CD _____ VPCD 1446
VP / Nov '95 / Jetstar.

ROUGHER THAN THEM
CD _____ VYDCD 08
Vine Yard / Sep '95 / Grapevine.

SEXY THING
CD _____ LG 21092
Lagoon / Apr '94 / Magnum Music Group / THE.

TRUTHS AND RIGHTS
CD _____ CDHB 3613
Heartbeat / Jul '92 / Greensleeves / Jetstar / Direct / ADA.

Osbourne, Ozzy

BARK AT THE MOON
Rock 'n' roll rebel / Bark at the moon / You're no different / Now you see it, now you don't / Forever / So tired / Waiting for darkness / Spiders
CD _____ 4816782
Epic / Nov '95 / Sony.

BARK AT THE MOON/BLIZZARD OF OZ (2CD Set)
CD Set _____ 4652112
Epic / Oct '95 / Sony.

BLIZZARD OF OZ
I don't know / Crazy train / Goodbye to romance / Dee / Suicide solution / Mr. Crowley / No bone movies / Revelation (mother earth) / Steal away (the night)
CD _____ 4816742
Epic / Nov '95 / Sony.

DIARY OF A MADMAN
Over the mountain / Flying high again / You can't kill rock and roll / Believer / Little doills / Tonight / S.A.T.O / Diary of a madman
CD _____ 4816772
Epic / Nov '95 / Sony.

LIVE AND LOUD (2CD Set)
Intro / Paranoid / I don't want to change the world / Desire / Mr. Crowley / I don't know / Road to nowhere / Flying high again / Guitar solo / Suicide solution / Goodbye to romance / Shot in the dark / No more tears / Miracle man / Drum solo / War pigs / Bark at the moon / Mama I'm coming home / Crazy train / Black Sabbath / Changes
CD Set _____ 4737982
Epic / Sep '95 / Sony.

NO MORE TEARS
Mr. Tinkertrain / I don't want to change the world / Mama I'm coming home / Desire / No more tears / S.I.N / Hellraiser / Time after time / Zombie stomp / A.V.H. / Road to nowhere
CD _____ 4816752
Epic / Nov '95 / Sony.

NO REST FOR THE WICKED
Miracle man / Devil's daughter (Holy war) / Crazy babies / Breakin' all the rules / Bloodbath in paradise / Fire in the sky / Tattooed dancer / Demon alcohol
CD _____ 4816812
Epic / Nov '95 / Sony.

OZZMOSIS
Tomorrow / Dental / My little man / Mr Jekyll doesn't hide / Old la / Tonight / Perry Mason / I just want you / Ghost behind my eyes / Thunder tonight / See you on the other side
CD _____ 4802812
Epic / Oct '95 / Sony.

SPEAK OF THE DEVIL
Sympton of the universe / Snow blind / Black Sabbath / Fairies wear boots / War pigs / Wizard / Never say die / Sabbath bloody Sabbath / Iron man/Children of the grave / Paranoid
CD _____ 4816792
Epic / Nov '95 / Sony.

TRIBUTE
I don't know / Crazy train / Believer / Mr. Crowley / Flying high again / Revelation (mother earth) / Steal away (the night) / Suicide solution / Iron man / Children of the grave / Paranoid / Goodbye to romance / No bone movies / Dee

---

CD _____ 4815162
Epic / Nov '95 / Sony.

TRUST ME THE INTERVIEW
CD P.Disc _____ CBAK 4062
Baktabak / Feb '94 / Baktabak.

ULTIMATE SIN
Ultimate sin / Secret loser / Never know why / Thank God for the bomb / Never / Lightning strikes / Killer of giants / Fool like you / Shot in the dark
CD _____ 4816802
Epic / Nov '95 / Sony.

Osby, Greg

BLACK BOOK
Pillars / Mr. Freeman / Rocking chair / Buried alive / Poetry in motion / Black book / Smokescreen / Brewing poetry / Intuition / Fade to black medley (A brother and a token/In a city blues/Urbanite kodes)
CD _____ CDP 8292662
Blue Note / Oct '95 / EMI.

GREG OSBY AND SOUND THEATRE (Osby, Greg & Sound Theatre)
You big / Daigoro / Return to now / Shohachi bushi - oyamako bushi / Calculated risk / For real moments / Gyrhthmitoid
CD _____ JMT 872011
Watt / Oct '87 / New Note.

Oscar, John

JOHN OSCAR, EDDIE MILLER & GEORGE NOBLE (Oscar, John & Eddie Miller/George Noble)
CD _____ DOCD 5191
Blues Document / Oct '93 / Swift / Jazz Music / Hot Shot.

Oscar's Not Wild

WINDOW IN TIME, A
CD _____ ONW 1995
Oscar's Not Wild / May '96 / Else.

O'Shamrock, Barney

IRISH ACCORDION, THE
Slievenamon / Old flames / Doonaree / Rose of Tralee / Rose of Mooncoin / Wild colonial boy / Irish American (medley) / How can you buy Killarney / Maggie / Fields of Athenry / Galway Bay / Molly Malone / Bunch of thyme / Danny boy / Hannigan's hooley / Banks of my own lovely Lee / When Irish eyes are smiling / Did your mother come from Ireland / Old bog road / Forty shades of green / Irish medley
CD _____ PLATCD 11
Platinum Music / Jul '89 / Prism / Ross.

O'Shea, Tessie

I'M READY, I'M WILLING
CD _____ PASTCD 7078
Flapper / Sep '95 / Pinnacle.

Osibisa

CELEBRATION - THE BEST OF OSIBISA
CD _____ AIM 1036CD
Aim / Oct '93 / Direct / ADA / Jazz Music.

HAPPY CHILDREN
Happy children / We want to know / Kotuku / Adwoa / Bassa-Bassa / Somaja / Fire
CD _____ 7599268632
WEA / Jan '96 / Warner Music.

HEADS
Kokoroko / Wango wango / So ro mi la ne / Sweet America / Ye tie wo / Che che Kule / Mentumi / Sweet sounds / Do you know
CD _____ AIM 1047
Aim / Apr '95 / Direct / ADA / Jazz Music.

MOVEMENTS
In Akustik / Mar '95 / Magnum Music Group.
CD _____ INAK 8902

MYSTIC ENERGY
Meeting point / Celebration / Africa we go go / Orebo (magic people) / Moving on / Mama (I will be back) / Pata pata / Fatima / Obinkabimame
CD _____ MAUCD 614
Mau Mau / Feb '92 / Pinnacle.

OSIBIROCK
Who's got the paper / Why / Osibrock / Celele / Atinga bells / African jive / We belong / Komfo (High Priest) / Kangaroo / Home affairs
CD _____ 7599268642
WEA / Jan '96 / Warner Music.

OSIBISA
Dawn / Music for Gong Gong / Ayiko Bia / Akwaaba / Oranges / Phallus C / Think about the people
CD _____ AIM 1045
Aim / Apr '95 / Direct / ADA / Jazz Music.

OSIBISA'S FIRST
Line / Sep '94 / CM / Grapevine / ADA / Conifer / Direct.
CD _____ LCCD 901266

SUPERFLY TNT
CD _____ RMCCD 0196
Red Steel Music / Feb '95 / Grapevine.

UNLEASHED IN INDIA
CD _____ RMCCD 0200
Red Steel Music / Jul '95 / Grapevine.

Osiris

FUTURITY AND HUMAN DEPRESSIONS
CD _____ SHARK 027CD
Shark / Jan '92 / Plastic Head.

Oskar, Lee

BEST OF LEE OSKAR
Promised land / Sunshine Kerl / San Francisco bay / Before the rain / More than words can say / Song for my son / Document / Feeling happy / My road
CD _____ 74321305292
Avenue / Sep '95 / BMG.

LEE OSKAR
I remember home (a peasant's symphony) / The journey; The immigrant; The promised land) / Blisters / BLT / Sunshine Kerl / Down the Nile / Starkite
CD _____ 74321305282
Avenue / Sep '95 / BMG.

Osmium

RISE UP
CD _____ DMCD 1032
Demi-Monde / Feb '92 / Disc / Magnum Music Group.

Osmond, Donny

TWELFTH OF NEVER
CD _____ BX 425-2
BR Music / Jul '94 / Target/BMG.

Osmonds

GREATEST HITS
CD _____ BX 424-2
BR Music / Jul '94 / Target/BMG.

OSMOND FAMILY ALBUM, THE
CD Set _____ DBP 102007
Double Platinum / May '95 / Target/BMG.

Ossian

BEST OF OSSIAN
St. Kilda wedding/Perrie werrie reel/Honourable Mrs. Moll's / 'S gann gunn d'irich mi chaoidh / Road to Drumleman / Sound of sleat/Aandowin' at the bow/Old reel / Will ye go to Flanders/Lord Lovat's lament / Duncan Johnstone/The duck/The curlew / Drunk at night, dry in the morning / I will set my ship in order / Rory Dall's sister's lament / Johnny Todd/Far from home / Jamie Raeburn/Broomielaw / Mrs. Stewart of Grantully/Be sud an'gille truagh/Harris danc
CD _____ IRCD 023
Iona / Mar '94 / ADA / Direct / Duncans.

BORDERS
Troy's wedding / Biddy from sligo / Rory Dall's sisters / Lament / Chairlie, oh Chairlie / I will set my ship in order / John Macdonald's / Sandpit / Bide ye yet / 'Neath the gloamin / Star at e'en / New house in St Peter's / Ewe wi' the crookit horn / Willie Murray's
CD _____ IRCD 007
Iona / Aug '91 / ADA / Direct / Duncans.

DOVE ACROSS THE WATER
Duck / Duncan Johnstone / Curlew / Braw sailin' on the sea / Drunk at night, dry in the morning / Will ye go to Flanders / Take the begpin / Mile Marbhaig / I'nye across the water / Iona theme / March; The cunning workmen / Columbia / Iona theme (reprise)
CD _____ IRCD 004
Iona / Aug '91 / ADA / Direct / Duncans.

LIGHT ON A DISTANT SHORE
Johnny Todd / Far from home / It was a' for our rightful king / Le chanson des livrees / Sun rises bright in France / Mrs. Stewart of Grantully / Be sud an' gille truagh / Calum Johnston's harris dance / Jamie Raeburn/Broomielaw / Light on a distant shore / New York harbour / At work on the land / In the new world
CD _____ IRCD 009
Iona / Sep '91 / ADA / Direct / Duncans.

SEAL SONG
Sound of sleat / Aandowin' at the bow / Old reel / To pad the road wi, me / Coilsfield house / Heilandmen cam doon the hill / Thornton jig / Aye waukin' o / Corn rigs / Lude's supper / Road to Drumleman / Fisherman's song for attracting seals / Lieutenant / Maguire walking / Floor / Mull of the mountains
CD _____ IRCD 002
Iona / Aug '91 / ADA / Direct / Duncans.

St KILDA WEDDING
St Kilda wedding / Perrie werrie (reel) / Honourable Mr's Moll's reel / Give me a lass wi a lump o'land / lomramh eadar il' a's uist / Dean cadalan samhach / Gala water David Manson / 'S gann gunn d'irich mi chaoidh / Farewell to whiskey / My love is the fair lad / Fourth bridge / Pretty peg / Braes o'strathblane / More grog coming / Tilley plump, Da / Foostra
CD _____ IRCD 001
Iona / Aug '91 / ADA / Direct / Duncans.

Ostanek, Walter

GERMAN BEER DRINKING SONGS
CD _____ HADCD 191
Javelin / Nov '95 / THE / Henry Hadaway Organisation.

Ostroushko, Peter

HEART OF THE HEARTLAND
CD _____ RRHCD 70
Red House / Oct '95 / Koch / ADA.

SIUZ DUZ MUSIC
CD _____ ROUC 0204
Rounder / Aug '95 / CM / Direct / ADA / Cadillac.

Ó Súilleabháin,...

BETWEEN WORLDS (Ó Súilleabháin, Mícheál)
Oiche nollag/Christmas Eve / An tseangh liath/The old grey goose / An cailin deas caras na mbo/The pretty milkmaid / Casadh na graige/The turning of the road / An mhaigdean cheansa/The gentle maiden / Fiach an mhada rua/The fox chase / Brian Boru / Idir eatarthu/Between worlds / Woodbrook / Ah, sweet dancer / Eleanor Plunkett / Heartwork / (Must be more) Crispy / River of sound / Lumen
CD _____ CDVE 926
Venture / Aug '95 / EMI.

CASADH/TURNING (Ó Súilleabháin, Mícheál)
By golly / Wexford carol / Brian Boru / Londubh agus an cheirseach / Blackbird and the thrush / Rolling wave / Casadh na graige / Turning of the road / King of the blind / Fairy queen / Planxty Irwin / Fanny power / Cearc agus coileach / Hen and the cock / Lady Maisterton
CD _____ CDVE 904
Virgin / Jun '91 / EMI.

DOLPHIN WAY, THE (Ó Súilleabháin, Mícheál)
Christmas Eve / Plains of Boyle / Gentle fair Elly (Eiblhi gheal chiuin) / Old grey goose / Pretty milkmaid / Snowy breasted pearl (Pearls an bhrollaig bhain) / Carolan's concerto / Merrily kiss the quaker / Little fair haired child / Fox chase / Molly Halpin (Mollai ni ailpin) / Planxty Irwin / Gentle maiden
CD _____ CDVE 1
Venture / '88 / EMI.

GAISEADH / FLOWING (Ó Súilleabháin, Mícheál)
Woodbrook / Flowansionnamare (In three parts i)Flowan ii)Sionna iii)Mare.) / Eleanor Plunkett / Angel face / Crispy / Through an eye of stone / At the still point of the turning world
CD _____ CDVE 915
Venture / Nov '92 / EMI.

MÍCHEÁL Ó SÚILLEABHÁIN (Ó Súilleabháin, Mícheál)
CD _____ CEFCD 046
Gael Linn / Jan '92 / Roots / CM / Direct / ADA.

OILEAN/ISLAND (Ó Súilleabháin, Mícheál)
Heartwork / Ah sweet dancer / Idir eatarthu / Between worlds / Carolan's farewell to music / Oilean/island / First movement / Second movement / Third movement / Ah sweet dancer (version)
CD _____ CDVE 40
Virgin / May '89 / EMI.

O'Sullivan, Bernard

CLARE CONCERTINAS (O'Sullivan, Bernard & Tommy McMahon)
Babes in the wood / Cooraclare polka / Clare dragoons / Sandy groves of Piedmont / Humours of Ennistymon / Old torn petticoat / Tommy People's favourite / Mount Fabus hunt / Ollie Conway's selection / Kilrush races / Clogher reel / Burren reel / Bonaparte's retreat / Bonaparte's march / Barron's jig / Jackson's jig / Miltown jig / Rodney's glory / Tommy McMahon's reel / Over the waves / Can't left behind me / Maggie in the wood / Martin Taltry's jig / Thomas Fresh'j jig / Joe Cunnean's jig / Sean Ryan's hornpipe / Danganella hornpipe / Job of journeywork / Ash plant / Maid of Mount Cisco
CD _____ GL 3092CD
Green Linnet / Sep '94 / Roots / CM / Direct / ADA.

O'Sullivan, Gilbert

BY LARRY
CD _____ PRKCD 25
Park / Mar '94 / Pinnacle.

EVERY SONG HAS ITS PLAY
Overture / Showbiz (featuring Nicky Henson) / Dear diman / I wish I could cry / Nothing to fear (featuring Mike Dore) / Pretty Polly / Can't find my way home / Dishonourable profession / You don't own me/If I know you (featuring Val Stokes & Mike Dore) / Nobody wants to know (featuring Barry Esson) / Young at heart (we'll always remain) / I've never been short of a smile / Showbiz (reprise) / If you commence before the start
Are you happy / Not that it bothers me / Sometimes / It's easy to see when you're blind / Having said that / Can't think straight / Best love I ever had / Divorce Irish style / Came and went / I'm not too young / I can give you / Can't think straight (Japanese version)
CD _____ PARKCD 19
Park / Mar '93 / Pinnacle.

O'Sullivan, Jerry

INVASION, THE
CD _____ GLCD 1074
Green Linnet / Feb '92 / Roots / CM / Direct / ADA.

O'Sullivan, Maire

FROM THERE TO HERE
CD _____ CIC 076CD
Clo Iar-Chonnachta / Nov '93 / CM.

Oswald, John

PLEXURE
CD _____ AVAN 016
Avant / Sep '93 / Harmonia Mundi / Cadillac.

Other Half

MR. PHARMACIST & THE LOST SINGLES
CD _____ 842093
EVA / May '94 / Direct / ADA.

Other Two

OTHER TWO AND YOU, THE
Tasty fish / Greatest thing / Selfish / Movin' on / Ninth configuration / Feel this love / Spirit level / Night voice / Innocence / Loved it (The other track)
CD _____ 520028-2
Factory / Nov '93 / PolyGram.

Otherside

BURN BABY BURN
CD _____ JRVCD 101
Vous / Oct '95 / Jetstar.

Otis, Johnny

JOHNNY OTIS SHOW/CREEPING WITH THE CATS (Otis, Johnny Show)
Midnight creeper (part 1) / Driftin' blues / Ali Baba's boogie / Let the sunshine in my life (once more) / Hey hey hey hey / Dog face (part 1) / Dog face (part 2) / Show me the way to go home / Sleepy shines butt shuffle / Organ grinder swing / Someday / Sadie / Butterball / Wa wa (part 1) / My eyes are full of tears / Turtle dove / Groove juice / Trouble on my mind / Number 69/ number 21 / Creeper returns / Stop, look and love me / Night is young (and you're so fine)
CD _____ CDCHD 325
Ace / Jul '91 / Pinnacle / Cadillac / Complete / Direct / ADA.

LET'S LIVE IT UP
Let's rock (let's surf awhile) / Hand jive one more time / It must be love / I say I love you / She's alright / Baby I got news for you / California mash (the hash) / Darling / I'll be true / Let's live it up / That's the chance you've got to take / Hey hey song / Somebody call the station / Early in the morning blues / You better love me / Queen of the twist / Oh my soul / Wilted rose buds / I know my love is true / Cold cold heart / Bye bye baby (I'm leaving you) / Yes / In the evening
CD _____ CDCHARLY 269
Charly / Nov '92 / Charly / THE / Cadillac.

LIVE AT MONTEREY (Otis, Johnny Show)
Willie and the hand jive / Cry me a river / Cleanheads blues / I got a gal / Baby you don't know / Preacher's blues / Good rockin' tonight / Time machine / Margie's boogie / Little Esther's blues / Blowtop blues / T-Bone blues / Jelly jelly / Kidney stew / Things I used to do / R.M. blues / Shuggie's blues / You better look out / Goin' back to L.A. / Plastic man / Boogie woogie bye bye
CD _____ ED CD 266
Edsel / May '88 / Pinnacle / ADA.

NEW JOHNNY OTIS SHOW, THE
Drinkin' wine spo-dee-o-dee / Every beat of my heart / Jonella and Jack / What else can
I do / Half steppin' woman / Why don't you do right / Big time scoop / I never felt this way before / Don't deceive me / So fine
CD _____ ALCD 4726
Alligator / May '93 / Direct / ADA.

ORIGINAL JOHNNY OTIS, THE
Harlem nocturne / My baby's business / Around the clock / Preston love's mansion / Boogie guitar / Little red hen / Hangover blues / New Orleans shuffle / If it's so baby / Rain in my eyes / I found out my troubles / I'm living OK / Ain't no use beggin' / You're fine but not my kind / Turkey hop part 1 / Turkey hop part 2 / Blues nocturne / Cry baby / Mistrustin' blues / Dreamin' blues / Cool and easy / Wedding boogie / Sunset to dawn / Honky tonk boogie / ALI nite long / Deceiving blues / Three magic words
CD _____ SV 0266
Savoy Jazz / Apr '95 / Conifer / ADA.

OTISOLOGY
Hand jive / Roll with me Henry / Let's go Johnny / I'm ready for love / I'm scared of you / Fonkitup / I can't help myself / I wanna come over / Nut pony
CD _____ CDMF 095
Magnum Force / Jan '96 / Magnum Music Group.

SPIRIT OF THE BLACK TERRITORY BANDS
CD _____ ARHCD 384
Arhoolie / Apr '95 / ADA / Direct / Cadillac.

Otis, Jon

SAND, THE MOON & THE STARS, THE
CD _____ LAKE 3060
Lakeside / Aug '95 / Magnum Music Group.

Otis, Shuggie

SHUGGIE'S BOOGIE: SHUGGIE OTIS PLAYS THE BLUES
12.15 Slow goonbash blues / Shuggie's boogie / Gospel groove / Hawks / Me and my woman / I can't stand to see you die / I got the walking blues / Purple (Edited version) / Cold shot / Sweet thang / Bottie cooler / Shuggie's old time dee-di
CD _____ 4767262
Legacy / May '94 / Sony.

Ottawan

VERY BEST OF OTTAWAN, THE
CD _____ KWEST 5407
Disky / Feb '93 / THE / BMG / Discovery / Pinnacle.

Otto, Hans

DAS BUCH DER KLANGE
CD Set _____ CDKUCK 069/070
Kuckuck / '86 / CM / ADA.

Otway, John

COR, BABY THAT'S REALLY ME
Misty mountain / Gypsy / Murder man / Louisa on a horse / Really free / Geneve / Cheryl's going home / Beware of the flowers 'cause I'm sure they're going to get y / Baby's in the club / Best dream / Frightened and scared / D.K. 50/80 / Green grass of home / Turning point / Headbutts / Montreal / In dreams / Middle of winter / Jerusalem / Last of the mochicans / Racing cars / Jet spotter of the track)
CD _____ SBR 004CD
Strike Back / Oct '95 / Vital / Grapevine.

LIVE
In dreams / Misty mountain / Cor baby that's really free / Bluey green / Racing cars / Beware of the flowers / Josephine / Louisa on a horse / Baby's it's real thing / Two little boys / Best dream / Frightened and scared / Cheryl's goin' home / House of the rising sun / Geneve
CD _____ OTCD 4001
Amazing Feet / Apr '95 / Grapevine / Vital.

OTWAY & BARRETT/DEEP AND MEANINGLESS (Otway, John & Wild Willy Barrett)
CD _____ TMC 9302
Eclectic / Jan '96 / Pinnacle.

PREMATURE ADULATION
Judgement day / Poetry and jazz / Duet / We know what she's doing (she's in love) / Saddest sound since the blues / Entertainment (not) / Photograph / Please don't read my poetry / Nothing at all / God's camera / Willy (in the air) / Typewriter
CD _____ OTCD 4004
Amazing Feet / Apr '95 / Grapevine / Vital.

TWO LITTLE BOYS
CD _____ OTWAYS 1
Music Of Life / Sep '92 / Grapevine.

UNDER THE COVERS & OVER THE TOP
CD _____ OTWAY 1 CD
Music Of Life / Oct '92 / Grapevine.

Out Of Body Experience

ILLEGAL STATE OF MIND, AN
CD _____ VP 17
Spinefarm / Feb '94 / Plastic Head.

Out Of Darkness

CELEBRATION CLUB SESSION, THE
Walk on the water / Love to love / Worldpool / Cocaine / Valley (I'm gonna follow) / Child of the universe
CD _____ PCDN 138
Plankton / Aug '93 / Plankton.

Out Ov Kontrol

OUT OV CONTROL
CD _____ WRA 8121CD
Wrap / Apr '94 / Koch.

Outback

BAKA
Air play / Baka / An dro nevez / Other side / Hold on / On the streets / Buenaventura / Dingo go
CD _____ HNCD 1357
Hannibal / Apr '90 / Vital / ADA.

DANCE THE DEVIL AWAY
CD _____ HNCD 1369
Hannibal / Sep '91 / Vital / ADA.

Outcasts

BLOOD AND THUNDER
CD _____ ROSE 16CD
New Rose / '84 / Direct / ADA.

OUTCASTS PUNK SINGLES COLLECTION
You're a disease / Don't want to be no adult / Frustration / Just another teenage rebel / Love is for sops / Cops are comin' / Self conscious over you / Love you for ever / Cyborg / Magnum force / Gangland warfare / Programme love / Beating and screaming part 1 / Beating and screaming part 2 / Mania / Angel face / Gangland warfare (version 2) / Nowhere left to run / Running's over, time to pray / Ruby / Seven deadly sins / Swamp fever / 1969 / Psychotic shakedown / Blue murder
CD _____ CDPUNK 62
Anagram / Sep '95 / Pinnacle.

SELF CONSCIOUS OVER YOU
Self conscious over you / Clinical love / One day / Love is for sops / You're a disease / Love you for never / Princess grew up a frog / Cyborg / School teacher / Spiteful Sue / Cops are comin' / Just another teenage rebel
CD _____ DOJOCD 182
Dojo / Feb '94 / BMG.

Outhere Brothers

1 POLISH, 2 BISCUITS & A FISH SANDWICH
CD _____ 0630105852
Eternal / May '95 / Warner Music.

PARTY ALBUM
CD _____ 0630127812
Eternal / Dec '95 / Warner Music.

Outkast

SOUTHERNPLAYALISTICADILLACHMUSIZ
Peaches (Intro) / Myintrotoletuknow / Ain't no thang / Welcome to Atlanta / Southernplayalisticadillacchmusiz / Call of the wild (Featuring The Goody Mob) / Player's ball (Original) / Claimin' true / Club donkey ass / Funky ride / Git up, git out(Featuring The Goody Mob) / Dat true / Crumblin' erb / Hootie hoo / D.E.E.P. Player's ball (Reprise) / Flim flam
CD _____ 73008260102
Arista / Jul '94 / BMG.

Outlaws

DREAM OF THE WEST
Dream of the west / Outlaws / Husky team / Rodeo / Smoke signals / Ambush / Barbecue / Spring is near / Indian brave / Homeward bound / Western sunset / Tune for short cowboys
CD _____ BGOCD 118
Beat Goes On / Sep '91 / Pinnacle.

RIDE AGAIN (Singles A's and B's)
CD _____ SEECD 303
See For Miles/C5 / '90 / Pinnacle.

Outlines

BLIND ALLEY
CD _____ L 8909302
Danceteria / Jan '90 / Plastic Head / ADA.

Outrage

SPIT
Mr. Rightman / Faith / To you / Smoke / How bad / Key / Never make the same / Live my life / Inner strength / Eagle
CD _____ 450994308-2
WEA / Feb '94 / Warner Music.

Outrider

NO WAY OUT
CD _____ CDSGP 001
Prestige / Aug '91 / Total/BMG.

Outside

ALMOST IN
CD _____ DORO 18CD
Dorado / Dec '93 / Disc.

ROUGH AND THE SMOOTH
CD _____ DOR 43CD
Dorado / Jul '95 / Disc.

Outsider

OUTSIDER MEETS THE ROOTS DYNAMICS (Outsider & Roots Dynamics)
CD _____ JW 011CD
Jah Works / Apr '94 / Roots Collective.

Outsiders

RIPPED SHIRT
CD _____ PLAN 004CD
Planet / Mar '94 / Grapevine / ADA / CM.

Outskirts Of Infinity

INCIDENT AT PILATUS
CD _____ DSKCD 002
Dark Skies / Aug '94 / Disc.

STONE CRAZY
CD _____ CDINF 002
Infinity / May '90 / Pinnacle.

Oval

94 DISKONT
CD _____ EFA 006632
Mille Plateau / May '95 / SRD.

SYSTEMISCH
CD _____ EFA 006592
Mille Plateau / Nov '94 / SRD.

Ovans, Tom

TALES FROM THE UNDERGROUND
Let it rain / Mr. Blue / Uncle Joe / Dance with me girl / Sailor / Angelou / Echoes of the fall / Lucky to be alive / Brakeman's blues / Real bono / Nine below zero / Waiting on you
CD _____ SUR437CD
Survival / May '95 / Pinnacle.

Ovarian Trolley

CROCODILE TEARS
See what happens / Rogue / Crocodile tears / Senorita / Lost girls / Serenity / Death / Puppy / Coin op / Dream
CD _____ BOOT 003
Shimmy Disc / Feb '94 / Vital.

Overdose

PROGRESS OF DECADENCE
CD _____ CDFLAG 83
Under One Flag / Nov '94 / Pinnacle.

Overkill

FEEL THE FIRE
CD _____ CDMFN 127
Music For Nations / Oct '92 / Pinnacle.

HORRORSCOPE
Coma / Infectious / Blood money / Thanx for nothin' / Bare bones / Horrorscope / New machine / Frankenstein / Live young die free / Nice day... / Solitude
CD _____ 7567822832
Atlantic / Aug '91 / Warner Music.

I HEAR BLACK
Dreaming in Columbian / I hear black / World of hurt / Feed my head / Shades of grey / Spiritual void / Ghost dance / Weight of the world / Ignorance and innocence / Undying / Just like you
CD _____ 756782476-2
Atlantic / Apr '93 / Warner Music.

TRIUMPH OF WILL
CD _____ SST 038 CD
SST / Oct '93 / Plastic Head.

Overlanders

MICHELLE
CD _____ REP 4095-WZ
Repertoire / Aug '91 / Pinnacle / Cadillac.

Owens, Buck

BLUE LOVE
House down the block / You're for me / Down on the corner of love / Blue love / It don't show on me / Three dimension love / Why don't Mommy stay with Daddy and me / When I hold you / Country girl / I will love you always / Right after the dance / I'm gonna blow / Higher and higher and higher / Honeysuckle / Learnin' dirty tracks
CD _____ CDSD 055
Sundown / Jan '93 / Magnum Music Group.

BUCK OWENS STORY 1956-1964 (Volume 1)
CD _____ PRS 23017
Personality / Feb '95 / Target/BMG.

BUCK OWENS STORY 1964-1968 (Volume 2)
CD _____ PRS 23018
Personality / Feb '95 / Target/BMG.

BUCK OWENS STORY 1969-1989 (Volume 3)
CD _____ PRS 23019
Personality / May '95 / Target/BMG.

LIVE AT CARNEGIE HALL 1966 (Owens, Buck & The Buckaroos)
Act naturally / Together again / Love's gonna live here / Medley (I don't care; My heart skips a beat; Gonna have love) / Medley #2 (In the palm of her hand; Cryin' time; Don't let her know; Only you) / Waitin' in your welfare line / Buckaroo / Streets of Laredo / I've got a tiger by the tail / Fun 'n' games (With Don & Doyle) / Twist and shout / Medley #3 (Under your spell again; Above & beyond; Excuse me; Foolin' around; Truck drivin' man)
CD _____ CMFCD 012
Country Music Foundation / Jan '93 / Direct / ADA.

Owens, Calvin

TRUE BLUE
True blue / Hot burning fever / Don't you want a man like me / Texas stomp / Sitting here / Sweet meat / Cherry red / Woke up screaming / Lick or split / Deviation / Don't you want a woman like me / Dreams come true
CD _____ IMP 707
Topcat / Sep '95 / Discovery.

Owens, Jack

IT MUST HAVE BEEN THE DEVIL (Owens, Jack & Bud Spires)
CD _____ TCD 5016
Testament / Mar '95 / Complete/Pinnacle / ADA / Koch.

Owens, Jay

BLUES SOUL OF JAY OWENS
Come to my house / Steppin' stone / Bottom line / Chasing my dreams / Lake city, fla / Wishing well / Back row / Why do you treat me this way / Can't do the same thing again / Crosstown love / Missing you blues / My kind of woman / We're human
CD _____ 4509965962
WEA / Jan '95 / Warner Music.

MOVIN' ON
CD _____ 4509990612
Warner Bros. / Feb '95 / Warner Music.

Owens, Tex

CATTLE CALL
Cattle call / Pride of the prairie / Dude ranch party (part 1) / Dude ranch party (part 2) / Rockin' alone in an old rocking chair / Two sweethearts / By the rushing waterfall / Give me the plains at night / Let me ride the range / Porcupine serenade / Lost indian call / Grandpa and the lovebug / Daddy's old rocking chair / I'll be happy / Lonesome for you / Red roses bring memories of you / Yesterday's roses / Lonely for you, oh so long / Cowboy call / While I'm nearly home / Don't hide your tears darling / Cattle call (theme song)
CD _____ BCD 15777
Bear Family / May '94 / Rollercoaster / Direct / CM / Swift / ADA.

Oxbow

LET ME BE A WOMAN
CD _____ EFA 127201
Crippled Dick Hot Wax / Apr '95 / SRD.

Oxford Pro Music Singers

AMONG THE LEAVES SO GREEN
Among the leaves so green / Bushes and briars / Black sheep / Bobby Shaftoe / Dashing away / Early one morning / Greensleeves / Londonderry air / My sweetheart's like Venus / O waly, waly / She's like the swallow / Sourwood mountain / Afton water / Brigg fair / Ca' the yowes / Faithful Johnny / I love my love / Strawberry fair / Swansea Town / Keel row / Oak and the ash / Sailor and young Nancy / Three ravens / Turtle dove / Yarmouth fair
CD _____ PROUCD 137
Proudsound / Apr '95 / Conifer.

Oxford, Vernon

KEEPER OF THE FLAME (5CD Set)
Watermelon time in Georgia / Roll big wheels roll / Woman let me sing you a song / Move to town in the fall / Nashville women / Goin' home / Let's take a cold shower / Field of flowers / Hide / Stone by stone / Behind every good man there's a woman / Forgetfulness for sale / Baby sister / Goin'

home (2) / Honky tonk girls / Babies, stop your crying / Blues come in / Treat yourself right / Little sister throw your red shoes away / Old folk's home / That's the way I talk / Touch of God's hands / Come back and see us / This woman is mine / Mansion on the hill / Wedding bells / Don't let a little thing like that / You win again / Touch of God's hands (2) / Come back and see us (2) / Nashville women (2) / What will I live on tomorrow / Wine, women and songs / I'd rather see you wave goodbye / This is where I came in / What color is wine? / Hazard County Saturday night / Rise of Seymour Simmons / How high does the cotton grow mama / I've got to get Peter off your mind / We came awfully close to sin / Love and Pearl and me / She's always there / I wish you would leave me alone / We sure danced us some goodn's / Woman you've got a hold of me / Soft and warm / Surprise birthday party / Shadows of my mind / Country singer / Anymore / God keeps the wild flowers blooming / Giving the pill / Beautiful junk / Mowing the lawn / Wait a little longer please Jesus / Clean your own tables / Your waiting me is gone / Don't be late / Leave me alone with the blues / One more night to spare / Only the shadows know / Redneck / Good old fashioned Saturday night honky / Midnight memories / Red hot women (and ice cold beer) / Backslider's wine / Redneck roots / Songs that losers choose / Images / Brother jukebox / Kaw liga / Your cheatin' heart / Hey good lookin' / When God comes and gathers his jewels / Baby we're really in love / Wedding bells (2) / Cold cold heart / I saw the light / Setting the woods on fire / I can't help it / You win again (2) / Jambalaya / I'm so lonesome I could cry / Mansion on the hill (2) / Funeral / Nobody's child / Who were Ann and Louis Adams / There's a better place / Joanna / Mommy do you think I'll get to heaven / State of depression / Woman / Maggie the baby is crying / If I had my wife to love over / I'll forgive you for the last time / If there was no country music / Cattle call / I love to sing / Walkin' my blues away / If kisses could talk / Gonna ease my worried mind / No one else is listening / Turn the record over / I think living is sweet / Blanket of stars / Great Stoneface / Rainy day / Somebody to love me / Let your light shine / Bringing Mary home / Bad moon risin' / Letters have no arms / Mother's not dead, she's only sleeping / Honky tonk troubles / Daughter of the vine / They'll never take her love from me / Angel band / Have you loved your woman today / Lonesome rainin' city / Veil of white lace / Sweeter than the flowers / Busiest memory in town / Wings of a dove / This world holds nothin' since you're gone / Family bible / Always true / Where the soul of man never dies / Lord, I've tried everything but you / Better way of life / Uncloudy day / His and hers / House of gold / Baby sister (2) / Sad situation / Dust on the bible / Early morning rain / Last letter / You're the reason / Are they gonna make us outlaws again / Long black veil / I feel chained
CD Set _____ BCD 15774 EI
Bear Family / Oct '95 / Rollercoaster / Direct / CM / Swift / ADA.

O'Yaba

GAME IS NOT OVER, THE
CD _____ SHCD 45005
Greensleeves / Apr '93 / Total/BMG / Jetstar / SRD.

ONE FOUNDATION
CD _____ PLTRCD 523
Timbuktu / Feb '94 / Pinnacle.

Oyster Band

DESERTERS
CD _____ COOKCD 041
Cooking Vinyl / Mar '92 / Vital.

HOLY BANDITS
When I'm up I can't get down / Road to Santiago / I look for you / Gone west / We shall come home / Cry cry / Here's to you / Moving on / Ramblin' Irishman / Fire is burning / Blood wedding
CD _____ COOKCD 058
Cooking Vinyl / Feb '95 / Vital.

LITTLE ROCK TO LEIPZIG
Jail song two / Gonna do what I have to do / Galopade / I fought the law / New York girls / Oxford girl / Too late now / Red barn stomp / Coal not dole / Johnny Mickey Barry's
CD _____ COOKCD 032
Cooking Vinyl / Apr '90 / Vital.

RIDE
Too late now / Polish plain / Heaven to Calcutta / Tincans / This year, next year / New York girls / Gamblers / Take me down / Cheekbone City / Love vigilantes / My dog (CD only.) / Sins of a family (CD only.)
CD _____ COOKCD 020
Cooking Vinyl / Feb '95 / Vital.

Oz

ROLL THE DICE
CD _____ BMCD 11
Black Mark / '92 / Plastic Head.

Ozark Mountain Daredevils

MODERN HISTORY
Everywhere she goes / Love is calling / I'm still dreaming / Turn it up / True love / Lonely knight / Over again / Heating up / River / Heart of the country / Wild the days
CD _____ CDRR 303
Request / Jan '90 / Jazz Music.

Ozkan, Talip

ART OF THE TANBUR, THE
CD _____ C 560042
Ocora / May '94 / Harmonia Mundi / ADA.

MYSTERIES OF TURKEY
CD _____ CDT 115
Topic / Apr '93 / Direct / ADA.

Ozone, Makoto

STARLIGHT
Starlight / Riverside expressway / Night spark / 03 / I love to be face to face (Malta) / Sky / Spring stream / Chega de saudade / Moonstone / Tenderly
CD _____ JD 3323
JVC / Nov '90 / New Note.

Ozric Tentacles

ARBORESCENCE
CD _____ DOVECD 7
Dovetail / Jun '94 / Pinnacle.

BECOME THE OTHER
CD _____ DOVECD 8
Dovetail / Oct '95 / Pinnacle.

BITS BETWEEN THE BITS
CD _____ OTCD 6
Dovetail / Feb '92 / Pinnacle.

ERPLAND
CD _____ DOVECD 1
Dovetail / Jul '90 / Pinnacle.

ERPSONGS
CD _____ OTCD 1
Dovetail / Apr '93 / Pinnacle.

JURASSIC SHIFT
CD _____ DOVECD 6
Dovetail / Apr '93 / Pinnacle.

LIVE ETHEREAL CEREAL
CD _____ OTCD 3
Dovetail / Feb '92 / Pinnacle.

LIVE UNDERSLUNKY
CD _____ DOVECD 5
Dovetail / Apr '92 / Pinnacle.

SLIDING GLIDING WORLDS
CD _____ OTCD 5
Dovetail / Feb '92 / Pinnacle.

STRANGEITUDE
CD _____ DOVECD 3
Dovetail / Sep '91 / Pinnacle.

TANTRIC OBSTACLES
CD _____ OTCD 2
Dovetail / Apr '93 / Pinnacle.

THERE IS NOTHING
CD _____ OTCD 4
Dovetail / Feb '94 / Pinnacle.

SHOUTING END OF LIFE, THE

We'll be there / Blood red roses / Jam tomorrow / By northern lights / Shouting end of life / Long dark street / Our lady of the battle / Everywhere I go / Put out the lights / Voices / Don't slit your wrists / World turned upside down
CD _____ COOKCD 091
Cooking Vinyl / Oct '95 / Vital.

STEP OUTSIDE
Hal-an-Tow / Flatlands / Another quiet night in England / Milly Bond / Bully in the alley / Day that the ship goes down / Gaol song / Old dance / Bold Riley / Ashes to ashes (CD only.)
CD _____ BAKECD 001
Cooking Vinyl / May '90 / Vital.

TRAWLER
Hal-an-tow / Another quiet night in England / We could leave right now / Blood wedding / Oxford girl / Granite years / Ramblin' Irish-man / Hal-an-tow (CD only.) / Flatlands / 20th April / Lost and found / One green hill / Coal not dole / Bells of rhymney
CD _____ COOKCD 078
Cooking Vinyl / Oct '94 / Vital.

WIDE BLUE YONDER
Generals are born again / Pigsty Billy / Oxford girl / Following in father's footsteps / Lost and found / Coal creek mine / Rose of England / Careless life / Early days of a better nation / Hal-an-tow (CD only.) / Flatlands (CD only.) / Another quiet night in England (CD only.)
CD _____ COOKCD 006
Cooking Vinyl / Aug '87 / Vital.

509

P.E.Z.

WAITING
Into nothing / Downtown / Play this round / Slave fire / Nice present / Down forever / Makeshift / Shame / Up to you / Glass globe / 5 A.M. / Love = death / Waiting / Plaid rock
CD _____ R 3582
Rough Trade / Oct '94 / Pinnacle.

P.G.R.

CHEMICAL BRIDE, THE
CD _____ SR 9218
Silent / Jul '94 / Plastic Head.

GRAVE (P.G.R./Merzbow/Asmus Tietchens)
CD _____ SR 9114
Silent / Jul '94 / Plastic Head.

P.O.W.E.R.

DEDICATED TO WORLD REVOLUTION
Revolution / Power to the people / Race-mixer / Modern day slavery / Guerilla warfare / Tribute to the native Americans / Death machine / Future shock / U.S. Peace plan / Legally insane / United snakes / May-day / Out of control / Potential criminals / Class war / Let's kill 'em
CD _____ NET 050CD
Nettwerk / Apr '94 / Vital / Pinnacle.

Pablo All Stars

MONTREUX '77
Cote D'Azur / Pennies from heaven / Camba de orfue / God bless the child / Sweethearts on parade
CD _____ OJCCD 380
Original Jazz Classics / Apr '93 / Wellard / Jazz Music / Cadillac / Complete/Pinnacle.

Pablo, Augustus

AUTHENTIC GOLDEN MELODIES
CD _____ CDRP 002
Rockers International / Oct '92 / Jetstar / THE / SRD.

BLOWING WITH THE WIND
CD _____ GRELCD 149
Greensleeves / Sep '90 / Total/BMG / Jetstar / SRD.

EAST MAN DUB
Only Jah Jah dub / Eastman dub / Look within dub / Isn't it time (dub) / It up to Jah dub / Big great connection / African step / Original scientist / Corner stone
CD _____ GRELCD 109
Greensleeves / '88 / Total/BMG / Jetstar / SRD.

HEARTICAL CHART
CD _____ CDRP 004
Rockers Production / May '93 / Jetstar.

ITAL DUB
Big rip off / Roadblock / Curly dub / Well red / Gun trade / Shake up / Hihate airstrip / Barbwire disaster / Mr. Big / Ell's move / House raid / Shake down
CD _____ TRCD 805
A & A Productions / Jun '95 / Jetstar.

ORIGINAL ROCKERS VOLUME 2
555 Crown Street / Rockers rock / Burial dub / Pablo satta / Pablo meets Mr. Bassie / Havendale rock / Golden seal / Power of the trinity / West Abyssinia
CD _____ AP 001CD
Rockers International / May '95 / Jetstar / THE / SRD.

PABLO & FRIENDS
CD _____ RASCD 3220
Ras / Nov '92 / Jetstar / Greensleeves / SRD / Direct.

PRESENTS AUTHENTIC GOLDEN MELODIES
CD _____ CDRP 003
Greensleeves / Nov '92 / Total/BMG / Jetstar / SRD.

PRESENTS CULTURAL SHOWCASE
CD _____ CDRP 001
Greensleeves / Nov '92 / Total/BMG / Jetstar / SRD.

PRESENTS KING TUBBY
CD _____ RNCD 2082
Rhino / Dec '94 / Jetstar / Magnum Music Group / THE.

PRESENTS ROCKERS INTERNATIONAL II
CD _____ GRELCD 168
Greensleeves / Nov '92 / Total/BMG / Jetstar / SRD.

REBEL ROCK RADIO
CD _____ CDHB 34
Heartbeat / Aug '88 / Greensleeves / Jetstar / Direct / ADA.

RISING SUN
Dub wiser / Hopi land / Rising sun / Fire red / Jah wind / Pipers of Zion / Day before the riot / African frontline / Melchesedec (the high priest) / Signs and wonders
CD _____ SHCD 44009
Shanachie / Jun '91 / Koch / ADA / Greensleeves.

ROCKERS MEET KING TUBBY IN A FIRE HOUSE
CD _____ SHANCD 43001
Shanachie / Apr '88 / Koch / ADA / Greensleeves.

THIS IS AUGUSTUS PABLO (Rebel Rock Reggae)
CD _____ HBCD 34
Heartbeat / '88 / Greensleeves / Jetstar / Direct / ADA.

THIS IS...AUGUSTUS PABLO
CD _____ ARM 2001
Above Rock / Jul '95 / SRD.

Pablo's Eyes

YOU LOVE CHINESE FOOD
CD _____ XCD 031
Extreme / May '95 / Vital/SAM.

Pace Bend

LIKE A DRINK
CD _____ CMR 2012
Blue Rose / Nov '95 / 3MV.

Pacheco, Johnny

PACHECO'S PARTY
Dile / Los compadres seguiran / La esencia del guaguanco / Latin gravy / Noche buena (Christmas eve) / Son del Callejon / Tango uncarinito / Samrose / Como el guarapo / Tu barriga / El polverete / Amor en el arena / Danza del cocoye / Como cambian los tiempos / Anoranzas / Asi son bonco
CD _____ CDHOT 512
Charly / Sep '94 / Charly / THE / Cadillac.

Pacheco, Tom

BIG STORM COMIN' (Pacheo, Tom & Steinar Albrigtsten)
CD _____ RTMCD 53
Round Tower / Jun '93 / Pinnacle / ADA / Direct / BMG / CM.

EAGLE IN THE RAIN
CD _____ TPCD 1
Round Tower / Feb '94 / Pinnacle / ADA / Direct / BMG / CM.

SUNFLOWERS AND SCARECROWS
CD _____ RTMCD 30
Round Tower / Apr '91 / Pinnacle / ADA / Direct / BMG / CM.

TALES FROM THE RED LAKE
CD _____ RTMCD 42
Round Tower / Feb '93 / Pinnacle / ADA / Direct / BMG / CM.

Pacher, Yves

MUSIQUE BUISSONNIERE
CD _____ Y 225210CD
Silex / Oct '93 / ADA.

Packes, Jimmy

AXXE TO GRIND
CD _____ AZJ 001-2
Azimuth Jag / Feb '94 / Plastic Head.

Paczynski, Georges

8 YEARS OLD (Paczynski/Levinson/Jenny-Clark)
CD _____ BBRC 9209
Big Blue / Jan '93 / Harmonia Mundi.

Page 12

REVENGE AND MORE
Revenge and more
CD _____ EFA 125342
Celtic Circle / Dec '95 / SRD.

Page, Hot Lips

CLASSICS 1940-44
CD _____ CLASSICS 809
Classics / Apr '95 / Discovery / Jazz Music.

HOT LIPS PAGE
CD _____ CD 14558
Jazz Portraits / Jul '94 / Jazz Music.

PLAY THE BLUES IN 'B'
CD _____ 3801172
Jazz Archives / Feb '93 / Jazz Music / Discovery / Cadillac.

Page, Jimmy

NO INTRODUCTION NECESSARY (Page, Jimmy & Friends)
Lovin' up a storm / Everything I do is wrong / Think it over / Boll weevil song / Livin' lovin' wreck / One long kiss / Dixie fried / Down the line / Fabulous / Breathless / Rave on / Lonely weekends / Burn up
CD _____ CDTB 007
Magnum Music / Apr '93 / Magnum Music Group.

NO QUARTER (Page, Jimmy & Robert Plant)
Nobody's fault but mine / Thank you / No quarter / Friends / Yallah / City don't cry / Since I've been loving you / Battle of Evermore / Wonderful one / Wah wah / That's the way / Gallows pole / Four sticks / Kashmir
CD _____ 5263622
Fontana / Oct '94 / PolyGram.

SESSION MAN VOL 1
CD _____ AIPCD 1041
AIP / May '90 / Disc.

SESSION MAN VOL 2
CD _____ AIPCD 1053
AIP / Jul '90 / Disc.

SMOKE AND FIRE
Wailing sounds / Because I love you / Flashing lights / Gutty guitar / Would you believe / Smoke and fire / Thumping beat / Union Jack car / One for you baby / L.O.N.D.O.N. / Brightest lights / Baby come back
CD _____ CDTB 2.022
Thunderbolt / '86 / Magnum Music Group.

Page, Larry

KINKY MUSIC (Page, Larry Orchestra)
Tired of waiting / Come on now / Something better beginning / You really got me / Don't ever change / Got my feet on the ground / All day and all of the night / One fine day / I go to sleep / Just can't go to sleep / Revenge / I took my baby home / Everybody's gonna be happy
CD _____ MONDE 17CD
Cherry Red / Oct '93 / Pinnacle.

Page, Patti

WOULD I LOVE YOU
Now that I'm in love / Would I love you / Send my baby back to me / This is my song / Breeze / My lonely world / (How much is that) doggie in the window / I let a song go out of my heart / The whole world is singing my song / What a dream / Don't get around much anymore / Cross over the bridge / Steam heat / It's a wonderful world / I cried
CD _____ JASCD 315
Jasmine / May '94 / Wellard / Swift / Conifer / Cadillac / Magnum Music Group.

Page, Tommy

FROM THE HEART
Whenever you close your eyes / Under the rainbow / Madly in love / You are my heaven / I still believe (prelude) / I still believe in you and me / Written all over my heart / My shining star / Can't get you outta my mind / I'll never forget you / Never gonna fall in love again
CD _____ 7599265832
WEA / Jul '91 / Warner Music.

Pahinui Brothers

PAHINUI BROTHERS, THE
Mele of my tutu e / Isa lei / Jealous guy / O kamawailua lani / My old friend the blues / Do you love me / Kowali / Waimamalo blues / Panin pua kea / Come go with me / Hehehene ko aka
CD _____ 01005820982
Private Music / Aug '92 / BMG.

Pahinui, Gabby

GABBY PAHINUI HAWAIIAN BAND
Alhoa ka mamo / Ku 'U pua lei mokihana / Pu' uanahulu / Moani ke'ala / Blue Hawaiian moonlight / Moonlight lady / E nihi ka hele / Hawaiian love / Wahini U'l / Oli komo – chant / Ipo lei manu
CD _____ EDCD 241
Edsel / Sep '91 / Pinnacle / ADA.

Paich, Marty

ARRANGER, CONDUCTER, PIANO
It don't mean a thing / Just in time / Moanin' / I've grown accustomed to her face / It's alright with me / Things ain't what they used to be / Move / I love Paris / No more / Love for sale / Warm valley / Groovin' high / Four brothers / Walkin' / Doggin' around / Swingin' the blues / All the things you are / Marty's blues
CD _____ CD 53251
Giants Of Jazz / Jan '96 / Target/BMG / Cadillac.

PICASSO OF BIG BAND JAZZ, THE
CD _____ CCD 9031
Candid / May '89 / Cadillac / Jazz Music / Wellard / Koch.

Paige, Elaine

CHRISTMAS
Walking in the air / Peace on Earth / Father Christmas eyes / Ave Maria / Wishing on a star / Santa Claus is coming to town / Coventry carol / Coldest night of the year / Light of the stable / I believe in Father Christmas / Thirty two feet and eight little tails / Winter's tale
CD _____ 2292420402
WEA / Jul '95 / Warner Music.

CINEMA
Windmills of your mind / Out here on my own / Prisoner / Sometimes / Do you know where you're going to (Theme from 'Mahogany') / Up where we belong / Unchained melody / Bright eyes / Alfie / Missing / Way we were / Rose
CD _____ 2292405112
WEA / Jul '95 / Warner Music.

COLLECTION
Sometimes / Rose / MacArthur Park / Windmills of your mind / Without you / Walking in the air / Secrets / Last one to leave / Memory / Winter's tale / Ave Maria / Another suitcase in another hall / So sad (to watch good love go bad) / If you don't want my love for you / Hot as sun / Way we were
CD _____ PWKS 4021
Carlton Home Entertainment / Sep '90 / Carlton Home Entertainment.

ELAINE PAIGE
If you don't want my love for you / Far side of the bay / So sad (to watch good love go bad) / Secrets / I want to marry you / Second time / Falling down to earth / Hot as sun / Last one to leave / How the heart approaches what it yearns / Miss my love today
CD _____ 2292462042
WEA / Jul '95 / Warner Music.

ENCORE
CD _____ 0630104762
East West / Jun '95 / Warner Music.

LOVE CAN DO THAT
Love can do that / Oxygen / Heart don't change my mind / Same train / You don't own me / I only have eyes for you / Well almost / True colours / If I loved you / He's out of my life / Only the very best / Grow young
CD _____ 74321 22880-2
RCA / Sep '94 / BMG.

LOVE HURTS
Love hurts / Sorry seems to be the hardest word / This is where I came in / All things considered / MacArthur Park / For you / My man and me / Without you / Apple tree / Shaking you / I know him so well
CD _____ 2292407962
WEA / Jul '95 / Warner Music.

MEMORIES
I have dreamed / Amything goes / Heart don't change my mind / Another suitcase another hall / Rose / Love hurts / What'll I do/Who / I only have eyes for you / He's out of my life / I know him so well / Don't cry for me Argentina / Memory (Mixes)
CD _____ 74321339382
Camden / Jan '96 / BMG.

PIAF
La vie en rose / La goualante du pauvre jean / Hymne a l'amour / C'est a hambourg / Les trois cloches / Mon dieu / Les amants d'un jour / La belle histoire d'amour / Je sais comment / Non, je ne regrette rien / L'accordeoniste
CD _____ 450994641-2
WEA / Nov '94 / Warner Music.

QUEEN ALBUM, THE
Bohemian rhapsody / Kind of magic / Love for life / Who wants to live forever / My melancholy blues / You take my breath away / Las palabras de amor (the words of love) / One year of love / Is this the world we created / Radio ga ga
CD _____ CDVIP 106
Virgin VIP / Nov '93 / Carlton Home Entertainment / THE / EMI.

ROMANCE AND THE STAGE
They say it's wonderful / I got lost in his arms / As time goes by / Feeling good / More than you know / With every breath I

take / Mad about the boy / I gaze in your eyes / Kismet suite / Stranger in paradise / He's in love / This is my beloved / Long before I knew you / How long has this been going on / Smoke gets in your eyes / September song / Song of a summer night
CD _____ 74321 13615-2
RCA / Sep '94 / BMG.

STAGES
Memory / Be on your own / Another suitcase in another hall / Send in the clowns / Running back for more / Good morning starshine / Don't cry for me Argentina / I don't know how to love him / What I did for love / One night only / Losing my mind / Tomorrow
CD _____ K 2402282
WEA / Jul '95 / Warner Music.

Paillard, Jean Francois

JAPANESE MELODIES
Hamabe no uta / Komoro magouta / Aka tombo / Toryanse / Kojo no tsuki / Nanatsu no ko / Yasho no mi / Kokiriko / Oboro Zukiyo / Matsushima Ondo / Chin-chin chidori / Yuyake koyake
CD _____ C 377330
Denon / '88 / Conifer.

Pain Teens

BEAST OF DREAMS
CD _____ TR 41CD
Trance / Nov '95 / SRD.

DESTROY THE LOVER
CD _____ TRA 17CD
Trance / Jun '93 / SRD.

STIMULATION FESTIVAL
CD _____ TR 10CD
Trance / Jul '92 / SRD.

Paine Brothers

HONKY HELL
CD _____ ROSECD 291
New Rose / Sep '92 / Direct / ADA.

Painkiller

BURIED SECRETS
CD _____ MOSH 062CD
Earache / Oct '92 / Vital.

Pajama Slave Dancers

FULL METAL UNDERPANTS
CD _____ ROSE 271CD
New Rose / Dec '91 / Direct / ADA.

Pajeaud, Willie

WILLIE PAJEAUD AND HIS NO. BAND '55 (Pajeaud, Willie & His No. Band '55)
CD _____ 504CD 31
504 / Feb '92 / Wellard / Jazz Music / Target/BMG / Cadillac.

Pal, Asit

RHYTHMICALLY YOURS
CD _____ CDJP 1038
Jazz Point / Jan '94 / Harmonia Mundi / Cadillac.

Palace Brothers

PALACE BROTHERS
CD _____ WIGCD 14
Domino / Sep '94 / Pinnacle.

THERE IS NO ONE WHAT WILL TAKE CARE OF YOU
CD _____ ABBCD 050
Big Cat / Aug '95 / SRD / Pinnacle.

VIVA LAST BLUES
More brother rides / Viva ultra / Brute choir / Work hard, play hard / New partner / Cat's blues / We all will ride / Old Jerusalem
CD _____ WIG CD21
Domino / Aug '95 / Pinnacle.

Palace Songs

HOPE
CD _____ WIGCD 18
Domino / Nov '94 / Pinnacle.

Paladins

LET'S BUZZ
CD _____ ALCD 4782
Alligator / May '93 / Direct / ADA.

PALADINS
Hold on / Make it / Honky tonk all night / Let's go / Lucky man / Lover's rock / Daddy yar / Come on home / Bad case of love / Let 'er roll / Slow down
CD _____ CDWIK 64
Big Beat / Apr '88 / Pinnacle.

TICKET HOME
CD _____ SECTOR 10003
Sector 2 / Jul '94 / Direct / ADA.

YEARS SINCE YESTERDAY
CD _____ ALCD 4762
Alligator / Apr '93 / Direct / ADA.

Pale Fountains

FROM ACROSS THE KITCHEN TABLE
Shelter / Stole the love / Jean's not happening / Bicycle thieves / Limit / Twenty last chances / get back home / Bruised arcade / These are the things / It's only hard / From across the kitchen table / Hey / September sting
CD _____ CDV 2333
Virgin / Jul '89 / EMI.

PACIFIC STREET
Reach / Something on my mind / Unless / Southbound excursion / Natural / Faithful pillow (part 1) / You'll start a war / Beyond Friday's field / Abergele next time / Crazier / Faithful pillow (part 2)
CD _____ CDV 2274
Virgin / Nov '89 / EMI.

Pale Saints

COMFORTS OF MADNESS
Way the world is / Sea of sound / Little hammer / Deep sleep for Steven / Fell from the sun / Time thief / You tear the world in two / True coming dream / Insubstantial / Language of flowers / Sight of you
CD _____ CAD 0002CD
4AD / Feb '90 / Disc.

IN RIBBONS
CD _____ CAD 2004CD
4AD / Mar '92 / Disc.

SLOW BUILDINGS
King Fade / Angel (Will you be my) / One blue hill / Henry / Under your nose / Little gestures / Song of Solomon / Fine friend / Gesture of a fear / Always I / Suggestion
CD _____ CAD 4014CD
4AD / Aug '94 / Disc.

Paley's Watch

NOVEMBER
CD _____ PCDN 144
Plankton / Aug '94 / Plankton.

Palladinos

TRAVELLING DARK
In this place here / Northern flashes / I'll keep you in mind / Rocking the black road / Down at the station / I won't be going South (for a while) / Boom town / Saturday night / In my city heart / Moon on the motorway
CD _____ 540244-2
A&M / May '94 / PolyGram.

Pallas

KNIGHTMOVES TO WEDGE
CD _____ CENCD 002
Centaur / Oct '93 / Complete/Pinnacle.

SENTINEL
CD _____ CENCD 001
Centaur / Oct '93 / Complete/Pinnacle.

Palm Court Theatre...

PICNIC PARTY, THE (Palm Court Theatre Orchestra)
There's a ring around the Moon / Black eyes / Grasshoppers dance / Silver bird / Fiddlesticks rag / I'm forever blowing bubbles / Petite tonkinoise / Whistle for me / In the shadows / Polly / Down in Zanzibar / Ragtime bass player / Two little sausages / In a Persian market
CD _____ CHAN 8437
Chandos / Mar '87 / Chandos.

Palmer, David

ORCHESTRAL SGT. PEPPER
Sergeant Pepper's lonely hearts club band / With a little help from my friends / Lucy in the sky with diamonds / Getting better / Fixing a hole / She's leaving home / Being for the benefit of Mr. Kite / When I'm sixty four / Lovely Rita / Sergeant Pepper's lonely hearts club band (reprise) / Day in the life
CD _____ CDDPR 125
Premier/MFP / Oct '94 / EMI.

SYMPHONIC MUSIC OF YES
CD _____ 09026619382
RCA / Jan '94 / BMG.

Palmer, Michael

JOINT FAVOURITES (Palmer, Michael & Half Pint)
Crazy girl / What's going down / Tell me this tell me that / Day I can't forget / Freedom fighters / You're safe / Belly lick / Read your Bible / I don't know why / Saw you at the dance
CD _____ GRELCD 89
Greensleeves / Mar '95 / Total/BMG / Jetstar / SRD.

Palmer, Robert

ADDICTIONS VOL.1
Bad case of lovin' you (Doctor Doctor) / Pride / Addicted to love / Sweet lies / Woke up laughing / Looking for clues / Some guys have all the luck / Some like it hot / What's it take / Every kinda people / Johnny and Mary / Simply irresistible / Style kills

CD _____ CID 9944
Island / Oct '89 / PolyGram.

ADDICTIONS VOL.1/VOL.2 (2CD Set)
Bad case of lovin' you / Pride / Addicted to love / Sweet lies / Woke up laughing / Looking for clues / Some guys have all the luck / Some like it hot / What's it take / Every kinda people / Johnny and Mary / Simply irresistible / Style kills / Remember to remember / Sneakin' Sally through the alley / Maybe it's you / You are in my system / I didn't mean to turn you on / Can we still be friends / Men smart, women smarter / Too good to be true / Every kinda people #2 / She makes my day / Best of both worlds / Give me an inch / You're gonna get what's coming / I dream of wires / Silver gun
CD Set _____ ISDCD 2
Island / Nov '95 / PolyGram.

ADDICTIONS VOL.2
Remember to remember / Sneakin' Sally through the alley / Maybe it's you / You are in my system / I didn't mean to turn you on / Can we still be friends / Man smart, woman smarter / Too good to be true / Every kinda people / She makes my day / Best of both worlds / Give me an inch / You're gonna get what's coming / I dream of wires / Silver gun
CD _____ CIDTV 4
Island / Sep '91 / PolyGram.

CLUES
Looking for clues / Sulky girl / Johnny and Mary / What do you care / I dream of wires / Woke up laughing / Not a second time / Found you now
CD _____ IMCD 21
Island / Jun '89 / PolyGram.

DON'T EXPLAIN
Your mother should have told you / Light years / You can't get enough of a good thing / Dreams to remember / You're amazing / Mess around / Happiness / History / I'll be your baby tonight / Housework / Mercy mercy me/I want you / Don't explain / Aeroplane / People will say we're in love / Not a word / Top 40 / You're so desirable / You're my thrill
CD _____ CDEMX 1018
EMI / Nov '90 / EMI.

DOUBLE FUN
Every kinda people / Best of both worlds / Where can it go / Night people / Love can run faster / You overwhelm me / You really got me / Your gonna get what's coming
CD _____ IMCD 23
Island / Jun '89 / PolyGram.

HEAVY NOVA
Simply irresistable / More than ever / Change his ways / Disturbing behaviour / Early in the morning / It could happen to you / She makes my day / Between us / Casting a spell / Tell me I'm not dreaming
CD _____ CDEMD 1007
EMI / Feb '94 / EMI.

HONEY
Honey A / Honey B / You're mine / Know by now / Nobody but you / Love takes time / Honeymoon / You blow me away / Close to the edge / Closer to the edge / Girl u want / Wham bam boogie / Big trouble / Dreams come true
CD _____ CDEMD 1069
EMI / Sep '94 / EMI.

MAYBE IT'S LIVE
Every kinda people / Sneakin' Sally through the alley / Some guys have all the luck
CD _____ 5500682
Spectrum/Karussell / May '93 / PolyGram / THE.

PRESSURE DROP
Give me an inch / Work to make it work / Back in my arms / Riverboat / Pressure drop / Here with you tonight / Trouble / Fine time / Which of us is the fool
CD _____ IMCD 24
Island / Aug '89 / PolyGram.

PRIDE
Pride / Deadline / Want you more / Dance for me / You are in my system / It's not difficult / Say you will / You can have it (take my heart) / What you waiting for / Silver gun
CD _____ IMCD 22
Island / Jun '89 / PolyGram.

RIDIN' HIGH
Love me or leave me / Tender trap / You're my thrill / Want you more / Baby, it's cold outside / Aeroplane / Witchcraft / What a little moonlight can do / Don't explain / Chance / Good goody / Do nothin' 'til you hear from me / Honeysuckle rose / No not much / Riding high / Hard head
CD _____ CDEMD 1038
EMI / Sep '92 / EMI.

RIPTIDE
Riptide / Hyperactive / Addicted to love / Trick bag / Get it through your heart / I didn't mean to turn you on / Flesh wound / Discipline of love / Riptide (reprise)
CD _____ IMCD 25
Island / Jun '89 / PolyGram.

SECRETS
Bad case of lovin' you (Doctor Doctor) / Too good to be true / Can we still be friends / In walks love again / Mean ol' world / Love

stop / Jealous / Under suspicion / Woman you're wonderful / What's it take / Remember to remember
CD _____ IMCD 26
Island / Aug '89 / PolyGram.

SNEAKIN' SALLY THROUGH THE ALLEY
Sailing shoes / Hey Julia / Sneakin' Sally through the alley / Get outside / How much fun / From a whisper to a scream / Through it all there's you
CD _____ IMCD 20
Island / Aug '89 / PolyGram.

SOME PEOPLE CAN DO WHAT THEY LIKE
One last look / Keep in touch / Man smart, woman smarter / Spanish moon / Have mercy / Gotta get a grip on you (part 2) / What can you bring me / Hard head / Off the bone / Some people can do what they like
CD _____ IMCD 69
Island / Nov '89 / PolyGram.

VERY BEST OF ROBERT PALMER
Addicted to love / Bad case of loving you / Simple irresistable / Get it on / Some guys have all the luck / I didn't mean to turn you on / Looking for clues / U R in my system / Some like it hot / Respect yourself / I'll be your baby tonight / Johnny & Mary / She makes my day / Know by now / Every kinda people / Mercy mercy me/I want you
CD _____ CDEMD 1088
EMI / Oct '95 / EMI.

Palmieri, Charlie

MONTUNO SESSION, THE
Tema de maria cerantes / Tumba palo (CD only.) / Descarga charanson / 6-8 Modal latin jazz / Talking about the Danzon (CD only.) / Paracachero / Que no muera (CD only.) / Son de mi vida (CD only.) / Oriente (CD only.)
CD _____ MRBCD 004
Mr. Bongo / Oct '95 / New Note.

Palmieri, Eddie

ARETE
Don't stop the train / Definitely in / Sisters / Crew / Waltz for my grandchildren / Sixes in motion / Oblique / Carribbean mood
CD _____ 66058087
Tropi / Feb '96 / New Note.

LA VERDAD (The Truth)
El cuarto / Congo yambumba / La verdad / Lisa / Noble cruise / Buscandote
CD _____ CDCHARLY 147
Charly / Nov '88 / Charly / THE / Cadillac.

PACHANGA TO JAZZ
El molestoso / Muneca / Mi mujer spiritual / Pa los congos / Bomba de corazon / Pensando en ti / La verdad / Lisa / Conga yumbambo / Buscandote
CD _____ CDHOT 519
Charly / Apr '95 / Charly / THE / Cadillac.

PALMAS
Palmas
Elektra Nonesuch / Dec '94 / Warner Music.

SALSA BRAVA
Palo pa rumba / 1983 / Bomba de corazon / Bajo con tumbao / Pensando en ti / Venezuela / Solito / Lindo Yambu
CD _____ CDHOT 505
Charly / Oct '93 / Charly / THE / Cadillac.

SALSA MEETS JAZZ
Vamanos na'l monte / Prohibition de pelota / Que lindo bambu / Sabroso guaguanco / Dieciseite punto uno / Azucar / Justicia / Yo no soy guapo / Cara vez que te veo / El cuarto / Noble cruise
CD _____ CDHOT 511
Charly / Sep '94 / Charly / THE / Cadillac.

SUENO
Variations on a given theme / Azucar / Just a little dream / Covarde / Humpty Dumpty / La liberatad
CD _____ INT 30082
Intuition / Apr '90 / New Note.

Pameljer, Pam

PAM PAMEIJER & HIS NEW JAZZ WIZARDS
CD _____ SOSCD 1281
Stomp Off / Mar '95 / Jazz Music / Wellard.

Pammi, Parmijit

BALLE BALLE
CD _____ DMUT 1268
Multitone / Jan '94 / BMG.

Pan

OLOLY
CD _____ ABBCD 049
Big Cat / Jun '93 / SRD / Pinnacle.

Pan African Orchestra

OPUS 1
Wia concerto no. 1 (First movement in four parts) / Yaa yaa kole / Mmenson / Explorations - high life structures / Akan drum-

ming / Sisala sebrew / Explorations - ewe 6/8 rhythms / Box dream / Adawura kasa
CD _____ CDRW 48
Realworld / Apr '95 / EMI / Sterns.

Pan Head

TRIBUTE TO PAN HEAD
CD _____ CRCD 29
Charm / Mar '94 / Jetstar.

Pan Pipes

FLIGHT OF THE CONDOR
CD Set _____ DCDCD 211
Castle / Nov '95 / BMG.

PLAY THE BEATLES BALLADS
For no one / Michelle / Strawberry fields forever / Here, there and everywhere / In my life / And I love her / If I fall / Long and winding road / Something / Fool on the hill / Day in the life / She's leaving home / You've got to hide your love away / Imagine / My love / Blackbird / Mother nature's son / Across the universe / Yesterday
CD _____ 30360 00262
Carlton Home Entertainment / Jan '96 / Carlton Home Entertainment.

Pan Thy Monium

DREAM 11
CD _____ CDAV 008
Avant Garde / May '95 / Plastic Head.

KHAOOHS
CD _____ OPCD 14
Osmose / Oct '93 / Plastic Head.

Panaché Culture

TRAVEL IN A DREAM
CD _____ RN 0038
Runn / Oct '95 / Jetstar / SRD.

Panama Jazz Band

ORIGINAL DIXIELAND ONE STEP
CD _____ BCD 275
GHB / Oct '92 / Jazz Music.

Panasonic

VAKIO
CD _____ BFFP 118CD
Blast First / Sep '95 / Disc.

Panatella, Slim

SLIM PANATELLA & THE MELLOW VIRGINIANS (Panatella, Slim & The Mellow Virginians)
Acoustics / Aug '95 / Conifer / Direct / ADA.
CD _____ CDACS 024

SLIM PANATELLA AND THE MELLOW VIRGINIANS (Panatella, Slim & The Mellow Virginians)
Blues for Dixie / Looking after business / Heat of the moment / Lime rock / Sweet Lorraine / Cow cow boogie / Blue skies / Miles and miles of Texas / When you say you love me / Peach pickin' time / Texas hambone blues / Stay a little longer / Fool about a cigrette / Dill pickle rag
CD _____ ACS 024
Acoustic Music / Jan '95 / ADA.

Pandora's Box

ORIGINAL SIN
Invocation / Original sin (the natives are restless tonight) / Twentieth century fox / Safe sex (when it comes 2 loving U) / Good girls go to heaven (bad girls go everywhere) / Requiem metal / I've been dreaming up a storm lately / It's all coming back to me now / Opening of the box / Want ad / My little red book / It just won't quit / Pray lewd / Future ain't what it used to be
CD _____ CDV 2605
Virgin / Sep '89 / EMI.

Pandoras

IT'S ABOUT TIME
CD _____ VOXXCD 2021
Voxx / Jan '94 / Else / Disc.

Pane, Febian Reza

DREAMS OF GANESHA
Dreams of Ganesha / Salsare / Grazie, madre / Borobudur / Resistencia dos Quilombos / Full moon won't smile / Memories of Taketi-Jima / For your peaceful night
CD _____ CY 78998
Savoy Jazz / Nov '95 / Conifer / ADA.

Panic

EPIDEMIC
CD _____ CDZORRO 24
Metal Blade / Jul '91 / Pinnacle.

FACT
Die tryin' / Close my eyes and jump / Burn one / Nonchalance / Two things (XYZ) / Hit and dragged / Rotator / Gone bad / Hell no fuck yes / Think about it
CD _____ CDZORR 060
Metal Blade / May '93 / Pinnacle.

Pankow

FREIHEIT FUR DIE SKLAVEN
Gimme more (dub) / Girls and boys / In Heaven / Sickness takin' over / Freiheit fur die sklaven / Gimme more / She's gotta be mine / Nice bottom (schoener arsch) (Mixes) / Touch (I'm your bastard)
CD _____ CONTECD 113
Contempo / Jun '88 / Plastic Head.

GISELA
CD _____ CONTE 131 CD
Contempo / Oct '89 / Plastic Head.

OMNE ANIMAL TRISTE POST COITUM
CD _____ CONTECD 161
Contempo / Oct '90 / Plastic Head.

TREUE HUNDE
CD _____ CONTE 171CD
Contempo / Jun '92 / Plastic Head.

Pansy Division

DEFLOWERED
CD _____ LOOKOUT 87CD
Lookout / Oct '94 / SRD.

PILE UP
CD _____ DAMGOOD 60CD
Damaged Goods / Mar '95 / SRD.

UNDRESSED
CD _____ LOOKOUT 70CD
Lookout / Oct '94 / SRD.

Pantera

COWBOYS FROM HELL
Cowboys from hell / Primal concrete sledge / Psycho holiday / Cemetery gates / Shattered / Medicine man / Sleep / Heresy / Domination / Clash with reality / Message in blood / Art of shredding
CD _____ 7567913722
East West / Jul '90 / Warner Music.

FAR BEYOND DRIVEN
Strength beyond strength / Becoming / Five minutes alone / I'm broken / Good friends and a bottle of Pils / Hard lines, sunken cheeks / Slaughtered / Twenty five years / Shedding skin / Use my third arm / Throes of rejection / Planet caravan
CD _____ 756792302-2
Atco / Mar '94 / Warner Music.

VULGAR DISPLAY OF POWER, A
Mouth for war / New level / Walk / Fucking hostile / This love / Rise / No good for no one / Live in a hole / Regular people / By demons be driven / Hollow
CD _____ 7567917582
Atco / Feb '92 / Warner Music.

Pants

PANTS, THE
CD _____ HIPCD 6
Hipster / Aug '95 / SRD.

Papa Brittle

OBEY, CONSUME, MARRY & REPRODUCE
Trailer / Status Quo / Greed is good / Global intensified Nationalism / Heist your mind / Jesus in a crack / Crackdown 80's, 90's / Unsafe / Twenty seconds of noise / Enemy of the Brotherhood / Dissection of the great British public / Klan in the neighbourhood / Subconscious distortion of perception and sensation / Twisted and feckless
CD _____ NET 055CD
Nettwerk / Apr '94 / Vital / Pinnacle.

Papa Doo Run Run

CALIFORNIA PROJECT
CD _____ CD 70501
Telarc / '88 / Conifer / ADA.

Papa Ladji

LES BALLET AFRICAINS
CD _____ LYRCD 7419
Lyrichord / Aug '93 / Roots / ADA / CM.

Papa Levi

BACK TO BASICS
Jah rastafari selassie I / Nuff black / One night stand / Jah mi fear / Back to basics / Can't impress / Pretty she pretty / Narcotic
CD _____ ARICD 103
Ariwa Sounds / Apr '94 / Jetstar / SRD.

CODE OF PRACTICE
CD _____ ARICD 060
Ariwa Sounds / Sep '90 / Jetstar / SRD.

Papa San

D.J. RULE - 3 THE HARD WAY (Papa San/Tulloch T/Double Ugly)
CD _____ RNCD 2029
Rhino / Oct '93 / Jetstar / Magnum Music Group / THE.

FIRE INNA DANCEHALL
CD _____ 790032
Pippers / Nov '92 / Jetstar.

GI MI DI LOVING
CD _____ 794512
Melodie / Dec '95 / Triple Earth / Discovery / ADA / Jetstar.

PRAY FI DEM
Ras / Apr '93 / Jetstar / SRD.
CD _____ RASCD 3115

SISTEM, THE
CD _____ PWD 7415
Sir George / Jul '93 / Jetstar / Pinnacle.

Papadimitriou, Sakis

PIANO ORACLES
CD _____ CDLR 163
Leo / Oct '94 / Wellard / Cadillac / Impetus.

Papaila, Dan

POSITIVELY!
Lover man / Prisms / Things ain't what they used to be / When a man loves a woman / Rush hour / Positively / That's the way of the world
CD _____ CDSJP 403
Timeless Jazz / Sep '93 / New Note.

Papalote

CHISELLED IN STONE
CD _____ LARRCD 283
Larrikin / Jun '94 / Roots / Direct / ADA / CM.

Papa's Culture

PAPA'S CULTURE BUT...
Swim / It's me / Time fekill 1 / Muffin man / Toes / Sometimes / Top 40 / Put me down / (Who is) Mack daddy love / Bronze / Time fekill 2 / Fire
CD _____ 755961432-2
Elektra / Dec '93 / Warner Music.

Papasov, Ivo

BALKANOLOGY
Miladeshki dance / Hristianova kopanitsa / Istoria na edna / Ivo's ruchenitsa / Song for Baba Nedelya / Ergenski dance / Mominsko horo / Tziganska ballada / Veseli Zborni / Proleten dance / Kasapsko horo
CD _____ HNCD 1363
Hannibal / May '91 / Vital / ADA.

ORPHEUS ASCENDING (Papasov, Ivo & His Bulgarian Wedding Band)
CD _____ HNCD 1347
Hannibal / May '89 / Vital / ADA.

Paper Bags

MUSIC TO TRASH
CD _____ SST 200 CD
SST / May '93 / Plastic Head.

Paphiti, Savvas

GREEK POPULAR SONGS (Paphiti, Savvas & George Gregoriou)
CD _____ EUCD 1236
ARC / Nov '93 / ARC Music / ADA.

Paquette, David

OUTRAGEOUS
CD _____ SACD 105
Solo Art / Apr '94 / Jazz Music.

Paquito D'Rivera

CARIBBEAN JAZZ PROJECT, THE
CD _____ INAK 9038
In Akustik / Oct '95 / Magnum Music Group / THE.

NIGHT IN ENGLEWOOD, A (Paquito D' Rivera & United Nations Orchestra)
CD _____ MES 158292
Messidor / Jul '94 / Koch / ADA.

Parachute Men

EARTH, DOGS AND EGGSHELLS
CD _____ FIRE 33024
Fire / Oct '91 / Disc.

INNOCENTS, THE
CD _____ FIRE 33014
Fire / Oct '91 / Disc.

Parachute Regiment

PARAS, THE (Massed Bands Of The Parachute Regiment)
Green light / Airborne warrior / Red beret / Arnhem / Paras / Bruneval raid / Longest day / Sailing / Mount longdon / Marche des parachutist / Belges / Screaming eagles / Red devils / Aslo ran / Pomp and circumstance march No.4 / Ride of the valkyries / Delta wing / Three para songs / Songs of World War Two / American patrol / Elvis Presley, his greatest hits / Out of the sky / Echoes of an era / Space medley
CD _____ BNA 5039
Bandleader / '91 / Conifer.

Paradis, Vanessa

VANESSA PARADIS
Natural high / Waiting for the man / Silver and gold / Be my baby / Lonely rainbows / Sunday mornings / Your love has got a handle on my mind / Future song / Paradise / Just as long as you are there / Lenny Kravitz
CD _____ 5139542
Polydor / Sep '92 / PolyGram.

VANESSA PARADIS LIVE
CD _____ 521693-2
Polydor / Mar '94 / PolyGram.

Paradise Jazz Band

BLOWIN' THE BLUES AWAY
CD _____ JCD 229
Jazzology / Jan '94 / Swift / Jazz Music.

Paradise Lost

DRACONIAN TIMES
Enchantment / Hallowed land / Last time / Forever failure / Once solemn / Shadowkings / Elusive cure / Yearn for change / Hands of reason / See your face / Jaded
CD _____ MFNP 184
Music For Nations / Aug '95 / Pinnacle.

GOTHIC
CD _____ CDVILE 26
Peaceville / Mar '95 / Pinnacle.

ICON
CD _____ CDMFN 152
Music For Nations / Sep '93 / Pinnacle.

PARADISE LOST
Intro / Deadly inner sense / Paradise lost / Our saviour / Rotting misery / Frozen illusion / Breeding fear / Lost paradise
CD _____ CDVILE 17
Peaceville / Apr '95 / Pinnacle.

SHADES OF GOD
CD _____ CDMFN 135
Music For Nations / Jun '92 / Pinnacle.

Paradogs

HERE COMES JOEY
CD _____ PRD 70312
Provogue / Nov '91 / Pinnacle.

Paragons

25 YEARS OF THE PARAGONS
CD _____ RNCD 2099
Rhino / Mar '95 / Jetstar / Magnum Music Group / THE.

GOLDEN HITS
CD _____ LG 21028
Lagoon / Jun '93 / Magnum Music Group / THE.

HEAVEN & EARTH
CD _____ CDSGP 075
Prestige / May '94 / Total/BMG.

MY BEST GIRL WEARS MY CROWN
Happy go lucky girl / I want to go back / When the lights are low / On the beach / Island in the sun / Riding on a high and windy day / Silver bird / Same song / Tide is high / I wanna be with you / Mercy mercy mercy / Wear you to the ball / I'm a worried man / My best girl / You mean the world to me / Only a smile / Paragons medley
CD _____ CDTRL 299
Trojan / Mar '94 / Jetstar / Total/BMG.

RIDING HIGH
CD _____ RNCD 2085
Rhino / Dec '94 / Jetstar / Magnum Music Group / THE.

Paralysed Age

BLOODSUCKER
CD _____ EFA 112702
Glasnost / Dec '94 / SRD.

Paramor, Norrie

GOLDEN PIANO HITS
CD _____ MATCD 247
Castle / Dec '92 / BMG.

Paramount Jazzband Of...

AIN'T CHA GLAD (Paramount Jazzband Of Boston)
CD _____ SOSCD 1205
Stomp Off / Aug '90 / Jazz Music / Wellard.

PARAMOUNT JAZZ BAND, THE (Paramount Jazzband Of Boston)
Dans la rue d'antibes / Jelly roll / Joint is jumpin' / What a difference a day makes / You / Until the real thing comes along / It's a sin to tell a lie / I would do 'most anything for your love / Nevertheless (I'm in love with you) / Some of these days
CD _____ CDTTD 596
Timeless Jazz / Aug '95 / New Note.

Paramount Singers

WORK & PRAY ON
CD _____ ARHCD 382

Arhoolie / Apr '95 / ADA / Direct /
Cadillac.

Paramounts

WHITER SHADES OF R & B
Poison ivy / I feel good all over / Little bitty
pretty one / Certain girl / I'm the one who
loves you / It won't be long / Bad blood /
Do I / Blue ribbons / Cuttin' in / You never
had it so good / Don't ya like my love / Draw
me closer / Turn on your love light / You've
got what I want / Freedom
CD _____ EDCD 112
Edsel / Aug '91 / Pinnacle / ADA.

Paranoise

START A NEW RACE
CD _____ OZOO 3CD
Ozone / Jul '93 / SRD.

Paranonia

PARANONIA
CD _____ NZCD 021
Nova Zembla / Sep '95 / Plastic Head.

Paranza Di Somma...

**SCENNENNO D'A MUNTAGNA (Paranza
Di Somma Vesuviana)**
CD _____ NT 6719
Robi Droli / Jan '94 / Direct / ADA.

Paras, Fabio

BIRTH OF SHIVA SHANTI, THE
CD _____ SHANTI 1CD
Junk Rock / Oct '93 / Disc.

Pardesi Music Machine

SHAKE YOUR PANTS
CD _____ CDST 015
Star / May '90 / Pinnacle / Sterns.

Parenti, Tony

**STRUT YO' STUFF (Tony Parenti &
Bands 1925-29)**
That's plenty / Cabaret echoes / Dizzy
Lizzie / French market blues / La vida med-
ley / Be yourself / 12th street blues (1 & 2)
/ Creole blues / Strut yo' stuff / Midnight
Papa / I need some lovin' / Cabaret echoes
#2 / Up jumped the devil / Weary blues /
New crazy blues #1/#2 / African echoes / In
the dungeon / When you and I were pals /
Gumbo / You made me like it baby / Old
man rhythm
CD _____ DGF 4
Frog / May '95 / Jazz Music / Cadillac /
Wellard.
TONY PARENTI & HIS NEW ORLENIANS
CD _____ JCD 1
Jazzology / Oct '92 / Swift / Jazz Music.

Parga, Mario

MAGICIAN, THE
CD _____ PCOM 1116
President / Sep '91 / Grapevine / Target/
BMG / Jazz Music / President.

Parham, Tiny

1926-1928
CD _____ DOCD 5341
Blues Document / May '95 / Swift / Jazz
Music / Hot Shot.
**TINY PARHAM & HIS MUSICIANS 1929-
1940 (Parham, Tiny & His Musicians)**
CD _____ CLASSICS 691
Classic Jazz Masters / May '93 / Wellard /
Jazz Music / Jazz Music.

Pariah

BLAZE OF OBSCURITY
Missionary of mercy / Puppet regime / Ca-
nary / Retaliate / Hypochondriac / Enemy
within
CD _____ 857595
Steamhammer / Jun '89 / Pinnacle / Plastic
Head.
KINDRED, THE
CD _____ 857528
Steamhammer / '89 / Pinnacle / Plastic
Head.

Paris

GUERRILLA FUNK
Prelude / It's real / One time fo' ya mind /
Guerrilla funk / Blacks and blues / Bring it
to ya / Outta my life / What'cha see / Forty
ounces and a fool / Back in the days / Guer-
rilla funk (Deep fo' real mix) / It's real (Mix)
/ Shots out
CD _____ CDPTY 108
Priority/Virgin / Nov '94 / EMI.

Paris, Jackie

**JACKIE PARIS/CARLOS FRANZETTI/
MARC JOHNSON**
CD _____ ACD 158
Audiophile / Jan '94 / Jazz Music / Swift.

NOBODY ELSE BUT ME
CD _____ ACD 245
Audiophile / Mar '95 / Jazz Music / Swift.

Paris, Jeff

LUCKY THIS TIME
CD _____ NTHEN 6
Now & Then / Sep '95 / Plastic Head.

Paris, Mica

CONTRIBUTION
Contribution / South of the river / If I love u
2 nite / Just to be with you / Take me away
/ Truth and honesty / Deep Afrika / More
love / You can make a wish / Just make me
the one / I've been watching you / Who can
we blame / One world
CD _____ IMCD 184
Island / Mar '94 / PolyGram.
SO GOOD
Where is the love / My one temptation / Like
dreamers do / Breathe life into me / Nothing
hits your heart like soul music / Sway /
Don't give me up / I'd hate to love you /
Great impersonation / So good
CD _____ IMCD 209
Island / Apr '95 / PolyGram.
WHISPER A PRAYER
I never felt like this before / I wanna hold on
to you / You put a move on my heart / We
were made for love / Whisper a prayer / Too
far apart / I bless the day / Two in a million
/ Positivity / Can't seem to make up my
mind / You got a special way / Love keeps
coming back
CD _____ IMCD 221
Island / Mar '96 / PolyGram.

Paris Washboard

TRUCKIN'
CD _____ SOSCD 1293
Stomp Off / Nov '95 / Jazz Music /
Wellard.

Parisa

**PARISA AT THE ROYAL FESTIVAL HALL
(Persian Classical Music)**
CD _____ PS 65155
Playasound / Oct '95 / Harmonia Mundi /
ADA.

Parker, Billy

BILLY PARKER AND FRIENDS
Something old, something new / Memory
number one / Too many irons in the fire /
Who said love was fair / I believe I'm enti-
tled to you / Milk cow blues / Tomorrow
never comes / When I need bread bad /
Honky tonk girls / Love don't know a lady /
Take me back to Tulsa / Last country song
/ It's not me / If I ever need a lady / I see
an angel every day / I'll drink to that / Why
do I keep calling you honey, honey / Can I
have what's left / What's a nice girl like you
/ One more last time / Hello out there
CD _____ BCD 15521
Bear Family / Oct '90 / Rollercoaster / Direct
/ CM / Swift / ADA.

Parker, Bobby

BENT OUT OF SHAPE
CD _____ BT 1086CD
Black Top / May '93 / CM / Direct / ADA.
SHINE ME UP
CD _____ BT 1119CD
Black Top / Aug '95 / CM / Direct / ADA.

Parker, Charlie

**1949 CONCERT AND ALLSTARS 1950-
51**
CD _____ UCD 19009
Forlane / Jun '95 / Target/BMG.
AUTUMN IN NEW YORK
CD _____ LEJAZZCD 3
Le Jazz / Mar '93 / Charly / Cadillac.
BEST OF CHARLIE PARKER
CD _____ DLCD 4021
Dixie Live / Mar '95 / Magnum Music
Group.
BEST OF THE BIRD, THE
CD _____ 17020
Laserlight / May '94 / Target/BMG.
BIRD
CD _____ GOJCD 53069
Giants Of Jazz / Mar '90 / Target/BMG /
Cadillac.
**BIRD - THE ORIGINAL RECORDINGS
OF CHARLIE PARKER**
Now's the time / Laura / Mohawk / Kim /
Blues for Alice / Laird baird / K.C. Blues /
Lover man / Just friends / Bird / April in
Paris / Lester leaps in
CD _____ 837 176-2
Verve / Nov '88 / PolyGram.
BIRD AT BIRDLAND (4CD Set)
CD Set _____ CDDIG 16
Charly / Jun '95 / Charly / THE / Cadillac.

BIRD AT St. NICK'S
CD _____ OJCCD 041
Original Jazz Classics / Jun '95 / Wellard /
Jazz Music / Cadillac / Complete/Pinnacle.
BIRD IN CONCERT 1946 - 1952
CD Set _____ CDB 1215
Giants Of Jazz / Jul '92 / Target/BMG /
Cadillac.
BIRD LIVES
Move / Ornithology / Out of nowhere / Hot
house / How high the moon / Be bop /
Scrapple from the apple / Street beat /
Midnight / Koko / Groovin high
CD _____ CDCD 1011
Charly / Mar '93 / Charly / THE / Cadillac.
**BIRD MEETS DIZ (Parker, Charlie &
Dizzy Gillespie)**
CD _____ LEJAZZCD 21
Le Jazz / Feb '94 / Charly / Cadillac.
BIRD OF PARADISE
CD _____ JHR 73531
Jazz Hour / Sep '93 / Target/BMG / Jazz
Music / Cadillac.
**BIRD OF PARADISE BE-BOP GENIUS
1947**
CD _____ CD 56029
Jazz Roots / Nov '94 / Target/BMG.
BIRD RETURNS, THE
Chasin' the bird / Thriving on a riff / Koko /
Half nelson / Scrapple from the apple /
Cheryl / Barbados
CD _____ SV 0155
Savoy Jazz / Apr '92 / Conifer / ADA.
BIRD SYMBOLS
Moose the mooche / Yardbird suite / Orni-
thology / Night in Tunisia / Bird's nest / Cool
blues / Bird of paradise / Embraceable you
/ My old flame / Scrapple from the apple /
Out of nowhere / Don't blame me
CD _____ RHCD 5
Rhapsody / Jul '91 / President / Jazz Music
/ Wellard.
BIRD YOU NEVER HEARD, THE
CD _____ STCD 582
Stash / Jun '94 / Jazz Music / CM /
Cadillac / Direct / ADA.
BIRD'S BEST
CD _____ 5274522
Verve / Oct '95 / PolyGram.
BIRD'S EYES VOL. 20
CD _____ W 8502
Philology / Apr '95 / Harmonia Mundi /
Cadillac.
BIRD'S EYES VOL. 7
CD _____ 214 W57-2
Philology / Aug '91 / Harmonia Mundi /
Cadillac.
BIRD'S EYES VOL. 8
CD _____ CD 241 W80-2
Philology / May '92 / Harmonia Mundi /
Cadillac.
BIRD'S EYES VOL. 9
CD _____ W 120-2
Philology / Sep '93 / Harmonia Mundi /
Cadillac.
BIRD'S EYES VOL.10
CD _____ W 200-2
Philology / Sep '93 / Harmonia Mundi /
Cadillac.
BIRD'S EYES VOL.11
CD _____ W 622-2
Philology / Apr '94 / Harmonia Mundi /
Cadillac.
BIRD'S EYES VOL.12
CD _____ W 842-2
Philology / Apr '94 / Harmonia Mundi /
Cadillac.
BIRD'S EYES VOL.13
CD _____ W 843-2
Philology / May '94 / Harmonia Mundi /
Cadillac.
BIRD'S EYES VOL.14
CD _____ W 844-2CD
Philology / Jul '94 / Harmonia Mundi /
Cadillac.
BIRD'S EYES VOL.15
CD _____ PHIL 845-2
Philology / Oct '94 / Harmonia Mundi /
Cadillac.
BIRD'S EYES VOL.16
CD _____ PHIL 846-2
Philology / Oct '94 / Harmonia Mundi /
Cadillac.
BIRD'S EYES VOL.19
CD _____ W 8492
Philology / Apr '95 / Harmonia Mundi /
Cadillac.
BIRD'S THE WORD 1944-52
CD Set _____ JWD 102308
JWD / Oct '94 / Target/BMG.
BLUEBIRD
CD _____ JHR 73532
Jazz Hour / Sep '93 / Target/BMG / Jazz
Music / Cadillac.

BROADCAST PEFORMANCES
CD _____ ESP 3001-2
ESP / Jan '93 / Jazz Horizons / Jazz
Music.
**CARNEGIE HALL CONCERTS 1949 -
1950**
CD _____ CD 53111
Giants Of Jazz / Jun '92 / Target/BMG /
Cadillac.
CARNEGIE HALL, CHRISTMAS '49
CD _____ JASSCD 16
Jass / '88 / CM / Jazz Music / ADA /
Cadillac.
CHARLIE PARKER (2CD Set)
CD Set _____ R2CD 4016
Deja Vu / Jan '96 / THE.
**CHARLIE PARKER & JAY MCSHANN
(1940-44) (Parker, Charlie & Jay
McShann & His Orchestra)**
CD _____ STCD 542
Stash / Feb '91 / Jazz Music / CM /
Cadillac / Direct / ADA.
CHARLIE PARKER 1945-53
CD _____ GOJCD 53051
Giants Of Jazz / Mar '92 / Target/BMG /
Cadillac.
CHARLIE PARKER 1947-50
CD _____ CD 14549
Jazz Portraits / Jul '94 / Jazz Music.
**CHARLIE PARKER AT BIRDLAND &
CAFE SOCIETY**
CD _____ C&BCD 108
Cool 'n' Blue / Oct '93 / Jazz Music /
Discovery.
CHARLIE PARKER COLLECTION
CD _____ COL 028
Collection / Jun '95 / Target/BMG.
CHARLIE PARKER GOLD (2CD Set)
CD Set _____ D2CD 4016
Deja Vu / Jun '95 / THE.
CHARLIE PARKER MEMORIAL VOL.1
Another hair do / Bluebird / Bird gets the
worm / Barbados / Constellation / Parker's
mood / Ah leu cha / Perhaps / Marmaduke
/ Steeplechase / Merry go round / Buzzy
CD _____ CY 78982
Savoy Jazz / Nov '95 / Conifer / ADA.
CHARLIE PARKER MEMORIAL VOL.2
Barbados / Constellation / Parker's mood /
Perhaps / Marmaduke / Donna Lee /
Chasin' the bird / Buzzy / Milestones / Half
nelson / Slippin' at Bells / Billie's bounce /
Thriving on a riff
CD _____ CY 78984
Savoy Jazz / Nov '95 / Conifer / ADA.
CHARLIE PARKER STORY, THE
Billie's bounce / Warming up a riff / Now's
the time / Thriving on a riff / Meandering /
Koko
CD _____ CY 78990
Savoy Jazz / Nov '95 / Conifer / ADA.
CHARLIE PARKER STORY: VOL.1, THE
CD _____ STBCD 2602
Stash / Aug '95 / Jazz Music / CM /
Cadillac / Direct / ADA.
CHARLIE PARKER STORY: VOL.2, THE
CD _____ STBCD 2603
Stash / Aug '95 / Jazz Music / CM /
Cadillac / Direct / ADA.
CHARLIE PARKER WITH MILES DAVIS
CD _____ 30017
Giants Of Jazz / Sep '92 / Target/BMG /
Cadillac.
CHASIN' THE BIRD
How high the moon / Moose the mooch /
Be bop a lula / Yardbird suite / Crazeology
/ Slow boat to China / Riff raff / Scrapple
from the apple / Star eyes / Sly mongoose
/ Round Midnight / Theme / Rocker / Don't
blame me / Relaxin' at Camarillo / Constel-
lation / Bluebird / Parker's mood / Marma-
duke / Bird of paradise / My old flame /
Chasin' the Bird
CD _____ CDGRF 063
Tring / '93 / Tring / Prism.
COLE PORTER SONGBOOK
Easy to love / Begin the beguine / Night and
day / What is this thing called love / In the
still of the night / I get a kick out of you /
Just one of those things / My heart belongs
to daddy / I've got you under my skin / Love
for sale / I love Paris
CD _____ 8232502
Verve / Feb '91 / PolyGram.
COMPLETE BIRTH OF BEBOP 1940-42
CD _____ STCD 535
Stash / Oct '91 / Jazz Music / CM /
Cadillac / Direct / ADA.
COMPLETE SESSIONS, THE
Diggin' diz / Moose and mooche / Yardbird
suite / Ornithology / Night in Tunisia / Max
making wax / Lover man / Gypsy / Be bop
/ Home cooking / Lullaby in rhythm / Blues
on the sofa / Kopely plaza blues / This is
always / Dark shadows / Bird's nest / Cool
blues / Relaxin' at Camarillo / Cheers / Car-
vin' the bird / Stupendous / Dexterity /
Bongo bop / Dewey Square / Hymn / Bird
of paradise / Embraceable you / Bird feathers / Klactoveesedstein / Scrapple from the

apple / My old flame / Out of nowhere / Don't blame me / Drifting on a reed / Quasimado / Charlie's wig / Bongo beep / Crazeology / How deep is the ocean
CD _____ SPJCD 4-101
Spotlight / May '93 / Braveworld Video.

EVENING AT HOME WITH THE BIRD, AN (Jazz Immortal Series Vol. 1)
There's a small hotel / These foolish things / Fine and dandy / Hot house
CD _____ SV 0154
Savoy Jazz / Apr '92 / Conifer / ADA.

FROM DIZZY TO MILES
CD _____ GOJCD 53052
Giants Of Jazz / Mar '90 / Target/BMG / Cadillac.

GENIUS OF BE-BOP
Bird of paradise / Embraceable you / Crazeology / Dewey Square / My old flame / Relaxin' at Camarillo / Hymn / Klacto-veesdstein / Don't blame me / Scrapple from the apple / Quasimado / Dexterity / Night in Tunisia / Ornithology / Lover man / Yardbird suite / Moose the mooche / Gypsy / Be bop / Bird's nest / Out of nowhere / Cheer / Stupendous / K.C. blues / Au privave / Oscar for treadwell, An / Bloomdido / Leapfrog / My melancholy baby / Mohawk / Relaxin' with Lee / She rote / Compulsion / Summertime / Just friends / Star eyes / What is this thing called love / I can't get started (with you) / Half Nelson / Milestones / Dizzy atmosphere / Hot house / Visa / Diverse / Passport / Now's the time / Song is you / Kim / Blues / Cosmic rays / I remember you / Chi chi / I'm in the mood for love / Just one of those things / Swedish schnapps / Parker's mood / Merry go round / Marmaduke / Koko / Cool blues / Chasin' the bird / Drifting on a reed / Donna Lee / Cheryl / Constellation / Buzzy / Blue bird / Bongo beep / Billie's bounce
CD Set _____ CDB 1202
Giants Of Jazz / '92 / Target/BMG / Cadillac.

GENIUS OF CHARLIE PARKER, THE
Bird gets the worm / Bluebird / Klaunstance / Barbados / Merry go round / Donna Lee / Chasin' the Bird / Koko / Perhaps / Warming up a riff / Slim's jam / Poppity pop / Dizzy boogie / Flat foot floogie
CD _____ SV 0104
Savoy Jazz / Apr '94 / Conifer / ADA.

GITANES - JAZZ 'ROUND MIDNIGHT
CD _____ 5109112
Polydor / Oct '91 / PolyGram.

HIGHEST FLYING BIRD (14 Of His Classic Recordings)
Moose the mooche / Yardbird smile / Orthinology / Scrapple from the apple / Rocker / Sly mongoose / Star eyes / This time the dream's on me / Cool blues / My little suede shoes / Lester leaps in / Laura
CD _____ PAR 2002
Parade / May '90 / Koch / Cadillac.

IMMORTAL CHARLIE PARKER, THE
Little Willie leaps / Donna Lee / Chasin' the Bird / Cheryl / Milestones / Half Nelson / Slippin' at Bells / Tiny's tempo / Red cross / Now's the time / Buzzy / Marmaduke
CD _____ CY 78983
Savoy Jazz / Nov '95 / Conifer / ADA.

IN A SOULFUL MOOD
CD _____ MCCD 205
MCI / Jul '95 / Disc / THE.

IN SWEDEN 1950
CD _____ STCD 4031
Storyville / Oct '87 / Jazz Music / Wellard / CM / Cadillac.

JAM SESSION 1952
CD _____ CD 53120
Giants Of Jazz / Jan '94 / Target/BMG / Cadillac.

JAZZ AT THE PHILHARMONIC 1946
CD _____ CD 53107
Giants Of Jazz / May '92 / Target/BMG / Cadillac.

JAZZ AT THE PHILHARMONIC 1949
CD _____ 519803-2
Verve / Feb '94 / PolyGram.

JAZZ MASTERS
CD _____ 519827-2
Verve / Feb '94 / PolyGram.

JAZZ PORTRAITS
Dizzy atmosphere / Hot house / Billie's bounce / Koko / Moose the mooche / Yardbird suite / Ornithology / Night in Tunisia / Lover man / Gypsy / Be bop / Bird's nest / Cool blues / Relaxin' at Camarillo / Cheers / Carvin' the bird / Stupendous / Donna Lee
CD _____ CD 14504
Jazz Portraits / May '94 / Jazz Music.

LEGENDARY DIAL MASTERS. VOL 1
CD _____ STCD 23
Stash / Mar '90 / Jazz Music / CM / Cadillac / Direct / ADA.

LEGENDARY DIAL MASTERS. VOL 2
CD _____ STCD 25
Stash / Mar '90 / Jazz Music / CM / Cadillac / Direct / ADA.

LIVE AT St. NICKS
CD _____ OJCCD 41
Original Jazz Classics / Jun '95 / Wellard / Jazz Music / Cadillac / Complete/Pinnacle.

LIVE AT TRADE WINGS
CD _____ LEJAZZCD 48
Le Jazz / Nov '95 / Charly / Cadillac.

LIVE IN LOS ANGELES 1947
CD _____ 550082
Jazz Anthology / Jan '94 / Harmonia Mundi / Cadillac.

LIVE PERFORMANCES
CD _____ ESP 3000-2
ESP / Jan '93 / Jazz Horizons / Jazz Music.

LOVER MAN
CD _____ CDSGP 064
Volume / Sep '93 / Total/BMG / Vital.

MASTERWORKS 1946-47
Bird of paradise / Embraceable you / Crazeology / Dewey Square / My old flame / Relaxin' at Camarillo / Hymn / Klacto-veesdstein / Don't blame me / Scrapple from the apple / Quasimodo / Dexterity / Night in Tunisia / Ornithology / Lover man / Yardbird suite / Moose the mooche / Gypsy / Be bop / Bird's nest / Out of nowhere / Cheers
CD _____ CD 53007
Giants Of Jazz / Mar '92 / Target/BMG / Cadillac.

NEWLY DISCOVERED SIDES BY THE IMMORTAL CHARLIE PARKER
52nd Street (theme) / Night in Tunisia / Slow boat to China / Groovin' high / Big foot / Hot house
CD _____ SV 0156
Savoy Jazz / Apr '92 / Conifer / ADA.

ORIGINAL CHOICE TAKES
Diggin' diz / Moose the mooche / Yardbird suite / Ornithology / Night in Tunisia / Max making wax / Loveman / Gypsy / Be bop / This is always / Dark shadows / Bird's nest / Hot blues / Cool blues / Relaxin' at Camarillo / Cheers / Carvin' the bird / Stupendous / Dexterity / Bongo bop / Dewey Square / Hymn / Bird of paradise / Embraceable you / Scrappel from the apple / My old flame / Out of nowhere / Don't blame me / Drifting on a reed / Quasimado / Charlie's wig / Bongo beep / Carazeology / How deep is the ocean
CD Set _____ SPJCD 1092
Spotlite / May '95 / Cadillac / Jazz Horizons / Swift.

PARKER'S MOOD 1947-1950
CD _____ CD 56036
Jazz Roots / Jul '95 / Target/BMG.

RARE BIRD
CD _____ STCD21
Stash / Mar '90 / Jazz Music / CM / Cadillac / Direct / ADA.

RARITIES FROM PRIVATE COLLECTION - 1947-50
CD _____ JZ-CD311
Suisa / Feb '91 / Jazz Music / THE.

RARITIES FROM PRIVATE COLLECTION - 1950-53
CD _____ JZ-CD312
Suisa / Feb '91 / Jazz Music / THE.

SAVOY RECORDINGS
CD _____ VGCD 650107
Vogue / Jan '93 / BMG.

SAVOY RECORDINGS VOL. 2
CD _____ VGCD 650108
Vogue / Jan '93 / BMG.

STREET BEAT
CD _____ CDSGP 088
Prestige / May '94 / Total/BMG.

TRIUMPH OF CHARLIE PARKER
CD _____ CDCH 380
Milan / Jan '89 / BMG / Silva Screen.

UNHEARD CHARLIE PARKER: BIRDSEED VOL. 1 (1947-50)
CD _____ STB 2500
Stash / Apr '95 / Jazz Music / CM / Cadillac / Direct / ADA.

WITH STRINGS (The Master Takes)
CD _____ 5239842
Verve / Feb '95 / PolyGram.

YARDBIRD SUITE
CD _____ CD 56011
Jazz Roots / Aug '94 / Target/BMG.

Parker, Elaine

S'WONDERFUL
Some of my best friends / Touch of your lips / In a sentimental mood / 'S Wonderful / Stardust / I did it all for you / Little girl blue / Carioca / They can't take that away from me / We could be flying / They say it's wonderful / Ol' man river / There's a small hotel / Joy / My foolish heart / Like a lover / Love for sale
CD _____ JHCD 027
Ronnie Scott's Jazz House / Jan '94 / Jazz Music / Magnum Music Group / Cadillac.

Parker, Evan

50TH BIRTHDAY CONCERT
CD _____ CDLR 212/3
Leo / Jan '95 / Wellard / Cadillac / Impetus.

ATLANTA (Parker, Evan Trio)
CD _____ IMPCD 18617
Impetus / '90 / CM / Wellard / Impetus / Cadillac.

CONIC SECTIONS
Conic section 1 / Conic section 2 / Conic section 3 / Conic section 4 / Conic section 5
CD _____ AHUM 015
Ah-Um / Jul '93 / New Note / Cadillac.

CORNER TO CORNER (Parker, Evan & John Stevens)
CD _____ OGCD 005
Ogun / May '94 / Cadillac / Jazz Music / Charly.

IMAGINARY VALUES (Parker, Evan Trio)
CD _____ MCD 9401
Maya / Oct '94 / Complete/Pinnacle / Direct / Cadillac.

PROCESS & REALITY
CD _____ FMPCD 37
FMP / Oct '87 / Cadillac.

SAXOPHONE SOLOS
CD _____ CPE 20022
Chronoscope / Jun '95 / Harmonia Mundi / Wellard / Cadillac.

Parker, Graham

12 HAUNTED EPISODES
CD _____ GRACD 204
Grapevine / Apr '95 / Grapevine.

ALONE IN AMERICA (LIVE)
White honey / Black honey / Soul corruption / Gypsy blood / Back in time / Change is gonna come / Watch the moon come down / Protection / Back to schooldays / Durban poison / You can't be too strong / Don't let it break you down
CD _____ FIENDCD 141
Demon / Apr '89 / Pinnacle / ADA.

BURNING QUESTIONS
CD _____ FIEND CD 721
Demon / Aug '92 / Pinnacle / ADA.

GRAHAM PARKER
CD Set _____ GRAHAM 1
Demon / '91 / Pinnacle / ADA.

HOWLING WIND/HEAT TREATMENT (2 CDs)
White honey / Nothing's gonna pull us apart / Silly thing / Gypsy blood / Between you and me / Back to schooldays / Soul shoes / Lady doctor / You've got to be kidding / Howling wind / Not if it pleases me / Don't ask me questions / Heat treatment / That's what they all say / Turned up too late / Black honey / Hotel chambermaid / Pourin' it all out / Back door love / Something you're goin' thru / Help me shake it / Fools' gold
CD Set _____ 5286032
Vertigo / Aug '95 / PolyGram.

HUMAN SOUL
Little Miss Understanding / My love's strong / Dancing for money / Call me your doctor / Big man on paper / Soultime / Everything goes / Sugar gives you energy / Daddy's a postman / Green monkeys / I was wrong / You got the word (right where you want it) / Slash and burn
CD _____ FIENDCD 163
Demon / Oct '89 / Pinnacle / ADA.

LIVE - ALONE IN JAPAN
That's what they all say / Platinum blonde / Mercury poisoning / Sweet sixteen / No woman, no cry / Lunatic fringe / Long stem rose / Discovering Japan / Don't ask me questions / Watch the moon come down (revisited) / Just like Hermann Hesse / Too many knots to untangle / Chopsticks / Short memories
CD _____ FIENDCD 735
Demon / Aug '93 / Pinnacle / ADA.

LIVE ON THE TEST
CD _____ WHISCD 002
Windsong / May '94 / Pinnacle.

MONA LISA'S SISTER
Don't let it break you down / Under the mask of happiness / Back in time / I'm just your man / OK Hieronymous / Get started, start a fire / Girl isn't ready / Blue highway / Success / I don't know / Cupid
CD _____ FIENDCD 122
Demon / Jun '88 / Pinnacle / ADA.

PARKERILLA
CD _____ 8422632
Vertigo / Jan '94 / PolyGram.

STRUCK BY LIGHTNING
CD _____ FIENDCD 201
Demon / Jan '91 / Pinnacle / ADA.

UP ESCALATOR, THE
No holding back / Devil's sidewalk / Stupefaction / Love without greed / Jolie Julie / Endless night / Paralysed / Manoeuvres / Empty lives / Beating of another heart

CD _____ FIENDCD 121
Demon / Jun '90 / Pinnacle / ADA.

Parker, Junior

LITTLE JUNIOR PARKER
CD _____ CDC 9002
LRC / Oct '90 / New Note / Harmonia Mundi.

Parker, Kim

SOMETIMES I'M BLUE
CD _____ SN 1133
Soul Note / '86 / Harmonia Mundi / Wellard / Cadillac.

Parker, Knocky

KNOCKY PARKER & GALVANISED WASHBOARD BAND
CD _____ BCD 1
GHB / Jan '94 / Jazz Music.

Parker, Leon

ABOVE AND BELOW
Body movement / Bemsha swing / You don't know what love is / All my life / Above and below / Celebration / Epistrophy / B.B.B.B. / Evy / It's only a paper moon / Body movement II
CD _____ 4781982
Epicure / Feb '95 / Sony.

Parker, Maceo

DOING THEIR OWN THING (Parker, Maceo & All The Kings Men)
Maceo / Got to getcha / Southwick / Funky woman / Shake it baby / Better half / Don't waste this world away / (I remember) Mr. Banks / Thank you for letting me be myself again (On CD only)
CD _____ CPCD 8041
Charly / Jun '94 / Charly / THE / Cadillac.

FUNKY MUSIC MACHINE (Parker, Maceo & All The Kings Men)
Funky music machine / I want to sing / Dreams / Feeling alright / Something / Born to wander / T.S.U / For no one / Make it with you / Funky tale to tell
CD _____ CDSEWM 087
Southbound / Nov '93 / Pinnacle.

SOUNDTRACK
CD _____ MM 801046
Minor Music / Feb '95 / Vital/SAM.

Parker, Ray Jnr.

BEST OF RAY PARKER JNR (Parker, Ray Jnr.& Raydio)
Ghostbusters / You can't change that / Woman needs love (just like you do) / More than one way to love a woman / Stay the night / Let me go / Betcha can't love me just once / Jack and Jill / Other woman / Two places at the same time / Loving you / Girls are more fun / Is this a love thing / For those who like to groove
CD _____ 260.365
Ariola / Dec '89 / BMG.

COLLECTION, THE
Jack and Jill / You can't change that / Girls are more fun / Other woman / Is this a love thing / Still in the groove / Loving you / Bad boy / It's time to party now / Honey I'm rich / Two places at the same time / That old song / Let me go / Jamie / People next door / Ghostbusters
CD _____ 74321139862
Arista / Jul '93 / BMG.

Parker, Robert

BAREFOOTIN'
Barefootin' / Let's go baby (where the action is) / Little bit of something / Sneakin' Sally through the alley / Better luck in the summertime / You see me / You can be the country side of life / Get right down / Get ta steppin' / Hiccup / Hot and cold / Skinny dippin' / I like what you do to me / Disco doctor
CD _____ CPCD 8013
Charly / Feb '94 / Charly / THE / Cadillac.

Parker, Rupert

DOUBLE HARP
CD _____ MSPCD 9301
Mabley St. / Sep '93 / Grapevine.

ELECTRIC HARP - ORIGINAL WORKS
CD _____ MSPCD 9504
Mabley St. / Sep '95 / Grapevine.

SOLO
CD _____ MSPCD 9401
Mabley St. / Feb '94 / Grapevine.

SONGS FROM THE HARP
Bridge over troubled water / Lady in red / Saving all my love / Daniel / Jealous guy / Careless whisper / Jameela / Moondance / Without you / Can't help falling in love with you / Stay with me 'til dawn / Music of the night / Throwing it all away / Wonderful tonight / Could it be magic / Up where we belong / He was beautiful / Since I don't have you / Long and winding road / Nobody does it better / Annie's song / Bright eyes / Weather with you / Vincent / Variation on a

dream / Hello / I heard it through the grape-vine / Power of love
CD Set _____ MSPCD 9404
Mabley St. / Nov '94 / Grapevine.

WELL PLUCKED/WITH THE FLOW
Everything I do (I do it for you) / Sacrifice / Unchained Melody / Always A Woman / Three Times A Lady / She's not there / More Than Words / Wonder Why / One Day I'll Fly Away / Albatross / Eternal Flame / Best of my love / Oxygene / Miss You Nights
CD Set _____ VCD 3078
Victory Disques / Nov '92 / Grapevine.

Parker, William

IN ORDER TO SURVIVE
CD _____ 1201592
Black Saint / Jan '96 / Harmonia Mundi / Cadillac.

Parkin, Eric

MARIGOLD (Piano Impressions Of Billy Mayer)
Legends of King Arthur / Almond blossom / April's fool / Harp of the winds / Marigold / Railroad rhythm / Shallow waters / From a Spanish lattice / Song of the fir tree / Nimble fingered gentleman / Evening primrose / Ace of diamonds / Ace of hearts / Joker
CD _____ CHAN 8560
Chandos / '89 / Chandos.

Parkins, Zeena

URSA'A DOOR
CD _____ VICTOCD 018
Victo / Nov '94 / These / ReR Megacorp / Cadillac.

Parkinson, Chris

OUT OF HIS TREE
CD _____ PAN 147CD
Pan / Apr '94 / ADA / Direct / CM.

Parks, Van Dyke

CLANG OF THE YANKEE REAPER
Clang of the Yankee reaper / City on the hill / Pass that stage / Another dream / You're a real sweetheart / Love is the answer / Iron man / Tribute to Spree / Soul Train / Cannon in D
CD _____ 7599261852
WEA / Jan '96 / Warner Music.

DISCOVER AMERICA
Jack Palance / Introduction / Bing Crosby / Steelband music / Four Mills brothers / Be careful / John Jones / F.D.R. in Trinidad / Sweet Trinidad / Occapella / Sailin' shoes / Riverboat / Ode to Tobago / Your own comes first / G man hoover / Stars and stripes forever
CD _____ 7599261452
WEA / Jan '96 / Warner Music.

IDIOSYNCRATIC PATH
Donovan's colours / John Jones / Pass that stage / Ode to Tobago / Attic / Clang of the Yankee reaper / Four mills brothers / You're a real sweetheart / Sailin' shoes / Vine street / Palm desert / Tribute to spree / Iron man / Sweet Trinidad / Be careful / Bing Crosby / Steelband music / Your own comes first / Stars and stripes forever
CD _____ DIAB 807
Diabolo / Oct '95 / Pinnacle.

JUMP
Jump / Opportunity for two / Come along / I ain't going home / Many a mile to go / Tang / Invitation to sin. An / Home / After the ball / Look away / Hominy grove
CD _____ 7599238292
WEA / Jan '96 / Warner Music.

SONG CYCLE
Vine Street / Palm desert / Widow's walk / Laurel Canyon Boulevard / All golden / Van Dyke Parks / Public domain / Donovan's colours / Attic / By the people / Potpourri
CD _____ EDCD 207
Edsel / Jul '88 / Pinnacle / ADA.

TOKYO ROSE
America / Tokoyo rose / Yankee go home / Cowboy / Manzanar / Calypso / White chry-santhemum / Trade war / Out of love / One home run
CD _____ 7599259682
WEA / Jan '96 / Warner Music.

Parlan, Horace

JOE VAN ENKHUIZEN MEETS THE RHYTHM SECTION
CD _____ CDSJP 249
Timeless Jazz / Jan '88 / New Note.

PANNONICA
No greater love / Pannonica / C jam blues / Hi fly / Who cares
CD _____ ENJ 40762
Enja / Jul '93 / New Note / Vital/SAM.

Parliament

CLONES OF DR. FUNKENSTEIN, THE
Prelude / Gamin' on ya / Dr. Funkenstein / Children of production / Gettin' to know you / Do that stuff / Everybody is on the one / I've been watching you / Funkin' for fun

CD _____ 8426202
Casablanca / Feb '91 / PolyGram.

DOPE DOGS
CD _____ HOTHCD 1
Hot Hands / Apr '95 / Total/BMG.

GIVE UP THE FUNK (The Best Of Parliament)
CD _____ 5269952
Mercury / Sep '95 / PolyGram.

I WANNA TESTIFY
Testify / Time / Good ole music / I can feel the ice melting / Don't se sore at me / All your goodies are gone / Little man / Goose that laid the golden egg / What you been growing / Look at what I almost missed / New day beings / Fellow's let's make it last / All your goodies are gone (inst) / Baby I owe you something good (inst) / I'll wait / I'll wait (inst)
CD _____ GSCD 052
Goldmine / Oct '94 / Vital.

RHENIUM
Breakdown / Call my baby pussycat / Little ole country boy / Moonshine Heather / Oh Lord, why Lord - prayer / Red hot mama / My automobile / Nothing before me but rain / Funky woman / Come in out of the rain / Silent boatman
CD _____ HDH CD 008
HDH / Feb '90 / Pinnacle.

Parmerley, David

I KNOW A GOOD THING
I know a good thing when I feel it / Grand-pa's radio / Have you come to say goodbye / She keeps hanging on / Someone took my place with you / Morristown / Excuse me / Down home / Someone on her mind / Sometimes silence says it all / Live and let live / From cotton to satin (Features on CD only.)
CD _____ SHCD 3777
Sugarhill / '89 / Roots / CM / ADA / Direct.

Parnell, Jack

LIVE FROM RONNIE'S
Horatio Nelson / Jul '95 / THE / BMG / Avid/BMG / Koch.
CD _____ CDSIV 1142

MEMORIES
Memories / Stardust / Touch of your lips / Shadow of your smile / I can't get started (with you) / Very thought of you / Serenade / I'll never smile again / Yesterdays / I had the craziest dream / Serenata / All the things you are / Remember / Way we were / Laura / Street of dreams
CD _____ 2MEM 1
Berkeley / Jan '89 / Jazz Music.

Parnell, Lee Roy

LOVE WITHOUT MERCY
What kind of fool do you think I am / Back in my arms again / Rock / Ain't no short way home / Love without mercy / Road scholar / Night after night / Done deal / Tender mo-ment / Rollercoaster
CD _____ 07822186842
Arista / Jan '94 / BMG.

ON THE ROAD
CD _____ 07822187392
Arista / Jun '94 / BMG.

WE ALL GET LUCKY SOMETIMES
Little bit of you / Knock yourself out / Heart's desire / When a woman loves a man / If the house is rockin' / We all get lucky sometimes / Saved by the grace of your love / Givin' water to a drowning man / I had to let it go / Squeeze me in / Catwalk
CD _____ 07822187902
Arista / Aug '95 / BMG.

Parr, John

JOHN PARR
Magical / Naughty naughty / Love grammar / Treat me a like an animal / She's gonna love you to death / Revenge / Heartbreaker / Somebody stole my thunder / Don't leave your mark on me / St. Elmo's fire
CD _____ 826 384-2
London / Oct '85 / PolyGram.

MAN WITH A VISION
CD _____ CDMFN 129
Music For Nations / Jan '93 / Pinnacle.

RUNNING THE ENDLESS MILE
Two hearts / Don't worry 'bout me / King of lies / Running the endless mile / Don't leave your mark on me / Scratch / Do it again / Blame it on the radio / Story still remains the same / Steal you away
CD _____ 830 401 2
London / Oct '86 / PolyGram.

Parrondo, Jose

RECITAL DE CANTE FLAMENCO
(Parrondo, Jose & Miguel Iven)
Malagueñas / Tientos y tangos / Solea / Tonas / Peteneras / Seguiriyas / Bulerias
CD _____ 93052
Emocion / Jul '95 / New Note.

Parry, Harry

GONE WITH THE WIND
Basin Street ball / Crazy rhythm / Sophis-ticated lady / Mr. Five by Five / If I had you / I can't dance / Don't you know I care (or don't you care to) / Who's sorry now / So-meone's in the kitchen with Dinah / Star-dust / I never knew / Boogie rides to Yorke / Onm the sunny side of the street / Don't be that way / Angry / Darktown strutter's ball / Blues around my bed / Champagne / My favourite dream / Blue Lou / Bounce me brother with a solid four / Honeysuckle rose / Gone with the wind / Parry party
CD _____ RAJCD 840
Empress / Feb '95 / THE.

Parsons, Alan Project

AMMONIA AVENUE
Prime time / Let me go home / One good reason / Since the last goodbye / Don't an-swer me / Dancing on a high wire / You don't believe / Pipeline / Ammonia Avenue
CD _____ 258885
Arista / '88 / BMG.

BACK2BACK
CD Set _____ 74321292082
RCA / Sep '95 / BMG.

BEST OF ALAN PARSONS PROJECT
I wouldn't want to be like you / Eye in the sky / Games people play / Time / Pyramania / You wouldn't believe / Lucifer / Psychob-abble / Damned if I do / Don't let it show / Can't take it with you / Old and wise
CD _____ 610052
Arista / Aug '95 / BMG.

EVE
Lucifer / You lie down with the dogs / I'd rather be a man / You won't be there / Winding me up / Damned if I do / Don't hold back / Secret garden / If I could change your mind
CD _____ 258981
Arista / '88 / BMG.

I ROBOT
I wouldn't want to be like you / Some other time / Breakdown / Don't let it show / Voice / Nucleus / Day after day / Total eclipse / Genesis ch.1 vs.32 / I robot
CD _____ 259651
Arista / Mar '89 / BMG.

PYRAMID
Voyager / What goes up... / Eagle will rise again / One more river / Can't take it with you / In the lap of the gods / Pyramania / Hyper gamma spaces / Shadow of a lonely man
CD _____ 258983
Arista / Apr '88 / BMG.

TALES OF MYSTERY
Dream within a dream / Raven / Tell-tale heart / Cask of Amontillado / Dr. Tarr and Professor Fether / Fall of the House of Usher / To one in Paradise
CD _____ 832 820 2
London / Jun '92 / PolyGram.

TRY ANYTHING ONCE
Three of me / Turn it up / Wine from the water / Breakaway / Jigue / Mr. Time / Siren song / Back against the wall / Re-jigue / Oh life (there must be more) / I'm talking to you (Not available on LP) / Dreamscape (Not available on LP)
CD _____ 74321167302
Arista / Nov '93 / BMG.

TURN OF A FRIENDLY CARD
Turn of a friendly card / Gold bug / Time / Games people play / I don't wanna go home / Nothing left to lose / May be a price to pay
CD _____ 258982
Arista / '88 / BMG.

VULTURE CULTURE
Let's talk about me / Separate lives / Days are numbers (The traveller) / Sooner or later / Vulture culture / Hawkeye / Somebody out there / Same old song and dance
CD _____ 258884
Arista / '88 / BMG.

Parsons, Gram

COSMIC AMERICAN MUSIC
Song for you (1) / Kentucky blues / Streets of Baltimore / Folsom prison blues / Love-sick blues / New soft shoe / How much I've lied / Still feeling blue / Ain't no Beatle, ain't no Rolling Stone / How can I forget you/Cry one more time / Song for you (2) / Streets of Baltimore #2 / That's all it took (1) / So-mebody's back in town / More and more / Teaching Emmy to sweep out the ashes / Daddy's fiddle / We'll sweep out the ashes in the morning / Cold cold heart / That's all it took (2) / Song for you (3)
CD _____ CDSD 071
Sundown / Jun '95 / Magnum Music Group.

G.P./GRIEVOUS ANGEL
Still feeling blue / We'll sweep out the ashes in the morning / Song for you / Streets of Baltimore / She / That's all it took / New soft shoe / Kiss the children / Cry one more time / Return of the grievous angel / Hearts on fire / I can't dance / Brass buttons / Thousand dollar wedding / Cash on the barrelhead /

Hickory wind / Love hurts / Ooh Las Vegas / In my hour of darkness
CD Set _____ 759926108-2
WEA / Jan '94 / Warner Music.

SAFE AT HOME (Parsons, Gram International Submarine Band)
Blue eyes / I must have been somebody else / You've known a satisfied mind / Fol-som Prison blues / That's all right / Millers cave / I still miss someone / Luxury liner / Strong boy / Do you know how it feels to be lonesome
CD _____ CDSD 071
Sundown / Jan '91 / Magnum Music Group.

WARM EVENINGS, PALE MORNINGS AND BOTTLED BLUES 1963-1973
Zah's blues / Blue eyes / Strong boy / Truck driving man / Hot burrito / Christine's tune / Sin City / Dark end of the street / Wild horses / She / New soft shoe / We'll sweep out the ashes in the morning / Brass but-tons / Return of the grievous angel / Drug store truck drivin' man / Brand new heart-ache / Love hurts / I'm your toy
CD _____ RVCD 24
Raven / Jun '92 / Direct / ADA.

Parsons, Longineu

WORK SONG
Work song / Search for the new land / Party in Morocco / Song for Dr. Drew / Passing dance / Soyuz dance / One for Daddy-O / Spaced part II / Lost in the black forest / My funny valentine / Gathering
CD _____ TCB 94302
TCB / Jun '94 / New Note.

Parsons, Niamh

LOOSELY CONNECTED
Katie Campbell's rambles / Streets of Forbes / Tinkerman's daughter / Little big time / Lover's ghost / Man of Arran / North Amerikay / We two people / One morning in May / Play a merry jig / Where are you (tonight I wonder) / Don't give your heart away
CD _____ CDTRAX 052
Greentrax / May '92 / Conifer / Duncans / ADA / Direct.

Parton, Dolly

ANTHOLOGY - DOLLY PARTON
Jolene / Old flames / Two doors down / My blue ridge mountain boy / Save the last dance for me / Put it off until tomorrow / Something fishy / I've lived my life / Coat of many colours / Daddy come and get me / My Tennessee mountain home / Nine to Five / In the good old days / Joshua / But you know I love you / Daddy won't be home anymore / Happy, happy birthday baby / Dumb blonde / Company you keep / Too lonely too long / Down from Dover / Love is like a butterfly
CD _____ VSOPCD 165
Connoisseur / Jul '91 / Pinnacle.

COLLECTION, THE
CD _____ CCSCD 353
Castle / Nov '92 / BMG.

COLLECTION, THE
Save the last dance for me / I walk the line / Turn, turn, turn / Downtown / We had it all / She don't love you (like I love you) / We'll sing in the sunshine / I can't help myself / Elusive butterfly / Great pretender / Harper Valley PTA / D.I.V.O.R.C.E. / I will always love you / Jolene / Nine to Five / Here you come again
CD _____ 74001 10097 2
RCA / Jul '93 / BMG.

COUNTRY GIRL
Jolene / My Tennessee mountain home / Bargain store / Love is like a butterfly / Just the two of us / I will always love you / Touch your woman / Seeker / Travelling man / Daddy come and get me / My blue tears / Coat of many colours / Joshua / Washday blues / Mule skinner blues (Blue yodel #8) / Coming for to carry me home / Afraid to love again (CD only.) / I washed my face in the morning dew (CD only)
CD _____ CDMFP 5914
Music For Pleasure / Apr '91 / EMI.

DOLLY PARTON - FAVOURITES
CD _____ PWKS 4116
Carlton Home Entertainment / Sep '92 / Carlton Home Entertainment.

EAGLE WHEN SHE FLIES
If you need me / Rockin' years / Country road / Silver and gold / Eagle when she flies / Best woman wins / What a heartache / Runaway feelin' / Dreams do come true / Family / Wildest dreams
CD _____ 4678542
Columbia / May '91 / Sony.

GREATEST HITS, THE
CD _____ TCD 2739
Telstar / Oct '94 / BMG.

GREATEST HITS: DOLLY PARTON
Here you come again / Think about love / Baby I'm burning / Love is like a butterfly / But you know I love you / Nine to Five / Islands in the stream (duet with Kenny Rog-ers) / Don't call it love / Old flames cant

515

hold a candle to you / Bargain store / Real love (with Kenny Rogers) / Potential new boyfriend / Jolene / I will always love you / I really got the feeling (Not on LP) / Starting over again (Not on LP) / We had it all (CD only) / You're the only one (CD only)
CD _____ PD 90407
RCA / Dec '89 / BMG.

HEART SONG
Heart song / I'm thinking tonight of my blue eyes / Mary of the wild moor / In the pines / My blue tears / Applejack / Coat of many colours / Smoky mountain memories / Night train to Memphis / What a friend we have in Jesus / Hold fast to the right / Walter Henry Hagan / Barbara Allen / Brave little soldier / To Daddy / True blue / Longer than always / Wayfaring stranger / My Tennessee mountain home / Heart song (reprise) / Cas Walker theme / Black draught theme / PMS blues
CD _____ 477276 2
Columbia / Nov '94 / Sony.

HONKY TONK ANGELS (Parton, Dolly/ Tammy Wynette/Loretta Lynn)
It wasn't God who made honky tonk angels / Put it off until tomorrow / Silver threads and golden needles / Please help me, I'm falling / Sittin' on the front porch swing / Wings of a dove / I forgot more than you'll ever know / Wouldn't it be great / That's the way it could have been / Let her fly / Lovesick blues / I dreamed of a hillbilly heaven
CD _____ 474626 2
Columbia / Nov '93 / Sony.

JOLENE
Jolene / When someone wants to leave / River of happiness / Early morning breeze / Highlight of my life / I will always love you / Randy / Living on memories of you / Lonely comin' down / It must be you
CD _____ WMCD 5638
Disky / May '94 / THE / BMG / Discovery / Pinnacle.

LOVE ALBUM, THE
You are / Heartbreaker / Bargain store / I will always love you / Love is like a butterfly / Coat of many colours / Islands in the stream / Here you come again / Send me the pillow that you dream on / It's all wrong but it's all right / Jolene / One of those days
CD _____ ND 90307
RCA / Feb '89 / BMG.

LOVE ALBUM, THE Vol.2
We used to / You're the only one / But you know I love you / We had it all / Sweet music man / My girl (my love) / Almost in love / Sandy's song / I really don't want to know / Sweet summer lovin' / Love I used to call mine / Starting over again
CD _____ ND 90455
RCA / Nov '90 / BMG.

ONCE UPON A CHRISTMAS (Parton, Dolly & Kenny Rogers)
I believe in Santa Claus / Sleighride / Winter wonderland / Christmas without you / Christmas song / Christmas to remember / With bells on / Silent night / Greatest gift of all / White Christmas / Once upon a Christmas
CD _____ ND 90615
Arista / Oct '94 / BMG.

SLOW DANCING WITH THE MOON
Full circle / Romeo / Heartache tonight / What will baby be / More where that came from / Put a little love in your heart / Why can't we / I'll make your bed / Whenever forever comes / Cross my heart / Slow dancing with the moon / High and mighty
CD _____ 472944 2
Columbia / Mar '93 / Sony.

SOMETHING SPECIAL
Crippled bird / Something special / Change / I will always love you / Green eyed boy / Speakin' of the Devil / Jolene / No good way of saying goodbye / Seeker / Teach me to trust
CD _____ 4807542
Columbia / Sep '95 / Sony.

TRIO (Parton, Dolly/Linda Ronstadt/ Emmylou Harris)
Pain of loving you / Making plans / To know him is to love him / Hobo's meditation / Wildflowers / Telling me lies / My dear companion / Those memories of you / I've had enough / Rose wood casket / Farther along
CD _____ 9254912
WEA / Feb '95 / Warner Music.

WORLD OF DOLLY PARTON, THE
Dumb blonde / Your ole handy man / I don't want to throw ice / Put it off until tomorrow / I wasted my tears / Something fishy / Fuel to the flame / Giving and the taking / I'm in no condition / Company you keep / I've lived my life / Little things / Why why why / I wound easy / I don't want you around me anymore / Hillbilly Willy / This boy has been hurt / Daddy won't be home anymore / As long as I love / Habit I can't break / I'm not worth the tears / I don't trust me around you / I couldn't wait forever / Too lonely too long
CD _____ 983317 2
Pickwick/Sony Collector's Choice / Oct '93 / Carlton Home Entertainment / Pinnacle / Sony.

Partridge, Andy

THROUGH THE HILL (Partridge, Andy & Harold Budd)
Hand 19 / Through the hill / Great valley of gongs / Western island of apples / Anima mundi / Hand 20 / Place of odd glances / Well for the sweat of the moon / Tenochtitlan's numberless bridges / Ceramic avenue / Hand 21 / Missing pieces in the game of salt and onyx / Mantle of peacock bones / Bronze coins showing genitals / Bearded aphrodite / Hand 22
CD _____ ASCD 021
All Saints / Jan '95 / Vital / Discovery.

Party Boppers

SINGALONG ROCK 'N' ROLL PARTY
(We're gonna) rock around the clock / Shake, rattle and roll / See you later alligator / Shake, rattle and roll (reprise) / Bye bye love / Wake up little Susie / All I have to do is dream / Bird dog / Everyday / Heartbeat / Oh boy / That'll be the day / Peggy Sue / Rave on / Raining in my heart / It's my heart / Locomotion / Stupid cupid / Sweet nothin's / Lipstick on your collar / Ma, he's making eyes at me / Ain't that a shame / Blueberry hill / Great balls of fire / Tutti frutti / Long tall Sally / Good golly Miss Molly / Whole lotta shakin' goin' on / C'mon everybody / Weekend / Summertime blues / Three steps to heaven / Hound dog / All shook up / Let me be your teddy bear / Blue suede shoes / Jailhouse rock / Return to sender / Wooden heart / Love me tender / Wonder of you
CD _____ CDMFP 5834
Music For Pleasure / Oct '93 / EMI.

Party Diktator

WORLDWIDE
CD _____ DEP 003CD
Dead Eye / Nov '92 / SRD.

Party Poppers

40 SING-ALONG FAVOURITES
Down at the old Bull And Bush / Daisy bell / Two lovely black eyes / Joshua / Oh oh Antonio / I'm forever blowing bubbles / Hello hello, who's your lady friend / You must have been a beautiful baby / Daddy wouldn't buy me a bow-wow / Waiting at the church / It's a long way to Tipperary / Pack up your troubles in your old kit back / Goodbye Dolly Gray / Bless 'em all / Hold your hand out, naughty boy / I do like to be beside the seaside / Lilly of Laguna / Tip toe thru' the tulips with me / Honeysuckle and the bee / Roamin' in the gloamin' / On mother Kelly's doorstep / Roll out the barrel / Who were you with last night / Don't dilly dally on the way / When you're smiling / Ma, he's making eyes at me / Side by side / (In) a shanty in old Shanty Town / On a slow boat to China / Bye bye blackbird / I'm shy, Mary Ellen, I'm shy / Let me call you sweetheart / When I grow too old to dream / On moonlight bay / By the light of the silvery moon / If you were the only girl in the world / You were meant for me / Ain't she sweet / Nellie Dean / Show me the way to go home
CD _____ CDMFP 6105
Music For Pleasure / Jan '94 / EMI.

LET'S HAVE A PARTY
Let's have a party / Agadoo / Let's twist again / March of the Mods / Birdie song / Simon says / Lambeth walk / Boomps a daisy / Y viva Espana / Paloma blanca / La Bamba / I came, I saw, I conga'd / Knees up mother Brown / Can can / Hi ho silver lining / Last waltz / Auld lang syne
CD _____ CDMFP 5948
Music For Pleasure / Oct '92 / EMI.

SING-ALONG CHRISTMAS PARTY
White Christmas / I saw Mommy kissing Santa Claus / Let it snow, let it snow, let it snow / Frosty the snowman / Happy holiday / That's what I'd like for Christmas / When Santa got stuck up the chimney / It's the most wonderful time of the year / We three kings of Orient are / Jingle bells / Good King Wenceslas / Kings' horses / Santa Claus is coming to town / Rudolph the red nosed reindeer / Holiday season / Mary's boy child / When a child is born / Silent night / Deck the halls with boughs of holly / Stop the cavalry / Have yourself a merry little Christmas / Christmas song / Do you hear what I hear / Christmas medley / Little donkey / Winter wonderland / It's beginning to look like Christmas / I saw three ships / All I want for Christmas (is my two front teeth) / Silver bells / Sleigh ride / Joy to the world / I wish it could be Christmas every day / Merry Christmas everybody / We wish you a Merry Christmas / Auld lang syne / Christmas alphabet (CD only.) / Fairy on the Christmas tree (CD only.) / Jolly old St. Nicholas (CD only.) / Mr. Santa (CD only.) / Mistletoe and wine (CD only.) / Little drummer boy (CD only.) / O little town of Bethlehem (CD only.) / It came upon a midnight clear (CD only.) / God rest ye merry gentlemen (CD only.)
CD _____ CDMFP 5795
Music For Pleasure / Dec '94 / EMI.

SING-ALONG CHRISTMAS PARTY VOL.2

Good Christian men rejoice / Here we come a-wassailing / I believe in Father Christmas / Rockin' around the Christmas tree / Mary had a baby boy / Jingle bell rock / Baby it's cold outside / Go tell it on the mountain / Twelve days of Christmas / Hark the herald angels sing / O come all ye faithful / One in royal David's city / See amid the winter's snow / Angels from the realms of Glory / Saviour's day / Wonderful Christmas time / Ding dong merrily on high / On Christmas night all Christians sing / O Christmas tree / First Noel / Away in a manger / Happy Christmas (war is over) / Do they know it's Christmas / Scarlet ribbons / Coventry carol / While shepherds watched their flocks by night / Rocking carol / Rise up shepherd and follow / Last Christmas / Merry Christmas everyone / Rockin' around the Christmas tree (reprise)
CD _____ CDMFP 6180
Music For Pleasure / Nov '95 / EMI.

SINGALONG 60'S PARTY
Sergeant Pepper's lonely hearts club band / Mighty Quinn / Downtown / Summer holiday / When I'm sixty four / Little lovin' / With a little help from my friends / King of the road / I want to hold your hand / Winchester Cathedral / Sugar sugar / Hard day's night / Ob la di ob la da / World without love / Ferry 'cross the Mersey / Yellow submarine / Can't buy me love / Carnival is over / Hey Jude / Have I the right / Baby, now that I've found you / Oh pretty woman / Release me / Green green grass of home / I can't stop loving you / Crying in the chapel / Young ones / I like it / There's a kind of hush / I only want to be with you / How do you do it / Bachelor boy / Delilah / You'll never walk alone / Are you lonesome tonight / Last waltz
CD _____ CDMFP 5892
Music For Pleasure / Sep '90 / EMI.

Pasadena Roof Orchestra

BEST OF THE PASADENA ROOF ORCHESTRA
CD _____ MATCD 313
Castle / Jun '95 / BMG.

BEST OF THE PASADENA ROOF ORCHESTRA, THE
CD _____ TRTCD 199
TrueTrax / Jun '95 / THE.

BREAKAWAY
Breakaway / Jeepers creepers / Piccolo Pete / Very thought of you / Continental / Temptation rag / Sweet Georgia Brown / Ain't misbehavin' / Play that hot guitar / Rockin' chair / That's a plenty / Zing went the strings of my heart / Tom Thumb's drum / Love is good for anything that ails you / Stompin' at the Savoy / Just one more chance / Man from the South
CD _____ CD PRO 3
Pasadena Roof Orchestra / Oct '91 / New Note.

COLLECTION: PASADENA ROOF ORCHESTRA
It don't mean a thing if it ain't got that swing / Bye bye blackbird / Black bottom / Charleston / Temptation rag / Blue skies / What is this thing called love / Lullaby of Broadway / Nobody's sweetheart / You're the cream in my coffee / Singin' in the rain / Top hat, white tie and tails / I won't dance / Three little words / Stormy weather / Don't be that way / I'll see you again / Pasadena / Georgia / Whispering / Paddlin' Madelin' home / Varsity drag / Here's to the next time / Cheek to cheek
CD _____ CCSCD 189
Castle / Jul '88 / BMG.

FIFTEEN YEARS ON
I can't dance / Yes yes (my baby says yes) / You took advantage of me / Varsity drag / Very thought of you / Casa loma stomp / Pasadena / Lambeth walk / Solitude / I heard / Don't bring Lulu / Ain't she sweet / Five foot two, eyes of blue / Charleston / Here's to the next time
CD _____ 825 649-2
Pasadena Roof Orchestra / May '87 / New Note.

HAPPY FEET
Happy feet / Nightingale sang in Berkeley Square / I got rhythm / Georgia on my mind / Cotton Club stomp / I'm crazy 'bout my baby / When it's sleepy time down South / Oh Donna Clara / Makin' wickey wackey down in Waikiki / Just squeeze me / Bei mir bist du schon
CD _____ CDPRO 1
Pasadena Roof Orchestra / Feb '88 / New Note.

PASADENA - THE 25TH ANNIVERSARY
You ought to see Sally on sunday / Lullaby of broadway / Old man river / By the fireside / Puttin' on the ritz / Kansas city kitty / Old man blues / Happy days are here again / Home in Pasadena / You're my everything / Me and Jane in a plane / I want to be happy / Maple leaf ray / Some of these days / As time goes by / St. Louis blues
CD _____ CDPRO 4
Pasadena Roof Orchestra / Mar '94 / New Note.

PASADENA ROOF ORCHESTRA GREATEST HITS
CD _____ CD 845006
Bluebird / Jan '94 / BMG.

PASADENA ROOF ORCHESTRA, THE
Pasadena / It don't mean a thing if it ain't got that swing / Isn't it romantic / Nagasaki / Singin' in the rain / Everything stops for tea / Mississipi mud / Cheek to cheek / Dream a little dream of me / Creole love call / Don't be that way / Sing, sing, sing / Shokiaan / Come on baby
CD _____ 8217452
Pasadena Roof Orchestra / May '87 / New Note.

SENTIMENTAL JOURNEY
CD _____ NCCD 110
Music Club / Jun '93 / Disc / THE / CM.

STEPPING OUT
Who walks in my melancholy baby / How 'm doin / Creole love call / Sahara / Skirts / Pennies from Heaven / Latin from Manhattan / Business in 'F' / I can't get started (with you) / Louisiana / Golden wedding / I only have eyes for you / Minnie the moocher / Stepping out / Pasadena
CD _____ CDPRO 2
Pasadena Roof Orchestra / Jan '90 / New Note.

Pasadenas

TO WHOM IT MAY CONCERN
Funny feeling / Living in the footsteps of another man / Enchanted lady / New love / Riding on a train / Give a little peace / Tribute (right on) / I really miss you / Justice for the world / Something else
CD _____ 4628772
Columbia / Oct '91 / Sony.

Pascoal, Hermann

PASCOAL (Pascoal, Hermann & Crupo)
CD _____ WWCD 009
West Wind / Oct '88 / Swift / Charly / CM / ADA.

Pascoal, Hermeto

BRAZIL ADVENTURE
CD _____ MCD 6006
Muse / Sep '92 / New Note / CM.

FESTA DOS DEUSES
CD _____ 5104072
Philips / May '93 / PolyGram.

Pass, Joe

APPASSIONATO
Relaxin' at Camarillo / Grooveyard / Body and soul / Nica's dream / Tenderly / When it's sleepy time down South / Red door / Gee baby ain't I good to you / Li'l darlin' / That's Earl brother / Stuffy / You're driving me crazy
CD _____ CD 2310946
Pablo / Apr '94 / Jazz Music / Cadillac / Complete/Pinnacle.

AT AKRON UNIVERSITY
It's a wonderful world / Body and soul / Bridgework / Tarde / Time in / Duke Ellington medley / Joy spring / I'm glad there's you
CD _____ CD 2308249
Pablo / May '94 / Jazz Music / Cadillac / Complete/Pinnacle.

BETTER DAYS
CD _____ EFA 120682
Hotwire / May '95 / SRD.

BLUES FOR FRED
Cheek to cheek / Night and day / Blues for Fred / Oh lady be good / Foggy day / Be myself / They can't take that away from me / Dancing in the dark / I concentrate on you / Way you look tonight
CD _____ CD 2310931
Pablo / Apr '94 / Jazz Music / Cadillac / Complete/Pinnacle.

CHECKMATE (Pass, Joe & Jimmy Rowles)
What's your story Morning Glory / So rare / As long as I live / Marquita / Stardust / We'll be together again / Can't we be friends / Deed I do / 'Tis Autumn / God bless the child
CD _____ CD 2310865
Pablo / May '94 / Jazz Music / Cadillac / Complete/Pinnacle.

CHOPS (Pass, Joe & Niels Pederson)
Have you met Miss Jones / Oleo / Lover man / Five pound blues / Come rain or come shine / Quiet nights / Tricotism / Old folks / Yardbird suite / Your own sweet way
CD _____ OJCCD 786-2
Original Jazz Classics / Jun '94 / Wellard / Jazz Music / Cadillac / Complete/Pinnacle.

EXIMIOUS (Pass, Joe Trio)
Foxy chick and a cool cat / Robbin's nest / Lush life / Serenata / We'll be together again / You to me are everything / Love for sale / Everything I got belongs to you / Night and day / Speak low
CD _____ CD 2310877
Pablo / Apr '87 / Jazz Music / Cadillac / Complete/Pinnacle.

I REMEMBER CHARLIE PARKER
Just friends / Easy to love / Summertime / April in Paris / Everything happens to me / Laura / They can't take that away from me / I didn't know what time it was / If I should lose you / Out of nowhere (concept 1) / Out of nowhere (concept 2)
CD _____ OJCCD 602
Original Jazz Classics / Nov '95 / Wellard / Jazz Music / Cadillac / Complete/Pinnacle.

IRA, GEORGE AND JOE (Joe Pass Loves Gershwin)
Bidin' my time / How long has this been going on / Soon / Lady be good / But not for me / Foggy day / It ain't necessarily so / Love is here to stay / 'S wonderful / Nice work if you can get it / Embraceable you
CD _____ OJCCD 8282
Original Jazz Classics / Jun '95 / Wellard / Jazz Music / Cadillac / Complete/Pinnacle.

JOY SPRING
Joy spring / Some time ago / Night that has a thousand eyes / Relaxin' at Camarillo / There is no greater love
CD _____ CDP 8352222
Pacific Jazz / Jan '96 / EMI.

LIVE AT DONTE'S (Pass, Joe Trio)
What have they done to my song Ma / You stepped out of a dream / Time for love / Donte's inferno / You are the sunshine of my life / Secret love / Sweet Georgia Brown / Stompin' at the Savoy / Dam that dream / Milestones / Lullaby of the leaves / What are you doing the rest of your life / Blues for Pam
CD _____ CD 2620114
Pablo / Apr '87 / Jazz Music / Cadillac / Complete/Pinnacle.

LIVE AT LONG BEACH COLLEGE
Wave / Blues in G / All the things you are / Round Midnight / Here's that rainy day / Duke Ellington's sophisticated lady melange / Blues dues / Bluesette / Honeysuckle rose
CD _____ CD 2308239
Pablo / Apr '87 / Jazz Music / Cadillac / Complete/Pinnacle.

MY SONG
Telarc / Aug '93 / Conifer / ADA.
CD _____ CD 83326

ONE FOR MY BABY
Bluesology / One for my baby (and one more for the road) / J.P. blues / Poinciana / I don't stand a ghost of a chance with you / I remember you / Bay city blues / Song is you
CD _____ CD 2310936
Pablo / May '94 / Jazz Music / Cadillac / Complete/Pinnacle.

PORTRAITS OF DUKE ELLINGTON
Satin doll / I let a song go out of my heart / Sophisticated lady / I got it bad and that ain't good / In a mellow tone / Solitude / Don't get around much anymore / Do nothin' 'til you hear from me / Caravan
CD _____ CD 20027
Pablo / May '86 / Jazz Music / Cadillac / Complete/Pinnacle.

SUMMER NIGHTS
Summer nights / Anouman / Douce ambience / For Django / D-Joe / I got rhythm / E blue eyes / Belleville / In my solitude / Tears / In a sentimental mood / Them there eyes
CD _____ CD 2310939
Pablo / Apr '94 / Jazz Music / Cadillac / Complete/Pinnacle.

VIRTUOSO
Night and day / Stella by starlight / Here's that rainy day / My old flame / How high the moon / Cherokee / Sweet Lorraine / Have you met Miss Jones / Round Midnight / All the things you are / Blues for Alican / Song is you
CD _____ CD 2310708
Pablo / May '94 / Jazz Music / Cadillac / Complete/Pinnacle.

VIRTUOSO LIVE
Stompin' at the Savoy / Just the way you are / Eric's smoozies blues / Beautiful love / Daquilo que eu sei / In the wee small hours of the morning / Love for sale / Mack the knife / So what's new / (Back home again in) Indiana
CD _____ CD 2310948
Pablo / Jul '94 / Jazz Music / Cadillac / Complete/Pinnacle.

WHITESTONE
Light in your eyes / Shuffle city / Estate / Daquilo que eu sei / Whitestone / Lovin' eyes / Amancer / I can't help it / Tarde / Fleeting moments
CD _____ CD 2310912
Pablo / May '94 / Jazz Music / Cadillac / Complete/Pinnacle.

Passaggio

PASSAGGIO (QUINTET CELEA COUTURIER)
L'Ibere / Lucculus / Arno / Ole rafafa / Gala / Norvegian flamenco / Hip / Warm canto / Hep / My foolish heart / Tabato / L'autre
CD _____ LBLC 6567
Label Bleu / Nov '95 / New Note.

Passion Fodder

FAT TUESDAY
Extra extra / I.O.U. / So this is love / My world is empty without you / I want it to be real / Dream / Move / Luz blanca / St. Helens / Heart hunters / Mardi gras / Skin poetry / In the echo / Hot waltz away / In the moodswing / Hard work / As you dig your hole / Tomorrow is a long time (MC only) / Paname song / Violations (MC only) / Dirt (MC only) / God couldn't fight his way out of a wet brown bag
CD _____ BBL 83CD
Beggars Banquet / Feb '90 / Warner Music / Disc.

LOVE, WALTZES AND ANARCHY
Polished off / Pascal's waltz / Kill me Hannah / Hunger burns / Orwell cooks / Spokane / Struggle for love / Pray, anarchist / Girl that I marry
CD _____ BBL 94CD
Beggars Banquet / '92 / Warner Music / Disc.

WOKE UP THIS MORNING
Little wolf / My body betrays me she said / Happy new year / Letter from '38 / Man is a man / Love burns / Los Cuatro / Between ten and noon / Ventoline blues / I'd sell my soul to God
CD _____ BBL 105CD
Beggars Banquet / '92 / Warner Music / Disc.

Passos, Monica

CASAMENTO
CD _____ FPC 100
EMP / Nov '93 / Harmonia Mundi.

Pastels

MOBILE SAFARI
CD _____ WIGCD 17
Domino / Feb '95 / Pinnacle.

SUCK ON THE PASTELS
CD _____ CRELP 031CD
Creation / Jul '88 / 3MV / Vital.

TRUCKLOAD OF TROUBLE
CD _____ PAPCD 008
Paperhouse / Jun '93 / Disc.

Pastor, Guy

ITS MAGIC
CD _____ USACD 584
USA / Feb '89 / Charly / Jazz Music.

Pastor, Tony

TONY PASTOR & ORCHESTRA 1941-45
CD _____ CCD 31
Circle / Aug '95 / Jazz Music / Swift / Wellard.

TONY PASTOR & ORCHESTRA 1945-1950
CD _____ CCD 121
Circle / Aug '95 / Jazz Music / Swift / Wellard.

Pastorius, Jaco

HOLIDAY FOR PANS
CD _____ SSCD 8001
Sound Hills / Feb '94 / Harmonia Mundi / Cadillac.

HONESTLY
CD _____ CDJP 1032
Jazz Point / Nov '91 / Harmonia Mundi.

JACO (Pastorius, Jaco/Metheney/Ditmas/Bley)
CD _____ 1238462
IAI / Feb '93 / Harmonia Mundi / Cadillac.

JACO PASTORIUS
Donna Lee / Come on come over / Continuum / Kuru/Speak like a child / Portrait of Tracy / Opus pocus / Okonkole y trompa / (Used to be a) cha-cha / Forgotten love
CD _____ CD 81453
Sony Jazz / Jan '95 / Sony.

JAZZ STREET (Pastorius, Jaco & Brian Melvin)
No oback / Miles modes / Wedding waltz / Drums of Yadzarah / Jazz Street / May day / Out of the night
CD _____ CDSJP 258
Timeless Jazz / Jun '89 / New Note.

LIVE IN ITALY
CD _____ CDJP 1031
Jazz Point / Nov '91 / Harmonia Mundi / Cadillac.

Pate, Johnny

AT THE BLUE NOTE
CD _____ PS 008CD
P&S / Sep '95 / Discovery.

Pathologist

GRINDING OPUS OF FORENSIC MEDICAL PROBLEMS
CD _____ MAB 008
MAB / May '95 / Plastic Head.

PUTREFACTIVE AND CADAVEROUS ODES ABOUT NECROTICISM
CD _____ MABCD 002
Plastic Head / Jun '93 / Plastic Head.

Patinkin, Mandy

DRESS CASUAL
Doodle doodle doo (medley) / On the Atchison, Topeka and the Santa Fe / Bein' green / Triplets / I'm always chasing rainbows / Evening primrose / Pal Joey (suite) / Sorry grateful / Being alive / Ya got trouble (in River City) / Giants in the sky / Mr. Arthur's place / Yossel, yossel / Hollywood (medley)
CD _____ CD 45998
Columbia / May '91 / Sony.

EXPERIMENT
CD _____ 7559793302
Elektra Nonesuch / Jul '95 / Warner Music.

MANDY PATINKIN
Over the rainbow / Coffee in a cardboard cup / Pretty lady / Brother can you spare a dime / Love unrequited / No more / Me and my shadow / No one is alone / Sonny boy / Rock-a-bye your baby with a Dixie melody / Casey (medley) / And the band played on / Marie / Once upon a time / Anyone can whistle / Soliloquy / I'll be seeing you / There's a rainbow 'round my shoulder / Top hat, white tie and tails / Puttin' on the ritz / Alexander's ragtime band / Swanee / My mammy / Handful of keys / Pennies from Heaven
CD _____ CD 44943
CBS / Apr '89 / Sony

Patino, Deborah

NOCTURNAL
CD _____ NAR 081CD
SST / Mar '95 / Plastic Head.

Patitucci, John

ANOTHER WORLD
Ivory coast #2 / Ivory coast #4 / Another world / My summer vacation / Soho steel / I saw you / Hold that thought / Norwegian sun / Griot / Showtime / Peace prayer / Shanachie / Till then / Ivory coast / Ivory coast #3
CD _____ GRP 97252
GRP / Aug '93 / BMG / New Note.

HEART OF THE BASS
Concerto for jazz bass and orchestra / Heart of the bass / Four hands / Mullagh / Bach prelude in G major / Miniatures for solo bass
CD _____ GRS 10012
GRP / Aug '92 / BMG / New Note.

MISTURA FINA
Mistura fina / Bate balaio / Puccini / Samba nova / Four loves / Assim nao da / Joys and sorrows / Aqua mae agua / Soul song / Varadero / love story / Barra da Tijuca (Tijuca bay) / Samba school
CD _____ GRP 98022
GRP / Mar '95 / BMG / New Note.

SKETCHBOOK
Spaceships / Joab / If you don't mind / Songville / Greatest gift / From a rainy night / Junk man / Two worlds / Backwoods / They heard it twice / Trane / Through the clouds
CD _____ GRP 96172
GRP / Aug '90 / BMG / New Note.

Patto

QUEEN OF THE PACK
Hardcore side / Hardcore / Think (about it) / Queen of the pack / Poor people's song / Wok the money / Romantic call / Cool-running side / Woman war / Sexual feeling / Be protected / Whining skill / Knock knock / In the mood
CD _____ 474184 2
Epic / Oct '93 / Sony.

SCENT OF ATTRACTION
Pull up to the bumper / Dip and fall back / Hot stuff / Banana / Mek me hot / Scent of attraction / Goin' 2 the chapel / Time fi wine / Undercover lover / You want it / Deep inside
CD _____ 4807052
Epic / Oct '95 / Sony.

Patrick Street

ALL IN GOOD TIME
Walsh's polkas / Prince among men (Only a miner) / Frank Quinn's reel / Lintheads / Pride of the Springfield Road / Lawrence Common / Goodbye Monday blues / Light and airy/All in good time / Mouth of Tobique/Billy Wilson / Girls along the road / Thames hornpipe / Fairy Queen / Dennis Murphy's reel/Bag of spuds/MacFarley's reel / Carrowclare / Lynch's barndances
CD _____ SPDCD 1049
Special Delivery / Apr '93 / ADA / CM / Direct.

ALL IN GOOD TIME
CD _____ GLCD 1125
Green Linnet / Oct '93 / Roots / CM / Direct / ADA.

BEST OF PATRICK STREET
CD _____ NTMCD 503
Nectar / Jun '95 / Pinnacle.

IRISH TIMES
CD _____ SPCD 1033
Special Delivery / Mar '90 / ADA / CM / Direct.

IRISH TIMES
CD _____ GLCD 1105
Green Linnet / May '95 / Roots / CM / Direct / ADA.

NO.2 PATRICK STREET
John McKenna's jigs / Braes of Moneymore / Hard by Seifin/Woodcock Hill / Tom Joad / Benton's jig/Benton's dream / William Taylor / Caherlistrane/Gallowglass/Kanturk jigs / Facing the chair / Sweeney's reel
CD _____ GLCD 1088
Green Linnet / Feb '90 / Roots / CM / Direct / ADA.

PATRICK STREET
CD _____ GLCD 1071
Green Linnet / Apr '88 / Roots / CM / Direct / ADA.

PATRICK STREET/ALL IN GOOD TIME
CD _____ 5016272104921
Special Delivery / Apr '93 / ADA / CM / Direct.

Patrick, David M.

GREAT EUROPEAN ORGANS NO. 28 (Plays the Organ of Blackburn Cathedral)
CD _____ PRCD 371
Priory / Jul '92 / Priory.

Patrick, Johnny

GIRL FROM IPANEMA, THE
CD _____ MATCD 243
Castle / Nov '93 / BMG.

HAMMOND ORGAN HITS
CD _____ MATCD 243
Castle / Mar '93 / BMG.

Patterson, Bobby

I GET MY GROOVE FROM YOU
I get my groove from you / Make sure you get the pick / Everything good to you (don't have to be good for you) / How do you spell love / Recipe for peace / She don't have to see you (to see through you) / Right on Jody / Quiet, do not disturb / I just love you because I wanted to / One ounce of prevention / Whole funky world is a ghetto / What goes around comes around / It takes two to do wrong / Take time to know the truth / I'm the wrong / If love can't do it (it can't be done) / I got a suspicion / Right place, wrong time
CD _____ CPCD 8123
Charly / Oct '95 / Charly / THE / Cadillac.

TAKING CARE OF BUSINESS
Till you give in / You just got to understand / What's your problem baby / If I didn't have you / Long ago / Soul is our music / Let them talk / Sock some lovin' at me / I'm Leroy, I'll take her / Broadway ain't funky no more / I met my match / Don't be so mean / Good ol' days / Busy busy bee / Sweet taste of love / T.C.B. or T.Y.A. / What a wonderful night for love / My thing is your thing / Keeping it in the family / My baby's coming back to me / Guess who / Knockout power of love / Trial of Mary McGuire / If a man ever loved a woman / You taught me how to love / I'm in love with you / Married lady / If I didn't know better / Who wants to fall in love
CD _____ CDKEND 098
Kent / Apr '91 / Pinnacle.

Patterson, Jordan

GIVE ME A CHANCE
Funky thang / Those pretty eyes / Life of misery / No educated woman / Thing I do for you / Black hole / Give me a chance / Your love is killing me / Fast lane / Natural
CD _____ JSPCD 263
JSP / Nov '95 / ADA / Target/BMG / Cadillac / Complete/Pinnacle.

Patterson, Kellee

KELLEE
CD _____ HUBCD 3
Hubbub / Oct '95 / SRD / BMG.

Patterson, Ottilie

BACK IN THE OLD DAYS (Patterson, Ottilie & Chris Barber)
Hot time in the old town tonight / Lordy Lord / Basin Street blues / T'aint what you do / Bad spell blues / Squeeze me
CD _____ CBJBCD 4001
Chris Barber Collection / Apr '88 / New Note / Cadillac.

OTTILIE PATTERSON & CHRIS BARBER'S JAZZBAND 1955-58
CD _____ LA 30CD
Lake / Oct '93 / Target/BMG / Jazz Music / Direct / Cadillac / ADA.

Patto

SENSE OF THE ABSURD
Hold your fire / You, you point your finger / How's your Father / See you at the dance tonight / Give it all away / Air raid shelter / Tell me where you've been / Magic door / Beat the drum / Bad news / Man / Hold me back / Time to die / San Antone / Red glow / Government man / Money bag / Sittin' back easy / Hanging rope
CD _____ 5286962
Mercury / Oct '95 / PolyGram.

Patton, Big John

BLUE PLANET MAN
Congo chant / Popeye / Funky Mama / What's your name / Claudette / U-Jama / Chip / Bama
CD _____ KICJ 168
King/Paddle Wheel / Nov '93 / New Note.

ORGANISATION - BEST OF BIG JOHN PATTON
Along came John / Silver meter / Bermuda clay house / Hot sauce / Fat Judy / Amanda / Turnaround / Latona / Footprints / Jerry (CD only) / Chitting com came (CD only) / Freedom jazz dance (CD only) / Ain't that peculiar (LP only) / Barefootin' (LP only) / Dirty fingers (LP only) / Man from Tanganyika (LP only) / Memphis (LP only)
CD _____ CDP 8307282
Blue Note / Sep '94 / EMI.

Patton, Charlie

CHARLIE PATTON, VOL 1 (1929)
CD _____ DOCD 5009
Blues Document / Feb '92 / Swift / Jazz Music / Hot Shot.

CHARLIE PATTON, VOL 2 (1929)
CD _____ DOCD 5010
Blues Document / Feb '92 / Swift / Jazz Music / Hot Shot.

CHARLIE PATTON, VOL 3 (1929 - 1934)
CD _____ DOCD 5011
Blues Document / Feb '92 / Swift / Jazz Music / Hot Shot.

FOUNDER OF DELTA BLUES
CD _____ YAZCD 2010
Yazoo / Apr '95 / CM / ADA / Roots / Koch.

REMAINING TITLES 1929-34
CD _____ WSECD 103
Wolf / Nov '90 / Jazz Music / Swift / Hot Shot.

Patton, John

BOOGALOO
Boogaloo / Milk and honey / Barefootin' / Shoutin' but not poutin' / Spirit / B and J (two sisters)
CD _____ CDP 8318782
Blue Note / Apr '95 / EMI.

UNDERSTANDING
Ding dong / Congo chant / Alfie's theme / Soul man / Understanding / Chitlins con carne
CD _____ CDP 8312232
Blue Note / Mar '95 / EMI.

Pattullo, Gordon

GOLDEN SOUND OF SCOTTISH MUSIC FROM STARS PAST AND PRESENT
CD _____ CDGR 149
Ross / Jun '95 / Ross / Duncans.

SCOTTISH ACCORDION HITS
Sailor's hornpipe / College hornpipe / Lowe's hornpipe / Chester hornpipe / Trumpet hornpipe / Cuckoo waltz / Painter's choice / Para handy / Miss Suzanne Barbour / Jean's fancy / Boys of the Lough / Tony Reid of Balnakilly / Mist covered mountains of home / Alpine holiday / New ashludie rant / Elizabeth Adair / Princess Margaret's jig / Jimmy Stephen / Lochanside / Battle's o'er / Heather bells / Happy hours polka / Dashing white sergeant / Lord Saltoun / Catchin' rabbits / Inchmickery / Misty islands of the highlands / Crossing the minch / Banjo breakdown / Les triolets / Dark island / Pigeon pie / Moors of Perth / Shufflin' Samuel/Whistling Rufus / Memories of Willie snaith of Hexham / Dancing fingers
CD _____ GRCD 57
Grasmere / Jun '93 / Target/BMG / Savoy.

Paul

PAUL
CD _____ GRAVITYCD 2
Sugar / Sep '95 / Disc.

Paul & Margie

TWENTY BEST FOLK SONGS OF AMERICA
CD _____ EUCD 1202
ARC / Sep '93 / ARC Music / ADA.

Paul, Billy

360 DEGREES OF BILLY PAUL
Brown baby / I'm just a prisoner / It's too late / Me and Mrs. Jones / Am I black

enough for you / Let's stay together / Your song / I'm gonna make it this time
CD _____ 983378 2
Carlton Home Entertainment / Feb '94 / Carlton Home Entertainment.

FIRST CLASS
CD _____ KWEST 5405
Disky / Mar '93 / THE / BMG / Discovery / Pinnacle.

LATELY
Fire in her love / Sexual therapy / Lately / I search no more / I only have eyes for you / Hot date / Get down to lovin' / Let me in / Me and you / On a clear day
CD _____ FL 85711
Total Experience / Sep '85 / PolyGram.

WIDE OPEN
CD _____ CDICH 1025
Ichiban / Sep '88 / Koch.

Paul, Bollenback

ORIGINAL VISIONS
CD _____ CHR 70022
Challenge / Sep '95 / Direct / Jazz Music / Cadillac / ADA.

Paul, Frankie

20 MASSIVE HITS
CD _____ SONCD 0008
Sonic Sounds / Oct '90 / Jetstar.

BACK TO THE ROOTS
CD _____ RNCD 2043
Rhino / Apr '94 / Jetstar / Magnum Music Group / THE.

CAN'T GET YOU OUT OF MY MIND
CD _____ RRTGCD 7780
Rohit / Jul '90 / Jetstar.

DANCE HALL DUO (Paul, Frankie & Pinchers)
CD _____ RASCD 3237
Ras / Aug '88 / Jetstar / Greensleeves / SRD / Direct.

DON MAN
CD _____ HBCD 146
Greensleeves / Sep '93 / Total/BMG / Jetstar / SRD.

F.P. THE GREATEST
CD _____ FADCD 025
Fashion / Sep '92 / Jetstar / Grapevine.

FIRE DEH A MUS MUS TAIL
CD _____ BDCD 001
Greensleeves / Nov '92 / Total/BMG / Jetstar / SRD.

FOREVER
CD _____ RNCD 2128
Rhino / Nov '95 / Jetstar / Magnum Music Group / THE.

FREEDOM
CD _____ CRCD 46
Charm / Nov '95 / Jetstar.

I'VE GOT THE VIBES
CD _____ DBTXCD 3
Digital B / Nov '95 / Jetstar.

IF YOU WANT ME GIRL
CD _____ CDTRL 354
Trojan / Jun '95 / Jetstar / Total/BMG.

LOVE LINE
CD _____ GGCD 003
Glory Gold / Jun '89 / Jetstar.

PASS THE TU-SHENG-PENG/TIDAL WAVE
CD _____ GRELCD 502
Greensleeves / '88 / Total/BMG / Jetstar / SRD.

SHOULD I
CD _____ CDHB 113
Heartbeat / Feb '92 / Greensleeves / Jetstar / Direct / ADA.

SLOW DOWN
CD _____ VPCD 1034
VP / Apr '89 / Jetstar.

TALK ALL YOU WANT
CD _____ VPCD 1363
VP / Aug '94 / Jetstar.

TIMELESS
CD _____ TYCD 003
Tan Yah / Oct '92 / Jetstar.

TURBO CHARGE (Paul, Frankie & Pinchers)
I need you / Kuff / Chat mi back / Life is a gamble / Traveller / I'm in love again / Musical calamity / Memories of love
CD _____ SUPCD 1
Super Supreme / Mar '89 / Jetstar.

WARNING
Tato / Tickle me / Don't pressure me / Raggamuffin / Hungry belly / Warning / She's a maniac / Give me what we want / Rock you / Lady love
CD _____ RASCD 3027
Ras / Nov '87 / Jetstar / Greensleeves / SRD / Direct.

Paul, Les

CAPITOL YEARS: LES PAUL AND MARY FORD (Best of) (Paul, Les & Mary Ford)
Whispering / World is waiting for the sunrise / Lover / Mockin' Bird Hill / Nola / That old feeling / Little Rock getaway / Bye bye blues / Twelfth St. rag / I'm sitting on top of the world / Chicken reel / How high the moon / Walkin' and whistlin' blues / How deep is the ocean / Tico-tico / Vaya con dios
CD _____ CDEMS 1309
Capitol / Jan '89 / EMI.

WORLD IS WAITING FOR THE SUNRISE, THE (Paul, Les & Mary Ford)
CD _____ 15436
Laserlight / Jan '93 / Target/BMG.

Paulsen, Ralf

JUBILAUMS AUSGABE
CD _____ 15126
Laserlight / Aug '91 / Target/BMG.

Pauly, Danielle

FLEUR DU JURA
Reve gourmand (Waltz) / L'epatante (Polka) / Ballade matinale (March) / Delice Catalan (Tango) / Rapide digitale (Polka) / Carte postale (Waltz) / Ballade Vosgienne (Polka) / Clin d'oeil (Java) / File Indienne (March) / Piccolo rag (Rag) / Fleur du Jura (Polka) / Exotic samba (Samba) / Souffle Andalou (Tango) / Matin tonique (Not a military march,more suited to bombing along a m-way at an early hr) / Eclats de rire (Novelty foxtrot) / Melody bolero (Bolero) / Valse des lucioles (Waltz)
CD _____ CDSDL 353
Saydisc / Mar '94 / Harmonia Mundi / ADA / Direct.

Pausini, Laura

LAURA PAUSINI
CD _____ 4509998852
East West / Jun '95 / Warner Music.

Pavement

CROOKED RAIN, CROOKED RAIN
CD _____ ABB 56CD
Big Cat / Aug '95 / SRD / Pinnacle.

SLANTED AND ENCHANTED
CD _____ ABB 34CD
Big Cat / Aug '95 / SRD / Pinnacle.

WESTING (BY MUSKET AND SEXTANT)
CD _____ ABB 40CD
Big Cat / Aug '95 / SRD / Pinnacle.

WOWEE ZOWEE
We dance / Rattled by the rush / Black out / Brinks job / Grounded / Serpentine pal / Motion suggest itself / Lovermont / Extradition / Best friends arm / Grve architecture / At and T / Flux rad / Fight this generation / Kennel district / Spanos country rag / Half a canyon / Western homes
CD _____ ABB 84CD
Big Cat / Apr '95 / SRD / Pinnacle.

Pavlov's Dog

PAMPERED MENIAL
Julia / Late November / Song dance / Fast gun / Natchez trace / Subway Sue / Episode / Preludin / Of once and future kings
CD _____ 4690852
Columbia / Feb '95 / Sony.

Pavone, Mario

TOULON DAYS
CD _____ 804202
New World / Sep '92 / Harmonia Mundi / ADA / Cadillac.

Paw

DEATH TO TRAITORS
CD _____ 5403912
A&M / Aug '95 / PolyGram.

DRAGLINE
Gasoline / Sleeping bag / Jessie / Bridge / Couldn't know / Pansy / Lolita / Dragline / Veronica / One more bottle / Sugarcane / Hard pig
CD _____ 540 065-2
A&M / Mar '94 / PolyGram.

Pax

MAY GOD...
CD _____ HBG 123/4
Background / Apr '94 / Background.

Paxarino, Javier

TEMURA - THE MYSTERY OF SILENCE
Conductus mundi / Cortesanos / Preludio y danza / Canto del viento / Suspiro del moro / Reuda de juglar / Tierra baja / Reyes y reinas / Temura / Mater aurea
CD _____ 892172
Act / Oct '94 / New Note.

Paxton, Tom

AND LOVING YOU
Last hobo / Nothing but time / Home to me / Love changes the world / Missing you / You are love / And lovin' you / Every time / Bad old days / Panhandle wind / When we were good / All coming together
CD _____ FF 70414
Flying Fish / Jul '95 / Roots / CM / Direct / ADA.

EVEN A GREY DAY
Even a grey day / I give you the morning / Love of loving you / When Annie took me home / Dance in the shadows / Annie's going to sing her song / Corrymeela / Outward bound / Wish I had a troubador / Hold on to me babe / Last thing on my mind
CD _____ FF 70280
Flying Fish / Jul '95 / Roots / CM / Direct / ADA.

IT AIN'T EASY
CD _____ FF 70574
Flying Fish / Jul '95 / Roots / CM / Direct / ADA.

ONE MILLION LAWYERS AND OTHER DISASTERS
CD _____ FF 70356
Flying Fish / Jul '95 / Roots / CM / Direct / ADA.

POLITICS - LIVE
CD _____ FF 70486
Flying Fish / Jul '95 / Roots / CM / Direct / ADA.

STORYTELLER
CD _____ STFCD 4
Start / Dec '89 / Koch.

VERY BEST OF TOM PAXTON
CD _____ FF 70519
Flying Fish / Jul '95 / Roots / CM / ADA / Direct.

WEARING THE TIME
CD _____ SHCD 1045
Sugarhill / Oct '94 / Roots / CM / ADA / Direct.

Paycheck, Johnny

GREATEST HITS: JOHNNY PAYCHECK
Take this job and shove it / Slide off your satin sheets / Somebody loves me / Motel time again / In memory of memory / Mr. Love maker / A11 / She's all I got For a minute there / Only hell my mama ever raised / Loving you beats all I ever seen / Song and dance man / Keep on lovin' me / Jukebox Charlie / Something about you I love / Someone to give my love to / Green green grass of home / Don't monkey with another monkey's monkey / Heaven's almost as big as Texas / Close all the honky tonks / Almost persuaded / Release me / All the time / Crazy arms / Heartaches by the number / Apartment no. 9
CD _____ CDGRF 070
Tring / Feb '93 / Tring / Prism.

SURVIVOR
Buried treasures / He left it all / I.Q. blues / I can't quit drinkin' / Everything is changing / OI pay ain't checked out yet / Palimony / You're every step I take / I never got over you / I'm a survivor
CD _____ VD 102
Dixie Frog / Sep '90 / Magnum Music Group.

TAKE THIS JOB AND SHOVE IT
Take this job and shove it / From cotton to satin / Spirits of St. Louis / 4 F blues / Barstool Mountain / Georgia in a jug / Fool strikes again / Man from Bowling Green / When I had a home to go to / Colorado cool aid
CD _____ 15483
Laserlight / May '93 / Target/BMG.

Payne, Cecil

CASBAH
CD _____ STCD 572
Stash / Mar '94 / Jazz Music / CM / Cadillac / Direct / ADA.

CERUPA
CD _____ DE 478
Delmark / Aug '95 / Hot Shot / ADA / CM / Direct / Cadillac.

PATTERNS OF JAZZ
This time the dream's on me / How deep is the ocean / Chessman's delight / Arnetta / Saucer eyes / Man of moods / Bringing up Father / Groovin' high
CD _____ SV 0135
Savoy Jazz / Apr '94 / Conifer / ADA.

ZODIAC - THE MUSIC OF CECIL PAYNE
Martin Luther King, Jr. - I know love / Girl, you got a home / Slide Hampton / Follow me / Flying fish
CD _____ 66051021
Strata East / Aug '93 / New Note.

Payne, Freda

DEEPER AND DEEPER - THE BEST OF FREDA PAYNE

Unhooked generation / I left some dreams back there / Rock me in the cradle of love / Cherish what is dear to you / Mama's gone goodbye / Bring the boys home / You brought the joy / I'm not getting any better / You've got to love somebody / Road we didn't take / He's my life / Band of gold / Deeper and deeper / Easiest way to fall / Now is the time to say goodbye / Just a woman / Through the memory of my mind / World don't owe you a thing / Suddenly it's yesterday / How can I live without my life / Odds and ends / You're the only bargain I've got
CD _____ HDH CD 005
HDH / Aug '89 / Pinnacle.

Payne, Jack

I'LL STRING ALONG WITH YOU
This'll make you whistle / My song for you / Tina / I'll string along with you / Little valley in the mountains / Over my shoulder / Guilty / Isle of Capri / Close your eyes / Until the real thing comes along / Nun-yuff and sun-yuff / Juba / Organ grinder swing / Shadows on the pavement / When your hair has turned to silver / When it's springtime in the Rockies / Just imagine / Sunny days
CD _____ 2 BUR 008
Burlington / Sep '88 / CM.

Payne, Jimmy

NEW YORK FUNK VOL I
Streets of New York / She's a reptile / Bathtub club / Love letters / Bone dance / Talking chicken / Oh the walrath / Waiting for you / Bottom line / Planet X / Far from home / Last chance
CD _____ GCD 79489
Gramavision / Dec '95 / Vital/SAM / ADA.

NEW YORK FUNK VOL II
CD _____ GCD 79504
Gramavision / Dec '95 / Vital/SAM / ADA.

Payton, Nicholas

FROM THIS MOMENT
CD _____ 5270732
Verve / May '95 / PolyGram.

Payvar, Faramarz

PERSIAN HERITAGE, A (Classical Music Of Iran) (Payvar, Faramarz Ensemble & Khatereh Parvaneh)
CD _____ 7559720602
Elektra Nonesuch / Jan '95 / Warner Music.

Paz

BEST OF PAZ, THE
AC-DC-3 / Time stood still / Laying eggs / Yours is the light / Crotales / Iron works / Bell tree / Buddha
CD _____ SPJCD 554
Spotlite / Oct '95 / Cadillac / Jazz Horizons / Swift.

LOVE IN PEACE
CD _____ CHECD 00102
Master Mix / Jan '92 / Wellard / Jazz Music / New Note.

MESSAGE, THE
Xenon / Message / Party / Citron presse / Slide time / Nylon stockings
CD _____ CDCHE 6
Master Mix / Aug '89 / Wellard / Jazz Music / New Note.

PEACE IS LOVE
Kandeen love song / Look inside / Amour em Paz / Dream sequence / Singing bowl / I can't remember / Bags
CD _____ CDCHE 102
Master Mix / Dec '91 / Wellard / Jazz Music / New Note.

Pazuzu

AND ALL WAS SILENT
CD _____ HNF 004CD
Head Not Found / Oct '95 / Plastic Head.

PD31 Syncopated

DOES ANYBODY KNOW WHY
CD _____ PDCD 001
Scratch / Oct '94 / BMG.

Peace, Love & Pitbulls

PEACE LOVE AND PITBULLS
(I'm the) Radio king kong / Dog church / Be my T.V. / Reverberation nation / Elektrik '93 / What's wrong / Nutopia / Futurehead / This is trash / Psycho / Hitch hike to Mars (remix)
CD _____ BIAS 238CD
Play It Again Sam / Apr '93 / Vital.

RED SONIC UNDERWEAR
Itch / Das neue konzept / Warzaw / 2000 Ways of gettin' drunk / G.O.D. (on vacation) / Animals / His head is spinnin' off / Good morning / War in my livin' room / Discussing the artist in pain / Pig machine / Skinny and white / Other life form / Complete guide (imitating a bulldozer) / Endless masturbation
CD _____ BIAS 291CD
Play It Again Sam / Oct '94 / Vital.

Peach

GIVING BIRTH TO A STONE
CD _____ MADMIN 009CD
Mad Minute / May '94 / Pinnacle / Disc.

Peacock, Annette

ABSTRACT CONTACT
CD _____ IRONIC 5CD
Ironic / Aug '88 / Cadillac.

I HAVE NO FEELINGS
Nothing ever was, anyway / Butterflies / I'm not perfect / I have no feelings / Cynic / Carousel / You've left me / Sincereless / Freefall / This almost spring / Feeling's free / Personal revolution / Not enough
CD _____ IRONIC 4CD
Ironic / Feb '86 / Cadillac.

SKY-SKATING
CD _____ IRONIC 2CD
Ironic / Jul '89 / Cadillac.

Peacock, Gary

GUAMBA
Guamba / Requiem / Celina / Thyme time / Lila / Introending / Gardenia
CD _____ 8330392
ECM / Oct '87 / New Note.

ORACLE (Peacock, Gary & Ralph Towner)
CD _____ ECM 1490
ECM / Jun '94 / New Note.

RALPH TOWNER/ORACLE
Gaya / Flutter step / Empty carrousel / Inside inside / St. Helens / Oracle / Burly hello / Palermo ballad
CD _____ 5213502
ECM / Feb '94 / New Note.

SHIFT IN THE WIND
So green / Fractions / Last first / Shift in the wind centers / Caverns beneath the zoth / Valentine
CD _____ 8201592
ECM / Aug '86 / New Note.

TALES OF ANOTHER
Vignette / Tone field / Major / Trilogy / Trilogy (II) / Trilogy (III)
CD _____ 8274182
ECM / Feb '86 / New Note.

Pearce, Alison

MY LAGAN LOVE (AND OTHER SONGS OF IRELAND) (Pearce, Alison & Susan Drake)
Castle of Dromore / She moved through the fair / Next market day / Gartan mothers lullaby / I have a bonnet trimmed with blue / Little boats / I will walk with my love / Star of the County Down
CD _____ CDH 88023
Helios / May '89 / Select.

SONGS OF THE HEBRIDES (Pearce, Alison & Susan Drake)
Isle of my heart / Leaping galley / Spinning song / Sea longing / Crone's reel / Caristiona / Ullapool sailor's song / Eriskay lullaby / Reiving ships / O heartling of my heart / Birlinn of the white shoulders / Islay reapers' song / Ailein Duinn / Ship at sea / Loch Broom love song / Kirsteen / Sea wandering / Uncanny mannikin of the cattlefold / Death farewell
CD _____ CDH 88024
Helios / Feb '89 / Select.

Pearce, Bob

KEEP ON KEEPIN' ON
CD _____ TRCD 9913
Tramp / Apr '93 / Direct / ADA / CM.

Pearce, Dick

BIG HIT
CD _____ FMRCD 17
Future / Aug '95 / Harmonia Mundi / ADA.

Pearce, Ian

IAN PEARCE/PAUL FURNISS/S. GRANT
CD _____ TLACD 03
Tasmanian Jazz Composers / Mar '95 / Jazz Music.

Pearce, Monty

COUNTRY STYLE MIX
Blanket on the ground/'57 chevrolet / Seven lonely days/Anytime/Quicksilver / There goes my everything/Are you lonesome tonight / Hasta luego/Marcheta / I love you because/Just out of reach / Stand by your man / I'm a fool to care/I can't stop loving you / Distant drums/Nobody's darlin' but mine / Help me make it through the night/Make the world go away / South of the border/Mexicali rose / Angelo / Tango tears from your eyes / Anna Marie/Oh! How I miss you tonight / It the world stopped loving/Love me tender / Room full of roses/Someday (You'll want me to want you) / My grandfather's clock / Sioux City Sue/You are my sunshine / Pistol packin' mama/The yellow rose of Texas / Blue bayou / Rosanna

CD _____ SAV 176CD
Savoy / Jul '92 / THE / Savoy.

EASY DANCING
CD _____ SAV 186CD
Savoy / May '93 / THE / Savoy.

EASY DANCING 5
CD _____ SAV 237CD
Savoy / Dec '95 / THE / Savoy.

KING OF THE ROAD
Heartaches by the number / Shades of gold / Crystal chandeliers / Welcome to my world / King of the road / One has my name (the other has my heart) / Hello Mary Lou / Oh Lonesome me / I love you so much it hurts / After all these years / From a Jack to a King / Candy kisses / Take these chains from my heart
CD _____ SAV 182CD
Savoy / Feb '93 / THE / Savoy.

Pearl Jam

TEN
Once / Even flow / Alive / Why go / Black / Jeremy / Oceans / Porch / Garden / Deep / Release / Master/Slave
Epic / Feb '92 / Sony.
CD _____ 4688842

VITALOGY
Last exit / Spin the black circle / Not for you / Tremor Christ / Nothingman / Whipping / Pry, To / Corduroy / Bugs / Satan's bed / Better man / Ave davanita (LP only) / Immortality (LP only) / Stupid mop (LP only)
CD _____ 477861-2
Epic / Nov '94 / Sony.

VS
Go / Animal / Daughter / Glorified G / Dissident / W.M.A. / Blood / Rear view mirror / Rats / Elderly woman behind the counter in a small town / Leash / Indifference
CD _____ 474549 2
Epic / Oct '93 / Sony.

Pearlfishers

ZA ZA'S GARDEN
CD _____ IGCD 204
Iona / Sep '93 / ADA / Direct / Duncans.

Pearson, Duke

BAG'S GROOVE
Black Lion / Jul '91 / Jazz Music / Cadillac / Wellard / Koch.
CD _____ BLC 760149

Pearson, John

BUSY BOOTIN' (Pearson, John & Roger Hubbard)
Busy bootin' / As I went down the railroad track / Write me a few lines / Wort Worth and Dallas blues / Barrelhouse woman / Streamline train / Jesus on the mainline / Jitterbug swing / East St. Louis fare thee well / Cigarette blues / Don't take everybody to be your friend / Stealin' / Walkin' blues
CD _____ TX 1007CD
Taxim / Jan '94 / ADA.

Pearson, Johnny

SLEEPY SHORES
Sleepy shores / Nadia's theme / Heather / Concerto d'aranjuez / Feelings / Annie's song / All creatures great and small / Vincent / Just the way you are / Misty sunset / You don't bring flowers / What's another year / Theme from the deerhunter / First time ever I saw your face / Killing me softly with his song / Winner takes it all / If
CD _____ BR 1322
BR Music / Dec '95 / Target/BMG.

THEMES AND DREAMS (Pearson, Johnny Orchestra)
Godfather / House of Caradus (theme) / All creatures great and small / Love dream / Chi mai / First love / Triangle (love theme and intro) / Chariots of fire / You are the one / Seduction / Love dreamer / Cavatina / I wish I knew (how it would feel to be free) / Love story (theme)
CD _____ PRCD 132
President / Jun '89 / Grapevine / Target/ BMG / Jazz Music / President.

Pedersen, Herb

LONESOME FEELING
Last thing on my mind / Childish love / Fields have turned brown / Homecoming / Easy ride / Lonesome feeling / Willow garden / It's worth believing / Even the worst of us / Your love is like a flower
CD _____ SHCD 3738
Sugarhill / Jul '95 / Roots / CM / ADA / Direct.

SOUTHWEST
Paperback writer / Rock 'n' roll cajun / If I can sing a song / Our baby's gone / Harvest home / Hey boys / Juses once again / Younger days / Can't you hear me callin' / Wait a minute
CD _____ 900929
Line / Oct '94 / CM / Grapevine / ADA / Conifer / Direct.

Pedersen, Leonardo

I WANT A ROOF (Pedersen, Leonardo Jazzkapel)
CD _____ MECCACD 1047
Music Mecca / Nov '94 / Jazz Music / Cadillac / Wellard.

Pedersen, Niels-Henning..

ETERNAL TRAVELLER, THE (Pedersen, Niels-Henning Orsted)
Moto perpetu / En elefant kom marcherende / Jeg gik mig ud en sommerdag at hore / Det haver so nyeligen regnet / His hvor vejen slar en bugt / Jeg ved en Laerkerede / Sig manen langsomt haever / Dawn / Eternal traveller / Skul gammel venskab / Rejn forgo / Moto perpetuo
CD _____ CD 2310 910
Pablo / May '94 / Jazz Music / Cadillac / Complete/Pinnacle.

VIKING, THE (Pedersen, Niels-Henning Orsted)
Puzzle / My funny valentine / Marie / Nuages / Air power / Dancing girls / September start / Little train / Stella by starlight / I fall in love too easily
CD _____ CD 2310894
Pablo / Apr '87 / Jazz Music / Cadillac / Complete/Pinnacle.

Pedicin, Mike

JIVE MEDICIN (Pedicin, Mike Quintet)
Mambo rock / I want to hug you, kiss you, squeeze you / Rock-a-bye / I'm hip / Large, large house (2) / Rock-a-bye (2) / Hotter than a pistol / Teenage fairy tale / Beat / Save us, Preacher Davis / Close all the doors / Td's boogie / Hucklebuck / Calypso rock / Hi'yo Silver / Tiger rag / Ain't that a shame / Crazy ball / I want you to be my baby / Night train / Sweet Georgia Brown / Rock-a-bye (3) / Hotter than a pistol (live)
CD _____ BCD 15738
Bear Family / Oct '93 / Rollercoaster / Direct / CM / Swift / ADA.

Peebles, Ann

FLIPSIDE
CD _____ HIUKCD 144
Hi / Aug '93 / Pinnacle.

GREATEST HITS
Ninety nine pounds / Walk away / Give me some credit / Heartaches, heartaches / Somebody's on your case / I still love you / Part time love / Generation gap between us / Slipped, tripped and fell in love / Trouble heartaches and sadness / I feel like breaking up somebody's home / I pity the fool / Do I need you / One way street / I can't stand the rain / Beware / Love vibration / Dr. Love Power / It was jealousy / Being here with you / I'm gonna tear your playhouse down / When in your arms / Good day for lovin' / Come to Mama / Old man with young ideas / If this is heaven
CD _____ HIUKCD 119
Hi / Apr '88 / Pinnacle.

LOOKIN' FOR A LOVIN'
Respect / Make me yours / It's your thing / Won't you try me / My man (mon homme) / I'll get along / What you laid on me / You keep me hangin' on / Love played a game / I needed somebody / You're gonna make me cry / Bip, bam, Thank you mam / Handwriting on the wall / Livin' in lovin' out / Lookin' for a lovin' / You've got the papers (I've got the man) / I didn't take your man / Heartaches / Be for me / Mon belle amour / I'd rather leave while I'm in love
CD _____ HIUKCD 105
Hi / Aug '90 / Pinnacle.

STRAIGHT FROM THE HEART/I CAN'T STAND THE RAIN
Slipped, tripped and fell in love / Trouble, heartaches and sadness / What you laid on me / How strong is a woman / Somebody's on your case / I feel like breaking up somebody's home / I've been there before / I pity the fool / Ninety nine pounds / I take what I want / I can't stand the rain / Do I need you / Until you came into my life / You keep me hangin' on / Run run run / If we can't trust each other / Love vibration / You got to feed the fire / I'm gonna tear your playhouse down / One way street
CD _____ HIUKCD 137
Hi / Jan '93 / Pinnacle.

TELLIN IT/IF THIS IS HEAVEN
Come to Mama / I don't lend my man / I needed somebody / Stand by woman / It was jealousy / Dr. Love Power / You can't hold a man / Beware / Put yourself in my place / Love played a game / If this is heaven / Good day for lovin' / I'm so thankful / Being here with you / Boy I gotta have you / When I'm in your arms / You're gonna make me cry / Games / Lovin' you wihtout love / It must be love
CD _____ HIUKCD 138
Hi / Jan '93 / Pinnacle.

THIS IS ANN PEEBLES
CD _____ HIUKCD 139
Hi / Jun '93 / Pinnacle.

US R&B CHARTS HITS
CD _____ HILOCD 13
Hi / Jan '95 / Pinnacle.

Peeping Tom

EYES HAVE IT, THE
Room in the loft / Meeting of the waters / First of May / French polka / Be minor baby / Steamboat quickstep / Mote and beam / Beamish Mary / Tower green / Salty dog pokas / Annie's hornpipe / Liquor hornpipe / Highland hunt / Highland hunt 2 / Duke of Grafton / Treat / Oscar Wood's jig / Serpent dance / Knockabower No.2 / Cobbler / Paddy and dandy / Wellington's advance / Connaught man's rambles / Lullaby waltzes / Prowed C / Mystery jig / Breach of Killiecrankie / Britches full of stitches / Showman's fancy / Alexander's favourite / Gaspe reel / Malarky / Redcar reel / Johnny comes marching home / Swallow's nest / Istanbull / Gighouse shuffle
CD _____ FSCD 26
Folksound / Aug '94 / Roots / CM.

SIGHT FOR SORE EYES, A
Camels are coming / Lizzie Lichine / Abbeyfield / Woolaton park / Charlie Stewart / Victors return / Routier 66 / Whirlpool / Les filles de St. Nicolas / MacMahon's march / Night on the gin / Bedbreaker / Rag on reels / Jolly Geordies / Ranting Ross / Catchgate crapshooter / Buttonhole / Rig-a-jig / Mother's ruin / Chateau / Enrico / Tuxedo junction / Boanupstekker / Jackanory jig / Scottish de lea / Miss Sayers Allemande
CD _____ FSCD 21
Accolade / Aug '92 / Roots / CM.

Peers, Donald

IN A SHADY NOOK
In a shady nook / Don't sweetheart me / You're in love / It's love love love / By the river of roses / You fascinating you / London pride / I met her on a Monday / Isabel loves a soldier / I'm all right / Johnny and Mary / Lights out till reveille / Forever and a day / Just a little cottage / Russian rose / St. Mary's in the twilight / Tangerine / Moonlight cocktail / Three little sisters / Hey little hen / Nevada / Sing everybody sing / Marie Elena
CD _____ RAJCD 846
Empress / Feb '95 / THE.

VERY BEST OF DONALD PEERS
CD _____ SOW 907
Sound Waves / May '93 / Target/BMG.

Peg Leg Sam

MEDICINE SHOW MAN
Who's that left her 'while ago / Greasy greens / Reuben / Irene, tell me, who do you love / Skinny woman blues / Lost John / Ode to bad Bill / Ain't but one thing give a man the blues / Easy ridin' buggy / Peg's fox chase / Before you give it all away / Fast freight train / Nasty old trail / Born in hard luck
CD _____ TRIX 3302
Trix / Jun '94 / New Note.

Pegboy

EARWIG
CD _____ QS 28CD
Quarter Stick / Nov '94 / SRD.

STRONG REACTION
CD _____ QS 007CD
Quarter Stick / '94 / SRD.

Pege, Aladar

SOLO BASS, JAZZ AND CLASSIC
CD _____ RST 91532
RST / Feb '91 / Jazz Music / Hot Shot.

Peggio

ALTERAZIONE DELLA STRUTTURA
CD _____ WD 012CD
Plastic Head / Jun '92 / Plastic Head.

Pegram, George

GEORGE PEGRAM
CD _____ ROUCD 0001
Rounder / Feb '95 / CM / Direct / ADA / Cadillac.

Peguri, Charles

COMPOSITIONS 1907-30
CD _____ FA 021CD
Fremeaux / Nov '95 / Discovery / ADA.

Pekka Pohjola

KATKAVAARAN LOHIKAARME
CD _____ 450996415
F-Music / Dec '94 / Direct.

KEESOJEN LEHTO
CD _____ LRCD 219
Love / Dec '94 / Direct / ADA.

Pele

A-LIVE-A-LIVE-O
Don't worship me / Fair blows the wind for France / Swinging from a tree / Oh Lord part

II / Chosen one / Mairas wedding / King's ransom / Fireworks / In the beginning
CD _____ MAGCD 1049
M&G / Jun '94 / 3MV / Sony.

SPORT OF KINGS, THE
CD _____ MAGCD 1043
M&G / Dec '93 / 3MV / Sony.

Pelican Daughters

BLISS
CD _____ SR 9456
Silent / Jul '94 / Plastic Head.

Peligro

PELIGRO
Coffee shop / King of the road / Love hate war / Hellations from hell / Spazztic nerve / Cat burglar / Cornfed knuckle head / Black bean chili thing / I spy / Hellnation / Beloved infidels / No TV show / Dirty / No way / Cat swing / Mystery
CD _____ VIRUS 165CD
Alternative Tentacles / May '95 / Pinnacle.

Pell, Axel Rudi

BALLADS, THE
CD _____ SPV 084-76642
Steamhammer / Jul '93 / Pinnacle / Plastic Head.

BETWEEN THE WALLS
CD _____ SPV 08476822
Nosferatu / Jun '94 / Plastic Head.

LIVE IN GERMANY
CD _____ SPV 08576972
SPV / May '95 / Plastic Head.

Pell Mell

BUMPER CROP
CD _____ SST 158 CD
SST / May '93 / Plastic Head.

Pelland, Paul

PAUL PELLAND & BOB PILSBURY (Pelland, Paul & Bob Pilsbury)
CD _____ SOSCD 1212
Stomp Off / Oct '92 / Jazz Music / Wellard.

Pellegrino, Antonio

CELESTIAL CHRISTMAS 2
CD _____ CDCEL 13038
Celestial Harmonies / Oct '91 / ADA / Select.

Pellen, Jaques

CELTIC PROCESSION
CD _____ Y225028
Silex / Jun '93 / ADA.

PELLEN/ DEL FRA/ GRITZ/ WHEELER
CD _____ DSC 25015-2
Diffusion Breizh / Apr '94 / ADA.

Pelzl, Stefan

TALES OF SISYPHOS (Pelzl, Stefan 'Ju Ju' & Idris Muhammad)
CD _____ RST 91580
RST / Mar '95 / Jazz Music / Hot Shot.

Pemarwan, Gender Wayang

MUSIC FOR THE BALINESE SHADOW PLAY
Gending petegak "Sekar Gendontan" / Gending pemungkah / Gending angkat - Angkatan / Gending mesem / Gending angkat-angkatan, Batel / Gending delem, Batle / Gending rebong / Gending langiang
CD _____ CMPCD 3014
CMP / Oct '94 / Vital/SAM.

Pena, Miles

MILES PENA
Un sueno prohibido / Es mi culpa / Corazon partido / Dame tu perdon / Un sentimental / Aire no viciado en mi existir / Habale / Cuenta conmigo
CD _____ 66058066
RMM / Jul '95 / New Note.

Pena, Paco

ART OF PACO PENA
CD _____ NI 7011
Nimbus / Sep '94 / Nimbus.

AZAHARA
CD _____ NI 5116
Nimbus / Sep '94 / Nimbus.

ENCUENTROS (Pena, Paco & Eduardo Falu)
CD _____ NI 5196
Nimbus / Sep '94 / Nimbus.

FABULOUS FLAMENCO (Nice 'N' Easy Series)
CD _____ 8206922
Eclipse / Mar '92 / PolyGram.

MISA FLAMENCA
CD _____ NI 5288
Nimbus / Sep '94 / Nimbus.

Penal Colony

PUT YOUR HANDS DOWN
CD _____ CLEO 10942
Cleopatra / Jun '94 / Disc.

Penance

PARALLEL CORNERS
CD _____ CM 77077CD
Century Media / Oct '94 / Plastic Head.

ROAD LESS TRAVELLED, THE
CD _____ RISE 007CD
Rise Above / Jul '92 / Vital / Plastic Head.

Pencil

SKANTRON
CD _____ GROW 019-2
Grass / Jun '94 / SRD.

Pendergrass, Teddy

JOY
Joy / 2 a.m. / Good to you / I'm ready / Love is the power / This is the last time / Through the falling rain / Can we be lovers
CD _____ 7559607752
Pickwick/Warner / Oct '94 / Pinnacle / Warner Music / Carlton Home Entertainment.

LITTLE MORE MAGIC, A
Believe in love / Slip away / I'm always thinking about you / I choose you / Voodoo / Tender / Can't help nobody / Little more magic / My father's child / Say it / No one like you / Reprise - my father's child
CD _____ 7559614972
WEA / Oct '94 / Warner Music.

STAR COLLECTION
CD _____ STCD 1004
Disky / Jun '93 / THE / BMG / Discovery / Pinnacle.

TEDDY PENDERGRASS
CD _____ 7559603172
WEA / Jan '96 / Warner Music.

TRULY BLESSED
She knocks me off my feet / It should've been you / Don't you ever stop / It's over / Glad to be alive / How can you mend a broken heart / I find everything in you / Spend the night with you / We can't keep going on (like this) / Truly blessed
CD _____ 7559608912
Elektra / Mar '91 / Warner Music.

Pendragon

9.15 LIVE
Victims of life / Circus / Leviathan / Red shoes / Alaska / Black Knight / Please / Fly high fall far / Higher circles
CD _____ PEND 3CD
Toff / '91 / Pinnacle.

FALLEN DREAMS AND ANGELS
Third World in the UK / Dune / Sister Bluebird / Fallen dreams and angels
CD _____ MOB 2CD
Toff / Mar '95 / Pinnacle.

JEWEL
Higher circles / Pleasure of hope / Leviathan / At home with the earth / Snowfall / Circus / Oh Divineo / Black night / Fly high fall far / Victims of life
CD _____ PEND 2CD
Toff / '91 / Pinnacle.

KOWTOW
I walk the rope / Solid heart / A.M. / Time for a change / Total recall / Haunting / Kowtow
CD _____ PEND 1CD
Toff / Nov '88 / Pinnacle.

REST OF PENDRAGON, THE
CD _____ PEND 4CD
Toff / Jun '91 / Pinnacle.

VERY VERY BOOTLEG-LIVE IN LILLE, THE
Excalibur / Totall recall / Queen of hearts / We'll go hunting deer / Solid heart
CD _____ MOB 1CD
Toff / Feb '95 / Pinnacle.

WINDOW OF LIFE
CD _____ PEND 6CD
Toff / Oct '93 / Pinnacle.

WORLD, THE
CD _____ PEND 5CD
Toff / Oct '91 / Pinnacle.

Penetration

DON'T DICTATE (The Best Of Penetration)
Come into the open / Lifeline / Firing squad / Never / Life's a gamble / V.I.P. / Danger signs / Stone heroes / Don't dictate / Free money / Shout above the noise / She is the slave / Party's over / Future daze
CD _____ CDOVD 450
Virgin / Feb '95 / EMI.

MOVING TARGETS
Future daze / Life's a gamble / Lovers of outrage / Vision / Silent community / Stone heroes / Movement / Too many friends / Reunion / Nostalgia / Freemoney
CD _____ CDV 2109
Virgin / '89 / EMI.

Penetration

PENETRATION
Duty free technology / Firing squad / Race against time / In the future / Free money/ Never / V.I.P. / Don't dictate / Silent community / She is the slave / Danger signs / Last saving grace / Movement / Stone heroes / Vision / Future daze / Come into the open / Lovers of outrage / Too many friends / Killed in the rush
CD _____ PILOT 001
Trident / Sep '93 / Pinnacle.

Penguin Cafe Orchestra

BROADCASTING FROM HOME
Music for a found harmonium / Prelude and yodel / More milk / Sheep dip / White mischief / In the back of a taxi / Music by numbers / Another one from the colonies / Air / Heartwind / Isle of view (music for helicopter pilots) / Now nothing
CD _____ EEGCD 38
EG / Apr '92 / EMI.

CONCERT PROGRAMME
CD Set _____ ZOPFD 002
Zopf / Jul '95 / PolyGram.

MUSIC FROM THE PENGUIN CAFE
Chartered flight / Hugebaby / Penguin Cafe single / Sound of someone you love / Zopf (from the colonies) (From the colonies/Coronation/Giles Farnaby's dream/In a Sydney motel/Pop/Surface tension/Milk)
CD _____ EEGCD 27
EG / Apr '92 / EMI.

PENGUIN CAFE ORCHESTRA
Air a danser / Number 1-4 / Salty bean fumble / Yodel 1 / Telephone and rubber band / Cutting branches for a temporary shelter / Pythagoras' trousers / Yodel 2 / Paul's dance / Ecstasy of dancing fleas / Walk don't run / Flux / Simon's dream / Harmonic necklace / Steady state
CD _____ EEGCD 11
EG / Apr '92 / EMI.

SIGNS OF LIFE
Bean fields / Southern jukebox music / Horns of the bull / Oscar tango / Snake and the lotus / Rosasolis / Sketch / Perpetuum mobile / Swing the cat / Wildlife / Dirt
CD _____ EEGCD 50
EG / '87 / EMI.

WHEN IN ROME - LIVE
Air a danser / Yodel 1 / From the colonies / Southern jukebox music / Numbers 1-4 / Bean fields / Paul's dance / Oscar tango / Music for a found harmonium / Isle of view (music for helicopter pilots) / Prelude and yodel / Giles Farnaby's dream / Air (CD & Cassette only) / Dirt (CD & cassette only) / Cutting branches for a temporary shelter (CD & cassette only) / Telephone and rubber band (CD & Cassette only)
CD _____ EEGCD 56
EG / Sep '88 / EMI.

Penguins

EARTH ANGEL
Don't do it / Promises, promises, promises / She's gone, gone, gone / Okey ook / Walkin' down Broadway / Hey senorita / Cool baby cool / Ice / Jingle jangle / Christmas prayer / Earth angel / It only happens with you / Be mine / My troubles are not at an end / Love will make your mind go wild / Dealer of dreams / Will you be mine / Devil that I see / Peace of mind / Earth angel (2)
CD _____ CDCH 249
Ace / Nov '90 / Pinnacle / Cadillac / Complete/Pinnacle.

Peniston, Ce Ce

FINALLY
We got a love thang / Finally (Mixes) / Inside that I cried / Lifeline / It should have been you / Keep on walkin' / Crazy love / I see love / You win, I win, we lose / Virtue
CD _____ 3971822
A&M / Apr '95 / PolyGram.

THOUGHT 'YA KNEW
Searchin' / I'm in the mood / Hit by love / Whatever it is / Forever in my heart / I'm not over you / Anyway you wanna go / Give what I'm givin' / Through those doors / Let my love surround you / Keep givin' me your love / If you love me, I will love you / Maybe it's the way
CD _____ 540 138-2
A&M / Jan '94 / PolyGram.

Penn, Dan

DO RIGHT MAN
CD _____ 936245519-2
Warner Bros. / Oct '94 / Warner Music.

Penn, Dawn

NO NO NO
I want a love I can see / I'm sorry / You don't know me (no no no) / Night and day / My love takes over / First cut is the deepest / I'll do it again / Hurt / Samfi boy / Keep in touch / My man / Blue yes blue
CD _____ 756792365-2
Warner Bros. / Jun '94 / Warner Music.

Penn, Michael

FREE FOR ALL
Long way down (look what the cat drug in) / Free time / Coal / Seen the doctor / By the book / Drained / Slipping my mind / Strange season / Bunker hill / Now we're even
CD _____ 07863611132
RCA / Nov '93 / BMG.

Pennou Skoulm

PENNOU SKOULM
CD _____ CD 854
Diffusion Breizh / Jan '95 / ADA.

Pennywise

ABOUT TIME
CD _____ 864372
Epitaph / Jun '95 / Plastic Head / Pinnacle.

PENNYWISE
CD _____ E 864122
Epitaph / Nov '92 / Plastic Head / Pinnacle.

UNKNOWN ROAD
CD _____ E 864292
Epitaph / Aug '93 / Plastic Head / Pinnacle.

WILD CARD (A Word From The Wise)
CD _____ TS 003CD
Semaphore / May '95 / Plastic Head.

Pensyl, Kim

WHEN YOU WERE MINE
CD _____ SH 5010
Shanachie / Dec '94 / Koch / ADA / Greensleeves.

Pentagram

BE FOREWARNED
Live free and burn / Too late / Ask no more / World will love again / Vampyre love / Life blood / Wolf's blood / Frustration / Bride of evil / Nightmare gown / Petrified / Timeless heart / Be forewarned
CD _____ CDVILE 42
Peaceville / Mar '95 / Pinnacle.

DAY OF RECKONING
Day of reckoning / Broken vows / Madman / When the screams come / Burning saviour / Evil seed / Wartime
CD _____ VILE 040CD
Peaceville / Aug '93 / Pinnacle.

RELENTLESS
Death row / All your sins / Sign of the wolf / Ghoul / Relentless / Run my course / Sinister / Deist / You're lost, I'm free / Dying world / Twenty buck spin
CD _____ VILE 038CD
Peaceville / Apr '93 / Pinnacle.

RELENTLESS/DAY OF RECKONING
CD _____ CDVILE 40
Peaceville / May '95 / Pinnacle.

TRAIL BLAZER
CD _____ SULH 70178
Nuclear Blast / Jan '95 / Plastic Head.

Pentangle

ANNIVERSARY
CD _____ HY 200122CD
Hypertension / Sep '93 / Total/BMG / Direct / ADA.

BASKET OF LIGHT
Light flight / Once I had a sweetheart / Springtime promises / Lyke wyke dirge / Train song / Hunting song / Sally go round the roses / Cuckoo / House carpenter
CD _____ 9005550
Line / Jun '94 / CM / Grapevine / ADA / Conifer / Direct.

CRUEL SISTER
Maid that's deep in love / When I was in my prime / Lord Franklin / Cruel sister / Jack Orion
CD _____ TACD 900558
Line / Oct '94 / CM / Grapevine / ADA / Conifer / Direct.

ESSENTIAL PENTANGLE, THE (VOL. 1)
Once I had a sweetheart / Hear my call / Hole in the coal / Omie wise / Waltz / Trees they do grow high / Sweet child / Woman like you / Reflection / Will the circle be unbroken / Watch the stars / Helping hand / Goodbye pork pie hat / When I was in my prime
CD _____ TRACD 602
Transatlantic / Jul '87 / BMG / Pinnacle / ADA.

ESSENTIAL PENTANGLE, THE (VOL. 2)
Pentangling / Bruton Town / Shake shake mama / Let no man steal your thyme / Soho / Cruel sister / Bells / Wedding dress / I've got a feeling / Three part thing / Rain and snow / Way behind the sun / When I get home / Time has come / When I was in my prime
CD _____ TRACD 606
Transatlantic / Sep '87 / BMG / Pinnacle / ADA.

IN YOUR MIND
CD _____ 295942
Ariola / Oct '94 / BMG.

LIVE 1994
CD _____ HYCD 200152
Hypertension / Jun '95 / Total/BMG / Direct / ADA.

LIVE AT THE BBC
Cuckoo song / Hunting song / Light flight / People on the highway / No love is sorrow / Cherry tree carol / Jump baby jump / Lady of Carlisle / Train song / In time / House carpenter / I've got a feeling
CD _____ BOJCD 013
Strange Fruit / Aug '95 / Pinnacle.

MAID THAT'S DEEP IN LOVE, A
CD _____ SH 79066 CD
Shanachie / Jul '90 / Koch / ADA / Greensleeves.

PENTANGLE, THE
CD _____ 9005490
Line / Jun '94 / CM / Grapevine / ADA / Conifer / Direct.

PEOPLE ON THE HIGHWAY
Pentangling / Travelling song / In time / Bells / Way behind the sun / Waltz / Time has come (Live) / Sweet child / Moon dog / I saw an angel / Light flight / Sakky goes round the roses / Train song / Once I had a sweetheart / Wedding dress / Helping hand / Rain and snow / When I get home / Cold mountain
CD _____ TDEM 12
Trandem / Mar '94 / CM / ADA / Pinnacle.

SWEET CHILD
CD _____ ESMCD 354
Essential / Jan '96 / Total/BMG.

THINK OF TOMORROW
CD _____ HY 200112CD
Hypertension / Mar '95 / Total/BMG / Direct / ADA.

Pentatonik

ANTHOLOGY
CD _____ DVNT 1CD
Deviant / Jul '95 / Vital.

PENTATONIK
Movements: Parts 1 to 4 / About that / La verite / Solution / Create / Sleeper / Part 4 live / Detox / Real / Green / Passion / Prophesy / Pantatonik melody
CD Set _____ DVNT 001CD
Deviant / Sep '95 / Vital.

Pentti Rasankangas

ANKKAPAALLIKKO
CD _____ OMCD 52
Olarin Musiiki Oy / Dec '93 / ADA / Direct.

People Like Us

GUIDE TO BROADCASTING
CD _____ STCDMCD 002
Staalplaat / Sep '95 / Vital/SAM.

People Without Shoes

THOUGHTS OF AN OPTIMIST
CD _____ RGE 102-2
Enemy / Nov '94 / Grapevine.

Peoples, Tommy

HIGH PART OF THE ROAD (Peoples, Tommy & Paul Brady)
CD _____ SHANCD 34007
Shanachie / Jan '95 / Koch / ADA / Greensleeves.

IRON MAN, THE
CD _____ SHCD 79044
Shanachie / May '95 / Koch / ADA / Greensleeves.

TRANQUIL IRISH MUSIC PLAYED ON THE FIDDLE
CD _____ TRADCD 008
GTD / Mar '91 / Else / ADA.

Peoplespeak

PEOPLESPEAK
Agitate the gravel / Rain / Wanawaki / Say it, do it / Others / Sometime / Burma / January
CD _____ PS 1001
PS Records / Sep '92 / New Note.

Pepl, Harry

CRACKED MIRRORS (Pepl, Harry/ Herbert Joos/ Jon Christensen)
Wolkenbilder 1 / Reflections in a cracked mirror / Schikaneder delight / Die alte mar und das mann / More far out than east / Wolkenbilder 2 / Tintenfisch inki / Purple light
CD _____ 8334722
ECM / Jul '88 / New Note.

Peplowski, Ken

CONCORD DUO SERIES...
Blue room / Why / Changes / Chasin' the Bird / Deep purple / You're my everything / s'posin' / Two not one / If I should lose you / In the dark / Just one of those things

---

CD _____ CCD 4556
Concord Jazz / Jun '93 / New Note.

DOUBLE EXPOSURE
(I would do) anything for you / There's no you / Lava / Blame it on my youth / Segment / High and flighty / Don't you know I care (or don't you care to) / Jubilee / Careless love / Imagination
CD _____ CCD 4344
Concord Jazz / Jul '88 / New Note.

ILLUMINATIONS
June night / Trubbel / Panama / Between the Devil and the deep blue sea / How long has this been going on / Jim Dawg / Smada / Alone together (Only on CD.) / Did I remember / Nancy with the laughing face / Best things in life are free / If we never meet again (Only on CD.)
CD _____ CCD 4449
Concord Jazz / Mar '91 / New Note.

IT'S A LONESOME OLD TOWN
More than ever / They can't take that away from me / It's a lonesome old town / These foolish things / Supposin' / Bonicrates de mutelas / It never entered my mind / In my life / Last night when we were young / Eternal triangle / Zingaro / Crimehouse
CD _____ CCD 4673
Concord Jazz / Nov '95 / New Note.

LIVE AT AMBASSADOR AUDITORIUM
Kirk's works / Nuts / I don't stand a ghost of a chance with you / Best things in life are free / At long last love / Menina flor / I brung you frijans for your zarf / Why try to change me now / Exactly like you
CD _____ CCD 4610
Concord Jazz / Sep '94 / New Note.

MR. GENTLE AND MR. COOL (Peplowski, Ken Quintet)
Mr. Gentle and Mr. Cool / Please be kind / You do something to me / Body and soul / Makin' whoopee (Only on CD.) / Stray horn (Only on CD.) / Follow your heart / On a misty night / Syeeda's song flute / There'll be some changes made / Count your blessings instead of sheep / When day is done
CD _____ CCD 4419
Concord Jazz / Jul '90 / New Note.

NATURAL TOUCH (Peplowski, Ken Quintet)
I'll close my eyes / One I love (belongs to someone else) / Guess I'll hang my tears out to dry / Evidence / Evening / You never know / You must believe in spring / Flunk blues / Circles of theme / My buddy / How deep is the ocean / Say it isn't so / I thought about you
CD _____ CCD 4517
Concord Jazz / Aug '92 / New Note.

SONNY SIDE (Peplowski, Ken Quintet)
CD _____ CCD 4376
Concord Jazz / May '89 / New Note.

STEPPIN' WITH PEPS
Steppin' / Courtship / Among my souvenirs / Lotus blossom / No problems / Johnny come lately / Blue mood / Antigua / Lady's in love with you / Pretend / Huggles / Turn around
CD _____ CCD 4569
Concord Jazz / Sep '93 / New Note.

Pepper, Art

AMONG FRIENDS
What is this thing called love / Round Midnight / What's new / I'll remember April / Among friends / I'm getting sentimental over you / Blue bossa / Besame mucho
CD _____ STCD 1107
Storyville / Feb '90 / Jazz Music / Wellard / CM / Cadillac.

ART IN L.A. (1957-58)
Breeze and I / Without a song / Long ago and far away / Fascinatin' rhythm / I can't believe that you're in love with me / Webb City / Begin the beguine
CD _____ WW 2064
West Wind / Apr '91 / Swift / Charly / CM / ADA.

ART PEPPER & ZOOT SIMS ALL STARS (Pepper, Art & Zoot Sims)
CD _____ WW 2071
West Wind / Mar '93 / Swift / Charly / CM / ADA.

ART PEPPER MEETS THE RHYTHM SECTION
You'd be so nice to come home to / Red pepper blues / Imagination / Waltz me blues / Straight life / Jazz me blues / Tin tin deo / Star eyes / Birk's works
CD _____ OJCCD 3382
Original Jazz Classics / Sep '93 / Wellard / Jazz Music / Cadillac / Complete/Pinnacle.

ARTHUR'S BLUES
Donna Lee / Road waltz / For Freddie / But beautiful / Arthur's blues
CD _____ OJCCD 680
Original Jazz Classics / May '93 / Wellard / Jazz Music / Cadillac / Complete/Pinnacle.

COMPLETE GALAXY RECORDINGS, THE
CD Set _____ GCD 1016
Galaxy / Nov '92 / Pinnacle.

FRIDAY NIGHT AT THE VILLAGE VANGUARD
CD _____ OJCCD 695
Original Jazz Classics / Nov '95 / Wellard / Jazz Music / Cadillac / Complete/Pinnacle.

GETTIN' TOGETHER (Pepper, Art & Conte Candoli)
CD _____ OJCCD 169
Original Jazz Classics / May '93 / Wellard / Jazz Music / Cadillac / Complete/ Pinnacle.

INTENSITY
I can't believe that you're in love with me / I love you / Come rain or come shine / Long ago and far away / Gone with the wind / I wished on the moon / Too close for comfort
CD _____ OJCCD 3872
Original Jazz Classics / Feb '92 / Wellard / Jazz Music / Cadillac / Complete/Pinnacle.

LAURIE'S CHOICE
CD _____ 17012
Laserlight / Aug '93 / Target/BMG.

LIVE AT DONTE'S 1968 (2 CD) (Pepper, Art Quintet)
CD _____ FSCD 1039
Fresh Sound / Nov '95 / Jazz Music / Discovery.

LIVING LEGEND
Orphelia / Here's that rainy day / What Laurie likes / Mr. Yohe / Lost life / Samba mom-mom
CD _____ OJCCD 408
Original Jazz Classics / Apr '93 / Wellard / Jazz Music / Cadillac / Complete/Pinnacle.

MEMORIAL COLLECTION VOL 1
CD _____ STCD 4128
Storyville / Feb '90 / Jazz Music / Wellard / CM / Cadillac.

MEMORIAL COLLECTION VOL 2
CD _____ STCD 4129
Storyville / Feb '90 / Jazz Music / Wellard / CM / Cadillac.

MEMORIAL COLLECTION VOL 3
CD _____ STCD 4130
Storyville / Feb '90 / Jazz Music / Wellard / CM / Cadillac.

MEMORIAL COLLECTION VOL 4
CD _____ STCD 4146
Storyville / Feb '90 / Jazz Music / Wellard / CM / Cadillac.

MODERN JAZZ CLASSICS (Pepper, Art + Eleven)
Move / Groovin' high / Opus de funk / Round Midnight / Four brothers / Shaw nuff / Bernie's tune / Walkin' shoes / Anthropology / Airegin / Walkin' / Donna Lee
CD _____ OJCCD 341
Original Jazz Classics / Jun '94 / Wellard / Jazz Music / Cadillac / Complete/Pinnacle.

NO LIMIT
CD _____ OJCCD 411
Original Jazz Classics / Nov '95 / Wellard / Jazz Music / Cadillac / Complete/Pinnacle.

PEPPER RETURNS
Pepper returns / Broadway / I surrender dear / Art's opus / What is this thing called love / Foggy day / I can't give you anything but love / You go to my head / You and the night and the music / Abstract art / Val's pal / Pepper pot / Blues at twilight / Angel wings / Minority / Walkin' out blues
CD _____ CD 53237
Giants Of Jazz / Jan '96 / Target/BMG / Cadillac.

ROADGAME
Roadgame / Road waltz / When you're smiling / Everything happens to me
CD _____ OJCCD 774
Original Jazz Classics / Sep '93 / Wellard / Jazz Music / Cadillac / Complete/Pinnacle.

SATURDAY NIGHT AT THE VILLAGE VANGUARD
CD _____ OJCCD 696
Original Jazz Classics / Nov '95 / Wellard / Jazz Music / Cadillac / Complete/Pinnacle.

STRAIGHT LIFE
Chili pepper / Cinnamon / Tickle toe / Suzy the poodle / Everything happens to me / Nutmeg / Deep purple / What's new / Thyme time / Art's oregano / Way you look tonight / Straight life
CD _____ OJCCD 475
Original Jazz Classics / Nov '95 / Wellard / Jazz Music / Cadillac / Complete/Pinnacle.

SURF RIDE
Tickle toe / Chili pepper / Susie the poodle / Brown gold / Holiday flight / Surf ride / Straight life / Cinnamon / Thyme time / Way you look tonight / Nutmeg / Art's oregano
CD _____ SV 0115
Savoy Jazz / Apr '93 / Conifer / ADA.

THURSDAY NIGHT AT THE VILLAGE VANGUARD
CD _____ OJCCD 694
Original Jazz Classics / Nov '95 / Wellard / Jazz Music / Cadillac / Complete/Pinnacle.

TRIP, THE
Trip / Song for Richard / Sweet love of mine / Junior cat / Summer knows / Red car
CD _____ OJCCD 4102

PEPPER, ART

TWO ALTOS (Pepper, Art & Sonny Redd)
Deep purple / Watkins production / Everything happens to me / Redd's head / These foolish things / What's new
CD _____ SV 0161
Savoy Jazz / Jan '94 / Conifer / ADA.

WINTER MOON
Our song / Here's that rainy day / That's love / Winter moon / When the sun comes out / Blues in the night / Prisoner (love theme from 'Eyes of Laura Mars')
CD _____ OJCCD 677
Original Jazz Classics / Nov '95 / Wellard / Jazz Music / Cadillac / Complete/Pinnacle.

Pepper, Jim

COMIN' AND GOIN'
Witchi ta to / Ya na ho / Squaw song / Goin' down to Muskogee / Comin' and goin' / Lakota song / Water / Custer gets it / Malinyea
CD _____ 29031029
Bellaphon / Nov '95 / New Note.

Pepsi & Shirlie

HEARTACHE
Goodbye stranger / Can't give me love / What's going on inside your head / All right now / Lover's revolution / High time / Heartache / It's a shame / Surrender / Feels like the first time / Crime of passion / Someday
CD _____ 5500092
Spectrum/Karussell / May '93 / PolyGram / THE.

Percy X

SPYX
CD _____ SOMACD 4
Soma / Feb '96 / Disc.

Pere Ubu

390 DEGREES OF SIMULATED STEREO (Live Volume 1)
CD _____ ROUGHCD 23
Rough Trade / Mar '89 / Pinnacle.

ART OF WALKING, THE
CD _____ ROUGHCD 14
Rough Trade / Mar '89 / Pinnacle.

CLOUDLAND
Breath / Cry / Waiting for Mary / Bus called Happiness / Lost Nation Road / Flat / Pushin' / Race the sun / Why go it alone / Ice cream truck / Love love love / Nevada / Waltz / Monday night
Fontana / May '89 / PolyGram.
CD _____ 8382372

DUB HOUSING
CD _____ CDR 6002
Rough Trade / Feb '89 / Pinnacle.

FOLLY OF YOUTH
Folly of youth / Ball 'n' chain / Down by the river II / Memphis
CD _____ FRYCD 043
Cooking Vinyl / Oct '95 / Vital.

MODERN DANCE, THE/TERMINAL TOWER (2 CDs)
Non-alignment pact / Modern dance / Laughing / Street waves / Chinese radiation / Life stinks / Real world / Over my head / Sentimental journey / Humor me / Heart of darkness / 30 seconds over Tokyo / Final solution / Cloud 149 / Untitled / My dark ages / Heaven / Humor me (live) / Book is on the table / Not happy / Lonesome Cowboy Dave
CD Set _____ MPG 74178
Movieplay Gold / Nov '95 / Target/BMG.

NEW PICNIC TIME
CD _____ CDR 6003
Rough Trade / Feb '89 / Pinnacle.

ONE MAN DRIVES (WHILE THE OTHER ONE SCREAMS)
CD _____ ROUGHCD 093
Rough Trade / Feb '89 / Pinnacle.

RAY GUN SUITCASE
Folly of youth / Electricity / Beach boys / Turquoise fins / Vaccum in my head / Memphis / Three things / Horse / Don't worry / Ray gun suitcase / Surfer girl / Red sky / Montana / My friend is a stooge of the media priests / Down by the river
CD _____ COOKCD089
Cooking Vinyl / Jul '95 / Vital.

SONG OF THE BAILING MAN, THE
CD _____ ROUGHCD 033
Rough Trade / Mar '89 / Pinnacle.

Peregoyo Y Su Combo...

TROPICALISMO (Peregoyo Y Su Combo Vacana)
CD _____ WCD 015
World Circuit / Dec '89 / New Note / Direct / Cadillac / ADA.

Peress, Cindy

WORLD IS WATCHING, THE
CD _____ SHAM 1013CD
Shamrock / May '93 / Wellard / ADA.

Perez, Danilo

DANILO PEREZ
Panama libre / Serenata / Alfonsina y el mar / Solo contigo basta / Irremediablemente solo / Body and soul / Caludio / Time on my hands / Friday morning / Skylark
CD _____ 01241631482
Novus / Mar '93 / BMG.

JOURNEY, THE
Capture / Morning / Forest / Taking chains / Voyage / Arrival / Awakening / New vision / Panama 2000 / Reminisce / Flight to freedom / Anticipation / Flight / African wave / Libre spirits
CD _____ 1241 63166-2
RCA / Jul '94 / BMG.

Perez, Pocho

EL NEGRITO
CD _____ TUMICD 034
Tumi / '92 / Sterns / Discovery.

Perfect Disaster

HEAVEN SCENT
CD _____ FIRE 33027
Fire / Oct '90 / Disc.

UP
CD _____ FIRE 33018
Fire / Oct '91 / Disc.

Perfect Houseplants

CLEC
CD _____ EFZ 1011
EFZ / Jan '95 / Vital/SAM.

PERFECT HOUSEPLANTS
These foolish times / Somewhere in England / Salvadors / Knees / Last summer / With hindsight / Fedora / When/Starry eyed / Going home
CD _____ AHUM 014
Ah-Um / Jul '93 / New Note / Cadillac.

Perfect, Christine

CHRISTINE PERFECT
Crazy about you baby / I'm on my way / Let me go (Leave me alone) / Wait and see / Close to me / I'd rather go blind / When you say / And that's saying a lot / No road is the right road / For you / I'm too far gone (To turn around) / I want you
CD _____ 4747002
Blue Horizon / Feb '95 / Sony.

Perfume Tree

DUST
CD _____ ZULU 006CD
Zulu / Oct '95 / Plastic Head.

Perkins, Bill

BILL PERKINS SEPTET & VICTOR FELDER (Perkins, Bill & Victor Felder)
CD _____ OJCCD 17662
Original Jazz Classics / Jun '95 / Wellard / Jazz Music / Cadillac / Complete/Pinnacle.

FRONT LINE, THE (Perkins, Bill & Pepper Adams)
CD _____ STCD 4166
Storyville / Feb '90 / Jazz Music / Wellard / CM / Cadillac.

I WISHED ON THE MOON
I wished on the moon / Remember / Beautiful love / Besame mucho / Opals / No more / Last port of call / Rockin' chair / Summer knows / Caravan
CD _____ CCD 79524
Candid / Oct '92 / Cadillac / Jazz Music / Wellard / Koch.

REMEMBERANCE OF DINO'S
CD _____ IPCD 8606
Interplay / Apr '94 / Jazz Music.

WARM MOODS (Perkins, Bill & Frank Strazzeri)
CD _____ FSRCD 191
Fresh Sound / Dec '92 / Jazz Music / Discovery.

Perkins, Carl

BEST OF AND THE REST OF, THE
(We're gonna) Rock around the clock / That's alright mama / Kaw-liga / Tutti frutti / Yes it's me and I'm in love again / Blue suede shoes / Be bop a lula / Maybellene / Whole lotta shakin' goin' on / Hang up my rock 'n' roll shoes / shake, rattle and roll
CD _____ CDAR 1025
Action Replay / Mar '91 / Tring.

BEST OF CARL PERKINS, THE
CD _____ MATCD 324
Castle / Feb '95 / BMG.

BLUE SUEDE SHOES
CD _____ CDSGP 0164
Prestige / Aug '95 / Total/BMG.

BOPPIN' BLUE SUEDE SHOES
Movie magg / Let the jukebox keep on playing / Sure to fall / Honey don't / Blue suede shoes / Boppin' the blues / Dixie fried / Put your cat clothes on / Right string baby, but the wrong yo-yo / Everybody's tryin' to be my baby / That don't move me / Caldonia / Sweethearts or strangers / I'm so sorry, I'm not sorry / Matchbox / Roll over Beethoven / That's right / Forever yours / Your true love / Y.O.U. / Pink pedal pushers / I care / Lend me your comb / Look at that moon / Glad all over
CD _____ CPCD 8102
Charly / Jun '95 / Charly / THE / Cadillac.

CLASSIC CARL PERKINS (5 CD Box Set)
Honky tonk babe / Movie Magg / Honky tonk gal / runaround / Turn around / Let the jukebox keep on playing / What you doin' when you're cryin' / You can't make love to somebody / Gone gone gone / Dixie bop / Perkin's wiggle / Blue suede shoes (take 1) / Blue suede shoes (take 2) / Blue suede shoes (take 3) / Honey don't (takes 1-3) / Tennessee / Sure to fall / All Mama's children / Everybody's tryin' to be my baby / Boppin' the blues / Put your cat clothes on / Only you / Right string baby, but the wrong yo-yo / All mama's children (false start) / Dixie fried / Dixie fried (false start) / I'm sorry I'm not sorry / That don't move me / Lonely street / Drink up and go home / Pink pedal pushers / Way you're living is breaking my heart / Take back my love / Somebody tell me / Instrumental (1 & 2) / Red wing / Down by the riverside / Her love rubbed off / Caldonia / You can do no wrong / Sweethearts or strangers / Be honest with me / Your true love / Matchbox / Your true love (original tempo) / Keeper of the key / Roll over Beethoven / Try my heart out / That's right / Forever yours / Y.O.U. / I care / Lend me your comb / Look at the moon / Glad all over / Tutti frutti / Whole lotta shakin' goin' on / That's alright / Where the Rio de Rosa flows / Shake, rattle and roll / Long tall Sally / I got a woman / Hey good lookin' / Sittin' on top of the world / Good rockin' tonight / Jive after five / Rockin' record hop / Just tonight I'd call / Ready Teddy / Jenny Jenny / You were there / Because you're mine / Pop, let me have the car / Levi jacket and a longtail shirt / When the moon comes over the mountain / Sister twister / Ham bone / This life I live / Please say you'll be mine / Honey 'cause I love you / I don't see me in your eyes anymore / Highway of love / Pointed toe shoes / One-way ticket to lonliness / Drifter / Too much for a man to understand / LOV-EVILLE / Big bad blues / Say when / Lonely heart / Love I'll never win / Let my baby be / Monkey shine / Mama of my song / One of these days / I wouldn't have you / Help me find my baby / After sundown / For a little while / Just for you / When the night time comes along / Fool I used to be / Forget me (next time around) / Hollywood city / I've just got back from there / Unhappy girls / Someday, somewhere someone waits for me / Anyway the wind blows
CD Set _____ BCD 15494
Bear Family / Feb '90 / Rollercoaster / Direct / CM / Swift / ADA.

COUNTRY BOY'S DREAM (The Dollie Masters)
Country boy's dream / If I could come back / Star of the show / Poor boy blues / Detroit city / Dream on little dreamer / Stateside / Sweet misery / Unmitigated gall / Shine shine shine / Without you / You can take the boy out of the... / Almost love / Old fashioned singalong / Old number one / My old hometown / Back to Tennessee / It's you / I'll go wrong again / Dear Abby / Lake country, cotton country / All you need to know / Quite like you / Just as long #2 / Just as long / Baby I'm hung on you / Tom / Mary Jane / Mama and Daddy / Valda
CD _____ BCD 15593
Bear Family / Apr '92 / Rollercoaster / Direct / CM / Swift / ADA.

DIXIE FRIED
Honey don't / Boppin' the blues / Blue suede shoes / Put your cat clothes on / Dixie fried / Matchbox / Pink pedal pushers / Thats right / I'm sorry I'm not sorry / Roll over Beethoven / Glad all over / Right string baby, but the wrong yo-yo / Everybody's tryin' to be my baby / Gone gone gone / Lend me your comb / All Mama's children / Sweet hearts or strangers / Your true love / Movie Magg / Tennessee / Sure to fall / Honky tonk gal / Turn around / Let the jukebox keep on playing
CD _____ CDCHARLY 2
Charly / Mar '86 / Charly / THE / Cadillac.

FIRST KING OF ROCK 'N' ROLL, THE
Blue suede shoes / Honey don't / I'm walkin' / Matchbox / Suzie Q / Memphis / Maybellene / Slippin' and slidin' / Be bop a lula / Roll over Beethoven / Hound dog / Whole lotta shakin' goin' on / That's alright mama / Bird dog / Rock Island line
CD _____ ECD 3107
K-Tel / Jun '95 / K-Tel.

FRIENDS FAMILY & LEGENDS
CD _____ CDMF 084
DRG / Jan '93 / New Note.

HOUND DOG
CD _____ MU 5062
Musketeer / Oct '92 / Koch.

LEGENDARY, THE
Born to boogie / I can feel it / Don't get off gettin' it on / Take me back / Redneck / Hurt put on by you / Sweeter than candy / Boppin' the blues / We did in '54 / Mama / Standing in the need of love / What am I living for / Twenty one / Country soul / Georgia court room / I didn't want to fall in love again
CD _____ PWK 4037
Carlton Home Entertainment / Feb '91 / Carlton Home Entertainment.

MAN AND THE LEGEND, THE
Blue suede shoes / Honey don't / I'm walkin' / Matchbox / Suzie Q / Memphis / Maybellene / Slippin' and slidin' / Be bop a lula / Roll over Beethoven / Hound dog / Whole lotta shakin' goin' on / Lucille / Jailhouse rock / All shook up / That's alright mama / Bird dog / Rock Island line / Singin' the blues / Got my mojo working
CD _____ CDMF 039
Magnum Force / May '95 / Magnum Music Group.

PEARLS FROM THE PAST VOL. 2 - CARL PERKINS
CD _____ KLMCD 016
Scratch / May '94 / BMG.

ROCKABILLY KING, THE
CD _____ CDCD 1252
Charly / Jun '95 / Charly / THE / Cadillac.

ROCKIN' GUITARMAN
Blue suede shoes / Roll over Beethoven / Sweethearts and strangers / Perkin's wiggle / Honky tonk gal / You can do no wrong / What do you want when you're crying / Boppin' the blues / Caldonia / Lonely street / I care / Y.O.U. / Glad all over / Honey don't / Dixie fried / Her love rubbed off
CD _____ CDCD 1052
Charly / Mar '93 / Charly / THE / Cadillac.

SUN SESSIONS, THE
CD _____ MCCD 191
Music Club / Nov '94 / Disc / THE / CM.

SUN YEARS, THE
Honky tonk gal / Movie Magg (2 takes) / Turn around (2 takes) / You can't make love to somebody / Gone gone gone / Let the jukebox keep on playing / What ya doin' when you're cryin' / Drink up and go home / Blue suede shoes (3 takes) / Honey don't (2 takes) / Sure to fall / Tennessee / Perkin's wiggle / Boppin' the blues (2 takes) / All Mama's children / Everybody's tryin' to be my baby / Somebody tell me (plus Carl Perkins in Memphis - radio plug) / Dixie fried / I'm sorry I'm not sorry / Sweethearts or strangers / Keeper of the key / Be honest with me / That don't move me / Lonely street / Pink pedal pushers (2 takes) / Matchbox (2 takes) / Your true love / Caldonia / Her love rubbed off / You can do no wrong / Roll over Beethoven / Put your cat clothes on (2 takes) / Only you / That's right (2 takes) / Glad all over / Right string baby, but the wrong yo-yo / Honky tonk babe
CD Set _____ SUN BOX 2
Sun / Feb '90 / Charly.

TENNESSEE BOP
Blue suede shoes / Honky tonk gal / Glad all over / Perkin's wiggle / Honey don't / Matchbox / Put your cat clothes on / Everybody's tryin' to be my baby / Lend me your comb / Dixie fried / Boppin' the blues / Tennessee / Gone gone gone / All Mama's children
CD _____ CDINS 5019
Instant / Feb '90 / Charly.

UP COUNTRY VOL.2
CD _____ SOV 021CD
Sovereign / Sep '93 / Target/BMG.

UP THROUGH THE YEARS '1954-1957'
Honky tonk gal / Movie magg / Turn around / Gone gone gone / Let the jukebox keep on playing / You can't make love to somebody / Blue suede shoes / Honey don't / Tennessee / Boppin' the blues / All Mama's children / Everybody's tryin' to be my baby / Dixie fried / I'm sorry I'm not sorry / You can do no wrong / Matchbox / Your true love / Put your cat clothes on / Only you / Pink pedal pushers / That's right / Lend me your comb / Glad all over / Right string baby, but the wrong yo-yo
CD _____ BCD 15246
Bear Family / Nov '86 / Rollercoaster / Direct / CM / Swift / ADA.

Perkins, Pinetop

AFTER HOURS
CD _____ CD 73088
Blind Pig / Mar '90 / Hot Shot / Swift / CM / Roots / Direct / ADA.

BOOGIE WOOGIE KING
CD _____ ECD 260112
Evidence / Jan '92 / Harmonia Mundi / ADA / Cadillac.

LIVE TOP
CD _____ DELD 3010
Deluge / Dec '95 / Direct / ADA.

ON TOP
CD _____ DELCD 3002
Deluge / Jan '96 / Koch.

PINETOP'S BOOGIE WOOGIE
CD _____ ANTCD 0020
Antones / Nov '93 / Hot Shot / Direct / ADA.

Perko, Jukka

GARDEN OF TIME (Perko, Jukka & Severi Pyysalo)
CD _____ ODE 4012
Ondine / Feb '94 / Koch / ADA.

Pernice, Laurent

AXIDENT
CD _____ PER 018
Semantic / Feb '94 / Plastic Head.

EXIT TO THE CITY
CD _____ PPP 113
PDCD / Oct '93 / Plastic Head.

Peron, Carlos

IMPERSONATOR 3
CD _____ EFA 02852 CD
A.L.L. / Nov '92 / SRD.

IMPERSONATOR II
CD _____ BIASCD 116
Play It Again Sam / Aug '89 / Vital.

Perri, Joel

EL CONDOR DEL INDIO
CD _____ EUCD 1067
ARC / '89 / ARC Music / ADA.

EL CONDOR PASA (Magic of the Indian Flute)
CD _____ EUCD 1173
ARC / '91 / ARC Music / ADA.

EL CONDOR PASA
CD _____ EUCD 1055
ARC / '89 / ARC Music / ADA.

MANDOLINE
CD _____ EUCD 1047
ARC / '89 / ARC Music / ADA.

MASTER OF THE INDIAN FLUTES
CD _____ EUCD 1329
ARC / Nov '95 / ARC Music / ADA.

SOUFFLE DE VENTE
CD _____ EUCD 1029
ARC / '89 / ARC Music / ADA.

TARANTELLA DEL DIAVOLO
CD _____ EUCD 1077
ARC / '89 / ARC Music / ADA.

Perry, Al

RETRONUEVO (Perry, Al & Dan Stuart)
CD _____ NORM 169CD
Normal/Okra / Dec '94 / Direct / ADA.

Perry, Demetrius

ANOTHER WORLD
Another world / Can do can do (anything for you) / Breathless / Betcha don't know / Use me / I'll take you there / Are you lonely / I'll be true / Everything a man could want
CD _____ 466 878 2
Tabu / Jun '90 / Sony.

Perry, Frank

BELOVODYE - LAND OF THE WHITE WATERS
CD _____ IS 03CD
Isis / Apr '94 / ADA / Direct.

Perry, Joe

LET THE MUSIC DO THE TALKING (Perry, Joe Project)
Let the music do the talking / Conflict of interest / Discount dogs / Shooting star / Break song / Rockin' train / Mist is rising / Ready on the firing line / Life at a glance
CD _____ 4809672
Columbia / Aug '95 / Sony.

Perry, John G.

UNCLE SEABIRD
CD _____ VP 169CD
Voice Print / Feb '95 / Voice Print.

Perry, Lee 'Scratch'

BLACK ARK EXPERRYMENTS (Perry, Lee 'Scratch' & Mad Professor)
Thank you / Super ape in good shape / Jungle safari / From heaven above / Heads of government / Open door / Black ark experryments / Poop song / Come back
CD _____ ARICD 114
Ariwa Sounds / Jun '95 / Jetstar / SRD.

BLOOD VAPOUR
CD _____ LACD 007
La / May '94 / Plastic Head.

BUILD THE ARK (Perry, Lee 'Scratch' & The Upsetters)
My little Sandra / Dubbing Sandra / Long long time / White belly rat / Freedom street / Land of love / Crossover / Travelling / Green Bay incident / Thanks and praise / Feelings / Wah dat / White belly rat (version) / Peace and love / Think so / At the feast / Ethiopian land / Brother nosh / Mr. Money Man
CD Set _____ CDPRY 003
Trojan / Mar '94 / Jetstar / THE.

DUB AROUND THE WORLD
CD _____ SFCD 5
Sprint / Nov '95 / Jetstar / THE.

DUB CONFRONTATION VOL.2 (Perry, Lee 'Scratch' & King Tubby)
CD _____ LG 21107
Lagoon / Apr '95 / Magnum Music Group / THE.

EXCALIBURMAN
CD _____ SLCD 6
Seven Leaves / Sep '93 / Roots Collective / SRD / Greensleeves.

EXPERRYMENTS AT THE GRASS ROOTS OF DUB (Perry, Lee 'Scratch' & Mad Professor)
Jungle roots dub / Dubbing with the super ape / Alien in out a space / Sky high dub / Nucleus dub / Dub it wide open / Dub wise experryments / Pooping dub song / Black Ark come again
CD _____ ARICD 115
Ariwa Sounds / Oct '95 / Jetstar / SRD.

FROM THE HEART OF THE CONGO
CD _____ RN 0029CD
Runn / Apr '94 / Jetstar / SRD.

GIVE ME POWER (Perry, Lee 'Scratch' & Friends)
Sick and tired / Rasta no pickpocket / Don't cross the nation / Give me power / News flash / Justice to the people / Babylon burning / Ring of fire / Dig the grave / Thanks we get / Public enemy no.1 / Mid East rock / Forward up / Hot tip / To be a lover
CD _____ CDTRL 254
Trojan / Mar '94 / Jetstar / Total/BMG.

GLORY DUB
CD _____ RB 3015
Reggae Best / Oct '95 / Magnum Music Group / THE.

GOOD, THE BAD AND THE UPSETTERS, THE (Perry, Lee 'Scratch' & The Upsetters)
CD _____ LG 21083
Lagoon / Aug '93 / Magnum Music Group / THE.

GUITAR BOOGIE DUB
CD _____ RNCD 2057
Rhino / May '94 / Jetstar / Magnum Music Group / THE.

HEART OF THE ARK
CD _____ SLCD 1
Seven Leaves / Jul '94 / Roots Collective / SRD / Greensleeves.

HEAVY MANNERS (Perry, Lee 'Scratch' & The Upsetters)
CD _____ RB 3001
Reggae Best / May '94 / Magnum Music Group / THE.

HOLD OF DEATH
CD _____ RNCD 2007
Rhino / May '93 / Jetstar / Magnum Music Group / THE.

KUNG FU MEETS THE DRAGON (Perry, Lee 'Scratch' & The Upsetters)
CD _____ LG2 1112
Lagoon / Aug '95 / Magnum Music Group / THE.

KUNG FU MEETS THE DRAGON
CD _____ JLCD 5000
Justice League / Jun '95 / SRD.

LARKS FROM THE ARK
Conscious man / Nuh fe run down / Freedom / Brotherly love / Groovy situation / Them don't know love / Rastafari / Forward with love / Such is life / Elaine / School girl dub / Don't be afraid / Cool down / I've never had it so good / Four & twenty dreadluck / What's the use / African freedom / Colour
CD _____ NTMCD 511
Nectar / Sep '95 / Pinnacle.

LEE PERRY MEETS MAD PROFESSOR IN DUB 1 & 2 (Perry, Lee 'Scratch' & Mad Professor)
CD _____ ANGCD 8/9
Angella / Jan '91 / Jetstar.

LORD GOD MUZIK
CD _____ ZSCDII0
Heartbeat / Sep '91 / Greensleeves / Jetstar / Direct / ADA.

MEET AT KING TUBBY'S (Perry, Lee 'Scratch' & The Upsetters)
CD _____ RNCD 2027
Rhino / Dec '93 / Jetstar / Magnum Music Group / THE.

MEETS BULLWACKIE IN SATANS DUB
CD _____ RE 178CD
Reach Out International / Nov '94 / Jetstar.

MEETS MAFIA & FLUXY IN JAMAICA (Perry, Lee 'Scratch' & The Upsetters)
CD _____ LG 21025
Lagoon / Jul '93 / Magnum Music Group / THE.

MEETS THE MAD PROFESSOR (CHAPTER ONE)
CD _____ LG 21068
Lagoon / Feb '93 / Magnum Music Group / THE.

MEETS THE MAD PROFESSOR (CHAPTER TWO)
CD _____ LG 21069
Lagoon / Feb '93 / Magnum Music Group / THE.

MEGATON DUB VOLUME 1
Seven Leaves / '92 / Roots Collective / SRD / Greensleeves.
CD _____ SLCD 11

MEGATON DUB VOLUME 2
CD _____ SLCD 10
Seven Leaves / Apr '92 / Roots Collective / SRD / Greensleeves.

MILLIONAIRE LIQUIDATOR (Perry, Lee 'Scratch' & The Upsetters)
Introducing myself / Drum song / Grooving / All things are possible / Show me that river / I'm a madman / Judgar / Happy birthday / Sexy lady / Time marches on
CD _____ CDTRL 227
Trojan / Mar '94 / Jetstar / Total/BMG.

MYSTIC WARRIOR
CD _____ AROCD 054
Ariwa Sounds / Aug '90 / Jetstar / SRD.

ON THE WIRE
CD _____ CDTRL 348
Trojan / Apr '95 / Jetstar / Total/BMG.

OPEN THE GATES (Perry, Lee 'Scratch' & Friends)
CD _____ CDPRY 2
Trojan / Mar '94 / Jetstar / Total/BMG.

ORIGINAL BLACK BOARD JUNGLE DUB
CD _____ ORCHCD 1
Red Honey / May '94 / Disc.

OUT OF MANY - THE UPSETTER
CD _____ CDTRL 297
Trojan / Mar '94 / Jetstar / Total/BMG.

PEOPLE FUNNY BOY
CD _____ CDTRL 339
Trojan / Mar '94 / Jetstar / Total/BMG.

PHOENIX OF PEACE (Perry, Lee 'Scratch' & Earl Sixteen)
CD _____ SLCD 8
Seven Leaves / Aug '93 / Roots Collective / SRD / Greensleeves.

PRESENTS BLACK ARK ALMIGHTY DUB
CD _____ BCD 403
Black Ark / Dec '94 / Jetstar.

PUBLIC JESTERING 1974-76
CD _____ CDAT 108
Attack / Jul '94 / Jetstar / Total/BMG.

REGGAE GREATS
Party time / Police and thieves / Groovy situation / Soul fire / War in a Babylon / Wisdom / To be a lover / Roast fish and cornbread / Croaking lizard / Dreadlocks in moonlight
CD _____ RRCD 10
Reggae Refreshers / Sep '90 / PolyGram / Vital.

REMINAH DUB (Perry, Lee 'Scratch' & The Upsetters)
CD _____ OMCD 11
Original Music / Mar '93 / SRD / Jetstar.

REVOLUTION DUB
CD _____ RNCD 2120
Rhino / Sep '95 / Jetstar / Magnum Music Group / THE.

SCRATCH THE UPSETTERS AGAIN
CD _____ CDTRL 352
Trojan / Apr '95 / Jetstar / Total/BMG.

SENSI DUB VOLUME 2 (Perry, Lee 'Scratch' & King Tubby)
CD _____ OMCD 15
Original Music / Jul '93 / SRD / Jetstar.

SENSI DUB VOLUMES 2 & 3 (Perry, Lee 'Scratch' & King Tubby)
CD Set _____ OMCD 015/16
Original Music / Sep '90 / SRD / Jetstar.

SOME OF THE BEST (Perry, Lee 'Scratch' & The Upsetters)
CD _____ HBCD 37
Heartbeat / Jul '88 / Greensleeves / Jetstar / Direct / ADA.

SOUNDS FROM THE HOTLINE
CD _____ HBCD 70
Heartbeat / Nov '92 / Greensleeves / Jetstar / Direct / ADA.

SUPER APE (Perry, Lee 'Scratch' & The Upsetters)
Zion's blood / Croaking lizard / Black vest / Underground / Curly dub / Dread lion / Three in one / Patience / Dub along / Super ape in good shape
CD _____ RRCD 13

Reggae Refreshers / Sep '90 / PolyGram / Vital.

SUPER APE IN THE JUNGLE
CD _____ ARICD 112
Ariwa Sounds / Jul '95 / Jetstar / SRD.

TIME BOOM
CD _____ ONUCD 43
On-U Sound / Mar '94 / SRD / Jetstar.

UPSETTER COLLECTION (Upsetters (1))
Cold sweat / Return of Django / Check him out / Django shoots first / Kill them all / Vampire / Drugs and poison / Sipreano / Black I.P.A. / Bucky skank / Words of my mouth / Tipper special / Cow thief skank / French connection / Better days / Freak out skank
CD _____ CDTRL 195
Trojan / Mar '94 / Jetstar / Total/BMG.

UPSETTER COMPACT SET, THE (Perry, Lee 'Scratch' & Friends)
CD Set _____ CDPRY 1
Trojan / Mar '94 / Jetstar / Total/BMG.

Perry, Phil

PURE PLEASURE
One touch / Way that I want U / After the love has gone / If only you knew / I love it, I love it / When it comes to love / Heaven / You say, I say / Angel of the night / Love don't love nobody
CD _____ GRM 40272
GRP / Oct '94 / BMG / New Note.

Perry, Rich

BEAUTIFUL LOVE
CD _____ SCCD 31360
Steeplechase / May '95 / Impetus.

Perry, Steve

FOR THE LOVE OF STRANGE MEDICINE
You better wait / Young hearts forever / I am / Stand up (before it's too late) / For the love of strange medicine / Donna please / Listen to your heart / Tuesday heartache / Missing you / Somewhere there's hope / Anyway
CD _____ 4771962
Columbia / Aug '94 / Sony.

Persip, Charlie

CHARLIE PERSIP & SUPERBAND
CD _____ NI 4028
Natasha / Jun '94 / Jazz Music / ADA / CM / Direct / Cadillac.

Person, Eric

ARRIVAL
CD _____ 121237-2
Soul Note / Apr '93 / Harmonia Mundi / Wellard / Cadillac.

PROPHECY
CD _____ 121287-2
Soul Note / May '94 / Harmonia Mundi / Wellard / Cadillac.

Person, Houston

GOODNESS
CD _____ OJCCD 332
Original Jazz Classics / Dec '95 / Wellard / Jazz Music / Cadillac / Complete/Pinnacle.

LION AND HIS PRIDE, THE
Dig / I remember Clifford / Dear Heart / Sweet love / You are too beautiful / Like someone in love / Our day will come / Captain Hook
CD _____ MCD 5480
Muse / Sep '94 / New Note / CM.

NOW'S THE TIME (Person, Houston & Ron Carter)
Bermsha swing / spring can really hang you up the most / Einbahnstrasse / Memories of you / Quiet nights / If you could see me now / Now's the time / Since I fell for you / Little waltz
CD _____ MCD 5421
Muse / Aug '93 / New Note / CM.

PERSONALITY
Kittitian carnival / Funky sunday afternoon / Pain / Shotgun / Touch of the bad stuff / He'll fight my battles / All in love is fair / Mayola / Until it's time for you to go / You are the sunshine of my life / Don't go to strangers / Easy walker
CD _____ CDBGPD 070
BGP / Mar '93 / Pinnacle.

SOMETHING IN COMMON (Person, Houston & Ron Carter)
Blue seven / I thought about you / Mack the knife / Joy Spring / Good morning heartache / Anthropology / Once in a while / Blues for two
CD _____ MCD 5376
Muse / Apr '91 / New Note / CM.

TALK OF THE TOWN
CD _____ MCD 5331
Muse / Sep '92 / New Note / CM.

WHY NOT?
Why not / As time goes by / Namely you / Joey's blues / Blue gardenia / Deed I do

CD _____ MCD 5433
Muse / Jan '92 / New Note / CM.

Persson, Bent

I REMEMBER CLIFFORD (Persson, Bent & Ludwigsson/Lundgren Quintet)
CD _____ PACD 94081
Pama / Dec '94 / Jazz Music / Cadillac.

LOUIS ARMSTRONG'S 50 HOT CORNET CHORUSES VOLS.3 & 4
Copenhagen / Someday sweetheart / Sidewalk blues / Jackass blues / Easy rider / Chant / Sugarfoot stomp / Grandpa's spells / Dixieland blues / Chicago breakdown / 29th and dearborn / Chattanooga stomp / Mr. Jelly Lord / Darktown shuffle / Panama blues / Dallas stomp / Stomp your stuff / Tampeekoe
CD _____ CKS 3413
Kenneth / Apr '94 / Wellard / Cadillac / Jazz Music.

Persuaders

THIN LINE BETWEEN LOVE & HATE
CD _____ 7567804142
Atlantic / Jan '96 / Warner Music.

Persuasions

NO FRILLS
You can have her / Under the boardwalk / Sand in my shoes / I was wrong / I woke up in love this morning / I wonder do you love the Lord like I do / Still ain't got no band / Victim / Treasure of love / Sweet was the wine / What are you doing New Year's Eve / Slip slidin' away
CD _____ CD 3083
Rounder / Aug '88 / CM / Direct / ADA / Cadillac.

RIGHT AROUND THE CORNER
CD _____ BBCD 9556
Bullseye Blues / Oct '94 / Direct.

Peruna Jazzmen

PERUNA JAZZMEN VOL. 1 & 2
CD _____ SOSCD 1003
Stomp Off / Dec '94 / Jazz Music / Wellard.

Perverted

POETIC TERRORISM IN AN ERA OF GRIEF
CD _____ GAP 028
Gap Recordings / Jun '95 / SRD.

Pestilence

SPHERES
Mind reflections / Multiple beings / Level of perception / Aurian eyes / Soul search / Personal energy / Voices from within / Spheres / Changing perspective / Phileas / Demise of time
CD _____ CD RR 9081 2
Roadrunner / Aug '93 / Pinnacle.

Pet Shop Boys

ACTUALLY
One more chance / Shopping / Rent / Hit music / What have I done to deserve this / It couldn't happen here / It's a sin / I want to wake up / Heart / King's Cross
CD _____ CDPCSD 104
Parlophone / Sep '87 / EMI.

ALTERNATIVE
In the night / Man could get arrested / That's my impression / Was that what is was / Paninaro / Jack the lad / You know where you went wrong / New life / I want a dog / Do I have to / I get excited (you get excited to) / Don Juan / Sound of the atom splitting / One of the crowd / You funny uncle / It must be obvious / We all feel better in the dark / Bet she's not your girlfriend / Losing my mind / Music for boys / Miserabilism / Hey headmaster / What keeps mankind alive / Shameless / Too many people / Violence / Decadence / If love were all / Euroboy / Some speculation
CD _____ CDPCSDS 166
CD Set _____ CDPSCSD 166
Parlophone / Aug '95 / EMI.

BEHAVIOUR
Being boring / This must be the place I waited years to leave / To face the truth / How can you expect to be taken seriously / Only the wind / My October symphony / So hard / Nervously / End of the world / Jealousy
CD _____ CDPCSD 113
Parlophone / Oct '90 / EMI.

DISCO 2
Absolutely fabulous (2 mixes) / I wouldn't normally do this kind of thing (Beatmasters/DJ Pierre mixes) / Go West (Farley & Heller mix) / Liberation (E Smoove 12" mix) / So hard (Moralaes mix) / Can you forgive her (Rollo dub) / Yesterday, when I was mad (Junior Vasquez/Coconut 1/Jam & Spoon mixes) / We all feel better in the dark (After hours climax)
CD _____ CDPCSD 159
Parlophone / Sep '94 / EMI.

DISCOGRAPHY - THE COMPLETE SINGLES COLLECTION

West End girls / Love comes quickly / Opportunities (let's make lots of money) / Suburbia / It's a sin / What have I done to deserve this / Always on my mind / Heart / Domino dancing / Left to my own devices / It's alright / So hard / Being boring / Where the streets have no name / Jealousy / D.J. culture / Was it worth it
CD _____ CDPMTV 3
Parlophone / Oct '91 / EMI.

INTROSPECTIVE
Left to my own devices / I want a dog / Domino dancing / I'm not scared / Always on my mind / It's alright / In my house
CD _____ CDPCS 7325
Parlophone / Feb '94 / EMI.

PET SHOP BOYS: INTERVIEW COMPACT DISC
CD P.Disc _____ CBAK 4021
Baktabak / Nov '89 / Baktabak.

PLEASE
Two divide by zero / West End girls / Opportunities (Lets make lots of money) / Love comes quickly / Suburbia / Tonight is forever / Violence / I want a lover / Later tonight / Why don't we live together
CD _____ CDP 746 271 2
Parlophone / Jun '86 / EMI.

VERY
Can you forgive her / I wouldn't normally do this kind of thing / Liberation / Different point of view / Dreaming of the Queen / Yesterday, when I was mad / Theatre / One and one make five / To speak is a sin / Young offender / One in a million / Go west
CD _____ CDPCSD 143
Parlophone / Sep '93 / EMI.

Petards

PETARDS, THE
CD _____ BTCD 971404
Beartracks / Apr '92 / Rollercoaster.

Peter & Gordon

EP COLLECTION, THE
Leave my woman alone / Hurtin' is loving / Long time gone / Lady Godiva / I got to pieces / Woman / Flower lady / Night in rusty armour / Sunday for tea / Start trying someone else / Love me baby / Lucille / If I were you / Pretty Mary / World without love / Tell me how / You don't have to tell me / Tears don't stop / Soft as the dawn / Leave me alone / Roving rambler / I don't want to see you again / Devant toi je suis sans voix (in front of you I am without a / True love ways / Ne me plains pas (don't feel sorry for me) / Le temps va le temps court (time is going, time is running) / L'unconnue (the unknown)
CD _____ SEECD 426
See For Miles/C5 / May '95 / Pinnacle.

Peter & The Test Tube...

JOURNEY TO THE CENTRE OF JOHNNY CLARKE'S HEAD (Peter & The Test Tube Babies)
CD _____ WB 31242
We Bite / May '95 / Plastic Head.

LIVE AND LOUD (Peter & The Test Tube Babies)
Keep Britain untidy / Boozana / Every second counts / Spirit of Keith Moon / Guest list / Goodbye forever / Blown out again / Ghost in my bedsit / Maniac / Banned from the pubs / Elvis is dead / September part 3 / Moped lads / Vicars / Key to the city / He's on the whiskey / Louise wouldn't like it / Jinx / Pissed punks (go for it) / Run like hell / Leader of the gang
CD _____ LINK CD 108
Street Link / Aug '92 / BMG.

LOUD BLARING PUNK ROCK CD, (Peter & The Test Tube Babies)
Oral Annie / We're too drunk / Pick yer nose (And eat it) / Vicars / Snakebite / I lust for the disgusting things in life / Tupperware party / Breast cancer / TQBBJ's / Student wankers / Big mouth / Child molester / Porno queen / Being sick / Excuses / Beat up the mods / Get 'em in (and get 'em off) / Rock 'n' roll is shit
CD _____ WB 31252
We Bite / May '95 / Plastic Head.

MATING SOUNDS OF THE SOUTH AMERICAN FROG, THE (Peter & The Test Tube Babies)
September part 1 / Guest list / One night stand / Let's burn / Jinx / Blown out again / Wimpeez / Easter bank holiday '83 / No invitation / Pissed punks (go for it) / Never made it / September part 2
CD _____ WB 31232
We Bite / May '95 / Plastic Head.

PISSED AND PROUD (Peter & The Test Tube Babies)
Moped lads / Banned from the pubs / Elvis is dead / Up yer bum / Smash and grab / Run like hell / Shit stirrer / Intensive care / Keep Britain untidy / Transvestite / Maniac / Disco / I'm the leader of the gang (I am)
CD _____ CDPUNK 3
Anagram / Apr '95 / Pinnacle.

PUNK SINGLES COLLECTION, THE (Peter & The Test Tube Babies)
Banned from the pubs / Moped lads / Peacehaven wild kids / Run like hell / Up yer bum / Zombie creeping flesh / No invitation / Smash and grab / Jinx / Trapper ain't got a bird / Wimpeez / Never made it / Blown out again / Rotting in the fart sack / Ten deadly sins / Spirit of Keith Moon / Boozanza / Alchohol / Key to the city / Vicar's wank too
CD _____ CDPUNK 64
Anagram / Oct '95 / Pinnacle.

SOBERPHOBIA (Peter & The Test Tube Babies)
Keys to the city / Louise / Spirit of keith moon / Allergic to life / All about love / Every time I see her / Ghost in my bedsit / Every second counts
CD _____ WB 31282
We Bite / May '95 / Plastic Head.

SUPERMODELS (Peter & The Test Tube Babies)
CD _____ WB 11392
We Bite / Nov '95 / Plastic Head.

TEN DEADLY SINS (Peter & The Test Tube Babies)
CD _____ WB 31272
We Bite / May '95 / Plastic Head.

TOTALLY TEST TUBED (Peter & The Test Tube Babies)
Banned from the pubs / Moped lads / Peacehaven wild kids / Maniac / Transvestite / Elvis is dead (Live) / I lust for the disgusting things / TQGGBJ / Run like hell / Up yer bum / Vicar's wank too (Live) / Jinx / Trapper ain't got a bird / Blown out again / Never made it / Pissed punks (go for it) / Spirit of Keith Moon / Zombie creeping flesh / Keys to the city / Louise wouldn't like it / Every second counts / All about love / September part 2
CD _____ WB 31262
We Bite / May '95 / Plastic Head.

Peter, John

JOHN PETER & RED HOT SEVEN (Featuring Wally Fawkes) (Peter, John & Red Hot Seven)
CD _____ JCD 176
Jazzology / Oct '91 / Swift / Jazz Music.

Peter, Paul & Mary

C'MON FOLKS
CD _____ TC 022
That's Country / Mar '94 / BMG.

PETER, PAUL & MARY
CD _____ 7599271572
WEA / Jan '96 / Warner Music.

Peters & Lee

PETERS AND LEE
CD _____ PTLM 1098
President / Aug '89 / Grapevine / Target/ BMG / Jazz Music / President.

THROUGH ALL THE YEARS
Welcome home / I'm confessin' that I love you / Let it be me / Love will keep us together / Air that I breathe / Suspicious minds / Brand new / Don't stay away / Endless love / Always on my mind / Rainbow / Hello / Hey Mr. Music Man / Through all the years
CD _____ PWKS 4214
Carlton Home Entertainment / Oct '94 / Carlton Home Entertainment.

Peters, Brian

SEEDS OF TIME, THE
Manchester jig - welcome home / History lesson / Living in the past that never was / Cropper lads / Killy Fisher / My lad's over bonny for the coal trade / Coffee and tea / Lowlands of Holland / Box in the attic / Northern Nanny / Low flier / Servant of the company / Sir William Stanier's favourite / Lovely Joan / Oyster girl / Lad with the trousers on / Mad Moll / False foudrage / Old hollie hornpipe / Padlocks / Ruins by the shore / Dark island / Arran boat
CD _____ HARCD 021
Harbour Town / May '92 / Roots / Direct / CM / ADA.

SQUEEZING OUT SPARKS
CD _____ PUG 001CD
Pugwash / Apr '94 / ADA.

Peters, Mike

AER (Welsh Language Version Of 'Breathe') (Peters, Mike & The Poets)
CD _____ CRAICD 047
Crai / Dec '94 / ADA / Direct.

BREATHE (Peters, Mike & The Poets)
Poetic justice / All I wanted / If I can't have you / Breathe / Love is a revolution / Who's gonna make the peace / Spiritual / What the world can't give me / Levis and bibles / Beautiful thing / Into the 21st century / This is war / Message / Back into the system (LP) / It just don't get any better than this (LP) / Train a comin' / New chapter (reprise)

CD _____ CRAI 042CD
Crai / Oct '94 / ADA / Direct.

Petersen, Pete

PLAYIN' IN THE PARK (Petersen, Pete & Collection Jazz Orchestra)
CD _____ CMD 8109
CMJ / Aug '89 / Jazz Music / Wellard.

STRAIGHT AHEAD (Petersen, Pete & Collection Jazz Orchestra)
CD _____ CMCD 8020
CMJ / '88 / Jazz Music / Wellard.

Peterson, James

TOO MANY KNOTS
Fish ain't bitin' / Flip floppin' my love / Call before you come home / Long handled spoon / Slob on the knob / Too many knots / Jacksonville / Every goodbye ain't gone / More than one way to skin a cat / Blind can't lead the blind / Killer rock
CD _____ CDICH 1130
Ichiban / Oct '93 / Koch.

Peterson, Lucky

LUCKY STRIKES
Over my head / Can't get no loving on the telephone / Lucky strikes / Bad feeling / Earlene / Pounding of my heart / She spread her wings / Dead cat on the line / Heart attack
CD _____ ALCD 4770
Alligator / May '93 / Direct / ADA.

RIDIN'
Ridin' / Don't answer the door / Farther up the road / Kinda easy like / Baby, what you want me to do / Green onions / Little red rooster / You don't have to go
CD _____ ECD 260332
Evidence / Sep '93 / Harmonia Mundi / ADA / Cadillac.

TRIPLE PLAY
Let the chips fall where they may / Your lies / On o'clock blues / Repo man / I found a love / Jammin' in the jungle / Locked out of love / I'm free / Don't cloud up on me / Funky Ray
CD _____ ALCD 4789
Alligator / May '93 / Direct / ADA.

Peterson, Marvin

ONE WITH THE WIND (Peterson, Marvin 'Hannibal')
Nile's song / God bless the child / One with the wind / Misty / Change is going to come / Glow / Revelation / Since she went away / Echoes
CD _____ MCD 5523
Muse / Dec '94 / New Note / CM.

Peterson, Master Joe

MASTER JOE PETERSEN (The Phenomenal Boy Singer)
Smilin' through / My ain folk / No souvenirs / Rainbow valley / It's a sin to tell a lie / Old rugged cross / Memories of childhood days / When they sound the last All Clear / You don't have to tell me / Two little tears / Badge from your coat / Perfect day / Little grey home in the west / My heart's in Old Killarney / Broken hearted clown / Choir boy / Goodnight my love
CD _____ LCOM 5233
Lismor / May '94 / Lismor / Direct / Duncans / ADA.

Peterson, Oscar

1959 (Peterson, Oscar Trio)
CD _____ CD 53190
Giants Of Jazz / Sep '94 / Target/BMG / Cadillac.

AN OSCAR PETERSON CHRISTMAS
CD _____ 83372CD
Telarc / Nov '95 / Conifer / ADA.

AT STRATFORD SHAKESPEAREAN FESTIVAL
CD _____ 5137522
Verve / Jul '93 / PolyGram.

DIGITAL AT MONTREUX
Old folks / Soft winds / (Back home again in) Indiana / That's all / Younger than Springtime / Caravan / Rockin' in rhythm / C jam blues / Solitude / Satin doll / Caravan (reprise) / On the trail
CD _____ CD 2308224
Pablo / May '94 / Jazz Music / Cadillac / Complete/Pinnacle.

ENCORE AT THE BLUE NOTE (Peterson, Oscar Trio)
CD _____ CD 83356
Telarc / Oct '93 / Conifer / ADA.

FOR MY FRIENDS
CD _____ 5138302
Verve / Apr '92 / PolyGram.

GOOD LIFE, THE
CD _____ OJCCD 6272
Original Jazz Classics / Feb '92 / Wellard / Jazz Music / Cadillac / Complete/Pinnacle.

HALLELUJAH TIME
CD _______ MCD 0502
Moon / Nov '93 / Harmonia Mundi / Cadillac.

HISTORY OF AN ARTIST
R.B. blues / I wished on the moon / You can depend on me / This is where it's at / Okie blues / I want to be happy / Texas blues / Main stem / Don't get around much anymore / Swamp fire / In a sentimental mood / Greasy blues / Sweetie blues / Gay's blues / Good life / Richard's round / Lady of the lavender mist
CD _______ CD 2310895
Pablo / Oct '92 / Jazz Music / Cadillac / Complete/Pinnacle.

JAM AT MONTREUX '77
CD _______ OJCCD 378
Original Jazz Classics / Feb '92 / Wellard / Jazz Music / Cadillac / Complete/Pinnacle.

JAZZ 'ROUND MIDNIGHT
CD _______ 5110362
Verve / Apr '92 / PolyGram.

JAZZ MASTERS
CD _______ 5163202
Verve / Apr '93 / PolyGram.

JAZZ PORTRAIT OF FRANK SINATRA, A
You make me feel so young / Come dance with me / Learnin' the blues / Witchcraft / Tender trap / Saturday night is the loneliest night of the week / Just in time / It happened in Monterey / I get a kick out of you / All of me / Birth of the blues / How about you
CD _______ 8257692
Verve / Mar '93 / PolyGram.

LAST CALL AT THE BLUE NOTE (Peterson, Oscar Trio)
CD _______ CD 83314
Telarc / Sep '92 / Conifer / ADA.

LIKE SOMEONE IN LOVE (Peterson, Oscar Trio)
CD _______ JHR 73570
Jazz Hour / Nov '93 / Target/BMG / Jazz Music / Cadillac.

LIVE (Peterson, Oscar Trio)
CD _______ CD 2310940
Pablo / Apr '94 / Jazz Music / Cadillac / Complete/Pinnacle.

LIVE 1953 (Peterson, Oscar Quartet & Buddy De Franco)
CD _______ EBCD 2111-2
Jazzband / Dec '89 / Jazz Music / Wellard.

LIVE AT THE NORTH SEA JAZZ FESTIVAL, 1980
Caravan / Straight no chaser / Like someone in love / There is no you / You stepped out of a dream / City lights / I'm old fashioned / Time for love / Bluesology / Goodbye / No greater love
CD _______ CD 2620115
Pablo / Apr '94 / Jazz Music / Cadillac / Complete/Pinnacle.

LIVE IN 1953 (Peterson, Oscar Quartet & Buddy De Franco)
CD _______ EBCD 21112
Flyright / Feb '94 / Hot Shot / Wellard / Jazz Music / CM.

LLUBJANA 1964
CD _______ CD 53203
Giants Of Jazz / May '95 / Target/BMG / Cadillac.

LLUBJANA 1964 II
CD _______ CD 53204
Giants Of Jazz / May '95 / Target/BMG / Cadillac.

LOUIS ARMSTRONG MEETS OSCAR PETERSON (The Silver Collection) (Peterson, Oscar & Louis Armstrong)
CD _______ 8257132
Verve / Mar '92 / PolyGram.

MEETS DIZZY GILLESPIE
Caravan / Mozambique / Autumn leaves / Close your eyes / Blues for Bird / Dizzy atmosphere / Alone together / Con Alma
CD _______ J33J 20015
Pablo / Jul '86 / Jazz Music / Cadillac / Complete/Pinnacle.

MORE I SEE YOU, THE
In a mellow tone / Gee baby ain't I good to you / Squatty Roo / More I see you / When my dreamboat comes home / Ron's blues / For all we know / On the trail / Blues for L.S.A.
CD _______ CD 83370
Telarc / Jul '95 / Conifer / ADA.

MOTIONS AND EMOTIONS
Sally's tomato / Sunny / By the time I get to Phoenix / Wanderin' / This guy's in love with you / Wave / Dreamsville / Yesterday / Eleanor Rigby / Ode to Billy Joe
CD _______ 821 289-2
Polydor / Jul '90 / PolyGram.

NIGERIAN MARKETPLACE (Peterson, Oscar Trio)
Nigerian marketplace / Au privave / Nancy with the laughing face / Misty / Waltz for Debbie / Cake walk / You look good to me
CD _______ CD 2308231
Pablo / Jun '93 / Jazz Music / Cadillac / Complete/Pinnacle.

OSCAR PETERSON & STEPHANE GRAPPELLI (Peterson, Oscar & Stephane Grappelli Quartet)
Them there eyes / Blues for musidisc / Makin' whoopee / Thou swell / Walkin' my baby back home / Autumn leaves / Looking at you / Folks who live on the hill / I won't dance / Time after time / My one and only love / My heart stood still / Flamingo / If I had you / Let's fall in love
CD _______ 403292
Accord / Nov '93 / Discovery / Harmonia Mundi / Cadillac.

OSCAR PETERSON 1951
CD _______ JAS 9501
Just A Memory / Dec '95 / Harmonia Mundi.

OSCAR PETERSON AND HARRY EDISON (Peterson, Oscar & Harry Edison)
Easy living / Days of wine and roses / Gee baby ain't I good to you / Basie / Mean to me / Signify / Willow weep for me / Man I love / You go to my head
CD _______ OJCCD 738
Original Jazz Classics / May '93 / Wellard / Jazz Music / Cadillac / Complete/Pinnacle.

OSCAR PETERSON AND ROY ELDRIDGE (Peterson, Oscar & Roy Eldridge)
Little Jazz / She's funny that way / Way you look tonight / Sunday / Bad hat blues / Between the Devil and the deep blue sea / Blues for Chu
CD _______ OJCCD 727
Original Jazz Classics / Nov '95 / Wellard / Jazz Music / Cadillac / Complete/Pinnacle.

OSCAR PETERSON CD COLLECTION (10 CD Box Set)
CD Set _______ PACD 0012
Pablo / '93 / Jazz Music / Cadillac / Complete/Pinnacle.

OSCAR PETERSON CHRISTMAS, AN
Winter wonderland / Santa Claus is coming to town / Let it snow, let it snow, let it snow / Silent night / Jingle bells / White Christmas / Have yourself a merry little Christmas / Christmas waltz / I'll be home for Christmas / Away in a manger / O Christmas tree / O little town of Bethlehem / God rest ye merry gentlemen / What child is this
CD _______ CD 83372
Telarc / Nov '95 / Conifer / ADA.

OSCAR PETERSON IN CONCERT
Bag's groove / I've got the world on a string / Daahoud / Gai / Sweet Georgia Brown / Tenderly / C jam blues / Pompton turnpike / Seven come eleven / Love for sale / Lollobrigida / Swingin' 'til the girls come home / Nuages / Avalon / Come to the Mardi Gras / Baby, baby, all the time / Easy does it / Sunday / Falling in love with love / Noreen's nocturne / Gypsy in my soul / Flamingo / Love you madly / 52nd Street (theme)
CD _______ RTE 10022
RTE / Apr '95 / ADA / Koch.

OSCAR PETERSON IN CONCERT
CD Set _______ 710443CD
RTE / Apr '95 / ADA / Koch.

OSCAR PETERSON PLAYS BROADWAY
CD _______ 5168932
Verve / Apr '94 / PolyGram.

OSCAR PETERSON TRIO WITH CLARK TERRY (Peterson, Oscar Trio & Clark Terry)
Brotherhood of man / Jim / Blues for Smedley / Roundalay / Mumbles / Mack the knife / They didn't believe me / Squeaky's blues / I want a little girl / Incoherent blues
CD _______ 8188402
Emarcy / Jun '85 / PolyGram.

OSCAR PETERSON, HARRY EDISON & EDDIE 'CLEANHEAD' VINSON (Peterson, Oscar/Harry Edison/Eddie 'Cleanhead' Vinson)
Stuffy / This one's for jaws / Everything happens to me / Broadway / Slooo drag / What's new / Satin doll
CD _______ CD 2310927
Pablo / Apr '94 / Jazz Music / Cadillac / Complete/Pinnacle.

PETERSON
CD _______ OJCCD 3832
Original Jazz Classics / Feb '92 / Wellard / Jazz Music / Cadillac / Complete/Pinnacle.

PORGY AND BESS (Peterson, Oscar & Joe Pass)
Summertime / Bess, you is my woman now / My man's gone now / It ain't necessarily so / I got plenty o' nuttin' / Oh, Bess, oh where's my Bess / I loves you Porgy / They pass by singin' / There's a boat that's leaving shortly for New York / Strawberry woman
CD _______ CD 2310779
Pablo / Apr '94 / Jazz Music / Cadillac / Complete/Pinnacle.

SATCH AND JOSH (Peterson, Oscar & Count Basie)
Bun's blues / These foolish things / R.B. burning / Exactly like you / Jumpin' at the woodside / Louis B. / Lester leaps in / Big stockings / S and J blues
CD _______ CD 2310722
Pablo / Apr '94 / Jazz Music / Cadillac / Complete/Pinnacle.

SATURDAY NIGHT AT BLUE NOTE (Peterson, Oscar Trio)
CD _______ CD 83306
Telarc / Sep '91 / Conifer / ADA.

SIDE BY SIDE (Peterson, Oscar & Itzhak Perlman)
Dark eyes / Stormy weather / Georgia on my mind / Blue skies / Misty / Mack the knife / Night time / I loves you Porgy / On the trail / Yours is my heart alone / Makin' whoopee / Why think about tomorrow
CD _______ CD 83341
Telarc / Oct '94 / Conifer / ADA.

SILVER COLLECTION, THE
My foolish heart / Round Midnight / Someday my Prince will come / Come Sunday / Nightingale / My ship / Sleeping bee / Portrait of Jennie / Goodbye / Con Alma / Maidens of Cadiz / My heart stood still / Woody 'n' you
CD _______ 8234472
Verve / Feb '92 / PolyGram.

SKOL (Peterson, Oscar/Stephane Grappelli/Joe Pass)
Nuages / How about you / Someone to watch over me / Makin' whoopee / That's all / Skol blues
CD _______ OJCCD 496-2
Original Jazz Classics / Feb '92 / Wellard / Jazz Music / Cadillac / Complete/Pinnacle.

STRATFORD, ONTARIO, CANADA
CD _______ CD 53209
Giants Of Jazz / Nov '95 / Target/BMG / Cadillac.

THREE ORIGINALS
CD Set _______ 5210592
Verve / Apr '93 / PolyGram.

TIME AFTER TIME
Cool walk / Love ballade / Soft winds / Who can I turn to / Without a song / Time after time
CD _______ CD 2310947
Pablo / May '94 / Jazz Music / Cadillac / Complete/Pinnacle.

TIMEKEEPERS (Peterson, Oscar & Count Basie)
I'm confessin' that I love you / Soft winds / Rent party / (Back home again in) Indiana / Hey Raymond / After you've gone / That's the one
CD _______ OJCCD 790
Original Jazz Classics / Sep '93 / Wellard / Jazz Music / Cadillac / Complete/Pinnacle.

TRIBUTE TO MY FRIENDS, A
Blueberry Hill / Sometimes I'm happy / Stuffy / Birk's works / Cotton tail / Lover man / Tisket-a-tasket / Rockin' chair / Now's the time
CD _______ CD 2310902
Pablo / May '94 / Jazz Music / Cadillac / Complete/Pinnacle.

TRIO, THE
Blues etude / Chicago blues / Easy listening blues / Come Sunday / Secret love
CD _______ 8230082
Verve / Feb '94 / PolyGram.
CD _______ CD 2310701
Pablo / May '94 / Jazz Music / Cadillac / Complete/Pinnacle.

TRUMPET SUMMIT MEETS THE OSCAR PETERSON BIG FOUR (Peterson, Oscar Big 4)
Daahoud / Chicken wings / Just friends / Champ
CD _______ OJCCD 603-2
Original Jazz Classics / Mar '92 / Wellard / Jazz Music / Cadillac / Complete/Pinnacle.

VIENNA CONCERT 1968
CD _______ W 34-2CD
Philology / Apr '94 / Harmonia Mundi / Cadillac.

WILL TO SING, THE
Fine and dandy / Tenderly / Facsinating rhythm / Swingin' till the girls come home / Gypsy in my soul / When lights are low / Con alma / Ill wind / In the wee small hours of the morning / Daahoud / C Jam blues / Nightingale / Place St. Henri / I've got a crush on you / Lulu's back in town / Wave / Child is born / Younger than springtime
CD Set _______ 847 203-2
Polydor / May '91 / PolyGram.

Peterson, Ralph

RECLAMATION PROJECT, THE
Further fo / Song of serenity / Long journey home / Insanity / Bottom / Turn it over / Just for today / Acceptance / For all my tomorrows / Keep it simple
CD _______ ECD 22113
Evidence / Jun '95 / Harmonia Mundi / ADA / Cadillac.

Peterson, Ricky

SMILE BLUE
CD _______ GOJ 60042
Go Jazz / Sep '95 / Vital/SAM.

TEAR CAN TELL, A
CD _______ GOJ 60162
Go Jazz / Oct '95 / Vital/SAM.

Petra

NO DOUBT
CD _______ 701962460X
Word / Oct '95 / Total/BMG.

Petri, Michala

MOONCHILD'S DREAM
CD _______ 09026625432
RCA / Jul '95 / BMG.

Petrie, Robin

CONTINENTAL DRIFT (Petrie, Robin & Danny Carnahan)
CD _______ FF 70442
Flying Fish / '88 / Roots / CM / Direct / ADA.

Petrucciani, Michel

AU THEATRE DES CHAMPS-ELYEES
Medley of my favourite songs / Night sun in Blois / Radio dial / I mean you/Round about midnight / Even mice dance / Caravan / Love letter / Besame mucho
CD Set _______ FDM 365702
Dreyfus / Mar '95 / ADA / Direct / New Note.

BLUE NOTE YEARS, THE (The Best Of Michel Petrucciani)
Looking up / September song / Miles Davis licks / Play me / Home / Lullaby / La champagne / She did it again / Our tune / Bimini / Brazilian suite / O nana oye
CD _______ CDP 7899162
Blue Note / Nov '93 / EMI.

CONFRENCE DE PRESSE VOL.2 (Petrucciani, Michel & Eddy Louiss)
Autumn leaves / Hub art / Caravan / Naissance / Rachid / Caraibes / Au p'tit jour / Summertime
CD _______ FDM 365732
Dreyfus / Dec '95 / ADA / Direct / New Note.

LIVE
Black magic / Miles Davis licks / Contradictions / Bite / Rachid / Looking up / Thank you note / Estate
CD _______ CDP 7805892
Blue Note / Oct '94 / EMI.

LIVE: MICHEL PETRUCCIANI
CD _______ CCD 43006
Concord Jazz / '88 / New Note.

MARVELLOUS
Manhattan / Charlie Brown / Even mice dance / Why / Hidden joy / Shooting stars / You are my waltz / Dumb breaks / 92's Last / Besame mucho
CD _______ FDM 365642
Dreyfus / Mar '94 / ADA / Direct / New Note.

PROMENADE WITH DUKE
Caravan / Lush life / Take the 'A' train / African flower / In a sentimental mood / Hidden joy / One night in a hotel / Satin doll / C jam blues
CD _______ CDP 7805902
Blue Note / Feb '93 / EMI.

Petters, John

BOOGIE WOOGIE & ALL THAT JAZZ (Petters, John & His Rhythm)
CD _______ RRCD 003
Roots / Apr '93 / Pinnacle.

Pettersson, Andreas

LIVE IN FINLAND
CD _______ DRCD 238
Dragon / Jan '87 / Roots / Cadillac / Wellard / CM / ADA.

Petteway, Al

WATERS & THE WILD, THE
CD _______ MMCD 205
Maggie's Music / Dec '94 / CM / ADA.

WHISPERING STONES
CD _______ MMCD 206
Maggie's Music / Dec '94 / CM / ADA.

Pettiford, Oscar

MONTMARTRE BLUES
CD _______ BLC 760124
Black Lion / Feb '89 / Jazz Music / Cadillac / Wellard / Koch.

VIENNA BLUES
CD _______ BLC 760104
Black Lion / Oct '94 / Jazz Music / Cadillac / Wellard / Koch.

VIENNA BLUES -- THE COMPLETE SESSION
Cohn's limit / Gentle art of love / All the things you are / Stalag 414 / Vienna blues / Oscar's blues / Stardust / There will never be another you / Blues in the closet
CD _______ BLCD 760104
Black Lion / Jun '88 / Jazz Music / Cadillac / Wellard / Koch.

Pettis, Pierce

TINSELTOWN
Moments / Can't get away from my love / So many words / Mickey Leland / Flannery's Georgia / You need a love / Little man / Swimming / Grandmother's song / From way up here / Infernal equinox / Tinseltown
CD _____ 103112
High Street / Jul '91 / ADA.

Petty, Norman

15 CLASSIC MEMORIES VOL.1
Mood indigo / Jambalaya / If you see me crying / Pretty's little polka / I'll string along with you / Oh you pretty woman / Hey good lookin' / Gimme a little kiss, will ya, huh / Jax boogie / It's been a long, long time / Little black samba / Half as much / Echo polka / Dream is a wish your heart makes / My blue heaven
CD _____ CDCHM 443
Ace / Jul '94 / Pinnacle / Cadillac / Complete/Pinnacle.

Petty, Tom

DAMN THE TORPEDOES
Refugee / Here comes the girl / Even the losers / Century city / Don't do me like that / What are you doin' in my life / Louisiana rain
CD _____ MCLD 19014
MCA / Apr '92 / BMG.

FULL MOON FEVER
Free fallin' / I won't back down / Love is a long road / Feel a whole lot better / Yer so bad / Depending on you / Apartment song / Alright for now / Mind with a heart of it's own / Zombie zoo
CD _____ DMCG 6034
MCA / May '89 / BMG.

HARD PROMISES
Waiting / Woman in love / Nightwatchman / Something big / Kings Road / Letting you go / Thing about you / Insider / Criminal kind / You can still change your mind
CD _____ MCLD 19077
MCA / Nov '91 / BMG.

INTO THE GREAT WIDE OPEN
CD _____ MCAD 10317
MCA / Jul '91 / BMG.

LET ME UP (I'VE HAD ENOUGH) (Petty, Tom & The Heartbreakers)
Jammin' me / Runaway train / Damage you've done / It'll all work out / My life / Think about me / All mixed up / Self made man / Ain't love strange / How many more days / Your world / Let me up (I've had enough)
CD _____ MCLD 19141
MCA / Nov '92 / BMG.

LONG AFTER DARK
One story town / You got lucky / Deliver me / Change of heart / Finding out / We stand a chance / Straight into darkness / Same old you / Between two worlds / Wasted life
CD _____ MCLD 19078
MCA / Jun '92 / BMG.

PACK UP THE PLANTATION
CD _____ MCLD 19142
MCA / Nov '91 / BMG.

PLAYBACK (6CD Set)
Big jangle / Breakdown / American girl / Hometown blues / Anything that's rock 'n' roll / I need to know / Listen to her heart / When the time comes / Too much ain't enough / No second thoughts / Baby's a rock 'n' roller / Refugee / Here comes my girl / Even the losers / Shadow of a doubt / Don't do me like that / Waiting / Woman in love / Something big / Thing about you / Insider / You can still change your mind / Spoiled and mistreated / You got lucky / Change of heart / Straight into darkness / Same old you / Rebels / You don't come around here no more / Southern accents / Make it better (forget about me) / Best of everything / So you want to be a rock 'n' roll star / Don't bring me down / Jammin' me / It'll all work out / Mikes life, Mikes world / Think about me / Self made man / Good booty / Free fallin' / I won't back down / Love is a long road / Runnin' down a dream / Yer so bad / Alright for now / Learning to fly / Into the great wide open / All or nothin' / Out in the cold / Built to last / Mary Jane's last dance / Christmas all over again / Outer sides / Casa dega / Heartbreaker's beach party / Trailer / Cracking up / Psychotic reactions / I'm tired Joey boy / Lonely weekends / Gator on the lawn / Make that connection / Down the line / Peace in LA / It's raining again / Somethin' else / I don't know what to say to you / Kings highway / Through the cracks / On the street / Depot street / Cry to me / I can't fight it / Since you said you loved me / Louisiana rain / Keeping me alive / Turning point / Stop draggin' my heart around / Apartment song / Big boss man / Image of me / Moon pie / Damage you've done / Nobody's children / Got my mind made up / Ways to be wicked / Can't get her out / Waiting for tonight / travelin' / baby, let's play house / Wooden heart / God's gift to man / You get me high / Come on down to

my house / You come through / Up in Mississippi tonight
CD Set _____ MCAD 611375
MCA / Nov '95 / BMG.

SOUTHERN ACCENTS
Rebels / It ain't nothin' to me / Don't come around here no more / Southern accents / Make it better / Spike / Dogs on the run / Mary's new car / Best of everything
CD _____ MCLD 19079
MCA / Nov '90 / BMG.

TOM PETTY & THE HEARTBREAKERS (Petty, Tom & The Heartbreakers)
Rockin' around (with you) / American girl / Luna / Mystery man / Fooled again (I don't like it) / Stranger in the night / Anything that's rock 'n' roll / Forever / Wild one / Home town blues / Breakdown
CD _____ MCLD 19012
MCA / Apr '92 / BMG.

TOM PETTY'S GREATEST HITS (Petty, Tom & The Heartbreakers)
American girl / Breakdown / Anything that's rock 'n' roll / Listen to her heart / I need to know / Refugee / Don't do me like that / Even the losers / Here comes my girl / Waiting / You got lucky / Don't come around here no more / I won't back down / Runnin' down a dream / Free fallin' / Learning to fly / Into the great wide open / Mary Jane's last dance / Something in the air
CD _____ MCD 10964
MCA / Oct '93 / BMG.

WILDFLOWERS
CD _____ 936245759-2
WEA / Oct '94 / Warner Music.

YOU'RE GONNA GET IT (Petty, Tom & The Heartbreakers)
When the time comes / You're gonna get it / Hurt / Magnolia / Too much ain't enough / I need to know / Listen to her heart / No second thoughts / Restless / Baby's a rock'n'roller
CD _____ MCLD 19013
MCA / Apr '92 / BMG.

PFR

GREAT LENGTHS
Great lengths / Wonder why / Merry go round / Love I know / Stay / Walk away from love / Trials turned to gold / Blind man, deaf boy / See the sun again / Spinnin' round / Last breathe / Life goes on
CD _____ CDEMC 3703
EMI / Aug '95 / EMI.

Phair, Liz

EXILE IN GUYVILLE
Six foot one / Help me Mary / Glory / Dance of the seven veils / Never said / Soap star Joe / Explain it to me / Canary / Mesmerizing / Fuck and run / Girls, girls, girls / Divorce song / Shatter / Flatter / Flower / Johnny sunshine / Gunshy / Stratford-on-Guy / Strange loop
CD _____ OLE 051-2
Matador / Aug '93 / Vital.

JUVENILIA
Jealousy / Turning Japanese / Animal girl / California / South Dakota / Batmobile / Dead shark / Easy
CD _____ OLE 1292
Matador / Jul '95 / Vital.

WHIPSMART
Chopsticks / Supernova / Support system / X-ray man / Shane / Nashville / Go west / Cinco de mayo / Dogs of L.A. / Whipsmart / Jealousy / Crater lake / Alice springs / May Queen
CD _____ 756792429-2
Warner Bros. / Sep '94 / Warner Music.

Phallus Dei

CYBERFLESH
CD _____ PA 02CD
Dark Vinyl / Sep '93 / Plastic Head.

LUXURIA
CD _____ PA 08CD
Dark Vinyl / May '95 / Plastic Head.

ORPHEUS AND EURYDICE
CD _____ PA 017CD
Resurrection / Jan '96 / Plastic Head.

PORNOCRATES
CD _____ PA 06CD
Paragoric / Mar '95 / Plastic Head.

Phantom

PHANTOM
CD _____ SHARK 023CD
Shark / Jan '92 / Plastic Head.

Phantom 309

SINISTER ALPHABET, A
CD _____ TUPCD 003
Tupelo / Jul '89 / Disc.

Phantom Blue

BUILT TO PERFORM
CD _____ RR 90272
Roadrunner / Oct '93 / Pinnacle.

PHANTOM BLUE
CD _____ RR 9469 2
Roadrunner / Jun '89 / Pinnacle.

Phantom Payn Act

BAD VIBES, ANYONE
CD _____ GRCD 329
Glitterhouse / Sep '94 / Direct / ADA.

TROUBLE WITH GHOSTS
CD _____ GRCD 221
Glitterhouse / Sep '94 / Direct / ADA.

Phantom Rockers

BORN TO BE WILD
CD _____ TBCD 2002
Nervous / Mar '93 / Nervous / Magnum Music Group.

Pharcyde

BIZARRE RIDE II THE PHARCYDE
4 better or 4 worse (interlude) / Oh shit / It's jigaboo time / 4 better or 4 worse / I'm that type of nigga / If I were President / Soul flower / On the DL / Pack the pipe (interlude) / Officer / Ya mama / Passing me by / Otha fish / Quinton's on the way / Pack the pipe / Return of the B-Boy
CD _____ 756792222-2
Delicious Vinyl / Oct '93 / PolyGram.

Phase 5

MENTALE VERWANDLUNG
CD _____ EFA 120562
Rap Nation / Apr '94 / SRD.

Phauss

GOD T PHAUSS
CD _____ SR 9459
Silent / Aug '94 / Plastic Head.

PHAUSS, KARKOWSKI & BILTING (Phauss, Karkowski & Bilting)
CD _____ SR 9217
Silent / Jul '94 / Plastic Head.

Phenobaridols

FISH LOUNGE
CD _____ SFTR 1348CD
Sympathy For The Record Industry / Oct '95 / Plastic Head.

Phenonema 3

INNER VISION
CD _____ CDPAR 002
Parachute Music / Nov '92 / THE.

PHI

SOUND IS SOUND
CD _____ NZ 008CD
Nova Zembla / Jan '95 / Plastic Head.

Philadelphia Bluntz

BLUNTED AT BIRTH
Blunt chronicles / Hostility / Mosquito / I like that / Shaky shaky / Slidehead (mixes) / Transformer / Jugs / Dum dum dum
CD _____ ZEN 005CD
China / Jul '95 / Pinnacle.

Philadelphia...

LET'S CLEAN UP THE GHETTO (Philadelphia International All Stars)
Trade winds / Let's clean up the ghetto / Ooh child / Now is the time to do it / Year of decision / Big gangster / New day / New world comin' / Old people / Save the children / Everybody's here
CD _____ 12218
Laserlight / May '94 / Target/BMG.

Philharmonic Chamber...

ALL IN THE APRIL EVENING (Philharmonic Chamber Choir)
All in the April evening / Isle of Mull / Steal away / Dashing white sergeant / Were you there / Banks o'Doon / Peat fire / Smooring prayer / Loch Lomond / King Arthur / Belmont / Iona boat song / Herdmaiden's song / Bluebird / Faery song from "The Immortal Hour" / An eriskay love lilt
CD _____ CDH 88008
Helios / May '88 / Select.

Philharmonic Pop...

CLASSIC LOVE SONGS (Philharmonic Pop Orchestra)
CD _____ TRTCD 178
TrueTrax / Feb '96 / THE.

DOUBLE IMAGES (Philharmonic Pop Orchestra)
CD _____ ISCD 111
Intersound / Jun '95 / Jazz Music.

PHILHARMONIC POP ORCHESTRA (Philharmonic Pop Orchestra)
CD _____ ISCD 118
Intersound / '91 / Jazz Music.

POP CLASSICS (Philharmonic Pop Orchestra)
CD _____ DCD 5303
Disky / Dec '93 / THE / BMG / Discovery / Pinnacle.

POP TO THE PAST (Philharmonic Pop Orchestra)
CD _____ ISCD 106
Intersound / Jun '95 / Jazz Music.

Philip & Lloyd

BLUES BUSTERS, THE
CD _____ RNCD 2122
Rhino / Nov '95 / Jetstar / Magnum Music Group / THE.

Philip, Michael

AT THE RIVERSIDE (Philip, Michael Ceilidh Band)
CD _____ SP 1035CD
Springthyme / May '93 / Direct / Roots / CM / Duncans / ADA.

Philippe, Louis

APPOINTMENT WITH VENUS
La pluie fait des claquettes / Man down the stairs / When I'm an astronaut / We live on an island / Orchard / Heaven is above me / Rescue the Titanic / Touch of evil / Ballad of Sophie Sololil / Angelica my love / I will / Exporado tales / Apertivo / Fires rise and die
CD _____ ACME 5 CD
El / Jul '89 / Pinnacle.

CLARET
You Mary you / Domenica / What if a day / Monsieur Leduc / Man down the stairs / Red shoes ballet suite / Anna / Anna s'en va / With you and without you / Aperitivo / La pluie fait des claquettes / I collect stamps / Guess I'm dumb / Ruben's room / All stands still / Did you say her name was Peg / Night talk / Fires and rise and die / Yuri Gagarin
CD _____ MONDE 4CD
Richmond / May '92 / Pinnacle.

YURI GAGARIN
Diamond / Did you say her name was Peg / She's great / Endless September / Vision / Goodbye again / Anna s'en va / Jean and me / I collect stamps / Sunday morning / Camden Town / Another boy / Yuri Gagarin
CD _____ ACME 23CD
El / Oct '89 / Pinnacle.

Philips, Glen

ELEVATOR
Micro / Sex messiah / Inca silver metallic / Ario / John Marshall / Vista cruiser / D.N.A. / I ran / Rememory / Tower of babel / Rain tonight / Death ship
CD _____ SST 136 CD
SST / May '93 / Plastic Head.

Philistines Jnr.

SINKING OF THE SS DANEHOWER, THE
CD _____ DOT 9CD
Dot / Nov '95 / EMI.

Phillipe, Louis

DELTA KISS
CD _____ ANA 001
Humbug / Oct '93 / Pinnacle.

SUNSHINE
CD _____ BAH 23
Humbug / Oct '95 / Pinnacle.

Phillips, Anthony

1984
Prelude 84 / 1984 (pts 1 & 2) / Anthem 1984
CD _____ CDOVD 321
Virgin / '89 / EMI.

ANTHOLOGY
Women were watching / Prelude '84 / Anthem from Tarka / Lucy wild / Tregenna afternoons / Unheard cry / Catch at the tables / Lights on the hill / Now what / Um and aargh / Slow dance / Tears on a rainy day / God if I saw her now / Nightmare / Last goodbyes / Collections / Sleepfall: The geese fly west
CD _____ BP 201CD
Blueprint / Oct '95 / Pinnacle.

FINGERPAINTING
CD _____ BP 209CD
Blueprint / Oct '95 / Pinnacle.

GEESE AND THE GHOST, THE
CD _____ CDOVD 315
Virgin / Nov '90 / EMI.

GYPSY SUITE (Phillips, Anthony & Harry Williamson)
First light / Siesta / Evening circle / Crystal ball / Early years / Streams river and salmon hunting / Dunes and estuary / Moonfield - Postscript
CD _____ VP 189CD
Voice Print / Jan '95 / Voice Print.

INVISIBLE MEN
Sally / Golden bodies / Going for broke / It's not easy / Traces / Guru / My time has come / Love in a hot air balloon / I want your heart / Falling for love / Women were watching
CD _______________ BP 211CD
Blueprint / Oct '95 / Pinnacle.

MISSING LINKS
CD _______________ PRO 012
Progress / Jul '92 / Vital.

MISSING LINKS VOL. 2 (The Sky Road)
Exile / Lifeboat suite / Bitter suite / Across the river Styx / Flock of souls / Along the towpath / Sky road / Tears on a rainy day / Tiwai: Island of the apes / Wild voices, quiet water / Suite / Serenita / Timepiece / Field of eternity / Beggar and the thief
CD _______________ BWKD 212
Brainworks / May '94 / Pinnacle.

PRIVATE PARTS AND PIECES I
CD _______________ BP 202CD
Blueprint / Oct '95 / Pinnacle.

PRIVATE PARTS AND PIECES II (Back To The Paviliion)
CD _______________ BP 203CD
Blueprint / Oct '95 / Pinnacle.

PRIVATE PARTS AND PIECES III (Antiques)
CD _______________ BP 204CD
Blueprint / Nov '95 / Pinnacle.

PRIVATE PARTS AND PIECES V (Twelve)
January / February / March / April / May / June / July / August / September / October / November / December
CD _______________ BP 206CD
Blueprint / Dec '95 / Pinnacle.

PRIVATE PARTS AND PIECES VI (Ivory Moon)
Sunrise over Sienna / Basking shark - sea dog's air / Safe havens / Tara's theme / Winter's thaw / Old house / Moonfall / Rapids / Let us now make love
CD _______________ BP 207CD
Blueprint / Jan '96 / Pinnacle.

PRIVATE PARTS AND PIECES VII
CD _______________ BP 208CD
Blueprint / Jan '96 / Pinnacle.

PRIVATE PARTS AND PIECES VIII
Aubade / Infra dig / Santuary / La dolorosa / New England suite (I) / New England suite (II) / New England suite (III) / Last goodbyes / Sunrise and sea monsters / Iona / Cathedral woods / If I could tell you / Jaunty roads / Spirals / Pieces of eight (I) Pressgang / Pieces of eight (II) Sargasso / Pieces of eight (III) Sea-shanty / In the maze / Unheard cry / Now they're all gone
CD _______________ BP 212CD
Blueprint / Jan '96 / Pinnacle.

SAIL THE WORLD (Music From The Whitbread Race 1994)
Opening theme / Fast work / Dark seas / Cool sailing / Wildlife choir / I wish this would never end / Salsa / Roaring forties / Lonely whales / Icebergs / Majestic whales / In the Southern ocean / Freemantle doctor / Long way from home / Wildlife flotilla / Big combers / Cool sailing II / Cape horn / Amongst mythical birds / Salsa II / Into the tropics / In the doldrums / Heading for home and victory
CD _______________ RES 102CD
Voice Print / May '94 / Voice Print.

SIDES
CD _______________ BP 210CD
Blueprint / Nov '95 / Pinnacle.

WISE AFTER THE EVENT
CD _______________ CDOVD 322
Virgin / '89 / EMI.

Phillips, Barre

AQUARIAN RAIN
Bridging / Flow / Ripples edge / Inbetween I and E / Ebb / Promenade de Memoire / Eddies / Early tide / Water shed / Aquarian rain
CD _______________ 5115132
ECM / Mar '92 / New Note.

CAMOUFLAGE
CD _______________ VICTOCD 08
Victo / Nov '94 / These / ReR Megacorp / Cadillac.

JOURNAL VIOLONE II
CD _______________ 8473282
ECM / Mar '94 / New Note.

THREE DAY MOON
A-i-a / Ms. P. / La folle / BRD / Ingul-Buz / S.C. and W.
CD _______________ 8473262
ECM / Jun '92 / New Note.

Phillips, Eddie

RIFFMASTER OF THE WESTERN WORLD
CD _______________ PL 102152
Promised Land / Oct '90 / Kingdom / Direct.

Phillips, Esther

BAD BAD GIRL
Ring-a-ding doo / I'm a bad bad girl / Deacon moves in / Looking for a man / Hound dog / Cherry wine / Turn the lamps down low / Flesh blood and bones / Last laugh blues / You took my love too fast / Saturday night daddy / Mainliner / Hollerin' and screamin' / Storm / Ramblin' blues / Aged and mellow blues
CD _______________ CDCHARLY 47
Charly / Jan '87 / Charly / THE / Cadillac.

CONFESSIN' THE BLUES
I'm gettin' 'long alright / Ronettes / Confessin' the blues / Romance in the dark / C.C. rider / Cherry red / In the evening / I love Paris / It could happen to you / Bye bye blackbird / Blow top blues / Jelly jelly blues / Long John blues
CD _______________ 7567906702
Atlantic / Jul '93 / Warner Music.

CONFESSIN' THE BLUES
CD _______________ RSACD 807
Sequel / Oct '94 / BMG.

I PAID MY DUES
Better beware / Hold me / Somebody new / Bring my lovin' back to me / I paid my dues / Sweet lips / Love oh love / I'll be there (at your beck and call) / Street lights / Heart to heart / Tell him that I need him / Summertime / Cryin' blues / Other lips, other arms / Don't make a fool out of me / Cryin' and singin' the blues
CD _______________ SING 81156
Sing / May '88 / Charly.

LIVE AT THE RISING SUN
CD _______________ RS 0007CD
Rising Sun / Jul '95 / ADA.

WAY TO SAY GOODBYE, A
It's all in the game / Mama said / Going in circles / Nowhere to run / We are through / Fa fa fa fa fa (sad song) / Mr. Bojangles / Shake this off / Way to say goodbye
CD _______________ MCD 5302
Muse / Feb '87 / New Note / CM.

Phillips, Flip

FLIP PHILLIPS AND SCOTT HAMILTON (Phillips, Flip & Scott Hamilton)
CD _______________ CCD 4334
Concord Jazz / Dec '87 / New Note.

FLIP PHILLIPS AT THE HELM 1993
CD _______________ CRD 127
Chiara Scuro / Feb '95 / Jazz Music / Kudos.

FLIP WAILS - THE BEST OF THE VERVE YEARS
CD _______________ 521645-2
Verve / Jun '94 / PolyGram.

Phillips, John

JOHN THE WOLF KING OF L.A.
CD _______________ EDCD 372
Edsel / Nov '92 / Pinnacle / ADA.

Phillips, Simon

PROTOCOL
Street wise / Protocol / V8 / Red rocks / Slofunk / Wall Street
CD _______________ GRUB 10 MCD
Food For Thought / Dec '88 / Pinnacle.

Phillips, Sonny

SURF NUFF/ BLACK MAGIC
Sure nuff sure nuff / Be yourself / Oleo / Mobile to Chicago / Other blues / Make it plain / Wakin' up / Over the rainbow / Bean pie / I'm an old cowhand (from the Rio Grande) / Brotherhood
CD _______________ CDBGPD 063
BGP / Jun '93 / Pinnacle.

Phillips, Steve

BEEN A LONG TIME GONE (Phillips, Steve & The Famous Five)
CD _______________ CL 001CD
Clarion / Jul '95 / ADA / Hot Shot.

STEEL RAIL BLUES
CD _______________ BRAVE 9 CD
UnAmerican Activities / Dec '89 / Hot Shot / Swift.

Phillips, Stu

JOURNEY THROUGH THE PROVINCES, A
Village blacksmith / Champlain and St. Lawrence line / En roulant ma boule / Donkey riding / Legend of Perce rock / Horse trader / Canadee-i-o / Phantom priest / Dollard les ormeaux / Madelaine De Vecheres / Winter camp / Priest who slept one hundred years / Riverboat captain / Okanagan valley / Simon gun-a-noot / Mountain boy / Bill miner / Cartherine O'Hare Schubert / When the iceworms nest again / Legend of the fernie fire / Grand hotel / Bill Barker's party / Alexander Mackensie / Moon over the rockies / Fraser's valley / Star child / Almighty voice / Albert Johnson / Chief's lament / Ernest Cashel / White stallion legend / Nigger John / Bull train / Banff cave / Fireworks
CD _______________ BCD 15721
Bear Family / Aug '93 / Rollercoaster / Direct / CM / Swift / ADA.

Phillips, Utah

WE HAVE FED YOU ALL A THOUSAND YEARS
Boss / We have fed you all a thousand years / Sheep and goats / Timberbeast's lament / Dump the bosses off your back / Lumberjack's prayer / Mr. Block / Preacher and the slave / Popular wobbly / Casey Jones - the union scab / Where the fraser river flows / Bread and roses / Joe Hill / Union burying ground / Two bums / Hallelujah / I'm a bum / Solidarity forever / There's power in a union
CD _______________ PHCD 1076
Philo / May '93 / Direct / CM / ADA.

Phillips, Washington

I AM BORN TO PREACH THE GOSPEL
CD _______________ CD 2003
Yazoo / Sep '92 / CM / ADA / Roots / Koch.

Philly Groove Orchestra

SOUNDS OF PHILLY
CD _______________ HADCD 186
Javelin / Nov '95 / THE / Henry Hadaway Organisation.

Phlebotomized

IMMENSE INTENSE SUSPENSE
CD _______________ CYBERCD 12
Cyber / Jan '95 / Plastic Head.

Phobia

RETURN TO DESOLATION
CD _______________ RR 6093-2
Relapse / Oct '94 / Plastic Head.

Phoenix Jig

S.T.
CD _______________ SOHO 15CD
Suburbs Of Hell / Aug '94 / Pinnacle / Plastic Head / Kudos.

Phoenix Sax Quartet

RETURN OF BULGY GOGO
Two cod pieces / Dance variations / In memoriam Scott Fitzgerald / Pantomine / In memoriam Django Reinhardt / Patterns / Flying birds / Fugue in G minor / Saxe blue / What then is love / Mock Joplin / Three musical mishaps / Quincey's rag / Return of the pink panther
CD _______________ URCD 106
Upbeat / Apr '92 / Target/BMG / Cadillac.

Phunk Junkees

INJECTED
CD _______________ 6544925562
WEA / Sep '95 / Warner Music.

Phychodrama

ILLUSION, THE
CD _______________ MASSCD 079
Massacre / Nov '95 / Plastic Head.

Piaf, Edith

30EME ANNIVERSAIRE
La vie en rose / J'm'en fous pas mal / Les trois cloches / Les amants de Paris / Bal dans ma rue / Plus bleu que tes yeux / Hymne a l'amour / Jezebel / Padam padam / Hymn to love / Bravo pour le clown / Johnny tu n'es pas un ange / La goualante du pauvre Jean / Le ca Ira / L'accordeoniste / C'est a Hambourg / L'homme a la moto / Les amants d'un jour / Autumn leaves / Dans les prisons de Nantes / Pour moi toute seule / Il y avait / La foule / Mon manage a moi / Fais comme ci / Je sais comment / Milord / Non, je ne regrette rien / Les flons flons du bal / Le vieux piano / Mon vieux Lucien / Mon dieu / Sous le ciel de Paris / Les amants / A quoi ce sert l'amour / Une valse / Emporte-moi / L'homme de Berlin / Legende / A l'eneigne de la fille sans coeur / La valse de l'amour / Les mots d'amour
CD Set _______________ CDS 8270972
EMI / Nov '93 / EMI.

CHANSOPHONE 1936-42
CD _______________ 701272
Chansophone / Jun '93 / Discovery.

EDITH PIAF AT THE PARIS OLYMPIA
Milord / Heureuse / Avec ce soleil / C'est a Hambourg / Legende / Enfin le printemps / Padam padam / Hymne a l'amour / L'accordeoniste / Mon manege a moi / Bravo pour le clown / Les mots d'amour / Les flons flons du bal / T'es l'homme qu'il me faut / Mon dieu / Mon vieux Lucien / Non, je ne regrette rien / La ville inconnue (CD only.) / La belle histoire d'amour (CD only.) / Les blouses blanches (CD only.)
CD _______________ CZ 315
EMI / Jun '90 / EMI.

EDITH PIAF IN CONCERT
CD _______________ 3456001
RTE / Oct '95 / ADA / Koch.

EDITH PIAF TRIBUTE (Various Artists)
La vie en rose / Hymn to love (L'hymme a l'amour) / Jezebel / When I see her (Fallait-il) / Effect you have on me (L'effet que tu me fais) / Lovers of one day (Les amants d'un jour) / Carousel for two (Mon manege a moi) / No regret (Non je ne regrette rien) / Three bells (Les trois cloches) / My legionnaire (Mon legeionnaire) / Black denim and motorcycle boots (L'homme a la moto) / In memory
CD _______________ DSHCD 7014
D-Sharp / May '94 / Pinnacle.

ESCALE
CD _______________ CDCD 3010
Charly / Sep '94 / Charly / THE / Cadillac.

ETOILES DE LA CHANSON 1935-42
CD _______________ 878162
Music Memoria / Jun '93 / Discovery / ADA.

FAIS-MOI VALSER
CD _______________ CDCD 3006
Charly / Sep '94 / Charly / THE / Cadillac.

HER GREATEST RECORDINGS 1935-1942
Mon legionnaire / Un coin tout bleu / Mon coeur est au coin d'une rue / Le grand voyage du pauvre negre / Ballade de Mr. Browning / D'etait une histoire d'amour / On danse sur ma chanson / De l'autre cote de la rue / C'est toi le plus fort / Fais-moi valser / Paris - Mediterranee / Mon apero / Le fanion de la legion / Mon amant de la coloniale / Entre se ouen et clignancourt / L'etranger / C'etait un jour de fete / Les momes de la cloche / Elle frequentait la rue pigalle / C'est lui que mon coeur a choisi / L'accordeoniste
CD _______________ CDAJA 5165
ASV / Apr '95 / Koch.

INTEGRALE 1946-1963
J'm'en fous pas mal / Le petit homme / Unrefrain courait dans la rue / Celine / Le roi a fait battre tambour / Dans les prisons de Nantes / Les trois cloches / Adieu mon coeur / Le chant du pirate / C'est marveilleux / Mariage / Un homme comme les autres / Qu'as-tu fait John / C'est pour ca / Il pleut / Monsieur Lenoble / Les amants de Paris / Il a chante / Dany / Pour moi toute seule / Bal dans ma rue / Le prisonnier de la tour / Paris / L'orgue des amoureux / Pleure pas / La petite Marie / Tous les amoureux chantent / Hymne a l'amour / Le ciel est ferme / Il fait bon t'aimer / Le chavelaier de Paris / C'est un gars / C'est d'la faute a tes yeux / La fete continue / Hymn to love / Three bells / La vie en rose / Simply a waltz / Il y avait / Chante moi / Chanson bleue / Plus bleu que tes yeux / Une enfant / Jezebel / Le noel de la rue / A l'eneigne de la fille sans coeur / Telegramme / Je hais les dimanches / Si, si, si, si / Du matin jusqu'au soir / Demain / C'est toi / L'homme que j'aimerai / Avant l'heure / Rien de rien / La valse de l'amour / Padam padam / La rue aux chansons / Chanson de Catherine / Mon ami m'a donne / Je t'ai dans la peau / Monsieur et madame / Ca guele ca Madame / Au bal de la chance / Notre Dame de Paris / Elle a dit / Jean et Martine / Les amants de Venise / Les croix / Bravo pour le clown / Johnny tu n'es pas un ange / Et moi... / Soeur Anne / Heureuse / N'y vas pas Manuel / L'effet qu'tu m'fais / Pour qu-'elle soit jolie ma chanson / Le bel indifferent / La goualante du pauvre Jean / Le "ca ira" / Avec ce soleil / Mea culpa / Enfin le printemps / L'homme au piano / Sous le ciel de Paris / L'accordeoniste / Retour / Serenade de Pave / Le chemin des Forains / Un grand amour qui s'acheve / Misericorde / legende / C'est a Hambourg / L'homme a la moto / Soudain une vallee / Avant nous / Toi qui sais / Une dame / Et pourtant / Marie la Francaise / Les amants d'un jour / Autumn leaves / One little man / Heaven a mercy / My lost melody / I shouldn't care / Don't cry / Chante-moi / Because I love you / la Foule / Salle d'attente / Les prisons du Roy / Opinion publique / Les grognards / Comme toi / Mon manege a moi / Les amants de demain / Fais comme si / Les nieges de Finlande / Tant qu'il y aura des jours / Un etranger / Le ballet des coeurs / Eden blues / Je sais comment / Le gitan et la fille / Les orgues de Barbarie / Je me souviens d'une chanson / C'est un homme terrible / Tatave / T'es beau tu sais / Milord / C'est l'amour / Ouragan / Cri du coeur / kiosque a journaux / Le metro de Paris / Non la vie n'est pas triste / Non, je ne regrette rien / Les flons flons du bal / Les mots d'amour / La ville inconnue / Des histoires / Les blouses blanches / T'es l'homme qu'il me faut / Mon dieu / La belle histoire d'amour / Je suis a toi / Les amants merveilleux / Le vieux piano / Boulevard du crime / Jerusalem / Je m'imagine / La vie, l'amour / Les bleuets d'azur / Quand tu dors / Toujours aimer / Le billard electrique / Mon vieux Lucien / No regrets / Exodus / Dans leur baiser / Faut pas qu'il se figure / Le bruit des villes / Marie trottoir / Les amants / Qu'il etait triste cet Anglais / C'est peut-etre ca / Carmen's story / Toi, tu l'entends pas / Polichinelle / Fallait-il / A quoi ca sert

l'amour / Une valse / Ca fait drole / On cherche un Auguste / Emporte-moi / Musique a tout va / Le diable de la Bastille / Inconnu excepte de dieu / Quatorze Juillet "Les enfants de Teruel" / Le petit brouillard / Le droit d'aimer / Roulez tambours / Le rendez-vous / Monsieur incognito / Le chant d'amour / J'en ai tant vu / C'etait pas moi / Margot coeur gros / Les gens / Traque / Tiens, v'la un marin / L'homme de Berlin / Le chemin de forains
CD Set _____ CDS 4790642
EMI / Nov '93 / EMI.

L'IMMORTELLE
La vie en rose / Les trois cloches / Hymne a l'amour / Mon dieu / Jezebel / Le noel de la rue / Padam padam / La chanson de Catherine / Bravo pour le clown / Johnny tu n'es pas un ange / Heureuse / La goualante du pauvre Jean / Enfin le printemps / L'accordeoniste / Le chant d'amour / C'est a Hambourg / Les amants d'un jour / La foule / Mon manege a moi / Milord / La ville inconnue / A quoi ca sert l'amour / Le diable de la Bastille / Non, je ne regrette rien
CD _____ CDEMC 3674
EMI / Mar '94 / EMI.

LA FANION DE LA LEGION
CD _____ CDCD 3008
Charly / Sep '94 / Charly / THE / Cadillac.

LA MOME EARLY RECORDINGS 1936-44
CD _____ PASTCD 7068
Flapper / Apr '95 / Pinnacle.

LA MOME PIAF
CD _____ 105012
Musidisc / Mar '90 / Vital / Harmonia Mundi / ADA / Cadillac / Discovery.

LA MOME PIAF VOL.1
Les momes de la cloche / L'etranger / Reste / La fille et le chien / La julie jolie / Moi valser / Mon amant de la coloniale / Il n'est pas distingue / La java de cezique / Mon apero / Les hiboux / Je suis mordue / Fais / Va danser / Y avaid du soleil / Les deux menetriers
CD _____ 104 552
Musidisc / Mar '90 / Vital / Harmonia Mundi / ADA / Cadillac / Discovery.

LA MOME PIAF VOL.2
Mon legionnaire / Chants d'habits / Entre saint - queen et clingnancourt / Browning / Un jeune homme chantait / Le fanion de la legion / Tout fout le camp le chacal / Madeleine qu'avait du coeur / Le contrebandier / La petite boutique / Correcq et reguyer / Paris mediterranee / C'est toi le plus fort / Ding din dong / Le chacal
CD _____ 104 562
Musidisc / Mar '90 / Vital / Harmonia Mundi / ADA / Cadillac / Discovery.

LA MOME PIAF VOL.3
CD _____ 104 572
Musidisc / Mar '90 / Vital / Harmonia Mundi / ADA / Cadillac / Discovery.

LEGENDARY EDITH PIAF, THE
Heureuse / Non, Je ne regrette rien / La goualante du pauvre Jean / Padam padam / L'accordeoniste / La vie en rose / Les amants d'un jour / A quoi ca sert l'amour (CD only.) / Mon manege a moi (CD only.) / La foule (CD only.) / Les mots d'amour (CD only.) / Comme moi (CD only.) / Le droit d'aimer (CD only.) / Les feuilles mortes / Les flons flons du bal / Enfin le printemps / Mon dieu / C'est a Hambourg / Milord / Hymne a l'amour (If you love me, really love me)
CD _____ CDMFP 6071
Music For Pleasure / Jun '89 / EMI.

NON JE NE REGRETTE RIEN
CD _____ CD 0201
Entertainers / Mar '92 / Target/BMG.

Piano Red

ATLANTA BOUNCE
CD _____ ARHCD 379
Arhoolie / Apr '95 / ADA / Direct / Cadillac.

BLUES,BLUES,BLUES
CD _____ BLCD 760181
Black Lion / Apr '93 / Jazz Music / Cadillac / Wellard / Koch.

DOCTOR IS IN, THE
Jumpin' the boogie / Rockin' with Red / Let's have a time tonight / Red's boogie / Right string baby, but the wrong yo-yo / My gal Jo / Baby, what's wrong / Well, well baby / Just right bounce / Diggin' the boogie / Layin' the boogie / Bouncin' with Red / It makes no difference now / Hey good lookin' / Count the days I'm gone / My boogie / Sales tax boogie / Voo doopee doo / Daybreak / She walks right in / I'm gonna tell everybody / I'm gonna rock some more / She's dynamite / Everybody's boogie / Your mouth's got a hole in it / Right and ready / Taxi, taxi 6963 / Decatur Street boogie / Sober / She knocks me out / Going away baby / Chittlin' hop / Decatur Street blues / I ain't fattenin' frogs for snakes / Big rock Joe from Kokomo / Play it no mind / Jump man jump / She love me / Peach tree parade / Red's blues / Six o'clock bounce / Jumpin' with daddy / Gordy's rock / Real good thing / Goodbye/Please tell me

baby / You were mine for a while / Sweetest little something / Since I fell for you / Wooee / Rock baby / Teach me to forget / Wild fire / Please don't talk about me when I'm gone / South / Coo cha / Dixie roll / Boston scored / One glimpse of heaven / Blues blues / Work with it / Eighter from Decatur / Please come back home / Comin' on / Ain't nobody's fool / Don't get around much anymore / Umph-umph-umph / Got you on my mind / It's time to boogie / That's my desire / Teen-age bounce / Pay it no mind / Get up mare / 1-2-3 / My baby / Rock 'n' roll boogie / Nighttime / So worried / Blues, blues / Boogie re-bop / This old world / I feel good / Talk to me / Believe in me / Guitar walk / I've been rockin' / So shook up / Dr. Feelgood / Mr. Moonlight / Swabble / I'll be home one day / Sea breeze / I ain't gonna be a lowdown log no more / Don't let me catch you wrong / What's up doc / I'll give anything / Love is amazing / Bald headed Lena / It's a sin to tell a lie / Same old things keep happening / My gal Joe / Blang dong / I don't mind / Doctor's boogie / I'm the house rock on / Doctor of love / It's sin to tell a lie / Good guys / Goodbye (I can't forget) / Don't tell me no dirty / Where did you go
CD Set _____ BCD 15685
Bear Family / Nov '93 / Rollercoaster / Direct / CM / Swift / ADA.

Pianorama

CHRISTMAS CRACKER, A
Jingle bells medley / Sleigh ride / Home for the holidays (medley) / It's beginning to look like Christmas / Snowy white snow and jingle bells / Hark the herald angels sing (medley) / Silent night / Winter wonderland / I saw Mommy kissing Santa Claus (medley) / Mistletoe and holly medley / Christmas song / Does Santa Claus sleep on his whiskers / Once upon a wintertime/Mary's boy child / White Christmas / God rest ye merry gentlemen (medley)
CD _____ DLCD 112
Dulcima / Nov '90 / Savoy / THE.

LET YOURSELF GO
Let's face the music and dance / Is it true what they say about dixie / You brought a new kind of love / Swinging down the lane
CD _____ DLCD 111
Dulcima / Sep '91 / Savoy / THE.

SENSATIONAL SIXTIES, THE (2)
CD _____ DLCD 108
Dulcima / Sep '90 / Savoy / THE.

SHOW TIME IN DANCE TIME
Put me on a happy face/Me and my girl / Lambeth walk / On the street where you live/Dancing on the ceiling/If I rul / Mr. Snow/If I loved you/When the children are asleep / There's a small hotel / I'm gonna wash that man right outa my hair (medley with Honey Bun/Happy) / I whistle a happy tune/Shall we dance/I want to be happy / Glamorous night/Waltz of my heart / Someday I'll find you/I'll see you again / Anything you can do / Surrey with the fringe on top / There's no business like shoe business / Best of times/June is bustin' out all over / We kiss in a shadow/I have dreamed / Bewitched, bothered and bewildered / Wonderful guy/Wunderbar / They say it's wonderful/I won't send roses/Younger than spri / Edelweiss/This nearly was mine / Who do I love you/People will say we're in love/Doi what co
CD _____ DLCD 114
Dulcima / May '94 / Savoy / THE.

WARTIME FAVOURITES
We're gonna hang out the washing on the Siegfried line / Run rabbit run / Hey little hen / Let the people sing / I've got sixpence / Roll out the barrel / Praise the lord and pass the ammunition / Mairzy doats and dozy doats / In the quartermaster's stores / I left my heart at the stage door canteen / If I had my way / I don't want to set the world on fire / You are my sunshine / Sgt Major's serenade / Don't sit under the apple tree / Dearly beloved / I'll be seeing you / Something to remember you by / Sailor with the navy blue eyes / Coming in on a wing and a prayer / I'm gonna get lit up (when the lights go on in London) / Fleet's in / That lovely weekend / Room 504 / Nightingale sang in Berkeley Square / It's foolish but it's / Elmer's tune / Lili Marlene / Yours / Jingle jangle / Deep in the heart of Texas / Oh Johnny oh / Nightingale will make it so) / Tangerine / Long ago and far away / Our love affair / It's a lovely day tomorrow / Wish me good luck as you wave goodbye / Kiss me goodnight, Sergeant Major / Nursie nursie / Ma, I miss your apple pie / You'll never know (Available CD only) / Beneath the lights of home (Available CD only) / Silver wings in the moonlight (Available CD only) / Moonlight becomes you (Available CD only) / When the lights go on again (Available CD only) / All over the place (Available CD only) / Down forget-me-not lane (Available CD only) / White cliffs of Dover / We'll meet again
CD _____ DLCD 106
Dulcima / Apr '95 / Savoy / THE.

Pianosauras

GROOVY NEIGHBOURHOOD
CD _____ CD 9010
Rounder / '88 / CM / Direct / ADA / Cadillac.

Piazza, Rod

BLUES IN THE DARK (Piazza, Rod & The Mighty Flyers)
Black Top / '92 / CM / Direct / ADA. _____ BT 1062CD

HARPBURN
Black Top / Apr '93 / CM / Direct / ADA. _____ BT 1087CD

LIVE AT BB KING'S, MEMPHIS (Piazza, Rod & The Mighty Flyers)
Big Mo / Jul '94 / Direct / ADA. _____ BIGMO 1026

Piazzolla, Astor

5 TANGO SENSATIONS (Piazzolla, Astor & Kronos Quartet)
CD _____ 7599792542
Elektra Nonesuch / Jan '95 / Warner Music.

ADIOS NONINO
CD _____ CD 12508
Music Of The World / Nov '92 / Target/ BMG / ADA.

BALADA PARA UN LOCO AMELITA
CD _____ CD 3508
Cameo / Nov '95 / Target/BMG.

CENTRAL PARK CONCERT, THE
Verano porteno / Jundado / Milonga del angel / Muerte del angel / Astor's speech / La camorra / Mumuki / Adios nonino / Contra bajilsmo / Michelangelo / Concierto para quinteto
CD _____ JD 107
Chesky / Feb '94 / Complete/Pinnacle.

CONCERTO FOR BANDONEON & ORCHESTRA
CD _____ 7559791742
Elektra Nonesuch / Jan '95 / Warner Music.

LA CAMORRA
La Camorra 1 / La Camorra 2 / La Camorra 3 / Soledad / Fugata / Sur: Los Suenos / Sur: Regresso al amor
CD _____ AMCL 1021CD
American Clave / Jan '94 / New Note / ADA / Direct.

LATE MASTERPIECES
CD _____ AMCL 1022
American Clave / Jan '94 / New Note / ADA / Direct.

LIBERTANGO
Libertango / Meditango / Undertango / Adios nonino / Violentango / Novi tango / Amelitango / Tristango
CD _____ CD 62037
Saludos Amigos / Nov '93 / Target/BMG.

LIVE IN VIENNA
Fracanapa / Verano Porteno / Caliente / Decarisimo / Libertango / Revirado / Invierno porteno / Adois nonino
CD _____ 159222
Ronnie Scott's Jazz House / Jun '89 / Jazz Music / Magnum Music Group / Cadillac.

LUNA (Piazzolla, Astor & The New Tango Sextet)
Hora cero / Tanguedia 3 / Milonga del angel / Camorra 3 / Preludio y fuga / Sex-tet / Luna
CD _____ CDEMC 3723
Hemisphere / Oct '95 / EMI.

MILONGA DEL ANGEL
CD _____ CD 62036
Saludos Amigos / Oct '93 / Target/BMG.

PIAZZOLLISSIMO - 1974-1983
CD Set _____ JAM 9103/5-2
Just A Memory / Mar '92 / Harmonia Mundi.

ROUGH DANCER AND THE CYCLICAL NIGHT
CD _____ AMCL 1019CD
American Clave / Jan '94 / New Note / ADA / Direct.

SADNESS OF A DOUBLE A, THE
CD _____ 15970
Messidor / Apr '89 / Koch / ADA.

TANGAMENTE
CD Set _____ JAM 9107/9-2
Just A Memory / Sep '93 / Harmonia Mundi.

TANGO PIAZZOLLA
CD _____ MCCD 165
MCI / Jul '94 / Disc / THE.

TANGO: ZERO HOUR
Tanguedia III / Milonga del angel / Concierto para quinteto / Milonga loca / Michelangelo '70 / Countrabajissimo / Mumuki
CD _____ AMCL 1013CD
American Clave / Jan '94 / New Note / ADA / Direct.

Pic & Bill

TAKING UP THE SLACK
CD _____ BAN 4109CD
Haven/Backs / Sep '91 / Disc / Pinnacle.

Picasso Trigger

BIPOLAR COWBOY
Serve this / Jack rabbit / Hod rod luvr / Towel song / Narcon milk shakes on sale today / Fried fish and cole slaw / Coco w / Skimmed milk / OCS / Reverend Money Waters / Club joiner / T-rash soundtrack for a t-rash heart / Jiminy slim / Riot girls taste like chicken / Let you down / Jerry bomber / City slut slander / You are / Carteret country castes / Buckshot goodbyes
CD _____ A 081D
Alias / Aug '95 / Vital.

FIRE IN THE HOLE
Rub a dub / Expect / Valentine / Get up / Matarcher / Beanpole / Sheltie / We're going down / Man's fault / Remind us / Queenie / TV mind / Mi lapizes muy grande / Colossal man / Count to ten
CD _____ A 056D
Alias / Mar '94 / Vital.

T'AIN'T
Lo-fi Tennesse mountain angel / 455 / Infinite belching boy / Red headed retard / Kiss me where it counts / Anti'd
CD _____ A 077D
Alias / Jan '95 / Vital.

Piccadilly Dance...

SHALL WE DANCE (Piccadilly Dance Orchestra)
CD _____ VIRCD 8326
TER / Mar '94 / Koch.

Piccolo, Greg

HEAVY JUICE
Hammer / Baby I'm gone / Bolo blues / Freeze / It's obdacious / Mushmouth / Brother Jug's sermon / Plaid laces / Count your blessings / Highballin' daddy / Hawk's barrel house / Pic's gospel groove / Big boss man
CD _____ FIENDCD 202
Demon / Oct '90 / Pinnacle / ADA.

Pickett, Dan

DAN PICKETT/SLIM TARHEEL 1949 (Pickett, Dan & Slim Tarheel)
Baby how long / You got to do better / Ride to funeral / Decoration day / Drivin' that thing / That's grieving me / Chicago blues / Somebody changed the lock / You're a little too slow / Get on the road to glory
CD _____ FLYCD 25
Flyright / Oct '90 / Hot Shot / Wellard / Jazz Music / CM.

Pickett, Lenny

LENNY PICKETT & THE BORNEO HORNS (Pickett, Lenny & The Borneo Horns)
Dance music for Borneo Horns (1-5) / Solo for saxaphone / Septer / Dance suite / Landscape
CD _____ HNCD 1321
Hannibal / May '89 / Vital / ADA.

Pickett, Wilson

AMERICAN SOUL MAN
Thing called love / When your heart speaks / Love never let me down / Man of value / (I wanna) make love to you / In the midnight hour / Don't turn away / Just let her know / Can't stop now
CD _____ 5501782
Spectrum/Karussell / Mar '94 / PolyGram / THE.

BEST OF WILSON PICKETT
In the midnight hour / 634 5789 / I found a love / Mustang Sally / ninety nine and a half (won't do) / Everybody needs somebody to love / Don't fight it / I'm a midnight mover / Funky Broadway / Soul dance number three / I'm in love / Land of 1000 dances
CD _____ 7567817372
WEA / Mar '93 / Warner Music.

HEY JUDE
Save me / Hey Jude / Back in your arms / Toe hold / Night owl / My own style of loving / Man and a half / Sit down and talk this over / Search your heart / Born to be wild / People make the world
CD _____ 7567803752
Atlantic / Jan '96 / Warner Music.

I'M IN LOVE
Jealous love / Stagger Lee / That kind of love / I'm in love / Hello sunshine / Don't let no woman / We've got to have love / Bring it on home / She is looking good / I've come a long way
CD _____ 8122722182
Atlantic / Jan '96 / Warner Music.

IN PHILADELPHIA
CD _____ 8122722192
Atlantic / Jan '96 / Warner Music.

IN THE MIDNIGHT HOUR
In the midnight hour / Terdrops will fall / Take a little love / For better or worse / I found a love / That's a man's way / I'm gonna cry / Don't fight it / Take this love / I've got / Come home baby / I'm not tired / Let's kiss and make up
CD _____ 8122712752
East West / Jul '94 / Warner Music.

MAN AND A HALF, A
I found a love / Let me be your boy / If you need me / It's too late / I'm gonna cry / Come home baby / In the midnight hour / Don't fight it / I'm not tired / That's a man's way / 634 5789 / Ninety nine and a half (won't do) / Land of 1000 dances / Mustang Sally / Three time loser / Everybody needs somebody to love / Soul dance number three / You can't stand alone / Funky broadway / Fire and water / Call my name, I'll be there / Don't let the green grass fool you / Get me back on time / Cole, Cooke and Redding / She said yes / You keep me hangin' on / Hey Joe / Toe hold / Mini skirt Minnie / Hey Jude / Man and a half / She's looking good / I found a true love / I'm a midnight mover / I've come a long way / Jealous love / Stagger / I'm in love
WEA / Jul '93 / Warner Music.

VERY BEST OF WILSON PICKETT, THE
In the midnight hour / 634 5789 / Land of 1000 dances / Mustang Sally / Funky broadway / I'm in love / She's looking good / Hey Jude / Sugar sugar / Engine No.9 / Don't let the green grass fool you / Don't knock my love / Fire and water / I'm a midnight mover / I found a love / Everybody needs somebody to love
CD _____ 812271212-2
Atlantic / Jun '93 / Warner Music.

Picketts

WICKED PICKETTS, THE
CD _____ ROUCD 9046
Rounder / Aug '95 / CM / Direct / ADA / Cadillac.

Pickford, Andy

MAELSTROM
Voyager / Cathedral / Blue world / Tetsuo / Synbiosis / Raumfaire / Oblivion / Hell's gate
CD _____ CENCD 010
Centaur / Apr '95 / Complete/Pinnacle.

REPLICANT
CD _____ CENCD 004
Centaur / Oct '93 / Complete/Pinnacle.

TERRAFORMER
CD _____ CENCD 008
Centaur / Jun '94 / Complete/Pinnacle.

Pictures Of Tom

RIDICULOUS POSITIONS
CD _____ BAH 19
Humbug / Aug '94 / Pinnacle.

Pie Finger

DALI SURPRISE, A
CD _____ CRELPCD 122
Creation / Apr '92 / 3MV / Vital.

Piece Dogs

EYES FOR EYES
CD _____ RR 90582
Roadrunner / May '93 / Pinnacle.

Pied Pipers

CAPITOL COLLECTORS SERIES: PIED PIPERS
Pistol packin' mama / Deacon Jones / Mairzy doats and dozy doats / Trolley song / Dream / There's a fella waitin' in Poughkeepsie / Lily Belle / We'll be together again / Personality / Aren't you glad you're you / In the middle of May / Open the door Richard / Mam'selle / Freedom train / I'm a walkin' / Penny / Katrina / Ok'l baby dok'l / My happiness
CD _____ CZ 492
Capitol / Feb '92 / EMI.

Scottish & Irish Music

CD _____ EUCD 1009
ARC / Sep '93 / ARC Music / ADA.

Pieranunzi, Enrico

ISIS (Pieranunzi, Enrico Quartet & Quintet)
CD _____ 121021-2
Soul Note / Jan '94 / Harmonia Mundi / Wellard / Cadillac.

NO MAN'S LAND (Pieranunzi, Enrico Trio)
CD _____ 121 221 2
Soul Note / Oct '90 / Harmonia Mundi / Wellard / Cadillac.

Pierce, Billie

NEW ORLEANS-THE LIVING LEGENDS (Pierce, Billie & Joseph 'De De')
CD _____ OBCCD 534
Original Blues Classics / Nov '92 / Complete/Pinnacle / Wellard / Cadillac.

ONE FOR CHUCK
CD _____ SSC 1053D
Sunnyside / Nov '91 / Pinnacle.

Pierce, Dede

DEDE PIERCE STOMPERS VOL. 1
CD _____ AMCD 81
American Music / Feb '95 / Jazz Music.

DEDE PIERCE STOMPERS VOL. 2
CD _____ AMCD 82
American Music / Feb '95 / Jazz Music.

Pierce, Jeffrey Lee

RAMBLIN' JEFFREY LEE & CYPRESS GROVE
CD _____ 527901220
Solid / Jun '93 / Vital.

Pierce, Joshua

PORTRAIT OF BROADWAY, A (Pierce, Joshua & Dorothy Jonas)
CD _____ CDPC 5003
Prestige / Aug '90 / Total/BMG.

Pierce, Nat

BOSTON BUST OUT, THE
What can I say (after I'm sorry) / You were never gone / King Edward the flatted fifth / That's the kinda girl / What's new / Paradise / Pat / Sheba
CD _____ HEPCD 13
Hep / Nov '95 / Cadillac / Jazz Music / New Note / Wellard.

EASY SWING (Pierce, Nat & Mel Powell)
CD _____ 662 133
Vanguard / May '94 / Complete/Pinnacle / Discovery.

Pierce, Webb

HONKY TONK SONG
CD _____ CTS 55423
Country Stars / Jun '94 / Target/BMG.

KING OF THE HONKY-TONK
CD _____ CMFCD 019
Country Music Foundation / Sep '94 / Direct / ADA.

ONE AND ONLY WEBB PIERCE, THE
CD _____ KCD 00648
King/Paddle Wheel / Feb '93 / New Note.

WONDERING BOY, THE 1951-1958
Drifting Texas sand / If crying would make you care / California blues / You scared the love right out of me / New silver bells / Wondering / You know I'm still in love with you / I'm gonna see my baby / That heart belongs to me / I just can't be true / So used to loving you / I haven't got the heart / I'll always take care of you / Backstreet affair / I'm only wishin' / Slowly / Last waltz / Bow thy head / Country church / I'll go on alone / That's me without you / Broken engagement / We'll find a way / It's been so long / Don't throw your life away / Too late to worry now / There stands the glass / There's a better home / Mother call my name in prayer / I'm walking the dog / You just can't be true / Slowly (2) / Broken engagement (2) / Slowly (3) / Even tho' / Sparkling brown eyes / Bugle call from Heaven / Thank you dear Lord / Kneel at the cross / Leaning on the everlasting arms / You're not mine anymore / I'm gonna fall out of love with you / Your good for nothing heart / Just imagination / I love you dear / More and more / I found someone that's true / Waltz you saved for me / One day later / In the jailhouse now / Sneakin' all around / I don't care / Just how long / Why baby why / Yes I know why / I found a true love / Because I love you / Little Rosa / Let forgiveness in / Any old time / You make love to everyone / Teenage boogie / I'm really glad you hurt me / Teenage boogie (2) / Oh so many years / One week later / When I'm with you / Can I find it in your heart / Crying over you / I'm tired / It's my way / Slowdang / Honky tonk song / I care no more / Bye bye love / Missing you / Let forgiveness in (2) / Who wouldn't love you / New panhandle rag / I know it was you /

Don't do it darlin' / Holiday for love / How long / New raunchy / I'll get by somehow / English sweetheart / Down Panama way / Foreign love / You'll come back / New love affair / Falling back to me / Sittin' alone / I'm letting you go / Tupelo County jail / Waiting a lifetime / True love never dies / I think of you / I won't be cryin' anymore / I owe it to my heart / Violet and a rose / After the boy gets the girl / You make me love you again / Crazy arms / Pick me up on your way down / Life to go / My shoes keep walking back to you
CD Set _____ BCD 15522
Bear Family / Sep '90 / Rollercoaster / Direct / CM / Swift / ADA.

Pierre, Marie

LOVE AFFAIR
Choose me / Can't go through (with life) / I believe / Somebody else's man / Nothing gained (for loving you) / Humanity / Roving / My best friend / Walk away / Over reacting
CD _____ CDTRL 177
Trojan / Nov '95 / Jetstar / Total/BMG.

Pierron, Gerard

GASTON COUTE
CD _____ LDX 274947
La Chant Du Monde / Nov '92 / Harmonia Mundi / ADA.

Pig

POKE IN THE EYE, A
CD _____ EFA 2228 CD
Yellow / Feb '89 / SRD.

Pigalle, Anne

EVERYTHING COULD BE SO PERFECT
Why does it have to be this way / Via vagabond / Looking for love / Intermission / Souvenir d'un Paris / Crack in the ocean / 1000 colours waltz
CD _____ 450994750-2
ZTT / Mar '94 / Warner Music.

Pigbag

BEST OF PIGBAG
Papa's got a brand new pigbag / Weak at the knees / Hit the O deck / Getting up / Brazil nuts / Jump the line / Another orangutango / Sunny day / Big bean / Can't see for looking / Six of one / Big bag / Listen listen little man
CD _____ KAZ CD 3
Kaz / Nov '87 / BMG.

Pigeonhead

PIGEONHED
CD _____ SPCD 101/273
Sub Pop / Jul '93 / Disc.

Pigface

FEELS LIKE HEAVEN SOUNDS LIKE SHIT
CD _____ INV 034CD
Invisible / Nov '95 / Plastic Head.

FOOK
CD _____ CDDVN 18
Music For Nations / Oct '92 / Pinnacle.

GUB
Tapeworm / Bushmaster / Cylinder head world / Point blank / Suck / Symphony for taps / Greenhouse / Little sisters / Tailor made / War ich nicht immer ein guter junge / Blood and sand / Weightless
CD _____ CDDVN 2
Devotion / Apr '91 / Pinnacle.

LEAN JUICY PORK
CD _____ INV 012-2
Invisible / Jul '93 / Plastic Head.

NOTES FROM THEE UNDERGROUND
Asshole / Divebomber / Your own you own / Fuck it up / Hagseed / Exclusaway / Empathy / Magazine / Think / Trivial scene / Slut / Blood/Pain / Psalm springs eternal / Steamroller / Your music is garbage
CD _____ CDDVN 29
Devotion / May '94 / Pinnacle.

TRUTH WILL OUT
CD _____ CDDVN 25
Devotion / Jan '94 / Pinnacle.

WELCOME TO MEXICO...ASSHOLE
CD _____ CDTDVN 3
Devotion / Nov '91 / Pinnacle.

Piggott, Mavis

LATE BLOOM
CD _____ FLY 009
Blue Rose / Jan '96 / 3MV.

Pike, Dave

DAVE PIKE AND CHARLES MCPHERSON (Pike, Dave & Charles McPherson)
Scrapple from the apple / Off minor / Piano trio medley / Embraceable you / Up jumped Spring / Big bloop
CD _____ CDSJP 302
Timeless Jazz / Jun '89 / New Note.

PIKE'S GROOVE (Pike, Dave & Cedar Walton Trio)
CD _____ CRISS 1021CD
Criss Cross / Oct '92 / Cadillac / Harmonia Mundi.

TIMES OUT OF MIND
Dance of the Grebes / Wee / Times out of mind / Djalama / Morning in the park / I love my cigar
CD _____ MCD 5446
Muse / May '92 / New Note / CM.

Pilc, Jean Michel

BIG ONE
CD _____ EPC 890
European Music Production / Jan '94 / Harmonia Mundi.

Pilgrim Travelers

BEST OF VOLS. 1 AND 2
I was there when the spirit came / Blessed be the name / Standing on the highway / Jesus hits like the atom bomb / I've got a mother gone home / Jesus I'm thankful / Straight street / Mother bowed / Old rugged cross / Something within me / Soldier's plea / Satisfied with Jesus / My old home / Jesus met the woman at the well / What a blessing in Jesus I've found / I want my crown / God shall wipe all tears away / Weary traveller / I'll tell it wherever I go / He will remember me / Lord help me carry on / Now Lord (yes, my Lord) / Lord hold my hand
CD _____ CDCHD 342
Ace / May '91 / Pinnacle / Cadillac / Complete/Pinnacle.

BETTER THAN THAT
I could do better than that / Please watch over me / Long ago (wooden church) / I know Jesus loy before / Leaning on the everlasting arms / I'm going through / How about you / I'll be there (in that number) / All the way (I'm willing to run) / Your mother is your friend / Gonna walk right out / Move up to heaven / What a friend we have in Jesus / Hard road to travel / Look down that lonesome road / Go ahead / In my heart / I love Jesus / He's my friend / I love you save may be your own (the safety song) / Troubles in my home will have to end / Every prayer will find it's answer / Close to thee / Troubled in mind / Bless us today / Hold on / After while
CD _____ CDCHD 564
Ace / Mar '94 / Pinnacle / Cadillac / Complete/Pinnacle.

WALKING RHYTHM
What are they doing (my lord) / Stretch out / My prayer / Good news / Dig a little deeper / Everybody's gonna have a wonderful time up there / Nothing can change me (since I found the lord) / Jesus / Thank you jesus / What a friend we have in Jesus / It's a blessing / Not a one / He's pleading in glory / Jesus gave me water / Jesus he's the one / King jesus will roll all burdens away / My eternal-home / Pass me not, o gentle saviour / Footprints of Jesus / When i join the jubilee / Call him by his name / Welcome home / My road's so rough and rocky / I love the lord / Deliver me from evil / Jesus is the first line of defence / Peace of mind / Angels tell mother / WDIA plug
CD _____ CDCHD 463
Ace / Mar '93 / Pinnacle / Cadillac / Complete/Pinnacle.

Pilgrim, Billy

BILLY PILGRIM
Get me out of here / Insomniac / Try / Here we go again / Halfway home / Hula hoop / Hurricane season / Lost and found in tinseltown / Too many people / Mama says
CD _____ 756782515-2
Warner Bros. / May '94 / Warner Music.

Pilot

BEST OF PILOT, THE
CD _____ C5CD-563
See For Miles/C5 / Jan '91 / Pinnacle.

FROM THE ALBUM OF THE SAME NAME
CD _____ C5CD 567
See For Miles/C5 / Jun '91 / Pinnacle.

MORIN HEIGHTS
CD _____ C5CD 569
See For Miles/C5 / Jun '91 / Pinnacle.

SECOND FLIGHT
CD _____ C5CD 568
See For Miles/C5 / Jun '91 / Pinnacle.

Pinchers

TWO ORIGINALS (Pinchers & Tweety Bird)
CD _____ 790022
Pippers / Nov '92 / Jetstar.

Pinckney, St. Clair

PRIVATE STOCK
Private stock / From the book / Joy life / Stranded / Night stroller / From the head / Summer night / I'm in love with you

CD _____ CDICH 1036
Ichiban / Jul '89 / Koch.

Pincock, Dougie

SOMETHING BLEW
Gem so small / Piper's piper / Eric Big-stones' leaky boat / Douglas Adams' fancy / Fastest gasman / Video kid / Miss Cara Spencer / Return to Kashmagiro / Balnain household / Tanks for the memory / Macrmmon's sweetheart / Rest / Unrest / Twins / January girl / Handyman's legacy / Rogart refusal / Songs for Chris
CD _____ CDTRAX 080
Greentrax / Nov '94 / Conifer / Duncans / ADA. / Direct.

Pine, Courtney

DESTINY'S SONG & THE IMAGE OF PURSUANCE
Beyond the thought of my last reckoning / In pursuance / Vision / Guardian of the flame / Round Midnight / Sacrifice / Prismic omnipotence / Alone / Raggamuffin's tale / Mark of the time
CD _____ IMCD 114
Island / May '91 / PolyGram.

JOURNEY TO THE URGE WITHIN
Mis-interpret / I believe / Peace / Delores St. S.F / As we would say / Children of the ghetto / When, where, how and why / C.G.C. / Seen / Sunday song
CD _____ IMCD 112
Island / May '91 / PolyGram.

MODERN DAY JAZZ STORIES
CD _____ 5290282
Talkin' Loud / Jan '96 / PolyGram.

TO THE EYES OF CREATION
Healing song / Zaire (Interlude) / Country dance / Psalm / Eastern standard time / X-calibur (Interlude) / Meditation of contem-plation / Life goes round / Ark of Mark (In-terlude) / Children hold on / Cleopatra's needle / Redemption song / Holy grail
CD _____ IMCD 210
Island / Mar '95 / PolyGram.

VISION'S TALE, THE
Introduction / In a mellow tone / Just you, just me / Raggamuffin's stance / No greater love / Skylark / I'm an old cowhand (from the Rio Grande) / God bless the child / And then (a warrior's tale) / Our descendants' descendants / C.P.'s theme
CD _____ IMCD 192
Island / Mar '95 / PolyGram.

WITHIN THE REALMS OF OUR DREAMS
Sepia love song / Una muy bonita / Donna Lee / Up behind the beat / Time to go home / Delfeayo's dilemma / Raggamuffin and his lance / Slave's tale
CD _____ IMCD 193
Island / Jul '94 / PolyGram.

Pingxin, Xu

ART OF THE CHINESE DULCIMER, THE
CD _____ EUCD 1293
ARC / Nov '95 / ARC Music / ADA.

Pinhead Gunpowder

JUMP SALTY
CD _____ LOOKOUT 105
Lookout / '94 / SRD.

Pini, Mick

MICK WILDMAN PINI (Pini, Mick 'Wildman')
Collector / Onion rings / You can make it / Unknown destination / It's got to be the blues / More than I could chew / Free load / Like mother like daughter / Freddy's mid-nite dream / Too many mountains
CD _____ STCD 900846
Line / Oct '94 / CM / Grapevine / ADA / Conifer / Direct.

Pink, Celinda

UNCHAINED
I don't need no lover boy / You ain't leaving me without you / Hound dog / Pack your lies and go / I've changed since I've been unchained / Love her right off your mind / Taking my freedom / Found me a backdoor man / You better quit it / Sneakin' up your backdoor / Love you till the cows come home / Me and Bobby McGee / I've earned the right to sing the blues
CD _____ SORCD 0085
D-Sharp / Aug '95 / Direct.

Pink Fairies

KILL 'EM N' EAT' EM
Broken statue / Fear of love / Undercover of confusion / Waiting for the ice cream to melt / Taking LSD / White girls on amphet-amine / Seeing double / Food about you / Bad attitude / I might be lying
CD _____ FIENDCD 105
Demon / Oct '90 / Pinnacle / ADA.

LIVE AT THE ROUNDHOUSE
City kids / Waiting for the man / Lucille / Uncle Harry's last freakout / Going down

CD _____ CDWIK 965
Big Beat / Jul '91 / Pinnacle.

OUT OF THE BLUES AND INTO THE PINK
CD _____ HTDCD 46
HTD / Jan '96 / Pinnacle.

Pink Floyd

ANIMALS
Pigs on the wing 1 / Dogs / Pigs (three dif-ferent ones) / Sheep / Pigs on the wing 2
CD _____ CDEMD 1060
EMI / Aug '94 / EMI.

ATOM HEART MOTHER
Atom heart mother / If / Summer '68 / Fat old sun / Alan's psychedelic breakfast
CD _____ CDEMD 1072
EMI / Oct '94 / EMI.

COLLECTION OF GREAT DANCE SONGS, A
One of these days / Money / Another brick in the wall pt 2 / Wish you were here / Shine on you crazy diamond / Sheep
CD _____ CDP 790 732 2
EMI / Nov '88 / EMI.

DARK SIDE OF THE MOON
Speak to me / Breathe / On the run / Time / Great gig in the sky / Money / Us and them / Any colour you like / Brain damage / Eclipse
CD _____ CDEMD 1064
EMI / Aug '94 / EMI.

DELICATE SOUND OF THUNDER
Shine on you crazy diamond / Learning to fly / Yet another movie / Round and around / Sorrow / Dogs of war / On the turning away / One of these days / Time / Wish you were here / Us and them (CD/MC only) / Money (LP/CD only) / Another brick in the wall pt 2 / Comfortably numb / Run like hell
CD Set _____ CDEQ 5009
EMI / Nov '88 / EMI.

DIVISION BELL, THE
Cluster one / What do you want from me / Poles apart / Marooned / Great day for free-dom / Wearing the inside out / Take it back / Coming back to life / Keep talking / Lost for words / High hopes
CD _____ CDEMD 1055
EMI / Apr '94 / EMI.

FINAL CUT, THE
Post war dream / Your possible pasts / One of the few / Hero's return / Gunner's dream / Paranoid eyes / Get your filthy hands off my desert / Fletcher memorial home / Southampton dock / Final cut / Not now John / Two suns in the sunset / Hero's re-turn (part 2) (TCEMD 1070 only)
CD _____ CDEMD 1070
EMI / Oct '94 / EMI.

LONDON '66-'67
Interstellar overdrive / Nick's boogie
CD _____ SFMDP 3
See For Miles/C5 / Sep '95 / Pinnacle.

MEDDLE
One of these days / Pillow of winds / Fear-less (interpolating You'll Never Walk Alone) / San Tropez / Seamus / Echoes
CD _____ CDEMD 1061
EMI / Aug '94 / EMI.

MOMENTARY LAPSE OF REASON, A
Signs of life / Learning to fly / Dogs of war / One slip / On the turning away / Yet an-other movie / Round and around / New ma-chine (part 1) / Terminal frost / New ma-chine (part 2) / Sorrow
CD _____ CDEMD 1003
EMI / Sep '87 / EMI.

MOON REVISITED, THE (Tribute To Dark Side Of The Moon) (Various Artists)
Speak to me / Breathe / On the run / Time / Great gig in the sky / Money / Us and them / Any colour you like / Brain Damage / Eclipse
CD _____ RR 89162
Roadrunner / Oct '95 / Pinnacle.

MORE
Cirrus minor / Nile song / Crying song / Up the Khyber / Green is the colour / Cymba-line / Party sequence / Main theme / Ibiza bar / More blues / Quicksilver / Spanish piece / Dramatic theme
CD _____ CDP 7463862
EMI / Mar '87 / EMI.

OBSCURED BY CLOUDS
Obscured by clouds / When you're in / Burning bridges / Gold it's in the... / Wot's... uh the deal / Mudmen / Childhood's end / Free four / Stay / Absolutely curtains
CD _____ CDP 746 385 2
EMI / Mar '87 / EMI.

PINK FLOYD: INTERVIEW PICTURE DISC
CD P.Disc _____ CBAK 4013
Baktabak / Apr '88 / Baktabak.

PIPER AT THE GATES OF DAWN, THE
Astronomy domine / Lucifer Sam / Matilda mother / Flaming / Pow R Toc H / Take up thy stethoscope and walk / Interstellar over-drive / Gnome / Chapter 24 / Scarecrow / Bike

CD _____ CDEMD 1073
EMI / Oct '94 / EMI.

PLAYS THE HITS OF PINK FLOYD (Royal Philharmonic Orchestra)
Shine on you crazy diamond / Money / Us and them / Hey you / Another brick in the wall pt 2 / Wish you were here / Time / Great gig in the sky / In the flesh
CD _____ EDL 28382
Edel / Dec '94 / Pinnacle.

PULSE
Shine on you crazy diamond / Astronomy domine / What do you want from me / Learning to fly / Keep talking / Coming back to life / Hey you / Great day for freedom / Sorrow / High hopes / Another brick in the wall pt 2 / One of these days (Not on CD) / Speak to me / Breathe / On the run / Time / Great gig in the sky / Money / Us and them / Any colour you like / Brain damage / Comfortably numb / Run like hell
CD Set _____ CDEMD 1078
EMI / Jun '95 / EMI.

SAUCERFUL OF PINK, A (Various Artists)
Set the controls for the heart of the sun / Another brick in the wall pt 2 / One of these days / Wot's... uh the deal / Interstellar overdrive / Learning to fly / To Roger Wa-ters, wherever you are / Jugband blues / On the run / Hey you / Careful with that axe, Eugene / Lucifer Sam / Pigs on the wing 1 / Let there be more light / Young lust / Sau-cerful of secrets / Point me at the sky / Nile song
CD _____ CDBRED 120
Anagram / Jun '95 / Pinnacle.

SAUCERFUL OF SECRETS, A
Let there be more light / Remember a day / Set the controls for the heart of the sun / Corporal Clegg / Saucerful of secrets / See saw / Jugband blues
CD _____ CDEMD 1063
EMI / Aug '94 / EMI.

SHINE ON (9 CDs)
Arnold Layne / Candy and a currant bun / See Emily play / Scarecrow / Apples and oranges / Paintbox / It would be so nice / Julia dream / Point me at the sky / Careful with that axe, Eugene / Let there be more light / Remember a day / Set the controls for the heart of the sun / Corporal Clegg / Saucerful of secrets / See saw / Jugband blues / One of these days / Pillow of winds / Fearless / San Tropez / Seamus / Echoes / Speak to me / Breathe / On the run / Time / Great gig in the sky / Money / Us and them / Any colour you like / Brain damage / Eclipse / Shine on you crazy diamond / Welcome to the machine / Have a cigar / Wish you were here / Pigs on the wing 1 / Dogs / Pigs (three different ones) / Sheep / Pigs on the wing 2 / In the flesh / Thin ice / Another brick in the wall pt 1 / Happiest days of our lives / Another brick in the wall pt 2 / Mother / Goodbye blue sky / Empty spaces / Young lust / One of my turns / Don't leave me now / Another brick in the wall pt 3 / Goodbye cruel world / Hey you / Is there anybody out there / Nobody home / Vera / Bring the boys back home / Com-fortably numb / Show must go on / In the flesh (2) / Run like hell / Waiting for the worms / Trial / Outside the wall / Signs of life / Learning to fly / Dogs of war / One slip / On the turning away / Yet another movie / Round and around / New machine 1 / Terminal frost / New machine 2 / Sorrow
CD Set _____ PFBOX 1
EMI / Nov '92 / EMI.

UMMAGUMMA
Astronomy domine / Careful with that axe, Eugene / Set the controls for the heart of the sun / Saucerful of secrets / Sysyphus / Grantchester meadows / Several species of small furry animals gathered together... / Narrow way / Grand Vizier's garden party
CD Set _____ CDEMD 1074
EMI / Oct '94 / EMI.

WALL, THE
In the flesh / Thin ice / Another brick in the wall pt 1 / Happiest days of our lives / An-other brick in the wall pt 2 / Mother / Good-bye blue sky / Empty spaces / Young lust / One of my turns / Don't leave me now / Another brick in the wall pt 3 / Goodbye cruel world / Hey you / Is there anybody out there / Nobody home / Vera / Bring the boys back home / Comfortably numb / Show must go on / In the flesh (2) / Run like hell / Waiting for the worms / Trial / Outside the wall
CD Set _____ CDEMD 1071
EMI / Oct '94 / EMI.

WISH YOU WERE HERE
Shine on you crazy diamond / Welcome to the machine / Have a cigar / Wish you were here
CD _____ CDEMD 1062
EMI / Aug '94 / EMI.

Pink Turns Blue

MUZAK
CD _____ RTD 19519452
Our Choice / Jul '95 / Pinnacle.

CD _____ CDEMD 1073
EMI / Oct '94 / EMI.

PERFECT SEX
CD Set _____ RTD 19519032
Our Choice / Apr '94 / Pinnacle.

Pinky & Perky

PIG ATTRACTION, THE
CD _____ CDSR 032
Telstar / Nov '93 / BMG.

Piolot, Maxime

BRETON QUAND MEME
CD _____ RSCD 212
Keltia Musique / Apr '95 / ADA / Direct / Discovery.

Pioneers

20 ORIGINAL FAMOUS HITS
CD _____ TPCD 001
Pioneer / Apr '92 / Jetstar.

KICK DE BUCKET
CD _____ RNCD 2064
Rhino / Nov '94 / Jetstar / Magnum Music Group / THE.

LONG SHOT KICK DE BUCKET
CD _____ CDTRL 347
Trojan / Mar '95 / Jetstar / Total/BMG.

Pipes & Drums of the...

TUNES OF GLORY (Pipes & Drums of the Scottish Regiments)
CD _____ MOICD 006
Moidart / Jun '94 / Conifer / ADA.

Pirates

DON'T MUNCHEN IT-LIVE IN EUROPE
CD _____ RPM 110
RPM / Jul '93 / Pinnacle.

FISTFUL OF DUBLOONS, A
Linda Lou / Honey hush / Put your cat clothes on / Sweet love on my mind / Lone-some train / Milk cow blues / Casting my spell / Tricky Dicky / Tear it up / Kaw-Liga
CD _____ EDCD 102
Edsel / Aug '92 / Pinnacle / ADA.

FROM CALYPSO TO COLLAPSO
Jezebel / Good drink / Bad woman / Ar-mageddon / Burning rubber / Turn up the heat / Lost and found / Slow down / Don't munchen it / Down to the bone / Friends for life
CD _____ CDTB 156
Thunderbolt / Nov '94 / Magnum Music Group.

LIVE IN JAPAN
All by myself / Ain't got no money / I can tell / Lonesome train / Money honey / Don't munchen it / Can't believe you wanna leave / Goin' back home / Please don't touch / Honey hush / Peggy Sue / Burnin' rubber / Shakin' all over / All in it together
CD _____ CDTB 143
Magnum Music / Apr '93 / Magnum Music Group.

SAILING THROUGH FRANCE
CD _____ 422265
New Rose / May '94 / Direct / ADA.

Pirchner, Werner

EU
Sonate vom rauhen leben / Streichquartett fur blaserquintett / Good news from the Ziller family / Kammer-symphonie 'Soiree Tyrolienne' / Do you know Emperor Joe / Two war and peace choirs / Kleine mes um 'c' fur den lieben gott / Solo sonata for bass-vibes
CD _____ 8294632
ECM / '86 / New Note.

Pirnales

AQUAS
CD _____ KICD 27
Digelius / Jun '93 / Direct.

BEST BEFORE
CD _____ OMCD 60
Olarin Musiiki Oy / Dec '94 / ADA / Direct.

Piron, A.J.

DECEMBER ISSUE (Piron, A.J. New Orleans Orchestra)
Bouncin' around / Kiss me sweet / New Or-leans wiggle / West Indies blues / Sud bus-tin' blues / West Indies blues (1) / Do double oom / West Indies blues (2) / Gnost of the blues / Bright star blues / Lou'siana swing / Sitting on the curbstone blues / Southern woman blues / Seawall special blues / Jail-house blues / Kiss me sweet #2 / Red man blues / Red man blues #2 / Do just as I say / Bad bad mama / Willie Jackson's blues / She keeps it up all the time / Old New Or-leans blues / Mama's gone goodbye
CD _____ AZCD 13
Azure / Nov '93 / Jazz Music / Swift / Wel-lard / Azure / Cadillac.

Piss Drunks

URINE IDIOT
CD _____ RNR 001CD
Ransom Note / Oct '95 / Plastic Head.

Pitbull

CASUALTY
CD _____ LF 049CD
Lost & Found / Aug '93 / Plastic Head.

NEW ALL TIME LOW
CD _____ LF 128CD
Lost & Found / May '95 / Plastic Head.

PITBULL
CD _____ LF 093CD
Lost & Found / May '94 / Plastic Head.

Pitch Shifter

DESENSITIZED
Lesson one / Diable / Ephemerol / Triad / To die is to gain / (A higher form of) killing / Lesson two / Cathode / N/A / Gatherer of data / N.C.M. / Routine
CD _____ MOSH 075CD
Earache / Oct '93 / Vital.

INDUSTRIAL
CD _____ CDVILE 56
Peaceville / Mar '95 / Pinnacle.

SUBMIT
CD _____ MOSH 066CD
Earache / Apr '92 / Vital.

Pitchblende

AU JUS
Nine volt / Your own arturo / Ambient noise / Karoshi / Cupcake Jones / Tourniquet / X's for I's / Human lie / Detector / Showroom / Practice song / Short term / Talking / Psychic power control
CD _____ OLE 1022
Matador / Feb '95 / Vital.

Pitney, Gene

22 GREATEST HITS, THE
Louisiana mama / Only love can break a heart / Man who shot Liberty Valance / It hurts to be in love / I'm gonna be strong / Half heaven half heartache / Mecca / Town without pity / Last chance to turn around / Every breath I take / Just a smile / Twenty four hours from Tulsa / True love never runs smooth / Dream / Just one smile / Princess in rags / (I wanna) love my life away / Yesterday's hero / She lets her hair down / If I didn't have a dime / She's a heartbreaker
CD _____ CD 38
Bescol / Jul '87 / CM / Target/BMG.

24 HOURS FROM TULSA
Twenty four hours from Tulsa / Something's gotten hold of my heart / (I wanna) Love my life away / Town without pity / That girl belongs to yesterday / I'm gonna be strong / I must be seeing things / Looking through the eyes of love / Princess in rags / Backstage / It hurts to be in love / 24 Sycamore / Maria Elena / Yours until tomorrow / Somewhere in the country / Cold light of day / Just one smile / Nobody needs your love
CD _____ MUCD 9021
Start / Apr '95 / Koch.

BACKSTAGE (The Greatest Hits & More)
Something's gotten hold of my heart / Twenty four hours from Tulsa / That girl belongs to yesterday / I'm gonna be strong / I must be seeing things / Looking through the eyes of love / Princess in rags / Nobody needs your love / Just one smile / In my life / Only one woman / First cut is the deepest / We've got tonight / Let the heartaches begin / There is no distance / Fool (if you think it's over) / All by myself / Town without pity (Only on CD and cassette.) / Something's gotten hold of my heart (original) (CD/MC only)
CD _____ 847 119-2
Polydor / Oct '90 / PolyGram.

BEST OF GENE PITNEY
CD _____ MATCD 262
Masterpiece / Nov '93 / BMG.

COLLECTION: GENE PITNEY
Something's gotten hold of my heart / Man who shot Liberty Valance / Twenty four hours from Tulsa / Mecca / Maria Elena / Backstage (I'm lonely) / I'm gonna be strong
CD _____ CLACD 369
Castle / '90 / BMG.

EP COLLECTION: GENE PITNEY
CD _____ SEECD 313
See For Miles/C5 / Apr '91 / Pinnacle.

ESSENTIAL COLLECTION
CD Set _____ LECD 611
Wisepack / Apr '95 / THE / Conifer.

GENE PITNEY - 20 GREATEST HITS
wanna love my life away / Twenty four from Tulsa / That girl belongs to yesterday / It hurts to be in love / I'm gonna be strong / I must be seeing things / Looking through the eyes of love / Princess in rags / Backstage (I'm lonely) / Nobody needs your love

---

more than I do / Just one smile / Something's gotten hold of my heart / Somewhere in the country / Yours until tomorrow / Maria Elena / 24 Sycamore / Hello Mary Lou
CD _____ PLATCD 3904
Platinum Music / Dec '88 / Prism / Ross.

HITS & MISSES
Man who shot Liberty Valance / Twenty four hours from Tulsa / Town without pity / Hello Mary Lou / Today's teardrops / Surefire bet / Donna means heartbreak / If I didn't have a dime / (I wanna) Love my life away / Every breath I take / Mecca / True love never runs smoothly / Teardrop by teardrop / Dream for sale / Half heaven half heartache / Only love can break a heart / Bleibe bei mir (Town without pity) (German version) / I'll find you / Cradle of my arms / Please come back, baby / I'm going back to my love / Classical rock 'n' roll / Snuggle up baby / Strolling (through the park) / Faithful our love / Make believe lover (demo)
CD _____ BCD 15724
Bear Family / Feb '95 / Rollercoaster / Direct / CM / Swift / ADA.

LEGENDS IN MUSIC - GENE PITNEY
CD _____ LECD 078
Wisepack / Jul '94 / THE / Conifer.

MR. HITMAKER
CD _____ CDCD 1044
Charly / Mar '93 / Charly / THE / Cadillac.

PEARLS FROM THE PAST - GENE PITNEY
CD _____ KLMCD 007
Scratch / Nov '93 / BMG.

TWENTY FOUR HOURS FROM TULSA
Twenty four hours from Tulsa / Nobody needs your love / 24 sycamore / Princess in rags / Half heaven half heartache / Shady lady / I must be seeing things / Looking through the eyes of love / It hurts to be in love / Somewhere in the country / Something's gotten hold of my heart / Man who shot liberty valance / Maria Elena / Backstage (I'm lonely) / I'm gonna be strong / Last chance to turn around / Just one smile / Yours until tomorrow / Only love can break a heart / Town without pity
CD _____ TRTCD 157
TrueTrax / Oct '94 / THE.

VERY BEST OF GENE PITNEY, THE
Twenty four hours from Tulsa / Something's gotten hold of my heart / Cold light of day / Yours until tomorrow / Backstage (I'm lonely) / Somewhere in the country / Town without pity / Looking through the eyes of love / Girl belongs to yesterday / I'm gonna be strong / Princess in rags / Nobody needs your love / Shady lady / I must be seeing things / Maria Elena / Street called hope / Just one smile / (I wanna) Love my life away / It hurts to be in love / Man who shot liberty valance
CD _____ MCCD 155
Music Club / May '94 / Disc / THE / CM.

Pixies

BOSSANOVA
Cecilia Ann / Velouria / Is she weird / All over the world / Down to the well / Blown away / Stormy weather / Rock music / Allison / Ana / Dig for fire / Happening / Hang wire / Havalina
CD _____ CADCD 0010
4AD / Aug '90 / Disc.

DOOLITTLE
Debaser / Wave of mutilation / Dead / Mr. Grieves / La la I love you / There goes my gun / Silver / Tame / Here comes your man / Monkey gone to heaven / Crackity Jones / Number 13 baby / Hey / Gouge away
CD _____ CADCD 905
4AD / Feb '89 / Disc.

SURFER ROSA
Bone machine / Something against you / Gigantic / Where is my mind / Tony's theme / Vamos / Brick is red / Break my body / Broken face / River Euphrates / Cactus / Oh my golly / I'm amazed / Caribou (CD only) / Vamos (2) (CD only) / Isla de Incanta (CD only) / Ed is dead (CD only) / Holiday song (CD only) / Nimrod's song (CD only) / I've been tired (CD only) / Levitate me (CD only)
CD _____ CAD 803CD
4AD / Mar '88 / Disc.

TROMPE LE MONDE
Trompe le monde / Planet of sound / Alec Eiffel / Sad punk / Head on / U-mass / Palace of the Brine / Letter to Memphis / Bird dream of the Olympus Mons / Space (I believe in) / Subbacultcha / Distance equals rate times time / Lovely day / Motorway to Roswell / Navajo know
CD _____ CADCD 1014
4AD / Sep '91 / Disc.

Pizzarelli, Bucky

BUCKY PLAYS BIX
CD Set _____ DAPCD 238
Audiophile / Apr '89 / Jazz Music / Swift.

MEETS SLAM STEWART AND RED NORVO
CD _____ STCD 18
Stash / Aug '90 / Jazz Music / CM / Cadillac / Direct / ADA.

MEMORIAL, A
CD _____ STCD 551
Stash / '92 / Jazz Music / CM / Cadillac / Direct / ADA.

NIRVANA
Azure'te / Sing, sing, sing / Little world called home / Pick yourself up / Nuages / Honeysuckle rose / Willow weep for me / Tangerine / It's been a long time / Don't take your love from me / Two funky people / Come rain or come shine / Stompin' a the Savoy
CD _____ CDC 9090
LRC / Aug '95 / New Note / Harmonia Mundi.

SOLO FLIGHT 1981/86
CD _____ STCD 573
Stash / Feb '94 / Jazz Music / CM / Cadillac / Direct / ADA.

Pizzarelli, John

ALL OF ME
Three little words / If I had you / More I see you / 'S Wonderful / This will make you laugh / All of me / River is blue / I know that you know / For all we know / Love falls into place / My baby just cares for me / Roslyn
CD _____ PD 90619
Novus / Apr '92 / BMG.

DEAR MR. COLE
Style is coming back in style / What can I say after I say I'm sorry / Little girl / You must be blind / Sweet Georgia Brown / It's only a paper moon / September song / On the sunny side of the street / Nature boy / This way out / Too marvelous for words / Route 66 / Sweet Lorraine / Straighten up and fly right / L.O.V.E. / Unforgettable / Portrait of Jenny / Honeysuckle rose
CD _____ 01241631822
Novus / Apr '95 / BMG.

HIT THAT JIVE, JACK
CD _____ STB 2508
Stash / Sep '95 / Jazz Music / CM / Cadillac / Direct / ADA.

I LIKE JERSEY BEST
CD _____ STB 2501
Stash / Apr '95 / Jazz Music / CM / Cadillac / Direct / ADA.

NATURALLY
Splendid splinter / I'm confessin' that I love you / Lady be good / When I grow too old to dream / Gee baby ain't I good to you / Baby, baby, all the time / Midnight blue / Seven on Charlie / Slappin' the cakes on me / Nuage / I cried for you / Naturally / You stepped out of a dream / Headed out to Vera's / Your song is with me
CD _____ 01241631512
Novus / Mar '93 / BMG.

NEW STANDARDS
Fools fall in love / Oh how my heart beats for you (Swing) / Beautiful moons ago / I'm your guy / Come on-a-my house / Beautiful Maria of my soul / I only want some / I'm alright now / Just a skosh / Why do people fall in love / Hearts like mine are broken every day / Better run before it's spring / Give me your heart / Look at us / Oh how my heart beats for you
CD _____ 1011 69170 0
RCA / Jul '94 / BMG.

Pizzicato 5

5 X 5
Pizzicatomania / Twiggy, Twiggy / Baby love child / Me Japanese boy / This years girl # 2
CD _____ OLE 096-2
Matador / Aug '94 / Vital.

MADE IN U.S.A
I / Sweet soul revue / Magic carpet ride / Readymade FM / Baby love child / Twiggy twiggy/Twiggy Vs. James Bond / Go go dancer / Catchy / Peace music
CD _____ OLE 099-2
Matador / Aug '94 / Vital.

PJ & Duncan

PSYCHE
CD _____ TCD 2746
Telstar / Nov '94 / BMG.

TOP KATZ
CD _____ TCD 2793
Telstar / Nov '95 / BMG.

PJ Harvey

4 TRACK DEMOS
Rid of me / Legs / Reeling / Snake / Hook / Fifty foot Queenie / Driving / Ecstasy / Hardly wait / Rub 'til it bleeds / Easy / M Bike / Yuri-G / Goodnight
CD _____ IMCD 170
Island / Oct '93 / PolyGram.

DRY
Oh my lover / O Stella / Dress / Victory / Happy and bleeding / Sheela na gig / Hair / Joe / Plants and rags / Fountain / Water
CD _____ PURECD 010
Too Pure / Mar '92 / Vital.

RID OF ME
Rid of me / Missed / Legs / Rub 'til it bleeds / Hook / Man size sextet / Highway 61 revisited / Fifty foot queenie / Yuri-G / Man size / Dry / Me Jane / Snake / Ecstasy
CD _____ CID 8002
Island / Apr '93 / PolyGram.

TO BRING YOU MY LOVE
To bring you my love / Meet ze monsta / Working for the man / C'mon Billy / Teclo / Long snake moan / Down by the water / I think I'm a mother / Send his love to me / Dancer
CD _____ CID 8035
Island / Feb '95 / PolyGram.

TO BRING YOU MY LOVE/THE B-SIDES ALBUM
To bring you my love / Meet ze monsta / Working for the man / C'mon Billy / Teclo / Long snake moan / Down by the water / I think I'm a mother / Send his love to me / Dancer / Reeling / Daddy / Lying in the sun / Somebody's down, somebody's name / Darling be there / Maniac / One time too many / Harder / Goodnight
CD _____ CIDZ 8035
Island / Nov '95 / PolyGram.

Pla, Roberto

ROBERTO PLA'S LATIN JAZZ ENSEMBLE
CD _____ TUMICD 051
Tumi / Aug '95 / Sterns / Discovery.

Placebo Effect

GALLERIES OF PAIN
CD _____ EFA 11204
Danse Macabre / Apr '93 / SRD.

MANIPULATED MIND CONTROL
CD _____ EFA 053242
Ausfahrt / Oct '94 / SRD.

Plainsong

AND WHAT'S THAT
CD _____ TX 2002CD
Taxim / Dec '93 / ADA.

DARK SIDE OF THE ROOM
CD _____ LICD 901247
Line / Dec '92 / CM / Grapevine / ADA / Conifer / Direct.

ON AIR
CD _____ BOJCD 005
Band Of Joy / Nov '92 / ADA.

VOICE ELECTRIC
Gravy train / Unreal dreams / Where the coyotes roam / Steal the beat / Rat and the snake / Gunga din / Christoforo's eyes / Clearances / William's canon / It's not just the stars that fall
CD _____ LICD 901288
Line / Sep '94 / CM / Grapevine / ADA / Conifer / Direct.

Planet

SPLITTING THE HUMIDITY
CD _____ FOCUS 6CD
Focus / Oct '95 / Pinnacle.

Planet Gong

FLOATING ANARCHY 1991
Floating anarchy radio / It's the time of your life / Stoned innocent Frankenstein / New age transformation my / Poet to take / Astral alien / Pot head pixies / Much too old / Change the world / Teeth / Allez Ali Baba blacksheep / Mushroom song / Opium for the people
CD _____ AGAS 003CD
Gas / Oct '95 / Vital.

Planet Rockers

COMING IN PERSON
CD _____ NOHITCD 005
No Hit / Jan '94 / SRD.

INVASION OF THE PLANET ROCKERS
CD _____ NOHITCD 007
No Hit / Jan '94 / SRD.

Planetary Assault Systems

ARCHIVES
In from the night / Twilight / Trek / Flightdrop / Manipulator / Gated / Booster / Electric / Starway ritual
CD _____ PF 039CD
Peacefrog / Feb '96 / Disc.

Plant, Robert

FATE OF NATIONS
Calling to you / Down to the sea / Come into my life / I believe / Twenty nine palms / Memory song (Hello, hello) / If I were a carpenter / Colours of a shade / Promised land / Greatest gift / Great spirit / Network news

CD _____ 514 867-2
Fontana / May '93 / PolyGram.

MANIC NIRVANA
Hurting kind (I've got my eyes on you) / SSS and Q / Nirvana / Your ma said you cried in your sleep last night / Liars dance / Big love / I cried / Tie dye on the highway / Anniversary / Watching you
CD _____ WX 339CD
Atlantic / Mar '90 / Warner Music.

NOW AND ZEN
Heaven knows / Dance on my own / Tall cool one / Way I feel / Helen of Troy / Billy's revenge / Ship of fools / Why / White, clean and neat
CD _____ 790 863-2
Es Paranza / Feb '88 / Warner Music.

PICTURES AT ELEVEN
Burning down one side / Moonlight in Samosa / Pledge pin / Slow dancer / Worse than Detroit / Fat lip / Like I've never been gone / Mystery title
CD _____ SK 259418
Swansong / '86 / Warner Music.

PRINCIPAL OF MOMENTS
Other arms / In the mood / Messin' with the Mekon / Wreckless love / Through with the two step / Horizontal departure / Big log / Stranger here than over there
CD _____ 790101 2
WEA / Jul '83 / Warner Music.

SHAKEN 'N' STIRRED
Hip to hoo / Kallalou / Too loud / Trouble your money / Pink and black / Little by little / Doo doo a do do / Easily lead / Sixes and sevens
CD _____ 790265 2
WEA / Jun '85 / Warner Music.

Planxty

AFTER THE BREAK
CD _____ TARACD 3001
Tara / Oct '89 / CM / ADA / Direct / Conifer.

COLD BLOW AND THE RAINY NIGHT
Johnny Cope / Reels / Cold blow and the rainy night / P stands for Paddy, I suppose / Polkas / Bansea's green glade / Nominsko horo / Little drummer / Lakes of Ponchartrain / Jigs / Green fields of Canada
CD _____ SH 79011 CD
Shanachie / '90 / Koch / ADA / Greensleeves.

WELL BELOW THE VALLEY, THE
CD _____ SH 79010 CD
Shanachie / '88 / Koch / ADA / Greensleeves.

WOMAN I LOVED SO WELL, THE
True love knows no season / Out on the ocean/Tiocfaidh tu abhaile liom / Roger O'Hehir / Tailor's twist / Kellswater / Johnny of Brady's lea / Woman I never forgot/Pullet/Ladies pantalettes / Little musgrave
CD _____ TARACD 3005
Tara / Jan '92 / CM / ADA / Direct / Conifer.

Plasmatics

NEW HOPE FOR THE WRETCHED
Tight black pants / Monkey suit / Living dead / Test tube babies / Won't you / Concrete shoes / Squirm (live) / Want you baby / Dream lover / Sometimes / Corruption / Butcher baby
CD _____ DOJOCD 79
Dojo / Feb '94 / BMG.

Plass, Wesley

I'LL BE THERE
CD _____ ISCD 120
Intersound / '91 / Jazz Music.

Plastic Ono Band

LIVE PEACE IN TORONTO 1969
Blue suede shoes / Dizzy Miss Lizzy / Yer blues / Cold turkey / Give peace a chance / Don't worry Kyoko / John John
CD _____ CDP 7904282
Apple / May '95 / EMI.

Plasticland

DAPPER SNAPPINGS
CD _____ EFA 156602
Repulsion / Feb '95 / SRD.

Plastikman

MUSIK
CD _____ CDNOMU 37
Nova Mute / Nov '94 / Disc.

SHEET ONE
CD _____ NOMU 22CD
Mute / Oct '93 / Disc.

Platinum Dance Orchestra

STRICT TEMPO (64 great dance melodies)
Quickstep medley / Slow fox-trot medley / Samba medley / Barn dance medley / Tango medley / Palma waltz medley / Gypsy tap medley / Old time waltz medley / Rumba medley / Pride of Erin / Cha cha medley
CD _____ PLATCD 03
Platinum Music / Dec '88 / Prism / Ross.

Platters

ALL THE HITS AND MORE
CD _____ DBG 53041
Double Gold / Apr '95 / Target/BMG.

AUDIO ARCHIVE
Great pretender / Smoke gets in your eyes / Magic touch / Only you / Twilight time / Wonder of you / I get the sweetest feeling / I'm sorry / I love you 1000 times / Red sails in the sunset / Sweet sweet lovin' / Delilah / Harbour lights / My prayer / Washed ashore / Heaven on earth / I love you yes I do / All my love belongs to you / More I see you / Sayonara
CD _____ CDAA 007
Tring / Jan '92 / Tring / Prism.

BEST OF THE PLATTERS, THE
Smoke gets in your eyes / Great pretender / My dream / Twilight time / You'll never never know / (You've got) The magic touch / One in a million / Enchanted / I'm sorry / Only you / Harbour lights / Red sails in the sunset / I wish / Sleepy lagoon / Ebb tide / Heaven on Earth / Remember when / My prayer
CD _____ 5517312
Spectrum/Karussell / Nov '95 / PolyGram / THE.

ENCHANTED
Great pretender / Enchanted / You'll never never know / Little things mean a lot / I'll never smile again / Magic touch / Sixteen tons / I'm sorry / September song / Where / You're making a mistake / My dream / Trees / Winner takes all
CD _____ 5500922
Spectrum/Karussell / Oct '93 / PolyGram / THE.

ESSENTIAL COLLECTION
CD Set _____ LECD 619
Wisepack / Apr '95 / THE / Conifer.

FOUR PLATTERS AND ONE LOVELY DISH
Bark, battle and ball / I wanna / Why should I / Only you (and you alone) / Great pretender / I'm just a dancing partner / Winner takes all / Magic touch / My prayer / Someone to watch over me / I'm sorry / At your beck and call / Heaven on earth / Bewitched, bothered and bewildered / On my word of honor / Glory of love / Have mercy / Remember when / You'll never, never know / One in a million / I give you my word / It isn't right / You've changed / He's mine / I'll get by / I don't know why / Heart of stone / I'd climb the highest mountain / Temptation / In the still of the night / September in the rain / Wagon wheels / You can depend on me / Take me in your arms / You're making a mistake / My dream / Low / Darktown strutter's ball / Mean to me / You are too beautiful / No power on earth / I'm gonna sit right down and write myself a letter / Time and tide / Love you funny thing / In the middle of nowhere / When you return / Let's start all over again / Oh promise me / Don't forget / Only because / Sweet sixteen / Mystery of you / Indiff'rent / Sixteen tons / Goodnight sweetheart, it's time to go / My serenade / Try a little tenderness / My old flame / Sleepy time gal / Don't blame me / Wish me love / Helpless / I wish / No matter what you are / Twilight time (1) / Twilight time (2) / That old feeling / I'll take you home again Kathleen / It's raining outside / For the first time / Whispering wind / But not like you / Out of my mind / Don't let go / You don't say / Are you sincere / If I didn't care / Smoke gets in your eyes / Thanks for the memory / I can't get started (with you) / Somebody loves me / My blue heaven / Love in bloom / Prisoner of love / Until the real thing comes along / I'll never smile again / Tisket-a-tasket / Hula hop / Wish it were me / Enchanted / Where / Love of a lifetime / Sound and the fury / To each his own / Harbor lights / By the sleepy lagoon / By the river Sainte Marie / Rainbow on the river / Sad river / Ebb tide / Reflections in the water / My secret / What does it matter / Whispering grass / I'll be with you in apple blossom time / Lullaby of the leaves / Jeannine / Tumbling tumbleweeds / Trees / Orchids in the moonlight / Little white gardenia / Honeysuckle rose / Life is just a bowl of cherries / When you wore a tulip / Roses of picardy / Movin' in / One love / Immortal love / Love your magic spell is everywhere / Love is just around the corner / Love me or leave me / It's love love love / Let's fall in love / Advertise it / Who wouldn't love you / (I'm afraid) the masquerade is over / Nearness of you / You'll never know / It's magic / I love you truly / Love is / Love is the sweetest thing / Love is a many splendoured thing / Don't let me fall in love / True lover / Rear view mirror / I miss you so / I just got rid of a heartache / Reaching for a star / All the things you are / Song for the lonely / Say a prayer / How will I know / Keep me in love / If only you knew / Summertime / Embraceable you / People will say we're in love / Poor butterfly / Stormy weather / Every little movement / More than

you know / September song / That old black magic / My heart belongs to daddy / Sometimes I'm happy / But not for me / I heartbreak / Memories / Moon over Miami / On the top of my mind / In a little Spanish town / Shine on harvest moon / Oh how I miss you tonight / I'll see you in my dreams / Moonlight memories / Moonlight and roses / My reverie / Full moon and empty arms / Once in a while / Sentimental journey / It might as well be spring / But beautiful / I only have eyes for you / Pennies from heaven / Singin' in the rain / Blues in the night / As time goes by / My romance / Moonlight and shadows / Sweet Leilani / Stay as sweet as you are / Here comes heaven again / Viva jujuy / Cuando calienta el sol / Maria Elena / Solamente tu / Siboney / Amor / Aquellos ojos verdes / Aquarela do Brazil / Tu dolce voz / La hora del crepusculo / Besame mucho / Malaguena salerosa / Strangers / Winter wonderland / White Christmas / Silent night / Santa Claus is coming to town / I'll be home for Christmas / For Auld Lang Syne / Rudolph the red nosed reindeer / All I want for Christmas (is my two front teeth) / Come home for Christmas / Jingle bell rock / Jingle bells jingle / Blue Christmas / Christmas time / Sincerely / P.S. I love you / Hut sut song / Banana boat song (Day O) / Mississippi mud / False hearted lover / Michael, row the boat ashore / Crying in the chapel / Java jive / Three coins in the fountain / Way down yonder in New Orleans / Three bells / Song from Moulin Rouge / Little things mean a lot / (We're gonna) Rock around the clock / Don't be cruel / Tammy / Volare / Mack the knife / Summer place / Exodus song / Twist / Love me tender / Anniversary song / Gypsy / When I fall in love / Big forget / Soothe me / Easy street / It could happen to you / Blues serenade / These foolish things / Somewhere along the line / Love / House of the rising sun / Hard hearted Hannah (the vamp of Savannah)
CD _____ BCD 15741
Bear Family / Jan '94 / Rollercoaster / Direct / CM / Swift / ADA.

GOLDEN HITS COLLECTION
CD _____ PWK 071
Carlton Home Entertainment / Sep '88 / Carlton Home Entertainment.

GOLDENS HITS, THE
CD _____ 826 447-2
Mercury / '86 / PolyGram.

GREATEST HITS
CD _____ GRF 215
Tring / Mar '93 / Tring / Prism.

GREATEST HITS: PLATTERS
CD _____ CDSGP 014
Prestige / Oct '92 / Total/BMG.

MUSICOR YEARS, THE
With this ring / I love you 1000 times / I can't get used to sharing you / Don't hear, speak, see no evil / Washed ashore / Doesn't it ring a bell / Devri / Why do you wanna make me blue / Think before you walk / So many tears / Alone in the night / How beautiful our love is / Hard to get thing called love / Sweet sweet lovin' / Going back to Detroit / Run while it's dark / Fear of losing you / Not my girl / Get a hold of yourself / Shing-a-ling-a-loo / Baby baby / Love must go on / I'll be home / If I had a love / What name shall I give you my love / Magic touch / Sonata / Why
CD _____ CDKEND 116
Kent / Jul '94 / Pinnacle.

ONLY YOU
CD _____ CDCD 1045
Charly / Mar '93 / Charly / THE / Cadillac.

ONLY YOU
CD _____ 15077
Laserlight / Aug '92 / Target/BMG.

PERFECT HARMONY
CD _____ CDCD 1112
Charly / Jul '93 / Charly / THE / Cadillac.

PLATTERS
CD _____ LECD 040
Dynamite / May '94 / THE.

PLATTERS, THE
CD _____ KCD 651
King/Paddle Wheel / Mar '90 / New Note.

PLATTERS, THE
CD _____ KLMCD 043
Scratch / Apr '95 / BMG.

PLATTERS/DRIFTERS ESSENTIALS (Platters & Drifters)
CD _____ LECDD 626
Wisepack / Aug '95 / THE / Conifer.

REMEMBER WHEN
CD _____ AIM 1026CD
Aim / Oct '93 / Direct / ADA / Jazz Music.

SINCERELY
Only you (And you alone) / Smoke gets in your eyes / Thanks for the memory / Red sails in teh sunset / I wish / I wanna / I only have eyes for you / On a slow boat to China / To each his own / Heaven on earth / I wish it were me / Glory of love / Lazy river / Sincerely
CD _____ 5500522

Spectrum/Karussell / May '93 / PolyGram / THE.

SMOKE GETS IN YOUR EYES
Great pretender / Only you / Harbour lights / Pledging my love / With this ring / My prayer / Smoke gets in your eyes / Twilight time / I'm sorry / If I had you / Red sails in the sunset / I'll be home / I love you 1000 times / Sweet sweet lovin' / Delilah / Washed ashore / Magic touch / Heaven on earth / I love you, yes I do / All my love belongs to you
CD _____ CDINS 5045
Charly / Sep '91 / Charly / THE / Cadillac.

Plaxico, Lonnie

IRIDESCENCE
CD _____ MCD 5427
Muse / Nov '91 / New Note / CM.

WITH ALL YOUR HEART
With all your heart / When you went away / Ray / Basement jammin' / Sixteenth Movement / Avonelle / Southside soul / As I gaze / Since we parted
CD _____ MCD 5525
Muse / Jul '95 / New Note / CM.

Play Dead

COMPANY OF JUSTICE
CD _____ FREUDCD 41
Jungle / Sep '93 / Disc.

FIRST FLOWER
CD _____ CLEO 7519CD
Cleopatra / Jan '94 / Disc.

Players

CHRISTMAS
CD _____ EXPALCD 6
Expression / Nov '91 / Pinnacle.

Playground

BENT, LOST OR BROKEN
CD _____ HABITCD 001
IFA / Oct '95 / Plastic Head.

RESILIENCES
CD _____ DPROMCD 5
Dirter Promotions / Nov '93 / Pinnacle.

Playle, Jerry

BEYOND SILENCE
Another time / Riders on the storm / Toys / Nice pair / Senorina latina / World suite / Praying for rain / Mirage / Managua tormenta / Aries rising / Beyond silence
CD _____ 33 JAZZ 022
33 Jazz / Apr '95 / Cadillac / New Note.

Pleasant Gehman

RUINED
CD _____ NAR 086 CD
SST / Aug '93 / Plastic Head.

Pleasure

BEST OF PLEASURE, THE
Bouncy lady / Straight ahead / Sassafras girl / Let me be the one / Two for one / Tune in / Foxy lady / Ghettos of the mind / Joyous / Glide / Strong love / Ladies night out / Pleasure for your pleasure / No matter what / Selim
CD _____ CDBGPD 036
BGP / Jun '92 / Pinnacle.

Pleasure Barons

LIVE IN LAS VEGAS
CD _____ HCD 8044
Hightone / Jul '94 / ADA / Koch.

Pleasure Elite

BAD JUJU
CD _____ CDVEST 13
Bulletproof / Jun '94 / Pinnacle.

Plethyn

BLAS Y PRIDD/GOLAU TAN GWMWL
Y gwlliaid / Ffarwel i blwy Llangywer / Ifan Pant y Fedwen / Can y cathreiniwr / Y morwr / Y sgyttan / Helyntion caru / Lluen / Merch o blwy Penderyn / Cystal gen i wdi gwmwl / Y deryn du a'i blufyn sidan / Lodes lan / Gwaed ar eu dwylo / Un peth rwy'n ei garu / Y cryman bach / Pelydrau / Adar man y mynydd / Ye ferch yn ffair Llanidloes / Gwenno Penygelli / Deio bach / Tan yn Llyn
CD _____ SAIN 6045CD
Sain / Aug '94 / Direct / ADA.

DRWS AGORED
Cwm y coed / Myn Mair / Breuddwyd Glyndwr / Rho wen yn dy gwsg / La Rochelle / Philomela / Hon yw fy Olwen i / Y ceidwad / Ffarwel i Aberystwyth / Wylaf dros lwerddon / Y deryn pur / Cysga di fy mhlentyn tlws / Tafarn fach glyd ar y cei
CD _____ SAIN 4033CD
Sain / Aug '94 / Direct / ADA.

SEIDIR DDOE
CD _____ SCD 2083
Sain / Dec '94 / Direct / ADA.

Plews, Steve

LIVE 95 - MADE IN MANCHESTER
Idsong / God's mates / Riley's death / Sleepwalker / An idle person in love / Too much apple pie
CD _____ ASCCD 6
ASC / Jan '96 / New Note / Cadillac.

SECRET SPACES
Idsong / Humorists / Secret spaces / Fanfare for a pit pony / Free fantasia / Ivov / 188 / Pavanne for JW
CD _____ ASCCD 3
ASC / Sep '95 / New Note / Cadillac.

Plexi

CD EP
CD _____ IFACD 003
IFA / Nov '95 / Plastic Head.

Pliers

I WANNA BE YOUR MAN
CD _____ RNCD 2066
Rhino / Aug '94 / Jetstar / Magnum Music Group / THE.

Plimsouls

ONE NIGHT IN AMERICA
Hush hush / How long will it take / I want what you got / In this town / Help yourself / I'll get lucky / Now / Million miles away / Time won't let me / One more heartache / Dizzy Miss Lizzy / Come on now
CD _____ 422266
New Rose / May '94 / Direct / ADA.

Plummer, Tonya

I'M READY
CD _____ JBR 001
Johnny Boy / Oct '94 / Else.

Plunk

SWELL
CD _____ GAP 026
Gap Recordings / Jun '95 / SRD.

Pluto

PLUTO...PLUS
I really want it / Crossfire / And my old rocking horse / Down and out / She's innocent / Road to glory / Stealing my thunder / Beauty Queen / Mr. Westwood / Something that you loved / Rag a bone Joe / Bare lady
CD _____ SEECD 265
See For Miles/C5 / Oct '89 / Pinnacle.

Pluto

RISING
CD _____ ITPAL 002CD
ITP / Jul '95 / Jumpstart / Kudos.

Pluznick, Michael

RHYTHM HARVEST (Pluznick, Michael Group)
Echoes of time / Capilonga / Kongo / Le bolero haitien / Jungle jam / L'Artibonite / Haitian rumba / Mozambique / Rara / Rumbacito / Rhythm realm / Giant step / Yemaya- Blue currents / Echoes of time (Reprise)
CD _____ ND 63022
Narada / Nov '92 / New Note / ADA.

RM Down

BLISS ALBUM, THE
CD _____ IMCD 222
Island / Mar '96 / PolyGram.

JESUS WEPT
CD _____ GEECD 16
Gee Street / Oct '95 / PolyGram.

OF THE HEART, OF THE SOUL, OF THE CROSS
Intro / Reality used to be a friend of mine / Paper doll / To serenade a rainbow (Tony Love mix) / Comatose / Watchers point of view (7" youth mix) / Even after I die / Ode to a forgetful mind (The more than words mix) / Twisted mellow / Paper doll (Flute mix) / In the presence of mirrors / Set adrift on memory bliss / Shake / If I wuz U
CD _____ GECDX 7
Gee Street / Mar '92 / PolyGram.

Po

DUCKS & DRAKES
CD _____ RUTCD 001
Rutland / Oct '93 / Disc.

Pocket Fishermen

FUTURE GODS OF ROCK
CD _____ SECTOR 210016
Sector 2 / Aug '95 / Direct / ADA.

Poco

BLUE AND GREY
CD _____ MCAD 22068
One Way / Apr '94 / Direct / ADA.

Cowboys and Englishmen

COWBOYS AND ENGLISHMEN
CD _____ MCAD 22067
One Way / Apr '94 / Direct / ADA.

CRAZY EYES
Blue water / Fool's gold / Here we go again / Brass buttons / Right along / Crazy eyes / Magnolia / Let's dance tonight
CD _____ EK 66968
Epic / Jul '95 / Sony.

PICKIN' UP THE PIECES
Foreward / What a day / Nobody's fool / Calico lady / First love / Make me a smile / Short changed / Pickin' up the pieces / Grand junction / Oh yeah / Just in case it happens / Yes indeed / Tomorrow / Consequently so long / Do you feel it
CD _____ EK 66227
Epic / Jul '95 / Sony.

ROSE OF CIMARRON
Stealaway / Just like me / Rose of Cimarron / Company's coming / Slow poke / Too many nights too long / When you come around / Starin' at the sky / All alone together / Tulsa turnaround
CD _____ MCAD 22076
One Way / Apr '94 / Direct / ADA.

SEVEN
Drivin' wheel / Rocky mountain breakdown / Just call my name / Skatin' / Faith in the families / Krikkit's song / Angel / You've got your reasons
CD _____ EK 66985
Epic / Jul '95 / Sony.

Podewell, Polly

POLLY PODEWELL
CD _____ ACD 276
Audiophile / Aug '95 / Jazz Music / Swift.

Podium Trio

MEET THE PODIUM 3
Blues for Dolphy / Mr. Monk / Mo's mood / High life
CD _____ CDSJP 421
Timeless Jazz / May '94 / New Note.

Poem Rocket

FELIX CULPA
Eject / Deus absconditus / Animal planter / Contrail de l'avion / Small white animal / Flaw / Milky white entropy / Period / Pretty baby / Blue chevy impala
CD _____ PCP 0292
PCP / Nov '95 / Vital.

Pogatschar, Helga

MARS REQUIEM
CD _____ EFA 155892
Gymnastic / Dec '95 / SRD.

Pogues

BEST OF THE POGUES, THE
Fairytale of New York / Sally Maclennane / Dirty old town / Irish rover / Pair of brown eyes / Streams of whiskey / Rainy night in Soho / Fiesta / Rain street / Misty morning / Albert Bridge / White City / Thousands are sailing / Broad majestic Shannon / Body of an American
CD _____ 9031754052
WEA / Oct '91 / Warner Music.

HELL'S DITCH
Sunny side of the street / Sayonara / Ghost of a smile / Hell's ditch / Lorca's novena / Summer in Siam / Rain street / Rainbow man / Wake of the Medusa / House of the Gods / Five green Queens and Jean (CD only) / Maidrin rua / Six to go
CD _____ 9031725542
WEA / Mar '94 / Warner Music.

IF I SHOULD FALL FROM GRACE WITH GOD
If I should fall from grace with God / Turkish song of the damned / Bottle of smoke / Fairytale of New York / Metropolis / Thousands are sailing / South Australia / Fiesta / Recruiting sergeant / Rocky road to Dublin / Galway races (medley) / Streets of sorrow/Birmingham six / Lullaby of London / Battle march / Sit down by the fire / Broad majestic Shannon / Worms
CD _____ K 2444932
WEA / Oct '95 / Warner Music.

PEACE AND LOVE
Gridlock / Young Ned of the hill / Cotton fields / Down all days / Lorelei / Boat train / Night train to Lorca / White City / Misty morning Albert Bridge / Blue heaven / U.S.A. / Gartloney rats / Tombstone / London you're a lady
CD _____ K 2460862
WEA / Mar '94 / Warner Music.

POGUE MAHONE
CD _____ 0630112102
WEA / Oct '95 / Warner Music.

RED ROSES FOR ME
Transmetropolitan / Battle of Brisbane / Auld triangle / Waxie's dargle / Sea shanty / Dark streets of London / Streams of whiskey / Poor Paddy / Dingle regatta / Greenland whale fisheries / Down in the ground where the dead men go / Kitty

CD _____ K 2444942
WEA / Mar '94 / Warner Music.

REST OF THE BEST, THE
If I should fall from grace with God / Sick bed of Cuchulainn / Old main drag / Boys from the county hell / Young Ned of the hill / Dark streets of London / Repeal of the licensing laws / Yeah yeah yeah yeah yeah / London girl / Honky tonk women / Summer in siam / Turkish song of the damned / Sunny side of the street / Hell's ditch
CD _____ 903177341-2
East West / Mar '94 / Warner Music.

RUM, SODOMY AND THE LASH
Sick bed of Cuchulainn / Old main drag / Wild cats of Kilkenny / Man you don't meet every day / Pair of brown eyes / Sally Maclennane / Dirty old town / Jesse James / Navigator / Billy's bones / Gentleman soldier / And the band played waltzing Matilda / Pistol for Paddy Garcia
CD _____ K 2444952
WEA / Mar '94 / Warner Music.

WAITING FOR HERB
Tuesday morning / Smell of petroleum / Haunting / Once upon a time / Sittin' on top of the world / Drunken boat / Big city / Girl from the Wadi Hammamat / Modern world / Pachinko / My baby's gone / Small hours
CD _____ 450993463-2
WEA / Sep '93 / Warner Music.

Poindexter, Pony

PLAYS 'THE BIG ONES'/GUMBO
Midnight in Moscow / Moon river / Twistin' USA / Poinciana / Love me tender / Green eyes / Fly me to the moon / San Antonio rose / Front o' town / Happy strut / Creole girl / 4-11-44 / Back o' town / Muddy dust / French market / Gumbo fillet
CD _____ CDBGPD 077
BGP / Sep '93 / Pinnacle.

Poindexter, Steve

MAN AT WORK
CD _____ ACVCD 104
ACV / Dec '95 / Plastic Head / SRD.

Pointed Sticks

PART OF THE NOISE
CD _____ ZULU 015CD
Zulu / Oct '95 / Plastic Head.

Pointer Sisters

BACK2BACK
CD Set _____ 74321291462
RCA / Sep '95 / BMG.

BREAK OUT
Jump / Automatic / I'm so excited / I need you / Dance electric / Neutron dance / Easy persuasion / Baby come and get it / Telegraph your love / Operator
CD _____ ND 90206
RCA / Aug '88 / BMG.

COLLECTION, THE
Yes we can-can / Fairytale / Fire / Happiness / He's so shy / Slow hand / I'm so excited / American music / Should I do it / If you wanna get back / Your lady / I need you / Jump / Automatic / Neutron dance / Baby come and get it / Dare me / Twist my arm / Goldmine
CD _____ 74321 13957-2
RCA / Jul '93 / BMG.

JUMP (Best Of The Pointer Sisters)
Jump / Someday we'll be together / Automatic / He's so shy / Should I do it / Slow hand / Heart to heart / Telegraph your love / I'm so excited / Goldmine / Back in my arms / I need you / Neutron dance / Dare me / See how the love goes / Overnight success (Not on LP) / I'm ready for love (Not on LP) / Fire (CD only)
CD _____ 74321289862
RCA / Aug '95 / BMG.

POINTER SISTERS
Twist my arm / Hey you / Pound pound pound / Back in my arms / Burn down the night / Bodies and souls / Contact / Dare me / Freedom
CD _____ PD 85487
Planet / Nov '85 / Grapevine / ADA / CM.

Pointer, Noel

NEVER LOSE YOUR HEART
CD _____ SHCD 5007
Shanachie / Dec '93 / Koch / ADA / Greensleeves.

Poison

FLESH AND BLOOD
Strange days of uncle Jack / Valley of lost souls / (Flesh and blood) sacrifice / Swamp juice (soul-o) / Unskinny bop / Let it play / Life goes on / Come hell or high water / Ride the wind / Don't give up an inch / Something to believe in / Ball and chain / Life loves a tragedy / Poor boy blues
CD _____ CDEST 2126
Capitol / Jul '90 / EMI.

OPEN UP AND SAY AHH
Love on the rocks / Nothin' but a good time / Back to the rocking horse / Good love / Tearin' down the walls / Look but you can't touch / Fallen angel / Every rose has its thorn / Your mama don't dance / Bad to be good
CD _____ CDEST 2059
Capitol / Feb '94 / EMI.

Poison 13

WINE IS RED POISON IS BLUE
CD _____ SP 273B
Sub Pop / Nov '94 / Disc.

Poison Chang

FROM JA TO UK - MC CLASH VOL.3 (Poison Chang & Top Cat)
CD _____ FADCD 027
Fashion / Jul '93 / Jetstar / Grapevine.

RUMBLE IN THE JUNGLE VOL.2 (Poison Chang & Cutty Ranks)
CD _____ JFCD 02
Fashion / Aug '95 / Jetstar / Grapevine.

Poison Girls

STATEMENT (The Complete Recordings 1977-1989)
Revenge / Cat's eye / Piano lessons / Closed shop / I wanted the moon / Old tarts song / Crisis / Ideologically unsound / Bremen song / Political love / Jump Mama jump / Under the doctor / Reality attack / Persons unknown / State control / Bully boys / Tension / SS Snoopers / Promenade immortelle / Another hero / Hole in the wall / Underbitch / Alienation / Pretty Polly / Good time / Other / Daughters and sons / Tender love / Dirty work / Statement / Don't go home tonight / Fuckin' Mother / Where's the pleasure / Lovers are they worth it / Done it all before / Whiskey voice / Menage abbatoir / Take the toys / Soft touch / Toys no more / Mandy is having a baby / Fear is freedom / Happy now / Cinnamon garden / Offending article / Perfect crime / Tell the children / Cream dream / Real woman / Hot for love / Riot in my mind / Feeling the pinch / Desperate days / Voodoo pappadollar / Too close for comfort / Rockface / No more lies / Too proud / Price of grain / Stonehenge / Jenny / Girls over there / Let it go / Cupid / Mirror and glass / Abort the system / All the waystate banjo
CD Set _____ COOKCD 087
Cooking Vinyl / May '95 / Vital.

Poison Idea

KINGS OF PUNK
CD _____ TG 9284 2
Roadrunner / Sep '91 / Pinnacle.

PAJAMA PARTY
Kick out the jams / Vietnamese baby / We got the beat / Motorhead / Endless sleep / Laudy Miss. Clawdy / Jailhouse rock / Up front / Harder they come / Green onions
CD _____ SOLO 34 CD
Vinyl Solution / Aug '92 / Disc.

RECORD COLLECTORS ARE PRETENTIOUS ASSHOLES
CD _____ TG 9299 2
Roadrunner / Sep '91 / Pinnacle.

WAR ALL THE TIME
Temple / Romantic self destruction / Push the button / Ritual chicken / Nothing is final / Motorhead / Hot time / Steel rule / Typical / Murderer / Marked for life
CD _____ SOL 40CD
Vinyl Solution / Sep '94 / Disc.

Poisoned Electrick Head

BIG EYE AM
CD _____ ABT 098CD
Abstract / Apr '94 / Pinnacle / Total/BMG.

POISONED ELECTRICK HEAD
Immortal / Unborn / What ya gonna be son / Garden of Eden / Creature feature / Twentieth Century man/President's reply / Mortal
CD _____ PROBEHEAD 033C
Probe Plus / Jun '92 / Vital.

Pokkela, Martti

OLD AND NEW KANTELE
CD _____ EUCD 1040
ARC / '89 / ARC Music / ADA.

Pokrovsky, Dmitri

LES NOCES
CD _____ 7559793352
Elektra Nonesuch / Jan '95 / Warner Music.

Poland, Chris

RETURN TO METALOPOLIS
CD _____ RR 9348-2
Roadrunner / Sep '90 / Pinnacle.

Polara

POLARA
CD _____ 892762
Clean Up / Feb '95 / Vital.

Polcer, Ed

COAST TO COAST SWINGIN' JAZZ
(Polcer, Ed & His All Stars)
CD _____ JCD 198
Jazzology / '91 / Swift / Jazz Music.

Polecat, Tim

VIRTUAL ROCKABILLY
Thunder and lightnin' / Tornado / Jigsawman / Lady Medusa / Rockin' bones / Catman returns / Panic / Boys are back in town / Head on / Guardian angel / Shiver shiver / Rock until you drop / Pit / Jungle of the bass
CD _____ NERCD 078
Nervous / Aug '94 / Nervous / Magnum Music Group.

Polecats

CULT HEROES
CD _____ NERCD 001
Nervous / Oct '91 / Nervous / Magnum Music Group.

LIVE & ROCKIN'
CD _____ DOJOCD 172
Dojo / Jun '94 / BMG.

Police

GHOST IN THE MACHINE
Spirits in the material world / Every little thing she does is magic / Invisible sun / Hungry for you / Demolition man / Too much information / Rehumanise yourself / One world / Omega man / Secret journey / Darkness
CD _____ CDMID 162
A&M / Oct '92 / PolyGram.

GREATEST HITS
Roxanne / Can't stand losing you / So lonely / Message in a bottle / Walking on the moon / Bed's too big without you / Don't stand so close to me / De Do Do Do De Da Da Da / Every little thing she does is magic / Invisible Sun / Spirits in the material world / Synchronicity II / Every breath you take / King of pain / Wrapped around your finger / Tea In The Sahara
CD _____ 5400302
A&M / Sep '92 / PolyGram.

MESSAGE IN THE BOX
Nothing achieving / Fallout / Dead end job / Next to you / So lonely / Roxanne / Hole in my life / Peanuts / Can't stand losing you / Truth hits everybody / Born in the 50s / Be my girl Sally / Masoko tanga / Landlord / Message in a bottle / Regatta de blanc / It's alright for you / Bring on the night / Deathwish / Walking on the moon / On any other day / Bed's too big without you / Contact / Does everyone stare / No time this time / Visions of the night / Friends / Don't stand so close to me / Driven to tears / When the world is running down (you make the best of what's still around) / Canary in a coalmine / Voices inside my head / Bombs away / De do do do de da da da / Behind my camel / Man in a suitcase / Shadows in the rain / Other way of stopping / Sermon / Shamelle / Spirits in the material world / Every little thing she does is magic / Invisible sun / Hungry for you (J'aurais toujours faim de toi) / Demolition man / Too much information / Rehumanise yourself / One world (not three) / Omega man / Secret journey / Darkness / Finale everything / Low life / How stupid Mr. Bates / Kind of loving / Synchronicity / Walking in your footsteps / One God / Mother / Miss Gradenko / Synchronicity II / Every breath you take / King of pain / Wrapped around your finger / Tea in the Sahara / Murder by numbers / Someone to talk to / Don't stand so close to me '86 / Once upon a daydream / I burn for you
CD Set _____ 5401502
A&M / Nov '93 / PolyGram.

OUTLANDOS D'AMOUR
Next to you / So lonely / Hole in my life / Roxanne / Peanuts / Can't stand losing you / Truth hits everybody / Born in the 50s / Be my girl Sally / Masoko Tango
CD _____ CDMID 126
A&M / Aug '91 / PolyGram.

POLICE LIVE, THE
Next to you / So lonely / Truth hits everybody / Walking on the moon / Hole in my life / Fall out / Bring on the night / Message in a bottle / Bed's too big without you / Peanuts / Roxanne / Can't stand losing you / Landlord / Born in the 50's / Be my girl Sally / Synchronicity I / Synchronicity II / Walking in your footsteps / Message in a bottle (1) / O my God / De do do do de da da da / Wrapped around your finger / Tea in the Sahara / Spirits in the material world / King of pain / Don't stand so close to me / Every breath you take / Roxanne #2 / Can't stand losing you (1)
CD Set _____ 5402222
A&M / May '95 / PolyGram.

Polce

REGATTA DE BLANC
Message in a bottle / Regatta de blanc / It's alright for you / Bring on the night / Deathwish / Walking on the moon / On any other day / Bed's too big without you / Contact / Does everyone stare / No time this time
CD _____ CDMID 127
A&M / Oct '92 / PolyGram.

ZENYATTA MONDATTA
Don't stand so close to me / Driven to tears / When the world is running down (you make the best of what's still around) / Canary in a coalmine / Voices inside my head / Bombs away / De do do do De da da da / Behind my camel / Man in a suitcase / Shadows in the rain / Other way of stopping
CD _____ CDMID 128
A&M / Oct '92 / PolyGram.

Polish Nightingales

MOST BEAUTIFUL CHRISTMAS CAROLS, THE
CD _____ DCD 5231
Hermanex / Nov '92 / THE.

Polka Dogs

ENTERTAINERS, THE
CD _____ CDPAN 137
Pan / Apr '93 / ADA / Direct / CM.

Polkemmet Grorud Pipe...

PIPE BANDS OF DISTINCTION
(Polkemmet Grorud Pipe Band)
CD _____ CD MON 808
Monarch / Jul '90 / CM / ADA / Duncans / Direct.

Pollack, Ben

BEN POLLACK & HIS PICK-A-RIB BOYS
CD _____ JCD 224
Jazzology / Oct '93 / Swift / Jazz Music.

Pollard, Lisa

I SEE YOUR FACE BEFORE ME
Stuffy / Nightingale sang in Berkley Square / Stalking / I let a song go our of my heart / Things we did last summer / Namely you / Old folks / All blues / Sometimes I'm happy / I see your face before me
CD _____ CCD 4681
Concord Jazz / Feb '96 / New Note.

Pollen

BLUETTE
CD _____ GROW 252
Grass / Sep '94 / SRD.

COLOURS AND MAKE BELIEVE
CD _____ DANCD 028
Danceteria / Feb '90 / Plastic Head / ADA.

Poltergeist

BEHIND THE MASK
CD _____ 8497152
Century Media / Feb '91 / Plastic Head.

Polvo

CELEBRATE THE NEW DARK AGE
CD _____ TQ 133CD
Touch & Go / May '94 / SRD.

THIS ECLIPSE
CD _____ TG 156 CD
Touch & Go / Nov '95 / SRD.

TODAYS ACTIVE LIFESTYLES
CD _____ TG 114D
Touch & Go / Apr '93 / SRD.

Poly Styrene

TRANSLUCENCE
Dreaming / Talk in toytown / Skydive / Day that time forgot / Shades / Essence / Hip city hip / Bicycle song / Sub tropical / Translucence / Age / Goodbye
CD _____ RRCD 128
Receiver / Apr '90 / Grapevine.

Polygon

REFUGE
CD _____ EFA 112852
Glasnost / Jan '96 / SRD.

Polygon Window

SURFING ON SINE WAVES
CD _____ WARPCD 7
Warp / Jan '93 / Disc.

Polyphemus

SCRAPBOOK OF MADNESS
CD _____ BBQCD 134
Beggars Banquet / May '93 / Warner Music / Disc.

STONEHOUSE
CD _____ BBQCD 171
Beggars Banquet / Sep '95 / Warner Music / Disc.

Polyphonic Size

OVERNIGHT DAY, THE
CD _____ ROSE 150CD
New Rose / Aug '88 / Direct / ADA.

Polyyanka Russian Gypsy..

PLAY BALALAIKA PLAY (Polyyanka Russian Gypsy Ensemble)
CD _____ MCD 71371
Monitor / Jun '93 / CM.

Pond

POND
CD _____ SPCD 66/233
Sub Pop / Feb '93 / Disc.

PRACTICE OF JOY BEFORE DEATH, THE
CD _____ SPCD 143357
Sub Pop / Feb '95 / Disc.

Ponder, Jimmy

JUMP
CD _____ MCD 5347
Muse / Sep '92 / New Note / CM.

MEAN STREETS
CD _____ MCD 5324
Muse / Sep '92 / New Note / CM.

SOUL EYES
Kansas city / Soul eyes / All blues / Sun song / I didn't know what time it was / You are too beautiful / Love can be a lonley place / You don't have to go
CD _____ MCD 5514
Muse / Apr '95 / New Note / CM.

Ponomarev, Valery

LIVE AT SWEET BASIL
CD _____ RSRCD 131
Reservoir Music / Oct '94 / Cadillac.

MEANS OF IDENTIFICATION
CD _____ RSRCD 101
Reservoir Music / Dec '94 / Cadillac.

PROFILE
CD _____ RSRCD 119
Reservoir Music / Nov '94 / Cadillac.

TRIP TO MOSCOW
CD _____ RSRCD 107
Reservoir Music / Oct '89 / Cadillac.

Ponsford, Jan

VOCAL CHORDS
View / When the birds start to sing / Universal love / Turn your whole world / Are we there yet / Your eyes / Clip-clop song / Prejudice groove / Prejudice
CD _____ ASCCD 5
ASC / Oct '95 / New Note / Cadillac.

Ponta Box

PONTA BOX
Nothing from nothing well, you needn't / Fairy tale / Pin tuck / Fill in / Nabi's napping / Fifteen / Hero inn / Nefertiti-pinocchio / Concrete / Pooh song
CD _____ JVC 2002
JVC / Jul '95 / New Note.

Pontarddulais Male Choir

SOFTLY AS I LEAVE YOU
Softly as I leave you / Ride the chariot / Doilch I'r 'or / Finnish forest / Windmills of your mind / Thanks be to God / Evening's pastorale / Bryn myrddin / Christus redemptor (hyfrydol) / My Lord, what a morning / Memory / Lord's prayer / Bywyd y bugail / Mil harddach wyt na'r rhosyn gwyn / Comrades in arms
CD _____ GRCD 8
Grasmere / May '94 / Target/BMG / Savoy.

Pontiac Brothers

DOLL HUT/FIESTA EN LA BIBLIOTECA
CD _____ 346372
Frontier / Nov '92 / Vital.

FUZZY LITTLE PICTURE
CD _____ 346442
Alias / Nov '92 / Vital.

JOHNSON
CD _____ 46142
Frontier / Jul '91 / Vital.

Ponty, Jean-Luc

AURORA
Is once enough / Renaissance / Aurora (part 1) / Aurora (part 2) / Passenger of the dark / Lost forest / Between you and me / Waking dream
CD _____ 756781543-2
Atlantic / Jun '93 / Warner Music.

COSMIC MESSENGER
Cosmic messenger / Art of happiness / Don't let the world pass you by / I only feel good with you / Puppets' dance / Fake paradise / Ethereal mood / Egocentric molecules
CD _____ 756781550-2
WEA / Mar '93 / Warner Music.

Poop

ENIGMATIC OCEAN
Overture / Trans love express / Mirage / Enigmatic ocean (parts 1 and 2) / Nostalgic lady / Struggle of the turtle to the sea parts 1,2,3
CD _____ 756781512-2
WEA / Mar '93 / Warner Music.

FABLES
Infinite pursuit / Elephants in love / Radioactive legacy / Cats' tales / Perpetual rondo / In the kingdom of peace / Plastic idols
CD _____ 756781276-2
WEA / Mar '93 / Warner Music.

IMAGINARY VOYAGE
New country / Gardens of Babylon / Wandering on the milky way / Once upon a dream / Tarantula / Imaginary voyage (pts 1 & 2)
CD _____ 756781535-2
Atlantic / Jun '93 / Warner Music.

LIVE AT DONTE'S
Hypomode de sol / People / California / Eight-one / Foosh / Sara's theme / Pamukkale / Cantaloupe island
CD _____ CDP 8356352
Pacific Jazz / Jan '96 / EMI.

NO ABSOLUTE TIME
No absolute time / Savannah / Lost illusions / Dance of the spirits / Forever together / Caracas / African spirits / Speak out / Blue mambo / Child in you
CD _____ 592213
FNAC / May '94 / Discovery.

TCHOKOLA
CD _____ 4685222
Sony Jazz / Jan '95 / Sony.

Pony

COSMOVALIDATOR
CD _____ FIRECD 41
Fire / Aug '94 / Disc.

Pooh Sticks

GREAT WHITE WONDER, THE
CD _____ CHEREE 18 CD
Cheree / May '91 / SRD.

MULTIPLE ORGASM
CD _____ FRIGHT 047CD
Fierce / Mar '92 / Disc.

OPTIMISTIC FOOL
Opening night / Cool in a crisis / Starfishing / Optimistic fool / Who was it / Bad morning girl / Miss me / Working on a beautiful thing / Up on the roof / Prayer for my demo / All things must pass / Song cycle / First of a million love songs
CD _____ 925132
Seed / May '95 / Vital.

TRADEMARK OF QUALITY
CD _____ FRIGHT 048CD
Fierce / Feb '92 / Disc.

Pooka

POOKA
City sick / Bluebell / Car / Graham Robert Wood / Breeze / Nothing in particular / Dream / Boomerang / Demon / Rollin' stone / Between my knees / Sleepwalking
CD _____ 4509935152
WEA / Sep '93 / Warner Music.

Pool, Hamilton

RETURN TO ZERO
CD _____ WMCD 1031
Watermelon / Apr '95 / ADA / Direct.

Poor

WHO CARES
Poison / Dirty money / Man of war / Tell someone who cares / More wine waiter please / Ain't on the chain / Downtown / Hair of the dog / Liar / Ride / Only the night
CD _____ 475967 2
Columbia / Sep '94 / Sony.

Poor Righteous Teachers

BLACK BUSINESS
144 K / Da rill shit / Nobody move / Ni fresh / Here we go again / Selah / Black business / Get off the crack / None can test / Ghetto we love / Rich mon time / Lick shots
CD _____ FILECD 443
Profile / Aug '93 / Pinnacle.

HOLY INTELLECT
Can I start this / Strictly ghetto / Time to say peace / So many teachers / Butt naked booty bless / Rock dis funky joint / Holy intellect / Style dropped / Word from the wise / Poor righteous teachers
CD _____ FILECD 289
Profile / Apr '90 / Pinnacle.

PURE POVERTY
CD _____ FILERCD 415
Profile / Sep '91 / Pinnacle.

Poorboys

POORBOYS
CD _____ APCD 057
Appaloosa / '92 / ADA / Magnum Music Group.

Poors Of Reign

WRECKED
CD _____ FUCTCD 1
Fat Terry / Sep '91 / Pinnacle.

Poozies

CHANTOOZIES
We built fires / Mountaineer's sect / Les femmes chaussees / Willie's old trousers / Honesty / Foggy mountain top / Crazy raven / Waking up in wonderful wark / Dhearainn sugradh / Love on a farmboy's wages / Another train
CD _____ HY 200132CD
Hypertension / Mar '95 / Total/BMG / Direct / ADA.

DANSOOZIES
CD _____ HYCD 200150
Hypertension / May '95 / Total/BMG / Direct / ADA.

Pop Will Eat Itself

CURE FOR SANITY
Incredible PWEI vs the moral majority / Dance of the mad bastards / Eighty eight seconds and still counting / X, Y and Zee / City Zen Radio 1990/2000 FM / Dr. Nightmare's medication time / Touched by the hand of Cicciolina / 1000 times no / Psychosexual / Axe of men / Another man's rhubarb / Medicine man speaked with forked tongue / Nightmare at 20,000 feet / Very metal noise pollution / 92 degrees F (the 3rd degree) / Lived in splendour, died in chaos / Beat that refused to die
CD _____ 74321 15791-2
RCA / Nov '93 / BMG.

DOS DEDOS MIS AMIGOS
CD _____ INFECT 10CD
CD _____ INFECT 10CDX
Infectious / Sep '94 / Disc.

LOOKS OR THE LIFESTYLE
England's finest / Eat me, drink me, love me, kill me / Mother / Get the girl, kill the baddies / Always been a coward baby / To-ken drug song / Karmadrome / Urban futuristic / Pretty, pretty / I was a teenage grandad / Harry Dean Stanton
CD _____ 74321157902
RCA / Nov '93 / BMG.

NOW FOR A FEAST
Black Country chainstore massacre / Monogamy / Oh Grebo I think I love you / Titanic clown / B-6-B-6 / Breakdown / Sweet sweet pie / Like an angel / I'm sniffin' with you hoo / Sick little girl / Mesmerized / There's a psychopath in my soup / Candydiosis / Devil inside / Orgone accumulator
CD _____ CHAPCD 33
Chapter 22 / Nov '88 / Vital.

SIXTEEN DIFFERENT FLAVOURS OF HELL
Urban futuristic / Get the girl, kill the baddies / Wise up sucker / Inject me / Axe of men / Can U dig it / Always been a coward baby / Karmadrome / Dance of the mad bastards / Another man's rhubarb / X, Y and Zee / F / Touched by the hand of Cicciolina / Bullet proof / Def con one / Wake up, time to die / Pweization (Available on CD only) / Eat me, drink me, love me, kill me (Available on CD only) / Preaching to the perverted (Available on CD only)
CD _____ 74321153172
RCA / Oct '93 / BMG.

THIS IS THE DAY, THIS IS THE HOUR
PWEI is a four letter word / Preaching to the perverted / Wise up sucker / Sixteen different flavours of hell / Inject me / Can U dig it / Fuses have been lit / Poison to the mind / Def con one / Radio PWEI / Shortwave transmission on up to the minuteman / Satellite ecstatica / Now now James we're busy / Wake up, time to die / Wise up sucker (remix) (Only on CD format.)
CD _____ 74321157922
RCA / Nov '93 / BMG.

TWO FINGERS MY FRIEND
CD _____ INFECT 10CDR
Infectious / Feb '95 / Disc.

WEIRD'S BAR & GRILL
England's finest / Eat me, drink me, love me, kill me / Get the girl, kill the baddies / Wise up sucker / Eighty eight seconds and counting / Karadrome / Token drug song / Mother / Preaching to the perverted / Axe of men / Nightmare at 20,000 feet / Harry Dean Stanton (Features on CD and MC only.) / Always been a coward baby / Can U dig it / Bullet proof / Urban futuristic / Teenage grandad (Features on CD and MC only.) / There is no love between us anymore / Def con one
CD _____ 74321133432
Arista / Mar '93 / BMG.

Popa Chubby

BOOTY AND THE BEAST
Palace of the king / Lookin' back / Healing in her hands / Sweet goddess of love and beer / Stoop down baby / Trouble / Same old blues / Anything you want me to do / Low down and dirty / Waitin' for the light / Angel on my shoulder / You rub me the wrong way / Secret Chubby / Sweat / Chubby's goodnight
CD _____ 4803582
Epic / Jul '95 / Sony.

Pope, Mal

COPPER KINGDOM
CD _____ CDWM 111
Westmoor / Oct '95 / Target/BMG.

Pope, Odean

EPITOME (Pope, Odean Saxophone Choir)
CD _____ 121279-2
Soul Note / Nov '94 / Harmonia Mundi / Wellard / Cadillac.

Popguns

LOVE JUNKY
I'll take you down / Get out / Star / Second time around / Someone to dream of / Under starlight / Miserable boy / How to face it / Here in heaven / Over your head / So cold
CD _____ STONE 016CD
3rd Stone / Feb '95 / Vital / Plastic Head.

Popinjays

BANG UP TO DATE WITH THE POPINJAYS
CD _____ TPCD 28
One Little Indian / Apr '90 / Pinnacle.

TALES FROM THE URBAN PRAIRIE
Queen of the parking lot / Feelin' / When I believed in you / Moonheart / Slowly I reach / Hurricane / Kentish Town / Buffalo / Down / Drive the train
CD _____ TPLP 48CD
One Little Indian / May '94 / Pinnacle.

Poppi UK

MISFIT HOME MUSIC
CD _____ SCH 8908CD
Schemer / Nov '90 / Vital.

Poppies

HONEYBEE
She is revolution / That's what we'll do / Love trippin' / Hello Saturday / Without freedom / All tomorrow's parties / Friends for life / La de da (a trilogy) / Wonderdrug / Soulflower / Mother groove / Love amplifier / Everyone's song
CD _____ 450993068-2
East West / Jul '93 / Warner Music.

Poppy, Andrew

ALPHABED (A Mystery Dance)
Forty five is / Goodbye Mr. G / Amusement
CD _____ 450994752-2
ZTT / Mar '94 / Warner Music.

BEATING OF WINGS
Object is a hungry wolf / Thirty two frames for orchestra / Listening in / Cadenza
CD _____ 450994751-2
ZTT / Mar '94 / Warner Music.

Pops Mohamed

ANCESTRAL HEALING
Mbira jive / Shona dawn / Cup O' "Jo" (burg) / Communal well / Lolly's song / Election day serenade / Idube / Salaam / Ancestral healing
CD _____ BW 069
B&W / Sep '95 / New Note.

Popsicle

ABSTINENCE
CD _____ 4509956792
Warner Bros. / Feb '95 / Warner Music.

Popul Vuh

BEST OF POPUL VUH
CD _____ CDCH 042
Milan / Feb '90 / BMG / Silva Screen.

CITY RAGA
CD _____ 239752
Milan / Oct '95 / BMG / Silva Screen.

SING FOR SONG DRIVES AWAY THE WOLVES
CD _____ 139142
Milan / May '93 / BMG / Silva Screen.

Porcelain Bus

FRAGILE
CD _____ CGASS 14 CD
Citadel / Jul '90 / ADA.

TALKING TO GOD
CD _____ CGAS 804CD
Citadel / Apr '89 / ADA.

Porch

PORCH
Damn I'm lazy / Little white cracker / My ragin' ragged / Booty / Expectorant / Your hair / Dip / Bum holy / Iceberg / Bulbous head / Tattoed love boys / Palm hair
CD _____ MR 0942
Mammoth / Feb '95 / Vital.

Porcupine

LOOK BUT DON'T TOUCH
Moonwatch / Armed response / Adventures of Cal Ipso / Not in this lifetime / Look but don't touch / Games of summer / Los Angeles / Akwaba / If not now when
CD _____ 101S 8770552
101 South / Apr '95 / New Note.

Porcupine Tree

ON THE SUNDAY OF LIFE
CD _____ DELECCD 008
Delerium / May '92 / Vital.

SKY MOVES SIDEWAYS, THE
Sky moves sideways (part one) / Dislocated day / Moon touches your shoulder / Prepare yourself / Moonloop / Sky moves sideways (part two)
CD _____ DELECCD 028
Delerium / Jan '95 / Vital.

STAIRCASE INFINITIES
Cloud zero / Jokes on you / Navigator / Rainy taxi / Yellow hedgerow / Dreamscape
CD _____ BP 217CD
Blueprint / Oct '95 / Pinnacle.

UP THE DOWNSTAIR
CD _____ DELECCD 020
Delerium / Jun '93 / Vital.

YELLOW HEDGEROW DREAMSCAPE
Mute / Landscare / Prayer / Daughter in excess / Delightful suicide / Split image / No reason to live, no reason to die / Wastecoat / Towel / Execution of the will of The Marquis De Sade / Track eleven / Radioactive toy / Am empty box / Cross/Yellow hedgerow dreamscape / Music for the head
CD _____ MG 4291325
Metropnenee / Aug '94 / Vital.

Pore

NOTATION
CD _____ CDPPP 117
PDCD / Feb '94 / Plastic Head.

Porn Orchard

URGES & ANGERS
CD _____ CZ 039CD
C/Z / Jan '92 / Plastic Head.

Porno For Pyros

PORNO FOR PYROS
Sadness / Porno for pyros / Meija / Cursed female / Cursed male / Pets / Bad shit / Packin' 25 / Black girlfriend / Blood rag / Orgasm
CD _____ 936245228-2
Warner Bros. / Apr '93 / Warner Music.

Portastatic

I HOPE YOUR HEART IS NOT BRITTLE
CD _____ ELM 17CD
Elemental / Feb '94 / Disc.

Porter, Art

POCKET CITY
CD _____ 5118772
Verve / Feb '92 / PolyGram.

Porter, Cole

COLE PORTER
CD _____ DVX 08082
Deja Vu / May '95 / THE.

COLE PORTER SONG BOOK (20 Instrumental Tracks)
Another opening another show / Begin the beguine / C'est magnifique / From this moment on / I love Paris / It's all right with me / It's de-lovely / My heart belongs to daddy / Night and day / So in love / True love / What is this thing called love / Wunderbar / Allez-vous en / Why can't you behave / Can can / Where is the life that late I led / If I loved you truly / Were thine that special face / Well did you evah
CD _____ CDGRF 109
Tring / '93 / Tring / Prism.

FIFTY MILLION FRENCHMEN
CD _____ 804172
New World / Aug '92 / Harmonia Mundi / ADA / Cadillac.

Porter, Larry

MARCH BLUES
CD _____ ENJACD 80922
Enja / Sep '95 / New Note / Vital/SAM.

Portion Control

MAN WHO DID BACKWARDS SOMERSAULTS
CD _____ TEQM 4003
TEQ / May '95 / Plastic Head.

Portishead

DUMMY
Mysterons / Sour times / Strangers / It could be sweet / Wandering star / Numb / Roads / Pedestal / Biscuit / Glory box
CD _____ 8285222
Go Discs / Aug '94 / PolyGram.

Portnoy, Jerry

HOME RUN HITTER (Portnoy, Jerry & The Streamliners)
CD _____ IGOCD 2026
Indigo / Jul '95 / Direct / ADA.

POISON KISSES (Portnoy, Jerry & The Streamliners)
CD _____ MBCD 1202
Modern Blues / Sep '94 / Direct / ADA.

Portrait

ALL THAT MATTERS
Here's a kiss / I can call you / All that matters / All natural girl / Friday night / Hold me close / Lovin' u is ah-ight / How deep is your love / Me oh my / Lay you down / Heartstrings / Much too much
CD _____ CDEST 2251
Capitol / Apr '95 / EMI.

Posey, Sandy

BEST OF SANDY POSEY & SKEETER DAVIS, VOL 2 (Posey, Sandy & Skeeter Davis)
CD _____ BTBCD 002
Sound Waves / Jul '93 / Target/BMG.

VERY BEST OF SANDY POSEY
Single girl / I take it back / What a woman in love won't do / Just out of reach / It's all in the game / Hey mister / Don't touch me / I've been loving you too long / Born a woman / Sunglasses / Twelfth of never / Satin pillows / Arms full of sin / Here comes my baby again / Blue is my best color / Are you never coming home
CD _____ SOWCD 705
Sound Waves / May '93 / Target/BMG.

Posies

DEAR 23
My big mouth / Apology / You avoid parties / Help yourself / Everyone moves away / Golden blunders / Any other way / Suddenly Mary / Mrs. Green / Flood of sunshine
CD _____ GFLD 19223
Geffen / Aug '93 / BMG.

FAILURE
CD _____ PLCD 2323
Pop Llama / Feb '95 / 3MV.

FROSTING ON THE BEATER
Dream all day / Solar sister / Flavor of the month / Love letter boxes / Definite door / Burn and shine / Earlier than expected / Twenty Questions / When mute tongues can speak / Lights out / She lied by living / Coming right along
CD _____ GFLD 19298
Geffen / Oct '95 / BMG.

Position Alpha

GREETINGS FROM THE RATS
CD _____ DRCD 199
Dragon / Jan '88 / Roots / Cadillac / Wellard / CM / ADA.

TITBITS
CD _____ DRCD 252
Dragon / Oct '94 / Roots / Cadillac / Wellard / CM / ADA.

Positive Black Soul

SALAAM
Def lo xam / Le rat des villes, le rat des champs / Boul fale / Respect the Nubians / Bon a rien / Djoko / Le bourreau est mort / Ataya / Return of the diallo / Ja na oulo pao / Peurs / Nel oh / President d'Afrique
CD _____ CIDM 1114
Mango / Oct '95 / Vital / PolyGram.

Positive Dub

TRIBULATION VOL.3
CD _____ WSPCD 007
WSP / Aug '95 / Jetstar.

Positive K

SKILLS DAT PAY DA BILLS, THE
Intro (Pos K theme) / Pass the mic / One 2 the head / Shakin' / How the fuck would you know / Carhoppers / Nightshift / Intro (Back the fuck up) / I got a man / Ain't no crime / Shout out / Friends / Minnie the moocher / Nightshift (Remix) / Flower grows in Brooklyn / It's all over
CD _____ BRCD 598
4th & Broadway / Apr '93 / PolyGram.

Possum Dixon

POSSUM DIXON
Nerves / In buildings / Watch the girl destroy me / She drives / We're all happy / Invisible / Pharmaceutical itch / Executive slacks / Regina / John struck lucky / Elevators
CD _____ 654492291-2
Interscope / Apr '94 / Warner Music.

Poster Children

DAISYCHAIN REACTION
CD _____ CRECD 131
Creation / Jul '92 / 3MV / Vital.

FLOWER POWER
CD _____ 346332
Frontier / Feb '92 / Vital.

JUNIOR CITIZEN
CD _____ 9362457372
Warner Bros. / Mar '95 / Warner Music.

Potato Five

FIVE ALIVE
Shuttle disaster / Spit 'n' polish / Call me master / Live up / Jail me / Stop that train / Harvest in the east / Hi-Jacked / Stopped by a cop / Do the jerk / Western special / Got to go
CD _____ DOJOCD 181
Dojo / Jun '94 / BMG.

Pothead

DESSICATED SOUP
CD _____ EFA 127592
Orangehaus / Jul '95 / SRD.

RUMELY OIL PULL
CD _____ EFA 11973 2
Orangehaus / Sep '94 / SRD.

Potlatch

GRINGO
CD _____ DOLCD 015
Delores / Feb '95 / Plastic Head.

Potter, Chris

CONCENTRIC CIRCLES
El Morocco / Klee / Blues in concentric circles / Dusk / Lonely moon / You and the night and the music / Mortal coils / In a sentimental mood / Aurora
CD _____ CCD 4595
Concord Jazz / May '94 / New Note.

PURE
Salome's dance / Checking out / Resonance / Bad guys / Boogie stop shuffle / Second thoughts / That's what I said / Fool on the hill / Bonnie rose / Easy to love / Distant present / Every time we say goodbye
CD _____ CCD 4637
Concord Jazz / Apr '95 / New Note.

SUNDIATA
CD _____ CRISS 1107
Criss Cross / Dec '95 / Cadillac / Harmonia Mundi.

Potter, Gary

GRACENOTES
Move / Toutes directions / Cannonball rag / Wooper snooper / Misty / Moppin' the bride / Grace / Daisy Daisy / Blue drag / J'attendrai / Provenance / Sim / Swing / It don't mean a thing it it ain't got that swing
CD _____ FJCD 104
Fret / Nov '94 / New Note / Cadillac.

Potter, Nic

BLUE ZONE, THE
CD _____ VP 103CD
Voice Print / Dec '90 / Voice Print.

LONG HELLO VOLUME 1, THE
CD _____ ZOMCD 004
Zomart / Mar '94 / Total/BMG.

MOUNTAIN MUSIC & SKETCHES IN SOUND
CD _____ ZOMCD 006
Zomart / Mar '94 / Total/BMG.

Potts, Tommy

LIFFEY BANKS, THE
CD _____ CC 13CD
Claddagh / Jun '95 / ADA / Direct.

Pound & Koch

ELECTRONIC DUB
CD _____ RSNCD 21
Rising High / Aug '94 / Disc.

Pousseur, Henri

ACOUSMATRIX 4
CD _____ BVHAASTCD 9010
Bvhaast / Dec '89 / Cadillac.

POV

HANDIN' OUT BEATDOWNS
Nuff of the ruff stuff / U got what I want / Anutha luv / Good lovin' / Tell me / Summer nights / Never believe / Let me do u / U R the only 1 / Sitting here waiting / Settle down / All thru the nite / Ball ya fist
CD _____ 74321159462
Giant / Feb '94 / BMG.

Poverty Stinks

ANOTHER WORLD
You're going away / Another World / Only One / You can't give enough / There Must Be / Hitch hiker / She / Take Me Home / Man Like Anyone Else / Don't Follow Me / Getting deeper / One Love / Waltz / Poverty Stinks

CD _____ SNAP 004
Soap / Nov '92 / Vital.

Powdered Rhino Horns

BLOW JOB (GATEWAY TO A RHINO'S WORLD)
Astral visions / Charge of the large Brigade / Inner consternation (Hustlers of Culture) / Size of an elephant / Edge of a wave / Theme from Tokyo bullet / Break the equation / Inner consternation / Charge of the large Brigade (Off road mix) / Other side
CD _____ TNGCD 003
Tongue 'n' Groove / Mar '94 / Vital.

Powell, Baden

BADEN POWELL LIVE IN HAMBURG
CD _____ BEST 1037CD
Acoustic Music / Nov '93 / ADA.

MELANCOLIE
CD _____ 139 213
Accord / '86 / Discovery / Harmonia Mundi / Cadillac.

Powell, Bryan

I.T.O.Y.
I think of you / I commit / It's alright / Friends / All my love / Hurtin' / Natural / Night and day / Lady in my life / Smile / Faith / Like U do
CD _____ 518065-2
Talkin' Loud / Nov '93 / PolyGram.

Powell, Bud

'ROUND ABOUT MIDNIGHT AT THE BLUE NIGHT
Shawnuff / Lover man / There will never be another you / Monk's mood / Night in Tunisia / Round Midnight / Thelonious / 52nd Street (theme)
CD _____ FDM 365002
Dreyfus / Oct '93 / ADA / Direct / New Note.

1953 - AUTUMN BROADCASTS
CD _____ ESP 3024-2
ESP / Jan '93 / Jazz Horizons / Jazz Music.

1953 - SPRING BROADCASTS
CD _____ ESP 3022-2
ESP / Jan '93 / Jazz Horizons / Jazz Music.

1953 - SUMMER BROADCASTS
CD _____ ESP 3023-2
ESP / Jan '93 / Jazz Horizons / Jazz Music.

1953 - WINTER BROADCASTS
CD _____ ESP 3021-2
ESP / Jan '93 / Jazz Horizons / Jazz Music.

AMAZING BUD POWELL, VOL 1
Un poco loco (first take) / Un poco loco (second take) / Dance of the infidels / 52nd Street (theme) / It could happen to you (LP only.) / Night in Tunisia (LP only.) / Wail / Ornithology / Bouncing with Bud / Parisian thoroughfare (LP only.) / Wail (alt. take (CD only.) / Dance of the infidels (alt. take CD only.) / You go to my head (CD only.) / Ornithology (alt. master) (CD only.) / Un poco loco (alt. take 2) (CD only.) / Over the rainbow (CD only.)
CD _____ CDP 7815032
Blue Note / Mar '95 / EMI.

BEST OF BUD POWELL ON VERVE, THE
CD _____ 5233922
Verve / Mar '94 / PolyGram.

BIRDLAND, NEW YORK 1956
Tea for two / Lover come back to me / I want to be happy / I've got you under my skin / Hallelujah / It could happen to you / Lullaby of Birdland / Embraceable you / Ornithology / How high the moon
CD _____ 550202
Jazz Anthology / Feb '94 / Harmonia Mundi / Cadillac.

BLUE NOTE CAFE PARIS 1961
CD _____ ESP 1066-2
ESP / Jan '93 / Jazz Horizons / Jazz Music.

BLUES FOR BOUFFEMONT
In the mood for a classic / Una noche con frances / Relaxin' at Camarillo / Moose the mooche / Blues for Bouffemont / Little Willie leaps / My old flame / Star eyes / There will never be another you
CD _____ BLCD 760135
Black Lion / Apr '90 / Jazz Music / Cadillac / Wellard / Koch.

BOUNCING WITH BUD (Powell, Bud Trio)
CD _____ DD 406
Delmark / Nov '89 / Hot Shot / ADA / CM / Direct / Cadillac.

BUD POWELL TRIO PLAYS, THE (Powell, Bud Trio)
I'll remember April / (Back home again in) Indiana / Somebody loves me / I should care / Bud's bubble / Off minor / Nice work if you can get it / Everything happens to me / Embraceable you / Burt covers Bud / My heart stood still / You'd be so nice to come

home to / Bag's groove / My devotion / Stella by starlight / Woody 'n' you
CD _____ CDROU 1011
Roulette / Feb '90 / EMI.

CELIA 1947-57
CD _____ GOJCD 53075
Giants Of Jazz / Mar '92 / Target/BMG / Cadillac.

COMPLETE BLUE NOTE & ROOST RECORDINGS, THE
I'll remember April / (Back home again in) Indiana / Somebody loves me / I should care / Bud's bubble / Off minor / Nice work if you can get it / Everything happens to me / Bouncing with Bud (alt. take 1) / Bouncing with Bud (alt. take 2) / Bouncing with Bud / Wail (alt. take) / Wail / Dance of the infidels (alt. take) / Dance of the infidels / 52nd Street (theme) / Ornithology (alt. take) / Un poco loco (alt. take 1) / Un poco loco (alt. take 2) / Un poco loco / Over the rainbow / Night in Tunisia / Night in Tunisia (alt. take) / It could happen to you / It could happen to you (alt. take) / Parisian thoroughfare / Autumn in New York / Reets and I / Reets and I (alt. take) / Sure thing / Collard greens and black eyed peas (alt. take) / Collard greens and black eyed peas / Polka dots and moonbeams / I want to be happy / Audrey / Glass enclosure / Embraceable you / Burt covers Bud / My heart stood still / You'd be so nice to come home to / Bag's groove / My devotion / Stella by straight / Woody 'n' you / Blue pearl / Blue pearl (alt. take) / Keepin' in the groove / Some soul / Frantic fancies / Bud on Bach / Idaho / Don't blame me / Moose the mooche / John's abbey (alt. take) / Sub City (alt. take) / Sub City / John's abbey / Buster rides again / Like someone in love / Dry soul / Marma lade / Monopoly / Time waits / Scene changes / Down with it / Comin' up (alt. take) / Comin' up / Dual deed / Cleopatra's dream / Gettin' there / Crossin' the channel / Danceland / Borderick
CD Set _____ CDP 8300832
Blue Note / Oct '94 / EMI.

COMPLETE ESSENTIAL JAZZ FESTIVAL CONCERT, THE
Shaw 'nuff / Blues in the closet / Willow weep for me / John's abbey / Salt peanuts / All the things you are / Just you, just me / Yesterdays / Stuffy
CD _____ BLCD 760105
Black Lion / Jul '88 / Jazz Music / Cadillac / Wellard / Koch.

COMPLETE VERVE RECORDINGS, THE
CD _____ 521669-2
Verve / Nov '94 / PolyGram.

INNER FIRES
I want to be happy / Somebody loves me / Nice work if you can get it / Salt peanuts / Conception / Lullaby of Birdland / Little Willie leaps / Hallelujah / Lullaby of Birdland (alt.) / Sure thing / Woody 'n' you / Bud Powell interviews
CD _____ 1046710072
Discovery / May '95 / Warner Music.

PIANOLOGY (Powell, Bud & Thelonious Monk)
CD _____ MCD 0552
Moon / Apr '94 / Harmonia Mundi / Cadillac.

PORTRAIT OF THELONIOUS
Off minor / There will never be another you / Ruby / My dear / No name blues / Thelonious / Monk's mood / I ain't fooling / Squattyroo
CD _____ 4723512
Sony Jazz / Jan '95 / Sony.

SALT PEANUTS
CD _____ BLCD 760121
Black Lion / Aug '89 / Jazz Music / Cadillac / Wellard / Koch.

STRICTLY CONFIDENTIAL
CD _____ BLCD 760196
Koch / Nov '94 / Koch.

SWINGIN' WTH BUD (Powell, Bud Trio)
Another dozen / Almost like being in love / Salt peanuts / She / Swedish pastry / Shaw 'nuff / Oblivion / In the blue of evening / Get it / Birdland blues / Midway
CD _____ 74321 13041-2
RCA / Sep '93 / BMG.

TIME WAITS
Buster rides again / Sub city / Time waits / Marmalade / Monopoly / John's abbey / Dry soul / Sub city (alt. take) / John's abbey (alt. Take)
CD _____ BNZ 76
Blue Note / Aug '87 / EMI.

Powell, Cozy

SOONER OR LATER
Sooner or later / 633 squadron / Cat moves / Blister / Right side / Formula one / Hot rock / Prince town / Living a lie / Dartmoor / Jekyll and Hyde / Rattler
CD _____ ELITE 018CDP
Elite/Old Gold / Aug '91 / Carlton Home Entertainment.

Powell, Doc

INNER CITY BLUES
Bahama Mama / All this love / Alone with you / Mr. Magic 1994 / Song for you / New day / Inner city blues / For old times sake / On the other side / Soul strut / Sade's song / We'll make it last
CD _____ 101 S 873624
101 South / Feb '95 / New Note.

Powell, Jimmy

MANDOLIN MOMENTS
Lara's theme / Sealed with a kiss / Spanish eyes / Godfather / Milanese waltz / Skye boat song / Certain smile / Serenata / Autumn leaves / LA paloma / Song for the seashore / Forever and ever / O sole mio / Breeze and I
CD _____ PLATCD 32
Platinum Music / Jul '92 / Prism / Ross.

R & B SENSATION
Sugar man / House of the rising sun / Captain Man / Nine live wire / Witness to a war / Progressive talking blues / I'm a rocker / On the beach / I can go down / Sugar baby / Slow down / Gonna find a cave / Strangers on a train / Slow lovin' man / Back in the U.S.S.R / Out of time / Ivory / Real cool / Hipster / Hold on / Rosavelt and Iralee / Do you really have a heart
CD _____ SEECD 337
See For Miles/C5 / Feb '92 / Pinnacle.

Powell, Keith

KEITH POWELL STORY, THE
Come and join the party / Answer is no / Tore up / You better let him go / I should know better / Too much monkey business / Walkin' and cryin' / New Orleans / People get ready / Paradise / Beyond the hill / Come home baby / Goodbye girl / It was easier to hurt her / When you move you lose / Tastes sour don't it / Victory / Some people only / Two little people / You don't know like I know / Swinging tight / That's really some good / Song of the moon / It keeps rainin'
CD _____ NEMCD 717
Sequel / Nov '94 / BMG.

Powell, Marilyn

SEEDS
Seeds / Hurt / No one's gonna be a fool forever / Time for peace / Tonight / Why didn't I think of that / Old lover / Once upon a time / Up in the world / Crazy / For you / Like no one else / Music / If you're looking for a heartache / Star
CD _____ PCOM 1130
President / Oct '93 / Grapevine / Target/ BMG / Jazz Music / President.

Powell, Mel

BORDERLINE/THINGAMAGIG (Powell, Mel & Nat Pierce)
CD _____ 662223
Vanguard / Jan '94 / Complete/Pinnacle / Discovery.

Powell, Roy

BIG SKY, A
Magic mountain / Moonchild / Roast ghost / Each day / Hidden agenda / For Alice / Lorenzo / Venus and Eve
CD _____ TOTEMCD 101
Totem / Oct '94 / New Note / Jazz Music.

Power

JUSTICE OF FIRE
CD _____ RTN 41206
Rock The Nation / Feb '95 / Plastic Head.

Power, Brendan

NEW IRISH HARMONICA
CD _____ PM 002CD
Punch Music / Jan '96 / ADA / Roots.

STATE OF THE HARP
CD _____ TCJAY 335
Jayrem / Jul '94 / CM.

Power, Duffy

BLUES POWER
Hell hound / Mary open the door / Holiday / Little boy blue / Open the door / I need you / Midnight special / Gin house blues / Fox and geese / Exactly like you / Fixing a hole / Roll over Beethoven / I've been lonely baby / Lawdy Miss Clawdy / Lily / Little man you've had a busy day / City woman / Half-way / Louisiana blues / One night / Leaving blues
CD _____ SEECD 356
See For Miles/C5 / Sep '92 / Pinnacle.

JUST STAY BLUE
Love's gonna go / There's no living without your loving / I'm so glad you're mine / Dollar Mamie / Little boy blue / Little girl / Mary open the door / Hound dog / Rags and old iron / Just stay blue / Lilly / Hell hound / Love is shelter / Lawdy Miss Clawdy / Love's prescription / Halfway / Corine / Songs about Jesus / Lover's prayer / Swansong / River

CD _____ RETRO 802
RPM / Jun '95 / Pinnacle.

LITTLE BOY BLUE
Rosie / Leaving blues / It's funny / God bless the child / Coming round no more / Give me one / Mary open the door / Help me / Louisiana blues / Little boy blue / Exactly like you / One night / There you go / Red, white and blue
CD _____ EDCD 356
Edsel / Sep '92 / Pinnacle / ADA.

Power Of Dreams

IMMIGRANTS, EMIGRANTS AND ME
Jokes on me / Does it matter / Had you listened / Never told you / Never been to Texas / Maire I don't love you / Mothers eyes / Talk / Much too much / Stay / Bring you down / Where is the love / 100 ways to kill a man / My average day
CD _____ 843 258-2
Polydor / Jul '90 / PolyGram.

Power Of Expression

POWER OF EXPRESSION, THE
CD _____ LF 107CD
Lost & Found / Oct '94 / Plastic Head.

Power Pack Orchestra

YOUR 40 ALL-TIME DANCE HITS
In the mood / Opus one / Don't get around much anymore / I'm beginning to see the light / American patrol / Touch of your lips / Spanish harlem / My cherie amour / Shadow of your smile / Guitar boogie shuffle / Nut rocker / Goody goody / Deep in the heart of Texas / Honky tonk moon / Lara's theme / You made me love you / Limehouse blues / St. Louis Blues / Body and soul / Stranger on the shore / Moonlight serenade / Mood indigo / Tuxedo Junction / It happened in Monterey / String of pearls / Brazil / Sucu sucu / Caravan / Copacabana / Lipstick on your collar / Let there be drums / Never on a Sunday / Spanish flea / Hernando's hideaway / New fangled tangle / Get happy / Continental / Last waltz
CD _____ CDMFP 6083
Music For Pleasure / Mar '90 / EMI.

Power Rangers

POWER RANGERS
Go go Power Rangers (Long version) / Fight / Lord Zedd / Hey Rita / We need a hero / Combat / Go green ranger go / 5-4-1 / Zords / I will win / Go go Power Rangers (TV version) / White ranger tiger power / Power Rangers
CD _____ 74321252982
RCA / Dec '94 / BMG.

Power Station

POWER STATION
Some like it hot / Murderess / Lonely tonight / Communication / Get it on / Go to zero / Harvest for the world / Still in your heart
CD _____ CDPRG 1011
Parlophone / Aug '93 / EMI.

Power Steppers

BASS ENFORCEMENT
CD _____ WWCD 15
Wibbly Wobbly / Nov '95 / SRD.

Powerhouse

NIGHTLIFE/LOVIN' MACHINE
CD _____ PRD 70182
Provogue / Nov '90 / Pinnacle.

Powerlord

AWAKENING, THE
Masters of death / Malice / Silent terror / Invasion of the Lords / Merciless Titans / Powerlord
CD _____ SHARK 008 CD
Shark / Jun '88 / Plastic Head.

Powers, Johnny

NEW SPARK (FOR AN OLD FLAME), A
Rattled / Rock you around the world / Something about you / Rocker Billy / Bigger heartaches / Trouble / Please please do / It'll be me / Honky tonkin' Saturday night / You win again / Singin' the blues / Stuck on you / Love to burn / New spark (for an old flame) / Love business / Say it / Help me I'm in need
CD _____ NEXCD 259
Sequel / Oct '93 / BMG.

Powersurge

POWERSURGE
CD _____ RR 93112
Roadrunner / Jul '91 / Pinnacle.

Powrie, Glenna

ASHA
CD _____ MCD 5392
Muse / Sep '92 / New Note / CM.

Pozo, Chano

LEGENDARY SESSIONS (Pozo, Chano & Arsenio Rodriguez/Machito & Orchestra)
CD _____ TCD 017
Fresh Sound / Dec '92 / Jazz Music / Discovery.

Prado, Perez

BESAME MUCHO
CD _____ OD 02004
Saludos Amigos / Apr '94 / Target/BMG.

CILIEGI ROSA
CD _____ CD 62004
Saludos Amigos / Apr '94 / Target/BMG.

GO GO MAMBO (Prado, Perez & His Orchestra)
CD _____ TCD 013
Fresh Sound / Dec '92 / Jazz Music / Discovery.

GREATEST HITS
CD _____ CD 845004
Bluebird / Apr '94 / BMG.

KING OF MAMBO (Prado, Perez 'Prez')
Patricia / Ruletero / Mambo no.8 / Guaglione / Mambo no.5 / Paris / Cherry pink and apple blossom white / Caballo negro (mambo batri) / In a little Spanish town / My Roberta / Why wait / Mambo jambo / Rockambo baby / La rubia / San Remo / One night / Adios pampa mia
CD _____ ND 90424
RCA / May '95 / BMG.

LATINO
Jumbo jumbo / Ni hablar / Muchachita / La rubia / Marichita / Mama Y tata / Mambo del 65 / Latino / Jing a ling, jing a lang / Al compas del mambo / La nina popof / Paso bakan / Mi gallo / Ole mambo / Peanut vendor / Ritmo de chunga / Gateando / Oh Caballo
CD _____ CD 62079
Saludos Amigos / Jan '96 / Target/BMG.

MAMBO JAMBO
CD _____ CD 62001
Saludos Amigos / Apr '94 / Target/BMG.

MAMBO MANIA/HAVANA 3 AM
Cherry pink and apple blossom white / Ballin' the Jack / Tomcat mambo / April in Portugal / Mambo a la Kenton / High and mighty / Marilyn Monroe mambo / St. Louis blues mambo / Skokiaan / Mambo a la Billy May / Mambo de chattanooga / Mambo en sax / La comparsa / Desconfianza / La faraona / Besame mucho / Freeway mambo / Granada / Almendra / Bacoa / Peanut vendor / Baia / Historia de un amor / Mosaico cubano
CD _____ BCD 15462
Bear Family / Feb '90 / Rollercoaster / Direct / CM / Swift / ADA.

MAMBOS (Prado, Perez & Benny More)
CD _____ CD 62051
Saludos Amigos / May '94 / Target/BMG.

VOODOO SUITE/EXOTIC SUITE OF THE AMERICAS
Voodoo suite / St. James Infirmary / In the mood / I can't get started (with you) / Jumpin' at the woodside / Stompin' at the Savoy / Music makers / Exotic suite of the Americas / Midnight in Jamaica / Mama yo quiero / Son of a gun / Jacqueline and Caroline / El relicario / I could have danced all night
CD _____ BCD 15463
Bear Family / Feb '90 / Rollercoaster / Direct / CM / Swift / ADA.

Praise Space Electric

2 LEAVING SESSIONS
Doc's groove / Sinnerman / Rhythm rhythm / Singing the same song / Diggin' at the dig in / Freedom / 300,000 million years / Waves of joy / Drain your wobbles away (Available on CD only) / Cybergenetic experiment X (Available on CD only) / Pebbles (Available on CD only)
CD _____ DELECCD 015
Delerium / Apr '94 / Vital.

Pram

SARGASSO SEA
Loose threads / Little scars / Earthling and protection / Cotton candy / Three wild Georges / Serpentine / Crystal tips / Crooked tiles / Eels / Sea swells and distant squalls
CD _____ PURECD 046
Too Pure / Sep '95 / Vital.

STARS ARE SO BIG, THE EARTH IS SO SMALL
CD _____ PURECD 026
Too Pure / Sep '93 / Vital.

Prasit Thawon Ensemble

THAI CLASSICAL MUSIC
CD _____ NI 5412CD
Nimbus / Oct '94 / Nimbus.

Praxis

TRANSMUTATION
Blast/War machine dub / Interface/Stimulation loop / Crash victim/Black science navigator / Animal behaviour / Dead man walking / Seven laws of woo / Interworld and the new innocence / Giant robot/Machines in the modern city / After shock (Chaos never died)
CD _____ 5123382
Axiom / Sep '92 / PolyGram / Vital.

Praying Mantis

CRY FOR THE NEW WORLD, A
CD _____ CDFLAG 80
Under One Flag / Sep '93 / Pinnacle.

PREDATOR IN DISGUISE
Can't see the angels / She's hot / This time / Time slipping away / Listen what your heart says / Still want you / Horn / Battle royal / Only you / Borderline / Can't wait forever
CD _____ CDFLAG 77
Under One Flag / Feb '93 / Pinnacle.

Preacher Boy

PREACHER BOY & THE NATURAL BLUES
CD _____ BPCD 5017
Blind Pig / Feb '95 / Hot Shot / Swift / CM / Roots / Direct / ADA.

Prefab Sprout

FROM LANGLEY PARK TO MEMPHIS
King of rock 'n' roll / Cars and girls / I remember that / Enchanted / Nightingales / Hey Manhattan / Knock on wood / Golden calf / Nancy let your hair down for me / Venus of the soup kitchen
CD _____ 4601242
Columbia / Oct '91 / Sony.

JORDAN - THE COMEBACK
Looking for Atlantis / Wild horses / Machine gun Ibiza / We let the stars go / Carnival 2000 / Jordan: The comeback / Jesse James symphony / Jesse James bolero / Moon dog / All the world loves lovers / All boys believe anything / Ice maiden / Paris Smith / Wedding march / One of the broken / Michael / Mercy / Scarlet nights / Doo wop in Harlem
CD _____ KWCD 142
Columbia / Apr '94 / Sony.

LIFE OF SURPIRISES, A/STEVE MCQUEEN
CD Set _____ 4718862 D
Columbia / Feb '93 / Sony.

LIFE OF SURPRISES, A
King of rock 'n' roll / When love breaks down / Sound of crying / Faron Young / Carnival 2000 / Goodbye Lucille / Cruel / I remember that / Cars and girls / We let the stars go / Life of surprises / Appetite / If you don't love me / Wild horses / Hey Manhattan / All the world loves lovers
CD _____ 4718862
Columbia / Jun '92 / Sony.

PROTEST SONGS
World awake / Life of surprises / Horsechimes / Wicked things / Dublin / Tiffanys / Talkin' scarlet / Till the cows come home / Pearly gates
CD _____ 4651182
Columbia / May '91 / Sony.

STEVE MCQUEEN
Faron young / Bonny / Appetite / When love breaks down / Goodbye Lucille / Cruel / I remember that / Cars and girls / Life of surprises / Appetite / If you don't love me / Wild horses / Hey Manhattan / All the world loves lovers
CD _____ 4663362
Columbia / Nov '92 / Sony.

STEVE MCQUEEN/FROM LANGLEY PARK TO MEMPHIS
Faron Young / Bonny / When love breaks down / Goodbye Lucille / No. 1 / Hallelujah / Appetite / Moving the river / Horsin' around / Desire as / Blueberry pies / When the angels / King of rock 'n' roll / Cars and girls / I remember that / Enchanted / Nightingales / Hey Manhattan / Knock on wood / Golden calf / Nancy (let your hair down for me) / Venus of the soup kitchen
CD Set _____ 4784822
Columbia / Mar '95 / Sony.

SWOON
Don't sing / Cue fanfare / Green Isaac / Here on the eerie / Cruel / Couldn't bear to be special / I never play basketball now / Ghost town blues / Elegance / Technique
CD _____ 4609082
Columbia / Jun '91 / Sony.

Prego

MOCHA EXPRESS
Mocha Express / Norbert's/Turn of the wheel / Grandjean/Laurel / Doigts de Carmen/Trois / Ami / Chasse a la Becasse / Madame Nuds Tarantella / Georgian twist / Littel green hat / Bailiffs bouree/Marijean/Jeanmari / Trois matelots/Chemin du village / Adeles / Mexican hatstand/Winter sunshine / Boeing 747/Berceuse
CD _____ FSCD 24
Folksound / Aug '94 / Roots / CM.

Prelude

AFTER THE GOLDRUSH
CD _____ PACD 7015
Disky / Sep '93 / THE / BMG / Discovery / Pinnacle.

Premature Ejaculation

ANESTHESIA
CD _____ DV 18CD
Dark Vinyl / Sep '93 / Plastic Head.

ASSERTIVE DISCIPLINE
CD _____ DV 023CD
Dark Vinyl / Jan '95 / Plastic Head.

NECESSARY DISCOMFORTS
CD _____ CLEO 7593-2
Cleopatra / Mar '94 / Disc.

Premi

10 YEARS ON
CD _____ DMUT 1212
Multitone / Aug '93 / BMG.

Premier Accordian Band

GO COUNTRY
CD _____ PLATCD 3924
Prism / May '94 / Prism.

GO HAWAIIAN
Clap clap sound / Aloha oe / Highland hulu / Beyond the reef / Now is the hour
CD _____ PLATCD 3925
Prism / May '94 / Prism.

GO SCOTTISH
CD _____ PLATCD 3926
Prism / May '94 / Prism.

Presencer, Alain

SINGING BOWLS OF TIBET
Invocation / Bowl voices / Shepherd's song / Lullaby / Bon-po chant / Lamentation / Symphony of the bowls
CD _____ CDSDL 326
Saydisc / Mar '94 / Harmonia Mundi / ADA / Direct.

Presidents Of The USA

PRESIDENTS OF THE USA
Kitty / Feather pluckn / Lump / Stranger / Boll weevil / Peaches / Dune buggy / We are not going to make it / Kick out the jams / Body / Back porch / Candy / Naked and famous
CD _____ 4810392
Columbia / Oct '95 / Sony.

Presley

AFRICAN SWIM
CD _____ SHCD 6018
Sky High / Jul '95 / Jetstar.

Presley, Elvis

50,000,000 ELVIS FANS CAN'T BE WRONG
Big hunk o' love / My wish came true / Fool such as I / I need your love tonight / Don't / I beg of you / Santa bring my baby back to me / Party / Paralysed / One night / I got stung / Kong Creole / Wear my ring around your neck / Don't cha think it's time
CD _____ ND 89429
RCA / May '90 / BMG.

ALL TIME GREATEST HITS, THE
Heartbreak hotel / Blue suede shoes / Hound dog / Love me tender / Too much / All shook up / Teddy bear / Paralysed / Party / Jailhouse rock / Don't / Wear my ring around your neck / Hard headed woman / King Creole / One night / Fool such as I / Big hunk o' love / Stuck on you / Girl of my best friend / It's now or never / Are you lonesome tonight / Wooden heart / Surrender / His latest flame / Can't help falling in love / Good luck charm / She's not you / Return to sender / Devil in disguise / Crying in the chapel / Love letters / If I can dream / In the ghetto / Suspicious minds / Don't cry Daddy / Wonder of you / I just can't help believin' / American trilogy / Burning love / Always on my mind / My boy / Suspicion / Moody blue / Way down / It's only love
CD _____ PD 90100
RCA / Sep '94 / BMG.

ALOHA FROM HAWAII
What now my love / Fever / Welcome to my world / Suspicious minds / C.C. rider / Burning love / Hound dog / I'll remember you / Long tall Sally / Whole lotta shakin' goin' on / American trilogy / Big hunk o' love / Can't help falling in love / Something / You gave me a mountain / Steamroller blues / My way / Love me / Johnny B. Goode / It's over / Blue suede shoes / I'm so lonesome I could cry / I can't stop loving you
CD _____ 74321289872
RCA / Aug '95 / BMG.

ALTERNATIVE ALOHA
Also sprach Zarathustra (Introduction) / C.C. rider / Something / You gave me a mountain / Steamroller blues / My way / It's over / Blue suede shoes / I'm so lonesome I could cry / What now my love / Fever / Welcome to my world / Suspicious

minds / I'll remember you / American trilogy / Big hunk o' love / Can't help falling in love / Blue Hawaii / Hound dog / Hawaiian wedding song / Ku-u-i-po (Available on Compact Disc only)
CD _____ PD 86985
RCA / Aug '88 / BMG.

AMAZING GRACE (His Greatest Sacred Performances)
I believe / peace in the valley / Take my hand precious Lord / It is no secret / Milky white way / His hand in mine / I believe in the man in the sky / He knows just what I need / Mansion over the hilltop / In my father's house / Joshua fit de Battle of Jericho / Swing low, sweet chariot / I'm gonna walk dem golden stairs / If we never meet again / Known only to him / Working on the building / Crying in the chapel / Run on / How great thou art / Stand by me / Where no one stands alone / So high / Farther along / By and by / In the garden / Somebody bigger than you and I / Without him / If the Lord wasn't walking by my side / Where could I go but to the Lord / We call on him / You'll never walk alone / Only believe / Amazing grace / Miracle of the rosary / Lead me, guide me / He touched me / I've got confidence / Evening prayer / Seeing is believing / Thing called love / Put your hand in the hand / Reach out to Jesus / He is my everything / There is no God but God / I, John / Bosom of Abraham / Help me / If that isn't love / Why me Lord / You better run / Lead me / Nearer my God to thee
CD _____ 07863 66421-2
RCA / Oct '94 / BMG.

AT THE WORLD'S FAIR/FUN IN ACAPULCO
Beyond the bend / Relax / Take me to the fair / They remind me too much of you / One broken heart for sale (Film version) / I'm falling in love tonight / Cotton candy land / World of our own / How would you like to be / Happy ending / One broken heart for sale / Fun in Acapulco / Vino, dinero y amor / Mexico / El toro / Marguerita / Bullfighter was a lady / No room to rhumba in a sports car / I think I'm gonna like it here / Bossa nova baby / You can't say no in Acapulco / Guadalajara
CD _____ 74321134312
RCA / Mar '93 / BMG.

BACK IN MEMPHIS
Inherit the wind / This is the story / Stranger in my own hometown / Little bit of green / And the grass won't pay no mind / Do you know who I am / From a jack to a king / Fair's moving on / You'll think of me / Without love (there is nothing)
CD _____ ND 90599
RCA / Oct '91 / BMG.

BLUE HAWAII
Blue Hawaii / Almost always true / Aloha oe / No more / Can't help falling in love / Rock-a-hula baby / Moonlight swim / Ku-u-i-po / Ito eats / Slicin' sand / Hawaiian sunset / Beach boy blues / Island of love / Hawaiian wedding song
CD _____ ND 83683
RCA / Oct '87 / BMG.

COLLECTION: ELVIS PRESLEY VOL.3
Wooden heart / Surrender / Wild in the country / Can't help falling in love / Rock-a-hula baby / His latest flame / Follow that dream / Good luck charm / She's not you / Return to sender
CD _____ PD 89472
RCA / Feb '85 / BMG.

COLLECTION: ELVIS PRESLEY VOL.4
Guitar man / U.S. male / If I can dream / In the ghetto / Suspicious minds / Don't cry daddy / Wonder of you / American trilogy / Burning love / Always on my mind / It's only love
CD _____ PD 89473
RCA / Feb '85 / BMG.

COLLECTOR'S GOLD (Hollywood Album/Nashville Album/Live in Las Vegas 1969)
G.I. blues / Pocket full of rainbows / Big boots / Black star / Summer kisses, Winter tears / I slipped, I stumbled, I fell / Lonely man / What a wonderful life / Whistling tune / Beyond the bend / One broken heart for sale / You're the boss / Roustabout / Girl happy / So close, yet so far / Stop, look and listen / Am I ready / How can you lose what you never had / Like a baby / There's always me / I want you with me / Gently / Give me the right / I met her today / Night rider / Just tell her Jim said hello / Ask me / Memphis, Tennessee / Love me tonight / Witchcraft / Come what may / Love letters / Going home / Blue suede shoes / I got a woman / Heartbreak hotel / Love me tender / Baby, what you want me to do / Runaway / Surrender/Are you lonesome tonight / Rubber neckin' / Memories / Introduction by Elvis Presley / Jailhouse rock/Don't be cruel / Inherit the wind/This is the story / Mystery train / Tiger man / Funny how time slips away / Loving you/Reconsider baby / What I'd say
CD Set _____ PD 90574
RCA / Aug '91 / BMG.

COMMAND PERFORMANCE
CD Set _____ 07863666012
RCA / Jul '95 / BMG.

COMMAND PERFORMANCES (The Essential 60s Masters 2 - 2CD Set)
G.I. blues / Wooden heart / Shoppin' around / Doin' the best I can / Flaming star / Wild in the country / Lonely man / Blue Hawaii / Rock-a-hula baby / Can't help falling in love / Beach boy blues / Hawaiian wedding song / Follow that dream / Angel / King of the whole wide world / I got lucky / Girls, girls, girls / Because of love / Return to sender / One broken heart for sale / I'm falling in love tonight / They remind me too much of you / Fun in Acapulco / Bossa Nova baby / Marguerita / Mexico / Kissin' cousins / One boy two little girls / Once is enough / Viva Las Vegas / What'd I say / Roustabout / Poison Ivy League / Little Egypt / There's a brand new day on the horizon / Girl happy / Puppet on a string / Do the clam / Harem holiday / So close, yet so far / Frankie and Johnny / Please don't stop loving me / Paradise Hawaiian style / This is my heaven / Spinout / All that I am / I'll be back / Easy come, easy go / Double trouble / Long legged girl with the short dress on / Clambake / You don't know me / Stay away / Joe / Speedway / Your time hasn't come yet, baby / Let yourself go / Almost in love / Little less conversation / Edge of reality / Charro! / Clean up your own backyard
CD Set _____ 07863666012
RCA / Jun '95 / BMG.

COMPLETE SUN SESSIONS, THE
That's alright mama / Blue moon of Kentucky / Good rockin' tonight / I don't care / the sun don't shine / Milkcow blues boogie / You're a heartbreaker / Baby let's play house / I'm left, you're right, she's gone / Mystery train / I forgot to remember to forget / I love you because / Blue moon / Tomorrow's night / I'll never let you go / Just because / Trying to get to you / Harbour lights / When it rains it really pours
CD _____ PD 86414
RCA / Jul '87 / BMG.

DATE WITH ELVIS, A
Blue moon of Kentucky / Young and beautiful / Baby I don't care / Milk cow blue boogie / Baby let's play house / Good rockin' tonight / Is it so strange / I forgot to remember to forget
CD _____ ND 90360
RCA / Sep '89 / BMG.

EASY COME, EASY GO/SPEEDWAY (Double Feature Vol. 9)
Easy come, easy go / Love machine / Yoga is as yoga does / You gotta stop / Sing you children / I'll take love / She's a machine / Love machine (alternate take) / Sing you children (alternate take) / She's a machine (alternate take 13) / Suppose (alternate master) / Speedway / There ain't nothing like a song / Your time hasn't come yet, baby / Who are you, who am I / He's your uncle, not your dad / Let yourself go / Five sleepy heads / Suppose / Your groovy self
CD _____ 07863665582
RCA / Mar '95 / BMG.

ELVIS - THE ALBUM
CD _____ SGCD 001
Dynamite / Nov '94 / THE.

ELVIS - THE FOOL ALBUM
Fool / Where do I go from here / It's impossible / It's still here / I will be true / I'll take you home again Kathleen / That's what you get) for lovin' me / Padre / Don't think twice, it's alright / Love me love the life I lead
CD _____ 07863 50283-2
RCA / Feb '94 / BMG.

ELVIS ELVIS ELVIS
That's alright mama / Blue moon of Kentucky / Heartbreak hotel / Long tall Sally / I was the one / Money, honey / I've got a woman / Blue suede shoes / Hound dog / Baby let's play house / Maybellene / There're good rockin' tonight / Tweedle dee
CD _____ MUCD 9017
Start / Apr '95 / Koch.

ELVIS FOR EVERYONE
Your cheatin' heart / Summer kisses, Winter tears / Finders keepers / In my way / Tomorrow night / Memphis, Tennessee / For the millionth and the last time / Forget me never / Sound advise Santa Lucia / Met her today / When it rains it really pours
CD _____ 7863534502
RCA / Apr '95 / BMG.

ELVIS GOSPEL 1957-1971
Peace in the valley / Take my hand / Precious Lord / I'm gonna walk dem golden stairs / I believe in the man in the sky / Joshua fit de Battle of Jericho / Swing low, sweet chariot / Stand by me / Run on / Where could I go but to the Lord / So high / We call on him / Who am I / Lead me, guide me / Known only to him
CD _____ 74321 18753-2
RCA / Feb '94 / BMG.

ELVIS IN CONCERT
Elvis fans comment / Opening riff / 2001 / C.C. rider / That's alright / Are you lonesome tonight / You gave me a mountain / Jailhouse rock / How great thou art / I really don't want to know / Elvis introduces his father / Hurt
CD _____ 74321114693-2
RCA / Jul '93 / BMG.

ELVIS IN PERSON
Blue suede shoes / Johnny B. Goode / All shook up / Are you lonesome tonight / Hound dog / I can't stop loving you / My babe / Mystery train tiger man / Words / In the ghetto / Suspicious minds / Can't help falling in love
CD _____ ND 83892
RCA / Oct '91 / BMG.

ELVIS IS BACK
Make me know it / Fever / Girl of my best friend / I will be home again / Dirty, dirty feeling / Thrill of your love / Soldier boy / Such a night / It feels so right / Girl next door / Like a baby / Reconsider baby
CD _____ ND 89013
RCA / Feb '89 / BMG.

ELVIS LIVE AT MADISON SQUARE GARDEN
2001 / That's alright mama / Proud Mary / Never been to Spain / You don't have to say you love me / You've lost that lovin' feelin' / Polk salad Annie / Love me / All shook up / Heartbreak hotel / Impossible dream / Hound dog / Suspicious minds / For the good times / American trilogy / Funny how time slips away / I can't stop loving you / Can't help falling in love / Why me Lord / How great thou art / Blueberry Hill / Can't stop loving you / Help me / Let me be there / My baby left me / Lawdy Miss Clawdy / Closing vamp
CD _____ ND 90663
RCA / Apr '92 / BMG.

ELVIS NBC SPECIAL (TV soundtrack)
Trouble / Guitar man / Lawdy Miss Clawdy / Baby, what you want me to do / Heartbreak hotel / Hound dog / All shook up / Can't help falling in love / Jailhouse rock / Love me tender / Where could I go but to the Lord / Up above my head / Saved / Blue Christmas / One night / Memories / Nothingville / Big boss man / Little Egypt / If I can dream
CD _____ ND 83894
RCA / Mar '91 / BMG.

ELVIS NOW
Help me make it through the night / Miracle of the rosary / Hey Jude / Put your hand in the hand / Until it's time for you to go / We can make the morning / Early morning rain / Sylvia / Fools rush in / I was born ten thousand years ago
CD _____ 7432114831-2
RCA / Jul '93 / BMG.

ELVIS PRESLEY
Blue suede shoes / I love you because / Tutti frutti / I'll never let you go / Money honey / I'm counting on you / I got a woman / One-sided love affair / Just because / Trying to get to you / I'm gonna sit right down and cry over you / Blue moon
CD _____ ND 89046
RCA / Oct '88 / BMG.

ELVIS PRESLEY LIVE ON STAGE IN MEMPHIS
C.C. rider / I got a woman / Love me / Trying to get to you / Long tall Sally (Medley) / Flip flop and fly / Jailhouse rock / Hound dog / Why me Lord / How great Thou art / Blueberry Hill (Medley) / Help me / American trilogy / Let me be there / My baby left me / Lawdy Miss Clawdy / Can't help falling in love / Closing vamp
CD _____ 07863506062
RCA / Feb '94 / BMG.

ELVIS PRESLEY SUN COLLECTION
That's alright mama / Blue moon of Kentucky / I don't care if the sun don't shine / Good rockin' tonight / Milk cow blue boogie / You're a heartbreaker / I'm left, you're right, she's gone / Baby let's play house / Mystery train / I forgot to remember to forget / I love you because / Trying to get to you / Blue moon / Just because / I'll never let you go
CD _____ ND 89107
RCA / '88 / BMG.

ELVIS SINGS THE WONDERFUL WORLD OF CHRISTMAS
O come all ye faithful (Adeste Fidelis) / First Noel / On a snowy Christmas night / Winter wonderland / Wonderful world of Christmas / It won't seem like Christmas (without you) / I'll be home on Christmas day / If I get home on Christmas day / Holly leaves and Christmas trees / Merry Christmas baby / Silver bells
CD _____ ND 81936
RCA / Nov '93 / BMG.

ELVIS TAPES, THE
Ace / Jul '91 / Pinnacle / Cadillac / Complete/Pinnacle.

ELVIS' CHRISTMAS ALBUM
Santa Claus is back in town / White Christmas / Here comes Santa Claus / I'll be home for Christmas / Blue Christmas / Santa bring my baby back to me / Little town of Bethlehem / Silent night / Peace in the valley / I believe / Take my hand, precious Lord / It is no secret
CD _____ ND 90300
RCA / Nov '93 / BMG.

ELVIS' GOLDEN RECORDS VOL.3
It's now or never / Stuck on you / Fame and fortune / I gotta know / Surrender / I feel so

bad / Are you lonesome tonight / His latest flame / Little sister / Good luck charm / Anything that's part of you / She's not you
CD _____ ND 82765
RCA / Oct '90 / BMG.

ELVIS' GOLDEN RECORDS VOL.4
Love letters / It hurts me / What I'd say / Please don't drag that string around / Indescribably blue / Devil in disguise / Lonely man / Mess of blues / Ask me / Ain't that lovin' you baby / Just tell her Jim said hello / Witchcraft
CD _____ ND 83921
RCA / Nov '90 / BMG.

ESSENTIAL COLLECTION, THE
Heartbreak hotel / Blue suede shoes / Hound dog / Don't be cruel / Love me tender / All shook up / Teddy bear / Jailhouse rock / King Creole / Girl of my best friend / It's now or never / Are you lonesome tonight / Wooden heart / His latest flame / Can't help falling in love / Good luck charm / She's not you / Return to sender / Devil in disguise / Crying in the chapel / In the ghetto / Suspicious minds / Wonder of you / I just can't help believin' / American trilogy / Burning love / Always on my mind / Moody blue
CD _____ 74321 22871-2
RCA / Aug '94 / BMG.

ESSENTIAL ELVIS VOL. 2 (Stereo 57)
I beg of you / Have I told you lately that I love you / Blueberry Hill / Peace in the valley / is it so strange / It is no secret / Mean woman blues / That's when your heartache begins
CD _____ PD 90250
RCA / Jan '89 / BMG.

ESSENTIAL ELVIS VOL.3 (Hits Like Never Before)
King Creole / Fool such as I / Your cheatin' heart / Don't cha think it's time / Lover doll / Danny / Crawfish / Ain't that lovin' you baby / I need your love tonight / I got stung / As long as I have you / Wear my ring around your neck / Big hunk o' love / Steadfast, loyal and true / King Creole (instrumental)
CD _____ PD 90486
RCA / May '90 / BMG.

FIFTIES INTERVIEWS, THE
Truth about me / Jacksonville, Florida / WMPS, Memphis / Witchita Falls, Texas / LaCrosse, Wisconsin / Little Rock, Arkansas / KLAC-TV, Memphis / New Orleans / New Orleans (2) / St. Petersburg, Florida
CD _____ CDMF 074
Magnum Force / Feb '91 / Magnum Music Group.

FLAMING STAR/WILD IN THE COUNTRY/FOLLOW THAT DREAM (Double Feature Vol. 8)
Flaming star / Summer kisses, winter tears / Britches a cane and a high starched collar / Black star / Flaming star (end title version) / Wild in the country / I slipped, I stumbled, I fell / Lonely man / In my way / Forget me never / Lonely man (solo) / I slipped, I stumbled, I fell (Alternate master) / Follow that dream / Angel / What a wonderful life / I'm not the marrying kind / Whistling tune / Sound advice
CD _____ 07863665572
RCA / Mar '95 / BMG.

FOR LP FANS ONLY
That's all right / Lawdy Miss Clawdy / Mystery train / Playing for keeps / Poor boy / Money honey / I'm counting on you / My baby left me / I was the one / shake, rattle and roll / I'm left, you're right, she's gone / You're a heartbreaker / Tryin' to get to you / Blue suede shoes
CD _____ ND 90359
RCA / Sep '89 / BMG.

FRANKIE AND JOHNNY/PARADISE, HAWAIIAN STYLE
Frankie and Johnny / Come along / Petunia, the gardener's daughter / Chesay / What every woman lives for / Look out, Broadway / Beginner's luck / Down by the riverside / When the saints go marching in / Shout it out / Hard luck / Please don't stop loving me / Everybody come aboard / Paradise, Hawaiian style / Queenie Wahine's papaya / Scratch my back / Drums of the islands / Datin' / Dog's life / House of sand / Stop where you are / This is my heaven / Sand castles
CD _____ 07863663602
RCA / Jun '94 / BMG.

FROM ELVIS IN MEMPHIS
Wearin' that loved on look / Only the strong survive / I'll hold you in my heart / Long black limousine / It keeps right on a-hurtin' / I'm movin' on / Power of my love / Gentle on my mind / After loving you / True love travels on a gravel road / Any day now / In the ghetto
CD _____ ND 90548
RCA / Mar '91 / BMG.

FROM ELVIS PRESLEY BOULEVARD, MEMPHIS, TENNESSEE
Hurt / Never again / Blue eyes cryin' in the rain / Danny boy / Last farewell / For the heart / Bitter they are / Solitaire / Love coming down / I'll never fall in love again

CD _____ 7432114691-2
RCA / Jul '93 / BMG.

FROM NASHVILLE TO MEMPHIS (The Essential 60s Masters I)

Make me know it / Soldier boy / Stuck on you / Fame and fortune / Mess of blues / It feels so right / Fever / Like a baby / It's now or never / Girl of my best friend / Dirty, dirty feeling / Thrill of your love / I gotta know / Such a night / Are you lonesome tonight / Girl next door went a'walking / I will be home again / Reconsider baby / Surrender / I'm coming home / Gently / In your arms / Give me the right / I feel so bad / It's a sin / I want you with me / There's always me / Starting today / Sentimental me / Just for the blame on me / Kiss me quick / That's someone you never forget / I'm yours / His latest flame / Little sister / For the millionth and last time / Good luck charm / Anything that's part of you / I met her today / Night rider / Something blue / Gonna get back home somehow / (Such an) Easy question / Fountain of love / Just for old times sake / You'll be gone / I feel that I've known you forever / Just tell her Jim said hello / Suspicion / She's not you / Echoes of love / Please don't drag that string around / Devil in disguise / Never ending / What'd I say / Witchcraft / Finders keepers / Love me tonight / (It's a) Long lonely highway / Western Union / Slowly but surely / Blue river / Memphis, Tennessee / Ask me / It hurts me / Down the alley / Tomorrow is a long time / Love letters / Beyond the reef / Come what may / Fools fall in love / Indescribably you / I'll remember you (unedited master) / Why me when like Christmas / Suppose / Guitar man/What'd I say (Original unedited master) / Big boss man / Mine / Just call me lonesome / Hi-heel sneakers (original unedited master) / You don't know me / Singing trees / Too much monkey business / U.S. male / Long black limousine / This is the story / Wearin' that loved on look / You'll think of me / Little bit of green / Gentle on my mind / I'm movin' on / Don't cry daddy / Inherit the wind / Mama liked the roses / My little friend / In the ghetto / Rubberneckin' / From a Jack to a King / Hey Jude / Without love (there is nothing) / I'll hold you in my heart / I'll be there / Suspicious minds / True love travels on a gravel road / Stranger in my own hometown / And the grass won't pay no mind / Power of my love / After loving you / Do you know who I am / Kentucky rain / Only the strong survive / It keep right on hurtin' / Any day now / If I'm a fool (For loving you) / Rain is moving on / Who am I / This time/I can't stop loving you (Informal recording) / In the ghetto (alt. take) / Suspicious minds (Alternate take 6) / Kentucky rain (Alt Take) / Big boss man #2 / Down the alley (Alternate take 1) / Memphis, Tennessee (Alternate take) / I'm yours (alt. take) / His latest flame (Alternate take 4) / That's someone you never forget (alternate take) / Surrender (Alternate take 1) / It's now or never (Original undubbed master) / Love me tender/Witchcraft (From the 'Frank Sinatra Timex Spe
CD Set _____ 74321 15430-2
RCA / Oct '93 / BMG.

GI BLUES

Tonight is so right for love / What's she really like / Frankfurt special / Wooden heart / G.I. blues / Pocket full of rainbows / Shoppin' around / Big boots / Didja ever / Blue suede shoes / Doin' the best I can
CD _____ ND 83735
RCA / Oct '87 / BMG.

GOOD TIMES

Take good care of her / Loving arms / I got a feelin' in my body / If that isn't love / She wears my ring / I got a thing about you baby / My boy / Spanish eyes / Talk about the good times / Good time Charlie's got the blues
CD _____ 07863 50475-2
RCA / Feb '94 / BMG.

GREAT PERFORMANCES

My happiness / That's all right / Shake, rattle and roll / Flip flop and fly / Heartbreak hotel / Blue suede shoes / Ready teddy / Don't be cruel / Got a lot of livin' to do / Jailhouse rock / Treat me nice / King Creole / Trouble / Fame and fortune / Return to sender / Always on my mind / American trilogy / If I can dream / Unchained melody / Memories
CD _____ PD 82227
RCA / Aug '90 / BMG.

HARUM SCARUM/GIRL HAPPY

Harem holiday / My desert serenade / Go eat young man / Mirage / Kismet / Shake that tambourine / Hey little girl / Golden coins / So close, yet so far / Animal instinct / Wisdom of the ages / Girl happy / Spring fever / Fort Lauderdale chamber of commerce / Startin' tonight / Wolf call / Do not disturb / Cross my heart and hope to die / Meanest girl in town / Do the clam / Puppet on a string / I've got to find my baby
CD _____ 74321 13433-2
RCA / Mar '93 / BMG.

HE TOUCHED ME

He touched me / I've got confidence / Amazing grace / Seeing is believing / He is my everything / Bosom of Abraham / Evening prayer / Lead me, guide me / There is

no God but God / Thing called love / I, John / Reach out to Jesus
CD _____ ND 90661
RCA / Apr '92 / BMG.

HIS HAND IN MINE

His hand in mine / I'm gonna walk dem golden stairs / My father's house / Milky white way / Known only to him / I believe / Joshua fit de battle of Jericho / Jesus knows what I need / Swing low, sweet chariot / Mansion over the hilltop / If we never meet again / Working on the building
CD _____ ND 83935
RCA / Oct '88 / BMG.

HOW GREAT THOU ART

How great Thou art / In the garden / Somebody bigger than you and I / Farther along / Stand by me / Without him / So high / Where could I go but to the Lord / By and by / If the Lord wasn't walking by my side / Run on / Where do you come from / Crying in the chapel
CD _____ ND 83758
RCA / Apr '88 / BMG.

I WISH YOU A MERRY CHRISTMAS

O come all ye faithful (Adeste Fidelis) / First Noel / On a snowy Christmas night / Winter wonderland / Wonderful world of Christmas / It won't seem like Christmas (without you) / I'll be home on Christmas Day / If I get home on Christmas Day / Holly leaves and Christmas trees / Merry Christmas baby / Silver bells / Santa Claus is back in town / White Christmas / Here comes Santa Claus / I'll be home for Christmas / Blue Christmas / Santa bring my baby back to me / O little town of Bethlehem / Silent night / Peace in the valley / I believe / Take my hand, precious Lord / It is no secret
CD _____ ND 89474
RCA / '87 / BMG.

I'M 10,000 YEARS OLD (Elvis Country)

Snowbird / Tomorrow never comes / Little cabin home on the hill / Whole lotta shakin' goin' on / Funny how time slips away / I really don't want to know / There goes my everything / It's your baby / Fool / Faded love / I washed my hands in muddy water / Make the world go away / I was born ten thousand years ago
CD _____ 7432114692-2
RCA / Jul '93 / BMG.

IF EVERY DAY WAS LIKE CHRISTMAS

If every day was like Christmas / Blue Christmas / Here comes Santa Claus / White Christmas / Santa bring my baby back to me / I'll be home for Christmas / O little town of Bethlehem / Santa Claus is back in town / It won't seem like Christmas (without you) / If I get home on Christmas day / Holly leaves and Christmas trees / On a snowy Christmas night / Winter wonderland / Wonderful world of Christmas / O come all ye faithful (Adeste Fidelis) / First Noel / It won't seem like Christmas (without you) (alt. take) / If I get home on Christmas day (unreleased alternate take) / Christmas message from Elvis / Silent night / Holly leaves and Christmas trees (unreleased alternate take)
CD _____ 07863664822
CD _____ 07863665062
RCA / Nov '95 / BMG.

IN THE BEGINNING (Elvis, Scotty & Bill)

Biff Collie interview / There's good rockin' tonight / Baby let's play house / Blue moon of Kentucky (I got a woman / That's alright mama / Elvis Presley interview / Tweedlee dee / Maybellene
CD _____ CDCD 1020
Charly / Mar '93 / Charly / THE / Cadillac.

IT FEELS SO RIGHT

World Music / '88 / Pinnacle.
CD _____ CD 88003

IT'S NOW OR NEVER (The Tribute To Elvis) (Various Artists)

Mercury / Jan '95 / PolyGram.
CD _____ 5240722

JAILHOUSE ROCK

Ariola Express / Oct '94 / BMG.
CD _____ 295051

KID GALAHAD/GIRLS GIRLS GIRLS

King of the whole wide world / This is living / Riding the rainbow / Home is where the heart is / I got lucky / Whistling tune / Girls, girls - girls - girls, girls / I don't wanna be tied / Where do you come from / I don't want to / We'll be together / Boy like me, a girl like you / Return to sender / Because of love / Thanks to the rolling sea / Song of the shrimp / Walls have ears / We're coming in loaded / Mama / Plantation rock / Dainty little moonbeams / Girls, girls, girls
CD _____ 74321 13430-2
RCA / Mar '93 / BMG.

KING CREOLE

King Creole / As long as I have you / Hard headed woman / Trouble / Dixieland rock / Don't ask me why / Lover doll / Crawfish / Young dreams / Steadfast, loyal and true / New Orleans
CD _____ ND 83733
RCA / Oct '87 / BMG.

KING OF ROCK 'N' ROLL, THE (The Complete 50's Masters)

CD Set _____ PD 90689
RCA / Jul '92 / BMG.

KISSIN' COUSINS/CLAMBAKE/STAY AWAY, JOE

Kissin' cousins #2 / Smoky mountain bay / There's gold in the mountains / One boy two little girls / Catchin' on fast / Tender feeling / Anyone (could fall in love with you) / Barefoot ballad / Once is enough / Kissin' cousins / Clambake / Who needs money / House that has everything / Confidence / Hey hey hey / You don't know me / Girl I never loved / How can you lose what you never had / Clambake (Reprise) / Stay away, Joe / Dominic / All I needed was the rain / Goin' home / Stay away
CD _____ 07863663622
RCA / Jun '94 / BMG.

LIVE A LITTLE.../TROUBLE WITH GIRLS/CHANGE OF HEART/CHARRO

Almost in love / Little less conversation / Wonderful world / Edge of reality / Little less conversation (album version) / Charro / Let's forget about the stars / Clean up your own backyard / Swing low, sweet chariot #2 / Swing low, sweet chariot / Signs of the zodiac / Almost / Whiffenpoof song / Violet / Clean up your own backyard (undubbed version) / Almost (undubbed version) / Have a happy / Let's be friends / Change of habit / Let us pray / Rubberneckin'
CD _____ 07863665592
RCA / Mar '95 / BMG.

LOVE LETTERS FROM ELVIS

Love letters / When I'm over you / If I were you / Get my mojo working / Heart of Rome / Only believe / This is our dance / Cindy Cindy / I'll never know / It ain't no big thing (but it's growing) / Life
CD _____ ND 89011
RCA / Jun '88 / BMG.

LOVE ME TENDER

CD _____ 295 052
RCA / May '95 / BMG.

LOVING YOU

Mean woman blues / Teddy bear / Got a lot of livin' to do / Lonesome cowboy / Hot dog / Party / Blueberry Hill / True love / Don't leave me now / Have I told you lately that I love you / I need you so / Loving you
CD _____ ND 81515
RCA / Oct '87 / BMG.

MEMPHIS RECORD, THE

Stranger in my own hometown / Power of love / Only the strong survive / Any day now / Suspicious minds / Long black limousine / Wearin' that loved on look / I'll hold you in my heart / After loving you / Rubberneckin' / I'm movin' on / Gentle on my mind / True love travels on a gravel road / It keeps right on a-hurtin' / You'll think of me / Mama like the roses / Don't cry daddy / In the ghetto / Fair is movin' on / Inherit the wind / Kentucky rain / Without love (there is nothing) / Who am I
CD _____ 74321 18754-2
RCA / Feb '94 / BMG.

MOODY BLUE

Unchained melody / If you love me (let me know) / Little darlin' / He'll have to go / Let me be there / Way down / Pledging my love / Moody blue / She thinks I still care
CD _____ ND 90252
RCA / '88 / BMG.

ON STAGE (February 1970)

See rider blues / Release me / Sweet Caroline / Runaway / I wonder if you / Polk salad Annie / Yesterday / Proud Mary / Walk a mile in my shoes / Let it be me
CD _____ ND 90549
RCA / Mar '91 / BMG.

ONE AND ONLY, THE

Heartbreak hotel / Long tall Sally / I was the one / Money honey / I got a woman / Blue suede shoes / Hound dog / Interviews (Arkansas 1965) / Baby let's play house / Maybellene / That's alright mama / Blue moon of Kentucky / There's good rockin' tonight / I got a woman (2) / Tweedle dee
CD _____ HADCD 151
Javelin / May '94 / THE / Henry Hadaway Organisation.

POT LUCK WITH ELVIS

Kiss me quick / Just for old times sake / Gonna get back home somehow / (Such an) Easy question / Steppin' out of line / I'm yours / Something blue / Suspicion / I feel I've known you forever / Night rider / Fountain of love / That's someone you never forget
CD _____ ND 89098
RCA / Apr '88 / BMG.

PROMISED LAND

Promised land / There's a honky tonk angel (who will take me) / Help me / Mr. Songman / Love song of the year / It's midnight / Your love's been a long time coming / If you talk in your sleep / Thinking about you / You ask me to
CD _____ ND 90598
RCA / Oct '91 / BMG.

RAISED ON ROCK

Raised on rock / Are you sincere / Find out what's happening / I miss you / Girl of mine

/ For ol' times sake / If you don't come home / Just a little bit / Sweet Angeline / Three corn patches
CD _____ 07863 50388-2
RCA / Feb '94 / BMG.

RECONSIDER BABY

Reconsider baby / Tomorrow night / So glad you're mine / When it rains it really pours / My baby left me / Ain't that lovin' you baby / I feel so bad / Down in the alley / Hi-heel sneakers / Stranger in my own hometown / Merry Christmas baby
CD _____ AFL1 5418
RCA / Jan '86 / BMG.

ROCK 'N' ROLL NO. 2

Rip it up / Love me / When my blue moon turns to gold again / Long tall Sally / First in line / Paralysed / So glad you're mine / Old Shep / Ready Teddy / Any place is paradise / How's the world treating you / How do you think I feel
CD _____ ND 81382
RCA / May '90 / BMG.

SOMETHING FOR EVERYBODY

There's always me / Give me the right / It's a sin / Sentimental me / Starting today / I'm yours / Gently / I'm coming home / In your arms / Put the blame on me / Judy / I want you with me / I slipped, I stumbled, I fell
CD _____ ND 84116
RCA / Nov '90 / BMG.

SPINOUT/DOUBLE TROUBLE

Stop, look and listen / Adam and evil / All that I am / Never say yes / Am I ready / Beach shack / Spinout / Smorgasbord / I'll be back / Double trouble / Baby, if you'll give me all your love / Could I fall in love / Long legged girl with the short dress on / City by night / Old MacDonald / I love only one girl / There's so much world to see / It won't be long
CD _____ 07863663612
RCA / Jun '94 / BMG.

THAT'S THE WAY IT IS

I just can't help believin' / Twenty days and twenty nights / How the web was woven / Patch it up / Mary in the morning / You don't have to say you love me / You've lost that lovin' feelin' / I've lost you / Just pretend / Stranger in the crowd / Next step is love / Bridge over troubled water
CD _____ 7432114690-2
RCA / Jul '93 / BMG.

TODAY

T-R-O-U-B-L-E / And I love you so / Susan when she tried / Woman without love / Shake a hand / Pieces of my life / Fairytale / I can help / Bringing it back / Green green grass of home
CD _____ ND 90660
RCA / Apr '92 / BMG.

VIVA LAS VEGAS/ROUSTABOUT

Viva Las Vegas / If you think I don't need you / If you need somebody to lean on / You're the boss / What I'd say / Do the Vega / C'mon everybody / Lady love me (With Ann Margaret) / Night life / Today, tomorrow and forever / Yellow rose of Texas / The eyes of Texas / Santa Lucia / Roustabout / Little Egypt / Poison ivy league / Hard knocks / It's a wonderful world / Big love, big heartache / One track heart / It's carnival time / Carny town / There's a brand new day on the horizon / Wheels on my heels
CD _____ 74321 13432-2
RCA / Mar '93 / BMG.

WALK A MILE IN MY SHOES - THE ESSENTIAL 70'S MASTERS (5 CD Set)

Wonder of you / I've lost you / Next step is love / You don't have to say you love me / Patch it up / I really don't want to know / There goes everything / Rags to riches / Where did they go / Life / I'm leavin' / Heart of Rome / It's only love / Sound of your cry / I just can't help believin' / How the web was woven / Until it's time for you to go / We can make the morning / An American trilogy / First time ever I saw your face / Burning love / It's a matter of time / Separate ways / Always on my mind / Fool / Steamroller blues / Raised on rock / For ol' times sake / I've got a thing about you baby / Take good care of her / If you talk in your sleep / Promised land / It's midnight / Loving arms / T-R-O-U-B-L-E / Mr Songman / Bringing it back / Pieces of my life / Green, green grass of home / Thinking about you / Hurt / For the heart / Moody blue / She thinks I still care / Way down / Pledging my love / Twenty days and twenty nights / I was born about ten thousand years ago / Fool (2) / Hundred years from now / Little cabin on the hill / Cindy Cindy / Bridge over troubled water / Got my mojo workin' / Keep your hands off it / It's your baby, you rock it / Stranger in the crowd / Mary in the morning / It ain't no big thing (but it's growing) / Just pretend / Faded love / Tomorrow never comes / Make the world go away / Funny how time slips away / I wash my hands in muddy water / Snowbird / Whole lotta shakin' goin' on / Amazing Grace / (That's what you get) For lovin' me / Lady Madonna / Merry Christmas baby / I shall be released / Don't think it's alright / It's still here / I'll take you home Kathleen / I will be true / My way / For the good times / Just a little bit / It's different now / Are you sincere

/ I got a feelin' in my body / You asked me to / Good time Charlie's got the blues / Talk about the good times / Tiger man / She thinks I still care (2) / Danny boy / Love coming down / He'll have to go / See see rider / Men with broken hearts / Walk a mile in my shoes / Polk salad Annie / Let it be me / Proud Mary / Something / You've lost that lovin' feelin' / Heartbreak hotel / Is the one / One night / Never been to Spain / You gave me a mountain / It's impossible / Big hunk o'love / It's over / Impossible dream / Reconsider baby / I'll remember you / I'm so lonesome I could cry / Suspicious minds / Unchained melody / Twelfth of never / Softly as I leave you / Alla' en el Rancho Grande / Froggie went a-courtin' / Stranger in my home town

CD Set _____ 74321303312
RCA / Sep '95 / BMG.

Press Gang

BURNING BOATS
CD _____ PUSS 0002CD
Cat / Apr '94 / ADA.

FIRE
CD _____ EFA 611012
Twah / Nov '95 / SRD.

Pressure

PRESSURE FEATURING RONNIE LAWS
That's the thing to do / Hold on / Fantastic dreams / Can you feel it / Shove it in the oven / Peaceful stream / Stay together / I promise
CD _____ 74321305272
Avenue / Sep '95 / BMG.

Pressure Of Speech

ART OF THE STATE
CD _____ POS 100CD
North South / May '94 / Pinnacle.

Pressure Zone

NEW JAZZ FUNK
CD _____ BFRCD 11
Beat Farm / Jun '94 / Total/BMG.

Preston Orpheus Choir

SONGS SACRED AND SECULAR
CD _____ CDCA 928
SCS Music / Oct '93 / Conifer.

Preston, Billy

ENCOURAGING WORDS
Right now / Little girl / Use what you got / My sweet Lord / Let the music play / Same thing again / I've got a feeling / Sing one for the Lord / When you are mine / I don't want you to pretend / Encouraging words / All things must pass / You've been acting strange / As long as I got my baby (Not on LP) / All that I've got (I'm gonna give to you) (Not on LP)
CD _____ CDP 7812792
Apple / Mar '93 / EMI.

Preston, Jimmy

JIMMY PRESTON - 1948 to 1950
Messin' with Preston / Chop Suey Louie / Hucklebuck Daddy / Rock the joint / Early morning blues
CD _____ FLYCD 33
Flyright / Apr '91 / Hot Shot / Wellard / Jazz Music / CM.

Preston, Johnny

RUNNING BEAR.
Charming Billy / Running bear / Cradle of love / Chief heartbreak / My heart knows / That's all I want / Just little boy blue / Leave my kitten alone / Sitting here crying / I want a rock and roll guitar / Hearts of stone / Do what you did / I played around with my love / Chosen few / Up in the air / Kissin' tree / Four letter word / Feel so fine / She once belonged to me / New baby for christmas / City of tears / I'm startin' to go steady with the blues / Dream / Madre de dios / You'll never walk alone / Danny Boy / Broken heart anonymous
CD _____ BCD 15473
Bear Family / '88 / Rollercoaster / Direct / CM / Swift / ADA.

Pretenders

DON'T GET ME WRONG
Don't get me wrong / Never do that / Room full of mirrors / Wait / Money (live) / Cuban slide / Sense of purpose / Thin line between love and hate / Porcelain / Time the avenger / Tattooed love boys / Louie Louie / Watching the clothes / Brass in pocket
CD _____ 4509 918852
Carlton Home Entertainment / Jun '94 / Carlton Home Entertainment.

GET CLOSE
My baby / When I change my life / Light of the moon / Dance / Tradition of love / Don't get me wrong / I remember you / How much did you get for your soul / Chill factor / Hymn to her / Room full of mirrors

CD _____ 240976 2
WEA / Oct '86 / Warner Music.

LAST OF THE INDEPENDENTS
Hollywood perfume / Night in my veins / Money talk / 977 / Revolution / All my dreams / I'll stand by you / I'm a mother / Tequila / Every mother's son / Rebel rock me / Colours / Forever young
CD _____ 450095822-2
WEA / May '94 / Warner Music.

LEARNING TO CRAWL
Middle of the road / Back on the chain gang / Time the avenger / Show me / Watching the clothes / Thumbelina / My city was gone / Thin line between love and hate / I hurt you / 2000 miles
CD _____ 923980 2
WEA / Jan '84 / Warner Music.

LIVE AT THE ISLE OF VIEW
CD _____ 0630120592
WEA / Oct '95 / Warner Music.

PACKED
Never do that / Let's make a pact / Millionaires / May this be love / No guarantee / When will I see you / Sense of purpose / Downtown / How do I miss you / Hold a candle to this / Criminal
CD _____ 9031714032
East West / Nov '94 / Warner Music.

PRETENDERS 2
Adultress / Bad boys get spanked / Message of love / I go to sleep / Birds of paradise / Talk of the town / Pack it up / Waste not, want not / Day after day / Jealous dogs / English rose / Louie Louie
CD _____ 256924
WEA / Jul '93 / Warner Music.

PRETENDERS, THE
Precious / Phone call / Up to the neck / Tattooed love boys / Space invaders / Wait / Stop your sobbing / Kid / Private life / Lovers of today / Brass in pocket / Mystery achievement
CD _____ 256774
WEA / '83 / Warner Music.

SINGLES, THE
Stop your sobbing / Kid / Brass in pocket / Talk of the town / I go to sleep / Day after day / Message of love / Back on the chain gang / Middle of the road / 2000 miles / Show me / Thin line between love and hate / Don't get me wrong / Hymn to her / My baby / I got you babe / What you gonna do about it
CD _____ 242229 2
WEA / Dec '87 / Warner Music.

Pretty Maids

SCREAM
CD _____ MASSCD 0472
Massacre / Mar '95 / Plastic Head.

SCREAMIN' LIVE
CD _____ MASSCD 081
Massacre / Nov '95 / Plastic Head.

Pretty Things

1967-1971
Defecting Grey / Mr. Evasion / Talkin' about the good times / Walking through my dreams / Private sorrow / Balloon burning / Good Mr. Square / Blue serge blues / October 26 / Cold stone / Summertime / Circus mind / Stone hearted mama
See For Miles/C5 / Oct '89 / Pinnacle.

CHICAGO BLUES JAM - 1991 (Pretty Things & Yardbird Blues Band)
You can't judge a book by the cover / Down in the bottom / Hush hush / Can't hold out / Spoonful / She fooled me / Time is on my side / Long tall shorty / Diddley daddy / Ain't got you / Caress me baby / Here's my picture / Chain of fools / Don't start cryin' now
CD _____ FIENDCD 708
Demon / Oct '91 / Pinnacle / ADA.

COLLECTION
CD _____ IMCD 900986
Line / Oct '92 / CM / Grapevine / ADA / Conifer / Direct.

ELECTRIC BANANA
CD _____ REP 4088-WZ
Repertoire / Aug '91 / Pinnacle / Cadillac.

MIDNIGHT TO 6
Don't bring me down / Children / Cry to me / Judgement day / We'll be together / Moon is rising / Progress / Midnight to six man / Get the picture / Roadrunner / I can never say / Mama keep your big mouth shut / I want your love / Raining in my heart
CD _____ 5501862
Spectrum/Karussell / Mar '94 / PolyGram / THE.

MORE ELECTRIC BANANA
CD _____ REP 4089-WZ
Repertoire / Aug '91 / Pinnacle / Cadillac.

ON AIR
Don't bring me down / Hey mamma / Midnight to six man / Buzz the jerks / LSD / Big boss man / Defecting grey / Cold stone / Sickle clowns / She's a lover

CD _____ BOJCD 3
Band Of Joy / Mar '92 / ADA.

OUT OF THE ISLAND
CD _____ INAK 8708
In Akustik / May '95 / Magnum Music Group.

PARACHUTE
Scene one / Good Mr. Square / She was tall, she was high / In the square / Letter / Rain / Miss Fay regrets / Cries from the midnight circus / Grass / Sickle clowns / She's a lover / What's the use / Parachute
CD _____ EDCD 289
Edsel / Sep '88 / Pinnacle / ADA.

PRETTY THINGS, THE
Roadrunner / Judgement day / 13 Chester Street / Big city / Unknown blues / Mama keep your big mouth shut / Honey I need / Oh baby doll / She's fine, she's mine / Don't you lie to me / Moon is rising / Pretty thing
CD _____ 8460542
Fontana / Jul '90 / PolyGram.

UNREPENTANT - BLOODY BUT UNBOWED
Rosalyn / Don't bring me down / Get yourself home / Roadrunner / Judgement day / Honey, I need / You don't believe me / Buzz the jerk / Cry to me / Midnight to six man / L.S.D. / Death of a socialite / Growing in my mind / Defecting grey / S.F. sorrow is born / Private sorrow / Balloon burning / Old man going / Loneliest person / Scene one / In the square / Letter / Rain / Grass / Parachute / October 26 (Revolution) / Summertime / Peter / Rip off train / Havana bound / Dream/Joey / Bridge of God / Is it only love / Singapore silk torpedo / Under the volcano / Sad eye / Remember that boy / It's been so long / I'm calling / Office love / She don't / No future / God give me the strength (to carry on)
CD Set _____ FRA 005D
Fragile / Oct '95 / Grapevine.

WHITER SHADE OF DIRTY WATER, A
He's waitin' / Strychnine / Pushin' too hard / kicks / Candy / louie Louie / 96 tears / Let's talk about girls / Sometimes good guys don't wear white / I'm a man / Red River rock / Midnight to 6 man
CD _____ CDKVL 9031
Kingdom / May '94 / Kingdom.

WINE, WOMEN & WHISKEY (Pretty Things & Yardbird Blues Band)
Wine, women and whiskey / Sure look good to me / No questions / Amble / It's all over now / Bad boy / Spoonful / French champagne / My back scratcher / Can't hold you / Diddley daddy / I'm cryin' / Gettin' all wet
CD _____ FIENDCD 748
Demon / Jan '94 / Pinnacle / ADA.

Previn, Andre

4 TO GO (Previn, Andre & Herb Ellis/ Shelly Manne/Ray Brown)
No moon at all / Bye bye blackbird / Life is a ball / It's easy to remember / You're impossible / Oh what a beautiful mornin' / I know you oh so well / Intersection / Like someone in love / Don't sing
CD _____ 4773392
Columbia / Nov '94 / Sony.

ANDRE PREVIN & FRIENDS PLAY SHOWBOAT
CD _____ 4476392
Deutsche Grammophon / May '95 / PolyGram.

KING SIZE (Previn, Andre Jazz Trio)
Original Jazz Classics / Nov '95 / Wellard / Jazz Music / Cadillac / Complete/Pinnacle.

PLAY A CLASSIC AMERICAN SONGBOOK (Previn, Andre & Thomas Stevens)
It might as well be spring / My funny valentine / Slowly/Laura / Bewitched, bothered and bewildered / I could write a book / It could happen to you/Here's that rainy day / You go to my head / Cabin in the sky/ Takin' a chance on love / I didn't know what time it was/Little girl blue / Easy living
CD _____ DRGCD 5222
DRG / Apr '94 / New Note.

PREVIN AT SUNSET
I got it bad and that ain't good / Body and soul / Sunset in blue / All the things you are / Something to live for / Good enough to keep / That old blue magic / Blue skies / I found a new baby / Variations on a theme / Mulholland Drive
CD _____ BLCD 760189
Black Lion / Jun '94 / Jazz Music / Cadillac / Wellard / Koch.

Previn, Dory

IN SEARCH OF MYTHICAL KINGS (THE UA YEARS)
Mythical Kings and Iguanas / Ester's first communion / When a man wants a woman / Yada yada la scala / Lady with the braid / Beware of young girls / Angels and devils that following day / Don't put him down / Dopplegang er / Left hand lost / New enzyme detergent demise of Ali McGraw / Twenty mile zone / Midget's lament / Michael Mile / I ain't his child / Stone for

Bessie Smith / Starlet starlet on the screen who will follow Norma Jean / Mary C. Brown and the Hollywood sign / King Kong / Play it again Sam / Going home
CD _____ CDGO 2045
EMI / Feb '93 / EMI.

Previte, Bobby 'Weather..

CLAUDE'S LATE MORNING (Previte, Bobby 'Weather Clear')
CD _____ GCD 79447
Gramavision / Sep '95 / Vital/SAM / ADA.

HUE & CRY (Previte, Bobby 'Weather Clear')
Hubbub / Smack dab / More heaven and earth / 700 Camels / Valerie / Hue and cry / For John Laughlan and all that we stood for
CD _____ ENJ 80642
Enja / Nov '94 / New Note / Vital/SAM.

MOSCOW CIRCUS (Previte, Bobby 'Weather Clear')
CD _____ GCD 79466
Gramavision / Sep '95 / Vital/SAM / ADA.

Prevost, Eddie

SUPER SESSION (Prevost, Eddie, Parker, Guy & Rowe)
CD _____ MR 17
Matchless / '90 / These / ReR Megacorp / Cadillac.

Prezident Brown

BIG BAD & TALENTED
CD _____ RN 0032
X-Rated / Jun '95 / Jetstar.

Price, Alan

BEST OF ALAN PRICE, THE
CD _____ MCCD 109
Music Club / Jun '93 / Disc / THE / CM.

GIGSTER'S LIFE FOR ME, A (Price, Alan & Electric Blues Company)
CD _____ IGOCD 2048
Indigo / Nov '95 / Direct / ADA.

LIVE IN CONCERT
CD _____ GRF 209
Tring / Mar '93 / Tring / Prism.

PRICE AND FAME TOGETHER (Price, Alan & Georgie Fame)
Rosetta / Yellow man / Dole song / Time I moved on / John and Mary / Here and now / Home is where the heart is / Ballad of Billy Joe / That's how long my love is / Blue condition / I can't take it much longer
CD _____ 4809722
Columbia / Aug '95 / Sony.

PRICE OF FAME, THE (Price, Alan & Georgie Fame)
Yeh yeh / Simon Smith and his amazing dancing bear / Get away / Hi-li hi-lo / Sitting in the park / Barefootin' / Let the sun shine in / Shame / Ride your pony / Jarrow song / That's got a brand new bag / I put a spell on you / In the meantime / House that Jack built / Sunny / Falling in love again / My girl / Baby of mine / Let the good times roll / Don't stop the carnival
CD _____ 5509312
Spectrum/Karussell / Oct '95 / PolyGram / THE.

PRICELESS
CD _____ EMPRCD 593
Emporio / Oct '95 / THE / Disc / CM.

Price, Lloyd

HEAVY DREAMS
Chee-koo baby / Coo-ee baby / Oooh-oooh-oooh / Restless heart / Tell me pretty baby / They say / I'm too young / Ain't it a shame / Jimmie Lee / Baby, don't turn your back on me / Old echo song / Too late for tears / Carry me home / Little Bea / Night and day / Oh love / Woe ho ho / Breaking my heart (All over again) / Iyi yi gomen-a-sai / Country boy rock / Heavy dreams / Why / I'm goin' back
CD _____ CDCHD 512
Ace / Jan '94 / Pinnacle / Cadillac / Complete/Pinnacle.

LAWDY
Lawdy Miss Clawdy / Mailman blues / Chee koo baby / Oo-ee baby / So long / Operator / Laurelle / What's the matter now / If crying was murder / Walkin' the track / Where you at / Lord, lord, amen / Carry me home / Frog legs / I wish your picture was you / Let me come home baby / Tryin' to find someone to love / Night and day blues / All alone / What a fire / Rock 'n' roll dance / I'm glad, glad / Baby please come home / Forgive me Clawdy
CD _____ CDCHD 360
Ace / Nov '91 / Pinnacle / Cadillac / Complete/Pinnacle.

Price, Maryann

ETCHED IN SWING
CD _____ WM 1014CD
Watermelon / May '94 / ADA / Direct.

Price, Ray

HONKY TONK YEARS 1950-1966, THE (10CD Set) (Price, Ray & The Cherokee Cowboys)

Jealous lies / Your wedding corsage / If you're ever lonely darling / I saw my castles fall today / You've got my troubles now / I get the short end every time / Hey la la / Answer to The Last Letter / Till death do us part / Beyond the last mile / Heart aching blues / Weary blues (from waiting) / I made a mistake and I'm sorry / We crossed our heart / Your heart is too crowded / I lost the only one I knew / I've got to hurry hurry hurry / Talk to your heart / I know I'll never win your love again / Road of no return / You're under arrest (for stealing my heart) / Move on in and stay / I can't escape from you / Won't you please be mine / Don't let the stars get in your eyes / My old scrap-book / Price of loving you / That's what I get for loving you / Cold shoulder / You weren't ashamed to kiss me last night / Wrong side of town / Time / Start the music / Gone again / Way you've treated me / Wrong side of town (2) / Who stole that train / Let your heart decide / You always get by / Leave her alone / Wall around your heart / Release me / I'll be there (if you ever want me) / Last letter / Much too young to die / I love you so much I let you go / I could love you more / What if he don't love you / If you don't somebody else will / I'm alone because I love you / Oh yes darling / One broken heart (don't mean a thing) / Sweet little Miss Blue Eyes / Way she got away / Let me talk to you / Call the Lord and he'll be there / Man called Peter / As strange as it seems (I still love you) / I can't go home like this / Don't you know me anymore / I don't want it on my conscience / Run boy / You never will be true / Don't tempt me / Slowly dying / Crazy arms / You done me wrong / Wild and wicked world / Crazy / Are you wasting my time / Fallin' fallin' fallin' / Wasted words / I've got a new heartache / Don't do this to me / Letters have no arms / I'll sail my ship alone / Mansion on the hill / I can't help it / Remember me (I'm the one who loves you) / I saw my castles fall today (2) / Let me talk to you (2) / Please don't leave me / Blues stay away from me / Pins and needles (in my heart) / I love you because / Many tears ago / I'll be there (when you get lonely) / It's all your fault / My shoes keep walking back to you / Faded love / Gone / Bye bye love / Four walls / Fallen star / Don't do this to me (2) / Walls of tears / Curtain in the window / Talk to your conscience / There'll be no teardrops tonight / Driftwood on the river / Deep water / I'll keep on loving you / I love you so much it hurts / I told you so / Ice cold heart / I've gotta have my baby back / Please don't leave me (2) / Talk to your heart (2) / I'm tired / Wondering / Walkin' the floor / Invitation to the blues / I've got to know / Heartaches must be your name / City lights / Kissing your picture (is so cold) / That's what it's like to be lonesome / Punish me tomorrow / Heartaches by the number / Wild and wicked world (2) / Beyond the last mile (2) / Same old me / Under your spell again / Broken hearts will haunt your soul / One more time / Who'll be the first / City lights (2) / Old rugged cross / In the garden / How big is God / Until then / I flew through my unbelief / When I take my vacation in heaven / Faith / Rock of ages / Softly and tenderly / When the roll is called up yonder / Just as I am / Where he leads me (I will follow) / Now the day is over / I can't run away from myself / I wish I could fall in love today / Heart over mind / Twenty-fourth hour / Walkin' slow and thinking 'bout her / Soft rain / Here we are again / You're stranger than me / This cold war with you / Imagination's wonderful thing / Walkin' slow (and thinking about her) (2) / Soft rain (2) / San Antonio Rose / Maiden's prayer / My confession / Whose heart are you breaking now / Roly poly / Bubbles in my beer / Home in San Antone / You don't love me (but I'll always care) / You don't care what happens to me / Time changes everything / Kinda love I can't forget / Hang your head in shame / Night life / Lonely street / Wild side of life / Sittin' and thinkin' / Girl in the night / There's no fool like a young fool / If she could see me now / Bright lights and blonde haired women / Are you sure / Let me talk to you (3) / This cold war with you (2) / I've just destroyed the world / Walkin' slow (and thinking 'bout her) (2) / Pride / Big shoes / Walk me to the door / You took her off my hands / Be a good girl / Make the world go away / I'll find a way (to free myself of you) / Let me talk to you (4) / I've still got room (for one more heartache) / That's all that matters / Burning memories / Each time / Way to free myself / How long is forever / This cold war with you (3) / Take me as I am (or let me go) / All right (I'll sign the papers) / I fall to pieces / Please talk to my heart / Cold cold heart / Still / I don't know why (I keep loving you) / Same old memories / Here comes my baby back again / Together again / Thing called sadness / Soft rain (3) / Release me (3) / Devil's dream / Linda Lou / Crazy arms (2) / Lil' Liza Jane / Rubber dolly / Burnt fingers / Twinkle, twinkle little star / Maiden's prayer (2) / Your old loveletters / Spanish two step / Liberty bells / Sing a sad song / Other woman / Tearful

earful / Last letter (2) / Born to lose / Just call me lonesome / Don't you ever get tired of hurting me / Funny how time slips away / Rose coloured glasses / Unloved, unwanted / Eye for an eye / Too much love is spoiling you / After effects (from loving you) / I'm not crazy yet / Way to survive / Another bridge to burn / Legend in my time / Take these chains in my heart / Don't touch me / Go away / I'd fight the world / I want to hear it from you / It should be easier now / Don't you believe her / Healing hands of time / Too late / Each time (2) / Touch my heart / There goes my everything / It's only love / I lie a lot / Enough to lie / Swinging doors / Am I that easy to forget / Same two lips / Just for the record / I'm still not over you / I let my heart wander / Danny Boy

CD Set _____ BCD 15843 JK

Bear Family / Nov '95 / Rollercoaster / Direct / CM / Swift / ADA.

PORTRAIT OF A SINGER

You're nobody 'til somebody loves you / Once in a while / Sentimental journey / Because of you / You'll never know / All the way / Smile / Bummin' around / You always hurt the one you love / Had to be you / I can't give you anything but love / I'm confessin' that I love you / Always / Mona Lisa / Young at heart / I'm in the mood for love / Love me tender / As time goes by / Don't get around much anymore / Please don't talk about me when I'm gone

CD _____ SORCD 0009

D-Sharp / Oct '94 / Pinnacle.

Price, Sammy

1929-1941

CD _____ CLASSICS 696

Classics / Jul '93 / Discovery / Jazz Music.

BARRELHOUSE & BLUES

Honey Grove Blues / Rosetta / St. James Infirmary / Real End boogie / In the evening / Keepin' out of mischief now / Struttin' with Georgia

CD _____ BLCD 760159

Black Lion / Oct '92 / Jazz Music / Cadillac / Wellard / Koch.

BLUES & BOOGIE (Price, Sammy & Jay McShann)

CD _____ 74321115092

Vogue / Jul '93 / BMG.

KING OF BOOGIE WOOGIE (Price, Sammy Trio)

King Boogie parts 1 and 2 / Makin' whoopee / Keepin' out of mischief now / Bass and piano talking / Please don't talk about me when I'm gone / My blue heaven / Saint James infirmary / Boogie woogie French style / Baby, won't you please come home / Trouble in mind / Blues in my heart

CD _____ STCD 5011

Storyville / Dec '94 / Jazz Music / Wellard / CM / Cadillac.

Price, Toni

HEY

CD _____ 1046770222

Warner Bros. / Jan '96 / Warner Music.

SWIM AWAY

Daylight / Throw me a bone / Richest one / In care of the blues / Just to hear / Twelve bar blues / Moonlight blues / I doubt if it does to you / Chain of love / Hell on love / Thinkin' 'bout lovin' you again / Lucky / Swim away

CD _____ 1046770032

Warner Bros. / Jan '96 / Warner Music.

Prichard, Peter

HARMONIC PIANO

CD _____ WCL 11001

White Cloud / May '94 / Select.

Pride & Glory

PRIDE AND GLORY

Losin' your mind / Horse called war / Shine on / Lovin' woman / Harvester of pain / Chosen one / Sweet Jesus / Troubled wine / Machine gun man / Cry me a river / Toe'n the line / Found a friend / Fadin' away / Hate your guts

CD _____ GED 24703

Geffen / May '94 / BMG.

Pride, Charley

AMY'S EYES

White houses / Moody woman / Amy's eyes / After me, after you / I made love to you in my mind / Whole lotta love on the line / Nickles and dimes and love / Look who's looking / I wrote the songs that broke her heart / You hold my world together / Right one / Plenty good lovin'

CD _____ RITZCD 525

Ritz / Apr '93 / Pinnacle.

BEST OF CHARLEY PRIDE, THE

CD _____ MATCD 330

Castle / Feb '95 / BMG.

CLASSIC COUNTRY

CD _____ CDSR 070

Telstar / May '95 / BMG.

CLASSICS WITH PRIDE

Most beautiful girl in the world / Always on my mind / You've got to stand for something / After all these years / I don't know why I love you but I do / If tomorrow never comes / Ramblin' rose / You'll never walk alone / Please help me, I'm falling / Here in the real world / Walk on by / I love you because / Four in the morning / It's just a matter of time / Ramona / What's another year

CD _____ CD 0064

Ritz / Feb '92 / Pinnacle.

CRYSTAL CHANDELIERS

CD _____ MU 3009

Start / Oct '94 / Koch.

GREATEST HITS

Kaw-liga / I'm so afraid of losing you again / Oklahoma morning / It's going to take a little bit longer / Crystals chandeliers / Does my ring hurt your finger / Too good to be true / I'd rather love you / All I have to offer you is me / I wonder could I live there anymore / Is anybody going to San Antone / I'm just me / Shutters and boards / Happiness of having you / My eyes can only see as far as you / Kiss an angel good morning / Let me live in the light of his light / Mississippi cotton picking Delta town / Help me make it through the night / Louisanna man / There goes my everything / Lovesick blues / Me and Bobby McGee

CD _____ MU 5070

Musketeer / Oct '94 / Koch.

KISS AN ANGEL GOOD MORNING

CD _____ WMCD 5699

Disky / Oct '94 / THE / BMG / Discovery / Pinnacle.

VERY BEST OF CHARLEY PRIDE, THE

I'd rather love you / Is anybody going to San Antone / I'm so afraid of losing you again / Kiss an angel good morning / Just between you and me / All I have to offer you is me / Wonder could I live there anymore / I can't believe that you've stopped loving me / I'm just me / Crystal chandeliers / Amazing love / Happiness of having you / Easy part's over / I know one / Does my ring hurt your finger / For the good times / Kaw-liga / My eyes can only see as far as you / She's just an old love turned memory / Someone loves you honey

CD _____ 74321272142

RCA / May '95 / BMG.

Pride, Dickie

SHEIK OF SHAKE, THE

Don't make me love you / You're singin' our love song to somebody else / Fabulous cure / Betty Betty (go steady with me) / Primrose Lane / Anything goes / Isn't this a lovely day (to be caught in the rain) / You turned the tables on me / Loch Lomond / Falling in love / Give the simple life / Slippin' and slidin' / Bye bye blackbird / Midnight oil / No John / Frantic / It's only a paper moon / I could write a book / Too close for comfort / There's a small hotel / They can't take that away from me / Lulu's back in town

CD _____ SEECD 344

See For Miles/C5 / Mar '92 / Pinnacle.

Pride Of Murray Pipe Band

BEST OF SCOTTISH PIPES AND DRUMS

CD _____ EUCD 1164

ARC / Jun '91 / ARC Music / ADA.

Priest, Maxi

BEST OF ME, THE

CD _____ DIXCD 111

10 / Oct '91 / EMI.

BONAFIDE

Just a little bit longer / Close to you / Never did say goodbye / Best of me / Space in my heart / Human work of art / Temptress / Peace throughout the world / You / Sure fire love / Life / Prayer for the world

CD _____ DIXCD 92

10 / Jun '90 / EMI.

COLLECTION, THE

Strollin' on / Some guys have all the luck / How can we ease the pain / Groovin' in the midnight / Love don't come easy / Just a little bit longer / One more chance / Pretty little girl / Should I (put my trust in you) / Human work of art / Sure fire love / Fatty fatty

CD _____ CDVIP 138

Virgin VIP / Sep '95 / Carlton Home Entertainment / THE / EMI.

FE REAL

Can't turn away / Promises / Just wanna know / Groovin' in the midnight / Make my day / Ten to midnight / Careless whispers (Featuring Carla Marshall) / One more chance / Sublime / Amazed are we / Hard to get

CD _____ DIXCD 113

10 / Nov '92 / EMI.

INTENTIONS

Love train / Woman in you / Crazy love / Jehovah / Cry me a river / Strollin' on / Pretty little girl / Let me know / Festival time / Must be a way

CD _____ DIXCD 32

10 / '88 / EMI.

MAXI

Wild world / Suzie - you are / Goodbye to love again / You're only human / Same old story / Marcus / How can we ease the pain / It ain't easy / Some guys have all the luck / Problems (CD & Cassette only) / Reasons (CD & Cassette only)

CD _____ OVEDC 347

10 / Mar '91 / EMI.

YOU'RE SAFE

Should I / Hey little girl / Dancing mood / Sensi / Caution / Stand up and fight / In the Springtime / Fatty fatty / You're safe / Throw me corn

CD _____ DIXCD 11

10 / '86 / EMI.

Priestley, Brian

SALUTES 15 JAZZ PIANO GREATS

CD _____ CD 90995

Spirits Of Jazz / Dec '95 / Harmonia Mundi.

YOU TAUGHT MY HEART TO SING

CD _____ SOJCD 9

FMR/Spirit Of Jazz / Dec '95 / Harmonia Mundi / Cadillac.

Prima, Louis

BUONA SERA

CD _____ RMB 75076

Remember / Oct '95 / Total/BMG.

CAPITOL COLLECTORS SERIES: LOUIS PRIMA

Just a gigolo/I ain't got nobody / Oh Marie / Buona sera / Jump, jive and wail / Basin Street blues / When it's sleepy time down South / Lip / Whistle stop / Five months, two weeks, two days / Banana split for my baby / There'll be no next time / When you're smiling / The sheik of Araby / Baby, won't you please come home / I've got the world on a string / Pennies from Heaven / Angelina/Zooma zooma / Beep beep / Embraceable you/I got it bad and that ain't good / Sing, sing, sing / That old black magic / Music goes 'round and around / Hey boy, hey girl / Lazy river / I've got you under my skin / You're just in love / Twist all night / St. Louis blues

CD _____ CZ 423

Capitol / May '91 / EMI.

CAPITOL RECORDINGS, THE (Louis Prima With Keely Smith & Sam Butera)

Buona sera / Oh Marie / Just a gigolo / I ain't got nobody / Body and soul / Jump, jive and wail / Nothing's too good for my baby #2 / (I'll be glad when you're dead) you rascal you / Basin Street blues / When it's sleepy time down South / Night train / Lip / Whistle stop / Five months, two weeks, two days / Banana split for my baby / Be mine (little baby) / When you're smiling / Sheik of araby / Birth of the blues / Blow red blow / When the saints go marching in / Sentimental journey / There'll be no next time / Closer to the bone / I've got the world on a string / Much too young to lose my mind / Don't let a memory / Pennies from heaven / Baby, won't you please come home / Autumn leaves / Pump song / Boulevard of broken dreams / Natural guy / Beep beep / If you were the only girl in the world / Bourbon street blues / Sing, sing, sing / That old black magic / Judy / Felica no capicai / That's my home / Moonglow / Gotta see baby tonight / Fee fie foo / Music goes round and round / Fever / Don't you take your love from me / Hey boy, hey girl / Lazy river / Hey boy, hey girl (reprise) / Nothing's too good for my baby / Oh Marie (alternate take) / I've got you under my skin / Don't take your love from me / You're just in love / Harlem nocturne / Glow worm / Just one of those things / All night long / Lover come back to me / Everybody knows / Ain't misbehavin' / Way down yonder in New Orleans / Three handed woman / St. Louis blues / Twist all night / John ping pong / Ooh look what you've done to me / Big Daddy / Sunday lover / Little girl blue / Scuba diver / I want you to be my baby / Shadrack / Next time / Lady of Spain / Hello lover, goodbye tears / Undecided / Come rain or come shine / Go back where you stayed last night / On the sunny side of the street / Exactly like you / Foggy day / How high the moon / Angelina / Zooa somma (medley) / Don't worry bout me / In the mood for love / Come back to sorrento / I gotta right to sing the blues / Robin Hood / Close to you / Honeysuckle rose / Tiger rag / Just because / Embraceable you / I got it bad and that ain't in love / Should I / I can't believe that you're in love with me / White cliffs of Dover / Holiday / Greenback dollar bill / Love of my life (o sole mio) / Too marvelous for words / I wish you love / I would do most anything for you / Shy / Rock-a-doodle-doo / Young and in love / Someone to watch over me / Nearness of you / Indian love call / Just as much / Sometimes / You are my love / Whip-poor-will / I understand / If we never meet again / Mr. Wonderful / When day is done / All the things you are / When your lover has gone / You go to my head / Imagination / Fools rush in / As you desire me / You better go now / Good behaviour / You'll never know / Man I love / It's magic / What is this thing called love / Stormy weather (keeps rainin'

all the time) / There'll never be another you / It's been a long, long time / You're driving me crazy / Stardust / What can I say after I say I'm sorry / Nitey nite / Hurt me / I keep forgetting / High school affair / Nothing in common / How are you fixed for love / s'posin' / Song is you / I'll get by (as long as I have you) / Never knew / I'll never smile again / Sweet and lovely / All the way / Lullaby of the leaves / East of the sun and west of the moon / I can't get started (with you) / Cocktails for two / Bim bam / Twinkle in your eye / Ten little women / Equator / Seven out / Kiss your hand madame / Love charm / Love nest / Put your mind at ease / It's better than nothing at all / Hold out for love / Good gracious baby / Handle with care / Dig that crazy chick / Hey there / I love Paris / On the street where you live / Song from Moulin Rouge / Three coins in the fountain / Too young / Rock-a-bye your baby with a Dixie melody / Love is a many splendoured thing / Around the world / La vie en rose / Bugs / Tennessee waltz / French poodle / Chantilly lace / Up jumped a rabbit / Just say I love her / Easy rockin' / Honey love / Street scene / Perdido / Kansas city / Love of my life (o sole mio 2nd version) / Ol' man river / Smilin' Billy / Skinny Minnie / Better twist now baby / Twistin' the blues / Continental twist / Tag that twistin' dolly / Come and do the twist / O ma-ma twist / I feel good all over / Later, baby, later / Ol' man river
CD Set _____ BCDHI 15776
Bear Family / Sep '94 / Rollercoaster / Direct / CM / Swift / ADA.

HIS GREATEST HITS
Lady in red / Music goes round and round / I'm an old cowhand (from the Rio Grande) / I'll be seeing you / I'll walk alone / My dreams are getting better all the time / Josephine please no lean on my bell / Hey ba ba re bop / Brooklyn boogie / Civilisation / Thousand island song / My cucuzza
CD _____ JASCD 316
Jasmine / Oct '94 / Wellard / Swift / Conifer / Cadillac / Magnum Music Group.

LOUIS & KEELY (Prima, Louis & Keely Smith)
Night and day / All I do is dream of you / Make love to me / I don't know why / Tea for two / And the angels sing / I'm confessin' that I love you / Why do I love you / You're my everything / Cheek to cheek / I've grown accustomed to her face / Bei mir bist du schon
CD _____ JASCD 326
Jasmine / Jan '95 / Wellard / Swift / Conifer / Cadillac / Magnum Music Group.

LOUIS PRIMA - VOLUME 1
CD _____ JSPCD 339
JSP / Nov '92 / ADA / Target/BMG / Direct / Cadillac / Complete/Pinnacle.

ON STAGE (Prima, Louis & Keely Smith)
CD _____ JASCD 331
Jasmine / Nov '95 / Wellard / Swift / Conifer / Cadillac / Magnum Music Group.

REMEMBER (Prima, Louis & His Orchestra)
Robin Hood / Sun blues / I'll walk alone / Angeline / Some Sunday morning / I don't wanna be loved / You gotta see baby tonight / White cliffs of Dover / Just a gigolo / I ain't got nobody
CD _____ DAWE 12
Magic / Nov '93 / Jazz Music / Swift / Wellard / Cadillac / Harmonia Mundi.

RETURN OF THE WILD WEST (Prima, Louis & Keely Smith)
South of the border / Come back to Sorrento / South Rampart street parade / I love you / For you / After you've gone / Absent minded lover / I have but one heart / Ol' man lover / Chinatown, my Chinatown
CD _____ JASCD 330
Jasmine / Oct '94 / Wellard / Swift / Conifer / Cadillac / Magnum Music Group.

TOGETHER (Prima, Louis & Keely Smith)
Together / Paradise / Teach me tonight / Nyow nyow nyow (the pussycat song) / They can't take that away from me / I can't give you anything but love / When my baby smiles at me / Let's get away from it all / Mashuga / Let's call the whole thing off / Mutual admiration society / Begin the beguine
CD _____ JASCD 325
Jasmine / Feb '94 / Wellard / Swift / Conifer / Cadillac / Magnum Music Group.

Prima Materia

MUSIC OF JOHN COLTRANE
CD _____ KFWCD 158
Knitting Factory / Feb '95 / Grapevine.

Primal Scream

GIVE OUT, BUT DON'T GIVE UP
Jailbird / Rocks / (I'm gonna) Cry myself blind / Funky jam / Big jet plane / Free / Call on me / Struttin' / Sad and blue / Give out but don't give up / I'll be there
CD _____ CRECD 146
Creation / Mar '94 / 3MV / Vital.

PRIMAL SCREAM
Ivy Ivy Ivy / You're just dead skin to me / She power / You're just too dark to care / I'm losing more than I'll ever have / Gimme gimme teenage head / Kill the King / Lone Star girl
CD _____ CRECD 054
Creation / Sep '89 / 3MV / Vital.

SCREAMADELICA
Movin' on up / Slip inside this house / Don't fight it, feel it / Higher than the sun / Come together / Damaged / Loaded / Shine like stars / Inner flight / I'm coming down
CD _____ CRELPCD 076
Creation / Sep '91 / 3MV / Vital.

SONIC FLOWER GROOVE
Gentle Tuesday / Treasure trip / May the sun shine bright for you / Sonic sister love / Silent spring / Imperial / Love you / Leaves / Aftermath / We go down slowly rising
CD _____ 2292421822
WEA / Jun '91 / Warner Music.

Prime Movers

ARC
Immortal / Interloper / Sheep / Crystalline (Features on CD only.) / Revelation / Obsession / Rollercoaster (Features on CD only.) / Sublime / Aural sea / Misled (Features on CD only.) / Prelude: Dawn of love / Mandrake root / Breed 'n' burn
CD _____ CND 005CD
Cyanide / Mar '93 / Vital.

Primer, John

REAL DEAL, THE
CD _____ 0630108382
East West / Nov '95 / Warner Music.

Primevals

LIVE A LITTLE
St. Jack / Justify / Cotton head / Fertile mind / Prairie chain / Heya / Sister
CD _____ ROSE 123CD
New Rose / Sep '87 / Direct / ADA.

Primich, Gary

MR. FREEZE
CD _____ FF 649CD
Flying Fish / Nov '95 / Roots / CM / Direct / ADA.

TRAVELIN' MOOD
CD _____ FF 70635
Flying Fish / Nov '94 / Roots / CM / Direct / ADA.

Primitive Instinct

FLOATING TANGIBILITY
Heaven / 11-11 / Circles / Keep on running / Friend / Hypnotic / Slaves / One way man / Shame / Triludan
CD _____ CYCL 003
Cyclops / Feb '94 / Pinnacle.

Primitives

BOMBSHELL
Crash / Stop killing me / Sick of it / Way behind me / Thru the flowers / Lead me astray / Secrets / Out of reach / You are the way / Empathise / Earth thing / All the way down / Don't want anything to change / Way behind me (Acoustic) / Stop killing me (Acoustic) / As tears go by / Secrets (Demo) / Crash (Demo)
CD _____ 74321 22635-2
RCA / Sep '94 / BMG.

Primrose, Christine

AITE MO GHAOIL (PLACE OF MY HEART)
CD _____ COMD 1006
Temple / Feb '94 / CM / Duncans / ADA / Direct.

STU NAM CHUMHNE
CD _____ COMD 2024
Temple / Apr '95 / CM / Duncans / ADA / Direct.

Primus

FRIZZLE FRY
To defy the laws of tradition / Too many puppies / Frizzle fry / You can't kill Michael Malloy / Pudding time / Spaghetti western / To defy / Ground hog's day / Mr. Know it all / John the fisherman / Toys go winding down / Sathington Willoby / Harold of the rocks
CD _____ CARCD 10
Caroline / Jul '90 / EMI.

PORK SODA
Pork chop's little ditty / My name is mud / Welcome to this world / Bob / DMV / Ol' diamond back sturgeon / Nature boy / Wounded knee / Pork soda / Pressman / Mr. Krinkle / Air is getting slippery / Hamburger train / Hail santa
CD _____ 756792257-2
Interscope / Mar '93 / Warner Music.

PUNCH BOWL
CD _____ 6544925532
Interscope / Jun '95 / Warner Music.

SAILING THE SEAS OF CHEESE
Seas of cheese / Here come the bastards / Sgt. Baker / American life / Jerry was a race car driver / Eleven / Is it luck / Grandad's little ditty / Tommy the cat / Sathington waltz / Those damned blue-collar tweekers / Fish on (fisherman chronicles, chapter II) / Los bastardos
CD _____ 7567916592
East West / May '91 / Warner Music.

SUCK ON THIS
John the fisherman / Ground hog's day / Heckler / Pressman / Jellikit / Tommy the cat / Pudding time / Harold of the rocks / Frizzle fry
CD _____ 7567918332
Interscope / Apr '92 / Warner Music.

Prince

1999
1999 / Little red corvette / Delirious / Let's pretend we're married / D.M.S.R. / Automatic / Something in the water / Free / Lady cab driver / All the critics love you in New York / International lover
CD Set _____ 923720 2
WEA / Nov '84 / Warner Music.

AROUND THE WORLD IN A DAY
Around the world in a day / Paisley Park / Condition of the heart / Raspberry beret / Tambourine / America / Pop life / Ladder / Temptation
CD _____ 925286 2
WEA / May '85 / Warner Music.

BATMAN
Future / Electric chair / Arms of Orion / Partyman / Vicki waiting / Trust / Lemon crush / Scandalous / Batdance
CD _____ 9259362
WEA / Feb '95 / Warner Music.

COME
Come / Space / Pheromone / Loose / Papa / Race / Dark / Solo / Letitgo / Orgasm
CD _____ 936245700-2
Paisley Park / Aug '94 / Warner Music.

CONTROVERSY
Private joy / Ronnie talk to Russia / Let's work / Annie Christian / Jack U off / Sexuality / Controversy / Do me baby
CD _____ K 256 950
WEA / '84 / Warner Music.

DIAMONDS AND PEARLS (Prince & The New Power Generation)
Thunder / Daddy pop / Diamonds and pearls / Cream / Strollin' / Willing and able / Gett off / Walk don't walk / Jughead / Money don't matter 2 night / Push / Insatiable / Live 4 love
CD _____ 7599253792
Paisley Park / Feb '95 / Warner Music.

DIRTY MIND
Dirty mind / When you were mine / Do it all night / Gotta broken heart again / Uptown / Head / Sister / Party up
CD _____ K 256 862
WEA / Jan '86 / Warner Music.

FOR YOU
For you / In love / Soft and wet / Crazy you / Just as long as we're together / Baby / My love is forever / So blue / I'm yours
CD _____ K2 56989
WEA / Oct '87 / Warner Music.

GOLD EXPERIENCE, THE
Pussy control / Endorphinmachine / Shhh / We march / Most beautiful girl in the world / Dolphin / Now / 319 / Shy / Billy Jack Bitch / I hate U / Gold
CD _____ 9362450992
Warner Bros. / Oct '95 / Warner Music.

GRAFFITI BRIDGE
Can't stop this feeling I.got / Question of U / Round and round / Joy in repetition / Tick tick bang / Thieves in the temple / Melody cool / Graffiti bridge / Release it / Elephants and flowers / We can funk / Love machine / Shake / Latest fashion / Still would stand all time / New power generation (pts I and II)
CD _____ 7599274932
WEA / Aug '90 / Warner Music.

HITS & B-SIDES, THE
When doves cry / Pop life / Soft and wet / I feel for you / Why you wanna treat me so bad / When you were mine / Uptown / Let's go crazy / 1999 / I could never take the place of your man / Nothing compares 2 U / Adore / Pink cashmere / Alphabet Street / Sign o' the times / Thieves in the temple / Diamonds and pearls / 7 / Controversy / Dirty mind / I wanna be your lover / Head / Do me baby / Delirious / Little red corvette / I would die 4 U / Raspberry beret / If I was your girlfriend / Kiss / Peach / U got the look / Sexy M.F. / Gett off / Cream / Pope / Purple rain / Sexy dancer / Shockadelica / Irresistible bitch / Scarlet pussy / La la la he he hee / She's always in my hair / Seventeen days / How come U don't call me anymore / Another lonely Christmas / God 4 The tears in your eyes / Power fantastic
CD Set _____ 9362454402
Paisley Park / Sep '93 / Warner Music.

HITS 1, THE
When doves cry / Pop life / Soft and wet / I feel for you / Why you wanna treat me so bad / When you were mine / Uptown / Let's go crazy / 1999 / I could never take the place of your man / Nothing compares 2 U / Adore / Pink cashmere / Alphabet Street / Sign o' the times / Thieves in the temple / Diamonds and pearls / 7
CD _____ 9362454312
Paisley Park / Sep '93 / Warner Music.

HITS 2, THE
Controversy / Dirty mind / I wanna be your lover / Head / Do me baby / Delirious / Little red corvette / I would die 4 U / Raspberry beret / If I was your girlfriend / Kiss / Peach / U got the look / Sexy M.F. / Gett off / Cream / Pope / Purple rain
CD _____ 9362454352
Paisley Park / May '93 / Warner Music.

LOVESEXY
I no / Alphabet Street / Glam slam / Anna Stesia / Dance on / Lovesexy / When 2 R in love / I wish U heaven / Positivity
CD _____ 925720 2
Paisley Park / May '88 / Warner Music.

MINNEAPOLIS GENIUS (94 East)
If you feel like dancin' / Lovin' cup / Just another sucker / Dance to the music of the world / One man jam
CD _____ CLACD 132
Castle / '87 / BMG.

PARADE (Original Soundtrack - Under The Cherry Moon) (Prince & The Revolution)
Christopher Tracy's parade / New position / I wonder U / Under the cherry moon / Girls and boys / Life can be so nice / Venus de Milo / Mountains / Do U lie / Kiss / Anotherloverholenyohead / Sometimes it snows in April
CD _____ 925395 2
WEA / Apr '86 / Warner Music.

PRINCE
I wanna be your lover / Why you wanna treat me so bad / Sexy dancer / When we're dancing close and slow / With you / Bambi / Still waiting / I feel for you / It's gonna be lonely
CD _____ K256772
WEA / '86 / Warner Music.

PRINCE: INTERVIEW COMPACT DISC
CD P.Disc _____ CBAK 4018
Baktabak / Nov '89 / Baktabak.

PURPLE RAIN (Prince & The Revolution)
Let's go crazy / Take me with U / Beautiful ones / Computer blue / Darling Nikki / When doves cry / I would die 4 U / Baby I'm a star / Purple rain
CD _____ 9251102
WEA / '86 / Warner Music.

SIGN O' THE TIMES
Play in the sunshine / Housequake / Ballad of Dorothy Parker / It / Starfish and coffee / Slow love / Hot thing / Forever in my life / U got the look / If I was your girlfriend / Strange relationship / I could never take the place of your man / Cross / It's gonna be a beautiful night / Adore / Sign o' the times
CD Set _____ 925 577 2
Paisley Park / Apr '87 / Warner Music.

SYMBOL
My name is Prince / Sexy M.F. / Love 2 the 9s / Morning papers / Max / Segue / Blue light / I wanna melt with U / Sweet baby / Continental / Damn U / Arrogance / Flow / 7 / And God created woman / Three chains o' gold / Sacrifice of Victor
CD _____ 9362450372
Paisley Park / Oct '92 / Warner Music.

SYMBOLIC BEGINNINGS (94 East)
CD Set _____ CPCD 8104
Charly / Jul '95 / Charly / THE / Cadillac.

Prince Buster

FABULOUS GREATEST HITS
Earthquake / Texas hold-up / Freezing up / Orange Street / Free love / Julie / Take it easy / Judge dread / Too hot / Ghost dance / Ten commandments / Al Capone / Barrister pardon
CD _____ SPCD 007
Westmoor / Aug '92 / Target/BMG.

FABULOUS GREATEST HITS (REMASTERED)
Madness / Al Capone / Wash wash / God son / It's Burke's law / Ten commandments / Blackhead Chinaman / Thirty pieces of silver / Hard man fe dead / Pharaoh house crash / Judge dread / Ghost dance / Take it easy / Too hot / My girl / This is a hold up / Shaking up Orange Street / Big 5 / Rough rider / Wreck a pum pum / Julie on my mind / Pharoah house crash / Tie the donkey's tail / Finger
CD _____ NEXCD 253
Sequel / Oct '93 / BMG.

JUDGE DREAD ROCK STEADY/SHE WAS A ROUGH RIDER
Judge dread / Shearing you / Nothing takes the place of you / Ghost dance / Rock with feeling / Sweet appeal / Dark street / Judge dread dance / Show it now / Raise your hands / Change is gonna come / Rough rider / Dreams to remember / Scorcher /

Hypocrites / Walk with love / Taxation / Bye bye baby / Tenderness / Wine or grind / Can't keep on running / Closer together / Going to the river
CD _____ LOMAC D 21
Loma / Feb '94 / BMG.

ORIGINAL GOLDEN OLDIES VOL 1
CD _____ PBCD 9
Prince Buster / Feb '89 / Jetstar.

ORIGINAL GOLDEN OLDIES VOL 2
CD _____ PBCD 10
Prince Buster / May '93 / Jetstar.

PROPHET, THE
CD _____ LG 21100
Lagoon / Sep '94 / Magnum Music Group / THE.

Prince Charles

GREATEST HITZ
CD _____ RE 115CD
Reach Out International / Nov '94 / Jetstar.

Prince Far-I

BLACKMAN LAND
Message from the king / Dream / Reggae music moving / Black man land / Marble stone / Wish I have a wing / Armageddon / Commandment of drugs / Badda card / Moses Moses / Some with roof / Foggy road / Put it out / King of kings / Ghetto living / River of Jordan
CD _____ CDFL 9005
Frontline / Sep '90 / EMI / Jetstar.

CRY FREEDOM DUB
CD _____ TWCD 1053
Tamoki Wambesi / Jun '94 / Jetstar / SRD / Roots Collective / Greensleeves.

CRY TUFF DUB CHAPTER 3 (Prince Far-I & The Arabs)
CD _____ PSCD 007
Pressure Sounds / Jan '96 / SRD / Jetstar.

CRY TUFF DUB ENCOUNTER
CD _____ RE 129CD
Reach Out International / Nov '94 / Jetstar.

DUB TO AFRICA (Prince Far-I & The Arabs)
CD _____ PSCD 002
Pressure Sounds / Apr '95 / SRD / Jetstar.

DUBWISE
Throw away your gun / Love divine dub / If you want to do ya dub / Jah do that dub / No more war / Suru lere dub / Anambra dub / Kaduna dub / Oyo dub / Borno dub / Bendel dub / Ondo dub / Ogun dub
CD _____ CDFL 9019
Frontline / Jun '91 / EMI / Jetstar.

IN THE HOUSE OF VOCAL DUB (Prince Far-I & King Tubby)
CD _____ LJCD 001
Graylan / May '95 / Jetstar / Grapevine / THE.

MUS REVUE, THE (Prince Far-I & Suns Of Arqa)
CD _____ RE 161CD
Reach Out International / Nov '94 / Jetstar.

PSALMS FOR I
CD _____ CGCD 1002
Carib Jems / Jul '94 / Jetstar.

SPEAR OF THE NATION (Umkhonto We Sizwe)
Survival / Ask ask / African queen / Stop the war / Jerry doghead / Special request
CD _____ TWCD 1013
Tamoki Wambesi / Jul '93 / Jetstar / SRD / Roots Collective / Greensleeves.

UNDER HEAVY MANNERS
CD _____ CRCD 2
Crocodisc / May '95 / THE / Magnum Music Group.

VOICE OF THUNDER
Ten commandments / Tribute to Bob Marley / Hold the fort / Everytimo I hoar the word / Head of the Buccaneer / Shall not dwell in wickedness / Give I strength / Kingdom of God / Coming from the rock / Skinhead
CD _____ CDTRLS 204
Trojan / May '90 / Jetstar / Total/BMG.

Prince Hammer

RESPECT I MAN
CD _____ TWCD 1026
Tamoki Wambesi / Oct '95 / Jetstar / SRD / Roots Collective / Greensleeves.

Prince Ital Joe

LIFE ON THE STREETS (Prince Ital Joe & Marky Mark)
Life in the streets (intro) / United / Rastaman vibration / Happy people / To be important / In love / Babylon / Love of a mother / Into the light / In the 90's / Prankster / Life in the streets
CD _____ 450996318-2
East West / Mar '95 / Warner Music.

Prince Jammy

DANCEHALL KILLERS VOL 1
CD _____ 792062
Greensleeves / Nov '92 / Total/BMG / Jetstar / SRD.

HIS MAJESTY'S DUB (Prince Jammy & King Tubby)
CD _____ SJCD 003
Sky Juice / Apr '93 / Jetstar / SRD.

SLENG TENG EXTRAVAGANZA
CD _____ 792042
Greensleeves / Nov '92 / Total/BMG / Jetstar / SRD.

Prince Of Wales...

YORKIES IN STEP, THE (Prince Of Wales Yorkshire Regiment)
CD _____ MMCD 423
Music Masters / Jun '92 / Target/BMG.

Princess

PRINCESS
In the heat of a passionate moment / I'll keep on loving you / After the love has gone / Say I'm your number one / If it makes you feel good / Tell me tomorrow / Anytime's the right time / Just a tease
CD _____ CDSU 1
Supreme / Jul '86 / Pinnacle.

Princess Sharifa

HERITAGE
CD _____ ARICD 093
Ariwa Sounds / Jan '94 / Jetstar / SRD.

Principal Edwards Magic..

SOUNDTRACK & ASMOTO RUNNING BAND (Principal Edwards Magic Theatre)
Enigmatic insomniac machine / Sacrifice / Death of Don Quixote / Third sonnet to sundry notes of music / To a broken guitar / Pinky / McAlpine's dream / McAlpine verses the asmoto / Asmoto running band / Asmoto celebration / Further asmoto celebration / Total glycerol esther / Freef (R') all / Autumn lady dancing / Kettering song / Weirdsong of breaking through at last
CD _____ SEECD 412
See For Miles/C5 / Oct '94 / Pinnacle.

Principato, Tom

BLAZING TELECASTERS (Principato, Tom & Friends)
Honey hush (talkin' woman) / Blue mood / Quiet village / Cherokee / If you only knew / Didn't think twice / It's all right / Been 'n' gone
CD _____ POW 4036 CD
Power House / Nov '90 / Direct.

HOT STUFF
Congo square / Rolene / Here I come / Blue lights / My baby worships me / Never make your love too soon / I know what you're thinkin' / Try to reach you / Slipped, tripped and fell in love
CD _____ POW 4106CD
Power House / Jul '91 / Direct.

IN ORBIT
Nobody / In orbit / Arms around my honey / Deep in the heart of Texas / Same old blues / My baby don't love no-one but me / You slipped up / In a dream / You're not alone / All she wants to do is rock / Mama your daughter lied
CD _____ POW 4002 CD
Power House / Jul '90 / Direct.

Principle

DAMNED, THE (Principle & Silent Eclipse)
CD _____ HAUS 2
Tribehaus Recordings / Jan '94 / Plastic Head.

Principle, Peter

REVAUX AU BONGO
CD _____ MTM 2CD
Made To Measure / Nov '88 / Grapevine.

SEDIMENTAL JOURNEY
CD _____ MTM 4CD
Made To Measure / May '93 / Grapevine.

TONE POEMS
CD _____ MTM 18CD
Made To Measure / Nov '88 / Grapevine.

Principles Of Soul

PRINCIPLES OF SOUL
Strange land / Easy / Sammy / Blues for star eyes / People / Live and love / Nine to five / Bad reputation / POS / Mr. Comeback Man
CD _____ URG 002CD
Urban Groove / Jul '95 / Vital.

Prine, John

GERMAN AFTERNOONS
I just want to dance with me / Love love love / Bad boys / They'll never take her love from me / Paradise / Lulu walls / Speed of

the sound of loneliness / Sailin' around / If she were you / Linda goes to Mars
CD _____ FIENDCD 103
Demon / Aug '87 / Pinnacle / ADA.

GREAT DAYS - THE JOHN PRINE ANTHOLOGY
Illegal smile / Spanish pipedream / Hello in there / Sam Stone / Paradise / Donald and Lydia / Late John Garfield blues / Yes I guess they should name a drink after me / Great compromise / Sweet revenge / Please don't bury me / Christmas in prison / Dear Abby / Blue umbrella / Common sense / Come back to us Barbara Lewis Hare Krishna Beauregard / Saddle in the rain / He was in heaven before he died / Fish and whistle / That's the way that the world goes round / Bruised orange (chain of sorrow) / Sabu visits the twin cities alone / Automobile / Killing the blues / Down by the side of the road / Living in the future / Dear Abby / Storm windows / One red rose / Souvenirs / Aimless love / Oldest baby in the world / People putting people down / Unwed Fathers / Angel from montgomery / Linda goes to Mars / Bad boy / Speed of the sound of loneliness / It's a big old goofy world / Sins of Memphisto / All the best
CD Set _____ 812271400-2
Atlantic / Feb '94 / Warner Music.

LOST DOGS AND MIXED BLESSINGS
New train / Ain't hurtin' nobody / All the way with you / We are the lonely / Lake Marie / Humidity built the snowman / Day is done / Quit hollerin' at me / Big fat love / Same thing happend to me / This love is real / Leave the lights on / He forgot that it was Sunday / I love you so much it hurts
CD _____ RCD 10333
Rykodisc / Sep '95 / Vital / ADA.

MISSING YEARS, THE
Picture show / All the best / Sins of Memphisto / Everybody wants to feel like you / It's a big old goofy world / I want to be with you always / Daddy's like pumpkin / Take a look at my heart / Great run / Way back then / Unlonely / You got cold / Everything is cool / Jesus the missing years
CD _____ 512774-2
This Way Up / '92 / PolyGram / SRD.

PRIME PRINE
WEA / Feb '91 / Warner Music.
CD _____ 7567815042

Prinknash Abbey Monks

CHRISTMAS CHANT (Prinknash Abbey Monks & Stanbrook Abbey Nuns)
Laetundebus (Sequence) / Christus factus est (Invitatory (from Matins as are all tracks to Alma Redemptoris Mater)) / Christe Redemptor (Hymn (Melody from Ely manuscript)) / Dominus dixit #2 (Antiphon) / Isiah ch.9, vv.1-6 (Lesson) / Verbum Caro (Responsory) / Alma Redemptoris Mater (Marian anthem. end s1) / Dominus dixit (Introit - Midnight Mass (all tracks to In splendoribus are Mass chants)) / Kyrie eleison (Missa IV: Cunctipotens) / Gloria in excelsis / Omnes de Saba (Gradual for Epiphany) / Alleluia (Dawn Mass) / Laetentur (Offortory - Midnight Mass) / Sanctus (and Benedictus) / Agnus Dei / In splendoribus (Communion - Midnight Mass) / Angelus ad Virginem (Hymn) / Ecce Nomen (Anthem) / Quem Vidistis (Antiphon) / Angelus ad pastores (Antiphon) / Hodie Christus natus est (Antiphon (II vespers of Christmas)) / Puer natus (Recessional)
CD _____ CDSDL 369
Saydisc / Oct '88 / Harmonia Mundi / ADA / Direct.

Printed At Bismark's

TEN MOVEMENTS (Printed At Bismark's Death)
CD _____ EFA 11225-2
Danse Macabre / Jan '94 / SRD.

Printemp, Marcus

SONG FOR THE BEAUTIFUL WOMAN
Inquiry / I remember April / Song for the beautiful woman / Trauma / Presontation / Lonely heart / Minor ordeal / Speak low / Dahomey dance
CD _____ CDP 8307902
Blue Note / Jul '95 / EMI.

Prior, Andy

ALRIGHT, OK YOU WIN
Alright O.K. you win / Nevertheless (I'm in love with you) / I've got you under my skin / I'm a fool to want you / Beware the man / When you're in his eyes / Love changes everything / Our summer of love / You make me feel so young / All the things you are / Lover / In this world with you / Almost like being in love / Yeh yeh / Dream is a wish
CD _____ CDG 10
DG / Nov '94 / 3MV.

SHOT IN THE DARK, A (Prior, Andy & His Night Owls)
River stay 'way from my door / Hot toddy / Nightingale sang in Berkeley Square / Naked gun / I wish I were in love again / South Rampart street parade / That old black magic / Too little time / Peter Gunn / Puttin'

on the ritz / Dragnet / Where or when / Warm breeze / Mack the knife / Victor and Hugo / Serenade in blue / Pennsylvania 6-5000 / Learning the blues
CD _____ CDG 7
DG / '93 / 3MV.

Prior, Maddy

CAROLS AND CAPERS (Prior, Maddy & The Carnival Band)
Boar's head / Away in a manger / My dancing day / Monsieur Charpentier's Christmas stomp / See amid the winter's snow / Boy was born / Poor little Jesus / Turkey in the straw/Whiskey before breakfast / Wassail / Joy to the world / Cradle song / Shepherds rejoice / Old Joe Clark
CD _____ PRK CD9
Park / Nov '95 / Pinnacle.

CHANGING WINDS
To have and to hold / Pity the poor / Night porter / Bloomers / Acappella Stella / Canals / Sovereign prince / Ali Baba / Mountain / In fighting / Another drink
CD _____ BGOCD 213
Beat Goes On / Dec '93 / Pinnacle.

HANG UP SORROW AND CARE
Prodigal's resolution / Playford tunes / World is turned upside down / Jovial begger / Leathern bottel / lantha / An thou were my Ain Thing / Oh that I had but a fine man / Now O now I needs must part / Man is for the woman made / Northern catch/Little Barley Corne / Granny's delight/My Lady Foster's delight / Round of three country dances in one / Youth's the oaaoon made for joys / In the days of my youth / Never weatherbeaten saile / Old Simon the king
CD _____ PRKCD 31
Park / Oct '95 / Pinnacle.

HAPPY FAMILIES (Prior, Maddy & Rick Kemp)
CD _____ PRKCD 4
Park / Aug '91 / Pinnacle.

SING LUSTILY AND WITH GOOD COURAGE (Prior, Maddy & The Carnival Band)
Who would true valour see / As pants the hart / How firm a foundation / Light of the world / O worship the king / O for a thousand tongues / Lo he comes
CD _____ CDSDL 383
Saydisc / Mar '94 / Harmonia Mundi / ADA / Direct.

TAPESTRY OF CAROLS, A (Prior, Maddy & The Carnival Band)
Sans Day carol / In dulci jubilo / God rest ye merry Gentlemen / It came upon a midnight clear / Holly and the ivy / Coventry carol / Ding dong merrily on high / Angel Gabriel / Angels from the realms of glory / Infant Holy / Virgin most pure / Unto us a boy is born / Rejoice and be merry / Joseph dearest / Personent Hodie / On Christmas night (Sussex Carol.)
CD _____ CDSDL 366
Saydisc / Mar '94 / Harmonia Mundi / ADA / Direct.

WOMAN IN THE WINGS
Woman in the wings / Cold flame / Mother and child / Gutter geese / Rollercoaster / Deep water / Long shadows / I told you so / Rosettes / Cats' eyes / Baggy pants
CD _____ BGOCD 215
Beat Goes On / Mar '94 / Pinnacle.

YEAR
CD _____ PRKCD 20
Park / Oct '93 / Pinnacle.

YEAR/HAPPY FAMILIES
CD Set _____ PRKCD 33
Park / Dec '95 / Pinnacle.

Prior, Snooky

IN THIS MESS UP TO MY CHEST
CD _____ ANT 0028CD
Antones / Sep '94 / Hot Shot / Direct / ADA.

Prison

DISCIPLINE
CD _____ LF 163CD
Lost & Found / Jul '95 / Plastic Head.

Prisonaires

JUST WALKIN' IN THE RAIN
Just walking in the rain / Baby please / Dreaming of you / That clock's too young to fry / Softly and tenderly / My god is real / Prisoner's prayer / No more tears / I know / If I were king / I wish / Don't say tomorrow / What'll you do next / Two strangers / What about Frank Clemen / Friends call me a fool / Lucille / I want you / Surleen / All alone and lonely / Rockin' horse
CD _____ BCD 15523
Bear Family / Aug '91 / Rollercoaster / Direct / CM / Swift / ADA.

JUST WALKIN' IN THE RAIN
CD _____ CPCD 8120
Charly / Aug '95 / Charly / THE / Cadillac.

Prisoners

LAST FOURFATHERS, THE
Nobody wants your love / Night of the Nazgul / Thinking of you (broken pieces) / I am the fisherman / Mrs. Fothergill / Take you for a ride / Drowning / F.O.P. / Whenever I'm gone / Who's sorry now / Explosion on Uranus / I drink the ocean
CD _____ OWNUPU 003CD
Own Up / Jan '94 / Vital.

TASTE OF PINK, A
Better in black / Taste of pink / Maybe I was wrong / Creepy crawlies / There can't be a place / Pretend / Coming home / Threw my heart away / Come to the mushroom / Till the morning light / Say your prayers / Don't call my name
CD _____ OWNUPU 002CD
Own Up / Jan '94 / Vital.

WISERMISERDEMELZA, THE
Go go / Hurricane / Somewhere / Think of me / Love me lies / Tonight / Here come the misunderstood / Dream is gone / For now and forever / Unbeliever / Far away
CD _____ CDWIKD 937
Big Beat / May '90 / Pinnacle.

Prisonshake

FAILED TO MENACE
Last time I looked / Either way evil eye / Brilliant idea / Ever and ever / Some chick you fucked / Stumble / Asiento / Cigarette day / (Not without) Grace / Nothing has to hurt / Humor
CD _____ OLE 085-2
Matador / Jul '94 / Vital.

Pritchard, Bill

DEATH OF BILL POSTERS
CD _____ TMCD 004
Third Mind / Aug '88 / Pinnacle / Third Mind.

Pro-Pain

FOUL TASTE OF FREEDOM
CD _____ RR 90682
Roadrunner / Apr '93 / Pinnacle.

TRUTH HURTS
Make war (Not love) / Bad blood / Truth hurts / Put the lights out / Denial / Let sleeping dogs lie / One man army / Down in the dumps / Beast is back / Switchblade knife / Death on the dancefloor (Features on MC only.) / Pound for pound (Features on MC only.) / Foul taste of freedom (Features on MC only.)
CD _____ RR 89852
Roadrunner / Aug '94 / Pinnacle.

Proby, P.J.

CALIFORNIA LICENSE (Jett Powers)
Bop ting a ling / Blue moon medley / Linda tu / Stranded in the jungle / Tomorrow night / Stagger Lee / Caledonia / Mia amore / Hound dog / Forever my darling / Daddy's home / Rockin' pneumonia and the boogie woogie flu
CD _____ SEECD 390
See For Miles/C5 / Dec '93 / Pinnacle.

I AM P.J. PROBY/P.J. PROBY
Whatever will be will be (Que sera sera) / It's no good for me / Rockin' pneumonia and the boogie woogie flu / Woogie flu / (I'm afraid) the masquerade is over / Glory of love / I'll go crazy / Question / You don't love me no more / Don't worry baby / Just call and I'll be there / Louisiana man / Cuttin' in / My prayer / I will / Mission bell / Nearness of you / Lonely weekends / If I loved you / When I fall in love / She cried / Secret love / I will come to you / Lonely teardrops / With these hands / Just holding on / Mama hold me not to come / Work with me Annie / Ling ting tong / Honey hush / Straight up / Butterfly high / She's looking good / You can't come home again (if you leave me now) / Pretty girls everywhere / Good rockin' tonight / Sanctification / When love has passed you by / I'm coming home / Give me time / Turn her away / Mary in the morning / It's your day today / I shall be released / Cry baby / Why baby why / I've got my eyes on you / I apologise / Judy in the junkyard
CD _____ C5HCD 605
See For Miles/C5 / Jan '96 / Pinnacle.

IN TOWN/ENIGMA
What kind of fool am I / To make a big man cry / No other love / Walk hand in hand / People / It ain't necessarily so / Some enchanted evening / Come back to me / We kiss in a shadow / If I ruled the world / Maria / I could write a book / Niki Hoeky P and L / Reach out, I'll be there / Out of time / People that's why (I sing my song) / I'm twenty eight / I can't make it alone / Shake, shake, shake / That's the tune / Don't forget about me / I wanna thank you baby / Angelica / You make me feel like someone
CD _____ C5HCD 606
See For Miles/C5 / Jan '96 / Pinnacle.

ROUGH VELVET
Maria / I will / My prayer / To make a big man cry / What kind of fool am I / No other love / I apologise / When I fall in love / With these hands / I will come to you / Some enchanted evening / If I loved you / Rain on snow / I'm coming home / Turn her away / Somewhere / I can't make it alone / Per questo voglio te / What's wrong with my world / When love has passed you by / If I ruled the world / You've come back / We kiss in a shadow / It's your day today / Hold me / I'll go crazy / Just call and I'll be there / Linda Lou / Glory of love / Together / Question / Rockin' pneumonia and the boogie woogie flu / Stagger lee / Zing went the strings of my heart / (I'm afraid) The masquerade is over / Whatever will be will be (Que sera sera) / Hold what you've got / Cuttin' in / Let the water run down / That means a lot / Niki hoeky / I wanna thank you baby / That's the tune / Butterfly high / Day that Lorraine came down / Honey hush / Pretty girls everywhere / She's looking good / You can't come home again (if you leave me now) / Stranded in the jungle / Mary Hopkins never had days like this
CD _____ CDEM 1464
EMI / Oct '92 / EMI.

THREE WEEK HERO
CD _____ BGOCD 87
Beat Goes On / Oct '90 / Pinnacle.

Proclaimers

HIT THE HIGHWAY
Let's get married / More I believe / What makes you cry / Follow the money / These arms of mine / Shout shout / Light / Hit the highway / Long long time ago / I want to be a christian / Your childhood / Don't turn out like your mother
CD _____ CDCHR 6066
Chrysalis / Feb '94 / EMI.

SUNSHINE ON LEITH
I'm gonna be (500 miles) / Cap in hand / Then I met you / My old friend the blues / Sean / Sunshine on leith / Come on nature / I'm on my way / What do you do / It's Saturday night / Teardrops / Oh Jean
CD _____ CD25CR 18
Chrysalis / Mar '94 / EMI.

THIS IS THE STORY
Throw the 'r' away / Over and done with / Misty blue / Part that really matters / (I'm gonna) burn your playhouse down / Letter from America / Sky takes the soul / It broke my heart / First attack / Make my heart fly / Beautiful truth / Joyful Kilmarnock blues
CD _____ CCD 1602
Chrysalis / Mar '93 / EMI.

Proctor, Chris

STEEL STRING STORIES
CD _____ FF 554CD
Flying Fish / '92 / Roots / CM / Direct / ADA.

TRAVELOGUE
CD _____ FF 70633CD
Flying Fish / Apr '94 / Roots / CM / Direct / ADA.

Procul Harum

BEST OF PROCUL HARUM
CD _____ BRCD 106
BR Music / Jan '95 / Target/BMG.

COLLECTION: PROCUL HARUM
Whiter shade of pale / Homburg / Too much between us / Salty dog / Devil came from Kansas / Whaling stories / Good Captain Clack / All this and more / Quite rightly so / Shine on brightly / Grand hotel / Bringing home the bacon / Toujours l'amour / Broken barricades / Power failure / Conquistador / Nothing but the truth / Butterfly Boys / Pandora's box / Simple sister
CD _____ CCSCD 120
Castle / '86 / BMG.

EARLY YEARS, THE
Whiter shade of pale / Lime Street blues / Homburg / Monsieur Armand / Seem to have the blues all the time / Conquistador / She wandered through the garden fence / Quite rightly so / In the wee small hours of sixpence / Shine on brightly / Magdalene / Skip softly my moonbeams / Salty dog / Long gone geek / Boredom / Devil came from Kansas / Whiskey train / About to die / Nothing I didn't know / Still there'll be more
CD _____ EARLD 6
Castle / Nov '92 / BMG.

EXOTIC BIRDS AND FRUIT
Nothing but the truth / Beyond the pale / As strong as Samson / Idol / Thin end of the wedge / Monsieur R.Monde / Fresh fruit / Butterfly boys / New lamps for old
CD _____ ESMCD 291
Essential / Oct '95 / Total/BMG.

GRAND HOTEL
Grand hotel / Roberts box / Fires (which burn brightly) / For liquorice John / Bring home the bacon / Souvenir of London / T.V. Caesar / Rum tale / Toujours l'amour
CD _____ ESMCD 290
Essential / Oct '95 / Total/BMG.

HOMBURG AND OTHER HATS (Best Of Procul Harum)
CD _____ ESSCD 295
Essential / Oct '95 / Total/BMG.

HOME
Whisky train / Dead man's dream / Still there'll be more / Nothing that I didn't know / About to die / Barnyard story / Piggy pig pig / Whaling stories / Your own choice
CD _____ CLACD 292
Castle / Apr '89 / BMG.

PROCUL HARUM
Whiter shade of pale / Salty dog / Shine on brightly / Wreck of the Hesperus / Long gone geek / Whaling stories / Homburg / Conquistador / Whisky train / Good Captain Clack / Barnyard story / Kaleidoscope
CD _____ CUCD 05
Disky / Oct '94 / THE / Discovery / Pinnacle.

PROCUL'S NINTH
Taking the time / Pandora's box / Fools gold / Uniquiet zone / Final thrust / I keep forgetting / Without a doubt / Piper's tune / Typewriter torment
CD _____ ESMCD 292
Essential / Oct '95 / Total/BMG.

SALTY DOG
Salty dog / Milk of human kindness / Too much between us / Devil came from Kansas / Boredom / Juicy John Pink / Wreck of the Hesperus / All this and more / Crucifiction Lane / Pilgrims progress
CD _____ CLACD 289
Castle / Jul '92 / BMG.

SHINE ON BRIGHTLY
Quite rightly so / Shine on brightly / Skip softly my moonbeams / Wish me well / Rambling on / Magdalena / In held 'twas in I / Glimpses of Nirvana / 'Twas tea time at the circus / In the Autumn of my madness / Look to your soul / Grand finale / Whisky train / Dead man's dreams / Still there'll be more / Nothing that I didn't know / About to die / Barnyard story / Piggy pig pig / Whaling stories / Your own choice
CD _____ CLACD 321
Castle / Nov '92 / BMG.

SOMETHING MAGIC
Something magic / Skating on thin ice / Wizard man / Mark of the claw / Strangers in space / Worm and the tree (1 to 3)
CD _____ ESMCD 293
Essential / Oct '95 / Total/BMG.

WHITER SHADE OF PALE, A
Whiter shade of pale / Conquistador / She wandered through the garden fence / Something following me / Mabel / Cerdes / Christmas camel / Kaleidoscope / Salad days / Good Captain Clack / Repent / Walpurgis
CD _____ CLACD 188
Castle / Aug '90 / BMG.

Prodigy

EXPERIENCE
CD _____ XLCD 110
XL / Nov '92 / Warner Music.

MUSIC FOR THE JILTED GENERATION
CD _____ XLCD 114
XL / Jul '94 / Warner Music.

Product, Clive

FINANCIAL SUICIDE
CD _____ UTIL 002 CD
Utility / Jun '90 / Grapevine.

Professor Blues

PROFESSOR STRUT (Professor Blues Review)
CD _____ DD 650
Delmark / Jan '93 / Hot Shot / ADA / CM / Direct / Cadillac.

Professor Frisky

ROUGHER
CD _____ RN 0041
X-Rated / Apr '95 / Jetstar.

Professor Griff

PAWNS IN THE GAME (Professor Griff & The Last Asiatic Disciples)
Pawns in the game / Verdict / Suzi wants to be a rock star / Real African people (pt 1) / Pass the ammo / Real African people (pt 2) / Love thy enemy / Rap terrorist / 1-900 stereotype / Last Asiatic disciples / Word of God / Fifth amendment / Interview / It's a blax thanx
CD _____ CDXR 111
Skywalker / Apr '90 / Pinnacle.

Professor Longhair

BIG CHIEF
Big chief / Hey little girl / How long has that train been gone / I'm movin' on / Mess around / She walks right in / Shake, rattle and roll / Sick and tired / Tipitina / Little blues / Her mind is gone / Stagger Lee / I've got my mojo working / Rum and coca cola / Mardi gras in New Orleans
CD _____ 598 1093 20
Tomato / Aug '93 / Vital.

BIG EASY, THE
Big chief / Tipitina / Gone so long / How long has that train been gone / Messin'

around / She ain't got no hair / Going to the mardi gras / Big chief (Alt.) / Her mind is gone / Baldhead
CD _____ CDBM 094
Blue Moon / Feb '94 / Magnum Music Group / Greensleeves / Hot Shot / ADA / Cadillac / Discovery.

COMPLETE LONDON CONCERT, THE
Mess around / Hey now baby / Whole lotta lovin' / Go to the Mardi Gras / Bald head / Tipitina / Big chief / Every day I have the blues / Hey little girl / Rockin' pneumonia and the boogie woogie flu
CD _____ JSPCD 202
JSP / Jul '87 / ADA / Target/BMG / Direct / Cadillac / Complete/Pinnacle.

CRAWFISH FIESTA
CD _____ ALCD 4718
Alligator / May '93 / Direct / ADA.

HOUSEPARTY NEW ORLEANS STYLE (The Lost Sessions 1971-72)
No buts and maybes / Gone so long / She walked right in / Thank you pretty baby / 501 boogie / Tipitina / Gonna leave this town / Cabbagehead / Hey little girl / Big chief / Cherry pie / Junco partner / Everyday I have the blues / G jam / Dr. Professor Longhair
CD _____ ROUCD 2057
Rounder / Jun '95 / CM / Direct / ADA / Cadillac.

LAST MARDI GRAS
CD _____ 7567814062
Atlantic / Jun '95 / Warner Music.

LIVE ON THE QUEEN MARY
Tell me pretty baby / Mess around / Everyday I have the blues / Tipitina / I'm movin' on / Mardi Gras in New Orleans / Cry to me / Gone so long / Stagger Lee
CD _____ S21 56844
One Way / Apr '94 / Direct / ADA.

NEW ORLEANS HOUSEPARTY
No buts and no maybes / Gone so long / She walk right in / Thank you pretty baby / 501 boogie / Tipitina / Gonna leave this town / Cabbagehead / Hey little girl / Big chief / Cherry pie / Junco partner / Every day I have the blues / G jam / Dr. Professor Longhair
CD _____ FIENDCD 189
Demon / Aug '90 / Pinnacle / ADA.

NEW ORLEANS PIANO
CD _____ RSACD 808
Sequel / Oct '94 / BMG.

NEW ORLEANS PIANO BLUES - VOL.2
CD _____ 756781419-2
Atlantic / Jun '93 / Warner Music.

ROCK 'N' ROLL GUMBO
CD _____ 5197462
Verve / Apr '93 / PolyGram.

RUM AND COKE
Everyday I have the blues / Jambalaya / Rum and coca cola / She walks right in / Shake, rattle and roll / Roberta / Mardi gras in New Orleans / Whole lotta lovin' / Gone so long / Doin' it / How long has that train been gone (version 2) / Hey now baby / 501 boogie / Junco partner / She ain't got no hair / Gone so long (second conversation)
CD _____ 598 1092 30
Tomato / Aug '93 / Vital.

Profit, Clarence

SOLO & TRIO SIDES
CD _____ CDMOIR 504
Memoir / Aug '93 / Target/BMG.

Profound Effect

LASHING OUT
CD _____ LF 156CD
Lost & Found / Aug '95 / Plastic Head.

Prohibition

NOBODINSIDE
CD _____ 059012
Distortion / Jun '94 / Plastic Head.

Project

FROM ACROSS THIS GRAY LAND NO.3
CD _____ HY 3910033CD
Hyperium / Nov '92 / Vital.

Project D

SYNTHESIZER ALBUM, THE
CD _____ CDSR 020
Telstar / Sep '93 / BMG.

Project G-5

TRIBUTE TO WES MONTGOMERY
Wes / Days of wine and roses / Four on six / Darn that dream / Besame mucho / Gone with the wind / West coast blues / Yesterdays / Body and soul / End of a love affair / Naptown blues
CD _____ KICJ 146
King/Paddle Wheel / Sep '93 / New Note.

Project G-7

TRIBUTE TO WES MONTGOMERY, A
Impressions / Remembering Wes / Groove yard / Canadian sunset / Fried pies / Road song / Some rain or come shine / Serena / Yesterdays
CD _____ ECD 22049
Evidence / Jul '93 / Harmonia Mundi / ADA / Cadillac.

TRIBUTE TO WES MONTGOMERY, VOL 2
More blues for Wes / Bock to bock / For heaven's sake / Montgomery blue / Finger pickin' / Never again / Polka dots and moonbeams / Samba Wes / West coast blues - three quarters of the house
CD _____ ECD 22051
Evidence / Jul '93 / Harmonia Mundi / ADA / Cadillac.

Project Pitchfork

LAM BRAS
CD _____ HY 21030
Hypertension / Nov '92 / Total/BMG / Direct / ADA.

RENASCENCE
CD _____ SPV 05522063
SPV / Oct '94 / Plastic Head.

SOULS ISLAND
CD _____ HY 210519
Hypertension / Jul '93 / Total/BMG / Direct / ADA.

Project X

STRAIGHT EDGE REVENGE
CD _____ LF 072
Lost & Found / Feb '94 / Plastic Head.

Prolapse

BACK SATURDAY
CD _____ LISSCD 8
Lissy's / Nov '95 / SRD.

POINTLESS WALKS TO DISMAL PLACES
Serpico / Headless in a beat motel / Surreal Madrid / Doorstop rhythmic bloc / Burgundy spine / Black death ambulance / Chill blown / Hungarian suicide song / Tina this is Matthew stone
CD _____ CDBRED 116
Cherry Red / Oct '94 / Pinnacle.

Promise

PROMISE, THE
CD _____ NTHEN 14
Now & Then / Sep '95 / Plastic Head.

Prong

CLEANSING
Another worldly device / Whose fist is this anyway / Snap your fingers, snap your neck / Cut rate / Broken peace / One outnumbered / Out of this misery / No question / Not of this earth / Home rule / Sublime / Test
CD _____ 474796 2
Epic / Feb '94 / Sony.

Propaganda

1, 2, 3, 4
Vicious circle / Heaven give me words / Your wildlife / Only one word / How much love / Vicious / Ministry of fear / Wound in my heart / La carne la morte o il diavolo
CD _____ CDV 2625
Virgin / Apr '92 / EMI.

SECRET WISH, A
Dream within a dream / Murder of love / Jewel duel / P machinery / Power force push drive / Dr. Mabuse / Sorry for laughing
CD _____ 450994749-2
ZTT / Mar '94 / Warner Music.

WISHFUL THINKING (DISTURB DANCES)
Dr. Mabuse / P. Machinery / Sorry for laughing / Jewelled / Murder of love
CD _____ 450994748-2
ZTT / Mar '94 / Warner Music.

Propaghandi

HOW TO CLEAN EVERYTHING
CD _____ FAT 506CD
Fat Wreck Chords / Aug '93 / Plastic Head.

SPLIT CD
CD _____ FAT 666CD
Fat Wreck Chords / Jul '95 / Plastic Head.

Proper Grounds

DOWNTOWN CIRCUS GANG
Black noize / Mind tempest / Joker E double / Jezebel / Money in the depths of a plagueless man / Downtown circus gang / 2 Kill a clown / Backwards mass/Black noize / I'm drowning / D-views man / Nature song / Fuck the blues / Purgatory / Seventh House on the bank / Black noize (reprise)
CD _____ 936245256-2
Sire / Mar '93 / Warner Music.

Prophecy Of Doom

MATRIX
CD _____ CORE 11CD
Metalcore / Jun '92 / Plastic Head.

Prophet, Chuck

BALINESE DANCER
CD _____ WOLCD 1031
China / Feb '93 / Pinnacle.

BROTHER ALDO
CD _____ FIRE 33022
Fire / Oct '91 / Disc.

FEAST OF HEARTS
CD _____ WOLCD 1061
China / May '95 / Pinnacle.

Prophet, Michael

GUNMAN
CD _____ GRELCD 509
Greensleeves / Apr '91 / Total/BMG / Jetstar / SRD.

LOVE IS AN EARTHLY THING
Rich man, poor man / Instructions / Never fall in love / Baby baby / Reggae music all right / Love is an earthly thing / It's a girl / Pretty face / Fussing and fighting
CD _____ CPCD 8136
Charly / Oct '95 / Charly / THE / Cadillac.

SERIOUS REASONING
Fight to the top / Hear I prayer / Turn me loose / Gates of Zion / Praise you jah jah / Love and unity / Warn them / Conscious man / Give thanks / Serious reasoning
CD _____ RRCD 48
Reggae Refreshers / Jul '94 / PolyGram / Vital.

Prophets Of Da City

UNIVERSAL SOULJAZ
CD _____ NATCD 54
Nation / Jun '95 / Disc.

Pros & Concept

PRECREATIONS
Peanut gallery / W.O.T.R. / Checkin' the mike / Do you know / P. Fossil / Alone in this field / Lyrical drippin' / Roll call on the 1 and 2's / Brothers / Expressions in the shower / It's dope
CD _____ 4783792
Epic / Jul '95 / Sony.

Protector

GOLEM
CD _____ ATOMH 007CD
Atom / '90 / Cadillac.

HERITAGE, THE
CD _____ CC 020462CD
Major / Jan '94 / Plastic Head.

LOST IN ETERNITY
CD _____ CC 030057CD
Major / Aug '95 / Plastic Head.

Protocal

FORCE MAJEURE
Gooz / Force majeure / Two socks / Harlem nights / Cosmos / Blue shoes, no dance / Bottom line / Street wise / One for C.J. / Outback
CD _____ BW 021
B&W / Aug '93 / New Note.

Druidia

DESIGNER KARMA
CD _____ ILLCD 030
Imaginary / Jun '91 / Vital.

Prud'Homme, Emile

INOUBLIABLES DE L'ACCORDEON
CD _____ 882422
Music Memoria / Aug '93 / Discovery / ADA.

Pryor, Snooky

TOO COOL TO MOVE
Keyhole in your door / Can I be your friend / Bottle it up and go / Hold me in your arms / Don't you want to know / Cheatin' and lyin' / Walkin' with Snooky / Fire, Fire / Coal black mare / Lovin' you is killin' me / Boogie twist / My baby been gone / Please be careful
CD _____ ANTCD 0017
Antones / Nov '91 / Hot Shot / Direct / ADA.

Psychedelic Furs

ALL OF THIS AND NOTHING
President gas / All that money wants / Imitation of christ / Sister Europe / Love my way / Highwire days / Dumb waiters / Pretty in pink / Ghost in you / Heaven / Heartbreak beat / All of this and nothing
CD _____ 4611102
CBS / Apr '91 / Sony.

B SIDES & LOST GROOVES
Aeroplane / Another edge / Badman / Birdland / Goodbye / I don't want to be your shadow / Heartbeat / Mack the knife / New dream / Here come cowboys / Heartbreak beat / Angels don't cry / Shock / President gas / No easy street
CD _____ 4803632
Columbia / Apr '95 / Sony.

COLLECTION: PSYCHEDELIC FURS
India / Sister Europe / We love you / Flowers / Dumb waiters / Sleep comes down / Mr. Jones / Love my way / Forever now / Danger / Shadow / Pretty in pink / Mack the knife / Heaven / Heartbeat / No release / Angels don't cry
CD _____ CCSCD 308
Castle / Oct '91 / BMG.

MIRROR MOVES
Ghost in You / Here come cowboys / Heaven / Heartbeat / My time / Like a stranger / Alice's house / Only a game / Highwire days
CD _____ 450356 2
Columbia / May '94 / Sony.

WORLD OUTSIDE
Valentine / In my head / Until she comes / Don't be a girl / Sometimes / Tearing down / There's a world / Get a room / Better days / All about you
CD _____ 9031746692
East West / Feb '95 / Warner Music.

Psychedelic Warriors

WHITE ZONE
Frenzzy (Mixes) / Am I fooling / Pipe dreams / Heart attack / Time and space / White zone / Bay of Bengal / Moonbeam / Pulsating pussy / Love in space
CD _____ EBSSCD 113
Emergency Broadcast System / Feb '95 / Vital.

Psychic Pawn

DECADENT DELIRIUM
CD _____ NIHIL 2CD
Vinyl Solution / Aug '95 / Disc.

Psychic TV

ALLEGORY AND SELF
CD _____ TOPY 038CD
Temple / Aug '91 / Pinnacle / Plastic Head.

BEAUTY FROM THEE BEAST
Roman P / Good vibrations / Hex sex / Godstar / Je t'aime / United 94 / Ev ov destruction / S.M.I.L.E. / I.C. Water / Horror house / Back to reality
CD _____ VICD 006
Visionary/Jettisoundz / Sep '95 / THE / Pinnacle.

BEYOND THEE INFINITE BEAT
Money for E / S.M.I.L.E. / Bliss / Horror house / I.C. water / Stick insect
CD _____ VICD 004
Cherry Red / Oct '94 / Pinnacle.

CATHEDRAL ENGINE
CD _____ EFA 084672
Dossier / Mar '95 / SRD.

DESCENDING
CD _____ SSCD 001
Semantic / Jan '94 / Plastic Head.

ELECTRIC NEWSPAPER
CD _____ EFA 08459-2
Dossier / Jan '95 / SRD.

ELECTRIC NEWSPAPER ISSUE 2
CD _____ EFA 08470-26
Dossier / Jul '95 / SRD.

ELECTRONIC NEWSPAPER
CD _____ EFA 084762
Dossier / Nov '95 / SRD.

GODSTAR THE SINGLES PART II
CD _____ CLEO 9518CD
Cleopatra / Apr '95 / Disc.

HEX SEX
CD _____ CLEO 6508-2
Cleopatra / Mar '94 / Disc.

HOLLOW COST, A
CD _____ VICD 003
Visionary/Jettisoundz / Oct '94 / THE / Pinnacle.

KONDOLE
CD _____ SR 9332
Silent / Jan '94 / Plastic Head.

KONDOLE/COPYCAT
CD _____ TOPYCD 46
Temple / Jul '89 / Pinnacle / Plastic Head.

LISTEN TODAY
CD _____ SSCDV 01
Semantic / Jan '94 / Plastic Head.

LIVE AT THEE BERLIN WALL VOL.1
CD _____ TOPYCD 052 CD
Temple / Sep '90 / Pinnacle / Plastic Head.

LIVE AT THEE BERLIN WALL VOL.2
CD _____ TOPYCD 053 CD
Temple / Sep '90 / Pinnacle / Plastic Head.

LIVE IN BREGENZ
CD _____ TOPY 020CD
Temple / Jan '91 / Pinnacle / Plastic Head.

MEIN GOTTINGEN
CD _____ EFA 06446-2
Dossier / Jun '94 / SRD.

MOUTH OF THE NIGHT
CD _____ VAULT 23
Trident / Nov '93 / Pinnacle.

PAGAN DAY
Catalogue / W kiss / Opium / Cold steel / Los Angeles / Iceland / Translucent carriages / Paris / Baby's gone away / Alice / New sexuality / Farewell
CD _____ CLEO 94692
Cleopatra / Jun '94 / Disc.

PEAK HOUR
CD _____ TOPY 068 CD
Temple / Apr '95 / Pinnacle / Plastic Head.

RARE AND ALIVE
CD _____ TIBCD 10
Temple / Aug '93 / Pinnacle.

SINGLES PART ONE, THE
CD _____ CLEO 65082
Jungle / Apr '95 / Disc.

SIRENS
Stargods / Skreemer / Reunited / Sirens
CD _____ VICD 005
Cherry Red / Mar '95 / Pinnacle.

THEE TRANSMUTION OV MERCURY
CD _____ EFA 08454-2
Dossier / Mar '94 / SRD.

TOWARDS THEE INFINITE BEAT
Infinite beat / Bliss / Drone zone / S.M.I.L.E. / I.C.Water / Black rainbow / Short sharp taste ov mistress mix / Horror house / Jigsaw / Alien be-in / Stick insect / Money for E
CD _____ VICD 002
Visionary/Jettisoundz / Sep '94 / THE / Pinnacle.

ULTRADRUG
Scoring / Tempted / Swallow / Bloodstream / B on E / Constant high / Back to reality / Eagle has landed / S.U.C.K. or know / Tempter / Still B on E / Gone paranoid / Loose nuts
CD _____ VICD 001
Visionary/Jettisoundz / Sep '94 / THE / Pinnacle.

Psychik Warriors Ov Gaia

OBSIDIAN
Obsidian / Challenge / Patience
CD _____ KK 090CD
KK / Dec '92 / Plastic Head.

OV BIOSPHERES
CD _____ KK65 CDD
KK / Apr '94 / Plastic Head.

OV SACRED GROOVES
CD _____ KK 065 CDD
Foundation 2000 / '91 / Plastic Head.

RECORD OF BREAKS, A
CD _____ KK 118CD
KK / Oct '95 / Plastic Head.

Psycho Bunnies

VAMPIRE MISTRESS
And it hurts / Outsiders / Vampire mistress / Searchin' / I don't want you / Jolene / Fallen angels / Rock against romance / Not with you / He's 17 / Hey big Daddy / Blood and roses
CD _____ RAGECD 110
Rage / Feb '93 / Nervous / Magnum Music Group.

Psycho Motel

STATE OF MIND
CD _____ RAWCD 108
Raw Power / Jan '96 / BMG.

Psychograss

PSYCHOGRASS
Love on three levels / Little Jaco / Pleasant pheasant / Whiter shade of pale / Real dragon / Frogs on ice / Song for Kaila / Flanders rock / Dawn chorus / Wedges
CD _____ 01934111322
Windham Hill / Nov '93 / Pinnacle / BMG / ADA.

Psychomuzak

EXSTASIE, THE
Exstasie / Diamond zombie / Far in / Concentrate (over concentration) / Concentration
CD _____ DELECCD 018
Delerium / Feb '95 / Vital.

Psychopomps

IN THE SKIN
CD _____ HY 859210595
Hyperium / Jun '94 / Plastic Head.

Psychosis

SQUIRM
CD _____ MASSCD 018
Massacre / Nov '93 / Plastic Head.

Psychotic Waltz

MOSQUITO
CD _____ CDVEST 27
Bulletproof / Sep '94 / Pinnacle.

Psychotic Youth

BAMBOOZLE
CD _____ SPV 08056922
SPV / May '95 / Plastic Head.

BE IN THE SUN
CD _____ RA 91792
Roadrunner / Mar '92 / Pinnacle.

Psychrist

ABYSMAL FIEND
CD _____ WHCD 004
Modern Invasion / Apr '95 / Plastic Head.

Psyclone Rangers

DEVIL MAY CARE
CD _____ WDOM 015CD
World Domination / Mar '95 / Pinnacle.

FEEL NICE
I wanna be Jack Kennedy / Spinnin' my
head / Christie indecision / I feel nice / Hate
noise / Stephen / Heaven / Riot girl / Bigger
than a gun / Devil's down there / Perfect
engine / You're not Edie Sedgwick
CD _____ WDOM 005CD
World Domination / May '94 / Pinnacle.

Psylons

GIMP
CD _____ CSA 102
RPM / Jun '94 / Pinnacle.

Ptacek, Rainer

WORRIED SPIRITS
CD _____ FIENDCD 723
Demon / Oct '93 / Pinnacle / ADA.

Pterodactyl

SNARE PRESSURE VOL.1
CD _____ DBASSCD 01
D.Bass / Nov '95 / Total/BMG.

Public Enemy

**APOCALYPSE '91 (The Enemy Strikes
Black)**
Lost at birth / Rebirth / Can't truss it / I don't
wanna be called yo niga / How to kill a radio
consultant / By the time I get to Arizona /
Move / Million bottlebags / More news at
11 / Shut 'em down / Letter to the New York
Post / Get the fuck outta Dodge / Bring the
noise (with Anthrax) / Nightrain
CD _____ 5234792
Def Jam / Jul '95 / PolyGram.

FEAR OF A BLACK PLANET
Contract on the world love jam / Brothers
gonna work it out / 911 is a joke / Incident
at 66.6 FM / Welcome to the terrordome /
Meet the G that killed me / Pollywanacraka
/ Anti-nigger machine / Burn Hollywood
burn / Power to the people / Who stole the
soul / Fear of a black planet / Revolutionary
generation / Can't do nuttin' for ya man /
Reggie Jax / Leave this off your fuckin'
charts / B side wins again / War at 33 1/3
/ Final count of the collision between us and
them
CD _____ 5234462
Def Jam / Jul '95 / PolyGram.

GREATEST MISSES
Tie goes to the runner / Hit da road Jack /
Gett off my back / Gotta do what I gotta do
/ Air hoodlum / Hazy shade of criminal / Me-
gablast / Louder than a bomb / You're
gonna get yours / How to kill a radio con-
sultant / Who stole the soul / Party for your
right to fight
CD _____ 5234872
Def Jam / Jul '95 / PolyGram.

**IT TAKES A NATION OF MILLIONS TO
HOLD US BACK**
Countdown to Armageddon / Bring the
noise / Don't believe the hype / Cold lampin' wit' Flavor / Terminator X to the edge
of panic / Mind terrorist / Louder than a
bomb / Caught, can we get a witness /
Show 'em whatcha got / She watch Channel Zero / Night of the living baseheads /
Black steel in the hour of chaos / Security
of the first world / Rebel without a pause /
Prophets of rage / Party for your right to
fight
CD _____ 5273582
Def Jam / Jul '95 / PolyGram.

MUSE SICK-N-HOUR MESS AGE
Whole lotta love goin' on in the middle of
hell / Theater part intro / Give it up / What
side you on / Bedlam 13:13 / Stop in the
name / What kind of power we got / So
what'cha gonna do now / White heaven/
Black hell / Race against time / They used
to call it dope / Ain'tnuttinbuttersong / Live

and undrugged (pts 1 & 2) / Thin line be-
tween law and rape / I ain't madd at all /
Death of a carjacka / I stand accused /
Godd complexx / Hitler day / Harry Allen's
interactive super highway phone call to
Chuck / Livin' in a zoo (remix/Not on MC)
CD _____ 523 362-2
Def Jam / Aug '94 / PolyGram.

YO, BUM RUSH THE SHOW
You're gonna get yours / Sophisticated
bitch / Miuzi weighs a ton / Time bomb /
Too much posse / Rightstarter (message to
a black man) / Public enemy no.1 / M.P.E.
/ Yo, bum rush the show / Raise the roof /
Megablast / Terminator X speaks with his
hands
CD _____ 5274412
Def Jam / Jul '95 / PolyGram.

Public Image Ltd

ALBUM
F.F.F. / Rise / Fishing / Round / Bags /
Home / Ease
CD _____ CDV 2366
Virgin / Feb '86 / EMI.

FLOWERS OF ROMANCE
Four enclosed walls / Track 8 / Phenagen /
Flowers of romance / Under the house / Hy-
mies him / Banging the door / Go back /
Francis massacre
CD _____ CDV 2189
Virgin / Apr '90 / EMI.

LIVE IN TOKYO
Annalisa / Religion / Low life / Flowers of
romance / Death Disco / Solitaire / This is
not a love song / Bad life / Banging the door
/ Under the house
CD _____ VGDCD 3508
Virgin / Apr '92 / EMI.

**PARIS AU PRINTEMPS (PARIS IN
SPRING)**
Theme / Chant / Careering / Bad baby / At-
tack / Poptones / Lowlife
CD _____ CDV 2183
Virgin / Apr '90 / EMI.

PUBLIC IMAGE
Theme / Religion 1 / Religion 2 / Annalisa /
Fodderstompt / Low life / Public image /
Attack
CD _____ CDV 2114
Virgin / Jun '88 / EMI.

SECOND EDITION
Albatross / Memories / Swan lake / Pop
tones / Careering / Socialist / Graveyard /
Suit / Bad baby / No birds do sing / Chant
/ Radio 4
CD _____ CDVD 2512
Virgin / Jun '92 / EMI.

THAT WHAT IS NOT
Acid drops / Luck's up / Cruel / God / Cov-
ered / Love hope / Unfairground / Think
tank / Emperor / Good things
CD _____ CDV 2681
Virgin / Feb '92 / EMI.

Pucho

**BEST OF PUCHO, THE (Pucho & His
Latin Soul Brothers)**
Cantaloupe island / Vietnam mambo / Soul
yamie / Something black / Shuckin' and
jivin' / Got myself a good man / Maiden voy-
age / Strange thing mambo / Groover / Psy-
chedelic pucho / Let love find you / Yambo
/ Swamp people / Dateline / Cloud 9 /
Swing thing / Big stick
CD _____ CDBGPD 069
BGP / Feb '93 / Pinnacle.

**HEAT/JUNGLE FIRE (Pucho & His Latin
Soul Brothers)**
Heat / Georgia on my mind / Presence of
your heart / Psychedelic Pucho / I can't
stop loving you / Wanderin' rose / Let love
find you / Candied yam / Payin' dues /
Friendship train / Got myself a good man /
Spokerman / Cloud 9 / Jamilah
CD _____ CDBGPD 047
BGP / Nov '92 / Pinnacle.

**RIP A DIP (Pucho & His Latin Soul
Brothers)**
CD _____ CDBGPD 102
BGP / Feb '96 / Pinnacle.

Puente, Tito

12 MAMBOS & TAKE FIVE
CD _____ WW 002216
West Wind / Dec '93 / Swift / Charly / CM
/ ADA.

BARBARABATIRI
CD _____ CD 62053
Saludos Amigos / May '94 / Target/BMG.

**BLUE GARDENIA NEW YORK 1958
(Puente, Tito & Woody Herman)**
CD _____ 17031
Laserlight / May '94 / Target/BMG.

**EL REY (Puente, Tito & His Latin
Ensemble)**
Oye como va / Autumn leaves / Ran kan
kan / Rainfall / Giant steps / Linda Chicana
/ Medley: Stella by starlight / Delirio / Equi-
noxe / El rey del timbal
CD _____ CCD 4250
Concord Jazz / Jan '87 / New Note.

**GOLDEN LATIN JAZZ ALL STARS (Live
At The Village Gate)**
Intro / New arrival / Sunflower / Afro blue /
Skin jam / I loves you Porgy / Oye como va
/ Milestones
CD _____ 66058021
RMM / Aug '93 / New Note.

GOZA MI TIMBAL
Airegin / Cha cha cha / Pent-up house /
Picadillo a lo Puente / All blues / Ode to
Cachao / Straight no chaser / Lambada
timbales
CD _____ CCD 4399
Concord Picante / Jan '90 / New Note.

IN SESSION
Teach me tonight / Flight to Jordan / In a
heart beat / Un poco mas / Thunderbird /
Miami girl / Obsession / Tigimo + 2 / Tritone
/ Mood's mood for love
CD _____ 66058037
RMM / Jul '94 / New Note.

MAMA INEZ
CD _____ CD 62028
Saludos Amigos / Apr '94 / Target/BMG.

**MAMBO DIABLO (Puente, Tito & His
Latin Ensemble)**
Mambo diablo / Take five / Lush life / Pick
yourself up / Lullaby of Birdland / No pien-
ses asi / China / Eastern joy dance
CD _____ CCD 4283
Concord Picante / Sep '86 / New Note.

MAMBO GOZON
CD _____ CD 62008
Saludos Amigos / Oct '93 / Target/BMG.

MAMBO OF THE TIMES
Things to come / Jitterbug waltz / Mambo
king / Passion flower / Baqueteo / Japan
mambo / Mambo of the times / If you could
see me now / Best is yet to come / El Titan
CD _____ CCD 4499
Concord Jazz / Mar '92 / New Note.

MAMBO Y CHA CHA CHA
CD _____ CD 312
Entertainers / Feb '95 / Target/BMG.

**MAMBURAMA (Puente, Tito & His
Orchestra)**
Mambo típico / Mambo Inn / Mambolino /
Mambo rumbon / Mambo rama / Mambo
lenko / Ran kan kan / Mambo with me-
mambo gallego / Que lindo el mambo /
Mambiando / Titoro / La guira / Este tumbao / Mambo suavecito / Bamaram bam
bam / Penjamo / El ray del timbal / Esto es
coco camina camaron / Tatalibaba / Guajeo
en dominate / Picao y tostao / Coco seco
CD _____ CDCHARLY 253
Charly / Oct '91 / Charly / THE / Cadillac.

**MASTER TIMBALERO (Puente, Tito &
His Latin Ensemble)**
Old arrival / Enchantment / Sakura / Azu ki
ki / Espresso por favor / Nostalgia in Times
Square / Chow mein / Creme de menthe /
Sun goddess / Vaya puente / Master Tim-
baleo / Bloomdido
CD _____ CCD 4594
Concord Picante / May '94 / New Note.

NIGHT BEAT/MUCHO PUENTE
Live a little (let's face it) / Late late scene /
Midnight lament (minor moods) / Night
hawk (minor moods) / Night hawk (coconut
and rice) / Malibu beat / Mambo beat /
Night ritual / Floozie / Poor butterfly / Lull-
aby of the leaves / Duerme (time was) / No-
che de ronda (be mine tonight) / Ecstasy /
Tea for two / Son de la Loma / Tito's guajira
/ Almendra / La ola marina / Un poquito de
tu amor / What a difference a day makes /
Night beat (mono) / Emerald beach / Caro-
oca (mono)
CD _____ BCD 15686
Bear Family / May '93 / Rollercoaster /
Direct / CM / Swift / ADA.

**ON BROADWAY (Puente, Tito & His
Latin Ensemble)**
T.P.'s special / Sophisticated lady / Blue-
sette / Soul song / On Broadway / Maria
Cervantes / Jo je ti / First light
CD _____ CCD 4193
Concord Picante / Sep '88 / New Note.

PARE COCHERO
Caney / Nov '95 / ADA / Discovery. CCD 508

PUENTE GOES JAZZ
Whats this thing called love / Tiny-not
Ghengis / What are you doin' honey / Lotus
land / Lucky dog / Birdland after dark /
That's a Puente / Yesterdays / Terry cloth /
Tito'in
CD _____ 7863 66148-2
Bluebird / Apr '93 / BMG.

ROYAL'T
Donna Lee / Tokyo blues / Virgo / Moanin'
/ Stompin' at the Savoy / Enquentro /
Mambo gallego / Second wind / Royal't /
Slam bam
CD _____ CCD 4553
Concord Picante / Jun '93 / New Note.

SALSA MEETS JAZZ
CD _____ CCD 4354
Concord Jazz / Sep '88 / New Note.

SENSATION
Fiesta a la king / Guajira for cal / Round
Midnight / Que sensacion / Jordu / Cantigo
en la distancia / Morning / Spain
CD _____ CCD 4301
Concord Picante / Apr '87 / New Note.

**TITO'S IDEA (Puente, Tito & His Latin
Ensemble)**
Woody 'n' you / Asia mood / I concentrate
on you / Tito's idea / Nica's tempo / Para
el rey / Mambo sentimental / Joy spring /
Yeah / Eight Timbales
CD _____ 66058071
RMM / Aug '95 / New Note.

TOP PERCUSSION/DANCE MANIA
Elequana / Bragada / Obatala yeza /
Alaumba clemencie / Oguere madeo / Ob-
raricosu / Four by two, part 1 / Conga ale-
gre / Ti mon bo / Mambo / Hot timbales / El
cayuco / Complication / Mambo gozon /
Saca tu mujer / Llego mijan / Agua limpia
todo / Cuando te vea / Mi chiquita quiere
bembe / 3-D mambo / Varsity drag / Hong
Kong mambo / Estoy siempre junto a ti
CD _____ BCD 15687
Bear Family / May '93 / Rollercoaster /
Direct / CM / Swift / ADA.

**UN POCO LOCO (Puente, Tito & His
Latin Ensemble)**
Un poco loco / Swinging shepherd blues /
Alma con alma / El timbalon / Chang /
Machito forever / Prelude to a kiss / Killer
Joe / Triton
CD _____ CCD 4329
Concord Picante / Oct '87 / New Note.

YAMBEQUE
Yambeque / Guataca / Suave asi / Esper-
ame / Delisse / Estoy siempre junto a ti /
Plaza stomp / El yoyo / Oye lo que tiene el
mambo / Ricci Ricci / Friquilandia / Arrol-
lando / Cuban mambo / Guaguanco en tropicana / Preparen candela / Mambo en
blues
CD _____ CD 62081
Saludos Amigos / Jan '96 / Target/BMG.

Puerto Rico All Stars

DE REGRESO
De regreso / Tito, el rey / Quien dijo miedo
/ Pensar ser numbero / Boricua hasta la
muerte / Chango ta beni / Despierta boricua
/ Un saludo / Cuban fantasy
CD _____ 66058088
RMM / Feb '96 / New Note.

Pui-Yeun, Lui

MUSIC OF THE PIPA
CD _____ 7559720852
Elektra Nonesuch / Jan '95 / Warner
Music.

Pukwana, Dudu

COSMICS CHAPTER 90
Mra khali / Hamba (go away) / Big apple /
Cosmics / Blues for Nick / Zwelistsha
CD _____ AHUM 005
Ah-Um / Aug '90 / New Note / Cadillac.

**IN THE TOWNSHIPS (Pukwana, Dudu &
Spear)**
Baloyi / Ezialini / Zukude / Sonia / Angel
Nemali / Nobomyu / Sekela khuluma
CD _____ CDEWV 5
Earthworks / '87 / EMI / Sterns.

Pullen, Don

CAPRICORN RISING
CD _____ 1200042
Black Saint / Oct '90 / Harmonia Mundi /
Cadillac.

LIFE LINE (Pullen, Don Quartet)
Great escape, or run John Henry run / Seriously appealing / Soft seas / Nature's children / Protection / Newcomer; seven years
later
CD _____ CDSJP 154
Timeless Jazz / Jan '92 / New Note.

RESOLUTION (Pullen, Don & H. Bluiett)
CD _____ 1200142
Black Saint / Oct '90 / Harmonia Mundi /
Cadillac.

SACRED COMMON GROUND
Eagle staff in first / Common ground / River
song / Reservation blues / Messgae in
smoke / Resting on the road / Reprise / Still
here
CD _____ CDP 8328002
Blue Note / Jan '96 / EMI.

**SIXTH SENSE, THE (Pullen, Don
Quintet)**
CD _____ BSR 0088
Black Saint / '86 / Harmonia Mundi /
Cadillac.

Pulp

DIFFERENT CLASS
Mis-shapes / Pencil skirt / Common people
/ I-spy / Disco 2000 / Live bed show /
Something changed / Sorted for E's and
wizz / F.E.E.L.I.N.G.C.A.L.L.E.D.L.O.V.E. /
Underwear / Monday morning / Bar Italia
CD _____ CID 8041
Island / Oct '95 / PolyGram.

FREAKS
CD _____ FIRECD 5
Fire / Apr '93 / Disc.

HIS 'N' HERS
Joyriders / Lipgloss / Acrylic afternoons / Have you seen her lately / She's a lady / Happy endings / Do you remember the first time / Pink glove / Someone like the moon / David's last summer
CD _____ CID 8025
Island / Apr '94 / PolyGram.

INTRO - THE GIFT RECORDINGS
Space / O.U. (12" Mix) / Babies / Styloroc (Nites of suburbia) / Razzamatazz / Sheffield: Sex city / Inside Susan: A story in 3 songs
CD _____ IMCD 159
Island / Oct '93 / PolyGram.

IT
My lighthouse / Wishful thinking / Joking aside / Boats and trains / Blue girls / Love love / In many ways / Looking for life / Everybody's problem / There was
CD _____ REFIRECD 15
Fire / Nov '94 / Disc.

MASTERS OF THE UNIVERSE
CD _____ FIRECD 36
Fire / Jun '94 / Disc.

SEPARATIONS
CD _____ FIRE 33026
Fire / Oct '91 / Disc.

Pulse

SURFACE TENSIONS
CD _____ HHCD 7
Harthouse / Aug '94 / Disc / Warner Music.

Pulsinger, Patrick

PORNO
CD _____ EFA 122752
Disko B / May '95 / SRD.

Punaruu, Tamarii

KAINA MUSIC TRADITION
CD _____ S 65812
Manuiti / Feb '93 / Harmonia Mundi.

Puncture

PUNCTURE
CD _____ CDVEST 29
Bulletproof / Aug '94 / Pinnacle.

Pungent Stench

BEEN CAUGHT BUTTERING
CD _____ NB 052CD
Nuclear Blast / Jan '92 / Plastic Head.

CLUB MONDO BIZARRE
CD _____ NB 079CD
Nuclear Blast / Mar '94 / Plastic Head.

DIRTY RHYMES AND PYSCOTRONIC
CD _____ NB 078CD
Nuclear Blast / Jun '93 / Plastic Head.

FOR GOD YOUR SOUL
CD _____ 842973
Nuclear Blast / Aug '90 / Plastic Head.

Punishable Act

INFECT
CD _____ NO 2462
Noise/Modern Music / Sep '94 / Pinnacle / Plastic Head.

Punishers

BEAT ME
CD _____ RUMBCD 015
Rumble / Aug '92 / Nervous.

Punishment Of Luxury

LAUGHING ACADEMY
Puppet life / Funk me / Message / All white jack / Obsession / Radar bug/Metropolis /

British baboon / Babalon / Excess bleeding heart / Laughing academy / Secrets / Brain bomb / Engine of excess / Jellyfish
CD _____ DOJOCD 147
Dojo / Sep '93 / BMG.

Pura Fe & Ulali

CAUTION TO THE WIND
CD _____ SHCD 5013
Shanachie / May '95 / Koch / ADA / Greensleeves.

Purdie, Bernard

PURDIE GOOD/SHAFT
Cold sweat / Montego bay / Purdie good / Wasteland / Everybody's talkin' / You turn me on / Shaft / Way back home / Attica / Them changes / Summer melody / Butterfingers
CD _____ CDBGPD 050
BGP / Mar '93 / Pinnacle.

Pure Gold

PURE GOLD
CD _____ MAUCD 635
Mau Mau / Apr '93 / Pinnacle.

YOU LIGHT UP MY LIFE
CD _____ GBCD 001
Pure Gold / Nov '95 / Jetstar.

Puressence

PURESSENCE
Near distance / I suppose / Mr. Brown / Understanding / Fire / Traffic jam in Memory Lane / Casting lazy shadows / You're only trying to twist my arm / Every house on every street / India
CD _____ CID 8046
Island / Jan '96 / PolyGram.

Purim, Flora

BUTTERFLY DREAMS
CD _____ OJCCD 315-2
Original Jazz Classics / Feb '92 / Wellard / Jazz Music / Cadillac / Complete/Pinnacle.

FLIGHT, THE
Aviao (Airplane) / Perfume de cebola (Fragrance of onion) / My song for you / Maca / Branco e preto (White and black) / Meu mestre coracao (Tutor heart) / Rainha da noite (Queen of the night) / Tarde (late afternoon) / Radio experiencia / Dois irmaos / Dona olympia (Mrs Olympia) / Finale
CD _____ BW 048
B&W / Mar '94 / New Note.

LOVE REBORN
CD _____ FCD 6209095
Fantasy / Nov '86 / Pinnacle / Jazz Music / Wellard / Cadillac.

MILESTONE MEMORIES
Moon Dreams / Vera Cruz / Windows / Cravo E Canela / What can I say / Casa Forte / Samba Michel / Open your eyes you can fly / Overture
CD _____ CDBGP 1008
BGP / Mar '93 / Pinnacle.

SPEED OF LIGHT
Secret from the sea / Wings / Portal da cor / Rhythm runner / Light as my flo' / Mojave crossing / O canto da sereira / This world is mine / Overture / Goddess of thunder / What you see / Maiasta (miraculous bird)
CD _____ BW 044
B&W / Mar '95 / New Note.

STORIES TO TELL
CD _____ OJCCD 619-2
Original Jazz Classics / Feb '92 / Wellard / Jazz Music / Cadillac / Complete/Pinnacle.

WELCOME BACK '95
Wings / Portal da cor / Rhythm runner / Light as my flo'
CD _____ BW 5068
B&W / Jan '95 / New Note.

Purim, Yana

BRASILYANAS VOL.1
Luiza / Atraz da porta / Romance de amor / Isto aqui o que e (what is this) / Pra voce (just for you) / Eu e a brisa / Cancao do amanhecer (song of the sunrise) / My foolish heart / O que tinha de ser (what is supposed to be) / Amor, amigo / Sambra da pergunta / Retrado em branco e preto (picture in black and white)
CD _____ BW 043
B&W / May '95 / New Note.

Purna Das Baul

BAULS OF BENGAL
CD _____ CRAW 11
Crammed World / Jan '96 / New Note.

Purnell, Alton

ALTON PURNELL/KEITH SMITH'S CLIMAX JAZZ BAND (Purnell, Alton & Keith Smith)
CD _____ BCD 264
GHB / Aug '95 / Jazz Music.

Purnell, Nick

ONE, TWO, THREE
Helena / See you on the weekend / 1-2-3 / P.S. / Fowler's band / Yes or no / As you / Vinceable / Hi ho / Will I ever
CD _____ AHUM 006
Ah-Um / Feb '91 / New Note / Cadillac.

Purple Helmets

RIDE AGAIN
Brand new Cadillac / I'm crying / Rosalyn / She's not there / First I look at the purse / Get yourself home / Oh pretty woman / Homework / Don't you like what I do / Money / Under the sun / Baby let me take you home / She la la (Only on CD.) / Baby (Only on CD.) / Everything's alright (Only on CD.)
CD _____ 422283
New Rose / Jan '95 / Direct / ADA.

Purple Outside

MYSTERY LANE
CD _____ NAR 052 CD
New Alliance / Sep '90 / Pinnacle.

Purrone, Tony

ELECTRIC POETRY (Purrone, Tony Trio)
Melrose Avenue / Lakewood / Lost and found / Norwegian wood / Hybrid / Checks / Everything happens to me / Mesopotamia
CD _____ BW 028
B&W / Oct '93 / New Note.

Purtenance

MEMBER OF IMMORTAL DAMNATION
CD _____ DL 011CD
Drowned / Jun '93 / Plastic Head.

Pusching, Wolfgang

PIECES OF A DREAM
CD _____ 837322-2
Amadeo / Oct '94 / PolyGram.

Pussy

PUSSY
CD _____ HBG 123/5
Background / Apr '94 / Background.

Pussy Crush

TORMENTING THE EMOTIONALLY FRAIL
Mindless / Postcard / She ain't the one / Kill you / Do it / Beat your heart out / Witch bitch / Ghost of am empty bottle / Irrespectable / Fun, fun, fun / Loop / Come back to me / Grunk / Mainline / That girl / Roof surfing
CD _____ LADIDA 039CD
La-Di-Da / Nov '94 / Vital.

Pussy Galore

CORPSE LOVE
CD _____ HUT 013CD
Hut / Feb '92 / EMI.

HISTORIA DELLA MUSICA-ROCK
CD _____ ROUGHCD 149
Rough Trade / Apr '90 / Pinnacle.

RIGHT NOW
CD _____ PRODCD 19
Product Inc. / Feb '88 / Vital.

Pussycat

STAR PORTRAIT: PUSSYCAT
CD _____ 16028
Laserlight / '93 / Target/BMG.

Pussycat Trash

NON-STOP HIP ACTION
CD _____ SLAMPT 25CD
Slampt Underground / Mar '95 / SRD.

Putrefy Factor 7

TOTAL MIND COLLAPSE
CD _____ EFA 125232
Celtic Circle / Aug '95 / SRD.

Putrid Offal

EXULCERATION
CD _____ CDAB 002
Adipocre / Feb '94 / Plastic Head.

PVC

PVC AFFAIR
CD _____ DIVINE 006CD
Taste / Nov '95 / Plastic Head.

PVH

WHITE
CD _____ CDCB 0201
Carbon Base / Jun '95 / Plastic Head.

Pyewackett

MAN IN THE MOON DRINKS CLARET, THE
CD _____ MW 4007CD
Music & Words / Jan '95 / ADA / Direct.

Pylon

CHAIN
CD _____ SKY 72020CD
Sky / Sep '94 / Koch.

Pylon King

CITIZEN Z COUNTDOWN TO THE CONTINUUM
CD _____ FIRECD 050
Fire / Jul '95 / Disc.

Pyogenesis

SWEET X-RATED NOTHINGS
CD _____ NB 113-2
Nuclear Blast / Oct '94 / Plastic Head.

TWINALEBLEBLOOD
CD _____ NB 136CD
Nuclear Blast / Nov '95 / Plastic Head.

Pyrexia

SERMON OF MOCKERY
CD _____ DC 017
Drowned / Apr '94 / Plastic Head.

Pyrolator

WUNDERLAND
CD _____ EFA 037632
Atatak / Feb '94 / SRD.

Q

Q Squad

PSYCHED
CD _____ NO 2562
Noise/Modern Music / Jul '95 / Pinnacle / Plastic Head.

Q-Tips

LIVE AT LAST (Q-Tips & Paul Young)
CD _____ RPM 102
RPM / Oct '92 / Pinnacle.

Q5

WHEN THE MIRROR CRACKS
CD _____ CDMFN 64
Music For Nations / Dec '87 / Pinnacle.

Qasimov, Alim

MUGHAM OF AZERBAIDJAN, THE
CD _____ C 560013
Ocora / Sep '93 / Harmonia Mundi / ADA.

QFX

FREEDOM
CD _____ EPICD 3
Epidemic / Apr '95 / Grapevine / Mo's Music Machine.

Qntal

QNTAL 3
CD _____ EFA 155912
Gymnastic / Dec '95 / SRD.

Quakes

NEW GENERATION
New generation / How brave are you / Stranded in the streets / Anonymous / Suburbia / Dateless night / Wonderin' / Behind the wheel / It's gone / Your castle / Gothic girl / Now I wanna / Lover's curse
CD _____ NERCD 073
Nervous / Sep '93 / Nervous / Magnum Music Group.

VOICE OF AMERICA
CD _____ NERDCD 058
Nervous / Aug '90 / Nervous / Magnum Music Group.

Quarte, Chris

TEXAS STREET SUGAR STRAT MAGIK
CD _____ ORECD 534
Silvertone / Mar '95 / Pinnacle.

Quarterman, Sir Joe

FREE SOUL
CD _____ CPCD 8079
Charly / Mar '95 / Charly / THE / Cadillac.

Quartette Indigo

QUARTETTE INDIGO
Ragtime dance / Naima / Andromeda / Footprints / Efua / Saturday night on Beale Street / Come Sunday / Ladies blues / Ruby my dear / Lift every voice and sing
CD _____ LCD 15362
Landmark / Mar '94 / New Note.

Quatermass

QUATERMASS
CD _____ REP 4044-WZ
Repertoire / Aug '91 / Pinnacle / Cadillac.

Quatre

EARTHCAKE
CD _____ LBLC 6539
Label Bleu / Jan '92 / New Note.

Quatro, Suzi

ROCK HARD
Rock Hard / Glad all over / Love is ready / State of mind / Woman cry / Lipstick / Hard headed / Ego in the night / Lonely is the hardest / Lay me down / Wish upon me
CD _____ CSAPCD 102
Connoisseur / Jun '90 / Pinnacle.

WILD ONE - GREATEST HITS, THE
Can the can / 48 crash / Daytona demon / Devil gate drive / Too big / Wild one / Your mama won't like me / I bit off more than I could chew / I may be too young / Tear me apart / Roxy roller / If you can't give me love / Race is on / She's in love with you / Ma-ma's boy / I've never been in love / Rollin' stone (CD only.) / All shook up (CD only.) / Keep a knockin' (CD only.) / Wake up little Susie (CD only.)
CD _____ CZ 281
EMI / Apr '90 / EMI.

Quazar

ZODIAC TRAX
Sunflower / Wanderlight / Khedan / Moonflower / Time / Gemini / Arrow / Rhythm dog / Zodiac trax / U.S.A. / Deeper and higher / 110
CD _____ STAR 006CD
Seven Stars / Jun '95 / Vital.

Qubism

QUBISM
CD _____ EMIT 2294
Time Recordings / Sep '94 / Pinnacle.

Que

GOOD LOVE (Que & Ruby Turner)
CD _____ BCQCD 1001
Black Current / Oct '92 / Grapevine.

Quebec, Ike

BLUE AND SENTIMENTAL
Blue and sentimental / Minor impulse / Don't take your love from me / Blues for Charlie / Like / Count every star / That old black magic (CD only.) / It's all right with me (CD only.)
CD _____ CDP 7840982
Blue Note / Mar '95 / EMI.

HEAVY SOUL
Acquitted / Just one more chance / Que's dilemma / Brother can you spare a dime / Man I love / Heavy soul / I want a little girl / Nature boy / Blues for Ike
CD _____ CDP 8320902
Blue Note / May '95 / EMI.

Queen

DAY AT THE RACES, A
Long away / Millionaire waltz / You and I / Somebody to love / White man / Good old fashioned lover boy / Drowse / Teo torriate / Tie your mother down / You take my breath away
CD _____ CDPCSD 131
Parlophone / Sep '93 / EMI.

GAME, THE
Play the game / Dragon attack / Another one bites the dust / Need your loving tonight / Crazy little thing called love / Rock it (prime jive) / Don't try suicide / Sweet sister / Coming soon / Save me
CD _____ CDPCSD 134
Parlophone / Feb '94 / EMI.

GREATEST HITS II
Kind of magic / Under pressure / I want it all / I want to break free / Innuendo / Breakthru' / Who wants to live forever / Headlong / Miracle / I'm going slightly mad / Invisible man / Hammer to fall / Friends will be friends / Show must go on
CD _____ CDPMTV 2
Parlophone / Oct '91 / EMI.

GREATEST HITS VOLS. 1 & 2
Bohemian rhapsody / Another one bites the dust / Killer queen / Fat bottomed girls / Bicycle race / You're my best friend / Don't stop me now / Save me / Crazy little thing called love / Somebody to love / Now I'm here / Good old fashioned lover boy / Play the game / Flash / Seven seas of Rhye / We will rock you / We are the champions / Kind of magic / Under pressure / Radio gaga / I want it all / I want to break free / Innuendo / It's a hard life / Breakthru' / Who wants to live forever / Headlong / Miracle / I'm going slightly mad / Invisible man / Hammer to fall / Friends will be friends / Show must go on / One vision
CD Set _____ CDPCSD 161
Parlophone / Oct '94 / EMI.

GREATEST HITS: QUEEN
Bohemian rhapsody / Another one bites the dust / Killer queen / Fat bottomed girls / Bicycle race / You're my best friend / Don't stop me now / Save me / Crazy little thing called love / Now I'm here / Good old fashioned lover boy / Play the game / Flash / Seven seas of Rhye / We will rock you / We are the champions / Somebody to love
CD _____ CDPCSD 141
Parlophone / Jun '94 / EMI.

HOT SPACE
Staying power / Dancer / Back chat / Body language / Action this day / Put out the fire / Life is real (song for Lennon) / Calling all girls / Las palabras de amor (the words of love) / Cool cat / Under pressure
CD _____ CDPCSD 135
Parlophone / Feb '94 / EMI.

INNUENDO
Innuendo / I'm going slightly mad (edit) (LP only) / I'm going slightly mad (Not on LP) / Headlong / I can't live with you / Ride the wild wind / All God's people / These are the days of our lives / Delilah / Don't try so hard

(edit) (LP only) / Don't try so hard (Not on LP) / Hitman (edit) (LP only) / Hitman (Not on LP) / Bijou (edit) (LP only) / Bijou (Not on LP) / Show must go on
CD _____ CDPCSD 115
Parlophone / Feb '91 / EMI.

INTERVIEW COLLECTION, THE
CD P.Disc _____ CBAK 4957
Baktabak / Feb '94 / Baktabak.

JAZZ
Mustapha / Fat bottomed girls / Jealousy / Bicycle race / If you can't beat them / Let me entertain you / Dead on time / In only seven days / Dreamers ball / Fun it / Leaving home ain't easy / Don't stop me now / More of that jazz
CD _____ CDPCSD 133
Parlophone / Feb '94 / EMI.

KIND OF MAGIC, A
Princes of the universe / Kind of magic / One year of love / Pain is so close to pleasure / Friends will be friends / Who wants to live forever / Gimme the prize / Don't lose your head / One vision / Friends will be friends (2) (CD) / Forever (CD)
CD _____ CDP 7462672
EMI / Jun '88 / EMI.

LIVE AT WEMBLEY '86
One vision / Tie your mother down / In the lap of the Gods / Seven seas of Rhye / Tear it up / Kind of magic / Under pressure / Another one bites the dust / Who wants to live forever / I want to break free / Impromptu / Brighton rock solo / Now I'm here / Love of my life / Is this the world we created / Baby I don't care / Hello Mary Lou / Tutti frutti / Gimme some lovin' / Bohemian rhapsody / Hammer to fall / Crazy little thing called love / Big spender / Radio ga ga / We will rock you / Friends will be friends / We are the champions / God save the Queen
CD Set _____ CDPCSP 7251
Parlophone / Jun '92 / EMI.

LIVE KILLERS
We will rock you / Let me entertain you / Death on two legs / Killer queen / Bicycle race / I'm in love with my car / Get down make love / You're my best friend / Now I'm here / Dreamers ball / Love of my life / '39 / Keep yourself alive / Don't stop me now / Spread your wings / Brighton rock / Bohemian rhapsody / Tie your mother down / Sheer heart attack / We are the champions / God save the Queen
CD _____ CDPCSD 138
Parlophone / Apr '94 / EMI.

LIVE MAGIC
One vision / Tie your mother down / Seven seas of Rhye / Another one bites the dust / I want to break free / Is this the world we created / Bohemian rhapsody / Hammer to fall / Radio ga ga / We will rock you / Friends will be friends / We are the champions / God save the Queen / Kind of magic / Under pressure
CD _____ CDP 746 413 2
Parlophone / Jan '87 / EMI.

MADE IN HEAVEN
It's a beautiful day / Made in Heaven / Let me live / Mother love / My life has been saved / I was born to love you / Heaven for everyone / Too much love will kill you / You don't fool me / Winter's tale
CD _____ CDPCSD 167
Parlophone / Nov '95 / EMI.

MIRACLE, THE
Party / Khashoggi's ship / Miracle / I want it all / Invisible man / Breakthru' / Rain must fall / Scandal / My baby does me / Was it all worth it / Hang on in there (On CD only) / Chinese torture (On CD only)
CD _____ CDPCSD 107
Parlophone / May '89 / EMI.

NEWS OF THE WORLD
We will rock you / We are the champions / Sheer heart attack / All dead all dead / Spread your wings / Fight from the inside / Get down make love / Sleeping on the sidewalk / Who needs you / It's late / My melancholy blues
CD _____ CDPCSD 132
Parlophone / Sep '93 / EMI.

NIGHT AT THE OPERA, A
Death on two legs / Lazing on a Sunday afternoon / I'm in love with my car / Sweet lady / Seaside rendezvous / Good company / '39 / Prophet's song / Love of my life / Bohemian rhapsody / God save the Queen
CD _____ CDPCSD 130
Parlophone / Jul '93 / EMI.

PHOTO SESSION
CD Set _____ QU 2
UFO / Nov '92 / Pinnacle.

QUEEN
Keep yourself alive / Doing alright / Great King Rat / My fairy King / Liar / Night comes

down / Modern times rock 'n' roll / Son and daughter / Jesus / Seven seas of Rhye
CD _____ CDPCSD 139
Parlophone / Apr '94 / EMI.

QUEEN II
Procession / Father to son / White Queen (as it began) / Some day one day / Loser in the end / Ogre battle / Fairy feller's masterstroke / Nevermore / March of the black Queen / Funny how love is / Seven seas of Rhye
CD _____ CDPCSD 140
Parlophone / Apr '94 / EMI.

QUEEN: INTERVIEW COMPACT DISC
CD P.Disc _____ CBAK 4022
Baktabak / Nov '89 / Baktabak.

SHEER HEART ATTACK
Brighton rock / Tenement funster / Flick of the wrist / Lily of the valley / Now I'm here / In the lap of the gods / Stone cold crazy / Bring back that Leroy Brown / She makes me (stormtrooper in stilettos) / In the lap of the gods...revisited / Killer queen / Dear friends / Misfire
CD _____ CDPCSD 129
Parlophone / Jul '93 / EMI.

ULTIMATE QUEEN (18 CDs - from Queen to Made In Heaven)
CD Set _____ QUEENBOX 20
Parlophone / Nov '95 / EMI.

WORKS, THE
Radio ga ga / Tear it up / It's a hard life / Man on the prowl / Machines (or Back to humans) / I want to break free / Keep passing the open windows / Hammer to fall / Is this the world we created
CD _____ CDPCSD 136
Parlophone / Feb '94 / EMI.

Queen, B.B.

IN THE MOOD (FOR SOMETHING GOOD)
I'm in the mood (for something good) / Now love me / Blueshouse (Radio mix) / Try to find me back / No time to hesitate / We gonna rock this house / Love you nights / I wanna be next to you / Soultrain / Hey B.B. be careful out there in the jungle / Blueshouse ballad
CD _____ CDEMC 3591
EMI / May '91 / EMI.

Queen Elizabeth

QUEEN ELIZABETH
CD _____ ESPCD 2
Echo / Nov '94 / Pinnacle. EMI.

Queen Ida

CAUGHT IN THE ACT (Queen Ida & Her Zydeco Band)
CD _____ GNPD 2181
GNP Crescendo / '88 / Silva Screen.

COOKIN' WITH QUEEN IDA
Zydeco / Gator man / C'est moi / Love is the answer / La bas two step / 1-10 express / Dancing on the bayou / Ranger's waltz / Hard headed woman / Lady be mine
CD _____ GNPD 2197
GNP Crescendo / Sep '95 / Silva Screen.

MARDI GRAS
Comment ca va / Oh, what can you do / Home on the bayou / Since you been gone / Louisiana / Where are you now / Mardi Gras / Object of my affection / Cajun cookin' / Mr. Fine / Papa on the fiddle / Molina / New kid on the bayou / I can see clearly now
CD _____ GNPD 2227
GNP Crescendo / Sep '95 / Silva Screen.

ON A SATURDAY NIGHT (Queen Ida & The Bon Temps Zydeco Band)
Capitaine Gumbo / La Louisiane / Le Mazuka / Grand Basile / P'tit fille o'paradis / Bran back that Leroy Brown / La femme du doight / Vieux Paris / On a Saturday night / Bonjour tristesse / Creole de lake Charles / Celimene / Mal d'amour / Chere duloone / My tu tu / Hey negress / Jolie Blon / Cotton eyed Joe
CD _____ 600256
GNP Crescendo / Jun '91 / Silva Screen.

QUEEN IDA & THE BON TEMPS BAND ON TOUR (Queen Ida & The Bon Temps Zydeco Band)
CD _____ GNPD 2147
GNP Crescendo / '88 / Silva Screen.

Queen Latifah

BLACK REIGN
CD _____ 5302722
Motown / Jan '94 / PolyGram.

NATURE OF A SISTA
Latifah's had it up 2 here / Nuff of the ruff stuff / One mo time / Give your love to me

/ Love again / Bad as a mutha / Fly girl / Sexy fancy / Nature of a sista / That's the way we flow / If you don't know / How do I love thee
CD _____ GEECD 8
Gee Street / Sep '91 / PolyGram.

Queen Majeeda

CONSCIOUS
CD _____ HBCD 90
Heartbeat / Jun '93 / Greensleeves / Jetstar / Direct / ADA.

Queen Sylvia

MIDNIGHT BABY
I'm hurtin' / Life and troubles / New York bound / Baby, What do I do / Midnight baby / Party / Can't get along / Why wonder / You treat me so mean / I love you
CD _____ ECD 260572
Evidence / Sep '94 / Harmonia Mundi / ADA / Cadillac.

Queen's College Choir

ORGAN OF QUEEN'S COLLEGE, OXFORD, THE (Queen's College Choir, Oxford)
CD _____ CDCA 925
Alpha / '91 / Abbey Recording.

Queen's Royal Lancers

INTO HISTORY (16th/5th Queen's Royal Lancers)
CD _____ BNA 5082
Bandleader / Aug '93 / Conifer.

Queen's Royal Scots...

QUEEN'S ROYAL SCOTS PIPERS, THE (Queen's Royal Scots Pipers)
CD _____ EUCD 1312
ARC / Jul '95 / ARC Music / ADA.

Queensryche

EMPIRE
Best I can / Thin line / Jet city woman / Della Brown / Another rainy night / Empire / Re-sistgance / Silent lucidity / Hand on heart / One and only / Anybody listening
CD _____ COMTL 1058
EMI Manhattan / Sep '90 / EMI.

PROMISED LAND
9.28 a.m. / I am I / Damaged / Out of mind / Bridge / Promised land / Disconnected / Lady Jane / My global mind / One more time / Someone else
CD _____ CDMTL 1081
EMI Manhattan / Oct '94 / EMI.

RAGE FOR ORDER
Walk in the shadows / I dream in infrared / Whisper / Gonna get close to you / Killing words / Surgical strike / Neue regal / Chemical youth (We are rebellion) / London / Screaming in digital / I will remember
CD _____ CDAML 3105
EMI Manhattan / Aug '91 / EMI.

WARNING, THE
Warning / En force / Deliverance / No sanc-tuary / NM 156 / Take hold of the flame / Before the storm / Child of fire / Roads to madness
CD _____ CDP 7465572
EMI Manhattan / Feb '87 / EMI.

Queers

BEAT OFF
CD _____ LOOKOUT 81CD
Lookout / Jul '95 / SRD.

GROW UP
CD _____ LOOKOUT 009CD
Lookout / Jul '95 / SRD.

LOVE SONGS
CD _____ LOOKOUT 66CD
Lookout / Jul '95 / SRD.

MOVE BACK HOME
CD _____ LOOKOUT 114CD
Lookout / Jul '95 / SRD.

Quench

SEQUENCHAL
CD _____ INFECT 20CD
Infectious / Nov '94 / Disc.

Quest

LIVE AT THE MONTMARTRE
CD _____ STCD 4121

Storyville / Feb '90 / Jazz Music / Wellard / CM / Cadillac.

NATURAL SELECTION
As always / Natural selection / Nocturnal / Amethyst suite / Fahamivu / Michiyo / Moody time / Nighty-nite
CD _____ ECD 220822
Evidence / Feb '94 / Harmonia Mundi / ADA / Cadillac.

OF ONE MIND
CD _____ CMPCD 047
CMP / '95 / Vital/SAM.

QUEST
CD _____ STCD 4158
Storyville / Feb '90 / Jazz Music / Wellard / CM / Cadillac.

Quest

DO YOU BELIEVE
CD _____ NTHEN 5
Now & Then / Sep '95 / Plastic Head.

Question Mark

96 TEARS (Question Mark & The Mysterians)
CD _____ RE 137CD
Reach Out International / Nov '94 / Jetstar.

Quick Change

CIRCUS OF DEATH
Will you die / Show no mercy / Sea witch / Circus of death / Injected / What's next / Sludge / A.T.L. / Leave it to the beaver / Battle your fear / Death games / Plowed
CD _____ RR 95032
Roadrunner / Feb '89 / Pinnacle.

Quicksand

MANIC COMPRESSION
Backward / Delusional / Divorce / Simpleton / Skinny (it's overflowing) / Thorn in my side / Landmine spring / Blister / Brown gargan-tuan / East 3rd Street / Supergenius / It would be cooler if you did
CD _____ CIRD 1005
Island Red / Apr '95 / PolyGram / Vital.

Quicksilver Messenger...

ANTHOLOGY (Quicksilver Messenger Service)
Pride of man / Dino's song / Fool / Bears / Mona / Edward, the mad shirt grinder / Three or four feet from home / Fresh air / Just for love / Spindrifter / Local color / What about me / Don't cry my lady love / Hope / Fire brothers / I found love
CD _____ BGOCD 270
Beat Goes On / Mar '95 / Pinnacle.

COMIN' THRU (Quicksilver Messenger Service)
Doin' time in the USA / Chicken / Changes / California state correctional facility blues / Forty days / Mojo / Don't lose it
CD _____ BGOCD 88
Beat Goes On / Jul '91 / Pinnacle.

HAPPY TRAILS (Quicksilver Messenger Service)
Who do you love (part one) / When you love / Where you love / How do you love / Which do you love / Who do you love (part two) / Mona / Maiden of the cancer moon / Cal-vary / Happy trails
CD _____ BGOCD 151
Beat Goes On / Sep '92 / Pinnacle.

JUST FOR YOU (Quicksilver Messenger Service)
CD _____ BGOCD 141
Beat Goes On / Jun '92 / Pinnacle.

QUICKSILVER (Quicksilver Messenger Service)
CD _____ BGOCD 217
Beat Goes On / Jan '94 / Pinnacle.

QUICKSILVER MESSENGER SERVICE (Quicksilver Messenger Service)
Pride of man / Light your windows / Dino's song / Gold and silver / It's been too long / Fool
CD _____ EDCD 200
Edsel / May '92 / Pinnacle / ADA.

SHADY GROVE (Quicksilver Messenger Service)
Shady grove / Flute song / Three or four feet from home / Too far / Holy moly / Joseph's coat / Flashing lonesome / Words can't say / Edward, the mad shirt grinder
CD _____ EDCD 208
Edsel / Sep '90 / Pinnacle / ADA.

SOLID SILVER (Quicksilver Messenger Service)
CD _____ EDCD 376
Edsel / Aug '93 / Pinnacle / ADA.

ULTIMATE JOURNEY (Quicksilver Messenger Service)
Who do you love / Pride of man / Codine / Dino's song / Gold and silver / Joseph's coat / Shady grove / Fresh air / Too far / Stand by me / What about me / Mona
CD _____ SEECD 61
See For Miles/C5 / Apr '93 / Pinnacle.

WHAT ABOUT ME (Quicksilver Messenger Service)
CD _____ BGOCD 58
Beat Goes On / Oct '90 / Pinnacle.

Quiet Boys

BOSH
Righteous / Take four / Deeper / Blue 4 royal T / Inner sense / Prayer mat / Boshin' around / Conguero wronguero / Ghetto life / Never change / Love will find a way / Astral space
CD _____ JAZIDCD 121
Acid Jazz / Apr '95 / Pinnacle.

CAN'T HOLD THE VIBE
Inside your mind / Let it go / Give it all u got / Make me say it again girl / Roaring fast / Long way from me / Sim ting / Att etude / Modal / Can't hold the vibe / Mellow blow
CD _____ JAZIDCD 045
Acid Jazz / Mar '92 / Pinnacle.

Quiet Elegance

YOU GOT MY MIND MESSED UP
After you / Mama said / Do you love me / Something you got / I'm afraid of losing you / You brought the sun back into my life / I need love / Tired of being alone / Will you be my man (in the morning) / You got my mind messed up / Your love is strange / Roots of love / Love will make you feel bet-ter / Have you been making out OK / Set the record straight / How's your love life baby
CD _____ HIUKCD 109
Hi / Dec '89 / Pinnacle.

Quiet Riot

CONDITION CRITICAL
Sign of the times / Mama weer all crazee now / Party all night / Stomp your hands, clap your feet / Winners take all / Condition critical / Scream and shout / Red alert / Bad boy / Born to rock
CD _____ 4678342
Epic / Sep '94 / Sony.

RANDY RHOADS YEARS, THE
Trouble / Laughing gas / Afterglow of your love / Killer girls / Picking up the pieces / Last call for rock 'n' roll / Breaking up is a heartache / Force of habit / It's not so funny / Look in any window
CD _____ 8122714452
Atlantic / Feb '94 / Warner Music.

Quigg, Stephen

VOICE OF MY ISLAND
Steal away / Gallant Murray / Voice of my island / Almost every circumstance / Strong women rule us with their fears / Freewheel-ing now / Work o' the weavers / Come by the hills / Whatever you say say nothing / Annie McKelvie / Willie's gane tae Melville Castle / Last leviathan
CD _____ CDTRAX 066
Greentrax / Jul '93 / Conifer / Duncans / ADA / Direct.

Quinichette, Paul

KID FROM DENVER, THE
CD _____ BCD 136
Biograph / Aug '95 / Wellard / ADA / Hot Shot / Jazz Music / Cadillac / Direct.

Quinn

QUINN
Crown of life / Sacred revelation / In a per-fect world / Prophecy / These four walls / In reverie / Autonomous / All alone / Lotus / Lavender moonlight / Red sky / Bardo thodol
CD _____ SR 4001
PLR / Jun '95 / Pinnacle.

Quinn, Brendan

MELODIES AND MEDLEYS
My lady from Glenfarne / Lovely leitrim / My lovely rose of Clare / My heart skips a beat

/ Turn out the lights and love me tonight / Some broken hearts never mend / I recall a gypsy woman / Dublin in the rare old times / Any tipperary town / Among the Wicklow hills / He'll have to go / I won't forget you / I love you because
CD _____ RITZRCD 515
Ritz / Apr '92 / Pinnacle.

Quinn, Freddy

1956-1965
Sie hiess Mary Ann / Heimweh / Bel sante / Cigarettes and whisky / Junge kommen bald wieder / So geht das jede nacht / Don't forbid me / At the hop / Stood up / Lone-some star / Heimatlos / Ein armer mulero / Ich bin bald wieder hier / Die gitarre und das meer / Unter fremden sternen / Guitar play-ing Joe / La guitarra Brasiliana / Der boss ist nicht hier / Ein schiff voll whiskey / You, you, you / Blue mirage / I'll hold you in my heart / By the way / Spanish eyes
CD _____ BCD 15403
Bear Family / Jul '87 / Rollercoaster / Direct / CM / Swift / ADA.

Quinn, Jackie

DON'T FORCE THE RIVER
Deep water / Reconcile / Love rain / Miracle / Love will break the chains / Instincts / Free / Love or lose / Nothing matters / Trigonon / Mother / Ultimate love (song) / Trigon my life
CD _____ DIXCD 105
10 / Jun '91 / EMI.

Quinn, Paul

PHANTOMS AND THE ARCHETYPES (Quinn, Paul & The Independent Group)
Phantoms and the Archetypes / Born on the wrong side of town / What can you do to me now / Should've known by now / Punk Rock Hotel / Superstar / Call my name / Damage Is Done / Darling I Can't Fight / Hangin' On
CD _____ DUBH 921CD
Postcard / Sep '92 / Vital.

WILL I EVER BE INSIDE OF YOU (Quinn, Paul & The Independent Group)
Will I ever be inside of you / Have you been seen / Lover that's you all over / Moorereffloc (misty thought) / Passing thought / Outre / Misty blue / Stupid thing / At the end of the night
CD _____ DUBH 945CD
Postcard / Oct '94 / Vital.

Quintessence

SELF/INDWELLER
Cosmic surfer / Wonders of the universe / Hari om / Vishnu narain / Hallelujah / Celes-trial procession / Self / Freedom / Water Goddess / Jesus is my life / Butterfly / It's all the same / Indweller / Portable realm / Holy roller / On the other side of the wall / Dedication / Bliss trip / Mother of the universe
CD _____ DOCD 1982
Drop Out / May '95 / Pinnacle.

Quintetto Vocale Italiano

FREEDOM JAZZ DANCE
CD _____ 121247-2
Soul Note / Nov '92 / Harmonia Mundi / Wellard / Cadillac.

Quireboys

BITTER SWEET AND TWISTED
Tramps and thieves / Can't get through / Ain't love blind / King of New York / White trash blues / Sweet little girl / Wild wild wild / Take no revenge / Can't park here / Ode to you (baby just walk) / Hates to please / Last time
CD _____ CDFA 3307
Fame / Nov '94 / EMI.

FROM TOOTING TO BARKING
CD _____ ESSCD 222
Essential / Sep '94 / Total/BMG.

MINI CD
CD _____ SURCD 014
Survival / Sep '91 / Pinnacle.

Quorthon

QUORTHON
CD _____ BMCD 6669
Black Mark / May '94 / Plastic Head.

R

R. Cajun

NO KNOWN CURE (R. Cajun & The Zydeco Brothers)
CD _____ BCAT 03CD
Bearcat / Jun '93 / Direct / ADA.

THAT CAJUN THING (R. Cajun & The Zydeco Brothers)
CD _____ BCAT 05CD
Bearcat / Aug '94 / Direct / ADA.

R. Kelly

12 PLAY
CD _____ CHIP 144
Jive / Nov '94 / BMG.

BORN INTO THE 90'S (R. Kelly & Public Announcement)
CD _____ CHIP 123
Jive / Feb '92 / BMG.

R. KELLY
CD _____ CHIP 166
Jive / Dec '95 / BMG.

R.A.C.

DIVERSIONS
CD _____ WARPCD 22
Warp / Apr '94 / Disc.

R.A.F.

ODE TO A TRACTOR
Pork / Stay where you are / Freezing dessert / Land of the dead and dying / Suburb of hell / Head of a monk / Ode to a tractor / Buchlain in Australia / Chant / Konkret
CD _____ DEMCD 030
Day Eight Music / Jun '93 / New Note.

R.E.M.

AUTOMATIC FOR THE PEOPLE
Drive / Try not to breathe / Sidewinder sleeps tonite / Everybody hurts / New Orleans Instrumental No.1 / Sweetness follows / Monty got a raw deal / Ignoreland / Star me kitten / Man on the moon / Nightswimming / Find the river
CD _____ 9362450552
WEA / Sep '92 / Warner Music.

BEST OF R.E.M., THE
Carnival of sorts / Radio free Europe / Perfect circle / Talk about the passion / So. Central rain / (Don't go back to) Rockville / Pretty persuasion / Green grow the rushes / Can't get there from here / Driver 8 / Fall on me / I believe / Cuyahoga / One I love / Finest worksong / It's the end of the world as we know it (and I feel fine)
CD _____ DMIRH 1
MCA / Aug '91 / BMG.

BIRTH OF A MONSTER - INTERVIEW
CD _____ VP 001
RPM / Oct '94 / Pinnacle.

DEAD LETTER OFFICE
Crazy / There she goes again / Burning down / Voice of Harold / Burning hell / White Tornado / Toys in the attic / Windout / Ages of you / Pale blue eyes / Rotary ten / Bandwagon / Femme fatale / Walter's theme / King of the road / Wolves, lower (CD only) / Gardening at night (CD only) / Carnival of sorts (boxcars) (CD only) / 1,000,000 (CD only) / Stumble (CD only)
CD _____ CDMID 195
A&M / '94 / PolyGram.

DOCUMENT
Finest worksong / Welcome to the occupation / Exhuming McCarthy / Disturbance at the Heron House / Strange / It's the end of the world as we know it (and I feel fine) / One I love / Fireplace / Lightnin' Hopkins / King of birds / Oddfellows local 151
CD _____ IRLD 19144
MCA / Oct '92 / BMG.

EPONYMOUS
Gardening at night / So. Central rain / Driver 8 / Fall on me / Finest worksong / Talk about the passion / Can't get there from here / Romance / One I love / It's the end of the world as we know it (and I feel fine) / Radio free Europe / (Don't go back to) Rockville
CD _____ DMIRG 1038
MCA / Aug '92 / BMG.

FABLES OF THE RECONSTRUCTION
Feeling gravity's pull / Maps and legends / Driver 8 / Life and how to live it / Old man Kensey / Can't get there from here / Green grow the rushes / Kohoutek / Auctioneer (another engine) / Good advice / Wendell Gee
CD _____ IRLD 19016
MCA / Apr '92 / BMG.

GREEN
Pop song '89 / Get up / You are the everything / Stand / World leader pretend / Wrong child / Orange crush / Turn you inside out / Hairshirt / I remember California / Untitled
CD _____ 9257952
WEA / Nov '88 / Warner Music.

LIFE'S RICH PAGEANT
Begin the begin / These days / Fall on me / Cuyahoga / Hyena / Underneath the bunker / Flowers of Guatemala / I believe / What if we give it away / Just a touch / Swan swan H / Superman
CD _____ IRLD 19080
MCA / Nov '92 / BMG.

MONSTER
What's the frequency, Kenneth / Crush with eyeliner / King of comedy / I don't sleep, I dream / Star 69 / Strange currencies / Tongue / Bang and blame / I took your name / Let me in / Circus envy / You
CD Set _____ 936245763-2
WEA / Oct '94 / Warner Music.
CD _____ 936245740-2
WEA / Sep '94 / Warner Music.

MURMUR
Radio free Europe / Pilgrimage / Laughing / Talk about the Passion / Moral kiosk / Perfect circle / Catapult / Sitting still / 9-9 / Shaking through / We walk / West of the fields
CD _____ CDMID 129
A&M / Oct '92 / PolyGram.

OUT OF TIME
Radio song / Losing my religion / Low / Near wild Heaven / Endgame / Shiny happy people / Belong / Half a world away / Texarkana / Country feedback / Me in honey
CD _____ 7599264962
WEA / Mar '91 / Warner Music.

RECKONING
Harborcoat / Seven Chinese brothers / So. central rain (I'm sorry) / Pretty persuasion / Time after time / Second guessing / Letter never sent / Camera / (Don't go back to) Rockville / Little America
CD _____ CDMID 194
A&M / Oct '94 / PolyGram.

SHINY CHATTY PEOPLE (Interview disc)
CD P.Disc _____ CBAK 4041
Baktabak / Jan '92 / Baktabak.

SURPRISE YOUR PIG (A Tribute To R.E.M.) (Various Artists)
CD _____ SG 001
Plastic Head / Jul '92 / Plastic Head.

R.I.C.

DISTANCE
CD _____ EFA 006554
Mille Plateau / Sep '94 / SRD.

R.N.C. Chapel Choir

20 FAVOURITE HYMNS
Lead us heavenly father, lead us / All people that on earth do dwell / Immortal love for ever full / When I survey the wondrous cross / Ye holy angels bright / Alleluia, sing to Jesus / Christ is made the sure foundation / There is a green hill far away / Just as I am / Love divine, all love excelling / O God, our help in ages past / Guide me O thou great redeemer / O worship the king / Holy holy holy / Lord enthroned in heavenly splendour / Eternal father strong to save / Praise to the holiest / Now thank we all our God / Dear lord and father of mankind / Day thou gavest Lord is ended
CD _____ CDMVP 826
SCS Music / Apr '94 / Conifer.

R.N.C. Wind Orchestra

EDWARD GREGSON WIND MUSIC (R.N.C. Wind Orchestra/Manchester Boys Choir)
Celebration / Metamorphoses / Missa brevis pacem / Sword and the crown / Festivo
CD _____ DOYCD 043
Doyen / Sep '95 / Conifer.

GALLIMANFRY
Illyrian dances / S.P.Q.R. / Suite Francaise / Mockbeggar variations / Deo gracias / Full fathom five / Galliman
CD _____ DOYCD 042
Doyen / Sep '95 / Conifer.

R.O.C.

Desert wind / Excised / God willing / Hey you chick / Balloon / Real time / Plastic Jesus / I want you I need you I miss you / Gold bug / La heredia / 13 Summers / Hey Nicky / Sylvia's thighs / Ascension / Clouds
CD _____ SETCD 022
Setanta / Jan '96 / Vital.

Rabbitt, Eddie

ALL TIME GREATEST HITS
CD _____ 7599264672
Elektra / Jan '96 / Warner Music.

Rabin, Oscar

TWO IN LOVE
No souvenirs / I understand / Moonlight avenue / I'd know you anywhere / I ain't got nobody / Deep in the heart of Texas / Angeline / At the woodchopper's ball / Bluebirds in the moonlight / I fall in love whit you every day / My wubba dolly / Starlight serenade / Predigree on pomander walk / Daddy / Down Argentina way / My sisters and I / Two in love / Sweet madness / Who's taking you home tonight
CD _____ RAJCD 871
Empress / Oct '95 / THE.

Race, Hugo

EARLS WORLD (Race, Hugo & The True Spirit)
CD _____ NORMAL 125CD
Normal/Okra / May '94 / Direct / ADA.

RUE MORGUE BLUES (Race, Hugo & The True Spirit)
CD _____ NORMAL 118CD
Normal/Okra / May '94 / Direct / ADA.

SECOND REVELATOR (Race, Hugo & The True Spirit)
CD _____ NORMAL 135
Normal/Okra / May '94 / Direct / ADA.

SPIRITUAL THIRST (Race, Hugo & The True Spirit)
CD _____ NORMAL 155
Normal/Okra / May '94 / Direct / ADA.

Racer X

SECOND HEAT
CD _____ RR 349601
Roadrunner / Dec '87 / Pinnacle.

Rachell, Yank

CHICAGO STYLE
CD _____ DD 649
Delmark / Nov '93 / Hot Shot / ADA / CM / Direct / Cadillac.

Rachels

HANDWRITING
CD _____ QS 30CD
Quarter Stick / May '95 / SRD.

Racing Cars

BBC LIVE IN CONCERT - RACING CARS
CD _____ WINCD 015
Windsong / Apr '92 / Pinnacle.

Radakka

MALICE OF TRANQUILITY
CD _____ CM 77111CD
Century Media / Jan '96 / Plastic Head.

Radcliff, Bobby

THERE'S A COLD GRAVE IN YOUR WAY
CD _____ BT 1110CD
Black Top / Nov '94 / CM / Direct / ADA.

Radha Krishna Temple

RADHA KRISHNA TEMPLE
Govinda / Sri Guruvastak / Bhaja Bhakata/ Arotrika / Hare Krsna mantra / Sri Isopanisad / Bhaja Hure Mana / Govinda Jai Jai / Prayer to the spiritual masters
CD _____ CDP 7812552
Apple / Mar '93 / EMI.

Radial Blend

ABANDON TIME
CD _____ SOHO 19CD
Suburbs of Hell / Jan '95 / Pinnacle / Plastic Head / Kudos.

ENOUGH ROADS
CD _____ SOH 021CD
Suburbs of Hell / Jul '95 / Pinnacle / Plastic Head / Kudos.

Radial Spangle

ICE CREAM HEADACHE
CD _____ MINTCD 8
Mint Tea / Jun '93 / Disc.

SYRUP MACRANE
Syrup macrane
CD _____ BBQCD 163

Beggars Banquet / Aug '94 / Warner Music / Disc.

Radiators

COCKLES AND MUSSELS (The Best Of The Radiators)
Television screen / Love detective / Sunday world / Prison bars / Party line / Roxy girl / Enemies / Try and stop me / Million dollar hero / Let's talk about the weather / Johnny Jukebox / Confidential / They're looting in the town / Who are the strangers / Kitty Ricketts / Ballad of the faithful departed / Walking home alone again / Dead the beast, dead the poison / Stranger than fiction / Dancing years / Under Cleary's clock / Chinese poem / Rogue trooper (live mix) / Plura Belle
CD _____ CDWIKS 156
Chiswick / Oct '95 / Pinnacle.

Radical Dance Faction

BORDERLINE CASES
Surplus people / Borderline / Four chuck chant / Riverwise / Sorepoint for a sickman / Back in the same place / Hot on the wire / Firepower
CD _____ EZ1 CD
Earthzone / Jul '94 / SRD.

RAGGAMUFFIN STATEMENT
CD _____ CD 4DS 4A
Inna State / May '95 / SRD.

Radical Retard

ONCE I WOKE UP
CD _____ C 6201CD
R / Mar '94 / Plastic Head.

Radio Big Band

SPECIAL EDITION
Chicago / Auf wiedersehen sweetheart / I remember Clifford / Body and soul / For you, for me, for evermore / Broadway / Easy living / Oh I do like to be beside the seaside / Imagination / Big band treasure chest
CD _____ RBB 002
Radio Big Band / Feb '95 / New Note.

Radio Four

THERE'S GONNA BE JOY
Earnest prayer / If you miss me from praying / How much I owe / Building a home / I feel the spirit / Road's rocky / There's gonna be joy / That's all I need / Road's rough and rocky / How about you / When he calls / Whisper to Jesus / I received my blessings / One more river / What's he done for me / Walk around my bedside / Jesus never left me alone / What kind of man Jesus is / In my father's house / Believe every word he says / On my journey now / One day / Heaven is my goal / Jesus is my friend
CD _____ CDCHD 448
Ace / Jun '93 / Pinnacle / Cadillac / Complete/Pinnacle.

Radio Massacre...

FROZEN NORTH (2CD Set) (Radio Massacre International)
CD _____ CENCD 012
Centaur / Nov '95 / Complete/Pinnacle.

Radio Moscow

GET A NEW LIFE
CD _____ RMCD 104
Status / May '93 / PolyGram.

Radio Stars

SOMEWHERE (THERE'S A PLACE FOR US)
CD _____ CDWIKD 107
Chiswick / May '92 / Pinnacle.

Radio Waves

RADIO WAVES
CD _____ RSNCD 32
Rising High / Apr '95 / Disc.

Radiohead

BENDS, THE
Planet Telex / Bends / High and dry / Fake plastic trees / Bones / Nice dream / Just / My iron lung / Bullet proof... I wish I was / Black star / Sulk / Street spirit (fade out)
CD _____ CDPCS 7372
Parlophone / Mar '95 / EMI.

PABLO HONEY
You / Creep / How do you / Stop whispering / Thinking about you / Anyone can play guitar / Ripcord / Vegetable / Prove yourself / I can't / Lurgee / Blow out
CD _____ CDPCS 7360
Parlophone / Mar '93 / EMI.

Radium Cats

OTHER WORLDS
Martian hop / Six foot down / Freak / Mygirl isIike uranium / Idol with the golden head / Great shakin' fever / Return of the mystery train / Well I knocked (bim bam) / Strange, baby strange / Eraserhead / Let it rot / Zuvembi stroll / Pink hearse / Surfin' D.O.A.
CD _____ NERCD 068
Nervous / May '92 / Nervous / Magnum Music Group.

Radu, Dinu

ROMANTIC PAN PIPES (Radu, Dinu & G.S.O.)
I have a dream / Strawberry fields forever / Dark side of the moon / Scarborough fair / Sailing / Unchained melody / Amazing grace / If you leave me now / Something / Feelings / Here comes the sun / Sara / Yesterday / MacArthur park / Bird of paradise / House of the rising sun / Don't cry for me Argentina / Banks of the Ohio / Autumn dream / Let it be
CD _____ CD 6002
It's Music / Nov '95 / Total/BMG.

Rae, Dashiell

SONG WITHOUT WORDS
CD _____ NAGE 4CD
Art Of Landscape / Feb '86 / Sony.

Rae, John

OPUS DE JAZZ VOL.2
Potlicker blues / Ah-leu-cha / Roll on down / Back yard blues / By my side / Parker's mood / Beat and blue
CD _____ SV 0179
Savoy Jazz / Aug '93 / Conifer / ADA.

Raeburn, Boyd

1944-1945: MORE BOYD RAEBURN (Raeburn, Boyd Orchestra)
CD _____ CCD 113
Circle / Mar '95 / Jazz Music / Swift / Wellard.

1944: BOYD RAEBURN
CD _____ CCD 22
Circle / Mar '95 / Jazz Music / Swift / Wellard.

BOYD MEETS STRAVINSKY
Night in Tunisia / March of the Boyd / Summertime / You got me crying again / Boyd's nest / Blue prelude / Temptation / Dalvatore Sally / Boyd meets Stravinsky / I only have eyes for you / Over the rainbow / Body and soul / Blues echoes
CD _____ SV 0185
Savoy Jazz / Oct '92 / Conifer / ADA.

JEWELLS
Tonsilectomy / Forgetful / Rip Van Winkle / Yerxa / Temptation / Dalvatore Sally / Boyd meets Stravinsky / I only have eyes for you / Over the rainbow / Body and soul / Blue echoes / Little Boyd blue / Hep Boyd's / Man with a horn / Prelude to the dawn / Duck waddle / Love tales / Soft and warm / Lady is a tramp / How high the moon / Trouble is a man / St. Louis blues / It never entered my mind / Wait till you see her / It can't be wrong / When love comes
CD _____ SVOCD 273
Savoy Jazz / Nov '95 / Conifer / ADA.

JUBILEE PERFORMANCES 1946 (Raeburn, Boyd & His Orchestra)
Tonsillectomy / Rip Van Winkle / Caravan / How deep is the ocean / Boyd meets Stravinsky / Dalvatore Sally / Night in Tunisia / Hep boyds
CD _____ HEPCD 1
Hep / Oct '95 / Cadillac / Jazz Music / New Note / Wellard.

TRANSCRIPTION PERFORMANCES 1946
Boyd's nest / Blue prelude / High tide / Picnic in the wintertime / Are you livin' old man / Tush / Concerto for Duke / Where you at / Out of this world / Boyd meets Stravinsky / Personality / Dalvatore Sally / Blue echoes / I only have eyes for you / Two spoos in an igloo / Temptation / I can't believe that you're in love with me / I don't know why / More than you know / Amnesia / Cartaphilius / Night in Tunisia / I cover the waterfront / Foolish little boy
CD _____ HEPCD 42
Hep / Nov '93 / Cadillac / Jazz Music / New Note / Wellard.

Raekwon The Chef

ONLY BUILT FOR HUMANS
CD _____ 07863666632
RCA / Jul '95 / BMG.

Rafferty, Gerry

CITY TO CITY
Ark / Baker Street / Right down the line / City to city / Sealin' time / Mattie's rag / Whatever's written in your heart / Home and dry / Island / Waiting for the day
CD _____ CDFA 3119
Fame / Jul '89 / EMI.

EARLY COLLECTION
Look over the hill and far away / Patrick / Rick rack / Her father didn't like me anyway / Please sing a song for us / Blood and glory / Coconut tree / Steam boat row / Shoe shine boy / All the best people do it / Song for Simon / Keep it to yourself / Can I have my money back / New street blues / Didn't I / Don't count me out / Make you break you / To each and everyone / Mary Skeffington / Half a chance / Where I belong
CD _____ TRACD 601
Transatlantic / Jul '87 / BMG / Pinnacle / ADA.

NIGHT OWL
Days gone down / Night owl / Way that you do it / Why won't you talk to me / Get it right now / Take the money and run / Family tree / Already gone / Tourist / It's gonna be a long night
CD _____ CDFA 3147
Fame / Jul '89 / EMI.

ON A WING AND A PRAYER
Time's caught up on you / I see red / It's easy to talk / I could be wrong / Don't speak of my heart / Get out of my life woman / Don't give up on me / Hang on / Love and affection / Does he know what he's taken on / Light of love / Life goes on
CD _____ 517495-2
A&M / Feb '93 / PolyGram.

ONE MORE DREAM
CD _____ 5292792
PolyGram TV / Oct '95 / PolyGram.

OVER MY HEAD
CD _____ 5235992
A&M / Jul '95 / PolyGram.

RIGHT DOWN THE LINE (The Best Of Gerry Rafferty)
Baker Street / Whatever's written in your heart / Bring it all home / Right down the line / Get it right next time / Way that you do it (CD only.) / Tired of talking (CD only.) / Garden of England (CD only.) / Sleepwalking (CD only.) / Night owl / As wise as a serpent (CD only.) / Dangerous age / Family tree / Shipyard town / Right moment / Look at the moon (Not on CD.)
CD _____ CDUAG 330333
United Artists / Oct '89 / EMI.

TRANSATLANTIC YEARS, THE
CD _____ CCSCD 428
Castle / Mar '95 / BMG.

Rage

BEYOND THE WALL
CD _____ NO 2023
Noise/Modern Music / Nov '92 / Pinnacle / Plastic Head.

MISSING LINK
CD _____ NO 2172
Noise/Modern Music / Aug '93 / Pinnacle / Plastic Head.

TEN YEARS IN RAGE
CD _____ N 0291-2
Noise/Modern Music / Sep '94 / Pinnacle / Plastic Head.

Rage

SAVIOUR
CD _____ PULSECD 9
Pulse 8 / Mar '93 / Pinnacle / 3MV.

Rage Against The Machine

RAGE AGAINST THE MACHINE
Bombtrack / Killing in the name / Take the power back / Settle for nothing / Bullet in the head / Know your enemy / Wake up / Fistful of steel / Township rebellion / Freedom
CD _____ EPC 472224 2
Epic / Mar '93 / Sony.

Ragga Twins

FREEDOM TRAIN
CD _____ SUADCD 006
Shut Up & Dance / Feb '93 / SRD.

REGGAE OWES ME MONEY
CD _____ SUADCD 002
Shut Up & Dance / Mar '91 / SRD.

RINSIN' LYRICS
Money / Zodiac / Return / Street life / One thing / Love a marriage / Lock up / Freedom train / L.I.F.E. / Gun / Mash it up
CD _____ CDTIVA 1009
Positiva / Oct '95 / EMI.

Raging Slab

DYNAMITE MONSTER BOOGIE CONCERT
Anywhere but here / Weatherman / Pearly / So help me / What have you done / Take a hold / Laughin' and cryin' / Don't worry about the bomb / Lynne / Lord have mercy / National dust / Ain't ugly non
CD _____ 74321287592
American / Jun '95 / BMG.

Ragnarok

RAGNAROK
CD _____ SRS 3613CD
Silence / Jul '95 / ADA.

Ragtime Millionaires

MAKING A MILLION
National seven / B flattened by the blues / Dark road blues / Snowy morning blues / Stone cold sober / Buckets of rain / Making a million / Rivers of beer / Corine Corina / Diddy wah diddy / Everywhere I go / Hi-heel sneakers / Warm summer rain / Old man's bike / Things we do / Highway robbery / Over the river / Ragtime millionaire / Where does all the money go
CD _____ FECD 095
Fellside / Jan '94 / Target/BMG / Direct / ADA.

Rah Band

BEST OF THE RAH BAND, THE
CD _____ MCCD 217
Music Club / Oct '95 / Disc / THE / CM.

Raices, Grupo

QUE VIVA LA SALSA
Se va el caiman / Asi eres tu / Dejala que se vays / Que viva la salsa / Mentiras tuyas / Cancion para ti / No me provoques / Guaguanco pa' la calle
CD _____ 6605080
RMM / Nov '95 / New Note.

Railroad Jerk

ONE TRACK MIND
Gun problem / Bang the drum / Pollerkoaster / Riverboat / What did you expect / Home = hang / Forty minutes / Ballad of Railroad Jerk / Big white lady / Help yourself / Zero blues / Some girls waved / You better go now
CD _____ OLE 127-2
Matador / Mar '95 / Vital.

Railway Children

LISTEN ON (The Best Of The Railway Children)
Every beat of the heart / Everybody / Give it away / Music stop / What she wants / Something so good / Hours go by / After the rain / You're young / Collide / Somewhere south / Listen on / Over and over / Gentle sound / Monica's light / So right / In the meantime
CD _____ CDOVD 451
Virgin / Feb '95 / EMI.

Rain, Billy

SALAD DAYS
CD _____ 450996189-2
Oval 2 / Oct '94 / Warner Music.

Rain Parade

EMERGENCY THIRD RAIL POWER TRIP/ EXPLOSIONS IN THE GLASS ...
CD _____ MAUCD 611
Mau Mau / Apr '92 / Pinnacle.

Rainbow

BEST OF RAINBOW, THE (2CD Set)
All night long / Man on the silver mountain / Can't happen here / Lost in Hollywood / Since you've been gone / Stargazer / Catch the rainbow / Kill the king / Sixteenth century greensleeves / I surrender / Long live rock 'n' roll / Eyes of the world / Starstruck / Light in the black / Mistreated
CD Set _____ 800 074-2
Polydor / '83 / PolyGram.

DIFFICULT TO CURE
I surrender / Spotlight kid / No release / Magic / Vielleicht das nachster zeit (Maybe next time.) / Can't happen here / Freedom fighter / Midtown tunnel vision / Difficult to cure
CD _____ 800 018 2
Polydor / Aug '84 / PolyGram.

DOWN TO EARTH
All night long / Eyes of the world / No time to lose / Making love / Since you've been gone / Love's no friend / Danger zone / Lost in Hollywood
CD _____ 823 705-2
Polydor / Dec '86 / PolyGram.

FINYL VINYL (2CD Set)
Spotlight kid / I surrender / Miss Mistreated / Jealous lover / Can't happen here / Tearin' out my heart / Since you've been gone / Bad girl / Difficult to cure / Stone cold / Power / Long live rock 'n' roll / Weiss heim / Man on the silver mountain
CD Set _____ 827 987-2
Polydor / Feb '86 / PolyGram.

LIVE IN GERMANY 1976 (2CD Set)
Kill the king / Mistreated / Sixteenth century greensleeves / Catch the rainbow / Man on the silver mountain / Stargazer / Still I'm sad / Do you close your eyes
CD _____ DPVSOPCD 155
Connoisseur / Oct '90 / Pinnacle.

Long Live Rock 'N' Roll

LONG LIVE ROCK 'N' ROLL
Long live rock 'n' roll / Lady of the lake / L.A. connection / Gates of Babylon / Sensitive to light / Kill the King / Shed / Rainbow eyes
CD _____ 8250902
Polydor / Jan '93 / PolyGram.

ON STAGE
Kill the king / Man on the silver mountain / Blues / Starstruck / Catch the Rainbow / Mistreated / Sixteenth century Greensleeves / Still I'm sad
CD _____ 823 656-2
Polydor / Nov '86 / PolyGram.

RAINBOW FAMILY TREE, THE (Various Artists)
CD _____ VSOPCD 195
Connoisseur / Apr '94 / Pinnacle.

RAINBOW RISING
Tarot woman / Run with the wolf / Starstruck / Do you close your eyes / Stargazer / Light in the black
CD _____ 823 655-2
Polydor / Nov '86 / PolyGram.

RITCHIE BLACKMORE'S RAINBOW
Man on the silver mountain / Self portrait / Black sheep of the family / Catch the rainbow / Snake charmer / Temple of the king / If you don't like rock'n'roll / Sixteenth century greensleeves / Still I'm sad
CD _____ 8250902
Polydor / Jan '93 / PolyGram.

STRAIGHT BETWEEN THE EYES
Death Alley driver / Stone cold / Bring on the night / Tite squeeze / Tearin' out my heart / Power / Miss Mistreated / Rock fever / Eyes on fire
CD _____ 521709-2
Polydor / Apr '94 / PolyGram.

STRANGER IN US ALL
Wolf to the moon / Cold hearted woman / Hunting humans (insatiable) / Stand and fight / Ariel / Too late for tears / Black masquerade / Silence / Hall of the mountain king / Still I'm sad
CD _____ 74321303372
Arista / Sep '95 / BMG.

Rainbow, Tucker

PUSH ME TO WAR
CD _____ ARICD 094
Ariwa Sounds / Dec '94 / Jetstar / SRD.

Raincoats

MOVING
No-one's little girl / Ooh ooh la la la / Dance of hopping mad / Balloon / Mouth of a story / I saw a hill / Overheard / Rainstorm / Body / Animal rhapsody
CD _____ R 3062
Rough Trade / Feb '94 / Pinnacle.

ODY SHAPE
Shouting out loud / Family treat / Only loved at night / Dancing in my head / Ody shape / And then it's O.K. / Baby song / Red shoes / Go away
CD _____ R 3042
Rough Trade / Jan '94 / Pinnacle.

RAINCOATS, THE
Fairytale in the supermarket / No side to fall in / Adventures close to home / Off duty trip / Lola / Void / Life on the line / You're a million / In love / No looking
CD _____ R 3022
Rough Trade / Sep '93 / Pinnacle.

Raindance

RAINDANCE
CD _____ 5298622
PolyGram TV / Dec '95 / PolyGram.

Raindrops

COMPLETE RAINDROPS, THE
What a guy / Hanky panky / I won't cry / It's so wonderful / Da doo ron ron / When the boy's happy (the girl's happy too) / Kind of boy you can't forget / Isn't that love / Every little beat / Even though you can't dance / That boy's messin' up my mind / Not too young to get married / That boy John / Book of love / Let's go together / You got what I like / One more tear / Another boy like mine / Don't let go / Do wah diddy diddy / More than a man / Talk about me / Can't hide the hurtin'
CD _____ NEMCD 713
Sequel / Nov '94 / BMG.

Rainer & Das Combo

BAREFOOT ROCK
CD _____ FIEND 756
Demon / Oct '94 / Pinnacle / ADA.

NOCTURNES
CD _____ GRCD 363
Glitterhouse / Jun '95 / Direct / ADA.

POWDERKEG
CD _____ TEX 1
Demon / Jul '93 / Pinnacle / ADA.

TEXAS TAPES, THE
Power of delight / One man crusade / It's a matter of taste / Merciful God / (Making the)

trains (run on time) / What's wrong romeo / Powder keg / Mush mind blues / Drive drive drive / Another man / That's how things get done / I am a sinner
CD _____ FIENDCD 734
Demon / Jun '93 / Pinnacle / ADA.

Rainey, Ma

MA RAINEY
Jealous hearted blues / See see rider blues / Jelly bean blues / Countin' the blues / Slave to the blues / Chain gang blues / Bessemer bound blues / Wringin' and twistin' blues / Mountain Jack blues / Trust no man / Morning hour blues / Ma Rainey's black bottom / New boweavil blues / Black cat - Hoot owl blues / Hear me / Talking to you / Prove it on me blues / Victim of the blues / Sleep talking blues / Blame it on the blues / Daddy - Goodbye blues / Sweet rough man / Black eye blues / Leavin' this morning / Runaway blues
CD _____ MCD 47021
Milestone / Jan '93 / Jazz Music / Pinnacle / Wellard / Cadillac.

MA RAINEY'S BLACK BOTTOM (Rainey, Gertrude 'Ma')
Ma rainey's black bottom / Don't fish in my sea / Booze and blues / Farewell Daddy blues / Oh papa blues / Blues oh blues / Shave 'em dry / Lucky rock blues / Screetch owl blues / Georgia cake walk / Sleep talking blues / Yonder come the blues
CD _____ YAZCD 1071
Yazoo / Apr '91 / CM / ADA / Roots / Koch.

PARAMOUNT SESSIONS #1 (Rainey, Gertrude 'Ma')
CD _____ HCD 12001
Black Swan / Oct '92 / Jazz Music.

PARAMOUNT SESSIONS #5
CD _____ HCD 12005
Black Swan / May '95 / Jazz Music.

Rainwater, Marvin

CLASSIC MARVIN RAINWATER (4CD Set)
I gotta go get my baby / Baby's glad you came home / Albino pink-eyed stallion / Sticks and stones / Tea bag Romeo / Tennessee houn' dog yodel / Dem low down blues / Where do we go from here / Hot and cold / Mr. Blues / Get off the stool / What am I supposed to do / I feel like leaving town (sometimes) / Why did you have to go and leave me / Gonna find me a bluebird / Because I'm a dreamer #2 / So you think you've got troubles / Look for me (I'll be waiting for you) / Wayward angel / My brand of blues / My love is real / Lucky star / Majesty of love / You my darling you / Whole lotta woman (undubbed version) / Whole lotta woman / That's the way I feel / Baby don't go / Two fools in love / Because I'm a dreamer / Down in the cellar / Crazy love / Moanin' the blues / Gamblin' man / I dig you baby / Dance me daddy / Nothin' needs nothin' (like I need you) / Need for love (there's always) / No good runaround / Late for love (don't be) / Last time / Can I count on your love / Let me live again / Lonely island / Born to be lonesome / Love me baby (like there's no tomorrow) / That's when I'll stop loving you / Song of new love / Half breed / Valley of the moon / Young girls / Pale faced Indian (lament of the Cherokee) / Hard luck blues / She's gone / Yesterday's kisses / You're not happy / I can't forget / Boo hoo / Tough top cat / Honky tonk in your heart (There's a) / Hey good lookin' / Do it now / It wasn't enough / That little house / Part time love / That aching heart / Love's prison / Bad girl / I saw your new love today / My old home town / Branded / Sing the girls a song / Indian burial / Black sheep / Troubles my little boy had / Sorrow brings a good man down / I want your heart / Talk to me / Run for your life boy / Old gang's gone / Cold woman / Oklahoma hills / Wedding rings / I love my country / Burning bridges / Black Jack McClain / Heart's hall of fame / Hit and run lover / Korea's mountain northland / Tainted gold / Don't tell my boy (in prison living a lie) / Don't try to change your little woman / Do you want to know / Engineer's song (the boy and the engineer) / Freight train blues / Key / Let's go on a picnic / Moment's of love / So long / Teardrops / Wanderer in me / What you got, you don't want / Would your mother be proud of you / You can't keep a secret
CD Set _____ BCD 15600
Bear Family / Nov '93 / Rollercoaster / Direct / CM / Swift / ADA.

ROCKIN' ROLLIN' RAINWATER
Hot and cold / Mr. Blues / Get off the stool / There's a honky tonk in your heart / My brand of blues / Whole lotta woman / That's the way I feel / Baby don't go / Down in the cellar / Crazy love / Moanin' the blues / Gamblin' man / I dig you baby / Dance me Daddy / (There's always) A need for love / Don't be Late for love / Last time / Love me baby (like there's no tomorrow) / Valley of the moon / Young girls / Hard luck blues / I can't forget / Boo hoo / Tough top cat / Oklahoma Hills / Henryetta, Oklahoma
CD _____ BCDAH 15182

Bear Family / Jun '94 / Rollercoaster / Direct / CM / Swift / ADA.

WHOLE LOTTA WOMAN
I dig you baby / Whole lotta woman / Baby don't go / Moanin' the blues / Crazy love / Mr. Blues / Hot and cold / Get off the stool / Down in the cellar / That's the way I feel / Dance me Daddy / Love me baby (Like there's no tomorrow) / (There's always) A need for love / (Dont' be late) For love / Last time / Young girls / Boo hoo / Tough top cat / (There's a) Honky tonk in your heart / I can't forget / Gamblin' man (Roving gambler) / My brand of blues / Valley of the moon / Hard luck blues / Oklahoma hills / Henryetta, Oklahoma / Oklahoma
CD _____ BCD 15812-AH
Bear Family / Jul '94 / Rollercoaster / Direct / CM / Swift / ADA.

Raised Fist

YOUR NOT LIKE ME
CD _____ BHR 017
Burning Heart / Feb '95 / Plastic Head.

Raitt, Bonnie

COLLECTION: BONNIE RAITT
Finest lovin' man / Women be wise / Love me like a man / I feel the same / Angel from Montgomery / My first night alone without you / Louise / Runaway / Wild for you baby / True love is hard to find / Give it up or let me go / Under the falling sky / Love has no pride / Guilty / What is success / Sugar mama / About to make me leave home / Glow / Willya wontcha / No way to treat a lady
CD _____ 7599262422
WEA / Sep '90 / Warner Music.

GIVE IT UP
Give it up or let me go / Nothing seems to matter / I know / If you gotta make a fool of somebody / Love me like a man / Stayed too long at the fair / Under the falling sky / You got to know how / You told me baby / Love has no pride
CD _____ 759927642
WEA / Feb '93 / Warner Music.

GLOW, THE
I thank you / Your good thing / Standin' by the same old love / Sleep's dark and silent gate / Glow / Bye bye baby / Boy can't help it / Best old friend / You're gonna get what's comin' / Wild for you baby
CD _____ 7599274032
WEA / Jun '94 / Warner Music.

HOME PLATE
What do you want the boy to do / Good enough / Run like a thief / Fool yourself / My first night alone without you / Walk out the front door / Sugar mama / Pleasin' each other / I'm blown away / Your sweet and shiny eyes
CD _____ 7599272922
WEA / Jun '94 / Warner Music.

LONGING IN THEIR HEARTS
Love sneakin' up on you / Longing in their hearts / You / Cool clear water / Circle dance / I sho do / Dimming of the day / Feeling of falling / Steal your heart away / Storm warning / Hell to pay / Shadow of doubt
CD _____ CDEST 2227
Capitol / Apr '94 / EMI.

LUCK OF THE DRAW
Something to talk about / Good man, good woman / I can't make you love me / Tangled and dark / Come to me / No business / One part be my lover / Not the only one / Papa come quick (Jody and Chico) / Slow ride / Luck of the draw / All at once
CD _____ CDEST 2145
Capitol / Jun '91 / EMI.

NICK OF TIME
Nick of time / Thing called love / Love letters / Cry on my shoulder / Real man / Nobody's girl / Have a heart / Too soon to tell / I will not be denied / I ain't gonna let you break my heart again / Road's my middle name
CD _____ CDEST 2095
Capitol / Apr '89 / EMI.

ROAD TESTED
Thing called love / Something to talk about / Never make your move too soon / Shake a little / Matters of the heart / Love me like a man / Kokomo medley / My opening farewell / Dimming of the day / Longing in their hearts / Love sneakin' up on you / Burning down the house / I can't make you love me / I believe I'm in love with you / Rock steady / Angel from Montgomery
CD _____ CDEST 2274
Capitol / Nov '95 / EMI.

STREETLIGHTS
That song about the midway / Rainy day man / Angel from Montgomery / I got plenty / Street lights / What is success / Ain't nobody home / Everything that touches you / Got you on my mind / You gotta be ready for love (if you wanna be)
CD _____ 927286 2
WEA / '89 / Warner Music.

TAKIN' MY TIME
You've been in love too long / I gave my love a candle / Let me in / Everybody's

cryin' mercy / Cry like a rainstorm / Wah she go do / I feel the same / I thought I was a child / Write me a few of your lines / Kokomo blues / Guilty
CD _____ 7599272752
WEA / Feb '94 / Warner Music.

Raja-Nee

HOT AND READY
Quick / Turn it up / Taunted / Walking away with it / Who's been givin' it up / Sex in a jeep / Hot and ready / Give it to me / Take your time / Dance hall druglord / I wanna get next to you / Bitchism
CD _____ 5490142
Perspective / Feb '95 / PolyGram.

Rakasha Mancham

PHYIDAR
CD _____ EEE 013CD
Musica Maxima Magnetica / Sep '93 / Plastic Head.

Rake's Progress

ALTITUDE
CD _____ ALMOCD 003
Almo Sounds / Oct '95 / Pinnacle.

CHEESE FOOD PROSTITUTE
CD _____ ALMOCD 001
Almo Sounds / May '95 / Pinnacle.

Rakha, Ustad Alla

TABLA DUET (Rakha, Usted Alla & Zakir Hussain)
CD _____ MR 1001
Moment / Apr '95 / ADA / Koch.

Rakotozafy

MADAGASIKARA 4 (Valihala Malazi - Historical Recordings From The 1960's)
Salama 'nareo tompoko o / Ramanjareo / O zaza ny fandeha diasa / Botofetsy / Tonga teto lala / Hitako o / Mandrosoa lahy mahaeva / Isa, roa, telo / Rey lahy, rey lahy / Varavaranakely / Sega vaovao valiha malaza / Mandihiza raha manan' eratra / Iadiavan janako aho rafozako / Ny fitiavana raho vao miaraka / Miasa tsara raha manambady (CD only) / Tangalamena (CD only) / Lekatseka (CD only) / Samy faly (CD only) / Fisaorana (CD only)
CD _____ CDORBD 029
Globestyle / Jul '95 / Pinnacle.

Raksha Mancham

CHOS KHOR
CD _____ EEE 17
Musica Maxima Magnetica / Aug '94 / Plastic Head.

Ramani, Dr. N.

MUSIC IN THE RAGAS...
CD _____ NI 5257
Nimbus / Sep '94 / Nimbus.

Ramases

SPACE HYMNS
CD _____ REP 4108-WP
Repertoire / Aug '91 / Pinnacle / Cadillac.

Ramazzotti, Eros

MUSICA E
CD _____ 259174
Arista / Aug '95 / BMG.

TUTTE STORIE
Cose della vita / A mezza via / Un altra te / Memorie / In compagnia / Un grosso no / Favola / Non c'e piu fantasia / Nostalgong / Niente di male / Esodi / L'ulti ma rivoluzione / Silver e missile
CD _____ 74321 14329-2
Arista / Jan '94 / BMG.

Ramblers Dance Band

HIT SOUND OF THE RAMBLERS DANCE BAND
CD _____ FLTRCD 526
Timbuktu / Oct '95 / Pinnacle.

Ramirez, Humberto

ASPECTS
Aspects / Chapter 27 / Rumbero siempre / At peace / El ministro / Amanda / Golden view / Camino azul / Touch of beauty
CD _____ 66058039
RMM / Mar '94 / New Note.

PORTRAIT OF A STRANGER
El principe / Sanjuanero / Cuando estoy contigo (madrigal) / Catalina / Sonando con puerto rico / Un tipo con suerte / Ball players / My funny valentine / To the king / Portrait of a stranger / Cristina / Atmospheres
CD _____ 66058091
Tropi / Feb '96 / New Note.

Ramirez, Louie

OTRA NOCHE CALIENTE (Ramirez, Louie & Ray De La Paz)

Otra noche caliente / El / Suddenly / Definitivamente / Soy feliz / Yo soy la rumba / Medley: Noche caliente hits
CD _____ 66058008
RMM / Sep '93 / New Note.

Ramleh

BE CAREFUL WHAT YOU WISH FOR
CD _____ SFTRI 397CD
Sympathy For The Record Industry / Jan '96 / Plastic Head.

HOMELESS
CD _____ FRR 006
Freek / Jul '94 / SRD.

Ramlosa Kvallar

NIGHTS WITH NO FRAMES
CD _____ RESCD 507
Resource / Oct '93 / ADA.

Ramones

ACID EATERS
Journey to the centre of the mind / Substitute / Out of time / Shape of things to come / When I was young / Seven and seven is / My back pages / Can't seem to make you mine / Have you ever seen the rain / I can't control myself / Surf city
CD _____ CDCHR 6052
Chrysalis / Nov '93 / EMI.

ADIOS AMIGOS
I don't want to grow up / Making monsters for my friends / It's not for me to know / Crusher / Life's a gas / Take the pain away / I love you / Cretin family / Have a nice day / Scattergun / Got a lot to say / She talks to rainbows / Born to die in Berlin
CD _____ CDCHR 6104
Chrysalis / Jun '95 / EMI.

ALL THE STUFF (AND MORE) #1 (2CD Set)
Blitzkrieg bop / Beat on the brat / Judy is a punk / Now I wanna sniff some glue / Don't go down the basement / Loudmouth / Havana affair / 53rd and 3rd / I don't wanna walk around with you / I wanna be sedated / Glad to see you go / I remember you / Sheena is a punk rocker / Pinhead / Swallow my pride / California sun / I wanna be your boyfriend / You're gonna kill that girl / Babysitter / Listen to my heart / Let's dance / Today your love, tomorrow the world / I can't be / Gimme gimme shock treatment / Oh oh I love her so / Suzy is a headbanger / Now I wanna be a good boy / What's your game / Commando / Chainsaw / You should never have opened that door / California sun (live)
CD _____ 759926204
Sire / Aug '90 / Warner Music.

BRAIN DRAIN
I believe in miracles / Punishment fits the crime / Pet Sematary / Merry Christmas / Learn to listen / Zero zero UFO / All screwed up / Can't get you outta my mind / Ignorance is bliss
CD _____ CCD 1725
Chrysalis / Jul '89 / EMI.

END OF THE CENTURY
Do you remember rock 'n' roll radio / I'm affected / Danny says / Chinese rocks / Return of Jackie and Judy / Let's go baby / Baby I love you / I can't make it on time / This ain't Havanna
CD _____ E59927429-2
Sire / Mar '94 / Warner Music.

HALFWAY TO SANITY
Wanna live / Bop 'till you drop / Garden of serenity / Weasel face / Go lil' Camaro go / I know better now / Death of me / I lost my mind / Real cool time / I'm not Jesus / Bye bye baby / Worm man
CD _____ BEGA 89 CD
Beggars Banquet / Dec '87 / Warner Music / Disc.

IT'S ALIVE
Rockaway beach / Teenage labotomy / Blitzkrieg bop / I wanna be well / Glad to see you go / Gimme gimme shock treatment / You're gonna kill that girl / I can't care / Sheena is a punk rocker / Havana affair / Commando / Here today, gone tomorrow / Surfin' bird / Cretin hop / Listen to my heart / California sun / I don't wanna walk around with you / Pinhead / Suzy is a headbanger / Let's dance / Oh oh I lover her so / Now I wanna sniff some glue / We're a happy family
CD _____ 9362460452
Sire / Jan '96 / Warner Music.

LOCO LIVES (2CD Set)
Good, the bad, the ugly / Durango 95 / Teenage labotomy / Psychotherapy / Blitzkreig bop / Rock 'n' roll radio / I believe in miracles / Gimme gimme shock treatment / I wanna hold my high school / I wanna be sedated / KKK took my baby away / I wanna live / Bonzo goes to Bitberg / Too touch to die / Sheena is a punk rocker / Rockaway beach / Pet sematary / Don't bust my chops / Palisades park / Mama's boy / Animal boy / War hog / Surfin' bird / Cretin hop / Cretin family / Psycho therapy / Commando / Someday put something in my drink

552

/ Beat on the brat / Judy is a punk / Chinese
rocks / Love kills / Ignorance is bliss
CD _____ CCD 1901
Chrysalis / Oct '91 / EMI.

PLEASANT DREAMS
We want the airwaves / All's quiet on the
eastern front / KKK took my baby away /
Don't go / You sound like you're sick / It's
not my place / She's a sensation / 7-11 /
You didn't mean anything to me / Come on
now / This business is killing me / Sitting in
my room
CD _____ 759923571-2
Sire / Mar '94 / Warner Music.

RAMONES MANIA (2CD Set)
I wanna be sedated / Teenage lobotomy /
Do you remember rock 'n' roll radio /
Gimme gimme shock treatment / Beat on
the brat / Sheena is a punk rocker / I wanna
live / Pinhead / Blitzkrieg bop / Cretin hop /
Rockaway beach / Commando / I wanna be
your boyfriend / Mama's boy / Bop 'till you
drop / We're a happy family / Bonzo goes
to Bitburg / Outsider / Psychotherapy / Wart
hog / Animal boy / Needles and pins / Howling at the moon (sha la la) / Somebody put
something in my drink / We want the airwaves / Chinese rocks / I just want to have
something to do / KKK took my baby away /
Indian giver / Rock 'n' roll high school
CD _____ 925709 2
Sire / Jun '88 / Warner Music.

SUBTERRANEAN JUNGLE
Little bit of soul / I need your love / Outsider
/ What'd ya do / Highest trails above /
Somebody like mo / Psychotherapy / Time
has come today / My kind of a girl / In the
park / Time bomb / Everytime I eat
vegetables...
CD _____ 759923800-2
Sire / Mar '94 / Warner Music.

Ramos, Kid

TWO HANDS, ONE HEART
CD _____ BM 9031
Black Magic / Jul '95 / Hot Shot / Swift /
CM / Direct / Cadillac / ADA.

Rampage

PRIORITY 1
CD _____ ALMOCD 005
Almo Sounds / Nov '95 / Pinnacle.

Rampling, Danny

IN THE MIX
CD Set _____ DRCD 1
Metropole / Nov '95 / 3MV.

Rampolokeng, Lesego

**END BEGINNINGS (Rampolokeng,
Lesego & Kalahari Surfers)**
CD _____ LRSCD 1
ReR Megacorp / Jul '93 / These / ReR
Megacorp.

Ramsey, Bill

SOUVENIRS
Wumba tumba schokoladeneisverkaufer /
Casa bambu / Erwar vom Konstantinopoli-
tanischen / Gesangverein / Cecilia / Mach
keinen heck meck / Go man go / Souvenirs
/ Hier konn matrosen vor anker gehn / Te-
lefon aus Paris / Gina, Gina / Jeden tag 'ne
andre party / Die welt ist rund / Pigalle (die
groue musikaffär) / Das is hinfäll / Das
mädchen mit dem aufregenden gang /
Zuckerpuppe (aus der Bauchtanz truppe) /
Mach ein foto davon / Weit weg von hier /
Missouri cowboy / Yes, fanny, ich tu das /
So ein strudl in tirol / Nichts gegen die wei-
ber / Got a call from Paris / Rockin' moun-
tain / Gina Gina / Pigalle / Telefon fra Paris
CD _____ BCD 15672
Bear Family / Jun '92 / Rollercoaster / Direct
/ CM / Swift / ADA.

Ramsey, Bill

**WHEN I SEE YOU (Ramsey, Bill & Toots
Thielemans)**
CD _____ BLR 84 022
L&R / May '91 / New Note.

Ramsey, Jack

FULL COURT PRESS
CD _____ ISS 004CD
SST / Sep '94 / Plastic Head.

Ramshackle

DEPTHOLOGY
CD _____ BLRCD 30
Big Life / Nov '95 / Pinnacle.

Ramzy, Hossam °

BALADI PLUS
CD _____ EUCD 1083
ARC / '91 / ARC Music / ADA.

**BEST OF ABDUL HALIM HAFIZ (Ramzy,
Hossam & His Egyptian Ensemble)**
CD _____ EUCD 1195
ARC / Apr '92 / ARC Music / ADA.

**BEST OF OM KOLTHOUM (Ramzy,
Hossam & His Egyptian Ensemble)**
CD _____ EUCD 1194
ARC / Apr '92 / ARC Music / ADA.

**EGYPTIAN RAI (Ramzy, Hossam &
Ensemble)**
CD _____ EUCD 1132
ARC / '91 / ARC Music / ADA.

EL SULTAAN
CD _____ EUCD 1122
ARC / '91 / ARC Music / ADA.

ESHTA
CD _____ EUCD 1121
ARC / '91 / ARC Music / ADA.

**INTRODUCTION TO EGPTIAN DANCE
RHYTHMS**
CD _____ EUCD 1081
ARC / '91 / ARC Music / ADA.

KOUHAIL
CD _____ EUCD 1120
ARC / '91 / ARC Music / ADA.

**LATIN AMERICAN HITS FOR
BELLYDANCE**
CD _____ EUCD 1259
ARC / Mar '94 / ARC Music / ADA.

RHYTHMS OF THE NILE
CD _____ EUCD 1104
ARC / '91 / ARC Music / ADA.

**RO-HE - CLASSICAL EGPTIAN
BELLYDANCE**
CD _____ EUCD 1082
ARC / '91 / ARC Music / ADA.

SAMYA, BEST OF FARID AL ATRASH
CD _____ EUCD 1232
ARC / Nov '93 / ARC Music / ADA.

SOURCE OF FIRE
CD _____ EUCD 1305
ARC / Jul '95 / ARC Music / ADA.

**ZEINA, BEST OF MOHAMMED ABDUL
WAHAB**
CD _____ EUCD 1231
ARC / Nov '93 / ARC Music / ADA.

Ranaldo, Lee

FROM HERE TO INFINITY
CD _____ SST 113 CD
SST / May '93 / Plastic Head.

Ranch Romance

BLUE BLAZES
Heartaches / What's wrong with you / Blue
blazes / Indeed I do / Arizona moon / Racin'
/ Burnin' bridges / Buckaroo / Lost heart /
Cuttin' a rug / Trouble / Baby doll / Lucky
one
CD _____ FIENDCD 709
Demon / Dec '91 / Pinnacle / ADA.

FLIP CITY
CD _____ SH 3813CD
Sugarhill / Jan '94 / Roots / CM / ADA /
Direct.

WESTERN DREAM
When the bloom is on the sage / Lovesick
blues / Baby's on the town / St. Louis blues
/ Cowboys and indians / St. James Avenue
/ Gotta lot of rhythm in my soul / Ain't no
ash will burn / Why don't you love me (Like
you used to) / Birmingham fling / Last one
to know / Western dream
CD _____ SHCD 3799
Sugarhill / '92 / Roots / CM / ADA / Direct.

Rancho Diablo

CHICKEN WORLD
CD _____ THIRTEENCD 1
13th Hour / Feb '95 / Disc.

Rancid

LET'S GO
CD _____ E 864342
Epitaph / Jan '95 / Plastic Head /
Pinnacle.

RANCID
CD _____ E 064282
Epitaph / Jun '93 / Plastic Head /
Pinnacle.

Rancid Hell Spawn

AXE HERO
CD _____ STUNCH 6
Wrench / Sep '93 / SRD.

Randall, Jon

WHAT YOU DON'T KNOW
This heart / If blue tears were silver / I came
straight to you / If I hadn't reached for the
stars / To pieces / Tennessee blues / What
if you don't know / Only game in town /
They're gonna miss when I'm gone / Just
like you
CD _____ 74321272972
RCA / Mar '95 / BMG.

Randles, Philip

HEAR MY SONG
CD _____ CDTS 040
Maestro / Nov '93 / Savoy.

ORGAN DANCE BONANZA
CD _____ CDTS 052
Maestro / Dec '95 / Savoy.

PARTY DANCE BONANZA
CD _____ CDTS 055
Maestro / Dec '95 / Savoy.

Randolph, Boots

YAKETY SAX
Percolator / Yakety sax (mono) / Hey Elvis
/ Difficult / I'm getting the message baby /
Little big horn / Big daddy / Blue guitar /
Greenback dollar / Sweet talk / Red light /
La golondrina / Temptation / Battle of New
Orleans / Sleepwalk / After you've gone /
Little big horn (2) / Sleep / So rare / Teach
me tonight / Happy whistler / Estrelita / Big
daddy (2) / Bongo band / Yakety sax
(stereo) / Hey Elvis (2)
CD _____ BCD 15459
Bear Family / Apr '89 / Rollercoaster / Direct
/ CM / Swift / ADA.

Random Damage

RANDOM DAMAGE
CD _____ M 7014CD
Mascot / Oct '95 / Vital.

Random Killing

RANDOM KILLING
CD _____ BMCD 078
Black Mark / Nov '95 / Plastic Head.

THOUGHTS OF AGGRESSION
CD _____ BMCD 074
Black Mark / Jun '95 / Plastic Head.

Randy

**NO CARROTS FOR THE
REHABILITATED**
CD _____ DOLCD 011
Delores / Feb '95 / Plastic Head.

THERE'S NO WAY
CD _____ DOLO 16CD
Dolores / Aug '95 / Plastic Head.

**THERE'S NO WAY WE'RE GONNA FIT
IN**
CD _____ DOLCD 016
Delores / Feb '95 / Plastic Head.

Raney, Doug

GUITAR, GUITAR, GUITAR
CD _____ SCCD 31212
Steeplechase / Jul '88 / Impetus.

**MEETING THE TENORS (Raney, Doug
Sextet)**
CD _____ CRISS 1006CD
Criss Cross / Feb '94 / Cadillac /
Harmonia Mundi.

Raney, Jimmy

BUT BEAUTIFUL (Raney, Jimmy Trio)
CD _____ CRISS 1065CD
Criss Cross / Oct '92 / Cadillac /
Harmonia Mundi.

JAZZ GUITAR RARITIES
CD _____ JZCD 377
Recording Arts / Jun '93 / THE / Disc.

MASTER, THE (Raney, Jimmy Quartet)
CD _____ CRISS 1009CD
Criss Cross / Nov '90 / Cadillac /
Harmonia Mundi.

**STOLEN MOMENTS (Raney, Jimmy &
Doug Raney Quartet)**
CD _____ SCCD 31118
Steeplechase / Jul '88 / Impetus.

WISTARIA (Raney, Jimmy Trio)
CD _____ CRISS 1019CD
Criss Cross / Nov '91 / Cadillac /
Harmonia Mundi.

Raney, Wayne

SONGS OF THE HILLS
CD _____ KCD 588
King/Paddle Wheel / Feb '93 / New Note.

Ranft, Richard

RAINFOREST REQUIEM
CD _____ MANCD 1
Mankind / Jun '93 / Koch.

Rangell, Nelson

DESTINY
Road ahead / Grace / Street wise / House
is not a home / Crazy all the way / Rainbow
shadows / Little dream girl / (On the) Phone
/ Sonora / Joie de vivre / Destiny
CD _____ GRP 98142
GRP / Apr '95 / BMG / New Note.

TO BEGIN AGAIN
CD _____ 1390072
Gaia / May '89 / New Note.

YES THEN YES
Yes then yes / Looking forward / Never forgotten / Love is / Star stream / Swingin' for
the fence / One heart calling / Runaround /
Child's play / Time will tell

CD _____ GRP 97552
GRP / Jan '94 / BMG / New Note.

Ranglin, Alvin

HOLY GROUND
CD _____ CDHB 62
Heartbeat / Sep '90 / Greensleeves /
Jetstar / Direct / ADA.

Rankin Family

ENDLESS SEASONS
As I roved out / River / Natives / Oganaich
an or-fhuilt Bhuide/Am braighe / Forty days
and nights / Eyes of Margaret / You feel the
same way too / Endless seasons / Padstow
/ Blue eyed Suzie / Your boat's lost at sea
CD _____ CDEST 2275
Capitol / Jan '96 / EMI.

FARE THEE WELL LOVE
CD _____ LCOM 9001
Lismor / Mar '92 / Lismor / Direct /
Duncans / ADA.

NORTH COUNTRY
Fare thee well love / North Country / Oich
u agus h-iuraibh eile (love song) / Borders
and time / Mull river shuffle / Golden rod jig
/ Lisa Brown / Ho ro my nut brown maiden
/ Tramp miner / Rise again / Boat song /
Christy Campbell medley / Betty Lou's reel
/ Turn that boat around
CD _____ CDEST 2214
Capitol / Nov '93 / EMI.

RANKIN FAMILY
CD _____ CDEST 2185
Capitol / Oct '92 / EMI.

RANKIN FAMILY, THE
CD _____ LCOM 8901
Lismor / Mar '92 / Lismor / Direct /
Duncans / ADA.

Rankin File

FOR THE RECORD
Call on me / Sense of kind / Words and
wisdom / Canadian trilogy / Leaving home
/ Whispy / Leaving is the story of my life /
Carefully / Lost it on the road / Met her on
the shap / Drank his son to death / Circle
turns again / Mrs. Mann and me / Mr. Sax
CD _____ CDTRAX 057
Greentrax / Dec '92 / Conifer / Duncans /
ADA / Direct.

Rankin, Iain

OUT OF THE BLUE
Teardrop on the ocean / Thirty storeys high
/ We're still here / Out of nowhere / Go to
hell but turn right / Daddy was a miner /
McGingle's violin / Make love to me / One
time you talk to heaven / Wild horses / Let's
do it all over again
CD _____ CDTRAX 069
Greentrax / Dec '93 / Conifer / Duncans /
ADA.

Rankine, Alan

DAYS AND DAYS
CD _____ TWI 8872
Les Disques Du Crepuscule / '90 /
Discovery / ADA.

Rannenberg, Christian

**LONG WAY FROM HOME (Rannenberg,
Christian & Pink Piano Allstars)**
CD _____ BEST 1006CD
Acoustic Music / Nov '93 / ADA.

Rant

MIXING IT
CD _____ CMCD 074
Celtic Music / Jul '94 / CM / Roots.

Raped

**COMPLETE RAPED PUNK
COLLECTION, THE**
Moving target / Raped / Escalator hater /
Normal / B.I.C. / E.C.T. / Foreplay play-
ground / Cheap night out / Babysitting / Shit
/ L.O.N.D.O.N. / Slits / Cheap trash / Knock
on wood
CD _____ CDPUNK 35
Anagram / Jun '94 / Pinnacle.

Rapeman

TWO NUNS AND A PACK MULE
CD _____ BFFP 33CD
Blast First / Nov '88 / Disc.

Rapiers

BACK TO THE POINT
CD _____ FCD 3034
Fury / Aug '94 / Magnum Music Group /
Nervous.

Rapoon

FALLEN GODS
CD _____ STCD 086
Staalplaat / May '95 / Vital/SAM.

553

Rappin' 4-Tay

DON'T FIGHT THE FEELIN'
Back again / Black season / Keep one in the chambra / Can u buckem / Just 'cause I called you a bitch / Playaz club / She's a sell out / I'll be around / Tear the roof off / Sucka free / Call it what you want / I got cha back / This is what I know / Gift / Out 4000 / Playaz club (sucka 3 remix) / I'll be around (wicked mix) / I'll be around (Al's brother 2 brother mix)
CD _____ CTCD 45
Cooltempo / Jul '95 / EMI.

Rapscallion

CHAMELEON DROOL
CD _____ CDZORRO 41
Metal Blade / Jul '90 / Pinnacle.

Rara Machine

VOUDOU NOU
CD _____ SHCD 64054
Shanachie / Oct '94 / Koch / ADA / Greensleeves.

Rare Air

HARD TO BEAT
CD _____ GLCD 1073
Green Linnet / Feb '93 / Roots / CM / Direct / ADA.

PRIMEVAL
CD _____ GLCD 1104
Green Linnet / Feb '91 / Roots / CM / Direct / ADA.

SPACE PIPER
CD _____ GLCD 1115
Green Linnet / '92 / Roots / CM / Direct / ADA.

Rare Bird

SYMPATHY
Sympathy / You went away / Nature's fruit / Bird on a wing / What you want to know / Beautiful scarlet / Hammerhead / I'm thinking / As your mind flies by
CD _____ CDOVD 280
Charisma / Apr '90 / EMI.

Rare Earth

DIFFERENT WORLD
CD _____ 341002
Koch / Feb '93 / Koch.

RARE EARTH
Big John / Big brother / Born to wander / All or nothing / Tobacco Road / Smiling faces / I'm losing you / Can't stop / Get ready / Celebrate
CD _____ 900065
Line / Jul '95 / CM / Grapevine / ADA / Conifer / Direct.

RARE EARTH
CD _____ KLMCD 052
Scratch / May '95 / BMG.

Ras Command

IN DUB
CD _____ SPVCD 55462
Red Arrow / May '95 / SRD / Jetstar.

Ras Iley

KING OF THE STAGE
CD _____ WCD 395
JW / Feb '94 / Jetstar.

Ras Ivi

ARK OF COVENANT (Ras Ivi & The Family Of Rastafari)
CD _____ SZCD 003
Surr Zema Musik / Apr '95 / Jetstar.

Ras Michael

FREEDOM SOUND (Ras Michael & The Sons Of Negus)
CD _____ RNCD 2015
Rhino / Sep '93 / Jetstar / Magnum Music Group / THE.

KIBIR AM LAK (Ras Michael & The Sons Of Negus)
CD _____ CC 2712
Crocodisc / Jul '94 / THE / Magnum Music Group.

KNOW NOW (Ras Michael & The Sons Of Negus)
CD _____ SHANCD 64019
Shanachie / May '90 / Koch / ADA / Greensleeves.

LOVE THY NEIGHBOUR (Ras Michael & The Sons Of Negus)
CD _____ LLCD 001
Greensleeves / Mar '93 / Total/BMG / Jetstar / SRD.

NEW NAME (Ras Michael & The Sons Of Negus)
CD _____ RB 3007
Reggae Best / May '94 / Magnum Music Group / THE.

NYAHBINGHI (Ras Michael & The Sons Of Negus)
CD _____ CC 2710
Crocodisc / Apr '94 / THE / Magnum Music Group.

RAS MICHAEL-ZION TRAIN (Ras Michael & Zion Train)
CD _____ SST 168 CD
SST / May '93 / Plastic Head.

RASTAFARI (Ras Michael & The Sons Of Negus)
CD _____ GRELCD 153
Greensleeves / Feb '91 / Total/BMG / Jetstar / SRD.

RASTAFARI DUB (Ras Michael & The Sons Of Negus)
CD _____ RE 162CD
Reach Out International / Nov '94 / Jetstar.

Rascoe, Moses

BLUES LIVE
CD _____ FF 454CD
Flying Fish / May '93 / Roots / CM / Direct / ADA.

Raskinen, Minna

REVELATIONS
CD _____ OMCD 64
Olarin Musiiki Oy / Nov '95 / ADA / Direct.

Rasle, Jean-Pierre

CORNERMUSIQUE
CD _____ CMCD 058
Celtic Music / Mar '94 / CM / Roots.

Rasmussen, Valdemar

DEN SIGNEDE DAG
CD _____ MECCACD 1017
Music Mecca / Nov '94 / Jazz Music / Cadillac / Wellard.

ET YNDIGT LAND
CD _____ MECCACD 1029
Music Mecca / Nov '94 / Jazz Music / Cadillac / Wellard.

SONDERJYSK KAFFEBORD
CD _____ MECCACD 1016
Music Mecca / Nov '94 / Jazz Music / Cadillac / Wellard.

VELKOMMEN IGEN
CD _____ MECCACD 1004
Music Mecca / Nov '94 / Jazz Music / Cadillac / Wellard.

Ratos De Paraos

ANARKOPHOBIA
CD _____ RO 93262
Roadrunner / Apr '91 / Pinnacle.

Rattle 'N' Reel

OUTRAGEOUS
CD _____ RNR 001CD
RNR / Oct '94 / ADA.

Rattlers

PLEASURES IN MISADVENTURES
CD _____ PRMCD 10
Pagan / Aug '95 / Total/BMG.

SCARE ME TO DEATH
Scare me to death / Little red / Mine all mine / Cat crept in / Blue zoot / Hey baby / Always yours yours / You're my baby / Rattlin' boogie / Knife edge baby
CD _____ NERCD 047
Nervous / Sep '93 / Nervous / Magnum Music Group.

Rattlesnake Kiss

RATTLESNAKE KISS
Railroad / Sad Suzie / Angel / Alright by me / Nothing this good (could be real) / Wake up / Taste it / Don't make it right / All to me (that I was to you) / Kiss this
CD _____ SOV 106CD
Sovereign / '92 / Target/BMG.

Rattus

RATTUS 1981-1984
CD _____ RATCD 1
Poko / Nov '93 / Plastic Head.

Raux, Richard

UNDER THE MAGNOLIAS (Raux, Richard Quartet)
CD _____ CDLLL 27
La Lichere / Aug '93 / Discovery / ADA.

Rava, Enrico

PILGRIM & THE STARS, THE
Pilgrim and the stars / Parks / Bella / Pesce naufrago / Surprise hotel / By the sea / Blancasnow
CD _____ 8473222
ECM / Jul '95 / New Note.

PLOT, THE
Tribe / On the red side of the street / Amici / Dr. Ra and Mr. Va / Foto di famiglia / Plot
CD _____ 5232822
ECM / Jul '95 / New Note.

QUARTET
Lavari casalinghi / Fearless five / Tramps / Round Midnight / Blackmail
CD _____ 5232832
ECM / Jul '95 / New Note.

VOLVER (Rava, Enrico & Dino Saluzzi Quintet)
Bout de soufle / Minguito / Luna-volver / Tiempos de ausencias / Ballantine for valentine visions
CD _____ 8313952
ECM / Feb '88 / New Note.

Raven

ALL FOR ONE
Take control / Mind over metal / Sledgehammer rock / All for one / Run silent, run deep / Hung drawn and quartered / Break the chain / Take it away / Seek and destroy / Athletic rock
CD _____ NEATCD 1011
Neat / '85 / Plastic Head.

GLOW
CD _____ SPV 08412092
SPV / Jun '95 / Plastic Head.

ROCK UNTIL YOU DROP
Hard ride / Hell patrol / Don't need your money / Over the top / 39-40 / For the future / Rock until you drop / Nobody's here / Hellraiser / Action / Lambs to the slaughter / Tyrant of the airways
CD _____ CLACD 257
Castle / '91 / BMG.

Raven, Michael

SHROPSHIRE LAD, A (Raven, Michael & Joan Mills)
CD _____ MR 69
MR / Apr '94 / CM.

Ravens

GREATEST VOCAL GROUP OF THEM ALL
For you / Write me a letter / Until the real thing comes along / September song / Always / I'm afraid of you / Fool that I am / Together / It's too soon to know / White Christmas / Silent night / Deep purple / There's nothing like a woman in love / Careless love / If you didn't mean it / Someday / Lilacs in the rain / I've been a fool / I'm gonna paper my walls with your love letters / Sylvia / Tea for two / Without a song / It's the talk of the town / No more kisses for baby / Moonglow / Who's sorry how / I've got the world on a string
CD _____ SV 0270
Savoy Jazz / Sep '95 / Conifer / ADA.

OLD MAN RIVER
Old man river / Summertime / Once in a while / I don't know why I love you like I do / House I live in / Get wise baby / Send for me if you need me / County every star / Be I bumblebee or not / Leave my gal alone / Rooster / I don't have to ride no more / Time is marching on / Marie / Rickey's blues
CD _____ SV 0260
Savoy Jazz / Nov '94 / Conifer / ADA.

RARITIES
Until the real thing comes along / Once in a while / Phantom stage coach / Please believe me / I'm gonna take to the road / Comin' back home / Bless you / Cadillac song / I'm afraid of you / Tea for two / Get wise baby / House I live in / Ricky's blues / Sylvia
CD _____ SV 0261
Savoy Jazz / Nov '94 / Conifer / ADA.

Ravers, Pat

BBC RADIO 1 IN CONCERT
CD _____ WINCD 017
Windsong / May '92 / Pinnacle.

Raw Breed

LUNE TUNZ
CD _____ CDCTUM 5
Under One Flag / Oct '93 / Pinnacle.

Raw Material

RAW MATERIAL
CD _____ HBG 123/2
Background / Apr '94 / Background.

Raw Power

FIGHT
CD _____ GOD 014CD
Godhead / Jul '95 / Plastic Head.

Too Tough To Burn

CD _____ BABECD 7
Rosemary's Baby / Sep '93 / Plastic Head.

Raw To The Core

IN THE MOOD VOL.2
CD _____ ITM 001 CD
KGR / Oct '95 / Jetstar.

Rawhead, Jason

BACKFIRE
CD _____ KKUK 005CD
KK / '90 / Plastic Head.

COLLISON HYPE
CD _____ KK 61CD
KK / Jul '91 / Plastic Head.

JASON RAWHEAD
CD _____ KK 024 CD
KK / '89 / Plastic Head.

Rawicz & Landauer

THEIR GREAT PIANO HITS
CD _____ PASTCD 7040
Flapper / May '94 / Pinnacle.

Rawls, Lou

FOR YOU MY LOVE
For you my love / If I had my life to live over / Nobody but me / Whispering grass / Gee baby I'd good to you / If it's the last thing I do / Blues for the weepers / That's your red wagon / Just squeeze me / It's you / I love you yes I do / Ronettes / Wee baby blues / I wonder where our love has gone
CD _____ CDP 8289792
Capitol Jazz / Oct '94 / EMI.

LOU RAWLS IN THE HEART
CD _____ 847 948-2
Polydor / May '91 / PolyGram.

STAR COLLECTION
CD _____ STCD 1002
Disky / Jun '93 / THE / BMG / Discovery / Pinnacle.

YOU'LL NEVER FIND
CD _____ WMCD 5700
Disky / Oct '94 / THE / BMG / Discovery / Pinnacle.

Rawside

POLICE TERROR
CD _____ WH 1133CD
We Bite / Nov '95 / Plastic Head.

Ray & Glover

PICTURE HAS FADED
Tell me Mama / Jimmy Bell / Can't see your face / Downtown blues / Sittin' on top of the world / Long haired donkey / Ice blue / Going away blues / Afraid to trust 'em / Mellow chick swing / Saturday blues / New Buddy Brown / If it looks like jelly / As the years go passing by
CD _____ TK 92CD036
T/K / Aug '94 / Pinnacle.

Ray, James

DIOS ESTA DE NUESTRO LADO (Ray, James Gangwar)
Rev rev lowrider / Heart surgery / 35,000 times / Badlands / Hardwar / Cadillac coming / Bad gin / Santa Susana / Coz ca choo
CD _____ MRAY 341 CD
Merciful Release / Apr '92 / Warner Music.

NEW KIND OF ASSASSIN, A (Ray, James Gangwar)
Mexico sundown blues / Texas / Mountain voices (remix) / Dust boat / Edie Sedgwick / Mexico sundown blues (edit)
CD _____ MRAY 089 CD
Merciful Release / Aug '92 / Warner Music.

THIRD GENERATION (Ray, James Gangwar)
Cobalt blue / Sinner / Fuelled up / Take it / Third generation / Blue lover / Strange / Luxury / Ridge
CD _____ SURG 001CD
Surgury / Jun '93 / Vital.

Ray, Johnnie

16 MOST REQUESTED SONGS
Cry / Walkin' my baby back home / All of me / Whiskey and gin / Let's walk that way / Don't blame me / Little cloud that cried / Just walking in the rain / Tell the lady I said goodbye / Why should I be sorry / Glad rag doll / Hey there / Please Mr. Sun / Such a night / As time goes by
CD _____ 4720492
Columbia / Jul '92 / Sony.

AT THE PALLADIUM
Please don't talk about me / Glad / Rag doll / Hundred years from now / Somebody stole my gal / With these hands / Walkin' my baby back home / As time goes by / Such a night
CD _____ BCD 15666
Bear Family / Jun '92 / Rollercoaster / Direct / CM / Swift / ADA.

BEST OF JOHNNIE RAY/FRANKIE LAINE (Ray, Johnnie & Frankie Laine)
CD _____ BTBCD 001
Soundsrite / Jun '93 / THE / Target/BMG.

CRY
Yes tonight Josephine / Just walking in the rain / I've got so many million years / Johnnie's comin' home / Look homeward angel / Up above my head / Good evening friends / Up until now / How long blues / You don't owe me a thing / No wedding today / Build your love / Streets of memories / Miss me, just a little / Texas tambourine / Pink sweater angel / Soliloquy of a fool / Endlessly / Plant a little seed / I'll make you mine / Papa loves mambo / Ooo aah oh / Flip flop and fly / Alexander's ragtime band / Little white cloud that cried / Pa sez / Full time job / Such a night / Hernando's hideaway
CD _____ BCD 15450
Bear Family / May '90 / Rollercoaster / Direct / CM / Swift / ADA.

PORTRAIT OF A SONG STYLIST
Just walking in the rain / Hey there / I'm beginning to see the light / If you believe / Nethertheless I'm in love with you / Hands across the table / Walkin' my baby back home / Cry / I'm confessin' that I love you / All of me / Too marvellous for words / They can't take that away from me / Little white cloud that cried / Alexander's ragtime band / Yes tonight Josephine / Shake a hand / Who's sorry now / It all depends on you
CD _____ HARCD 103
Masterpiece / Apr '89 / BMG.

Ray, Michael

MICHAEL RAY & THE COSMIC KREWE (Ray, Michael & The Cosmic Krewe)
Rhythm and muse / Discipline / Carefree / Champions / Charlie B's / 3-22-93 / Anthology / Beans and rice / Island in space / Echoes of boat people
CD _____ ECD 220842
Evidence / May '94 / Harmonia Mundi / ADA / Cadillac.

Raye, Collin

EXTREMES
That's my story / Man of my word / My kind of girl / Little rock / Bible and a bus ticket home / Nothin' a little love won't cure / If I were you / To the border and beyond / Angel of no mercy / Dreaming my dreams with you
CD _____ 474799 2
Epic / Apr '94 / Sony.

IN THIS LIFE
What they don't know / In this life / Big river / Somebody else's Moon / You can't take it with you / That was a river / I want you bad (And that ain't good) / Latter day cowboy / Many a mile / Let it be me
CD _____ 472314 2
Epic / Feb '93 / Sony.

Raymond Listen

LICORICE ROOT ORCHESTRA
September in the night / Cloud symphonies / Saturn rise / Lemon peel medallion / Tangled weeds / Ocean's long floor/spell on this room / Sunday theme of petals / Coronation day / Let darkness fall / Everyday supernatural / Garden of Chalcedony / Black eyed Susans / Firmament
CD _____ SHIMMY 069CD
Shimmy Disc / Feb '94 / Vital.

Razor

SHOTGUN JUSTICE
CD _____ FPD 3094
Fringe / Mar '95 / Plastic Head.

VIOLENT RESTITUTION
CD _____ 857 571
Steamhammer / '89 / Pinnacle / Plastic Head.

Razor Baby

TOO HOT TO HANDLE
Danger / Rock this place / Downtown / Outta hand sister / Move me / Too hot to handle / Got me running / Low down and dirty
CD _____ HMAXD 102
Heavy Metal / Aug '89 / Sony.

Razorbacks

I'M ON FIRE
CD _____ FCD 3026
Fury / Aug '93 / Magnum Music Group / Nervous.

Razorcuts

WORLD KEEPS TURNING, THE
CD _____ CRECD 045
Creation / Feb '89 / 3MV / Vital.

Re-Animator

CONDEMNED TO ETERNITY
Don't eat the yellow snow / St. Alphonzo's pancake breakfast / Cosmik debris / Apostrophe / Stink foot / In the slime / 50/50 /

Dinah moe hum / Nanook rubs it / Father O'Blivion / Excentrifugal forz / Uncle Remus / Camarillo brillo / Dirty love / Zomby woof / Montana
CD _____ CDFLAG 37
Under One Flag / Oct '89 / Pinnacle.

LAUGHING
CD _____ CDFLAG 53
Under One Flag / Feb '91 / Pinnacle.

THAT WAS THEN, THIS IS NOW
Take me away / 2 CV / Cold sweat / Hope / Last laugh / Kick back / Listen up / Sunshine / That was then...This is now / D.U.A.F. (Features on CD only.)
CD _____ CDFLAG 67
Under One Flag / Oct '92 / Pinnacle.

Rea, Chris

AUBERGE
Auberge / Gone fishing / You're not a number / Heaven / Set me free / Red shoes / Sing a song of love to me / Every second counts / Looking for the summer / And you my love / Mention of your name
CD _____ 9031756932
Magnet / Feb '91 / Warner Music.

CHRIS REA
Loving you / If you choose to go / Guitar Street / Do you still dream / Every beat of my heart / Goodbye little Columbus / One sweet tender touch / Do it for your love / Just want to be with you / Runaway / When you know your love has died
CD _____ 242 371 2
Magnet / Feb '88 / Warner Music.

DANCING WITH STRANGERS
Joys of Christmas / I can't dance to that / Windy town / Gonna buy a hat / Curse of the traveller / Let's dance / Que sera / Josie's tune / Loving you again / That girl of mine / September blue / I don't care anymore (Extra track on CD only) / Donahue's broken wheel (Extra track on CD only.) / Danielle's breakfast (Extra track on CD only.)
CD _____ 242 378 2
Magnet / Sep '87 / Warner Music.

DELTICS
Twisted wheel / Things lovers should do / Dance (don't think) / Raincoat and a rose / Cenotaph - letter from Amsterdam / Deltics / Diamonds / She gave it away / Don't want your best friend / No qualifications / Seabird
CD _____ 242 369 2
Magnet / Feb '88 / Warner Music.

ESPRESSO LOGIC
Espresso logic / Red / Soup of the day / Johnny needs a fast car / Between the devil and the deep blue sea / Julia / Summer love / New way / Stop / She closed her eyes
CD _____ 4509943112
Magnet / Nov '93 / Warner Music.

GOD'S GREAT BANANA SKIN
Nothing to fear / Miles is a cigarette / God's great banana skin / Nineties blues / Too much pride / Boom boom / I ain't the fool / There she goes / I'm ready / Black dog / Soft top, hard shoulder
CD _____ 4509909952
Magnet / Nov '92 / Warner Music.

NEW LIGHT THROUGH OLD WINDOWS (The Best Of Chris Rea)
Let's dance / Working on it / Ace of hearts / Josephine / Candles / On the beach / Fool (if you think it's over) / I can hear your heartbeat / Shamrock diaries / Stainsby girls / Windy town / Driving home for Christmas / Steel river
CD _____ 243841-2
Magnet / Oct '88 / Warner Music.

ON THE BEACH
On the beach / Little blonde plaits / Giverney / Lucky day / Just passing through / It's all gone / Hello friend / Two roads / Light of hope / Auf immerund ewig / Bless them all (Casette and compact disc only) / Freeway (Casette and compact disc only) / Crack that mould (Casette and compact disc only)
CD _____ MAGD 5069
Magnet / '88 / Warner Music.

ROAD TO HELL
Road to hell / Road to hell #2 / You must be evil / Texas / Looking for a rainbow / Your warm and tender love / Daytona / That's what they always say / I just wanna be with you / Tell me there's a heaven
CD _____ 2462852
Magnet / Feb '95 / Warner Music.

SHAMROCK DIARIES
Steel river / Stainsby girls / Chisel Hill / Josephine / One golden rule / All summer long / Stone / Shamrock diaries / Love turns to lies / Hired gun
CD _____ 242 374 2
Magnet / Jun '88 / Warner Music.

TENNIS
Tennis / Sweet kiss / Since I don't see you anymore / Dancing girls / No work today / Every time I see you smile / For ever and ever / Good news / Friends across the water / Distant summers / Only with you / Stick it
CD _____ 242 370 2
Magnet / Feb '88 / Warner Music.

VERY BEST OF CHRIS REA, THE
Road to hell / Josephine / Let's dance / Fool if you think it's over / Auberge / Julia / Stainsby girls / If you were me / On the beach / Looking for the summer / Driving / Go your own way / God's great banana skin / Winterson / Gone fishing / Tell me there's a heaven
CD _____ 450998040-2
Magnet / Oct '94 / Warner Music.

WATER SIGN
Nothing's happening by the sea / Deep water / Candles / Love's strange ways / Texas / Let it loose / I can hear your heartbeat / Midnight blue / Hey you / Out of the darkness
CD _____ 242 372 2
Magnet / Feb '88 / Warner Music.

WHATEVER HAPPENED TO BENNY SANTINI?
Whatever happened to Benny Santini / Closer you get / Because of you / Dancing with Charlie / Bows and bangles / Fool (if you think it's over) / Three angels / Just one of those days / Standing in your doorway / Fires of spring
CD _____ 2292 423682
Carlton Home Entertainment / Jan '93 / Carlton Home Entertainment.

WIRED TO THE MOON
Bombollini / Touche d'amour / Shine shine shine / Wired to the moon / Reasons / I don't know what it is but I love it / Ace of hearts / Holding out / Winning
CD _____ 242 373 2
Magnet / Dec '88 / Warner Music.

React 2 Rhythm

WHATEVER YOU DREAM
CD _____ GRCD 002
Guerilla / Mar '92 / Pinnacle.

Reactor

REVELATION
CD _____ 1MF 37700332
Invisible / Jul '93 / Plastic Head.

Reader, Eddi

HUSH
Right place / Patience of angels / Dear John / Scarecrow / East of us / I'm laughing) / Exception / Red face big sky / Howling in ojai / When I watch you sleeping / Wonderful lie / Siren
CD _____ 450996177-2
Warner Bros. / Jun '94 / Warner Music.

MIRMAMA
What you do with what you've got / Honeychild / All or nothing / Hello in there / Dolphins / Blacksmith / That's fair / Cinderellas downfall / Pay no mind / Swimming song / My old friend the blues
CD _____ 74321 15865-2
RCA / Sep '94 / BMG.

Reading, Bertice

TED EASTON'S JAZZBAND & QUARTET
CD _____ ACD 80
Audiophile / Apr '93 / Jazz Music / Swift.

Real Cool Killers

ILLUSIONS
Just for fun / Knife / Daddy's footsteps / Judgement day / Myrtle Gordon / Bitter end / I much more than a liar / Illusion / Stupid lines / Open the night
CD _____ SUR 453CD
Survival / Jun '94 / Pinnacle.

Real Life

HEARTLAND
CD _____ INT 847 710
Interchord / '88 / CM.

LITTLE PIECE OF HEAVEN, A
CD _____ CANDRCD 80101
Candor / Nov '94 / Else.

Real McCoy

ANOTHER NIGHT
Another night / Come and get your love / If you should ever be lonely / Runaway / Sleeping with an angel / Ooh boy / Love and devotion / Automatic lover / Operator / I want you / Megablast
CD _____ 74321280972
Arista / May '95 / BMG.

Real Thing

YOU TO ME ARE EVERYTHING
You to me are everything / What'cha say, what'cha do / Can't get by without you / Love's such a wonderful thing / I want you back / You can feel the force / Lady I love you all the time / Whenever you want my love / Love is a playground / Lightning strikes again / Boogie down / She's a groovy freak / You can't force the funk / You're missing / Dance with me / Watch out Carolina / Rainin' through my sunshine / Children of the ghetto
CD _____ 5507402

Spectrum/Karussell / Sep '94 / PolyGram / THE.

Reality

REGGAE, REGGAE, REGGAE
Stand up and be counted / Donna / Set me free / Peaceful man / Rasta man / Singer skin / Wintersong / Gone fishing / Tell me there's a heaven / OK / Gonna live my life / Steppin' out
CD _____ SOV 008CD
Sovereign / '92 / Target/BMG.

Rebello, Jason

KEEPING TIME
Swings and roundabouts / Coral beads / Close your eyes / Silver surfer / Wind in the willows / Wind in the willows (piano) / Eraserhead (old piano) / Eraserhead (new piano) / Keeping time / Spider / Silver surfer (no sax) / Permanent love (full) / Permanent (edited) / Little man / Tic toc / Future / Untitled / Solo piece 1 / Solo piece 2
CD _____ 7432112904-2
Novus / Feb '93 / BMG.

LAST DANCE (Rebello, Jason & Roy Rose)
Wind in the willows / Every little thing / Life is her friend / Play piano play / Last dance / Soul eyes / I am what you see / Tears / What is this thing called love / Foggy day / Adrian's wall / God bless the child
CD _____ ATJR 001
All That / May '95 / New Note.

MAKE IT REAL
When words fail / Summertime / Compared to what / Wake up / It's alright / Message / Wait and see / Beautiful day / It's at times like these / Heartless monster / Dolphin dance / When words fail (Reprise)
CD _____ 74321 22408-2
Novus / Sep '94 / BMG.

Rebello, Simone

FASCINATING RHYTHM
CD _____ DOYCD 024
Doyen / Aug '93 / Conifer.

SECRET PLACE, A
Secret place / Leyenda / Saturday's child / Ensemble / Jupiter's dance / Marimba spiritual
CD _____ DOYCD 040
Doyen / Jun '95 / Conifer.

Rebirth Brass Band

REBIRTH KICKIN' IT LIVE
CD _____ ROUCD 2106
Rounder / Dec '94 / CM / Direct / ADA / Cadillac.

ROLLIN'
CD _____ ROUCD 2132
Rounder / Oct '94 / CM / Direct / ADA / Cadillac.

Rebroff, Ivan

KALINKA MALINKA
CD _____ WMCD 5692
Disky / May '94 / THE / BMG / Discovery / Pinnacle.

VERY BEST OF IVAN REBROFF
Evening chimes / Song of the Volga boatmen / Hava nagila / Im tiefen keller / Two white doves / Perestroika / Grosser alter stern / Dark eyes / Sohto nom gorje / Roi zyganka / Somewhere my love / Ol' man river / Kalinka malinka / La calunnia / Ach natascha / On the way from Petersburgh to Nowgorod / Cossack patrol
CD _____ MDMCD 001
Moidart / Jun '93 / Conifer / ADA.

VERY BEST OF IVAN REBROFF VOLUME II, THE
Mutterchen Russland / Hej Andrushka / If I were a rich man / My yiddishe momme / Lonely chimes / Barcarolle / Sah ein Knabein / Rosen steh'n / Elizabethan serenade / Moscow nights / Ach varmaeland / Mit der troike in die grosse Stadt / Ech dorogi / Ave Maria - plaisir d'amour / Cossacks must ride / Ode to joy
CD _____ MDMCD 002
Moidart / Jun '94 / Conifer / ADA.

Reckless Abandon

RECKLESS
CD _____ CUS 41592CD
Ichiban / May '94 / Koch.

Recoil

BLOODLINE
CD _____ CDSTUMM 94
Mute / Apr '92 / Disc.

Records

SMASHES, CRASHES AND NEAR MISSES
Starry eyes / Girl in golden disc / Teenarama / Up all night / I don't remember your name / Girls that don't exist / Hearts will be broken / All messed up and ready to go / Hearts in her eyes / Girl / Spent a week with

you last night / Held up high / Rumour sets the woods alight / Same mistakes / Selfish love / Not so much the time / Affection rejected / Paint her face / Imitation jewellery / Rock 'n' roll love letter
CD _____ CDOVD 456
Virgin / Feb '95 / EMI.

Recycle Or Die

SILK
Dimension X / Inner peace / Desert bean / Passion and hope / Oceans of infinity
CD _____ 450994061-2
WEA / Oct '93 / Warner Music.

Red Alert

WE'VE GOT THE POWER
We've got the power / They came in force / Crisis / You've got nothing / SPG / Art of brutality / Industrial slide
CD _____ AHOYCD 12
Captain Oi / Jan '94 / Plastic Head.

Red Army Choir

RED ARMY CHOIR, THE
La Chant Du Monde / Jan '94 / Harmonia Mundi / ADA. _____ LDX 274768

Red Army Ensemble

RED ARMY ENSEMBLE AT THE ROYAL ALBERT HALL
British national anthem / Russian national anthem / Russian fields / Volga boat song / Festive overture / My motherland / Parade on Red Square / Barinya / Live and don't be sad / Above clear fields / Yesterday / Di quella pira / La donna e mobile / No, John, no / Brave soldiers / Unharness your horses, oh guys / Cossack dance / Variyag / Quiet, quiet / Korobeiniki / Serenade of the stutterer / Cossack goes to the Danbube / O sole mio / Amapola / Kalinka / Soldier's friendship / Auld lang syne / Kalinka (reprise)
CD _____ 353.278
RCA / May '88 / BMG.

RUSSIAN CAVALCADE
CD _____ CDSR 063
Telstar / Oct '94 / BMG.

Red Aunts

 # 1 CHICKEN
CD _____ E 86446
Epitaph / Mar '95 / Plastic Head / Pinnacle.

Red Beards From Texas

HAVIN' A BALL
CD _____ RRCD 108
Receiver / Jan '90 / Grapevine.

Red Chair Fade Away

MESMERIZED
CD _____ ENG 1012
English Garden / Apr '94 / Background.

Red Clay Ramblers

LIE OF THE MIND, A
Run Sister run / South of the border/In the pines / Honey babe / I love you a thousand ways / Home is where the heart is / Seeing it now / Blue Jay/The gal I left behind / Light years away / Cumberland mountain deer chase / Red rocking chair / Montana underscoring / Killing floor / I can't live without 'em blues / Folding the flag/Hard times
CD _____ SHCD 8501
Sugarhill / '86 / Roots / CM / ADA / Direct.

RAMBLER
Cotton eyed Joe / Cajun Billy / Black smoke train / Saro Jane / Annie Oakley / Queen of Skye / Ninety and Nine / Mile long medley / Darlin' say/Pony cart / Hiawatha's lullaby / What does the deep sea say / Ryan's/Jordan reel / Barbeque / One rose/Hot buttered rum / Olkas
CD _____ SHCD 3798
Sugarhill / '92 / Roots / CM / ADA / Direct.

Red, Danny

RIDDIMWIZE
Can't live it up / Be grateful / Mystic lady / Don't cry soundboy / Rollin' stone / Rise up / Riddimwize / Teaser / Cool bad boy / Tell me why / Riddimwize #2 / Can't live it dub / Rise up dub / Be dubful
CD _____ 477774 2
Columbia / Sep '94 / Sony.

Red Dawn

NEVER SAY SURRENDER
CD _____ NTHEN 10
Now & Then / Sep '95 / Plastic Head.

Red Devils

KING KING
CD _____ 5144922
Phonogram / Jan '94 / PolyGram.

Red Dragon

BUN THEM
CD _____ VPCD 1350
VP / Mar '94 / Jetstar.

Red Eye

TIME FRAME ANARCHY
CD _____ AFTER CD4
After 6am / Dec '94 / Plastic Head.

Red Fox

AS A MATTER OF FOX
Born again black man / Dry head shakira Pt 1 / Good body runs in ya family / No condom, no fun / Girl's vineyard (all fruits ripe) / I'm gonna take you home / Ghetto gospel / Pressure dem / Golden axe / Dry head shakira Pt 2 / Dem a murderer / Hey Mr. Rude bwoy / Dance hall scenario / Ya can't test me again
CD _____ 7559615312
Warner Bros. / Sep '93 / Warner Music.

Red Fun

RED FUN
CD _____ CDMFN 173
Music For Nations / Dec '94 / Pinnacle.

Red Guitars

SEVEN TYPES OF AMBIQUITY
CD _____ RPM 109
RPM / Jul '93 / Pinnacle.

Red Harvest

MASTER NATION
CD _____ VOW 046CD
Voices Of Wonder / Jul '95 / Plastic Head.

NOMANSLAND
Cure / Righteous majority / Acid / No next generation / Machines way / (Live and pay) / The holy way / Crackman / Face the fact / Wrong arm of the law
CD _____ BMCD 019
Black Mark / Apr '92 / Plastic Head.

THERE'S BEAUTY IN THE PURITY OF SADNESS
CD _____ VOW 39C
Voices Of Wonder / Apr '94 / Plastic Head.

Red Hot 'n' Blue

HAVIN' A BALL
CD _____ FCD 3033
Fury / '94 / Magnum Music Group / Nervous.

Red Hot Chili Peppers

BLOOD SUGAR SEX MAGIK
Power of equality / If you have to ask / Breaking the girl / Funky monks / Suck my kiss / I could have lied / Mellowship slinky in B major / Righteous and the wicked / Under the bridge / Naked in the rain / Apache rose peacock / Greeting song / My lovely man / Sir psycho sexy / They're red hot
CD _____ 7599266812
Warner Bros. / Oct '91 / Warner Music.

FREAKY STYLEY
Jungle man / Hollywood (Africa) / American ghost dance / If you want me to stay / Nevermind / Freaky styley / Blackeyed blonde / Brothers cup / Battle ship / Lovin' and touchin' / Catholic school girls rule / Sex rap / Thirty dirty birds / Yertle the turtle
CD _____ CDFA 3309
Fame / Nov '94 / EMI.

MOTHER'S MILK
Good time boys / Higher ground / Subway to Venus / Magic Johnson / Nobody weird like me / Knock me down / Taste the pain / Stone cold bush / Fire / Pretty little ditty / Punk rock classic / Sexy Mexican maid / Johnny kick a hole in the sky
CD _____ CDMTL 1046
EMI / Aug '89 / EMI.

ONE HOT MINUTE
CD _____ 9362457332
Warner Bros. / Sep '95 / Warner Music.

OUT IN LA
Higher ground (12" mix) / Hollywood (Africa) (extended) / If you want me to stay / Behind the sun / Castles made of sand (live) / Special secret song inside (live) / FU (live) / Get up and jump (demo) / Out in LA (demo) / Green heaven (demo) / Police helicopter (demo) / Nevermind (demo) / Sex rap (demo) / Blues for meister / You always sing the same / Stranded / Flea fly / What it is / Deck the halls with boughs of holly
CD _____ CDMTL 1082
EMI / Nov '94 / EMI.

PLASMA SHAFT
Give it away (demo) / If you have to ask (mixes) / Nobody weird (live) / Sikamikanico / Breaking the girl (radio edit) / Fela's cock / Soul to squeeze
CD _____ 9362456649-2
Warner Bros. / Oct '94 / Warner Music.

RED HOT CHILI PEPPERS
True men don't kill coyotes / Baby appeal / Buckle down / Get up and jump / Why don't you love me / Green heaven / Mommy, where's daddy / Out in LA / Police helicopter / You always sing / Grand pappy du plenty
CD _____ CDFA 3297
Fame / May '93 / EMI.

RED HOT CHILI PEPPERS/FREAKY STYLEY/UPLIFT MOFO PARTY PLAN (3CD Set)
True men don't kill coyotes / Baby appeal / Buckle down / Get up and jump / Why don't you love me / Green heaven / Mommy where's daddy / Out in LA / Police helicopter / You always sing the same / Grand Pappy du plenty / Jungleman / Hollywood (Africa) / American ghost dance / If you want me to stay / Never mind / Freaky styley / Blackeyed blonde / Brother's cup / Battleship / Lovin' and touchin' / Catholic schoolgirls rule / Sex rap / 30 dirty birds / Yertle the turtle / Fight like a brave / Funky crime / Me & my friends / Backwoods / Skinny sweaty man / Behind the sun / Subterranean homesick blues / Special secret song inside / No chump love sucker / Walkin' on down the road / Love trilogy / Organic anti-beatbox band
CD Set _____ CDOMB 004
EMI / Oct '95 / EMI.

UPLIFT MOFO PARTY PLAN, THE
Fight like a brave / Funky crime / Me and my friends / Backwoods / Skinny sweaty man / Behind the sun / Subterranean homesick blues / Special secret song inside / No chump love sucker / Walkin' on down the road / Love trilogy / Organic anti-beat box band
CD _____ CDAML 3125
EMI / Aug '90 / EMI.

WHAT HITS
Higher ground / Fight like a brave / Behind the sun / Me and my friends / Backwoods / True men don't kill coyotes / Fire / Get up and jump / Knock me down / Under the bridge / Show me your soul / If you want me to stay / Hollywood (Africa) / Jungle man / Brothers cup / Taste the pain / Catholic school girls rule / Johnny kick a hole in the sky
CD _____ CDMTL 1071
EMI / Oct '92 / EMI.

Red House Painters

DOWN COLORFUL HILL
Twenty four / Medicine bottle / Down colorful hill / Japanese to English / Lord kill the pain / Michael
CD _____ CAD 2014CD
4AD / Aug '92 / Disc.

OCEAN BEACH
Cabezon / Summer dress / San Geronimo / Shadows / Over my head / Long distance runaround (LP only.) / Red carpet / Brockwell park / Moments / Drop
CD _____ CAD 5005CD
4AD / Mar '95 / Disc.

RED HOUSE PAINTERS
Grace Cathedral Park / Down through / Katy song / Mistress / Things mean a lot / Fun house / Take me out / Rollercoaster / New Jersey / Dragonflies / Mistress (piano version) / Mother / Strawberry Hill / Brown eyes
CD _____ DAD 3008CD
4AD / May '93 / Disc.

RED HOUSE PAINTERS
Evil / Bubble / I am a rock / Helicopter / New Jersey / Uncle Joe / Blindfold / Star spangled banner
CD _____ CAD 3016CD
4AD / Oct '93 / Disc.

Red Jasper

ACTION REPLAY
CD _____ HTDDWCD 9
HTD / Nov '92 / Pinnacle.

STING IN THE TALE
Faceless people / Guy Fawkes / TV screen / Second coming / Old Jack / Company director / Secret society / Magpie / I can hew
CD _____ HTD CD 3
HTD / Dec '90 / Pinnacle.

Red Lorry Yellow Lorry

BEST OF RED LORRY YELLOW LORRY
CD _____ CLEO 9404
Cleopatra / Jun '94 / Disc.

BLASTING OFF
CD _____ DW 23556CD
Deathwish / Nov '92 / Plastic Head.

NOTHING WRONG
Nothing wrong / Do you understand / Calling (Extra track on 12".) / Big stick / Hands off me / She said / Sayonara / World around / Hard-away / Only dreaming / Never know / Pushing on / Time is tight
CD _____ SITU 20 CD
Situation 2 / May '88 / Pinnacle.

Beating my head / I'm still waiting / Take it all away / Happy / He's red / See the fire / Monkey's on juice / Push / Silence / Hollow eyes / Feel a piece / Chance / Generation / Spinning around / Hold yourself down / Regenerate / Walking on your hands / Which side / Jipp (instrumental mix) / Cut down / Burning fever / Pushed me / Crawling mantra / Hangman / All the same / Shout at the sky
CD _____ CDMRED 109
Cherry Red / Feb '94 / Pinnacle.

SMASHED HITS
Beating my head / He's red / Monkeys on juice / Spinning round / Cut down / Take it all / Hollow eyes / Generation / Hold yourself down / Chance
CD _____ DOJOCD 210
Dojo / May '95 / BMG.

TALK ABOUT THE WEATHER/PAINT YOUR WAGON
CD _____ CDMRED 115
Cherry Red / Jun '94 / Pinnacle.

Red Moon Joe

ARMS OF SORROW
CD _____ RRACD 013
Haven/Backs / Oct '91 / Disc / Pinnacle.

Red Onion Jazzband

CREOLE RHAPSODY
CD _____ BCD 309
GHB / Jul '93 / Jazz Music.

Red Red Meat

RED RED MEAT
CD _____ RRM 001
Sub Pop / Feb '95 / Disc.

Red River

TEXAS ADVICE
Ride ride ride / Comin' to you live / Eight chrome and wings / Come on over / Dry business blues / Ain't workin' no more / Broke again / Lucky tonight / Cheap thrills / Texas advice / At the roadhouse tonite / I'll drink your booze / Talkin' to me / Something's gotta give / Goin' down / Mercury / Fools paradise / City doesn't weep
CD _____ ROSE 210CD
New Rose / Aug '90 / Direct / ADA.

Red Rodney

BIRD LIVES
CD _____ MCD 5371
Muse / Sep '92 / New Note / CM.

FIERY
Star eyes / You better go now / Stella by starlight / Red arrow / Box 2000 / Ubas
CD _____ SV 0148
Savoy Jazz / Jan '94 / Conifer / ADA.

NO TURN ON RED (Red Rodney Quintet)
No turn on red / Bishop / Young and foolish / Observation and celebration / Answered prayer / But, but, what if / Red giant / Quick pick / Greensleeves
CD _____ CY 73149
Denon / Apr '89 / Conifer.

RED GIANT
CD _____ SCCD 31233
Steeplechase / '88 / Impetus.

SOCIETY RED (Red Rodney & The Danish Jazz Army)
Music Mecca / Oct '89 / Jazz Music / Cadillac / Wellard. _____ MECCACD 1003

Red Rooster

STRAIGHT FROM THE HEART
CD _____ MAPCD 93005
Music & Words / Aug '94 / ADA / Direct.

Red Sekta

ANODIZE
CD _____ EFA 125102
Celtic Circle / May '95 / SRD.

Red Shoe Diaries

RED SHOE DIARIES
CD _____ WWRCD 6001
Wienerworld / Jun '95 / Disc.

Red Snapper

REELED AND SKINNED
CD _____ WARPCD 33
Warp / Jun '95 / Disc.

Red Stripe Ebony Steel...

BEST OF STEELDRUMS (Red Stripe Ebony Steel Band)
CD _____ EUCD 1110
ARC / '91 / ARC Music / ADA.

PRESENTS: POPULAR BEATLES SONGS (Red Stripe Ebony Steel Band)
CD _____ EUCD 1152
ARC / '91 / ARC Music / ADA.

Red Sun

THEN COMES THE WHITE TIGER (Red Sun & Samul Nori)
CD _____ 5217342
ECM / Oct '94 / New Note.

Red Thunder

MAKOCE WAKAN
CD _____ 379162
Koch International / Dec '95 / Koch.

Red Velvet Trio

MILLION TEARS
CD _____ TBCD 2007
Nervous / Mar '93 / Nervous / Magnum Music Group.

Redagain P

GIGANTOCHELONIA
Tretcho Inc / Soid a sonic / Troitanica / Cyclips / Aclipted inquesting / Zoola trique / X-Clewats / Therapeu-dance
CD _____ 950119CD
Source / Jul '95 / Vital.

Redbone, Leon

CHRISTMAS ISLAND
White Christmas / Winter wonderland / Frosty the snowman / Blue Christmas / There's no place like home for the holidays / Toyland / Christmas Island / That old Christmas moon / I'll be home for Christmas / Let it snow, let it snow, let it snow / Christmas ball blues
CD _____ AS 8890CD
August / Jan '94 / Direct.

RED TO BLUE
CD _____ SHCD 3840
Sugarhill / Aug '95 / Roots / CM / ADA / Direct.

SUGAR
Ghost of the Saint Louis blues / Roll along Kentucky moon / Right or wrong / Laughing blues / Breeze / Whistling colonel / Sugar / Pretty baby / When I take my sugar to tea / What you want me to do / Messin' around / So relax / 14th Street blues
CD _____ 260 555
Private Music / Mar '90 / BMG.

UP A LAZY RIVER
Play gypsy play / At the chocolate bon bon ball / Lazy river / When Dixie stars are playing peek-a-boo / Mr. Jelly Roll Baker / Gotta shake that thing / You're a heartbreaker / Bittersweet waltz / Goodbye Charlie blues / That old familiar blues / Dreamer's holiday / I'm going home
CD _____ 262666
Private Music / Apr '92 / BMG.

WHISTLING IN THE WIND
Dancin' on Daddy's shoes / When I kissed that girl goodbye / Bouquet of roses / Truckin' 101 / Sittin' by the fire / Crazy over Dixie / Little grass shack / Love letters in the sand / You're gonna lose your gal / If I could be with you one hour tonight / Crazy about my baby / I ain't got nobody
CD _____ 100582117-2
Private Music / Apr '94 / BMG.

Redcell

ESOTERIK/BLUE BINARY (Redcell/Cmetric)
CD _____ B12CD 2
B12 / Jan '96 / Kudos.

Redd Kross

PHASESHIFTER
CD _____ 5181672
Phonogram / Jan '94 / PolyGram.

Redd, Sharon

ESSENTIAL DANCEFLOOR ARTISTS VOL. 3
CD _____ DGPCD 696
Deep Beats / Jun '94 / BMG.

SHARON REDD COLLECTION
CD _____ CCSCD 388
Castle / Oct '93 / BMG.

Redding, Noel

MISSING ALBUM, THE (Redding, Noel Band)
CD _____ MSCD 005
Mouse / Feb '95 / Grapevine.

Redding, Otis

DOCK OF THE BAY (The Definitive Collection)
Shake / Mr. Pitiful / Respect / Love man / Satisfaction / I can't turn you loose / Hard to handle / Fa fa fa fa (sad song) / My girl / I've been loving you too long / Try a little tenderness / That's how strong my love is / Pain in my heart / Change is gonna come / (Sittin' on) the dock of the bay / Cigarettes and coffee (CD only) / These arms of mine (CD only) / Tramp (CD only)
CD _____ 9548317092
Atlantic / Nov '92 / Warner Music.

I'VE BEEN LOVIN' YOU TOO LONG
CD _____ TS 022
That's Soul / Mar '94 / BMG.

IMMORTAL OTIS REDDING, THE
I've got dreams to remember / You made a man out of me / Nobody's fault but mine / Thousand miles away / Happy song / Think about it / Waste of time / Champagne and wine / Fool for you / Amen
CD _____ 7567802702
Atlantic / Mar '95 / Warner Music.

IT'S NOT JUST SENTIMENTAL
Trick or treat / Loving by the pound 1 / There goes my baby / Remember me / Send me some lovin' / She's alright / Cupid / Boston monkey / Don't be afraid of love / Little ol' me / Loving by the pound 2 / You got good lovin' / Gone again / I'm coming home / (Sittin' on) the dock of the bay (Not on LP) / Respect (Not on LP) / Open the door (Not on LP) / I've got dreams to remember (Not on LP) / Come to me (Not on LP) / Try a little tenderness (Not on LP) / Stay in school (Not on LP)
CD _____ CDSXD 041
Stax / Jan '92 / Pinnacle.

KING AND QUEEN (Redding, Otis & Carla Thomas)
CD _____ 7567822562
Atlantic / Nov '92 / Warner Music.

LIVE AT THE WHISKEY-A-GO-GO #1
I can't turn you loose / Pain in my heart / Just one more day / Mr. Pitiful / Satisfaction / I'm depending on you / Any ole way / These arms of mine / Papa's got a brand new bag / Respect
CD _____ 8122703802
Pickwick/Warner / Oct '94 / Pinnacle / Warner Music / Carlton Home Entertainment.

LIVE AT THE WHISKEY-A-GO-GO #2 (Good To Me)
Introduction / I'm depending on you / Your one and only man / Good to me / Chained and bound / Ol' man trouble / Pain in my heart / These arms of mine / I can't turn you loose / I've been loving you too long / Security / Hard day's night
CD _____ CDSX 089
Stax / Apr '93 / Pinnacle.

LIVE IN EUROPE
Respect / I can't turn you loose / I've been loving you too long / My girl / Shake / Satisfaction / Fa fa fa fa (Sad song) / These arms of mine / Day tripper / Try a little tenderness
CD _____ 7567903952
Pickwick/Warner / Feb '95 / Pinnacle / Warner Music / Carlton Home Entertainment.

LOVE MAN
I'm a changed man / (Your love has lifted me) Higher and higher / That's a good idea / I'll let nothing separate us / Direct me / Love man / Groovin' time / Your feeling is mine / Got to get myself together / Free me / Lover's question / Look at that girl
CD _____ 8122702942
Atlantic / Nov '92 / Warner Music.

OTIS (The Definitive Otis Redding/4CD Set)
CD Set _____ 8122714392
Atlantic / Oct '93 / Warner Music.

OTIS BLUE
Ole man trouble / Respect / Change is gonna come / Down in the valley / I've been loving you too long / Shake / My girl / Wonderful world / Rock me baby / Satisfaction / You don't miss your water
CD _____ 7567803182
Atlantic / Nov '92 / Warner Music.

OTIS REDDING DICTIONARY OF SOUL
Fa fa fa fa (sad song) / I'm sick y'all / Tennessee waltz / My sweet Lorene / Try a little tenderness / Day tripper / My lover's prayer / She put the hurt on me / Ton of joy / You're still my baby / Hawg for you / Love have mercy
CD _____ 7567917072
Atlantic / Nov '92 / Warner Music.

OTIS REDDING STORY, THE (3CD Set)
These arms of mine / That's what my heart needs / Mary's little lamb / Pain in my heart / Something is worrying me / Security / Come to me / I've been loving you too long / Change is gonna come / Shake / Rock me baby / Respect / You don't miss your water / Satisfaction / Chain gang / My lover's prayer / It's growing / Fa fa fa fa (sad song) / I'm sick y'all / Sweet Lorene / Try a little tenderness / Day tripper / Stay in school / You left the water running / Happy song / Hard to handle / Amen / I've got dreams to remember / Champagne and wine / Direct me / Your one and only man / Chained and bound / That's how strong my love is / Mr. Pitiful / Keep your arms around me / For your precious love / Woman, a lover, a friend / Home in your heart / Ole man trouble / Down in the valley / I can't turn you loose / Just one more day / Papa's got a brand new bag / Good to me / Cigarettes and coffee / Ton of joy / Hawg for you / Tramp / Knock on wood / Lovey dovey / New year's resolution / Ooh Carla ooh Otis / Merry Christmas baby / White

Christmas / Love man / Free me / Look at that girl / Match game / Tell the truth / (Sittin' on) the dock of the bay
CD Set _____ 756781762-2
Atlantic / Mar '93 / Warner Music.

PAIN IN MY HEART
Pain in my heart / Dog / Stand by me / Hey hey baby / You send me / I need your lovin' / These arms of mine / Louie Louie / Something is worrying me / Security / That's what my heart needs / Lucille
CD _____ 756780253-2
Atlantic / Jun '93 / Warner Music.

SOUL ALBUM, THE
Just one more day / It's growing / Cigarettes and coffee / Chain gang / Nobody knows you (when you're down and out) / Good to me / Scratch my back / Treat her right / Everybody makes a mistake / Any ole way / 634 5789
CD _____ 7567917052
Atlantic / Nov '92 / Warner Music.

SOUL BALLADS
That's how strong my love is / Chained and bound / Woman, a lover, a friend / Your one and only man / Nothing can change this love / It's too late for your precious love / I want to thank you / Come to me / Home in your heart / Keep your arms around me / Mr. Pitiful
CD _____ 7567917062
Atlantic / Nov '92 / Warner Music.

TELL THE TRUTH
Demonstration / Tell the truth / Out of sight / Give away none of my love / Wholesale love / I got the will / Johnny's heartbreak / Snatch a little piece / Slippin' and slidin' / Match game / Little time / Swingin' on a string
CD _____ 8122702952
Atlantic / Nov '92 / Warner Music.

Reddog

AFTER THE RAIN
CD _____ TX 1008CD
Taxim / Jan '94 / ADA.

Reddy, Helen

FEEL SO YOUNG (The Helen Reddy Collection)
Angie baby / You make me feel so young / Let's go up / I am woman / That's all / Ain't no way to treat a lady / Lost in the shuffle / Looks like love / Here in my arms / You and me against the world
CD _____ CDSGP 0124
Prestige / Apr '95 / Total/BMG.

VERY BEST OF HELEN REDDY
Angie baby / Raised on rock / Leave me alone (ruby red dress) / Delta dawn / Peaceful / Our house / Emotion / I don't know how to love him / Crazy love / How / Lady of the night / Keep on singing / Somewhere in the night / Bluebird / Come on John / Don't mess with a woman / Candle on the water (live) / You're my world / I can't hear you no more / You and me against the world / Ain't no way to treat a lady / I am woman
CD _____ CDGO 2044
Capitol / Sep '92 / EMI.

Redman

DARE IZ A DARKSIDE
CD _____ 5238462
RAL / Dec '94 / PolyGram.

WHUT THEE ALBUM
Psycho ward / Time 4 sum aksion / Da funk / News break / So ruff / Rated R / Watch yo nuggets / Psycho dub / Jam 4 U / Blow your mind / Hardcore / Funky uncles / Redman meets Reggie Noble / Tonight's da night / Blow your mind (remix) / I'm a bad / Sessed one night / How to roll a blunt / Sooper lover interview / Day of sooperman lover / Encore
CD _____ 462259 2
Sony Music / Dec '92 / Sony.

Redman, Dewey

AFRICAN VENUS
African Venus / Venus and Mars / Mr. Sandman / Echo prayer / Satin doll / Take the 'A' train / Turnaround
CD _____ ECD 220932
Evidence / Jul '94 / Harmonia Mundi / ADA / Cadillac.

CHOICES
Le cut / Everything happens to me / O'besso / Imagination / For mo
CD _____ ENJACD 70732
Enja / Jan '95 / New Note / Vital/SAM.

LIVING ON THE EDGE (Redman, Dewey Quartet)
CD _____ 1201232
Black Saint / Oct '90 / Harmonia Mundi / Cadillac.

Redman, Don

1931-1933
CD _____ CLASSICS 543
Classics / Dec '90 / Discovery / Jazz Music.

1932-33 (Redman, Don & His Orchestra)
CD _____ 3801052
Jazz Archives / Feb '93 / Jazz Music / Discovery / Cadillac.

1936-1939 (Redman, Don & His Orchestra)
Moonrise on the lowlands / I gotcha / Who wants to sing my love song / Too bad / We don't know from nuthin' / Bugle call rag / Stormy weather / Exactly like you / Man on the flying trapeze / On the sunny side of the street / Swingin' with the fat man / Sweet Sue, just you
CD _____ CLASSICS 574
Classics / Oct '91 / Discovery / Jazz Music.

DOIN' WHAT I PLEASE
Beau Koo Jack / Bugle call rag / Cherry / Chant of the weed / Doin' what I please / Gee baby ain't I good to you / Got the jitters / Henderson stomp / Hot and anxious / Hot mustard / How'm I doin' / I got rhythm / Miss Hannah / Nagasaki / Paducah / Rocky Road / Save it pretty Mama / Shakin' the African / Sophisticated lady / Sugarfoot stomp / Sweet Leilani / Sweet Sue, just you / Swingin' with the fat man / That's how I feel today / Whiteman stomp
CD _____ CDAJA 5110
Living Era / Sep '93 / Koch.

Redman, Joshua

LIVE AT THE VANGUARD
CD _____ 9362459232
Warner Bros. / Aug '95 / Warner Music.

MOOD SWING
CD _____ 936245643-2
Warner Bros. / Sep '94 / Warner Music.

WISH
Turnaround / Soul dance / Make sure you're sure / Deserving many / We had a sister / Moose the mooche / Tears in heaven / Whittlin' / Wish / Blues for Pat (Live)
CD _____ 9362453652
Warner Bros. / Dec '93 / Warner Music.

Rednex

SEX AND VIOLINS
CD _____ KGBD 502
Internal Affairs / Mar '95 / BMG.

Redouane, Aicha

EGYPTE
CD _____ C 560020
Ocora / Jan '94 / Harmonia Mundi / ADA.

Redpath, Jean

FINE SONG FOR SINGING, A
I will make you brooches / Up the Noran water / Caprice song of Mary Stuart / Wild geese / Capernaum / Now the die is cast / South wind / Song of wandering aengus / Rohallion / Tryst / John O'Dreams / Broom o'the Cowdenknowes / Annie Laurie / Broken brook
CD _____ CDPH 1110
Philo / '88 / Direct / CM / ADA.

FIRST FLIGHT
CD _____ R 11556CD
Rounder / Jul '90 / CM / Direct / ADA / Cadillac.

JEAN REDPATH
CD _____ CDPH 2015
Philo / '90 / Direct / CM / ADA.

LEAVING THE LAND
Leaving the land / Miss Admiral Gordon's Strathspey / Scarborough settler's lament / Un Canadien errant / Last minstrel show / Snow goose / Next time round / Sonny's dream / Maggie / Halloween / Leaving Lerwick harbour / Now I'm easy / Wild lass
CD _____ CDTRAX 029
Greentrax / Nov '90 / Conifer / Duncans / ADA / Direct.

LOWLANDS
CD _____ PH 1066CD
Philo / Aug '94 / Direct / CM / ADA.

SONGS OF ROBERT BURNS VOLUME 7
Mauchline lady / O merry hae I been / Gallant weaver / Young highland rover / Cauld is the e'enin blast / My father was a farmer / My love / She's but a lassie yet / Ode to Spring / O' guid ale comes / Bonnie lass o'Albanie / O, for ane-and-twenty, Tam / Where are the joys
CD _____ CDTRAX 039
Greentrax / Nov '90 / Conifer / Duncans / ADA / Direct.

SONGS OF THE SEAS
CD _____ PHCD 1054
Philo / Aug '94 / Direct / CM / ADA.

Redskins

LIVE
CD _____ DOJOCD 188
Dojo / Jun '94 / BMG.

Redway, Mike

MOONLIGHT AND LOVE SONGS
CD _____ RKD 14
Redrock / Dec '94 / THE / Target/BMG.

THOSE BEAUTIFUL BALLAD YEARS
Lark in the clear air / Rose of Killarney / Passing by / On the banks of the Wabash / I love the moon / Barbara Allen / I dream of Jeannie with the light brown hair / Just aweary'n for you / I'll be your sweetheart / When you and I were young Maggie / Mighty like a rose
CD _____ RKD 7
Redrock / Dec '94 / THE / Target/BMG.

Reece, Dizzy

BLUES IN TRINITY
Blues in trinity / I had the craziest dream / Close up / Shepherd's serenade / Color blind / Round Midnight / Eboo (CD only.) / Just a penny (CD only.)
CD _____ CDP 8320932
Blue Note / Aug '95 / EMI.

Reed, A.C.

I GOT MONEY (Reed, A.C. & M. Vaughn)
CD _____ BLE 597272
Black & Blue / Oct '94 / Wellard / Koch.

I'M IN THE WRONG BUSINESS
I'm in the wrong business / I can't go on this way / Fast food Annie / This little voice / My buddy buddy friends / She's fine / These blues is killing me / Miami strut / Things I want you to do / Don't drive drunk / Hard times / Going to New York / Moving out of the ghetto
CD _____ ALCD 4757
Alligator / May '93 / Direct / ADA.

Reed, Dalton

LOUISIANA SOUL MAN
Read me my rights / Blues of the month club / Keep on loving me / Last to understand / Heavy love / Full moon / Keep the spirit / I'm only guilty of loving you / Party on the farm / Chained and bound
CD _____ CDBB 9517
Bullseye Blues / Sep '92 / Direct.

WILLING AND ABLE
CD _____ BB 9547
Bullseye Blues / Apr '94 / Direct.

Reed, Eric

SOLDIER'S HYMN
CD _____ CCD 9511
Candid / Nov '93 / Cadillac / Jazz Music / Wellard / Koch.

SWING AND I, THE
CD _____ 5304682
Mo Jazz / May '95 / PolyGram.

Reed, Jimmy

BEST OF JIMMY REED
CD _____ GNPD-10006
GNP Crescendo / Jan '88 / Silva Screen.

BRIGHT LIGHTS, BIG CITY (Charly Blues - Masterworks Vol 17)
You don't have to go / I don't go for that / Ain't that lovin' you baby / Can't stand to see you go / I love you baby / You've got me dizzy / Honey / Where you going / Little rain / Sun is shining / Honest I do / Down in Virginia / I'm gonna get my baby / Baby, what you want me to do / I love you / Hush hush / Big boss man / Bright lights big city / Aw shucks hush your mouth / Good lover / Shame, shame, shame
CD _____ CDBM 1324
Charly / Apr '92 / Charly / THE / Cadillac.

CARESS ME BABY
CD _____ CDSGP 086
Prestige / Oct '93 / Total/BMG.

GREATEST HITS
Sun is shining / Honest I do / Down in Virginia / Baby, what you want me to do / Found love / Hush hush / Bright lights big city / Close together / Big boss man / Aw shucks hush your mouth / Good lover / Shame, shame, shame / I ain't got you / I'm forty upside your head / Pretty ring
CD _____ CDCD 1040
Charly / Mar '93 / Charly / THE / Cadillac.

GUITAR, HARMONICA AND FEELING
High and lonesome / Jimmie's boogie / You don't have to go / Boogie in the dark / You upset my mind / She don't want me no more / I don't go for that / Ain't that lovin' you baby / You got for that / You got me dizzy / Honest I do / Sun is shining / End and odds / My bitter seed / Going to New York / Take out some insurance / Baby, what you want me to do / Hush hush / Found love / You gonna need my help / Found joy / Kind of lonesome / Blue Carnagie / Big boss man / Sugar sugar / Jimmy's rock / Bright lights big city / I'm going upside your head
CD _____ CD 52012
Blues Encore / '92 / Target/BMG.

JIMMY REED - THE VEE JAY RECORDS (6CD Set)
High and lonesome / Jimmie's boogie / I found my baby / Roll and rhumba / You don't have to go / Boogie in the dark / Shoot my baby / Rockin' with Reed / You upset my mind / I'm gonna ruin you / Pretty thing / I ain't got you / She don't want me no more / Come on baby / I don't go for

that / Baby, don't say that no more / Ain't that lovin' you baby / Can't stand to see you go / When you left me / I love you baby / My first plea / You got me dizzy / Honey don't let me go / Untitled instrumental / It's you baby / Honey where you going / Do the thing / Little rain / Signals of love / Sun is shining / Baby, what's on your mind / Honest I do / State street boogie / Odds and ends / My baby (Down in Virginia) / You're something else / String to your heart / Go on to school / You got me crying / Moon is rising / Down in Virginia / I'm gonna get my baby / I wanna be loved / Caress me baby / I know it's a sin / You'n that sack / Going to New york / I told you baby / take out some insurance / I'm nervous / You know I love you / Baby, what you want me to do / Goin' by the river (1) / Goin' by the river (2) / Where can you be / Hush hush / I was so wrong / Blue blue water / Please don't / Found love / You gonna need my help / Hold me close / Come love / Big boss man / Meet me / I got the blues / Sugar sugar / Got me chasing you / Down the road / Want to be with you baby / Jimmy's rock / Tell the world I do / You're my baby / Ain't gonna cry no more / Close together / You know you're looking good / Laughing at the blues / I'm a love you / Kind of lonesome / Found joy / Tell me you love me / Bright lights / Baby what's wrong / Aw shucks / Hush your mouth / I'm Mr. Luck / Blue Carnegie / Take it slow / Good lover / Down in Mississippi / Too much / I'll change my style / Let's get together / In the morning / You can't hide / Back home at noon / Lookin' for you baby / Kansas city baby / Oh John / Shame, shame, shame / Cold and lonesome / There'll be a day / Ain't no big deal / Mary Mary / Upside the wall / Baby's so sweet / I'm gonna help you / Up tight / Mixed up / I'm trying to please you / Five long years / See see sider / Outskirts of town / Trouble in mind / Comebacks / How long blues / Roll 'em Pete / Cherry red / Wee wee baby / St. Louis blues / Worried life blues / Blues for 12 strings / New Chicago blues / Wear something green / Help yourself / Heading for a fall / Going fishing / Left handed woman / I wanna be loved (Crazy love) / Fifteen years / New leaf / When you're doing all right / I'm going upside your head / Devil's shoestring 2 / You've got me waiting / I'm the man down there / When girls do it / Don't think I'm through
CD Set _____ CDREDBOX 9
Charly / Feb '94 / Charly / THE / Cadillac.

TAKE OUT SOME INSURANCE
CD _____ CDRB 13
Charly / Jul '93 / Charly / THE / Cadillac.

VERY BEST OF JIMMY REED, THE (& Roots Of The Blues #5 Compilation/3CD Set)
I found my baby / You don't have to go / I'm gonna ruin you / She don't want me no more / I don't go for that / Ain't that lovin' you baby / Can't stand to see you go / I love you baby / You got me dizzy / Honey, where you going / Do the thing / Little rain / Sun is shining / Odds and ends / Honest I do / My bitter seed / Moon is rising / Down in Virginia / I'm gonna get my baby / I wanna be loved / Take out some insurance / What do you want me to do / Hush-hush / Found love / Come love / Big boss man / Close together / Tell me you love me / Bright lights / Big city / Baby / What's wrong / Aw shucks / Hush your mouth / Good lover / Too much / I'll change my style / Let's get together / Shame, shame, shame / When you're doing all right / I'm going upside your head / I'm the man down there / St Louis Blues / Matchbox / Big road blues / Got the blues can't be satisfied / Going up the country / Spoonful blues / Sugar Mama blues / Honky tonk train blue / Lead pencil blues / Sweet home Chicago / Just a dream / Jeremona blues / Good morning blues / Country jail blues / country blues
CD Set _____ VBCD 1325
Charly / Jul '95 / Charly / THE / Cadillac.

Reed, Kay

WE ARE ONE
CD _____ GBW 006
GBW / Jan '93 / Harmonia Mundi.

Reed, Lou

BELLS, THE
CD _____ 262918
RCA / Aug '92 / BMG.

BERLIN
Berlin / Lady Day / Men of good fortune / Caroline says / How do you think it feels / Oh Jim / Caroline says II / Kids / Bed / Sad song
CD _____ ND 84388
RCA / Jun '86 / BMG.

BETWEEN THOUGHT AND EXPRESSION (Lou Reed Anthology Box Set/3CD Set)
I can't stand it / Lisa says / Ocean / Walk on the wild side / Satellite of love / Vicious / Caroline says (1) / How do you think it feels / Oh Jim / Caroline says (2) / Kids / Sad song / Sweet Jane / Kill your sons / Coney Island baby / Nowhere at all / Kicks

/ Downtown dirt / Rock 'n' roll heart / Vicious circle / Temporary thing / Real good time together / Leave me alone / Heroin / Here comes the bride / Street hassle / Metal machine music / Bells / America / Think it over / Teach the gifted children / Gun / Blue mask / My house / Waves of fear / Little sister / Legendary hearts / Last shot / New sensations / My friend George / Doin' the things that we want to / Original wrapper / Video violence / Tell it to your heart / Voices of freedom
CD Set _____ PD 906213
RCA / Mar '92 / BMG.

CONEY ISLAND BABY
Crazy feeling / Charley's girl / She's my best friend / Kicks / Gift / Oooh baby / Nobody's business / Coney Island baby
CD _____ ND 83807
RCA / Dec '86 / BMG.

GROWING UP IN PUBLIC
How do you speak to an angel / My old man / Keep away / Standing on ceremony / So alone / Love is here to stay / Power of positive drinking / Smiles / Think it over / Teach the gifted children
CD _____ 262917
Arista / Aug '92 / BMG.

LEGENDARY HEARTS
Legendary hearts / Don't talk to me about work / Make up / Martial law / Last shot / Turn out the light / Pow wow / Betrayed / Bottoming out / Home of the brave / Rooftop garden
CD _____ ND 89843
RCA / Apr '91 / BMG.

LOU REED AND THE VELVET UNDERGROUND (Reed, Lou & Velvet Underground)
CD _____ RADCD 21
Global / Oct '95 / BMG.

LOU REED LIVE
Vicious / Satellite of love / Walk on the wild side / I'm waiting for the man / Oh Jim / Sad song
CD _____ ND 83752
RCA / Feb '90 / BMG.

MAGIC AND LOSS
Dorita / What's good / Power and glory / Magician / Sword of damocles / Goodby mass / Cremation / Dreamin' / No change / Warrior king / Harry's circumcision / Grassed and stoked / Power and glory part II / Magic and loss
CD _____ 7599266622
Sire / Jan '92 / Warner Music.

NEW YORK
Romeo and Juliet / Halloween parade / Dirty boulevard / Endless cycle / There is no time / Last great American whale / Beginning of a great mystery / Busload of faith / Sick of you / Hold on / Good evening Mr. Waldheim / Christmas in February / Strawman / Dime store mystery
CD _____ 7599258292
Sire / Feb '95 / Warner Music.

ROCK AND ROLL HEART
I believe in love / Banging on my drum / Follow the leader / You wear it so well / Ladies pay / Rock 'n' roll heart / Temporary thing
CD _____ 262271
Arista / Feb '93 / BMG.

SALLY CAN'T DANCE
Ride Sally ride / Animal language / Baby face / NY stars / Kill your sons / Billy / Sally can't dance / Ennui
CD _____ ND 90308
RCA / Feb '89 / BMG.

SET THE TWILIGHT REELING
CD _____ 9362461592
Sire / Feb '96 / Warner Music.

STREET HASSLE
Gimme some good times / Dirt / Street hassle / I wanna be black / Real good time together / Shooting star
CD _____ 262270
Arista / Feb '93 / BMG.

TRANSFORMER
Vicious / Andy's chest / Perfect day / Hangin' around / Walk on the wild side / Make up / Satellite of love / Wagon wheel / New York telephone conversation / I'm so free / Goodnight ladies
CD _____ ND 83806
RCA / Aug '95 / BMG.

WALK ON THE WILD SIDE (Best Of Lou Reed)
Satellite of love / Wild child / I love you / How do you think it feels / New York telephone conversation / Walk on the wild side / Sweet Jane / White light, white heat / Sally can't dance / Nowhere at all / Coney Island baby / Vicious
CD _____ ND 83753
RCA / Oct '91 / BMG.

Reed, Lucy

BASIC REEDING
CD _____ ACD 273
Audiophile / Apr '93 / Jazz Music / Swift.

Reed, Lulu

BLUE AND MOODY
CD _____ KCD 604
King/Paddle Wheel / Mar '90 / New Note.

BOY GIRL BOY (Reed, Lulu, Freddy King & Sonny Thompson)
CD _____ KCD 777
King/Paddle Wheel / Mar '90 / New Note.

Reed, Preston

ROAD LESS TRAVELLED, THE
CD _____ FF 70423
Flying Fish / Oct '89 / Roots / CM / Direct / ADA.

Reedstorm Saxophone...

JAZZ STANDARDS (Reedstorm Saxophone Quartet)
CD _____ BEST 1075CD
Acoustic Music / Nov '95 / ADA.

Reedus, Tony

FAR SIDE, THE
Far side / Song of Gideon / Never let me go / You and the night and the music / I just can't stop loving you / On Green Dolphin Street / Stumbling block / Summer night / End of a love affair / Calvary
CD _____ 66053016
Jazz City / Mar '91 / New Note.

Reedy, Winston

GOLD
CD _____ RNCD 2049
Rhino / Mar '94 / Jetstar / Magnum Music Group / THE.

Reef

REPLENISH
Feed me / Naked / Good feeling / Repulsive / Mellow / Together / Replenish / Choose to live / Comfort / Loose / End
CD _____ 4806982
Sony Soho2 / Jun '95 / Sony.

Reefa

LOVE LIFE LIVE LOVE
CD _____ STRSCD 4
Stress / Oct '94 / Pinnacle.

Reegs

RETURN OF THE SEA MONKEY
CD _____ ILLCD 029
Imaginary / May '91 / Vital.

ROCK THE MAGIC ROCK
J.J. 180 / Blind denial / Goodbye world / Dream police / Nasty side / Dolphin's enemy / In disbelief / Oil and water / Running to a standstill / Nasty side (instrumental)
CD _____ ILLCD 045
Imaginary / Oct '93 / Vital.

Reel 2 Real

MOVE IT (Reel 2 Real & The Mad Stuntman)
I like to move it (mixes) / Can you feel it (On LP only) / Raise your hands / One life to live / Stuntman's anthem / Erick More's anthem (Can you feel it) / Conway / Wine your body / R.E.X. / Toety / Go on move
CD _____ CDTIVA 1003
Positiva / Oct '94 / EMI.

REEL 2 REMIXED (Reel 2 Real & The Mad Stuntman)
Go on move (Mixes) / Can you feel it (Mixes) / I like to move it (Mixes) / Conway (Mixes) / Raise your hands (Mixes) / Stuntman's anthem (Mixes)
CD _____ CDTIVA 1007
Positiva / Aug '95 / EMI.

Reel Union

BROKEN HEARTED I'LL WANDER
CD _____ CLUNCD 033
Mulligan / Nov '86 / CM / ADA.

Reeltime

REELTIME
CD _____ GL 1154CD
Green Linnet / Jul '95 / Roots / CM / Direct / ADA.

Reese, Della

LIVE 1963 GAURD SESSIONS (Reese, Della & Duke Wellington)
CD _____ EBCD 21102
Flyright / Feb '94 / Hot Shot / Wellard / Jazz Music / CM.

Reese Project

FAITH, HOPE & CLARITY
CD _____ TRPCD 1
Network / Nov '92 / Sony / 3MV.

Reeves, Dianne

QUIET AFTER THE STORM
Hello haven't I seen you before / Comes love / Smile / Jive samba / Country preacher / Detour ahead / Vermonja / Sargaco mar / Nine / In a sentimental mood / When morning comes / Both sides now / Sing my heart
CD _____ CDP 8295112
Blue Note / Jun '95 / EMI.

Reeves, Goebel

HOBO'S LULLABY
Tramp's mother / I learned about women from her / Drifter (part 1) / Drifter (part 2) / When the clock struck seventeen / Blue undertaker's blues (part 1) / Blue undertaker's blues (part 2) / Fortunes galore / My mountain gal / Song of the sea / In the land of never was / Texas drifter's warning / Cowboy's lullaby / Hobo's lullaby / Drifter's buddy (drifter's prayer) / Cowboy's prayer / Happy days (I'll never leave old Dixieland) / Wayward son / Reckless Tex / Soldier's return / Miss Jackson, Tennessee / My mountain girl / Cold and hungry / Meet me at the crossroads, pal / Yodeling teacher / Kidnapped baby
CD _____ BCD 15680
Bear Family / Nov '94 / Rollercoaster / Direct / CM / Swift / ADA.

Reeves, Jim

BEST OF JIM REEVES, THE
CD _____ MATCD 317
Castle / Dec '94 / BMG.

CHRISTMAS COLLECTION
CD _____ ARC 94842
Arcade / Nov '92 / Sony / Grapevine.

CLASSIC COUNTRY
CD _____ CDSR 068
Telstar / May '95 / BMG.

COLLECTION, THE
Memories are made of this / Have you ever been lonely / My happiness / Mexicali rose / Take my hand, precious Lord / Charmaine / Distant drums / Goodnight Irene / I fall to pieces / Mary's boy child / I love you because / It's only a paper moon / Maria Elena / Have thine own way / White cliffs of Dover / You're free to go / Moon river / Auf wiedersehen sweetheart
CD _____ 74321142292
RCA / Jul '93 / BMG.

DEAR HEARTS AND GENTLE PEOPLE
Have I told you lately that I love you / Just call me lonesome / How's the world treating you / If heartaches are the fashion / Home / Dear hearts and gentle people / I'm beginning to forget you / Roly poly / Wind up doll / Sweet evening breeze / Your old love letters / Till the end of the world / Making believe / Oaklahoma hills
CD _____ CDSD 073
Sundown / Jun '92 / Magnum Music Group.

DISTANT DRUMS
Distant drums / I won't forget you / Is it really over / I missed me / Snowflake / Letter to my heart / Losing your love / This is it / Not until the next time / Good morning self / Where does a broken heart go / Overnight / Gods were angry with me
CD _____ WMCD 5635
Disky / May '94 / THE / BMG / Discovery / Pinnacle.

GENTLEMAN JIM (4CD Set)
I'm hurtin' inside / If you were mine / That's a sad affair / Yonder comes a sucker / Jimbo Jenkins / My lips are sealed / Your old love letters / Waltzing on top of the world / Beyond a shadow of a doubt / Love me a little bit more / According to my heart / Each time you leave / Highway to nowhere / Breeze (blow my baby back to me) / Roly poly / Tweedle o'twill / Have I told you lately that I love you / Oklahoma hills / Pickin' a chicken / I've got just the thing for you / I'm the mother of a honky tonk girl / Am I losing you / Don't tell me / I can't fly / Don't ask me why / Waiting for a train / Look behind you / Four walls / Honey, won't you please come home / Gods were angry with me / I know (and you know) / Young hearts / I heard my heart break last night / Image of me / Anna Marie / Seabreeze / Blue without my baby / I love you more / Theme of love (I love to say I love you) / Wishful thinking / Two shadows on your window / Everywhere you go (single version) / Teardrops in my heart / Yours / I don't see me in your eyes anymore / I get the blues when it rains / I care no more / Final affair / You belong to me / My happiness / Everywhere you go / Blues in my heart / Need me / That's my desire / He'll have to go / In a mansion stands my love / Billy Bayou / I'd like to be partners / I'm beginning to forget you / If heartaches are the fashion / Home after awhile / Overnight blue boy / Charmaine / Mona Lisa / Marie / Goodnight Irene / Linda / Maria Elena / My Mary Ramona / Margie / My Juanita / Sweet Sue, just you / Just you / Snowflake / But you love me daddy / But you love me daddy (2) / Throw another log on the fire / Making believe / Till the end of the world / How's the world treating you

/ Someday (you'll want me to want you) / Just call me lonesome / Fool such as I / May the good Lord bless and keep you / Dear hearts and gentle people / Satan can't hold me / Scarlet ribbons / How long has it been / Teach me how to pray / Evening prayer / Padre of old San Antone / Suppertime / It is no secret / God be with you / Beautiful life / In the garden / Precious memories / Whispering hope / Flowers / Sunset, the trees
CD Set _____ BCD 15439
Bear Family / Jun '89 / Rollercoaster / Direct / CM / Swift / ADA.

GENTLEMAN JIM (2CD Set)
CD Set _____ DBG 53031
Double Gold / Apr '94 / Target/BMG.

HAVE I TOLD YOU LATELY
CD _____ MU 5046
Musketeer / Oct '92 / Koch.

HE'LL HAVE TO GO
He'll have to go / Bimbo / I'd like to be / Billy Bayou / In a mansion stands my love / I'm getting better / I know one / I missed me / Yonder comes a sucker / Waiting for a train / Am I losing you / According to my heart / Four walls / Mexican Joe / Anna Marie / Blue boy / Softly and tenderly / Peace in the valley
CD _____ MUCD 9022
Start / Apr '95 / Koch.

I LOVE YOU MORE (Live)
If you were only mine / I love you more / Have I told you lately that I love you / Everywhere you go / Sweet evening breeze / Oklahoma hills where I was born / Evening prayer / Dear hearts and gentle people / I've lived a lot in my time / If heartaches are the fashion / Home / How's the world treating you / I'm beginning to forget you / Roly poly / Wind up / Your old love letters / Till the end of the world / Making believe / Just call me lonesome / Highway to nowhere / Beyond the shadow of a doubt
CD _____ DATOM 3
A Touch Of Magic / Apr '94 / Harmonia Mundi.

I LOVE YOU MORE
CD _____ CTS 55433
Country Stars / Oct '95 / Target/BMG.

INTIMATE JIM REEVES, THE
Dark moon / OH how I miss you tonight / Take me in your arms and hold me / I'm getting better / Almost / You're free to go / You're the only good thing / Have I stayed away too long / No one to cry to / I was just walking out the door / Room full of roses / We could
CD _____ 74321260482
RCA / Jun '95 / BMG.

JIM REEVES - SPECIAL EDITION
CD _____ CD 90244
RCA / Nov '94 / BMG.

JIM REEVES IN CONCERT
Yonder comes a sucker / Blue boy / Just call me lonesome / In a mansion stands my love / He'll have to go / Have I told you lately that I love you / I know one / Am I losing you / Your old love letters / Anna Marie / I'm beginning to forget you / I love you more / Waiting for a train / Mexican Joe / I missed me / According to my heart / Four walls / Bimbo / When God dips his love in my heart / Billy Bayou / If heartaches are the fashion / Peace in the valley
CD _____ TRTCD 122
TrueTrax / Dec '94 / THE.

JIM REEVES LIVE AT THE OPRY
CD _____ SSLCD 208
Savanna / Jun '95 / THE.

LEGENDS IN MUSIC - JIM REEVES
CD _____ LECD 060
Wisepack / Jul '94 / THE / Conifer.

LIVE AT THE OPRY
Yonder comes a sucker / Waiting for a train / Am I losing you / When God dips his love in my heart / According to my heart / Four walls / Mexican Joe / Anna Marie / Blue boy / Softly and tenderly Jesus is calling / He'll have to go / Bimbo / I'd like to be / Peace in the valley / Billy Bayou / In a mansion stands my love / I'm getting better / Give me that old time religion / I know one / I missed me
CD _____ CMFCD 008
Country Music Foundation / Oct '94 / Direct / ADA.

MEXICAN JOE
CD _____ CTS 55420
Country Stars / Jun '94 / Target/BMG.

REMEMBERING
Distant drums / He'll have to go / I love you because / I won't forget you / Adios amigo / There's a heartache following me / I won't come in while he's there / Have you ever been lonely / Missing you / I can't stop loving you / Fool such as I / From a Jack to a King / Nobody's fool / Mona Lisa / Tennessee
CD _____ PWKS 4120
Carlton Home Entertainment / Oct '92 / Carlton Home Entertainment.

SPOTLIGHT ON JIM REEVES
Have I told you lately that I love you / Just call me lonesome / How's the world treating you / If heartaches are the fashion / Home / Dear hearts and gentle people / I'm beginning to forget you / Roly poly / Wind up doll / Sweet evening breeze / Your old love letters / Till the end of the world / Making believe / Oklahoma hills / Highway to nowhere / If you were mine
CD _____ HADCD 126
Javelin / Feb '94 / THE / Henry Hadaway Organisation.

TWELVE SONGS OF CHRISTMAS
Jingle bells / Blue Christmas / Senor Santa Claus / Old Christmas card, An / Merry Christmas polka / White Christmas / Silver bells / C-H-R-I-S-T-M-A-S / O little town of Bethlehem / Mary's boy child / O come all ye faithful (Adeste Fidelis) / Silent night
CD _____ ND 82758
RCA / Oct '94 / BMG.

VERY BEST OF JIM REEVES VOL. 2, THE
Bimbo / Yonder comes a sucker / My lips are sealed / Four walls / Anna Maria / Billy Bayou / How can I write on paper (what I feel in my heart) / Losing your love / Adios amigo / I'm gonna change everything / Blue side of lonesome / I won't come in while he's there / I heard my heart break last night / That's when I see the blues (in your pretty brown eyes) / Angels don't lie / Missing you / How long has it been / This world is not my home / But you love me daddy / Old tige / Jim Reeves medley
CD _____ ND 90568
RCA / Aug '91 / BMG.

VERY BEST OF JIM REEVES, THE
He'll have to go / Distant drums / When two worlds collide / I missed me / Blizzard / This is it / Moonlight and roses / You're the only good thing (that's happened to me) / I love you because / I won't forget you / There's heartache following me / I hurt so much to see you go / Not until the next time / Is it really over / Snowflake / Guilty / I'd fight the world / Trying to forget / Nobody's fool / Welcome to my world
CD _____ ND 89017
RCA / Apr '90 / BMG.

WELCOME TO MY WORLD (14CD Set)
My heart's like a welcome mat / Teardrops of regret / Chicken hearted / I've never been so blue / What were you doing last night / Wagon load of love / I could cry / Mexican Joe / Butterfly love / Let me love you just a little / El rancho del rio / It's hard to love just one / Bimbo / Gypsy heart / Echo bonita / There I'll stop loving you / Beatin' on a ding dong / My rambling heart / Padre of old San Antone / Mother went a-walkin / I love you (and Ginny Wright) / I'll follow you / Penny candy / Where does a broken heart go / Wilder your heart beats (False start) / Wilder your heart beats / Drinking tequila / Red eyed and rowdy / Tahiti / Give me one more kiss / Are you the one / How many / Hillbilly waltz / Let me remember (Things I can't forget) / Spanish violins / Woman's love / Whispering willow / If you love me don't leave me / Each beat of my heart / Let me love you just a little (Alternative) / Then I'll stop loving you (Alternative) / Hillbilly waltz (Alternative) / Mexican Joe (Alternative) / Marriage of Mexican Joe / You're the sweetest thing / I've forgotten you / Sand in my shoes / There's someone who loves you / Heartbreaking baby / Did you darling / Standhy / I'll always love you / I never take no for an answer / Please leave my darling alone / You're slipping away from me / I'm hurtin' inside / If you were mine / That's a sad affair / Jimbo Jenkins / I've lived a lot in my time / Ichabod Crane / My lips are sealed / Your old love letters / Waltzing on top of the world / Beyond a shadow of a doubt / Love me a little bit more / According to my heart / Each time you leave / Highway to nowhere / Breeze (blow my baby back to me) / Roly poly / Tweedle o'twill / Have I told you lately that I love you / Oklahoma hills / Pickin' a chicken / I've got just the thing for you / Mother of a honky tonk girl / Am I losing you / Don't tell me / I can't fly / Don't ask me why / Waiting for a train / Look behind you / Four walls / Honey, won't you please come home / Gods were angry with me / I know (and you know) / Please come home / Young hearts / Image of me / Two shadows on your window / Teardrops in my heart / Yours / I don't see me in your eyes anymore / I get the blues when it rains / I care no more / Final affair / You belong to me / My happiness / Everywhere you go (LP master) / Everywhere you go (Single master) / Blues in my heart / Need me / That's my desire / Anna Marie / Seabreeze / Blue without my baby / I love you more / Theme of love (I love to say I love you) / Wishful thinking / Charmaine / Mona Lisa / Marie / Goodnight Irene / Linda / Maria Elena / My Mary / Ramona / Margie / My Juanita / Sweet Sue, just you / From the how to pray / Evening prayer / Suppertime / It is no secret / God be with you / Beautiful life / In the garden / Precious memories / Whispering hope / Flowers, the sunset, the trees / I'd like to be / Billy Bayou / Throw another log on the fire / Making believe / Till the end of the world / How's the world

treating you / Someday (you'll want me to want you) / Just call me lonesome / Fool such as I / May the good lord bless and keep you / Dear hearts and gentle people / Satan can't hold me / Scarlet ribbons / If heartaches are the fashion / Home / Partners / I'm beginning to forget you / He'll have to go / In a mansion stands my love / After a while / Snowflake / But you love me Daddy / You'll never be mine again / Stand at your window / What would you do / Don't you want to be my girl (Poor little doll) / Dark moon / You're free to go / You're the only good thing (that's happened to me) / No one to cry to / OH how I miss you tonight / I'm getting better / Have I stayed away too long / Room full of roses / I was just walking out the door / We could / Take me in your arms and hold me / Almost / I missed me / I know one / Fool's paradise / Blizzard / Wreck of number nine / Letter edged in black / Tie that binds / Danny boy / Streets of Laredo / Rodger Young / Mighty everglades / It is nothing to me / That silver haired Daddy of mine / Wild rose / It hurts so much (to see you go) / Trouble in the amen corner / I'm waiting for ships that never come in / Farmer and the Lord / Gun / Spell of the Yukon / Shifting whispering sands / Seven days / Old tige / Annabel Lee / Why do I love you / Too many parties and too many pals / Men with broken hearts / Somewhere along the line / Missing angel / How can I write on paper (what I feel in my heart) / I never pass there anymore / Losing your love / Railroad bum / When two worlds collide / Fallen star / Most of the time / Blue side of lonesome / I won't forget you / New All dressed up and lonely / Welcome to my world / Be honest / I fall to pieces / Just wanting in the rain / Blue skies / I'm a fool to care / It's no sin / Am I that easy to forget / Adios amigo / I'll fly away / Where do I go from here / This world is not my home / Oh gentle shepherd / Where we'll never grow old / I'd rathere have Jesus / Have thine own way / Night watch / Across the bridge / My cathedral / Take my hands precious Lord / We thank thee / I catch myself crying / (That's when I see the blues) In your pretty brown eyes / Where do I go to throw a picture away / Letter to my heart / Pride goes before a fall / Little ole you / I'm gonna change everything / Bolandse nooientjie / Ek verlang na jou / Die ou kalahari / Roses are red / Just out of reach / Memories are made of this / Stand in / After loving you / One that got away / I'd fight the world / When you are gone / Once upon a time / O little town of Bethlehem / Old Christmas card / Silent night / Mary's boy child / O come all ye faithful (Adeste fidelis) / White Christmas / Jingle bells / Merry Christmas polka / Blue Christmas / Senor Santa Claus / C-H-R-I-S-T-M-A-S / Daar doer in die bosveld / Ding dong / Draf maar aan ou ryperd / Die blonde matroos / JY is my liefling / Indie skadu van ou tafelberg / Sarie Marais / Geboorteplaas / Net 'n stille uurtjie / Nooientjie van die ou transvaal / Verre land / My blinde hart / Good morning self / Is this me / Teardrops on the rocks / Heartbreak in silhouette / Auf wiedersehen sweetheart / Golden memories and silver tears / Blue canadian rockies / White cliffs of Dover / Guilty / Hawaiian wedding song / True / Old Kalahari / I'm crying again / You are my love / Lonely music / There's a heartache following me / You kept me awake last night / Talking walls / Before I died / Little ole dime / Bottle take effect / World you left behind / I've enjoyed as much of this as I can stand / I don't let you mess over / From a Jack to a King / Silver bells / Born to be lucky / Kimberly Jim / Could I be falling in love / Search is ended / Strike it rich / I grew up / Diamonds in the sand / Stranger's just a friend / Roving gambler / Dolly with the dimpled knees / Nickel piece of candy / Love is no excuse / Look who's talking / Mexicali Rose / Carolina moon / Moon river / When I lost you / It's only a paper moon / Roses / There's a new moon over my shoulder / One dozen roses / Moonlight and roses / What's in it for me / Rosa Rio / Oh what it seemed to be / I guess I'm crazy / Angels dont' lie / Not until the next time / I won't come in while he's there / This is it / Make the world go away / There's that smile again / You'll never know / Is it really you / I can't stop loving you / In the misty moonlight / Missing you / Maureen / Distant drums / Storm / Trying to forget / I heard my heart break last night / Nobody's fool / Gypsy feet / Writing's on the wall / I love you because / It's nothing to me #2 / Jim Reeves medley / When did you leave Heaven / Christmas alone / once upon a time / Jesus is calling / Wagon load of love (1) / Wagon load of love (2) / I'll tell the world I love you / Girl I left behind / Chittlin' blues / Dissatisfied / Penny for your thoughts / Near the cross / Humpty Dumpty heart / Naughty Angeline / Got you on my mind / Tijuana / Yonder comes a sucker / Mary Carter paint (3) / Mary Carter paint (2) / Mary Carter paint (3) / Mary Carter paint (4) / I'm glad you're better / Please forgive / Right words / You darling you / One little Rose / I'd rather not know / Ballad of 96 / Lonesome waltz / Your wedding / Read this letter / I let the world pass me by / Send me back my love / My hands are clean / Crying in my sleep / Deep dark water / Before you came along / Crying is

my favourite mood / He will / Make me won-
derful in her eyes / Beyond the clouds
CD Set _____ BCDPI 15656
Bear Family / Jul '94 / Rollercoaster / Direct
/ CM / Swift / ADA.

WELCOME TO MY WORLD
Welcome to my world / Distant drums / Blizzard / I won't come while he's there / I love
you because I won't forget you / He'll have
to go / You're the only good thing (that's
ever happend to me) / Adios amigo / There's a heartache follow me / It hurts too
much to see you go
CD _____ 74321339412
Camden / Jan '96 / BMG.

YOUR OLD LOVE LETTERS
Have I told you lately that I love you / Just
call me lonesome / How's the world treating
you / If heartaches are the fashion / Home
/ Dear hearts and gentle people / I'm begin-
ning to forget you / Roly poly / Wind up /
Sweet evening breeze / Your old love letters
/ Till the end of the world / Making believe
/ Oklahoma blues / Highway to nowhere / If
you were mine / Everywhere you go / I love
you more / I've lived a lot in my time
CD _____ GRF 199
Tring / Jan '93 / Tring / Prism.

Reeves, Martha

**24 GREATEST HITS: MARTHA & THE
VANDELLAS (Reeves, Martha & The
Vandellas)**
CD _____ 530040-2
Motown / Jan '92 / PolyGram.

**DANCING IN THE STREET (Reeves,
Martha & The Vandellas)**
Dancing in the street / Heatwave / Jimmy
Mack / In the midnight hour / I want you
back / Come see about me / Gotta see
Jane / Nowhere to run / Spooky / It's the
same old song / I say a little prayer / Get
ready / I heard it through the grapevine
CD _____ CDCD 1140
Charly / Nov '93 / Charly / THE / Cadillac.

**DANCING IN THE STREETS (Reeves,
Martha & The Vandellas)**
Dancing in the street / Nowhere to run /
Heatwave / I'm ready to love / Third finger
left hand / Jimmy Mack / Motoring / You've
been in love too long / My baby loves me /
I gotta let you go / Come and get these
memories / Love like yours (Don't come
knocking everyday) / Forget me not /
Quicksand
CD _____ 530230-2
Motown / Jan '92 / PolyGram.

**WE MEET AGAIN/GOTTA KEEP
MOVING**
Free again / You're like sunshine / I feel like
magic / One line from every love song /
Love don't come no stranger / What are you
doing the rest of your life / Dedicated to be
your woman / Special to me / Skating in the
streets / That's what I want / Really like your
rap / Gotta keep moving / Then you came
/ If it wasn't for my baby
CD _____ CDSEWD 083
Southbound / Jul '93 / Pinnacle.

Reeves, Reuben

**REUBEN REEVES & OMER SIMEON
(1929-33) (Reeves, Reuben 'River' &
Omer Simeon)**
CD _____ JPCD 1516
Jazz Perspectives / May '95 / Jazz Music
/ Hot Shot.

Reflexionen

LIVE AT MONTREUX 1987
Mood 20 / Mountain song 1 / Waves
CD _____ BW 016
B&W / Sep '93 / New Note.

Refused

THIS IS THE NEW DEAL
CD _____ BHR 002
Burning Heart / Oct '94 / Plastic Head.

THIS JUST MIGHT BE...
CD _____ WB 31162
We Bite / Jan '95 / Plastic Head.

Regan Youth

REGAN YOUTH
CD _____ NRA 13CD
New Red Archives / Apr '92 / Plastic
Head.

Regenerator

REGENERATOR
CD _____ HY 39100902
Hyperium / Jun '94 / Plastic Head.

Regents

ALBUM, THE
CD _____ RRCD 202
Receiver / Jun '95 / Grapevine.

Reggio, Felice

I REMEMBER CHET
CD _____ CD 214W1112

Philology / Mar '92 / Harmonia Mundi /
Cadillac.

Regredior

FORBIDDEN TEARS
CD _____ SHR 010CD
Shiver / Aug '95 / Plastic Head.

Rei, Panta

DANCE CONTINUES, THE
CD _____ DRCD 185
Dragon / Jan '88 / Roots / Cadillac /
Wellard / CM / ADA.

Reich, Steve

CAVE, THE
CD _____ 7559791012
Elektra Nonesuch / Jan '95 / Warner
Music.

DESERT MUSIC, THE
CD _____ 9791012
Elektra Nonesuch / '86 / Warner Music.

**DESERT MUSIC/DIFFERENT TRAINS/
SEXTET & SIX MARIMBAS/TEHILLIM
(4CD Set)**
CD Set _____ 7559793762
Elektra Nonesuch / Jan '95 / Warner
Music.

**DIFFERENT TRAINS (Reich, Steve & The
Kronos Quartet)**
Different trains / Electric counterpoint
CD _____ 979176 2
Elektra Nonesuch / Jun '89 / Warner Music.

DRUMMING
Part 1 / Part 2 / Part 3 / Part 4
CD _____ 919170 2
Elektra Nonesuch / Mar '88 / Warner Music.

EARLY WORKS
Come out 1966 / Piano phrase / Clapping
music / It's gonna rain
CD _____ 7559791692
Elektra Nonesuch / Jan '95 / Warner Music.

FOUR ORGANS - PHASE PATTERNS
CD _____ 642090MAN90
Mantra / Nov '94 / Direct / Discovery.

MUSIC FOR 18 MUSICIANS
CD _____ 8214172
ECM / '84 / New Note.

**OCTET MUSIC FOR A LARGE
ENSEMBLE**
Music for a large ensemble / Violin phase /
Octet
CD _____ 8272872
ECM / '85 / New Note.

SIX MARIMBAS
CD _____ 979 1382
Elektra Nonesuch / Jan '87 / Warner
Music.

TEHILLIM
Parts I and II (Performed by Steve Reich
and Musicians conducted by George Man-
ahan.) / Parts III and IV
CD _____ 8274112
ECM / '90 / New Note.

Reicha, Anton

ANTON REICHA
CD _____ 999 061-2
CPO / Jul '92 / Koch.

Reichel, Hans

**ANGEL CARVER (Reichel, Hans & Tom
Cora)**
CD _____ FMPCD 5
FMP / Dec '87 / Cadillac.

DAWN OF THE DACHSMAN...PLUS
CD _____ FMPCD 60
FMP / Oct '94 / Cadillac.

SHANGHAIED ON TOR ROAD
CD _____ FMPCD 46
FMP / Aug '86 / Cadillac.

SOLO - COCO BOLO NIGHTS
CD _____ FMPCD 10
FMP / Feb '85 / Cadillac.

STOP COMPLAINING
CD _____ FMPCD 36
FMP / Nov '87 / Cadillac.

Reid, Duke

BA BA BOOM
CD _____ CDTRL 265
Trojan / Nov '94 / Jetstar / Total/BMG.

**DUKE REID'S BOOM SHAKA LAKA
(Various Artists)**
CD _____ RNCD 2095
Rhino / Mar '95 / Jetstar / Magnum Music
Group / THE.

**DUKE REID'S KINGS OF SKA (Various
Artists)**
CD _____ RNCD 2098
Rhino / Mar '95 / Jetstar / Magnum Music
Group / THE.

**DUKE REID'S ROCKING STEADY
(Various Artists)**
CD _____ RNCD 2100
Rhino / Mar '95 / Jetstar / Magnum Music
Group / THE.

**DUKE REID'S TREASURE ISLE (Various
Artists)**
CD _____ CDHB 095/096
Heartbeat / Aug '92 / Greensleeves /
Jetstar / Direct / ADA.

FROM BOOGIE TO NYAMBINGHI
CD _____ LG 21082
Lagoon / Jun '93 / Magnum Music Group
/ THE.

IT'S ROCKIN' TIME
CD _____ CDTRL 279
Trojan / Mar '92 / Jetstar / Total/BMG.

JAMAICAN BEAT
CD _____ LG 21038
Lagoon / Jul '93 / Magnum Music Group /
THE.

MIDNIGHT CONFESSION
CD _____ LG 21084
Lagoon / Aug '93 / Magnum Music Group
/ THE.

TRIBUTES TO SKATALITES
CD _____ LG 21015
Lagoon / Jun '93 / Magnum Music Group /
THE.

VERSION AFFAIR VOL 1
CD _____ LG2 1062
Lagoon / Nov '92 / Magnum Music Group
/ THE.

VERSION AFFAIR VOL 2
CD _____ LG2 1066
Lagoon / Mar '93 / Magnum Music Group /
THE.

Reid, Jim

**FREEWHEELING NOW (Reid, Jim &
John Huband)**
Hey Donald / Whar the dichty rins / Queer
fowk / Cruachan Ben / O Gin I were a Bar-
on's heir / Great storm is over / Music on
his mind / Back in Scotland / Balaena / An
t-eilean muileach / Lassie o' the morning /
Moothie man / Oh dear me / Scattered /
There's no indispensable man / Auld beech
tree / Freewheeling now
CD _____ SPRCD 1030
Springthyme / Dec '93 / Direct / Roots / CM
/ Duncans / ADA.

Reid, Junior

**DOUBLE TOP (Reid, Junior & Cornell
Campbell)**
CD _____ TWCD 1033
Tamoki Wambesi / Jun '94 / Jetstar / SRD
/ Roots Collective / Greensleeves.

**JUNIOR REID & THE BLOODS (Reid,
Junior & The Bloods)**
CD _____ RASCD 3154
Ras / Jul '95 / Jetstar / Greensleeves /
SRD / Direct.

ONE BLOOD
One blood / Nuh so / Who done it / When
it shows / Searching for better / Married life
/ Eleanor Rigby / Gruppie Diana / Sound /
Dominant
CD _____ JRCD 1
Big Life / Feb '90 / Pinnacle.

Reid, Lou

WHEN IT RAINS
Ain't it funny / Cry cry darlin' / Hand of the
higher power / You better hold onto your
heart / Red, white and blue / Summer your
name / Mom's old picture book / One track
man / Absence makes the heart grow
fonder / First step to heaven / Nobody's
loves like mine
CD _____ SHCD 3788
Sugarhill / '91 / Roots / CM / ADA / Direct.

Reid, Terry

BANG BANG YOU'RE
CD _____ BGOCD 164
Beat Goes On / Dec '92 / Pinnacle.

DRIVER, THE
Fifth of July / There's nothing wrong / Right
to the end / Whole of the moon / Hand of
dimes / Driver #1 / If you let her / Turn
around / Gimme some lovin' / Laugh at life
/ Driver #2
CD _____ 9031749052
WEA / Nov '94 / Warner Music.

ROGUE WAVES
Ain't no shadow / Baby I love you / Stop
and think it over / Rogue wave / Walk away
Renee / Believe in the magic / Then I kissed
her / Bowangi / All I have to do is dream
CD _____ BGOCD 140
Beat Goes On / Apr '92 / Pinnacle.

SEED OF MEMORY
Faith to arise / Seed of memory / Brave
awakening / To be treated right / Ooh baby
(makes me feels so young) / Way you walk
/ Frame / Fooling you
CD _____ EDCD 425
Edsel / May '95 / Pinnacle / ADA.

TERRY REID
Superlungs my supergirl / Silver white light
/ July / Marking time / Stay with me baby /
Highway 61 revisited/Friends / May fly /
Speak now or forever hold your peace /
Rich kids blues / Hand don't fit the glove /
This time / Better by far / Fire's alive
CD _____ BGOCD 168
Beat Goes On / Dec '92 / Pinnacle.

Reiersrud, Knut

TRAMP
CD _____ FX 129CD
Kirkelig Kultuverksted / Apr '95 / ADA.

Reign

EMBRACE
CD _____ 9040162
Mausoleum / Mar '95 / Grapevine.

Reigndance

PROBLEM FACTORY
Second time around / Temporarily an eter-
nity / No room / Why divide / I'd tell you /
Lazybones / You're wrong / Things will be
different now / Luxury / Out of the question
/ Open arms / Better than I
CD _____ RTD 15717602
World Service / Jun '94 / Vital.

Reilly, Robert

TEMPTATION
Half a chance / Gone too long / Praying for
rain / Long distance / North wind / Temptation / Towns like mine / Save me / After
all these years / All I want
CD _____ SCARTCD 3
Scarlett Recordings / Jul '90 / Pinnacle.

Reilly, Tommy

**THANKS FOR THE MEMORY (Reilly,
Tommy & James Moody)**
CD _____ CHAN 8645
Chandos / Oct '88 / Chandos.

Reimer, Jan

POINT OF NO RETURN, THE
CD _____ BEST 1020CD
Acoustic Music / Nov '93 / ADA.

Rein Sanction

MARIPOSA
CD _____ SP 43/208CD
Sub Pop / Sep '92 / Disc.

Reincarnation

SEED OF HATE
CD _____ RPS 008MCD
Repulse / Oct '95 / Plastic Head.

Reinders, Ge

AS'T D'R OP AAN KUMP
CD _____ MW 1005CD
Music & Words / Aug '94 / ADA / Direct.

Reinhardt, Babik

ALL LOVE
CD _____ 400012
Melodie / Aug '94 / Triple Earth /
Discovery / ADA / Jetstar.

LIVE
CD _____ CDSW 8431
DRG / Sep '91 / New Note.

LIVE
CD _____ 400032
Melodie / Aug '94 / Triple Earth /
Discovery / ADA / Jetstar.

VIBRATION
CD _____ 400452
Melodie / Sep '95 / Triple Earth /
Discovery / ADA / Jetstar.

Reinhardt, Django

1935-1939
CD _____ CD 56061
Jazz Roots / Jul '95 / Target/BMG.

**ART OF DJANGO, THE/THE
UNFORGETTABLE**
Mystery Pacific / little love, a little kiss /
Running wild / Body and soul / Hot lips /
Solitude / When day is gone / Tears / Rose
room / Sheikh of Araby / Liebestraum no. 3
/ Exactly like you / Miss Annabelle Lee /
Ain't misbehavin' / Sweet Georgia Brown /
Minor swing / Double scotch / Artillerie
Lourde / St. James Infirmary / C Jam blues
/ Honeysuckle Rose / Dream of you / Begin
the beguine / How high the moon / Nuages
/ I can't get started (with you) / I can't give
you anything but love / Manoir de mes
reves
CD _____ BGOCD 198
Beat Goes On / Jul '93 / Pinnacle.

ART OF GREAT JAZZ GUITAR, THE
CD _____ CD 411
Bescol / May '95 / CM / Target/BMG.

ATC BIG BAND LIVE 1945
CD _____ JCD 628
Jass / Mar '87 / CM / Jazz Music / ADA /
Cadillac / Direct.

CLASSICS 1935-1936
CD _____ CLASSICS 739
Classics / Feb '94 / Discovery / Jazz
Music.

CLASSICS 1937
CD _____ CLASSICS 748
Classics / Aug '94 / Discovery / Jazz
Music.

CLASSICS 1937 #2
CD _____ CLASSICS 762
Classics / Jun '94 / Discovery / Jazz
Music.

CLASSICS 1937-1939
CD _____ CLASSICS 777
Classics / Mar '95 / Discovery / Jazz
Music.

CLASSICS 1938-1939
CD _____ CLASSICS 793
Classics / Jan '95 / Discovery / Jazz
Music.

CLASSICS 1939-1940
CD _____ CLASSICS 813
Classics / May '95 / Discovery / Jazz
Music.

CONTINENTAL STYLE (Reinhardt, Django & Stephane Grappelli)
What a difference a day makes / Avalon /
Blue moon / Stardust / It's a muggin / I can't
give you anything but love / Oriental shuffle
/ It was so beautiful / Chasing shadows /
Nocturne / Djangology / Don't worry 'bout
me / I've got my love to keep me warm /
Man I love / Louise / Ultrafox / I've had my
moments / Please be kind / Louise /
Improvisation
CD _____ PAR 2023
Parade / Jul '94 / Koch / Cadillac.

DEFINITIVE DJANGO REINHARDT #1 (First Original Hot Club Recordings 1934-1935)
CD _____ JSPCD 341
JSP / Feb '93 / ADA / Target/BMG / Direct
/ Cadillac / Complete/Pinnacle.

DEFINITIVE DJANGO REINHARDT #2 (London Decca Recordings 1938-1939)
Honeysuckle rose / Sweet Georgia Brown /
Night and day / My sweet / Souvenirs /
Daphne / Black and white / Stompin' at the
Decca / Tornerai / If I had you / It had to be
you / Nocturne / Flat foot floogie / Lambeth
walk / Why shouldn't I / I've got my love to
keep me warm / Please be kind / Louise /
Improvisation no.2 / Undecided / HCQ strut
/ Don't worry 'bout me / Man I love
CD _____ JSPCD 342
JSP / Jan '94 / ADA / Target/BMG / Direct
/ Cadillac / Complete/Pinnacle.

DEFINITIVE DJANGO REINHARDT #3
Billets doux / Swing from Paris / Them there
eyes / Three little words / Appel direct /
Hungaria / Jeepers creepers / Swing '39 /
Japanese sandman / I wonder were my
baby is tonight / Tea for two / My melan-
choly baby / Time on my hands / Twelfth
year
CD _____ JSPCD 343
JSP / Apr '94 / ADA / Target/BMG / Direct
/ Cadillac / Complete/Pinnacle.

DEFINITIVE DJANGO REINHARDT #4
CD _____ JSPCD 344
JSP / Oct '94 / ADA / Target/BMG / Direct
/ Cadillac / Complete/Pinnacle.

DEFINITIVE DJANGO REINHARDT #5
CD _____ JSPCD 349
JSP / May '95 / ADA / Target/BMG /
Direct / Cadillac / Complete/Pinnacle.

DJANGO
Lady be good / Dinah / Confessin' / I saw
stars / Tiger rag / Continental / Blue drag /
Sweet Sue, just you / Sunshine of your
smile / Nuages / Swanee river / Night and
day / September song / Testament / Brazil
/ Manoir de mes reves / Blues for Ike / In-
sensibilement / Gypsy with a song
CD _____ CDHD 234
Happy Days / Mar '94 / Conifer.

DJANGO AND HIS AMERICAN FRIENDS VOLS 1 & 2
Avalon / Rosetta / Honeysuckle rose /
Sweet Georgia Brown / I got rhythm / Japanese sandman / I ain't got nobody / Bill
Coleman blues / I'm coming Virginia / Mont-
martre / I know that you know me / What a
difference a day makes / Stardust / Crazy
rhythm / Bugle call rag / Sweet Sue, just
you / Eddie's blues / Baby, won't you
please come home / Somebody loves me /
Farewell blues / Low cotton / Solid old man
/ Object of my affection / Out of nowhere /
Between the devil and the deep blue sea /
Hangin' around Boulden / Big Boy Blues / I
can't believe that you're in love with me /
Blue light blues / Finesse
CD _____ BGOCD 249
Beat Goes On / Dec '94 / Pinnacle.

DJANGO REINHARDT & HIS AMERICAN SWING BAND
CD _____ JASSCD 628
Jass / Oct '92 / CM / Jazz Music / ADA /
Cadillac / Direct.

DJANGO REINHARDT 1935
CD _____ OJCCD 772
Original Jazz Classics / Dec '93 / Wellard /
Jazz Music / Cadillac / Complete/Pinnacle.

DJANGO REINHARDT 1935-39
CD _____ CD 14555
Jazz Portraits / Jul '94 / Jazz Music.

DJANGO REINHARDT 1938-1939
CD _____ JSP 343
JSP / Jun '94 / ADA / Target/BMG / Direct
/ Cadillac / Complete/Pinnacle.

DJANGO REINHARDT AND FRIENDS
(I'll be glad when you're dead) you rascal
you / Stephen's blues / Sugar / Sweet
Georgia Brown / Tea for two / Younger
generation / I'll see you in my dreams / Ech-
oes of Spain / Naguine / What a difference
a day makes / Tears / Limehouse blues /
Daphne / At Jimmy's bar / Rosetta / Nuages
/ Pour vous (exactly like you) / Vendredi 13
/ Petits mesonges (little white lies) / Star-
dust / Sweet Sue, just you / Swing de Paris
CD _____ PASTCD 9792
Flapper / Jun '92 / Pinnacle.

DJANGO REINHARDT AND STEPHANE GRAPPELLI (Reinhardt, Django & Stephane Grappelli)
CD _____ CD 14580
Complete / Nov '95 / THE.

DJANGO REINHARDT ET SON QUINTETTE DU HOT CLUB DE FRANCE (Quintette Du Hot Club De France)
CD _____ 403222
Musidisc / Nov '93 / Vital / Harmonia
Mundi / ADA / Cadillac / Discovery.

DJANGO REINHARDT PLAYS THE STANDARDS
You're driving me crazy / Solitude / Ain't
misbehavin' / Shine / Exactly like you /
Body and soul / Nagasaki / When day is
done / Running wild / Crazy rhythm / Hon-
eysuckle rose / Out of nowhere / St. Louis
blues / Georgia on my mind / Lady be good
/ After you've gone / Limehouse blues /
Sweet Georgia brown / Begin the beguine /
I can't give you anything but love / Sweet
Sue, just you / All of me
CD _____ RAJCD 808
Empress / Nov '93 / THE.

DJANGO REINHARDT/STEPHANE GRAPPELLI (Reinhardt, Django & Stephane Grappelli)
CD _____ PASTCD 9738
Flapper / Sep '91 / Pinnacle.

DJANGO REINHARDT/STEPHANE GRAPPELLI (Reinhardt, Django & Stephane Grappelli)
CD _____ GNPD 9053
GNP Crescendo / Jul '94 / Silva Screen.

DJANGO'S MUSIC
Tears / Limehouse blues / Daphne / At the
Jimmy's bar / Festival swing '41 / Stock-
holm / Nympheas / Feerie / Seul ce soir /
Bei dir war es immer so schoen / Nuages /
Djangology / Eclats de culvres / Django rag
/ Dynamisme / Tons' D ebene / Chez moi a
six heures / Bellville / Oubli / Zuiderzee
blues / ABC / Galement / Melodie au cre-
pescule / Blues d'autrefois / Place de
brouckere
CD _____ HEPCD 1041
Hep / Oct '94 / Cadillac / Jazz Music / New
Note / Wellard.

DJANGOLOGY
CD _____ CD 53002
Giants Of Jazz / Mar '92 / Target/BMG /
Cadillac.

DJANGOLOGY
Dinah / Tiger rag / Lady be good / I saw
stars / Lily belle May June / Sweet Sue, just
you / Confessin' / Continental / Blue drag /
Swanee river / Ton doux sourire / Ultrafox /
Avalon / Smoke rings / Clouds / Believe it,
beloved / I've found a new baby / St. Louis
blues / Crazy rhythm / Sheikh of Araby /
Chasing shadows / I've had my moments /
Some of these days / Djangology
CD _____ CDGRF 089
Tring / '93 / Tring / Prism.

DJANGOLOGY 1937-39
After you've gone / Limehouse blues / Nagasaki / Honeysuckle rose / Crazy rhythm /
Out of nowhere / Chicago / Georgia on my
mind / Shine / Sweet Georgia Brown / Bugle
call rag / Between the Devil and the deep
blue sea / Exactly like you / Charleston /
You're driving me crazy / Farewell blues / I
got rhythm / I know that you know / Ain't
misbehavin' / Rose room / Japanese sandman / Swing guitars / Minor swing / Nuages
CD _____ GOJCD 0219
Giants Of Jazz / '88 / Target/BMG /
Cadillac.

DJANGOLOGY 49
World is waiting for the sunrise / Hallelujah
/ I'll never be the same / Honeysuckle rose
/ All the things you are / Djangology /
Daphne / Beyond the sea / Lover man / Ma-
rie / Minor swing / Ou est tu mon amour /
Swing '42 / After you've gone / I got rhythm
/ I saw stars / Heavy artillery (artillerie
lourde) / It's only a paper moon / Bricktop
CD _____ ND 90448
RCA / Apr '90 / BMG.

DJANGOLOGY/USA (Reinhardt, Django & Quintette Du Hot Club De France)
CD Set _____ CDSW 8421/2
DRG / Jan '89 / New Note.

GIPSY GENIUS, THE
CD _____ ENTCD 219
Entertainers / '89 / Target/BMG.

GUITAR GENIUS
I can't give you anything but love / Swing
guitars / Sweet chorus / Rose room / Chi-
cago / Sweet Georgia brown / I got rhythm
/ Lady be good / In a sentimental mood / It
had to be you / Limehouse blues / Nuages
CD _____ CDCD 1048
Charly / Mar '93 / Charly / THE / Cadillac.

I GOT RHYTHM
I got rhythm / Crazy rhythm / My melan-
choly baby / Jeepers creepers / Sweet
Georgia Brown / Honeysuckle rose / Liza /
Nauges / Nuits de saint germain de press /
Just one of those things / I cover the wa-
terfront / I wonder where my baby is tonight
CD _____ CDSGP 0106
Prestige / Jun '94 / Total/BMG.

I GOT RHYTHM (Reinhardt, Django & Stephane Grappelli)
Dinah / I'm confessin' that I love you / Swa-
nee river / Sunshine of your smile / Believe
it, beloved / Chasing shadows / I've had my
moments / Some of these days / I got
rhythm / Sheikh of araby / It don't mean a
thing if it ain't got that swing / Viper's dream
/ Running wild / Ain't misbehavin' / Tears /
Miss Annabelle Lee / Djangology / Daphne
/ Billets doux / Swing '39 / Tea for two / My
melancholy baby / Younger generation /
HCQ strut
CD _____ PPCD 78110
Past Perfect / Feb '95 / THE.

IN PARIS, 1935-36
Nagasaki / Oriental shuffle / After you've
gone / Moong low / In the still of the night
/ Shine / Chasing shadows / It was so
beautiful / I've had my moments
CD _____ DOLD 12
Old Bean / Dec '90 / Jazz Music / Wellard.

INDISPENSABLE DJANGO REINHARDT (1949-50)
Minor swing / Beyond the sea / World is
waiting for the sunrise / Django's castle /
Dream of you / Menilmontant / It's only a
paper moon / I saw stars / Nuages / Swing
guitars / All the things you are / Tisket-a-
tasket / September song / Heavy artillery
(Artillerie lourde) / Improvisation / Djangol-
ogy / Daphne / I'll never be the same / Marie
/ Jersey bounce / I surrender dear / Halle-
lujah / Honeysuckle rose / After you've gone
/ Swing '42 / Stormy weather / Brick top /
Lover man / I got rhythm / Honeysuckle
rose / St. Louis blues
CD _____ ND 70929
RCA / Mar '94 / BMG.

JAZZ MASTERS
CD _____ 5169312
Verve / Apr '94 / PolyGram.

JAZZ PORTRAITS
Limehouse blues / Nagasaki / After you've
gone / You're driving me crazy / Ain't misbehavin' / Chicago / Georgia on my mind /
China / Honestly this / confessin' that love /
room / When day is done / Running wild
(course movementee) / Swing guitars / Minor swing / Oriental shuffle / I can't give you
anything but love / Sweet chorus
CD _____ CD 14509
Jazz Portraits / May '94 / Jazz Music.

KING OF THE GYPSIES
Swing guitars / Georgia on my mind /
Charleston / Ain't misbehavin' / Limehouse
blues / Hot lips
CD _____ BSTCD 9101
Best Compact Discs / May '92 / Complete/
Pinnacle.

LE QUINTETTE DU HOT CLUB DE FRANCE (Quintette Du Hot Club De France)
Limehouse blues / Nagasaki / After you've
gone / You're driving me crazy / Ain't mis-
behavin' / Chicago / Georgia on my mind /
Shine / Exactly like you / Charleston / Rose
room / When day is done / Running wild /
Swing guitars / Minor swing / Oriental shuf-
fle / I can't give you anything but love /
Sweet chorus
CD _____ 56020
Carlton Home Entertainment / Nov '92 /
Carlton Home Entertainment.

LE QUINTETTE DU HOT CLUB DE FRANCE (Quintette Du Hot Club De France)
CD _____ CD 56020
Jazz Roots / Aug '94 / Target/BMG.

LONDRES 1938, PARIS 1938 (Reinhardt, Django & Stephane Grappelli)
CD _____ 879482
Music Memoria / Jun '93 / Discovery /
ADA.

MUSIC OF DJANGO REINHARDT
CD _____ NI 4029
Natasha / Jun '94 / Jazz Music / ADA /
CM / Direct / Cadillac.

NUAGES (Reinhardt, Django & Stephane Grappelli)
Avalon / Blue drag / Confessin' / Continen-
tal / Dinah (2 versions) / Djangology / I saw
stars / Improvisation / I've had my moments
/ Jive bomber / Low cotton / Nagasaki /
Nocturne / Nuages / Oh Lady be good /
Rose room / Smoke rings / Solid old man /
Swanee river / Sweet chorus / Tiger rag /
Ultrafox / When day is done
CD _____ CDAJA 5138
Living Era / Aug '94 / Koch.

PARIS 1939, LONDRES 1939 (Reinhardt, Django & Stephane Grappelli)
CD _____ 879492
Music Memoria / Jun '93 / Discovery /
ADA.

QUINTET OF THE HOT CLUB OF FRANCE (Quintette Du Hot Club De France)
CD _____ CWNCD 2010
Javelin / Jun '95 / THE / Henry Hadaway
Organisation.

RARE DJANGO
CD _____ CDSW 8119
DRG / Aug '91 / New Note.

RARE RECORDINGS
CD _____ JZCD 376
Recording Arts / Jun '93 / THE / Disc.

ROME SESSIONS, 1949-50: VOL 1
Waiting for the sunrise / Hallelujah / I'll never
be the same / Honeysuckle rose / All the
things you are / Daphne / La mer / Lover
man / Marie / Anniversary song / Stormy
weather / Russian songs medley / Jersey
bounce / Sophisticated lady / Dream of you
/ At the Darktown strutter's ball / Royal Garden blues
CD _____ 8274472
Jazztime / Jan '95 / Discovery / BMG.

SOUVENIRS (Reinhardt, Django & Stephane Grappelli)
Honeysuckle Rose / Night and day / Sweet
Georgia Brown / Souvenirs / My sweet /
Liza (all the clouds'll roll away) / Stomping
at Decca / Love's melody / Daphne / Lam-
beth walk / Nuages / H.C.Q. Strut / Man I
love / Improvisation no.2 / Undecided /
Please be kind / Nocturne / I've got my love
to keep me warm / Louise / Don't worry
'bout me
CD _____ 8205912
London / Jun '88 / PolyGram.

SWING DE PARIS (4CD Box Set)
CD Set _____ CDDIG 12
Charly / Apr '95 / Charly / THE / Cadillac.

SWING FROM PARIS (Recordings From 1935-39) (Reinhardt, Django & Stephane Grappelli)
Miss Annabelle Lee / Chasing shadows /
Stomping at Decca / Solitude / Appel direct
/ J'attendrai / After you've gone / Nagasaki
/ Night and day / Avalon / Running wild /
Djangology / Shine / Sweet chorus / Them
there eyes / Some of these days / If I had
you / Three little words / Little love, a little
kiss / Swing from Paris
CD _____ CDHD 165
Happy Days / '89 / Conifer.

SWING FROM PARIS (Reinhardt, Django & Stephane Grappelli)
I got rhythm / St. Louis blues / Appel direct
/ Honeysuckle rose / Black and white / Limehouse blues / Moonglow / Billets doux /
Daphne / China boy / Night and day / My
sweet / It don't mean a thing if it ain't got
that swing / Sweet Georgia Brown / Swing
from Paris / I've found a new baby / Lambeth walk / Them there eyes / It was so
beautiful / Three little words / HCQ strut /
Swing '39
CD _____ CD AJA 5070
Living Era / Apr '90 / Koch.

SWINGIN' WITH DJANGO (Reinhardt, Django & Stephane Grappelli)
CD _____ CDCD 1182
Charly / Apr '94 / Charly / THE / Cadillac.

UNFORGETTABLE DJANGO REINHARDT
China boy / Tornerai / My sweet / Souvenirs
/ Honeysuckle rose / Stompin' at Decca /
I've found a new baby / Night and day / I've
got my love to keep me warm / Improvisa-
tion / Limehouse blues / Them there eyes /
Man I love / My melancholy baby / Hungaria
/ Appel direct / Three little words / Daphne
/ Tea for two / Billets doux / Ultrafox / I've
had my moments
CD _____ RHCD 6
Rhapsody / Dec '93 / President / Jazz Mu-
sic / Wellard.

Reininger, Blaine

BOOK OF HOURS
CD _____ TWI 8452
Les Disques Du Crepuscule / '89 /
Discovery / ADA.

COLORADO SUITE (Reininger, Blaine & Mikel Rouse)
CD _____ MTM 3CD
Made To Measure / Nov '88 / Grapevine.

LIVE IN BRUSSELS
CD _____ TWICD 637
Les Disques Du Crepuscule / Jan '87 / Discovery / ADA.

Reis, Rosani

CAFUSO
CD _____ CDSGP 0138
Prestige / Jul '95 / Total/BMG.

Reischman, John

NORTH OF THE BORDER
CD _____ ROU 315CD
Rounder / Jan '94 / CM / Direct / ADA / Cadillac.

Reisel, Jacqueline

SONGS IN YIDDISH & LADINO 2
CD _____ YILADI 8803
Yiladi / Sep '94 / Direct.

Reiter, Jorg

CAN'T STOP IT
CD _____ ISCD 102
Intersound / '88 / Jazz Music.

Rejuvenate

MOMENT OF TRUTH
CD _____ LF 082CD
Lost & Found / Sep '94 / Plastic Head.

Rejuvination

INTRODUCTION
CD _____ SOMACD 2
Soma / May '95 / Disc.

Relativity

GATHERING PACE
Blackwell court / Gathering pace / Rose catha na mumhan / Miss Tara Macadam / Ma theid tu unaonaigh / Siun ni dhuibhir / When she sleeps / Monday morning reel / Ceol Anna
CD _____ GLCD 1076
Green Linnet / May '88 / Roots / CM / Direct / ADA.

Rembetika

TALKING TO CHAROS
CD _____ EUCD 1169
ARC / '91 / ARC Music / ADA.

Rembrandts

LP
CD _____ 7559617522
East West / Sep '95 / Warner Music.

REMBRANDTS, THE
Just the way it is / Baby / Save me / Someone / Show me your love / New King / Every secret thing / If not for misery / Moonlight on Mt. Hood / Goodnight / Burning timber / Confidential information / Everyday people / Follow you down
CD _____ 7567914122
East West / Jun '91 / Warner Music.

UNTITLED
CD _____ 7567922002
East West / Jan '96 / Warner Music.

Remler, Emily

EAST TO WEST
Daahoud / Sweet Georgie Fame / East to West / Snowfall / Hot house / Softly as in a morning sunrise
CD _____ CCD 4356
Concord Jazz / Sep '88 / New Note.

FIREFLY
Strollin' / Look to the sky / Perk's blues / Firefly / Movin' along / Taste of honey / Inception / In a sentimental mood
CD _____ CCD 4162
Concord Jazz / Sep '92 / New Note.

JUST FRIENDS VOL.2 (A Gathering In Tribute To Emily Remler) (Various Artists)
CD _____ JR 005032
Justice / Dec '92 / Koch.

RETROSPECTIVE #1 (Standards)
Daahoud / How insensitive / Strollin' / Hot house / In your own sweet way / Joy Spring / Softly as in a morning sunrise / Afro blue / Del sasser / In a sentimental mood
CD _____ CCD 4453
Concord Jazz / Mar '91 / New Note.

RETROSPECTIVE #2 (Compositions)
Macha spice / Nunca mais / Waltz for my grandfather / Catwalk / Blues for herb / Transitions / Firefly / East to West / Antonio / Mozambique
CD _____ CCD 4463
Concord Jazz / May '91 / New Note.

TAKE TWO (Remler, Emily Quartet)
Cannonball / In your own sweet way / For regulars only / Search for peace / Pocket

west / Waltz for my grandfather / Afro blue / Eleuthra
CD _____ CCD 4195
Concord Jazz / Sep '92 / New Note.

THIS IS ME
CD _____ JR 005012
Justice / Sep '92 / Koch.

Remy, Tony

BOOF
Glide / Boof / Mercy mercy me / Different people / Reginald Miller / Fewtcha funk / Geraldine / Our love grows / Trio / Hazel's dream / It's been a long time / Return of the pork pie
CD _____ GRP 97362
GRP / Dec '93 / BMG / New Note.

Rena Rama

INSIDE - OUTSIDE
CD _____ 1182
Caprice / Oct '90 / CM / Complete/ Pinnacle / Cadillac / ADA.

JAZZ IN SWEDEN 1973
CD _____ 1049
Caprice / Mar '90 / CM / Complete/ Pinnacle / Cadillac / ADA.

Renaissance

AZURE D'OR
Jekyll and Hyde / Winter tree / Only angels have wings / Golden key / Forever changing / Secret mission / Kalynda / Discovery / Friends / Flood at Lyons
CD _____ 7599265172
WEA / Jan '96 / Warner Music.

BLESSING IN DISGUISE (Haslam, Annie Renaissance)
Blessing in disguise / Pool of tears / Love lies, love dies / Can't turn the night off / In another life / Raindrops and leaves / Whisper from Marseilles / I light this candle / What he seeks / See this through your eyes / Sweetest kiss / Children (Of Medellin) / New life / After the oceans are gone
CD _____ CDTB 151
Thunderbolt / Jul '95 / Magnum Music Group.

CAMERA CAMERA
CD _____ HTCD 43
HTD / Oct '95 / Pinnacle.

DEATH OF ART
CD _____ SHR 006CD
Shiver / Aug '95 / Plastic Head.

FIRST/ILLUSION
Kings and queens / Innocence / Island / Wanderer / Bullet / Love goes on / Golden thread
CD Set _____ LICD 921163
Line / Jan '92 / CM / Grapevine / ADA / Conifer / Direct.

NOVELLA
Can you hear me / Sisters / Midas man / Captive heart / Touching once (is so hard to keep)
CD _____ 7599265162
WEA / Jan '96 / Warner Music.

OTHER WOMAN, THE
Northern lights / Love / Other woman / So blase / Love lies / Somewhere west of here / Lock in on love / Deja vu / Don't talk / Quicksilver
CD _____ HTDCD 27
HTD / Jan '95 / Pinnacle.

RENAISSANCE FIRST
CD _____ LICD 900421
Line / Sep '94 / CM / Grapevine / ADA / Conifer / Direct.

SONG FOR ALL SEASONS, A
Opening out / Day of the dreamer / Closer than yesterday / Kindness (at the end) / Back home once again / She is love / Northern lights / Song for all seasons
CD _____ 7599259592
WEA / Jan '96 / Warner Music.

TIME LINE
Flight / Missing persons / Chagrin Boulevard / Richard the IX / Entertainer / Electric avenue / Majik / Distant horizons / Orient express / Auto tech
CD _____ HTDCD 42
HTD / Oct '95 / Pinnacle.

TURN OF THE CARDS
Running hard / I think of you / Things I don't understand / Black flame / Cold is being / Mother Russia
CD _____ HTDCD 51
HTD / Jan '96 / Pinnacle.

Renault, Philippe

BOSSA POUR SEPTEMBRE (Renault, Philippe Nonet)
CD _____ BBRC 9105
Big Blue / Dec '91 / Harmonia Mundi.

Renbourn, John

BLACK BALLOON, THE
Moon shines bright / English dance / Bouree / Mist covered mountains of home / Orphan / Tarboulton / Pelican / Black balloon

CD _____ PENT 001CD
Pentangle / Oct '93 / ADA.

COLLECTION, THE
CD _____ CCSCD 429
Castle / Mar '95 / BMG.

ESSENTIAL COLLECTION VOL 1 (The Soho Years)
Judy / Candy man / Lost lover blues / East wind / Nobody's fault but mine / Wildest pig in captivity / I know my babe / After the dance / No exit / Lord Franklin / Cuckoo / Another Monday / Country blues / Waltz / White House blues / My dear boy / Hermit / Buffalo skinners / Sweet potato / Kokomo blues / So clear
CD _____ TRACD 603
Transatlantic / Jul '87 / BMG / Pinnacle / ADA.

ESSENTIAL COLLECTION VOL 2 (Moon Shines Bright)
Gypsy dance / Lady Nothinge's toye puffe / Lady and the unicorn / Lady goes to church / Trees they do grow high / Watermill / Moon shines bright / My Johnny was a shoemaker / Alman / Melancholy galliard / Pelican / Three pieces by O'Carolan / Morgana part 1 and 2 / Earl of Salisbury / English dance / Pavanne / Jew's dance / Tourdion
CD _____ TRACD 605
Transatlantic / Sep '87 / BMG / Pinnacle / ADA.

ESSENTIAL JOHN RENBOURN
CD _____ TDEM 10
Trandem / Mar '94 / CM / ADA / Pinnacle.

LADY AND THE UNICORN, THE
Lady and the unicorn / Trotto / Saltarello / Lamento di tristan / La rotta / Veri floris / Triple ballade / Bransie gay / Bransie de bourgogne / Alman / Melancholy galliard / Sarabande / My Johnny was a shoemaker / Westron wynde / Scarborough Fair
CD _____ SHANCD 97022
Shanachie / '92 / Koch / ADA / Greensleeves.

LIVE IN AMERICA (Renbourn, John Group)
CD _____ FF 103CD
Flying Fish / May '93 / Roots / CM / Direct / ADA.

MAID IN BEDLAM, A
Black waterside / Nacht tanz/Shaeffertanz / Maid in bedlam / Gypsy dance/Jews dance / John Barleycorn / Reynardine / My Johnny was a shoemaker / Death and the Lady / Battle of Augrham/5 / In a line / Talk about suffering
CD _____ TACD 900777
Line / Sep '94 / CM / Grapevine / ADA / Conifer / Direct.

NINE MAIDENS
CD _____ FF 70378
Flying Fish / '88 / Roots / CM / Direct / ADA.

SHIP OF FOOLS
CD _____ FF 466CD
Flying Fish / Apr '94 / Roots / CM / Direct / ADA.

SIR JOHN A LOT...
CD _____ SHANCD 97012
Shanachie / '92 / Koch / ADA / Greensleeves.

WHEEL OF FORTUNE (Renbourn, John Group & Robin Williamson)
CD _____ FIENDCD 746
Demon / Nov '93 / Pinnacle / ADA.

Rendell, Don

IF I SHOULD LOSE YOU (Rendell, Don & His Big Eight)
If I should lose you / Calas vinas / All too soon / I can dream, can't I / Out of my window / Under pressure blues / Blues house effect / Hard knott pass / Relaxing at Loweswater / Jumpin' at the lakeside
CD _____ SPJCD 546
Spotlite / May '93 / Cadillac / Jazz Horizons / Swift.

Renegade

LOST ANGELS
CD _____ 15392
Laserlight / Aug '91 / Target/BMG.

Renegade Soundwave

NEXT CHAPTER OF DUB, THE
CD _____ CDSTUMM 90
Mute / Apr '95 / Disc.

RENEGADE SOUNDWAVE IN DUB
CD _____ CDSTUMM 85
Mute / Oct '90 / Disc.

SOUNDCLASH
CD _____ CDSTUMM 63
Mute / Feb '90 / Disc.

Renegades Steel Orchestra

BUMP AND WINE
CD _____ 795872
Melodie / Dec '95 / Triple Earth / Discovery / ADA / Jetstar.

Reno & Smiley

GOOD OLD COUNTRY BALLADS
CD _____ KCD 621
King/Paddle Wheel / Mar '93 / New Note.

Reno, Don

VARIETY OF COUNTRY SONGS, A (Reno, Don & Red Smiley)
CD _____ KCD 646
King/Paddle Wheel / Nov '92 / New Note.

Rent Party

PIC NIC
CD _____ 422495
New Rose / Nov '94 / Direct / ADA.

Rent Party Revellers

SHE WAS JUST A SAILOR'S SWEETHEART
CD _____ SOSCD 1220
Stomp Off / Oct '92 / Jazz Music / Wellard.

Rentals

RETURN OF THE RENTALS
CD _____ 9362460932
Warner Bros. / Jan '96 / Warner Music.

Renzi, Mike

PROVIDENCE JAM (A Beautiful Friendship)
CD _____ STB 2506
Stash / Sep '95 / Jazz Music / CM / Cadillac / Direct / ADA.

REO Speedwagon

BEST FOOT FORWARD
Roll with the changes / Take it on the run / Don't let him go / Live every moment / Keep on loving you / Back on the road again / Wherever you're goin' (it's alright) / Can't fight this feeling / Shakin' it loose / Time for me to fly / Keep pushin' / I wish you were there
CD _____ 4686032
Epic / Oct '91 / Sony.

HI-INFIDELITY
Don't let him go / Keep on loving you / Follow my heart / In your letter / Take it on the run / Tough guys / Out of season / Shakin' it loose / Someone tonight / I wish you were there
CD _____ CD 84700
Epic / '88 / Sony.
CD _____ EK 66233
Epic / May '95 / Sony.

HITS, THE
I don't want to lose you / Here with me / Roll with the changes / Keep on loving you / That ain't love / Take it on the run / Don't let him go / Can't fight this feeling / Keep pushin' / In my dreams / Time for me to fly / Ridin' the storm out
CD _____ 4655952
Epic / Jan '95 / Sony.

REO SPEEDWAGON
CD _____ 9829672
Pickwick/Sony Collector's Choice / Jun '93 / Carlton Home Entertainment / Pinnacle / Sony.

Repeat

REPEATS
End up / Q thing / Tuesday's hot hit / Lilt A / Fish stew / Hurricane felix / Tomorrow's people / Death-bed visions / Drifting sounds of Wikiki
CD _____ AA 002CD
A13 Productions / Oct '95 / Vital.

Repercussions

EARTH AND HEAVEN
CD _____ 9362456442
Warner Bros. / Feb '95 / Warner Music.

Replacements

ALL SHOOK DOWN
Merry go round / Nobody / Sadly beautiful / When it began / Attitude / Torture / Last / One wink at a time / Bent out of shape / Someone take the wheel / All shook down / Happy town / My little problem
CD _____ 7559262982
Sire / Feb '95 / Warner Music.

DON'T TELL A SOUL
Talent show / Back to back / We'll inherit the earth / Achin' to be / They're blind / Anywhere's better than here / Asking me lies / I'll be you / I won't / Rock 'n' roll ghost / Darlin' one
CD _____ 7599258312
Sire / Mar '94 / Warner Music.

HOOTENANNY
Hootenanny / Run it / Color me impressed / Will power / Take me down to the hospital / Mr. Whirly / Within your reach / Buck hill / Love lines / You lose / Hayday / Treatment bound
CD _____ TTR 83322
Twin Tone / Feb '95 / Pinnacle.

LET IT BE
I will dare / Favourite thing / We're comin' out / Tommy gets his tonsils out / Androgynous / Black diamond / Unsatisfied / Seen your video / Gary's got a boner / Sixteen blue / Answering machine
CD _____ TRR 84412
Twin Tone / Feb '95 / Pinnacle.

PLEASED TO MEET ME
I.O.U. / Alex Chilton / I don't know / Nightclub jitters / Ledge / Never mind / Valentine / Shooting dirty pool / Red red wine / Skyway / Can't hardly wait
CD _____ 7599255572
Sire / Jul '93 / Warner Music.

SORRY MA FORGOT TO TAKE OUT THE TRASH
Takin' a ride / Careless / Customer / Hanging downtown / Kick your door down / Otto / I bought a headache / Rattlesnakes / I hate music / Johnny's gonna die / Shiftless when idle / More cigarettes / Don't ask why / Somethin' to du / I'm in trouble / Love you till Friday / Shutup / Raised in the city
CD _____ TTR 81232
Twin Tone / Feb '95 / Pinnacle.

STINK
Kids don't follow / Fuck school / Stuck in the middle / God damn job / White and lazy / Dope smokin' moran / Go / Gimme noise
CD _____ TTR 82282
Twin Tone / Feb '95 / Pinnacle.

TIM
Hold my life / I'll buy / Kiss me on the bus / Dose of thunder / Waitress in the sky / Swingin' party / Bastards of young / Lay it down clown / Left of the dial / Little mascara / Here comes a regular
CD _____ 7599253302
Sire / Jul '93 / Warner Music.

Repo, Teppo
HERDSMAN'S MUSIC FROM INGRIA
CD _____ KICD 7
Kansanmusiikki Instituutti / Dec '94 / Direct / ADA.

Reptile
FAME AND FOSSILS
CD _____ PLAY CD 13
Workers Playtime / May '90 / Pinnacle.

Reptilicus
O
CD _____ STCD 089
Staalplaat / Dec '95 / Vital/SAM.

Repulsion
HORRIFIED
Stench of burning death / Acid bath / Radiation sickness / Splattered cadavers / Festering boils / Eaten alive / Slaughter of the innocent / Pestilent decay / Decomposed
CD _____ RR 6063CD
Relapse / Jun '93 / Plastic Head.

Requiem
REQUIEM BY ROUGH TRADE
CD _____ 35JS 104
Rough Trade / '88 / Pinnacle.

SOUL MACHINE
CD _____ SHARK 105CD
Shark / May '95 / Plastic Head.

Resa
HAPPY NIGHTMARE
CD _____ 1213
Caprice / Nov '91 / CM / Complete/Pinnacle / Cadillac / ADA.

Residents
DUCK STAB
CD _____ TORSOCD 406
Torso / Oct '87 / SRD.

ESKIMO
CD _____ TORSOCD 404
Torso / Jul '87 / SRD.

FINGERPRINCE
CD _____ TORSOCD 407
Torso / Dec '87 / SRD.

GOD IN THREE PERSONS
Hard and tenderly / Devotion / Thing about them / Their early years / Loss of a loved one / Touch / Service / Confused / Fine fat flies / Time / Silver sharp / Kiss of flesh / Pain and pleasure
CD _____ TORSOCD 055
Torso / '88 / SRD.

LIVE IN HOLLAND
CD _____ CD 018
Torso / Jul '87 / SRD.

MEET THE RESIDENTS
CD _____ CD 416
Torso / Dec '88 / SRD.

Resistance D
INEXHAUSTIBILITY
CD _____ HHSP 005CD

Harthouse / Nov '94 / Disc / Warner Music.

ZTRING 2 OF LIFE
CD _____ HHCD 4
Harthouse / Mar '94 / Disc / Warner Music.

Resolution
SEATTLE BROTHERHOOD
CD _____ LF 147CD
Lost & Found / Jun '95 / Plastic Head.

Resonance Vox
RESONANCE VOX
CD _____ 5218792
Verve / May '95 / PolyGram.

Rest In Pieces
MY RAGE
CD _____ LF 081CD
Lost & Found / May '94 / Plastic Head.

Restless
BEAT MY DRUM
CD _____ NUTACD 001
Madhouse / Dec '88 / Nervous.

DO YOU FEEL RESTLESS ?
CD _____ NERCD 015
Nervous / '90 / Nervous / Magnum Music Group.

EARLY YEARS 1981-83, THE
CD _____ NERCD 026
Nervous / '90 / Nervous / Magnum Music Group.

FIGURE IT OUT
Road to paradise / Guitar man / Nowhere to go / Just an echo / Empty hands / Better than nothing / Still waiting / I go wild / Shopping around / Going back / His latest flame / Memoir blue
CD _____ NERCD 072
Nervous / Jun '93 / Nervous / Magnum Music Group.

NO.7
CD _____ NUTACD 6
Madhouse / Oct '91 / Nervous.

WHY DON'T YOU JUST ROCK
CD _____ NERCD 004
Nervous / Jan '92 / Nervous / Magnum Music Group.

Restless Heart
BEST OF RESTLESS HEART, THE
You can depend on me / Fast movin' train / Tender lie / Bluest eyes in Texas / Familiar pain / Wheels / That rock won't roll / Till I loved you / Why does it have to (wrong or right) / I'll still be loving you
CD _____ PD 90608
RCA / Feb '92 / BMG.

BIG IRON HORSES
Mending fences / We got the love / As far as I can tell / When she cries / Meet on the other side / Tell me what you dream / Blame it on love / Born in a high wind / Just in time / Big iron horses
CD _____ 74321 13899-2
RCA / Apr '93 / BMG.

MATTERS OF THE HEART
In this little town / Love train / Mind over matters of the heart / Baby needs new shoes / Hold you now / She's still in love / You're a stronger man than I am / Hometown boys / Sweet whiskey lies / I'd cross the line
CD _____ 07863663972
RCA / Jun '94 / BMG.

Retros
STRINGS AND SKINS
CD _____ APLCD 002
Scratch / Jul '95 / BMG.

Return To Khafji
RETURN TO KHAFJI
CD _____ ABCD 004
Resurrection / Jan '96 / Plastic Head.

Return To Sender
FESTIVAL TOUR
CD _____ NORMAL 175
Normal/Okra / Apr '95 / Direct / ADA.

Return To Zero
RETURN TO ZERO
Face the music / There's another side / All you've got / This is my life / Rain down on me / Every door is open / Devil to pay / Until your love comes back around / Livin' for the rock 'n' roll / Hard time (in the big house) / Return to zero
CD _____ 07599244222
Giant / Apr '92 / BMG.

Rev Hammer
BISHOP OF BUFFALO
Lamb / Tranquility of solitude / Etain / Ellan vannin / Circular blues / (Worse and worse)

---

like the son of a goat / Every step of the way / Drunkard's waltz / Blood whisky (LP only) / Spanish lullaby (LP only) / Shanty / Chase
CD _____ COOKCD 063
Cooking Vinyl / Feb '94 / Vital.

INDUSTRIAL SOUNDS AND MAGIC
CD _____ COOKCD 046
Cooking Vinyl / Jun '92 / Vital.

Rev, Martin
CHEYENNE
CD _____ FM 1006CD
Marilyn / Jul '92 / Pinnacle.

Revelation
ADDICTED
Jack's in the box / Addiction / Jack the lad / Wicked woman / Witches and wizards / Freewheeling
CD _____ CDR 108
Red Hot / Jun '95 / THE.

Revelation
NEVER COMES SILENCE
CD _____ HELL 020CD
Hellhound / Dec '92 / Plastic Head.

SALVATION'S ANSWER
CD _____ RISE 006CD
Rise / Mar '92 / Plastic Head.

YET SO FAR
Soul barer / Eternal search / Little faith / Grasping the nettle / Morning sun / Fallen / Alone / Natural steps / Yet so far
CD _____ H 00362
Hellhound / Feb '95 / Plastic Head.

Revelators
AMAZING STORIES
What does it take (to win your love) / Oh darlin' / Do right woman, do right man / Caribbean wind / El Salvador / Hot Burrito / Louisiana blues / I've got to find a way to win Maria back / If I could be there / Tupelo honey / Walk that line
CD _____ FIENDCD 729
Demon / Jun '93 / Pinnacle / ADA.

Revenants
HORSE OF A DIFFERENT COLOUR
CD _____ LONCD 931
Hunter / Sep '93 / Grapevine.

Revere, Paul
ESSENTIAL RIDE 1963-67, THE (The Best Of Paul Revere & The Raiders) (Revere, Paul & The Raiders)
Louie, Louie / Mojo workout / Over you / Crisco party / Walking the dog / Steppin' out / Just like me / Stepping stone / Kicks / Ballad of a useless man / Louie, go home / Take a look at yourself / Hungry / (You're a) Bad girl / Louise / Great airplane strike / In my community / Good thing / Why why why (is it so hard) / Ups and downs / Him or me, who's it gonna be
CD _____ CD 48949
Columbia / Jul '95 / Sony.

Reverend Horton Heat
FULL CUSTOM, THE
CD _____ SPCD 248
Sub Pop / Apr '93 / Disc.

LIQUOR TO THE FRONT
Big sky / Baddest of the bad / One time for me / Five-o-ford / In your wildest dreams / Entertainer / Rockin' dog / Jezebel / I can't surf / Liquor, beer and wine / I could get used to it / Cruisin' for a bruisin' / Yeah right
CD _____ 654492364-2
East West / Jul '94 / Warner Music.

SMOKE 'EM IF YOU GOT 'EM
Bullet / I'm mad / Bad reputation / It's a dark day / Big dwarf rodeo / Psychobilly freakout / Put it to me straight / Marijuana / Baby, you know who / Eat steak / D for Dangerous / Love whip
CD _____ SPCD 25/177
Sub Pop / '90 / Disc.

Reversing Hour
RIDDLE OF THE MONKEYSUIT
CD _____ LFP 0003
Ichiban / Sep '94 / Koch.

Revolting Cocks
BEERS, STEERS AND QUEERS
CD _____ DVNCD 4
Devotion / Apr '92 / Pinnacle.

BIG SEXY LAND
CD _____ CDDVN 6
Devotion / Mar '92 / Pinnacle.

LINGER FICK'EM GOOD
CD _____ CDDVN 22
Devotion / Sep '93 / Pinnacle.

YOU GODDAMNED SON OF A BITCH
CD _____ CDDVN 8
Devotion / Apr '92 / Pinnacle.

Revolution 9
YOU MIGHT AS WELL LIVE
You don't know what love is / Giving up the ghost / Now that your lover has gone / Winter song / You broke my heart / Damaged goods / Jessica / Jealousy / Amen to that / Song noir / Living with you / Patron Saint of lonliness / Shining guiding star
CD _____ HABCD 1
Habana / Jul '95 / Pinnacle.

Revolutionaries
BLACK ASH DUB
Marijuana / Herb / Collie / Lambs bread / Rizla / LSD / Acapulco / Cocaine
CD _____ CDTRL 186
Trojan / Jun '94 / Jazz / Total/BMG.

MACCA POSTMAN DUB
CD _____ JMC 200218
Jamaica Gold / Apr '95 / THE / Magnum Music Group / Jetstar.

Revolutionary Army Of...
GIFT OF TEARS (Revolutionary Army Of The Infant Jesus)
CD _____ PROBECD 012
Probe Plus / Dec '93 / Vital.

GIFT OF TEARS/MIRROR/LITURGIE (Revolutionary Army Of The Infant Jesus)
CD _____ EFA 015512
Apocalyptic Vision / Oct '95 / Plastic Head / SRD.

Revolutionary Dub...
RE-ACTION DUB PART 1 - DELIVERANCE (Revolutionary Dub Warriors)
CD _____ ONUCD 68
On-U Sound / Oct '94 / SRD / Jetstar.

Revolver
BABY'S ANGRY
CD _____ HUTCD 015
Hut / Apr '92 / EMI.

COLD WATER FLAT
Cool blue / Shakesdown / Cradle snatch / I wear your chain / Nothing without you / Bottled out / Coming back / Cold water flat / Makes no difference all the same / Wave
CD _____ CDHUT 8
Hut / Apr '93 / EMI.

Revolving Paint Dream
MOTHER WATCH ME BURN
CD _____ CRECD 039
Creation / May '94 / 3MV / Vital.

Revs
REVS, THE
Just ask why / We're so modern / Stay with me / Julie got a raise / Selfish / Making time / Joyrider / Ten seconds of temptation
CD _____ MASKCD 018
Vinyl Japan / Jan '93 / Vital.

REX
REX
CD _____ 185302
Southern / Apr '95 / SRD.

Rey, Alvino
BY REQUEST
CD _____ HCD 249
Hindsight / Jan '95 / Target/BMG / Jazz Music.

Reyes, Jorge
FLAYED GOD, THE
CD _____ STCD 069
Staalplaat / May '95 / Vital/SAM.

MORT AUX VACHES
CD _____ STCD 007
Staalplaat / Sep '95 / Vital/SAM.

NIERIKA
CD _____ PS 9326
Silent / Oct '93 / Plastic Head.

Reykjavik Jazz Quartet
REYKJAVIK JAZZ QUARTET
Changing weather / Alone together / So young / Flight 622 / Dark thoughts / Tongue in cheek / All the time / Hot house
CD _____ JHCD 032
Ronnie Scott's Jazz House / Jul '94 / Jazz Music / Magnum Music Group / Cadillac.

Reynoso, Juan
PLAYS SONES AND GUSTOS
CD _____ CO 105
Corason / Jan '94 / CM / Direct / ADA.

Rez Band
SILENCE SCREAMS
CD _____ OCE D 8123
Nelson Word / Jan '89 / Nelson Word.

Rezillos

CAN'T STAND THE REZILLOS
Flying saucer attack / No / Someone's gonna get their head kicked in tonight / Top of the pops / 2000 AD / It gets me / Can't stand my baby / Glad all over / My baby does good sculptures / I like it / Gettin' me down / Cold wars / Bad guy reaction
CD _____ 7599269422
Sire / Jan '96 / Warner Music.

LIVE AND ON FIRE IN JAPAN (Revillos)
Secret of the shadow / Bongo brain / Rock-a-boom / She's fallen in love with a monster man / Where's the boy for me / Rev up / Bitten by a lovebug / Mad from birth to death / Bobby come back to me / Fiend / Scuba scuba / My baby does good / Sculptures / Do the mutilation / Somebody's gonna get their head kicked in tonight / Yeah yeah
CD _____ ASKCD 046
Vinyl Japan / May '95 / Vital.

MOTORBIKE BEAT (Revillos)
Motorbike / Where's the boy for me / Fiend / Rev up / Rock-a-boom / Bobby come back to me / Yeah yeah / On the beach / Bitten by a loved bug / Cat call / Midnight / Z-X-7
CD _____ MAUCD 643
Mau Mau / Jul '95 / Pinnacle.

RF7

ALL YOU CAN EAT
CD _____ GTA 001CD
Grand Theft Auto / Aug '95 / Plastic Head.

Rhabstallion

DAY TO DAY
Hard luck man / Chain reaction / Breadline / Day to day / I could not believe my eyes / Times ain't so bad / Runaway / Driving seat / Stranger stranger / Shock 'n' roll / Day go disco / Sioux child / You're to blame (Live) / Stranger stranger (Live)
CD _____ ETHEL 1
Vinyl Tap / Dec '94 / Vinyl Tap.

Rhatigan

LATE DEVELOPER
CD _____ ORGAN 018CD
Org / Jan '96 / Pinnacle.

Rheostatics

INTRODUCING HAPPINESS '94
CD _____ 936245670-2
Warner Bros. / Aug '94 / Warner Music.

Rhodes, Bill

MIND BREAK
CD _____ 710 123
Innovative Communication / Jan '91 / Magnum Music Group.

SCULPTURES
CD _____ 710 124
Innovative Communication / Jan '91 / Magnum Music Group.

TWILIGHT ZONE
CD _____ 710 122
Innovative Communication / Jan '91 / Magnum Music Group.

Rhodes, Kimmie

WEST TEXAS HEAVEN
CD _____ 422505
New Rose / Jan '95 / Direct / ADA.

Rhodes, Sonny

BLUES IS MY BEST FRIEND
CD _____ KS 022
Flying Fish / Nov '94 / Roots / CM / Direct / ADA.

DISCIPLE OF THE BLUES
You can look for me / Blue funky down / Ain't nothing but the blues / Cigarette blues / Are we losing our thing / Ain't no blues in town / Ya ya / Blue shadows falling / Blue thunder
CD _____ ICH 9002 CD
Ichiban / Apr '91 / Koch.

I DON'T WANT MY BLUES COLOURED BRIGHT
CD _____ BM 9029
Black Magic / May '94 / Hot Shot / Swift / CM / Direct / Cadillac / ADA.

JUST BLUES
I can't lose / Things I used to do / Please love me / House without love / Think / Cigarette blues / Strange things happening / It hurts me too / East Oakland stomp
CD _____ ECD 26060
Evidence / Mar '95 / Harmonia Mundi / ADA / Cadillac.

Rhody, Alan

DREAMER'S WORLD
CD _____ TX 3005CD
Taxim / Jan '94 / ADA.

Rhos Male Voice Choir

WITH A VOICE OF SINGING
CD _____ BNA 5083
Bandleader / Aug '93 / Conifer.

Rhyne, Melvin

BOSS ORGAN (Rhyne, Melvin Quartet)
CD _____ CRISS 1080CD
Criss Cross / May '94 / Cadillac / Harmonia Mundi.

LEGEND, THE
CD _____ CRISS 1059CD
Criss Cross / May '92 / Cadillac / Harmonia Mundi.

TELL IT LIKE IT IS (Rhyne, Melvin & The Tenor Triangle)
CD _____ 1089CD
Criss Cross / Mar '95 / Cadillac / Harmonia Mundi.

TO CANNONBALL WITH LOVE
Introduction to samba / Marline / We'll be together again / Work song / Nippon soul / Mercy mercy mercy / Light little love / You and the night and the music
CD _____ KICJ 147
King/Paddle Wheel / Sep '93 / New Note.

Rhythm Cadillacs

SHAKE THIS SHAK
CD _____ ROCK CD 8808
Rockhouse / Oct '88 / Charly / CM / Nervous.

Rhythm Collision

CLOBBER
CD _____ DSR 039
Dr. Strange / Nov '95 / Plastic Head.

Rhythm Devils

APOCALYPSE NOW (sessions)
Compound / Trenches / Street gang / Beast / Steps / Tar / Lance / Cave / Hell's bells / Kurtz / Napalm for breakfast
CD _____ RCD 10109
Rykodisc / Sep '91 / Vital / ADA.

Rhythm Invention

INVENTURES IN WONDERLAND
CD _____ WARPCD 15
Warp / Aug '93 / Disc.

Rhythm Zone

RHYTHM ZONE 2
CD _____ KOOLCD 002
Kool Kat / Oct '89 / Pinnacle.

Rhythmaires

10TH ANNIVERSARY
CD _____ RAUCD 006
Raucous / May '93 / Nervous / Disc.

Rhythmatic

SPLAT, WHAT A BEAUTIFUL MESS
CD _____ SPLATCD 1
Network / Nov '91 / Sony / 3MV.

Rhythmstick

RHYTHMSTICK
Caribe / Friday night at the Cadillac Club / Quilombo / Barbados / Waiting for Angela / Nana / Softly as in a morning sunrise / Colo de Rio / Palisades in blue / Wamba
CD _____ ESJCD 230
Essential Jazz / Oct '94 / BMG.

Rias Orchestra

ORCHESTRAL COLOURS
CD _____ ISCD 119
Intersound / Jul '91 / Jazz Music.

Ribot, Marc

DON'T BLAME ME
CD _____ DIW 902
DIW / Dec '95 / Harmonia Mundi / Cadillac.

SHREK
CD _____ AVAN 033CD
Avant / Jul '94 / Harmonia Mundi / Cadillac.

Ricardos Jazzmen

OLE MISS
CD _____ MECCACD 1022
Music Mecca / Nov '94 / Jazz Music / Cadillac / Wellard.

Ricchizzi, Gianni

RAGA YAMAN/RAGA BHUPALI
CD _____ NI 5431
Nimbus / Apr '95 / Nimbus.

Rice

FUCK YOU, THIS IS RICE
CD _____ LOOKOUT 93CD
Lookout / Nov '94 / SRD.

Rice Brothers

RICE BROTHERS 2, THE
CD _____ ROUCD 0286
Rounder / Nov '94 / CM / Direct / ADA / Cadillac.

RICE BROTHERS, THE
Grapes on the vine / This ole house / Original unlimited / Teardrops in my eyes / You're drifting away / Don't think twice, it's alright / Let it ride / Keep the light on Sadie / Soldier's joy / Whisper my name / Life is like a mountain railroad
CD _____ CD 0256
Rounder / '89 / CM / Direct / ADA / Cadillac.

Rice, Daryle

FROM NOW ON
CD _____ AP 100CD
Appaloosa / Jun '94 / ADA / Magnum Music Group.

Rice, Gene

JUST FOR YOU
Love is calling you / You're gonna get served / No one can love you like I love you / Let's do it again / Let's get away / You're a victim / I believe / It's too late / So far away / I'll be right here waiting on you
CD _____ PD 83159
RCA / Aug '91 / BMG.

Rice, Tony

ACOUSTICS
CD _____ ROU 0317CD
Rounder / Jul '94 / CM / Direct / ADA / Cadillac.

BACKWATERS (Rice, Tony Unit)
CD _____ CD 0167
Rounder / Aug '88 / CM / Direct / ADA / Cadillac.

COLD ON THE SHOULDER
Cold on the shoulder / Wayfaring stranger / John Hardy / Fare thee well / Bitter green / Mule skinner blues / Song for life / Why don't you tell me so / If you only knew / Likes of me / I think it's going to rain today
CD _____ CD 0183
Rounder / Dec '86 / CM / Direct / ADA / Cadillac.

DEVLIN (Rice, Tony Unit)
CD _____ CD 11531
Rounder / '88 / CM / Direct / ADA / Cadillac.

MANZANITA
CD _____ CD 0092
Rounder / '88 / CM / Direct / ADA / Cadillac.

ME AND MY GUITAR
CD _____ CD 0201
Rounder / Aug '88 / CM / Direct / ADA / Cadillac.

NATIVE AMERICAN
Shadows / St. James hospital / Night flyer / Why you been so long / Urge for going / Go my way / Nothin' like a hundred miles / Changes / Brother to the wind / John Wilkes Booth / Summer wages
CD _____ CD 0248
Rounder / Aug '88 / CM / Direct / ADA / Cadillac.

PLAYS & SINGS BLUEGRASS
CD _____ ROU 253CD
Rounder / Jan '94 / CM / Direct / ADA / Cadillac.

RIVER SUITE FOR TWO GUITARS (Rice, Tony & John Carlini)
CD _____ SHCD 3837
Sugarhill / May '95 / Roots / CM / ADA / Direct.

TONY RICE
CD _____ CD 0085
Rounder / '88 / CM / Direct / ADA / Cadillac.

Rice, Wyatt

NEW MARKET GAP
CD _____ CDROU 272
Rounder / Dec '90 / CM / Direct / ADA / Cadillac.

Rich, Buddy

BUDDY AND SOUL
Love and peace / St. Petersburg race / Soul lady / Street kiddie / Greensleeves / Soul kitchen / Hello I love you / Comin' home baby / Meaning of the blues / Buddy
CD _____ BGOCD 23
Beat Goes On / Jun '94 / Pinnacle.

BUDDY RICH & HIS BIG BAND AT THE STADSHALLE LEONBERG, 1986
CD _____ EBCD 2119-2
Jazzband / Oct '94 / Jazz Music / Wellard.

BUDDY RICH AND HIS ORCHESTRA (Rich, Buddy & His Orchestra)
CD _____ 15758
Laserlight / Aug '92 / Target/BMG.

BURNING FOR BUDDY (A Tribute To Buddy Rich) (Various Artists)
CD _____ 7567826992
Warner Bros. / Jan '95 / Warner Music.

EASE ON DOWN THE ROAD (Rich, Buddy Big Band)
Time check / Backwoods sideman / Nuttville / Playhouse / Senator Sam / Big Mac / Three day sucker / Ease on down the road / Tommy (medley) / Pieces of dreams / Lush life / Nik-nik / Layin' it down
CD _____ CDC 8511
LRC / Sep '93 / New Note / Harmonia Mundi.

EUROPE 77 (Rich, Buddy & His Orchestra)
CD _____ DAWE 60
Magic / Nov '93 / Jazz Music / Swift / Wellard / Cadillac / Harmonia Mundi.

HIS LEGENDARY 1947-1948 ORCHESTRA
I've got news for you / Man could be a wonderful thing / Good bait / Blue skies / Just you, just me / I believe / What is this thing called love / Daily double / Nellie's nightmare / Little white lies / You go to my head / Queer Street / Fine and dandy / That's rich / I may be wrong, but I think you're wonderful / Robbin's nest / Four rich brothers / Carioca
CD _____ HEPCD 12
Hep / Aug '91 / Cadillac / Jazz Music / New Note / Wellard.

LIONEL HAMPTON PRESENTS BUDDY RICH (Rich, Buddy & Lionel Hampton)
Moment's notice / Giant steps / Buddy's Cherokee / Take the 'A' train / I'll never be the same / Latin silk / Buddy's rock (CD only.) / My funny valentine (CD only.)
CD _____ CDGATE 7011
Kingdom Jazz / Jun '87 / Kingdom.

MASTER OF DRUMS
Moment's notice / Giant steps / Buddy's cherokee / Take the 'A' train / I'll never be the same / Latin silk
CD _____ 722 005
Scorpio / May '93 / Complete/Pinnacle.

NO JIVE
You gotta try / Tales of Rhoda Rat / No jive / Lush life / Party time / Medley (i) Storm at sunup. ii) Love me now. iii) Yearnin' learnin'.) / Piece of the road suite (i) Pipe dreams. ii) Countin' them long white lines. iii) A piece of the road. iv) Back of the bus.)
CD _____ 01241660612
Novus / Oct '92 / BMG.

PHILADELPHIA 1986 (Rich, Buddy & His Big Band)
CD _____ EBCD 2126
Jazzband / Dec '95 / Jazz Music / Wellard.

PLAYTIME
Lulu's back in town / Playtime / Will you still be mine / Fascinating rhythm / Makin' whoopee / Marbles / Misty / Cheek to cheek / Four / If I were a bell / In a prescribed manner / I don't wanna be kissed
CD _____ LEJAZZCD 47
Le Jazz / Oct '95 / Charly / Cadillac.

RICH AND FAMOUS
Red snapper / Time will tell / Ballad of the matador / Dancing man / Cotton tail / One and only love / Manhattan - the city / Manhattan - central park
CD _____ CDMT 004
Meteor / Jul '95 / Magnum Music Group.

SWINGIN NEW BIG BAND/KEEP THE CUSTOMERS SATISFIED
Readymix / Basically blues / Critic's choice / My mans gone now / Up tight / Sister Sadie / More soul / West side story Medley: (Overture, Cool, Something's coming, Somewhere.) / Keep the customer satisfied / Long days journey / Midnight cowboy medley (Midnight cowboy, He quit me, Everybody's talkin, Tears and joys.) / Celebration / Groovin' hard / Juicer is wild / Winning the west
CD _____ BGOCD 169
Beat Goes On / Feb '93 / Pinnacle.

SWINGIN' NEW BIG BAND
Readymix / Basically blues / Critic's choice / My man's gone now / Up tight (everything's alright) / Sister Sadie / More soul / West Side Story medley / What'd I say / Step right up / Apples / In a mellotone / Lament for Lester / Naptown blues / Hoe down
CD _____ CDP 8352322
Pacific Jazz / Jan '96 / EMI.

TAKE IT AWAY (Rich, Buddy & His Big Band)
CD _____ BGOCD 210
Beat Goes On / Oct '93 / Pinnacle.

TUFF DUDE
Donna Lee / Chameleon / Second Avenue blue / Jumpin' at the woodside / Sierra lonely / Nica's dream / Billie's bounce
CD _____ DC 8543
Denon / Apr '89 / Conifer.

Rich, Charlie

BOSS MAN
CD _____ 340502
Koch / Aug '95 / Koch.

FABULOUS CHARLIE RICH, THE
CD _____ 340492
Koch / May '95 / Koch.

GREATEST HITS: CHARLIE RICH
Most beautiful girl / Very special love song / Since I fell for you / My elusive dreams / Every time you touch me (I get high) / Behind closed doors / Life has its little ups and downs / All over me / I love my friend / We love each other / Daddy don't you walk so fast / She / Sunday kind of woman / Rollin' with the flow / Almost persuaded / Spanish eyes
CD _____ 4721242
Epic / Sep '95 / Sony.

MOST BEAUTIFUL GIRL IN THE WORLD
CD _____ CTS 55426
Country Stars / Jun '94 / Target/BMG.

MOST BEAUTIFUL GIRL, THE
Behind closed doors / Most beautiful girl / Sunday kind of woman / Stay / There won't be anymore / Whu oh why / Field of yellow daisies / I take it on home / If you wouldn't be my lady / Very special love song / Everytime you touch me / We love each other / You never really wanted me / Till I can't take it anymore / I love my friend / Life has its little ups and downs / Since I fell for you / She
CD _____ PWKS 4168
Carlton Home Entertainment / Jan '94 / Carlton Home Entertainment.

REBOUND
Rebound / Whirlwind / Break up / Philadelphia baby / Big man / Everything I do is wrong / Lonely weekends / You never know about love / School days / There won't be anymore / Juanita / Little woman friend of mine / C.C. rider / Easy money / Gonna be waitin' / There's another place I can't go / Who will the next fool be / Sittin' and thinkin' / Midnight blues / Unchained melody / You finally found out / Stay / My baby done left me / Charlie's boogie
CD _____ CDCHARLY 52
Charly / Feb '87 / Charly / THE / Cadillac.

SET ME FREE
CD _____ 340482
Koch / May '95 / Koch.

SINGS HANK WILLIAMS
My heart would know / Take these chains from my heart / Half as much / You win again / I can't help it / Hey good lookin' / Your cheatin' heart / Cold cold heart / Nobody's lonesome for me / I'm so lonesome I could cry / Wedding bells / They'll never take her love from me / Love is after me / Pass on by / Hurry up freight train / Only me / When something is wrong with my baby / Don't tear me down / Can't get it right / I'll shed no tears / To fool a fool / Who will the next fool be / Big time operator / Renee / Motels, hotels
CD _____ DIAB 810
Diabolo / Oct '95 / Pinnacle.

THAT'S RICH
CD _____ CPCD 8146
Charly / Nov '95 / Charly / THE / Cadillac.

Rich, Dave

AIN'T IT FINE
Your pretty blue eyes / Ain't it fine / I'm glad / Didn't work out did it / I'm sorry goodbye / Darling I'm lonesome / Tuggin' on my heart strings / I love 'em all / I forgot / I think I'm gonna die / Lonely street / Our last night together / City lights / Rosie let's get cozy / Burn on love fire / Red sweater / I've learned / Red beads / School blues / Sunshine in my heart / Chicken house / That's what this whole world needs / Saved from sin / Brand new feeling / Where else would I want to be / Key to my heart / I've thought it over / Just like mine
CD _____ BCDAH 15763
Bear Family / Nov '94 / Rollercoaster / Direct / CM / Swift / ADA.

Rich Kids

GHOSTS OF PRINCES IN TOWERS
Strange one / Hung on you / Ghosts of princes in towers / Cheap emotion / Marching men / Put you in the picture / Young girls / Bullet proof lover / Rich kids / Lovers and fools / Burning sounds
CD _____ DOJOCD 151
Dojo / Sep '93 / BMG.

Rich Kids On LSD

RICHES TO RAGS
CD _____ E 86445-2
Epitaph / Jan '95 / Plastic Head / Pinnacle.

ROCK 'N' ROLL
CD _____ E 864262
Epitaph / Jun '92 / Plastic Head / Pinnacle.

Rich, Robert

TRANCES/DRONES
CD _____ XLTD 001
Extreme / May '95 / Vital/SAM.

Richard, Cliff

31ST OF FEBRUARY STREET, THE/I'M NEARLY FAMOUS
31st of February street opening / Give me back that old familiar feeling / Leaving / Travellin' light / There you go again / Our love could be so real / No matter what / Fireside song / Going away / Long long time / You will never know / Singer / 31st of February street closing / I can't ask for anymore than you / It's no use pretending / I'm nearly famous / Lovers / Junior cowboy / Miss you nights / I wish you'd change your mind / Devil woman / Such is the mystery / You've got to give me all your lovin' / If you walked away / Alright, it's alright
CD _____ CDEMC 3642
EMI / Nov '93 / EMI.

32 MINUTES AND 17 SECONDS/WHEN IN SPAIN
It'll be me / So I've been told / How long is forever / I'm walking the blues / Turn around / Blueberry hill / Let's make a memory / When my dreamboat comes home / I'm on my way / Spanish harlem / You don't know / Falling in love with love / Who are we to say / I wake up cryin' / Perfidia / Amor amor amor / Frenesi / Solamente una vez / Me lo dijo adela / Maria no mas / Tus besos / Quizas quizas quizas / Te quiero dijiste / Cancion de orfeo / Quien sera
CD _____ CDEMC 3630
EMI / Oct '92 / EMI.

CAROLS
Saviour's day / Silent night / Little town / In the bleak mid-Winter / Sweet little Jesus boy / While shepherds watched / Mary / What you gonna name that pretty little baby / Joseph / God rest you merry gentlemen / Unto us a child is born / Can it be true / O little town of Bethlehem
CD _____ ALD 025
Alliance Music / Oct '95 / EMI.

CLIFF RICHARD AND THE SHADOWS BOX SET (Richard, Cliff & The Shadows)
Omoide no nagisa / Giniro no michi / Londonderry air / Kimi to itsumademo / Boys #2 / Boys / Foot tapper / Round and round / Les girls / Frenesi / Shazam / Guitar boogie / Sleepwalk / F.B.I. / Bongo blues / Ranka chank / Flyder and the spy / Autumn / Chinchilla / Walkin' / Look in my eyes, Maria / If I give my heart to you / Maria / Secret love / Love letters / I only have eyes for you / All I do is dream of you / When I grow too old to dream / My heart is an open book / Boom boom (that's how my heart goes) / Moonlight bay / Forever kind of love / La mer / J'attendrai / Shrine on the second floor / Where the four winds blow / Solitary man / Things we said today / Carnival (from Black Orpheus) / Little rag doll / Pefidia / 36-24-36 / All day / My grandfather's clock / Lady Penelope / Zero X theme / Thunderbirds theme / Finders keepers / Shane / Giant (theme from) / Shotgun / Las tres carabelas / Adios muchachos / Valencia / Granada / Tonight / Fandango / Little princess / Gonzales / Jet black / Driftin' (live)
CD Set _____ MAGPIE 1
See For Miles/C5 / Apr '92 / Pinnacle.

CLIFF RICHARD THE ALBUM
Peace in our time / Love is the strongest emotion / I still believe in you / Lean on you / Salvation / Only angel / Handle my heart with love / Little mistreater / You move heaven / I need love / Hold us together / Human work of art / Never let go / Healing love / Brother to brother
CD _____ CDEMD 1043
EMI / Apr '93 / EMI.

CLIFF SINGS/ME AND MY SHADOWS
Blue suede shoes / Snake and the bookworm / I gotta know / Here comes summer / I'll string along with you / Embraceable you / As time goes by / Touch of your lips / Twenty flight rock / Pointed toe shoes / Mean woman blues / I'm walkin' / I don't know why / Little things mean a lot / Somewhere along the way / That's my desire / I'm gonna get you / You and I / I cannot find a true love / Evergreen trees / She's gone / Left out again / You're just the one to do it / Lamp of love / Choppin 'n' changin / We have it made / Tell me / Gee whiz it's you / I love you so / I'm willing to learn / I don't know / Working after school
CD _____ CDEMC 3628
EMI / Oct '92 / EMI.

DON'T STOP ME NOW/GOOD NEWS
Shout / One fine day / I'll be back / Heartbeat / I saw her standing there / Hang on to a dream / You gotta tell me / Homeward bound / Good golly Miss Molly / Don't make promises / Move it / Don't / Dizzy Miss Lizzy / Baby, it's you / My babe / Save the last dance for me / Good news / It is no secret / We shall be changed / 23rd Psalm (Crimond) / Go where I send thee / What a friend we have in Jesus / All glory, laud and honour / Just a closer walk with thee / King of love my shepherd is / Mary what you gonna name that pretty little baby boy / When I survey the wondrous cross / Take

my hand, precious Lord / Get on board little children / May the good Lord bless and keep you
CD _____ CDEMC 3635
EMI / Nov '92 / EMI.

DRESSED FOR THE OCCASION (Richard, Cliff & Philharmonic Orchestra)
Green light / We don't talk anymore / True love ways / Softly as I leave / Carrie / Miss you nights / Galadriel (spirit of starlight) / Maybe someday / Thief in the night / Up in the world / Treasure of love / Evil woman (reprise)
CD _____ CZ 187
EMI / May '89 / EMI.

ESTABLISHED 1958/THE BEST OF
Minute you're gone / On my word / Time in between / Wind me up (let me go) / Blue turns to grey / Visions / Time drags by / In the country / It's all over / I'll come runnin' / Day I met Marie / All my love / Congratulations / Girl, you'll be a woman soon
CD _____ CDEMC 3637
EMI / Nov '92 / EMI.

EVENT BOXSET, THE
CD Set _____ CDCRTVB 31
EMI / Nov '90 / EMI.

EVERY FACE TELLS A STORY/SMALL CORNERS
My kinda life / Must be love / When two worlds drift apart / You got me wondering / Every face tells a story / Try a smile / Hey Mr. Dream Maker / Give me love your way / Up in the world / Don't turn the light out / Spider Man / Why should the devil have all the good music / I love / Why me / I've got news for you / Hey, watcha say / I wish we'd all been ready / Joseph / Good on the sally army / Goin' home / Up in Canada / Yes, He lives / When I survey the wondrous cross
CD _____ CDEMC 3643
EMI / Nov '93 / EMI.

FINDERS KEEPERS/CINDERELLA
Finders keepers / Time drags by / Washerwoman / La la song / My way / Oh senorita / Spanish music fiesta / This day / Paella / Finders keepers/My way/Paella/Fiesta / Run to the door / Where did the summer go / Into each life some rain must fall / Welcome to stoneybroke / Why wasn't I born rich / Peace and quiet / Flyder and the spy / Poverty / Hunt / In the country / Come Sunday / Dare I love him like I do / If our dreams came true / Autumn / King's place / Peace and quiet (Reprise) / She needs him more than me / Hey doctor man
CD _____ CDEMC 3634
EMI / Oct '92 / EMI.

GREEN LIGHT/THANK YOU VERY MUCH
Young ones / Do you wanna dance / Day I met marie / Shadoogie / Green light / Under lock and key / She's a gypsy / Count me out / Please remember me / Never even thought / Free my soul / Start all over again / While she's young / Can't take the hurt anymore / Easy along / Atlantis / Nivram / Apache / Please don't tease / Miss you nights / Move it / Willie and the hand jive / All shook up / Devil woman / Why should the devil have all the good music / End of the show
CD _____ CDEMC 3644
EMI / Nov '93 / EMI.

HIT LIST, THE (The Best Of 35 Years)
CD Set _____ CDEMTVD 84
EMI / Oct '94 / EMI.

I'M NO HERO
Take another look / Anything I can do / Little in love / Here (so doggone blue) / Give a little bit more / In the night / I'm no hero / Dreamin' / Heart will break / Everyman
CD _____ CDFA 3148
Fame / Jul '88 / EMI.

LISTEN TO CLIFF/21 TODAY
CD _____ CDEMC 3629
EMI / Nov '93 / EMI.

LOVE IS FOREVER/KINDA LATIN
Everyone needs someone to love / Long ago and far away / (All of a sudden) my heart sings / Have I told you lately that I love You / Fly me to the moon / Summer place / I found a rose / My foolish heart / Through the eye of a needle / My coloring book / I'll walk alone / Someday (you'll want me to want you) / Paradise lost / Look homeward angel / Blame it on the bossa nova / Blowin' in the wind / Quiet nights of quiet stars / Eso beso / Girl from Ipanema / One note samba / Our day will come / Quando, quando, quando / Come closer to me / Meditation / Concrete and clay
CD _____ CDEMC 3633
EMI / Nov '92 / EMI.

LOVE SONGS: CLIFF RICHARD
Miss you nights / Constantly / Up in the world / Carrie / Voice in the wilderness / Twelfth of never / I could easily fall / Day I met Marie / Can't take the hurt anymore / Little in love / Minute you're gone / Visions / When two worlds drift apart / Next time / It's all in the game / Don't talk to him / When the girl in your arms (is the girl in your heart) / Theme for a dream / Fall in love with you / We don't talk anymore

CD _____ CDEMTV 27
EMI / Mar '88 / EMI.

MY KINDA LIFE
Born to rock 'n' roll / Hotshot / Devil woman / Remember (when two worlds drift apart) / Carrie / Lean on you / We don't talk anymore / Monday thru' Friday / Lucille / You've got wondering / Never even thought / Two hearts / Language of love / My kinda life
CD _____ CDEMD 1034
EMI / Jun '92 / EMI.

NOW YOU SEE ME, NOW YOU DON'T
Only way out / First date / Thief in the night / Where do we go from here / Son of thunder / Little town / It has to be you / Water is wide / Now you see me, now you don't / Be in my heart / Discovering
CD _____ CZ 2
EMI / Oct '87 / EMI.

PRIVATE COLLECTION (His Personal Best 1979-1988)
Some people / Wired for sound / All I ask of you / Carrie / Remember me (Album & Cass. only.) / True love ways / Dreamin' / Green light (Album & cassette only.) / She means nothing to me / Heart user (Album & Cassette only.) / Little in love / Daddy's home / We don't talk anymore / Never say die (give a little bit more) / Only way out / Suddenly / Slow rivers (Album & cassette only.) / Please don't fall in love / Little town / My pretty one / Ocean deep / She's so beautiful / Two hearts (Album & cassette only.) / Mistletoe and wine
CD _____ CDCRTV 30
EMI / Nov '88 / EMI.

ROCK 'N' ROLL SILVER/ROCK CONNECTION
Silver's home tonight / Hold on / Never say die (give a little bit more) / Locked inside your prison / Please don't fall in love / Baby you're dynamite / Love stealer / Golden days are over / Ocean deep / Move it / Donna / Lucille / Little bitty pretty one / Never be anyone else but you / It'll be me / Heart user / Willie and the hand jive / Lovers and friends / La Gonave / Over you / Shooting from the heart / Learning how to rock 'n' roll / Dynamite / She means nothing to me / Makin' history
CD _____ CDEMC 3645
EMI / Nov '93 / EMI.

ROCK ON WITH CLIFF RICHARD
Move it / High class baby / My feet hit the ground / Living doll / Mean streak / Never mind / Apron strings / Dynamite / Blue suede shoes / Twenty flight rock / Mean woman blues / Willie and the hand jive / Please don't tease / Nine times out of ten / D in love / Mumblin' Mosie / Gee whiz it's you / What'd I say / Got a funny feeling / Forty days / Tough enough / We say yeah / Do you wanna dance / It'll be me / Dancing shoes
CD _____ CDMFP 6005
Music For Pleasure / Oct '87 / EMI.

SINCERLEY CLIFF RICHARD/LIVE AT THE TALK OF THE TOWN
In the past / Always / Will you still love me tomorrow / You'll want me / I'm not getting married / Time / For Emily, wherever I may find her / Baby I could be so good loving you / Sam / London's not too far / Take miles / Take good care of her / When I find You / Punch and Judy
CD _____ CDEMC 3638
EMI / Nov '92 / EMI.

SUMMER HOLIDAY (Richard, Cliff & The Shadows)
Seven days to a holiday / Summer holiday / Let us take you for a ride / Les girls / Foot tapper / Round and round / Stranger in town / Orlando's mime / Bachelor boy / Swingin' affair / Really waltzing / All at once / Dancing shoes / Yugoslav wedding / Next time / Big news
CD _____ CDMFP 6021
Music For Pleasure / Apr '88 / EMI.

TAKE ME HIGH/HELP IT ALONG
It's only money / Midnight blue / Hover (instrumental) / My life / Driving / Game / Brumburger duet / Take me high / Antibrotherhood of man / Winning / Driving (instrumental) / Join the band / Word is love / Brumburger finale / Day by day / Celestial houses / Jesus / Silvery rain / Jesus loves you / Fire and rain / Yesterday, today, forever / Mr. Business man / Help it along / Amazing grace / Higher ground / Sing a song of freedom
CD _____ CDEMC 3641
EMI / Nov '93 / EMI.

TOGETHER WITH CLIFF
Have yourself a merry little Christmas / O come all ye faithful (Adeste Fidelis) / We should be together / Mistletoe and wine / Christmas never comes / Christmas alphabet / Saviour's day / Christmas song / Scarlet ribbons / Silent night / White Christmas / This New Year
CD _____ CDEMD 1028
EMI / Oct '91 / EMI.

TRACKS 'N GROVES/THE BEST OF CLIFF RICHARD - VOL.2
Early in the morning / As I walk into the morning of your life / Love, truth and Emily Stone / My head goes around / Put my

mind at ease / Abraham, Martin and John /
Girl can't help it / Bang bang (my baby shot
me down) / I'll make it all up to you / I'd just
be fool enough / Don't let tonight ever end
/ What a silly thing to do / Your heart's not
in your love / Don't ask me to be friends /
Are you only fooling me / Goodbye Sam,
hello Samantha / Marianne / Throw down a
line / Jesus / Sunny honey girl / I ain't got
time anymore / Flying machine / Sing a
song of freedom / With the eyes of a child
/ Good times (better times) / I'll love you
forever today / Joy of living / Silvery rain /
Big ship
CD Set _____ CDEMC 3640
EMI / Nov '93 / EMI.

WINNER, THE
Winner / Wild geese / Such is the mystery
/ Reunion of the heart / Discovering / There's more to life / Peace in our time / Under
the gun / Yesterday, today, forever / Where
you are / Be in my heart / Fighter / Thief in
my heart / From a distance
CD _____ ALD 020
Alliance Music / May '95 / EMI.

WIRED FOR SOUND
Wired for sound / Once in a while / Better
than I know myself / Oh no don't let me go
/ 'Cos I love that rock 'n' roll / Broken doll
/ Lost in a lonely world / Summer rain /
Young love / Say you don't mind / Daddy's
home
CD _____ CDFA 3159
Fame / Oct '87 / EMI.

**YOUNG ONES, THE (Richard, Cliff &
The Shadows)**
Friday night / Got a funny feeling / Peace
pipe / Nothing's impossible / Young ones /
All for one / Lessons in love / No one for
me but Nicky / What d'you know, we've got
a show / Vaudeville routine / Mambo / Sav-
age / We say yeah
CD _____ CDMFP 6020
Music For Pleasure / Apr '88 / EMI.

Richards, Ann

I'M SHOOTING HIGH
I'm shooting high / Moanin' low / Nightingale / Blues in my heart / I've got to pass
your house to get to my house / Deep night
/ Poor little rich girl / Should I / I'm in the
market for you / Absence makes the heart
grow fonder / Lullaby of Broadway / Will you
still be mine
CD _____ JASCD 310
Jasmine / May '90 / Wellard / Swift / Conifer
/ Cadillac / Magnum Music Group.

Richards, Goff

**GOFF RICHARDS & THE BRITISH
NUCLEAR FUEL BAND (Richards, Goff
& BNFL Band)**
CD _____ QPRL 055D
Polyphonic / Apr '93 / Conifer.

Richards, Johnny

**LIVE IN HI-FI STEREO 1957-58
(Richards, Johnny Big Band)**
CD _____ JH 1010
Jazz Hour / '91 / Target/BMG / Jazz
Music / Cadillac.

Richards, Keith

**LIVE AT THE HOLLYWOOD PALLADIUM
'88 (Richards, Keith & The X-Pensive
Winos)**
Take it so hard / How I wish / I could have
stood you up / Too rude / Make no mistake
/ Time is on my side / Big enough / Whip it
up / Locked away / Struggle / Happy / Con-
nection / Rockawhile
CD _____ CDVUS 7
Virgin / Feb '92 / EMI.

MAIN OFFENDER
999 / Wicked as it seems / Eileen / Words
of wonder / Yap yap / Bodytalks / Hate it
when you leave / Runnin' too deep / Will
but you won't / Demon
CD _____ CDVUS 59
Virgin / Oct '92 / EMI.

TALK IS CHEAP
Big enough / Take it so hard / Struggle / I
could have stood you up / Make no mistake
/ You don't move me / How I wish / Rock-
awhile / Whip it up / Locked away / It means
a lot
CD _____ CDV 2554
Virgin / '88 / EMI.

Richards, Red

DREAMY
CD _____ SKCD 23053
Sackville / Aug '94 / Swift / Jazz Music /
Jazz Horizons / Cadillac / CM.

**GROOVE MOVE (Richards, Red &
George Kelly Sextet)**
CD _____ JP 1045
Jazz Point / May '95 / Harmonia Mundi /
Cadillac.

LULLABY IN RHYTHM
CD _____ SKCD 23044
Sackville / Jun '93 / Swift / Jazz Music /
Jazz Horizons / Cadillac / CM.

MY ROMANCE
CD _____ CDJP 1042
Jazz Point / May '94 / Harmonia Mundi /
Cadillac.

SWING TIME
CD _____ CDJP 1041
Jazz Point / May '94 / Harmonia Mundi /
Cadillac.

Richards, Sue

GREY EYED MORN
CD _____ MMCD 201
Maggie's Music / Dec '94 / CM / ADA.

MORNING AIRE
CD _____ MMCD 204
Maggie's Music / Dec '94 / CM / ADA.

Richards, Terrie

**I CRIED FOR YOU (Richards, Terrie &
Harry Allen/Howard Alden)**
CD _____ CHECD 00107
Master Mix / Oct '93 / Wellard / Jazz
Music / New Note.

Richards, Tim

**OTHER SIDE, THE (Richards, Tim Trio &
Quartet)**
CD _____ SPJCD 548
Spotlite / May '93 / Cadillac / Jazz
Horizons / Swift.

Richards, Trevor

**TREVOR RICHARDS NEW ORLEANS
TRIO**
CD _____ SOSCD 1222
Stomp Off / Oct '92 / Jazz Music /
Wellard.

Richardson, Geoffrey

VIOLA MON AMOUR
Rhapsodic uke / Blossomville / Borrowed
kalimba / On the beech / Life drawing /
Blossomville (reprise) / Viola mon amour /
Diogenes and Alexander / Well tempered
ukelele / Fifty four homes / Rhapsodic uke
(reprise) / Diogenes and Alexander (reprise)
CD _____ VP 132CD
Voice Print / Jun '93 / Voice Print.

Richardson, Jim

**UP JUMPED LUNCH (Richardson, Jim
Quartet)**
CD _____ SPJCD 541
Spotlite / May '93 / Cadillac / Jazz
Horizons / Swift.

Richie, Lionel

BACK TO FRONT
Do it to me / My destiny / Love oh love / All
night long / Easy / Still / Endless love / Running with the night / Dancing on the ceiling
/ Sail on / Hello / Truly / Penny lover / Stuck
on you / Say you, say me / Three times a
lady
CD _____ 5300182
Motown / May '92 / PolyGram.

CAN'T SLOW DOWN
All night long / Stuck on you / Penny lover
/ Hello / Love will find a way / Running with
the night / Only one / Can't slow down
CD _____ 530023-2
Motown / Jan '92 / PolyGram.

DANCING ON THE CEILING
Sela / Ballerina girl / Don't stop / Deep river
woman / Love will conquer all / Tonight will
be alright / Say you, say me / Night train
(Smooth alligator) (Cassette and Compact
Disc only.) / Dancing on the ceiling / Love
will find a way
CD _____ 530024-2
Motown / Jan '92 / PolyGram.

LIONEL RICHIE
Serves you right / Wandering stranger / Tell
me / My love / Round and round / Truly /
You are / You mean more to me / Just got
some love in your heart
CD _____ 530026-2
Motown / Jan '92 / PolyGram.

Richies

PET SUMMER
CD _____ WB1-106-2
We Bite / Dec '93 / Plastic Head.

WINTER WONDERLAND
CD _____ 846 119
We Bite / Jul '90 / Plastic Head.

Richman, Jonathan

COLLECTION
CD _____ CCSCD 397
Castle / Apr '94 / BMG.

I, JONATHAN
CD _____ ROUCD 9036
Rounder / Jan '94 / CM / Direct / ADA /
Cadillac.

JONATHAN RICHMAN
Malaguena de Jojo / Everyday clothes /
Blue moon / I eat with gusto, damn you bet
/ Sleepwalk / Mistake today for my / Action

packed / Fender Statocaster / Closer / Mir-
acles will start to happen / Que reste t'll de
nos amours / Cerco
CD _____ ROUCD 9021
Special Delivery / Sep '94 / ADA / CM /
Direct.

**JONATHAN RICHMAN & BARRENCE
WHITFIELD (Richman, Jonathan &
Barrence Whitfield)**
CD _____ CDS 1
Rounder / '88 / CM / Direct / ADA /
Cadillac.

**JONATHAN RICHMAN & THE MODERN
LOVERS (Richman, Jonathan & Modern
Lovers)**
Rockin' shopping centre / Back in the U.S.A
/ Important in your life / New England /
Lonely financial zone / Hi dear / Abominable
snowman in the market / Hey there little in-
sect / Here come the Martian Martians /
Springtime / Amazing grace
CD _____ CREV 008CD
Rev-Ola / Jan '93 / 3MV / Vital.

JONATHAN, TE VAS A EMOCIONAR
CD _____ ROU 9040CD
Rounder / Apr '94 / CM / Direct / ADA /
Cadillac.

**LIVE AT THE LONGBRANCH SALOON
(Modern Lovers)**
CD _____ 422439
New Rose / May '94 / Direct / ADA.

MODERN LOVERS (Modern Lovers)
Roadrunner / Astral plane / Old world /
Pablo picasso / I'm straight / She cracked
/ Hospital / Someone I care about / Girl-
friend / Modern world / Dignified and old /
Government centre
CD _____ CREV 007CD
Rev-Ola / Nov '92 / 3MV / Vital.

**MODERN LOVERS 88 (Richman,
Jonathan & Modern Lovers)**
Dancin' late at night / When Harpo played
his harp / Gail loves me / New kind of neigh-
borhood / African lady / I love hot nights /
California desert party / Everything's gotta
be right / Circle 1 / I have come out to play
/ Moulin rouge theme
CD _____ FIENDCD 106
Demon / Jan '88 / Pinnacle / ADA.

PLEA FOR TENDERNESS, A
CD _____ NTMCD 506
Nectar / Jun '95 / Pinnacle.

**PRECISE MODERN LOVERS ORDER
(Modern Lovers)**
CD _____ ROUCD 9042
Rounder / Apr '95 / CM / Direct / ADA /
Cadillac.

**ROCK 'N' ROLL WITH THE MODERN
LOVERS (Richman, Jonathan & Modern
Lovers)**
Sweeping wind / Ice cream man / Rockin'
rockin' leprechauns / Summer morning / Af-
ternoon / Fly into the mystery / South Amer-
ican folk song / Rollercoaster by the sea /
Dodge Veg-O-matic / Egyptian reggae /
Coomyah / Wheels on the bus / Angels
watching over me
CD _____ CREV 009CD
Rev-Ola / Feb '93 / 3MV / Vital.

YOU MUST ASK THE HEART
CD _____ ROUCD 9047
Rounder / May '95 / CM / Direct / ADA /
Cadillac.

Richmond, Dannie

LAST MINGUS BAND A.D., THE
Cumbia and jazz fusion / Feel no evil / April
Denise / Seven words / Cumbia and jazz
fusion (alternate take)
CD _____ LCD 15372
Landmark / Sep '94 / New Note.

Richmond, Kim

PASSAGES
Passages / Old acquaintances / Passcaglia/
My funny valentine / Melon bells / Street of
dreams / Soft feelings / Chic-a-brac / Im-
ages and likeness / Indian Summer / Nardis
CD _____ CDSB 2043
Sea Breeze / Jul '92 / Jazz Music.

Richrath

ONLY THE STRONG SURVIVE
After all / Captured / Heart on fire / In your
letter / Murder by suicide / Only the strong
survive / If the nite don't get'cha / Tragedy
/ Outlaws / Where I pray / Today / Searchin'
/ Holly would
CD _____ GNPD 2027
GNP Crescendo / Apr '92 / Silva Screen.

Ricks, Glen

OH CAROLINA
CD _____ LG 21089
Lagoon / Sep '93 / Magnum Music Group
/ THE.

Ricky & The Rockets

HOOKED ON ROCK 'N' ROLL
CD _____ ND 75264
RCA / Apr '92 / BMG.

Rico

**BLOW YOUR HORN/BRIXTON CAT
(Rico & The Rudies)**
CD _____ CDTRL 361
Trojan / Jun '96 / Jetstar / Total/BMG.

RISING IN THE EAST
CD _____ JOVECD 3
Jove Music / Sep '94 / Jetstar / SRD.

ROOTS TO THE BONE
Children of Sanchez / Midnight in Ethiopia
/ Free ganja / Take five / Far East / No pol-
itician / Firestick / Matches Lane / This day
/ Ramble / Lumumba / Africa / Man from
Wareika / Over the mountain / Dial Africa
CD _____ RRCD 54
Reggae Refreshers / Apr '95 / PolyGram /
Vital.

Riddle, Leslie

STEP BY STEP
Little school girl / Frisco blues / Broke and
weary blues / Hilltop blues / Motherless
children / Titanic / I'm out on the ocean a-
sailing / I'm working on a building / I know
what it means to be lonesome / Red river
blues / One kind favor / If you see my saviour / Cannonball / Step by step
CD _____ ROU 0299CD
Rounder / May '93 / CM / Direct / ADA /
Cadillac.

Riddle, Nelson

CAPITOL YEARS: NELSON RIDDLE
Let's face the music and dance / You are
the night and the music / Younger than
springtime / You leave me breathless /
You're an old smoothie / Then I'll be happy
/ I get along without you very well / I can't
escape from you / Have you got any castles, baby / Darn that dream / Let yourself
go / Jeannine / Without a song / September
in the rain / S'posin' / Am I blue / Rain / I'll
get by (as long as I have you) / Diga diga
doo / For all we know / Time was / Something to remember you by / Get happy
CD _____ CDEMS 1489
Capitol / Apr '93 / EMI.

Ride

CARNIVAL OF LIGHT
CD _____ CRECD 147
Creation / Jun '94 / 3MV / Vital.

GOING BLANK AGAIN
CD _____ CRELD 124
Creation / Jan '92 / 3MV / Vital.

NOWHERE
Seagull / Kaleidoscope / In a different place
/ Polar bear / Dreams burn down / Decay /
Paralysed / Vapour trail / Taste / Here and
now / Nowhere
CD _____ CRECD 074
Creation / Oct '90 / 3MV / Vital.

SMILE
Chelsea Girl / Drive Blind / All I can see /
Close my eyes / Like A Daydream / Silver /
Furthest Sense / Perfect time
CD _____ CRECD 126
Creation / May '94 / 3MV / Vital.

Riders In The Sky

**ALWAYS DRINK UPSTREAM FROM THE
HERD**
CD _____ ROUCD 0360
Rounder / Jan '96 / CM / Direct / ADA /
Cadillac.

BEST OF THE WEST
CD _____ CD 11517
Rounder / '88 / CM / Direct / ADA /
Cadillac.

BEST OF THE WEST RIDERS AGAIN
CD _____ CD 11524
Rounder / '88 / CM / Direct / ADA /
Cadillac.

SADDIE PAIS
CD _____ CD 8011
Rounder / '88 / CM / Direct / ADA /
Cadillac.

Ridgley, Tommy

**NEW ORLEANS KING OF THE STROLL,
THE**
New Orleans king of the stroll / Double eyed
whammy / Is it true / Should I ever love
again / My ordinary girl / I've heard that
story before / Heavenly / Girl from Kooka
Monga / In the same old way / Three times
/ Only girl for me / I love you yes I do /
Please hurry home
CD _____ CD 2079
Rounder / CM / Direct / ADA / Cadillac.

SHE TURNS ME ON
CD _____ MBCD 1203
Modern Blues / Jun '93 / Direct / ADA.

SINCE THE BLUES BEGAN
CD _____ BT 1115CD
Black Top / May '95 / Direct / ADA.

Ridley, Larry

**LIVE AT RUTGERS UNIVERSITY (Ridley,
Larry & the Jazz Legacy Ensemble)**

Vamp / Ypso factor / Bock to bock / Ugly beauty / Ossie Mae / On a clear day / Dr. Feelgood / Breakthrough
CD _____ 66051020
Strata East / Aug '93 / New Note.

Ridout, Bonnie

CELTIC CIRCLES
CD _____ MMCD 209
Maggie's Music / Dec '94 / CM / ADA.

SOFT MAY MORN
CD _____ MMCD 208
Maggie's Music / Dec '94 / CM / ADA.

Riessler, Michael

HELOISE
CD _____ WER 8008-2
Wergo / Nov '93 / Harmonia Mundi / ADA / Cadillac.

MOMENTUM MOBILE
Anekdoten / La rage / Ein ittlige sprag / Luigi / Marathon / Ba binga / Marsch der ketzer / Ost - west / Old Orleans, New Orleans / Song mecanique
CD _____ ENJ 90032
Enja / Mar '95 / New Note / Vital/SAM.

TENTATIONS D'ABELARD
CD _____ WER 8010
Wergo / Dec '95 / Harmonia Mundi / ADA / Cadillac.

Riff, Nick

CLOAK OF IMMORTALITY
Cloak of immortality / Creature feature / Way out / Staring into space / Like a zen stray / Something indside / Temple of dreams / Ghost / Tribal elders / From beyond they speak (Features on CD only.) / Go far go wide
CD _____ DELECCD 017
Delerium / Apr '95 / Vital.

FREAK ELEMENT
CD _____ DELECD 001
Delerium / Jun '92 / Vital.

Riffburglars

SHORTLIST/SWAG
Free, single and disengaged / Can't stand it / Bring it on home / Strange brew / Slow down / Big leg woman / Shadow knows / Who do you love / Peter Gunn / Harlem shuffle / Mama told me not to come / Treat her right
CD Set _____ LICD 921158
Line / Jun '92 / CM / Grapevine / ADA / Conifer / Direct.

Rifkin, Joshua

SCOTT JOPLIN'S PIANO RAGS
CD _____ 7559791592
Warner Bros. / Jan '95 / Warner Music.

Rig

BELLY TO THE GROUND
CD _____ CRZ 035CD
Cruz / Feb '94 / Pinnacle / Plastic Head.

Rigai, Amiram

AMIRAM RIGAI PLAYS LOUIS MOREAU GOTTSCHALK
CD _____ 0DSF 40000
Smithsonian Folkways / Oct '93 / ADA / Direct / Koch / CM / Cadillac.

Riggan, Tracey

FRIENDS
Amazing grace / Challenge / Arms of the Father / Special friend / Never gonna look back / Security / Free / Dance of fire / Hide no more / Celebration
CD _____ MYRCD 1283
Myrrh / Jan '92 / Nelson Word.

Right Direction

ALL OF A SUDDEN
CD _____ LF 133CD
Lost & Found / May '95 / Plastic Head.

Right Said Fred

UP
CD _____ SNOGCD 1
Gut / Mar '92 / Total/BMG.

Righteous Brothers

INSPIRATIONS
Soul and inspiration / What now my love / Ebb tide / White cliffs of Dover / Go ahead and cry / Just once in my life / Stranded in the middle of no place / Great pretender / He will break your heart / Island in the sun / (I love you) for sentimental reasons / That lucky old sun / My darling Clementine / Georgia on my mind
CD _____ 5501972
Spectrum/Karussell / Mar '94 / PolyGram / THE.

ORIGINAL ALBUMS
CD _____ DCD 5285
Disky / Dec '93 / THE / BMG / Discovery / Pinnacle.

UNCHAINED MELODY
CD _____ AVC 513
Avid / Dec '92 / Avid/BMG / Koch.

Rights Of The Accused

KICK-HAPPY, THRILL-HUNGRY, RECKLESS AND WILLING
CD _____ N 0167-2
Noise/Modern Music / '91 / Pinnacle / Plastic Head.

Rigid Containers Band

ENGLISH LANDSCAPES
CD _____ HARCD 1125
Harlequin / Jul '95 / Magnum Music Group.

Rigo, Sandor Buffo

BEST OF TRADITIONAL, THE (Rigo, Sandor Buffo & His Hungarian Gypsy Band)
CD _____ SYNCD 148
Topic / Apr '93 / Direct / ADA.

Riisnaes, Knut

GEMINI TWINS
CD _____ GMCD 175
Gemini / Oct '89 / Cadillac.

Riley, Billy Lee

CLASSIC RECORDINGS 1956-1960
Rock with me baby / Troublebound / Flyin' saucer rock 'n' roll / I want you baby / Red hot / Pearly Lee / Wouldn't you / Baby, please don't go / Rockin' on the moon / Is that all to the ball, Mr Hall / Itchy / Thunderbird / Down by the riverside / No name girl / Come back baby / Got the water boiling / Open the door Richard / Dark muddy bottom / Repossession blues / That's what I want to do / Too much woman for me / Flyin' saucer rock 'n' roll #2 / I want you (version) / She's my baby / Pearly Lee (unissued) / Red hot (unissued) / That's right / Searchin' / Chatter and college man / Your cash ain't nothin' but trash / Swanee river rock / Betty and Dupree / Let's talk about us / Got the water boiling (unissued) / Saturday night fish fry / Folsom prison blues / Billy's blues / When a man gets the blues / Sweet William / Red hot (version) / Mud Island / My baby's got love
CD Set _____ BCD 15444
Bear Family / Jul '90 / Rollercoaster / Direct / CM / Swift / ADA.

ROCKIN' WITH BILLY (3CD Set)
CD Set _____ CDSUNBOX 3
Sun / Feb '93 / Charly.

Riley, Howard

BERNE CONCERT, THE (Riley, Howard & Keith Tippett)
CD _____ FMRCD 08
Future / Mar '91 / Harmonia Mundi / ADA.

FLIGHT
CD _____ FMRCD 26
Future / Dec '95 / Harmonia Mundi / ADA.

WISHING ON THE MOON
CD _____ FMRCD 14
Future / Aug '95 / Harmonia Mundi / ADA.

Riley, Jimmy

20 CLASSIC HITS
CD _____ SONCD 0053
Sonic Sounds / Aug '93 / Jetstar.

Riley, Philip

VISIONS AND VOICES
CD _____ WCL 110122
White Cloud / May '95 / Select.

Riley, Steve

'TIT GALOP POUR MAMA (Riley, Steve & Mamou Playboys)
CD _____ ROU 6048CD
Rounder / Dec '90 / CM / Direct / ADA / Cadillac.

LA TOUSSAINT (Riley, Steve & Mamou Playboys)
CD _____ ROUCD 6068
Rounder / Jan '96 / CM / Direct / ADA / Cadillac.

LIVE (Riley, Steve & Mamou Playboys)
CD _____ ROU 6058CD
Rounder / May '94 / CM / Direct / ADA / Cadillac.

TRACE OF TIME (Riley, Steve & Mamou Playboys)
Bayou noir / Mon vieux wagon / Old home waltz / Church point breakdown / Parlez-nous a boire / Lover's waltz / Sur le courtableau / La valse du regret / La Point-au-pic / Corner post / Zarico est pas sale
CD _____ ROUCD 6053

Rounder / Jul '93 / CM / Direct / ADA / Cadillac.

Riley, Terry

CADENZA ON THE NIGHT PLAIN (Riley, Terry & The Kronos Quartet)
CD _____ GCD 79444
Gramavision / Sep '95 / Vital/SAM / ADA.

PERSIAN SURGERY DERVISHES
CD _____ NT 6715
Robi Droli / Jan '94 / Direct / ADA.

RAINBOW IN CURVED AIR
CD _____ 477849 2
Columbia / Oct '94 / Sony.

Rimmington, Sammy

CHRISTMAS IN NEW ORLEANS
CD _____ BCD 209
GHB / Jan '94 / Jazz Music.

GINGER PIG NEW ORLEANS JAZZ BAND
CD _____ BCD 232
GHB / Oct '92 / Jazz Music.

ON TOUR (Rimmington, Sammy & His Band)
CD _____ BCD 211
GHB / Jun '95 / Jazz Music.

ONE SWISS NIGHT
CD _____ MECCACD 1021
Music Mecca / Jun '93 / Jazz Music / Cadillac / Wellard.

SAMMY RIMMINGTON & HIS BAND (Rimmington, Sammy & His Band)
CD _____ BCD 288
GHB / Aug '94 / Jazz Music.

Rincon Surfside Band

SURFING SONGBOOK
CD _____ VSD 5481
Varese Sarabande/Colosseum / Jan '95 / Pinnacle / Silva Screen.

Ringer, Jim

GOOD TO GET HOME
CD _____ CIC 069CD
Clo lar-Chonnachta / Nov '93 / CM.

Ringo

EYEWITNESS
CD _____ LG 21102
Lagoon / Apr '95 / Magnum Music Group / THE.

Ringtailed Snorter

SEXUAL CHILD ABUSE
CD _____ ZOTCD 19
Talitha / Aug '93 / Plastic Head.

Ringworm

FLATLINE, THE
CD _____ LF 135CD
Lost & Found / Mar '95 / Plastic Head.

Rinpoche, Chogyal

CHOD: CUTTING THROUGH DUALISM
CD _____ ARNR 0193
Amiata / Sep '93 / Harmonia Mundi.

Rin

RIO
CD _____ BLIPCD 102
Urban London / Mar '94 / Jetstar.

Riot

FIRE DOWN BELOW
CD _____ 7559605762
Elektra / Jan '96 / Warner Music.

LIVE
CD _____ 7559679692
Elektra / Jan '96 / Warner Music.

NIGHTBREAKER
CD _____ SPV 084 62222
Rising Sun / Jun '94 / Plastic Head.

RESTLESS BREED
Restless breed / Hard lovin' man / CIA / When I was young / Loved by you / Loneshark / Over to you / Showdown / Dream away / Violent crimes
CD _____ 7559601342
Elektra / Jan '96 / Warner Music.

RIOT LIVE
CD _____ CDZORRO 55
Metal Blade / Jul '92 / Pinnacle.

ROCK CITY
Desperation / Warrior / Rock city / Overdrive / Angel / Tokyo rose / Heart of fire / Gypsy queen / This is what I get
CD _____ CDMZORRO 54
Metal Blade / Feb '93 / Pinnacle.

Riot City

RIOT CITY PUNK SINGLES COLLECTION

Fuck the tories / We are the Riot Squad / Civil destruction / Riots in the city / Why should we / Religion doesn't mean a thing / Lost cause / Suspicion / Unite and fight / Police power / Society's fodder / In the future / Friday night hero / There ain't no solution / Government somewhere / No potential threat / Ten years time / Hate the law / Hidden in fear / Lost cause (demo) / Unite and fight (demo)
CD _____ CDPUNK 41
Anagram / Jan '95 / Pinnacle.

Riot Clone

STILL NO GOVERNMENT
CD _____ RCR 005CD
Riot Clone / Aug '95 / Plastic Head.

Riot Squad

ANYTIME
I take it we're through / Bittersweet love / How is it done / Jump / It's never too late to forgive / Working man / Not a great talker / Anytime / Try to realise / Gonna make you mine / Gotta be the first time / Nevertheless / I wanna talk about my baby
CD _____ REP 4192-WZ
Repertoire / Aug '91 / Pinnacle / Cadillac.

Riou

EXHIBITION OF THE SAMPLES
CD _____ KKCD 137
KK / Sep '95 / Plastic Head.

Ripe

PLASTIC HASSLE
CD _____ BBQCD 149
Beggars Banquet / Apr '94 / Warner Music / Disc.

Riperton, Minnie

CAPITOL GOLD: THE BEST OF MINNIE RIPERTON
Perfect angel / Lover and friend (Single version) / Memory lane / Woman of heart and mind / Loving you / Young willing and able / Can you feel what I'm saying / Stick together / Wouldn't matter where you are / Stay in love / Inside my love / Here we go / Give me time (Single version) / You take my breath away / Adventures in paradise / Simple things / Light my fire
CD _____ CDP 7805162
Capitol / Aug '93 / EMI.

COME TO MY GARDEN
Les fleurs / Completeness / Come to my garden / Memory band / Rainy day in centerville / Close your eyes and remember / Oh by the way / Expecting / Only when I'm dreaming
CD _____ CDBM 080
Blue Moon / May '95 / Magnum Music Group / Greensleeves / Hot Shot / ADA / Cadillac / Discovery.

Ripped Shirt

OUTSIDERS, THE
CD _____ PLAN 004
Planet / Mar '94 / Grapevine / ADA / CM.

Ripping Corpse

DREAMING WITH THE DEAD
CD _____ CDFLAG 57
Music For Nations / Jun '91 / Pinnacle.

Rippingtons

LIVE IN L.A.
Indian summer / Aspen / Curves ahead / Weekend in Monaco / One summer night in Brazil / High roller / Dream of sirens / Once in a lifetime love / Tourists in paradise
CD _____ GRP 97182
GRP / Jul '93 / BMG / New Note.

WEEKEND IN MONACO
Weekend in Monaco / St. Tropez / Vienna / Indian summer / Place for lovers / Carnival / Moka java / High roller / Where the road will lead us
CD _____ GRP 96812
GRP / Aug '92 / BMG / New Note.

WELCOME TO THE St. JAMES' CLUB
Welcome to The St James Club / Soul mates / I watched her walk away / Affair in San Miguel / Who's holding her now / Kenya / Wednesday's child / Tropic of Capricorn / Passion fruit / Victoria's secret
CD _____ GRP 96182
GRP / Aug '90 / BMG / New Note.

Ripple

RIPPLE
You were right on time / Be my friend / I don't know what it is but it sure is funky / I'll be right there trying / Get off / See the light in the window / Funky song / Willie pass the water / Dance lady dance / Ripplin'
CD _____ CPCD 8093
Charly / Apr '95 / Charly / THE / Cadillac.

Riqueni, Rafael

MAESTROS
El bohio / Noches de cadix / Inspiration / Con salero y garbo / De chiclana a cai / Nostalgia flamenco / Recuerdo a sevilla / Sentir del sacromonte / Perfil flamenco / Mantilla e feria / Estrella amargura
CD _____ EMO 93062
Act / Oct '94 / New Note.

Rishell, Paul

BLUES ON A HOLIDAY
CD _____ TONECOOLCD 1144
Tonecool / May '94 / Direct / ADA.

SWEAR TO TELL THE TRUTH
CD _____ TONECOOLCD 1148
Tonecool / May '94 / Direct / ADA.

Rising Sons

RISING SONS, THE
Statesboro blues / If the river was whiskey / By and by (poor me) / Candy man / Let the good times roll / 44 blues / 11th street overcrossing / Corine Corina / Tulsa county / Walkin' down the line / Girl with green eyes / Sunny's dream / Spanish lace blues / Devil's got my woman / Take a giant step / Flyin' so high / Dust my broom / Last fair deal gone down / Baby, what you want me to do / I got a little
CD _____ 472865 2
Columbia / May '93 / Sony.

Risk

DIRTY SURFACES
CD _____ 0876234
Steamhammer / Aug '90 / Pinnacle / Plastic Head.

HELL'S ANIMALS
Monkey business / Perfect kill / Dead or alive / Secret of our destiny / Sicilian showdown / Torture and pain / Mindshock / Megalomania / Russian nights / Epilogue
CD _____ 85-7593
Steamhammer / Jun '89 / Pinnacle / Plastic Head.

Risk, Laura

JOURNEY BEGUN (Risk, Laura & Athena Tergis)
CD _____ CUL 105CD
Culburnie / Oct '95 / Ross / ADA.

Ritchie, Jean

MOST DULCIMER, THE
CD _____ GR 70714
Greenhays / Dec '94 / Roots / Jazz Music / Duncans / CM / ADA.

NONE BUT ONE/HIGH HILLS & MOUNTAINS
CD _____ GR 70708
Greenhays / Dec '94 / Roots / Jazz Music / Duncans / CM / ADA.

Rite Of Strings

RITE OF STRINGS
Indigo / Renaissance / Song to John / Chilean pipe song / Topanga / Morocco / Change of life / La cancion de sofia / Memory canyon
CD _____ CDP 8341672
IRS / Aug '95 / PolyGram / BMG / EMI.

Ritenour, Lee

BANDED TOGETHER
Operator (Thief on the line) / Other love / Sunset drivers / Mandela / Ameretto / Rit variations II / Be good to me / I'm not responsible / Shadow dancing / Heavenly bodies
CD _____ 1046710182
Discovery / May '95 / Warner Music.

BEST OF LEE RITENOUR
Sun song / Captain fingers / Caterpillar / Three days of the condor / Fly by night / Little bit of this and a little bit of that / Wild rice / Isn't she lovely
CD _____ EK 36527
Sony Jazz / Jul '95 / Sony.

CAPTAIN'S JOURNEY, THE
Captain's journey / Captain's journey #2 / Morning glory / Sugar loaf express / Matchmakers / What do you want / That's enough for me / Etude
CD _____ 1046710152
Discovery / May '95 / Warner Music.

FEEL THE NIGHT
Feel the night / Market place / Wicked wine / French roast / You make me half way / You should know better / Midnight lady / Uh oh
CD _____ 1046710102
Discovery / May '95 / Warner Music.

FIRST COURSE
CD _____ 4670942
Sony Jazz / Jan '95 / Sony.

FRIENDSHIP
Sea dance / Woody creek / Crystal morning / It's a natural thing / Samurai night fever / Life is the song we sing
CD _____ JMI 20092
JVC / Nov '93 / New Note.

GENTLE THOUGHTS
Captain caribe/Getaway / Chanson / Meiso / Captain fingers / Feel like makin' love / Gentle thoughts
CD _____ JMI 20072
JVC / Apr '94 / New Note.

LARRY & LEE (Ritenour, Lee & Larry Carlton)
Crosstown kids / Low steppin' / L.A. Underground / Closed door jam / After the rain / Remembering J.P. / Fun in the dark / Lota about nothin' / Take that / Up and adam / Reflections of a guitar player
CD _____ GRP 98172
GRP / Apr '95 / BMG / New Note.

RIT
Mr. Briefcase / Tell me pretty lies / No sympathy / Is it you / Dream walk / Good question / On the slow glide
CD _____ 1046710132
Discovery / May '95 / Warner Music.

RIT 2
Cross my heart / Voices / Dreamwalkin' / Keep it alive / Malibu / Tied up / Roadrunner / Promises, promises / On the Boardwalk / Fantasy
CD _____ 1046710172
Discovery / May '95 / Warner Music.

STOLEN MOMENTS
Uptown / Stolen moments / 24th Street blues / Haunted heart / Waltz for Carmen / St. Bart's / Blue in green / Sometime ago
CD _____ GRP 96152
GRP / Apr '90 / BMG / New Note.

WEST BOUND
West bound / Boss city / Four on six / Little bumpin' / Waiting in vain / Goin' on to Detroit / New day / Ocean Ave / Road song / West coast blues / N.Y. Times
CD _____ GRP 97052
GRP / Mar '93 / BMG / New Note.

Ritmo Oriental

RITMO ORIENTAL IS CALLING YOU
Nena, asi no se vale / Yo traigo panatela / Que rico bailo yo / Martiza / La ritmo suena a areito / La ritmo te esta llamando / Maria baila el son / El que no sabe, sabe / Advertencia para todos / Si no hay posibilidad me voy
CD _____ CDORB 034
Globestyle / Jan '89 / Pinnacle.

Ritta, Canzoniere Della

MALEVENTO
CD _____ NT 6734CD
Robi Droli / Apr '95 / Direct / ADA.

Ritter, Julie

MEDICINE SHOW
CD _____ NAR 122CD
SST / Jul '95 / Plastic Head.

Ritter, Tex

HIGH NOON
High noon (1) (Movie soundtrack - rare British Capitol recording.) / Boogie woogie cowboy / Pecos Bill / Dallas darling / Eyes of Texas / Night Herding song / Pony express / High noon (2) (1st Capitol recording) / He's a cowboy auctioneer / Billy the kid / Texas rangers / Cattle call / Goodbye my little cherokee / There's a goldstar in her window / In case you change your mind (Previously unissued.) / I was out of my mind (Previously unissued.) / Dark days in Dallas (Previously unissued.Tribute to J.F.Kennedy)
CD _____ BCD 15634
Bear Family / Feb '92 / Rollercoaster / Direct / CM / Swift / ADA.

Ritual Device

HENGE
CD _____ RED 9-2
Redemption / Jun '93 / SRD.

Ritz

ALMOST BLUE (Ritz & Clark Terry)
Blue and sentimental / Mood indigo / Almost blue / Meditation / Come Sunday / Beautiful friendship / Last night when we were young / Lotus blossom / Lament / Love so strong / Heart's desire
CD _____ CY 77999
Denon / '90 / Conifer.

FLYING
Full moon / Flying / Meet me half way / You should know better / Walking on a thin line / Skylark / To you / What's this / Never never land / Fall too far
CD _____ CY 73673
Denon / Oct '89 / Conifer.

MOVIN' UP
Movin' up / Mr. flat five / South of the border / My foolish heart / Perdido / Vine Street Bar and grille / Basically blues / Jeru / Rhythm-a-ning / Shake rattle 'n' roll
CD _____ CY 72526
Denon / Oct '88 / Conifer.

RITZ, THE
All the things you are / Saturday night fish fry / Summer burn / Walkin' / It never entered my mind / Invitation / Scrapple from the apple / Child is born / Old folks / Golden rule / Ooh yah / Music in the air / Best is yet to come / It ain't necessarily so
CD _____ CY 1839
Denon / Oct '88 / Conifer.

SPIRIT OF CHRISTMAS, THE
Silent night / Have yourself a merry little Christmas / Sleigh ride / Spirit of Christmas / Wonderful Christmas time / What child is this / Christmas song / Carol of the bells / Christmas time is here
CD _____ CY 72663
Denon / Nov '89 / Conifer.

Rivas, Antonio

LA PERLA DE ARSEGUEL
CD _____ MW 3002CD
Music & Words / Jun '92 / ADA / Direct.

River City Brass Band

CONCERT IN THE PARK
El capitan / Daisy bell / Sweet and low / Belle of chicago / Maple leaf rage / Whirlwind polka / Grand dutchess / Semper fidelis / Fireman's polka / On with the motley / William Tell overture / Love's old sweet song / Lassus trombone / Washington post / Lost chord / Believe me if / All those endearing / Young charms / Liberty bell / 12th Street rag / Stars and stripes forever
CD _____ QMPR 604D
Polyphonic / Mar '94 / Conifer.

FOOTLIFTERS
CD _____ QPRL 057D
Polyphonic / Mar '93 / Conifer.

River City People

SAY SOMETHING GOOD
What's wrong with dreaming / Walking on ice / Under the rainbow / Carry the blame / Say something good / Thirsty / When I was young / No doubt / I'm still waiting / Home and dry / Huskisson St. (CD only.) / Find a reason (CD only.)
CD _____ CDFA 3295
Fame / May '93 / EMI.

Rivera, Hector

AT THE PARTY WITH HECTOR RIVERA
At the party / Shingaling baby / My foolish heart / Pra voz wilma / I got my eye on you / Got to make up your mind / Playing it cool / Crown my heart / Calypso number 10 / Do it to me / Asia minor / I want a chance for romance / Hueso E. Pellenjo / Angue tu mamino querra (aka Lily)
CD _____ CDBGPD 082
BGP / Jan '94 / Pinnacle.

Rivera, Johnny

DEJAME INTENTARIO
Yo sin tu amor / Se parecia tanto a ti / Te me perdiste / Esa chica / Por falta de amor / Dejame intentario / Sin ella / Y donde estas / Renuciar a tu amor
CD _____ 66058062
RMM / May '95 / New Note.

Rivera, Luis

BATTLE OF THE ORGANS
DB / Hay ride / Soft one / Grinding / Deep purple / I want a little girl / Memories of you / LR / Tangerine / Fat stocking / Heavy hips / Bobby sox / Manhattan / Milano blues
CD _____ KCD 631
King/Paddle Wheel / Mar '90 / New Note.

Rivera, Willie

EL DIA QE ME DEJES
El amor corre por mi cuenta / Puerto querido / Amiga mia / No podras escaparte / Dejate querer / Todo por quererte / El dia que me dejas / Ella quiere volver
CD _____ 66058068
RMM / Dec '95 / New Note.

Riverdales

RIVERDALES, THE
CD _____ LOOKOUT 120
Lookout / Sep '95 / SRD.

Rivers, Blue

BLUE BEAT IN MY SOUL (Rivers, Blue & His Maroons)
Guns of Navarone / Too much / Mercy mercy mercy / Phoenix city / Witchcraft man / Searching for you baby / I've been pushed around
CD _____ SEECD 318
See For Miles/C5 / May '91 / Pinnacle.

Rivers, James

BEST OF NEW ORLEANS RHYTHM & BLUES VOL. 3
CD _____ MG 9009
Mardi Gras / Feb '95 / Jazz Music.

Rivers, Johnny

LIVE AT THE WHISKY A GO GO/HERE WE A GO GO AGAIN
Memphis / It won't happen with me / Oh lonesome me / Lawdy Miss Clawdy / Whisky A Go Go / Walking the dog / Brown eyed handsome man / You can have her / Multiplication / Medley: La Bamba/Twist and shout / Maybelliene / Dang me / Hello Josephine / Hi-heel sneakers / Can't buy me love / I've got a woman / Baby, what you want me to do / Midnight special / Roll over Beethoven / Walk myself on home / Johnny B. Goode / Whole lotta shakin' goin' on
CD _____ BGOCD 241
Beat Goes On / Feb '95 / Pinnacle.

ROCKS THE FOLK/MEANWHILE BACK AT THE WHISKY A GO GO
Tom Dooley / Long time man / Michael (row the boat ashore) / Blowin' in the wind / Green green / Where have all the flowers gone / If I had a hammer / Tall oak tree / Catch the wind / 500 miles / Mr Tambourine Man / Jailer bring me water / Seventh son / Greenback dollar / Stop in the name of love / Un-Square dance / Silver threads and golden needles / Land of 1000 dances / Parchment Farm / I'll cry instead / Break up / Work song / Stagger Lee / Susie Q
CD _____ BGOCD 299
Beat Goes On / Oct '95 / Pinnacle.

Riverside Ceilidh Band

FIRST FOOTING
Gay Gordons / Gay Gordons (encore) / Strip the willow / Strip the willow (encore) / Dashing white sergeant / Dashing white sergeant (encore) / Song / Military two step / Pride of Erin waltz / Pride of Erin waltz (encore) / Eightsome reel / Highland schottische / Highland schottische (encore) / St. Bernard's waltz (Mixes) / St. Bernard's waltz (encore) / Canadian barn dance / Canadian barn dance encore
CD _____ LISMOR 5241
Lismor / Jan '95 / Lismor / Direct / Duncans / ADA.

HORSES FOR COURSES
CD _____ LCOM 9035
Lismor / Apr '91 / Lismor / Direct / Duncans / ADA.

Riverside Reunion Band

MOSTLY MONK
Bemsha swing / West coast blues / Round Midnight / Well you needn't / Gemini / Ruby my dear / In walked bud / Four on six / Work song
CD _____ MCD 9216
Milestone / Aug '94 / Jazz Music / Pinnacle / Wellard / Cadillac.

Rizzetta, Sam

SEVEN VALLEYS - HAMMERED DULCIMER
CD _____ FF 70489
Flying Fish / Jan '90 / Roots / CM / Direct / ADA.

Roach, Archie

JAMU DREAMING
CD _____ D 30851
Mushroom / Mar '94 / BMG / 3MV.

Roach, Max

DEEDS, NOT WORDS
CD _____ OJCCD 304
Original Jazz Classics / Feb '93 / Wellard / Jazz Music / Cadillac / Complete/Pinnacle.

DRUMS UNLIMITED
Drum also waitzes / Nommo / Drums unlimited / St. Louis blues / For big Sid / In the red
CD _____ 7567813612
Atlantic / Apr '95 / Warner Music.

EASY WINNERS (Roach, Max Double Quartet)
Bird says / Sis / Little booker / Easy winners
CD _____ SNCD 1109
Soul Note / '86 / Harmonia Mundi / Wellard / Cadillac.

FREEDOM NOW SUITE
CD _____ CCD 79002
Candid / Oct '83 / Cadillac / Jazz Music / Wellard / Koch.

HISTORIC CONCERTS (Roach, Max & Cecil Taylor)
CD Set _____ 121100/1-2
Soul Note / Nov '93 / Harmonia Mundi / Wellard / Cadillac.

IN THE LIGHT (Roach, Max Quartet)
CD _____ SNCD 1053
Soul Note / '86 / Harmonia Mundi / Wellard / Cadillac.

IT'S CHRISTMAS AGAIN
CD _____ 1211532
Soul Note / May '95 / Harmonia Mundi / Wellard / Cadillac.

MAX ROACH AND FRIENDS
CD _____ COD 018
Jazz View / Mar '92 / Harmonia Mundi.

MAX ROACH AND FRIENDS VOL.2
CD _____ COD 019
Jazz View / Aug '92 / Harmonia Mundi.

MAX ROACH TRIO (Roach, Max Trio)
CD _____ 7567822732
Atlantic / Apr '95 / Warner Music.

MOP MOP
Kardouba / Stop motion / Night mountain / Cecillana / Mop mop / Jordu / Sophisticated lady / Who will buy / Love for sale / Long as you're living
CD _____ LEJAZZCD 44
Le Jazz / Jun '95 / Charly / Cadillac.

SCOTT FREE
Scott free (part 1) / Scott free (part II)
CD _____ SNCD 1103
Soul Note / '86 / Harmonia Mundi / Wellard / Cadillac.

SPEAK, BROTHER, SPEAK
Original Jazz Classics / Nov '95 / Wellard / Jazz Music / Cadillac / Complete/Pinnacle.

SURVIVORS
Survivors / Third eye / Billy the kid / Jasme / Drum also waltzes / Sassy Max (self portrait) / Smoke that thunders
CD _____ SNCD 1093
Soul Note / May '85 / Harmonia Mundi / Wellard / Cadillac.

Roach, Michael

AIN'T GOT ME NO HOME
CD _____ ST 001CD
Stella / Mar '94 / ADA.

Roach, Nancy

DOUBLE SCOTCH
CD _____ CIC 066CD
Clo Iar-Chonnachta / Nov '93 / CM.

Roachford

GET READY
Get ready / Survival / Funkee chile / Stone city / Wanna be loved / Bayou / Innocent eyes / Hand of fate / Takin' it easy / Higher / Vision of the future / Get ready (reprise)
CD _____ 4681362
Columbia / Apr '95 / Sony.

PERMANENT SHADE OF BLUE
Only to be with you / Johnny / Emergency / Lay your love on me / Ride the storm / This generation / I know you don't love me / Gus's blues (Intro) / Do we wanna live together / Cry for me / Guess I must be crazy / Higher love
CD _____ 475842 2
Columbia / Apr '94 / Sony.

ROACHFORD
Give it up / Family man / Cuddly toy / Find me another love / No way / Kathleen / Beautiful morning / Lying again / Since / Nobody but you
CD _____ 4606302
Columbia / Apr '92 / Sony.

Roadside Picnic

LA FAMILLE
La famille (theme) / Precious metal / New travelling tune / Quazar / Truth in you / Frozen night / La famille / Promido / I'mmin
CD _____ BW 067
B&W / Aug '95 / New Note.

Robbins, Marty

1951-1958
Tomorrow you'll be gone / I wish somebody else loves me / Love me or leave me alone / Cryin' 'cause I love you / I'll go on alone / Pretty words / You're breaking my heart / I can get along / I couldn't keep from crying / Just in time / Crazy little heart / After you leave / Lorelei / Castle in the sky / Your hearts turn to break / Why keep wishing / Half way chance with you / Sing me something sentimental / At the end of a long lonely day / Blessed Jesus, Should I fall don't let me lay / Kneel and let the Lord take your load / Don't make me ashamed / It's a long, long ride / It looks like I'm just in your way / I'm happy 'cause you're hurtin' / My isle of golden dreams / Have thine own way / God understands / Aloha oe / What made you change your mind / Way of a hopeless love / Pain and misery / Juarez / I'm too big to cry / Call me up / It's a pity what money can do / Time goes by / This broken heart of mine / I'll love you 'til the day I die / Don't let me hang around / Pray for me mother of mine / Daddy loves you / That's all right / Gossip / Maybellene / Pretty mama / Mean mama blues / Long gone lonesome blues / I can't quit (I've gone too far) / Singing the blues / Tennessee toddy / Baby I need you (2) / Long tall Sally / Mr. Teardrop / Respectfully Miss Brooks / You don't owe me a thing / I'll know your gone / How long will it be / Where d'ya go / Most of the time / Same two lips / Your heart of blue is showing through / Knee deep in the blues / Little rosewood casket

/ Letter edged in black / Twenty one years / Convict and the rose / Bus stop song / Dream the miner's child / Little box of pine in the 7:29 / Wreck of number nine / Sad lover / Little shirt my mother made for me / My mother was a lady / When it's lamplighting time in the valley / Wreck of the 12:56 / It's too late now / I never let you cross my mind / I'll step aside / Bouquet of roses / I'm so lonesome I could cry / Lovesick blues / Moanin' the blues / Rose of ol' Pawnee / I hang my head and cry / Have I told you lately that I love you / All the world is lonely now / You only want me when you're lonely / Crying steel guitar waltz / Beautiful Ohio / Now is the hour / Down where the tradewinds blow / Sweet leilani / Beyond the reef / Constancy / Don't sing aloha when I go / Song of the Islands / Moonland / Island echoes / Faded petal from a beautiful bouquet / When I turned and slowly walked away / Jody / House with everything but love / Nothing but sweet lies / Baby I need you / Kaw-liga / Paper / Face / Many tears ago / Address unknown / Waltz of the wind / Hands you're holding now / Wedding bells / Shackles and chains / Oh how I miss you / Footprints in the snow / It's driving me crazy
CD Set _____ BCD 15570
Bear Family / Aug '91 / Rollercoaster / Direct / CM / Swift / ADA.

ALL AROUND COWBOY
All around cowboy / Dreamer / Pride and the badge / Restless cattle / When I'm gone / Buenos dias Argentina / Lonely old bunkhouse / San Angelo / Tumbling tumbleweeds / Ballad of a small man
CD _____ PWKS 565
Carlton Home Entertainment / Feb '90 / Carlton Home Entertainment.

COUNTRY 1960-1966 (5 CDST)
Devil woman / It's your world / Lonely too long / Over high mountain / Fly, buterfly, fly / Because it's wrong / Like all other times / Little Robin / It kinda reminds me / Address unkown / Yesterday's roses / Each night at nine / People's valley / No one will ever know / I'm not ready yet / I feel another heartbeat coming on / Ribbon of darkness / Robing garden / Foggy foggy river / Lolene / Just before the battle Mother / Beautiful dreamer / Long, long ago / Melba from Melbourne / Change that dial / Only a picture stops time / Southern Dixie flyer / Everybody's darling plus mine / She means nothing to me now / Making excuses / Rainbow / I've lived a lifetime in a day / You won't have her long / Things I don't know / Urgently needed / I'll have to make some changes / Nine tenth of the law / Sorting memories / Hello heartache / One window, four walls / Working my way through a heartache / Would you take me back again / Do me a favor / Sixteen weeks / Seconds to remember / Another lost weekend / Last night about this time / This song / Hello baby / Don't worry / Time and a place for everything / Sixtyfwo's most promising fool / Too far gone / April fool's day / Rich man, rich man / I've got a woman's love / Never look back / I'm beginning to forget you / Progressive love / Hands your holding now / Ain't life a crying shame / Kinda halfway feel / Little rich girl / Will the circle be unbroken / Little spot in heaven / Evening prayer / With his hands on my shoulder / There's power in the blood / When the roll is called up yonder / Where should I go (but to the lord) / Almost persuaded / What God has done / You gotta climb / Great speckled bird / Who at my door is standing / Have thine own way, Lord / Cigarettes and cone blues / No tears milady / Wine flowed freely / Shoe goes on the other foot tonight / Not so long ago / I hope you learn a lot / Beginning to love / In the ashes of an old love affair / Love's a hurtin game / Worried / Time can't make me forget / Baby talk to me / Pieces of your heart / It kinda reminds me of me / My own native land / Private Wilson White / Ain't it right / You gave me a mountain / To be in love with her / Matilda / It's finally happened / They'll never take her love from me
CD Set _____ BCD 15655
Bear Family / Nov '95 / Rollercoaster / Direct / CM / Swift / ADA.

ESSENTIAL MARTY ROBBINS, THE
CD Set _____ 4689092
Legacy / May '94 / Sony.

HAWAII'S CALLING ME
Lovely Hula hands / Sea and me / Night I came to shore / Echo island / Kuu ipo Lani (my sweetheart Lani) / Beyond the reef / Hawaiian wedding song / Drowsy waters / Hawaiian bells / My wonderful one / Blue sand / Hawaii's calling me / Ku lu a (love song of kalua) / Drowsy waters (Wailana) / Song of the Islands / Don't sing aloha when i go / Crying steel guitar waltz / My isle of golden dreams / Now is the hours (Maori Farewell song) / Sweet leilani / Down where the tradewinds blow / Aloha oe / Island echoes / Moonland / Constancy
CD _____ BCD 15568
Bear Family / May '91 / Rollercoaster / Direct / CM / Swift / ADA.

IN CONCERT
CD _____ CDCD 1262
Charly / Nov '95 / Charly THE / Cadillac.

MUSICAL JOURNEY TO THE CARIBBEAN AND MEXICO
Girl from Spanish Town / Kingston girl / Sweet bird of paradise / Jamaica farewell / Calypso girl / Back to Montego Bay / Girl from Spanish Town (2) / Kingston girl (2) / Woman gets her way / Mango song / Calypso vacation / Blue sea / Bahama Mama / Tahitian boy / Native girl / Girl from Spanish Town (3) / Yours / You belong to my heart / La Borachita / La paloma / Quiereme / No quiero / Adios mariquita Llinda / Amor / Camellia
CD _____ BCD 15571
Bear Family / May '91 / Rollercoaster / Direct / CM / Swift / ADA.

ROCKIN' ROLLIN' ROBBINS
That's all right / Maybellene / Pretty mama / Mean mama blues / Tenessee Toddy / Singin' the blues / I can't quit (I've gone too far) / Long tall sally / Mr. Teardrop / Respectfully Miss Brooks / You don't owe me a thing / Baby I need you / Pain and misery / Footprints in the snow / It's driving me crazy / It's a long, long ride / Call me up (and I'll come calling on you)
CD _____ BCD 15566
Bear Family / May '91 / Rollercoaster / Direct / CM / Swift / ADA.

ROCKIN' ROLLIN' ROBBINS VOL.2
White sports coat and a pink carnation / Grown up tears / Please don't blame me / Teenage dream / Story of my life / Once a week date / Just married / Stairway of love / She was only seventeen / Sittin' in a tree house / Ain't I the lucky one / Last time I saw my heart / Hanging tree / Blues country style / Jeannie and Johnnie / Foolish decision
CD _____ BCD 15567
Bear Family / May '91 / Rollercoaster / Direct / CM / Swift / ADA.

ROCKIN' ROLLIN' ROBBINS VOL.3
Ruby Ann (chart version) / Sometimes I'm tempted / No signs of loneliness here / While you're dancing / Teenager's Dad / Ruby Ann / Cap and gown (fast) / Last night about this time / I hope you learn a lot / Love can't wait / Cigarettes and coffee / Little rich girl / Hello baby (goodbye baby) / Baby's gone / Cap and gown (slow) / Whole lot easier / She was young and she was pretty / Cap and gown (New york recording) / Sweet cora / Ain't live a cryin' shame / Silence and tears / You've been so busy baby
CD _____ BCD 15569
Bear Family / Nov '93 / Rollercoaster / Direct / CM / Swift / ADA.

UNDER WESTERN SKIES (4 CDST)
El Paso / Cool water / In the valley / Running gun / Big iron / Master's call / Little green valley / Hundred and sixty acres / Billy the kid / Strawberry roan / They're hanging me tonight / Utah Carol / Saddle tramp / She was young and she was pretty / Streets of Laredo / Little Joe / Wrangler / I've got no use for the woman / Billy Venero / This peaceful sod / Five brothers / San Angelo / Ballad of the alamo (thirteen days of glory) / Hanging tree / Jimmy Martinez / Ghost train / Song of the bandit / Wind / Prairie fire / My love / Ride cowboy ride / Red river valley / Bend in the river / When the work's all done this fall / Abilene rose / Dusty winds / Old red / Doggone cowboy / Small man / Red hill of Utah / Tall handsome stranger / Fastest gun around / Man walks among us / Johnny Fedavo / Cowboy in the continental suit / I'm gonna be a cowboy / Cry stampede / Oh, Virginia / Meet me tonight in Loredo / Take me to the prairie / Wind goes / An old pal / Real pal / Feleena (from El Paso) / Never tie me down / Lonely old bunkhouse / Night time on the desert / Cottonwood tree / Mister shorty / When it's lamplighting time in the valley / Is there anything else I can say / Tonight Carmen / Waiting in Reno / Mission in Guadalajaro / Love's gone away / Bound for Old Mexico / Chaple bell chime / Don't go away Senor / In the valley of the Rio Grand / (Girl with) Gardenias in her hair / Spanish lullaby / That silver haired daddy of mine / Preach of the wanderer / (Ghost) Riders in the sky / South of the border / Sundown (ballad of Bill Thaxton) / Queen of the big rodeo / Ava Maria Morales / Outlaws / El Paso city / I'm kin to the wind / Trail dreamin' / She's just a drifter / Way out there / Tumbling tumbleweeds / Pride and the badge / All around cowboy / Restless cattle / Dreamer / Lonely old bunkhouse / Shotgun rider
CD Set _____ BCD 15646
Bear Family / Nov '95 / Rollercoaster / Direct / CM / Swift / ADA.

Robert & Johnny

WE BELONG TOGETHER
We belong together / Broken hearted man / I don't stand a ghost of a chance with you / Baby come home / You're mine / Eternity with you / Dream girl / Oh my love / Million dollar bills / I got you / Give me the key to your heart / Wear this ring / Gosh oh gee / Don't do it / I believe in you / God knows / Bad Dan / Indian marriage / Your kisses / Baby baby / I hear my heartbeat / Togetherness / I'm truly truly yours / Please me

please / Try me pretty baby / Baby girl of mine / Train to paradise
CD _____ CDCHD 384
Ace / Apr '93 / Pinnacle / Cadillac / Complete/Pinnacle.

Robert, George

LIVE AT Q4 (Robert, George Quintet)
Snapper / Michelle / Samba de jump / On Green Dolphin Street / Simple waltz / Joan / Mumbles
CD _____ TCB 90802
TCB / Apr '95 / New Note.

LIVE AT THE CHORUS
Jeanine / Dolphin dance / Remembering Henri / Voyage / Village / Upper Manhattan Medical Group U.M.M.G. / Sandu
CD _____ TCB 95102
TCB / Sep '95 / New Note.

TRIBUTE (Robert, George Quintet)
CD _____ JFCD 004
Jazz Focus / Dec '94 / Cadillac.

Robert, Yves

TOUT COURT
CD _____ ZZ 84103
Deux Z / Jan '94 / Harmonia Mundi / Cadillac.

Roberts, Andy

BEST OF ANDY ROBERTS
CD _____ CRESTCD 014
Mooncrest / Mar '92 / Direct / ADA.

Roberts, Howard

REAL HOWARD ROBERTS, THE
Dolphin dance / Darn that dream / Lady wants to know / Gone with the wind / Serenata / Angel eyes / All blues
CD _____ CCD 4053
Concord Jazz / Apr '94 / New Note.

Roberts, Juliet

NATURAL THING
Caught in the middle / Free love / Tell me / Life goes around / Someone like you / Force of nature / Save it / Again / I want you / September / Eyes of a child / Natural thing
CD _____ CTCD 39
Cooltempo / Mar '94 / EMI.

Roberts, Malcolm

BEST OF THE EMI YEARS, THE
Love is all / We can make it girl / Why did I fall for love / You, no one but you / Please forgive me / And this is my beloved / Because you're mine / May I have the next dream with you / Where did I go wrong / My way / Lovingly / Tra la la / This is my life / Ebb tide / Medley (They long to be) Close to you, We've only just begun) / I thought I knew / Impossible dream / If ever I would leave you / When there's no you / Let's be me the one the one / Love me Ave Maria
CD _____ CDEMS 1484
EMI / Apr '93 / EMI.

Roberts, Marcus

ALONE WITH THREE GIANTS
Jungle blues / Mood indigo / Solitude / I got it bad and that ain't good / Trinkle tinkle / Misterioso / Pannonica / New Orleans blues / Prelude to a kiss / Shout 'em Aunt Tillie / Balck and tan fantasy / Monk's mood / In walked Bud / Crepuscule with Nellie / Crave
CD _____ PD 83109
Novus / Mar '91 / BMG.

AS SERENITY APPROACHES
Cherokee / Slippin' and slidin' / Blues in the evening time / First come, first serve / Nigh Eve / As serenity approaches / Jitterbug waltz / St. Louis blues / I remember you / Preach, Reverend preach / Tint of blue / When the morning comes / Where or when / King Porter stomp / Creole blues / Broadway / Angel
CD _____ PD 90624
Novus / Apr '92 / BMG.

GERSHWIN FOR LOVERS
Foggy day / Man I love / Our love is here to stay / Summertime / Someone to watch over me / It ain't necessarily so / Nice work if you cna get it / They can't take that away from me / How long has this been going on / But not for me
CD _____ 477752 2
Columbia / Oct '94 / Sony.

IF I COULD BE WITH YOU
Just a closer walk with thee / Maple leaf rag / Arkansas blues / Carolina shout / Embraceable you / Moonlight in Vermont / Keep off the grass / Rippling waters / Sweet repose / Country blues / If I could be with you one hour tonight / Let's call this / Every time we say goodbye / What is this thing called love / Mood indigo / Preach / Reverend preach / Snowy morning blues / Fascination / In a southern sense
CD _____ 01241631492
Novus / Apr '93 / BMG.

Roberts, Paul

WURLITZER SHOWTIME
CD _____ CDSR 034
Telstar / Nov '93 / BMG.

Roberts, Paul Dudley

FROM RAGS TO RICHES
CD _____ DLD 1034
Dance & Listen / May '93 / Savoy.

I GOT RHYTHM
CD _____ DLD 1035
Dance & Listen / Mar '93 / Savoy.

Robertson, B.A.

HITS & PIECES
CD _____ VSOPCD 223
Connoisseur / Jan '96 / Pinnacle.

Robertson, Jeannie

JEANNIE ROBERTSON
Bonnie wee lassie who never said no / What a voice / My plaidie's awa' / Gypsy laddie / When I was no' but sweet sixteen / MacCrimmon's lament / Roy's wife of Aldivalloch / Lord Lovat
CD _____ OSS 92CD
Ossian / Aug '94 / ADA / Direct / CM.

Robertson, Robbie

NATIVE AMERICANS
Coyote dance / Mahk tchi (Heart of the people) / Ghost dance / Vanishing breed / It's a good day to die / Golden feather / Akua Tutu / Words of fire, deeds of blood / Cherokee morning song / Skinwalker / Ancestor song / Twisted hair
CD _____ CDEST 2238
EMI / Oct '94 / EMI.

ROBBIE ROBERTSON
Fallen angel / Showdown at big sky / Broken arrow / Sweet fire of love / American roulette / Somewhere down the crazy river / Hell's half acre / Sonny got caught in the moonlight / Testimony
CD _____ GFLD 19294
Geffen / Oct '95 / BMG.

STORYVILLE
CD _____ GFLD 19295
Geffen / Oct '95 / BMG.

Robertson, Sherman

HEAR AND NOW
CD _____ 0630122782
Warner Bros. / Oct '95 / Warner Music.

I'M THE MAN
I'm the man / Somebody's messin' / Am I losing you / Special kind of loving / Make it rain / Out of sight out of mind / Linda Lou / Home of the blues / Our good thing is through / Vacating the blues / Helping hand / Take a message
CD _____ 450995726-2
Warner Bros. / Jun '94 / Warner Music.

Robeson, Paul

BIG FELLA
Lazy bones / Scarecrow / Fat li'l feller / Wagon wheels / Deep river / My curly headed baby / Carry me back to green pastures / Old folks at home / High water / My heart is where the mohawk flows tonight / Plantation songs medley / So early in the morning / Carry me back to old Virginny / Old folks at home / Goodnight ladies / Away down in Dixie / Poor old Joe / Oh, Susanna / My old Kentucky home / River / Stay down south / Hail the crown / Love song / Killing song / Black emperor / I don't know what's wrong / Lazin' / You didn't oughta do such things / Ecantadora Maria / David of the white rock / Thora / Love at my heart / Ebenezer / King Joe / Little black boy
CD _____ CDHD 245
Happy Days / Sep '94 / Conifer.

GLORIOUS VOICE OF PAUL ROBESON, THE
Lonesome road / River stay 'way from my door / Mighty lak' a rose / My curly headed baby / Ol' man river / Round the bend of the road / Lazybones / Waterboy / Song of freedom / Sleepy river / Carry me back to green pastures / Canoe song / I still suits me / Lonely road / Passing by / My way / Summertime / It ain't necessarily so / All through the night / Just a wearyin' for you / Perfect day / Deep river
CD _____ CZ 310
EMI / May '90 / EMI.

GREAT VOICES VOL.2
CD _____ CDMOIR 426
Memoir / Nov '94 / Target/BMG.

GREEN PASTURES
St. Louis blues / Rockin' chair / Mary had a baby, yes Lord / Love song / All God's chillun got wings / Banjo song / Bear the burden / Shortnin' bread / Snowball / Fat li'l feller with his mammy's eyes / Canoe song / River stay 'way from your door

CD _____ CD AJA 5047
Living Era / Oct '88 / Koch.

LONESOME ROAD, A
Ol' man river / My curly headed baby / Waterboy / I'm goin' to tell God all o' my troubles / Oh didn't it rain, little pal / There's no hiding place / Poor old Joe / Scandalise my name / Ezekiel saw de wheel / Sinner please doan' let this harves' pass / Jus' keepin' on / Mah Lindy Lou / Steal away / Mighty lak' a rose / Deep river / Hear the lambs a-cryin' / Git on board, li'l chilun / Old folks at home (Swanee river) / Witness / Oh rock me Julie / Li'l gal / I got a home in that rock / Lonesome road
CD _____ CD AJA 5027
Living Era / Oct '88 / Koch.

OL' MAN RIVER
CD _____ CD 12519
Music Of The World / Feb '95 / Target/ BMG / ADA.

OLE MAN RIVER
CD _____ RMB 75024
Remember / Nov '93 / Total/BMG.

PAUL ROBESON
Lazybones / It ain't necessarily so / Sleepy river / My way / I don't know what's wrong / Song of the Volga boatmen / Canoe song / Roll up sailorman / That's why darkies were born / Swing low, Sweet chariot / Mammy's little kinky headed boy / Roll away clouds / Just a wearyin' for you / Deep river / Sea fever / Absent / Mighty lak' a rose / On ma journey / Just keepin' on / Woman is a sometime thing / You didn't oughta do such things / Lazin' / Ol' man river
CD _____ PASTCD 7009
Flapper / May '93 / Pinnacle.

PAUL ROBESON I
Sonny boy / It takes a long pull to get there / Summertime / Woman is a sometime thing / It ain't necessarily so / Congo lullaby / Canoe song (From 'Sanders Of The River') / Mood indigo / Solitude / At dawning / All through the night / Lazy bones / St. Louis blues / Old folks at home (Swanee River) / My old Kentucky home / My curly headed baby / Mighty lak' a rose / Swing low, sweet chariot / Just a wearyin' for you / Ol' man river (from 'Showboat')
CD _____ GEMM CD 9356
Pearl / '90 / Harmonia Mundi.

PAUL ROBESON II
Down in lovers' lane / Swing along / Bear the burden / All God's chillun got wings / Joshua fit de battle of Jericho / De ole ark's a movering / Ezekiel saw de wheel / Scandalise my name / Sinner please doan' let this harves' pass / Work all de summer / Didn't my Lord deliver Daniel / Dere's a man goin' roun' takin' names / Shenendoah / Little pal / Lonesome Road / Roll away clouds / Ho Ho / Climbing up / Song of freedom / Sleepy river / Trees / No John no / Song of the Volga boatmen / There is a green hill / Nearer, my God to thee / Fat li'l feller with his mammy's eyes / Mama's little baby love
CD _____ GEMM CD 9382
Pearl / '90 / Harmonia Mundi.

Robic, Ivo

MIT SIE BZEHN FANGT DAS LEBEN ERST AN
Morgen / Mit siebzehn fangt das leben erst an / Rot ist der Wein / Muli song / Rhondaly / Ay ay ay Paloma / Endlich / Auf der sonnenseite der welt / So allein / In einer bar in buffalo / Liebeleer / Du bist niemand, wenn niemand dich lieb hat / Traume vom Gluck / Schau dich night um / Ich denk nuran's wiedersehn / Wenn ich in deine augen schau / Tiefes blaues meer / Glaub daran (das leben ist schon) / Jezebel / Lass dein little girl nie weinen / Geh zu ihm / Ein ganzes leben lang / Fremde in der nacht / Mond guter freund / Happy muleteer / So alone / Endless / On the sunny side of the world
CD _____ BCD 15671
Bear Family / Jun '92 / Rollercoaster / Direct / CM / Swift / ADA.

Robillard, Duke

PLEASURE KING/TOO HOT TO HANDLE (2 albums on 1 CD)
CD _____ FIENDCD 707
Demon / Sep '91 / Pinnacle / ADA.

ROCKIN' BLUES (Robillard, Duke & The Pleasure Kings)
CD _____ CD 11548
Rounder / '88 / CM / Direct / ADA /

SWING
Cadillac Slim / Jumpin' blues / Exactly like you / Glide on / Zot / I'll always be in love with you / Shuffin' with some barbeque / Durn tottin' / You'd better change your ways / Jim jam
CD _____ FIENDCD 191
Demon / Aug '90 / Pinnacle / ADA.

TEMPTATION
Rule the world / (You got my love) Sewed up / Live to give / Change is on / Life's funny / When my love comes down / This

dream (still coming true) / Temptation / Never been satisfied / Born to love you / What's wrong
CD _____ VPBCD 20
Virgin / Sep '94 / EMI.

YOU GOT ME (Robillard, Duke & Guests)
CD _____ CD 3100
Rounder / '88 / CM / Direct / ADA / Cadillac.

Robin, Jennifer

FISH UP A TREE
CD _____ CY 77059
Denon / Feb '91 / Conifer.

Robin, Roger

REFLECTIONS
CD _____ LOVCD 005
Love Injection / Apr '95 / Jetstar.

UNDILUTED
CD _____ LOVCD 004
Spider Ranks / Nov '93 / Jetstar.

Robin S

SHOW ME LOVE
CD _____ CHAMCD 1028
Champion / Oct '94 / BMG.

Robin, Thierry

GITANS
CD _____ Y 225035CD
Silex / Mar '94 / ADA.

Robine, Marc

LES TEMPS DES CERISES
CD _____ 983462
EPM / Jul '95 / Discovery / ADA.

Robinson, David

NEVER STOP LOVIN'
CD _____ RYTCD 4188
Ichiban / Jun '94 / Koch.

Robinson, Elzadie

ELZADIE ROBINSON VOL. 1 1926-1928
CD _____ DOCD 5248
Blues Document / May '94 / Swift / Jazz Music / Hot Shot.

ELZADIE ROBINSON VOL. 2 1928-1929
CD _____ DOCD 5249
Blues Document / May '94 / Swift / Jazz Music / Hot Shot.

Robinson, Fenton

I HEAR SOME BLUES DOWNSTAIRS
I hear some blues downstairs / Just a little bit / West side baby / I'm so tired / I wish for you / Tell me what's the reason / Going west / Killing floor / As the years go passing by
CD _____ ALCD 4710
Alligator / May '93 / Direct / ADA.

MELLOW FELLOW (Charly Blues - Masterworks Vol. 41)
CD _____ CDBM 41
Charly / Jun '93 / Charly / THE / Cadillac.

NIGHTFLIGHT
CD _____ ALCD 4736
Alligator / May '93 / Direct / ADA.

SOMEBODY LOAN ME A DIME
CD _____ ALCD 4705
Alligator / May '93 / Direct / ADA.

SPECIAL ROAD
7-11 Blues / Love is just a gamble / Special road / Too many drivers / Baby, please don't go / Crying the blues / Find a way / R.M. Blues / Slick and greasy / Blue Monday / Money problem / Nothing but a fool / Little torch
CD _____ ECD 260252
Evidence / Feb '93 / Harmonia Mundi / ADA / Cadillac.

Robinson, Jim

CLASSIC NEW ORLEANS JAZZ VOL. 2
CD _____ BCD 128
Biograph / Oct '93 / Wellard / ADA / Hot Shot / Jazz Music / Cadillac / Direct.

Robinson, Jimmie Lee

LONELY TRAVELLER
CD _____ DD 665
Delmark / May '94 / Hot Shot / ADA / CM / Direct / Cadillac.

Robinson, Justin

JUSTIN TIME
CD _____ 5132542
Verve / Mar '92 / PolyGram.

Robinson, Orphy

VIBES DESCRIBES, THE
Once upon a time / Annavas / Free to the power of M / Loneliest monk / Chunky but funky / For time to time / Monica / Make a

change / Where's Winston / Eternal spirit / An and Vas / Juxtafusician / Golden brown / Krossover point / Savannah
CD _____ CDBLT 1009
Blue Note / May '94 / EMI.

WHEN TOMORROW COMES
All at sixes and sevens / Bass of bad intentions - Part 1 - Deep / Bass of bad intentions - Part 2 - Dirty / Bass of bad intentions - Part 3 - Dirty / Jigsaw / Let's see what tomorrow brings - Part 1 / Let's see what tomorrow brings - Part 2 / Let's see what tomorrow brings - Part 3 / Let's see what tomorrow brings - Part 4 / Let's see what tomorrow brings - Part 5 / Bach to 1st bass / Bads means beautiful / Jigsaw (reprise)
CD _____ CDBLT 1004
Blue Note / Jan '92 / EMI.

Robinson, Perry

CALL TO THE STARS (Robinson, Perry Quartet)
CD _____ WWCD 2052
West Wind / Jan '91 / Swift / Charly / CM / ADA.

FUNK DUMPLING (Robinson, Perry Quartet)
Moon over Moscow / Sprites delight / Wahayla / Farmer Alfalfa / Margareta / Funk dumpling / Home is where the hearth is
CD _____ SV 0255
Savoy Jazz / Nov '94 / Conifer / ADA.

KUNDALINI (Robinson, Perry/Nana Vasconcelos/Badal Roy)
CD _____ 123856-2
IAI / Sep '93 / Harmonia Mundi / Cadillac.

NIGHTMARE ISLAND
CD _____ WWCD 2026
West Wind / May '89 / Swift / Charly / CM / ADA.

Robinson, Reginald G.

STRONGMAN, THE
CD _____ DDCD 662
Delmark / Nov '93 / Hot Shot / ADA / CM / Direct / Cadillac.

Robinson, Reverend...

SOMEONE TO CARE (Robinson, Reverend Cleophus)
Get away Jordan / Before this time another year / Morning and evening / Someone to care / Let the church roll on / Near the cross / It won't hurt you to speak / Peace in the valley / When the sun goes down / Grace made a change / I know prayer changes things / Jesus met the woman at the well / Until I found the Lord / I'm going to leave you in the hands of the Lord / Going over yonder / Strange things happening / Consecrated / You've got to love everybody / No more than you can bear / I can't help it / We'll understand it better by and by / Farthar along / Lord I'm in your care / When the saints go marching in / Sometimes I feel like a motherless child / Waiting for Jesus
CD _____ CDCHD 566
Ace / Mar '94 / Pinnacle / Cadillac / Complete/Pinnacle.

Robinson, Smokey

BEING WITH YOU
Being with you / Food for thought / If you wanna make love / Who's sad / Can't fight love / You are forever / As you do / I hear the children singing
CD _____ 5302192
Motown / Sep '93 / PolyGram.

CHRISTMAS WITH THE MIRACLES (Robinson, Smokey & The Miracles)
Santa Claus is coming to town / Let it snow, let it snow, let it snow / Winter wonderland / Christmas everyday / I'll be home for Christmas / Christmas song / White Christmas / Silver bells / Noel / O holy night
CD _____ 5504052
Spectrum/Karussell / Nov '94 / PolyGram / THE.

GREATEST HITS, THE (Robinson, Smokey & The Miracles)
Being with you / Tracks of my tears / I second that emotion / I'm the one you need / Mickey's monkey / Going to a go go / I don't blame you at all / if you can want / Just to see her / Shop around my soul responding (On MC/CD only) / Tears of a clown / Abraham, Martin and John / You've really got a hold on me / Shop around / What's so good about goodbye / Ooo baby baby / Love I saw in you was just a mirage / Quiet storm / One heartbeat / Baby, baby, don't cry / Cruisin' (On MC/CD only)
CD _____ 5301212
PolyGram TV / Nov '92 / PolyGram.

SMOKEY'S SONGBOOK (Various Artists)
Tears of a clown / Tracks of my tears / Shop around / My girl / More love / Hunter gets captured by the game / You beat me to the punch / You really got a hold on me / Way you do the things you do / Don't mess with the bill / My guy / Since I lost my baby / Going to a go go / From head to toe / Whole lotta shakin' in my head / Get ready / What's easy for two is so hard for one /

Goodbye cruel love / My baby must be a magician / My smile is just a frown
CD _____ 3035990042
Motor City / Oct '95 / Carlton Home Entertainment.

TEARS OF A CLOWN (Robinson, Smokey & The Miracles)
Tears of a clown / You ain't livin' till you're lovin' / Save me / Medley: Something / We had a love so strong / You've lost that lovin' feelin' / My girl / Hunter gets captured by the game / More, more, of your love / I'm the one you need / You must be love / I can't stand to see you cry / It will be alright / Composer
CD _____ 5500732
Spectrum/Karussell / May '93 / PolyGram THE.

TRACKS OF MY TEARS - THE VERY BEST OF SMOKEY ROBINSON (LIVE)
CD _____ DINCD 17
Dino / '93 / Pinnacle / 3MV.

WHAT EVER MAKES YOU HAPPY (More Best Of Smokey Robinson & The Miracles 1961-71) (Robinson, Smokey & The Miracles)
Money / Won't you take me back / Mighty good lovin' / I need a change / From head to toe / More, more, more of your love / Swept for you baby / Beauty is only skin deep / Don't think it's me / Dancing's alright / You only build me up to tear me down / I'll take you any way that you come / My world is empty without you / Dreams dreams / Backfire / Flower girl / Faces
CD _____ 812271181-2
WEA / Jun '93 / Warner Music.

Robinson, Spike

IN TOWN WITH ELAINE DELMAR
Too close for comfort / You've changed / Just one of those things / In a sentimental mood / 'S Wonderful / Get out of town / Little girl blue / Everything I love / Young and foolish / Will you still be mine
CD _____ HEPCD 2035
Hep / Jun '93 / Cadillac / Jazz Music / New Note / Wellard.

JUSA BIT O' BLUES (Robinson, Spike & Harry Edison Quintet)
One I love / Autumn leaves / Elaine / Just in time / 'Tis Autumn / Slow boat to China / Jus' a bit o' blues / Stars fell on Alabama / Time after time
CD _____ 74012
Capri / Nov '93 / Wellard / Cadillac.

JUSA BIT O' BLUES VOL.2 (Robinson, Spike & Harry Edison Quintet)
CD _____ 74013
Capri / Sep '89 / Wellard / Cadillac.

ODD COUPLE, THE (Robinson, Spike & Rob Mullins)
CD _____ 74008
Capri / Oct '90 / Wellard / Cadillac.

PLAYS HARRY WARREN
This heart of mine / At last / Boulevard of broken dreams / There will never be another you / I had the craziest dream / Shadow waltz / Serenade in blue / This is always / More I see you / Chattanooga choo choo / Cheerful little earful / I only have eyes for you / Lulu's back in town / I wish I knew
CD _____ HEPCD 2056
Hep / Oct '94 / Cadillac / Jazz Music / New Note / Wellard.

SPIKE ROBINSON & GEORGE MASSO PLAY ARLEN (Robinson, Spike & George Masso)
Let's fall in love / Right as rain / I gotta right to sing the blues / Taking a chance on love / This time the dream is on me / Happiness is a thing called Joe / When the sun comes out / Last night when we were young / My shining hour / As long as I live / Come rain or come shine / Between the devil and the deep blue sea
CD _____ HEPCD 2053
Hep / Oct '92 / Cadillac / Jazz Music / New Note / Wellard.

STAIRCASE TO THE STARS
Gone with the wind / Beautiful love / Gypsy sweetheart / It's always you / It's a blue world / Summer thing / From here to eternity / Stairway to the stars / It should happen to you
CD _____ HEPCD 2049
Hep / Oct '91 / Cadillac / Jazz Music / New Note / Wellard.

THREE FOR THE ROAD (Robinson, Spike & Louis Stewart)
They didn't believe me / Dearly beloved / If you were mine / Yes sir that's my baby / Only a rose / My buddy / Song is you / For Heaven's sake / They say that falling in love is wonderful
CD _____ HEPCD 2045
Hep / Oct '90 / Cadillac / Jazz Music / New Note / Wellard.

Robinson, Tad

ONE TO INFINITY
CD _____ DE 673
Delmark / Feb '95 / Hot Shot / ADA / CM / Direct / Cadillac.

Robinson, Tom

BACK IN THE OLD COUNTRY
Listen to the radio: Atmospherics / Too good to be true / Up against the wall / Northern rain / I shall be released / Mary Lynne / 2-4-6-8 Motorway / Drive all night / Don't take no for an answer / Where can we go tonight / Back in the old country / Alright all night / War baby / Power in the darkness / Crossing over the road / Rikki don't lose that number / Bitterly disappointed / Looking for a bonfire / Hard cases / Still loving you / Not ready / Bully for you / Long hot summer
CD _____ VSOPCD 138
Connoisseur / Oct '89 / Pinnacle.

GLAD TO BE GAY CABARET/LAST TANGO
Pub hassle / Cold Harbour Lane / Baby you're an angel / Glad to be gay / TR: (tell them) / Stand together / Trance / Closing a door / 1967 (so long ago) / Even Steven / Sartorial eloquence / Mad about the boy / Easy Street / Atmospherics / Tango an der wand / Surabaya Johnny / War baby / 2-4-6-8 Motorway / Back in the old country / Night tide / I wanna be your cabin boy / Old friend / Glad to be gay '87
CD _____ LICD 921215
Line / Jun '92 / CM / Grapevine / ADA / Conifer / Direct.

GLAD TO BE GAY/LAST TANGO
Pub hassle / Coldharbour Lane / Baby you're an angel / Glad to be gay (1978) / Tr: (tell them) / Stand together / Truce / Closing a door / 1967 (so long ago) / Even Steven / Sartorial eloquence / Mad about the boy / Easy street / Atmospherics / Listen to the radio / Tango an der wand / Surabaya Johnny / War baby / 2-4-6-8 Motorway / Back in the old country / Night tide / I wanna be your cabin boy / Old friend / Glad to be gay (87)
CD Set _____ 921215
Line / Aug '95 / CM / Grapevine / ADA / Conifer / Direct.

LIVING IN A BOOM TIME
CD _____ COOKCD 052
Cooking Vinyl / Feb '95 / Vital.

LOVE OVER RAGE
Roaring / Hard / Loved / Days / Driving green / Green / DDR / Fifty / Silence / Chance
CD _____ COOKCD 066
Cooking Vinyl / Mar '94 / Vital.

MOTORWAY
Number one protection / Winter of '79 / You gotta survive / Too good to be true / Martin / We didn't know (what was going on) / Up against the wall / Glad to be gay / Power in the darkness / 2-4-6-8 Motorway / Atmospherics / Listen to the radio / War baby
CD _____ MSCD 6
Magnum Music / May '95 / Magnum Music Group.

POWER IN THE DARKNESS (Robinson, Tom Band)
Up against the wall / Grey Cortina / Too good to be true / Ain't gonna take it / Long hot summer / Winter of '79 / Man you never saw / Better decide which side you're on / You gotta survive / Power in the darkness
CD _____ COOKCD 076
Cooking Vinyl / Oct '94 / Vital.

TRB TWO (Robinson, Tom Band)
Alright all night / Why should I mind / Black angel / Let my people be / Blue murder / Bully for you / Crossing over the road / Sorry Mr. Harris / Law and order / Days of rage / Hold out
CD _____ COOKCD 77
Cooking Vinyl / Oct '94 / Vital.

Robson & Jerome

ROBSON & JEROME
Unchained melody / Daydream believer / I believe / Sun ain't gonna shine anymore / Up on the roof / Amazing grace / Danny boy / (There'll be bluebirds over) The white cliffs of Dover / This boy / Little latin Lupe Lu / Love you forever / I'll come running back to you / If I can dream
CD _____ 74321323902
RCA / Nov '95 / BMG.

Roby, Charlie

UTOPIA IS NOT HERE
CD _____ MAL 0102CD
Maladrin Music / Aug '95 / ADA.

Rocchi, Riccardo

IT'S JUST A MELTING POT OF EMOTIONS
CD _____ ACVD 011
ACV / Nov '95 / Plastic Head / SRD.

Roccisano, Joe

LEAVE YOUR MIND BEHIND
Fax of life / Quill / Round midnight / Goodbye look / It seems like yesterday / Throw back the little ones / Changes / Avarice / Take five / Leave your mind behind / Adios nonino / La muerta del anel

CD _____ LCD 15412
Landmark / Aug '95 / New Note.

SHAPE I'M IN, THE (Roccisano, Joe & His Orchestra)
Borderland / New beginning / Mornings glory's story / Synthesis / Prism / Isabel / Shape I'm in / Piece of the pie / Don't stop now / Earth day / Blue Lou
CD _____ LCD 15352
Landmark / Nov '93 / New Note.

Roche, Ives

TAHITI COOL, VOL. 4
CD _____ PS 65806
Playasound / Nov '91 / Harmonia Mundi / ADA.

Roches

ANOTHER WORLD
CD _____ 7599253212
WEA / Jan '96 / Warner Music.

CAN WE GO HOME NOW
Great gaels / Move / You (make my life come true) / Christlike / Home away from home / Can we go home now / When you're ready / I'm someone who loves you / So / My winter coat / Holidays
CD _____ RCD 10299
Rykodisc / Sep '95 / Vital / ADA.

KEEP ON DOING
Hallelujah chorus / Losing true / Steady with the maestro / Largest Elizabeth in the world / On the road to Fairfax country / I fell in love / Scorpion lament / Want not want not / Sex is for children / Keep on doing what you do / Jerks on the loose
CD _____ 7599237252
WEA / Jan '96 / Warner Music.

NURDS
Nurds / It's bad for me / Louis / Bobby's song / Boat family / My sick mind / Death of Suzzy Roche / Factory girl / One season / This femine position
CD _____ 7599234752
WEA / Jan '96 / Warner Music.

ROCHES, THE
We / Hammond song / Mr. Sellack / Damned old dog / Troubles / Train / Married men / Runs in the family / Quitting time / Pretty and high
CD _____ 7599273902
WEA / Jan '96 / Warner Music.

Rock & Pop Revival

ROCK AND POP REVIVAL PLAYS ELTON JOHN
CD _____ RPR 9401
Scratch / Mar '95 / BMG.

ROCK AND POP REVIVAL PLAYS PINK FLOYD
CD _____ RPR 9402
Scratch / Mar '95 / BMG.

ROCK AND POP REVIVAL PLAYS THE BEATLES
CD _____ RPR 9403
Scratch / Mar '95 / BMG.

Rock, Dickie

20 GREATEST HITS: DICKIE ROCK
Every step of the way / Yours / Till / I'll hide my teardrops / There's always me / Coward of the county / Angeline / Candy store / Mandy / Just for all times / take it Come back to stay / I left my heart in San Francisco / She believes in me / You're my world / Love me tender / Back home again / You don't have to say you love me / How could you go / I write the songs / Wonder of you
CD _____ DHCD 717
Homespun / May '89 / Homespun Records / Ross / Wellard.

Rock Goddess

YOUNG & FREE
Young and free / Hello / So much love / Jerry / Streets of the city / Party never ends / Love has passed me by / Raiders / Love is a bitch / Boys will be boys / Sexy eyes / Rumour / Turn me loose / Hey lover
CD _____ CDTB 155
Magnum Music / Jul '94 / Magnum Music Group.

Rock Melons

STRONGER TOGETHER
CD _____ TVD 93360
Mushroom / Jan '95 / BMG / 3MV.

Rock, Pete

MAIN INGREDIENT, THE (Rock, Pete & C.L. Smooth)
In the house / Carmel city / Physical / Sun won't come out / I got a love / Escapism / Main ingredient / World wide / All the places / Tell me / Take you there / Searching / Chick it out / In the flesh / It's on you / Get on the mic
CD _____ 755961661-2
Warner Bros. / Nov '94 / Warner Music.

MECCA AND THE SOUL BROTHER (Rock, Pete & C.L. Smooth)
Return to the Mecca / For Pete's sake / Ghettos of the mind / Lots of lovin' / Act like you know / Straighten it out / Soul brother no.1 / Wig out / Anger in the nation / They reminisce over you (T.R.O.Y.) / On and on / It's like that / Can't front on me / Basement / If it ain't rough, it ain't right / Skinz
CD _____ EKT 105 CD
Elektra / May '92 / Warner Music.

Rock, Salt & Nails

MORE AND MORE
Don't know about you/Friday card school / Someday / Jack broke da prison door / Life / Lucy Bain / More and more / Uneasy ride / Tilly plump set / Grandmother's eyes / Forced to return/Spootiskerry / Lucy Bain reprise
CD _____ IRCD 030
Iona / May '95 / ADA / Direct / Duncans.

WAVES
Man who ate mountains / Slockit light - Waiting for the Federals / Happy to be here / Jack broke da prison door / Faroe rum / Oliver Jack / Willafjord / Iron horse / Arkansas traveller / Welcome / Central house / Square da Mizzen / Doon hingin' tie / Waves / Hut on Staffin Island / Barmaid / Music for a found harmonium
CD _____ IRCD 025
Iona / Jan '94 / ADA / Direct / Duncans.

Rockabilly Mafia

ANOTHER DRUNKEN NIGHT
CD _____ RUMBCD 002
Rumble / Aug '92 / Nervous.

Rockats

LAST CRUSADE
CD _____ TBCD 2005
Nervous / Mar '93 / Nervous / Magnum Music Group.

Rocker, Lee

ATOMIC BOOGIE HOUR (Rocker, Lee & Big Blue)
CD _____ BT 1121CD
Black Top / Sep '95 / CM / Direct / ADA.

LEE ROCKER'S BIG BAND
CD _____ BT 1105CD
Black Top / Sep '94 / CM / Direct / ADA.

Rockers Hi-Fi

ROCKERS TO ROCKERS
Push push / Rockers to rockers / What a life / More and more (The hidden persuader) / D.T.I. (Don't stop the music) / What a life (live) (MC only) / Dick from outaspace / Round reversion / Look for a spark / Stoned / Seven shades of dub
CD _____ BRCD 615
4th & Broadway / May '95 / PolyGram.

Rocket From The Crypt

SCREAM DRACULA SCREAM
CD _____ ELM 34CD
Elemental / Jan '96 / Disc.

Rockets

OUT OF THE BLUE
I got the same old blues / Why I sing the blues / Sweet little angel / Smokestack lightnin' / I got a mind to travel / Stop breaking down / When the war is over / Every day I have the blues / I'm ready / Look over yonder's wall / Great balls of fire
CD _____ CDLR 42077
L&R / Jun '94 / New Note.

Rockin' Bandits

WATCH OUT...WE'RE GONNA 'JUMP BACK'
Jump back boogie / Gonna rock with ya baby / Ain't gonna be your crazy cat / Long black train / Pretty little baby / I'm in love with you baby / Cruisin' blues / Oakie boogie / Angel girl / Lonely country girl / Two lane black top / My little baby / Folsom prison blues / Rock-a-baby rock / Midnight shift / Rock 'n' roll Mama / I don't care / Everybody's tryin' to be my baby
CD _____ FCD 3036
Fury / Mar '95 / Magnum Music Group / Nervous.

Rockin' Berries

BOWL OF BERRIES
CD _____ REP 4181-WZ
Repertoire / Aug '91 / Pinnacle / Cadillac.

IN TOWN
CD _____ REP 4099-WZ
Repertoire / Aug '91 / Pinnacle / Cadillac.

Rockin' Dopsie

FEET DON'T FAIL ME NOW
CD _____ AIMA 1
Rounder / Oct '95 / CM / Direct / ADA / Cadillac.

Rockin' Ramrods

BEST OF THE ROCKIN' RAMRODS
Jungle call / I wanna be your man / I'll be on my way / Don't fool with Fu Manchu / Tears melt the stones / Play it / Bright lit blue skies / Mr. Wind / Can't you see / Mary Mary / Flowers in my mind / Vacuum / Trees / Rainy days / Looking in my window / Who do you think you are / Or not being able to sleep / Dead thoughts of Alfred / I sure need you / When I wake up in the morning / Go with you / Changes / My vision has cleared / I don't want to, I will / Troubles
CD _____ CDWIKD 151
Big Beat / May '95 / Pinnacle.

Rockin' Sidney

LIVE WITH THE BLUES
CD _____ JSPCD 213
JSP / Mar '88 / ADA / Target/BMG / Direct / Cadillac / Complete/Pinnacle.

MY TOOT TOOT
My toot toot / My zydeco shoes / Joy to the south / Don't be a wallflower (On LP only) / Alligator waltz / Rock 'n' roll me baby (On LP only) / Joe Pete is in the bed / You ain't nothing but fine / If it's good for the gander / Twist to the zydeco / Dance and show off / Let me take you to zydeco / I got the blues for my baby (On LP only) / Louisiana creole man (On LP only) / If I could I would / No good woman (On CD only) / Send me some lovin' / Past bedtime (On CD only) / No good man (On CD only) / You don't have to go (On CD only) / Something's wrong (On CD only) / My little girl (On CD only) / Wasted days and wasted nights (On CD only) / Ya ya (On CD only) / Jalapena lena (On CD only) / Sweet lil' woman (On CD only) / Once is not enough (On CD only) / Cochon de lait (On CD only)
CD _____ CDCH 160
Ace / Jun '93 / Pinnacle / Cadillac / Complete/Pinnacle.

Rockin' Vickers

LIFELINES (The Complete Collection)
I go ape / Someone like me / Zing went the strings of my heart / Stella / It's alright / Stay by me / Dandy / I don't need your kind / Baby never say goodbye / I just stand there / Say Mama / Shake, rattle and roll / What's the matter Jane / Little Rosey
CD _____ RETRO 803
RPM / Jul '95 / Pinnacle.

Rockin' Vincent

UNRELEASED
Grand hotel / Dixie boogie / Chantilly lace / End of the road / Music box swing / Ain't nobody's business / Rockin' hearts / 42nd Street / Twenty flight rock / Puttin' on the ritz / Maxin's boogie / Some of these days / Let the good times roll / That's life
CD _____ CDDS 9252
White Label/Bear Family / Apr '94 / Bear Family / Rollercoaster.

Rockingbirds

WHATEVER HAPPENED TO THE ROCKINGBIRDS
Roll on forever / I like winter / Everybody lives with us / Band of dreams / We had it all / I woke up one morning / High part / Bitter tear / Before we got to the end / Hell / Let me down slow
CD _____ COOKCD 084
Cooking Vinyl / Mar '95 / Vital.

Rockpile

SECONDS OF PLEASURE
Teacher teacher / If sugar was as sweet as you / Heart / Now and always / Knife and fork / Play that fast thing / Wrong way / Pet you and hold you / Oh what a thrill you / When I write the book / Fool too long / You ain't nothing but fine
CD _____ FIENDCD 28
Demon / Oct '90 / Pinnacle / ADA.

Rocks

COMBAT ZONE
CD _____ KR 004CD
Kangaroo / Aug '95 / Plastic Head.

Rockwell, Bob

ON THE NATCH (Rockwell, Bob Quartet)
CD _____ SCCD 31229
Steeplechase / Jul '88 / Impetus.

RECONSTRUCTION
CD _____ SCCD 31270
Steeplechase / Nov '90 / Impetus.

Rodan

RUSTY
CD _____ QS 24CD
Quarter Stick / Apr '94 / SRD.

Roddy, Ted

FULL CIRCLE
CD _____ HCD 8065
Hightone / Oct '95 / ADA / Koch.

Roden, Jess

JESS RODEN
Reason to change / I'm on your side / Feelin easy / Sad story / On broadway / Ferry cross / Trouble in the mind / What the hell
CD _____ IMCD 143
Island / Aug '91 / PolyGram.

Rodgers Melnick, Peter

ARCTIC BLUE
Arctic blue / Tundra / Breakaway / Wolf / Take off / Dream / Dixie's revenge / Looking for trouble / Living and the dead / No man's land / Return to Devil's cauldron / Cut to the chase / Mitchell dies / Mine / Up in flames / Trappers and hunters / In the shadows / Viking Bob / Freeing the wolf
CD _____ ND 63030
Narada / Nov '94 / New Note / ADA.

Rodgers, Jimmie

AMERICA'S BLUE YODELER, 1930-1931
Blue yodel No. 8 / Jimmie's mean mama blues / I'm lonesome too / Mystery of number five / One rose / In the jailhouse now No.2 / For the sake of days gone by / Blue yodel No. 9 / T.B. blues / Travellin' blues / Why there's a tear in my eye / Jimmie the kid / Wonderful city / Let me be your sidetrack
CD _____ CDROU 1060
Rounder / Sep '91 / CM / Direct / ADA / Cadillac.

DOWN THE OLD ROAD (1931-32)
Looking for a new mama / When the cactus is in bloom / Jimmie Rodgers visits the Carter Family / Carter Family and Jimmie Rodgers in Texas / Gambling dot blues / Southern cannonball / Roll along Kentucky moon / What's it my time ain't long / Hobo's meditation / Ninety nine years blues / Mississippi moon / Down the old road to home call / Mother the queen of my heart
CD _____ CDROU 1061
Rounder / Sep '91 / CM / Direct / ADA / Cadillac.

FIRST SESSIONS, 1927-1928
Blue yodel / Soldier's sweetheart / Ben Dewberry's final run / Sleep, baby sleep / Mother was a lady / Dear old sunny south by the sea / Away out on the mountain / Treasures untold / Blue yodel no. 11 / Sailor's plea / In the jailhouse now / Memphis yodel / Brakeman's blues / Blue yodel no. 3
CD _____ CDROU 1056
Rounder / '90 / CM / Direct / ADA / Cadillac.

LAST SESSIONS, 1933
Blue yodel No. 12 / Dreaming with tears in my eyes / Cowhand's last ride / I'm free from the chain gang now / Yodeling my way back home / Jimmie Rodgers' last blue yodel / Yodeling ranger / Old pal of my heart / Years ago / Somewhere below the Mason Dixon line / Old love letters / Mississippi delta blues
CD _____ CDROU 1063
Rounder / Mar '92 / CM / Direct / ADA / Cadillac.

MY OLD PAL
Blue yodel no. 1 (T for Texas) / Away out on the mountain / Frankie and Johnny / Gamblin' bar room blues / When the cactus is in bloom / Sleep, baby, sleep / My old pal / Daddy and home / My Carolina sunshine girl / Why there's a tear in my eye / We miss him when the evening shadows fall / Never no no' blues / Blue yodel no. 5 / Any old time / Lullaby yodel / Looking for a new mama
CD _____ CD AJA 5058
Living Era / Mar '89 / Koch.

NO HARD TIMES, 1932
Blue yodel No. 10 / Whippin' that old T.B. / Rock all our babies to sleep / Home call / Mother, the queen of my heart / No hard times / Peach pickin' time in Georgia / Long tall mama blues / Gamblin' bar room blues / I've only loved three women / In the hills of Tennessee / Old pal of my heart / Mississippi moon / Sweet Mama hurry home
CD _____ CDROU 1062
Rounder / Feb '92 / CM / Direct / ADA / Cadillac.

ON THE WAY UP, 1929
High powered Mama / Tuck away my lonesone blues / Frankie and Johnny / I'm sorry we met / Train whistle blues / Everybody does it in Hawaii / Blue yodel No. 6 / Yodeling cowboy / My rough and rowdy ways / Land of my boyhood dreams / Whisper your mother's name / I've ranged, I've roamed, I've travelled / Hobo Bill's last ride
CD _____ CDROU 1059
Rounder / '91 / CM / Direct / ADA / Cadillac.

RIDING HIGH, 1929-1930
Anniversary blue yodel / That's why I'm blue / Mississippi river blues / She was happy till she met you / Blue yodel no. 11 / Drunkard's child / Nobody knows but me /

Moonlight and the skies / Why did you give me your love / Pistol packin' papa / Why should I be lonely / Take me back again / Those gambler's blues / My blue eyed Jane
CD _____ CDROU 1059
Rounder / '91 / CM / Direct / ADA / Cadillac.

SINGING BRAKEMAN, THE
Soldier's sweetheart / Sleep, baby, sleep / Ben Dewberry's final run / Mother was a lady / Blue yodel / Away out on the mountain / Dear old sunny south by the sea / Treasures untold / Brakeman's blues / Sailor's plea / In the jailhouse now / Blue yodel No. 2 / Memphis yodel / Blue yodel No. 3 / My old pal / Mississippi moon / My little old home down in New Orleans / You and my old guitar / Daddy and home / My little lady / I'm lonely and blue / Lullaby yodel / Never mo' blues / My Carolina sunshine girl / Blue yodel No. 4 / Waiting for a train / Desert blues / Any old time / Blue yodel No. 5 / High powered mama / I'm sorry we met / Everybody does it in Hawaii / Tuck away my lonesome blues / Train whistle blues / Jimmie's Texas blues / Frankie and Johnny / Homecall / Whisper your mother's name / Land of my boyhood dreams / Blue yodel No. 6 / Yodeling cowboy / My rough and rowdy ways / I've ranged, I've roamed, I've travelled / Hobo Bill's last ride / Mississippi river blues / Nobody knows but me / Anniversary blue yodel / She was happy till she met you / Blue yodel No. 11 / Drunkard's child / That's why I'm blue / Why did you give me your love / My blue eyed Jane / Why should I be lonely / Moonlight and skies / Pistol packin' papa / Take me back again / Those gambler's blues / I'm lonesome too / One rose / For the sake of days gone by / Jimmie's mean mama blues / Mystery of number five / Blue yodel No. 8 / Blue yodel No. 9 / T.B. blues / Travellin' blues / Jimmie the kid / Why there's a tear in my eye / Wonderful city / Let me be your sidetrack / Jimmie Rodgers visits the Carter Family / Carter Family and Jimmie Rodgers in Texas / When the cactus is in bloom / Gambling polka dot blues / Looking for a new mama / What's it / My good gal's gone / Southern cannonball / Roll along Kentucky moon / Hobo's meditation / My time ain't long / Ninety nine year blues / Down the old road to home / Blue yodel No. 10 / Home call / Mother the queen of my heart / Rock all my babies to sleep / Whippin' that old T.B. / No hard times / Long tall mama blues / Peach pickin' time in Georgia / Gamblin' bar room blues / I've only loved three women / In the hills of Tennessee / Prairie lullaby / Miss the Mississippi and you / Sweet mama hurry home / Blue yodel No. 12 / Dreaming with tears in my eyes / Cowhand's last ride / I'm free from the chain gang now / Dream with tears in my eyes / Yodeling my way back home / Jimmie Rodgers' last blue yodel / Yodeling ranger / Old pal of my heart / Old love letters / Mississippi Delta blues / Somewhere below the Mason Dixon line / Years ago / Singing brakeman / Pullman porters / In the jailhouse now No.2 / Mule skinner blues / Mother, the queen of my heart / Never no no' blues / Blue yodel No. 1
CD Set _____ BCD 15540
Bear Family / Mar '92 / Rollercoaster / Direct / CM / Swift / ADA.

TRAIN WHISTLE BLUES
Jimmie's mean mama blues / Southern Cannonball / Jimmie the kid / Travellin' blues / Mystery of number five / Memphis yodel / Blue yodel no. 4 (California blues) / Hobo Bill's last ride / Waiting for a train / Ben Dewberry's final run / My rough and rowdy ways / Blue yodel no. 7 (Anniversary blue yodel) / Brakeman's blues / Let me be your sidetrack / Hobo's meditation / Train whistle blues
CD _____ CD AJA 5042
Living Era / Jun '86 / Koch.

YODELLING RANGER, THE
Jimmie the kid / Roll along Kentucky moon / Looking for a new Mama / Round up time out West / Sleep, baby, sleep / Yodelling my way back home / Gamblin' bar room blues / In the hills of Tennessee / Old pal of my heart / My lovin' gal Lucille / Standin' on the corner / She was happy till she met you / Peach pickin' time in Georgia / I've lonesome too / Jimmie Rodgers last blue yodel / Yodelling ranger / Mississippi moon / Prairie lullaby / Down the old road to home / Jimmie Rodgers visits the Carter family / Carter family and Jimmie Rodgers
CD _____ RAJCD 806
Empress / Oct '92 / THE.

Rodgers, Jimmie

KISSES SWEETER THAN WINE
CD _____ PWK 011
Carlton Home Entertainment / '88 / Carlton Home Entertainment.

Rodgers, Nile

B MOVIE MATINEE
Groove master / Let's go out tonight / Stay out of the light / Same wavelength / Plan number 9 / State your mind / Face in the window / Doll squad
CD _____ 7599252902
WEA / Jan '96 / Warner Music.

Rodgers, Paul

MUDDY WATER BLUES.
CD _____ 828424-2
London / Jun '93 / PolyGram.

Rodgers, Richard

RICHARD RODGERS BALLET MUSIC (Various Artists)
Ghost town / Slaughter on 10th Avenue / Princess Zenobia ballet
CD _____ TERCD 1114
TER / Jun '94 / Koch.

Roditi, Claudio

MILESTONES
Milestones / I'll remember April / But not for me / Pent-up house / Brussels in the rain / Mr. P.C.
CD _____ CCD 79515
Candid / Apr '92 / Cadillac / Jazz Music / Wellard / Koch.

TWO OF SWORDS
CD _____ CCD 790504
Candid / Apr '91 / Cadillac / Jazz Music / Wellard / Koch.

Rodrigues, Amalia

COIMBRA
CD _____ CD 12502
Music Of The World / Nov '92 / Target/BMG / ADA.

LIVE AT THE OLYMPIA
CD _____ MCD 71442
Monitor / Jun '93 / CM.

QUEEN OF THE FADO
CD _____ SOW 90107
Sounds Of The World / Sep '93 / Target/BMG.

Rodriguez

PROUD HEART
CD _____ CSC 1002
Continental / Oct '95 / Direct.

Rodriguez, David

LANDIN '92
CD _____ BRAM 199235-2
Brambus / Nov '93 / ADA / Direct.

TRUE CROSS, THE
CD _____ DJD 3202
Dejadisc / May '94 / Direct / ADA.

Rodriguez, Tito

MAMBO MONA (Rodriguez, Tito y Los Lobos del Mamboa)
CD _____ TCD 014
Fresh Sound / Dec '92 / Jazz Music / Discovery.

Roea, Jude

MYSTIC IN THE MAKING
CD _____ CDSGP 082
Prestige / Oct '94 / Total/BMG.

Roedelius, Hans Joachim

AFTER THE HEAT
CD _____ SKYCD 3021
Sky / Nov '94 / Koch.

AUF LEISEN SOHLEN
CD _____ SKYCD 3048
Sky / Feb '95 / Koch.

DURCH DIE WUSTE
CD _____ SKYCD 3051
Sky / May '95 / Koch.

LUSTWANDEL
CD _____ SKYCD 3058
Sky / Feb '95 / Koch.

THEATRE WORKS
CD _____ MRC 016
Staalplaat / May '95 / Vital/SAM.

WEEN DER SUDWIND WEHT
CD _____ SKYCD 3064
Sky / Feb '95 / Koch.

Rogers, Billy

GUITAR ARTISTRY OF BILLY ROGERS, THE
CD _____ STCD 566
Stash / May '93 / Jazz Music / CM / Cadillac / Direct / ADA.

Rogers, Jimmy

BILL'S BLUES (Rogers, Jimmy/Hubert Sumlin/Big Bill Hickey)
CD _____ ATD 1112CD
Atomic Theory / Dec '94 / ADA.

FEELIN' GOOD
CD _____ BPCD 5018
Blind Pig / Feb '95 / Hot Shot / Swift / CM / Roots / Direct / ADA.

HARD WORKING MAN (Charly Blues - Masterworks Volume 3)
I used to have a woman / Hard working man / My little machine / Give love another

chance / What's the matter / Blues leave me alone / Sloppy drunk / If it ain't me / One kiss / I can't believe / What have I done / Trace of you / Don't turn me down / Don't you know my baby
CD _____ CD BM 3
Charly / Apr '92 / Charly / THE / Cadillac.

JIMMY ROGERS WITH RONNIE EARL & THE BROADCASTERS
CD _____ CCD 11033
Crosscut / Jan '94 / ADA / CM / Direct.

LUDELLA
CD _____ 422294
New Rose / May '94 / Direct / ADA.

SLOPPY DRUNK
Sloppy drunk / I can't sleep for worrying / Mistreated baby / Slick chick / Pretty baby / Left me with a broken heart / I lost the good woman / You're so sweet / Last time / Shelby county / Tricky woman / Sloppy drunk (2) / Gold tailed bird / Walking by myself / That's alright / Ludella
CD _____ ECD 260362
Evidence / Sep '93 / Harmonia Mundi / ADA / Cadillac.

THAT'S ALL RIGHT
That's all right / Ludella / Goin' away baby / Today today blues / World's in a tangle / She loves another man / Money, marbles and chalk / Chance to love / Back door friend / Crying shame / Mistreated baby / Last time / Out on the road / Left me with a broken heart / Act like you love me / Chicago bound / You're the one / Walking by myself / My baby don't love me no more / This has never been / Rock this house / My last meal / You don't know / Can't keep from worrying
CD _____ CDRED 16
Charly / Sep '89 / Charly / THE / Cadillac.

Rogers, Kenny

BEST OF KENNY ROGERS (And the First Edition)
CD _____ CTS 55402
Country Stars / Jan '92 / Target/BMG.

COLLECTION
CD _____ COL 031
Collection / Oct '95 / Target/BMG.

COUNTRY COLLECTION (Rogers, Kenny & The First Edition)
For the good times / She even woke me up to say goodbye / Me and Bobby McGee / King of Oak Street / Ticket to nowhere / Tell it all brother / Way it used to be / Just dropped in / Heed the call / Church without a name / But I know I love you / Poem for my little lady / Hurry up love / Run thru your mind / Sleep comes easy / Always leaving, always gone / I believe in music / Ruby, don't take your love to town
CD _____ MUCD 9023
Start / Apr '95 / Koch.

DAYTIME FRIENDS (The Very Best Of Kenny Rogers)
Gambler / Daytime friends, nightime lovers / Lucille / Ruby, don't take your love to town / Don't fall in love with a dreamer / Coward of the county / You decorated my life / Reuben James / She believes in me / Long arm of the law / Till I make it on my own / Son of Hickory Holler's tramp / Sweet music man / Green green grass of home / We've got tonight / Something's burning / Desperado / Lady / Abraham, Martin and John / Everytime two fools collide
CD _____ CDEMTV 79
EMI / Sep '93 / EMI.

DUETS (Rogers, Kenny & Dottie West)
All I ever need is you / Till I can make it on my own / Just the way you are / You needed me / Let it be me / Together again / Midnight flyer / You've lost that lovin' feelin' / Let's take the long way around the world / Hey won't you play another somebody done somebody wrong song / Every time two fools collide / You and me / What's wrong with us today / Beautiful lies / That's the way it could have been / Why don't we go somewhere and love / Baby I'm a want you / Anyone who isn't me tonight / Loving gift / We love each other
CD _____ CDMFP 6111
Music For Pleasure / Mar '94 / EMI.

ESSENTIAL COLLECTION
CD Set _____ LECD 615
Wiseback / Apr '95 / THE / Conifer.

EYES THAT SEE IN THE DARK
This woman / You and I / Buried treasure / Islands in the stream / Living with you / Evening star / Hold me / Midsummer night / I will always love you / Eyes that see in the dark
CD _____ ND 90084
RCA / Oct '87 / BMG.

FABULOUS KENNY ROGERS,THE
Ruby, don't take your love to town / Tulsa turnaround / Where does Rosie go / Love woman / Reuben James / I'm gonna sing you a sad song Susie / Me and Bobby McGee / Molly / Something's burning / Elvira / Tell it all brother / King of Oak Street
CD _____ PWK 019

Carlton Home Entertainment / Feb '88 / Carlton Home Entertainment.

GOLD COLLECTION, THE
CD _____ D2CD 28
Recording Arts / May '94 / THE / Disc.

KENNY ROGERS
CD _____ 15342
Laserlight / Nov '92 / Target/BMG.

KENNY ROGERS STORY, THE (20 Golden Greats)
Lucille / Lady / Long arm of the law / You decorated my life / Sweet music man / Ruby, don't take your love to town / Love or something like it / Through the years / You are so beautiful / Don't fall in love with a dreamer / Gambler / Daytime friends / We've got tonight (With Sheena Easton) / Love lifted me / Coward of the county / Reuben James / Desperado / She believes in me / Something's burning / Blaze of glory
CD _____ CDEMTV 39
Liberty / Dec '87 / EMI.

KENNY ROGERS/WILLIE NELSON ESSENTIALS (Rogers, Kenny & Willie Nelson)
CD _____ LECDD 637
Wisepack / Aug '95 / THE / Conifer.

LEGENDS IN MUSIC - KENNY ROGERS
CD _____ LECD 106
Wisepack / Sep '94 / THE / Conifer.

LOVE SONGS: KENNY ROGERS
Always leavin' always alone / What am I gonna do / Girl get a hold of yourself / I found a reason / It's gonna be better / She even woke me up to say goodbye / Last few wanna give my love to you / Last few threads of love / Way it used to be / I'm gonna sing you a sad song Susie / But you know I love you / Shadow in the corner of your mind / Stranger in my place / Sunshine / Once again she's all alone / My Washington woman / Hurry up love / Homemade lies / Poem for my little lady
CD _____ PWK 070
Carlton Home Entertainment / Jun '89 / Carlton Home Entertainment.

LOVE SONGS: KENNY ROGERS
Lady / Ruby, don't take your love to town / Lucille / She believed in me / Together again / Don't fall in love with a dreamer / You decorated my life / Every time two fools collide / All I ever need is you / You needed me / Why don't we go somewhere and love / Love or something like it / Hey won't you play another somebody done somebody wrong song / My world begins and ends with you / You and me / We love each other / You've lost that lovin' feelin' / But you know I love you / Love lifted me / Just the way you are
CD _____ CDMFP 5880
Music For Pleasure / Apr '90 / EMI.

PEARLS FROM THE PAST - KENNY ROGERS
CD _____ KLMCD 006
Scratch / Nov '93 / BMG.

RUBEN JAMES
CD _____ WMCD 5663
Disky / May '94 / THE / BMG / Discovery / Pinnacle.

RUBY
CD _____ AVC 510
Avid / Dec '92 / Avid/BMG / Koch.

RUBY DON'T TAKE YOUR LOVE TO TOWN
Ticket to nowhere / Conditions (Just dropped in) / She even woke me up to say goodbye / My Washington woman / Run thru your mind / Something's burning / Hurry up love / Trying just as hard / Ruby, don't take your love to town / Heed the call / we all got to help each other / Poem for my little lady / Where does Rosie go / Sunshine / Reuben James / Loser / Church without a name / Green green grass of home / Sweet music man / Daytime friends
CD _____ MU 5066
Musketeer / Oct '93 / BMG.

RUBY DON'T TAKE YOUR LOVE TO TOWN
Ruby, don't take your love to town / Reuben James / Shine on Ruby mountain / Ticket to nowhere / Conditions (just dropped in) / She even woke me up to say goodbye / My Washington woman / Run thru your mind / Sleep comes easy / After all / For the good times / Something's burning / Hurry up love / Trying just as hard / Heed the call / we all got to help each other / Poem for my little lady / Where does Rosie go / Sunshine / Loser / Church without a name / He and Bobby McGee / Always leaving, always gone / Calico silver / Way it used to be / Goodtime liberator
CD _____ CDGRF 027
Tring / Feb '93 / Tring / Prism.

RUBY DON'T TAKE YOUR LOVE TO TOWN (Rogers, Kenny & The First Edition)
CD _____ CDSGP 094
Prestige / Mar '94 / Total/BMG.

RUBY DON'T TAKE YOUR LOVE TO TOWN
CD _____ CDCD 1245
Charly / Jun '95 / Charly / THE / Cadillac.

RUBY, DON'T TAKE YOUR LOVE TO TOWN
Ruby, don't take your love to town / Green green grass of home / Sweet music man / Love or something like it / You and me / King of Oak Street / Reuben James / Puttin' in overtime at home / Daytime friends / Let it be me / Buried treasure / Son of Hickory Holler's tramp / I wasn't man enough (CD only) / Mother country music (CD only) / Lay down beside me (CD only) / Lucille (CD only)
CD _____ CDMFP 6001
Music For Pleasure / Sep '88 / EMI.

RUBY, DON'T TAKE YOUR LOVE TO TOWN
CD _____ 15075
Laserlight / Aug '91 / Target/BMG.

SPOTLIGHT ON KENNY ROGERS
Ruby, don't take your love to town / Me and Bobby McGee / Poem for my lady / For the good times / Good lady of Toronto / Where does Rosie go / What am I going to do / All God's lovely children / Lay it down / Tulsa turn around / Tell it all brother / Love woman / I'm going to sing a sad song Suzie / King of Oak Street / Shine on Ruby Mountain / Heed the call / Molly / Camptown ladies / We all got to help each other / After all
CD _____ HADCD 104
Javelin / Feb '94 / THE / Henry Hadaway Organisation.

VERY BEST OF KENNY ROGERS, THE
What I did for love / Ruby, don't take your love to town / Don't fall in love with a dreamer / Gambler / Daytime friends / Love is strange / She believes in me / Lucille / Lady / Coward of the county / You decorated my life / Love lifted me / Something's burning / Islands in the stream
CD _____ 7599264572
WEA / Nov '90 / Warner Music.

Rogers, Roy

BLUES ON THE RANGE
CD _____ CCD 11026
Crosscut / '92 / ADA / CM / Direct.

SLIDE ZONE
Get back in line / Spent money / House of blue dreams / Lover's moon / Livin' on borrowed time / Ode to the Delta / Not fade away / Slide zone / Lookin' up at downside / Rough house / Still a long ways to go / Off the cuff
CD _____ CDP 8294172
Liberty / Sep '94 / EMI.

TRAVELLIN' TRACKS (Rogers, Roy & Norton Buffalo)
CD _____ BPCD 5003
Blind Pig / Jan '93 / Hot Shot / Swift / CM / Roots / Direct / ADA.

Rogers, Sally

CLOSING THE DISTANCE (Rogers, Sally & Claudia Schmidt)
CD _____ FF 425CD
Flying Fish / May '93 / Roots / CM / Direct / ADA.

WE'LL PASS THEM ON
CD _____ RHRCD 71
Red House / Aug '95 / Koch / ADA.

WHEN HOWIE MET SALLY (Rogers, Sally & Howie Bursen)
CD _____ FF 538CD
Flying Fish / '92 / Roots / CM / Direct / ADA.

Rogers, Shorty

AMERICA THE BEAUTIFUL (Rogers, Shorty & Bud Shank)
CD _____ CCD 79510
Candid / Dec '91 / Cadillac / Jazz Music / Wellard / Koch.

BIG SHORTY ROGERS EXPRESS, THE
Blues express / Pink squirrel / Coop de graas / Infinity promenade / Short stop / Boar-jibu / Pay the piper / Home with sweets / Tales of an African lobster / Contours / Chiquito loco / Sweetheart of Sigmund Freud
CD _____ 74321 18519-2
RCA / Jul '94 / BMG.

EIGHT BROTHERS (Rogers, Shorty & Bud Shank / Lighthouse All Stars)
CD _____ CCD 79521
Candid / Mar '93 / Cadillac / Jazz Music / Wellard / Koch.

PORTRAIT OF SHORTY (Rogers, Shorty & His Giants)
Saturnian slaigh ride / Martian's lullaby / Line backer / Grand slam / Playboy / Geophisical ear / Red dog play / Bluezies
CD _____ 74321218222
RCA Victor / Nov '94 / BMG.

Rogers, Stan

BETWEEN THE BREAKS - LIVE
CD _____ FOG 002CD
Fogerty's Cove / Jul '94 / ADA.

FOGERTY'S COVE
CD _____ FOG 1001CD
Fogerty's Cove / Jul '94 / ADA.

FOR THE FAMILY
CD _____ R 002CD
Folk Tradition Canada / Jul '95 / ADA.

FROM FRESH WATER
CD _____ FOG 007CD
Fogerty's Cove / Jul '94 / ADA.

NORTHWEST PASSAGE
CD _____ FOG 004CD
Fogerty's Cove / Jul '94 / ADA.

TURNAROUND
CD _____ FOG 001CD
Fogerty's Cove / Jul '94 / ADA.

Rogers, Tammy

IN THE RED (Rogers, Tammy & Don Heffington)
CD _____ DR 0002
Dead Reckoning / Oct '95 / Direct.

Rogie, S.E.

DEAD MEN DON'T SMOKE MARIJUANA
Kpindigbee / Time in my life / Nor weigh me down / Jaimgba tutu / Koneh pelawoe / Jojo yalah jo / Nyalomei luange / African gospel / Nyalimagutee / Dieman noba smoke tafee
CD _____ CDRW 46
Realworld / May '94 / EMI / Sterns.

PALM WINE SOUNDS OF S.E. ROGIE
CD _____ PLAY 009CD
Workers Playtime / Jun '89 / Pinnacle.

Roland, Joe

JOLTIN' JOE
Gene's stew / Spice / Garrity's flight / Indian summer / Half nelson / Love is just a plaything / Music house / Joyce's choice / I've got the world on a string / Stephanie's dance / Sally is gone / Deedee's dance
CD _____ SV 0215
Savoy Jazz / Jun '93 / Conifer / ADA.

Roland, Paul

DANSE MACABRE
Witchfinder General / Madame Guillotine / Great Edwardian air raid / Hanging judge / Still falls the snow / Matilda mother / Gabrielle / Requiem / Buccaneers / In the opium den / Twilight of the rock
CD _____ 422296
New Rose / May '94 / Direct / ADA.

DUEL
CD _____ 422297
New Rose / May '94 / Direct / ADA.

HOUSE OF DARK SHADOWS
CD _____ 422299
New Rose / May '94 / Direct / ADA.

STRYCHNINE
CD _____ 422431
New Rose / May '94 / Direct / ADA.

Rollerskate Skinny

HORSE DRAWN WISHES
LP _____ 0630150100
WEA / Feb '96 / Warner Music.

SHOULDER VOICES
CD _____ PILLCD 3
Placebo / May '93 / Disc.

Rolling Stones

12 X 5
Around and around / Confessin' the blues / Empty heart / Time is on my side / Good times, bad times / It's all over now / 2120 South Michigan Avenue / Under the boardwalk / Congratulations / Grown up wrong / If you need me / Suzie Q
CD _____ 8444612
London / Jun '95 / PolyGram.

AFTERMATH
Mother's little helper / Stupid girl / Lady Jane / Under my thumb / Don't cha bother me / Goin' home / Flight 505 / High and dry / Out of time (long version) / It's not easy / I am waiting / Take it or leave it / Think / What to do
CD _____ 8444662
London / Jun '95 / PolyGram.

BEGGARS BANQUET
Sympathy for the devil / No expectations / Dear Doctor / Parachute woman / Jigsaw puzzle blues / Street fighting man / Prodigal son / Stray cat blues / Factory girl / Salt of the Earth
CD _____ 8444712
London / Jun '95 / PolyGram.

BETWEEN THE BUTTONS
Let's spend the night together / Yesterday's papers / Ruby Tuesday / Connection / She smiled sweetly / Cool calm and collected / All sold out / My obsession / Who's been

sleeping here / Complicated / Miss Amanda Jones / Something happened to me yesterday
CD _____ 8444682
London / Jun '95 / PolyGram.

BIG HITS (High Tide And Green Grass)
Have you seen your mother, baby, standing in the shadow / Paint it black / It's all over now / Last time / Heart of stone / Not fade away / Come on / Satisfaction / Get off my cloud / As tears go by / Nineteenth nervous breakdown / Lady Jane / Time is on my side / Little red rooster
CD _____ 8444652
London / Jun '95 / PolyGram.

BLACK AND BLUE
Hot stuff / Hand of fate / Cherry oh baby / Memory motel / Hey Negrita / Fool to cry / Crazy mama / Melody (inspiration by Billy Preston)
CD _____ CDV 2736
Virgin / Aug '94 / EMI.

DECEMBER'S CHILDREN (AND EVERYBODY'S)
She said yeah / Talkin' 'bout you / You better move on / Look what you've done / Singer not the song / Route 66 / Get off my cloud / I'm free / As tears go by / Gotta get away / Blue turns to grey / I'm movin' on (live)
CD _____ 8444642
London / Jun '95 / PolyGram.

DIRTY WORK
One hit (to the body) / Fight / Harlem shuffle / Hold back / Too rude / Winning ugly / Back to zero / Dirty work / Had it with you / Sleep tonight
CD _____ CDV 2743
Virgin / Aug '94 / EMI.

EMOTIONAL RESCUE
Summer romance / Send it to me / Let me go / Indian girl / Where the boys go / Down in the hole / Emotional rescue / She's so cold / All about you / Dance (part 1)
CD _____ CDV 2737
Virgin / Aug '94 / EMI.

EXILE ON MAIN STREET
Rocks off / Rip this joint / Casino boogie / Tumbling dice / Sweet Virginia / Torn and frayed / Sweet black angel / Loving cup / Shake your hips / Happy / Turd on the run / Ventilator blues / I just want to see his face / Let it loose / All down the line / Stop breaking down / Shine a light / Soul survivor
CD _____ CDV 2731
Virgin / Aug '94 / EMI.

FLOWERS
Ruby Tuesday / Have you seen your mother, baby, standing in the shadow / Let's spend the night together / Lady Jane / Out of time / My girl / Backstreet girl / Please go home / Mother's little helper / Take it or leave it / Ride on baby / Sittin' on a fence (version 1)
CD _____ 8444692
London / Jun '95 / PolyGram.

GET YER YA-YA'S OUT (Rolling Stones Live In Concert)
Jumpin' Jack Flash / Carol / Stray cat blues / Love in vain / Midnight rambler / Sympathy for the devil / Live with me / Little Queenie / Honky tonk women / Street fighting man
CD _____ 8444742
London / Jun '95 / PolyGram.

GOATS HEAD SOUP
Dancing with Mr. D / 100 years ago / Coming down again / Doo doo doo doo (Heartbreaker) / Angie / Silver train / Hide your love / Winter / Can you hear the music / Star star
CD _____ CDV 2735
Virgin / Aug '94 / EMI.

GOT LIVE IF YOU WANT IT
Under my thumb / Get off my cloud / Lady Jane / Not fade away / I've been loving you too long / Fortune teller / Last time / Nineteenth nervous breakdown / Time is on my side / I'm alright / Have you seen your mother, baby, standing in the shadow / Satisfaction
CD _____ 8444672
London / Jun '95 / PolyGram.

HOT ROCKS 1964-1971
Satisfaction / Get off my cloud / Paint it black / Under my thumb / Ruby Tuesday / Let's spend the night together / Jumpin' Jack Flash / Sympathy for the devil / Honky tonk women / Gimme shelter / You can't always get what you want / Brown sugar / Time is on my side / Heart of stone / Play with fire / As tears go by / Mother's little helper / Nineteenth nervous breakdown / Street fighting man / Midnight rambler / Wild horses
CD Set _____ 8444752
London / Jun '95 / PolyGram.

IT'S ONLY ROCK 'N' ROLL
If you can't rock me / Ain't too proud to beg / It's only rock 'n' roll / Till the next goodbye / Luxury / Time waits for no one / Dance little sister / If you really want to / Short and curlies / Fingerprint file
CD _____ CDV 2733
Virgin / Aug '94 / EMI.

JAGGER AND RICHARDS SONGBOOK (Various Artists)
Last time / Nineteenth nervous breakdown / Street fighting man / Heart of stone / Mother's little helper / Ruby Tuesday / Out of time / Congratulations / Wild horses / Tell me / Silver train / Sympathy for the devil / Lady Jane / Take it or leave it / Sleepy city / That girl belongs to yesterday / As tears go by / Honky tonk women / So much in love / Will you be my lover tonight / Sitting on a fence / Satisfaction / Connection / Sister Morphine
CD _____ VSOPCD 159
Connoisseur / Apr '91 / Pinnacle.

JAMMING WITH EDWARD (Hopkins/Cooder/Jagger/Wyman/Watts)
Boudoir stomp / It hurts me too / Edward's thrump up / Blow with Ry / Interlude a la el mojo / Loveliest night of the year / Highland fling
CD _____ CDV 2779
Virgin / May '95 / EMI.

JUMP BACK (The Best Of The Rolling Stones 1971-1993)
Harlem shuffle / Start me up / Brown sugar / It's only rock 'n' roll / Mixed emotions / Angie / Tumbling dice / Fool to cry / Rock and a hard place / Miss you / Hot stuff / Emotional rescue / Respectable / Beast of burden / Waiting on a friend / Wild horses / Bitch / Undercover of the night
CD _____ CDV 2726
Virgin / Dec '93 / EMI.

LET IT BLEED
Gimme shelter / Love in vain / Country honk / Live with me / Let it bleed / Midnight rambler / You got the silver / Monkey man / You can't always get what you want
CD _____ 8444732
London / Jun '95 / PolyGram.

MORE HOT ROCKS (Big Hits And Fazed Cookies)
Tell me / Not fade away / Last time / It's all over now / Good times, bad times / I'm free / Out of time / Lady Jane / Sittin' on a fence / Have you seen your mother, baby, standing in the shadow / Dandelion / She's a rainbow / 2000 light years from home / Child of the moon / No expectations / Let it bleed / What to do / Money / Come on / Fortune teller / Poison ivy / Bye bye Johnny / I can't be satisfied / Long long while
CD Set _____ 8444782
London / Jun '95 / PolyGram.

OUT OF OUR HEADS
She said yeah / Mercy mercy / Hitch hike / That's how strong my love is / Good times / Gotta get away / Talkin bout you / Cry to me / Oh baby / Heart of stone / Under assistant West Coast promotion man / I'm free
CD _____ 8444632
London / Jun '95 / PolyGram.

ROLLING STONES
Route 66 / I just want to make love to you / Honest I do / I need you baby / Now I've got a witness / Little by little / I'm a king bee / Carol / Tell me (you're coming back) / Can I get a witness / You can make it if you try / Walking the dog
CD _____ 8444602
London / Jun '95 / PolyGram.

ROLLING STONES BOX SET
CD Set _____ RS 1
UFO / Oct '92 / Pinnacle.

ROLLING STONES NOW, THE
Everybody needs somebody (version 2) / Down home girl / You can't catch me / Heart of stone / What a shame / I need you baby / Down the road apiece / Off the hook / Pain in my heart (version 1) / Oh baby (we got a good thing goin') (version 1) / Little red rooster / Surprise surprise
CD _____ 8444622
London / Jun '95 / PolyGram.

SINGLES COLLECTION: THE LONDON YEARS
Come on / I want to be loved / I wanna be your man / Stoned / Not fade away / Little by little / It's all over now / Good times, bad times / Tell me / I just want to make love to you / Time is on my side / Congratulations / Little red rooster / Off the hook / Heart of stone / What a shame / Last time / Play with fire / Satisfaction / Under assistant West coast promotion man / Spider and the fly / Get off my cloud / I'm free / Singer not the song / As tears go by / Gotta get away / Nineteenth nervous breakdown / Sad day / Paint it black / Stupid girl / Long long while / Mother's little helper / Lady Jane / Have you seen your mother, baby, standing in the shadow / Who's driving your plane / Let's spend the night together / Ruby Tuesday / We love you / Dandelion / She's a rainbow / 2000 light years from home / In another land / Lantern / Jumpin' Jack Flash / Child of the moon / Street fighting man / No expectations / Surprise surprise / Honky tonk women / You can't always get what you want / Memo from Turner / Brown sugar / Wild horses / I don't know why / Try a little harder / Out of time / Jiving sister Fanny / Sympathy for the devil
CD Set _____ 8444812
London / Jun '95 / PolyGram.

SOME GIRLS
Miss you / When the whip comes down / Just my imagination / Some girls / Lies / Faraway eyes / Respectable / Before they make me run / Beast of burden / Shattered
CD _____ CDV 2734
Virgin / Aug '94 / EMI.

STEEL WHEELS
Sad, sad, sad / Mixed emotions / Terrifying / Hold on to your hat / Hearts for sale / Blinded by love / Rock and a hard place / Can't be seen / Almost hear you sigh / Continental drift / Break the spell / Slippin' away
CD _____ CDV 2742
Virgin / Aug '94 / EMI.

STICKY FINGERS
Brown sugar / Sway / Wild horses / Can't you hear me knocking / You gotta move / Bitch / I got the blues / Sister Morphine / Dead flowers / Moonlight mile
CD _____ CDV 2730
Virgin / Aug '94 / EMI.

STRIPPED
Street fighting man / Like a rolling stone / Not fade away / Shine a light / Spider and the fly / I'm free / Wild horses / Let it bleed / Dead flowers / Slipping away / Angie / Love in vain / Sweet Virginia / Little baby
CD _____ CDV 2801
Virgin / Nov '95 / EMI.

SYMPHONIC MUSIC OF THE ROLLING STONES (Various Artists)
Street fighting man / Paint it black / Under my thumb / As tears go by / Sympathy for the devil / Dandelion / Ruby Tuesday / Angie / She's a rainbow / Gimme shelter / Jumpin' Jack Flash
CD _____ 09026625262
RCA / Jun '94 / BMG.

TATTOO YOU
Start me up / Hang fire / Slave / Little T and A / Black limousine / No use in crying / Neighbours / Worried about you / Tops / Heaven / Waiting on a friend
CD _____ CDV 2732
Virgin / Aug '94 / EMI.

THEIR SATANIC MAJESTIES REQUEST
Citadel / In another land / Sing this all together (see what happens) / She's a rainbow / Lantern / Gomper / 2000 light years from home / On with the show / 2000 man
CD _____ 8444702
London / Jun '95 / PolyGram.

THROUGH THE PAST DARKLY (Big Hits Vol. 2)
Paint it black / Ruby Tuesday / She's a rainbow / Jumpin' Jack Flash / Mother's little helper / Let's spend the night together / Honky tonk women / Dandelion / 2000 Light years from home / Have you seen your mother, baby, standing in the shadow / Street fighting man
CD _____ 8444722
London / Jun '95 / PolyGram.

UNDER COVER
Too much blood / Pretty beat up / Too tough / All the way down / It must be hell / Undercover of the night / She was hot / Tie you up (The pain of love) / Wanna hold you / Feel on baby
CD _____ CDV 2741
Virgin / Aug '94 / EMI.

VOODOO LOUNGE
Love is strong / You got me rocking / Worst / Out of tears / I go wild / Brand new car / Sweethearts together / Suck on the jugular / Blinded by rainbows / Baby break it down / Thru and thru / Mean disposition (CD only) / New faces / Moon is up / Sparks will fly
CD _____ CDV 2750
Virgin / Jul '94 / EMI.

WHO ARE THE STONES (Interview picture disc)
CD P.Disc _____ CBAK 4008
Baktabak / Apr '88 / Baktabak.

Rollinghead

LONG BLACK FEELING
CD _____ GROW 007-2
Grass / Apr '94 / SRD.

Rollini, Adrian

ADRIAN ROLLINI GROUPS 1924-27
CD _____ VILCD 0232
Village Jazz / Sep '92 / Target/BMG / Jazz Music.

BOUNCIN' IN RHYTHM
CD _____ TPZ 1027
Topaz Jazz / Sep '95 / Pinnacle / Cadillac.

Rollins, Henry

BIG UGLY MOUTH
CD _____ QS 9CD
Quarter Stick / Jul '92 / SRD.

BOXED LIFE, THE (Spoken Word Performances Parts 1 & 2)
Bone tired / Airplanes / Airport courtesy phone / Jet lag / Hating someone's guts, part 1 / Funny guy / Love in Venice / Strength, part 1 / Strength, part 2 / Odd ball / Hating someone's guts, part 2 / Blues / Big knowledge / Good advice / Vacation in

England / Condos / Trade secrets / I know you / Odd ball gets a big laugh
CD _____ 72787210092
Imago / Jan '93 / BMG.

DEEP THROAT BOX SET
CD Set _____ QS 13CD
Quarter Stick / Jul '92 / SRD.

DO IT (Rollins, Henry Band)
CD _____ 986978
Intercord / Jan '94 / Plastic Head.

GET IN THE VAN
CD Set _____ 74321242382
Imago / Nov '94 / BMG.

HARD VOLUME
CD _____ 986979
Intercord / Jan '94 / Plastic Head.

HOT ANIMAL MACHINE
CD _____ 986976
Intercord / Jan '94 / Plastic Head.

HUMAN BUTT
CD _____ QS 12CD
Quarter Stick / Jul '92 / SRD.

LIFE TIME (Rollins, Henry Band)
Burned beyond recognition / What am I doing here / 1000 times beyond / Lovely / Wreckage / Gun in mouth blues / You look at you / If you're alive / Turned out
CD _____ 986977
Intercord / Jan '94 / Plastic Head.

LIVE AT MCCABES
CD _____ QS 11CD
Quarter Stick / Jul '92 / SRD.

SWEAT BOX
CD _____ QS 10CD
Quarter Stick / Jul '92 / SRD.

TURNED ON (Rollins, Henry Band)
Lonely / Do it / What have I got / Tearing / Out there / You didn't need / Hard / Followed around / Mask / Down and away / Turned inside out / Deitmar song / Black and white / What do you do / Crazy lover
CD _____ QS 02CD
Quarter Stick / Dec '90 / SRD.

Rollins, Sonny

AIREGIN 1951-56
CD _____ GOJCD 53060
Giants Of Jazz / Mar '92 / Target/BMG / Cadillac.

ALL THE THINGS YOU ARE
Yesterdays / Summertime / Lover man / Round Midnight / Afternoon in Paris / It could happen to you / All the things you are / Just friends / At McKies / Now's the time / My one and only love / Trav'lin' light
CD _____ ND 82179
Bluebird / Jul '90 / BMG.

BEST OF SONNY ROLLINS
Decision / Poor butterfly / Why don't I (CD only.) / Misterioso / Tune up / How are things in Glocca Morra / Sonnymoon for two / Softly as in a morning sunrise (CD only.) / Striver's row (CD only.)
CD _____ CDP 7932032
Blue Note / Jan '96 / EMI.

BRIDGE, THE
Without a song / Where are you / John S / Bridge / God bless the child / You do something to me
CD _____ 74321185262
RCA Victor / Oct '94 / BMG.

COMPLETE PRESTIGE RECORDINGS, THE
CD Set _____ 7PCD 4407
Prestige / Jun '92 / Complete/Pinnacle / Cadillac.

CUTTING EDGE, THE
CD _____ OJCCD 468
Original Jazz Classics / Nov '95 / Wellard / Jazz Music / Cadillac / Complete/Pinnacle.

DANCING IN THE DARK
Just Once / O T Y O G / Promise / I'll String Along With You / Allison
CD _____ MCD 9155
Milestone / Oct '93 / Jazz Music / Pinnacle / Wellard / Cadillac.

EAST BROADWAY RUN DOWN
East Broadway run down / Blessings in disguise / We kiss in a shadow
CD _____ IMP 11612
GRP / Sep '95 / BMG / New Note.

ESSENTIAL, THE
Pannonica / La villa / Dearly beloved / Every time we say goodbye / Cutie / Last time I saw Paris / Happiness is a thing called Joe / Someday I'll find you / Freedom suite
CD _____ FCD 60020
Fantasy / Oct '93 / Pinnacle / Jazz Music / Wellard / Cadillac.

FALLING IN LOVE WITH JAZZ
CD _____ MCD 9179
Milestone / Oct '93 / Jazz Music / Pinnacle / Wellard / Cadillac.

FIRST RECORDINGS 1957
Sunny moon for two / Like someone in love / Theme from Tchaikovsky's symphony pathetic / Lust for life / I got it bad / Ballad medley: Flamingo (Medley includes: If you

were mine, I'm through with love, Love walked in.)
CD _____ 550142
Jazz Anthology / Feb '94 / Harmonia Mundi / Cadillac.

FREEDOM SUITE
CD _____ OJCCD 067
Original Jazz Classics / Oct '92 / Wellard / Jazz Music / Cadillac / Complete/Pinnacle.

FREEDOM SUITE, THE (1956-58)
CD _____ GOJCD 53062
Giants Of Jazz / Mar '92 / Target/BMG / Cadillac.

G-MAN
CD _____ MCD 9150
Milestone / Oct '93 / Jazz Music / Pinnacle / Wellard / Cadillac.

HERE'S TO THE PEOPLE
Why was I born / I wish I knew / Here's to the people / Dr. Phil / Someone to watch over me / Young Roy / Lucky day / Long ago and far away
CD _____ MCD 9194-2
Milestone / Mar '92 / Jazz Music / Pinnacle / Wellard / Cadillac.

HORN CULTURE
CD _____ OJCCD 314
Original Jazz Classics / Sep '93 / Wellard / Jazz Music / Cadillac / Complete/Pinnacle.

IN DENMARK VOL.1
CD _____ MCD 0372
Moon / Aug '92 / Harmonia Mundi / Cadillac.

IN DENMARK VOL.2
CD _____ MCD 0382
Moon / Aug '92 / Harmonia Mundi / Cadillac.

LIVE AT GREENWICH VILLAGE (Rollins, Sonny/Elvin Jones & Wilbur Ware)
CD _____ GOJCD 53044
Giants Of Jazz / Mar '90 / Target/BMG / Cadillac.

LIVE IN FRANCE
CD _____ LS 2929
Landscape / Nov '92 / THE.

LIVE MID 60'S
CD _____ LS 2915
Landscape / Nov '92 / THE.

LOVE AT FIRST SIGHT
Little lulu / Dream that we fell out of / Strode rode / Very thought of you / Caress / Double feature
CD _____ OJCCD 753
Original Jazz Classics / Apr '93 / Wellard / Jazz Music / Cadillac / Complete/Pinnacle.

MOVING OUT
CD _____ OJCCD 058-2
Original Jazz Classics / Feb '92 / Wellard / Jazz Music / Cadillac / Complete/Pinnacle.

NEWK'S TIME
Tune up / Asiatic races / Wonderful, wonderful / Surrey with the fringe on top / Blues for Philly Joe / Namely you
CD _____ CDP 7840012
Blue Note / Mar '95 / EMI.

NEXT ALBUM
CD _____ OJCCD 312-2
Original Jazz Classics / Apr '92 / Wellard / Jazz Music / Cadillac / Complete/Pinnacle.

OLD FLAMES
Darn that dream / Where is love? / My old flame / Time slimes / I see you face before me / Delia / Prelude to a kiss
CD _____ MCD 9215
Milestone / Jan '94 / Jazz Music / Pinnacle / Wellard / Cadillac.

OLEO
CD _____ JHR 73552
Jazz Hour / Jan '93 / Target/BMG / Jazz Music / Cadillac.

ON THE OUTSIDE
Dearly beloved / Doxy / Oleo / I could write a book / You are my lucky star / There will never be another you
CD _____ ND 82496
Bluebird / Apr '91 / BMG.

PLUS FOUR
CD _____ OJCCD 243-2
Original Jazz Classics / Feb '92 / Wellard / Jazz Music / Cadillac / Complete/Pinnacle.

QUARTETS, FEATURING JIM HALL
God bless the child / John S / You do something to me / Where are you / Without a song / Bridge / If ever I would leave you / Night has a thousand eyes
CD _____ ND 85643
Bluebird / Apr '88 / BMG.

ROLLINS MEETS CHERRY, VOL.1
CD _____ MCD 0532
Moon / May '94 / Harmonia Mundi / Cadillac.

ROLLINS MEETS CHERRY, VOL.2
CD _____ MCD 0542
Moon / Apr '94 / Harmonia Mundi / Cadillac.

ROLLINS PLAYS FOR BIRD (Rollins, Sonny Quintet)
CD _____ OJCCD 214-2
Original Jazz Classics / Mar '93 / Wellard / Jazz Music / Cadillac / Complete/Pinnacle.

SAXOPHONE COLOSSUS
CD _____ OJCCD 291-2
Original Jazz Classics / Feb '92 / Wellard / Jazz Music / Cadillac / Complete/Pinnacle.

SONNY BOY
CD _____ OJCCD 348
Original Jazz Classics / May '93 / Wellard / Jazz Music / Cadillac / Complete/Pinnacle.

SONNY ROLLINS & CO 1964
Django / Afternoon in Paris / Now's the time / Four / Blue 'n' boogie / Night and day / Three little words / My ship / Love letters / Long ago and far away / Winter wonderland / When you wish upon a star / Autumn nocturne
CD _____ 7863665302
Bluebird / Apr '95 / BMG.

SONNY ROLLINS 1951 - 1958
CD Set _____ CDB 1213
Giants Of Jazz / Jul '92 / Target/BMG / Cadillac.

SONNY ROLLINS AND THE CONTEMPORARY LEADERS PLUS
CD _____ OJCCD 340-2
Original Jazz Classics / Apr '86 / Wellard / Jazz Music / Cadillac / Complete/Pinnacle.

SONNY ROLLINS WITH THE MODERN JAZZ QUARTET (Rollins, Sonny & Modern Jazz Quartet)
Stopper / Almost like being in love / No Moe / In a sentimental mood / Scoops / With a song in my heart / Newk's fadeaway / Time on my hands / This love of mine / Shadrack / On a slow boat to China / Mambo bounce / I know
CD _____ OJCCD 011
Original Jazz Classics / Sep '93 / Wellard / Jazz Music / Cadillac / Complete/Pinnacle.

SONNY ROLLINS/VOL.2/NEWK'S TIME
Decision / Bluesnote / Plain Jane / Sonnysphere / How are things in Giocca Morra / Why don't I / Wail march / Misterioso / Reflections / You stepped out of a dream / Poor butterfly / Tune up / Asiatic raes / Wonderful wonderful / Surrey with the fringe on top / Blues for Philly Joe / Namely you
CD Set _____ CDOMB 008
Blue Note / Oct '95 / EMI.

SOUND OF SONNY, THE
Last time I saw Paris / Toot toot tootsie / Dearly beloved / Cutie / Mangoes / Just in time / What is there to say / Every time we say goodbye / It could happen to you
CD _____ OJCCD 029-2
Original Jazz Classics / Feb '92 / Wellard / Jazz Music / Cadillac / Complete/Pinnacle.

STOCKHOLM 1959
CD _____ DRCD 229
Dragon / Jan '88 / Roots / Cadillac / Wellard / CM / ADA.

TENOR MADNESS
CD _____ OJCCD 124
Original Jazz Classics / Feb '92 / Wellard / Jazz Music / Cadillac / Complete/Pinnacle.
CD _____ GOJCD 53061
Giants Of Jazz / Mar '92 / Target/BMG / Cadillac.

TENOR MADNESS AND SAXOPHONE COLOSSUS
Saxophone colossus - St. Thomas / You don't know what love is / Strode rode / Moritat / Blue seven / Tenor madness, tenor madness / When your lover has gone / Paul's Pal / My reverie / Most beautiful girl in the world
CD _____ CDJZD 002
Prestige / Jan '91 / Complete/Pinnacle / Cadillac.

THIS LOVE OF MINE
CD _____ CD3GP 043
Prestige / Mar '93 / Total/BMG.

TOUR DE FORCE
CD _____ OJCCD 095
Original Jazz Classics / Sep '93 / Wellard / Jazz Music / Cadillac / Complete/Pinnacle.

WHAT'S NEW
CD _____ 07863525722
Novus / Jul '93 / BMG.

WORK TIME
CD _____ OJCCD 007-2
Original Jazz Classics / Mar '93 / Wellard / Jazz Music / Cadillac / Complete/Pinnacle.

Romance, Lance

FORTUNE AND FAME
Don't cheat lady / Fortune and fame / Headache / Concentrate on you / Treat you right / There you go again / Baby tonight / Ain't that a shame / On my mind
CD _____ WRA 8101 CD
Wrap / Nov '91 / Koch.

Romane

QUINTET
CD _____ JSL 023
JSL Green / Jan '95 / Discovery.

SWING FOR NININE
CD _____ BPE 127
Kardum / Nov '92 / Discovery.

Romano, Aldo

CARNET DE ROUTES
Standing ovation / Vol / Daoulaged / Boroko dance / Annonbon / Les petits lits blancs / Flash memoire / Korokoro / Entrave
CD _____ LBLC 6569
Label Bleu / Nov '95 / New Note.

NON DIMENTICAR
CD _____ 518264-2
PolyGram / May '94 / PolyGram.

Romanos, Carlos

DANSAN YEARS VOL. 8 (Romanos, Carlos & Berry Lipman)
CD _____ DACD 8
Dansan / Mar '95 / Savoy / President / Target/BMG.

Romantics

MADE IN DETROIT
You and your folks, me and my folks / Love it up / I wanna know / Runaway / Leave her alone
CD _____ CDSEWT 705
Westbound / Mar '93 / Pinnacle.

Romeo, Max

CROSS OR THE GUN
CD _____ TZ 018
Tappa / Apr '94 / Jetstar.

MCCABEE VERSION
CD _____ SONCD 0078
Sonic Sounds / May '95 / Jetstar.

ON THE BEACH
CD _____ LG 21042
Rhino / Feb '93 / Jetstar / Magnum Music Group / THE.

WET DREAM
CD _____ CC 2705
Crocodisc / Aug '93 / THE / Magnum Music Group.

Romeo's Daughter

DELECTABLE
CD _____ CDMFN 153
Music For Nations / Oct '93 / Pinnacle.

ROMEO'S DAUGHTER
Heaven in the back seat / I cry myself to sleep at night / Hymn (look through golden eyes) / Inside out / Colour you a smile / Don't break my heart / Wild child / Velvet tongue / I like what I see
CD _____ CHIP 69
Jive / Mar '89 / BMG.

Romer, Hanne

AKIJAVA (Romer, Hanne & Marietta Wandall Duo)
CD _____ MECCACD 1012
Music Mecca / Nov '94 / Jazz Music / Cadillac / Wellard.

Romiosini

PICTURES OF CRETE
CD _____ EUCD 1049
ARC / '89 / ARC Music / ADA.

SONGS AND DANCES FROM GREECE
CD _____ EUCD 1163
ARC / Aug '94 / ARC Music / ADA.

Ron-E Was Another 1

SEXOCET
CD _____ REVXD 182
FM / Mar '93 / Sony.

Rondat, Patrick

RAPE OF THE EARTH
CD _____ CDGRUB 20
Food For Thought / Jun '91 / Pinnacle.

Rondo Veneziano

POESIA DI VENEZIA
CD _____ 259826
Private Music / Aug '95 / BMG.

VISIONI DI VENEZIA
CD _____ 260213
Private Music / Aug '95 / BMG.

Rondstadt, Linda

GREATEST HITS
You're no good / Silver threads and golden needles / Desperado / Love is a rose / That'll be the day / Long long time / Different drum / When will I be loved / Love has no pride / Heatwave / It doesn't matter anymore / Tracks of my tears
CD _____ 253055
WEA / Jul '94 / Warner Music.

Ronettes

BEST OF THE RONETTES
Be my baby / Why don't they let us fall in love / Baby I love you / Best part of breaking up / So young / When I saw you / Do I love you / You baby / How does it feel / Born to be together / Is this what I get for loving you / Paradise / Here I sit / I wish I never saw the sunshine / Everything under the sun / You came, you saw, you conquered
CD _____ PSCD 1006
Phil Spector Int. / Oct '92 / EMI.

COMPLETE COLPIX & BUDDAH SESSIONS, THE
He did it / Silhouettes / Good girls / Memory / You bet I would / I'm gonna quit while I'm ahead / I'm on the wagon / Recipe for love / My guiding angel / I want a boy / Sweet sixteen / Getting nearer / Lover lover / Go out and get it / I wish I never saw the sunshine / I wonder what he's doing / Silhouettes (Overdub session)
CD _____ NEMCD 620
Sequel / Jul '92 / BMG.

Roney, Antoine

TRAVELER, THE
Traveler / Cry of.... / Chief rahab / Mayan owl / Tempus fugit / On Green Dolphin street / Estate / Weaver of dreams / Bean and the boys
CD _____ MCD 5469
Muse / Jul '94 / New Note / CM.

WHIRLING
CD _____ MCD 5546
Muse / Feb '96 / New Note / CM.

Roney, Wallace

CRUNCHIN'
Woody 'n' you / What's new / Angel eyes / Swing spring / Time after time / We see / You stepped out of a dream / Misterioso
CD _____ MCD 5518
Muse / Feb '94 / New Note / CM.

INTUITION
CD _____ MCD 5346
Muse / Sep '92 / New Note / CM.

MUNCHIN'
Solar / Ah leu cha / Bemsha swing / Lost / Daahound / Whims of chambers / Smooch / Love for sale
CD _____ MCD 5533
Muse / Sep '95 / New Note / CM.

SETH AIR
Melchizedek / Breath of Seth Air / Black people suffering / 28 rue pigalle / Lost / People / Gone / Wives and lovers
CD _____ MCD 5441
Muse / Sep '92 / New Note / EMI.

STANDARD BEARER, THE
CD _____ MCD 5372
Muse / Sep '92 / New Note / CM.

VERSES
CD _____ MCD 5335
Muse / Sep '92 / New Note / CM.

Ronny & The Daytonas

BEST OF RONNY & THE DAYTONAS
G.T.O. / Sandy / California bound / Beach boy / I'll thing of summer / Bucket T / Teenage years / Somebody to love / Antique '32 Studebaker Dictator Coupe / Surfin' in the summertime / Teen's clown / Little scrambler / Hot rod baby / Be good to your baby / Little stingray that could / Hold me baby / No wheels / Little rail job / Goodbye baby / Back in the U.S.A
CD _____ 262528
Arista / Jun '92 / BMG.

Ronson, Mick

HEAVEN AND HULL
Don't look down / Like a rolling stone / When the world falls down / Trouble with me / Life's a river / You and me / Colour me / Take a long line / Midnight love / All the young dudes
CD _____ 474742 2
Epic / May '94 / Sony.

ONLY AFTER DARK
Love me tender / Growing up and I'm fine / Only after dark / Music is lethal / I'm the one / Pleasure man / Hey Ma get Papa / Slaughter on 10th Avenue / Leave my heart alone (live) / Love me tender (live) / Slaughter on 10th Avenue (Live) / Billy Porter / Angel number nine / This is for you / White light, white heat / Play don't worry / Hazy days / Girl can't help it / Empty bed (lo me no andrei) / Woman / Seven days (B'side) / Stone love / I'd rather be me
CD Set _____ GY 003SP
Trident / May '95 / Pinnacle.

Ronstadt, Linda

CRY LIKE A RAINSTORM, HOWL LIKE THE WIND
Still within the sound of my voice / Cry like a rainstorm / All my life / Don't know much / Adios / Trouble again / I keep it hid / So right, so wrong / Shattered / When some-

575

thing is wrong with my baby / Goodbye my
friend
CD _____ 9608722
Elektra / Oct '89 / Warner Music.

FEELS LIKE HOME
CD _____ 7559617032
Warner Bros. / Mar '95 / Warner Music.

FOR SENTIMENTAL REASONS
When you wish upon a star / Bewitched,
bothered and bewildered / You go to my
head / But not for me / My funny valentine
/ I get along without you very well / Am I
blue / (I love you) for sentimental reasons /
Straighten up and fly right / Little girl blue /
Round Midnight
CD _____ 960 474-2
Asylum / Sep '86 / Warner Music.

GREATEST HITS: LINDA RONSTADT
You're no good / Silver threads and golden
needles / Desperado / Love is a rose /
That'll be the day / Long long time / Different drum / When will I be loved / Love has
no pride / Heatwave / It doesn't matter anymore / Tracks of my tears
CD _____ 253 055
Asylum / '84 / Warner Music.

HASTEN DOWN THE WIND
Lose again / Tattler / If he's ever near /
That'll be the day / Lo siento me vida / Has-
ten down the wind / Rivers of Babylon /
Give one heart / Try me again / Crazy /
Down so low / Someone to lay down beside
me
CD _____ K 9606102
WEA / Sep '89 / Warner Music.

**LINDA RONSTADT GREATEST HITS
VOL.2**
It's so easy / I can't let go / Hurt so bad /
Blue bayou / How do I make you / Back in
the U.S.A / Ooh baby baby / Poor, poor pit-
iful me / Tumbling dice / Just one look /
Someone to lay down beside me
CD _____ 252255
WEA / Jul '94 / Warner Music.

MAS CANCIONES
Tata dios / El toro relajo / Mi ranchito / LA
mariquita / Gritenme piedras del campo /
Siempre haco frio / El crucifijo de piedra /
Palomita de ojos negros / Pena de los
amores / El camino / El gustito / El sueno
CD _____ 7559612392
WEA / Nov '91 / Warner Music.

ROUND MIDNIGHT
What's new / You've got a crush on you /
Guess I'll hang my tears out to dry / Crazy
he calls me / Someone to watch over me /
I don't stand a ghost of a chance with you
/ What'll I do / Lover man / Goodbye / When
I fall in love / Skylark / I've never entered my
mind / Mean to me / When your lover has
gone / I'm a fool to want you / You took
advantage of me / Sophisticated lady /
Can't we be friends / My old flame / Falling
in love again / Lush life / When you wish
upon a star / Bewitched, bothered and
bewildered / You go to my head / But not
for me / My funny valentine / I get along
without you very well / Am I blue / (I love
you) for sentimental reasons / Straighten up
and fly right / Little girl blue / Round
Midnight
CD _____ 9604892
WEA / Jul '94 / Warner Music.

WINTER LIGHT
Heartbeats accelerating / Do what you
gotta do / Anyone who had a heart / Don't
talk (put your head on my shoulder) / Oh
no, not my baby / It's too soon to know / I
just don't know what to do with myself /
River for him / Adonde voy / You can't treat
the wrong man right / Winter light
CD _____ 755961545-2
WEA / Dec '93 / Warner Music.

Room

HALL OF MIRRORS
CD _____ CD 700
Music & Arts / Sep '92 / Harmonia Mundi
/ Cadillac.

Roomful Of Blues

DANCE ALL NIGHT
CD _____ BBCD 9955
Bullseye Blues / Jul '94 / Direct.

DRESSED UP TO GET MESSED UP
Money talks / What happened to the sugar
/ Let's ride / Yes indeed / Albi's boogie /
Last time / Oh oh / Dressed up to get
messed up / He knows the rules / Whiplash
CD _____ CDVR 018
Varrick / '88 / Roots / CM / Direct / ADA.

FIRST ALBUM, THE
CD _____ CDVR 035
Varrick / '88 / Roots / CM / Direct / ADA.

HOT LITTLE MAMA
Hot little mama / Big question / New Or-
leans shuffle / Sufferin' mind / Caravan /
Loan me a helping hand / Long distance
operator / Something to remember you by
/ Two bones and a pick / Little healthy
thing / Sugar coated love / Jeep's blues
CD _____ CDCHM 39
Ace / Jul '91 / Pinnacle / Cadillac / Com-
plete/Pinnacle.

TURN IT ON, TURN IT UP
CD _____ CDBB 9566
Bullseye Blues / Oct '95 / Direct.

Rooney, Jim

BRAND NEW TENNESSEE WALTZ
Brand new Tennessee waltz / Be my friend
tonight / Amanda / Heaven become a
woman / We must believe in magic / Fish
and whistle / Dreaming my dreams / Six
white horses / Satisfied mind
CD _____ AP 067CD
Appaloosa / Jul '94 / ADA / Magnum Music
Group.

Roos, Randy

PRIMALVISION
Ancestor / Black elk / Raven's light / Craft-
man's prelude / Chameleon's dance /
Craftsman / Between states / Desert vision
/ Badlands / View from the summit / An-
cestor's reprise
CD _____ ND 62015
Narada / Oct '95 / New Note / ADA.

Root Boy Slim

ROOT 6
Everybody's got a problem / Burger row /
Hey Mr. President / I wanna be a business-
man / Eight ball boogie / Sex with a capital
X / You excite me / Our little mistake / Party
at the Berlin Wall / Big yellow streetsweeper
CD _____ CDNAK 6002
Naked Language / Feb '92 / Koch.

Rootless

ROTTEN WOOD FOR SMOKING BEES
CD _____ WALLCD 8
Wall Of Sound / May '95 / Disc / Soul
Trader.

Roots

DO YOU WANT MORE
Intro / There's something goin' on / Proceed
/ Distortion to static / Mellow my man / I
remain calm / Datskat / Lazy afternoon / vs
Rahzel / Do you want more / What goes on
part 7 / Essaywhuman / Swept away / You
ain't fly / Silent treatment / Lesson part 1 /
Unlocking
CD _____ GED 24708
Geffen / Nov '94 / BMG.

FROM THE GROUND UP
It's comin' / Distortion to static / Mellow my
man / Dat scat / Worldwide / Do you want
more
CD _____ 5189412
Talkin' Loud / Jun '94 / PolyGram.

ORGANIX
Root is comin' / Pass the popcorn / Anti-
circle / Writers block / Good music (prelude)
/ Good music / Grits / Leonard I-V / I'm out
deah
CD _____ RRCD 001
Remedy / Jun '95 / Vital.

Roots Radics

FREELANCE
Earsay / Rainbow / I'm not a king / Too
much fuss / Party time / Everywhere Natty
go / Dance with me / Midnight / Mash it up
/ Reggae on Broadway
CD _____ CD KVL 9021
Kingdom / Jan '87 / Kingdom.

LIVE AT CHANNEL ONE
CD _____ LAP 100CD
Live & Love / Jul '95 / Jetstar.

Roots, Randy

LIQUID SMOKE
Summer's decision / South of some border
/ Ferry / Copan / Ray's passage / Twelve
three / Precipice / Newfoundland / Not so
far / Rest assured
CD _____ ND 63028
Narada / Jun '94 / New Note / ADA.

Roots Syndicate

GARVEY - ROOTS OF DUB 1
CD _____ DTCD 19
Disctex / Nov '93 / SRD.

MANDELA THE ROOTS OF DUB VOL.3
CD _____ DTCD 20
Discotex / May '94 / Jetstar.

Rootsman

IN DUB WE TRUST
CD _____ TEMCD 002
Third Eye / Jul '95 / SRD.

INTERNATIONAL LANGUAGE OF DUB
CD _____ TEMCD 04
Third Eye / Jan '96 / SRD.

Roparz, Gwenola

**BRETON MUSIC FOR THE CELTIC
HARP**
CD _____ CD 130
Diffusion Breizh / Jan '95 / ADA.

Ros, Edmundo

CELEBRATION
Cuban love song / South America take it
away / Come closer to me / Amapola /
Wedding samba / What a difference a day
makes / Guantanamera / Brazil / I, yi, yi, yi,
yi / Alma llanera / Papa says / I'm grown
accustomed to her face / Girl from Ipanema
/ Mala Guena / Forbidden games / Peanut
vendor / Laughing samba / How near is love
/ Colonel Bogey / Coffee song
CD _____ 844 052 2
Eclipse / Jan '91 / PolyGram.

EDMUNDO ROS - 1939-41
CD _____ HQCD 15
Harlequin / '92 / Swift / Jazz Music /
Wellard / Hot Shot / Cadillac.

TROPICAL MAGIC
CD _____ HQCD 50
Harlequin / Mar '95 / Swift / Jazz Music /
Wellard / Hot Shot / Cadillac.

Ros, Lazaro

OLORUN
CD _____ GLCD 4022
Green Linnet / Nov '94 / Roots / CM /
Direct / ADA.

Rosa Mota

DRAG FOR A DRAG
CD _____ PILLMCD 2
Placebo / Jun '93 / Disc.

WISHFUL SINKING
CD _____ 13 THCD 2
Mute / Jan '95 / Disc.

Rose, Alan

PAST AND PRESENT
CD _____ FRCD 033
Foam / Oct '94 / CM.

Rose Among Thorns

BUTTERFLY DREAMS
Plaids deep stained in red / Don't cry for
me / Hero / Don't turn around / Journeys
from afar / I'm going to get there / Run run
run / Stepping stones / Butterfly dreams /
My homelands calling me
CD _____ HTDCD 31
HTD / Mar '95 / Pinnacle.

ROSE AMONG THORNS
Prologue / Journey / Keep me warm / Danc-
ing drum / Lady of Hay / Heart and Soul /
So much to tell / Losers 'n' Dreamers / Lu-
nar love / Hold on / Sail away / Take me
home
CD _____ HTDCD 6
HTD / May '91 / Pinnacle.

THIS TIME IT'S REAL
CD _____ HTDCD 8
HTD / Jul '92 / Pinnacle.

Rose Chronicles

SHIVER
Dwelling / Glide (free above) / Nothing's real
/ Deirdre / Brick and glue / Undertow / Bot-
tle song / Visions / Shiver / Forgotten /
Awaiting eternity
CD _____ NET 051CD
Nettwerk / Mar '94 / Vital / Pinnacle.

Rose, Dan

CONVERSATIONS
Fiber optic lover / Great harbour / Marcia /
Conversations / Carla, Carla, Carla / Back
burner / Designer in you / Across the divide
/ Shall we dance / Care and feeding
CD _____ ENJACD 80062
Enja / Oct '93 / New Note / Vital/SAM.

Rose, David

**STRIPPER & OTHER FAVOURITES, THE
(Rose, David & His Orchestra)**
CD _____ EMPRCD 501
Emporio / Apr '94 / THE / Disc / CM.

Rose, Jon

VIOLIN MUSIC FOR RESTAURANTS
CD _____ RERBJRCD
Recommended / '90 / These / ReR
Megacorp.

Rose Marie

BEST OF ROSE MARIE
CD _____ MATCD 217
Castle / Dec '92 / BMG.

COLLECTION: ROSE MARIE
CD _____ CCSCD 277
Castle / Oct '90 / BMG.

HEARTBREAKERS
It's a heartache / Sometimes when we
touch / Crazy / Without you / Let the heartaches begin / Cry me a river / Heartbreaker
/ Heartaches / Crying / There's nothing in
my life / You don't know me / I will always
love you / She's got you / True love ways
CD _____ CDDPR 121
Premier/MFP / May '94 / EMI.

ROSE MARIE SINGS JUST FOR YOU
Make the world go away / Hurt / Old rugged
cross / When your old wedding ring was
new / Answer to everything / This is my
mother's day / Legend in my time / When I
leave the world behind / Pal of my cradle
days / You'll never know / I apologise / Sunshine of your smile / If I had my life to live
over / Cry / My mother's eyes / Let the rest
of the world go by
CD _____ CLACD 229
Castle / Mar '91 / BMG.

SENTIMENTALLY YOURS
I don't know why I love you but I do / Let
me call you sweetheart / Who's sorry now
/ Good luck, good health, God bless you /
What do you want to make those eyes at
me for / Jerusalem / At the end of the day
/ Just one more chance / You're nobody 'til
somebody loves you / Please don't go /
Have you ever been lonely / Crazy / Beauti-
ful dreamer / Love letters in the sand / Anni-
versary waltz / I'll be seeing you
CD _____ CLACD 300
Castle / '92 / BMG.

SO LUCKY
Is it too late / Anniversary song / Let by-
gones be bygones / You're breaking my
heart / My world keeps getting smaller
every day / Harbour lights / So lucky /
Sweet sixteen / St. Therese of the roses /
All the love in the world / My Yiddishe
momma
CD _____ CLACD 228
Castle / Mar '91 / BMG.

TAKE IT TO THE LIMIT
Take it to the limit / It must be him / When
I leave the world behind / Danny boy
CD _____ PWK 066
Carlton Home Entertainment / '88 / Carlton
Home Entertainment.

TEARDROPS AND ROMANCE
Wheel of fortune / After all these years /
Dear daddy / Pal must be a pal forever /
Just for the old times sake / Wekking / Little
one / Danny boy / Mistakes / Child of mine
/ When I grow too old to dream / Ave Maria
/ I fall to pieces / I'll never fall in love again
/ Now is the hour / We'll meet again
CD _____ CLACD 230
Castle / Mar '91 / BMG.

TOGETHER AGAIN
Way old friends are / Among my souvenirs
/ I'll be your sweetheart / So deep is the
night / Strollin' underneath the arches / Behind the footlights / Nobody's child / Abide
with me / Mama / You always hurt the one
you love / Just out of reach / Someday / I'm
sorry / Love is all / Last waltz
CD _____ CLACD 296
Castle / Mar '92 / BMG.

WHEN I LEAVE THE WORLD BEHIND
When I leave the world behind / Danny boy
/ Take it to the limit / It must be him / It
comes from the heart / Too darn bad / It
ain't easy bein' easy / Rock 'n' roll waltz /
You can never stop me loving you / Looking
for love / Right to sing it blue / It's a sin to
tell a lie / You'll never walk alone / No
regrets
CD _____ MCCD 064
Music Club / '92 / Disc / THE / CM.

**WHEN YOUR OLD WEDDING RING WAS
NEW**
When your old wedding ring was new /
Make the world go away / This is my moth-
er's day / Old rugged cross / When I leave
the world behind / Wheel of fortune / When
I grow too old to dream / We'll meet again
/ Legend in my time / Just for old times sake
/ Pal of my cradle days / Sunshine of your
smile / My mother's eyes / Answer to every-
thing / Let the rest of the world go by / After
these years / Ave Maria / My blue heaven
/ Danny Boy / Now is the hour
CD _____ TRTCD 152
TrueTrax / Oct '94 / THE.

Rose, Michael

MICHAEL ROSE
CD _____ CDHB 144
Heartbeat / Apr '95 / Greensleeves /
Jetstar / Direct / ADA.

RISING STAR
CD _____ RFCD 003
Record Factory / Oct '95 / Jetstar.

VOICE OF THE GHETTO
CD _____ VPCD 1431
VP / Aug '95 / Jetstar.

Rose, Ndiaye Doudou

DJABOTE
Ligue nu ndeye / Cheikh anta diop / Rose
rhythm / Sidati aidara / Baye kene ndiaye /
Chants du burgam / Khine sine / Khine sal-
oume / Walo / Tabala ganar / Diame /
Ndiouk
CD _____ CDRW 43
Realworld / Feb '94 / EMI / Sterns.

Rose Of Avalanche

ALWAYS THERE
CD _____ FIRE 33007
Fire / Oct '91 / Disc.

LIVE AT THE TOWN AND COUNTRY
Stick in the works / Just like yesterday / Mainline man / Velveteen / 1000 landscapes / Waiting for the sun / Always there / Dreamland / Too many castles / Gimme some lovin'
CD _____ CONTECD 104
Contempo / Nov '88 / Plastic Head.

Rose Royce

ROSE ROYCE
CD _____ JHD 103
Tring / Aug '93 / Tring / Prism.

WISHING ON A STAR
CD _____ 9548 317242
Carlton Home Entertainment / Jan '93 / Carlton Home Entertainment.

Rose, Sammy

FOOL'S GOLD
You're gonna miss me / One in the red dress / Destination heartbreak / Rose's lament / My heart can't take the beating / Jealous bone / Cold heart stare / Till I'm over you / Backside view / Sugar please / Fool's gold
CD _____ BCD 15876
Bear Family / Mar '95 / Rollercoaster / Direct / CM / Swift / ADA.

Rose Tattoo

ASSAULT AND BATTERY
Out of this place / All the lessons / Let it go / Assault and battery / Magnum maid / Rock 'n' roll is king / Manzil madness / Chinese Dunkirk / Sidewalk Sally / Suicide city
CD _____ REP 4011-WZ
Repertoire / Aug '91 / Pinnacle / Cadillac.

BEST OF ROSE TATTOO, THE
Rock 'n' roll outlaw / Remedy / Nice boys / One of the boys / Bad boy for love / Butcher and fast Eddy / Manzil madness / All the lessons / Assault and battery / Rock 'n' roll is king / Branded / Scarred for life / It's gonna work itself out / We can't be beaten / Southern stars / I wish / Death or glory / Saturday's rage / Freedom's flame
CD _____ DOJOCD 126
Dojo / Jun '95 / BMG.

ROCK 'N' ROLL OUTLAWS
Rock 'n' roll outlaw / Nice boys / Butcher and fast Eddy / One of the boys / Remedy / Bad boy for love / T.V. / Stuck on you / Tramp / Astra wally
CD _____ REP 4010-WZ
Repertoire / Aug '91 / Pinnacle / Cadillac.

ROSE TATTOO
CD _____ REP 4103-WZ
Repertoire / Aug '91 / Pinnacle / Cadillac.

SCARRED FOR LIFE
Scarred for life / We can't be beaten / Juice on the loose / Who's got the cash / Branded / Texas / It's gonna work itself out / Sydney girls / Dead set / Revenge
CD _____ REP 4049-WZ
Repertoire / Aug '91 / Pinnacle / Cadillac.

SOUTHERN STARS
Southern stars / Let us live / Freedom's flame / I wish / Saturday's rage / Death or glory / Pirate song / You've been told / No secrets / Radio said rock 'n' roll is dead
CD _____ REP 4050-WZ
Repertoire / Aug '91 / Pinnacle / Cadillac.

Rose, Tim

GAMBLER, THE
I just want to make love to you / He was born to be a lady / Dance on ma belle / It'll be alright on the night / Runaway / Moving targets / Gambler / Blow me back Santa Ana / So much to lose / Is there something 'bout the way I hold my gun / Bowery Avenue / Laurie
CD _____ PCOM 1117
President / Nov '91 / Grapevine / Target / BMG / Jazz Music / President.

Rose, Wally

RAGS, BLUES, JOYS
CD _____ SACD 109
Solo Art / Jul '93 / Jazz Music.

Rose, Winston 'Saxon'

SOUNDS OF FREEDOM
CD _____ RRCD 012
Roots Collective / May '95 / SRD / Jetstar / Roots Collective.

Rosebud

ROSEBUD
My baby, your baby / Landslide / Eye of the hurricane / Fire / Fool for a broken heart / Dynamite / Too late now / Hot 'n' heavy / Love you till the day I die
CD _____ MMT 3304 CD
Shark / Jul '90 / Plastic Head.

Rosenberg Trio

CARAVAN
CD _____ 523030-2
Verve / Aug '94 / PolyGram.

Rosengren, Bernt

BIG BAND
CD _____ 1214
Caprice / Jul '89 / CM / Complete / Pinnacle / Cadillac / ADA.

UG, THE
CD _____ DRCD 211
Dragon / Jan '88 / Roots / Cadillac / Wellard / CM / ADA.

Rosenthal, Ted

MAYBECK RECITAL HALL SERIES VOL.38
It's all right with me / Long ago and far away / Lennie's pennies / Better you than me / You're a joy / Jesu joy of man's desiring / Drop me a line / 117th Street / Gone with the wind / Hallucinations / You've got to be modernistic
CD _____ CCD 4648
Concord Jazz / Jun '95 / New Note.

NEW TUNES, NEW TRADITIONS
(Rosenthal, Ted Trio)
San Francisco holiday / N.T.N.T. / Roll down, roll on / Valse desesperee / Rhythm-a-ning / Round Midnight / Let's call this / Hackensack / New light / Straight beyond
CD _____ 66056003
Ken Music / Jan '92 / New Note.

Rosetta Stone

ADRENALINE
CD _____ CLEO 12752
Cleopatra / Feb '95 / Disc.

EYE FOR THE MAIN CHANCE
CD _____ MIN 01CD
Minority/One / Aug '94 / Pinnacle.

FOUNDATION STONES
CD _____ CLEO 9323CD
Cleopatra / Jan '94 / Disc.

ON THE SIDE OF ANGELS
CD _____ MIN 02CD
Minority/One / Aug '94 / Pinnacle.

TYRANNY OF INACTION
CD _____ MIN 03CD
Minority/One / Jan '95 / Pinnacle.

URBAN DOGS
CD _____ CLEO 93232
Cleopatra / Jun '94 / Disc.

Rosicrucian

NO CAUSE FOR CELEBRATION
CD _____ BMCD 57
Black Mark / Aug '94 / Plastic Head.

SILENCE
Column of grey / Way of all flesh / Within the silence / Esoteric traditions / Autocratic faith / Nothing but something remains / Aren't you bored enough / Back in the habit / Defy the oppression / Do you know who you're crucifying
CD _____ BMCD 025
Black Mark / Oct '92 / Plastic Head.

Ross, Andy

COME DANCING
You make me feel so young / Nice and easy does it / Day in, day out / Night and day / Jean / If this were the last song / Blue tango / Golden tango / Light Cavalry / September song / Feed the birds / Nice work if you can get it / Fascinatin' rhythm / Mr. Melody / Copacabana / Save the best for last / Speak softly love / Amparita Roca / Fat man boogie / Bill / Over the rainbow / Innuendo / Bohemian rhapsody / Radio Ga Ga / We are the champions
CD _____ 475642 2
Columbia / Jun '94 / Sony.

COME DANCING (Ross, Andy & His Orchestra)
Let's face the music and dance / People will say we're in love / Flight of the foo birds / That old feeling / What now my love / Jesse / Weekend in New England / Guitar tango / Delilah / Hey daddy / On Broadway / September / Brazil / Copacabana / All in love is fair / History of love / El adorno / Leroy Brown / It had to be you / As if we never said goodbye
CD _____ CDMFP 6183
Music For Pleasure / Oct '95 / EMI.

DANCING FEET (Ross, Andy Orchestra)
Dancing feet / I can't get started with you / Toujours l'amour toujours / It don't mean a thing if it ain't got that swing / Railway children / Spinning wheel / Embraceable you / How lucky you are / Thou swell / Portrait of you / Teach me tonight / (We're gonna) Rock around the clock / Time after time / May each day / Sing, sing, sing / White rose of Athens / Opportunity
CD _____ PCOM 1107
President / Jul '91 / Grapevine / Target / BMG / Jazz Music / President.

LIVE AT THE INTERNATIONAL (Ross, Andy & His Orchestra)
Strike up the band / South Rampart street parade / Thou swell / Bye bye blues / Danse schon / Golden tango / Jealousy / L'amour toujours l'amour / May each day / Belle of the ball / La ronde / Moonglow / Am I blue / La player / Portrait of my love / I only want to be with you / Winchester Cathedral / Lucretia Macevil / Happy birthday sweet sixteen / April in Portugal / Matrimony / Toreador / Baker Street / Battle of New Orleans / Go away little girl / Resurrection shuffle
CD _____ PCOM 1123
President / Jul '92 / Grapevine / Target / BMG / Jazz Music / President.

Ross, Annie

SINGS A HANDFUL OF SONGS
CD _____ FSCD 61
Fresh Sound / Oct '90 / Jazz Music / Discovery.

Ross, Billy

BILLY ROSS & JOHN MARTIN (Ross, Billy & John Martin)
Hut on Staffin Island/Lone bush / Smith's a gallant fireman / Battle of Sheriffmuir / Dheanainn sugradh / Lass from Erin's Isle / Dr. MacInnes' fancy/Lexy MacAskill / Avondale / Scandinavian polkas / Bold reuin man / Braes of Lochel / Jenny Dang the weaver/Malcolm the tailor / Auld meal mill
CD _____ SPRCD 1029
Springthyme / Feb '94 / Direct / Roots / CM / Duncans / ADA.

Ross, Diana

ALL THE GREAT LOVE SONGS
I'm still waiting / My man (mon homme) / All of my life / Love me / After you / All night lover / Sparkle / It's my turn / Cryin' in my heart out for you / Endless love
CD _____ 530056-2
Motown / Jan '93 / PolyGram.

ANTHOLOGY - DIANA ROSS (Volumes 1 & 2)
Reach out and touch / Ain't no mountain high enough / Remember me / Reach out, I'll be there / Surrender / I'm still waiting / Good morning heartache / Touch me in the morning / You're a special part of me / Last time I saw him / My mistake (was to love you) / Sleepin' / Sorry doesn't always make it right / Do you know where you're going to / I thought it took a little time (but today I fell in love) / One love in my lifetime / Baby, I love your way / Young mothers / Brown baby/Save the children / Love hangover / Gettin' ready for love / Your love is so good for me / You got it / Top of the world / Lovin', livin' and givin' / What you gave me / Boss / It's my house / Upside down / I'm coming out / It's my turn / One more chance / Cryin' my heart out for you / My old piano / My man (mon homme) / Endless love / Imagine / Too shy to say
CD Set _____ 530199-2
Motown / Jan '93 / PolyGram.

ANTHOLOGY - DIANA ROSS & THE SUPREMES (Volume 1 & 2) (Ross, Diana & The Supremes)
Your heart belongs to me / Let me go the right way / Breathtaking guy / When the lovelight starts shining through his eyes / Standing at the crossroads of love / Where did our love go / Come see about me / Back in my arms again / Nothing but heartaches / My world is empty without you / Love is like an itching in my heart / You can't hurry love / Love is here and now you've gone / Happening / Hard day's night / Funny how time slips away / Falling in love with love / Forever came today / Some things you never get used to / I'm gonna make you love me / I'm livin' in shame / Composer / I'll try something new / No matter what sign you are / Someday we'll be together / Up the ladder to the roof / Everybody's got the right to love / Automatically sunshine / Your wonderful sweet sweet love / I guess I'll miss the man / Bad weather / It's all been said before / I'm gonna let my heart do the walking / Reflections / In and out of love / Love child / Composer #2 / Young folks / Stoned love / Nathan Jones / Floy joy / Touch / Run run run / Baby love / Ask any girl / Stop in the name of love / I hear a symphony / You keep me hangin' on / You send me / I'm the greatest star
CD Set _____ 5301962
Motown / Jan '93 / PolyGram.

DIANA EXTENDED (The remixes)
Boss (93 remix) / Love hangover (Classic mix) / Upside down (Mixes) / Someday we'll be together (Def mix) / I'm coming out (Maurice's club mix) / Chain reaction (Low end mix/CD & MC) / You're gonna love it (Radio edit/CD & MC) / Love hangover #2 / Boss (Dub/BYC) (LP) / I'm coming out (Monstrumental) (LP) / Someday we'll together (Dub) (LP)
CD _____ CDDREX 1
EMI / Apr '94 / EMI.

EATEN ALIVE
Eaten alive / Oh teacher / Experience / Chain reaction / More and more / I'm watching you / Love on the line / I love being in love with you / Crime of passion / Don't give up on each other / Eaten alive (extended)
CD _____ CDEMD 1051
EMI / Nov '93 / EMI.

FORCE BEHIND THE POWER
Change of heart / When you tell me that you love me / Battlefield / Blame it on the sun / You're gonna love it / Heavy weather / Force behind the power / Heart don't change my mind / Waiting in the wings / You and I (Not on LP) / One shining moment / If we hold on together (Not on LP) / No matter what you do (CD only)
CD _____ CDEMD 1023
EMI / Aug '91 / EMI.

FOREVER DIANA
When the lovelight starts shining through his eyes / Breathtaking guy / Where did our love go / Baby love / Come see about me / Stop in the name of love / Back in my arms again / You send me / Nothing but heartaches / Put on a happy face / I hear a symphony / My world is empty without you / Love is like an itching in my heart / I hear a happy symphony / You can't hurry love / You keep me hangin' on / Love is here and now you're gone / Happening / Reflections / In and out of love / Forever came today / Love child / I'm gonna make you love me / Try it baby / I'm livin' in shame / Someday we'll be together / Reach out and touch / Ain't no mountain high enough / Remember me / Reach out, I'll be there / Surrender / I'm still waiting / Lady sings the blues / Good morning heartache / God bless the child / Touch me in the morning / Brown baby/Save the children (medley) / Last time I saw him / You are everything / My mistake (was to love you) / Do you know where you're going to (theme from Mahogany) / Love hangover / Confide in me / Come in from the rain / Gettin' ready for love / Home / Boss / It's my house / I ain't been licked / Upside down / I'm coming out / It's my turn / Endless love / My old piano / Why do fools fall in love / Mirror mirror / Work that body / Muscles / Missing you / Swept away / Eaten alive / Chain reaction / Family / Ninety nine and a half (Won't do) / What a wonderful world / Amazing Grace / If we hold on together / Workin' overtime / This house / Force behind the power / When you tell me that you love me / One shining moment / Waiting in the wings / Where did we go wrong / Back to the future / Let's make every moment count / Your love / It's a wonderful life / Best years of my life
CD Set _____ DRBOX 1
EMI / Oct '93 / EMI.

MERRY CHRISTMAS
CD _____ 5504032
Spectrum/Karussell / Nov '94 / PolyGram / THE.

MOTOWN'S GREATEST HITS: DIANA ROSS
Ain't no mountain high enough / Touch me in the morning / I'm still waiting / I'm gonna make you love me / Upside down / My old piano / You keep me hangin' on / Happening / Reflections / Baby love / You can't hurry love / Where did our love go / Stop in the name of love / All of my life
CD _____ 5300132
Motown / Feb '92 / PolyGram.

ONE WOMAN - THE ULTIMATE COLLECTION
Where did our love go / Baby love / You can't hurry love / Reflections / Reach out and touch / Ain't no mountain high enough / Touch me in the morning / Love hangover / I'm still waiting / Upside down / Do you know where you're going to (theme from Mahogany) / Endless love / Why do fools fall in love / Chain reaction / When you tell me that you love me / One shining moment / If we hold on together / Best years of my life / Your love / Let's make every moment count
CD _____ CDONE 1
EMI / Oct '93 / EMI.

SILK ELECTRIC
Muscles / So close / Still in love / Fool for your love / Turn me over / Who / Love's lies / In your arms / Anywhere you run to / I am me
CD _____ CDEMD 1050
EMI / Nov '93 / EMI.

STOLEN MOMENTS - THE LADY SINGS JAZZ & BLUES LIVE
Fine and mellow / Them there eyes / Don't explain / What a little moonlight can do / Mean to me / Lover man / Gimme a pigfoot and a bottle of beer / Little girl blue / There's a small hotel / I cried for you / God bless the child / Love is here to stay / You've changed / Strange fruit / Good morning heartache / Ain't nobody's business / My man (mon homme) / Fine and mellow / Reprise / Where did we go wrong
CD _____ CDEMD 1044
EMI / Apr '93 / EMI.

STOP IN THE NAME OF LOVE
Baby love / Heatwave / Heartaches don't last always / Mother dear / Always in my heart / Get ready / Everything is good about you / Shake me, wake me (when it's over) / Who could ever doubt my love / Honey boy / Ask any girl / I'm in love again / Any girl in love (knows what I'm going through) / Stop in the name of love
CD _____ 5500712
Spectrum/Karussell / May '94 / PolyGram / THE.

TAKE ME HIGHER
If you're not gonna love me right / I never loved a man before / Swing it / Keep it right there / Don't stop / Gone / I thought that we were still in love / Voice of the heart / Only love can conquer all / I will survive
CD _____ CDEMD 1085
EMI / Sep '95 / EMI.

TOUCH ME IN THE MORNING
Touch me in the morning / All of my life / We need you / Leave a little room / I won't last a day without you / Little girl blue / My baby / Imagine / Brown baby / Save the children
CD _____ 530165-2
Motown / Jan '93 / PolyGram.

VERY SPECIAL SEASON, A
Winter wonderland / White Christmas / Wonderful Christmas time / What the world needs now / Happy Christmas (war is over) / Let it snow, let it snow, let it snow / Amazing grace / His eye is on the sparrow / Silent night / Overjoyed / O holy night / Someday at Christmas / Ave Maria / Christmas song
CD _____ CDEMD 1075
EMI / Nov '94 / EMI.

WHY DO FOOLS FALL IN LOVE
Why do fools fall in love / Sweet surrender / Mirror mirror / Endless love / It's never too late / Think I'm in love / Sweet nothin's / Two can make it / Work that body
CD _____ CDEMD 1049
EMI / Nov '93 / EMI.

Ross, Dr. Isiah

BOOGIE DISEASE
CD _____ ARHCD 371
Arhoolie / Apr '95 / ADA / Direct / Cadillac.

CALL THE DOCTOR
CD _____ TCD 5009
Testament / Oct '94 / Complete/Pinnacle / ADA / Koch.

I WANT ALL MY FRIENDS TO KNOW
My little woman / Cat squirrel / I want all my friends to know / Boogie for the doctor / Hobo blues / Little school girl / That's alright mama
CD _____ JSPCD 243
JSP / Apr '91 / ADA / Target/BMG / Direct / Cadillac / Complete/Pinnacle.

Ross, Jerry

JERRY ROSS SYMPOSIUM, THE
Ma belle amie / Everything is beautiful / When love slips away / For the love of him / Let me love you one more time / Little green bag / But for love / Montego love theme / If you do believe in love / Venus / How can I be happy / Take it out on me / I saw the light/Life and breath / Superwoman / If we only have love/Oh girl / It happened on a Sunday morning / Too late to turn back now/I wanna be where you are / Brandy (you're a fine girl) / It's the same old love / Too young / Duck you sucker (movie theme)
CD _____ NEMCD 722
Sequel / May '95 / BMG.

Ross, Malcolm

LOW SHOT
CD _____ MA 14
Marina / Sep '95 / SRD.

Rosselson, Leon

GUESS WHAT THEY'RE SELLING AT THE HAPPINESS COUNTER
Hugga mugga chugga lugga humbugga boom chit / Story line / Barney's epic homer / Boys will be boys / My daughter, my son / Do you remember / Abiezer coppe / On her silver jubilee / Ugly ones / Susie / Invisible married breakfast blues / Years grow tall / Invisible man / Pills / Across the hills / Battle hymn of the new socialist party / World's police / Voices / Voice that lives inside you
CD _____ CFCD 003
Fuse / Feb '88 / Direct / Roots / CM / ADA.

INTRUDERS
CD _____ CFCD 005
Fuse / Nov '95 / Direct / Roots / CM / ADA.

ROSSELSONGS
Tim McGuire / Penny for the guy / Palaces of gold / We sell everything / Stand up for Judas / Sing a song to please us / She was crazy, he was mad / Not quite but nearly / Let your hair hang down / Don't get married, girls / I didn't mean it / No-one is responsible / Still is the memory green in my mind / Whoever invented the fishfinger / Who reaps the profits, who pays the price / It wasn't me, I didn't do it / Bringing the news from nowhere / World turned upside down
CD _____ CFCD 1
Fuse / '88 / Direct / Roots / CM / ADA.

WO SIND DIE ELEFANTEN
Neighbours' cat / Poet, the wife and the monkey / Wo sind die elefanten / Juggler / Whatever happened to Nanneri / Song of the old communist / Where's the enemy /

William / General Lockjaw briefs the british media / Out of the fires and smoke of history
CD _____ CFCD 002
Fuse / Feb '89 / Direct / Roots / CM / ADA.

Rossendale Male Voice

VALLEY OF SONG, THE (Rossendale Male Voice Choir)
Ma belle marguerite / Donkey serenade / I gave my love a cherry / Phil the fluter's ball / Down in the valley / What shall we do with the drunken sailor / Hippopotamus song / Muss I denn / There is nothin' like a dame / I will give my love an apple / Ghost's high noon / Yesterday / Mad dogs and English-men / Cease thy affections / Lighthouse keeper and the mermaid / Blow the wind southerly / Old superb
CD _____ CHAN 6602
Chandos / Jun '94 / Chandos.

Rosser, Neil

GWYNFYD (Rosser, Neil A'i Bartneriaid)
CD _____ CRAICD 043
Crai / Dec '94 / ADA / Direct.

Rossi, Tino

HISTOIRES D'AMOUR
Voulez-vous, madame / Rien qu'un chant d'amour / Pres du feu qui chante / Au bal de l'amour / Le chant du gardian / Toi que mon coeur appelle / Maria / Un soir, une nuit / Le matin meme / J'ai deux mots dans mon coeur / Paquita / Donne moi ton sou-rire / Serenade sans espoir / J'attendrai / Tu etais la plus belle / Tristesse / Serenade pres de Mexico / Dites-lui de ma part / Soir de pluie / Ce soir
CD _____ UCD 19110
Forlane / Nov '95 / Target/BMG.

J'ATTENDRAI: THE BEST OF TINO ROSSI
J'attendrai / Vieni vieni / O corse, ille d'amour / Tant qu'il y aura des etoiles / Bella ragazzina / Reginella / Chant d'amour de Tahiti / Reviens / Tchi-tchi / Marinella / Tristesse (l'ambre s'enfuit) / Quand to rev-erras ton village / Le chant du gardian / Petit papa Noel / Serenade sur Paris / Mediter-ranee / Potpourri: Au pays du soleil / Ajac-clo / Le tango nous invite / Cerisier rose et pommier blanc / Ma joie / La vie commence a 60 ans
CD _____ CDEMS 1444
EMI / Apr '92 / EMI.

L'INCOMPARABLE
CD _____ UCD 19053
Forlane / Jun '95 / Target/BMG.

PARIS VOICI PARIS
CD _____ CDAJA 5168
Living Era / Dec '95 / Koch.

Rossy

ONE EYE ON THE FUTURE, ONE EYE ON THE PAST
CD _____ SHCD 64046
Shanachie / May '93 / Koch / ADA / Greensleeves.

Rostock Vampires

TRANSYLVANIAN DISEASE
CD _____ NB 014CD
Nuclear Blast / Oct '89 / Plastic Head.

Rosvett

FATAL
CD _____ BIRD 045CD
Birdnest / Oct '94 / Plastic Head.

Roswoman, Michele

OCCASION TO RISE (Roswoman, Michele Trio)
Lazy bird / Sweet eye of hurricane Sally / Occasion to rise / Prelude to a kiss / Weird nightmare / First trip / We are / Nite flite / Eee-yaa / West Africa
CD _____ ECD 22042
Evidence / Mar '93 / Harmonia Mundi / ADA / Cadillac.

Rota, Nino

HARMONIA ENSEMBLE
CD _____ JSL 015
JSL Green / Aug '93 / Discovery.

Rotary Connection

SONGS
Respect / Weight / Sunshine of your love / I've got my mojo working / Burning of the midnight lamp / Tales of brave Ulysses / This town / We're going wrong / Salt of the Earth
CD _____ CDARC 520
Charly / Mar '95 / Charly / THE / Cadillac.

Roth, Arlen

GUITAR
CD _____ CD 11538
Rounder / '88 / CM / Direct / ADA / Cadillac.

Roth, David

DIGGING THROUGH THE CLOSET
CD _____ FE 1414
Folk Era / Dec '94 / CM / ADA.

RISISNG IN LOVE
CD _____ FE 1410
Folk Era / Dec '94 / CM / ADA.

Roth, David Lee

CRAZY FROM THE HEAT
Easy Street / Just a gigolo / I ain't got no-body / California girls / Coconut grove
CD _____ 7599252222
WEA / Jul '92 / Warner Music.

EAT 'EM AND SMILE
Yankee rose / Shy boy / I'm easy / Ladies nite in Buffalo / Goin' crazy / Tobacco Road / Elephant gun / Big trouble / Bump and grind / That's life
CD _____ 925470 2
WEA / Aug '86 / Warner Music.

LITTLE AIN'T ENOUGH, A
Little ain't enough / Shoot it / Lady luck / Hammerhead shark / Tell the truth / Baby's on fire / Forty below / Sensible shoes / Last call / Dogtown shuffle / It's showtime / Drop in the bucket
CD _____ 7599264772
WEA / Jan '91 / Warner Music.

SKYSCRAPER
Hot dog and a shake / Stand up / Hina / Perfect timing / Two fools a minute / Knuck-lebones / Just like paradise / Bottom line / Skyscraper / Damn good / California girls (Reissues only) / Just a gigolo (Reissues only)
CD _____ 925824 2
WEA / Jan '89 / Warner Music.

YOUR FILTHY LITTLE MOUTH
She's my machine / Everybody's got the monkey / Big train / Experience / Little luck / Cheatin' heart cafe / Hey, you never know / No big 'ting / You're breathin' it / Your filthy little mouth / Land's edge / Night life / Sunburn
CD _____ 936245391-2
Warner Bros. / Mar '94 / Warner Music.

Rothenberg, Ned

POWER LINES
CD _____ 804762
New World / Jan '96 / Harmonia Mundi / ADA / Cadillac.

Rotting Christ

PASSAGE TO ACTURO
CD _____ USRDEC 003CD
Unisound / Nov '95 / Plastic Head.

PASSAGE TO ARCTURO
CD _____ DEC 003
Decapitated / Nov '93 / Plastic Head.

SATANAS TEDEUM
CD _____ USR 015CD
Unisound / Nov '95 / Plastic Head.

Rottrevore

INIQUITOUS
CD _____ DC 016
Drowned / Apr '94 / Plastic Head.

Rough Silk

WALLS OF NEVER
CD _____ 9041032
Mausoleum / Mar '95 / Grapevine.

Roulettes

STAKES AND CHIPS
CD _____ BGOCD 130
Beat Goes On / Apr '92 / Pinnacle.

Roupe

STROM
CD _____ INMCD 002
General Production Recordings / Mar '95 / Pinnacle.

Rouse, Charlie

CINNAMON FLOWER
CD _____ RCD 10053
Rykodisc / '91 / Vital / ADA.

EPISTROPHY
Nutty / Blue monk / Epistrophy / Ruby my dear / Round Midnight
CD _____ LCD 15212
Landmark / Jun '89 / New Note.

LES JAZZ MODES
CD _____ BCD 134/135
Biograph / Aug '95 / Wellard / ADA / Hot Shot / Jazz Music / Cadillac / Direct.

TWO IS ONE
Bitchin' / Hiopscotch / In a funky way / Two is one / In his presence searching
CD _____ 66051012
Strata East / Jul '95 / New Note.

Rouse, Mikel

WALK IN THE WOODS (Rouse, Mikel & Broken Consort)
CD _____ MTM 6CD
Made To Measure / Sep '88 / Grapevine.

Roussos, Demis

FAVOURITE RARITIES
CD _____ RA 95012
BR Music / Sep '94 / Target/BMG.

GREEK, THE
CD _____ BR 1292
BR Music / May '94 / Target/BMG.

LOST IN LOVE
Happy to be an island in the sun / Forever and ever / Can't say much how I love you / When forever has gone / Goodbye my love goodbye / My reason / Lost in love / I just don't know what to do with myself / Lost in a dream / Velvet mornings / Midnight is the time I need you / Gypsy lady / Senora (I need you) / Cancion de boda (The wedding song)
CD _____ 5500692
Spectrum/Karussell / May '93 / PolyGram / THE.

MY FRIEND THE WIND
Rain and tears / We shall dance / Forever and ever (and ever) / My friend the wind / My reason / Goodbye my love goodbye / Follow me / Summer wine / Marie Jolie / Summer in her eyes / Greater love / Tropi-cana bay / Island of love / Lovely lady of Arcadia / I found you (CD only.) / Spring Summer Winter and Fall (CD only.) / I want to live (CD only.) / End of the world (CD only.)
CD _____ CDMFP 6074
Music For Pleasure / Aug '89 / EMI.

TOO MANY DREAMS
Morning has broken / Tous les je vous aime / Oxygen / Too many dreams / Les mots qui font peur / Adagio / Italian song / Take me home / Spleen sergueii
CD _____ MSCD 5
Music De-Luxe / Jun '94 / Magnum Music Group.

Routledge, Keith

PRAISE HIM ON THE PIANO
CD _____ SOPD 2049
Spirit Of Praise / May '92 / Nelson Word.

Rova

WORKS, THE
CD _____ 1201762
Black Saint / Sep '95 / Harmonia Mundi / Cadillac.

Rova Saxophone Quartet

CHANTING THE LIGHT OF FORESIGHT
CD _____ NA 064CD
New Albion / May '94 / Harmonia Mundi / Cadillac.

CROWD, THE (Rova)
CD _____ ARTCD 6098
Hat Art / Apr '92 / Harmonia Mundi / ADA / Cadillac.

FROM THE BUREAU OF BOTH
CD _____ 120135-2
Black Saint / Apr '93 / Harmonia Mundi / Cadillac.

SAXOPHONE DIPLOMACY (Rova)
CD _____ ARTCD 6068
Hat Art / Nov '91 / Harmonia Mundi / ADA / Cadillac.

THIS TIME WE ARE BOTH
CD _____ NA 041 CD
New Albion / Aug '91 / Harmonia Mundi / Cadillac.

Row, Porter

FREE 'N' EASY
CD _____ FRCD 032
Foam / Oct '94 / Pinnacle.

Rowallan Consort

NOTES OF JOY
CD _____ COMD 2058
Temple / Feb '95 / CM / Duncans / ADA / Direct.

Rowan, Peter

ALL ON A RISING DAY
Midnight highway / Last train / Howlin' at the moon / Mr. Time clock / Behind these prison walls of love / Deal with the devil / Undying love / Wheel of fortune / All on a rising day / Freedom walkabout / Prayer of a homeless wanderer / John O'Dreams
CD _____ SH 3791CD
Sugarhill / Oct '94 / Roots / CM / ADA / Direct.

AWAKE ME IN THE NEW WORLD
Shaman's vision / Dreams of the sea / Pul-cinella sails away / Caribbean woman / Dance with no shoes / Sugarcane / For Gods, for Kings and for gold / Awake me in the new world / All my relations / Remember

that I love you / Maria de las Rosas / African banjo / Sailing home dance of Pulcinella
CD _____ SH 3807CD
Sugarhill / May '93 / Roots / CM / ADA / Direct.

BACKROADS
Roving gambler / Lone pilgrim / Raglan Road / Going up on the mountain / Casey's last ride / Old old house / Hiroshima mon amour / Willow garden / Moonshiner / Thirsty in the rain / Walls of time / Olains of Waterloo
CD _____ SHCD 3722
Sugarhill / '91 / Roots / CM / ADA / Direct.

DUST BOWL CHILDREN
Dust bowl children / Before the streets were paved / Electric blanket / Little mother / Barefoot country road / Seeds my daddy sowed / Tumbleweed / Dream of a home / Rainmaker
CD _____ SHCD 3781
Sugarhill / '90 / Roots / CM / ADA / Direct.

FIRST WHIPPERWILL, THE
I'm on my way back to the old home / I'm just a used to be / I believed in you darling / Sweetheart you done me wrong / When the golden leaves begin to fall / I was left on the street / Goodbye old pal / When you are lonely / First whipperwill / Sitting alone in the moonlight / Boat of love / It's mighty dark to travel
CD _____ SHCD 3749
Sugarhill / '93 / Roots / CM / ADA / Direct.

NEW MOON RISING (Rowan, Peter & The Nashville Bluegrass Band)
That high lonesome sound / Trail of tears / Memories of you / Moth to a flame / I'm gonna love you / One way / New moon rising / Jesus made the wine / Cabin of love / Meadow green
CD _____ SHCD 3762
Sugarhill / Nov '94 / Roots / CM / ADA / Direct.

PETER ROWAN AND RED HOT PICKERS
Hobo song / Old old house / Willow garden / Jimmie Brown the newsboy / Wild Billy Jones / Hiroshima mon amour / Come ye tender hearted / Oh Susanna / Rosalie McFall / Good woman's love
CD _____ SHCD 3733
Sugarhill / Dec '95 / Roots / CM / ADA / Direct.

TREE ON A HILL (Rowan, Peter Band)
CD _____ SHCD 2823
Sugarhill / Jun '94 / Roots / CM / ADA / Direct.

WILD STALLIONS
CD _____ AP 016CD
Appaloosa / Apr '94 / ADA / Magnum Music Group.

Rowe, Keith

DIMENSION OF PERFECTLY ORDINARY, A
CD _____ MR 19
Matchless / '90 / These / ReR Megacorp / Cadillac.

Rowles, Jimmy

LILAC TIME
Music music everywhere / Lullaby of the leaves / Theme from Arrest and Trial / Accent on youth / flight in Tunisia / Emily / I'm old fashioned / Morning lovely / Jeannine, I dream of lilac time / Belfast / Maurcie / After school / Time out / I wonder where love has gone / Chloe / Maids of Cadiz / Summer night
CD _____ KOKO 1297
Kokopelli / Oct '94 / New Note.

LOOKING BACK (Rowles, Jimmy & Stacey)
Good bait / Dirty butt blues / Lullaby of the leaves / Looking back / You don't know what love is / I fall in love too easily / East of the sun and west of the moon / Emily
CD _____ DE 4009
Delos / Mar '90 / Conifer.

PEACOCKS (Rowles, Jimmy & Michael Hashim)
CD _____ STB 2511
Stash / Sep '95 / Jazz Music / CM / Cadillac / Direct / ADA.

PROFILE (Rowles, Jimmy & Michael Moore)
CD _____ 4745562
Sony Jazz / Jan '95 / Sony.

REMEMBER WHEN
Lady be good / Peacocks / Things are looking up / Outsity / Come Sunday / Let's fall in love / Remember when / Just like a butterfly / Grooveyard
CD _____ CDCHE 11
Master Mix / Oct '91 / Wellard / Jazz Music / New Note.

TRIO (Rowles, Jimmy, Red Mitchell & Donald Bailey)
CD _____ 740092
Capri / '90 / Wellard / Cadillac.

Rowsome, Leo

CLASSICS OF IRISH PIPING VOL.1
Boil the breakfast early/Heather breeze / Savoureen deelish/Clare's dragoons / Blackbird / St. Patrick's day / Boolavogue/ Old Bog road / Boys of Wexford/Kelly the boy from Killane / Rights of man/Wexford/ Dunphy's hornpipe / Broom/Star of Munster/Milliner's daughter / Collier's reel/The maid of Tramore / Independent hornpipe/ The star hornpipe / Frieze breeches / Tomorrow morning/Cloone hornpipe / Cook in the kitchen/Rakes of kildare / Sweep's hornpipe/The friendly visit / Jockey to the fair / My darling asleep/Tongues of fire / Higgin's hornpipe/The queen of May / Larie's revels/I won't be a nun / Shandon bells/ Haste, to the wedding / Rocky road to Dublin
CD _____ TSCD 471
Topic / Sep '93 / Direct / ADA.

Rox Diamond

ROX DIAMOND
CD _____ CDATV 23
Active / Jul '92 / Pinnacle.

Roxette

CRASH, BOOM, BANG
Harleys and Indians (riders in the sky) / Crash boom bang / Fireworks / Run to you / Sleeping in my car / Vulnerable / First girl on the moon / Place your love / I love the sound of crashing guitars / What's she like / Do you wanna go the whole way / Lies / I'm sorry / Love is all (shine your light on me) / Go to sleep
CD _____ CDEMD 1056
EMI / Apr '94 / EMI.

DON'T BORE US, GET TO THE CHORUS
June afternoon / You don't understand me / Look / Dressed for success / Listen to your heart / Dangerous / It must have been love / Joyride / Fading like a flower / Big L / Spending my time / How do you do / Almost unreal / Sleeping in my car / Crash boom bang / Vulnerable / She doesn't live here anymore / I don't want to get hurt
CD _____ CDEMTV 98
EMI / Oct '95 / EMI.

JOYRIDE
Joyride / Hotblooded / Fading like a flower (every time you leave) / Knockin' on every door / Spending my time / I remember you (Not on album) / Watercolours in the rain / Big L / Soul deep (Not on album) / (Do you get) excited / Church of your heart (Not on album) / Small talk / Physical fascination / Things will never be the same / Perfect day
CD _____ CDEMD 1019
EMI / Mar '91 / EMI.

LOOK SHARP
Look / Dressed for success / Sleeping single / Paint / Dance away / Cry / Chances / Dangerous / Half a woman, half a shadow / View from a hill / I could never give you up (CD only.) / Shadow of a doubt / Listen to your heart
CD _____ CDEMC 3557
EMI / Apr '89 / EMI.

Roxxi

DRIVE IT TO YA HARD
CD _____ RH 1491
FM / May '91 / Sony.

Hoxy Music

AVALON
More than this / Space between / India / While my heart is still beating / Main thing / Take a chance with me / Avalon / To turn you on / True to life / Tara
CD _____ EGCD 50
EG / Apr '92 / EMI.

COMPACT COLLECTION
CD Set _____ TPAK 34
Virgin / Oct '94 / EMI.

COUNTRY LIFE
Thrill of it all / Three and nine / All I want is you / Out of the blue / If it takes all night / Bittersweet / Triptych / Casanova / Really good time / Prairie rose
CD _____ EGCD 16
EG / Jan '87 / EMI.

FLESH AND BLOOD
In the midnight hour / Oh yeah / Same old scene / Flesh and blood / My only love / Over you / Eight miles high / Rain rain rain / Running wild / No strange delight
CD _____ EGCD 46
EG / Sep '91 / EMI.

FOR YOUR PLEASURE
Do the Strand / Beauty Queen / Strictly confidential / Editions of you / In every dream home a heartache / Bogus man / Grey lagoons / For your pleasure
CD _____ EGCD 8
EG / Sep '91 / EMI.

HEART STILL BEATING (LIVE)
India / Can't let go / While my heart is still beating / Out of the blue / Dance away / Impossible guitar / Song for Europe / Love is the drug / Like a hurricane / My only love

/ Both ends burning / Avalon / Editions of you / Jealous guy
CD _____ EGCD 77
EG / Oct '90 / EMI.

MANIFESTO
Ain't that so / Cry cry cry / Dance away / Manifesto / My little girl / Spin me round / Still falls the rain / Trash / Stronger through the years
CD _____ EGCD 38
EG / Sep '91 / EMI.

ROXY MUSIC
Bitters end / Bob / Chance meeting / If there is something / Ladytron / Re-make/Re-model / 2HB / Would you believe / Sea breezes
CD _____ EGCD 6
EG / Sep '91 / EMI.

ROXY MUSIC COMPACT COLLECTION
CD _____ TPAK23
Virgin / Jan '93 / EMI.

STRANDED
Street life / Just like you / Amazon / Psalm / Serenade / Song for Europe / Mother of pearl / Sunset
CD _____ EGCD 10
EG / Sep '91 / EMI.

THRILL OF IT ALL, THE (Roxy Music 1972-1982/4CD Set)
Re-make/Re-model / Ladytron / If there is something / 2HB / Chance meeting / Sea breezes / Do the Strand / Beauty Queen / Strictly confidential / Editions of you / In every dream home a heartache / Bogus man / For your pleasure / Street life / Just like you / Amazona / Song for Europe / Mother of pearl / Sunset / Thrill of it all / Three and nine / All I want is you / Out of the blue / Bitter sweet / Casanova / Really good time / Prairie Rose / Love is the drug / Sentimental fool / Could it happen to me / Both ends burning / Just another high / Manifesto / Trash / Angel eyes / Stronger through the years / Ain't that so / Dance away / Oh yeah / Same old scene / Flesh and blood / My only love / Over you / No strange delight / More than this / Avalon / While my heart is still beating / Take a chance with me / To turn you on / Tara / Virginia Plain / Numberer / Pyjamarama / Pride and the pain / Manifesto (remake) / Hula kula / Trash 2 / Your application's failed / Lover / Sultanesque / Dance away (remix) / South Downs / Always unknowing / Main thing / India / Jealous guy
CD Set _____ CDBOX 5
Virgin / Nov '95 / EMI.

VIVA ROXY MUSIC
Out of the blue / Pyjamarama / Bogus man / Chance meeting / If there is something / In every dream home a heartache / Do the Strand / Can't let go / My only love / Like a hurricane / Jealous guy
CD _____ EGCD 25
EG / Sep '91 / EMI.

Roy, Harry

GREETINGS FROM YOU
Tangerine / Hold your hats on / Oh the pity of it all / Humpty Dumpty heart / When I love I love / Was it love / Sentimental interlude / You bring the boogie woogie out in me / Greetings from you / Zoot suit / Do you care / When daddy comes home / Darling Daisy / Elmer's tune / Madelaine / Chattanooga choo choo / Tica ti tica ta / It's funny to everyone but me / In the middle of a dance / Blues in the night / Green eyes / Shrine of St. Cecilia
CD _____ RAJCD 803
Empress / Oct '93 / THE.

HARRY ROY
Tiger rag / Canadian capers / Who walks in when I walk out / If I can't have Anna in Cuba / When I told the village belle / Campesina / Ever so quiet / Every time I look at you / Bugle call rag / Mr. Magician / My dog love's your dog / Nasty man / Harry Roy's new stage show / Valentina / Becky, play your violin / World is so small / Coconut oil (mama don't want)
CD _____ PASTCD 0741
Flapper / Sep '91 / Pinnacle.

Roy, Kalyani

VIRTUOSO OF SITAR, THE
Raga / Yaman / Yaman (Gat II) / Bhatiali (Boat song of Bengal) / Durga / Mishra Kamaj
CD _____ DC 8560
Denon / Dec '89 / Conifer.

Roy, Larry

QUARTER TO THREE (Roy, Larry & Marilyn Lerner)
CD _____ JTR 8437-2
Justin Time / Oct '92 / Harmonia Mundi / Cadillac.

Royal Air Force

70 YEARS (Royal Air Force Central Band)
Brave defenders / Royal Air Force march past / Spitfire prelude and fugue / Lawrence of Arabia / Four caballeros / TV sports

themes / Oor Wullie / Fanfare on the RAF call / March and dance of the comedians / Little light music / Viva musica / Introduction and march from the Battle of Britain / Those magnificent men in their flying machines / Concert march- Cockleshell heroes / Elegy / March: Uxbridge
CD _____ BNA 5009
Bandleader / Jun '87 / Conifer.

AIRMEN, THE (Bands Of The Royal Air Force)
Fanfare on the RAF call / Royal Air Force march past / Dam busters / Keepers of the peace / Out of the blue / Holyrood / Those magnificent men in their flying machines / Songs of the early airmen / Grand March 'RAF' / Tiger squadron / Swing squadron / Cavalry of the clouds / Jolly airmen / Spitfire prelude and fuge / Tornado / Squadron / Battle of Britain march / When the squads go marching / Celebration march / Battle in the air
CD _____ STACD 7003
Valentine / Jan '94 / Conifer.

BIG BAND SPECTACULAR (Royal Air Force Squadronaires Band)
There's something in the air / Lover / Splanky / John Brown's other body / Stardust / Doin' Basie's thing / Autumn leaves / Sweet Georgia Brown / Glenn Miller Medley / In the mood / Little brown jug / String of pearls / Moonlight serenade / St. Louis blues march / Song of India / All the things you are / Captiva sound / That warm feeling / South Rampart street parade / Switch in time / Pennsylvania 6-5000 / Scott's place / Basie straight ahead / Bedtime for drums / Sounds familiar
CD _____ BNA 5007
Bandleader / Jun '87 / Conifer.

BRANDENBURG GATE (Band Of The RAF Germany)
Under the double eagle / Hoch und deutschmeister / Old comrades / Berliner luft / Celebration march / Colonel Bogey / Buck private / Bridge too far / Marche des parachutistes belges / B.B. and C.F. / Black adder / Entrance of the court / Auf der alm / Plaisir d'amour / Swiss miss / Suite Francaise / Brandenburg gate / Night flight to Madrid / Armenian dances
CD _____ BNA 5046
Bandleader / '91 / Conifer.

CELEBRATION (Staff Band Of WRAC)
ATS March / Preludium and fugue / Nimrod / Last past and reveille / Jubilant prelude / Crown imperial / Colonel Bogey / Tara eagle strut / Songs of World War Two / Auld lang syne / Furchtlos und treu / Clarinet carousel / Cornet carillon / Where no man has gone before / You needed me / Lassus trombone / Sabre dance / Tyrolean tuba / Living in the UK / Stage centre / WRAC March
CD _____ BNA 5036
Bandleader / '91 / Conifer.

FESTIVAL OF MUSIC 1987 (Massed Bands Of The Royal Air Force)
Fanfare and National Anthem / Jaguar / Marvin Hamlish showcase / Trumpet concerto-3rd movement (Hadyn) / Those magnificent men in their flying machines / Eleanor Rigby / Overture: Prince Igor / Marching with Sousa / Pines of the Appian Way (from 'The pines of Rome')
CD _____ QPRM 112D
Polyphonic / '88 / Conifer.

FESTIVAL OF MUSIC 1992 (Massed Bands Of The Royal Air Force)
CD _____ QPRM 118D
Polyphonic / Jan '93 / Conifer.

FESTIVAL OF MUSIC 1994 (Massed Bands Of The Royal Air Force)
Fanfare for the common man / March of friendship / Time piece / African symphony / Weber / Second concerto for clarinet / Travelogue / Big country / European excursion / Sahra omania / 1812 Overture
CD _____ QPRM 122D
Polyphonic / Jan '95 / Conifer.

GRAND PARADE (Royal Air Force Central Band)
Tiger squadron / Mad major / March of the bowmen / Pathfinder's march / Touchdown / March: The love of three oranges / Flight of the tees / Grand parade / Oak and the ash / Black Hole (theme) / March: Things to come / Spirals / Adagio / Detectives - Hill Street Blues / Kojak / Cagney and Lacey / Dempsey and makepeace
CD _____ BNA 5028
Bandleader / '88 / Conifer.

HEROES OF THE AIR (Royal Air Force Central Band)
Battle of Britain suite (Walton) / Spitfire prelude and fugue / Conquest of the air / Battle of Britain suite (Josephs) / Coastal command
CD _____ CDPR 500
Premier/MFP / Jul '92 / EMI.

MARCHES OF THE ROYAL AIR FORCE (Royal Air Force Central Band)
Royal Air Force March past / Jolly airman / Aircrew on parade / High flight / Skywatch / Strike command march past / Tornado / Aces high / Royal air force college march / Songs of the early airmen / Acorn / Call to

adventure / Royal Air Force Association march / Newcomers / Militant miss / Skywriter / Keepers of the peace / Radio / Jaguar / Holyrood / Per ardua ad astra / Grand march 'RAF'
CD _____ BNA 5037
Bandleader / Apr '95 / Conifer.

MARCHING THROUGH THE 20TH CENTURY (Band Of The Royal Air Force College Cranwell)
CD _____ BNA 5103
Bandleader / Mar '94 / Conifer.

MASSED BANDS OF THE R.A.F
Fantasy of RAF call / Knights of the air / Spitfire prelude / Bugler's holiday / Skyliner / Cheek to cheek / Conquest of the air / Flute concerto (Ibert) / Coastal command / Call of the trumpet / Dam busters march / Cavalry of the clouds / Colditz march / Clarinet candy / Battle for freedom / Salute to British songs (medley) / Pathfinder's march / Reach for the sky / RAF march past
CD _____ QPRM 121D
Polyphonic / Jan '94 / Conifer.

MUSIC FROM THE 1992 ROYAL TOURNAMENT
CD _____ BNA 5092
Bandleader / Jun '92 / Conifer.

OUT OF THE BLUE (Royal Air Force Western Band)
Out of the blue / Eagle squadron march / Cavalry of the clouds / Blue devils / Howard's Way / Blue rondo a la turk / Swan / Doyen / Homage fanfare / Glorious victory / Middy march / Down in the skullery / Cryptic message / What are you doing for the rest of your life / Cowboys
CD _____ BNA 5024
Bandleader / '88 / Conifer.

REACH FOR THE SKY (Bands Of The Royal Air Force)
CD _____ MU 5007
Musketeer / Oct '92 / Koch.

SALUTE TO HEROES (50th Anniversary Album) (Royal Air Force Central Band)
Royal Air Force march past / Pathfinder's march / Dambusters march / Those magnificent men in their flying machines / Reach for the sky / Out of the blue / Crown imperial / 633 squadron / Colditz march / Cavalry of the clouds / Secret army / Aces high / Spitfire prelude / Battle of Britain / We'll meet again / Valiant years (CD only.) / White cliffs of Dover (CD only.) / Run rabbit run (CD only.)
CD _____ CDRAF 1
Premier/MFP / Jul '90 / EMI.

SALUTE TO THE RAF (Royal Air Force Central Band)
Spitfire / Viscount Trenchard / Fanfare on the Royal Air Force call / Soldiers of the Queen / It's a long way to Tipperary / Pack up your troubles in your old kit bag / Goodbye-ee / Take me back to dear old Blighty / Gunfire / Army, Navy and Airforce / AVRO 540k / I don't want to join the Air Force / Bold aviator / Bless 'em all / AVRO Lancaster / Air raid warning siren / Winston Churchill / September 15th 1940 / B.B.C. Announcement- "The Squadronaires" / Music in the air / We'll meet again / Big Ben / I'm gonna get lit up (when the lights go on in London) / Air raid / Coming in on a wing and a prayer / We're gonna hang out the washing on the Siegfried Line / nightingale sang in berkeley square / Run rabbit run / I've got sixpence / Kiss me goodnight / Sergeant Major / White cliffs of Dover / There'll always be an England / Lancaster returns / Dambusters march / Aerial combat / Reach for the sky / Aerial combat (2) / Battle of Britain / Aerial combat (3) / 633 Squadron / All clear siren / Speedbird salutes the few / RAF call / Evening hymn / Last Post sunset / March of the Royal Air Forces Association / Reveille / Ad Astra - An airman's hymn / Viscount Trenchard (2) / Royal Air Force march past / Lightning
CD _____ CDPR 105
Premier/MFP / Mar '93 / EMI.

SQUADS AWAY (Royal Air Force Squadronaires Band)
CD _____ BNA 5081
Bandleader / Apr '93 / Conifer.

SWING SQUADRON (Royal Air Force Squadronaires Band)
There's something in the air / Opus 1 / Satin doll / Sheikh of Araby / Body and soul / Volando / String of pearls / When the squads go marching in / I've got my love to keep me warm / Beyond the bar / In the mood / Wind machine / Swing squadron / Here's that rainy day / Best blue / Bones away / Li'l darlin' / Flying home
CD _____ BNA 5043
Bandleader / '91 / Conifer.

SWORD AND THE CROWN, THE
CD _____ QPRM 120D
Polyphonic / Aug '93 / Conifer.

TRIBUTE TO THE FEW (Massed Bands Of The Royal Air Force)
CD _____ QPRM 116F
Polyphonic / Jun '91 / Conifer.

WE WILL REMEMBER THEM
CD _____ SRCD 322
Souvenir / Jul '94 / Target/BMG.

Royal Artillery

CALL FOR THE GUNS (Royal Artillery Band)
Call for the guns / Overture- The force of destiny / Nocturne / Blaze away / Lucy Long / Washington post / Festive overture / Gymnopedie No.1 / March: la pere la victoire / March: Rapier / Selections from Barnum / Regimental quick march / Regimental slow march
CD _____ BNA 5054
Bandleader / Apr '91 / Conifer.

CHRISTMAS FESTIVAL, A (Royal Artillery Orchestra)
Christmas festival / Sleigh ride / Pie Jesu / Postman's knock / Shepherd's hymn / Pie in the face polka / Stop the cavalry / Walking in the air / Dance of the snowmen / Frosty sleigh ride / Gesu bambino / Have a merry Christmas
CD _____ SRCD 316
Souvenir / Nov '95 / Target/BMG.

MARCHES FOR EUROPE (Royal Artillery Band)
CD _____ BNA 5080
Bandleader / Apr '93 / Conifer.

Royal, Billy Joe

BILLY JOE ROYAL
CD _____ 7567823272
Atlantic / Jan '96 / Warner Music.

DOWN IN THE BOONDOCKS
CD _____ MMCD 5741
Mammoth / Jun '92 / Vital.

SPOTLIGHT ON BILLY JOE ROYAL
Down in the boondocks / Cherry Hill park / I knew you when / Up on the roof / On Broadway / Save the last dance for me / Stand by me / Hush / To love somebody / Tulsa / Campfire girls / I gotta be somebody / Raindrops keep falling on my head / Please come to Boston
CD _____ HADCD 101
Javelin / Feb '94 / THE / Henry Hadaway Organisation.

Royal British Legion Band

HERITAGE OF BRITAIN
CD _____ SRCD 324
Music Masters / Mar '95 / Target/BMG.

THANKS FOR THE MEMORIES
CD _____ SRCD 318
Music Masters / May '93 / Target/BMG.

Royal Choral Society

CAROL COLLECTION
Once in Royal David's city / In dulci jubilo / I saw three ships / Fist nowell / Holly and the ivy / O little town of Bethlehem / God rest you merry gentlemen / Silent night / While shepherds watch'd / Good King Wenceslas / Bethlehem down / Coventry carol / O come all ye fathful / Hark the herald angels sing
CD _____ 30367 00022
Carlton Home Entertainment / Oct '95 / Carlton Home Entertainment.

CAROL CONCERT (Live From The Royal Albert Hall)
Boar's head carol / Adeste fideles / Gabriel's message / Mary had a baby / Crown of roses / With gladness men of old / In dulci jubilo / Once in Royal David's city / Unto us is born a son / Noel nouvelet / Hark the herald angels sing / While shephers watch'd / Truth from above / Mary's lullaby / O little town of Bethlehem / Adam lay ybounden / It came upon the midnight clear / Spiritual: I can tell the world / God rest you merry gentlemen / Stille nacht / First nowell
CD _____ PCD 1026
Carlton Home Entertainment / Oct '95 / Carlton Home Entertainment.

Royal Corps/Signals

SIGNALLER, THE (Band Of The Royal Corps Of Signals)
Regimental quick march / Begone dull care / Signaller / Swift and sure / Regimental slow march / H.R.H. Princess Royal / On Richmond Hill bah'at / Donkey serenade / Lassus trombone / Vimy ridge / Master / Jubilee overture / Largo al factotum / Blandford suite / Nessun dorma / Rondo for horns / Carnival of Venice / Concerto for drum set / Farandole / History of the Royal Corps of Signals
CD _____ BNA 5114
Bandleader / Aug '95 / Conifer.

Royal Corps/Transport

CONCERT BANDSTAND (Band Of The Royal Corps Of Transport)
CD _____ BNA 5071
Bandleader / Aug '92 / Conifer.

MUSIC FROM THE GREAT HORSE SHOWS (Staff Band Of The Royal Corps Of Transport)
Fanfare / Tribute to next milton / Trotting medley / Television horse show themes / Music for heavy horses / Interval music / Another show / Cantering medley / Hunters,

the judging music / Hunting medley / Quadrille time / Tribute to the horse / Finale
CD _____ BNA 5035
Bandleader / '91 / Conifer.

Royal Crescent Mob

GOOD LUCKY KILLER
CD _____ EMY 143-2
Enemy / Nov '94 / Grapevine.

Royal Doulton Band

HYMNS FOR BAND
Praise my soul the king of heaven / Onward christian soldiers / King of love my shepherd is / Day thou gavest Lord is ended / All things bright and beautiful / Lord's my shepherd / Amazing grace / Immortal, invisible, God only wise / Holy city / Now the day is over / He who would valiant be / All people that on earth do dwell / Old rugged cross / Now thank we all our God / Ave Maria / O praise ye the lord / Let us with a gladsome mind / Abide with me / Jerusalem / How sweet the name of Jesus sounds
CD _____ BNA 5008
Bandleader / Jul '87 / Conifer.

HYMNS FOR BAND, VOL. 2
Holy holy holy / Glorious things of thee are spoken / Therr is a green hill far away / Dear Lord and Father of mankind / I will sing the wondrous story / Thine is the glory / Pie Jesu / All the toil and sorrow done / Fill thou my life / Guide me o thou great Jehovah / Fight the good fight / Morning has broken / Jesus Christ is risen today / Be thou my guardian and my guide / Rejoice the Lord is King / Stand up, stand up for Jesus / Jesu joy of man's desiring / We plough the fields and scatter / Nearer my God to thee / I vow to thee my country
CD _____ BNA 5034
Bandleader / '91 / Conifer.

MARCHING FORWARD
CD _____ BNA 5049
Bandleader / Feb '91 / Conifer.

Royal Dragoon Guards

FAME AND RENOWN
CD _____ BNA 5111
Bandleader / Oct '94 / Conifer.

FESTIVO (Band Of Her Majesty's Dragoon Guards)
Regimentsgruss / Namur / Marche Lorraine / Barman and Bailey's favourite / Welshman / Yorkshire overture / Rhapsody on the minstrel boy / Queen Elizabeth march set / Rhapsody for euphonium / Celtic folk / Rhosymedre / Finnegan's wake / Ensigh ewart's air / Three dale dances / Pipes and drums medley / Sicilienne / Festivo / Regimental marches / Radetzky march / Three DG's - Fare ye well Inniskilling
CD _____ BNA 518
Bandleader / Aug '95 / Conifer.

Royal Engineers

QUALITY PLUS
March / Quality plus / Stage centre / Michael / I just can't stop loving you / Way you make me feel / Man in the mirror / Stardust / Arnhem
CD _____ BNA 5068
Bandleader / May '92 / Conifer.

Royal Family

STRAIGHT FROM THE UNDERGROUND
CD _____ SPOCK 2CD
Music Of Life / Oct '90 / Grapevine.

Royal Folkloric Troupe...

COCO'S TAMAEVA (Royal Folkloric Troupe Of Tahiti)
CD _____ S 65808
Manuiti / Mar '92 / Harmonia Mundi.

COCO'S TEMAEVA - VOL. 2 (Royal Folkloric Troupe Of Tahiti)
CD _____ S 65815
Manuiti / Feb '94 / Harmonia Mundi.

Royal Highland Fusiliers

AFORE YE GO
Fanfare / March / Song for Suzanne / March: Birkenhead / Pipe dreams / March: Be ye also ready / Scottish serenade / Victory salute / Oft in the stilly night / Pipe set / Bays of Harris / Sunset salute / Seventy Ninth Farewell to Gibraltar / My own land / Tenth HLI crossing the Rhine / Misty morn / March: Assaye / Seventy Fourth Officers' mess call / Company marches (pipes) / Regimental marches (pipes) / Regimental slow march / Regimental quick march / March medley
CD _____ BNA 5102
Bandleader / Jan '94 / Conifer.

Royal Highland Regiment

PROUD HERITAGE
Reveille / Company marches / Headquarter company marches / Working day calls / Daily parade calls / Battalion parade tunes / Crimean long reveille / Retreat marches /

Officer's mess blues night / Officer's mess guest night / March off parade / Lights out
CD _____ LCOM 5221
Lismor / Sep '93 / Lismor / Direct / Duncans / ADA.

Royal Hussars

COLONEL IN CHIEF (Regimental Band Of The Royal Hussars)
Colonel-in-chief (fanfare) / Merry month of May / Moses in Egypt / John Peel / Coburg / Light of foot / Old grey mare / God bless the Prince of Wales / As pants the hart/Thy will be done / Men of Harlech / Guidon 90 / Standard of St. George Punjab / Trombone king / San Lorenzo / Belphegor / Trafalgar / Cougar conquest / Take the 'A' train / Shadow of your smile / Profiles in courage
CD _____ BNA 5044
Bandleader / '91 / Conifer.

SABRE AND SPURS (Royal Hussars Regiment Band)
Fanfare - Arrival / Princess of Wales march / Sabre and spurs / With sword and lance / Cavalry walk / Parade / March of the 18th Hussars / Golden spurs / Cavalry of the Steppes / Step lightly / New Colonial / Old Panama / Ca ira / Light of foot / Waveney manar / British eights / Rogue's march / Lincolnshire poacher / Regimental quick and slow marches
CD _____ BNA 5033
Bandleader / Aug '89 / Conifer.

Royal Kushite P.O.

KUSH KUSH KUSH
CD _____ MMCD 4
Melody Muzik / Nov '95 / SRD.

MELODY MUZIK
CD _____ MMCD 001
Melody Muzik / Feb '95 / SRD.

Royal Logistic Corps

ON PARADE (Band Of The Royal Logistic Corps)
On parade / Wait for the wagon / Village blacksmith / Pioneer corps / Sugar and spice / First post / Sostenare / Oregon / Concerto for cornet / Flugelhorn and trumpet / Concerto for band / You'd be so nice to come home to / Concerto for clarinet / Power and glory / Forest of Arden
CD _____ BNA 5117
Bandleader / Aug '95 / Conifer.

Royal Marines

ANYTHING GOES
CD _____ MMCD 426
Music Masters / Jul '92 / Target/BMG.

ASHOKAN FAREWELL, THE
Ashokan farewell / Rhapsody for trombone / Traumerei / Rhapsody for euphonium / Clarinet concerto in C / Gabriel's oboe / Trumpet concerto / Xylophonist's apprentice / Swan / Bach flute sonata no.4 in C / Evening breeze
CD _____ CLCD 10595
Clovelly / Nov '95 / Target/BMG.

BEATING RETREAT AND TATTOO
Fanfare / Salute to heroes / Soldiers to the sea / March and air / Silver bugles / Army of the Nile / Marines' walk / Sea soldier / Montafortabeek / Top mald / Dunkirk veterans / Famous songs of the British Isles / Evening hymn and sunset / Britannic salute / God save the Queen / Heart of Oak / Fanfara alla danza / Admiral's regiment / Westering home / Per mare / Per terram / Wee Mac / Maranatha / Claymore / Semper / Supremus / Sussex by the sea / Commando patrol / At the close of the day / Lost post / Nimrod / Marines' hymn / Life on the ocean wave
CD _____ GRCD 45
Grasmere / '91 / Target/BMG / Savoy.

BEST OF THE ROYAL MARINES
Strike up the band / Radetsky march / Sailing / March: Things to come / March of youth / Anything goes / Thunderbirds / Gibraltar march / My way / Symphonic marches of John Williams / Hearts of oak/ A life on the ocean wave/Prelude and sunset / SSAFA march / Jerusalem / Navy day / Unchained melody / Holyrood / Cockleshell heroes / Here's a health unto her Majesty / Big country / On the quarterdeck
CD _____ PWKS 4202
Carlton Home Entertainment / May '94 / Carlton Home Entertainment.

BEST OF THE ROYAL MARINES (2)
Marche Lorraine / Pomp and circumstance march No.1 / El Capitan / Solid men to the front / Thunderer / King Cotton / Army and Marine / Le pere la Victoire / National emblem / Hands across the sea / Invincible eagle / Old comrades / Under the double eagle / L'entente cordiale / Semper fidelis / Bugler's holiday / Contemptibles
CD _____ CDM 769 935 2
HMV / May '89 / EMI.

BEST OF THE ROYAL MARINES (3)
CD _____ MMCD 424
Music Masters / Jun '92 / Target/BMG.

BY LAND AND SEA
National emblem / Preobrakensky march / Top malo / Concert march- Cockleshell heroes / Captain general / President elect / By land and sea / Anchors aweigh / Post horn gallop / Picconautical / In party mood / Falcon crest / Overture- Monte Carlo or bust / Barwick Green / Elizabeth Tudor
CD _____ BNA 5030
Bandleader / '88 / Conifer.

CELEBRATION
Fanfare for a festival / Festival prelude / Serenade for wind band Op.22 / Choral and rockout / Fanfares / Bolero / Prelude for an occasion / Fanfare for the common man / Festive overture Op.96 / Army with the flaxen hair / Toccata in D minor / Finale from five Burns sketches / Symphonic marches of John Williams / Prelude and sunset / Grate gate of Kiev
CD _____ MMCD 410
Music Masters / Nov '95 / Target/BMG.

COMPLETE MARCHES OF KENNETH ALFORD
CD _____ CLCD 102
Clovelly / Jan '94 / Target/BMG.

GLOBE AND LAUREL
On parade / Globe and laurel / Officer of the day / Cavalry of the Steppes / Uncle Sammy / Dad's army march / Belphegor / Advance guard / My regiment / Brass buttons / Gladiator's farewell / Punjab / Contemptibles / Voice of the guns / Robinson's grand entree / Dunedin / Vimy ridge / On the square
CD _____ BNA 5023
Bandleader / Aug '89 / Conifer.

HIGHLAND CATHEDRAL (Royal Marines Band, Scotland)
CD _____ MMCD 441
Music Masters / Aug '94 / Target/BMG.

KALEIDOSCOPE (Royal Marines Commando Forces Band)
March: Royal buglers / Jubilee overture / Londonderry air / Shepherd's hey / Valdres / March / Irish washerwoman / West Side story selection / Can't buy me love / Passion eyes / Time after time / All through the night / Kaleidoscope / Black is black / Lady in red / Blue rondo a la turk / Whiter shade of pale
CD _____ BNA 5064
Bandleader / May '92 / Conifer.

LIFE ON THE OCEAN WAVE
Life on the ocean wave / Salute the sovereign / Portsmouth / Evening hymn - the day / Thou gavest Lord is ended/Sunset / By land and sea / Bugle fanfare / Drum display / Victory / On the quarterdeck / Greensleeves / Men of action / Cockleshell heroes / Hands across the sea / Warship / Anchors aweigh / Officers of the day / Picconautical / Troika / Post horn gallop / Salute to James Last / Nobilmente
CD _____ MCCD 073
Music Club / Jun '92 / Disc / THE / CM.

MARCHES OF THE SEA
CD _____ CLCD 101
Clovelly / Jan '94 / Target/BMG.

MARTIAL MUSIC OF SIR VIVIAN DUNN, THE
CD _____ CLCD 10394
Clovelly / Dec '94 / Target/BMG.

MEN OF ACTION
Life on the ocean wave / On the quarter deck / Overture, the marriage of Figaro / Salute to James Last / Jeu joy of man's desiring / Slavonic rhapsody / State occasion / Greensleeves / Purple pageant / Chimes of liberty / Flying eagle / Men of action / Nobilmente / General Mitchell / Heralds of victory / Marche vanier / Barnum and Bailey's favourite / Trombone king
CD _____ BNA 5010
Bandleader / Oct '87 / Conifer.

MEN OF MUSIC
CD _____ MMCD 425
Music Masters / Nov '94 / Target/BMG.

MUSIC THAT STIRS THE NATION
CD _____ MU 5008
Musketeer / Oct '92 / Koch.

OLD COMRADES - NEW COMRADES
Old comrades / In the Bristol fashion / Lichfield / Cairo Road / Ventis secundis / Sea shanties / Parade of brass / Blue devils / New comrades / H.M. jollies / Broadlands / Little swiss piece / HMY Britannia / Nation / Up periscope / Glorious victory
CD _____ GRACC 1
Grasmere / May '94 / Target/BMG / Savoy.

PORTSMOUTH
Heart of oak / Portsmouth / Warship / Splice the mainbrace / Nelson touch / Trafalgar / Viscount Nelson / Hands across the sea / Under the white ensign / Sea songs / Victory / Salute to the sovereign / Bugle fanfare / Drum display / Evening hymn / Sunset / Fantasia on British sea songs / Land of hope and glory
CD _____ BNA 5020
Bandleader / Jun '93 / Conifer.

SEA SOLDIER, THE
CD _____ STACD 7002
Valentine / Nov '93 / Conifer.

SPECTACULAR SOUNDS OF, THE (Royal Marines & Argyll & Sutherland Highlanders)
Fanfare royal occasion / Life on the ocean wave / Highland laddie / Famous songs of the British Isles medley / Fine old English gentleman / To be a farmer's boy / Here's a health unto His Majesty / British Grenadiers / Minstral boy / Annie Laurie / Men of Harlech / Pipe selection / Gordon boy (lang) / Barren rocks of Aden / Brown haired maiden / Marie's wedding / Major A.C.S. Boswell / Captain D P Thomson / Lieutenant Colonel H. L. Clark / Sea shanties medley / What shall we do with the drunken sailor / Portsmouth / Rovin' / Hornpipe / Highland fling / Dornoch links / Marquis of Huntly / Man's a man for a' that / Arrival / Black bear / Fanfare no.1 / Royal salute / Drumbeatings / Time off / Argyll broadswords / Glendaavel highlanders / O'er the bows to Ballindalloch / Miss Ada Crawford / Because he was a bonny lad / Piper o'Drummond / Sleepy Maggie / All the blue bonnets are over the mountain / Soldiers return / Chariots of fire / Crown imperial / Day thou gavest Lord is ended / Sunset / Rule Britannia / Auld lang syne / Scotland the brave / Campbells are coming
CD _____ CDMFP 6043
Music For Pleasure / Sep '88 / EMI.

THAT'S ENTERTAINMENT
CD _____ MMCD 438
Music Masters / Jul '94 / Target/BMG.

VERY BEST OF THE ROYAL MARINES BAND
Colonel Bogey / Standard of St. George / Great little army / El abanico / National Emblem / Anchors Aweigh / Semper fidelis / Cockershell heroes / Espana / Life on the ocean wave / Warship / On the square / This guy's in love with you / Sutherland's law theme / Shadow of your smile / Troika / Eye level / What the world needs now is love / On the track / When the saints go marching in
CD _____ CDMFP 5789
Music For Pleasure / Jun '90 / EMI.

Royal Military School Of.

KNELLER HALL (Kneller Hall R.M.S. Band)
Blow away the morning dew / Pinapple poll suite No.1 / Great little army / First suite in Eb for military band / Three humouresques / Tocatta mariale / H.R.H. The Duke Of Cambridge / Sir Godfrey Kneller / Original suite / Serenade / Celebration
CD _____ BNA 5109
Bandleader / Aug '94 / Conifer.

SULLIVAN SALUTE (Kneller Hall R.M.S. Band)
Procession March / Overture Iolanthe / Three little maids from school / Incidental music to Henry VIII / March / King Henry's song / Graceful dance / Danish march / Overture the yeomen of the guard / Absent Minded Beggar / Lost Chord / Battle of St.Gertrude / March of the Peers / Overture / Di Ballo
CD _____ BNA 5067
Bandleader / Aug '92 / Conifer.

Royal Philharmonic...

CLASSICS OF LOVE (Royal Philharmonic Orchestra)
Three times a lady / If you leave me now / Up where we belong / You don't bring me flowers / Imagine / Weekend in New England / Miss you nights / One day I'll fly away / Memory / With you I'm born again / One day in your life / Sun ain't gonna shine anymore
CD _____ CDMFP 5792
Music For Pleasure / Apr '90 / EMI.

COLOURS (Royal Philharmonic Orchestra)
Ochre / Red / Green / Sienna / Black / Mauve / Gold / Azure / Yellow / Grey
CD _____ PWK 1143
PWK Classics / Mar '90 / Carlton Home Entertainment / Complete/Pinnacle.

DREAMS (Royal Philharmonic Orchestra)
Unchained melody / Groovy kind of love / Everything I do (I do it for you) / Show me heaven / Take my breath away / My girl / Twin Peaks (Falling) / Second time (Bilitis) / Wind beneath my wings / It must have been love / Love changes everything / Music of the night / Any dream will do / Memory / Cavatina / Chariots of fire / Up where we belong / Hopelessly devoted to you / I've had the time of my life / Arthur's theme
CD _____ MOCD 3003
More Music / Feb '95 / Sound & Media.

GERSHWIN GOLD (Gershwin 50th Anniversary Tribute) (Royal Philharmonic Orchestra & Andrew Litton)
Rhapsody in blue / Swanee / Nobody but you / Do it again / Clap yo' hands / Who cares / Strike up the band / Sweet and low down / Somebody loves me / Bidin' my time / 'S wonderful / That certain feeling / Do do do / Lady be good / Man I love / I'll build a stairway to paradise / Embraceable

you / Fascinating rhythm / My one and only / Liza / I got rhythm
CD _____ CDRPD 9002
Carlton Home Entertainment / May '91 / Carlton Home Entertainment.

HOOKED ON CLASSICS, THE ULTIMATE COLLECTION (Royal Philharmonic Orchestra)
Symphony of the seas / Hooked on Mendelssohn / Hooked on classics (pts 1-3) / Dance of the furies / Hooked on romance / Hooked on Rodgers and Hammerstein / Night at the opera / Also sprach Zarathustra / Hooked on Bach / Journey through the classics / Scotland the brave / Tales of the Vienna woods / Can't stop the classics / Hooked on romance (part 2) / Hooked on baroque
CD _____ MCCD 003
Music Club / Feb '91 / Disc / THE / CM.

PLAY ABBA/BEATLES/QUEEN (Royal Philharmonic Orchestra)
CD _____ HRCD 8011
Kenwest / Nov '92 / THE.

PLAYS THE ROLLING STONES (Royal Philharmonic Orchestra)
CD _____ DCD 5296
Disky / Sep '93 / THE / BMG / Discovery / Pinnacle.

POP CLASSICS (Royal Philharmonic Orchestra)
CD Set _____ 24306
Laserlight / May '94 / Target/BMG.

POP GO THE BEATLES (Royal Philharmonic Pops Orchestra)
Maxwell's silver hammer / Strawberry fields / Something / Got to get you into my life / Imagine / Lady Madonna / Norwegian wood / Sergeant Pepper suite / I want to hold your hand / Can't buy me love / If I fell / Penny Lane / Jet / Ob la di ob la da / Michelle / Here, there and everywhere / Get back
CD _____ CO 33324
Denon / Oct '89 / Conifer.

St. PAUL'S CHRISTMAS CONCERT (Royal Philharmonic Orchestra)
Fantasy on Christmas carols (the holly and the ivy) / Sleepers, wake / Sussex mummers' Christmas carol / Legend / Spotless rose / Sleigh ride / Noble stem of Jesse / Est ist ein ros ensprungen / Christmas sequence / Bethlehem down / Maid peerless / New Year Carol / In Bethlehem city / I sing of a maiden / Christmas day
CD _____ CDRPO 7021
Carlton Home Entertainment / Oct '95 / Carlton Home Entertainment.

THEMES FOR LOVERS (Royal Philharmonic Orchestra)
CD _____ PWKS 4239
Carlton Home Entertainment / Feb '95 / Carlton Home Entertainment.

VERY BEST OF HOOKED ON CLASSICS (Clark, Louis & Royal Philharmonic Orchestra)
Hooked on classics (parts 1 & 2) / Hooked on Tchaikovsky / Hooked on a can can / Journey through the classics / Hooked on Haydn / If you knew sousa / Can't stop the classics / Hooked on romance (opus 3) / Hooked on romance / Hooked on a song / Hooked on Mozart / Journey through the classics #2
CD _____ PWKS 4017
Carlton Home Entertainment / Oct '90 / Carlton Home Entertainment.

Royal Scots Dragoon...

AMAZING GRACE (Royal Scots Dragoon Guards)
Amazing grace / Scotland the brave / Cornet carillon / Russian imperial anthem / Abide with me / Dark island / Ode 'An die Freude" (Song of joy) / Scottish soldier / Road to the isles / Drummer's call / Belmont (by cool Siloam's shady rill) / Bunessan / Banda / Little drummer boy / Standchen / Day is ended / Wooden heart / Going home
CD _____ ND 74884
RCA / Jun '91 / BMG.

AMAZING GRACE (Royal Scots Dragoon Guards)
CD _____ MATCD 249
Castle / Dec '92 / BMG.

AMAZING GRACE (Royal Scots Dragoon Guards)
Medley / Speed your journey (Song of the Hebrew slaves) / Moonliner rock march / Medley #7 / Y viva Espana / Medley #2 / Barock '75 / Medley #3 / Brazil / Tribute to Duthart / Medley #4 / Amazing grace / Una banda chacoa / 6/8 marches / Rock 'n' roll march / Largo / Theme in glory / Retreat airs / Rockout / 4/4 marches / Medley #5
CD _____ TRTCD 134
TrueTrax / Dec '94 / THE.

AMAZING GRACE (Royal Scots Dragoon Guards)
CD _____ 74321292802
RCA / Jul '95 / BMG.

IN THE FINEST TRADITION (Royal Scots Dragoon Guards Pipes & Drums)
Amazing grace / Three DG's / Send in the clowns / Symphonic marches of John Wil-

liams / Way old friends do / McPhedran's strathspey / Highland whiskey / Mermaid song / Troy's wedding / Mason's apron / Seventy Ninth farewell to Gibraltar / Highland cathedral / Scotland the brave / Black bear / Carillon / Going home / My home / Skye boat song / Irish air / Ballochmyle / Mrs. Lily Christie / Farewell to the creeks / Garb of old gaul / Moonstar
CD _____ BNA 5017
Bandleader / Jul '88 / Conifer.

ROYAL SCOTS DRAGOON GUARDS (Royal Scots Dragoon Guards)
Amazing grace / Gallowa' hills / Lili Marlene / Skye boat song / Black Watch polka / Battle of the Somme / Highland wedding / Mill in the Glen / Hills of home / Crossing the Rhine / Dovecote Park
CD _____ MCCD 105
MCI / May '93 / Disc / THE.

SCOTTISH SALUTE (Royal Scots Dragoon Guards)
CD _____ CDITV 455
Scotdisc / Jul '89 / Duncans / Ross / Conifer.

SECOND TO NONE (Royal Scots Dragoon Guards)
CD _____ LCOM 5248
Lismor / Aug '95 / Lismor / Direct / Duncans / ADA.

TUNES OF GLORY (Royal Scots Dragoon Guards)
CD _____ CDLOC 1069
Lochshore / Sep '94 / ADA / Direct / Duncans.

VERY BEST OF THE ROYAL SCOTS DRAGOON GUARDS, THE (Royal Scots Dragoon Guards)
Amazing grace / Little drummer boy / Scotland the brave / Highland laddie / Morning has broken / Ode to joy (ode 'an die freude) / Day is ended / Reveille / Scottish waltz / Hayken's serenade / Russian imperial anthem / Going home
CD _____ 74321339362
Camden / Jan '96 / BMG.

Royal Scottish Orchestra

CHRISTMAS FANFARE, A
Jingle bells / II est ne / Jesus ahatonia / We wish you a Merry Christmas / Ding dong merrily on high / Past 3 o'clock / O come, all ye faithful / Once in royal David's City / Torches / Christmas fantasy / Hark the herald angels sing / Good King Wenceslas / Great and mighty wonder / Christmas piece / Schneewalzer / Two Christmas pieces / Caribbean Christmas / Christmas song
CD _____ CDCA 923
Alpha / Nov '91 / Abbey Recording.

Royal Society Jazz...

ROYAL SOCIETY JAZZ ORCHESTRA (Royal Society Jazz Orchestra)
CD _____ SOSCD 1208
Stomp Off / Jan '93 / Jazz Music / Wellard.

Royal Tahitian Dance Co.

ROYAL TAHITIAN DANCE CO.
CD _____ MCD 71758
Monitor / Jun '93 / CM.

Royal Tank Regiment

IN CONCERT
CD _____ MMSB 444
Music Masters / May '95 / Target/BMG.

Royal, Teddy

KEEP ON MOVING ON
Smooth talk / Grits and gravy / Domani ti amo / London blues / Chickadee / Keep on moving on / Blossoms / Artie / Buck's groove
CD _____ SP 1002
Morning Groove / Dec '95 / New Note.

Royal Trux

CATS & DOGS
CD _____ WIGCD 6
Domino / Jul '93 / Pinnacle.

ROYAL TRUX
CD _____ WIGCD 5
Domino / Jun '93 / Pinnacle.

THANK YOU
Night to remember / Sewers of Mars / Ray O Vac / Map of the city / Granny grunt / Lights on the levee / Fear strikes out / (Have you met) Horror James / You're gonna lose / Shadow of the wasp
CD _____ CDHUT 23
Hut / Feb '95 / EMI.

TWIN INFINITIVES
CD _____ WIGCD 8
Domino / Jan '94 / Pinnacle.

Royal Ulster Constabulary

PIPE BANDS OF DISTINCTION
CD _____ CDMON 814
Monarch / Jul '94 / CM / ADA / Duncans / Direct.

Royal Welsh Fusiliers

TO THE BEAT OF A DRUM (Royal Welsh Fusiliers & Blaenavon Male Voice Choir)
Fanfare - the 300th / Men of Glamorgan / Lilliburlero / Grenadiers slow march / How stands the glass around / Quick march of the 23rd regiment / Marquis of Granby / Sospan fach / My Lord what a morning / Girl I left behind me / Lass of Richmond Hill / Calon lan / Soldiers of the Queen / Goodbye Dolly Gray / U.S. Marine Corps hymn / Myfyrmwy / We'll keep a welcome / Vive la Canadienne / Keep the home fires burning / It's a long way to Tipperary / March of the Grenadiers / Royal Welch Fusiliers / Wish me luck as you wave me goodbye / Rachie / Cwm Rhondda / That astonishing infantry / British Grenadiers / Men of Harlech / Land of my fathers (Hen wlad fy nhadau) / God save the Queen
CD _____ BNA 5026
Bandleader / Aug '89 / Conifer.

Roza, Lita

SOMEWHERE, SOMEHOW, SOMEDAY
That's the beginning of the end / I've got my eyes on you / Oh dear what can the matter be / But beautiful / I'll never say Never Again again / End of a love affair / Not mine / As children do / There's nothing better than love / Allentown jail / Once in a while / Nel blu di pinto di blu / This is my town / Maybe you'll be there / Sorry, sorry, sorry / I could have danced all night / All alone / Other woman / Love can change the stars
CD _____ C5CD-552
See For Miles/C5 / Jan '90 / Pinnacle.

Rozalla

EVERYBODY'S FREE - STYLE 1993
CD _____ PULSECD 11
Pulse 8 / Oct '93 / Pinnacle / 3MV.

LOOK NO FURTHER
I love music / You never love the same way twice / This time I found love / Baby / Look no further / Do you believe / Work me / If love is a dream / All that I need / Love work music (Mix) / Baby (Mix) / You never love the same way twice (Mix)
CD _____ 4779829
Epic / Mar '95 / Sony.

Rozario

SPANISH SONG RECITAL (Rozario/ Troop)
CD _____ 30522
Collins Classics / Aug '92 / Conifer.

Rua

AO-TEA-ROA
Music from the jungles of Caledonia / Raider / Jeltic music / Moon & St. Christopher / Caribbean celts / Allelujah / HAyfever / College boy / Band on the run / Eleanor Rigby / Waltzuraka / Winter's rage / Arrival in Auckland / Highland cream
CD _____ CDTRAX 103
Greentrax / Nov '95 / Conifer / Duncans / ADA / Direct.

HOMELAND
CD _____ CDTRAX 061
Greentrax / Mar '93 / Conifer / Duncans / ADA / Direct.

LIVE IN THE CATHEDRAL
CD _____ CDODE 1391
Ode / Jul '94 / CM / Discovery.

Rub Ultra

LIQUID BOOTS AND BOILED SWEETS
Brown box nitro (dog's life) / Blasted freak / Health horror and the vitamin urge / Oily man eel / Your nasty hair / Generate / Whale boy / Free toy / Cat's gone underground / Suspend your belief / Castles / Voodoo accident
CD _____ FLATCD 21
Hi Rise / Oct '95 / EMI / Pinnacle.

Rubalcaba, Gonzalo

DIZ
Hot house / Woody 'n' you / I remember Clifford / Donna Lee / Bouncing with Bud / Smooch / Ah-leu-cha / Night in Tunisia / Con Alma

CD _____ CDP 8304902
Blue Note / Sep '95 / EMI.

GIRALDILLA
Rumbero / Proyecto latino / Giraldilla / Campo finda / Encuentros / Presidente / Comienzo
CD _____ MES 158012
Messidor / Apr '93 / Koch / ADA.

IMAGINE - LIVE IN AMERICA
Imagine / Contagio / First song / Woody 'n' you / Circuilo II / Perfidia / Mima
CD _____ CDP 8304912
Blue Note / Jan '96 / EMI.

LIVE IN HAVANA 1986
CD _____ MES 158302
Messidor / May '95 / Koch / ADA.

LIVE IN HAVANA VOLS 1 & 2
CD _____ 15960
Ronnie Scott's Jazz House / Aug '89 / Jazz Music / Magnum Music Group / Cadillac.

MI GRAN PASION
CD _____ 15999
Messidor / Apr '89 / Koch / ADA.

Rubbersmell

INDIAN FLESH - INDIAN DOME
CD _____ CHILLUM 001
Chill Um / Jan '96 / Plastic Head.

Rubella Ballet

AT THE END OF THE RAINBOW
CD _____ BND 2CD
One Little Indian / Feb '90 / Pinnacle.

GREATEST TRIPS
CD _____ BND 3 CD
One Little Indian / Feb '90 / Pinnacle.

Ruben & The Jets

CON SAFOS
CD _____ EDCD 405
Edsel / Jan '95 / Pinnacle / ADA.

FOR REAL
CD _____ EDCD 406
Edsel / Nov '94 / Pinnacle / ADA.

Rubettes

BEST OF THE RUBETTES
Sugar baby love / Tonight / Under one roof / Judy run run / I'm just dreaming / I can do it / Jukebox jive / Little darlin' / Julia / Foe dee oh dee / You're the reason why / Sha na na song
CD _____ 843 896-2
Polydor / Sep '90 / PolyGram.

JUKE BOX JIVE
CD _____ GRF 213
Tring / Mar '93 / Tring / Prism.

Rubicon

ROOM 101
CD _____ BBQCD 170
Beggars Banquet / Apr '95 / Warner Music / Disc.

Rubin, Ruth

YIDDISH SONGS OF THE HOLOCAUST: A LECTURE/RECITAL
CD _____ GV 150CD
Global Village / May '94 / ADA / Direct.

Rubin, Vanessa

I'M GLAD THERE IS YOU (A Tribute To Carmen McRae)
Yardbird suite / I'm glad there is you / Midnight sun / Inside a silent tear / No strings attached / Alfie / Speak low / Easy living / Child is born / Send in the clowns
CD _____ 1241 63170-2
RCA / Jul '94 / BMG.

PASTICHE
In a sentimental mood / Simone / I'm just a lucky so and so / When love is new / Black Nile / I only have eyes for you / Mosaic / Estoy siempre junto a ti / Weekend / Crazy love / Arise and shine
CD _____ 01241631522
Novus / Apr '93 / BMG.

Ruby

SALT PETER
CD _____ CRECD 166
Creation / Oct '95 / 3MV / Vital.

Ruby Blue

GLANCES ASKANCES
Give us our flag back / Quiet mind / Just relax / So unlike me / Walking home / Meaning of life / Wintery day / Sitting in a cafe / Bless you
CD _____ RFCD 2
Red Flame / Feb '91 / Pinnacle.

Rucker, Vernis

STRANGER IN THE SHEETS
Fishin' for a man / You've been good for me / He's cheating on you / There must be

someone for me / Fever / There's a hurt where my heart used to be / Put love first / Then came you / Stormy Monday / Dead to right / Strangers in the sheets
CD _____ CDCH 508
Ace / Jan '94 / Pinnacle / Cadillac / Complete/Pinnacle.

Rude Boys

RUDE AWAKENINGS
Come on let's do this / Written all over your face / I feel for you / Heaven / Pressure / I'm going thru / Are you lonely for me / Fool for you / Never get enough of it (Not available on LP) / I need you (Not available on LP)
CD _____ 7567821212
East West / Jul '91 / Warner Music.

Rude Girls

MIXED MESSAGES
CD _____ FF 511CD
Flying Fish / '92 / Roots / CM / Direct / ADA.

Rudimentary Peni

DEATH CHURCH
CD _____ BOOB 004CD
Outer Himalayen / Apr '94 / SRD.

E.P.'S OF R.P.
CD _____ BOOB 003CD
Outer Himalayen / Sep '94 / SRD.

POPE ADRIAN 37TH PSYCHRISTIATRIC
CD _____ BOOB 005CD
Outer Himalayen / Sep '95 / SRD.

Rudolph, Adam

GIFT OF THE GNAWA
CD _____ FF 571CD
Flying Fish / May '93 / Roots / CM / Direct / ADA.

MOVING PICTURES
CD _____ FF 612CD
Flying Fish / Feb '93 / Roots / CM / Direct / ADA.

Ruf Der Heimat

RUF DER HEIMAT
CD _____ EFA 127652
Konnex / Aug '95 / SRD.

Ruff 2 Da Smoove

RUFF 2 DA SMOOVE
CD _____ CDBR 10
Body Rock / Feb '95 / Jetstar.

Ruffin, Jimmy

GREATEST MOTOWN HITS
What becomes of the broken hearted / Baby I've got it / I've passed this way before / Gonna give her all the love I've got / World so wide, nowhere to hide / Don't you miss me a little bit baby / Everybody needs love / It's wonderful (to be loved by you) / Gonna keep on tryin' till I win your love / This guy's in love with you / Farewell is a lonely sound / Stand by me / As long as there is l-o-v-e love / Sad and lonesome feeling / I'll say forever my love / Don't let him take your love from me / Maria / Living in a world I created for myself / Let's say goodbye tomorrow / He ain't heavy, he's my brother
CD _____ 530057-2
Motown / Jan '93 / PolyGram.

SON OF A PREACHER MAN
It's wonderful (to be loved by you) / 96 Tears / Things we have to do / Honey come back / You got what it takes / Turn back the hands of time / How can I say I'm sorry / Farewell is a lonely sound / I will never let you get away / Set 'em up (move in for the thrill) / I want her love / Since I've lost you / Your love was worth waiting for / Lonely, lonely man am I
CD _____ 5504092
Spectrum/Karussell / Aug '94 / PolyGram / THE.

Ruffins, Kermit

BIG BUTTER & EGG MAN, THE
CD _____ JR 11022
Justice / Jun '94 / Koch.

WORLD ON A STRING
CD _____ JR 001101
Justice / Apr '93 / Koch.

Ruffner, Mason

EVOLUTION
CD _____ PRD 70632
Provogue / May '94 / Pinnacle.

Ruffnexx Sound System

RUFFNEXX
CD _____ 9362456052
Warner Bros. / Jul '95 / Warner Music.

Ruins

BURNING STONE
Grubandgo / Onyx / Misonta / Power shift / Sac / Gold stone / Negotiation / Zasca coska / Praha in Spring / Spazm cambilist / Real jam / Burning stone / Vexoprakta
CD _____ SHIMMY 057CD
Shimmy Disc / Aug '92 / Vital.

STONEHENGE
CD _____ SDE 9025CD
Shimmy Disc / Jan '91 / Vital.

Ruiz, Hilton

HANDS ON PERCUSSION
Ornithology / Blues for cos / Mambo for vibes / Round Midnight / Cotton tail / Jack's tune / Like Sonny / Maneguitos way / Salute to Eddie
CD _____ 66058061
RMM / May '95 / New Note.

HEROES
Round Midnight / Sonny mood / Guataca / Little suede shoes / Lover man / For Maz / Maiden voyage / Con alma / Tune up / Praise
CD _____ CD 83338
Telarc / May '94 / Conifer / ADA.

LIVE AT BIRDLAND (Ruiz, Hilton Sextet)
CD _____ CCD 79532
Candid / Jul '93 / Cadillac / Jazz Music / Wellard / Koch.

SOMETHING GRAND (Ruiz, Hilton Ensemble)
Home cooking / Puerto Rican children / Four west / Something grand / Sunrise over Madarao / One step ahead
CD _____ PD 83011
RCA / Nov '87 / BMG.

STRUT
Sidewinder / Going back to New Orleans / Bluz / Aged in soul / All my love is yours / Soca serenade / Why don't you steal my blues / Lush life (Only on CD.)
CD _____ PD 83053
RCA / May '89 / BMG.

Ruiz, Jim

OH BROTHER WHERE ART THOU (Ruiz, Legendary Jim Group)
CD _____ MF 11
Minty Fresh / Jun '95 / SRD / Pinnacle.

Rule 62

LOVE AND DECLINE
Lonely / Life goes on / Still I pay / Belong here / I run / I believed / Don't ignore me / Obsolete machine / Friends / Stormy sea / Broken down
CD _____ AG 0752
Noise/Modern Music / Nov '95 / Pinnacle / Plastic Head.

Rum & Black

WITHOUT ICE
CD _____ SUADCD 3
Shut Up & Dance / Sep '91 / SRD.

Rumbata

ENCUENTROS
CD _____ CHR 70032
Challenge / Nov '95 / Direct / Jazz Music / Cadillac / ADA.

Rumbel, Nancy

NOTES FROM THE TREE OF LIFE
Tree of life / Lullaby / Night tribe / Anansi / Passing fancy / Song of hope / Dona nobis pacem / Coyote dance / Delicate balance / Satie
CD _____ ND 61050
Narada / Dec '95 / New Note / ADA.

Rumble

RUMBLE
Safe / Dontress / Suspect / Take me / Look at the kid / All I know / Serious ting / Crack song / Black man wagon / Follow me / Booyaka booyaka
CD _____ GEECD 12
Gee Street / Nov '93 / PolyGram.

Rumillajta

CITY OF STONE
CD _____ TUMICD 001
Tumi / '92 / Sterns / Discovery.

HOJA DE COCA
CD _____ TUMICD 002
Tumi / '92 / Sterns / Discovery.

PACHAMAMA
CD _____ TUMICD 003
Tumi / '92 / Sterns / Discovery.

WIRACOCHA
CD _____ RUM 1871CD
Rumillajta / Jan '90 / Sterns.

Rumors Of The Big Wave

BURNING TIMES
Nightmare / Only green world / Needle full of dreams / Stranger to you / Burning times / I choose life / Love has a body / Tenderness / Echo of a scream / Spirit in the wasteland
CD _____ 936242535-2
Warner Bros. / Jun '93 / Warner Music.

Rumour

FROGS SPROUTS CLOGS AND KRAUTS
CD _____ REP 4219-WY
Repertoire / Aug '91 / Pinnacle / Cadillac.

RUMOUR
Frogs / Sprouts / Clogs / Krauts
CD _____ STIFFCD 14
Disky / Jan '94 / THE / BMG / Discovery / Pinnacle.

Rump

HATING BRENDA
CD _____ CARCD 24
Caroline / Apr '94 / EMI.

Rumsey, Howard

LIGHTHOUSE ALL STARS
CD _____ OJCCD 154
Original Jazz Classics / Jun '95 / Wellard / Jazz Music / Cadillac / Complete/Pinnacle.

LIGHTHOUSE ALL STARS VOL. 6
CD _____ OJCCD 386
Original Jazz Classics / Jun '95 / Wellard / Jazz Music / Cadillac / Complete/Pinnacle.

MUSIC FOR LIGHTHOUSEKEEPING
(Rumsey, Howard Lighthouse All Stars)
CD _____ OJCCD 636-2
Original Jazz Classics / Feb '92 / Wellard / Jazz Music / Cadillac / Complete/Pinnacle.

Run C & W

ROW VS. WADE
Let me in / Medley: Hot corn, cold corn/I like it like that/Reach out / Hold what you've got / Signed, sealed, delivered (I'm yours) / Papa was a rollin' stone / Spanish Harlem / I second that emotion / Chain of fools / Bring it on home to me
CD _____ MCAD 11041
MCA / Nov '94 / BMG.

Run DMC

BACK FROM HELL
Sucker DJ's / What's it all about / Faces / Pause / Back from hell / Groove to the sound / Naughty / Not just another groove / Ave / Bob your head / Kick the frama lama lama / Word is born / Don't stop / P upon a tree / Livin' the city / Party time
CD _____ FILECD 401
Profile / Nov '90 / Pinnacle.

DOWN WITH THE KING
Down with the king / C'mon everybody / Can I get it yo / Hit 'em hard / To the maker / In the head / Ooh what ya gonna do / Big Willie / Three little indians / In the house / Kick it (can I get a witness) / Get open / What's next / Wreck shop / For ten years
CD _____ FILECD 440
Profile / May '93 / Pinnacle.

RUN D.M.C.
Hard times / Rock box / Jam-master Jay / It's like that (Crush-groove mix) / Sucker M.C.'s (Krush-groove 1) / It's like that / Wake up / Thirty days / Jay's game
CD _____ FILERCD 202
Profile / Apr '91 / Pinnacle.

RUN DMC TOGETHER FOREVER
(Greatest Hits 1983 - 91)
CD _____ FILERCD 419
Profile / Sep '91 / Pinnacle.

Run Dog Run

BEAUTY SCHOOL DROPOUT
CD _____ VOW 040CD
Voices Of Wonder / May '94 / Plastic Head.

HOWLING SUCCESS, A
CD _____ VOW 032C
Voices Of Wonder / Dec '93 / Plastic Head.

Run Westy Run

HARDLY, NOT EVEN
CD _____ SST 192 CD
SST / May '93 / Plastic Head.

RUN WESTY RUN
CD _____ SST 199 CD
SST / Feb '89 / Plastic Head.

Runaways

AND NOW...THE RUNAWAYS
Saturday night special / Eight days a week / Mama weer all crazee now / I'm a million / Right now / Take over / My buddy and me / Little lost girls / Black leather
CD _____ CDMGRAM 63
Cherry Red / Jun '93 / Pinnacle.

BORN TO BE BAD
CD _____ FM 1004CD
Marilyn / Jul '92 / Pinnacle.

Rundgren, Todd

ADVENTURES IN UTOPIA (Utopia)
Road to Utopia / You make me crazy / Second nature / Set me free / Caravan / Last of the new wave riders / Shot in the dark / Very last time / Love alone / Rock love
CD _____ 812270872-2
WEA / Mar '93 / Warner Music.

ANOTHER LIFE (Utopia)
Another life / Wheel / Seven ray's / Intro (Mister Triscuits) / Something's coming / Heavy metal kids / Do ya / Just one victory
CD _____ 8122708672
WEA / Jul '93 / Warner Music.

ANTHOLOGY (Utopia)
CD _____ 8122708922
Rhino / May '95 / Warner Music.

ANTHOLOGY
Open my eyes / We gotta get you a woman / Wailing wall / Be nice to me / Hello it's me / I saw the light / It wouldn't have made any difference / Couldn't I just tell you / Sometimes I don't know what to feel / Just one victory / Dream goes on forever / Last ride / Don't you ever learn / Real man / Black and white / Love of the common man / Cliches / All the children sing / Can we still be friends / You cried wolf / Time heals / Compassion / Hideaway / Bang the drum all day / Drive / Johnee jingo / Something to fall back on
CD _____ 8122714912
WEA / Jul '93 / Warner Music.

BACK TO BARS
CD _____ 812271109-2
WEA / Mar '93 / Warner Music.

BACK TO THE BARS
Real man / Love of the common man / Verb: To love / Love in action / Dream goes on forever / Sometimes I don't know what to think / Range war / Black and white / Last ride / Cliches / Don't you ever learn / Never never land / Black Maria / Zen archer / I'm so proud / Oh baby baby / La la means I love you / I saw the light / It wouldn't have made any difference / Eastern intrigues / Initiation / Couldn't I just tell you / Hello it's me
CD _____ 8122711092
East West / Feb '93 / Warner Music.

BALLAD OF TODD RUNDGREN
Long flowing robe / Ballad (Denny and Jean) / Bleeding / Wailing wall / Range war / Chain letter / Long time a long way to go / Boat on the Charles / Be nice to me / Hope I'm around / Parole / Remember me
CD _____ 812270863-2
WEA / Mar '93 / Warner Music.

DEFACE THE MUSIC (Utopia)
I just want to touch you / Crystal ball / Where does the world to go hide / Silly boy / Alone / That's not right / Take it home / Hoi poloi / Life goes on / Feel too good / Always take / All smiles / Everybody else is wrong
CD _____ 812270873-2
WEA / Mar '93 / Warner Music.

EVER POPULAR TORTURED ARTIST EFFECT, THE
Hideway / Influenza / Don't hurt yourself / There goes your baybay / Tin soldier / Emporer of the highway / Bang the drum all day / Drive / Chant
CD _____ 812270876-2
WEA / Mar '93 / Warner Music.

FAITHFUL
Happenings ten years time ago / Good vibrations / Rain / Most likely you'll go your way / Most likely you'll go mine / It was a lie now / Strawberry Fields forever / Black and white / Love of the common man / When I pray / Cliches / Verb: To love / Boogies (hamburger hell)
CD _____ 812270868-2
WEA / Mar '93 / Warner Music.

HEALING
Healer / Pulse / Flesh / Golden goose / Compassion / Shine / Healing (pts 1-3)
CD _____ 812270874-2
WEA / Mar '93 / Warner Music.

INITIATION, THE
Real man / Born to synthesize / Death of rock and roll / Eastern intrigues / Initiation / Fair warning / Treatise on cosmic fire / Fire in mind or solar fire / Fire of spirit or electric fire / Internal fire or fire by friction
CD _____ 812270866-2
WEA / Mar '93 / Warner Music.

NO WORLD ORDER LITE
CD Set _____ CDGRUB 30
Food For Thought / Sep '94 / Pinnacle.

OOPS SORRY WRONG PLANET (Utopia)
Trapped / Windows / Love in action / Martyr / Abandon city / Gangreen / Crazy lady blue / Back on the street / Marriage of heaven and hell / Mount Angel / Rape of the young / Love is the answer
CD _____ 812270870-2
WEA / Mar '93 / Warner Music.

RA (Utopia)
Overture (inst) from journey to the centre of the / Communion with the sun / Magic dragon theatre / Jealousy / Eternal love / Sunburst finish / Hiroshima / Singring and the glass guitar
CD _____ 812270869-2
WEA / Mar '93 / Warner Music.

REDUX 92: LIVE IN JAPAN (Utopia)
Fix your gaze / Zen machine / Trapped / Princess of the universe / Abandon city / Hammer in my heart / Swing to the right / Ikon / Hiroshima / Back on the street / Only human / Love in action / Caravan / Last of the new wave riders / One world / Love is the answer
CD _____ 812271185-2
WEA / Jun '93 / Warner Music.

RUNT
Broke down and busted / Believe in me / We got to get you a woman / Who's that man / Once burned / Devil's bite / I'm in the clique / There are no words / Let's swing / Birthday you said / Don't tie my hands / Birthday carol
CD _____ 812270862-2
WEA / Mar '93 / Warner Music.

SOMETHING ANYTHING
I saw the light / I wouldn't have made any difference / Wolfman Jack / Cold morning light / It takes two to tango / Sweeter memories / Intro / Breathless / Night the carousel burned down / Saving grace / Marlene / Song of the viking / I went to the mirror / Black Maria / One more day (no word) / Couldn't I just tell you / Torch song / Little red lights / Overture / Money: messin' with the kid / Dust in the wind / Piss Aaron / Hello it's me / Some folks is even whiter than me / You left me sore / Slut
CD _____ 812271107-2
WEA / Mar '93 / Warner Music.

SWING TO THE RIGHT (Rundgren, Todd & Utopia)
Swing to the right / Lysistrata / Up / Junk rock (million monkey's) / Shinola / For the love of money / Last dollar on earth / Fahrenheit 451 / Only human / One world
CD _____ 812270875-2
WEA / Mar '93 / Warner Music.

TODD
How about a little fanfare / I think you know / Spark of life / Elpee's worth of toons / Dream goes on forever / Lord Chancellor's nightmare / Drunken blue rooster / Last number 1 lowest common denomination / Useless begging / Sidewalk cafe / Izzat love / Heavy metal kids / In and out of the chakras we go / Don't you ever learn / Sons of 1984
CD _____ 812271108-2
WEA / Mar '93 / Warner Music.

TODD RUNDGREN'S UTOPIA
Utopia theme / Freak parade / Freedom fighters / Ikon
CD _____ 812270865-2
WEA / Mar '93 / Warner Music.

UTOPIA (Utopia)
Libertine / Bad little actress / Feet don't fail me now / Neck on up / Say yeah / Call it what you will / I'm looking at you but I'm talking to myself / Hammer in my heart / Burn three times / There goes my inspiration
CD _____ 8122707132
WEA / Jul '93 / Warner Music.

WIZARD, A TRUE STAR, A
International feel / Never never land / Tic tick tick it wears off / You / Need your head / Rock 'n' roll / Pussy / Dogfight giggle / You don't have to camp around / Flamingo / Zen archer / Just another onionhead / Da da dali / When the shit hits the fan / Sunset Boulevard / Le feel internacionale / Sometimes I don't know what to feel / Does anybody love you / I'm so proud / Ooo baby baby / La la means I love you / Cool jerk / Hungry for love / I don't want to tie you down / Is it my name / Just one victory
CD _____ 812270864-2
WEA / Mar '93 / Warner Music.

Rundqvist, Gosta

GOSTA RUNDQVIST & KRISTER ANDERSON (Rundqvist, Gosta & Krister Andersin)
CD _____ SITCD 9212
Sittel / Aug '94 / Cadillac / Jazz Music.

Runners

PHONETIC
Secret world / Crooked man / Journeying / Funk talk / C Sands / Phonetic / Hours / Stomp
CD _____ CDEYE 0010
i2i / Sep '95 / New Note.

Running Wild

BLACKHAND INN
CD _____ NCD 007
Noise / Jan '96 / Koch.

BLAZON STONE
CD _____ NCD 005
Noise / Jan '96 / Koch.

DEATH OR GLORY
Riding the storm / Renegade / Evilution / Running blood / Highland glory (the eternal flight) / Marooned / Bad to the bone / Tortuga bay / Death or glory / Battle of Waterloo / March on (CD only)
CD _____ NCD 004
Noise / Jan '96 / Koch.

FIRST YEARS OF PIRACY, THE
CD _____ N01842
Noise/Modern Music / Jan '92 / Pinnacle / Plastic Head.

MASQUERADE
CD _____ NO 2619
CD _____ NO 2612
Noise/Modern Music / Oct '95 / Pinnacle / Plastic Head.

PILE OF SKULLS
CD _____ NCD 006
Noise / Jan '96 / Koch.

Runrig

AMAZING THINGS
Amazing things / Wonderful / Greatest flame / Move a mountain / Pog aon oidche earraich (One kiss one spring evening) / Dream fields / Song of the earth / Forever eyes of blue / Sraidean na roinn Eorpa (Streets of Europe) / Canada / Ard / On the edge
CD _____ CDCHR 2000
Chrysalis / Mar '93 / EMI.

BIG WHEEL, THE
Headlights / Healer in your heart / abhainn an t-aluaigh / Always the winner / This beautiful pain / An cuibhle mor/The big wheel / Edge of the world / Hearthammer / I'll keep coming home / Flower of the West
CD _____ CCD 1858
Chrysalis / Jun '91 / EMI.

CUTTER AND THE CLAN, THE
Alba / Cutter / Hearts of olden glory / Pride of the summer / Worker for the wind / Rocket to the moon / Only rose / Protect and survive / Our earth was once green / Aubhal as airds
CD _____ CCD 1669
Chrysalis / May '95 / EMI.

HEARTLAND
CD _____ RRCD 005
Ridge / Feb '86 / Direct / Roots / Duncans / CM / ADA.

HIGHLAND CONNECTION, THE
CD _____ RRCD 001
Ridge / Aug '89 / Direct / Roots / Duncans / CM / ADA.

MARA
Day in a boat / Nothing but the sun / Mighty Atlantic/Mara theme / Things that are / Road and the river / Meadhan oidche air on acairseid / Wedding / Dancing floor / Thairis air a ghleann / Lighthouse
CD _____ CDCHR 6111
Chrysalis / Nov '95 / EMI.

ONCE IN A LIFETIME
Dance called America / Protect and survive / Chiu mi'n geamradh / Rocket to the moon / Going home / Cnoc na feille / Nightfall on Marsco / S to mo leannan / Skye / Loch Lomond
CD _____ CCD 1695
Chrysalis / Nov '88 / EMI.

PLAY GAELIC
Dusig mo run / Sguaban arbhair / Tillidh mi / Cnngal cridhn / Mach nponach peird a tha e / Sunndach / Air an traigh / De ni mi and puirt / An ros / Ceol an dannsa / Chiu mi'n geamradh / Cum 'ur n'airie
CD _____ LCOM 9026
Lismor / Jul '95 / Lismor / Direct / Duncans / ADA.

RECOVERY
CD _____ RRCD 002
Ridge / Aug '89 / Direct / Roots / Duncans / CM / ADA.

SEARCHLIGHT
News from Heaven / Every river / City of lights / Eirinn / Tir a'mhurain / World appeal / Tear down these walls / Only the brave / Siol ghoraidh / That final mile / Smalltown / Precious years
CD _____ CCD 1713
Chrysalis / Sep '89 / EMI.

TRANSMITTING LIVE
Urlar / Ard / Edge of the world / Greatest flame / Harvest moon / Wire / Precious years / Every river / Flower of the West / Only the brave / Alba / Pog aon oidche earraich (one kiss one spring evening)
CD _____ CDCHR 6090
Chrysalis / Nov '94 / EMI.

Rupaul

SUPERMODEL OF THE WORLD
Supermodel / Miss Lady DJ / Free your mind / Supernatural / House of love / Thinkin' bout you / Back to my roots / Prisoner of love / Stinky dinky / All of a sudden / Everybody dance / Shade shadey (now prance)
CD _____ CDUCR 2
Union City / Jul '93 / EMI.

Rupkina, Yanka

KALIMENKO DENKO
CD _____ HNCD 1334
Hannibal / May '89 / Vital / ADA.

Rusby, Kate

KATE RUSBY & KATHRYN ROBERTS
(Rusby, Kate & Kathryn Roberts)
CD _____ PRCD 01
Pure / May '95 / Direct.

Rush

2112
Lessons / Passage to Bangkok / Something for nothing / Tears / Twilight zone / 2112 overture / Temples of Syrinx / Discover / Presentation / Oracle / Dream / Soliloquy / Grand finale
CD _____ 822 545-2
Mercury / Apr '87 / PolyGram.

ALL THE WORLD'S A STAGE
Anthem / Bastille day / By-Tor and the snow dog / At the tobes of Hades / Across the Styx / Of the battle / Epilogue / Fly by night / In the mood / In the end / Lakeside park / Something for nothing / 2112 overture / Temples of syrinx / Presentation / Soliloquy / Grand finale / What you're doing / Working man / Finding my way
CD _____ 822 552-2
Mercury / Apr '87 / PolyGram.

CARESS OF STEEL
Bastille day / Fountain of Lamneth / In the valley / Didacts and narpets / No one at the bridge / Panacea / Bacchus plateau / Fountain / I think I'm going bald / Lakeside park / Necromancer / Into the darkness / Under the shadow / Return of the Prince
CD _____ 822 543-2
Mercury / Apr '87 / PolyGram.

CHRONICLES
Finding my way / Fly by night / Bastille day / 2112 overture / Temples of syrinx / Farewell to kings / Trees / Freewill / Tom Sawyer / Limelight / Subdivisions / Distant early warning / Big money / Force ten / Mystic rhythms (live) / Working man / Anthem / Lakeside Park / What you're doing (live) / Closer to the heart / La villa strangiato / Spirit of radio / Red Barchetta / Passage to Bangkok / New world man / Red sector A / Manhattan Project / Time stand still / Show don't tell
CD Set _____ 8389362
Vertigo / Sep '90 / PolyGram.

COUNTERPARTS
Animate / Stick it out / Cut to the chase / Nobody's hero / Between sun and moon / Alien shore / Speed of love / Double agent / Leave that thing alone / Cold fire / Everyday glory
CD _____ 756782528-2
WEA / Oct '93 / Warner Music.

EXIT... STAGE LEFT
Spirit of radio / Red Barchetta / YYZ / Passage to Bangkok / Closer to the heart / Beneath, between and behind / Jacob's ladder / Broon's bane / Trees / Xanadu / Freewill / Tom Sawyer / La villa strangiato
CD _____ 822 551-2
Mercury / Apr '87 / PolyGram.

FAREWELL TO KINGS, A
Farewell to Kings / Xanadu / Closer to the heart / Cinderella man / Madrigal / Cygni X-1
CD _____ 822 546-2
Mercury / Apr '87 / PolyGram.

FLY BY NIGHT
Anthem / Beneath, between and behind / Best I can / By-Tor and the snow dog / At the tobes of Hades / Across the Styx / Of the battle / Epilogue / Fly by night / In the end / Making memories / Rivendell
CD _____ 822 542-2
Mercury / Apr '87 / PolyGram.

GRACE UNDER PRESSURE
Distant early warning / After image / Red sector A / Enemy within / Body electric / Kid gloves / Red lenses / Between the wheels
CD _____ 818 476 2
Vertigo / Apr '84 / PolyGram.

HEMISPHERES
Mercury / Apr '87 / PolyGram.
CD _____ 822 547-2

HOLD YOUR FIRE
Force team / Time stand still / Open secrets / Prime mover / Lock and key / Tai Shan / High water
CD _____ 832 464 2
Vertigo / '88 / PolyGram.

MOVING PICTURES
Tom Sawyer / Red Barchetta / YYZ / Limelight / Camera / Witch hunt / (Part III of Fear) / Vital signs
CD _____ 800 048-2
Mercury / '83 / PolyGram.

PERMANENT WAVES
Spirit of radio / Freewill / Jacob's ladder / Entre nous / Different strings / Natural science
CD _____ 822 548-2
Mercury / Jan '83 / PolyGram.

POWER WINDOWS
Big money / Grand design / Manhattan Project / Marathon / Territories / Middletown dreams / Emotion detector / Mystic rhythms
CD _____ 826 098-2
Vertigo / Nov '85 / PolyGram.

PRESTO
Show don't tell / Chain lightning / Pass / War paint / Scars / Presto / Super conductor / Anagram (for Mongo) / Red tide / Hand over fist / Available light
CD _____ 782 040-2
Atlantic / Dec '89 / Warner Music.

ROLL THE BONES
Dreamline / Bravado / Roll the bones / Face up / Where's my thing / Big wheel / Heresy / Ghost of a chance / Neurotica / You bet your life
CD _____ 7567822932
Atlantic / Sep '91 / Warner Music.

RUSH
Before and after / Finding my way / Here again / In the mood / Need some love / Take a friend / What you're doing / Working man
CD _____ 822 541-2
Mercury / Apr '87 / PolyGram.

RUSH: INTERVIEW PICTURE DISC
CD P.Disc _____ CBAK 4055
Baktabak / Apr '92 / Baktabak.

SHOW OF HANDS, A
Big money / Subdivisions / Marathon / Turn the page / Manhattan project / Mission / Distant early warning / Mystic rhythms / Witch hunt / Rhythm method (drum solo) / Force ten / Time stands still / Red sector A / Closer to the heart
CD _____ 846 346-2
Vertigo / Jan '89 / PolyGram.

SIGNALS
Subdivisions / Analog kid / Chemistry / Digital man / Weapon / New world man / Losing it / Countdown
CD _____ 810 002-2
Mercury / '83 / PolyGram.

Rush, Bobby

I AIN'T STUDDIN' YOU
I ain't studdin' you / You, you, you (know what to do) / Hand jive / Blues singer / Thank you (for what you done) / You make me feel so good / Money honey / Time to the road again
CD _____ URG 4117 CD
Urgent / Nov '91 / Koch.

Rush, Jennifer

JENNIFER RUSH
Madonna's eyes / Twenty five lovers / Come give me your hand / Nobody move / Never gonna turn back again / Ring of ice / Into my dreams / I see a shadow (not a fantasy) / Surrender / Power of love
CD _____ 4609472
CBS / Oct '90 / Sony.

POWER OF JENNIFER RUSH, THE
Destiny / Heart over mind / Ring of ice / Ave Maria (Survivors of a different kind) / Power of love / Higher ground / Flames of paradise / Twenty five lovers / I come undone / Same heart / If you're ever gonna lose my love
CD _____ 4691632
Columbia / Feb '92 / Sony.

Rush, Otis

AIN'T ENOUGH COMIN' IN
Don't burn down the bridge / That will never do / Somebody have mercy / Fool for you / Homework / My jug and I / She's a good 'un / It's my own fault / Ain't enough comin' in / If I had any sense, I'd go back home / Ain't that good news / As the years go passing by
CD _____ 518769-2
This Way Up / Apr '94 / PolyGram / SRD.

CLASSIC RECORDINGS
All your love / Three times a fool / She's a good 'un / It takes time / Double trouble / My love will never die / My baby is a good 'un / Checking on my baby / Jump sister Bessie / I can't quit you baby / If you were mine / Groaning the blues / Keep on loving me baby / Sit down baby / Love that woman / Violent love / So many roads, so many trains / I'm satisfied / So close / You know my love / I can't stop baby
CD _____ CDCHARLY 217
Charly / Apr '90 / Charly / THE / Cadillac.

COLD DAY IN HELL
CD _____ DD 638
Delmark / Jul '93 / Hot Shot / CM / Direct / Cadillac.

DOUBLE TROUBLE (Charly Blues - Masterworks Vol. 24)
All your love / Three times a fool / She's a good 'un / It takes time / Double trouble / My love will never die / My baby is a good 'un / Checking on my baby / Jump sister Bessie / I can't quit you baby / If you were mine / Groaning the blues / Keep on loving me baby / Sit down baby / Love that woman / Violent love
CD _____ CDBM 24
Charly / Apr '92 / Charly / THE / Cadillac.

DOUBLE TROUBLE - LIVE IN JAPAN 1986
Introduction/Tops / All your love / Please, please, please / Killing floor / Stand by me / Lonely man / Double trouble / Right place, wrong time / Got my mojo working / Gambler's blues
CD _____ NEGCD 217
Sequel / Oct '95 / BMG.

LIVE IN EUROPE
Cut you loose / All your love / You're breaking my heart / I wonder why / Feel so bad / Society woman/Love is just a gamble / Crosscut saw / I can't quit you baby / I'm tore up / Looking back
CD _____ ECD 260342
Evidence / Sep '93 / Harmonia Mundi / ADA / Cadillac.

LOST IN THE BLUES
Hold that tiger / You've been an angel / Little red rooster / Trouble, trouble / Please love me / You don't have to go / Got to be some changes made / You got me runnin' / I miss you so
CD _____ ALCD 4797
Alligator / Aug '92 / Direct / ADA.

SCREAMIN' & CRYIN'
CD _____ ECD 260142
Evidence / Jan '92 / Harmonia Mundi / ADA / Cadillac.

SO MANY ROADS
CD _____ DE 643
Blind Pig / Dec '95 / Hot Shot / Swift / CM / Roots / Direct / ADA.

TOPS
Right place, wrong time / Crosscut saw / Tops / Feels so bad / Gambler's blues / Keep on loving me baby / I wonder why
CD _____ BP 3188CD
Blind Pig / May '94 / Hot Shot / Swift / CM / Roots / Direct / ADA.

Rush, Tom

BLUES, SONGS AND BALLADS
Duncan and Brady / I don't want your millions mister / San Francisco Bay blues / Mole's moan / Rye whiskey / Big fat woman / Nine pound hammer / Diamond Joe / Mobile Texas line / Joe Turner / Every day in the week / Alabamy bound / More pretty girls / I wish I could shimmy like my sister Kate / Original talking blues / Pallet on the floor / Drop down mama / Rag mama / Barb'ry Allen / Cocaine / Come back baby / Stagger Lee / Baby, please don't go
CD _____ CDWIK 948
Big Beat / Aug '90 / Pinnacle.

CIRCLE GAME
Tin angel / Something in the way she moves / Urge for going / Sunshine sunshine / Glory of love / Shadow dream song / Circle game / No regrets / Rockport Sunday / So long
CD _____ 755960659-2
WEA / Oct '93 / Warner Music.

Rushing, Jimmy

BLUES SINGER 1929-37, THE
CD _____ JZCD 344
Suisa / Jan '93 / Jazz Music / THE.

BLUES SINGER 1937-38, THE
CD _____ JZCD 345
Suisa / Jan '93 / Jazz Music / THE.

MR. FIVE BY FIVE
CD _____ TPZ 1017
Topaz Jazz / May '95 / Pinnacle / Cadillac.

TWO SHADES OF BLUE (Rushing, Jimmy & Jack Dupree)
Way I feel / In the moonlight / She's mine, she's yours / Go get some more you fool / Somebody's spoiling these women / Walking the blues / Harelip blues / Overhead blues / Silent partner / Everybody's blues
CD _____ TKOCD 022
TKO / May '92 / TKO.

YOU AND ME THAT USED TO BE, THE
You and me that used to be / Fine and mellow / When I grow too old to dream / I surrender dear / Linger awhile / Bei mir bist du schon / My last affair / All God's chillun got rhythm / More than you know / Home / Thanks a million
CD _____ ND 86460
Bluebird / Apr '89 / BMG.

Russell Family

OF DOOLIN, COUNTY CLARE
Campbell's reel / Heather breeze/The Traveller / St. Kevin of Glendalough / Potlick/The Peeler's jacket / Five mile chase / Russell's hornpipe/Fisher's hornpipe / Poor little fisher boy / Walls of Liscarroll/The battering ram / Garrett Barry's reel / Tommy glenny's reel / Connemara stockings/The Westmeath hunt / When Musheen went to Bunnan / Tatter Jack Walsh / De'il among the tailors / Roscrea cows / Fair haired boy/The black haired lass / Off to California / Give the girl her fourpence / Nora Daly
CD _____ GLCD 3079
Green Linnet / May '93 / Roots / CM / Direct / ADA.

RUSSELL FAMILY OF DOOLIN, CO. CLARE, THE
Campbell's reel / Heather breeze/The traveller / St. Kevin of Glendalough / Potlick/The peeler's jacket / Five mile chase / Russell's hornpipe/Fisher's hornpipe / Poor little fisher boy / Walls of Liscarroll/The battering ram / Garrett Barry's reel / Tommy Glenny's reel / Connemara stockings/The westmeath hunt / When Musheen went to Bunnan / Tatter Jack Walsh / De'il among the tailors / Roscrea cows / Fair haired boy/The black haired lass / Off to California / Give the girl her fourpence / Nora Daly
CD _____ OSS 8CD
Ossian / Jan '94 / ADA / Direct / CM.

Russell, Brenda

GREATEST HITS
Piano in the dark / So good, so right / Gravity / Kiss me with the wind / Get here / Dinner with Gershwin / Stop running away / In the thick of it / If only for one night / Way back when / Justice in truth / Le restaurant
CD _____ CDMID 171
A&M / Oct '92 / PolyGram.

Russell, Calvin

CRACK IN TIME, A
Crack in time / Big brother / Nothin' / Behind the eight ball / Automated / North Austin slim / One step ahead / Living at the end of a gun / I should have been home / My way / This is my life / Little stars / Moments / Wagon to stars
CD _____ 422303
New Rose / May '94 / Direct / ADA.

DREAM OF THE DOG
CD _____ 422020
Last Call / Apr '95 / Direct.

LE VOYAGEUR
CD _____ 422489
New Rose / Jan '95 / Direct / ADA.

SOLDIER
CD _____ 422422
New Rose / May '94 / Direct / ADA.

SOUNDS FROM THE FOURTH WORLD
CD _____ 422306
New Rose / Nov '94 / Direct / ADA.

Russell, Devon

DARKER THAN BLUE
CD _____ CSCD 2
Sweetest / Nov '93 / Jetstar / Roots Collective.
CD _____ CDSGP 0142
Prestige / Apr '95 / Total/BMG.

MONEY SEX AND VIOLENCE
CD _____ RNCD 0010
RN / Jan '91 / Jetstar.

Russell, George

ELECTRONIC SONATA FOR SOULS LOVED BY NATURE (1968)
Part 1 / Part 2
CD _____ 121034-2
Soul Note / Jan '94 / Harmonia Mundi / Wellard / Cadillac.

EZZ-THETICS (Russell, George Sextet)
CD _____ OJCCD 070
Original Jazz Classics / Oct '92 / Wellard / Jazz Music / Cadillac / Complete/Pinnacle.

LIVE IN AN AMERICAN TIME SPIRAL (Russell, George New York Band)
CD _____ SNCD 1049
Soul Note / '86 / Harmonia Mundi / Wellard / Cadillac.

LONDON CONCERT VOL. 1 (Russell, George Living Time Orchestra)
CD _____ STCD 560
Stash / May '93 / Jazz Music / CM / Cadillac / Direct / ADA.

LONDON CONCERT VOL. 2 (Russell, George Living Time Orchestra)
CD _____ STCD 561
Stash / May '93 / Jazz Music / CM / Cadillac / Direct / ADA.

LONDON CONCERT, THE (Live at Ronnie Scott's, August 1928-31) (Russell, George Living Time Orchestra)
CD Set _____ LBLC 6527/8
Label Bleu / Nov '95 / New Note.

NEW YORK BIG BAND
CD _____ SNCD 1039
Soul Note / '86 / Harmonia Mundi / Wellard / Cadillac.

OTHELLO BALLET SUITE/ELECTRONIC ORGAN SONATA 1
CD _____ 121 014 2
Soul Note / Oct '90 / Harmonia Mundi / Wellard / Cadillac.

OUTER VIEW
CD _____ OJCCD 616
Original Jazz Classics / Jun '95 / Wellard / Jazz Music / Cadillac / Complete/Pinnacle.

VERTICAL FORM VI
CD _____ 1210192
Soul Note / Nov '90 / Harmonia Mundi / Wellard / Cadillac.

Russell, Hal

CONSERVING NRG (Russell, Hal & NRG Ensemble & Charles Tyler)
Rusty nails / Blue over you / OJN / Pontiac / Sine die / Overbite / Song singing to you / Swing sting / Linda's rock vamp
CD _____ PJP CD02
Principally Jazz / Feb '91 / Cadillac.

FINISH SWISS TOUR, THE
Monica's having a baby / Aila/35 basic / Temporarily / Raining violets / For MC / Dance of the spider people / Ten letters of love / Hal the weenie / Linda's rock vamp / Mars theme
CD _____ 5112612
ECM / Oct '91 / New Note.

GENERATION (Russell, Hal & NRG Ensemble & Charles Tyler)
Sirus up / Poodle cut / Sponge / Tatwas / Cascade / Generation
CD _____ CHIEFCD 5
Chief / Jun '89 / Cadillac.

HAL RUSSELL STORY
Intro and fanfare / Toy parade / Trumpet march / Riverside jump / Krupa / You're blase / Dark rapture / World class / Wood chips / My little grass shack / O and B / For M / Gloomy Sunday / Hair male / Bossa G / Mildred / Dope music / Two times two / Ayler song / Rehcabnettul / Steve's freedom principle / Lady in the lake / Oh well
CD _____ 5173642
ECM / Jun '93 / New Note.

Russell, Janet

BRIGHT SHINING MORNING
CD _____ HARCD 026
Harbour Town / Oct '93 / Roots / Direct / CM / ADA.

DANCIN' CHANTIN' (Russell, Janet & Christine Kydd)
Rattlin' roarin' Willie / Fisherman's wife / Logan water / Les filles des forges / Maire Nighean Alastair / Up and awa' wi' the laverock / Duncan Gray / Lady Mary Anne / Reel o' stumpie / Tail toddle / Terror time / Strathmartine Braes / Clerk Saunders / La Caille / Pride's awa' / Bluebell polka / Parting glass / Jock since ever
CD _____ CDTRAX 077
Greentrax / Sep '94 / Conifer / Duncans / ADA / Direct.

JANET RUSSELL AND CHRISTINE KYDD (Russell, Janet & Christine Kydd)
Buy broom besoms / Dainty Davie / Up wi' the Carls o'Dysart / De'il is awa' wi' tha exciseman / Deja mal Mariee / Bonnie at morn / Children of Africa / My Donald / Ode to big blue / Tae the weavers gin ye gang / Old and strong / Mountain song / Do you love an apple / Last carol / Stand up fight for your rights / Everyone 'neath a vine and fig tree
CD _____ CDTRAX 011
Greentrax / Aug '93 / Conifer / Duncans / ADA / Direct.

Russell, Luis

1930-34 (Russell, Luis & His Orchestra)
CD _____ CLASSICS 606
Classics / Oct '92 / Discovery / Jazz Music.

COLLECTION 1926-34, THE
CD _____ COCD 7
Collector's Classics / May '93 / Cadillac / Complete/Pinnacle.

LUIS RUSSELL (1926-1929)
CD _____ CLASSICS 588
Classics / Aug '91 / Discovery / Jazz Music.

LUIS RUSSELL AND HIS ORCHESTRA VOL. 1 (Russell, Luis & His Orchestra)
CD _____ VILCD 0182
Village Jazz / Aug '92 / Target/BMG / Jazz Music.

SAVOY SHOUT
CD _____ JSPCD 308
JSP / Aug '80 / ADA / Target/BMG / Direct / Cadillac / Complete/Pinnacle.

Russell, Micho

LIMESTONE ROCK, THE
CD _____ GTDHCD 104
GTD / Jul '93 / Else / ADA.

MAN FROM CLARE, THE
CD _____ TRADHCD 011
GTD / Jul '93 / Else / ADA.

Russell, Pee Wee

INDIVIDUALISM OF PEE WEE RUSSELL, THE
Love is just around the corner / Squeeze me / Ballin' the Jack / I'd do most anything for you / California here I come / St. James infirmary / Baby, won't you please come home / Lady's in love with you / Struttin' with some barbecue / St. Louis blues / Sweet Lorraine / Sentimental journey / If I had you / Coquette / Lady is a tramp
CD _____ SV 0271
Savoy Jazz / Sep '95 / Conifer / ADA.

Russell, Tom

JAZZ REUNION (Russell, Pee Wee & Coleman Hawkins)
If I could be with you one hour tonight / Tin tin deo / Mariooch / All too soon / 29th and 8th / What am I here for
CD _____ CCD 9020
Candid / Jul '88 / Cadillac / Jazz Music / Wellard / Koch.

LAND OF JAZZ
CD _____ TPZ 1018
Topaz Jazz / Apr '95 / Pinnacle / Cadillac.

PORTRAIT OF PEE WEE
CD _____ FSCD 126
Fresh Sound / Jan '91 / Jazz Music / Discovery.

WE'RE IN THE MONEY
CD _____ BLCD 760909
Black Lion / Jan '89 / Jazz Music / Cadillac / Wellard / Koch.

Russell, Tom

BEYOND St. OLAV'S GATE 1979-1992 (Best Of Tom Russell)
CD _____ RTMCD 40
Round Tower / Apr '93 / Pinnacle / ADA / Direct / BMG / CM.

BOX OF VISIONS
CD _____ RTMCD 54
Round Tower / May '93 / Pinnacle / ADA / Direct / BMG / CM.

COWBOY REEL
El Liano / Bad half hour / Basque / Claude Dallas / Navajo rug / Indian cowboy / Gallo del cielo / Rayburn Crane / Sonora's death row / Zane grey / Roanie
CD _____ MRCD 161
Munich / '92 / CM / ADA / Greensleeves / Direct.

HEART ON A SLEEVE
One and one / Heart on a sleeve / Blinded by the light of love / Touch of grey / Wild hearts / St. Olav's gate / Gallo del cielo / Mandarin oranges / Cropduster / Canadian whiskey / Chinese silver / Bowl of red
CD _____ BCD 15243
Bear Family / Aug '86 / Rollercoaster / Direct / CM / Swift / ADA.

HURRICANE SEASON (Russell, Tom Band)
Black pearl / Lord of the trains / Beyond the blues / Jack Johnson / Chocolate cigarette / Winnipeg / Evangeline hotel / Dollars worth of gasoline / Hurricane season / Haley's comet
CD _____ RTMCD 49
Round Tower / Jan '93 / Pinnacle / ADA / Direct / BMG / CM.

POOR MAN'S DREAM (Russell, Tom Band)
Blue wing / Heart of the working man / Veteran's day / Walkin' on the moon / Outbound plane / Bergenfield / Spanish burgundy / Gallo del cielo / La frontera / Navajo rug / Under the gun / White trash song
CD _____ RTMCD 48
Round Tower / Apr '94 / Pinnacle / ADA / Direct / BMG / CM.

ROAD TO BAYAMON (Russell, Tom Band)
Home before dark / U.S. Steel / Downtown train / Love makes a fool of the wise / Definition of a fool / As the crow flies / Road to Bayamon / Alkali / Wise blood / Joshua tree / Mescal / William Faulkner in Hollywood / Fire
CD _____ PH 1116CD
Philo / '89 / Direct / CM / ADA.

ROSE OF THE SAN JOAQUIN, THE
CD _____ RTMCD 71
Round Tower / Oct '95 / Pinnacle / ADA / Direct / BMG / CM.

Russki Color

RUSSKI COLOR (Traditional folk melodies from Russia)
CD _____ LDX 274955
La Chant Du Monde / Jan '93 / Harmonia Mundi / ADA.

Russo, Marc

WINDOW, THE
Southern tale / Shake / Intro / Window / Crooked numbers / Elizabeth / Whatever you want / Weekend / School / In the rain / Notes next to the notes
CD _____ JVC 20352
JVC / Jul '94 / New Note.

Russo, Rafa

DESPITE MYSELF
CD _____ MAUVE D002
Mauve / Mar '94 / Pinnacle.

Rustavi Choir

GEORGIAN VOICES
CD _____ 7559792242
Elektra Nonesuch / Jan '95 / Warner Music.

Rusted Root

WHEN I WOKE
Drum trip / Ecstasy / Send me on my way / Cruel sun / Cat turned blue / Beautiful people / Martyr / Rain / Food and creative love / Lost in a crowd / Laugh as the sun / Infinite tamboura / Back to the Earth
CD _____ 5227132
Mercury / Aug '95 / PolyGram.

Rustichelli, Paolo

MYSTIC JAZZ
CD _____ 5134152
PolyGram Jazz / Apr '92 / PolyGram.

Ruth Ruth

LAUGHING GALLERY
Uninvited / Uptight / All ready down / Bald Marie / Mission idiot / Amnesia / Neurotica / Don't shut me out / Pervert / I killed Meg the prom Queen / I grew up / EQ master
CD _____ 74321302772
American / Nov '95 / BMG.

Rutherford, Mike

SMALLCREEPS DAY
Between the tick and the tock / Working in line / After hours / Cats and rats in this neighbourhood / Smallcreep alone / Out into the daylight / At the end of the day / Moonshine / Time and time again / Romani / Every road / Overnight job
CD _____ CASCD 1149
Charisma / Jun '89 / EMI.

Rutherford, Paul

1989 AND ALL THAT (Rutherford, Paul & George Haslam)
CD _____ SLAMCD 301
Slam / Oct '90 / Cadillac.

Ruthless Blues

RUTHLESS BLUES
Fine, fine, fine / Better things to do / Never told me why / Too many drivers / Solid gold mustang / Tie me up / Maintenance man / Tightrope blues / Ain't no love in the heart of the city
CD _____ PCOM 1102
President / Mar '93 / Grapevine / Target/BMG / Jazz Music / President.

SURE ENOUGH
Stomp (is that the blues) / Rollin' drunk / Can I see you tonight / Handle / This time / Bad case of lovin' you (Doctor Doctor) / Nursery rhyme blues / Break my back / Women problems / Born under a bad sign / Lowdown blues
CD _____ PCOM 1122
President / Jun '92 / Grapevine / Target/BMG / Jazz Music / President.

Ruthless Rap Assassins

THINK - IT AIN'T ILLEGAL YET
What did you say your name was / Listen to the hit / Why me / Think / Hard and direct / I got no time / Radio / Down and dirty / No tale, no twist / Pick up the pace / (I try to) flow it out / Less mellow
CD _____ CDEMC 3604
Murdertone / Oct '91 / Pinnacle.

Ruts

CRACK, THE
Babylon's burning / Dope for guns / O.U.O. / Something that I said / You're just a... / It was cold / Savage circle / Jah war / Criminal mind / Backwater / Out of order / Human punk
CD _____ CDV 2132
Virgin / Jul '90 / EMI.

DEMOLITION DANCING
CD _____ RRCD 182
Receiver / Apr '94 / Grapevine.

LIVE AND LOUD
Something that I said / H-Eyes / Gotta little number / I ain't sophisticated / Babylon's burning / Backbiter / Out of order / Jah war / Criminal mind / In a rut / Blue suede shoes / Ditty part 1 / Society / Love song / Ditty part 2
CD _____ LINK CD 013
Street Link / Oct '92 / BMG.

PEEL SESSIONS: RUTS (Complete Sessions 1979-81)
Savage circle / Babylon's burning / Dope for guns / Black mans pinch / Criminal mind / S.U.S. / Society / You're just a... / It was cold / Something that I said / Staring at the rude boys / Demolition dancing / In a rut / Secret soldiers
CD _____ SFRCD 109
Strange Fruit / Jun '90 / Pinnacle.

RHYTHM COLLISION DUB VOL.1 (Ruts D.C. & Mad Professor)
CD _____ RE 151CD
Reach Out International / Nov '94 / Jetstar.

RULES
CD _____ EFA 12303-2
Vince Lombard / Jul '94 / SRD.

Ryder, Mitch

SOMETHING THAT I SAID (The best of The Ruts)
In a rut / H-eyes / Babylon's burning / Dope for guns / S.U.S. / Something that I said / You're just a... / It was cold / Savage circle / Jah war / Criminal mind / Backbiter / Out of order / Human punk / Staring at the rude boys / Love in vain / West one (Shine on me)
CD _____ CDOVD 454
Virgin / Feb '95 / EMI.

Ruzicka, Karel

YOU'RE NEVER ALONE
CD _____ CR 0012-2
Czech Radio / Nov '95 / Czech Music Enterprises.

Ryan, Barry

ELOISE
Love is love / Kitsch / Hunt / My mama / I'm sorry Susan / From my head to my toe / Can't let you go / Eloise / Colour of my love / We did it together / It is written / Caroline / Love always comes tomorrow / Goodbye
CD _____ 5503852
Spectrum/Karussell / Jan '95 / PolyGram / THE.

Ryan, Marion

AT HER BEST
CD _____ C5MCD 614
See For Miles/C5 / Jun '94 / Pinnacle.

Ryan, Seán

MINSTREL'S FANCY
CD _____ CEFCD 169
Gael Linn / Dec '95 / Roots / CM / Direct / ADA.

TAKE THE AIR
CD _____ CEFCD 142
Gael Linn / Jan '94 / Roots / CM / Direct / ADA.

Ryce, Daryle

UNLESS IT'S YOU
CD _____ ACD 271
Audiophile / Apr '93 / Jazz Music / Swift.

Rydell, Bobby

BEST OF BOBBY RYDELL
CD _____ CDSGP 0156
Prestige / Jul '95 / Total/BMG.

Ryder, Anna

EYE TO EYE
CD _____ RM 01CD
Rowdy / Oct '93 / ADA.

Ryder, Mitch

BREAKOUT (Ryder, Mitch & The Detroit Wheels)
Walking the dog / I had it made / In the midnight hour / Ooh poo pah doo / I like it like that / Little latin lupe lu / Medley (Devil with a blue dress on/Good golly Miss Molly) / Shakin' with Linda / Stubborn kind of fellow / You get your kicks / Any day now / Breakout
CD _____ CDSC 6008
Sundazed / Jan '94 / Rollercoaster.

DETROIT MEMPHIS EXPERIMENT, THE
CD _____ REP 4117-WZ
Repertoire / Aug '91 / Pinnacle / Cadillac.

HOW I SPENT MY VACATION/NAKED BUT NOT DEAD
CD Set _____ LICD 921192
Line / Mar '92 / CM / Grapevine / ADA / Conifer / Direct.

LA GASH
It must be in her genes / Argyle / Do you feel alright / Child of rags / Bye bye love / Dr. Margaret Smith / It's your birthday / Arms without love / Correct me if I'm wrong / One thing / Almost bigamy / Terrorist / Long neck goose
CD _____ LICD 901180
Line / Apr '92 / CM / Grapevine / ADA / Conifer / Direct.

MITCH RYDER
CD _____ CSAPCD 111
Connoisseur / Oct '92 / Pinnacle.

RITE OF PASSAGE
See her again / Sex you up / Actually 101 / It wasn't me / Are we helpless / Into the blue / Mercy / Too sentimental / Let it shine / Herman's garden / I'm starting all over again / By the feel
CD _____ 901285
Line / Sep '94 / CM / Grapevine / ADA / Conifer / Direct.

SOCK IT TO ME (Ryder, Mitch & The Detroit Wheels)
Sock it to me baby / I can't hide it / Takin' all I can get / Slow fizz / Walk on by / I never had it better / Shakedown / Face in the crowd / I'd rather go to jail / Wild child / Medley (Too many fish in the sea/Three little

fishes) / You are my sunshine / Ruby baby and peaches on a cherry tree
CD _____ CDSC 6009
Sundazed / Jan '94 / Rollercoaster.

TAKE A RIDE (Ryder, Mitch & The Detroit Wheels)
Shake a tail feather / Come see about me / Let your love light shine / Just a little bit / I hope / Jenny take a ride / Please please please / I'll go crazy / I got you / Sticks and stones / Bring it on home to me / Baby Jane (mo-mo Jane) / Joy
CD _____ CDSC 6007
Sundazed / Jan '94 / Rollercoaster.

Ryerson, Ali

BLUE FLUTE
CD _____ 4715762
Sony Jazz / May '94 / Sony.

PORTRAIT IN SILVER
Windows / Beatrice / Ausencia / Shadow-light / Beautiful love / Zingaro / Very early / Jardin de la paresse / Lament / Summer knows
CD _____ CCD 4638
Concord Jazz / Apr '95 / New Note.

Rykers

BROTHER AGAINST BROTHER
CD _____ LF 102CD
Lost & Found / Oct '94 / Plastic Head.

FIRST BLOOD
CD _____ LF 187CD
Lost & Found / Oct '95 / Plastic Head.

PAYBACK TIME
CD _____ LF 080CD
Lost & Found / Jun '94 / Plastic Head.

Ryman, John

ARTIFICE AND ARCHITECTURE
CD _____ MILL 006MCD
Millenium / Nov '94 / Plastic Head.

Rymes With Orange

PEEL
CD _____ RW 08882
TKO / Sep '94 / TKO.

Rypdal, Terje

AFRICA PEPPERBIRD (Rypdal, Terje & Jan Garbarek)
Sharabee / Mahjong / Beast of Kommodo / Blow away zone / MYB / Concentus / Africa pepperbird / Blupp
CD _____ 8434752
ECM / Oct '90 / New Note.

AFTER THE RAIN
Autumn breeze / Air / Now and then / Wind / After the rain / Kjare maren / Little bell / Vintage year / Multer / Like a child, like a song
CD _____ 5231592
ECM / Jul '95 / New Note.

BLUE (Rypdal, Terje & Chasers)
Curse / Kompet Gar / I disremember quite well / Og hva synes vi om det / Last nite / Blue / Tanga / Om bare
CD _____ 8315162
ECM / Jul '87 / New Note.

CHASER
Ambiguity / Once upon a time / Geysir / Closer look / Orion / Chaser / Transition / Imagi (theme)
CD _____ 8272562
ECM / Dec '85 / New Note.

DESCENDRE
Askjed / Circles / Innseiling / Men of mystery / Speil
CD _____ 8291182
ECM / Jun '86 / New Note.

EOS (Rypdal, Terje & David Darling)
Eos / Bedtime story / Light years / Melody / Mirage / Adagietto / Laser
CD _____ 8153332
ECM / Sep '88 / New Note.

IF MOUNTAINS COULD SING
Return of per ulv / It's in the air / But on the other hand / If mountains could sing / Private eye / Foran peisen / Dancing without reindeers / One for the roadrunner / Blue angel / Genie / Lonesome guitar
CD _____ 5239872
ECM / Feb '95 / New Note.

ODYSSEY
CD _____ 8353552
ECM / Sep '88 / New Note.

Q.E.D
Quod erat demonstradum opus 52 1st-5th movements / Largo Opus 55
CD _____ 5133742
ECM / Jan '92 / New Note.

RYPDAL/VITOUS/DEJOHNETTE (Rypdal, Terje/Miroslav Vitous/Jack Dejohnette)
Sunrise / Den forste sne / Will / Believer / Flight / Seasons
CD _____ 8254702
ECM / Aug '85 / New Note.

SART (Rypdal, Terje/Stenson/Jan Garbarek)
CD _____ 8393052
ECM / Nov '89 / New Note.

SINGLES COLLECTION, THE
CD _____ 8377492
ECM / Apr '89 / New Note.

TERJE RYPDAL
Keep it like that tight / Rainbow / Electric fantasy / Lontano II / Tough enough
CD _____ 5276452
ECM / Jul '95 / New Note.

TO BE CONTINUED (Rypdal, Terje/Miroslav Vitous/Jack Dejohnette)
Maya / Mountains in the clouds / Morning-lake / To be continued / This morning / Top-plue, vooter and skjerf / Uncomposed appendix
CD _____ 8473332
ECM / Mar '92 / New Note.

UNDISONUS
CD _____ 837 755 2
New Note / Mar '90 / New Note / Cadillac.

WAVES
Per ulv / Karusell / Stenskoven / Waves / Dain curse / Charisma
CD _____ 8274192
ECM / Feb '86 / New Note.

WHAT COMES AFTER
CD _____ 8393062
ECM / Nov '89 / New Note.

WHENEVER I SEEM TO BE AWAY
Silver bird is heading for the sun / Hurt / Whenever I seem to be far away
CD _____ 8431662
ECM / Jun '92 / New Note.

WORKS: TERJE RYPDAL
Waves / Den forste sne / Hung / Better off without you / Innseiling / Rainbow / Top-plue, vooter and skjerf / Descendre
CD _____ 8254282
ECM / Jun '89 / New Note.

Rzewski, Frederic

NORTH AMERICAN BALLADS & SQUARES
CD _____ ARTCD 6089
Hat Art / Jan '92 / Harmonia Mundi / ADA / Cadillac.

S

S.D.I.

SIGN OF THE WICKED
CD _____ 15390
Laserlight / Aug '91 / Target/BMG.

S.D.L.

SPACE AGE FRONTIER
CD _____ DBMLABCD 5
Labworks / Oct '95 / SRD / Disc.

S.E.T.I.

KNOWLEDGE
CD _____ ASH 2.1CD
Ash International / Jan '95 / These /
Kudos.

S.N.F.U.

**ONE VOTED MOST LIKELY TO
SUCCEED, THE**
CD _____ E 86441-2
Epitaph / Mar '95 / Plastic Head /
Pinnacle.

**SOMETHING GREEN AND LEAFY THIS
WAY COMES**
CD _____ E 86430CD
Epitaph / Dec '93 / Plastic Head /
Pinnacle.

S.O.B.

WHAT'S THE TRUTH
CD _____ RISE 4 CD
Rise / Dec '90 / Pinnacle.

S.O.S. Band

DIAMOND IN THE RAW
CD _____ 4607352
Epic / Nov '89 / Sony.

HIT MIXES, THE
Just be good to me (Vocal remix) / Borrowed love (Extended version) / Just the
way you like it (Long version) / Finest (Extended version) / No lies (Special version) /
No lies (Dub mix) / Take your time (do it
right)
CD _____ 4601892
Tabu / Nov '87 / Sony.

S.U.N.

HYPNOTIKI
Xenon '88 / Dictorobotary / We love you /
Spirality / L.S. dream / Vision / Hardware
junky / Mezmorised / Hypnotiki / Big (CD
only)
CD _____ OUTCD 003
Flat / Jan '95 / Direct / Else / ADA.

S.W.E.D.

CROSSTALK
CD _____ EFA 034072
Muffin / Oct '94 / SRD.

S.W.V.

REMIXES, THE
CD _____ 07863664012
Arista / Jun '94 / BMG.

S.Y.P.H.

WIELEICHT
CD _____ EFA 037622
Atatak / Apr '94 / SRD.

S.Y.T.

CUBIC SPACE
CD _____ MEYCD 12
Magick Eye / Nov '95 / SRD.

Sababougnouma

**SABABOUGNOUMA (Balafons &
Africans Drums)**
CD _____ PS 65156
Playasound / Oct '95 / Harmonia Mundi /
ADA.

Sabia

LIVE IN CULVER CITY
CD _____ FF 70494
Flying Fish / Jul '89 / Roots / CM / Direct /
ADA.

Sablon, Jean

JEAN SABLON IN PARIS
CD _____ CDXP 606
DRG / Jan '89 / New Note.

SI TU MAINES
CD _____ PASTCD 7058
Flapper / Apr '95 / Pinnacle.

Sabres Of Paradise

DEEP CUTS (Various Artists)
Ooh baby / Roy revisited / Musical science
/ Internal / Take the book / X / Vega God /
Sugar Daddy / Smokebelch II
CD _____ SOP 001CD
Sabres Of Paradise / Oct '93 / Vital.

HAUNTED DANCEHALL
Bubble and slide / Bubble and slide II /
Duke of Earlsfield / Flight path estate /
Planet D / Wilmot / Tow truck / Theme /
Theme 4 / Return to Planet D / Ballad of
Nicky McGuire / Jacob Street 7am / Chapel
Street market 9am / Haunted dancehall
CD _____ WARPCD 26
Warp / Nov '94 / Disc.

**PINK ME UP (A Sabrettes Compilation)
(Various Artists)**
Let's go to work / Vernal equinox / Altitude
/ Spike it / Bunny new guinea pig / Through
the floor / Quadrafunk / Blacknuss /
Guitarambience
CD _____ SBR 001CD
Sabres Of Paradise / Aug '94 / Vital.

SABRESONIC 2
CD _____ WARPCD 34
Warp / Jul '95 / Disc.

Sabri Brothers

YAH HABIB
Saqia aur pila / Ya sahib ul jamal / Allah hi
allah tan mein tar / Kal kamaliya wale
CD _____ CDRW 12
Realworld / '89 / EMI / Sterns.

Sabri, Sarwar

MASTER DRUMMER OF INDIA
CD _____ EUCD 1138
ARC / '91 / ARC Music / ADA.

Sabu, Paul

IN DREAMS
CD _____ NTHEN 18
Now & Then / Apr '95 / Plastic Head.

Saccharine Trust

PAST LIVES
CD _____ SST 149 CD
SST / May '93 / Plastic Head.

Sachdev, G.S

LIVE IN CONCERT AT HAYWARD CA
CD _____ LYRCD 7422
Lyrichord / Dec '94 / Roots / ADA / CM.

SOLO BANSURI
CD _____ LYRCD 7405
Lyrichord / '91 / Roots / ADA / CM.

Sachse, Joe

SOLO - EUROPEAN HOUSE
CD _____ FMPCD 41
FMP / Aug '87 / Cadillac.

Sack

YOU ARE WHAT YOU EAT
CD _____ LEMON 014CD
Lemon / Aug '94 / Vital / Pinnacle.

Sackville All Stars

CHRISTMAS RECORD
Santa Claus is coming to town / We three
kings / At the Christmas ball / Winter won-
derland / Go tell it on the mountain / Good
King Wenceslas / Santa Claus came in the
spring / Silent night / Let it snow, let it snow,
let it snow / Old time religion
CD _____ SKCD 2-3038
Sackville / Jun '93 / Swift / Jazz Music /
Jazz Horizons / Cadillac / CM.

SATURDAY NIGHT FUNCTION
John Hardy's wife / Trouble in mind / Jive
at five / Russian lullaby / Good Queen Bess
/ Arkansas blues / Saturday night function
/ Rosalie
CD _____ SKCD 2-3028
Sackville / Jun '93 / Swift / Jazz Music /
Jazz Horizons / Cadillac / CM.

TRIBUTE TO LOUIS ARMSTRONG
Song of the islands / (I'll be glad when
you're dead) you rascal you / Save it pretty
Mama / On the sunny side of the street /
Willie the weeper / I gotta right to sing the
blues / Kiss to build a dream on / Big butter
and eggman / Pennies from heaven / Kee-
pin' out of mischief now / Sweethearts on
parade
CD _____ SKCD 2-3042
Sackville / Feb '89 / Swift / Jazz Music /
Jazz Horizons / Cadillac / CM.

Sacramentum

FINIS MALORUM
CD _____ CDAR 023
Adipocre / Mar '95 / Plastic Head.

Sacred Cowboys

TROUBLE FROM PROVIDENCE
CD _____ CGAS 806 CD
Citadel / May '89 / ADA.

Sacred Denial

SIFTING THROUGH THE WRECKAGE
Sifting through the wreckage / When I sleep
/ Brothers inventions / Some curiosity /
Conquer / No way / Take a look around /
Violent affection
CD _____ 082955
Nuclear Blast / '90 / Plastic Head.

Sacred Hearts

BROKEN DREAMS
CD _____ TWISTBIG 3CD
Twist / Mar '94 / SRD.

Sacred Mushroom

SACRED MUSHROOM, THE
CD _____ EVA 852125B30
EVA / Nov '94 / Direct / ADA.

Sacred Reich

AMERICAN WAY, THE
Love ..... hate / Crimes against humanity / I
don't know / State of emergency / American
way / Way it is / Flavors
CD _____ R093925
Roadrunner / Jun '91 / Pinnacle.

HEAL
CD _____ 398414106CD
Metal Blade / Jan '96 / Plastic Head.

IGNORANCE
Death squad / Victim of demise / Layed to
rest / Ignorance / No believers / Violent so-
lutions / Rest in peace / Sacred Reich / Ad-
ministrative decisions
CD _____ CDZORRO 30
Music For Nations / Sep '91 / Pinnacle.

SURF NICARAGUA
CD _____ CDZORRO 47
Music For Nations / Aug '92 / Pinnacle.

Sacred Spirit

**CHANTS AND DANCES OF THE NATIVE
AMERICANS**
How the West was lost (intro & prelude) /
Winter ceremony (Tor-cheney-nahana) /
Counterclockwise circle dance (Ly-o-lay ale
loya) / Celebrate wild rice (Ya-na-hana) /
Cradlesong (Dawa) / Advice for the young
(Gitchi-manidoo) / Interiblal song to stop
prosperity (Yeha-noha) / Elevation (Ta-was-
hee) / Heal the soul (Shamanic chant no.5)
/ Brandishing the tomahawk (Yo-hey-o-hee)
UD _____ 8DVII AY88
Virgin / Oct '95 / EMI.

Sacrifice

APOCALYPSE INSIDE
My eyes see red / Apocalypse inside / Flesh
/ Salvation / Beneath what you see / Incar-
cerated / Ruins of the old / Love / Freedom
Slave
CD _____ CDZORRO 62
Metal Blade / Jul '93 / Pinnacle.

Sacrilege

BEYOND THE REALMS OF MADNESS
Lifeline / At death's door / Sacred / Out of
sight out of mind
CD _____ CORECD 8
Metalcore / Nov '91 / Plastic Head.

TURN BACK TRILOBITE
CD _____ CDFLAG 29
Under One Flag / Jan '89 / Plastic Head.

Sacrosanct

TRAGIC INTENSE
CD _____ 1MF 37700322
Invisible / Jul '93 / Plastic Head.

Sad Cafe

POLITICS OF EXISTING
I didn't want you / Midnite / Trying to reach
you / Saving grace / Clocks / Refugees /
Only love / Keep us together / Heart / China
seize
CD _____ CLACD 273
Castle / '92 / BMG.

Whatever It Takes

WHATEVER IT TAKES
Whatever it takes / This heart's on fire / Stay
with me tonight / Back to zero / So cold /
Take me / Don't give up on love / Blood on
the sand / Universe / I won't leave
CD _____ CLACD 273
Castle / Jun '92 / BMG.

Sad Whisperings

SENSITIVE TO AUTUMN
CD _____ FDN 2007-2
Foundation 2000 / Dec '93 / Plastic Head.

Sadana

MUSIC FROM CATALONIA
CD _____ SYNCD 147
Topic / May '93 / Direct / ADA.

Saddar Bazaar

CONFERENCE OF THE BIRDS, THE
Sukoon / Arc of ascent (part 1) / Kiff riff /
Garden of essence / Sukoon (reflection) /
Shamsa (sunburst) / Baraka / Arc of ascent
(part 2) / Freedom rider / Neelum blue
CD _____ DELECCD 034
Delerium / Jul '95 / Vital.

Sade

BEST OF SADE, THE
Your love is king / Hang on to your love /
Smooth operator / Jezebel / Sweetest ta-
boo / Is it a crime / Never as good as the
first time / Love is stronger than pride /
Paradise / Nothing can come between us /
No ordinary love / Like a taboo / Kiss of life
/ Please send me someone to love / Cherish
the day / Pearls
CD _____ 477793-2
Epic / Oct '94 / Sony.

DIAMOND LIFE
Smooth operator / Your love is king / Hang
on to your love / When am I gonna make a
living / Frankie's first affair / Cherry pie /
Sally / I will be your friend / Why can't we
live together
CD _____ 4811782
Epic / Oct '95 / Sony.

LOVE DELUXE
No ordinary love / Feel no pain / I couldn't
love you more / Like a tattoo / Kiss of life /
Cherish the day / Pearls / Bullet proof soul
/ Mermaid
CD _____ 4726262
Epic / Oct '92 / Sony.

PROMISE
Is it a crime / Sweetest taboo / War of the
hearts / Jezebel / Mr. Wrong / Never as
good as the first time / Fear / Tar baby /
Maureen / You're not the man (MC only) /
Punch drunk (MC only)
CD _____ 4655752
Epic / Mar '90 / Sony.

STRONGER THAN PRIDE
Love is stronger than pride / Paradise /
Nothing can come between us / Haunt me
/ Turn my back on you / Keep looking /
Clean heart / Give it up / I never thought I'd
see the day / Siempre hay esperanza
CD _____ 4604972
Epic / May '88 / Sony.

Sadist

ABOVE THE LIGHT
CD _____ NOSF 001CD
Nosferatu / Jun '95 / Plastic Head.

Sadistik Exekution

WE ARE DEATH FUCK YOU
CD _____ CD 022
Osmose / Oct '94 / Plastic Head.

Sadolikar, Shruti

RAGA MIYAN KI TODI/RAGA BIBHAS
CD _____ NI 5346
Nimbus / Sep '94 / Nimbus.

Saetas

SONGS FROM ANDALUZA
CD _____ B 6785
Auvidis/Ethnic / Oct '94 / Harmonia Mundi.

Saffire

BROADCASTING
CD _____ ALCD 4811
Alligator / May '93 / Direct / ADA.

**HOT FLASH (Saffire The Uppity Blues
Woman)**
Two in the bush is better than one in the
hand / Sloppy drunk / One good man / Dirty
sheets / Tom cat blues / Learn to settle for
less / You'll never get me out of your mind
/ (Mr Insurance man) take out that thing /

Hopin' it'll be alright / Little bit of your loving goes a very long way / Shopping for love / Elevator man / Torch song / Torch song (part 2) / Why don't you do right / Prove me wrong / (No need) Pissin' on a skunk
CD _____ ALCD 4796
Alligator / May '93 / Direct / ADA.

OLD, BORROWED AND BLUE (The Uppity Blue Woman)
CD _____ ALCD 4826
Alligator / Dec '94 / Direct / ADA.

UPPITY BLUES WOMAN, THE
CD _____ ALCD 4780
Alligator / May '93 / Direct / ADA.

Safri

GET REAL
CD _____ DMUT 1292
Multitone / Jul '94 / BMG.

Sage, Carson

FINAL KITCHEN BLOWOUT (Sage, Carson & The Black Riders)
CD _____ EFA 11393D
Musical Tragedies / Jul '93 / SRD.

Sage, Greg

SACRIFICE (FOR LOVE)
CD _____ LS 92372
Roadrunner / Nov '91 / Pinnacle.

Sagittarius

SANITY OF MADNESS
CD _____ VOW 049CD
Voices Of Wonder / Jul '95 / Plastic Head.

Sagoo, Bally

BALLY SAGOO ON THE MIX - THE STORY SO FAR
CD _____ SAGOO 2-1
Mango / Jul '93 / Vital / PolyGram.

BOLLYWOOD FLASHBACK
Chura liya / Yeh sama hai pyar ka / O saathi / Quarbani quarbani / Mehbooba mehbobba / Roop tera mastana / jab hum jawan honge / Waada na tod / Choli ke peeche
CD _____ 477697 2
Columbia / Sep '94 / Sony.

Sahm, Doug

BEST OF THE ATLANTIC SESSIONS, THE
CD _____ RSACD 813
Sequel / Oct '94 / BMG.

TEXAS TORNADO - BEST OF
CD _____ 8122710322
WEA / Jul '93 / Warner Music.

Sahotas

RIGHT TIME, THE
Out of reach / Love fire / She runs / Eyes for me / Hass hogia / Right time / Feeling high / Your name is enough / Be with you / No escape
CD _____ EIRSCD 1070
IRS / May '95 / PolyGram / BMG / EMI.

Sahraoui, Cheb

N'SEL FIK (Sahraoui, Cheb & Chaba Fadela)
N'sel fik / La verite / Hala la la / Rah galbi mrid / Ya eli nsitini / N'sel fik (Nouvelle version) / Ma andi zhar maak / Ana melit / Loukene ma nebghih / Mazal naachak
CD _____ COOKCD 057
Cooking Vinyl / Oct '95 / Vital.

Saigon Kick

FIELDS OF RAPE
One step closer / Space oddity / Water / Torture / Fields of rape / I love you / Sgt. Steve / My heart / On and on / Way / Sentimental girl / Close to you / When you were mine / Reprise
CD _____ 756792300-2
WEA / Oct '93 / Warner Music.

LIZARD, THE
Cruelty / Hostile youth / Feel the same way / Freedom / God of 42nd Street / My dog / Peppermint tribe / Love is on the way / Lizard / All alright / Sleep / All I want / Body bags / Miss Jones / World goes round / Chanel
CD _____ 7567921582
Atlantic / Jun '92 / Warner Music.

SAIGON KICK
New world / What you say / What do you do / Suzy / Colours / Coming home / Love of God / Down by the ocean / Acid rain / My life / Month of Sundays / Ugly / Come take me now / I.C.U.
CD _____ 7567916342
East West / Apr '91 / Warner Music.

WATER
One step closer / Space oddity / Water / Torture / Fields of rape / I love you / Sgt. Steve / My heart / On and on / Way / Sentimental girl / Close to you / Whne you were mine / Reprise

CD _____ 7567923002
East West / Jun '94 / Warner Music.

Saih Pitu, Gamelan

HEAVENLY ORCHESTRA OF BALI, THE
CD _____ CMP CD 3008
CMP / Jul '92 / Vital/SAM.

Sainkho

OUT OF TUVA
CD _____ CRAW 6
Crammed World / Jan '96 / New Note.

Saint & Campbell

TIME ON THE MOVE
CD _____ COPCD 2
Copasetic / Feb '95 / Jetstar / Pinnacle / Grapevine.

Saint Preux

LA TERRA MONDO
CD _____ WOLCD 1066
China / Jan '96 / Pinnacle.

Saint Vitus

DIE HEALING
CD _____ HOO 352
Noise/Modern Music / Jan '95 / Pinnacle / Plastic Head.

Saint-Paul, Lara

MAMMA
CD _____ PCOM 1141
President / Nov '95 / Grapevine / Target / BMG / Jazz Music / President.

Sainte-Marie, Buffy

COINCIDENCE (AND LIKELY STORIES)
Big ones get away / Fallen angels / Bad end / Emma Lee / Starwalker / Priests of the Golden Bull / Disinformation / Getting started / I'm going home / Bury my heart at Wounded Knee / Goodnight
CD _____ CCD 1920
Ensign / Mar '92 / EMI.

IT'S MY WAY
CD _____ VMD 79142
Start / Oct '92 / Koch.

SHE USED TO WANT TO BE A BALLERINA
CD _____ VND 79311
Vanguard / Oct '95 / Complete/Pinnacle / Discovery.

Saints

ETERNALLY YOURS
CD _____ 422309
New Rose / May '94 / Direct / ADA.

MOST PRIMITIVE BAND IN THE WORLD LIVE FROM THE TWILIGHT ZONE
Wild about you / Do the robot / One way street / Knock on wood / Erotic neurotic / River deep, mountain high / Lies / Misunderstood / Messin' with the kid / Stranded
CD _____ HOT 1035CD
Hot / Jul '95 / Vital.

NEW ROSE YEARS, THE (Greatest hits)
CD _____ FC 060 CD
Fan Club / Feb '90 / Direct.

PREHISTORIC SOUNDS
CD _____ 422312
New Rose / May '94 / Direct / ADA.

Sakamoto, Ryuichi

BEAUTY
You do me / Calling from Tokyo / Rose / Asadoya yunta / Futique (Only on MC and CD) / Amore / We love you / Diabaram / Pile of time (Only on MC and CD) / Romance (Only on MC and CD) / Chinsagu no hana
CD _____ CDVUS 14
Virgin / Aug '91 / EMI.

HEARTBEAT
Heartbeat / Rap the world / Triste / Lulu / High tide / Song lines / Nuages / Sayonara / Borom gal / Epilogue / Heartbeat (Tainai Kaiki) / Returning to the womb / Cloud #9
CD _____ CDVUS 46
Virgin / Jun '92 / EMI.

MUSICAL ENCYCLOPEDIA
Field work (Featuring Thomas Dolby) / Etude / Paradise lost / M.A.Y. in the backyard / Steppin' into Asia / Tibetan dance / Zen-gun / In a forest of feathers
CD _____ DIXCD 34
10 / Jul '87 / EMI.

SWEET REVENGE
Tokyo story / Moving on / Sentimental / Regret / Pounding at my heart / Love and hate / Sweet revenge / Seven Seconds / Same dream, same destination / Interruptions / Waters edge
CD _____ 755961680-2
East West / Aug '94 / Warner Music.

Sakhile

AFRICAN ECHOES
Maluti / Mshandira phamwe / Crossroads / Song for bra zakes / Phambili / Mantenga falls / Same time next year / Tears of joy
CD _____ KAZ CD 17
Kaz / Oct '91 / BMG.

Salad

DRINK ME
Motorbike to heaven / Drink the elixir / Granite statue / Machine of menace / Overhear me / Shepherd's isle / Muscleman / Your ma / Warmth of your heart / Gertrude Campbell / Nothing happens / Noi's cooking / Man with a box / Insomnia
CD _____ CIRD 1002
Island / May '95 / PolyGram.

SINGLES BAR
Kent / King of love / Heaven can wait / Mistress / Diminished clothes / Clear my name / Come back tomorrow / On a leash / What do you say about that then / Planet in the ocean / Problematique
CD _____ CIRM 1000
Island Red / Oct '94 / PolyGram / Vital.

Salah, Sadaoui

ANTHOLOGY OF ARAB MUSIC VOL.1
CD _____ AAA 106
Club Du Disque Arabe / Sep '95 / Harmonia Mundi / ADA.

Salas Humara, Walter

LAGARTIJA
CD _____ ROUGHCD 144
Rough Trade / Apr '90 / Pinnacle.

LEAN
CD _____ RTS 9
Normal/Okra / Jul '94 / Direct / ADA.

Salas, Patricia

CHRISTMAS IN LATIN AMERICA
CD _____ EUCD 1088
ARC / '91 / ARC Music / ADA.

Salassie, Iauwata

ISES
CD _____ CDLINC 009
Lion Inc. / Dec '95 / Jetstar / SRD.

Salem

KADDISH
CD _____ MRO 15CD
Morbid Sounds / Apr '95 / Plastic Head.

Salem, Kevin

SOMA CITY
CD _____ RR 89792
Roadrunner / Oct '95 / Pinnacle.

Salgan, Horacio

TANGO VOL.1
CD _____ MAN 4830
Mandala / May '94 / Mandala / Harmonia Mundi.

Salim, A.K.

BLUES SUITE
Payday / Joy box / Full moon / Blue baby / Sultan / Blues shout / Like how long baby
CD _____ SV 0142
Savoy Jazz / Jan '94 / Conifer / ADA.

Salim, Abdel Gadir

NUJUM AL-LAIL - STARS OF THE NIGHT
Gidraishinna / Al-lemoni / Nujum al-lail / Nitlaga nitlaga / Jeenaki / A'abir sikkah
CD _____ CDORB 039
Globestyle / May '89 / Pinnacle.

Salisbury Cathedral Choir

HOW LOVELY ARE THY DWELLINGS
CD _____ CDE 84288
Meridian / Aug '94 / Nimbus.

Salmon, Kim

ESSENCE (Salmon, Kim & Surrealists)
CD _____ REDCD 21
Normal/Okra / May '94 / Direct / ADA.

HELL IS WHERE MY HEART LIVES
CD _____ REDCD 34
Normal/Okra / Jun '94 / Direct / ADA.

HEY BELIEVER
CD _____ GRCD 349
Glitterhouse / Nov '94 / Direct / ADA.

JUST BECAUSE YOU CAN'T SEE IT (Salmon, Kim & Surrealists)
CD _____ BLACKCD 9
Normal/Okra / May '94 / Direct / ADA.

KIM SALMON & THE SURREALISTS (Salmon, Kim & Surrealists)
CD _____ GRCD 381
Glitterhouse / Nov '95 / Direct / ADA.

SIN FACTORY (Salmon, Kim & Surrealists)

CD _____ REDCD 33
Normal/Okra / Mar '94 / Direct / ADA.

Salonga, Lea

LEA SALONGA
CD _____ 756782534-2
Warner Bros. / Sep '94 / Warner Music.

Salsa Blanca

MANUELA
CD _____ TUMICD 035
Tumi / '93 / Sterns / Discovery.

Salsoul Orchestra

NICE 'N' NAASTY
It's good for the soul / Nice 'n' naasty / It don't have to be funky (To be a groove) / Nightcrawler / Don't beat around the bush / Standing and waiting on love / Salsoul 3001 / We've only just begun/Feelings / Ritzy mambo / Jack and Jill
CD _____ CPCD 8077
Charly / Mar '95 / Charly / THE / Cadillac.

SALSOUL ORCHESTRA, THE
CD _____ CPCD 8059
Charly / Nov '94 / Charly / THE / Cadillac.

STREET SENSE
Zambesi / Burning spear / Somebody to love / Street sense / 212 North 12th / Sun after the rain
CD _____ CPCD 8098
Charly / Apr '95 / Charly / THE / Cadillac.

Salt 'N' Pepa

BLACK'S MAGIC
Expression / Doper than dope / Negro wit' an ego / You showed me / Do you want me / Swift / Life is party / Black's magic / Start the party / Let's talk about sex / I don't know / Live and let die / Independent / Expression (Brixton bass mix) (Only on CD or cassette)
CD _____ 8281642
FFRR / Nov '91 / PolyGram.

BLITZ OF SALT 'N' PEPA HITS, A (REMIX)
Push it / Expression / Independent / Shake your thang (It's your thing) / Twist and shout / Let's talk about sex / Tramp / Do you want me / My mic sounds nice / I'll take your man / I gotcha (once again) / You showed me
CD _____ 8282692
FFRR / Oct '91 / PolyGram.

GREATEST HITS: SALT 'N' PEPA
Push it / Expression / Independent / Shake your thang (it's your thing) / Twist and shout / Let's talk about sex / I like it like that / Tramp / Do you want me / My mic sounds nice / I'll take your man / I gotcha / I am down / You showed me
CD _____ 8282912
London / Oct '91 / PolyGram.

HOT COOL VICIOUS
Beauty and the beat / Tramp / I'll take your man / It's all right / Chick on the side / I desire / Showstopper / My mic sounds nice
CD _____ 8282962
FFRR / Nov '91 / PolyGram.

SALT WITH A DEADLY PEPA
Intro jam / Salt with a deadly pepa / I like it like that / Solo power / Shake your thang (it's your thing) / I gotcha / Let the rhythm run / Everybody get up / Spinderella's not a fella / Solo power (Syncopated soul) / Twist and shout / Hyped on the mic / Push it
CD _____ 5500412
Spectrum/Karussell / May '93 / PolyGram / THE.

VERY NECESSARY
Groove me / No one does it better / Somebody's gettin' on my nerves / Whatta man / None of your business / Step / Shoop / Heaven or hell / Big shot / Sexy noises turn me on / Somma time man / Break of dawn / PSA we talk / Shoop (radio mix) / Start me up
CD _____ 828377-2
FFRR / Oct '93 / PolyGram.

Salty Dogs Jazzband

LONG, DEEP & WIDE
CD _____ BCD 237
GHB / Jan '93 / Jazz Music.

Saluzzi, Dino

KULTRUM
Kultrum pampa / Gabriel kondor / Agua de paz / Pajaros Y ceibos / Ritmo arauca / El rio Y el abuelo / Pasos que quedan / Por el sol Y por la lluvia
CD _____ 8214072
ECM / May '92 / New Note.

MOJOTORO (Saluzzi, Dino Group)
Mojotoro / Tango a mi padre / Mundos / Lustrin / Viernes santo / Milonga (la punalada) / El camino
CD _____ 5119522
ECM / May '92 / New Note.

ONCE UPON A TIME - FAR AWAY IN THE SOUTH
Jose, Valeria and Matias / And the Father said... / Revelation / Silence / And he loved his brother, till the end / Far away in the south... / We are the children
CD _____ 8277682
ECM / Apr '86 / New Note.

RIOS
Los men / Minguito / Fulano de tal / Sketch / He loved his brother 'til the end / Penta y uno / JAD / Lunch with pancho villa / My one and only love / Rios
CD _____ VBR 21562
Intuition / Nov '95 / New Note.

SOLO BANDONEON (Saluzzi, Dino & Andina)
CD _____ 8371862
ECM / Feb '89 / New Note.

Salvador, Sal

SAL SALVADOR AND CRYSTAL IMAGE
CD _____ ST-CD 17
Stash / Nov '90 / Jazz Music / CM / Cadillac / Direct / ADA.

Salvagnini, Massimo

VERY FOOL
CD _____ CDSGP 095
Prestige / Jul '95 / Total/BMG.

Salvatore, Sergio

TUNE UP
Autumn leaves / Footprints / Tune up / Locked up combination / Times place / Moments in Montreal / Au private / Sea journey / Almost home / Somewhere over the rainbow
CD _____ GRP 97632
GRP / May '94 / BMG / New Note.

Sam & Dave

GREATEST HITS SOUL MAN
CD _____ MU 5034
Musketeer / Feb '95 / Koch.

HOLD ON I'M COMING
Hold on I'm comin' / If you got the loving / I take what I want / Ease me / I got everything I need / Don't make it so hard on me / It's a wonder / Don't help me out / Just me / You got it made / You don't know like I know / Blame me (don't blame me)
CD _____ 7567802552
Atlantic / Jul '91 / Warner Music.

I THANK YOU
I thank you / Everybody got to believe in somebody / These arms of mine / Wrap it up / If I didn't have a girl like you / You don't your heater on / Talk to the man / Love is after me / Ain't that a lot of love / Don't waste that love / That lucky old sun
CD _____ 812271012-2
WEA / Mar '93 / Warner Music.

LEGENDS IN MUSIC - SAM & DAVE
CD _____ LECD 063
Wisepack / Jul '94 / THE / Conifer.

R & B
CD _____ RLBTC 001
Realisation / Oct '93 / Prism.

SAM & DAVE
It feels so nice / I got a thing going on / My love belongs to you / Listening for my name / No more pain / I found out / It was so nice while it lasted / You ain't no big thing baby / New love / She's alright / Keep a walkin' / I'll still it still have me / Garden of Earth (On CD only) / Azethoth (On CD only) / Crown Street gang (On CD only) / Clean innocent fun (On CD only) / Metempsychosis (On CD only)
CD _____ EDCD 388
Edsel / Jun '94 / Pinnacle / ADA.

SAM & DAVE
CD _____ KLMCD 035
Scratch / Nov '94 / BMG.

SOUL BROTHERS
CD _____ CDCD 1244
Charly / Jun '95 / Charly / THE / Cadillac.

SOUL KINGS VOL.2
Don't pull your love / Hold on I'm comin' / Said I wasn't gonna tell anybody / I thank you / You don't know like I know / You got / Nathveth / When something is wrong / Soul sister/Brown sugar / Can't you find another way / Soul man / Soothe me / You don't know what you mean to me
CD _____ SMS 057
Carlton Home Entertainment / Oct '92 / Carlton Home Entertainment.

SOUL MEN
Soul man / May I baby / Broke down piece of man / Let it be me / Hold it baby / I'm with you / Don't knock it / Just keep holding on / Good runs the bad way / Rich kind of poverty / I've seen what loneliness can do
CD _____ 8122702962
Atlantic / Jul '93 / Warner Music.

SWEAT AND SOUL
Place nobody can find / Goodnight baby / I take what I want / You don't know like I know / Hold on I'm comin' / I got everything

---

I need / Don't make it so hard on me / Blame me (Don't blame my heart) / You got me hummin' / When something is wrong with my baby / Small portion of your love / I don't need nobody (to tell me bout my baby) / That's the way it's gotta be / Said I wasn't gonna tell nobody / Soothe me / I can't stand up for falling down / Toe hold / Soul man / May I baby / Just keep holding on / Good runs the bad way / Rich kind of poverty / I've seen what loneliness can do / My reason for living / I thank you / Wrap it up / Broke down piece of man / Shop around / Stop / Starting over again / Jody Ryder got killed / Don't pull your love / Knock it out the park / Standing in the safety zone / Baby baby don't stop now / One part love, two part pain / I'm not an indian giver / Holdin' on / You left the water running / Born again / Soul sister brown sugar / Don't you turn your heater on / Ain't that a lot of love / Can't you find another way of doing it / Everybody got to believe in somebody / You don't know what you mean to me / This is your world / Come on in / Hold it baby
CD Set _____ 812271253-2
Warner Bros. / Dec '93 / Warner Music.

SWEET SOUL MUSIC
CD _____ 15076
Laserlight / Aug '91 / Target/BMG.

Sam Black Church

LET IN LIFE
CD _____ TAANG 77CD
Taang / Dec '93 / Plastic Head.

SAM BLACK CHURCH
CD _____ TAANG 76CD
Taang / Jun '93 / Plastic Head.

Samael

1987 - 92
CD Set _____ CM 7708522
Century Media / Jan '95 / Plastic Head.

BLOOD RITUAL
CD _____ 84 97374
Century Media / Dec '92 / Plastic Head.

CEREMONY OF OPPOSITES
CD _____ CM 77064CD
Century Media / Mar '94 / Plastic Head.

Samaroo Jets

QUINTESSENCE
Meditation / Tico tico / Everything I do (I do it for you) / Bee's melody / I'll be there / Alma llanera / Portrait of Trinidad / Coming in from the cold / O mere sona / Memory / Unforgettable / Two to go / Heal the world / One moment in time / Pan rising
CD _____ DE 4024
Delos / Jul '94 / Conifer.

Sambeat, Perico

DUAL FORCE
Body / Luso / Wonderful, wonderful / Lament / Dual force / Ask me now / Plot
CD _____ JHCD 031
Ronnie Scott's Jazz House / Jun '94 / Jazz Music / Magnum Music Group / Cadillac.

Sambora, Richie

STRANGER IN THIS TOWN
Rest in peace / Church of desire / Stranger in this town / Ballad of youth / One light burning / Mr. Bluesman / Rosie / River of love / Father time / Annuya... / I'll still it still have me
CD _____ 8488952
Phonogram / Sep '91 / PolyGram.

Samiam

CLUMSY
CD _____ 756782642-2
East West / Aug '94 / Warner Music.

Samla Mammas Manna

MALTID
CD _____ RESCD 505
Resource / Oct '93 / ADA.

Sammy

DEBUT ALBUM
CD _____ FIRECD 40
Fire / Jun '94 / Disc.

Sample, Joe

ASHES TO ASHES
Ashes to ashes / Road less travelled / Mother's eyes / Last child / Born in trouble / Strike two / I'll love you / Born to be bad / Phoenix
CD _____ 7599263182
WEA / Mar '94 / Warner Music.

COLLECTION: JOE SAMPLE
Carmel / Woman you're driving me mad / Rainy day in Monterey / Sunrise / There are many stops along the way / Rainbow seeker / Fly with the wings of love / Burning up the carnival / Night flight / Oasis
CD _____ GRP 96582
GRP / Oct '91 / BMG / New Note.

DID YOU FEEL THAT
CD _____ 936245729-2
East West / Aug '94 / Warner Music.

Sampson, Don Michael

COPPER MOON
CD _____ AP1102
Appaloosa / Jan '96 / ADA / Magnum Music Group.

CRIMSON WINDS
Cherokee river / Long black train / Six string healing wheel / Old black guitar case / Fighter / Song in the wind
CD _____ R 103 CD
Red Horse / Aug '90 / BMG.

Samson

BURNING EMOTION
Burning emotion / Tramp / Tell me / No turning back / Stranger / Don't turn away / Tomorrow / Silver screen / Too late / Don't close your eyes / Can't live without your love / Don't tell me it's over / Room 109 / Good to see you / Fight for your life
CD _____ CDTB 169
Thunderbolt / Apr '95 / Magnum Music Group.

HEAD ON
Hard times / Take it like a man / Vice versa / Manwatcher / Too close to rock / Thunderburst / Hammerhead / Hunted / Take me to your leader / Walking out on you
CD _____ REP 4037-WZ
Repertoire / Aug '91 / Pinnacle / Cadillac.

LIVE AI READING '81
CD _____ REP 4040-WP
Repertoire / Aug '91 / Pinnacle / Cadillac.

REFUGE
Good to see you / Can't live without your love / Turn on the lights / Love this time / Room 109 / Sate of emergency / Don't tell me it's over / Look to the future / Someone to turn to / Too late / Samurai sunset / Silver screen
CD _____ CDTB 163
Thunderbolt / Sep '95 / Magnum Music Group.

SAMSON
CD _____ CMGCD 008
Communique / Aug '93 / Plastic Head.

SHOCK TACTICS
CD _____ REP 4038-WZ
Repertoire / Aug '91 / Pinnacle / Cadillac.

SURVIVORS
It's not as easy as it seems / I wish I was the saddle of a devil / Big brother / Tomorrow or yesterday / Koz / Six foot under / Wrong side of time / Mr. rock 'n' roll / Primrose shuffle / Telephone / Leavin' you
CD _____ REP 4039-WZ
Repertoire / Aug '91 / Pinnacle / Cadillac.

THANK YOU AND GOODNIGHT
CD _____ CDTB 160
Thunderbolt / Mar '95 / Magnum Music Group.

Samson, Paul

JOINT FORCES
Burning emotion / No turning back / Russians / Tales of the fury / Reach out to love / Chosen few / Tramp / Power of love / Tell me
CD _____ CDTB 148
Magnum Music / Oct '94 / Magnum Music Group.

LIVE AT THE MARQUEE
Burning emotion / Stranger / Vice versa / Fighting man / Matter of time / Afraid of the light / Tell me / Turn on the lights / Earth Mother / Tomorrow / Don't turn away
CD _____ CDTB 157
Thunderbolt / Nov '94 / Magnum Music Group.

Samurai & Hardbartle

SYNTRONIC MEGAHITS
CD _____ 710 099
Innovative Communication / Aug '90 / Magnum Music Group.

San Francisco Starlight..

DOIN' THE RACOON (San Francisco Starlight Orchestra)
CD _____ SOSCD 1271
Stomp Off / Apr '94 / Jazz Music / Wellard.

San Miguel, Tomas

CON TXALAPARTA
CD _____ 15641
Nuevos Medios / Jan '95 / ADA.

Sanabria, Bobby

NEW YORK CITY ACHE (Sanabria, Bobby & Ascension)
CD _____ FF 630CD
Flying Fish / Dec '93 / Roots / CM / Direct / ADA.

Sanborn, David

ANOTHER HAND
First song / Monica Jane / Come to me / Nina / Hobbies / Another hand / Jesus / Weird / Cee / Medley / Dukes and Counts
CD _____ 7559610882
Elektra / Sep '91 / Warner Music.

AS WE SPEAK
Port of call / Better believe it / Rush hour / Over and over / Back again / As we speak / Straight to the heart / Rain on Christmas / Love will come someday
CD _____ 923650 2
WEA / Oct '87 / Warner Music.

BACKSTREET
I told U so / When you smile at me / Believer / Backstreet / Tear for crystal / Bums cathedral / Blue beach / Neither one of us
CD _____ 923906 2
WEA / Oct '87 / Warner Music.

BEST OF DAVID SANBORN
CD _____ 9362457682
WEA / Nov '94 / Warner Music.

CHANGE OF HEART, A
Chicago song / Imogene / High roller / Tin tin / Breaking point / Change of heart / Summer / Dream
CD _____ 925479 2
WEA / Jan '87 / Warner Music.

CLOSE UP
Slam / J.T. / Leslie Ann / Goodbye / Same girl / Pyramid / Tough / So far away / You are everything / Camel island
CD _____ 9257152
WEA / Jul '94 / Warner Music.

HEARSAY
Savannah / Long goodbye / Little face / Got to give it up / Jaws / Mirage / Big foot / Back to Memphis / Ojiji
CD _____ 755961620 2
WEA / Jun '94 / Warner Music.

LOVE SONGS
CD _____ 9362460022
Warner Bros. / Nov '95 / Warner Music.

PEARLS
CD _____ 7559617592
Warner Bros. / Mar '95 / Warner Music.

STRAIGHT TO THE HEART
Hideaway / Straight to the heart / Run for cover / Smile / Lisa / Love and happiness / Lotus blossom / Hundred ways
CD _____ 9251 502
WEA / Jan '86 / Warner Music.

UPFRONT
Snakes / Benny / Crossfire / Full house / Soul serenade / Hey / Bang bang / Ramblin'
CD _____ 7559612722
Elektra / May '92 / Warner Music.

VOYEUR
Let's just say goodbye / It's you / Wake me when it's over / One in a million / Run for cover / All I need is you / Just for you
CD _____ 256 900
WEA / Dec '81 / Warner Music.

Sanchez

BOOM BOOM BYE BYE
CD _____ GRELCD 186
Greensleeves / Jul '93 / Total/BMG / Jetstar / SRD.

BROWN EYE GIRL
CD _____ VPCD 1392
VP / Aug '95 / Jetstar.

CAN WE TALK
CD _____ GRELCD 211
Greensleeves / Dec '94 / Total/BMG / Jetstar / SRD.

FOREVER
CD _____ CRCD 44
Charm / Oct '95 / Jetstar.

I CAN'T WAIT
CD _____ VYDCD 2
Vine Yard / Sep '95 / Grapevine.

MISSING YOU
CD _____ NWSCD 8
New Sound / Mar '94 / Jetstar.

NUMBER ONE DUB
CD _____ RE 173CD
Reach Out International / Mar '95 / Jetstar.

SANCHEZ & FRIENDS
CD _____ RNCD 2036
Rhino / Jan '94 / Jetstar / Magnum Music Group / THE.

SANCHEZ MEETS COCOA T (Sanchez & Cocoa T)
CD _____ SONCD 0051
Sonic Sounds / Jul '93 / Jetstar.

SANCHEZ VOL.1
CD _____ PHCD 2008
Penthouse / Aug '94 / Jetstar.

SANCHEZ VOL.2
CD _____ PHCD 2011
Penthouse / Aug '94 / Jetstar.

SWEETEST GIRL, THE
CD _____ RRTGCD 7708
Rohit / May '89 / Jetstar.

Sanchez, David

DEPARTURE, THE
Ebony / Woody 'n' you / Interlude 1 / You got it diz / Santander / I'll be around / Departure / Nina's mood / Cara De Payaso / Interlude 2 / CJ / Postlude
CD _____ 476507 2
Columbia / Jul '94 / Sony.

SKETCHES OF DREAMS
Africa Y Las Americas / Bomba blues / Falling in love / Extensions / Tu y mi cancion / Mal social / Sketches of dreams / Easy to remember / Little Melanie
CD _____ 4803252
Sony Jazz / May '95 / Sony.

Sanchez, Paul

JET BLACK AND JEALOUS
CD _____ LFP 0002
Ichiban / Sep '94 / Koch.

Sanchez, Poncho

BIEN SABROSO
Ahora / Bien sabroso / Nancy / Keeper of the flame / Brisa / Sin timbal / Una mas / Half and half / I can
CD _____ CCD 4239
Concord Picante / Jul '88 / New Note.

EL CONGUERO
Siempre me va bien / Mi negra / Shiny stockings / Si no hay amor / Yumbambo / Agua dulce / Night walk / Tin tin deo / Cuidado
CD _____ CCD 4286
Concord Picante / Jul '88 / New Note.

EL MEJOR
Just a few / Son son charari / Suenos / Lip smacker / Angel / Monk / El jamaiquino / Dichoso / Suave cha / Typhoon
CD _____ CCD 4519
Concord Picante / Sep '92 / New Note.

FUERTE - STRONG
Fuerte / Baila mi gente / It could happen to you / Lo llores, mi corazon / Ixtapa / Co co my my / Siempre te amare / Alafia / Daahoud
CD _____ CCD 4340
Concord Picante / May '88 / New Note.

LA FAMILIA
CD _____ CCD 4369
Concord Jazz / Feb '89 / New Note.

NIGHT WITH PONCHO SANCHEZ, A
Siempre me va bien / Bien sabroso / Alafia / Time for love / Sonando / Tito medley / La familia
CD _____ CCD 4558
Concord Picante / Jul '93 / New Note.

PARA TODOS
Five brothers / Cold duck time / Ugetsu / Angue tu / Cha cha / Happy blues / Lament / Ven morena / Rapture / Meeker's blues / Afro blue
CD _____ CCD 4600
Concord Picante / Jun '94 / New Note.

SONANDO
Night in Tunisia / Sonando / Summer knows / Con tres tambores bata / Almendra / Sueno / Cals pals / Peruchin / Este san
CD _____ CCD 4201
Concord Picante / Nov '89 / New Note.

TRIBUTE TO CAL TJADER
Soul sauce / Tripocville / I showed them / Somewhere in the night / Song for Cal / Morning / Tu crees que / Leyte / Song for Pat / Liz-Anne / Poinciana cha cha / Oran (On CD only.)
CD _____ CCD 4662
Concord Jazz / Oct '95 / New Note.

Sanchez, Roger

D.J.'S TAKE CONTROL VOL.2 (Various Artists)
CD _____ ORCD 026
One / Jul '95 / Total/BMG.

HARD TIMES (2CD Set)
CD Set _____ NACD 002
Narcotic / Nov '95 / Vital / Disc.

SECRET WEAPONS VOLUME 1
Spirit lift you up (Mixes) / Boom / Fill me / D-Day / Free your body / There it iz / Never give up / Rejoice (Available on CD only) / I need you (Available on CD only)
CD _____ ORCD 013
One / Feb '94 / Vital.

Sand

DYNAMIC CURVE
CD _____ CRECD 089
Creation / May '94 / 3MV / Vital.

FIVE GRAINS
CD _____ CREDCD 127
Creation / Nov '92 / 3MV / Vital.

Sandals

CRACKED
Changed / Osocurioso / Shake the brain / Joy / Arden's bud phase 3 / Cracked / Wake the brain / Open
CD _____ 8285732
Open Toe / Oct '94 / PolyGram.

RITE TO SILENCE
Feet / Nothing / No movement / Change / Arden's bud / We wanna live / We don't wanna be the ones to take the blame / Lovewood / Here comes the sign / Profound dub
CD _____ 828488-2
London / Apr '94 / PolyGram.

Sandberg, Ulf

ULF SANDBERG QUARTET, THE (Sandberg, Ulf Quartet)
Bolivia / Blue reflections / I mean you / Manhattan transfusion / Driftin' / Samba for someone / Like a child / Carlton in and out / Bolivia (alternative version) / Tildess (CD only)
CD _____ JAZIDCD 074
Acid Jazz / Jun '93 / Pinnacle.

Sanders, John Lee

WORLD BLUE
CD _____ HYCD 295155
Hypertension / Jul '95 / Total/BMG / Direct / ADA.

Sanders, Pharoah

AFRICA
You've got to have freedom / Naima / Origin / Speak low / After the morning / Africa
CD _____ CDSJP 253
Timeless Jazz / Feb '91 / New Note.

HEART IS A MELODY
Ole / On a misty night / Heart is a melody of time (Hiroko's song) / Goin' to Africa / Naima / Rise 'n' shine
CD _____ ECD 220632
Evidence / Nov '93 / Harmonia Mundi / ADA / Cadillac.

JOURNEY TO THE ONE
Greetings to Idris / Doktor Pitt / Kazuko (peace child) / After the rain / Soledad / You've got to have freedom / Yemenja / Easy to remember / Think about the one / Bedria
CD _____ ECD 220162
Evidence / Jul '92 / Harmonia Mundi / ADA / Cadillac.

KARMA
Creator has a master plan / Creator has a master plan #2 / Colours
CD _____ IMP 11532
Impulse Jazz / Nov '95 / BMG / New Note.

MOONCHILD
Moon child / Moon rays / Night has a thousand eyes / All or nothing at all / Soon / Mananberg
CD _____ CDSJP 326
Timeless Jazz / Aug '90 / New Note.

PRAYER BEFORE DAWN, A
Light at the edge of the world / Dedication to James W Clark / Softly for Shyla / After the rain / Greatest love of all / Midnight at Yoshi's / Living space / In your own sweet way / Christmas song
CD _____ ECD 22047
Evidence / Mar '93 / Harmonia Mundi / ADA / Cadillac.

REJOICE
CD _____ ECD 220202
Evidence / Jul '92 / Harmonia Mundi / ADA / Cadillac.

SHUKURU
CD _____ ECD 220222
Evidence / Aug '92 / Harmonia Mundi / ADA / Cadillac.

WELCOME TO LOVE
You don't know what love is / Nearness of you / My one and only love / I want to talk about you / Soul eyes / Nancy / Polka dots and moonbeans / Say it (over and over again) / Lament / Bird song
CD _____ CDSJP 358
Timeless Jazz / May '91 / New Note.

Sanders, Ric

CARRIED AWAY (Sanders, Ric/Vikki Clayton & Fred T. Baker)
CD _____ SVL 03CD
Speaking Volumes / Apr '95 / ADA.

WHENEVER
CD _____ NP 001CD
Nico Polo / Aug '89 / Roots / Direct / ADA.

Sanderson, Tommy

KEEP ON DANCING (Sanderson, Tommy & His Orchestra)
CD _____ CDTS 003
Maestro / Aug '93 / Savoy.

Sandira

ISHMAL DU BACH
CD _____ INDO 002
Plastic Head / Jul '92 / Plastic Head.

Sandke, Randy

CHASE, THE
Lullaby of Broadway / Jordu / Ill wind / Booker / Chase / Folks who live on the hill / Primordial blooze / Oh miss Hannah / Hyde Park / So in love / Randy's Rolls Royce
CD _____ CCD 4642
Concord Jazz / May '95 / New Note.

GET HAPPY
Get happy / Tuscaloosa / Sicilienne / Humph / Sonata / Let me sing and I'm happy / You / Regret / Deception / Black beauty / Owl eyes / Boogie stop shuffle / Me and my shadow
CD _____ CCD 4598
Concord Jazz / Jun '94 / New Note.

I HEAR MUSIC
Wildfire / Thanks a million / Say it / Dream song / Muddy water / With a song in my heart / See you later / I gotta right to sing the blues / Domino / I hear music / I love Louis / Lullaby for Karen / BG postscript
CD _____ CCD 4566
Concord Jazz / Aug '93 / New Note.

NEW YORKERS
CD _____ JCD 222
Jazzology / Oct '93 / Swift / Jazz Music.

RANDY & JORDAN SANDKE & SANDKE BROTHERS
CD _____ STCD 575
Stash / Feb '94 / Jazz Music / CM / Cadillac / Direct / ADA.

Sandler, Albert

ALBERT SANDLER AND HIS ORCHESTRA (Sandler, Albert & His Orchestra)
Portrait of a toy soldier / Casino Tanze - Valse / Kisses in the dark / Faust - Selection / Rosa Mia - Tango serenade / Minuetto from Mozart's symphony #39 / Yvonne (waltz) / Allegro (Violin solo) / Salut d'amour / From me to you / Folk tune and fiddle dance / By the sleepy lagoon / With you / Fairies' gavotte / Melody at dusk (Violin solo) / Souvenir d'Ukraine / Always in my heart / Boccherini's minuet in A / Japansy - Intermezzo / Biens Aimes - Waltz / King steps out
CD _____ PASTCD 9732
Flapper / '90 / Pinnacle.

Sandoval, Arturo

CLASSICAL ALBUM
CD _____ GRK 75002
GRP / May '94 / BMG / New Note.

DAN-ZON
Conga / Gypsy / Groovin' high / A mis abuelos / Tres palabras / Dance on / Suavito / Conjunto / Guaguanco / Coconut groove / Conga (revisited) / Tres palabras (instrumental)
CD _____ GRP 97642
GRP / May '94 / BMG / New Note.

DREAM COME TRUE
CD _____ GRP 97022
GRP / May '93 / BMG / New Note.

FLIGHT TO FREEDOM
Flight to freedom / Last time I saw you / Caribeno / Samba de amore / Psalm / Rene's song / Body and soul / Tanga / Caprichosos de la habana / Marianela
CD _____ GRP 96342
GRP / Mar '91 / BMG / New Note.

I REMEMBER CLIFFORD
Daahoud / Joy spring / Parisian thoroughfare / Cherokee / I remember Clifford / Blues walk / Sandu / I get a kick out of you / Jordu / Caravan / I left this space for you
CD _____ GRP 96682
GRP / Mar '92 / BMG / New Note.

JUST MUSIC
El misterioso / Sambeando / Georgia on my mind / Libertao carnaval / Saving all my love / Al chicoy / My love
CD _____ JHCD 008
Ronnie Scott's Jazz House / Jan '94 / Jazz Music / Magnum Music Group / Cadillac.

LATIN TRAIN, THE
Be bop / La guarapachanga / Marte belona / Waheera / I can't get started (with you) / La P.P. / Royal poinciana / Latin train / Candela/Quimbombo / Drume negrita / Orula
CD _____ GRP 98202
GRP / May '95 / BMG / New Note.

NO PROBLEM
Nuestro blues / Los elefantes / Donna Lee / Rimsky / Campana / Fiesta mojo
CD _____ JHCD 001
Ronnie Scott's Jazz House / Jan '94 / Jazz Music / Magnum Music Group / Cadillac.

STRAIGHT AHEAD (Sandoval, Arturo & Chucho Valdes)
King Pete's heart / My funny valentine / Mambo influenciado / Claudia / Blues '88 / Blue monk

CD _____ JHCD 007
Ronnie Scott's Jazz House / Feb '94 / Jazz Music / Magnum Music Group / Cadillac.

TUMBAITO
CD _____ MES 158742
Messidor / Apr '93 / Koch / ADA.

Sandow

ANSCHLAG
CD _____ FL 82
Fluxus / Nov '94 / Plastic Head.

STATION EINER SUCHT
CD _____ FLOOO3-2
Fluxus / Jun '94 / Plastic Head.

Sandoz

DARK CONTINENT
CD _____ TONE 4
Touch / Oct '95 / These / Kudos.

DIGITAL LIFEFORMS
CD _____ TO 21
Touch / Oct '95 / These / Kudos.

EVERY MAN GOT DREAMING
CD _____ TO 28
Touch / Oct '95 / These / Kudos.

INTENSELY RADIOACTIVE
CD _____ TO 23
Touch / Jun '94 / These / Kudos.

Sandpipers

GUANTANAMERA
Guantanamera / Carmen / La bamba / La mer (beyond the sea) / Louie, Louie / Things we said today / Enamorado / What makes you dream, pretty girls / Stasera gli angeli non volano (for the last time) / Angelica
CD _____ 5404152
A&M / Sep '95 / PolyGram.

Sandra

CLOSE TO SEVEN
CD _____ CDVIR 13
Virgin / Mar '92 / EMI.

PAINTINGS IN YELLOW
Hiroshima / Life may be a big insanity / Johnny wanna live / Lovelight in your eyes / One more night / Skin I'm in / Paintings in yellow / Journey / Cold out here / I'm alive / Paintings / Come alive / End
CD _____ CDV 2636
Virgin / Oct '90 / EMI.

Sands Family

SANDS FAMILY COLLECTION
CD _____ SC 1030CD
Spring / Jan '94 / Direct / ADA.

Sands, Tommy

BEYOND THE SHADOWS
CD _____ GLCD 3068
Green Linnet / Jun '93 / Roots / CM / Direct / ADA.

HEART'S A WONDER, THE
CD _____ GLCD 1158
Green Linnet / Dec '95 / Roots / CM / Direct / ADA.

SINGING OF THE TIMES
CD _____ GLCD 3044
Green Linnet / Oct '93 / Roots / CM / Direct / ADA.

Sands, Tommy

WORRYIN' KIND, THE (The Capitol Recordings)
Worryin' kind / Ring my phone / Blue ribbon baby / Man like wow / One day later / I ain't gettin' rid of you / Every little once in a while / I love you because / Ring-a-ding-ding / Rock light / Maybellene / Hearts of stone / Oop shoop / Hey Miss Fannie / Tweedle dee / Such a night / Honey love / Little mama / Chicken and the hawk / Big date / Soda pop pop / Sing boy sing / Teen age crush / Wicked woman / Is it ever gonna happen / Goin' steady / Bigger than Texas / Hawaiian rock / Jimmy's song / Wrong side of love
CD _____ BCD 15643
Bear Family / Mar '94 / Rollercoaster / Direct / CM / Swift / ADA.

Sandunga

VALIO LA PENA ESPERAR
CD _____ TUMICD 042
Tumi / May '91 / Sterns / Discovery.

Sandvik Small Band

SANDVIK SMALL BAND
CD _____ SITCD 9217
Sittel / Feb '95 / Cadillac / Jazz Music.

Sanford, Don

SAPPHIRE IN SEQUENCE #2 (Sanford, Don & Tommy Sanderson)
CD _____ CDTS 053
Maestro / Dec '95 / Savoy.

Sangare, Oumou

KO SIRA
CD _____ WCD 036
World Circuit / May '95 / New Note /
Direct / Cadillac / ADA.

MOUSSOLOU
Djama kaissoumou / Diarabi / Woula bara
diagna / Moussolou / Diya gneba / Ah ndiya
CD _____ WCD 021
World Circuit / May '95 / New Note / Direct
/ Cadillac / ADA.

Sangeet, Apna

JAM TO THE BHANGRA
CD _____ DMUT 1242
Multitone / Aug '93 / BMG.

Sangsters

BEGIN
Jesse / Feed the children / Heart like a
wheel / Chorus song / Lea rig / White cock-
ade / Sheath and knife / C-rap / Some kind
of love / Will ye gang love / Steal away /
Helen of Kirkconnel / Simple melody /
Golden, golden / Silence and tears / Quiet
comes in
CD _____ CDTRAX 065
Greentrax / Jul '93 / Conifer / Duncans /
ADA / Direct.

Sanne

LANGUAGE OF THE HEART
CD _____ CDV 2744
Virgin / Jul '94 / EMI.

Sansone, Maggie

**ANCIENT NOELS (Sansone, Maggie &
Ensemble Galilei)**
CD _____ MMCD 108
Maggie's Music / Dec '94 / CM / ADA.

DANCE UPON THE SHORE
CD _____ MMCD 109
Maggie's Music / Dec '94 / CM / ADA.

MIST AND STONE
CD _____ MMCD 106
Maggie's Music / Dec '94 / CM / ADA.

**MUSIC IN GREAT HALL (Sansone,
Maggie & Ensemble Galilei)**
CD _____ MMCD 107
Maggie's Music / Dec '94 / CM / ADA.

TRADITIONS
CD _____ MMCD 104
Maggie's Music / Dec '94 / CM / ADA.

Santamaria, Mongo

AFRO ROOTS
Afro blue / Che que re que che que / Rezo
/ Ayanye / Onyaye / Bata / Meta rumba /
Chano pozo / Los Conquitos / Monte Ad-
entro / Imaribayo / Mazacote / Yeye / Con-
gobel / Macunsere / Timbales y bongo /
Yambu / Bricamo / Longoito / Conga pa
Gozar / Mi Guaguanco / Columbia
CD _____ PCD 24018
Pablo / Oct '93 / Jazz Music / Cadillac /
Complete/Pinnacle.

AT THE VILLAGE GATE
CD _____ OJCCD 490-2
Original Jazz Classics / Feb '92 / Wellard /
Jazz Music / Cadillac / Complete/Pinnacle.

LIVE AT JAZZ ALLEY
Home / Bonita / Philadelphia / Para II (Only
on CD) / Manteca / Ponce / Come Candola
Ibiano (Only on CD) / Juan Jose (Only on
CD) / Afro blue
CD _____ CCD 4427
Concord Picante / Aug '90 / New Note.

MAMBOMONGO
Mambomongo / Happy as a fat rat in a
cheese factory / Gabrielle / Jelly belly /
That's so good / New one / Amancecer / Good
Doctor (dedicated to Dr. Allen H. Cashman)
/ Little T / Manteca
CD _____ CDHOT 501
Charly / Oct '93 / Charly / THE / Cadillac.

**MONGO EXPLODES/WATERMELON
MAN**
Skins / Fatback / Hammer head / Dot dot
dot / Cornbread guajira / Watermelon man /
Sweet potato pie / Bembe blue / Dulce amor / Ta-
cos / Para ti / Watermelon man / Funny
money / Cut that cane / Get the money /
Boogie cha cha blues / Don't bother me no
more / Love oh love / Yeh yeh / Peanut ven-
dor / Bayou root / Suavito
CD _____ CDBGPD 062
BGP / Apr '93 / Pinnacle.

**MONGO INTRODUCES LA LUPE
(Santamaria, Mongo Orchestra)**
Besito pa ti / Kiniqua / Canta bajo / Uncle
Calypso / Montuneando / Que lindas son /
Oye este guaguanco / Este mambo (this is
my mambo) / Quiet stroll
CD _____ MCD 9210
Milestone / Apr '94 / Jazz Music / Pinnacle
/ Wellard / Cadillac.

MONGO'S MAGIC
Dr. Gasca / O mi shango / Lady Marmalade
/ Iberia / Naked / Funk up / Secret admirer

/ Song for you / Princess / What you don't
know / Funk down / Leah
CD _____ CDHOT 516
Charly / Apr '95 / Charly / THE / Cadillac.

OLE OLA
CD _____ CCD 4387
Concord Picante / Aug '89 / New Note.

OUR MAN IN HAVANA
CD _____ FCD 24729
Fantasy / Oct '93 / Pinnacle / Jazz Music /
Wellard / Cadillac.

SABROSO
Que maravilloso / En la felicidad / Pachanga
pa ti / Tulibamba / Mambo de cuco / El bote
/ Pito pito / Guaguanco mania / Ja ja ja /
Tula hula / Dimelo / La luna me voy / Para
ti
CD _____ OJCCD 281
Original Jazz Classics / Sep '93 / Wellard /
Jazz Music / Cadillac / Complete/Pinnacle.

SKINS
CD _____ MCD 47038
Milestone / Oct '93 / Jazz Music /
Pinnacle / Wellard / Cadillac.

SOCA ME NICE
Con mi ritmo / Cookie / Cu-bop alert / Day
tripper / Kathy's waltz / Quiet fire / Soca me
nice / Tropical breeze
CD _____ CCD 4362
Concord Jazz / Nov '88 / New Note.

SOY YO
La manzana (the apple) / Sweet love / Soy
yo (that's me) / Salazar / Mayeya / Oasis /
Smooth operator / Un dia de playa (a day
at the beach)
CD _____ CCD 4327
Concord Picante / Oct '87 / New Note.

WATERMELON MAN
CD _____ EMPRCD 569
Emporio / May '95 / THE / Disc / CM.

Y SU ORQUESTA
Che que re que che que / Pachanga pa ti /
Tulibamba / Para ti / Guaguanco mania /
Pito pito / Monte adentro / Ye ye / Mambo
de cuco / Ja ja ja / El bote / Tula hula /
Conga pa gozar / En la felicidad / Que mar-
avilloso / La luna me voy
CD _____ CD 62067
Saludos Amigos / Apr '95 / Target/BMG.

Santana

ABRAXAS
Singing winds / Crying beasts / Black magic
woman / Gypsy queen / Oye como va / Incident at Neshabur / Se acabo / Mother's
daughter / Samba pa ti / Hope you're feeling better / El nicoya
CD _____ CD 32032
CBS / Mar '91 / Sony.

ACAPULCO SUNRISE
Acapulco sunrise / Coconut grove / Hawaii
/ Hot tamales / El corazon manda / Studio
jam No. 1 / Studio jam No. 2 / With a little
help from my friends / Travellin' blues
CD _____ CDTB 087
Thunderbolt / '91 / Magnum Music Group.

BEST OF SANTANA
She's not there / Black magic woman/
Gypsy queen / Carnaval / Let the children
play / Jugando / Vera Cruz / No one to de-
pend on / Evil way / Oye como va / Jin-go-
lo-ba (MC only) / Soul sacrifice / Europa /
Dealer / One chain (don't make no prison)
(MC only) / Samba pa ti / Dance, sister,
dance / Hold on (MC only) / Lightening in
the sky / Aquamarine
CD _____ 4682672
Columbia / Jun '92 / Sony.

BORBOLETTA
Spring manifestations / Cantos de los flores
/ Life is anew / Give and take / One with
the sun / Aspirations / Practice what you
preach / Mirage / Here and now / Flor de
canela / Promise of a fisherman / Borboletta
CD _____ 983300 2
Carlton Home Entertainment / Nov '93 /
Carlton Home Entertainment.

CARAVANSERAI
Eternal caravan of reincarnation / Waves
within / Look up (to see what's coming
down) / Just in time to see the sun / Song
of the wind / All the love of the universe /
Future primitive / Stone flower / La fuente
del ritmo / Every step of the way
CD _____ CD 65299
CBS / '88 / Sony.

**DANCE OF THE RAINBOW SERPENT (3
CDs)**
Evil ways / Soul sacrifice (from Woodstock
1) / Black magic woman/Gypsy queen / Oye
como va / Samba pa ti / Everybody's everything / Song of the wind / Toussaint
l'overture / In a silent way (live) / Waves within
/ Flame sky / Naima / I love you too much
/ Blues for Salvador / Aqua marine / Bella /
River / I'll be waiting / Love is you / Europa
/ Move on / Somewhere in Heaven / Open
invitation / All I ever wanted / Hannibal /
Brightest star / Wings of grace (live) / Fe
lie l'amo-kere kere (with Olatunji) / Mud-
bone / Healer / Chill out (things gonna
change) (with John Lee Hooker) / Sweet
black cherry pie (with Larry Graham) / Every

now and then (with Vernon Reid) / This is
this (with Weather Report)
CD Set _____ C3K 64605
Columbia / Sep '95 / Sony.

EARLY YEARS, THE
CD _____ MU 5025
Musketeer / Oct '92 / Koch.

EVOLUTION
Jingo / El corazon manda / La puesta del
sol / Persuasion / As the years go by / Soul
sacrifice / Fried neckbone and home fries
/ Latin tropical / Let's get ourselves together
/ Acapulco sunrise / Coconut grove / Hawaii
/ Hot tamales / Jam in E / Jammin' home /
With a little help from my friends / Travellin'
blues
CD _____ CDTB 502
Thunderbolt / Feb '94 / Magnum Music
Group.

GREATEST HITS: SANTANA
Evil ways / Jin-go-lo-ba / Hope you're feeling better / Samba pa ti / Persuasion / Black
magic woman / Oye como va / Everything's
coming up roses / Se acabo / Everybody's
everything
CD _____ 4032386
Columbia / Jun '92 / Sony.

LATIN ROCK FUSION
CD _____ CDCD 1187
Charly / Sep '94 / Charly / THE / Cadillac.

LATIN TROPICAL
Soul sacrifice / Fried neckbones and home
fries / Santana jam / Latin tropical / Let's
get ourselves together
CD _____ CDTB 079
Thunderbolt / Jun '95 / Magnum Music
Group.

LOTUS
Meditation / Going home / A1 funk / Every
step of the way / Black magic woman /
Gypsy queen / Oye como va / Yours is the
light / Batukada / Xibaba (she-ba-ba) /
Stone flower / Waiting / Castillos de'arena /
Se acabo / Samba pa ti / Savor / Toussaint
l'overture / Incident at Neshabur / Lotus
CD Set _____ 4679432
Columbia / Jul '91 / Sony.

MOONFLOWER
Dawn-go within / Carnaval / Let the children
play / Jugando / I'll be waiting / Zulu / She's
not there / Bahia / Black magic woman /
Gypsy queen / Dance, sister, dance / Europa / Flor d'luna / Soul sacrifice / El Morocco / Transcendance / Savor / Toussaint
l'overture
CD _____ CD 332 80
CBS / Apr '89 / Sony.

PERSUASION
Jingo / El corazon manda / La puesta del
sol / Persuasion / As the years go by
CD _____ CDTB 071
Thunderbolt / Jun '89 / Magnum Music
Group.

SACRED FIRE (Live In South America)
Angels all around us / Vive la vida / Esper-
ando / No one to depend on / Black magic
woman/Gypsy queen / Oye como va /
Samba pa ti / Guajira / Make somebody
happy / Toussaint l'overture / Soul sacrifice/
Don't try this at home / Europa / Jingo
CD _____ 521 082-2
Polydor / Nov '93 / PolyGram.

SALSA, SAMBA & SANTANA
Samba de sausalito / Touchdown raiders /
Brotherhood / Carnaval / Song of the wind
/ E para re / Wham / Flora de canela / Angel
negro / Hannibal / Para los rumheros / Ma-
ria caraoles / Bailando / Free as the morning
sun / Neuva York / Le fuente del ritmo /
Primera invasion / Toussaint l'overture
CD _____ 983259 2
Pickwick/Sony Collector's Choice / Aug '93
/ Carlton Home Entertainment / Pinnacle /
Sony.

SAMBA PA TI
Earth's cry heaven's smile / Moonflower / I
love you much too much / Guru's song /
Illuminations / Transformation day / Samba
pa ti / Aquamarine / Tales of Kilimanjaro /
Life is a lady / Holiday / Revelations /
Lightnin'
CD _____ 983322 2
Pickwick/Sony Collector's Choice / Nov '93
/ Carlton Home Entertainment / Pinnacle /
Sony.

SANTANA
Waiting / Evil ways / Shades of time / Savor
/ Jin-go-lo-ba / Persuasion / Treat / You just
don't care / Soul sacrifice
CD _____ CK 64212
Columbia / Nov '94 / Sony.

SANTANA BOXSET (3 CDST)
Jingo / El corazon manda / La puesta del
sol / Persuasion / As the years go by / Soul
sacrifice / Santana jam / Let's get ourselves
together / Fried neckbones and home
fries / Latin tropical / Jam in E / Jam in G
minor / With a little help from my friends /
Travelin' blues / Everyday I have the blues
/ Jammin' home
CD Set _____ KBOX 346
Collection / Nov '95 / Target/BMG.

SANTANA/ABRAXAS
Waiting / Evil ways / Shades of time / Savor
/ Jin-go-lo-ba / Persuasion / Treat / You just
don't care / Soul sacrifice / Singing winds /
Crying beasts / Black magic woman /
Gypsy queen / Oye como va / Incident at
Neshabur / Se acabo / Mother's daughter /
Samba pa ti / Hope you're feeling better /
El nicoya
CD Set _____ 4652212
Columbia / Jun '93 / Sony.

SANTANA/ABRAXAS/3RD
CD Set _____ 4673892
CBS / Dec '90 / Sony.

VIVA SANTANA - LIVE
Everybody's everything / Black magic
woman/Gypsy queen / Guajira / Jungle
strut / Jingo / Ballin' / Bambara / Angel negro / Incident at Neshabur / Just let the music speak / Super boogie/Hong Kong blues
/ Song of the wind / Abi cama / Vilato / Paris
finale / Brotherhood / Open invitation / Ag-
uamarine / Dance, sister, dance / Europa /
Peraza 1 / She's not there / Bambele / Evil
ways / Daughter of the night / Peraza II /
Black magic woman/Gypsy queen (Live) /
Oye como va / Persuasion / Soul sacrifice
CD _____ 4625002
CBS / Oct '88 / Sony.

Santana

SUCH IS LIFE
Mr. President / Black European / Beware /
Make a joyful noise / Call on me / Call on
me dub / Signs of the times / Wonderful
world / You're my woman / My woman dub
/ Such is life
CD _____ NGCD 540
Twinkle / Feb '94 / SRD / Jetstar / Kingdom.

Santana Brothers

BROTHERS
Transmutation / Industrial / Thoughts / Luz
amor y vida / En aranjuez con tu amor /
Contigo (with you) / Blues latino / La danza
/ Brujo / Trip / Reflections / Morning in
Marin
CD _____ CID 8034
Island / Sep '94 / PolyGram.

Santing, Mathilde

**CARRIED AWAY (Santing, Mathilde
Ensemble)**
Real Man / Polka dots and moonbeams /
It's Not Unusual / Overnite / Word girl /
Oblivious / Pretending To Care / Bad influ-
ence / Only A Motion / Yes the river knows
CD _____ 527900520
Solid / Nov '92 / Vital.

Santos, John

**MACHETE (Santos, John & The
Machete Ensemble)**
CD _____ XENO 4029
Xenophile / Mar '95 / Direct / ADA.

Santos, Turibio

VALAS AND CHORUS
CD _____ CDCH 574
Milan / Nov '91 / BMG / Silva Screen.

Sanvoisen

EXOTIC WAYS
CD _____ NO 2212
Noise/Modern Music / Jan '95 / Pinnacle /
Plastic Head.

Sapphires

BEST OF THE SAPPHIRES
Where is Johnny now / Your true love / Who
do you love / Oh so soon / I found out too
late / I've got mine you better get yours /
Where is your heart (Moulin Rouge) / Gotta
be more than friends / Wild child / Come on
and love me / Baby you've got me / Hearts
are made to be broken / Let's break up for
a while / Our love is everything / Thank you
for loving me / Gotta have your love / Gee
I'm sorry baby / Evil one / How could I say
goodbye / Gonna be a big thing / You'll
never stop me from loving you / Slow fizz
CD _____ NEMCD 676
Sequel / Aug '94 / BMG.

Saprize

NO
CD _____ RTD 19519162
Our Choice / Nov '94 / Pinnacle.

Saquito, Nico

GOOD-BYE MR CAT
Al vaiven de mi carreta / Me tenian amarrado con fe / Maria cristina / Meneame la
cuna, ramon / A orillas del cauto / Me tanian
amarrado con fe / Estoy hecho tierra / Que
lio company / Adios company gato
CD _____ WCD 035
World Circuit / Feb '94 / New Note / Direct
/ Cadillac / ADA.

Saraceno, Blues

PLAID
Last train out / Remember when / Elvis talking (you think it's over but it's not) / Never look back / Full tank / Scratch / Jaywalkin' / Friday's walk / Deliverance / Little more cream please / Shakes / Girth / Before the storm / Lighter shade of plaid / Funk 49 / Cat's squirrel / Jitter blast / L.A. Vignette / Frazzin' / Exit 21 / Tommy gun
CD _____ 592228
Semetery / Nov '93 / New Note.

Sarasota Slim

BOURBON TO BEALE
CD _____ APCD 069
Appaloosa / '92 / ADA / Magnum Music Group.

Sarbib, Saheb

IT COULDN'T HAPPEN WITHOUT YOU
Conjunctions / It couldn't happen without you / Watchmacallit / You don't know what love is / East 11th Street / Sasa's groove / Crescent
CD _____ SN 121098-2
Soul Note / Oct '94 / Harmonia Mundi / Wellard / Cadillac.

Sarcofago

LAWS OF SCOURGE
CD _____ CDFLAG 66
Music For Nations / Apr '92 / Pinnacle.

Sardaby, Michel

NIGHT CAP (Sardaby, Michel Trio)
CD _____ SSCD 8004
Sound Hills / Nov '93 / Harmonia Mundi / Cadillac.

Sargent, Gray Trio

SHADES OF GREY
Let's get lost / Gray haze / Don't take your love from me / I know why / My foolish heart / A.P. in the P.M. / You don't know what love is / Nightingale sang / This time the dream's on me / My ideal / Long ago and far away / Love is a many splendoured thing
CD _____ CCD 4571
Concord Jazz / Sep '93 / New Note.

Sarkoma

COMPLETELY DIFFERENT
CD _____ GC 189805
Recommended / Jul '92 / These / ReR Megacorp.

INTERGRITY
CD _____ CDVEST 16
Bulletproof / Jun '94 / Pinnacle.

Sarpila, Antti

HOT TIME IN UMEA (Tribute To Benny Goodman) (Sarpila, Antti/Ulf Johansson/Ronnie Gardiner)
Body and soul / After you've gone / So rare / Running wild / Man I love / Exactly like you / I want to be happy / These foolish things / It had to be you / China boy / Indian summer / Sweet Sue, just you / Stealin' apples / I've found a new baby / Memories of you
CD _____ NCD 8833
Phontastic / Aug '94 / Wellard / Jazz Music / Cadillac.

ORIGINAL ANTTI SARPILA
CD _____ ASCD 1
Hep / Oct '94 / Cadillac / Jazz Music / New Note / Wellard.

SWINGING ANTTI SARPILA
CD _____ ASCD 4
Hep / Oct '94 / Cadillac / Jazz Music / New Note / Wellard.

Sarstedt, Peter

ASIA MINOR (Sarstedt, Peter & Clive)
Dream pilot / Teradactyl walk / Glider / India / River / Corigador / Vaguely connected
CD _____ CMMR 923
Music Maker / May '93 / Grapevine / ADA.

PETER SARSTEDT/AS THOUGH IT WERE A MOVIE
I am a cathedral / Sons of Cain are Abel / No more lollipops / Stay within myself / You are my life / Sayonara / Where do you go to my lovely / Blagged / My Daddy is a millionaire / Once upon an everyday / Mary Jane / Time was leading us home / Many coloured semi precious Easter eggs / Time, love, hope, life / Overture / As though it were a movie / Open a tin / Step into the candlelight / Take off your clothes / Letter to a friend / Overture (2) / Boulevard / Sunshine is expensive / Artist / Friendship song / Juan / I'm a good boy / National anthem / Frozen orange juice / Aretusa loser
CD _____ BGOCD 274
Beat Goes On / May '95 / Pinnacle.

Sasajima, Akio

AKI OUSTICALLY SOUND
Darn that dream / Waltz from Brazil / I fall in love too easily / Akiology / Gentle rain / I love you / God bless the child
CD _____ MCD 5448
Muse / Sep '95 / New Note / CM.

HUMPTY DUMPTY
Humpty dumpty / Peace / Eyes of the dragon / Wheeler dealer / Seven souls / Alone together
CD _____ ENJ 80322
Enja / Nov '93 / New Note / Vital/SAM.

Sash, Leon

TRIO - I REMEMBER NEWPORT
CD _____ DD 416
Delmark / Nov '81 / Hot Shot / ADA / CM / Direct / Cadillac.

Sasha

QAT COLLECTION VOL. 2
CD _____ 7432122336-2
De-Construction / Aug '94 / BMG.

Sasha

ALL OR NOTHING
CD _____ DMUT 1270
Multitone / Nov '93 / BMG.

Satan

SUSPENDED SENTENCE/INTO THE FUTURE
CD _____ 851 819
Steamhammer / '89 / Pinnacle / Plastic Head.

Satan & Adam

MOTHER MOJO
Intro / Mother Mojo / Seventh avenue / Ain't nobody better than nobody / Heartbreak / Watermelon man / Funky thing / Silly little things / Freedom for my people / Crawdad hole / Mr. Contrell / Cry to me
CD _____ FIENDCD 738
Demon / Aug '93 / Pinnacle / ADA.

Satanic Surfers

HERO OF OUR TIME
CD _____ BHR 027CD
Burning Heart / Oct '95 / Plastic Head.

KEEP OUT
CD _____ BHR 018
Burning Heart / Feb '95 / Plastic Head.

Satans Pilgrims

SOUL PILGRIMS
CD _____ ES 1226CD
Estrus / Nov '95 / Plastic Head.

Satchel

EDC
Mr. Brown / Equilibrium / Taste it / Trouble come down / More ways than 3 / Hollywood / O / Mr. Pink / Built 4 it / Mr. Blue / Willow / Roof almighty / Suffering
CD _____ 477314-2
Epic / Sep '94 / Sony.

Satchmo Legacy Band

SALUTE TO POPS VOL. 1
CD _____ 121116-2
Soul Note / Sep '89 / Harmonia Mundi / Wellard / Cadillac.

SALUTE TO POPS VOL.2
CD _____ 1211662
Soul Note / Jan '93 / Harmonia Mundi / Wellard / Cadillac.

Satriani, Joe

DREAMING II
Crush of love / Ice nine / Memories / Hordes of locusts
CD _____ 473604 2
Relativity / May '93 / Sony.

EXTREMIST, THE
Friends / Extremist / War / Cryin' / Rubina's blue sky happiness / Summer song / Tears in the rain / Why / Motorcycle driver / New blues
CD _____ 4716722
Epic / Aug '92 / Sony.

FLYING IN A BLUE DREAM
Flying in a blue dream / Mystical potato head groove thing / Can't slow down / Headless / Strange / I believe / One big rush / Big bad moon / Feeling / Phone call / Day at the beach / Back to Shalla-bal / Ride / Forgotten (pts 1 & 2) / Bells of Lal (pts 1 & 2) / Into the light
CD _____ 465995 2
Relativity / May '93 / Sony.

JOE SATRIANI
Cool # 9 / Down, down, down / Luminous flesh giants / S.M.F. / Look my way / Home / Moroccan sunset / Killer bee bop / Slow down blues / (You're) My world / Sittin' around

CD _____ 4811022
Epic / Oct '95 / Sony.

JOE SATRIANI 3 ALBUM SET
Not of this Earth / Snake / Rubina / Memories / Brother John / Enigmatic / Driving at night / Hordes of locusts / New day / Headless horseman / Surfing with the alien / Ice nine / Crushing day / Always with me, always with you / Satch boogie / Hill of the skulls / Circles / Lords of Karma / Midnight / Echo / Flying in a blue dream / Mystical potato head groove thing / Can't slow down / Headless / Strange / I believe / One big rush / Big bad moon / Feeling / Phone call / Day at the beach (New rays from the ancient sun) / Back to Shalla-bal / Ride / Forgotten Pt. 1 / Forgotten Pt. 2 / Bells of lal Pt. 1 / Bells of lal Pt. 2 / Into the light
CD Set _____ 477519-2
Relativity / Oct '94 / Sony.

NOT OF THIS EARTH
Not of this Earth / Snake / Rubina / Memories / Brother John / Enigmatic / Driving at night / Hordes of locusts / New day / Headless horseman
CD _____ 462972 2
Relativity / May '93 / Sony.

SURFING WITH THE ALIEN
Surfing with the alien / Ice 9 / Crushing day / Always with me, always with you / Satch boogie / Hill of the skull / Circles / Lords of Karma / Midnight / Echo
CD _____ 462973 2
Relativity / May '93 / Sony.

TIME MACHINE
Time machine / Mighty turtle head / All alone / Banana mango (2) / Crystal / Crazy / Speed of light / Baroque / Dweller on the threshold / Banana mango / Dreaming / I am become death / Saying goodbye / Woodstock jam / Satch boogie / Summer song / Flying in a blue dream / Cryin' / Crush of love / Tears in the rain / Always with me, always with you / Big bad moon / Surfing with the alien / Rubina / Circles / Drum solo / Lords of karma / Echo
CD _____ 474515 2
Relativity / Oct '93 / Sony.

Satyricon

DARK MEDIEVIL
CD _____ FOG 001
Panorama / Sep '94 / Melcot Music.

ENSALVED
CD _____ FOG 009CD
Moonfog / Jan '96 / Plastic Head.

SHADOWTHRONE, THE
CD _____ FOG 003
Moonfog / Nov '94 / Plastic Head.

Saulis, Jannis

SOUVENIRS FROM GREECE
CD _____ 90683-2
PMF / Jul '92 / Kingdom / Cadillac.

Saunders, Kevin

KEVIN SAUNDERS PRESENTS KMS
CD Set _____ KMSCD 1
Network / Oct '94 / Sony / 3MV.

Sausage

RIDDLES ARE ABOUND TONIGHT
Prelude to fear / Riddles are abound tonight / Here's to the man / Shattering song / Toyz 1988 / Temporary phase / Girls for single men / Recreating / Caution should be used while driving.........
CD _____ 654492361-2
Interscope / Apr '94 / Warner Music.

Savage

HOLY WARS
CD _____ NM 004CD
Neat / Nov '95 / Plastic Head.

Savannah Jazzband

I CAN'T ESCAPE FROM YOU
CD _____ LACD 29
Le Jazz / Jul '93 / Charly / Cadillac.

IT'S ONLY A BEAUTIFUL PICTURE
CD _____ LACD 51
Lake / Jun '95 / Target/BMG / Jazz Music / Cadillac / ADA.

SAVANNAH JAZZ BAND
I can't escape / Funky kinklets / Sing on / I don't see me / All alone / Smiles / Gravier street / Shake it and break it / Miner's dream of homes / Lead me saviour / Buddy's habit / Curse of an aching heart / Trog's blues / At the cross / South Rampart Street parade
CD _____ LACD 99
Fellside / Jun '93 / Target/BMG / Direct / ADA.

Savatage

DEAD WINTER DEAD
CD _____ 086202RAD
CD Set _____ 086252RAD
Edel / Oct '95 / Pinnacle.

DUNGEONS ARE CALLING, THE

CD _____ CDMFN 42
Music For Nations / Mar '85 / Pinnacle.

EDGE OF THORNS
Edge of thorns / He carves his stone / Lights out / Skraggy's tomb / Labyrinths / Follow me / Exit music / Degrees of sanity / Conversation piece / All that I bleed / Damien / Miles away / Sleep
CD _____ 756782488-2
Atlantic / Mar '93 / Warner Music.

GUTTER BALLET
Of rage and war / Temptation revelation / Silk and steel / Hounds / Mentally yours / Gutter ballet / When the crowds are gone / She's in love / Unholy / Summer's rain
CD _____ K 782 008 2
Atlantic / Jun '92 / Warner Music.

HANDFUL OF RAIN
CD _____ CDVEST 32
Bulletproof / Aug '94 / Pinnacle.

JAPAN LIVE '94
CD _____ IRS 993011CD
Intercord / Jan '96 / Plastic Head.

SIRENS
Sirens / Holocaust / I believe / Rage / On the run / Twisted little sister / Living for the night / Scream murder / Out on the streets
CD _____ CDMFN 48
Music For Nations / Sep '85 / Pinnacle.

SIRENS/DUNGEONS ARE CALLING
CD _____ CDZORRO 83
Metal Blade / Nov '94 / Pinnacle.

Savia Andina

SAVIA ANDINA
CD _____ TUMICD 040
Tumi / '93 / Sterns / Discovery.

Savitt, Jan

LIVE IN HI-FI 1938 (Savitt, Jan & The Top Hatters)
CD _____ JH 1024
Jazz Hour / Feb '93 / Target/BMG / Jazz Music / Cadillac.

Savoy Brown

BEST OF SAVOY BROWN
Train to nowhere / Mr. Downchild / Stay with me baby / Shake 'em on down / Leavin' again / Needle and spoon / Hellbound train / Coming your way / Made up my mind / Let it rock / Highway blues
CD _____ C5CD-504
See For Miles/C5 / May '90 / Pinnacle.

BRING IT HOME
CD _____ CTC 0107
Coast To Coast / Jul '95 / Koch / Grapevine.

KINGS OF BOOGIE
CD _____ GNPD 2196
GNP Crescendo / Jul '94 / Silva Screen.

MAKE ME SWEAT
Limehouse boogie / Just for kicks / Good time lover / Goin' down / Hard way to go / Don't tell me it's over / Running with a bad crowd / Tell Mama / Shot in the head / Breakin' up / On the prowl
CD _____ GNPD 2193
GNP Crescendo / Jun '92 / Silva Screen.

SAVAGE RETURN
CD _____ 8442432
Deram / Jan '96 / PolyGram.

Savoy Havana Band

CHARLESTON (Savoy Havana Band/Savoy Orpheans/Sylvians)
Charleston / Headin' for Louisville / Blue room / Where'd you get those eyes / Hard hearted Hannah / Five foot two, eyes of blue / Fascinating rhythm / You're in Kentucky sure as you're born / Side by side / Masculine women, feminine men / Pasadena / Dinah / Turkish towel Charleston / San Francisco / Crazy words crazy tune / She don't wanna / Baby face / I love my chilli bon bon / Someone to watch over me / Whisper song
CD _____ CDHD 160
Happy Days / Jun '88 / Conifer.

Savoy Jazzmen

30TH ANNIVERSARY (1962 - 1992)
CD _____ 322909
Koch / Feb '93 / Koch.

Savoy, Marc

BENEATH A GREEN OAK TREE (Savoy, Marc & Dewey Balfa/D.L. Menard)
CD _____ ARHCD 312
Arhoolie / Apr '95 / ADA / Direct / Cadillac.

HOME MUSIC WITH SPIRITS (Savoy-Doucet Cajun Band)
CD _____ ARHCD 389
Arhoolie / Apr '95 / ADA / Direct / Cadillac.

LIVE AT THE DANCE (Savoy-Doucet Cajun Band)
CD _____ ARHCD 418
Arhoolie / Apr '95 / ADA / Direct / Cadillac.

TWO-STEP D'AMEDE (Savoy-Doucet Cajun Band)
CD _____ ARHCD 316
Arhoolie / Apr '95 / ADA / Direct / Cadillac.

Saw Doctors

ALL THE WAY FROM TUAM
Green and red of mayo / You got me on the run / Pied piper / My heart is livin' in the sixties still / Hay wrap / Wake up sleeping / Midnight express / Broke my heart / Exhilarating sadness / All the way from Tuam / F.C.A. / Music I love / Yvonne / Never mind the strangers
CD _____ SAWDOC 002CD
Shamtown / Oct '94 / Pinnacle.

IF THIS IS ROCK AND ROLL I WANT MY OLD JOB BACK
I useta lover / Only one girl / Why do I always want you / It won't be tonight / Irish post / Sing a powerful song / Freedom fighters / That's what she said last night / Don't let me down / Twenty five / What a day / n17 / I hope you meet again
CD _____ SAWDOC 001CD
Shamtown / Oct '94 / Pinnacle.

SAME OUL TOWN
CD _____ SAWDOC 004CD
Shamtown / Feb '96 / Pinnacle.

THAT'S WHAT SHE SAID LAST NIGHT
CD _____ ROKCD 751
Solid / Nov '91 / Grapevine.

Sawhney, Nitin

SPIRIT DANCE
River pulse / Skylight / Taste / Pieces of ten / Wind and rain / Twilight daze / Chase the sun / Spirit dance (Mixes)
CD _____ SDCD 7001
Spirit Dance / Mar '94 / New Note / Direct.

Sawyer Brown

SAWYER BROWN - GREATEST HITS
CD _____ CURCD 013
Curb / Jan '95 / PolyGram.

Sax & Ivory

BEST OF SAX & IVORY
CD _____ PKCD 61194
K&K / Sep '94 / Jetstar.

Sax Appeal

FLAT OUT
Dervish / Wasps / Smiffy / Trains / Semi conscious / Kites / Sand in my shoes / Chee o wa wa cha cha
CD _____ HEPCD 2050
Hep / Oct '91 / Cadillac / Jazz Music / New Note / Wellard.

LET'S GO
Zoot suit / Wild river / Let's go / Makambo triangle / Longshore drift / One step further / Monkish / Rio / Stompin' on the saveloy / Midnight
CD _____ JITCD 9401
Jazzizit / Jul '94 / New Note.

Sax, Mostafa

BEST OF EGYPTIAN BELLY DANCE MUSIC
CD _____ EUCD 1131
ARC / '91 / ARC Music / ADA.

Saxon

BACK ON THE STREETS
Power and the glory / Backs to the wall / Watching the sky / Midnight rider / Never surrender / Princess of the night / Motorcycle man / 747 (Strangers in the night) / Wheels of steel / Nightmare / Back on the streets / Rock 'n' roll gypsy / Broken heroes / Devil rides out / Party 'til you puke / Rock the nations / Waiting for the night / Ride like the wind / I can't wait anymore / We are the strong
CD _____ VSOPCD 147
Connoisseur / Jan '90 / Pinnacle.

BEST OF SAXON
Eagle has landed / Ride like the wind / Crusader / Rainbow theme/Frozen rainbow / Midas touch / Denim and leather / Broken heroes / Dallas 1pm / 747 (strangers in the night) (Live) / Princess of the night (Live) / And the bands played on (CD only.) / Never surrender (CD only.) / This town rocks (CD only.) / Strong arm of the law (Live (CD only)) / Heavy metal thunder (Live (CD only))
CD _____ CDEMS 1390
EMI / Mar '91 / EMI.

DOGS OF WAR
CD _____ HTDCD 35
HTD / May '95 / Pinnacle.

FOREVER FREE
CD _____ WARCD 10
Warhammer / May '93 / Grapevine.

GREATEST HITS LIVE: SAXON
Opening theme / Heavy metal thunder / Rock 'n' roll gypsy / And the bands played on / Twenty thousand feet / Ride like the wind / Motor cycle man / 747 (Strangers in the night) / See the light shining / Frozen rainbow / Princess of the night / Wheels of steel / Denim and leather / Crusader / Rockin' again / Back on the streets again
CD _____ ESMCD 132
Essential / May '95 / Total/BMG.

LIVE AT THE MONSTERS OF ROCK
CD _____ IRS 933011CD
Intercord / Jan '96 / Plastic Head.

Saxon, Al

HOOKED ON THE 40S (Saxon, Al '40s Band)
CD _____ EMPRCD 515
Emporio / Jul '94 / THE / Disc / CM.

Saxon, Sky

IN SEARCH OF BRIGHTER COLORS (Saxon, Sky & Fire Wall)
I hear the mountains crash / Lightning lightning / Put something sweet between your lips / Barbie doll look / Big screen / Baby baby / Come on pretty girl / Kick kick / Paisley rocker / Come a here right now
CD _____ ROSE 155CD
New Rose / Dec '88 / Direct / ADA.

Saxtet

SAFER SAX
CD _____ SERCD 8000
Serendipity / Aug '93 / Koch.

Sayama, Masahiro

PLAY ME A LITTLE MUSIC
CD _____ JD 3305
JVC / Jul '88 / New Note.

Sayer, Leo

ALL THE BEST
When I need you / Show must go on / One man band / Long tall glasses / Moonlighting / You make me feel like dancing / How much love / Thunder in my heart / I can't stop loving you (Though I try) / Raining in my heart / More than I can say / Have you ever been in love / Heart (Stop beating in time) / Orchard Road / Living in a fantasy / Giving it all away
CD _____ CDCHR 1980
Chrysalis / Feb '93 / EMI.

ENDLESS FLIGHT
Hold on to my love / You make me feel like dancing / Reflections / When I need you / No business like love business / I hear the laughter / Magdalena / How much love / I think we fell in love too fast / Endless flight
CD _____ CD25CR 09
Chrysalis / Mar '94 / EMI.

Sayles, Charlie

I GOT SOMETHING TO SAY
CD _____ JSPCD 261
JSP / Nov '95 / ADA / Target/BMG / Direct / Cadillac / Complete/Pinnacle.

NIGHT AIN'T RIGHT
CD _____ JSPCD 241
JSP / '89 / ADA / Target/BMG / Direct / Cadillac / Complete/Pinnacle.

Sayles Silverleaf...

SAYLES SILVERLEAF RAGTIMERS (Sayles Silverleaf Ragtimers)
CD _____ BCD 8
GHB / Aug '95 / Jazz Music.

Sayyah, Emad

MODERN BELLY DANCE MUSIC FROM LEBANON
CD _____ EUCD 1099
ARC / '91 / ARC Music / ADA.

MODERN BELLY DANCE MUSIC FROM LEBANON VOL.2
CD _____ EUCD 1226
ARC / Sep '93 / ARC Music / ADA.

Scabs

SKINTIGHT
CD _____ BIASCD 102
Play It Again Sam / '89 / Vital.

Scaggiari Trio

STEFAN ITELY
Just in time / I'm old fashioned / Icarus / All of me / Honeysuckle rose / Samba de bunda / Old folks / Where or when / Bittersweet / I've got the world on a string / Golden lady / Windswept high
CD _____ CCD 4570
Concord Jazz / Sep '93 / New Note.

Scaggiari, Stefan

STEFAN OUT
Love walked in / Felix / Love for sale / Make me a memory / Willow weep for me / Ill wind / Bolivia / When you're around / I am singing / If I could / Windows / For all we know
CD _____ CCD 4659
Concord Jazz / Aug '95 / New Note.

Scaggs, Boz

SILK DEGREES
What can I say / Georgia / Jump street / What do you want the girl to do / Harbour lights / Lowdown / It's over / Love me tomorrow / Lido shuffle / We're all alone
CD _____ CK 64420
Columbia / Feb '95 / Sony.

SLOW DANCER
Slow dancer / Angel lady come just in time / There is someone / Hercules / Pain of love / Sail on / White moon / Let it happen / I got your number / Take it for granted
CD _____ 982986-2
Pickwick/Sony Collector's Choice / Mar '94 / Carlton Home Entertainment / Pinnacle / Sony.

SOME CHANGE
You got my letter / Some change / I'll be the one / Call me / Fly like a bird / Sierra / Lost it / Time / Illusion / Follow that man
CD _____ CDVUS 73
Virgin / Jun '94 / EMI.

Scalaland

BREATHING DOWN THE NECK OF MEANING
Call me / Snow white lies / Burn the wish / Shots / Global village idiot blues / Born and raised and failing / Softly, softly / Foxgirl and ostrichboy / Babyfake / Insomnia mon amour
CD _____ MUMCD 9502
Mother / Sep '95 / PolyGram.

Scamps

MAY DAY
CD _____ NERCD 062
Nervous / '91 / Nervous / Magnum Music Group.

Scanner

MENTAL RESERVATION
CD _____ MASSCD 058
Massacre / Oct '95 / Plastic Head.

Scanner

SCANNER
CD _____ ASH 1.1
Ash International / Jan '95 / These / Kudos.

SCANNER #2
CD _____ ASH 1.2
Ash International / Jan '95 / These / Kudos.

SPORE
Full fathom / 915.675 / 394 / Strom / Lacuna / R.F. radiation / Silver / Flyjazz / Pudenda / Naked / At the end of the day / Axy
CD _____ ELEC 1001
New Electronica / Mar '95 / Pinnacle / Plastic Head.

Scarce

DEADSEXY
Honey simple / Freakshadow / Days like this / Stella / Glamourising / Cigarettes / Girl through me / Karona krome / All sideways / Thrill me / Sense of quickness / Given / Obviously midnight
CD _____ PDOXCD 001
Paradox / Jul '95 / PolyGram / Vital.

RED
CD _____ ABB 79
Big Cat / Aug '95 / SRD / Pinnacle.

Scarecrow

TOUCH OF MADNESS, A
CD _____ CDVEST 43
Bulletproof / Feb '95 / Pinnacle.

Scarecrow's Shadow

SCARECROW'S SHADOW
CD _____ NAK 6004CD
Naked Language / Sep '94 / Koch.

Scarface

DIARY, THE
Intro / White sheet / No tears / Jesse James / G's / I seen a man die / One / Goin' down / One time / Hand of the dead body / Mind playin' tricks '94 / Diary / Outro
CD _____ CDVUS 81
Virgin / Oct '94 / EMI.

Scarfo

SCARFO
Eyesore / Coin op / Skinny / Backwater / Car chase / Thow it all / Wailing words

CD _____ BLUFF 017CD
Deceptive / Oct '95 / Vital.

Scarlet

NAKED
CD _____ 450997643-2
WEA / Feb '95 / Warner Music.

Scarlet

RED ALERT
CD _____ 086 804
We Bite / Nov '89 / Plastic Head.

Scarp

SCARP
CD _____ BNQ 94CD
Arax Pan Global / Jul '94 / Direct / ADA.

Scat Opera

ABOUT TIME
CD _____ CDMFN 111
Music For Nations / Feb '91 / Pinnacle.

FOUR GONE CONFUSION
CD _____ CDMFN 140
Music For Nations / Oct '92 / Pinnacle.

Scatman John

SCATMAN'S WORLD
Welcome to Scatland / Scatman's world / Only you / Quiet desperation / Scatman / Sing now / Popstar / Time (take your time) / Mambo jambo / Everything changes / Song of Scatland / Hi Louis / Scatman (remix)
CD _____ 74321298792
RCA / Sep '95 / BMG.

Scatterbrain

MINDUS INTELLECTUALIS
Write that hit / Beer muscles / Everybody does it / Funny thing / How could I love you / Dead man blues / Down with the ship
CD _____ CDVEST 33
Bulletproof / Sep '94 / Pinnacle.

Scelsi, Giacinto

BOT-BA (Scelsi, Giacinto & Marianne Schroeder)
CD _____ ARTCD 6092
Hat Art / Oct '92 / Harmonia Mundi / ADA / Cadillac.

Schafer, Peter

FOREIGN WORLDS
CD _____ 710 097
Innovative Communication / Aug '90 / Magnum Music Group.

Schatz, Lesley

BANJO PICKIN' GIRL
Winter it is past / Trouble in mind / Cruel sister / Barbara Allen / little Joe the wrangler / Zebra Dun / Streets of Laredo / Jesse James / Tom Dula / Banjo pickin' girl / Early one morning / Arthur McBride / Jack O'Hazlegreen / Great Silkie / Silver dagger / Rowan tree / White coral bells / Flor del pino / Tumbalalaika / Will the circle be unbroken
CD _____ BCD 15729
Bear Family / May '93 / Rollercoaster / Direct / CM / Swift / ADA.

BRAVE WOLFE
Red river valley / Gypsy Davey / Oh Susanna / Brave Wolfe / Banks of the Ohio / I never will marry / Greensleeves / Greenpeace / I ride an old paint / Shady grove / Rising sun blues / Train that carried my man from town / Shortnin' bread / Cripple creek / Mole in the ground / Old Joe Clarke / Nine pound hammer / Turkey in the straw / Sinner man / Careless love / Pretty little horses
CD _____ BCD 15735
Bear Family / May '93 / Rollercoaster / Direct / CM / Swift / ADA.

COYOTE MOON/ RUN TO THE WIND
It's about time / Alberta blue / Freight train bound / Way she would sing / Printed word / Coyote moon / Boppin' at the gamble / Going home / Old tin pot / Les' wish / Alberta waltz / Molly and tenbrooks / To each his own / I'll be on the road again / Run to the wind / Chinese silver / Slow dance / Wind (stay away) / Only sound you'll hear / Empty hands
CD _____ BCD 15513
Bear Family / May '90 / Rollercoaster / Direct / CM / Swift / ADA.

HELLO STRANGER
Hello stranger / Shenandoah / Wayfaring stranger / Apple blossom time / Beautiful river valley / Sweetest gift / Water is wide / Somewhere in Tennessee / Froggie went a-courtin' / Farewell to Nova Scotia / Home on the range / Down in the valley / Whiskey in the jar / Girl I left behind / Lily of the west / Did he mention my name / Spanish is a loving tongue / Cancion de cuna / La source / Brahms lullaby
CD _____ BCD 15725
Bear Family / May '93 / Rollercoaster / Direct / CM / Swift / ADA.

WALLS, HEARTS AND HEROES
Walls and borders / Gotta go (Bremen Train) / Dry land / Lonely bird / Back to your arms / Girl gone wild / Old old doll / Take a stand (for the children) / I can hear ya callin' / Foothill's lullaby / My heart stands (at your door) / Gypsy blue / Wastin' the moon / Merlin and the cowboy / I can dance (like Arthur Murray) / New crescent moon / Once a dream / Way o' walkin' / Old Wooley / Christmas wish / In the cabin walls / Un Canadien errant
CD _____ BCD 15674
Bear Family / Jun '92 / Rollercoaster / Direct / CM / Swift. ADA.

Schatz, Mark
BRAND NEW OLD TYME WAY
CD _____ ROUCD 0342
Rounder / Jun '95 / CM / Direct / ADA / Cadillac.

Schechter, Gregori
DER REBE ELIMELECH (Schechter, Gregori Klezmer Festival Band)
CD _____ EUCD 1324
ARC / Nov '95 / ARC Music / ADA.

Scheetz, Jeff
WOODPECKER STOMP
CD _____ RR 00012
Re-flexx / Nov '90 / Re-flexx.

Schell, Daniel
IF WINDOWS THEY HAVE (Schell, Daniel & Kara)
Un celte / Remi sace an lacis dore / Vienna Carmen / Moustiquaires / If windows they have / Bigna zomer en ik loop altjid / Listen to short wave: Je suis dans / Tapi la nuit / Buches/logs/holz
CD _____ MTM 13CD
Made To Measure / Sep '88 / Grapevine.

Schenker, Michael
BBC LIVE IN CONCERT (Schenker, Michael Group)
Armed and ready / Cry for the nations / Mad axeman / But I want more / Heavy blues / Instrumental guitar / Let sleeping dogs lie / Lost horizons / Doctor doctor
CD _____ WINCD 043
Windsong / Sep '93 / Pinnacle.

BEST OF MICHAEL SCHENKER GROUP, THE (Schenker, Michael Group)
Armed and ready / Cry for the nations / Victim of illusion / Into the arena (Overture) / Are you ready to rock / Attack of the mad axeman / On and on / Assault attack / Dancer / Searching for a reason / Desert song / Rock my nights away / Captain Nemo / Let sleeping dogs lie / Bijou pleasurette / Lost horizons
CD _____ MCCD 160
Music Club / May '94 / Disc / THE / CM.

COLLECTION: M.S.G. (Schenker, Michael Group)
Armed and ready / Lost horizons / Buou pleasurette / Ready to rock / Let sleeping dogs lie / But I want more / Into the arena / Attack of the mad axeman / Never trust a stranger / Dancer / Desert song / Broken promises / Rock my nights away / Captain Nemo / Walk the stage
CD _____ CCSCD 294
Castle / Jul '91 / BMG.

Scherman, Theo
CHAMPAGNE IN THE STARLIGHT
CD _____ RTCD 901151
Line / Sep '92 / CM / Grapevine / ADA / Conifer / Direct.

Schifrin, Lalo
MORE JAZZ MEETS THE SYMPHONY
Sketches of miles / Down here on the ground / Chano / Begin the beguine / Django / Old friends / Madrigal / Portrait of Louis Armstrong
CD _____ 450995589-2
Warner Bros. / Aug '94 / Warner Music.

Schimmerman, Rolf
JENESAIQUOI VOL.1
Caravan of wonder / Faster and higher / Soul of the desert / Finally / Spinning / Thank you / Radio guga / Knide magic / Jam tomorrow / Dream of up / I miss you / Take me home (Parts 1 and 2)
CD _____ BW 017
B&W / Sep '94 / New Note.

SURU
Ainat / Passages / Traces / Take six / Endless longing / Pole star
CD _____ BW 009
B&W / Mar '93 / New Note.

Schinjuku Thief
WITCH HAMMER, THE
CD _____ DOROBO 003CD
Dorobo / Oct '95 / Plastic Head.

Schizo
SOUNDS OF COMING
CD _____ AVRCD 008
Nosferatu / Jun '94 / Plastic Head.

Schlippenbach, Alexander
ELF BAGATELLEN (Schlippenbach Trio)
CD _____ FMPCD 27
FMP / Aug '86 / Cadillac.

PHYSICS (Schlippenbach Trio)
CD _____ FMPCD 50
FMP / Dec '89 / Cadillac.

Schloss, Cynthia
SAD MOVIES
CD _____ REVCD 3002
Revue / Feb '94 / Jetstar.

THIS IS LOVE
CD _____ CRCD 26
Charm / Nov '93 / Jetstar.

Schlott, Volker
DAY BEFORE, THE (Schlott, Volker Quartett)
CD _____ BEST 1026CD
Acoustic Music / Nov '93 / ADA.

Schmidt, Claudia
CLAUDIA SCHMIDT
CD _____ FF 70066
Flying Fish / Mar '89 / Roots / CM / Direct / ADA.

IT LOOKS FINE FROM HERE
CD _____ RHRCD 64
Red House / Jul '95 / Koch / ADA.

MIDWESTERN HEART
CD _____ FF 241CD
Flying Fish / May '93 / Roots / CM / Direct / ADA.

Schmidt, Irmin
ANTHOLOGY (Soundtracks)
CD Set _____ SPOONCD 3233
Grey Area / Oct '94 / Pinnacle.

Schnaufer, David
DULCIMER SESSIONS
If she's gone, let her go / Blackberry blossom / Sandy / Down yonder / Lady Jane / Juley Calhoun / All I have to do is dream / Spaced out and blue / packington's pound/ The Almaine / Orphan's picnic / Wait a minute / Santiago's shottis / Spanish Harlem / Wheeling / Ebeneezer/Fly around my pretty little Miss / Colours / Fisher's hornpipe
CD _____ SFL 005
SFL Tapes & Discs / Jul '92.

Schneider, Maria
EVANESCENCE (Schneider, Maria Jazz Orchestra)
Wyrgly / Evanescence / Gumba blue / Some circles / Green piece / Gush / My lament / Dance you monster to my soft song / Last season
CD _____ ENJ 80482
Enja / Apr '94 / New Note / Vital/SAM.

Schneiderman, Rob
DARK BLUE
CD _____ RSRCD 132
Reservoir Music / Oct '94 / Cadillac.

NEW OUTLOOK
CD _____ RSRCD 106
Reservoir Music / Oct '89 / Cadillac.

RADIO WAVES
CD _____ RSRCD 120
Reservoir Music / Nov '94 / Cadillac.

SMOOTH SAILING
CD _____ RSRCD 114
Reservoir Music / Nov '94 / Cadillac.

STANDARDS
CD _____ RSRCD 126
Reservoir Music / Nov '94 / Cadillac.

Schnitt Acht
SLASH & BURN
CD _____ CDDVN 23
Devotion / Sep '93 / Pinnacle.

SUBURBAN MINDS
CD _____ HY 391009CD
Hyperium / Nov '92 / Plastic Head.

Schnyder, Daniel
NUCLEUS
Angry blackbird / Soleil noir / Mystified churchgoer / Scherzo / Retrogradus ex machina / Teiresias / Triplex / No opera / Do re mi / Collectors choice
CD _____ ENJ 80682
Enja / Mar '95 / New Note / Vital/SAM.

Schoenberg, Loren
JUST A-SETTIN' AND A-ROCKIN'
CD _____ MM 5039
Music Masters / Oct '94 / Nimbus.

SOLID GROUND (Schoenberg, Loren Orchestra)
Midriff / They say it's wonderful / Solid ground / Coquette / After all / Maid with the flaccid air / Bulgar (and other balkan-type inventions) / You are / Only trust your heart / This one's for Basie / I double dare you / Blue monk
CD _____ CIJD 60186F
Music Masters / '89 / Nimbus.

TIME WAITS FOR NO ONE
CD _____ MM 5032
Music Masters / Aug '94 / Nimbus.

Scholl, Bernd
SECRET GARDEN
CD _____ SKYCD 8703052
Sky / Sep '95 / Koch.

Schonherz & Scott
UNDER A BIG SKY
Gathering / Little amnesia / Daydreams / Gold and ivory or purple / Love just is / I remember / Heart of the matter / Seven sisters / Sin ken ken / Who do I belong to
CD _____ WD 1105
Windham Hill / Jul '91 / Pinnacle / BMG / ADA.

Schoolly D
ADVENTURES OF SCHOOLLY D
CD _____ RCD 20050
Rykodisc / May '92 / Vital / ADA.

Schramm, Dave
VI
CD _____ RTS 6
Normal/Okra / Jul '94 / Direct / ADA.

Schrammel & Slide
DEUX
CD _____ BEST 9011CD
Acoustic Music / Nov '95 / ADA.

Schramms
LITTLE APOCALYPSE
CD _____ OKRACD 33022
Normal/Okra / May '94 / Direct / ADA.

ROCK, PAPER, SCISSORS, DYNAMITE
CD _____ OKRACD 33017
Normal/Okra / Mar '94 / Direct / ADA.

WALK TO DELPHI
CD _____ OKRA 007
Normal/Okra / Nov '94 / Direct / ADA.

Schroeder, Robert
BODY LOVE
CD _____ RRK 715025
Racket / May '86 / CM.

BRAIN VOYAGER
CD _____ CD 715030
Racket / '86 / CM.

COMPUTER VOICE
CD _____ CD 715025
Racket / Oct '86 / CM.

HARMONIC ASCENDENT
CD _____ 715 020
Racket / Apr '90 / CM.

PARADISE
In memory of paradise / Moments / Deep dream / Balance / Future memories / Skywalker / Time machine / Timeless
CD _____ RRK 715024
Racket / '86 / CM.

PEGASUS
CD _____ 710 093
Racket / Apr '90 / CM.

TIMEWAVES
Turn of a dream / Waveshape attack / Waveshape decay / Love and emotion / Message / Imagine
CD _____ 715033
Racket / Jan '89 / CM.

Schubert
TOILET SONGS
CD _____ 9041542
Mausoleum / Feb '95 / Grapevine.

Schubert, Matthias
BLUE AND GREY SUITE
Nichol's dime / La maitre / Blue and grey suite / Wariatka
CD _____ ENJ 90452
Enja / Oct '95 / New Note / Vital/SAM.

Schuler, Manfred
SOUND OF AUSTRIA, A (Schuler, Manfred Zither & Folk Music Ensemble)
CD _____ DIS 80116
Dorian Discovery / Jan '94 / Conifer.

Schulkowsky, Robyn
HASTENING WESTWARD (Schulkowsky, Robyn & Nils Petter Molvaer)
CD _____ 4493712
ECM / Nov '95 / New Note.

Schuller, Ed
ELEVENTH HOUR, THE (Schuller, Ed Band)
O zone / Eleventh hour (pts 1 & 2) / PM in the AM / Keeping still / Mountain / Love lite / Shamal / For dodo
CD _____ TUTUCD 888124
Tutu / May '92 / Vital/SAM.

Schulz, Bob
TOGETHER AGAIN (Schulz, Bob & The Riverboat Ramblers)
CD _____ BCD 279
GHB / Jul '93 / Jazz Music.

TRIBUTE TO TURK MURPHY (Schulz, Bob & His Frisco Band)
CD _____ SOSCD 1288
Stomp Off / Nov '95 / Jazz Music / Wellard.

Schulze, Klaus
AUDENTITY
CD _____ CDTB 505
Thunderbolt / Mar '95 / Magnum Music Group.

BABEL
Nebuchadnezzar's dream / Foundation / Tower raises / First clouds / Communication problems / Gap of alienation / Immuring insanity / Heaven under feet / Deserted stones / Facing abandoned tools / Vanishing memories / Sinking into oblivion / Far from earth
CD _____ CDVE 5
Venture / May '94 / EMI.

BEYOND RECALL
Grongo Nero / Trancess / Brave old sequence / Big fall / Airlight
CD _____ CDVE 906
Venture / Mar '93 / EMI.

BODY LOVE
CD _____ CDTB 123
Thunderbolt / Jan '90 / Magnum Music Group.

DIG IT
CD _____ CDTB 144
Thunderbolt / Mar '94 / Magnum Music Group.

DOME EVENT, THE
Dome event / Andante / Nachtmusik. Schattenhaft / Allegro / Energisch. In gemesenem schritt / Sehr behaglich / Unbeschwert / Ohne hast / Scherzo: Un poco loco / Event: Rhythmisch uppig, Dann vergnugt. Bewegt / Presto / Ubermutig, Sturmisch bewegt. Heftig / Un poco loco (Reprise) / Crescendo / Finale: Tuttu synthi / After eleven
CD _____ CDVE 918
Venture / Mar '93 / EMI.

DREAMS
Classical move / Five to four / Dreams / Klaustrophony
CD _____ CDTB 039
Thunderbolt / Aug '95 / Magnum Music Group.

DRESDEN PERFORMANCE/DRESDEN IMAGINARY SCENES
CD _____ CDVED 903
Venture / Nov '90 / EMI.

DRIVE INN (Schulze, Klaus & Rainer Bloss)
Drive Inn / Sightseeing / Truckin' / Highway / Racing / Road to clear / Drive out
CD _____ CDTB 028
Thunderbolt / May '86 / Magnum Music Group.

DUNE
Dune / Shadows of ignorance
CD _____ CDTB 145
Thunderbolt / '86 / Magnum Music Group.

EN = TRANCE
En=trance / A-numerique / Fm delight / Velvet system
CD Set _____ CDTB 061
Thunderbolt / '89 / Magnum Music Group.

IRRLICHT
CD _____ CDTB 133
Thunderbolt / '86 / Magnum Music Group.

MIDTERRANEAN PADS
Decent changes / Miditerranean pads / Percussion / Piriante
CD _____ CDTB 081
Thunderbolt / Jan '90 / Magnum Music Group.

MIRAGE
Aeronef / Eclipse / Exvasion / Lucidinterspace / Destinationvoid / Xylotones / Crom-waves / Willowdreams / Liquidmirrors / Springdance
CD _____ CDTB 033
Thunderbolt / Nov '86 / Magnum Music Group.

594

MOONDAWN
Floating / Mindphaser
CD _____ CDTB 093
Thunderbolt / Feb '91 / Magnum Music Group.

PICTURE MUSIC
Totem / Mental door
CD _____ CDTB 098
Thunderbolt / Jan '91 / Magnum Music Group.

POLAND LIVE 83
CD _____ CDTB 504
Thunderbolt / Nov '94 / Magnum Music Group.

ROYAL FESTIVAL HALL VOL I
CD _____ CDVE 916
Venture / Nov '92 / EMI.

ROYAL FESTIVAL HALL VOL II
CD _____ CDVE 917
Venture / Nov '92 / EMI.

TIMEWIND
Bayreuth return / Wahnfried 1883
CD _____ CDCA 2006
Virgin / Jun '88 / EMI.

TRANCEFER
CD _____ CDTB 146
Thunderbolt / Jun '94 / Magnum Music Group.

X
CD _____ CDTB 501
Thunderbolt / Jan '93 / Magnum Music Group.

Schurr, Diane

DIANE SCHUUR & THE COUNT BASIE ORCHESTRA (Schurr, Diane & Count Basie Orchestra)
CD _____ GRP 95502
GRP / Feb '92 / BMG / New Note.

DIANE SCHUUR COLLECTION
CD _____ GRP 95912
GRP / Jun '89 / BMG / New Note.

HEART TO HEART (Schurr, Diane & B.B. King)
No one ever tells you / I can't stop loving you / You don't know me / It had to be you / I'm putting all my eggs in one basket / Glory of love / Try a little tenderness / Spirit in the dark / Freedom / At last / They can't take that away from me
CD _____ GRP 97722
GRP / May '94 / BMG / New Note.

Schutz, Michael

DON'T LOOK BACK (Schutz, Michael & Marco Bronzini)
CD _____ ISCD 115
Intersound / Oct '91 / Jazz Music.

Schutze, Paul

APART
Rivers of mercury / Skin of air and tears / Sleeping knife dance / Visions of a sand drinker / Coldest light / Eyeless and naked / Ghosts of animals / Taken (apart) / Consequence / Memory of water (pt 2) / Throat full of stars / Sleep (pts 1-3)
CD _____ AMBT 6
Virgin / Feb '95 / EMI.

DEUS EX MACHINA
■■ _____ ■■■ ■■■
Extreme / May '95 / Vital/SAM.

ISABELLE EBRAHARDT: THE OBLIVION SEEKER
CD _____ SDV 031CD
SDV / Nov '94 / Plastic Head.

RAPTURES OF METALS, THE
CD _____ SDV 027CD
SDV / Oct '94 / Plastic Head.

SURGERY OF TOUCH
CD _____ SNTX 175
Sentrax Corporation / Sep '94 / Plastic Head.

Schwartz, Jonathan

ALONE TOGETHER
You and the night and music / I see your face before me / New sun in the sky / Then I'll be tired of you / I'm like a new broom / I guess I'll have to change my plan / Where do I go from you / Be myself / Something to remember you by / Alone together
CD _____ MCD 5143
Muse / Dec '95 / New Note / CM.

ANYONE WOULD LOVE YOU
CD _____ MCD 5325
Muse / Sep '92 / New Note / CM.

Schwartz, Radam

ORGAN-IZED
Big Daddy and the boys / Lament / Sweet love / Shaw as can be / Polka dots and moonbeams / Radam steps / Night travelling / Eyewitness blues
CD _____ MCD 5497
Muse / Apr '95 / New Note / CM.

Schwarz, Rudy

SALMON DAVE
CD _____ EFA 11388-2
Musical Tragedies / May '94 / SRD.

Schweitzer, Irene

LES DIABOLIQUES
CD _____ INTAKTCD 033
Intakt / Oct '94 / Cadillac / SRD.

Schwitters, Kurt

URSONATE
CD _____ ARTCD 6109
Hat Art / May '92 / Harmonia Mundi / ADA / Cadillac.

Sciaky, Carla

AWAKENING
CD _____ GLCD 2115
Green Linnet / Feb '95 / Roots / CM / Direct / ADA.

Scialfa, Patti

RUMBLE DOLL
Rumble doll / Come tomorrow / In my imagination / Valerie / As long as I (can be with you) / Big black heaven / Love's glory / Lucky girl / Charm light / Baby don't / Talk to me like the rain / Spanish dancer
CD _____ 473874 2
Columbia / Jul '93 / Sony.

Scientist

FREEDOM FIGHTERS DUB (Scientist & The Force Of Music)
CD _____ TWCD 1051
Tamoki Wambesi / Jun '95 / Jetstar / SRD / Roots Collective / Greensleeves.

HIGH PRIEST OF DUB
Hail him in dub / Gad man the prophet / Reuben first born / Ethiopian high priest / Repatriation is a must / Their hands in blood / Vatican / President / Forgive them, oh Jah / Mass murder and corruption
CD _____ TWCD 1050
Tamoki Wambesi / Jun '95 / Jetstar / SRD / Roots Collective / Greensleeves.

INTERNATIONAL HEROES DUB
CD _____ TWCD 1022
Tamoki Wambesi / Aug '94 / Jetstar / SRD / Roots Collective / Greensleeves.

KING OF DUB
11 Guava Road dub / 13 Bread Lane dub / Burning Lane dub / 18 Drumalie Avenue (dub) / Gad man the prophet / Rise with version / Next door dub / Forgive them oh Jah / Mass murder and corruption / King Tub-by's hi-fi / Raw dub / Jack Ruby's hi power / Cultural vibes / Everlasting version / Knockout version / King Sturgav
CD _____ CD KVL 9029
Kingdom / Mar '87 / Kingdom.

REPATRIATION DUB
CD _____ TWCD 1058
Tamoki Wambesi / Nov '95 / Jetstar / SRD / Roots Collective / Greensleeves.

SCIENTIST ENCOUNTERS PAC-MAN
Under surveillance / Pac-man's wrath / Space invaders re-group / World cup squad lick their wounds / Vampire initiative / Malicious intent / Dark secret of the box / S.O.S. / Man trap / Look out + behind you
CD _____ GRELCD 46
Greensleeves / Mar '94 / Total/BMG / Jetstar / SRD.

SCIENTIST WINS THE WORLD CUP
Five dangerous matches Pt. 1 / Five dangerous matches Pt. 2
CD _____ GRELCD 37
Greensleeves / Mar '94 / Total/BMG / Jetstar / SRD.

Scientists

ABSOLUTE
CD _____ REDCD 23
Normal/Okra / May '94 / Direct / ADA.

Scissormen

MUMBO JUMBO
CD _____ BACCYCD 003
Diversity / Sep '95 / 3MV / Vital.

NITWIT
CD _____ EVRCD 16
Eve / Nov '92 / Grapevine.

Sclavis, Louis

ACCOUSTIC QUARTET
Sensible / Bafouee / Abrupto / Elke / Hop / Seconde / Beata / Rhinoceros
CD _____ 5213492
ECM / Feb '94 / New Note.

ROUGE (Sclavis, Louis Quintet)
One / Nacht / Kali la nuit / Reflet / Reeves / Les bouteilles / Moment donne / Face nord / Rouge / Yes love
CD _____ 5119292
ECM / Mar '92 / New Note.

Scobey, Bob

BOB SCOBEY'S FRISCO BAND
CD _____ CD 53143
Giants Of Jazz / Jan '94 / Target/BMG / Cadillac.

DIRECT FROM SAN FRANCISCO
CD _____ GTCD 12023
Good Time Jazz / Oct '93 / Jazz Music / Wellard / Pinnacle / Cadillac.

SCOBEY & CLANCY (Scobey, Bob & Clancy Hayes)
CD _____ GTCD 12009
Good Time Jazz / Oct '93 / Jazz Music / Wellard / Pinnacle / Cadillac.

Scofield, John

BLUE MATTER
Blue matter / Trim / Heaven hill / So you say / Now she's blonde / Make me / Nag / Time marches on
CD _____ GCD 79403
Gramavision / Sep '95 / Vital/SAM / ADA.

ELECTRIC OUTLET
Big break / Best Western / Pick hits / Filibustero / Thanks again / King for a day / Phone home / Just my luck
CD _____ GCD 79404
Gramavision / Sep '95 / Vital/SAM / ADA.

FLAT OUT
Cissy strut / Secret love / All the things you are / In the cracks / Softly / Science and religion / Boss's car / Evansville / Rockin' pneumonia and the boogie woogie flu
CD _____ GCD 79400
Gramavision / Sep '95 / Vital/SAM / ADA.

GROOVE ELATION
Lazy / Peculiar / Let the cat out / Kool / Old soul / Groove elation / Carlos / Soft shoe / Let it shine / Bigtop
CD _____ CDP 8328012
Blue Note / Nov '95 / EMI.

HAND JIVE
I'll take Les / Dark blue / Do like Eddie / She's so lucky / Checkered past / Seventh Floor / Golden daze / Don't shoot the messenger / Whip the mule / Out of the city
CD _____ CDP 8273272
Blue Note / Aug '94 / EMI.

I CAN SEE YOUR HOUSE FROM HERE (Scofield, John & Pat Metheny)
I can see your house from here / Red one / No matter what / Everybody's party / Message to my friend / No way Jose / Say the brothers name / S.C.O. / Quite rising / One way to be / You speak my language
CD _____ CDP 8277652
Blue Note / Mar '94 / EMI.

LIQUID FIRE
CD _____ GCD 79501
Gramavision / May '95 / Vital/SAM / ADA.

LIVE
CD _____ ENJACD 30132
Enja / Nov '94 / New Note / Vital/SAM.

LOUD JAZZ
Tell you what / Dance me home / Signature of Venus / Dirty rice / Wabash / Loud jazz / Otay / True love / Igetthepicture / Spy Vs. spy
CD _____ GCD 79402
Gramavision / Sep '95 / Vital/SAM / ADA.

MEANT TO BE (Scofield, John Quartet)
Big fan / Keep me in mind / Go blow / Chariots / Guinness spot / Mr. Coleman to you / Eisenhower / Meant to be / Some nerve / Lot in space / French flics
CD _____ CDP 795 479 2
Blue Note / Mar '91 / EMI.

OUT LIKE A LIGHT
CD _____ ENJA 40382
Enja / Nov '94 / New Note / Vital/SAM.

PICK HITS
CD _____ GCD 79405
Gramavision / Sep '95 / Vital/SAM / ADA.

PICK HITS LIVE
Picks and pans / Heaven will / Blue matter / Trim / Make me / Pick hits / Protocol / Thanks again / Georgia on my mind
CD _____ GRV 88052
Gramavision / Feb '91 / Vital/SAM / ADA.

ROUGH HOUSE
CD _____ ENJA 30332
Enja / Nov '94 / New Note / Vital/SAM.

SLO SCO
CD _____ GV 794302
Gramavision / Dec '90 / Vital/SAM / ADA.

STILL WARM
Techno / Still warm / High and mighty / Protocol / Rule of thumb / Picks and pans / Gil b 643
CD _____ GCD 79401
Gramavision / Sep '95 / Vital/SAM / ADA.

Scooter

BEATS GOES ON
CD _____ 0060962CLU
Edel / Nov '95 / Pinnacle.

Scorn

COLOSSUS
Endless / Crimson seed / Blackout / Sky is loaded / Nothing hunger / Beyond / Little angel / White irises blind / Scorpionic / Night ash black / Sunstroke
CD _____ MOSH 091CD
Earache / Jun '93 / Vital.

ELLIPSIS
Silver rain fell / Exodus / Dreamscape / Night ash black / Night tide / Falling / End / Automata / Light trap / Dreamscape 2 (On LP)
CD _____ SCORNCD 001
Earache / Jun '95 / Vital.

EVANESCENCE
Silver rain fell / Light trap / Falling / Automata / Days passed / Dreamspace / Exodus / Night tide / End / Slumber
CD _____ MOSH 113CD
Earache / Jun '94 / Vital.

GYRAL
Six hours one week / Time went slow / Far in out / Stairway / Forever turning / Black box / Hush / Trondheim - Gaule
CD _____ SCORNCD 002
Earache / Nov '95 / Vital.

VAE SOLIS
CD _____ MOSH 054CD
Earache / Apr '92 / Vital.

Scorpio Rising

PIG SYMPHONY
Talking backwards / Breathing underwater / Beautiful people / Watermelon girl / Oceanside / Silver surfing / Evelyn / Little pieces / Goofball / Sleeping sickness / Fountain of you
CD _____ 936245270-2
Warner Bros. / May '93 / Warner Music.

Scorpions

ANIMAL MAGNETISM
Make it real / Don't make no promises (your body can't keep) / Hold me tight / Twentieth century man / Lady starlight / Falling in love / Only a man / Zoo / Animal magnetism
CD _____ CDFA 3217
Fame / May '89 / EMI.

BEST OF ROCKERS 'N' BALLADS
Rock you like a hurricane / Can't explain / Rhythm of love / Big city nights / Lovedrive / Is there anybody there / Holiday / Still loving you / No one like you / Blackout / Another piece of meat / You give me all I need / Hey you / Zoo / China white
CD _____ CDFA 3262
Fame / Oct '91 / EMI.

BEST OF THE SCORPIONS
Steam rock fever / Pictured life / Robot man / Back stage queen / Speedy's coming / Hellcat / He's a woman, she's a man / In trance / Dark lady / Sails of Charon / Virgin killer
CD _____ ND 74006
RCA / Feb '89 / BMG.

BEST OF THE SCORPIONS VOL.2
Top of the bill / They need a million / Longing for fire / Catch your train / Speedy's coming (Live) / Crying days / All night long / This is my song / Sun in my hand / We'll burn the sky
CD _____ ND 74517
RCA / Feb '90 / BMG.

BLACKOUT
Blackout / Can't live without you / You give me all I need / Now / Dynamite / Arizona / China white / When the smoke is going down
CD _____ CDFA 3126
Fame / Nov '88 / EMI.

CRAZY WORLD
Tease me please me / To be with you in heaven / Restless night / Kicks after six / Money and fame / Don't believe her / Wind of change / Lust or love / Hit between the eyes / Send me an angel
CD _____ 846908 2
Vertigo / Nov '90 / PolyGram.

DEADLY STING
Coming home / Rock you like a hurricane / No one like you / Lovedrive / Bad boys running wild / I'm leaving you / Passion rules the game / China white / Walking on the edge / Coast to coast / Loving you Sunday morning / Another piece of meat / Dynamite / Can't live without you / Edge of time
CD _____ CDEMC 3698
EMI / Feb '95 / EMI.

HOT AND HARD
Top of the bill / Drifting sun / Sun in my hand / Longing for fire / Catch your train / Virgin killer / Hell cat / Polar nights / I've got to be free / Riot of your times / He's a woman, she's a man / Steam rock fever / Suspender love (live) / Hound dog (live) / Long tall Sally (live) / Fly to the rainbow
CD _____ 74321151192
RCA / Sep '93 / BMG.

HOT AND SLOW (Best Of The Ballads)
In trance / Life's like a river / Yellow raven / Born to touch your feeling / In search of the peace of mind (live) / Far away / In your

park / Crying days / Fly people fly / We'll burn the sky / Living and dying / Kojo no tsuki
CD _____ ND 75029
RCA / Dec '91 / BMG.

HURRICANE ROCK
Fly to the rainbow / Speedy's coming / In trance / Robot man / Polar nights / We'll burn the sky / Steamrock fever / He's a woman, she's a man / Another piece of meat / Coast to coast / Love drive / Zoo / Blackout / Can't live without you / When the smoke is going down / Dynamite / Rock you like a hurricane / Still loving you / Coming home / Rhythm of love
CD _____ VSOPCD 156
Connoisseur / Dec '90 / Pinnacle.

LIVE BITES
Mercury / Apr '95 / PolyGram. 5269032

LOVE AT FIRST STING
Bad boys running wild / Rock you like a hurricane / I'm leaving you / Coming home / Same thrill / Big city nights / As soon as the good times roll / Crossfire / Still loving you
CD _____ CDFA 3224
Fame / Aug '89 / EMI.

LOVEDRIVE
Loving you Sunday morning / Another piece of meat / Always somewhere / Coast to coast / Can't get enough / Is there anybody there / Lovedrive / Holiday
CD _____ CDFA 3080
Fame / Nov '88 / EMI.

SCORPIONS CD SET
Countdown / Coming home / Blackout / Bad boys running wild / Loving you Sunday morning / Make it real / Big city nights / Coast to coast / Holiday / Still loving you / Rock you like a hurricane / Can't live without you / Zoo / No one like you / Dynamite / Don't stop at the top / Rhythm of love / Passion rules the game / Media overkill / Walking on the edge / We let it rock (you let it roll) / Every minute of the day / Love on the run / Believe in love / Can't explain / Lovedrive / Is there anybody there / Another piece of meat / You give me all I need / Hey you / China white
CD Set _____ CDS 7979632
EMI / Oct '91 / EMI.

Scotrail Vale Of Atholl..

BOTH SIDES OF THE TRACKS (Scotrail Vale Of Atholl Pipe Band)
CD _____ LAPCD 115
Lapwing / Dec '88 / CM.

NO RESERVATIONS (Scotrail Vale Of Atholl Pipe Band)
Zito the bubbleman / Marjorie Lowe / Gallowglass / Jig / House in St. Peter's / Monymusk / Mrs. Stewart of Grantully / Miss Monaghan's / Maggie's pancakes / Hawk / March, strathspey and reel / John MacDonald of Glencoe / Athol cummers / John Morrison of Assynt House / Isobel Blackley / Sweeney's Reel / Molly Rankine's / Hogties' reel / Kenny the Sparrowman / Boys of Ballmote / Double Rise / Brest St. Mark jig / Hag at the churn / Smeceno Horo / Mountains of Pomeroy / Thomas Maxwell of Briarsbush / Garba Chriochan / Snug in the blanket / Congress reel / John Keith Laing / Hills of Kowloon / L.L. Wade's Welcome to Inverness / Lyndhurst / Killoran Bay / St. Jean-des-Vignes / Summertime / Big parcel / Jim Blakeley / Mrs. Macleod of Raasay / Galician jigs
CD _____ LAP CD 122
Lapwing / '89 / CM.

Scots Guards Bands

FROM THE HIGHLANDS (Band Of The Scots Guards)
Alma / Highland gathering / Tam O'shanter / Wee MacGregor / Nairn / Loch Lomond / Hebrides / Swing O'the kilt / Four scottish dances / Land of the mountain and the flood / Celtic melody / From the highlands
CD _____ BNA 5038
Bandleader / '91 / Conifer.

ON PARADE (Scots Guards Pipes & Drums Band)
CD _____ CC 292
Music For Pleasure / Jun '93 / EMI.

PIPES & DRUMS (Scots Guards Pipes & Drums Band)
March medley / March, strathspey and reel / Solo pipes / Slow march medley / Drum display / Regimental quick march
CD _____ BNA 5012
Bandleader / Feb '88 / Conifer.

Scott, Audrey

STEP BY STEP
CD _____ CDSGP 0133
Prestige / Mar '95 / Total/BMG.

Scott, Bobby

FOR SENTIMENTAL REASONS
(I love you) for sentimental reasons / Night lights / Lovewise / More I see you / Gee baby ain't I good to you / I keep going back to Joe's / Mamselle / That's all / That Sunday that summer / Nature boy

CD _____ MM 5025
Music Masters / Oct '94 / Nimbus.

SLOWLY
CD _____ MM 5053
Music Masters / Aug '94 / Nimbus.

Scott, Bon

EARLY YEARS (Scott, Bon & The Valentines)
To know you is to love you / She said / Everyday I have to cry / I can't dance with you / Peculiar hole in the sky / Love makes sweet music / I can hear raindrops / Why me / Sookie sookie
CD _____ C5CD-520
See For Miles/C5 / Sep '91 / Pinnacle.

HISTORICAL DOCUMENT (Scott, Bon & The Spectors)
CD _____ SEACD 6
See For Miles/C5 / Oct '92 / Pinnacle.

Scott, E.C.

COME GET YOUR LOVE
CD _____ BPCD 75019
Blind Pig / Jul '95 / Hot Shot / Swift / CM / Roots / Direct / ADA.

Scott, Jack

CLASSIC SCOTT
Greaseball / Baby she's gone / You can bet your bottom dollar / Two timin' woman / I need your love / My true love / Leroy / With your love / Indiana waltz / No one will ever know / I can't help it / I'm dreaming of you / Midgie / Save my soul / Geraldine / Goodbye baby / Way I walk / I never felt like this / Bella / Go wild little Sadie / What am I living for / There'll come a time / Baby Marie / Baby baby / What in the world's come over you / Goo deal Lucille / Oh little one / So used to loving you / Cruel world / Window shopping / Burning bridges / Your cheatin' heart / I can't escape from you / Cold cold heart / I could never be ashamed of you / They'll never take her love from me / Crazy heart / You win again / Half as much / I'm sorry for you my friend / Take these chains from my heart / My heart would know / May you never be alone / It's my way of loving you / My King / I'm satisfied with you / Am I the one / It only happened yesterday / True love is blind / Part where I cried / When the Saints go marching in (take 8) / Swing low, sweet chariot / Ezekiel saw de wheel / Joshua fit de battle of Jericho / Little David play your harp / Roll Jordan roll / Down by the riverside / Old time religion / Gospel train / I want to be ready / Just a closer walk with thee / He'll understand and say Well Done / Lonesome Mary / Patsy / Is there something on your mind / Found a woman / Little feeling called love / Now that I / True true love / One of these days / Strange desire / My dream come true / Steps one and two / Sad story / You only see what you wanna see / I can't hold your letters (in my arms) / Cry cry cry / Grizzly bear / Part where I cried / Green green valley / Strangers / Laugh and the world laughs with you / Meo myo / All I saw is blue / Jingle bell slide / There's trouble brewin' / Thou shalt not steal / I knew you first / I prayed for an angel / Blue skies (movin' in on me) / What a wonderful night out / Wiggle on out / Tall tales / Flakey John / Seperation's now granted / I don't believe in tea leaves / Standing on the outside looking in / Looking for Linda / I hope, I think, I wish / Gone again / Let's learn to live and love again / Don't hush the laughter / With your love (stereo) / Indiana waltz (stereo) / No one will ever know (stereo) / I'm dreaming of you (stereo) / Geraldine (stereo) / Goodbye baby (stereo) / Way I walk (stereo) / If only (takes 8 & 15) / When the Saints go marching in (take 19) / Go away from here (crying in my beer) / Before the bird flies / Insane / My special angel / I keep changing my mind / Hard luck Joe / Billy Jack / Mary marry me / Face to the wall / I still love you enough / As you take a walk through my mind / You make it hard not to love you / You're just not gettin' better / Apple blossom time / Blues stay away from me / Stones / Bo's going to jail / Country witch
CD Set _____ BCD 15534
Bear Family / Aug '92 / Rollercoaster / Direct / CM / Swift / ADA.

JACK SCOTT/WHAT IN THE WORLD'S COME OVER YOU
Save my soul / With your love / Leroy / No one will ever know / Geraldine / I can't help it / Indiana waltz / Midgie / My true love / Way I walk / I'm dreaming of you / Goodbye baby / What in the world's come over you / Oh, little one / Am I the one / I'm satisfied with you / My King / It's my way of loving you / Burning bridges / Baby, baby / So used to loving you / Cruel world / Good deal Lucille / Window shopping
CD _____ BGOCD 303
Beat Goes On / Nov '95 / Pinnacle.

SCOTT ON GROOVE
Flakey John / Jingle bell slide / There's trouble brewin' / Tall tales / Wiggle on out / I

knew you first / Blue skies (moving in on me) / I prayed for an angel / Separation's now granted / Thou shalt not steal / Road keeps winding (Previously unissued) / Let's learn to live and love again / Don't hush the laughter / This is where I came in (Previously unissued) / Looking for Linda / I hope, I think, I wish / Standing on the outside looking in (Previously unissued) / Gone again (Previously unissued) / I don't believe in tea leaves / What a wonderful night out
CD _____ BCD 15445
Bear Family / '88 / Rollercoaster / Direct / CM / Swift / ADA.

WAY I WALK, THE
Leroy / Midgie / Way I walk / Goodbye baby / Go wild Little Sadie / Geraldine / Save my soul / Baby she's gone / Two timin' woman / I never felt like this / My true love / I'm dreaming of you / With your love / I can't help it / No one will ever know / Indiana waltz / Baby Marie / Bella / There comes a time / I need your love / You can bet your bottom dollar / What am I living for / There's trouble brewin' / Lonesome Mary / Greaseball
CD _____ RCCD 3002
Rollercoaster / Aug '90 / CM / Swift.

Scott, Jimmy

ALL OVER AGAIN
Sometimes I feel like a motherless child / Evening in Paradise / If I ever lost you / (I'm afraid) the masquerade is over / Please forgive me / How else / If you are but a dream / Way you look tonight / Things that are love / Everybody's somebody's fool / Once / What good would it be / Imagination / How can I go on without you / Time on my hands / Very truly yours / Show goes on / Someone to watch over me / Street of dreams / Don't cry baby / Why don't you open your heart / Everybody needs somebody / Guilty / When did you leave Heaven
CD _____ SV 0263
Savoy Jazz / Apr '95 / Conifer / ADA.

DREAM
Don't take you love from me / It shouldn't happen to a dream / I cried for you / So long / You never miss the water / It's the talk of the town / I'm through with love / Laughing on the outside / Dream
CD _____ 936245629-2
Warner Bros. / Jul '94 / Warner Music.

LITTLE JIMMY SCOTT - VERY TRULY YOURS
Imagination / How can I go on / Time on my hands / When did you leave Heaven / Guilty / Everybody needs somebody / Why don't you open your heart / Don't cry baby / Street of dreams / Someone to watch over me / Show goes on / Very truly yours
CD _____ SV 0239
Savoy Jazz / Jan '94 / Conifer / ADA.

LOST AND FOUND
I have dreamed / Stay with me / Folks who live on the hill / For once in my life / Dedicated to you / Day to day / Unchained melody / Sometimes I feel like a motherless child / Exodus / I wish I knew
CD _____ RSACD 804
Sequel / Dec '94 / BMG.

Scott, Mike

BRING 'EM ALL IN
Bring 'em all in / Iona song / Edinburgh Castle / What do you want me to do / I know she's in the building / City full of ghosts (Dublin) / Wonderful disguise / Sensitive children / Learning to love him / She is so beautiful / Wonderful disguise (reprise) / Long way to the light / Building the city of light
CD _____ CDCHR 6108
Chrysalis / Sep '95 / EMI.

Scott, Peggy

BEST OF PEGGY SCOTT AND JO JO BENSON, THE (Scott, Peggy & Jo Jo Benson)
CD _____ SCL 2103
Ichiban Soul Classics / Aug '95 / Koch.

Scott, Raymond

POWERHOUSE, VOL. 1
CD _____ STCD 543
Stash / '92 / Jazz Music / CM / Cadillac / Direct / ADA.

Scott, Ronnie

JAZZMAN (CD/Book Set)
CD _____ BKB 002
Elm Tree / Jun '95 / Magnum Music Group.

NEVER PAT A BURNING DOG (Scott, Ronnie Quintet)
Contemplation / I'm glad there is you / White caps / All the things you are / This love of mine / When love is new / Little sunflower (CD only)
CD _____ JHCD 012
Ronnie Scott's Jazz House / Jan '94 / Jazz Music / Magnum Music Group / Cadillac.

Scott, Shirley

BLUES EVERYWHERE
CD _____ CCD 79525
Candid / Apr '93 / Cadillac / Jazz Music / Wellard / Koch.

OASIS
CD _____ MCD 5388
Muse / Sep '92 / New Note / CM.

SKYLARK (Scott, Shirley Trio)
CD _____ CCD 79536
Candid / Sep '94 / Cadillac / Jazz Music / Wellard / Koch.

Scott, Sonny

COMPLETE RECORDINGS (1933)
CD _____ SOB 035252
Story Of The Blues / Dec '92 / Koch / ADA.

Scott, Stephen

AMINAH'S DREAM
CD _____ 517996-2
Verve / Jul '93 / PolyGram.

Scott, Tom

DESIRE
Desire / Sure enough / Only one / Stride / Johnny B. Badde / Meet somebody / Maybe I'm amazed / Chunk of funk
CD _____ 7599601622
Elektra / Mar '93 / Warner Music.

FLASHPOINT
CD _____ GRP 95712
GRP / Oct '88 / BMG / New Note.

NIGHT CREATURES
Night creatures / Don't get any better / Bhop / Anytime anyplace / We'll be together / Mazin' / Yeah / Refried / Daybreak / We'll be together (instrumental)
CD _____ GRP 98042
GRP / Feb '95 / BMG / New Note.

TARGET
Target / Come back to me / Aerobia / He's too young / Got to get out of New York / Biggest part of me / Burindi bump
CD _____ 756780106-2
Atlantic / Jun '93 / Warner Music.

Scott, Tommy

COUNTRY HOLIDAY
I never loved no one but you / Does my ring hurt your finger / I'd rather love you / All I have to offer you / Rose Marie / Distant drums / This world is not my home / Cry / Any time / Someday you'll want me to want you / Crying time / Together again / But when I dream / Lovesick blues / Rock of ages / Kiss an angel good morning / There goes my everything / Pretty woman / Blanket on the ground / Stop / If I had my life to live over / Let me be there
CD _____ LCDITV 606
Scotdisc / Nov '95 / Duncans / Ross / Conifer.

GOING HOME
CD _____ CDITV 564
Scotdisc / Oct '92 / Duncans / Ross / Conifer.

HAIL HAIL CALEDONIA
CD _____ CDITV 597
Scotdisc / Nov '94 / Duncans / Ross / Conifer.

ORIGINAL HOPSCOTCH
CD _____ PLATCD 3923
Prism / May '94 / Prism.

PIPES & STRINGS OF SCOTLAND
Pride of bonnie Scotland / Ode to joy / Abide with me / Scottish banner / 'Tis a gift (to be simple) / Bonnie Mary of Argyle / Send in the clowns / Jesu joy of man's desiring / Rose of Kelvingrove / Song of the wind / Scott's choice / Light of the morning / Little drummer boy / Carnival is over
CD _____ CDITV 456
Scotdisc / Aug '89 / Duncans / Ross / Conifer.

SCOTLAND FOREVER
CD _____ CDITV 545
Scotdisc / Sep '91 / Duncans / Ross / Conifer.

TOMMY SCOTT AND HIS PIPES AND DIXIE BANDS
CD _____ CDITV 521
Scotdisc / Nov '90 / Duncans / Ross / Conifer.

TOMMY SCOTT COLLECTION
Scotland forever / My ain folk / Going home / Old Scots mother mine / Glencoe / Rowan tree / Abide with me / Road to Dundee / Amazing grace / Flower of Scotland / Bonnie Mary of Argyle / Auld lang syne
CD _____ CDITV 431
Scotdisc / Nov '87 / Duncans / Ross / Conifer.

TOMMY SCOTT'S COUNTRY HOP
CD _____ CDITV 569
Scotdisc / May '94 / Duncans / Ross / Conifer.

TOMMY SCOTT'S HOPSCOTCH CEILIDH PARTY
CD _____ CDITV 528
Scotdisc / Dec '90 / Duncans / Ross / Conifer.

TOMMY SCOTT'S ROYALE HIGHLAND SHOWBAND (Scott, Tommy's Royale Highland Showband)
Red river rose / March march march all the way / Morag of Dunvegan / Mingulay boat song / Maggie may / Day is ended / P.K.'s salute / Pigeon on the gate / Pipes O'Drummond / De'il among the tailors / Kilt is my delight / Pipers patrol / Mount Fuji / Water is wide / Flute salad / Dark island / May kway o'may kway / High road to Linton
CD _____ CDITV 426
Scotdisc / Jun '87 / Duncans / Ross / Conifer.

TOMMY SCOTT'S SCOTLAND
Annie Laurie / Dark Lochnagar / Great Glen / Skye boat song / Amazing grace / Flower of Scotland / Will ye no' come back again / Scotland forever / My love is like a red red rose / Flowers of the forest / Rowan tree / Green trees of Tyrol / My Ain folk / Auld lang syne
CD _____ CD ITV 411
Scotdisc / Dec '86 / Duncans / Ross / Conifer.

Scott, Toni

CHIEF, THE
CD _____ CHAMPCD 1022
Champion / Feb '90 / BMG.

Scott, Tony

1957 (Scott, Tony & Bill Evans)
CD _____ CD 53202
Giants Of Jazz / May '95 / Target/BMG / Cadillac.

CLARINET ALBUM, THE (Scott, Tony Quartet)
CD _____ W 113-2
Philology / Nov '93 / Harmonia Mundi / Cadillac.

DIALOGUE WITH MYSELF, LIKE A CHILD'S WHISPER
CD _____ W 76-2
Philology / Dec '95 / Harmonia Mundi / Cadillac.

MUSIC FOR ZEN MEDITATION
Is not all one / Murmuring sound of the mountain / Quivering leaf, ask the wind / After the snow the fragrance / To drift like clouds / Za-zan (meditation) / Prajna paramita hridya sutra / Sanzan (moment of truth) / Satori (enlightenment)
CD _____ 8172092
Verve / Jan '93 / PolyGram.

SUNG HEROES
Misery (to lady day) / Portrait of Anne Frank / Remembrance of Art Tatum / Requiem for 'Hot Lips' Page / Blues for an African friend / For Stefan Wolpe / Israel / Memory of my father / Lament to manolete
CD _____ SSC 1015D
Sunnyside / Sep '86 / Pinnacle.

Scott-Heron, Gil

GLORY (The Gil Scott Heron Collection)
Johannesburg / Revolution will not be televised / Blue collar / New York City / Hello Sunday, hello road / We almost lost Detroit / Angel dust / Bottle / Winter in America / Delta man / South Carolina (Barnwell) / Inner city blues / Showbizness / B Movie / Lady Day and John Coltrane / I think I'll call it morning / You can depend on (the train from Washington) / Shut 'em down / Ain't no such thing as superman / Klan / Fast lane / Race track in France / Storm music / Save the children / Song for Bobby Smith / Beginnings / Legend in his own mind
CD _____ 353913
Arista / Nov '90 / BMG.

MINISTER OF INFORMATION
CD _____ CCSCD 403
Castle / Apr '94 / BMG.

REVOLUTION WILL NOT BE TELEVISED, THE
Revolution will not be televised / Sex education - ghetto style / Get out of the ghetto blues / No knock / Lady Day and John Coltrane / Pieces of a man / Home is where the hatred is / Brother / Save the children / Whitey on the moon / Did you hear what they said / When you are who you are / I think I'll call it morning / Sign of the ages / Or down you fall / Needle's eye / Prisoner
CD _____ ND 86994
Bluebird / Apr '89 / BMG.

SPIRITS
Message to the messengers / Spirits / Give her a call / Lady's song / Spirits past / Other side (parts 1-3) / Work for peace / Don't give up
CD _____ MUMCD 9415
Mother / Aug '94 / PolyGram.

Scottish Fiddle Orchestra

LEGENDARY SCOTTISH FIDDLE ORCHESTRA, THE (Scottish Fiddle Orchestra & John Mason)
CD _____ RECD 498
REL / Apr '95 / THE / Gold / Duncans.

Scottish Gas Caledonia...

OUT OF THE BLUE (Scottish Gas Caledonia Pipe Band)
2/4 marches / March / Strathspey and reel / Irish hornpipe rhythms / Pipe band medley / Irish set / Reels / Slow air / Hornpipes and reels / Jigs
CD _____ CDTRAX 064
Greentrax / Nov '93 / Conifer / Duncans / ADA / Direct.

Scottish National Pipe &.

SCOTLAND THE BRAVE (Scottish National Pipe & Drum Corps)
CD _____ CNCD 5958
Disky / Jul '93 / THE / BMG / Discovery / Pinnacle.

Scottish Philharmonic...

PSALMS OF SCOTLAND (Scottish Philharmonic Singers)
Psalm 23 Crimond / Psalm 100 Old 100th / Paraphrase 18 Glasgow / Psalm 136 Crofts' 136th / Paraphrase 18 Glasgow / Psalm 43 Martyrs / Psalm 24 St George's, Edinburgh / Psalm 46 Stroudwater / Paraphrase 48 St Andrew / Paraphrase 65 Desert / Psalm 148 St John / Psalm 130 Martyrdom / Psalm 124 Old 124th / Psalm 23 Orlington / Psalm 103 Coleshill / Psalm 36 London new / Psalm 95 Bon Accord / Paraphrase 2 Salzburg / Psalm 12 French / Psalm 72 Effingham
CD _____ SCSCD 2830
SCS Music / Apr '94 / Conifer.

SCOTTISH PHILHARMONIC SINGERS (Scottish Philharmonic Singers)
In praise of Islay / Rosebud by my early walk / Johnny Cope / Fairy lullaby / Scots wha hae / Island herdsmaid / Duncan Gray / Iona boat song / Ossianic processional / Flow gently sweet Afton / Charlie is my darling / Skye boat song / Fife fisher song / Ye banks and braes o' bonnie Doon / Ca' the Yowes / Loch Lomond / Island sheiling song / Eriskay love lilt / Flowers o' the forest / Donald Ewan's wedding
CD _____ LCOM 9043
Lismor / Apr '91 / Lismor / Direct / Duncans / ADA.

Scottish Power Pipe Band

TARTAN WEAVE
CD _____ CDMON 836
Monarch / Aug '95 / CM / ADA / Duncans / Direct.

Scottish Regiment

PIPES & DRUMS OF THE SCOTTISH REGIMENT
CD _____ CC 295
EMI / May '93 / EMI.

Scotto, Renata

GREAT VOICE
CD Set _____ HR 4291/92
New Note / Mar '91 / New Note / Cadillac.

Scram C Baby

TASTE
CD _____ GAP 018
Gap Recordings / Feb '94 / SRD.

Scrawl

BLOODSUCKER
CD _____ SMR 17D
Simple Machines / May '93 / SRD.

HE'S DRUNK
One green beer ready / For your sister / I feel your pain / Small day / Major, minor / Breaker breaker / Believe / Let it all hang out / Rocky top
CD _____ ROUGHCD 138
Rough Trade / Aug '89 / Pinnacle.

SMALLTOOTH
CD _____ ROUGHCD 150
Rough Trade / Mar '90 / Pinnacle.

Scream

FUMBLE/BANGING THE DRUM
CD _____ DIS 82D
Dischord / Jul '93 / SRD.

SCREAM: LIVE
CD _____ YCLS 010CD
Your Choice / Jun '94 / Plastic Head.

STILL SCREAMING/THIS SIDE UP
CD _____ DIS 81D
Dischord / Jul '93 / SRD.

Scream

NO MORE CENSORSHIP
CD _____ RASCD 4001

Ras / Dec '88 / Jetstar / Greensleeves / SRD / Direct.

Screamin' Cheetah...

SCREAMIN' CHEETAH WHEELIES (Screamin' Cheetah Wheelies)
Shakin' the blues / Ride the tide / Something else / This is the time / Slow burn / Leave your pride (at the front door) / Jami / Sister mercy / Majestic / Moses brown / Let it flow
CD _____ 756782507-2
WEA / Mar '94 / Warner Music.

Screaming Blue Messiahs

BBC LIVE IN CONCERT
CD _____ WINCD 022
Windsong / Jul '92 / Pinnacle.

Screaming Iguanas Of Love

GLAD YOU WEREN'T THERE
CD _____ NAK 6003CD
Naked Language / Sep '94 / Koch.

WILD WILD WILD
Wild wild wild / Never let you fall / Hole in my soul / Girl stuff / Let it down / Back together / Punch it / Madison / Ain't a thing about it / Our gang / I think of you / Let me explain / Stone's throw away / Stuck to you
CD _____ NAK 6001 CD
Naked Language / Nov '91 / Koch.

Screaming Lord Sutch

MURDER IN THE GRAVEYARD
CD _____ FCD 3023
Fury / Mar '95 / Magnum Music Group / Nervous.

Screaming Trees

ANTHOLOGY
CD _____ SST 260 CD
SST / May '93 / Plastic Head.

BUZZ FACTORY
Black sun morning / Flower web / End of the universe
CD _____ SST 248 CD
SST / Mar '89 / Plastic Head.

CHANGE HAS COME
Change has come / Days / Flashes / Time speaks her golden tongue / I've seen you before
CD _____ GRCD 80
Sub Pop / May '93 / Disc.

EVEN IF AND ESPECIALLY WHEN
Transfiguration / Straight out to any place / World painted / Don't look down / Girl behind the mask / Flying / Cold rain / Other days and different planets / Pathway / You know where it's at / Back together / In the forest
CD _____ SST 132 CD
SST / May '93 / Plastic Head.

INVISIBLE LANTERN
CD _____ SST 188 CD
SST / Sep '88 / Plastic Head.

OTHER WORLDS
CD _____ SST 105 CD
SST / May '93 / Plastic Head.

SWEET OBLIVION
Shadow of the season / Nearly lost you / Dollar bill / More or less / Butterfly / Secret kind / Winter song / Troubled times / No one knows / Julie paradise
CD _____ 4717242
Sony Music / '91 / Sony.

Screaming Tribesmen

BONES AND FLOWERS
CD _____ RCD 1007
Rykodisc / Jun '92 / Vital / ADA.

I'VE GOT A FEELING
CD _____ RCD 1006
Rykodisc / May '93 / Vital / ADA.

Screams For Tina

SCREAMS FOR TINA
CD _____ CDSATE 11
Zoth Ommog / Nov '94 / Plastic Head.

Screeching Weasel

ANTHEM FOR A NEW TOMORROW
CD _____ LOOKOUT 76CD
Lookout / Oct '94 / SRD.

HOW TO MAKE ENEMIES
CD _____ LOOKOUT 97CD
Lookout / Jun '95 / SRD.

KILL THE MUSICIANS
CD _____ LOOKOUT 095CD
Lookout / Jun '95 / SRD.

Screw Radio

TALK RADIO VIOLENCE
CD _____ SST 324CD
SST / Jan '96 / Plastic Head.

Screwdriver

TEACH DEM
CD _____ GS 70037 CD
Greensleeves / Apr '92 / Total/BMG / Jetstar / SRD.

Script

21 SYNTHESIZER SPACE HITS
CD _____ CDCH 076
Milan / Feb '91 / BMG / Silva Screen.

Scritti Politti

CUPID AND PSYCHE '85
Word girl / Small talk / Absolute / Little knowledge / Don't work that hard / Perfect way / Lover to fall / Wood beez (pray like Aretha Franklin) / Hypnotize / Flesh and blood (CD/MC only) / Absolute (version) (CD/MC only) / Hypnotize (version) (CD/MC only) / Wood Beez (version) (CD/MC only)
CD _____ CDV 2350
Virgin / Jun '85 / EMI.

PROVISION
Boom there she was / Overnite / First boy in this town (Lovesick) / All that we are / Best thing ever / Oh Patti (don't feel sorry for loverboy) / Bam salute / Sugar and spice / Philosophy now / Oh Patti (don't feel sorry for loverboy) (extended) (CD/MC only) / Boom there she was (dub) (CD/MC only)
CD P.Disc _____ CDVP 2515
Virgin / Dec '88 / EMI.

SONGS TO REMEMBER
Asylums in Jerusalem / Slow soul / Jacques Derrida / Lions after slumber / Faithless / Sex / Rock-a-boy blue / Gettin', havin' and holdin' / Sweetest girl
CD _____ ROUGHCD 20
Rough Trade / May '87 / Pinnacle.

Scuba

UNDERWATER SYMPHONIES
CD _____ CRECD 136
Creation / Oct '95 / 3MV / Vital.

Scud

EDWIN INCIDENT, THE
CD _____ BGR 009
BGR / Mar '95 / Plastic Head.

Scum

MOTHER NATURE
CD _____ BMCD 46
Black Mark / Aug '94 / Plastic Head.

Scum Of Toytown

STRIKE
CD _____ WOWCD 41
Words Of Warning / Mar '95 / SRD.

Scum Rats

GO OUT
CD _____ RUMBCD 001
Rumble / Aug '92 / Nervous.

LIVE AT THE BIG RUMBLE
CD _____ RUMBCD 014
Rumble / Aug '92 / Nervous.

Sea & Cake

BIZ
CD _____ EFA 121152
Moll / Oct '95 / SRD.

NASSAU
CD _____ EFA 121122
Moll / May '95 / SRD.

SEA AND CAKE, THE
Jacking the ball / Polio / Bring my car I need to smash it / Flat lay the waters / Choice blanket / Culabra cut / Bombay / Showboat angel / So long to the captain / Lost in autumn
CD _____ R 3102
Rough Trade / Feb '94 / Pinnacle.

Sea Horses

LISTEN
Asking heaven and heart / Salute to the sun / Exaltations / Angles of incidence / Pray / Satori / Kissing flowers / For our emotions / Open veins / Insufferance / Confession
CD _____ SH 777
Mandala / Apr '91 / Mandala / Harmonia Mundi.

Sea Nymphs

SEA NYMPHS, THE
CD _____ ALPHCD 021
Alphabet Business Concern / May '95 / Plastic Head.

Sea Train

MARBLEHEAD MESSENGER, THE
CD _____ S21 57661
One Way / Apr '94 / Direct / ADA.

Sea Urchins

LIVE FROM LONDON
CD _____ FRIGHT 061
Fierce / Mar '94 / Disc.

STARDUST
CD _____ SARAH 609CD
Sarah / Mar '95 / Vital.

Seaford College Chapel...

CAROLS FOR THE FAMILY (Seaford College Chapel Choir)
CD _____ CDFRC 522
Conifer / Dec '89 / Conifer.

FOR THE BEAUTY OF THE EARTH (Seaford College Chapel Choir)
CD _____ GRCD 71
Grasmere / Nov '95 / Target/BMG / Savoy.

Seal

SEAL
Beginning / Deep water / Crazy / Killer / Whirlpool / Future love paradise / Wild / Show me / Violet
CD _____ ZTT 9CD
ZTT / May '91 / Warner Music.

SEAL II
Bring it on / Prayer for the dying / Dreaming in metaphors / Don't cry / Fast changes / Kiss from a rose / People asking why / Newborn friend / If I could / I'm alive / Bring it on (reprise)
CD _____ 450996256-2
ZTT / May '94 / Warner Music.

Seal, Joseph

WURLITZER
CD _____ TRTCD 184
TrueTrax / May '95 / THE.

Seals & Crofts

SUMMER BREEZE
Hummingbird / Funny little man / Say / Summer breeze / East of ginger trees / Fiddle in the sky / Boy down the road / Euphrates / Advance guards / Yellow dirt
CD _____ 7599267442
Warner Bros. / May '95 / Warner Music.

Seals, Son

BAD AXE
Don't pick me for your fool / Going home (where women got meat on their bones) / Just about to lose your clown / Friday again / Cold blood / Out of my way / I think you're foolin' me / I can count on my blues / Can't stand to see her cry / Person to person
CD _____ ALCD 4738
Alligator / May '93 / Direct / ADA.

CHICAGO FIRE
CD _____ ALCD 4720
Alligator / May '93 / Direct / ADA.

LIVE & BURNING
CD _____ ALCD 4712
Alligator / May '93 / Direct / ADA.

LIVING IN THE DANGER ZONE
Frigidaire woman / I can't lose the blues / Woman in black / Tell it to another fool / Ain't that some shame / Arkansas woman / Danger zone / Last four nickels / My time now / Bad axe / My life
CD _____ ALCD 4798
Alligator / May '93 / Direct / ADA.

MIDNIGHT SON
CD _____ ALCD 4708
Alligator / May '93 / Direct / ADA.

NOTHING BUT THE TRUTH
CD _____ ALCD 4822
Alligator / Sep '94 / Direct / ADA.

SON SEALS BLUES BAND (Seals, Son Blues Band)
Mother-in-law blues / Sitting at my window / Look now baby / Your love is a cancer / All you love / Cotton pickin' blues / Hot sauce / How could she leave me / Going home tomorrow / Now that I'm down
CD _____ ALCD 4703
Alligator / Feb '94 / Direct / ADA.

Seam

ARE YOU DRIVING ME CRAZY
CD _____ EFA 049602
City Slang / Jul '95 / Disc.

HEADSPARKS
CD _____ EFA 0407626
City Slang / Apr '92 / Disc.

PROBLEM WITH ME
CD _____ EFA 0492326
City Slang / Sep '93 / Disc.

Seance

FORNEVER LAID TO REST
Who will not be dead / Reincarnage / Blessing of death / Sin / Haunted / Fornever laid to rest / Necronomicon / Wind of Gehenna / Inferna cabbala
CD _____ BMCD 017
Black Mark / Jun '92 / Plastic Head.

SALTRUBBED EYES
CD _____ BMCD 44
Black Mark / Jan '94 / Plastic Head.

Searchers

30TH ANNIVERSARY COLLECTION
CD Set _____ NEXCD 170
Sequel / Feb '92 / BMG.

BEST OF THE SEARCHERS 1963-1964, THE
Sweets for my sweet / Stand by me / Love potion no.9 / Some other guy / Where have all the flowers gone / Money (that's what I want) / Missing you / Sugar and spice / Needles and pins / It's in her kiss (Shoop shoop song) / When you walk in the room / Saints and searchers / What have they done to the rain / Someday we're gonna love again / All my sorrows / Don't throw your love away
CD _____ PWKS 4076
Carlton Home Entertainment / Aug '91 / Carlton Home Entertainment.

EP COLLECTION: SEARCHERS
When you walk in the room / Missing you / Oh my lover / This empty place / No one else could love me / What have they done to the rain / Goodbye my love / Till I met you / Can't help forgiving you / I don't want to go on without you / Till you say you'll be mine / Sweets for my sweet / Since you broke my heart / Two many miles / Take me for what I'm worth / Take it or leave it / Someday we're gonna love again / Bumble bee / System / Love potion no.9 / Money / Alright / Just like me (CD only) / Everything you do (CD only) / If I could find someone (CD only) / It's all been a dream (CD only) / Hungry for love (CD only) / Sea of heartbreak (CD only) / Ain't gonna kiss ya (CD only) / Don't cha know (CD only)
CD _____ SEECD 275
See For Miles/C5 / Jul '89 / Pinnacle.

GERMAN, FRENCH AND RARE RECORDINGS
CD _____ REP 4102-WZ
Repertoire / Aug '91 / Pinnacle / Cadillac.

IT'S THE SEARCHERS
Sea of heartbreak / Glad all over / It's in her kiss (Shoop shoop song) / Livin' lovin' wreck / Where have you been / Shimmy shimmy / Needles and pins / This empty place / Gonna send you back to Georgia / I count the tears / Hi-heel sneakers / Can't help forgiving you / Sho' know a lot about love / Don't throw your love away
CD _____ CLACD 167
Castle / Dec '89 / BMG.

MEET THE SEARCHERS
Sweets for my sweet / Alright / Love potion no.9 / Farmer John / Stand by me / Money / Da doo ron ron / Ain't gonna kiss ya / Since you broke my heart / Tricky Dicky / Where have all the flowers gone / Twist and shout
CD _____ CLACD 165
Castle / Dec '89 / BMG.

MIKE PENDER'S SEARCHERS
CD _____ GRF 185
Tring / Jan '93 / Tring / Prism.

SEARCHERS, THE
Sweets for my sweet / Sugar and spice / Needles and pins / Saints and sinners / Missing you / Goodbye my love / Glad all over / Have you ever loved somebody / Love potion no.9 / Take it or leave it / When you walk in the room / What have they done to the rain / It's all been a dream / Someday we're gonna love again / Don't throw your love away / He's got no love / Take me for what I'm worth / Alright / Money / When I get home
CD _____ CDMFP 5922
EMI / Oct '91 / EMI.

SEARCHERS, THE
CD _____ KLMCD 031
Scratch / Nov '94 / BMG.

SUGAR AND SPICE
Sugar and spice / Don't cha know / Some other guy / One of these days / Listen to me / Unhappy girls / Just like me / Oh my lover / Saints and searchers / Cherry stones / All my sorrows / Hungry for love
CD _____ CLACD 166
Castle / Dec '89 / BMG.

SWEETS FOR MY SWEET
Sweets for my sweet / He's got no love / Take me for what I'm worth / What have they done to the rain / Someday we're gonna love again / Take it or leave it / Needles and pins / Have you ever loved somebody / Don't throw your love away / When you walk in the room / Sugar and spice / Goodbye my love
CD _____ 5507412
Spectrum/Karussell / Sep '94 / PolyGram / THE.

Sears, Al

SEAR-IOUSLY
125th Street, New York / Shake hands / Tan skid lad / Brown boy / Huffin' and puffin' / Sear-iously / Mag's alley / Fo yah / In the good old summertime / Ivory cliffs / Easy Ernie / Vo sa / Goin' uptown / Tweedle dee

/ Come and dance with me / Come a runnin' / Tom, Dick 'n' Henry / Tina's canteen / Right now, right now / Midnight wail / Love call / Rock 'n' roll ball / Here's the beat / Great googa mooga / Fo ya
CD _____ BCD 15668
Bear Family / Jun '92 / Rollercoaster / Direct / CM / Swift / ADA.

Seaton, B.B.

EVERYDAY PEOPLE
Now I know / Good to me / Just a little more time / Private lessons / Everyday people / Gimme little love / Tell me if you're ready / Still look sexy / Some day I'll be free / Photographs and souvenirs
CD _____ RNCD 2012
Rhino / Jul '93 / Jetstar / Magnum Music Group / THE.

Seatrain

WATCH
Pack of fools / Freedom is the reason / Bloodshot eyes / We are your children too / Abbeville fair / Northcoast / Scratch / Watching the river flow / Flute thing
CD _____ 900898
Line / Oct '94 / CM / Grapevine / ADA / Conifer / Direct.

Seaweed

FOUR
CD _____ SPCD 110/286
Sub Pop / Sep '93 / Disc.

SEAWEED
CD _____ TUPCD 028
Tupelo / Oct '91 / Disc.

Sebadoh

BAKESALE
CD _____ WIGCD 11
Domino / Jun '95 / Pinnacle.

BUBBLE AND SCRAPE
CD _____ WIGCD 4
Domino / Jun '95 / Pinnacle.

ROCKING THE FOREST
CD _____ WIGCD 2
Domino / Jun '95 / Pinnacle.

SEBADOH III
CD _____ HMS 1682
Homestead / Jul '94 / SRD.

SEBADOH VS HELMET
CD _____ WIGCD 3
Homestead / '94 / SRD.

WEED FORRESTIN
CD _____ HMS 1582
Homestead / '94 / SRD.

Sebastian, John B.

JOHN B SEBASTIAN
Red eye express / She's a lady / What she thinks about / Magical connection / You're a big boy / Rainbows all over your blues / How have you been / Baby, don't ya get crazy / Room nobody lives in / Fa-fana-fa / I had a dream
CD _____ EDCD 304
Edsel / Jan '90 / Pinnacle / ADA.

Sebestyen, Marta

KISMET
Devoika mome / Sino moi / Leaving Derry Quay / Eleni / Gold, silver or love / Hindu lullabye / Shores of loch brann / Hazafele / If I were a rose (ha en rozsa velnek) / Imam sluzhba (the conscript)
CD _____ HNCD 1392
Hannibal / Feb '96 / Vital / ADA.

MARTA SEBESTYEN AND MUZIKAS (Sebestyen, Marta & Muzikas)
CD _____ HNCD 1330
Hannibal / May '88 / Vital / ADA.

Sebo, Ferenc

HUNGARIAN FOLK MUSIC (Sebo, Ferenc Ensemble)
CD _____ ROU 5005CD
Rounder / Feb '93 / CM / Direct / ADA / Cadillac.

Secada, Jon

HEART, SOUL & A VOICE
Whipped / Take me / If you go / Good feelings / Where do I go from you / Fat chance / Mental picture / Stay / La la / Don't be silly / Eyes of a fool / Si te vas (If you go) / Tuyo (Take me)
CD _____ SBKCD 29
SBK / Feb '95 / EMI.

JON SECADA
Just another day / Dreams that I carry / Angel / Do you believe in us / One of a kind / Time heals / Do you really want me / Misunderstood / Always something / I'm free / Otro dia mas sin verte / Angel (Spanish version)
CD _____ SBKCD 19
SBK / Aug '92 / EMI.

Secola, Keith

CIRCLE
CD _____ NORMAL 162CD
Normal/Okra / Mar '94 / Direct / ADA.

Secombe, Harry

FAVOURITE CHRISTMAS CAROLS (Secombe, Harry & Westminster City Choir)
O come all ye faithful (Adeste Fidelis) / Once in Royal David's city / Silent night / Away in a manger
CD _____ PWKS 520
Carlton Home Entertainment / Dec '88 / Carlton Home Entertainment.

HIGHWAY FAVOURITES
CD _____ KMCD 832
Kingsway / May '95 / Total/BMG / Complete/Pinnacle.

HIGHWAY OF LIFE
CD _____ CDSR 021
Telstar / Sep '93 / BMG.

IF I RULED THE WORLD
Be my love / Bless this house / Falling in love with love / I believe in love / If / I'll ruled the world / Mama / O Sole Mio / Speak to me of love / This is my song / Younger than Springtime
CD _____ PWK 095
Carlton Home Entertainment / '89 / Carlton Home Entertainment.

MY FAVOURITE CAROLS
Here we come a-wassailing / While shepherds watched their flocks by night / Good King Wenceslas / Silent night / First Noel / O come all ye faithful (Adeste Fidelis) / That's what I'd like for Christmas / Mary's boy child / Once in Royal David's City / Holly and the ivy / God rest ye merry gentlemen / White Christmas / Ave Maria / Nessun dorma
CD _____ 5509302
Spectrum/Karussell / Nov '94 / PolyGram / THE.

SIR HARRY
CD _____ PRCD 143
President / May '93 / Grapevine / Target/BMG / Jazz Music / President.

THIS IS MY SONG
This is my song / Younger than springtime / When you wish upon a star / Story of a starry night / Father of girls / Falling in love with love / September song / Three coins in the fountain / Impossible dream / Come back to Sorrento / Catari, catari / Some enchanted evening / O sole mio / Nessun dorma
CD _____ 5501882
Spectrum/Karussell / Mar '94 / PolyGram / THE.

VERY BEST OF SIR HARRY SECOMBE, THE
Onward Christian soldiers / Battle hymn of the Republic / Guide me o thou great / Jehovah / How sweet the name of Jesus sounds / When I survey / Somewhere / Jerusalem / I vow to thee my country / Holy city / Old rugged cross / How great thou art / Lord's prayer / When you look back / On your life / Cover me with love / You'll never walk alone
CD _____ WSTCD 9724
Nelson Word / Apr '92 / Nelson Word.

YOURS SINCERELY
Love changes everything / Sunrise sunset / Amazing grace / Impossible dream / September song / Land for all seasons / If / I'll see you again / Nessun dorma / Colours of my life / Cover me with love / Right to sing / Father of girls / What kind of fool am I / We'll keep a welcome / If I loved you / What a wonderful world / And yet
CD _____ 5107322
Philips / Nov '91 / PolyGram.

Second Decay

TASTE
CD _____ SPV 0848472-2
Lost & Found / Oct '94 / Plastic Head.

Second Hand

DEATH MAY BE YOUR SANTA CLAUS
CD _____ BFTP 004CD
UFO / Aug '91 / Pinnacle.

Second Imij

NATIVE
CD _____ SI 005
Second Image Records / Nov '92.

Second Voice

APPROACHING LUNA
CD _____ HY 39100682
Hyperium / Nov '93 / Plastic Head.

Secrecy

RAGING ROMANCE
CD _____ N 0182-2
Noise/Modern Music / '91 / Pinnacle / Plastic Head.

Secret Affair

GLORY BOYS BEHIND CLOSED DOORS
Glory boys / Shake and shout / Going to a
go go / Time for action / New dance / Days
of change / Don't look down / One way
world / Let your heart dance / I'm not free
(but I'm cheap)
CD _____ 74321276182
RCA / Jul '92 / BMG.

Secret Life

SOLE PURPOSE
CD _____ PULSE 18CD
Pulse 8 / Feb '95 / Pinnacle / 3MV.

Secret Shine

UNTOUCHED
Suck me down / Temporal / Spellbound /
So close I come / Into the ether / Toward
the sky / Underworld / Sun warmed water
CD _____ SARAH 615CD
Sarah / Mar '95 / Vital.

Section

SECTION, THE
CD _____ 7599265412
WEA / Jan '96 / Warner Music.

Section Brain

HOSPITAL OF DEATH
CD _____ MABCD 005
MAB / Jan '94 / Plastic Head.

Sector

ORANGE
CD _____ AT 06CD
Atmosphere / Jan '96 / Plastic Head.

Sedaka, Neil

BEST OF NEIL SEDAKA, THE
CD _____ 74321113142
RCA / Aug '94 / BMG.

BREAKING UP IS HARD TO DO
CD _____ WMCD 5698
Disky / Oct '94 / THE / BMG / Discovery /
Pinnacle.

CLASSICALLY SEDAKA
Prologue / Moscow night / Turning back the
hands of time / Keeper of my heart / Never
ending serenade / Steel blue eyes / Santiago / I'm always chasing rainbows / There
is a place / Clair De Lune / I'll sing you a
song / Honey of my life / Gentle as a summer's day / Goodnight my love, goodnight
/ Kiska my angel
CD _____ VISCD 5
Vision / Oct '95 / Pinnacle.

GREATEST HITS
Sing me / Standing on the inside / Laughter
in the rain / Oh, Carol / Stairway to heaven
/ Hey little devil / Happy birthday sweet six-
teen / Cardboard California / Let's go
steady again / New York city blues /
Love will keep us together / Solitaire /
Lonely night (angel face) / Sad eyes / Bad
blood / Immigrant / Breaking up is hard to
do
CD _____ PLATCD 365
Prism / '91 / Prism.

GREATEST HITS LIVE
CD _____ MU 5028
Musketeer / Oct '92 / Koch.

GREATEST HITS: NEIL SEDAKA
I go ape / Oh Carol / Stairway to heaven /
Run Samson run / You mean everything to
me / Calendar girl / I must be dreaming /
Little devil / Happy birthday sweet sixteen /
Next door to an angel / Let's go steady
again
CD _____ ND 89171
RCA / Apr '90 / BMG.

HIS GREATEST HITS OF THE 60'S
Oh Carol / Oh Carol / I go ape / Happy
birthday sweet sixteen / Breaking up is hard
to do / Calendar girl / Stairway to heaven /
Next door to an angel / King of clowns / You
mean everything to me / One way ticket (to
the blues) / Sweet little you
CD _____ CDMFP 5819
Music For Pleasure / Oct '91 / EMI.

HOLLYWOOD CONCERT
CD _____ CD 3504
Cameo / Aug '94 / Target/BMG.

LAUGHTER AND TEARS
Standing on the outside / Love will keep us
together / Solitaire / Other side of me / little
lovin' / Lonely nights / Brighton / I'm a song,
sing me / Breaking up is hard to do / Laughter in the rain / Cardboard California / Bad
blood / Queen of 1964 / Hungry years /
Betty Grable / Beautiful you / That's when
the music takes me / Our last song together
CD _____ 5500322
Spectrum/Karussell / May '93 / PolyGram /
THE.

LEGENDS IN MUSIC - NEIL SEDAKA
CD _____ LECD 073
Wisepack / Jul '94 / THE / Conifer.

LOVE WILL KEEP US TOGETHER
Love will keep us together / Rainy day bells
/ My son and I / Clown time / When a love

affair is through / My Athena / Desiree / Going nowhere / I'm a song, sing me / Little
lovin' / Steppin' out / Betty Grable / I go ape
/ Stupid cupid / Number one with a heartache / You turn me on / Can't get you out
of my mind / Blinded by your love / No getting over you
CD _____ 5173512
Polydor / Oct '92 / PolyGram.

NEIL SEDAKA (2)
CD _____ 295054
Ariola Express / Jul '92 / BMG.

OH CAROL
CD _____ WMCD 5650
Disky / May '94 / THE / BMG / Discovery /
Pinnacle.

ORIGINALS - GREATEST HITS
Oh Carol / Happy birthday sweet sixteen /
Little Devil / I go ape / Diary / You mean
everything to me / King of clowns / Let's go
steady again / Sunny / I'm a song, sing me
/ Next door to an angel / Stupid cupid / Girl
for me / Crying my heart out for you / Run
Samson run / One way ticket
CD _____ PWKS 4119
Carlton Home Entertainment / Oct '92 /
Carlton Home Entertainment.

SINGER & HIS SONGS, THE
Oh Carol / Breaking up is hard to do / Rainy
day bells / Little devil / Can't get you out of
my mind / Happy birthday sweet sixteen /
No getting over you / I go ape / Betty grable
/ Calendar girl / When a love affair is
through / Next door to an angel / Clown
time / Stairway to heaven / One way ticket
(to the blues) / You turn me on / My son
and I / Miracle song
CD _____ MCCD 148
Music Club / Feb '94 / Disc / THE / CM.

SOLITAIRE
Prelude / Solitaire / Silent movies / Rose-
mary blues / Little song / God bless Joanna
/ Cardboard California / Gone with the
morning / I wish I had a carousel / Adven-
tures of a boy child wonder / Is anybody
going to miss you / Better days are coming
/ What have they done to the moon / One
more mountain to climb / Home / I'm a song
/ Don't let it mess your mind / Beautiful you
/ That's when the music takes me
CD _____ MUCD 9024
Start / Apr '95 / Koch.

SPOTLIGHT ON NEIL SEDAKA
Rosemary blue / One more mountain to
climb / Silent movies / What have they done
to the moon / Super bird / Cardboard Cal-
ifornia / God bless Joanna / Little song /
Prelude / Gone with the morning / Ring-a-
rock / While I dream
CD _____ HADCD 118
Javelin / Feb '94 / THE / Henry Hadaway
Organisation.

**TIMELESS (The very best of Neil
Sedaka)**
Happy birthday sweet sixteen / Breaking up
is hard to do / Calender girl / Our last song
together / Oh Carol / I go ape / One way
ticket (to the blues) / Next door to an angel
/ Standing on the inside / Immigrant /
Laughter in the rain / Hungry years / That
when the music takes me (live) / Solitaire /
Love will keep us together / Queen of 1964
/ Little devil / Other side of me / Stairway to
heaven / Miracle song
CD _____ 5114422
Polydor / Oct '91 / PolyGram.

VERY BEST OF NEIL SEDAKA, THE
Calendar girl / Oh Carol / King of clowns /
Next door to an angel / Let's go steady
again / Breaking up is hard to do / Happy
birthday sweet sixteen / Little devil / I go
ape / Stairway to heaven / Diary / You mean
everything to me
CD _____ 74321339402
Camden / Jan '96 / BMG.

Seddiki, Sidi

SHOUFI
Shouffin qouna / Maliki / Liam / Haram alou
/ Bent nass / Galbi / Zin / Melkoum / Qaoun
allah / Lachir
CD _____ CDORB 063
Globestyle / Oct '90 / Pinnacle.

Seed

VERTICLE MEMORY
CD _____ RBADCD 12
Beyond / Aug '95 / Kudos / Pinnacle.

Seeds

**BAD PART OF TOWN/LIVE ALBUM
BEDTIME (Seeds/Sky Saxon)**
CD _____ 842110
EVA / May '94 / Direct / ADA.

EVIL HOODOO
March of the flower children / Wind blows
your hair / Tripmaker / Try to understand /
Evil hoodoo / Chocolate river / Pushin' too
hard / Falling off the edge / Mr. Farmer / Up
in her room / Can't seem to make you mine
/ Pictures and designs / Flower lady and her
assistant / Rollin' machine / Out of the
question / Satisfy you
CD _____ DOCD 1998
Drop Out / Jul '91 / Pinnacle.

FADED PICTURE, A
CD _____ DOCD 1992
Drop Out / Sep '91 / Pinnacle.

TRAVEL WITH YOUR MIND
Satisfy you / Wind blows your hair / Pretty
girl / Chocolate river / Out of the question /
March of the flower children / Other place /
Fallin' off the edge (of my mind) / Flower
lady and her assistant / Pushin' too hard /
Thousand shadows / Wild blood / Now a
man / Travel with your mind / Daisy Mae /
900 Million people daily (all making love) /
Nobody spoil my fun / Sad and alone /
Fallin'
CD _____ GNPD 2218
GNP Crescendo / Jul '95 / Silva Screen.

Seefeel

QUIQUE
CD _____ PURECD 028
Too Pure / Oct '93 / Vital.

SUCCOUR
CD _____ WARPCD 28
Warp / Mar '95 / Disc.

Seeger, Mike

3RD ANNUAL REUNION
CD _____ ROU 0313CD
Rounder / Jan '95 / CM / Direct / ADA /
Cadillac.

FRESH OLD TIME MUSIC
CD _____ CD 0262
Rounder / Aug '88 / CM / Direct / ADA /
Cadillac.

THIRD ANNUAL FAREWELL REUNION
CD _____ ROUCD 0313
Rounder / Nov '94 / CM / Direct / ADA /
Cadillac.

Seeger, Peggy

**AMERICAN FOLK SONGS FOR
CHILDREN (Seeger, Peggy & Mike)**
CD _____ CD 11544
Rounder / '88 / CM / Direct / ADA /
Cadillac.

**AMERICAN FOLK SONGS FOR
CHRISTMAS (Seeger, Peggy & Mike)**
CD _____ R 0268/69CD
Rounder / '90 / CM / Direct / ADA /
Cadillac.

**MIKE & PEGGY SEEGER (Seeger, Peggy
& Mike)**
CD _____ CD 11543
Rounder / '88 / CM / Direct / ADA /
Cadillac.

**SONGS OF LOVE AND POLITICS (The
Folkways Years 1955-1992)**
CD _____ SFWCD 40048
Smithsonian Folkways / Nov '94 / ADA /
Direct / Koch / CM / Cadillac.

Seeger, Pete

AMERICAN FOLK SONG, THE
CD _____ ENTCD 241
Entertainers / Mar '92 / Target/BMG.

AMERICAN INDUSTRIAL BALLADS
CD _____ SF 40058CD
Smithsonian Folkways / Aug '94 / ADA /
Direct / Koch / CM / Cadillac.

**DARLING COREY & GOOFING OFF
SUITE**
CD _____ SFLCD 40018
Smithsonian Folkways / Jun '93 / ADA /
Direct / Koch / CM / Cadillac.

FEEDING THE FLAME
CD _____ FF 541CD
Flying Fish / '92 / Roots / CM / Direct /
ADA.

LIVE AT NEWPORT 1960'S
CD _____ VCD 77008
Vanguard / Oct '94 / Complete/Pinnacle /
Discovery.

TRADITIONAL CHRISTMAS CAROLS
CD _____ SFWCD 40024
Smithsonian Folkways / Dec '94 / ADA /
Direct / Koch / CM / Cadillac.

YANKEE DOODLE
CD _____ CD 12504
Music Of The World / Nov '92 / Target/
BMG / ADA.

Seekers

**CARNIVAL OF HITS (Durham, Judith &
The Seekers)**
Morningtown Ride / World of our own / Island of dreams / Red rubber ball / Colours
of my life / Georgy girl / Land is your land /
Carnival is over / When will the good apples
fall / Someday one day / Kumbaya / 59th
Street Bridge song (Feelin' groovy) / Walk
with me / Leaving of Liverpool / I'll never
find another you / Little light of mine / Times
they are a-changin' / We shall not be moved
/ One world love / Keep a dream in your
pocket
CD _____ CDEMTV 83
EMI / Apr '94 / EMI.

**LIVE IN CONCERT (25 Year Reunion
Celebration) (Durham, Judith & The
Seekers)**
When the stars begin to fall / With my swag
all on my shoulder / Plaisir d'amour / Morn-
ingtown ride / I've my spirit / Kumbaya /
Gospel medley (This little light of mine/Open
up them pearly gates/We shall not be
moved) / Come the day / One world love /
You / Colours of my life / Time and again /
Red rubber ball / I am Australian / I'll never
find another you / Georgy girl / World of our
own / Carnival is over / Keep a dream in
your pocket
CD _____ CDDPR 130
Premier/MFP / Mar '95 / EMI.

SEEKERS, THE
I'll never find another you / World of our
own / Carnival is over / Some day one day
/ Walk with me / Morningtown ride / Georgy
girl / When will the good apples fall / Em-
erald City / We shall not be moved / Island
of dreams / Open up them pearly gates /
Kumbaya / Blowin' in the wind / Wreck of
of 97 / Lemon tree / Whiskey in the jar /
Five hundred miles / Gypsy Rover / South
Australia / Danny boy / Waltzing Matilda /
Water is wide
CD _____ CC 226
Music For Pleasure / Sep '88 / EMI.

Seelenwinter

SEELENWINTER
CD _____ MASSCD 048
Massacre / Mar '95 / Plastic Head.

Seelos, Ambros

**DANCE GALA '90 (Seelos, Ambros
Orchestra)**
CD _____ 322287
Koch / Dec '92 / Koch.

**DANCE GALA '91 (Seelos, Ambros
Orchestra)**
CD _____ 322462
Koch / Dec '92 / Koch.

**DANCE GALA '92 (Seelos, Ambros
Orchestra)**
CD _____ 322665
Koch / Dec '92 / Koch.

**DANCE GALA '93 (Seelos, Ambros
Orchestra)**
CD _____ 322863
Koch / Dec '92 / Koch.

**DANCE GALA VOL.1 : FORMAL
BALLROOM DANCING (Seelos, Ambros
Orchestra)**
CD _____ 340052
Koch / Apr '93 / Koch.

TANZ GALA (Seelos, Ambros Orchestra)
CD _____ CD 395703
Koch / Nov '93 / Koch.

**TYPICAL LATIN (Seelos, Ambros
Orchestra)**
CD _____ 340092
Koch / Aug '93 / Koch.

Seelyhoo

FIRST CAUL, THE
CD _____ CDTRAX 102
Greentrax / Jan '96 / Conifer / Duncans /
ADA / Direct.

Seers

PSYCH OUT
Wildman / Rub me out / One summer / Welcome to deadtown / I'll be there / You keep
me praying / Walk / Sun in the sky / Fly
away / Breathless / Freedom trip / (All late
nite) tequila drinking blues / Magic potion /
Lightning strikes
CD _____ CDBRED 86
Cherry Red / Feb '90 / Pinnacle.

Seersucker

PUSHING ROPE
CD _____ SKY 75010CD
Sky / Sep '94 / Koch.

Seffer, Debora

SILKY
CD _____ CDLLL 157
La Lichere / Aug '93 / Discovery / ADA.

Segal, Misha

ZAMBOOKA
CD _____ MM 65068
Music Masters / Oct '94 / Nimbus.

Seger, Bob

**AGAINST THE WIND (Seger, Bob & The
Silver Bullet Band)**
Horizontal bop / You'll accompany me / Her
strut / No man's land / Long man's land /
Long twin silver line / Against the wind /
Good for me / Betty Lou's gettin' out to-
night / Fire lake / Shinin' brightly
CD _____ CDP 746 060 2
Capitol / Feb '95 / EMI.

BOB SEGER GREATEST HITS
Roll me away / Night moves / Turn the page / You'll accomp'ny me / Hollywood nights / Still the same / Mainstreet / Old time rock 'nd' roll / We've got tonight / Against the wind / Fire inside / Like a rock C'est la vie / In your time
CD _____ CDEST 2241
Capitol / Feb '95 / EMI.

DISTANCE, THE (Seger, Bob & The Silver Bullet Band)
Even now / Makin' Thunderbirds / Boom-town blues / Shame on the moon / Love's the last to know / Roll me away / House behind a house / Comin' home / Little victories
CD _____ CZ 403
Capitol / Mar '91 / EMI.

FIRE INSIDE, THE (Seger, Bob & The Silver Bullet Band)
Take a chance / Real love / Sightseeing / Always in my heart / Fire inside / Real at the time / Which way / Mountain / Blind love / She can't do anything wrong
CD _____ CDEST 2149
Capitol / Feb '95 / EMI.

IT'S A MYSTERY (Seger, Bob & The Silver Bullet Band)
Rite of passage / Lock and load / By the river / Manhattan / I wonder / It's a mystery / Revisionism Street / Golden boy / I can't save you Angelene / Sixteen shells from a 30-6 / West of the moon / Hands in the air
CD _____ CDEST 2271
Capitol / Nov '95 / EMI.

LIVE BULLET
Nutbush City Limits / Travellin' man / Beautiful loser / Jody girl / Looking back / Get out of Denver / Let it rock / I've been working / Turn the page / U.M.C. / Bo Diddley / Ramblin' gamblin' man / Heavy music / Katmandu
CD _____ CDP 746 085 2
EMI / Feb '95 / EMI.

NIGHT MOVES
Rock 'n' roll never forgets / Night moves / Fire down below / Sunburst / Sunspot baby / Mainstreet / Come to poppa / Ship of fools / Mary Lou
CD _____ CDP 746 075 2
EMI / Feb '95 / EMI.

NINE TONIGHT
Nine tonight / Trying to live my life without you / You'll accompany me / Hollywood nights / Night moves / Rock 'n' roll never forgets / Let it rock / Old time rock 'n' roll / Mainstreet / Against the wind / Fire down below / Her strut / Feel like a number / Fire lake / Betty Lou's gettin' out tonight / We've got tonight
CD _____ CDP 7460862
EMI / Feb '95 / EMI.

STRANGER IN TOWN
Hollywood nights / Still the same / Old time rock 'n' roll / Till it shines / Feel like a number / Ain't got no money / We've got tonight / Brave strangers / Famous final scene
CD _____ CDP 746 074 2
EMI / Feb '95 / EMI.

Seiler, Peter

SENSITIVE TOUCH
Still the same sun / Reef moods / Journey to nowhere / I'm on my way / Mountain peaks / Her song / Sensitive touch
CD _____ 710 069
Thunderbolt / '89 / Magnum Music Group.

Seis Del Solar

ALTERNATE ROOTS
CD _____ MES 158312
Messidor / Apr '95 / Koch / ADA.

DECISION
Sentimento de cancion / Island walk / Una sola casa / Un nuevo dia / Decision / Sea dance / Mirage / Entregate / Heart dues / Newtown
CD _____ 158212
Messidor / Aug '92 / Koch / ADA.

Seka

LOVES HYMN
CD _____ TG 92972
Roadrunner / Jul '91 / Pinnacle.

Seka, Monique

OKAMAN
CD _____ 503842
Declic / Apr '95 / Jetstar.

Selassie, Bunny

EYES CAN SEE
CD _____ MTXCD 0001
Mantrax / Jan '96 / SRD.

Selassie, Kebra

THROUGH DEEP MEDITATION
CD _____ CDLINC 004
Lion Inc. / Mar '95 / Jetstar / SRD.

Seldom Scene

ACT FOUR
CD _____ SHCD 3709
Sugarhill / Nov '95 / Roots / CM / ADA / Direct.

AFTER MIDNIGHT
Lay down Sally / Hearts overflowing / Old hometown / Stompin' at the Savoy / Border incident / After midnight / If I had left it up to you / Heartsville Pike / Stolen love / Let old Mother Nature have her way
CD _____ SHCD 3721
Sugarhill / Dec '94 / Roots / CM / ADA / Direct.

AT THE SCENE
Girl I know / Jamaica say you will / Open up the window, Noah / Winter wind / Heal it / Weary pilgrim / It turns inside out / Champion / Born of the wind / Peaceful dreams
CD _____ SHCD 3726
Sugarhill / '92 / Roots / CM / ADA / Direct.

CHANGE IN SCENERY, A
Breaking new ground / Casting a shadow in the road / Settin' me up / Alabama clay / I'll be a stranger there / West Texas wind / Satan's choir / In despair / What goes on / One way ticket
CD _____ SHCD 3763
Sugarhill / '88 / Roots / CM / ADA / Direct.

LIKE WE USED TO BE
CD _____ SH 3822CD
Sugarhill / Mar '94 / Roots / CM / ADA / Direct.

LIVE: CELEBRATION 15TH ANNIVERSARY
Sittin' on top of the world / Big train from Memphis / Lorena / Dark as a dungeon / Blue Ridge / Raised by the railroad line / Don't know my mind / Drifting too far from the shore / Those memories of you / Keep me from blowing away / Wheels / Carolyn at the broken wheel inn / If I needed you / Rose of old Kentucky / I couldn't find my walkin' shoes / Workin' on a building / Say you lied / High on a hilltop / Sweetest gift / Take me on your life boat
CD _____ SHCD 2202
Sugarhill / '88 / Roots / CM / ADA / Direct.

SCENE 20 20TH ANNIVERSARY SPECIAL
Intro (Haven't I got the right to love you) / Gardens and memories / House of gold / Picture's of life's other side / Satan's jewelled crown / Will you ready to go home / Were you there / Weary pilgrim / Leavin' harlan / Take him in / Stompin' at the Savoy / Something in the wind / Muddy water / Open up the window / Breakin' new ground / Old train / Wait a minute / Blue ridge cabin home / Gypsy moon / In the pines / And on bass / Another lonesome day / Have mercy on my soul / House of the rising sun/Walk don't run / In the midnight hour
CD _____ SH-CD-2501 02
Sugarhill / '92 / Roots / CM / ADA / Direct.

SCENIC ROOTS
If you ever change your mind / Lost in your memory / Wrath of God / Before I met you / Red Georgia Clay / I've cried my last tear / Not in my arms / Highway of heartache / Long black veil / Last call to glory / Distant train / How mountain girls can love
CD _____ SHCD 3785
Sugarhill / '90 / Roots / CM / ADA / Direct.

Selecter

HAIRSPRAY
CD _____ TX 51214CD
Triple X / Oct '95 / Plastic Head.

HAPPY ALBUM
CD _____ FIENDCD 751
Demon / May '94 / Pinnacle / ADA.

LIVE INJECTION
Live injection / Whip them down / Three minute hero / California screaming / Everyday / I want justice / Missing words / Neurotica / Selector / James Bond / Train to Skaville / On my radio / Too much pressure / Murder / Orange street / My sweet collie / Madness
CD _____ CDBM 108
Blue Moon / Jan '96 / Magnum Music Group / Greensleeves / Hot Shot / ADA / Cadillac / Discovery.

PRIME CUTS (Black, Pauline & The Selecter)
Something's burning / Coming up / Dial my number / Woke up laughing / Touissants children / Whisper of the rain / Nameless / Use me up / I really didn't have the time / Clear water / No regrets / On my radio (Live)
CD _____ CDBM 103
Blue Moon / Nov '94 / Magnum Music Group / Greensleeves / Hot Shot / ADA / Cadillac / Discovery.

PRIME CUTS 2
On my radio / Three minute hero / Whisper / Shoorah, shoorah / Celebrate the bullet / Missing words / Out on the streets / Tell me what the others do / Street feeling / Selecter / Best of both worlds / Too much pressure
CD _____ CDBM 106

Blue Moon / Sep '95 / Magnum Music Group / Greensleeves / Hot Shot / ADA / Cadillac / Discovery.

PUCKER
CD _____ DOJOCD 218
Dojo / Sep '95 / BMG.

RARE SELECTER
CD _____ DOJOCD 199
Dojo / Nov '94 / BMG.

RARE SELECTER VOL. 2
CD _____ DOJOCD 201
Dojo / Mar '95 / BMG.

RARE SELECTER VOL. 3 (Versions)
CD _____ DOJOCD 205
Dojo / May '95 / BMG.

Self, Ronnie

BOP A LENA
Bop a Lena / I ain't going nowhere / You're so right for me / Ain't I'm a dog / Too many lovers (unissued) / Date bait / Big blon' baby / Petrified / Flame of love / Big fool / Black night blues / Pretty bad blues / Three hearts later / Rocky Road blues / Do it now / Bless my broken heart / This must be the place / Big town / Some other world / Instant man / Oh me, oh my / Whistling words / Past, present and future / So high / I've been there / Moon burn (unissued) / Some things you can't change / Houdini / Go go cannibal (unissued) / Ugly stick (unissued)
CD _____ BCD 15436
Bear Family / Jul '90 / Rollercoaster / Direct / CM / Swift / ADA.

Self Transforming...

BITONE (Self Transforming Machine Elves)
CD _____ NZCD 025
Nova Zembla / Apr '95 / Plastic Head.

Sellers Engineering Band

WE LOVE A PARADE
Entry of the Gladiators / Seventy six Trombones / Royal trophy / Dam busters march / Toeador's march / Arromanches / Marche militaire / Parade of the tin soldiers / Marche slave / Punchinello / I love a parade / Gladiator's farewell / Musical joke / Shield of Liberty / Radetzky march / Rhapsody on Scottish marches / Coronation march
CD _____ CHAN 4527
Chandos / Aug '93 / Chandos.

Semantics

BONE OF CONTENTION
CD _____ SST 167 CD
SST / May '88 / Plastic Head.

Sembello, Michael

BOSSA NOVA HOTEL
Maniac / Superman / Talk / First time / Cowboy / Cadillac / It's over / Automatic man / Lay back / Godzilla
CD _____ 7599239202
WEA / Jan '96 / Warner Music.

Sempiternal Death Reign

SPOOKY GLOOM, THE
CD _____ FDN 8099CD
Plastic Head / Jan '92 / Plastic Head.

Senate

SOCK IT TO YOU ONE MORE TIME
Sock it to 'em JB / Summertime / Girls are out to get you / Love is after me / Sweet thing / Try a little tenderness / What is soul / Knock on wood / Intro 5 bars (who's afraid of Virginia Woolf) / How sweet is it / You don't know like I know / Shake / Please stay / Can't stop / Invitation / Hold on I'm comin'
CD _____ RTCD 901146
Line / Apr '92 / CM / Grapevine / ADA / Conifer / Direct.

Senator Flux

STORYKNIFE
CD _____ EM 92632
Roadrunner / Oct '91 / Pinnacle.

Senators

LOVELY
Best friend / East of here / Forty nights / Hosing down the strand / Disbelieve it / Strange sound / Port in my storm / Late train home / Simple game / Strange house / Another love song / Girl I adore / End
CD _____ 8283192
Go Discs / Apr '92 / PolyGram.

Senensky, Bernie

HOMELAND
New life blues / Leira / Guys and dolls / Falling / Doron / Kiki / Homeland / J.C. / More than that
CD _____ CDSJP 426
Timeless Jazz / May '95 / New Note.

WHEEL WITHIN A WHEEL
Bop-be / No more tears / Adam / Silver trane / Lolito's theme / Floating / What is happening here / Eye of the hurricane / Soul eyes / Wheel within a wheel
CD _____ CDSJP 410
Timeless Jazz / Nov '93 / New Note.

Sensation

BORN TO LOVE YOU
CD _____ WRCD 36
Techniques / Nov '92 / Jetstar.

Sensefield

KILLED FOR LESS
CD _____ REVEL 32CD
Revelation / May '94 / Plastic Head.

SENSEFIELD
CD _____ REVEL 033CD
Revelation / Oct '94 / Plastic Head.

Senseless Things

EMPIRE OF THE SENSELESS
Homophobic asshole / Keepsake / Tempting Kate / Hold it down / Counting friends / Just one reason / Cruel moon / Primary instinct / Rise (Song for Dean and Gene) / Ice skating at the Milky Way / Say what you will / Runaways
CD _____ 473525 2
Epic / Mar '93 / Sony.

PEEL SESSIONS
CD _____ SFRCD 127
Strange Fruit / Jan '94 / Pinnacle.

TAKING CARE OF BUSINESS
Christine Keeler / Something to miss / Page 3 valentine / Any which way / Marlene / Touch me on the heath / Wanted / Dead sun / Way to the drugstore
CD _____ 4783682
Epic / Feb '95 / Sony.

Senser

STACKED UP
CD _____ TOPPCD 008
Ultimate / Mar '94 / 3MV / Vital.

Sensorama

WELCOME
CD _____ LADOCD 2022
Ladomat / Oct '95 / Plastic Head.

Sensurreal

NEVER TO TELL A SOUL
CD Set _____ BMU 005CD
Beam Me Up / Feb '95 / Vital.

Sentenced

AMOK
CD _____ CM 77076CD
Century Media / Apr '95 / Plastic Head.

LOVE AND DEATH
CD _____ CM 77101
Century Media / Oct '95 / Plastic Head.

SHADOWS OF THE PAST
CD _____ CM 7716CD
Century Media / Jan '96 / Plastic Head.

Seppuku

TAXI GIRL
Les armees de la nuit / N'importe quel soir / Musee tong / Les damnes (chant des enfants morts) / Les armees de la nuit (instrumental) / Armies of the night / Scarlet woman / Tong museum / Viviane vog / Avenue du crime / John Doe 85 / Treizime section / La femme ecarlate / On any evening / Avenue of crime
CD _____ FC 047 CD
Fan Club / May '89 / Direct.

September When

ONE EYE OPEN
No simple reason / Fish song / Can I trust you / Street jam / Let the rain fall / Comes around / Not my day / Nightflight / What you give is what you get / Pretty lonely star / Beauty of it
CD _____ 450991814-2
East West / May '93 / Warner Music.

Septeto Hananero

75 YEARS LATER
CD _____ CORA 126
Corason / Nov '95 / CM / Direct / ADA.

Septic Flesh

MYSTIC PLACES OF DAWN
CD _____ HOLY 5CD
Holy / May '94 / Plastic Head.

SEPTIC FLESH
CD _____ HOLY 12CD
Holy / Jun '95 / Plastic Head.

Sepultura

ARISE
CD _____ RO 93282
Roadrunner / Jul '95 / Pinnacle.

BENEATH THE REMAINS
CD _____ RO 95112
Roadrunner / Jul '95 / Pinnacle.

CHAOS A.D.
Refuse/Resist / Territory / Slave new world / Amen / Kaiowas / Propaganda / Biotech is Godzilla / Nomad / We are not as others / Manifest / Hunt / Clenched fist / Policia / Inhuman nature
CD _____ RR 90002
Roadrunner / Jul '95 / Pinnacle.

MORBID VISIONS
CD _____ RO 92762
Roadrunner / Jul '95 / Pinnacle.

MORBID VISIONS/CEASE TO EXIST
CD _____ SHARK 012 CD
Shark / Nov '89 / Plastic Head.

SCHIZOPHRENIA
CD _____ RO 93602
Roadrunner / Jul '95 / Pinnacle.

Sepulveda, Charlie

NEW ARRIVAL, THE
CD _____ ANCD 8767
Antilles/New Directions / Aug '91 / PolyGram.

Sequentia

DANTE AND THE TROUBADOURS
CD _____ 05472772272
BMG / Aug '95 / BMG.

EL SABIO
CD _____ 05472771732
BMG / Nov '92 / BMG.

VOICE OF THE BLOOD
CD _____ 05472773462
Total / Nov '95 / Total/BMG.

VOX IBERICA BOX SET
CD Set _____ 05472773332
BMG / Feb '94 / BMG.

Serban, Andrei

ROMANIAN FOLK MUSIC (Serban, Andrei & His Orchestra)
CD _____ SYN CD 150
Syncoop / Apr '93 / ADA / Direct.

Sereba, Kouame Gerard

KILIMANDJARO
CD _____ KGS 004CD
Musikk Distribujson / Dec '94 / ADA.

Serenata Mexicana

CANCIONES DE MEXICO
CD _____ MRM 004
Modern Blues / Feb '94 / Direct / ADA.

Serenity

THEN CAME SILENCE
CD _____ HOLY 010CD
Holy / Feb '95 / Plastic Head.

Sergeant Benjamin

NATTY DREAD SOLDIER
CD _____ RRCD 017
Roots Collective / Nov '95 / SRD / Jetstar / Roots Collective.

Sergeant Fury

TURN THE PAGE
CD _____ SPV 08412082
SPV / Apr '95 / Plastic Head.

Serious Drinking

HITS, THE MISSES AND OWN GOALS, THE
CD _____ PLAYCD 14
Workers Playtime / Jul '90 / Pinnacle.

Sermon, Erick

DOUBLE OR NOTHING
Intro / Bomdigi / Freak out / In the heat / Tell 'em / In the studio / Boy meets world / Welcome / Live in the backyard / Set it off / Focus / Move on / Smooth thought / Do your thing / Man above / Message / Open fire
CD _____ 5292862
RAL / Nov '95 / PolyGram.

NO PRESSURE
Payback II / Stay real / Imma gitz mine / Hostile / Do it up / Safe sex / Hittin' switches / Erick Sermon / Hype / Li'l grazy / Stll in' / Swing it over here / All in the mind / Female species (On CD only)
CD _____ 5279772
Def Jam / Jan '96 / PolyGram.

Serrie, John

AND THE STARS GO WITH YOU
Gentle, the night / Fantasy passages / And the stars go with you / Far river / Stratos
CD _____ MPCD 2001
Miramar / Jun '93 / New Note.

MIDSUMMER CENTURY
Lookback / Moon is a harsh mistress / Timelines / Distant moment / Velvet / Century seasons / Ancient of days / Land of Lyss / Last secret
CD _____ MPCD 2005
Miramar / Aug '94 / New Note.

PLANETARY CHRONICLES VOL.1
Mystery road / Dawn trader / Straits of Madigann / Starmoods / Auran vector
CD _____ MPCD 2004
Miramar / Nov '94 / New Note.

PLANTARY CHRONICLES, VOL 2
First night out / Vista range / Aftervisions / Continuum / On a frontier of fables
CD _____ MPCD 2006
Miramar / Oct '94 / New Note.

Sertl, Doug

JOY SPRING
CD _____ STCD 565
Stash / May '93 / Jazz Music / CM / Cadillac / Direct / ADA.

Servants

DISINTERESTED
Move out / Restless / Thin skinned / Hush now / Hey Mrs. John / Big future / Power of woman / Third wheel / Self destruction / They should make a statue / Look like a girl / Afterglow
CD _____ PAPCD 005
Paperhouse / Jul '90 / Disc.

Servat, Giles

A-RAOK MONT KUIT
CD _____ KM 45
Keltia Musique / Sep '94 / ADA / Direct / Discovery.

Seti

PHAROS
CD Set _____ IAE 001
Instinct Ambient Europe / Apr '95 / Plastic Head.

Setters

SETTERS, THE
CD _____ WM 1020
Watermelon / Jul '94 / ADA / Direct.

Setzer, Brian

BRIAN SETZER ORCHESTRA, THE (Setzer, Brian Orchestra)
Lady luck / Ball and chain / Sittin' on it all the time / Good rockin' Daddy / September skies / Brand new cadillac / There's a rainbow 'round my shoulder / Route 66 / Your true love / Nightingale sang in Berkeley Square / Straight up / Drink that bottle down
CD _____ 74321195772
Arista / Apr '94 / BMG.

Sevag, Oystein

GLOBAL HOUSE
CD _____ 01934111482
Windham Hill / Sep '95 / Pinnacle / BMG / ADA.

LINK
CD _____ 01934111232
Windham Hill / Sep '95 / Pinnacle / BMG / ADA.

Seven Day Diary

SKIN AND BLISTER
CD _____ 9362458702
Warner Bros. / May '95 / Warner Music.

Seven Little Sisters

COW TROUSERS
CD _____ RGB 5012
BGR / Mar '95 / Plastic Head.

Seven Seconds

CREW, THE
CD _____ BY 0005CD
Better Youth Organisation / Nov '93 / SRD.

NEW WIND
CD _____ BY 0014CD
Better Youth Organisation / Nov '93 / SRD.

OURSELVES
CD _____ 722762
Restless / Feb '95 / Vital.

SOUL FORCE REVOLUTION
CD _____ 723442
Restless / Feb '95 / Vital.

Seven Sioux

ANOTHER
CD _____ XM 029CD
X-Mist / Apr '92 / SRD.

Sevenchurch

BLEAK INSIGHT
Perceptions / Low / Surreal wheel / Crawl line / Sanctum / Autobituary
CD _____ N 0222-2
Noise/Modern Music / Sep '93 / Pinnacle / Plastic Head.

Seventh Avenue Stompers

FIDGETY FEET
Fidgety feet / Basin Street blues / Muskrat ramble / How come you do me like you do / Struttin' with some barbecue / St. Louis blues / Yellow dog blues / Sunday / Ferry boat romp / Blues like they used to be
CD _____ SV 0252
Savoy Jazz / Nov '94 / Conifer / ADA.

Severed Heads

BIG CAR
CD _____ W2-3043
Nettwerk / '89 / Vital / Pinnacle.

BULKHEAD
Dead eyes opened / Greater reward / Hot with fleas / Goodbye tonsils / Twenty deadly diseases / Propellor / Petrol
CD _____ NTCD 041
Nettwerk / Mar '09 / Vital / Pinnacle.

CITY SLAB HORROR
CD _____ W 230033
Nettwerk / May '91 / Vital / Pinnacle.

COME VISIT THE BIG BIGOT/DEAD EYES OPENED
CD _____ NTCD 31
Nettwerk / '89 / Vital / Pinnacle.

CUISINE (WITH PISCATORIAL)
Pilot in hell / Seven of oceans / Finder / Estrogen / King of the sea / Host of quadrille / Life in the whale / Twister / Ugly twenties / Piggy smack / Golden height / I'm your antidote / Tingler they shine within / Goodbye / Her teeth the ally / Skippy roo kangaroo / Ottoman / Quest for oom pa pa / Wonder of all the world
CD _____ NET 028CD
Nettwerk / Mar '92 / Vital / Pinnacle.

SINCE THE ACCIDENT
CD _____ W2-30039
Nettwerk / '89 / Vital / Pinnacle.

SINGLES - SEVERED HEADS
CD _____ NTCD 033
Nettwerk / '88 / Vital / Pinnacle.

Severin

ACID TO ASHES
CD _____ DIS 72VCD
Dischord / Sep '92 / SRD.

Severinsen, Doc

GOOD MEDICINE
Brass roots / Good medicine / Prelude 'Come sweet death' / Love story / Liberia / Godfather waltz / Rhapsody for now / Medley
CD _____ 07863660622
Bluebird / Oct '92 / BMG.

UNFORGETTABLY DOC
What is this thing called love / Love / Unforgettable / Lush Life / Georgia On My Mind / Speak Low / Music Of The Night / Bad and the beautiful / Someone to watch over me / Misty / Wind beneath my wings / Memory
CD _____ CD 80304
Telarc / Sep '92 / Conifer / ADA.

Sewing Room

NICO
CD _____ DEADELVIS 005
Dead Elvis / Nov '95 / Disc.

Sex Gang Children

BLIND
CD _____ CLEO 51222
Cleopatra / Jun '94 / Disc.

ECSTASY AND VENDETTA OVER NEW YORK
CD _____ CLEO 3833
Cleopatra / Aug '94 / Disc.

MEDEA
CD _____ CDSATE 07
Talitha / Dec '93 / Plastic Head.

PLAY WITH CHILDREN
CD _____ CLEO 6957
Cleopatra / May '94 / Disc.

Sex Love & Money

ERA
CD _____ CDMFN 180
Music For Nations / Jan '95 / Pinnacle.

Sex Pistols

ALIVE
CD _____ ESDCD 321
Essential / Oct '95 / Total/BMG.

BETTER LIVE THAN DEAD
CD _____ DOJOCD 73
Dojo / Feb '94 / BMG.

EARLY DAZE - THE STUDIO COLLECTION
I wanna be me / No feelings / Anarchy in the U.K. / Satellite / Seventeen / Submission / Pretty vacant / God save the queen / Liar / EMI / New York / Problems
CD _____ DOJOCD 119
Dojo / May '93 / BMG.

FLOGGING A DEAD HORSE
Anarchy in the U.K. / I wanna be me / God save the Queen / Did you no wrong / Pretty vacant / Holidays in the sun / No fun / My way / Something else / Silly thing / C'mon everybody / Stepping stone / Great rock 'n' roll swindle / No one is innocent
CD _____ CDV 2142
Virgin / Oct '86 / EMI.

GREAT ROCK 'N' ROLL SWINDLE, THE (Highlights)
God save the Queen (Symphony) / Great rock 'n' roll swindle / You need hands / Silly thing / Lonely boy / Something else / (We're gonna) Rock around the clock / C'mon everybody / Who killed Bambi / No one is innocent / L'anarchie pour le UK / My way
CD _____ CDVDX 2510
Virgin / Jan '92 / EMI.

KISS THIS
Anarchy in the U.K. / God Save The Queen / Pretty vacant / Holidays In The Sun / I wanna be me / Did you no wrong / Satellite / Don't give me no lip child / Stepping stone / Bodies / No feelings / Liar / Problems / Seventeen / Submission / EMI / My Way / Silly thing / Anarchy in the U.K. (live) / I Wanna Be Me (Live) / Seventeen (Live) / New York (Live) / EMI (live) / No fun (Mixes) / Problems (live) / God save the Queen (live)
CD _____ CDV 2702
CD Set _____ CDVX 2702
Virgin / Oct '92 / EMI.

LIVE AT CHELMSFORD PRISON
Lazy sod / New York / No lip / Stepping stone / Suburban kids / Submission / Liar / Anarchy in the U.K. / Did you no wrong / Substitute / No fun / Pretty vacant / Problems / I wanna be me
CD _____ DOJOCD 66
Dojo / Mar '93 / BMG.

NEVER MIND THE BOLLOCKS, HERE'S THE SEX PISTOLS
Holidays in the sun / Bodies / No feelings / Liar / God save the Queen / Problems / Seventeen / Anarchy in the U.K. / Submission / Pretty vacant / New York / EMI
CD _____ CDVX 2086
Virgin / Oct '86 / EMI.

ORIGINAL PISTOLS LIVE
No feelings / Anarchy in the U.K. / I'm a lazy sod / Liar / Dolls (New York) / Don't give me no lip child / Substitute / Pretty vacant / I wanna be me / Problems / Submission / No fun
CD _____ CDFA 3149
Fame / Jul '89 / EMI.

PIRATES OF DESTINY
CD _____ DOJOCD 222
Dojo / Jan '96 / BMG.

PRETTY VACANT
CD Set _____ RRCD 004
Receiver / Jul '93 / Grapevine.

WANTED
CD _____ DOJOCD 216
Dojo / Jun '95 / BMG.

Sexepil

SUGAR FOR THE SOUL
CD _____ 0630107692
East West / Feb '96 / Warner Music.

Sexpod

HOME
CD _____ PILLMCD 6
Placebo / Jan '95 / Disc.

Sexteto Habanero

SEXTETO HABANERO 1926-1931
CD _____ HQCD 53
Harlequin / Aug '95 / Swift / Jazz Music / Wellard / Hot Shot / Cadillac.

Sexton, Ann

YOU'RE GONNA MISS ME
I had a fight with love (and I lost) / I'm his wife, you're just a friend / You got to use what you got / Color my world blue / I want to be loved / You've been doing me wrong for so long / What's gonna love you / You can't win / Love love love / You're letting me down / You've been gone too long / Come back home / Keep on holding on / Loving you, loving me / You're gonna miss me / If I work my thing on you / You're los-

ing me / Sugar Daddy / Be serious / Have a little mercy
CD _____ CPCD 8012
Charly / Feb '94 / Charly / THE / Cadillac.

Seymour, Daren

AUROBINDO: INVOLUTION (Seymour, Daren & Mark Van Hoen)
CD _____ ASH 2.4CD
Ash International / Jan '95 / These / Kudos.

SF Seals

NOWHERE
Back again / Don't underestimate me / 8's / Janine's dream / Still / Day 12 / Winter song / Baby blue / Demons on the corner / Missing
CD _____ OLE 089-2
Matador / Jun '94 / Vital.

TRUTH WALKS IN SLEEPY SHADOWS
S.F. sorrow / Ladies of the sea / Ipecec / Locked out / Bold letters / Flashback caruso / Pulp / Soul of Patrick Lee / Kid's pirate ship / How did you know / Stellar lullabye
CD _____ OLE 162-2
Matador / Sep '95 / Vital.

Shabazz, Lakim

PURE RIGHTEOUSNESS
CD _____ SDCD 1
Jetstar / Mar '89 / Jetstar.

Shabba Ranks

A MI SHABBA
Ram dancehall / Shine eye gal / Spoil me appetite / Well done / Fattie fattie / Rough life / Let's get it on / Ice cream love / High seat / Gal nuh ready / Medal and certificate / Original woman
CD _____ 4774822
Epic / Jun '95 / Sony.

AS RAW AS EVER
Trailor load a girls / Where does slackness come from / Woman tangle / Gun pon me / Gone up / Ambi get scarce / Housecall / Flesh axe / Mi di girls dem love / Fist a ris / Jame / Park yu benz
CD _____ 4681022
Epic / Apr '95 / Sony.

BEST BABY FATHER/JUST REALITY
CD _____ VYDCD 06
Vine Yard / Sep '95 / Grapevine.

CAAN DUNN (The Best Of Shabba Ranks)
CD _____ VPCD 1450
VP / Dec '95 / Jetstar.

GOLDEN TOUCH
CD _____ GRELCD 141
Greensleeves / Apr '90 / Total/BMG / Jetstar / SRD.

KING OF DANCEHALL
CD _____ 080892
Melodie / Sep '94 / Triple Earth / Discovery / ADA / Jetstar.

LOVE PUNANNY BAD
CD _____ 080862
Jammy's / Apr '93 / Jetstar.

MR. MAXIMUM
CD _____ GRELCD 172
Greensleeves / Jun '92 / Total/BMG / Jetstar / SRD.

RAPPING WITH THE LADIES
CD _____ GRELCD 150
Greensleeves / Aug '90 / Total/BMG / Jetstar / SRD.

ROUGH AND READY, VOL. 1
Mr. Loverman / Pirate's anthem / Wicked in bed / Wootop / Gal yuh good / Just reality / Hard and stiff / Raggamuffin
CD _____ 4714422
Epic / Aug '92 / Sony.

ROUGH AND READY, VOL. 2
Housecall (Your body can't lie to me) / Girls whine / Ting a ling a school pickney sing ting / Telephone love deh pon mi mind / Get up stand up and rock / Mr. Tek it back / Jam / Roots and culture / Twice my age / Pay down pon it / Respect / Ting-a-ling (the original)
CD _____ 474231 2
Epic / Nov '93 / Sony.

X-TRA NAKED
Ting a ling a school pickney sing ting / Slow and sexy / Will power / Muscle grip / Rude boy / Cocky rim / What'cha gonna do / Beroom bully / Another one program / Readyready,goody-goody / Two breddrens / S-F Man
CD _____ 472333-5
Epic / Apr '93 / Sony.

Shack

WATERPISTOL
CD _____ MA 16
Marina / Nov '95 / SRD.

Shades Of Black

SHADES OF DUB
CD _____ ACTCD 003
Abba Christos Tafari / Jan '96 / SRD / Jetstar.

Shades Of Kenton Jazz...

ROUND MIDNIGHT (Shades Of Kenton Jazz Orchestra)
Here's that rainy day / Chiapas / Painted rhythm / Artistry in boogie / Intermission riff / Hey there / Stella by starlight / Stairway to the stars / Reuben's blues / Over the rainbow / Swinghouse / Artistry in rhythm
CD _____ HEPCD 2043
Hep / Feb '89 / Cadillac / Jazz Music / New Note / Wellard.

Shades Of Rhythm

SHADES
CD _____ 9031741042
ZTT / Dec '91 / Warner Music.

SHADES OF RHYTHM
Exactly / Sweet sensation / Homicide / Everybody / Lonely days, lonely nights / Sound of eden / Lies / Armageddon / Exorcist / Summer of '89
CD _____ 9031762762
WEA / Jan '92 / Warner Music.

Shadow

SHADOW MEETS NANNY GOAT (Shadow & Nanny Goat)
CD _____ VPCD 1236
VP / Jul '92 / Jetstar.

Shadow Gallery

SHADOW GALLERY
Dance of Fools / Darktown / Mystified / Question at hand / Final hour / Sat goodbye to the morning / Queen of the city of ice
CD _____ RR 91442
Roadrunner / Sep '92 / Pinnacle.

Shadowfax

ESPERANTO
CD _____ CDEB 2523
Earthbeat / May '93 / Direct / ADA.

SHADOWDANCE
New electric India / Watercourse way / Ghost bird / Distant voices / Shadowdance / Brown rice/ Karmapa chenno / Song for my brother
CD _____ WD 1029
Windham Hill / '88 / Pinnacle / BMG / ADA.

TOO FAR TO WHISPER
Too far to whisper / What goes around / China blue / Orang-utan gang / Road to Hanna / Street noise / Slim limbs akimbo / Tsunami / Maceo / Ritual
CD _____ CDW 1051
Windham Hill / '88 / Pinnacle / BMG / ADA.

WHAT GOES AROUND (THE BEST OF SHADOWFAX)
Angel's flight / Vajra / Thousand teardrops / New electric india / Shadowdance / Brown rice/Karmapa chenno / Another country / Dreams of children / Shaman song / What goes around / Orangutan gang (strikes back) / Road to Hanna
CD _____ WD 1104
Windham Hill / May '91 / Pinnacle / BMG / ADA.

Shadows

20 GOLDEN GREATS: SHADOWS
Apache / Frightened city / Guitar tango / Kon-Tiki (From the film "Summer Holiday".) / Genie with the light brown lamp / Warlord / Place in the sun / Atlantis / Wonderful land / F.B.I. / Savage (From the film "The Young Ones".) / Geronimo / Shindig / Stingray / Theme for young lovers (From the film "Wonderful Life".) / Rise and fall of Flingel Bunt / Maroc 7 / Dance on / Man of mystery / Foot tapper
CD _____ CDP 746 243 2
EMI / Aug '87 / EMI.

ANOTHER STRING OF HOT HITS AND MORE
Wonderful land / Atlantis / Black is black / Goodbye yellow brick road / River deep, mountain high / Rise and fall of Flingel Bunt / Midnight cowboy / Pinball wizard / See me, feel me / Apache / God only knows / Stardust / Walk don't run / Most beautiful girl / Good vibrations / Something / Superstar / Trains and boats and planes / Honky tonk women / F.B.I. / Kon-Tiki
CD _____ CDMFP 6002
Music For Pleasure / Oct '87 / EMI.

AT THEIR VERY BEST
Apache / Man of mystery / Shindig / Wonderful land / Rise and fall of flingel bunt / Deer hunter / Boys / Frightened city / Theme for young lovers / Dance on / Savage / F.B.I. / Guitar tango / Genie with the light brown lamp / Atlantis / Foot tapper / Don't cry for me Argentina / Kon-Tiki / Geronimo / Stranger
CD _____ 841520-2
Polydor / Apr '94 / PolyGram.

BEST OF HANK MARVIN & THE SHADOWS (Marvin, Hank & The Shadows)
Another day in paradise / Every breath you take / Jessica / Rise and fall of Flingel Bunt / Atlantis / I will always love you / Foot tapper / Cavatina / Heartbeat / Everything I do (I do it for you) / Riders in the sky / Dance on / Hot rox / Sylvia / Moonlight shadow / Apache / Mrs. Robinson / Walking in the air / Lady in red / Don't cry for me Argentina / Guitar tango / Wonderful land / Kon-Tiki / FBI
CD _____ 523821-2
PolyGram / Oct '94 / PolyGram.

COLLECTION: SHADOWS
Just the way you are / Turning point / Midnight creepin' / Shady lady / Thing me jig / Johnny Staccato / Stack it / If you leave me now / Equinoxe part 5 / Change of address / Fender bender / Temptation / Fourth man / Summer love / Mozart forte / Albatross
CD _____ PWKS 559
Carlton Home Entertainment / Dec '89 / Carlton Home Entertainment.

DANCE ON
CD _____ 16090
Laserlight / Oct '95 / Target/BMG.

DANCE WITH THE SHADOWS/SOUND OF THE SHADOWS
Chattanooga choo choo / Blue shadows / Tonight (From West Side Story.) / That's the way it goes / Big B / In the mood / Lonely bull / Dakota / French dressing / High and mighty / Don't it make you feel good / Zambesi / Temptation / Brazil / Lost city / Little bitty tear / Blue sky, blue sea, blue me / Bossa roo / Five hundred miles / Cotton pickin' / Deep purple / Santa Anna / Windjammer / Dean's theme / Breakthru' / Let it be me / National provincial samba / Fandango
CD _____ CZ 379
EMI / Feb '91 / EMI.

DANCING IN THE DARK
Dancing in the dark / Life in the jungle / Queen of hearts / Cat 'n' mouse / I will return / Shoba / No dancing / High noon / Telstar / More than I can say / Outdigo / Spot the ball / Time is tight / Elevenis / Mountains of the moon / Whiter shade of pale
CD _____ PWKS 4031P
Carlton Home Entertainment / Apr '91 / Carlton Home Entertainment.

DARK SIDE OF THE SHADOWS, THE
CD _____ DOG 9109
Ichiban / Aug '95 / Koch.

DIAMONDS
Diamonds / Imagine/Woman / Missing (Theme from) / You rescue me / Hats off to Wally / Nut rocker / I'm gonna be your guardian angel / Up where we belong / This ole house / Africa / Arty's party / Can't play your game / Old romantics / Our Albert / Cowboy cafe / We don't talk anymore
CD _____ PWKS 4018P
Carlton Home Entertainment / Sep '90 / Carlton Home Entertainment.

DREAMTIME
Medley: Imagine / Three times a lady / Just the way you are / I you leave me now / Up where we belong / Misty / Careless whisper / I guess that's why they call it the blues / I just called to say I love you / Always on my mind / Sealed with a kiss / Walking in the air / Going home (theme from Local Hero) / Skye boat song
CD _____ 5500942
Spectrum/Karussell / Oct '93 / PolyGram THE.

EARLY YEARS, THE
Feelin' fine / Don't be a fool with love / Driftin' / Jet black / Chinchilla / Saturday dance / Lonesome fella / Bongo blues / Apache / Quartermaster's stores / Stranger / Man of mystery / Mustang / Shana (Theme) / Shotgun / Giant (Theme) / F.B.I. / Midnight / Frightened city / Back home / Kon-Tiki / 36-24-36 / Shadoogie / Blue star / Nivram / Baby my heart / See you in my drums / All my sorrows / Gonzales / Find me a golden street / Theme from a filleted place / That's my desire / My resistance is low / Sleep walk / Big boy / Peace pipe / Wonderful land / Stars fell on Stockton / Guitar tango / Sweet dreams / Boys / Rumble / Bandit / Cosy / 1861 / Perfidia / Little B / Bo Diddley / South of the Border / Spring is nearly here / Are they all like you / Tales of a raggy tramline / Some are lonely / Kinda cool / Some are lonely (French version) / Dance on / All day / Foot tapper / Atlantis / I want you to want me / Geronimo / Shindig / It's been a blue day / Big B / In the mood / Lonely bull / Dakota / French dressing / High and mighty / Don't it make you feel good / Zambesi / Temptation / Walkin' / Rhythm and greens / Ranka chank / Main theme / Drum number / Lute number / Miracle / Genie with the

light brown lamp / Little princess / Friends / Evening comes / Mary Anne / Chu chi / Stingray / Alice in Sunderland / Don't make my baby blue / My grandfather's clock / War lord / I wish I could shimmy like my sister Arthur / I met a girl / Late night set / Place in the sun / Will you be there / Dreams / I dream / Scotch on the socks / My way
CD Set _____ CDSHAD 1
EMI / Sep '91 / EMI.

EP COLLECTION: SHADOWS
Perfidia / 36-24-36 / All day / My grandfather's clock / Lady Penelope / Zero X theme / Thunderbird / Finders keepers / Mustang / Shane / Giant (theme from) / Shotgun / Las tres carabelas / Adios muchachos / Valencia / Granada / Tonight / Fandango / Little princess / Gonzales / Jet black / Driftin' (live)
CD _____ SEECD 246
See For Miles/C5 / '88 / Pinnacle.

EP COLLECTION: SHADOWS VOL. 2
Omoide no nagisa / Londonderry air / Boys #2 / Foot tapper / Les girls / Shazam / Sleepwalk / Bongo blues / Flyder and the spy / Chinchilla / Gin iro no michi / Kimi to itsumademo / Boys / Round and round / Friends / Guitar boogie / F.B.I. / Ranka chank / Autumn / Walkin'
CD _____ SEECD 296
See For Miles/C5 / Sep '90 / Pinnacle.

EP COLLECTION: SHADOWS VOL. 3
Quartermaster's stores / It's been a blue day / I wish I could shimmy like my sister Arthur / Sweet dreams / Driftin' / Don't be a fool with love / Be bop a lula / Late night set / 1861 / Spring is nearly here / Back home / Some are lonely / Alice in Sunderland / Blue star / Jet black / Feelin' fine / Saturday dance / Perfidia / Chu chi / Find me a golden street / Bongo blues / It's a man's man's man's world
CD _____ SEECD 375
See For Miles/C5 / Oct '93 / Pinnacle.

FIRST 20 YEARS AT THE TOP (75 Classic Original Recordings 1959-1979)
Feelin' fine / Don't be a fool with love / Driftin' / Jet black / Saturday dance / Lonesome fella / Apache / Quartermaster's stores / Stranger / Man of mystery / F.B.I. / Midnight / Frightened city / Back home / Kon-Tiki / 36-24-36 / Savage / Peace pipe / Wonderful land / Stars fell on Stockton / Guitar tango / What a lovely tune / Boys / Dance on / All day / Foot tapper / Breeze and I / Atlantis / I want you to want me / Shindig / It's been a blue day / Geronimo / Shazam / Theme for young lovers / This hammer / Rise and fall of Flingel bunt / It's a man's man's man's world / Rhythm and greens / Miracle / Genie with the light brown lamp / Little princess / Mary Anne / Chu chi / Stingray / Alice in Sunderland / Don't make my baby blue / My grandfather's clock / War lord / I wish I could shimmy like my sister Arthur / Arthur / I met a girl / Late night set / Place in the sun / Will you be there / Dreams / I dream / Scotch on the socks / Maroc 7 / Bombay duck / Tomorrow's cancelled / Somewhere / Running out of world / Dear old Mrs Bell / Trying to forget the one you love / Slaughter on 10th Avenue / Turn around and touch me / Jungle jam / Let me be the one / Run Billy run / It'll be me babe / Another night / Love deluxe / Don't cry for me Argentina / Cavatina / En aranjuez con tu amor / Heart of glass / Riders in the sky
CD Set _____ CDSHAD 2
EMI / May '95 / EMI.

FROM HANK, BRIAN, BRUCE AND JOHN
Snap, crackle and how's your dad / Thing of beauty / Letter / Holy cows / Holy cow / Last train to Clarksville / Day I met Marie / Evening glow / Naughty nippon lights / San Francisco / Tokaido line / Alentjo / Let me take you there / Mister, you're a better man than I
CD _____ BGOCD 20
Beat Goes On / Apr '90 / Pinnacle.

GREATEST HITS: SHADOWS
Apache / Man of mystery / F.B.I. / Midnight / Frightened city / Kon-Tiki / 36-24-36 / Savage / Peace pipe / Wonderful land / Stars fell on Stockton / Guitar tango / Boys / Dance on / Stranger
CD _____ CZ 189
EMI / May '89 / EMI.

JIGSAW
Jigsaw / Prelude in E major / Cathy's clown / Friday on my mind / Chelsea boot / With a hmm hmm on my knee / Tennessee waltz / Stardust / Semi-detached suburban Mr. James / Winchester cathedral / Maria Elena / Green eyes
CD _____ BGOCD 66
Beat Goes On / '89 / Pinnacle.

LIFE IN THE JUNGLE
Life in the jungle / High noon / Missing / Treat me nice / Cat 'n' mouse / Chariots of fire / No dancing / Riders on the range / Old romantics / You rescue me / Lili Marlene / Raunchy
CD _____ PWKS 4134
Carlton Home Entertainment / Nov '92 / Carlton Home Entertainment.

LIVE AT THE PARIS OLYMPIA
Shazam / Man of mystery / Lady of the morning / Shadoogie / Guitar tango / Faithful / Tiny Robin / Honourable puff-puff / Sleepwalk / Marmaduke / Foot tapper / Apache / Rise and fall of Flingel Bunt / Dance on / Lonesome mole / Nivram / Turn around and touch me / Music make my day / Frightened city
CD _____ CZ 484
EMI / Jan '92 / EMI.

MOONLIGHT SHADOWS
Moonlight shadow / Walk of life / I just called to say I love you / Every breath you take / Nights in white satin / Hello / Power of love / Three times a lady / Against all odds / Hey Jude / Dancing in the dark / I know him so well / Memory / Imagine / Sailing / Whiter shade of pale
CD _____ 829 358-2
Polydor / May '86 / PolyGram.

MORE TASTY
Cricket bat boogie / Return to the Alamo / Goodbye yellow brick road / Another night / Honky tonk woman / Montezuma's revenge / Walk don't run / Superstar / Bermuda triangle / Brazil / Autumn girl / Creole nights / Black is black / Air that I breathe / Sweet Saturday night / Rusk
CD _____ CZ 513
EMI / Sep '92 / EMI.

ORIGINAL CHART HITS 1960-1980, THE
Apache / Man of mystery / Stranger / F.B.I. / Midnight / Frightened city / Kon-Tiki / Savage / Peace pipe / Shadoogie / Wonderful land / Sleepwalk / Guitar tango / Boys / Dance on / Foot tapper / Atlantis / Shindig / Geronimo / Theme for young lovers / Perfidia (CD only.) / Mustang (CD only.) / Cosy (CD only.) / Nivram (CD only.) / Little B (CD only.) / Rise and fall of Flingel Bunt / Rhythm and greens / Genie with the light brown lamp / Mary Anne / Stringray / Don't make my baby blue / Warlord / I met a girl / Place in the sun / Dreams I dream / Maroc 7 / Bombay duck / Tomorrow's cancelled / Dear old Mrs Bell / Slaughter on 10th Avenue / Turn around and touch me / Let me be the one / Don't cry for me Argentina / Deer hunter / Riders in the sky (CD only.) / Thunderbirds theme (CD only.) / Little princess (CD only.) / Tonight (CD only.) / Flyder and the spy (CD only.) / Chatta nooka choo choo (CD only.)
CD Set _____ CDEM 1354
EMI / Feb '90 / EMI.

REFLECTION
Eye of the tiger / Crockett's theme / Right here waiting / Every little thing she does is magic / Sealed with a kiss / Uptown girl / Strawberry Fields forever / Riders in the sky / Flashdance / Something's gotten hold of my heart / Love changes everything / Nothing's gonna stop us now / Bilitis / You'll never walk alone / Always on my mind
CD _____ 847 120-2
Polydor / Oct '90 / PolyGram.

ROCKIN' WITH CURLY LEADS
CD _____ BGOCD 84
Beat Goes On / Oct '90 / Pinnacle.

SHADOW MUSIC/SHADES OF ROCK
I only want to be with you / Fourth street / Magic doll / Stay around / Maid marion's theme / Benno-san / Don't stop now / In the past / Fly me to the moon / Now that you're gone / One way to love / Razzamatazz / Sigh / March to Drina / Proud Mary / My babe / Lucille / Johnny B. Goode / Paperback writer / Satisfaction / Bony Moronie / Get back / Something / River deep, mountain high / Memphis / What'd I say
CD _____ CZ 477
EMI / Feb '92 / EMI.

SHADOWS AND FRIENDS, THE
CD _____ BR 1372
BR Music / May '94 / Target/BMG.

SHADOWS IN THE 60'S, THE
Dance on / Foot tapper / Guitar tango / Man of mystery / Stranger / Midnight / 36-24-36 / Peace pipe / Stars fell on Stockton / Boys / Mary Anne / Don't make my baby blue / Frightened city / Savage / Shindig / Breeze and I / All day / What a lovely tune / Bo Diddley / Quartermaster's stores / Bandit (CD only.) / Little B (CD only.) / South of the border (CD only.) / Shazam (CD only.)
CD _____ CDMFP 6076
Music For Pleasure / Sep '89 / EMI.

SHADOWS IN THE NIGHT
Lady in red / Love changes everything / Power of love / Winner takes it all / Sealed with a kiss / All I ask of you / One moment in time / Careless whisper / I just called to say I love you / I want to know what love is / I guess that's why they call it the blues / Missing (theme) / Going home (theme from Local Hero) / Right here waiting / Chi Mai / Dancing in the dark
CD _____ 843 798-2
PolyGram TV / Apr '93 / PolyGram.

SHADOWS, THE//OUT OF THE SHADOWS
Shadoogie / Blue star / Nivram / Baby my heart / See you in my drums / All my sorrows / Stand up and say that / Gonzales / Find me a golden street / Theme from a filleted place / That's my desire / My resistance is low / Sleepwalk / Big boy / Rumble

---

/ Bandit / Cosy / 1861 / Perfidia / Little B / Bo Diddley / South of the border / Spring is nearly here / Are they all like you / Tales of a raggy tramline / Some are lonely / Kinda cool
CD _____ CZ 378
EMI / Feb '91 / EMI.

SIMPLY SHADOWS
I know you were waiting (for me) / We don't need another hero / Walking in the air / Careless whisper / Don't give up / I guess that's why they call it the blues / Heart will break tonight / Lady in red / Pulaski / Take my breath away / Eastenders / I want to know what love is / Skye boat song / Jealous guy / Chain reaction / Howard's Way
CD _____ 833 682-2
Polydor / Oct '87 / PolyGram.

SPECIAL COLLECTION, A
CD Set _____ BOXD 8
Carlton Home Entertainment / Nov '91 / Carlton Home Entertainment.

STEP FROM THE SHADOWS (Marvin, Welch & Farrar)
Marmaduke / Lady of the morning / Time to come / Lonesome mole / Black eyes / Brownie Kentucky / Skin deep / Faithful / You never can tell / Hard to live with / Music makes my day / Mistress fate and father time / Silvery rain / Wish you were here / Thousand conversations / Tiny Robin / please / Thank heavens I've got you / Please Mr. please
CD _____ SEECD 78
See For Miles/C5 / Apr '93 / Pinnacle.

STEPPIN' TO THE SHADOWS
You win again / I wanna dance with somebody (who loves me) / He ain't heavy, he's my brother / Candle in the wind / Farewell my lovely / Mountains of the moon / Nothings gonna change my love for you / Heaven is a place on earth / When the going gets tough / Alone / All I ask of you / Stack it / Shoba / You keep me hangin' on / Some people / One moment in time
CD _____ 839 357 2
Roll Over Records / May '89 / PolyGram.

STRING OF HITS
Riders in the sky / Parisienne walkways / Classical gas / Deer hunter / Bridge over troubled water / You're the one that I want / Heart of glass / Don't cry for me Argentina / Song for Duke / Bright eyes / Rodrigo's guitar concerto de aranjuez / Baker Street
CD _____ CDMFP 5724
Music For Pleasure / Nov '91 / EMI.

THEMES AND DREAMS
Crockett's theme / Up where we belong / Take my breath away / Deer hunter / Walking in the air / If you leave me now / One day I'll fly away / Africa / Every breath you take / Memory / Nights in white satin / Candle in the wind / You win again / Sailing / Just the way you are / Moonlight shadow
CD _____ 5113742
Roll Over Records / Nov '91 / PolyGram.

Shady

WORLD
Beggars Banquet / Nov '94 / Warner Music / Disc.

Shady Grove Band

CHAPEL HILLBILLY WAY
CD _____ FF 70639
Flying Fish / Feb '95 / Roots / CM / Direct / ADA.

MULBERRY MOON
CD _____ FF 544CD
Flying Fish / '92 / Roots / CM / Direct / ADA.

Shafer, Ted

ORIGINAL JELLY BLUES (Shafer, Ted Jelly Roll Jazz Band)
CD _____ SOSCD 1278
Stomp Off / May '95 / Jazz Music / Wellard.

SAN FRANCISCO (Shafer, Ted Jelly Roll Jazz Band)
CD _____ MMRC-CD 4
Merry Makers / '93 / Jazz Music.

Shaffer, Doreen

SUGAR SUGAR
CD _____ JFCD 4648
Joe Frazier / Mar '95 / Jetstar.

Shaggs

SHAGGS, THE
CD _____ CREV 019CD
Rev-Ola / Nov '94 / 3MV / Vital.

Shaggy

BOOMBASTIC
In the summertime / Boombastic / Something different / Forgive them father / Heartbreak Suzie / Finger Smith / Why you treat me so bad / Woman a pressure / Train is coming / Island lover / Day oh / Jenny / How much more / Gal you a pepper

---

CD _____ CDV 2782
Virgin / Oct '95 / EMI.

ORIGINAL DOBERMAN
Kibbles and bits / Bullet proof buddy / Chow / Alimony / Wildfire / P.H.A.T. / Glamity power / Get down to it / Man a yard / Soldering / Lately / Jump and rock / We never danced to the rub-a-dub sound
CD _____ GRELCD 208
Greensleeves / Nov '94 / Total/BMG / Jetstar / SRD.

PURE PLEASURE
Soon be done / Give thanks and praise / Lust / Oh Carolina / Tek set / Bedroom bounty hunter / Nice and lovely / Love how them flex / All virgins / Ah-e-a-oh / It bun me / Big up / Bow wow wow / Follow me / Mampie / Oh Carolina (Raas bumba claat version)
CD _____ GRELCD 184
Greensleeves / Jul '93 / Total/BMG / Jetstar / SRD.

Shah

BEWARE
Total devastation / Coward / Save the human race / Threshold of pain / Beware / Bloodbrothers / Age of dismay / Say hi to Anthrax
CD _____ ATOMH 009CD
Atom / '90 / Cadillac.

Shaheen, Simon

TURATH
CD _____ CMP CD 3006
CMP / Jul '92 / Vital/SAM.

Shai

IF I EVER FALL IN LOVE
Sexual interlude / Comforter / If I ever fall in love / Sexual / Together forever / If I ever fall in love (accapella) / Flava / Baby, I'm yours / Waiting for the day / Changes / Don't wanna play / Lord I've come
CD _____ MCD 10762
MCA / Jan '93 / BMG.

Shaikl, Adham

JOURNEY TO THE SUN
CD _____ IAE 006CD
Instinct Ambient Europe / Jul '95 / Plastic Head.

Shaka Shamba

NAMEBRAND
CD _____ GRELCD 203
Greensleeves / Apr '94 / Total/BMG / Jetstar / SRD.

Shaka, Tom

HIT FROM THE HEART
CD _____ CCD 11025
Crosscut / '92 / ADA / CM / Direct.

HOT 'N' SPICY
CD _____ CCD 11036
Crosscut / Jan '94 / ADA / CM / Direct.

TIMELESS IN BLUES
CD _____ CDST 03
Stumble / Nov '95 / Direct.

Shakatak

CHRISTMAS ALBUM, THE
Happy Christmas to ya / Winter wonderland / White Christmas / O little town of Bethlehem / Silent night / Christmas time again / Christmas in Rio / Good King Wenceslas / Let it snow, let it snow, let it snow / Sing (Little one) / God rest ye merry gentlemen / Lonely on Christmas day / Jingle bells / Christmas song / Away in a manger / Auld lang syne
CD _____ CDINZ 3
Debut / Dec '93 / Pinnacle / 3MV / Sony.

CITY RHYTHM
Invitations / City rhythm / Climbing high / China Bay / Rio nights / Brazilian dawn / Doctor doctor / Down on the street / Takin' off / Covina / Night moves / Out of the blue / Fly the wind / Feels like the right time / Night bird
CD _____ PWKS 4103P
Carlton Home Entertainment / Mar '92 / Carlton Home Entertainment.

FULL CIRCLE
Brazilian love affair / Catwalk / Out of my sight / Sweet Sunday / You are / Walk in the night / Haze / Diamond in the night / Midnight temptation / Havana express / Tonight's the night / Blue azure
CD _____ CDINZ 2
Inside Out / Feb '95 / 3MV / Sony.

ON THE STREET
Down on the street / Easier said than done / Invitations / Out of this world / Holding on / Lights on my life / Lady (To Billie Holiday) / Dark is the night / Doctor doctor / Something special / Mr. Manic and Sister cool / Turn the music up / Bittersweet / You'll never know
CD _____ 5500082

Spectrum/Karussell / May '93 / PolyGram / THE.

OUT OF THIS WORLD
Dark is the night / Don't say that again / Slip away / On nights like tonight / Out of this world / Let's get together / If you can see me now / Sanur
CD _____ OW 30014
One Way / Sep '94 / Direct / ADA.

STREET LEVEL
One day at a time / Street level / Sleepin' alone / Siberian breeze / Anyway you want it / Night ain't over yet / Watchin' the rain / Without you / Jump 'n' pump / Empty skies / Calm before the storm / Vibe tribe
CD _____ CDINZ 1
Debut / Mar '93 / Pinnacle / 3MV / Sony.

UNDER THE SUN
Soul destination / Don't walk away / Paradise island / Rest of your life / Crosstown / On for the boyz / Beyond the reach / Can't stop running / Sweat / It's over / Fly by night / Shine your light
CD _____ CDINZ 2
Debut / Nov '92 / Pinnacle / 3MV / Sony.

Shakedown Club

SHAKEDOWN CLUB, THE
CD _____ BDV 9403CD
Babel / Jul '94 / ADA / Harmonia Mundi / Cadillac / Diverse.

Shakespears Sister

HORMONALLY YOURS
Goodbye cruel world / I don't care / My 16th apology / Are we in love yet / Emotional thing / Stay / Black sky / Trouble with Andre / Moonchild / Catwoman / Let me entertain you / Hello (turn your radio on)
CD _____ 8282662
London / Feb '92 / PolyGram.

SACRED HEART
Heroine / Run silent / Run deep / Dirty mind / Sacred heart / Heaven in your arms / You're history / Break my heart / Red rocket / Electric moon / Primitive love / Could you be loved / Twist the knife (Only on CD.) / You made me come to this (Only on CD.)
London / May '92 / PolyGram.
_____ 828 131-2

Shalamar

NIGHT TO REMEMBER, A
Night to remember / There it is / I can make you feel good / Over and over / My girl loves me / Amnesia / Leave it all up to love / Whenever you need me / Uptown festival / Second time around / Lovely lady / Work it out / Sweeter as the days go by / On top of the world / Don't try to change me / You won't miss love (until it's gone)
CD _____ 5507542
Spectrum/Karussell / Mar '95 / PolyGram / THE.

VERY BEST OF SHALAMAR, THE
Friends / Take that to the bank / Second time around / There it is / Make that move / I can make you feel good / I owe you one / Uptown festival / Dancing in the sheets / Disappearing act / Night to remember / Dead giveaway / Amnesia / Deadline USA / My girl loves me / Over and over / Circumstantial evidence / Sweeter as the days go by
CD _____ CCSCD 803
Renaissance Collector Series / Sep '95 / BMG.

Shalawambe

SAMORA MACHEL
Mulemeleni / Abantu balafwa / Twansanswa / Umpele njibikile / Kambelenkele / Samora machel / Ifilamba / Icupo cha perm / Mulamu
CD _____ DIAB 817CD
Diabolo / Nov '95 / Pinnacle.

Shaljean, Bonnie

FAREWELL TO LOUGH NEAGH
Rosie Castle / Captain O'Neill / Colonel O'Hara / Sir Festus Burke / Foweles in the frith / Ecb beo thu / Reverie queme / Summer is icumen in / Clocks back reel / Kilburn jig / Diarmuid's well / Wild Irishman / Her mantle so green / Planxty Drew / Mary O'Neill / Maid of Derry
CD _____ CDSDL 372
Saydisc / Mar '94 / Harmonia Mundi / ADA / Direct.

Sham 69

BBC LIVE IN CONCERT
CD _____ WINCD 049
Windsong / Oct '93 / Pinnacle.

BEST OF SHAM 69, THE
CD Set _____ ESDCD 350
Essential / Nov '95 / Total/BMG.

COMPLETE LIVE
Hurry up Harry / I don't wanna / If the kids are united / Borstal breakout / Angels with dirty faces / They don't understand / Rip and tear / Day tripper / That's life / Poor cow / Give a dog a bone / Questions and

answers / Tell us the truth / Hersham boys / Vision and the power / White riot
CD _____ CLACD 153
Castle / Oct '89 / BMG.

FIRST, THE BEST AND THE LAST
Borstal breakout / Hey little rich boy / Angels with dirty faces / Cockney kids are innocent / If the kids are united / Sunday morning nightmare / Hurry up Harry / Questions and answers / Give the dog a bone / Hersham boys / Tell the children / Unite and win
CD _____ 513429-2
Polydor / Apr '94 / PolyGram.

INFORMATION LIBRE
Break on through / Uptown / Planet trash / Information libertaire / Caroline's suitcase / Feel it / King Kong drinks cocacola / Saturdays and strangeways / Breeding dinosaurs / Wild and wonderful
CD _____ DOJOCD 236
Dojo / Jan '96 / BMG.

KINGS AND QUEENS (The Best Of Sham 69)
CD _____ DOJOCD 235
Dojo / Jun '95 / BMG.

LIVE AT THE ROXY
CD _____ RRCD 133
Receiver / Jul '93 / Grapevine.

LIVE IN JAPAN
CD _____ DOJOCD 105
Dojo / Feb '94 / BMG.

SHAM'S LAST STAND
What have we got / I don't wanna / They don't understand / Angels with dirty faces / Tell us the truth / That's life / Rip off / Cockney kids are innocent / Voices / Borstal breakout / Pretty vacant / White riot / If the kids are united / Hurry up Harry / Hersham boys / Questions and answers
CD _____ DOJOCD 95
Dojo / Apr '93 / BMG.

SOAPY WATER AND MR. MARMALADE
CD _____ AICD 001
Scratch / Jul '95 / BMG.

VOLUNTEER
Outside the warehouse / Wicked tease / Wall paper / Mr. Know It All / As black as sheep / How the West was won / Rip and tear / Bastard club / Volunteer / Ad lib Anglais
CD _____ CLACD 274
Castle / '92 / BMG.

Shamen

AXIS MUTATIS
CD _____ TPLP 52CD
CD _____ TPLP 52CDL
One Little Indian / Oct '95 / Pinnacle.

DIFFERENT DRUM
CD _____ TPLP 42CDR
One Little Indian / Nov '93 / Pinnacle.

DROP
Something about you / Passing away / Young 'til yesterday / World theatre / Through with you / Where do you go / Do what you will / Happy days / Through my window / Velvet box / I don't like the way the world is / Other side / Four letter girl
CD _____ MAUCD 613
Mau Mau / Nov '91 / Pinnacle.

EN-TACT
CD _____ TPLP 22CD
One Little Indian / Oct '90 / Pinnacle.

IN GORBACHEV WE TRUST
Synergy / Raspberry infundibulum / Adam strange / Transcendental / Raptyouare / Sweet young thing / War prayer / Jesus loves Amerika / Misinformation / In Gorbachev we trust
CD _____ FIENDCD 666
Demon / Jan '89 / Pinnacle / ADA.

ON AIR -THE BBC SESSIONS
Human Energy/Omega Amigo / Progen/ Make it mine / Hyperreal / Make it mine / Possible worlds / In the bag / Spacetime / Make it mine (Live USA) / Boss drum / Ebeneezer Goode
CD _____ BOJCD 006
Band Of Joy / Sep '93 / ADA.

Shampoo

WE ARE SHAMPOO
Trouble / Delicious / Viva la megababes / Dirty old love song / Skinny white thing / Glimmer globe / Shiny black taxi cab / Me hostage / Game boy / House of love / Shampoo you / Saddo
CD _____ FOODCD 12
Food / Aug '95 / EMI.

Shanahan, Bernie

BERNIE SHANAHAN
CD _____ K 781934-2
WEA / May '89 / Warner Music.

Shand, Jimmy

KING OF THE MELODEON MEN
Punch bowl / My love she's but a lassie yet / Fair maid of Perth / Drunken piper / Laird of Drumblair / De'il among the tailors / Ma-

chine without horses / My wife's a wanton wee thing / Glendaurel highlanders / Cairdin 'ot / Jock O'Hazeldean / We'd better bide a wee / My Nannie's awa / Auld Scotch sangs / Dundee hornpipe / Millicent's favourite / Staten island / Speed the plough / Wind that shakes the barley / Mrs. McLeod / Bluebell polka / Bonnie Dundee / Rock and wee pickle tow / Athol gathering / Merrily danc'd the Quacker's wife / Dumfries house / Bonnie doon / Miss Betty Fitchets wedding / New rigged ship / Off she goes / Kinloch of Kinloch / Queen Mary waltz / La valeta / Londonderry and high level hornpipes / Primrose polka / Petronella / Duke of Perth / This is not my ain lassie / Wandering drummer / Bonnie Ann / Inverness gathering / Braes of Tullymet / Kitty high / Agnes waltz
CD _____ CDEMS 1530
EMI / Jul '94 / EMI.

LAST TEN YEARS, THE (Shand, Jimmy & His Band)
Georgina Catherine MacDonald's fancy / Lord Randal's bride / Calton Hill reel / Lady Elgin of Broomhall / Lord Elgin of Broomhall / Green glens of Antrim / Come back to Erin / Bryce Laing's welcome to Auchtermuchty / John and Mary's Young's golden wedding anniversary / Threave Castle polka / Major Norman Orr Ewing / Crossing the new Forth Bridge / Seventy second Highlanders' farewell to Aberdeen / Jimmy Shand's 80th year / Now is the hour / At the end of a perfect day / MacKenzie highlanders / Glengarry quickstep / Teribus / Sweet maid of Glendaruel / Francis Wright's waltz / Suptd. Ian Thompson's farewell to the Fife police / Jimmy Shand's compliments to Willie Laird / Guardians of the Gulf / Royal Guard Regiment of H.M. Sultan Of Oman / Heather mixture twostep / Badge of Scotland / Fifty first Highland Division / Hills of Alva / MacNeils of Ugadale / John D. Burgess / Hugh MacPherson / Piper's weird / Flower o' the Quern / Cradle song / Lochanside / Bill Dickman of Stonehouse / Woodlands polka / Scottish horse / Bugle horn / MacDonald's awa' tae the war / Gentle maiden / Believe me, if all those endearing young charms / Come back Paddy Reilly to Ballyjamesduff / James Duff / Rose of Tralee / Ian Powrie's welcome to Dunblane / Jimmy Shand's compliments to Ian Powrie / Whitley chapel barn dance / Miss Elder / John MacDonald of Glencoe / Maresland twostep
CD _____ WGRCD 13
Ross / Dec '89 / Ross / Duncans.

LEGENDARY JIMMY SHAND, THE
Muckin' o' Geordie's byre / Lady Nellie Wemyss / Braidley's house / Major Mackie / Scotland the brave / Thistle of Scotland / We're no awa' tae bide awa' / Cailin mo ruin-sa / Leaving barra / Morag of Dunvegan / Cock o' the North / Jeannie King / Bluebell polka / If you're Irish come into the parlour / With my shillelagh under me arm / Royal Scots polka / Lord Lyndoch / Duke of Gordon / Laird o' Thrums / Lady Anne Hope / Gordon B. Cosh / Kinkell braes / Ythan bar / Northern lights of Aberdeen / Black dance / Thurso wedding / Wandering drummer / Breadalbane reel / Miss Bennetts jig / John Mearn's favourite / Balcomie House / Threave castle polka / Mrs. Cholmondely's reel / Lass o' paties mill / O Harveston Castle / Deveron reel / Blow the wind southerly / O hey ye seen the roses blow / Cushie butterfield / Cullercoats fish lass / Peter's peerie boat / Boonie doon / Jeanie's blue e'en / Neidpath castle / Tom's highland fling / Scotch mist / Lamb skinnet / John Grumlie / I lo'ed nae a lassie but Ane / Brinkie braes / Aunice Gillie's farewell to Loch Gilphead / John Bain Mackenzie / Galloway house reel / Georgina Catherine MacDonald's fancy
CD _____ CC 248
Music For Pleasure / Sep '89 / EMI.

PLAYS JIMMY SHAND
CD _____ EXC 102
Exclusive / Dec '95 / Target/BMG.

SCOTTISH FANCY, A (Shand, Jimmy & His Band)
White heather jig / Grosvenor House strathspey / Campbells are coming / Balmoral strathspey / Miss Hadden's reel / Quiet and snug strathspey / Forper's jig / Waltz country dance / Galloway House reel / Express (CD only.) / La tempete (CD only.) / Marie's wedding (CD only.) / Road to the isles (CD only.) / Waverley (CD only.)
CD _____ GRCD 37
Grasmere / Sep '89 / Target/BMG / Savoy.

Shangaie

CHANSON MARINEES
CD _____ CD 857
Diffusion Breizh / Aug '95 / ADA.

Shanghai Folk Orchestra

BUTTERFLY LOVERS, THE
CD _____ 8.240 277
Impetus / '88 / CM / Wellard / Impetus / Cadillac.

Shangoya

COLLECTION
CD _____ MPD 6006
Flying Fish / Nov '94 / Roots / CM / Direct / ADA.

Shangri-Las

COLLECTION
CD _____ COL 043
Collection / Mar '95 / Target/BMG.

HIT SINGLE COLLECTABLES
CD _____ DISK 4512
Disky / Apr '94 / THE / BMG / Discovery / Pinnacle.

LEADER OF THE PACK
CD _____ CDCD 1057
Charly / Mar '93 / Charly / THE / Cadillac.

MYRMIDONES OF MELODRAMA
Remember (walkin' in the sand) / It's easier to cry / Leader of the pack / What is love / Give him a great big kiss / Maybe / Out in the streets / Boy / Give us your blessings / Heaven only knows / Right now and not later / Train from Kansas city / I can never go home anymore / Bulldog / Long live our love / Sophisticated boom boom / He cried / Dressed in black / Past, present and future / Love you more than yesterday / Paradise / Never again / I'm blue / What's a girl supposed to do / Dum dum ditty / You cheated, you lied / Give him a great big kiss (alt take) / Dating courtesy Pt 1 / Dating courtesy Pt 2 / Hate to say I told you so / Wishing well
CD _____ RPM 136
RPM / Apr '95 / Pinnacle.

PEARLS FROM THE PAST VOL. 2 - THE SHANGRI-LAS
CD _____ KLMCD 013
Scratch / May '94 / BMG.

REMEMBER
Leader of the pack / Give him a great big kiss / Maybe / Out in the streets / Give us your blessing / Right now and not later / Remember (walkin' in the sand) / I can never go home anymore / Long live our love / Past, present and future / Train from Kansas City / Shout / Twist and shout / I'm blue / You cheated, you lied / So much in love
CD _____ CDINS 5021
Instant / Feb '90 / Charly.

Shanice

21 WAYS TO GROW
Ways to grow / I care / Don't break my heart / Turn down the lights / Somewhere / Ace boon coon / I like / I'll be there / I wish / When I say that I love you / I wanna give it to you / Never changing love / Needing me
CD _____ 530345-2
Motown / Jun '94 / PolyGram.

Shank, Bud

BUD SHANK PLAYS CONCERTO FOR ALTO SAX AND ORCHESTRA (Shank, Bud & The Royal Philharmonic Orchestra)
Here's that rainy day / Body and soul / Concerto for jazz alto saxophone and orchestra
CD _____ MOLECD 12
Mole Jazz / Apr '87 / Jazz Horizons / Jazz Music / Cadillac / Wellard / Impetus.

CRYSTAL COMMENTS (Shank, Bud & Bill Mays, Alan Broadbent)
Scrapple from the apple / How are things in glocca morra / I'll take romance / Solar / Body and soul / On green dolphin street
CD _____ CCD 4126
Concord Jazz / Feb '94 / New Note.

DOCTOR IS IN, THE
CD _____ CCD 79520
Candid / Nov '93 / Cadillac / Jazz Music / Wellard / Koch.

DRIFTING TIMELESSLY
CD _____ 75001
Capri / Jun '87 / Wellard / Cadillac.

I TOLD YOU SO
CD _____ CCD 79533
Candid / Dec '93 / Cadillac / Jazz Music / Wellard / Koch.

LOST CATHEDRAL, THE
CD _____ ITMP 970087
ITM / Oct '95 / Tradelink / Koch.

NEW GOLD (Shank, Bud Sextet)
CD _____ CCD 79707
Candid / '94 / Cadillac / Jazz Music / Wellard / Koch.

SUNSHINE EXPRESS
CD _____ CCD 6020
Concord Jazz / Sep '91 / New Note.

TALES OF THE PILOT
CD _____ CAPR 74025
Capri / Jan '89 / Wellard / Cadillac.

Shankar, Lakshminarayana

LAKSHMI SHANKAR EVENING CONCERT
CD _____ RSMCD 102
Ravi Shankar Music Circle / Apr '94 / Conifer.

M.R.C.S.

Adagio / March / All I care / Reasons / Back again / Al's hallucinations / Sally / White buffalo / Ocean waves
CD _____ 8416422
ECM / Jun '91 / New Note.

NOBODY TOLD ME
Chittham irangaayo / Chodhanai thanthu / Nadru dri dhom - tillana
CD _____ 8396232
ECM / Nov '89 / New Note.

PANCHA NADAI PALLAVI
Ragam tanam pallavi / Ragam: Sankarabharanam / Talam mahalakshmi tala / 9/12 beats / Pancha nadai pallavi
CD _____ 8416412
ECM / Jun '90 / New Note.

SONG FOR EVERYONE
CD _____ 8237952
ECM / Apr '85 / New Note.

WHO'S TO KNOW
Ragam tanam pallavi / Ananda nadamaadum tillai sankara
CD _____ 8272692
ECM / Dec '85 / New Note.

Shankar, Ravi

AT THE WOODSTOCK FESTIVAL
Raga puriya-Dhanashri / Gat in Sawarital / Tabla solo in Jhaptal / Raga manj-khama
CD _____ BGOCD 117
Beat Goes On / Jul '91 / Pinnacle.

CONCERT FOR PEACE LIVE AT THE ROYAL ALBERT HALL
CD Set _____ MRCD 1013
Moment / Oct '95 / ADA / Koch.

FESTIVAL FROM INDIA
CD _____ BGOCD 301
Beat Goes On / Nov '95 / Pinnacle.

FROM INDIA
CD _____ CD 12522
Music Of The World / Feb '95 / Target/ BMG / ADA.

IMPROVISATIONS
CD _____ BGOCD 115
Beat Goes On / Jul '91 / Pinnacle.

IN NEW YORK
CD _____ BGOCD 144
Beat Goes On / Jun '92 / Pinnacle.

IN SAN FRANCISCO
CD _____ BGOCD 197
Beat Goes On / Dec '93 / Pinnacle.

INDIA'S MASTER MUSICIAN
CD _____ BGOCD 218
Beat Goes On / Jan '94 / Pinnacle.

INSIDE THE KREMLIN
Prarambh / Shanti mantra / Three ragas in D minor / Shankhya / Tarana / Bahu-rang
CD _____ 259620
Arista / Feb '89 / BMG.

LIVE AT MONTEREY 1967
Raga todi / Rupak tal (7 beats) / Tabla solo in ektal (12 beats)
CD _____ RSMCD 101
Ravi Shankar Music Circle / Apr '94 / Conifer.

LIVE AT THE MONTEREY FESTIVAL
Raga Bhimpalasi / Tabla solo in Ektal / Dhun
CD _____ BGOCD 99
Beat Goes On / Jul '93 / Pinnacle.

PANDIT RAVI SHANKAR
CD _____ C558 674
Ocora / '88 / Harmonia Mundi / ADA.

PORTRAIT OF A GENIUS
CD _____ BGOCD 99
Beat Goes On / '91 / Pinnacle.

RAGAS
CD _____ FCD 24714
Fantasy / Oct '93 / Pinnacle / Jazz Music / Wellard / Cadillac.

RAVI SHANKAR
CD _____ C 570000CD
Ocora / Jul '95 / Harmonia Mundi / ADA.

SOUND OF THE SITAR
Raga Malkauns / Tala Sawari (Tabla Solo) / Pahari Dhun
CD _____ BGOCD 171
Beat Goes On / Apr '93 / Pinnacle.

TANA MANA (Shankar, Ravi Project)
Chase / Tana mana / Village dance / Seven and 10 1/2 / Friar park / Romantic voyage / Memory of Uday / West eats meat / Reunion / Supplication
CD _____ 259.962
Private Music / Nov '89 / BMG.

TRANSMIGRATION MACABRE
Madness / Anxiety / Submission / Transmigration / Reflection / Fantasy / Torment / Death / Retribution
CD _____ C5CD 596
See For Miles/C5 / Jan '93 / Pinnacle.

Shanley, Eleanor

ELEANOR SHANLEY
CD _____ GRACD 206
Grapevine / Apr '95 / Grapevine.

Shannon

BEST OF SHANNON, THE
Let the music play / Sweet somebody / Stronger together / My heart's divided / Give me tonight / Do you wanna get away / Urgent / Prove me right / Dancin' / You put a spark in my life / Give me the music
CD _____ DGPCD 738
Deep Beats / Nov '95 / BMG.

COLLECTION
CD _____ CCSCD 394
Castle / Apr '94 / BMG.

Shannon Singers

60 SHADES OF GREEN
CD _____ CDIRISH 002
Outlet / Jan '95 / ADA / Duncans / CM / Ross / Direct / Koch.

CHRISTMAS PARTY
CD _____ CCSCD 801
Outlet / Oct '95 / ADA / Duncans / CM / Ross / Direct / Koch.

GOLDEN COLLECTION OF IRISH SONGS
CD _____ CDIRISH 008
Outlet / Oct '95 / ADA / Duncans / CM / Ross / Direct / Koch.

Shannon, Del

DEL SHANNON GREATEST HITS
Runaway / Hats off to Larry / Little town flirt / Swiss maid / Hey little girl / Two kinds of teardrops / So long baby / She's gotta be mine / From me to you / Handyman / Do you want to dance / Big hurt / Keep searchin' / Stranger in town / Break up / Cry myself to sleep / Two silouettes / Don't gild the lily / Lily / Ginny in the mirror / I go to pieces
CD _____ CPCD 8001
Charly / Oct '93 / Charly / THE / Cadillac.

GREATEST HITS
CD _____ MU 5017
Musketeer / Oct '92 / Koch.

LIVE IN ENGLAND/AND THE MUSIC PLAYED ON
Hats off to Larry / Handyman / Swiss maid / Hey little girl / Little town flirt / Kelly / Crying / Two kinds of teardrops / Coopersville yodel / Answer to everything / Keep searchin' / What's the matter baby / So long baby / Runaway / It's my feeling / Mind over matter / Silently / Cut and come again / My love has gone / Led along / Life is nothing / Music plays on / Easy to say / Friendly you behind / Raindrops / He cheated / Leaving you behind / Runaway '67
CD _____ BGOCD 280
Beat Goes On / Jun '95 / Pinnacle.

LOOKING BACK
Runaway / Hats off to Larry / Don't gild the lily, Lily / So long baby / Answer to everything / Hey little girl / I don't care anymore / You never talked about me / I won't be there / Ginny in the mirror / Cry myself to sleep / Swiss maid / Little town flirt / Two kinds of teardrops / Kelly / Two silhouettes / From me to you / Sue's gonna be mine / That's the way love is / Mary Jane / Handyman / World without love / Do you wanna dance / Keep searchin' / Broken promises / I go to pieces / Stranger in town / Break up / Why don't you tell him / Hats off to over
CD _____ VSOPCD 161
Connoisseur / Apr '91 / Pinnacle.

PEARLS FROM THE PAST - DEL SHANNON
Scratch / Nov '93 / BMG.
CD _____ KLMCD 002

ROCK ON
CD _____ ORECD 514
Silvertone / Mar '94 / Pinnacle.

RUNAWAY
CD _____ RMB 75027
Remember / Nov '93 / Total/BMG.

RUNAWAY HITS
Little town flirt / Runaway / Jody / Hats off to Larry / So long baby / Swiss maid / Answer to everything / Hey little girl / Cry myself to sleep / Two kinds of teardrops / Kelly / Handyman / Two silouettes / Sue's gotta be mine / Keep searchin' / Stranger in town
CD _____ EDCD 121
Edsel / Nov '86 / Pinnacle / ADA.

THIS IS MY BAG/TOTAL COMMITMENT
CD _____ BGOCD 307
Beat Goes On / Feb '96 / Pinnacle.

Shannon, Hugh

TRUE BLUE HUGH
CD _____ ACD 140
Audiophile / Apr '93 / Jazz Music / Swift.

Shannon, Mem

CAB DRIVER'S BLUES, A
5th Ward horseman / Play the guitar son / 17.00 Brunette / You ain't nothin' nice / My baby's been watching TV / Me and my bed / Ode to Benny Hill / Taxicab driver / Miserable bastard / One hot night / Dick tie

---

commandos / Boogie man / Maxine / Older broad / Got to go / Chantelle / If this ain't the blues / Food drink and music
CD _____ HNCD 1387
Hannibal / Jan '96 / Vital / ADA.

Shannon, Preston

BREAK THE ICE (Shannon, Preston Band)
CD _____ BB 9545CD
Bullseye Blues / Aug '94 / Direct.

Shannon, Sharon

OUT THE GAP
CD _____ ROCDG 14
Grapevine / Jan '95 / Grapevine.

SHARON SHANNON
Glentown / Blackbird / Queen of the West / Retour des hirondelles/Tune for a found harmonium / Miss Thomson and Derry reel / Munster hop / Tickle her leg / Marguerita suite / Coridinio / Anto's cajun cousins / Comphiopa corafinne and skidoo / Marbhna luimni / Phil Cunningham sets / Woodchoppers/Reel des Voyguers
CD _____ ROCDG 8
Grapevine / Jan '95 / Grapevine.

Shannon, Tom

ROCKIN' REBELS
Tom Shannon show logo / Wild weekend / Rockin' crickets / Whole lotta shakin' goin' on / Another wild weekend / Rumble / Hully gully rock / Flibbity jibbitt / Honky tonk / Happy popcorn / Monday morning / Sweet little sixteen / Buffalo blues / Tequila / Wild rebel / Third man theme / Wild weekend cha cha / Ram-bunk-shush / Telstar / Donkey walk / Stripper / Coconuts / Loaded dice / Anyway you want me / Theme from the rebel / Wild weekend theme
CD _____ CDCHD 426
Ace / May '94 / Pinnacle / Cadillac / Complete/Pinnacle.

Shanti, Oliver

TAI CHI
CD _____ SKV 006CD
Sattva Art / Jul '95 / THE.

Shaolin Wooden Men

SHAOLIN WOODEN MEN
CD _____ NZ 013
Nova Zembla / Jul '94 / Plastic Head.

Shapeshifter

MYSTERY OF BEING
CD _____ HY 85921054
Hyperium / Apr '94 / Plastic Head.

Shapiro, Helen

BEST OF THE EMI YEARS: HELEN SHAPIRO
Tip toe through the tulips / Don't treat me like a child / You don't know / Walkin' back to happiness / Birth of the blues / Tell me what he said / Little Miss Lonely / St. Louis blues / Teenager in love / Keep away from other girls / Let's talk about love / Lipstick on your collar / Little devil / Queen for tonight / I want to be happy / Look who it is / Woe is me / All alone am I / Fever / Walk on by
CD _____ CDEMS 1398
EMI / May '91 / EMI.

EP COLLECTION: HELEN SHAPIRO
Little devil / I don't care / Don't treat me like a child / You don't know / Teenager in love / Lipstick on your collar / Beyond the sea / Little Miss Lonely / Day the rains came / Tell me what he said / Walkin' back to happiness / I apologise / Let's talk about love / When I'm with you / Because they're young / St. Louis blues / Goody goody / Birth of the blues / Keep away from other girls / After you've gone
CD _____ SEECD 272
See For Miles/C5 / Oct '89 / Pinnacle.

HELEN IN NASHVILLE
Not responsible / I cried myself to sleep last night / Young stranger / Here today and gone tomorrow / It's my party / No trespassing / I'm tickled pink / I walked right in (with my eyes wide open) / Sweeter than sweet / You'd think he didn't know me / When you hurt me / I cry / Woe is me
CD _____ C5CD-545
See For Miles/C5 / Jul '89 / Pinnacle.

HELEN SHAPIRO
Don't treat me like a child / You don't know / Walkin' back to happiness / Tell me what he said / Let's talk about love / Little Miss Lonely / Keep away from other girls / Queen for tonight / Woe is me / Look who it is / Fever / Look over your shoulder / Tomorrow is another day / When I'm with you / Marvellous lie / Kiss 'n' run / I apologise / Sometime yesterday / I don't care / Cry my heart out / Daddy couldn't get me one of those / Walking in my dreams / Ole Father Time / He knows how to love me / I walked right in (with my eyes wide open) (CD only) / You won't come home (CD only) / I was

---

only kidding (CD only) / It's so funny I could cry (CD only)
CD _____ CC 259
Music For Pleasure / Oct '90 / EMI.

IMMER DIE BOYS
Frag'mich nicht warum / Komm sei wieder gut / Den ton kenn'ich schon / Gestern nachmittag / Ich war der star heute nacht / Glaube mir, Jonny / Schlafen kann ich nie / Warum gerade ich / Immer die boys / Rote rosen und vergissmeinnicht / Sag dass es schonist / Ich such mir meinen brautigam alleine aus / Der weg zu die inern herzen / Das ist nicht die feine englische art / Walkin' back to happiness / Don't treat me like a child / Tout ce qu'il voudra / J'ai tant de remords / Parlons d'amour / Sans penser a rien
CD _____ BCD 15509
Bear Family / Jul '90 / Rollercoaster / Direct / CM / Swift / ADA.

KADOSH
CD _____ MANNACD 041
Manna Music / Sep '93 / BMG.

NOTHING BUT THE BEST
CD _____ ICCD 13530
ICC / May '95 / Total/BMG.

SENSATIONAL
Teenager sings the blues / Blues in the night / Are you lonesome tonight / Tearaway Johnny / Without your love / Aren't you the lucky one / Every one but the right one / It's alright without me / Lookin' for my heart / Basin Street blues / You must be readin' my mind / Till I hear the truth from you / Sensational / Easy come, easy go / Remember me / End of the world / It might as well rain until September / Here in your arms / Only once / Just a line / Forget about the bad things / Wait a little longer / In my calendar / Empty house
CD _____ RPM 151
RPM / Jul '95 / Pinnacle.

Shapiro, Jaacov

BEST OF YIDDISH FOLK SONGS
Kinder jorn / Vu bistu geven / Aroiskumen zolstu main meidl / Shabes shabes / Unter eltern / Abisl zin abisl reign / Rebe elimelech / Shlof stoin main jankele / Idish gesl / Kadish / Di zun is fargangen / Skeshenever shtikele / Hobn mir a meidl / Hop maine humentashn
CD _____ EUCD 1216
ARC / Sep '93 / ARC Music / ADA.

Shareh, Oku

TURTLE DANCE SONGS OF SAN JUAN PEBLO
CD _____ 803012
New World / Sep '92 / Harmonia Mundi / ADA / Cadillac.

Sharif, Jamil

PORTRAITS OF NEW ORLEANS
CD _____ UKJ 128
Dalya / Oct '93 / Jazz Music.

Shark Taboo

BLACK ROCK SANDS
CD _____ PLASCD 021
Plastic Head / Nov '89 / Plastic Head.

Sharkboy

MATINEE
CD _____ NUDECD 2
Nude / Apr '94 / Disc.

VALENTINE TAPES
CD _____ NUDECD 4
Nude / Sep '95 / Disc.

Sharkey, Feargal

FEARGAL SHARKEY
Good heart / You little thief / Ghost train / Ashes and diamond / Made to measure / Someone to somebody / Don't leave it to nature / Love and hate / Bitter man / It's all over now
CD _____ CDV 2360
Virgin / Jun '88 / EMI.

Sharks

COLOUR MY FLESH
Hanger 84 / Grave robber / Desire calls / Time bomb / Blue water, white death / Rat race / Man with the x-ray eyes / Jet boy / On the run / Too little, too late / Parasite / Sgt rock
CD _____ CDGRAM 100
Anagram / Feb '96 / Pinnacle.

LIKE A BLACK VAN PARKED IN A DARK CURVE
CD _____ BH 003
Bubblehead / Nov '95 / Total/BMG.

PHANTOM ROCKERS
CD _____ NERCD 008
Nervous / Oct '91 / Nervous / Magnum Music Group.

RECREATIONAL KILLER
Screw / Bye bye girl / Charlie (93 version) / Recreational killer / Dealer / Hooker / Surf-

---

caster / Morphine daze / Publican gullican / Gettin' even with you / Something in my basement / Blockhouse / I'm hooked on you / Schizoid man / Charlie 2 / Scratchin' my way out
CD _____ CDGRAM 72
Cherry Red / Oct '93 / Pinnacle.

Sharma, Shivkumar

CALL OF THE VALLEY
Rag pahadi / Ghara dadra / Dhun mishra / Bageshwari / Rag piloo / Bhoop / Rag des
CD _____ CDEMC 3707
EMI / Apr '95 / EMI.

RAG MADHUVANTI/RAG MISRA TILANG
CD _____ NI 5110
Nimbus / Sep '94 / Nimbus.

Sharon, Ralph

MAGIC OF COLE PORTER (Sharon, Ralph Trio)
You're the top / All through the night / Easy to love / Get out of town / You'd be so nice to come home to / I concentrate on you / I've got you under my skin / Down in the depths / So in love / Anything goes / Let's do it / From this moment on / What is this thing called love / Do I love you / Night and day / I love Paris / Love for sale / I love you / It's all right with me / All of you / I get a kick out of you / Why should I / Just one of those things / Long last love / Begin the beguine / Sorta Porter
CD _____ CDSIV 1123
Horatio Nelson / Jul '95 / THE / BMG / Avid/BMG / Koch.

MAGIC OF GEORGE GERSHWIN, THE (Sharon, Ralph Trio)
Fascinating rhythm / They all laughed / Somebody loves me / 'S Wonderful / But not for me / Soon / I loves you Porgy / I get rhythm / They can't take that away from me / Someone to watch over me / Man I love / Love is here to stay / There's a boat dat's leavin' soon for New York / Rhapsody in blue / Foggy day / Embraceable you / Liza (all the clouds'll roll away) / How long has this been going on / Swanee / Love walked in / Oh lady be good
CD _____ CDSIV 1116
Horatio Nelson / Jul '95 / THE / BMG / Avid/BMG / Koch.

MAGIC OF IRVING BERLIN, THE (Sharon, Ralph Trio)
CD _____ CDSIV 1134
Horatio Nelson / Jul '95 / THE / BMG / Avid/BMG / Koch.

MAGIC OF JEROME KERN, THE (Sharon, Ralph Trio)
CD _____ CDSIV 1138
Horatio Nelson / Apr '93 / THE / BMG / Avid/BMG / Koch.

MAGIC OF RICHARD RODGERS, THE (Songs Composed with Lorenz Hart) (Sharon, Ralph Trio)
I didn't know what time it was / Falling in love with love / Most beautiful girl in the world / Lover / Wait till you see her / Slaughter on 10th Avenue / You are too beautiful / I wish I were in love again / Bewitched, bothered and bewildered / Ten cents a dance / Have you met Miss Jones / It's easy to remember / Where or when / Mountain greenery / I could write a book / Mimi / On your toes / Thou swell / My funny valentine / Lady is a tramp / There's a small hotel / Little girl blue / Isn't it romantic / Blue room / I never entered my mind / Blues for Rodgers and Hart
CD _____ CDSIV 6130
Horatio Nelson / Jul '95 / THE / BMG / Avid/BMG / Koch.

SWINGS THE SAMMY CAHN SONGBOOK (Sharon, Ralph Trio & Gerry Mulligan)
My king of town / Teach me tonight / Mario Lanza medley - Be my love / Guess I'll hang my tears out to dry / It's magic / It's you or no one / Call me irresponsible / Blues for Sammy / Things we did last summer / Autumn in Rome / I should care / All the way / Time after time / Tender trap
CD _____ DRGCD 5232
DRG / Feb '95 / New Note.

Sharp 9

UNTIMED
CD _____ 9041532
Mausoleum / Feb '95 / Grapevine.

Sharp, Brian

AMOR AMOR
CD _____ CDGRS1247
Grosvenor / Feb '93 / Target/BMG.

FREEWAY
CD _____ CDGRS1212
Grosvenor / Feb '93 / Target/BMG.

SHARP IMPRESSIONS
Annan polka / We'll gather lilacs / What kind of fool am I / Who can I turn to / Walk in the Black Forest / Spanish harlequin / Root beer rag / All the things you are / Chorus of the Hebrew slaves / Spanish disco / Pop

looks Bach / All the world's a stage / Grass-hoppers dance / Midnight in Mayfair / How high the moon / Alias Smith and Jones / Moonlight fiesta / Perchance to dream / Amigos para siempra / Syncopated clock (CD only) / Rag a de rag (CD only) / Old rugged cross (CD only) / Dream theme (CD only)
CD _____ CDGRS 1267
Grosvenor / Feb '95 / Target/BMG.

Sharp, Elliott

ABSTRACT REPRESSIONISM 1990-99
CD _____ VICTOCD 019
Victo / Nov '94 / These / ReR Megacorp / Cadillac.

DATACIDE
CD _____ EMY 1162
Enemy / Nov '92 / Grapevine.

HAMMER, ANVIL, STIRRUP (Sharp, Elliott & The Soldier String Quartet)
CD _____ SST 232 CD
SST / Dec '89 / Plastic Head.

IN THE LAND OF THE YAHOOS
CD _____ SST 128 CD
SST / Feb '88 / Plastic Head.

MONSTER CURVE
CD _____ SST 208 CD
SST / May '93 / Plastic Head.

PSYCHO-ACOUSTIC (Sharp, Elliot & Zeena Parkins)
CD _____ VICTOCD 026
Victo / Oct '94 / These / ReR Megacorp / Cadillac.

TECTONICS
CD _____ EFA 127622
Atonal / Jun '95 / SRD.

TOCSIN (Sharp, Elliott & Carbon)
CD _____ EMY 134-2
Enemy / Nov '94 / Grapevine.

Sharpe, Jack

CATALYST (A Tribute To Tubby Hayes) (Sharpe, Jack Big Band)
Milestones / You know I care / Sharpe edge / Suddenly last Tuesday / Keith / Souriya / Alisamba
CD _____ CDFRG 716
Frog / Jun '89 / Jazz Music / Cadillac / Wellard.

ROARIN' (Sharpe, Jack Big Band)
I'm beginning to see the light / Old folks / Mayfly / Wait and see (CD only.) / 100 degrees proof / Skylark / All the things you are / K and J (CD only.) / J and B (CD only.)
CD _____ JHCD 016
Ronnie Scott's Jazz House / Jan '94 / Jazz Music / Magnum Music Group / Cadillac.

Sharpe, Ray

LINDA LU
Linda Lu / Monkey's uncle / Oh my baby's gone / That's the way I feel / Kewpie doll / Red sails in the sunset / Silly Dilly Millie / Bus song / T.A. blues / Long John / Gonna let it go this time / Bermuda / Give'n up / For you my love / Justine / On the street where you love / There'll come a day / Dallas / So sorry / Hey little girl / Thank you so much / New Linda Lu / T.A. blues (2) / Long John (2) / Kewpie doll (2) / On the street where you love (2) / Red sails in the sunset (2)
CD _____ BCD 15888
Bear Family / Nov '95 / Rollercoaster / Direct / CM / Swift / ADA.

Sharpe, Rocky

FABULOUS ROCKY SHARPE & THE REPLAYS (Sharpe, Rocky & The Replays)
Rama lama ding dong / Imagination / Love will make you fail in school / Martian hop / Shout (knock yourself out) / Heart / Never / Come on let's go / Looking for an echo / Teenager in love / Never be anyone else but you / Get a job
CD _____ CDFAB 009
Ace / Oct '91 / Pinnacle / Cadillac / Complete/Pinnacle.

SO HARD TO LAUGH (Sharpe, Rocky & The Razors)
I wonder why / Drip drop / Daddy cool / Devil or angel / One summer night / So hard to laugh so easy to cry / What's your name / Mathilda / Poison ivy / Thats my desire / Pretty little angel eyes / As long as I'm moving / Whole lotta shakin' goin' on / Splish splash
CD _____ CDWIKM 116
Chiswick / Mar '93 / Pinnacle.

Sharriff, Imam Omar

RAVEN, THE
CD _____ ARHCD 365
Arhoolie / Apr '95 / ADA / Direct / Cadillac.

Sharrock, Linda

LIKE A RIVER
CD _____ 5230152
Amadeo / Mar '95 / PolyGram.

Sharrock, Sonny

GUITAR
CD _____ EMY 102-2
Enemy / Nov '94 / Grapevine.

SEIZE THE RAINBOW
CD _____ EMY 104-2
Enemy / Nov '92 / Grapevine.

SONNY SHARROCK: LIVE IN NEW YORK
CD _____ EMY 108-2
Enemy / Nov '94 / Grapevine.

Shaskeen

IRISH TRADITIONAL MUSIC AND SONG
CD _____ CDIRISH 010
Outlet / Oct '95 / ADA / Duncans / CM / Ross / Direct / Koch.

SILVER JUBILEE COLLECTION
CD _____ FA 3509CD
GTD / Jul '95 / Else / ADA.

Shatner, William

TRANSFORMED MAN, THE
King Henry The Fifth / Elegy For The Brave / Theme From Cyrana / Mr. Tambourine Man / Hamlet / It Was A Very Good Year / Romeo And Juliet / How Insensitive / Spleen / Lucy In The Sky With Diamonds / Transformed man
CD _____ CREV 004CD
Rev-Ola / Nov '92 / 3MV / Vital.

Shava Shava

DIGGIN' THE ROOTS
CD _____ DMUT 1248
Multitone / Jan '94 / BMG.

Shave The Monkey

DRAGONFLY
CD _____ APE 3002CD
Pecheron / Oct '94 / ADA.

UNSEELIE COURT
CD _____ APE 3001CD
Pecheron / Oct '94 / ADA.

Shaver, Billy Joe

RESTLESS WIND
Texas uphear Tennessee / Good Lord knows / Ride me down easy / When I get my wings / Ain't no good in Mexico / Love you till the cows come home / Woman is the wonder of the world / When the word was thunderbird / America, you are my woman / Restless wind / Evergreen / Billy B. Damned / We stayed too long at the fair / Honky tonk heroes / I'm going crazy in 3/4 time / Gypsy boy / Chicken on the ground / Everything, everywhere's / Slow rollin' low / Silver wings of time / Believer / You asked me to / Lately I've been leaning towards the blues / I couldn't be me without you / Music city U.S.A.
CD _____ BCDAH 15775
Bear Family / Jun '94 / Rollercoaster / Direct / CM / Swift / ADA.

Shavers, Charlie

BLUES SINGERS
Freight train blues / My Daddy rocks me / I am a woman / Low down dirty groundog / Jive is here / Downhearted blues
CD _____ CBC 1025
Timeless Jazz / Sep '95 / New Note.

Shaw, Artie

1938 VOL.1 (Shaw, Artie & Rhythm Makers)
CD _____ TAX 37092
Tax / Aug '94 / Jazz Music / Wellard / Cadillac.

22 ORIGINAL BIG BAND RECORDINGS (Shaw, Artie & His Orchestra)
CD _____ HCD 401
Hindsight / Jun '95 / Target/BMG / Jazz Music.

ARTIE SHAW
CD _____ 22705
Music / Nov '95 / Target/BMG.

ARTIE SHAW & HIS ORCHESTRA (Shaw, Artie & His Orchestra)
'S wonderful / Man and his dream / April in Paris / Summertime / I cover the waterfront / Blues (end s1) / I could write a book / Don't take your love from me / Beyond the blue horizon / Maid with the flaccid air / Time on my hands / Deep purple / Prelude in C major
CD _____ 15757
Laserlight / Aug '92 / Target/BMG.

ARTIE SHAW & HIS ORCHESTRA VOL.2 (Shaw, Artie & His Orchestra)
Stardust / They say / My heart stood still / Begin the beguine / Dancing in the dark / Serenade to a savage / Day in, day out / I

don't want to walk without you / Rockin' chair / Temptation / Carioca / Out of no-where / Softly as in a morning sunrise / Blues in the night / Back bay shuffle / Jungle drums / All the things you are / Someo-ne's rocking my dreamboat / I poured my heart into a song / Rose room / Smoke gets in your eyes / My blue heaven
CD _____ PASTCD 7038
Flapper / Mar '94 / Pinnacle.

ARTIE SHAW & HIS RHYTHM MAKERS - 1938 (Shaw, Artie & Rhythm Makers)
Toy trumpet / Any old time / Powerhouse / Call of the freaks / Lost in the shuffle / If dreams come true / 'S wonderful / Meade Lux special / Sweet and low / Indian love call
CD _____ TAXCD 3709
Tax / May '90 / Jazz Music / Wellard / Cadillac.

ASTONISHING ARTIE SHAW, THE
Love and learn / Free wheeling / Rose room / Fee fi fo fum / Lady be good / I've a strange new rhythm in my heart / Just you, just me / I surrender Dear / Vilia / Let'er go / You can tell she comes from Dixie / It ain't right / Streamline / Cream puff / Non-stop flight / Sweet Adeline / Blues / I'll be with you in apple blossom time / Prosschai
CD _____ PAR 2027
Parade / Jul '94 / Koch / Cadillac.

BEGIN THE BEGUINE
Nightmare / Indian love call / Back bay shuffle / Any old time / Traffic jam / Comes love / What is this thing called love / Begin the beguine / Lady be good / Frenesi / Ser-enade to a savage / Deep purple / Special delivery stomp / Summit Ridge Drive / Temptation / Stardust / Blues (parts 1 and 2) / Moonglow / Moon ray / Carioca
CD _____ ND 86274
Bluebird / Apr '88 / BMG.

BEGIN THE BEGUINE
Begin the beguine / Back bay shuffle / In-dian love call / Nightmare / What is this thing called love / Deep purple / Traffic jam / Comes love / Serenade to a savage / Oh lady be good / Frenesi / Special delivery stomp / Summit ridge drive / Temptation / Stardust / Moonglow
CD _____ CDCD 1007
Charly / Mar '93 / Charly / THE / Cadillac.

BEGIN THE BEGUINE
Any old time / April in Paris / Back bay shuf-fle / Begin the beguine / Concerto for clari-net / Dancing in the dark / Deep purple / Donkey serenade / Frenesi / I surrender dear / Moonglow / Nightmare / Oh Lady be good / Rosalie / Special delivery stomp / St. James infirmary / Stardust / Summit Ridge Drive / Traffic jam / Yesterdays
CD _____ CD AJA 5113
Living Era / Aug '93 / Koch.

BEST OF THE BIG BANDS
Japanese sandman / Pretty girl is like a mel-ody / I used to be above love / No regrets / South sea island magic / It ain't right / Sugarfoot stomp / Thou swell / You're giv-ing me a song and a dance / Darling not without you / 1-2 Button your shoe / Let's call a heart a heart / Skeleton in the closet / There's something in the air / Take another guess / There's frost on the moon
CD _____ 4669592
CBS / Sep '90 / Sony.

BIG BAND BASH (Shaw, Artie & His Orchestra)
CD _____ GOJCD 53093
Giants Of Jazz / Mar '92 / Target/BMG / Cadillac.

CONCERTO FOR CLARINET (Shaw, Artie & His Orchestra)
One night stand / Traffic jam / Summit ridge drive / Prosschai / I surrender Dear / Mari-nella / Lady be good / You can tell she comes from Dixie / Darling not without you / Moonlight and shadows / Concerto for clarinet / You're a sweet little headache / Sometimes I feel like a motherless child / Monsoon / Non stop flight / I have eyes / You're giving me a song and a dance / Spe-cial delivery stomp / Why begin again / Free for all
CD _____ RAJCD 830
Empress / Jul '94 / THE.

CREAM OF ARTIE SHAW & HIS ORCHESTRA, THE
Stardust / They say / My heart stood still / Begin the beguine / Dancing in the dark / Serenade to a savage / Day in, day out / I don't want to walk without you / Rockin' chair / Temptation / Carioca / Out of no-where / Softly as in a morning sunrise / Blues in the night / Back bay shuffle / Jun-gle drums / All the things you are / Someo-ne's rocking my dreamboat / I poured my heart into a song / Rose room / Smoke gets in your eyes / My blue heaven
CD _____ PASTCD 9779
Flapper / Nov '92 / Pinnacle.

FRENESI
Begin the beguine / Back bay shuffle / Nightmare / Traffic jam / Oh Lady be good / Frenesi / Star dust / Any old time / These (parts 1 and 2) / Moonglow
CD _____ ND 90628
Bluebird / Apr '92 / BMG.

GLOOMY SUNDAY (Shaw, Artie & His Orchestra)
Begin the beguine / Moonglow / Lady be good / Gloomy Sunday / Man I love / Temp-tation / Night/Mare / Diga diga doo / Cari-oca / Donkey serenade / Frenesi / Serenade to a savage / Deep purple / I didn't know that time it was / Yesterdays / Rosalie / In-dian love call / Jungle drums
CD _____ CD 56003
Jazz Roots / Aug '94 / Target/BMG.

GREAT ARTIE SHAW & HIS ORCHESTRA, THE
CD _____ CWNCD 2001
Javelin / Jun '95 / THE / Henry Hadaway Organisation.

IN THE BEGINNING - 1936
CD _____ HEPCD 1024
Hep / Dec '87 / Cadillac / Jazz Music / New Note / Wellard.

IN THE BLUE ROOM/IN THE CAFE ROUGE
Nightmare / Together / My reverie / Sobbin' blues / Jeepers creepers / In the mood / Non-stop flight / Begin the beguine / Old stamping ground / Chant / Stardust / Cari-oca / At sundown / I'm sorry for myself / Maria, my own / Diga diga doo / Moonray / Everything is jumpin' / St. Louis blues / I've got my eye on you / My blue heaven / El Rancho Grande / Sweet Sue, just you / Man from Mars
CD _____ 74321185272
RCA Victor / Oct '94 / BMG.

INDIAN LOVE CALL (Shaw, Artie & His Orchestra)
CD _____ JHR 73535
Jazz Hour / May '93 / Target/BMG / Jazz Music / Cadillac.

INDISPENSABLE ARTIE SHAW VOLS.5 & 6 (1944-45) (Shaw, Artie & His Orchestra)
Lady Day / Jumpin' on the merry-go-round / I'll never be the same / 'S wonderful / Bed-ford drive / Grabtown grapple / Sad sack / Little jazz / Tea for two / Summertime / Time on my hands / Foggy day / Man I love / I could write a book / Thrill of a lifetime / Lucky number / Love walked on / Soon / Natch / They can't take that away from me / Someone to watch over me / Things are looking up / Maid with the flaccid air / No one but you / Dancing on the ceiling / I can't get started (with you) / Just floatin' along / I can't escape from you / Scuttlebutt / Gen-tle drifter / Mysterioso / Hop, skip and jump
CD Set _____ ND 89914
RCA / Nov '94 / BMG.

INTRODUCTION TO ARTIE SHAW 1937-42
CD _____ BEST 4016
Best Of Jazz / Apr '95 / Discovery.

IT GOES TO YOUR FEET
Love and learn / Moon face / Same old line / You can tell she comes from Dixie / Sob-bin' blues / Copenhagen / Cream puff / My blue heaven / Streamline / Sweet Lorraine / Love is good for anything / No more tears / Moonlight and shadows / Was it rain / All alone / All God's chillun got rhythm / It goes to your feet / Because I love you
CD _____ 4736572
Columbia / Sep '93 / Sony.

JAZZ PORTRAITS (Shaw, Artie & His Orchestra)
Begin the beguine / Moonglow / Lady be good / Gloomy Sunday / Man I love / Temp-tation / Nightmare / Diga diga doo / Carioca / Donkey serenade / Frenesi / Serenade to a savage / Deep purple / I didn't know what time it was / Yesterdays / Rosalie / Indian love call / Jungle drums
CD _____ CD 14501
Jazz Portraits / May '93 / Jazz Music.

LAST RECORDINGS, THE (Rare And Unreleased)
Pied piper theme / Love of my life / Rough ridin' / Yesterdays / Lyric / Bewitched, both-ered and bewildered / Lugubrious / S'posin' / Tenderly / When the quail come back to San Quentin / Imagination / Besame mucho / My funny valentine / Too marvellous for words / I can't get started (with you) / Sad sack / Dancing on the ceiling / Someone to watch over me / Mysterioso / Chaser
CD Set _____ 8208472
Limelight / May '92 / PolyGram.

LET'S GO FOR SHAW
Stardust / Blues / Moonglow / Blues in the night / Rockin' chair / Solid Sam / Someo-ne's rocking my dreamboat / Special deliv-ery stomp / Dancing in the dark / Smoke gets in your eyes / Begin the beguine / Back bay shuffle / Fresnesi / Deep purple / Don't take your love from me / What is there to say / Deep in a dream / Rosalie / All the things you are / Concerto for clarinet
CD _____ AVC 523
Avid / Apr '93 / Avid/BMG / Koch.

LIVE IN 1938-39 VOL.I
CD _____ PHONTCD 7609
Phontastic / Apr '94 / Wellard / Jazz Music / Cadillac.

LIVE IN 1938-39 VOL.II
CD _____ PHONTCD 7613
Phontastic / Apr '94 / Wellard / Jazz
Music / Cadillac.

LIVE IN 1938-39 VOL.III
CD _____ PHONTCD 7628
Phontastic / Apr '94 / Wellard / Jazz
Music / Cadillac.

LIVE IN HI-FI
CD _____ JH 1031
Jazz Hour / Jul '93 / Target/BMG / Jazz
Music / Cadillac.

**LIVE PERFORMANCES 1938-39 (Shaw,
Artie & His Orchestra)**
CD _____ HBCD 502
Hindsight / Nov '93 / Target/BMG / Jazz
Music.

**MORE LAST RECORDINGS - THE FINAL
SESSIONS**
CD Set _____ MM 65101/2
Music Masters / Oct '94 / Nimbus.

**OLD GOLD SHOWS - 1938-39 (Shaw,
Artie & His Orchestra)**
CD _____ JH 1009
Jazz Hour / '91 / Target/BMG / Jazz
Music / Cadillac.

**RADIO YEARS, THE (Volume 1, 1938)
(Shaw, Artie & His Orchestra)**
Nightmare (theme) / Sobbin' blues / I can't
believe that you're in love with me / They
say / It had to be you / My revenue / Sweet
Adeline / Who blew out the flame / Copen-
hagen / Nightmare (closing theme) / Night-
mare (theme) (1) / Begin the beguine /
You're a sweet little headache / Old stamp-
ing ground / What is this thing called love /
Jungle drums / It had to be you (1) / Thanks
for everything / Copenhagen #2 / Nightmare
(closing theme) (1)
CD _____ JUCD 2018
Jazz Unlimited / Nov '94 / Wellard /
Cadillac.

TRAFFIC JAM
Man I love / Muchodenada / Love is the
sweetest thing / Love walked in / You're
mine / Oh you crazy moon / Serenade to a
savage / Sweet little headache / What is this
thing called love / Thanks for everything /
Mood in question / Orinoco / Traffic jam /
I'm coming Virginia / Last two weeks in July
/ Lilacs in the rain
CD _____ NI 4013
Natasha / May '93 / Jazz Music / ADA / CM
/ Direct / Cadillac.

Shaw Brothers

COLLECTION
CD _____ FE 2041
Folk Era / Dec '94 / CM / ADA.

Shaw, Eddie

IN THE LAND OF THE CROSSROADS
CD _____ R 72624CD
Rooster / Feb '93 / Direct.

MOVIN' & GROOVIN' MAN
Highway bound / Blues dues / Blues for to-
mako / Dunkin' donut woman / Louisiana
blues / Movin' and groovin' man / Sad and
lonesome / Big leg woman / I've got to tell
somebody / My baby and me
CD _____ ECD 260282
Evidence / Feb '93 / Harmonia Mundi / ADA
/ Cadillac.

Shaw, Ian

GHOSTSONGS
Danny boy / Spinning wheel / When Sassy
sings / Broken blue heart / Me, myself and
I / Some other time/People will say we're in
love / Lover man / Calling you / Sophisti-
cated lady/I've got it bad and that ain't
good / Somewhere / Goodbye pork pie hat
/ Blame it on my youth
CD _____ JHCD 025
Ronnie Scott's Jazz House / Jan '94 / Jazz
Music / Magnum Music Group / Cadillac.

TAKING IT TO HART
CD _____ JHCD 036
Ronnie Scott's Jazz House / Mar '95 /
Jazz Music / Magnum Music Group /
Cadillac.

Shaw, Marlena

**FEEL THE SPIRIT (Shaw, Marlena & Joe
Williams)**
In the beginning / My Lord / Feel the spirit
/ Go down Moses / Wade in the water /
Great camp meeting / Were you there /
Walk with me / I couldn't hear nobody pray
/ In my heart / Little David / His eye is on
the sparrow / Pass it on / Lord's prayer /
Doxology
CD _____ CD 83362
Telarc / Jun '95 / Conifer / ADA.

LIVE AT MONTREUX
Show has begun / Song is you / You are
the sunshine of my life / Twisted / But for
now / Save the children / Woman of the
ghetto
CD _____ CDP 8327492
Blue Note / Jun '95 / EMI.

Shaw, Pat

**LIES & ALIBIS (Shaw, Pat & Julie
Matthews)**
CD _____ FATCAT 001CD
Fat Cat / Jun '93 / Direct / ADA / CM.

Shaw, Robert

MA GRINDER, THE
CD _____ ARHCD 377
Arhoolie / Apr '95 / ADA / Direct /
Cadillac.

Shaw, Sandie

CHOOSE LIFE
Dragon king's daughter / Mermaid / Let
down your hair / East meets west / Bark
back at dogs / Life is like a star / Moontalk
/ Sister sister / Wish I was
CD _____ RETRO 801
RPM / Jun '95 / Pinnacle.

CLASSIC ARTISTS
CD _____ JHD 048
Tring / Jun '92 / Tring / Prism.

COLLECTION, THE
CD _____ COL 067
Collection / Jan '95 / Target/BMG.

COLLECTION: SANDIE SHAW
Puppet on a string / Everybody loves a lover
/ I'll stop at nothing / As long as you're
happy baby / If you ever need me / Tomorrow / Long live love / Nothing comes easy
/ I'd be far better off without you / Lemon
tree / You don't love me no more / Think
sometimes about me / No moon / Message
understood / Had a dream last night / Tell
the boys / Run / Girl don't come / Gotta see
my baby every day / How can you tell / Stop
feeling sorry for yourself / I don't need anything / You won't forget me / Always
something there to remind me
CD _____ CCSCD 251
Castle / Feb '90 / BMG.

COMPLETE SANDIE SHAW, THE
As long as you're happy / Ya-Ya-Da-Da /
Always something there to remind me /
Don't you know / Girl don't you know / I'd
be far better off without you / Everybody
loves a lover / Gotta see my baby every day
/ Love letters / Stop feeling sorry for yourself / Always / Don't be that way / It's in his
kiss (Shoop shoop song) / Downtown / You
won't forget me / Lemon tree / Talk about
love / I'll stop at nothing / You can't blame
him / Long live love / I've heard about him
/ Message understood / Don't you count on
it / You don't love me no more / I don't need
that kind of lovin' / Down dismal ways / Oh
no he don't / When he was a child / Do you
mind / How glad am I / I know / Till the night
begins to die / Too bad you don't want me
/ One day / When I fall in love / How can
you tell / If ever you need me / Tomorrow /
Hurting you / Nothing ever comes easy /
Stop before start / Run / Long walk home /
Think sometimes about me / Hide all emotion / I don't need anything / Keep in touch
/ Puppet on a string / Had a dream last
night / Ask any woman / I don't think you
want me anymore / No moon
CD Set _____ NEDCD 230
Sequel / May '93 / BMG.

EP COLLECTION: SANDIE SHAW
CD _____ SEECD 305
See For Miles/C5 / '90 / Pinnacle.

LONG LIVE LOVE
CD _____ WMCD 5611
Disky / May '94 / THE / BMG / Discovery /
Pinnacle.

LOVE ME PLEASE LOVE ME
Love me please love me / One note samba
/ Smile / Yes my darling daughter / Ne me
quitte pas / Every time we say goodbye /
Way that I remember him / Hold 'im down
/ I get a kick out of you / Time after time /
That's why / By myself / Tonight in Tokyo /
You've been seeing her again / You've not
changed / Don't make me cry / Today /
London / Don't run away / Stop
CD _____ RPM 124
RPM / Mar '94 / Pinnacle.

**NOTHING LESS THAN BRILLIANT - THE
BEST OF SANDIE SHAW**
Always something there to remind me /
Long live love / Girl don't come / Message
understood / Nothing less than brilliant /
Hand in glove / Are you ready to be heartbroken / Girl called Johnny / I'll stop at
nothing / Heaven knows I'm missing him
now / You've not changed / Monsieur Du-
pont / Don't owe you anything / Anyone
who had a heart / Comrade in arms / Hello
angel / Strange bedfellows / Words / Every
time we say goodbye / Your time is gonna
come / Frederick / Please help the cause
against loneliness / Tomorrow / Nothing
comes easy / Puppet on a string
CD _____ VTCD 34
Virgin / Nov '94 / EMI.

PUPPET ON A STRING
Always something there to remind me / It's
in his kiss (Shoop shoop song) / Always /
Long live love / I've heard about him / When
I fall in love / Do you mind / Baby I need
your loving / Nothing comes easy / Love
letters / Puppet on a string / Had a dream

last night / Downtown / Run / You won't
forget me / I don't need anything / Tell the
boys / I'll cry myself to sleep / Tomorrow
CD _____ 5507552
Spectrum/Karussell / Sep '94 / PolyGram /
THE.

REVIEWING THE SITUATION
CD _____ RPM 101
RPM / Jul '93 / Pinnacle.

SANDIE SHAW SUPPLEMENT, THE
Route 66 / Homeward bound / Scarborough
Fair / Right to cry / Same things / Our song
of love / Satisfaction / Words / Remember
me / Change of heart / Aranjuez mon amour
/ What now my love / Show me / One more
lie / Together / Turn on the sunshine / Those
were the days / Make it go / Monsieur Du-
pont / Voice in the crowd
CD _____ RPM 112
RPM / Oct '93 / Pinnacle.

SANDIE/ME
Everybody loves a lover / Gotta see my
baby everyday / Love letters / Stop feeling
sorry for yourself / Always / Don't be that
way / It's in his kiss / Downtown / You won't
forget me / Lemon tree / Baby, I need your
loving / Talk about love / You don't love me
no more / I don't need that kind of lovin' /
Down dismal ways / Oh no he don't / When
I was a child / Do you mind / How glad I
am / I know / Till the night begins to die /
Too bad you don't want me / One day /
When I fall in love
CD _____ SEECD 436
See For Miles/C5 / Oct '95 / Pinnacle.

Shaw, Thomas

BORN IN TEXAS
CD _____ TCD 5027
Testament / Oct '95 / Complete/Pinnacle /
ADA / Koch.

Shaw, Woody

IMAGINATION
CD _____ MCD 5338
Muse / Sep '92 / New Note / CM.

IN MY OWN SWEET WAY
CD _____ IOR 70032
In & Out / Sep '93 / Vital/SAM.

MOONTRANE, THE
Moontrane / Are they only dreams / Tap-
scott's blues / Sanyas / Katrina ballerina
CD _____ MCD 5472
Muse / May '95 / New Note / CM.

TIME IS RIGHT, THE
CD _____ 123168-2
Red / Apr '93 / Harmonia Mundi / Jazz
Horizons / Cadillac / ADA.

Shazar, Pal

THERE'S A WILD THING IN THE HOUSE
Falling is a form of flying / Penny for your
thoughts / San Francisco Bay / Three
sheets to the wind / Small talk with the
ticket man / If it's you that I got here / Ain't
nobody's mistress but my own / Then I met
Anna / Scared / Wade went wild / Sentimental breakdown
CD _____ TRACD 113
Transatlantic / Oct '95 / BMG / Pinnacle /
ADA.

Shea, David

SHOCK CORRIDOR
CD _____ AVAN 013
Avant / Nov '92 / Harmonia Mundi /
Cadillac.

Shearing, George

**ALONE TOGETHER (Shearing, George &
Marian McPartland)**
O grande amor / To Bill Evans / All through
the night / Born to be blue / They say it's
Spring / Alone together / There'll be other
times / Nobody else but me / Chasing
shadows / Improvisation on a theme
CD _____ CCD 4171
Concord Jazz / Feb '91 / New Note.

BEST OF GEORGE SHEARING, THE
Midnight in the air / Have you met Miss
Jones / Dancing on the ceiling / Cuban love
song / Folks who live on the hill / Nothing
ever changes my love for you / Friendly per-
suasion (thee I love) / Later / Cheek to
cheek / Sand in my shoes / Kinda cute /
September in the rain / East of the sun /
Estampa Cubano / Ship without a sail /
Laura / Bernie's tune / Canadian sunset
CD _____ CDP 8335702
Capitol Jazz / Nov '95 / EMI.

BLUES ALLEY JAZZ
One for the woofer / Autumn in New York /
(I'm afraid) the masquerade is over / Soon
it's gonna rain / High and inside / For every
man there's a woman / This couldn't be the
real thing / Up a lazy river
CD _____ CCD 4110
Concord Jazz / Nov '89 / New Note.

BREAKIN' OUT (Shearing, George Trio)
CD _____ CCD 4335
Concord Jazz / Dec '87 / New Note.

**COCKTAILS FOR TWO (Shearing,
George Quintet)**
CD _____ JW 77016
JWD / May '93 / Target/BMG.

DEXTERITY
You must believe in Spring /
Sakura / Long ago and far away / Can't we
be friends / As long as I live / Please send
me someone to love / Duke Ellington
medley
CD _____ CCD 4346
Concord Jazz / Jul '88 / New Note.

**ELEGANT EVENING, AN (Shearing,
George & Mel Torme)**
I'll be seeing you / Love and the moon / Oh
you crazy moon / No moon at all / After the
waltz is over / This time the dream is on me
/ Last night when we were young / You
changed my life / I had the craziest dream
/ Darn that dream / Brigg fair / My foolish
heart / You're driving me crazy
CD _____ CCD 4294
Concord Jazz / Jul '87 / New Note.

**EVENING AT CHARLIE'S, AN (Shearing,
George & Mel Torme)**
Just one of those things / On Green Dolphin
Street / Dream dancing / I'm hip / Then I'll
be tired of you / Caught in the middle of my
years / Welcome to the club / Nica's dream
/ Chase me Charlie / Love is just around the
corner
CD _____ CCD 4248
Concord Jazz / Sep '84 / New Note.

**EVENING WITH GEORGE SHEARING,
AN (Shearing, George & Mel Torme)**
All God's chillun got rhythm / Born to be
blue / Give me the simple life / Good morn-
ing heartache / Manhattan hoedown /
You'd be so nice to come home to / Night-
ingale sang in Berkeley Square / Love / It
might as well be Spring / Lullaby of Birdland
CD _____ CCD 4190
Concord Jazz / Mar '87 / New Note.

**GEORGE SHEARING IN DIXIELAND
(Shearing, George & Dixie Six)**
Clap your hands / Truckin' / New Orleans /
Take five / Blue monk / Alice in Dixieland /
Mighty like the blues / Destination moon /
Soon / Lullaby of Birdland / Desafinado
CD _____ CCD 4388
Concord Jazz / Sep '89 / New Note.

GRAND PIANO
When a woman loves a man / It never en-
tered my mind / Mack the knife / Nobody
else but me / Imitations / Taking a chance
on love / If I had you / How insensitive /
Easy to love / While we're young
CD _____ CCD 4281
Concord Jazz / Sep '86 / New Note.

**HOW BEAUTIFUL IS THE NIGHT
(Shearing, George & The Robert Farnon
Orchestra)**
CD _____ CD 83325
Telarc / May '93 / Conifer / ADA.

**I HEAR A RHAPSODY (Live At The Blue
Note)**
Bird feathers / Dreamsville / End Of A Love
Affair / Zingaro / Duke / I hear a rhapsody
(I'm afraid) the masquerade is over / Hom-
zon / Just a mood / Wait / Too Late Now
CD _____ CD 83310
Telarc / Sep '92 / Conifer / ADA.

JAZZ MOMENTS
Makin' whoopee / What is this thing called
love / What's new / Like someone in love /
Heart of winter / Blues in the A / Symphony /
When Danny gets blue / Wonder why /
Mood is mellow / Gone with the wind / It
could happen to you
CD _____ CDP 8320852
Capitol Jazz / Aug '95 / EMI.

**LIVE AT THE CAFE CARLYLE (Shearing,
George & Don Thompson)**
Pent-up house / Shadow of your smile /
Teach me tonight / Cheryl / Blues for break-
fast / P.S. I love you / I cover the waterfront
/ Tell me a bedtime story / Stratford stomp
/ Inside
CD _____ CCD 4246
Concord Jazz / '88 / New Note.

LONDON YEARS 1939-1943
How come you like me like you do / Stomp
in F / Squeezing the blues / Southern fried
/ Missouri scrambler / Overnight hop / De-
layed action / Beat me Daddy, eight to the
bar / How could you / Pretty girl is like a
melody / These foolish things / More than
you know / Softly as in a morning sunrise /
You stepped out of a dream / Spoodle woo-
gie / Moon ray / Rosetta / I'll never let a day
pass me by / Coquette / Out of nowhere /
Can't we be friends / Ghost of a chance /
Guilty / I found a new boogie / Sweet
Lorraine
CD _____ HEPCD 1042
Hep / Feb '95 / Cadillac / Jazz Music / New
Note / Wellard.

MIDNIGHT ON CLOUD 69
Sorry wrong rumba / Cotton top / Be bop's
fables / Midnight on cloud 69 / Little white
lies / I'm yours / Moon over Miami / Cher-
okee / Life with feather / Four bars short /
Time and tide / Night and day
CD _____ SV 0208
Savoy Jazz / Apr '93 / Conifer / ADA.

MORE GRAND PIANO (solo piano)
My silent love / Change partners / My favourite things / You don't know what love is / Ramona / People / East of the sun and west of the moon / I can't get started (with you) / Dream / Wind in the willows
CD _____ CCD 4318
Concord Jazz / Jul '87 / New Note.

MUSIC OF COLE PORTER, THE (Shearing, George & Barry Tuckwell)
I concentrate on you / Everything I love / I've got you under my skin / Easy to love / In the still of the night / Every time we say goodbye / But in the morning no / So in love / After you / All through the night / Do I love you
CD _____ CCD 42010
Concord Concerto / Oct '86 / Pinnacle.

ON A CLEAR DAY (Shearing, George & Brian Torff)
Love for sale / On a clear day / Brasil '79 / Don't explain / Happy days are here again / Have you met Miss Jones / Lullaby of Birdland
CD _____ CCD 4132
Concord Jazz / Dec '93 / New Note.

ONCE AGAIN THAT SHEARING SOUND
East of the sun and west of the moon / I like to recognise the tune / I'll never smile again / I hear music / Girl talk / Autumn serenade / Consternation / Stars in my eyes / Strollin / Very early / Conception / Peace / Lullaby of birdland
CD _____ CD 83347
Telarc / Sep '94 / Conifer / ADA.

PERFECT MATCH, A (Shearing, George & Ernestine Anderson)
CD _____ CCD 4357
Concord Jazz / Oct '88 / New Note.

PIANO
It had to be you / Daisy / Thinking of you / Sweet and lovely / It's you or no one / Wendy / Am I blue (CD only.) / Miss Invisible (CD only.) / You're my everything / John O'Groats / Waltz for Claudia / For you / Children's waltz / Happiness is a thing called Joe
CD _____ CCD 4400
Concord Jazz / Jan '90 / New Note.

SATIN AFFAIR/CONCERTO FOR MY LOVE
Early autumn / You were never lovelier / Star dust / Baubles, bangles and beads / It's not you / Party's over / Midnight sun / Here's what I'm here for / I like to recognise the tune / My own / My romance / Bolero no.3 / Portrait of Jennie / I'm in the mood for love / Answer me my love / I wish you love / Love letters / I fall in love too easily / Love is the sweetest thing / Portrait of my love / P.S. I love you / Lady love be mine / In love in vain / Love child
CD _____ BGOCD 269
Beat Goes On / Apr '95 / Pinnacle.

SHEARING ON STAGE
September in the rain / On the street where you live / Roses of Picardy / Little Niles / Caravan / I'll remember April / Little white lies / East of the sun and west of the moon / Nothing be de best / Love is just around the corner / Walkin' / I cover the waterfront / Love walked in / Bel-Air
CD _____ CDREN 004
Renaissance / '89 / Wellard / Jazz Music.

SWINGIN'S MUTUAL, THE (Shearing, George & Nancy Wilson)
Things we did last Summer / All night long / My gentleman friend / Born to be blue / I remember Clifford / On Green Dolphin Street / Let's live again / Whisper not / Nearness of you / Evansville / Don't call me / Inspiration / You are there / Wait till you see her / Blue Lou / Oh, look at me now / Lullaby of Birdland
CD _____ CDP 7991902
Blue Note / Mar '95 / EMI.

TWO FOR THE ROAD (Shearing, George & Carmen McRae)
I don't stand a ghost of a chance with you / Gentleman friend / Cloudy morning / If I should lose you / What is there to say / You're all I need / More than you know / Too late now / Ghost of yesterday / Two for the road
CD _____ CCD 4128
Concord Jazz / '89 / New Note.

WALKIN'
That's earl, brother / My one and only love / Pensativa / Walkin' / When she makes music / Celia / Subconscious Lee / Suddenly / Bag's groove / Every time we say goodbye / Loot to loot
CD _____ CD 83333
Telarc / Apr '95 / Conifer / ADA.

Shearing, Peter G.

VIKING DREAM
CD _____ CDSGP 9006
Prestige / Apr '95 / Total/BMG.

Shed Seven

CHANGE HEAVEN
Dirty soul / Speakeasy / Long time dead / Head and hands / Casino girl / Missing out

---

/ Dolphin / Stars in your eyes / Mark / Ocean pie / On an island with you
CD _____ 523615-2
Polydor / Sep '94 / PolyGram.

Sheehan, Chris

OUT OF THE WOODS
CD _____ 0630120432
Anxious / Oct '95 / Warner Music.

Sheehan, Stephen

EYES OF THE WILDERNESS
CD _____ ROSE 199 CD
New Rose / Nov '90 / Direct / ADA.

Sheep On Drugs

GREATEST HITS
Uberman / Acid test / Fifteen minutes of fame / Track X / Suzie Q / Catch 22 / Mary Jane / Motorbike / TV USA / Chard / Cheep
CD _____ CID 8006
Island / Mar '93 / PolyGram.

ON DRUGS
Intro / Chasing dreams / English rose / Let the good times roll / Beefcake / Segway / A2H / Clucking / Slap happy / Slim Jim / Lolita / Slow suicide / Hi-fi low-life / Dirtbox blues
CD _____ CID 8020
Island / Apr '94 / PolyGram.

Sheer Taft

ABSOLUTELY SHEER
CD _____ CRELPCD 121
Creation / Jun '92 / 3MV / Vital.

Sheer Terror

LOVE SONGS FOR THE UNLOVED
Love song for the unloved / Tale of moran / Jimmy's high life / Not waving, drowning / Rock bottom on the kitchen floor / Skinhead girl / Drunk, divorced and downhill fast / Broken / Outro / College boy / For Rudy / The Kraut / Walnut St / Be still my heart / Walls / Everything's life / Goodbye farewell
CD _____ BLK 023ECD
Blackout / Aug '95 / Vital.

Sheffield Harmony

BEST OF THE BARBERSHOP, THE
Wonderful day like today / Give me a barbershop song / Sing me that song again / Oh you beautiful doll / The me to your apron strings again / South Rampart street parade / Don't leave me mammy / Rock-a-bye your baby with a dixie melody / Hush / Nightingale sang in Berkeley Square / That great come and get it day / Crossing Jordan river / Fare thee well / Waiting for the Robert E. Lee / April showers / Operator / Play a vaudeville song tonight / Little pal / There is nothin' like a dame / Love at home / Carolina in the morning / Only you / Wonderful day like today (reprise)
CD _____ CDMFP 5944
Music For Pleasure / Aug '92 / EMI.

Sheik Chinna Moulana

NADHASWARAM
CD _____ SM 1507-2
Wergo / Nov '92 / Harmonia Mundi / ADA / Cadillac.

Sheik, Kid

CLEVELAND & BOSTON 1960-1961
CD _____ AMCD 69
American Music / Aug '94 / Jazz Music.

REAL NEW ORLEANS JAZZ 1960 (Sheik, Kid & Charlie Love)
When you're smiling / Waltz of the bells / Don't go 'way nobody / Sheik's blues / Corine Corina / Georgia camp meeting / Then I'll be happy / What a friend we have in Jesus / Sheikh of araby / Near the cross / Over in the glory land / Cado blues / Down in honky tonk town / Bill Bailey, Won't you please come home / Indian Sagua
CD _____ 504CDS 21
504 / Jan '95 / Wellard / Jazz Music Target/BMG / Cadillac.

Sheldon, Jack

HOLLYWOOD HEROES (Sheldon, Jack Quintet)
Joint is jumpin' / Pardon my southern accent / Poor butterfly / Lover / Rosetta / I thought about you / I want to be happy
CD _____ CCD 4339
Concord Jazz / May '88 / New Note.

ON MY OWN (Sheldon, Jack & Ross Tomkins)
Accentuate the positive / Love of mine / Blues in the night / How about you / Day drama / Opus one / Losing my mind / I can't get started (with you) / New York medley (Manhattan, Autumn in New York, New York New York.) / Laughing on the outside / Avalon / Over the rainbow
CD _____ CCD 4529
Concord Jazz / Oct '92 / New Note.

Shellac

AT ACTION PARK
CD _____ TG 141CD
Touch & Go / Nov '94 / SRD.

Shelley, Pete

HOMOSAPIEN
CD _____ GRACD 201
Grapevine / Aug '94 / Grapevine.

XL-1
CD _____ GRACD 202
Grapevine / Aug '94 / Grapevine.

Shelleyan Orphan

BUMROOT
CD _____ R 2792
Rough Trade / Mar '92 / Pinnacle.

CENTURY FLOWER
CD _____ ROUGHCD 137
Rough Trade / Apr '89 / Pinnacle.

HELLEBORINE
CD _____ ROUGHCD 97
Rough Trade / '87 / Pinnacle.

Shelter

MANTRA
CD _____ RR 89382
Roadrunner / Oct '95 / Pinnacle.

PERFECTION
CD _____ REVEL 016CD
Revelation / Jan '96 / Plastic Head.

Shelton, Anne

EARLY YEARS OF ANNE SHELTON, THE
CD _____ SWNCD 003
Sound Waves / Oct '95 / Target/BMG.

LET THERE BE LOVE
While the music plays on / Daddy / Better not roll those blue blue eyes / Minnie from Trinidad / Russian rose / St. Louis blues / Yes my darling daughter / Until you fall in love / Little steeple pointing to a star / Let there be love / Amapola / Tomorrow's sunrise / Fools rush in / Always in my heart / How about you / How green was my valley / I don't want to walk without you / My devotion / Taxi driver's serenade / South wind / Only you / My yiddishe Momme
CD _____ RAJCD 815
Empress / Jul '94 / THE.

NIGHTINGALE SANG, A
I'll be with you in apple blossom time / Last time I saw Paris / Daddy, blues in the night / Kiss the boys goodbye / Begin the beguine / You'd be so nice to come home to
CD _____ PASTCD 7048
Flapper / Aug '94 / Pinnacle.

NOW HEAR THIS
Now hear this / Hurry home / Where can I go / Great pretender / Souvenir d'italie / Too young to go steady / Carnival is closed today / Volare / Sail along silv'ry moon / Where were you when I needed you / It's you / Harbour lights / Dancing with tears in my eyes / Nein nein fraulein / Daydreams / My one and only love / Forever / Tonights my night / Tread softly (you're treading on my heart) / How green was my valley / Village of St. Bernadette / I hear that song again / You're not living in vain / Lay down your arms
CD _____ C5MCD 624
See For Miles/C5 / Jun '95 / Pinnacle.

SENTIMENTAL JOURNEY
Crazy / Tangerine / Sentimental journey / Nightingale sang in Berkeley Square / Don't fence me in / I'll walk alone / Run rabbit run / When the lights go on again / White cliffs of Dover / You'll never know / After all / Don't sit under the apple tree / I left my heart at the stage door canteen / Roll out the barrel / I'll get by (as long as I have you) / Boogie woogie bugle boy / I'll be seeing you / Chattanooga choo choo / Lili Marlene / Just look around
CD _____ PLCD 537
President / Nov '94 / Grapevine / Target/ BMG / Jazz Music / President.

SOLDIER'S SWEETHEART MEMORIAL ALBUM, THE
I'll never smile again / I'll be seeing you / There goes that song again / Yes my darling daughter / Fools rush in / I don't want to walk without you / You'd be so nice to come home to / Coming in on a wing and a prayer / Last time I saw paris / I don't want to set the world on fire / Nightingale sang in Berkeley Square / Saying a chance on love / Only you / Daddy / My yiddishe momme / Until you fall in love / Amapola / St. Louis blues / Kiss the boys goodbye / Lili Marlene
CD _____ PAR 2061
Start / Mar '95 / Koch.

Shelton, Ricky Van

LOVE AND HONOR
Wherever she is / Complicated / Lola's love / I thought I'd heard it all / Then for them / Baby, take a picture / Love without you / Been there, done that / Love and honor /

Where the tall grass grows / Thanks a lot / Where was I
CD _____ 477680 2
Columbia / Oct '94 / Sony.

Shelton, Roscoe

SHE'S THE ONE
CD _____ AP 114
Appaloosa / Oct '95 / ADA / Magnum Music Group.

Shepherd, Dave

GOOD ENOUGH TO KEEP
CD _____ BLCD 760514
Black Lion / Nov '95 / Jazz Music / Cadillac / Wellard / Koch.

Shepherd, James

RHYTHM AND BLUES (Shepherd, James Versatile Brass)
Arrival of the Queen of Sheba / Moonlight in Vermont / Long John's hornpipe / Lazybone blues / Three English dances / Rhythm and blues / Little white donkey / Fantasy and vibrations / Three miniatures
CD _____ QPRL 035D
Polyphonic / '88 / Conifer.

VERSATILE BRASS
CD _____ DOYCD 031
Doyen / Nov '93 / Conifer.

Shepp, Archie

BALLADS FOR TRANE (Shepp, Archie Quartet)
Soul eyes / You don't know what love is / Wise one / Where are you / Darn that dream / Theme for Ernie
CD _____ DC 8570
Denon / '90 / Conifer.

BLASE
My angel / There is a balm in Gilead / Sophisticated lady / Touareg / Blase
CD _____ LEJAZZCD 26
Le Jazz / Aug '94 / Charly / Cadillac.

DAY DREAM
Don't you know I care (or don't you care to) / Caravan / Daydream / Satin doll / I got it bad and that ain't good / Prelude to a kiss
CD _____ DC 8547
Denon / Jun '89 / Conifer.

DUET (Shepp, Archie & Dollar Brand)
Fortunato / Barefoot boy from Queens Town / Left alone / Proof of the man / Ubu suku / Moniebah
CD _____ DC 8561
Denon / Aug '94 / Conifer.

FIFTH OF MAY (Shepp, Archie & Jasper Van't Hof)
CD _____ CDLR 45.004
L&R / Jul '88 / New Note.

FIRE MUSIC
Ham bone / Malcolm Malcolm Semper Malcolm / Los Olvidados
CD _____ MCAD 39121
Impulse Jazz / Jun '89 / MCA / New Note.

FREEDOM (Shepp, Archie Quintet)
CD _____ JMY 1007-2
JMY / Aug '91 / Harmonia Mundi.

GOIN' HOME (Shepp, Archie & Horace Parlan)
CD _____ SCCD 31079
Steeplechase / Jul '88 / Impetus.

I KNOW ABOUT THE LIFE
CD _____ SKCD 2-3026
Sackville / Jun '93 / Swift / Jazz Music / Jazz Horizons / Cadillac / CM.

IN MEMORY OF ARCHIE SHEPP (Shepp, Archie & Chet Baker)
CD _____ CDLR 45.006
L&R / Jul '88 / New Note.

LADY BIRD (Shepp, Archie Quartet)
Donna Lee / Relaxin' at Camarillo / Now's the time / Ladybird / Flamingo
CD _____ DC 8546
Denon / Jun '89 / Conifer.

LOVER MAN
CD _____ CDSJP 287
Timeless Jazz / Jun '89 / New Note.

MAMA ROSE
CD _____ SCCD 31169
Steeplechase / Jul '88 / Impetus.

MONTREUX 1
Lush life / U-jamaa / Crucificado / Miss Toni
CD _____ FCD 741027
Freedom / Sep '88 / Jazz Music / Swift / Wellard / Cadillac.

ON GREEN DOLPHIN STREET (Shepp, Archie Quartet)
On Green Dolphin Street / Enough / Scene is clean / In a mellow blues / I thought about you
CD _____ DC 8587
Denon / Sep '91 / Conifer.

PARLAN DUO REUNION (Shepp, Archie & Horace Parlan)
CD _____ CDLR 45.003
L&R / Oct '88 / New Note.

PASSPORT TO PARADISE (Archie Shepp plays Sydney Bechet)
CD _____ WWCD 002
West Wind / Jul '88 / Swift / Charly / CM / ADA.

RISING SUN
CD _____ RS 0005
Just A Memory / Oct '94 / Harmonia Mundi.

SEA OF FACES, A
CD _____ 1200022
Black Saint / Sep '95 / Harmonia Mundi / Cadillac.

SPLASHES (Shepp, Archie Quartet)
Arrival / Reflexions / Groovin' high / Steam / Manhattan
CD _____ CDLR 45.005
L&R / Jul '88 / New Note.

STREAM
CD _____ JHR 73520
Jazz Hour / Sep '93 / Target/BMG / Jazz Music / Cadillac.

THERE'S A TRUMPET IN MY SOUL
There's a trumpet in my soul suite (part 1) / Samba da rua / Zaid (part 1) / Down in Brazil / There's a trumpet in my soul suite (part 2) / Zaid (part 2) / It is the year of the rabbit / Zaid (part 3)
CD _____ FCD 41016
Freedom / Dec '87 / Jazz Music / Swift / Wellard / Cadillac.

TRAY OF SILVER (Shepp, Archie Quintet)
No smokin' / If you could see me now / Nica's dream / Cookin' at the Continental
CD _____ DC 8548
Denon / Jun '89 / Conifer.

TRUMPET IN MY SOUL
CD _____ FCD 74106
Freedom / Oct '89 / Jazz Music / Swift / Wellard / Cadillac.

YASMINA, A BLACK WOMAN
Yasmina, a black woman / Sonny's back / Body and soul
CD _____ LEJAZZCD 51
Le Jazz / Oct '95 / Charly / Cadillac.

Sheppard, Andy

ANDY SHEPPARD
Java jive / Esme / Twee / Sol / Coming second / Want a toffee / Liquid
CD _____ IMCD 115
Antilles/New Directions / May '91 / PolyGram.

ANDY SHEPPARD & INCLASSIFICABLE (Sheppard, Andy & Inclassificable)
Where we going / Slow boat / Hush hush / R.C.A. / Ocean view / Is everything alright up there / Too close to the flame / Ships in the night / Sharp practice
CD _____ LBLC 6583
Label Bleu / Jul '95 / New Note.

DELIVERY SUITE
Delivery suite / Part 1 - perambulator / Part 2 - Inside information / Part 3 - Gas and air / Multi media / So...
CD _____ CDBLT 1008
Blue Note / Mar '94 / EMI.

IN-CO-MOTION
ASAP / Eargliding / Backstage passes / Movies / Upstate / Let's lounge / Pinky
CD _____ IMCD 195
Island / Jul '94 / PolyGram.

INTRODUCTIONS IN THE DARK
Romantic / Rebecca's / Optics / Conversations / Forbidden fruit
CD _____ IMCD 113
Antilles/New Directions / May '91 / PolyGram.

RHYTHM METHOD
Sofa safari / Undercovers / Access all areas / So / Well kept secret / Hop dreams
CD _____ CDBLT 1007
Blue Note / Nov '93 / EMI.

SOFT ON THE INSIDE
Soft on the inside / Rebecca's silk stockings / Carla, Carla, Carla / Adventures in the rave trade
CD _____ IMCD 194
Island / Jul '94 / PolyGram.

Sheppard, Bob

TELL TALE SIGNS
Hidden agenda / Might as well be / Once removed / Tell tale signs / Point of departure / Shifting sands / Echoes / You betta' off / A.J. / How deep is the ocean
CD _____ WD 0129
Windham Hill / May '91 / Pinnacle / BMG / ADA.

Sherburn, Chris

LAST NIGHT'S FUN (Sherburn, Chris & Denny Bartley)
CD _____ SOM 002
Sound Out Music / Oct '95 / Direct / ADA.

Sheridan, Tony

FIRST (Sheridan, Tony & The Beatles)
Ain't she sweet / Cry for a shadow / When the saints go marching in / Why / If you love me baby / What'd I say / Sweet Georgia Brown / Let's dance / Ruby baby / My Bonnie / Nobody's child / Ready Teddy / Ya ya / Kansas city
CD _____ 5500372
Spectrum/Karussell / May '93 / PolyGram / THE.

HAMBURG 1961 (Sheridan, Tony & The Beatles)
Why can't you love me again / Cry for a shadow / Let's dance / Ya ya / What'd I say / Ruby baby / Take out some insurance / Sweet Georgia brown
CD _____ CDCD 1018
Charly / Mar '93 / Charly / THE / Cadillac.

Sherman, Bim

CRAZY WORLD
CD _____ CENTURY 1600CD
Century / Apr '92 / Total/BMG / Jetstar.

CRUCIAL CUTS VOL.1
CD _____ CEND 400
Century / Sep '94 / Total/BMG / Jetstar.

EXPLOITATION
CD _____ RDL 1100 CD
RDL / Jul '89 / RDL.

IN A RUB A DUB STYLE
CD _____ OMCD 013
Original Music / May '95 / SRD / Jetstar.

LION HEART DUB
CD _____ 1800 CD
Century / Mar '93 / Total/BMG / Jetstar.

REALITY (Sherman, Bim & Dub Syndicate)
CD _____ CENTURY 1700CD
Century / Nov '92 / Total/BMG / Jetstar.

TAKEN OFF
CD _____ CEND 2001
Century / Nov '94 / Total/BMG / Jetstar.

Shew, Bobby

TRUMPETS NO END (Shew, Bobby & Chuck Findley)
CD _____ DCD 4003
Delos / Mar '90 / Conifer.

Shicheng, Lin

ART OF THE PIPA
CD _____ C 560046
Ocora / Nov '93 / Harmonia Mundi / ADA.

Shields, Chris

HAUNT ME
Haunt me / Fool / Talking 'bout that feeling / Never the same again / Gently fade away / In another time / Your tender touch / Things you do to me / Thousand dreams / Secret love / But the neighbours ain't / Mother love
CD _____ CRAZCD 195
Go Crazy / Sep '93 / Go Crazy Music.

Shihab, Sahib

CONVERSATIONS
CD _____ BLCD 760169
Black Lion / Oct '93 / Jazz Music / Cadillac / Wellard / Koch.

JAZZ SAHIB
S.M.T.W.T.F.S blues / Jamilla / Moors / Blu-a-round / Le'sneak / Ballad to the East / Ba-dut-du-dat
CD _____ SV 0141
Savoy Jazz / Jan '94 / Conifer / ADA.

Shihad

CHURN
Factory / Screwtop / Scacture / Stations / Clapper-loader / I only said / Derail / Bone orchard / Happy meal
CD _____ N 0249-2
Noise/Modern Music / Jul '94 / Pinnacle / Plastic Head.

KILLJOY
CD _____ NO 2542
Noise/Modern Music / Apr '95 / Pinnacle / Plastic Head.

Shijuku Thief

SCRIBBLER, THE
CD _____ DOROBO 002CD
Dorobo / Sep '95 / Plastic Head.

Shindell, Richard

BLUE DIVIDE
CD _____ SH 8014
Shanachie / Dec '94 / Koch / ADA / Greensleeves.

Shine, Brendan

ALWAYS A WELCOME
CD _____ CDPLAY 1031
Play / Dec '92 / Avid/BMG.

COLLECTION: BRENDAN SHINE
CD _____ PLACD 101
Play / Oct '94 / Avid/BMG.

I WANNA STAY WITH YOU
I wanna stay with you / Lay down beside me / When the lovin' is through / Hello Darlin' / One more chance / Saints and sinners / Drive me to drink / Walkin' on new grass / Squeeze box / Shoe the donkey / It doesn't matter anymore / Some broken hearts never mend / Dad / Goodbye / (There's) The door / If tomorrow never comes / Love bug / Rock 'n' roll kids / Not counting you / When two lovers meet
CD _____ 3036000082
Carlton Home Entertainment / Nov '95 / Carlton Home Entertainment.

LOVIN YOU
CD _____ AVC 543
Avid / Jul '94 / Avid/BMG / BMG / ADA.

MEMORIES
Danny boy / If I were a blackbird / Old bog road / Dublin in the rare old times / Mountains of Mourne / Banks of my own lovely Lee
CD _____ CDPLAY 3
Play / Dec '92 / Avid/BMG.

Shinehead

SIDEWALK UNIVERSITY
Try my love / Jamaican in New York / Rainbow / Peace and love / Sidewalk university / Should I
CD _____ 7559611392
Elektra / Aug '92 / Warner Music.

TRODDIN'
CD _____ 755961667-2
Warner Bros. / Sep '94 / Warner Music.

Shines, Johnny

JOHNNY SHINES
CD _____ HCD 8028
Hightone / Jul '94 / ADA / Koch.

JOHNNY SHINES WITH BIG WALTER HORTON (Shines, Johnny & Big Walter Horton)
CD _____ TCD 5015
Testament / Mar '95 / Complete/Pinnacle / ADA / Koch.

MASTERS OF MODERN BLUES SERIES
CD _____ TCD 5002
Testament / Aug '94 / Complete/Pinnacle / ADA / Koch.

MR COVER SHAKER
CD _____ BCD 125
Biograph / Jan '93 / Wellard / ADA / Hot Shot / Jazz Music / Cadillac / Direct.

STANDING AT THE CROSSROADS
CD _____ TCD 5022
Testament / Mar '95 / Complete/Pinnacle / ADA / Koch.

TRADITIONAL DELTA BLUES
CD _____ BCD 121
Biograph / '92 / Wellard / ADA / Hot Shot / Jazz Music / Cadillac / Direct.

Shiney Gnomes

MC CREATRIX
CD _____ RTD 19519172
Our Choice / Feb '95 / Pinnacle.

Shining Path

NO OTHER WORLD
Freedom / No other world / They may be blind / Kiss of death / It was my turn to lose / This is my punishment / Kill / Wrath of God / End
CD _____ DEMCD 029
Day Eight Music / Jun '93 / New Note.

Shiny Gnomes

ORANGE
CD _____ RTD 19515482
Our Choice / Jun '93 / Pinnacle.

Ship Of Fools

CLOSE YOUR EYES (FORGET THE WORLD)
In the wake of / Where is here / Passage by night / L = SD2 / S.O.L.93 / Starjumper / Western lands / Close your eyes (forget the world)
CD _____ KTB 013CD
Dreamtime / Jun '93 / Kudos / Pinnacle.

OUT THERE SOMEWHERE
Elevator / Diesel spaceship / First light / Guidance is internal / Out there somewhere / From time / Eternal guidance
CD _____ CDKTB 18
Dreamtime / Apr '95 / Kudos / Pinnacle.

Shipp, Matthew

CIRCULAR TEMPLE (Shipp, Matthew Trio)
CD _____ 74321327582
RCA / Oct '95 / BMG.

ZO (Shipp, Matthew Duo)
CD _____ RR 126-2
Rise / Dec '94 / Pinnacle.

Shipway, Michael

BENEATH FOLLY
Arrival / Folly / Caravan / Celebration / Dream / Flying machine / After dark / Procession / Secrets / Watchkeeper / Departure / Return to battle
CD _____ REAL 094
Surreal / Sep '92 / Surreal To Real / C & D Compact Disc Services.

Shirelles

21 GREATEST HITS, THE
Soldier boy / Will you still love me tomorrow / Dedicated to the one I love / Foolish little girl / Mama said / Baby, it's you / Everybody loves a lover / Big John / Maybe tonight / Mad mad world / Welcome home / Don't say goodnight and mean goodbye / Stop the music / Tonight's the night / I met him on a Sunday / What does girl do / Thank you baby / Sha la la / To know him is to love him / Boys / My heart belongs to you
CD _____ CD 37
Bescol / May '87 / CM / Target/BMG.

BABY IT'S YOU
Baby, it's you (Original mono single version) / Irresistible you / Thing I want to hear (pretty words) / Big John / Same old story / Voice of experience / Soldier boy / Thing of the past / Twenty one / Make the night a little longer / Twisting in the U.S.A. / Putty in your hands
CD _____ CDSC 6012
Sundazed / Jan '94 / Rollercoaster.

BEST OF THE SHIRELLES, THE
Dedicated to the one I love / Look a here baby / Tonight's the night / Will you still love me tomorrow / Boys / Mama said / Thing of the past / What a sweet thing that was / Big John / Putty in your hands / Baby, it's you / Soldier boy / Welcome home baby / Mama here comes the bride / Stop the music / It's love that really counts / Everybody loves a lover / Foolish little girl / Abracadabra / Don't say goodnight and mean goodbye / What does a girl do / Don't let it happen to us / Girl is not a girl / Sha la la / His lips get in the way / Thank you baby / Doomsday / Maybe tonight / Shades of blue / Don't go home (My little darling) / Last minute miracle / Wait till I give the signal
CD _____ CDCHD 356
Ace / Apr '91 / Pinnacle / Cadillac / Complete/Pinnacle.

COLLECTION: SHIRELLES
CD _____ CCSCD 238
Castle / Apr '90 / BMG.

FABULOUS SHIRELLES
Will you still love me tomorrow / Soldier boy / Dedicated to the one I love / Foolish little girl / Mama said / Baby, it's you / Big John / Welcome home baby / Everybody loves a lover / Don't say goodnight and mean goodbye / Tonight's the night / What does a girl do
CD _____ CDFAB 011
Ace / Oct '91 / Pinnacle / Cadillac / Complete/Pinnacle.

GIVE A TWIST PARTY (Shirelles & King Curtis)
Mama here comes the bride / Take the last train home (instr.) / Welcome home baby / I've got a woman / I still want you / Take the last train home (vocal) / Love is a swingin' thing / Ooh poo pah doo / New Orleans / Mr. Twister / Potato chips
CD _____ CDSC 6013
Sundazed / Jan '94 / Rollercoaster.

LEGENDS IN MUSIC - SHIRELLES
CD _____ LECD 077
Wisepack / Sep '94 / THE / Conifer.

LOST & FOUND
Good good time / Long day, short night / You'll know when the right boy comes along / Rocky / Go tell her / Remember me / For my sake / Celebrate your victory / Hands off, he's mine / Crossroads in your heart / He's the only guy I'll ever love / One of the flower people / I'm feeling it too / If I had you / There goes my heart / Shh, I'm watching the movie
CD _____ CDCHD 521
Ace / May '94 / Pinnacle / Cadillac / Complete/Pinnacle.

SHIRELLES, THE
CD _____ KLMCD 039
Scratch / Nov '94 / BMG.

WILL YOU LOVE ME TOMORROW
Dedicated to the one I love / Tonight's the night / Will you still love me tomorrow / Boys / Mama said / Thing of the past / What a sweet thing that was / Big John / Baby, it's you / Soldier boy / Welcome home baby / Stop the music / It's love that really counts / Everybody loves a lover / Foolish little girl / Don't say goodnight and mean goodbye / What does a girl do / Sha la la / Thank you baby / Maybe tonight
CD _____ CDCHARLY 173
Charly / Jan '89 / Charly / THE / Cadillac.

Shirley, Roy

BLACK LION NEGUS RASTAFARI
CD _____ CDLINC 011
Lion Inc. / Dec '95 / Jetstar / SRD.

CONTROL THEM VOL.1
CD _____ GR 004CD
Sprint / May '95 / Jetstar / THE.

Shiv & Hari

YUGAL BANDI
Raga jhinjhoti / Raga mshira piloco
CD _____ RSMCD 104
Ravi Shankar Music Circle / May '94 /
Conifer.

Shivers

SHIVERS, THE
CD _____ GRCD 372
Glitterhouse / Aug '95 / Direct / ADA.

Shizzoe, Hank

LOW BUDGET
CD _____ CCD 11046
Crosscut / Nov '94 / ADA / CM / Direct.

Sho

TROUBLE MAN (Sho & Willie D)
CD _____ WRA 8125CD
Wrap / Apr '94 / Koch.

Sho Nuff

FROM THE GUT TO THE BUTT
Funkasize you / Steppin' out / You chose
me / Thinking of you / Get it together /
Watch me do it / I live across the street /
Come on / Mix match man / Total answer
CD _____ CDSXE 092
Stax / Aug '93 / Pinnacle.

Shock Box

DROPPIN' THE BOMB
CD _____ RTN 41211CD
Rock The Nation / Jan '96 / Plastic Head.

Shock Therapy

DARK YEARS, THE
CD _____ EFA 08440CD
Dossier / Oct '92 / SRD.

HATE IS A FOUR LETTER WORD
CD _____ SPV 08419572
SPV / May '95 / Plastic Head.

HEAVEN AND EARTH
CD _____ EFA 08455-2
Dossier / Mar '94 / SRD.
CD _____ SPV 08419552
SPV / Jun '95 / Plastic Head.

Shockabilly

VIETNAM/ HEAVEN
CD _____ SDE 9026CD
Shimmy Disc / Dec '90 / Vital.

Shocked, Michelle

ARKANSAS TRAVELER
33 rpm Soul / Come a long way / Secret to
a long life / Contest coming (Cripple creek)
/ Over the waterfall / Shaking hands (Sol-
dier's joy) / Jump Jim crow / Hold me back
(Frankie and Johnny) / Strawberry jam /
Prodigal daughter (Cotton eyes Joe) /
Blackberry blossom / Weaving way / Arkan-
sas traveller / Woody's rag
CD _____ 5121892
London / Apr '92 / PolyGram.

CAPTAIN SWING
Ged is a real estate developer / On the
greener side / Silent ways / Sleep keeps me
awake / Cement lament / (Don't you mess
around with) my little sister / Looks like
Mona Lisa / Too little, too late / Street corner ambassador / Must be luff
CD _____ 838 878 2
London / Jun '92 / PolyGram.

TEXAS CAMPFIRE TAPES
5 a.m. in Amsterdam / Secret admirer / Incomplete image / Who cares / Down on
Thomas St. Fogtown / Steppin' out / Hep
cat / Necktie / (Don't you mess around with)
my little sister / Ballad of patched eye and
Meg / Secret to a long life / Chain smoker
(CD only) / Stranded in a limousine (CD
only) / Goodnight Irene (CD only)
CD _____ COOKCD 022
Cooking Vinyl / Apr '88 / Vital.

Shocking Blue

20 GREATEST HITS
CD _____ REP 4125-WZ
Repertoire / Aug '91 / Pinnacle / Cadillac.

AT HOME
CD _____ REP 4041-WZ
Repertoire / Aug '91 / Pinnacle / Cadillac.

BEST OF SHOCKING BLUE
CD _____ CSAPCD 113
Connoisseur / Jan '94 / Pinnacle.

SCORPIO'S DANC
CD _____ REP 4086-WZ
Repertoire / Aug '91 / Pinnacle / Cadillac.

Shoenfelt, Phil

BACKWOODS CRUCIFIXION
Garden of Eden / Light that surrounds you
/ Devil's hole / Walkaway / Marianne, I'm
falling / Psyche / Hateful heart / Salvation
Hotel
CD _____ PAPCD 002
Paperhouse / May '90 / Disc.

**GOD IS THE OTHER FACE OF THE
DEVIL**
Charlotte's room / Gambler / Alchemy /
Hospital / Black rain / Only you / Martha's
well / Killer inside / Well of souls / Pale light
shining
CD _____ BAH 11
Humbug / Oct '93 / Pinnacle.

Shoes

BLACK VINYL SHOES
Boys don't lie / Do you wanna get lucky /
She'll disappear / Tragedy / Writing a post-
card / Not me / Someone finer / Capital gain
/ Fatal running start / Okay it really hurts /
Fire for a while / If you'd stay / Nowhere so
fast
CD _____ CREV 016CD
Rev-Ola / Sep '93 / 3MV / Vital.

STOLEN WISHES
CD _____ ROSE 202CD
New Rose / May '90 / Direct / ADA.

Shonen Knife

LET'S KNIFE
Riding the rocket / Bear up bison / Twist
Barbie / Tortoise theme 2 / Antonio baka
guy / Ah Singapore / Flying jelly attack /
Black bass / Cycling is fun / Watchin' girl /
I am a cat / Tortoise theme 1 / Devil house
/ Insect collector / Burning farm
CD _____ RUST 1 CD
August / Jan '93 / Vital.

ROCK ANIMALS
CD _____ RUST 009CD
August / Jan '94 / Vital.

WE ARE VERY HAPPY YOU CAME
Lazybone / Public bath / Goose steppin'
mama / I wanna eat choco bars / Suzy is a
headbanger / Boys / Red kross
CD _____ RUST 004CD
August / Apr '93 / Vital.

Shooglenifty

VENUS IN TWEED
Pipe tunes / Horace / Point Road / Venus
in tweeds / Waiting for Conrad / Two fifty
to Vigo / Paranoia / Buying a blanket / Tam-
mienorrie / Point Road (mix)
CD _____ CDTRAX 076
Greentrax / Aug '94 / Conifer / Duncans /
ADA / Direct.

Shook, Travis

TRAVIS SHOOK
CD _____ 4737702
Sony Jazz / Jan '95 / Sony.

Shootyz Groove

JAMMIN IN VICIOUS ENVIRONMENTS
CD _____ ABT101CD
Abstract / May '95 / Pinnacle / Total/BMG.

Shopping Trolley

SHOPPING TROLLEY
CD _____ HNCD 1349
Hannibal / Jan '90 / Vital / ADA.

Shore, Dinah

16 MOST REQUESTED SONGS
Laughing on the outside / All that glitters is
not gold / You keep coming back like a
song / I wish I didn't love you so / You do
/ Gentlemen is a dope / Golden earrings /
How soon (will I be seeing you) / Best things
in life are free / Little white lies / Far away
places / So in love / Forever and ever / It's
so nice to have a man around the house
CD _____ CK 66141
Columbia / May '95 / Sony.

BLUES IN THE NIGHT
As we walk into the sunset / Blues in the
night / Body and soul / Boy in khaki, a girl
in lace / Chloe / Down Argentina way / He's
my guy / Honeysuckle rose / Manhattan
serenade / Memphis blues / Mocking Bird
lament / Mood indigo / Murder he says / My
man / Skylark / Smoke gets in your eyes /
Somebody loves me / Something to remember you by / Sophisticated lady / Stardust / Three little sisters / Yes my darling
daughter / You and I / You'd be so nice to
come home to
CD _____ CDAJA 5136
Living Era / Jun '94 / Koch.

DINAH'S SHOW TIME 1944-47
You're a builder upper / Can't you read be-
tween the lines / Sometimes I'm happy /
Linger in my arms a little longer / Rainy night
in Rio / Laura / Just one of those things /
Love me or leave me / Dreamer / Tallahas-
see / How high the moon / Night and day /
Dixieland band: Button up your overcoat /
I've got the world on a string / Way you look

tonight / Smoke gets in your eyes / Shoo,
shoo baby / Yesterdays / Man I love / Zing
went the strings of my heart / I'll walk alone
/ Tess's torch song / Lover come back to
me / Gotta be this or that
CD _____ HEPCD 45
Hep / Feb '95 / Cadillac / Jazz Music / New
Note / Wellard.

LIKE SOMEONE IN LOVE
I thought about you / Last night / Imagina-
tion / Say it / Jim / You can't brush me off
/ My man / Is it taboo / All I need is you / I
don't want to walk without you / Maybe /
Something to remember you by / Now I
know / Night is young and your so beautiful
/ I'll walk alone / My romance / Like some-
one in love / I can't tell why I love you but
I do / Sleigh ride in July
CD _____ ROYCD 201
Flare / Nov '95 / Target/BMG.

MAD ABOUT YOU, SAD WITHOUT YOU
Thrill of a new romance / I like to recognise
the tune / That dream / Smoke gets in
your eyes / Outside of that I love you / How
come you do me like you do / Somebody
loves me / Mocking bird lament / I'm
through with love / Somebody nobody
loves / All alone / Not mine / Skylark / One
dozen roses / I can't give you anything but
love / Mad about him, sad without him /
Dearly beloved / Boy in khaki, a girl in lace
/ Murder, he says / You'd be so nice to
come home to
CD _____ HQCD 43
Harlequin / Jun '94 / Swift / Jazz Music /
Wellard / Hot Shot / Cadillac.

SPOTLIGHT ON DINAH SHORE
It all depends on you / It had to be you /
Somebody loves me / I'm old fashioned /
It's all right with me / It's so nice to have a
man around the house / My funny valentine
/ One I love / I'll be seeing you / Blues in
the night / Takin' a chance on love / My
buddy / Lover come back to me / Sleepy
time gal / Our love is here to stay / I only
have eyes for you / Bye bye blues
CD _____ CDP 8285142
Capitol / Apr '95 / EMI.

VERY BEST OF DINAH SHORE, THE
CD _____ SWNCD 006
Sound Waves / Oct '95 / Target/BMG.

**WHEN DINAH SHORE RULED THE
EARTH**
CD _____ VJCD 1052
Vintage Jazz Classics / Feb '94 / Direct /
ADA / CM / Cadillac.

WORLD WAR II
CD _____ VJC 1052
Vintage Jazz Classics / Apr '94 / Direct /
ADA / CM / Cadillac.

Short, Bobby

LIVE AT THE CARLYLE
Do I hear you saying I love you / Tea for two
/ Night and day / Too marvellous for words
/ Love is here to stay / Drop me off in Harlem / Body and soul / I can't give you anything but love / I can dream, can't I / I get
a kick out of you / Satin doll / Nearness of
you / Paradise / Easy to love / After you,
who / Every time we say goodbye
CD _____ CD 83311
Telarc / Mar '92 / Conifer / ADA.

Shorter, Wayne

ATLANTIS
Endangered species / Three Marias / Last
silk hat / When you dream / Who goes there
/ Atlantis / Shere Khan / Criancas / On the
eve of departure
CD _____ 4816172
Sony Jazz / Dec '95 / Sony.

ETCETERA
Etcetera / Penelope / Toy tune / Barracudas
/ Indian song
CD _____ CDP 8335812
Blue Note / Oct '95 / EMI.

NATIVE DANCER
Ponta de Areia / Beauty and the beast /
Tarde / Miracle of the fishes / Diana / Ana
Maria / Lilia / Joanna's theme
CD _____ 4670952
Columbia / Jan '95 / Sony.

SCHIZOPHRENIA
Tom Thumb / Go / Schizophrenia / Kryp-
tonite / Miyako / Playground
CD _____ CDP 8320962
Blue Note / Aug '95 / EMI.

SECOND GENESIS
Ruby and the pearl / Pay as you go / Sec-
ond Genesis / Mr. Chairman / Tenderfoot /
Albatross / Getting to know you / I didn't
know what time it was
CD _____ LEJAZZCD 9
Le Jazz / Mar '93 / Charly / Cadillac.

SPEAK NO EVIL
Fee fi fo fum / Dance cadaverous / Speak
no evil / Infant eyes / Wild flower / Out to
lunch / Straight up and down / Witch hunt
CD _____ CDP 7465092
Blue Note / Mar '95 / EMI.

WAYNE SHORTER
CD _____ GNPD 2075
GNP Crescendo / Jul '94 / Silva Screen.

Shortino, Paul

BACK ON TRACK
Kid is back in town / Body and soul / Girls
like you / Pieces / Bye bye to love / Everybody can fly / Give me love / Remember
me / Rough life / Forgotten child / When
there's a life
CD _____ CDVEST 3
Bulletproof / Mar '94 / Pinnacle.

Shorty

FRESH BREATH
CD _____ GR 14CD
Skingraft / Jun '94 / SRD.

THUMB DAYS
CD _____ GB 06-2
Gasoline Boost / Jul '93 / Plastic Head.

Shotgun Messiah

SECOND COMING, THE
CD _____ RR 92392
Roadrunner / Nov '91 / Pinnacle.

Shotgun Rationale

ROLLERCOASTER
CD _____ EFA 11894 CD
Vince Lombard / Jun '93 / SRD.

Shotts & Dykehead...

**ANOTHER QUIET SUNDAY (Shotts &
Dykehead Caledonia Pipe Band)**
CD _____ COMD 2037
Temple / Feb '94 / CM / Duncans / ADA /
Direct.

**BY THE WATERS EDGE (Shotts &
Dykehead Caledonia Pipe Band)**
Hornpipe - The walrus / March, strathspey
and reel / Slow air "By the waters edge" /
Jigs and slow air / Slow air "Farewell to
camraw" / Strathspey and reel / Medley /
Slow air "Piper alpha" / Dance jigs / 6/8
Marches / Retreat marches
CD _____ LCOM 5229
Lismor / Aug '94 / Lismor / Direct / Duncans
/ ADA.

Shoukichi, Kina

**MUSIC POWER FROM OKINAWA
(Shoukichi, Kina & Champroose)**
Haisai ojisan / Uwaki bushi / Red ojisan /
Bancho guwa / Agarizachi / Sukuchinamun
/ Ichimushiguwanu yuntaku / Bashaguwa
suncha / Shimaguwa song / Tokyo sanbika
CD _____ CDORBD 072
Globestyle / Oct '91 / Pinnacle.

Shoulders

TRASHMAN'S SHOES
Charm / On Sunday / Trashman shoes /
Beckoning bells / Weatherman / I'll take
what's left / Lula's bar and pool / Unle achin
/ whole way to the halfway house / All the
nights to come / Fare thee well
CD _____ DJD 3208
Dejadisc / May '94 / Direct / ADA.

Shout

IN YOUR FACE
Borderline / Give me an answer / Getting
ready / Getting on with life / Ain't givin' up
/ When the love is gone / Faith hope and
love / In your face / Moonlight sonata /
Waiting on you
CD _____ CDMFN 92
Music For Nations / May '89 / Pinnacle.

IT WON'T BE LONG
CD _____ CDMFN 58
Music For Nations / Aug '89 / Pinnacle.

Show & AG

GOODFELLAS
Never less than ill / You know now / Check
it out / Add on / Next level / Time for ... /
Got the flava / Neighborhood sickness / All
out / Medicine / Got ya back / Next level (2)
/ You want it
CD _____ 8286412
FFRR / Oct '95 / PolyGram.

Show Of Hands

BACKLOG 1987-1991
CD _____ CDIS 08
Isis / Mar '94 / ADA / Direct.

BEAT ABOUT THE BUSH
Beat about the bush / Cousin of Seventy
Three / Armadas / Nine hundred miles /
Shadows in the dark / Galway farmer /
White tribes / Day has come / Hook of love
/ Cars / Blue cockade / Mr. May's/Glouces-
ter hornpipe / Oak
CD _____ CDIS 05
Isis / Mar '94 / ADA / Direct.

COLUMBUS (DIDN'T FIND AMERICA)
Columbus (Didn't find America) / Exile /
Breakfast for Altan / Scattering tears

CD _____ CDIS 07
Isis / Apr '94 / ADA / Direct.

LIE OF THE LAND
CD _____ CDIS 09
Isis / Oct '95 / ADA / Direct.

SHOW OF HANDS 'LIVE'
Silver dagger / Blind fiddler / Don't it feel good / I still wait / Exile / Yankee clipper / Man of war / Bonnie Light Horseman / I'll put a stake through his heart / Low down in the broome / Six o'clock waltz / Sit you down / Wolf at the door / Caught in the rain / Santiago / It's all your fault
CD _____ CDIS 06
Isis / Mar '95 / ADA / Direct.

Showaddywaddy

25 STEPS TO THE TOP
CD _____ REP 4171-WZ
Repertoire / Aug '91 / Pinnacle / Cadillac.

JUMP, BOOGIE AND JIVE
Hang up my rock 'n' roll boots / Red hot / Another sad and lonely night / Pretty little angel eyes / I'm walkin' / Tutti frutti
CD _____ PCOM 1112
President / Jul '91 / Grapevine / Target/ BMG / Jazz Music / President.

ROCK 'N' ROLL FAVOURITES
Charly / Feb '94 / Charly / THE / Cadillac.
CD _____ CDCD 1150

VERY BEST OF SHOWADDYWADDY, THE
CD _____ 100166
Scratch / Oct '94 / BMG.

Showmen

SOME FOLKS DON'T UNDERSTAND IT
It will stand / Country fool / This misery / Wrong girl / Fate planned it this way / For you my darling / Valley of love / Owl sees you / Swish fish / I'm coming home / Strange girl / I love you, can't you see / Let her feel it in your kiss / True fine mama / 39-21-40 shape
CD _____ CDCHARLY 226
Charly / Jul '90 / Charly / THE / Cadillac.

Shreeve, Mark

ASSASSIN
Assassin / Angel of fire / Tyrant / System six
CD _____ CENCD 005
Centaur / Jun '94 / Complete/Pinnacle.

CRASH HEAD
Crash head / Darkness comes / Edge of darkness / Dead zone / Shrine / Angels of death / It / Night church / Hellraiser
CD _____ CENCD 007
Centaur / Sep '94 / Complete/Pinnacle.

LEGION
Legion / Storm column / Flags / Sybex factor / Domain 7 / Con / Stand
CD _____ CENCD 006
Centaur / Sep '94 / Complete/Pinnacle.

Shriekback

BEST OF SHRIEKBACK, THE
CD _____ 7432122636-2
RCA / Sep '94 / BMG.

GO BANG
Intoxication / Shark walk / Nighttown / Dust and shadow / Go bang / New man / Big fun
CD _____ IMCD 87
Island / '89 / PolyGram.

NATURAL HISTORY - THE VERY BEST OF SHRIEKBACK
CD Set _____ ESDCD 217
Essential / Sep '94 / Total/BMG.

PRIESTS AND KANIBALS
Nemesis (7") / Hammerheads / All lined up / My spine is a base line / Hand on my heart / Achtung / Mercy dash (7") / Suxck / Health and knowledge and wealth and power / Nerve / Only thing that shines / Coelacanth / Nemesis (Arch deviant) / Cloud of nails (Pimp up a storm) / Mercy dash (12" Extended version) / Fish below the ice (Mixes)
CD _____ 07822226362
RCA / Sep '94 / BMG.

SACRED CITY
CD _____ SHRIEK 1CD
World Domination / Feb '94 / Pinnacle.

Shrieve, Michael

FASCINATION
CD _____ CD 67
CMP / May '95 / Vital/SAM.

TWO DOORS
CD _____ CMPCD 074
CMP / Jan '96 / Vital/SAM.

Shrimp Boat

CAVALE
Pumpkin lover / Duende suite / Line song / Blue green song / What do you think of love / Swinging shell / Creme brulee / I'll name it Sue / Free love overdrive / Dollar bill / Apples / Smooth ass / Small wonder / Oranges / Henny penny

CD _____ R 3002
Rough Trade / Jul '93 / Pinnacle.

Shrivastav, Baluji

CLASSICAL INDIAN RAGAS
CD _____ EUCD 1101
ARC / '91 / ARC Music / ADA.

CLASSICAL INDIAN SITAR AND SURBAHAR RAGAS
CD _____ EUCD 1139
ARC / '91 / ARC Music / ADA.

Shrubs

VESSELS OF THE HEART
CD _____ DOM 2CD
Public Domain / Nov '88 / Disc.

Shu, Shomyo Shingon

BUDDHIST RITUAL "LIVE"
CD _____ LDX 274976
La Chant Du Monde / May '94 / Harmonia Mundi / ADA.

Shu-De

VOICES FROM THE DISTANT STEPPE
Sygyt khoomei kargyraa / Aian dudal (Songs of devotion and praise) / Beezhinden (Coming back from Beijing) / Buura / Durgen chugaa (Tongue twisters) / Throat singing and sigit / Yraazhy kys (The singing girl) / Shyngyr-shyngyr / Baian-dudai / Khomus solo / Meen khemchiim / Opei yry (A lullaby) / Tyva-uruankhai / Chasphy-khem (The river chashby) / Kadarchynying / Kham
CD _____ CDRW 41
Realworld / Jan '94 / EMI / Sterns.

Shudder To Think

FUNERAL AT THE MOVIES
CD _____ DIS 54CD
Dischord / '94 / SRD.

GET YOUR GOAT
CD _____ DIS 67CD
Dischord / '94 / SRD.

LIVE
CD _____ YCLS 020
Your Choice / Aug '94 / Plastic Head.

PONY EXPRESS RECORD
CD _____ ABB 65CD
Big Cat / Aug '95 / SRD / Pinnacle.

Shuffle Demons

BOP RAP
CD _____ SP 1124CD
Stony Plain / Oct '93 / ADA / CM / Direct.

STREETNIKS
CD _____ SP 1128CD
Stony Plain / Oct '93 / ADA / CM / Direct.

WHAT DO YOU WANT
CD _____ SP 1152CD
Stony Plain / Oct '93 / ADA / CM / Direct.

Shull, Tad

DEEP PASSION
CD _____ CRISS 1047CD
Criss Cross / May '91 / Cadillac / Harmonia Mundi.

Shut Up & Dance

BLACK MEN UNITED
CD _____ PULSE 22CD
Pulse 8 / Oct '95 / Pinnacle / 3MV.

DEATH IS NOT THE END
CD _____ SUADCD 005
Shut Up & Dance / Jun '92 / SRD.

Shutdown

EMITS A REAL BRONZE CHEER
CD _____ CDHOLE 003
Golf / Mar '95 / Plastic Head.

Shy

WELCOME TO THE MADHOUSE
CD _____ GRCD 1
Granite / Oct '94 / BMG / Pinnacle.

Shy FX

JUST AN EXAMPLE
CD _____ SOURCDLP 4
SOUR / Oct '95 / SRD.

Siam

LANGUAGE OF MENACE, THE
CD _____ NTHEN 11
Now & Then / Sep '95 / Plastic Head.

Sibbles, Leroy

IT'S NOT OVER
CD _____ VPCD 1452
VP / Dec '95 / Jetstar.

Siberry, Jane

SUMMER IN THE YUKON
Life is the red wagon / Miss Punta Blanca / Calling all angels / Above the treeline / In the blue light / Seven steps to the wall / Mimi on the beach / Walking / Very large hat / Lobby / Red high heels / Map of the world / Taxi ride
CD _____ 7599269362
WEA / Apr '92 / Warner Music.

WHEN I WAS A BOY
Temple / Calling all angels / Love is everything / Sail across the water / All the candles in the world / Sweet incarnadine / Gospel according to darkness / Angel stepped down / Vigil / At the beginning of time / Love is everything (version)
CD _____ 7599268242
Atlantic / Jul '93 / Warner Music.

Sick Of It All

JUST LOOK AROUND
CD _____ RR 91912
Roadrunner / Apr '95 / Pinnacle.

LIVE IN A WORLD FULL OF HATE
CD _____ LF 073CD
Lost & Found / Dec '93 / Plastic Head.

REVELATION RECORDINGS 1987-89, THE
CD _____ LF 083CD
Lost & Found / May '94 / Plastic Head.

SCRATCH THE SURFACE
CD _____ 7567024222
WEA / Nov '94 / Warner Music.

SPREADING THE HARDCORE REALITY
CD _____ LF 084MCD
Lost & Found / May '94 / Plastic Head.

Sickler, Don

MUSIC OF KENNY DORHAM (Sickler, Don/Jimmy Heath/Cedar Walton)
CD _____ RSRCD 111
Reservoir Music / Nov '94 / Cadillac.

Sicko

YOU CAN FEEL THE LOVE
CD _____ EFA 12358-2
Empty / Mar '94 / Plastic Head / SRD.

Side By Side

YOUR ONLY YOUNG ONCE
CD _____ LF 040CD
Lost & Found / Sep '95 / Plastic Head.

Sideral

MIL PARSECS
CD _____ PODUKCD 023
Pod England / Jan '96 / Plastic Head.

Sidewalk

NON STOP HIT MIX
Tragedy / I'm alive / I close my eyes and count to ten / I heard it through the grapevine / I feel love / 1-2-3 / Rescue me / Y.M.C.A. / High energy / Dancing in the street / Funky town / Locomotion / Lay all your love on me / Lost in music / Everlasting love / Flashdance (what a feeling)
CD _____ PWK 122
Carlton Home Entertainment / Jul '89 / Carlton Home Entertainment.

Sidi Bou Said

BROOOCH
CD _____ TOPPCD 5
Ultimate / Jul '94 / 3MV / Vital.

Sidibe, Sali

FROM TIBUKTU TO GAO
CD _____ SHAN 65011CD
Shanachie / Oct '93 / Koch / ADA / Greensleeves.

Sidney, Anthony

ANTHOLOGY - ANTHONY SIDNEY
St. Patrick's Day / Snail stepper / Prologo / My classic soul / Changing shadow / April / Line of women in white / Wonder world / Peru / Little David
CD _____ CONTECD 149
Contempo / Oct '90 / Plastic Head.

Sidran, Ben

COOL PARADISE
She steps into a dream / Searching for a girl like you / If someone has to wreck your life / Lip service / Language of the blues / Cool paradise / Desire of love / Bye bye blackbird / Walking with the blues / So long
CD _____ GOJ 60012
Go Jazz / Sep '95 / Vital/SAM.

ENIVRE D'AMOUR
Shine a light on me / Enivre d'amour / Everything happens to me / Freedom jazz dance / On the sunny side of the street / Critics / Pepper / Too hot too touch / Longing for Bahia / I wanna be a bebopper

CD _____ GOJ 60102
Go Jazz / Sep '95 / Vital/SAM.

GOOD TRAVEL AGENT, A
Doctor's blues / Broad daylight / Piano players / Turn to the music / Good travel agent / There they go / Lover man / Mitsubishi boy / On the cool side / Space cowboy / Last dance
CD _____ GOJ 60082
Go Jazz / Sep '95 / Vital/SAM.

HEAT WAVE
Mitsubishi boy / Lover man / Lover man (pt.2) / Brown eyes / On the cool side / Old Hoagy / Heatwave / Take it easy greasy / Up a lazy river / That's what the note said / Lost in the stars
CD _____ GOJ 60092
Go Jazz / Sep '95 / Vital/SAM.

LIFE'S A LESSON
Eliyahu / Oseh shalom / Life's a lesson / Ani ma'amin / Avinu Malchenu / Tree of life / B'rosh hashana / Eli Eli / Shofar shogood / Y'did nefesh / Kol Nidre / Hashiveni / Hatikvah / Face your fears / Hine ma tov
CD _____ GOJ 60132
Go Jazz / Sep '95 / Vital/SAM.

Siebel, Paul

JACK-KNIFE GYPSY
Jasper and the miners / If I could stay / Jack knife gypsy / Prayer song / Legend of the captian's daughter / Chips are down / Pinto pony / Hillbilly child / Uncle dudley / Miss Jones / Jeremiah's song
CD _____ 90051
Line / Oct '94 / CM / Grapevine / ADA / Conifer / Direct.

PAUL SIEBEL
CD _____ CDPH 1161
Philo / Nov '95 / Direct / CM / ADA.

Siebert, Budi

PYRAMID CALL
Life power / Sunrise / Feather of thruth / Third eye / Sphinx / Flight of the falcon / Voice of the heart / Cosmic soul / Golden kobra / Sunset / Illuminated pyramid / Ankh of the earth / Life dream / Horus / Remember all
CD _____ CD 256
Narada / Jun '95 / New Note / ADA.

WILD EARTH
Wild earth / Dancing with the bear / Beauty within / Black rain - Grey snow / Winds from the south / Silent earth / Phoenix rises / Round my way / On your shores / Gentle earth
CD _____ ND 63031
Narada / Mar '95 / New Note / ADA.

Siegal Schwall

SIEGAL SCHWALL REUNION CONCERT, THE
You don't love me like that / Devil / Leaving / Hey, Billie Jean / I wanna love ya / I think it was the wine / I don't want you to be my girl / When I've been drinking / Hush hush
CD _____ ALCD 4760
Alligator / May '93 / Direct / ADA.

Siegel, Corky

CHAMBER BLUES
CD _____ ALCD 4824
Alligator / Nov '94 / Direct / ADA.

Siegel, Janis

SLOW HOT WIND
CD _____ VSD 5552
Varese Sarabande/Colosseum / May '95 / Pinnacle / Silva Screen.

Sierra, Fredy

VALLENATO (Sierra, Fredy & Eglio Vega)
CD _____ TUMICD 041
Tumi / Jun '93 / Sterns / Discovery.

Sierra Maestra

DUNDUNBANZA
Juana pena / Dundubanza / No me llores / Mi guajira son / Cangrejo fue a estudiar / Kila qique y chocolate / El gago / El reloj de pastora
CD _____ WCD 041
World Circuit / Oct '94 / New Note / Direct / Cadillac / ADA.

Sierra, Ruben

IMAGEN VIVA
Cuando la recuerdo / Eres mia / Imagen viva / Voy a dejarle lina cancion / Lo mismo que ayer / Esta es tru cama / Demliestame / Mi fanatica mayor / Eso eres tu
CD _____ 66058056
RMM / Feb '95 / New Note.

Siffre, Labi

IT MUST BE LOVE
CD _____ MCCD 141
Music Club / Nov '93 / Disc / THE / CM.

MAKE MY DAY
Make my day / Watch me / For the children / Prayer / Nothing in the world like love / Some say / Just a little more line / Words / Maybe tomorrow / I love you / Maybe / Talk about / Too late / My song / It must be love / Crying, laughing, loving, lying / If you have faith / Fool me a good night / Give love / Something on my mind / I don't know what's happened to... / Bless the telephone / Who do you see / Cannock Chase
CD _____ VSOPCD 137
Connoisseur / Jul '89 / Pinnacle.

MAN OF REASON
CD _____ WOLCD 1015
China / May '91 / Pinnacle.

Sigh

SCORN DEFEAT
CD _____ ANTI-MOSH 007CD
Voices Of Wonder / Apr '94 / Plastic Head.

Siglo XX

FEAR AND DESIRE
Fear and desire / Everything is on fire / Lost in violence / Sorrow and pain / Thirty five poems / On the third day / My sister called silence / Pain came
CD _____ CDBIAS 087
Play It Again Sam / '88 / Vital.

FLOWERS FOR THE REBELS
Sister in the rain / Fear / No one is innocent / Afraid to tell / Sister suicide / Till the act is done / Shadows / Flesh and blood / Ride
CD _____ CDBIAS 051
Play It Again Sam / '88 / Vital.

UNDER A PURPLE SKY
CD _____ BIAS 145CD
Play It Again Sam / Jan '90 / Vital.

Sigue Sigue Sputnik

FIRST GENERATION, THE
Rockit miss USA / Sex bomb boogie / 21st century boy / Teenage thunder / She's my man / Love missile F1-11 / Jayne Mansfield / Ultra violence / Krush groove girls / Rock-a-jet baby / Rebel rebel
CD _____ FREUDCD 35
Jungle / Dec '90 / Disc.

Silberman, Benedict

TRADITIONAL JEWISH MELODIES
CD _____ CD 395
Bescol / Aug '94 / CM / Target/BMG.

Silberstein, Moshe

SHALOM ISRAEL
CD _____ CNCD 5953
Disky / Jul '93 / THE / BMG / Discovery / Pinnacle.

Sileas

BEATING HARPS
Pipers / Silver whistle / Oh wee white rose of Scotland / Solos / Puirt a buel / Shore of Gruinard / Ca' The Yowes / Dogs / Beating harps
CD _____ GLCD 1089
Green Linnet / Oct '93 / Roots / CM / Direct / ADA.

DELIGHTED WITH HARPS
Brigs / Cadal chan fhaigh mi (I can get no sleep) / Reels / Eppie Morrie / Air and reel / Da day dawn / Little cascade / Tha mulad / 'S coltach mi ri craobh gun duilleag / John Anderson, my Jo / Judges dilemma / Inverness gathering
CD _____ LAPCD 113
Lapwing / Dec '88 / CM.

Silencers

BLUES FOR BUDDHA
Answer me / Scottish rain / Real McCoy / Blues for Buddha / Walk with the night / Razor blades of love / Skin games / Wayfaring stranger / Sacred child / Sand and stars / My love is like a wave
CD _____ PD 71859
RCA / Nov '88 / BMG.

DANCE TO THE HOLY MAN
Singing ginger / Robinson Crusoe in New York / Bullet proof heart / Art of self-deception / I want you / One inch of heaven / Hey Mr. Bank Manager / This is serious/ John the revelator / Afraid to love / Rosanne / Electric storm / When the night comes down / Robinson rap / Just can't be bothered (Track on cassette/ CD only.) / Cannons and collisseums (Track on cassette/ CD only.)
CD _____ PD 74924
RCA / Mar '91 / BMG.

LETTER FROM ST.PAUL, A
Painted moon / I can't cry / Bullets and blue eyes / God's gift / I see red / I ought to know / Letter from St. Paul / Blue desire / Possessed
CD _____ PD 71336
RCA / Jun '87 / BMG.

SECONDS OF PLEASURE
I can feel it / Cellar of dreams / Small mercy / It's only love / Misunderstood / Life can be fatal / Unhappiest man / Walkmans and magnums / Street walker song / My prayer / Unconcious
CD _____ 74321141132
RCA / May '93 / BMG.

SO BE IT
CD _____ PERMCD 31
Permanent / Mar '95 / Total/BMG.

Silent Death

STONE COLD
CD _____ MASSCD 044
Massacre / Jan '95 / Plastic Head.

Silent Eclipse

DON'T JUDGE A BOOK BY ITS COVER
Best at slavery / Baptism, war and satellite / Don't judge a book by it's cover / Government piss off, parliament spin / Psychological enslavement / How many die / What ya gonna do / Policing as a tool / One in ya body / Story to tell
CD _____ BRCD 604
4th & Broadway / Aug '95 / PolyGram.

Silent Partners

IF IT'S ALL RIGHT, IT'S ALL RIGHT
CD _____ ANTCD 0010
Antones / Jan '93 / Hot Shot / Direct / ADA.

Silent Phase

THEORY OF SILENT PHASE, THE
Waterdance / Body rock / Air puzzle / Meditive fusion / Earth (interlude) / Spirit of sankofa / Spirit journey / Fire (prelude) / Psychotic funk / Electric relaxation / Love comes & goes / Forbidden dance
CD _____ TMT 001CD
R & S / Nov '95 / Vital.

Silk

SMOOTH AS SILK/SILK
Things haven't changed / I'll be waiting / Answer my prayer / Gone away / Get ready for the day / Simply beautiful / People / I never had love (like this before) / Dogs of war / I know I didn't do you wrong / Give yourself to me / Leaving me
CD _____ NEMCD 745
Sequel / Aug '95 / BMG.

Silk

LOSE CONTROL
Interlude / Happy days / Don't keep me waiting / Girl U for me / Freak me / When I think about you / Baby, it's you / Lose control / It had to be you / I gave to you
CD _____ 755961394-2
Keia / Mar '93 / Warner Music.

SILK
CD _____ 7559618492
Keia / Nov '95 / Warner Music.

Silkworm

FIREWATER
Nerves / Drink / Wet firecracker / Slow hands / Cannibal, cannibal / Tarnished angel / Quicksand / Ticket tulane / Don't make plans this Friday / Caricature of a joke / Killing my ass / River / Miracle mile / Lure of beauty / Severence pay / Swings
CD _____ OLE 1582
Matador / Feb '96 / Vital.

Silly Sisters

NO MORE TO THE DANCE
Blood and gold / Cake and ale / Fine horseman / How shall I / Hedger and ditcher / Agincourt Carol / Barring of the door / What'll we do / Almost every circumstance / Old miner
CD _____ TSCD 450
Topic / Aug '88 / Direct / ADA.

SILLY SISTERS
Burnin' o'Auchidoon / Lass of roch royal / Seven joys of Mary / My husband's got no courage in him / Singing the travels / Silver whistle / Grey funnel line / Geordie / Seven wonders / Four loom weaver / Game of cards / Dame Durden
CD _____ BGOCD 214
Beat Goes On / Jan '94 / Pinnacle.

Silly Wizard

GLINT OF SILVER, A
CD _____ GLCD 1070
Green Linnet / Mar '87 / Roots / CM / ADA.

KISS THE TEARS AWAY
Queen of Argyl / Golden golden / Finlay M Macrae / Banks of the Lee / Sweet Dublin Bay / Mo nighean donn / Gradh mo chroidhe / Banks of the Bann / Greenfields of Glentown / Galtee reel / Bobby Casey's number two / Wing commander Donald MacKenzie's reel / Loch Tay boat song
CD _____ SHANCD 79037

Shanachie / Apr '88 / Koch / ADA / Greensleeves.

LIVE AT CENTER STAGE
CD _____ GLV 1
Green Linnet / Mar '95 / Roots / CM / Direct / ADA.

LIVE WIZZARDRY
CD _____ GLCD 3036/37
Green Linnet / Oct '93 / Roots / CM / Direct / ADA.

Silmarils

SILMARILS
CD _____ 0630104542
East West / Feb '96 / Warner Music.

Silos

ASK THE DUST
CD _____ NORMAL 166CD
Normal/Okra / Jun '95 / Direct / ADA.

DIABLO
CD _____ NORMAL 163
Normal/Okra / May '94 / Direct / ADA.

HASTA LA VICTORIA
CD _____ NORMAL 143
Normal/Okra / May '94 / Direct / ADA.

Silva, Alan

ALAN SILVA
CD _____ ESP 1091-2
ESP / Jan '93 / Jazz Horizons / Jazz Music.

MY COUNTRY (Silva, Alan & Celestrial Communication Orchestra)
CD _____ CDLR 302
Leo / Apr '89 / Wellard / Cadillac / Impetus.

Silva, Chelo

LA REINA TEJANA DEL BOLERO
CD _____ ARHCD 423
Arhoolie / Jan '96 / ADA / Direct / Cadillac.

Silvadier, Pierre-Michel

D'AMOUR FOU D'AMOUR
CD _____ A XVI
Seventh / Dec '95 / Harmonia Mundi / Cadillac.

Silveira, Ricardo

STORYTELLER
Francesca / Upon a time / Storyteller / Island magic / Still think of you / Puzzle Fountains / After the rain / Always there / That day in Tahiti
CD _____ KOKO 1307
Kokopelli / Nov '95 / New Note.

Silver Birch

SILVER BIRCH
CD _____ DORIS 3
Vinyl Tap / Jan '96 / Vinyl Tap.

Silver, Horace

1952-1954
CD _____ CD 53131
Giants Of Jazz / Sep '94 / Target/BMG / Cadillac.

BAGHDAD BLUES, THE
CD _____ CD 53138
Giants Of Jazz / Jan '95 / Target/BMG / Cadillac.

BEST OF HORACE SILVER (Blue Note Years)
Opus de funk / Doodlin' / Room 608 (CD only.) / Preacher / Senor blues / Cool eyes (CD only.) / Home cooking / Soulville (CD only.) / Cookin' at the continental / Peace / Sister Sadie / Blowin' the blues away (CD only.)
CD _____ CDP 791 143 2
Blue Note / Dec '95 / EMI.

IT'S GOT TO BE FUNKY (Silver, Horace & The Silver Brass Ensemble)
Funky bunky / Dufus rufus / Lunceford legacy / Hillbilly bebopper / Walk around / Look up and down song / It's got to be funky / Basically blue / Song for my father / When you're in love / Put me in the basement / Little mama / Yo' Mamma's mambo
CD _____ 473877 2
Columbia / Apr '94 / Sony.

LIVE 1964
CD _____ EMRCD 101
Emerald / Jan '88 / Direct.

NATIVES ARE RESTLESS, THE
CD _____ EMRCD 1003
Emerald / Feb '87 / Direct.

PENCIL PACKIN' PAPA
Pencil packin' Papa / I got the dancin' blues / Soul mates / I need my baby / My Mother's waltz / Red beans and rice / Blues for brother blue / Let it all hang out / Senor blues / Viva amour
CD _____ 476979 2
Columbia / Jul '94 / Sony.

SENOR BLUES
CD _____ CD 53134
Giants Of Jazz / Nov '92 / Target/BMG / Cadillac.

SILVER'S BLUE
Silver's blue / To beat or not to beat / How long has this been going on / I'll know / Shoutin' out / Hank's tune / Night has a thousand eyes
CD _____ 4765212
Sony Jazz / Dec '95 / Sony.

SONG FOR MY FATHER (Silver, Horace Quintet)
Song for my father / Natives are restless to-night / Calcutta cutie / Que pasa / Kicker / Lonely woman / Sanctimonious Sam (CD only.) / Sighin' and cryin' (CD only.) / Silver threads among the soul (CD only.)
CD _____ CDP 7841852
Blue Note / Mar '95 / EMI.

Silver Jews

STARLITE WALKER
CD _____ WIGCD 15
Domino / Oct '94 / Pinnacle.

Silver Leaf Jazz Band

STREETS & SCENES OF NEW ORLEANS
CD _____ GTCD 15001
Good Time Jazz / May '95 / Jazz Music / Wellard / Pinnacle / Cadillac.

Silver Leaf Quartette Of.

COMPLETE RECORDED WORKS (Silver Leaf Quartette Of Norfolk)
CD _____ DOCD 5352
Blues Document / Jun '95 / Swift / Jazz Music / Hot Shot.

Silver, Mike

DEDICATION
CD _____ SR 0194CD
Silversound / Apr '95 / Roots / ADA.

ROADWORKS (LIVE)
Too many lies / Angel in deep shadow / Pretoria / Heatwave / Somebody's angel / Old fashioned Saturday night / Where would you rather be tonight / Let it be so / Not that easy / N.A.S.A. / Down South / Circle of stones / Nothing to do with me (Not on album) / Sailors all (Not on album) / Certain something (Only on CD) / Time for leaving (Only on CD) / Mine for ever more (Only on CD)
CD _____ SRO 190CD
Silversound / Aug '90 / Roots / ADA.

Silverchair

FROGSTOMP
Israel's son / Tomorrow / Faultline / Pure massacre / Shade / Blind / Leave me out / Suicidal dream / Madman / Undecided / Cicada / Findaway
CD _____ 4803402
Murmur / Sep '95 / Sony.

Silverfish

FAT AXL
CD _____ WIJ 006CD
Wiiija / Jan '91 / Vital.

ORGAN FAN
CD _____ CRECD 118
Creation / May '92 / 3MV / Vital.

Silverhead

FIRST/16 AND SAVAGE
Long legged Lisa / Underneath the light / Ace supreme / Johnny / In your eyes / Rolling with my baby / Wounded heart / Sold me down the river / Rock 'n' roll band / Silver boogie / Hello New York / More than your mouth can hold / Only you / Bright light / Heavy hammer / Cartoon princess / Rock out Claudette rock out / This ain't a parody / Sixteen and savage
CD Set _____ LICD 921174
Line / Mar '92 / CM / Grapevine / ADA / Conifer / Direct.

Silverheel

7000 DAYS 9000 SUNSETS
CD _____ FOCUSCD 9
Focus / Oct '95 / Pinnacle.

Silvers, Jim

MUSIC MAKIN' MAMA FROM MEMPHIS
Cannonball yodel / Paul's saloon / My, my, my / Each season changes you / Goodbye California (Hello Illinois) / You gotta let all the girls know you're a cowboy / I wanna see Las Vegas / Waltz across Texas / Model 2017 / Old faithful / Music makin' mama from Memphis / Last to get the news / Julie / Cash on the barrelhead / For your own good / I ate the whole damn hog / Call me a cab / Blue night / Cryin' my heart out over you / Ain't it strange / Last to get the news (2) / Music makin' mama from Memphis (2) / Losin' you (might be the best thing yet) / Scrap of paper and a 20 cent pen / Ocean of dreams

CD _____ BCD 15555
Bear Family / Jan '92 / Rollercoaster / Direct
/ CM / Swift / ADA.

Silvester, Victor

BEST OF THE DANSAN YEARS, VOL 1
(Silvester, Victor & His Ballroom
Orchestra)
CD _____ DACD 1001
Dansan / Jul '92 / Savoy / President /
Target/BMG.

**COME DANCE WITH ME - 20
BALLROOM FAVOURITES** (Silvester,
Victor & His Ballroom Orchestra)
I can dream, can't I / Come dance with me
/ C'est si bon / Always true to you in my
fashion / Waltz of my heart / Autumn leaves
/ I wonder where my baby is tonight / C'est
magnifique / Unforgettable / Tea for two /
Whisper while you waltz / By candle light /
Lady is a tramp / 'S Wonderful / Till there
was you / Moonlight serenade / Charleston
/ Mr. Sandman / April in Paris / It happened
in Monterey
CD _____ CC 8233
Music For Pleasure / Jan '94 / EMI.

COME DANCING VOL.1
CD _____ MU 3007
Musketeer / Oct '92 / Koch.

COME DANCING VOL.2
CD _____ MU 3008
Musketeer / Oct '92 / Koch.

DANCE, DANCE, DANCE
CD _____ MATCD 234
Castle / Dec '92 / BMG.

IN A DANCING MOOD (Silvester, Victor
& His Ballroom Orchestra)
CD _____ MATCD 283
Castle / Sep '93 / BMG.

IN STRICT TEMPO
s'posin' / You're in Kentucky sure as you're
born / Green eyes / So rare / At dusk / Sleep
tight / It's a sin to tell a lie / Paul Jones /
You're here, you're there / Will you remember / Can I forget you / Carelessly / You
needn't have kept it a secret / House
beautiful / Maria, my own / Goodnight to
you all / Don't say goodbye
CD _____ 2 BUR 006
Burlington / Sep '88 / CM.

LET'S DANCE (Silvester, Victor & His
Ballroom Orchestra)
On your toes / My blue heaven / Very
thought of you / If I had you / It happened
in Monterey / One night of love / I once had
a heart Margarita / You know it all smarty /
Kiss the boys goodbye / June in January /
September song / Roses of Picardy / Ra-
mona / Could be / Gotta be this or that /
Apple for the teacher / Time on my hands /
Stella by starlight / Love is my reason / Love
everlasting / Nice work if you can get it /
Moonlight and roses / You couldn't be cuter
/ Deep purple / Once in a while / Luna rossa
(Blushing moon) / Goody goody / Zing went
the strings of my heart
CD Set _____ CDDL 1197
EMI / Nov '92 / EMI.

STRICT TEMPO DANCING (Silvester,
Victor & His Ballroom Orchestra)
CD Set _____ MBSCD 405
Castle / Nov '93 / BMG.

STRICTLY BALLROOM (Silvester, Victor
& His Ballroom Orchestra)
Too close for comfort / Lady's in love with
you / Call me irresponsible / You're my
everything / Amore baciami / I give my heart
/ Belle of the ball / Gotta be this or that /
Old devil moon / My foolish heart / It can't
be wrong / Foggy day / Boy next door /
Around the world / At the jazz band ball /
Cerveza / One / Al di la / Copacabana / La
cumparsita / I'll go where your music takes
me / You were never lovelier / One I love
(Belongs to somebody else)
CD _____ TRTCD 150
TrueTrax / Dec '94 / THE.

STRICTLY BALLROOM
Born free / Walk in the Black Forest / Guantanamera / Gentle on my mind / You're
dancing on my heart / Quando, quando,
quando / Second time around / Love me
tonight / Lovely lady / Call me / Look of love
/ Mi amigo / Tijuana taxi / Stars in my eyes
/ Ob la di ob la da / Skirl o' the pipes / I'd
rather Charleston / Acapulco 1922 / Yeh
yeh / Desert song
CD _____ 5507682
Spectrum/Karussell / Mar '95 / PolyGram /
THE.

TRULY GREAT DANCE MELODIES
(Silvester, Victor & His Ballroom
Orchestra)
CD _____ DCD 5365
Disky / Apr '94 / THE / BMG / Discovery /
Pinnacle.

Silvestri, Alan

SHATTERED
CD _____ 262208
Milan / Nov '91 / BMG / Silva Screen.

Simbi

VODOU BEAT
CD _____ XENO 4038
Xenophile / Dec '95 / Direct / ADA.

Simeon, Omer

OMER SIMEON 1926-29
CD _____ 157752
Hot 'n' Sweet / Jul '93 / Discovery.

Simien, Terrance

THERE'S ROOM FOR US ALL
CD _____ BT 1096CD
Black Top / Jan '94 / CM / Direct / ADA.

ZYDECO ON THE BAYOU
Zydeco on the bayou / Back in my baby's
arms / Stop the train / Zydeco zambada /
Don't cry no more / I'll do it all over again /
Intro / Ta casse mon coeur / Love we
shared / I'll say so long / Will the circle be
unbroken / Moi su pas tracasser
CD _____ FIENDCD 715
Demon / Apr '92 / Pinnacle / ADA.

Simion, Nicholas

BLACK SEA
Black sea / Blues for Bird / Africa / Red /
Song for Leo / Solomon / Mr. McCoy
CD _____ TUTUCD 888134
Tutu / May '92 / Vital/SAM.

Simmons, Sonny

BACKWOODS SUITE
CD _____ WWCD 2074
West Wind / Mar '93 / Swift / Charly / CM
/ ADA.

Simms, Ginny

GINNY SIMMS MEMORIAL ALBUM, THE
CD _____ VN 150
Viper's Nest / Nov '94 / Direct / Cadillac /
ADA.

Simon & Garfunkel

BOOKENDS
Bookends / Save the life of my child / America / Overs / Voice of old people / Old
friends / Fakin' it / Punky's dilemma / Hazy
shade of winter / At the zoo / Mrs. Robinson
CD _____ CD 63101
CBS / Dec '85 / Sony.

**BOOKENDS/ BRIDGE OVER TROUBLED
WATER/ SOUND OF SILENCE**
CD Set _____ 4673962
CBS / Dec '90 / Sony.

BRIDGE OVER TROUBLED WATER
Bridge over troubled water / El condor pasa
/ Cecilia / Keep the customer satisfied / So
long, Frank Lloyd Wright / Boxer / Baby
driver / Only living boy in New York / Why
don't you write me / Bye bye love / Song
for the asking
CD _____ 4804182
Columbia / Jul '95 / Sony.

CONCERT IN CENTRAL PARK
Mrs. Robinson / Homeward bound / America / Me and Julio down by the schoolyard /
Scarborough Fair / April come she will /
Wake up little Susie / Still crazy after all
these years / American tune / Late in the
evening / Kodachrome / Maybellene / Bridge
over troubled water / 59th Street Bridge song (Feeling
groovy) / Late in the evening / I do it for
your lover / Boxer / Old friends / Feeling
groovy / Sound of silence
CD _____ CD 96008
Geffen / May '88 / BMG.

**DEFINITIVE SIMON AND GARFUNKEL,
THE**
Wednesday morning 3am / Sound of silence / Homeward bound / Kathy's song / I
am a rock / For Emily, wherever I may find
her / Scarborough Fair/Canticle / 59th
Street Bridge song / Seven o'clock news/
Silent night / Hazy shade of winter / El condor pasa (If I could) / Mrs. Robinson / America / At the zoo / Old friends / Bookends
theme / Cecilia / Boxer / Bridge over troubled water / Song for the asking
CD _____ MOODCD 21
Columbia / Nov '91 / Sony.

**GREATEST HITS: SIMON &
GARFUNKEL**
Mrs. Robinson / For Emily, wherever I may
find her / Boxer / Feeling groovy / Sound of
silence / I am a rock / Scarborough Fair /
Canticle / Homeward bound / Bridge over
troubled water / America / Kathy's song / If
I could / Bookends / Cecilia
CD _____ CD 69003
CBS / Mar '87 / Sony.

**PARSLEY, SAGE, ROSEMARY AND
THYME**
Scarborough Fair / Patterns / Cloudy / Big
bright green pleasure machine / 59th Street
Bridge song / Dangling conversation / Flowers never bend with the rainfall / Simple
desultory philippic / For Emily, wherever I
may find her / Poem on the underground
wall / Seven o'clock news / Silent night
CD _____ CD 32031
CBS / Apr '89 / Sony.

**SIMON & GARFUNKEL COLLECTION,
THE**
I am a rock / Homeward bound / America /
59th Street Bridge song / Wednesday
morning 3am / El condor pasa / At the zoo
/ Scarborough Fair / Boxer / Sound of si-
lence / Mrs. Robinson / Keep the customer
satisfied / Song for the asking / Hazy shade
of Winter / Cecilia / Old friends / Bookends
/ Bridge over troubled water
CD _____ CD 24005
CBS / Apr '88 / Sony.

SOUND OF SILENCE
Sound of silence / Leaves that are green /
Blessed / Somewhere they can't find me /
Kathy's song / Homeward bound / Most
peculiar man / I am a rock / Richard Cory /
April come she will
CD _____ CD 62690
CBS / Dec '85 / Sony.

WEDNESDAY MORNING, 3AM
You can tell the world / Last night I had the
strangest dream / Bleecker Street / Sparrow
/ Benedictus / Peggy-O / He was my
brother / Sound of silence / Go tell it on the
mountain / Sun is burning / Times they are
a changin' / Wednesday morning 3am
CD _____ 982639 2
Pickwick/Sony Collector's Choice / Aug '91
/ Carlton Home Entertainment / Pinnacle /
Sony.

Simon & The Bar Sinisters

LOOK AT ME I'M COOL
CD _____ CD 023
Upstart / Aug '95 / Direct / ADA.

Simon, Arletty Michel

LA COMPILATION
CD _____ UCD 19087
Forlane / Jun '95 / Target/BMG.

Simon, Carly

BEST OF CARLY SIMON
That's the way I've always heard / Right
thing to do / Mockingbird / Legend in your
own time / Haven't got time for the pain /
You're so vain / No secrets / Night owl /
Anticipation / Attitude dancing
CD _____ 9548304602
WEA / May '91 / Warner Music.

COMING AROUND AGAIN
Itsy bitsy spider / If it wasn't love / Coming
around again / Give me all night / As time
goes by / Do the walls come down / It
should have been me / Stuff that dreams
are made of / Two hot girls / You have to
hurt / All I want is you / Hold what you've
got
CD _____ 261038
Arista / Nov '90 / BMG.

FIRST ALBUM
CD _____ 7559606722
Elektra / Jan '96 / Warner Music.

GREATEST HITS LIVE: CARLY SIMON
You're so vain / Nobody does it better /
Coming around again / It happens every
day / Anticipation / Right thing to do / Do
the walls come down / You belong to me /
Two hot girls / All i want is you / Never been
gone
CD _____ 259196
Arista / Aug '95 / BMG.

LETTERS NEVER SENT
Intro / Letter never sent / Lost in your love
/ Like a nun / Time works on all the wild
young men / Touched by the sun / Davy /
Halfway 'round the world / What about a
holiday / Reason / Private / Catch it like a
fever / Born to break my heart / I'd rather it
was you
CD _____ 07822187522
Arista / Nov '94 / BMG.

MY ROMANCE
My romance / By myself / I see your face /
When your lover is gone / In the wee small
hours of the morning / My funny valentine /
Something wonderful / Little girl blue / He
was good to me / What has she got / Be-
witched, bothered and bewildered / Danny
boy / Time after time
CD _____ 262019
Arista / Jan '92 / BMG.

NO SECRETS
Right thing to do / Carter family / You're so
vain / His friends are more than fond of
Robin / We have no secrets / Embrace me,
you child / It was so easy / Waited so long
/ Night owl / When you close your eyes
CD _____ 7559606842
WEA / Jul '93 / Warner Music.

SPOILED GIRL
My new boyfriend / Come back home / To-
night and forever / Spoiled girl / Tired of be-
ing blonde / Wives are in Connecticut / An-
yone but me / Make me feel something /
Can't give up / Black honeymoon
CD _____ 9825892
Pickwick/Sony Collector's Choice / Jun '91
/ Carlton Home Entertainment / Pinnacle /
Sony.

Simon, Edward

BEAUTY WITHIN
Mastery of all situations / Beauty within /
Rare days / In search of power / Reprise 1
/ El Dia que me quieras / Homecoming /
Calling / Reprise 2
CD _____ AQCD 1025
Audioquest / Sep '95 / New Note.

EDWARD SIMON
Colega / Alma llanera, part 1 / Alma llanera,
part 2 / Caballo viejo / Slippin' and slidin' /
Stop looking to find (it finds you) / Magic
between us / Teen's romance
CD _____ KOKO 1305
Kokopelli / Nov '95 / New Note.

Simon, Joe

DROWNING IN THE SEA OF LOVE
Glad to be your lover / Something you can
do today / I found my dad / Mirror don't lie
/ Ole night owl / You are everything / If / Let
me be the one (the one who loves you) /
Pool of bad luck
CD _____ CDSEW 021
Southbound / Apr '90 / Pinnacle.

LOOKING BACK (Best Of Joe Simon)
Chokin' kind / My special prayer / No sad
songs / San Francisco is a lonely town /
Message from Maria / Look of love / Baby
don't be looking in my mind / Teenagers'
prayer / Nine pound steel / You keep me
hangin' on / Put your trust in me / It's hard
to get along / Misty blue / Farther on down
the road / Yours love / That's the way I want
our love
CD _____ CDCHARLY 144
Charly / Nov '88 / Charly / THE / Cadillac.

MOOD, HEART AND SOUL/ TODAY
Neither one of us / I would still be there /
Good time Charlie's got the blues / Cover-
ing the same old ground / Walking down
lonely street / Best time of my life / What
we gonna do now / I'm in the mood for you
/ Carry me / Come back home / Let's spend
the night forever / I just want to make love
to you / Let the good times roll / Come get
to this / What a wonderful world / I need
you, you need me / I'll take care of you /
Music for my lady
CD _____ CDSEWD 971
Southbound / Apr '91 / Pinnacle.

MY ADORABLE ONE
CD _____ CDRB 28
Charly / Aug '95 / Charly / THE / Cadillac.

SOUNDS OF SIMON
To lay down beside you / I can't see no-
body / Most of all / No more me / Your time
to cry / Help me make it through the night
/ My woman, my woman, my wife / I love
you more / Georgia blue / All my hard times
CD _____ CDSEWD 954
Southbound / Oct '90 / Pinnacle.

SOUNDS OF SIMON/ SIMON COUNTRY
To lay down beside you / I can't see nobody / Most of all / No more me / Your time
to cry / Help me make it through the night
/ My woman, my woman, my wife / I love
you more than anything / Georgia blue / All
my hard times / Do you know what it's like
to be lonesome / You don't know me / To
get to you / Before the next teardrop falls /
Someone to give my love to / Good things
/ Kiss an angel good morning
CD _____ CDSEW 954
Southbound / Oct '90 / Pinnacle.

Simon, Jona

PIANO AFTER MIDNIGHT (Simon, Jona
Trio)
CD _____ CDSGP 0140
Prestige / Apr '95 / Total/BMG.

Simon, Paul

ANTHOLOGY
Sound of silence / Cecilia / El condor pasa
/ Boxer / Mrs. Robinson / Bridge over trou-
bled water / Me and julio down by the
schoolyard / Peace like a river / Mother and
child reunion / American tune / Loves me
like a rock / Kodachrome / Gone at last /
Still crazy after all these years / Something
so right / Fifty Ways to leave your lover /
Slip slidin' away / Late in the evening /
Hearts and bones / Rene and Georgette
Magritte with their dog after the war
CD _____ 9362454082
Warner Bros. / Oct '93 / Warner Music.

**CONCERT THE PARK - AUGUST 15TH,
1991**
Obvious child / Boy in the bubble / She
moves on / Kodachrome / Born at the right
time / Train in the distance / Me and Julio
down by the schoolyard / I know what I
know / Cool cool river / Bridge over troubled
water / Proof / Coast / Graceland / You can
call me Al / Still crazy after all these years /
Loves me like a rock / Diamonds on the soles of her shoes / Hearts and bones / Late
in the evening / America / Boxer / Cecelia /
Sound of silence
CD _____ 7599267372
WEA / Nov '91 / Warner Music.

GRACELAND
Boy in the bubble / Graceland / I know what
I know / Gumboots / Diamonds on the soles

SIMON, PAUL (continued)

of her shoes / You can call me Al / Under African skies / Homeless / Crazy love Vol 2 / All around the world or the myth of fingerprints
CD _____ 925447 2
WEA / Sep '86 / Warner Music.

HEARTS AND BONES
Think too much / Train in the distance / Cars are cars / Late great Johnny Ace / Allergies / Hearts and bones / When numbers get serious / Song about the moon / Rene and Georgette Magritte with their dog after the war
CD _____ 923942 2
WEA / '83 / Warner Music.

LIVE RHYMIN' - IN CONCERT
Me and Julio down by the schoolyard / Homeward bound / American tune / El condor pasa / Duncan / Boxer / Mother and child reunion / Sound of silence / Jesus is the answer / Bridge over troubled water / Loves me like a rock / America
CD _____ 925590 2
WEA / Dec '87 / Warner Music.

ONE TRICK PONY
Late in the evening / That's why God made the movies / One-trick pony / How the heart approaches what it yearns / Oh Marion / Ace in the hole / Nobody / Jonah / God bless the absentee / Long long day
CD _____ 256846
WEA / Feb '94 / Warner Music.

PAUL SIMON
Mother and child reunion / Duncan / Everything put together falls apart / Run that body down / Armistice Day / Me and Julio down by the schoolyard / Peace like a river / Papa hobo / Hobo blues / Paranoia blues / Congratulations / Kodachrome / Tenderness / Take me to the Mardi Gras / Something so right / One man's ceiling is another man's floor / American tune / Was a sunny day / Learn how to fall / St. Judy's comet / Loves me like a rock
CD _____ 925588 2
WEA / Dec '87 / Warner Music.

PAUL SIMON SONGBOOK (Various Artists)
CD _____ VSOPCD 173
Connoisseur / Jun '92 / Pinnacle.

RHYTHM OF THE SAINTS
Obvious child / Boy in the bubble / She moves on / Kodachrome / Born at the right time / Train in the distance / Me and Julio down by the schoolyard / I know what I know / Cool cool river / Bridge over troubled water / Proof / Coast / Graceland / Further to fly
CD _____ 7599260982
WEA / Oct '90 / Warner Music.

STILL CRAZY AFTER ALL THESE YEARS
Still crazy after all these years / My little town / I do it for your love / Fifty ways to leave your lover / Night game / Gone at last / Some folk's lives roll easy / Have a good time / You're kind / Silent eyes
CD _____ 925591 2
WEA / Dec '87 / Warner Music.

THERE GOES RHYMIN' SIMON
Kodachrome / Tenderness / Take me to the Mardi Gras / Something so right / One man's ceiling is another man's floor / American tune / Was a sunny day / Learn how to fall / St. Judy's comet / Loves me like a rock
CD _____ 925589 2
WEA / Dec '87 / Warner Music.

Simon, Tito

I CRIED A TEAR
I cried a tear / Every beat of my heart / I'd rather go blind / River of tears / That's where it's at / Tell it like it is / After loving you / Hold on to what you've got
CD _____ FECD 10
First Edition / Apr '93 / Jetstar.

Simona, Tiziana

GIGOLO (Simona, Tiziana & Kenny Wheeler)
CD _____ ITM 0014CD
ITM / '89 / Tradelink / Koch.

Simone, Nina

60'S VOL 1, THE
CD _____ 838543-2
Mercury / Apr '94 / PolyGram.

BALTIMORE
Baltimore / Everything must change / Family / My father / Music for lovers / Rich girl / That's all I want from you / Forget / Balm in Gilead / If you pray right
CD _____ 4769062
Sony Jazz / Jan '95 / Sony.

BEST OF NINA SIMONE
In the morning / I shall be released / Day and night / It be's that way sometimes / I want a little sugar in my bowl / My man's gone now / Why (the king of love is dead) / Compensation / I wish I knew (how it would feel to be free) / Go to hell / Do what you gotta do / Suzanne

CD _____ ND 90376
RCA / Sep '89 / BMG.

BEST OF NINA SIMONE - THE COLPIX YEARS
Children go where I send you / It might as well be spring / Willow weep for me / Other woman / Fine and mellow / Wild is the wind / You can have him / I loves you Porgy / Forbidden fruit / Gin house blues / Work song / House of the rising sun / I got it bad and that ain't good / Solitude / It don't mean a thing if it ain't got that swing / Twelfth of never / Baubles, bangles and beads / Gimme a pigfoot / Every time we say goodbye
CD _____ CDROU 1048
Roulette / Mar '92 / EMI.

BLUES, THE
Do I move you / Day and night / In the dark / Real real / My man's gone now / Backlash blues / I want a little sugar in my bowl / Buck / Since I fell for you / House of the rising sun / Blues for Mama / Pusher / Turn me on / Nobody's fault but mine / Go to hell / I shall be released / Gin house blues
CD _____ ND 83101
Novus / Apr '91 / BMG.

BROADWAY, BLUES, BALLADS
Don't let me be misunderstood / Night song / Laziest girl in town / Something wonderful / Don't take all night / Nobody / I am blessed / Of this I'm sure / See line woman / Our love / How can I / Last rose of summer
CD _____ 518190-2
Verve / Feb '94 / PolyGram.

DO NOTHIN' TILL YOU HEAR FROM ME
Just in time / House of the rising sun / It don't mean a thing if it ain't got that swing / I loves you Porgy / Gin house blues / Assingment song / Solitude / Sea lion woman / No opportunity necessary, no experience needed / Black is the colour of my true love's hair / Wild is the wind / Nobody / Don't let me be misunderstood / Do nothin' till you hear from me / I got it bad and that ain't good / Hey Buddy Bolden / My way
CD _____ CDGRF 022
Tring / '93 / Tring / Prism.

FEELING GOOD (THE VERY BEST OF NINA SIMONE)
CD _____ 522669 2
Polydor / Jul '94 / PolyGram.

IN CONCERT
CD _____ RMB 75011
Remember / Nov '93 / Total/BMG.

LET IT BE ME (Live At Vine Street)
My baby just cares for me / Sugar in my bowl / fodder on her wings / Be my husband / Just like a woman / Balm in Gilead / Stars / If you pray right (Heaven belongs to you) / If you knew / Let it be me / Baltimore
CD _____ 831 437-2
Verve / May '87 / PolyGram.

LIVE (Early 80's recording)
CD _____ CDCD 1232
Charly / Jun '95 / Charly / THE / Cadillac.

MY BABY JUST CARES FOR ME
My baby just cares for me / Don't smoke in bed / Mood indigo / He needs me / Love me or leave me / I loves you Porgy / You'll never walk alone / Good bait / Central Park blues / Plain gold ring / Little girl blue / My baby just cares for me (Ext.version) / My baby just cares for me (mix)
CD Set _____ CPCD 8002
Charly / Feb '95 / Charly / THE / Cadillac.

MY BABY JUST CARES FOR ME
CD _____ ENTCD 266
Entertainers / Mar '92 / Target/BMG.

MY BABY JUST CARES FOR ME (live at Ronnie Scott's)
God, God, God / If you knew / Mr. Smith / fodder on her wings / Be my husband / I loves you Porgy / Other woman / Mississippi goddam / Moon over Alabama / For a while / My baby just cares for me / See live woman / I sing just to know that I'm alive
CD _____ CLACD 331
Castle / Mar '94 / BMG.

NINA SIMONE
CD _____ 295055
Ariola / Feb '95 / BMG.

NINA'S BACK
It's cold out here / Porgy / I sing just to know that I'm alive / For a while / Fodder on her wings / Touching and caring / Saratoga / You must have another lover
CD _____ CDMT 019
Meteor / '85 / Magnum Music Group.

RISING SUN COLLECTION
CD _____ RSCD 004
Just A Memory / Apr '94 / Harmonia Mundi.

SINGLE WOMAN
Single woman / Lonesome cities / If I should lose you / Folks who live on the hill / Love's been good to me / Papa, can you hear me / Il n'y a pas d'amour / Just say I love him / More I see you / Marry me
CD _____ 755961503-2
Elektra / Aug '93 / Warner Music.

SONGS OF THE POETS
Just like a woman / Backlash blues / Just like Tom Thumb's blues / I shall be released / Here comes the sun / Times they are a changin' / I want a little sugar in my bowl / To be young gifted and black
CD _____ EDCD 347
Edsel / Feb '92 / Pinnacle / ADA.

SPOTLIGHT ON NINA SIMONE
Work song / Angel of the morning / Ain't got no...I got life / You can have him / Lovin' woman / Little Liza Jane / Here comes the sun / My way / Fine and mellow / Nina's blues / Porgy
CD _____ HADCD 109
Javelin / Feb '94 / THE / Henry Hadaway Organisation.

Simopoulos, Nana

GAIA'S DREAM
Koula koula / White bird / Artemis' silver bow / Journey / Hunga cheeda (flying eagle) / Marry moons / Like you / Open moons / Raphael / Tonight
CD _____ BW 013
B&W / Mar '93 / New Note.

Simper, Nick

SLIPSTREAMING/FUTURE TIMES
Candice Larene / Rocky road blues / Independent man (Hey Mama) / Slipstreaming / Schoolhouse party / Sister / Mississippi lady / Time will tell / Pull out and start again / Get down, lay down / She was my friend / Future times / Undercover man / Something's burning / Hard drink and easy women
CD _____ RPM 125
RPM / Mar '94 / Pinnacle.

Simpkins, Nat

COOKIN' WITH SOME BARBECUE
Our love is here to stay / Deep blue sea / Now houston / Shadow of your smile / God bless the children / Shuffle the deck / Nicole's waltz / When Sunny gets blue / Arnett left town
CD _____ MCD 5510
Muse / Sep '95 / New Note / CM.

Simple Agression

FORMULATIONS IN BLACK
Quiddity / Formulation in black / Lost / Phychoradius / Sea of eternity / Of winter / Simple aggression / Frenzy / Madd / Spiritual voices / Jedi mind trick / Share your pain
CD _____ CDVEST 1
Bulletproof / Mar '94 / Pinnacle.

Simple Minds

CELEBRATION
Life in a day / Chelsea girl / Premonition / Factory / Calling your name / I travel / Changeling / Celebrate / Thirty frames a second / Kaleidoscope
CD _____ CDV 2248
Virgin / Apr '90 / EMI.

EMPIRES AND DANCE
I travel / Today / I died again / This fear of Gods / Celebrate / Constantinople line / Twist, run, repulsion / Thirty frames a second / Kant-kino / Room / Capital city
CD _____ CDV 2247
Virgin / Jun '88 / EMI.

GLITTERING PRIZE (1981-'92)
Waterfront / Don't you forget about me / Alive and kicking / Sanctify yourself / Love Song / Someone, somewhere in summertime / See the lights / Belfast child / American / All the things she said / Promised you a miracle / Ghostdancing / Speed your love to me / Glittering prize / Let there be love / Mandela Day
CD _____ SMTVD 1
Virgin / Oct '92 / EMI.

GOOD NEWS FROM THE NEXT WORLD
She's a river / Night music / Hypnotised / Great leap forward / Seven deadly sins / And the band played on / My life / Criminal world / This time
CD _____ CDV 2760
Virgin / Jan '95 / EMI.

LIFE IN A DAY
Someone / Life in a day / Sad affair / All for you / Pleasantly disturbed / No cure / Chelsea girl / Wasteland / Destiny / Murder story
CD _____ VMCD 6
Virgin / Jul '87 / EMI.

LIVE-IN THE CITY OF LIGHT
Ghostdancing / Big sleep / Waterfront / Promised you a miracle / Someone, somewhere in summertime / Oh jungleland / Alive and kicking / Don't you forget about me / Once upon a time / Book of brilliant things / East at Easter / Sanctify yourself / Love song / Sun city / Dance to the music / New gold dream
CD Set _____ CDSM 1
Virgin / '87 / EMI.

NEW GOLD DREAM (81-82-83-84)
Someone, somewhere in summertime / Colours fly and catherine wheel / Promised you a miracle / Big sleep / Somebody up there likes you / New gold dream / Glittering

prize / Hunter and the hunted / King is white and in the crowd
CD _____ CDV 2230
Virgin / Apr '92 / EMI.

ONCE UPON A TIME
Once upon a time / All the things she said / Ghostdancing / Alive and kicking / Oh jungleland / I wish you were here / Sanctify yourself / Come a long way
CD _____ CDV 2364
Virgin / Oct '85 / EMI.

REAL LIFE
Real life / See the lights / Let there be love / Woman / Stand by love / Let the children speak / African skies / Ghost rider / Banging on the door / Travelling man / Rivers of ice / When two worlds collide
CD _____ CDV 2660
Virgin / Apr '91 / EMI.

REEL TO REAL CACOPHONY
Real to real / Naked eye / Citizen (dance of youth) / Veldt / Carnival (shelter in a suitcase) / Factory / Cacophony / Premonition / Changeling / Film theme / Calling your name / Scar
CD _____ CDV 2246
Virgin / '86 / EMI.

SIMPLE MINDS: BOX SET
CD Set _____ TPAK 2
Virgin / Oct '90 / EMI.

SONS AND FASCINATION
In trance as mission / Sweat in bullet / Seventy cities as love brings the fall / Boys from Brazil / Love song / This earth that you walk upon / Sons and fascination / Seeing out the angel / Theme for great cities (Not on LP) / American (Not on LP) / Twentieth century promised land (Not on LP) / Wonderful in young life (Not on LP) / Careful in career (Not on LP)
CD _____ CDV 2207
Virgin / Apr '86 / EMI.

SPARKLE IN THE RAIN
Up on the catwalk / Book of brilliant things / Speed your love to me / Waterfront / East at Easter / Street hassle / White hot day / C moon / Kick inside of me / Shake off the ghosts / Cry like a baby
CD _____ CDV 2300
Virgin / Mar '92 / EMI.

STREET FIGHTING YEARS
Street fighting years / Wall of love / Take a step back / Let it all come down / Belfast child / Soul crying out / This is your land / Kick it in / Mandela day / Biko
CD _____ MINDD 1
Virgin / May '89 / EMI.

Simply Red

LIFE
You make me believe / So many people / Lives and loves / Fairground / Never never love / So beautiful / Hillside Avenue / Remembering the first time / Out on the range / We're in this together
CD _____ 0630120692
East West / Oct '95 / Warner Music.

MEN AND WOMEN
Right thing / Infidelity / Suffer / I won't feel bad / Every time we say goodbye / Let me have it all / Love fire / Move on out / Shine / Maybe someday
CD _____ 2420712
WEA / Feb '95 / Warner Music.

NEW FLAME, A
It's only love / New flame / You've got it / To be with you / More / Turn it up / Love lays it's tune / She'll have to go / If you don't know me by now / Enough / I asked for water (10" and 12" only) / Woman (10" and 12" only) / Funk on out (instr./10")
CD _____ 244689 2
WEA / Feb '89 / Warner Music.

PICTURE BOOK
Come to my aid / Sad old red / Look at you now / Heaven / Jericho / Money's too tight to mention / Holding back the years / Open up the red box / No direction / Picture book
CD _____ 90331769932
East West / Mar '92 / Warner Music.

STARS
Something got me started / Stars / Thrill me / Your mirror / She's got it bad / For your babies / Model / How could I fall / Freedom / Wonderland
CD _____ 9031752842
East West / Oct '91 / Warner Music.

Simpson, Carole

ALL ABOUT CAROLE
You make me feel so young / Listen little girl / You forgot your gloves / Sure thing / Gentleman friend / Your name is love / Everytime / Oh look at me now / Time / I'll be around / There will never be another you / Just because we're kids
CD _____ JASCD 309
Jasmine / Jul '95 / Wellard / Swift / Conifer / Cadillac / Magnum Music Group.

Simpson, Martin

CLOSER WALK WITH THEE, A
Weary blues / Old rugged cross / Salutation march / Spinning wheel / Savoy blues / Moose march / If I had my life to live over / East coast trot / Just a closer walk with thee / Marie / Chimes blues / Wreck of ol' 97 / Does Jesus care / Dinah / Saratoga swing
CD _____ FLE 1007CD
Fledg'ling / Jul '94 / CM / ADA / Direct.

COLLECTION, THE
First cut is the deepest / Roving gambler / This war may last you for years / Masters of war / Reuben's train / Handsome Molly / Moonshine / Green linnet/Grinning in your face / Shawnee town / Moth / For Jessica, sad or high kicking / No depression in heaven / Stillness in company / Lakes of Ponchartrain / Doney girl / Essequibo river / Keel row
CD _____ SHCD 79089
Shanachie / Jun '94 / Koch / ADA / Greensleeves.

RED ROSES (Simpson, Martin & Jessica)
We were all the heroes / Dreamtime / Spare change / The gypsies / How I wanted to / Icarus / Company you keep / Mermaid / Seven sisters / Turtle and the sea / Gardeners child / Red roses
CD _____ RHYD 5001
Rhiannon / May '94 / Vital / Direct / ADA.

SMOKE AND MIRRORS
Poormouth / See that my grave is kept clean / Droke down engine / New kitchen blues / Hard love / I want my crown / Will this house be blessed / Delia / Lock, stock and barrel / Spoonful / Me and my chauffeur / Big road blues / Road kill / Gone fishing
CD _____ RHYD 5011
Rhiannon / Oct '95 / Vital / Direct / ADA.

SPECIAL AGENT
CD _____ FLED 3005
Fledg'ling / Nov '95 / CM / ADA / Direct.

Simpsons

SIMPSONS SING THE BLUES, THE
School day / Born under a bad sign / Moanin' Lisa blues / Deep deep trouble / God bless the child / I love to see you smile / Springfield soul stew / Look at all those idiots / Sibling rivalry / Do the Bartman
CD _____ GFLD 19201
Geffen / Mar '93 / BMG.

Sims, Frankie Lee

LUCY MAE BLUES
Lucy Mae blues / Don't take it out on me / Married woman / Wine and gin bounce / Boogie 'cross the country / Jelly roll baker / I'm so glad / Long gone / Raggedy and dirty / Yeh, baby / No good woman / Walking boogie / Frankie's blues / Crying won't help you / I done talked and I done talked / Lucy Mae blues (Part 2) / Rumba my boogie / I'll get along somehow / Hawk shuffle / Frankie Lee's 2 O' Clock jump
CD _____ CDCHD 423
Ace / Sep '92 / Pinnacle / Cadillac / Complete/Pinnacle.

Sims, Joyce

COME INTO MY LIFE
Come into my life / Love makes a woman / It wasn't easy / All and all / Lifetime love / Change in you / Walk away / All and all (the UK remix) / All and all (Megamix) (Track only on CD.)
CD _____ 828 077.2
London / Dec '87 / PolyGram.

Sims, Kym

TOO BLIND TO SEE IT
Too blind to see it / Take my advice / Little bit more / Take me to the groove / One look / I found love / Shoulda known better / In my eyes / Never shoulda let you go / I can't stop / Too blind to see it (soul mix)
CD _____ 7567921042
Atco / Apr '92 / Warner Music.

Sims, Willie

STORY TELLER
CD _____ NAR 113CD
SST / Nov '94 / Plastic Head.

Sims, Zoot

AT RONNIE SCOTTS '61 (Sims, Zoot Quartet)
CD _____ FSRCD 134
Fresh Sound / Dec '90 / Jazz Music / Discovery.

BIG STAMPEDE, THE
You're my girl / Purple cow / Ill wind / Big stampede / Too close for comfort / Jerry's jaunt / How now blues / Bye ya
CD _____ CDMT 017
Meteor / Aug '89 / Magnum Music Group.

BLUES FOR TWO (Sims, Zoot & Joe Pass)
Blues for two / Dindi / Remember / Poor butterfly / Black and blue / Pennies from Heaven / I hadn't anyone till you / Take off
CD _____ OJCCD 635-2
Original Jazz Classics / Feb '92 / Wellard / Jazz Music / Cadillac / Complete/Pinnacle.

BOHEMIA AFTER DARK
Jazz Hour / May '94 / Target/BMG / Jazz Music / Cadillac.
CD _____ JHR 73578

FOR LADY DAY
Easy living / That old devil called love / Some other Spring / I cover the waterfront / You go to my head / I cried for you / Body and soul / Travelin' light / You're my man / No more / My man (mon homme)
CD _____ CD 2310942
Pablo / Jan '94 / Jazz Music / Cadillac / Complete/Pinnacle.

HAPPY OVER HOAGY (Sims, Zoot & Al Cohn Septet)
CD _____ JASSCD 5
Jass / '88 / CM / Jazz Music / ADA / Cadillac / Direct.

HOAGY & COLE (Sims, Zoot & Al Cohn)
CD _____ JCD 5
Jass / Sep '87 / CM / Jazz Music / ADA / Cadillac / Direct.

I HEAR A RHAPSODY
CD _____ ATJCD 5967
All That's Jazz / Aug '92 / THE / Jazz Music.

IF I'M LUCKY (Sims, Zoot & Jimmy Rowles)
Where our love has gone / Legs / If I'm lucky / Shadow waltz / You're my everything / It's all right with me / Gypsy sweetheart / I hear a rhapsody
CD _____ OJCCD 683
Original Jazz Classics / Nov '95 / Wellard / Jazz Music / Cadillac / Complete/Pinnacle.

IN COPENHAGEN
CD _____ STCD 8244
Storyville / May '95 / Jazz Music / Wellard / CM / Cadillac.

ON THE KORNER
CD _____ 2310953
Pablo / Nov '95 / Jazz Music / Cadillac / Complete/Pinnacle.

RARE DAWN SESSIONS
CD _____ BCD 131
Biograph / Oct '94 / Wellard / ADA / Hot Shot / Jazz Music / Cadillac / Direct.

SOMEBODY LOVES ME
Summerset / Honeysuckle rose / Summer thing / Somebody loves me / Gee baby / Ain't I good to you / Nirvana / (Back home again in) Indiana / Memories of you / Come rain or come shine / Up a lazy river / Send in the clowns / Airmail special / Ham hock blues / Ring dem bells
CD _____ DC 8514
Denon / '88 / Conifer.

SUDDENLY IT'S SPRING
Brahm's...I think / I can't get started (with you) / MacGuffie's blues / In the middle of a kiss / So long / Never let me go / Suddenly it's spring / Emaline
CD _____ OJCCD 742
Original Jazz Classics / May '93 / Wellard / Jazz Music / Cadillac / Complete/Pinnacle.

SUMMER THING A
CD _____ 15754
Laserlight / Aug '92 / Target/BMG.

TENORLY
Night and day / Slingin' hash / Tenorly / Zoot and Zoot / I understand / Don't worry 'bout me / Crystal / Toot's suite / Late Tiny Kahn / Call it anything / Once in a while / Great drums
CD _____ 74321134132
Vogue / Jul '93 / BMG.

TONITE'S MUSIC TODAY (Sims, Zoot & Bob Brookmeyer)
CD _____ BLCD 760907
Black Lion / Jun '88 / Jazz Music / Cadillac / Wellard / Koch.

ZOOT SIMS & THE GERSHWIN BROTHERS
Man I love / How long has this been going on / Lady be good / I've got a crush on you / I got rhythm / Embraceable you / 'S wonderful / Someone to watch over me / Isn't it a pity / Summertime
CD _____ OJCCD 444
Original Jazz Classics / Feb '93 / Wellard / Jazz Music / Cadillac / Complete/Pinnacle.

ZOOT SIMS AND BOB BROOKMEYER (Sims, Zoot & Bob Brookmeyer)
King / Lullaby of the leaves / I can't get started (with you) / Snake eyes / Morning fun / Whooeeeeee / Someone to watch over me / My old flame / Boxcars
CD _____ BLCD 760914
Black Lion / '88 / Jazz Music / Cadillac / Wellard / Koch.

ZOOT SIMS IN PARIS
CD _____ CDSW 8417
DRG / Jan '89 / New Note.

Sin E

SIN E
Freeze, bitches / Houmous of green lanes / Come and watch me / Estelle's peppers / Snows they melt the soonest / Barnsley abacus / Maid of Coolmore / Reels for Luke / Kama / Lust / Sh jigs
CD _____ RHYD 5006
Rhiannon / Nov '95 / Vital / Direct / ADA.

Sinatra, Frank

16 MOST REQUESTED SONGS
All or nothing at all / You'll never know / Saturday night is the loneliest night of the week / Dream / Put your dreams away / Day by day / Nancy with the laughing face / Oh what it seemed to be / Sology (part 1 and 2) / Five minutes more / Things we did last summer / Coffe song (they've got a awful lot of coffee in Brazil) / Time after time / Mam'selle / Fools rush in / Birth of the blues
CD _____ 4805132
Columbia / May '95 / Sony.

1949 LITE UP TIME SHOWS
CD _____ EBCD 21162
Flyright / Feb '94 / Hot Shot / Wellard / Jazz Music / CM.

20 CLASSIC TRACKS: FRANK SINATRA
Come fly with me / Around the world / French Foreign Legion / Moonlight in Vermont / Autumn in New York / Let's get away from it all / April in Paris / London by night / It's nice to go travellin' / Come dance with me / Something's gotta give / Just in time / Dancing in the dark / Too close for comfort / I could have danced all night / Saturday night is the loneliest night of the week / Cheek to cheek / Baubles, bangles and beads / Day in, day out
CD _____ CDMFP 50530
Music For Pleasure / Mar '92 / EMI.

AT THE MOVIES
From here to eternity / Three coins in the fountain / Young at heart / She's funny that way / Just one of those things / Someone to watch over me / Not as a stranger / Tender trap / Our town / Impatient years / Love and marriage / Look to your heart / Johnny Concho theme (Wait for me) / All the way / Chicago / Monique / They came to Cordura / High hopes / All my tomorrows
CD _____ CDP 7993742
Capitol / Apr '93 / EMI.

BEGIN THE BEGUINE
CD _____ MU 5043
Musketeer / Oct '92 / Koch.

BEST OF FRANK SINATRA
CD _____ DLCD 4007
Dixie Live / Mar '95 / Magnum Music Group.

CAPITOL COLLECTORS SERIES: FRANK SINATRA
I'm walking behind you / I've got the world on a string / From here to eternity / South of the border / Young at heart / Don't worry 'bout me / Three coins in the fountain / Melody of love / Learnin' the blues / Same old Saturday night / Love and marriage / Tender trap / How little it matters, how little we know / Hey jealous lover / Can I steal a little love / All the way / Chicago / Witchcraft / High hopes / Nice 'n' easy
CD _____ CZ 228
Capitol / Sep '89 / EMI.

CAPITOL YEARS: FRANK SINATRA
I've got the world on a string / Lean baby / I love you / Mouth of the border / From here to eternity / They can't take that away from me / I get a kick out of you / Young at heart / Three coins in the fountain / All of me / Taking a chance on love / Someone to watch over me / What is this thing called love / In the wee small hours of the morning / Learnin' the blues / Our town / Love and marriage / Tender trap / Weep they will / I thought about you / You make me feel so young / Memories of you / I've got you under my skin / Too marvellous for words / Don't like goodbyes / How little it matters, how little we know / Your sensational (Single version) / Hey jealous lover / Close to you / Stars fell on Alabama / I got plenty o' nuttin' / I wish I were in love again / Lady is a tramp / Night and day / Lonesome road / If I had you / Where are you / I'm a fool to want you / Witchcraft / Something wonderful happens in summer / All the way / Chicago / Let's get away from it all / Autumn in New York / Come fly with me / Everybody loves somebody / It's the same old dream / Put your dreams away / Here goes / Angel eyes / Guess I'll hang my tears out to dry / Ebb tide / Only the lonely / One for my baby / To love and be loved (Single version) / I couldn't care less / Song is you / Just in time / Saturday night is the loneliest night of the week / Come dance with me / French Foreign Legion / One I love (Belongs to someone else) / Here's that rainy day / High hopes / When no one cares / I'll never smile again / I've got a crush on you / Embraceable you / Nice 'n' easy / I can't believe that you're in love with me / French / Almost like being in love / I'll be seeing you / I gotta right to sing the blues
CD Set _____ C2 94317
Capitol / Nov '90 / EMI.

CHAIRMAN OF THE BORED (A Tribute To Frank Sinatra) (Various Artists)
CD _____ GROW 12122
Grass / Oct '93 / SRD.

CHRISTMAS SONGS
White Christmas / Silent night / Adeste fideles (O come all ye faithful) / Jingle bells / Have yourself a merrily little Christmas / Christmas dreaming (A little early this year) / It came upon the midnight clear / O little town of Bethlehem / Santa Claus is coming to town / Let it snow, let it snow, let it snow / Medley / Ave Maria / Winter wonderland / Lord's prayer
CD _____ 4782562
Columbia / Nov '95 / Sony.

CLASSIC YEARS VOLUME 2, THE
CD _____ CDSGP 0157
Prestige / Mar '95 / Total/BMG.

CLASSIC YEARS, THE
CD _____ CDSGP 091
Prestige / Nov '93 / Total/BMG.

CLOSE TO YOU
Close to you / P.S. I love you / Love locked out / Everything happens to me / It's easy to remember / Don't like goodbyes / With every breath I take / Blame it on my youth / It could happen to you / I've had my moments / I couldn't sleep a wink last night / End of a love affair / If it's the last thing I do / There's a flaw in my flute / Wait till you see her
CD _____ BU 19
Capitol / Mar '88 / EMI.

COLLECTION
CD _____ COL 051
Collection / Apr '95 / Target/BMG.

COME DANCE WITH ME
Come dance with me / Something's gotta give / Just in time / Dancing in the dark / Too close for comfort / I could have danced all night / Saturday night is the loneliest night of the week / Day in, day out / Cheek to cheek / Baubles, bangles and beads / Song is you / Last dance
CD _____ CDP 7484682
Capitol / Nov '92 / EMI.

COME FLY WITH ME
Come fly with me / Around the world / Isle of Capri / Moonlight in Vermont / Autumn in New York / On the road to Mandalay / Let's get away from it all / April in Paris / London by night / Brazil / Blue Hawaii / It's nice to go travellin'
CD _____ CDP 7484692
Capitol / Nov '92 / EMI.

COME SWING WITH ME
Day by day / Sentimental journey / Almost like being in love / Five minutes more / American beauty rose / Yes indeed / On the sunny side of the street / Don't take your love from me / That old black magic / Lover / Paper doll / I've heard that song before / I love you (CD only.) / Why should I cry over you (CD only.) / How could you do a thing like that to me (CD only.) / River stay 'way from my door (CD only.) / I gotta right to sing the blues (CD only.)
CD _____ CZ 391
Capitol / Mar '91 / EMI.

COMPLETE COLUMBIA RECORDINGS 1943-1952, THE (4CD Set)
Close to you / People will say we're in love / If you are but a dream / Saturday night (is the loneliest night of the week) / White Christmas / I fall in love too easily / Ol' man river / Stormy weather / Embraceable you / She's funny that way / My melancholy baby / Over the rainbow / If I loved you / Someone to watch over me / You go to my head / These foolish things (remind me of you) / House I live in / Nancy (with the laughing face) / Full moon and empty arms / Oh what it seemed to be / (I don't stand) A ghost of a chance / Why shouldn't I / Try a little tenderness / Begin the beguine / They say it's wonderful / That old black magic / How deep is the ocean (how blue is the sky) / Home on the range / Five minutes more / Things we did last summer / Among my souvenirs / September song / Blue skies / Guess I'll hang my tears out to dry / Lost in the stars / There's no business like show business / Time after time / Brooklyn bridge / Sweet Lorraine / Always / Mam'selle / Stella by starlight / My romance / If I had you / One for my baby (and one more for the road) / But beautiful / You're my girl / All of me / Night and day / S'posin' / Night we called it a day / Song is you / What'll I do / Music stopped / Fools rush in (where angels fear to tread) / I've got a crush on you / Body and soul / I'm glad there is you / Autumn in New York / Nature boy / Once in love with Amy / Some enchanted evening / Huckle-buck / Let's take an old fashioned walk / If I ever love again / Bye bye baby / Don't cry Joe (let her go, let her go, let her go) / That lucky old sun (just rolls around heaven all day) / Chattanoogie shoe shine boy / American beauty rose / Should I (reveal) / You do something to me / Lover / When you're smiling (the whole world smiles with you) / London by night / Meet me at the Copa / April in Paris / I guess I'll have to dream the rest / Never-
CD Set _____ C2 94317

theless / Am I loved / Hello, young lovers / We kiss in a shadow / I'm s fool to want you / Love me / Deep night / I could write a book / I hear a rhapsody / My girl / Birth of the blues / Azure-te (Paris blues) / Why try to change me now
CD Set _____ **C4K 64681**
Columbia / Nov '95 / Sony.

COMPLETE REPRISE STUDIO RECORDINGS, THE
CD _____ **9362460132**
Reprise / Jan '96 / Warner Music.

DORSEY YEARS, THE
CD _____ **CDCD 1133**
Charly / Mar '93 / Charly / THE / Cadillac.

DUETS
Lady is a tramp / What now my love / I've got a crush on you / Summer wind / Come rain or come shine / New York, New York / They can't take that away from me / You make me feel so young / I've one small hours of the morning / I've got the world on a string / Witchcraft / I've got you under my skin / All the way / One for my baby (and one more for the road)
CD _____ **CDEST 2218**
Capitol / Nov '93 / EMI.

DUETS II
For once in my life / Moonlight in Vermont / Foggy day / Come fly with me / Fly me to the moon / Embraceable you / House I live in / Luck be a lady / Bewitched, bothered and bewildered / Best it yet to come / How do you keep the music playing / Funny Val / When or where / My kind of town / Mack the knife / Christmas song
CD _____ **CDEST 2245**
Capitol / Nov '94 / EMI.

EARLY YEARS, THE
CD Set _____ **AVC 552**
Avid / Jan '96 / Avid/BMG / Koch.

ESSENTIAL COLLECTION
CD Set _____ **LECD 606**
Wisepack / Apr '95 / THE / Conifer.

FAMOUS CONCERTS, THE
CD _____ **15263**
Laserlight / Aug '91 / Target/BMG.

FOR YOU
CD _____ **3001042**
Scratch / Jul '95 / BMG.

FRANK SINATRA
CD _____ **CDCD 1063**
Charly / Mar '93 / Charly / THE / Cadillac.

FRANK SINATRA (2CD Set)
CD Set _____ **R2CD 4011**
Deja Vu / Jan '96 / THE.

FRANK SINATRA & BING CROSBY (Sinatra, Frank & Bing Crosby)
CD _____ **KLMCD 050**
Scratch / Nov '94 / BMG.

FRANK SINATRA COLLECTION, THE
Nice 'n' easy / Cheek to cheek / I'm gonna sit right down and write myself a letter / As time goes by / Witchcraft / I've got you under my skin / You make me feel so young / I can't get started with you) / I get a kick out of you / Chicago / Come fly with me / Lady is a tramp / Tender trap / My funny valentine / Night and day / You'd be so nice to come home to / Dancing in the dark / Let's get away from it all / Nice work if you can get it / One for my baby
CD _____ **CDEMTV 41**
EMI / Dec '87 / EMI.

FRANK SINATRA COLLECTOR'S EDITION
CD _____ **DVX 08032**
Deja Vu / Apr '95 / THE.

FRANK SINATRA ESSENTIALS
CD _____ **LECDD 606A**
Wisepack / Aug '95 / THE / Conifer.

FRANK SINATRA GOLD (2CD Set)
CD Set _____ **D2CD 4011**
Deja Vu / Jun '95 / THE.

FRANK SINATRA SINGS THE GREATS
Just one of those things / 'S Wonderful / On the sunny side of the street / Ol' man river / Somebody loves me / Music stopped
CD _____ **BSTCD 9102**
Best Compact Discs / May '92 / Complete/ Pinnacle.

FRANK SINATRA SINGS THE GREATS, VOL.2.
Swinging on a star / Lover come back to me / Girl that I marry / Come fly with me / I get a kick out of you / I've got you under my skin / Moonlight in Vermont / April in Paris / She's funny that way / Lady is a tramp / Willow weep for me / Just one of those things / Willow weep for me / Dancing in the dark / At long last love / All of me
CD _____ **BSTCD 9112**
Best Compact Discs / Apr '94 / Complete/ Pinnacle.

FRANK SINATRA SINGS THE SELECT COLE PORTER
I've got you under my skin / I concentrate on you / What is this thing called love / You

do something to me / At long last love / Anything goes / Night and day / Just one of those things / I get a kick out of you / You'd be so nice to come home to / I love Paris / From this moment on / C'est magnifique / It's all right with me / Mind if I make love to you / You're sensational
CD _____ **C2 96611**
Capitol / Aug '91 / EMI.

FRANK SINATRA SINGS THE SONGS OF SAMMY CAHN AND JULE STYNE
CD _____ **VJC 1045**
Vintage Jazz Classics / Feb '94 / Direct / ADA / CM / Cadillac.

FRANK SINATRA, DEAN MARTIN & SAMMY DAVIS JR. VOL.1 (Sinatra, Frank & Dean Martin/Sammy Davis Jr.)
CD _____ **JH 1033**
Jazz Hour / Oct '93 / Target/BMG / Jazz Music / Cadillac.

FRANK SINATRA, DEAN MARTIN & SAMMY DAVIS JR. VOL.2 (Sinatra, Frank & Dean Martin/Sammy Davis Jr.)
CD _____ **JH 1034**
Jazz Hour / Oct '93 / Target/BMG / Jazz Music / Cadillac.

GOLD COLLECTION, THE
CD _____ **D2CD11**
Recording Arts / Dec '92 / THE / Disc.

GOLDEN DAYS OF RADIO
CD _____ **PWKS 4225**
Carlton Home Entertainment / Nov '94 / Carlton Home Entertainment.

GOT THE WORLD ON A STRING
I've got the world on a string / Them there eyes / If I could be with you one hour to-night / Under a blanket of blue / Just you, just me / Let's fall in love / Hands across the table / You must have been a beautiful baby / Someone to watch over me / I'll string along with you / You swell / You took advantage of me / Where or when / This can't be love / Try a little tenderness / Platinum blues / I'm confessin' that I love you / Sometimes I'm happy / My funny valentine / That old black magic
CD _____ **CBSB 007**
Starburst / Jan '94 / Magnum Music Group.

GREAT FILMS AND SHOWS
Night and day / I wish I were in love again / I got plenty o' nuttin' / I guess I'll have to change my plan / Nice work if you can get it / I won't dance / You'd be so nice to come home to / I got it bad and that ain't good (CD only.) / From this moment on / Blue moon / September in the rain / It's only a paper moon / You do something to me / Taking a chance on love / Get happy / Just one of those things / I love Paris / Chicago / High hopes / I believe / Lady is a tramp / Let's do it (With Shirley MacLaine.) / C'est magnifique / Tender trap / Three coins in the fountain / Young at heart / Girl next door .They can't take that away from me / Someone to watch over me / Little girl blue / Like someone in love / Foggy day / I got plenty o' nuttin' / My funny valentine / Embraceable you / That old feeling / I've got a crush on you / Dream / September song / I'll see you again / As time goes by / There will never be another you / I'll remember April / Stormy weather / I can't get started (with you) / Around the world / Something's gotta give / Just in time / Dancing in the dark / Too close for comfort / I could have danced all night / Cheek to cheek / Song is you / Baubles, bangles and beads / Almost like being in love / Lover / On the sunny side of the street / That old black magic / I've heard that song before / You make me feel so young / Too marvellous for words / It happened in Monterey / I've got you under my skin / How about you / Pennies from Heaven / You're getting to be a habit with me / You ought to be in / I love Paris / Song is you / Love is here to stay / Old devil moon / Makin' whoopee / Anything goes / What is this thing called love / Glad to be unhappy / I get along without you very well / Dancing on the ceiling / Can't we be friends / All the way / To love and be loved / All my tomor-rows / I couldn't sleep a wink last night / Spring is here / One for my baby / Time after time / It's all right with me / It's the same old dream / Johnny Concho theme (wait for me) / Wait till you see her / Where are you / Lonely town / Where or when / I concentrate on you / Love and marriage
CD Set _____ **CDFS 1**
Capitol / Apr '89 / EMI.

GREATEST HITS, THE EARLY YEARS
If you are but a dream / Nancy (with the laughing face) / Girl that I marry / House I live in / Saturday night (is the loneliest night of the week) / Five minutes more / I have but one heart (O Marenariello) / Time after time / People will say we're in love
CD _____ **4625612**
Columbia / Dec '95 / Sony.

GREATEST HITS: FRANK SINATRA (The Early Years)
I've got a crush on you / If you are but a dream / Nancy with the laughing face / Girl that I marry / House that I live in / Dream / Saturday night is the loneliest night of the week / Five minutes more / Coffee song / Sunday, Monday or always / Put your dreams away

CD _____ **902128-2**
Carlton Home Entertainment / Jun '94 / Carlton Home Entertainment.

HELLO YOUNG LOVERS
Hello, young lovers / Farewell, farewell to love / Walking in the sunshine / Azure te / Mad about you / I concentrate on you / I dream of you (more than you dream I do) / We just couldn't say goodbye / I am loved / You do something to me / Music stopped / We kiss in a shadow / You're my girl / Sunday, Monday or always / Right girl for me / Almost like being in love / There but for you go I / Falling in love with you / How cute can you be / I only have eyes for you / That old black magic / That's how much I love you / Always / You'll never know
CD _____ **983335 2**
Pickwick/Sony Collector's Choice / Oct '93 / Carlton Home Entertainment / Pinnacle / Sony.

HELLO YOUNG LOVERS
Netherless / What can I say after I say I'm sorry / Hello, young lovers / Love me or leave me / You toook advantage of me / Let's fall in love / Them there eyes / Some-body loves me / On the sunny side of the street / 'S Wonderful / Under a blanket of blue / I don't know why / Thou swell / I'm confessin' that I love you / Out of nowhere / Hundred years from today / Between the devil and the deep blue sea / What is this thing called love / Night and day / Just you, just me
CD _____ **MUCD 9025**
Start / Apr '95 / Koch.

HIT PARADE SHOWS MAY 1949
CD _____ **JH 1036**
Jazz Hour / Aug '94 / Target/BMG / Jazz Music / Cadillac.

HOUSE I LIVE IN, THE (1943-46)
CD _____ **VJC 1007-2**
Victorious Discs / Aug '90 / Jazz Music.

I GET A KICK OUT OF YOU
CD _____ **ENTCD 231**
Entertainers / Mar '92 / Target/BMG.

I'LL BE SEEING YOU (Sinatra, Frank & Tommy Dorsey)
I'll be seeing you / Fools rush in (where an-gels fear to tread) / It's a lovely day today / Tomorrow / World is in my arms / We three (my echo, my shadow and me) / Dolores / Everything happens to me / Let's get away from it all / Blue skies / There are such things / Daybreak / You're part of my heart
CD _____ **0786366427-2**
Bluebird / Oct '94 / BMG.

I'VE GOT YOU UNDER MY SKIN
CD _____ **ENTCD 229**
Entertainers / '88 / Target/BMG.

IN CELEBRATION
CD _____ **EXC 101**
Exclusive / Nov '95 / Target/BMG.

IN THE WEE SMALL HOURS
In the wee small hours of the morning / Glad to be unhappy / I get along without you very well / Deep in a dream / I see your face before me / Can't we be friends / When your lover has gone / What is this thing called love / I'll be around / Ill wind / It never entered my mind / I'll never be the same / This love of mine / Last night when we were young / Dancing on the ceiling
CD _____ **CDP 7968262**
Capitol / Nov '92 / EMI.

KID FROM HOBOKEN
CD Set _____ **CDDIG 6**
Charly / Feb '95 / Charly / THE / Cadillac.

LEGENDS IN MUSIC - FRANK SINATRA
CD _____ **LECD 055**
Wisepack / Jul '94 / THE / Conifer.

LIGHT UP TIME - 1949
CD _____ **JRR 1492**
JR / Jul '92 / THE.

LIVE DUETS 1943-57
CD _____ **VCD 1101**
Voice / Jun '94 / Direct.

LIVE IN CONCERT
You are the sunshine of my life / What now my love / My heart stood still / What's new / For once in my life / If / In the still of the night / Soliloquy / Maybe this time / Where or when / You will be my music / Strangers in the night / Angel eyes / New York, New York / My way
CD _____ **CDEST 2272**
Premier / Dec '95 / EMI.

LIVE: FRANK SINATRA (Seattle, June 9, 1957)
CD _____ **JH 3001**
Jazz Hour / Jun '95 / Target/BMG / Jazz Music / Cadillac.

LONDON 1 JUNE 1962
CD _____ **JRR 1622**
JR / Apr '94 / THE.

MELBOURNE 19 JANUARY 1955
CD _____ **JRR 155-2**
JR / Nov '93 / THE.

MONTE CARLO 14 JUNE 1958
CD _____ **JRR 1582**
JR / Jul '92 / THE.

NEW YORK, NEW YORK (His Greatest Hits)
I get a kick out of you / Something stupid / Moon river / What now my love / Summer wind / Mrs. Robinson / My way / Strangers in the night / For once in my life / Yesterday / That's life / Girl from Ipanema / Lady is a tramp / Bad, Bad Leroy Brown / Ol' man river
CD _____ **923927 2**
WEA / '87 / Warner Music.

NIGHT & DAY
Remember / Nov '93 / Total/BMG.
CD _____ **RMB 75020**
CD _____ **LOK 01CD**
Night & Day / Jan '94 / Direct / ADA.

NIGHT AND DAY
Oh what a beautiful morning / If you please / Saturday night is the loneliest night of the week / Sunshine of your smile / East of the sun and west of the moon / Delores / I guess I'll have to dream the rest / Blue skies / I'll never smile again / Whispering / Take me / Be careful it's my heart / Without a song / This love of mine / Lamplighter's ser-enade / Night and day / If you are but a dream / Kiss me again / There's no you / I dream of you / I begged her / I fall in love too easily / Embraceable you / When your love has gone
CD _____ **CDHD 263**
Happy Days / Jun '95 / Conifer.

OLD GOLD SHOWS 1946
CD _____ **JH 1040**
Jazz Hour / Feb '95 / Target/BMG / Jazz Music / Cadillac.

POINT OF NO RETURN
When the world was young / I'll remember April / September song / Million dreams ago / I'll see you again / There will never be an-other you / Somewhere along the way / It's a blue world / These foolish things / As time goes by / I'll be seeing you / Memories of you
CD _____ **CDP 7483342**
Capitol / Nov '92 / EMI.

RADIO RARITIES 1943-49
CD _____ **VJC 1030-1**
Vintage Jazz Classics / '91 / Direct / ADA / CM / Cadillac.

RADIO YEARS
CD _____ **CDSR 017**
Telstar / Jun '93 / BMG.

RADIO YEARS 1939-1955, THE (6CD Set)
All or nothing / After all / I've got my eyes on you / Polka dots and moonbeams / Deep night / Whispering / Sky fell down / On the isle of May / It's a blue world / Fable of the rose / Marie / I'll get by / Lover is blue / Careless / I'll never smile again / Our love affair / East of the sun and west of the moon / One I love / Shadow on the sand / That's how it goes / I get a kick out of you / Let's get lost / Embraceable you / Night and day / Close to you / I couldn't sleep a wink last night / Falling in love with you / Music stopped / My ideal / Speak low / People will say we're in love / Long ago and far away / Sweet Lorraine / Swinging on a star / These foolish things / Very thought of you / All the things you are / My melancholy baby / Homesick / That's all / Till the end of time / What makes the sunset / I fall in love too easily / I begged her / Don't forget tonight tomorrow / That's for me / I found a new baby / I'm always chasing rainbows / Aren't you glad you're you / It might as well be spring / Lily belle / If I loved you / Slowly / Great day / I only have eyes for you / Oh what it seemed to be / Full moon and empty arms / Exactly like you / Summertime/it ain't neccessarily so / Bess, oh where's my bess / I fall in love with you every day / It's a good day / My sugar is so refined / Ole buttermilk sky / Lullaby of broadway / I won't dance
CD Set _____ **CDMT 901**
Meteor / Aug '95 / Magnum Music Group.

REHEARSALS AND BROADCASTS (1942-46)
CD _____ **VJC 1004-2**
Victorious Discs / Aug '90 / Jazz Music.

REPRISE YEARS COLLECTION, THE
I'm getting sentimental over you / Without a song / I get a kick out of you / Night and day / Come rain or come shine / All or noth-ing at all / Nightingale sang in Berkeley Square / All alone / I won't dance / Ol' man river / I've got you under my skin / In the wee small hours of the morning / Nancy / Way you look tonight / Fly me to the moon / All the way / Luck be a lady / I only miss her when I think of her / September of my years / This is all I ask / It was a very good year / Strangers in the night / Call me irre-sponsible / Moon love / Don't worry / One for my baby / My kind of town / Poor butter-fly / How insensitive / Dindi / By the time I get to Phoenix / Didn't we / Some-thing stupid / Love's been good to me / Man alone / Goin' out of my head / Some-thing / Train / Lady Day / Drinking angels / Send in the clowns / Let me try again / What are you doing the rest of your life / If / Put your dreams away / In the still of the night / Granada
CD Set _____ **7599265012**
Reprise / Feb '91 / Warner Music.

REPRISE YEARS, THE

All the way / Come rain or come shine / I get a kick out of you / Night and day / All or nothing at all / I've got you under my skin / Didn't we / Strangers in the night / It was a very good year / Call me irresponsible / One for my baby / My kind of town / September of my years / Luck be a lady / Something stupid / New York, New York / My way

CD _____ 759926522-2
Reprise / Dec '93 / Warner Music.

SALUTE TO SINATRA (Various Artists)

I'll never smile again / Night and day / All or nothing at all / Lovely way to spend an evening / Dream / Stella by starlight / Some enchanted evening / Learnin' the blues / Three coins in the fountain / Love and marriage / Tender trap / All the way / Lady is a tramp / Just one of those things / It's nice to go trav'ling / Me and my shadow / Strangers in the night / Somethin' stupid / My way / Send in the clowns

CD _____ 8440622
Eclipse / May '91 / PolyGram.

SCREEN SINATRA

From here to eternity / Three coins in the fountain / Young at heart / Just one of those things / Someone to watch over me / Not as a stranger / Tender trap / Wait for me (Johnny Concho theme) / All the way / Chicago / Monique-Song from Kings Go Forth / They came to Cordura / To love and be loved / High hopes / All my tomorrows / It's all right with me / C'est magnifique / Dream

CD _____ CDMFP 6052
Music For Pleasure / Mar '89 / EMI.

SINATRA (SOUNDTRACK) (Sountrack to the CBS mini-series.)

Where the blue of the night meets the gold of the day / Temptation / All or nothing at all / Shake down the stars / Without a song / Street of dreams / I'll be seeing you / I'll never smile again / Sing, sing, sing / Where or when / Stormy weather / Our love affair / I fall in love too easily / Hucklebuck / Fairy tale / Lover man / You go to my head / I'm a fool to want you / It was a very good year / Autumn in New York / It all depends on you / They can't take that away from me / Come fly with me / High hopes / One for my baby / You make me feel so young / That's life / All the way / New York, New York / My way

CD Set _____ 9362450912
WEA / Nov '92 / Warner Music.

SINATRA 80TH ALL THE BEST (2CD/MC Set)

Lean baby / I'm walking behind you / I've got the world on a string / From here to eternity / South of the border / Young at heart / Three coins in the fountain / Come fly with me / Someone to watch over me / Melody of love / Night and day / Learnin' the blues / Same old Saturday night / Love and marriage / Impatient years / (Love is) the tender trap / (How little it matters) How little we know / Johnny Concho theme (wait for me) / Lady is a tramp / Well did you evah / Hey jealous lover / I've got you under my skin / All the way / Chicago / Witchcraft / How are ya fixed for love / No one ever tells you / Time after time / In the wee small hours of the morning / You make me feel so young / I get a kick out of you / All my tomorrows / High hopes / What is this thing called love / Moon was yellow (and the night was young) / I love Paris / Blues in the night / Guess I'll hang my tears out to dry / Nice 'n' easy / Thye Christmas song

CD Set _____ GDFSTD 2
Premier / Dec '95 / EMI.

SINATRA ARCHIVES VOL. 2

CD _____ FAS 19402
JR / Jul '92 / THE.

SINATRA AT THE SANDS (Sinatra, Frank & Count Basie)

Come fly with me / I've got a crush on you (vocal only) / I've got you under my skin / Shadow of your smile / Street of dreams / One for my baby / You make me feel so young / All of me / September of my years / Get me to the church on time / It was a very good year / Don't worry 'bout me / Ma-kin' whoopee / Where or when / Angel eyes / My kind of town

CD _____ 9010192 2
Reprise / Nov '86 / Warner Music.

SINATRA CHRISTMAS ALBUM, THE

Jingle bells / Christmas song / Mistletoe and holly / I'll be home for Christmas / Have yourself a merry little Christmas / Christmas waltz / First Noel / Hark the herald angels sing / O little town of Bethlehem / O come all ye faithful (Adeste fidelis) / It came upon a midnight clear / Silent night / White Christmas (CD only) / Christmas waltz (alternate)

CD _____ CDMFP 5797
Music For Pleasure / Dec '94 / EMI.

SINATRA'S SWINGIN' SESSION

When you're smiling / Blue moon / S'posin' / It all depends on you / It's only a paper moon / My blue Heaven / Should I / September in the rain / Always / I can't believe that you're in love with me / I concentrate on you / You do something to me / Sentimental baby / Ol' MacDonald / Hidden persuasion

---

SINATRA: THE RADIO YEARS (1939-55)

All or nothing at all / After all / I've got my eyes on you / Polka dots and moonbeams / Deep night / Whispering / Sky fell down / On the isle of may / It's a blue world / Fable of the rose / Marie / Love is blue / Careless / I'll never smile again / Our love affair / East of the sun and west of the moon / One I love / Shadows on the sand / That's how it goes / I get a kick out of you / Let's get lost / Embraceable you / Night and day / Close to you / I couldn't sleep a wink last night / Falling in love with you / Music stopped / My ideal / Speak low / People will say we're in love / Long ago and far away / I'll get by / Sweet Lorraine / Swinging on a star / These foolish things / Very thought of you / All the things you are / My melancholy baby / Homesick that's all / Till the end of time / What makes the sunset / I fall in love too easily / I begged her / Don't forget tonight tomorrow / That's for me / I found a new baby / I'm always chasing rainbows / Aren't you glad you're you / It might as well be spring / Lily Belle / If I loved you / Slowly / Great day / I only have eyes for you / Oh,what it seemed to be / Full moon and empty arms / Exactly like you / I fall in love with you every day / It's a good day / My sugar is so refined / Ole buttermilk sky / Lullaby of broadway / I won't dance / Touch of your hand / Why was I born / All through the day / Make believe / Song is you / You can't see the sun when you're crying / Anniversary song / You do / Let it snow, let it snow, let it snow / I wish I didn't love you so / Wrap your troubles in dreams (and dream your troubles away) / Nature boy / My haunted heart / Little white lies / Tree in the meadow / It only happens when I dance with you / My happiness / O sole mio / It isn't fair / Body and soul / When you're smiling / I've got a crush on you / My foolish heart / Best things in life are free / I love you / Why remind me / Just you, just me / Somebody loves me / Sorry / Young at heart / Among my souvenirs / September song / As time goes by / Take a chance / Till we meet again / Meet me in dreamland / There's a long long trail / Don't blame me / 'S wonderful / It all depends on you / Somebody loves you / Nevertheless / On the sunny side of the street / Love me or leave me / Try a little tenderness / Out of nowhere / I've got my love to keep me warm / What can I say / Between the Devil and the deep blue sea / Hundred years from today / I'm in the mood for love / Tenderly / Hello, young lovers / She's funny that way / I don't know why / Come rain or come shine

CD Set _____ CDMTBS 001
Meteor / Mar '89 / Magnum Music Group.

SINGS THE SELECT JOHNNY MERCER

Too marvelous for words / Day in, day out / Laura / Jeepers creepers / Blues in the night / Something's gotta give / Fools rush in / P.S. I love you / When the world was young / That old black magic / Autumn leaves / I thought about you / Dream / One for my baby

CD _____ CDP 7803262
Capitol / Apr '95 / EMI.

SINGS THE SELECT RODGERS & HART

Lover / Glad to be unhappy / I didn't know what time it was / Where or when / It's easy to remember / There's a small hotel / Wait till you see her / Little girl blue / My funny valentine / It never entered my mind / Blue moon / I could write a book / Bandling on the ceiling / Lady is a tramp / Spring is here / I wish I was in love again / Bewitched, bothered and bewildered

CD _____ CDP 7803232
Capitol / Apr '95 / EMI.

SONG IS YOU, THE (Sinatra, Frank & Tommy Dorsey)

Sky fell down / Too romantic / Shake down the stars / Moments in the moonlight / I'll be seeing you / Say it / Polka dots and moonbeams / Fable of the rose / This is the beginning of the end / Hear my song Violetta / Fools rush in (where angels fear to tread) / Devil may care / April played the fiddle / I haven't time to be a millionaire / Imagination / Yours is my heart alone / You're lonely and I'm lonely / East of the sun and west of the moon / Head on my pillow / It's a lovely day tomorrow / I'll never smile again / All this and heaven too / Where do you keep your heart / Whispering / Trade winds / One I love (belongs to somebody else) / Call of the canyon / Love lies / I could make you care / I fall in love with my arms / Our love affair / Looking for yesterday / Tell me at midnight / We three (my echo, my shadow and me) / When you awake / Anything / Shadows on the sand / You're breaking my heart all over again / I'd know you anywhere / Do you know why / Long ago / Stardust / Oh look at me now / You might have belonged to another / You lucky people you / It's always you / I tried / Dolores / Without a song / Do I worry / Everything happens to me / Let's get away from it all / I'll never let a day pass me by / Love me as I am / This love of mine / I guess I'll have to dream the rest / You and I / Neiani / Free for all / Blue skies / Two in love / Pale moon / I think of you / How do you do

---

without me / Sinner kissed an angel / Violets for your furs / Sunshine of your smile / How about you / Snootie little cutie / Poor you / I'll take Tallulah / Last call for love / Somewhere a voice is calling / Just as though you were here / Street of dreams / There'll be careful it's my heart / In the blue of evening / Dig down deep / There are such things / Daybreak / It started all over again / Light a candle in the chapel / Too romantic (2) / Shake down the stars (2) / Hear my song Violetta (2) / You're lonely and I'm lonely (2) / Our love affair (2) / Violets for your fur (2) / Night we called it a day / Lamplighter's serenade / Song is you / Night and day / I'm getting sentimental over you / Who / I hear a rhapsody / I'll never smile again (2) / Half way down the street / Some of your sweetness (got into my heart) / Once in a while / Little love / It came to me / Only forever / Marie / Yearning / How am I to know / You're part of my heart / Announcements / You're stepping on my toes / You got the best of me / That's how it goes / When daylight dawns / When sleepy stars begin to fall / Goodbye lover, goodbye / One red rose / Things I love / In the blue of evening (2) / Just as though you were here (2) / Frank Sinatra's farewell to the Tommy Dorsey Orchestra / Song is you (2)

CD Set _____ 0786366353-2
Bluebird / Oct '94 / BMG.

SONGS FOR SWINGIN' LOVERS

Too marvellous for words / Old devil moon / Pennies from Heaven / Love is here to stay / I've got you under my skin / I thought about you / We'll be together again / Makin' whoopee / Swingin' down the lane / Any thing goes / How about you / You make me feel so young / It happened in Monterey / You're getting to be a habit with me / You brought a new kind of love to me

CD _____ BU 17
Capitol / Mar '88 / EMI.

SONGS FOR YOUNG LOVERS & SWING EASY

CD _____ CDP 7484702
Capitol / Nov '92 / EMI.

SPOTLIGHT ON FRANK SINATRA

I wonder who's kissing her now / I'll string along with you / Devil and the deep blue sea / Speak low / Mimi / At long last love / Lover is blue / Day by day / Five more minutes / After I say I'm sorry / Serenade of the bells / Long ago and far away / I wish I didn't love you so / You're the top / It's all up to you / Some other time

CD _____ HADCD 131
Javelin / Feb '94 / THE / Henry Hadaway Organisation.

SUNDAY MORNING OR ALWAYS

CD _____ CPCD 8157
Charly / Nov '95 / Charly / THE / Cadillac.

SWING EASY

Jeepers creepers / Taking a chance on love / Wrap your troubles in dreams (and dream your troubles away) / Lean baby / I love you / I'm gonna sit right down and write myself a letter / Get happy / All of me / How could you do a thing like that to me / Why should I cry over you / Sunday / Just one of those things

CD _____ CDMFP 5973
Music For Pleasure / Oct '92 / EMI.

SWINGIN' AFFAIR, A

Night and day / I wish I were in love again / I got plenty o' nuttin' / I guess I'll have to change my plan / Nice work if you can get it / Stars fell on Alabama / No one ever tells you / I won't dance / Lonesome road / At long last love / You'd be so nice to come home to / I got it bad and that ain't good / From this moment on / If I had you / Oh, look at me now

CD _____ CZ 393
Capitol / Mar '91 / EMI.

THAT'S LIFE

CD _____ 9010202 2
Reprise / Oct '86 / Warner Music.

THERE ARE SUCH THINGS (Sinatra, Frank & Tommy Dorsey)

Blue skies / Call of the canyon / Daybreak / East of the sun and west of the moon / Everything happens to me / Fools rush in / Hear my song Violetta / How about you / I'll never smile again / Imagination / Let's get away from it all / One I love (belongs to somebody else) / Polka dots and moonbeams / Sinner kissed an angel / Somewhere a voice is calling / Stardust / There are such things / This love of mine / Too romantic / Violets for your furs / Whispering / Without a song / Yours is my heart alone

CD _____ CDAJA 5106
Living Era / Apr '93 / Koch.

THERE'LL BE SOME CHANGES MADE

CD _____ VCD 1102
Voice / Jun '94 / Direct.

THIS IS FRANK SINATRA 1953-1957

I've got the world on a string / Three coins in the fountain / Love and marriage / From here to eternity / South of the border / Rain / Gal that got away / Young at heart / Learnin' the blues / My one and only love / Tender trap / Don't worry 'bout me / Look to your heart / Anytime anywhere / Not as a stranger / Our town / You, my love / Same

---

old Saturday night / Fairy tale / Impatient years / I could have told you / When I stop loving you / If I had three wishes / I'm gonna live till I die / Hey jealous lover / Everybody loves somebody / Something wonderful happens in summer / Half as lovely / You're cheating' yourself (if you're cheatin' on you) / You'll always be the one I love / You forgot all the words / How little it matters, how little we know / Time after time / Crazy love / Johnny Concho theme (wait for me) / If you are but a dream / So long, my love / It's the same old dream / I believe / Put your dreams away

CD Set _____ CDDL 1275
EMI / Nov '94 / EMI.

THIS LOVE OF MINE

CD _____ CDMOIR 511
Memoir / Sep '95 / Target/BMG.

THIS ONE'S FOR TOMMY

CD _____ VCD 1103
Viper's Nest / May '95 / Direct / Cadillac / ADA.

TIME AFTER TIME

Time after time / Our love / All or nothing at all / On a little street in Singapore / East of the sun / I'll never smile again / Everything happens to me / This love of mine / There are such things / Just as though you were there / People will say we're in love / Lovely way to spend an evening / I couldn't sleep a wink last night / Night and day / White Christmas / You'll never know / Long ago (and far away) / Guess I'll hang my tears out to dry / Saturday night / I'll walk alone / Exactly like you / I fall in love too easily / Body and soul / You'll be so nice to come home (you're in love with me / Day by day

CD _____ CECD 1
Collector's Edition / Oct '95 / Magnum Music Group.

TWENTY GOLDEN GREATS

That old black magic / Love and marriage / Fools rush in / Lady is a tramp / Swingin' down the lane / All the way / Witchcraft / It happened in Monterey / You make me feel so young / Nice 'n' easy / Come fly with me / High hopes / Let's do it (let's fall in love) / I've got you under my skin / Chicago / Three coins in the fountain / It's nice to go trav'ling / Young at heart / In the wee small hours of the morning / Tender trap

CD _____ CDEMTV 10
Capitol / May '92 / EMI.

UNHEARD FRANK SINATRA VOL. 4 - I'LL BE SEEING YOU

CD _____ VJCD 1051
Vintage Jazz Classics / Feb '94 / Direct / ADA / CM / Cadillac.

V DISCS - THE COLUMBIA YEARS, THE (1943-52) (2CD Set)

I only have eyes for you / Kiss me again / (There's gonna be a) Hot time in the town of Berlin / Music stopped / I couldn't sleep a wink last night / Way you look tonight / I'll be around / You've got a hold on me / Lovely way to spend an evening / She's funny that way / Speak low / Close to you / My shining hour / Long ago and far away / Some other time / Come out come out wherever you are / Put your dreams away / And then you kissed me / All the things you are / All of me / Nancy with the laughing face / Mighty lak' a rose / Falling in love without a song / Was the last time I saw you (the last time) / Don't forget tonight tomorrow / Oh - What it seemed to be / Over the rainbow / Where is my Bess / My romance / Song is you / That's all wonderful / You are too beautiful / Come rain or come shine / Stormy weather

CD Set _____ C2K 66135
Legacy / Oct '94 / Sony.

WASHINGTON DC APRIL 1973

CD _____ JRR 173-2
JR / Oct '94 / THE.

WHERE ARE YOU?

Where are you / Night we called it a day / I cover the waterfront / Maybe you'll be there / Laura / Lonely town / Autumn leaves / I'm a fool to want you / I think of you / Where is the one / There's no you / Baby, won't you please come home / I can read between the lines (CD only.) / It worries me (CD only.) / Rain (CD only) / Don't worry 'bout me (CD only)

CD _____ CZ 390
Capitol / Mar '91 / EMI.

YOU MAKE ME FEEL SO GOOD

CD _____ AVC 505
Avid / Dec '92 / Avid/BMG / Koch.

YOU MAKE ME FEEL SO YOUNG

Night and day / Laura / Somebody loves me / Little white lies / This can't be love / You make me feel so young / Speak low / You

do something to me / Begin the beguine /
Tenderly / On the sunny side of the street /
Love me or leave me / They didn't believe
me / Out of nowhere / I've got my love to
keep me warm / For you
CD _____ ENTCD 213
Entertainers / '88 / Target/BMG.

YOU MAKE ME FEEL SO YOUNG
You make me feel so young / 'S wonderful
/ Love me or leave me / On the sunny side
of the street / Blue skies / They say it's
wonderful / Begin the beguine / Ol' man
river / Don't blame me / It all depends on
you / I fall in love with you / Music stopped
/ I don't stand a ghost of a chance with you
/ You do something to me / Night and day
/ Somebody loves me / Just one of those
things / Nevertheless / You are love / They
did not believe me / Out of nowhere / I've
got my love to keep me warm / For you
CD _____ CDGRF 136
Tring / '93 / Tring / Prism.

YOUNG BLUE EYES
CD _____ CDGR 107
Charly / Jan '96 / Charly / THE / Cadillac.

YOUR HIT PARADE 1947
CD _____ JRR 1472
JR / Jul '92 / THE.

YOUR HIT PARADE 1948
CD _____ JRR 1482
JR / Jul '92 / THE.

YOUR HIT PARADE 1949
CD _____ JRR 2492
JR / Apr '94 / THE.

Sinatra, Nancy

GREATEST HITS
CD _____ PA 7112
Paradiso / Apr '94 / Target/BMG.

**GREATEST HITS: NANCY SINATRA
(Featuring Frank Sinatra & Lee
Hazlewood)**
Storybook children / These boots are made
for walking / Sugar town / Something stupid
/ How does that grab you, darlin' / Summer
wine / Sundown sundown / I've been down
so long / Sand / Oh lonesome me / Lady-
bird / Jackson / You've lost that lovin' feelin'
/ Some velvet morning / Did you ever / Elu-
sive dreams / Greenwich village folksong
man / So long, babe
CD _____ PLATCD 3903
Platinum Music / Oct '88 / Prism / Ross.

VERY BEST OF NANCY SINATRA, THE
CD _____ ANUECD 1
Boulevard / Nov '95 / Total/BMG.

Sinclair, Dave

MOON OVER MOON
Wanderlust / Tropical island / Mallorcan
dance / Make yourself at home / Harry /
Where have I gone / Make a brand new
start / Moving on / Lost in the woods / Re-
miniscermemoring / Honky dorry / Piano
player / Back for tea / Here to stay
CD _____ VP 119CD
Voice Print / May '93 / Voice Print.

Sinclair, Richard

CARAVAN OF DREAMS
CD _____ HTDCD 7
HTD / Nov '92 / Pinnacle.

EVENING OF MAGIC, AN
CD _____ HIDCD 17
HTD / Jan '94 / Pinnacle.

R.S.V.P.
CD _____ RSSCD 001
RRS / Jul '94 / Pinnacle.

Sincola

SINCOLA
CD _____ RR 123-2
Rise / Feb '94 / Pinnacle.

Sindelfingen

ODGIPIG
CD _____ HBG 122/10
Background / Apr '94 / Background.

Sinfield, Pete

STILLUSION
Can you forgive a fool / Night people / Will
it be you / Hanging fire / House of hopes
and dreams / Wholefood boogie / Piper /
Under the sky / Envelopes of yesterday /
Song of the sea goat / Still
CD _____ VP 152CD
Voice Print / Mar '94 / Voice Print.

Singabangqobi

GREATER IS HE
CD _____ FIFCD 1001
Friends In Fellowship / Oct '92 / Jetstar.

Singer, Hal

RENT PARTY
Cornbread / Teddy's dream / One for Willie
/ Neck bones / Rent party / Singer song /
Rice and red beans / Swing shift / Hot rod
/ Rock 'n' roll / Indian love call / Frog hop /

Hometown / Down for Dean / Easy living /
Hound's tooth / Mr. Movin's groovin' /
Crossroads
CD _____ SV 0258
Savoy Jazz / Nov '94 / Conifer / ADA.

Singers & Players

GOLDEN GREATS
CD _____ ONUCD 4
On-U Sound / Sep '89 / SRD / Jetstar.

GOLDEN GREATS VOL.2
CD _____ ONUCD 26
On-U Sound / Jul '93 / SRD / Jetstar.

LEAPS AND BOUNDS
CD _____ CDBRED 58
Cherry Red / Sep '91 / Pinnacle.

Singh, Kiran

RAGA SHREE
CD _____ DSAV 1026
Multitone / Dec '95 / BMG.

STRING OF ELEGANCE
CD _____ DSAV 1020
Multitone / Jun '95 / BMG.

Singh, Mangal

JAM TO THE BHANGRA VOL. 2
CD _____ DMUT 1263
Multitone / Jan '94 / BMG.

Singing Kettle

GREATEST HITS VOL.1
CD _____ KOP 27CD
Kettle / Aug '95 / Roots / CM / Ross /
Duncans.

Singing Sweet

DON'T SAY NO
CD _____ CFCD 2
Colin Fat / Apr '93 / Jetstar.

Single Cell Orchestra

DEAD VENT 7
CD _____ EFA 003182
Reflective / Jul '95 / SRD.

Single Gun Theory

EXORCISE THIS WASTELAND
CD _____ NTCD 039
Nettwerk / '88 / Vital / Pinnacle.

FLOW RIVER OF MY SOUL
CD _____ W 230088
Edel / May '95 / Pinnacle.

LIKE STARS IN MY HAND
CD _____ NETCD 020
Nettwerk / Nov '91 / Vital / Pinnacle.

Sinister

DIABOLICAL SUMMONING
CD _____ NB 081
Nuclear Blast / Aug '93 / Plastic Head.

HATE
CD _____ NB 131
Nuclear Blast / Jul '95 / Plastic Head.

Sinner

BOTTOM LINE
CD _____ 342612
No Bull / Oct '95 / Koch.

DANGEROUS CHARM
CD _____ N 0101 3
Noise/Modern Music / Nov '87 / Pinnacle /
Plastic Head.

NO MORE ALIBIS
CD _____ 9040082
Posh / Oct '92 / THE.

RESPECT
CD _____ 342702
No Bull / Dec '95 / Koch.

Sinners

TURN IT UP!
CD _____ MNWCD 213
MNW / Jan '92 / Vital / ADA.

Sinoath

STILL IN GREY DYING
CD _____ 1 STSINONCD
SPV / May '95 / Plastic Head.

Siouxsie & The Banshees

HYENA
Take me back / Running town / Pointing
bone / Blow the house down / Dazzle / We
hunger / Belladonna / Swimming horses /
Bring me the head of the preacher man
CD _____ 8215102
Wonderland / Mar '95 / PolyGram.

JOIN HANDS
Poppy day / Regal zone / Placebo effect /
Icon / Premature burial / Playground twist /
Mother / On mein papa / Lord's prayer
CD _____ 8390042
Wonderland / Mar '95 / PolyGram.

JU JU
Spellbound / Into the light / Arabian knights
/ Halloween / Monitor night shift / Sin in my
heart / Head cut / Voodoo dolly
CD _____ 8390052
Wonderland / Mar '95 / PolyGram.

KALEIDOSCOPE
Happy house / Tenant / Trophy / Hybrid /
Clockface / Lunar camel / Christine / Desert
kisses / Red light / Paradise place / Skin
CD _____ 8390062
Wonderland / Mar '95 / PolyGram.

KISS IN THE DREAMHOUSE, A
Cascade / Green fingers / Obsession /
She's a carnival / Circle / Melt / Painted bird
/ Cacoon / Slowdive
CD _____ 8390072
Wonderland / Mar '95 / PolyGram.

NOCTURNE
Intro (The rite of spring) / Israel / Dear Pru-
dence / Paradise place / Melt / Cascade /
Pulled to bits / Nightshift / Sin in my heart
/ Slowdive / Painted bird / Happy house /
Switch / Spellbound / Helter skelter / Eve
white, Eve black / Voodoo dolly
CD _____ 8390092
Wonderland / Mar '95 / PolyGram.

ONCE UPON A TIME 'THE SINGLES'
Hong Kong garden / Mirage / Staircase
(mystery) / Playground twist / Happy house
/ Christine / Israel / Spellbound / Arabian
knights / Fire works
CD _____ 8315422
Wonderland / May '89 / PolyGram.

PEEP SHOW
Peek-a-boo / Killing jar / Scarecrow / Car-
ousel / Burn-up / Ornaments of gold / Turn
to stone / Rawhead and bloody bones /
Last beat of my heart / Rhapsody
CD _____ 8372402
Wonderland / Mar '95 / PolyGram.

RAPTURE, THE
O Baby / Tearing apart / Stargazers / Fall
from grace / Not forgotten / Sick child /
Lonely one / Falling down / Forever / Rap-
ture / Double life / Love out me
CD _____ 523725-2
Wonderland / Oct '94 / PolyGram.

SCREAM, THE
Pure / Jigsaw feeling / Overground / Car-
cass / Helter skelter / Mirage / Metal post-
card / Nicotine stain / Surburban relapse /
Switch
CD _____ 8390082
Wonderland / Mar '95 / PolyGram.

SUPERSTITION
Kiss them for me / Fear (Of the unknown) /
Cry / Drifter / Little sister / Shadowtime /
Silly thing / Got to get up / Silver waterfalls
/ Softly / Ghost in you
CD _____ 8477312
Wonderland / Mar '95 / PolyGram.

THROUGH THE LOOKING GLASS
Hall of mirrors / Trust in me / This wheel's
on fire / Strange fruit / This town ain't big
enough for the both of us / You're lost little
girl / Passenger / Gun / Little Johnny Jewel
CD _____ 8314742
Wonderland / Mar '95 / PolyGram.

TINDERBOX
Candy man / Sweetest chill / This unrest /
Cities in dust / Cannons / Party's fall / 92 /
Land's end / Quarterdrawing of the dog /
Execution / Lullaby / Umbrella / Cities in
dust (Extended version)
CD _____ 8291452
Wonderland / Mar '95 / PolyGram.

TWICE UPON A TIME
CD _____ 5171602
Wonderland / Mar '95 / PolyGram.

Sipahi, Nesrin

**SHARKI LOVE SONGS FROM ISTANBUL
(Sipahi, Nesrin & The Kudsi Erguner
Ensemble)**
CD _____ CMP CD 3009
CMP / Jul '92 / Vital/SAM.

Siperkov

GIPSY MUSIC
CD _____ SYNCD 163
Syncoop / Jun '94 / ADA / Direct.

Sir Douglas Quintet

COLLECTION
CD _____ COL 060
Collection / Mar '95 / Target/BMG.

Sir Lancelot

LEGENDARY SIR LANCELOT, THE
CD _____ LYRCD 7406
Lyrichord / '91 / Roots / ADA / CM.

TRINIDAD IS CHANGING (1940's/1950's)
Century of the common man / Trinidad is
changing / Donkey City / Neighbour neigh-
bour leave me door / Night in Central Park
/ Ugly woman / Scandal in the family /
Young girls today / Oken karange / Sweet
like a honey bee / Pan American way /
Gimme crab and callaloo / Mary Ann / Take
me take me (to San Pedro) / Matilda Matilda
/ West Indian families

CD _____ FLYCD 942
Flyright / May '95 / Hot Shot / Wellard /
Jazz Music / CM.

Sir Mix-a-Lot

CHIEF BOOT KNOCKA
Sleepin' with my fonk / Take my stash /
Double my stash / Don't call me Da Da /
Just da pimpin' in me / Let it beaounce /
Brown shuga / Put 'em on the glass / Nast
dog / I checks my bank / Ride / What's real
/ Chief boot knocka / Monsta' mack
CD _____ 74321 243422
American / Aug '95 / BMG.

MACK DADDY
One time's got no case / Mack Daddy /
Baby got back / Swap meet lovie / Seattle
ain't bullshit / Lock jaw / Boss is back / Tes-
tarossa / Rapper's reputation / Spring on
the cat / Jack back / I'm your new God /
No holds barred
CD _____ 74321248472
American / Jun '95 / BMG.

SEMINAR
Seminar / Beepers / National anthem / My
hooptie / Goretex / (peek-a-boo) Game / I
got game / I'll roll you up / Something about
my benzo / My bad side
CD _____ 74321248462
American / Jun '95 / BMG.

SWASS
Buttermilk biscuits (keep on square dancin')
/ Posse on Broadway / Gold / Swass / Rip-
pin' / Attack on the stars / Mail dropper /
Hip hop solider / Iron man / Bremelo /
Square dance rap / Romantic interlude / F
the b's
CD _____ 74321248452
American / Jun '95 / BMG.

Sircle Of Silence

SUICIDE CANDYMAN
CD _____ 342142
No Bull / Dec '95 / Koch.

Siren

SIREN
CD _____ REP 4202-WP
Repertoire / Aug '91 / Pinnacle / Cadillac.

**STRANGE LOCOMOTION (Siren & Kevin
Coyne)**
CD _____ REP 4083-WP
Repertoire / Aug '91 / Pinnacle / Cadillac.

STRANGE LOCOMOTION & SIREN
Ze-ze-ze-ze / Get right church / Wake up
my children / Wasting my time / Sixteen
women / First time I saw your face / Gar-
dener man / And I wonder / Asylum / Bertha
Lee / I wonder where / Relaxing with Bonnie
Lou / Some dark day / Hot potato / Soon /
Gigolo / I'm all aching / Strange locomotion
/ Shake my hand / Lonesome ride / Fat
moaning minnie / Squeeze me
CD _____ SEECD 014
See For Miles/C5 / Oct '94 / Pinnacle.

Siren

LET'S DO IT
CD _____ DJC 002CD
Blueprint / Oct '95 / Pinnacle.

Sirtos Ensemble

FOLK MUSIC OF GREECE
CD _____ HMP 3903060
HM Plus/Quintana / Oct '94 / Harmonia
Mundi.

Sista

**4 ALL THE SISTAS AROUND THE
WORLD**
CD _____ 755961653-2
East West / Aug '94 / Warner Music.

Sister Aaron

PURIFICATION
CD _____ E 11399-2
Musical Tragedies / Dec '93 / SRD.

Sister Audrey

POPULATE
CD _____ ARICD 070
Ariwa Sounds / Nov '91 / Jetstar / SRD.

Sister Carol

BLACK CINDERELLA
CD _____ CDHB 173
Heartbeat / Dec '95 / Greensleeves /
Jetstar / Direct / ADA.

CALL MI SISTER CAROL
CD _____ HBCD 93
Heartbeat / Nov '94 / Greensleeves /
Jetstar / Direct / ADA.

Sister Double Happiness

HORSEY WATER
CD _____ SPCD 137337
Sub Pop / Nov '94 / Disc.

SISTER DOUBLE HAPPINESS
CD _____ SST 162 CD
SST / May '93 / Plastic Head.

UNCUT
San Diego / Will you come / Ashes / Whipping song / Doesn't make sense / Honey don't / Keep the city clean / Do what you gotta do / Where do we run / No good for you / Lightnin' / Louise
CD _____ SPCD 105277
Sub Pop / Jul '93 / Disc.

Sister George

DRAG KING
Sister George / Let's breed / Janey's block / Roccoco subversive / Handlebar / Krap / Virus envy / 100 times no
CD _____ PUSS 003CD
Catcall / Feb '94 / Vital.

Sister Grant

DOWN AT CROSS (Sister Grant & The Gospelettes)
CD _____ KGC 107
Kangaroo / Apr '94 / ADA.

HARBOUR IN JESUS (Sister Grant & The Gospelairs)
CD _____ KGC 104
Kangaroo / Apr '94 / ADA.

Sister Psychic

SURRENDER, YOU FREAK
Surrender you freak / Part of love / Velvet dug / I can't breathe / Happiness / Kim the waitress / Little bird / Death by fascination / Sleepwalking / Clapper (wish I was blind) / Blue river / Eddie Mars / On the floor
CD _____ 72744-2
Restless / Mar '94 / Vital.

Sister Sledge

ALL AMERICAN GIRLS
All American girls / He's just a runaway / If you really want me / Next time you'll know / Happy feeling / Ooh you caught my heart / Make a move / Don't you let me lose it / Music makes me feel good / I don't want to say goodbye
CD _____ 8122719142
Rhino / May '95 / Warner Music.

AND NOW...SISTER SLEDGE...AGAIN
CD _____ FMDX 190
FM / Mar '93 / Sony.

GREATEST HITS LIVE
Everybody dance / Thinking of you / He's the greatest dancer / True love / Frankie / Brother, brother, stop / Love of the Lord / We are family / Lost in music/Melody is good to me / Everybody dance/We are family/Frankie/Thinking of you
CD _____ MDCD 10
Music De-Luxe / Jun '95 / Magnum Music Group.

HITS OF SISTER SLEDGE
CD _____ KLMCD 025
Scratch / Apr '94 / BMG.

LOVE SOMEBODY TODAY
Got to love somebody / You fooled around / I'm a good girl / Easy street / Reach your peak / Pretty baby / How to love / Let's go on a vacation
CD _____ 8122719132
Rhino / May '95 / Warner Music.

SISTER SLEDGE
CD _____ STACD 083
Stardust / Apr '93 / Carlton Home Entertainment.

VERY BEST OF SISTER SLEDGE
We are family / He's the greatest dancer / All American girls / Pretty baby / Got to love somebody / Frankie / Lost in music / Thinking of you / Mama never told me / Reach your peak / Lost in music (mix)
CD _____ 9548318132
WEA / Feb '93 / Warner Music.

WE ARE FAMILY
He's the greatest dancer / Lost in music / Somebody loves me / Thinking of you / We are family / Easier to love / You're a friend to me / One more time
CD _____ 8122715872
Rhino / Jun '95 / Warner Music.

Sisters Of Glory

GOOD NEWS IN HARD TIMES
CD _____ 9362459902
Warner Bros. / Aug '95 / Warner Music.

Sisters Of Mercy

FIRST, LAST AND ALWAYS
Black planet / Walk away / No time to cry / Rock and a hard place / Marian (version) / First and last and always / Possession / Nine while nine / Amphetamine logic / Some kind of stranger
CD _____ 9031773792
Merciful Release / Jun '92 / Warner Music.

FIRST, LAST FOREVER
CD _____ CLEO 6642CD
Cleopatra / Jan '94 / Disc.

FLOODLAND
Dominion/Mother Russia / Flood I / Lucretia my reflection / 1959 / This corrosion / Flood II / Driven like the snow / Never land / Torch (CD/MC only) / Colours (CD only)
CD _____ 242 246 2
Merciful Release / Dec '87 / Warner Music.

GIFT (Sisterhood)
Jihad / Colours / Giving ground / Finland red, Egypt white / Rain from heaven
CD _____ 11316842
Merciful Release / Jun '94 / Warner Music.

SISTERS OF MERCY: INTERVIEW PICTURE DISC
CD P.Disc _____ CBAK 4010
Baktabak / Apr '88 / Baktabak.

SLIGHT CASE OF OVERBOMBING, A (Greatest Hits #1)
Under the gun / Temple of love / Vision thing / Detonation Boulevard / Dr. Jeep / More / Lucretia my reflection / Dominion/Mother Russia / This Corrosion / No time to cry / Walk away / Body and soul
CD _____ 450993579-2
Merciful Release / Aug '93 / Warner Music.

SOME GIRLS WANDER BY MISTAKE
Alive / Floorshow / Phantom / 1969 / Kiss the carpet / Lights / Valentine / Fix / Burn / Kiss the carpet (reprise) / Temple of love / Heartland / Gimme shelter / Damage done / Watch / Home of the hit-men / Body electric / Adrenochrome / Anaconda
CD _____ 9031764762
Merciful Release / Apr '91 / Warner Music.

VISION THING
Vision thing / Ribbons / Detonation Boulevard / Something fast / When you don't see me / Dr. Jeep / More / I was wrong
CD _____ 9031726632
Merciful Release / Oct '90 / Warner Music.

Sisters Unlimited

NO BED OF ROSES
CD _____ FECD 104
Fellside / Jun '95 / Target/BMG / Direct / ADA.

NO LIMITS
No going back / Promises / Breastfeeding baby in the park / Tomorrow / Mouth music / My better years / Working girl blues / Dance / Old and strong / My true love once / When I was single / On children / No man's momma / Forgive and forget / We were there
CD _____ HARCD 013
Harbour Town / Nov '91 / Roots / Direct / CM / ADA.

Sivertsen, Kenneth

REMEMBERING NORTH
Nimis (near but far) / Cock ones head / Remembering / Going home / Division / Sideblink / From Paris to Mosterhamn / Procession / Tony's rain / Journey / Rain
CD _____ NYC 60072
NYC / Aug '94 / New Note.

Six Feet Under

HAUNTED
CD _____ 398414093
Metal Blade / Oct '95 / Plastic Head.

Six Finger Satellite

PIGEON IS THE MOST POPULAR BIRD, THE
Untitled / Home for the holy day / Untitled (2) / Laughing Larry / Untitled (3) / Funny a clown / Untitled (4) / Deadpan / Untitled (5) / Hi lo jerk / Untitled (6) / (Love) via satellite / Untitled (7) / Save the last dance for Larry / Untitled (8) / Zeroes and ones / Untitled (9) / Neuro-harmonic conspiracy / Untitled (10) / Takes one to know one / Symphony in A
CD _____ SPCD 268
Sub Pop / Aug '93 / Disc.

SEVERE EXPOSURE
CD _____ SP 299B
Sub Pop / Jul '95 / Disc.

Six Ton Budgie

UNPLUCKED
CD _____ AXEL/VINTAP 1
Vinyl Tap / Jan '96 / Vinyl Tap.

Six Winds

ANGER DANCE
CD _____ BVHAASTCD 9305
Bvhaast / Feb '86 / Cadillac.

Six Yard Box

IMAGINATION IS GREATER THAN KNOWLEDGE
Sweet leaf / What's the point / K4R Part III / Cat is wiser / Clutter up buttering / Spellbound / K4R Part IV / Pictures of matchstick men (Reggae mix)
CD _____ MOSH 087CD
Earache / Apr '93 / Vital.

Sixteen Deluxe

BACKFEED MAGNETBABE
CD _____ TR 37CD
Trance / May '95 / SRD.

Sixths

WASP'S NESTS
CD _____ FACD 206
Factory Too / Jul '95 / Pinnacle.

Sjosten, Lars

IN CONFIDENCE
CD _____ DRCD 197
Dragon / Sep '88 / Roots / Cadillac / Wellard / CM / ADA.

SELECT NOTES
CD _____ CAPRICE 1216
Caprice / May '89 / CM / Complete/ Pinnacle / Cadillac / ADA.

Skaboosh

FREETOWN
Movin' up an' movin' on / Fanfare / Bareback ridin' / Freedom / Time / Startin from scratch / Spain / Ain't got any money / I want to grow old with you by my side
CD _____ VP128 CD
Voice Print / Feb '93 / Voice Print.

Skagarak

SKAGARACK
Move it in the night / I'm alone / Saying / Damned woman / Don't turn me upside down / Lies / Victim of the system / City child / Double crossed
CD _____ 829 446 2
IMS / Nov '86 / PolyGram.

Skaggs, Ricky

FAMILY AND FRIENDS
Lost and I'll never find the way / Two different worlds / River of memory / Talk about sufferin' / Think of what you've done / Toy heart / Hallelujah I'm ready / Say / Won't you be mine / Won't it be wonderful there / River of Jordan
CD _____ CD 0151
Rounder / Aug '88 / CM / Direct / ADA / Cadillac.

FAVOURITE COUNTRY SONGS
If that's the way you feel / Sweet temptation / I'll take the blame / Waitin' for the sun to shine / You may see me walkin' / Can't you hear me callin' / Your old love letters / Lost to a stranger / Wound time can't erase / Nothing can hurt you
CD _____ 9825872
Pickwick/Sony Collector's Choice / Jul '91 / Carlton Home Entertainment / Pinnacle / Sony.

LIVE IN LONDON: RICKY SKAGGS
Uncle Pen / Heartbroke / She didn't say why / Cajun moon / Country boy / I've got a new heartache / You make me feel like a man / Rockin' the boat / Honey (open that door) / Don't get above your raising
CD _____ PWKS 4048
Carlton Home Entertainment / Apr '91 / Carlton Home Entertainment.

ORIGINAL RECORDINGS
CD _____ CDSD 015
Magnum Music / Sep '94 / Magnum Music Group.

SOLID GROUND
CD _____ 7567828342
Atlantic / Jan '96 / Warner Music.

THAT'S IT
Red apple rag / At the Darktown strutter's ball / Florida blues / Bubble gum song / Whitesburg / Meeting house branch / Sweet Georgia Town / Hook and line / Southern moon / Twenty one fiddle salute / That's it / Evergreen shore
CD _____ CDSD 040
Sundown / Dec '86 / Magnum Music Group.

Skaos

BACK TO LIVE
CD _____ EFA 946252
Pork Pie / Dec '95 / SRD.

BEWARE/CATCH THIS BEAT
Going insane / After midnight / Destination skaville / J.B.'s / These boys / Munsters / I love to dance / Invisible seven / Jesse James / Prison / Frankenstein's party / Do the ska / Oh Sally / Straight to your heart / Brainkiller / Jungle beat / Everything (Girl) but you / Better beware / Bonehead (I just can't stand it) / Super hero / Living in Bavaria
CD _____ LOMACD 29
Dojo / Feb '94 / BMG.

Skatalites

HI BOP SKA
CD _____ SH 45019
Shanachie / Dec '94 / Koch / ADA / Greensleeves.

HOG IN A COCOA (Skatalites & Friends)
CD _____ LG 21016
Lagoon / May '93 / Magnum Music Group / THE.

LIBERATION SKA
CD _____ RNCD 2056
Rhino / May '94 / Jetstar / Magnum Music Group / THE.

STRETCHING OUT
CD _____ RE 141CD
Reach Out International / Nov '94 / Jetstar.

Skatenigs

OH WHAT A MANGLED WEB WE HAVE
CD _____ CDVEST 14
Bulletproof / Jun '94 / Pinnacle.

STUPID PEOPLE SHOULDN'T BREED
Chemical imbalance / Got it made / Stand tall / Shit authority / Horny for evil / Pound sauce / Fight da suckas / Loudspeaker / Roadkill
CD _____ VIRUS 105CD
Alternative Tentacles / Mar '92 / Pinnacle.

Skeaping, Lucie

RAISINS AND ALMONDS (Skeaping, Lucie & The Burning Bush)
Yoi m'enamori d'un aire (I fell in love with the charms) / Tum Balalaika (Play balalaika) / Chassidic melody No. 24 / Tsen kopikes (Ten kopeks) / Adio querida (Good bye my love) / Puncha, puncha (The perfumed rose) / Sha, Shtil (Sh, Quiet) / Una matica de ruda (a little bunch of rue) / Chassidic melody No. 13 / Di alte kashe (The eternal question) / Avrix mi galanica (Open, my sweet) / Gey ikh mir shpatsirn (As I went walking) / Una hija tiene el rey (The King has a daughter) / Di mezinke oysgegebn (My youngest daughter's married) / Mi padre era de Francia / Oyfn pripetchik (On the hearth) / Chassidic melody No. 10, La rose ellorece (The rose blooms) / Rozhinkes mit mandlen / Zog nit keynmol (Never say)
CD _____ CDSDL 395
Saydisc / Mar '94 / Harmonia Mundi / ADA / Direct.

Skee Lo

I WISH
CD _____ 5297892
Wild Card / Dec '95 / PolyGram.

Skeete, Beverley

ALL MY DREAMS
CD _____ CUTUPCD 008
Jump Cut / Jun '95 / Total/BMG / Vital/ SAM.

Skeletal Earth

DE-EVOLUTION
CD _____ DAR 017-2
Desperate Attempt / Mar '95 / SRD.

EULOGY FOR A DYING FOETUS
CD _____ FDNCD 8215
Plastic Head / Jan '92 / Plastic Head.

Skeletal Family

BURNING OIL
CD _____ LOMACD 40
Loma / May '95 / BMG.

SINGLES PLUS
Trees / Just a friend / Night / Waiting here / She cries alone / Wind blows / Eternal / Waiting here (version) / Night (version) / So sure / Batman / Lies / Promised land / Stand by me / Puppet / Waltz / Guilt
CD _____ CDMGRAM 75
Cherry Red / Mar '94 / Pinnacle.

Skeleton Crew

BLUE MANIA
Satisfaction guaranteed / Glory hunter / Watch your step / Can't buy love with money / Mother earth / Blues got me / Trail of tears / Chinese eyes / Mississippi burning / See me later / Walking in my sleep
CD _____ 109042
Musidisc / Mar '92 / Vital / Harmonia Mundi / ADA / Cadillac / Discovery.

Skeletons

IN THE FLESH/ROCKIN' BONES
Trans am / Tell her I'm gone / Very last day / Blood surfin' / Sour snow / Gas money / She drives me out of my mind / B gas accord / Crazy country hop / Outta my way / Older guys / Laugh at me / Waitin' for a slow dance / Meaning of the blues / I'm a little but I'm loud / Thirty days in the workhouse / I play the drums / Primitive / For every heart
CD _____ FIENDCD 178
Demon / Aug '90 / Pinnacle / ADA.

WAITING
CD _____ A 030D
Alias / Nov '92 / Vital.

Skellern, Peter

BEST OF PETER SKELLERN
CD _____ 74321292782
RCA / Jul '95 / BMG.

CHEEK TO CHEEK
Cheek to cheek / Continental / Puttin' on the Ritz / Top hat, white tie and tails / Stormy weather / All or nothing at all / Busy line / Love is the sweetest thing / Two sleepy people / Deep purple / Raining in my heart / Where do we go from here / They all laughed / Way you look tonight
CD _____ 74321 15219-2
Ariola Express / Sep '93 / BMG.

OASIS
Prelude / If this be the last time / I wonder why / Hold me / Oasis / Sirocco / Who knows / Weavers of moonbeams / Loved and lost / True love
CD _____ PWKS 557
Carlton Home Entertainment / Dec '89 / Carlton Home Entertainment.

SINGER & SONG, THE
You're a lady / Abdul abulbul amir / Lean back (and let it happen) / Georgia moon / She had to go and lose it at the astor / Our Jackie's getting married / Streaker / Hold on to love / Rockin' chair / Manifesto / Somebody call me tonight / Send my heart to San Francisco / All last night / That is the end of the news
CD _____ 5500302
Spectrum/Karussell / May '93 / PolyGram THE.

STARDUST MEMORIES
CD _____ 450998132-2
Warner Bros. / Mar '95 / Warner Music.

YOU'RE A LADY
You're a lady / Sad affair / Keep in your own backyard / Ain't life something / Don't it matter anymore / Manifesto / Now I've seen the light / Apollo II / Our Jackie's getting married / Every home should have one / Rock on / Roll on Rhoda / All last night / My lonely room / I don't know / Roll away / Somebody call me tonight / Sleep guitar / Goodnight / Symphonion
CD _____ PWK 135
Carlton Home Entertainment / May '90 / Carlton Home Entertainment.

Skelton, John

ONE AT A TIME
CD _____ PAN 146CD
Pan / Oct '93 / ADA / Direct / CM.

Sketch

COSMOSIS
CD _____ 33JAZZ 003CD
33 Jazz / Jun '93 / Cadillac / New Note.

Skew Siskin

SKEW SISKIN
If the walls could talk / Out of control / I wanna know / Livin' on the redline / In another world / I gotta go away / When the sun goes down / Sniffin' the dirt / Thank you for the time / All day and all of the night / Cheap trick / Shake down and roll
CD _____ 07599244592
Giant / Aug '92 / BMG.

Skid Row

B SIDE OURSELVES
Psychotherapy / C'mon and love me / Delivering the goods / What you're doing / Little wing
CD _____ 7567824312
Atlantic / Oct '92 / Warner Music.

SKID ROW
Big guns / Sweet little sister / Can't stand the heartache / Piece of me / Eighteen and life / Rattlesnake shake / Youth gone wild / Here I am / Makin' a mess / I remember you / Midnight tornado
CD _____ 7819362
Atlantic / Feb '95 / Warner Music.

SLAVE TO THE GRIND
Monkey business / Slave to the grind / Threat / Quicksand Jesus / Psycho love / Get the fuck out / Livin' on a chain gang / Creepshow / In a darkened room / Riot act / Mudkicker / Wasted time
CD _____ 7567822422
Atlantic / Jun '91 / Warner Music.

SUBHUMAN RACE
CD _____ 7567827302
Atlantic / Mar '95 / Warner Music.

Skid Row

34 HOURS
CD _____ 4805252
Columbia / May '95 / Sony.

SKID
Sandie's gone / Man who never was heading home again / Felicity / Un co-op showband blues / Morning star avenue / Oi'll tell you later / Virgo's daughter / New faces old places
CD _____ 477360-2
Columbia / Aug '94 / Sony.

SKID ROW (Gary Moore, Brush Shiels and Noel Bridgeman)

Benedict's cherry wine / Saturday morning man / Crystal ball / Mr. Deluxe / Girl called Winter / Morning Star Avenue / Silver bird
CD _____ CLACD 343
Castle / Jun '94 / BMG.

Skids

DUNFERMLINE
Into the valley / Charles / Saints are coming / Scared to dance / Sweet suburbia / Of one skin / Night and day / Animation / Working for the Yankee dollar / Charade / Masquerade / Circus games / Out of town / Goodbye civilian / Woman in Winter / Hurry on boys / Iona / Fields
CD _____ CDVM 9022
Virgin / Jul '93 / EMI.

SCARED TO DANCE
Into the valley / Scared to dance / Of one skin / Dossier (of fallibility) / Melancholy soldiers / Hope and glory / Saints are coming / Six times / Calling the tune / Integral plot / Scale / Charles
CD _____ CDV 2116
Virgin / Jun '90 / EMI.

SWEET SUBURBIA (The Best Of The Skids)
Into the valley / Charles / Saints are coming / Scared to dance / Sweet suburbia / Of one skin / Night and day / Animation / Working for the Yankee dollar / Charade / Masquerade / Circus games / Out of town / Goodbye civillian / Woman in winter / Hurry on boys / Iona / Fields
CD _____ CDOVD 457
Virgin / Feb '95 / EMI.

Skin & Bones

NOT A PRETTY SIGHT
CD _____ EQNCD 2
Equinox / Jul '90 / Total/BMG.

Skin

SKIN
Money / Shine your light / House of love / Colourblind / Which are the tears / Look but don't touch / Nightsong / Tower of strength / Revolution / Raised on radio / Wings of an angel / Unbelievable (CDST only) / Pump it up (CDST only) / Hangin' on the telephone (CDST only) / Express yourself (CDST only) / Funktified (CDST only) / Monkey (CDST only) / Should I stay or should I go (CDST only) / Dog eat dog (CDST only) / Down down down (CDST only) / Good good lovin' (CDST only)
CD _____ CDPCSD 151
Parlophone / May '94 / EMI.
CD Set _____ CDPCSDS 151
Parlophone / Oct '94 / EMI.

Skin

BLOOD, WOMAN, ROSES
CD _____ CDPROD 4
Product Inc. / '89 / Vital.

SHAME, HUMILITY, REVENGE
CD _____ CDPROD 11
Product Inc. / Mar '88 / Vital.

WORLD OF SKIN
CD _____ YGCD 002
Young God / Jul '95 / Vital.

Skin Chamber

TRIAL
On a drunk / Throb / Ripping fist / Torturous world / Sloven / Glisten / Slowcrime / Trial / Swallowing scrap metal Pt 5
CD _____ CDRR 9075 2
Roadrunner / Apr '93 / Pinnacle.

WOUND
CD _____ 92742
Roadrunner / Oct '91 / Pinnacle.

Skin The Peeler

FRIENDS AND LOVERS
CD _____ STP 101CD
Skindependent / Mar '94 / CM.

WORLD DANCE
CD _____ CDSTP 100
Skindependent / Dec '91 / CM.

Skin Yard

1000 SMILING KNUCKLES
CD _____ CRZ 017 CD
Cruz / May '93 / Pinnacle / Plastic Head.

FIST SIZED CHUNKS
CD _____ CRZ 009 CD
Cruz / Apr '90 / Pinnacle / Plastic Head.

INSIDE THE EYE
CD _____ CRZ 027 CD
Cruz / May '93 / Pinnacle / Plastic Head.

SKIN YARD
CD _____ CRZ 015 CD
Cruz / May '93 / Pinnacle / Plastic Head.

Skink

DEAF TO SUGGESTION
Deadlock / Undercurrents / Enemy / Violator / Drug called religion / Blood eagle / Dark side / Real deep shit / Hand comes down
CD _____ BGR 006
BGR / Mar '95 / Plastic Head.

Skinned Teen

BAZOOKA SMOOTH/JAIL BAIT CORE (Skinned Teen & Raooul)
Skinned teen anthem / Pillow case kisser / Starch / Black cat / Double D / Ex-boyfriend / Cub car / Geometry of twigs / Gumball / Pidgeon steps / I had Mark Owen / Dan / Dark coffee house / Rotten dead monkey / Stupid poser from hell / Possessed / Mastubatory / Spirit of '78 / I had Jesse Blatz
CD _____ LOOKOUT 088CD
Lookout / Jul '94 / SRD.

Skinner, Billy

KOSEN RUFU
CD _____ AC 3333CD
Accurate / Nov '93 / Cadillac.

Skinny Puppy

BACK AND FORTH SERIES TWO
Intro (Live in Winnipeg) / Sleeping beast / K-9 / Monster radio man / Quiet solitude / Pit / Sore in a masterpiece/Dead of winter / Unovis on a stick / To a baser nature / A.M./ Meat flavour / My voice sounds like shit / Smothered hop (Demo) / Explode the P.A. / Assimilate (Original Inst. Demo) / Dope of insanity
CD _____ W2-30078
Nettwerk / Jan '93 / Vital / Pinnacle.

CLEANSE, FOLD AND MANIPULATE
First aid / Addiction / Shadow cast / Draining faces / Mourn / Second touch / Tear or beat / Trauma hounds / Anger / Epilogue
CD _____ NETCD 019
Nettwerk / Nov '90 / Vital / Pinnacle.

LAST RIGHTS
Hinder / Killing game / Cancelled / Xception / Catbowl / Hurtful 2 / River's end / Fester / Premonition / Wrek / Epilogue 2
CD _____ NET 038CD
Nettwerk / Apr '92 / Vital / Pinnacle.

MIND: THE PERPETUAL INTERCOURSE
One time one place / God's gift / Three blind mice / Love / Stairs and flowers / Antagonism / 200 years / Dig it / Burnt with water
CD _____ NTCD 037
Nettwerk / '88 / Vital / Pinnacle.

RABIES
CD _____ NETCD 023
Nettwerk / Jul '90 / Vital / Pinnacle.

REMISSION AND BITES
CD _____ BIAS 048
Play It Again Sam / Jan '87 / Vital.

TESTURE
CD _____ CD3-15439
Nettwerk / '89 / Vital / Pinnacle.

TOO DARK PARK
CD _____ NET 026CD
Nettwerk / Sep '93 / Vital / Pinnacle.

VIVISECT VI
Dogshit / V.S. gas attack / Harsh stone white / Human disease (S.K.U.M.M.) / Who's laughing now / Tenure / State aid / Hospital waste / Fritter (Stella's home)
CD _____ NETCD 021
Nettwerk / Nov '90 / Vital / Pinnacle.

WORLOCK (Twelve Inch Anthology)
CD _____ W2-30041
Nettwerk / '89 / Vital / Pinnacle.

Skippies

WORLD UP
CD _____ NR 422455
New Rose / Jan '94 / Direct / ADA.

Skitzo

TERMINAL DAMAGE
CD _____ NERCD 039
Nervous / '88 / Nervous / Magnum Music Group.

Skjelbred, Ray

CHICAGO SESSIONS (Skjelbred, Ray Quartet)
CD _____ SACD 98
Solo Art / Jul '93 / Jazz Music.

Skolvan

SWING & TEARS
CD _____ KM 46
Keltia Musique / Oct '94 / ADA / Direct / Discovery.

Skorr

POPULAR UKRAINIAN DANCES (Skorr & Ukrainian Ensemble)
CD _____ MCD 71446
Monitor / Jun '93 / CM.

Skoubie Dubh Orchestra

SPIKE'S 23 COLLECTION
CD _____ LDL 1210CD
Klub / Jul '94 / CM / Ross / Duncans / ADA / Direct.

Skrapp Metal

SENSITIVE
CD _____ PAR 2008CD
PAR / Nov '92 / Charly / Wellard.

Skrew

DUSTED
CD _____ CDDVN 28
Devotion / May '94 / Pinnacle.

Skud

BULLGATOR
CD _____ BGR 017CD
BGR / Oct '95 / Plastic Head.

Skull

NO BONES ABOUT IT
CD _____ CDMFN 117
Music For Nations / Jun '91 / Pinnacle.

Skull Snaps

SKULL SNAPS
My hang up is you / Having you around / Didn't I do it to you / All of a sudden / It's a new day / I'm your pimp / I turn my back on love / Trespassing / I'm falling out of love
CD _____ CPCD 8094
Charly / Apr '95 / Charly / THE / Cadillac.

Skullflower

ARGON
CD _____ FRR 012
Freek / May '95 / SRD.

IIIRD GATEKEEPER
CD _____ HD 001
Headdirt / Nov '92 / SRD.

INFINITYLAND
CD _____ HD 9003CD
We Bite / May '95 / Plastic Head.

RUINS
CD _____ SX 006
Shock / '89 / Pinnacle / Cadillac.

TRANSFORMER
CD _____ SFTR 1325CD
Psychedelic Noise / Jan '96 / Plastic Head.

Skunk Anansie

PARANOID & SUNBURNT
CD _____ TPLP 55CD
One Little Indian / Oct '95 / Pinnacle.

Skunkhour

SKUNKHOUR
Pullatickin / Cow and a pig / Horse / Booty full / Back to basics / Sheep of Sam / Free man / Do you like it / State / Echinda
CD _____ JAZIDCD 113
Acid Jazz / Jul '95 / Pinnacle.

Sky

BEST OF SKY
Toccata / Westway / Sanara / Gymnopedie No.1 / Moonroof
CD _____ MCCD 172
Music Club / Sep '94 / Disc / THE / CM.

SKY
Westway / Carrillon / Danza / Gymnopedie No.1 / Cannonball / Where opposites meet
CD _____ MCCD 077
Music Club / Jun '92 / Disc / THE / CM.

SKY
CD _____ MER 008
Tring / Mar '93 / Tring / Prism.

SKY 2
Hotta / Dance of the little fairies / Sahara / Fifo / Vivaloi / Tuba smarties / Ballet-volta / Gavotte and variations / Andante / Tristan's magic garden / El cielo / Scipio (part 1 and 2) / Toccata
CD _____ MCCD 078
Music Club / Jun '92 / Disc / THE / CM.

SKY 2
CD _____ MER 009
Tring / Mar '93 / Tring / Prism.

SKY 3
Grace / Chiropodie no.1 / Westwind / Sarabande / Connecting rooms / Moonroof / Sister Rose / Hello / Dance of the big fairies / Meheeco / Keep me safe and keep me warm / Shelter me from darkness
CD _____ MCCD 079
Music Club / Jun '92 / Disc / THE / CM.

SKY WRITING
Toccata / Westway / Gymnopedie / Vivaldi / Skylark / Hotta / Masquerade / Dance of the little fairies / Keep me safe and keep me warm / Meheeco / Grace / Chiropodie No.1 / El cielo / Moonroof / Carrillon / Yelatso pedi / Ride of the valkyries
CD _____ MDCD 8

Music De-Luxe / '90 / Magnum Music Group.

Sky Cries Mary

RETURN TO THE INNER EXPERIENCE
Walla walla / Moving like water / Gone / 2000 Light years from home / When the fear stops / Lay down your head / Rain / Ocean which humanity is / Broken down / Rosaleen / Bus to gate / Joey's aria / We will fall
CD _____ WDOM 006CD
World Domination / May '94 / Pinnacle.

THIS TIMELESS TURNING
CD _____ WDOM 011CD
World Domination / Oct '94 / Pinnacle.

Sky High

AFRICAN VENGANCE (Sky High & The Mau Mau)
CD _____ CD 1004
Sky High / Sep '94 / Jetstar.

LION JUNGLE (Sky High & The Mau Mau)
CD _____ SHCD 2001
Ras / Jan '95 / Jetstar / Greensleeves / SRD / Direct.

MARCUS GARVEY CHANT (Sky High & The Mau Mau)
CD _____ RASCD 3107
Ras / Nov '92 / Jetstar / Greensleeves / SRD / Direct.

Sky Painter

LONG WINTER OF MARS
CD _____ RP 05CD
Red Planet / Jan '94 / Plastic Head.

Skyclad

BURNT OFFERING FOR THE BONE IDOL, A
War and disorder / Broken promised land / Spinning Jenny / Salt on earth (another man's poison) / Karmageddon (the suffering silence) / Ring stone round / Men of straw / R'vannith / Declaration of indifference / Alone in death's shadow
CD _____ NO 1862
Noise/Modern Music / Mar '92 / Pinnacle / Plastic Head.

IRRATIONAL ANTHEMS
CD _____ MASSCD 084
Massacre / Jan '96 / Plastic Head.

JONAH'S ARK
CD _____ NO 2092
Noise/Modern Music / May '93 / Pinnacle / Plastic Head.

PRINCE OF THE POVERTY LINE
CD _____ N 0239-2
Noise/Modern Music / Mar '94 / Pinnacle / Plastic Head.

SILENT WHALES OF LUNAR SEA
CD _____ NO 2282
Noise/Modern Music / Apr '95 / Pinnacle / Plastic Head.

Skylab

SKYLAB NO.1
River of bass / Seashell / Depart / Next / Ghost dance / Shhh / Indigo / Ah ee hu / Electric blue / Six nine / Tokyo 1 (On CD only) / Tetsuo plummer
CD _____ LATCD 21
L'Attitude / Dec '95 / PolyGram / Vital.

Skylark

ALL OF IT
Fair Jane/Townsend's jig/Captain White's jig / Pretty Susan / Tryst / Heel and toe / Siuil arun / Contradiction set / All of it / Ball and pin / In contempt / Teelin polkas / Braes of Balquhidder / Dewdrops on the corn/Pat McKenna's jig/Cook in the kitchen / For a new baby
CD _____ GLCD 3046
Green Linnet / Aug '92 / Roots / CM / Direct / ADA.

LIGHT AND SHADE
Mad French / Brown girl / Sunflower / Neil Mulligan's jig / Upon St. Nicholas boat / Cruel wars / O'Donnel's fancy/Get up old woman and shake yourself / Star above the garter / Little pack of tailors / Frank Quinn's and Peter McArdle's highlands / Factory girl / Up in smoke / Young and foolish / Munster bacon/The hawk/Paddy Kierce's jig / Boys of Mullaghbawn / Gypsy
CD _____ CC 57CD
Claddagh / Feb '92 / ADA / Direct.

Skyliners

SINCE I DON'T HAVE YOU
Since I don't have you / This I swear / I'll be seeing you / Lonely way to be / If I loved you / Warm / When I fall in love / Tired of me / Pennies from Heaven / It happened today / Zing went the strings of my heart / One night, one night / Tomorrow / Lorraine from Spain / I can dream, can't I
CD _____ CDCH 378

Ace / May '91 / Pinnacle / Cadillac / Complete/Pinnacle.

Skyscraper

SUPERSTATE
CD _____ DSCD 001
Dynosupreme / Nov '95 / SRD.

Slade

AMAZING KAMIKAZE SYNDROME, THE
My oh my / Run runaway / C'est la vie / Slam the hammer down / Cocky rock boys / In the doghouse / Ready to explode / Razzle dazzle man / Cheap 'n' nasty love / High and dry
CD _____ CLACD 381
Castle / Apr '93 / BMG.

COLLECTION
CD _____ CCSCD 372
Castle / Mar '93 / BMG.

CRACKERS
Let's dance / Santa Claus is coming to town / Hi ho silver lining (Not on Castle reissues) / We'll bring the house down / Cum on feel the noize / All join hands / Okey cokey / Merry Christmas everybody / Do you believe in miracles / Let's have a party / Get down and get with it / My oh my / Run runaway / Here's to (the New Year) / Do they know it's Christmas (Not on Castle reissues) / Auld lang syne / You'll never walk alone / Mama weer all crazee now (On Castle reissues only)
CD _____ CCSCD 401
Castle / Nov '93 / BMG.

NOBODY'S FOOL
CD _____ 8491832
Polydor / May '91 / PolyGram.

OLD, NEW, BORROWED AND BLUE
CD _____ 8491812
Polydor / May '91 / PolyGram.

ON STAGE
Rock 'n' roll preacher / When I'm dancin' / ain't fightin' / Take me bak 'ome / Everyday / Lock up your daughters / We'll bring the house down / Night to remember / Gudbuy t' Jane / Mama weer all crazee now / You'll never walk alone
CD _____ CLACD 388
Castle / Jun '93 / BMG.

PLAY IT LOUD
Raven / See us here / Dapple rose / Could I / One way hotel / Shape of things to come / Know who you are / I remember / Pouk hill / Angelina / Dirty joker / Sweet box
CD _____ 849 178-2
Polydor / May '91 / PolyGram.

ROGUES GALLERY
Hey ho wish you well / Little Sheila / Harmony / Mysterious Mizster Jones / Walking on water, running on alcohol / Year bitch / I'll be there / I win, you lose / Time to rock / All join hands
CD _____ CLACD 378
Castle / Apr '93 / BMG.

SLADE ALIVE
Hear me calling / In like a shot from my gun / Darling be home soon / Know who you are / Keep on rocking / Get down with it / Born to be wild
CD _____ 841 114-2
Polydor / Apr '91 / PolyGram.

SLADE ALIVE #2
CD _____ 8491792
Polydor / May '91 / PolyGram.

SLADE COLLECTION 1981-1987, THE
Run runaway / Everyday / We'll bring the house down / Ruby red / C'est la vie / Do you believe in miracles / Still the same / My oh my / All join hands / Wheels ain't coming down / Seven year bitch / Mysterious Mizter Jones / Lock up your daughters / Me and the boys / Gudbuy t' Jane (live) / Mama weer all crazee now (live) / Love is like a rock (Bonus track on CD only.)
CD _____ ND 74926
RCA / Apr '91 / BMG.

SLADE IN FLAME
How does it feel / Them kinda monkeys can't swing / So far, so good / Summer song / OK yesterday was yesterday / Far far away / This girl / Lay it down / Heaven knows / Standing on the corner
CD _____ 8491822
Polydor / May '91 / PolyGram.

SLADEST
Cum on feel the noize / Look wot you dun / Gudbuy t' Jane / One way hotel / Skweeze me pleaze me / Pouk Hill / Shape of things to come / Take me back 'ome / Coz I luv you / Wild winds are blowing / Know who you are / Get down and get with it / Look at last nite / Mama weer all crazee now
CD _____ 8371032
Polydor / May '93 / PolyGram.

SLAYED ?
How d'you ride / Whole world's goin crazee / Look at last nite / I won't let it appen agen / Move over / Gudbuy t' Jane / Gudbuy gudbuy / Mama weer all crazee now / I don't mind / Let the good times roll
CD _____ 8491802
Polydor / May '91 / PolyGram.

STORY OF SLADE VOL.2
Cum on feel the noize / Far far away / Everyday / Skweeze me, pleeze me / Don't blame me / Summer song / Get down and get with it / In for a penny / Just want a little bit / I'm mee, I'm now, an that's orl / Get on up / How does it feel
CD _____ BTCD 979412
Beartracks / Oct '90 / Rollercoaster.

TILL DEAF DO US PART
Rock 'n' roll preacher / Lock up your daughters / Till deaf do us part / Ruby red / She brings out the devil in me / Night to remember / M'hat m'coat / It's your body not your mind / Let the rock roll out of control / That was no lady that was my wife / Knuckle sandwich Nancy / Till deaf resurrected
CD _____ CLACD 377
Castle / Apr '93 / BMG.

WALL OF HITS
Radio wall of sound / Coz I luv you / Take me bak 'ome / Mama weer all crazee now / Cum on feel the noize / Skweeze me, pleeze me / Universe / Merry Christmas everybody / Get down and get with it / Look wot you dun / Gudbuy t' Jane / My friend Stan / Everyday / Bangin' man / Far far away / How does it feel (Not on LP) / Thanks for the memory (wham bam thank you mam) (Not on LP) / Let's call it quits / My oh my / Run run away
CD _____ 5116122
Polydor / Nov '91 / PolyGram.

WE'LL BRING THE HOUSE DOWN
We'll bring the house down / Night starvation / Wheels ain't coming down / Hold on to your hats / My baby's got it / When I'm dancin' I ain't fightin' / Dizzy mama / Nuts, bolts and screw / Lemme love into ya / I'm a rocker
CD _____ CLACD 380
Castle / Apr '93 / BMG.

WHATEVER HAPPENED TO SLADE
CD _____ 8491842
Polydor / May '93 / PolyGram.

YOU BOYZ MAKE BIG NOIZE
Love is like a rock / That's what friends are for / Still the same / Fools go grazy / She's heavy / We won't give in / Won't you rock with me / Ooh la la in L.A. / Me and the boys / Sing shout (knock yourself out) / Roaring silence / It's hard having fun nowadays / You boyz make big noize / Boyz (Instr.)
CD _____ CLACD 379
Castle / Apr '93 / BMG.

Slagle, Steve

SPREAD THE WORD
CD _____ SCCD 31354
Steeplechase / May '95 / Impetus.

Slags

TURN ON, TUNE IN, DROP OUT
CD _____ UGCD 5504
Unique Gravity / Oct '95 / Pinnacle / ADA.

Slant 6

INZOMBIA
CD _____ DIS 94CD
Dischord / May '95 / SRD.

SODA POP RIP OFF
CD _____ DIS 91CD
Dischord / Mar '94 / SRD.

Slapp Happy

ACNALBASAC NOOM
Casablanca moon / Me and Paravati / Mr. Rainbow / Michelangelo / Drum / Little something / Secret / Dawn / Half way there / Charlie 'n' Charlie / Slow moon's rose / Everybody's slimmin' / Blue eyed William / Karen / Messages
CD _____ RERSHCD
Recommended / '90 / These / ReR Megacorp.

CASABLANCA MOON / DESPERATE STRAIGHTS
Casablanca moon / Me and Paravati / Half way there / Michelangelo / Dawn / Mr. Rainbow / Secret / Little something / Drum / Haiku / Slow moon's rose / Some questions about hats / Owl / Worm is at work / Bad alchemy / Europa / Desperate straights / Riding tigers / Apes in capes / Strayed / Giants / Extracts from the Messiah / In the sickbay / Caucasian lullaby
CD _____ CDOVD 441
Virgin / Oct '91 / EMI.

Slapshot

16 VALVE HATE
CD _____ LF 195CD
Lost & Found / Aug '95 / Plastic Head.

BLAST FURNACE
CD _____ WB 2098CD
We Bite / Jun '93 / Plastic Head.

LIVE IN BERLIN
CD _____ WB 2111-2
We Bite / May '94 / Plastic Head.

STEP ON IT
CD _____ TAANG 028 CD
Taang / Jan '89 / Plastic Head.

STEP ON IT/BACK ON THE MAP
CD _____ TAANG 28CD
Taang / Nov '92 / Plastic Head.

SUDDEN DEATH
CD _____ TAANG 40CD
Taang / Nov '92 / Plastic Head.

UNCONSCIOUSNESS
We Bite / Oct '94 / Plastic Head.
CD _____ WB 2114CD

Slash's Snake Pit

IT'S 5'O CLOCK SOMEWHERE
Neither can I / Dime store rock / Beggers and hangers on / Good to be alive / What do you want to be / Monkey chow / Back and forth again / I hate everybody (but you) / Be the ball / Doin' fine / Take it away / Jizz da pit lower / Some city ward
CD _____ GED 24730
Geffen / Feb '95 / BMG.

Slater, Luke

FOUR CORNERED ROOM
CD _____ GPRCD 3
General Production Recordings / Feb '94 / Pinnacle.

MY YELLOW WISE RUG
CD _____ GPRCD 8
General Production Recordings / Sep '94 / Pinnacle.

X FRONT VOL 2
CD _____ PF 11CD
Peacefrog / Oct '93 / Disc.

Slatkin, Leonard

ANDERSON - THE TYPEWRITER
CD _____ 09026680482
RCA / Aug '95 / BMG.

Slaton, Wendi

TURN AROUND AND LOOK
CD _____ JR 006012
Justice / Nov '92 / Koch.

Slaughter

FEAR NO EVIL
CD _____ SPV 08576002
SPV / May '95 / Plastic Head.

Slaughter Joe

PIED PIPER OF FEEDBACK
CD _____ CRECD 084
Creation / May '94 / 3MV / Vital.

Slaughter, John

ALL THAT STUFF AIN'T REAL
Red tail light / Get some rest / Louisiana 1927 / I've got the proof / Something you got / Ready to fall / Lost and found / On my way to heaven / St James' infirmary / I can't swim / Don't fool yourself / Shame on you
CD _____ CDSJP 430
Timeless Jazz / Oct '95 / New Note.

NEW COAT OF PAINT, A (Slaughter Blues Band)
Riding with the king / Walking on sunset / I believe to my soul / Paint my mailbox blue / Watch your step / Cold cold feeling / Woke up this morning / Help me / Burn't go the strangers / New coat of paint
CD _____ CDSJP 313
Timeless Jazz / Jun '92 / New Note.

Slaughterback

SEA OF TRANQUILITY
CD _____ ESPCD 1
Echo / Oct '94 / Pinnacle / EMI.

Slava

KAGAN
CD _____ ORACD 1
AO / Dec '93 / Pinnacle.

Slave

FUNK STRIKES BACK, THE
CD _____ ICH 1144CD
Ichiban / Feb '94 / Koch.

MASTERS OF THE FUNGK
CD _____ D 2248622
Ichiban / Jan '96 / Koch.

REBIRTH
Are you ready / Way you dance / My everything / Everybody's talkin' / Thrill me / Victim of circumstance / I love you / Andy's ways / Behind closed doors / How is this love
CD _____ CDICH 1055
Ichiban / Oct '93 / Koch.

SLAVE '88'
CD _____ CDICH 1030
Ichiban / Dec '88 / Koch.

STELLAR FUNK (The Best Of Slave)
Slide / Party song / Stellar funk / Are you ready for love / Way out / Feel so real / Dan-

cin' in the key of life / Weak at the knees / Nobody can be you / Wait for me / Snap shot / Just a touch of love / Stolen jam
CD _____ 812271592-2
Atlantic / Mar '94 / Warner Music.

Slave Master

UNDER THE 6
Godless / Heal / Damnation / Come out / Day of requital / Final call / Walk the water / Down / Each one teach one / Freedom
CD _____ RCD 10302
Black Arc / Jun '94 / Vital.

Slaves

TALKING REGGAE
CD _____ 669122
Greensleeves / Nov '92 / Total/BMG / Jetstar / SRD.

Slawterhaus

LIVE
CD _____ VICTOCD 013
Victo / Nov '94 / These / ReR Megacorp / Cadillac.

Slayer

DECADE OF AGGRESSION
Hell awaits / Anti-christ / War ensemble / South of heaven / Raining blood / Altar of sacrifice / Jesus saves / Captor of sin / Born of fire / Post mortem / Spirit in black / Dead skin mask / Seasons in the abyss / Mandatory suicide / Angel of death / Hallowed point / Blood red / Die by the sword / Expendable youth / Chemical warfare / Black magic
CD _____ 74321248512
American / Dec '94 / BMG.

DIVINE INTERVENTION
Killing field / Sex murder act / Fictional reality / Ditto head / Divine intervention / Circle of beliefs / SS III / Serenity in murder / Two-thirteen / Mind control
CD _____ 74321236772
American / Oct '94 / BMG.

HELL AWAITS
Hell awaits / At dawn they sleep / Praise of death / Captor of death / Hardening of the arteries / Kill again / Haunting the chapel / Necrophiliac / Crypts of eternity
CD _____ CDZORRO 8
Metal Blade / Aug '90 / Pinnacle.

LIVE UNDEAD
CD _____ CDZORRO 29
Music For Nations / Sep '91 / Pinnacle.

REIGN IN BLOOD
Angel of death / Piece by piece / Necrophobic / Altar of sacrifice / Jesus saves / Criminally insane / Reborn / Epidemic / Post mortem / Raining blood
CD _____ 74321248482
American / Dec '94 / BMG.

SEASONS IN THE ABYSS
War ensemble / Blood red / Spirit in black / Expendable youth / Dead skin mask / Hallowed point / Skeletons of society / Temptation / Born of fire / Seasons in the abyss
CD _____ 74321248502
American / Dec '94 / BMG.

SHOW NO MERCY
Evil has no boundaries / Die by the sword / Metal storm / Black magic / Final command / Show no mercy / Anti-christ / Fight till death / Aggressive perfector / Tormentor / Crionics / Face the Slayer
CD _____ CDZORRO 7
Metal Blade / Aug '90 / Pinnacle.

SLATANIC SLAUGHTER (A Tribute To Slayer) (Various Artists)
CD _____ BS 03CD
Black Sun / Nov '95 / Plastic Head.

SOUTH OF HEAVEN
South of heaven / Silent scream / Live undead / Behind the crooked cross / Mandatory suicide / Ghosts of war / Read between the lies / Cleanse the soul / Dissident aggressor / Spill the blood
CD _____ 74321248492
American / Dec '94 / BMG.

Slazenger, Jake

MAKESARACKET
CD _____ CLR 410CD
Clear / Jun '95 / Disc.

Sledge, Percy

20 GREATEST HITS
CD _____ MU 5016
Musketeer / Oct '92 / Koch.

BLUE NIGHT
You got away with love / Love come knockin' / Why did you stop / I wish it would rain / Blue night / These ain't raindrops / Your love will save the world / First you cry / Going home tomorrow / Grand blvd. / I've got dreams to remember
CD _____ VPBCD 21
Pointblank / Nov '94 / EMI.

GREATEST HITS: PERCY SLEDGE
CD _____ CDSGP 044
Prestige / Apr '93 / Total/BMG.

IF LOVING YOU IS WRONG
(If loving you is wrong) I don't want to be right / When a man loves a woman / Take time to know her / Warm and tender love / It tears me up / Behind closed doors / Try a little tenderness / (Sittin' on) the dock of the bay / Tell it like it is / You send me / Bring it on home to me / My special prayer / I've been loving you too long / Cover me
CD _____ CDCD 1064
Charly / Mar '93 / Charly / THE / Cadillac.

IT TEARS ME UP (The Best Of Percy Sledge)
When a man loves a woman / I'm hanging up my heart for you / Put a little lovin' on me / Love me like you mean it / It tears me up / Warm and tender love / Love me tender / Dark end of the street / Take time to know her / Try a little tenderness / Bless your sweet little soul / True love travels on a gravel road / Sudden stop / Stop the world tonight / It's all wrong but it's all right / Drown in my own tears / Out of left field / Kind woman / Cover me / That's the way I want to live my life / Push Mr. Pride aside / It can't be stopped / Rainbow road
CD _____ 812270285-2
WEA / Mar '93 / Warner Music.

LEGENDS IN MUSIC - PERCY SLEDGE
CD _____ LECD 065
Wisepack / Jul '94 / THE / Conifer.

OUT OF LEFT FIELD
My special prayer / Take time to know her / My special prayer / Thief in the night / Out of left field / It tears me up / When a man loves a woman / You're pouring water on a drowning man / Just out of reach / Cover me / Warm and tender love
CD _____ TKOCD 008
TKO / '92 / TKO.

PERCY
Bring your lovin' to me / You had to be there / All night train / She's too pretty to cry / I still miss someone / Faithful kind / Home type thing / Personality / I'd put angels around you / Hard lovin' woman / When a man loves a woman
CD _____ CDCHARLY 95
Charly / Jul '87 / Charly / THE / Cadillac.

PERCY SLEDGE COLLECTION
CD _____ COL 048
Collection / Jun '95 / Target/BMG.

SPOTLIGHT ON PERCY SLEDGE
Warm and tender love / Cover me / You're pouring water on a drowning man / My special prayer / Take time to know her / My adorable one / Sudden stop / Good love / Walking in the sun / It tears me up / Make it good and make it last / Out of left field / Behind closed doors / Just out of reach / Thief in the night / When a man loves a woman
CD _____ HADCD 125
Javelin / Feb '94 / THE / Henry Hadaway Organisation.

WANTED AGAIN
Keep the fire burning / Kiss an angel good morning / If you've got the money honey / Today I started loving you again / Wabash cannonball / Wanted again / Hey good lookin' / He'll have to go / She thinks I still care / For the good times
CD _____ FIENDCD 140
Demon / Jul '89 / Pinnacle / ADA.

WHEN A MAN LOVES A WOMAN
When a man loves a woman / Warm and tender love / Bring it on home to me / Behind closed doors / Try a little tenderness / Tell it like it is / My special prayer / (Sittin' on) the dock of the bay / (If loving you is wrong) I don't want to be right / It tears me up / I've been loving you too long / Cover me / You send me
CD _____ ECD 3087
K-Tel / Jan '95 / K-Tel.

WHEN A MAN LOVES A WOMAN (2)
When a man loves a woman / Warm and tender love / Just out of reach / Dark end of the street / Cover me / My special prayer / Sudden stop / You're all around me / It tears me up / Out of left field / Take time to know her / Baby help me
CD _____ PWKS 547
Carlton Home Entertainment / Oct '89 / Carlton Home Entertainment.

Sleep

SLEEPS HOLY MOUNTAIN
Dragonaut / Druid / Evil gypsy / Some grass / Aquarian / Holy mountain / Inside the sun / From beyond / Nain's baptism
CD _____ MOSH 079CD
Earache / Mar '93 / Vital.

VOLUME ONE
CD _____ TUPCD 034
Tupelo / Feb '92 / Disc.

Sleep Chamber

SECRETS OV 23
CD _____ EEE 014CD

Musica Maxima Magnetica / Sep '93 / Plastic Head.

Sleeper

PREPARING FOR TOMORROW'S BREAKDOWN
CD _____ EXC 0122
Excursion / Jun '94 / SRD.

SMART
Inbetweener / Swallow / Delicious / Hunch / Amuse / Behead / Lady love your country-side / Vegas / Poor flying man / Alice in vain / Twisted / Pyrotechnician
CD _____ SLEEPCD 007
Indolent / Feb '95 / Vital / BMG / 3MV.

Sleeping Dogs Wake

SUGAR KISSES
CD _____ HY 39100832
Hyperium / Dec '93 / Plastic Head.

Sleepyhead

STAR DUSTER
CD _____ HMS 2142
Homestead / Dec '94 / SRD.

Sleight Of Hand

SECEDE
CD _____ HMRXD 196
Heavy Metal / Nov '95 / Sony.

Slick, Earl

IN YOUR FACE
CD _____ CDZORRO 34
Music For Nations / Sep '91 / Pinnacle.

Slick Rick

BEHIND BARS
CD _____ 5238472
Def Jam / Feb '95 / PolyGram.

GREAT ADVENTURES OF SLICK RICK, THE
Treat her like a prostitute / Ruler's back / Children's story / Moment I feared / Let's get crazy / Indian girl / Teenage love / Mona Lisa / Kit (what's the scoop) / Hey young world / Teacher teacher / Lick the balls
CD _____ 5273592
Def Jam / Jan '96 / PolyGram.

RULERS BACK, THE
CD _____ 5234802
Def Jam / Jan '96 / PolyGram.

Slickee Boys

FASHIONABLE LATE
CD _____ ROSE 147CD
New Rose / May '88 / Direct / ADA.

LIVE AT LAST
Gotta tell my why / Dream lovers / Missing part / Sleepless nights / Disconnected / Droppin' off to sleep / Brain that refused to die / Death lane / Life of the party / Pictures of matchstick men / When I go to the beach / Jailbait Janet / This party sucks / Here to stay
CD _____ ROSE 169CD
New Rose / Aug '89 / Direct / ADA.

Slimani, Abdel Ali

MRAYA
Laziza / Habibti / Zeyna / Mraya / Yasmin / Alger / Hadi / Ana guellile / Ana guellile (dub)
CD _____ CDRW 55
Realworld / Jan '96 / EMI / Sterns.

Slinger, Cees

LIVE AT THE NORTH SEA JAZZ FESTIVAL
CD _____ MCD 198244
Limetree / Oct '92 / New Note.

Slipstream

SIDE EFFECTS
CD _____ CHE 37CD
Che / Nov '95 / SRD.

SLIPSTREAM
CD _____ CHE 22CD
Che / Mar '95 / SRD.

Slits

CUT
Instant hit / So tough / Spend spend spend / Shoplifting / FM / Ping pong affair / Newtown / Love and romance / Typical girls / Adventures close to home
CD _____ IMCD 90
Island / Feb '90 / PolyGram.

Sloane, Carol

HEART'S DESIRE
Secret love / Memories of you / Heart's desire / September in the rain (CD only) / Devil may care / You must believe in Spring / Them there eyes / Never never land (CD only) / My ship (CD only) / He loves and she loves / Fairy tales / Robbin's nest / You'll see / For Susannah Kyle

CD _____ CCD 4503
Concord Jazz / May '92 / New Note.

SONGS CARMEN SANG
I'm gonna lock my heart (and throw away the key) / What can I say after I say I'm sorry / If the moon turns green / Sunday / Suppertime / Just you, just me / It's like reaching for the moon / What a little moonlight can do / Cloudy morning / Autumn nocturne / That old black magic / Folks who live on the hill / I'm a errand girl for rhythm
CD _____ CCD 4663
Concord Jazz / Sep '95 / New Note.

SWEET & SLOW
Sometime ago / One morning in May / I'm way ahead of the game / I'm getting sentimental over you / Until I met you / Sweet and slow / You're getting to be a habit / Woman's intuition / Baubles, bangles and beads / Older man / One hour / I got it bad and that ain't good
CD _____ CCD 4564
Concord Jazz / Aug '93 / New Note.

WHEN I LOOK IN YOUR EYES
Simple life / Isn't this a lovely day (to be caught in the rain) / Midnight sun / Take your shoes off, baby / I didn't know about you / Soon / Old devil moon / Let's face the music and dance / Something cool / Tulip or turnip / I was telling him about you / When I look in your eyes / Will you still be mine
CD _____ CCD 4619
Concord Jazz / Nov '94 / New Note.

Sloppy Seconds

DESTROYED
I don't wanna be a homosexual / Come back Traci / Take you home / Black roses / Runnin' from the C.I.A. / Horror of party beach / Black mail / So fucked up / Germany / Janie is a nazi / I want 'em dead / If I had a woman / Veronica / Candy man / Steal your beer / Time bomb
CD _____ CDZORR 071
Metal Blade / Mar '94 / Pinnacle.

KNOCK YOUR BLOCK OFF
CD _____ TAANG 71CD
Taang / Jun '93 / Plastic Head.

SLOPPY SECONDS
CD _____ TAANG 059CD
Taang / Jun '92 / Plastic Head.

WHERE THE EAGLES DARE
CD _____ MA 113231CD
Musical Tragedies / Nov '92 / SRD.

Slovenly

HIGHWAY TO HANNOS
CD _____ SST 287 CD
SST / May '93 / Plastic Head.

RIPOSTE
Way untruths are / Old / new / On the surface / Prejudice / Emma / Enormous critics / Myer's dark / Not mobile / As if it always happens / Little resolve
CD _____ SST 089 CD
SST / May '93 / Plastic Head.

WE SHOOT FOR THE MOON
CD _____ SST 209 CD
SST / Mar '89 / Plastic Head.

Slow Burn

CANDY FROM A STRANGER
CD _____ SPCD 04
Shadow Play / Nov '93 / Plastic Head.

Slowdive

JUST FOR A DAY
CD _____ CRELPCD 094
Creation / Aug '91 / 3MV / Vital.

PYGMALION
Rutti / Crazy for you / Miranda / Trellisaze / Cello / Just heaven / Visions of la / Blue skied an' clear / All of us
CD _____ CRECD 168
Creation / Feb '95 / 3MV / Vital.

SOUVLAKI
CD _____ CRECD 139
Creation / May '93 / 3MV / Vital.

Slowly

MING
CD _____ CHILLCD 003
Chillout / Oct '94 / Disc / Kudos.
CD _____ CHILLXCD 003
Chillout / Apr '95 / Disc / Kudos.

Slowpoke

MADCHEN
CD _____ GROW 222
Grass / Oct '94 / SRD.

Sludgeworth

SLUDGEWORTH
CD _____ LOOKOUT 131CD
Lookout / Nov '95 / SRD.

Slug

OUT SOUND, THE
X-Chest / Aurora F / Here and now / Crawl / Sung II meat / King of ghosts / Symbol for snack / Lofthouse / Co-ordinate points / Kitty thai spice
CD _____ PCP 013-2
Matador / Aug '94 / Vital.

Slugbait

MEDIUM TO HEAVY FLOW
CD _____ DPROMCD 26
Dirter Promotions / Jul '95 / Pinnacle.

Sluggy Ranks

GHETTO YOUTH BUST
Ghetto youth bust / Jah is calling I / Surrender your heart / Badness nah go work / Take the slug / 95% Black and 5% white / Girls time now / Loving Jah Jah / No money naah run / No pardon / Mi love oono bad / Badge
CD _____ FILECD 457
Profile / Oct '94 / Pinnacle.

Slum Turkeys

COMMUNICATE
CD _____ COX 029CD
Meantime / Apr '92 / Vital / Cadillac.

Slunk

COWBOY SONGS FOR COUNTRY LOVERS
Tura satana / Pigsty / Frauleins in uniform / Tim Turan / Twenty four track / Spouted / Drugs and pygmies / Wirehead / Total mekon / Sweet story / Jack it / Nothing can bring me down
CD _____ NISHI 221CD
Nightshift / Jun '92 / Vital.

Slutt

MODEL YOUTH
Angel / Breaking all the rules / Twisted / Women of the night / Revolution / Atomic envelope / T.K.O. / Thrill me / Shooting for love / Through the fire / Too far to run / Model youth / Blue suede shoes
CD _____ NEATCD 1043
Neat / '88 / Plastic Head.

Sly & Robbie

BLAZING HORNS IN DUB
CD _____ RNCD 2097
Rhino / Mar '95 / Jetstar / Magnum Music Group / THE.

CRUCIAL REGGAE (Driven By Sly & Robbie) (Various Artists)
Music is my desire / New age music / Just like that / Saturday evening / Reggae fever / One love jamdown / Rainbow culture / Jogging / Happiness / Some guys have all the luck
CD _____ RRCD 37
Reggae Refreshers / Jul '92 / PolyGram / Vital.

DUB ROCKERS DELIGHT
Leaving dub / Dub glory / Righteous dub / Dub to my woman / Night of dub / Dub softly / Doctor in dub / Bound in dub / Dub in government / Jah in dub
CD _____ CDBM 055
Blue Moon / '91 / Magnum Music Group / Greensleeves / Hot Shot / ADA / Cadillac / Discovery.

MONEY DUB
CD _____ RNCD 2063
Rhino / Jun '94 / Jetstar / Magnum Music Group / THE.

OVERDRIVE IN OVERDUB
CD _____ SONCD 0055
Sonic Sounds / Jan '94 / Jetstar.

PRESENT POWERMATIC VOLUME 1
CD _____ RASCD 3111
Greensleeves / Mar '93 / Total/BMG / Jetstar / SRD.

REGGAE GREATS (A Dub Experience)
Destination unknown / Assault on Station 5 / Joyride / Demolition city / Computer malfunction / Jailbreak / Skull and crossbones / Back to base
CD _____ RRCD 29
Reggae Refreshers / Sep '91 / PolyGram / Vital.

REMEMBER PRECIOUS TIMES
CD _____ RASCD 3109
Ras / Mar '93 / Jetstar / Greensleeves / SRD / Direct.

RHYTHM KILLERS
Fire / Boops (Here to go) / Let's rock / Yes we can can / Rhythm killer / Bank job
CD _____ 842 785 2
Island / '90 / PolyGram.

SLY & ROBBIE PRESENT JACKIE MITTOO (Sly & Robbie/Jackie Mittoo)
CD _____ RNCD 2108
Rhino / Jun '95 / Jetstar / Magnum Music Group / THE.

Sly and Robbie Hits 1987-1990

SLY AND ROBBIE HITS 1987-1990
CD _____ SONCD 0010
Sonic Sounds / Jan '91 / Jetstar.

SLY AND ROBBIE PRESENT THE PUNISHERS
CD _____ CIDM 1104
Mango / Nov '93 / Vital / PolyGram.

TAXI FARE
CD _____ HBCD 39
Heartbeat / Jul '87 / Greensleeves / Jetstar / Direct / ADA.

Sly & The Revolutionaries

SENSI DUB VOLUMES 1 & 7 (Sly & The Revolutionaries/Jah Power Band) (Sly & The Revolutionaries/Jah Power Band)
CD _____ OMCD 030
Original Music / Sep '95 / SRD / Jetstar.

Small

CAKES
CD _____ ROCK 6078-2
Rockville / Mar '93 / SRD.

CHIN MUSIC
Mona skips breakfast / Shaken, not stirred / Weather king / Tumble dry / Pretty side down / Toastmaster / My head is full of chocolate / Pet rock / Could you be on my side / Scenic route / Start with the victim
CD _____ A 061D
Alias / Oct '94 / Vital.

SILVER GLEAMING DEATH MACHINE
Steal some candy / Dert factor / Wind, the rain and the lava / Halter and flick / Vega and Boston / B is for bridge / Three-legged race / Do the math / Copping chords / Map of the stars / There's a hatchet buried around here somewhere / Shunned off, pissed off / Top of the hill
CD _____ A 089D
Alias / Oct '95 / Vital.

TRUE ZERO HOOK
True zero hook / Off balance / Noodles / Makes me high / Red comes up / Rechose / Finding it hard / Saturday / Wall to paint on / Before we forget / Get used to it / Chopsocky
CD _____ A 050D
Alias / Nov '93 / Vital.

Small Faces

AUTUMN STONE
Here comes the nice / Autumn stone / Collibosher / All or nothing / Red balloon / Lazy Sunday / Call it something nice / I can't make it / Afterglow of your love / Sha la la la lee / Universal / Rollin' over / If I were a carpenter / Every little bit hurts / My mind's eye / Tin soldier / Just passing / Itchycoo Park / Hey girl / Wide eyed girl on the wall / What'cha gonna do about it / Wam bam thank you mam
CD _____ CLACD 114
Castle / Nov '86 / BMG.

FROM THE BEGINNING
Runaway / My mind's eye / Yesterday, today and tomorrow / That man / My way of giving / Hey girl / Tell me, have you ever seen me / Come back and take this hurt off me / All or nothing / Baby don't do it / Plum Nellie / Sha la la la lee / You really got a hold on me / What'cha gonna do about it
CD _____ 8207662
London / May '91 / PolyGram.

GREATEST HITS: SMALL FACES
Itchycoo Park / Wham bam thank you ma-'am / Universal / Son of a baker / Rene / Here comes the nice / Tin soldier / Autumn stone / Afterglow of your love / Red balloon / All or nothing / Lazy Sunday
CD _____ CLACD 128
Castle / Apr '89 / BMG.

GREEN CIRCLES
CD _____ NEXCD 163
Sequel / Apr '91 / BMG.

HERE COMES THE NICE
CD _____ CD 12221
Laserlight / Apr '94 / Target/BMG.

HIT SINGLE COLLECTABLES
CD _____ DISK 4504
Disky / Apr '94 / THE / BMG / Discovery / Pinnacle.

IMMEDIATE YEARS, THE (4CD Set)
You really got me / Money money / What-cha gonna do about it / Sha la la la lee / Hey girl / My mind's eye / My mind's eye (2) / All or nothing / Yesterday, today & tomorrow / I can't make it / Just passing / Tin soldier / I feel much better / Lazy Sunday / Rollin' over / Universal / Donkey rides, a penny, a glass / Afterglow / Wham, bam, thank you Mam / I can't make it (2) / Just passing (2) / Here comes the nice (2) / Itchycoo Park (2) / I'm only dreaming (2) / Tin soldier (2) / I feel much better (2) / Universal (2) / Donkey rides, a penny, a glass (2) / Wham, bam, thank you Mam (2) / (Tell me) Have you ever seen me / Something I want to tell you / Feeling lonely / Happy boys happy / Things are going to get better / My way of giving / Green circles / Become like you / Get yourself to-gether / All our yesterdays / Talk to you / Show me the way / Up the wooden hills to Bedfordshire / Eddie's dreaming / Ogden's nut gone flake / Afterglow of / Long agos and world's apart / Rene / Song of a baker / Lazy Sunday (2) / Happiness Stan / Rollin' over (2) / Hungry intruder / Journey / Hap-pydaystoytown / Rollin' over (live) / If I were a carpenter / Every little bit hurts (live) / All or nothing (live) / Tin soldier (live) / Call it something nice / Autumn stone / Every little bit hurts / Collibosher / Red balloon / Don't burst my bubble / (Tell me) Have you ever seen me (2) / Green circles (2) / Picaninny / Pig trotters / War of the worlds / Wide-eyed girl on the wall / Tin soldier (instrumental) / Green circles (3) / Wham, bam, thank you Mam (3) / Collibosher (2) / Hungry intruder (2) / Red balloon (2) / Autumn stone (2) / Wide-eyed girl on the wall (2)
CD Set _____ CDIMMBOX 1
Immediate / Oct '95 / Charly / Target/BMG.

IT'S ALL OR NOTHING
Sha la la la lee / Sorry she's mine / All or nothing / Grow your own / Come on children / Don't stop what you're doing / Own up time / What's a matter baby / I've got mine / It's too late / Runaway / Almost grown / You better believe it / My minds eye
CD _____ 5500472
Spectrum/Karussell / May '93 / PolyGram / THE.

ITCHYCOO PARK
CD _____ CD 12208
Laserlight / Aug '93 / Target/BMG.

OGDEN'S NUT GONE FLAKE
Ogden's nut gone flake / Afterglow of your love / Long agos and worlds apart / Rene / Son of a baker / Lazy Sunday / Happiness Stan / Rollin' over / Hungry intruder / Journey / Mad John / Happy days toy town / Tin soldier (live)
CD _____ CDIMM 006
Charly / Feb '94 / Charly / THE / Cadillac.

SINGLES A'S AND B'S, THE
What'cha gonna do about it / Hey girl / My mind's eye / E to D / Itchycoo Park / Lazy Sunday / Wham bam thank you man / I'm only dreaming / I can't dance with you / Sha la la la lee / All or nothing / I can't make it / Here comes the nice / Tin soldier / Afterglow of your love / Talk to you / Donkey rides, a penny a glass / It's too late
CD _____ SEECD 293
See For Miles/C5 / Jun '90 / Pinnacle.

SMALL FACES
(Tell me) Have you ever seen me / Something I want to tell you / Feeling lonely / Happy boys happy / Things are going to get better / My way of giving / Green circles / Become like you / Get yourself together / All our yesterdays / Talk to you / Show me the way / Up the wooden hills to Bedfordshire / Eddie's dreaming
CD _____ CDIMM 004
Charly / Feb '94 / Charly / THE / Cadillac.

Small Factory

FOR IF YOU CANNOT FLY
CD _____ QUIGD 6
Quigley / Feb '95 / EMI.

Small, Fred

EVERYTHING POSSIBLE
CD _____ FF 70625CD
Flying Fish / Dec '93 / Roots / CM / Direct / ADA.

I WILL STAND FAST
CD _____ FF 704941
Flying Fish / Oct '89 / Roots / CM / Direct / ADA.

JAGUAR
CD _____ FF 570CD
Flying Fish / May '93 / Roots / CM / Direct / ADA.

NO LIMIT
CD _____ ROU 4018CD
Rounder / Jan '94 / CM / Direct / ADA / Cadillac.

Small, Judy

BEST OF - WORD OF MOUTH, THE
Alison and me / How many times / Mothers, daughters, wives / Manly ferry song / Walls and windows / Much too much trouble / Golden arches / Speaking hands, hearing eyes / One voice in the crowd / Song for Jacqueline / Alice Martin / Mary Parker's lament / Family maiden aunt / For women of our time / Futures exchange
CD _____ CDTRAX 050
Greentrax / Mar '92 / Conifer / Duncans / ADA / Direct.

BEST OF THE 80'S
CD _____ CMMCD 007
Larrikin / Jun '94 / Roots / Direct / ADA / CM.

SECOND WIND
CD _____ CMM 008CD
Larrikin / Jul '94 / Roots / Direct / ADA / CM.

Small, Michael

MOBSTERS
CD _____ VSD 5334
Varese Sarabande/Colosseum / Aug '91 / Pinnacle / Silva Screen.

Smart, Leroy

EVERY TIME
CD _____ RASCD 3139
Ras / Jun '94 / Jetstar / Greensleeves / SRD / Direct.

LEROY SMART & FRIENDS
CD _____ LG2 1113
Lagoon / Aug '95 / Magnum Music Group / THE.

LET EVERYONE SURVIVE
CD _____ JMC 200207
Jamaica Gold / May '89 / THE / Magnum Music Group / Jetstar.

PRIVATE MESSAGE
CD _____ DGVCD 2024
Greensleeves / Sep '93 / Total/BMG / Jetstar.

TALK'BOUT FRIEND
CD _____ VYDCD 09
Vine Yard / Sep '95 / Grapevine.

Smart Went Crazy

NOW WE'RE EVEN
CD _____ DISS 96CD
Dischord / Jan '96 / SRD.

Smarties

OPERATION THUNDERBUNNY
CD _____ 859 314
Steamhammer / Jun '89 / Pinnacle / Plastic Head.

SMASH

SELF ABUSED
Revisited no. 5 / Barrabas / Oh ovary / Altruism / Reflections of you (Remember me) / Self abused / Scream silent / Another love / Another shark in the deep end of my swimming pool / Real surreal / Dear Lou / Trainspotter (On FLATCD 6/FLATLPX 6 only) / A.L.L.Y.C. (On FLATCD 6/FLATLPX 6 only) / Trainspotter (On FLATLPX 6 only)
CD _____ FLATCD 6
Hi Rise / Sep '94 / EMI / Pinnacle.

Smashed Gladys

SMASHED GLADYS
CD _____ HMUSA 49
Heavy Metal / Nov '85 / Sony.

Smashers

LOUD, CONFIDENT AND WRONG
CD _____ AP 076CD
Appaloosa / Jun '92 / ADA / Magnum Music Group.

Smashing Pumpkins

GISH
I am one / Siva / Rhinoceros / Bury me / Crush / Snail / Fristessa / Window paine / Daydream / Suffer
CD _____ HUTCDX 2
Hut / May '94 / EMI.

MELLON COLLIE AND THE INFINITE SADNESS (2CD/MC Set)
Mellon Collie and the infinite sadness / Tonight tonight / Jellybelly / Zero / Here is no why / Bullet with butterfly wings / To forgive / Fuck you (an ode to no one) / Love / Cupid De Locke / Galapogos / Muzzle / Porcelina of the vast oceans / Take me down / Where boys fear to tread / Bodies / Thirty three / In the arms of sleep / 1979 / Tales of a scorched earth / Thru the eyes of Ruby / Stumbleine / X.Y.U. / We only come out at night / Beautiful / Lily (my one and only) / By starlight / Farewell and goodnight
CD Set _____ CDHUTD 30
Hut / Nov '95 / EMI.

SIAMESE DREAM
Cherub rock / Quiet / Today / Hummer / Rocket / Disarm / Soma / Geek U.S.A. / Mayonaise / Spaceboy / Silverfuck / Sweet sweet / Luna
CD _____ CDHUT 19
Hut / Jun '93 / EMI.

Smear, Pat

SO YOU FELL IN LOVE WITH A MUSICIAN
CD _____ SST 294 CD
SST / May '93 / Plastic Head.

Smersh

EMMANUELLE GOES TO BANGKOK
Touch of Venus / Great Ceasar's ghost / Burn / Titanic fantastic / Blonde devil / You remind me of summer / Armoured man / Under your hoop / Brown out / Riding with the Pharoahs / Discotes
CD _____ KK 47 CD
KK / Apr '90 / Plastic Head.

GREATEST STORY EVER DISTORTED, THE
Licorice rope / Jack your metal / Japanese princess / Bootie heaven / Spook house
CD _____ KK 019 CD
KK / Mar '89 / Plastic Head.

Smith & Mighty

BASS IS MATERNAL
CD _____ ZCDKR 2
More Rockers / Nov '95 / 3MV / Sony.

Smith, Al

HEAR MY BLUES
Night time is the right time / Pledging my love / I've got a girl / I'll be alright / Come on pretty baby / Tears in my eyes / Never let me go / I've got the right kind of lovin'
CD _____ OBCCD 514
Original Blues Classics / Apr '94 / Complete/Pinnacle / Wellard / Cadillac.

Smith, Barkin Bill

BLUEBIRD BLUES
CD _____ DD 652
Delmark / Mar '87 / Hot Shot / ADA / CM / Direct / Cadillac.

Smith, Bessie

BESSIE SMITH
CD _____ DVBC 9092
Deja Vu / May '95 / THE.

BESSIE SMITH 1925-33
CD _____ GOJCD 53090
Giants Of Jazz / Mar '92 / Target/BMG / Cadillac.

BLUE SPIRIT BLUES
I'm down in the dumps / Blue spirit blues / Kitchen man / Foolish man blues / Thinking blues / Devil's gonna git you / Send me to the 'lectric chair / I'm wild about that thing / You've got to give me some / Standing in the rain blues / He's got me goin' / Do your duty / Dyin' by the hour / Lock and key / Gimme a pigfoot / Take me for a buggy ride / I used to be your sweet mama / Trombone cholly / Alexander's ragtime band / Good man is hard to find
CD _____ CDGRF 102
Tring / '93 / Tring / Prism.

CLASSICS 1923
CD _____ CLASSICS 761
Classics / Jun '94 / Discovery / Jazz Music.

CLASSICS 1923-24
CD _____ CLASSICS 787
Classics / Nov '94 / Discovery / Jazz Music.

CLASSICS 1924-25
CD _____ CLASSICS 812
Classics / May '95 / Discovery / Jazz Music.

CLASSICS 1925-27
CD _____ CLASSICS 843
Classics / Nov '95 / Discovery / Jazz Music.

COMPLETE COLLECTION VOL.1, THE (2CD Set)
Downhearted blues / Gulf coast blues / Aggravatin' papa / Beale Street Mama / Baby, won't you please come home / Oh daddy blues / T'aint nobody's business if I do / Keeps on a-rainin' / Mama's got the blues / Outside of that / Bleeding hearted blues / Lady luck blues / Yodling blues / Midnight blues / If you don't, I know who will / Nobody in town can bake a sweet jelly roll like man / Jailhouse blues / St. Louis gal / Sam Jones blues / Graveyard dream blues / Cemetery blues / Far away blues / I'm going back to my used to be / Whoa, Tillie, take your time / My sweetie went away / Any woman's blues / Chicago bound blues / Mistreating daddy / Frosty morning blues / Haunted house blues / Eavesdropper's blues / Easy come, easy go blues / Sorrowful blues / Pinchbacks - Take 'em away / Rcoking chair blues / Ticket agent / Ease your window down / Boweavil blues / Hateful blues
CD Set _____ 4678952
Columbia / May '91 / Sony.

COMPLETE COLLECTION VOL.2, THE (2CD Set)
Frankie blues / Moonshine blues / Lou'siana low-down blues / Mountain top blues / Work house blues / House rent blues / Salt water blues / Rainy weather blues / Weeping willow blues / Bye bye blues / Sing sing prison blues / Follow the deal on down / Sinful blues / Woman's trouble blues / Love me daddy blues / Dying gambler's blues / St. Louis blues / Reckless blues / Sobbin' hearted blues / Cold in hand blues / You've been a good ole wagon / Cake walkin' babies from home / Yellow dog blues / Soft pedal blues / Dixie flyer blues / Nashville women's blues / Careless love blues / J.C. Holmes blues / I ain't got nobody / My man blues / Nobody's blues but mine / New gulf coast blues / Florida bound blues / At the Christmas ball / I've been mistreated and I don't like it

CD Set _____ 4687672
Columbia / May '93 / Sony.

COMPLETE COLLECTION VOL.4, THE (2CD Set)
Standin' in the rain blues / It won't be you / Spider man blues / Empty bed blues (part 1) / Empty bed blues (part 2) / Put it right here (Or keep it out there) / Yes indeed he do / Devil's gonna git you / You ought to be ashamed / Washwoman's blues / Slow and easy man / Poor man's blues / Please help me to get him out of my mind / Me and my gin / I'm wild about that thing / You've got to give me some / Kitchen man / I've got what it takes / Nobody knows when you're down and out / Take it right back / He's got me goin' / It makes my love come down / Wasted life blues / Dirty no-gooders blues / Blue spirit blues / Worn out Papa blues / You don't understand / Don't cry baby / Keep it to yourself / New Orleans hop skop blues / See if I'll care / Baby have pity on me / On revival day (A Rhythmic spiritual) / Moan you moaners / Hustlin' Dan / Black mountain blues / In the house blues / Long old road / Blue blues / Shipwreck blues
CD Set _____ 472934 2
Columbia / May '94 / Sony.

COMPLETE St. LOUIS BLUES
CD _____ JZ-CD308
Suisa / Mar '91 / Jazz Music / THE.

DO YOUR DUTY
CD _____ IGOCD 2008
Indigo / Nov '94 / Direct / ADA.

EMPRESS OF THE BLUES
Downhearted blues / T'aint nobody's business if I do / St. Louis blues / You've been a good ole wagon / I ain't gonna play no second fiddle / Young woman's blues / Muddy Waters / Empty red blues / Nobody knows when you are down and out / Black mountain blues / Do your duty / Gimme a pigfoot / Surf coast blues / Won't you please come home / Easy come, easy go blues / Rockin' chair blues
CD _____ CDCD 1030
Charly / Mar '93 / Charly / THE / Cadillac.

EMPRESS OF THE BLUES
Gimme a pigfoot and a bottle of beer / Downhearted blues / Yellow dog blues / Careless love / Good man is hard to find / St. Louis blues / Do your duty / Cold in hand blues / Send me to the 'lectric chair / Empty bed blues / Nobody's blues but mine / Alexander's ragtime band / Them's graveyard words / New Orleans hopscotch blues / One and two blues / Take me for a buggy ride / Squeeze me / Nobody knows you when you're down and out
CD _____ CBCD 001
Collector's Edition / Jan '96 / Magnum Music Group.

EMPRESS OF THE BLUES, THE (Charly Blues - Masterworks Vol. 31)
CD _____ CDBM 31
Charly / Jan '93 / Charly / THE / Cadillac.

GREATEST BLUES SINGER IN THE WORLD, THE
Downhearted blues / Gulf coast blues / Nobody in town can bake a sweet jelly roll like mine / Jailhouse blues / Graveyard dream blues / Cemetery blues / Frosty morning blues / Haunted house blues / Easy come, easy go blues / Follow the deal on down / Sinful blues / Lady luck blues / Reckless blues / Cold in hand blues / Mean old bed-bug blues / Yellow dog blues / Sweet mistreater / Empty bed blues / Blue spirit blues / Black mountain blues / In the house blues / Nashville woman's blues
CD _____ CD 52009
Blues Encore / '92 / Target/BMG.

MAMA'S GOT THE BLUES
CD _____ TPZ 1002
Topaz Jazz / Jul '94 / Pinnacle / Cadillac.

RECKLESS BLUES
CD _____ CD 14546
Jazz Portraits / Jan '94 / Jazz Music.

SINGS THE JAZZ 1923-33
CD _____ 157902
Jazz Archives / Jun '93 / Jazz Music / Discovery / Cadillac.

St. LOUIS BESSIE & ALICE MOORE VOL. 1 (1927-29)
CD _____ DOCD 5290
Blues Document / Dec '94 / Swift / Jazz Music / Hot Shot.

St. LOUIS BESSIE & ALICE MOORE VOL. 2 (1934-41)
CD _____ DOCD 5291
Blues Document / Dec '94 / Swift / Jazz Music / Hot Shot.

Smith, Brian

MOONLIGHT SAX
CD _____ NELCD 104
Timbuktu / Aug '93 / Pinnacle.

UNFORGETTABLE SAX
CD _____ NELCD 105
Timbuktu / Aug '93 / Pinnacle.

Smith, Bryan

BEST OF VOLUME 1, THE (Smith, Bryan & His Piano)
CD _____ CDTS 002
Maestro / Aug '93 / Savoy.

BRYAN'S CHRISTMAS BOX
CD _____ CDTS 017
Maestro / Dec '95 / Savoy.

DANCING FOR PLEASURE (Smith, Bryan & His Festival Orchestra)
Horse guards blue / Stella d'Italia (Star of Italy) / Closer / Once in a while / Edwardians / Sobre las olas (Over the waves) / I'll never say Never Again again / That's a plenty / Blue Tahitian moon / Just for a while / Suzy / Tango 65 / Egerland march / Bandstand march / Make believe / It looks like rain in Cherry Blossom Lane / Kind regards / Pink Colombine / Rags and tatters / Stumbling / Student Prince waltz / Anytime's kissing time / Tango hacienda / Tango sombrero
CD _____ CC 275
Music For Pleasure / Oct '91 / EMI.

DANSAN SEQUENCE COLLECTION VOL 1, THE (Smith, Bryan & His Concert Orchestra)
CD _____ DNSN 901
President / May '93 / Grapevine / Target/BMG / Jazz Music / President.

DANSAN SEQUENCE COLLECTION VOL 2, THE (Smith, Bryan & His Concert Orchestra)
CD _____ DNSN 902
Dansan / '93 / Savoy / President / Target/BMG.

MARCHING AND WALTZING
CD _____ DLCD 113
Dulcima / May '94 / Savoy / THE.

Smith, Byther

ADDRESSING THE NATION WITH BLUES
CD _____ JSPCD 254
JSP / Aug '94 / ADA / Target/BMG / Direct / Cadillac / Complete/Pinnacle.

I'M A MAD MAN
CD _____ BB 9527CD
Bullseye / May '93 / Bullseye / ADA.

Smith, Carrie

FINE AND MELLOW
CD _____ ACD 164
Audiophile / May '95 / Jazz Music / Swift.

Smith, Charlene

FEEL THE GOOD TIMES
Feel the good times / Count on me / Sometimes / I learned my lesson / Too much for me / Let it slide / I got what you need / World goes round / No more lies / What'cha do
CD _____ WOLCD 1069
China / Jul '95 / Pinnacle.

Smith, Cheikh M.

TOUBABOU
CD _____ WCOA 203CD
World Circuit / May '93 / New Note / Direct / Cadillac / ADA.

TOUBABOU BALAFOLA
CD _____ OA 203
PAM / Feb '94 / Direct / ADA.

Smith, Clara

CLARA SMITH #1 - 1923-24
CD _____ DOCD 5364
Document / Jul '95 / Jazz Music / Hot Shot / ADA.

CLARA SMITH #2 - 1924
CD _____ DOCD 5365
Document / Jul '95 / Jazz Music / Hot Shot / ADA.

CLARA SMITH #3 - 1925
CD _____ DOCD 5366
Document / Jul '95 / Jazz Music / Hot Shot / ADA.

CLARA SMITH #4 - 1926-27
CD _____ DOCD 5367
Document / Jul '95 / Jazz Music / Hot Shot / ADA.

CLARA SMITH #5 - 1927-29
CD _____ DOCD 5368
Document / Jul '95 / Jazz Music / Hot Shot / ADA.

CLARA SMITH #6 - 1930-32
CD _____ DOCD 5369
Document / Jul '95 / Jazz Music / Hot Shot / ADA.

Smith, Darden

LITTLE VICTORIES
Place in the sun / Loving arms / Little victories / Love left town / Hole in the river / Dream Intro / Dream's a dream / Precious time / Days on end / Levee song / Only one dream
CD _____ 473603-2
Columbia / Feb '94 / Sony.

NATIVE SOIL
Bus stop bench / Red sky / Little Maggie / Veteran's day / Sticks and stones / Keep an open mind / Wild West show / Painter's song / Two dollar novels / God's will / Clatter and roll
CD _____ WM 1009
Watermelon / Jun '93 / ADA / Direct.

Smith, Derek

DARK EYES (Smith, Derek Trio)
CD _____ PRSCDSP 204
Prestige / May '94 / Total/BMG.

DEREK SMITH PLAYS THE MUSIC OF JEROME KERN
Ol' man river / Fine romance / Folks who live on the hill / I'm old fashioned / Long ago and far away / Way you look tonight / I won't dance
CD _____ PCD 7055
Progressive / Jun '93 / Jazz Music.

PLAYS PASSIONATE PIANO
CD _____ MICH 4526
Hindsight / Sep '92 / Target/BMG / Jazz Music.

Smith, Gary

RHYTHM GUITAR
CD _____ IMPCD 18920
Impetus / Mar '92 / CM / Wellard / Impetus / Cadillac.

Smith, Gregg

PARTY WARRIOR
CD _____ CDSGP 013
Prestige / Mar '92 / Total/BMG.

Smith, Hal

CALIFORNIA HERE I COME
CD _____ JCD 182
Jazzology / Feb '91 / Swift / Jazz Music.

MILNEBURG JOYS
CD _____ BCD 277
GHB / Oct '92 / Jazz Music.

MUSIC FROM THE MAUVE DECADES (Smith, Hal & Keith Ingram/Bobby Gordon)
CD _____ SKCD 22033
Sackville / Aug '94 / Swift / Jazz Music / Jazz Horizons / Cadillac / CM.

Smith, Huey

PITTA PATTIN' (Smith, Huey 'Piano' & Friends)
Rockin' pneumonia and the boogie woogie flu / Through fooling around / It do me good / Don't you just know it / I'll never forget / Coo coo over you / Smile for me / You got to / We like mambo / Bury me dead / I do things come) naturally / What'cha bet / I've got everything / Baby you hurt me / Blues '67 / High blood pressure
CD _____ CDCHARLY 225
Charly / Dec '90 / Charly / THE / Cadillac.

Smith, Ivy

1927-1930 (Smith, Ivy & Cow Cow Davenport)
CD _____ BDCD 6039
Blues Document / May '93 / Swift / Jazz Music / Hot Shot.

Smith, Jabbo

CLASSICS 1929-38
CD _____ CLASSICS 669
Classics / Oct '92 / Discovery / Jazz Music.

COMPLETE 1928-38 SESSIONS
CD Set _____ 158112
Jazz Archives / Dec '93 / Jazz Music / Discovery / Cadillac.

Smith, Jack

ROCKABILLY PLANET
CD _____ FF 70510
Flying Fish / Jul '89 / Roots / CM / Direct / ADA.

Smith, Jimmy

AT CLUB 'BABY GRAND' WILMINGTON, DELAWARE OCTOBER 1956
CD _____ CD 53114
Giants Of Jazz / Jan '94 / Target/BMG / Cadillac.

BACK AT THE CHICKEN SHACK
Back at the Chicken Shack / When I grow too old to dream / Minor chant / Messy Bessy / On the sunny side of the street
CD _____ CDP 7464022
Blue Note / Mar '95 / EMI.

BEST OF JIMMY SMITH (Blue Note Years)
Sermon / Fungi mama (CD only.) / When Johnny comes marching home / Jumpin' the blues / Back at the chicken shack / Champ (CD only.) / All day long (CD only.)
CD _____ BNZ 147
Blue Note / Dec '88 / EMI.

CHRISTMAS COOKIN'
CD _____ 5137112
Verve / Apr '92 / PolyGram.

FOURMOST
CD _____ MCD 9184
Milestone / Oct '93 / Jazz Music / Pinnacle / Wellard / Cadillac.

FURTHER ADVENTURES OF JIMMY & WES (Smith, Jimmy & Wes Montgomery)
CD _____ 519802-2
Verve / Feb '94 / PolyGram.

I'M MOVIN' ON
I'm movin' on / Hotel happiness / Cherry / T'aint no use / Back talk / What kind of fool am I / Organic greenery / Day in, day out
CD _____ CDP 8327502
Blue Note / Jun '95 / EMI.

JAZZ MASTERS
CD _____ 5218552
Verve / Feb '94 / PolyGram.

MIDNIGHT SPECIAL
Midnight special / Subtle one / Jumpin' the blues / Why was I born / One o'clock jump
CD _____ BNZ 162
Blue Note / May '91 / EMI.

PRIME TIME
CD _____ MCD 9176
Milestone / Oct '93 / Jazz Music / Pinnacle / Wellard / Cadillac.

SUM SERIOUS BLUES
Sum serious blues / Around the corner / Hurry change if you're comin' / Sermon / You've changed / Moof's blues / Open for business / I'd rather drink Muddy Water
CD _____ MCD 9207
Milestone / Apr '94 / Jazz Music / Pinnacle / Wellard / Cadillac.

Smith, Johnny

LEGENDS (Smith, Johnny & George Van Eps)
I'm old fashioned / Macho's lullaby / Round Midnight / Wally's waltz / Black black black / Golden earrings / Romance de los pinos / Nortena / Maid with the flaxen hair / Waltz / Old castle / Sevilla / Cheek to cheek / Foggy day / Tangerine / Sunny / Why was I born / I didn't know what time it was / Tea for two / Man I love / For you / I hadn't anyone till you / I could write a book
CD _____ CCD 4616
Concord Jazz / Oct '94 / New Note.

Smith, Johnny

GEARS/FOREVER TAURUS (Smith, Johnny 'Hammond')
Tell me what to do / Los conquistadores chocolates / Lost on 23rd Street / Fantasy / Shifting gears / Can't we smile / Old devil moon / Countdown / Walk in sunshine / Ghetto samba / Cosmic voyager / My ship / Forever Taurus
CD _____ CDBPGD 037
BGP / Oct '92 / Pinnacle.

THAT GOOD FEELING / TALK THAT TALK (Smith, Johnny 'Hammond')
That good feeling / Bye bye blackbird / Autumn leaves / I'll remember April / Billie's bounce / My funny valentine / Puddin' / Talk that talk / Affair to remember / End of a love affair / Minors allowed / Riptide / Misty / Benny's diggin' / Portrait of Jennie
CD _____ CDBGPD 061
BGP / Jun '93 / Pinnacle.

Smith, Keely

BE MY LOVE
Be my love / You're nobody 'til somebody loves you / You made me love you / Smoke gets in your eyes / How deep is the ocean / Don't let the stars get in your eyes / I'd climb the highest mountain / Pretend / I'm gonna sit right down and write myself a letter / Fascination / My reverie / It's all in the game
CD _____ JASCD 321
Jasmine / Feb '94 / Wellard / Swift / Conifer / Cadillac / Magnum Music Group.

CAPITOL YEARS: KEELY SMITH (The Best Of Keely Smith)
Sweet and lovely / Cocktails for two / Song is you / I'll get by / Lullaby of the leaves / On the sunny side of the street / I can't get started (with you) / I'll never smile again / s'posin' / East of the sun and west of the moon / All the way / I never knew / I wish you love / You go to my head / Young lover has gone / Fools rush in / Don't take your love from me / Imagination
CD _____ CZ 305
Capitol / Apr '90 / EMI.

CHEROKEELY SWINGS
To each his own / Where is your heart (Moulin Rouge) / My heart cries for you / Yellow bird / That lucky old sun / Too young / True love / Secret love / Rags to riches / Young at heart / Stranger in paradise / My devotion
CD _____ JASCD 323
Jasmine / Jan '95 / Wellard / Swift / Conifer / Cadillac / Magnum Music Group.

DEARLY BELOVED
CD _____ JASCD 328
Jasmine / Nov '95 / Wellard / Swift / Conifer / Cadillac / Magnum Music Group.

KEELY CHRISTMAS
White Christmas / Christmas island / O little town of Bethlehem / Jingle bells / Here comes Santa Claus / O holy night / Silent night / Christmas song / Hark the herald angels sing / I'll be home for Christmas / Rudolph the red nosed reindeer / O come all ye faithful (Adeste fidelis) / Blue Christmas
CD _____ JASCD 329
Jasmine / Oct '94 / Wellard / Swift / Conifer / Cadillac / Magnum Music Group.

KEELY SMITH AND COUNT BASIE (Live 1963 Guard Session) (Smith, Keely & Count Basie)
CD _____ EBCD 21092
Jazzband / Feb '92 / Jazz Music / Wellard.

SPOTLIGHT ON KEELY SMITH
It's magic / You go to my head / Stardust / I can't get started (with you) / When your lover had gone / Sweet and lovely / Stormy weather / Fools rush in / Song is you / Mr. Wonderful / It's been a long, long time / I'll never smile again / Someone to watch over me / I'll get by (as long as I have you) / Don't take your love from me / Lullaby of the leaves / There will never be another you / Imagination / On the sunny side of the street / I wish you love
CD _____ CDP 7803272
Capitol / Apr '95 / EMI.

SWING YOU LOVERS
Swing you lovers / I love to you / Misty / I love you / If I could be with you one hour tonight / Hello, young lovers / All or nothing at all / All night long / Talk to me / Everybody loves a lover / They say it's wonderful / At long last love
CD _____ JASCD 322
Jasmine / Jul '94 / Wellard / Swift / Conifer / Cadillac / Magnum Music Group.

WHAT KIND OF FOOL AM I
What kind of fool am I / Fly me to the moon / More I see you / But not for me / What's new / Don't blame me / If I should lose you / Then I'll be tired of you / But beautiful / Love me tender / Nature boy / I love you so much it hurts
CD _____ JASCD 324
Jasmine / Jun '94 / Wellard / Swift / Conifer / Cadillac / Magnum Music Group.

Smith, Keith

KEITH SMITH & HIS CLIMAX BLUES BAND (Smith, Keith & His Climax Blues Band)
CD _____ BCD 27
GHB / Aug '94 / Jazz Music.

Smith, Kendra

FIVE WAYS TO DISAPPEAR
Aurelia / Bohemian zebulon / Temporarily Lucy / In your head / Space unadorned / Maggots / Drunken boat / Dirigible / Valley of the morning sun / Judge not / Get there / Saturn / Bold marauder
CD _____ CAD 5008CD
4AD / May '95 / Disc.

GUILD OF TEMPORAL ADVENTURERS, THE
Stars are in your eyes / Earth same breath / Waiting in the rain / She brings in the rain / Iridescence 31 / Wheel of the law
CD _____ FSC 001 CD
Fiasco / Aug '92 / Vital.

Smith, Leo

KULTURE JAZZ
Don't you remember / Kulture of jazz / Song of humanity / Fire-sticks, crysanthemums and moonlight / Seven rings of light in the Holy Trinity / Louis Armstrong counterpointing / Albert Ayler in a spiritual light / Kemet Omega reigns (for Billie Holiday) / Love supreme (for John Coltrane) / Mississippi delta sunrise (for Bobbie) / Mother: Sarah Brown-Smith-Wallace / Healer's voyage on the sacred river / Uprising
CD _____ 5190742
ECM / Jun '93 / New Note.

PROCESSION OF THE GREAT ANCESTRY
Blues: Jah Jah is the greatest love / Procession of the great ancestry / Flower that seeds the earth / Third world, grainery of pure earth / Who killed David Walker / Celestial sparks in the sanctuary / Nuru light: The prince of peace
CD _____ CHIEFCD 6
Chief / Jun '89 / Cadillac.

Smith, Little George

HARMONICA ACE
Rockin' / Telephone blues / Blues in the dark / Blues stay away / Have myself a ball / I found my baby / Oopin' doopin' doopin' / California blues / Hey Mr. Porter / Early one Monday morning (take 1) / Love life / Cross-eyed Suzie Lee / You don't love me / Early one Monday morning (take 2)
CD _____ CDCHD 337

Ace / Jun '91 / Pinnacle / Cadillac / Complete/Pinnacle.

Smith, Lonnie Liston

EXPANSIONS
Expansions / Dessert nights / Summer days / Voodoo woman / Peace / Shadows / My love
CD _____ ND 80934
RCA / Mar '94 / BMG.

LIVE AT THE CLUB MOZAMBIQUE
I can't stand it / Expressions / Scream / Play it back / Love bowl / Peace of mind / I want to thank you / Seven steps to heaven
CD _____ CDP 8318802
Blue Note / Apr '95 / EMI.

LOVE GODDESS
Love goddess / Obsession / Heaven / Monk's mood / Star flower / Giving you the best that I've got / Don't write cheques that your body can't cash / Dance floor / I'm your melody / Blue in green / Blue Bossa / Child is born
CD _____ STACD 4021
Star Track / Mar '94 / Koch.

VERY BEST OF LONNIE LISTON SMITH, THE
Space princess / Get down everybody (it's time for world peace) / Desert nights / Voodoo woman / Chance for peace / Visions of a new world / Song for the children / Fruit music / Quiet moments / Quiet dawn / Sunbeams / Expansions / Prelude (live) (Available on CD only) / Expansions (live) (Available on CD only)
CD _____ 74321 13761-2
RCA / Jul '93 / BMG.

WATERCOLORS
Watercolors / Sunset / Starlight and you / My love / Expansions / Song for love / Renaissance / Devika / Summer nights / Aspirations / Colors of the rainbow
CD _____ ND 83099
RCA / Jan '92 / BMG.

Smith, Mamie

MAMIE SMITH VOL.1 (1920-21)
CD _____ DOCD 5357
Blues Document / Jun '95 / Swift / Jazz Music / Hot Shot.

MAMIE SMITH VOL.2 (Get Hot)
CD _____ DOCD 5358
Blues Document / Jun '95 / Swift / Jazz Music / Hot Shot.

MAMIE SMITH VOL.3 (1922-1923)
CD _____ DOCD 5359
Blues Document / Jun '95 / Swift / Jazz Music / Hot Shot.

MAMIE SMITH VOL.4 (First Lady Of The Blues)
CD _____ DOCD 5360
Blues Document / Jun '95 / Swift / Jazz Music / Hot Shot.

Smith, Marvin

KEEPER OF THE DRUMS
Just have fun / Miss Ann / Love will find a way / Song of joy / Creeper / Now I know / Thinking of you / Simple samba song
CD _____ CCD 4325
Concord Jazz / Sep '87 / New Note.

ROAD LESS TRAVELLED, THE (Smith, Marvin 'Smitty')
Neighbourhood / Road less travelled where we meet with me part 1 / Gothic 17 / Road less travelled / I'll love you always / Salsa blue / Concerto in B.G. / Wish you were here with me part 2
CD _____ CCD 4379
Concord Jazz / Jul '89 / New Note.

Smith, Melvin

AT HIS BEST
Up on the hill / School boy blues / Reliefin' blues / They ain't come tell it right / Rampaging Mama / Homesick blues / Come back my darlin' / Real true gal / Everybody's got the blues / I remember / California baby / Looped / Baby I'll be there / I'm out of my mind / Woman trainer / Business man's blues / Sarah Kelly (from Plumnelly) / Six times six / Call me darling, call me sweetheart, dear / What's to become of me / Hot ziggety zag / Letter to my baby / I don't have to hunt no more / Every pound / Miss Brown / I feel like goin' home / It went down easy / Why do these things have to be / Things you oughta know / No baby / You can't stay here / Crazy baby
CD Set _____ BCDBH 15703
Bear Family / Nov '94 / Rollercoaster / Direct / CM / Swift / ADA.

Smith, Michael

TIME
CD _____ FF 70613
Flying Fish / Nov '94 / Roots / CM / Direct / ADA.

Smith, Michael W.

CHRISTMAS (Smith, Michael W/ Hollywood Presby. Choir/American Boys Choir)
Sing, choirs of angels / Lux venit (The Light comes) / Arise, shine, for your light has come / Anthem for Christmas / First snowfall (instrumental) / Christ the Messiah / No eye had seen / All is well / Memoirs (instrumental: The voice/Good King Wenceslas/Hark, the Herald Angels sing) / Gloria (rock version of Angels we have heard on high) / Silent night
CD _____ RRACD 0052
Reunion / Dec '89 / Nelson Word.

GO WEST YOUNG MAN
CD _____ RRACD 0063
Reunion / Jan '91 / Nelson Word.

Smith, Mike

SINATRA SONGBOOK
CD _____ DE 480
Delmark / Aug '93 / Hot Shot / ADA / CM / Direct / Cadillac.

TRAVELLER, THE (Smith, Mike Quintet)
CD _____ DDCD 462
Delmark / Nov '93 / Hot Shot / ADA / CM / Direct / Cadillac.

UNIT 7 - TRIBUTE TO CANNONBALL
CD _____ DD 444
Delmark / Oct '87 / Hot Shot / ADA / CM / Direct / Cadillac.

Smith, Patti

DREAM OF LIFE
People have the power / Going under / Up there, down there / Paths that cross / Dream of life / Where duty calls / Looking for you (I was) / Jackson song
CD _____ 262021
RCA / Jan '92 / BMG.

EASTER
Till victory / Space monkey / Because the night / Ghost dance / Babelogue / Rock 'n' roll nigger / Privilege / We three / Twenty fifth floor / Easter / Break it up / High on rebellion
CD _____ 251 128
RCA / Aug '88 / BMG.

HORSES
Gloria / Redondo beach / Birdland / Free money / Break it up / Land / Elegie / Kimberly / Land-horses / Land of 1000 dances / La mer
CD _____ 251 112
RCA / '88 / BMG.

Smith, Paul

BY THE FIRESIDE
Cupid took me for a ride / Way you look tonight / By the fireside / Wandering / Out of nowhere / "S Wonderful / Over the rainbow / Great lie / Jumper / Lauri Lou / Pick yourself up / I only have eyes for you
CD _____ SV 0225
Savoy Jazz / Oct '93 / Conifer / ADA.

SOFTLY BABY (Smith, Paul Quartet)
Softly / Taking a chance on love / Easy to love / Long live Phineas / I didn't know what time it was / I'll remember April / Invitation / I got rhythm / Man I love / Blues a la P.T.
CD _____ JASCD 311
Jasmine / May '90 / Wellard / Swift / Conifer / Cadillac / Magnum Music Group.

Smith, Ray

SHAKE AROUND
CD _____ CPCD 8117
Charly / Aug '95 / Charly / THE / Cadillac.

Smith, Slim

20 RARE GROOVES
CD _____ RNCD 2050
Rhino / Mar '94 / Jetstar / Magnum Music Group / THE.

20 SUPER HITS
CD _____ SONCD 0004
Sonic Sounds / Jan '91 / Jetstar.

RAIN FROM THE SKIES
Love power / It's alright / Don't tell your mama / Love and affection / Sunny side of the sea / Money love / Travel on / Stand up and fight / Sitting in the park / Turning point / Time has come / Take me back / Will you still love me / Burning fire / This feeling / Rain from the skies / Just a dream / Send me some lovin' / Blinded by love / Where do I turn / My conversation
CD _____ CDTRL 303
Trojan / Mar '94 / Jetstar / Total/BMG.

Smith, Steve

VITALIVE
CD _____ VBR 20512
Vera Bra / Dec '90 / Pinnacle / New Note.

Smith, Stuff

LIVE AT MONTMARTRE
CD _____ STCD 4142

625

Storyville / Feb '90 / Jazz Music / Wellard / CM / Cadillac.

LIVE IN PARIS 1965
CD _____ FCD 120
France's Concert / Oct '88 / Jazz Music / BMG.

STUFF SMITH, DIZZY GILLESPIE & OSCAR PETERSON (Smith, Stuff & Dizzy Gillespie/Oscar Peterson)
CD Set _____ 5216762
Verve / Feb '95 / PolyGram.

Smith, Tab

ACE HIGH
CD _____ DD 455
Delmark / Nov '92 / Hot Shot / ADA / CM / Direct / Cadillac.

BECAUSE OF YOU
CD _____ DD 429
Delmark / Dec '89 / Hot Shot / ADA / CM / Direct / Cadillac.

JUMP TIME 1951-52
CD _____ DD 447
Delmark / Jun '87 / Hot Shot / ADA / CM / Direct / Cadillac.

Smith, Tim

EXTRA SPECIAL OCEANLAND WORLD
CD _____ ALPHCD 020
Alphabet Business Concern / May '95 / Plastic Head.

Smith, Tommy

MISTY MORNING AND NO TIME
CD _____ AKD 040
Linn / May '95 / PolyGram.

PEEPING TOM
New road / Follow your heart / Merry go round / Slip of the tongue / Interval time (CD only.) / Simple pleasures (CD only.) / Peeping Tom / Quiet picnic (CD only.) / Affairs, please / Harlequin / Boats and boxes (CD only.) / Biting at the apple / Baked air (CD only.)
CD _____ CDBLT 1002
Blue Note / May '90 / EMI.

REMINISCENCE (Smith, Tommy & Forward Motion)
CD _____ AKD 024
Linn / Feb '94 / PolyGram.

Smith, Tony

BIG CAT
Renegade / Arabella / Botswana / Don't lose it / Dark bark / Cruisin' / Big cat / South wind / Angie
CD _____ JITCD 9502
Jazzizit / Sep '95 / New Note.

Smith, Trixie

1922-1924 VOL.1
CD _____ DOCD 5332
Blues Document / May '95 / Swift / Jazz Music / Hot Shot.

1925-1939 VOL.2
CD _____ DOCD 5333
Blues Document / May '95 / Swift / Jazz Music / Hot Shot.

Smith, TV

IMMORTAL RICH
CD _____ BAH 21
Humbug / Jan '95 / Pinnacle.

MARCH OF THE GIANTS
CD _____ COOKCD 047
Cooking Vinyl / Jul '92 / Vital.

R.I.P
CD _____ BAH 5
Humbug / Mar '93 / Pinnacle.

Smith, Warren

CALL OF THE WILD
Cave in / I don't believe I'll fall in love today / After the boy gets the girl / Whole lot of nothin' / Odds and ends / Call of the wild (unissued) / Old lonesome feeling / Call of the wild / Book of broken hearts / I fall to pieces / Foolin' around / Take good care of her / Pick me up on your way down / Just call me lonesome / Heartbreak Hotel / I still miss someone / Kissing my pillow / I can't stop loving you / Why baby why / Why I'm walkin' / Five minutes of the latest blues / Put me back together again / Bad news gets around / Hundred and sixty pounds of hurt / That's why I sing in a honky tonk / Big city ways / Blue smoke / Judge and jury / Future x / She likes attention
CD _____ BCD 15495
Bear Family / Apr '90 / Rollercoaster / Direct / CM / Swift / ADA.

CLASSIC SUN RECORDINGS
Rock 'n' roll Ruby / I'd rather be safe than sorry / Black Jack David / Ubangi stomp / Darkest cloud / So long I'm gone / Who took my baby / I couldn't take the chance / Miss Froggie / Red Cadillac and a black moustache / Stop the world (and let me off) / I fell in love / Got love you want it / Old

lonesome feeling (incomplete) / Tell me who / Tonight will be the last night / Dear John / Hank Snow medley / Do I love you / Uranium rock / Goodbye Mr. Love / Sweet sweet girl / I like your kind of love / My hanging day
CD _____ BCD 15514
Bear Family / Apr '92 / Rollercoaster / Direct / CM / Swift / ADA.

ROCKABILLY LEGEND
CD _____ CPCD 8119
Charly / Aug '95 / Charly / THE / Cadillac.

Smith, Wayne

WICKED IN A DANCE HALL
CD _____ RRTGCD 7785
Rohit / Jul '90 / Jetstar.

Smith, Whispering

WHISPERING SMITH
CD _____ PASTCD 7074
Flapper / Oct '95 / Pinnacle.

Smith, Willie

1938-40 (Smith, Willie 'The Lion')
CD _____ CLASSICS 692
Classic Jazz Masters / May '93 / Wellard / Jazz Music / Cadillac.

HARLEM JOYS (Smith, Willie 'The Lion')
There's gonna be the devil to pay / Streamline girl / What can I do with a foolish girl like you / Harlem joys / Echo of spring / Breeze (blow my baby back to me) / Swing brother swing / Sittin' at the table (opposite you) / Swamp land (is calling me) / More than that / I'm all out of breath / I can see you all over the place / Get acquainted with yourself / Knock wood / Peace brother peace / Old stomping ground / Blues why don't you let me alone / I've got to think it over / Achin' hearted blues / Honeymoonin' on a dime
CD _____ CDAFS 1032
Charly / Jun '93 / Charly / THE / Cadillac.

LION ROARS AGAIN (Smith, Willie 'The Lion')
CD _____ CBC 1012
Bellaphon / Jun '93 / New Note.

LION'S IN TOWN, THE (Smith, Willie 'The Lion')
Don't you hit that lady dressed in green / Maple leaf rag / Don't you dare to strike me again / Shine / At the Darktown strutter's ball / Pork and beans / Chevy Chase / Oh you devil rag / When I walk by with Billy / Buddy Bolden's blues / Passionette / Can you hear me / Trains and planes / Conversations on Park Avenue / Pretty baby / Sweet Sue, just you / Cuttin' out / Echoes of spring / Here comes the band / Relaxin' / Contrary motions / Zig zag / 12th Street rag / Late hours / Portrait of the Duke / Dardanella / La madelon
CD _____ 74321115062
Vogue / Jul '93 / BMG.

PORK AND BEANS (Smith, Willie 'The Lion')
Pork and beans / Moonlight cocktail / Spanish Venus / Junk man rag / Squeeze me / Love will find a way / I'm just wild about Harry / Memories of you / Alexander's ragtime band / All of me / Ain't misbehavin' / Man I love / Summertime / Ain't she sweet
CD _____ BLCD 760144
Black Lion / Jan '85 / Jazz Music / Cadillac / Wellard / Koch.

Smither, Chris

HAPPIER BLUE
Happier blue / Memphis in the meantime / Devil's real / No more cane on the Brazos / Mail order mystics / No reward / Already gone / Killing the blues / Rock 'n' roll doctor / Magnolia / Honeysuckle dog / Take it all / Time to spend
CD _____ FIENDCD 739
Demon / Mar '94 / Pinnacle / ADA.

UP ON THE LOWDOWN
CD _____ HCD 8060
Hightone / Apr '95 / ADA / Koch.

Smiths

BEST 1
This charming man / William, it was really nothing / What difference does it make / Stop me if you think you've heard this one before / Girlfriend in a coma / Half a person / Rubber ring / How soon is now / Hand in glove / Shoplifters of the world unite / Sheila take a bow / Some girls are bigger than others / Panic / Please please please let me get what I want
CD _____ 4509900442
WEA / Aug '92 / Warner Music.

BEST OF THE SMITHS
CD _____ 4509941642
WEA / Oct '93 / Warner Music.

BEST..2
Boy with the thorn in his side / Headmaster ritual / Heaven knows I'm miserable now / Ask / Oscillate wildly / Nowhere fast / Still ill / That joke isn't funny anymore / Shakespeare's sister / Girl afraid / Reel around

the fountain / Last night I dreamt somebody loved me / There is a light that never goes out
CD _____ 4509904062
WEA / Nov '92 / Warner Music.

HATFUL OF HOLLOW
William, it was really nothing / What difference does it make / These things take time / This charming man / How soon is now / Handsome devil / Hand in glove / Still ill / Heaven knows I'm miserable now / This night has opened my eyes / Accept yourself / Girl afraid / Back to the old house / Reel around the fountain / Please, please, please let me get what I want
CD _____ 4509918932
WEA / Nov '92 / Warner Music.

LOUDER THAN BOMBS
Is it really so strange / Sheila take a bow / Shoplifters of the world unite / Sweet and tender hooligan / Half a person / London / Panic / Girl afraid / Shakespeare's sister / William, it was really nothing / You just haven't earned it yet baby / Heaven knows I'm miserable now / Ask / Golden lights / There is a light that never goes out
CD _____ 4509938332
WEA / Feb '95 / Warner Music.

MEAT IS MURDER
Headmaster ritual / Barbarism begins at home / Rusholme ruffians / I want the one I can't have / What she said / Nowhere fast / That joke isn't funny anymore / Well wonder / Meat is murder
CD _____ 4509918952
WEA / Feb '95 / Warner Music.

QUEEN IS DEAD, THE
Frankly, Mr. Shankly / I Know it's over / Never had no one ever / Cemetery gates / Big mouth strikes again / Vicar in a tutu / There is a light that never goes out / Some girls are bigger than others / Queen is dead / Boy with the thorn in his side
CD _____ 4509918962
WEA / Feb '95 / Warner Music.

RANK
Queen is dead / Panic / Vicar in a tutu / Ask / Rusholme ruffians / What she said / Cemetery gates / London / Big mouth strikes again / Draize Train / Boy with the thorn in his side / Is it really so strange / I know it's over / Still ill / His latest flame
CD _____ 4509919002
WEA / Feb '95 / Warner Music.

SMITHS SINGLES
CD _____ 4509990902
WEA / Feb '95 / Warner Music.

SMITHS, THE
Reel around the fountain / You've got everything now / Miserable lie / Pretty girls make graves / Hard that rocks the cradle / This charming man / Still ill / Hand in glove / What difference does it make / I don't owe you anything / Suffer little children
CD _____ 4509918922
WEA / Feb '95 / Warner Music.

SMITHS: INTERVIEW COMPACT DISC
CD P.Disc _____ CBAK 4025
Baktabak / Nov '89 / Baktabak.

STRANGEWAYS HERE WE COME
Rush and a push and the land is ours / I started something I couldn't finish / Death of a disco dancer / Girlfriend in a coma / Stop me if you think you've heard this one before / Last night I dreamt somebody loved me / Unhappy birthday / Paint a vulgar picture / Death at one's elbow / I won't share you
CD _____ 4509918992
WEA / Feb '95 / Warner Music.

WORLD WON'T LISTEN, THE
Panic / Ask / London / Big mouth strikes again / Shakespeare's sister / There is a light that never goes out / Shoplifters of the world unite / Boy with the thorn in his side / Asleep / Unloveable / Half a person / Stretch out and wait / That joke isn't funny anymore / You haven't earned it yet baby / Rubber ring / Oscillate wildly / Money changes everything
CD _____ 4509918982
WEA / Feb '95 / Warner Music.

Smog

BURNING KINGDOM
CD _____ EFA 049462
City Slang / Nov '94 / Disc.

JULIUS CAESAR
Strawberry rash / Your wedding / Thirty seven push-ups / Stalled on the tracks / One less star / Golden / When you talk / I am Star Wars / Connections / When the power goes out / Chosen one / What kind of angel / Stick in the mud
CD _____ OLE 097-2
Matador / Jul '94 / Vital.

WILD LOVE
CD _____ EFAD 49522
Skunk / Mar '95 / Pinnacle.

Smokehouse

LET'S SWAMP AWHILE
It's goin' on / Braggin' 'bout your baby / Big mistake / Fork in the road / Sweet little woman / I didn't know / Poontang blues / Evil woman / Skin is back / Day Jack Frost killed Parson Brown
CD _____ ICH 9003 CD
Ichiban / Apr '91 / Koch.

SWAMP JIVE
CD _____ ICH 9017CD
Ichiban / Oct '93 / Koch.

Smokie

ALICE
CD _____ WAGCD 247
Now / Nov '95 / Total/BMG.

BEST OF SMOKIE
CD _____ TCD 2455
Telstar / Nov '90 / BMG.

COLLECTION VOL.2, THE (The Complete B-Sides 1975-1978)
Couldn't live / Talking her round / Train song / Loser / Miss you / Run to you / Here lies a man / Now you think you know / No one coul ever love you more / Going tomorrow / Will you love me / You took me by surprise / Stranger with you
CD _____ 74321 23294-2
Ariola / Nov '94 / BMG.

COLLECTION, THE
Living next door to Alice / Mexican girl / Wild wild angels / Something's been making me blue / If you think you know how to love me / For a few dollars more / Don't play your rock 'n' roll to me / Needles and pins / It's your life / Baby, it's you / Changing all the times / Lay back in the arms of someone / Oh Carol / I'll meet you at midnight
CD _____ 262538
Arista / Jun '92 / BMG.

PARTY HITS, THE
Who the fuck is Alice / Oh Carol / Surfin / Needles and pins / Tambourine man / Take good care of my baby / Naked love (baby love me) / It's your life / Respect / Relying on you / Derry girl / Somethings been making me blue / Don't play your rock 'n' roll to me / Lay back in the arms of someone
CD _____ CDEMS 1581
Premier / Dec '95 / EMI.

SMOKIE GREATEST HITS LIVE
I'll meet you at midnight / Lay back in the arms of someone / Medley / Something's making me blue / Wild angels / If you think you know how to love me / Don't play myour rock 'n' roll to me / Rock away your teardrops / Cry in the night / Oh Carol / Needles and pins / Living next door to Alice / Whiskey in the jar
CD _____ PLATCD 3916
Prism / Apr '93 / Prism.

Smooth

SMOOTH
CD _____ CHIP 162
Jive / Aug '95 / BMG.

Smoothies

PICKLE
CD _____ 185292
Southern / Sep '95 / SRD.

Smothers, Smokey

BOSSMAN
CD _____ BM 9022
Black Magic / Jun '93 / Hot Shot / Swift / CM / Direct / Cadillac / ADA.

Smudge

HOT SMOKE AND SASSAFRAS
CD _____ WIGCD 19
Domino / Feb '95 / Pinnacle.

MANILOW
CD _____ WIGCD 7
Domino / Feb '94 / Pinnacle.

TEA, TOAST & TURMOIL
Spoilt brat / Straight face down / Outside / Make all our dreams come true / Pulp / Plug it up / Divan / Alison / Don't want to be Grant McLennan / Stranglehold / Dabble / Leroy de Foix / Tea, toast and turmoil / Foccacia / Steak and chips / Babaganouj
CD _____ SALD 207
Shake / Oct '93 / Vital.

Smulyan, Gary

LURE OF BEAUTY, THE (Smulyan, Gary Quintet)
CD _____ CRISS 1049CD
Criss Cross / Nov '91 / Cadillac / Harmonia Mundi.

SAXOPHONE MOSAIC (Smulyan, Gary Nonet)
CD _____ 1092CD
Criss Cross / Jan '95 / Cadillac / Harmonia Mundi.

Smut

BLOOD, SMUT AND TEARS
Cave / Alone / Spirit / Symphony #1 / No
sacrifice / Women / Baby Jack / Emotional
suicide / Take back the night / Object of
intentions / Autumn storm / Goodness, no
grief
CD _____ 89240-2
Spanish Fly / Apr '94 / Vital.

Smyth, Gilli

EVERY WITCHES WAY
Simple / Bold and brazen / Show is over /
We who were raging / Beltaine / Four horse-
men / Medicine woman / Animal / Magic /
Lammas / I am witch / Lady wise / Simples
CD _____ VP 139CD
Voice Print / Jun '93 / Voice Print.

Smyth, Sean

BLUE FIDDLE, THE
CD _____ LUNCD 060
Mulligan / Apr '94 / CM / ADA.

Snafu

**IF YOU SWEAR, YOU'LL CATCH NO
FISH**
CD _____ BY 0017CD
Better Youth Organisation / Nov '93 /
SRD.

Snagapuss

WHAP DEM MERLENE
CD _____ SVCD 4
Shocking Vibes / Feb '94 / Jetstar.

Snagga

LINE UP ALL THE GIRKS DEM
CD _____ HCD 7007
Hightone / Aug '94 / ADA / Koch.

Snail, Azalia

BLUE DANUBE
CD _____ NORMAL 197CD
Normal/Okra / Jan '96 / Direct / ADA.

Snake Corps

SPICE
Science kills / Nothing / This is seagull /
Come the glorious day / House of man /
Calling you / Strangers / Man in the mirror
/ More than the ocean / Yesterday with you
/ In flux / Colder than the kiss / Party's over
/ Sky in your eyes / Dreamland
CD _____ CDMGRAM 97
Anagram / Oct '95 / Pinnacle.

Snake Finger

NIGHT OF DESIRABLE OBJECTS
CD _____ AIM 1011CD
Aim / Oct '93 / Direct / ADA / Jazz Music.

Snap

WELCOME TO TOMORROW
Green grass grows (earth follows) / It's a
miracle (people need to love one another) /
Rame / Dream on the moon / Welcome to
tomorrow (are you ready) / World in my
hands (we are one) / First last eternity (till
the end) / Waves / Where are the boys,
where are the girls (CD) / It's not over (CD)
CD _____ 74681 22301 6
Arista / Oct '94 / BMG.

WORLD POWER
Power / Cult of snap / I'm gonna get you
(to whom it may concern) / Many had a little
boy / Ooops up / Believe the hype / Witness
the strength / Blase blase
CD _____ 260682
Arista / Aug '95 / BMG.

Snapcase

SNAPCASE
CD _____ VR13-2
We Bite / Apr '94 / Plastic Head.

Snatch It Back

DYNAMITE
CD _____ TRCD 9904
Tramp / Nov '93 / Direct / ADA / CM.

EVIL
CD _____ TRCD 9907
Tramp / Nov '93 / Direct / ADA / CM.

Sneak's Noyse

CHRISTMAS NOW IS DRAWING NEAR
Good people all this Christmastide / Sweet
was the song the virgin sang / Down in yon
forest / Holly and the ivy / Joseph was an
old man / Angelus ad Virginem / Hail Mary
full of grace / Tomorrow shall be my dancing day / Furry dag carol / Deck the halls
with boughs of holly / God bless you merry
gentlemen
CD _____ CDSDL 371
Saydisc / Oct '86 / Harmonia Mundi / ADA
/ Direct.

Sneetches

LIGHTS OUT WITH THE SNEETCHES
I need someone / In my car / Lonelei / Fifty
four hours / I don't expect her for you /
Home again / No one knows / Only for a
moment
CD _____ CRECD 077
Creation / Apr '91 / 3MV / Vital.

OBSCUREYEARS
CD _____ CREV 031CD
Rev-Ola / Nov '94 / 3MV / Vital.

SOMETIMES THAT'S ALL WE HAVE
CD _____ CRECD 043
Creation / May '94 / 3MV / Vital.

STARFUCKER
CD _____ BUS 10062
Bus Stop / May '95 / Vital.

Snell, Adrian

ALPHA AND OMEGA
CD _____ MYRCD 1210
Myrrh / '86 / Nelson Word.

Snell, Howard

FOUR SEASONS, THE
CD _____ QPRZ 007D
Polyphonic / Sep '91 / Conifer.

JEUX D'ENFANTS (Snell, Howard Brass)
CD _____ QPRZ 010D
Polyphonic / Feb '93 / Conifer.

Snenska Hotkvinetten

SVENSKA HOTKVINETTEN
CD _____ DRCD 223
Dragon / Jan '88 / Roots / Cadillac /
Wellard / CM / ADA.

Snetberger, Ferenc

SIGNATURE
Toni's carnival II / Passages / Obsession /
Tangoa free / Poems for my people / Sur-
prise / Variation
CD _____ ENJ 90172
Enja / May '95 / New Note / Vital/SAM.

Snidero, Jim

STORM RISING
Fast lane / Takin' it easy / Storm rising /
Beatrice / Break away / Virgo / Reluctance
/ Depressions
CD _____ 66056006
Ken Music / Mar '92 / New Note.

**WHILE YOU'RE HERE (Snidero, Jim
Quartet)**
CD _____ 1232412
Red / Mar '92 / Harmonia Mundi / Jazz
Horizons / Cadillac / ADA.

Sniff 'N' The Tears

BEST OF SNIFF 'N' THE TEARS, A
Driver's seat / What can daddy do / Thrill of
it all / Looking for you / One love / Driving
beat / Night life / Snow White / Roll 'em
blues / Poison pen mail / Hungry eyes /
Steal my heart / Ride blue divide
CD _____ CDWIK 102
Chiswick / Aug '91 / Pinnacle.

FICKLE HEART
Driver's seat / New lines on love / Carve
your name on my door / This side of the
blue horizon / Sing / Rock 'n' roll music /
Fight for love / Thrill of it all / Slide away /
Last dance / Looking for you
CD _____ CDWIKM 9
Chiswick / Aug '91 / Pinnacle.

GAMES UP, THE
Game's up / Moment of weakness / What
can daddy do / Night life / If I knew then /
One love / Five and zero / Poison pen mail
/ Rodeo drive
CD _____ CDWIKM 92
Chiswick / Aug '90 / Pinnacle.

LOVE/ACTION
Driving beat / Put your money where your
mouth is / Snow White / For what they
promise / Without love / Steal my heart /
That final love / Don't frighten me / Love
action / Shame
CD _____ CDWIKM 96
Chiswick / Feb '91 / Pinnacle.

NO DAMAGE DONE
CD _____ PRD 70482
Provogue / Jan '92 / Pinnacle.

RIDE BLUE DIVIDE
Hand of fate / Hungry eyes / Roll the weight
away / Like wildfire / Trouble is my business
/ You may find your heart / Gold / Ride blue
divide / Company man
CD _____ CDWIKM 97
Chiswick / Apr '91 / Pinnacle.

Snoop Doggy Dogg

DOGGY STYLE
Bathtub / G funk intro / Gin and juice / Tha
shiznit / Lodi Dodi / Murder was the case /
Serial killa / Who am I (What's my name) /
For all my niggaz and bitches / Ain't no fun
/ Doggy dogg world / Gz and hustlas /
Pump pump

CD _____ 6544922792
Interscope / Sep '93 / Warner Music.

Snow

12 INCHES OF SNOW
Runaway / Champion sound / Lonely Monday morning / Drunken styles / Girl, I've
been hurt / Hey pretty love / Informer / Creative child / Lady with the red dress / Uhh
in you / Can't get enough / Ease up / Fifty
five / Lonely Monday morning (remix)
CD _____ 756792207-2
East West / Mar '93 / Warner Music.

MURDER LOVE
CD _____ 7567617372
East West / Mar '95 / Warner Music.

Snow, Hank

**SINGING RANGER VOL. 1 (The
Complete Early 50's Hank Snow/4CD
Set)**
I'm movin' on / With this ring / Rumba boogie / Paving the highway with tears / Golden
rocket / Your lockwet has broken my heart /
Unwanted sign upon my heart / (I wish
upon) my little golden horseshoe / Confused with the blues / You pass me by /
Love entered the iron door / I cried but my
tears were too late / One more ride / Hobo
Bill's last ride / Wreck of ol' 97 / Ben Dew-
berry's final run / Mystery of number five /
Engineer's child / Law of love / Nobody's
child / I wonder where you are tonight / Star
spangled waltz / Blind boy's dog / Marriage
vow / Only rose / Anniversary of my broken
heart / Music makin' mama from Memphis
/ Highest bidder / Gold rush is over / Love's
game of let's pretend / Bluebird Island /
Down the trail of aching hearts / Lady's man
/ Fool such as I / Why do you punish me /
Chattin' with a chick in Chattanooga /
Greatest sin / Married by the Bible, divorced
by the law / There wasn't an organ at our
wedding / Zeb Turner's gal / Golden river /
Moanin' / I knew that we'd meet again / Yodeling cowboy / On that old Hawaiian shore
with you / On that old Hawaiian shore with
you (2) / I'm movin' on to glory / Jesus wept
/ Pray / These things shall pass / He'll un-
derstand and say well done / I just telephone upstairs / I'm in love with Jesus / Gal
who invented kissin' / Spanish fireball /
Honeymoon on a rocketship / Between fire
and water / Boogie woogie flying cloud / I
can't control my heart / For now and always
/ Message from the tradewinds / I traded
love / Next voice you hear / When Mexican
Joe met Jole Blon / I went to your wedding
/ Jimmie the kid / My blue eyed Jane /
When Jimmie Rodgers said goodbye /
Southern Cannonball / Anniversary blue yo-
del / Why did you give me your love / Mis-
sissippi river blues / In daddy's footsteps /
Gloryland march / Christmas roses / Reindeer boogie / Frosty the snowman / Silent
night / My mother / Just keep a movin' / My
sweet Conchita / Panamama / Unfaithful /
Wabash blues / It's you, only you that I love
/ Would you mind / In old Dutch garden
/ Owl and I / I don't hurt anymore / Stolen
moments / Hilo march / Act 1, act 2, act 3
/ Yellow roses / No longer a prisoner /
Sweet Marie / My Arabian baby / Bill is falling due / Blossoms in the springtime / I'm
glad I'm on the inside (looking out) / When
it's reveille time in Heaven / My religion's
not old fashioned / Invisible hands / Little
children / Alphabet / God's little candles #2
/ God's little candles
CD Set _____ BCD 15426
Bear Family / Nov '88 / Rollercoaster /
Direct / CM / Swift / ADA.

SINGING RANGER VOL. 2 (4CD Set)
Love's call from the mountain (unissued) /
I've forgotten you / That crazy mambo thing
/ Let me go, lover / Old spinning wheel / At
the Darktown strutter's ball / Silver bell /
Under the double eagle / It's you, only you
that I love / Keep your promise, Willie Thomas / Crying, waiting, hoping / Someone
mentioned your name / I'm glad to see you
once again / Mainliner (the hawk of the
West) / Cuba rhumba / Scale to measure
love / Blue sea blues / Twelfth Street rag /
Rainbow boogie / vaya con dios / Madison
madness / Can't have you blues / Doe bone
(unissued) / Born to be happy / Golden
rocket / Hobo Bill's last ride / Stolen moments / Pray / Nothing but sweet lies
(unissued) / Conscience I'm guilty / Hula
rock / Two won't care / Party of the second
part (unissued) / These hands / Reminiscin'
/ New Spanish two-step / In an old Dutch
drawing room / La cucaracha / Born to lose
(unissued) / I'm movin' in / Sunshine serenade / El rancho grande / Grandfather's
clock / Lover's farewell / Carnival of Venice
/ Old Doc Brown / That pioneer mother of
mine / Blind boy's prayer / Lazy bones /
What do I know today / Trouble, trouble,
trouble / First nighters / How to play the
guitar / Little britches / What is father / Horse's prayer / Wedding bells / Loose talk / I
never been anywhere / Sonny boy / Indian
love call / Unchained melody / Beautiful
dreamer / My Isle of golden dreams /
Brahms lullaby / Blue tango / Dark moon /
Vaya con dios / In an old Dutch garden / By
an old Dutch mill / I can't stop loving you /
Convict and the rose / Limbo rock / Hold
me tight / Tammy / Everybody does it in
Hawaii / I saw the light / Green leaves of
Summer / Difficult / Wheels / Tiptoeing /
Waltz you saved for me / Lay my head beneath the rose / Whispering hope / Wabash
blues / Sentimental journey / Am I losing
you / I get the blues when it rains / Sweet
Marie / Birth of the blues / White Christmas
/ Little stranger (in a manger) / Christmas
roses / Silent night / C-H-R-I-S-T-M-A-S /
Blue Christmas / Reindeer boogie / Frosty
the snowman / Christmas wants / Rudolph
the red nosed reindeer / God is my Santa
Claus / Long eared Christmas donkey /
Cremation of Sam McGee / Spell
McGrew / Cremation of Sam McGee / Spell
of the Yukon / Ballad of blasphemous Bill /

ground / New blue velvet band / Calypso
sweetheart / I'm hurtin' all over (unissued) /
My memory (unissued) / Party of the second part marriage and divorce / Unfaithful
(unissued) / Tangled mind / My arms are a
house / Love's call from the mountain / On
a Tennessee Saturday night (unissued) / Big
wheels / Woman captured me / I heard my
heart break last night / I wish I was the
moon / My lucky friend / Whispering rain /
I'm hurtin' all over / I'm here to get my baby
out of jail / Don't make me go to bed and
I'll be good / Convict and the rose / There's
a little box of pine on the 7.29 / Put my little
shoes away / Letter edged in black / Old
Shep / Prisoner's prayer / Drunkard's child
/ Little Buddy / Nobody's child / Blue Danube / Waltz, Kitty waltz (unissued) / Brahms
lullaby / Sleepy Rio Grande / Brahms lullaby
(2)
CD Set _____ BCD 15476
Bear Family / Apr '90 / Rollercoaster / Direct
/ CM / Swift / ADA.

SINGING RANGER VOL. 3 (12CD Set)
Casey Jones was his name / Southbound /
Streamlined cannonball / (I heard that)
Lonesome whistle / Waiting for a train /
Wreck of the number nine / Pan American
/ Big wheels / Ghost trains / Chattanooga
choo choo / Last ride / Crazy engineer /
One more ride / Wreck of ol' 97 / Crazy little
train of love / Any old time / Blue yodel no.
10 / Travelin' blues / Never no' mo' blues /
Gambling polka dot blues / You and my old
guitar / Roll along Kentucky moon / Moonlight and skies / One rose (that's left in my
heart) / Tuck away my lonesome blues /
Down the old road to home / I'm sorry we
met / Chasin' a rainbow / Doggone that
train / Father time and mother love / I heard
my heart break last night / Walkin' and
talkin' / Rockin' rollin' ocean / Miller's cave
/ Dreamer's island / Change of the tide / I'm
movin' on / Golden rocket / My mother / I
don't hurt anymore / Conscience I'm guilty
/ I'm asking for a friend / Bluebird Island /
Fool such as I / Marriage vow / With this
ring / thee wed / My Nova Scotia home /
Tramp's story / Lifetime blues / Maple
leaves / Casey's washerwoman boogie /
Hawaiian sunset / Man who robbed the
bank of Santa Fe / Man behind the gun /
Restless one / Call of the wild / Laredo /
Way out there / Patanio, the pride of the
plains / Queen of Draw Poker Town / On
the rhythm range / Chant of the wanderer /
Wayward wind / Following the sun all day /
Texas plains / Teardrops in my heart / Tumbling tumbleweeds / Heartbreak trail / Cool
water / Riding home / At the rainbow's end
/ It's a little more like Heaven / I went to
your wedding / Just a faded petal from a
beautiful bouquet / Blue roses / Human /
Breakfast with the blues / Down the trail of
aching hearts / Let me go, lover / Tangled
mind / Next voice you hear / Stolen moments / Gal who invented kissin' / Gold rush
is over / Ninety miles an hour (down a dead
end street) / My memories of you / Wishing
well / I stepped over the line / Ninety days
/ Wedding picture / I've cried a mile / Listen
/ Friend / When today is a long time ago /
Black diamond / Ancient history / You're
easy to love / You're the reason / Poor
little Jimmie / Beggar to a king / Countdown
/ Down at the pawnshop / I know you / You
take the future (and I'll take the past) / Dog
bone / If I try hard enough / Poison love /
Legend in my time / Bury me deep /
Fraulein / Mansion on the hill / Send me the
pillow that you dream on / On a petal from
a faded rose / Return to me / Heart belongs
to me / I'll go no more / I care no more / I
love you because / Address unknown /
Rumba boogie / Music makin' Mama from
Memphis / These hands / Letter from Vietnam to mother / Born for you / Late and
great love of my heart / Promised to John /
If today were yesterday / For sale / Rose of
old Monterey / My adobe hacienda / I never
will marry / Mockin' Bird Hill / No letter today / I dreamed of an old love affair / If it's
wrong to love you / When my blue moon
turns to gold again / Let's pretend / Pair of
broken hearts / I've been everywhere / Jamaica farewell / Blue Canadian Rockies /
Geisha girl / When it's Springtime in Alaska
/ Galway Bay / My Filipino rose / Lili Marlene / Melba from Melbourne / Atlantic
coastal line / Isle of Sicily / Gypsy and me
/ I ain't been anywhere / Sonny boy / Indian

627

The ballad of one eyed Mike / Ballad of hard luck Henry / My friends / He'll understand and say well done / I saw a man / Rich man am I / Jesus wept / I'm movin' on to glory / Gloryland march / Farther along / Invisible hands / Last mile of the way / Sweet hour of prayer / These things shall pass / His hands / What then / Lord's way of sayin' goodnight / Dear Lord / Remember me / I see Jesus / My religion's not old fashioned / I'm glad I'm on the inside (looking out) / Runt / How big is God / Shop worn / Man who is wise / This train / I'll go marching into glory / I'd rather be on the inside looking out / Lord it's me again / Lord I do believe / Learnin' a new way of life / Wildflower / Little Joe / Put your arms around me / Color song / Your little band of gold / Prisoner's song / A star spangled banner waving / Old Rover / Mother I thank you for the bible you gave / Prisoner's song / Walking the last mile / Rockin' alone in an old rocking chair / Lonesome / She wears my ring / White silver sands / Trouble in mind / Mary Ann regrets / Six days on the road / Bummin' around / From a Jack to a King / Handcuffed to love / What more can I say / I wish my heart could talk / Hula love / Cry my guitar, cry on / Beyond the reef / To you my sweetheart, aloha when I go / Hawaiian cowboy / My little grass shack in Kealakekua, Hawaii / On the beach in Waikiki / Tradewinds / Pearly shells / On that old Hawaiian shore with you / Now is the hour / Tears in the tradewinds / King's serenade / Whispering tradewinds / Spanish fireball / Cross the Brazos at Waco / El Paso / Caribbean / Senorita Rosalita / Cuba rhumba / Nuevo laredo / Blue rose of the Rio / Maria Elena / Adios amigo / Among my souvenirs / Miami snow / Springtime in the Rockies / Blossoms in the Springtime / At the first fall of snow / Snowbird / Seasons / Roses in the snow / Flying South / January / You're as welcome as the flowers in May / Peach pickin' time in Georgia / All nite cafe / Tip of my fingers / He dropped the world in my hands / Blue blue day / It kinda reminds me of me / All the time / Blue side of lonesome / There goes my everything / Once more you're mine again / Million and one / Green green grass of home / Wound time can't erase / I just wanted to know how the wind was blowin' / Who will answer / Cure for the blues / That's when the hurtin' sets in / Rome wasn't built in a day / Name of the game was love

CD Set _____ **BCD 15502**
Bear Family / Jun '92 / Rollercoaster Direct / CM / Swift / ADA.

SINGING RANGER VOL. 4 (9CD Set)
If I ever get back to Georgia / Gentle on my mind / Honey / Sweet dreams / Break my mind / Where has all the love gone / Green green green / Oh lonesome me / Like a bird / I really don't want to know / (As love goes) so goes my heart / Vanishing breed / It's a hard wind that blows / Brand on my heart / Francesca / When today is a long time ago / Come the morning / I wish it was mine / Cure for the blues / Crying time / There's the chair / Snowbird / I thew away the rose / Me and Bobby McGee / Just bidin' my time / I'm moving / Silver rails / Go with my heart / Wabash cannonball / Engineer's child / Casey Jones was his name / Fire ball mail / Folsom prison blues / Lonely train / That same old dotted line / I'm movin' in / Train my woman's on / Durquesne, Pennsylvania / Canadian pacific / Crack in the box car door / North to Chicago / City of New Orleans / Texas silver zephyr / Get on my love train / My blue river rose / Blue velvet band / Wanderin' on / Old doc brown / Stolen moments / When that someone you love doesn't love you / My mother / Nobody's child / Little buddy / Hobo's meditation / My rough and rowdy ways / Frankie and Johnny / She was happy till she met you / Away out on the mountain / Cowhand's last ride / Everybody does it in Hawaii / I've ranged, I've roamed, I've travelled / Ninety nine year blues / Mother, the queen of my heart / Whisper your mother's name / Home call / My blue eyed Jane / Waiting for a train / Pistol packin' Papa / T.B. Blues / My little old home down in New Orleans / Why did you give me your love / In the jailhouse now / Gambling polka dot blues / One rose (that's left in my heart) / Hobo Bill's last ride / Nobody knows but me / Hello love / One minute past eternity / No one will ever know / For the good times / Sunday morning coming down / Everytime I love her / Seashores of old Mexico / Gypsy feet / Ribbon of darkness / My way / Bob / Friend / Governor's hand / Rolling thunder in my mind / I'm not at all sorry for you / My dreams tell it like it was / It's over, over nothing #2 / Till the end of time / Four in the morning / I've got ot give it all to you / Daisy a day / Today I started loving you again / I have you and that's enough for me / I washed my hands in muddy water / It just happened that way / Last thing on my mind / Big silver screen at the Strand / Six string Tennessee flat top box / Somewhere my love / Why me Lord / Born to be with you / I keep dreaming of you all the time / Birth of the blues / Hijack / Come live with me / That's you and me / Paper roses / Why do you punish me / Mama tried / Prisoner's song / All I can hold to / You're easy to love / Just want you to

know / Right or wrong / Colorado country morning / Top of the morning / She even woke me up to say goodbye / So good to be back with you / Follow me / Merry go round of love / Almost lost my mind / You're wondering why / Ninety miles an hour (down a dead end street) / Breakfst with the blues / Trying to get my baby off my mind / Trouble in mind / I'm gonna bid my blues goodbye / Love is so elusive / I've done at least one thing / Don't rock the boat / If you could just remember / That heart belongs to me / I'm still moving on / Inside out / Somewhere, someone is waiting for you / I put her on (and wore her time) / Who's been here since I've been gone / That's when he dropped the world in my mind / Night I stole Sammy Morgan's gin / I wonder where you are tonight / I takes to long / Nevertheless / Forever and one day / Just one of a kind / My happiness / Mysterious lady from St.Martinique / Ramblin' rose / Good gal is good to find / Hula love / Things / Pain didn't show / It was love / All I want to do is touch you / There is something about you / What we had is over / Stay a while / Hasn't it been good together / After the love has gone / Check / Forbidden lovers / Love takes two / It's too far gone / It's over, over nothing / First hurt / Golden rocket / I've been everywhere / I almost lost my mind / Caribbean / I'm movin' on / Send me the pillow that you dream on / I don't hurt anymore / Fools such as I / It makes no difference now / Spanish eyes / Sweetheart of sigma / Over the rainbow (instr) / Tradewinds over Mamala Bay (instr) / Indian love call (instrumental) / You belong to me / Wabash blues (instr) / King's serenade / Make the world go away (instr) / Oh wonderful world (instr) / My isle of golden dreams (instr) / Tuck away my lonesome blues (instr) / Tammy (instr) / Beautiful Ohio (instr) / Song of India / Sunrise serenade (Inst) / Misty dawn (instr) / Vaya con dios / I remember you love in my prayers (instrumental) / I'm movin' on (live) / Send me the pillow you dream on (live) / In the misty moonlight (live) / Orange blossom special (Live) / Tammy / Black diamond / Whispering tradewinds (snow in Hawaii) / Hawaiian sunset

CD Set _____ **BCD 15787**
Bear Family / Apr '94 / Rollercoaster Direct / CM / Swift / ADA.

THESAURUS TRANSCRIPTIONS, THE (5CD Set)
Weary river / Bury me deep / Let's pretend / Address unknown / Golden river / Blue yodel no. 12 / I'm here to get my baby out of jail / Brand on my heart / With this ring I thee wed / I wonder where you are tonight / Fire on the mountain / Draggin' / Steel guitar rag / Wabash blues / I'm movin' on / Handcuffed to love / Convict and the rose / Anniversary blue yodel / Frankie and Johnny / Closed for repairs / End of the world / I wonder if you feel the way I do / Pins and needles / Where romance calls / Streamlined cannonball / Trouble in mind / Last letter / Headin' down the wrong highway / Lonely / Blue eyes cryin' in the rain / These tears are not for you / Jealous heart / Hawaiian cowboy / I'm thinking tonight of my blue eyes / Whispering hope / It is no secret / Molly darling / I'll remember you love in my prayers / Blue dreams / Blow yo' whistle freight train / Lonely river / I'll never let you go little darling / Texas plains / Born to lose / Too many tears / Travellin' blues / Faded rose, a broken heart / Yodeling ranger / Roll along Kentucky moon / Zeb Turner's gal / Sun has gone down on our love / I walk alone / Old Shep / Mississippi river blues / Linda Lou / My good gal's gone / Breeze / This cold war with you / I love you Nellie / Beautiful dreamer / 12th Street rag / Bye bye blues / Hilo march / Orange blossom special / Beaumont ride / Just when I needed you / Ninety nine years blues / My blue eyed Jane / Yodeling cowboy / Cannonball / It's been so long darling / Lover's farewell / You nearly lose your mind / Kentucky waltz / There's a pony standing in his stall / Among my souvenirs / Little old home down in New Orleans / Go on alone / Cowhand's last ride / I almost lost my mind / Patanio, the pride of the plains / That heart belongs to me / Peach pickin' time in Georgia / Alabama jubilee / Farewell blues / In an old dutch garden / Sally Goodin / Arkansas traveller / Petal from a faded rose / It's a sin / Wedding bells / At mail call today / Those blue eyes don't sparkle anymore / Have I stayed away too long / San Antonio rose / Each minute seems a million years / Blue steel blues / Then I turned and walked slowly away / Blue rose of the Rio / My wubba dolly / Tuck away my lonesome blues / Land of my childhood dreams / Wreck of ol' 97 / My life with you / One rose (that's left in my heart) / I'm coming home / Song of the saddle / Easter parade / Peter Cottontail / My rough and rowdy ways / Sing me a song of the Islands / Little Joe / White Christmas / Blue Christmas / Making believe / Any old time / Never no mo' blues / When my blue moon turns to gold again / Katy Hill / Put your arms around me / I was sorta wonderin' / Over the waves / Do right daddy blues / As long as I live / Loose talk / Waltz you saved for me / Memories are made of this / I really

don't want to know / Wayward wind / Chant of the wanderer / Put on your old grey bonnet / When you and I were young Maggie / Sentimental journey / Birth of the blues

CD Set _____ **BCD 15488**
Bear Family / Feb '91 / Rollercoaster Direct / CM / Swift / ADA.

YODELLING RANGER, THE 1936-1947 (5CD Set)
Prisoned cowboy / Lonesome blue yodel / Blue for old Hawaii / We met down in the hills of old Wyoming / My San Antonio Mama / My little swiss maiden / Was there ever a pal like you / Blue velvet band / Someday you'll care / I'll ride back to lonesome valley / Bluer than blue / Yodelling back to you / There's a picture on Pinto's bridle / Texas cowboy / On the Mississippi shore / Under Hawaiian skies / She's a rose from the Garden of Prayer / Wanderin' on / Broken wedding ring / You didn't have to tell me / His message home / Answer to The Blue Velvet Band / I'll tell the world I love you / Polka dot blues / Alphabet song / Galveston rose / Broken dreams / Let's pretend / Days are long, I'm weary / I traded my saddle for a rifle / When that someone you love doesn't love you / Rainbow's end / We'll never say goodbye, Just say so long / I'm sending you red roses / Goodnight little buckaroos / When my blue moon turns to gold again / Dream tide / Seal our parting with a kiss / You'll regret those words my darling / You promised to love me to the end of the world / Just across the bridge of gold / There's a pony that's lonely tonight / Old moon of Kentucky / Rose of the Rio / Lonely and heartsick / Your last kiss has broken my heart / When it's over I'll be coming back to you / Mother is praying / Soldier's last letter / Riding along, singing a song / Don't hang around me anymore / Only a rose from my mother's grave / Too many tears / Your little band of gold / Sunny side of the mountain / You broke the chain that held our hearts / My blue river rose / You played love on the strings of my heart / How she could yodel / Headin' home / Dry those tears little girl and don't cry / In memory of you dear old pal / Can't have you blues / Just waiting for you / Just wanting for you (2) / My kalua sweetheart / I'll not forget my mother's prayer / Darling I'll always love you / Blue ranger / Just a faded petal from a beautiful bouquet / My sweet Texas Bluebonnet Queen / I'm gonna bid my blues goodbye / Down where the dark waters flow / Answer to Galveston Rose / Brand on my heart / No golden tomorrow / On that old Hawaiian shore with you / You've broken my heart / Linda Lou / My mother / Drunkard's son / Within this broken heart of mine / My Filipino rose / Night I stole Sammy Morgan's gin / My two timin' woman / Wasted love / Broken hearted / You sad kiss goodbye / Somewhere along life's highway / Out on the open range / Little buddy / Journey my baby back home / I knew that we'd meet again / Within this broken heart of mine (Alt) / My two timin' woman (Alt) / Wasted love (Alt) / Life story, Part 1 / Life story, Part 2 / Marriage and divorce / I don't hurt anymore

CD Set _____ **BCD 15587**
Bear Family / Mar '93 / Rollercoaster Direct / CM / Swift / ADA.

Snowboy

BEST OF SNOWBOY, THE (Snowboy & The Latin Section)
Night in Tunisia / Wild spirit / Mr. PC / Beyond the snowstorm / Mambito / Where's the one / Snow snow quick quick snow / In the wee small hours of the morning / Flintstones / 42nd and Broadway / Anarchy in the U.K. / Something's coming
CD _____ **JAZIDCD 102**
Acid Jazz / Nov '94 / Pinnacle.

DESCARGA MAMBITA (Snowboy & The Latin Section)
CD _____ **JAZIDCD 040**
Acid Jazz / Sep '91 / Pinnacle.

PIT BULL LATIN JAZZ (Snowboy & The Latin Section)
CD _____ **JAZIDCD 126**
Acid Jazz / Oct '95 / Pinnacle.

SOMETHING'S COMING
September rains / Salute to elegua / Flintstones / Dreamstate / Greeting from Southend / 42nd and Broadway / Interlude in son / Dilo como yo / Anarchy in the U.K. / Something's coming / Chant to aggayu / Somewhere
CD _____ **JAZIDCD 092**
Acid Jazz / Jan '94 / Pinnacle.

Snowmen

SOUNDPROOF
CD _____ **NORMAL 172CD**
Normal/Okra / Feb '95 / Direct / ADA.

Snuff

DEMMAMUSSABEBONK
Martin / Defeat / Dick trois / Nick Northern / Look mum there's vikings on the Tundra again / Batten down the hatches / Gone to the dogs / Sunny places / Horse and cart / Squirrels / Cricklewood / B / Punchline / Who

CD _____ **BLUFF 023CD**
Deceptive / Jan '96 / Vital.

KILBURN NATIONAL 27.11.90
Somehow / Porro / Hairy womble / City crusty is attacked by soap / Damage is done / I see / What kind of love / Hazy shade of winter / Day of the PX's / Do nothing / Too late / Win some lose some
CD _____ **ASKCD 048**
Vinyl Japan / Jan '95 / Vital.

So Much Hate

LIES
CD _____ **XM 040**
X-Mist / Dec '93 / SRD.

Soap

DUMB FUNK RESISTANCE
CD _____ **HHUKCD 002**
Harthouse / Oct '95 / Disc / Warner Music.

Soares, Fernando Machado

FADO FROM COIMBRA
CD _____ **C 559 041**
Ocora / Feb '89 / Harmonia Mundi / ADA.

Sober

FIRST STEP
CD _____ **BIRD 49CD**
Burning Heart / Nov '94 / Plastic Head.

Sobin A'r Smaeliaid

A RHAW
CD _____ **SCD 2017**
Sain / Feb '95 / Direct / ADA.

Sobule, Jill

JILL SOBULE
CD _____ **7567926202**
Atlantic / Nov '95 / Warner Music.

Social Disorder

GOIN' THE DISTANCE
CD _____ **LF 153CD**
Lost & Found / Jul '95 / Plastic Head.

Social Interiors

WORLD BEHIND YOU, THE
CD _____ **XCD 029**
Extreme / Feb '95 / Vital/SAM.

Social Justice

UNITY IS STRENGTH
CD _____ **LF 136CD**
Lost & Found / May '95 / Plastic Head.

Sodom

BETTER OFF DEAD
Eye for an eye / Saw is the law / Capture the flag / Never healing wound / Resurrection / Shellfire defense / Turn your head around / Bloodtrials / Better off dead / Stalinogel
CD _____ **8476261**
Steamhammer / Nov '90 / Pinnacle / Plastic Head.

GET WHAT YOU DESERVE
CD _____ **SPV 0847676-2**
SPV / May '94 / Plastic Head.

IN THE SIGN OF EVIL
Outbreak of evil / Blasphemer / Burst command 'til war / Sepulchral voice / Witching metal
CD _____ **607 598**
SPV / Jul '89 / Plastic Head.

MAROONED - LIVE
CD _____ **SPV 08476852**
SPV / Nov '94 / Plastic Head.

MASQUERADE IN BLOOD
CD _____ **SPV 08576962**
SPV / Jul '95 / Plastic Head.

OBSESSED BY CRUELTY
CD _____ **857 533**
Steamhammer / '88 / Pinnacle / Plastic Head.

PERSECUTION MANIA
CD _____ **857 509**
Steamhammer / Jun '88 / Pinnacle / Plastic Head.

THIS WAY OF LIFE
CD _____ **847576**
Steamhammer / '90 / Pinnacle / Plastic Head.

Sod's Opera

COME ON LADS
I haven't seen old Hitler / D-Day dodgers / Go a Gezira lovely / Tins / Ballad of Wadi Maktila / Dying soldier / Service police song / Kiss me goodnight, Sergeant Major / Thanks for the memory / Come on chaps / Firth of Forth / Down the mine / Sailor's wife / Longmoor / I don't want to join the army / Bloody Orkney / We are the boys / Africa star / Sinking of the Graf Spee / My bomber lies over the ocean / When this

bloody war is over / Gay Caballero / Onward 15th Army group / Highland division's farewell to Sicily / Bless 'em all
CD _____ BEJOCD 7
Beautiful Jo / Jun '95 / ADA.

Sofa Glue

SMILE
CD _____ RNR 004CD
Ransom Note / Oct '95 / Plastic Head.

Sofa Head

PRE MARITAL PREDICAMENT
CD _____ COXCD 001
Meantime / Jan '91 / Vital / Cadillac.

Sofia Singers

TRADITION SINGS ON
CD _____ 925992CD
Buda / Aug '94 / Discovery / ADA.

Soft Boys

CAN OF BEES
CD _____ RCD 20231
Rykodisc / Nov '92 / Vital / ADA.

INVISIBLE HITS
CD _____ RCD 20233
Rykodisc / Nov '92 / Vital / ADA.

SOFT BOYS 1976-81
Wey wey hep uh hole / It's not just the size of a walnut / Ugly Nora / Yodelling hoover / Hear my Brane / Face of death / Wading through a ventilator / Give it to The Soft Boys / I want to be an angelpoise lamp / Tarman's son / Where are the prawns / Psychedelic love / Heartbreak hotel / Caroline says / We like bananas / Pigworker / Do the chisel / Return of the sacred crab / That's when your heartache begins / Book of love / Sandra's having her brain out / Leppo and the jooves / Rat's prayer / Have a heart, Betty (I'm not fireproof) / Mystery train / He's a reptile / Rock 'n' roll toilet / Insanely jealous / Underwater moonlight / I wanna destroy you / Queen of eyes / Kingdom of love / Positive vibrations / Gigolo aunt / Train around the bend / Only the stones remain
CD _____ RCD 10234/35
Rykodisc / Aug '93 / Vital / ADA.

UNDERWATER MOONLIGHT
I wanna destroy you / Kingdom of love / Positive vibrations / I got the hob / Insanely jealous / Tonight / You'll have to go sideways / I'm an old pervert / Queen of eyes / Underwater moonlight
CD _____ RCD 20232
Rykodisc / Nov '92 / Vital / ADA.

Soft Cell

ART OF FALLING APART
Forever the same / Where the heart is / Numbers / Heat / Kitchen sink drama / Baby doll / Loving you hating me / Art of falling apart
CD _____ 5102962
Some Bizarre/Mercury / Sep '92 / PolyGram.

DOWN IN THE SUBWAY
Where did our love go / Memorabilia / Torch / Entertain me / Fun city / Secret life / Kitchen sink drama / Down in the subway / Baby doll / Where the heart is / I feel love / Seedy films / Loving you, hating me / Soul inside
CD _____ 5501892
Spectrum/Karussell / Mar '94 / PolyGram / THE.

MEMORABILIA - THE SINGLES (Soft Cell & Marc Almond)
Memorabilia / Tainted love / Bedsitter / Say hello, wave goodbye / What / Torch / Soul inside / Where the heart is / I feel love / Tears run rings / Lover spurned / Something's gotten hold of my heart
CD _____ 8485122
Some Bizarre/Mercury / Apr '91 / PolyGram.

NON STOP ECSTATIC DANCING
Memorabilia / Where did our love go / What / Man could get lost / Chips on my shoulder / Sex dwarf
CD _____ 5102952
Some Bizarre/Mercury / Sep '92 / PolyGram.

NON STOP EROTIC CABARET
Frustration / Tainted love / Seedy films / Youth / Sex dwarf / Entertain me / Chips on my shoulder / Bedsitter / Say hello / Secret life / Wave goodbye
CD _____ 800 061 2
Some Bizarre/Mercury / Mar '92 / PolyGram.

SINGLES 1981-1985, THE
Memorabilia / Tainted love / Bedsitter / Say hello, wave goodbye / Torch / What / Where the heart is / Numbers / Soul inside / Down in the subway
CD _____ 8307082
Some Bizarre/Mercury / Nov '86 / PolyGram.

Soft Machine

ALIVE AND WELL RECORDED IN PARIS
White kite / Eos / Odds bullets and blades, pt I / Odds bullets and blades, pt II / Song of the sunbird / Puffin' / Huffin / Number three / Nodder / Surrounding silence / Soft space
CD _____ SEECD 290
See For Miles/C5 / Jan '90 / Pinnacle.

AS IF
Facelift / Slightly all the time / Kings and Queens / Drop / Chloe and the pirates / As if
CD _____ ELITE 006 CD
Elite/Old Gold / Aug '93 / Carlton Home Entertainment.

BBC RADIO 1 LIVE IN CONCERT
CD _____ WINCD 056
Windsong / May '94 / Pinnacle.

BUNDLES
Hazard profile (pts 1-5) / Gone sailing / Bundles / Land of the bag snake / Man who waved at trains / Peff / Four gongs two drums / Floating world
CD _____ SEECD 283
See For Miles/C5 / '89 / Pinnacle.

COMPLETE PEEL SESSIONS: SOFT MACHINE (1969-1971)
Moon in June / Esther's nose job / Mousetrap / Noisette / Backwards / Reprise / Slightly all the time / Out-bloody-rageous / Eamonn Andrews / Facelift
CD _____ SFRCD 201
Strange Fruit / Jul '90 / Pinnacle.

HARVEST YEARS, THE (The Best Of Soft Machine)
Hazard profile (pt 1) / Gone sailing / Bundles / Land of the bag snake / Man who waved at trains / Peff / Four gongs two drums / Songs of Aeolus / Kayoo / Aubade / Second bundle / Camden tandem / One over the eight / Number three / Nodder / Soft space
CD _____ C5MCD 623
See For Miles/C5 / Jul '95 / Pinnacle.

LIVE AT THE PARADISO
Movieplay Gold / Jan '95 / Target/BMG.

LIVE AT THE PROMS
Out-rageous / Facelift / Esther's nosejob / Pig / Orange skin food / Door opens and closes / Pigling bland / 10.30 returns to the bedroom
CD _____ CDRECK 3
Reckless / Aug '88 / Pinnacle.

RUBBER RIFF
Crunch / Ravan / Joubles / Little fighting music / Hi power / Little Miss B / Splot / Rubber riff / Sam's short shuffle / Melina / City steps / Gentle turn/Porky/Travelogue
CD _____ VP 190CD
Voice Print / Nov '94 / Voice Print.

SOFT MACHINE VOL.1 & 2
Hope for happiness / Joy of a toy / Hope for happiness (reprise) / Why am I so short / So boot if at all / Certain kind / Save yourself / Priscilla / Lullaby letter / We did it again / Plus belle qu'une poubelle / Why are we sleeping / Box 25/4 / Pataphysical introduction Part 1 / Concise British alphabet Part 1 / Hibou, anemone and bear / Concise British alphabet Part 2 / Hulloder / Dada was here / Thank you Pierrot Lunaire / Have you ever bean green / Pataphysical introduction Part 2 / Out of tunes / As long as he lies perfectly still / Dedicated to you but you weren't listening / Fire engine passing with bells clanging / Pig / Orange skin food / Door opens and closes / 10.30 returns to the bedroom
CD Set _____ CDWIKD 920
Big Beat / Sep '89 / Pinnacle.

SOFTS
Aubade / Tale of taliesin / Ban ban caliban / Song of Aeolus / Out of season / Second bundle / Kayoo / Camden tandem / Nexus / One over the eight / Etika
CD _____ SEECD 285
See For Miles/C5 / Jan '90 / Pinnacle.

THIRD
Facelift / Slightly all the time / Moon in June / Out bloody rageous
CD _____ BGOCD 180
Beat Goes On / Mar '93 / Pinnacle.

Softballetforms

REMIX FOR ORDINARY PEOPLE
CD _____ SSR 160CD
Crammed Discs / Feb '96 / Grapevine / New Note.

Softies

IT'S LOVE
CD _____ KLP 43 CD
K / Oct '95 / SRD.

Software

CHIP MEDITATION
CD _____ 710 050
Innovative Communication / Apr '90 / Magnum Music Group.

Digital Dance

Oceans breath / Magnificent shore / Waking voice / Island sunrise / Magic beach / Seagulls audience / Digital dance
CD _____ 710 071
Thunderbolt / Mar '88 / Magnum Music Group.

LIVE
CD _____ 710084
Magnum Music / Nov '89 / Magnum Music Group.

OCEAN
CD _____ 710 088
Innovative Communication / Apr '90 / Magnum Music Group.

Soig Siberil

DIGOR
CD _____ GWP 005CD
Gwerz Productions / Aug '93 / ADA.

Sol Y Canto

SANCOCHO
CD _____ ROUCD 6055
Rounder / Dec '94 / CM / Direct / ADA / Cadillac.

Sola, Payita

SONG OF ARGENTINA - THE PERCUSSIONS OF GUINEA
CD _____ 825012
Buda / Apr '91 / Discovery / ADA.

Solal, Martial

IMPROVISE POUR FRANCE MUSIQUE
Just you, just me / Don't blame me / L'ami remy est effare / Ballade / Cheek to cheek / Round Midnight / Ah non / Woodin' you / Cuivre a la mer / Tout va tres bien madame la marquise / Somebody loves me / Night in Tunisia / Hommage a tea a very / Tea for two / Lover man / Cumparsita / Darn that dream / Take the 'A' train / I can't get started (with you) / Corcovado
CD Set _____ JMS 186382
JMS / Dec '95 / BMG / New Note.

LIVE 1959/85
CD _____ 239 963
Accord / '86 / Discovery / Harmonia Mundi / Cadillac.

TRIANGLE
Round about twelve / Isicele / Soliloc / Antheme (theme for Anna) / Night in Venizia / Monostome / Viennoiserie / Cygne d'etang / French lick / Triangle
CD _____ JMS 186742
JMS / Nov '95 / BMG / New Note.

VOGUE RECORDINGS, THE - VOLUME 1
Dinah / La chaloupee / Ramona / Once in a while / Poinciana / Champ / Farniente / Pennies from heaven / Paris je t'aime d'amour / Tout bleu / Sadi's sad / Love walked in / Tenderly / Ridikool / Time on my hands / I cover the waterfront / Yoga / Cross your heart / There's a small hotel / Everything I got is yours
CD _____ 74321115142
Vogue / Jul '93 / BMG.

VOGUE RECORDINGS, THE - VOLUME 2
I only have eyes for you / You stepped out of a dream / Love that dream / I litry you / look tonight / Signal / Midi / Just one of those things / You're not the kind of boy / All God's chillun got rhythm / But not for me / Caravan / Everything happens to me / Have you met Miss Jones / Cherokee / Frenesi / Love me or leave me / Fascinating rhythm / There's a small hotel / Don't blame me / Too marvellous for words / I can't get started (with you) / Blues for Albert
CD _____ 74321115152
Vogue / Jul '93 / BMG.

VOGUE RECORDINGS, THE - VOLUME 3
My funny valentine / Song is you / Ridikool / Studio fagon / Fantasque / Special club / Derniere minute / Middle jazz / Tourmente / Blouse bleu / Midi 1/4 / Alhambra / Yes or no / In the moon / Horloge parlante / Au quatrieme top / You go to my head
CD _____ 74321131112
Vogue / Jul '93 / BMG.

Solar Eclipse

FROM HERE
CD _____ AFTERCD 003
After 6am / Jan '95 / Plastic Head.

Solid Gold Hell

SWINGIN' HOT MURDER
CD _____ FNCD 298
Flying Nun / Sep '94 / Disc.

Solid Senders

EVERYTHING'S GONNA BE ALRIGHT
CD _____ TR 9920CD
Tramp / Aug '94 / Direct / ADA / CM.

Solidor, Suzi

1933-39
CD _____ 121
Chansophone / Nov '92 / Discovery.

Solis, Sebastian

EL GAUCHO, EL INKA
CD _____ EUCD 1033
ARC / '89 / ARC Music / ADA.

FESTIVAL LATINO (Solis, Sebastian, Patricia Salas & Pablo Carcamo)
CD _____ EUCD 1074
ARC / '91 / ARC Music / ADA.

FROM CUBA TO TIERRA DEL FUEGO
CD _____ EUCD 1066
ARC / '89 / ARC Music / ADA.

Solitaire

RITUAL GROUND
CD _____ SR 9341
Silent / Jan '94 / Plastic Head.

Solitaires

WALKING ALONG WITH
Walking alone / Wedding / How long / I really love you so (honey babe) / Please remember my heart / Blue valentine / Later for you baby / Honeymoon / Angels sang / Girl is gone / I don't stand a ghost of a chance with you / Chances I've taken / Give me one more chance / Please kiss this letter / You've sinned / What did she say / Wonder why / South of the border / Fine little girl / Nothing like a little girl / At night / When will the lights shine for me / Light a candle in the chapel / My dear / Come back my love / Stranger in paradise / Time is here
CD _____ CDCHD 383
Ace / Oct '92 / Pinnacle / Cadillac / Complete/Pinnacle.

Solitude

FROM WITHIN
CD _____ CDVEST 18
Bulletproof / Nov '94 / Pinnacle.

Solitude Aeturnus

THROUGH THE DARKEST HOUR
CD _____ CDVEST 35
Bulletproof / Nov '94 / Pinnacle.

Solo

SOLO
What a wonderful world / Back 2 da street / Blowin' my mind / Cupid / Heaven / Xxtra / It's such a shame / He's not good enough / Another Saturday night/Everybody loves to cha cha / Where do u want me to put it / Keep it right here / I'm sorry / Under the boardwale / In bed / (Last night I made love) Like never before / Prince Street / Holdin' on / Change is gonna come / Solo strut
CD _____ 5490172
Perspective / Dec '95 / PolyGram.

Solo, Napoleon

SHOT
CD _____ BBSCD 006
Blue Beat / Oct '89 / Magnum Music Group / THE.

Soloff, Lew

LITTLE WING
CD _____ 66055015
Sweet Basil / Jul '92 / New Note.

MY ROMANCE
Oregon / Time shelter / My romance / Samba dese days / I love you more than you'll ever know / Laura and Lena / Whatever possessed me / Drop me off in Harlem / Face in the mirror / Depraw / Cavatina (Deerhunter)
CD _____ K32Y 6278
King/Paddle Wheel / Aug '91 / New Note.

YESTERDAYS
CD _____ K32Y 6120
King/Paddle Wheel / Oct '87 / New Note.

Soloman Grundy

SOLOMAN GRUNDY
CD _____ NAR 049 CD
New Alliance / Sep '90 / Pinnacle.

Solstice

PRAY
CD _____ SPV 08476902
SPV / May '95 / Plastic Head.

Solstice

LAMENTATIONS
CD _____ CANDLE 007CD
Candlelight / Aug '94 / Plastic Head.

Solvent Drag

INSENTIENT
CD _____ GBO4 CD
Gasoline Boost / Nov '92 / Plastic Head.

Soma

HOLLOW EARTH
CD _____ XCD 028
Extreme / Feb '95 / Vital/SAM.

Some More Crime

ANOTHER DOMESTIC DRAMA
CD _____ ZZ 009
Hyperium / Jul '93 / Plastic Head.

Somerville, Jimmy

DARE TO LOVE
Heartbeat / Hurt so good / Cry / Love thing / By your side / Dare to love / Someday we'll be together / Alright / Too much of a good thing / Dream gone wrong / Come lately / Safe in these arms / Because of him
CD _____ 8285402
London / Jun '95 / PolyGram.

READ MY LIPS
Comment te dire adieu / You make me feel (mighty real) / Perfect day / Heaven here on earth (with your love) / Don't know what to do / Read my lips / My heart is in your hands / Control / And you never thought this could happen to you / Rain
CD _____ 5500422
Spectrum/Karussell / May '93 / PolyGram / THE.

SINGLES COLLECTION, THE
Smalltown boy / Don't leave me this way / It ain't necessarily so / Comment te dire adieu / Never can say goodbye / Why / You are my world / For a friend / I feel love / There's more to love / So cold the night / Mighty real / To love somebody / Run from love / Tomorrow (Not on LP) / Disenchanted (Not on LP) / Read my lips / You make me feel (Mighty real)
CD _____ 8282682
London / Aug '91 / PolyGram.

Something Happens

BEDLAM A GO-GO
CD _____ CDV 2695
Virgin / Jul '92 / EMI.

BEEN THERE, SEEN THAT, DONE THAT
Beach / Incoming / Take this with you / Forget Georgia / Way I feel / Both men crying / Burn clear / Give it away / Tall girls club / Shoulder high / Here comes the only one again / Be my love / Promised (CD only) / Seven days 'til 4 a.m. (CD only) / Free and easy (CD only)
CD _____ CDV 2561
Virgin / Oct '88 / EMI.

STUCK TOGETHER WITH GOD'S GLUE
What now / Hello hello hello hello hello (petrol) / Parachute / Esmerelda / I had a feeling / Kill the roses / Brand new God / Room 29 / Patience business / Devil in Miss Jones / Good time coming / Feel good / Skyrockets
CD _____ CDV 2628
Virgin / May '90 / EMI.

Something Pretty...

SOMETHING PRETTY BEAUTIFUL
(Something Pretty Beautiful)
CD _____ CRECD 075
Creation / May '94 / 3MV / Vital.

Sommerfolk

BEHAKLICHKEIT
CD _____ BEST 1009CD
Acoustic Music / Nov '93 / ADA.

Son Of Crackpipe

BENEVOLENCE OF DOGS AND EVOLUTIONARY ACCIDENTS
CD _____ BGRO 15CD
BGR / Oct '95 / Plastic Head.

Son Of Noise

ACCESS DENIED - BULLSHIT AND POLITICS PART 1
CD _____ COM 102152
Tribehaus Recordings / Sep '95 / Plastic Head.

Sonar Nation

CYLINDERS IN BLUE
CD _____ ABT100CD
Abstract / May '95 / Pinnacle / Total/BMG.

Sondheim, Alan

RITUAL
CD _____ ESP 1048-2
ESP / Jan '93 / Jazz Horizons / Jazz Music.

T'OTHER LITTLE TUNE
CD _____ ESP 1082-2
ESP / Jan '93 / Jazz Horizons / Jazz Music.

Sonerien Du

TREDAN
CD _____ CD 829
Diffusion Breizh / Apr '95 / ADA.

Sonetic Vet

PEER
Boys peeking / Shut me down / Fanatic / Winklewagon / Out of your cocoon / Horny preaches / Niger zip / Zifia stocking / Hangover Davey
CD _____ BIT 005CD
Bittersweet / Oct '94 / Vital.

Songmakers' Almanac

VOICES OF THE NIGHT
CD _____ CDA 66053
Hyperion / Feb '89 / Select.

Songrien Du

TRADITION VIBRANTE
CD _____ KMCD 004
Keltia Musique / Jul '90 / ADA / Direct / Discovery.

Sonic Experience

DEF TILL DAWN
CD _____ STUCD 2
Strictly Underground / Nov '93 / SRD.

Sonic Sufi

SACRAMENTAL
CD _____ PSY 018CD
PSY Harmonics / Oct '95 / Plastic Head.

Sonic Violence

TRANSFIXION
CD _____ KTB 004CD
Dreamtime / May '92 / Kudos / Pinnacle.

Sonic Voyager

ENDLESS MISSION
CD _____ APR 006CD
April / May '95 / Plastic Head.

Sonic Walters

MEDICATION
CD _____ RA 91782
Roadrunner / Apr '92 / Pinnacle.

Sonic Youth

BAD MOON RISING
CD _____ BFFP 1 CD
Blast First / Nov '86 / Disc.

CONFUSION IS SEX/KILL YOUR IDOLS
CD _____ BFFP 113CD
Blast First / Oct '88 / Disc.

DAYDREAM NATION
CD _____ BFFP 34 CD
Blast First / Oct '88 / Disc.

DIRTY
100% / Swimsuit issue / Theresa's sound world / Drunken butterfly / Shoot / Wish fulfillment / Sugar kane / Orange rolls, angel's spit / Youth against facism / Nic fit / On the strip / Chapel hill / Stalker / J.C. / Purr creme brulee
CD _____ GFLD 19296
Geffen / Oct '95 / BMG.

E.V.O.L.
CD _____ BFFP 4CD
Blast First / Nov '86 / Disc.

EXPERIMENTAL JET SET
Winner's blues / Bull in the heather / Starfield road / Skink / Screaming skull / Self-obssessed and sexxee / Bone / Androgynous mind / Quest for the cup / Waist / Doctor's orders / Tokyo eye / In the mind of the bourgeois reader / Sweet shine
CD _____ GED 24632
Geffen / May '94 / BMG.

GOO
Dirty boots / Tunic (song for Karen) / Mary Christ / Kool thing / Mote / My friend Goo / Disappearer / Mildred Pierce / Cinderella's big score / Scooter and Jinx / Titanium expired
CD _____ GFLD 19297
Geffen / Oct '95 / BMG.

MADE IN THE USA
CD _____ 8122715912
Warner Bros. / Mar '95 / Warner Music.

SCREAMING FIELDS OF SONIC LOVE
CD _____ BFFP 119CD
Blast First / Apr '95 / Disc.

SISTER
CD _____ BFFP 20CD
Blast First / Jun '87 / Disc.

SONIC DEATH (Early Sonic Youth - Live 1981-1983)
CD _____ BFFP 32CD
Blast First / '89 / Disc.

WASHING MACHINE
Becuz / Junkie's promise / Saucer-like / Washing machine / Unwind / Little trouble girl / No Queen blues / Panty lies / Skip tracer / Diamond sea
CD _____ GED 24825
Geffen / Oct '95 / BMG.

WHITEY ALBUM, THE (Ciccone Youth)

Needle gun / G force / Platform 11 / Me and Jill / Hi everybody / Children of Satan / Moby Dick / Into the groovy / March of the Ciccone robots / Macbeth / Burning up / Two cool rock chicks listening to Neu / Addicted to love / Making the nature scene / Tuff titty rap
CD _____ BFFP 28CD
Blast First / Mar '88 / Disc.

Sonics

HERE ARE THE SONICS/BOOM
CD _____ 422331
New Rose / May '94 / Direct / ADA.

PSYCHO-SONIC
Witch / Do you love me / Roll over beethoven / Boss hoss / Dirty robber / Have love will travel / Psycho / Money (that's what I want) / Walking the dog / Night time is the right time / Strychnine / Good golly Miss Molly / Hustler / Psycho (Live) / Cinderella / Don't be afraid of the dark / Skinny Minnie / Let the good times roll / Don't you just know it / Jenny Jenny / He's waiting / Louie Louie / Since I fell for you / Hitch hike / It's alright / Shot down / Keep on knockin' / Witch (Live) / Witch (2)
CD _____ CDWIKD 115
Big Beat / Feb '93 / Pinnacle.

Sonnier, Jo El

CAJUN LIFE
Cajun life / Tes yeux bleu / Allons a Lafayette / Bayou teche / Les flames d'enfer / Lacassine special / Chere Alice / Louisiana blues / Les grande bois / Perrodin two step
CD _____ CD 3049
Rounder / Aug '88 / CM / Direct / ADA / Cadillac.

CAJUN ROOTS
CD _____ ROU 6059CD
Rounder / Jul '94 / CM / Direct / ADA / Cadillac.

Sonny & Cher

BEAT GOES ON, THE
CD _____ 7567917962
Atlantic / Mar '93 / Warner Music.

SONNY & CHER COLLECTION
Gypsies / Tramps and thieves / Dark lady / Way of love / I got you babe / Baby don't go / All I ever need is you / Laugh at me / Dead ringer for love / Beat goes on / Little man / Half breed / What now my love / But you're mine / Cowboy's work is never done
CD _____ 9548301522
Atlantic / Dec '94 / Warner Music.

Sonora Majestad

LA NEGRA TOMASA
CD _____ TUMICD 026
Tumi / '91 / Sterns / Discovery.

Sonora Matancera

EN GRANDE
CD _____ TUMICD 022
Tumi / '91 / Sterns / Discovery.

Sonora Poncena

OPENING DOORS
Bamboleo / La rumba es mia / Dejala que siga / Conga yumbambe / A la patria mia / Son matamoroscelia / La mora / Ese animal / Ese mar es mio / No me cambie camino / Cobarde / Quitate la mascara
CD _____ CDHOT 514
Charly / Sep '94 / Charly / THE / Cadillac.

Sons Of Blues

LIVE '82
Never make your move to soon / Did you ever love a woman / Eyesight to the blind / Sweet little angel / My kind of woman / Reconsider baby / Detroit, Michigan / Goin' on main street
CD _____ ECD 260492
Evidence / Sep '94 / Harmonia Mundi / ADA / Cadillac.

Sons of Selina

NOUR D'OUR
Climb / Life is but / Existing services / Gamato manopano / Of the first water (Features on CD only.) / Once every so often (Features in CD only.) / Four plus twenty / Growing bold (Features on CD only.) / Anxiety / It's a boy / On a promise / Dreamshadow
CD _____ DELECCD 025
Delerium / Aug '94 / Vital.

Sons Of The Pioneers

WAGON WEST (4CD Set)
Forgive and forget / Cool water / Timber trail / Stars and stripes on Iwo Jima / You're getting tired of me / Gold star mother with silvery hair / You'll be sorry when I'm gone / I wear your memory in my heart / Cowboy camp meetin' / Tumbling tumbleweeds / Out California way / Grievin' my heart out for you / No one to cry to / Everlasting hills of Oklahoma / Chant of the wanderer / Blue

prairie / Trees / Letter marked unclaimed / Baby doll / Penny for your thoughts / Have I told you lately that I love you / Let's pretend / Cigarettes, whiskey and wild, wild women / Teardrops in my heart / My best to you / Will there be sagebrush in Heaven / You don't know what lonesome is / You never miss the water / Lead me gently home father / Too high, too wide, too low / Out in pioneertown / Hundred and sixty acres / Seawaker / Read the bible every day / Last round-up / Two eyes, two lips but no heart / Cowboy country / Bar-none ranch (in the sky) / Where are you / Calico apron and a gingham gown / Happy birthday polka / Let me share your name / Wind / Whiffenpoof song / Old rugged cross / Power in the blood / Touch of God's hand / Rounded up in glory / Santa Fe, New Mexico / Down where the Rio flows / My feet takes me away / Red River valley / Serenade to a coyote / Missouri is a devil of a woman / No rodeo dough / Sentimental, worried and blue / Little grey home in the West / I still do / Riders in the sky / Room full of roses / No one here but you / Lie low little doggies (the cowboy's prayer) / Let's go west again / Love at the country fair / Wedding bells (from your wedding cake) / Outlaws / Roses / Eagle's heart / Land beyond the sun / I told them all about you / Wagons west / Rollin' dust / Song of the wagonmaster / Chuckawalla swing / Old man atom / What this country needs / Baby, I ain't gonna cry no more / Little white cross / America forever / Daddy's little cowboy / Moonlight and roses / Bring your roses to her now / San Antonio rose / Mexican rose / Lonesome / Wonderous word / Resurrectus / Haste of roses / Lord's prayer / Heartbreak hill / Holeo / Diesel smoke / Almost / Empty saddles / There's a goldmine in the sky / Old pioneer / Home on the range / If you would only be mine / Sierra Nevada / River of no return / Lilies grows high / Lonely little
CD Set _____ BCD 15640
Bear Family / Aug '93 / Rollercoaster / Direct / CM / Swift / ADA.

Sonz Of A Loop Da Loop...

FLOWERS IN MY GARDEN (Sonz Of A Loop Da Loop Era)
CD _____ SUBBASE 19 CD
Suburban Base / Mar '93 / SRD.

Soon E MC

POINT DE VUE
Inter diction / Au nom des miens / Repugnant / O.P.I.D. / O.P. Reaction / Abattu / A mort / Tort sur le boulevard du rythm' funky / Sur le boulevard / Quelque chose qui cloche / 500 One for all / Combattre c'est etre / Sa motivation / Chauffer de taxi groove / Seme monsieur Lution / Elucider ce mystere / Point de vue / Rap jazz soul / Wadchie wadcha / Eh a biento
CD _____ CDPCSD 155
Parlophone / Aug '94 / EMI.

Sopor Aeternus

ICH TOTE
CD _____ EFA 01552
Apocalyptic Vision / Dec '95 / Plastic Head / SRD.

TODESWUNSCH
CD _____ EFA 015592
Apocalyptic Vision / Dec '95 / Plastic Head / SRD.

Sopwith Camel

HELLO HELLO AGAIN
CD _____ NEMCD 601
Sequel / Apr '90 / BMG.

Sorabji/Marek/Buso

CATHEDRALS IN SOUND
CD _____ AIRCD 9043
New Note / Aug '92 / New Note / Cadillac.

Sorbye, Lief

SPRINGDANCE
CD _____ EUCD 1056
ARC / '89 / ARC Music / ADA.

Sorrels, Rosalie

ALWAYS A LADY
CD _____ GLCD 2110
Green Linnet / May '93 / Roots / CM / Direct / ADA.

BE CAREFUL THERE'S A BABY IN THE HOUSE
CD _____ GLCD 2100
Green Linnet / '92 / Roots / CM / Direct / ADA.

BORDERLINE HEART
CD _____ GLCD 2119
Green Linnet / Sep '95 / Roots / CM / ADA.

MISCELLANEOUS RECORD NO. 1
CD _____ GLCD 1042
Green Linnet / Nov '88 / Roots / CM / Direct / ADA.

THEN CAME THE CHILDREN
CD _____ GLCD 2099
Green Linnet / '92 / Roots / CM / Direct /
ADA.

TRAVELIN' LADY RIDES
CD _____ GLCD 2109
Green Linnet / May '93 / Roots / CM /
Direct / ADA.

WHAT DOES IT MEAN TO LOVE
CD _____ GL 2113
Green Linnet / Feb '94 / Roots / CM /
Direct / ADA.

Sorrow

FORGOTTEN SUNRISE
CD _____ R 09262
Roadrunner / Sep '91 / Pinnacle.

TAKE A HEART
CD _____ REP 4093-WZ
Repertoire / Aug '91 / Pinnacle / Cadillac.

Sort Of Quartet

PLANET MAMON
CD _____ SST 315CD
SST / Jul '95 / Plastic Head.

Sortie

SORTIE
CD _____ JUST 47-2
Justin Time / Oct '92 / Harmonia Mundi /
Cadillac.

Soskin, Mark

OVERJOYED
CD _____ 66053020
Jazz City / Mar '91 / New Note.

Soul Asylum

AND THE HORSE THEY RODE IN ON
Spinnin / Bitter pill / Veil of tears / Nice guys
(Don't get paid) / Something out of nothing
/ Gullible's travels / Brand new shine / Easy
street / Grounded / Be on your way / We 3
/ All the king's friend
CD _____ CDMID 190
A&M / Nov '93 / PolyGram.

CLAM DIP & OTHER DELIGHTS
Just plain evil / Chains / Secret no more /
Artificial heart / P-9 / Take it to the root
CD _____ TTR 881442
Twin Tone / Feb '95 / Pinnacle.

GRAVE DANCERS UNION
Somebody to shove / Black gold / Runaway
train / Keep it up / Homesick / Get on out /
New world / April fool / Without a trace /
Growing into you / 99% / Sun maid
CD _____ 472253-2
Columbia / Oct '92 / Sony.

HANG TIME
Down on up to me / Little too clean / Sometime to return / Cartoon / Beggars and
choosers / Endless farewell / Standing in
the doorway / Marionette / Ode / Jack of all
trades / Twiddly dee / Heavy rotation
CD _____ CDMID 189
A&M / Nov '93 / PolyGram.

LET YOUR DIM LIGHT SHINE
Misery / No own devices / Shut down /
Hope up / Promises broken / Bittersweet /
String of pearls / Crawl / Caged rat / Eyes
of a child / Just like anyone / Tell me when
/ Nothing to write home about / I did my
best
CD _____ 4803202
Columbia / Jun '95 / Sony.

MADE TO BE BROKEN
Tied to the tracks / Ship of fools / Can't go
back / Another world another day / Made
to be broken / Never really been / Whoa /
New feelings / Growing pains / Long way
home / Lone rider / Ain't that tough / Don't
it...
CD _____ TTR 86662
Twin Tone / Feb '95 / Pinnacle.

**SAY WHAT YOU WILL, CLARENCE,
KARL SOLD THE TRUCK**
Draggin' me down / Long day / Money talks
/ Voodoo doll / Stranger / Do you know /
Sick of that song / Religiavision / Space-
head / Walkin' / Broken glass / Masquerade
/ Happy / Black and blue
CD _____ TTR 84392
Twin Tone / Feb '95 / Pinnacle.

WHILE YOU WERE OUT
Freaks / Carry on / No man's land / Crash-
ing down / Judge / Sun don't shine / Closer
to the stars / Never too soon / Miracle mile
/ Lap of luxury / Passing sad daydream
CD _____ TTR 86912
Twin Tone / Feb '95 / Pinnacle.

Soul Brothers

SOUL OF SOWETO
Umlohla / Siyayi dudula / Indlada / Umlenze
/ Kuyeza nakuwe / Bazobuya (Mixes) /
Jzongihumbula / Ngixolele / Inhlonipho /
Ennandi / Uthando Iwenu / Hamba ntombi
CD _____ MOU 40332
Mountain / Oct '95 / CM.

Soul Cages

SOUL CAGES
CD _____ MASSCD 032
Massacre / Jun '94 / Plastic Head.

Soul Children

FRICTION/ BEST OF TWO WORLDS
I'll be the other woman / What's happening
baby / Can't let you go / It's out of my
hands / Just one moment / We're gettin' too
close / Love makes it right / Bring it here /
Thanks for a precious nothing / Put your
world in my world (best of two worlds) /
Give me one good reason / Got to get away
from it all / Hang ups of holding on / Wrap
it up tonight / Let's make a sweet thing
sweeter / Finish me off / Don't break away
CD _____ CDSXD 056
Stax / Jun '93 / Pinnacle.

SINGLES, THE/OPEN DOOR POLICY
Don't take my kindness for weakness / It
ain't always what you do (it's who you let
see you do it) / Hold on I'm comin' / Make
it good / Ridin' on love's merry go-round /
Love is a hurtin' thing / Poem on the school
house door / Come back kind of love /
Signed, sealed, delivered (I'm yours) / I
don't know what this world is coming to /
Hearsay / Stir up the boogie, Part II / Who
you used to be / Strangers / Summer in the
shade / Can't give up a good thing / Butt la
rose / Hard living with a man / believing
CD _____ CDSXD 101
Stax / Jan '94 / Pinnacle.

SOUL CHILDREN/GENESIS
I'll understand / Move over / When tomorrow comes / Sweeter he is / Sweeter he is
(part 2) / Tighten up my thang / Give 'em
love / Doing our thang / Take up the slack
/ Super soul / My baby specializes / I want
to be loved / Don't take my squeeze /
Hearsay / All that shines ain't gold / It hurts
me to my heart / I'm loving you more everyday / Just the one I've been looking for /
Never get enough of your love / All day
preaching / Get up about yourself
CD _____ CDSXD 944
Stax / Aug '90 / Pinnacle.

Soul Circus

INSIDE
CD _____ DRCCD 42002
Ichiban / Mar '95 / Koch.

Soul Coughing

RUBY VROOM
Is Chicago, is not Chicago / Sugar free jazz
/ Casiotone nation / Blue eyed devil / Bus
to Beelzebug / True dreams of Wichita /
Screenwriter's blues / Moon Sammy / Su-
pra genius / City of motors / Un zoom zip /
Down to this / Mr. Bitterness / Janine
CD _____ 828555-2
Slash / Sep '94 / PolyGram.

Soul, David

BEST OF DAVID SOUL, THE
Don't give up on us / Tattler / Silver lady /
I wish I was / It sure brings out the love in
your eyes / Seem to miss so much (coalminer's song) / Let's have a quiet night in /
Going in with my eyes open / One more
mountain to climb / Topanga / 1927 Kansas
city / Landlord / Nobody but a fool or a
preacher / Bird on the wire
CD _____ MCCD 152
Music Club / Feb '94 / Disc / THE / CM.

Soul Defenders

SOUL DEFENDERS AT STUDIO ONE
CD _____ CDHB 066
Heartbeat / Jun '91 / Greensleeves /
Jetstar / Direct / ADA.

Soul Family Sensation

BURGER HABIT
CD _____ TPLP 45CD
One Little Indian / Sep '93 / Pinnacle.

NEW WAVE
CD _____ TPLP 35CD
One Little Indian / Sep '91 / Pinnacle.

Soul For Real

CANDY RAIN
Candy rain / Every little thing I do / All in my
mind / If you want it / I wanna be your friend
/ Ain't no sunshine / Spend the night / I
don't know / I only you knew / Thinking of
you / Piano interlude
CD _____ MCD 11125
MCA / Mar '95 / BMG.

Soul II Soul

VOLUME I - CLUB CLASSICS
Keep on movin' / Back to life / Feel free /
Live rap / Dance / Jazzie's groove / Fairplay
/ Happiness / Holdin' on Bambelaa / African
dance / Acapella
CD _____ DIXCD 82
10 / Mar '89 / EMI.

VOLUME II - 1990 A NEW DECADE
Get a life / Jazzie B / Daddae Harvey / Love
comes through / People / Missing you /
Courtney blows / 1990 a new decade /
Dreams a dream / Time (untitled) / In the
heat of the night / Our time has now come
/ Nomsa caluza / Sonti mndebele
CD _____ DIXCD 90
10 / Apr '92 / EMI.

VOLUME III - JUST RIGHT
Joy / Take me higher / Storm / Direction /
Just right / Move me no mountain / Intelli-
gence / Future / Mood / Everywhere
CD _____ DIXCD 100
10 / Apr '92 / EMI.

**VOLUME IV - THE CLASSIC SINGLES
1988-93**
Back to life / Keep on movin' / Get a life /
Dreams a dream / Missing you / Just right
/ Move me no mountain / People / Fairplay
(Mixes) / Jazzie's groove / Wish / Joy / Keep
on movin' (mixes) / Back to life (mixes)
CD _____ CDV 2724
Virgin / Oct '93 / EMI.

VOLUME V - BELIEVE
Love everlight / Ride on / How long / Feeling /
Universal love / Be a man / Zion / Don't you
dream / Game dunn / Sunday / Pride / I care
/ B groove / Believe
CD _____ CDV 2739
Virgin / Jul '95 / EMI.

Soul Immigrants

**HEALTHY VIBE FOR A MOOD
WORLDWIDE, A**
CD _____ 3AXCD 010
Saxology / Aug '95 / Harmonia Mundi /
Cadillac.

Soul, Jimmy

IF YOU WANNA BE HAPPY
If you wanna be happy / I can't hold out
any longer / Some kinda nut / Twistin' Matilda (and the channel) / Take me to Los Angeles / Call me / When I get my car / Everybody's gone ape / Guess things happen
that way / She's alright / Church Street in
the summertime / I want to know if you love
me / You're nothing / I hate you baby / My
little room / You can't have your cake / I
know why dreamers cry / Hands off / I love
you so / Treat 'em tough / I need your love
/ Tell me why / Don't release me / When
Matilda comes back / Go 'way Christina
CD _____ CDCH 593
Ace / Jan '96 / Pinnacle / Cadillac / Com-
plete/Pinnacle.

**IF YOU WANT TO BE HAPPY (The Very
Best Of Jimmy Soul)**
If you want to be happy / I can't hold out
any longer / Some kinda nut (take 1) / Never
hold (and the channel) / Take me to Los Angeles / Call me / When I get my car / Everybody's gone ape / Guess things happen
that way / She's alright / Church street in
the summertime / Church street in summertime / I want to know if you love me /
You're nothin' / I hate you baby / My little
room / You can't have your cake / I know
why dreamers cry / Hands off / I love you
so / Treat 'em rough / I need your love / Tell
me why / Don't release me / When Matilda
comes / Go 'way Christina
CD _____ CDCHD 593
Ace / Mar '94 / Pinnacle / Cadillac / Com-
plete/Pinnacle.

Soul Stirrers

HEAVEN IS MY HOME
Christ is all / He's my rock (wait on Jesus)
(takes 2 & 3) / In a few more days / Golden
bells (takes 1 & 2) / Sinner run to Jesus /
Heaven is my home (take 1) / Heaven is my
home (Take 2) / Till then / Out on a hill (take
1) / Swing low, sweet chariot (takes 1 & 2)
/ Loved ones are waiting / Love of God
(takes 2, 3 & 4) / When the gates swing
open / Lord laid his hands on me / That's
all I need to know / My life belongs to him
/ There's not a friend like Jesus / Heaven is
my home
CD _____ CDCHD 478
Ace / Jul '93 / Pinnacle / Cadillac / Com-
plete/Pinnacle.

JESUS GAVE ME WATER
Jesus gave me water / Christ is all / Come
let us go back to god / I'm on the firing line
/ How far am I from canaan / Jesus done
just what he said / He's my rock (wait on
jesus) / Joy joy to my soul / I'm gonna build
on that shore / Until Jesus calls me home /
Jesus will lead me to that promised land /
It wont' be long / Let me go home / Someday somewhere / Jesus paid the debt / End
of my journey / He's my friend (until the end)
/ I have a friend above all others / I gave up
everything to follow him / Come and go to
that land / Any day now / Jesus I'll never
forget / All right now / Pray / Come to go to
that land / I'm so happy in the service of the
lord
CD _____ CDCHD 464
Ace / Mar '93 / Pinnacle / Cadillac / Com-
plete/Pinnacle.

LAST MILE OF THE WAY, THE
Last mile of the way / Mean old way / That's
heaven to me / Were you there (false starts)

/ Were you there / Lord remember me / Pilgrim of sorrow / He's my guide / He's my
guide (incomplete) / Last mile of the way
(incomplete) / All right now / He'll make a
way / Jesus I'll never forget / Come and go
to that land / Just as I am / He'll welcome
me / He's my friend (until the end) / Jesus
paid the debt / Jesus will lead me to that
promised land #2 / Jesus will lead me to that
promised land / It won't be very long /
How far am I from Canaan (incomplete) /
How far am I from Canaan / Let me go
home
CD _____ CDCHD 563
Ace / Mar '94 / Pinnacle / Cadillac / Com-
plete/Pinnacle.

LIVE IN CONCERT
Introduction / He's my friend / Be with me,
Jesus / I'm travelling on and on / Wade in
the water / God is able / Lord remember me
/ When the gates swing open / Touch the
hem of his garment / He's my friend / Jesus
/ Raise your hand / Amazing grace / I will
trust in the Lord
CD _____ MIR 5025CD
Miracle / Nov '90 / Disc.

Soul Survivors

SOUL SOUNDS
Jump back / See saw / You can't sit down
/ How sweet it is (to be loved by you) / Soul
soup / Sunshine superman / Last night /
When something is wrong with my baby / I
feel good / Philly dog / Soul survival / Night
train
CD _____ RTCD 901145
Line / Sep '94 / CM / Grapevine / ADA /
Conifer / Direct.

Soul Syndicate

**MOODIE DUB I (Soul Syndicate & Black
Slate)**
CD _____ MMLP 95-2
Moodie / Mar '94 / Jetstar / SRD.

MOODIE IN DUB VOL.3
CD _____ MMCD 1032
Moodie / Sep '94 / Jetstar / SRD.

Soul Train

JAZZ IN SWEDEN 1986
CD _____ 1335
Caprice / Feb '90 / CM / Complete/
Pinnacle / Cadillac / ADA.

Soul Whirling Somewhere

EATING THE SEA
CD _____ HY 39100892
Hyperium / Apr '94 / Plastic Head.

Souled American

FLUBBER
CD _____ ROUGHCD 141
Rough Trade / Apr '89 / Pinnacle.

FROZEN
CD _____ EFA 121072
Moll / Dec '94 / SRD.

Souls At Zero

TASTE FOR THE PEVERSE, A
CD _____ 086272CTR
Edel / Oct '95 / Pinnacle.

Souls Of Mischief

93 TIL INFINITY
CD _____ CHIP 138
Jive / Oct '93 / BMG.

NO MAN'S LAND
CD _____ CHIP 163
Jive / Oct '95 / BMG.

Soulside

SOON COME HAPPY
CD _____ DISCHORD 51
Dischord / Feb '91 / SRD.

Sound

THUNDER UP
CD _____ CDBIAS 053
Play It Again Sam / Apr '87 / Vital.

Soundgarden

BADMOTORFINGER
Rusty cage / Outshined / Slaves and bull-
dozers / Jesus christ pose / Face pollution
/ Somewhere / Searching with my good eye
closed / Room a thousand years wide /
Mind riot / Drawing flies / Holy water / New
damage
CD _____ 395374 2
A&M / Oct '91 / PolyGram.

LOUDER THAN LOVE
Ugly truth / Hands all over / Gun / Power
trip / Get on the snake / Full on Kevin's
Mom / Loud love / I wake / Now wrong no
right / Uncovered / Big dumb sex
CD _____ CDA 5252
A&M / Sep '89 / PolyGram.

SOUNDGARDEN

LOUDER THAN LOVE/ BADMOTORFINGER
CD _____ CDA 24118
A&M / Oct '93 / PolyGram.

SCREAMING LIFE
CD _____ SPCD 12B
Sub Pop / Oct '93 / Disc.

SCREAMING LIFE/FOPP
Hunted down / Entering / Tears to forget / Nothing to say / Little Joe / Hand of God / Kingdom of come / Swallow my pride / Fopp / Fopp (dub)
CD _____ SPCD 12A/B
Sub Pop / Feb '94 / Disc.

SUPERUNKNOWN
Let me drown / My wave / Fell on black days / Mailman / Superunknown / Head down / Black hole sun / Spoonman / Limo wreck / Day I tried to live / Kickstand / Fresh tendrils / 4th of July / Half / Like suicide / She likes surprises
CD _____ 540215-2
A&M / Mar '94 / PolyGram.

ULTRAMEGA OK
Flower / All your lies / 665 / Beyond the wheel / 667 / Mood for trouble / Circle of power / He didn't / Smokestack lightnin' / Nazi driver / Head injury / Incessant mace / One minute of silence
CD _____ SST 201 CD
SST / Nov '88 / Plastic Head.

Sounds From The Ground

KIN
CD _____ WWCD 14
Wibbly Wobbly / Nov '95 / SRD.

Sounds Incorporated

SOUNDS INCORPORATED
Spartans / Detroit / Rinky dink / My little red book / Hall of the mountain king / One mint julep / Last night / Crane / Emily / Mogambo / Bullets / Spanish Harlem / Little bird / If we loved on top of a mountain / Old and the new / Grab this thing / Boil over / I'm comin' through / Fingertips / I'm in love again
CD _____ SEECD 371
See For Miles/C5 / Mar '93 / Pinnacle.

Sounds Of Blackness

AFRICA TO AMERICA: THE JOURNEY OF THE DRUM
Hold on (Part 1) / I'm going all the way / Ah been 'buked (Part 1) / I believe / Hold on (Part 2) / Everything's gonna be alright / Sun up to sundown / Lord will make a way / He took away all my pain / Place in my heart / Harder they are, the bigger they fall / Drum (Africa to America) / Royal Kingdoms/Rise/ My Native Land / Very special love / Strange fruit / Black butterfly / You've taken by blues and gone / Livin' the blues / Ah been 'buked (Part 2) / I'm going all the way (Brixton flavour)
CD _____ 549009-2
Perspective / Apr '94 / PolyGram.

EVOLUTION OF GOSPEL
Chains / Optimistic / Ah been workin' / Pressure (pt.1) / Pressure / Stand / Pressure (pt.2) / Your wish is my command / Hallelujah Lord / We give you thanks / He holds the future / What shall I call him / Better watch your behaviour / Please take my hand / I'll fly away / Harambee
CD _____ 3953612
Perspective / Oct '91 / PolyGram.

NIGHT BEFORE CHRISTMAS, THE
Born in a manger / Soul holidays / It's Christmas time / Away in a manger / O come all ye faithful (Adeste Fidelis) / O' Holy night / Peace on earth for everyone / Children go / Santa's comin' to town / Dance, chitlins, dance / Holiday love / Santa won't you come by / Jolly one's here / Dash away all/ Reindeer revolt / Give us a chance / Santa watch yo' step / Why don't you believe in me / Merry Christmas to the world
CD _____ 549 000-2
Perspective / Oct '92 / PolyGram.

Sounds Of The Future

FEAR OF THE FUTURE EP
CD _____ FORM 28
Formation / Sep '93 / SRD.

Sounds Orchestral

BEST OF SOUNDS ORCHESTRAL
CD _____ MATCD 225
Castle / Dec '92 / BMG.

CAST YOUR FATE TO THE WIND
CD _____ NEMCD 617
Sequel / Nov '91 / BMG.

Soup Dragons

HOTWIRED
CD _____ BLRCD 15
Big Life / May '92 / Pinnacle.

HYDROPHONIC
One way street / Don't get down (Get down) / Do you care / May the force be with you / Contact high / All messed up / Time is now / Freeway / Rest in peace / J.F. junkie /
CD _____ LECD 901952
Line / Oct '94 / CM / Grapevine / ADA / Conifer. Direct.

Automatic speed queen / Out of here / Motherfunker / Painkilla / Cruel lust / Black and blues / Hypersonic re-entry
CD _____ 522781-2
Mercury / Sep '94 / PolyGram.

LOVEGOD
CD _____ SOUPCD 2R
Big Life / Jul '90 / Pinnacle.

Source

ORGANISED NOISE
Vagator / Eclipse / Neuromancer / Real thing / Squeeze / Analysis / Release it / Beyond time
CD _____ RS 93005CD
R & S / May '93 / Vital.

Source Experience

DIFFERENT JOURNEYS
Unkown territory / Gate 41 (Features on LP only.) / Point zero / Pressure drop / Diatonic shift / Intruder / X-ray / Night shift / Voices of the spirit
CD _____ RS 94056CD
R & S / Nov '94 / Vital.

Souskay

SOUSKAY
CD _____ CD 69812
Melodie / '91 / Triple Earth / Discovery / ADA / Jetstar.

South African National...

CLASSIC UNCHAINED MELODIES (South African National Symphony Orchestra)
CD _____ CDSGP 1098
Prestige / Sep '95 / Total/BMG.

South, Eddie

EDDIE SOUTH 1923-37
CD _____ CLASSICS 707
Classics / Jul '93 / Discovery / Jazz Music.

EDDIE SOUTH 1937-41
CD _____ CLASSICS 737
Classics / Feb '94 / Discovery / Jazz Music.

EDDIE SOUTH IN PARIS 1929 & 1937
Doin' the raccoon / Two guitars / Eddie's blues / Sweet Georgia Brown / Lady be good / Dinah / Daphne / Somebody loves me / I can't believe that you're in love with me / Swing interpretation of the first movement of the concerto / Fiddle blues / Improvisations on the first movement of the concerto
CD _____ DRGCD 8405
DRG / Sep '93 / New Note.

South 'Frisco Jazz Band

BROKEN PROMISES
CD _____ SOSCD 1180
Stomp Off / Aug '90 / Jazz Music / Wellard.

GOT EVERYTHING, DON'T WANT ANYTHING
CD _____ SOSCD 1240
Stomp Off / Nov '92 / Jazz Music / Wellard.

SAGE HEN STRUT
CD _____ SOSCD 1143
Stomp Off / Apr '94 / Jazz Music / Wellard.

SOUTH 'FRISCO JAZZ BAND
CD _____ MMRC CD 4
Merry Makers / Feb '94 / Jazz Music.

SOUTH 'FRISCO JAZZ BAND - VOL.2
CD _____ MMRC CD 7
Merry Makers / Feb '94 / Jazz Music.

SOUTH 'FRISCO JAZZ BAND VOL. 1
CD _____ SOSCD 1027
Stomp Off / Dec '94 / Jazz Music / Wellard.

THESE CATS ARE DIGGIN' US
CD _____ SOSCD 1035
Stomp Off / Mar '95 / Jazz Music / Wellard.

Souther, J.D.

HOME BY DAWN
CD _____ 7599250812
Elektra / Jan '96 / Warner Music.

SOUTHER-HILLMAN-FURAY (Souther-Hillman-Furay)
CD _____ 7559611642
Elektra / Jan '96 / Warner Music.

TROUBLE IN PARADISE (Souther-Hillman-Furay)
Trouble in paradise / Move me real slow / For someone I love / Mexico / Love and satisfy / On the line / Prisoner in disguise / Follow me through / Somebody must be wrong

---

Southern Exposure

SMALL TOWN
Little company / Walls of time / Wheel hoss / Gypsy breeze / African breeze / I'm just a used to be / Green light / Moonshine whiskey / Wild Bill Jones / Bonaparte's retreat / Small town
CD _____ GRP 002
Get Real Productions / Sep '93 / Get Real Productions.

Southern Pacific

COUNTY LINE
CD _____ 7599258952
WEA / Jan '96 / Warner Music.

ZUMA
Midnight highway / Honey I dare you / New shade of blue / Dream on / Invisible man / Wheels on the line / Just hang on / All is lost / Bail out / Trail of tears
CD _____ 7599256092
WEA / Jan '96 / Warner Music.

Southern Sons

DEEP SOUTH GOSPEL
CD _____ ALCD 2802
Alligator / Oct '93 / Direct / ADA.

Southern, Jeri

SOUTHERN BREEZE
CD _____ FSRCD 104
Fresh Sound / Jan '93 / Jazz Music / Discovery.

Southern, Sheila

WITH LOVE (Southern, Sheila & Royal Philharmonic Orchestra)
What are you doing the rest of your life / My funny valentine / My coloring book / How beautiful is night / Nearness of you / Losing my mind / Country girl / My one and only love / Memory / Touch me in the morning / She's out of my life
CD _____ CDSIV 1107
Horatio Nelson / Jul '95 / THE / BMG / Avid/ BMG / Koch.

Southside Johnny

BEST OF SOUTHSIDE JOHNNY & THE ASBURY JUKES (Southside Johnny & The Asbury Jukes)
I don't want to go home / Fever / This time it's for real / Love on the wrong side of town / Without love / Having a party / Got to get you off my mind / Snatchin' it back / Sweeter than honey / You mean so much to me / Little by little / Got to be a better way home / This time baby's gone for good / Hearts of stone / Take it inside / Talk to me / Next to you / Trapped again
CD _____ 4735882
Sony Music / '89 / Sony.

Souvenir, William

TIN TELE, A
CD _____ MW 3010CD
Music & Words / Jul '95 / ADA / Direct.

Soviet Army Chorus

POPULAR SELECTIONS (Soviet Army Chorus & Band)
CD _____ MCD 71500
Monitor / Jun '93 / CM.

SONG OF YOUTH (Soviet Army Chorus & Band)
Song of youth / Birch tree in a field did stand / Far away / Volga boat song / You are always beautiful / Along Peter's street / Tipperary / Ah lovely night / Kamarinskaya / Annie Laurie / Song of the plains / Kalinka / Bandura / Oh no, John / Snow flakes / Ukrainian poem / Soldier's chorus (From the Decembrists.)
CD _____ CDC 747 833 2
Angel / Aug '87 / EMI.

Soviet France

ELSTRE
CD _____ CHARRMCD 5
Charrm / Jul '90 / Plastic Head.

MOHNOMISCHE
CD _____ CHARRMCD 4
Charrm / '84 / Plastic Head.

POPULAR SOVIET SONS AND YOUTH MUSIC
CD _____ STCD 024
Staalplaat / Sep '95 / Vital/SAM.

Space Cowboys

LOCKED 'N' LOADED
CD _____ RTD 19512672
Our Choice / Nov '92 / Pinnacle.

Space Streakings

7-TOKU
CD _____ GR 18CD
Skingraft / Nov '94 / SRD.

Spacebow

BIG WAVES
CD _____ NW 50012
Extreme / May '95 / Vital/SAM.

Spacehog

RESIDENT ALIEN
CD _____ 7559618342
East West / Jan '96 / Warner Music.

Spacemen 3

DREAM WEAPON
CD _____ ORBIT 001CD
Space Age / Oct '95 / Plastic Head.

FOR ALL THE FUCKED UP CHILDREN OF THE WORLD
CD _____ SFTRI 1368CD
Sympathy For The Record Industry / May '95 / Plastic Head.

LIVE IN EUROPE
CD _____ ORBIT 002CD
Space Age / Oct '95 / Plastic Head.

LOSING TOUCH
CD _____ MR 011CD
Munster / Apr '92 / Plastic Head.

PEFORMANCE
CD _____ REF 33011
Fire / Oct '91 / Disc.

PERFECT PRESCRIPTIONS
Take me to the other side / Walking with Jesus / Ode to street hassle / Ecstasy symphony / Transparent radiation / Feel so good / Things'll never be the same / Come down easy / Call the doctor
CD _____ REF 33006
Fire / Oct '91 / Disc.

PLAYING WITH FIRE
CD _____ FIRE 33016
Fire / Oct '91 / Disc.

RECURRING
Big City / Just to see you smile #2 / I love you / Set me free/I've got the key / Set me free / Why couldn't I see / Just to see you smile / When tomorrow hits / Feel so sad (Reprise) / Hypnotised / Sometimes / Feeling just fine (head full of shit) / Billy Whizz/ Blue 1 / Drive/Feel so sad / Feeling just fine (alternative mix)
CD _____ FIRE 33023
Fire / Oct '91 / Disc.

REVOLUTION OR HEROIN
CD _____ FRIGHT 053
Fierce / Oct '95 / Disc.

SOUND OF CONFUSION
CD _____ RED 33005
Fire / Oct '91 / Disc.

SPACEMEN ARE GO
CD _____ BCD 4044
Bomp / May '95 / Pinnacle.

TAKING DRUGS TO MAKE MUSIC
CD _____ BCD 4047
Bomp / Nov '94 / Pinnacle.

TRANSLUCENT FLASHBACKS (The Glass Singles)
CD _____ FLIPCD 003
Fire / Jun '95 / Disc.

Spacetime Continuum

EMIT ECAPS
CD _____ REFCD 7
CD _____ REFSCD 7
Reflective / Jan '96 / SRD.

Spahn Ranch

BLACKMAIL STARTERS KIT
CD _____ CLEO 94772
Cleopatra / Jun '94 / Disc.

BREATH & TAXES
CD _____ CDZOT 116
Zoth Ommog / Aug '94 / Plastic Head.

Spain

BLUE MOODS OF SPAIN, THE
So it's true / Ten nights / Dreaming of love / Untitled / Her used-to-been / Ray of light / World of blue / I lied / Spiritual
CD _____ 729102
Restless / Sep '95 / Vital.

Spain, Johnnie

BOHEMIAN HOLIDAY
Don't tell Franz / Little Spanish madness / Bohemian holiday / Head honcho / Alfie / Dago red / Heart of a cowboy / Quiet elegance
CD _____ CDSGP 011
Prestige / Jan '93 / Total/BMG.

Spand, Charlie

1929-31
CD _____ DOCD 5108
Blues Document / Nov '92 / Swift / Jazz Music / Hot Shot.

Spandau Ballet

BEST OF SPANDAU BALLET, THE
To cut a long story short / Freeze / Muscle-bound / Chant no.1 (I don't need this pressure on) / Paint me down / She loved like diamond / Instinction / Lifeline / True / Gold / Only when you leave / I'll fly for you / Highly strung / Round and round / Fight for ourselves / Through the barricades / How many lies / Raw / Be free with your love
CD _____ CCD 1894
Chrysalis / Sep '91 / EMI.

SINGLES COLLECTION, THE
Gold / Lifeline / Round and round / Only when you leave / Instinction / Highly strung / True / Communication / I'll fly for you / To cut a long story short / Chant no.1 (I don't need this pressure on) / She loved like diamond / Paint me down / Freeze / Musclebound
CD _____ CCD 1498
Chrysalis / Apr '86 / EMI.

THROUGH THE BARRICADES
Barricades - introduction / Cross the line / Man in chains / How many lies / Virgin / Fight for ourselves / Swept / Snakes and lovers / Through the barricades / With pride
CD _____ 4502592
CBS / Feb '94 / Sony.

TRUE
Gold / Pleasure / Communication / Code of love / Lifeline / Heaven is a secret / Foundation / True
CD _____ CD25CR 11
Chrysalis / Mar '94 / EMI.

TWELVE INCH MIXES
Gold / Lifeline / Round and round / Only when you leave / Instinction / Highly restrung / True / Communication / I'll fly for you / To cut a long story short / Chant no.1 (I don't need this pressure on) / She loved like diamond / Paint me down / Freeze / Musclebound
CD _____ CCD 1574
Chrysalis / Feb '94 / EMI.

Spanier, Herbie

ANTHOLOGY 1962-93
CD _____ JUST 55-2
Justin Time / Feb '94 / Harmonia Mundi / Cadillac.

Spanier, Muggsy

1939 (The Ragtime Band Sessions)
Big butter and egg man / Someday sweetheart / Eccentric (That eccentric rag) / That da da strain / At the jazz band ball / I wish I could shimmy like my sister Kate / Dippermouth blues / Livery stable blues / Riverboat shuffle / Relaxin' at the Touro / At sundown / Bluin' the blues / Lonesome road / What did I do to be so black and blue / Mandy, make up your mind
CD _____ 7863665502
Bluebird / Jun '95 / BMG.

GREAT 16! - MUGGSY SPANIER'S RAGTIME BAND
Relaxin' at the Touro / Mandy, make up your mind / Bluin' the blues / That da da strain / I wish I could shimmy like my sister Kate / At sundown / Lonesome road / Eccentric / At the jazz band ball / Dinah / Big butter and egg man / Livery stable blues / What did I do to be so black and blue / Riverboat shuffle / Someday sweetheart / Dippermouth blues
CD _____ 74321 13039-2
Bluebird / Sep '93 / BMG.

LITTLE DIXIE PLAY YOUR HARP
(Spanier, Muggsy & His Orchestra)
CD _____ 3801302
Jazz Archives / Oct '92 / Jazz Music / Discovery / Cadillac.

MUGGSHOT
At Sundown / Baby, won't you please come home / Bluin' the blues / Bullfrog blues / Chicago / China boy / Dallas blues / Dark town strutter's ball / Down to Steamboat Tennessee / Four or five times / Friars Point Shuffle / Hesitating blues / I wish I could shimmy like my sister Kate / I've found a new baby / Mobile blues / Nobody's sweetheart / Relaxin' at the Touro / Royal Garden blues / Sugar / That's a plenty / There'll be some changes made / Why can't it be poor little me / (I'll be glad when you're dead) you rascal you / You're bound to look like a monkey
CD _____ CDAJA 5102
Living Era / Mar '93 / Koch.

MUGGSY SPANIER & TESCHEMACHER'S CHICAGOANS
(Spanier, Muggsy & Frank Teschemaker)
CD _____ VILCD 001-2
Village Jazz / Nov '93 / Target/BMG / Jazz Music.

MUGGSY SPANIER 1939-42
CD _____ CLASSICS 709
Classics / Jul '93 / Discovery / Jazz Music.

MUGGSY SPANIER 1939-44
CD _____ CD 14570
Jazz Portraits / May '95 / Jazz Music.

MUGGSY SPANIER VOL. 1 - 1924-27
CD _____ KJ 107FS
King Jazz / Oct '93 / Jazz Music / Cadillac / Discovery.

MUGGSY SPANIER VOL. 2 - 1928-29
CD _____ KJ 108FS
King Jazz / Oct '93 / Jazz Music / Cadillac / Discovery.

MUGGSY, TESCH AND THE CHICAGOANS (Spanier, Muggsy & Frank Teschemaker)
CD _____ VILCD 0142
Village Jazz / Aug '92 / Target/BMG / Jazz Music.

Spanish Fly

ANYTHING YOU WANT
CD _____ 9362459262
Warner Bros. / Jun '95 / Warner Music.

RAGS TO BRITCHES
CD _____ KFWCD 114
Knitting Factory / Feb '95 / Grapevine.

Spanish Gipsy

CON AMOR
CD _____ EUCD 1190
ARC / Apr '92 / ARC Music / ADA.

Spann, Otis

BIGGEST THING SINCE COLOSSUS
(Spann, Otis & Fleetwood Mac)
My love depends on you / Walkin' / It was a big thing / Temperature is rising (100.2 F) / Dig you / No more doggin' / Ain't nobody's business / She needs some loving / I need some air / Someday baby
CD _____ 4759722
Blue Horizon / Feb '95 / Sony.

BLUES IS WHERE IT'S AT, THE
Popcorn man / Brand new house / Chicago blues / Steel mill blues / Down on Sarah Street / T'ain't nobody's business if I do / Nobody knows Chicago like I do / My home is on the Delta / Spann blues
CD _____ BGOCD 221
Beat Goes On / Mar '94 / Pinnacle.

BLUES NEVER DIE
Blues never die / I got a feeling / One more mile to go / Feeling good / After while / Dust my broom / Straighten up baby / Come on / Must have been the Devil / Lightning / I'm ready
CD _____ OBCCD 530
Original Blues Classics / Nov '92 / Complete/Pinnacle / Wellard / Cadillac.

BLUES OF OTIS SPANN, THE
Rock me Mama / Keep your hand out of my pocket / Sarah Street / Country boy / Meet me in the bottom / I got a feeling / You're gonna need my help / I came from Clarksdale / Spann's boogie / Blues don't like nobody / Pretty girls everywhere / Lost sleep in the fold / Jangle boogie / Natural days / Stirs me up
CD _____ SEECD 389
See For Miles/C5 / Oct '93 / Pinnacle.

BOTTOM OF THE BLUES, THE
I feel bundled with trouble / Dirty dealin' / Shimmy baby / Looks like twins / I'm a fool / My man / Down to earth / Nobody knows / Dr. blues
CD _____ BGOCD 94
Beat Goes On / Nov '90 / Pinnacle.

CHICAGO BLUES
CD _____ TCD 5005
Testament / Oct '94 / Complete/Pinnacle / ADA / Koch.

CRYIN' TIME
Home to Mississippi / Blues is a botheration / You said you'd be on time / Crying time / Blind man / Someday / Twisted snake / Green flowers / New boogaloo / Mule kicking in my stall
CD _____ VMD 6514
Vanguard / Feb '96 / Complete/Pinnacle / Discovery.

OTIS SPANN IS THE BLUES
Hard way / Take a little walk with me / Otis in the dark / Little boy blue / Country boy / Beat-up team / My daily wish / Great Northern stomp / I got rambling on my mind / Worried life blues
CD _____ CCD 9001
Candid / Sep '87 / Cadillac / Jazz Music / Wellard / Koch.

WALKING THE BLUES
It must have been the devil / Otis blues / Going down slow / Half ain't been told / Monkey face woman / This is the blues / Evil ways / Come day go day / Walking the blues
CD _____ CCD 9025
Candid / Jul '87 / Cadillac / Jazz Music / Wellard / Koch.

Spanner Banner

CHILL
Universal love / Baby don't leave me / Chill / Slow motion / Cheater / You gotta be / Michelle / What we need is love / Sweet angel / Little bit of rain
CD _____ IJCD 3006
Island / Jul '95 / PolyGram.

Spare Snare

LIVE AT HOME
Thorns (version 1) / Shine on now / Wired for sound / Super slinky / As a matter of fact / Skateboard punk rocker / Bugs / My better half (Features on CD.) / Call the birds / Thorns (version 2)
CD _____ CHUTECD 005
Chute / May '95 / Vital.

Sparks

BIG BEAT
Big boy / I want to be like everybody else / Nothing to do / I bought Mississippi river / Fill-er up / Everybody's stupid / Thrown her away (and get a new one) / Confusion / Screwed up / White woman / I like girls / Tearing the place apart / Gone with the wind
CD _____ IMCD 201
Island / Jul '94 / PolyGram.

GRATUITOUS SAX & SENSELESS VIOLINS
Gratuitous sax / When do I get to sing 'My Way' / (When I kiss you) I hear Charlie Parker playing / Frankly Scarlett I don't give a damn / I thought I told you to wait in the car / Hear no evil, see no evil, speak no evil / Now that I own the BBC / Tsui Hark (featuring Tsui Hark & Bill Kong) / Ghost of Liberace / Let's go surfing / Senseless violins
CD _____ 74321232672
Arista / Mar '95 / BMG.

HALF NELSON
CD _____ 8122713002
WEA / Jul '93 / Warner Music.

IN THE SWING
This town ain't big enough for the both of us / Hasta manana Monsieur / Amateur hour / Lost and found / Never turn your back on mother earth / I like girls / I want to hold your hand / Get in the swing / Looks, looks, looks / England / Big boy / Something for the girl with everything / Marry me / Gone with the wind
CD _____ 5500652
Spectrum/Karussell / May '93 / PolyGram / THE.

INDISCREET
Hospitality on parade / Happy hunting ground / Without using hands / Get in the swing / Under the table with her / How are you getting home / Pineapple / Tits / This ain't 1918 / Lady is lingering / In the future / Looks, looks, looks / Miss the start, miss the end / Profile / I want to hold your hand / England
CD _____ IMCD 200
Island / Jul '94 / PolyGram.

INTERIOR DESIGN
So important / I just got back from heaven / Lots of reasons / You got a hold of my heart / Love-o-rama / Toughest girl in town / Let's make love / Stop me if you've heard this before / Walk down memory lane / Madonna / Big brass ring (CD only)
CD _____ CDTB 141
Thunderbolt / '88 / Magnum Music Group.

KIMONO MY HOUSE
This town ain't big enough for the both of us / Amateur hour / Falling in love with myself again / Here in heaven / Thank God it's not Christmas / Hasta manana Monsieur / Talent is an asset / Complaints / In my family / Equator / Barbecutie / Lost and found
CD _____ IMCD 198
Island / Jul '94 / PolyGram.

MAEL INTUITION - THE BEST OF SPARKS 1974-76 (It's a Mael, Mael, Mael World)
This town ain't big enough for the both of us / Hasta manana monsieur / Tearing the place apart / At home, at work, at play / Never turn your back on Mother Earth / Get in the swing / Amateur hour / Looks, looks, looks / Thanks but no thanks / Gone with the wind / Something for the girl with everything / Thank God it's not Christmas
CD _____ IMCD 88
Island / Feb '90 / PolyGram.

PROPAGANDA
Propaganda / At home, at work, at play / Reinforcements / B.C. / Thanks but no thanks / Don't leave me alone with her / Never turn your back on Mother Earth / Something for the girl with everything / Achoo / Who don't like kids / Bon voyage / Alabamy right / Marry me
CD _____ IMCD 199
Island / Jul '94 / PolyGram.

SO IMPORTANT
CD _____ 12571
Laserlight / Oct '95 / Target/BMG.

Sparks

SPARKS
CD _____ REP 4052-WZ
Repertoire / Aug '91 / Pinnacle / Cadillac.

SPARKS/WOOFER IN A TWEETER'S CLOTHING
Wonder girl / Fa la fa lee / Roger / High C / Fletcher honorama / Simple ballet / Slow-boat / Biology 2 / Saccarin and the war / Big bands / (Nor more) / Girl from Germany / Beaver O'Lindy / Nothing is sacred / Here comes Bob / Moon over Kentucky / Do re mi / Angus desire / Underground / Louvre / Batteries not included / Whippings and apologies
CD _____ LOMACD 23
Loma / Feb '94 / BMG.

WOOFER IN TWEETERS CLOTHING, A
CD _____ REP 4051-WZ
Repertoire / Aug '91 / Pinnacle / Cadillac.

Sparks Brothers

SPARKS BROTHERS 1932-35
CD _____ DOCD 5315
Blues Document / Dec '94 / Swift / Jazz Music / Hot Shot.

Sparks, Melvin

SPARKS/AKILAH
Thank you / I didn't know what time it was / Charlie Brown / Stinker / Spill the wine / Love the life you live / On the up / All wrapped up / Akilah / Blues for J.B. / Image of love
CD _____ CDBGPD 064
BGP / Jan '93 / Pinnacle.

TEXAS TWISTER
Whip whop / Gathering together / Judy's groove / Texas twister / Ain't no woman (Like the one I got) / I want to talk about you / Star in the crescent / I've got to have you / Mocking bird / Looking for a love / Get ya some / Get down with the get down / Bump & stomp / In the morning / If you want my love
CD _____ CDBGPD 092
BGP / Aug '95 / Pinnacle.

Sparks, Tim

NUTCRACKER SUITE
CD _____ BEST 1028CD
Acoustic Music / Nov '93 / ADA.

Sparrow

CARNIVAL JAMBACK SOCA BALLADS
CD _____ BLS 1019CD
BLS / Aug '95 / Jetstar.

ONLY A FOOL
CD _____ JMC 200111
Jamaica Gold / Jun '94 / THE / Magnum Music Group / Jetstar.

Sparrow

HATCHING OUT
I'm coming back / Well I can tell you / Don't ask me / Nightmare / Many things are clear / Rollercoaster / Dream song / Rainsung song / Break my heart again / Round and round
CD _____ SEECD 434
See For Miles/C5 / Aug '95 / Pinnacle.

Sparrow Dragon

AGAIN
CD _____ RNCD 2011
Rhino / Jun '93 / Jetstar / Magnum Music Group / THE.

Sparrow, Johnny

DANCIN' TIME VOL. 3
CD _____ SAV 240CD
Savoy / Dec '95 / THE / Savoy.

Spasm

SPASM
CD _____ INV 048CD
Invisible / Jan '96 / Plastic Head.

Spasmodique

HAVEN
CD _____ SCH 9014CD
Schemer / Sep '91 / Vital.

Spaulding, James

BLUES NEXUS
Hipsippy blues / Gerkin from perkin / John charles / Rue prevail / Gypsy blues / Vaunex / Soul station / Chamber mates / Bleeker street blues / Public eyes
CD _____ MCD 5467
Muse / Feb '95 / New Note / CM.

BRILLIANT CORNERS
CD _____ MCD 5369
Muse / Sep '92 / New Note / CM.

GOTSTABE A BETTER WAY
CD _____ MCD 5413
Muse / Sep '92 / New Note / CM.

Speake, Martin

IN OUR TIME
Understatement / Hidden vision / Twisted tungo / Sugar loaf / Benjamin / Blackwell / Trust / Spring dance / Intention
CD _____ TJL 005CD
The Jazz Label / Feb '95 / New Note.

Speaking Canaries

SONGS FOR THE TERRESTRIALLY CHALLENGED
CD _____ SCT 0392
Scat / Feb '95 / Vital.

Spear Of Destiny

BBC LIVE IN CONCERT
Land of shame / Strangers in our town / Pumpkin man / Embassy song / Never take me alive / Outlands / Was that you / Miami Vice / Rocket ship / Once in her lifetime / All you young men / Mickey / Liberator
CD _____ WINDCD 055
Windsong / Mar '94 / Pinnacle.

COLLECTION: SPEAR OF DESTINY
CD _____ CCSCD 297
Castle / Oct '91 / BMG.

LIVE AT THE LYCEUM - 22.12.85.
Rainmaker / Rocket ship / Attica / Come back / Up all night / Mickey / Young men / World service / Playground of the rich / Grapes of wrath / I can see / Liberator / Prisoner of love / Incinerator / These days are gone / Do you believe in the westworld
CD _____ MAUCD 638
Mau Mau / Jun '93 / Pinnacle.

TIME OF OUR LIVES (The Best Of Spear Of Destiny)
Never take me alive / Outlands / Traveller / Strangers in our town / Miami Vice / Time of our lives / Man that never was / So in love with you / March or die / I remember / Radio radio / Life goes on / If the guns / Was that you
CD _____ CDOVD 449
Virgin / Feb '95 / EMI.

Spearhead

HOME
People in the middle / Love is da shit / Piece o' peace / Positive / Of course you can / Hole in the bucket / Home / Dream team / Runfayalifel crime to be broke in America / 100,000 miles / Red beans and rice / Caught without an umbrella
CD _____ CDEST 2236
Capitol / Sep '94 / EMI.

Spearman's Double Trio

SMOKEHOUSE
CD _____ 120157-2
Black Saint / Oct '94 / Harmonia Mundi / Cadillac.

Spears, Billie Jo

16 COUNTRY FAVOURITES
You're my man / One more chance / Cheatin' kind / I'll take a melody / Look what they've done to my song Ma / If it ain't love / Ease the want in me / Dallas / It makes no difference now
CD _____ PWK 069
Carlton Home Entertainment / Sep '88 / Carlton Home Entertainment.

BILLIE JO SPEARS EMI COUNTRY MASTERS
I love you because / He's got more love in his little finger / Help me make it through the night / Marty Gray / I'll share my world with you / I stayed loving you again / Today I started loving you again / It coulda been me / Snowbird / See the funny little clown / Harper Valley PTA / Blanket on the ground / Rose garden / Stay away from the apple tree / Lay down beside me / Silver wings and golden rings / Livin' in a house full of love / What I've got in mind / Apartment no. 9 / On the rebound / Faded love / Never did like whiskey / Your old love letters / I'm not easy / Yours love / If you want me / Heart over mind / Too much is not enough / Mr. walker, it's all over / Lonely hearts club / Tips and tables / Teardrops will kiss the morning dew / True love / I've got to go / Take me to your world / '57 Chevrolet / Stand by your man / Love ain't gonna wait for us / Price I pay to stay / Yesterday / I will survive / Livin' our love together / Games people play / Sing me an old fashioned song / Rainy days and rainy nights / Standing tall / Misty blue / Your good girl's gonna go bad / For the good times / What the world needs now is love
CD Set _____ CDEM 1481
EMI / Apr '93 / EMI.

GREATEST HITS
CD _____ WMCD 5680
Disky / Nov '93 / THE / BMG / Discovery / Pinnacle.

LOVE SONGS
Blanket on the ground / What I've got in mind / Today I started loving you again / Don't ever let go of me / All I want is you / I've never loved anyone before / Say it again / I fall to pieces / True love / Love ain't the question (love ain't the answer) / Every time I sing a love song / I've got to go / Since I fell for you / Come on home / What a love I have in you / There's more to a tear than meets the eye / What the world needs now is love / Love ain't gonna wait for us / I love you because / Put a little love in your heart
CD _____ CDMFP 6112
Music For Pleasure / Mar '94 / EMI.

MAGIC OF BILLIE JO SPEARS, THE
CD _____ TKOCD 002
TKO / '92 / TKO.

MISTY BLUE
CD _____ 15476
Laserlight / Nov '92 / Target/BMG.

QUEEN OF COUNTRY MUSIC, THE
Cry / Country roads / Make the world go away / Slow hand / I believe / Love letters in the sand / You light up my life / Heartaches by the number / Always on my mind / Raindrops keep falling on my head / Misty / Paper roses / If you love me (let me know) / Amazing grace
CD _____ CDDPR 123
Premier/MFP / Nov '94 / EMI.

SINGS THE COUNTRY GREATS
'57 Chevrolet / Loving him was easier / He won't you play another somebody done somebody wrong song / Till something better comes along / Sing me an old fashioned song / Every time I sing a love song / See the funny little clown / That's what friends are for / Blanket on the ground / Ode to Billy Joe / Misty blue / I don't wanna play house / Hurt / Stand by your man / He's got more love in his little finger / Take me to your world
CD _____ CDMFP 5784
Music For Pleasure / May '91 / EMI.

STAND BY YOUR MAN
CD _____ CDCD 1099
Charly / Apr '93 / Charly / THE / Cadillac.

UNMISTAKABLY
Every time I close my eyes / One smokey rose / Mutual aquaintance / I got this train to ride / If wishes were wings / We need to walk / Keep me from dreamin' / Star / We're over / It won't be long
CD _____ ETCD 194
Etude / Sep '92 / Grapevine.

Special A

SPECIAL A. ENCOUNTERS MIXMAN
CD _____ BLKMCD 008
Blakamix / Dec '94 / Jetstar / SRD.

Special Ed

LEGAL
CD _____ FILERCD 297
Profile / Sep '90 / Pinnacle.

Special EFX

BODY LANGUAGE
Bodyheat / Seduction / Sunset / Night rhythm / Till we meet again / Spy vs spy / When love cries / Papa jinda / Mikes D / Free
CD _____ JVC 20512
JVC / Nov '95 / New Note.

CATWALK
Nitty gritty / Mercy mercy me / Passions / Dancing cobra / Siana / George can't dance / So happy, so sad / Hip hop bop / Forever this love / Concrete jungle
CD _____ JVC 20382
JVC / Oct '94 / New Note.

SPECIAL DELIVERY
Safari / Sambuca nights / Much too soon / Forever hold your peace / Foggy streets of London / Slug / Waiting / Katalin
CD _____ FCD 0004
Limetree / Nov '95 / New Note.

Specials

LIVE AT THE MOONLIGHT CLUB
It's up to you / Do the dog / Monkey man / Blank expressions / Nite klub / Concrete jungle / Too hot / Too much too young / Little bitch / Longshot kick de bucket
CD _____ CCD 5011
Chrysalis / Apr '92 / EMI.

SPECIALS LIVE IN CONCERT
CD _____ WINCD 030
See For Miles/C5 / Dec '92 / Pinnacle.

SPECIALS, THE
Message to you Rudy / Do the dog / It's up to you / Nite klub / Doesn't make it alright / Concrete jungle / Too hot / Monkey man / (Dawning of a) New era / Blank expression / Stupid marriage / Too much too young / Little bitch / You're wondering now
CD _____ CD25CR 02
Chrysalis / Mar '94 / EMI.

Species Of Fish

SONGS OF A DUMB VOICE
CD _____ KIP 006
Staalplaat / Dec '95 / Vital/SAM.

Speckled Red

SPECKLED RED - 1929-30
Blues Document / Oct '93 / Swift / Jazz Music / Hot Shot.
CD _____ DOCD 5205

Speckmann

SPECKMANN
CD _____ NB 056CD
Nuclear Blast / Feb '92 / Plastic Head.

Specter, Dave

BLUEPLICITY (Specter, Dave & The Bluebirds)
CD _____ DD 664
Delmark / May '94 / Hot Shot / ADA / CM / Direct / Cadillac.

LIVE IN EUROPE (Specter, Dave & The Bluebirds)
CD _____ CCD 11047
Crosscut / Nov '95 / ADA / CM / Direct.

Spector, Phil

CHRISTMAS GIFT FOR YOU FROM PHIL SPECTOR, A (Various Artists)
White Christmas / Frosty the snowman / Bells of St. Mary's / Santa Claus is coming to town / Sleigh ride / Marshmallow world / I saw Mommy kissing Santa Claus / Rudolph the red nosed reindeer / Winter wonderland / Parade of the wooden soldiers / Christmas (baby please come home) / Here comes Santa Claus / Silent night
CD _____ PSCD 1005
EMI / Dec '95 / EMI.

PHIL SPECTOR - BACK TO MONO (1958-1969/4CD Set) (Various Artists)
To know him is to love him / Corrine Corina / Spanish harlem / Pretty little angel eyes / Every breath I take / I love how you love me / Under the moon of love / There's no other (like my baby) / Uptown / He hit me (and it felt like a kiss) / He's a rebel / Zip a dee doo dah / Puddin' 'n' tain / He's sure the boy I love / Why do lovers break each others hearts / Today I met the boy I'm gonna marry / Da doo ron ron / Heartbreaker / Why don't they let us fall in love / Chapel of love / Not too young to get married / Wait 'til my Bobby gets home / All grown up / Be my baby / Then he kissed me / Fine fine boy / Baby I love you / Ronettes / Girls can tell / Little boy / Hold me tight / Best part of breaking up / Soldier baby of mine / Strange love / Stumble and fall / When I saw you / So young / Do I love you / Keep on dancin' / You baby / Woman in love (with you) / Walking in the rain / You've lost that lovin' feelin' / Born to be together / Just once in my life / Unchained melody / Is this what I get for loving you / Long way to be happy / (I love you) for sentimental reasons / Ebb tide / This could be the night / Paradise / River deep, mountain high / I'll never need more than this / Love like yours (don't come knockin' everyday) / Save the last dance for me / I wish I never saw the sunshine / You came, you saw, you conquered / Black pearl / Love is all I have to give / White Christmas / Frosty the snowman / Bells of St. Mary's / Santa Claus is coming to town / Sleigh ride / Marshmallow world / I saw Mommy kissing Santa Claus / Rudolph the red nosed reindeer / Winter wonderland / Parade of the wooden soldiers / Christmas (baby please come home) / Here comes Santa Claus / Silent night
CD Set _____ CDP 7980632
EMI / Nov '91 / EMI.

Spector, Ronnie

DANGEROUS
CD _____ RVCD 48
Raven / Sep '95 / Direct / ADA.

Spectrum

HIGH LOWS & HEAVENLY BLOWS
CD _____ ORECD 532
Silvertone / Oct '94 / Pinnacle.

SOUL KISS (GLIDE DIVINE)
CD _____ ORECD 518
Silvertone / Jun '92 / Pinnacle.

Specula

ERUPT
Desolation nightmare / She walks in sunshine / Hello pain / Forever loving you / Can't we all / Stand by / Rock stepper / Inertia / Steal your love / Dual
CD _____ SCT 0422
Scat / Aug '95 / Vital.

Spedding, Chris

CAFE DAYS
CD _____ 422340
New Rose / Nov '94 / Direct / ADA.

CHRIS SPEDDING
Jump in my car / Hungry man / Motor bikin' / Catch that train / Nervous / Boogie City / New girl in the neighbourhood / School days / Sweet disposition / Bedsit girl / Guitar jamboree
CD _____ FC 051CD
Fan Club / '90 / Direct.

ENEMY WITHIN
CD _____ ROSE 94CD
New Rose / Sep '86 / Direct / ADA.

GUITAR GRAFITTI
Video life / Radio times / Time warp / Midnight boys / Bored, bored, walkin' / Breakout / Frontal lobotomy / Hey Miss Betty / More lobotomy
CD _____ FC 054CD
Fan Club / Aug '89 / Direct.

GUITAR JAMBOREE
CD _____ 422343 FC
Fan Club / '90 / Direct.

HURT
Wild in the street / Silver bullet / Lone ruler / Woman trouble / I ain't superstitious / Wild wild women / Roadrunner / Stay dumb / Get outa my pagoda / Hurt by love
CD _____ FC 052CD
Fan Club / '90 / Direct.

I'M NOT LIKE EVERYBODY ELSE
I'm not like everybody else / Box number / I got a feeling / Crying game / Depravity / Musical press / Contract / Counterfeit / Shot of rhythm and blues / Mama coco
CD _____ FC 055CD
Fan Club / Aug '89 / Direct.

JUST PLUG HIM IN
CD _____ FC 081
Fan Club / Nov '94 / Direct.

MEAN AND MOODY
For what we are about to hear / Backwood progression / Only lick I know / Listen while I sing my song / Saw you yesterday / Hill / Don't leave me / White lady / She's my friend / London town / Dark end of the street / Please Mrs. Henery / Never carry mor than you can eat / Words don't come / Backwood theme
CD _____ SEECD 372
See For Miles/C5 / Mar '93 / Pinnacle.

Speedfreak

DESTRUCTION BY SPEED
CD _____ EFA 007502
Shockwave / Sep '94 / SRD.

Speedy J

G SPOT
CD _____ WARPCD 27
Warp / Mar '95 / Disc.

GINGER
CD _____ WARPCD 14
Warp / Jun '93 / Disc.

LIVE
CD _____ HHCD 015
Harthouse / Nov '95 / Disc / Warner Music.

Speegle, David

DIM LIGHTS & CANDLES
CD _____ CDSGP 017
Prestige / Jan '93 / Total/BMG.

Spell

MISSISSIPPI
Dixie / Seems to me / Superstar / More / Straight to hell / 4-B / Hazel Motes / Safe / Mom / Bring the old man / Three
CD _____ CIRD 1003
Island Red / Apr '95 / PolyGram / Vital.

SEASONS IN THE SUN
CD _____ CDSTUMM 126
Mute / Oct '93 / Disc.

Spelmansforbund, Blekinge

SONGS AND DANCES FROM SWEDEN
CD _____ EUCD 1108
ARC / '91 / ARC Music / ADA.

Spence, Bill

HAMMERED DULCIMER RETURNS, THE
CD _____ FHR 041CD
Front Hall / Nov '95 / ADA.

HAMMERED DULCIMER, THE
CD _____ FHR 302CD
Front Hall / Nov '95 / ADA.

Spence, Joseph

BAHAMIAN GUITARIST
CD _____ ARHCD 349
Arhoolie / Apr '95 / ADA / Direct / Cadillac.

OUT ON THE ROLLING SEA (A Tribute To Joseph Spence) (Various Artists)
CD _____ HPR 2004CD
Hokey Pokey / Jul '94 / ADA / Direct.

Spencer, Joel

BRIGHTER SIDE, THE (Spencer, Joel & Kelly Sill)
Fear of foley / Rosebud / Greater fool / Additional dialogue / Naomi / Brighter side / Ironic line / Charlie's tonic

CD _____ TJA 10026
Jazz Alliance / Feb '96 / New Note.

Spencer, John B.

BACK PAGES 1: THE LOUT'S LP
CD _____ RTMCD 34
Round Tower / Nov '90 / Pinnacle / ADA /
Direct / BMG / CM.

BACK PAGES 2: BLUE SMARTIES
CD _____ RTMCD 35
Round Tower / Nov '93 / Pinnacle / ADA /
Direct / BMG / CM.

BACK PAGES 4: JUDAS AND THE OBSCURE
CD _____ RTMCD 37
Round Tower / Nov '93 / Pinnacle / ADA /
Direct / BMG / CM.

OUT WITH A BANG
Out with a bang / Funny honey / Gingham
white and blue / Acceptable losses / Plaisir
d'amour / Forgotten the blues / Hold on to
your heartache / Cry baby cry / Flesh and
blood / Chris is in love again / One more
whiskey / Sad reunion / Answer only with
your eyes
CD _____ RTMCD 36
Round Tower / Jan '94 / Pinnacle / ADA /
Direct / BMG / CM.

PARLOUR GAMES
Parlour games / Billy / Slow beers / Sweet
Lucinda / Poor little rich boy / Drive-in mov-
ies / Behold the king is dead / Dead man's
shoes / Alone together / Left hand of love /
Count ten / London I knew / Going down
South / Quiet nights
CD _____ RTMCD 23
Round Tower / Feb '91 / Pinnacle / ADA /
Direct / BMG / CM.

SUNDAY BEST
CD _____ RTMCD 39
Round Tower / May '92 / Pinnacle / ADA /
Direct / BMG / CM.

Spencer, Jon

CRYPT STYLE (Spencer, Jon Blues Explosion)
CD _____ EFA 115022
Crypt / Jan '94 / SRD.

EXTRA WIDTH (Spencer, Jon Blues Explosion)
Afro / History of lies / Back slider / Soul let-
ter / Soul typecast / Pant leg / Hey mom /
Big road / Train #2 / Inside the world of the
Blues Explosion / World of sex
CD _____ OLE 052-2
Matador / Aug '93 / Vital.

JON SPENCER BLUES EXPLOSION, THE
CD _____ HUTCD 003
Hut / Apr '92 / EMI.

ORANGE (Spencer, Jon Blues Explosion)
Bell bottoms / Ditch / Dang / Very rare /
Sweat / Cowboy / Orange / Brenda / Dis-
sect / Blues X man / Full grown / Flavor /
Greyhound
CD _____ OLE 105-2
Matador / Sep '94 / Vital.

Spencer, Sarah

LAISSEZ LES BONS TEMPS ROULER (Spencer, Sarah Rue Conti Jazz Band)
Mardi Gras in New Orleans / My life will be
sweeter / Somebody else is taking my place
/ In the garden / Whoopin' blues / Mama
Inez / What a friend we have in Jesus /
Junco partner / Bogalousa strut / Lead me
saviour / Sweet fields
CD _____ LACD 22
Fellside / Jan '93 / Target/BMG / Direct /
ADA.

Spendel, Christoph

COOL STREET
Cool Street / Pismo Beach / New York in
July / Neptune Hotel / She's got it going on
/ Runnin Vera Cruz / Coney Island / Travel-
ling / Stella by starlight (intro) / Stella by
starlight / Handsups on Bleeker Street / Cal-
ifornia / Mr. Big Band
CD _____ TCB 01012
TCB / Aug '93 / New Note.

OUT OF TOWN
Out of town / I heard it through the grapevine / Spendel EFX / Rainbound / Night letter / Ever again / Cat / Tried to my soul /
Techno jazz / San Diego nights / Weekend
in San Francisco / Nice to meet you / Life
is a beach / First class
CD _____ TCB 01032
TCB / Apr '95 / New Note.

READY FOR TAKE OFF
Salsito / Carly / Ready for take off / Monday
in July / Rain / Queen's plaza / Downtown
/ Tapsi strikes again
CD _____ CDLR 45010
L&R / Dec '88 / New Note.

SPENDEL
White cars / New York P.M. / Mr. Cameo /
Midnight / Columbus circle / Byton funk /
Banana republic / Eilat / Otto's magic bus /

Hugo update / Suite 11F / Piano graffity /
Manhattan candlelight
CD _____ CDLR 45014
L&R / Jan '90 / New Note.

Spermbirds

EATING GLASS
CD _____ XM032CD
X-Mist / Apr '92 / SRD.

NOTHING IS EASY
CD _____ 851 280
We Bite / '88 / Plastic Head.

RICH MAN'S HIGH
CD _____ IRS 5977055
Community / Feb '94 / Plastic Head.

THANKS
CD _____ DEP 02CD
Dead Eye / Jun '93 / SRD.

Sphere

PUMPKIN'S DELIGHT
CD _____ 123207-2
Red / Apr '93 / Harmonia Mundi / Jazz
Horizons / Cadillac / ADA.

Spice Lab

DAY ON PLANET EARTH, A
CD _____ HHCD 9
Harthouse / Oct '94 / Disc / Warner
Music.

LOST IN SPICE
CD _____ HARTUKCD 2
Harthouse / Oct '93 / Disc / Warner
Music.

Spice, Mikey

CLOSE THE DOOR
Way you are / What the world need now /
Close the door / Deeper and deeper / Am I
losing you / Can't get enough / Loving you
/ Baby come back / Real good men / Sun-
day morning / Winter of a loving heart / Be
my friend
CD _____ CRCD 2
Charm / Jan '96 / Jetstar.

HAPPINESS
CD _____ RN 0042
Runn / Apr '95 / Jetstar / SRD.

Spiders

COMPLETE IMPERIAL RECORDINGS, THE (2CD Set)
I didn't want to do it / You're the one for a
thrill / Mellow Mama / Lost and bewildered
/ Tears begin to flow / Why do I love you /
Love's all I'm puttin' down / I'll stop crying
/ Mmm mmm baby (hey baby) / Walking
around in circles / I'm searchin' / Real thing
/ She keeps me wondering / Three times
seven equals twenty one / That's enough /
Sukey Sukey Sukey / Bells in my heart / Am
I the one / Don't knock / True (you don't
love me) / Witchcraft / You played the part
/ Is it true / How I feel / That's the way to
win my heart / Goodbye / I'll be free / Don't
pity me / Dear Mary / A1 in my heart / With-
out love / Someday bye and bye / That's
my desire / Better be on my way / Honey
bee / I'm glad for your sake / Poor boy /
Bells are ringing / I miss you times / You're
the one / Tennessee Slim
CD Set _____ BCD 15673
Bear Family / Jun '92 / Rollercoaster / Direct
/ CM / Swift / ADA.

Spiegl, Steve

THEN AND NOW (Spiegl, Steve Big Band)
CD _____ 71002-2
Capri / Oct '94 / Wellard / Cadillac.

Spier, Bernd

OHNE EIN BESTIMMTES ZIEL
Memphis, Tennessee / Ohn ein bestimmtes
Ziel / Hey Mr. Postman / Heut' bei mir-Und
dann / Ein dufte party / Das kannst dur mir
nicht verbieten / Was ich an der am meis ten
liebe / Das war mein schonster Tanz / Sag
nicht goodbye / Chone Madchen muss man
lieben / Keiner weiss, dass wir uns lieben /
Ich bin nicht schuld daran / Du bist schoner
als die ander'n / Einmal gibt der Vorhang
zu / Du bizt fur mich geboren / Der neue tag
beginnt / Wenn erst der abend kommt /
Danke schon / Julia / Wird eph es wunderbar
/ Komm zu mir / Two strangers / I only came
to dance with you / Million and one times /
Rose Marie / Pretty Belinda / Klopf dreimal
/ Lass dein little girl nie weinen
CD _____ BCD 15591
Bear Family / Mar '92 / Rollercoaster /
Direct / CM / Swift / ADA.

Spike

GLOBAL 2000
CD _____ BLCCD 9
Blanc / Feb '95 / Pinnacle.

Spillane, Davy

ATLANTIC BRIDGE
Atlantic Bridge / Davie's reels / Daire's
dream / Tribute to Johnny Doran / O'Neill's
statement / Sliverish / By the river of gems
/ Pigeon on the gate / In my life / Lans-
downe blues
CD _____ COOKCD 009
Cooking Vinyl / Aug '88 / Vital.

OUT OF THE AIR
Atlantic bridge / Daire's dream / Mystic sea-
cliffs / Litton Lane / River of gems / Storm
/ Road to Ballyalla / One for Phil
CD _____ COOKCD 016
Cooking Vinyl / Oct '88 / Vital.

PIPEDREAMS
Shifting sands / Undertow / Shorelines /
Call across the canyon / Midnight walker /
Mistral / Rainmaker / Stepping in silence /
Morning wings / Corcomroe
CD _____ TARACD 3026
Tara / Oct '94 / CM / ADA / Direct / Conifer.

PLACE AMONG THE STONES, A
Darklight / Promised rain / Place among the
stones / Western whisper / Starry night /
Elgeebar / Callow Lake / Forever frozen /
Always travelling / Near the horizon
CD _____ 4769302
Columbia / Oct '95 / Sony.

SHADOW HUNTER, THE
Lucy's tune / Indiana drones / Carron
streams / Watching the clock / Walker of
the snow / Hidden ground / White crow /
Moyasta junction / Journeys of a dreamer /
One day in June / Equinox / Host of the air
CD _____ COOKCD 030
Cooking Vinyl / Apr '90 / Vital.

Spin Doctors

HOMEBELLY GROOVE
What time is it / Off my line / Freeway of
the plains / Lady Kerosene / Yo baby / Little
Miss can't be wrong / Shinbone Alley / Refrigerator car / Sweet widow / Stepped on
a crack / Yo mama's a pajama / Rosetta
stone
CD _____ 472896 2
Epic / Dec '93 / Sony.

POCKET FULL OF KRYPTONITE
Jimmy Olsen's blues / What time is it / Little
miss can't be wrong / Forty or fifty / Refrigerator car / More than she knows / Two
princes / Off my line / How could you want
him (When you know you could have me) /
Shinbone Alley / Hard to exist
CD _____ 468250 2
Epic / Mar '93 / Sony.

TURN IT UPSIDE DOWN
Big fat funky booty / You let your heart go
too fast / Cleopatra's cat / Hungry Hamed's
/ Biscuit head / Indifference / Bags of dirt /
Mary Jane / More than meets the ear / Lar-
aby's gang / At this hour / Someday all this
will be road / Beasts in the woods
CD _____ 476886 2
Epic / Jun '94 / Sony.

Spina Bifida

ZIYADHA
CD _____ CDAR 010
Adipocre / Feb '94 / Plastic Head.

Spinal Tap

THIS IS SPINAL TAP
Hell hole / Tonight I'm gonna rock you /
Heavy duty / Rock 'n' roll creation / America
/ Cups and cakes / Big bottom / Sex farm
/ Stonehenge / Gimme some money /
Flower people
CD _____ 817 846-2
Polydor / Aug '90 / PolyGram.

Spinanes

MANOS
CD _____ SPCD 114292
Sub Pop / Nov '93 / Disc.

NOEL, JONAH AND ME
CD _____ SPCD 328
Sub Pop / May '94 / Disc.

STRAND
CD _____ SPCD 345
Sub Pop / Feb '96 / Disc.

Spine

TRANSITION
Ride my own spine / N.A.C. / Irreversible /
Sickness to insanity / Salt the sores / But
now that I'm gone / We are theirs / Leave
neveragaining
CD _____ SST 302-2
SST / Mar '94 / Plastic Head.

Spinners

BEST OF THE SPINNERS
CD _____ PWK 103
Carlton Home Entertainment / '91 /
Carlton Home Entertainment.

BEST OF THE SPINNERS
CD _____ MATCD 228
Castle / Dec '92 / BMG.

ONE AND ONLY, THE

Lord of the dance / All day singing / Blaydon races / Land before my mind / Amazing grace / We shall not be moved / Guantanamera / Jamaica farewell / To be a
farmer's boy / Foggy dew / Greensleeves /
Lovely Joan / North country maid / Liverpool hornpipes / Collier's rant / Dane the
flora / Banks of the Ohio / Shepherd lad /
Waters o' Tyne / Lamorna / Bucket of the
mountain dew / When I first came to this
land / So long (it's been good to know yuh)
CD _____ CC 8239
EMI / Nov '94 / EMI.

SPINNERS IN CONCERT, THE
All day singing / Moonshiner / William
Brown / Bleacher lass o' Kelvinhaugh / Jane
and Louisa / Tom Brown / Castles in the air
/ Calico printer's clerk / Guantanamera /
Deep blue sea / Poverty knock / Lamorna /
Cobbler's song / Ring of iron / Waltzing Ma-
tilda / Little boy / Mule skinner blues / So
long, it's been good to know you
CD _____ CC 212
Music For Pleasure / May '88 / EMI.

Spiral Jetty

BAND OF GOLD
CD _____ OUT 1102
Brake Out / Jan '93 / Vital.

DOGSTAR
CD _____ ILLCD 018
Imaginary / Sep '90 / Vital.

Spirea X

FIREBLADE SKIES
CD _____ CAD 1017CD
4AD / Oct '91 / Disc.

Spirit

CLEAR
Dark eyed woman / Apple orchard / So little
time to fly / Ground hog / Policeman's ball
/ Ice / Give a life take a life / I'm truckin' /
Clear / Caught / New dope in town / Cold
wind
CD _____ EDCD 268
Edsel / Mar '88 / Pinnacle / ADA.

COLLECTION: SPIRIT
CD _____ CCSCD 319
Castle / Oct '91 / BMG.

FAMILY THAT PLAYS TOGETHER, THE
I got a line on you / It shall be / Poor Richard
/ Sikly Sam / Drunkard / Darlin' / All the
same / Jewish / Dream within a dream / She
smiled / Aren't you glad
CD _____ 477355-2
Epic / Aug '94 / Sony.

POTATOLAND
We've got a lot to learn / Potatoland / Open
up your hand / Information suite / Mashed
potatoes / Midnight train / Oil slick / Hollow
years
CD _____ LICD 900092
Line / Oct '92 / CM / Grapevine / ADA /
Conifer / Direct.

SPIRIT
Fresh garbage / Uncle Jack / Mechanical
world / Taurus / Girl in your eyes / Straight
arrow / Topanga windows / Gramophone
man / Water woman / Great canyon fire in
general / Elijah
CD _____ 4809652
Epic / Aug '95 / Sony.

TIME CIRCLE (2CD Set)
Fresh garbage / Uncle Jack / Mechanical
world / Taurus / Girl in your eye / Straight
arrow / Topanga windows / Gramophone
man / Great canyon fire in general / I got a
line on you / It shall be / Poor Richard / Sikly
Sam / Sherozode / All the same / Dream
within a dream / Aren't you glad / Eventide
/ Green gorilla / Rehearsal theme / Fog /
Now or anywhere / Dark eyed woman / So
little time to fly / Ground hog / Ice / I'm
truckin' / New dope in town / 1984 / Sweet
Stella baby / Nothin' to hide / Nature's way
/ Animal zoo / Love has found a way / Why
can't I be free / Mr. Skin / When I touch you
/ Street worm / Morning will come / Turn to
the right
CD Set _____ 4712662
Legacy / Mar '92 / Sony.

TWELVE DREAMS OF DR. SARDONICUS
Nothin' to hide / Nature's way / Animal zoo
/ Love has found a way / Why can't I be
free / Mr. Skin / Space child / When I touch
you / Street worm / Life has just begun /
Morning will come / Soldier / We've got a
lot to learn / Potatoland (theme) / Open up
your heart / Morning light / Potatoland (prelude) / Potatoland (introduction) / Turn to the
right / Donut house / Fish fry road / Information / My friend
CD _____ 476603 2
Epic / Apr '94 / Sony.

Spirit Feel

SPIRIT FEEL
CD _____ TPLP 77CD
One Little Indian / Mar '95 / Pinnacle.

Spirit Level

NEW YEAR
CD _____ FMRCD 03
Future / Jan '89 / Harmonia Mundi / ADA.

ON THE LEVEL
Over the moon / Spiral staircase / Seventh heaven / Tollbridge / Merhaba mustafa / Y ya la quiero / Sometime never / You and I / Looking on the bright side / La dolce vita
CD _____ 33 JAZZ 021
33 Jazz / Apr '95 / Cadillac / New Note.

Spirit Of The Day

LABOUR DAY
Darkhouse / Profiteers / Run boy / Expensive/Cinema of pain / Take it from the source / Political / Hounds that wait outside your door / Drinking man / Gottingen street
CD _____ SP 1123CD
Stony Plain / Oct '93 / ADA / CM / Direct.

Spirit Of The West

OLD MATERIAL 1984-86
CD _____ SP 1141CD
Stony Plain / Oct '93 / ADA / CM / Direct.

TRIPPING UP THE STAIRS
CD _____ CMCD 035
Celtic Music / Mar '94 / CM / Roots.

Spirit Traveller

PLAYING HITS FROM MOTOR CITY
Signed, sealed, delivered (I'm yours) / Since I lost my baby / Ain't that peculiar / Ain't nothing like the real thing / You keep me hangin' on / OOO baby baby / Tracks of my tears / Ain't no mountain high enough / I love you / It's growing / You've really got a hold on me
CD _____ JVC 20292
JVC / Feb '94 / New Note.

Spiritualized

PURE PHASE (Spiritualized Electric Mainline)
CD _____ DEDCD 017S
CD _____ DEDCD 017
Dedicated / Jan '95 / Vital.

Spirogyra

BELLS BOOTS AND SHAMBLES
CD _____ REP 4137-WZ
Repertoire / Aug '91 / Pinnacle / Cadillac.

OLD BOOT WINE
CD _____ REP 4173-WZ
Repertoire / Aug '91 / Pinnacle / Cadillac.

St. RADIGUNS
Future won't be long / Island / Magical Mary / Captain's log / At home in the world / Cogwheels, crutches and cyanide / Time will tell / We were a happy crew / Love is a funny thing / Duke of Beaufoot
CD _____ REP 4070-WZ
Repertoire / Aug '91 / Pinnacle / Cadillac.

Spit The Pips

SHOW-BIZ-TOOL-SHED
CD _____ PSQK 4
Scratch / Mar '95 / BMG.

Spitfire

FEVERISH
CD _____ DANCD 097
Danceteria / Mar '95 / Plastic Head / ADA.

SEX BOMB
CD _____ PAPCD 21
Paperhouse / Sep '93 / Disc.

Spitfire Band

SPITFIRE BAND SWINGS FROM STAGE TO SCREEN
CD _____ ACD 2500
Attic Records / '88 / Swift.

Spitters

SUN TO SUN
Sun to sun / Days into a week / Cradle / Living things / Impasse / Swipe / Strange / Throat
CD _____ PCP 0302
PCP / Jan '96 / Vital.

Spivak, Charlie

CHARLIE SPIVAK
CD _____ CCD 017
Circle / Oct '93 / Jazz Music / Swift / Wellard.

FOR SENTIMENTAL REASONS (Spivak, Charlie & His Orchestra)
CD _____ VJC 1041
Vintage Jazz Classics / Feb '93 / Direct / ADA / CM / Cadillac.

UNCOLLECTED, THE (1943-46) (Spivak, Charlie & His Orchestra)
Stardreams / Mean to me / Serenade in blue / I used to love you / Cuddle up a little closer / Blue Lou / Laura / More than you know / Stardust / Accentuate the positive / Solitude / Travelin' light / Blue champagne

---

/ Let's go home / It's the same old dream / Saturday night
CD _____ HCD 105
Hindsight / Oct '95 / Target/BMG / Jazz Music.

Spivey, Victoria

VICTORIA SPIVEY VOL. 1 1926-27
CD _____ DOCD 5316
Blues Document / Mar '95 / Swift / Jazz Music / Hot Shot.

VICTORIA SPIVEY VOL. 2 1927-29
CD _____ DOCD 5317
Blues Document / Mar '95 / Swift / Jazz Music / Hot Shot.

VICTORIA SPIVEY VOL. 3 1929-36
CD _____ DOCD 5318
Blues Document / Mar '95 / Swift / Jazz Music / Hot Shot.

VICTORIA SPIVEY VOL. 4 1936-37
CD _____ DOCD 5319
Blues Document / Mar '95 / Swift / Jazz Music / Hot Shot.

WOMAN BLUES (Spivey, Victoria & Lonnie Johnson)
CD _____ OBCCD 566
Original Blues Classics / Jul '95 / Complete/Pinnacle / Wellard / Cadillac.

Spizz

UNHINGED (Spizz Energi)
CD _____ DAMGOOD 36
Damaged Goods / Mar '94 / SRD.

SPK

C.D. BOX SET
CD Set _____ SPKBOX 1
Grey Area / Jun '92 / Pinnacle.

DIGITALIS AMBIGUA, GOLD AND POISON
CD _____ NTCD 035
Nettwerk / Feb '88 / Vital / Pinnacle.

INFORMATION OVERLOAD UNIT
CD _____ SPKCD 1
Grey Area / Sep '92 / Pinnacle.

LEICHENSCHRE
CD _____ SPKCD 2
Grey Area / Aug '92 / Pinnacle.

OCEANIA
Oceania / Doctrine of eternal ice / Breathless / Mouth to mouth / Kambuja / Crack / Seduction / Dies irae
CD _____ DFX 01
Side Effects / Jun '88 / Pinnacle.

ZAMI LEHMANNI
CD _____ SPKCD 3
Grey Area / Sep '92 / Pinnacle.

Splatcats

RIGHT ON
CD _____ PRD 70092
Provogue / May '90 / Pinnacle.

Splatter

FROM HELL TO ETERNITY
CD _____ SECTOR 210010
Sector 2 / Aug '95 / Direct / ADA.

Splendora

IN THE GRASS
CD _____ 379122
Koch International / Dec '95 / Koch.

Splintered

JUDAS CRADLE
CD _____ DPROMCD 17
Dirter Promotions / Dec '93 / Pinnacle.

Split Enz

ANNIVERSARY
CD _____ D 98010
Mushroom / Apr '95 / BMG / 3MV.

BEST OF SPLIT ENZ, THE
Titus / Late last night / Matinee idyll 129 / Amy (darling) / Lovey dovey / Time for a change / Crossroads / Another great divide / Bold as brass / My mistake / I see red / I got you / One step ahead / History never repeats / Six months in a leaky boat / Message to my girl
CD _____ CDCHR 6059
Chrysalis / Jan '94 / EMI.

HISTORY NEVER REPEATS - THE BEST OF SPLIT ENZ
CD _____ CDMID 175
A&M / Oct '92 / PolyGram.

TRUE COLOURS
Shark attack / I got you / Whats the matter with you / Double happy / I wouldn't dream of it / I hope I never / Nobody takes me seriously / Missing person / Poor boy / How can I resist her / Choral sea
CD _____ CDMID 130
A&M / Oct '92 / PolyGram.

Split Up

FATES GOT A DRIVER
CD _____ DOG 031CD
Doghouse / Aug '95 / Plastic Head.

Splodgenessabounds

NIGHTMARE ON RUDE STREET
CD _____ RRCD 148
Receiver / Oct '91 / Grapevine.

Spolier

CRASHPAD
Something for nothing / Up above / Crashpad / Custom fit / Where to / Small stone / Prism 23 / Four walls / Moving in theory / Numero
CD _____ PCP 015-2
Matador / Oct '94 / Vital.

Sponge

ROTTING PINATA
Pennywheels / Rotting pinata / Giants / Neenah Menasha / Miles / Plowed / Drownin' / Molly / Fields / Rainin'
CD _____ 4769822
Columbia / Sep '95 / Sony.

Spontaneous Music...

KARYOBIN (Spontaneous Music Ensemble)
CD _____ CPE 2001-2
Chronoscope / Jan '94 / Harmonia Mundi / Wellard / Cadillac.

SUMMER '67 (Spontaneous Music Ensemble)
CD _____ EM 4005
Emanem / Dec '95 / Cadillac / Harmonia Mundi.

Spooky

GARGANTUAN
Don't panic / Schmoo / Aqualung / Little bullet part 1 / Little bullet part 2 / Land of Oz / Something's got to give / Orange coloured liquid / Schmoodub (On CD & MC only.) / Let go (On CD & MC only.)
CD _____ GRCD 006
Guerilla / Jul '94 / Pinnacle.

Spooky Tooth

BEST OF SPOOKY TOOTH
Tobacco Road / Better by you, better than me / It's all about a roundabout / Waitin' for the wind / Last puff / Evil woman / That was only yesterday / I am the walrus / Self seeking man / All sewn up / Times have changed / As long as the world keeps turning / Weight
CD _____ 842 688 2
Island / Mar '94 / PolyGram.

BEST OF SPOOKY TOOTH, THE
CD _____ IMCD 74
Island / '89 / PolyGram.

MIRROR, THE
CD _____ 90009
Line / Oct '94 / CM / Grapevine / ADA / Confex / Direct.

Spooned Hybrio

SPOONED HYBRIO
CD _____ GU 5CD
Guernica / Oct '93 / Pinnacle.

Spore

FEAR GOD
CD _____ TAANG 75CD
Taang / Dec '93 / Plastic Head.

GIANT
CD _____ TANNG 81
Taang / Aug '94 / Plastic Head.

SPORE
CD _____ TAANG 74CD
Taang / Jun '93 / Plastic Head.

Sposito, John

VOYAGER IV
CD _____ CDSGP 9017
Prestige / Jun '95 / Total/BMG.

VOYAGER V
CD _____ CDSGP 9027
Prestige / Jun '95 / Total/BMG.

VOYAGER VI
CD _____ CDSGP 9028
Prestige / Jun '95 / Total/BMG.

Spot 1019

SPOT 1019
CD _____ 346342
Frontier / Feb '92 / Vital.

Spotnicks

HIGHWAY BOOGIE
Highway boogie / Lost property / Could it be love / Mighty bump / Love is a symphony / Truck driver's dream / Just another boy / Dolly H. / Let it roll roll roll / Besame mucho

---

CD _____ CDMF 036
Magnum Force / Jun '86 / Magnum Music Group.

Sprague, Carl T.

CLASSIC COWBOY SONGS
Home on the range / It is no secret / Following the cowtrail / Girl I loved in sunny Tennessee / When the work's all done this fall / Kissing / Club meeting / Bad companions / Rounded up in glory / Red river valley / Roll on little dogies / Last great roundup / Last fierce charge / Gambier / Boston burglar / Orphan girl / Utah Carol / Just break the news to mother / Chicken / Cowman's prayer / Sarah Jane / My Carrie Lee / Zebra Dun / Mormon cowboy / Cowboy's meditation / Kicking mule
CD _____ BCD 15456
Bear Family / Dec '88 / Rollercoaster / Direct / CM / Swift / ADA.

Spriguns

JACK WITH A FEATHER (Spriguns Of Tolgus)
CD _____ HBG 122/9
Background / Apr '94 / Background.

Spring Heel Jack

THERE ARE STRINGS
Only you / Masquerade / Flying again / Oceola / Where do you fit in / Derek / There are strings / Colonades / Lee Perry part 1 / Day of the dead
CD _____ R 3533
Rough Trade / Aug '95 / Pinnacle.

Springer, Mark

SWANS AND TURTLES (Springer, Mark & Sarah Sarhandi)
Torreador / Scattered gloves / Desire / Inner secret / Nothing serious / Swans and turtles / Yellow / Brown / Road into the forest
CD _____ CDVE 902
Venture / Feb '91 / EMI.

Springfield, Dusty

BLUE FOR YOU
I just don't know what to do with myself / Your hurtin' kinda love / Will you still love me tomorrow / Every day I have to cry / Some of your lovin' / No easy way down / If you go away / Goin' back / Morning please don't come / How can I be sure / What do you do when love dies / I can't make it alone / My colouring book / Yesterday when I was young
CD _____ 5500052
Spectrum/Karussell / May '93 / PolyGram / THE.

DUSTY - THE LEGEND OF DUSTY SPRINGFIELD (4CD Set)
How can I be sure / Stay awhile / I just don't know what to do with myself / Son of a preacher man / All cried out / I will come to you / Some of your lovin' / Give me time / I'm coming home again / What's it gonna be / Losing you / Nothing has been proved / Yesterday when I was young / Your hurtin' kinda love / I only want to be with you / All I see / I'll try anything / I close my eyes and count to ten / Brand new me / Your love still brings me to my knees / Magic garden / What good is I love you / You don't have to say you love me / Baby don't you know / Wishin' and hopin' / Corrupt ones / Tanto so che moi me passa / How can I learn to say goodbye / Summer is over / Where am I going / Something in your eyes / I only wanna laugh / Sweet lover no more / Meditation / Come for a dream / Once upon a time / Will you still love me tomorrow / Goodbye / Lose again / I want to be a free girl / Don't say it baby / Heartbeat / He's got something / What do you do when love dies / Time after time / Softcore / When the midnight train leaves for Alabam / La bamba / Love like yours / Go ahead on / What have I done to deserve this / In the middle of nowhere / Another night / Little by little / That's the kind of love I've got for you / In private / I just wanna be there / Mama's little girl / I can't give back the love I feel for you / Oh no not my baby / Donnez moi / Reputation / Mockingbird / Am I the same girl / When the lovelight starts shining / Take me for a little while / Bring him back / Every ounce of strength / Blind sheep / Goin' back / I think it's going to rain today / Tupelo honey / Chained to a memory / Who can I turn to / If you go away / What are you doing the rest of your life / Love me / No easy way down / Never love again / I just fall in love again / That's how heartaches are made / I don't want to hear it anymore / I wish I'd never loved you / Just a little lovin' / Who will take my place / I'd rather leave while I'm in love / Sandra / I've been wrong before / If it hadn't been for you / I had a talk with my man / Second time around / Close to you / Look of love
CD Set _____ 522254-2
Philips / Aug '94 / PolyGram.

DUSTY IN MEMPHIS
Just a little lovin' / So much love / Son of a preacher man / I don't want to hear it anymore / Don't forget about me / Breakfast in bed / Just one smile / Windmills of your

---

mind / In the land of make believe / No easy way down / I can't make it alone / Willie and Laura Mae Jones (reissue only) / That old sweet roll (Hi de ho) (reissue only) / What do you do when love dies (reissue only)
CD _____ 5286872
Mercury / Sep '95 / PolyGram.

DUSTY SONGBOOK
I close my eyes and count to ten / I start counting / Summer is over / Your hurtin' kinda love / Who gets your love / Where am I going / Son of a preacher man / Am I the same girl / What's it gonna be / Morning please don't come / Yesterday when I was young / Breakfast in bed / Magic garden / Give me time / Spooky / I will come to you / Brand new me / I'll try anything / Colour of your eyes / Learn to say goodbye
CD _____ PWKS 580
Carlton Home Entertainment / Jun '90 / Carlton Home Entertainment.

DUSTY'S SOUNDS OF THE 60'S
CD _____ PWK 104
Carlton Home Entertainment / '89 / Carlton Home Entertainment.

EVERYTHING'S COMING UP DUSTY
CD _____ BGOCD 74
Beat Goes On / '89 / Pinnacle.

GOIN' BACK (The Best Of Dusty Springfield 1962-1994)
CD _____ 848789-2
Philips / May '94 / PolyGram.

LOVE SONGS: DUSTY SPRINGFIELD
You don't have to say you love me / I've been wrong before / I can't make it alone / Come back to me / Let's talk it over / This girl's in love with you / Some of your lovin' / Don't let me lose this dream / Broken blossoms / It was easier to hurt him / That's how heartaches are made / All I see is you / I just don't know what to do with myself / Who (will take my place) / So much love / I can't give back the love I feel for you / Never love again / Losing you / Look of love / My colouring book / I think it's going to rain today / Just a little lovin' / How can I be sure / If you go away
CD _____ PWK 120
Carlton Home Entertainment / Jul '89 / Carlton Home Entertainment.

REPUTATION
Reputation / Send it to me / Arrested by you / Time waits for no one / I was born this way / In private / Daydreaming / Nothing has been proved / I want to stay here / Occupy your mind
CD _____ CDFA 3320
Fame / Apr '95 / EMI.

SOMETHING SPECIAL (2CD Set)
Something special / Reste encore un instant / Je ne peux pas t'en vouloir / I'll love you for a while / Needle in a haystack / Tu che ne sai / Di fronte a l'amore / I will always want you / I'm gonna leave you / Small town girl / I've got a good thing / Don't forget about me / No stranger am I / Don't speak of love / Earthbound gypsy / Wasn't born to follow / Song for you / Haunted / I am your child / You set my dreams to music / Give me the night / Baby blue / Your love still brings me to my knees / It goes like it goes / Just one smile / Something in your eyes / I'd rather leave while I'm in love / Let me love you before you go / Tupelo honey / I just fall in love again / What are you doing the rest of your life / Who will take my place / Who can I turn to / Joe / Who could be lovin' you other than me / I've been wrong before / I can't make it alone / They long to be close to you / My colouring book / If you go away / Sandra / No easy way down / Breakfast in bed / Long after tonight is all over / This girl's in love with you / I think it's gonna rain today / Love me by name / Look of love
CD _____ 5288182
Mercury / Oct '95 / PolyGram.

VERY FINE LOVE, A
Roll away / Very fine love / Wherever would I be / Go easy on me / You are the storm / I can't help the way I don't feel / All I have to offer you is love / Lovin' proof / Old habits die hard / Where is A
CD _____ 4785082
Columbia / Jun '95 / Sony.

Springfield, Rick

GREATEST HITS: RICK SPRINGFIELD
Jessie's girl / I've done everything for you / Love is alright tonight / Don't talk to strangers / What kind of fool am I / Affair of the heart / Human touch / Love somebody / Bop 'till you drop / Celebrate youth / State of the heart / Rock of life
CD _____ 74321289892
RCA / Aug '95 / BMG.

Springsteen, Bruce

BORN IN THE U.S.A.
Cover me / Born in the USA / Darlington County / Working on the highway / Downbound train / I'm on fire / No surrender / Bobby Jean / I'm goin' down / Glory days / Dancing in the dark / My hometown
CD _____ CD 86304
CBS / Aug '84 / Sony.

BORN TO RUN
Spirit in the night (In box set) / Because the night (In box set) / 10th Avenue freeze out / Thunder road / Born to run / Back streets / She's the one / Meeting across the river / Jungleland / Night
CD _____ CD 69170
CBS / '83 / Sony.
CD _____ 4804162
Columbia / Jul '95 / Sony.

DARKNESS ON THE EDGE OF TOWN
Badlands / Adam raised a Cain / Something in the night / Candy's room / Racing in the street / Promised land / Factory / Streets of fire / Prove it all night / Darkness on the edge of town
CD _____ CD 86061
CBS / Jul '84 / Sony.

DARKNESS ON THE EDGE OF TOWN/ NEBRASKA (2CD Set)
CD _____ 4716072
Columbia / Jul '94 / Sony.

DARKNESS ON THE EDGE OF TOWN/ WILD, THE INNOCENT../GREETINGS. (3CD Set)
CD Set _____ 4673842
CBS / Dec '90 / Sony.

GHOST OF TOM JOAD, THE
Ghost of Tom Joad / Straight time / Highway 29 / Youngstown / Sinola cowboys / Line / Balbo Park / Dry lightning / New timer / Across the border / Galveston Bay / Best was never enough
CD _____ 4816502
Columbia / Nov '95 / Sony.

GREATEST HITS
Born to run / Thunder road / Badlands / River / Hungry heart / Atlantic City / Dancing in the dark / Born in the USA / My hometown / Glory days / Brilliant disguise / Human touch / Better days / Streets of Philadelphia / Secret garden / Murder incorporated / Blood brothers / This hard land
CD _____ 4785552
Columbia / Feb '95 / Sony.

GREETINGS FROM ASBURY PARK,N.J
Blinded by the light / Growing up / Mary Queen of Arkansas / Does this bus stop at 82nd Street / Lost in the flood / Angel for you / Spirit in the night / It's hard to be a saint in the city
CD _____ CD 65480
CBS / Nov '82 / Sony.

HUMAN TOUCH
Human touch / Soul driver / Fifty seven channels (and nothin' on) / Cross my heart / Gloria's eyes / With every wish / Real world / All or nothing at all / Man's job / I wish I were blind / Long goodbye / Real man / Pony boy
CD _____ 4714232
Columbia / Mar '92 / Sony.

LIVE 1975-1985 (3CD Set) (Springsteen, Bruce & The E Street Band)
Thunder road / Adam raised a Cain / Spirit in the night / 4th of July, Asbury Park (Sandy) / Paradise by the 'c' / Fire / Growing up / It's hard to be a saint in the city / Backstreets / Rosalita / Raise your hand / Hungry heart / Two hearts / Cadillac ranch / You can cook (but you'd better not touch) / Independence day / Badlands / Because the night / Candy's room / Racing in the street / This land is your land / Nebraska / Johnny 99 / Reason to believe / Born in the USA / Seeds / River / War / Darlington County / Working on the highway / Promised land / Cover me / I'm on fire / Bobby Jean / My home town / Born to run / No surrender / 10th Avenue freeze out / Jersey girl
CD _____ 4502272
CBS / Nov '86 / Sony.

LUCKY TOWN
Better days / Lucky town / Local hero / If I should fall behind / Leap of faith / Big muddy / Living proof / Book of dreams / Souls of the departed / My beautiful reward
CD _____ 4714242
Columbia / Mar '92 / Sony.

NEBRASKA
Nebraska / Atlantic city / Mansion on the hill / Johnny 99 / Highway patrolman / State trooper / Used cars / Open all night / My father's house / Reason to believe
CD _____ 4633602
CBS / Feb '89 / Sony.

PLUGGED - MTV IN CONCERT
Red headed woman / Better days / Atlantic city / Darkness on the edge of town / Man's job / Human touch / Lucky town / I wish I were blind / Thunder road / Light of day / If I should fall behind / Living proof / My beautiful reward
CD _____ 473860 2
Columbia / Apr '93 / Sony.

RIVER, THE (2CD Set)
Ties that bind / Sherry darling / Jackson Cage / Two hearts / Independence day / Hungry Heart / Out in the street / Crush on you / You can look (but you'd better not touch) / I wanna marry you / River / Point blank / Cadillac Ranch / I'm a rocker / Fade away / Stolen car / Ramrod / Price you pay / Wreck on the highway

CD Set _____ 477376-2
Columbia / Sep '94 / Sony.

TUNNEL OF LOVE
Ain't got you / Tougher than the rest / All that heaven will allow / Spare parts / Cautious man / Walk like a man / Tunnel of love / Two faces / Brilliant disguise / One step up / When you're alone / Valentine's day
CD _____ 4602702
CBS / Oct '87 / Sony.

WILD, THE INNOCENT AND THE E.STREET SHUFFLE, THE
E Street shuffle / 4th of July, Asbury Park (Sandy) / Kitty's back / Wild Billy's circus / Incident on 57th Street / Rosalita / New York City serenade
CD _____ CD 32363
CBS / Apr '89 / Sony.

Sprinkler

MORE BOY, LESS FRIEND
CD _____ SP 211CD
Sub Pop / Nov '92 / Disc.

Sproton Layer

WITH MAGNETIC FIELDS DISRUPTED
CD _____ NAR 055 CD
New Alliance / May '93 / Pinnacle.

Sproule, Daithi

HEART MADE OF GLASS, A
Lonely Waterloo / Turkish revery / Gabham molta bride / Patty's tune / Bold Belfast shoemaker / Banks of Claudy / September / Gleanntain ghlas ghaoth dobhair / House carpenter / Beaver brig / Bonny bunch of roses / Cailin na gruaige doinne/Little star
CD _____ GLCD 1123
Green Linnet / May '93 / Roots / CM / Direct / ADA.

Sprouse, Blaine

INDIAN SPRINGS (Sprouse, Blaine & Kenny Baker)
Oh demi slippers / Molly darlin' / Owensboro / Avalon / September waltz / Three days in Dublin / Coker creek / K and W waltz / Cotton town breakdown / Indian springs
CD _____ ROUNDER 0259CD
Rounder / '89 / CM / Direct / ADA / Cadillac.

Spudmonsters

STOP THE MADNESS
CD _____ MASSCD 017
Massacre / Jun '95 / Plastic Head.

Spunk

SPUNK
CD _____ VIRION 101
Sound Virus / Sep '94 / Plastic Head.

Spyro Gyra

DREAMS BEYOND CONTROL
Walk the walk / Patterns in the rain / Breakfast at Igor's / Waltz for Isabel / South beach / Send me one line / Bahia / Kindred spirit / Birks law / Same difference / Delicate prey / Friendly fire
CD _____ GRP 97432
GRP / Sep '93 / BMG / New Note.

LOVE & OTHER OBSESSIONS
Lost and found / Ariana / Serengeti / Fine time to explain / Third street / Group therapy / Horizon's edge / Let's say goodbye / On liberty road (for South Africa) / Rockin' a heart place / Baby dreams / Open season
CD _____ GRP 98112
GRP / Mar '95 / BMG / New Note.

MORNING DANCE
Morning dance / Jubilee / Rasul / Song for Lorraine / Starburst / It doesn't matter / Little Linda / End of Romanticism / Heliopolis
CD _____ 7432120261-2
MCA / May '94 / BMG.

THREE WISHES
Pipo's song / Introduction to breathless / Breathless / Heal time / Jennifer's lullaby / Whitewater / Inside your love / Nothing to lose / Three wishes / Gliding / Yemanja / Rollercoaster / Three wishes (reprise)
CD _____ GRP 96742
GRP / May '92 / BMG / New Note.

Squadronaires

THERE'S SOMETHING IN THE AIR
There's something in the air / South Rampart Street parade / C jam blues / Pompton turnpike / Ringle dingle / Anchors aweigh / Commando patrol / Boston bounce / Ring dem bells / Cow cow boogie / High society / Mistakes / Mission on Moscow / That's a plenty
CD _____ HEPCD 44
Hep / Dec '90 / Cadillac / Jazz Music / New Note / Wellard.

THERE'S SOMETHING IN THE AIR
Chattanooga choo chou / Beat me Daddy, eight to the bar / Blues in the night / Pennyslyania polka / Me and Melinda / Be careful it's my heart / Jersey bounce / Tropical magic / Jealous / Lover's lullaby / String of

pearls / Cow cow boogie / Commando patrol / Drummin' man / Darktown strutter's ball / Boogie woogie bugle boy / My mother would love you / (Back home again) in Indiana / Lament to love / All of me / There's something in the air
CD _____ RAJCD 816
Empress / Feb '94 / THE.

THERE'S SOMETHING IN THE AIR
All of me / Anchors aweigh / Blue Lou / Bounce me brother with a solid four / Chattanooga choo choo / Cherokee / Darktown strutter's ball / Daybreak / Dolores / Drummin' man / Goodnight sweet neighbour / How sweet you are / (Back home again) in Indiana / Jazz me blues / Jersey bounce / Ringle dingle / Sinner kissed an angel / Some sunny day / South Rampart Street parade / String of pearls / That day it rained / That's a-plenty / There's something in the air / Way down yonder in New Orleans / You're my baby
CD _____ CDAJA 5128
Living Era / Mar '94 / Koch.

WARTIME MEMORIES
There's something in the air tonight / Skyliner / We're gonna hang out the washing on the Siegfried Line / Nightingale sang in Berkeley Square / White cliffs of Dover / Foggy day / South Rampart Street parade / Lili Marlene / I'll be seeing you / We'll meet again / Little brown jug / You'll never know / I'm gonna get lit up (when the lights go on in London) / News bulletins from throughout the war
CD _____ CDMFP 6123
Music For Pleasure / May '94 / EMI.

Squeeze

BABYLON AND ON/EASTSIDE STORY
CD _____ CDA 24120
A&M / Jul '92 / PolyGram.

COOL FOR CATS
Slap and tickle / Revue / Touching me touching you / It's not cricket / It's so dirty / Hop, skip and jump / Up the junction / Hard to find / Slightly drunk / Goodbye girl / Cool for cats / Up the junction (live)
CD _____ CDMID 131
A&M / Oct '92 / PolyGram.

EAST SIDE STORY
In quintessence / Someone else's heart / Tempted / Piccadilly / There's no tomorrow / Woman's world / Is that Love / F-hole / Labelled with love / Someone else's bell / Mumbo Jumbo / Vanity fair / Messed around
CD _____ CDMID 132
A&M / Oct '92 / PolyGram.

GREATEST HITS: SQUEEZE
Take me I'm yours / Goodbye girl / Cool for cats / Up the junction / Slap and tickle / Another nail in my heart / Pulling mussels (from the shell) / Tempted / Labelled with love / Black coffee in bed / Annie get your gun / Last time forever / Hourglass / Trust me to open my mouth / Footprints / If it's love / Is that love (CD only.) / King George street (CD only.) / No place like home (CD only.) / Love circles (CD only.)
CD _____ 3971812
A&M / May '92 / PolyGram.

PLAY
Satisfied / Crying in my sleep / Letting go / Day I get home / Truth / House of love / Cupid's toy / Gone to the dogs / Walk a straight line / Sunday street / Wicked and cruel / There in a ruine
CD _____ 7599266442
Reprise / Sep '91 / Warner Music.

RIDICULOUS
CD _____ 5404402
A&M / Nov '95 / PolyGram.

SOME FANTASTIC PLACE
Everything in the world / Some fantastic place / Third rail / Loving you tonight / It's over / Cold shoulder / Talk to him / Jolly comes home / Images of loving / True colours (the storm) / Pinocchio
CD _____ 540140-2
A&M / Oct '93 / PolyGram.

Squire

BIG SMASHES
CD _____ TANGCD 4
Tangerine / Aug '92 / Disc.

GET READY TO GO
CD _____ TANGCD 5
Tangerine / Aug '94 / Disc.

Squire, Chris

FISH OUT OF WATER
Hold out your hand / You by my side / Silently falling / Lucky seven / Safe (canon song)
CD _____ 7567815002
Atlantic / Jan '96 / Warner Music.

Squire, Nikki

ESQUIRE
CD _____ WCPCD 1011
West Coast / Aug '94 / BMG.

Squires, Dorothy

BEST OF DOROTHY SQUIRES, THE
CD _____ SOW 713
Sound Waves / Nov '94 / Target/BMG.

WITH ALL MY HEART
Gypsy / It's a pity to say goodnight / When you lose the one you love / I'll close my eyes / Changing partners / Danger ahead beware / Don't search for love / White wings / With all my heart / When I grow too old to dream / Yes I'll be here / Torremolinos / Tree in the meadow / I still believe / In all the world / Come home to my arms / Safe in my arms / Sorrento and you / Mother's day / Coming home / I'm walking behind you / Someone to love / Blue blue water / Reflections on the water
CD _____ C5CD 604
See For Miles/C5 / Aug '93 / Pinnacle.

Squires, Rosemary

ELLA FITZGERALD SONGBOOK (Squires, Rosemary & Maxine Daniels & Babrbara Jay)
Tisket-a-tasket / It don't mean a thing if it ain't got that swing / But not for me / They all laughed / This cant' be love / Someone to watch over me / Soon / Every time we say goodbye / Foggy day / That old black magic / Miss Otis regrets / Love for sale / Take a chance on love / Cheek to cheek / Frim fram sauce / Ten cents a dance / Manhattan / Thou swell / Looking for a boy / Fine romance / How about you / Anything goes / They can't take that away from me / I concentrate on you / Dream dancing / You do something to me / Airmail special / Mack the knife
CD _____ SPJCD 556
Spotlite / Oct '94 / Cadillac / Jazz Horizons / Swift.

Squirrel Nut Zippers

INEVITABLE, THE
Lover's lane / Danny Diamond / I've found a new baby / Anything but love / Good enough for Grandad / Wished for you / Plenty more / You're driving me crazy / Wash Jones / Clun limbo / Lugubrious whing whang / La grippe
CD _____ MR 105-2
Mammoth / Apr '95 / Vital.

Squirtgun

SHENADIGANS
CD _____ LOOKOUT 118
Lookout / Oct '95 / SRD.

Srinivas, U.

DREAM (Srinivas, U. & Michael Brook)
Dance / Think / Run / Dream
CD _____ CDRW 47
Realworld / May '95 / EMI / Sterns.

MODERN MANDOLIN MAESTRO
Ghananayakam / Ninnvvina / Arulseya / Ragam madhyamavati / Thanam / Palinchu kamakshi / Saravana bhava / Malai pozudinile / Folk note
CD _____ CDORBD 068
Globestyle / Mar '91 / Pinnacle.

RAMA SREERAMA
CD _____ CDRW 39
Realworld / Jul '94 / EMI / Sterns.

SSD

POWER
CD _____ TAANG 050CD
Taang / Jun '92 / Plastic Head.

St. Christopher

DIG DEEP BROTHER 1984-90
Forevermore starts here / To the mountain / Charmelle / Who's next on Cupid's hit list / Climb on forever / If I could capture / My fond farewell / Even the sky seems blue / Rivers run dry / Awe / I wish I hadn't seen her / Remember me to her / Tell the world / Our secret / Crystal clear / Rollercoaster / Where in the world / Josephine why / All of a tremble / On the death of my son / Sinking ships / For one so weak / My fortune / How can you tell / Wanda
CD _____ ASKCD 026
Vinyl Japan / Jun '93 / Vital.

LOVE YOU TO PIECES
Away / Leader / Crush / Baptise me baby / Wildest dreams / Everything now / Magic spell / Liberty / For the world to see / Dive / Stars belong to me / Pieces
CD _____ ASKCD 027
Vinyl Japan / Feb '94 / Vital.

MAN I COULD SCREAM
CD _____ ASK 6CD
Vinyl Japan / Feb '94 / Vital.

St. Clair, Isla

INHERITANCE
Flowers of the forest / Ye Jacobites by name / Smile in your sleep / Farewell tae tarwathie / Fear a'bhata / MacCrimmon's lament / Fifty first highland division's farewell to Sicily / Come ye o'er frae france /

Hush ye noo / Norland wind / Freedom come-all-ye / Hills of Ardmorn
CD _____ MOICD 008
Moidart / May '93 / Conifer / ADA.

St. Clement Danes Choir

MOST BEAUTIFUL CHRISTMAS SONGS, THE
CD _____ DCD 5133
Hermanex / Nov '92 / THE.

TRADITIONAL ENGLISH CHRISTMAS CAROLS
CD _____ CNCD 5934
Hermanex / Nov '92 / THE.

St. Etienne

FOXBASE ALPHA
CD _____ HVNCD 1
Heavenly / Sep '91 / Vital.

SO TOUGH
Mario's cafe / Railway Jam / Date with spelman / Calico / Avenue / You're in a bad way / Memo to pricey / Hobart paving / Leafhound / Clock milk / Conichita matrinez / No rainbows for me / Here come clown feet / Junk the morgue / Chicken soup
CD _____ HVNLP 6CD
Heavenly / Jan '93 / Vital.

TIGER BAY
CD _____ HVNLP 8CD
Heavenly / Feb '94 / Vital.

TOO YOUNG TO DIE
CD _____ HVNLP 10CDX
CD _____ HVNLP 10CD
Heavenly / Nov '95 / Vital.

YOU NEED A MESS OF HELP TO STAND ALONE
Who do you think you are / Archway people / California snow story / Kiss and make up / Duke duvet / Filthy / Join our club / Paper / People get real / Some place else / Speedwell
CD _____ HVNLP 7CD
Heavenly / Nov '93 / Vital.

St. Germain

BOULEVARD
Deep in it / Thank U Mum (4 everything you did) / Street scene / Easy to remember / Sentimental mood / What's new / Dub experience II / Forget it
CD _____ F 002CD
F-Communications / Jul '95 / Vital.

St. John's Cambridge

CHRISTMAS CAROLS (St. John's College Cambridge Choir)
God rest ye merry gentlemen / Ding dong merrily on high / O little town of Bethlehem / Unto us a boy is born / Good King Wenceslas / Holly and the ivy / I sing of a maiden / Two Welsh carols / Silent night / Hark the herald angels sing / Jesus Christ the apple tree / In the bleak midwinter / O come all ye faithful (Adeste Fidelis) / Shepherd's pipe carol / On Christmas night / Away in a manger / There is no rose / Balulalow
CD _____ CHAN 8485
Chandos / '86 / Chandos.

St. John, Bridget

ASK ME NO QUESTIONS
CD _____ REP 4203-WP
Repertoire / Aug '91 / Pinnacle / Cadillac.

ASK ME NO QUESTIONS/SONGS FOR THE GENTLEMEN
To B without a hitch / Autumn lullaby / Curl your toes / Like never before / Curious crystals of unusual purity / Barefeet and hot pavements / I like to be with you in the sun (Song for the Laird of Connaught Hall) / Lizard-long-tongue-boy / Hello again (of course) / Many happy returns / Broken faith / Ask me no questions / Day a way / City crazy / Back to stay / Seagull Sunday / It you's been there / Song for the Laird of Connaught Hall (part 2) / Making losing better / Lady and the gentle man / Downderry daze / Pebble and the man / It seems very strange
CD Set _____ SEECD 408
See For Miles/C5 / Sep '94 / Pinnacle.

JUMBLEQUEEN
Sparrowpit / Song for the waterden widow / I don't know if I can take it / Some kind of beautiful / Last goodnight / Curious and woolly / Want to be with you / Jumblequeen / Sweet painted lady / Long long time
CD _____ BGOCD 260
Beat Goes On / Feb '95 / Pinnacle.

TAKE THE FIFTH
CD _____ RGFCD 026
Road Goes On Forever / Oct '95 / Direct.

THANK YOU FOR
Nice / Thank you for / Lazarus / Good baby goodbye / Love minus zero, no limit / Silver coin / Happy day / Fly high / To leave your cover / Every day / Song as long as it wants to go on
CD _____ SEECD 428
See For Miles/C5 / Jul '95 / Pinnacle.

St. John, Kate

INDESCRIBABLE NIGHT
There is sweet music here that softer falls / Paris skies / Now the night comes stealing in / Fireflies / Le premier bonheur du jour / Green park blues / Wherefore art thou / Variety lights / On the dodge / Indescribable night / Shadows of doubt / Chat voyeur / Mr. Goodbyes
CD _____ ASCD 025
All Saints / Jun '95 / Vital / Discovery.

St. Johnny

HIGH AS A KITE
CD _____ R 2966
Rough Trade / Feb '93 / Pinnacle.

St. Louis Ragtimers

St. LOUIS RAGTIMERS
CD _____ SOSCD 1267
Stomp Off / Oct '93 / Jazz Music / Wellard.

St. Paul's Cathedral...

CAROLS FROM St. PAUL'S CATHEDRAL (Choir Of St Paul's & The Trumpeters Of The Life Guards)
O come all ye faithful (Adeste Fidelis) / Away in a manger / First nowell / Ding dong merrily on high / Holly and the ivy / O little town of Bethlehem / Joy to the world / In dulci jubilo / Once in Royal David's City / Sussex carol / See amid the winter's snow / In the bleak midwinter / Mary's lullaby / Silent night / Hark the herald angels sing /
CD _____ CDPR 124
Premier/MFP / Nov '94 / EMI.

St. Peters, Crispian

FOLLOW ME
CD _____ REP 4199-WZ
Repertoire / Aug '91 / Pinnacle / Cadillac.

St. Vitus

BORN TOO LATE
CD _____ SST 082 CD
SST / Oct '87 / Plastic Head.

HEAVIER THAN THOU
CD _____ SST 266 CD
SST / May '93 / Plastic Head.

MOURNFUL CRIES
CD _____ SST 161 CD
SST / Sep '88 / Plastic Head.

V
Living backwards / When emotion dies / Ice monkey / Angry man / I bleed black / Patra / Jack Frost / Mind food
CD _____ H 0005-2
Hellhound / Apr '90 / Plastic Head.

Stabbing Westward

UNGOD
Lost / Control / Nothing / ACF / Lies / UnGod / Throw / Violent moodswings / Red on white / Can't happen here
CD _____ 475735 2
Columbia / May '94 / Sony.

Stackhouse, Houston

CRYIN' WON'T HELP YOU
CD _____ EDCD 383
Edsel / Oct '94 / Pinnacle / ADA.

Stackridge

RADIO 1 LIVE IN CONCERT
CD _____ WINCD 019
Windsong / Jun '92 / Pinnacle.

STACKRIDGE
Grande piano / Percy the penguin / Three legged table / Dora the female explorer / Essence of porphyry / Marigold conjunction / 32 West Mall / Marzo plod / Slark
CD _____ BGOCD 65
Beat Goes On / Dec '89 / Pinnacle.

Stackwaddy

BUGGER OFF
Rosalyn / Willie the pimp / Hoochie coochie man / It's all over now / Several yards / You really got me / I'm a lover not a fighter / Meat pies 'ave come but band's not here yet / It ain't easy / Long tall shorty / Repossession boogie / Girl from Ipanema
CD _____ REP 4082-WP
Repertoire / Aug '91 / Pinnacle / Cadillac.

STACK WADDY/BUGGER OFF
Roadrunner / Bring it to Jerome / Mothballs / Sure nuff 'N' yes I do / Love story / Suzie Q / Country line special / Rollin' stone / Mystic eyes / Kentucky / Rosalyn / Willie the pimp / Hoochie coochie man / It's all over now / Several yards / You really got me / I'm a lover not a fighter / Meat pies 'ave come but band's not here yet / It ain't easy / Long tall shorty / Repossession boogie
CD _____ SEECD 407
See For Miles/C5 / Sep '94 / Pinnacle.

Stacy Cats

ROCKJIVE
CD _____ RKCD 9312
Rockhouse / May '93 / Charly / CM / Nervous.

Stacy, Jess

JESS STACY (20 Great Piano Performances 1935-1945)
Barrelhouse / Rhythm rhythm (I got rhythm) / Take me to the land of jazz / Rose of Washington Square / I got rhythm / Blue room / Carnegie jump / Darktown strutter's ball / Mad house / Roll 'em / Big John special / Opus 3/4 / Vultee special / Ec-Stacy / Spain / Down to steamboat Tennessee / In a mist / Candlelights / In the dark / I ain't got nobody / Blue fives / Ridin' easy / Sing, sing, sing
CD _____ CDAJA 5172
ASV / May '95 / Koch.

STACY JESS 1935-39
CD _____ CLASSICS 795
Classics / Mar '95 / Discovery / Jazz Music.

Stadacona Band

ON THE QUARTER DECK
On the quarter deck / Parade of the tall ships / Helen Creighton folk songs / Vedette / Overture to an unwritten comedy / Concertino for flute / Seven seas overture / Les arrivals / Gladiator's farewell / You needed me / Shadows in the moonlight / I just fall in love again / Processions of the nobles / Nova scotia farewell / Barrett's privateers / H.M. Jollies / Heart of oak
CD _____ BNA 5113
Bandleader / Jun '95 / Conifer.

Stafford, Jo

CAPITOL COLLECTORS SERIES: JO STAFFORD
Old acquaintance / How sweet you are / Long ago and far away / I love you / It could happen to you / Trolley song / There's no you / That's for me / Symphony / Ridin' on the gravy train / This is always / Things we did last summer / Smoke dreams / Temptation (Timtayshun) / You so right tonight / Serenade of the bells / I never love anyone / He's gone away / Congratulations / Once and for always / Some enchanted evening / Whispering hope / Ragtime cowboy Joe / Scarlet ribbons / It's great to be alive / No other love
CD _____ CZ 414
Capitol / Apr '91 / EMI.

CAPITOL YEARS: JO STAFFORD
Best things in life are free / Long ago and far away / On the sunny side of the street / Boy next door / I'll be with you in apple blossom time / Ragtime cowboy Joe / There's no you / diamonds are a girl's best friend / Play a simple melody / Let's take the long way home / Shrimp boats / Georgia on my mind / Jambalaya / Come rain or come shine / Day by day / Gentleman is a dope / I'll be seeing you / Trolley song
CD _____ CDEMS 1371
Capitol / Feb '91 / EMI.

DRIFTING & DREAMING (Stafford, Jo & Dick Haynes)
CD _____ VJC 1040
Vintage Jazz Classics / Nov '92 / Direct / ADA / CM / Cadillac.

FOR YOU
CD _____ CDMOIR 513
Memoir / Nov '95 / Target/BMG.

ONE AND ONLY, THE
I promise you / Friend of yours / Why can't you behave / This is the moment / Roses of Picardy / Smiling through / Last mile home / Red River Valley / If I ever love again / Happy times / On the outgo tide / If I loved you / Goodnight Irene / Autumn leaves / Some time / La vie en rose / Our very own / I hate men / Congratulations / Old rugged cross
CD _____ CDSL 8276
Music For Pleasure / Nov '95 / EMI.

SOLDIERS' SWEETHEARTS (3CD Set) (Stafford, Jo/Vera Lynn/Anne Shelton)
You belong to me / Allentown jail / Come rain or come shine / On London Bridge / As I love you / Make love to me / Shrimp boats / Tennessee waltz / I'll be seeing you / Whispering hope / Teach me tonight / Jambalaya / Thank you for calling, goodbye / Ay round the corner / If / Keep it secret / Stardust / Hawaiian war chant / If you've got the money, I've got the time / Embraceable you / Every night when the sun goes in / I should care / It is no secret / St. Louis blues / We'll meet again / Wishing (will make it so) / Mexicali Rose / I paid for the lie that I told you / I shall be waiting / Little Sir Echo / Little boy that Santa Claus forgot / Goodnight children everywhere / My own / Who's taking you home tonight / Bells of St. Mary's / Harbour lights / It's a sin to tell a lie / Lonely sweetheart / Memory of a rose / It's a lovely day tomorrow / I'll pray for you / Nightingale sang in Berkeley Square /

Medley (I hear a dream/You're here, you're there, you're everywhere/So rare) / Wish me luck as you wave me goodbye / I'll never smile again / There goes that song again / Yes my darling daughter / Fools rush in / I don't want to walk without you / You'd be so nice to come home to / Coming in on a wing and a prayer / Last time I saw Paris / A chance on love / Only you / Daddy / My Yiddishe momma / Until you fall in love / Amapola / Kiss the boys goodbye / Lili Marlene / I'll be seeing you (2)

CD Set _____ **PAK 905**
Parade / May '95 / Koch / Cadillac.

VERY BEST OF JO STAFFORD, THE
You belong to me / Allentown jail / Come rain or come shine / On London Bridge / As I love you / Make love to me / Shrimp boats / Tennessee waltz / I'll never love again / Whispering hope / Teach me tonight / Jambalaya / Thank you for calling, goodbye / Ay round the corner / If / Keep it a secret / Stardust / Hawaiian war chant / If you've got the money, I've got the time / Embraceable you / Every night when the sun goes in / I should care / It is no secret / St. Louis blues

CD _____ **PAR 2014**
Parade / Sep '94 / Koch / Cadillac.

Stafford, Terell

TIME TO LET GO
CD _____ **CACD 797022**
Candid / Dec '95 / Cadillac / Jazz Music / Welland / Koch.

Stagg, Richard

JAPANESE BAMBOO FLUTE, THE
CD _____ **EUCD 1103**
ARC / '91 / ARC Music / ADA.

Stahl, Jeanie

MYSTERIES
CD _____ **DARINGCD 3017**
Daring / Nov '95 / Direct / CM / ADA.

Staines, Bill

GOING TO THE WEST
CD _____ **RHR 56**
Red House / Oct '95 / Koch / ADA.

LOOKING FOR THE WIND
CD _____ **RHRCD 79**
Red House / Dec '95 / Koch / ADA.

Stainsby, Trevor

RHYTHM OF RETURN, THE
CD _____ **HWYLCD 3**
Hwyl / May '89 / Hwyl.

Stalag 13

IN CONTROL
CD _____ **LF 058**
Lost & Found / Aug '93 / Plastic Head.

Stallings, Mary

I WAITED FOR YOU (Stallings, Mary & Gene Harris)
When or where / Love dance / I waited for you / Blues in my heart / Dedicated to you / It's crazy / Serenade in blue / But not for me / I wanna be loved / Only trust your heart / T'ain't nobody's business if I do
CD _____ **CCD 4620**
Concord Jazz / Nov '94 / New Note.

Stallone, Frank

CLOSE YOUR EYES
CD _____ **DSHCD 7008**
D-Sharp / May '93 / Pinnacle.

Stamm, Marvin

BOP BOY
CD _____ **MM 65065**
Music Masters / Oct '94 / Nimbus.

MYSTERY MAN
CD _____ **MM 65085**
Music Masters / Oct '94 / Nimbus.

Stanciu, Simon

MUSIQUE TZIGANE EN ROUMAINE
CD _____ **ARN 64236**
Arion / Aug '93 / Discovery / ADA.

Stand Up

WORDS IN MOTION
CD _____ **CI 005-2**
CI / Mar '93 / SRD.

Standells

DIRTY WATER
Medication / Little Sally Tease / There is a storm comin' / Nineteenth nervous breakdown / Dirty water / Pride and devotion / Sometimes good guys don't wear white / Hey Joe / Why did you hurt me / Rari / Why pick on me / Paint it black / Mi ha fatto innamorare / Black hearted woman / Girl and the moon / Mr. Nobody / My little red

book / Mainline / Have you ever spent the night in jail
CD _____ **CDSC 6019**
Sundazed / Apr '94 / Rollercoaster.

DIRTY WATER THE HOT ONES
CD _____ **EVA 842121B5**
EVA / Nov '94 / Direct / ADA.

HOT ONES, THE
Last train to Clarksville / Wild thing / Sunshine superman / Sunny afternoon / Li'l Red Riding Hood / Eleanor Rigby / Black is black / Summer in the city / You were the one / Trip to paradise / St James infirmary / Ten o'clock scholar / When I was a cowboy / Don't ask me what to do / Misty lane / Standell's love theme
CD _____ **CDSC 6021**
Sundazed / Apr '94 / Rollercoaster.

HOT ONES, THE/TRY IT
Last train to Clarksville / Wild thing / Sunshine superman / Sunny afternonn / Li'l Red Riding Hood / Eleanor rigby / Black is black / Summer in the city / Nineteenth nervous breakdown / Dirty water / Can't help but love you / Ninety nine and a half (won't do) / Trip to paradise / St. James infirmary / Try it / Barracuda / Did you ever have that feeling / All fall down / Poor shell of a man / Riot on sunset strip
CD _____ **CDWIKD 112**
Big Beat / Mar '93 / Pinnacle.

IS THIS THE WAY YOU GET YOUR HIGH
Dirty water / Rari / Sometimes good guys don't wear white / Medication / There is a storm comin' / Ninotoonth nervous breakdown / Why did you hurt me / Why pick on me / Paint it black / Black hearted woman / Mainline / Mr. Nobody / Wild thing / Riot on Sunset Strip / Try it / Barracuda / Poor shell of a man / Can't help but love you / Ninety nine and a half (won't do) / Animal girl / Soul drippin' / enimal girl
CD _____ **CDWIKD 114**
Big Beat / Jun '93 / Pinnacle.

STANDELLS RARITIES (& Riot On Sunset Strip)
Riot on sunset strip / Sunset Sally / Sunset theme / Old country / Don't need your lovin' / Children of the night / Make the music pretty / Get away from here / Like my baby / Sitting there standing / Love me / Batman / Our candidate / Boy who is lost / It's all in your mind / School girl / I hate to leave you / Looking at tomorrow / Don't say nothing at all / Try it (Alternate vocal) / Rari (Extended version)
CD _____ **CDWIKD 113**
Big Beat / Jun '93 / Pinnacle.

TRY IT
Can't help but love you / Ninety nine and a half (won't do) / Trip to paradise / St. James infirmary / Try it / Did it ever have the feeling / All fall down / Poor shell of a man / Riot on sunset.strip / Get away from here / Animal girl / Soul drippin' / Can you dig it
CD _____ **CDSC 6022**
Sundazed / Apr '94 / Rollercoaster.

WHY PICK ON ME
Why pick on me / Paint it black / Mi ha fatto innamorare / I hate to leave / Black hearted woman / Sometimes good guys don't wear white / Girl and the moon / Looking at tomorrow / Mr. Nobody / My little red book / Mainline / Have you ever spent the night in jail / Our candidate / Don't say nothing at all / Boy who is lost
CD _____ **CDSC 6020**
Sundazed / Apr '94 / Rollercoaster.

Stanford Prison...

GATO HUNCH (Stanford Prison Experiment)
You're the Vulgarian / Repeat removal / (Very) Put out / Cansado / Flap / So far, so good / El nuevo / Accomplice / Harcord idiot / Swoon / Worst case scenario
CD _____ **WDOM 020CD**
World Domination / Aug '95 / Pinnacle.

STANFORD PRISON EXPERIMENT (Stanford Prison Experiment)
CD _____ **WDOM 009CD**
World Domination / Jun '94 / Pinnacle.

Stanko, Tomasz

BALLADYNA
First song / Tale / Num / Duet / Balladyna / Last song / Nenaliina
CD _____ **5192892-2**
ECM / Nov '93 / New Note.

MATKA JOANNA
CD _____ **5239862**
ECM / Oct '95 / New Note.

TWET
CD _____ **PBR 33860**
Power Bros. / Aug '95 / Harmonia Mundi.

Stanley & The Turbines

BIG BAMBOO
CD _____ **JMC 200203**
Jamaica Gold / Feb '93 / THE / Magnum Music Group / Jetstar.

Stanley Brothers

HYMNS AND SACRED SONGS
CD _____ **KCD 645**
King/Paddle Wheel / Nov '92 / New Note.

STANLEY BROTHERS & THE CLINCH MOUNTAIN BOYS (2CD Set) (Stanley Brothers & The Clinch Mountain Boys)
Won't you be mine / This weary heart you stole away / I'm lonesome without you / Our last goodbye / Poison lies / Dickson County breakdown / I long to see the old folks / Voice from on high / Memories of mother / Could you love me (one more time) / Nobody's love is like mine / I just got wise / Blue moon of Kentucky / Close by / Calling from heaven / Harbor love / Hard times / Baby girl / Say you'll take me back / I worship you / You're still on my mind / I hear my saviour calling / Just a little talk with Jesus / So blue / You'd better get right / Tragic love / Lonesome and blue / Orange blossom special / Clinch mountain blues / Big Tilda / Will he wait a little longer / Angel Band / Cry from the cross / Who will call you sweetheart / I'm lost, I'll never find the way / Let me walk, Lord, by your side / Lonesome night / Flood / Fling ding / I'll never grow tired of you / Loving you too well / Daybreak in Dixie / If that's the way you feel / Life of sorrow / I'd rather be forgotten / No school bus in heaven / Meet me tonight / Nobody's business
CD _____ **BCD 15681**
Bear Family / Oct '93 / Rollercoaster / Direct / CM / Swift / ADA.

STANLEY BROTHERS & THE CLINCH MOUNTAIN BOYS 1949-1952 (Stanley Brothers & The Clinch Mountain Boys)
Vision of mother / White dove / Gathering flowers for the master's bouquet / Angels are singing / It's never too late / Have you someone (in Heaven waiting) / Little glass of wine / Let me be your friend / We'll be sweethearts in Heaven / I love no one but you / Too late to cry / Old home / Drunkard's hell / Fields have turned brown / Hey hey hey / Lonesome river / I'm a man of constant sorrow / Pretty Polly / Life of sorrow / Sweetest love / Wandering boy / Let's part the best of friends
CD _____ **BCD 15564**
Bear Family / Nov '93 / Rollercoaster / Direct / CM / Swift / ADA.

Stanley, Ralph

MASTERS OF THE BANJO (Stanley, Ralph & Tony Ellis/Seleshe Damassae)
CD _____ **ARHCD 421**
Arhoolie / Apr '95 / ADA / Direct / Cadillac.

RALPH STANLEY - SATURDAY NIGHT AND SUNDAY MORNING (2CD Set)
CD Set _____ **FRC 9001**
Freeland Recording Company / Oct '93 / Direct / ADA.

Stansfield, Lisa

AFFECTION
This is the right time / Mighty love / Sincerity / Love in me / All around the world / What did I do to you / Live together / You can't deny it / Poison / When are you coming back / Affection / Wake up baby (Only on cassette and CD.) / Way you want it
CD _____ **260379**
Arista / Aug '95 / BMG.

REAL LIFE
Change / Real love / Set your loving free / I will be waiting / All woman / Soul deep / Make love to u / Time to make you mine / Symptoms of loneliness and heartache / It's got to be real / First joy (Only on cassette and CD.) / Tenderly (Only on cassette and CD.) / Little more love
CD _____ **262300**
Arista / Nov '91 / BMG.

SO NATURAL
So natural / I give you everything / Marvellous and mine / Little bit of heaven / Goodbye / Sweet memories / She's always there / Turn me on / Never set me free / Wish I could always be this way / In all the right places
CD _____ **74321172312**
Arista / Nov '93 / BMG.

Stanshall, Vivian

TEDDY BOYS DON'T KNIT
King Kripple / Slave value / Gums / Biwilderbeeste / Calypso to calapso / Tube / Ginger geezer / Cracks are showing / Flung a dummy / Possibly an arm chair / Fresh faced boys / Terry keeps his clips on / Bass Macaw and broken bottles / Nose hymn / Everyday I have the blues / Smoke signals at night / Nouveau riffe
CD _____ **CASCD 1153**
Charisma / Jun '91 / EMI.

Staple Singers

BEALTITUDE: RESPECT YOURSELF
This world / Respect yourself / Name the missing word / I'll take you there / This old town / We the people / Are you sure / Who do you think you are / I'm just another soldier / Who

Stanley Brothers

STANLEY BROTHERS & THE CLINCH MOUNTAIN BOYS
CD _____ **CDSXE 001**
Stax / May '91 / Pinnacle.

GREAT DAY
Gloryland / Everybody will be happy / Here me call, here / Nobody knows the trouble I've seen / I'm willin' (pts 1 & 2) / Great day / Do you know him / New-born soul / Dying man's plea / New home / Wish I had answered / Better home / Old time religion / Swing low, sweet chariot / Motherless children / Gamblin' man / I know I've been changed / Jesus is all / You got shoes / What are they doing (in heaven today) / Will the Lord rememeber me / My dying bed / Let Jesus lead you / Praying time / I can't help from cryin' sometime / Masters of war
CD _____ **CDCH 391**
Ace / May '92 / Pinnacle / Cadillac / Complete/Pinnacle.

RESPECT YOURSELF - THE BEST OF THE STAPLE SINGERS
Heavy makes you happy / Long walk to D.C. / This world / Respect yourself / I see it / We'll get over / Take you there / Oh la de da / Are you sure / If you're ready (come go with me) / Touch a hand, make a friend / City in the sky / People come out of your shell / You've got to earn it (Available on CD only) / Love is plentiful (Available on CD only) / Got to be some changes made (Available on CD only) / Be what you are (Available on CD only) / This old town (Available on CD only) / Slow train (Available on CD only) / My main man (Available on CD only)
CD _____ **CDSX 006**
Stax / Oct '07 / Pinnacle.

SOUL FOLK IN ACTION/WE'LL GET OVER
We've got to get ourselves together / (Sittin' on) the dock of the bay / Top of the mountain / Slow train / Weight / Long walk to D.C. / Got to be some changes made / Ghetto / People, my people / I see it / This year / We'll get over / Give a damn / Everyday people / End of our road / Tend to your own business / Solon bushi / Challenge / God bless the children / Games people play / Wednesday in your garden / Gardener / When will be paid (For the work we did)
CD _____ **CDSXD 109**
Stax / Jul '94 / Pinnacle.

STAPLE SWINGERS
This is a perfect world / What's your thing / You've got to earn it / You're gonna make me cry / Little boy / How do you move a mountain / Almost / I'm a lover / Love is plentiful / Heavy makes you happy / I like the things about you / Give a hand take a hand
CD _____ **CDSXE 035**
Stax / Feb '91 / Pinnacle.

UNCLOUDY DAY
Uncloudy day / Let me ride / Help me Jesus / I'm coming home / God's wonderful love / Low is the way / Ain't that good news / This may be the last time / I had a dream / Going away / I know I got religion / Will the circle be unbroken / Stand by me / Come up in glory / Pray on / Somebody save me / Each day / So soon / Too close / Let's go home
CD _____ **CPCD 8087**
Charly / Apr '95 / Charly / THE / Cadillac.

Staples, Mavis

DON'T CHANGE ME NOW
Ready for the heartbreak / Sweet things you do / Chokin' kind / House is not a home / Security / Good to me / You send me / I'm tired / Why can't I be like it used to be (CD only) / You're the fool (CD only) / You're all I need / I have learned to do without you / How many times / Endlessly / Since I fell for you / Since you became a part of my life / Don't change me now / You're driving me (to the arms of a stranger) (CD only) / Pick up the pieces (CD only) / Chains of love (CD only) / What happened to the real me (CD only) / It makes me wanna cry
CD _____ **CDSX 014**
Stax / Aug '88 / Pinnacle.

VOICE, THE
CD _____ **0060542**
Edel / Nov '95 / Pinnacle.

Staples, Pops

FATHER FATHER
Father Father / Why am I treated so bad / Too big for your britches / Jesus is going to make up (My dying bed) / Downward road / People get ready / Hope in a hopeless world / You got to serve somebody / Waiting for my child / Simple man / Glory glory
CD _____ **VPBCD 19**
Pointblank / May '94 / EMI.

PEACE IN THE NEIGHBORHOOD
CD _____ **VPBCD 8**
Pointblank / Mar '92 / EMI.

Star Accordion Band

INSPIRATIONAL FAVOURITES
CD _____ **CDSLP 616**
Igus / Dec '89 / CM / Ross / Duncans.

SCOTTISH FAVOURITES
I belong to Glasgow / Amazing grace / Roamin' in the gloamin' / Star o' Rabbie Burns / Rowan tree / Westering home / Mairi's wedding / Ye banks and braes o' bonnie Doon / Loch Lomond / Scotland again / Auld lang syne
CD _____ CDSLP 602
Igus / Jun '87 / CM / Ross / Duncans.

SENTIMENTAL FAVOURITES
CD _____ CDSLP 611
Igus / Nov '88 / CM / Ross / Duncans.

Star Pimp

SERAPHIM 280Z
Slave girl / Size zero / Yoko Phono / Snowball / Little tattoo / Pee test / Greatest hits of love / Human dolphin / Palmolive / Vegan pussy / Gold / Titty / Vocal fader
CD _____ TUP 050-2
Tupelo / Jan '94 / Disc.

Star Sounds Orchestra

INTER PLANETARY AMBIENCE
CD _____ AEOS 001CD
ITP / Sep '95 / Jumpstart / Kudos.

Starclub

STARCLUB
Hard to get / Let your hair down / Call my name / Forever / All falls down / World keeps turning / Bad machine / We believe / Question / Answer / Pretty thing
CD _____ CID 9995
Island / Mar '93 / PolyGram.

Stardust, Alvin

HITS GO ON
CD _____ STIFFCD 18
Disky / Nov '93 / THE / BMG / Discovery / Pinnacle.

JEALOUS MIND
CD _____ 4509 918812
Carlton Home Entertainment / Jan '93 / Carlton Home Entertainment.

Starfish Enterprises

SONIC SYMPHONY NO.1
CD _____ EL 112CD
Electrip / Nov '94 / Plastic Head.

Starfish Pool

AMPLIFIED TONES
CD _____ NZ 034
Nova Zembla / May '95 / Plastic Head.

CHILL OUT N CONFUSED
CD _____ NZ 016
Nova Zembla / Oct '94 / Plastic Head.

Starfish TX

STELLAR SONIC SOLUTIONS
CD _____ TR 40CD
Trance / Oct '95 / SRD.

Stargazers

BACK IN ORBIT
Crazy but true / Loretta / It's only a paper moon / Baby, baby, baby / Got that beat / Walking beat / Sweet Georgia Brown / Dig that rock'n'roll / Stargazer's blues / Crazy man crazy / Every cloud has a silver lining / Feeling happy
CD _____ CDCH 312
Ace / Mar '91 / Pinnacle / Cadillac / Complete/Pinnacle.

SPEAKING CLOCK SAYS...ROCK, THE
Lights out / Rockin' Robin / In a little Spanish town / See you later alligator / Pete's beat / Stop beatin' around the mulberry bush / Cat / Just go wild over rock 'n' roll / Lady killer / Florida twist / Shake, rattle and roll / Eat your heart out Annie
CD _____ JRCD 004
Jappin' & Rockin' / Jan '93 / Vital.

Starkweather

CROSSBEARER
CD _____ TOODAMNHY 32
Too Damn Hype / May '94 / SRD.

Starlights

SOLDERING
CD _____ HBCD 102
Heartbeat / Jan '94 / Greensleeves / Jetstar / Direct / ADA.

Starling, John

LONG TIME GONE
Long time gone / Turned you to stone / Half a man / Jordan / White line / Hobo on a freight train to heaven / Last thing I needed / Brother juke box / Carolyn at the Broken Wheel Inn / He rode all the way to Texas / Drifting too far from the shore / Dark hollow (Only on CD) / (I heard that) Lonesome whistle (Only on CD) / Roads and other reasons (Only on CD) / Sin City (Only on CD)
CD _____ SHCD 3714
Sugarhill / '88 / Roots / CM / ADA / Direct.

WAITIN' ON A SOUTHERN TRAIN
New Delhi freight train / We know better / Carolina star / Other side of life / Waitin' on a southern train / Heart trouble / Homestead in my heart / Hey bottle of whisky / Those memories of you / Slow movin' freight train
CD _____ SHCD 3724
Sugarhill / Aug '95 / Roots / CM / ADA / Direct.

Starlings

TOO MANY DOGS
CD _____ 450995195-2
Anxious / Apr '94 / Warner Music.

VALID
Now take that / That's it you're in trouble / Unhealthy / Start again / Bad Dad / Right school / Shoot up hill / Sick puppy / Jack
CD _____ 450990285 2
Anxious / Aug '92 / Warner Music.

Starmarket

STARMARKET
CD _____ DOL 022CD
Dolores / Jun '95 / Plastic Head.

Starpoint

HAVE YOU GOT WHAT IT TAKES
Elektra / Apr '90 / Warner Music.
CD _____ 7559609232

HOT TO TOUCH
Fresh start / Tough act to follow / Hot to the touch / After all is said and done / Park it / One step closer to your love / Say you will / Swept away / Heart attack
CD _____ K 960810 2
Elektra / Oct '88 / Warner Music.

Starr, Andy

DIG THEM SQUEAKY SHOES
She's a going Jessie / One more time / Rockin' rollin' stone / Deacon Jones / No room for your kind / Round and round / I wanna go south / Give me a woman / Dig them squeaky shoes / Dirty bird song / Do it right / Rockin' reelin' country style / Tell me why / For the want of your love / Love is a simple thing / Me and the fool / Lover man / Knee shakin' / Evil Eye / Little bitty feeling / Lost in a dream / Pledge of love / Do it right now / I'm seeing things (I shouldn't see) / Somali Dolly / I waited for you to remember
CD _____ BCDAH 15890
Bear Family / Jun '95 / Rollercoaster / Direct / CM / Swift / ADA.

Starr, Edwin

20 GREATEST MOTOWN HITS
Stop her on sight (S.O.S.) / Twenty five miles / Headline news / Agent double o soul / Backstreet / I want my baby back / Funky music sho nuff turns me on / Soul master / You've got my soul on fire / Who's right, who's wrong / War / Stop the war now / Way over there / Take me clear from here / Cloud 9 / There you go / Gonna keep on tryin' till I win your love / Time / My weakness is you / Harlem
CD _____ 530064-2
Motown / Jan '93 / PolyGram.

STOP HER ON SIGHT (S.O.S.)
Stop her on sight (S.O.S.) / Headline news / Time is passin' by / I am the man for you baby / Love is my destination / We'll find a way / Oh how happy / You beat me to the punch / Twenty-five miles / Backyard lovin' man / Running back and forth / Mighty good lovin' / All around the world / I'm glad you belong to me / She should have been home / I am your man
CD _____ 5512862
Spectrum/Karussell / Aug '95 / PolyGram / THE.

Starr, Freddie

AFTER THE LAUGHTER
It's only make believe / Fever / I don't want to talk about it / Love hurts / Halfway to paradise / You got it / I will / Sun ain't gonna shine anymore / Teddy bear / I love how you love me / Run to my lovin' arms / I'm lost without you
CD _____ CDMFP 5909
Music For Pleasure / Apr '91 / EMI.

Starr, Kay

1947: KAY STARR
CD _____ HCD 214
Hindsight / Jun '94 / Target/BMG / Jazz Music.

CAPITOL COLLECTORS SERIES: KAY STARR
I'm the lonesomest gal in town / You've got to see mama ev'ry night / You were only fooling (while I was falling in love) / So tired / Bonaparte's retreat / Hoop dee doo / Mississippi / I'll never be free / I waited a little too long / Wheel of fortune / Fool, fool, fool / Kay's lament / Side by side / Comes a-long-a-love / When my dreamboat comes home / Half a photograph / Allez-vous en / Changing partners / If you love me (really

love me) / Man upstairs / Toy or treasure / Lazy river / Foolin' around / Crazy / Rock 'n' roll waltz
CD _____ CZ 411
Capitol / Mar '91 / EMI.

GREAT LADIES OF SONG, THE
You're just in love / Nevertheless (I'm in love with you) / When a woman loves a man / I've got the world on a string / More than you know / I should care / I love Paris / After you've gone / Singin' the blues / Going to Chicago blues / P.S. I love you / Heart / I got it bad and that ain't good / Sunday / Lover man / Please don't talk about me when I'm gone / C'est magnifique / It had to be you
CD _____ CDP 8293922
Capitol Jazz / Aug '95 / EMI.

KAY STARR
Wheel of fortune / I'll always be in love with you / If you love me (really love me) / Comes a-long-a-love / Two brothers / Lovesick blues / Side by side / You've got to see Mama ev'ry night / If I could be with you one hour tonight / Mississippi / Bonaparte's retreat / You broke your promise / Half a photograph / Come on a my house / I wanna love you / Three letters / I wish I had a wishbone / tell me how long the trains been gone / Mama goes where Papa goes / Tonight you belong to me / Changing partners / Dancing on my tears / Waiting at the end of the road / I forgot to forget / Rock 'n' roll waltz
CD _____ CC 8238
EMI / Nov '94 / EMI.

MOONBEAMS AND STEAMY DREAMS
CD _____ STCD 534
Stash / Oct '91 / Jazz Music / CM / Cadillac / Direct / ADA.

MOVIN'
On a slow boat to China / I cover the waterfront / Around the world / Sentimental journey / Night train / Riders in the sky / Goin' to Chicago blues / (Back home again in) Indiana / Song of the wanderer / Swingin' down the lane / Lazy river / Movin'
CD _____ JASCD 307
Jasmine / Mar '95 / Wellard / Swift / Conifer / Cadillac / Magnum Music Group.

SWINGS THE STANDARDS
CD _____ CDCD 1264
Charly / Oct '95 / Charly / THE / Cadillac.

WHAT A DIFFERENCE A DAY MADE
Dixieland band / There's a lull in my life / Ain't misbehavin' / What a difference a day made / What can I say dear after I say I'm sorry / Nobody knows the trouble I've seen / What goes up must come down / Honeysuckle rose / My future just passed / Betcha I getcha / You're always there / Don't do something to someone else / Blame my absentminded heart / It's a great feeling
CD _____ HCD 229
Hindsight / Nov '95 / Target/BMG / Jazz Music.

Starr, Ringo

BEAUCOUPS OF BLUES
Beaucoups of blues / Love don't last long / Fastest growing heartache in the west / Coochy coochy / Silent homecoming / Waiting / Loser's lounge / I wouldn't have it any other way / Wine, women and and loud happy songs / Without her / Woman of the night / I'd be talking all the time / Fifteen dollar draw
CD _____ CDPAS 10002
Apple / May '95 / EMI.

LIVE FROM MONTREUX (Starr, Ringo & His All-Starr Band)
Really serious introduction / I'm the greatest / Don't go where the road don't go / Yellow submarine / Desperado / I can't tell you why / Life kath / Weight of the world / Bang the drum all day / Walking nerve / Black Maria / In the city / American woman / Boys / With a little help from my friends
CD _____ RCD 20264
Rykodisc / Oct '93 / Vital / ADA.

SENTIMENTAL JOURNEY
Sentimental journey / Night and day / Whispering grass / Bye bye blackbird / I'm a fool to care / Stardust / Blue turning grey over you / Love is a many splendoured thing / Dream / You always hurt the one you love / Have I told you lately that I love you / Let the rest of the world go by
CD _____ CDPCS 7101
Apple / May '95 / EMI.

Stars Of Faith

FAMOUS SPIRITUALS, NEGRO SPIRITUALS
CD _____ BB 3222
Black & Blue / Sep '95 / Wellard / Koch.

LIVE AT MONTREUX
CD _____ BLE 591862
Black & Blue / Apr '92 / Wellard / Koch.

Stars Of Heaven

SPEAK SLOWLY
CD _____ ROUGHCD 131
Rough Trade / Jun '88 / Pinnacle.

Starshooter

STARSHOOTER
CD _____ FC 039CD
Fan Club / '87 / Direct.

Starsound

BEST OF STARS ON 45
CD _____ MCCD 192
Music Club / Nov '94 / Disc / THE / CM.

STARS ON 45
Do you want to know a secret / Nowhere man / Eight days a week / My sweet lord / Hard day's night / Video killed the radio star / Cathy's clown / Bird dog / Sherry / Buona sera / At the hop
CD _____ CDMFP 6031
Music For Pleasure / Sep '88 / EMI.

STARS ON 45 - STARSOUND
CD _____ OG 3600
Old Gold / Nov '87 / Carlton Home Entertainment.

Starsound Orchestra

I'M IN THE MOOD FOR ROMANCE
CD _____ LPCD 1023
Disky / Apr '94 / THE / BMG / Discovery / Pinnacle.

Starspeed Transmission

METAMORPHIC ILLUMINATION
CD _____ NZ 012CD
Nova Zembla / Aug '94 / Plastic Head.

Starvation Army

MERCENARY POSITION
CD _____ RAVE 019CD
Rational / Sep '91 / Vital.

Stasis

INSPIRATION
Natural people / Sound files nos 68 / Inside / Exosphere / Sound files nos 13 / They shit chips don't they / Pork chop hill / Sound files nos 94 / World out of time / Inspiration / Sound files nos 7 / Welcome to the new age disco
CD _____ PF 028CD
Peacefrog / Aug '95 / Disc.

State

CONTROL
CD _____ SOS 1CD
Sound Sound / Mar '94 / Plastic Head.

SEARCHES FOR NAKED FORMS
CD _____ SOS 2CD
Sound Sound / Mar '94 / Plastic Head.

State Of Grace

JAMBOREEBOP
Whetherette / Smile / And love will fall / Flourescent sea / Hello / Mystery / Bitter sun / Different world / Rose / New fear / Truth / Jamboreebop
CD _____ STONE 014CD
3rd Stone / May '95 / Vital / Plastic Head.

PACIFIC MOTION
Sooner or later / Miss you IV / Camden / Love pain and passion II / Bitter sun II / Ruby sky / Head / P.S. High / Miss you (Arizona mix)
CD _____ STONE 008CD
3rd Stone / Mar '94 / Vital / Plastic Head.

State Street Ramblers

STATE STREET RAMBLERS VOL. 1 1927-31
CD _____ JPCD 1512
Jazz Perspectives / Dec '94 / Jazz Music / Hot Shot.

STATE STREET RAMBLERS VOL. 2 1931-36
CD _____ JPCD 1513
Jazz Perspectives / Dec '94 / Jazz Music / Hot Shot.

Statetrooper

STATETROOPER
Shape of things to come / Set fire to the night / Dreams of the faithful / Stand me up / Veni vidi vici / Last stop to heaven / She got the look / Too late / Armed and ready
CD _____ WKFMXD 91
FM / May '87 / Sony.

Static Seekers

BODY AUTOMATIC
CD _____ AXS 007CD
Axis / Sep '90 / Plastic Head.

Statman, Andy

ANDY'S RAMBLE
CD _____ ROUCD 0244
Rounder / Dec '94 / CM / Direct / ADA / Cadillac.

Staton, Candi

BEST OF CANDI STATON, THE
CD _____ 9362457302
Warner Bros. / Nov '95 / Warner Music.

GLORIFY
Sing a song / He is Lord / To glorify your name / It's not easy / Have you tried God / First face / I want to see / God's got it / He's coming back
CD _____ CDBM 075
Blue Moon / '91 / Magnum Music Group / Greensleeves / Hot Shot / ADA / Cadillac / Discovery.

NIGHTLITES
Love and be free / Suspicious minds / In the still of the night / Sunshine of our love / Hurry sundown / Tender hooks / Count on me
CD _____ NEMCD 624
Sequel / Jun '92 / BMG.

STAND UP AND BE A WITNESS
Stand up / I'm depending on you / You don't know / He's always there / Advance / God's got an answer / Until you make it through / Glory of Jesus / Hallel
CD _____ CDBM 077
Blue Moon / Apr '90 / Magnum Music Group / Greensleeves / Hot Shot / ADA / Cadillac / Discovery.

STANDING ON THE PROMISES
Blood rushes / No not one / There is the power in the word / Glory to his name / Living on the edge of time / Let not your heart be troubled / Oh I want to see him / When he reached down his hand for me / Finally, finally
CD _____ CDBM 096
Blue Moon / Oct '93 / Magnum Music Group / Greensleeves / Hot Shot / ADA / Cadillac / Discovery.

Staton, Dakota

DARLING PLEASE SAVE YOUR LOVE FOR ME
I thought about you / You've changed / I can't quit you baby / You better go now / Gone with the wind / Save your love for me / East of the sun and west of the moon / Walking the backstreets / I'm just a lucky so and so / Skylark / Your husband's cheating on us
CD _____ MCD 5462
Muse / Sep '92 / New Note / CM.

ISN'T THIS A LOVELY DAY
Isn't this a lovely day (to be caught in the rain) / I cover the waterfront / Gee baby ain't I good to you / My lean baby / If he walked into my life / I'll close my eyes / Close your eyes / (I'm afraid) the masquerade is over / Ain't no use
CD _____ MCD 5502
Muse / Sep '95 / New Note / CM.

LET ME OFF UPTOWN
When lights are low / Willow weep for me / But not for me / You don't know what love is / Best thing for you / Song is you / Avalon / Until the real thing comes along / If I should lose you / Gone with the wind / Let me off uptown / Anything goes / When Sunny gets blue / They all laughed / Too close for comfort / Cherokee / September in the rain / East of the sun and west of the moon / It's you or no one / Song is ended (but the melody lingers on) / Goodbye / Love walked in
CD _____ CDREN 005
Dessiennnee / '90 / Wolford / Jazz Music.

Statton, Alison

TIDAL BLUES (Statton, Alison & Spike)
Greater notion / In this world / Empty hearth / Open eyes / Take heart / Lemming time / Mr. Morgan / Hidden combat / Seaport town / Find and seek / Tidal blues / Alternations
CD _____ ASKCD 037
Vinyl Japan / Oct '94 / Vital.

Status Quo

AIN'T COMPLAINING
CD _____ 8346042
Vertigo / Feb '91 / PolyGram.

B SIDES AND RARITIES
I who have nothing / Neighbour neighbour / Hurdy gurdy man / Laticia / (We ain't got) nothin' yet / I want it / Almost but not quite there / Wait just a minute / Gentleman Joe's sidewalk cafe / To be free / When my mind is not alive / Make me stay a little bit longer / Auntie Nellie / Price of love / Little Miss Nothing / Down the dustpipe / Face without a soul / In my chair / Good thinking Batman / Time to fly / Do you live in fire / Josie
CD _____ CCSCD 271
Castle / Sep '90 / BMG.

BACK TO THE BEGINNING
CD Set _____ CDLIK 81
Decal / Sep '91 / Charly / Swift.

BEST OF 1968-71
Mean girl / Down the dustpipe / Spinning wheel blues / Need your love / Lazy poker blues / Daughter / In my chair / Railroad / Gerdundula / Hey little woman / Good

thinking batman / Josie / To be free / Shy fly / (April) spring, summer and wednesdays
CD _____ PWKS 4080
Carlton Home Entertainment / Aug '91 / Carlton Home Entertainment.

COLLECTION: STATUS QUO
Pictures of matchstick men / Green tambourine / Technicolour dreams / Sunny cellophane skies / Paradise flat / Clown / Antique Angelique / Ice in the sun / Lakky lady / Is it really me / Gerdundula / Neighbour neighbour / Paradise flat (2)
CD _____ CCSCD 114
Castle / '88 / BMG.

DOG OF TWO HEAD
Umleitung / Nanana / Something's going on in my head / Railroad / Gerdundula / Mean girl / Someone's learning
CD _____ CLACD 206
Castle / Sep '90 / BMG.

DON'T STOP
CD _____ 5310352
PolyGram TV / Feb '96 / PolyGram.

EARLY WORKS, THE (3CD Set)
I who have nothing / Neighbour, neighbour / Hurdy gurdy man / Laticia / (We ain't got) nothin' yet / I want it / Almost but not quite there / Wait just a minute / Pictures of matchstick men / Black veils of melancholy / To be free / Ice in the sun / When my mind is not alive / Elizabeth dreams / Paradise flat / Technicolour dreams / Spicks and specks / Sheila / Sunny cellophane skies / Green tambourine / Make me stay a little bit longer / Auntie Nellie / Are you growing tired of my love / So ends another life / Price of love / Face without a soul / You're just what I was looking for today / Antique Angelique / Poor old man / Mr. Mind Detector / Clown / Velvet curtains / Little Miss Nothing / When I awake / Nothing at all / Josie / Down the dustpipe / Time to fly / Do you live in fire (April) Spring, Summer and Wednesdays / Daughter / Everything / Lazy poker blues / Is it really me / Gotta go home / Junior's waiting / Shy fly / Lakky lady / Need your love / Spinning wheel blues / In my chair / Gerdundula (original version) / Tune to the music / Good thinking batman / Umleitung / Nanana / Something going on in my head / Mean girl / Railroad / Someone's learning / Nanana (2) / Nanana (3) / Gerdundula
CD Set _____ ESBCD 136
Essential / Dec '90 / Total/BMG.

FEW BARS MORE, A
Whatever you want / What you are proposing / Softer ride / Price of love / Drifting away / She don't fool me / Who gets the love / Let's work together / Bring it on home / Backwater / I saw the light / Don't stop me now / Come rock with me / Rockin' all over the world
CD _____ 5500022
Spectrum/Karussell / May '93 / PolyGram / THE.

HELLO
And it's better now / Blue eyed lady / Caroline / Claudie / Forty five hundred times / Reason for living / Roll over lay down / Softer ride
CD _____ 8481722
Vertigo / Feb '91 / PolyGram.

ICE IN THE SUN
CD _____ SSLCD 204
Savanna / Jun '95 / THE.

INTROSPECTIVE: STATUS QUO
Mean girl / Ice in the sun / Pictures of matchstick men / Interview part one / Down the dustpipe / Little Miss Nothing / Is it really me / Interview part two
CD _____ CINT 5003
Baktabak / Nov '90 / Baktabak.

IT'S ONLY ROCK & ROLL
Wanderer / Don't waste my time / Something 'bout you baby / Like / Blue eyed lady / Accident prone / Where am I / Little dreamer / Ain't complaining / Hard ride / Mess of blues / You don't own me / Your smiling face / Name of the game / Enough is enough
CD _____ 5501902
Spectrum/Karussell / Sep '94 / PolyGram / THE.

LIVE AT THE NEC
CD _____ 8189472
Vertigo / Feb '91 / PolyGram.

MA KELLY'S GREASY SPOON
Spinning wheel blues / Daughter / Everything / Shy fly / Junior's waiting / Lakky lady / Need your love / Lazy poker blues / Is it really me / Gotta go home / April, Spring, Summer and Wednesdays
CD _____ CLACD 169
Castle / Dec '89 / BMG.

NEVER TOO LATE/ BACK TO BACK
Never too late / Something bout you baby I like / Take me away / Falling in falling out / Carol / Long ago / Mountain lady / Don't stop me now / Enough is enough / Riverside / Mess of blues / Ol rag blues / Can't be done / Too close to the ground / No contract / Win or lose / Marguerita time / Going down town tonight

CD _____ 8480882
Vertigo / Feb '91 / PolyGram.

ON THE LEVEL
Broken man / Bye bye Johnny / Down down / I saw the light / Most of the time / Night ride / Over and one / What to do / Where am I
CD _____ 8481742
Vertigo / Feb '91 / PolyGram.

OTHER SIDE OF STATUS QUO, THE
Magic / Power of rock / Don't give it up / Rotten to the bone / Lost the love / Heartburn / Perfect remedy / A B Blues / Keep me guessing / Joanne / Doing it all for you / Lonely / That's alright / I wonder why / Gerundula (live) / Long legged girls / Forty five hundred times / Junior's wailing
CD _____ VSOPCD 213
Connoisseur / Feb '95 / Pinnacle.

PICTURES OF MATCHSTICK MEN
Down the dustpipe / Mean girl / Gerdundula / Price of love / Make me stay a little bit longer / Josie / Hurdy gurdy man / Something going on in my heart / Green tambourine / Pictures of matchstick men / Ice in the sun / Black veils of melancholy / Laticia / I who have nothing / Tune to the music / Spicks and specks / Umleitung / Nanana
CD _____ 5507272
Spectrum/Karussell / Mar '95 / PolyGram / THE.

PICTURESQUE MATCHSTICKABLE MESSAGES FROM THE STATUS QUO
Black veils of melancholy / When my mind is not alive / Ice in the sun / Elizabeth dreams / Gentleman Joe's sidewalk cafe / Paradise flat / Technicolour dreams / Spicks and specks / Sheila / Sunny cellophane skies / Green tambourine / Pictures of matchstick men
CD _____ CLACD 168
Castle / Dec '89 / BMG.

PILEDRIVER
All the reasons / Big fat mama / Don't waste my time / O baby / Paper plane / Roadhouse blues / Unspoken words / Year
CD _____ 8841712
Vertigo / Feb '91 / PolyGram.

QUO/ BLUE FOR YOU
Backwater / Just take me / Break the rules / Drifting away / Don't think it matters / Fine fine fine / Lonely man / Slow train / Is there a better way / Mad about the boy / Ring of a change / Blue for you / Rain / Rollin' home / That's a fact / Ease your mind / Mystery song
CD _____ 8480892
Vertigo / Feb '91 / PolyGram.

ROCK TIL YOU DROP
Like a zombie / All we really wanna do (Polly) / Fakin' the blues / One man band / Rock 'til you drop / Can't give you more / Warning what / Let's work together / Bring it on home / No problems / Good sign / Tommy / Nothing comes easy / Fame or money / Price of love / Forty five hundred times
CD _____ 5103412
Vertigo / Jan '93 / PolyGram.

ROCKIN' ALL OVER THE WORLD
Baby boy / Can't give you more / Dirty water / For you / Hard time / Hold you back / Let's ride / Rockin' all over the world / Too far gone / Who am I / You don't own me / Rockers rollin'
CD _____ 8481732
Vertigo / Feb '91 / PolyGram.

ROCKING ALL OVER THE YEARS
Pictures of matchstick men / Ice in the sun / Paper plane / Caroline / Break the rules / Down down / Roll over lay down / Rain / Wild side of life / Rockin' all over the world / Whatever you want / What you're proposing / Something 'bout you baby I like / Rock 'n' roll / Dear John / Ol' rag blues / Marguerita time / Wanderer / Rollin' home / In the army now / Burning bridges (on and off and on again) / Anniversary waltz
CD _____ 846 797 2
Vertigo / Oct '90 / PolyGram.

SPARE PARTS
Face without a soul / You're just what I was looking for today / Are you growing tired of my love / Antique Angelique / So ends another life / Poor old man / Mr. Mind detector / Clown / Velvet curtains / Little Miss Nothing / When I awake / Nothing at all
CD _____ CLACD 205
Castle / Sep '90 / BMG.

STATUS QUO
CD _____ MATCD 291
Castle / Mar '94 / BMG.

THIRSTY WORK
Goin' nowhere / I didn't mean it / Confidence / Point of no return / Sail away / Like it or not / Soft in the head / Queenie / Lover of the human race / Sherri don't fail me now / Rude awakening time / Back on my feet / Restless / Ciao ciao / Tango / Sorry
CD _____ 5236072
Vertigo / Oct '94 / PolyGram.

TWELVE GOLD BARS VOL.1
Rockin' all over the world / Down down / Caroline / Paper plane / Break the rules / Again and again / Mystery song / Roll over

lay down / Rain / Wild side of life / Whatever you want / Living on an island
CD _____ 800 062-2
Vertigo / Nov '84 / PolyGram.

WHATEVER YOU WANT/ JUST SUPPOSIN'
Whatever you want / Shady lady / Who asked you / Your smiling face / Living on an island / Come rock with me / Rockin' on / Runaway / Breaking away
CD _____ 8480872
Vertigo / Feb '91 / PolyGram.

Stauber, Beverly

NAIL MY FEET TO THE KITCHEN FLOOR
CD _____ NERCD 064
Nervous / '91 / Nervous / Magnum Music Group.

Steakknife

GODPILL
CD _____ EFA 120112
X-Mist / Nov '95 / SRD.

Stealer's Wheel

BEST OF STEALERS WHEEL (Featuring Gerry Rafferty)
Stuck in the middle with you / Nothing's gonna to change my mind / Star / This morning / Steamboat row / Next to me / Right or wrong / Go as you please / Benediction / Waltz / Blind faith / Late again / Wheelin' / Jose
CD _____ CSAPCD 106
Connoisseur / Jun '90 / Pinnacle.

STUCK IN THE MIDDLE
Stuck in the middle with you / Who cares / Benediction / Go as you please / Late again / Everything will turn out fine / Blind faith / Star / Outside looking in / Found my way to you / Right or wrong / You put something better inside of me
CD _____ CDMID 151
A&M / Oct '92 / PolyGram.

Steam Jenny

WELCOME BACK
CD _____ CDLOC 1082
Klub / Oct '94 / CM / Ross / Duncans / ADA / Direct.

Steamboat Band

RUMOURS & RIDERS
Got no tears / Died without sleeping / Everybody needs the morning rain / Fall from grace / Hit the bottle again / Take your hands off the wheel / Just like me / Running to Waycross / Goodbye Mary Jane / Take a little time (Off my hands) / Restless lullaby / She's coming my way / Let it pass me by
CD _____ 5274732
Polydor / Apr '95 / PolyGram.

Steamhammer

MOUNTAINS
CD _____ REP 4066-WZ
Repertoire / Aug '91 / Pinnacle / Cadillac.

SPEECH
CD _____ REP 4139-WZ
Repertoire / Aug '91 / Pinnacle / Cadillac.

Steaming Jungle

RUPUNI SAFARI
CD _____ ARICD 111
Ariwa Sounds / Sep '95 / Jetstar / SRD.

Steampacket

FIRST SUPERGROUP, THE
Can I get a witness / In crowd / Baby take me / Baby baby / Back at the chicken shack / Cry me a river / Oh baby, don't you do it / Holy smoke / Lord remember her
CD _____ CDCD 1031
Charly / Mar '93 / Charly / THE / Cadillac.

STEAMPACKET
CD _____ REP 4090-WZ
Repertoire / Aug '91 / Pinnacle / Cadillac.

Steamroller

DEAD MAN'S TAN
CD _____ CDSGP 0136
Prestige / Dec '94 / Total/BMG.

Stecher, Jody

STAY AWHILE (Stecher, Jody & Kate Brislin)
CD _____ ROUCD 0334
Rounder / Apr '95 / CM / Direct / ADA / Cadillac.

Steckar, Marc

PACKWORK (Steckar, Marc Tubapack)
CD _____ BBRC 9310
Big Blue / Jan '94 / Harmonia Mundi.

Steel

STEEL
CD _____ EFA 006662
Mille Plateau / Oct '95 / SRD.

Steel Band Des Caraibes

STEEL MUSIC FROM THE CARIBBEAN
CD _____ 824552
Buda / Nov '90 / Discovery / ADA.

Steel, Eric

BACK FOR MORE
911 / Something for nothing / Low down / Crazy lady / Stray cat blues / Back for more / Meant to be / Material law / Insert gently
CD _____ KILCD 1003
Killerwatt / Oct '93 / Kingdom.

Steel Fury

LESSER OF TWO EVILS
CD _____ 859 803
Steamhammer / '89 / Pinnacle / Plastic Head.

Steel Pole Bath Tub

LIVE
CD _____ YCLS 019
Your Choice / Jun '94 / Plastic Head.

LURCH
Christina / Hey you / Paranoid / I am Sam I am / Bee sting / Swerve / Heaven on dirt / Lime away / River / Time to die / Welcome aboard it's love / Hey Bo Diddley / Thru the windshield of love / Tear it apart
CD _____ TUPCD 16
Tupelo / Jul '94 / Disc.

MIRACLE OF SOUND IN MOTION, THE
Pseudoephendrine hydrochloride / Train to Miami / Exhale / Thumbnail / Down all the days / Carbon / Bozeman / Borstal / 594 / Waxl
CD _____ TUP 472
Tupelo / Apr '93 / Disc.

SCARS FROM FALLING DOWN
CD _____ 8286852
Slash / Jan '96 / PolyGram.

SOME COCKTAIL SUGGESTIONS
Ray / Living end / Slip / Hit it / Speaker phone / Wasp jar
CD _____ TUP 051-2
Tupelo / Jan '94 / Disc.

Steel Prophet

GODDESS PRINCIPLE, THE
CD _____ MASSE 001
Massacre / Aug '95 / Plastic Head.

Steel Pulse

HANDSWORTH REVOLUTION
Handsworth revolution / Bad man / Soldiers / Sound check / Prodigal / Ku klux klan / Prediction / Macka splaff
CD _____ RRCD 24
Reggae Refreshers / Nov '90 / PolyGram / Vital.

REGGAE GREATS
Sound system / Babylon makes the rules / Don't give in / Soldier / Prodigal son / Ku klux klan / Macka splaff / Drug squad / Reggae fever / Handsworth revolution
CD _____ IMCD 33
Island / Jul '89 / PolyGram.

TRIBUTE TO THE MARTYRS
Unseen guest / Sound system / Jah Pickney / Biko's kindred lament / Tribute to the martyrs / Babylon makes the rules / Uncle George / Blasphemy
CD _____ RRCD 17
Reggae Refreshers / Sep '90 / PolyGram / Vital.

Steele, Davy

SUMMERTIME
CD _____ CMCD 046
Celtic Music / Apr '94 / CM / Roots.

Steele, Jevetta

HERE IT IS
Say a little prayer for you / Baby are you / And how / You're gonna love me / Here it is / Calling you / In this man's world / Good foot / Skip 2 my u my darling / Where do we go from here / Love will follow
CD _____ 108772
Musicdisc / Mar '92 / Vital / Harmonia Mundi / ADA / Cadillac / Discovery.

Steele, Tommy

EP COLLECTION: TOMMY STEELE
Rock with the caveman / Wedding bells / Doomsday rock / Singin' the blues / Take me back baby / Handful of songs / Rebel rock / Will it be you / Happy guitar / Knee deep in the blues / Put a ring on her finger / Young love / Come on let's go / Elevator rock / Only man on the island / Time to kill / Little white ball / Number twenty two across the way / You gotta go / Singin' time / Cannibal pot / Build up /. Water, water

CD _____ SEECD 347
See For Miles/C5 / May '95 / Pinnacle.

HANDFUL OF SONGS, A
Handful of songs / Singin' the blues / Young love / Water water / Cannibal pot / It's all happening / Where have all the flowers gone / Nairobi / I put the lightie on / Georgia on my mind / Where's the birdie / Rock with the caveman / Butterfingers / Shiralee / What a little darlin' / She's too far above me / Hey you / Flash bang wallop
CD _____ 5500182
Spectrum/Karussell / May '93 / PolyGram THE.

ROCK 'N' ROLL YEARS, THE (Steele, Tommy & The Steelemen)
Rock with the caveman / C'mon let's go / Butterfly / Give give give / Elevator rock / Rebel rock / You gotta go / Build up / Put a ring on her finger / You were mine / Swallow tail coat / Singin' the blues / Doomsday rock / Knee deep in the blues / Two eyes / Take me back baby / Writing on the wall / Hey you / Teenage party / Plant a kiss / Rock around the town / Drunken guitar / Tallahassee lassie
CD _____ SEECD 203
See For Miles/C5 / May '95 / Pinnacle.

VERY BEST OF TOMMY STEELE
Nairobi / Tallahassie Lassie / Kookaburra / Flash bang wallop / She's too far above me / Happy guitar / Young love / Butterfingers / Green eye / Where have all the flowers gone / Handful of songs / Marriage type love / Georgia on my mind / Come on let's go / Sweet Georgia Brown / It's all happening / Only man on the island / Princess / Writing on the wall / What a mouth (what a North and South)
CD _____ PWKM 4071P
Carlton Home Entertainment / Aug '91 / Carlton Home Entertainment.

Steeler

STRIKE BACK
CD _____ 851 861
Steamhammer / '88 / Pinnacle / Plastic Head.

UNDERCOVER
CD _____ 857 512
Steamhammer / '89 / Pinnacle / Plastic Head.

Steeles

HEAVEN HELP US ALL
Heart in my hand / Tide keeps lifting me / Never get over you / Well done / I don't wanna be without U / Heaven help us all / It'll be alright / Oh what a gift / Those were the days / Big God
CD _____ 7559612902
Elektra Nonesuch / Aug '93 / Warner Music.

Steeleye Span

ALL AROUND MY HAT
Black jack David / Hard times of old England / Cadwith anthem / All around my hat / Gamble gold (Robin Hood) / Wife of Usher's well / Sum wavves (Tunes) / Dance with me / Bachelors hall
CD _____ CD25CR 21
Chrysalis / Mar '94 / EMI.

BACK IN LINE
CD _____ PRKCD 8
Park / Aug '91 / Pinnacle.

BEST OF & THE REST OF STEELEYE SPAN
CD _____ CDAR 1012
Action Replay / Oct '94 / Tring.

BEST OF LIVE IN CONCERT, THE
CD _____ PRK 27CD
Park / Oct '94 / Pinnacle.

BEST OF STEELEYE SPAN
Gaudete / All around my hat / Thomas the rhymer / Alison Gross / Little Sir Hugh / Cam ye o'er frae France / Long lankin / Gone to America / Let her go down / Black jack David / Bach goes to Limerick
CD _____ CCD 1467
Chrysalis / '88 / EMI.

COLLECTION IN CONCERT, THE
Blacksmith / Waterver / Spotted cow / One misty moisty morning / King Henry / Fox / Two butchers / Jack Hall / Canon / Shaking of the sheets / All around my hat / Tunes / Gaudete
CD _____ PRKCD 27
Park / Nov '94 / Pinnacle.

COLLECTION: STEELEYE SPAN
CD _____ CCSCD 292
Castle / Aug '91 / BMG.

NOW WE ARE SIX
Seven hundred elves / Edwin / Drink down the moon / Now we are six / Thomas the rhymer / Mooncoin jig / Long-a-growing / Two magicians / Twinkle twinkle little star / To know him is to love him
CD _____ BGOCD 157
Beat Goes On / Dec '92 / Pinnacle.

PARCEL OF ROGUES, A
One misty moisty morning / Alison Gross / Bold poachers / Ups and down / Robbery

with violins / Wee wee man / Weaver and the factory maid / Rogues in a nation / Can ye o'er frae France / Hares on the mountain
CD _____ SHAN 79045 CD
Shanachie / Nov '88 / Koch / ADA / Greensleeves.

SPANNING THE YEARS (2CD Set)
Blacksmith / My Johnny was a shoe maker / King / Lovely on the water / Marrowbones / Rave on / Gaudette / John Barleycorn / Alison Gross / Robbery with violins / Rogues in a nation / Cam ye o'er frae France / Thomas the rhymer / To know him is to love him / New York girls / Long lankin / Black jack David / Hard times of Old England / All around my hat / London / Fighting for strangers / Black freighter / Victory / False knight on the road / Rag doll / Let her go down / Sails of silver / Gone to America / My love / Lady diamond / Blackleg miner / One misty moisty morning / Fox / Following me / Tam lin
CD Set _____ CDCHR 6093
Chrysalis / Apr '95 / EMI.

STEELEYE SPAN - THE EARLY YEARS
Blacksmith / Marrowbones / Westron wynde / All things are quite silent / Lovely on the water / Boys of Bedlam / My Johnny was a shoemaker / Cold haily windy night / Horn of the hunter / Lark in the morning / Prince Charlie Stuart / Reels / Dark eyed sailor / Rave on / Brisk young butcher / Wee weaver / When I was on horseback / Female drummer / Skewball
CD _____ VSOPCD 132
Connoisseur / Apr '89 / Pinnacle.

Steely & Cleevie

PLAY STUDIO ONE VINTAGE
CD _____ CDHB 116
Heartbeat / May '92 / Greensleeves / Jetstar / Direct / ADA.

STEELY & CLEEVIE PRESENTS HARDCORE
CD _____ SCCD 2
Steely & Cleevie / Oct '93 / Jetstar.

Steely Dan

AJA
Black cow / Aja / Deacon blues / Peg / Home at last / I got the news / Josie
CD _____ MCLD 19145
MCA / Nov '90 / BMG.

ALIVE IN AMERICA
Babylon sister / Green earrings / Bodhisattva / Reelin' in the years / Josie / Book of liars / Peg / Third world man / Kid Charlemagne / Sign in stranger / Aja
CD _____ 74321286912
Giant / Oct '95 / BMG.

ASIA
CD _____ DMCA 102
MCA / Jan '85 / BMG.

BEST OF STEELY DAN - REMASTERED
Reelin' in the years / Rikki don't lose that number / Peg / FM (no static at all) / Hey nineteen / Deacon blues / Black Friday / Bodhisattva / Do it again / Haitian divorce / My old school / Midnite cruiser / Babylon sisters / Kid Charlemagne / Dirty work / Josie
CD _____ MCD 10967
MCA / Nov '93 / BMG.

CAN'T BUY A THRILL
Do it again / Dirty work / Kings / Midnite cruiser / Only a fool / Reelin' in the years / Fire in the hole / Brooklyn (owes the charmer and me) / Change of the guard / Turn that heartbeat over again
CD _____ MCLD 19017
MCA / Apr '92 / BMG.

CATALYST
Sun mountain / Barrytown / Take it out on me / Cave's of Altamira / Charlie Freak / You go where I go / Any world (that I'm welcome to) / Little with sugar / Android warehouse / More to come / Parker's band / Oh wow it's you again / Stone piano / Yellow peril / Roaring of the lamb / This seat's been taken / Ida Lee / Undecided / Horse in town
CD _____ CDTB 503
Thunderbolt / Jun '94 / Magnum Music Group.

CITIZEN 1972-1980 (The Best Of Steely Dan/4CD Set)
Do it again / Dirty work / Kings / Midnite cruiser / Only a fool would say that / Reelin' in the years / Fire in the hole / Brooklyn (owes the charmer under me) / Change of the guard / Turn that heartbeat over again / Bodhisattva / Razor boy / Boston rag / Your gold teeth / Showbiz kid / My old school / King of the world / Pearl of the quarter / Rikki don't lose that number / Night by night / Any major dude will tell you / Barrytown / East St. Louis toodle-oo / Parker's band / Through with buzz / Pretzel logic / With a gun / Charlie Freak / Monkey in your soul / Bodhisattva (live) / Black Friday / Bad sneakers / Rose darling / Daddy don't live in that New York City no more / Dr. Wu / Everyone's gone to the movies / Chain lightning / Your gold teeth II / Any world (that I'm welcome to) / Throw back the little one / Kid Charlemagne / Caves of Altmira / Don't take me alive / Sign in stranger / Fez

/ Green earrings / Haitian divorce / Everything you did / Royal scam / Here at the western world / Black cow / Aja / Peg / Deacon blues / Home at last / I got the news / When Josie comes home / FM / Babylon sisters / Hey nineteen / Glamour profession / Gaucho / Time out of mind / My rival / Third world man / Everyone's gone to the movies (demo)
CD Set _____ MCAD 410981
MCA / Jan '94 / BMG.

COUNTDOWN TO ECSTASY
Bodhisattva / Razor boy / Boston rag / Your gold teeth / Showbiz kid / My old school / Pearl of the quarter / King of the world
CD _____ MCLD 19018
MCA / Apr '92 / BMG.

GAUCHO
Babylon sisters / Hey nineteen / Glamour profession / Gaucho / Time out of mind / My rival / Third world man
CD _____ MCLD 19146
MCA / Oct '92 / BMG.

GOLD
Hey nineteen / Green earring / Deacon blues / Chain lightning / FM / Black cow / King of the world / Babylon sisters
CD _____ MCAD 10387
MCA / Aug '91 / BMG.

KATHY LIED
Black Friday / Bad sneakers / Rose darling / Daddy don't live in that New York City no more / Dr. Wu / Everyone's gone to the movies / Your gold teeth II / Chain lightning / Any world (that I'm welcome to) / Throw back the little ones
CD _____ MCLD 19082
MCA / Nov '92 / BMG.

OLD REGIME
Brain tap shuffle / Come back baby / Don't let me in / Old regime / Brooklyn / Mock turtle song / Soul rain / I can't function / Yellow peril / Let George do it
CD _____ CDTB 040
Thunderbolt / May '87 / Magnum Music Group.

PRETZEL LOGIC
Rikki don't lose that number / Night by night / Any major dude will tell you / Barrytown / East St. Louis toodle-oo / Parker's band / Thru with buzz / Pretzel logic / With a gun / Charlie freak / Monkey in your soul
CD _____ MCLD 19081
MCA / Nov '91 / BMG.

ROARING OF THE LAMB
Charly / Jul '93 / Charly / THE / Cadillac.
CD _____ CDCD 1116

ROYAL SCAM, THE
Kid Charlemagne / Sign in stranger / Fez / Caves of Altmira / Don't take me alive / Green earring / Haitian divorce / Everything you did / Royal scam
CD _____ MCLD 19083
MCA / Nov '92 / BMG.

SPOTLIGHT ON STEELY DAN
Braintap shuffle / Come back baby / Don't let me in / Stone piano / Brooklyn / Mock turtle song / Soul ram / I can't function / Yellow peril / Let George do it / Parker's band / Any world (that I'm welcome to) / Barrytown / Ida Lee
CD _____ HADCD 103
Javelin / Feb '94 / THE / Henry Hadaway Organisation.

STONE PIANO
Android warehouse / Horse in town / More to come / Parker's band / Ida Lee / Stone piano / Any world (that I'm welcome to) / Take it out on me / This seat's been taken / Barrytown
CD _____ CDTB 054
Thunderbolt / Apr '88 / Magnum Music Group.

SUN MOUNTAIN
Berry town / Android warehouse / More to come / Sun mountain / Ida Lee / Any world (that I'm welcome to) / Stone piano / Caves of Altmira / Horse in town / Roaring of the lamb / Parker's band / Oh wow it's you / You go where I go / This seat's been taken / Little with sugar / Take it out on me
CD _____ CDTB 139
Magnum Music / Nov '92 / Magnum Music Group.

Steffen, Bruno

CITY OF GLASS (Steffen/Althaus Quartet)
CD _____ BRAM 199013-2
Brambus / Nov '93 / ADA / Direct.

IN BETWEEN (Steffen, Bruno & Heiner Althaus)
CD _____ BRAM 199237-2
Brambus / Nov '93 / ADA / Direct.

Steidl, Bernd

PSYCHO ACOUSTIC OVERTURE
Irrlichter / Metamorphosis / Cobra Negra / Jeux D'eau / Death of Ludwig II / Eine Kleine Bassmusik / Walburg's night / Papillon / La campanella / Will-O-The-Wisp / In Venice

Steig, Jeremy

JIGSAW
CD _____ RR 9204 2
Triloka / Jun '92 / New Note.

SOMETHING ELSE (Steig, Jeremy & Jan Hammer)
Home / Cakes / Swamp carol / Down stretch / Give me some / Come with me / Dance of the mind / Up tempo thing / Elephant hump / Rock No.6 / Slow blues in G / Rock No.9 / Something else
CD _____ DC 8512
Denon / '88 / Conifer.

Stein

KONIGZUCKER
CD _____ RTD 19516982
Our Choice / Mar '95 / Pinnacle.

Stein, Hal

CLASSIC SESSIONS (Stein, Hal & Warren Fitzgerald)
CD _____ PCD 7050
Progressive / Jun '93 / Jazz Music.

Stein, Ira

CAROUSEL
Briarcombe / High country / Continuum / Who's say / Carousel / Another country (another soul) / Open door / Place without words / Sevilla / Johnathan's lullaby
CD _____ ND 61033
Narada / Nov '92 / New Note / ADA.

SPUR OF THE MOMENT
Way back when / Fiddletown / Footsteps / Tributaries / Continuum II / La source / Spur of the moment / Winter wind / Pinnacles / Horseshoe hill / Dominique
CD _____ ND 63029
Narada / Jul '94 / New Note / ADA.

Steinman, Jim

BAD FOR GOOD
Bad for good / Lost boys and golden girls / Love and death and an American guitar / Stark raving love / Out of the frying pan (and into the fire) / Surf's up / Dance in my pants / Left in the dark
CD _____ 4720422
Epic / Oct '92 / Sony.

Stelin, Tena

SACRED SONGS
CD _____ WRCD 08
World / Sep '94 / Jetstar / Total/BMG.

SUN AND MOON (Stelin, Tena & Centry)
CD _____ DUBVCD 010
Dub Vintage / Dec '94 / Jetstar.

TAKE A LOOK AT THE WORLD
CD _____ DUBVCD 011
Dub Vintage / Dec '94 / Jetstar.

Steltch

RHYTHM OF BUST
CD _____ SON 003 2
Sonic Noise / Mar '93 / SRD.

Stendal Blast

WAS VERDURRT
CD _____ EFA 155842
Gymnastic / May '95 / SRD.

Stenson, Bobo

REFLECTIONS
Enlightener / My man's gone now / Not / Dorrmattan / Q / Reflections in D / 12 Tones old / Mindiatyr
CD _____ 5231602
ECM / Feb '96 / New Note.

SOUNDS AROUND THE HOUSE, THE
CD _____ 1206
Caprice / Jan '89 / CM / Complete / Pinnacle / Cadillac / ADA.

Stensson, Ewan

PRESENT DIRECTIONS
CD _____ DRCD 218
Dragon / Aug '87 / Roots / Cadillac / Wellard / CM / ADA.

Stephens, Anne

TEDDY BEARS PICNIC
CD _____ PASTCD 7067
Flapper / Jun '95 / Pinnacle.

Stephens, Richie

MIRACLES
CD _____ CRCD 48
Charm / Jan '96 / Jetstar.

Stephenson, Martin

BOAT TO BOLIVIA (Stephenson, Martin & The Daintees)
Colleen / Little red bottle / Tribute to the late Reverend Gary Davis / Running water / Candle in the middle / Piece of the cake / Look down, look down / Slow lovin' / Caroline / Rain / Crocodile crier / Boat to Bolivia / Slaughter man / Wholly humble heart
CD _____ KWCD 005
Kitchenware / Mar '87 / Sony / PolyGram / BMG.

BOY'S HEART, THE (Stephenson, Martin & The Daintees)
CD _____ 8283242
Kitchenware / Nov '92 / Sony / PolyGram / BMG.

SALUTATION ROAD (Stephenson, Martin & The Daintees)
Left us to burn / Endurance / In the heat of the night / Big North lights / Long hard road / Heart of the city / Too much in love / We are storm / Migrants / Morning time / Salutation Road
CD _____ 8281982
Kitchenware / Apr '90 / Sony / PolyGram / BMG.

SWEET MISDEMEANOUR (The Best Of Martin Stephenson & The Daintees)
CD _____ FIEND 770CD
Demon / Nov '95 / Pinnacle / ADA.

THERE COMES A TIME (Stephenson, Martin & The Daintees)
CD _____ 8283982
Kitchenware / Jul '93 / Sony / PolyGram / BMG.

YOGI IN MY HOUSE
CD _____ FIENDCD 762
Demon / Feb '95 / Pinnacle / ADA.

Steppenwolf

BORN TO BE WILD
CD _____ MPG 74016
Movieplay Gold / May '93 / Target/BMG.

MONSTER
CD _____ BGOCD 126
Beat Goes On / Sep '91 / Pinnacle.

Steppes

ALIVE ALIVE OH
CD _____ VOXXCD 2065
Voxx / Feb '92 / Else / Disc.

HARPS AND HAMMERS
CD _____ VOXXCD 2064
Voxx / Feb '91 / Else / Disc.

Steps Ahead

LIVE IN TOKYO 1986
Beirut / Oops / Self portrait / Sumo / Cajun / Safari / In a sentimental mood / Trains
CD _____ NYC 60062
NYC / May '94 / New Note.

N.Y.C.
Well in that case / Lust for life / Red neon, go or give / Charanga / Get it / N.Y.C. / Stick jam / Absolutely maybe / Festival paradiso
CD _____ INT 30072
Intuition / Apr '90 / New Note.

VIBE
Buzz / From light to light / Penn station / Vibe / Green dolphin street / Miles away / Staircase / Renezvous / Crunch / Waxing and wanning / Miles away reprise (the gentle giant)
CD _____ IVB 881AA
NYC / Feb '95 / New Note.

YIN YANG
CD _____ NYC 60012
NYC / Jul '92 / New Note.

Stereo Maximus

QUILOMBO
CD _____ ABB 028CD
Big Cat / Oct '91 / SRD / Pinnacle.

Stereo MC's

33-45-78
On 33 / Use it / Gee street / Neighbourhood / Toe to toe / What is soul / Use it (part 2) / Outta touch / Sunday 19th March / This ain't a love song / Ancient concept / On the mike / Back to the future
CD _____ IMCD 127
Island / Apr '91 / PolyGram.

CONNECTED
Connected / Ground level / Everything / Sketch / Fade away / All night long / Step it up / Playing with fire / Pressure / Chicken shake / Creation / End
CD _____ BRCD 589
4th & Broadway / Oct '92 / PolyGram.

SUPERNATURAL
I'm a believer / Scene of the crime / Declaration / Elevate my mind / What'cha gonna do / Two horse town / Ain't got nobody / Goin' back to the wild / Lost in music / Life on the line / Other side / Set me loose / What's the word / Early one morning / Smokin' with the motherman / Relentless
CD _____ IMCD 185
Island / Mar '94 / PolyGram.

Stereolab

EMPEROR TOMATO KETCHUP
CD _____ DUHFCD 11
Duophonic / Mar '96 / Disc.

GROOP PLAYED SPACE AGE BACHELOR PAD MUSIC, THE
Avant garde (M.O.R.) / Groop played chord X / Space age bachelor pad music (Mixes) / Ronco symphony / We're not adult orientated / UMF-MFP / We're not adult orientated (2)
CD _____ PURECD 019
Too Pure / Mar '93 / Vital.

MARS AUDIAC QUINTET
CD _____ DUHFCD 05
Duophonic / Aug '94 / Disc.

PENG
CD _____ PURECD 011
Too Pure / May '92 / Vital.

REFRIED ECTOPLASM
CD _____ DUHFCD 09
Duophonic / Sep '95 / Disc.

SWITCHED ON
Super electric / Doubt / Au grand jour / Way will be opening / Brittle / Contact / High expectation / Light that will cease to fail / Changer
CD _____ PURE 001
Too Pure / Apr '92 / Vital.

TRANSIENT RANDOM NOISE BURSTS
CD _____ DUHFCD 02
Duophonic / Sep '93 / Disc.

Stereotaxic Device

STEREOTAXIC DEVICE
CD _____ KK 046CD
KK / Jan '91 / Plastic Head.

Stern, Leni

LIKE ONE
Bubbles / Blue cloud / Jessie's song / Bruze / Every breath you take / Leave softly / Court and spark / Light out / Back out
CD _____ LIP 890712
Lipstick / Feb '95 / Vital/SAM.

SECRETS
CD _____ ENJA 50932
Enja / Mar '92 / New Note / Vital/SAM.

TEN SONGS
Miss V / Talk to me / Mary Ellen / If anything / Shooting star / Trouble / Our man's gone now / Sparrows / More trouble / Glass
CD _____ LIP 890092
Lipstick / Feb '95 / Vital/SAM.

WORDS
CD _____ LIP 890282
Lipstick / May '95 / Vital/SAM.

Stern, Peggy

PLEIADES (Stern, Peggy Trio)
CD _____ W 82-2
Philology / Apr '94 / Harmonia Mundi / Cadillac.

Stetson Stompers

COUNTRY LINE DANCING MUSIC
CD _____ RBCD 531
Sharpe / Oct '95 / Target/BMG.

Stevens, Cat

BUDDAH AND THE CHOCOLATE BOX
Music / Oh very young / Sun/C79 / Ghost town / Jesus / Ready to love / King of trees / Bad penny / Home in the sky
CD _____ IMCD 70
Island / Nov '89 / PolyGram.

CATCH BULL AT FOUR
Sitting / Boy with a moon and star on his head / Angelsea / Silent sunlight / Can't keep it in / 18th Avenue (Kansas City nightmare) / Freezing steel / O'Caritas / Sweet scarlet / Ruins
CD _____ IMCD 34
Island / Jul '89 / PolyGram.

EARLY TAPES
I love my dog / First cut is the deepest / Bad night / I'm so sleepy / Blackness of the night / School is out / Northern wind / View from the top / Come on and dance / Where are you / Granny / Moonstone / Ceylon city / Kitty
CD _____ 5501082
Spectrum/Karussell / Oct '93 / PolyGram / THE.

FOREIGNER
Foreigner suite / Hurt / How many times / Later / Hundred I dream
CD _____ IMCD 72
Island / Nov '89 / PolyGram.

GREATEST HITS: CAT STEVENS
Wild world / Oh very young / Can't keep it in / Hard headed woman / Moonshadow / Two fine people / Peace train / Ready / Father and son / Sitting / Morning has broken / Another Saturday night
CD _____ IMCD 168
Island / Mar '93 / PolyGram.

Stevens, John

NEW COOL
Do be up / You're life / 2 Free 1 / Du du's gone
CD _____ TJL 006CD
The Jazz Label / Oct '94 / New Note.

Stevens, Kenni

YOU
Who's been lovin' you / Hurt this way / Never gonna give you up / 24-7-365 / You don't know / I bleed for you / You / Didn't mean to hurt you / Work me up (Extra track on cassette & CD.) / Anne (Extra track on cassette & CD.)
CD _____ CDDB 502
Debut / May '88 / Pinnacle / 3MV / Sony.

Stevens, Meic

ER COF AM BLANT Y CWM
Er cof am blant y cwm / Yr eglwys ar y cei / Tafarn Elfed / Sabots Bernie / Morwen y medd / Yfory y plant / Angau opera ffug y clon / Mae gen i gariad / Bwda Bernie / Breniny bop / Iraq
CD _____ CRAICD 036
Crai / Mar '94 / ADA / Direct.

Y BALEDL
CD _____ SCD 2001
Sain / Feb '95 / Direct / ADA.

Stevens, Mike

JOY
CD _____ DOMECD 5
Dome / Oct '95 / 3MV / Sony.

Stevens, Ray

BEST OF RAY STEVENS, THE
Everything is beautiful / Mr. Businessman / Unwind / Yakety yak / Bridget the Midget / Gitarzan / Ahnnn name Innes / Turn your radio on / Mama and a papa / Moonlight special / Streak / Time for us (love theme from Romeo & Juliet) / She belongs to me / Young love / Raindrops keep falling on my head / Indian love call / Something / Leaving on a jet plane / Bye bye love / Misty
CD _____ MOCD 3011
More Music / Feb '95 / Sound & Media.

HIT SINGLE COLLECTABLES
CD _____ DISK 4510
Disky / Apr '94 / THE / BMG / Discovery / Pinnacle.

Stevens, Shakin'

ALL THE HITS
This ole house / Shirley / Don't turn your back / Teardrops / It's late / Because I love you / Little boogie woogie (in the back of my mind) / Sea of love / Heartbeat / Rockin' good way / Tired of toin' the line / Love worth waiting for / Shame, shame, shame / Hot dog / Oh Julie / You drive me crazy / This time / I'm knockin' / Give me your heart tonight / Lawdy Miss Clawdy / Letter to you/Blue Christmas / What do you want to make those eyes at me for / Josephine / Merry Christmas everyone / With my heart / Whatever will be will be (Que sera sera) / Endless sleep / Green door / Shape I'm in / I'll be satisfied / Marie Marie / Lonely blue boy / It's raining / I'm gonna sit right down and write myself a letter / Your Ma said you cried in your sleep last night / Cry just a little bit / Turning away / Breaking up my heart / Treat her right / Lipstick, powder and paint / Mona Lisa
CD Set _____ BOXD 46
Carlton Home Entertainment / May '94 / Carlton Home Entertainment.

Stevens, Shakin'

MONA BONE JAKON
Lady D'Arbanville / Maybe you're / Pop star / I think I see the light / Trouble / Mona bone jakon / I wish I wish / Katmandu / Fill my eyes / Timer / Time / Lillywhite
CD _____ IMCD 35
Island / '89 / PolyGram.

TEA FOR THE TILLERMAN
Where do the children play / Hard headed woman / Wild world / Sad Lisa / Miles from nowhere / But I might die tonight / Longer boats / Into white / On the road to find out / Father and son / Tea for the tillerman
CD _____ IMCD 36
Island / '89 / PolyGram.

TEASER AND THE FIRECAT
Wind / Ruby love / If I laugh / Changes IV / How can I tell you / Tuesday's dead / Morning has broken / Bitter blue / Moon shadow / Peace train
CD _____ IMCD 104
Island / Mar '90 / PolyGram.

VERY BEST OF CAT STEVENS, THE
Where do the children play / Wild world / Tuesday's dead / Lady D'Arbanville / First cut is the deepest / Oh very young / Ruby love / Morning has broken / Moonshadow / Matthew and son / Father and son / Can't keep it in / Hard headed woman / Old school yard / I love my dog / Another Saturday night / Sad Lisa / Peace train
CD _____ 8401482
Island / Jun '95 / PolyGram.

GREATEST HITS: SHAKIN' STEVENS

This ole house / You drive me crazy / Letter to you. A / It's raining / Green door / Hot dog / Teardrops / Breaking up my heart / Oh Julie / Marie Marie / Love worth waiting for / It's late / Give me your heart tonight / Shirley / Blue Christmas / Cry just a little bit / Rockin' good way / I'll be satisfied
CD _____ 4669932
Epic / Sep '93 / Sony.

HITS, THE VOL.1

This ole house / Shirley / Don't turn your back / Teardrops / It's late / Because I love you / Little boogie woogie (in the back of my mind) / Sea of love / Heartbeat / Rockin' good way / Tired of toin' the line / Love worth waiting for / Shame, shame, shame / Hot dog
CD _____ PWKS 4179
Carlton Home Entertainment / Oct '93 / Carlton Home Entertainment.

ROCK 'N' ROLL

CD _____ CDSR 044
Telstar / Feb '94 / BMG.

SHAKIN' STEVENS

Roll over Beethoven / White lightning / One night with you / Hi-heel sneakers / Tallahassee lassie / Yakety yak / Maybellene / Hearts made of stone / Good rockin' tonight / At the hop / Walking on the water / Rip it up / Saturday night rock
CD _____ PWK 045
Carlton Home Entertainment / Jul '90 / Carlton Home Entertainment.

SHAKIN' STEVENS

CD _____ GRF 234
Tring / Aug '93 / Tring / Prism.

SHAKY - THE HITS 2

Oh Julie / You drive me crazy / This time / I'm knockin' / Give me your heart tonight / Letter to you / Merry Christmas everyone / Blue Christmas / Whatever will be will be (Que sera sera) / Josephine / Lawdy Miss Clawdy / What do you want to make those eyes at me for / With my heart / Endless sleep
CD _____ PWKS 4185
Carlton Home Entertainment / Nov '93 / Carlton Home Entertainment.

SHAKY - THE HITS 3

CD _____ PWKS 4190
Carlton Home Entertainment / Mar '94 / Carlton Home Entertainment.

THIS OLE HOUSE

CD _____ 9829662
Pickwick/Sony Collector's Choice / Jun '93 / Carlton Home Entertainment / Pinnacle / Sony.

UNIQUE ROCK'N'ROLL CHRISTMAS, THE

Rockin' little Christmas / White Christmas / Sure won't seem like Christmas / I'll be home this Christmas / Merry Christmas everyone / Silent night / It's gonna be a lonely Christmas / Best Christmas of them all / Merry Christmas pretty baby / Christmas wish / Blue Christmas / So long Christmas
CD _____ 4692602
Epic / Nov '91 / Sony.

Stevenson, Savourna

CUTTING THE CHORD

Aeolian / Basse Breton rhapsody / Cutting the chord / Harplands / Blues in 10
CD _____ ECLCD 9308
Eclectic / Jan '96 / Pinnacle.

TUSITALA, TELLER OF TALES

CD _____ ECLCD 9412
Eclectic / Jan '96 / Pinnacle.

TWEED JOURNEY

Source / Fording the tweed / Waulk from the tweed / Lost bells / Trows and Cowdieknowes / Percussion solo / Forest flowers / Tweed journey
CD _____ ECLCD 9001
Eclectic / Jan '96 / Pinnacle.

Stewart Family

STEWARTS O'BLAIR (Stewart, Belle & Family)

Come a' you jolly Ploomen / Lakes of Shillin / Bonnie hoose o'Airlie / Moving on song / Nobleman / Jock Stewart / Inverness-shire / Banks of the Lee / Betsy belle / Dawning of the day / My dog and gun / Berryfields o'Blair / I'm no coming oot the noo / Mickey's warning / Hatton woods / Parting song / Canntaireachd
CD _____ OSS 06CD
Ossian / Aug '94 / ADA / Direct / CM.

Stewart, Al

24 CARAT

Running man / Midnight rocks / Constantinople / Merlin's time / Mondo sinistro / Murmansk run/Ellis Island / Rocks in the ocean / Paint by numbers / Optical illusion (CD only) / Here in Angola (CD only) / Indian summer (CD only) / Pandora (CD only) / Delia's gone (CD only) / Princess Olivia (CD only)
CD _____ CZ 512
EMI / Aug '92 / EMI.

BETWEEN THE WARS

Night train to Munich / Age of rhythm / Sampan / Lindy comes to town / Three mules / League of notions / Between the wars / Betty Boop's birthday / Marion the Chatelaine / Joe the Georgian / Always the cause / Laughing into 1939 / Black Danube
CD _____ CDEMC 3710
EMI / Jun '95 / EMI.

CHRONICLES - THE BEST OF AL STEWART

Year of the cat / On the border / If it doesn't come naturally, leave it / Time passages / Almost Lucy / Song on the radio (Not on album) / Running man (Not on album) / Merlin's time / In Brooklyn / Soho (needless to say) (Not on album) / Small fruit song / Manuscript / Roads to Moscow (live) / Nostradamus - Pt. 1 / World goes to Riyadh (Nostradamus - Pt. 2)
CD _____ CDEMC 3590
EMI / Apr '91 / EMI.

FAMOUS LAST WORDS

CD _____ PERMCD 15
Permanent / Nov '93 / Total/BMG.

LAST DAYS OF THE CENTURY

Last days of the century / Real and unreal / King of Portugal / Where are they now / License to steal / Josephine Baker / Antarctica / Ghostly horses of the plain / Red toupee / Bad reputation / Fields of France
CD _____ CDENV 505
Enigma / Sep '88 / EMI.

MODERN TIMES

CD _____ BGOCD 156
Beat Goes On / Nov '92 / Pinnacle.

ORANGE

CD _____ BGOCD 154
Beat Goes On / Nov '92 / Pinnacle.

PAST, PRESENT AND FUTURE

Old admirals / Warren Harding / Soho (needless to say) / Last day of June 1934 / Post World War Two blues / Roads to Moscow / Terminal blues / Nostradamus
CD _____ BGOCD 155
Beat Goes On / Sep '92 / Pinnacle.

RHYMES IN ROOMS

Flying sorcery / Soho (needless to say) / Time passages / Josephine Baker / On the border / Nostradamus / Fields of France / Clifton in the rain / Small fruit song / Broadway hotel / Leave it / Year of the cat
CD _____ CDFA 3315
Fame / Feb '95 / EMI.

RUSSIANS AND AMERICANS

Lori don't go right now / Don't go right now / Gypsy and the rose / Accident on 3rd street / Strange girl / Russians and Americans / Cafe society / 1-2-3 / Candidate
CD _____ CZ 523
EMI / Jul '93 / EMI.

TIME PASSAGES

Valentina way / Life in dark water / Man for all seasons / Almost Lucy / Time passages / Palace of Versailles / Timeless skies / End of the day / Song on the radio
CD _____ CDFA 3312
Fame / Dec '94 / EMI.

TO WHOM IT MAY CONCERN (Al Stewart 1966 - 1970)

Elf / Turn into earth / Bedsitter images / Swiss Cottage manoeuvres / Carmichaels / Scandinavian girl / Pretty golden hair / Denise at sixteen / Samuel, oh how you've changed / Cleave to me / Long way down from Stephanie / Ivich / Belecka doodle day / Lover man / Clifton in the rain / In Brooklyn / Old Compton Street blues / Ballad of Mary Foster / Life and life only / You should have listened to Al / Love chronicles / My enemies have sweet voices / Small fruit song / Gethsemane, again / Burbling / Electric Los Angeles sunset / Manuscript / Black Hill / Anna / Room of roots / Zero she flies
CD _____ CDEM 1511
EMI / Nov '93 / EMI.

YEAR OF THE CAT

Lord Grenville / On the border / Midas shadow / Sand in your shoes / If it doesn't come naturally, leave it / Flying sorcery / Broadway hotel / One stage before / Year of the cat
CD _____ CDFA 3253
Fame / Apr '91 / EMI.

Stewart, Amii

DESIRE

My heart and I / Desire / Hurry to me / Come sail away / Here's to you / Song for Elena / One love / Saharan dream / Sean Sean / Could heaven be
CD _____ MSCD 16
Music De-Luxe / Mar '95 / Magnum Music Group.

Stewart, Andy

ANDY STEWART COLLECTION - 20 SCOTTISH FAVOURITES

Scottish soldier / Dr. Finlay / Cambeltown Loch / Battle's o'er / Haughmann's Umbrella / I'm off to Bonnie Scotland / Road to the Isles / Scotland yet / Farewell 51st farewell / Muckin' O' Geordie's byre / Donald, where's yer troosers / Girl from Glasgow town / Ho ro my nut brown maiden / Tunes

of glory / Wild rover / Road and the miles to Dundee / Courtin' in the kitchen / Lassie come and dance with me / I love to wear a kilt / Going doon the water
CD _____ CDMFP 5700
EMI / Mar '93 / EMI.

ANDY STEWART'S SCOTLAND

CD _____ CDITV 563
Scotdisc / May '93 / Duncans / Ross / Conifer.

FOREVER IN SONG

Donald, where's yer troosers / Highlandman's umbrella / Lock Marie island / Lovely Stornoway / Dancing in kyle / Song of the Clyde / In praise of Islay / Rothesay bay / Joy of my heart / Loch Lomond / Stop your ticklin' jock / Roamin' in the gloamin' / Wee Deoch an' Doris / Keep right on to the end of the road / Away up in Clachan / Gordon for me / Jock McKay / My ain hoose / Westering home / Wild mountain thyme / Horee - horo / Wild rover / Waggle o' the kilt / It's nice to get up in the morning / Tobermoray / Safest o' the family / I' foo the noo / Wedding of Sandy McNab / Will ye no' come back again / Skye boat song / Come ower the stream, Charlie / Rise and follow Charlie / Take me back / Barren rocks of Aden / Farewell 51st farewell / Jock Cameron / bee baw babbity / Queen Mary / Height starvation song / Do re mi / Ye canny shove yer granny aff a bus / Andy where's yer kilt / Hiking song / Ho ro my nut brown maiden / Uist tramping song / Marching through the heather / I belong to Glasgow / Sailup up the Clyde / We've got a baby in the house / Ninety four this morning / Johnny Lad / Bonnie wee Jeannie McColl / Soor milk cairt / Wee toon clerk / Dashing white sergeant / Tartan ball / Lassie come and dance with me / Country dance / There was a lad / Polly Stewart / De'il's awa' wi' tha excise-man / Man's a man for a' that / Tartan / Campbells are coming / Johnny cope / Piper O'Dundee / Old Scottish waltz / Bonnie wells o'wearie / Back in bonnie Scotland / Bonnie Scotland / Haste ye back / Scotland the brave / We're no awa' tae bide awa' / Mairi's wedding / Thistle of Scotland / Muckin' O' Geordie's byre / Lass O'Fyvie / Nickie tams / Barnyards o'delgaty / Auld lang syne
CD _____ PLATCD 3921
Prism / Nov '93 / Prism.

Stewart, Andy M.

AT IT AGAIN (Stewart, Andy M. & Manus Lunny)

CD _____ GLCD 1107
Green Linnet / Feb '92 / Roots / CM / Direct / ADA.

BY THE HUSH

CD _____ GLCD 3030
Green Linnet / Oct '93 / Roots / CM / Direct / ADA.

DUBLIN LADY (Stewart, Andy M. & Manus Lunny)

Take her in your arms / Where are you / Dublin Lady / Freedom is like gold / Bogie's bonnie belle / Dinny the piper / Heart of the home / Humours of whiskey / Tak' it man tak' it
CD _____ GLCD 1083
Green Linnet / Feb '92 / Roots / CM / Direct / ADA.

FIRE IN THE GLEN (Stewart, Andy M./ Phil Cunningham/Manus Lunny)

CD _____ SHAN 79062 CD
Shanachie / Oct '89 / Koch / ADA / Greensleeves.

MAN IN THE MOON

CD _____ GLCD 1140
Green Linnet / Apr '94 / Roots / CM / Direct / ADA.

SONGS OF ROBERT BURNS

CD _____ GLCD 3059
Green Linnet / '92 / Roots / CM / Direct / ADA.

Stewart, Billy

THINK BEFORE YOU THINK

Think before you think / Faces / Dewey said / When you're smiling / Goodbye / Processional / I'm gettin' sentimental over you / Rain / Deed-Lee-Yah / Little Niles
CD _____ 66053024
Jazz City / Jun '91 / New Note.

Stewart, Bob

IN A SENTIMENTAL MOOD

CD _____ STCD 3
Stash / Jul '87 / Jazz Music / CM / Cadillac / Direct / ADA.

WELCOME TO THE CLUB (Stewart, Bob & Hank Jones)

Day in, day out / I'll never be the same / Body and soul / September in the rain / Don't misunderstood / Fools rush in / Then I'll be tired of you / Just friends / Did I remember / When Sunny gets blue / What a little moonlight can do / Love look away / Every time we say goodbye / Very thought of you
CD _____ CDLR 45017
L&R / Aug '90 / New Note.

Stewart, Dave

AS FAR AS DREAMS (Stewart, Dave & Barbara Gaskin)

CD _____ 900894
Line / Feb '95 / CM / Grapevine / ADA / Conifer / Direct.

AS FAR AS DREAMS CAN GO (Stewart, Dave & Barbara Gaskin)

Locomotion / Lenina Crowe / I'm losing you / Roads girdle the globe / Do I still figure in your life / When the guards are asleep / Make me promises / Do we see the light of day / As far as dreams can go
CD _____ BRCD 9008940
Broken / '88 / Broken.

BIG IDEA, THE (Stewart, Dave & Barbara Gaskin)

Levi Stubbs' tears / My scene / Grey skies / Subterranean homesick blues / Heatwave / Crying game / Deep underground / Shadowland / Mr. Theremin / New Jerusalem
CD _____ BRCD 9009330
Broken / '90 / Broken.

BROKEN RECORDS - THE SINGLES (Stewart, Dave & Barbara Gaskin)

I'm in a different world / Leipzig / It's my party / Johnny Rocco / Lenina and son / Busy doing nothing / Rich for a day / Waiting in the wings / Emperor's new guitar / Hamburger song / Henry and James / World spins so slow
CD _____ BRCD 9008900
Broken / '87 / Broken.

SELECTED TRACKS (Stewart, Dave & Barbara Gaskin)

CD _____ STIFFCD 24
Disky / Jan '94 / THE / BMG / Discovery / Pinnacle.

SPIN (Stewart, Dave & Barbara Gaskin)

Miles high / day / Cloths of heaven / Eight miles high / Ameila / Trash planet / Golden rain / Your lucky star / Cast your fate to the wind / Louie Louie / Sixties never die / Star blind
CD _____ BRCD 9011400
Broken / Aug '92 / Broken.

UP FROM THE DARK (Stewart, Dave & Barbara Gaskin)

I'm in a different world / Leipzig / It's my party / Lenina Crowe / Do I still figure in your life / Busy doing nothing / I'm losing you / Roads girdle the globe / When the guards are asleep / World spins so slow / Siamese cat song / Do we see the light of day / Henry and James / As far as dreams can go
CD _____ BRCD 10011
Broken / '86 / Broken.

Stewart, David A.

GREETINGS FROM THE GUTTER

Heart of stone / Greeting from the gutter / Crazy sister / Chelsea lovers / Jealousy / St. Valentine's day / kinky sweetheart / Damien save me / Tragedy street / You talk a lot / Oh no, not you again
CD _____ 450997546-2
East West / Sep '94 / Warner Music.

Stewart, Gary

GARY'S GREATEST

CD _____ HCD 8030
Hightone / Jun '94 / ADA / Koch.

I'M A TEXAN

CD _____ HCD 8050
Hightone / Jul '94 / ADA / Koch.

OUT OF HAND

Drinkin' thing / Honky tonkin' / I see the want to in your eyes / This old heart won't let go / Draggin' shackles / She's actin' single (I'm drinkin' doubles) / Back sliders' wine / Sweet country red / Out of hand / Williamson County
CD _____ HCD 8026
Hightone / Sep '94 / ADA / Koch.

Stewart, Grant

DOWNTOWN SOUNDS (Stewart, Grant Quintet)

CD _____ CRISS 1085CD
Criss Cross / May '94 / Cadillac / Harmonia Mundi.

Stewart, Jermaine

WORD IS OUT

Word is out / I like it / In love again / Debbie / Reasons why / Get over it / Month of Mondays / You / Spies / Brilliance
CD _____ CDPSRN 14
Siren / Dec '88 / EMI.

Stewart, John

AIRDREAM BELIEVER

CD _____ SHCD 8015
Shanachie / Aug '95 / Koch / ADA / Greensleeves.

CALIFORNIA BLOODLINES...PLUS

California bloodlines / Razor back woman / She believes in me / Omaha rainbow / Pirates of Stone County Road / Shackles and chains / Heart full of woman and a bellyful of Tenness / Willard / Big Joe / Mother

country / Lonesome picker / You can't look back / Missouri birds / July you're a woman / Never goin' back / Friend of Jesus / Marshall wind
CD _____ SEECD 87
See For Miles/C5 / May '91 / Pinnacle.

CALIFORNIA BLOODLINES/WILLARD MINUS TWO
California bloodlines / Razor back woman / She believes in me / Omaha rainbow / Pirates of Stone County Road / Shackles and chains / Mother Country / Some lonesome picker / You can't look back / Missouri birds / July you're a woman / Never goin' back / Big Joe / Julie / Judy angel role / Belly full of Tennessee / Friend of Jesus / Clack clack / Hero from the war / Back in Pomona / Willard / Golden rollin' belly / All American girl / Oldest living son / Earth rider
CD _____ BCD 15468
Bear Family / Jul '89 / Rollercoaster / Direct / CM / Swift / ADA.

CANNONS IN THE RAIN/WINGLESS ANGELS
Durango / Chilly winds / Easy money / Anna on a memory / All time woman / Road away / Armstrong / Spirit / Wind dies down / Cannons in the rain / Lady and the outlaw / Hung on your heart / Rose water / Wingless / Angels / Some kind of love / Survivors / Summer child / Josie / Rise stone blind / Mazatlan / Let the big horse run
CD _____ BCD 15519
Bear Family / Oct '90 / Rollercoaster / Direct / CM / Swift / ADA.

CHILLY WINDS
Folk Era / Dec '94 / CM / ADA.
CD _____ FE 1401CD

COMPLETE PHOENIX CONCERTS, THE
Wheatfield lady / Kansas rain / You can't look back / Pirates of Stone County Road / Runaway fool of love / Roll away the stone / July you're a woman / Last campaign trilogy / Oldest living son / Little road and a stone to roll / Kansas / Cody / California bloodlines / Mother country / Cops / Never goin' back / Freeway pleasure / Let the big horse run
CD _____ BCD 15518
Bear Family / Feb '91 / Rollercoaster / Direct / CM / Swift / ADA.

LONESOME PICKER RIDES AGAIN
Just an old love song / Road shines bright / Touch of the sun / Bolinas / Freeway pleasure / Swift lizard / Wolves in the kitchen / Little road and a stone to roll / Daydream believer / Crazy / Wild horse run / All the brave horses
CD _____ 900948
Line / Feb '95 / CM / Grapevine / ADA / Conifer / Direct.

PUNCH THE BIG GUY
Shanachie / Mar '94 / Koch / ADA / Greensleeves.
CD _____ SHCD 08009

SUNSTORM
Kansas rain / Cheyenne / Bring it on home / Sunstorm / Arkansas breakout / Account of Haley's comet / Joe / Light come shine / Lonesome John / Drive again
CD _____ 900946
Line / Feb '95 / CM / Grapevine / ADA / Conifer / Direct.

Stewart, Louis

OVERDRIVE
All the things you are / Lady be good / Polka dots and moonbeams / Oleo / Yesterdays / Stompin' at the savoy / Body and soul / Walkin' / My shining hour
CD _____ HEPCD 2057
Hep / Aug '94 / Cadillac / Jazz Music / New Note / Wellard.

Stewart, Mark

CONTROL DATA
Mute / Mar '96 / Disc.
CD _____ CDSTUMM 93

MARK STEWART
Survival / Survivalist / Anger / Hell is empty / Stranger / Forbidden colour / Forbidden (Dub) / Fatal / Attraction
CD _____ CD STUMM 43
Mute / Oct '87 / Disc.

METATRON
Mute / Apr '90 / Disc.
CD _____ CD STUMM 62

Stewart, Rex

CHATTER JAZZ (Stewart, Rex & Dickie Wells)
Little Sir Echo / Together / Let's call the whole thing off / Gimme a little kiss, will ya, huh / Show me the way to go home / Frankie and Johnny / Let's do it / I may be wrong, but I think you're wonderful / Thou swell / Side by side / Ain't we got fun / Jeepers creepers
CD _____ 74321185252
RCA Victor / Oct '94 / BMG.

INTRODUCTION TO REX STEWART 1920-41
Best Of Jazz / Dec '93 / Discovery.
CD _____ 4005

REX MEETS HORN (Stewart, Rex & Friends)
Jazz & Jazz / Jan '92 / Target/BMG.
CD _____ CDJJ 621

Stewart, Rod

AMAZING GRACE (Stewart, Rod & The Faces)
Reason to believe / Dirty old town / That's alright / Handbags and gladrags / Street fighting man / Sweet little rock 'n' roller / Cut across shorty / Sailor / Old raincoat won't ever let you down / Pinball wizard / It's all over now (live) / Jealous guy / Stay with me (Live) / Amazing grace
CD _____ 5500262
Spectrum/Karussell / May '93 / PolyGram / THE.

ATLANTIC CROSSING
Three times a loser / Alright for an hour / All in the name of rock 'n' roll / Drift away / Stone cold sober / I don't want to talk about it / It's not the spotlight / This old heart of mine / Still love you / Sailing
CD _____ K2 56151
WEA / '89 / Warner Music.

BEST OF ROD STEWART, THE
Maggie May / You wear it well / Baby Jane / Do ya think I'm sexy / Sailing / This old heart of mine / Sailing / I don't want to talk about it / You're in my heart / Young Turks / What am I gonna do (I'm so in love with you) / First cut is the deepest / Killing of Georgie / Tonight's the night / Every beat of my heart / Downtown train
CD _____ 9260342
WEA / '89 / Warner Music.

BLONDES HAVE MORE FUN
Do ya think I'm sexy / Dirty weekend / Ain't love a bitch / Best days of my life / Is that the thanks I get / Attractive female wanted / Blondes have more fun / Last summer / Standing in the shadows of love / Scarred and scared
CD _____ 7599273762
WEA / Jan '91 / Warner Music.

BODY WISHES
Dancin' alone / Baby Jane / Move me / Body wishes / Sweet surrender / What am I gonna do / Ghetto blaster / Ready now / Strangers / Again / Satisfied
CD _____ 9238772
WEA / Jul '84 / Warner Music.

CAMOUFLAGE
Infatuation / All right now / Some guys have all the luck / Can we still be friends / Bad for you / Heart is on the line / Camouflage / Trouble
CD _____ 9250952
WEA / Jul '84 / Warner Music.

COAST TO COAST - OVERTURES AND BEGINNERS (LIVE) (Stewart, Rod & The Faces)
It's all over now / Cut across shorty / Too bad / Angel / Stay with me / I wish it would rain / I'd rather go blind / Borstal boys / Jealous guy / Every picture tells a story / Amazing grace
CD _____ 832 128-2
Mercury / Nov '87 / PolyGram.

EARLY YEARS, THE
I just got some / Bright lights big city / Ain't that lovin' you baby / Mapper's blues / Why does it go on / Shake / Keep your hands off her / Don't you tell nobody / Just like I treat you / Day will come / Little Miss Understood / Come home baby
CD _____ ECD 3109
K-Tel / Jan '95 / K-Tel.

EVERY BEAT OF MY HEART
Who's gonna take me home / Another heartache / Night like this / Red hot in black / Here to eternity / Love touch / In my own crazy way / Every beat of my heart / Ten days of rain / In my life / Trouble
CD _____ 925446 2
WEA / Jul '86 / Warner Music.

EVERY BEAT OF MY HEART (Music Of Rod Stewart - 16 Instrumental Hits) (Various Artists)
Carlton Home Entertainment / Sep '94 / Carlton Home Entertainment.
CD _____ 5708574-338127

EVERY PICTURE TELLS A STORY
Every picture tells a story / Seems like a long time / That's alright / Amazing grace / Tomorrow is such a long time / Maggie May / Mandolin wind / I'm losing you / Reason to believe
CD _____ 8223852
Mercury / Aug '95 / PolyGram.

FACE OF SIXTIES
Telstar / Jun '93 / BMG.
CD _____ CDSR 014

FOOTLOOSE AND FANCY FREE
Hot legs / You're insane / You're in my heart / Born loose / You keep me hangin' on / (If loving you is wrong) I don't want to be right / You gotta nerve / I was only joking

CD _____ 9273232
WEA / Jun '89 / Warner Music.

GASOLINE ALLEY
Gasoline alley / It's all over now / Only a hobo / My way of giving / Country comfort / Cut across shorty / Lady Day / Jo's lament / I don't want to discuss it
CD _____ 8469982
Mercury / Aug '95 / PolyGram.

HANDBAGS AND GLADRAGS (The Mercury Recordings 1970-1974/2CD Set)
Mercury / Oct '95 / PolyGram.
CD _____ 5288232

JUST A LITTLE MISUNDERSTOOD
M Classics / Nov '92 / Grapevine.
CD _____ CJESD 2

LEAD VOCALIST
I ain't superstitious / Handbags and gladrags / Cindy incidentally / Stay with me / True Blue / Sweet lady Mary / Hot legs / Stand back / Ruby Tuesday / Shotgun wedding / First I look at the purse / Tom Traubert's blues
CD _____ 9362452582
WEA / Feb '93 / Warner Music.

MAGGIE MAY
Maggie May / Sailing / Oh no, not my baby / Street fighting man / It's all over now / Mandolin wind / Man of constant sorrow / Reason to believe / Twistin' the night away / Angel / Girl from the North Country / Sweet little rock 'n' roller
CD _____ PWKS 586
Carlton Home Entertainment / Jul '90 / Carlton Home Entertainment.

MAGGIE MAY
Maggie May / Oh no not my baby / Twistin' the night away / Mandolin wind / Jodie / I'd rather go blind / Cindy's lament / Seems like a long time / Country comfort / (I know) I'm losing you / I wouldn't ever change a thing / Blind prayer / Hard road / I've grown accustomed to her face
CD _____ 5511102
Spectrum/Karussell / Jul '95 / PolyGram / THE.

NEVER A DULL MOMENT
True blue / Los Paraguayos / Mama you been on my mind / Italian girls / Angel / Interludings / You wear it well / I'd rather go blind / Twistin' the night away
CD _____ 8262632
Mercury / Aug '95 / PolyGram.

NIGHT ON THE TOWN, A
Ball trap / Pretty flamingo / Big bayou / Wild side of life / Trade winds / Tonight's the night / First cut is the deepest / Fool for you / Killing of Georgie
CD _____ K2 56234
WEA / '89 / Warner Music.

OLD RAINCOAT WON'T LET YOU DOWN, AN
Street fighting man / Man of constant sorrow / Blind prayer / Handbags and gladrags / Old raincoat won't ever let you down, An / I wouldn't ever change a thing / Cindy's lament / Dirty old town
CD _____ 8305722
Mercury / Aug '95 / PolyGram.

ONCE IN A BLUE MOON
WEA / Nov '92 / Warner Music.
CD _____ 9362451172

ORIGINAL FACE, THE
I just got some bright lights / Big city / Ain't that lovin' you baby / Moppers blues / Why does it go on / Shake / Keep your hands off her / Don't you tell nobody / Just like I treat you / Day will come / Just a little misunderstood / Baby come home / Sparky rides / Can I get a witness / Baby take me
CD _____ CDTB 085
Thunderbolt / Sep '90 / Magnum Music Group.

OUT OF ORDER
Lost in you / Wild horse / Lethal dose of love / Forever young / My heart can't tell you no / Dynamite / Nobody knows you (when you're down and out) / Crazy about her / Try a little tenderness / When I was your man
CD _____ 9256842
WEA / Jul '92 / Warner Music.

SMILER
Sweet little rock 'n' roller / Lochnagar / Farewell / Sailor / Bring it on home to me / Let me be your car / (You make me feel like) a natural man / Dixie toot / Hard road / I've grown accustomed to her face / Girl from the North Country / Mine for me
CD _____ 8320562
Mercury / Aug '95 / PolyGram.

SPANNER IN THE WORKS
Windy town / Downtown lights / Leave Virginia alone / Sweetheart / This / Lady Luck / You're the star / Muddy, Sam and Otis / Hang on St. Christopher / Delicious / Soothe me / Purple heather
CD _____ 9362458672
Warner Bros. / May '95 / Warner Music.

STORYTELLER (Complete Anthology 1964-1990/4CD Set)
Good morning little school girl / Can I get a witness / Shake / So much to say / Little

Miss understood / I've been drinking / I ain't superstitious / Shapes of things / In a broken dream / Street fighting man / Handbags and gladrags / Gasoline alley / Cut across shorty / Country comforts / It's all over now / Sweet lady Mary / Had me a real good time / Maggie May / Mandolin wind / I'm losing you / Reason to believe / Every picture tells a story / Stay with me / True blue / Angel / You wear it well / I'd rather go blind / Twistin' the night away / What made Milwaukee famous (has made a loser out of me) / Oh no not my baby / Pinball wizard / Sweet little rock 'n' roller / Let me be your car / You can make me dance / Sing or anything / Sailing / I don't want to talk about it / Stone cold sober / To love somebody / Tonight's the night / First cut is the deepest / Killing of Georgie / Get back / Hot legs / I was only joking / You're in my heart / Do ya think I'm sexy / Passion / Oh God / I wish I was home tonight / Tonight I'm yours (don't hurt me) / Young turks / Baby Jane / What am I gonna do (I'm so in love with you) / People get ready / Some guys have all the luck / Infatuation / Love touch / Every beat of my heart / Lost in you / My heart can't tell you no / Dynamite / Crazy about her / Forever young / This old heart of mine / Downtown train
CD Set _____ 9259872
WEA / Nov '89 / Warner Music.

TONIGHT I'M YOURS
Tonight I'm yours / How long / Tora tora tora / Tear it up / Only a boy / Just like a woman / Jealous / Sonny / Young Turks / Never give up on a dream
CD _____ 7500236022
WEA / Jul '93 / Warner Music.

UNPLUGGED...AND SEATED
Hot legs / Tonight's the night / Handbags and gladrags / Cut across shorty / Every picture tells a story / Maggie May / Reason to believe / People get ready / Have I told you lately that I love you / Tom Traubert's blues / First cut is the deepest / Mandolin wind / Highgate shuffle / Stay with me / Having a party
CD _____ 936245289-2
WEA / May '93 / Warner Music.

UP ALL NIGHT
Warner Bros. / Apr '95 / Warner Music.
CD _____ 9362458672

VAGABOND HEART
Rhythm of my heart / Rebel heart / Broken arrow / It takes two / When a man's in love / You are everything / Motown song / Go out dancing / No holding back / Have I told you lately that I love you / Moment of glory / Downtown train / If only
CD _____ 7599265982
WEA / Mar '91 / Warner Music.

Stewart, Sandy

SONGS OF JEROME KERN (Stewart, Sandy & Dick Hyman)
Audiophile / Jun '95 / Jazz Music / Swift.
CD _____ ACD 247

Stewart, Slam

SHUT YO' MOUTH
Delos / Mar '91 / Conifer.
CD _____ DE 1024

SLAM STEWART MEMORIAL ALBUM (Stewart, Slam & Bucky Pizzarelli)
Stash / Sep '95 / Jazz Music / CM / Cadillac / Direct / ADA.
CD _____ STB 2507

TWO BIG NICE (Stewart, Slam & Major Holley)
Black & Blue / Apr '91 / Wellard / Koch.
CD _____ BLE 591242

Stewart, Tinga

TINGA STEWART RETURNS WITH THE DANCE HALL D.J'S
Northless duci / Hip hop / Best that I can / Love can make you happy / We can dance / Moon / Gal over dehso / Out of your spell / Dreams / Play reggae music / Street side junkie / Have you ever been in love / Reggae down town
CD _____ CY 78937
Nyam Up / Mar '95 / Conifer.

Stewart, Wendy

ABOUT TIME
Hip hip bouree / Pheasant feathers; Bonawe highlanders / Stirling castle / Rachel Rose / Harp song of the Dane women (Medley inc. Love like near me/The Burning bing/Petronella/Polska from Orumunga/Silent rains/Roslin Castle) / Miss Gordon of Gight / St. Bride's coracle; The streams of Abernethy / Puinneagan Cail; William Joseph Guppy / King's house; Wild west waltz
CD _____ CDTRAX 059
Greentrax / Jan '93 / Conifer / Duncans / ADA / Direct.

Stex

SPIRITUAL DANCE
Chapter 22 / Take this feeling / If I were you / Not coming back / Moses / Still feel the

rain / Inside out / Free this innocent soul /
Pray / Never gonna see me
CD _____ SBZCD 004
Some Bizarre / Sep '92 / Pinnacle.

Stickmen

MUSICA
CD _____ K 7041CD
Studio K7 / Feb '96 / Disc.

Stiefel, Christopher

ANCIENT LONGING
CD _____ JL 111412
Lipstick / May '95 / Vital/SAM.

Stiff Kittens

EAT THE PEANUT
CD _____ PSYC 4
Psychic / Aug '94 / Pinnacle / 3MV.

Stiff Little Fingers

ALL THE BEST (2CD Set)
Suspect device / Wasted life / Alternative
Ulster / 78 rpm / Gotta get away / Bloody
Sunday / Straw dogs / You can't say crap
on the radio / At the edge / Running bear /
White Christmas / Nobody's hero / Tin sol-
diers / Back to front / Mr. Fire coal man /
Just fade away / Go for it / Doesn't make it
alright / Silver lining / Gate 49 / Listen /
Sad eyed people / Two guitars clash / Listen /
That's when your blood bumps / Good for
nothing / Talkback / Stands to reason / Bits
of kids / Touch and go / Price of admission
CD Set _____ CDEM 1428
EMI / Oct '91 / EMI.

ALTERNATIVE CHARTBUSTERS
Suspect device (Live) / Alternative Ulster /
Gotta getaway (Live) / At the edge (Live) /
Nobody's heroes (Live) / Tin soldier (Live) /
Just fade away (Live) / Silver lining (Live) /
Johnny was / Last time (Live) / Mr. Fire
Coalman (Live) / Two guitars clash (Live)
CD _____ AOK 103
Plastic Head / Jan '92 / Plastic Head.

BBC LIVE IN CONCERT
Roots, radicals, rockers and reggae / Just
fade away / Safe as houses / Gate 49 / Hits
and misses / Only one / Silver lining / Piccadilly circus
CD _____ WINCD 037
Windsong / Jul '93 / Pinnacle.

FLAGS AND EMBLEMS
CD _____ DOJOCD 243
Dojo / Jul '95 / BMG.

FLY THE FLAGS
Long way to paradise / Roots, radicals,
rockers and reggae / Nobody's hero / No
surrender / Gotta getaway / Just fade away
/ Cosh / Johnny 7 / Barbed wire love /
Stand up and shout / Johnny was / Wasted
life / Beirut moon / Fly the flag / Suspect
device / Doesn't make it alright / Each dollar
a bullet / Alternative Ulster
CD _____ DOJOCD 75
Dojo / Nov '92 / BMG.

GET A LIFE
CD _____ ESSCD 210
Essential / Feb '94 / Total/BMG.

GO FOR IT
Just fade away / Go for it / Only one / Hit
and misses / Kicking up a racket / Safe as
houses / Gate 49 / Silver lining / Piccadilly
Circus / Back to front (Extra track on Fame
release.)
CD _____ DOJOCD 148
Dojo / Sep '93 / BMG.

GREATEST HITS LIVE
Alternative Ulster / Roots, radicals, rockers
and reggae / Silver lining / Wait and see /
Gotta getaway / Just fade away / Wasted
life / Nobody's heroes / At the edge / Listen
/ Barbed wire love / Fly the flag / tin soldiers
/ No sleep til belfast / Suspect device /
eAlternative Ulster
CD _____ DOJOCD 110
Dojo / May '93 / BMG.

HANX
Nobody's hero / Gotta getaway / Wait and
see / Barbed wire love / Fly the flag / Alter-
native Ulster / Johnny was / At the edge /
Wasted life / Tin soldiers / Suspect device
CD _____ CDFA 3215
Fame / Feb '89 / EMI.

INFLAMMABLE MATERIAL
Suspect device / State of emergency / Here
we are nowhere / Wasted life / No more of
that / Barbed wire love / White noise /
Breakout / Law and order / Johnny was /
Alternative Ulster / Closed groove
CD _____ CZ 165
EMI / Mar '89 / EMI.

NO SLEEP TILL BELFAST
Alternative Ulster / Roots, radicals, rockers
and reggae / Silver lining / Wait and see /
Gotta getaway / Just fade away / Wasted
life / Only one / Nobody's heroes / At the
edge / Listen / Barbed wire love / Fly the
flag / Tin soldiers / Johnny was
CD _____ CCSCD 318
Castle / Jun '92 / BMG.

NOBODY'S HEROES
Gotta getaway / Wait and see / Fly the flag
/ At the edge / Nobody's hero / Bloody dub
/ Doesn't make it alright / I don't like you /
No change / Suspect device / Tin soldiers
CD _____ CZ 166
EMI / Mar '89 / EMI.

NOW THEN
Falling down / Won't be told / Love of the
common people / Price of admission /
Touch and go / Bits of kids / Welcome to
the whole week / Big city nights / Talkback
/ Is that what you fought the war for
CD _____ CDFA 3306
Fame / Nov '94 / EMI.

**PEEL SESSIONS: STIFF LITTLE
FINGERS (2)**
Johnny was / Law and order / Barbed wire
love / Suspect device / Wait and see / At
the edge / Nobody's hero / Straw dogs / No
change / I don't like you / Fly the flag /
Doesn't make it all right
CD _____ SFRCD 106
Strange Fruit / Dec '89 / Pinnacle.

PURE FINGERS LIVE
Go for it / Nobody's hero / At the edge / No
surrender / Love of the common people /
What if I want more / Fly the flag / Piccadilly
Circus / Wasted life / When the stars fall
from the sky / Road to Kingdom come /
Stand up and shout / Smithers Jones /
Barbed wire love / Long way to paradise /
Gotta getaway / Suspect device / Walk tall
/ Tin soldiers / Alternative Ulster
CD _____ DOJOCD 224
Dojo / Mar '95 / BMG.

STIFF LITTLE FINGERS
CD _____ SFRCD 1
Strange Fruit / Nov '89 / Pinnacle.

Stiffs

NIX NOT NOTHING
Chelsea / Sad song / 250624 / Space noth-
ing / Fairy tales / Generation crap /
Engineering / Blow away baby / Work /
Quick Wotson / Mary Pickford / Die mother
die / Fear in the night
CD _____ 74321279692
American / Jul '95 / BMG.

Stigers, Curtis

TIME WAS
This time / Keep me from the cold / Every
time you cry / Anything you want / There's
more to making love (than layin' down) /
Time was / Ghost of you and me / It never
comes / Cry / Somebody in love / Big one
/ New York is rockin' / There will always be
a place
CD _____ 74321282792
Arista / Jun '95 / BMG.

Stigma A Go Go

IT'S ALL TRUE
CD _____ GROW 0312
Grass / Feb '95 / SRD.

Stills, Stephen

**DOWN THE ROAD (Stills, Stephen
Manassas)**
Isn't it about time / Lies / Pensamiento / So
many times / Business on the street / Do
you rember the Americans / Down the
road / City junkies / Guaguanco de vero /
Rollin' my stone
CD _____ 7567814242
Atlantic / '93 / Warner Music.

**LONG MAY YOU RUN (Stills, Stephen &
Neil Young)**
Long may you run / Make love to you / Mid-
night on the bay / Black coral / Ocean girl /
Let it shine / 12/8 blues / Fontaine bleau /
Guardian angel
CD _____ 759927230-2
Reprise / Jun '93 / Warner Music.

MANASSAS (Stills, Stephen Manassas)
Song of love / Crazies / Cuban bluegrass /
Jet set / Anyway / Both of us (bound to
lose) / Fallen eagle / Jesus gave love away
for free / Colorado / So begins the task /
Hide it so deep / Don't look at my shadow
/ It doesn't matter / Johnny's garden /
Bound to fall / How far / Move around /
Love gangster / What to do / Right now /
Treasure (take one) / Blues man
CD _____ 7567828082
Atlantic / Nov '95 / Warner Music.

RIGHT BY YOU
50/50 / Stranger / Flaming heart / Love
again / Can't let go / No problem / Grey to
green / Only love can break your heart / No
hiding place / Right by you
CD _____ 7567801772
Atlantic / Jun '93 / Warner Music.

STEPHEN STILLS
Love the one you're with / Do for the others
/ Church (part of someone) / Old times,
good times / Go back home / Sit yourself
down / To a flame / Black Queen / Chero-
kee / We are not helpless
CD _____ 7567828092
Atlantic / Nov '95 / Warner Music.

Stiltskin

MIND'S EYE, THE
CD _____ WWD 1
White Water / Oct '94 / Sony / 3MV.

Stimela

KHULULANI
Siyaya phambili / Never seem to learn /
Song of hope / Song tells a story / Go on
living your life / Part to play / Khululani /
Confusion / Colours and shades / Take me
to the top / Nothing matters / You're the
one I love
CD _____ FLTRCD 506
Flame Tree / Feb '93 / Pinnacle.

Sting

BRING ON THE NIGHT
Bring on the night / Consider me gone /
Low life / We work the black seam / Driven
to tears / Dream of the blue turtles / Demolition man / One world / Love is the seventh wave / Moon over Bourbon Street / I
burn for you / Another day / Children's crusade / I've been down so long / Tea in the
Sahara
CD _____ CDMID 192
A&M / May '94 / PolyGram.

DREAM OF THE BLUE TURTLES, THE
If you love somebody set them free / Love
is the seventh wave / We work the black
seam / Russians / Children's crusade /
Shadows in the rain / Consider me gone /
Dream of the blue turtles / Moon over Bour-
bon Street / Fortress around your heart
CD _____ DREMD 1
A&M / Jun '85 / PolyGram.

**FIELDS OF GOLD - THE BEST OF
STING 1984-1994**
When we dance / If you love somebody set
them free / Fields of gold / They dance
alone (Queca solo) / If I ever lose my faith
in you / We'll be together / Nothing 'bout
me / Fragile / Englishman in New York / All
this time / Seven days / Mad about you /
Russians / Love is the seventh wave / It's
probably me / Demolition man / This cowboy song
CD _____ 5403072
A&M / Nov '94 / PolyGram.

NOTHING LIKE THE SUN
Lazarus heart / Be still my beating heart /
Englishman in New York / History will teach
us nothing / They dance alone / Fragile /
We'll be together / Straight to my heart /
Rock steady / Sister Moon / Little wing /
Secret marriage
CD _____ CDA 6402
A&M / Oct '87 / PolyGram.

SOUL CAGES, THE
Island of souls / All this time / Mad about
you / Jeremiah blues (Part 1) / Why should
I cry for you / Saint Agnes and the burning
train / Wild wild sea / Soul cages / When
the angels fall
CD _____ 396 405 2
A&M / Jan '91 / PolyGram.

TEN SUMMONER'S TALES
Prologue (If I ever lose my faith in you) /
Love is stronger than justice (The magnificent seven) / Fields of gold / Heavy cloud
no rain / She's too good for me / Seven
days / St. Augustine in hell / It's probably
me / Everybody laughed but you / Shape of
my heart / Something the boy said /
Epilogue (Nothing 'bout me)
CD _____ 540075-2
A&M / Mar '93 / PolyGram.

Stinga, Paul

**CHARMS OF THE ROMANIAN MUSIC
(Stinga, Paul & His Orchestra)**
Sirba de la seaca / Batrineasca / Tara-
neasca de la burau Jeni / Suite de Moldavie
I / Suite de Moldavie II / Purtata de la bis-
trica / Suite de muntenie / Hora din raso-
miresti / Joc din bihor / Suite de banat /
Suite de Transilvanie
CD _____ PV 787021
Disques Pierre Verany / May '87 / Kingdom.

Stitt, Sonny

AUTUMN IN NEW YORK
Stardust / Cherokee / Autumn in New York
/ Gypsy / Lover man / Matterhorns / Hello /
Nightwork
CD _____ BLCD 760130
Black Lion / Apr '90 / Jazz Music / Cadillac
/ Wellard / Koch.

BACK IN MY OWN HOME TOWN
(I'm afraid) the masquerade is over / Dozy
free / I can't get started (with you) / My little
suede shoes / Simon's blues / Streamline
Stanley / There will never be another you
CD _____ BLE 597542
Black & Blue / Dec '90 / Wellard / Koch.

**BATTLE OF THE SAXES (Stitt, Sonny &
Richie Cole)**
CD _____ AIM 1010CD
Aim / Oct '93 / Direct / ADA / Jazz Music.

CHAMP, THE
Champ / Sweet and lovely / Midgets / Eternal triangle / All the things you are / Walkin'

CD _____ MCD 5429
Muse / Sep '92 / New Note / CM.

CONSTELLATION
Constellation / I don't stand a ghost of a
chance with you / Webb City / By accident
/ Ray's idea / Casbah / It's magic / Topsy
CD _____ MCD 5323
Muse / Sep '92 / New Note / CM.

**GOOD LIFE, THE (Stitt, Sonny & The
Hank Jones Trio)**
Deuces wild / Autumn leaves / Angel eyes
/ Bye bye blackbird / Polka dots and moon-
beams / My funny valentine / As time goes
by / Ain't misbehavin' / Good life / Body and
soul
CD _____ ECD 220082
Evidence / Jun '94 / Harmonia Mundi / ADA
/ Cadillac.

**JUST FRIENDS (Stitt, Sonny & Red
Holloway)**
Way you look tonight / Forecast / You don't
know what love is / Getting sentimental
over you / Lester leaps in / Just friends / All
God's chillun got rhythm
CD _____ LEJAZZCD 40
Le Jazz / May '95 / Charly / Cadillac.

LAST STITT SESSIONS VOLS. 1 & 2
CD _____ MCD 6003
Muse / Sep '92 / New Note / CM.

MADE FOR EACH OTHER
CD _____ DD 426
Delmark / Jun '87 / Hot Shot / ADA / CM /
Direct / Cadillac.

MOONLIGHT IN VERMONT
West 46th Street / Who can I turn to /
Moonlight in Vermont / Flight cap blues / It
might as well be Spring / Constellation /
Blues for P.C.M.
CD _____ DC 8566
Denon / '90 / Conifer.

**SONNY'S BLUES (Archive Series - Live
At Ronnie Scott's)**
Ernest's blues / Home sweet home / Mother
/ My Mother's eyes / Sonny's theme song
/ Blues with Dick and Harry / It could hap-
pen to you / Oh Lady be good
CD _____ JHAS 603
Ronnie Scott's Jazz House / Jun '95 / Jazz
Music / Magnum Music Group / Cadillac.

**THERE IS NO GREATER LOVE (Stitt,
Sonny, Harry 'Sweets' Edison & Eddie
'Lockjaw' Davis)**
CD _____ JHR 73557
Jazz Hour / Jan '93 / Target/BMG / Jazz
Music / Cadillac.

TUNE UP
Tune-up / I can't get started (with you) /
Idaho / Just friends / Blues for Prez and Bird
/ Groovin' high / I got rhythm
CD _____ MCD 5334
Muse / Jun '93 / New Note / CM.

Stivell, Alan

A LANGONNET
CD _____ FDM 36203
Dreyfus / Oct '94 / ADA / Direct / New
Note.

AGAIN
CD _____ FDM 36198-2
Dreyfus / Oct '93 / ADA / Direct / New
Note.

BRIAN BORU
Brian Boru / Let the plinn / Mna na heireann
/ Ye banks and braes o' bonnie Doon / Mai-
ri's wedding / Ceasefire / De ha bla / Sword
dance / Parlamant lament / Lands of my
fathers
CD _____ FDM 362082
Dreyfus / Jul '95 / ADA / Direct / New Note.

CELTIC SYMPHONY (Tir Na Nog)
Journey to inner spaces / Nostalgia for the
past and future / Song and profound lake
that I interrogate / Dissolution in the great
all / Regaining consciousness / Vibratory
communion with the universe / In quest of
the Isle / Landing on the isle of the pure
world / First steps on the Isle / Discovery of
the radiant city / March towards the city /
Universal festival / Sudden return to the
relative and interrogative world
CD _____ CD 11523
Rounder / '88 / CM / Direct / ADA / Cadillac.

CHEMINS DE TERRE
CD _____ FDM 36202
Dreyfus / Oct '94 / ADA / Direct / New
Note.

HARPE CELTIQUE
CD _____ FDM 36200
Dreyfus / Oct '94 / ADA / Direct / New
Note.

HARPES DU NOUVEL AGE
CD _____ FDM 36206
Dreyfus / Oct '94 / ADA / Direct / New
Note.

JOURNEE A LA MAISON
CD _____ DRYF 8343164 2
Dreyfus / Jan '93 / ADA / Direct / New
Note.

LEGENDE
CD _____ FDM 36205
Dreyfus / Oct '94 / ADA / Direct / New Note.

REFLETS
CD _____ FDM 36201
Dreyfus / Oct '94 / ADA / Direct / New Note.

TERRE DES VIVANTS
CD _____ FDM 36204
Dreyfus / Oct '94 / ADA / Direct / New Note.

Stoa

URTHONA
CD _____ HY 39100592
Hyperium / Jul '93 / Plastic Head.

Stockhausen, Markus

COSI LONTANO...QUASI DENTRO (So Far Almost Inside)
CD _____ 8371112
ECM / Feb '89 / New Note.

POSSIBLE WORLDS
CD _____ CMPCD 68
CMP / Sep '95 / Vital/SAM.

SOL MESTIZO
Creation / Takirari / Emanacion / Reconciliation / Vanguardia / La conquista / In your mind / Adentro / Davindad / Zampona / Canto indio / Refelxion / Loncanao / Queca / Desolacion / Asfalto
CD _____ 92???
Act / Feb '96 / New Note.

TAGTRAUM (Stockhausen, Markus & Simon)
Glocken / Kuche / Passacaglia / Himmel auf / Ungewitter / Gamelan / Weltraum / Ping pong / Klangduo / Feuerwerk / Yeah / Zwei Bruder / Gran finale / Tagtraum / Miles mute / Wustenwind / Esprit / Bumerang
CD _____ UBM 1139
New Note / Dec '92 / New Note / Cadillac.

Stockholm Jazz Orchestra

JIGSAW
CD _____ DRCD 213
Dragon / Jan '88 / Roots / Cadillac / Wellard / CM / ADA.

Stockton's Wing

CROOKED ROSE, THE
Master's daughter / Some fools cry / Aaron's key / When you smiled / Angel / Humours of Clonmult / Black Hill / Prince's feather / Chasing down a rainbow / Catalina / Lonesome road / Stars in the morning East
CD _____ TARACD 3028
Tara / May '92 / CM / ADA / Direct / Conifer.

LETTING GO
Letting go / Maids of Castlebar / Jig mayhem / Another day / All the time / Eastwood / Rossclogher jigs / I'll believe again / Anyone out there / Sliabh Lucan polkas / Hold you forever
CD _____ TARA 3036
Tara / Nov '95 / CM / ADA / Direct / Conifer.

Stoddart, Pipe Major

GREATEST PIPERS VOL. 3
CD _____ LS 5151CD
Lismor / Apr '95 / Lismor / Direct / Duncans / ADA.

PIPERS OF DISTINCTION
CD _____ CDMON 806
Monarch / Jul '90 / CM / ADA / Duncans / Direct.

WORLD'S GREATEST PIPERS VOL. 3
CD _____ LCOM 5151
Lismor / Sep '95 / Lismor / Direct / Duncans / ADA.

Stojiljkovic, Jova

BLOW 'BESIR' BLOW
CD _____ CDORBD 038
Globestyle / Feb '96 / Pinnacle.

Stokes, Frank

CREATOR OF THE MEMPHIS BLUES
CD _____ YAZCD 1056
Yazoo / Jun '91 / CM / ADA / Roots / Koch.

FRANK STOKES DREAM (Memphis blues anthology)
CD _____ YAZCD 1008
Yazoo / Mar '92 / CM / ADA / Roots / Koch.

VICTOR RECORDINGS - 1928-29, THE
CD _____ DOCD 5013
Blues Document / Feb '92 / Swift / Jazz Music / Hot Shot.

Stoller, Rhet

EMBER LANE
Travelling song / Perpetual Summer / Sea breeze / Concerto for a rainbow / Lucky five / Ember lane / Tree top woman / Sandy's rave up / Ocean serenade / Down the line

---

CD _____ SEECD 348
See For Miles/C5 / Jul '92 / Pinnacle.

Stomp That Pussy

HATE IS THE MOVE
CD _____ LF 057
Lost & Found / Jan '94 / Plastic Head.

Stone

EMOTIONAL PLAYGROUND
Small tales / Home base / Last chance / Above the grey sky / Mad Hatter's den / Dead end / Adrift / Haven / Years after / Time dive / Missionary of charity / Emotional playground
CD _____ 8410562
Black Mark / Feb '92 / Plastic Head.

Stone Age

STONE AGE
Stoneage / Zo laret / Kervador / Ultra breizh / Yesterday's child / Kalon Marie / Sellet / Reel legend / Stone transe / Til plad
CD _____ 4772742
Columbia / Sep '95 / Sony.

Stone Age Project

FLINTSTONES, THE
Meet the Flintstones / Human Being (Bedrock Steady) / Hit and run holiday / Prehistoric daze / Rock with the caveman / I showed a caveman how to rock / Bedrock twitch / I wanna be a flintstone / In the days of the caveman / Anarchy in the U.K. / Walk the dinosaur / Bedrock anthem / Mesozic music
CD _____ AAOHP 93552
Start / Oct '94 / Koch.

Stone, Billy

WEST TEXAS SKY
Brand new shade of red / Into every life (A little love must fall) / When two people meet / Just like a diamond / West Texas sky / Was you / Pictures never lie / You just don't know what you've got / Holmes county home / Miz Leah / Family reunion / My heart jumped over the moon / All love needs / Love love love / That empty chair / Last Dallas cowboy / Walter petty / What in the world (Is this coming to) / This old / Grandma's old gas stove / Master electrician / Ain't no telling what a fool will do / What are we trying to prove / Sight for sore ears / Little brother
CD _____ BCD 15736
Bear Family / May '93 / Rollercoaster / Direct / CM / Swift / ADA.

Stone By Stone

I PASS FOR HUMAN
CD _____ SST 247 CD
SST / Jul '89 / Plastic Head.

Stone, Carl

MOM'S
CD _____ NA 049 CD
New Albion / Nov '92 / Harmonia Mundi / Cadillac.

Stone, Cliffie

TRANSCRIPTIONS - 1945-49
Draggin' the bow / Beautiful brown eyes / Mine all mine / Mule skinner blues / Little cabin home on the hill / Blue steel blues / Stuck up blues / Mandolin boogie / Bill Cheatham / Red's boogie / Freight train blues / After you've gone / Flop eared mule / Sugar hill / Cactus set-up / Daughter of Jolie Blon / Steel guitar rag / Free little bird / Honky tonkin' / Lady be good / Sally Goodin / Little rock getaway
CD _____ RFDCD 08
Country Routes / Oct '91 / Jazz Music / Hot Shot.

Stone, Doug

FROM THE HEART
Warning labels / Made for lovin' you / Leave me the radio / This empty house / Why didn't I think of that / Ain't your memory got no pride at all / Workin' end of a hoe / Too busy being in love / She's got a future in the movies / Left, leaving, goin' or gone
CD _____ 472131-2
Epic / Jan '93 / Sony.

Stone Funkers

HARDER THAN KRYPTONITE
Here we go-go / Talk / Bassrace / Sucker 4 your love / Message from da falcon / S.T.O.N.E.F.U.N.K. Theme / Rock city / Good time / We come to party / Slam da phunk / Massive party / Can U follow
CD _____ 9031715022
WEA / Jul '91 / Warner Music.

Stone, Lew

CREAM OF LEW STONE & HIS BAND, THE (Stone, Lew & His Band)
Undecided / Ups and downs / Coffee in the morning / Moon remembered, but you forgot / Shades of Hades / Flat foot floogie /

Apple blossom time / Why waste your tears / Nine pins in the sky / Dark clouds / Serenade for a wealthy widow / There's something wrong with the weather / Frog on the water-lily / Get happy / I get along without you very well / I want the waiter (with the water) / Lonely / Beale Street blues / Louisiana hayride / My wubba Dolly / Music maestro please / St. Louis blues
CD _____ PASTCD 7041
Flapper / Mar '94 / Pinnacle.

DINNER AND DANCE - 1937-39 (Stone, Lew & His Band)
CD _____ CDSVL 216
Saville / Oct '91 / Conifer.

RIGHT FROM THE HEART (Stone, Lew & His Orchestra)
CD _____ DOLD 3
Old Bean / Sep '93 / Jazz Music / Wellard.

Stone Roses

COMPLETE STONE ROSES, THE
So young / Tell me / Sally Cinnamon / All across the sands / Here it comes / Elephant stone / Full fathom five / Hardest thing in the world / Made of stone / Going down / She bangs the drum / Mersey paradise / Standing here / I wanna be adored / Waterfall / I am the resurrection / Where angels play / Fool's gold / What the world is waiting for / Something burning / One love
CD _____ ORECD 535
Silvertone / May '95 / Pinnacle.

SECOND COMING
Breaking into heaven / Driving South / Ten storey love song / Daybreak / Your star will shine / Straight to the man / Begging you / Tightrope / Good times / Tears / How do you sleep / Love spreads
CD _____ GED 24503
Geffen / Dec '94 / BMG.

STONE ROSES
I wanna be adored / Waterfall / She bangs the drum / Don't stop / Bye bye badman / Elizabeth my dear / (Song for my) Sugar spun sister / Made of stone / Shoot you down / This is the one / I am the resurrection
CD _____ ORECD 502
Silvertone / Mar '89 / Pinnacle.

TURNS INTO STONE
CD _____ ORECD 521
Silvertone / Jun '92 / Pinnacle.

WHAT A TRIP
CD P.Disc _____ CBAK 4045
Baktabak / Jan '91 / Baktabak.

Stone, Roland

REMEMBER ME
Go on feel / Lovey dovey / She's the one / Try the impossible / You can make it if you try / Remember me / Please don't leave me / Down the road / (I'm afraid) the masquerade is over / Ain't gonna do it
CD _____ 879372
Sky Ranch / Oct '93 / New Note.

Stone, Sly

AIN'T NOTHING BUT THE ONE WAY
CD _____ 7599237002
WEA / Jan '96 / Warner Music.

BACK ON THE RIGHT TRACK (Sly & The Family Stone)
Remember who you are / Back on the right track / If it's not addin' up / Same thing / It takes all kinds / Who's to say / Sheer energy
CD _____ 7599268582
WEA / Jan '96 / Warner Music.

BEST OF SLY AND THE FAMILY STONE (Sly & The Family Stone)
Dance to the music / I want to take you higher / Thank you (falettinme be mice elf agin) / I get high on you / Stand / M'lady / Skin I'm in / Everyday people / Sing a simple song / Hot fun in the summertime / Don't call me nigger, whitey / Brave and strong / Life / Everybody is a star / If you want me to stay / (You caught me) smilin' / Whatever will be will be (Que sera sera) / Running away / Family affair (Mixes)
CD _____ 4717582
Epic / Jul '92 / Sony.

COLLECTION: SLY & THE FAMILY STONE (Sly & The Family Stone)
CD _____ CCSCD 307
Castle / Sep '91 / BMG.

DANCE TO THE MUSIC (Sly & The Family Stone)
You're my only love / Heavenly angel / Oh what a night / You've forgotten me / Yellow moon / Honest / Nerves / Help me with my broken heart / Long time alone / Uncle Sam needs you my friend
CD _____ CDTB 1.029
Thunderbolt / Nov '87 / Magnum Music Group.

DANCE TO THE MUSIC (Sly & The Family Stone)
CD _____ 4809062
Epic / Jul '94 / Sony.

EVERY DOG HAS ITS DAY (Sly & The Family Stone)
CD _____ CDSGP 0125
Prestige / Dec '94 / Total/BMG.

FAMILY AFFAIR (Sly & The Family Stone)
My woman's head / New breed / As I get older / Somethin' bad / Fire in my heart / She's my baby / Free as a bird / Girl won't you go / Everything I need / Why can't you stay / Off the hook / Dance your pants off / Under the influence of love / Crazy love song / Seventh son
CD _____ CDTB 119
Thunderbolt / Apr '91 / Magnum Music Group.

GREATEST HITS: SLY & THE FAMILY STONE (Sly & The Family Stone)
I want to take you higher / Everybody is a star / Stand / Life / Fun / You can make it if you try / Dance to the music / Everyday people / Hot fun in the summertime / M'lady / Sing a simple song / Thank you (falettinme be mice elf agin)
CD _____ 4625242
Epic / Sep '90 / Sony.

IN THE STILL OF THE NIGHT (Sly & The Family Stone)
In the still of the night / Searchin' / Don't say I didn't warn you / Ain't that lovin' you baby / Swim / Every dog has his day / Suki suki (pts 1 & 2) / Seventh son / I can't turn you loose / Take my advice / Watermelon man / I ain't got nobody / I you were blue / Rock dirge / High love / Life of fortune and fame
CD _____ CDTB 129
Thunderbolt / Sep '91 / Magnum Music Group.

PEARLS FROM THE PAST - SLY STONE
CD _____ KLMCD 005
Scratch / Nov '93 / BMG.

PRECIOUS STONE: IN THE STUDIO WITH SLY STONE 1963-65 (Various Artists)
Swim / Scat swim / I taught him / Don't say I didn't warn you / Help me with my broken heart / Out of sight / Nerve of you / Every dog has his day / On Broadway / Searchin' / Lord, Lord / Seventh son / Jerk / That little old heartbreaker / I'll never fall in love again / Ain't that lovin' you baby / Buttermilk / Fake / Laugh / Little lupe lu / Dance all night / Temptation walk / Underdog / Radio spot / Can't you tell I love her / Life of fortune and fame / Take my advice / As I get older
CD _____ CDCHD 539
Ace / Aug '94 / Pinnacle / Cadillac / Complete/Pinnacle.

SHINE IT ON (Sly & The Family Stone)
Shine it on / Back on the right track / It takes all kinds / Do the rattleshake / Seventh son / Searchin' / Swim / Google eyes / Somebody to you / Things that'll make you laugh / If it's not addin' up / Buttermilk (part 1) / Remember who you are / In the still of the night / Ain't that lovin' you baby
CD _____ 16222CD
Success / Sep '94 / Carlton Home Entertainment.

SPOTLIGHT ON SLY & FAMILY STONE (Sly & The Family Stone)
Honest / Ain't that lovin' you baby / Watermelon man / Hi love / Life of fortune and fame / Don't say I didn't warn you / Take my advice / In the still of the night / If you were blue / Searchin' / Every dog has his day / I ain't got nobody (for real) / Seventh son / I can't turn you loose / Swim / Nerves
CD _____ HADCD 119
Javelin / Feb '94 / THE / Henry Hadaway Organisation.

STAND (Sly & The Family Stone)
Stand / Don't call me nigger, Whitey / I want to take you higher / Somebody's watching you / Sing a simple song / Everyday people / (Get up I feel like being a) sex machine / You can make it if you try
CD _____ EK 64422
Epic / Feb '95 / Sony.

THERE'S A RIOT GOIN' ON (Sly & The Family Stone)
Luv 'n' Haight / Just like a baby / Poet / Family affair / Africa talks to you - The Asphalt Jungle / There's a riot goin' on / Time / Spaced cowboy / Running away / Thank you for talking to me Africa
CD _____ 467063 2
Epic / Apr '94 / Sony.

WHOLE NEW THING, A (Sly & The Family Stone)
Underdog / If this room could talk / Run run run / Turn me loose / Let me hear it from you / Advice / I cannot make it / Trip to your heart / I hate to love her / Bad risk / That kind of person / Dog
CD _____ EK 66424
Epic / Jul '95 / Sony.

Stone Temple Pilots

CORE
Dead and bloated / Sex type thing / Wicked garden / No memory / Sin / Naked Sunday

647

/ Creep / Piece of pie / Plush / Wet my bed / Crackerman / Where the river goes
CD _____ 7567824182
WEA / Nov '92 / Warner Music.

PURPLE
Meat plow / Vasoline / Lounge fly / Interstate love song / Still remains / Pretty penny / Silvergun superman / Big empty / Unglued / Army ants / Kitchenware and candy bars
CD _____ 756782607-2
WEA / Jun '94 / Warner Music.

Stone The Crows

STONE THE CROWS
Big Jim Salter / Love 74 / Touch of your loving hand / Sad Mary / Good time girl / On the highway / Mr. Wizard / Sunset cowboy / Raining in your heart / Seven lakes
CD _____ CDTB 070
Thunderbolt / Jun '89 / Magnum Music Group.

Stoneflow

SCULPTURE
CD _____ CC 027054CD
Shark / May '95 / Plastic Head.

Stoneham, Harry

LIVE AT ABBEY ROAD (Stoneham, Harry Trio)
Oh lady be good / My foolish heart / Jersey bounce / East of the sun and west of the moon / I should care / Harlem nocturne / Strike up the band / Out of nowhere / Georgia on my mind / How high the moon / (Back home again in) Indiana / Moonlight in vermont / Now is the time
CD _____ GRCD 55
Grasmere / Oct '92 / Target/BMG / Savoy.

Stop

NEVER
CD _____ FOR 0010
Backs / Feb '96 / Disc.

Storey, Liz

ESCAPE OF THE CIRCUS PONIES
Broken arrow drive / Inside out / Escape of the circus ponies / Church of tress / Sounding joy / Another shore / Incision / Worth winning / Empty forest
CD _____ WD 1099
Windham Hill / May '91 / Pinnacle / BMG / ADA.

MY FOOLISH HEART
My foolish heart / Spring can really hang you up the most / How insensitive / My one and only love / My romance / My ship / I got it bad and that ain't good / You are too beautiful / In a sentimental mood / Someday my Prince will come / Never never land / Never will I know / All the things you are / Turn out the stars
CD _____ 01934111152
Windham Hill / Sep '95 / Pinnacle / BMG / ADA.

SPEECHLESS
Forgiveness / Frog park / Welcome home / Hermes dance / Speechless / Back porch / Vigil
CD _____ PD 83037
RCA / Mar '89 / BMG.

Storm

NORDAVIND
CD _____ FOG 004CD
Moonfog / May '95 / Plastic Head.

Storm, Gale

DARK MOON
CD _____ VSD 5523
Varese Sarabande/Colosseum / Nov '94 / Pinnacle / Silva Screen.

Stormwitch

BEAUTY AND THE BEAST
Call of the wicked / Beauty and the beast / Just for one night / Emerald eyes / Tears by the firelight / Tigers of the sea / Russia's on fire / Cheyenne / Welcome to Bedlam
CD _____ 15348
Laserlight / Aug '91 / Target/BMG.

SHOGUN
CD _____ SPV 8476842
SPV / Oct '94 / Plastic Head.

WALPURGIS NIGHT
CD _____ 15391
Laserlight / Aug '91 / Target/BMG.

Stormy Monday Band

LIVE AT 55
CD _____ BLUE 10102
Blues Beacon / Nov '91 / New Note.

Story

ANGEL IN THE HOUSE, THE
So much mine / Missing person afternoon / Gilded cage / When two and two are five / At the still point / Angel in the house / Mer-

maid / Barefoot ballroom / In the gloaming / Fatso / Love song / Amelia / Fatso, part 2
CD _____ 755961471-2
Elektra / Aug '93 / Warner Music.

GRACE IN GRAVITY
CD _____ 7559613212
Elektra / Jun '92 / Warner Music.

Story Board

STORY BOARD
CD _____ PMC 1113
Pan Music / Jan '93 / Harmonia Mundi.

Stotzem, Jacques

CLEAR NIGHT
CD _____ BEST 1030CD
Acoustic Music / Nov '93 / ADA.

STRAIGHT ON
CD _____ BEST 1013CD
Acoustic Music / Nov '93 / ADA.

Stover, Don

THINGS IN LIFE
CD _____ ROUCD 0014
Rounder / Feb '95 / CM / Direct / ADA / Cadillac.

Stradlin, Izzy

IZZY STRADLIN AND THE JU JU HOUNDS
Somebody knockin' / Pressure drop / Time gone by / Shuffle it all / Bucket o'trouble / Train tracks / How will it go / Cuttin' the rug / Take a look at the guy / Come on now inside
CD _____ GFLD 19288
Geffen / Oct '95 / BMG.

Stradling, Rod

RHYTHMS OF THE WORLD
CD _____ FMSD 5021
Rogue / Oct '91 / Sterns.

Strafe Feur Rebellion

LUFTHUNGER (Ten Catastrophes In The History Of The World & Music)
CD _____ TO 19
Touch / Mar '91 / These / Kudos.

Strait, George

EASY COME EASY GO
Stay out of my arms / Just look at me / Easy come, easy go / I'd like to have that one back / Lovebug / I wasn't fooling around / Without me around / Man in love with you / That's where my baby feels at home / We must be loving right
CD _____ MCAD 10907
MCA / Mar '94 / BMG.

HOLDING MY OWN
You're right I'm wrong / Holding my own / Gone as a girl can get / So much like my dad / Trains make me lonesome / All of me (loves all of you) / Wonderland of love / Faults and all / It's all right with me / Here we go again
CD _____ MCAD 10532
MCA / Jun '92 / BMG.

LEAD ON
You can't make a heart love somebody / Adalida / I met a friend of yours today / Nobody has to get hurt / Down Louisiana way / Lead on / What am I waiting for / Big one / I'll always be loving you / No one but you
CD _____ MCAD 11092
MCA / Jan '95 / BMG.

STRAIT OUT OF THE BOX (4CD Set)
I just can't let you go on dying like this / (That don't change) way I feel about you / I don't want to talk it over anymore / Unwound / Blame it on Mexico / Her goodbye hit me in the heart / If you're thinking you want a stranger (there's one coming h / Any old love won't do / Fool hearted memory / Marina Del Rey / I can't see Texas from here / Heartbreak / What would your memory do / Amarillo by morning / I thought I heard you calling my name / Fire I can't put out / You look so good in love / 80 Proof bottle of tear stopper / Right or wrong / Let's fall to pieces together / Does Fort Worth / Ever cross your mind / Cowboy rides away / Fireman / Chair / You're something special to me / Haven't you heard / In too deep / Lefty's gone / Nobody in his right mind would've left her / It ain't cool to be crazy about you / Ocean front property / Rhythm of the road / Six pack to go / All me Ex's live in Texas / Am I blue / Famous last words of a fool / Baby blue / If you ain't lovin' (you ain't livin) / Baby's gotten good at goodbye / Bigger man than me / Hollywood squares / What's going on in my world / Ace in the hole / Love without end, amen / Drinking champagne / I've come expect it from you / You know me better than that / Chill of an early fall / Lovesick blues / Milk cow blues / Gone as a girl can get / So much like my Dad / Trains make me lonesome / Wonderland of love / I cross my heart / Heartland / When did you stop loving me / Overnight male / King of broken hearts / Where the sidewalk ends / Easy come, easy go / I'd like to have that one back /

Lovebug / Man in love with you / Just look at me / Stay out of my arms / Big balls in Cowtown / Big one / Fly me to the moon / Check yes or no / I know she still loves me
CD Set _____ MCAD 411263
MCA / Nov '95 / BMG.

Straitjacket Fits

BLOW
CD _____ FNCD 251
Flying Nun / Sep '93 / Disc.

HAIL
CD _____ ROUGHCD 147
Rough Trade / Nov '89 / Pinnacle.

Strand, Leif

YEAR, THE/ 12 SEASONS
CD _____ 710 101
Innovative Communication / Apr '90 / Magnum Music Group.

ZODIAC/ 12 TEMPERAMENTS, THE
CD _____ 710 102
Innovative Communication / Apr '90 / Magnum Music Group.

Strandberg, Paul

FUTURISTIC RHYTHM
CD _____ SITCD 9210
Sittel / Aug '94 / Cadillac / Jazz Music.

Strange Advance

DISTANCE BETWEEN, THE
Till the stars fall / Love becomes electric / Who lives next door / Love is strange / This island earth / Hold you / Crying in the ocean / Wild blue / Rock and whirl / Ultimate angels / Alien time
CD _____ PCOM 1094
President / Aug '88 / Grapevine / Target/ BMG / Jazz Music / President.

Strange Brew

EARTH OUT
CD _____ CDROB 40
Rob's Records / Jan '96 / Pinnacle.

Strange Nature

WORLD SONG
CD _____ NATURECD 1
WEA / Jul '93 / Warner Music.

Strange Parcels

DISCONNECTION
CD _____ ONUCD 57
On-U Sound / Jul '94 / SRD / Jetstar.

Strange, Billy

RAILROAD MAN
CD _____ GNPD 2041
GNP Crescendo / Jan '92 / Silva Screen.

Strangelove

TIME FOR THE REST OF YOUR LIFE
Sixer / Time for the rest of your life / Quiet day / Sand / I will burn / Low life / World outside / Return of the real me / All because of you / Fire (show me light) / Hopeful / Kite / Is there a place
CD _____ FOODCD 11
Food / Aug '94 / EMI.

Strangeways

STRANGEWAYS AND THE HORSE
CD _____ JHMO 1001
JHM / Mar '95 / Total/BMG.

Stranglers

ABOUT TIME
Golden boy / Money / Face / Sinister / Little blue lies / Still life / Paradise row / She gave it all / Lies and deception / Lucky finger / And the boat sailed by
CD _____ WENCD 001
When / May '95 / BMG / Pinnacle.

AURAL SCULPTURE
Ice queen / Skin deep / Let me down easy / No mercy / North winds / Uptown / Punch and Judy / Spain / Laughing / Souls / Mad hatter
CD _____ 983285 2
Pickwick/Sony Collector's Choice / Mar '94 / Carlton Home Entertainment / Pinnacle / Sony.

BLACK AND WHITE
Tank / Nice 'n' sleazy / Outside Tokyo / Mean to me / Sweden (all quiet on the eastern front) / Hey (rise of the robots) / Toiler on the sea / Curfew / Threatened / Do you wanna / In the shadows / Enough time / Death and night and blood (Yukio) (CD only) / Tits (CD only) / Walk on by
CD _____ CZ 109
EMI / Aug '88 / EMI.

COLLECTION, THE (1977-82)
(Get a) grip (on yourself) / Peaches / Hangin' around / No more heroes / Duchess / Walk on by / Waltzinblack / Something better change / Nice 'n' sleazy / Bear cage / Who

wants the world / Golden brown / Strange little girl / La folie
CD _____ CDFA 3230
Fame / Aug '89 / EMI.

DREAMTIME
Always the sun / Dreamtime / Was it you / You'll always reap what you sow / Ghost train / Nice in Nice / Big in America / Shakin' like a leaf / Mayan skies / Too precious
CD _____ CD 26648
Epic / Oct '86 / Sony.

EARLY YEARS (1974-1976 - Rare, Live & Unreleased)
(Get a) grip (on yourself) / Bitching / Go Buddy go / (Get a) grip (on yourself) (live) / Sometimes (live) / Bitching (live) / Peasant in the big shitty (live) / Hanging around (live) / Peaches (live)
CD _____ CLACD 401
Castle / Jun '94 / BMG.

FELINE/AURAL SCULPTURE/ DREAMTIME (3CD Set)
CD Set _____ 4673952
Epic / Dec '90 / Sony.

GREATEST HITS: STRANGLERS (1977-1990)
Peaches / Something better change / No more heroes / Walk on by / Duchess / Golden brown / Strange little girl / European female / Skin deep / Nice in Nice / Always the sun / Big in America / All day and all of the night / 96 tears / No mercy (Not on LP)
CD _____ 4675412
Epic / Nov '90 / Sony.

LA FOLIE
Non-stop / Everybody loves you when you're dead / Tramp / Let me introduce you hate / Two to tango / Golden brown / How to find true love and happiness in the present day / La folie
CD _____ CDFA 3083
Fame / Nov '88 / EMI.

LIVE (X-CERT)
(Get a) grip (on yourself) / Dagenham Dave / Burning up time / Dead ringer / Hangin' around / Feel like a wog / Straight out / Do you wanna / Five minutes / Go buddy go / Peasant in the big shitty (CD only) / In the shadows (CD only)
CD _____ CDFA 3313
Fame / Dec '94 / EMI.

LIVE AT THE HOPE & ANCHOR (The Requests Show - Nov 22 1977)
Tits / Choosey Susie / Goodbye Toulouse / Bitching / School Mam / Peasant in the big shitty / In the shadows / Walk on by / Princess of the streets / Go buddy go / No more heroes / Straighten out / Peaches / Hangin' around / Dagenham Dave / Sometimes / Bring on the nubiles / London lady
CD _____ CDFA 3316
Fame / Feb '95 / EMI.

MENINBLACK
Waltzinblack / Just like nothing on Earth / Second coming / Waiting for the meninblack / Turn the centuries turn / Two sunspots / Four horsemen / Thrown away / Manna machine / Hallo to our men / Top secret (CD only)
CD _____ CDFA 3208
Fame / Sep '88 / EMI.

NO MORE HEROES
I feel like a wog / Bitching / Dead ringer / Dagenham Dave / Bring on the nubiles / Something better change / No more heroes / Peasant in the big shitty / Burning up time / English towns / School Mam / In the shadows
CD _____ CDFA 3190
Fame / Nov '88 / EMI.

OLD TESTAMENT, THE (The UA Studio Recordings 1977-1982/4CD Set)
Sometimes / Goodbye toulouse / London lady / Princess of the streets / Hangin' around / Peaches / (Get a) Grip (On yourself) #2 / Ugly / Down in the sewer / Choosey Susie / Go Buddy go / I feel like a wog / Bitching / Dead ringer / Dagenham Dave / Bring on the nubiles / Something better change / No more heroes / Peasant in the big shitty / Burning up time / English towns / School Mam / Straighten out / Tank / Nice 'n' sleazy / Outside Tokyo / Sweden (All quiet on the Eastern front) / Hey rise of the robots / Toiler of the sea / Curfew / Threatened / In the shadows / Do you wanna / Death and night and blood (yukio) / Enough time / Shut up / Walk on by / Mean to me / Old codger / Longships / Raven / Dead loss angeles / Ice / Baroque bordello / Nuclear device / Shah shah a go go / Don't bring Harry / Duchess / Meninblack / Genetix / Fools rush out / Yellowcake / Vietnamerica / Bear cage / Who wants the world / Waltzinblack / Just like nothing on Earth / Second coming / Waiting for the meninblack / Turn the centuries turn / Two sunspots / Four horsemen / Trown away / Manna machine / Hallow to our men / Top secret / Maninwhite / Non-stop / Everybody loves you when you're dead / Tramp / Let me introduce you to the family / Ain't nothin' to it / Man they love to hate / Pin up / It only takes two to tango / Golden brown / How to find true love and happiness in the present day / La Folie / Love 30 / Strange

little girl / Cruel garden / (Get a) Grip (on yourself)
CD Set _____ CDS 7999242
EMI / Sep '92 / EMI.

RADIO ONE
CD _____ ESSCD 283
Essential / Nov '95 / Total/BMG.

RATTUS NORVEGICUS (Stranglers IV)
Sometimes / Goodbye Toulouse / London lady / Princess of the streets / Hangin' around / Peaches / (Get a) Grip (on yourself) / Ugly / Down in the sewer: Falling / Down in the sewer: Trying to get out again / Rat's rally
CD _____ CDFA 3001
Fame / Apr '88 / EMI.

RAVEN, THE
Longships / Raven / Dead loss Angeles / Ice / Baroque bordello / Nuclear device / Shah shah a go go / Don't bring Harry / Duchess / Meninback / Genetix / Bear cage
CD _____ CDFA 3131
Fame / Aug '88 / EMI.

SATURDAY NIGHT AND SUNDAY MORNING
CD _____ ESSCD 194
Castle / Jun '93 / BMG.

SINGLES (The UA Years)
(Get a) grip (on yourself) / Peaches / Go buddy go / Something better change / Straighten out / No more heroes / Five minutes / Nice 'n' sleazy / Walk on by / Duchess / Nuclear device / Don't bring Harry / Bear cage / Who wants the world / Thrown away / Just like nothing on Earth / Let me introduce you to the family / Golden brown / La folie / Strange little girl
CD _____ CDEM 1314
Liberty / Feb '89 / EMI.

Strapping Young Lad

HEAVY AS A REALLY HEAVY THING
CD _____ CM 770922
Century Media / May '95 / Plastic Head.

Strasser, Hugo

60'S, THE (Strasser, Hugo & His Dance Orchestra)
CD _____ 16055
Laserlight / May '94 / Target/BMG.

HUGO STRASSER'S DANCE PARTY (Strasser, Hugo & His Dance Orchestra)
Crazy rhythm / Congratulations / Love story / I could have danced all night / Fascination / Ramona / Maria from Bahia / Samba cielito / Reet petite / Red roses for a blue lady / Moonlight and roses / Undecided / Frenesi / La cumparsita / Kiss of fire / Spanish gypsy dance / Y viva Espana / Wunderbar
CD _____ GRCD 38
Grasmere / Nov '89 / Target/BMG / Savoy.

LATIN RHYTHMS
CD _____ 16119
Laserlight / Jun '95 / Target/BMG.

STRICTLY DANCING (Strasser, Hugo & His Dance Orchestra)
CD _____ 26098
Laserlight / Nov '93 / Target/BMG.

Strata Institute

TRANSMIGRATION
CD _____ 4729752
Sony Jazz / Jan '93 / Sony.

Strathclyde Police Pipers

CHAMPION OF CHAMPIONS (Champions of The World)
Marches / Jigs / Strathspey and reel / Polkas / Hornpipes / Slow air
CD _____ LCDM 9028
Lismor / Aug '90 / Lismor / Direct / Duncans / ADA.

STRATHCLYDE POLICE PIPERS, THE
CD _____ LCOM 5201
Lismor / Jul '91 / Lismor / Direct / Duncans / ADA.

Stratovarius

FOURTH DIMENSION
Against the wind / Distant skies / Galaxies / Winter / Startovarious / Lord of the wasteland / 030366 / Nightfall / We hold the key / Twilight symphony / Call of the wilderness
CD _____ TT 0142
T&T / Feb '95 / Pinnacle / Koch.

TWILIGHT TIME
CD _____ TT 0022
T&T / '94 / Pinnacle / Koch.

Straus, Ste

STE REAL
Je suis prete / Met play - G mix / Yo boom / Trop dur pour un seul homme / Track cheul / Nee gangstaa / Met play - East coast mix
CD _____ 122053
Plug It / Nov '94 / Vital.

Stravaig

MOVIN' ON
Birken tree / (Back home again in) Indiana / Song of the gutters / Terror time / Pressers / Dumfries hiring fair / Dundee weaver / Bonnie wee lassie's answer / My aim countrie / Miller tae ma trade / Davey fae / Bonnie lass come ower the buru / Another clearing time / Di nanina
CD _____ CDTRAX 074
Greentrax / Jul '94 / Conifer / Duncans / ADA / Direct.

Straw Dogs

COMPLETE DISCOGRAPHY, THE
CD _____ LF 199CD
Lost & Found / Jan '96 / Plastic Head.

OWN WORST NIGHTMARE
CD _____ LF 034CD
Lost & Found / Apr '92 / Plastic Head.

UNDER THE HAMMER
CD _____ LF 030CD
Lost & Found / Apr '92 / Plastic Head.

Strawberry Alarm Clock

STRAWBERRIES MEAN LOVE
Incense and peppermints / Rainy day mushroom pillow / Sit with the guru / Tomorrow / Black butter - present / Love me again / Pretty song from psych out / World's on fire / Birds in my tree / Birdman of Alkatrash / Small package / They saw the fat one coming / Strawberries mean love
CD _____ CDWIKD 56
Big Beat / Jan '92 / Pinnacle.

Strawberry Story

CLAMMING FOR IT
Gone like summer / Pushbutton head / I still want you / Ashlands Road / Close my eyes / Kissamatic lovebubble / Chicken biscuit / Buttercups and daisys / Made of stone / Caroline / Twenty six / Shame about Alice / Behind this smile / Freight train / Midsummer's daydream / Tell me now
CD _____ ASKCD 025
Vinyl Japan / Jan '93 / Vital.

Strawbs

BBC RADIO 1 LIVE IN CONCERT
CD _____ WINCD 069
Windsong / Feb '95 / Pinnacle.

CHOICE SELECTION OF STRAWBS
Lay down / Lemon pie / Lady fuschia / Autumn / Glimpse of heaven / Hangman and the papist / New world / Round and round / I only want my love to grow in you / Benedictus / Hero and heroine / Song of a sad little girl / Tears and pavan / To be free / Part of the union / Down by the sea
CD _____ CDMID 173
A&M / Oct '92 / PolyGram.

GREATEST HITS LIVE
CD _____ RGFCD 015
Road Goes On Forever / Jul '95 / Direct.

HEARTBREAK HILL
CD _____ RGFWC 024
Road Goes On Forever / Apr '95 / Direct.

STRAWBS IN CONCERT, THE
CD _____ WIN 069
Windsong / Apr '95 / Pinnacle.

UNCANNED PRESERVES
CD Set _____ RGFCD 003
Road Goes On Forever / '92 / Direct.

Strawhead

TIFFIN
CD _____ DRCD 902
Dragon / '90 / Roots / Cadillac / Wellard / CM / ADA.

VICTORIAN BALLADS
CD _____ DRGNCD 941
Dragon / Mar '94 / Roots / Cadillac / Wellard / CM / ADA.

Strawman

LOTTERY, THE
CD _____ ALLIED 53
Allied / May '95 / Plastic Head.

Stray

HEARTS OF FIRE
CD _____ REP 4112-WZ
Repertoire / Aug '91 / Pinnacle / Cadillac.

STAND UP AND BE COUNTED
CD _____ REP 4136-WZ
Repertoire / Aug '91 / Pinnacle / Cadillac.

Stray Cats

BACK TO THE ALLEY (The Best Of The Stray Cats)
Stray cat strut / Rock this town / Rebels rule / Built for speed / Little Miss Prissy / Too hip, gotta go / My one desire / I won't stand in your way (Only on CD) / C'mon everybody / Fishnet stockings / Jeannie Jeannie Jeannie / You don't believe

me / Ubangi stomp (Only on CD) / Double takin' baby / Storm the embassy / Rumble in Brighton / Gonna ball
CD _____ 260963
Arista / Nov '90 / BMG.

CHOO CHOO HOT FISH
CD _____ 9070147
Dino / May '92 / Pinnacle / 3MV.

ORIGINAL COOL
CD _____ ESSCD 208
Essential / Feb '94 / Total/BMG.

ROCK THIS TOWN
Rock this town / C'mon everybody / Fishnet stockings / Crawl up and die / That mellow saxaphone / Lonely summer nights / You don't believe me / Stray Cat strut / Rumble in Brighton / Gonna ball / Little Miss Prissy / Rev it up and go / Crazy mixed up kid / Double talkin' baby
CD _____ RRCD 006
Receiver / Mar '95 / Grapevine.

STRAY CATS/GONNA BALL
Runaway boys / Fishnet stockings / Ubangi stomp / Jeannie Jeannie Jeannie / Storm the embassy / Rock this town / Rumble in Brighton / Stray Cat strut / Crawl up and die / Double talkin' baby / My one desire / That mellow saxaphone / Baby blue eyes / Little Miss Prissy / Wasn't that good / Crying shame / (She'll stay just) one more day / You won't believe me / Gonna ball / Wicked whisky / Rev it up and go / Lonely summer nights / Crazy mixed up kid
CD _____ 74321259552
Arista / Mar '95 / BMG.

TEAR IT UP
CD _____ RRCD 176
Receiver / Jul '93 / Grapevine.

Strayhorn, Billy

BILLY STRAYHORN PROJECT, THE
CD _____ STCD 533
Stash / Feb '91 / Jazz Music / CM / Cadillac / Direct / ADA.

LUSH LIFE
CD _____ 4722062
Sony Jazz / Nov '92 / Sony.

Strazzeri, Frank

I REMEMBER YOU (Strazzeri, Frank Trio)
CD _____ FSCD 123
Fresh Sound / Jan '91 / Jazz Music / Discovery.

Stream

TAKE IT OR LEAVE IT
CD _____ 342792
No Bull / Dec '95 / Koch.

Street Called Straight

STREET CALLED STRAIGHT
Reconciled / All you Madonnas / Destination / Count-down to eternity / Mary's eyes / World without end / Think / Think (reprise) / Rose of Sharon / What a wonderful night / You will answer
CD _____ FLD 9247
Frontline / Apr '92 / EMI / Jetstar.

Streetwalkers

RED CARD
CD _____ REP 4147-WR
Repertoire / Aug '91 / Pinnacle / Cadillac.

VICIOUS BUT FAIR...PLUS
Mama was mad / Chili con carne / Diceman / But you're beautiful / Can't come home / Belle star / Sam / Cross time woman / Downtown flyers / Gypsy moon / Crawfish / Raingame / Crazy charade / Shotgun messiah / Decadence code / Daddy rollin' stone
CD _____ SEECD 352
See For Miles/C5 / Jun '92 / Pinnacle.

Strehli, Angela

BLONDE & BLUE
CD _____ ROU 3127CD
Rounder / Jan '94 / CM / Direct / ADA / Cadillac.

Streisand, Barbra

BACK TO BROADWAY
Some enchanted evening / Everybody says don't / Music of the night / Speak low / As if we never said goodbye / Children will listen / I have a love / I've never been in love before / Luck be a lady / With one look / Man I love / Move on
CD _____ 473880 2
Columbia / Jun '93 / Sony.

BARBRA STREISAND ALBUM, THE
Cry me a river / My honey's loving arms / I'll tell the man in the street / Taste of honey / Who's afraid of the big bad wolf / Soon it's gonna rain / Happy days are here again / Keepin' out of mischief now / Much more / Come to the supermarket / Sleeping bee
CD _____ 474904 2
Columbia / Jan '94 / Sony.

BARBRA STREISAND LIVE (2CD Set)
Overture / As if we never said goodbye / Opening remarks / I'm still here/Everybody says don't/Don't rain on my parade / Can't help lovin' dat man / I'll know / People / Lover man / Therapist dialogue 1 / Will he like me / Therapist dialogue 2 / He touched me / Evergreen / Therapist dialogue 3 / Man that got away / On a clear day (you can see forever) / Entr'acte / Way we were / You don't bring me flowers / Lazy afternoon / Disney medley / Not while I'm around / Ordinary miracles / Yentl medley / Happy days are here again / My man for all we know / Somewhere
CD Set _____ 4775992
Columbia / Oct '94 / Sony.

BROADWAY ALBUM
Putting it together / If I loved you / Something's coming / Not while I'm around / Being alive / I have dreamed / We kiss in a shadow / Something wonderful / Send in the clowns / Pretty women / Ladies who lunch / Can't help lovin' dat man / I loves you Porgy / Porgy, I's your woman now / Somewhere
CD _____ CD 86322
CBS / Feb '86 / Sony.

CHRISTMAS ALBUM
Christmas song / Jingle bells / Have yourself a merry little Christmas / White Christmas / My favourite things / Best of gifts / Silent night / Gounod's Ave Maria / O little town of Bethlehem / I wonder as I wander / Lord's prayer
CD _____ 4605362
Columbia / Nov '95 / Sony.

COLLECTION OF GREATEST HITS AND MORE
We're not makin' love anymore / Woman in love / All I ask of you / Comin' in and out of your life / What kind of fool / Main event/Fight / Someone that I used to love / By the way / Guilty / Memory / Way he makes me feel / Somewhere
CD _____ 4658452
CBS / Nov '89 / Sony.

GREATEST HITS: BARBRA STREISAND VOL.2
Evergreen / Prisoner / My heart belongs to me / Songbird / You don't bring me flowers (With Neil Diamond) / Way we were / Sweet inspiration / Where you lead / All in love is fair / Superman / Stoney end
CD _____ CD 86079
CBS / '86 / Sony.

GUILTY
Guilty / Woman in love / Run wild / Promises / Love inside / What kind of fool / Life story / Never give up / Make it like a memory
CD _____ CD 86122
CBS / '83 / Sony.

HIGHLIGHTS FROM JUST FOR THE RECORD
You'll never know / Sleepin' bee / Miss Marmelstein / I hate music / Nobody's heart (belongs to me) / Cry me a river / Auld Garland medley / Get happy / Happy days are here again / People / Second hand rose / My name is Barbra / Act II medley / Best things are life are free / You wanna bet / Come rain or come shine / Don Rickles (monologue) / Sweetest sounds / You're the top / What are you doing the rest of your life / Crying time / Medley / Quiet thing / There won't be trumpets / Evergreen / Between yesterday and tomorrow / You don't bring me flowers / Papa, can you hear me / I know him so well / Warm all over
CD _____ 4/16402
Columbia / Jul '92 / Sony.

JUST FOR THE RECORD (4CD Set)
You'll never know / Jack Paar show / P.M. east, moon river / Miss Marmelstein / Happy days are here again / Bon soir, keepin' out of mischief now / I hate music / Nobody's heart (belongs to me) / Value / Cry me a river / Who's afraid of the big bad wolf / I had myself a true love / Lover come back to me / Spring can really hang you up the most / My honey's lovin' arms / Any place I hang my hat is home / When the sun comes out / Medley (With Judy Garland) / Medley #2 (With Judy Garland) / I'm the greatest star / My man (mon homme) / Auld lang syne / People / Second hand rose / Medley from My Name is Barbra / Give me the simple life / Nobody knows you (when you're down and out) / Best things in life are free / He touched me / You wanna bet / House of flowers / Ding dong / Witch is dead / Too long at the fair / Look at that face / Starting here, starting now / Belle of 14th street / Good man is hard to find / Some of these days / I'm always chasing rainbows / Happening in Central Park / Silent night / Don't rain on my parade / Funny girl / Come rain or come shine / Hello Dolly / On a clear day (you can see forever) / When you gotta go / In the wee small hours of the morning / Singer / I can do it / Stoney end / Close to you / We've only just begun / Since I fell for you / What's up doc / You're the top / What are you doing the rest of your life / If I close my eyes / Between yesterday and tomorrow / Hatikvah / Can you tell the moment / Way we were / Crying time / God bless the child / Quiet thing / There won't be trumpets / Star is born / Lost inside of

you / Evergreen / You don't bring me flowers / Yaw we are (live) / Guilty / Papa, can you hear me / Moon and I / Piece of sky / I know him so well / If I loved you / Putting it together / Voice / Over the rainbow / Theme from Nuts / Here we are at last / Back to Broadway / Warm all over
CD Set _____ 4687342
Columbia / Oct '91 / Sony.

LOVE SONGS: BARBRA STREISAND
Memory / You don't bring me flowers / My heart belongs to me / Wet / New York state of mind / Man I love / No more tears / Comin' in and out of your life / Evergreen / I don't break easily / Kiss me in the rain / Lost inside of you / Way we were / Love inside
CD _____ CD 10031
CBS / Sep '84 / Sony.

ON A CLEAR DAY YOU CAN SEE FOREVER
Hurry, it's lovely up here / Main title / On a clear day (you can see forever) / Love with all the trimmings / Melinda / Go to sleep / He isn't you / What did I have that I don't have / Come back to me
CD _____ 474907 2
Columbia / Jan '94 / Sony.

ONE VOICE
Somewhere / Evergreen / Something's coming / People / Over the rainbow / Guilty / Papa, you hear me / Way we were / It's a new world / Happy days are here again / America the beautiful
CD _____ 4508912
CBS / May '87 / Sony.

PEOPLE
Absent minded me / When in Rome / Fine and dandy / Suppertime / Will he like me / How does the wine taste / I'm all smiles / Autumn / My lord and master / Love is a bore / Don't like goodbyes
CD _____ 982638 2
Pickwick/Sony Collector's Choice / Apr '94 / Carlton Home Entertainment / Pinnacle / Sony.
CD _____ 4604982
Columbia / Oct '95 / Sony.

SECOND BARBRA STREISAND ALBUM, THE
Any place I hang my hat in Rome / Right as the rain / Down with love / Who will buy / When the sun comes out / Gotta move / My colouring book / I don't care much / Lover come back to me / I stayed too long at the fair / Like a straw in the wind
CD _____ 474908 2
Columbia / Jan '94 / Sony.

STAR IS BORN, A
Watch closely now / Queen Bee / Everything / Lost inside of you / Hellacious acres / Love theme / Woman in the moon / I believe in love / Crippled crow / With one more look at you
CD _____ 474905 2
Columbia / Jan '94 / Sony.

THIRD ALBUM, THE
My melancholy baby / Just in time / Taking a chance on love / Bewitched, bothered and bewildered / Never will I marry / As time goes by / Draw me a circle / It had to be you / Make believe / I had myself a true love
CD _____ 474909 2
Columbia / Jan '94 / Sony.

TILL I LOVED YOU
Places you find love / On my way to you / Till I loved you / Love light / All I ask of you / You and me for always / Why let it go / Two people / What were you thinking of / Some good things never last / One more time around
CD _____ 4629432
CBS / Nov '88 / Sony.

WHAT ABOUT TODAY
What about today / Ask yourself why / Honey pie / Punky's dilemma / Until it's time for you to go / That's a fine kind of freedom / Little tin soldier / With a little help from my friends / Alfie / Morning after / Goodnight
CD _____ 474901 2
Columbia / Jan '94 / Sony.

STRESSBALL
CD _____ IRSCD 981201
Intercord / Jan '94 / Plastic Head.

LIFEBLOOD
CD _____ REP 4087-WZ
Repertoire / Aug '91 / Pinnacle / Cadillac.

YOU CAN'T BEAT YOUR BRAIN FOR ENTER...
CD _____ REP 4200-WZ
Repertoire / Aug '91 / Pinnacle / Cadillac.

WORLD OF STRETCH
CD _____ COTINDCD 3
Cottage Industry / Jul '95 / Total/BMG.

STRICTLY INC.
Don't turn your back on me / Walls of sound / Only seventeen / Serpent said / Never let me know / Charity balls / Something to live for / Piece of you / Island in the darkness / Strictly incognito
CD _____ CDV 2790
Virgin / Sep '95 / EMI.

ONE TRUTH
CD _____ VE 16CD
Victory / Apr '95 / Plastic Head.

WHEELS
Wheels / Brass buttons / Should I / Scottie / Nearly sunrise / Sunday / My blue heaven / Mathilda / Skippin' / Mina bird / Happy melody / Panic button / Walk don't run / Summertime / Perfidia / Bulldog / Spinnin' my wheels / Red river twist / Take a minute / You don't have to go / Torquay / Harbour lights / Tell the world / Are you lonesome tonight / My babe / Heartaches / Replica
CD _____ CDCHD 390
Ace / Jan '93 / Pinnacle / Cadillac / Complete/Pinnacle.

MACHINE THAT CRIED, THE
CD _____ REP 4207-WP
Repertoire / Aug '91 / Pinnacle / Cadillac.

SUICIDE LIVE IN BERLIN' 94
CD _____ TRUCKCD 023
Terrapin Truckin' / Jul '95 / Total/BMG / Direct / ADA.

WARM EVENINGS
CD _____ CCD 4050
Concord Jazz / Nov '89 / New Note.

ASCENDANT
CD _____ STCD 532
Stash / Oct '91 / Jazz Music / CM / Cadillac / Direct / ADA.

BLUES
CD _____ 1201482
Black Saint / Sep '95 / Harmonia Mundi / Cadillac.

OCTAGON
CD _____ 120131
Black Saint / Apr '94 / Harmonia Mundi / Cadillac.

REBIRTH OF A FEELING
CD _____ 120068-2
Black Saint / May '94 / Harmonia Mundi / Cadillac.

STRING TRIO OF NEW YORK & JAY CLAYTON (String Trio of New York & Jay Clayton)
CD _____ WWCD 008
West Wind / Jul '88 / Swift / Charly / CM / ADA.

PATHFINDER
Pathfinder / Fortune green / Wendy blue / Catwalk / In sentimental mood / Samba for Liza / Paris / Softly as in a morning sunrise / Billie's bounce / Joker / Kia
CD _____ MSPCD 9501
Mabley St. / Apr '95 / Grapevine.

SPANISH EYES
CD _____ MATCD 246
Castle / Dec '92 / BMG.

BALLROOM DANCE FESTIVAL
CD _____ BMC 87117
Beautiful Music Collection / Jun '95 / Target/BMG.

PANFLUTE MEMORIES
CD _____ BMC 87125
Beautiful Music Collection / Jun '95 / Target/BMG.

STRITCH
Are you having any fun / You're getting to be a habit with me / That's the beginning of the end / Angels sing / Let it snow, let it snow, let it snow / That's my boy / I don't want to walk without you / Too many rings around Rosie / Object of my affection / Easy street / If / There's a lull in my life / You took avantage of me
CD _____ DRGCD 91434
DRG / Aug '95 / New Note.

CIRCLE NEVER ENDS
CD _____ BBA 11
Big Cat / Mar '94 / SRD / Pinnacle.

FOLLOW ME
Follow me / In your dreams / Joined at the hip / My number / Same world / Killing fields of love / Bad news on the mountain / Diamond shine / Judas kiss / Gun metal grey
CD _____ AKD 023
Linn / Oct '93 / PolyGram.

RIO DE LA PLATA
CD _____ 829052CD
Buda / Jul '95 / Discovery / ADA.

ANOTHER DAY IN PARADISE
CD _____ FAT 5172
Fat Wreck Chords / Jun '94 / Plastic Head.

AMERICAS (Strunz, Jorge & Adeshir Farah)
Caracol / El jaguar / Candela / Alas del sur / Americas / Luna suave (soft moon) / Balada (for Heideh) / Gypsy earrings / Rayo / Selva
CD _____ 812279041-2
WEA / May '93 / Warner Music.

FRONTERA (Strunz, Jorge & Adeshir Farah)
Quetzal / Zona liberada / Reng / Cassiopeia / Rio nuevo / Abrazo / Amritsar / Desira
CD _____ MCD 9123
Milestone / Nov '95 / Jazz Music / Pinnacle / Wellard / Cadillac.

GUITARS (Strunz, Jorge & Adeshir Farah)
CD _____ MCD 9136
Milestone / Jun '95 / Jazz Music / Pinnacle / Wellard / Cadillac.

SOLDIERS UNDER COMMAND
CD _____ CDMFN 72
Music For Nations / Aug '89 / Pinnacle.

TO HELL WITH THE DEVIL
Abyss (to hell with the devil) / To hell with the devil / Calling on you / Free / Honestly / Way / Sing along song / Rockin' the world / All of me / More than a man
CD _____ CDMFN 70
Music For Nations / Aug '87 / Pinnacle.

YELLOW AND BLACK ATTACK, THE
Loud 'n' clear / My love I'll always show / You know what to do / Common rock / You won't be lonely / Loving you / Reasons for the season
CD _____ CDMFN 74
Music For Nations / Aug '89 / Pinnacle.

MYSTERY OF TIME
Mighty call / Calling in the dark / Lost command / Desperate child / None of your business / Always lying / I'll never loose my way / Mystery of time
CD _____ ATOMH 011 CD
Atom / Apr '90 / Cadillac.

CAN O' WORMS
CD _____ NORMAL 189
Normal/Okra / May '95 / Direct / ADA.

RESTRONUEVO (Stuart, Dan & Al Perry)
CD _____ NORMAL 169CD
Normal/Okra / Aug '94 / Direct / ADA.

MARTY STUART
If it ain't got you / Whiskey ain't working / Hillbilly rock / Now that's country / Burn me down / Likes of me tempted / This one's gonna hurt you / Little things / Weight / Western girls / Don't be cruel
CD _____ MCD 11237
MCA / Mar '95 / BMG.

THIS ONE'S GONNA HURT YOU
Me and Hank and Jumping Jack Flash / High on a mountain top / This one's gonna hurt you / Down home / Always used me / Hey baby / Doin' my time / Now that's country / King of Dixie / Honky tonky crowd
CD _____ MCAD 10596
MCA / Mar '94 / BMG.

MORNING SONG
Blues for the moment / King of harts / So what / Morning song / Blue moon / Night in Lisbon / Shaw of Newark / In a sentimental mood / Slick stud and sweet thang / Here and there / Here's one

---

CD _____ ENJ 80362
Enja / Feb '94 / New Note / Vital/SAM.

SNAPPING NECKS
CD _____ CM 770882
Century Media / Mar '95 / Plastic Head.

OUTSIDE LOOKIN' IN (Studebaker John & the Hawks)
CD _____ BPCD 75022
Blind Pig / Jul '95 / Hot Shot / Swift / CM / Roots / Direct / ADA.

OFFICIUM TENEBRARUM
CD _____ CDCEL 022
Celestial Harmonies / Jul '88 / ADA / Select.

SEVEN SONGS
Sans titre / Ein blindenhund und ein / Bellydance on a chessboard / Hajime / Soly sombra / I don't hear anything / S.F.K.
CD _____ VBR 20562
Vera Bra / Jun '91 / Plastic Head / New Note.

PARADISE IN THE PICTUREHOUSE
CD _____ ROCD 005
Solid / Oct '90 / Grapevine.

RETARD PICNIC
CD _____ CLAYCD 117
Clay / Apr '94 / Cargo.

I LOVE TO POLKA
CD _____ ROUCD 6067
Rounder / Jun '95 / CM / Direct / ADA / Cadillac.

POLKA YOUR TROUBLES AWAY
CD _____ ROUCD 6057
Rounder / Oct '94 / CM / Direct / ADA / Cadillac.

BIG NOISE
CD _____ TRCD 9906
Tramp / Nov '93 / Direct / ADA / CM.

COST OF LIVING
It didn't matter / Right to go / Heavens above / Fairytales / Angel / Walking the night / Waiting / Cost of living / Woman's song
CD _____ 831 443-2
Polydor / Jan '87 / PolyGram.

ESSENTIAL COLLECTION, THE
Speak like a child / Headstart for happiness / Long hot Summer / Paris match / It just came to pieces in my hands / My ever changing moods / Whole point of no return / Ghosts of Dachau / You're the best thing / Big boss groove / Man of great promise / Homebreakers / Down in the Seine / Stones throw away / With everything to lose / Boy who cried wolf / Cost of loving / Changing of the guard / Why I went missing / It's a very deep sea
CD _____ 5294832
Polydor / Feb '96 / PolyGram.

HERE'S SOME THAT GOT AWAY
Love pains / Party chambers / Whole point of no return / Ghosts of dachau / Sweet loving ways / Casual affair / Woman's song / Mick's up / Waiting on a connection / Night after night / Piccadilly trail / When you call me / My very good friend / April's fool / In love for the first time / Big boss groove / Mick's company / Bloodsports / Who will buy / I ain't goin' under / I am leaving / Stone's throw away
CD _____ 519372-2
Polydor / Jun '93 / PolyGram.

HOME AND ABROAD (LIVE)
My ever changing moods / Lodgers / Head start for happiness / When you call me / Whole point of no return / With everything to lose / Homebreaker / Shout to the top / Walls come tumbling down / Internationalists
CD _____ 829 143-2
Polydor / Aug '86 / PolyGram.

INTRODUCING THE STYLE COUNCIL
Long hot summer / Head start for happiness / Speak like a child / Long hot summer (Club mix) / Paris match / Mick's up / Money go round (Club mix)
CD _____ 815 277-2
Polydor / PolyGram.

OUR FAVOURITE SHOP
Homebreaker / All gone away / Come to Milton Keynes / Internationalists / Stones throw away / Stand up comics instructions / Boy who cried wolf / Man of great promise

/ Down in the Seine / Lodgers / Luck / With everything to lose / Our favourite shop / Walls come tumbling down / Shout to the top
CD _____ 825 700-2
Polydor / Aug '90 / PolyGram.

SINGULAR ADVENTURES OF THE STYLE COUNCIL, THE (Greatest hits vol 1)
You're the best thing / Have you ever had it blue / Money go round / My ever changing moods / Long hot summer / Lodgers / Walls come tumbling down / Shout to the top / Wanted / It didn't matter / Speak like a child / Solid bond in your heart / Life at a top peoples health farm / Promised land / How she threw it all away (CD/MC only) / Waiting (CD/MC only) / Have you ever had it blue (12" mix) (CD only) / Long hot summer (12" mix) (CD only)
CD _____ 837 896-2
Polydor / Mar '89 / PolyGram.

Stylistics

BEST OF THE STYLISTICS, THE
Can't give you anything (but my love) / Let's put it all together / I'm stone in love with you / You make me feel brand new / Sing baby sing / Na na is the saddest word / Sixteen bars / Star on a TV show / Funky weekend / Break up to make up / Can't help falling in love / Peek-a-boo / 7000 Dollars and you / You'll never go to heaven (if you break my heart)
CD _____ 842 936 2
Mercury / May '90 / PolyGram.

GREAT LOVE HITS, THE
Rock 'n' roll baby / You make me feel brand new / I'm stone in love with you / Hey girl, come and get it / We can make it happen again / Peek-a-boo / You are everything / You'll never get to heaven (if you break my heart) / I will love you always / Love comes easy / Betcha by golly wow / If you are there / Break up to make up / People make the world go round
CD _____ PWK 139
Carlton Home Entertainment / Jul '90 / Carlton Home Entertainment.

LOVE TALK
CD _____ MYCD 301
Mythical Records / Feb '93 / Pinnacle.

SETTING THE SCENE
You make me feel brand new / Sing baby sing / You'll never get to heaven (if you break my heart) / You are everything / People make the world go round / I plead guilty / You are beautiful / Break up to make up / Only for the children / Jenny / Love at first sight / You're a big girl now / Stop, look, listen (to your heart) / Peek-a-boo
CD _____ 5500312
Spectrum/Karussell / May '93 / PolyGram / THE.

SPOTLIGHT ON THE STYLISTICS
CD _____ 8483392
Mercury / Jul '93 / PolyGram.

Styx

BOAT ON THE RIVER
CD _____ 3969592
A&M / Mar '95 / PolyGram.

PARADISE THEATRE
A.D. 1928 / Rockin' in paradise / Too much time on my hands / Nothing ever goes as planned / Best of times / Lonely people / Sho narre / Snowblind / Halfpenny, two penny / A.D. 1958 / State street Sadie
CD _____ CDMID 154
A&M / Oct '91 / PolyGram.

Subdudes

ANNUNCIATION
(You'll be) satisfied / Why can't I forget about you / Angel to be / I know / Late at night / Miss Love / Poverty / Message man / Save me / Fountains flow / Cold nights / Sugar pie / It's so hard
CD _____ 7290210323-2
Windham Hill / Jun '94 / Pinnacle / BMG / ADA.

Subhumans

EPLP
CD _____ FISH 14CD
Blurrg / Feb '92 / SRD.

WORLDS APART
CD _____ FISH 12CD
Blurrg / Feb '92 / SRD.

Submarine

KISS ME TILL YOUR EARS BURN OFF
CD _____ FAN 1022
Fantastick / Mar '94 / SRD.

SUBMARINE
CD _____ TOPPCD 007
Ultimate / Mar '94 / 3MV / Vital.

Subramaniam, Dr. L.

ELECTRIC MODES VOLS 1 & 2
CD _____ WLAES4
Waterlilly Acoustics / Nov '95 / ADA.

KALYANI
CD _____ WLAES 19CD
Waterlilly Acoustics / Nov '95 / ADA.

RAGA DHARMAVATI
Ragam and Tanam / Pallavi and tabla solo / Ragamalika
CD _____ RMSCD 106
Ravi Shankar Music Circle / May '94 / Conifer.

RAGA HEMEVATI
CD _____ NI 5227
Nimbus / Sep '94 / Nimbus.

SARASVATI
CD _____ WLAES 24CD
Waterlilly Acoustics / Nov '95 / ADA.

THREE RAGAS FOR SOLO VIOLIN
CD _____ NI 5323
Nimbus / Sep '94 / Nimbus.

Subramanium, Karaikudi

MASTERS OF RAGA
CD _____ SM 16082
Wergo / Sep '95 / Harmonia Mundi / ADA / Cadillac.

SUNADA (Subramaniam, Karaikudi & Trichy Sankaran)
Sarasasamadana / Varanarada / Ramachandra bhavayami / Nidu charanamule: Ragam / Nidu charanamule: Tanam and kriti / Tiruppugar: Iyal Isaiyum / Mayatita svarupini
CD _____ CDT 127
Topic / Apr '93 / Direct / ADA.

Subsurfing

FROZEN ANTS
Number readers / Face with corn / Frozen ants / Sleepless snake / Angel fish / She swims above the horizon / H.S.J. (Features on CD only.)
CD _____ AMB 5941CD
Apollo / Aug '91 / Vital.

Subterfuge

SYNTHETIC DREAM
Last dimension / Pain everlasting / Enchantress / Unconscious world / Ninety seconds of homelessness / Shadows of reality / City / Journey to eternity / Liquid eternity / Cosmopolis / Death of love
CD _____ PRIME 013CD
Prime / Nov '93 / Vital.

Subtle Plague

IMPLOSION
CD _____ NORM 159CD
Normal/Okra / Mar '94 / Direct / ADA.

Subtropic

HOMEBREW
CD _____ REFCD 6
Subtropic / Dec '95 / Disc.

Suburban Studs

COMPLETE STUDS COLLECTION
Suburban stud / Dissatisfied / Rumble / Resistor / I hate school / My generation / Traffic jam / Revenge / Questions / Necro / Razor blades / Two victims / Young power / Panda control / Bondage / Throbbing lust / No faith / Snipper / Hit and run / I hate school (live) / Sinkin down / Hudini charms / Questions / Questions (sax version) / No faith (sax version)
CD _____ CDPUNK 21
Anagram / Oct '93 / Pinnacle.

Subvert

SUBVERT
CD _____ SFLS 282
Selfless / Dec '94 / SRD.

Success-n-Effect

BACK-N-EFFECT
Angel dust / Blueprint / Robo's housin' / Seven Gs I'll flow / Slick the slick / Real deal (Holyfield) / Mack of the year / Jump 2 it (house from the South) / Slow flow / So many faces / Nuthin' but success (Mixes) / 360
CD _____ CDICH 1108
Ichiban / Oct '93 / Koch.

Succulent Blue Sway

SOUNDTRACK
CD _____ DOROBO 006CD
Dorobo / Oct '95 / Plastic Head.

Suchas

LOW LEVEL THERAPY
CD _____ CDVEST 47
Bulletproof / Apr '95 / Pinnacle.

Suckspeed

UNKNOWN GENDER
CD _____ WB 1099-2
We Bite / Aug '93 / Plastic Head.

Sudden, Nikki

BACK TO THE COAST
CD _____ CRECD 083
Creation / May '94 / 3MV / Vital.

DEAD MEN TELL NO TALES
When I cross the line / Before I leave you / Dog latin / Wooden leg / Dog rose / How many lies / Cup full of change / Kiss at dawn
CD _____ CRECD 016
Creation / Feb '91 / 3MV / Vital.

DEAD MEN TELL NO TALES/ TEXAS (Sudden, Nikki & The Jacobites)
CD _____ CRECD 018
Creation / Feb '91 / 3MV / Vital.

GROOVE
CD _____ CRECD 041
Creation / May '94 / 3MV / Vital.

GROOVE CREATION (Sudden, Nikki & The French Revolution)
CD _____ CRELP 041 CD
Creation / Apr '89 / 3MV / Vital.

JEWEL THIEF
CD _____ UFO 004CD
UFO / Oct '91 / Pinnacle.

KISS YOU KIDNAPPED CHARABANC (Sudden, Nikki & Roland S. Howard)
Wedding hotel / Rebel grave / Sob story / French revolution blues / Crossroads / Don't explain / Hello wolf (little baby) / Better blood / Debutante blues / Girl without a name / Wedding hotel (The Moooo)
CD _____ CRECD 022
Creation / Nov '90 / 3MV / Vital.

Sudden Sway

KO-OPERA
CD _____ ROUGHCD 142
Rough Trade / Feb '90 / Pinnacle.

Suddenly Tammy

TAMMY
CD _____ 936245524-2
Warner Bros. / May '94 / Warner Music.

WE GET THERE WHEN WE DO
Stacey's trip / Plant me / Way up / Pretty back / Bebee / No respect girl / Can't decide / Disease / Lamp / How me / Instrumental / Fearless / Ryan / Mount Rushmore
CD _____ 9362458312
Warner Bros. / Mar '95 / Warner Music.

Sudhalter, Dick

DICK SUDHALTER/ROY WILLIAMS/ KEITH NICHOLS/AL GAY
CD _____ CHR 70014
Challenge / Jun '95 / Direct / Jazz Music / Cadillac / ADA.

FRIENDS WITH PLEASURE
CD _____ ACD 159
Audiophile / Mar '95 / Jazz Music / Swift.

Suede

DOG MAN STAR
Introducing the band / We are the pigs / Heroine / Wild ones / Daddy's speeding / Power / New generation / This Hollywood life / Two of us / Black or blue / Asphalt world / Still life
CD _____ NUDECD 3
Nude / Oct '94 / Disc.

SUEDE
So young / Animal nitrate / She's not dead / Moving / Pantomine horse / Drowners / Sleeping pills / Breakdown / Metal Mickey / Animal lover / Next life
CD _____ NUDE 1CD
Nude / Mar '93 / Disc.

Suffer

GLOBAL WARMING
CD _____ NPR 002CD
Napalm / Mar '94 / Plastic Head.

Suffocation

BREEDING THE SPAWN
Beginning of sorrow / Breeding the spawn / Epitaph of the credulous / Marital decimation / Prelude to repulsion / Anomalistic offerings / Ornaments of decrepancy / Ignorant deprivation
CD _____ CD RR 9113 2
Roadrunner / Mar '93 / Pinnacle.

HUMAN WASTE
CD _____ NB 051CD
Nuclear Blast / Jul '91 / Plastic Head.

Sufi

LIFE'S RISING
Bluesunslide / Lover (versions) / Into the blue / Chrysalids / Desert flower / From slow syrup silence rise time tilted glances / Lostaday / Still pool reflects a clear moon / Beloved / Soon
CD _____ AMBT 9
Virgin / Jun '95 / EMI.

Sufit, Alisha

ALISHA THROUGH THE LOOKING GLASS
CD _____ SUF 010CD
Sufit / Apr '94 / ADA.

Sugar

BEASTER
Come around / Tilted / Judas cradle / J.C. auto / Feeling better / Walking away
CD _____ CRECD 153
Creation / Apr '93 / 3MV / Vital.

COPPER BLUE
Act we act / Good idea / Changes / Helpless / Hoover dam / Slim / If I can't change your mind / Fortune teller / Slick / Man on the moon
CD _____ CRECD 129
Creation / Jul '92 / 3MV / Vital.

FILE UNDER EASY LISTENING
Gift / Company book / Your favorite thing / What you want it to be / Gee Angel / Panama city motel / Can't help you anymore / Granny cool / Believe what you're saying / Explode and make up
CD _____ CRECD 172
Creation / Sep '94 / 3MV / Vital.

Sugar Blue

BLUE BLAZES
CD _____ RRCD 901301
Ruf / Dec '94 / Pinnacle / ADA.

FROM PARIS TO CHICAGO
CD _____ 157562
Blues Collection / Feb '93 / Discovery.

IN YOUR EYES
CD _____ TRIP 7711
Ruf / Oct '95 / Pinnacle / ADA.

Sugar Loaf Express

SUGAR LOAF EXPRESS (Sugar Loaf Express & Lee Ritenour)
Sugar loaf express / Morning glory / That's the way of the world / Slippin' in the back door / Tomorrow / Lady soul
CD _____ JMI 20082
JVC / Nov '93 / New Note.

Sugar Ray

KNOCKOUT (Sugar Ray & The Blue Tones)
CD _____ VRCD 037
Varrick / Sep '94 / Roots / CM / Direct / ADA.

LEMONADE AND BROWNIES
CD _____ 7567827432
Warner Bros. / Aug '95 / Warner Music.

Sugar Shack

I WANNA TAKE YOU HIGHER
CD _____ WIRED 219
Wired / Oct '95 / 3MV / Sony.

Sugarcubes

HERE TODAY, TOMORROW, NEXT WEEK
CD _____ TPCD15L
One Little Indian / Oct '89 / Pinnacle.

IT'S IT
CD _____ TPLP 40CD
One Little Indian / Sep '92 / Pinnacle.

LIFE'S TOO GOOD
Traitor / Motorcrash / Birthday / Delicious demon / Mama / Cold sweat / Blue eyed pop / Deus / Sick for toys / Fucking in rhythm and sorrow
CD _____ TPCD 5
One Little Indian / Apr '88 / Pinnacle.

STICK AROUND FOR JOY
Gold / Hit / Leash called love / Lucky night / Happy nurse / I'm hungry / Walkabout / Hetero scum / Vitamin / Chihuahua
CD _____ TPLP 30CD
One Little Indian / Feb '92 / Pinnacle.

Sugargliders

WE'RE ALL TRYING TO GET THERE
Letter from a lifeboat / Strong / Seventeen / Aloha street / Ahprahran / Theme from Boxville / Unkind / Trumpet play / Will we ever learn / Reinventing penicillin / 90 days of moths and rust / Top 40 sculpture
CD _____ SARAH 619CD
Sarah / Feb '94 / Vital.

Sugarhill Gang

BEST OF THE SUGARHILL GANG
Rapper's delight / Apache / Showdown with the furious five / Passion play / Hot hot summer day / Lover in you / Rapper's reprise / Eighth Wonder / Word is out / Kick it live from 9 to 5 / Livin' in the fast lane
CD _____ NEMCD 747
Sequel / Aug '95 / BMG.

Sugarsmack

TOP LOADER
CD _____ CDDVN 24
Devotion / Oct '93 / Pinnacle.

Sugartown

SWIMMING IN THE HORSEPOOL
CD _____ MA 9
Marina / Mar '95 / SRD.

Suhler, Jim

RADIO MOJO (Suhler, Jim & Monkey Beat)
CD _____ LUCKY 9203CD
Lucky Seven / May '93 / Direct / CM / ADA.

SHAKE (Suhler, Jim & Monkey Beat)
CD _____ LSCD 9207
Lucky Seven / Feb '95 / Direct / CM / ADA.

Suicidal Tendencies

CONTROLLED BY HATRED/FEEL LIKE SHIT...DEJA-VU
Master of no mercy / How will I laugh tomorrow / Just another love song / Waking the dead / Controlled by hatred / Choosing my own way of life / Feel like shit...deja vu / It's not easy / How will I laugh tomorrow (heavy emotion ver.)
CD _____ 4653992
Epic / Sep '94 / Sony.

F.N.G.
CD _____ CDVM 9003
Virgin / Jun '92 / EMI.

FIRST ALBUM
Suicide's an alternative/You'll be sorry / I shot the devil / Won't fall in love today / Memories of tomorrow / I saw your mommy.... / Two sided politics / Subliminal / Institutionalised / Possessed to skate (CD only) / Human guinea pig (CD only) / Two wrongs don't make a right (but they make me feel better) (CD only)
CD _____ CDV 2495
Virgin / Jan '88 / EMI.

HOW WILL I LAUGH TOMORROW WHEN I CAN'T EVEN SMILE TODAY
Trip at the brain / Hearing voices / Pledge your allegiance / How will I laugh tomorrow / Miracle / Surf and slam / If I don't wake up / Sorry / One too many times / Feeling's back / Suicyco mania (CD only)
CD _____ CDV 2551
Virgin / Sep '88 / EMI.

JOIN THE ARMY
Suicidal maniac / Join the army / You got, I want / Little each day / Prisoner / War inside my head / I feel your pain and I survive / Human guinea pig (CD only) / Possessed to skate / No name, no words / Cyco / Two wrongs don't make a right (but they make me feel better) / Looking in your eyes
CD _____ CDV 2424
Virgin / Jun '87 / EMI.

LIGHTS...CAMERA...REVOLUTION!
You can't bring me down / Lost again / Alone / Lovely / Give it revolution / Get whacked / Send me your money / Emotion no.13 / Disco's out / Murder's in / Go'n breakdown
CD _____ 4665692
Epic / Jun '90 / Sony.

SUICIDAL FOR LIFE
Invocation / Don't give a fuck / No fuckin' problem / Suicyco Muthafucka / Fucked up just right / No bullshit / What else could I do / What you need's a friend / I wouldn't mind / Depression and anguish / Evil / Love v. lonliness / Benediction
CD _____ 476885-2
Epic / Jun '94 / Sony.

Suicide

GHOST RIDERS
Rocket U.S.A. / Dream baby dream / Rock 'n' roll (is killing my life) / Sweet white lady / Ghost rider / Harlem
CD _____ RE 145CD
Danceteria / Mar '95 / Plastic Head / ADA.

HALF ALIVE
CD _____ CONTECD 148
Contempo / '90 / Plastic Head.

SUICIDE.
Ghost rider / Rocket USA / Cheree / Johnny / Girl / Frankie teardrop / Che
CD _____ FIENDCD 74
Demon / Jan '88 / Pinnacle / ADA.

WHY BE BLUE
CD _____ OUT 108-2
Brake Out / Nov '94 / Vital.

Suicide Twins

SILVER MISSILES & NIGHTINGALES
CD _____ ESMCD 276
Essential / Apr '95 / Total/BMG.

Sukay

HUAYRASAN - MUSIC OF THE ANDES
CD _____ FF 70501
Flying Fish / Jul '89 / Roots / CM / Direct / ADA.

INSTRUMENTAL, THE (Music Of The Andes)
CD _____ FF 70108
Flying Fish / Nov '94 / Roots / CM / Direct / ADA.

Sulam

KLEZMER MUSIC FROM TEL AVIV
CD _____ SM 1506-2
Wergo / Jul '92 / Harmonia Mundi / ADA / Cadillac.

Sulke, Stephan

AUSGEWAHITES
CD _____ INT 860 190
Interchord / '88 / CM.

LIEBE GIBT'S IM KINO
CD _____ INT 860 194
Interchord / '88 / CM.

Sullivan, Big Jim

BIG JIM'S BACK
Rubber hip gnome / Home / Arabella swampchild / Laid back rock 'n' roll song / Cascade / One fing 'n' anuvver / Takin it easy / Louisiana lovelips / Ballad of Billy Tyler / Country boy picker / If I could only play like that
CD _____ 901152
Line / Apr '95 / CM / Grapevine / ADA / Conifer / Direct.

TEST OF TIME
CD _____ EFA 132862
Ozone / Jul '94 / SRD.

Sullivan, Christine

IT'S ABOUT TIME
CD _____ LRJ 257
Larrikin / Oct '93 / Roots / Direct / ADA / CM.

Sullivan, Ira

NICKY'S TUNE (Sullivan, Ira Quintet)
Secret love / When Sunny gets blue / Nicky's tune / Wilbur's love
CD _____ DD 422
Delmark / Dec '94 / Hot Shot / ADA / CM / Direct / Cadillac.

TOUGH TOWN
CD _____ DD 446
Delmark / May '92 / Hot Shot / ADA / CM / Direct / Cadillac.

Sullivan, Jerry

JOYFUL NOISE, A (Sullivan, Jerry & Tammy)
Get up John / He called me baby / I'm working on a building / Soldiers of the cross / Gates of Zion / Think about that promise / When Jesus passed by / Brand new church / Gospel plow / What a wonderful saviour he is
CD _____ CMFCD 016
Country Music Foundation / Jan '93 / Direct / ADA.

Sullivan, Joe

CLASSICS 1933-1941
CD _____ CLASSICS 821
Classics / Jul '95 / Discovery / Jazz Music.

Sullivan, K.T.

CRAZY WORLD
CD _____ DRGCD 91413
DRG / Jun '93 / New Note.

SING MY HEART
Sing my heart / This time the dream's on me / Hit the road to dreamland / Let's take a walk around the block / Little drops of rain / Right as the rain / Ill wind I gotta right to sing the blues / Fun to be fooled / Sleepin' bee / Two ladies in the shade of de banana tree / Out of this world / My shining hour / I wonder what became of me / If I only had a brain / Don't like goodbyes / Silent spring / It's a new world
CD _____ DRGCD 91437
DRG / Dec '95 / New Note.

Sullivan, Maxine

CLOSE AS PAGES IN A BOOK (Sullivan, Maxine & Bob Wilber)
As long as I live / Gone with the wind / Rockin' rhythm / Darn that dream / Every time / Harlem butterfly / Loch Lomond / Too many tears / Jeepers creepers / Restless / You're driving me crazy / Close as pages in a book
CD _____ ACD 203
Audiophile / May '95 / Jazz Music / Swift.

GREAT SONGS OF THE COTTON CLUB, THE

Happy as the day is long / You gave me everything but love / As long as I live / Raisin' the rent / 'Neath the pale Cuban moon / Ill wind / Between the Devil and the deep blue sea / I love a parade / Harlem holiday / Get yourself a new broom / Stormy weather / In the silence of the night? / That's what I hate about love / Primitive prima donna / I've got the world on a string
CD _____ CD 270
Milan / Jul '87 / BMG / Silva Screen.

IT'S WONDERFUL
Loch Lomond / I'm coming Virginia / Annie Laurie / Blue skies / Easy to love / Folks who live on the hill / Darling Nellie Grey / Nice work if you can get it / 'S Wonderful / Dark eyes / Brown bird singing / You went to my head / Moments like this / Please be kind / It was a lover and his lass / Spring is here / Down the Old Ox Road / St. louis blues / L'amour toujours l'amour / Might and day / Kinda lonesome / It ain't necessarily so / Say it with a kiss
CD _____ CDAFS 1031
Affinity / Feb '92 / Charly / Cadillac / Jazz Music.

LOCH LOMOND (Sullivan, Maxine & John Kirby)
CD _____ CCD 47
Circle / Aug '94 / Jazz Music / Swift / Wellard.

MAXINE SULLIVAN & SCOTT HAMILTON (Sullivan, Maxine & Scott Hamilton)
CD _____ CCD 4351
Concord Jazz / Jul '88 / New Note.

MAXINE SULLIVAN 1944 - 1948
CD _____ LEGEND CD 6004
Fresh Sound / Dec '92 / Jazz Music / Discovery.

MAXINE SULLIVAN AT VINE STREET
I'm crazy 'bout my baby / Accentuate the positive / Say it with a kiss / Jeepers creepers / Old music master / Bob White / Personality
CD _____ CDSW 8436
DRG / Nov '92 / New Note.

MAXINE SULLIVAN CELEBRATES THE MUSIC OF HARRY WARREN
CD _____ DAPCD 229
Audiophile / Jan '93 / Jazz Music / Swift.

QUEEN, THE (VOL.5)
What a difference a day makes / Until the real thing comes along / You were meant for me / I'm in the mood for love / You're driving me crazy / Thanks for the memory / Fine and dandy / Song is you / Ghost of a chance / Should I / Very thought of you / There'll be some changes made / I hadn't anyone till you / After I say I'm sorry / Something to remember you by
CD _____ CKS 3406
Kenneth / Jun '94 / Wellard / Cadillac / Jazz Music.

SPRING IS NOT EVERYTHING
CD _____ APCD 229
Audiophile / '89 / Jazz Music / Swift.

UPTOWN (Sullivan, Maxine & Scott Hamilton Quintet)
You were meant for me / I thought about you / Goody goody / Something to remember you by / Wrap your troubles in dreams (and dream your troubles away) / You're a lucky guy / Georgia on my mind / By myself / I got the right to sing the blues / Just one of those things
CD _____ CCD 4288
Concord Jazz / '85 / New Note.

Sultans Of Ping FC

CASUAL SEX IN THE CINEPLEX
Back in a tracksuit / Indeed you are / Veronica / Two pints of rasa / Stupid kid / You talk too much / Give him a ball (and a yard of grass) / Karaoke queen / Let's go shopping / Kick me with your leather boots / Clitus Clarke
CD _____ 4724952
Epic / Feb '93 / Sony.

Sulzmann, Stan

FEUDAL RABBITS
Elephant house / Spider / Feudal rabbits / Owens field / Feeling bettison / Review / Three quarters in the afternoon / Barry Diddle / Ken Blake - Ending
CD _____ AHUM 011
Ah-Um / Nov '91 / New Note / Cadillac.

NEVER AT ALL (Sulzmann, Stan & Marc Copland)
CD _____ FMRCD 05
Future / Aug '82 / Harmonia Mundi / ADA.

Sumac, Yma

VOICE OF THE XTABY & OTHER DELIGHTS
CD _____ CREV 034CD
Rev-Ola / Jul '95 / 3MV / Vital.

YMA SUMAC

CD _____ ECD 2116
Fresh Sound / Jan '93 / Jazz Music / Discovery.

Sumen, Jimi

PAINTBRUSH, ROCK PENSTEMON
Crane / Curtain of twilight shimmer / Meant to ripen in straw / Deep in maze / Butterfly of wisdom / Jumpin' in obscure mind / Paintbrush, rock penstemon / Envelopes of dispair / Berperest brou
CD _____ CMPCD 61
CMP / Jul '94 / Vital/SAM.

Sumlin, Hubert

BLUES ANYTIME
It's you baby / Love you woman / Every time I get to drinking / When I feel better / Blues anytime / I love / Levee camp moan / My babe / Hubert's blues / We gonna jump / Big legged woman / Too late for me to pray
CD _____ ECD 260522
Evidence / Sep '94 / Harmonia Mundi / ADA / Cadillac.

BLUES GUITAR BOSS
All I can do / You got to help me / Blues is here to stay / Sometimes I'm right / Spanish greens / Still playing the blues / It could be you / Pickin' / Look don't touch / I've stopped crying
CD _____ JSPCD 239
JSP / Oct '90 / ADA / Target/BMG / Direct / Cadillac / Complete/Pinnacle.

BLUES PARTY
Hidden charms / West side soul / Soul that's been abused / Letter to my girlfriend / How can you leave me, little girl / Can't call you no more / Blue guitar / Down in the bottom / Poor me, poor me / Living the blues
CD _____ DIAB 803
Diabolo / Feb '94 / Pinnacle.

HEALING FEELING
I don't want to hear about yours / Healing feeling / Just like I treat you / Come back little girl / Play it cool / Without a friend like you / I don't want no woman / Blue shadows / Down the dusty road / Honey dumplins / Blues for Henry
CD _____ FIENDCD 193
Demon / Sep '90 / Pinnacle / ADA.

MY GUITAR AND ME
Happy with my french friends / Broke and hungry / Give the name Jacquot / My guitar and me / Groove / Easy, Hubert, easy / Don't forget / I wonder why / Broggin' all alone / Last boogie / I'll be home on Tuesday / Jerking in Paris
CD _____ ECD 260452
Evidence / Mar '94 / Harmonia Mundi / ADA / Cadillac.

Summer, Donna

ANOTHER PLACE AND TIME
This time I know it's for real / I don't wanna get hurt / In another place and time / Whatever your heart desires / If it makes you feel good / When love takes over you / Only one / Sentimental / Breakaway / Love's about to change my heart
CD _____ 255976 2
WEA / Jan '89 / Warner Music.

ANTHOLOGY (2CD Set)
Love to love you baby / Could it be magic / Try me I know we can make it / Spring affair / Love's unkind / I feel love / Once upon a time / Rumour has it / I love you / Last dance / Macarthur Park / Heaven knows / Hot stuff / Bad girls / Dim all the lights / Sunset people
CD Set _____ 5181442
Casablanca / Oct '93 / PolyGram.

BAD GIRLS
Hot stuff / Bad girls / Love will always find you / Walk away / Dim all the lights / Journey to the centre of your heart / One night in a lifetime / Can't get to sleep at night / On my honour / There will always be you / All through the night / My baby understands / One love / Lucky / Sunset people
CD _____ 822 557-2
Casablanca / Feb '87 / PolyGram.

BEST OF DONNA SUMMER, THE
I feel love / Macarthur park / Hot stuff / Wanderer / Love's unkind / On the radio / State of independence / Breakaway / Love is in control / Dinner with Gershwin / I don't wanna get hurt / This time I know it's for real / Love's about to change my heart (Not available on LP)
CD _____ 9031729092
WEA / Nov '90 / Warner Music.

DANCE COLLECTION
I feel love / With your love / Last dance / Macarthur Park / One of a kind / Heaven knows / Hot stuff / Walk away / Dim all the lights / No more tears (enough is enough)
CD _____ 8305042
Casablanca / Nov '90 / PolyGram.

DONNA SUMMER
Love is in control / Mystery of love / Woman in me / State of independence / Live in

America / Protection / (If it) hurts just a little / Love is just a breath away / Lush life
CD _____ K2 99163
WEA / Jul '82 / Warner Music.

DONNA SUMMER
CD _____ KLMCD 026
Scratch / May '94 / BMG.

DONNA SUMMER
CD _____ 12397
Laserlight / Sep '94 / Target/BMG.

ENDLESS SUMMER - THE BEST OF DONNA SUMMER
Melody of love (Wanna be loved) / Love to love you baby / Could it be magic / I feel love / Love's unkind / I love you / Last dance / MacArthur park / Hot stuff / Bad girls / No more tears (Enough is enough) / On the radio / Love is in control / State of independence / She works hard for the money / Unconditional love / This time I know it's for real / I don't wanna get hurt / Anyway at all
CD _____ 5262172
PolyGram / Nov '94 / PolyGram.

FOUR SEASONS OF LOVE
Spring affair / Summer fever / Autumn changes / Winter melody / Spring reprise
CD _____ 8262362
Casablanca / Aug '91 / PolyGram.

FUNSTREET
CD _____ HADCD 196
Javelin / Nov '95 / THE / Henry Hadaway Organisation.

I REMEMBER YESTERDAY
I remember yesterday / Love's unkind / Back in love again / Black lady / Take me / Can't we just sit down and talk it over / I feel love
CD _____ 8262372
Casablanca / '83 / PolyGram.

LOVE TO LOVE YOU BABY
Love to love you baby / Full of emptiness / Need-a-man blues / Whispering waves / Pandora's box / Full of emptiness (reprise)
CD _____ 8227922
Casablanca / '93 / PolyGram.

LOVE TRILOGY
Try me I know we can make it better / Could it be magic / Wasted / Prelude to love / Come with me
CD _____ 8227932
Casablanca / Feb '94 / PolyGram.

MISTAKEN IDENTITY
Get ethnic / Body talk / Work that magic / When love cries / Heaven's just a whisper away / Cry of a waking heart / Friends unknown / Fred Astaire / Say a little prayer / Mistaken identity / What is it you want / Let there be peace
CD _____ 9031751592
WEA / Sep '91 / Warner Music.

SHOUT IT OUT
Fun Street / Little Marie / Shout it out / They can't take away our music / Back off boogaloo / Jeannie / Nice to see you / Na na hey hey / Do what mothers do
CD _____ CDBM 078
Blue Moon / Oct '89 / Magnum Music Group / Greensleeves / Hot Shot / ADA / Cadillac / Discovery.

THIS TIME I KNOW IT'S FOR REAL
CD _____ 9548318232
Carlton Home Entertainment / Apr '93 / Carlton Home Entertainment.

WHOSE LAND IS IT ANYWAY
My father was a carpenter / Sally free and easy / Small song for the world / Cruel mother / Farewell friends / Laszlo feher / Remember the days / Man on the Clapham omnibus / Seasons / Farmer, the fox and the rambler / Settlers
CD _____ BHCD 9317
Brewhouse / Aug '94 / Complete/Pinnacle.

BEWITCHED (Summers, Andy & Robert Fripp)
Parade / What kind of man reads Playboy / Begin the day / Train / Bewitched / Maquillage / Guide / Forgotten steps / Image and likeness
CD _____ CDA 5011
A&M / '88 / PolyGram.

INVISIBLE THREADS (Summers, Andy & John Etheridge)
Broken brains / Moravia / Stoneless counts / Lolita / Nuages / Big gliss / Counting the days / Radiant lizards / Monks mood / Archimedes / Heliotrope / Little transgressions
CD _____ INAK 9024
In Akustik / Mar '95 / Magnum Music Group.

SYNAESTHESIA
CD _____ CMPCD 1011
CMP / Jan '96 / Vital/SAM.

SCHOOL OF ROCK & ROLL
School of rock and roll / Straight skirt / Nervous / Gotta lotta that / Twixteen / I'll

never be lonely / Dance, dance, dance / Almost 12 O'clock / Alabama shake / Wine, wine, wine / I've had it / Leroy / Lover please / Mad mad world / Loco cat / Mr. Rock and roll / Floppin' / Turnip greens / Hey my baby / Baby are you kiddin' / You're gonna be sorry / Honey hush / Rock-a-boogie shake / Big blue diamonds / Rockin' Daddy / Who stole the marker / Blue Monday / Big river / Rebel Johnny yuma
CD _____ CDCL 4420
White Label/Bear Family / '94 / Bear Family / Rollercoaster.

FULL OF LIFE
CD _____ DRCD 205
Dragon / Jan '88 / Roots / Cadillac / Wellard / CM / ADA.

LUG BURZ
CD _____ SPV 08423802
Napalm / Apr '95 / Plastic Head.

DAVID DONSON
CD _____ FFR 005CD
Freek / Feb '95 / SRD.

TORCH OF THE MYSTICS
Blue mambo / Tarmac / Esoterica of Abyssynia / Space prophet dogon / Shining path / Flower / Cafe batik / Radar 1941 / Papa legba / Vinegar stroke / Burial in the sky
CD _____ TUP 044-2
Tupelo / Oct '93 / Disc.

30.7.94 LIVE
CD _____ AMB 5938CD
Apollo / Feb '95 / Vital.

KITCHEN
U.F.O. / Entrance / Pitcheon / Sarotti / R gent / Sonification / Up the drain / Osram 509 / Qwertz / Beauty o'locco / Licherfelde
CD _____ RS 933CD
R & S / Nov '93 / Vital.

AVONDALE
Avondale / Show me / Sorcerer's apprentice / Variations on a tyrolean song / Masaniello / Tom marches on / Prisms / From the shores of the mighty pacific / Angels guard thee
CD _____ GRCD 41
Grasmere / Nov '90 / Target/BMG / Savoy.

ANGELS AND DEMONS AT PLAY/THE NUBIANS OF PLUTONIA (Sun Ra & His Myth Science Arkestra)
Tiny pyramids / Between two worlds / Music from the world tomorrow / Angels and demons at play / Urnack / Medicine for a nightmare / Call for all demons / Demon's lullaby / Plutonian nights / Golden lady / Star time / Nubia / Africa / Watusa / Aiethopia
CD _____ ECD 220662
Evidence / Nov '93 / Harmonia Mundi / ADA / Cadillac.

ATLANTIS (Sun Ra & His Arkestra)
Mu / Lemuria / Yucatan (Saturn version) / Yucatan (impulse version) / Bimini / Atlantis
CD _____ ECD 220672
Evidence / Nov '93 / Harmonia Mundi / ADA / Cadillac.

CONCERT FOR THE COMET KOHOUTEK
CD _____ ESP 3033-2
ESP / Jan '93 / Jazz Horizons / Jazz Music.

COSMIC TONES FOR MENTAL THERAPY
CD _____ ECD 220362
Evidence / Nov '92 / Harmonia Mundi / ADA / Cadillac.

DESTINATION UNKNOWN (Sun Ra & His Arkestra)
Carefree / Untitled (Echoes of the future) / Prelude to a kiss / Hocus pocus / Theme of the stargazers / Interstellar lo-ways / Calling planet earth / Satellites are spinning / 'S Wonderful / We travel the spaceways
CD _____ ENJACD 70712
Enja / Nov '94 / New Note / Vital/SAM.

FATE IN A PLEASANT MOOD/WHEN THE SUN COMES OUT (Sun Ra & His Myth Science Arkestra)
Others in their world / Space mates / Lights of a satelite / Distant stars / Kingdom of thunder / Fate in a pleasant mood / Ankhnation / Circe / Nile / Brazilian sun / We travel the spaceways / Calling planet earth / Dancing shadows / Rainmaker / When sun comes out / Dimensions in time
CD _____ ECD 220682
Evidence / Nov '93 / Harmonia Mundi / ADA / Cadillac.

FONDATION MAEGHT NIGHTS (Sun Ra & His Arkestra)
CD _____ COD 006
Jazz View / Mar '92 / Harmonia Mundi.

FUTURISTIC SOUNDS OF SUN RA
Bassism / Of wounds and something / What's that / Where is tomorrow / Beginning / China gates / New day / Tapestry from an asteroid / Jet flight / Looking outward / Space jazz reverie
CD _____ SV 0213
Savoy Jazz / Jun '93 / Conifer / ADA.

HOLIDAY FOR SOUL DANCE
CD _____ ECD 220112
Evidence / May '92 / Harmonia Mundi / ADA / Cadillac.

JAZZ IN SILHOUETTE
CD _____ ECD 220122
Evidence / May '92 / Harmonia Mundi / ADA / Cadillac.

LIVE AT THE HACKNEY EMPIRE (Sun Ra & The Year 2000 Myth Science Arkestra)
CD _____ CDLR 214/5
Leo / Feb '95 / Wellard / Cadillac / Impetus.

LIVE FROM SOUNDSCAPE (Sun Ra & His Arkestra)
CD _____ DIW 388
DIW / Feb '94 / Harmonia Mundi / Cadillac.

LIVE FROM SOUNDSCAPE/POSSIBILITY OF ALTERED DESTINY (Sun Ra & His Arkestra)
CD Set _____ DIW 388/2
DIW / Feb '94 / Harmonia Mundi / Cadillac.

LOVE IN OUTER SPACE (Sun Ra & His Arkestra)
CD _____ CDLR 154
Leo / Sep '88 / Wellard / Cadillac / Impetus.

MAGIC CITY, THE
Magic city / Shadow world / Abstract eye / Abstract 'I'
CD _____ ECD 220692
Evidence / Nov '93 / Harmonia Mundi / ADA / Cadillac.

MONORAILS AND SATELLITES
CD _____ ECD 220132
Evidence / May '92 / Harmonia Mundi / ADA / Cadillac.

MY BROTHER THE WIND, VOL.2
CD _____ ECD 220402
Evidence / Nov '92 / Harmonia Mundi / ADA / Cadillac.

NIGHT IN EAST BERLIN, A (Sun Ra & His Cosmo Discipline Arkestra)
CD _____ CDLR 149
Leo / Sep '87 / Wellard / Cadillac / Impetus.

OTHER PLANES OF THERE
CD _____ ECD 220372
Evidence / Nov '92 / Harmonia Mundi / ADA / Cadillac.

OUT THERE A MINUTE
CD _____ BFFP 42CD
Blast First / Mar '89 / Disc.

PURPLE NIGHTS
Journey towards star / Friendly galaxy / Love in outer space / Stars fell on Alabama / Of invisible them / Neverness / Purple night blues
CD _____ 395 324 2
A&M / Sep '90 / PolyGram.

QUIET PLACE IN THE UNIVERSE, A
CD _____ CDLR 198
Leo / Oct '94 / Wellard / Cadillac / Impetus.

SECOND STAR TO THE RIGHT (Salute To Walt Disney)
CD _____ CDLR 230
Leo / Oct '95 / Wellard / Cadillac / Impetus.

SOLO PIANO, VOL 1
CD _____ 123850-2
IAI / Nov '92 / Harmonia Mundi / Cadillac.

SOUND OF JOY (Sun Ra & His Arkestra)
CD _____ DD 414
Delmark / Dec '94 / Hot Shot / ADA / CM / Direct / Cadillac.

SOUND SUN PLEASURE
CD _____ ECD 220142
Evidence / May '92 / Harmonia Mundi / ADA / Cadillac.

SPACE IS THE PLACE
It's after the end of the world / Under different stars / Discipline / Watusa / Calling planet earth / I am the alter-destiny / Statelites are spinning / Cosmic forces / Outer spaceways incorporated / We travel the spaceways / Overseer / Blackman/Love in outer space / Mysterious crystal / I am the brother of the wind / We'll wait for you / Space is the place
CD _____ ECD 220702
Evidence / Nov '93 / Harmonia Mundi / ADA / Cadillac.

SPACEWAYS INCORPORATED
CD _____ BLCD 760191
Black Lion / Feb '94 / Jazz Music / Cadillac / Wellard / Koch.

St. LOUIS BLUES
CD _____ 123858-2
IAI / Nov '93 / Harmonia Mundi / Cadillac.

SUN RA SEXTET AT THE VILLAGE VANGUARD
CD _____ ROU 3124CD
Rounder / Jan '94 / CM / Direct / ADA / Cadillac.

SUN SONG
CD _____ DD 411
Delmark / '84 / Hot Shot / ADA / CM / Direct / Cadillac.

SUNRISE IN DIFFERENT DIMENSIONS
CD _____ ARTCD 6099
Hat Art / Dec '91 / Harmonia Mundi / ADA / Cadillac.

SUPER SONIC JAZZ (3CD Set)
CD _____ ECD 220152
Evidence / May '92 / Harmonia Mundi / ADA / Cadillac.

VISITS PLANET EARTH/INTERSTELLAR LOW WAYS
CD _____ ECD 220392
Evidence / Nov '92 / Harmonia Mundi / ADA / Cadillac.

WE TRAVEL THE SPACE WAYS/BAD AND BEAUTIFUL
CD _____ ECD 220382
Evidence / Nov '92 / Harmonia Mundi / ADA / Cadillac.

OLD TIME ROCK 'N' ROLL
CD _____ CDMF 073
Magnum Force / Feb '87 / Magnum Music Group.

OLD TIME ROCK 'N' ROLL (2)
Old time rock 'n' roll / Red hot / That's alright mama / Let it roll / Still rockin' / Don't send me no more drinks / You're a heartbreaker / Tutti frutti / Love my baby
CD Set _____ CDMF 2073
Magnum Force / Oct '89 / Magnum Music Group.

PIONEERS OF ROCK'N'ROLL
Pioneers of rock and roll / I'm so lonely / My love to remember / Hold you close / Greenback dollar / Rockabilly I back / Comin' back to Memphis / Boogie woogie rock 'n' roll / You're the reason / If I could write you a song / Jeannie Jeannie Jeannie / Ooh wee / Bye bye
CD _____ CDMF 085
Magnum Force / Dec '92 / Magnum Music Group.

MAMBO JAMBO
CD _____ CDGRS 1248
Grosvenor / Feb '93 / Target/BMG.

NIGHT & DAY
CD _____ CDGRS 1271
Grosvenor / Feb '95 / Target/BMG.

TUXEDO JUNCTION
CD _____ CDGRS 1233
Grosvenor / Feb '93 / Target/BMG.

GOOD SIDE
CD _____ GROW 014-2
Grass / Jun '94 / SRD.

SUNCHILDE UNIVERSITY
Sunny day / Change your life / Teacher teacher / Son / Feels like rain / Inside / Twilight drifter / Timing / Home / Room enough / Confident
CD _____ 4805972
Sony Soho2 / Jul '95 / Sony.

MUSIQUE ET CHANTS CLASSIQUE (Music From Java)
Ocora / Nov '95 / Harmonia Mundi / ADA.
CD _____ C 580064

UNDERGROUND CINEMA
CD _____ FIREMCD 49
Fire / Jul '95 / Disc.

BLIND
I feel / Goodbye / Life and soul / More / On earth / God made me / Love / What do you think / Twenty four hours / Blood on my hands / Medicine
CD _____ CDPCSD 121
Parlophone / Feb '94 / EMI.

READING, WRITING, ARITHMETIC
CD _____ ROUGHCD 148
Rough Trade / Jan '90 / Pinnacle.

Sundial

ACID YANTRA
CD _____ BBQCD 173
Sundial / Jun '95 / Disc.

LIBERTINE
CD _____ BBQCD 138
Beggars Banquet / Jun '93 / Warner Music / Disc.

OTHER WAY OUT
CD _____ UFO 1CD
UFO / Apr '91 / Pinnacle.

REFLECTOR
CD _____ UFO 008CD
UFO / Mar '92 / Pinnacle.

Sundogs

TO THE BONE
CD _____ ROU 9044CD
Rounder / Apr '94 / CM / Direct / ADA / Cadillac.

Sunkings

HALL OF HEADS
CD _____ GPRCD 7
General Production Recordings / Aug '94 / Pinnacle.

Sunny Day Real Estate

DIARY
CD _____ SPCD 121302
Sub Pop / May '94 / Disc.

SUNNY DAY REAL ESTATE
CD _____ SPCD 316
Sub Pop / Nov '95 / Disc.

Sunnyland Slim

CHICAGO JUMP (Sunnyland Slim Blues Band)
You used to love me / Halsted Street jump / Cryin' for my baby / Give you all my money / Calling out / I feel so bad / Got to stop this mess / From afar / Never picked no cotton / Chicago jump / Jammin' with Sam
CD _____ ECD 26067
Evidence / Jul '95 / Harmonia Mundi / ADA / Cadillac.

DECORATION DAY (Sunnyland Slim Blues Band)
Sun is going down / Past life / Decoration day / Boogie 'n' the blues / Depression blues / Tired of travelling / Canadian walk / Patience like Job / Sunnyland jump / Rock little Daddy / Every time I get to drinking / Sunnyland's New Orleans boogie / One room country shack / Tin pan alley / Dust my broom
CD _____ ECD 260532
Evidence / Sep '94 / Harmonia Mundi / ADA / Cadillac.

GIVE ME TIME
CD _____ DD 655
Delmark / Oct '84 / Hot Shot / ADA / CM / Direct / Cadillac.

SUNNYLAND TRAIN
Sunnyland train / Be my baby / Sometime I worry / Decoration day / All my life / Tin pan alley / Unlucky one / Pinetop's boogie woogie / Worried about my baby / Highway 61 / Backwater blues / Sad and lonesome / She used to love me / Sittin' here thinkin' / I feel so good / Patience like Job / Goin' down slow
CD _____ ECD 26066
Evidence / Jul '95 / Harmonia Mundi / ADA / Cadillac.

Suns Of Arqa

ALAP JOE JHALA
CD _____ ARKA 2102CD
Arka Sound / Feb '92 / Vital.

ARQAOLOGY
CD _____ ARKA 2105CD
Arka Sound / Jun '92 / Vital.

CRADLE
CD _____ CDEASM 004
Earthsounds / Aug '93 / Earthsounds.

JAGGERNAUT WHIRLING DUB
Bilawal / Yaman kalyan / Misra pahvadi / Bhairavi / Bhupali
CD _____ ARKA 2103CD
Arka Sound / Nov '94 / Vital.

LAND OF A THOUSAND CHURCHES
Truth lies / Govinda go / Open the door to your heart / La pucelle d'Orleans / Kalilotalove / Heavenly bodies / Govinda's house / Kyrie / Paradisum in dub / Give love / Truth lies there in / Libera me / Ark of the arquans / in paradisum / Sisters of wyrd / Govinda (I wait each day) / Les anciens mystiques / Erasmus meets the earthling / Deep journey
CD _____ ARKA 2101CD
Arka Sound / Apr '93 / Vital.

LIVE WITH PRINCE FAR I
Hey Jagunath / Bhoopali / Steppin' to the music / Throw away your guns / Brujo magic / 83 struggle / Transcedance music / Foggy road / What you gonna do / No song for Allah / Shamanism skank / Nah myoho renge kyo / Thunder bolt dark void

---

CD _____ ARKA 2100CD
Arka Sound / Mar '94 / Vital.

SHABDA
Tomorrow never knows / There is no danger here / Bharavi alap / Through the gate we go / Bharavi live / Pure reality / Great invocation / Basant alap / Basant dhrupad / Beyond the beyond / Great unique / Waterloo / Fire of life / Hear the call
CD _____ ARKA 2109CD
Arka Sound / Sep '95 / Vital.

TOTAL ECLIPSE OF THE SUNS REMIXES 1979-1995
Durga dub / Juggernaut / Gavati / Govinda's dream / Beyond the beyond / Inca man / Tabla school / Acid tabla / Sully's reel
CD _____ ARKA 2108CD
Arka Sound / Oct '95 / Vital.

Sunscreem

03
Portal / Pressure / B / Doved up / Love u more / Perfect motion / Chasing dreams / Your hands / Idaho / Walk on / Broken English / Release me / Psycho
CD _____ 472218 2
Sony Soho2 / Feb '93 / Sony.

Sunset Dance Orchestra

DANCING YEARS PART 1, THE
Blue skies / I'm putting all my eggs in one basket / Dancing cheek to cheek / China town, my China town / Bells of Saint Mary's / They can't take that away from me / After you've gone / White Christmas / Home on the range / Way you look tonight / Pretty baby / Pennies from heaven / Carolina in the morning / My mammy / Swingin' on a star / Pick yourself up / Let's face the music and dance / Anniversary song
CD _____ WRCD 5003
WRD / Nov '95 / Target/BMG.

DANCING YEARS PART 2, THE
Sunshine cake / Top hat, white tie and tails / I'm sittin' on top of the world / Toot toot tootsie goodbye / Moonlight becomes you / Smoke gets in your eyes / Swanee / Where the blue of the night meets the blue of the day / Fine romance / Back in your own back yard / Don't fence me in / Baby face / Wrap your troubles in dreams / Isn't this a lovely day to be in the rain / Continental / Sonny boy / Night and day / In the cool, cool, cool of the evening
CD _____ WRCD 5004
WRD / Nov '95 / Target/BMG.

Sunset Heights

TEXAX TEA
CD _____ KGBCD 1
KGB / Oct '94 / Total/BMG.

Sunset Stampede

SUNSET STAMPEDE
CD _____ WWRCD 6003
Wienerworld / Jun '95 / Disc.

Sunshine, Monty

GOTTA TRAVEL ON
You tell me your dream / Pretty baby / Sleep my little Prince / Down in Honky Tonk Town / Goin' home / Martha / Sheikh of Araby / Careless love / Wise guy / Pallet on the floor / Gotta travel on / Burgundy St. Blues / Joe Avery's blues
CD _____ CDTTD 570
Timeless Traditional / Nov '91 / New Note.

IN LONDON
CD _____ BLCD 760508
Black Lion / Oct '93 / Jazz Music / Cadillac / Wellard / Koch.

JUST A CLOSER WALK WITH THEE
CD _____ CDTTD 592
Timeless Traditional / Aug '95 / New Note.

NEW ORLEANS HULA (Great British Traditional Jazzband Vol.3) (Sunshine, Monty Jazz Band)
CD _____ LACD 47
Lake / May '95 / Target/BMG / Jazz Music / Direct / Cadillac / ADA.

SOUTH (Sunshine, Monty Jazz Band)
It's tight like that / Memphis blues / Ice cream / Wabash blues / All the girls / South / Bill Bailey, won't you please come home / Bugle boy march / Ups and downs / Carry me back to old virginity / If I ever cease to love / Isle of Capri / When I grow too old to dream
CD _____ CDTTD 583
Timeless Traditional / Jun '94 / New Note.

Sunshot

CAUGHT IN THE ACT OF ENJOYING OURSELVES
Nasties / She says / Big mistake / Stop me / Baby doll / Happy ever after / Play time / Twisting / Lose my grip / Brainstorm / Tank
CD _____ DVAC 005 CD
Deva / Sep '92 / Vital.

IRON BALL DIRECTION
Nasties / Baby doll / Kill or be killed / Big mistake / Tank / She says / Lose my grip /

Sally's ladders / Play time / Happy ever after
CD _____ DVAC 007
Trident / Jun '93 / Pinnacle.

Sunt

TWEEZ
CD _____ TG 138D
Touch & Go / May '93 / SRD.

Suonsaari, Klaus

REFLECTING TIMES (Suonsaari, Klaus Quintet)
CD _____ STCD 4125
Storyville / Feb '89 / Jazz Music / Wellard / CM / Cadillac.

Supahead

CAULK
CD _____ TOODAMNHY 42
Too Damn Hype / Feb '95 / SRD.

Super Cat

DON DADA
It fe done / Ghetto red hot / Them no care / Dolly my baby / Don't test / Must be bright / Don dada / Think me come fi play / Big and ready / Coke Don / Nuff man a dead / Oh it's you / Fight fi power / Yush talk
CD _____ 4715702
Columbia / Aug '92 / Sony.

SI BOOPS DEH
CD _____ WRCD 0021
Techniques / Nov '95 / Jetstar.

STRUGGLE CONTINUES, THE
Dance / Girlstown / Turn / Warning / Forgive me Jah / My girl Jospehine / "A" Class rub-a-dub / Too greedy / South central / Ready back / Every nigger is a star / Settlement / I hear dem seh
CD _____ 4772922
Columbia / Oct '95 / Sony.

Super Rail Band

NEW DIMENSIONS IN RAIL CULTURE (Super Rail Band of the Buffet de la Gare de Bamako, Mali)
Foliba / Bedianamogo / Tallassa / Konowale / Mali yo
CD _____ CDORB 001
Globestyle / Jul '90 / Pinnacle.

Super Star

GREATEST HITS VOL.1
CD _____ CRECD 134
Creation / Jun '92 / 3MV / Vital.

Superalmendrado

GOTTA GIVE IT UP
CD _____ DEDD 003CD
Dedicated / Feb '95 / Vital.

Superchunk

ALBUM
CD _____ EFA 049662
City Slang / Oct '95 / Disc.

FOOLISH
CD _____ EFA 49382
City Slang / Apr '94 / Disc.

INCIDENTAL MUSIC 1991-1995
CD _____ EFA 049592
City Slang / Jul '95 / Disc.

ON THE MOUTH
CD _____ EFA 04915262
City Slang / Jan '93 / Disc.

Superconductor

HIT SONGS FOR GIRLS
Scootin' / There goes Helen / For Kelly Freas / Nobody's cutie / Thorsen's eleven / Come on hot dog / E-Z bake oven / Lordy / I'm gonna knock your block off alistar / Feedbackin'
CD _____ TUP 0482
Tupelo / Aug '93 / Disc.

Supereal

ELIXIR
Body medusa / Aquaplane / Blue beyond belief / Mass motion / I almost love you / Terminal high rip / United state of love / One nation
CD _____ GRCD 005
Guerilla / Nov '92 / Pinnacle.

Supergrass

I SHOULD COCO
I'd like to know / Caught by the fuzz / Mansize rooster / Alright / Lose it / Lenny / Strange ones / Sitting up straight / She's so loose / We're not supposed to / Time / Sofa of my lethargy / Time to go
CD _____ CDPCS 7373
Parlophone / May '95 / EMI.

Supergroove

TRACTION
CD _____ 74321218462
RCA / Oct '95 / BMG.

Supermorris

MR SLAM
CD _____ RN 0030
Runn / Nov '93 / Jetstar / SRD.

Supernova

AGES 3 AND UP
CD _____ ARRCD 65008
Amphetamine Reptile / Nov '95 / SRD.

Superskill

SUPERIOR
CD _____ OUT 002CD
Wonderbrain / May '94 / Plastic Head.

Supersuckers

LA MANO CORUNDA
CD _____ SPCD 120301
Sub Pop / Apr '94 / Disc.

SACRILICIOUS
CD _____ SPCD 0303
Sub Pop / Sep '95 / Disc.

SONGS ALL SOUND THE SAME, THE
CD _____ EFA 11351
Musical Tragedies / Jul '92 / SRD.

Supertouch

EARTH IS FLAT, THE
CD _____ REVEL 021CD
Revelation / Apr '92 / Plastic Head.

Supertramp

AUTOBIOGRAPHY OF SUPERTRAMP, THE
Goodbye stranger / Logical song / Bloody well right / Breakfast in America / Take the long way home / Crime of the century / Dreamer / From now on / Give a little bit / It's raining again / Cannonball / Ain't nobody but me / Hide in your shell / Rudy
CD _____ TRACD 1
A&M / Oct '86 / PolyGram.

BREAKFAST IN AMERICA
Gone Hollywood / Logical song / Goodbye stranger / Breakfast in America / Oh darling / Take the long way home / Lord is it mine / Just another nervous wreck / Casual conversation / Child of vision
CD _____ CDA 63708
A&M / '82 / PolyGram.

CRIME OF THE CENTURY
School / Bloody well right / Hide in your shell / Asylum / Dreamer / Rudy / If everyone was listening / Crime of the century
CD _____ CDA 68258
A&M / '82 / PolyGram.

CRISIS ? WHAT CRISIS ?
Easy does it / Sister moonshine / Ain't nobody but me / Soapbox opera / Another man's woman / Lady / Poor boy / Just a normal day / Meaning / Two of us
CD _____ CDMID 133
A&M / Oct '92 / PolyGram.

EVEN IN THE QUIETEST MOMENTS
Give a little bit / Loverboy / Even in the quietest moments / Downstream / Babaji / From now on / Fool's overture
CD _____ CDMID 150
A&M / Oct '92 / PolyGram.

FAMOUS LAST WORDS
Crazy / Put on your old brown shoes / It's raining again / Bonnie / Know who you are / My kind of lady / C'est le bon / Waiting so long / Don't leave me now
CD _____ CDA 63732
A&M / Oct '82 / PolyGram.

INDELIBLY STAMPED
Your poppa don't mind / Travelled / Rosie had everything planned / Remember / Forever / Potter / Coming home to see you / Times have changed / Friend in need / Aries
CD _____ CDA 3149
A&M / '88 / PolyGram.

PARIS LIVE (2CD Set)
School / Ain't nobody but me / Logical song / Bloody well right / Breakfast in America / You started laughing / Hide in your shell / From now on / Dreamer / Rudy / Soapbox opera / Asylum / Take the long way home / Fool's overture / Two of us / Crime of the century
CD Set _____ CDD 6702
A&M / '88 / PolyGram.

SUPERTRAMP
It's a long road / Aubade / And I am not like other birds of prey / Words unspoken / Maybe I'm a beggar / Home again / Nothing to show / Shadow song / Try again / Surely
CD _____ CDA 3129
A&M / '88 / PolyGram.

SUPERTRAMP SONGBOOK, THE
CD _____ CCV 8919
Compact Club / Apr '94 / BMG.

VERY BEST OF SUPERTRAMP, THE
School / Goodbye stranger / Logical song / Bloody well right / Breakfast in America / Rudy / Take the long way home / Crime of the century / Dreamer / Ain't nobody but me / Hide in your shell / From now on / It's raining again / Give a little bit / Cannonball
CD _____ TRACD 1992
A&M / Jul '92 / PolyGram.

Supreme Dicks
WORKINGMAN'S DICK
CD _____ FFR 002CD
Freek / Aug '94 / SRD.

Supreme Love Gods
SUPREME LOVE GODS
CD _____ DABCD 2
Beggars Banquet / Jun '93 / Warner Music / Disc.

Supremes
GREATEST HITS AND RARE CLASSICS
Up the ladder to the roof / Nathan Jones / I guess I'll miss the man / Stoned love / Everybody's got the right to love / Floy joy / Bad weather / Automatically sunshine / Paradise / Tossin' and turnin' / Il voce de silenzio (Silent voices) / Love train / I had to fall in love / He's my man / Color my world blue / You turn me around / Sha-la bandit / This is why I believe in you / I'm gonna let my heart do the walking / You're my driving wheel / When I looked at your face / Another life from now now
CD _____ 530050-2
Motown / Jan '93 / PolyGram.

I'M GONNA MAKE YOU LOVE ME
(Supremes & Temptations)
I'm gonna make you love me / My guy, my girl / Uptight (everything's alright) / Sweet inspiration / I'll try something new / Ain't no mountain high enough / I second that emotion / Why (must we fall in love) / For better or worse / Weight / I'll be doggone / Stubborn kind of fellow
CD _____ 5500752
Spectrum/Karussell / May '93 / PolyGram / THE.

TOUCH
This is the story / Nathan Jones / Here comes the sunrise / Love it came to me this time / Johnny Raven / Have I lost you / Time and love / Touch / Happy (is a bumpy road) / It's so hard for me to say goodbye
CD _____ 530211-2
Motown / Jan '93 / PolyGram.

Surface
NICE TIME 4 LOVIN', A (The Best Of Surface)
Nice time 4 lovin' / Happy / Closer than friends / You are my everything / I missed (title song reprise) / Shower me with your love / First time / Never gonna let you down / World of own / Christmas time is here
CD _____ 4690542
Columbia / Oct '95 / Sony.

Surfaris
FUN CITY USA/WIPE OUT
CD _____ REP 4118-WZ
Repertoire / Aug '91 / Pinnacle / Cadillac.

SURF PARTY
Wipeout / Tequila / Shake'n stomp / Surfer Joe / Point panic / Pipeline / Summertime blues / Something else / Earthquake / Hiawatha / Louie Louie / Apache / Scatter shield / Let's go trippin' / Surfbeat / Misirolu
CD _____ GNPD 2239
GNP Crescendo / Aug '95 / Silva Screen.

WIPE OUT (The Best Of The Sufaris)
CD _____ VSD 5478
Varese Sarabande/Colosseum / Dec '94 / Pinnacle / Silva Screen.

Surgery
NATIONWIDE
CD _____ ARR 89201CD
Twin Tone / Sep '90 / Pinnacle.

SHIMMER
Bootywhack / Off the A list / Shimmer / Vibe out / Mr. Scientist / Low cut blues / D-Nice / Gulf coast / Nilla waif / Didn't I know you once / No 1 pistola
CD _____ 756782579
East West / '94 / Warner Music.

TRIM, 9TH WARD HIGH ROLLER
CD _____ ARRCD 35/225
Amphetamine Reptile / Jun '93 / SRD.

Surman, John
ADVENTURE PLAYGROUND
Only yesterday / Figfoot / Quadraphonic question / Trance said once / Just for now / As if we knew / Twisted roots / Duet for one / Seven
CD _____ 5119812
ECM / Sep '92 / New Note.

AMAZING ADVENTURES OF SIMON SIMON
Nestor's saga (the tale of the ancient) / Buccaneers / Kentish hunting (Lady Margaret's air) / Pilgrim's way (to the seventeenth walls) / Within the halls of Neptune / Phoenix and the fire / Fide et amore (by faith and love) / Merry pranks (the jester's song) / Fitting epitaph
CD _____ 8291602
ECM / Aug '86 / New Note.

BIOGRAPHY OF REV ABSALOM DAWE
First light / Countess journeys / Monastic calling / Druid's circle / 'Twas but piety / Three aspects / Long narrow road / Wayfarer / Far corners / An image
CD _____ 5237492
ECM / Sep '95 / New Note.

BRASS PROJECT, THE
Returning exile / Coastline / New one two / Special motive / Wider vision / Silent lake / Mellstock quire tantrum clangley / All for a shadow
CD _____ 5173622
ECM / May '93 / New Note.

ROAD TO SAINT IVES
Polperro / Tintagel / Trethevy quoit / Rame head / Mevagissey / Lostwithiel / Perranporth / Bodmin moor / Kelly Bray / Piperspool / Marazion / Bedruthan steps
CD _____ 8438492
ECM / Oct '90 / New Note.

STORAAS NORDIC QUARTET
Traces / Unwritten letter / Offshore piper / Gone to the dogs / Double trouble / Ved sorevatn / Watching shadows / Illusions / Wild bird
CD _____ 5271202
ECM / Mar '95 / New Note.

STRANGER THAN FICTION
CD _____ 5218502
ECM / Jan '89 / New Note.

SURMAN FOR ALL SAINTS
Round the round / Twelve alone / Electric plunger / Cascadence / Walls / Satisfied air / Matador / Saints alive / Barcarolle
CD _____ 8254072
ECM / Jan '89 / New Note.

UPON REFLECTION
Edges of illusion / Filigree / Caithness to Kerry / Beyond a shadow / Prelude and rustic dance / Lamp fighter / Following behind / Constellation
CD _____ 8254722
ECM / '82 / New Note.

Surman, Martin
LIVE AT WOODSTOCK TOWN HALL
(Martin, Stu & John Surman)
Harry Lovett - Man without a country / Are you positive you're negative / Wrested in mustard / Professor Goodly's implosion machine / Master of disaster / Don't leave me like this
CD _____ BGOCD 290
Beat Goes On / Nov '95 / Pinnacle.

Suryana, Ujang
INSTRUMENTALS VOL.1
CD _____ FLTRCD 516
Flame Tree / Sep '93 / Pinnacle.

INSTRUMENTALS VOL.2
CD _____ FLTRCD 517
Flame Tree / Sep '93 / Pinnacle.

Suso, Salieu
GRIOT
CD _____ LYRCD 7418
Lyrichord / Aug '93 / Roots / ADA / CM.

Suspiral
GREAT AND SECRET SHOW, THE
CD _____ NIGHTCD 007
Nightbreed / Nov '95 / Plastic Head.

Sutch, Screaming Lord
LIVE MANIFESTO
CD _____ JETCD 1004
Jet / Oct '92 / Total/BMG.

ROCK AND HORROR
Scream and scream / All black and hairy / Jack the ripper / Monster rock / Rock and shock / Murder in the graveyard / London rocker / Penny penny / Rockabilly madman / Oh well / Loonabilly / Go Berry go
CD _____ CDCHM 65
Ace / Jul '91 / Pinnacle / Cadillac / Complete/Pinnacle.

Sutherland Brothers
REACH FOR THE SKY (Sutherland Brothers & Quiver)
When the train comes / Dirty city / Arms of Mary / Something special / Love on the moon / Ain't too proud / Dr. Dancer / Reach for the sky / Moonlight lady / Mad trail
CD _____ 4805262
Columbia / May '95 / Sony.

Sutherland, Madge
HOME FREE
CD _____ CDJMI 2100
Jahmani / Dec '95 / Jetstar / Grapevine / THE.

Sutton Kurtis, Barbara
SOLO & DUETS (Sutton Kurtis, Barbara & Ralph Sutton)
CD _____ SKCD 2-2027
Sackville / Jun '93 / Swift / Jazz Music / Jazz Horizons / Cadillac / CM.

Sutton, Ralph
ALLIGATOR CRAWL
CD _____ SACD 92
Solo Art / Feb '93 / Jazz Music.

AT CAFE DES COPAINS
CD _____ SKCD 2-2019
Sackville / Jun '93 / Swift / Jazz Music / Jazz Horizons / Cadillac / CM.

EYE OPENER
Rippling waters / Viper's drag / Memories of you / Gone with the wind / June night / Old fashioned love / Cottage for sale / When I grow too old to dream / Clothes line ballet
CD _____ J&MCD 500
Collector's Items / Oct '91 / Swift / Wellard / Jazz Music.

LIVE AT MAYBECK RECITAL HALL, VOL. 30
Honeysuckle rose / In a mist / Clothes line ballet / In the dark / Ain't misbehavin' / Echo of Spring / Dinah / Love lies / Russian lullaby / St. Louis blues / Viper's drag / After you've gone
CD _____ CCD 4586
Concord Jazz / Dec '93 / New Note.

MORE SOLO PIANO
CD _____ SKCD 22036
Sackville / Aug '94 / Swift / Jazz Music / Jazz Horizons / Cadillac / CM.

PARTNERS IN CRIME (Sutton, Ralph & Bob & Len Barnard)
Swing that music / One morning in May / Old folks / Rain / I never knew / Slow boat to China / 'S wonderful / How can you face me / West End avenue blues / Diga diga doo
CD _____ SKCD 2-2023
Sackville / Jun '93 / Swift / Jazz Music / Jazz Horizons / Cadillac / CM.

RALPH SUTTON 1975
CD _____ FLYCD 911
Flyright / Feb '92 / Hot Shot / Wellard / Jazz Music / CM.

Suzuki, Yoshio Chin
MORNING PICTURE
CD _____ JD 3306
JVC / Jul '88 / New Note.

Sven Gali
IN WIRE
What you give / Keeps me down / Worms / Make me / Red moon / Tired of listening / Shallow truth / Rocking chair / Helen / Who said
CD _____ 74321282112
RCA / May '95 / BMG.

SVEN GALI
Under the influence / Tie dyed skies / Sweet little gypsy in my garden / Freaxz / Love don't live here anymore / Stiff competition / Real thing / Whisper in the rain / Twenty five hours a day / Here today, gone tomorrow / Disgusteen
CD _____ 74321114422
RCA / Mar '93 / BMG.

Svuci, Kalsijki
BOSNIAN BREAKDOWN
Oho ho sto je liepo / Ja te cekam milice / Crven fesic / Komsinice mila moja / Frula svira kosu kujem / Ramino kolo / Ako zelis mene / Inoco moja krivdoco / Otimas se branis se / Sedam puta lola se ozenio / Sota
CD _____ CDORB 074
Globestyle / Jan '92 / Pinnacle.

SWA
EVOLUTION 85-87
CD _____ SST 157 CD
SST / Aug '88 / Plastic Head.

VOLUME
CD _____ SST 282 CD
SST / May '93 / Plastic Head.

WINTER
CD _____ SST 238 CD
SST / Mar '89 / Plastic Head.

Swains
ELECTRIC SOUL
CD _____ KK 068CD
KK / Jun '92 / Plastic Head.

SONIC MIND JUNCTION
CD _____ KK 097
KK / Nov '93 / Plastic Head.

Swainson, Neil
FORTY NINTH PARALLEL (Swainson, Neil Quintet)
Forty ninth parallel / Port of Spain / Southern exposure / On the lam / Don't hurt yourself / Homestretch
CD _____ CCD 4396
Concord Jazz / Nov '89 / New Note.

Swaleh, Zuhura
JINO LA PEMBE (Swaleh, Zuhura & Maulidi Musical Party)
Shani / bado basi / Safari / Singetema / Kisu chako / Humvui alovikwa / Parare / Jino la pembe / Nalia na jito / Mdudu
CD _____ CDORBD 075
Globestyle / Sep '92 / Pinnacle.

Swallow
BLOW
CD _____ CAD 2010CD
4AD / Jul '92 / Disc.

Swallow, Steve
CARLA (Swallow, Steve Sextet)
Deep trouble / Crab alley / Fred and Ethel / Read my lips / Afterglow / Hold it against me / Count the ways / Last night
CD _____ 833 492 2
Watt / Oct '87 / New Note.

REAL BOOK
Bite your Grandmother / Second hand motion / Wrong together / Outfits / Thinking out loud / Let's eat / Better times / Willow / Muddy in the bank / Ponytail
CD _____ 5216372
Watt / Jun '94 / New Note.

SWALLOW
Belles / Soca symphony / Slender thread / Thrills and spills / William and Mary / Doin' it slow / Thirty five / Ballroom / Playing with water
CD _____ 5119602
Watt / Mar '92 / New Note.

Swamp Terrorists
GROW - SPEED INJECTION
Ratskin / Hidden (crab) / Vault I / Skizzo pierce / Rebuff / Vault II / Green blood / Braintrash / Vault III / Rawhead / S.S.M. / Drop the dig / Ratskin (floatmix) (Only on CD) / Drip the dog (Only on CD)
CD _____ MA 0092
Machinery / Mar '92 / Plastic Head.

Swamptrash
IT DON'T MAKE NO NEVER MIND
CD _____ FFUS 3301CD
Fast Forward / '88 / Fast Forward Records.

Swampwalk
STRANGLED AT BIRTH
CD _____ CDBLEED 6
Bleeding Hearts / Oct '93 / Pinnacle.

Swan Arcade
FULL CIRCLE
CD _____ 8108 0L
Cygnet / '90 / Probe Plus Records / Roots.

Swan, Billy
BILLY SWAN
I can help / You're the one / Ubangi stomp / Vanessa / Just want to taste your wine / Don't be cruel / Blue suede shoes / Swept away / Everything's the same (ain't nothin' changed) / Number one / (You just) Woman-handled my mind / I'm her fool / Overnite thing (usually) / Shake, rattle and roll / Lover please / Don't kill our love
CD _____ 474269-2
Monument / Sep '94 / Sony.

BOP TO BE
CD _____ PMPCD 1200
Carlton Home Entertainment / Jul '95 / Carlton Home Entertainment.

Swan, Jimmy
HONKY TONKIN' IN MISSISSIPPI
I had a dream / Juke joint mama / I love you too much / Trifflin' on me / Last letter / Little church / Mark of shame / Losers weepers / One more time / Lonesome daddy blues / Frost on my roof / Why did you change your mind / Hey baby, baby / It's your turn to cry / Good and lonesome / Country cattin' / Way that you're livin' / Lonesome man / I love you too much (2) / Don't conceal you're wedding ring / No one loves a broken heart / It takes a lonesome man / Rattlesnakin' Daddy / Asleep in the deep / Walkin' my dog / Good and lonesome (2) / Why did you change your mind (2)
CD _____ BCD 15758

655

Swan Silvertones

HEAVENLY LIGHT
Jesus is all the world to me / Love lifted me / I'm sealed / How I got over / Have thine own way / Shine on me / Heavenly light shine on me / Jesus keep me near the cross / He won't deny me / Every day and every hour / Four and twenty elders / Shine on me medley / My rock / Lord's prayer / Medley / I'm coming home / After a while
CD _____ CDCHD 482
Ace / Jul '93 / Pinnacle / Cadillac / Complete/Pinnacle.

LOVE LIFTED ME AND MY ROCK
Trouble in my way / How I got over / After a while / Prayer in my mouth / Glory to his name / I'm a rollin' / Let's go / Jesus changed this heart of mine / I'm coming home / Love lifted me / Heavenly light shine on me / Day will surely come / My rock / Since Jesus came into my heart / I cried / What do you know about Jesus / Milky white way / He won't deny me / Jesus is a friend / Motherless child / Man in Jerusalem / Keep my heart / Oh how I love Jesus / This little light of mine
CD _____ CDCHD 482
Ace / May '91 / Pinnacle / Cadillac / Complete/Pinnacle.

SINGING IN MY SOUL
Oh Mary don't you weep / Great day in December / Singin' in my soul / At the cross / He saved you / Why I love him so / Jesus is alright with me / Lord is coming / Nobody but you / Love lifted me / Call him Jesus / Leave your burden there / Cross for me / I'll be satisfied / Send my child / I thank you Lord / Come to Jesus / Without a mother / Search me Lord / Bible days
CD _____ CPCD 8089
Charly / May '95 / Charly / THE / Cadillac.

Swana, John

FEELING'S MUTUAL, THE
CD _____ 1090CD
Criss Cross / Jan '95 / Cadillac / Harmonia Mundi.

INTRODUCING JOHN SWANA
CD _____ CRISS 1045CD
Criss Cross / Apr '91 / Cadillac / Harmonia Mundi.

JOHN SWANA AND FRIENDS
CD _____ CRISS 1055CD
Criss Cross / May '92 / Cadillac / Harmonia Mundi.

Swans

BODY TO BODY JOB TO JOB
CD _____ YGCD 004
Young God / Jul '95 / Vital.

CHILDREN OF GOD
New mind / In my garden / Sex God sex / Blood and honey / Like a drug / You're not real, girl / Beautiful child / Blackmail / Trust me / Real love / Blind love / Children of God
CD _____ PRODCD 17
Product Inc. / Nov '87 / Vital.

COP
CD _____ KCCCD 001
K422 / Jan '89 / Vital.

COP / YOUNG GOD
Half Life / Job / Why Hide / Clayman / I Crawled / Raping A Slave / Your Property / Cop / Butcher / Thug / Young God / This Is Mine
CD _____ KCC 001CD
K422 / Aug '92 / Vital.

FILTH
CD _____ YGCD 1
Young God / Jul '95 / Vital.

GREAT ANNIHILATOR, THE
In / I am the sun / She lives / Celebrity lifestyle / Mother/Father / Blood promise / Mind, body, light, sound / My buried child / Warm / Alcohol the seed / Killing for company / Mothers milk / Where does a body end / Telepathy / Great annihilator / Out
CD _____ YGCD 009
Young God / Jan '95 / Vital.

GREED
CD _____ KCC 2 CD
K422 / Mar '86 / Vital.

HOLY MONEY
CD _____ KCCD 3
Some Bizarre / Feb '88 / Pinnacle.

LOVE OF LIFE
CD _____ YGCD 005
Young God / Jul '95 / Vital.

OMNISCIENCE
Mother's milk / Pow r sac / Will serve / Her / Black eyed dog / Amnesia / Love of life / Other side of the world / Rutting / God loves America / Omnipotent
CD _____ YGCD 007
Young God / Jul '95 / Vital.

REAL LOVE
CD _____ LOVETWOCD
Love / May '92 / Direct / ADA.

WHITE LIGHT FROM THE MOUTH OF INFINITY
CD _____ YGCD 3
Young God / Jul '95 / Vital.

Swarbrick, Dave

SWARBRICK AND SWARBRICK
CD _____ ESMCD 355
Essential / Jan '96 / Total/BMG.

Swartz, Harvey

IT'S ABOUT TIME (Swartz, Harvey & Urban Earth)
CD _____ 1390112
Gaia / Feb '89 / New Note.

Swat

DEEP INSIDE A COPS MIND
CD _____ ARRCD 54-334
Amphetamine Reptile / Aug '94 / SRD.

Sweat, Keith

GET UP ON IT
Interlude (how do you like it) / How do you like it / It gets better / Get up on it / Feels so good / How do you like it (part 2) / Intermission break / My whole world / Grind on you / When I give my love / Put your lovin' through the test / Telephone love / Come into my bedroom / For you (you got everything)
CD _____ 755961550-2
Elektra / May '94 / Warner Music.

I'LL GIVE ALL MY LOVE TO YOU
I'll give all my love to you / Make you sweat / Come back / Merry go round / Your love / Your love (part 2) / Just one of them thangs / I knew that you were cheatin' / Love to love you
CD _____ 7559608612
Elektra / Jun '90 / Warner Music.

KEEP IT COMIN'
Keep it comin' / Spend a little time / Why me baby / I really love you / Let me love you / I want to love you down / I'm gone for mine / (There you go) tellin' me no again / Give me what I want / Ten commandments of love / Keep it comin' (2)
CD _____ EKT 103CD
Elektra / Nov '91 / Warner Music.

MAKE IT LAST FOREVER
Something just ain't right / Right and a wrong way / Tell me it's me you want / I want her / Make it last forever / In the rain / How deep is your love / Don't stop your love
CD _____ 9607632
Elektra / Jul '88 / Warner Music.

Sweaty Nipples

BUG HARVEST
CD _____ CDVEST 37
Bulletproof / Jan '95 / Pinnacle.

Swedish String Quartet

LIVE AT SALSTA CASTLE
Poor butterfly / Avalon / Limehouse blues / I got rhythm / Tangerine / Have you met Miss Jones
CD _____ NCD 8803
Phontastic / '93 / Wellard / Jazz Music / Cadillac.

STOMPIN' AND FLYING
If I had you / Lover / Old folks / It could happen to you / Sweet Sue, just you / Flying home / Lady be good
CD _____ NCD 8805
Phontastic / '93 / Wellard / Jazz Music / Cadillac.

SWEDISH STRING QUARTET (feat. Ove Lars Erstrand)
Avalon / Poor butterfly / More than you know / Moonglow / Have you met Miss Jones / I got rhythm
CD _____ PHONT CD 8803
Phontastic / Apr '90 / Wellard / Jazz Music / Cadillac.

Swedish Swing Society

WINTER SWING
CD _____ SITCD 9213
Sittel / Mar '95 / Cadillac / Jazz Music.

Sweeney's Men

TIME WAS NEVER HERE 1968-1969
Rattlin' roarin' willie / Sullivan's John / Tom Dooley / Handsome cabin boy / Willie o' Winsbury / Dreams for me / Pipe on the hob / Brain jam / Hall of mirrors / Standing on the shore / Go by brooks / When you don't care for me / Afterthoughts / Hiram Hubbard / My dearest dear / House carpenter / Johnstone / Reynard the fox / Mistake no doubt / Dance to your Daddy / Pretty Polly / Sally Brown
CD _____ TDEM 11
Trandem / Apr '94 / CM / ADA / Pinnacle.

Sweet

A
CD _____ AIM 1048
Aim / Apr '95 / Direct / ADA / Jazz Music.

BALLROOM HITZ (The Best Of The Sweet)
CD _____ 5350012
PolyGram TV / Jan '96 / PolyGram.

BLOCKBUSTER (Live On Stage)
Hell raiser / Burning / Someone else / Rock 'n' roll disgrace / Need a lot of loving / Done me wrong alright / You're not wrong for loving me / Man with the golden arm / Wig wam bam / Little Willy / Teenage rampage / Keep on knockin' / Shakin all over / Great balls of fire / Reelin' and rockin' / Ballroom blitz / Blockbuster / FBI
CD _____ MDCD 013
Music De-Luxe / Jan '96 / Magnum Music Group.

BLOCKBUSTERS
Ballroom blitz / Hellraiser / New York connection / Little Willy / Burning / Need a lot of lovin' / Wig wam bam / Blockbuster / Rock 'n' roll disgrace / Chop chop / Alexander Graham Bell / Poppa Joe / Co co / Funny funny
CD _____ ND 74313
RCA / Dec '89 / BMG.

COLLECTION, THE
CD _____ 74321292752
RCA / Jul '95 / BMG.

COLLECTION: SWEET
Teenage rampage / Rebel rouser / Solid gold brass / Stairway to the stars / Turn it down / Six teens / Into the night / No you don't / Fever of love / Lies in your eyes / Fox on the run / Restless / Set me free / AC/DC / Sweet f.a. / Action / Peppermint twist / Heartbreak today / Lost angels / Lady Starlight
CD _____ CCSCD 230
Castle / Oct '89 / BMG.

DESOLATION BOULEVARD
Six teens / Fox on the run / Turn it down / Medusa / Solid gold brass / Lady Starlight / Man with the golden arm / Breakdown / My generation
CD _____ CLACD 170
Castle / Dec '89 / BMG.

FIRST RECORDINGS 1968-1971
CD _____ REP 4140-WZ
Repertoire / Aug '91 / Pinnacle / Cadillac.

GIVE US A WINK
CD _____ REP 4084-WZ
Repertoire / Aug '91 / Pinnacle / Cadillac.

GREATEST HITS LIVE
CD _____ AIM 1041
Aim / Apr '95 / Direct / ADA / Jazz Music.

GREATEST HITS: SWEET
CD _____ 290586
Ariola Express / Dec '92 / BMG.

HARD CENTRES - THE ROCK YEARS
Set me free / Sweet F.A. / Restless / Yesterday's rain / White mice / Cockroach / Keep it in / Live for today / Windy city / Midnight to daylight
CD _____ CDMZEB 11
Anagram / Sep '95 / Pinnacle.

IN CONCERT
Hell raiser / Burning / Someone will / Rock 'n' roll disgrace / Need a lot of loving / Done me wrong alright / You're not wrong for loving me / Man with golden arm / Wig wam bam / Little Willie / Teenage rampage / Keep on knockin' / Shakin' all over / Lucille / Great balls of fire / Reeling and rocking / Peppermint twist / Shout / Ballroom blitz / Blockbuster / F.B.I.
CD _____ HP 93462
Happy Price / Jan '96 / Target/BMG.

LEVEL HEADED
CD _____ REP 4234-WP
Repertoire / Aug '91 / Pinnacle / Cadillac.

LIVE FOR TODAY
CD _____ RRCD 175
Receiver / Nov '93 / Grapevine.

OFF THE RECORD
Fever of love / Lost angels / Midnight to daylight / Windy city / Live for today / She gimme lovin' / Laura Lee / Hard times / Funk it up
CD _____ REP 4085-WZ
Repertoire / Aug '91 / Pinnacle / Cadillac.

SWEET LIVE 1973, THE
Ballroom blitz / Little Willie / Rock 'n' roll disgrace / Done me wrong alright / Hellraiser / You're not wrong for loving me / Burning/Someone else will / Man with the golden arm / Need a lot of lovin' / Wig wam bam / Teenage rampage / Blockbuster / Keep on knockin' / Shakin' all over / Lucille / Great balls of fire / Reelin' and rockin' / Peppermint twist / Shout
CD _____ DOJOCD 89
Dojo / Mar '93 / BMG.

Sweet Diesel

KIDS ARE DEAD, THE
Empire strikes back / Supermarket / Morning breath / I hate the man / (I'm just a) Kid

---

in this town / You want it / Gallon man / Kids are dead / Enemy / Workers comp / What happend to my anger
CD _____ ENG 014ECD
Engine / Nov '95 / Vital.

Sweet Exorcist

SPIRIT GUIDE TO LOW TECH
CD _____ T 33.13
Touch / Oct '95 / These / Kudos.

Sweet Honey In The Rock

BREATHS (Best of Sweet Honey in the Rock)
Breaths / Stranger blues / Joanne little / Ella's song / More than a paycheck / Mandiacapella / Study war no more / Waters of Babylon (rivers of Babylon) / Oughta be a woman / On children / Chile your waters run red through Soweto / Azanian freedom song
CD _____ COOKCD 008
Cooking Vinyl / Feb '88 / Vital.

FEEL SOMETHING DRAWING ME ON
Waters of Babylon (rivers of Babylon) / In the upper room / Leaning and depending on the Lord / Try Jesus / Feel something drawing on me
CD _____ COOKCD 082
Cooking Vinyl / Mar '95 / Vital.

GOOD NEWS
Breaths / Chile your waters run red through Soweto / Good news / If you had lived / On children / Alla that's all right, but / Echo / Oh death / Biko / Oughta be a woman / Time on my hands / Sometime
CD _____ COOKCD 027
Cooking Vinyl / Aug '89 / Vital.

IN THIS LAND
CD _____ CDEB 2522
Earthbeat / May '93 / Direct / ADA.

LIVE AT CARNEGIE HALL
Beautitudes / Where are the keys to the kingdom / Emergency / Are my hands clean / Peace / My lament / Run run mourner run / Letter to Dr. Martin Luther King / Ode to the international debt / Your worries ain' like mine / Song of the exile / Denko / Drinking of the wine / Wade in the water (CD only.) / Our side won (CD only.)
CD _____ BAKECD 003
Cooking Vinyl / May '90 / Vital.

OTHER SIDE, THE
Mandiacapella / Step by step / Deportees / Moving on / Stranger blues / Venceremos / Other side / No images / Gift of love / Mae Frances / Let us go back to the old landmark / Tomorrow
CD _____ COOKCD 083
Cooking Vinyl / Mar '95 / Vital.

SACRED GROUND
CD _____ 9425802
Earthbeat / Jan '96 / Direct / ADA.

STILL ON THE JOURNEY
CD _____ EBCD 942536
Earthbeat / Nov '93 / Direct / ADA.

SWEET HONEY IN THE ROCK
Sweet honey in the rock / Sun will never go down / Dream variations / Let us all come together / Joanne Little / Jesus is my only friend / Are there any rights I'm entitled to / Going to see my baby / You make my day pretty / Hey mann / Doing things together / Travelling shoes / Sweet honey in the rock (2)
CD _____ COOKCD 080
Cooking Vinyl / Mar '95 / Vital.

WE ALL EVERYONE OF US
Study war no more / What a friend we have in Jesus / Sweet bird of youth / How long / More than a paycheck / Azanian freedom song / Listen to the rhythm / Testimony / Oh Lord hold my hand / Battle for my life / Ella's song / I'm gon' stand / We all every-one of us
CD _____ COOKCD 081
Cooking Vinyl / Mar '95 / Vital.

Sweet Inspirations

BEST OF THE SWEET INSPIRATIONS, THE
CD _____ SCLCD 2506
Ichiban Soul Classics / Mar '95 / Koch.

ESTELLE, MYRNA AND SYLVIA
Wishes and dishes / You roam when you don't get it at home / Slipped and tripped / All it takes is you and me / Pity yourself / Emergency / Call me when all else fails / Whole world is out / Why marry / Sweet inspiration / Why am I treated so bad
CD _____ CDSXE 062
Stax / Jul '92 / Pinnacle.

Sweet, Matthew

100% FUN
Sick of myself / Not when I need it / We're the same / Giving it back / Everything changes / Lost my mind / Come to love / Walk out / I almost forgot / Super baby / Get older / Smog moon
CD _____ 72445110812
Zoo Entertainment / Mar '95 / BMG.

ALTERED BEAST
Dinosaur act / Devil with the green eyes / Ugly truth / Time capsule / Someone to pull the trigger / Knowing people / Life without you / Ugly truth rock / In too deep / Reaching out / Falling / What do you know / Evergreen
CD _____ 72445110502
Zoo Entertainment / Jul '93 / BMG.

GIRLFRIEND
CD _____ PD 90644
Zoo Entertainment / Jun '92 / BMG.

Sweet, Michael

MICHAEL SWEET
CD _____ CD 02231
Way Hey / May '95 / Total/BMG.

Sweet People

SUMMER DREAM
Et les oiseaux chantaient / Heartstring / Un ete avec toi / Elodie / Lake como / Santorini / Balladepour tsi-co tsi co / Aria pour une voix / La foret enchantee / Barcarolle / Le grande large / Aria pour notre amour / Perce / Nuits blacnhes / Wonderful day
CD _____ 831213-2
Polydor / Apr '94 / PolyGram.

Sweet, Rachel

FOOL AROUND
CD _____ REP 4218-WY
Repertoire / Aug '91 / Pinnacle / Cadillac.

PROTECT THE INNOCENT
CD _____ STIFFCD 10
Disky / Jan '94 / THE / BMG / Discovery / Pinnacle.

Sweet Sister

FLORA & FAUNA
CD _____ CDFLAG 82
Under One Flag / Nov '94 / Pinnacle.

Sweet Talks

HOLLYWOOD HIGHLIFE PARTY
CD _____ ADC 301
PAM / Feb '94 / Direct / ADA.

Sweet Tooth

CRASH LIVE
CD _____ HD 002
PDCD / Apr '94 / Plastic Head.

Sweet Water

SUPERFRIENDS
CD _____ 7559617732
East West / Nov '95 / Warner Music.

Sweet William

KIND OF STRANGEST DREAM
CD _____ HY 39100282CD
Hyperium / Nov '92 / Plastic Head.

Sweetest Ache

GRASS ROOTS
Love me gently / Something we can find / Carry me home / Good days gone / One more time / Jayne / Nothing ever ends / Never gonna say goodbye / Honey / Little angel
CD _____ ASKCD 029
Vinyl Japan / Mar '94 / Vital.

Sweethearts Of The Rodeo

RODEO WALTZ
CD _____ SH 3819CD
Sugarhill / Apr '94 / Roots / CM / ADA / Direct.

SWEETHEARTS OF THE RODEO
Midnight girl/Sunset town / Hey doll baby / Since I found you / Gotta get away / Chains of gold / Chosen few / Everywhere I turn / I can't resist
CD _____ 4605312
CBS / Feb '88 / Sony.

Swell

41
CD _____ ARBCD 6
Beggars Banquet / Apr '94 / Warner Music / Disc.

WELL
Intro / At long last / Everything / Down / Turtle song / It's OK / Price / Showbiz / Tired / Wash your brain / Soda jerk fountain / Suicide fountain / Thank you, good evening
CD _____ MEANCD 002
Mean / Jun '92 / Vital.

Swell Maps

JANE FROM OCCUPIED EUROPE
CD _____ MAPS 002 CD
Grey Area / Jul '89 / Pinnacle.

TRAIN OUT OF IT
CD _____ MAPS 003CD
Grey Area / Aug '91 / Pinnacle.

TRIP TO MARINEVILLE, A
CD _____ MAPS 001 CD
Grey Area / Jul '89 / Pinnacle.

WHATEVER HAPPENS NEXT
CD _____ MAPS 004CD
Grey Area / Aug '91 / Pinnacle.

Swerdlow, Tommy

PRISONER OF THE GIFTED SLEEP
CD _____ NAR 074 CD
New Alliance / Dec '93 / Pinnacle.

Swervedriver

EJECTOR SEAT RESERVATIONS
CD _____ CRECD 157
Creation / Aug '95 / 3MV / Vital.

MEZCAL HEAD
For seeking heat / Duel / Blowin' cool / Mickey / Last train to Satansville / Harry and Maggie / Change is gonna come / Girl on a motorbike / Duress / You find it everywhere
CD _____ CRECD 143
Creation / Sep '93 / 3MV / Vital.

RAISE
CD _____ CRECD 093
Creation / Oct '91 / 3MV / Vital.

Swift, Duncan

BROADWAY CONCERT, THE
CD _____ ESSCD 258
Essential / Feb '95 / Total/BMG.

BROADWOOD CONCERT, THE
CD _____ BEARCD 34
Big Bear / Nov '91 / BMG.

OUT LOOKING FOR THE LION
CD _____ BEARCD 28
Big Bear / Jun '88 / BMG.

Swift, Jude

COMMON GROUND
CD _____ NOVA 9139
Nova / Jan '93 / New Note.

MUSIC FOR YOUR NEIGHBOURHOOD
CD _____ NOVA 8917
Nova / Jan '93 / New Note.

Swimwear Catalogue

NTUNXUN
CD _____ APR 005CD
April / Mar '95 / Plastic Head.

Swing Out Sister

GET IN TOUCH WITH YOURSELF
Get in touch with yourself / Am I the same girl / Incomplete without you / Everyday crime / Circulate / Who let the love out / Understand / Not gonna change / Don't say a word / Love child / I can hear you but can't see you (Inst.) / Everyday crime (Instrumental)
CD _____ 512 241-2
Fontana / May '92 / PolyGram.

IT'S BETTER TO TRAVEL
Breakout / Twilight world (superb, superb mix) / After hours / Blue mood / Surrender / Fooled by a smile / Communion / It's not enough / It's better to travel / Breakout (Nad mix) / Surrender (Stuff gun mix) / Twilight world (Remix) / Communion (Instrumental)
CD _____ 8322132
Fontana / Jul '93 / PolyGram.

KALEIDOSCOPE WORLD
You on my mind / Where in the world / Forever blue / Heart for hire / Tainted / Waiting game / Precious game / Masquerade / Between strangers / Kaleidoscope affair
CD _____ 8382932
Fontana / Jun '94 / PolyGram.

LIVING RETURN, THE
Better make it better / Don't let yourself down / Ordinary people / Mama didn't raise no fool / Don't give up on a good thing / Making the right move / La la (Means I love you) / Feel free / Stop and think it over / That's the way it goes / All in your mind / O pesadelo dos autores / Low down dirty business
CD _____ 522650-2
Fontana / Jun '94 / PolyGram.

Swingin' Haymakers

FOR RENT
CD _____ CCD 907
Circle / Aug '95 / Jazz Music / Swift / Wellard.

Swinging Blue Jeans

ALL THE HITS PLUS MORE
CD _____ CDPT 003
Prestige / Mar '94 / Total/BMG.

BEST OF THE SWINGING BLUE JEANS 1963-66, THE
Hippy hippy shake / It's too late now / Save the last dance for me / That's the way it goes / One of these days / Shakin' all over / roll / Angie / Good golly Miss Molly / Don't worry 'bout me / Sandy / You're no good / Do you know / Long tall Sally / Don't make

me over / Now the Summer's gone / Promise yu'll tell her / It isn't there / Lawdy Miss Clawdy
CD _____ CDSL 8254
EMI / Jul '95 / EMI.

BLUE JEANS ARE IN
CD _____ MOGCD 007
Moggie / Dec '94 / Else.

EMI YEARS: SWINGING BLUE JEANS (Best Of The Swinging Blue Jeans)
Three little fishes / Now I must go / Hippy hippy shake / It's too late now / Shaking feeling / Good golly Miss Molly / Ol' man Mose / Don't it make you feel good / Lawdy Miss Clawdy / You're no good / Long tall Sally / Shakin' all over / Tutti frutti / Make me know you're mine / Ready Teddy / Crazy about my baby / I've got a girl / Chug-a-lug / You're welcome to my heart / I wanna be there / Sidney, gotta draw the line / I want love / Don't make me over / What can I do today / Tremblin' / Rumours, gossip, words untrue / One woman man / Something's coming along / Don't go out into the rain (you're gonna melt) / What have they done to Hazel / Now that you've got me (you don't seem to want me) / Summer somes Sunday / Hey Mrs. Housewife / Big city
CD _____ CDEMS 1446
EMI / Apr '92 / EMI.

LIVE SHARIN'
Tulane / My life / Again and again / Good golly Miss Molly / Don't stop / I saw her standing there / She loves you / Caroline / You're no good / Heatwave / Shakin' all over / It's so easy / When will I be loved / Hard day's night / Hippy hippy shake
CD _____ CDPT 502
Prestige / Jul '90 / Total/BMG.

Swinging Utters

SOUNDS WRONG
CD _____ IFACD 010
IFA / Oct '95 / Plastic Head.

Swirl

PLUMPTUOUS
CD _____ AMUSE 014CD
Playtime / May '92 / Pinnacle / Discovery.

Swirlies

WHAT TO DO ABOUT THEM
CD _____ TAANG 65CD
Taang / Oct '92 / Plastic Head.

Swiss Dixie Stompers

PETITE FLEUR
CD _____ JCD 184
Jazzology / Oct '93 / Swift / Jazz Music.

Sybil

GOOD 'N' READY
CD _____ HFCD 28
PWL / May '93 / Warner Music / 3MV.

SYBILIZATION
CD _____ HFCD 17
PWL / Nov '90 / Warner Music / 3MV.

WALK ON BY
CD _____ HFCD 10
PWL / Feb '90 / Warner Music / 3MV.

Sykes, Roosevelt

BLUES BY ROOSEVELT "HONEYDRIPPER" SYKES
CD _____ SFWCD 40051
Smithsonian Folkways / Nov '95 / ADA / Direct / Koch / CM / Cadillac.

GOLD MINE
CD _____ DD 616
Delmark / Jul '93 / Hot Shot / ADA / CM / Direct / Cadillac.

HARD DRIVIN' BLUES
CD _____ DD 607
Delmark / Dec '95 / Hot Shot / ADA / CM / Direct / Cadillac.

HONEYDRIPPER, THE (1945-1960)
Miss Ida B / Mislead mother / I hate to be alone / Satellite baby / Raining my heart / Lucky blues / Hot boogie / Four o'clock boogie / Something like that / Walking the boogie / Sunnyland blues / Boogie skyes / Ruthie Lee / Hey big momma / Night time is the right time / Stompin the boogie / Hangover / Sweet old Chicago / Hush oh hush / I'm tired / Rock it / Drivin' wheel / Honeydripper
CD _____ CD 52014
Blues Encore / '92 / Target/BMG.

HONEYDRIPPER, THE
CD _____ SOB 35422
Story Of The Blues / Apr '93 / Koch / ADA.

HONEYDRIPPER, THE
CD _____ 5197272
Verve / Apr '93 / PolyGram.

HONEYDRIPPER, THE
CD _____ OBCCD 557
Original Blues Classics / Jul '95 / Complete/Pinnacle / Wellard / Cadillac.

MUSIC IS MY BUSINESS
CD _____ 157702
Blues Collection / Feb '93 / Discovery.

RETURN OF ROOSEVELT SYKES, THE
CD _____ OBCCD 546
Original Blues Classics / Nov '92 / Complete/Pinnacle / Wellard / Cadillac.

ROOSEVELT SYKES VOL. 1 (1929-30)
CD _____ DOCD 5116
Blues Document / Oct '92 / Swift / Jazz Music / Hot Shot.

ROOSEVELT SYKES VOL. 10 1951-57
CD _____ BDCD 6050
Blues Document / Sep '94 / Swift / Jazz Music / Hot Shot.

ROOSEVELT SYKES VOL. 2 (1930-31)
CD _____ DOCD 5117
Blues Document / Oct '92 / Swift / Jazz Music / Hot Shot.

ROOSEVELT SYKES VOL. 3 (1931-33)
CD _____ DOCD 5118
Blues Document / Oct '92 / Swift / Jazz Music / Hot Shot.

ROOSEVELT SYKES VOL. 4 (1934-36)
CD _____ DOCD 5119
Blues Document / Oct '92 / Swift / Jazz Music / Hot Shot.

ROOSEVELT SYKES VOL. 5 (1937-39)
CD _____ DOCD 5120
Blues Document / Oct '92 / Swift / Jazz Music / Hot Shot.

ROOSEVELT SYKES VOL. 6 (1939-40)
CD _____ DOCD 5121
Blues Document / Nov '92 / Swift / Jazz Music / Hot Shot.

ROOSEVELT SYKES VOL. 7 (1941-44)
CD _____ DOCD 5122
Blues Document / Oct '92 / Swift / Jazz Music / Hot Shot.

ROOSEVELT SYKES VOL. 8 1945-47
CD _____ BDCD 6048
Blues Document / Sep '94 / Swift / Jazz Music / Hot Shot.

ROOSEVELY SYKES VOL. 9 1947-51
CD _____ BDCD 6049
Blues Document / Sep '94 / Swift / Jazz Music / Hot Shot.

Sylvester

COLLECTION
CD _____ CCSCD 393
Castle / May '94 / BMG.

STAR - BEST OF SYLVESTER
Stars (everybody is one) / Dance / Down down down / I need somebody to love tonight / I who have nothing / You make me feel (mighty real) / My life is loving you / Can't stop dancing / Body strong (CD/MC only) / Over and over (CD/MC only) / Disco international (CD/MC only)
CD _____ CDSEW 007
Southbound / Jun '89 / Pinnacle.

SYLVESTER/STEP II
Over and over / I tried to forget you / Changes / Tipsong / Down down down / Loving grows up slow / I been down / Never too late / You make me feel (Mighty real) / Dance (Disco heat) / You make me feel (Mighty real) #2 / Grateful / I took my strength from you / Was it something that I said / Just you and me forever
CD _____ CDSEWD 104
Southbound / Jun '94 / Pinnacle.

Sylvian, David

BRILLIANT TREES
Pulling punches / Ink in the well / Nostalgia / Red guitar / Weathered wall / Back waters / Brilliant trees
CD _____ CDV 2290
Virgin / Jun '84 / EMI.

DAMAGE (Sylvian, David & Robert Fripp)
Damage / God's monkey / Brightness falls / Every colour you are / Firepower / Gone to earth / Twentieth Century dreaming (a shaman's song) / Wave / River man / Darshan (the road to Graceland) / Blinding light of heaven / First day
CD _____ DAMAGE 1
Virgin / Sep '94 / EMI.

DARSHAN (Sylvian, David & Robert Fripp)
Darshan (The road to Graceland) / Darshan
CD _____ SLYCD 1
Virgin / Feb '94 / EMI.

FLUX AND MUTABILITY
Flux (a big bright colour world) / Mutability (a new beginning in the offing)
CD _____ CDVE 43
Venture / Sep '89 / EMI.

GONE TO EARTH
Taking the veil / Laughter and forgetting / Before the bullfight / Gone to Earth / Wave / River man / Silver moon / Healing place / Answered prayers / Where the railroad meets the sea / Wooden cross / Silver moon over sleeping steeples / Campfire coyote country / Bird of prey vanishes into

a bright blue / Home / Sunlight seen through towering trees / Upon this earth
CD _____ CDVDL 1
Virgin / Apr '92 / EMI.

PLIGHT AND PREMONITION (Sylvian, David & Holger Czukay)
Plight (the spiralling of winter ghosts) / Premonition
CD _____ CDVE 11
Venture / Mar '88 / EMI.

SECRETS OF THE BEEHIVE
September / Boy with the gun / Maria / Orpheus / Devil's own / When poets dreamed of angels / Mother and child / Let the happiness in / Waterfront / Forbidden colours (CD only)
CD _____ CDV 2471
Virgin / Jul '91 / EMI.

Symarip

SKINHEAD MOONSTOMP
Skinhead moonstomp / Phoenix city / Skinhead girl / Try me best / Skinhead jamboree / Chicken merry / These boots are made for walking / Must catch a train / Skin flint / Stay with him / Fung shu / You're mine
CD _____ CDTRL 187
Trojan / Jan '95 / Jetstar / Total/BMG.

Symphonic Orchestra

ORCHESTRA ROCK 3 (The Love Classics)

With you I'm born again / Up where we belong / One day in your life / Three times a lady / Cavatina / You don't bring me flowers / Memory / One day I'll fly away / Imagine / Sun ain't gonna shine anymore / Hard to say I'm sorry / Miss you nights / I wish it would rain down / My funny valentine / It's raining again / All you need is love
CD _____ MCCD 075
Music Club / Jun '92 / Disc / THE / CM.

Symphonic Rock Orchestra

CLASSIC BEATLES
CD _____ 322879
Koch / Mar '93 / Koch.

Syncopace

SYNCOPACE
CD _____ CROCD 228
Black Crow / Jul '91 / Roots / Jazz Music / CM.

Synergy

RETURN TO RITUAL
CD _____ WHAD 1302
Word / Sep '95 / Total/BMG.

Synetics

PURPLE UNIVERSE, THE
CD _____ CAT 006CD
Rephlex / Jul '95 / Disc.

Syrinx

KALEIDOSCOPE OF SYMPHONIC ROCK
CD _____ CYBERCD 9
Cyber / Aug '94 / Plastic Head.

System 01

DRUGSWORK
CD _____ 74321250592
Tresor Berlin / Feb '95 / BMG.

System 7

777
CD _____ BFLCD 1
Big Life / Mar '93 / Pinnacle.

POINT 3: FIRE ALBUM
CD _____ BFLCA 11
Big Life / Oct '94 / Pinnacle.

POINT 3: WATER ALBUM
CD _____ BFLCB 11
Big Life / Oct '94 / Pinnacle.

SYSTEM 7
Sunburst / Freedom fighters / Habibi / Altitude / Bon humeur / Fractal liaison / Dog / Thunderdog / Listen / Strange quotations / Miracle / Over and out
CD _____ DIXCD 102
10 / Jun '91 / EMI.

Syzygy

MORPHIC RESONANCE
CD Set _____ RSNCD 22
Rising High / Sep '94 / Disc.

Szabo, Gabor

SORCERER, THE
CD _____ MCAD 33117
Impulse Jazz / Apr '90 / BMG / New Note.

Szabo, Sandor

SANCTIFIED LAND
Arrivers / Our presence and thirtyness / Equation of the existence / Ferdinandus / Miramare / Sikonda / Sanctified land / Departers
CD _____ HWYLCD 6
Hwyl / Jun '91 / Hwyl.

Szaszcsavas Band

FOLK MUSIC FROM TRANSYLVANIA
CD _____ QUI 903072
Quintana / Mar '92 / Harmonia Mundi.

Szelevenyi, Akosh

PANNONIA (Szelevenyi, Akosh Ensemble)
CD _____ EPC 891
European Music Production / Jan '94 / Harmonia Mundi.

T

T Power

SELF EVIDENT TRUTH OF AN INTUITIVE MIND, THE
CD _____ SOURCDLP 3
SOUR / Oct '95 / SRD.

T-Square

MEGALITH
CD _____ 4722982
Sony Jazz / Jan '95 / Sony.

T.A.G.C.

BURNING WATER
CD _____ DFX 17CD
Solielmoon Recordings / Mar '95 / Plastic Head.

T.G.V.T.

T.G.V.T.
CD _____ HY 39100972
Hyperium / Jun '94 / Plastic Head.

T.H.D.

MECHANICAL ADVANTAGE
CD _____ HY 859210588
Hypnobeat / Jun '94 / Plastic Head.

T.K.O.

BELOW THE BELT
CD _____ RR 349730
Roadrunner / '89 / Pinnacle.

T.S.O.L.

STRANGE LOVE
CD _____ LS 9392
Roadrunner / May '90 / Pinnacle.

THOUGHTS OF YESTERDAY
CD _____ EFA 122142
Poshboy / Nov '94 / Disc.

Tab Two

FLAGMAN AHEAD
MBN Trumpet intro / No flagman ahead (Mixes) / Wanna lay (on your side) / Swingbridge / (There's) Not a lot / What'cha gonna do / Scubertplatz / Vraimeort Pans / Tab jam / Curfew / Permanent protection
CD _____ CDVIR 34
Virgin / Aug '95 / EMI.

Tabackin, Lew

I'LL BE SEEING YOU (Tabackin, Lew Quartet)
I surrender dear / Wise one / I'll be seeing you / Ruby my dear / Chic lady / Perhaps / Isfahan / Lost in meditation / In walked bud
CD _____ CCD 4528
Concord Jazz / Oct '92 / New Note.

WHAT A LITTLE MOONLIGHT CAN DO
What a little moonlight can do / Easy living / I wished on the moon / Love letters / Poinciana / This time the dream's on me / Broken dreams / Leaves of absinthe / Dig
CD _____ CCD 4617
Concord Jazz / Oct '94 / New Note.

Tabane, Philip

UNH
CD _____ 7559792252
Elektra Nonesuch / Jan '95 / Warner Music.

Tabor, June

AGAINST THE STREAMS
Shameless love / I want to vanish / False, false / Pavanne / He fades away / Irish girl / Apples and potatoes / Beauty and the beast / Turn off the road / Windy city / Waiting for the lark
CD _____ COOKCD 077
Cooking Vinyl / Aug '94 / Vital.

ANGEL TIGER
CD _____ COOKCD 049
Cooking Vinyl / Feb '95 / Vital.

ANTHOLOGY
Mississippi summer / Verdi cries / Strange affair / She moves among men / Lay this body down / Band played waltzing Matilda / Night comes in / King of Rome / Lisbon / Month of January / Hard love / Dark eyed sailor / Heather down the moor / Cold and raw / Sudden waves / No man's land/Flowers of the forest
CD _____ MCCD 126
Music Club / Sep '93 / Disc / THE / CM.

ASHES AND DIAMONDS
Reynard the fox / Devil and bailiff McGlynn Streets of forbes / Lord Maxwell's last goodnight / Now i'm easy / Clerk Saunders Earl of Aboyne / Lisbon / Easter tree / Cold and raw / No mans's land / Flowers of the forest
CD _____ TSCD 360
Topic / Oct '92 / Direct / ADA.

CUT ABOVE, A
CD _____ TSCD 410
Topic / Nov '90 / Direct / ADA.

FREEDOM AND RAIN (Tabor, June & The Oyster Band)
Mississippi summer / Lullaby of London / Night comes in / Valentine's day is over / All tomorrow's parties / Dives and Lazarus / Dark eyed sailor / Pain or paradise / Susie Clelland / Finisterre
CD _____ COOKCD 031
Cooking Vinyl / Feb '95 / Vital.

SOME OTHER TIME
Some other time / Night and day / You don't know what love is / Body and soul / This is always / Pork pie hat / Solitude / I've got you under my skin / Man I love / Meditation / Sophisticated lady / Round Midnight
CD _____ HNCD 1346
Hannibal / Sep '89 / Vital / ADA.

Tackhead

FRIENDLY AS A HAND GRENADE
CD _____ WRCD 013
World / Nov '89 / SRD.

POWER INC VOL 1
CD _____ BLCCD 10
Blanc / Jun '95 / Pinnacle.

TACKHEAD TAPE TIME
Mind at the end of tether / Half cut again / Reality / M.O.V.E. / Hard left / Get this / Man in a suitcase / What's my mission now
CD _____ NTCD 036
Nettwerk / Feb '88 / Vital / Pinnacle.

Tacklebox

ON
CD _____ ROCK 6098-2
Rockville / Mar '93 / SRD.

Tacticos, Manos

MUSIC FROM THE GREEK ISLANDS (Tacticos, Manos & His Bouzoukis)
O Andonis (theme from 'Z') / Lefteris / Delfini - Delfinaki / Natane to Ikosiena / San sfiriksis tries fores / Nostalgia / Athena / Vrehi O Theos / Epipoleos (impulsive) / Tist' anathema in 'afto / Ela agapi mou / Stou kosmou tin aniforia / Strose to stroma sou yia thio / Afto to agori (that boy) / Siko horepse kouli mou / Siko horepse sirtaki / Falinrotissa / Laikos horos / Ta pedia tou pirea / Pai-pai / Ftochologia / Varka sto yialo / Ta thakria mou eene kafta
CD Set _____ CDDL 1029
Music For Pleasure / Nov '91 / EMI.

Tacuma, Jamaaladeen

BOSS OF THE BRASS
CD _____ GCD 79434
Gramavision / Sep '95 / Vital/SAM / ADA.

HOUSE OF BASS
CD _____ GCD 79502
Gramavision / Feb '95 / Vital/SAM / ADA.

JUKE BOX
CD _____ GCD 79436
Gramavision / Sep '95 / Vital/SAM / ADA.

MUSIC WORLD
Kimono queen / Tokyo cosmopolitaan / Matsuru / Rouge / Kismet / Creator has a master plan / Jamila's theme / One more night
CD _____ GCD 79437
Gramavision / Sep '95 / Vital/SAM / ADA.

RENAISSANCE MAN
Renaissance man / Flashback / Let's have a good time / Next stop / Dancing in your head / There he stood / Battle of images / Sparkle
CD _____ GCD 79438
Gramavision / Sep '95 / Vital/SAM / ADA.

SHOW STOPPER
Sunk in the funk / Rhythm box / From me to you / Animated creation / Bird of paradise / Show stopper / From the land of sand / Sophisticated us
CD _____ GCD 79435
Gramavision / Sep '95 / Vital/SAM / ADA.

Tad

8-WAY SANTA
Jinx / Giant killer / Wired god / Delinquent / Hedge hog / Flame tavern / Trash truck / Stumblin' man / Jack Pepsi / Candi / 3-D witch hunt / Crane's cafe / Plague years
CD _____ SPCD 8/122
Sub Pop / '91 / Disc.

INFRARED RIDINGHOOD
CD _____ 7559617892
Warner Bros. / Apr '95 / Warner Music.

INHALER
Grease box / Throat locust / Leafy incline / Luminol / Ulcer / Lycanthrope / Just bought the farm / Rotor / Paregoric / Pansy / Gouge
CD _____ 74321165702
Mechanic / Oct '93 / BMG.

LIVE ALIEN BROADCAST
CD _____ CDMFN 181
Music For Nations / Jan '95 / Pinnacle.

SALT LICK
Axe to grind / High on the hog / Loser / Hibernation / Glue machine / Potlatch / Wood goblins (CD only) / Cooking with gas (CD only) / Daisy (CD only)
CD _____ GRCD 76
Glitterhouse / Apr '90 / Direct / ADA.

Tad Morose

LEAVING THE PAST BEHIND
CD _____ BMCD 43
Black Mark / May '94 / Plastic Head.

PARADIGMA
CD _____ BMCD 085
Black Mark / Jan '96 / Plastic Head.

SENDER OF .....
CD _____ BMCD 056
Black Mark / Mar '95 / Plastic Head.

Tafari, Judah Eskender

RASTAFARI TELL YOU
CD _____ GPCD 007
Gussie P / Sep '95 / Jetstar.

Taff, Russ

WINDS OF CHANGE
CD _____ 9362456762
Warner Bros. / Jun '95 / Warner Music.

Tafolla, Joey

INFRA RED
CD _____ RR 93422
Roadrunner / Apr '91 / Pinnacle.

OUT OF THE SUN
CD _____ RR 9573 2
Roadrunner / '89 / Pinnacle.

Tag Team

AUDIO ENTERTAINMENT
CD _____ 0061322CLU
Edel / Nov '95 / Pinnacle.

WHOOMP (THERE IT IS)
Whoomp (There it is) (mixes) / Funkey / Kick da flow / Get nasty / Bring it on / Wreck da set / Gettin' phat / Just call me D.C. / Bobyhead / Drop 'em / It's somethin' / You go girl / Free style
CD _____ CLU 60062
Club Tools / Feb '94 / Grapevine.

Taggy Tones

LOST IN THE DESERT
I miss you / Monster bop / Big machine / People are strange / Wild girl / Double trouble / Saturday night / Trouble boys / Everybody's rockin' / Keep on waiting / Nose pickin' Mama / Lonely tonight / baby I don't care / Champagne for breakfast / Blue train / My first guitar / Kinky Miss Pinky
CD _____ NERCD 080
Nervous / Apr '95 / Nervous / Magnum Music Group.

VIKING ATTACK
So fine, so kind / B.C. stomp / 501 / John and Mary / Pretty eyes / Rebel cat / To my Dad / Paris, Copenhagen / Crazy love / Viking attack / Crazy kid / From me to you / C'mon Johnny / Sound of guns / Letter to my baby / Myggen svermer
CD _____ NERCD 070
Nervous / Feb '93 / Nervous / Magnum Music Group.

Tah, Geggy

GRAND OPENING
Last word (one for her) / Go / L.A. Lulah / Giddy up / P. Sluff / Tucked in / Fasterhan / Who's in a hurry / Intro / Ovary / Bomb fishing / Crack of dawn / Ghost of P. Sluff / Welcome to the world (Birthday song)
CD _____ 9362452542
Luaka Bop / Jul '94 / Warner Music.

Tahitian Choir

RAPA ITI
Oparo o oparo e / Morotiri nei / Himene tatou / Tarema / Ei reka e / Tatou ki ota / Te vahine ororagni / Te matamua / I te fenua / Tamaki a te mau ariki / Oparo / Tevaitau / Va hiti / Tau matamua / Te parau o eri rama
CD _____ SH 64055
Shanachie / Dec '94 / Koch / ADA / Greensleeves.

Tahitian Man Singers

TOP 20 "TANE"
CD _____ S 65813
Manuiti / Nov '93 / Harmonia Mundi.

Tai Pan

SLOW DEATH
CD _____ SHARK 108CD
Shark / Jun '95 / Plastic Head.

Taiko Drum Ensemble

SOH DAIKO
CD _____ LYRCD 7410
Lyrichord / '91 / Roots / ADA / CM.

Tailgators

HIDE YOUR EYES
CD _____ L3 93962
Roadrunner / Mar '90 / Pinnacle.

Taj Mahal

BIG BLUES (Live At Ronnie Scott's)
Big Blues / Mail box blues / Stagger Lee / Come on in my kitchen / Local local girl / Soothin' / Fishin' blues / Statesboro blues / Everybody is somebody
CD _____ CLACD 328
Castle / Apr '94 / BMG.

DANCING THE BLUES
Blues ain't nothin' / Hardway / Strut / Goin' to the river / Mockingbird / Blue light boogie / Hoochie coochie coo / That's how strong my love is / Down home girl / Stranger in my own hometown / Sittin' on top of the world / I'm ready
CD _____ 01005821122
Private Music / Mar '94 / BMG.

EVENING OF ACOUSTIC MUSIC, AN
CD _____ T&M 004
Tradition & Moderne / Nov '94 / Direct / ADA.

EVOLUTION
CD _____ 7599268112
WEA / Jan '96 / Warner Music.

GIANT STEP
Linin' Track / Country blues / Wild ox man / Little Rain Blues / Little soulful tune / Candy man / Cluck old hen / Colored aristocracy / Blind boy rag / Stagger Lee / Cajun tune / Fishin' Blues / Annie's lover
CD _____ EDCD 264
Edsel / Apr '88 / Pinnacle / ADA.

LIKE NEVER BEFORE
Don't call us / River of love / Scattered / Every wind (in the river) / Blues with a feeling / Squat that rabbit / Take all the time you need / Love up / Cake walk into town / Big legged mommas are back in style / Take a good time
CD _____ 261679
Private Music / Jun '91 / BMG.

LIVE AND DIRECT
Jorge Ben / Reggae no. 1 / You're gonna need somebody / Little brown dog / Take a giant step / L.O.V.E. Love / And who / Suva serenade / Airplay
CD _____ CDTB 121
Thunderbolt / Aug '95 / Magnum Music Group.

MULEBONE
Jubilee / Graveyard mule (hambone rhyme) / Me and the mule / Song for a banjo dance / But I rode some / Hey hey blues / Shake that thing / Intermission blues / Crossing (lonely day) / Bound no'th blues / Final
CD _____ GV 794322
Gramavision / Mar '91 / Vital/SAM / ADA.

MUSIC FUH YA
CD _____ 7599268102
WEA / Jan '96 / Warner Music.

NATCH'L BLUES, THE
Good morning Miss Brown / Corine Corina / Done changed my way of living / She caught the Katy / Cuckoo / You don't miss your water / Lot of love
CD _____ EDCD 231
Edsel / Feb '91 / Pinnacle / ADA.

RISING SUN COLLECTION
CD _____ RSCD 003
Just A Memory / Apr '94 / Harmonia Mundi.

TAJ
Everybody is somebody / Paradise / Do I love her / Light of the Pacific / Deed I do /

659

Soothin' / Pillow talk / Local local girl / Kauai
Kalypso / French letter
CD _____ GCD 79433
Gramavision / Sep '95 / Vital/SAM / ADA.

TAJ MAHAL
Leaving trunk / Statesboro blues / Checkin'
up on my baby / Everybody's got to change
sometime / Ezy ryder / Dust my broom /
Diving duck blues / Celebrated walkin'
blues
CD _____ 4809682
Columbia / Aug '95 / Sony.

TAJ'S BLUES
Leaving trunk / Statesboro blues / Every-
body's got to change / Sometime / Bound
to love me some / Frankie and Albert / East
Bay woman / Dust my broom / Corinna /
Jelly roll / Fishin' blues / Needed time /
Curiosity blues / Horse shoes / Country
blues
CD _____ 4716602
Columbia / Jul '92 / Sony.

Tajima, Tadashi

SHAKUHACHI
CD _____ CDT 124CD
Music Of The World / Jul '94 / Target/
BMG / ADA.

Takahashi, Ayuo

PRIVATE TAPES
CD _____ PSFD 64
PSF / Dec '95 / Harmonia Mundi.

Takahashi, Tatsuya

**TATSUYA TAKAHASHI PLAYS MILES
AND GIL**
CD _____ K32Y 6268
King/Paddle Wheel / Apr '89 / New Note.

Takano, Max

NEW YORK, NEW YORK
CD _____ CDGRS1205
Grosvenor / Feb '93 / Target/BMG.

SPIRIT OF MUSIC
When you wish upon a star / Superman /
Corner pocket / Carmina burana / Funeral
march of a Marionette / April fools / Green-
sleeves / Air water music / Merry Christmas
Mr. Lawrence / Stars and stripes / Moon-
light serenade / Cross my heart / Hooker's
hooker / Tap dance / Media luz, A (Medium
Light)
CD _____ CDGRS 1253
Grosvenor / Feb '95 / Target/BMG.

Takara

ETERNAL FAITH
CD _____ NTHEN 7
Now & Then / Sep '95 / Plastic Head.

Takase, Aki

CLAPPING MUSIC
CD _____ ENJACD 80902
Enja / Sep '95 / New Note / Vital/SAM.

PERDIDO
CD _____ ENJACD 40342
Enja / Sep '95 / New Note / Vital/SAM.

Takatina, He Toa

AUTHENTIC MAORI SONGS
CD _____ CDODE 1007
Ode / Feb '90 / CM / Discovery.

Take 6

JOIN THE BAND
Can't keep goin' on and on / All I need (is
a chance) / My friend / It's gonna rain / You
can never ask too much (of love) / I've got
life / Stay tuned (interlude) / Biggest part of
me / Badiyah (interlude) / Harmony / Four
Miles (interlude) / Even though / Why I feel
this way / Lullaby
CD _____ 936245497-2
Warner Bros. / Jun '94 / Warner Music.

SO MUCH 2 SAY
So much 2 say / I L-O-V-E U / Something
within me / Time after time (the savior is
waiting) / Come unto me / I'm on my way /
I believe / Sunday's on the way / Where do
the children play
CD _____ 7599258922
Reprise / Nov '90 / Warner Music.

Take That

EVERYTHING CHANGES
Everything changes / Pray / Wasting my
time / Relight my fire / Love ain't here any-
ymore / If this is love / Whatever you do to
me / Meaning of love / Why can't I wake up
with you / You are the one / Another crack
in my heart / Broken your heart / Babe
CD _____ 74321 16926-2
RCA / Oct '93 / BMG.

NOBODY ELSE
Sure / Back for good / Everyguy / Sunday
to Saturday / Nobody else / Never forget /
Hanging onto your love / Holding back the
tears / Hate it / Lady tonight / Day after
tomorrow

CD _____ 74321279092
RCA / May '95 / BMG.

TAKE THAT AND PARTY
I found heaven / Once you've tasted love /
It only takes a minute / Million love songs /
Satisfied / I can make it / Do what you like
/ Promises / Why can't I wake up with you
/ Never want to let you go / Give good feel-
ing / Could it be magic (CD only) / Take That
and party
CD _____ 74321109232
RCA / Aug '92 / BMG.

Takis & Anestos

GREEK FOLK DANCES
CD _____ MCD 71722
Monitor / Jun '93 / CM.

Tala'i, Daryoush

**TRADITION CLASSIQUE DE L'IRAN -
VOL. 2 (Tala'i, Daryoush & Djamchid
Chemirani)**
CD _____ HMA 1901031
Musique D'Abord / Nov '93 / Harmonia
Mundi.

Talamh, Sean

TRADITIONAL IRISH MUSIC
CD _____ EUCD 1252
ARC / Mar '94 / ARC Music / ADA.

Talas

SINK YOUR TEETH INTO THAT
Sink your teeth into that / Hit and run / NV
443345 / High speed on ice / Shy boy / King
of the world / Crystal clear / See me / See
my cry / Smart lady / Hick town
CD _____ CDGRUB 1
Food For Thought / Sep '91 / Pinnacle.

Talbert, Tom

**THINGS AS THEY ARE (Talbert, Tom
Septet)**
CD _____ CDSB 2038
Sea Breeze / Nov '88 / Jazz Music.

Tale

RIVERMAN VOL.1
CD _____ VPCD 1
Voyage Productions / Jun '94 / Plastic
Head.

Talila

PAPIROSSN
CD _____ LDX 274956
La Chant Du Monde / Jan '93 / Harmonia
Mundi / ADA.

Talisman

LIFE
CD _____ NTHEN 21
Now & Then / Oct '95 / Plastic Head.

Talk Talk

COLOUR OF SPRING, THE
Happiness is easy / I don't believe in you /
Life's what you make it / April 15th / Living
in another world / Give it up / Chameleon
day / Time it's time
CD _____ CDFA 3291
Fame / Apr '93 / EMI.

HISTORY REVISITED (The Remixes)
Living in another world ('91) / Such a shame
/ Happiness is easy (dub) / Today / Dum
dum girl / Life's what you make it / Talk Talk
/ It's my life / Living in another world (Curi-
ous world dub mix)
CD _____ CDPCS 7349
Parlophone / Feb '91 / EMI.

IT'S MY LIFE
Dum dum girl / Such a shame / Renee / It's
my life / Tomorrow / Started / Last time /
Call in the night boys / Does Caroline know
/ It's you
CD _____ CDFA 3274
Fame / Oct '92 / EMI.

LAUGHING STOCK
Myrrhman / Ascension day / After the flood
/ Tapehead / New grass / Rune
CD _____ 8477172
Polydor / Sep '91 / PolyGram.

**NATURAL HISTORY (Very Best Of Talk
Talk)**
Today / Talk talk / My foolish friend / Such
a shame / Dum dum girl / Living in another
world / It's my life / Happiness is easy / I believe
in you / Desire
CD _____ CDPCSD 109
Parlophone / May '90 / EMI.

PARTY'S OVER, THE
Talk talk / It's so serious / Today / Party's
over / Hate / Have you heard the news /
Mirror man / Another word / Candy
CD _____ CDFA 3187
Fame / Apr '88 / EMI.

SPIRIT OF EDEN
Rainbow / Eden / Desire / Inheritance / I
believe in you / Wealth

CD _____ CDFA 3293
Fame / Jun '93 / EMI.

Talking Heads

FEAR OF MUSIC
I Zimbra / Mind / Cities / Paper / Life during
wartime / Memories can't wait / Air /
Heaven / Animals / Electric guitar / Drugs
CD _____ 256707
WEA / '94 / Warner Music.

LITTLE CREATURES
And she was / Give me back my name /
Creatures of love / Lady don't mind / Per-
fect world / Stay up late / Walk it down /
Television man / Road to nowhere
CD _____ CDFA 3301
Fame / Nov '93 / EMI.

**MORE SONGS ABOUT BUILDINGS AND
FOOD**
Thank you for sending me an angel / With
our love / Good thing / Warning sign / Girls
want to be with the girls / Found a job /
Artists only / I'm not in love / Stay hungry /
Take me to the river / Big country
CD _____ K2 56531
Sire / Jan '87 / Warner Music.

NAKED
Blind / Mr. Jones / Totally nude / Ruby dear
/ Nothing but flowers / Democratic circus /
Facts of life / Mommy, daddy / Big daddy /
Cool water / Bill (Not on LP)
CD _____ CDFA 3300
Fame / Nov '93 / EMI.

REMAIN IN LIGHT
Great curve / Cross-eyed and painless /
Born under punches (heat goes on) /
Houses in motion / Once in a lifetime / Lis-
tening wind / Seen and not seen / Overload
CD _____ 256 867
Sire / '83 / Warner Music.

SAND IN THE VASELINE
Sugar on my tongue / I want to live / Love
building on fire / I wish you wouldn't say
that / Psycho killer / Don't worry about the
government / No compassion / Warning
sign / Take me to the river / Heaven / Memories can't wait / I zimbra / Once in a lifetime
/ Cross-eyed and painless / Burning down
the house / Swamp / This must be the place
(naive melody) / Life during wartime (live) /
Girlfriend is better (live) / And she was / Stay
up late / Road to nowhere / Wild wild life /
Love for sale / City of dreams / Mr. Jones /
Blind / Nothing but flowers / Sax and violins
/ Gangster of love / Lifetime piling up / Popsicle / Paris
CD _____ CDEQ 50101
Sire / Oct '92 / Warner Music.

SPEAKING IN TONGUES
Burning down the house / Making flippy
floppy / Swamp / Girlfriend is better / Slip-
pery people / I get wild / Pull up the roots /
Moon rocks / This must be the place
CD _____ 923883 2
Sire / '83 / Warner Music.

STOP MAKING SENSE
Psycho Killer / Swamp / Slippery people /
Burning down the house / Girlfriend is bet-
ter / Once in a lifetime / What a day that
was / Life during wartime / Take me to the
river
CD _____ CDFA 3302
Fame / Nov '93 / EMI.

**STOP MAKING SENSE/LITTLE
CREATURES/TRUE STORIES**
Psycho killer / Swamp / Slippery people /
Burning down the house / Girlfriend is bet-
ter / Once in a lifetime / What a day that
was / Life during wartime / Take me to the
river / And she was / Give me back my
home / Creatures of love / Lady don't mind
/ Perfect world / Stay up late / Walk it down
/ Television man / Road to nowhere / Love
for sale / Puzzlin' evidence / Hey now /
Papa Legba / Wild wild life / Radio head /
Dream operator / People like us / City of
dreams
CD Set _____ CDOMB 003
EMI / Oct '95 / EMI.

TALKING HEADS '77
Uh-oh, love comes to town / New feeling /
Tentative decisions / Happy day / Who is it
/ No compassion / Book I read / Don't worry
about the government / First week / Last
week... carefree / Psycho killer / Pulled up
CD _____ K 256 647
Sire / Feb '87 / Warner Music.

TRUE STORIES
Love for sale / Puzzlin' evidence / Hey now
/ Papa Legba / Wild wild life / Radio head /
Dream operator / People like us / City of
dreams / Wild wild life (remix) (CD only)
CD _____ CDFA 3231
Fame / Sep '89 / EMI.

Tallari

KONSTA
CD _____ KICD 31
Kansanmusiikki Instituutti / Dec '94 /
Direct / ADA.

Talley, James

AMERICAN ORIGINALS
Find somebody and love them / Bury me in
New Orleans / Baby she loves a rocker /
Whiskey on the side / Are they gonna make
us outlaws again / Way to say I love you /
New York town / Open all night / Montana
song / Ready to please / We're all one
family
CD _____ BCD 15244
Bear Family / '86 / Rollercoaster / Direct /
CM / Swift / ADA.

**BLACKJACK CHOIR/ AIN'T IT
SOMETHIN'**
Bluesman / Alabama summertime / Every-
body loves a love song / Magnolia boy /
Mississippi river whistle town / Daddy just
called it the blues / Up from Georgia / Mi-
grant Jesse Sawyer / You know I've got to
love her / When the fiddler packs his case
/ Ain't it somethin' / Only the best / We keep
tryin' / Dixie blues / Not even when it's over
/ Nine pounds of hashbrowns / Richland,
Washington / Middle C mama / Woman
troubles / Old time religion / Poets of the
West Virginia mines / What will there be for
the children
CD _____ BCD 15435
Bear Family / Jul '89 / Rollercoaster / Direct
/ CM / Swift / ADA.

**GOT NO BREAD/ TRYIN' LIKE THE
DEVIL**
W.Lee O'Daniel and the Light Crust Dough
Boys / Got no bread, no milk, no money /
Red river memory / Give him another bottle
/ Calico gypsy / To get back home / Big
taters in the sandy land / No openers
needed / Blue eyed Ruth and my Sunday
suit / Mehan, Oklahoma / Daddy's song /
Take me to the country / Red river reprise /
Forty hours / Deep country blues / Give my
love to Marie / Are they gonna make us out-
laws again / She tries not to cry / Tryin' like
the devil / She's the one / Sometimes I think
about Suzanne / Nothin' but the blues / You
can't ever tell
CD _____ BCD 15433
Bear Family / Nov '93 / Rollercoaster /
Direct / CM / Swift / ADA.

LIVE
Tryin' like the devil / Woman trouble / Whis-
key on the side / Dixie blues / W. Lee
O'Daniel and the light crust doughboys /
Not even when it's over / Nothin' take love /
Find somebody and love them / Survivors /
Bluesman / I can't surrender / We keep
tryin' / Are you gonna make us outlaws
again / Give my love to Mary / Alabama
summertime / Take me to the country /
Take a whirl on me
CD _____ BCDAH 15704
Bear Family / Jun '94 / Rollercoaster / Direct
/ CM / Swift / ADA.

LOVE SONGS AND THE BLUES
Your sweet love / Whatever gets you
through your life / I can't surrender / He
went back to Texas / Working girl / Little
child / Up from Georgia / All because of you
/ Collection of sorrows / 'Cause I'm in love
with you / May your dreams come true
CD _____ BCD 15464
Bear Family / Jul '89 / Rollercoaster / Direct
/ CM / Swift / ADA.

ROAD TO TORREON
Maria / Ramon estevan / H. John Tarragon
/ Demona / La rosa Montana / She was a
flower / Rosary / Storm / Little child / Anna
Maria / I had a love way out West
CD _____ BCD 15633
Bear Family / Jun '92 / Rollercoaster / Direct
/ CM / Swift / ADA.

Talulah Gosh

ROCK LEGENDS, VOL.69
Beatnik boy / My best friend / Steaming
train / Just a dream / Talulah gosh / Don't
go away / Escalator over the hill / My boy
says / Way of the world / Testcard girl /
Bringing up baby / I can't get no satisfaction (Thank god) / Strawberry girl
CD _____ ONLYCD 011
Avalanche / May '91 / Disc.

Tam Tam

DO IT TAM TAM
CD _____ CID 9983
Island / May '92 / PolyGram.

Tamarack

FIELDS OF ROCK AND SNOW
CD _____ FE 1407
Folk Era / Nov '94 / CM / ADA.

FROBISHER BAY
CD _____ FE 1409
Folk Era / Nov '94 / CM / ADA.

Tamas Laboratorium

LIVING STRUCTURES
CD _____ 710 125
Innovative Communication / Jan '91 /
Magnum Music Group.

Tambastics

TAMBASTICS
CD _____ CD 704
Music & Arts / Apr '93 / Harmonia Mundi /
Cadillac.

Tamia

SOLITUDES (Tamia & Pierre Favre)
CD _____ 8496454
ECM / Feb '92 / New Note.

Tammles

SANS BAGAGE
CD _____ BUR 832CD
Escalibur / '90 / Roots / ADA / Discovery.

Tampa Red

DON'T JIVE ME
CD _____ OBCCD 549
Original Blues Classics / Nov '92 /
Complete/Pinnacle / Wellard / Cadillac.

DON'T TAMPA WITH THE BLUES
CD _____ OBCCD 516
Original Blues Classics / Nov '92 /
Complete/Pinnacle / Wellard / Cadillac.

GUITAR WIZARD, THE
It's tight like that / Big fat Mama / No matter
how she done it / Reckless mama blues /
Don't leave me here / Dead cat on the line
/ Things' bout comin' my way No.2 / You
can't get that stuff no more / If you want
me to love you / Turpentine blues / Western
bound blues / That stuff is here / Sugar
Mama blues / Sugar Mama blues No.2 /
Black angel blues / Things 'bout coming my
way / Denver blues
CD _____ 475702 2
Columbia / May '94 / Sony.

IT HURTS ME TOO
CD _____ IGOCD 2004
Indigo / Oct '94 / Direct / ADA.

TAMPA RED VOL.1 1934-35
CD _____ BDCD 6044
Blues Document / May '93 / Swift / Jazz
Music / Hot Shot.

TAMPA RED VOL.2 1935-36
CD _____ BDCD 6045
Blues Document / May '93 / Swift / Jazz
Music / Hot Shot.

TAMPA RED, VOL. 1 (1928-29)
CD _____ DOCD 5073
Blues Document / '92 / Swift / Jazz Music
/ Hot Shot.

TAMPA RED, VOL. 10
CD _____ DOCD 5210
Blues Document / Oct '93 / Swift / Jazz
Music / Hot Shot.

TAMPA RED, VOL. 11
CD _____ DOCD 5211
Blues Document / Oct '93 / Swift / Jazz
Music / Hot Shot.

TAMPA RED, VOL. 12
CD _____ DOCD 5212
Blues Document / Oct '93 / Swift / Jazz
Music / Hot Shot.

TAMPA RED, VOL. 13
CD _____ DOCD 5213
Blues Document / Oct '93 / Swift / Jazz
Music / Hot Shot.

TAMPA RED, VOL. 14
CD _____ DOCD 5214
Blues Document / Oct '93 / Swift / Jazz
Music / Hot Shot.

TAMPA RED, VOL. 15
CD _____ DOCD 5215
Blues Document / Oct '93 / Swift / Jazz
Music / Hot Shot.

TAMPA RED, VOL. 2 (1929)
CD _____ DOCD 5074
Blues Document / '92 / Swift / Jazz Music
/ Hot Shot.

TAMPA RED, VOL. 3 (1929-30)
CD _____ DOCD 5075
Blues Document / '92 / Swift / Jazz Music
/ Hot Shot.

TAMPA RED, VOL. 4 (1929-30)
CD _____ DOCD 5076
Blues Document / '92 / Swift / Jazz Music
/ Hot Shot.

TAMPA RED, VOL. 5 (1931-34)
CD _____ DOCD 5077
Blues Document / Oct '93 / Swift / Jazz
Music / Hot Shot.

TAMPA RED, VOL. 6
CD _____ DOCD 5206
Blues Document / Oct '93 / Swift / Jazz
Music / Hot Shot.

TAMPA RED, VOL. 7
CD _____ DOCD 5207
Blues Document / Oct '93 / Swift / Jazz
Music / Hot Shot.

TAMPA RED, VOL. 8
CD _____ DOCD 5208
Blues Document / Oct '93 / Swift / Jazz
Music / Hot Shot.

TAMPA RED, VOL. 9
CD _____ DOCD 5209
Blues Document / Oct '93 / Swift / Jazz
Music / Hot Shot.

Tamplin

IN THE WITNESS BOX
CD _____ NTHEN 024CD
Now & Then / Jan '96 / Plastic Head.

Tams

BEST OF THE TAMS, THE
I've been hurt / Go away little girl / Take
away / Be young, be foolish, be happy / Hey
girl don't bother me / You lied to your
Daddy / Weep little girl / It's all night (you're
just in love) / Laugh it off / Shelter / What
kind of fool / Letter / Greatest love / All my
hard times
CD _____ CDSGP 0110
Prestige / Sep '94 / Total/BMG.

Tamulevich, David

**MUSTARD'S RETREAT (Tamulevich,
David & Michael Hough)**
CD _____ RHRCD 72
Red House / Aug '95 / Koch / ADA.

Tananas

ORCHESTRA MUNDO
CD _____ 342602
Koch International / Dec '95 / Koch.

TanaReid

**BLUE MOTION (Tana, Akira & Rufus
Reid)**
Day and night / Con alma / Blue motion /
Tata's dance / It's the nights I like / I con-
centrate on you / Medley (Salute to Duke/
Duke Ellington's sound of love) / With a
song in my heart / Amy Marie / Elvinesque
CD _____ ECD 220752
Evidence / Feb '94 / Harmonia Mundi / ADA
/ Cadillac.

**LOOKING FORWARD (Tana, Akira &
Rufus Reid)**
Billy / Gold minor / Duke / Skyline / Falling
in love / Bell / Third eye / Reminiscing / Love
dreams / Looking forward
CD _____ ECD 22114
Evidence / Jun '95 / Harmonia Mundi / ADA
/ Cadillac.

**PASSING THOUGHTS (Tana, Akira &
Rufus Reid)**
Hotel le hot / City slicker / Heroes / Cheek
to cheek / Sophisticated lady / Prelude to a
kiss / Hope for now / Passing thoughts /
Light blue / It's the magical look in your
eyes / Scufflestyle
CD _____ CCD 4505
Concord Jazz / May '92 / New Note.

Tanenbaum, David

ASTOR PIAZZOLLA - EL PORTENO
CD _____ NA 065CD
New Albion / May '94 / Harmonia Mundi /
Cadillac.

Tangerine

TANGERINE
CD _____ CRECD 061
Creation / May '94 / 3MV / Vital.

Tangerine Dream

220 VOLT LIVE
Oriental haze / Two bunch palms / 220 Volt
/ Homeless / Treasure of innocence / Sund-
ance kid / Backstreet hero / Blue bridge /
Hamlet / Dreamtime / Purple haze
CD _____ MPCD 2804
Miramar / Sep '93 / New Note.

ALPHA CENTAURI/ ATEM
Sunrise in the third system / Fly and colli-
sion of the comas sola / Alpha Centauri /
Atem / Fauni-gena / Circulation of events /
Wahn
CD _____ 88581-8069-2
Relativity (USA) / Oct '87 / Pinnacle.

ATMOSPHERICS
CD _____ EMPRCD 564
Emporio / Mar '95 / THE / Disc / CM.

BEST OF TANGERINE DREAM
Central Park (New York) / Livemiles (part 2)
(extract) / Song of the whale (part 1: from
dawn) / Le parc / Poland (extract) / Wahn /
Ashes to ashes / Tyger / Dolphin dance /
Song of the whale (part 2: from dusk) / Yel-
lowstone Park (Rocky mountains) / Astral
voyager / Sunrise in the third system / Zelt
CD _____ CHIP 75
Jive / Sep '89 / BMG.

BOOK OF DREAMS
CD Set _____ EDFCD 353
Essential / Nov '95 / Total/BMG.

COLLECTION: TANGERINE DREAM
Genesis / Circulation of events / Fauni-gena
/ Alpha Centauri / Fly and collision of the
comas sola / Journey through a burning
brain / Birth of liquid plejades / White clouds
CD _____ CCSCD 161
Castle / Jul '87 / BMG.

CYCLONE
Bent cold sidewalk / Rising runner missed
by endless sender / Madrigal meridian
CD _____ TAND 9
Virgin / Apr '95 / EMI.

ENCORE (Live)
Cherokee lane / Monolight / Coldwater can-
yon / Desert dream
CD _____ TAND 1
Virgin / Apr '95 / EMI.

FORCE MAJEURE
Force Majeure / Cloudburst flight / Thru
Metamorphic rocks
CD _____ TAND 10
Virgin / Apr '95 / EMI.

FROM DAWN 'TIL DUSK - 1973-88
Song of the whale (part 1: from dawn) /
Song of the whale (part 2: from dusk) / Bois
de Boulogne / Ride on the ray / Poland /
London / Le parc / Live miles (extract) /
Central Park / Zeit / Wahh
CD _____ MCCD 034
Music Club / Sep '91 / Disc / THE / CM.

GREEN DESERT
CD _____ CTANG 1
Jive / BMG.

HYPERBOREA
No man's land / Hyperborea / Cinnamon
road / Sphinx lightning
CD _____ TAND 4
Virgin / Jul '95 / EMI.

LILY ON THE BEACH
Too hot for my chinchilla / Lily on the beach
/ Alaskan summer / Desert drive / Mount
Shasta / Crystal curfew / Paradise cove /
Twenty nine palms / Valley of the kings /
Radio city / Blue Mango Cafe / Gecko /
Long island sunset
CD _____ 260.103
Private Music / Dec '89 / BMG.

**LOGOS (Live At The Dominion, London
1982)**
Logos / Dominion
CD _____ TAND 3
Virgin / Jul '95 / EMI.

OPTICAL RACE
Marrakesh / Atlas eyes / Mothers of rain /
Twin soul tribe / Optical race / Cat scan /
Sun gate / Turning of the wheel / Midnight
trail / Ghazal (Love song)
CD _____ 259557
Private Music / Aug '88 / BMG.

PHAEDRA
Phaedra / Mysterious semblance at the
strand of nightmares / Movements of a vi-
sionary / Sequent C
CD _____ TAND 5
Virgin / Feb '95 / EMI.

**PRIVATE MUSIC OF TANGERINE
DREAM, THE**
Melrose / Too hot for my chinchilla / Long
Island sunset / Atlas eyes / Sun gate / Roll-
ing down Cahuenga / Three bikes in the sky
/ After the call / Electric lion / Dolls in the
shadow / Beaver town / Roaring of the bliss
CD _____ 01005821052
Private Music / Feb '93 / BMG.

RICOCHET
Ricochet (pts 1 & 2) / Ricochet part 2
CD _____ TAND 7
Virgin / Feb '95 / EMI.

ROCKOON
CD _____ █████ █▀█
Essential / Feb '92 / Total/BMG.

RUBYCON
Rubycon (pts 1 & 2) / Rubycon part 2
CD _____ TAND 6
Virgin / Feb '95 / EMI.

STRATOSFEAR
Stratosfear / Big sleep in search of Hades /
3 a.m. at the border of the marsh / Invisible
limits
CD _____ TAND 8
Virgin / Feb '95 / EMI.

TANGENTS 1973-1983
Mojave plan (Desert part) / No man's land /
Kiew mission / Ricochet / Force majeure /
Logos (blue part) / Stratosfear / Mysterious
semblance at the strand of nightmares /
Cinnamon road / Tangram (solution part) /
White eagle / Phaedra / Logos (red part) /
Sphinx lightning / Desert dream / Invisible
limits / Exit / Mojave plan (canyon part) /
Tangram (puzzle part) / Monolight / Ruby-
con (The Decision) / Cloudburst flight / Pi-
lots of purple twilight / Logos (velvet part) /
Monolight (yellow part) / Tangram (future
part) / Rubycon (dice part) / Hyperborea /
Rubycon (crossing part) / Dominion / Per-
gamon (piano part) / Going West / Dream is
always the same / Alien goodbye / Call /
Run / Betrayal (Sorceror theme) / Rainbirds
move / Creation / Charly the kid / Journey
/ Scrap yard / Dirty cross roads / Search /
Highway patrol / Grind / Risky business /
Beach theme / Vulcano / Jogger / South
Dakota / Coppercoast / Great barrier reef /
Night at Ayers Rock / Afternoon on the Nile
/ Crane routing / Silver scale / Jamaican
monk
CD Set _____ CDBOX 4
Virgin / Oct '94 / EMI.

TANGRAM
CD _____ TAND 11
Virgin / Apr '95 / EMI.

WHITE EAGLE
Mojave plan / Midnight in Tula / Convention
of the 24 / White Eagle
CD _____ TAND 2
Virgin / Jul '95 / EMI.

Tangle Edge

IN SEARCH OF A NEW DAWN
CD _____ DMCD 1009
Demi-Monde / Mar '95 / Disc / Magnum
Music Group.

Tank

FILTH HOUNDS OF HADES
Shellshock / Struck by lightning / Run like
hell / Blood guts and beer / That's what
dreams are made of / Turn your head
around / Heavy artillery / Who needs love
songs / Filth hounds of Hades /
Stormtrooper
CD _____ REP 4149-WP
Repertoire / Aug '91 / Pinnacle / Cadillac.

POWER OF THE HUNTER
CD _____ REP 4150-WP
Repertoire / Aug '91 / Pinnacle / Cadillac.

Tank, John

SO IN LOVE
So in love / Address this issue / Snow place
/ West of the moon / Suite - peace / We'll
say hello again / Vengeance / Uptown lex /
Whipmarks
CD _____ TCB 95602
TCB / Dec '95 / New Note.

Tankard

STONE COLD SOBER
Jurisdiction / Broken image / Mindwild /
Ugly beauty / Centrefold / Behind the back
/ Stone cold sober / Blood guts and rock
'n' roll / Lost and found (tantrum part 2) /
Sleeping with the past / Tantrum part 2 /
people talking under Arabian skies
CD _____ NO 190-2
Noise/Modern Music / Jun '92 / Pinnacle /
Plastic Head.

TWO-FACED
CD _____ N 0233-2
Noise/Modern Music / Feb '94 / Pinnacle /
Plastic Head.

Tannahill Weavers

**BEST OF THE TANNAHILL WEAVERS
1979-1989, THE**
Geese in the bog/Jig of slurs / Auld lang
syne / Tranent muir / Highland laddie / Lucy
Cassidy/Bletherskate/Smith of Chilliechas-
sie / Farewell to Fiunary/Heather Island /
Roddie MacDonald's favourite / Gypsy lad-
die / Jamie Raeburn's farewell / Johnny
Cope/Atholl Highlanders / I once loved a
lass / Turf lodge/Cape Breton's fiddlers'
welcome to the Shetlands / Lady Margaret
Stewart/Flaggon
CD _____ GLCD 1100
Green Linnet / Jul '92 / Roots / Direct
/ ADA.

CAPERNAUM
CD _____ GLCD 1146
Green Linnet / Aug '94 / Roots / CM /
Direct / ADA.

CULLEN BAY
CD _____ GLCD 1108
Green Linnet / Mar '91 / Roots / CM /
Direct / ADA.

DANCING FEET
Turf lodge / Tranent Muir / Isabeaux S'y
Promene / Fisher row / Wild mountain
thyme / Maggie's pancakes / Mary Morrison
/ Campbeltown kiltie ball / Final trawl
CD _____ GLCD 1081
Green Linnet / Apr '92 / Roots / CM / Direct
/ ADA.

LAND OF LIGHT
Lucy Cassidy / Scottish settler's lament /
Ronald Maclean's farewell to Oban / Dun-
robin castle / Rovin' reelandman / Yellow
haired laddie / Land of light / Queen amang
the heather/Main Anne... / Bustles and bon-
nets / American stranger / Conon Bridge
CD _____ GLCD 1067
Green Linnet / Jun '88 / Roots / CM / Direct
/ ADA.

MERMAID'S SONG
Sweetbog side/Highland laddie/Pattie /
Logie o' Buchan / Elspeth Campbell/Kenny
Gilles of Portnalong/Skye/Malcolm Joh /
Mermaid's song/Herra boys/Captain Horn/
Fourth floor / Are ye sleeping Maggie/
Noose and the ghillie / A Bruxa / Come un-
der my plaidie / Campbell's farewell to Red-
castle / Flashmarket close / MacArthur/
Colonel Fraser/Swallow's tale / Ass in the
graveyard
CD _____ GLCD 1121
Green Linnet / Feb '89 / Roots / CM / Direct
/ ADA.

PASSAGE
Roddie MacDonald's favourite / Jamie Raeburn's farewell / Harris and the mare / Duntroon/Trip to Alaska / Highland laddie / At the end of a pointed gun / Lady Dysie / Coach house reel/Marie Christina / Phuktiphanno/John MacKenzie's fancy / Drink a round
CD _____ GLCD 3031
Green Linnet / Oct '93 / Roots / CM / Direct / ADA.

Tannas

HERITAGE
CD _____ CDLDL 1217
Lochshore / Nov '94 / ADA / Direct / Duncans.

RU-RA
CD _____ CDLDL 1231
Lochshore / Oct '95 / ADA / Direct / Duncans.

Tannehill, Frank

COMPLETE RECORDINGS 1932-1941
CD _____ SOB 035262
Story Of The Blues / Feb '93 / Koch / ADA.

Tanrikorur, Cinucen

CINUCEN TANRIKORUR
CD _____ C 580045
Ocora / Feb '94 / Harmonia Mundi / ADA.

Tans, J.C.

AROUND THE WORLD
CD _____ BVHAASTCD 8905
Bvhaast / Sep '92 / Cadillac.

Tansads

DRAG DOWN THE MOON
CD _____ TRACD 118
Transatlantic / Oct '95 / BMG / Pinnacle / ADA.

FLOCK
Band on a rainbow / Fear of falling / She's not gone / God on a string / Iron man / Waiting for the big one / Dance / Sunlight in the morning / G Man / Ship of fools / I know I can (but I won't) / Heading for the heart / Separate souls
CD _____ TRACD 1
Transatlantic / Oct '94 / BMG / Pinnacle / ADA.

SHANDYLAND
CD _____ ESMCD 351
Essential / Nov '95 / Total/BMG.

UP THE SHIRKERS
Eye of the average / Camelot / Brian Kant / Zig zag / Music down / Waste of space / Chip pan ocean / English rover / John John / Reason to be / Revolution / Turn on/tune up
CD _____ ESMCD 352
Essential / Nov '95 / Total/BMG.

Tansey, Seamus

BEST OF SEAMUS TANSEY
CD _____ PTICD 1007
Pure Traditional Irish / Jul '95 / ADA.

Tanzmusik

SINCEKAI
CD _____ RSNCD 26
Rising High / Jan '95 / Disc.

Tappin, Arturo

JAVA
Songbird / Java / Mista T / No woman, no cry / Step forward / Rhythm of love / Hello Africa / Ska-rol / Kingston rock / Cruzin' / Light my fire / Vibes surprise
CD _____ 8892795052
Sax Roots / Sep '95 / New Note.

STRICTLY ROOTS JAZZ
Blues reggae / Strange love / Steppers / Rock house / Alcatraz / Under cover / Breaking up / Shabeen rock / Steppers dub / Breaking dub / Shabeen dub
CD _____ SXR 001
Sax Roots / May '94 / New Note.

Tar

OVER AND OUT
CD _____ TGCD 145
Touch & Go / Oct '95 / SRD.

Tar Babies

DEATH TRIP
CD _____ SON 004-2
Sonic Noise / Jan '93 / SRD.

HONEY BUBBLE
CD _____ SST 236 CD
SST / Jul '89 / Plastic Head.

Tara

BOYS IN THE LANE
CD _____ EUCD 1019
ARC / '89 / ARC Music / ADA.

RIGS OF THE TIME
CD _____ EUCD 1006
ARC / '89 / ARC Music / ADA.

Tara Key

EAR AND ECHO
CD _____ HMS 2222
Homestead / May '95 / SRD.

Taraf De Carancebes

MUSICIENS DU BANAT - ROUMANIA
CD _____ Y225208
Silex / Jun '93 / ADA.

Taraf De Haidouks

HONOURABLE BRIGANDS MAGIC HORSES AND EVIL EYE
CD _____ CRAW 13
Crammed Discs / Apr '95 / Grapevine / New Note.

MUSIQUE DES TZIGANES DE ROUMANIE
CD _____ CRAW 2
Crammed World / Jan '96 / New Note.

Tarheel Slim

NO TIME AT ALL
So sweet, so sweet / Married woman blues / Guy with the 45 / No time at all / My baby's gone / Weeping willow / Walkin' / 'Fore day creep / Jitterbug rag / Some cold, rainy day / Screamin' and cryin' / Open nose / Dark shadows / Superstitious / 180 Days
CD _____ TRIX 3310
Trix / Jun '94 / New Note.

Tari Singers

SCOTTISH SINGALONG
CD _____ CDSLP 614
Igus / Dec '89 / CM / Ross / Duncans.

Tarika

BALANCE
CD _____ FMSD 5028
Rogue / Jan '94 / Sterns.

BIBIANGO
CD _____ GLCD 4028
Green Linnet / Jan '95 / Roots / CM / Direct / ADA.

FANAFODY
CD _____ FMSD 5024
Rogue / Oct '92 / Sterns.

Tarmey, Bill

GIFT OF LOVE, A
Nobody loves me like you do / Somewhere out there / In your eyes / Tonight I celebrate my love / It might be you / That's all / Save the best for last / Everything I do (I do it for you) / She loves me / Right here waiting / Hundred ways / Weekend in New England / If we hold on together / Wind beneath my wings
CD _____ CDEMC 3665
EMI / Nov '93 / EMI.

TIME FOR LOVE
Time for love / Don't it make my brown eyes blue / I.O.U. / I'm the one / If I thought you'd ever change your mind / If this is what love can do / Don't know much / Dance of love / Some people / Perfect year / One shining moment / Belonging / You and I / As long as you are there
CD _____ CDEMTV 85
EMI / Oct '94 / EMI.

Tarnation

GENTLE CREATURES
Game of broken hearts / Halfway to madness / Well / Big o motel / Tell me it's not so / Two wrongs / Lonely lights / Gentle creatures / Listen to the wind / Hand / Do you fancy me / Yellow birds / Burn again / Stranger in the mirror / It's not easy
CD _____ CAD 5010CD
4AD / Sep '95 / Disc.

Tarras, Dave

YIDDISH AMERICAN KLEZMER MUSIC
CD _____ YAZCD 7001
Shanachie / Apr '92 / Koch / ADA / Greensleeves.

Tarres, Fernando

SECRET RHYTHMS
Southern anger / Native spirit / Viene clarendo (As the sun rises) / Southern adventure / Colors of a dirty sky / Lines of your smile / Little carnival / Everness / La arena / Dave's mood
CD _____ MCD 5516
Muse / Jul '94 / New Note / CM.

Tartan Amoebas

IMAGINARY TARTAN MENAGERIE
Ska reggae / Sub heaven / Penguin blues / Road rage / New pipe order / Brief case shuffle / Clavershouse / I close my eyes / Adios amoebas

Tartan Lads

TARTAN LADS OF BONNIE SCOTLAND
CD _____ CDITV 540
Scotdisc / May '91 / Duncans / Ross / Conifer.

Tasby, Finis

PEOPLE DON'T CARE
CD _____ SHCD 9007
Shanachie / May '95 / Koch / ADA / Greensleeves.

Tashan

FOR THE SAKE OF LOVE
Tempted / Been a long time / Ecstatic / For the sake of love / Single and lonely / Still in love / Love is forever / Romantically inspired / Control of me / Insane / All I ever do / Love of my life
CD _____ 472411-2
Columbia / Mar '94 / Sony.

Tashian, Barry

LIVE IN HOLLAND (Tashian, Barry & Holly)
CD _____ SCR 27
Strictly Country / Jul '95 / ADA / Direct.

READY FOR LOVE (Tashian, Barry & Holly)
Ready for love / Let me see the light / Heaven with you / Heart full of memories / Hearts that break / Highway 86 / Price of pride / Diamond / Ring of gold / Memories remain / If I knew then / This old love
CD _____ ROU 0302CD
Rounder / May '93 / CM / Direct / ADA / Direct.

STRAW INTO GOLD (Tashian, Barry & Holly)
CD _____ ROUCD 0332
Rounder / Nov '94 / CM / Direct / ADA / Cadillac.

TRUST IN ME (Tashian, Barry & Holly)
Trust in me / Home / Blue eyes / Ramona / Making a change / You're running wild / Party doll / My favourite memory / Poor woman's epitaph / Look both ways / Boy who cried love / I can't dance
CD _____ CDRR 302
Request / Mar '92 / Jazz Music.

Tassilli Players

WONDERFUL WORLD OF WEED IN DUB, THE
CD _____ WWCD 11
Wibbly Wobbly / Sep '95 / SRD.

Taste

LIVE AT THE ISLE OF WIGHT
What's going on / Sugar mama / Morning sun / Sinner boy / I feel so good / Catfish
CD _____ 841602-2
Polydor / Apr '94 / PolyGram.

ON THE BOARDS
What's going on / Railway and gun / It's happened before, it'll happen again / If the day was any longer / Morning sun / Eat my words / On the boards / If I don't sing I'll cry / See here / I'll remember
CD _____ 841599-2
Polydor / Apr '94 / PolyGram.

TASTE
CD _____ 814 600-2
Polydor / Jul '94 / PolyGram.

Taste Of Fear

TASTE OF FEAR
CD _____ LF 118CD
Lost & Found / Feb '95 / Plastic Head.

Tate, Baby

SEE WHAT YOU DONE
CD _____ OBCCD 547
Original Blues Classics / Oct '95 / Complete/Pinnacle / Wellard / ADA.

Tate, Buddy

BALLAD ARTISTRY OF BUDDY TATE, THE
CD _____ SKCD 2-3034
Sackville / Oct '92 / Swift / Jazz Music / Jazz Horizons / Cadillac / CM.

JUMPING ON THE WEST COAST (Tate, Buddy & Friends)
CD _____ BLCD 760175
Black Lion / Mar '93 / Jazz Music / Cadillac / Wellard / Koch.

JUST JAZZ (Tate, Buddy & Al Grey)
CD _____ RSRCD 110
Reservoir Music / Dec '94 / Jazz Music.

SWINGING SCORPIO (Tate, Buddy & Humphrey Lyttelton)
CD _____ BLC 760165
Black Lion / '92 / Jazz Music / Cadillac / Wellard / Koch.

Texas Twister, The
CD _____ NW 352
New World / '88 / Harmonia Mundi / ADA / Cadillac.

Tate, Danny

DANNY TATE
CD _____ CDCUS 16
Charisma / Jan '92 / EMI.

Tate, Grady

BODY AND SOUL
CD _____ MCD 9208
Milestone / Jun '95 / Jazz Music / Pinnacle / Wellard / Cadillac.

Tater Totz

TATER COMES ALIVE
CD _____ ROCK 6054-2
Rockville / Jul '93 / SRD.

Taters & Pie

NO MORE PUTTING OFF
Let the white moon shine / Heather island / Catching flies / Where lies and land / Piskeflode / Sirens and screams / Fools never die out / Jamie foyers / East Anglian sunset / Sea fever / Chasing chickens / Highway to eternal night / Love is all he needs / Hands's have no tears to cry/Jonathan's hat / Farewell
CD _____ GFMSCDS 6
Green Fingers / Nov '93 / Green Fingers Music.

Tathak, Pandit Ashok

COLOURFUL WORLD OF PANDIT ASHOK TATHAK, THE
CD _____ CD 3301
Saraswati / Aug '94 / Direct.

Tattoo

BLOOD RED
CD _____ RR 94962
Roadrunner / Dec '88 / Pinnacle.

Tatum, Art

ART TATUM 1940-41
CD _____ CLASSICS 800
Classics / Mar '95 / Discovery / Jazz Music.

ART TATUM AT THE CRESCENDO VOL.1
CD _____ GNPD 9025
GNP Crescendo / Dec '91 / Silva Screen.

BODY AND SOUL
CD _____ JHR 73514
Jazz Hour / May '93 / Target/BMG / Jazz Music / Cadillac.

CLASSICS 1940
CD _____ CLASSICS 831
Classics / Sep '95 / Discovery / Jazz Music.

CLASSICS 1944
CD _____ CLASSICS 825
Classics / Sep '95 / Discovery / Jazz Music.

COMPLETE BRUNSWICK & DECCA SESSIONS 1932-1941 (3CD Set)
Strange as it seems / I'll never be the same / You gave me everything but love / This time it's love / Tea for two / St. Louis blues / Tiger rag / Sophisticated lady / Moonglow / (I would do) anything for you / When a woman loves a man / Emaline / Love me / Cocktails for two / After you've gone / Star dust / Ill wind / Shout / Beautiful love / Liza / I ain't got nobody / Boots and saddle / Body and soul / With plenty of money and you / What will I tell my heart / I've got my love to keep me warm / Gone with the wind / Stormy weather / Chloe / Sheikh of araby / Deep purple / Elegie / Humoresque / Sweet Lorraine / Get happy / Lullaby of the leaves / Begin the beguine / Rosetta / (Back home again in) Indiana / Wee baby blues / Stompin' at the Savoy / Last goodbye blues / Battery bounce / Lucille / Rock me mama / Corine Corina / Lonesome graveyard blues
CD _____ CDAFS 1035-3
Affinity / Apr '93 / Charly / Cadillac / Jazz Music.

COMPLETE CAPITOL RECORDINGS VOL.1
Willow weep for me / I cover the waterfront / Aunt Hagar's blues / Nice work if you can get it / Someone to watch over me / Dardanella / Time on my hands (you in my arms) / Sweet Lorraine / Somebody loves me / Don't blame me / September song / Melody in F / Tea for two / Out of nowhere
CD _____ CZ 278
Capitol / Jan '92 / EMI.

COMPLETE GROUP MASTERPIECES, THE (6 CDs) (Tatum, Art Trio)
CD Set _____ 6PACD 4401
Original Jazz Classics / Sep '93 / Wellard / Jazz Music / Cadillac / Complete/Pinnacle.

Iona / Nov '95 / ADA / Direct / Duncans.
CD _____ IRCD 034

COMPLETE PABLO SOLO MASTERPIECES, THE (7CD Set)
CD Set _____ 7PACD 4404-2
Pablo / Nov '92 / Jazz Music / Cadillac / Complete/Pinnacle.

GENIUS OF KEYBOARD, THE
Blue Lou / Gone with the wind / Foggy day / September song / Love for sale / You took advantage of me / Makin' whoopee / Willow weep for me / Hallelujah / Once in a while / This can't be love / All the things you are / My blue Heaven / I cover the waterfront / Somebody loves me
CD _____ GOJCD 53019
Giants Of Jazz / Jun '88 / Target/BMG / Cadillac.

IN PRIVATE
CD _____ FSCD 127
Fresh Sound / Jan '91 / Jazz Music / Discovery.

INTRODUCTION TO ART TATUM 1933-1944, AN
CD _____ 4022
Best Of Jazz / Jul '95 / Discovery.

JAZZ PORTRAITS
Tiger rag / St. Louis blues / Begin the beguine / (Back home again in) Indiana / Get happy / What will I tell my heart / Sheikh of Araby / Stormy weather / Tea for two / Sophisticated lady / I've got my love to keep me warm / Gone with the wind / Rosetta / Stompin' at the Savoy / Sweet Lorraine / I'll get by / Battery bounce / It had to be you
CD _____ CD 14523
Jazz Portraits / May '94 / Jazz Music.

LIVE AT THE CRESCENDO
It's only a paper moon / Just a gigolo / Three little words / I gotta right to sing the blues / On the sunny side of the street / Somebody loves me / Why was I born / If I could be with you one hour tonight / Mean to me / You took advantage of me / Body and soul / I guess I'll have to change my plan / Can't we be friends / Among my souvenirs / I'm gonna sit right down and write myself a letter / Stay as sweet as you are / Fine and dandy / I've got the world on a string / What is this thing called love / Crazy rhythm / Limehouse blues / All God's chillun got rhythm / I'm coming Virginia
CD _____ 655615
GNP Crescendo / May '91 / Silva Screen.

MASTERPIECES OF ART TATUM, THE
CD _____ 393502
Music Memoria / Aug '94 / Discovery / ADA.

MASTERPIECES VOL. 7
CD _____ CD 2405430
Pablo / Jun '95 / Jazz Music / Complete/Pinnacle.

PIANO GENIUS
Gone with the wind / Stormy weather / Chloe / Sheikh of araby / Tea for two / Deep purple / Elegie / Humoresque / Sweet Lorraine / Get happy / Lullaby of the leaves / Tiger rag / Emaline / Moonglow / Love me / Cocktails for two / St. Louis blues / Begin the beguine / Rosetta / (Back home again in) Indiana
CD _____ CDCD 1065
Charly / Mar '93 / Charly / THE / Cadillac.

PIANO SOLO - PRIVATE SESSIONS (New York 1952)
CD _____ 550052
Jazz Anthology / Jan '94 / Harmonia Mundi / Cadillac.

PIANO STARTS HERE
CD _____ 476546 2
Sony Jazz / May '94 / Sony.

RARE TEST PRESSINGS AND TRANSCRIPTIONS (1932-51)
CD _____ JZCD 360
Suisa / Feb '92 / Jazz Music / THE.

ROCOCO PIANO OF ART TATUM, THE
Gone with the wind / Stormy weather / Sheikh of araby / tea for two / Rosetta / Humoresque / Sweet Lorraine / Get happy / Lullaby of the leaves / Tiger rag / Sweet Emmalina / Emaline / Moon glow / Love me / Cocktails for two / St. louis blues / Begin the beguine / (Back home again in) Indiana / Stompin' at the savoy / Battery bounce / Rock me Mama / Corine Corina
CD _____ PASTCD 7031
Flapper / Jan '94 / Pinnacle.

St. LOUIS BLUES
Tiger rag / Tea for two / St. Louis blues / Strange as it seems / Sophisticated lady / I'll never be the same / When a woman loves a man / Shout / You gave me everything but love / This time it's love / Liza / I would do anything for you / After you've gone / Star dust / I ain't got nobody / Beautiful love
CD _____ CDGRF 085
Tring / '93 / Tring / Prism.

STANDARD TRANSCRIPTIONS, THE
CD Set _____ CD 673
Music & Arts / Jul '91 / Harmonia Mundi / Cadillac.

STANDARDS
CD _____ BLCD 760143
Black Lion / Nov '92 / Jazz Music / Cadillac / Wellard / Koch.

TATUM GROUP MASTERPIECES VOL.6
Just one of those things / More than you know / Some other Spring / If / Blue Lou / Love for sale / Isn't it romantic / I'll never be the same / I guess I'll have to change my plan / Trio blues
CD _____ CD 2405429
Pablo / Oct '93 / Jazz Music / Cadillac / Complete/Pinnacle.

TATUM GROUP MASTERPIECES VOL.7
Deep night / This can't be love / Memories of you / Once in a while / Foggy day / Lover man / You're mine / You / Makin' whoopee
CD _____ 2405420
Pablo / Nov '95 / Jazz Music / Cadillac / Complete/Pinnacle.

TATUM GROUP MASTERPIECES VOL.8
Gone with the wind / A foggy day are / Have you met Miss Jones / My one and only love / Night and day / My ideal / Where or when
CD _____ CD 2310737
Pablo / '94 / Jazz Music / Cadillac / Complete/Pinnacle.

TATUM GROUP MASTERPIECES, THE (Sept. 1956) (Tatum, Art & Ben Webster)
CD _____ CD 20034
Pablo / May '86 / Jazz Music / Cadillac / Complete/Pinnacle.

TEA FOR TWO
CD _____ BLCD 760192
Black Lion / Feb '94 / Jazz Music / Cadillac / Wellard / Koch.

TEA FOR TWO 1933-1940
CD _____ CD 56068
Jazz Roots / Jul '95 / Target/BMG.

TRIO DAYS
I got rhythm / Cocktails for two / I ain't got nobody / After you've gone / Moonglow / Deep purple / (I would do) anything for you / Liza / Tea for two / Honeysuckle rose / Man I love / Dark eyes / Body and soul / I know that you know / On the sunny side of the street / Flying home / Boogie / If I had you / Topsy / Soft winds
CD _____ LEJAZZCD 43
Le Jazz / Jun '95 / Charly / Cadillac.

V DISC YEARS, THE (1944-46)
CD _____ BLCD 760114
Black Lion / Apr '91 / Jazz Music / Cadillac / Wellard / Koch.

Tauber, Richard

GERMAN FOLK SONGS
CD _____ BLA 103002
Belage / Mar '95 / Target/BMG.

GREAT VOICES OF THE CENTURY
Prize song / Am stillen herd / Selig sind / Ach so fromm / Solo profugo / Ewig will ich dir gehoeren / Non plangere liu / Nessun dorma / Lug dursel lug / Addio fiorito asil / Lenski's aria / Adieu mignon / Di rigori armato / Flower song / Recondito armante / Lucevan le stelle
CD _____ TKOCD 020
TKO / May '92 / TKO.

OLD CHELSEA
CD _____ BLA 103003
Belage / Feb '95 / Target/BMG.

ONLY A ROSE
CD _____ CDMOIR 421
Memoir / Jun '93 / Target/BMG.

VIENNA, CITY OF MY DREAMS
CD _____ CDHD 189
Happy Days / Sep '92 / Conifer.

YOU ARE MY HEART'S DELIGHT
CD _____ PASTCD 7042
Flapper / May '94 / Pinnacle.

Taudi Symphony

TAUDI SYMPHONY
Aujack swing / Africa soul / T.O.D.I. / Caron style / Jam / Le lama el ritmo / Ludwig in the sunshine / Carcass / Royal Albert Hall / Loran's dance / Aktual / Africa soul (dub version)
CD _____ FR 346CD
Big Cheese / Apr '95 / Vital.

Tavares

CAPITOL GOLD: THE BEST OF TAVARES
What can I do / Check it out / That's the sound that lonely makes / Remember what I told you to forget / Too late / She's gone / It only takes a minute / Love I never had / Heaven must be missing an angel / Don't take away the music / Whodunit / Goodbye my love (pleasant dreams) / More than a woman / Never had love like this before / Bad times / Loveline
CD _____ C2 89380
Capitol / Aug '93 / EMI.

HITS OF TAVARES
CD _____ KLMCD 024
Scratch / Apr '94 / BMG.

LIVE HITS
CD _____ CDCD 1149
Charly / Feb '94 / Charly / THE / Cadillac.

TAVARES LIVE IN CONCERT
CD _____ JHD 104
Tring / Aug '93 / Tring / Prism.

Tawney, Cyril

DOWN THE HATCH
Charlie Mopp's / Early one evening / Bluey brink / Jug of this / Boozing / Oh good ale / Pint of contraception / Down where the drunkards roll / Sucking cider through a straw / As soon as the pub closes / On a Monday morning / All through the beer / Drunken maidens / Parting glass / Old pubs / Sparrow in the tree top / Farewell to the whiskey / Jolly roving tar / Come to Australia / Reunion / I mean to get jolly well drunk / Fathom the bowl / Barley mow
CD _____ NGL 101CD
Neptune / May '94 / Neptune Tapes / ADA.

Taxi Gang

HAIL UP THE TAXI
Crazy baldheads / Going home / Money / People listen / He said he said / Skin tight / One a wee, two a wee / No mama no cry / Easy and cool / Love my woman / Sweetie dear / Mechanic / Compliments on your kiss / Freak out
CD _____ IJCD 3002
Island / May '95 / PolyGram.

TAXI CHRISTMAS, A
CD _____ RASCD 3102
Greensleeves / Dec '92 / Total/BMG / Jetstar / SRD.

Taylor, Alex

DANCING WITH THE DEVIL
House of cards / Can't break the habit / Let the big dog eat / Birds of a feather / Change in me / Dancing with the devil / No life at all / Practice what you preach / Black sheep
CD _____ ICH 9007CD
Ichiban / Jul '91 / Koch.

Taylor, Allan

FADED LIGHT
CD _____ T 005CD
T / Nov '95 / CM / ADA.

LINES
CD _____ T 002CD
T / Aug '94 / CM / ADA.

SO LONG
CD _____ T 004CD
T / Aug '94 / CM / ADA.

Taylor, Art

WAILIN' AT THE VANGUARD (Taylor, Art Wailers)
CD _____ 519677-2
Verve / May '94 / PolyGram.

Taylor, Billy

HOMAGE
Homage (pts 1-3) / Step into my dream / Billy and Dave / On this lean, mean street / Barbados beauty / Kim's song / Hope and hostility / Uncle Bob / Two shades of blue / Dave and Billy / Back to my dream plus / It happens all the time / One for fun
CD _____ GRP 09062
GRP / Mar '95 / BMG / New Note.

Taylor, Bram

FURTHER HORIZONS
CD _____ FE 92CD
Fellside / Oct '93 / Target/BMG / Direct / ADA.

Taylor, Cecil

1955-1961
CD _____ CD 53172
Giants Of Jazz / Sep '94 / Target/BMG / Cadillac.

3 PHASIS
CD _____ NW 303
New World / Aug '92 / Harmonia Mundi / ADA / Cadillac.

AIR
CD _____ CCD 79046
Candid / Oct '90 / Cadillac / Jazz Music / Wellard / Koch.

ALMS/TIERGARTEN (SPREE) (Taylor, Cecil European Orchestra)
CD Set _____ FMPCD 08-9
FMP / Oct '85 / Cadillac.

CECIL TAYLOR UNIT
Idut / Serdab / Holiday en masque
CD _____ NW 201
New World / '88 / Harmonia Mundi / ADA / Cadillac.

CELEBRATED BLAZONS (Taylor, Cecil & Feel Trio)
CD _____ FMPCD 58
FMP / Oct '94 / Cadillac.

CELL WALK FOR CELESTE
CD _____ CCD 9034
Candid / May '89 / Cadillac / Jazz Music / Wellard / Koch.

CHINAMPAS
CD _____ CDLR 153
Leo / Mar '88 / Wellard / Cadillac / Impetus.

CROSSING
CD _____ JHR 73505
Jazz Hour / Sep '93 / Target/BMG / Jazz Music / Cadillac.

FONDATION MAEGHT NIGHTS
CD _____ COD 001
Jazz View / Mar '92 / Harmonia Mundi.

FONDATION MAEGHT NIGHTS, VOL. 2
CD _____ COD 002
Jazz View / Jun '92 / Harmonia Mundi.

FONDATION MAEGHT NIGHTS, VOL. 3
CD _____ COD 003
Jazz View / Jul '92 / Harmonia Mundi.

GARDEN PART 1
CD _____ ARTCD 6050
Hat Art / Nov '90 / Harmonia Mundi / ADA / Cadillac.

GREAT PARIS CONCERT, THE
Student studies / Student studies #2 / Amplitude / Niggle feuigle
CD _____ BLCD 760201
Black Lion / Apr '95 / Jazz Music / Cadillac / Wellard / Koch.

HEARTH, THE (Taylor, Cecil & Evan Parker/T. Tonsinger)
CD _____ FMPCD 11
FMP / Nov '84 / Cadillac.

IN EAST BERLIN (Taylor, Cecil & Gunter Sommer)
CD Set _____ FMPCD 13-14
FMP / Oct '86 / Cadillac.

INDENT
Indent: first layer / Indent: second layer (pts 1 & 2) / Indent: third layer
CD _____ FCD 41038
Freedom / Dec '87 / Jazz Music / Swift / Wellard / Cadillac.

IWONTUNWONSI
CD _____ SSCD 8065
Sound Hills / Jan '96 / Harmonia Mundi / Cadillac.

JUMPIN' PUNKINS
CD _____ CCD 9013
Candid / Dec '94 / Cadillac / Jazz Music / Wellard / Koch.

LEAF PLAM HAND (Taylor, Cecil & Tony Oxley)
CD _____ FMPCD 06
FMP / Jul '88 / Cadillac.

LIVE IN BOLOGNA (Taylor, Cecil Unit)
CD _____ CDLR 100
Leo / Mar '88 / Wellard / Cadillac / Impetus.

LOOKING (BERLIN VERSION)
CD _____ FMPCD 31
FMP / Dec '87 / Cadillac.

LOOKING (BERLIN VERSION) SOLO
CD _____ FMPCD 28
FMP / Mar '85 / Cadillac.

LOOKING - THE FEEL TRIO
CD _____ FMP CD 33
FMP / Jun '85 / Cadillac.

NEW YORK CITY RHYTHM AND BLUES (Taylor, Cecil & Buell Neidlinger)
OP / Cell walk for Celeste / Cindy's main mood / Things ain't what they used to be
CD _____ CD 79017
Candid / Mar '92 / Cadillac / Jazz Music / Wellard / Koch.

ONE TOO MANY SALTY SWIFT AND NOT GOODBYE
CD Set _____ ARTCD 26090
Hat Art / Dec '91 / Harmonia Mundi / ADA / Cadillac.

PLEISTOZAEN MIT WASSER (Taylor, Cecil & Derek Bailey)
CD _____ FMPCD 16
FMP / Aug '88 / Cadillac.

REGALIA (Taylor, Cecil & Paul Lovens)
CD _____ FMPCD 03
FMP / May '89 / Cadillac.

REMEMBRANCE (Taylor, Cecil & Louis Moholo)
CD _____ FMPCD 04
FMP / Dec '87 / Cadillac.

RIOBEC (Taylor, Cecil & Gunter Sommer)
CD _____ FMPCD 02
FMP / May '89 / Cadillac.

SILENT TONGUES
Abyss / Petals and filaments / Jitney / Taylor crossing part one / Crossing #2 / After all / Jitney No. 2 / After all No. 2
CD _____ FCD 41005
Freedom / Sep '87 / Jazz Music / Swift / Wellard / Cadillac.

TAYLOR, CECIL

SOLO - ERZULIE MAKETH SCENT
CD _____ FMPCD 18
FMP / Aug '89 / Cadillac.

SPOTS, CIRCLES & FANTASY (Taylor, Cecil & Han Bennink)
CD _____ FMPCD 05
FMP / Jan '88 / Cadillac.

SPRING OF TWO BLUE J'S (Taylor, Cecil Unit)
CD _____ COD 008
Jazz View / Aug '92 / Harmonia Mundi.

WINGED SERPENT (Taylor, Cecil Segments 11)
CD _____ SNCD 1089
Soul Note / '86 / Harmonia Mundi / Wellard / Cadillac.

WORLD OF CECIL TAYLOR, THE
CD _____ CCD 9006
Candid / Nov '87 / Cadillac / Jazz Music / Wellard / Koch.

Taylor, Dave

BOOGIE IN THE CITY
CD _____ CDCD 1114
Charly / Jul '93 / Charly / THE / Cadillac.

Taylor, David

PAST TELLS
CD _____ 804362
New World / Feb '94 / Harmonia Mundi / ADA / Cadillac.

Taylor, Derek

MY KIND OF JOLSON
CD _____ CDOK 3008
OK / Dec '89 / Ross.

Taylor, Eddie

BAD BOY (Charly Blues - Masterworks Vol. 35)
Bad boy / E.T. blues / Ride 'em on down / Big town playboy / You'll always have a home / Don't knock at my door / I'm gonna love you / Lookin' for trouble / Find my baby / Stroll out west / I'm sitting here / Do you want me to cry / Train fare / Leave this neighborhood / Somethin' for nothin'
CD _____ CDBM 35
Charly / Jan '93 / Charly / THE / Cadillac.

BAD BOY (Taylor, Eddie 'Big Town Playboy' & Vera Taylor)
CD _____ WCD 120711
Wolf / Jul '95 / Jazz Music / Swift / Hot Shot.

I FEEL SO BAD
CD _____ HCD 8027
Hightone / Sep '94 / ADA / Koch.

LONG WAY FROM HOME
CD _____ BPCD 5025
Blind Pig / Dec '95 / Hot Shot / Swift / CM / Roots / Direct / ADA.

MY HEART IS BLEEDING (Taylor, Eddie Blues Band)
My heart is bleeding / Going to Virginia / So bad / Lexington breakdown / Blow wind blow / Wreck on 83 Highway / Soul brother / There'll be a day / Lowdale blues / Gamblin' woman / I got a little thing they call it swing / One day I get lucky / Dust my broom
CD _____ CDLR 72008
L&R / Jul '94 / New Note.
CD _____ ECD 260542
Evidence / Sep '94 / Harmonia Mundi / ADA / Cadillac.

Taylor, Eric

ERIC TAYLOR
CD _____ WWMCD 1040
Watermelon / Nov '95 / ADA / Direct.

Taylor, Gary

ONE DAY AT A TIME
CD _____ XECD 3
Expansion / Jun '95 / Pinnacle / Sony / 3MV.

REFLECTIONS
CD _____ EXCDP 8
Expansion / Nov '94 / Pinnacle / Sony / 3MV.

SQUARE ONE
Hold me accountable / Irresistible love / A.P.B. / Pieces / Square one / Read between the lines / Never too blue / I need you now / Eye to eye / One and only
CD _____ EXCD 6
Expansion / Mar '93 / Pinnacle / Sony / 3MV.

TAKE CONTROL
Take control / Whatever / I need / In and out of love / Wishful thinking / Don't be so distant / I live 4 U / Sign my life away / Time after time
CD _____ EXCDP 5
Expansion / Jun '90 / Pinnacle / Sony / 3MV.

Taylor, Hound Dog

BEWARE OF THE DOG (Taylor, Hound Dog & The House Rockers)
Give me back my wig / Sun is shining / Kitchen sink boogie / Dust my broom / Comin' around the mountain / Let's get funky / Rock me / It's alright / Freddie's blues
CD _____ ALCD 4707
Alligator / May '93 / Direct / ADA.

GENUINE HOUSEROCKING MUSIC (Taylor, Hound Dog & The House Rockers)
Ain't got nobody / Gonna send you back to Georgia / Fender bender / My baby's coming home / Blue guitar / Sun is shining / Phillips goes bananas / What'd I say / Kansas City / Crossroads
CD _____ ALCD 4727
Alligator / May '93 / Direct / ADA.

HOUND DOG TAYLOR AND THE HOUSE ROCKERS (Taylor, Hound Dog & The House Rockers)
She's gone / Walking the ceiling / Held my baby last night / Taylor's rock / It's alright / Phillip's theme / Wild about you baby / I just can't make it / It hurts me too / 44 blues / Give me back my wig / 55th Street boogie
CD _____ ALCD 4701
Alligator / May '93 / Direct / ADA.

LIVE AT JOE'S PLACE
CD _____ 422174
New Rose / May '94 / Direct / ADA.

NATURAL BOOGIE (Taylor, Hound Dog & The House Rockers)
Take five / Hawaiian boogie / See me in the evening / You can't sit down / Sitting at home alone / One more time / Roll your moneymaker / Buster's boogie / Sadie / Talk to my baby / Goodnight boogie
CD _____ ALCD 4704
Alligator / May '93 / Direct / ADA.

Taylor, James

BEST LIVE
Sweet baby James / Handyman / Your smiling face / Steamroller blues / Mexico / Walking man / Country road / Fire and rain / How sweet it is (to be loved by you) / Riding on a railroad / Something in the way she moves / Sun on the moon / Up on the roof / Copperline / Slap leather / You've got a friend / That lonesome road
CD _____ 476657 2
Columbia / Apr '94 / Sony.

FLAG
Company man / Johnnie come back / Day tripper / I will not lie for you / Brother trucker / Is that the way you look / B.S.U.R. / Rainy day man / Millworker / Up on the roof / Chanson Francais / Sleep come free me
CD _____ 982987 2
Pickwick/Sony Collector's Choice / Aug '93 / Carlton Home Entertainment / Pinnacle / Sony.

GREATEST HITS: JAMES TAYLOR
Something in the way she moves / Carolina on my mind / Fire and rain / Sweet baby James / Country roads / You've got a friend / Don't let me be lonely tonight / Walking man / How sweet it is (to be loved by you) / Mexico / Shower the people / Steamroller
CD _____ 7599273362
WEA / '94 / Warner Music.

IN THE POCKET
Shower the people / Junkie's lament / Money machine / Slow burning love / Everybody has the blues / Daddy's all gone / Woman's gotta have it / Captain Jim's drunken dream / Don't be sad 'cause your sun is down / Nothing like a hundred miles / Family man / Golden moments
CD _____ 7599273012
WEA / '94 / Warner Music.

LIVE
Sweet baby James / Traffic jam / Handyman / Your smiling face / Secret of life / Shed a little light / Everybody has the blues / Steamroller blues / Mexico / Millworker / Country road / Fire and rain / Shower the people / How sweet it is (to be loved by you) / New hymn / Walking man / Riding on a railroad / Something / Sun on the moon / Night She thinks I still care / Copperline / Slap leather / Only one / You make it easy / Carolina on my mind / I will follow / You've got a friend / That lonesome road
CD _____ 474216 2
Columbia / Sep '93 / Sony.

NEW MOON SHINE
Copperline / Down in the hole / (I've got to) stop thinkin' 'bout that / Shed a little light / Frozen man / Slap leather / Like everyone she knows / One more go round / Everybody loves to cha cha / Native son / Oh brother / Water is wide
CD _____ 4689772
Columbia / Nov '91 / Sony.

YOU'VE GOT A FRIEND
CD _____ CJESD 1
M Classics / Nov '92 / Grapevine.

Taylor, James

BBC SESSIONS, THE (Taylor, James Quartet)
Blow up / Spyder / All about mine / Down by the river / Breakout / Bossa plante / Groovin' home / Mon oncle / Love the life / Tell it like it is
CD _____ CDNT 010
Strange Fruit / Oct '95 / Pinnacle.

DO YOUR OWN THING (Taylor, James Quartet)
Love the life / Killing time / Money / J.T.Q. theme / Ted's asleep / Always there / Oscar / Samba for Bill and Ben / Valhalla / Fat / Peace song
CD _____ 843 797-2
Polydor / Oct '90 / PolyGram.

GET ORGANIZED (Taylor, James Quartet)
Grooving home / Electric boogaloo / Stretch / It doesn't matter / Riding high / Touchdown / Breakout / Brothers batucada / Bluebird / Bossa pilante
CD _____ 839 405-2
Polydor / May '89 / PolyGram.

IN THE HAND OF THE INEVITABLE (Taylor, James Quartet)
CD _____ JAZIDCD 115
Acid Jazz / Feb '95 / Pinnacle.

Taylor, John

AMBLESIDE DAYS (Taylor, John & John Surman)
Lodore falls / Wandering / Ambleside days / Scale force / Coniston falls / Pathway / Clapperclowe / Dry stone
CD _____ AHUM 013
Ah-Um / Oct '92 / New Note / Cadillac.

BLUE GLASS (Taylor, John Trio)
Pure and simple / Spring is here / Q / Hermana guapa / Blue glass / How deep is the ocean / Fragment / Think before you think / Evansong (CD only) / Clapperclowe (CD only)
CD _____ JHCD 020
Ronnie Scott's Jazz House / Jan '94 / Jazz Music / Magnum Music Group / Cadillac.

PAUSE AND THINK AGAIN
CD _____ FMRCD 24
Future / Dec '95 / Harmonia Mundi / ADA.

Taylor, Johnnie

CHRONICLE
Who's making love / Take care of your homework / Testify / I could never be president / Love bones / Steal away / I am somebody / Jody's got your girl and gone / I don't wanna lose you / Hijackin' love / Standin' in for Jody / Doing my own thing (Part 2) / Doing my own thing / Stop doggin' me / I believe in you (You believe in me) / Cheaper to keep her / We're getting careless with our love / I've been born again / It's September / Try me tonight / Just keep on loving me
CD _____ CDSXE 084
Stax / Jul '93 / Pinnacle.

JOHNNIE TAYLOR PHILOSOPHY CONTINUES/ONE STEP BEYOND
Testify / Separation line / Love bones / Love is a hurtin' thing / I had a fight with love / I could never be president / It's amazing / Who can I turn to / Games people play / It's your thing / Time after time / Party life / Will you love me forever / I am somebody (pts 1 & 2) / I don't wanna lose you (pts 1 & 2) / Don't take my sunshine / Jody's got your girl and gone / Fool like me
CD Set _____ CDSXD 108
Stax / Jul '94 / Pinnacle.

RAW BLUES/LITTLE BLUEBIRD
CD _____ CDSXD 051
Stax / Jun '92 / Pinnacle.

SOMEBODY'S GETTIN' IT
Disco lady / Somebody's gettin' it / Pick up the pieces / Running out of lines / Did he make love to you / Your love is rated X / I'm just a shoulder to cry on / Love is better in the a.m. / Just a happy song / Right now
CD _____ CDCHARLY 160
Charly / Mar '89 / Charly / THE / Cadillac.

WANTED: ONE SOUL SINGER
I got to love somebody's baby / Just the one I've been looking for / Watermelon man / Where can a man go from here / Toe hold / Outside love / ain't that lovin' you / Blues in the night / I had a dream / Sixteen tons / Little bluebird
CD _____ 7567822532
Atlantic / Apr '95 / Warner Music.

Taylor, Koko

AUDIENCE WITH THE QUEEN, AN (Live From Chicago)
Let the good times roll / I'm a woman / Go back to luka / Devil's gonna have a field day / Come to Mama / I'd rather go blind / Let me love you / Wang dang doodle
CD _____ ALCD 4754
Alligator / May '93 / Direct / ADA.

EARTH SHAKER
CD _____ ALCD 4711
Alligator / May '93 / Direct / ADA.

FORCE OF NATURE
CD _____ ALCD 4817
Alligator / Feb '94 / Direct / ADA.

FROM THE HEART OF A WOMAN
Something strange is going on / I'd rather go blind / Keep your hands off him / Thanks but no thanks / If you got a heartache / Never trust a man / Sure had a wonderful time last night / Blow top blues / If walls could talk / It took a long time
CD _____ ALCD 4724
Alligator / May '93 / Direct / ADA.

I GOT WHAT IT TAKES
Trying to make a living / I got what it takes / Mama / Voodoo woman / Be what you want to be / Honky tonky / Big boss man / Blues never die / Find a fool / Happy home / What's what I'm crying
CD _____ ALCD 4706
Sonet / May '93 / ADA.

JUMP FOR JOY
CD _____ ALCD 4784
Alligator / Oct '93 / Direct / ADA.

QUEEN OF THE BLUES
CD _____ ALCD 4740
Alligator / Oct '93 / Direct / ADA.

SOUTH SIDE LADY
CD _____ ECD 260072
Evidence / Jan '92 / Harmonia Mundi / ADA / Cadillac.

Taylor, Little Johnny

GALAXY YEARS, THE
You'll need another favour / What you need is a ball / Part time love / Somewhere down the line / Since I found a new love / My heart is filled with pain / First class love / If you love me like you say / You win, I lose / Nightingale melody / I smell trouble / True love / For your precious love / I've never had a woman like you before / Somebody's got to pay / Help yourself / One more chance / Please come home for Christmas / All I want is you / Zig zag lightning / Things that I used to do / Big blue diamonds / I know you hear me calling / Drivin' wheel / Sometimey woman / Double or nothing
CD _____ CDCHD 967
Ace / Apr '91 / Pinnacle / Cadillac / Complete/Pinnacle.

PART-TIME LOVE
You're the one / As quick as I can / What you need is a ball / You gotta go on / She tried to understand / Since I found a new love / Darling believe me / She's yours, she's mine / Stay sweet / Somewhere down the line / Part time love
CD _____ CD 229
Wellard / Dec '87 / Wellard.

UGLY MAN
Have you ever been to Kansas City / Never be lonely and blue / LJT / Ugly man / It's my fault, darlin' / I enjoy you / How can a broke man survive / King size souvenir / Have you ever been to Kansas City (Reprise)
CD _____ CDICH 1042
Ichiban / Oct '93 / Koch.

Taylor, Lynn

I SEE YOUR FACE BEFORE ME
CD _____ PS 0011CD
P&S / Sep '95 / Discovery.

Taylor, Martin

ARTISTRY
Polka dots and moonbeams / Stella by starlight / Teach me tonight / Dolphin / Georgia on my mind / They can't that away from me / Here, there and everywhere / Just squeeze me / Gentle rain / Cherokee / That certain smile
CD _____ AKD 020
Linn / Mar '93 / PolyGram.

CHANGE OF HEART
73 Berkeley street / Gypsy / You don't know me / After hours / Change of heart / I get along without you very well / Angels's camp
CD _____ AKD 016
Linn / Nov '91 / PolyGram.

SARABANDA
CD _____ 1390182
Gaia / Feb '89 / New Note.

SPIRIT OF DJANGO
Chez Fernand / Minor swing / Night and day / Nuages / James / Django's dream / Swing '42 / Lady be good / Honeysuckle rose / Johnny and Mary
CD _____ AKD 030
Linn / Oct '94 / PolyGram.

Taylor, Matt

RADIO CITY BLUES
CD _____ MSECD 009
Mouse / Jun '95 / Grapevine.

TROUBLE IN THE WIND
CD _____ AIM 1034CD
Aim / Oct '93 / Direct / ADA / Jazz Music.

Taylor, Melvin

BLUES ON THE RUN
Travelin' man / Lowdown dirty shame / Escape / Cold cold feeling / Just like a woman / Chitlins con carne
CD _____ ECD 260412
Evidence / Mar '94 / Harmonia Mundi / ADA / Cadillac.

MELVIN TAYLOR AND THE SLACK BAND (Taylor, Melvin & The Slack band)
Texas flood / Depression blues / Grooving in New Orleans / Talking to Anna Mae / Tin pan alley / All your love / Don't throw your love on me so strong / T-bone shuffle / Voodoo chile (slight return) / Tequila
CD _____ ECD 260732
Evidence / Oct '95 / Harmonia Mundi / ADA / Cadillac.

PLAYS THE BLUES FOR YOU
Talking to Anna Mae, Part 1 / T.V. Mama / I'll play the blues for you / Born to lose / Tribute to Wes / Cadillac assembly line / Voodoo Daddy / Talking to Anna Mae, Part 2 / Groovin' in Paris
CD _____ ECD 260292
Evidence / Feb '93 / Harmonia Mundi / ADA / Cadillac.

Taylor, Mick

MICK TAYLOR
Leather jacket / Alabama / Slow blues / Baby I want you / Broken hands / Giddy up / S.W.5
CD _____ 477852 2
Columbia / Oct '94 / Sony.

MICK TAYLOR AND CARLA OLSON LIVE (Taylor, Mick & Carla Olson)
Who put the sting in the honeybee / Slow rollin' train / Trying to hold on / Rubies and diamonds / See the light / You can't move in / Broken hands / Sway / Hartley quits / Midnight mission / Silver train
CD _____ FIENDCD 197
Demon / Oct '90 / Pinnacle / ADA.

STRANGER IN THIS TOWN
CD _____ 844 649
Maze / Jul '90 / Plastic Head.

WITHIN AN ACE (Taylor, Mick & Carla Olson)
Justice / Dark horses / Why did you stop / World of pain / Fortune / Within an ace / Man once loved / How many days / Rescue fantasy / Is the lady gone
CD _____ FIENDCD 726
Demon / Jan '93 / Pinnacle / ADA.

Taylor, Rod

LIBERATE
CD _____ WSPCD 004
Word Sound & Power / Nov '93 / SRD.

Taylor, Roger

HAPPINESS
Nazis 1994 / Happiness / Revelations / Touch the sky / Foreign sand / Freedom train / You had to be there / The key / Everybody hurts sometime / Loneliness / Dear Mr. Murdoch / Old friends
CD _____ CDPCSD 157
Parlophone / Sep '94 / EMI.

Taylor, Rusty

RUSTY TAYLOR & STEVE LANE'S RED HOT PEPPERS (Taylor, Rusty & Steve Lane's Red Hot Peppers)
Cake walkin' babies from home / Wrap your troubles in dreams and dream your troubles away) / Trombone cholly / Just too bad / Do your duty / You've got to give me some / Baby, won't you please come home / Cheatin' on me / I've got what it takes / Alexander's ragtime band / There's a blue ridge round my heart, Virginia / Shine / I'm coming Virginia / Put it right here / Atlanta / Take me for a buggy ride / Spanish shawl / After you've gone
CD _____ AZMC 17
Azure / Apr '93 / Jazz Music / Swift / Wellard / Azure / Cadillac.

Taylor, Simon

IRISH GUITAR, THE
CD _____ OSS 1CD
Ossian / Jan '87 / ADA / Direct / CM.

Taylor, Steve

I PREDICT 1990
CD _____ MYRCD 6873
Myrrh / Jan '88 / Nelson Word.

Taylor, Tot

BOX OFFICE POISON
Australian / Arise Sir Tot / I was frank / Spoil her / Mr. Strings / Nevermore / Ballad of Jackie and Ivy / People will talk / I never rome / Babysitting / Mr. String's come back / My independant heart
CD _____ TOTE 3
Soundcakes / Oct '88 / 3MV / Sony.

INSIDE STORY, THE
CD _____ TOTE 2
Soundcakes / Oct '88 / 3MV / Sony.

MY BLUE PERIOD
Wrong idea / It must have been a craze / It's good for you / It's all a blur / Wild scene / I'll wait / Compromising life / Young world / I'll miss the lads / It's not a bad old place / Girl did this
CD _____ TOTE 4
Soundcakes / Oct '88 / 3MV / Sony.

PLAYTIME
CD _____ TOTE 1
Soundcakes / Oct '88 / 3MV / Sony.

Taylor, Tyrone

WAY TO PARADISE
CD _____ VPCD 1378
VP / Jan '95 / Jetstar.

Taylor, Vince

I'LL BE YOUR HERO
CD _____ 842132
EVA / Jun '94 / Direct / ADA.

Tchicai, John

LOVE IS TOUCHING
Breath bridge / Love is touching / 911-2 Days / Prayer for right guidance / Yam / Scientific Americans / Bless your heart / Salt lips city blues / You made me laugh / Ramana Maharshi / Lonesome abalone / Responsible fruit / Poetry department / Scholer's foundation of life / I skovens oyb
CD _____ BW 055
B&W / Oct '95 / New Note.

Tchinar, Ashik Feyzullah

SACRED CHANTS OF ANATOLIA
CD _____ C 580057
Ocora / Jan '96 / Harmonia Mundi / ADA.

Te Kanawa, Kiri

KIRI SIDETRACKS (The Jazz Album)
CD _____ 4340922
Philips / May '92 / PolyGram.

WORLD IN UNION
World in union / Pavanne (allez les blues) / Emerald eyes (Danny boy) / Italiana / Land of my fathers (hen wlad fy nhadau) / Emotion in motion / Swing low, sweet chariot (run with the ball) / Jupiter suite/World in union / Flower of Scotland / Australiana / Game of hearts / New world haka
CD _____ 4690472
Columbia / Apr '94 / Sony.

Te Track

LET'S GET STARTED/EASTMAN DUB (Te Track & Augustus Pablo)
CD _____ GRELCD 505
Greensleeves / Apr '90 / Total/BMG / Jetstar / SRD.

Tea Party

EDGES OF TWILIGHT, THE
Fire in the head / Bazaar / Correspondences / Badger / Silence / Sister awake / Turn the lamp down low / Shadows on the mountainside / Drawing down the moon / Inanna / Coming home / Walk with me
CD _____ CDCHR 6100
Chrysalis / Apr '95 / EMI.

SPLENDOR SOLIS
Rivue / Midsummer day / Certain slant of light / Winter solstice / Save me / Sun going down / In this time / Dreams of reason / Raven skies / Haze on the hills / Majestic song
CD _____ CDCHR 6072
Chrysalis / May '94 / EMI.

Teagarden, Jack

1944-1946: BIG T JUMP
CD _____ JCD 643
Jass / Aug '95 / CM / Jazz Music / ADA / Cadillac / Direct.

ACCENT ON TROMBONE
CD _____ FSRCD 138
Fresh Sound / Dec '90 / Jazz Music / Discovery.

BEST OF JACK TEAGARDEN
CD _____ DLCD 4022
Dixie Live / Mar '95 / Magnum Music Group.

BIG T
CD _____ TPZ 1001
Topaz Jazz / Jul '94 / Pinnacle / Cadillac.

BLUES SINGER 1931-41, THE
CD _____ JZCD 346
Suisa / Jan '93 / Jazz Music / THE.

CLASSICS 1934-39
CD _____ CLASSICS 729
Classics / Dec '93 / Discovery / Jazz Music.

CLASSICS 1939-40
CD _____ CLASSICS 758
Classics / Aug '94 / Discovery / Jazz Music.

CLASSICS 1940-41
CD _____ CLASSICS 839
Classics / Sep '95 / Discovery / Jazz Music.

CLEVELAND, OHIO 1958 (Teagarden, Jack Allstars)
CD _____ JCD 199
Jazzology / Oct '92 / Swift / Jazz Music.

HAS ANYBODY SEEN JACKSON VOL. 2
CD _____ JCD 637
Jass / Jan '93 / CM / Jazz Music / ADA / Cadillac / Direct.

I GOTTA RIGHT TO SING THE BLUES
That's a serious thing / I'm gonna stomp Mr. Henry Lee / Dinah / Never had a reason to believe in you / Tailspin blues / Dancing with tears in my eyes / Sheikh of Araby / Basin Street blues / (I'll be glad when you're dead) you rascal you / Two tickets to Georgia / I gotta right to sing the blues / Ain't cha glad / Texas tea party / Hundred years from today / Fare thee well to Harlem / Christmas night in Harlem / Davenport blues
CD _____ CD AJA 5059
Living Era / Feb '89 / Koch.

INDISPENSABLE JACK TEAGARDEN
She's a great, great girl / I'm gonna stomp Mr. Henry Lee / That's a serious thing / Tailspin blues / Never had a reason to believe in you / Buy buy for baby (or baby will bye bye you) / Sentimental baby / Futuristic rhythm / Louise / My kinda love / Sweetheart we need each other / From now on / Two tickets to Georgia / Fare thee well to Harlem / Christmas night in Harlem / Ain't misbehavin' / At the Darktown strutter's ball / Every now and then / Barrel house music / I'se a muggin' (pts 1 & 2) / St. Louis blues / Blues after hours / Jam session at Victor / Say it simple / There'll be some changes made / I cover the waterfront / You took advantage of me
CD Set _____ ND 89613
RCA / Mar '94 / BMG.

INTRODUCTION TO JACK TEAGARDEN 1928-1943
CD _____ 4025
Best Of Jazz / Sep '95 / Discovery.

IT'S TIME FOR TEA VOL. 1 (1941)
CD _____ JASSCD 624
Jass / '92 / CM / Jazz Music / ADA / Cadillac / Direct.

JACK TEAGARDEN & PEE WEE RUSSELL (Teagarden, Jack & Pee Wee Russell)
CD _____ OJCCD 1708
Original Jazz Classics / Jun '95 / Wellard / Jazz Music / Cadillac / Complete/Pinnacle.

JACK TEAGARDEN 1930-1934 (Teagarden, Jack & His Orchestra)
CD _____ CLASSICS 698
Classics / Jul '93 / Discovery / Jazz Music.

JAZZ ORIGINAL
King Porter stomp / Eccentric / Davenport blues / Original dixieland one-step / Bad actin' woman / Misery and the blues / High society / Music to love by / Meet me where they play the blues / Riverboat shuffle / Milenberg joys / Blue funk
CD _____ CDCHARLY 80
Charly / '87 / Charly / THE / Cadillac.

LIVE IN CHICAGO 1960-61 (Teagarden, Jack Sextet)
CD _____ EBCD 2111 2
Jazzband / Jul '93 / Jazz Music / Wellard.

MASTERS OF JAZZ VOL.10
CD _____ STCD 4110
Storyville / Feb '89 / Jazz Music / Wellard / CM / Cadillac.

TEAGARDEN PARTY, A
Muddy river blues / Somewhere a voice calling / Swingin' on a teagarden gate / Wolverine blues / (I'll be glad when you're dead) you rascal you / Plantation moods / Shake your hips / Somebody stole Gabriel's horn / Love me / I just couldn't take it baby / Hundred years from today / Blue river / Oi' Pappy / Fare-thee well to Harlem / Stars fell on Alabama / Junk man / Gotta right to sing the blues / Ain't cha glad / Dr. Heckle and Mr. Jibe / Texas tea party
CD _____ PAR 2013
Parade / Apr '94 / Koch / Cadillac.

TEXAS TROMBONE LIVE
CD _____ CDSG 403
Starline / Aug '89 / Jazz Music.

Teallach Ceilidh Band

CATCHING THE SUN RISE
Stool of repentance / Letham smiddy / Athol highlanders / Mountains of Pomeroy / Irish soldier laddie / Yellow's on the broom / John Barleycorn / Martin the Stout / All the blue bonnets are over the border / MacDonald's awa' tae the war / Rocks of bawn / David Ross of Rosehall / Major Manson at Clachantruical / Rainy day / Lark in the morning / Mysteries of knock / Barrowburn reel / Jack broke da prison door / Donald Blue / Sleep sound ida morning / Arthur McBride / Athol and Breadalbane / Cameron highlanders / Old skibbereen / Sean

O'Dwyer of the Glen / Royal Scots / Sleepy Maggie / Bessie McIntyre / All the way to Galway / Chris O'Callaghan / Hunting the hare / Shiramee / Back to the Haggard / Mo Dhachaidh (my home)
CD _____ LCOM 5208
Lismor / '91 / Lismor / Direct / Duncans / ADA.

DROPS OF BRANDY
CD _____ SPRCD 1028
Springthyme / Jan '90 / Direct / Roots / CM / Duncans / ADA.

Tear Ceremony

HOURGLASS OF OPALS, AN
CD _____ MA55-2
Machinery / Jun '94 / Plastic Head.

Tear Garden

BOUQUET OF BLACK ORCHIDS
Sheila liked the rodeo / Ophelia / Tear garden / My thorny thorny crown / Romulus and venus / White coats and haloes / Blobbo / Sybil the spider consumes himself / Ship named despair / Centre bullet / You and me and rainbows / Oo ee oo
CD _____ NET 047CD
Nettwerk / Jul '93 / Vital / Pinnacle.

LAST MAN TO FLY, THE
Hipper form / Running man / Turn me on dead man / Romulus and Venus / Great lie / Empathy with the devil / Love notes and carnations / Ship named despair / White coats and haloes / Isis veiled / Last post / Thirty technicolour scrambled egg trip down the hellhole
CD _____ NET 027 CD
Nettwerk / Apr '92 / Vital / Pinnacle.

TIRED EYES SLOWLY BURNING
Deja vu / Room with a view / Coma / Valium / You and me and rainbows / Ooh ee oo ee
CD _____ NTCD 034
Nettwerk / Feb '88 / Vital / Pinnacle.

Teardrop Explodes

EVERYBODY WANTS TO SHAG...THE TEARDROP EXPLODES
Ouch monkeys / Serious danger / Metranil Vavin / Count to ten and run for cover / In-psychopedia / Soft enough for you / You disappear from view / Challenger / Not my only friend / Sex / Terrorist / Strange house in the snow
CD _____ 8424392
Mercury / Mar '90 / PolyGram.

KILIMANJARO
Ha ha I'm drowning / Sleeping gas / Treason / Second head / Reward poppies / Went crazy / Brave boys keep their promises / Bouncing babies / Books / Thief of Baghdad / When I dream
CD _____ 8368972
Mercury / Jan '96 / PolyGram.

WILDER
Bent out of shape / Colours fly away / Seven views of Jerusalem / Pure joy / Falling down around me / Culture bunker / Tiny children / Passionate friend / Like Leila Khaled said / Great dominions
CD _____ 8368962
Mercury / Jan '96 / PolyGram.

WILDER/KILIMANJARO (2 CDs)
Ha ha I'm drowning / Sleeping gas / Treason / Second head / Reward / Poppies / Passionate friend / Tiny children / Like Leila Khaled said / Poll the lighting lakes over / Great dominions / Bent out of shape / Colours fly away / Seven views of Jerusalem / Pure joy / Falling down around me / Culture bunker / Went crazy / Brave boys keep their promises / Bouncing babies / Books / Thief of Baghdad / When I dream
CD Set _____ 5286012
Mercury / Aug '95 / PolyGram.

Tears For Fears

ELEMENTAL
CD _____ 514875-2
Fontana / Jun '93 / PolyGram.

HURTING, THE
Mad world / Pale shelter / Ideas as opiates / Memories fade / Suffer the children / Hurting / Watch me bleed / Change / Prisoner / Start of the breakdown
CD _____ 8110392
Fontana / Jan '88 / PolyGram.

HURTING, THE/SONGS FROM THE BIG CHAIR (2 CDs)
Hurting / Mad world / Pale shelter / Ideas as opiates / Memories fade / Suffer the children / Watch me bleed / Change / Prisoner / Start of the breakdown / Change (new) / Shout / Working hour / Everybody wants to rule the world / Mother's talk / I believe / Broken / Head over heels / Broken (live) / Listen
CD Set _____ 5285992
Fontana / Aug '95 / PolyGram.

RAOUL AND THE KINGS OF SPAIN
Raoul and the kings of Spain / Falling down / Secrets / God's mistake / Sketches of pain / Los reyes catalicos / Sorry / Humdrum and humble / I choose you / Me and my big ideas / Los reyes catalicos (reprise)

TEARS FOR FEARS

CD _____ 4809822
Epic / Oct '95 / Sony.

SEEDS OF LOVE, THE
Badman's song / Sowing the seeds of love / Advice for the young at heart / Standing on the corner of the third world / Swords and knives / Famous last words / Woman in chains
CD _____ 8387302
Fontana / Sep '89 / PolyGram.

SONGS FROM THE BIG CHAIR
Shout / Working hour / Everybody wants to rule the world / Mother's talk / I believe / Broken / Head over heels / Broken (live) / Listen
CD _____ 8243002
Fontana / Mar '85 / PolyGram.

TEARS ROLL DOWN (GREATEST HITS 1982-1992)
Sowing the seeds of love / Everybody wants to rule the world / Woman in chains / Shout / Head over heels / Mad world / Pale shelter / I believe / Laid so low (tears roll down) / Mother's talk / Change / Advice for the young at heart
CD _____ 5109392
Fontana / Mar '92 / PolyGram.

Tebot Piws

Y GORE A'R GWAETHA
CD _____ SCD 2049
Sain / Dec '94 / Direct / ADA.

Techniques

CLASSIC VOLUME 2
CD _____ WRCD 0019
Techniques / Nov '95 / Jetstar.

ROCK STEADY CLASSICS
CD _____ RNCD 2078
Rhino / Dec '94 / Jetstar / Magnum Music Group / THE.

RUN COME CELEBRATE
CD _____ HBCD 121
Greensleeves / Jun '93 / Total/BMG / Jetstar / SRD.

Techno

GO BANG 2.5
CD _____ TNO 5101CD
Ichiban / May '94 / Koch.

Techno Animal

RE-ENTRY
Flight of the hermaphrodite / Mighty atom smasher / Mastadon Americanus / City heathen dub / Narco Agent vs The Medicine Man / Demodex invasion / Evil spirits/Angel dust / Catatonia / Needle Park / Red Sea / Cape Canaveral / Resuscitator
CD _____ AMBT 8
Virgin / May '95 / EMI.

Technohead

HEADSEX
I wanna be a hippy / Headsex / Accelerator # 2 / Passion / Get high / Mary Jane / Get stoned / Keep the party going / Sexhead / Gabba hop
CD _____ DB 47919
Deep Blue / Feb '96 / Pinnacle.

Technotronic

GREATEST HITS: TECHNOTRONIC
CD _____ CCSCD 426
Castle / May '95 / BMG.

Technova

ALBUM
Firehorse one / Waiting / Sativa / Stalker / Transcience / Pacific highways / Third party / Alwah / Water margin / Yeah sister / Relentless / Forgotten
CD _____ SOP 006CD
Emissions / Nov '95 / Vital.

TANTRIC STEPS
Fema / Delta / Tetra / Tantra / Hydra / Shinobo / Data / Irezume / Plateau
CD _____ SOPCD 002
Sabres Of Paradise / Oct '94 / Vital.

Tedesco, Tommy

ROUMANIS JAZZ RHAPSODY
CD _____ 75002
Capri / Sep '89 / Wellard / Cadillac.

Tee Set

EMOTION
Just another hour / I go out of my mind / Don't you leave / Midnight hour / Nothing can ever change / Jet set / Willy nilly / Play that record / Can your monkey do the dog / So fine / For Miss Caulker / You better believe it / Early in the morning / Believe what I say / Don't go mess with Cupid / Long ago / Please call me / So I came back to you / Now's the time / Bring a little sunshine / What can I do / Colours of the rainbow / When I needed you so
CD _____ RPM 134
RPM / Aug '94 / Pinnacle.

Tee-Jay, Abdul Rokoto

KANKA KURU
CD _____ FMSD 5018
Rogue / Sep '89 / Sterns.

Teen Angels

DADDY
CD _____ SPCD 330
Sub Pop / Jan '96 / Disc.

Teen Kings

ARE YOU READY (Unissued 1956 Recordings)
Ooby dooby / Racker tracker / Blue suede shoes / Brown eyed handsome man / St. Louis Blues / Jam / Rock house / Singin' the blues / Pretend / Rip it up / Trying to get to you / TK Blues / Go go go / Bo Diddley / Do you remember
CD _____ RCCD 3012
Rollercoaster / Mar '95 / CM / Swift.

Teen Queens

EDDIE MY LOVE
Eddie my love / Red top / All my love / Billy boy / Zig zag / Till the day I die / Love sweet love / Just goofed / Rock everybody / Baby mine / So all alone / Teenage idol / Let's kiss / Riding / No other / Two loves and two lives / I miss you / My heart's desire
CD _____ CDCHD 581
Ace / Feb '95 / Pinnacle / Cadillac / Complete/Pinnacle.

Teenage Fanclub

BANDWAGONESQUE
Concept / Satan / December / What you do to me / I don't know / Star sign / Metal baby / Pet rock / Sidewinder / Alcoholiday / Guiding star / Is this music
CD _____ CRECD 106
Creation / Oct '91 / 3MV / Vital.

CATHOLIC EDUCATION, A
Heavy metal / Catholic education / Don't need a drum / Heavy metal II / Eternal light / Everybody's fool / Everthing flows / Too involved / Critical mass / Catholic education II / Every picture I paint
CD _____ PAPCD 4
Paperhouse / Mar '95 / Disc.

DEEP FRIED FAN CLUB
CD _____ FLIPCD 002
Fire / Feb '95 / Disc.

GRAND PRIX
About you / Sparky's dream / Mellow doubt / Don't look back / Verisimilitude / Neil Jung / Tears / Discolite / Say no / Going places / I'll make it clear / I gotta know / Hardcore/Ballad
CD _____ CRECD 173
Creation / May '95 / 3MV / Vital.

KING, THE
CD _____ CRELPCD 096
Creation / Aug '91 / 3MV / Vital.

PEEL SESSIONS: TEENAGE FANCLUB
CD _____ SFPCD 081
Strange Fruit / Dec '92 / Pinnacle.

THIRTEEN
Hang on / Cabbage / Radio / Norman 3 / Song to the cynic / 120 mins / Escher / Commercial alternative / Fear of flying / Tears are cool / Ret Liv Dead / Get funky / Gene Clark
CD _____ CRECD 144
Creation / Oct '93 / 3MV / Vital.

Teengenerate

GET ACTION
CD _____ EFACD 11586
Crypt / Dec '94 / SRD.

Teitelbaum, Richard

SEA BETWEEN, THE (Teitelbaum, Richard & Carlos Zingaro)
CD _____ VICTOCD 03
Victo / Nov '94 / These / ReR Megacorp / Cadillac.

Tek 9

IT'S NOT WHAT YOU THINK IT IS
CD _____ SSR 161CD
Crammed Discs / Mar '96 / Grapevine / New Note.

Tekno 2

NEVER ON TIME - THE LP
CD _____ DANCECD 001
D-Zone / Jun '92 / Pinnacle.

Tekton Motor Corporation

HUMAN RACE IGNITION
Cognitive magnitude / Ignition / Dreams / Horizon / Interactive turbulence / Champion 1st part / Spiral emotions / Champion 2nd part / Turning wheel / Cyber transducing / Mechanical spirit / Alert on the victory ahead / Dromologic mind

CD _____ CDKTB 11
Dreamtime / Apr '95 / Kudos / Pinnacle.

Telescopes

TASTE
CD _____ CHEREE 009CD
Cheree / Aug '90 / SRD.

UNTITLED
CD _____ CRECD 79
Creation / Mar '94 / 3MV / Vital.

Television

ADVENTURE
Glory / Days / Foxhole / Careful / Carried away / Fire / Ain't that nothin' / Dream's dream
CD _____ 7559605232
WEA / '92 / Warner Music.

BLOW UP, THE
Blow up / See no evil / Prove it / Elevation / I don't care / Venus De Milo / Foxhole / Ain't that nothin' / Knockin' on Heaven's door / Little Johnny Jewel / Friction / Marquee moon / Satisfaction
CD _____ RE 114CD
Reach Out International / Nov '94 / Jetstar.

MARQUEE MOON
See no evil / Venus / Friction / Marquee moon / Elevation / Guiding light / Prove it / Torn curtain
CD _____ 960616 2
WEA / '89 / Warner Music.

Tell Tale Hearts

HIGH TIDE ANTHOLOGY
CD _____ VOXXCD 2027
Voxx / Oct '94 / Else / Disc.

Telo

RITUAL DEBATE
CD _____ NZ 006-2
Nova Zembla / Apr '94 / Plastic Head.

Telson, Bob

WARRIOR ANT
Juices / Glow of the likeness / O shadow / I am / Welcome to me / Contessa / In the pavillion / Each time she takes one / All wars are lost / Ant alone / More juices / Little village
CD _____ GCD 79490
Gramavision / Sep '95 / Vital/SAM / ADA.

Telstar Ponies

IN THE SPACE OF A FEW MINUTES
CD _____ FIRECD 52
Fire / Oct '95 / Disc.

Tembang Sunda

SUNDANESE TRADITIONAL SONGS
CD _____ NI 5378CD
Nimbus / Oct '93 / Nimbus.

Temiz, Okay

FIS FIS TZIGANES
CD _____ CDLLL 107
La Lichere / Aug '93 / Discovery / ADA.

ISTANBUL DA EYLUL
CD _____ CDLLL 67
La Lichere / Aug '93 / Discovery / ADA.

MAGNET DANCE
Mus mus, mis mis / Ayiras / Komsu / Din din dina / Gulhane / Exmar / Namor / Izimrik / Gelen esme
CD _____ 8888192
Tiptoe / Aug '95 / New Note.

Tempchin, Jack

AFTER THE RAIN (Tempchin, Jack & The Seclusions)
CD _____ TX 2009CD
Taxim / Jan '94 / ADA.

Temperance Seven

33 NOT OUT
After you've gone / Home in Pasadena / Saratoga shout / Me and Jane in a plane / Cecelia / Mooche / Black bottom / Deep Henderson / Happy feet / Royal garden blues / Varsity drag / Seven and eleven / Borneo / Ziggy / Chili bom bom / Thirty four out / Mary / Button up your overcoat / You, you're driving me crazy
CD _____ URCD 103
Upbeat / Dec '90 / Target/BMG / Cadillac.

TEA FOR EIGHT
Waterloo Road / Charleston / I've had / Louisiana / Sahara / Running wild / Hard hearted Hannah / Charley my boy / My Momma's in town / Ukelele lady / Twelfth Street rag / 11.30 saturday night
CD _____ URCD 101
Upbeat / Mar '92 / Target/BMG / Cadillac.

WRITING ON THE WALL
Dog bottom / I can't sleep / From Monday On / Writing on the wall / Crying for the Carolines / Man I Love / Everybody loves my baby / San / Mornington Crescent / My baby just cares for me / Drum crazy / Mis-

sissippi Mud / Brown eyes / Ain't she sweet / There Ain't No Sweet man Worth the Salt Of My Tears / My Blue heaven / 'S Wonderful
CD _____ RRCD 108
Upbeat / Sep '92 / Target/BMG / Cadillac.

Temperley, Joe

CONCERTO FOR JOE
Hackensack / Snibor / Sentimental mood / Blues for Nat / East of the sun and west of the moon / Single petal of a rose / Cotton tail / Awright already / Blues / Slow for Joe / Day at a time / Sixes and sevens
CD _____ HEPCD 2062
Hep / Mar '95 / Cadillac / Jazz Music / New Note / Wellard.

NIGHTINGALE
Raincheck / Body and soul / Indian Summer / Sunset and a mocking bird / Petite fleur / Nightingale / It's you or no one / Creole love / Action / My love is like a red red rose
CD _____ HEPCD 2052
Hep / Mar '92 / Cadillac / Jazz Music / New Note / Wellard.

Tempest

TEMPEST/LIVING IN FEAR
Gorgon / Foyers of fun / Dark house / Brothers / Up and on / Grey and black / Strange her / Upon tomorrow / Funeral empire / Paperback writer / Stargazer / Dance to my tune / Living in fear / Yeah yeah yeah / Waiting for a miracle / Turn around
CD _____ NEXCD 159
Sequel / Dec '90 / BMG.

Tempest

SUNKEN TREASURE (Unreleased Tracks 1989-1992)
CD _____ FAM 10103CD
Firebird / Jul '95 / ADA.

SURFING TO MECCA
CD _____ FAM 10105CD
Firebird / Jul '95 / ADA.

Temple, Johnny

JOHNNY TEMPLE VOL. 1 1935-1938
CD _____ DOCD 5238
Blues Document / May '94 / Swift / Jazz Music / Hot Shot.

JOHNNY TEMPLE VOL. 2 1938-1940
CD _____ DOCD 5239
Blues Document / May '94 / Swift / Jazz Music / Hot Shot.

JOHNNY TEMPLE VOL. 3 1940-1949
CD _____ DOCD 5240
Blues Document / May '94 / Swift / Jazz Music / Hot Shot.

Temple Of The Dog

TEMPLE OF THE DOG
Say hello to heaven / Reach down / Hunger strike / Pushin' forward back / Call me a dog / Times of trouble / Wooden Jesus / Your savior / Four, walled world / All night thing
CD _____ 395 350-2
A&M / Jun '92 / PolyGram.

Temple, Shirley

LITTLE MISS WONDERFUL
On the good ship Lollipop / Baby take a bow / When I'm with you / Laugh, you son of a gun / At the codfish ball / Love's young dream / On accounta I love you / Goodnight my love / But definitely / In our little wooden shoes / Picture me without you / Sit on board, lit'l chilun / Animal crackers in my soup / That's what I want for Christmas / You've got to S-M-I-L-E (to be H-A double P-Y) / Early bird / He was a dandy / Right somebody to love / Hey, what did the blue jay say / Believe me, if all those endearing young charms / When I grow up / Oh my goodness / World owes me a living / Dixie-Anna / Toy trumpet / Polly Wolly Doodle
CD _____ CDHD 141
Happy Days / Nov '88 / Conifer.

ON THE GOOD SHIP LOLLIPOP
CD _____ PLCD 541
President / Aug '95 / Grapevine / Target/ BMG / Jazz Music / President.

Templegate

INNOCENCE
Innocence / Never be / Deep / Anger overload / Give / Salvation / Better off dead / Killing time / What I need / Wherever I fall / Suffer / Bastard son
CD _____ CDBLEED 13
Bleeding Hearts / Aug '95 / Pinnacle.

Templeton, Alec

BACH GOES TO TOWN
Three little fishes / Blues in the night / Lost chord / Shortest Wagnerian opera / Tea for two / Body and soul / Music goes round and around
CD _____ PASTCD 7057
Flapper / Feb '95 / Pinnacle.

Temptations

ALL DIRECTIONS
Funky music sho nuff turns me on / Run
Charlie run / Papa was a rollin' stone / Love
woke me up this morning / I ain't got nothin'
/ First time when I saw your face / Mother
nature / Do your thing
CD _____ 5301552
Motown / Sep '93 / PolyGram.

BEST OF THE TEMPTATIONS, THE
CD _____ 3127-2
Scratch / Oct '94 / BMG.

CLOUD NINE
Cloud 9 / I heard it through the grapevine /
Runaway child running wild / Love is a hurtin' thing / Hey girl (I like your style) / Why
did she have to leave me (why did she have
to go) / I need your lovin' / Don't let him
take your love from me / I gotta find a way
(to get you back) / Gonna keep on tryin' till
I win your love
CD _____ 5301532
Motown / Aug '93 / PolyGram.

EMPERORS OF SOUL
Come on / Oh mother of mine / Romance
without finance / Check yourself / Dream
come true / Mind over matter (I'm gonna
make you mine) / I'll love you 'til I die / Paradise / Slow down harri / I couldn't cry if I
wanted to / Witchcraft (for your love) / I
want a love I can see / Further you look the
less you see / Farewell my love / Tear from
a woman's eyes / Way you do the things
you do / I'll be in trouble / Girl's alright with
me / Girl (Why you wanna make me blue) /
Baby, baby I need you / My girl / (Talking
'bout) Nobody but my baby / It's growing /
You'll lose a precious love / Since I lost my
baby / You've got to earn it / My baby /
Don't look back / Get ready / Fading away
/ Ain't too proud to beg / Too busy thinking
about my baby / Who you gonna run to /
Beauty is only skin deep / I got heaven right
here on earth / I need you / All I need /
Sorry is a sorry word / I'm doing it all / No
more water in the well / You're my everything / Just one last look / Angel doll / It's
you that I need (Loneliness made me realize) / Don't send me away / Hello, young
lovers / Ol' man river / I wish it would rain /
I truly, truly believe / I could never love another (after loving you) / Please return your
love to me / How can I forget / For once in
my life (Live) / Cloud 9 / Why did she have
to leave me (Why did she have to go) / I'm
gonna make you love me / I'll try something
new / Runaway child running wild / Don't
let the Joneses get you down / I can't get
next to you / Message from a black man /
War / Psychedelic shack / Hum along and
dance / Ball of confusion / Ungena za ulimwengu (Unite the world) / Just my imagination / Take a look around / It's summer /
Superstar (Remember how you got where
you are) / I ain't got nothin' / Mother nature
/ Papa was a rollin' stone / Masterpiece /
Plastic man / Hey girl (I like your style) / Law
of the land / Let your hair down / Heavenly
/ You've got my soul on fire / Happy people
/ Memories / Keep holdin' on / Darling stand
by me (Song for my woman) / Who are you
/ In a lifetime / Power / Isn't the night fantastic / Aiming at your heart / Standing on
the top, part 1 / Sail away / Treat her like a
lady / My love is true (Truly for you) / Do
you really love your baby / Magic / Lady
soul / I wonder who she's seeing now /
Look what you started / Soul to soul / Special / My kind of woman / Hoops of fire /
Error of our ways / Givin' up the best / Elevator eyes / Blueprint for love
CD Set _____ 530338-2
PolyGram / Sep '94 / PolyGram.

FOR LOVERS ONLY
CD _____ 5305682
Motown / Sep '95 / PolyGram.

GREATEST HITS: TEMPTATIONS
CD _____ PA 714-2
Paradiso / Mar '94 / Target/BMG.

MASTERPIECE
Hey girl (I like your style) / Masterpiece / Ma
/ Law of the land / Plastic man / Hurry
tomorrow
CD _____ 530100-2
Motown / Jan '93 / PolyGram.

MILESTONE
Eeny meeny miney mo / Any old lovin' (just
won't do) / Hoops of fire / We should be
makin' love / Jones / Get ready / Corner of
my heart / Whenever you're ready / Do it
easy / Wait a minute / Celebrate (Cassette
& CD only.)
CD _____ 5300052
Motown / Jan '93 / PolyGram.

**MOTOWNS GREATEST HITS:
TEMPTATIONS**
CD _____ 5300152
Motown / Jan '93 / PolyGram.

Ten City

THAT WAS THEN, THIS IS NOW
Way you make me feel / Goin' up in smoke
/ When I'm gone, I'm gone / Love in a day
/ Whay my love can do / Interlude / Then /
Under you / All this love / Joy and pain / All

I want / Say something / Fantasy (Mixes) /
Now
CD _____ 474594 2
Columbia / May '94 / Sony.

Ten Foot Pole

REV
CD _____ E 86436-2
Epitaph / Jan '95 / Plastic Head /
Pinnacle.

Ten Sharp

FIRE INSIDE, THE
Where love lives / Dreamhome (dream on) /
Lines on your face / As I remember / Close
on your eyes / Rumours in the city / Wild-
flower / Fly away / Blue moon / Say it ain't
so
CD _____ 473886 2
Columbia / Aug '93 / Sony.

UNDER THE WATER-LINE
You / When the spirit slips away / Rich man
/ Ain't my beating heart / Lonely heart / Who
needs women / Some sails / Ray / When
the snow falls / Closing hour
CD _____ 4690702
Columbia / Apr '92 / Sony.

Ten Years After

COLLECTION: TEN YEARS AFTER
Hear me calling / No title / Spoonful / I can't
keep from crying sometimes / Standing at
the crossroads / Portable people / Rock
your mama / Love like a man (long version)
/ I want to know / Speed kills / Boogie on /
I may be wrong but I won't be wrong always
/ At the woodchoppers' ball / Spider in your
web / Summertime / Shantung cabbage /
I'm going home
CD _____ CCSCD 293
Castle / Jul '91 / BMG.

CRICKLEWOOD GREEN
Sugar the road / Working on the road /
50,000 miles beneath my brain / Year 3,000
blues / Me and my baby / Love like a man
/ Circles / As the sun still burns away
CD _____ CDCHR 1084
Chrysalis / Jul '94 / EMI.

**CRICKLEWOOD GREEN/WATT/A
SPACE IN TIME**
Sugar the road / Working on the road /
50,000 miles beneath my brain / Year 3000
blues / Me & my baby / Love like a man /
Circles / As the sun still burns away / I'm
coming on / My baby left me / Think about
the times / I say yeah / Band with no name
/ Gonna run / She lies in the morning /
Sweet little sixteen / One of these days /
Here they come / I'd love to change the
world / Over the hill / Baby won't you let me
rock'n'roll you / Once there was a time / Let
the sky fall / Hard monkeys / I've been there
too / Uncle Jam
CD Set _____ CDDOMB 011
Chrysalis / Oct '95 / EMI.

ESSENTIAL TEN YEARS AFTER
Rock 'n' roll music to the world / I'd love
to change the world / I'm going home /
Choo choo mama / Tomorrow / I woke up
this morning / Me and my baby / Good
morning little school girl / Goin' back to Birmingham / 50,000 miles beneath my brain
/ Sweet little sixteen / I'm coming on / Love
like a man / Baby won't you let me rock 'n'
roll to you
CD _____ CDCHR 1857
Chrysalis / Oct '92 / EMI.

LIVE AT READING '83
CD _____ FRSCD 003
Raw Fruit / Dec '90 / Pinnacle.

SSSSH
Bad scene / Two time Mama / Stoned
woman / Good morning little school girl / If
you should love me / I don't know that you
don't know my name / Stomp / I woke up
this morning
CD _____ CD25CR 05
Chrysalis / Mar '94 / EMI.

**TEN YEARS AFTER ORIGINAL
RECORDINGS**
I'm going home (live) / Portable people /
Speed kills / Going to try / Don't want you,
woman / Spider in your web (live) / Feel it
for me / Love until I die / Help me / Hear
me calling / Losing the dogs / Sounds
CD _____ SEECD 387
See For Miles/C5 / Oct '93 / Pinnacle.

Tenaglia, Danny

HARD & SOUL
Yesterday and today / Bottom heavy / Look
ahead / Work / World of plenty / Come to-
gether / Oh no / Money (that's what I want)
CD _____ TRIUK 005CD
Tribal UK / Mar '95 / Vital.

Tendekist Wanganui Band

CHAMPION BRASS
CD _____ CDODE 1306
Ode / Feb '90 / CM / Discovery.

Tender Fury

**IF ANGER WERE SOUL I'D BE JAMES
BROWN**
CD _____ TX 92582
Roadrunner / Nov '91 / Pinnacle.

Tenebrae

DYSANCHELIUM
CD _____ SPI 17CD
Spinefarm / Oct '94 / Plastic Head.

Tenko

AT THE TOP OF MT BROCKEN
CD _____ ACCDEC 48
Rec Rec / Mar '94 / Plastic Head / SRD /
Cadillac.

Tenney, Gerry

LET'S SING A YIDDISH SONG (Tenney,
Gerry & Betty Albert Schreck)
CD _____ GV 134CD
Global Village / Nov '93 / ADA / Direct.

Tennille, Toni

DO IT AGAIN (Tennille, Toni & Big Band)
Do it again / Close your eyes / Can't help
lovin' dat man / Our love is here to stay /
Let's do it / Daydream / Do nothin' 'til you
hear from me / More than you know / I got
it bad and that ain't good / I'll only miss him
when I think of him / Someone to watch
over me / I thought about you / Guess who
I saw today / But not for me
CD _____ CDPC 5006
Prestige / Jun '90 / Total/BMG.

Tenor, Jimi

EUROPA
CD _____ PUUCD 2
Still Bubbling / Sep '95 / Plastic Head.

Tenor Saw

TENOR SAW LIVES ON
CD _____ CD 005
Sky High / Jan '93 / Jetstar.

WITH LOTS OF SIGN (Tenor Saw & Nitty
Gritty)
CD _____ BR 002CD
Black Roots / Nov '94 / Jetstar.

Tenpole Tudor

EDDIE, OLD BOB, DICK & GARY
Swords of a thousand men / Go wilder / I
wish / Header now / There are boys / Wun-
derbar / Tell me more / Judy annual / I can't
sleep / Anticipation / What else can I do /
Confessions
CD _____ REP 4220-WY
Repertoire / Aug '91 / Pinnacle / Cadillac.

LET THE FOUR WINDS BLOW
Let the four winds blow / Throwing my baby
out with the bath water / Trumpeters / It's
easy to see / What you doing in Bombay /
Local animal / Her fruit is forbidden / To-
night is the night / Unpaid debt / King of
Siam / Sea of thunder
CD _____ STIFFCD 12
Disky / Jan '94 / THE / BMG / Discovery /
Pinnacle.

**WUNDERBAR (The Best Of Tenpole
Tudor)**
Three bulbs in a row / Swords of a thousand
men / Go wilder / Header now / Wunderbar
/ What else can I do / I can't sleep / Confessions / Tell me more / Throwing my baby
out with the bath water / Let the four winds
blow / Tonight is the night / What you doing
in Bombay / Her fruit is forbidden / Sea of
thunder / Hayrick song
CD _____ DOJOCD 76
Dojo / Nov '92 / BMG.

Tequila Sisters

OUT OF THE SHADOWS
CD _____ M3PCD 9403
Mabley St. / Jul '94 / Grapevine.

Ter Veldhuis, Jacob

DIVERSO IL TEMPO
CD _____ BVHAASTCD 9308
Bvhaast / Oct '94 / Cadillac.

Terem Quartet

CLASSICAL
Eine kleine nachtmusik / Ave Maria / Con-
certo grosso in G-minor / Waltz / Chardash
/ Oginsky's polonaise / Funeral march /
Nocturne 'Separation' / Flea waltz
CD _____ CDRW 49
Virgin / Oct '94 / EMI.

Terem

TEREM
Lyrical dance / Fantasy / Legend of the old
mountain man / Cossack's farewell / Toccata / Variations on Swan Lake / Simfonia
lubova / Old carousel / Two-step Nadya /
Tsiganka / Letni Kanikuli / Country improvisation / Valenki / Baryni
CD _____ CDRW 23
Realworld / Mar '92 / EMI / Sterns.

Terminal Cheesecake

KING OF ALL SPACEHEADS
CD _____ JAKCDX 8
CD _____ JAKCD 8
Jackass / Jul '94 / Pinnacle.

Terminator X

JEEP BEATS, THE
CD _____ 5234822
Def Jam / Jan '96 / PolyGram.

Termos, Paul

SHAKES & SOUNDS
CD _____ GEESTCD 05
Geest Gronden / Oct '87 / Cadillac.

Ternent, Billy

**UNMISTAKABLE SOUND OF BILLY
TERNENT VOL. 3** (Ternent, Billy & His
Orchestra)
CD _____ SAV 241CD
Savoy / Dec '95 / THE / Savoy.

**UNMISTAKABLE SOUND OF BILLY
TERNENT VOL. 4** (Ternent, Billy & His
Orchestra)
CD _____ SAV 242CD
Savoy / Dec '95 / THE / Savoy.

Terrasson, Jacky

JACKY TERRASSON
I love Paris / Just a blues / My funny valentine / Hommage a lili boulanger / Bye bye
blackbird / He goes on a trip / I fall in love
too easily / Time after time / For once in my
life / What a difference a day makes / Cum-
ba's dance
CD _____ CDP 8293512
Blue Note / Feb '95 / EMI.

Terrell

ANGRY SOUTHERN GENTLEMAN
Let's go for a ride / Straw dogs (Before the
fall) / Dreamed I was the devil / Newhope /
Angry southern gentleman / Piece of time /
Toystore / Redneck gigolo / Broken man /
Blacktop runaways / Long train / Come
down to me
CD _____ VPBCD 23
Pointblank / Apr '95 / EMI.

Terri & Monica

SYSTA
Uh huh / Lisa listen to me / Over it / Intentions / Supernatural thing / Next time / I've
been waiting / I need your love / Way you
make me feel / Temptation / Where are you
now / When the tables turn
CD _____ 477108 2
Epic / Jun '94 / Sony.

Terror Against Terror

PSYCHOLIGICAL WARFARE
CD _____ PA 01CD
Dark Vinyl / May '95 / Plastic Head.

Terror Fabulous

GLAMOUROUS
CD _____ NWSCD 7
New Sound / Mar '94 / Jetstar.

LYRICALLY ROUGH
CD _____ GRELCD 221
Greensleeves / Oct '95 / Total/BMG /
Jetstar / SRD.

YAGA YAGA
CD _____ 756792327-2
Warner Bros. / Aug '94 / Warner Music.

Terrorizer

WORLD DOWNFALL
After world obliteration / Tear of napalm /
Corporation pull in / Resurrection / Need to
live / Dead street / Injustice / Storm of
stress / Human prey / Condemned system
/ Enslaved by propaganda / Whirlwind
struggle / World downfall / Ripped to shreds
CD _____ MOSH 016CD
Earache / Nov '89 / Vital.

Terrorvision

FORMALDEHYDE
Problem solved / Ships that sink / American
TV / New policy one / Jason / Killing time /
Urban space crime / Hole for a snail / Don't
shoot my dog / Desolation town / My house
/ Human being
CD _____ VEGASCD 1
EMI / May '93 / EMI.

**HOW TO MAKE FRIENDS AND
INFLUENCE PEOPLE**
Alice, what's the matter / Oblivion / Stop the
bus / Discotheque wreck / Middle man / Stil
the rhythm / Ten shades of grey / Stab in
the back / Pretend best friend / Time o' the
signs / What the doctor ordered / Some
people say / What makes you tick
CD _____ VEGASCD 2
EMI / Apr '94 / EMI.

Terry

SILVERADO TRAIL (Terry & The Pirates)
Wish I was your river / Sweet emotions / I can't dance / Heartbeatin' away / Silverado trail / Follow her around / Risin' of the moon / Mustang ride / Gun metal blues / Inlaws and outlaws / Nighthawkin' the dawn
CD _____ CDWIK 89
Big Beat / Jan '90 / Pinnacle.

Terry, Clark

ALTERNATE BLUES (Terry, Clark/ Freddie Hubbard/Dizzy Gillespie/Oscar Peterson)
Alternate one / Alternate two / Alternate three / Alternate four / Wrap your troubles in dreams (and dream your troubles away) / Here's that rainy day / Gypsy / If I should lose you
CD _____ OJCCD 744
Original Jazz Classics / May '93 / Wellard / Jazz Music / Cadillac / Complete/Pinnacle.

COLOUR CHANGES
CD _____ CCD 9009
Candid / Jul '87 / Cadillac / Jazz Music / Wellard / Koch.

IN ORBIT (Terry, Clark Quartet & Thelonious Monk)
CD _____ OJCCD 302-2
Original Jazz Classics / Apr '92 / Wellard / Jazz Music / Cadillac / Complete/Pinnacle.

MELLOW MOODS
CD _____ PCD 24136
Pablo / Jun '95 / Jazz Music / Cadillac / Complete/Pinnacle.

POWER OF POSITIVE SWINGING (Terry, Clark & Bob Brookmeyer)
Dancing on the grave / Battle hymn of the Republic / King / Ode to a flugelhorn / Gal in Calico / Green stamps / Hawg jawz / Simple waltz / Just an old manuscript
CD _____ 4744152
Sony Jazz / Nov '93 / Sony.

SHADES OF BLUE
CD _____ CHR 70007
Challenge / Jun '95 / Direct / Jazz Music / Cadillac / ADA.

Terry, Gordon

LOTTA LOTTA WOMEN
Lotta lotta women / It ain't right / I had a talk with me / Queen of the seasons / Gonna go down the river / Lonely road / Honky tonk man / You remembered me / Reͥvenooer man / Long black limousine / Wild desire / Little ole you / How my baby can love / Fortune of love / Slow down old world / For old time's sake / You'll regret / Hook, line and sinker / Maybe / Keep on talking / Then I heard the bad news / I don't hurt anymore / Saddest day / All by my lonesome / Battle of New Orleans / Fifty stars / When they ring these wedding bells / Almost alone
CD _____ BCDAH 15881
Bear Family / Nov '95 / Rollercoaster / Direct / CM / Swift / ADA.

Terry, Lillian

DREAM COMES TRUE, A (Terry, Lillian & Tommy Flanagan)
CD _____ 121 047 2
Soul Note / Oct '90 / Harmonia Mundi / Wellard / Cadillac.

OO-SHOO-BE-DOO-BE....OO,OO
CD _____ SN 1147
Soul Note / '86 / Harmonia Mundi / Wellard / Cadillac.

Terry, Sonny

1958 LONDON SESSIONS, THE (Terry, Sonny & Brownie McGhee)
Just a dream / I've been treated wrong / Woman's lover blues / Climbing on top of the hill / Southern train / Black horse blues / Gone but not forgotten / I love you baby / Cornbread, peas and black molassas / You'd better mind / Brownie blues / Change the lock on my door / Auto-mechanics blues / Sonny's blues / Wholesale and retail / Fox chase / Way I feel / Hooray (this woman is killing me)
CD _____ NEXCD 120
Sequel / Apr '90 / BMG.

AT SUGAR HILL (Terry, Sonny & Brownie McGhee)
CD _____ OBCCD 536
Original Blues Classics / Nov '92 / Complete/Pinnacle / Wellard / Cadillac.

BACK TO NEW ORLEANS (Terry, Sonny & Brownie McGhee)
Let me be your big dog / Pawn shop / You don't know / Betty and dupree / Back to New Orleans / Stranger here / Fox hunt / I'm prison bound / Louise Louise / Baby how long / Freight train / I got a woman / Hold me in your arms / C.C. and the O blues / Devil's gonna git you / Don't you lie to me / That's why I'm walking / Wrong track / Blue feeling / House lady / I know better
CD _____ CDCH 372
Ace / May '92 / Pinnacle / Cadillac / Complete/Pinnacle.

BLUESMEN, THE (Terry, Sonny/Brownie McGee/Big Bill Broonzy)
CD _____ MATCD 250
Castle / May '93 / BMG.

BROWNIE MCGEE & SONNY TERRY SING (Terry, Sonny & Brownie McGhee)
CD _____ SFCD 40011
Smithsonian Folkways / Sep '94 / ADA / Direct / Koch / CM / Cadillac.

CALIFORNIA BLUES (Terry, Sonny & Brownie McGhee)
I got fooled / No need of running / I feel so good / Thinkin' and worrying / I love you baby / California blues / Walkin' and lyin' down / First and last love / Christine / I have had my fun / Whoppin' and Squalin' / Waterboy cry / Motherless child / Sportin' life / John Henry / I'm a stranger / Cornbread and peas / Louise / I done done / Meet you in the morning / Poor boy from home / Hudy Leadbelly / Something's wrong at home / Take this home / Take this hammer / Baby's gone / Lose your money
CD _____ CDCHD 398
Ace / May '93 / Pinnacle / Cadillac / Complete/Pinnacle.

DRINKING IN THE BLUES (Terry, Sonny & Brownie McGhee)
CD _____ CDCD 1109
Charly / Jul '93 / Charly / THE / Cadillac.

DUO, THE (Terry, Sonny & Brownie McGhee)
CD _____ CD 52032
Blues Encore / May '94 / Target/BMG.

FOLKWAYS YEARS 1944-1963, THE
CD _____ SFWCD 40033
Smithsonian Folkways / Dec '94 / ADA / Direct / Koch / CM / Cadillac.

HOMETOWN BLUES (Terry, Sonny & Brownie McGhee)
Mean ol' Frisco / Man ain't nothin' but a fool / Woman is killing me / Meet you in the morning / Stranger blues / Feel so good / Forgive me / Sittin' on top of the world / Crying the blues / Key to the highway / Ease my worried mind / Bulldog blues / C.C. rider / Going down slow / Bad blood / Lightnin's blues / Dissatisfied woman / Pawn shop blues
CD _____ 4744092
Sony Jazz / Dec '93 / Sony.

JUST A CLOSER WALK WITH THEE (Terry, Sonny & Brownie McGhee)
CD _____ OBCCD 541
Original Blues Classics / Nov '92 / Complete/Pinnacle / Wellard / Cadillac.

MIDNIGHT SPECIAL (Terry, Sonny & Brownie McGhee)
Sonny's squall / Red river blues / Gone gal / Blues before sunrise / Blues of happiness / I understand me / Jealous man / Midnight special / East Coast blues / Muddy water / Beggin' and cryin'
CD _____ CDCH 951
Ace / Aug '90 / Pinnacle / Cadillac / Complete/Pinnacle.

SONNY IS KING
CD _____ OBCCD 521
Original Blues Classics / Nov '92 / Complete/Pinnacle / Wellard / Cadillac.

SONNY TERRY 1938-45/ALONZO SCALES 1955 (Terry, Sonny & Alonzo Scales)
CD _____ DOCD 5230
Blues Document / Apr '94 / Swift / Jazz Music / Hot Shot.

SONNY TERRY AND BROWNIE MCGHEE (Terry, Sonny & Brownie McGhee)
CD _____ BGOCD 75
Beat Goes On / '89 / Pinnacle.

SONNY'S STORY
I ain't gonna be your dog no more / My baby done gone / Worried blues / High powered woman / Pepperheaded woman / Sonny's story / I'm gonna get on my feet after a while / Four o'clock blues / Telephone blues / Great tall engine
CD _____ OBCCD 503
Original Blues Classics / Nov '92 / Complete/Pinnacle / Wellard / Cadillac.

WHOOPIN' (Terry, Sonny/Johnny Winter/ Willie Dixon)
CD _____ ALCD 4734
Alligator / May '93 / Direct / ADA.

WHOOPIN' THE BLUES
Whoopin' the blues / All alone blues / Worried man blues / Leaving blues / Screamin' and cryin' blues / Riff and harmonica jump / Crow Jane blues / Beer garden blues / Hot headed woman / Custard pie blues / Early morning blues / Harmonica rag / Dirty mistreater, don't you know / Telephone blues / Madman blues (CD only) / Airplane blues (CD only)
CD _____ CZ 546
Capitol Jazz / Jul '95 / EMI.

Terry, Todd

BEST OF TODD TERRY'S UNRELEASED PROJECTS
CD _____ BB 042132CD
Broken Beat / Jan '96 / Plastic Head.

DAY IN THE LIFE OF TODD TERRY
CD _____ SOMCD 2
Ministry Of Sound / Jul '95 / 3MV / Warner Music.

TODD TERRY PROJECT (Terry, Todd Project)
CD _____ CHAMPCD 1027
Champion / May '92 / BMG.

Terzis, Michalis

MAGIC OF THE GREEK BOUZOUKI
Dance of the dolphins / Near the sea / Dance of the fisherman / Trikimia / Olympus / Morning breeze / Trip with Alexandra / Nocturno / Flight of the seagull / South wind / Dance of Captain Michalis / Sea dream / Mermaid on the boat
CD _____ EUCD 1206
ARC / Sep '93 / ARC Music / ADA.

NOSTIMON IMAR
CD _____ EUCD 1076
ARC / '89 / ARC Music / ADA.

Tesi, Riccado

COLLINE (Tesi/Vaillant)
CD _____ Y 225048CD
Silex / Apr '95 / ADA.

IL BALLO DELLA LEPRE
CD _____ CDMW 4001
Music & Words / Apr '93 / ADA / Direct.

Tesla

BUST A NUT
Gate / Invited / Solution / Shine away / Try so hard / She want she want / Need your lovin' / Action talks / Mama's fool / Cry / Earthmover / Lot to lose / Rubber band / Wonderful world / Games people play
CD _____ GED 24713
Geffen / Aug '94 / BMG.

FIVE MAN ACOUSTICAL JAM
CD _____ GEFD 24311
Geffen / Feb '91 / BMG.

PSYCHOTIC SUPPER
CD _____ GEFD 24424
Geffen / Aug '91 / BMG.

Test Department

BRITH GOF GODDIN
Sarff / Gwyr A Aeth Gatraeth / Arddyledog Ganu / Glasfedd Eu Hancwyn / Trichant Eurdochog / Yn Nydd Cadiawr / Truan Yw Gennyffi
CD _____ MOP 004CD
Ministry Of Power / Aug '92 / Disc / Vital.

ECSTASY UNDER DURESS
CD _____ RUSCD 8213
Roir USA / Oct '95 / Plastic Head.

GODODDIN
CD _____ MOP 4 CD
Ministry Of Power / Aug '89 / Disc / Vital.

GOODNIGHT OUT, A
Goodnight / Milk of human kindness / Generous terms / Victory / We shall return no more / Demonomania / Voice of reason
CD _____ MOP 003CD
Some Bizarre / Mar '94 / Pinnacle.

LEGACY (1990-93)
CD _____ FREUDCD 27
Jungle / Oct '94 / Disc.

LIVE ATONAL
CD _____ EFA 08438
Dossier / Jul '92 / SRD.

MATERIA PRIMA
CD _____ DEPTCD 1
Jungle / Jan '95 / Disc.

PAX BRITANNICA
CD _____ MOP 6CD
Ministry Of Power / Feb '91 / Disc / Vital.

TERRA FIRMA
Nadka / Siege / Current affairs / Dark eyes / Terra firma
CD _____ SUBCD 002-12
Sub Rosa / '88 / Vital / These / Discovery.

TOTALITY
CD _____ KK 140CD
KK / Nov '95 / Plastic Head.

Testament

LIVE AT THE FILLMORE
CD _____ CDMFN 186
Music For Nations / Jul '95 / Pinnacle.

PRACTICE WHAT YOU PREACH
Practice what you preach / Perilous nation / Envy time / Time is coming / Blessed in contempt / Greenhouse effect / Sins of omission / Ballad, The (A song of hope) / Nightmare (coming back to you) / Confusion fusion
CD _____ 7820092
Atlantic / Feb '95 / Warner Music.

RETURN TO THE APOCALYPSE CITY
Over the wall / So many lies / Disciples of the watch / Reign of terror / Return to serenity
CD _____ 756782487-2
WEA / Apr '93 / Warner Music.

RITUAL, THE
Sermon / As the seasons grey / Electric crown return to serenity / Ritual / Deadline / So many lies / Let go of my world / Agony / Troubled dreams / Signs of chaos / Electric crown / Return to serenity
CD _____ 756782392-2
East West / May '92 / Warner Music.

Testify

BALLROOM KILLER
CD _____ RTD 19519192
Our Choice / Jul '95 / Pinnacle.

TESTIFY
CD _____ RTD 19516392
Our Choice / Oct '93 / Pinnacle.

YOUR VISION
CD _____ RTD 19515923
Our Choice / Jul '93 / Pinnacle.

Testimony

SATISFACTION WARRANTED
CD _____ MABCD 006
MAB / Jan '94 / Plastic Head.

Tetes Noires

CLAY FOOT GODS
CD _____ CD 9008
Rounder / '88 / CM / Direct / ADA / Cadillac.

Tex, Joe

AIN'T GONNA BUMP NO MORE
Ain't gonna bump no more (With no big fat woman) / Be cool / Leaving you dinner / I mess eveything up / We held on / Music ain't got no colour / Loose caboose / Rub down / Congratulations / You can be my star / You might be diggin' the garden / Give the baby anything the baby wants / Takin' a chance / You're in too deep / God of love / Baby let me steal you / Woman cares / Love me right girl / I gotcha
CD _____ CDSEWD 043
Southbound / Jun '93 / Pinnacle.

BUMP TO THE FUNK
Papa was too / Men are getting scarce / You need me, baby / Anything you wanna know / We can't sit down now / I can't see you no more / You're right, Ray Charles / Give the baby anything the baby wants / I gotcha / You said a bad word / King Thaddeus / Cat's got her tongue / My body wants you / I'm goin' back again / I don't want you to love me (if you're gonna talk about it) / Ain't gonna bump no more (with no big fat women) / I mess up everything I get my hands on / Loose caboose / Who gave birth to the funk / Stick your key in (and start your car)
CD _____ CPCD 8081
Charly / Mar '95 / Charly / THE / Cadillac.

DIFFERENT STROKES
Have you ever / My neighbours got the gimmes / Mrs. Wiggles / Baby it's rainin' / Under your powerful love / Don't play with me / Same things it took to get me / All a man needs is his woman's love / When a woman stops loving a man / I can see everybody's baby / She said yeah / Time brings about a change / I don't want you to love me / I'm gonna try love again / This time we'll make it all the way / It's ridiculous / We're killing ourselves / Back off / Does it run in your family / Living in the last days / I've seen enough
CD _____ CDCHARLY 161
Charly / Jan '89 / Charly / THE / Cadillac.

I GOTCHA (His Greatest Hits)
Hold what you've got / You got what it takes / Woman can change a man / One monkey don't stop no show / I want to (do everything for you) / Sweet woman like you / Love you save (may be your own) / S.Y.S.L.J.F.M. (The letter song) / I believe I'm gonna make it / I've got to do a little bit better / Papa was, too (Tramp) / Show me / Woman like that, yeah / Woman's hands / Skinny legs and all / Men are getting scarce / I'll never do you wrong / Keep the one you got / Buying a book / I gotcha
CD _____ CPCD 8015
Charly / Feb '94 / Charly / THE / Cadillac.

SHOW ME THE HITS AND MORE
CD _____ ICH 1149CD
Ichiban / Jan '94 / Koch.

SKINNY LEGS AND ALL
S.Y.S.L.J.F.M. (The letter song) / Love you save (may be your own) / Show me / Hold what you've got / Heep see few know / Someone to take your place / One monkey don't stop no show / If sugar was as sweet as you / Meet me in church / You got what it takes / I had a good home but I left (part 1) / Don't let your left hand know / Woman can change a man / Papa was, too / Watch the one (that brings the bad news) / Truest woman in the world / Chicken crazy
CD _____ CDKEND 114
Kent / Mar '94 / Pinnacle.

STONE SOUL COUNTRY
Just out of reach / Detroit city / Set me free / Heartbreak Hotel / Together again / King of the road / Dark end of the street / I'll never do you wrong / Make the world go away / Funny how time slips away / Ode to Billy Joe / Release me / Skip a rope / Engine engine / Funny / By the time I get to Phoenix / Green green grass of home / Papa's dreams
CD _____ CDCHARLY 184
Charly / Jun '89 / Charly / THE / Cadillac.

VERY BEST OF JOE TEX, THE
Hold what you've got / One monkey don't stop no show / Woman (can change a man) / I want (do everything for you) / Don't make your children pay (for your mistakes) / Sweet woman like you / Love you save / You better leave it baby / I've got to do a little bit better / S.Y.S.L.J.F.M. (The letter song) / I believe I'm gonna make it / Woman sees a hard time (when her man is gone) / Watch the one (that brings the bad news) / Papa was too / Truest woman in the world / Show me / Woman like that, yeah / Woman's hands / Skinny legs and all / Men are getting scarce / I'll never do you wrong / Keep the one you've got / You need me, baby / Buying a book / It ain't sanitary / You're right, Ray Charles / I gotcha
CD _____ CDCHARLY 133
Charly / Jul '88 / Charly / THE / Cadillac.

YOU'RE RIGHT (King Of Downhome Soul)
You're right, Ray Charles / You need me, baby / Dark end of the street / Woman like that, yeah / Keep the one you got / Same things it took to get me / I'll never do you wrong / Take the fifth amendment / Sweet sweet woman / We can't sit down now / Buying a book / Sure is good / That's the way / Anything you wanna know / Only way / Grandma Mary / Take my baby a little love / I can see everybody's baby (but I can't see mine) / She said yeah / When a woman stops loving a man / Woman stealer / Funny how time slips away
CD _____ CDKEND 117
Kent / Jan '95 / Pinnacle.

Texas

SOUTHSIDE/RICK'S ROAD (2 CDs)
I don't want a lover / Tell me why / Everyday now / Southside / Prayer for you / Faith / Thrill has gone / Fight the feeling / Fool for love / One choice / Future is promises / So called friend / Fade away / Listen to me / You owe it all to me / Beautiful angel / So in love with you / You've got to give a little / I want to go to heaven / Hear me now / Fearing these days / I've been missing you / Winter's end
CD Set _____ 5286042
Vertigo / Aug '95 / PolyGram.

Texas Lone Star

DESPERADOS WAITING FOR A TRAIN
Good hearted woman / Here I am again / Friend of the devil / Desperados waiting for the train / Fast train / Me and my uncle / Wild horses / In my own way / Bluebirds are singing for you / Luckenbach, Texas (Back to the basics of love) / Painted ladies
CD _____ BCD 15692
Bear Family / Aug '92 / Rollercoaster / Direct / CM / Swift / ADA.

Texass

TEXASS
CD _____ IFACD 002
IFA / Oct '95 / Plastic Head.

Texier, Henri

PARIS BATIGNOLLES (Texier, Henri Quartet)
CD _____ LBLC 6506
Label Bleu / May '92 / New Note.

SCENE IS CLEAN, THE (Texier, Henri Trio)
CD _____ LBLC 6540
Label Bleu / Jun '91 / New Note.

Textones

BACK IN TIME
Trying to hold on / Slip away / Redemption song / I second that emotion / Through the canyon / Love out of control / What do you want with me / Back in time / Gotta get that feelin' back / Something to believe in / Jokers are wild / If I could be / We don't get along / Standing in the line
CD _____ FIENDCD 179
Demon / Jun '90 / Pinnacle / ADA.

Tez Fa Siyon

P YOURNESS
CD _____ CDLINC 010
Lion Inc. / Dec '95 / Jetstar / SRD.

Tezerdi

TEZERDI
CD _____ PAN 152
Pan / Oct '94 / ADA / Direct / CM.

Tha Chamba

MAKIN' ILLA NOIZE
CD _____ COR 4205
Ichiban / Apr '95 / Koch.

Thackeray, Jimmy

EMPTY ARMS MOTEL
CD _____ BPCD 5001
Blind Pig / Jan '93 / Hot Shot / Swift / CM / Roots / Direct / ADA.

SIDEWAYS IN PARADISE (Thackeray, Jimmy & John Mooney)
CD _____ BP 5006CD
Blind Pig / Mar '94 / Hot Shot / Swift / CM / Roots / Direct / ADA.

WILD NIGHT OUT (Thackery, Jimmy & The Drivers)
CD _____ BPCD 75021
Blind Pig / Jul '95 / Hot Shot / Swift / CM / Roots / Direct / ADA.

Thanatos

EMERGING FROM THE NETHERWORLDS
CD _____ SHARK 015 CD
Shark / Apr '90 / Plastic Head.

REALM OF ECSTASY
CD _____ SHARKCD 025
Shark / Jan '92 / Plastic Head.

Tharpe, Sister Rosetta

1938-1941 VOL.I
CD _____ DOCD 5334
Blues Document / May '95 / Swift / Jazz Music / Hot Shot.

1942-1944 VOL.2
CD _____ DOCD 5335
Blues Document / May '95 / Swift / Jazz Music / Hot Shot.

That Dog

THAT DOG
CD _____ GU 6CD
Guernica / Oct '93 / Pinnacle.

That Petrol Emotion

CHEMICRAZY
Hey venus / Blue to black / Mess of words / Sensitize / Another day / Gnaw mark / Scum surfin' / Compulsion / Tingle / Head staggered / Abandon / Sweet shiver burn
CD _____ CDV 2618
Virgin / Apr '90 / EMI.

END OF THE MILLENNIUM PSYCHOSIS
Sooner or later / Every little bit / Cellophane / Candy love satellite / Here it is...take it / Price of my soul / Groove check / Bottom line / Tension / Tired shattered man / Goggle box / Under the sky
CD _____ CDV 2550
Virgin / Oct '88 / EMI.

MANIC POP THRILL
Fleshprint / Can't stop / Lifeblood / Natural kind of joy / It's a good thing / Circusville / Mouth crazy / Tight lipped / Million miles away / Lettuce / Cheapskate / Blindspot
CD _____ FIENDCD 70
Demon / Jul '86 / Pinnacle / ADA.

That Uncertain Feeling

500/600
CD _____ GOODCD 5
Dead Dead Good / May '95 / Pinnacle.

Thatcher On Acid

PRESSING 1984-91
CD _____ DAR 013CD
Desperate Attempt / Nov '94 / SRD.

That's It

REALLY
CD _____ BY 0024CD
Better Youth Organisation / Nov '93 / SRD.

Thau

UTAH
CD _____ FROG 001-2
Pingo / May '95 / Plastic Head.

The The

BURNING BLUE SOUL
CD _____ HAD 113CD
4AD / Jun '84 / Disc.

DUSK
True happiness this way lies / Love is stronger than death / Dogs of lust / This is the night / Slow emotion replay / Helpline operator / Sodium light baby / Lung shadows / Bluer than midnight / Lonely planet
CD _____ 472468 2
Epic / Jan '93 / Sony.

HANKY PANKY
Honky tonkin' / Six more miles / My heart would know / If you'll be a baby to me / I'm a long gone daddy / Weary blues from waiting / I saw the light / Your cheatin' heart / I

can't get you off my mind / There's a tear in my beer / I can't escape from you
CD _____ 4781392
Epic / Feb '95 / Sony.

INFECTED
Infected / Out of the blue (into the fire) / Heartland / Sweet bird of truth / Slow train to dawn / Twilight of a champion / Mercy beat / Angels of deception / Disturbed
CD _____ CD 26770
Epic / May '87 / Sony.

MIND BOMB
Good morning beautiful / Armageddon days are here (again) / Violence of truth / Kingdom of rain / Beat(en) generation / August and September / Gravitate to me / Beyond love
CD _____ 4633192
Epic / Apr '94 / Sony.

SOUL MINING
I've been waiting for tomorrow / This is the day / Sinking feeling / Uncertain smile / Twilight hour / Soul mining / Giant / Perfect (Not on LP) / Three orange kisses from Kazan (Not on LP) / Nature of virtue (Not on LP) / Mental healing process (Not on LP) / Waitin' for the upturn (Not on LP) / Fruit of the heart (Not on LP)
CD _____ 4663372
Epic / Mar '90 / Sony.

Theatre Of Hate

COMPLETE SINGLES COLLECTION
Original sin / Legion / Rebel without a brain / My own invention / Nero / Incinerator / Do you believe in the Westworld / Propaganda / Hop / Conquistador / Eastworld / Assegai / Poppies / Brave new soldiers / Heathen / King of kings / Number twelve / Thalidomide / St Teresa / Abbatoir
CD _____ CDMGRAM 93
Cherry Red / May '95 / Pinnacle.

REVOLUTION
CD _____ MLCD 901280
Line / Sep '94 / CM / Grapevine / ADA / Conifer / Direct.

TEN YEARS AFTER
Hop / Americana / East world / Grapes of wrath / Solution / Omen / Aria / Murder of love / Black Madonna / Flying Scotsman / Man who tunes the drums
CD _____ MAUCD 637
Mau Mau / Jun '93 / Pinnacle.

WESTWORLD
CD _____ DOJOCD 220
Dojo / Jan '96 / BMG.

Theatricum Chemicum

VERSO LA LUCE
CD _____ EFA 148242
Glasnost / Oct '95 / SRD.

Thee Headcoatees

BALLAD OF THE INSOLENT PUP
What once was / This heart / Pretend / Ballad of the insolent pup / You'll be sorry now / All my feelings denied / It's bad / When you stop loving me / Two hearts beating / No respect / Again and again / Now is not the best time / I was led to believe / You'll never do it baby
CD _____ ASKCD 045
Vinyl Japan / Oct '94 / Vital.

HAVE LOVE WILL TRAVEL
CD _____ ASKCD 11
Vinyl Japan / Oct '92 / Vital.

SOUND OF THE BASKERVILLES (Thee Headcoatees & Thee Headcoats)
CD _____ OVER 42CD
Overground / Dec '95 / SRD.

Thee Headcoats

BEACH BUMS MUST DIE
CD _____ EFA 11563 D
Crypt / Apr '93 / SRD.

CONUNDRUM
CD _____ SCRAG 2CD
Hangman's Daughter / Sep '94 / Vital.

HEAVENS TO MURGATROYD EVEN, IT'S THEE HEADCOATS
CD _____ SPCD 6119
Sub Pop / May '93 / Disc.

LIVE IN LONDON (Thee Headcoats & Thee Headcoatees)
CD _____ DAMGOOD 30CD
Damaged Goods / Mar '94 / SRD.

Thee Hypnotics

LIVER THAN GOD
All night long / Let's get naked / Revolution stone / Rock me baby / Justice in freedom
CD _____ SP 54B
Sub Pop / Jan '94 / Disc.

VERY CRYSTAL SPEED MACHINE, THE
Keep rollin' on / Heavy liquid / Phil's drum acropolis / Goodbye / If the good lord love ya / Ray's baudelaire / Caroline inside out / Tie it up / Down in the hole / Peasant song / Fragile / Look what you've done / Broken morning has

CD _____ 74321264512
American / Jun '95 / BMG.

Thee Johanz

CONFIDENTIAL LP
CD _____ 53IRDTJ12CD
Irdial / Sep '95 / Disc.

Thee Madkatt Courtship

ALONE IN THE DARK
CD _____ 0090622DDX
Edel / Jul '95 / Pinnacle.

Thee Mighty Caesars

CAESAR'S PLEASURE
Wily cayote / Miss Ludella Black / Death of a mighty caesar / Why don't you try my love / It ain't no sin / You'll be sorry now / All of your love / Give it to me / Baby please / Little by little / What you've got / I've got everything indeed / When the night comes / You make me die / Loathsome 'n' will / don't need no baby / I was led to believe / Ain't taken from guts / Devious means / I've been waiting / True to you / I can't find pleasure / Come into my life / Double axe / Neat neat neat / She's just 15 years old / Everything I've got to give / Lie detector / Why can't you see / Cowboys are square
CD _____ CDWIKD 124
Big Beat / Feb '94 / Pinnacle.

SURELY THEY WERE THE SONS OF GOD
Wiley coyote / (Miss America) Got to get you outside my head / I don't need no baby / Stay the same / Double axe / I was led to believe / You make me die / Now I know / I've been waiting / Loathsome 'n' wild / You'll be sorry now / I can't find pleasure / Kinds of women / Lie detector / Confusion / Baby who mutilated everybody's heart / Suck the dog / Beat on the brat / Career opportunities / Because just because / Headcoats on / Somebody like you / Searching high and low / Don't wanna be ruled by women and money no more / Don't break my laws / Strange words / Signals of love / I've got everything indeed / Devious means / Why don't you try my love / Wise blood / It's you I hate to lose / Miss Loudella Black
CD _____ CD 0141823
Crypt / Jul '93 / SRD.

Thee Rayguns

REBEL ROCKERS
CD _____ RAUCD 013
Raucous / Feb '95 / Nervous / Disc.

Thee Waltons

DRUNK AGAIN
CD _____ RAUCD 69
Raucous / May '94 / Nervous / Disc.

GET OUT YER VEGETABLES
Get out yer vegetables / Rubber chicken / Kings of veg-a-billy / Barking up the wrong tree / Elvis P. / Devil in disguise / Hound dog / Famous / Devil's music / Drunk son / Tear it up
CD _____ CDGRAM 90
Cherry Red / Feb '95 / Pinnacle.

Theessink, Hans

BABY WANTS TO BOOGIE
CD _____ BG 1020CD
Blue Groove / Apr '94 / CM.

CALL ME
CD _____ MM 801022
Minor Music / Jul '92 / Vital/SAM.

CRAZY MOON
CD _____ MW 2018CD
Music & Words / Nov '95 / ADA / Direct.

HARD ROAD BLUES-SOLO
CD _____ SPINCD 155
Making Waves / Dec '94 / CM.

JOHNNY & THE DEVIL
CD _____ BG 2020CD
Blue Groove / Apr '94 / CM.

TITANIC
CD _____ BG 3020CD
Blue Groove / Apr '94 / CM.

Theis & Nyegaard Jazzband

THEIS/NYEGAARD JAZZBAND 1963/88 (The First 25 Years)
Chant / West End blues / Sidewalk blues / Sweet Georgia Brown / I don't mean a thing if it ain't got that swing / Blue turning grey over you / After you've gone / Someday you'll be sorry / Ain't misbehavin' / Willow weep for me / I found a new baby / Confessin' / Baby, won't you please come home / You can depend on me
CD _____ STCD 4174
Storyville / Feb '90 / Jazz Music / Wellard / CM / Cadillac.

Thelin, Eje

POLYGLOT
CD _____ 1291

Caprice / Dec '92 / CM / Complete/
Pinnacle / Cadillac / ADA.

Them

THEM
Mystic eyes / If you and I could be as two
/ Little girl / Just a little bit / I gave my love
a diamond / Gloria / You just can't win /
Route 66 / My little baby / Bright lights big
city / I'm gonna break in black / Go on home
baby / Don't look back / I like it like that
CD _____ 820 563-2
London / Feb '91 / PolyGram.

Themis, John

ATMOSPHERIC CONDITIONS
Emily / Trick / Post-hypnotic suggestions /
Cinderella's last waltz / Electric storm /
Transition / Black mamba samba / Trouble
CD _____ NAGE 1CD
Art Of Landscape / Jan '86 / Sony.

ENGLISH RENAISSANCE
Over the dark cloud / James I / Open Arms
/ Catrina / Cross crusader / English renais-
sance / Steed for a king / Don't wake the
dragon George
CD _____ NAGE 11CD
Art Of Landscape / Jul '86 / Sony.

Then Jerico

ELECTRIC
Big area / Word / Motive / Fault / Quiet
place (apathy and sympathy) / Clank
(countdown to oblivion) / Blessed days /
Electric / Prairie rose / Reeling / You ought
to know / Big sweep / One life / Darkest
hour
CD _____ 5501932
Spectrum/Karussell / Mar '94 / PolyGram /
THE.

Theodorakis, Mikis

BALLAD OF MAUTHAUSEN
CD _____ CD 7
Sound / '86 / Direct / ADA.

**BOUZOUKIS OF MIKIS THEODORAKIS,
THE**
Sto parathiri stekoussoun / Myrtia / Tou mi-
kou voria / Varka sto yialo / Marina / Yitonia
ton anghelon / Balanda tou andrikou / To
yelasto pedi / Apagoghi / To parathiro /
Mana mou ke panayia
CD _____ 111 692
Musidisc / May '90 / Vital / Harmonia Mundi
/ ADA / Cadillac / Discovery.

CANTO GENERAL
CD _____ INT 31142
Intuition / Jun '93 / New Note.

TROUBADOUR FROM GREECE, THE
CD _____ SOW 90104
Sounds Of The World / Sep '93 / Target/
BMG.

ZORBS - THE BALLET
CD _____ INT 31032
Intuition / Jul '92 / New Note.

Therapy

BABYTEETH
CD _____ 185072
Southern / Mar '93 / SRD.

HATS OFF TO THE INSANE
CD _____ 540139-2
A&M / Sep '93 / PolyGram.

INFERNAL LOVE
Epilepsy / Stories / Moment of clarity / Jude
the obscene / Bowels of love / Misery / Bad
mother / Me vs. you / Loose / Diane / Thirty
seconds
CD _____ 5403792
A&M / Jun '95 / PolyGram.

PLEASURE DEATH
CD _____ 185082
Southern / Apr '93 / SRD.

TROUBLEGUM
Knives / Screamager / Hellbelly / Stop it
you're killing me / Nowhere / Die laughing /
Unbeliever / Trigger inside / Lunacy booth /
Isolation / Turn / Femtex / Unrequited /
Brainsaw / You are my sunshine
CD _____ 540196-2
A&M / Nov '93 / PolyGram.

Thergothon

STEAM FROM THE HEAVENS
CD _____ CDAV 001
Avant Garde / May '94 / Plastic Head.

Therion

BEAUTY IN BLACK, THE
CD _____ NB 1252
Nuclear Blast / Mar '95 / Plastic Head.

BEYOND SANCTORIUM
CD _____ CDATV 23
Active / Jul '92 / Pinnacle.

LEPA KLIFFOTH
CD _____ NBCD 127
Nuclear Blast / May '95 / Plastic Head.

These Animal Men

COME ON JOIN THE HIGH SOCIETY
Sharp kid / Empire building / Ambulance /
This year's model / You're always right /
Flawed is beautiful (Edit) / This is the sound
of youth / Sitting tenant / Too sussed /
Come on join the high society / We are liv-
ing / High society (reprise)
CD _____ FLATCD 8
Hi Rise / Sep '94 / EMI / Pinnacle.

TAXI FOR THESE ANIMAL MEN
You're always right / Nowhere faces / My
human remains / False identification / Wait
for it
CD _____ FLATMCD 14
Hi Rise / Mar '95 / EMI / Pinnacle.

TOO SUSSED
CD _____ FLATMCD 4
Hi Rise / Jun '94 / EMI / Pinnacle.

These Immortal Souls

GET LOST (DON'T LIE)
Marry me (lie lie) / Hide / These immortal
souls / Hey little child / I ate the knife /
Blood and sand she said / One in shadow
one in sun / Open up and bleed / Blood and
sand she said (alternate) / I ate the knife
(alternate) / These immortal souls (alternate)
CD _____ CD STUMM 48
Mute / Oct '87 / Disc.

Thessalonians

SOULCRAFT
CD _____ PS 9334
Silent / Oct '93 / Plastic Head.

They Might Be Giants

APOLLO 18
Dig my grave / I palindrome I / She's actual
size / My evil twin / Mammal / Statue got
me high / Spider (The lion sleeps
tonight) / Dinner bell / Narrow eyes / Hall of
heads / Which describes how you're feeling
/ See the constellation / If I wasn't shy /
Turn around / Hypnotist of ladies / Fingertips / Space suit
CD _____ 7559612572
Elektra / Mar '92 / Warner Music.

DON'T LET'S START
CD _____ TPCD 14
One Little Indian / Nov '89 / Pinnacle.

FLOOD
Theme from flood / Lucky ball and chain /
Dead / Particle man / We want a rock / Bird-
house in your soul / Istanbul (not Constan-
tinople) / Your racist friend / Twisting
CD _____ 7559609072
WEA / '89 / Warner Music.

JOHN HENRY
Subliminal / Snail shell / Sleeping in the
flowers / Unrelated thing AKA driver / I
should be allowed to think / Extra savoir
faire / Why must I be sad / Spy / O do not
forsake me / No one knows my plan / Dirt
bike / Destination moon / Self called nowhere / Meet James Ensor / Thermostat /
Window out of jail / Stomp box / End of the
tour
CD _____ 755961654-2
Warner Bros. / Sep '94 / Warner Music.

LINCOLN
Ana ng / Cowtown / Lie still / Little bottle /
Purple toupee / Cage and aquarium / Where
your eyes don't go / Piece of dirt / MR. Me
/ Pencil rain / World's address / I've got a
match / Santa's beard / You'll miss me /
They'll need a crane / Shoehorn with teeth
/ Stand on your own head / Snowball in hell
/ Kiss me / Son of God
CD _____ 7559611452
Elektra / Jun '91 / Warner Music.

THEY MIGHT BE GIANTS
Everything right is wrong again / Put your
hand inside the puppet head / Number
three / Don't let's start / Footsteps / Toddler
hiway / Rabid child / Nothing's gonna
change my clothes / She was a hotel detective / She's an angel / Youth culture
killed / My dog / Boat of car / Absolutely
Bill's mood chess piece face / I hope that I
get old before I die / Alienation's for the rich
/ Day / Rhythm section want ad
CD _____ EKT 80 CD
Elektra / Nov '90 / Warner Music.

Thiele, Bob

LION HEARTED (Thiele, Bob Collective)
CD _____ 474982 2
Sony Jazz / May '94 / Sony.

**LOUIS SATCHMO (Thiele, Bob
Collective)**
CD _____ 471578 2
Sony Jazz / May '94 / Sony.

Thielemans, Toots

APPLE DIMPLE
Take the 'A' train / Sunday in New York /
Looking for Mr. Goodbar / Honesty / Mid-
night cowboy / Harlem nocturne / Still crazy
after all these years
CD _____ DC 8563
Denon / Aug '90 / Conifer.

BLUESETTE
CD _____ CDCH 303
Milan / Feb '91 / BMG / Silva Screen.

BLUESETTE
CD _____ CD 26604
Sony Jazz / Jan '95 / Sony.

BRASIL PROJECT, THE
Comecar de novo / Obi / Felicia and Bianca
/ O cantador / Joana Francesca / Coisa feita
/ Preciso aprender a so ser / Furta boa /
Coracao vagabundo / Manha de carnaval /
Casa forte / Moments / Bluesette
CD _____ 01005821012
Private Music / Aug '92 / BMG.

CONCERTO FOR HARMONICA
Prelude to a new life / Toots / Mo blues /
Song for Willy Graz / Ne me quitte pas /
Passionement / Asco / You just forgot that
I love you / Coda / Body and soul
CD _____ TCB 94802
TCB / Nov '94 / New Note.

**DO NOT LEAVE ME (Thielemans, Toots
& His American Band)**
CD _____ STCD 12
Stash / Aug '89 / Jazz Music / CM /
Cadillac / Direct / ADA.

EAST COAST, WEST COAST
CD _____ 1005821202
Private Music / Feb '95 / BMG.

**ESSENTIAL TOOTS THIELEMANS'
HARMONICA, THE**
CD _____ 4716882
Sony Jazz / Jan '95 / Sony.

**LIVE IN THE NETHERLANDS
(Thielemans, Toots, Joe Pass, Niels-
Henning Orsted Pedersen)**
Blues in the closet / Mooche / Thriving on
a riff / Autumn leaves / Someday my Prince
will come
CD _____ CD 2308233
Pablo / Apr '94 / Jazz Music / Cadillac /
Complete/Pinnacle.

**MAN BITES HARMONICA (Thielemans,
Jean 'Toots')**
CD _____ OJCCD 1738
Original Jazz Classics / Oct '92 / Wellard /
Jazz Music / Cadillac / Complete/Pinnacle.

ONLY TRUST YOUR HEART
CD _____ CCD 4355
Concord Jazz / Sep '88 / New Note.

TOOTS THIELEMANS
Giants Of Jazz / Nov '95 / Target/BMG /
CD _____ CD 53238
Cadillac.

TOOTS THIELEMANS IN TOKYO
What is this thing called love / Night in turin /
Fallin' in love with love / In the wee small
hours of the morning / Shade of love / Geor-
gia on my mind
CD _____ DC 8551
Denon / Jun '89 / Conifer.

TWO GENERATIONS
Bluesette / Be be creole / Monologue / Two
generations / Why did I choose you / Uncle
Charlie / Friday night / T T T / Inner journey /
L'eternal mari
CD _____ FCD 0003
Limetree / Nov '95 / New Note.

Thierry, Jacques

**HAWAIIAN GUITAR, VOL. 2, THE
(Thierry, Jacques & Trio Kailus)**
CD _____ PS 65081
Playasound / Nov '91 / Harmonia Mundi /
ADA.

Thieves

THIEVES
CD _____ CDHUT 12
Hut / May '94 / EMI.

Thigpen, Ed

MR. TASTE (Thigpen, Ed Trio)
CD _____ JUST 43-2
Justin Time / Oct '92 / Harmonia Mundi /
Cadillac.

YOUNG MEN AND OLD
Strike up the band / Yesterdays / Summer-
time / Night and day / Scramble / Shuffin'
long / Oh my gosh / Dark before the dawn
/ I should care
CD _____ CDSJP 330
Timeless Jazz / Aug '90 / New Note.

Thile, Chris

LEADING OFF...
CD _____ SH 3828CD
Sugarhill / Nov '94 / Roots / CM / ADA /
Direct.

Thilo, Jesper

FLAT FOOT BOOGIE
CD _____ MECCACD 1010
Music Mecca / Nov '94 / Jazz Music /
Cadillac / Wellard.

HALF NELSON (Thilo, Jesper Quartet)
CD _____ MECCACD 1009
Music Mecca / Jul '93 / Jazz Music /
Cadillac / Wellard.

**JESPER THILO QUARTET AND HARRY
EDISON (Thilo, Jesper Quartet)**
CD _____ STCD 4120
Storyville / Feb '89 / Jazz Music / Wellard
/ CM / Cadillac.

**JESPER THILO/CLARK TERRY (Thilo,
Jesper & Clark Terry)**
Just one of those things / Sophisticated
lady / Save your love for me / Rose room /
Wave / Ballad for Lester / Cherokee / Sun-
day / Did you call her today / Stardust /
Frog eyes / Body and soul
CD _____ STCD 8204
Storyville / Nov '94 / Jazz Music / Wellard /
CM / Cadillac.

PLAYS BASIE
CD _____ MECCACD 1035
Music Mecca / Nov '94 / Jazz Music /
Cadillac / Wellard.

SHUFFLIN'
CD _____ MECCACD 1015
Music Mecca / Nov '94 / Jazz Music /
Cadillac / Wellard.

**WE LOVE HIM MADLY (Thilo, Jesper
Quintet)**
CD _____ MECCACD 1025
Music Mecca / Jul '93 / Jazz Music /
Cadillac / Wellard.

Thin Lizzy

BAD REPUTATION
Bad reputation / Dancing in the moonlight /
Dear Lord / Downtown sundown / Killer
without cause / Opium train / Soldier of for-
tune / Southbound / That woman's gonna
break your heart
CD _____ 8424342
Vertigo / Apr '90 / PolyGram.

BBC RADIO ONE LIVE IN CONCERT
CD _____ WINCD 024
Windsong / Sep '92 / Pinnacle.

BLACK ROSE
Do anything you want to / Toughest street
in town / S and M / Waiting for an alibi /
Sarah / Got to give it up / Get out of here /
With love / Roisin dubh
CD _____ 8303922
Vertigo / Jun '89 / PolyGram.

CHINATOWN
We will be strong / Chinatown / Sweetheart
/ Sugar blues / Killer on the loose / Havin'
a good time / Genocide / Didn't I / Hey you
CD _____ 83033932
Vertigo / Jun '89 / PolyGram.

FIGHTING
Ballad of a hard man / Fighting my way
back / For those who love to live / Freedom
song / King's vengeance / Rosalie / Silver
dollar / Spirit slips away / Suicide / Wild one
CD _____ 842 433-2
Vertigo / Aug '83 / PolyGram.

JAILBREAK
Angel from the coast / Boys are back in
town / Cowboy song / Emerald / Fight or
fall / Jailbreak / Romeo and the lonely girl /
Running back / Warriors
CD _____ 8227852
Vertigo / Jun '89 / PolyGram.

JOHNNY THE FOX
Boogie woogie dance / Borderline / Don't
believe a word / Fool's gold / Johnny /
Johnny the fox meets Jimmy the weed /
Massacre / Old flame / Rocky / Sweet Marie
CD _____ 822 687 2
Vertigo / May '90 / PolyGram.

LIFE
Thunder and lightening / Waiting for an alibi
/ Jailbreak / Baby please don't go / Holy
war / Renegade / Hollywood / Got to give
it up / Angel of death / Are you ready / Boys
are back in town / Cold sweat / Don't believe a word / Killer on the loose / Sun goes
down / Emerald / Black rose / Still in love
with you / Rocker
CD _____ 812 882 2
Vertigo / Aug '90 / PolyGram.

LIVE AND DANGEROUS - IN CONCERT
Boys are back in town / Dancing in the
moonlight / Massacre / I'm still in love with
you / Me and the boys (Full title: Me and
the boys were wondering what you and the
girls were) / Don't believe a word / Warriors
/ Are you ready / Sha la la la / Baby drives
me crazy
CD _____ 8380302
Vertigo / Jun '89 / PolyGram.

LIZZY KILLERS
Do anything you want to / Sarah / Whiskey
in the jar / Jailbreak / Boys are back in town
/ Killer on the loose / Don't believe a word
/ Dancing in the moonlight / Waiting for an
alibi
CD _____ 800 060-2
Vertigo / '83 / PolyGram.

PEEL SESSIONS
Whiskey in the jar / Vagabond of the
Western world / Little girl in bloom / Little
darling / Still in love with you / Rosalie /

Suicide / Emerald / Cowboy song / Jail-break / Don't believe a word / Killer without a cause / Bad reputation / That woman's gonna break your heart / Dancing in the moonlight
CD _____ SFRCD 130
Strange Fruit / Sep '94 / Pinnacle.

RENEGADE
Angel of death / Renegade / Pressure will blow / Leave this town / Hollywood (down on your luck) / No one told him / Fats / Mexican blood / It's getting dangerous
CD _____ 842 435-2
Vertigo / Jun '90 / PolyGram.

THIN LIZZY
Friendly ranger at Clontarf Castle / Honesty is no excuse / Diddy levine / Ray gun / Look what the wind blue in / Eire / Return of the farmer's son / Clifton Grange Hotel / Saga of the ageing orphan / Remembering part 1 / Dublin / Remembering part 2 / Old moon madness / Thing's ain't working out down at the farm
CD _____ 8205282
Vertigo / Jan '89 / PolyGram.

THUNDER AND LIGHTNING
Thunder and lightning / This is the one / Sun goes down / Holy war / Cold sweat / Some-day / She is going to hit back / Baby, please don't go / Bad habits / Heart attack / Thunder and lightning
CD _____ 8104902
Vertigo / Jun '89 / PolyGram.

VAGABONDS OF THE WESTERN WORLD
Mama nature said / Hero and the madman / Slow blues / Rocker / Vagabond of the western world / Little girl in bloom / Gonna creep up on you / Song for while I'm away / Whiskey in the jar / Black boys on the corner / Randolph's tango / Broken dreams
CD _____ 820 969 2
Vertigo / May '91 / PolyGram.

WILD ONE (The Very Best Of Thin Lizzy)
Boys are back in town / Jailbreak / Don't believe a world / Waiting for an alibi / Rosalie/Cowgirl song (Live) / Cold sweat / Thunder and lightning / Out in the fields / Dancin' in the moonlight / Parisienne walkways / Sarah / Still in love with you (Live) / Emerald / Bad reputation / Killer on the loose / China town / Do anything you want to / Rocker / Whiskey in the jar
CD _____ 5281132
Mercury / Jan '96 / PolyGram.

Thin White Rope

EXPLORING THE AXIS
Down in the desert / Disney girl / Soundtrack / Lithium / Dead grammas on a train / Three song / Eleven / Roger's tongue / Real West / Exploring the axis
CD _____ 46072L
Frontier / Oct '92 / Vital.

ONE THAT GOT AWAY, THE
Down in the desert / Disney girl / Eleven / Not your fault / Wire animals / Take it home / Mr. Limpet / Elsie crashed the party / Red sun / Some velvet morning / Triangle song / Yoo doo right / Tina and Glen / Napkin song / Ants are cavemen / Fish song / Bartender's rag / Hunter's moon / Astronomy / Outlaw blues / It's OK / Wreck of ol' 97 / Roadrunner / Munich eunich / Silver machine / Clown song
CD Set _____ 346422
Frontier / Mar '93 / Vital.

RUBY SEA
CD _____ 346321
Frontier / Sep '91 / Vital.

SPOOR
Red sun / Town without pity / Man with the golden gun / They're hanging me tonight / Some velvet morning / Ants are cavemen / Little doll (live) / Outlaw blues / Burn the flames / Eye / Skinhead / Tina and Glen (Demo) / Munich eunich (demo) / Here she comes now (demo)
CD _____ 310642
Frontier / Feb '95 / Vital.

SQUATTER'S RIGHTS
CD _____ FCD 1035
Frontier / Jul '91 / Vital.

WHEN WORLDS COLLIDE
CD _____ MRCD 047
Munster / May '94 / Plastic Head.

Things To Come

I WANT OUT
Sweetgina / Mississippi dealer / I want out / Your down / Speak of the devil / Smokestack lightnin' / Character of Caruso / Tell me why / Tomorrow / Pushin' too hard (instr.) / Show me a place / I'm a man (instrumental) / Home to you / Your down (instr.) / Icicles on the roof / Sweetgina (instr.) / Behold now behemoth / Darkness
CD _____ CDSC 11017
Sundazed / Jan '94 / Rollercoaster.

Think About Mutation

HOUSE GRINDER
CD _____ DY 32
Dynamica / Oct '93 / Pinnacle.

HOUSEBASTARDS
CD _____ DY 102
Dynamica / Sep '94 / Pinnacle.

Thinking Fellas Union...

PORCELAIN ENTERTAINMENTS
(Thinking Fellas Union Local 282)
CD _____ RTS 21
Return To Sender / Jan '96 / Direct / ADA.

STRANGERS FROM THE UNIVERSE
(Thinking Fellas Union Local 282)
My pal the tortoise / Socket / Bomber pilot WWII / Hundreds of years / Guillotine / Uranium / February / Pull my pants up tight / Cup of dreams / Oxenmaster / Operation / Piston and the shaft / Communication / Noble experiment
CD _____ OLE 109-2
Matador / Oct '94 / Vital.

Thinking Plague

IN THIS LIFE
CD _____ RERTPCD
Recommended / '90 / These / ReR Megacorp.

Third & The Mortal

NIGHTSWAN
CD _____ VOW 047CD
Voices Of Wonder / Jun '95 / Plastic Head.

TEARS LAID IN EARTH
CD _____ VOW
Voices Of Wonder / Nov '94 / Plastic Head.

Third Ear Band

ALCHEMY
Mosaic / Ghetto raga / Druid one / Stone circle / Egyptian book of the dead / Area three / Dragon lines / Lark rise
CD _____ DOCD 1999
Drop Out / Apr '91 / Pinnacle.

BRAIN WAVES
Sirocco song / Midnight drums / Spell of the voodoo / Dances with dolphins / Water into wine / Alchemical raga / Psychedelic trance dance
CD _____ MASOCD 90045
Materiali Sonori / May '95 / New Note.

LIVE GHOSTS
Hope mosaic / Druid three / Ghetto raga / Live ghosts
CD _____ MASO 90004
Materiali Sonori / '90 / New Note.

MACBETH
Overture / Beach / Lady Macbeth / Inverness (Macbeth's return/Preparation/Duncan's arrival) / Banquet / Dagger and death / At the well/Prince's escape/Coronation/Come sealing night / Court dance / Fleance groom's dance / Bear baiting / Ambush / Banquo's ghost / Going to bed/Blind man's buff / Requiescant/Sere and yellow leaf / Cauldron / Prophesies / Wicca way
CD _____ BGOCD 61
Beat Goes On / Jan '89 / Pinnacle.

THIRD EAR BAND
Air / Earth / Fire / Water
CD _____ BGOCD 89
Beat Goes On / Dec '90 / Pinnacle.

VOICEPRINT RADIO SESSION
CD _____ VPR 017CD
Voice Print / Oct '94 / Voice Print.

Third Eye

ANCIENT FUTURE
CD _____ NZ 024-2
Third Eye / Oct '94 / Total/BMG.

DANCE OF CREATION
CD _____ NZ 023CD
Nova Zembla / Nov '94 / Plastic Head.

Third Person

BENDS, THE
CD _____ KFWCD 102
Knitting Factory / Nov '94 / Grapevine.

LUCKY WATER
Busy river / Cold call / Trick water / Bubble and crow / Bridge of a thousand tears / Globe trudgers / Old Grandad (doesn't smell too bad) / John Frum he come / Curlew's sad day / Cadillac bolero / Moro reflex / Hasten slowly
CD _____ KFWCD 156
Knitting Factory / Feb '95 / Grapevine.

Third World

REGGAE AMBASSADORS (20th anniversary collection)
Satta a masagana / Brand new beggar / Freedom song / Railroad track / 1865 / Rhythm of life / Dreamland / Now that we've found love / Journey to Addis / Cool meditation / Night heat / Talk to me / Irie ites / Always around / Uptown rebel / Jah glory (Live) / African woman (Live) / Breaking up is hard to do (Live) / Roots with quality / Dancing on the floor / Try Jah love / Lagos jump / Sense of purpose / Reggae radio

station / Forbidden love / Reggae ambassador / D.J. ambassador / Riddim haffe rule / Committed / Mi legal / Give the people what they need
CD _____ CRNCD 3
Island / Feb '94 / PolyGram.

REGGAE GREATS
Now that we've found love / Prisoner in the street / Always around / Talk to me / Cool meditation / Satta a masagana / Ninety six degrees in the shade / African woman / Rhythm of life
CD _____ CCD 9789
Mango / '88 / Vital / PolyGram.

ROCK THE WORLD
Rock the world / Spiritual revolution / Who gave you / Dub music / Shine like a blazing fire / Dancing on the floor / There's no need to question why / Peace and love / Standing in the rain / Hug it up
CD _____ 982988 2
Pickwick/Sony Collector's Choice / Sep '93 / Carlton Home Entertainment / Pinnacle / Sony.

Thirteen Moons

YOU WILL FIND MERCY ON YOUR ROAD
CD _____ WRCD 012
Wire / Oct '90 / Pinnacle.

This

LETTUCE SPRAY
Grooverang (intro) / Mind's eye / Michael / Criss cross world / Kite / Mentholated head balm / Tighter / Chicken run / Destiny / Swimming against the tide / Sandwich
CD _____ YM 002CD
Yellow Moon / Oct '93 / Vital.

This Ascension

LIGHT AND SHADE
CD _____ EFA 06481-2
Tess Europe / Mar '94 / SRD.

This Heat

DECEIT
CD _____ HEAT 2CD
Recommended / '91 / These / ReR Megacorp.

THIS HEAT
CD _____ HEAT 1CD
Recommended / '91 / These / ReR Megacorp.

This Lush Garden

BLACK TAPE FOR A BLUE GIRL
CD _____ HY 39100622CD
Hyperium / Aug '93 / Plastic Head.

This Mortal Coil

BLOOD
Lacemaker / Mr. Somewhere / Andialu / With tomorrow / Loose joints / You and your sister / Nature's way / I come and stand at every door / Bitter / Baby ray raby / Several times / Lacemaker II / Late night / Ruddy and wretched / Help me lift you up / Carolyn's song / D.D. and E. / Till I gain control again / Dreams are like water / I am the cosmos / (Nothing but) Blood
CD _____ DADCD 1005
4AD / Apr '91 / Disc.

FILIGREE AND SHADOW
Velvet belly / Jeweller / Ivy and neet / Meniscus / Tears / Tarantula / My father / Come here my love / At first and then / Strength of strings / Morning glory / Inchblue / I want to live / Mama K (1) / Filigree and shadow / Firebrothers / Thais (1) / I must have been blind / Heart of glass / Alone / Mama K (2) / Horizon bleeds and sucks its thumb / Drugs / Red rain / Thais (2)
CD _____ DAD 609 CD
4AD / Sep '86 / Disc.

IT'LL END IN TEARS
Kangaroo / Song to the siren / Holocaust / Fyt / Fond affections / Last ray / Waves become wings / Another day / Barramundi / Dreams made flesh / Not me / Single wish
CD _____ CAD 411 CD
4AD / '86 / Disc.

This Picture

CITY OF SIN
Great escape / High rise / Hands on my soul / Sycamore seeds / Face up to the facts / Fire in the house / City of sin / Outsider / Heart of another man / Maniac man / Prophet
CD _____ 74321 21034-2
Dedicated / Sep '94 / Vital.

Thistlethwaite, Anthony

AESOP WROTE A FABLE
Muddy waterboy / Let your conscience be your guide / Love that burns / Aesop wrote a fable / I just want to make love to you / Jenny / It don't make sense (You can't make peace) / Howling tom cat / Good

morning Mr. Customs man / Here in my arms / Flick-knife / Blues stars
CD _____ ACRE 001CD
Rolling Acres / Mar '93 / Vital.

CARTWHEELS
Cartwheels / Red jeans / Farming the right / Acres / Migrating bird / Cherry dress / Tower of love / Marie Dreslerova / Somewhere across the water / Communicating / Atlas / Back to the land
CD _____ ACRE 002CD
Rolling Acres / Jan '95 / Vital.

Thomas & Taylor

YOU CAN'T BLAME LOVE - AN ANTHOLOGY
City lights / Who can the winner be / I'll be waiting (mixes) / You can't blame love / Why don't you try me / Don't let it be (all in my mind) / I don't want to go through love again / Try me / My room / Love and affection / My life / Give it up / Snake in the grass (radio) / Freedom (Mixes) / Snake in the grass (extended) / I love you / Lonely (too long) / True love / Call me / Hey brother / Don't forget (who you are) / You can't blame love (extended mix)
CD Set _____ NED CD 227
Sequel / Oct '92 / BMG.

Thomas, Bill

PREACHER'S SON
CD _____ 422504
Last Call / May '05 / Direct.

Thomas, Blachman

BLACHMAN THOMAS MEETS AL AGAMI & REMEE
CD _____ YOCD 1
Mega / Mar '95 / 3MV.

Thomas, Carla

BEST OF CARLA THOMAS, THE
Where do I go / I've fallen in love / I like what you're doing (to me) / Strung out over you / Just keep on loving me / My life / I need you woman / I can't stop / Some other man (is beating your time) / Guide me well / Time for love (I'm going back to) living in the City / All I have to do is dream / I loved you like I love my very life / Hi de ho (that old sweet roll) / You've got a cushion to fall on / Love means you never have to say you're sorry / Sugar / I may not be all you want (but I'm all you got) / Love among people / I have a God who loves / Gee whiz / I'll never stop loving you
CD _____ CDSXD 093
Stax / Aug '93 / Pinnacle.

CARLA
CD _____ 7567823402
Atlantic / Jul '93 / Warner Music.

COMFORT ME
CD _____ 756780329-2
Atlantic / Jun '93 / Warner Music.

HIDDEN GEMS
I'll never stop loving you / I wonder about love / Little boy / Loneliness / Your love is a) lifesaver / Sweet sensation / You'll lose a good thing / I've made up my mind / My man believes in me / I like it / Runaround / Good good lovin' / That beat keeps disturbing my sleep / If it's not asking too much / I ain't no easy thing / Too hard / Good day n'hit / I can't hide it / Thump in my heart / Goodbye my love
CD _____ CDSXD 039
Stax / Oct '91 / Pinnacle.

LOVE MEANS
Didn't we / Are you sure / What is love / Daughter, you're still your daddy's child / Love means you never have to say you're sorry / You've got a cushion to fall on / Il est plus doux que / Cherish / I wake up wanting you
CD _____ CDSXE 060
Stax / Jul '92 / Pinnacle.

MEMPHIS QUEEN
I like what you're doing (to me) / Don't say no more / Strung out over you / Guide me well / Where do I go / I play for keeps / I've fallen in love / How can you throw my love away / Precious memories / Unyielding / More man than I ever had / He's beating your time
CD _____ CDSXE 027
Stax / Mar '90 / Pinnacle.

QUEEN ALONE, THE
CD _____ 8122710152
WEA / Jul '93 / Warner Music.

Thomas, Chris

21ST CENTURY BLUES... FROM DA HOOD
Intro / 21.cb / Hellhoundds / Kkkrossroads / Kickin' true blue / Up from da underground / Blues from da hood / Da gambler / Time bomb / Homesick blues / Phone interlude / My pain, your pleasure / Kill somebody tonight / Anotherdeadhomie
CD _____ 01005821232
Private Music / Jul '95 / BMG.

SIMPLE
CD _____ HCD 0043
Hightone / Jun '94 / ADA / Koch.

Thomas, Earl

BLUE NOT BLUES
CD _____ FIENDCD 740
Demon / Aug '93 / Pinnacle / ADA.

Thomas, Gary

EXILE'S GATE
CD _____ 514009-2
JMT / Dec '93 / PolyGram.

TILL WE HAVE FACES
CD _____ 5140002
JMT / Apr '92 / PolyGram.

Thomas, Guthrie

THROUGH THE YEARS
CD _____ TX 3001CD
Taxim / Jan '94 / ADA.

WRITER, THE
CD _____ TX 3002CD
Taxim / Dec '93 / ADA.

Thomas, Henry

COMPLETE RECORDINGS, THE
CD _____ YAZCD 1080
Yazoo / Apr '91 / CM / ADA / Roots /
Koch.

Thomas, Irma

DOWN AT MUSCLE SHOALS
We got something good / Good to me /
Here I am, take me / Security / Let's do it
over / Somewhere crying / Woman will do
wrong / Yours until tomorrow / I gave you
everything / I've been loving you too long /
Don't make me stop now / Cheater man /
Good things don't come easy (CD only)
CD _____ CDRED 28
Charly / Sep '91 / Charly / THE / Cadillac.

NEW RULES, THE
New rules / Gonna cry till my tears run dry
/ I needed somebody / Good things don't
come easy / Love of my man / One more
time / Thinking of you / Wind beneath my
wings / I gave you everything / Yours until
tomorrow
CD _____ 2046
Rounder / '86 / CM / Direct / ADA / Cadillac.

RULER OF HEARTS
I did my part / Cry on / For goodness sake
/ It's raining / Look up / It's too soon to
know / Somebody told you / Your love is
true / (You ain't) hittin' on nothing / Gone /
Two winters long / I done got over it / That's
all I ask / Ruler of my heart / Girl needs boy
CD _____ CDCHARLY 195
Charly / Aug '89 / Charly / THE / Cadillac.

SOUL QUEEN OF NEW ORLEANS
It's raining / Ruler of my heart / I did my
part / Cry on / Look up / It's too soon to
know / I done got over / That's all I ask /
For goodness sake / Gone / Somebody told
you / Two winters long / (You ain't) hittin'
on nothing / Girl needs boy / In between
tears (On CD only) / These four walls (On CD
only) / What's so wrong with you loving me
(On CD only) / You're the dog (I do the barking myself) (On CD only) / Coming from behind (On CD only) / Wish someone would
care (On CD only) / My world around
(On CD only)
CD _____ CPCD 8010
Charly / Feb '94 / Charly / THE / Cadillac.

WALK AROUND HEAVEN
CD _____ ROU 2128CD
Rounder / Apr '94 / CM / Direct / ADA /
Cadillac.

WAY I FEEL, THE
Old records / Baby I love you / Sorry wrong
number / You can think twice / Sit down
and cry / All I know is the way I feel / I'm
gonna hold you to your promise / I'll take
care of you / Dancing in the street / You
don't know nothin' about love
CD _____ FIENDCD 112
Demon / Sep '91 / Pinnacle / ADA.

Thomas Jefferson Slave...

**BAIT AND SWITCH (Thomas Jefferson
Slave Appartments)**
My mysterious death / Is she shy / Down to
High Street / Quarrel with the world / Chea-
ter's heaven / Cyclotron / Negative guestlist
/ Fire in the swimming girl / You can't kill
stupid / Rock 'n' roll hall of fame / Contract
dispute / Wrong headed
CD _____ 74321279652
American / Jul '95 / BMG.

Thomas, Jay

360 DEGREES
Cheryl / Waltz / All too soon / Wing span /
Why not / Aisha / Valse / Peacocks / Whims
of chambers / My ideal / Blues for McVouty
/ Isfahan
CD _____ HEPCD 2060
Hep / Feb '95 / Cadillac / Jazz Music / New
Note / Wellard.

BLUES FOR MCVOUTY
CD _____ STCD 562
Stash / May '93 / Jazz Music / CM /
Cadillac / Direct / ADA.

Thomas, Jesse

BLUE GOOSE BLUES
CD _____ IMP 704
Iris Music / Nov '95 / Discovery.

Thomas, John Charles

HOME ON THE RANGE
CD _____ GEMM CD 9977
Gemm / Sep '92 / Pinnacle.

Thomas, Kenny

VOICES
Outstanding / Best of you / Tender love /
Will I ever see your face / Something special
/ If you believe / Thinking about your love /
Voices / Girlfriend / Were we ever in love
CD _____ CD25CR 16
Chrysalis / Mar '94 / EMI.

WAIT FOR ME
Stay / Destiny / Piece by piece / Can't hide
love / Wait for me / Keep forgettin' / Trippin'
on your love / Hold you close / Separate
lives / Same old story / Garden of pain /
Reprise (wait for me)
CD _____ CTCD 36
Cooltempo / Sep '93 / EMI.

Thomas, Nicky

DOING THE MOONWALK
CD _____ CDTRL 288
Trojan / Apr '91 / Jetstar / Total/BMG.

Thomas, Pat

St. KATHERINE
CD _____ WSFASF 144
Normal/Okra / May '94 / Direct / ADA.

Thomas, Ramblin'

1928-32
CD _____ DOCD 5107
Blues Document / Nov '92 / Swift / Jazz
Music / Hot Shot.

Thomas, Rene

GUITAR GENIUS
All the things you are / Body and soul /
Deep purple / Day in day out / Just
friends / B like Bud / Round Midnight
CD _____ CDSGP 009
Prestige / Jan '94 / Total/BMG.

**GUITAR GROOVE (Thomas, Rene
Quintet)**
CD _____ OJCCD 1725
Original Jazz Classics / Nov '95 / Wellard /
Jazz Music / Cadillac / Complete/Pinnacle.

HOMMAGE A RENE THOMAS
My wife Maria / Jesus think of me / Star
eyes / Round Midnight
CD _____ CDSJP 398
Timeless Jazz / Aug '94 / New Note.

Thomas, Ruddy

WHEN I'VE GOT YOU
CD _____ HLCD 010
Hawkeye / Jun '94 / Jetstar.

Thomas, Rufus

**BEST OF RUFUS THOMAS - THE
SINGLES**
Funky Mississippi / So hard to get along
with / Funky way / I want to hold you / Do
the funky chicken / Preacher and the bear
/ Sixty minute man / Do the push and pull
(part 1) / Do the push and pull (part 2) /
World is round / Breakdown (part 1) /
Breakdown (part 2) / Do the funky penguin
(part 1) / Do the funky penguin (part 2) / 6-
3-8 (that's the number to play) / Itch and
scratch (part 1) / Funky robot (part 1) / I
know (I love you so) / I'll be your santa baby
/ Funky bird / Boogie ain't nuttin' (but gettin'
down) / Do the double bump / Jump back
'75 (part 1) / Looking for a love (part 1)
CD _____ CDSXD 094
Stax / Oct '93 / Pinnacle.

CAN'T GET AWAY FROM THIS DOG
Walking the dog / Can't get away from this
dog / Forty four long / Strolling Beale no.1
/ Cherry red blues / Carry me back to old
Virginny / Barefootin' / Story that's never
been told / Last clean shirt / Show me the
way to go home / Jump back / My girl /
We're gonna make it / Don't mess up a
good thing / I want to hold you / Can your
monkey do the dog / Stop kicking my dog
around / Wang dang doodle / Reconsider
baby
CD _____ CDSXD 038
Stax / Oct '91 / Pinnacle.

CROWN PRINCE OF DANCE
Git on up and do it / I know you don't want
me no more / Funkiest man alive / Tutti
Frutti / Funky robot / I wanna sang / Baby
it's real / Steal a little / I'm still in love with
you / Funky bird

CD _____ CDSXE 054
Stax / Nov '92 / Pinnacle.

DID YOU HEARD ME
Do the Push and pull (parts 1 & 2) / World
is round / (I love you) for sentimental reasons / Breakdown (part 1) / Breakdown
(part 2) / Love trap / Do the funky penguin
(part 1) / Do the funky penguin (part 2) /
Ditch digging / 6-3-8 (That's the number to
play)
CD _____ CDSXE 050
Stax / Nov '92 / Pinnacle.

DO THE FUNKY CHICKEN
Do the funky chicken / Let the good times
roll / Sixty minute man / Looking for a love
/ Bearcat / Old McDonald had a farm (parts
1 and 2) / Rufus Rastus Johnson Brown /
Soul food / Turn your damper down /
Preacher and the bear
CD _____ CDSXE 036
Stax / Mar '91 / Pinnacle.

**RUFUS THOMAS LIVE DOING THE
PUSH AND PULL AT PJ'S**
Monologue / Ooh poo pah do / Old Mc-
Donald had a farm / Walking the dog /
Preacher and the bear / Night time is the
right time / Push and pull / Do the funky
chicken / Breakdown (CD only) / Do the
funky chicken (2) (CD only) / Do the funky
chicken (CD only)
CD _____ CDSXE 121
Stax / Jul '95 / Pinnacle.

THAT WOMAN IS POISON
That woman is poison / Big fine hunk of
woman / Somebody's got to go / Walk /
Breaking my back / All night worker
CD _____ ALCD 4769
Alligator / May '93 / Direct / ADA.

TIMELESS FUNK
CD _____ CDSGP 036
Prestige / Nov '92 / Total/BMG.

Thompson Community...

**THROUGH GOD'S EYES (Brunson, Rev.
M. & Thompson Community Singers)**
CD _____ 701940660-2
Nelson Word / Dec '93 / Nelson Word.

Thompson Twins

BEST OF THE THOMPSON TWINS, THE
In the name of love ('88) / Lies / Love on
your side / Lay your hands on me / Gap /
Hold me now / Doctor doctor / You take me
up / King for a day / Get that love
CD _____ 261220
Arista / Mar '91 / BMG.

COLLECTION, THE
Hold me now / Sister of mercy / Don't mess
with Doctor Dream / Who can stop the rain
/ Perfect day / Day after day / Doctor doctor
/ You take me up / Lies / Follow your heart
/ Still waters / Emperor's clothes / Revolu-
tion / In the name of love
CD _____ 74321 15221-2
Ariola Express / Sep '93 / BMG.

Thompson, Barbara

**BARBARA THOMPSON'S SPECIAL
EDITION**
Country dance / Fear of spiders / City lights
/ Little Annie ooh / Fields of flowers / Dusk:
Nightwatch / Listen to the plants / Out to
lunch / Sleepwalker / Midday riser / Times
past / Voices behind locked doors
CD _____ VBR 20172
Vera Bra / Sep '93 / Pinnacle / New Note.

**BREATHLESS (Thompson, Barbara
Paraphernalia)**
Breathless / Sax rap / Jaunty / You must be
jokin' / Squiffy / Bad blues / Cheeky / Gra-
cey / Breathless (short cuts) / Sax rap (short
cuts) / Cheeky (short cuts)
CD _____ VBR 20572
Vera Bra / Sep '93 / Pinnacle / New Note.

**CRY FROM THE HEART, A (Live In
London) (Thompson, Barbara
Paraphernalia)**
CD _____ VBRCD 20212
Vera Bra / Sep '93 / Pinnacle / New Note.

EVERLASTING FLAME
Everlasting flame / Tatami / In the eye of a
storm / Ode to sappho / Emerald dusky
maiden / Night before culloden / Unity hymn
/ Ancient voices / So near, so far / Fanaid
grove
CD _____ VBR 20582
Vera Bra / Nov '93 / Pinnacle / New Note.

HEAVENLY BODIES
Le grand voyage / Extreme jonction / Requiem pour deux memoire / Entre le trous
de la memoire / Les barricades myster-
ieuses / Heavenly bodies / Love on the
edge of life / Elysian fields / Flights of fancy
/ Tibetan sunrise / Horizons new
CD _____ VBR 20152
Vera Bra / Sep '93 / Pinnacle / New Note.

**LIVE IN LONDON I CRY FROM THE
HEART (Thompson, Barbara
Paraphernalia)**
Joyride / L'extreme jonction / Cry from the
heart / Entre les trous de la memoire / Out
to lunch / Close to the edge / Voices behind

locked doors / Eastern Western promise
Part 1 / Eastern Western promise Part 11
CD _____ VBR 20212
Vera Bra / Sep '93 / Pinnacle / New Note.

Thompson, Bob

MAGIC IN YOUR HEART
CD _____ ICH 1165CD
Ichiban / Apr '94 / Koch.

Thompson, Butch

**BUTCH & DOC (Thompson, Butch &
Doc Cheatham)**
CD _____ CD 3012
Daring / Dec '94 / Direct / CM / ADA.

LINCOLN AVENUE BLUES
CD _____ DARINGCD 3019
Daring / Nov '95 / Direct / CM / ADA.

MINNESOTA WONDER
CD _____ DR 3004
Daring / Nov '95 / Direct / CM / ADA.

**PLAYS FAVORITES (Thompson, Butch
Trio)**
CD _____ SACD 113
Solo Art / Feb '93 / Jazz Music.

YULESTRIDE
CD _____ DARING 3010CD
Daring / Nov '94 / Direct / CM / ADA.

Thompson, Carroll

HOPELESSLY IN LOVE
CD _____ CGCD 15
Carib Jems / Jun '88 / Jetstar.

OTHER SIDE OF LOVE, THE
Other side of love / I go weak / Move me /
Walk away / Unity / Show some love /
Where is love / Where were you / Natural
woman / Lovers and strangers / Rock me
gently (Extra track on CD only.)
CD _____ ARICD 077
Ariwa Sounds / Dec '92 / SRD.

Thompson, Charles

ROBBIN'S NEST
Robbin's nest / You don't know what love
is / Solitude / For the ears / I love my baby
/ After hours / Centerpiece / My one and
only love / Corner pocket / Autumn leaves
/ Tickle toe
CD _____ KICJ 181
King/Paddle Wheel / Jun '94 / New Note.

Thompson, Danny

**SONGHAI (Thompson, Danny/Toumani
Diabate/Ketama)**
CD _____ HNCD 1323
Hannibal / May '89 / Vital / ADA.

SONGHAI 2
Sute monebo / Niani / Pozo del deseo /
Monte de los suspiros / Djamana djana / De
jerez a mali / Ndia / De la noche a la man-
ana / Mail sajio
CD _____ HNCD 1383
Rykodisc / Aug '94 / Vital / ADA.

WHATEVER
Idle Monday / Till Minne av jan / Yucateca
/ Lovely Joan / Swedish dance / Lament for
Alex / Crusader / Minor escapade
CD _____ HNCD 1326
Hannibal / Aug '87 / Vital / ADA.

WHATEVER NEXT
Dargai / Hopdance (invitation to dance) /
Beanpole / Wildfinger / Full English basket
/ Sandansko oro (Bulgarian dance) / Take it
off the top / Major escapade
CD _____ IMCD 117
Antilles/New Directions / May '91 /
PolyGram.

WHATEVER'S BEST
CD _____ WHAT 001CD
Whatdisc / Feb '95 / Vital.

Thompson, Eddie

**AT CHESTERS (Thompson, Eddie Trio &
Spike Robinson)**
'S Wonderful / Flamingo / Emily / I'm getting
sentimental over you / I should care / Ow
(CD only.) / Everything happens to me /
Please don't talk about me when I'm gone
CD _____ HEPCD 2028
Hep / Jan '92 / Cadillac / Jazz Music / New
Note / Wellard.

**AT CHESTERS VOL 2 (Thompson, Eddie
Trio & Spike Robinson)**
CD _____ HEPCD 2031
Hep / Jun '94 / Cadillac / Jazz Music /
New Note / Wellard.

**MEMORIES OF YOU (Thompson, Eddie
Trio & Spike Robinson)**
Rosetta / Memories of you / C Jam blues /
Misty / Paris mambo / Round Midnight /
Love will find a way / Satin doll / Memories
of you (alt. take) / Round midnight (Alt.) /
Love will find a way (alt. take)
CD _____ HEPCD 2021
Hep / Aug '94 / Cadillac / Jazz Music / New
Note / Wellard.

Thompson, Eric

ADAM & EVE HAD THE BLUES
(Thompson, Eric & Suzy)
CD _____ ARHCD 5041
Arhoolie / Apr '95 / ADA / Direct /
Cadillac.

Thompson, Linval

LOOK HOW ME SEXY
Are you ready / You're young / Look how
me sexy / Call me / Sure of the one you
love / Baby mother / I spy / Things couldn't
be the same / Holding on to my girlfriend /
Lick up the chalice
CD _____ GRELCD 515
Greensleeves / Aug '95 / Total/BMG / Jetstar / SRD.

Thompson, Lucky

BEGINNING YEARS, THE
CD _____ IAJRCCD 1001
IAJRC / Jun '94 / Jazz Music.

LUCKY MEETS TOMMY (Thompson,
Lucky & Tommy Flanagan)
CD _____ FSRCD 199
Fresh Sound / Jan '93 / Jazz Music /
Discovery.

LUCKY SESSIONS
I can't give you anything but love / Don't
blame me / East of the sun and west of the
moon / Our love is here to stay / I cover the
waterfront / My funny valentine / Undecided
/ Tenderly / But not for me / You go to my
head / Lullaby in rhythm / Indian summer /
World awakes / Lover man / Strike up the
band
CD _____ 74321115102
Vogue / Jul '93 / BMG.

LUCKY STRIKES
In a sentimental mood / Fly with the wind /
Midnite oil / Reminiscent / Mumba Neua / I
forgot to remember / Prey-loot / Invitation
CD _____ OJCCD 194
Original Jazz Classics / May '93 / Wellard /
Jazz Music / Cadillac / Complete/Pinnacle.

STREET SCENES (Thompson, Lucky &
Gigi Gryce)
Quick as a flash / Parisian knights / Street
scene / Angel eyes / To you dear one / But
not for tonight / Distant sound / Once upon
a time / Still waters / Theme for a brown
rose / Sunkissed rose / Portrait of Django /
Paris the beautiful / Purple shades / La rose
noire / Anna Marie / Hello / Evening in Paris
/ Strike up the band / Serenade to Sonny
CD _____ 74321154672
Vogue / Oct '93 / BMG.

Thompson, Malachi

BUDDY BOLDEN'S RAG
CD _____ DE 481
Delmark / Aug '95 / Hot Shot / ADA / CM
/ Direct / Cadillac.

JAZZ LIFE, THE
CD _____ DD 453
Delmark / Nov '92 / Hot Shot / ADA / CM
/ Direct / Cadillac.

LIFT EVERY VOICE (Thompson, Malachi
& African Brass)
CD _____ DDCD 463
Delmark / Nov '93 / Hot Shot / ADA / CM
/ Direct / Cadillac.

NEW STANDARDS
CD _____ DE 473
Delmark / Feb '95 / Hot Shot / ADA / CM
/ Direct / Cadillac.

SPIRIT
CD _____ DD 442
Delmark / '89 / Hot Shot / ADA / CM /
Direct / Cadillac.

Thompson, Prince Lincoln

UNITE THE WORLD
CD _____ BRMCD 026
Bold Reprive / '88 / Pinnacle / Bold
Reprive / Harmonia Mundi.

Thompson, Richard

ACROSS A CROWDED ROOM
When the spell is broken / You don't say /
I ain't going to drag my feet no more / Love
is a faithless country / Fire in the engine
room / Walking through a wasted land / Lit-
tle love number / She twists the knife again
/ Ghosts in the wind
CD _____ BGOCD 139
Beat Goes On / Mar '92 / Pinnacle.

AMNESIA
Turning of the tide / Gypsy love songs /
Reckless kind / Jerusalem on the jukebox /
I still dream / Don't tempt me / Yankee, go
home / Can't win / Waltzing's for dreamers
/ Pharaoh
CD _____ CZ 399
Capitol / Mar '91 / EMI.

BBC LIVE IN CONCERT
CD _____ WINCD 034
Windsong / May '93 / Pinnacle.

BEAT THE RETREAT (A Tribute To
Richard Thompson) (Various Artists)
Shoot the light / Wall of death / When the
spell is broken / Turning of the tide / For
shame of doing wrong / Beat the retreat / Genesis
hall / I misunderstood / Madness of love /
Just the motion / Valerie / Heart needs a
home / Dimming of the day / Farewell, farewell / Great Valerio
CD _____ CDEST 2242
EMI / Feb '95 / EMI.

DARING ADVENTURES
Bone through her nose / Valerie / Missie
how you let me down / Dead man's handle
/ Long dead love / Lover's lane / Nearly in
love / Jennie / Baby talk / Cash down never
never / How will I ever be simple again / Al
Bowlly's in heaven
CD _____ BGOCD 138
Beat Goes On / Mar '92 / Pinnacle.

FIRST LIGHT (Thompson, Richard &
Linda)
Restless highway / Sweet surrender / Don't
let a thief steal into your heart / Choice wife
/ Died for love / Strange affair / Layla / Pa-
vanne / House of cards / First light
CD _____ HNCD 4412
Rykodisc / Oct '92 / Vital / ADA.

GUITAR/VOCAL
Heart needs a home / Free as a bird / Night
comes in / Pitfall/Excursion / Calvary cross
/ Time will show the wiser / Throw away
street puzzle / Mr. Lacey / Ballad of easy
rider / Poor Will' and the jolly hangman /
Sweet little Rock 'n' roller / Dark end of the
street / It'll be me
CD _____ HNCD 4413
Hannibal / Mar '89 / Vital / ADA.

HAND OF KINDNESS
Poisoned heart and a twisted memory /
Tear stained letter / How I wanted to / Both
ends burning / Wrong heartbeat / Hand of
kindness / Devonside / Two left feet
CD _____ HNCD 1313
Hannibal / Jun '86 / Vital / ADA.

HENRY THE HUMAN FLY
Roll over Vaughan Williams / Nobody's
wedding / Poor ditching boy / Shaky Nancy
/ Angels took my racehorse away / Wheely
down / New St George / Painted ladies /
Cold feet / Mary and Joseph / Old changing
way / Twisted
CD _____ HNCD 4405
Hannibal / May '89 / Vital / ADA.

HOKEY POKEY (Thompson, Richard &
Linda)
Heart needs a home / Hokey pokey / I'll re-
gret it all in the morning / Smiffy's glass eye
/ Egypt / Never again / Georgie on a spree
/ Old man inside a young man / Sun never
shines on the poor / Mole in a hole
CD _____ HNCD 4408
Hannibal / May '89 / Vital / ADA.

**I WANT TO SEE THE BRIGHT LIGHTS
TONIGHT** (Thompson, Richard & Linda)
When I get to the border / Calvary cross /
Withered and died / I want to see the bright
lights tonight / Down where the drunkards
roll / We sing hallelujah / Has he got a friend
for me / Little beggar girl / End of the rain-
bow / Great Valerio
CD _____ IMCD 160
Island / Mar '93 / PolyGram.

MIRROR BLUE
For the sake of Mary / I can't wake up to
save my life / M.G.B. GT / Way that it shows
/ Easy there, steady now / King of Bohemia
/ Shane and Dixie / Brando mumble, Min-
gus eyes / I ride in your slipstream / Beeswa-
ing / Fastfood / Mascara tears / Taking my
business elsewhere
CD _____ CDEST 2207
Capitol / Jan '94 / EMI.

POUR DOWN LIKE SILVER (Thompson,
Richard & Linda)
Streets of paradise / For shame of doing
wrong / Poor boy is taken away / Night
comes in / Jet plane is a rocking chair / Beat
the retreat / Hard luck stories / Dimming of
the day / Dargai
CD _____ HNCD 4404
Hannibal / May '88 / Vital / ADA.

RUMOR AND SIGH
Read about love / Feel so good / I misun-
derstood / Behind grey walls / You dream
too much / Why must I plead / Vincent /
Backlash love affair / Mystery wind / Jimmy
Shand / Keep your distance / Mother knows
best / God loves a drunk / Psycho Street
CD _____ CDEST 2142
Capitol / May '91 / EMI.

SHOOT OUT THE LIGHTS (Thompson,
Richard & Linda)
Man in need / Walking on a wire / Don't
renege on our love / Just the motion / Shoot
out the lights / Backstreet slide / Did she
jump or was she pushed / Wall of death
CD _____ HNCD 1303
Hannibal / Dec '94 / Vital / ADA.

SMALL TOWN ROMANCE
Heart needs a home / Time to ring some
changes / Beat the retreat / Woman or man
/ For shame of doing wrong / Honky tonk
blues / Small town romance / I want to see
the bright lights tonight / Down where the

drunkards roll / Love is bad for business /
Great Valerio / Don't let a thief steal into
your heart / Never again
CD _____ HNCD 1316
Hannibal / Jun '86 / Vital / ADA.

STRICT TEMPO
Banish misfortune / Dundee hornpipe / Do
it for my sake / Rockin' in rhythm / Random
jig / Grinder / Will ye no' come back again
/ Cam o'er the steam Charlie / Ye banks
and braes o' bonnie Doon / Rufty tufty /
Nonsuch a la mode de France / Andalus /
Radio Marrakech / Knife edge
CD _____ TSCD 460
Topic / Aug '92 / Direct / ADA.

SUNNYVISTA (Thompson, Richard &
Linda)
Civilization / Borrowed time / Saturday rolling around / You're going to need somebody / Why do you turn your back / Sunnyvista / Lonely heart / Sisters / Justice in
the streets / Traces of my love
CD _____ HNCD 4403
Rykodisc / Oct '92 / Vital / ADA.

WATCHING THE DARK
Man in need / Can't win / Waltzing's for
dreamers / Crash the party / I still dream /
Bird in God's garden/Lost and found / Now
be thankful / Sailor's life / Genesis hall /
knife edge / Walking on a wire / Small town
romance / Shepherd's march/Maggie Cameron / Wall of death / For the shame of doing wrong / Back street slide / Strange affair
/ Wrong heartbeat / Borrowed time / From
Galway to Graceland / Tear stained letter /
Keep your distance / Boge's bonnie belle /
Poor wee Jockey Clarke / Jet plane is a
rocking chair / Dimming of the day / Old
man inside a young man / Never again /
Hokey pokey / Heart needs a home / Beat
the retreat / Al Bowlly's in heaven / Walking
through a wasted land / When the spell is
broken / Devonside / Little tipple number /
ain't going to drag my feet no more / Withered and died / Nobody's wedding / Poor
ditching boy / Great valerio / Twisted / Calvary cross / Jennie / Hand of kindness /
Two left feet / Shoot out the lights
CD Set _____ HNCD 5303
Hannibal / Apr '93 / Vital / ADA.

Thompson, Sir Charles

STARDUST
Stardust / St. Louis blues / I'm getting sen-
timental over you / Love me tender / Boogie
woogie / Gee baby ain't I good for you /
How high the moon / Tune us in / Groovin'
high / Georgia on my mind
CD _____ KICJ 225
King/Paddle Wheel / Mar '95 / New Note.

TAKIN' OFF
CD _____ DD 450
Delmark / Dec '89 / Hot Shot / ADA / CM
/ Direct / Cadillac.

Thompson, Sydney

CHA CHA CHA'S & JIVES (Thompson,
Sydney & His Orchestra)
CD Set _____ WRSTCD 5009
WRD / Aug '95 / Target/BMG.

CHA CHA CHA'S AND JIVES VOL.2
(Thompson, Sydney & His Orchestra)
CD _____ WRSTCD 5014
WRD / Oct '95 / Target/BMG.

QUICKSTEPS AND FOXTROTS
CD Set _____ WRSTCD 5003
WRD / Oct '95 / Target/BMG.

QUICKSTEPS AND FOXTROTS VOL. 2
(Thompson, Sydney & His Orchestra)
CD _____ WRSTCD 5010
WRD / Oct '95 / Target/BMG.

RUMBAS & SAMBAS (Thompson,
Sydney & His Orchestra)
CD Set _____ WRSTCD 5008
WRD / Aug '95 / Target/BMG.

RUMBAS & SAMBAS VOL.2 (Thompson,
Sydney & His Orchestra)
CD _____ WRSTCD 5013
WRD / Oct '95 / Target/BMG.

TANGOS AND PASO DOBLES
(Thompson, Sydney & His Orchestra)
CD Set _____ WRSTCD 5006
WRD / Aug '95 / Target/BMG.

TANGOS AND PASO DOBLES VOL.2
(Thompson, Sydney & His Orchestra)
CD _____ WRSTCD 5011
WRD / Oct '95 / Target/BMG.

WALTZES & VIENNESE WALTZES
(Thompson, Sydney & His Orchestra)
CD Set _____ WRSTCD 5007
WRD / Aug '95 / Target/BMG.

WALTZES & VIENNESE WALTZES VOL.2
(Thompson, Sydney & His Orchestra)
CD _____ WRSTCD 5012
WRD / Oct '95 / Target/BMG.

Thompson, Tony

SEXSATIONAL
CD _____ 74321276862
RCA / Jul '95 / BMG.

Thompson-Clarke, Robin

PRAISE HIM ON THE CELLO
All heaven declares / I love you Lord / Em-
manuel / I will sing the wondrous story /
There is a redeemer / In the night / When I
survey / Such love / Jesus you are changing
me / My Lord, what love is this (analyzing
love) / Send the rain Lord / Prayer of St.
Patrick
CD _____ SOPD 2052
Spirit Of Praise / Apr '92 / Nelson Word.

Thorburn, Billy

DON'T SWEETHEART ME
It's always you / Little steeple pointing to a
star / What more can I say / It's foolish but
it's fun / If I could learn to love / memory / Four
buddies / I'd never fall in love again / It
costs so little / I crossed the gypsy's hand
with silver / Don't sweetheart me / Sometimes / My dreams are getting better all the
time / I'm all alone / Echo of a serenade /
Somebody else is taking my place / Journey
to a star / I'll just close my eyes / There's a
land of beginning again / There'll come another day / I hear bluebirds / I'll be waiting
for you / Until you fall in love / Mem'ry of a
rose
CD _____ RAJCD 843
Empress / Feb '95 / THE.

Thore, Francke

ART OF RUMANIAN PAN FLUTE, THE
CD _____ CDCH 021
Milan / Feb '91 / BMG / Silva Screen.

PIPE DREAMS
Mon amour / Greensleeves for pipes / Solveig's song / Way he makes me feel / Entr'acte / Pipe dreams / Spain / Blue rondo
a la turk / Tretemps nippon / Thais meditation / Carillon / Thorn birds
CD _____ CDSGP 9009
Prestige / Mar '95 / Total/BMG.

Thorn, Tracey

DISTANT SHORE, A
Smalltown girl / Simply couldn't care / Sea-
scape / Femme fatale / Dreamy / Plain sail-
ing / New opened eyes / Too happy
CD _____ CDMRED 35
Cherry Red / Jul '93 / Pinnacle.

Thornhill, Claude

1947
CD _____ HCD 108
Hindsight / Aug '94 / Target/BMG / Jazz
Music.

**1984 TRANSCRIPTION PERFORMANCE,
THE**
Poor little rich girl / Adios / Where or when
/ Spanish dance / Anthropology / Raia /
Arab dance / Robbin's nest / Royal garden
blues / Polka dots and moonbeams / The-
re's a small hotel / I knew you when /
Someone to watch over me / Sometimes
I'm happy / I don't know why / April in Paris
/ Begin the beguine / Godchild / Song is you
/ La paloma / Lover man / To each his own
/ Elevation
CD _____ HEPCD 17
Hep / Oct '94 / Cadillac / Jazz Music / New
Note / Wellard.

TAPESTRIES
Snowfall / Stop, you're breaking my heart /
Portrait of a Guinea form / Autumn nocturne
/ I'm somebody nobody loves / Smiles /
Night and day / Buster's last stand / There's
a small hotel / I don't know why (I just do)
/ Under the willow tree / Arab dance / I get
the blues when it rains / Sunday kind of love
/ Early Autumn / La paloma / Warsaw con-
certo / Thriving on a riff (takes 1 & 2) / Sorta
kinda / Robbin's nest / Lover man / Polka
dots and moonbeams / Donna Lee / How
am I to know / Heaven's here nor's for heaven's sake / Whip-
poor-will / That old feeling / Coquette /
Yardbird suite / Let's call it a day
CD _____ CDCHARLY 82
Charly / Oct '87 / Charly / THE / Cadillac.

Thornton, Phil

WHILE THE GREEN MAN SLEEPS
(Thornton, Phil & Mandragora)
Sirocco / Penny drops / Xylem / Inside the
crystal circle / Dream catcher / Rainbow
chant
CD _____ RUNECD 015
Mystic Stones / Nov '93 / Vital.

Thornton, Willie Mae

BALL AND CHAIN (Thornton, Willie Mae
'Big Mama' & Lightnin' Hopkins)
CD _____ ARHCD 305
Arhoolie / Apr '95 / ADA / Direct /
Cadillac.

JAIL
CD _____ VND 79351
Vanguard / Oct '95 / Complete/Pinnacle /
Discovery.

ORIGINAL HOUND DOG, THE
Hound dog / Walkin' blues / My man called
me / Cotton pickin' blues / Willie Mae's
trouble / Big change / I smell a rat / I just

can't help myself / They call me Big Mama / Hard times / I ain't no fool either / You don't move me no more / Let your tears fall baby / I've searched the world over / Rock-a-bye baby / How come / Nightmare / Stop a hoppin' on me / Laugh laugh laugh / Just like a dog (barking up the wrong tree) / Fish / Mischievious boogie
CD _____ CDCHD 940
Ace / Jun '90 / Pinnacle / Cadillac / Complete/Pinnacle.

RISING SUN COLLECTION
CD _____ RSNCD 002
Just A Memory / Apr '94 / Harmonia Mundi.

SASSY MAMA
CD _____ 662217
Vanguard / Jan '94 / Complete/Pinnacle / Discovery.

Thorogood, George

BAD TO THE BONE (Thorogood, George & The Destroyers)
Back to Wentsville / Blue highway / Nobody but me / It's a sin / New boogie chillen / Bad to the bone / Miss Luann / As the years go passing by / No particular place to go / Wanted man
CD _____ BGOCD 94
Beat Goes On / Nov '90 / Pinnacle.

BADDEST OF GEORGE THOROGOOD AND THE DESTROYERS (Thorogood, George & The Destroyers)
Bad to the bone / Move it on over / I'm a steady rollin' man / You talk too much / Who do you love / Gear jammer / I drink alone / One bourbon, one scotch, one beer / If you don't start drinkin' (I'm gonna leave) / Treat her right / Long gone / Louis to Frisco
CD _____ CDMTL 1070
EMI / Sep '92 / EMI.

BOOGIE PEOPLE (Thorogood, George & The Destroyers)
If you don't start drinkin' (I'm gonna leave) / Long distance lover / Madman blues / Boogie people / Can't be satisfied / No place to go / Six days on the road / Born in Chicago / Oklahoma sweetheart / Hello little girl
CD _____ BGOCD 250
Beat Goes On / Dec '94 / Pinnacle.

BORN TO BE BAD
Shake your moneymaker / You talk too much / Highway 49 / Born to be bad / You can't catch me / I'm ready / Treat her right / I really like girls / Smokestack lightnin' / I'm movin' on
CD _____ BGOCD 224
Beat Goes On / May '94 / Pinnacle.

GEORGE THOROGOOD AND THE DESTROYERS (Thorogood, George & The Destroyers)
Who do you love / Bottom of the sea / Night time / I drink alone / One bourbon, one scotch, one beer / Alley oop / Madison blues / Bad to the bone / Sky is crying / Reelin' and rockin'
CD _____ CD 3013
Rounder / '88 / CM / Direct / ADA / Cadillac.

LIVE - LET'S WORK TOGETHER (Thorogood, George & The Destroyers)
No particular place to go / Ride on Josephine / Bad boy / Cocaine blues / If you don't start drinkin' (I'm gonna leave) / I'm ready / I'll change my style / Get a haircut / Gear jammer / Move it on over / You talk to much / Let's work together / St. Louis blues / Johnny B. Goode
CD _____ CDEMC 3718
EMI / Jul '95 / EMI.

LIVE: GEORGE THOROGOOD (Thorogood, George & The Destroyers)
Who do you love / Bottom of the sea / Night time / I drink alone / One bourbon, one scotch, one beer / Alley oop / Madison blues / Bad to the bone / Sky is crying / Reelin' and rockin'
CD _____ CDFA 3211
Fame / '93 / EMI.

MAVERICK (Thorogood, George & The Destroyers)
Gear jammer / I drink alone / Willie and the hand jive / What a price / Long gone / Dixie fried / Crawlin' kingsnake / Memphis Marie / Woman with the blues / Go go go / Ballad of Maverick
CD _____ BGOCD 223
Beat Goes On / Jun '94 / Pinnacle.

MORE GEORGE THOROGOOD & THE DESTROYERS (Thorogood, George & The Destroyers)
I'm wanted / Kids from Philly / One way ticket / Bottom of the sea / Night time / Tip on in / Goodbye baby / House of blue lights / Just can't make it / Restless
CD _____ FIEND CD 61
Demon / Mar '86 / Pinnacle / ADA.

MOVE IT ON OVER (Thorogood, George & The Destroyers)
Move it on over / Who do you love / Sky is crying / Cocaine blues / It wasn't me / That same thing / So much trouble / I'm just your Baby, please set a date / New Hawaiian boogie

CD _____ FIENDCD 58
Demon / May '90 / Pinnacle / ADA.

Those Darn Accordians

SQUEEZE THIS
CD _____ FF 70627
Flying Fish / Nov '94 / Roots / CM / Direct / ADA.

Those X-Cleavers

FIRST ALBUM/THE WAITING GAME
CD _____ OW 29313
One Way / Apr '94 / Direct / ADA.

Thought Industry

MODS CARVE THE PIG ASSASSINS
CD _____ CDZORRO 65
Metal Blade / Oct '93 / Pinnacle.

OUTER SPACE IS JUST A MARTINI AWAY
CD _____ 398414101CD
Metal Blade / Jan '96 / Plastic Head.

SONGS FOR INSERTS
CD _____ CDZORRO 45
Metal Blade / Jul '92 / Pinnacle.

Thoumire, Simon

EXHIBIT A (Thoumire, Simon & Fergus MacKenzie)
By the right / Green man / Interaction / Topless / Totally tropical / Experience the real (stop imagining) / Starjumping / Down / Overcast / Art of non-resistance
CD _____ IRCD 031
Iona / May '95 / ADA / Direct / Duncans.

WALTZES FOR PLAYBOYS
CD _____ ARADCD 102
Acoustic Radio / Mar '94 / CM.

Threadbare

FEELING OLDER FASTER
CD _____ DOG 028CD
Doghouse / Jul '95 / Plastic Head.

Threadgill, Henry

CARRY THE DAY
Come carry the day / Growing a big banana / Vivjanrondirkski / Between orchids, lillies, blind eyes and cricket / Hyla crucifer... silence of / Jenkins boys again / Wish somebody die / It's hot
CD _____ 4785062
Sony Music / Apr '95 / Sony.

MAKIN' A MOVE
Noisy flowers / Like it feels / Official silence / Refined poverty / Make hot and give / Mockingbird sin / Dirty in the right
CD _____ 4811312
Sony Jazz / Oct '95 / Sony.

SPIRIT OF NUFF...NUFF
CD _____ 120134-2
Black Saint / May '91 / Harmonia Mundi / Cadillac.

Three Blue Teardrops

ONE PART FIST
Sinner's spiritual / Rough and tumble world / Cadillac Jack / Switchblade pompadour / Wanted man / Red head gal / Ricochet rhythm rockabilly / In my own time / Jenny the generator / Vaporlock / Go, She devil / Rustbelt bop / Claimjumper blues / Another doggone Saturday night
CD _____ NERCD 075
Nervous / Mar '94 / Nervous / Magnum Music Group.

Three Chord Wonder

NOTHING MEANS NOTHING ANYMORE
CD _____ LF 155CD
Lost & Found / Sep '95 / Plastic Head.

Three Degrees

20 GREATEST HITS: THREE DEGREES
When will I see you again / Can't you see what you're doing to me / Toast of love / We're all alone / Long lost lover / Get your love back / I like being a woman / What I did for love / Standing up for love / Take good care of yourself / Dirty ol' man / Loving cup a woman needs a good man / T.S.O.P. (The sound of Philadelphia) / Another heartache / Distant lover / Together / Here I am / Year of decision (live)
CD _____ 982585-2
Pickwick/Sony Collector's Choice / Mar '94 / Carlton Home Entertainment / Pinnacle / Sony.

COLLECTION OF THEIR 20 GREATEST HITS, A
When will I see you again / Can't you see what you're doing to me / Toast of love / We're all alone / Long lost lover / Get your love back / I like being a woman / What I did for love / Standing up for love / Take good care of yourself / Dirty ol' man / Loving cup a woman needs / TSOP (The Sound Of Philadelphia) / Another heartache / Dis-

tant lover / Together / Here I am / Year of decision / Love train
CD _____ 4631882
Columbia / Oct '95 / Sony.

COMPLETE SWAN RECORDINGS
Gee baby (I'm sorry) / Do what you're supposed to do / Let's shindig / You're gonna miss me / How did that happen / Little red riding hood (that's what they call me) / I'm gonna need you / Just right for love / I'll weep for you / Don't (leave me lover) / Someone (who will be true) / Bongo's on the beach / Close your eyes / Gotta draw the line / Mine all mine / Are you satisfied / And in return / Heartbroken memories / Signs of love / Look in my eyes / Drivin' me mad / Maybe / Yours / Tales are true / I wanna be your baby / Love of my life
CD _____ NEMCD 631
Sequel / Nov '92 / BMG.

LET'S GET IT ON
Ebb tide / Trade winds / Maybe / I turn to you / Collage / I won't let you go / I do take you / Through misty eyes / You're the fool / Find my way / Grass will sing for you / Sugar on Sunday / Melting pot / Who is she (and what is she to you) / You're the one / Requiem / Stardust / Isn't it a pity / There's so much love all around me / Shades of green / Lowdown / Macarthur park
CD _____ NEMCD 753
Sequel / Sep '95 / BMG.

REALISATION
CD _____ RLBTC 004
Realisation / Oct '93 / Prism.

ROULETTE YEARS, THE
CD _____ CDICH 1041
Ichiban / Oct '93 / Koch.

THREE DEGREES... AND HOLDING, THE
Tie u up / Win, place or show / Make it easy on yourself / Lock it up / Vital signs / Tender lie / After the night is over / Are you that kind of guy
CD _____ CDICH 1041
Ichiban / Oct '93 / Koch.

VERY BEST OF THE THREE DEGREES, THE
CD _____ 74321279252
BMG / Jun '95 / BMG.

VERY BEST OF THE THREE DEGREES, THE
Sound of Philadelphia / Woman in love / Starlight / I'll never love this way again / Golden lady / When will I see you again / Dirty ol' man / Giving up, giving in / Just making love / Runner / Golden lady's theme / My simple heart / Jump the gun
CD _____ 74321339372
Camden / Jan '96 / BMG.

WHEN WILL I SEE YOU AGAIN
CD _____ HADCD 188
Javelin / Nov '95 / THE / Henry Hadaway Organisation.

WOMAN IN LOVE
CD _____ 290403
Ariola / Dec '92 / BMG.

Three Dog Night

20 GREATEST HITS
CD _____ MPG 74015
Movieplay Gold / May '93 / Target/BMG.

THAT AIN'T THE WAY TO HAVE FUN
Try a little tenderness / One / Easy to be hard / Eli's coming / Celebrate / Mama told me not to come / Out in the country / One man band / Joy to the world / Liar / Old fashioned love song / Never been to Spain / Family of man / Black and white / Pieces of April / Shamballa / Let me serenade you / Show must go on / Sure as I'm sitting / Play something sweet (brickyard blues) / Till the world ends
CD _____ VSOPCD 211
Connoisseur / Feb '95 / Pinnacle.

Three Johns

DEATH OF EVERYTHING
King is dead / Moonlight on Vermont / Spin me round / Humbug / Never and always / Bullshit, Aco / Go ahead bikini / Nonsense spews from my song machine / Down-hearted blues
CD _____ MOTCD 20
Tim / Oct '88 / Disc.

Three Man Army

MAHESHA
CD _____ REP 4057-WZ
Repertoire / Aug '91 / Pinnacle / Cadillac.

THIRD OF A LIFETIME, A
CD _____ REP 4071-QZ
Repertoire / Aug '91 / Pinnacle / Cadillac.

Three Suns

THREE SUNS VOL. 2 1949-1953
CD _____ CCD 145
Circle / Mar '95 / Jazz Music / Swift / Wellard.

THREE SUNS, THE (1949-1957)
CD _____ CCD 075
Circle / Oct '93 / Jazz Music / Swift / Wellard.

Threefold

CESARIUS ALVIM
CD _____ OMDCD 057
OMD / Sep '92 / Koch.

Threnody

AS THE HEAVENS FALL
CD _____ MASSCD 024
Massacre / Feb '94 / Plastic Head.

BEWILDERING THOUGHTS
CD _____ MASSCD 065
Massacre / Aug '95 / Plastic Head.

Threshold

LIVEDELICA
CD _____ GEPCD 1015
Giant Electric Pea / Jun '95 / Pinnacle.

PSYCHEDELICATESSEN
Sunseeker / Into the light / Under the sun / He is I am / Devoted / Tension of souls / Will to give / Babylon rising / Innocent
CD _____ GEPCD 1014
Giant Electric Pea / Feb '95 / Pinnacle.

WOUNDED LAND
Consume to live / Days of dearth / Sanity's end / Paradox / Surface of air / Mother earth / Siege of Baghdad / Keep it with mine
CD _____ GEPCD 1005
Giant Electric Pea / Aug '93 / Pinnacle.

Thrilled Skinny

SMELLS A BIT FISHY
CD _____ LOS 3CD
Artlos / Nov '93 / SRD.

Thriller U

LOVE RULE
CD _____ VPCD 1439
VP / Oct '95 / Jetstar.

ON AND ON
CD _____ MLCD 002
Mixing Lab / Jul '90 / Jetstar.

Thrillhammer

GIFTLESS
Pretty dead girl / Suffocation time / Bad trip / Laughing / Happy anniversary / Motor / Bleed / Magret / Dread / Alice's place / Jinx / Bride
CD _____ RTD 15714012
World Service / Apr '93 / Vital.

Throbbin Hoods

AMBUSH
CD _____ BMCD 076
Raw Energy / Jun '95 / Plastic Head.

Throbbing Gristle

ASSUME POWER FOCUS
CD _____ PA 016 CD
Paragoric / Nov '95 / Plastic Head.

ASSUMING POWER FOCUS
CD _____ PA 016CD
Resurrection / Jan '96 / Plastic Head.

FUNK BEYOND JAZZ
CD _____ EFA 08450CD
Dossier / Nov '93 / SRD.

GIFTGAS
CD _____ EFA 084582
Dossier / Sep '94 / SRD.

JOURNEY THROUGH A BODY
CD _____ TGCD 8
Grey Area / Oct '93 / Pinnacle.

LIVE - VOLUME 1
CD _____ TGCD 10
Grey Area / Apr '93 / Pinnacle.

LIVE - VOLUME 2
CD _____ TGCD 11
Grey Area / Apr '93 / Pinnacle.

LIVE - VOLUME 3
CD _____ TGCD 12
Grey Area / Apr '93 / Pinnacle.

LIVE - VOLUME 4
CD _____ TGCD 13
Grey Area / Apr '93 / Pinnacle.

ONCE UPON A TIME
CD _____ OBESSCD 2
Jungle / Oct '94 / Disc.

THROBBING GRISTLE
CD _____ TGCD 1
Mute / '88 / Disc.

Throne Of Ahaz

NIFELHEIM
CD _____ NFR 008
No Fashion / Oct '94 / Plastic Head.

Throneberry

TROT OUT THE ENCORES
On the strobe flume / Spellbinder / Nectarine / Hooray for everything / Unsere serenade / Cut to the chase / Widow / Drops of moxie / New year's routine / Sealboy / Truth serum / Sip of beauty

CD _____ A 086D
Alias / Jan '96 / Vital.

Throwing Muses

CURSE, THE
Manic depression / Counting backwards / Fish / Hate my way / Furious / Devil's roof / Snailhead / Fireplie / Finished / Take / Say goodbye / Mania / Two step / Delicate cutters / Cotton mouth / Pearl / Vic / Bea
CD _____ TAD 2019CD
4AD / Nov '92 / Disc.

HOUSE TORNADO
Colder / Mexican women / River / Juno / Marriage tree / Run letter / Saving grace / Drive / Downtown / Giant / Walking in the dark / Garoux des larmes (CD only) / Pools in eyes (CD only) / Feeling (CD only) / Soap and water (CD only) / And a she-wolf after the war (CD only) / You cage (CD only)
CD _____ CAD 802 CD
4AD / Mar '88 / Disc.

HUNKPAPA
Devil's roof / Dizzy / Dragonhead / Fall down / Angel / Burrow / Bea / No parachutes / Say goodbye / I'm alive / Mania / Take / Santa Claus (CD only)
CD _____ CAD 901CD
4AD / Jan '89 / Disc.

REAL RAMONA, THE
Counting backwards / Him dancing / Red shoes / Graffiti / Golden thing / Ellen West / Dylan / Honk in her head / Not too soon / Honeychain / Say goodbye / Two step
CD _____ CAD 1002C
4AD / Feb '91 / Disc.

RED HEAVEN
Furious / Fireplie / Dio / Dirty water / Stroll / Pearl / Summer St. / Vic / Backroad / Visit / Dovey / Rosetta stone / Carnival wig
CD _____ CAD 2013CD
4AD / Aug '92 / Disc.

THROWING MUSES
Call me / Green / Hate my way / Vicky's box / Rabbits dying / America (she can't say no) / Fear / Stand up / Soul soldier / Delicate cutters
CD _____ CAD 607 CD
4AD / Nov '86 / Disc.

UNIVERSITY
Bright yellow gun / Start / Hazing / Shimmer / Calm down, come down / Crabtown / No way in hell / Surf cowboy / That's all you wanted / Teller / University / Snakeface / Flood / Fever few
CD _____ CADD 5002CD
CD _____ CAD 5002CD
4AD / Jan '95 / Disc.

Thrum

RIFFERAMA
CD _____ FIRECD 38
Fire / Sep '94 / Disc.

Thug Life

THUG LIFE VOL. 1
Bury me a G / Don't get it twisted / Shit don't stop (featuring YNV) / Pour out a little liquor / Stay true / How long will they mourn me (featuring Nate Dogg) / Under pressure / Street fame / Cradle to the grave / Str8 ballin'
CD _____ 654492360-2
Interscope / Nov '94 / Warner Music.

Thulbion

TWILIGHT BOUND
King's reel/The perfect host/Boys of portaferry/Trad reel / Twilight / St. Gilbert's hornpipe/The fiddler's wife/Chromatic hornpipe / Annie / John D. Burgess/Major Nickerson's fancy/Dick Gossip's reel / James F. Dickie/J.F. Dickie's delight / Sheilis / Branden's centennial waltz / Waltz for Mary Ann / Raemona / Gravel walk / Andy Renwick's ferret / Old mountain road / Time for thought / Theodore Napier / Laird of Mackintosh / Earl of Lauderdale / Little daisy / North king street / Lady on the island / Kilavil reel / Far from home / Paddy on the turnpike / Loretta / Frank and Maureen Robb / Grew's hill / Duncan Black's hornpipe / Doon hingin' tie / Eeles' dream
CD _____ CDTRAX 088
Greentrax / Jan '95 / Conifer / Duncans / ADA / Direct.

Thunder

BACKSTREET SYMPHONY
She's so fine / Dirty love / Don't wait for me / Higher ground / Until my dying day / Backstreet symphony / Love walked in / Englishman on holiday / Girl's going out of her head / Gimme some lovin' / Distant thunder (Not on album.)
CD _____ CDEMC 3570
EMI / Feb '90 / EMI.

BACKSTREET SYMPHONY/
BACKSTREET SYMPHONY (LIVE)
She's so fine / Dirty love / Don't wait for me / Higher ground / Until my dying day / Backstreet symphony (Love walked in / Englishman on holiday, in / Girl's going out of her head / Gimme some lovin' / Distant thunder

/ Another shot of love (Live) / Girl's going out of her head (live) / Englishman on holiday (Live) / Until my dying day (live) / Fired up (Live) / Dirty love (live) / She's so fine (live) / Backstreet symphony (live) / Higher ground (live) / Don't wait for me (live)
CD Set _____ TOCP 6729
EMI / Oct '91 / EMI.

BEHIND CLOSED DOORS
Moth to the flame / Fly on the wall / I'll be waiting / River of pain / Future train / Till the river runs dry / Stand up / Preaching from a chair / Castles in the sand / Too scared to live / Ball and chain / It happened in this town
CD _____ CDEMD 1076
EMI / Jan '95 / EMI.

LAUGHING ON JUDGEMENT DAY
Does it feel like love / Everybody wants her / Low life in high places / Laughing on judgement day / Empty city / Today the world stopped turning / Long way from home / Fire to ice / Feeding the flame / Better man / Moment of truth / Flawed to perfection / Like a satellite / Baby I'll be gone
CD _____ CDEMD 1035
EMI / Feb '94 / EMI.

THEIR FINEST HOUR (AND A BIT)
Dirty love / River of pain / Love walked in / Everybody wants her / In a broken dream / Higher ground ('95) / Backstreet symphony / Better man / Gimme shelter / Like a satellite / Low life in high places / Stand up / Once in a lifetime / Gimme some lovin' / Castles in the sand / She's so fine
CD _____ CDEMD 1086
EMI / Sep '05 / EMI.

Thunderballs

SUMMER HOLIDAY
CD _____ SSHD 2
Hush / Jul '94 / Pinnacle.

Thunderclap Newman

HOLLYWOOD DREAM
Repertoire / Aug '91 / Pinnacle / Cadillac.
CD _____ REP 4065-WP

Thunderpussy

SAMPLER VOL. 1
CD _____ TNO 5102CD
Ichiban / Jan '94 / Koch.

Thunders, Johnny

BOOTLEGGING THE BOOTLEGGERS
You can't put your arms around a memory / Personality crisis / Sad vacation / I can tell / Little queenie / Stepping stone / As tears go by
CD _____ FREUDCD 30
Jungle / Jan '90 / Disc.

COPY CATS (Thunders, Johnny & Patti Palladin)
CD _____ FREUDCD 20
Jungle / Jun '88 / Disc.

D.T.K. (Thunders, Johnny & The Heartbreakers)
CD _____ FREUDCD 4
Jungle / Oct '94 / Disc.

HURT ME
CD _____ DOJOCD 217
Dojo / Jun '95 / BMG.

IN COLD BLOOD
CD _____ DOJOCD 221
Dojo / May '90 / BMG.

L.A.M.F. - The LOST '77 MIXES (Thunders, Johnny & The Heartbreakers)
CD _____ FREUDCD 044
Jungle / Jul '94 / Disc.

LIVE ALBUM
Pipeline / Countdown live / Personality crisis / Little bit of whore / M.I.A. / Stepping stone (Live) / So alone / Endless party / Copy cats (live) / Don't mess with cupid / Born to lose / Too much junkie business (live) / Chinese rocks / Pills
CD _____ CDGRAM 70
Cherry Red / Oct '93 / Pinnacle.

LIVE AT MOTHERS (Thunders, Johnny & The Heartbreakers)
CD _____ 422168
New Rose / May '94 / Direct / ADA.

LIVE IN JAPAN
CD _____ ESDCD 226
Essential / Nov '94 / Total/BMG.

QUE SERA SERA
CD _____ FREUDCD 049
Jungle / Nov '94 / Disc.

SO ALONE
Pipeline / You can't put your arms around a memory / Great big kiss / Ask me no questions / Leave me alone / Daddy rollin' stone / London boys / Untouchable / Subway train / Downtown / Dead or alive / Hurtin' / So alone / Wizard
CD _____ 7599269822
WEA / Aug '92 / Warner Music.

STATIONS OF THE CROSS
Wipeout / In cold blood / Just another girl / Too much junkie business / Sad vacation /

Who needs girls / Do you love me / So alone / Seven day weekend / Chinese rocks / Re-entry interlude / Voodoo dub / Surfer jam / Just because I'm white / One track mind (dub) / Little London boys / Stepping stone / I don't mind Mr. Kowalski / Creature from E.T. rap / Rather be with the boys
CD _____ RE 146CD
Reach Out International / Nov '94 / Jetstar.

STATIONS OF THE CROSS (REVISITED) (Thunders, Johnny & The Heartbreakers)
CD _____ RRCD 188
Receiver / Jun '94 / Grapevine.

TOO MUCH JUNKIE BUSINESS
CD _____ RE 118CD
Reach Out International / Nov '94 / Jetstar.

Thundersteel

THUNDERSTEEL
CD _____ BMCD 53
Black Mark / Aug '94 / Plastic Head.

Thuresson, Svante

LIVE
CD _____ SITCD 9203
Sittel / Aug '94 / Cadillac / Jazz Music.

Thurman

LUX
She's a man / English tea / Cheap holiday / Famous / Clowns / It would be / Now I'm a man / Flavour euphoria / Lewis Brightworth / Automatic thinker / Talk to myself / Strung out / Untitled
CD _____ RIGHT 005CD
Righteous / Oct '95 / Vital.

Ti Jaz

EN CONCERT
CD _____ Y225027
Silex / Jun '93 / ADA.

MUSIQUE BRETONNE AUJOURD 'HUI
CD _____ Y 225027CD
Silex / Aug '93 / ADA.

MUSIQUES DE BASSE BRETAGNE
CD _____ MW 4005CD
Music & Words / Jul '94 / ADA / Direct.

REVES SAUVAGES
CD _____ CD 834
Diffusion Breizh / May '93 / ADA.

Tia

TIA'S SIMCHA SONGS
CD _____ GV 167CD
Global Village / May '94 / ADA / Direct.

Tiajin Buddhist Music...

BUDDHIST MUSIC OF TIANJIN (Tiajin Buddhist Music Ensemble)
CD _____ NI 5416
Nimbus / Mar '95 / Nimbus.

Tiamat

ASTRAL SLEEP, THE
CD _____ CM 97222
Century Media / Sep '94 / Plastic Head.

SLEEPING BEAUTY (LIVE IN ISRAEL), THE
CD _____ CM 77065-2
Century Media / May '94 / Plastic Head.

SUMERIAN CRY
CD _____ CORE 009CD
Metalcore / Jan '92 / Plastic Head.

WILDHONEY
CD _____ CM 77080CD
Century Media / Oct '94 / Plastic Head.

Tibbetts, Steve

BIG MAP IDEA
Black mountain side / Black year / Big idea / Wish / Station / Start / Mile 234 / 100 moons / Wait / Three letters
CD _____ 8392532
ECM / Oct '89 / New Note.

EXPLODED VIEW
Name everything / Another year / Clear day / Your cat / Forget / Drawing down the moon / X festival / Metal summer / Assembly field
CD _____ 8311092
ECM / Jan '87 / New Note.

FALL OF US ALL, THE
Dzogchen punks / Full moon dogs / Nyemma / Formless / Roam and spy / Hellbound train / All for nothing / Fade away / Drinking lesson / Burnt offering / Travel alone
CD _____ 5211442
ECM / Apr '94 / New Note.

NORTHERN SONG
Form walking / Big wind / Aerial view / Nine doors, breathing space
CD _____ 8293782
ECM / Oct '89 / New Note.

SAFE JOURNEY
Test / Climbing / Running / Night again / My last chance / Vision / Any minute / Mission / Burning up / Going somewhere
CD _____ 8174382
ECM / Oct '89 / New Note.

YR
UR / Sphexes / Ten years / One day / Three primates / You and it / Alien lounge / Ten year dance
CD _____ 8352452
ECM / Aug '88 / New Note.

Tibetan Dixie

NOTHING TOO SERIOUS
CD _____ LRJ 263
Larrikin / Oct '93 / Roots / Direct / ADA / CM.

Tickell, Kathryn

BORDERLANDS
Mary the maid (Medley) / David's hornpipe (Medley) / Sidlaw Hills (Medley) / Brafferton Village / Stellgreen (Medley) / Loch rannoch (Medley) / Gypsy's lullaby (Medley) / Flowers of the forest (Medley) / Alston flower show (Medley) / Claudio's Polka (Medley) / Tents hornpipe (Medley) / Walker (Medley) / Lord Gordon's reel (Medley) / Robson (Medley) / Roly gentle (Medley) / Troy's wedding (Medley) / Tartar frigate (Medley) / Wark football team (Medley)
CD _____ CROCD 210
Black Crow / Feb '89 / Roots / Jazz Music / CM.

COMMON GROUND
Walsh's hornpipe / Dorrington lads / Richard Moscrop's waltzes / Another knight / Mrs. Bolowski's / Neil Gow's lament / Andrew Knight's favourite / Shining pool / Outclassed / Glen Ain / Bill Charlton's fancy / Fenham / Catch a penny fox / Bowmont water / Geoff Heslop's reel / New rigged ship / Remember me / Rafferty's reel / Wild hills o' Wannies
CD _____ CROCD 220
Black Crow / Feb '89 / Roots / Jazz Music / CM.

KATHRYN TICKELL BAND
CD _____ CROCD 227
Black Crow / Jun '91 / Roots / Jazz Music / CM.

NORTHUMBRIAN SMALL PIPES & FIDDLE
CD _____ CDSDL 343
Saydisc / Oct '92 / Harmonia Mundi / ADA / Direct.

SIGNS
CD _____ CROCD 230
Black Crow / Mar '94 / Roots / Jazz Music / CM.

Tickell, Mike

WARKSBURN (Tickell, Mike/Kathryn Tickell/Martin Simpson)
CD _____ CROCD 229
Black Crow / Dec '94 / Roots / Jazz Music / CM.

Tickled Pink

TICKLED PINK
CD _____ PINK 9301CD
Pink Kitten / Jan '94 / ADA.

Tierra Caliente

MESTIZA
CD _____ MW 3005CD
Music & Words / Aug '94 / ADA / Direct.

Tierre Sur

AMOR AND REBELLION
CD _____ CD 9402
Roots Collective / May '95 / SRD / Jetstar / Roots Collective.

Tiger

BAM BAM
CD _____ RASCD 3042
Ras / Sep '88 / Jetstar / Greensleeves / SRD / Direct.

LOVE AFFAIR
CD _____ RRTGCD 7787
Rohit / Jul '90 / Jetstar.

ME NAME TIGER
CD _____ RASCD 3021
Ras / '88 / Jetstar / Greensleeves / SRD / Direct.

RAM DANCEHALL
CD _____ VPCD 1052
VP / '89 / Jetstar.

TIGER
CD _____ RTCD 901153
Line / Nov '92 / CM / Grapevine / ADA / Conifer / Direct.

TOUCH IS A MOVE
CD _____ CIDM 1056
Mango / Aug '90 / Vital / PolyGram.

Tiger Lillies

BIRTHS, DEATHS & MARRIAGES
Beatman / Hell / Normal / Heroin and cocaine / Prison house blues / Jackie / Despite / Autumn leaves / Lager lout / Open your legs / Down and out / Tears / Her room / Flowers / War / Obscene / You're world / Sense of sentiment / Wake up / Repulsion / Sodsville / Bones / Circle line / Haunting me / Lili Marlene
CD _____ TIGER 1
Gee Street / Jul '94 / PolyGram.

Tiger Moth

HOWLING MOTH
Sloe benga / Polka volta / Olympia / Conquer your glasses / First wife / La bastringue / Gone with the lind / Flor marchita / Mustaphas horne schottische / Moth to California / Sestrina
CD _____ FMSD 5012
Rogue / Apr '88 / Sterns.

Tigertailz

BEZERK
Sick sex / Love bomb baby / I can fight dirty too / Noise level critical / Heaven / Love overload / Action city / Twist and shake / Squeeze it dry / Call of the wild
CD _____ CDMFN 96
Music For Nations / Jan '90 / Pinnacle.

YOUNG AND CRAZY
Star attraction / Hollywood killer / Living without you / Shameless / City kids / Shoot to kill / Turn me on / She's too hot / Young and crazy / Fall in love again
CD _____ CDMFN 78
Music For Nations / Aug '89 / Pinnacle.

Tight Fit

BACK TO THE 60'S - 60 NON STOP DANCING HITS
CD _____ CDMFP 6075
Music For Pleasure / Aug '89 / EMI.

BACK TO THE SIXTIES
Lion sleeps tonight / Dancing in the street / Satisfaction / You really got me / All day and all of the night / Do wah diddy diddy / Pretty flamingo / Back is black / Bend me, shape me / High in the sky / Mr. Tambourine man / Proud Mary / O prety woman / Letter / Baby let me take you home / Baby come back / How do you do it / I like it / Tossing and turning / Hippy hippy shake / Mony mony / Let's hang on / Sherry / Big girls don't cry / Walk like a man / Rag doll / Dawn / Yes I will / Stay / Just one look / Here I go again / I'm alive / There's a kind of hush / No milk today / Must to avoid / Hold tight / Legend of Xanadu / Sweets for my sweet / Sugar and spice / When you walk in the room / Needles and pins / Fantasy island
CD _____ 5501172
Spectrum/Karussell / Oct '93 / PolyGram / THE.

BEST OF TIGHT FIT, THE
CD _____ EMPRCD 570
Emporio / May '95 / THE / Disc / CM.

Tikaram, Tanita

ANCIENT HEART
Good tradition / Cathedral song / Sighing Innocents / I love you / World outside your window / For all these years / Twist in my sobriety / Poor cow / He likes the sun / Valentine heart / Preyed upon
CD _____ 2438772
WEA / Feb '95 / Warner Music.

ELEVEN KINDS OF LONELINESS
You make the whole world cry / Elephant / Trouble / I grant you / Heal you / To drink the rainbow / Out on the town / Hot stones / Men and women / Any reason / Love don't need no tyranny / Way that I want you
CD _____ 9031764272
East West / Mar '92 / Warner Music.

EVERYBODY'S ANGEL
Only the ones we love / Deliver me / This story in me / To wish this / Mud in any water / Sunface / Never known / This stranger / Swear by me / Hot pork sandwiches / Me in mind / Sometime with me / I love the heaven's solo / I'm going home
CD _____ 9031734982
East West / Feb '91 / Warner Music.

LOVERS IN THE CITY
CD _____ 4509988042
East West / Feb '95 / Warner Music.

SWEET KEEPER
Once and not speak / It all come back today / Sunset's arrived / I owe all to you / Harm in your hands / Thursday's child / We almost got it together / Little sister leaving town / Love story
CD _____ 9031708002
WEA / '89 / Warner Music.

Til, Sonny

SOLO FEATURING EDNA MCGRIFF
My prayer / I never knew (I could love anybody) / Fool's world / You never cared for me / For all we know / Blame it on yourself / Proud of you / No other love / Night has

come / I only have eyes for you / Once in a while / Good / Pick-a-dilly / That's how I feel without you / Lovebirds / Congratulations to someone / (Danger) Soft shoulders / Have you heard / Lonely wine / Come on home / First of Summer / Panama Joe / Night and day / Shimmy time / So long
CD _____ NEMCD 737
Sequel / Mar '95 / BMG.

Tilbury, John

DAVE SMITH'S FIRST PIANO CONCERT
CD _____ MR 14
Matchless / '90 / These / ReR Megacorp / Cadillac.

Tillet, Louis

CAST OF ASPERSIONS, A
CD _____ CGAS 812CD
Normal/Okra / May '94 / Direct / ADA.

EGO TRIPPING AT THE GATES OF HELL
CD _____ CGAS 802CD
Normal/Okra / May '94 / Direct / ADA.

LETTERS TO A DREAM
CD _____ CGAS 816CD
Normal/Okra / May '94 / Direct / ADA.

MIDNIGHT RAIN
CD _____ RTS 18
Return To Sender / Aug '95 / Direct / ADA.

RETURN TO SENDER FESTIVAL TOUR
CD _____ NORMAL 175CD
Normal/Okra / Nov '94 / Direct / ADA.

UGLY TRUTH
CD _____ RTS 5
Normal/Okra / Jul '94 / Direct / ADA.

Tillis, Pam

ALL OF THIS LOVE
Deep down / Mandolin rain / Sunset red and pale moonlight / It's lonely out there / River and the highway / You can't have a good time without me / Betty's got a bass boat / Tequila mockingbird / No two ways about it / All of this love
CD _____ 07822187992
Arista / Nov '95 / BMG.

HOMEWARD LOOKING ANGEL
How gone is goodbye / Shake the sugar tree / Do you know where your man is / Cleopatra, Queen of denial / Love is only human / Rough and tumble heart / Let that pony run / Fine, fine, very fine love / We've tried everything else / Homeward looking angel
CD _____ 07822186492
Arista / Oct '93 / BMG.

SWEETHEART'S DANCE
CD _____ 7822187582
RCA / Apr '95 / BMG.

Tillotson, Johnny

ALL HIS EARLY HITS - AND MORE
Poetry in motion / It keeps right on a-hurtin' / Send me the pillow that you dream on / Without you / You can never stop me loving you / We'll I'm your man / Dreamy eyes / True true happiness / Love is blind / Why do I love you so / Never let me go / Earth angel / Pledging my love / Princess, princess / Jimmy's girl / (Little sparrow) his true love said goodbye / Cutie pie / She gave sweet love to me / What'll I do / I can't help it (if I'm still in love with you) / I'm so lonesome I could cry / Out of my mind / Empty feeling / Judy Judy Judy / Funny how time slips away / Very good year for girls / Lonely street / I got a feeling / Lonesome town / I fall to pieces
CD _____ CDCHD 946
Ace / Jul '90 / Pinnacle / Cadillac / Complete/Pinnacle.

FABULOUS JOHNNY TILLOTSON, THE
Poetry in motion / It keeps right on a-hurtin' / Dreamy eyes / True true happiness / Why do I love you so / Jimmy's girl / Without you / Send me the pillow that you dream on / I can't help it (if I'm still in love with you) / Out of my mind / You can never stop me loving you / Funny how time slips away
CD _____ CDFAB 003
Ace / Aug '91 / Pinnacle / Cadillac / Complete/Pinnacle.

HIT SINGLE COLLECTABLES
Disky / Apr '94 / THE / BMG / Discovery / Pinnacle.
CD _____ DISK 4507

SHE UNDERSTANDS ME/THAT'S MY STYLE
She understands me / That's love / Busted / Willow tree / Tomorrow / Little boy / To be a child again / That's when it hurts the most / More than before / Island of dreams / Yellow bird / Take this hammer / Heartaches by the number / Without your sweet lips on mine / Countin' my teardrops / You don't want my love / Just one time / Race is on / Things / Me, myself and I / Oh, lonesome me / Then I'll count again / I've seen better days / Your mem'ry comes along
CD _____ CDCHD 345

Ace / Feb '92 / Pinnacle / Cadillac / Complete/Pinnacle.

TALK BACK TREMBLING LIPS/THE TILLOTSON TOUCH
Talk back trembling lips / Blue velvet / Danke schon / What am I gonna do / My little world / I can't stop loving you / Worried guy / Another you / Rhythm of the rain / All alone am I / Please don't go away / Blowin' in the wind / I rise, I fall / On the sunny side of the street / Then you can tell me goodbye / This ole house / Suff'rin from a heartache / I've got you under my skin / Worry / I'm watching my watch / When I lost you / Always / Cold cold heart / Jailer bring me water
CD _____ CDCHD 331
Ace / Aug '91 / Pinnacle / Cadillac / Complete/Pinnacle.

YOU'RE THE REASON
Talk back trembling lips / Another you / Worried guy / Please don't go away / I rise, I fall / Worry / Heartaches by the number / She understands me / Angel / Suff'rin from a heartache / (Wait 'till you see) My gidget / No love at all / More than before / Blue velvet / You're the reason / Dreamy eyes / Red roses for a blue lady / When I lost you / Oh, lonesome me / Danke schoen / It keeps right on a-hurtin' / You can tell me goodbye / Things / All alone am I / Cold, cold heart / Always / Without you / Race is on / I can't stop loving you / Rhythm of the rain
CD _____ CDCH 618
Ace / Jan '96 / Pinnacle / Cadillac / Complete/Pinnacle.

Tilston, Steve

AND SO IT GOES
CD _____ HR 01CD
Hubris / Jul '95 / ADA.

LIFE BY MISADVENTURE
These days / Nowhere to hide / Here comes the night / I call your name / Lazy tango / Life by misadventure / Lovers and dreamers / Polonaise / Tsetse fly shuffle / Sometimes in this life
CD _____ RRACD 001
Run River / Nov '90 / Direct / ADA / CM.

MUSIC OF O'CAROLAN, THE (Tilston, Steve & Duck Baker/Maggie Boyle/Ali Anderson)
CD _____ SHAN 97023CD
Shanachie / Aug '93 / Koch / ADA / Greensleeves.

OF MOOR AND MESA (Tilston, Steve & Maggie Boyle)
CD _____ GLCD 3087
Green Linnet / Feb '95 / Roots / CM / Direct / ADA.

SWANS AT COOLE
Rhapsody / Wind that shakes the barley / Ladies pantalettes / Planxty corcoron / Monaghan jig / Prelude / Ernie Clarke's lament / Lullaby
CD _____ RRACD 011
Run River / Nov '90 / Direct / ADA / CM.

Tilt

I PUT A SMELL ON YOU
CD _____ EFA 125412
Celtic Circle / Dec '95 / SRD.

TILL IT KILLS
CD _____ FAT 521CD
Fat Wreck Chords / Jun '95 / Plastic Head.

Timber

PARTS AND LABOR
There's always 1 and 9 / At the same time / I'm 30, I'm having a heart attack / Evidence is shifting (On CD only) / Bad education / Belay that (On CD only) / Crankcase (On CD only) / Fatal flaw (On CD only) / Move / Real NY (On CD only) / Stupid reasons / Deer slayer (On CD only) / Reversivle fortune / Puddle / Robins make eggs blus / Passage from Pakistan / Acid test/Pads / Sugary peppery (On CD only)
CD _____ R 3142
Rift / Mar '94 / Pinnacle.

Timbuk 3

HUNDRED LOVERS, A
Sunshine is dangerous / Hundred lovers / Just wanna funk with your mind / Legalize your love / Cynical / Not yet done / Prey / Inside out / Kitchen fire / Shotgun wedding
CD _____ 72902 103342
Windham Hill / Apr '95 / Pinnacle / BMG / ADA.

LIVE
CD _____ WM 1012
Watermelon / Jun '93 / ADA / Direct.

Time 1010

TIME 1010
CD _____ TIME 1010
Time / Apr '94 / Jetstar / Pinnacle.

Time Frequency

DOMINATION
CD _____ KGBD 500
Internal Affairs / Jun '94 / BMG.

Timeless All Stars

ESSENCE
CD _____ DCD 4006
Delos / '88 / Conifer.

Times

ALTERNATIVE COMMERCIAL CROSSOVER
Obligatory grunge song / Finnegans break / How honest are Pearl Jam / Sweetest girl / Ballad of Georgie Best / Lundi bleu (The Grid's Praise the Lord mix) / Palace in the sun / Sorry, I've written a melody / Finnegans break (Corporate rock mix) / Whole world's turning scarface / All I want is you to care
CD _____ CRECD 137
Creation / Apr '93 / 3MV / Vital.

BEAT TORTURE
CD _____ CRECD 038
Creation / May '94 / 3MV / Vital.

ENJOY/UP AGAINST IT
CD _____ CREV 029CD
Rev-Ola / Nov '93 / 3MV / Vital.

ET DIEU CREA LA FEMME
Septieme ciel / Chagrin d'amour / Baisers voles / Sucette / Extase / Aurore boreale / Volupte / Pour Kylie / 1990 Anee erotique
CD _____ CRECD 070
Creation / May '93 / 3MV / Vital.

GO WITH THE TIMES/POP GOES ART
Picture gallery / Biff bang pow / It's time / If now is the answer / New arrangement / Looking at the world through dark shades / I helped Patrick McGoohan escape / Pop goes art / Miss London / Sun never sets / Easy as pie / This is tomorrow / Red with purple flashes / My Andy Warhol poster / Pinstripes / Jokes on Zandra / Nowhere to run / No hard feelings / You can get it / Man from U.N.C.L.E. (theme) / Reflections in an imperfect mirror
CD _____ CREV 030CD
Rev-Ola / Jan '94 / 3MV / Vital.

I HELPED PATRICK MCGOOHAN ESCAPE
Big painting / Stranger than fiction / Danger man / I helped Patrick McGoohan escape / All systems are go / Up against it
CD _____ CREV 006CD
Rev-Ola / Nov '92 / 3MV / Vital.

LIVE AT THE ASTRADOME
CD _____ CRELPCD 123
Creation / Apr '92 / 3MV / Vital.

PINK BALL, BROWN BALL, RED BALL
CD _____ CRECD 073
Creation / Jul '91 / 3MV / Vital.

PURE
CD _____ CRECD 091
Creation / Mar '91 / 3MV / Vital.

THIS IS LONDON/HELLO EUROPE
CD _____ CREV 028CD
Rev-Ola / Oct '93 / 3MV / Vital.

Timeshard

CRYSTAL OSCILLATIONS
CD _____ BARKCD 004
Planet Dog / Jun '94 / 3MV / Vital.

Timmons, Bobby

THIS HERE IS BOBBY TIMMONS
CD _____ OJCCD 104
Original Jazz Classics / Oct '92 / Wellard / Jazz Music / Cadillac / Complete/Pinnacle.

Timmy T

TIME AFTER TIME
CD _____ TIMCD 1
Dino / Jul '91 / Pinnacle / 3MV.

Tin Machine

TIN MACHINE
Heaven's in here / Tin machine / Prisoner of love / Crack city / I can't read / Under the God / Amazing / Working class hero / Bus stop / Pretty thing / Video crime / Run (not on LP) / Sacrifice yourself (not on LP) / Baby can dance / Bus stop (live country version)
CD _____ CDVUS 99
Virgin / Nov '95 / EMI.

Tin Pots

DREAMS & NIGHTMARES
CD _____ TP 3
Tin Pot Productions / Apr '95 / SRD.

Tindersticks

LIVE AT THE BLOOMSBURY
El diabolo en el ojo / Night in / Talk to me / She's gone / My sister / No more affairs / City slickers / Sleepy song / Jism / Drunktank / Mistakes / Tiny tears / Raindrops / For those

CD _____ 5285972
This Way Up / Sep '95 / PolyGram / SRD.

SECOND ALBUM
El Diablo en El Ojo / Night in / My sister / Tiny tears / Snowy in F# minor / Seaweed / Vertrauen 2 / Talk to me / No more affairs / Singing / Travelling light / Cherry blossoms / She's gone / Mistakes / Vertrauen 3 / Sleepy song
CD _____ 5263032
This Way Up / Apr '95 / PolyGram / SRD.

TINDERSTICKS, THE
Nectar / Tyed / Sweet sweet man / Whiskey and water / Blood / City sickness / Patchwork / Marbles / Walt blues / Milky teeth / Pt two / Jism / Piano song / Tie dye / Raindrops / Pt three / Her / Tea stain / Drunk tank / Paco de Renaldo's dream / Not knowing
CD _____ 5183062
This Way Up / Oct '93 / PolyGram / SRD.

Ting, Li Xiang
SOUL OF CHINA
CD _____ CDSV 1337
Voyager / Jun '93 / Discovery.

Tingstad, Eric
GIVE AND TAKE (Tingstad, Eric & Nancy Rumbel)
CD _____ ND 61036
Narada / Jul '93 / New Note / ADA.

IN THE GARDEN (Tingstad, Eric & Nancy Rumbel)
Gardener / Bonsai picnic / Ghostwood / Parterre / Harvest / Hanging in Babylon / Big weather / Iris in moonlight / Medicine tree / Roses for Jassie / Monticello
CD _____ CD 4004
Narada / Jun '92 / New Note / ADA.

SENSE OF PLACE, A
Appalachia calling / Monogahela / Sense of place / Spirit of Rydal Mount / Magnolia / Sovereign of the sea / Castle by the lough / Sissinghurst / American blend / Craftsman / Moonlight blue
CD _____ ND 61048
Narada / Jul '95 / New Note / ADA.

STAR OF WONDER (Tingstad, Eric & Nancy Rumbel)
CD _____ ND 61043
Narada / Oct '94 / New Note / ADA.

Tinkerbell's Dope Ring
BEETMAKESPITPINK
CD _____ FLOP 2
Floppy Records / Jul '93 / Plastic Head.

Tinklers
CRASH
Hank Greenberg and Jackie Robinson / Guru / Born again / Samiland love story / Foreign exchange student / Tools of caution / Library song / Eileen / Knick knack paddywhack / Deep inside / Bats / Barney Clark / I'm stickin' with you / They call the wind Mariah / Fun, fun, fun in the sun, sun, sun / Dog sounds
CD _____ SHIMMY 065CD
Shimmy Disc / Aug '93 / Vital.

Tiny Tim
RESURRECTION - TIPTOE THROUGH THE TULIPS
Tiptoe through the tulips / Sweet Rosie O'Grady / Shine on harvest moon / Baby face / Till we meet again / It's a long way to Tipperary / Prisoner of love / Those were the days / Pennies from Heaven / When you wore a tulip / Tiny bubbles / When the saints go marching in / Just a gigolo / Happy days are here again / Bill Bailey, won't you please come home
CD _____ BCD 15409
Bear Family / Dec '87 / Rollercoaster / Direct / CM / Swift / ADA.

Tippett, Keith
DEDICATED TO YOU, BUT YOU WEREN'T
CD _____ REP 4227-WP
Repertoire / Aug '91 / Pinnacle / Cadillac.

MUJICIAN III (AUGUST AIR)
CD _____ FMPCD 12
FMP / Feb '89 / Cadillac.

Tir Na Nog
STRONG IN THE SUN
Free ride / Teesside / Strong in the sun / Wind was high / In the morning / Love lost / Most magical / Fall of day
CD _____ EDCD 336
Edsel / Oct '91 / Pinnacle / ADA.

TEAR AND A SMILE, THE
CD _____ EDCD 334
Edsel / Sep '91 / Pinnacle / ADA.

TIR NA NOG
Time is like a promise / Mariner blues / Daisy lady / Tir na nog / Aberdeen Angus / Looking up / Boat song / Our love will not

decay / Hey friend / Dance of years / Live a day / Piccadilly / Dante
CD _____ BGOCD 53
Beat Goes On / '89 / Pinnacle.

Tiramakhan Ensemble
SONGS FROM GAMBIA
CD _____ SOW 90128
Sounds Of The World / Sep '94 / Target/ BMG.

Titan Force
WINNER/LOSER
CD _____ SHARK 021CD
Shark / '92 / Plastic Head.

Titanic
TITANIC
CD _____ REP 4151-WZ
Repertoire / Aug '91 / Pinnacle / Cadillac.

Titiyo
THIS IS
This is / Back and forth / Hot gold / Deep down underground / Make my day / Way you make me feel / Spinnin' / Human climate / Defended / Never let me go / Rain in the moon
CD _____ 74321 18882-2
Arista / Jan '94 / BMG.

Tittle, Jimmy
GREATEST HITS
CD _____ 473924 2
Dixie Frog / Aug '93 / Magnum Music Group.

Titus Groan
TITUS GROAN...PLUS
It wasn't for you / Hall of bright carvings / Liverpool / I can't change / It's all up with us / Fuschia / Open the door homer / Woman of the world
CD _____ SEECD 260
See For Miles/C5 / Sep '89 / Pinnacle.

Tjader, Cal
A FUEGO VIVO
CD _____ CCD 4176
Concord Jazz / Jul '88 / New Note.

BLACK ORCHID
Mi china / Close your eyes / Mambo at the "M" / Contigo / Bonita / Lady is a tramp / Black orchid / Happiness is a thing called Joe / I've waited so long / Out of nowhere / Guajira at the blackhawk / I want to be happy / Nearness of you / Pete Kelly's blues / Minor goof / Undecided / Philadelphia mambo / Flamingo / Stompin' at the savoy / Laura / Lullaby of birdland
CD _____ FCD 24730
Fantasy / Jun '94 / Pinnacle / Jazz Music / Wellard / Cadillac.

GOOD VIBES
Guarachi guaro / Doxy / Shoshana / Speak low / Broadway / Cuban fantasy / Good vibes
CD _____ CCD 4247
Concord Picante / Apr '90 / New Note.

JAZZ MASTERS
CD _____ 5218582
Verve / Apr '94 / PolyGram.

LA ONDA VA BIEN
CD _____ CCD 4113
Concord Jazz / '88 / New Note.

MAMBO WITH TJADER
CD _____ OJCCD 271
Original Jazz Classics / Nov '95 / Wellard / Jazz Music / Cadillac / Complete/Pinnacle.

MONTEREY CONCERTS
CD _____ PCD 24026
Pablo / Oct '93 / Jazz Music / Cadillac / Complete/Pinnacle.

SOUL SAUCE
Soul sauce / Soul bird / Spring is here / Tanya / Joao / Maramoor mambo / Pantano / Somewhere is the night / Afro blue / Triste / Whiffenpoof song / Leyte / Mamblues / Curacao
CD _____ CD 62073
Saludos Amigos / Jan '96 / Target/BMG.

TLC
CRAZYSEXYCOOL
Intro-lude / Creep / Kick your game / Diggin' on you / Case of the fake people / Crazysexycool / Red light special / Waterfalls / Intermission-lude / Let's do it again / If I was your girlfriend / Sexy-interlude / Take our time / Can I get a witness / Switch / Sumthin' wicked this way comes
CD _____ 73008260092
Arista / May '95 / BMG.

OOOOOOOH... ON THE TLC TIP
Ain't 2 proud 2 beg / Shock dat monkey / Intermission / Hat 2 da bak / Das da way we like 'em / What about your friends / His story / Intermission 2 / Bad my myself / So- methin' you wanna know / Baby-baby-baby

/ This is how it should be done / Depend on myself / Conclusion
CD _____ 262 878
Arista / Aug '92 / BMG.

To Hell With Burgundy
3
CD _____ STIGCD 03
Stig / Aug '94 / Pinnacle / ADA.

ONLY THE WORLD
CD _____ STIGCD 05
Stig / Jul '94 / Pinnacle / ADA.

Toad The Wet Sprocket
FEAR
Walk on the ocean / Is it for me / Butterflies / Nightingale song / Hold her down / Pray your Gods / Before you were born / Something to say / In my ear / All I want / Stories I tell / I will not take these things for granted
CD _____ 4685022
Columbia / Mar '92 / Sony.

Toadies
PLEATHER
CD _____ ASS 001 2
Grass / May '93 / SRD.

Toasters
DUB 56
CD _____ EFA 046082
Pork Pie / Aug '94 / SRD.
CD _____ DOJOCD 214
Dojo / Jun '95 / BMG.

FRANKENSKA
CD _____ PHZCD 60
Unicorn / Nov '93 / Plastic Head.

LIVE IN L.A.
CD _____ EFA 046072
Pork Pie / Dec '94 / SRD.

NAKED CITY
CD _____ PHZCD 55
Unicorn / Oct '89 / Plastic Head.

NEW YORK FEVER
CD _____ EFA 04090 CD
Pork Pie / Jan '93 / SRD.

SKA BOOM
CD _____ EFA 046052
Pork Pie / Apr '94 / SRD.

Tobias, Nancy
BEAUTIFUL SOUNDS OF THE PANPIPE (Tobias, Nancy & Phil)
CD _____ HADCD 178
Javelin / Nov '95 / THE / Henry Hadaway Organisation.

Tobin, Christine
AILILIU
CD _____ BDV 9501CD
Babel / Jul '95 / ADA / Harmonia Mundi / Cadillac / Diverse.

Toby & The Whole Truth
IGNORANCE IS BLISS
CD _____ COTINDCD 5
Cottage Industry / Aug '95 / Total/BMG.

Today Is The Day
SUPERNOVA
CD _____ ARRCD 44/290
Amphetamine Reptile / Aug '93 / SRD.

WILLPOWER
CD _____ AARCD57 354
Amphetamine Reptile / Nov '94 / SRD.

Todd, Dick
HIS GREATEST HITS
CD _____ CDAJA 5179
Living Era / Dec '95 / Koch.

Toe Fat
TOE FAT
CD _____ REP 4416WY
Repertoire / Feb '94 / Pinnacle / Cadillac.

TOE FAT I AND II
That's my love for you / Bad side of the moon / Nobody / Wherefores and the whys / But I'm wrong / Just like all the rest / I can't believe / Working nights / You tried to take it all / Stick heat / Indian summer / Idol / There'll be changes / New way / Since you've been gone / Three time loser / Midnight sun
CD _____ BGOCD 278
Beat Goes On / Sep '95 / Pinnacle.

Toe Tag
REALITY
CD _____ CHERRY 22895-2
Cherrydisc / Jun '94 / Plastic Head.

Toe To Toe
THREATS AND FACTS
CD _____ KANG 006CD
Kangaroo / Nov '95 / Plastic Head.

Togashi, Masahiko
COLOUR OF DREAM
CD _____ TKOJ 1502
Take One / Jan '96 / Harmonia Mundi.

ISOLATION (Togashi, Masahiko & Mototeru Takagi)
CD _____ TKOJ 1503
Take One / Jan '96 / Harmonia Mundi.

SONG OF SOIL
CD _____ TKOJ 1501
Take One / Jan '96 / Harmonia Mundi.

Tognoni, Rob
STONES AND COLOURS
CD _____ PRD 70832
Provogue / Oct '95 / Pinnacle.

Toiling Midgets
SON
Faux pony / Fabric / Slaughter of Summer St. / Mr. Foster's shoes / Process words / Clinging firm/Clams / Third chair / Listen / Chains
CD _____ HUTCD 006
Hut / Jan '93 / EMI.

Token Entry
WEIGHT OF THE WORLD
CD _____ EM 93942
Roadrunner / Sep '90 / Pinnacle.

Token Women
OUT TO LUNCH
CD _____ NM 6CD
No Master's Voice / Jul '95 / ADA.

RHYTHM METHOD, THE
CD _____ NMV 2CD
No Master's Voice / Feb '93 / ADA.

Tokens
WIMOWEH - THE BEST OF THE TOKENS
Lion sleeps tonight / B'wanina (pretty girl) / La bamba / Hear the bells (ringing bells) / You're nothing but a girl / Tonight I met an angel / Sincerely / When I go to sleep at night / Thousand miles away / Please write / Dream angel good night / Somewhere there's a girl / I'll do my crying tomorrow / ABC 123 / Tonight, tonight / Dry your eyes / Sweet Laurie / My candy apple vette / My fiend's car / When summer is through
CD _____ 7863 66474-2
RCA / Nov '94 / BMG.

Toker, Bayram Bilge
BAYRAM
CD _____ CDT 122
Topic / Apr '93 / Direct / ADA.

Tokeya Inajin
DREAM CATCHER
CD _____ CDEB 2696
Earthbeat / May '93 / Direct / ADA.

Tokyo Blade
TOKYO BLADE
CD _____ RR 349883
Roadrunner / '89 / Pinnacle.

Tokyo Offshore Project
AEROTEK
Children of the rainbow / Soltaire / Magic melody (remix) / Aerotek / Running thunder / Gabriella / Solitaire
CD _____ SCIENCD 001
Scien / Sep '94 / Vital.

Tolliver, Charles
CHARLES TOLLIVER: THE RINGER
CD _____ BLC 760174
Black Lion / Dec '92 / Jazz Music / Cadillac / Wellard / Koch.

GRAND MAX
CD _____ BLC 760145
Black Lion / Apr '91 / Jazz Music / Cadillac / Wellard / Koch.

LIVE IN BERLIN (At the Quasimodo Vol 1)
Ruthie's heart / Ah I see / Stretch / On the Nile
CD _____ 66051001
Strata East / Dec '90 / New Note.

RINGER, THE
CD _____ BLCD 760174
Black Lion / Oct '93 / Jazz Music / Cadillac / Wellard / Koch.

WITH MUSIC INC. AND ORCH
Impact / Mother Wit / Grand Max / Plight / Lynnsome / Mournin' variations
CD _____ 6605 1004
Strata East / Feb '91 / New Note.

Tolman, Russ
ROAD MOVIE
CD _____ 422368
New Rose / May '94 / Direct / ADA.

TOTEM POLES AND GLORY HOLES
Lookin' for an angel / Talking hoover dam blues / Four winds / Everything you need and everything you want / Galveston mud / Better than before / I am not afraid / Nothin' slowing me down / Play hard to forget / Waitin' for rain
CD _____ DIAB 802
Diabolo / Oct '93 / Pinnacle.

Tolonen, Jukka

HOOK/HYSTERICA
CD _____ LRCD 113/149
Love / Dec '94 / Direct / ADA.

Tom Tom Club

TOM TOM CLUB
Wordy rappinghood / Genius of love / Tom Tom theme / L'elephant / As above so below / Lorelei / On on on on / Booming and zooming
CD _____ IMCD 103
Island / Feb '90 / PolyGram.

Tomita

BEST OF TOMITA
CD _____ PD 893 81
RCA / '88 / BMG.

FIREBIRD
Firebird suite / Prelude a l'apres midi d'un faune / Night on the bare mountain
CD _____ GD 60578
RCA / Oct '91 / BMG.

KOSMOS
Space fantasy / Unanswered question / Solveig's song / Hora staccato / Sea named Solaris
CD _____ GD 82616
RCA / Oct '91 / BMG.

PICTURES AT AN EXHIBITION
Gnome / Old castle / Tuileries / Bydlo / Ballet of the chicks in their shells / Samuel Goldenberg and Schmuyle / Limoges / Catacombs / Cum mortuis in lingua mortua / Hut of Baba Yaga / Great gate of Kiev
CD _____ GD 60576
RCA / Oct '91 / BMG.

SNOWFLAKES ARE DANCING
Snowflakes are dancing / Reverie / Gardens in the rain (estampes no 3) / Clair de Lune / Arabesque No.1 / Engulfed cathedral (preludes book no.8) / Golliwogg's cakewalk / Footprints in the snow(preludes book no.6)
CD _____ GD 60579
RCA / '85 / BMG.

Tommaso, Giovanni

VIA G.T. (Tommaso, Giovanni Quintet)
CD _____ 123196-2
Red / Apr '94 / Harmonia Mundi / Jazz Horizons / Cadillac / ADA.

Tomokawa, Kazuki

SHIBUYA APIA
CD _____ PSFD 65
PSF / Dec '95 / Harmonia Mundi.

Tomorrow

TOMORROW
My white bicycle / Colonel Brown / Real life permanent dream / Shy boy / Claremount lake / Revolution / Incredible journey of Timothy Chase / Auntie Mary's dress shop / Strawberry fields forever / Three jolly little dwarfs / Now your time has come / Hallucinations
CD _____ SEECD 314
See For Miles/C5 / Apr '91 / Pinnacle.

Tompkins, Ross

AKA THE PHANTOM
CD _____ PCD 7090
Progressive / Jun '93 / Jazz Music.

CELEBRATES THE MUSIC OF JULIE STYNE
CD _____ PCD 7103
Progressive / Aug '95 / Jazz Music.

Ton-Art

MAL VU, MAL DIT
CD _____ ARTCD 6088
Hat Art / Jan '92 / Harmonia Mundi / ADA / Cadillac.

Tone Loc

COOL HAND LOC
CD _____ BRCD 580
4th & Broadway / Oct '91 / PolyGram.

LOC'ED AFTER DARK
On fire (remix) / Wild thing / Loc'ed after dark / I got it going on / Cutting rhythms / Funky cold medina / Cheeba cheeba / Don't get close / Loc'in on the shaw / Homies
CD _____ IMCD 125
4th & Broadway / Apr '91 / PolyGram.

Toney, Kevin

LOVESCAPE
Kings / Aphrodisiac / Winds of romance / Lovescape / Sweet whispers / Intimate persuasion / Body language / Deeper shade of love / African knights / Twylight 2053 / Someone / Carnival / King's reprise
CD _____ ICH 1167CD
Ichiban / Jan '94 / Koch.

Tonight At Noon

DOWN TO THE DEVILS
John MacLean march / Hawks and eagles fly like doves / Travelling song / Wire the loom / People's will / Run run / Hell of a man / Down to the devils / Nae trust / Mission hall / Harry Wigwam's / Banks of marble / Jack the tanner / Rolling seas
CD _____ LCOM 9041
Lismor / Nov '90 / Lismor / Direct / Duncans / ADA.

Tonnerre, Michel

TI BEUDEFF - CHANT DE MARINS
CD _____ KMCD 39
Keltia Musique / Aug '93 / ADA / Direct / Discovery.

Tonooka, Sumi

HERE COMES KAI
CD _____ CCD 79516
Candid / Apr '92 / Cadillac / Jazz Music / Wellard / Koch.

TAKING TIME
CD _____ CCD 79502
Candid / Jul '91 / Cadillac / Jazz Music / Wellard / Koch.

Tony D

GET YOURSELF SOME (Tony D Band)
CD _____ TRCD 9919
Tramp / Nov '93 / Direct / ADA / CM.

Tony Rebel

DANCEHALL CONFRENCE (Tony Rebel & Garnet Silk)
CD _____ CDHB 152
Heartbeat / May '94 / Greensleeves / Jetstar / Direct / ADA.

MEET IN A DANCEHALL CONFERENCE (Tony Rebel & Garnet Silk)
CD _____ HBCD 152
Heartbeat / Jun '94 / Greensleeves / Jetstar / Direct / ADA.

REBELLIOUS
CD _____ RASCD 3097
Ras / May '92 / Jetstar / Greensleeves / SRD / Direct.

Tony Toni Tone

SONS OF SOUL
If I had no root / What goes around comes around / My ex-girlfriend / Tell me mama / Leavin' / Slow wine (slow grind) / Lay your head on my pillow / I couldn't keep it to myself / Gangsta groove / Tonyies! In the wrong key / Dance hall / Time Square 2:30 AM (Segue) / Fun / Anniversary / Castleers
CD _____ 514933-2
Polydor / Jul '93 / PolyGram.

Tonyall

NEW GIRL, OLD STORY
CD _____ CRZ 016 CD
Cruz / May '93 / Pinnacle / Plastic Head.

Too Strong

RABENSCHWARZE NACHT
CD _____ HAUS 1
Tribehaus Recordings / Jan '94 / Plastic Head.

Tool

OPIATE
Sweat / Hush / Part of me / Cold and ugly / Jerk off / Opiate
CD _____ 72445110272
Zoo Entertainment / Jul '92 / BMG.

UNDERTOW
Intolerance / Prison sex / Sober / Bottom / Crawl away / Swamp song / Undertow / Four degrees / Flood / Disgustipated
CD _____ 72445 11052-2
RCA / Apr '93 / BMG.

Toop, David

SCREEN CEREMONIES
Ceremonies behind screens / Darkened room / Dream fluid / Psychic / Howler monkeys thirst and roars / Butoh porno / Reverse world / Mica screen / I hear voices
CD _____ WIRE 9001
Wire Editions / Nov '95 / Vital.

Toots & The Maytals

BLA BLA BLA
CD _____ CC 2706

Crocodisc / Jan '94 / THE / Magnum Music Group.

DO THE REGGAE 1966-70
Bam bam / 54-46 (was my number) / Struggle / Reborn / Just tell me / Do the reggae / Hold on / Don't trouble trouble / Alidina / Oh yeah / Sweet and dandy / Johnny cool man / Night and day
CD _____ CDAT 103
Attack / May '94 / Jetstar / Total/BMG.

DON'T TROUBLE
CD _____ RB 3017
Reggae Best / Jan '96 / Magnum Music Group / THE.

FUNKY KINGSTON
Sit right down / Pomp and pride / Louie Louie / I can't believe / Redemption song / Daddy's home / Funky Kingston / It was written down
CD _____ RRCD 21
Reggae Refreshers / Nov '90 / PolyGram / Vital.

IN THE DARK
Got to be there / In the dark / Having a party / Time tough / I see you / Take a look in the mirror / Take me home country roads / Fever / Love gonna walk out on me / Revolution / 54-46 (was my number) / Sailing on
CD _____ CDTRL 202
Trojan / Mar '94 / Jetstar / Total/BMG.

REGGAE GREATS
54-46 (was my number) / Reggae got sould / Monkey man / Just like that / Funky Kingston / Sweet and dandy / Take me home country oads / Time tough / Spititual healing / Pressure drop / Peace perfect peace / Bam bam
CD _____ IMCD 38
Island / Jun '89 / PolyGram.

ROOTS REGGAE
CD _____ RNCD 2132
Rhino / Oct '95 / Jetstar / Magnum Music Group / THE.

SENSATIONAL SKA EXPLOSION
CD _____ JMC 200112
Jamaica Gold / Jun '94 / THE / Magnum Music Group / Jetstar.

Top Cat

9 LIVES OF THE CAT
CD _____ NLDCD 01
9 Lives / Feb '95 / Jetstar.

CAT O NINE TALES
CD _____ NLDCD 002
9 Lives / Dec '95 / Jetstar.

Torch, Sidney

SIDNEY TORCH
CD _____ PASTCD 9747
Flapper / Jun '91 / Pinnacle.

Torch Song

TOWARD THE UNKNOWN REGION
CD _____ 4509896962
Warner Bros. / Apr '95 / Warner Music.

Torchure

BEYOND THE VEIL
CD _____ 1MF3770026
1 MF / Nov '92 / Plastic Head.

Torkanowsky, David

STEPPIN' OUT
CD _____ CD 2090
Rounder / '88 / CM / Direct / ADA / Cadillac.

Torkildsen, Murray

SEX, LIES & VIDEOGAMES
CD _____ AMZT 4003
Amazing Feet / Feb '95 / Grapevine / Vital.

Torme

DEMOLITION BALL
Fallen angel / Black sheep / Action / Ball and chain / Slip away / Long time coming / Spinnin' your wheels / Don't understand / Industry / Draw the line / U.S. made / Let it go / Walk it / Man o' means
CD _____ CDBLEED 2
Bleeding Hearts / Apr '93 / Pinnacle.

Torme, Bernie

BACK TO BABYLON
All around the world / Star / Eyes of the world / Burning bridges / Hardcore / Here I go / Family at war / Front line / Arabia / Mystery train / T.V.O.D. (CD only.) / Kerrap (CD only.) / Love, guns and money (CD only.)
CD _____ CDZEB 6
Zebra / Jul '91 / Pinnacle.

OFFICIAL BOOTLEG
Front line / Turn out the lights / Hardcore / Star / Burning bridges / T.V.O.D. / My baby loves a vampire / New Orleans / Love, guns

and money / All around the world / Mystery train / Front line 2
CD _____ CDTB 112
Thunderbolt / '91 / Magnum Music Group.

Torme, Mel

16 MOST REQUESTED SONGS
P.S. I love you / Second time around / Haven't we met / Nearness of you / My romance / Do I love you because you're beautiful / Isn't it a pity / I know your heart / I've got you under my skin / That's all / What is there to say / Folks who live on the hill / Everyday's a holiday / You'd better love me / Strangers in the night / Christmas song
CD _____ 474398 2
Columbia / Feb '94 / Sony.

CAPITOL YEARS: MEL TORME
Do do do / Stompin' at the Savoy / You're getting to be a habit / Blue moon / Again / It's too late now / Sonny boy / Oh you beautiful doll / Skylark / Lullaby of the leaves / Piccolino / Bewitched, bothered and bewildered / I've got a feeling I'm falling in love / Cariola / On a street in Singapore / I like to recognise the tune / Stranger in town / Heart and soul / My buddy
CD _____ CDEMS 1447
Capitol / Jun '92 / EMI.

CHRISTMAS SONGS
CD _____ CD 83315
Telarc / Sep '92 / Conifer / ADA.

EASY TO REMEMBER
CD _____ HCD 253
Hindsight / May '94 / Target/BMG / Jazz Music.

FUJITSU-CONCORD JAZZ FESTIVAL (Japan '90)
Shine on your shoes / Looking at you/Look at that face / Nightingale sang in Berkeley Square / Wave / Star dust / Don't cha go 'way mad/Come to baby do / Christmas song/Autumn leaves / You're driving me crazy (what did I do) / Sent for you yesterday / Swingin' the blues / New York state of mind
CD _____ CCD 4481
Concord Jazz / Oct '91 / New Note.

GREAT AMERICAN SONGBOOK, THE
Stardust / You make me feel so young / Riding high / All God's chillun got rhythm / I'm gonna go fishin' / Don't get around much anymore / Sophisticated lady/I don't know about you / Rockin' in rhythm / It don't mean a thing if it ain't got that swing / Lovely way to spend an evening / I'll remember April/I concentrate on you / Autumn in New York / You gotta try / Just one of those things/On Green Dolphin Street / Party's over / I'll be a song go out of my heart
CD _____ CD 83328
Telarc / Dec '93 / Conifer / ADA.

IN CONCERT - TOKYO (Torme, Mel & Marty Paich Dektette)
It don't mean a thing if it ain't got that swing / Cotton tail / More than you know / Sweet Georgia Brown / Just in time / When the sun comes out / Carioca / Too close for comfort / City / Bossa nova pot pourri / On the street where you live
CD _____ CCD 4382
Concord Jazz / Jun '89 / New Note.

LIVE AT THE CRESCENDO (CHARLY)
Love is just a bug / Nobody's heart / It's only a paper moon / What is this thing called love / Got plenty o' nuttin' / Taking a chance / One for my baby / Nightingale sang in Berkeley Square / Just one of those things / Autumn leaves / Girl next door / Lover come back to me / I'm beginning to see the light / Looking at you / Tender trap / Tenderly / I wish I was in love again / It's de-lovely / It's all right with me / Home by the sea / Manhattan
CD _____ CDCHARLY 60
Charly / '87 / Charly / THE / Cadillac.

LULU'S BACK IN TOWN
CD _____ GOJCD 53010
Giants Of Jazz / Mar '90 / Target/BMG / Cadillac.

MAGIC OF MEL TORME, THE
CD _____ MCCD 198
Music Club / Mar '95 / Disc / THE / CM.

MEL AND GEORGE 'DO' WORLD WAR II (Torme, Mel & George Shearing)
Lili Marlene / I've heard that song before / I know why / Love / Aren't you glad you're you / Ellington medley / Walk medley / I could write a book / Lovely way to spend an evening / On the swing shift/Five o'clock whistle / Accentuate the positive / This is the army Mister Jones / We mustn't say goodbye
CD _____ CCD 4471
Concord Jazz / Jul '91 / New Note.

MEL TORME/ROB MCCONNELL AND BOSS BRASS (Torme, Mel/Rob McConnell/Boss Brass)
Just friends / September song / Don't cha go 'way mad / House is not a home / Song is you / Cow cow boogie / Handful of stars / Stars fell on Alabama / It don't mean a thing if it ain't got that swing / Do nothin' 'til you hear from me / Mood indigo / Take the 'A' train / Sophisticated lady / Satin doll

CD _____ CCD 4306
Concord Jazz / Jan '87 / New Note.

NIGHT AT THE CONCORD PAVILION
Sing for your supper / Sing, sing, sing / Sing (sing a song) / You make me feel so young / Early Autumn / Guys and dolls medley / I could have told you / Losing my mind / Deep in a dream / Goin' out of my head / Too darn hot / Day in, day out / Down for double / You're driving me crazy / Sent for you yesterday
CD _____ CCD 4433
Concord Jazz / Nov '90 / New Note.

NOTHING WITHOUT YOU (Torme, Mel & Cleo Laine)
CD _____ CCD 4515
Concord Jazz / Jul '92 / New Note.

RETROSPECTIVE, A (1956-68)
CD _____ STCD 4
Stash / '88 / Jazz Music / CM / Cadillac / Direct / ADA.

REUNION (Torme, Mel & Marty Paich Dektette)
Sweet Georgia Brown / I'm wishing / Blues / Trolley song / More than you know / For whom the bell tolls / When you wish upon a star / Walk between raindrops / Bossa nova pot porri / Get me to the church on time / Goodbye look / Spain (I can recall)
CD _____ CCD 4360
Concord Jazz / Jul '90 / New Note.

SPOTLIGHT ON MEL TORME
Oh you beautiful doll / My buddy / Stompin' at the Savoy / Blue moon / I love each move you make / You're getting to be a habit with me / It's too late now / Heart and soul / Lullaby of the leaves / Du do do / Sonny boy / Bewitched, bothered and bewildered / You're a heavenly thing / Skylark / Careless hands / I hadn't anyone till you / I've got a feeling I'm falling in love / Recipe for romance
CD _____ CDP 7899412
Capitol / Apr '95 / EMI.

TORME
All in love is fair / First time ever I saw your face / New York state of mind / Stars / Send in the clowns / Ordinary fool / When the world was young / Yesterday when I was young / Bye bye blackbird
CD _____ RHCD 3
Rhapsody / Jan '87 / President / Jazz Music / Wellard.

TRIBUTE TO BING CROSBY (Paramount's Greatest Singer)
This is my night to dream / It must be true / Moonlight becomes you / I can't escape from you (Features on CD only.) / With every breath I take (Features on CD only.) / Man and his dream / Without a word of warning / May I / Please / Thanks (On CD only.) / Don't let that moon get away / Soon / It's easy to remember / Love in bloom / Day you came along / Pennies from heaven / Learn to croon
CD _____ CCD 4614
Concord Jazz / Oct '94 / New Note.

VELVET AND BRASS
Liza (all the clouds'll roll away) / Swing shift / I'll be around / Sweety / Love walks in / These are the things / If you could see / High & low / Have you met Miss Jones / Nobody else / Autumn serenade / I get a kick out of you / Still of the night / I'm glad
CD _____ CCD 4667
Concord Jazz / Oct '95 / New Note.

Torment

HYPNOSIS
CD _____ NERDCD 057
Nervous / Jul '90 / Nervous / Magnum Music Group.

Torn, David

BEST LAID PLANS
Before the bitter wind / Best laid plans / Hum of its parts / Removable tongue / In the fifth direction / Two face flash / Angle of incidents
CD _____ 8236422
ECM / Mar '85 / New Note.

CLOUD ABOUT MERCURY
Suyafhu skin..snapping the hollow reed / Mercury grid / Three minutes of pure entertainment / Previous man / Network of sparks
CD _____ 8311082
ECM / Mar '87 / New Note.

DOOR X
Time bomb / Lion of Boaz / Voodoo chile / Others / Diamond mansions / Good morning Mr. Wonderful / Brave light of sun / Promise / Taste of roses / Door X
CD _____ WD 1096
Windham Hill / Jun '91 / Pinnacle / BMG / ADA.

POLYTOWN
Honey sweating / Palms for Lester / Open letter to the heart of Diaphora / Bandaged by dreams / Warrior horsemen... / Snail hair dune / This is the abduction scene / Red sleep / Res majuko / City of the dead
CD _____ CMPCD 1006
CMP / May '94 / Vital/SAM.

Tornados

ORIGINAL 60'S HITS, THE
CD _____ MCCD 161
MCI / Jul '94 / Disc / THE.

Torner, Gosta

TRUMPET PLAYER
CD _____ PHONTCD 9301
Phontastic / Jun '94 / Wellard / Jazz Music / Cadillac.

Toro, Yomo

GRACIAS
CD _____ CIDM 1034
Mango / Mar '90 / Vital / PolyGram.

Toronto Children's Chorus

CHRISTMAS CAROLS
Prelude - harp solo / Angelus ad virginem / Virgin most pure / Personal hodle / Interlude - harp solo / There is no rose / Coventry carol / Tomorrow shall be my dancing day / Angel's carol / Noel nouvelet / Robin / Donkey carol / Promptement levez-vous / Mary and Joseph / Noel des enfants / Christmas / Huron carol / D'ou veins tu, bergere / Stille nacht / Tweleve days of Christmas
CD _____ PCD 2049
Carlton Home Entertainment / Oct '95 / Carlton Home Entertainment.

Torr, Michele

GRANDS SUCCES
CD _____ MCD 339 207
Accord / '88 / Discovery / Harmonia Mundi / Cadillac.

Torres, Jaime

CHARANGO
Chimba chica / La diablada / Naupaj tiempos jinan tatay / Mambo de machahuay / Ch'isi / Caminos en la puna / La peregrinacion / El dia que me quieras / Chacarera del tiempo / Zamba de la candeleria / Sirvinaco / Milonga de mis amores
CD _____ 1115949
Messidor / Jan '87 / Koch / ADA.

Torres, Juan Pablo

TROMBONE MAN
Sweet cherry pie / From John to Johnny / Who's smoking / Fiesta for Juan Pablo / Foot tapping / Samba for Carmen / At daybreak / Four and como fue / Memories / Banana split / For Elsa
CD _____ 66058085
Barbington / Feb '96 / New Note.

Torres, Marcelo

EDAD LUZ
CD _____ F 1037CD
Sonifolk / Jun '94 / ADA / CM.

Tors Of Dartmoor

HOUSE OF SOUNDS
CD _____ HY 39100642
Hyperium / Jul '93 / Plastic Head.

Tortharry

WHEN MEMORIES ARE FREE
CD _____ TAGA 001CD
MAB / Nov '94 / Plastic Head.

Tortoise

MILLIONS NOW LIVING
CD _____ EFA 049722
City Slang / Jan '96 / Disc.

RHYTHMS, RESOLUTIONS AND CLUSTERS
CD _____ EFA 049572
City Slang / Jun '95 / Disc.

TORTOISE
CD _____ EFA 049502
Sub Pop / Jan '95 / Disc.

Toscanini, Arturo

ARTURO TOSCANINI & BENNY GOODMAN PLAY GEORGE GERSHWIN (Toscanini, Arturo & Benny Goodman)
CD _____ VJC 1034-2
Vintage Jazz Classics / Oct '92 / Direct / ADA / CM / Cadillac.

Tosh, Andrew

MAKE PLACE FOR THE YOUTH
CD _____ 269672-2
Tomato / Apr '90 / Vital.

ORIGINAL MAN, THE
Same dog bite / Too much rat / Heathen rage / My enemies / Maga dog / I'm the youngest / Poverty is a crime / Original man / My enemies (dub version) / Poverty is a

crime (dub version) / Original man (dub version)
CD _____ CDHB 140
Heartbeat / Apr '94 / Greensleeves / Jetstar / Direct / ADA.

Tosh, Peter

BUSH DOCTOR
You gotta walk don't look back / Pick myself up / I'm the toughest / Soon come / Moses the prophet / Bush doctor / Stand firm / Dem ha fe get a beatin' / Creation
CD _____ CDTRP 100
Trojan / Nov '90 / Jetstar / Total/BMG.

EQUAL RIGHTS
Get up stand up / Downpressor man / I am that I am / Stepping razor / Equal rights / African / Jah guide / Apartheid
CD _____ CDV 2081
Virgin / Nov '88 / EMI.

LEGALIZE IT
Legalize it / Burial / What'cha gonna do / No sympathy / Why must I cry / Igziabeher (Let Jah be praised) / Ketchy shuby / Till your well runs dry / Brand new secondhand
CD _____ CDV 2061
Virgin / Aug '88 / EMI.

Toss The Feathers

AWAKENING
Fever / Sunset / Awakening / Lonely man / Heritage / Requiem for the innocent / Thorn and nail / Drifting apart / Seven / Dr. Jekyll and Mrs. Hyde / Sail away / Long forgotten line
CD _____ FC 003CD
Fat Cat / Feb '93 / Vital.

Total

SKY BLUE VOID
CD _____ FRR007
Freek / Sep '94 / SRD.

TANZMUSIC DER RENAISSANCE, THE
CD _____ FRR 017
Freek / Dec '95 / SRD.

Total Chaos

PATRIOTIC SHOCK
CD _____ 864502
Epitaph / May '95 / Plastic Head / Pinnacle.

PLEDGE OF DEFIANCE
CD _____ E 86438-2
Epitaph / Apr '94 / Plastic Head / Pinnacle.

Total Eclipse

DELTA AQUARIDS
CD _____ BR 2 CD
Blue Room Released / Oct '95 / SRD.

Toto

ABSOLUTELY LIVE
Hydra / Rosanna / Kingdom of desire / Georgie Porgie / Ninety nine / I won't hold you back / Don't stop me now / Africa / Don't chain my heart / I'll be over you / Home of the brave / Hold the line / With a little help from my friends
CD _____ 474514 2
Columbia / Nov '93 / Sony.

KINGDOM OF DESIRE
Gypsy train / Don't chain my heart / Never enough / How many times / Two hands / Wings of time / She knows the devil / Other side / Only you / Kick down the walls / Kingdom of desire / Jake to the bone
CD _____ 4716339
Sony Music / Feb '93 / Sony.

TOTO - PAST TO PRESENT (1977-1990)
Love has the power / Africa / Hold the line / Out of love / Georgie Porgie / I'll be over you / Can you hear what I'm saying / Rosanna / I won't hold you back / Stop loving you / Ninety nine / Pamela / Animal
CD _____ 4659882
CBS / Sep '90 / Sony.

TOTO IV
Rossana / Make believe / I won't hold you back / Good for you / It's a feeling / Afraid of love / Lovers in the night / We made it / Waiting for your love / Africa
CD _____ 4500882
CBS / Mar '91 / Sony.

TOTO/TURN BACK/HYDRA
CD Set _____ 4673862
CBS / Dec '90 / Sony.

Toto Bissainthe

TOTO BISSAINTHE
CD _____ LDX 274014
La Chant Du Monde / Oct '95 / Harmonia Mundi / ADA.

Touch

TOUCH
CD _____ CDMFN 107
Music For Nations / Aug '90 / Pinnacle.

Touchstone

JEALOUSY
Mooncoin jig/High reel/Plover's wing / Cuach mo lonndubh bui/Three sea captains / Last chance / Lonely wanderer / Primrose lass/Keel row/Green grow the rushes o / Garcon a marier/Orgies nocturnes/Dans fisel / Jealousy / King's favourite/Cook in the kitchen/Din Turrant's polka / Invisible wings/Faolean / Green gates/Pinch of snuff / White snow
CD _____ GLCD 1050
Green Linnet / Feb '90 / Roots / CM / Direct / ADA.

NEW LAND, THE
Kilmoulis jig/The maid at the spinning wheel / Jack Haggerty / Flowing tide/Cooley's hornpipe / Susanna Martin / Flying reel/My Maryann/Game of love / Casadh carn na Feadanraighe / Three polkas / Farewell to Nova Scotia / Song in F / Bolen's fancy/Dunmore lasses/Glass of beer / New land
CD _____ GLCD 1040
Green Linnet / Feb '88 / Roots / CM / Direct / ADA.

Toure, Ali Farke

SOURCE, THE
CD _____ WCD 030
World Circuit / Jun '92 / New Note / Direct / Cadillac / ADA.

TALKING TIMBUKTU (Toure, Ali Farke & Ry Cooder)
Blonde / Soukora / Gomni / Sega / Amandrai / Lasidan / Keito / Banga / Ai du / Diarabi
CD _____ WCD 040
World Circuit / Mar '94 / New Note / Direct / Cadillac / ADA.

Tournesol

KOKOTSU
Imeat / Electric church / Henka / Orange planet / Draagmad Ultramarine (On CD only) / Cathedral / Holy cow
CD _____ AMB 4931CD
Apollo / Mar '94 / Vital.

MOONFUNK
Inside angel / Chords of rhythm / Junglemovie / Sunny blow / Interplanetary zonecheck / Electrowaltz / Scapeland / Break 'n' space / Voltage / Mapping your mind / Belagean / 2095 / Clockworking clockwork clock
CD _____ RS 95074CD
R & S / Aug '95 / Vital.

Toussaint, Allen

20 GOLDEN LOVE THEMES (Movie Themes) (Toussaint, Allen Orchestra)
CD _____ MU 5036
Musketeer / Oct '92 / Koch.

50'S MASTERS, THE
Whirlaway / Happy times / Up the crek / Tim tam / Me and you / Bono / Java / Wham tousan / Nowhere to go / Nashua / Po' boy walk / Pelican parade / Chico / (Back home again in) Indiana / Second liner / Cow cow blues / Moo moo / Sweetie pie (twenty years later) / You didn't know, did you / Up right / Blue mood / Lazy day / Naomi / Real churchy / Real church (2)
CD _____ BCD 15641
Bear Family / Mar '92 / Rollercoaster / Direct / CM / Swift / ADA.

FROM A WHISPER TO A SCREAM (Retro 87-88)
From a whisper to a scream / Chokin' kind / Sweet touch of love / What is success / Working in a coalmine / Everything I do gonh be funky / Either / Louie / Cast your fate to the wind / Number nine / Pickles
CD _____ CDKENM 036
Kent / Mar '91 / Pinnacle.

LIFE, LOVE AND FAITH
Victims of the darkness / Am I expecting too much / My baby is the real thing / Goin' down / Soul sister / Out of the city / Soul sister / Fingers and toes / I've got to convince myself / On your way down / Gone too far / Electricity
CD _____ 7599266082
Reprise / Jan '96 / Warner Music.

MOTION
Night people / Just a kiss away / With you in mind / Lover of love / To be with you / Motion / Viva la money / Declaration of love / Happiness / Optimism blues
CD _____ 7599268972
Reprise / Jan '96 / Warner Music.

SOUND OF MOVIES, THE (Toussaint, Allen Orchestra)
CD _____ MU 5038
Musketeer / Oct '92 / Koch.

SOUTHERN NIGHTS
Last train / Worldwide / Back in baby's arms / Country John / Basic lady / Southern nights / You will not lose / What do you want the girl to do / When the party's over / Cruel way to go down
CD _____ 7599265962
Reprise / Jan '96 / Warner Music.

WILD SOUNDS OF NEW ORLEANS
Up the creek / Tim Tam / Me And You / Bono / Java / Happy Times / Nowhere to go / Nashua / Po' Boy Walk / Pelican parade
CD _____ EDCD 275
Edsel / Apr '91 / Pinnacle / ADA.

Toussaint, Jean

LIFE I WANT
Blue funk / It's for you / Island man / Life I want / Crouch End afternoon / Soho strut / Gangway / Short straw / Grooving at the hall / London / Red cross
CD _____ NNCD 1001
New Note / Oct '95 / New Note / Cadillac.

WHAT GOES AROUND
CD _____ WCD 029
World Circuit / May '92 / New Note / Direct / Cadillac / ADA.

WHO'S BLUES
Opening gambit / Who's blues / London / Visiting / Body language / Yanar's dance / Soundtrack / Chameleon
CD _____ JHCD 019
Ronnie Scott's Jazz House / Jan '94 / Jazz Music / Magnum Music Group / Cadillac.

Tovey, Frank

CIVILIAN
CD _____ CDSTUMM 56
Mute / Jun '88 / Disc.

FAD GADGET SINGLES
Back to nature / Box / Ricky's hand / Fireside favourite / Insecticide / Lady shave / Saturday night special / King of the flies / Life on the line / 4M / For whom the bells toll / Love parasite / I discover love / Collapsing new people / One man's meat
CD _____ CDSTUMM 37
Mute / '86 / Disc.

SNAKES AND LADDERS
CD _____ CDSTUMM 23
Mute / '86 / Disc.

TYRANNY AND THE HIRED HAND
'31 depression blues / Hard times in the cotton mill / John Henry/Let your hammer ring / Blanfyre explosion / Money cravin' folks / All I got's gone / Midwife song / Sam Hall / Dark as a dungeon / Men of good fortune / Sixteen tons / North country blues / Buffalo skinners / Black lung song / Pastures of plenty / Joe hill
CD _____ CDSTUMM 73
Mute / Aug '89 / Disc.

Towa Tei

FUTURE LISTENING
CD _____ 7559671612
Warner Bros. / Sep '95 / Warner Music.

Tower Of Power

BUMP CITY
You got to funkifize / What happend to the world that day / Flash in the pan / Gone / You strike my main nerve / Down to the nightclub (bump city) / You're still a young man / Skating on thin ice / Of the earth
CD _____ 7599263482
Warner Bros. / Sep '93 / Warner Music.

IN THE SLOT
Just enough and too much / Treat me like your man / If I play my cards right / As surely as I stand here / Fanfare-matanuska / On the serious side / Ebony jam / You're so wonderful, so marvellous / Vuela por noche / Essence of innocence / Soul of a child / Drop it in the slot
CD _____ 7599263502
Warner Bros. / Sep '93 / Warner Music.

SOULED OUT
Souled out / Taxed to the max / Keep comin' back / Soothe you / Do you wanna (make love to me) / Lovin' you forever / Gotta make a change / Diggin' on James Brown / Sexy soul / Just like you / Once you get a taste / Undercurrent
CD _____ 4809422
Epic / Sep '95 / Sony.

URBAN RENEWAL
Only so much oil in the ground / Come back baby / It's not the crime / I won't leave unless you want me to / Maybe it'll rub off / (To say the least) you're the most / Willing to learn / Give me the proof / It can never be the same / I believe in myself / Walkin' up hip street
CD _____ 7599263492
Warner Bros. / Sep '93 / Warner Music.

Towering Inferno

KADDISH
Rose / Prayer / Dachau / 4 By 2 / Edvard Kiraly / Memory / Not me / Reverse field / Occupation / Sto Mondo Rotondo / Organ loop / Toll (I) / Toll (II) / Ruin / Juden / Pogrom / Partisans / Modern times / Bell / Kaddish / Weaver
CD _____ CID 8039
CD _____ CIDX 8039
Island / Aug '95 / PolyGram.

Townend, Rick

MAKE THE OLD TIMES NEW (Townend, Rick & Rosie Davis)
British Bluegrass / Nov '95 / Direct / ADA.
CD _____ BOBB 001CD

Towner, Ralph

BATIK
Waterwheel / Shades of Sutton Hoo / Trellis / Batik / Green room
CD _____ 8473252
ECM / Oct '89 / New Note.

BLUE SUN
CD _____ 8291622
ECM / Oct '86 / New Note.

CITY OF EYES
CD _____ 8377542
ECM / May '89 / New Note.

DIARY
Dark spirit / Entry in a diary / Images unseen / Icarus / Mon enfant / Ogden road / Erg / Silence of a candle
CD _____ 8291572
ECM / Aug '86 / New Note.

LOST AND FOUND
Harbringer / Trill ride / Elan vital / Summer's end / Col legno / Soft landing / Flying cows / Mon enfant / Breath away / Scrimshaw / Midnight blue...red shift / Moonless / Sco cone / Tattler / Taxi's waiting
CD _____ 5293472
ECM / Feb '96 / New Note.

MATCHBOOK (Towner, Ralph & Gary Burton)
CD _____ 8350142
ECM / Oct '88 / New Note.

OLD FRIENDS, NEW FRIENDS
CD _____ 8291962
ECM / Oct '86 / New Note.

OPEN LETTER
Sigh / Wistful thinking / Adrift / Infection / Alar / Short 'n' stout / Waltz for Debbie / I fall in love too easily / Magic touch / Magnolia Island / Nightfall
CD _____ 5119802
ECM / Jun '92 / New Note.

SARGASSO SEA (Towner, Ralph & John Abercrombie)
CD _____ 8350152
ECM / Sep '88 / New Note.

SLIDE SHOW (Towner, Ralph & Gary Burton)
Maelstrom / Vessel / Around the bend / Blue in green / Beneath an evening sky / Donkey jamboree / Continental breakfast / Charlotte's tangle / Innocenti
CD _____ 8272572
ECM / Feb '86 / New Note.

SOLO CONCERT
Spirit lake / Ralph's piano waltz / Train of thought / Zoetrope / Nardis / Chelsea courtyard / Timeless
CD _____ 8276682
ECM / Dec '85 / New Note.

SOLSTICE
Oceanus / Visitation / Drifting petals / Numbus / Winter solstice / Piscean dance / Red and black / Sand
CD _____ 8254582
ECM / '82 / New Note.

SOUND AND SHADOWS
Distant hills / Balance beam / Along the way / Arion / Song of the shadows
CD _____ 8293862
ECM / Oct '89 / New Note.

TRIOS AND SOLOS (Towner, Ralph & Glen Moore)
CD _____ 8333282
ECM / Jul '88 / New Note.

WORKS: RALPH TOWNER
Oceanus / Blue sun / New moon / Beneath an evening sky / Prince and the sage / Nimbus
CD _____ 8232682
ECM / Jun '89 / New Note.

Townes, Billy

LIVIN' FOR YOUR LOVE
Moroccan pasta / Minutes to go / Low gear / For my friend / Snowbound / Hypnotique / And the beat goes where / Sea breeze / Sun city at night / Dawn / Livin' for your love
CD _____ 101S 71422
101 South / Nov '93 / New Note.

Towns, Colin

MASK ORCHESTRA, THE
Smack and thistle / Music to type to / Tears for a traveller / Sixpence is a long shilling / Dream of pain / Magnificent whittling stomp / Completely lost / Not waving but drowning / Truth, beauty, compassion, dignity / Bolt from the blue / Solitude
CD _____ TJL 001CD
The Jazz Label / Feb '94 / New Note.

Townshend, Pete

CHINESE EYES
Stop hurting people / Sea refuses no river / Slit skirts / Somebody saved me / North country girl / Uniforms (crop d'esprit) / Stardom in Acton / Communication / Exquisitely bored / Face dances part two / Prelude
CD _____ 7567828122
Atlantic / Jan '96 / Warner Music.

EMPTY GLASS
Rough boys / I am an animal / And I moved / Let my love open the door / Jools and Jim / Keep on working / Cats in the cupboard / Little is enough / Empty glass / Gonna getcha
CD _____ 7567828112
Atco / Nov '95 / Warner Music.

PSYCHODERELICT
English boy / Meher baba M3 / Let's get pretentious / Meher baba M4 (signal box) / Early morning dreams / I want that thing / Dialogue introduction to Outlive The Dinosaur / Outlive the dinosaur / Flame (demo) / Now and then / I am afraid / Don't try to make me real / Dialogue introduction to Predictable / Predictable / Flame / Meher baba m5 / Fake it / Dialogue introduction to Now And Then (Reprise) / Now and then (reprise) / Baba O'Riley (demo) / English boy (reprise)
CD _____ 756782494-2
Atco / Jun '93 / Warner Music.

WHITE CITY
Second home love / Give blood / Brilliant blues / Crashing by design / Lonely words / White City fighting / Face the face / All shall be well / Hiding out / Closing sequence
CD _____ 252 392-2
Atco / Apr '86 / Warner Music.

WHO CAME FIRST
Pure and easy / Evolution / Forever's no time at all / Let's see action / Time is passing / There's a heartache following me / Sheraton Gibson / Content / Parvardigar / His hands / Seeker / Day of silence / Sleeping dog / Loved man / Latern cabin
CD _____ RCD 20246
Rykodisc / Oct '92 / Vital / ADA.

Toxik

WORLD CIRCUS
Heart attack / Social overload / Pain and misery / Voices / Door to hell / World circus / Forty seven seconds of sanity / False prophets / Haunted earth / Victims
CD _____ RR 349572
Roadrunner / Mar '88 / Pinnacle.

Toy Dolls

BARE FACED CHEEK
Bare faced cheek / Yul Bryner was a skinhead / How do you deal with Neal / Howza bouta kiss babe / Fisticuffs in Frederick Street / A.Diamond / Quick to quit the Quentin / Nowt can compare to Sunderland Fine-Fare / Ashbrooke launderette
CD _____ CLACD 280
Castle / Feb '93 / BMG.

COLLECTION: TOY DOLLS
CD _____ CCSCD 335
Castle / Jun '92 / BMG.

DIG THAT GROOVE BABY
Theme tune / Dig that groove baby / Dougy Giro / Spiders in the dressing room / Glenda and the test tube baby / Up the garden path / Nellie the elephant / Poor Davey / Stay mellow / Queen Alexandra Road / Worse things happen at sea / Blue suede shoes / Firey Jack
CD _____ RRCD 166
Receiver / Sep '92 / Grapevine.

FAR OUT DISC, A
Far out theme tune / she goes to fino's / Razzamatazz / Modern school of motoring / Carol Dodds is pregnant / You and a box of henkerchiefs / Bless you my son / My girlfriend's dad's a vicar / Come back Jackie / Do you want to finish....Or what / Commercial break / Chartbuster/Razzamatazz outro / We're mad / Wipeout / Florence is deaf (But there's no need to shout) / Far out theme tune (Final track)
CD _____ RRCD 164
Receiver / Sep '92 / Grapevine.

RECEIVER YEARS, THE
CD Set _____ RRCDX 504
Receiver / Sep '95 / Grapevine.

SINGLES 1983-84
Cheerio and toodle pip / H.O. / Alfie from the Bronx / Hanky panky / We're mad / Rupert the bear / Deirdre's a slag
CD _____ RRCD 167
Receiver / Jul '93 / Grapevine.

TEN YEARS OF TOYS
Florence is deaf (But there's no need to shout) / Glenda and the test tube baby / Idle gossip / Carol Dodds is pregnant / Tommy Knowey's car / Peter practise's practise place / Dierdre's a slag / Blue suede shoes / Dig that groove baby / Lambrusco kid / Doughy giro / Bless you my son / My girlfriend's Dad's a vicar / she goes to fino's / Firey Jack

Toyah

BEST OF TOYAH, THE
It's a mystery / Good morning universe / I want to be free / Neon womb / Be proud, be loud, be heard / Bird in flight / Rebel run / Brave new world / Dawn chorus / Victims of the riddle / Vow / Tribal look / Thunder in the mountains / Angel and me / Danced / Ieya
CD _____ CSAPCD 115
Connoisseur / Feb '94 / Pinnacle.

DREAMCHILD
Now and then / Let me go / Unkind / Out of the blue / Dreamchild / World of tension / Lost and found / Over you / I don't know / Disappear / Tone poem
CD _____ TOYCD 1001
Cryptic Enterprises / Feb '94 / Pinnacle.

Toyama, Yoshio

DUET (Toyama, Yoshio & Ralph Sutton)
CD _____ JCD 226
Jazzology / Apr '94 / Swift / Jazz Music.

Toyota Pipes & Drums

AMAZING GRACE
March, strathspey and reel / Slow air, jig and hornpipe / 6/8 Marches / Amazing grace / By the rivers of Babylon / Mount Fuji / Greatest hits medley / Sands of time / Magnificent seven / Send in the clowns / Salute to America
CD _____ LCOM 5133
Lismor / Jun '93 / Lismor / Direct / Duncans / ADA.

T'Pau

BRIDGE OF SPIES
Heart and soul / I will be with you / China in your hand / Friends like these / Sex talk / Bridge of spies / Monkey house / Valentine / Thank you for goodbye / You give up / China in your hand (reprise)
CD _____ CDSRN 8
Siren / Aug '91 / EMI.

HEART AND SOUL - THE VERY BEST OF T'PAU
Heart and soul / Valentine / Only a heartbeat / Whenever you need me / Secret garden / Sex talk / Road to our dream / This girl / Only the lonely / Bridge of spies / I will be with you / China in your hand
CD _____ TPAU 1
Virgin / Mar '93 / EMI.

PROMISE, THE
Soul destruction / Whenever you need me / Walk on air / Made of money / Hold on to love / Strange place / One direction / Only a heartbeat / Promise / Place in my heart / Man and woman / Purity
CD _____ CDVIP 124
Virgin VIP / Mar '94 / Carlton Home Entertainment / THE / EMI.

Tracey, Clark

FULL SPEED SIDEWAYS
Revenge of Sam Tracet / They're lovely / Sherman at the Copthorne / Sphere my dear / Mark nightingale song / Arnie's barnie / Chased out
CD _____ 33 JAZZ 018
33 Jazz / Apr '95 / Cadillac / New Note.

WE'VE BEEN EXPECTING YOU (Tracey, Clark Quintet)
CD _____ 33JAZZ 007CD
33 Jazz / Jun '93 / Cadillac / New Note.

Tracey, Stan

DUETS (SONATINAS /TNT)
Three against one / Still on the run / Murphy's dream / Fleeting glances / Summer hobo / Chalk blue / Ominoso / Dance 1 / Dance 2 / Skipover / Biformis / TNT
CD _____ CDP 7894502
Blue Note / May '93 / EMI.

GENESIS AND MORE... (Tracey, Stan & His Orchestra)
Beginning / Light / Firmament / Gathering / Sun, moon and the stars / Feather, fin and limb / Sixth day
CD _____ SJCD 114
Steam / Nov '89 / Cadillac / Wellard / Jazz Music.

LIVE AT THE QEH
Triple celebration / Come Sunday / Some other blues / Easy living / Devil's acre / Mary Rose / Cuban connection / Sixth day / Sophisticated lady
CD _____ CDBLT 1010
Blue Note / Oct '94 / EMI.

PLAYS DUKE ELLINGTON
I let a song go out of my heart / Prelude to a kiss / Satin doll / In a mellow tone / Daydream / Great times / Sophisticated lady / Black butterfly / Lotus blossom
CD _____ MOLECD 10
Mole Jazz / Jan '90 / Jazz Horizons / Jazz Music / Cadillac / Wellard / Impetus.

CD _____ DOJOCD 171
Dojo / Jun '94 / BMG.

PORTRAITS PLUS
Newk's fluke / Rocky mount / One for Gil /
Clinkscales / Spectrum No. 2 / Mainframe
CD _____ CDBLT 1006
EMI / Dec '92 / EMI.

**UNDER MILK WOOD (Jazz Suite
Inspired By Dylan Thomas)**
Cockle row / Starless and bible black / I lost
my step in Nantucket / No good boyo /
Penpals / Llareggub / Under Milk Wood /
A.M. Mayhem
CD _____ CDP 7894492
Blue Note / May '93 / EMI.

**WE STILL LOVE YOU MADLY (Tribute
To Duke Ellington) (Tracey, Stan & His
Orchestra)**
I'm beginning to see the light / Mood indigo
/ Blue feeling / I let a song go out of my
heart / Stomp, look and listen / Festival
junction / In a sentimental mood / Just
squeeze me / Lay by
CD _____ MOLECD 13
Mole Jazz / Apr '89 / Jazz Horizons / Jazz
Music / Cadillac / Wellard / Impetus.

Tractor

TRACTOR
All ends up / Little girl in yellow / Watcher /
Ravenscroft's 13 bar boogie / Shubunkin' /
Hope in favour / Every time it happens /
Make the journey
CD _____ REP 4081-WP
Repertoire / Aug '91 / Pinnacle / Cadillac.

Tractors

**HAVE YOURSELF A TRACTOR
CHRISTMAS**
Santa Claus is coming to town / Jingle my
bells / Shelter / Rockin' this Christmas /
Santa looked a lot like Daddy / Christmas
is coming / Santa Claus is comin' (in a boo-
gie woogie choo choo train) / Baby wanna
be by you / Swingin' home for Christmas /
White Christmas / Santa Claus boogie / Si-
lent night / Christmas blue
CD _____ 07822188052
Arista / Nov '95 / BMG.

TRACTORS, THE
Tulsa shuffle / Fallin' apart / Thirty days /
I've had enough / Little man / Baby likes to
rock it / Badly bent / Blue collar rock / Do-
reen / Settin' the woods on fire / Tryin' to
get to New Orleans / Tulsa shuffle
(Revisited)
CD _____ 07822187282
Arista / Aug '94 / BMG.

Tracy, Arthur

ALWAYS IN SONG
CD _____ PLATCD 36
Prism / Mar '95 / Prism.

MARTA
Across the great divide / Broken hearted
clown / East of the sun and west of the
moon / Greatest mistake of my life / I'll see
you again / I'll sing you a thousand love
songs / In a little gypsy tea room / Love's
last word is spoken / My curly headed baby
/ Marta / Music, maestro, please / Old sailor
/ Red maple leaves / Roses of Picardy /
September in the rain / Smilin' through /
South Sea island magic / Stay awhile /
When I grow too old to dream / Where are
you / Whistling waltz / You are my heart's
delight
CD _____ CDAJA 5095
Living Era / Sep '92 / Koch.

STREET SINGER, THE
There's a goldmine in the sky / Waltz for
those in love / Giannina mia / Water lilies in
the moonlight / When the organ played 'O
promise me' / Halfway to heaven / Song of
songs / Smilin' through / Faithful forever /
Just a wearyin' for you / Hills of old
Wyomin' / Along the Santa Fe trail / We
three (my echo, my shadow and me) /
Breeze and I / Shepherd's serenade / Say
it (over and over again) / Shrine of St. Cecilia
/ When the roses bloom again / Last time I
saw Paris / Somewhere in France with you
/ White cliffs of Dover / Marta
CD _____ PASTCD 7006
Flapper / Mar '93 / Pinnacle.

SWEETEST SONG IN THE WORLD, THE
Marta / Auf wiedersehen my dear / Play fiddle play / When a pal bids a pal goodbye /
I'll have the last waltz with mother / Everything I have is yours / How was I to know /
If I didn't care / Love me forever / It's easy
to remember / It's my Mother's birthday today / Leave me with a love song / Trees /
As long as our hearts are young / Old ship
o' mine / Keep calling me sweetheart /
When the poppies bloom again / Moonlight
on the waterfall / Goodnight angel / Little
lady make believe / Sweetest song in the
world / Grandma said / I paid for the lie I
told you / To Mother, with love / Faithful
forever
CD _____ CDHD 229
Happy Days / Sep '93 / Conifer.

**VERY BEST OF ARTHUR TRACY - THE
STREET SINGER**
CD _____ SOW 906
Sound Waves / May '93 / Target/BMG.

**VERY BEST OF THE STREET SINGER
VOL.2**
CD _____ SWNCD 002
Sound Waves / May '95 / Target/BMG.

Tracy, Jeanie

IT'S MY TIME
CD _____ PULSE 17CD
Pulse 8 / Nov '95 / Pinnacle / 3MV.

Tracy, Steve

GOING TO CINCINNATI
CD _____ BSCD 4707
Blue Shadow / '92 / Swift.

Trader Horne

MORNING WAY...PLUS
CD _____ SEECD 308
See For Miles/C5 / '90 / Pinnacle.

Trafalgar Squares

DIXIELAND GREATS
CD _____ PWK 039
Carlton Home Entertainment / '88 /
Carlton Home Entertainment.

Traffic

BEST OF TRAFFIC
Paper sun / Heaven is in your mind / No
face, no name, no number / Coloured rain
/ Smiling phases / Hole in my shoe / Med-
icated goo / Forty thousand headmen /
Feeling alright / Shanghai noodle factory /
Dear Mr. Fantasy
CD _____ IMCD 169
Island / Mar '93 / PolyGram.

FAR FROM HOME
Riding high / Here comes a man / Far from
home / Nowhere is their freedom / Holy
ground / Some kinda woman / Every night,
every day / This train won't stop / State of
grace / Mozambique
CD _____ CDV 2727
Virgin / May '94 / EMI.

JOHN BARLEYCORN MUST DIE
Glad / Freedom rider / Empty page /
Stranger to himself / John Barleycorn /
Every mother's son
CD _____ IMCD 40
Island / Sep '89 / PolyGram.

LAST EXIT
Just for you / Shanghai noodle factory / Something's got a hold of my toe / Withering
tree / Medicated goo / Feeling good / Blind
man
CD _____ IMCD 41
Island / Sep '89 / PolyGram.

**LOW SPARK OF HIGH-HEELED BOYS,
THE**
Hidden treasure / Low spark of high heeled
boys / Light up or leave me alone / Rock 'n'
roll stew / Many a mile to freedom /
Rainmaker
CD _____ IMCD 42
Island / Sep '89 / PolyGram.

MR. FANTASY
Heaven is in your mind / Berkshire poppies
/ House for everyone / No face, no name,
no number / Dear Mr. Fantasy / Dealer /
Utterly simple / Coloured rain / Hope I never
find me there / Giving to you
CD _____ IMCD 43
Island / Sep '89 / PolyGram.

ON THE ROAD
Glad/Freedom rider / Tragic magic / (Some-
times I feel so) Inspired / Shoot out at the
fantasy factory / Light up or leave me alone
/ Low spark of high heeled boys
CD _____ IMCD 183
Island / Mar '94 / PolyGram.

**SHOOT OUT AT THE FANTASY
FACTORY**
Shoot out at the fantasy factory / Roll right
stones / Evening blue / Tragic magic /
Sometimes I feel so uninspired
CD _____ IMCD 44
Island / Sep '09 / PolyGram.

TRAFFIC
You can all join in / Pearly queen / Don't be
sad / Who knows what tomorrow may bring
/ Feeling alright / Vagabond virgin / Forty
thousand headmen / Cryin' to be heard /
No time to live / Means to an end
CD _____ IMCD 45
Island / '89 / PolyGram.

**WELCOME TO THE CANTEEN
(Recorded Live)**
Medicated goo / Sad and deep / As you /
Forty thousand headmen / Shouldn't have
took more than you gave / Dear Mr. Fantasy
/ Gimme some lovin'
CD _____ IMCD 39
Island / '89 / PolyGram.

WHEN THE EAGLE FLIES
Something new / Dream Gerrard / Graveyard people / Walking in the wind / Memories of a rock and rolla / L.O.V.E. / When
the eagle flies
CD _____ IMCD 142
Island / Aug '91 / PolyGram.

Traffic Sound

1968-1969
CD _____ HBG 122/4
Background / Mar '94 / Background.

TRAFFIC SOUND
CD _____ HBG 122/13
Background / Apr '94 / Background.

Tragic Error

KLATCH IN DIE HANDEN
CD _____ WHOS 022CD
Who's That Beat / '90 / Vital.

Tragic Mulatto

ITALIANS FALL DOWN LOOK UP
CD _____ VIRUS 74CD
Alternative Tentacles / Jun '89 / Pinnacle.

Tragically Hip

DAY FOR NIGHT
Grace, too / Daredevil / Greasy jungle /
Yawning or snarling / Fire in the hole / So
hard done by / Nautical disaster / Thugs /
Inevitability of death / Scared / Inch an hour
/ Emergency / Titanic terrarium /
Impossibilium
CD _____ MCD 11140
MCA / Nov '94 / BMG.

FULLY COMPLETELY
Courage / Looking for a place to happen /
At the hundreth meridan / Pigeon camera /
Lionized / Locked in the trunk of a car /
We'll go too / Fully completely / Fifty mis-
sion cap / Wheat kings / Wherewithal /
Eldorado
CD _____ MCLD 19314
MCA / Oct '95 / BMG.

ROAD APPLES
CD _____ MCAD 10173
MCA / May '91 / BMG.

Trains & Boats & Planes

ENGULFED
CD _____ RAIN 002
Cloudland / Jan '94 / Plastic Head / SRD.

HUM
CD _____ UFO 010CD
UFO / Mar '92 / Pinnacle.

MINIMAL STAR
Parents' place / I like cars / Private party /
Minimal star / She had us / All we got /
Wake / Playback / Kitty Wu / Genius spider
/ Fat is free / You hear my dear / Timelove
CD _____ SHIMMY 070CD
Shimmy Disc / Feb '94 / Vital.

Trammell, Bobby Lee

YOU MOSTEST GIRL
Shirley Lee / I sure do love you baby / You
mostest girl / Uh oh / Should I make
amends / My Susie Jane my Susie Jane /
Martha Jane / Jenny Lee / It's all your fault
/ Couldn't believe my eyes / You stand a
chance of losing what you've got / Love
don't let me down / Twenty four hours / Am
I satisfying you / I tried / Just let me love
you one more time / Come on and love me
/ If you don't wanna you don't have to /
Give me that good lovin' / New dance in
France / Long Tall Sally
CD _____ BCD 15887
Bear Family / Nov '95 / Rollercoaster /
Direct / CM / Swift / ADA.

Trammps

LEGENDARY ZING ALBUM, THE
Penguin at the big apple/Zing went the
strings of my heart / Pray all you sinners /
Sixty minute man / Scrub board / Tom's
song / Rubber band / Hold back the night
/ Penguin at the big apple
CD _____ CDKENM 088
Kent / Oct '88 / Pinnacle.

Tramp

BRITISH BLUES GIANTS
Own up / What you gonna do when the
road comes through / Somebody watching
me / Baby, what you want me to do / On
the scene / Hard work / Too late for that
now / What you gonna do / You gotta move
/ Funky money / Maternity orders (keep on
rolling in) / Same old thing / Too late now /
Street walking blues / Month of Sundays /
Another day / Now I ain't a junkie anymore
/ Like you used to do / Put a record on /
Beggar by your side / It's over
CD _____ SEECD 354
See For Miles/C5 / Sep '92 / Pinnacle.

Trance

ROCKERS
CD _____ 367 0002.2
Mausoleum / Oct '91 / Grapevine.

Trance Groove

SOLID GOLD EASY ACTION
Reebop / Character / Bladerunner / Waiting
man / Funland / Driving south / Swamp / Air
Afrique / Mamboo moon / Water / Low tide
/ Bladerunner II / Reebop radio edit

Trans-Europe Express

CD _____ VBR 21432
Vera Bra / Jun '94 / Pinnacle / New Note.

Trance Induction

ELECTRICKERY
Ambienta / Nada brahma / New edge /
Heaven / New age heartcore / Spinner /
Bombay / Infotask / Cyberlog / Robogroove
3 / Lit by doctor life
CD _____ GPCD 001
Guerilla / Jan '94 / Pinnacle.

Trance To The Sun

GHOST FOREST
CD _____ EFA 06482-2
Tess Europe / Apr '94 / SRD.

Transcendental Anarchists

CLUSTER ZONE
CD _____ SR 9462CD
Silent / Jan '95 / Plastic Head.

Tranceport

TRANCEGLOBAL
Future foundation / Invisible anaconda /
Light tunnel / Whicker pacific / Solar inter-
ference / Colour of magic / Swimming in the
blue moon / Night geometry / Arc of
trancendance
CD _____ REAL 093
Surreal / Apr '93 / Surreal To Real / C & D
Compact Disc Services.

Trans-Europe Express

TRANS - EUROPE EXPRESS
CD _____ CLEO 5878CD
Cleopatra / Jan '94 / Disc.

Transambient...

**PRAZE-AN-BEEBLE (Transambient
Communications)**
Seabeams / Ocean waves at sunset / They
shoot geese don't they / Alaska pt.1 / Ar-
cades / Mauve / Iceman / Alaska pt.2 /
What is muzik / River
CD _____ STONE 015CD
3rd Stone / Sep '95 / Vital / Plastic Head.

Transcend

2001-2008 FULL LENGTH
2001 / 2002 / 2003 / 2004 / 2005 / 2006 /
2007 / 2008
CD _____ NTONECD 007
Ntone / Sep '95 / Vital.

VERSION 8.5
CD _____ SSR 005CD
Stormstrike / Jul '95 / Plastic Head.

Transcendental Love...

**ORGASMATRONIC (Transcendental
Love Machine)**
Hydrogen Dukebox / Apr '94 / Vital / 3MV.

Transglobal Underground

DREAM OF 100 NATIONS
CD _____ NR 021CD
Nation / Oct '93 / Disc.

INTERNATIONAL TIMES
CD _____ NATCD 38
Nation / Oct '94 / Disc.

INTERPLANETARY MELTDOWN
CD _____ NATCD 57
Nation / Oct '94 / Disc.

Transmetal

BURIAL AT SEA
CD _____ GCI 89804
Plastic Head / Jun '92 / Plastic Head.

Transmisia

DUMBSHOW
CD _____ INV 027CD
Invisible / Jun '94 / Plastic Head.

Transvision Vamp

POP ART
Trash city / I want your love / Sister moon
/ Psychosonic Cindy / Revolution baby / Tell
that girl to shut up / Wild star / Hanging out
with Halo Jones / Andy Warhol's dead / Sex
kick
CD _____ MCLD 19211
MCA / Sep '93 / BMG.

VELVETEEN
Baby I don't care / Only one / Landslide of
love / Falling for a goldmine / Down on you
/ Song to the stars / Kiss their sons / Born
to be sold / Pay the ghosts / Bad valentine
/ Velveteen
CD _____ MCLD 19215
MCA / Aug '93 / BMG.

Trapeze

HIGH FLYERS (The Best Of Trapeze)
CD _____ 8209572
Deram / Jan '96 / PolyGram.

TRAPEZE

MEDUSA
Black cloud / Jury / Your love is alright / Touch my life / Seagull / Mates you wanna cry / Medusa
CD _____ 820 955-2
London / Feb '94 / PolyGram.

TRAPEZE
It's only a dream / Giants dead, hoorah / Over / Nancy Gray / Fairytale / Verily verily / It's my life / Am I / Suicide / Wings / Another day / Send me no more letters
CD _____ 820 954-2
London / Feb '94 / PolyGram.

YOU ARE THE MUSIC, WE'RE THE BAND
Keepin' time / Coast to coast / What is a woman's role / Way back to the bone / Feelin' so much better now / Will our love end / Loser / We are the music
CD _____ 820 956-2
London / Feb '94 / PolyGram.

Trasante, Negrito

UNTIL DAWN
CD _____ 972
Kardum / Aug '93 / Discovery.

Trash Can Sinatras

CAKE
CD _____ 8282012
Go Discs / Jul '90 / PolyGram.

I'VE SEEN EVERYTHING
Easy road / Hayfever / Bloodrush / Worked a miracle / Perfect reminder / Killing the cabinet / Orange fell / I'm immortal / Send for Benny / Iceberg / One at a time / I've seen everything / Hairy years / Earlies
CD _____ 828408-2
Go Discs / May '93 / PolyGram.

Trashmen

LIVE BIRD 1965-1967
Let's go trippin' / Baja / Lovin' up a storm / Malaguena / Green onions / Surfin' bird / Henrietta / Rumble / Bird dance beat / King of the surf / The / Mashed potatoes / Ubangi stomp / Dai Winslow interview / Same lines / Keep your hands off my baby
CD _____ CDSC 11006
Sundazed / Jan '94 / Rollercoaster.

Traum, Artie

CAYENNE
CD _____ CD 3084
Rounder / CM / Direct / ADA / Cadillac.

LETTERS FROM JOUBEE
CD _____ SHAN 5008CD
Shanachie / Dec '93 / Koch / ADA / Greensleeves.

Travelin' Light

CHRISTMAS WITH TRAVELIN' LIGHT
Let it snow, let it snow, let it snow / Sleigh ride / Frosty the Snowman / Twelve days of Christmas / Carol of the bells / Have yourself a merry little Christmas / We wish you a Merry Christmas / Jingle bells / Rudolph the red nosed reindeer / Here comes Santa Claus / Winter wonderland / Christmas song / Silver bells / Silent night
CD _____ CD 83330
Telarc / Nov '93 / Conifer / ADA.

COOKIN' WITH FRANK & SAM
Manior de mes beves / Monk's dream / Dark eyes / Deep purple / Say it's so / Under Paris blues / Dig / Mood indigo / Alice's fax / Nuages / FDR Jones / Smoke gets in your eyes / Song d'automne / Loser
CD _____ CCD 4647
Concord Jazz / Jun '95 / New Note.

MAKIN' WHOOPEE
CD _____ CD 83324
Telarc / Feb '93 / Conifer / ADA.

Traveling Wilburys

TRAVELING WILBURYS
Handle with care / Dirty world / Rattled / Last night / Not alone anymore / Congratulations / Heading for the light / Margarita / Tweeter and the monkey man / End of the line
CD _____ 925 796 2
Wilbury / Oct '88 / Warner Music.

TRAVELING WILBURYS VOLUME 3
She's my baby / Inside out / If you belonged to me / Devil's been busy / Seven deadly sins / Poor house / Where were you last night / Cool dry place / New blue moon / You took my breath away / Wilbury twist
CD _____ 7599263242
Wilbury / Nov '90 / Warner Music.

Travers, Pat

BLUES TRACKS
CD _____ RR 91472
Roadrunner / Sep '92 / Pinnacle.

BOOM BOOM
Snorting whiskey, drinking cocaine / Life in London / It's a la love you / Getting better / What'cha gonna do without me / Daddy long legs / Heat in the street / School of hard knocks / Help me / Stevie / Ready or not / Boom boom / Born under a bad sign / Guitars from hell
CD _____ ESMCD 140
Essential / May '95 / Total/BMG.

HALFWAY TO SOMEWHERE
CD _____ PRD 70842
Provogue / Oct '95 / Pinnacle.

JUST A TOUCH
CD _____ RR 90452
Roadrunner / Oct '93 / Pinnacle.

Travis Cut

SERIAL INCOMPETENCE
CD _____ DAMGOOD 68CD
Damaged Goods / Apr '95 / SRD.

Travis, Merle

COUNTRY HOEDOWN SHOWS AND FILMS OF THE 1940S/50'S
CD _____ RFCD 14
Country Routes / Feb '95 / Jazz Music / Hot Shot.

FOLKSONGS OF THE HILLS
Nine pound hammer / That's all / John Bolin / Muskrat / Dark as a dungeon / John Henry / Sixteen tons / Possum up a Simmon tree / I am a pilgrim / Over by number nine / Barbara Allen / Lost John / Black gold / Harlan County boys / Pay day comes too slow / Browder explosion / Bloody Brethitt County / Here's to the operators, Boys / Miner's wife / Courtship of second cousin Claude / Miner's strawberries / Paw walked behind us with a cabride lamp / Preacher lane / Dear old Halifax
CD _____ BCD 15636
Bear Family / May '93 / Rollercoaster / Direct / CM / Swift / ADA.

GUITAR RAGS & A TOO FAST PAST
You'll be lonesome too / Steppin' out kind / When Mussolini laid his pistol down / Two time Annie / What will I do / So long, farewell, goodbye / God put a rainbow in the clouds / It may be too late / Be on your way / Rainin' on the mountains / Give me your hand / Out on the open range / Ridin' down to Santa Fe / Hominy grits / That's all / Used to work in Chicago / Boogie woogie boy / Boogie woogie boy (Alt) / Merle's buck dance / Steel guitar stomp / I used to work in Chicago / I'm all thru trusting you / Weary lonesome me / No vacancy / Cincinnati Lou / Two is a couple (And three is a crowd) / What a shame / T For Texas (Blue yodel) / Missouri / Divorce me C.O.D. / Fool at the steering wheel / Nine pound hammer / Sixteen tons / Dark as a dungeon / Over by number nine / John Henry / Muskrat / I am a pilgrim / This world is not my home / Covered wagon rolled right along / Oh why oh why did I ever leave Wyoming / Little too far / When Rosie Riccoola do the Hoola Ma Boola / Steel guitar rag (Alt) / Honey bunch (Alt) / Sweet temptation / Don't hand me that line / Steel guitar rag / Honey bunch / So round, so firm, so fully packed / Alimony bound / Follow thru / Three time's seven / I'm sick and tired of you little darlin' / Sunshine's back in town / Devil to pay / Lucky, what a gal / Sioux City Sue / Fat gal (False start) / Fat gal / I like my chicken fryin' size / Merle's boogie woogie (Alt) / Merle's boogie woogie / Dapper Dan / When my baby double talks to me / I'm pickin up the pieces of my heart / Information please / Any old time / Kentucky means paradise / Leave my honey bee alone / I'm a natural born gamblin' man / Get along blues / Too fast past / Crazy boogie / You better try another man / Deck of cards / Wabash cannonball / Blues stay away from me / Philosophy / I got a mean old woman / Petticoat fever / Start even / Cane bottom chair / I'm knee deep in trouble / Little Miss Sherlock Holmes / Too much sugar for a dime / Spoonin' moon / Trouble, trouble / El Reno / Won't cha be my baby / Dry bread / Lost John Boogie / Deep south / Boogie in minor / Let's settle down (To runnin' around together) / Done rovin' / Faithful fool / Love must be kept / Ain't that a cryin' shame / Rainy day feelin' / Ain't that a cryin' shame / I'll see you in my dreams / Cannonball rag / I'll have myself a ball / Bayou baby (Cajun lullaby) / Green Cheese / Louisiana boogie / Saturday night shuffle / Waltz you saved for me / Crazy about you / Re-enlistment blues / Dance of the golden road / Gambler's guitar / Shut up and drink your beer / Seminole girl / Jolie fille / I can't afford the coffee / Blue bell / Memphis blues / Sheikh of araby / On a bicycle made for two (Daisy Belle) / Black diamond blues / Blue smoke / Walking the strings / Sleepy time gal / Tuck me to sleep in my old 'Tucky home / Rock-a-bye rock / Bugle call rag / Cuddle up a little closer / Beer barrel polka / Turn my picture upside down / If you want it, I've got it / Lazy river / Hunky dory
CD Set _____ BCDEI 15637
Bear Family / Jun '94 / Rollercoaster / Direct / CM / Swift / ADA.

MERLE TRAVIS COMPILATION
Cincinnati Lou / No vacancy / Divorce me C.O.D. / Missouri / So round, so firm, so fully packed / Sweet temptation / Steel guitar rag / Three times seven / Sixteen tons / Nine pound hammer / I am a pilgrim / Dark as a dungeon / John Henry / Fat gal / Merle's boogie woogie / Crazy boogie / I'm a natural born gamblin' man / I'm sick and tired of you little darlin' / Sioux City Sue / What a shame / Kinfolks in Carolina (Featuring Joe Maphis). / Re-enlistment blues / Wildwood flower (Featuring Hank Thompson.) / Blues stay away from me / Kentucky means paradise / John Henry Jr. / Guitar rag / Way down yonder in New Orleans
CD _____ CDEMS 1468
Capitol / Nov '92 / EMI.

Travis, Mike

EH 15
Regarding Nelson / Grandfather clock menace / Cycle time / Forethought / L'allegria / Moonlight over joppa / Shall we Mr.Witherspoon / Backtalk
CD _____ ECL 9105 CD
Eclectic / Jun '93 / Pinnacle.

Travis, Randy

ALWAYS AND FOREVER
Too gone too long / My house / Good intentions / What'll you do about me / I won't need you anymore / Forever and ever, Amen / I told you so / Anything / Truth is lyin' next to you / Tonight we're gonna tear down the walls
CD _____ WX 107CD
WEA / Aug '90 / Warner Music.

BEST OF RANDY TRAVIS
CD _____ 9548334612
Warner Bros. / Apr '95 / Warner Music.

HIGH LONESOME
Let me try / Oh what a time to be me / Heart of hearts / Point of light / Forever together / Better class of losers / I'd surrender all / High lonesome / Allergic to the blues / I'm gonna have a little talk
CD _____ 759926612
WEA / Oct '91 / Warner Music.

NO HOLDING BACK
Mining for coal / Singin' the blues / When your world was turning for me / He walked on water / No stoppin' us now / It's just a matter of time / Card carryin' fool / Somewhere in my broken heart / Hard rock bottom of your heart / Have a nice rest of your life
CD _____ 9259882
WEA / Feb '95 / Warner Music.

OLD 8 BY 10
Forever and ever, amen / Honky tonk moon / Deeper than a holler / It's out of my hands / Is it still over / Written in stone / Blues in black and white / Here in my heart / We ain't out of love yet / Promises
CD _____ WX 162CD
WEA / Jul '88 / Warner Music.

STORMS OF LIFE
On the other hand / Storms of life / My heart cracked / Diggin' up bones / No place like home / 1982 / Send my body / Messin with my mind / Reasons I cheat / There'll always be a honky tonk somewhere
CD _____ 925435 2
WEA / Mar '87 / Warner Music.

THIS IS ME
Honky tonk side of town / Before you kill us all / That's where I draw the line / Whisper my name / Small y'all / Runaway train / This is me / Box / Gonna walk that line / Oscar / Angel
CD _____ 936245501-2
Warner Bros. / Apr '94 / Warner Music.

Travis, Theo

2AM
CD _____ 33JAZZ 011
33 Jazz / Jun '93 / Cadillac / New Note.

VIEW FROM THE EDGE
Fort Dunlop / Love for sale / Ghosts of Witley Court / Freedom / View from the edge / Psychgroove / I'm coming home / Empathy / Purple sky
CD _____ 33JAZZ 019CD
33 Jazz / May '95 / Cadillac / New Note.

Travis, Tom

TOM TRAVIS BLUEGRASS BAND
CD _____ BOBB 003CD
British Bluegrass / Nov '95 / Direct / ADA.

Travolta, John

BEST OF JOHN TRAVOLTA, THE
Sandy / Girl like you / Whenever I'm away from you / All strung out on you / Let her in / Never gonna fall in love again / Rainbows / Razzamatazz / I don't know what I like about you baby / Big trouble / Goodnight Mr. Moon / Baby, I could be so good at lovin' you / Slow dancin' / Can't let you go / Easy evil / Back doors crying / What would they say / Right time of the night / Moonlight lady / Settle down / You set my dreams to music
CD _____ 30359 00072
Essential Gold / Feb '96 / Carlton Home Entertainment.

GREASED LIGHTNIN' (70's Recordings)
CD _____ CDCD 1260
Charly / Jun '95 / Charly / THE / Cadillac.

JOHN TRAVOLTA
CD _____ EMPRCD 524
Empress / Sep '94 / THE.

Trax Beyond Subconscious

AMBIENT CUT-OUTS VOL 1
CD _____ LABUKCD 3
Labworks / Oct '94 / SRD / Disc.

Treacherous Human...

VICE (Treacherous Human Underdogs)
CD _____ RGE 103-2
Enemy / Nov '94 / Grapevine.

Treacherous Jaywalkers

SUNRISE
CD _____ SST 126 CD
SST / May '93 / Plastic Head.

Treacherous Three

OLD SCHOOL FLAVA
CD _____ WRA 8128CD
Wrap / Mar '94 / Koch.

Treatment

CIPHER CAPUT
Hidden attack / Boing song / Risky / Dissolving / Designer / Cigarettes and starling (On CD only) / Doubt / Better future for Britain / Big I am / Decay / Damage / Holding on
CD _____ DELECCD 026
Delerium / Nov '93 / Vital.

Trebunia Family Band

POLAND
CD _____ NI 5437
Nimbus / Jul '95 / Nimbus.

Treepeople

SOMETHING VICIOUS
CD _____ CZ 040CD
C/Z / Mar '92 / Plastic Head.

Trees

GARDEN OF JANE DELAWNEY
Nothing special / Great silkie / Garden of Jane Delawney / Lady Margaret / Glasgerion / She moved through the fair / Road / Epitaph / Snail's lament
CD _____ BGOCD 172
Beat Goes On / Apr '93 / Pinnacle.

ON THE SHORE
Soldiers three / Murdoch / Streets of Derry / Sally free and easy / Fool / Adams toon / Geordie / While the iron is hot / Little Sadie / Polly on the shore
CD _____ BGOCD 173
Beat Goes On / Mar '93 / Pinnacle.

Treme Brass Band

GIMME MY MONEY BACK
CD _____ ARHCD 417
Arhoolie / Jan '96 / ADA / Direct / Cadillac.

Tremeloes

GOLD
CD _____ GOLD 208
Disky / Apr '94 / THE / BMG / Discovery / Pinnacle.

HERE COME THE TREMELOES
One of the boys / My friend Delaney / Sad goodbye / I want it easy / September November December / Hard woman / Lonely Dolly / Big bad boogie / Love song / Help
CD _____ CLACD 250
Castle / '92 / BMG.

MASTER
Wait for me / Long road / Now's the time / Try me / But then / I / Before I sleep / Boola boola / I swear / Baby / By the way / Willow tree / Me and my life
CD _____ CLACD 251
Castle / '91 / BMG.

SILENCE IS GOLDEN
Even the bad times are good / Call me number one / Helule helule / Candy man / Yellow river / Silence is golden / Suddenly you love me / Me and my life / Here comes my baby / Last word / Someone / Mu little lady (non Il girti mi) / words
CD _____ 15067
Laserlight / Aug '92 / Target/BMG.

SILENCE IS GOLDEN
Call me number one / Even the bad times are good / Here comes my baby / Alli-oop / Do you love me / Ain't nothing but a house party / Reach out, I'll be there / I shall be released / Yellow river / My little lady / Silence is golden / I like it that way / Cool jerk / Every day / Peggy Sue / Rag doll / Twist and shout / Every little bit hurts
CD _____ 5507422
Spectrum/Karussell / Jan '95 / PolyGram / THE.

SINGLES, THE

Goodday sunshine / Here comes my baby / Silence is golden / Even the bad times are good / Be mine / Suddenly you love me / Helule helule / My little lady / I'm gonna try / I shall be released / Hello world / Once on a Sunday morning / (Call me) Number one / By the way / Me and my life / Right wheel, left hammer sham / Hello Buddy / Too late (to be saved) / I like it that way / Blue suede / Ride on / Make it break it / You can't touch Sue / Do I love you / Say OK / Be boppin boogie
CD _____ BX 4572
BR Music / Dec '95 / Target/BMG.

STORY OF THE TREMELOES, THE
CD _____ BS 80182
BR Music / Jul '94 / Target/BMG.

Trenchmouth

CONSTRUCTION OF NEW ACTION
CD _____ SR 89222CD
Skene / Nov '92 / SRD.

Trend

BITCH
CD _____ RRS 946CD
Progress / Nov '95 / Plastic Head.

Trends Of Culture

TRENDZ
CD _____ 530207-2
Polydor / Jul '93 / PolyGram.

Trenet, Charles

EXTRAORDINARY GARDEN, THE (Very Best Of Charles Trenet)
Boum (Orchestra Wal-Berg.) / L'ame des poetes (Orchestra dir. Trenet and quartet.) / Moi j'aime le music hall (Orchestra Guy Luypaerts.) / Vous qui passez sans me voir (Orchestra Hubert Rostaing.) / La jolie sardane (Orchestra Jo Boyer.) / En Avril a Paris (Orchestra Wal-Berg.) / Coin de rue (Orchestra Jacques Helian.) / Mes jeunes annes (Orchestra Albert Lasry with the Raymond St. Paul Chorus.) / A la porte du garage (Orchestra Guy Luypaerts.) / France Dimanche (Orchestra Albert Lasry.) / Qur reste t'll de nos amours (Orchestra Leo Chauliac.) / Y'a d'la Joie (Charles Trenet & His Orchestra.) / Douce France (Orchestra Albert Lasry.) / La polka du roi (Orchestra Trenet.) / Revoir Paris (Orchestra Albert Lasry.) / La folie complainte (Orchestra Jo Boyer.) / Le grand cafe (Orchestra Charles Trenet.) / La mer (Orchestra Albert Lasry.) / Menilmontant (Orchestra Wal-Berg. CD only.) / Vous oubliez votre cheval (Orchestra Wal-Berg. CD only.) / La maison du poete (CD only.) / La famille musicienne (Orchestra Guy Luypaerts. CD only.) / Le chante (Orchestra Wal-Berg. CD only.)
CD _____ CZ 314
EMI / Jun '90 / EMI.

L'AIME DES POETES
CD _____ CD 314
Entertainers / Feb '95 / Target/BMG.

Treniers

COOL IT BABY
You're killing me / Day old bread / Squeeze me / Flip your wins / Rock bottom / Give a little time / Hey you / Log of the blues so bad / Straighten up baby / Cool it baby / Drinkin' wine spo-dee-o-dee / Margie / Madune / Sorrento / Lover come back to me / We want a rock and roll president / Longest walk / Ain't nothing wrong with that baby
CD _____ BCD 15418
Bear Family / Dec '88 / Rollercoaster / Direct / CM / Swift / ADA.

HEY SISTER LUCY
Hey sister Lucy / Buzz buzz buzz / But I'd rather / Hey boys better get yourself an extra / Oooh look a there ain't she pretty / Near to me / No baby no / Sometimes I'm happy / I'll follow you / It's a quiet town / Convertable cadillac / Ain't she mean / Sure had a wonderful time last night / I miss you so / Hey jacobia / Why / Lady luck / When you're finished talkin' (let's make some love)
CD _____ BCD 15419
Bear Family / Dec '88 / Rollercoaster / Direct / CM / Swift / ADA.

Trent, Jackie

TWO OF US, THE (Trent, Jackie & Tony Hatch)
Downtown / Where are you now / My love / Joanna / What would I be / Call me / Who am I / Forget him / Colour my world / Thank you for loving me / I know a place / Opposite your smile / You're everything / Other man's grass / I couldn't live without your love / Let's do it again / Look for a star / Don't sleep in the subway / Sign of the times / Two of us
CD _____ PRCD 144
President / Nov '94 / Grapevine / Target/BMG / Jazz Music / President.

Treorchy Male Choir

SHOWSTOPPERS
Another opening another show / Just one of those things / You do something to me / So in love / Who wants to be a millionaire / Love changes everything / Bring him home / Anthem (Chess) / Climb every mountain / Somewhere / Do you hear the people sing / How to handle a woman / Impossible dream / Send in the clowns / On the street where you live
CD _____ CDMFP 5906
Music For Pleasure / Apr '91 / EMI.

TREORCHY SING QUEEN
Overture / We are the champions / Radio ga ga / Save me / Crazy little thing called love / Flash / You're best friend / Play the game / Good old fashioned lover boy / Don't stop me now / We will rock you / Bohemian rhapsody
CD _____ CDMFP 5996
Music For Pleasure / Nov '93 / EMI.

Treponem Pal

EXCESS & OVERDRIVE
CD _____ CD RR 9076 2
Roadrunner / Jun '93 / Pinnacle.

Trettine, Caroline

BE A DEVIL
CD _____ UTIL 008 CD
Utility / Feb '90 / Grapevine.

Trian

TRIAN II
CD _____ GLCD 1159
Green Linnet / Dec '95 / Roots / CM / Direct / ADA.

Triarchy

BEFORE YOUR VERY EARS
CD _____ ETHEL 5
Vinyl Tap / Jan '96 / Vinyl Tap.

Tribal Draft

COLLECTIVE JOURNEYS
CD _____ CHILLCD 006
Chillout / Nov '95 / Disc / Kudos.

Tribal Tech

FACE FIRST
Face first / Canine / After hours / Revenge stew / Salt lick / Uh...yeah Ok / Crawling horror / Boiler room / Boat gig / Precipice / Wounded
CD _____ R2 79190
Bluemoon / Apr '94 / New Note.

REALITY CHECK
Nite club / Premonition / Jakarta / Susie's digsbums / Stella by starlight / Stella in-frared high-particle nuetron beam / Hole in the head / Giddy up go
CD _____ 92549
Bluemoon / May '95 / New Note.

Tribe Called Quest

LOW END THEORY
Excursions / Buggin' out / Rap promoter / Butter / Verses from the abstract / Showbusiness / Vibes and stuff / Infamous date rape / Check the rhyme / Everything is fair / Jazz (We got the) / Sky pager / What / Scenario
CD _____ CHIP 117
Jive / Oct '91 / BMG.

MIDNIGHT MARAUDERS
CD _____ CHIP 143
Jive / Oct '93 / BMG.

PEOPLE'S INSTINCTIVE TRAVELS & THE PATHS OF RHYTHM
Push it along / Luck of Lucien / After hours / Footprints / I left my wallet in El Segundo / Pubic enemy / Bonita Applebum / Can I kick it / Youthful expression / Rhythm (Devoted to the art of moving butts) / Mr. Muhammad / Ham 'n' eggs / Go ahead in the rain / Description of a fool
CD _____ CHIP 96
Jive / May '90 / BMG.

Tribe Of Dan

SHOOK UP, SHOOK UP
CD _____ MRM 003CD
Mister M Records / Apr '92 / Plastic Head.

Tribulation

CLOWN OF THORNS
Borka intro / Born bizarre / My world is different / Rise of prejudice / Everything's floating / Safe murder of emotions / Angst / Decide (take a stand) / angel in a winterpile / Beautiful views / Landslide of losers / Down my lungs / Pick an image (make sure it sells) / Herr Ober / Tiny little skeleton / Disgraceland / Dogmother (LP only)
CD _____ 8410602
Black Mark / Feb '92 / Plastic Head.

SPICY
CD _____ BHR 010
Burning Heart / Oct '94 / Plastic Head.

Tribulation All Stars

DUB LIBERATION
CD _____ WSPCD 005
Word Sound & Power / Apr '94 / SRD.

POSITIVE DUB
CD _____ WSPCD 7
Word Sound & Power / Aug '95 / SRD.

Tribute

NEW VIEWS
CD _____ EUCD 1042
ARC / '89 / ARC Music / ADA.

Trice, Willie

BLUE & RAG'D
Trying to find my baby / You have mistreated me / New diddey wah diddey / Troublesome mind / Shine on / I love you, sweet baby / I've had trouble / Good time boogie / New careless love blues / Goin' to the country / She's coming on the C and O / My baby's ways
CD _____ TRIX 3305
Trix / Mar '95 / New Note.

Tricia & The Boogies

BREAKAWAY
Everybody's gonna be happy / Your love is mine / Woman child (You can't know what I know) / We fit together / Make it easy / It's my turn / Mistaken identity / Nowhere to run / Breakaway / I don't mind
CD _____ PCOM 1099
President / '89 / Grapevine / Target/BMG / Jazz Music / President.

Trickett, Katie

NEXT TIME, THE
Next time / Autumn eyes / I'll never change this lovin' feelin' / When you were here / Playin' against the beat / Don't say don't / Lonley road home / She danced alone / Dancin' on the edge of a razor
CD _____ FIENDCD 768
Demon / Aug '95 / Pinnacle / ADA.

Tricky

MAXINQUAYE
Overcome / Ponderosa / Black steel / Hell is round the corner / Pumpkin / Aftermath / Abbaon fat track / Brand new you're retro / Suffocated love / You don't / Strugglin' / Feed me
CD _____ BRCD 610
4th & Broadway / Feb '95 / PolyGram.

Triffids

AUSTRALIAN MELODRAMA
CD _____ D 31182
Mushroom / Oct '94 / BMG / 3MV.

BORN SANDY DEVOTIONAL
CD _____ D 19457
Mushroom / Mar '95 / BMG / 3MV.

CALENTURE
Trick of the night / Bury me deep in love / Kelly's blues / Home town farewell kiss / Unmade love / open for you / Holy water / Blinder by the hour / Vagabond holes / Jerdacuttup man / Calenture / Save what you can
CD _____ D 19458
Mushroom / Feb '95 / BMG / 3MV.

IN THE PINES
Suntrapper / In the pines / Kathy knows / Twenty five to five / Do you want me near you / Once a day / Just might fade away / Better off this way / Only one life / Keep your eyes on the hole / One soul less on your fiery list / Born Sandy Devotional / Love and affection
CD _____ D 19480
Mushroom / Feb '95 / BMG / 3MV.

STOCKHOLM
CD _____ D 30231
Mushroom / Feb '95 / BMG / 3MV.

Trigger Happy

KILLATRON 2000
CD _____ BMCD 073
Raw Energy / Jun '95 / Plastic Head.

Trilobites

AMERICAN TV
CD _____ CGAS 808 CD
Citadel / Sep '89 / ADA.

Trimble, Gerald

CROSS CURRENTS
Bedding of the bride / Adieu my lovely Nancy / Rolling spey/Green hills of Tyrol/ Bob Walters / Blessed be (the lady's token) / Frank Gilruth/Jack Danielson's reel / Trimble's compliments to the city of Philadelphia / Breakdown / Christina Marie / Shifting paradigms
CD _____ GLCD 1065
Green Linnet / Jul '93 / Roots / CM / Direct / ADA.

FIRST FLIGHT
CD _____ GLCD 1043
Green Linnet / Nov '88 / Roots / CM / Direct / ADA.

HEARTLAND MESSENGER
Kail pot/Fisher's rant/Morayshire farmer's club/General Long / Miss Wharton Duff's jig / Coates hall/Amazon / Miss Stewart's jig/ Mrs. Rose of Kilravock/Donald MacLean / Ostinelli's reel/Miss Gunning's fancy / Heartland Messsenger trilogy
CD _____ GLCD 1054
Green Linnet / Oct '93 / Roots / CM / Direct / ADA.

Trinity

BIG BIG MAN
CD _____ LG 21057
Lagoon / May '93 / Magnum Music Group / THE.

Trinity Boys Choir

CHRISTMAS COLLECTION, A
Jingle bell rock / Sleigh ride / Have yourself a merry little Christmas / Sailing / Winter wonderland / Christmas song / Let it be / Amazing grace / Christmas waltz / When a child is born / I'll be home for Christmas / White Christmas / Windmills of your mind / Away in a manger / Bridge over troubled water / Eleanor Rigby / Over the rainbow / Jerusalem
CD _____ PWKM 4032
Carlton Home Entertainment / Oct '95 / Carlton Home Entertainment.

Trio

CONFLAGRATION
CD _____ BGOCD 253
Beat Goes On / Oct '95 / Pinnacle.

TRIO, THE
Oh, Dear / Dousing Rod / Silvercloud / Incantation / Caractacus / Let's stand / Foyer hall / Portes des lilas / Veritably / In between / Sixes and sevens / Green walnut / Billy the kid / Dee tune / Centering / Joachim / Drum
CD _____ BGOCD 231
Beat Goes On / Aug '94 / Pinnacle.

Trio Azteca

BEST OF MEXICAN FOLK SONGS
CD _____ EUCD 1109
ARC / '91 / ARC Music / ADA.

Trio Bulgarka

FOREST IS CRYING
CD _____ HNCD 1342
Hannibal / May '88 / Vital / ADA.

MISSA PRIMI - MUSIC OF PALESTRINA
CD _____ 669512CD
Melodie / Apr '95 / Triple Earth / Discovery / ADA / Jetstar.

Trio Da Paz

BLACK ORPHEUS
Felicidade / Frevo / Manha de carnaval / O nosso amor / Chao de estrelas / Samba de Orfeu / Don Maria / Numacumba / Hugs and kisses
CD _____ KOKO 1005
Kokopelli / Mar '95 / New Note.

Trio Idea

NAPOLI CONNECTION (Trio Idea & Jerry Bergonzi)
CD _____ 123261-2
Red / Apr '94 / Harmonia Mundi / Jazz Horizons / Cadillac / ADA.

Trio Los Duques

MOST BEAUTIFUL MEXICAN LOVE SONGS VOL.1
Llorarás / Nuestro amor / la Malaguena salaerosa / Cielito lindo / El reloj / Contigo aprendi / Pensando en ti / Besos de fuego / Duda / Cansado de ti
CD _____ 90764-2
PMF / May '94 / Kingdom / Cadillac.

Trio Mexico

MEXICAN LANDSCAPES VOL. 1
CD _____ PS 65901
Playasound / Jan '92 / Harmonia Mundi / ADA.

Trio Pantango

TANGO ARGENTINO POPULAR
CD _____ EUCD 1257
ARC / Mar '94 / ARC Music / ADA.

Trio Pellen-Molard

TRYPTICH
CD _____ GWP 002CD
Gwerz Productions / Aug '93 / ADA.

Trio Pennec

JAVADAO
CD _____ CD 847
Diffusion Breizh / Apr '94 / ADA.

Trio Trabant A Roma

STATE OF VOLGOGRAD
CD _____ FMPCD 57
FMP / Oct '94 / Cadillac.

Tripmaster Monkey

GOODBYE RACE
Albert's twisted memory bank / Pecola / Shutter's closed / Faster than Dwight / Valium / Roman catholic haircut / Is that my bag / Dad / Gravity / Key / Night of day / Not quite sure / Depravation test
CD _____ 936245674-2
Warner Bros. / Jul '94 / Warner Music.

Tripping Daisy

BILL
My umbrella / One through four / Lost and found / Change of mind / On the ground / Morning / Blown away / Brown eyed pickle boy / Miles and miles of pain / Triangle
CD _____ CIRD 1001
Island Red / May '94 / PolyGram / Vital.

I AM AN ELASTIC FIRE CRACKER
Rocket pop / Song / I got a girl / Piranha / Motivation / Same dress new day / Trip along / Raindrop / Step behind / Noose / Prick / High
CD _____ CIRD 1004
Island Red / Feb '96 / PolyGram / Vital.

Tripsichord

TRIPSICHORD
CD _____ 852124
EVA / May '94 / Direct / ADA.

Triptych

SLEEPLESS
CD _____ GAP 031
Gap Recordings / Nov '95 / SRD.

.Trisan

TRISAN
Triangle / Big trouble in old ballymore E / May yo I / Dragon / Mother and son / Wintermoon / River of life / Tri le cheile
CD _____ CDRW 32
Realworld / Nov '92 / EMI / Sterns.

Trisaxual Soul Champs

GO GIRL
Go girl / She said / I messed up / Coffee break / Costume party / Blue Di / Misirlou / Cool face / Blue am I / Can't keep up with you / Fatman blues / Cherry race
CD _____ FIENDCD 186
Demon / Jun '90 / Pinnacle / ADA.

Trischka, Tony

ALONE & TOGETHER
CD _____ BRAM 199124-2
Brambus / Nov '93 / ADA / Direct.

DUST ON THE NEEDLE
CD _____ CD 11508
Rounder / '88 / CM / Direct / ADA / Cadillac.

FIRE OF GRACE (Trischka, Tony & Skyline)
CD _____ FF 479CD
Flying Fish / Jun '94 / Roots / CM / Direct / ADA.

GLORY SHONE AROUND
CD _____ ROUCD 0354
Rounder / Oct '95 / CM / Direct / ADA / Cadillac.

ROBOT PLANE FLIES OVER ARKANSAS, A
CD _____ ROU 0171CD
Rounder / May '94 / CM / Direct / ADA / Cadillac.

SOLO BANJO WORKS (Trischka, Tony & Bela Fleck)
Ruben's wah wah / Fourteen / Liberec / Free improvision no.2 / Assunta / Old Joe Clark/June Apple / Max and Gus / Beaumont rag / Kingfisher's wing / Earl Scrugg's medley: Nashville Skyline/Ground speed/ Shuckin / Jeff Davies medley: Jeff Davies/ Fort Monroe/Danville Days / Yaha yaha / Beatles medley / Rings of saturn / Green Willis/Whiskey before breakfast / Killer bees of caffeine / Oma and Opa / Solaris / Flapperette/Reed pepper - Spicy rag / Triplet fever / Bach violin partitain D minor / Did you ever meet Gary Owen, Uncle Joe / Middle Eastern medley: Improv/Hilmi rit/George and Gladys ka / Twisted teen / Au lait
CD _____ ROU 0247CD
Rounder / Feb '93 / CM / Direct / ADA / Cadillac.

WORLD TURNING
CD _____ ROU 294CD
Rounder / Oct '93 / CM / Direct / ADA / Cadillac.

Triskell

HARPES CELTIQUES
CD _____ KMCD 60
Keltia Musique / Jul '95 / ADA / Direct / Discovery.

Trisomie 21

DISTANT VOICES
Shine ola / Touch sweet pleasure / Again and again (what a regular world) / Perfect side of doubt / Badlands / Is anybody home (part 4) / Distant voices / Soft brushing speed / Jazz / Long rider
CD _____ BIAS 212 CD
Play It Again Sam / Oct '92 / Vital.

SONGS BY TRISOMIE 21 VOL.1, THE
Perfect side of doubt / Again and again (What a regular world) / New outset / Bamboo / Missing piece / Betrayed / Story so far / Sharing sensation / Sunken lives / Night flight / Last song / Waiting for / Moving by you / Is anybody home (pt 1) / Logical animals / Il se noie
CD _____ BIAS 281CD
Play It Again Sam / May '94 / Vital.

T21 PLAYS THE PICTURES
CD _____ BIAS 152 CD
Play It Again Sam / Apr '90 / Vital.

Trisquel

AMANDI
CD _____ 20052CD
Sonifolk / Dec '94 / ADA / CM.

O CHAPEU DE MERLIN
CD _____ J 1023CD
Sonifolk / Jun '94 / ADA / CM.

Tristan Park

AT THE END OF THE DAY
Once you've been to heaven / Precious designs / Different this time / Way it should be / It could have been today / Someone else's dream / Another pretty face
CD _____ ANTRIMCD 1
Cyclops / Sep '95 / Pinnacle.

Tristano, Lennie

FEATURING LEE KONITZ
CD _____ CD 53155
Giants Of Jazz / May '95 / Target/BMG / Cadillac.

LENNIE TRISTANO/THE NEW TRISTANO
Line up / Requiem / Turkish mambo / East 32nd / These foolish things / You go to my head / If I had you / Ghost of a chance / All the things you are / Becoming / You don't know what love is / Deliberation / Scene and variations / Love lines / G minor complex
CD _____ 271595-2
Atlantic / Jun '94 / Warner Music.

TRIO, QUARTET, QUINTET & SEXTET
CD _____ CD 53149
Giants Of Jazz / Sep '94 / Target/BMG / Cadillac.

Tristitia

ONE WITH DARKNESS
CD _____ HOLY 11CD
Holy / May '95 / Plastic Head.

Tritt, Travis

GREATEST HITS
CD _____ 9362460012
Warner Bros. / Oct '95 / Warner Music.

TEN FEET TALL & BULLETPROOF
Ten feet tall and bulletproof / Walkin' all over my heart / Foolish pride / Outlaws like us / Hard times and misery / Tell me I was dreaming / Wishful thinking / Between an old memory and me / No vacation from the blues / Southern justice
CD _____ 936245603-2
Warner Bros. / May '94 / Warner Music.

Troggs

ARCHAEOLOGY
CD _____ 5129362
Phonogram / Jan '93 / PolyGram.

ATHENS ANDOVER
Crazy Annie / Together / Tuned into love / Deja vu / Dust bowl / I'm in control / Don't you know / What's your game / Suspicious / Hot stuff
CD _____ BR 1542
BR Music / Nov '94 / Target/BMG.

AU
CD _____ ROSE 186 CD
New Rose / May '90 / Direct / ADA.

BLACK BOTTOM
CD _____ ROSE 4CD
New Rose / Mar '85 / Direct / ADA.

DOUBLE HITS COLLECTION (Troggs/ Dave Dee, Dozy, Beaky, Mick & Tich)
CD _____ PLATCD 3908
Platinum Music / Oct '89 / Prism / Ross.

GREATEST HITS - WILD THING
CD _____ MU 5022
Musketeer / Oct '92 / Koch.

LEGENDS IN MUSIC - THE TROGGS
CD _____ LECD 074
Wisepack / Jul '94 / THE / Conifer.

LIVE AT MAX'S KANSAS CITY
Got love if you want it / Satisfaction / Love is all around / Give it to me / Feels like a woman / Strange movie / Summertime / Walking the dog / Memphis / No particular place to go / Wild thing / Gonna make you / I do I do / Call me
CD _____ MKCD 1001
President / Oct '94 / Grapevine / Target/ BMG / Jazz Music / President.

LOVE IS ALL AROUND
Love is all around / Wild thing / Give it to me / Hi hi Hazel / Night of the long grass / Seventeen / Kitty cat song / Little girl / I just sing / Jingle jangle / When I'm with you / Let me tell you babe / You can cry if you want to / Ride your pony / Lost girl / Hip hip hooray / I can only give you everything / Louie Louie
CD _____ 5510452
Spectrum/Karussell / Jul '95 / PolyGram THE.

TROGGS - GREATEST HITS, THE
Wild thing / Love is all around / With a girl like you / I want you / I can't control myself / Gonna make you / Good vibrations / Anyway that you want me / Give it to me / Night of the long grass / Girl in black / Hi hi Hazel / Little girl / Cousin Jane / Don't you know / Together / Nowhere Road / I'm in control / Summertime / Hot stuff / Dust bowl / I'll buy you an island / Crazy Annie / Jingle jangle / Deja vu
CD _____ 522739-2
PolyGram TV / Jul '94 / PolyGram.

TROGGS AU ALBUM
CD _____ HADCD 195
Javelin / Nov '95 / THE / Henry Hadaway Organisation.

TROGGS, THE
CD _____ KLMCD 030
Scratch / Nov '94 / BMG.

WILD THING
CD _____ 15081
Laserlight / Aug '91 / Target/BMG.

WILD THINGS
I got lovin' if you want it / Good vibrations / No particular place to go / Summertime / Satisfaction / Full blooded band / Memphis, Tennessee / Peggy Sue / Wild thing / Get you tonight / Different me / Down South in Georgia / After the rain / Rock 'n' roll lady / Walking the dog / We rode through the night / Gonna make you / Supergirl / I'll buy you an island / Rollin' stone
CD _____ SEECD 256
See For Miles/C5 / Aug '94 / Pinnacle.

WILD THINGS
CD _____ CDCD 1147
Charly / Feb '94 / Charly / THE / Cadillac.

Troi

TROI
CD _____ JUCCD 02
Juce / Oct '95 / Grapevine.

Troise

TROISE & HIS MANDOLIERS (Troise & His Mandoliers)
CD _____ PASTCD 7051
Flapper / Feb '95 / Pinnacle.

Trojans

CELTIC SKA
CD _____ GAZCD 11
Gaz's Rockin' Records / Nov '94 / Pinnacle.

REBEL BLUES
CD _____ GAZCD 10
Gaz's Rockin' Records / Oct '93 / Pinnacle.

SKALALITUDE
CD _____ GAZCD 007
Gaz's Rockin' Records / Sep '91 / Pinnacle.

STACK-A-DUB
CD _____ GAZCD 12
Gaz's Rockin' Records / Jul '95 / Pinnacle.

WILD & FREE
CD _____ GAZCD 008
Gaz's Rockin' Records / Jun '93 / Pinnacle.

Troka

TROKA
CD _____ OMCD 54
Olarin Musiiki Oy / Dec '94 / ADA / Direct.

Trom

EVIL
CD _____ SR 9506CD
Shiadarshana / Sep '95 / Plastic Head.

Tronzo, David

NIGHT IN AMNESIA (Tronzo, David & Reeves Gabrels)
CD _____ UPSTART 018
Upstart / Jul '95 / Direct / ADA.

Tronzo Trio

ROOTS
CD _____ KFWCD 154
Knitting Factory / Feb '95 / Grapevine.

Trooper, Greg

EVERYWHERE
CD _____ CBM 009CD
Cross Border Media / Mar '94 / Direct / ADA.

Trotsky Icepick

BABY
CD _____ SST 197 CD
SST / Sep '88 / Plastic Head.

CARPETBOMB THE RIFF
CD _____ SST 295CD
SST / Sep '93 / Plastic Head.

DANNY AND THE DOORKNOBS
CD _____ SST 254 CD
SST / Sep '90 / Plastic Head.

EL KABONG
CD _____ SST 246 CD
SST / Jul '89 / Plastic Head.

HOT POP HELLO
CD _____ SST 286CD
SST / May '94 / Plastic Head.

POISON SUMMER
Gaslight / Nightingale drive / Just the end of the world / Clowns on fire / Ivory tour / Commissioner / Big dreams / Drawing fire / Hit parade / You look like something Goya drew
CD _____ SST 239 CD
SST / Dec '89 / Plastic Head.

ULTRA-VIOLET CATASTROPHE, THE
CD _____ SST 279 CD
SST / Oct '91 / Plastic Head.

Trottel

FINAL SALUTE
CD _____ XM 028CD
X-Mist / Apr '92 / SRD.

Trotwood

KERRI JIGS, REEL, POLKAS
CD _____ CD 413
Bescol / May '95 / CM / Target/BMG.

Trouble

PLASTIC GREEN HEAD
CD _____ CDVEST 45
Bulletproof / Apr '95 / Pinnacle.

PSALM 9/THE SKULL
CD Set _____ ZORRO 19 CD
Music For Nations / Apr '91 / Pinnacle.

RUN TO THE LIGHT
Misery show / Thinking of the past / Peace of mind / Born in a prison / Tuesdays child / Beginning
CD _____ CDMZORRO 74
Metal Blade / May '94 / Pinnacle.

Trouble Funk

DROP THE BOMB
Hey fellas / Get on up / Let's get hot / Drop the bomb / Pump me up / Don't try to use me / My love (burning love) / Caravan to midnight / I'm out to get you / Lost in love / Fool / It's for you / Birthday boy / King of the dances / Sail on / Supergrit (On CD only) / Hey Fellas (2) (On CD only)
CD _____ NEBCD 663
Sequel / Oct '93 / BMG.

Troubles

TROUBLES
CD _____ LARRCD 316
Larrikin / Nov '94 / Roots / Direct / ADA / CM.

Troup, Bobby

BOBBY TROUP 1955/59/67
CD _____ SLCD 9009
Starline / Dec '94 / Jazz Music.

IN A CLASS BEYOND COMPARE
CD _____ ACD 98
Audiophile / Apr '93 / Jazz Music / Swift.

KICKS ON 66
(Get your kicks on) Route 66 / Girl talk / It happened once before / Please belong to me / For once in my life / Jack 'n' Jill / Watch what happens / Thou swell / Hungry man / Tangerine / Bright lights and you girl / (Back home again in) Indiana / Try a little tenderness / Lemon twist / Misty / Lulu's back in town
CD _____ HCD 607
Hindsight / Nov '95 / Target/BMG / Jazz Music.

Troupe, Quincy

ROOT DOCTOR
CD _____ NAR 109CD
SST / Jan '95 / Plastic Head.

Trout, Jimbo

JIMBO TROUT & THE FISH PEOPLE
(Trout, Jimbo & The Fishpeople)
CD _____ EFA 800382
Twah / Sep '95 / SRD.

Trout, Walter

BREAKING THE RULES (Trout, Walter Band)
CD _____ PRD 70762
Provogue / Jun '95 / Pinnacle.

LIFE IN THE JUNGLE (Trout, Walter Band)
Good enough to eat / Mountain song / Life in the jungle / Spacefosh / Red house / She's out there somewhere / Frederica (I don't need you) / In my mind / Cold cold feeling / Serve me night to suffer
CD _____ PRD 70202
Provogue / '90 / Pinnacle.

NO MORE FISH JOKES (Trout, Walter Band)
CD _____ PRD 70512
Provogue / May '93 / Pinnacle.

PRISONER OF A DREAM (Trout, Walter Band)
CD _____ PRD 70262
Provogue / Oct '91 / Pinnacle.

TELLIN STORIES (Trout, Walter Band)
I can tell / Tremble / I wanna see the morning / I need to belong / Runnin' blues / On the rise / Time for movin' on / Head hung down / Please don't go / Tellin' stories / Somebody's crying / Take care of your business
CD _____ ORECD 530
Silvertone / Mar '94 / Pinnacle.

TRANSITION (Trout, Walter Band)
CD _____ PRD 70442
Provogue / Nov '92 / Pinnacle.

Trovesi, Gianluigi

FROM G TO G (Trovesi, Gianluigi Octet)
CD _____ 121231-2
Soul Note / Nov '92 / Harmonia Mundi / Wellard / Cadillac.

Trower, Robin

20TH CENTURY BLUES
CD _____ FIENDCD 753
Demon / Aug '94 / Pinnacle / ADA.

ANTHOLOGY
CD _____ VSOPCD 197
Connoisseur / Apr '94 / Pinnacle.

BBC LIVE IN CONCERT
CD _____ WINCD 013
Windsong / Feb '92 / Pinnacle.

BRIDGE OF SIGHS
Day of the eagle / Bridge of sighs / In this place / Fool and me / Too rolling stoned / About to begin / Lady love / Little bit of sympathy
CD _____ CD25CR 15
Chrysalis / Mar '94 / EMI.

COLLECTION: ROBIN TROWER
CD _____ CCSCD 291
Castle / Aug '91 / BMG.

PASSION
Caroline / Secret doors / If forever / Won't even think about you / Passion / No time / Night / Bad time / One more word
CD _____ GNPD 2187
GNP Crescendo / Jun '92 / Silva Screen.

Trowers, Robert

POINT OF VIEW
Have you met Miss Jones / Minority / Riff / Statement / Spleen bop / St. Thomas / Holiday for strings / R 'n' B / Duet / Jo / Joint is jumpin' / End of a love affair
CD _____ CCD 4656
Concord Jazz / Jul '95 / New Note.

Troy, Doris

JUST ONE LOOK (The Best Of Doris Troy)
What'cha gonna do about it / Bossa nova blues / Just one look / Trust in me / Lazy days / Are you coming home / Somewhere along the way / Draw me closer / School for fools / Be sure / Someone ain't right / Stormy weather / Time
CD _____ SLC 2504
Ichiban / Apr '95 / Koch.

Trubee, John

WORLD OF LIVING PIGS
CD _____ EFA 11336-2
Musical Tragedies / Feb '94 / SRD.

Truce

NOTHING BUT THE TRUCE
CD _____ BLRCD 29
Big Life / Oct '95 / Pinnacle.

Trudell, John

AKA GRAFFITI MAN
CD _____ RCD 51028
Rykodisc / Sep '92 / Vital / ADA.

JOHNNY DAMAS AND ME
Rant 'n' roll / See the woman / Raptor / Shadow over sisterland / Baby doll's blues / That love / Johnny Damas and me / Across my heart / Something about you / After all these years / All there is to it
CD _____ RCD 10286
Rykodisc / Feb '94 / Vital / ADA.

Trudy

TUNE-IN TO THE TRUDY LOVE-RAY
CD _____ TDYCD 054
Planet Miron / May '90 / Pinnacle.

True Believers

HARD ROAD
Tell her / Ring the bell / So blue about you / Rebel kind / Train round the bend / Lucky moon / Hard road / We're wrong / I get excited / Sleep enough to dream / Rain won't help you when it's over / She's got / All mixed up / One moment to another / Who calls my name / Outside your door / Wild eyed and wound up / Nobody's home / Only a dream / Please don't tade away
CD _____ RCD 40287
Rykodisc / Mar '94 / Vital / ADA.

True Grit

GET EDUCATED
Get educated / I decorated your house / You've got something on your mind / Give me your love / Just good friends / Fool on love / Everyday blues / Fatman sings rock'n'roll / Living in the real world
CD _____ SPAC 001 CD
Space Station / Sep '90 / Pinnacle.

True West

HOLLYWOOD HOLIDAY/ DRIFTERS
CD _____ ROSE 23CD
New Rose / Sep '90 / Direct / ADA.

Truman's Water

GOD SPEED THE PUNCHLINE
CD _____ ELM 12
Elemental / Feb '94 / Disc.

MILKTRAIN TO PAYDIRT
CD _____ HMS 2212
Homestead / Aug '95 / SRD.

OF THICK TUM
CD _____ HMS 192-2
Homestead / Mar '93 / SRD.

PEEL SESSION
CD _____ SFRCD 133
Strange Fruit / Apr '95 / Pinnacle.

SPASM SMASH XXX OX OX OX & ASS
CD _____ ELM 9CD
Elemental / Mar '93 / Disc.

Trusty

GOODBYE DR FATE
CD _____ DIS 93CD
Dischord / May '95 / SRD.

Trynin, Jennifer

COCKAMAMIE
CD _____ 9362459312
Warner Bros. / Jun '95 / Warner Music.

Tryolia Singers

SOUND OF TYROL
CD _____ 321680
Koch / Sep '92 / Koch.

Tschanz, Mark

BLUE DOG
CD _____ 0630106062
East West / Jul '95 / Warner Music.

Tse Tse Fly

MUD FLAT JOEY
M 1 / Jonah / Talk to me / Pog eared / On purpose / Lido / Roo mole suit / Itchy / Some pay soon / Non-ferrous / Kitchen / Hogwash
CD _____ CDBRED 117
Cherry Red / Oct '94 / Pinnacle.

Tsiboe, Nana

ASEM NIL TROUBLE DAT
Bue bue / Kai onyame / Adum / Nana ewusi / Odumankumah boa mi / Kokofu nene mba / Ghana muntye
CD _____ TD 8001
World Circuit / Feb '94 / New Note / Direct / Cadillac / ADA.

Tsibone, Nana

ANSEM NI
CD _____ WCD 8001
Topic / Apr '93 / Direct / ADA.

Tsinandali Choir

TABLE SONGS OF GEORGIA
Kakhun mravaljamieri / Makruli / Shashvi, Kakabi / Orovela / Turpani skhedan / Zamtari / Diamhego / Shemodzakhili / Berikatsi var / Charkrulo
CD _____ CDRW 28
Realworld / Jan '93 / EMI / Sterns.

Tsunami

DEEP END
CD _____ SMR 13D
Simple Machines / May '93 / SRD.

HEART'S TREMOLO
CD _____ SMR 25CD
Simple Machines / Jun '94 / SRD.

WHO IS IT
CD _____ DYN 101
Nova / Sep '93 / New Note.

WORLD TOUR AND OTHER DESTINATIONS
CD _____ SMR 33CD
Simple Machines / Apr '95 / SRD.

Tsurata, Kinshi

PLAYS SATSUMA BIWA
CD _____ C559067
Ocora / May '91 / Harmonia Mundi / ADA.

Tubb, Ernest

IT'S COUNTRY TIME 1
CD _____ 12245
Laserlight / Jul '94 / Target/BMG.

IT'S COUNTRY TIME 2
CD _____ 12246
Laserlight / Jul '94 / Target/BMG.

IT'S COUNTRY TIME 3
CD _____ 12247
Laserlight / Jul '94 / Target/BMG.

LET'S SAY GOODBYE LIKE WE SAY HELLO
You hit the nail right on the head / Two wrongs don't make a right / That wild and wicked look in your eye / Lonely heart knows / Don't your face look red / Answer to Rainbow At Midnight / Watching my past go by / Woman has wrecked many a good man / Headin' down the wrong highway / Let's say goodbye like we say hello / Takin' it easy here / Seaman's blues / How can I forget you / Yesterday's winner is a loser today / I'm with a crowd but so alone / Waiting for a train / Forever is ending today / Have you ever been lonely / Till the end of the world / Daddy, when is mommy coming home / Don't rob another man's castle / I'm biting my fingernails and thinking of you / My Filipino rose / My Tennessee baby / Slippin' around / Warm red wine / Driftwood on the river / Tennessee border #2 / Letters have no arms / I'll take a back seat for you / Throw your love my way / Don't be ashamed of your age / Stand by me / Old rugged cross / What a friend we have in Jesus / Wonderful city / When I take my vacation in heaven / Farther along / I love you because / Give me a little old-fashioned love / Unfaithful one / Hillbilly fever (no.2) / You'll recuperate / Soldier's last letter / You won't have to be a baby to cry / Mother, the Queen of my heart / Goodnight Irene / Remember me, I'm the one who loves you / I need attention bad / I'm lonely and blue / Why did you give me your love / I'm free from the chain gang now / Why should I be lonely / Hobo's meditation / Good morning Irene / Love bug itch / Don't stay too long / I'm steppin' out of the picture / May the good lord bless and keep you / When it's prayer meetin' time in the hollow / Drunkard's child / Any old time / If you want some lovin' / So long (it's been good to know yuh) / Chicken song / Strange little girl / Kentucky waltz / Hey la la / Rose of the mountains / Precious little baby / So many times / My mother must have been a girl like you / Somebody's stolen my honey / Heartsick soldier on a heartbreak ridge / I'm in love with Molly / You old to cut the mustard / Missing in action / I will miss you when you go / Fortunes in memories / Dear judge / Don't brush them on me / I love everything you do / Somebody loves you / Don't trifle on your sweetheart / Hank, it will sunset the same without you / beyond the sunset / When Jimmie Rodgers said goodbye / Jimmie Rodgers' last thoughts / My wasted past / Counterfeit kisses / Honeymoon is over / No help wanted #2 / You're a real good friend / Dear John letter / Double datin' / It's the mileage that's slowin' us down / Divorce granted / Honky tonk / I'm not looking for an angel / I met a friend / When Jesus calls / Too old to tango / Dr. Ketchum / Love lifted me / White Christmas / Blue Christmas / Christmas Island / C-H-R-I-S-T-M-A-S / We need God for Christmas / Merry Christmas you all / Blue snowflakes / I'm trimming my Christmas tree with teardrops

CD Set _____ BCD 15498
Bear Family / Feb '91 / Rollercoaster / Direct / CM / Swift / ADA.

NASHVILLE 1946/NBC 1950 (Tubb, Ernest & T. Texas Tyler)
CD _____ CDMR 1141
Radiola / Oct '90 / Pinnacle.

THANKS A LOT
CD _____ PWKS 4234
Carlton Home Entertainment / Jul '95 / Carlton Home Entertainment.

WALTZ ACROSS TEXAS
Waltz across Texas / When the world has turned you down / Let's say goodbye like we say hello / Answer the phone / Journey's end / Walkin' the floor over you / Half a mind / Jealous loving heart / Rainbow at midnight / Set up two glasses, Joe / You nearly lose your mind / You're the only good thing / Filipino baby / Jimmie Rodgers' last blue yodel / Seaman's blues
CD _____ PWKS 4217
Carlton Home Entertainment / Jul '95 / Carlton Home Entertainment.

YELLOW ROSE OF TEXAS, THE
Till we two are one / Your Mother, your darling, your friend / Baby your mother (Like she babied you) / Jealous loving heart / Two glasses, Joe / Woman's touch / Journey's end / Kansas city blues / Lonely Christmas eve / I'll be walking the floor this Christmas / Have you seen my boogie woogie baby / It's a lonely world / I got the blues for Mammy / (I'm gonna make my home) A million miles from here / Yellow rose of Texas / Thirty days / Doorstep to heaven / Will you be satisfied that way / Steppin' out / If I never have anything else / So doggone lonesome / Old love letters (Bring memories of you) / Jimmie Rodgers' last blue yodel / Travelin' blues / You're the only good thing (that's happened to me) / I've got the blues for Mammy / I dreamed of an old love affair / (I know my baby loves me) in her own peculiar way / Mississippi gal / There's no fool like a young fool / I new the moment I lost you / You're breaking my heart / When a soldier knocks and finds nobody home / This troubled mind o'mine / My hillbilly baby / Daisy May / Loving you is my weakness / Answer the phone / Tennessee baby / All of those yesterdays / Walking the floor over you / When the world has turned you down / I'll always be glad to take you back / It's been so long Darling / Careless Darlin' / Though the days were only seven / Last night I dreamed / Slippin' around / I love you because / There's nothing more to say / There's a little bit of everything in Texas / You nearly lose your mind / Blue Christmas / Don't rob another man's castle / What I didn't know about her / I melted her / Let's say goodbye like we say hello / Driftwood on the river / I wonder why you said goodbye / Tomorrow never comes / Filipino baby / I'd rather be / Letters have no arms / Rainbow at midnight / Have you ever been lonely / I will miss you when you go / Live it up / (I've lost you) So why should I care / Accidently on purpose / Do it now / He'll have to go / Mr. Blues / Kind of love she gave to me / Pick me up on your way down / This ain't the blues (Instrumental) / You win again / I believe I'm entitled to you / Guy named Joe / Who will buy the wine / Why I'm walkin' / White silver sands / Am I that easy to forget / Everybody's somebody's fool / Let the little girl dance / Candy kisses / It happened when I really needed you / Wondering / Cold cold heart / Four walls / Bouquet of roses / Crazy arms / I love you so much it hurts / I walk the line / Little ole band of gold / Wabash cannonball / I'm movin' on / Tennessee Saturday night / Signed, sealed, delivered (I'm yours) / Thoughts of a fool / Girl from Abilene / Same thing as me / Christmas is just another day / I hate to see you go / I'm sorry now / What will you tell them / It is no secret / Don't just stand there / Big blue diamonds / I'll just have another cup of coffee
CD Set _____ BCD 15688
Bear Family / May '93 / Rollercoaster / Direct / CM / Swift / ADA.

Tubb, Justin

ROCK ON DOWN TO MY HOUSE
I'm a darn good man / Story of my life / Ooh la la / Give three cheers for my baby / Somebody ughed on you / Something called the blues / I'm looking for a date tonight / You're the prettiest thing that ever

happend to me / Who will it be / Sufferin' heart / Looking back to see / Miss you so / My heart's not for little girls to play with / Little bit waltz / I'm sorry I stayed away so long / Sure fire kisses / Fickel heart / Waterloo / I gotta go get my baby / Chugachuga, chica maugal / I'm a damn good man / All alone / Within your arms / Pepper hot baby / Lucky lucky someone else / You nearly lose your mind / Oh how I miss you / Desert blues / Miss the Mississippi and you / It takes a lot of heart / I'm just fool enough / I'm a big boy now / Life I have to live / Bachelor man / Party is over (For me) / Tears of angels / If you'll be my love / Someday, you'll want me to want you / I saw your face in the moon / Try me one more time / I'd trade all of my tomorrows / Silver dew on the bluegrass / Bonaparte's retreat / There'll be no teardrops tonight / Gone and left my blues / My Mary / Into each life some rain must fall / I've gotta have my baby back / Hang your head in shame / Sugar lips / Rock it down to my house / Mine is a lonely life / Almost lonely / Giveway girl / Heart's command / Buster's gang / I wish I could love that much / I know you do

CD Set _____ BCDBH 15761
Bear Family / Jun '94 / Rollercoaster / Direct / CM / Swift / ADA.

Tube, Shem

ABANA BA NASERY (Tube, Shem/Justo Osala/Enos Okola)
Atisa wangu / Khwatsia ebunangwe / Servanus andai / Nilimwacha muke risavu / Mapenzi kama karata / Noah libuko / Omukhana meri / Abasiratsi muhulire / Ndakhomela / Ebijana bie bubayi / Mushalo ebutula / Rosey wangu / Willison oluhambo
CD _____ CDORB 052
Globestyle / Nov '89 / Pinnacle.

Tubes

COMPLETION BACKWARD PRINCIPLE,THE
Talk to ya later / Let's make some noise / Matter of pride / Mr. Hate / Attack of the 50 foot woman / Think about me / Sushi girl / Don't want to wait anymore / Power tools / Amnesia / When I see you / Politics / Slave trade / Could be her ... could be you / Make believe / Don't go away / Price / Animal laugh / Anything is good enough / Product of... / Perfect game / Vendredi saint
CD _____ BGOCD 100
Beat Goes On / Mar '91 / Pinnacle.

LOVE BOMB
Piece by piece / Stella / Come as you are / One good reason / Bora Bora 2000 / Love bomb / Night people / Say hey / Eyes / Muscle girls / Theme from a wooly place / For a song / Say hey (part 2) / Feel it / Night people (reprise)
CD _____ BGOCD 188
Beat Goes On / Jul '93 / Pinnacle.

OUTSIDE/INSIDE
She's a beauty / No not again / Out of the business / Monkey time / Glasshouse / Wild women of Wongo / Tip of my tongue / Fantastic delusion / Drums / Theme park / Outside looking in
CD _____ BGOCD 133
Beat Goes On / Mar '92 / Pinnacle.

Tubuai Choir

POLYNESIAN ODYSSEY
CD _____ SHAN 64049CD
Shanachie / Dec '93 / Koch / ADA / Greensleeves.

Tuck & Patti

BEST OF TUCK & PATTI, THE
CD _____ 01934111562
Windham Hill / Oct '94 / Pinnacle / BMG / ADA.

DREAM
Dream / One hand, one heart / Togetherness / Friends in high places / Voodoo music / From now on we're one / I wish / Sitting in limbo / High heel blues / All the love / As time goes by
CD _____ 01934101302
Windham Hill / Nov '93 / Pinnacle / BMG / ADA.

LEARNING TO FLY
Live in the light / Heaven down here / Learning how to fly / Strength / Woodstock / Drum / Up from the skies / Tossin' and turnin' / Getaway / In my life / Yeah yeah / Wide awake / Still tossin' and turnin
CD _____ 4783992
Sony Soho2 / Apr '95 / Sony.

LOVE WARRIORS
Love warriors / Honey pie / They can't take that away from me / Hold out hold up and hold on / Cantador (like a lover) / On a clear day / Europa / Castles made of sand / Little wing / Glory glory / If it's magic
CD _____ WD 0116
Windham Hill / May '91 / Pinnacle / BMG / ADA.

Tucker, Colin Lloyd

REMARKABLE
CD _____ BAH 2
Humbug / Apr '93 / Pinnacle.

SONGS OF LIFE, LOVE & LIQUID
CD _____ BAH 17
Humbug / Oct '95 / Pinnacle.

Tucker, Junior

LOVE OF A LIFETIME
CD _____ VPCD 1314
VP / Aug '93 / Jetstar.

SECRET LOVER
CD _____ CRCD 35
Charm / Nov '94 / Jetstar.

Tucker, Luther

LUTHER TUCKER & THE FORD BLUES BAND (Tucker, Luther & The Ford Blues Band)
CD _____ CCD 11040
Crosscut / Nov '95 / ADA / Direct.

SAD HOURS
CD _____ ANT 0026CD
Antones / Apr '94 / Hot Shot / Direct / ADA.

Tucker, Marshall

FINEST SOUTH ROCK (Tucker, Marshall Band)
CD _____ 12363
Laserlight / May '94 / Target/BMG.

FIRE ON THE MOUNTAIN (Tucker, Marshall Band)
CD _____ MPG 74018
Movieplay Gold / May '93 / Target/BMG.

HEARD IT IN A LOVE SONG (Tucker, Marshall Band)
CD _____ MPG 74019
Movieplay Gold / Jun '93 / Target/BMG.

Tucker, Mickey

GETTIN' THERE
CD _____ SCCD 31365
Steeplechase / Dec '95 / Impetus.

Tucker, Moe

DOGS UNDER STRESS
CD _____ NR 422492
New Rose / Mar '94 / Direct / ADA.

I SPENT A WEEK THERE THE OTHER NIGHT
CD _____ 422373
New Rose / May '94 / Direct / ADA.

LIFE IN EXILE AFTER ABDICATION
CD _____ CREV 011CD
Rev-Ola / Mar '93 / 3MV / Vital.

OH NO, THEY'RE RECORDING THIS SHOW
CD _____ 422418
New Rose / May '94 / Direct / ADA.

Tucker, Sophie

LEGENDARY SOPHIE TUCKER, THE
I'm the last of the red hot mammas / Some of these days / Aren't women wonderful / Louisville Lou / Oh you have no idea / Life begins at forty / 'Cause I feel low-down / You can't sew a button on a heart / What good am I without you / Older they get, the younger they want them / Fifty million Frenchmen can't be wrong / After you've gone / Washing the blues from my soul / Follow a star / Who wants them tell, Dard and Handsome / My Yiddishe momme / That man of my dreams / Man I love / He hadn't up 'til yesterday / Some of these days (2)
CD _____ PAR 2031
Parade / Sep '94 / Koch / Cadillac.

Tucker, Tanya

FIRE TO FIRE
Come in out of the world / I'll take the memories / I bet she knows / Find out what's happening / Fire to fire / Between the two of them / Nobody dies from a broken heart / Love will / Love you gave to me / I'll take today
CD _____ CDEST 2254
Liberty / Apr '95 / EMI.

HITS: TANYA TUCKER
San Antonio stroll / Don't believe my heart can stand another you / Jamestown ferry / Here's some love / Would you lay with me (in a field of stone) / Blood red and going down / Pecos promenade / What's your mama's name child / O Texas (when I die) / Just another love / I won't take less than your love / Daddy and home / It don't come easy / Strong enough to bend / It won't be me / I'll come back as another woman / Love me like you used to / Down to my last teardrop / My arms stay open all night / Walking shoes / Don't go out
CD _____ CDESTU 2169
Liberty / Apr '92 / EMI.

LIZZIE AND THE RAINMAN
CD _____ CDCOT 108
Cottage / Mar '94 / THE / Koch.

SOON
You just watch me / I love you anyway / Soon / Black water bayou / Let the good times roll / Strong enough to bend / Hangin' in / As long as there's a heartbeat / Oh what it did to me / Sneaky moon / Come on honey / We don't have to do this / Silence is king / Blue guitar
CD _____ C2 27577
Liberty / Nov '93 / EMI.

Tucker, Tommy

TOMMY TUCKER & HIS ORCHESTRA 1941-47
CD _____ CCD 15
Circle / Mar '95 / Jazz Music / Swift / Wellard.

Tud

DEUS KERNE
CD _____ CD 851
Diffusion Breizh / Jul '94 / ADA.

Tudor Lodge

TUDOR LODGE
CD _____ REP 4064-WP
Repertoire / Aug '91 / Pinnacle / Cadillac.

Tuff

RELIGIOUS FIX
CD _____ 9041672
Mausoleum / May '95 / Grapevine.

Tuff, Mikey

NAH LEF JAH JAH
CD _____ RMCD 012
Roots Man / Dec '92 / Jetstar.

Tumbao

SALSA PA' GOZAR!
CD _____ EUCD 1188
ARC / Apr '92 / ARC Music / ADA.

Tumor Circus

TUMOR CIRCUS
CD _____ VIRUS 87CD
Alternative Tentacles / Oct '91 / Pinnacle.

Tungsten

183.85
CD _____ IRSCD 981202
Intercord / Jan '94 / Plastic Head.

Tunjung, Gamelan Seker

MUSIC OF K.R.T. WASITODININGRAT
CD _____ CMP CD 3007
CMP / Jul '92 / Vital/SAM.

Tunnell, Jimi

TRILATERAL COMMISSION
Cross stick / Zalimo / Not 4 / A B C / True west / Slime / M O C / Nice west / Big pig / South West
CD _____ 101 S877083
101 South / Jan '96 / New Note.

Tupaia, Andy

HITS SELECTION VOL.2
CD _____ S 65810
Manuiti / Sep '92 / Harmonia Mundi.

Turbinton, Earl

BROTHERS FOR LIFE
CD _____ CD 2064
Rounder / '88 / CM / Direct / ADA / Cadillac.

Turbo

DEAD END
CD _____ CDFLAG 47
Under One Flag / Sep '90 / Pinnacle.

Turbonegro

HELTA SKELTA
CD _____ EFA 15665CD
Repulsion / Jun '93 / SRD.

Turmoil

CHOKE
CD _____ CM 770752
Century Media / Sep '94 / Plastic Head.

Turner, Big Joe

BEST OF BIG JOE TURNER, THE
CD _____ PACD 2405404
Pablo / Jan '95 / Jazz Music / Cadillac / Complete/Pinnacle.

BIG JOE TURNER RIDES AGAIN
CD _____ RSACD 810
Sequel / Oct '94 / BMG.

BIG JOE TURNER'S GREATEST HITS

Chill is on / After my laughter came tears / Bump Miss Suzie / Chains of love / I'll never stop loving you / Sweet sixteen / Baby I still want you / Honey hush / Crawdad hole / Oke she moke she pop / Shake, rattle and roll / Well all right / Hide and seek / Flip flop and fly / Chicken and the hawk / Boogie woogie country girl / Corrine Corrina / Midnight special train / Red sails in the sunset / Feeling happy / Blues in the night
CD _____ RSACD 809
Sequel / Oct '94 / BMG.

BIG THREE, THE (Turner, Big Joe & Joe Houston/L.C. Williams)
CD _____ CDBM 095
Blue Moon / Jul '93 / Magnum Music Group / Greensleeves / Hot Shot / ADA / Cadillac / Discovery.

BLUES BOSS, THE
Roll 'em Pete / Cherry red / Morning glories / How long blues / St. Louis blues / Piney Brown blues / Ti ri lee / In the evening / Midnight cannonball / Sweet sixteen / Low down dog / Wee baby blues / Jump for joy / Poor lover's blues / Chili is on / TV mama / Hollywood bed / Miss Brown blues / Chains of love / Don't you cry / Married woman
CD _____ CD 52008
Blues Encore / '92 / Target/BMG.

BLUES SINGER 1938-42, THE
CD _____ JZCD 347
Suisa / Jan '93 / Jazz Music / THE.

BLUES TRAIN (Turner, Big Joe & Roomful Of Blues)
Crawdad hole / Red sails in the sunset / Cock-a-doodle-doo / Jumpin' for Joe / I want a little girl / I know you love me / Last night / I love the way (my baby sings the blues) / Blues train
CD _____ MCD 5293
Muse / Feb '87 / New Note / CM.

BOSS OF THE BLUES (That's Jazz Vol.14)
Cherry red / Roll 'em Pete / I want a little girl / Low down dog / Wee baby blues / You're driving me crazy / How long blues / Morning glories / St. Louis blues / Piney Brown blues
CD _____ 756781459-2
Atlantic / Jun '93 / Warner Music.

EVERY DAY I HAVE THE BLUES
Stormy Monday / Piney Brown blues / Martin Luther King southside / Everyday / Shake, rattle and roll / Lucille
CD _____ OJCCD 634
Original Jazz Classics / Jan '95 / Wellard / Jazz Music / Cadillac / Complete/Pinnacle.

FLIP, FLOP AND FLY (Turner, Big Joe & Count Basie Orchestra)
CD _____ PACD 23109372
Pablo / Jan '92 / Jazz Music / Cadillac / Complete/Pinnacle.

HAVE NO FEAR, BIG JOE IS HERE
S.K. blues / Watch that jive / Howling wind / Low down dog / Mad blues / Playboy blues / My gal's a jockey / Sally Zu-Zazz / Oowee baby blues / Lucille Lucille / Careless love / Hollywood bed / Johnson and Turner blues / I got love for sale
CD _____ SV 0265
Savoy Jazz / Apr '95 / Conifer / ADA.

HONEY HUSH
Shake, rattle and roll / Chains of love / Roll 'em Hawk / Piney Brown blues / Cherry red / Honey hush / Roll 'em / Honey hush / Corine Corina / T.V. Mama / Wee baby blues / Squeeze me baby
CD _____ CDMF 064
Magnum Force / Mar '95 / Magnum Music Group.

I DON'T DIG IT
Goin' to Chicago blues / I can't give you anything but love / Blues in the night / Rocks in my bed / Sun risin' blues / Mardi gras boogie / Cry baby blues / Rainy weather blues / I don't dig it / Boogie woogie baby / My heart belongs to you / Born to gamble / I love you, I love you / Oo-ouch-stop / Wish I had a dollar / Fuzzy wuzzy honey
CD _____ RBD 618
Mr. R&B / Oct '91 / Swift / CM / Wellard.

KANSAS CITY HERE I COME
Down home blues / Call the plumber / Since I fell for you / Kansas City I come / Big legged woman / Sweet sixteen / Time after time
CD _____ OJCCD 743
Original Jazz Classics / Jan '95 / Wellard / Jazz Music / Cadillac / Complete/Pinnacle.

LA SELECTION 1938-41
CD _____ 700102
Art Vocal / Nov '92 / Discovery.

LIFE AIN'T EASY
CD _____ OJCCD 809
Original Jazz Classics / Jan '95 / Wellard / Jazz Music / Cadillac / Complete/Pinnacle.

MIDNIGHT SPECIAL
I left my heart in San Francisco / I'm gonna sit right down and write myself a letter / I can't give you anything but love / You're driving me crazy / So long / After my laugh-

ter came tears / Midnight special / Stoop down baby
CD _____ PACD 2310844
Original Jazz Classics / Jan '95 / Wellard / Jazz Music / Cadillac / Complete/Pinnacle.

NOBODY IN MIND (Turner, Big Joe & Milt Jackson/Roy Eldridge)
CD _____ OJCCD 729
Original Jazz Classics / Jan '95 / Wellard / Jazz Music / Cadillac / Complete/Pinnacle.

STORMY MONDAY
Long way from home / Somebody loves me / Stormy Monday / Time after time / Love is like a faucet / Things that I used to do
CD _____ CD 2310 843
Pablo / Jun '93 / Jazz Music / Cadillac / Complete/Pinnacle.

TELL ME PRETTY BABY (Turner, Big Joe & Pete Johnson Orchestra)
CD _____ ARHCD 333
Arhoolie / Apr '95 / ADA / Direct / Cadillac.

TEXAS STYLE
CD _____ BLE 595472
Black & Blue / Oct '94 / Wellard / Koch.

Turner, Bruce

THAT'S THE BLUES, DAD
CD _____ LACD 49
Lake / Nov '95 / Target/BMG / Jazz Music / Direct / Cadillac / ADA.

Turner, Geraldine

STEPHEN SONDHEIM SONGBOOK, THE
Like it was / Old friends / Losing my mind / Not while I'm around / Could I leave you / With so much to be sure of / Miller's son / Buddy's blues / I remember / Parade in town / There won't be trumpets / Being alive / Anyone can whistle / Another hundred people / Goodbye for now
CD _____ SILVAD 3009
Silva Treasury / '95 / Conifer / Silva Screen.

Turner, Ike

RHYTHM ROCKIN' BLUES (Turner, Ike & The Kings Of Rhythm)
Rocket 88 / Way you used to treat me / I miss you so / Nobody wants me / Wild one / All the blues, all the time (Medley) / Stirring and wondering / Early times / World is yours / Suffocate / Talking about me / Walk my way back home / I ain't drunk / Road travel / Night howler / Woman won't just do / I'm tired of being dogged around / You got me way down here / Love is scarce / Nobody seems to want me
CD _____ CDCHD 553
Ace / Oct '95 / Pinnacle / Cadillac / Complete/Pinnacle.

TRAILBLAZER (Turner, Ike & The Kings Of Rhythm)
Big question / Just one more time / Mistreater / No coming back / You found the time / She made my blood run cold / I'm tore up / Trail blazer / You've changed my love / Let's call it a day / Another miserable / Do you mean it / Gonna wait for my chance / If I never had known you / Rock-a-bucket / Sad as a man can be / What can it be / Do right baby / My baby's tops / Take your fine frame home
CD _____ CDCHARLY 263
Charly / Feb '91 / Charly / THE / Cadillac.

Turner, Ike & Tina

BEST OF IKE & TINA TURNER, THE
CD Set _____ LOXCD 2
Low Price Music / Oct '95 / Total/BMG.

COLLECTION: IKE AND TINA TURNER
Mississippi rolling stone / Living for the city / Golden empire / I'm looking for my mind / Shake a hand / Bootsie Whitelaw / Too much man for one woman / I know you don't want me no more) / Rockin' and rollin' / Never been to spain / Sugar sugar / Push / Raise your hand / Tinas prayer / Chicken / If you want it / Let's get it on / You're up to something / You're still my baby / Jesus
CD _____ CCSCD 170
Castle / '88 / BMG.

GOLDEN EMPIRE
CD Set _____ 24052
Laserlight / Sep '92 / Target/BMG.

GOOD OLD TIMES
Let's get it on / Mr. Right / Bootsie Whitelaw / Oh my my / Games people play / So fine / Something / Soul deep / You got to work it / I can't believe what you say / Stormy weather / Night time is the right time / It's gonna work out fine / Proud Mary / Endlessly
CD _____ 662171
FNAC / Dec '92 / Discovery.

IKE & TINA TURNER/SLY & THE FAMILY STONE ESSENTIALS (Turner, Ike & Tina/Sly & The Family Stone)
CD _____ LECDD 636
Wisepack / Aug '95 / THE / Conifer.

IT'S ALL OVER
CD _____ CDSGP 058
Prestige / Oct '93 / Total/BMG.

LEGENDS IN MUSIC - IKE & TINA TURNER

CD _____ LECD 102
Wisepack / Sep '94 / THE / Conifer.

LET THE GOOD TIMES ROLL
Nothing you can do boy / Cussin' cryin' and carryin' on / Make em wait / You got what you wanted / I smell trouble / Rock me baby / So blue over you / Beauty is just skin deep / Funky mule / I'm fed up / I've been loving you too long / I'm a merciless child / Bold soul sister / Hunter / I know / Early in the morning / You're still my baby / You got me running / Reconsider baby / Honest I do / Good times
CD _____ MDCD 11
Music De-Luxe / Sep '95 / Magnum Music Group.

M.R.S
CD _____ GRF 218
Tring / Mar '93 / Tring / Prism.

MOVIN' ON
CD _____ CDCD 1134
Charly / Mar '93 / Charly / THE / Cadillac.

NUTBUSH CITY LIMITS
Nutbush City Limits / Locomotion / It's gonna work out fine / I'm blue / River deep, mountain high / I'm falling in love / Fool in love / I idolize you / Come together / Shake, rattle and roll / If you can hully gully (I can hully gully too) / Fool for you / You can't blame me / This man's crazy / Good good lovin' / Stagger Lee
CD _____ 16217CD
Success / Oct '94 / Carlton Home Entertainment.

NUTBUSH CITY LIMITS
CD _____ CDCD 1274
Charly / Nov '95 / Charly / THE / Cadillac.

PEARLS FROM THE PAST
CD _____ KLMCD 019
Scratch / Apr '94 / BMG.

PROUD MARY (And Other Hits)
CD _____ 15090
Laserlight / Aug '91 / Target/BMG.

PROUD MARY - THE BEST OF IKE & TINA TURNER (Legendary Masters Series)
Fool in love / I idolize you / I'm jealous / It's gonna work out fine / Poor fool / Tra la la la la / You shoulda treated me right / Come together / Honky tonk women / I want to take you higher / Workin' together / Proud Mary / Funkier than a mosquita' tweeter / Ooh poo pa doo / I'm yours (use me anyway you wanna) / Up in heah / River deep, mountain high / Nutbush City Limits / Sweet Rhode Island Red / Sexy Ida (part 1) / Sexy Ida (part 2) / Baby - get it on / Acid Queen
CD _____ CZ 422
EMI / Apr '91 / EMI.

RIVER DEEP, MOUNTAIN HIGH
River deep, mountain high / I idolize you / Love like yours / Fool in love / I make 'em wait / Hold on baby / Save the last dance for me / Oh baby / Everyday I have to cry / Such a fool for you / It's gonna work out fine / I'll never need more than this
CD _____ CDMID 134
A&M / Oct '92 / PolyGram.

SHAKE
CD _____ MU 5068
Musketeer / Oct '92 / Koch.

SINGS HITS OF THE 60'S
CD _____ CDCD 1275
Charly / Nov '95 / Charly / THE / Cadillac.

SPOTLIGHT ON IKE & TINA TURNER
It's gonna work out fine / Fool for you / Crazy about you baby / I can't stop loving you / Somebody somewhere needs you / Too hot to hold / Cussin', cryin' and carryin' on / I know / It sho' ain't me / You got what you wanted / Ain't nobody's business / Betcha can't kiss me (Just one time) / I smell trouble / It's all over / Nothing you can do buy / All I do Is cry
CD _____ HADCD 222
Javelin / Feb '94 / THE / Henry Hadaway Organisation.

THOSE WERE THE DAYS
Sugar sugar / Never been to Spain / Too much for one woman / Stormy weather / Into it / Trying to find my mind / I want to take you higher / Fool in love / I idolize you / Poor fool / Lay it down / Freedom to stay / Loving him was easier / Rescue me / Father alone / What a friend / When the saints go marching in / Near the cross / Nutbush City Limits
CD _____ 662172
FNAC / Dec '92 / Discovery.

TOO HOT TO HOLD
CD _____ CDCD 1042
Charly / Mar '93 / Charly / THE / Cadillac.

WHAT YOU SEE (IS WHAT YOU GET)
What you see / Down in the valley / Proud Mary / Shake / Locomotion / I know
CD _____ SMCD 18
Start / Oct '88 / Koch.

Turner, Joe

JOE TURNER
CD _____ SACD 106
Solo Art / Oct '93 / Jazz Music.

SWEET AND LOVELY
Hallalujah / Sweet and lovely / Between the Devil and the deep blue sea / I cover the waterfront / I've got the world on a string / You're the cream in my coffee / Tea for two / Frankie and Johnny / Wedding boogie / Rita
CD _____ 74321115072
Vogue / Jul '93 / BMG.

Turner, Joe Lynn

NOTHING'S CHANGED
Promise of love / Baby's got a habit / Nothing's changed / Knock knock / I believe / Satisfy me / Liviana / Bad blood / All or nothing / Last thing / Imagination / Save a place / Let me love you
CD _____ CDMFN 189
Music For Nations / Oct '95 / Pinnacle.

Turner, Ken

BEST OF THE DANSAN YEARS, VOL 4 (Turner, Ken & His Orchestra)
CD _____ DACD 1004
Dansan / Jul '92 / Savoy / President / Target/BMG.

BEST OF THE DANSAN YEARS, VOL 5 (Turner, Ken & His Orchestra)
CD _____ DACD 1005
Dansan / Jul '92 / Savoy / President / Target/BMG.

Turner, Mark

YAM YAM
CD _____ CRISS 1094
Criss Cross / Apr '95 / Cadillac / Harmonia Mundi.

Turner, Nik

NEW ANATOMY (Turner, Nik & Inner City Unit)
Young girls / Convoy / Beyond the stars / Help sharks / Birdland / Lonesome train / Forbidden planet / Stop the city / Dr. Strange / Wildhunt
CD _____ CDTB 096
Thunderbolt / Mar '93 / Magnum Music Group.

PROPHETS OF TIME
CD _____ CLEO 69082
Cleopatra / Jun '94 / Disc.

SPACE RITUAL
CD Set _____ CLEO 95062
Cleopatra / Feb '95 / Disc.

SPHYNX
CD _____ CLEO 21352
Cleopatra / Feb '94 / Disc.

Turner, Ruby

BEST OF RUBY TURNER, THE
CD _____ EMPRCD 566
Emporio / May '95 / THE / Disc / CM.

RESTLESS MOODS
CD _____ MAGCD 1058
M&G / Aug '95 / 3MV / Sony.

WITH LOVE
What becomes of the broken hearted / I'd rather go blind / Tracks of my tears / Just my imagination / Ooh baby baby / Bye baby / Still waters run deep / Signed, sealed, delivered (I'm yours) / Baby I need your loving / How sweet it is (to be loved by you) / It's a crying shame / Surrender / Someday soon / Still on my mind
CD _____ 5501152
Spectrum/Karussell / Oct '93 / PolyGram / THE.

Turner, Tina

ACID QUEEN
Under my thumb / Let's spend the night together / Acid queen / I can see for miles / Whole lotta love / Baby git on / Bootsie Whitelaw / Pick me tonight / Rockin' and rollin'
CD _____ CDEST 2232
Capitol / Aug '94 / EMI.

BREAK EVERY RULE
What you get is what you see / Change is gonna come / Addicted to love / In the midnight hour / 634 5789 / Land of 1000 dances / Typical male / Two people / Till the right man comes along / Afterglow / Girls / Back where you started / Break every rule / Overnight sensation / Paradise is here / I'll be thunder
CD _____ CDP 746 323 2
Capitol / Sep '86 / EMI.

COLLECTED RECORDINGS: SIXTIES TO NINETIES, THE
Fool in love / It's gonna work out fine / I idolize you / Poor fool / Letter from Tina / Finger poppin' / River deep, mountain high / Crazy about you baby / I've been loving you too long / Bold soul sister / I want to take you higher / Come together / Honky

tonk women / Proud Mary / Nutbush city limits / Sexy Ida (part 1) / Sexy Ida (part 2) / It ain't right (lovin) to be lovin' / Acid Queen / Whole lotta love / Ball of confusion / Change is gonna come / Johnny and Mary / Games (unreleased demos) / When I was young / Total control (unreleased master) / Let's pretend we're married / It's only love / Don't turn around / Legs (live at the Blockbuster Pavilion) / Addicted to love (live) / Tearing us apart / It takes two / Let's stay together (LP edit) / What's love got to do with it (LP edit) / Better be good to me / Private dancer (LP edit) / I can't stand the mud / Don't need another hero / Typical male (LP edit) / What you get is what you see / Paradise is here / Back where you started / Best / Steamy windows (LP edit) / Foreign affair (Mixes) / It don't wanna fight
CD Set _____ CDEST 2240
CD Set _____ CDESTX 2240
Capitol / Nov '94 / EMI.

COUNTRY CLASSICS
Lay it down / Lovin' him was easier / Good hearted woman / If this was our last time / Stand by your man / Freedom to stay / We had it all / Soul deep / If it's alright with you / You ain't woman enough to take my man
CD _____ HADCD 166
Javelin / May '94 / THE / Henry Hadaway Organisation.

COUNTRY SIDE OF TINA TURNER
Star Collection / Apr '95 / BMG.

FOREIGN AFFAIR
Steamy windows / Best / You know who (is doing you know what) / Undercover agent for the blues / Look me in the heart / Be tender with me baby / You can't stop me loving you / Ask me how I feel / Falling like rain / I don't wanna lose you / Not enough romance / Foreign affair
CD _____ CDESTU 2103
Capitol / Sep '89 / EMI.

LIVE IN EUROPE
What you get is what you see / Break every rule / I can't stand the rain / Two people / Typical male / Better be good to me / Addicted to love / Private dancer / We don't need another hero / What's love got to do with it / Let's stay together / Show some respect / Land of 1000 dances / In the midnight hour / 634 5789 / Change is gonna come / Tearing us apart / Proud Mary / Help / Tonight / It's only love / Nutbush City Limits / Paradise is here / Let's dance / Girls (Not on LP) / Back where you started (Not on LP) / River deep, mountain high (Not on LP) / Overnight sensation (Not on LP)
CD Set _____ CDESTD 1
Capitol / Mar '88 / EMI.

PRIVATE DANCER
I might have been queen / Whats love got to do with it / Show some respect / I can't stand the rain / Private dancer / Let's together / Better be good to me / Steel claw / Help
CD _____ CDP 746 041 2
Capitol / Jun '84 / EMI.

ROUGH
Fruits of the night / Bitch is back / Woman I'm supposed to be / Viva la money / Funny how time slips away / Earthquake hurricane / Root root undisputable rock 'n' roller / Fire down below / Sometimes when we touch / Woman in a man's world / Night time is the right time
CD _____ CDP 1362132
Capitol / Aug '95 / EMI.

SIMPLY THE BEST
Best / What's love got to do with it / I don't wanna lose you / Nutbush City Limits / Let's stay together / Private dancer / We don't need another hero / Better be good to me / River deep, mountain high / Steamy windows / Typical male / It takes two / Addicted to love / Be tender with me baby / I want you near me / Love thing
CD _____ CDESTV 1
Capitol / Oct '91 / EMI.

Turner, Titus

JAMIE RECORDINGS, THE
CD _____ BCD 15532
Bear Family / Feb '92 / Rollercoaster / Direct / CM / Swift / ADA.

Turning Point

FEW AND THE PROUD, THE
CD _____ LF 172CD
Lost & Found / Jul '95 / Plastic Head.

Turntable Symphony

MINI LP, THE
Instructions of life (mixes) / Remix of life / Can't stop / It'll make you go ooh / Techno love
CD _____ HAPPYCD 001
Happy Music / May '93 / Vital.

Turquoise

TURQUOISE TRAIL, THE
CD _____ TURQUOISE 1995
Turquoise / Aug '95 / Vital.

Turre, Steve

FIRE AND ICE
CD _____ STCD 7
Stash / '88 / Jazz Music / CM / Cadillac / Direct / ADA.

VIEWPOINT AND VIBRATIONS
CD _____ STCD 2
Stash / '88 / Jazz Music / CM / Cadillac / Direct / ADA.

Turrentine, Stanley

PIECES OF A DREAM
CD _____ OJCCD 831
Original Jazz Classics / Nov '95 / Wellard / Jazz Music / Cadillac / Complete/Pinnacle.

Turtle Island String...

BY THE FIRESIDE (Turtle Island String Quartet)
CD _____ 01934111752
Windham Hill / Nov '95 / Pinnacle / BMG / ADA.

METROPOLIS (Turtle Island String Quartet)
CD _____ WD 0114
Windham Hill Jazz / Mar '92 / New Note.

ON THE TOWN (Turtle Island String Quartet)
Love for sale / Body and soul / Fascinatin' rhythm / Manoir de mes reves/Blues en mineur / Angel eyes / Smooth one / Oh lady be good / Li'l darlin' / Rachel's dream / In a sentimental mood / I love you / Cheek to cheek
CD _____ 101322
Windham Hill Jazz / Aug '91 / New Note.

SHOCK TO THE SYSTEM, A (Turtle Island String Quartet)
CD _____ WD 0123
Windham Hill Jazz / Mar '92 / New Note.

SKYLIFE (Turtle Island String Quartet)
Skylife / Senor Mouse / You noticed too / Blues for Oaktown / Gettysburg / Dexteriors / Tremors / Mr. Twitty's chair / Grant Wood / Ensenada / Crossroads
CD _____ WD 0126
Windham Hill / Jun '91 / Pinnacle / BMG / ADA.

TURTLE ISLAND STRING QUARTET (Turtle Island String Quartet)
CD _____ WD 0110
Windham Hill Jazz / Mar '92 / New Note.

WHO DO YOU (Turtle Island String Quartet)
CD _____ 01934101462
Windham Hill / Sep '95 / Pinnacle / BMG / ADA.

Turtles

CALIFORNIA GOLD
CD _____ 12380
Laserlight / Sep '94 / Target/BMG.

HAPPY TOGETHER (The Very Best Of The Turtles)
Happy together / She'd rather be with me / Too young to be one / Me about you / Think I'll run away / Can I get to know you better / Guide for the married man / Elenore / It ain't me babe / You baby / Let me be / She's my girl / You don't have to walk in the rain / You know what I mean / Lady O / You showed me / There you sit lonely / Outside chance / Buzz saw / Sound asleep
CD _____ MCCD 046
Music Club / Sep '91 / Disc / THE / CM.

Tuscadero

PINK ALBUM, THE
Heat lightnin' / Candy song / Game song / Latex dominatrix / Just my size / Dime a dozen / Lovesick / Mount Pleasant / Nancy Drew / Hollywood handsome / Leather idol / Crayola
CD _____ OLE 1592
Matador / Aug '95 / Vital.

STEP INTO MY WIGGLE ROOM
Holidays R hell / Angel in a half shirt / Poster boy / Dreams of the tanker / Sways / Given up / Sonic yogurt / Palmer: All Star jam
CD _____ TB 1792
Teenbeat / Oct '95 / SRD.

Tuu

1000 YEARS
CD _____ SDV 027CD
SDV / May '94 / Plastic Head.

ALL OUR ANCESTORS
CD _____ RBADCD 9
Beyond / Oct '94 / Kudos / Pinnacle.

Tuva

ECHOES FROM THE SPIRIT WORLD
CD _____ PANCD 2013
Pan / May '93 / ADA / Direct / CM.

VOICES FROM THE CENTRE OF ASIA
CD _____ SFWCD 40017
Smithsonian Folkways / May '95 / ADA / Direct / Koch / CM / Cadillac.

Tuxedo Moon

BEST OF TUXEDO MOON
What use / No tears / Cage / Some guys / Dark companion / In a manner of speaking / Atlantis / Waltz / L'etranger / Tritone (musica diablo) / East/jinx / Desire / You
CD _____ CBOY 1313
Crammed Discs / Jan '94 / Grapevine / New Note.

TV Personalities

AND DON'T THE KIDS JUST LOVE IT
CD _____ REF 33007
Fire / Oct '91 / Disc.

CHOCOLAT-ART LIVE 1984
CD _____ EFA 04320 CD
Pastell / Jun '93 / SRD.

CLOSER TO GOD
You don't know how lucky you are / Hard luck story no.39 / Little works of art / Razor blades and lemonade / Coming home soon / Me and my big ideas / Honey for the bears / I see myself in you / Goodnight Mr. Spaceman / My very first nervous breakdown / We will be your gurus / You are special and you always will be / Not for the likes of us / You're younger than you know / Very dark today / I hope you have a nice day / This heart's not made of stone / Baby, you're only as good as you should be / Closer to God
CD _____ FIRECD 32
Fire / Oct '92 / Disc.

I WAS A MOD BEFORE YOU WAS A MOD
CD _____ OVER 41CD
Overground / Jul '95 / SRD.

MUMMY, YOU'RE NOT WATCHING ME
CD _____ REF 33008
Fire / Oct '91 / Disc.

PAINTED WORD THE
CD _____ REF 33010
Fire / Oct '91 / Disc.

PRIVILEGE
Paradise is for the blessed / Conscience tells me no / All my dreams are dead / Man who paints the rainbows / Sad Mona Lisa / Sometimes I think you know me / Privilege / Good and faithful servant / My hedonistic tendencies / Salvador Dali's garden party / What if it's raining / Engine driver song / Better than I know myself
CD _____ FIRE 33021
Fire / Oct '91 / Disc.

THEY COULD HAVE BEEN BIGGER THAN THE BEATLES
Psychedelic holiday / David Hockney's diary / Boy in the paisley shirt / When Emily cries
CD _____ REF 33009
Fire / Oct '91 / Disc.

YES DARLING BUT IS IT ART
CD _____ FLIPCD 001
Fire / Jan '95 / Disc.

Twardzik, Richard

PACIFIC JAZZ (Twardzik, Richard Trio)
You stepped out of a dream / Bock's tops / At last / Laugh cry / Lullaby in rhythm / Joey Joey Joey / Albuquerque social swim / Yellow tango / I'll remember April / Crutch for the crab (alt.) / Don't worry 'bout me / Yesterday's gardenias / Backfield in motion / Eye opener / Party's over / Woody's dot / Bess, you is my woman now / Round Midnight / Crutch for the crab / Just one of those things
CD _____ CZ 245
Pacific Jazz / Apr '90 / EMI.

Tweed, Karen

DROPS OF SPRINGWATER
CD _____ DMP 9401CD
Punch Music / Jan '96 / ADA / Roots.

SHHH (Tweed, Karen & Ian Carr)
CD _____ HYCD 200147
Hypertension / Mar '95 / Total/BMG / Direct / ADA.

SILVER SPIRE, THE
CD _____ DMP 9402CD
Punch Music / Jan '96 / ADA / Roots.

TUNES FOR THE ACCORDION VOL. 1
CD _____ PMCD 003
Punch Music / Aug '94 / ADA / Roots.

TUNES FOR THE ACCORDION VOL. 2
CD _____ PMCD 004
Punch Music / Aug '94 / ADA / Roots.

Twelth Night

COLLECTORS ITEM
CD _____ CDGRUB 18
Food For Thought / Feb '91 / Pinnacle.

Twice A Man

COLLECTION OF STONES
CD _____ YELLOW 16
Yellow / Aug '88 / SRD.

FROM THE NORTHERN SHORE
CD _____ YELLOW 01CD
Yellow / '89 / SRD.

Twilight Circus

IN DUB VOL.1
CD _____ MREC 1CD
M / Nov '95 / Pinnacle.

Twilight Earth

INTERNATIONAL SOIREE
CD _____ TIME 002CD
Timebase / Nov '94 / Plastic Head.

Twink

MR. RAINBOW
CD _____ TWKCD 1
Twink / Jul '90 / Disc / Pinnacle.

Twinkle

GOLDEN LIGHTS
CD _____ RPM 108
RPM / Jul '93 / Pinnacle.

Twinkle Brothers

BABYLON RISE AGAIN
CD _____ NGCD 528
Twinkle / Apr '92 / SRD / Jetstar / Kingdom.

CHANT DOWN BABYLON
CD _____ NGCD 547
Twinkle / Oct '95 / SRD / Jetstar / Kingdom.

DJ SELECTION
CD _____ NGCD 545
Twinkle / Dec '94 / SRD / Jetstar / Kingdom.

DUB FEELING PROGRAMME DUB MASSACRE 6
CD _____ NGCD 543
Twinkle / Jun '94 / SRD / Jetstar / Kingdom.

DUB MASSACRE #1/#2
CD _____ NGCD 7102
Twinkle / Dec '94 / SRD / Jetstar / Kingdom.

DUB MASSACRE #3/#4
CD _____ NGCD 505
Twinkle / Jan '96 / SRD / Jetstar / Kingdom.

DUB PLATE
CD _____ NGCD 546
Twinkle / Dec '94 / SRD / Jetstar / Kingdom.

DUB WITH STRINGS
CD _____ NGCD 535
Twinkle / Nov '92 / SRD / Jetstar / Kingdom.

ENTER ZION
CD _____ NGCD 503
Twinkle / Jan '96 / SRD / Jetstar / Kingdom.

EQUALITY AND JUSTICE
Equality and justice / Rejoice / Lamb to the slaughter / We nah go let Jah go / Blood on their hands / Wicked them a go run / Lightning and thunder / You're bound / I will praise Jah
CD _____ NGCD 541
Twinkle / Feb '94 / SRD / Jetstar / Kingdom.

FREE AFRICA
I don't want to be lonely anymore / Free Africa / Love / I love you so / Gone already / Solid as a rock / Come home / Shu be dub (you can do it too) / Patoo / Never get burn / Dread in the ghetto / Watch the hypocrites / Jahovah / Since I threw the comb away / One head / Free us
CD _____ CDFL 9008
Frontline / Sep '90 / EMI / Jetstar.

ME NO YOU
CD _____ NGCD 632
Twinkle / Jul '94 / SRD / Jetstar / Kingdom.

NEW SONGS FOR JAH
CD _____ NGCD 518
Twinkle / Jan '96 / SRD / Jetstar / Kingdom.

OTHER SIDE, THE (Twinkle Brothers & Ralston Grant)
CD _____ RGCD 5805
Twinkle / Oct '95 / SRD / Jetstar / Kingdom.

RASTA PON TOP
CD _____ NGCD 532
Twinkle / Apr '92 / SRD / Jetstar / Kingdom.

TWINKLE LOVE SONGS VOL.2
CD _____ NGCD 536
Twinkle / Feb '93 / SRD / Jetstar / Kingdom.

Twinz

CONVERSATION
Conversation / Round and round / Good times / Eyes 2 heads / Jump ta this / East-

side LB / Sorry I kept you / Conversation # 2 / Journey wit me / Hollywood / Pass it on / Don't get it twisted / 1st Round draft pick
CD _____ 5278832
RAL / Aug '95 / PolyGram.

Twisted Roots

TURN TO STONE
CD _____ CHERRY 228932
Cherrydisc / Dec '94 / Plastic Head.

Twisted Sister

BIG HITS AND NASTY CUTS
We're not going to take it / I wanna rock / I am (I'm me) / Price / You can't stop rock 'n' roll / Kids are back / Shoot 'em down / Under the blade / I'll never grow up now / Feel so fine / Let the good times roll / It's only rock 'n' roll / Tear it loose / What you don't know / Be chrool to your scuel
CD _____ 7567823802
East West / Mar '92 / Warner Music.

LIVE AT HAMMERSMITH
What you don't know / Kids are back / Stay hungry / Destroyer / We're not gonna take it / You can't stop rock 'n' roll / Knife in the back / Shoot 'em down / Under the blade / Burn in hell / I am (I'm me) / I wanna rock / S.M.F. / We're gonna make it / Jailhouse rock / Train kept a rollin'
CD _____ CDMFN 170
Music For Nations / Oct '94 / Pinnacle.

Twitty, Conway

BEST OF CONWAY TWITTY, THE
It's only make believe / Hello darlin' / Fifteen years ago / Danny boy / You've never been this far before / Touch of the hand / To see an angel cry / She needs someone to hold her (when she cries) / I'll try / After all the good is gone / After our last date / As soon as I hang up the phone / Baby's gone / I can't see me without you / I'm not through loving you yet / I've hurt her more than she loves me / (Lying here with) Linda on my mind / Games that Daddies play / Don't cry Joni / (I can't believe) She gives it all to me
CD _____ CD 3558
Cameo / Nov '95 / Target/BMG.

CONWAY TWITTY
Guess my eyes were bigger than my heart / Look into my teardrops / I don't want to be with me / Image of me / To see my angel cry / Hello darlin' / I can't see me without you / (Lost her love) On our last date / You've never been this far before / I'm not through loving you yet / Linda on my mind / (I can't believe) She gives it all to me / I've already loved you in my mind / Boogie grass band / Don't take it away / I'd just love to lay you down / Tight fittin' jeans / Slow hand / Rose / I don't know a thing about love / Don't call him a cowboy / Desperado love / That's my job / Goodbye time / She's got a single thing in mind
CD _____ MCLD 19236
MCA / May '94 / BMG.

CONWAY TWITTY
CD _____ LECD 043
Dynamite / May '94 / THE.

FINAL RECORDINGS OF HIS GREATEST HITS
CD _____ PWKS 4263
Carlton Home Entertainment / Jul '95 / Carlton Home Entertainment.

I NEED YOUR LOVIN'
CD _____ CDCD 1110
Charly / Jul '93 / Charly / THE / Cadillac.

ROAD THAT I WALK, THE
CD _____ CDSGP 0170
Prestige / Sep '95 / Total/BMG.

SPOTLIGHT ON CONWAY TWITTY
Fifteen years ago / To see my angel cry / I see the want to in your eyes / I'm not through loving you yet / Linda on my mind / Don't cry Joni / I've already loved you in my mind / Play guitar, play / It's only make believe / Let me be the judge / Ever since you went away / Big town / Sitting in a dim cafe
CD _____ HADCD 121
Javelin / Feb '94 / THE / Henry Hadaway Organisation.

Two Bit Thief

ANOTHER SAD STORY IN THE BIG CITY
CD _____ 846129
We Bite / Feb '91 / Plastic Head.

GANGSTER REBEL BOP
CD _____ WB 2093CD
We Bite / Nov '92 / Plastic Head.

ONE MORE FOR THE ROAD
CD _____ WB 3103-2
We Bite / Apr '94 / Plastic Head.

Two Tons

TWO TONS O'FUN/BACKATCHA
Do you wanna boogie huh / Just us / I got the feelin' / Gone away / Earth can be just like heaven / Make someone feel happy today / Taking away your space / One-sided love affair / Never like this / I depend on you

/ Your love is gonna see me through / It's true I do / Can't do it by myself / Cloudy with a chance of rain / I've got to make it on my own / I been down
CD _____ CDSEWD 082
Southbound / Jul '93 / Pinnacle.

Two Tunes

RAINDROPS TALKING
CD _____ BRAM 199127-2
Brambus / Nov '93 / ADA / Direct.

Two Witches

AGONY OF THE UNDEAD VAMPIRE PIT II
CD _____ CANDY 1112CD
Candy / Nov '92 / Plastic Head.

VAMPIRE KISS, THE
CD _____ CDSATE 02
Talitha / Jul '93 / Plastic Head.

Two Worlds

QUIET FORCE
CD _____ 710 114
Innovative Communication / Apr '90 /
Magnum Music Group.

Ty Gwydr

292 YMLAEN AT Y FILIWN
CD _____ ANKST 045CD
Ankst / Feb '94 / SRD.

Tygers Of Pan Tang

FIRST KILL
Slave to freedom / Angel / Straight as a die / Final answer / Euthanasia / Shakespeare Road / Don't take nothing / Alright on the night / Bad times / Small town flirt
CD _____ CLACD 258
Castle / '91 / BMG.

SPELLBOUND
Gangland / Take it / Minotaur / Hellbound / Mirror / Silver and gold / Tyger Bay / Story so far / Black Jack / Don't stop by
CD _____ REP 4015-WZ
Repertoire / Aug '91 / Pinnacle / Cadillac.

WILD CAT
Euthanasia / Slave to freedom / Don't touch me there / Money / Killers / Fireclown / Wild cat / Badger badger / Insanity
CD _____ REP 4014-WZ
Repertoire / Aug '91 / Pinnacle / Cadillac.

Tyketto

SHINE
Jamie / Rawthigh / Radio Mary / Get me there / High / Ballad of Ruby / Let it go / Long cold winter / I won't cry / Shine
CD _____ CDMFN 195
Music For Nations / Nov '95 / Pinnacle.

STRENGTH IN NUMBERS
Strength in numbers / Rescue me / End of the summer days / Ain't that love / Catch my fall / Last sunset / All over me / Write your name in the sky / Meet me in the night / Why do you cry / Inherit the wind / Standing alone
CD _____ CDMFN 157
Music For Nations / Feb '94 / Pinnacle.

Tyla

LIFE AND TIMES OF A BALLAD MONGER
CD _____ REVYD 107
Revolver / Nov '95 / Revolver Music / Sony.

Tyler, Alvin 'Red'

GRACIOUSLY
CD _____ CD 2061
Rounder / '88 / CM / Direct / ADA / Cadillac.

HERITAGE
CD _____ CD 2047
Rounder / '88 / CM / Direct / ADA / Cadillac.

Tyler, Bonnie

BONNIE TYLER
CD _____ MATCD 255
Castle / Apr '93 / BMG.

BONNIE TYLER LOVE SONGS
CD _____ SSLCD 206
Savanna / Jun '95 / THE.

COLLECTION: BONNIE TYLER
CD _____ CCSCD 285
Castle / Feb '93 / BMG.

COMEBACK SINGLE COLLECTION
Fools lullaby / Bitterblue / Back home / Sally comes around / Say goodbye / Against the wind / Silhouette in red / Angel heart / Send me the pillow that you dream on / James Dean / Stay / Race to the fire / Fire in my soul / Call me / God gave love to you / From the bottom of my lonely heart / It's a heartache / Lost in France
CD _____ 74321233062
RCA / Feb '95 / BMG.

Tyler, Charles

EASTERN MAN ALONE
CD _____ ESP 1059-2
ESP / Jan '93 / Jazz Horizons / Jazz Music.

Tyler, Chris

SMILER, THE
CD _____ SOSCD 1258
Stomp Off / Dec '93 / Jazz Music / Wellard.

Tyler, T. Texas

GREAT TEXAN, THE
CD _____ KCD 000689
King/Paddle Wheel / Dec '92 / New Note.

FASTER THAN THE SPEED OF NIGHT
Have you ever seen the rain / Faster than the speed of night / Getting so excited / Total eclipse of the heart / It's a jungle out there / Going through the motions / Tears / Take me back / Straight from the heart
CD _____ CD 32747
CBS / Oct '92 / Sony.

GOODBYE TO THE ISLAND
I'm just a woman / We danced on the ceiling / Wild love / Closer you get / Sometimes when we touch / Goodbye to the island / Wild side of life / Whiter shade of pale / Sitting on the edge of the ocean / I believe in your sweet love
CD _____ CLACD 288
Castle / Jul '92 / BMG.

GREATEST HITS: BONNIE TYLER
Total eclipse of the heart / Faster than the speed of the night / Have you ever seen the rain / If you were a woman (and I was a man) / Here she comes / Loving you's a dirty job but someone's got to do it / Getting so excited / Save up all your tears / Best / Holding out for a hero / Married men / Rockin' good way / More than a lover / Don't turn around / Lovers again / Lost in France / It's a heartache / To love somebody
CD _____ 478047 2
Columbia / Oct '94 / Sony.

HEAVEN AND HELL (Tyler, Bonnie & Meatloaf)
Bat out of hell / Faster than the speed of night / You took the words right out of my mouth / Have you ever seen the rain / Read 'em and weep / Total eclipse of the heart / Two out of three ain't bad / Holding out for a hero / Dead ringer for love / If you were a woman (and I was a man) / If you really want to / Straight from the heart / Loving you's a dirty job but somebody's got to do it / Heaven can wait
CD _____ 473666 2
Columbia / May '93 / Sony.

IT'S A HEARTACHE
It's a heartache / Louisiana rain / Married men / Love of a rolling stone / Blame me / My guns are loaded / Heaven / If I sing you a love song / Whiter shade of pale / Piece of my heart / If you ever need me again / Eyes of a fool / I believe in your sweet love / Living for the city / Baby I remember you / Wild side of life
CD _____ 5507282
Spectrum/Karussell / Aug '94 / PolyGram THE.

LOST IN FRANCE
Sometimes when we touch / More than a lover / (You make me feel like) a natural woman / Goodbye to the island / Sitting on the edge of the ocean / Don't stop the music / Here I am / Get out of my head / Lost in France / Closer you get / Come on give me loving / I'm just a woman / Give me your love / Got so used to loving you / Here's Monday / Love tangle
CD _____ 5507292
Spectrum/Karussell / Mar '95 / PolyGram THE.

NATURAL FORCE
It's a heartache / Blame me / Living for the city / If I sing you a love song / Heaven / Yesterday dreams / Hey love / (You make me feel like) a natural woman / Here I am / Baby goodnight
CD _____ CLACD 232
Castle / Apr '91 / BMG.

SECRET DREAMS AND FORBIDDEN FIRE
Ravishing / If you were a woman (and I was a man) / Loving you's a dirty job but somebody's got to do it / No way to treat a lady / Band of gold / Rebel without a clue / Lovers again / Holding out for a hero
CD _____ 4719202
Columbia / Oct '92 / Sony.

STRAIGHT FROM THE HEART
CD _____ CCSCD 801
Castle / Aug '95 / BMG.

WORLD STARTS TONIGHT, THE
Got so used to loving you / Love of a rolling stone / Lost in France / Piece of my heart / More than a lover / Give me your love / World starts tonight / Here's Monday / Love tangle / Let the show begin
CD _____ CLACD 231
Castle / Apr '91 / BMG.

T. Texas Tyler

CD _____ KCD 721
King/Paddle Wheel / Apr '93 / New Note.

Tyndall, Nik

AMBIENT MUSIC
CD _____ SKYCD 3049
Sky / Feb '95 / Koch.

Tyner, McCoy

4 X 4 (Tyner, McCoy Quartets)
Inner glimpse / Manha de carnaval / Paradox / Backward glace / Forbidden land / Pannonica / I wanna stand over there / Seeker / Blues in the minor / Stay as sweet as you are / It's you or no one
CD _____ MCD 55007
Milestone / Apr '94 / Jazz Music / Pinnacle / Wellard / Cadillac.

44TH STREET SUITE
CD _____ 469284 2
Sony Jazz / May '94 / Sony.

ATLANTIS
CD _____ MCD 55002
Milestone / Oct '93 / Jazz Music / Pinnacle / Wellard / Cadillac.

BLUE BOSSA
CD _____ CDC 9033
LRC / Jul '91 / New Note / Harmonia Mundi.

BON VOYAGE
Bon voyage / Don't blame me / Summertime / You stepped out of a dream / Jazz walk / Yesterdays (On CD only)
CD _____ CDSJP 260
Timeless Jazz / Jul '91 / New Note.

DOUBLE TRIOS
Latino suite / Li'l darlin' / Dreamer / Satin doll / Down home / Sudan lover / Lover man / Rhythm a ring
CD _____ CY 1128
Denon / Oct '88 / Conifer.

FLY WITH THE WIND
CD _____ FCD 6019067
Fantasy / Nov '86 / Pinnacle / Jazz Music / Wellard / Cadillac.

INCEPTION
Inception / Blues for Gwen / Speak / We'll be together again / For heaven's sake / Blue monk / Days of wine and roses / There is no greater love / Sunset effendi / Satin doll / Round Midnight / Star eyes / Groove waltz
CD _____ MVCZ 76
Telstar / Oct '95 / BMG.

INFINITY (Tyner, McCoy & Michael Brecker)
Flying high / I mean you / Where is love / Changes / Happy days / Impressions / Mellow minor / Good morning heartache
CD _____ IMP 11712
Impulse Jazz / Sep '95 / BMG.

JOURNEY
CD _____ 5199412
Birdology / Apr '92 / PolyGram.

LIVE AT NEWPORT
CD _____ MVCZ 77
Telstar / Oct '95 / BMG.

LIVE AT WARSAW JAZZ FESTIVAL 1991
CD _____ CD 66050008
Bellaphon / Jul '93 / New Note.

PARIS BOSSA (Tyner, McCoy Quintet)
CD _____ MO□ □□1□
Moon / Jan '92 / Harmonia Mundi / Cadillac.

PLAYS ELLINGTON
Duke's place / Caravan / Solitude / Searchin' / Mr. Gentle and Mr. Cool / Satin doll / Gypsy without a song / It don't mean a thing if it ain't got that swing / I got it bad and that ain't good / Gypsy without a song (Alternate take)
CD _____ MCAD 33124
Impulse Jazz / Dec '90 / BMG / New Note.

REAL MCCOY, THE
Passion dance / Contemplation / Four by five / Search for peace / Blues on the corner
CD _____ CDP 7465122
Blue Note / Mar '95 / EMI.

SAHARA
CD _____ OJCCD 311-2
Original Jazz Classics / Apr '92 / Wellard / Jazz Music / Cadillac / Complete/Pinnacle.

SONG FOR MY LADY
CD _____ OJCCD 313-2
Original Jazz Classics / Apr '92 / Wellard / Jazz Music / Cadillac / Complete/Pinnacle.

SUPER TRIOS
CD _____ MCD 55003
Milestone / Oct '93 / Jazz Music / Pinnacle / Wellard / Cadillac.

TURNING POINT, THE
CD _____ 5131632
Verve / Jan '93 / PolyGram.

UPTOWN DOWNTOWN (Tyner, McCoy Big Band)
Love surrounds us / Three flowers / Genesis / Uptown / Lotus flower / Blues for Basie

---

CD _____ MCD 9167
Milestone / Apr '94 / Jazz Music / Pinnacle / Wellard / Cadillac.

WHAT'S NEW
CD _____ JHR 73564
Jazz Hour / Jan '93 / Target/BMG / Jazz Music / Cadillac.

Type O Negative

ORIGIN OF THE FECES
CD _____ RR 90062
Roadrunner / Oct '94 / Pinnacle.

SLOW DEEP AND HARD
CD _____ RO 93132
Roadrunner / May '91 / Pinnacle.

Tyrell, Sean

CRY OF A DREAMER
Mattie / Coast of Malabar / Demolition Dan / Isle of Inisfree / House of delight / November rain / Blue-green bangle / Message of peace / Cry of the dreamer / Only from day to day / No-go / Connie's song / Fortune for the finder / 12th Of July
CD _____ LMCD 001
L-MCD / Jun '94 / ADA.
CD _____ HNCD 1391
Hannibal / Nov '95 / Vital / ADA.

Tyrrall, Gordon

BRIDGE FLOWS, THE
CD _____ PM 001CD
Punch Music / Jun '94 / ADA / Roots.

WHERE THE RIVER FLOWS
CD _____ PMCD 001
Punch Music / Aug '94 / ADA / Roots.

Tyrrel Corporation

NORTH EAST OF EDEN
Bottle / Six o'clock / Ballad of British justice / Freedom / Going home / One day / Waking with a stranger / Lies before breakfast / Grapes of wrath / Cheated
CD _____ CTCD 29
Cooltempo / Oct '92 / EMI.

PLAY FOR TODAY
Ask me tomorrow / Better days ahead / April in Kings Cross / Practice what you preach / Never say never / You're not here / Turn around / I've had enough / No easy answers / This land is your land
CD _____ CTCD 43
Cooltempo / Feb '95 / EMI.

Tyson, Ian

AND STOOD THERE AMAZED
CD _____ SP 1168CD
Stony Plain / Oct '93 / ADA / CM / Direct.

FOUR STRONG WINDS (Tyson, Ian & Sylvia)
Jesus met the woman at the well / Tomorrow is a long time / Katy dear / Poor Lazarus / Four strong winds / Ella Speed / Long lonesome road / V' la l'bon vent / Royal canal / Lady Carlisle / Spanish is a loving tongue / Greenwood side / Every night when the sun goes down / Every time I feel the spirit
CD _____ VND 2149
Vanguard / '87 / Complete/Pinnacle / Discovery.

OLD CORRALS AND SAGEBRUSH & OTHER COWBOY CLASSIC
Gallo del cielo / Alberta's child / Old double diamond / Windy Bill / Montana waltz / Whoopie ti yi yo / Leavin' Cheyenne / Old corrals and sagebrush / Old Alberta moon / Night rider's lament / Oklahoma hills / Tom Blasingame / Colorado trial / Hot summer tears / What does she see / Rocks begin to roll / Will James / Murder steer
CD _____ BCD 15437
Bear Family / Aug '88 / Rollercoaster / Direct / CM / Swift / ADA.

ONE JUMP AHEAD OF THE DEVIL
What does she see / Beverly / Turning thirty / Newtonville waltz / Lone star and coors / One too many / Texas / I miss you / Goodness of Shirley / Freddie Hall / Half a mile to hell
CD _____ SPCD 1177
Stony Plain / Jun '93 / ADA / CM / Direct.

Tyson, Sylvia

GIPSY CADILLAC
CD _____ RTMCD 65
Round Tower / Nov '94 / Pinnacle / ADA / Direct.

YOU WERE ON MY MIND
Pepere's mill / Slow moving heart / Rhythm of the road / Walking on the moon / Thrown to the wolves / Night the Chinese restaurant burned down / You were on my mind / Sleep on my mind / Trucker's cafe / River Road / Last call / Le Moulin a Pepere / Blind fiddler's waltz
CD _____ SP 1140CD
Stony Plain / Oct '93 / ADA / CM / Direct.

Tytot, Angelin

GIITU

CD _____ **MIPU 204CD**

Mipu / Dec '93 / ADA / Direct.

Tzuke, Judie

BEST OF JUDIE TZUKE

New friends again / Black furs / Sukarita / Sports car / For you / These are the laws / Welcome to the cruise / Come hell or waters high / Higher and higher / Chinatown / Stay with me 'til dawn / Bring the rain

CD _____ **811 392-2**

Phonogram / Feb '94 / PolyGram.

CAT IS OUT, THE

How sweet is it / Who do you really love / Love like fire / I'll be the one / Girl without a name / This side of heaven / Harbour lights / You / Falling / Racing against time

CD _____ **CLACD 275**

Castle / Feb '92 / BMG.

LIVE IN CONCERT

You are the phoenix / Sukarita / Higher and higher / Stay with me till dawn / Flesh is week / Southern smiles / Kateira island / Ladies night / City of swimming pools / China town / Black furs / Sports car / Understanding

CD _____ **WINCD 077**

Windsong / Aug '95 / Pinnacle.

RITMO

Face to face / Nighthawks / How do I feel / Another country / Jeannie no / She don't live here anymore / Shoot from the heart / Walk don't walk / Push push / Chinatown / City of swimming pools

CD _____ **BGOCD 225**

Beat Goes On / Jun '94 / Pinnacle.

ROAD NOISE (The official bootleg)

Heaven can wait / Chinatown / I'm not a loser / Information / Flesh is weak / Sports car / For you / Come hell or waters high / Southern smiles / Kateria Island / Love on the border / Black furs / City of swimming pools / Bring the rain / Sukarita / Stay with me 'til dawn / Hunter

CD _____ **BGOCD 212**

Beat Goes On / Dec '93 / Pinnacle.

SHOOT THE MOON

Heaven can wait / Love on the border / Information / Beacon Hill / Don't let me sleep / I'm not a loser / Now there is no love at all / Late again / Liggers at your funeral / Water in motion / Shoot the moon

CD _____ **BGOCD 226**

Beat Goes On / Oct '94 / Pinnacle.

STAY WITH ME TILL DAWN

Stay with me till dawn / Bring the rain / Ladies night / Welcome to the cruise / We'll go dreaming / Let me be the pearl / Dominique / Turning stones / Choice you've made / Understanding / Living on the coast / Sports car / Higher and higher / I never know where my heart is / Come hell or waters high / Black furs

CD _____ **5508962**

Spectrum/Karussell / Aug '95 / PolyGram / THE.

U

U-Men

STEP ON A BUG
Whistlin' Pete / Three year old could do that / Flea circus / Willie Dong hurts dogs / Pay the bubba / Two times four / Juice party / Too good to be food / Papa doesn't love his children anymore
CD _____ TUPCD 012
Tupelo / Jun '90 / Disc.

U-Roy

DREAD IN A BABYLON
Runaway girl / Chalice in the palace / I can't love another / Dreadlocks dread / Great psalms / Natty don't fear / African message / Silver bird / Listen to the teacher / Trench Town rock
CD _____ CDFL 9007
Frontline / Sep '90 / EMI / Jetstar.

FLASHING MY WHIP
CD _____ RNCD 2130
Rhino / Nov '95 / Jetstar / Magnum Music Group / THE.

MUSIC ADDICT
I originate / Come fe warn them / King Tubby's skank / Reggae party / I feel good / Music addict / Jah Jah call you / Haul and pull / Waterboat
CD _____ RASCD 3024
Ras / Aug '87 / Jetstar / Greensleeves / SRD / Direct.

MUSICAL VISION
CD _____ LG 21080
Lagoon / Nov '93 / Magnum Music Group / THE.

NATTY REBEL
Babylon burning / Natty rebel / So Jah Jah say / Natty kung fu / If you should leave me / Do you remember / Travelling man / Have mercy / Badie boo / Go there natty / Fire in a Trench Town
CD _____ CDFL 9017
Virgin / Apr '83 / EMI.

ORIGINAL DJ
Babylon burning / Natty rebel / Evil doers / Jah Jah / Rule the nation / On the beach / Tide is high / Rock away / Peace and love in the ghetto / Say you / I can't love another / Trench town rock / Hot pop / Wear you to the ball / True confession / Everybody bawling / Words of wisdom / Great psalms / African message / Listen to the teacher / Control tower / Runaway girl / Natty don't fear / Chalice in the palace / Come home little girl
CD _____ CDFL 9020
Frontline / Jun '95 / EMI / Jetstar.

RASTA AMBASSADOR
Control tower / Wear you to the ball / Evil doers / Mr. Slave Driver / Small axe / Come home little girl / Say you / No more war / Tide is high / Jah Jah
CD _____ CDFL 9016
Frontline / Jun '91 / EMI / Jetstar.

SMILE A WHILE (U-Roy & Yabby U)
CD _____ ARICD 085
Ariwa Sounds / May '93 / Jetstar / SRD.

SUPER BOSS
CD _____ LG 21024
Lagoon / Jul '93 / Magnum Music Group / THE.

TEACHER MEETS THE STUDENT, THE (U-Roy & Josie Wales)
CD _____ SONCD 0028
Sonic Sounds / Apr '92 / Jetstar.

TRUE BORN AFRICAN
CD _____ AIRCD 071
Ariwa Sounds / Sep '91 / Jetstar / SRD.

VERSION OF WISDOM
Your ace from outer space / Rule the nation / Honey come forward / Version galore / Things you love / Wear you to the ball / On the beach / Rock away / True confession / Everybody bawling / Wake the town / Words of wisdom / Treasure isle skank / Same song / Tide is high / Hot pop / Tom drunk / Drive her home / Merry go round / What is catty
CD _____ CDFL 9003
Frontline / Jul '90 / EMI / Jetstar.

WAKE THE TOWN
CD _____ RNCD 2114
Rhino / Jul '95 / Jetstar / Magnum Music Group / THE.

WITH A FLICK OF MY MUSICAL WRIST (U-Roy & Friends)
CD _____ CDTRL 268
Trojan / Sep '94 / Jetstar / Total/BMG.

YOUR ACE FROM SPACE
CD _____ CDTRL 359
Trojan / Aug '95 / Jetstar / Total/BMG.

u-Ziq

IN PINE EFFECT
Mr. Angry / Melancho / Wailing song / Iced jem / Funky pipecleaner / Phiescope / Old fun no.1 / Pine effect / Dauphine / Roy Castle / Within a sound / Rain (LP only) / Tungsten carbide (LP only) / Frank (LP only) / Problematic / Green crumble
CD _____ FLATCD 20
Hi Rise / Oct '95 / EMI / Pinnacle.

TANGO N'VECTIF
CD _____ CAT 013CD
Rephlex / May '94 / Disc.

U.N.L.V.

NO LONGER VIRGINS
CD _____ WRA 8119CD
Wrap / Feb '94 / Koch.

U.N.V.

SOMETHING'S GOIN ON
UNV thang / When will I know / Who will it be / Close tonight / Gonna give U what U want / Something's goin' on / 2 B or not 2 B / Straight from my heart / Hold on / No one compares to you
CD _____ 93624528742
WEA / Nov '93 / Warner Music.

UNIVERSAL NUBIAN VOICES
CD _____ 9362458392
WEA / Jul '95 / Warner Music.

U.S. Maple

LONG HAIR IN 3 STAGES
CD _____ GR 33CD
Skingraft / Nov '95 / SRD.

U.V.X.

DOUBLE HELIX
CD _____ EYECDLP 7
Magick Eye / Aug '94 / SRD.

U2

ACHTUNG BABY
Zoo station / Even better than the real thing / One / Until the end of the world / Who's gonna ride your wild horses / So cruel / Fly / Mysterious ways / Tryin' to throw your arms around the world / Ultraviolet / Acrobat / Love is blindness
CD _____ CIDU 28
Island / Oct '91 / PolyGram.

BOY
Twilight / An cat dubh / Out of control / Stories for boys / Ocean / Day without me / Another time another place / Electric Co / Shadows and tall trees / I will follow
CD _____ IMCD 211
Island / Apr '95 / PolyGram.

JOSHUA TREE, THE
Where the streets have no name / I still haven't found what I'm looking for / With or without you / Bullet the blue sky / Running to stand still / Red hill mining town / In God's country / Trip through your wires / One tree hill / Exit / Mothers of the disappeared
CD _____ CIDU 26
Island / Mar '87 / PolyGram.

OCTOBER
Gloria / I fall down / I threw a brick through a window / Rejoice / Fire / Tomorrow / October / With a shout (Jerusalem) / Stranger in a strange land / Scarlet / Is that all
CD _____ IMCD 223
Island / Mar '96 / PolyGram.

ORIGINAL SOUNDTRACKS 1 (Passengers (2))
United colours / Slug / Your blue room / Always forever now / Different kind of blue / Beach sequence / Miss Sarajevo / Ito okashi / One minute warning / Corpse (These chains are way too long) / Elvis ate America / Plot 180 / Theme from The Swan / Theme from Lets Go Native
CD _____ CID 8043
Island / Oct '95 / PolyGram.

PHILADELPHIA INTERVIEWS, THE
CD P.Disc _____ CBAK 4006
Baktabak / Apr '88 / Baktabak.

RATTLE AND HUM
Helter skelter / Hawkmoon 269 / Van Diemen's land / Desire / Angel of Harlem / I still haven't found what I'm looking for / When love comes to town / God pt II / Bullet the blue sky / Silver and gold / Pride (in the name of love) / Love rescue me / Heartland / Star spangled banner / All I want is you / All along the watchtower
CD _____ CIDU 27
Island / Oct '88 / PolyGram.

UNDER A BLOOD RED SKY (Live)
Eleven o'clock tick tock / I will follow / Party girl / Gloria / Sunday Bloody Sunday / Electric Co / New Year's Day / 40
CD _____ CID 113
Island / May '86 / PolyGram.

UNFORGETTABLE FIRE, THE
Sort of homecoming / Pride (in the name of love) / 4th of July / Wire / Unforgettable fire / Promenade / Indian Summer sky / M.L.K. / Elvis Presley and America
CD _____ CID 102
Island / Sep '84 / PolyGram.

WAR
Sunday bloody Sunday / Seconds / Like a song / New Year's Day / Two hearts beat as one / Refugee / Drowning man / Red light / 40 / Surrender
CD _____ IMCD 141
Island / Aug '91 / PolyGram.

WIDE AWAKE IN AMERICA
Bad / Sort of homecoming / Three sunrises / Love comes tumbling
CD _____ IMCD 75
Island / Nov '89 / PolyGram.

ZOOROPA
Zooropa / Babyface / Numb / Lemon / Stay (Faraway, so close) / Daddy's gonna pay for your crashed car / First time / Some days are better than others / Dirty day / Wanderer
CD _____ CIDU 29
Island / Jun '93 / PolyGram.

UB40

BAGGARIDDIM
King step / Buzz feeling / Lyric officer Mk.2 / Demonstrate / Two in a one mk.1 / Hold your position Mk3 / Hip hop lyrical robot / Style Mk.4 / V's version / Don't break my heart / I got you babe / Mi spliff / Fight fe come in Mk.2
CD _____ DEPCD 10
DEP International / Oct '85 / EMI.

BEST OF UB40 VOL.1, THE
Red red wine / I got you babe / One in ten / Food for thought / Rat in mi kitchen / Don't break my heart / Cherry oh baby / Many rivers to cross / Please don't make me cry / If it happens again / Sing our own song / Maybe tomorrow / My way of thinking / King
CD _____ DUBTV 1
DEP International / Oct '87 / EMI.

BEST OF UB40 VOL.2, THE
Breakfast in bed / Where did I go wrong / I would do for you / Homely girl / Here I am (come and take me) / Wear you to the ball / Can't help falling in love / Higher ground / Bring me your cup / C'est la vie / Reggae music / Superstition / Until my dying day
CD _____ DUBTV 2
DEP International / Oct '95 / EMI.

COMPACT COLLECTION (Present Arms/Baggariddim/CCCP Live In Moscow) (3CD Set)
CD Set _____ TPAK 30
Virgin / Nov '91 / EMI.

COMPACT COLLECTION (Signing Off/ Rat In The Kitchen/Present Arms In Dub) (3CD)
CD Set _____ TPAK 35
Virgin / Oct '94 / EMI.

GEFFREY MORGAN
Riddle me / As always you were wrong again / If it happens again / D.U.B. / Pillow / Nkomo a go-go / Seasons / You're not an army / I'm not fooled so easily / You're eyes were open
CD _____ DEPCD 6
DEP International / Oct '84 / EMI.

GROOVIN' JAMAICA PAYS TRIBUTE TO UB40 (Various Artists)
CD _____ RNCD 2065
Rhino / Oct '94 / Jetstar / Magnum Music Group / THE.

LABOUR OF LOVE
Johnny too bad / Guilty / Sweet sensation / Many rivers to cross / Red red wine / Please don't make me cry / She caught the train / Keep on moving / Cherry oh baby / Version girl
CD _____ DEPCD 5
DEP International / Jul '86 / EMI.

LABOUR OF LOVE I & II
Cherry oh baby / Keep on moving / Please don't make me cry / Johnny too bad / Johnny too bad / Red red wine / Guilty / She caught the train / Version girl / Many rivers to cross / Here I am (come and take me) / Tears from my eyes / Groovin' / Way you do the things you do / Wear you to the ball / Singer man / Kingston town / Baby / Wedding day / Sweet cherrie / Stick by me

/ Just another girl / Homely girl / Impossible love
CD Set _____ DEPDDX 1
DEP International / Oct '94 / EMI.

LABOUR OF LOVE II
Here I am (come and take me) / Tears from my eyes / Groovin' / Way you do the things you do / Wear you to the ball / Singer man / Kingston town / Baby / Wedding day / Sweet cherrie / Stick by me / Just another girl / Homely girl / Impossible love
CD _____ DEPCD 14
DEP International / Nov '89 / EMI.

PRESENT ARMS
Present arms / Sardonicus / Don't let it pass you by / Wild cat / One in ten / Don't slow down / Silent witness / Lambs bread / Don't walk on the grass / Dr. X
CD _____ DEPCD 1
DEP International / Apr '88 / EMI.

PRESENT ARMS IN DUB
Present arms in dub / Smoke it / B line / King's row / Return of Dr. X / Walk out / One in ten / Neon haze
CD _____ DEPCD 2
DEP International / '88 / EMI.

PROMISES AND LIES
C'est la vie / Desert sand / Promises and lies / Bring me your cup / Higher ground / Reggae music / Can't help falling in love / Now and then / Things ain't like they used to be / It's a long, long way / Sorry
CD _____ DEPCD 15
DEP International / Jul '93 / EMI.

RAT IN MI KITCHEN
All I want to do / You could meet somebody / Tell it like this / Elevator / Watchdogs / Rat in mi kitchen / Looking down at my reflection / Don't blame me / Sing our own song
CD _____ DEPCD 11
DEP International / Apr '92 / EMI.

SIGNING OFF
Tyler / King / Twelve Bar / Burden of shame / 25% / Food for thought / Little by little / Signing off / Madame Medusa / Strange fruit / Reefer madness
CD _____ CDOVD 439
DEP International / Oct '93 / EMI.

UB40
Dance with the devil / Come out to play (On 7" & CD only) / Breakfast in bed / You're always pulling me down / I would do for you / 'Cause it isn't true / Where did I go wrong / Contaminated minds / Matter of time / Music so nice / Dance with the devil (reprise)
CD _____ DEPCD 13
DEP International / Jul '88 / EMI.

UB40 FILE, THE
Tyler / King / Twelve bar / Burden of shame / Adella / I think it's going to rain today / 25% / Food for thought / Little by little / Signing off / Madame Medusa / Strange fruit / Reefer madness / My way of thinking / Earth dies screaming / Dream a lie
CD _____ VGDCD 3511
DEP International / Jul '88 / EMI.

UB40 LIVE
Food for thought / Sardonicus / Don't slow down / Politician / Tyler / Present arms / Piper calls the tune / Love is all is alright / Burden of shame / One in ten
CD _____ DEPCD 4
DEP International / '88 / EMI.

UB44
So here I am / I won't close my eyes (remix) / Forget the cost / Love is all is alright (remix) / Piper calls the tune / Key / Don't do the crime / Politician (remix) / Prisoner
CD _____ DEPCD 3
DEP International / Apr '86 / EMI.

Ubik

JUST ADD PEOPLE
CD _____ ZOOMCD 1
Zoom / Jul '92 / Disc.

UFO

BBC LIVE IN CONCERT
CD _____ WINCD 016
Windsong / Apr '92 / Pinnacle.

DOCTOR DOCTOR
Ain't life sweet / One of those nights / Running up the highway / Back door man / Revolution / Too hot to handle (live) / Only you can rock me (live) / Lights out (live) / Doctor doctor (live) / Rock bottom (live) / Shoot shoot (live) / C'mon everybody (live) / Borderline / Let the good times roll
CD _____ 5507432
Spectrum/Karussell / Mar '95 / PolyGram / THE.

EARLY YEARS
Unidentified flying object / C'mon everybody / Shake it all about / Timothy / Who do you love / Evil silver bird / Coming of Prince Kajuuku / Loving cup (live) / Boogie for George (live)
CD _____ EARLD 9
Dojo / Nov '92 / BMG.

ESSENTIAL UFO
Doctor doctor / Rock bottom / Out in the street / Mother Mary / Natural thing / I'm a loser / Only you can rock me / Lookin' out for no.1 / Cherry / Born to lose / Too hot to handle / Lights out / Love to love / This kid's / Let it roll / Shoot shoot
CD _____ CDCHR 1888
Chrysalis / Oct '92 / EMI.

HEAVEN'S GATE LIVE
CD _____ MNMCD 1
M&M / Nov '95 / Total/BMG.

LIGHTS OUT
Too hot to handle / Just another suicide / Try me / Lights out / Gettin' ready / Alone again or / Electric chase / Love to love
CD _____ ACCD 1127
Chrysalis / '87 / EMI.

LIGHTS OUT IN TOKYO - LIVE
CD _____ ESSCD 191
Castle / Apr '93 / BMG.

NO HEAVY PETTING/LIGHTS OUT
Natural thing / I'm a loser / Can you roll her / Belladonna / Reasons love / Highway lady / On with the action / Fool in love / Martian landscape / Too hot to handle / Just another suicide / Try me / Lights out / Gettin' ready / Alone again or / Electric chase / Love to love
CD _____ BGOCD 228
Beat Goes On / Aug '94 / Pinnacle.

OBSESSION/NO PLACE TO RUN
Only you can rock me / Pack it up (and go) / Arbory hill / Ain't no baby / Lookin' out for no.1 / Hot 'n' ready / Cherry / You don't fool me / Lookin' out for No.1 (Reprise) / One more for the rodeo / This / Mystery train / This fire burns tonight / Gone in the night / Young blood / No place to run / Take it or leave it / Money, money / Any day
CD _____ BGOCD 229
Beat Goes On / May '94 / Pinnacle.

PHENOMENON/FORCE IT
Too young to no / Crystal light / Doctor Doctor / Space child / Rock bottom / Oh my / Time on my hands / Built for comfort / Lipstick traces / Queen of the deep / Let it roll / Shoot shoot / High flyer / Love lost love / Out in the street / Mother Mary / Too much of nothing / Dance your life away / This kid's
CD _____ BGOCD 227
Beat Goes On / Oct '94 / Pinnacle.

STRANGERS IN THE NIGHT
Natural thing / Out in the street / Only you can rock me / Doctor doctor / Mother Mary / This kid's / Love to love / Lights out / Rock bottom / Too hot to handle / I'm a loser / Let it roll / Shoot shoot
CD _____ CD25CR 22
Chrysalis / Mar '94 / EMI.

TOO HOT TO HANDLE (The Best Of UFO)
Only you can rock me (live) / Too hot to handle / Long gone / Profession of violence / We belong to the night (live) / Let it rain (live) / Lonely heart / This time / Lettin' go / Lights out (live) / Natural thing / Blinded by a lie / Wreckless / When it's time to rock / Shoot shoot / Young blood / Let it roll / Doctor doctor (live)
CD _____ MCCD 153
Music Club / Feb '94 / Disc / THE / CM.

WILD, THE WILLING AND THE INNOCENT/MECHANIX
Chains chains / Long gone / Wild, the willing and the innocent / It's killing me / Makin' moves / Lonely heart / Couldn't get it right / Profession of violence / Writer / Something else / Back into my life / You'll get love / Doing it all for you / We belong to the night / Let it rain / Terri / Feel it / Dreaming
CD _____ BGOCD 230
Beat Goes On / Sep '94 / Pinnacle.

Ugarte, Enrique

ENRIQUE UGARTE, ACCORDION CHAMPION (Ugarte, Enrique 'Kike')
Bolero / Sabre dance / Czardas
CD _____ EUCD 1151
ARC / Jun '91 / ARC Music / ADA.

FOLKLORE VASCO (Ugarte, Enrique 'Kike')
CD _____ EUCD 1157
ARC / Jun '91 / ARC Music / ADA.

VALSE MUSETTE (Ugarte, Enrique 'Kike')
CD _____ EUCD 1114
ARC / '91 / ARC Music / ADA.

VALSE MUSETTE II (Ugarte, Enrique 'Kike')
CD _____ EUCD 1200
ARC / Sep '93 / ARC Music / ADA.

Ugly Kid Joe

AMERICA'S LEAST WANTED
Neighbor / Goddamn devil / Come tomorrow / Panhandlin prince / Busy bee / Don't go / So damn cool / Same side / Cats in the cradle / I'll keep tryin' / Everything about you / Madman ('92 Re-mix) / Mr. Record man
CD _____ 5125712
Mercury / Nov '92 / PolyGram.

AS UGLY AS THEY WANNA BE
Madman / Whiplash / Too bad / Everything about you / Sweet leaf / Funky fresh country club / Heavy metal
CD _____ 8688232
Mercury / May '92 / PolyGram.

MESSAGE TO SOBRIETY
CD _____ 5282822
Mercury / Jun '95 / PolyGram.

Ugly Mustard

UGLY MUSTARD
CD _____ 0086302CTR
Edel / Nov '95 / Pinnacle.

Uglystick

UGLYSTICK
CD _____ CDVEST 46
Bulletproof / Mar '95 / Pinnacle.

Uí Cheallaigh, Áine

CUIMHNI CEOIL
CD _____ CIC 077CD
Clo Iar-Chonnachta / Nov '93 / CM.

IN TWO MINDS
CD _____ CEFCD 158
Gael Linn / Jan '94 / Roots / CM / Direct / ADA.

UK Subs

ANOTHER KIND OF BLUES
C.I.D. / I couldn't be you / I love in a car / Tomorrow's girls / Killer / World War / Rockers / I.O.D. / TV blues / Blues / Lady esquire / All I wanna know / Crash course / Young criminals / B.I.C. / Disease / Stranglehold
CD _____ DOJOCD 226
Dojo / Jun '95 / BMG.

BRAND NEW AGE
You can't take it anymore / Brand new age / Public servant / Warhead / Barbie's dead / Organised crime / Rat race / Emotional blackmail / Kicks / Teenage / Dirty girls / 500 cc / Bomb factory
CD _____ DOJOCD 228
Dojo / Jun '95 / BMG.

CRASH COURSE (Live)
C.I.D. / I couldn't be you / I live in a car / Tomorrows girls / Left for dead / Kicks / Rat race / New York State police / Warhead / Public servant / Telephone numbers / Organised crime / Rockers / Brand new age / Dirty girls / Same thing / Crash course / Teenage / Killer / Emotional blackmail
CD _____ DOJOCD 229
Dojo / Jun '95 / BMG.

DIMINISHED RESPONSIBILITY
You don't belong / So what / Confrontation / Fatal / Time and matter / Violent city / Too tired / Party in Paris / Gangster / Face the machine / New order / Just another jungle / Collision cult
CD _____ DOJOCD 232
Dojo / Jun '95 / BMG.

DOWN ON THE FARM
C.I.D. / I live in a car / Bic / Down on the farm / Endangered species / Countdown / Plan of action / Living dead / Ambition / Fear of girls / Lie down and die / Sensitive boys / Ice age / I Robot / Flesh wound / I don't need your love / Motivator / Combat zone / Fascist regime
CD _____ DOJOCD 117
Dojo / Apr '93 / BMG.

DOWN ON THE FARM - A COLLECTION OF THE LESS OBVIOUS
C.I.D. / I live in a car / B.I.C. / Down on the farm / Endangered species / Countdown / Plan of action / Living dead / Ambition / Fear of girls / Lie down and die / Sensitive boys / Eight times five / Ice age / I Robot / Flesh wound / I don't need your love / Motiovator / Combat zone / Fascist regime
CD _____ STR CD 017
Street Link / Oct '92 / BMG.

FLOOD OF LIES/SINGLES 1982-85
CD _____ FALLCD 18
Fallout / '95 / Disc.

GREATEST HITS LIVE
Emotional blackmail / Endangered species / Fear of girls / New York State Police / Rock 'n' roll savage / Does she suck / Organised crime / Bic / You don't belong / Confrontation street / Barbie's dead / Keep on running / Warhead / Police state / Teenage / Telephone numbers / I couldn't be you / I live in a car / Party in Paris / Crash course / Blues / Killer / Rat race / Young criminals / Left for dead / Rockers / Between the eyes / SK8 Tough / C.I.D. / Tomorrow's girls / Stranglehold / New barbarians

CD _____ DOJOCD 130
Dojo / Jun '93 / BMG.

GROSS OUT USA
CD _____ FALLCD 031
Fallout / '95 / Disc.

JAPAN TODAY
CD _____ FALLCD 045
Fallout / Mar '93 / Disc.

KILLING TIME
CD _____ FALLCD 047
Fallout / Mar '89 / Disc.

LEFT FOR DEAD, ALIVE IN HOLLYWOOD
CD _____ RE 412CD
Reach Out International / Nov '94 / Jetstar.

LIVE AT THE ROXY
CD _____ RRCD 146
Receiver / Jul '93 / Grapevine.

MAD COW FEVER
CD _____ FALLCD 048
Fallout / Jan '91 / Disc.

NORMAL SERVICE RESUMED
CD _____ FALLCD 050
Fallout / Jun '93 / Disc.

PUNK IS BACK, THE
Organised crime / Bomb factory / Dirty girls / Waiting for the man / Rat race / Teenage / Warhead / Sensitive boys / C.I.D. / Tomorrow's girls / Left for dead / She's not here / Kicks / I don't need your love / Limo life / Cocaine
CD _____ CD 430002
Voice Print / Apr '95 / Voice Print.

PUNK SINGLES COLLECTION, THE
CID / Stranglehold / Tomorrows girls / She's not there / Warhead / Teenage / Party in Paris / Keep on running / Countdown / Self destruct / Another typical city / Private army / Gun says / Motivator / Sabre dance / Hey Santa / Here comes Alex / Barmy London army / Freaked / New barbarians / Limo life
CD _____ CDPUNK 66
Anagram / Aug '95 / Pinnacle.

SCUM OF THE EARTH
CD _____ MCCD 120
Music Club / Aug '93 / Disc / THE / CM.

SINGLES 1978-1982, THE
CD _____ GBR 001 CD
Get Back / Apr '93 / Pinnacle.

Ukamau

FOLKLORE DE BOLIVIA
CD _____ EUCD 1023
ARC / '91 / ARC Music / ADA.

MUSICA DE BOLIVIA
CD _____ EUCD 1207
ARC / Sep '93 / ARC Music / ADA.

Ukrainians

KULTURA
Polityka / Ukrain America / Kievskiy express / Smert / Horilka / Slava / Europa / Kinets / Tycha voda / Zillya zeleneke / Ya / Tsyhanochka / Dyakuyu i dobranich
CD _____ COOKCD 070
Cooking Vinyl / Sep '94 / Vital.

UKRAINIANS, THE
Divchino / Te moyi radoshchi / Zavtra / Slave kobzarya / Dity plachut / Cherez richku, cherez hai / Pereyidu / Tebe zhdu / Son
CD _____ COOKCD 044
Cooking Vinyl / Feb '95 / Vital.

VORONY
Vorony / Chlib / Koroleva Ne Pomerla / Chi skriptsi hrayu / She Raz / Nadia Pishla / Doroha / Rospryahaite / Durak / Sertsem I dusheyu / Dvi Lebidky / De ye moya mila / Teper mi hovorymo / Chekannya (Venus in furs)
CD _____ COOKCD 054
Cooking Vinyl / Feb '95 / Vital.

Ulanbator

SPUTNIK
Sputnik / Zoom boom / My brain / Trans experience / Laika / M.D.K.S. / World / Serengal / Sky / Love this way / You are different / Obsessive / Himalaya
CD _____ ZENCD 008
Ninja Tune / Feb '94 / Vital / Kudos.

Ullman, Tracey

BOBBY'S GIRL - VERY BEST OF TRACEY ULLMAN
CD _____ 12374
Laserlight / Sep '94 / Target/BMG.

HIT SINGLE COLLECTABLES
CD _____ DISK 4513
Disky / Apr '94 / THE / BMG / Discovery / Pinnacle.

VERY BEST OF TRACY ULLMAN
CD _____ STIFFCD 19
Disky / Jan '94 / THE / BMG / Discovery / Pinnacle.

YOU CAUGHT ME OUT
You caught me out / Little by little / Bad motorcycle / Loving you is easy / Sunglasses / Helpless / If I had you / Where the boys are / I know what boys like / Give him a great big kiss / Baby I lied
CD _____ STIFFCD 08
Disky / Jan '94 / THE / BMG / Discovery / Pinnacle.

Ullmann, Gebhard

BASEMENT RESEARCH
CD _____ 1212712
Soul Note / Apr '95 / Harmonia Mundi / Wellard / Cadillac.

Ulloa, Francisco

MERENGUE!
La tijera / Agua de tu fuente / La situacion / El beso robao / Tongoneate / Ramonita / Manana por la manana / Los caballos / Linda Mujer / Lucas y radhames / La lengua / San Francisco / Homenaje a bolo
CD _____ CDORB 020
Globestyle / Jul '90 / Pinnacle.

Ulmer, James 'Blood'

BLACK AND BLUES
CD _____ DIW 845
DIW / Jul '91 / Harmonia Mundi / Cadillac.

BLUES PREACHER
CD _____ 4742972
Sony Jazz / Jan '95 / Sony.

HARMOLODIC GUITAR WITH STRINGS
CD _____ DIW 878
DIW / Feb '94 / Harmonia Mundi / Cadillac.

LIVE AT THE BAYERISCHER
Burning up / Church / Crying / Let me take you home / Boss lady / Street bride / Timeless / Make it night
CD _____ IOR 770182
In & Out / May '95 / Vital/SAM.

Ultimate Kaos

ULTIMATE KAOS
Intro (Age ain't nuthin' but a number) / Hoochie booty / Some girls / This heart belongs to you / Skip to my Lou / Misdemeanour / Show a little love / Weekend girl / Cool out alley / Believe in us / Age ain't nuthin' but a number / Uptown / Falling in love / Right here
CD _____ 5274442
Wild Card / May '95 / PolyGram.

Ultimate Spinach

BEHOLD AND SEE
Behold and see / Mind flowers / Where you're at / What you're thinking of / Fragmentary march of green / Genesis of beauty suite / Fifth horseman of the apocalypse
CD _____ CDWIKD 148
Big Beat / Oct '93 / Pinnacle.

ULTIMATE SPINACH
Ego trip / Sacfifice of the moon (In four parts) / Plastic raincoats / Hung up minds / (Ballad of the) Hip death goddess / Your head is reeling / Dove in Hawk's clothing / Baaroque no.1 / Funny freak parade / Pamela
CD _____ CDWIKD 142
Big Beat / Apr '95 / Pinnacle.

Ultra Nate

BLUE NOTES IN THE BASEMENT (Basement Boys)
Blue notes / Sands of time / Is it love / Deeper love (missing you) / You and me together / It's over now / Scandal / Rejoicing / Rain / Love hungover / It's my world / Funny (how things change)
CD _____ 9031747042
WEA / Jun '91 / Warner Music.

ONE WOMAN'S INSANITY
How long / You're not the only one / Show me / I'm not afraid / Incredibly you / Joy / I specialize in loneliness / One woman's insanity / Feelin' fine / Love is a many splendoured thing
CD _____ 9362453302
WEA / Oct '93 / Warner Music.

Ultra Sonic

GLOBAL TEKNO
CD _____ DCSR 007
Clubscene / Oct '95 / Clubscene / Mo's Music Machine / Grapevine.

TECHNO JUNKIES 1992-94
CD _____ DCSR 002
Clubscene / Sep '94 / Clubscene / Mo's Music Machine / Grapevine.

Ultra Vivid Scene

JOY 1967-1990
It happens every time / Three stars / Grey turns white / Guilty pleasure / Beauty No. 2 / Praise the love / Staring at the sun / Special one / Poison / Extraordinary / Kindest cut / Lightning

CD _____ CAD CD 0005
4AD / Apr '90 / Disc.

ULTRA VIVID SCENE
She screamed / Crash / You didn't say
please / Lynne-Marie 2 / Nausea / Mercy
seat / Dream of love / Lynne-Marie / This
isn't real / Whore of God / Bloodline / How
did it feel / Hail Mary
CD _____ CAD 809CD
4AD / Oct '88 / Disc.

Ultrahead

DEFINITION AGGRO
CD _____ CDVEST 4
Bulletproof / Feb '95 / Pinnacle.

Ultrahigh

VIEW OF ULTRAHIGH
CD _____ FIM 1015
Force Inc / Mar '95 / SRD.

Ultramarine

BEL AIR
CD _____ 0630112062
Blanco Y Negro / Aug '95 / Warner Music.

EVERY MAN AND WOMAN IS A STAR
CD _____ R 2892
Rough Trade / Jun '92 / Pinnacle.

FOLK
CD _____ OSHCD 1
Offshore / Jan '95 / Disc.

UNITED KINGDOMS
Source / Kingdom / Queen of the moon /
Prince Rock / Happy land / Urf / English
heritage / Instant kitten / Badger / Hooter /
Dizzy fox / No time
CD _____ 4509934252
Blanco Y Negro / Sep '93 / Warner Music.

Ultramarine

DE
Djanea / U song / Dub it / Ivory coast / De
/ Bod kan'nal / Modakofa
CD _____ 500052
Musidisc / Mar '90 / Vital. Harmonia Mundi
/ ADA / Cadillac / Discovery.

E SI MALA
CD _____ 500242
Musidisc / Nov '93 / Vital / Harmonia
Mundi / ADA / Cadillac / Discovery.

Ultras

**COMPLETE HANDBOOK OF
SONGWRITING**
CD _____ TX 92792
Roadrunner / Sep '91 / Pinnacle.

Ultraviolence

LIFE OF DESTRUCTOR
I am destructor / Electric chair / Joan /
Hardcore motherfucker / Digital selling /
Only love / We will break / Hiroshima / Des-
tructor's fall / Death of a child
CD _____ MOSH 103CD
Earache / Jun '94 / Vital.

PSYCHODRAMA
Birth - Jessica / Reject / Disco boyfriend /
Pimp / Psychodrama / Birth hitman / Stone
faced / Murder academy / Hitman's heart /
Contract / Curves / Suicide pact / God's
mistake / Searching hell / Heaven is oblivion
CD _____ MOSH 142CD
Earache / Jan '96 / Vital.

Ultravox

COLLECTION: ULTRAVOX
Dancing with tears in my eyes / Hymn / Thin
wall / Voice / Vienna / Passing strangers /
Sleepwalk / Reap the wild wind / All stood
still / Visions in blue / We came to dance /
One small day / Love's great adventure /
Lament
CD _____ CCD 1490
Chrysalis / Mar '85 / EMI.

DANCING WITH TEARS IN MY EYES
Sleepwalk / Waiting / Passing strangers /
Vienna / Passionate reply / Voice / Hymn /
Monument / We came to dance / Dancing
with tears in my eyes / Reap the wild wind
/ Love's great adventure / White china / All
fall down / Dreams / All in one day
CD _____ CDMFP 6175
Music For Pleasure / Sep '95 / EMI.

HA HA HA
Rock work / Frozen ones / Fear in the
western world / Distant smile / Man who
dies everyday / Artificial life / While I'm still
alive / Hiroshima mon amour
CD _____ IMCD 147
Island / Jul '92 / PolyGram.

INGENUITY
Ingenuity / There goes a beautiful world /
Give it all back / Future picture forever / Si-
lent cries / Distance / Ideals / Who'll save
you / Way out-a way through / Majestic
CD _____ RES 109CD
Resurgence / Oct '95 / Vital.

MONUMENT
Monument / Reap the wild wind / Voice /
Vienna / Mine for life / Hymn

CD _____ CCD 1452
Chrysalis / '86 / EMI.

RARE VOL. 1
Waiting / Face to face (Live) / King's lead
hat (Live) / Passionate reply / Herr X / Alles
klar / Keep talking / I never wanted to begin
/ Paths and angles / Private lives (live) / All
stood still / Hosanna (in Excelsis deo) /
Monument / Thin wall (Live) / Break your
back / Reap the wild wind (live) / Overlook
CD _____ CDCHR 6053
Chrysalis / Nov '93 / EMI.

RARE VOL. 2
Easterly / Building / Heart of the country
(mixes) / White china / Man of two worlds /
Three / All in one day / Dreams / All fall
down (Instrumental) / All fall down (Live) /
Dream on (Live) / Prize (Live) / Stateless /
One small day (Final mix)
CD _____ CDCHR 6078
Chrysalis / Aug '94 / EMI.

SLOW MOTION
Young savage / Rock work / Cross fade / I
want to be a machine / Life at rainbow's
end / Slip away / Just for a moment / Slow
motion / Dangerous rhythm / Quiet men /
Distant smile / While I'm still alive / My sex
/ Wild, the beautiful and the damned
CD _____ 5501122
Spectrum/Karussell / Oct '93 / PolyGram /
THE.

THREE INTO ONE
Young savage / Rock work / Dangerous
rhythm / Man who dies everyday / Wild, the
beautiful and the damned / Slow motion /
Just for a moment / Quiet men / My sex /
Hiroshima mon amour
CD _____ IMCD 301
Island / '89 / PolyGram.

ULTRAVOX
Ultravox / Saturday night in the city of the
dead / Life at rainbow's end / Slip away / I
want to be a machine / Wide boy / Dangerous rhythm / Lonely hunter / Wild, the
beautiful and the damned / My sex
CD _____ IMCD 144
Island / Jul '92 / PolyGram.

**ULTRAVOX/HA HA HA/SYSTEMS OF
ROMANCE (3CD Set)**
Saturday night in the city of the dead / Life
at the rainbow's end / Slip away / I want to
be a machine / Wide boys / Dangerous
rhythm / Lonely hunter / Wild, the beautiful
and the damned / My sex / Rockwrok / Frozen ones / Fear in the Western world / Distant smile / Man who dies everyday / Artificial life / While I'm still alive / Hiroshima
mon amour / Slow motion / Can't stay long
/ Someone else's clothes / Blue light /
Some of them / Quiet men / Dislocation /
Maximum acceleration / When you walk
through me / Just for a moment
CD Set _____ 5241522
Island / Nov '95 / PolyGram.

VIENNA
Astradyne / New Europeans / Private lives
/ Passing strangers / Mr. X / Sleepwalk /
Western promise / Vienna / All stood still
CD _____ CCD 1296
Chrysalis / Jul '94 / EMI.

Ultrbide

GOD IS GOD, PUKE IS PUKE
CD _____ K 162C
Konkurrel / Nov '85 / SRD.

Ulver

BERGTATT
CD _____ HNF 005CD
Head Not Found / Aug '95 / Plastic Head.

KVELDSSANGER
CD _____ HNF 014CD
Head Not Found / Jan '96 / Plastic Head.

Umbra Et Imago

GEDANKEN EINES VAMPIRES
CD _____ DW 075CD
Deathwish / Jan '96 / Plastic Head.

Umbrella Heaven

DO YOU HATE ME
CD _____ BWL 017
Boogle Wonderland / Sep '95 / SRD.

Umezu, Kazutoki

ECLECTICISM
CD _____ KFWCD 130
Knitting Factory / Feb '95 / Grapevine.

Unaminated

GOD OF EVIL
CD _____ NFR 009CD
No Fashion / Mar '95 / Plastic Head.

**IN THE FOREST OF THE DREAMING
DEAD**
CD _____ NFR 004
No Fashion / Oct '94 / Plastic Head.

Uncanny

SPLENIUM NYKTOPHBIA
CD _____ USR 008CD
Unisound / Nov '95 / Plastic Head.

Uncle Festive

PAPER AND THE DOG, THE
Paper and the dog / Road to Kent / Jessica
/ Boy King / Fantastic then / Super / Green
village / Sunday thoughts / All rise / Up and
down (and speedin' all over) / Not for
nothin'
CD _____ R2791692
Bluemoon / Nov '91 / New Note.

THAT WE DO KNOW
That we do know / Not for nothing / Incog-
nito / Trail of the wind / Goin' back / Con-
sider me gone / Dara Bueno / Three house
/ Yes you have / Horses
CD _____ CY 73671
Denon / Oct '89 / Conifer.

YOUNG PEOPLE WITH FACES
El tio / King Kent / Northern night / Monks
/ Young people with faces / All those with
wings / Soup of the day / Uncle Sandwich
/ To you
CD _____ CY 2135
Denon / Jun '88 / Conifer.

Uncle Sam

FOURTEEN WOMEN
CD _____ CMGCD 010
Communique / Nov '93 / Plastic Head.

HEAVEN OR HOLLYWOOD
Live for the day / Don't be shy / Alice D /
No reason why / Candy man / Don't you
ever / All alone / Peace of mind, piece of
body / Under sedation / Heaven or Holly-
wood / Steppin stone / Train keep a rollin'
CD _____ 3MC3
Skeller / Nov '90 / Pinnacle.

Uncle Slam

WHEN GOD DIES
When God dies / My mother's son / Pro-
creation / Smoke 'em if you got 'em / Of-
fering to a daity / Age of agression / End of
the line / Lightless sky / Summer in space
/ Bombs away
CD _____ 727732
Restless / Jan '95 / Vital.

Uncle Tupelo

ANODYNE
Slate / Acuff-Rose / Long cut / Give back
the key to my heart / Chickamauga / New
Madrid / Anodyne / We've been had / Fif-
teen keys / High water / No sense in lovin'
/ Steal the crumbs
CD _____ 9362454242
WEA / Oct '93 / Warner Music.

STILL FEEL GONE
Gun / Looking For A Way Out / Fall Down
Easy / Nothing / Still Be Around / Watch me
fall / Punch Drunk / D. Boon / True To Life
/ Cold shoulder / Discarded / If that's alright
CD _____ BUFF 001CD
Yellow Moon / May '93 / Vital.

Uncle Wiggly

**ACROSS THE ROOM AND INTO YOUR
LAP**
Stick up your smile / Nerve / Morphine and
ice-cream / Hope so, hope soon / Build
your own monster / That piece of string /
Express / Best boy
CD _____ SHIMMY 051CD
Shimmy Disc / Jul '92 / Vital.

THERE WAS AN ELK
There was an elk / Behold / Guadaloupe /
Frog / Weeping girder / Irresponsible pants
/ Sunny afternoon in the forest / Golden
moss / Trust / Hamsters / Crow (as in eat)
/ Toadstool / Sneaky pig / Man / Peaking
over the fence / Everything's pre-
tend / Small factory / Nostalgia / Elephant
fly / Mice w/rice / House of insect worship
/ Fruit salad
CD _____ SHIMMY 061CD
Shimmy Disc / Aug '93 / Vital.

Uncurbed

MENTAL DISORDER
CD _____ LF 094CD
Lost & Found / Jan '95 / Plastic Head.

STRIKE OF MANKIND
CD _____ LF 061CD
Lost & Found / Aug '93 / Plastic Head.

Under The Sun

UNDER THE SUN
CD _____ MABEL 2
Vinyl Tap / Jan '96 / Vinyl Tap.

Underbelly

**EVERYONE LOVES YOU WHEN YOU'RE
DEAD**
CD _____ SEVE 003CD
7 / Jul '95 / Pinnacle / Warner Music.

MUMBLY PEG

CD _____ OUT 114-2
Brake Out / Nov '94 / Vital.

Undercover

CHECK OUT THE GROOVE
CD _____ HFCD 26
PWL / Nov '92 / Warner Music / 3MV.

Underground Lovers

LEAVES ME BLIND
Leaves me blind
CD _____ GUCD 2
Guernica / Oct '92 / Pinnacle.

Undernation

ANGER
CD _____ OUT 1112
Brake Out / Nov '94 / Vital.

SOMETHING ON THE TV
CD _____ OUTCD 106
Brake Out / Sep '91 / Vital.

Understand

**BURNING BUSHES AND BURNING
BRIDGES**
CD _____ 0630119422
East West / Nov '95 / Warner Music.

Undertakers

UNEARTHED
CD _____ CDWIKD 163
Big Beat / Feb '96 / Pinnacle.

Undertones

**CHER O'BOWLIES (Pick Of The
Undertones)**
Teenage kicks / True confessions / Get over
you / Family entertainment / Jimmy Jimmy
/ Here comes the summer / You got my
number (why don't you use it) / My perfect
cousin / See that girl / Tearproof / Wednes-
day week / It's going to happen / Julie
Ocean / You're welcome / Forever paradise
/ Beautiful friend / Save me / Love parade /
Valentine's treatment / Love before
romance
CD _____ CDFA 3226
Fame / Oct '89 / EMI.

HYPNOTISED
More songs about chocolate and girls /
There goes Norman / See that girl / Whizz
kids / Under the boardwalk / Way girls talk
/ Hard luck / My perfect cousin / Boys will
be boys / Tearproof / Wednesday week /
Nine times out of ten / Girls that don't talk
/ What's with Terry
CD _____ DOJOCD 192
Dojo / May '94 / BMG.

PEEL SESSIONS: UNDERTONES
Listening in / Family entertainment / Billy's
third / Here comes the summer / Girls that
don't talk / Tear proof / What's with Terry /
Rock 'n' roll / Untouchable / Love parade /
Luxury / Sin of pride
CD _____ SFRCD 103
Strange Fruit / Feb '94 / Pinnacle.

POSITIVE TOUCH
Fascination / Julie Ocean / Life's too easy /
Crises of mine / You're welcome / His good
looking girlfriend / Positive touch / When
Saturday comes / It's going to happen /
Sign and explode / I don't know / Hannah
Doot / Boy wonder / Forever paradise
CD _____ DOJOCD 193
Dojo / May '94 / BMG.

SIN OF PRIDE, THE
Got to have you back / Untouchable / Val-
entine's treatment / Love before romance /
Luxury / Bye bye baby blue / Love parade
/ Soul seven / Conscious / Chain of love /
Save me / Sin of pride
CD _____ DOJOCD 194
Dojo / May '94 / BMG.

**TEENAGE KICKS (The Best Of The
Undertones)**
CD _____ CTVCD 121
Castle / Sep '93 / BMG.

UNDERTONES
Family entertainment / Girls don't like it /
Male model / I gotta getta / Teenage kicks
/ Wrong way / Jump boys / Here comes the
summer / Get over you / Billy's third /
Jimmy Jimmy / True confessions / She's a
runaround / I know a girl / Listening in /
Casbah rock
CD _____ DOJOCD 191
Dojo / May '94 / BMG.

Undertow

EDGE OF QUARREL
CD _____ LF 152CD
Lost & Found / May '95 / Plastic Head.

Underworld

DUB NO BASS WITH MY HEAD MAN
CD _____ JBOCD 1
Junior Boys Own / Jan '94 / Disc.

SECOND TOUGHEST IN THE INFANTS
CD _____ JBOCD 4
Junior Boys Own / Mar '96 / Disc.

Undivided Roots

UNDIVIDED ROOTS
Party Nite / Duke of Earl / Never get away / Mystic man / Mad about you / Stranger to my eyes / Someone to love / Rock dis ya music / To love again / Nature of love
CD _____ CIDM 1042
Mango / Jul '90 / Vital / PolyGram.

Ungod

CIRCLE OF THE 7 INFERNAL PACTS
CD _____ MRCD 001
Merciless / Oct '94 / Plastic Head.

Unholy

SECOND RING OF POWER, THE
CD _____ CDAV 005
Avant / Aug '94 / Harmonia Mundi / Cadillac.

Uniform Choice

STARING AT THE SUN
CD _____ LF 176CD
Lost & Found / Jul '95 / Plastic Head.

STRAIGHT AND ALERT
CD _____ LF 175CD
Lost & Found / Jul '95 / Plastic Head.

Union

UNION, THE
CD _____ GROW 0422
Grass / Feb '95 / SRD.

Union Jack

THERE WILL BE NO ARMAGEDDON
CD _____ PLAT 15CD
Platipus / Jul '95 / SRD.

Uniques

BEST OF THE UNIQUES (1967-1969)
CD _____ CDTRL 340
Trojan / Jun '94 / Jetstar / Total/BMG.

Unit 4+2

CONCRETE AND CLAY
CD _____ 8442962
London / Jan '93 / PolyGram.

Unit Pride

CAN I KILL A DREAM
CD _____ LF 158CD
Lost & Found / Jun '95 / Plastic Head.

United Future...

NO SOUND IT TOO TABOO (United Future Organisation)
Mistress of the dance / Stolen moments / Sunday folk tale / Future light / Make it better / Magic wand of love / Bar f out / Doop-sylalolic / Tears of gratitude / United future airlines
CD _____ 5222712
Talkin' Loud / Sep '94 / PolyGram.

SOUNDTRACK, THE (United Future Organisation)
CD _____ APR 003CD
April / May '95 / Plastic Head.

Unitone Rockers

MAGIC PLANET
CD _____ BFRCD 010
Beat Farm / Apr '93 / Total/BMG.

Unity

BLOOD DAYS
CD _____ LF 103CD
Lost & Found / Aug '94 / Plastic Head.

Universal Being

HOLISTIC RHYTHMS
CD _____ HOLCD 23
Kudos / Jan '96 / Kudos / Pinnacle.

Universal Congress Of

ELEVENTH HOUR SHINE ON
CD _____ EMY 1362
Enemy / Nov '92 / Grapevine.

MECOLODICS
CD _____ SST 204 CD
SST / May '93 / Plastic Head.

SAD & TRAGIC DEMISE OF THE BIG FINE HOT SALTY BLACK WIND
CD _____ EMY 1172
Enemy / Nov '92 / Grapevine.

Universal Indicator

COMPILATION I - IV
CD _____ MKS 80
Rephlex / May '94 / Disc.

University Of Wisconsin..

UNIVERSITY OF WISCONSIN/EAU CLAIRE SYMPHONY BAND (University Of Wisconsin Band)
CD _____ SOSCD 1284
Stomp Off / Dec '94 / Jazz Music / Wellard.

Unleashed

ACROSS THE OPEN SEA
CD _____ CM 77055-2
Century Media / Nov '93 / Plastic Head.

LIVE IN VIENNA
CD _____ CM 77056
Century Media / Jan '94 / Plastic Head.

VICTORY
CD _____ CM 770902
Century Media / May '95 / Plastic Head.

WHERE NO LIFE DWELLS
CD _____ CM 9718CD
Century Media / '92 / Plastic Head.

Unleashed Power

QUINTET OF SPHERES
CD _____ RS 101
S.O.R.T. / Nov '93 / Plastic Head.

Unlimited Dream Company

VOLTAGE
CD _____ CDTOT 24
Jumpin' & Pumpin' / Apr '95 / 3MV / Sony.

Unmen

LOVE UNDERWATER (AND OTHER MOTION PICTURE MUSIC)
Dig that crazy grave / Man from the bomb / Love under water / Gay scenes / Dooms of Mars / Unsleep (pt 1) / Wind from no-where / Soft way / Gay scenes (remix) / Unsleep (pt 2) / Tomorrow and tomorrow
CD _____ SBZCD 010
Some Bizarre / Apr '92 / Pinnacle.

MUSIC IN MOTION
Brief encounter / Trafic / Fast trafic / Swarm / Prepare to bomb the countryside / Also with you (Traditional mix) / Honey siege / Alive with you
CD _____ LEBCD 034
Handlebar / Jun '95 / Vital.

Unorthodox

ASYLUM
CD _____ HELL 0021CD
Hellhound / '90 / Plastic Head.

BALANCE OF POWER
CD _____ HELL 0030CD
Hellhound / Apr '94 / Plastic Head.

Unpure

UNPURE
CD _____ NPR 011CD
Napalm / Jun '95 / Plastic Head.

Unrest

B.P.M. (1991-1994)
June / Cath Carroll / When it all / So so sick / Hydrofoil #4 / Winina XY / Winona XX / Folklore / Imperial (excerpt) / Cherry, Cherry / Hey London / Bavarain mods / Vibe out / Hi-tec theme / Wednesday and proud
CD _____ TB 1752
Teenbeat / Aug '95 / SRD.

FUCK PUSSY GALORE (AND ALL HER FRIENDS)
So you want to be a rock 'n' roll star / Scott and Zelda / Hill / Happy song / Rigor mortis / Can't sit still / Cats / Die grunen / Holiday in Berlin / 91st Century schizoid man / Hil, part 2 / Picnic at Hanging Rock / Live on a hot August night / Chastity ballad / Judy says / Tundra / Wild thang / Laughter / S. Street shuffle (with a beat) / Over the life / Hope / Communist tart / She makes me free to be me / Sammy's mean mustard / Greg Hershey where are you / Egg cheer
CD _____ OLE 0242
Matador / Jan '94 / Vital.

IMPERIAL
CD _____ GU 1CD
Guernica / Aug '92 / Pinnacle.

PERFECT TEETH
CD _____ CAD 3012CD
4AD / Jun '93 / Disc.

Unruly Child

UNRULY CHILD
On the raw / Take me down nasty / Who cries now / To be your everything / Tunnel of love / When love is gone / Lay down your arms / Is it over / Wind me up / Let's talk about love / Criminal / Long hair woman
CD _____ 7567921012
Interscope / Apr '92 / Warner Music.

Unsane

PEEL SESSIONS
CD _____ SFRCD 123
Strange Fruit / Oct '93 / Pinnacle.

SCATTERED, SMOTHERED AND COVERED
CD _____ 08445782
SPV / Dec '95 / Plastic Head.

SINGLES 89-92
CD _____ EFA 04913CD
City Slang / Nov '92 / Disc.

TOTAL DESTRUCTION
CD _____ EFA 049262
City Slang / Jan '94 / Disc.

Untouchables

AGENT DOUBLE O SOUL
Agent double o soul / Stripped to the bone / World gone crazy / Cold city / Education / Let's get together / Airplay / Under the boardwalk / Sudden attack / Shama lama ding dong
CD _____ 723422
Restless / Feb '95 / Vital.

DECADE OF DANCE (Live)
CD _____ 725072
Restless / Feb '95 / Vital.

Unwound

FUTURE OF WHAT
CD _____ KRS 245CD
Kill Rock Stars / Jul '95 / Vital.

NEW PLASTIC IDEAS
Entirely different / Matters / What was wound / Envelope / Fiction friction / Abstraktions / Arboretum / Usual dosage / All souls day / Hexenszene
CD _____ KRS 223CD
Kill Rock Stars / Mar '94 / Vital.

Up & Running

NOT FOR SALE
Why do you kick her while she's down / Is this the start / This one is for you / Boom / Silent but deadly / Baby, baby, babe / Thunder / No more tears / Gangland / Absolute fool / Don't set me up / Red man blues
CD _____ PCOM 1142
President / Oct '95 / Grapevine / Target / BMG / Jazz Music / President.

Up Front

PSALMS
CD _____ RASCD 3093
Ras / Oct '92 / Jetstar / Greensleeves / SRD / Direct.

Upchurch, Phil

ALL I WANT
Poison / When we need it bad / 12/25 / 516 / Grace / What will I do / All I want from you / I god it gowin on
CD _____ ICH 1127CD
Ichiban / Jan '94 / Koch.

LOVE IS STRANGE (Upchurch, Phil & Chaka Khan)
CD _____ GOJ 60142
Go Jazz / Sep '95 / Vital/SAM.

WHATEVER HAPPENED TO THE BLUES
CD _____ GOJ 60062
Go Jazz / Sep '95 / Vital/SAM.

Upfront

SPIRIT
CD _____ LF 087CD
Lost & Found / Jun '94 / Plastic Head.

Upp

UPP
Bad stuff / Friendly street / It's a mystery / Get down in the dirt / Give it to you / Jeffs one / Count to ten
CD _____ 4809642
Epic / Aug '95 / Sony.

Upper Crust

LET THEM EAT ROCK
CD _____ UPSTART 026
Upstart / Oct '95 / Direct / ADA.

Uppsala Big Band

IN PROGRESS
CD _____ SITCD 9208
Sittel / Jun '94 / Cadillac / Jazz Music.

RADIO UPPLAND BIG BAND 93
CD _____ SITCD 9207
Sittel / Jun '94 / Cadillac / Jazz Music.

Upsetters

IN DUB AROUND
CD _____ SFCD 005
Sprint / Jan '96 / Jetstar / THE.

Upsetters A Go Go

UPSETTERS A GO GO
CD _____ CDHB 136
Heartbeat / Nov '95 / Greensleeves / Jetstar / Direct / ADA.

Upsetting The Nation

UPSETTING THE NATION
Eight for eight / Outer space / To love somebody / Soulful I / Man from M.I.5 / I'll be waiting / Ten to twelve / Kiddy O / Medical operation / Night Doctor / Self control / Crying about you / Thunderball / One punch / Vampire / Build my whole world around you / Prisoner of love / I was wrong
CD _____ CDTRL 330
Trojan / Mar '94 / Jetstar / Total/BMG.

Upshaw, Dawn

KNOXVILLE
CD _____ 9791872
Elektra / '89 / Warner Music.

Upsidedown Cross

EVILUTION
CD _____ TAANG 70CD
Taang / Jun '93 / Plastic Head.

Uralski All Stars

RUSSIAN ROULETTE
Mishka, mishka / South Rampart Street parade / C'est si bon / Cabaret / Fine flowers in the spring garden / I've been dreaming of you for three years / My blue heaven / Katusha / Midnight in Moscow / Stenjka razin – Ah, Odessa / Mjasoedowskaya uliza
CD _____ CDTTD 597
Timeless Jazz / Sep '95 / New Note.

Uralsky All Stars

WE'LL MEET AGAIN
Volga boatman's song / Back home again in Indiana / Dream a little dream of me / Nobody's sweetheart / Just a gigolo / I ain't got nobody / Night train / Amapola / Night and day / Struttin' with some barbecue / Meet me tonight in dreamland / We'll meet again
CD _____ CDTTD 595
Timeless Jazz / Feb '96 / New Note.

Urban Cookie Collective

HIGH ON A HAPPY VIBE
CD _____ PULSE 13CD
Pulse 8 / Mar '94 / Pinnacle / 3MV.

Urban Dance Squad

LIFE N' PERSPECTIVES OF A GENUINE CROSSOVER
Come back / Gates of the big fruit / Life 'n' perspectives / Mr. Ezway / Thru the eyes of Jason / Routine / Son of the culture clash / Careless / Grand black citizen / Harvey quinnt / Duck ska / For the plasters / Wino the medicineman / Bureaucrat of Flaccostreet
CD _____ 261 994
Arista / Oct '91 / BMG.

MENTAL FLOSS FOR THE GLOBE
Fast lane / No kid / Deeper shade of soul / Brainstorm on the U.D.S. / Big apple / Piece of rock / Prayer for my demo / Devil / Famous when you're dead / Mental floss of the globe / Hitchhike H.D. / God blasts the Queen
CD _____ 260325
Arista / Mar '90 / BMG.

PERSONA NON GRATA
Demagogue / Good grief / No honestly / Alienated / Candy strip exp / Self sufficient snake / (Some) Chit chat / Burnt up cigarette / Self styled / Mugshot / Hangout / Downer
CD _____ CDHUT 19
Hut / Jun '94 / EMI.

Urban Knights

URBAN KNIGHTS
On the radio / Wanna be with you / Chill / Hearts of longing / Friendship / Miracle / Rose / Urban samba / Forever more / Senegal
CD _____ GRP 98152
GRP / May '95 / BMG / New Note.

Urban Sax

SPIRAL
CD _____ FCD 1125
EPM / Jul '91 / Discovery / ADA.

URBAN SAX
CD _____ FDC 1124
EPM / Jul '91 / Discovery / ADA.

Urban Turban

URBAN TURBAN
CD _____ SRS 4722CD
Silence / Dec '94 / ADA.

Urban Waste

URBAN WASTE
Urban waste
CD _____ LF 062
Lost & Found / Jan '94 / Plastic Head.

Urbanator

URBANATOR
CD _____ HIBD 8001
Hip Bop / Apr '95 / Conifer / Total/BMG /
Silva Screen.

Urbani, Massimo

BLESSING, THE
CD _____ 123257-2
Red / Nov '93 / Harmonia Mundi / Jazz
Horizons / Cadillac / ADA.

Urbaniak, Michal

**FRIDAY NIGHT AT THE VILLAGE
VANGUARD**
CD _____ STCD 4093
Storyville / Feb '89 / Jazz Music / Wellard
/ CM / Cadillac.

TAKE GOOD CARE OF MY HEART
CD _____ SCCD 31195
Steeplechase / Jul '88 / Impetus.

Ure, Midge

**IF I WAS: THE VERY BEST OF MIDGE
URE & ULTRAVOX**
If I was / No regrets / Love's great adven-
ture / Dear God / Cold cold heart / Vienna
/ Call of the wild / Dancing with tears in my
eyes / All fall down / Yellow pearl / Fade to
grey / Reap the wild wind / Answers to
nothing / Do they know it's Christmas
CD _____ CDCHR 1987
Chrysalis / Feb '93 / EMI.

Urge Overkill

10 YEARS OF WRECKING (2CD/LP Set)
CD Set _____ 86132RAD
Edel / Jul '95 / Pinnacle.

AMERICRUISER
CD _____ TGCD 52
Touch & Go / Nov '94 / SRD.

EXIT THE DRAGON
Jaywalkin' / Break / Need some air / Some-
body else's body / Honesty files / This is no
place / Mistake / Take me / View of the rain
/ Last night / Tomorrow / Tin foil / Monopoly
/ You'll say / Digital black epilogue
CD _____ GED 24818
Geffen / Aug '95 / BMG.

SATURATION
Sister Havana / Tequila sundae / Positive
bleeding / Back on me / Woman 2 woman
/ Bottle of fur / Crackbabies / Stalker / Drop-
out / Erica Kane / Nite and grey / Heaven
90210
CD _____ GED 24529
Geffen / Jun '93 / BMG.

STULL (EP)
CD _____ NECKMCD 009
Roughneck / Feb '95 / Disc.

SUPERSONIC STORYBOOK
CD _____ TG 70CD
Touch & Go / Nov '94 / SRD.

Uriah Heep

ABOMINOG
Too scared to run / Chasing shadows / On
the rebound / Hot night in a cold town /
That's the way it is / Prisoner sell your soul
/ Hot persuasion / Think it over / Running
all night (with the lion)
CD _____ CLACD 110
Castle / Nov '86 / BMG.

COLLECTION: URIAH HEEP
Love machine / Look at yourself / Firefly /
Return to fantasy / Rainbow demon / That's
the way it is / Love is blind / On the rebound
/ Easy livin' / July morning / Running all
night (with the lion) / Been away too long /
Gypsy / Wake up (set your sights) / Can't
keep a good band down / All of my life
CD _____ CCSCD 226
Castle / Jul '89 / BMG.

CONQUEST
Carry on / Feelings / Fools / Imagination / It
ain't easy / No return / Out on the street /
Won't have to wait too long
CD _____ CLACD 208
Castle / Dec '90 / BMG.

DEMONS AND WIZARDS
Wizard / Traveller in time / Easy livin' /
Poet's justice / Circle of hands / Rainbow
demon / All my life / Paradise / Spell
CD _____ ESMCD 319
Essential / Jan '96 / Total/BMG.

DIFFERENT WORLD
Blood on stone / Which way will the wind
blow / All god's children / All for one / Dif-
ferent world / Step by step / Seven days /
First touch / One in one / Cross that line /
Stand back
CD _____ CLACD 279
Castle / Feb '93 / BMG.

DREAM ON
CD Set _____ CDHTD 102
HTD / Oct '95 / Pinnacle.

ECHOES IN THE DARK

Echoes in the dark / Wizard / Come away
Melinda / Devil's daughter / Hot persuasion
/ Showdown / I'm alive / Look at yourself /
Spider woman / Woman of the night / I want
to be free / Gypsy / Sunrise / Bird of prey /
Love machine / Lady in black
CD _____ ELITE 020 CD
Carlton Home Entertainment / Aug '93 /
Carlton Home Entertainment.

FALLEN ANGEL
Woman of the night / Falling in love / One
more night / One more night (Last farewell)
/ Put your love on / Come back to me /
Whad'ya say / Save it / Love or nothing /
I'm alive / Fallen angel
CD _____ CLACD 176
Castle / Feb '90 / BMG.

FIREFLY
Hanging tree / Been away too long / Who
needs me / Wise man / Do you know / Rol-
lin' on / Sympathy / Firefly
CD _____ CLACD 190
Castle / Mar '91 / BMG.

HEAD FIRST
Other side of midnight / Stay on top /
Lonely nights / Sweet talk / Love is blind /
Roll overture / Red lights / Rollin' the rock /
Straight through the heart / Weekend
warriors
CD _____ CLACD 209
Castle / Dec '90 / BMG.

HIGH AND MIGHTY
One way or another / Weep in silence /
Misty eyes / Midnight / Can't keep a good
band down / Woman of the world / Foot-
prints in the snow / Can't stop singing /
Make a little love / Confession
CD _____ CLACD 191
Castle / Mar '91 / BMG.

INNOCENT VICTIM
Keep on ridin' / Flyin' high / Roller / Free 'n'
easy / Illusion / Free me / Cheat and lie /
Dance / Choices
CD _____ CLACD 210
Castle / Jan '90 / BMG.

LADY IN BLACK
Lady in black / Easy livin' / Gypsy / Spider
man / Sympathy / Carry on / Think it over /
Traveller in time / Shady lady / Lonely nights
/ Fallen angel / Come back to me / Love
stealer / Stay on top
CD _____ 5507302
Spectrum/Karussell / Jan '95 / PolyGram /
THE.

LANSDOWNE TAPES
Born in a trunk / Simon the bullet freak /
Here I am / Magic lantern / Why / Astranaz
/ What's within my heart / What should be
done / Lucy blues / I want you babe / Cel-
ebrate / Schoolgirl / Born in a trunk (instru-
mental) / Look at yourself
CD _____ RPM 115
RPM / Jul '93 / Pinnacle.

LIVE 1973
Sunrise / Sweet Lorraine / Traveller in time
/ Easy livin' / July morning / Tears in my
eyes / Gypsy / Circle of hands / Look at
yourself / Magician's birthday / Love ma-
chine / Rock 'n' roll medley
CD _____ CCSCD 317
Castle / Oct '91 / BMG.

LIVE AT SHEPPERTON '74
Easy livin' / So tired / I won't mind / Some-
thing or nothing / Stealin' / Love machine /
Easy road / Rock 'n' roll medley (Roll over
Beethoven/Blue suede shoes/I found you)
CD _____ CLACD 192
Castle / Dec '88 / BMG.

LIVE IN EUROPE,1979
Easy livin' / Look at yourself / Lady in black
/ Free me / Stealin' / Wizard / July morning
/ Falling in love / Woman of the night / I'm
alive / Who needs me / Sweet Lorraine /
Free'n'easy / Gypsy
CD _____ RAWCD 030
Raw Power / '87 / BMG.

LIVE IN MOSCOW (Cam B Mockba)
Bird of prey / Stealin' / Too scared to run /
Corinna / Mr. Majestic / Wizard / July morn-
ing / Easy livin' / That's the way that it is /
Pacific highway
CD _____ CLACD 276
Castle / '92 / BMG.

LOOK AT YOURSELF
Look at yourself / I wanna be free / July
morning / Tears in my eyes / Shadows of
grief / What should be done / Love machine
CD _____ ESMCD 318
Essential / Jan '96 / Total/BMG.

MAGICIAN'S BIRTHDAY, THE
Sunrise / Spider woman / Blind eye / Ech-
oes in the dark / Rain / Sweet Lorraine /
Tales / Magician's birthday
CD _____ ESMCD 339
Essential / Jan '96 / Total/BMG.

RAGING SILENCE
Hold your head up woman / Blood red
roses / Voice on my TV / Rich kids / Cry

freedom / Bad bad man / More fool you /
When the war is over / Lifeline
CD _____ CLACD 277
Castle / Feb '93 / BMG.

RARITIES FROM THE BRONZE AGE
CD _____ NEXCD 184
Sequel / Feb '92 / BMG.

RETURN TO FANTASY
Return to fantasy / Shady lady / Devil's
daughter / Beautiful dream / Prima donna /
Your turn to remember / Showdown / Why
did you go / Year or a day
CD _____ CLACD 175
Castle / Feb '90 / BMG.

SALISBURY
Bird of prey / Park / Time to live / Lady in
black / High priestess / Salisbury
CD _____ ESMCD 317
Essential / Jan '96 / Total/BMG.

SEA OF LIGHT
CD _____ HTCD 33
HTD / Mar '95 / Pinnacle.

STILL 'EAVY, STILL PROUD
Gypsy / Lady in black / July morning / Easy
livin' / Easy road / Free me / Other side of
midnight / Mr. Majestic / Rich kid / Blood
red roses
CD _____ CLACD 278
Castle / '93 / BMG.

SWEET FREEDOM
Dreamer / Stealin' / One day / Sweet free-
dom / If I had the time / Seven stars / Circus
/ Pilgrim
CD _____ ESMCD 338
Essential / Jan '96 / Total/BMG.

TWO DECADES IN ROCK
July morning / Sweet Lorraine / Gypsy /
Look at yourself / Easy livin'
CD Set _____ ESBCD 022
Essential / Jun '90 / Total/BMG.

URIAH HEEP STORY, THE
CD _____ ROHACD 2
EMI / Feb '90 / EMI.

URIAH HEEP VOL.2 - FREE ME
Wizard / Something or nothing / On the re-
bound / I'm so tired / Been away too long
/ One way or another / Return to fantasy /
Free me / Woman of the world / Love or
nothing / That's the way that it is / Wise
man / Prima donna / Dreams
CD _____ 5507312
Spectrum/Karussell / Mar '95 / PolyGram /
THE.

VERY 'EAVY, VERY 'UMBLE
Gypsy / Walking in your shadow / Come
away Melinda / Lucy blues / Dreammare /
Real turned on / I'll keep on trying / Wake
up (set your sights)
CD _____ ESMCD 316
Essential / Jan '96 / Total/BMG.

WONDERWORLD
Wonderworld / Suicidal man / Shadows and
the wind / So tired / Easy road / Something
or nothing / I won't mind / We got we /
Dreams
CD _____ CLACD 184
Castle / Aug '90 / BMG.

Urlich, Margaret

CHAMELEON DREAMS
CD _____ TIMBCD 604
Timbuktu / Aug '95 / Pinnacle.

US 3

HAND ON THE TORCH
Cantaloop (Flip fantasia) / I got it goin' on /
Different rhythms, different people / It's like
that / Just another brother / Cruisin' / I go
to work / Tukka yoot's riddim / Knowledge
of self / Lazy day / Eleven long years / Make
tracks / Dark side
CD _____ CDEST 2230
Capitol / Jun '94 / EMI.

HAND ON THE TORCH (The Jazz Mixes)
CD Set _____ CDESTX 2195
Capitol / May '94 / EMI.

USA All Stars

IN BERLIN FEBRUARY 1955
CD _____ EBCD 21132
Flyright / Feb '94 / Hot Shot / Wellard /
Jazz Music / CM.

Usher, Raymond

USHER
I'll make it right / Can you get wit it / Think
of you / Crazy / Slow love / Many ways / I'll
show you love / Love was here / Whispers
/ You took my heart / Smile again / Final
goobye / Interlude / Interlude 2 (Can't stop)
CD _____ 73008260082
Arista / Oct '94 / BMG.

Usherhouse

FLUX
CD _____ CLEO 94612
Cleopatra / Apr '94 / Disc.

MOLTING
CD _____ SATE 05
Talitha / Aug '93 / Plastic Head.

Usry, Johnny

HEALING
Healing / Forgotten heroes / Johnny's rap
(give peace a chance) / Chu-lai Charlie /
Healing (reprise) / Girl of the night / When
love is gone / Mom / Homeless / Girl of the
night (instrumental)
CD _____ CDUSC 4006
Ichiban / Jul '89 / Koch.

Ut

IN GUT'S HOUSE
CD _____ BFFP 17CD
Blast First / Disc.

Utah Saints

UTAH SAINTS
New Gold Dream / What can you do for me
/ Soulution / Believe in me / Too much to
swallow part 1 / What can you do for me
(2) / Something good / I want you / States
of mind / Trance atlantic glide / Kinetic synthetic / My mind must be free
CD _____ 8283792
FFRR / Jun '93 / PolyGram.

UTE

FREE TO BE...FREE TO BREATHE
CD _____ 33JAZZ 009CD
33 Jazz / Jun '93 / Cadillac / New Note.

Uthanda

GROOVE
Be my friend / Sweet soul salvation / Found
out the hard way / Look away / Change in
my world / Don't let me be misunderstood
/ To be loved / You groove / Mercy mercy
/ Way you are / Red September
CD _____ CD 08794
Broken / Jan '92 / Broken.

Uttal, Jai

BEGGARS AND SAINTS
Lake of exploits / Hara shiva shankara / Be
with you / Gopala / Rama bolo / Radhe
radhe / Menoka / Beggars and saints / Lake
of exploits pt.2 / Conductor / Coda
CD _____ 3202082
Triloka / Nov '94 / New Note.

FOOTPRINTS
Footprints / Caranan / Andobar Island /
Raghupati / Madzoub / Pahari / Snowview
/ Taking the dust / Raghupati II / Bus has
come
CD _____ 3201832
Triloka / Jun '92 / New Note.

MONKEY
CD _____ 3201942
Triloka / Sep '92 / New Note.

Uys, Tessa

PIANO MUSIC
CD _____ URCD 107
Upbeat / Nov '92 / Target/BMG / Cadillac.

Uzeb

LIVE IN EUROPE
Time Square / Mile O / 4 p.m., gate 26 / Le
baiser sale / 60 Rue Des Lombards / New
Funk / Slinky / La ballade bleue / Bull's nos-
tril blues
CD _____ JMS 186282
Cream / May '95 / Rollercoaster / Swift.

Uzect Plaush

MORE BEAUTIFUL HUMAN LIFE
Violet cell edit / Wind from nowhere / Wet-
zone rapture / Falling dream / Auto-radia /
Boiling horizon / Discrete global / Sky rolled
back
CD _____ AMB 4932CD
Apollo / Apr '94 / Vital.

Uzeda

PEEL SESSION
CD _____ SFPSCD 090
Strange Fruit / Oct '94 / Pinnacle.

UZI

SLEEP ASYLUM
CD _____ PILLMCD 4
Placebo / Feb '94 / Disc.

Uzzell Edwards, Charles

OCTOPUS
CD _____ PS 0879CD
Fax / Nov '95 / Plastic Head.

V

V

SOME MOVING, SOME STOOD STILL
CD _____ GIFTCD 1
4AD / May '95 / Disc.

V Flo

YA DOWN OR YA NOT
CD _____ PLA 41652CD
Ichiban / May '94 / Koch.

V.S.O.P.

LIVE UNDER THE SKY
One of another kind / Teardrop / Pee wee / Para oriente / Fragile / Domp / Stella by starlight/On green dolphin street
CD _____ 471063 2
Columbia / Nov '93 / Sony.

Vache, Allan

ATLANTA JAZZ PARTY
CD _____ ACD 270
Audiophile / Apr '93 / Jazz Music / Swift.

ONE FOR MY BABY (Vache, Allan Quintet)
CD _____ ACD 255
Audiophile / '91 / Jazz Music / Swift.

Vache, Warren Jnr.

EASY GOING (Vache, Warren Sextet)
Little girl / Easy going bounce / Warm valley / You'd be so nice to come home to / Michelle / It's been so long / Was I to blame for falling in love with you / London by night / Mandy, make up your mind / Moon song (That wasn't meant for me)
CD _____ CCD 4323
Concord Jazz / Jul '87 / New Note.

FIRST TIME OUT
CD _____ ACD 196
Audiophile / Jan '94 / Jazz Music / Swift.

HORN OF PLENTY
Eternal triangle / Struttin' with some barbecue / Long ago and far away / Nancy's fancy / All blues / Bix fix / Joy spring / Buddy Bolden's blues / Swing samba / I can't get started (with you) / Liza
CD _____ MCD 5524
Muse / Jul '94 / New Note / CM.

WARREN VACHE AND THE BEAUX-ARTS STRING QUARTET (Vache, Warren & The Beaux-Arts String Quartet)
CD _____ CCD 4392
Concord Jazz / '89 / New Note.

Vache, Warren Sr.

TALK TO ME BABY
CD _____ MCD 5547
Muse / Feb '96 / New Note / CM.

WARREN VACHE & SYNCOPATIN' 7
CD _____ CCD 57
Circle / Apr '94 / Jazz Music / Swift / Wellard.

Vada

VADA
CD _____ MASS 64CD
Mass Productions / Jul '95 / ADA.

Vader

ULTIMATE INCANTATION
CD _____ MOSH 059CD
Earache / Nov '92 / Vital.

Vagtazo Halottkemek

HAMMERING AT THE DOOR OF NOTHINGNESS
CD _____ VIRUS 110CD
Alternative Tentacles / Mar '92 / Pinnacle.

JUMPING OUT OF THE WORLD
CD _____ VIRUS 92CD
Alternative Tentacles / '92 / Pinnacle.

Vai, Steve

ALIEN LOVE SECRETS
Mad horsie / Juice / Die to live / Boy from Seattle / Ya yo galak / Kill the guy with the ball / Good eaters / Tender surrender
CD _____ 4785862
Relativity / Apr '95 / Sony.

FLEX-ABLE
Little green men / Viv women / Lovers are crazy / Salamanders in the sun / Boy / Girl song / Attitude song / Call it sleep / Junkie / Bill's private parts / Next stop earth / There's something dead in here
CD _____ CDGRUB 3
Food For Thought / '89 / Pinnacle.

PASSION AND WARFARE
Liberty / Erotic nightmares / Animal / Answers / Riddle / Ballerina 12/24 / For the love of God / Audience is listening / I would love to / Blue powder / Greasy kids stuff / Alien water kiss / Sisters / Love secrets
CD _____ 467109 2
Relativity / Oct '93 / Sony.

SEX AND RELIGION
Earth dweller's return / Here and now / In my dreams with you / Still my bleeding heart / Sex and religion / Dirty black hole / Touching tongues / State of grace / Survive / Pig / Road to Mt. Calvary / Deep down into the pain / Rescue me or bury me
CD _____ 473947-2
Relativity / Jul '93 / Sony.

Vaiana, Pierre

SHAKRA
CD _____ CELPC 23
CELP / Sep '93 / Harmonia Mundi / Cadillac.

Vain

MOVE ON IT
Breakdown / Whisper / Long time ago / Ivy's dream / Hit and run / Family / Planets turning / Get up / Crumpled glory / Resurrection / Ticket outta here
CD _____ HMRXD 194
Heavy Metal / Sep '94 / Sony.

Val, Joe

DIAMOND JOE
CD _____ ROUCD 11537
Rounder / Nov '95 / CM / Direct / ADA / Cadillac.

Valdes, Bedo

BEDO RIDES AGAIN
CD _____ MES 158342
Messidor / Jul '95 / Koch / ADA.

Valdes, Carlos

MASTERPIECE
CD _____ MES 158272
Messidor / Dec '93 / Koch / ADA.

Valdes, Chucho

LUCUMI
CD _____ MES 158762
Messidor / Apr '93 / Koch / ADA.

Valdes, Merceditas

TUMI CUBA CLASSICS 2 - AFRO CUBAN
CD _____ TUMICD 050
Tumi / Aug '95 / Sterns / Discovery.

Vale, Jerry

16 MOST REQUESTED SONGS
Have you looked into your heart / Mama / Two purple shadows / Old cape cod / You don't know me / Al di la / Be my love / Tears keep on falling / Mala femmina / Dommage dommage / Pretend you don't see her / O sole mio (my sunshine) / Impossible dream / Arrivederci Roma / Love is a many splendoured thing / Innamorata (Sweetheart) / Amore, scusami
CD _____ CK 40216
Columbia / May '95 / Sony.

Valens, Ritchie

BEST OF RITCHIE VALENS
Come on let's go / La bamba / Donna / Bluebirds over the mountain / Fast freight / Cry cry cry / That's my little Suzie / Stay beside me / Big baby blues / Little girl / Hurry up / Bony Moronie / We belong together / Malaguena / Framed / In a turkish town / Dooby dooby wah / Ooh my head
CD _____ CDCHM 387
Ace / Mar '92 / Pinnacle / Cadillac / Complete/Pinnacle.

LOST TAPES, THE
We belong together / Blues with drum / Ritchie's blues / Come on let's go / In a turkish town / Dooby dooby wah / Bluebirds over the mountain / That's my little Suzie / Let's rock 'n' roll / Donna / Blues instrumental / Cry cry cry / Malaguena / Blues - slow / Stay beside me / Rhythm song / Guitar instrumental / Rock lil darlin' / La bamba / Ooh my head
CD _____ CDCHD 317
Ace / May '92 / Pinnacle / Cadillac / Complete/Pinnacle.

RITCHIE VALENS STORY, THE
Bony Moronie / Come on let's go / That's my little Suzie / Rock little Darlin' / Bluebirds over the mountain / La bamba / Let's rock

'n' roll / Donna / Summertime blues / In a Turkish town / Paddiwack song / Big baby blues / Malaguena / Stay beside me
CD _____ CDCHD 499
Ace / Jan '94 / Pinnacle / Cadillac / Complete/Pinnacle.

RITCHIE VALENS/RITCHIE
That's my little Suzie / In a Turkish town / Come on let's go / Donna / Bony Moronie / Ooh my head / La Bamba / Bluebirds over the mountain / Hi-tone / Framed / We belong together / Dooby dooby wah / Stay beside me / Cry cry cry / Big baby blues / Paddiwack song / My darling is gone / Hurry up / Little girl / Now you're gone / Fast freight / Ritchie's blues / Rockin' all night
CD _____ CDCHD 953
Ace / Oct '90 / Pinnacle / Cadillac / Complete/Pinnacle.

Valente, Caterina

INTERNATIONAL, THE
Guardando Il cielo / Zeeman / Koini tsukarete / Adam et eve / el bardo / Hava nagila / Nessuno mai / Tintarella di luna / Es mi amor / Tra-la-la-la-la / Das weisse hchzeitskleid / Diz me em setemro / Mijn souvenir / Leccion de twist / Weil die sehnsucht so gross war / Don Quixote / Dindi / Hana / Morgen wird's schoner sein / Me importas tu / Caro mio / Dammi retta / Oyedo nihonbashi / Una lagrima del yuo dolore / Parlezmoi d'amour / Napule ca se sceta / Ein stern ging verloren / Scandinavian folk song
CD _____ BCD 15604
Bear Family / Oct '91 / Rollercoaster / Direct / CM / Swift / ADA.

ONE AND ONLY, THE
Ola, ola, ola / Un p'tit beguine / Tornera / Das kommt vom kussen / Bruxeria / Adios Panama / Habame no Utah / Amo solo te / When in Rome / Und dann kam der Mondenschein / Q Erotas pou makousse / Broadway conga / La otra cara / Kumono nagareni / Twist a Napoli / Zuviel tequila / Dia de fiesta / I Melenia I yiftopoula / Amor prohibido / Kom lat ons dansen / Im Kabarett der illusionen / Una sera di Tokyo / Cua cua cua / Israeli lullaby
CD _____ BCD 15601
Bear Family / Oct '90 / Rollercoaster / Direct / CM / Swift / ADA.

Valentine Brothers

MONEY'S TOO TIGHT TO MENTION
CD _____ TKOCD 016
TKO / '92 / TKO.

Valentine Saloon

SUPER DUPER
CD _____ PIPECD 001
Pipeline / Mar '93 / Pinnacle.

Valentine, Cal

TEXAS ROCKER, THE
CD _____ BMCD 9027
Black Magic / Dec '94 / Hot Shot / Swift / CM / Direct / Cadillac / ADA.

Valentine, Dickie

BEST OF DICKIE VALENTINE, THE
CD _____ SOW 704
Sound Waves / May '94 / Target/BMG.

DICKIE VALENTINE & FRIENDS
CD _____ MATCD 279
Castle / Sep '93 / BMG.

MR. SANDMAN
Wanted / Stay awhile / Second time around / With these hands / For all we know / Lost dreams and lonely hearts / Wait for me / No such luck / My word / In times like these / Once in each life / Build yourself a dream / Mona Lisa / It's better to have loved / Nothing but the best / Free me / Old devil moon / Come another day another time / Dreams can tell a lie / Cry my soul / Something good / Song of the trees / Kiss to build a dream on / Mr. Sandman
CD _____ C5MCD 625
See For Miles/C5 / Jul '95 / Pinnacle.

MY FAVOURITE SONGS
CD _____ SSLCD 202
Savanna / Jun '95 / THE.

THIS IS DICKIE VALENTINE
Venus / La Rosita / Song of the trees / You touch my hand / Sometimes I'm happy / Just in time / Teenager in love / King of dixieland / Hold me in your arms / Get well soon / Homecoming waltz / Dreams can tell a lie / Long before I knew you / Blossom fell / Broken wings / Climb every mountain (CD only.) / Roundabout (CD only.) / My favourite song (CD only.) / Finger of suspicion / Mr. Sandman / Fool that I am / All the time and ev'rywhere / Ronettes / One more sun-

rise / No such luck / Where (in the old hometown) / Old pi-anna rag / Clown who cried / I'll never love again / You belong to me / Chapel of the roses / Standing on the corner / Endless / How unlucky can you be (CD only) / Once, only once (CD only) / Shalom (CD only)
CD Set _____ CDDL 1224
Music For Pleasure / Apr '92 / EMI.

Valentine, Kid Thomas

DANCE HALL YEARS
CD _____ AMCD 48
American Music / Jan '94 / Jazz Music.

KID THOMAS
CD _____ AMCD 010
American Music / Oct '93 / Jazz Music.

KID THOMAS & HIS DIXIELAND BAND 1960
CD _____ 504CD 33
504 / Feb '95 / Wellard / Jazz Music / Target/BMG / Cadillac.

KID THOMAS AT THE MOOSE HALL
CD _____ BCD 305
GHB / Oct '93 / Jazz Music.

KID THOMAS IN CALIFORNIA
CD _____ BCD 296
GHB / Jan '94 / Jazz Music.

KID THOMAS/EMANUEL PAUL/BARRY MARTYN BAND
CD _____ BCD 257
GHB / Mar '95 / Jazz Music.

NEW ORLEANS TRADITIONAL JAZZ LEGENDS
CD _____ MG 9004
Mardi Gras / Feb '95 / Jazz Music.

TRUMPET KING
CD _____ MG 9003
Mardi Gras / Feb '95 / Jazz Music.

Valentino, Vinny

VINNY VALENTINO & HERE NO EVIL
Distance between two lines / Venice / Don't blame me / Blues for a while / Secret hiding place / Full moon over the Mediterranean / Veins / Song is you / As you said / When the feeling moves you / Lu / Old folks
CD _____ PAR 2016
PAR / Aug '93 / Charly / Wellard.

Valhal

MOONSTONE
CD _____ HNF 009CD
Head Not Found / Mar '95 / Plastic Head.

Vali, Justin

TRUTH, THE (Vali, Justin Trio)
Malagasy intro / Ny marina (The truth) / Sova (Malagasy rap) / Sariaka (Joy) / Rambala / Tsondrao (Benediction) / Tsingy (Sacred mountain) / Bilo (Malagasy voodoo) / Relahy / Ray sy Reny (Mum and Dad) / Manga ny Lanitr'i / Kintana (The open roof) / Vato malaza / Sova (Repeat) / Bongo lava (The broad mountain range) / Malagasy folk dance medley / Surprise tunnel track
CD _____ CDRW 51
Realworld / Jan '95 / EMI / Sterns.

Valitsky, Ken

SPECIES COMPATIBILITY
CD _____ KFWCD 135
Knitting Factory / Nov '94 / Grapevine.

Valland, Asne

DEN LJOSE DAGEN
CD _____ FXCD 139
Musikk Distribusjon / Jan '95 / ADA.

Valle, Marcus

ESSENTIAL MARCUS VALLE, THE
CD _____ MRBCD 003
Mr. Bongo / May '95 / New Note.

Vallee, Rudy

HEIGH-HO EVERYBODY, THIS IS RUDY VALLEE
Heigh ho everybody, heigh ho / Betty co-ed / If I had a girl like you / Let's do it / I still remember / Salaaming the rajah / My heart belongs to the girl who belongs to somebody else / One in the world / I'll be reminded of you / You'll do it someday, so why not now / Kitty from Kansas City / That's when I learned to love you / Outside / Dream sweetheart / Love made a gypsy out of me / Perhaps / Little kiss each morning a little kiss each night / Verdict is life with you / Lover come back to me / Stein song
CD _____ CDAJA 5009

696

Living Era / Jul '92 / Koch.
CD _____ PASTCD 7077
Flapper / Sep '95 / Pinnacle.

SING FOR YOUR SUPPER
Naturally / Flying down to Rio / Sing for your supper / Stranger in Paree / Vieni vieni / Whiffenpoof song / Nasty man / You and me that used to be / Drunkard song / I'm just a vagabond lover / Me minus you / Latin Quarter / Orchids in the moonlight / Life is a song / This can't be love / Ha cha cha (funktion) / I wanna go back to Bali / Goodnight my love
CD _____ CMSCD 005
Movie Stars / Oct '91 / Conifer.

Vallenato

PRE - LOG
CD _____ TOPYCD 074
Temple / May '94 / Pinnacle / Plastic Head.

Valli, Frankie

20 GREATEST HITS: FRANKIE VALLI & FOUR SEASONS (Valli, Frankie & Four Seasons)
Sherry / Big girls don't cry / Walk like a man / Dawn / Rag doll / Stay / Let's hang on / Working my way back to you / Opus 17 (Don't you worry about me) / I've got you under my skin / C'mon Marianne / You're ready now / Who loves you / December 1963 (Oh what a night) / Silver star / My eyes adored you / Swearin' to God / Fallen angel / Grease / Can't take my eyes off you
CD _____ PLATCD 4902
Platinum Music / Dec '88 / Prism / Ross.

AIN'T THAT A SHAME/LIVE ON STAGE (Four Seasons)
Candy girl / Happy, happy birthday baby / Honey love / Soon (I'll be home again) / Stay / Dumb drum / Marlena / Long lonely nights / New Mexican rose / That's the only way / Melancholy / Ain't that a shame / Silver wings / Starmaker / Blues in the night / Just in time / Little boy (In grown up clothes) / I can dream, can't I / How do you make a hit song / By myself / Jada / We three / Day in, day out / My mother's eyes / Mack the knife / Come si bella / Brotherhood of man
CD _____ CDCHD 596
Ace / Jun '95 / Pinnacle / Cadillac / Complete/Pinnacle.

BIG HITS/NEW GOLD HITS (Four Seasons)
CD _____ CDCHD 620
Ace / Feb '96 / Pinnacle / Cadillac / Complete/Pinnacle.

CHRISTMAS ALBUM/BORN TO WANDER (Four Seasons)
We wish you a merry Christmas / Angels from the realms of glory / Hark the herald angels sing / It came upon a midnight clear / What child is this / Carol of the bells / Deck the walls / Excelsis deo / O come all ye faithful / Little drummer boy / First noel / O holy night / Silent night / Deck the halls / God rest ye merry gentlemen / Away in a manger / Joy to the world / Santa Claus is coming to town / Christmas tears / I saw Mommy kissing Santa Claus / Christmas song / Jingle bells / White Christmas / Born to wander / Don't cry, Elena / Where have all the flowers gone / Cry myslef to sleep / Ballad for our time / Silence is golden / New town / Golden ribbon / Little pony get along / No surfin' today / Searching wind / While
CD _____ CDCHD 615
Ace / Oct '95 / Pinnacle / Cadillac / Complete/Pinnacle.

DAWN (GO AWAY)/RAG DOLL (Four Seasons)
Big man's world / You send me / Mountain high / Life is but a dream / Church bells may ring / Dawn / Only yesterday / Sixteen candles / Breaking up is hard to do / Earth angel (will you be mine) / Don't let go / Do you want to dance / Save it for me / Touch of you / Danger / Marcie / No one cares / Rag doll / Angel cried / Funny face / Huggin' my pillow / Setting sun / Ronnie / On broadway tonight
CD _____ CDCHD 554
Ace / Sep '94 / Pinnacle / Cadillac / Complete/Pinnacle.

FOUR SEASONS ENTERTAIN YOU/ WORKING MY WAY BACK TO YOU (Four Seasons)
Show girl / Where is love / One clown cried / My prayer / Little Darlin' / Bye bye baby (baby goodbye) / Betrayed / Somewhere / Living just for you / Little angel / Big man in town / Sunday kind of love / Toy soldier / Girl come running / Let's hang on / Working my way back to you / Pity / I woke up / Beggar's parade / Can't get enough of you baby / Sundown / too many memories / Comin' up in the world / Everybody knows my name
CD _____ CDCHD 582
Ace / Feb '95 / Pinnacle / Cadillac / Complete/Pinnacle.

GOLD
CD _____ GOLD 212
Disky / Apr '94 / THE / BMG / Discovery / Pinnacle.

ORIGINAL HITS 1962-1972, THE (Four Seasons)
CD _____ DCD 5367
Disky / Apr '94 / THE / BMG / Discovery / Pinnacle.

SHERRY & 15 OTHERS (Four Seasons)
CD _____ DCD 5409
Disky / Oct '94 / THE / BMG / Discovery / Pinnacle.

SHERRY & BIG GIRLS DON'T CRY (Four Seasons)
Sherry / I've cried before / Yes sir that's my baby / Peanuts / La dee dah / Teardrops / You're the apple of my eye / Never on a Sunday / I can't give you anything but love / Girl in my dreams / Oh Carol / Lost lullabye / Walk like a man / Silhouettes / Why do fools fall in love / Tonite, tonite / Lucky ladybug / Alone / One song / Sincerely / Since I don't have you / My sugar / Hi Lili hi lo / Big girls don't cry
CD _____ CDCHD 507
Ace / Apr '94 / Pinnacle / Cadillac / Complete/Pinnacle.

SOLO/TIMELESS
My funny valentine / Cry for me / (You're gonna) Hurt yourself / Ivy / Secret love / Can't take my eyes off you / My Mother's eyes / This is goodbye / Sun ain't gonna shine anymore / Trouble with me / Proud one / You're ready now / By the time I get to Phoenix / Expression of love / For all we know / Sunny / Watch where you walk / To give (the reason I live) / Eleanor Rigby / September rain (here come's the rain) / Make the music play / Stop and say hollo / Donnybrook / I make a fool of myself
CD _____ CDCHD 538
Ace / Jun '94 / Pinnacle / Cadillac / Complete/Pinnacle.

VERY BEST OF FRANKIE VALLI & THE FOUR SEASONS (Valli, Frankie & Four Seasons)
Sherry / Big girls don't cry / Walk like a man / Ain't that a shame / Rag doll / Dawn / Silence is golden (Not on album) / Let's hang on / Working my way back to you / Who loves you / Opus 17 (Don't you worry about me) / I've got you under my skin / Can't take my eyes off you / Night / My eyes adored you / You're ready now / Swearin' to God / December 1963 (Oh what a night) / Silver star / Fallen angel / We can work it out / Sun ain't gonna shine anymore (Not on album) / Down the hall / Grease
CD _____ 5131192
PolyGram TV / Feb '92 / PolyGram.

VERY BEST OF THE FOUR SEASONS, THE (Four Seasons)
CD _____ MCCD 211
Music Club / Oct '95 / Disc / THE / CM.

Value

PULLING LEGS OFF FLIES
CD _____ BBA 10CD
Big Cat / Feb '94 / SRD / Pinnacle.

Vamp

HORISONTER
CD _____ MS 1121CD
Musikk Distribujson / Dec '94 / ADA.

Van Basten

PERIMITIVE
CD _____ BRUCD 1
Brute / Oct '93 / Disc.

Van Der Graaf Generator

1ST GENERATION
Darkness / Killer / Man erg / Theme one / Pioneers over C / Pictures/Lighthouse / Eyewitness / S.H.M. / Presence of the night / Kosmos tours / (Custards) last stand / Clot thickens / Land's end / We go now / Refugees
CD _____ COMCD 2
Virgin / Feb '87 / EMI.

GODBLUFF
Undercover man / Scorched earth / Arrow / Sleepwalkers
CD _____ CASCD 1109
Charisma / Apr '88 / EMI.

H TO HE, WHO AM THE ONLY ONE
Killer / With no door / Emperor in his war room / Lost / Pioneers over C
CD _____ CASCD 1027
Charisma / Nov '88 / EMI.

I PROPHESY DISASTER
Afterwards / Necromancer / Refugees / Boat of millions of years / Lemmings (including cog) / Arrow / La rossa / Ship of fools / Medley (Parts of "A plague of light-house keepers" and "The sleepwalkers")
CD _____ CDVM 9026
Virgin / Aug '93 / EMI.

LEAST WE CAN DO IS WAVE TO EACH OTHER, THE
Darkness / Refugees / White hammer / Whatever would Robert have said / Out of my book / After the flood
CD _____ CASCD 1007
Charisma / '87 / EMI.

MAIDA VALE
Band Of Joy / May '94 / ADA.
CD _____ BOJCD 008

NOW AND THEN
Liquidator / Gentlemen prefer blondes / Main slide / Spooks / Saigon roulette / Tropic of conversation / Tarzan the epilogue
CD _____ CDTB 042
Thunderbolt / May '88 / Magnum Music Group.

PAWN HEARTS
Lemmings (including Cog) / Man erg / Pictures/Lighthouse / Eyewitness / S.H.M. / Kosmos tours / Clot thickens / Land's end / We go now / Presence of the night / (Custards) last stand
CD _____ CASCD 1051
Charisma / Apr '88 / EMI.

QUIET ZONE PLEASURE DOME
Lizard play / Habit of the broken heart / Siren song / Last frame / Wave / Cat's eye, yellow fever (running) / Sphinx in the face / Chemical world / Sphinx returns
CD _____ CASCD 1131
Charisma / '87 / EMI.

STILL LIFE
Pilgrims / Still life / La Rossa / My room (waiting for wonderland) / Childlike faith in childhood's end
CD _____ CASCD 1116
Charisma / Apr '87 / EMI.

TIME VAULTS
Liquidator / Rift valley / Tarzan / Coil night / Time vaults / Drift / Roncevaux / It all went red / Faint and forsaken / (In the) Black room
CD _____ CDTB 106
Magnum Music / Dec '92 / Magnum Music Group.

VITAL
Ship of fools / Still life / Last frame / Mirror images / Medley / Plague of lighthouse keepers / Pioneers over C / Sci finance / Door / Urban / Killer / Urban (part 2) / Nadir's big chance
CD _____ CVLCD 101
Virgin / '89 / EMI.

WORLD RECORD
When she comes / Place to survive / Masks / Meurglys 111 (The songwriters guild) / Wondering
CD _____ CASCD 1120
Charisma / Aug '88 / EMI.

Van Duser, Guy

AMERICAN FINGER STYLE GUITAR
CD _____ CD 11533
Rounder / '88 / CM / Direct / ADA / Cadillac.

GUY & BILLY (Van Duser, Guy & Billy Novick)
CD _____ CD 3014
Daring / Dec '94 / Direct / CM / ADA.

Van Dyke, Leroy

HITS AND MISSES
Walk on by / If a woman answers (hang up the phone) / Black cloud / Happy to be unhappy / Night people / Big man in a big house / Faded love / Save me the moonlight / My world is caving in / Handful of friends / I got a conscience / Broken promise / Dim dark corner / I sat back and let it happen / Geh'nicht vorbei / Just before dawn / Now I lay me down / Heartaches by the number / Sea of heartbreak / Love letters in the sand / Sugartime / Don't forbid me / Honeycomb / How long must you keep me a secret / Party doll / Conscience I'm guilty / Day the preacher comes / Fireball mail / If you don't, somebody else will / Put your little hand in mine
CD _____ BCD 15779
Bear Family / Jan '94 / Rollercoaster / Direct / CM / Swift / ADA.

ORIGINAL AUCTIONEER, THE
Auctioneer / I fell in love with a pony tail / Leather jacket / I'm movin' on / My good mind (went bad on me) / Heartbreak can nonball / Chicken shack / Poor boy / What this old work needs / Every time I ask my heart / Pocketbook song / Down at the south end of town / Honky tonk song / One heart
CD _____ BCD 15647
Bear Family / Nov '93 / Rollercoaster / Direct / CM / Swift / ADA.

WALK ON BY
Walk on by / If a woman answers (Hang up the phone) / Black cloud / Happy to be unhappy / Night people / Big man in a big house / Faded love / Save me the moonlight / My world is caving in / Handful of friends / I got a conscience / Broken promise / Dim dark corner / I sat back and let it happen / Geh'nicht vorbei / Just before dawn / Now I lay me down / Heartaches by the number / Sea of heartbreak / Love letters in the sand / Sugartime / Don't forbid me / Honeycomb / How long must you keep me a secret / Party doll / Conscience I'm guilty / Day the preacher comes / Fireball mail / If you don't, somebody else will / Put your little hand in mine
CD _____ BCD 15779-AH

Bear Family / Jul '94 / Rollercoaster / Direct / CM / Swift / ADA.

Van Halen

1984
1984 / Jump / Panama / Top Jimmy / Drop dead legs / Hot for teacher / I'll wait / Girl gone bad / House of pain
CD _____ 9239852
WEA / Feb '95 / Warner Music.

5150
Good enough / Why can't this be love / Get up / Dreams / Summer nights / Best of both worlds / Love walks in / 5150 / Inside
CD _____ 9253942
WEA / Feb '95 / Warner Music.

BALANCE
CD _____ 9362457602
Warner Bros. / Jan '95 / Warner Music.

DIVER DOWN
Where have all the good times gone / Hang 'em high / Cathedral / Secrets / Intruder / Pretty woman / Dancing in the street / Little guitar (intro) / Little guitars / Big bad Bill is sweet William now / Bull bug / Happy trails
CD _____ K257 003
WEA / Jan '84 / Warner Music.

FAIR WARNING
Mean street / Dirty movies / Sinner's swing / Hear about it later / Unchained / Push comes to shove / So this is love / Sunday afternoon in the park / One foot out of the door
CD _____ K 9235402
WEA / Jun '89 / Warner Music.

FOR UNLAWFUL CARNAL KNOWLEDGE
Pound cake / Judgement day / Spanked / Runaround / Pleasure dome / In 'n' out / Man on a mission / Dream is over / Right now / 316 / Top of the world
CD _____ 7599265942
WEA / Jun '91 / Warner Music.

LIVE - RIGHT HERE, RIGHT NOW
Right now / One way to rock / Why can't this be love / Give to live / Finish what ya started / Best of both worlds / 316 / You really got me / Won't get fooled again / Jump / Top of the world / Pound cake / Judgement day / When it's love / Spanked / Ain't talkin' 'bout love / In 'n' out / Dreams / Man on a mission / Ultra bass / Pleasure dome (drum solo) / Panama / Love walks in / Runaround
CD _____ 9362451982
WEA / Feb '93 / Warner Music.

OU812
And all mine / When it's love / A.F.U. (naturally weird) / Cabo wabo / Source of infection / Feels so good / Come back and finish what you started / Black and blue / Sucker in a 3 piece
CD _____ K 925732 2
WEA / Jun '88 / Warner Music.

VAN HALEN
You really got me / Jamie's cryin' / On fire / Runnin' with the Devil / I'm the one / Ain't talkin' 'bout love / Little dreamer / Feel your love tonight / Atomic punk / Eruption / Ice cream man
CD _____ K256470
WEA / Feb '95 / Warner Music.

VAN HALEN II
You're no good / Dance the night away / Somebody get me a doctor / Bottoms up / Outta love again / Light up the sky / D.O.A. / Women in love / Spanish fly / Beautiful girls
CD _____ 256 616
WEA / Mar '87 / Warner Music.

WOMEN AND CHILDREN FIRST
Tora tora / Cradle will rock / Romeo delight / Fools / In a simply rhyme / Could this be magic / Loss of control / Take your whiskey home / Everybody wants some
CD _____ K 9234152
WEA / Jun '89 / Warner Music.

Van Helsingen, Bart

PERCUSSION DUO (Van Helsingen, Bart & Hans Hasebos)
CD _____ HH 001
Bvhaast / Apr '92 / Cadillac.

Van Maasakkers, Gerard

ZONDER TITEL
CD _____ MW 1002CD
Music & Words / Jun '92 / ADA / Direct.

Van Meter, Sally

ALL IN GOOD TIME
High country / Blues for your own / Tyson's dream / Crazy creek / Anne's waltz / Weary lonesome blues / Bird that I held in my hand / Amor de mi vida / Road to Columbus / Damien Miley / The idlers of Belltown / We're not over yet
CD _____ SHCD 3792
Sugarhill / '91 / Roots / CM / ADA / Direct.

Van Ronk, Dave

FOLKWAYS YEARS 1959-1961
CD _____ SFCD 40041

Smithsonian Folkways / Sep '94 / ADA /
Direct / Koch / CM / Cadillac.

Van Senger, Dominik

FIRST, THE
CD _____ VBR 20072
Vera Bra / Dec '90 / Pinnacle / New Note.

Van Zandt, Townes

AT MY WINDOW
Snowin' on Raton / Blue wind blew / At my
window / For the sake of the song / Ain't
leavin' your love / Buckskin stallion blues /
Little sundance / Still lookin' for you / Gone
gone blues / Catfish song
CD _____ SH 1020CD
Sugarhill / Apr '94 / Roots / CM / ADA /
Direct.

FIRST ALBUM
For the sake of the song / Tecumseh valley
/ Many a fine lady / Quick silver daydreams
of Maria / Waitin' around to die / I'll be there
in the morning / Sad Cinderella / Velvet
voices / Talkin' karate blues / All your young
servants / Sixteen summers, fifteen falls
CD _____ 598 1091 29
Tomato / Aug '93 / Vital.

FLYIN' SHOES
Loretta / No place to fall / Flyin' shoes /
Who do you love / When she don't need
me / Dollar bill blues / Rex's blues / Pueblo
waltz / Brother flower / Snake song
CD _____ CDCHARLY 193
Charly / Jul '89 / Charly / THE / Cadillac.

LIVE AND OBSCURE (Live In Nashville 1985)
Dollar bill blues / Many a fine lady / Pueblo
waltz / Talking Thunderbird blues / Loretta
/ Snake Mountain blues / Waitin' around to
die / Tecumseh Valley / Pancho and Lefty /
You are not needed now
CD _____ SH 1026CD
Sugarhill / Apr '94 / Roots / CM / ADA /
Direct.

LIVE AT THE OLD QUARTER, HOUSTON, TEXAS
Announcement / Pancho and Lefty / Mr.
Mudd and Me / Bad boy / Don't you take it too
bad / Tow girls / Fraternity blues / If I needed
you / Brand new companion / White freight-
liner blues / To live is to fly / She came and
she touched me / Talking thunderbird blues
/ Rex's blues / Nine pound hammer / For
the sake of the song / No place to fall /
Loretta / Kathleen / Tower song / Waitin'
around to die / Tecumseh valley / Lungs /
Only him or me
CD _____ CDCHARLY 183
Decal / Oct '89 / Charly / Swift.

NASHVILLE SESSIONS, THE
At my window / Rex's blues / No place to
fall / Buckskin stallion blues / White freightliner blues / Snake song / Loretta / Two
girls / Spider song / When she don't need
me / Pueblo waltz / Upon my soul
CD _____ 598 1079 29
Tomato / Aug '93 / Vital.

NO DEEPER BLUE
CD _____ SHCD 1046
Sugarhill / Aug '95 / Roots / CM / ADA /
Direct.

PONCHO & LEFTY (Live & Obscure)
Dollar bill blues / Many a fine lady / Nothin'
/ Pueblo waltz / Talking thunderbird blues /
Rex's blues / White freightliner blues / Lor-
etta / Snake Mountain blues / Waitin' round
to die / Tecumseh Valley / Pancho and Lefty
/ You are not needed now
CD _____ EDCD 344
Edsel / Jan '92 / Pinnacle / ADA.

RAIN ON A CONGA DRUM (Live In Berlin)
Mr. Mudd and Mr. Gold / If I needed you /
Buckskin stallion blues / Short haired
woman blues / Ain't leavin' your love / Pancho and Lefty / Dollar bill blues / Fraulein /
Shrimp song / Blaze's blues / No place to
fall / To live is to fly / Lungs / Nothin' / Tecumseh Valley / Dead flowers / White
freightliner blues / Catfish song
CD _____ 269 575 2
Silenz / Apr '94 / Direct / ADA.

REAR VIEW MIRROR
CD _____ IRS 993150
Roadsongs / Dec '94 / Direct / ADA.

ROADSONGS
CD _____ SH 1042CD
Sugarhill / Apr '94 / Roots / CM / ADA /
Direct.

TOWNES VAN ZANDT
For the sake of the song / Columbine /
Waiting around to die / Don't take it too bad
/ Colorado girl / Lungs / I'll be here in the
morning / Fare thee well, Miss Carousel /
(Quick silver day dreams of) Maria / None
but the rain
CD _____ CDCHARLY 119
Decal / Jun '88 / Charly / Swift.

Vandals

FEAR OF A PUNK PLANET
CD _____ TX 51094CD
Triple X / '95 / Plastic Head.

LIVE FAST DIARRHOEA
CD _____ 158022
Nitro / May '95 / Plastic Head.

LIVE FATS
CD _____ NITRO 15802CD
Nitro / Sep '95 / Plastic Head.

SWEATIN' TO THE OLDIES
CD _____ TX 51154CD
Triple X / Jul '95 / Plastic Head.

Vander, Christian

65 (Vander, Christian Trio)
CD _____ A 10
Seventh / Nov '93 / Harmonia Mundi /
Cadillac.

OFFERING
CD _____ A 9
Seventh / Sep '93 / Harmonia Mundi /
Cadillac.

OFFERING, PARTS 1 & 2
CD _____ A 1/2
Seventh / Mar '93 / Harmonia Mundi /
Cadillac.

OFFERING, PARTS 3 & 4
CD _____ A 5/6
Seventh / Mar '93 / Harmonia Mundi /
Cadillac.

SONS - DOCUMENT 1973 - LE MANOR (Vander/Top/Blasquiz/Garber)
CD _____ AKT 2
AKT / Jan '93 / Harmonia Mundi /
Cadillac.

Vander, Stella

D'EPREUVES D'AMOUR
CD _____ A 8
Seventh / Mar '93 / Harmonia Mundi /
Cadillac.

Vandermark, Ken

STEEL WOOD TRIO
CD _____ OD 12005
Okka Disk / Aug '95 / Harmonia Mundi /
Cadillac.

Vandoni, Chris

RAIN FOREST, THE
CD _____ BRAM 199119-2
Brambus / Nov '93 / ADA / Direct.

Vandross, Luther

BEST OF LUTHER VANDROSS, THE (The best of love)
Searching / Glow of love / Never too much
/ If this world were mine / Bad boy / Having
a party / Since I lost my baby / Promise me
/ Till my baby comes home / In only for one
night / Creepin' superstar / Until you come
back to me / Stop to love / So amazing /
There's nothing better than love / Give me
the reason / Any love / I really didn't mean
it / Love won't let me wait / Treat you right
/ Here and now
CD _____ 4658012
Epic / Oct '89 / Sony.

GIVE ME THE REASON/NEVER TOO MUCH
CD Set _____ 4501342
Epic / Feb '93 / Sony.

GREATEST HITS 1981-1995
Never too much / Sugar and spice / She's
a super lady / House is not a home / Give
me the reason / So amazing / Stop to love
/ See me / I really didn't mean it / Any love
/ Here and now / Power of love (love power)
/ Best things in life are free / Love the one
you're with / Power of love (love power)
(mix) / Thrill I'm in
CD _____ 4811002
LV / Oct '95 / Sony.

LUTHER VANDROSS
Bad boy / Having a party / Since I lost my
baby / She loves me back / House is not a
home / Never too much / She's a super lady
/ Sugar and spice / Better love / You're the
sweetest one
CD _____ 4606972
Epic / Feb '92 / Sony.

NEVER LET ME GO
Little miracles (happen every day) / Heaven
knows / Love me again / Can't be doin' that
now / Too far down / Love is on the way /
Hustle / Emotion eyes / Lady luck / Medley:
How deep is your love/Love don't love
nobody
CD _____ 473598 2
Epic / Jun '93 / Sony.

NEVER TOO MUCH
Never too much / Sugar and spice / Don't
you know that / I've been working / She's
a super lady / You stopped loving me /
House is not a home
CD _____ 32807 2
Epic / May '90 / Sony.

NIGHT I FELL IN LOVE, THE
Till my baby comes home / Night I fell in
love / If only for one night / Creepin' / It's
over now / Wait for love / My sensitivity
(Gets in the way) / Other side of the world

CD _____ 4624892
Epic / Mar '90 / Sony.

POWER OF LOVE
She doesn't mind / Power of love/Love
power / I'm gonna start today / Rush / I
want the night to stay / Don't want to be a
fool / I can tell you that / Sometimes it's only
love / Emotional love / I who have nothing
CD _____ 4680122
Epic / May '91 / Sony.

SONGS
Love the one you're with / Killing me softly
/ Endless love / Evergreen / Reflections /
Hello / Ain't no stoppin' us now / Always
and forever / Going in circles / Since you've
been gone / All the woman I need / What
the world needs now / Impossible
CD _____ 4766562
Epic / Sep '94 / Sony.

THIS IS CHRISTMAS
With a Christmas heart / This is Christmas
/ Mistletoe jam (everybody kiss somebody)
/ Every year, every Christmas / My favourite
things / Have yourself a merry little Christ-
mas / I listen to the bells / Please come
home for Christmas / Kiss for Christmas /
O come all ye faithful
CD _____ 4813122
LV / Dec '95 / Sony.

TWELVE INCH MIXES
Never too much / I gave it up (when I fell in
Love) / It's over now / Never too much (mix)
CD _____ 468986-2
Epic / Nov '92 / Sony.

Vangelis

ALBEDO 0.39/HEAVEN AND HELL
Pulstar / Freefall / Mare tranquillitatis / Main
sequence / Sword of orion / Alpha nucleo-
genesis / Albedo 0.39 / Heaven and hell (pts
1 & 2) / Symphony to the powers / Second
Movement / Third Movement / So long ago
/ So clear / Including intestinal bat / Needles
and bones / Twelve o'clock / Arise and
away
CD Set _____ 74321259542
RCA / Mar '95 / BMG.

BEAUBOURG
CD _____ ND 74516
RCA / Feb '90 / BMG.

BEST OF VANGELIS
Pulstar / Bacchanale / Aries / Beaubourg
excerpt / So long ago so'clear
CD _____ 74321138852
RCA / May '93 / BMG.

BEST OF VANGELIS
CD _____ 74321292812
RCA / Jul '95 / BMG.

CHINA
Chung kuo (the long march) / Dragon / Him-
alaya / Little fete / Long march / Plum blos-
som / Summit / Tao of love / Yin and Yang
/ Chung kuo
CD _____ 813 653-2
Polydor / '83 / PolyGram.

CITY
Dawn / Morning papers / Nerve centre /
Side streets / Good to see you / Twilight /
Red lights / Procession
CD _____ 9031730262
East West / Nov '90 / Warner Music.

COLLECTION, THE
CD _____ 7432122415-2
RCA / Aug '94 / BMG.

DIRECT
Motion of stars / Will of the wind / Metallic
rain / Elsewhere / Glorianna (hymn a la
femme) / Rotations logic / Oracle of apollo
/ Message / Ave / First approach / Dial out
/ Intergalactic radio station
CD _____ 259 149
Arista / Feb '91 / BMG.

HEAVEN AND HELL
Heaven and hell (pts 1 & 2) / So long long
ago so'clear
CD _____ ND 71148
RCA / Sep '89 / BMG.

INVISIBLE CONNECTIONS
Invisible connections / Atom blaster /
Thermo vision
CD _____ 4151962
Deutsche Grammophon / Mar '85 /
PolyGram.

L'APOCALYPSE DES ANIMAUX
Apocalypse des animaux / Generique / Petite fille de la mer (la) / Sing bleu (le) / Mort
du loup / Ours musicien / Creation du
monde / Mer recommence
CD _____ 831 503-2
Polydor / '88 / PolyGram.

MASK
Movements 1-6
CD _____ 825 245-2
Polydor / Apr '85 / PolyGram.

SOIL FESTIVITIES
Movement (pts 1-5) / Movement 2 / Move-
ment 3 / Movement 4 / Movement 5
CD _____ 823 396-2
Polydor / Sep '84 / PolyGram.

Vangelis

SPIRAL
Spiral / Ballad / Dervish D / To the unknown
man / Three plus three
CD _____ ND 70568
RCA / Oct '89 / BMG.

VANGELIS BOX SET
CD Set _____ ND 74378
RCA / Nov '90 / BMG.

VOICES
CD _____ 0630127862
East West / Feb '96 / Warner Music.

Vanguard Jazz Orchestra

TO YOU, A TRIBUTE TO MEL LEWIS
CD _____ MM 5054
Music Masters / Oct '94 / Nimbus.

Vanian, Dave

DAVE VANIAN & THE PHANTOM CHORDS
Voodoo doll / Screamin' kid / Big town /
This house is haunted / You and I / Whiskey
and me / Fever in my blood / Frenzy /
Shooting Jones / Jezebel / Tonight we ride
/ Johnny Guitar / Chase the wild wind /
Swamp thing
CD _____ CDWIKD 140
Big Beat / Mar '95 / Pinnacle.

Vanilla Fudge

NEAR THE BEGINNING
CD _____ REP 4127-WZ
Repertoire / Aug '91 / Pinnacle / Cadillac.

PSYCHEDELIC SUNDAE (The Best Of Vanilla Fudge)
You keep me hangin' on / Where is my mind
/ Look of love / Ticket to ride / Come by
day, come by night / Take me for a little
while / That's what makes a man / Season
of the witch / Shotgun / Thoughts / Faceless people / Good good lovin' / Some velvet morning / I can't make it alone / Lord in
the country / Need love / Street walking
woman / All in your mind
CD _____ 812271154-2
Atlantic / Mar '93 / Warner Music.

RENAISSANCE
CD _____ REP 4126-WZ
Repertoire / Aug '91 / Pinnacle / Cadillac.

ROCK 'N' ROLL
CD _____ REP 4168-WZ
Repertoire / Aug '91 / Pinnacle / Cadillac.

VANILLA FUDGE
Ticket to ride / People get ready / She's not
there / Bang bang (my baby shot me down)
/ You keep me hangin' on / Take me for a
little while / Eleanor Rigby
CD _____ 756790390-2
Atlantic / Mar '93 / Warner Music.

Vanilla Trainwreck

MORDECAI
Alex / Pink smoke / Sister / Pearl / Forget
/ Quagmire / Lie detector / Florida / Col-
lidiscope / Kiss me / Nothing I suppose /
Telefood / Drownt
CD _____ MR 076-2
Mammoth / Mar '94 / Vital.

Vanity Fare

SUN, THE WIND AND OTHER THINGS, THE
CD _____ REP 4155-WZ
Repertoire / Aug '91 / Pinnacle / Cadillac.

Vann, Stevie

STEVIE VANN
CD _____ ORECD 539
Silvertone / Oct '95 / Pinnacle.

Vannelli, Gino

BIG DREAMERS NEVER SLEEP
CD _____ FDM 362112
Dreyfus / Oct '93 / ADA / Direct / New
Note.

BLACK CARS
Black cars / Other man / It's over / Here she
comes / Hurts to be in love / Total stranger
/ Just a motion away / Imagination / How
much
CD _____ FDM 362102
Dreyfus / Oct '93 / ADA / Direct / New Note.

Van't Hof, Jasper

AT THE CONCERTGEBOUW
CD _____ CHR 70010
Challenge / Aug '95 / Direct / Jazz Music /
Cadillac / ADA.

EYEBALL
Bax / Viber snake / Eyeball I / Hyrax /
Schwester Johanna / Laur / One leg miss-
ing / Eyeball II / Rev
CD _____ FCD 0002
Limetree / Oct '95 / New Note.

FACE TO FACE
Kusini / Three doors / Get down / Zaire / Il
Piacere / As well / Echoes / Krise / You dare
CD _____ VBR 20632
Vera Bra / Dec '94 / Pinnacle / New Note.

Vanwarmer, Randy

EVERY NOW AND THEN
Stories, trophies and memories / Ain't nothin' coming / Every now and then / You were the one / Tomorrow would be better / She's the reason / Appaloosa night / Beautiful rose / Just when I needed you most / Love is a cross you bear / Safe harbour / I never got over you
CD _____ ETCD 190
Etude / Apr '90 / Grapevine.

I WILL WHISPER YOUR NAME
I guess it never hurts to hurt sometimes / I'm in a hurry / Vital spark / Used cars / Velvet vampire / Time and money / Just when I needed you most / Silence of her dreams / Echoes / There's a rhythm / Don't look back / I will whisper your name
CD _____ KCD 377
Irish / Jan '96 / Target/BMG.

THIRD CHILD
Follow that car / Romeo's heart / Don't want to think about it / As if my heart was not my own / Just when I needed you most / Third child / Something beautiful / Two strangers on a train / Damn this night / Whispers of emotion / Diamonds in the light
CD _____ FIENDCD 765
Demon / May '95 / Pinnacle / ADA.

VITAL SPARK, THE
CD _____ ALCD 194
Etude / Feb '94 / Grapevine.

WARMER
Losing out on love / Just when I needed you most / Your light / Gotta get out of here / Convincing lies / Call me / Forever loving you / I could sing / Deeper and deeper / One who loves you
CD _____ 8122713982
Rhino / Jun '95 / Warner Music.

Vanzyl

CELESTIAL MECHANICS
CD _____ CENCD 003
Centaur / Oct '93 / Complete/Pinnacle.

Varathron

HIS MAJESTY AT THE SWAMP
CD _____ CYBERCD 8
Cyber / Mar '94 / Plastic Head.

WALPURGISNACHI
CD _____ USR 017CD
Unisound / Jan '96 / Plastic Head.

Varga

PROTOTYPE
Unconscience / Greed / Wawnan mere / Freeze don't move / Self proclaimed / Thief / Bring the hammer down / Cast into the shade / Strong / Film at eleven / Goodbye boogaloo (Instrumental) / Freeze don't move (Krash's psycho mix)
CD _____ 74321 19080-2
RCA / Aug '94 / BMG.

Varttina

SELENIKO
CD _____ 51746-6
Spirit Feel / May '93 / Koch.

Varukers

BLOODSUCKERS/PREPARE FOR THE ATTACK
Protest and survive / Nowhere to go / No masters no slaves / Don't conform / Android / March of the SAS / Nodda (contraceptive machine) / Government's to blame / Tell us what we all want to hear / Don't wanna be a victim / What the hell do you know / School's out (maybe) / Killed by man's own hands / Animals / Enter a new phase / Stop the killing now / Instru-mental / Thatcher's fortress / Massacred millions / Nuclear / State enemy / Will they never learn / Bomb blast / Die for your government (Live) / Soldier boy (Live)
CD _____ CDPUNK 56
Anagram / Oct '95 / Pinnacle.

DEADLY GAMES
CD _____ ABBT 806CD
Abstract / Sep '94 / Pinnacle / Total/BMG.

STILL BOLLOX AND STILL HERE
CD _____ WB 11362
We Bite / Nov '95 / Plastic Head.

Vasconcelos, Nana

STORYTELLING
Curtain (Cortina) / Fui fuio, na praca / Uma tarde no norte (An afternoon in the north) / Um dia no Amazonas (A day in the Amazon) / Clementina, no terreiro / Vento chamando vento / Tu nem quer saber (You don't want to know) / Nordeste (Northeast) / Tiroleo / Note das estrelas (Night of stars)
CD _____ CDEMC 3712
EMI / Jun '95 / EMI.

Vaselines

ALL THE STUFF AND MORE
Son of a gun / Rory ride me raw / You think you're a man / Dying for it / Molly's lips /

Teenage Jesus superstar / Jesus doesn't want me for a sunbeam / Let's get ugly / Sex bus (amen) / Dum dum / Oliver twisted / Monster pussy / Day I was a horse / Bitch / Slushy / No hope / Hairy / Dying for some blues / Lovecraft
CD _____ ONLYCD 013
Avalanche / Sep '95 / Disc.

COMPLETE HISTORY, A
CD _____ SPCD 145
Sub Pop / Mar '94 / Disc.

Vasen

ESSENCE
CD _____ B 6787
Auvidis/Ethnic / Oct '94 / Harmonia Mundi.

Vasmalom

VASMALOM 2
CD _____ MW 4012CD
Music & Words / Nov '95 / ADA / Direct.

Vath, Sven

ACCIDENT IN PARADISE
Ritual of life / Caravan of emotions / L'es-peranca / Sleeping invention / Mellow illu-sion / Merry go round somewhere / Acci-dent in paradise / Drifting like whales in the darkness / Coda
CD _____ 450991193-2
Eye Q / May '93 / Disc / Warner Music.

REMIX LP
CD _____ 4509997022
Eye Q / Mar '95 / Disc / Warner Music.

ROBOT, THE HARLEQUIN & THE BALLETDANCER, THE
Intro / Harlequin plays bells / Harlequin / Beauty and the beast / Harlequin's medi-tation / Birth of Robby / Robot / Ballet ro-mance / Ballet fusion / Ballet dancer
CD _____ 450997534-2
Eye Q / Sep '94 / Disc / Warner Music.

Vatten

DIGGIN' THE ROOTS
You'll never know / Looking back / Status quo / Crossroads / Pretty woman / Stumble / First sight phenomenon / Black cat moan / Walkin' by myself / Don't try your jive on me / Prisons on the road / Little girl / Baby, baby, baby / Ernvik boogie / Killing floor
CD _____ GUTS 008CD
Gutta / Mar '93 / Plankton.

Vaughan, Jimmie

STRANGE PLEASURE
Boom-papa-boom / Don't cha know / Hey yeah / Flamenco dancer / (Everybody's got) Sweet soul vibe / Tilt a whirl / Six strings down / Just like putty / Two wings / Love the world / Strange pleasure (Modern back-port duende)
CD _____ 474268 2
Epic / Jun '94 / Sony.

Vaughan, Sarah

16 MOST REQUESTED SONGS
Black coffee / That lucky old sun (Just rolls around heaven all day) / Summertime / Nearness of you / Goodnight my love / Can't get out of this mood / It might as well be spring / Come rain or come shine / Thinking of you / These things I offer you (For a lifetime) / Vanity / Pinky / Sinner or saint / My tormented heart / Linger awhile / Spring will be a little late this year
CD _____ 474399 2
Columbia / Feb '94 / Sony.

1960-1964
CD _____ CD 53176
Giants Of Jazz / Sep '94 / Target/BMG / Cadillac.

1963 (Vaughan, Sarah & Woody Herman)
CD _____ EBCD 21082
Jazzband / Oct '91 / Jazz Music / Wellard.

20 JAZZ CLASSICS
Serenata / Baubles, bangles and beads / Star eyes / Wrap your troubles in dreams (and dream your troubles away) / My fa-vourite things / Come spring / Taste of honey / Fly me to the moon / This can't be love / Goodnight sweetheart / On Green Dolphin Street / I'm gonna live till I die / Ma-ria / Until I met you / Moonglow / I don't know about you / All I do is dream of you / Because
CD _____ CDMFP 6160
Music For Pleasure / May '95 / EMI.

AT MR KELLY'S
September in the rain / Willow weep for me / Just one of those things / Be anything but darling be mine / Thou swell / Stairway to the stars / Honeysuckle rose / Just a gigolo / How high the moon / Dream / I'm gonna sit right down and write myself a letter / It's got to be love / Alone / If this isn't love / Embraceable you / Lucky in love / Dancing in the dark / Poor butterfly / Sometimes I'm happy / I cover the waterfront
CD _____ 8327912
Emarcy / Mar '92 / PolyGram.

BEST OF SARAH VAUGHAN
You're blase / I've got the world on a string / Midnight sun / I gotta right to sing the blues / From this moment on / Ill wind / All too soon / Lush life / In a sentimental mood / Dindi
CD _____ CD 2405416
Pablo / Jun '93 / Jazz Music / Cadillac / Complete/Pinnacle.

BEST OF SARAH VAUGHAN
CD _____ DLCD 4016
Dixie Live / Mar '95 / Magnum Music Group.

BODY AND SOUL
CD _____ HADCD 187
Javelin / Nov '95 / THE / Henry Hadaway Organisation.

COPACABANA
Copacabana / Smiling hour / To say good-bye / Dreamer / Gentle rain / Tete / Dindi / Double rainbow / Bonita
CD _____ CD 2312125
Pablo / Jan '92 / Jazz Music / Cadillac / Complete/Pinnacle.

CRAZY AND MIXED UP
I didn't know what time it was / That's all / Autumn leaves / Love dance / Island / In love in vain / Seasons / You are too beautiful
CD _____ CD 2312137
Pablo / Apr '94 / Jazz Music / Cadillac / Complete/Pinnacle.

DIVINE
CD _____ ENTCD 225
Entertainers / '88 / Target/BMG.

DIVINE MISS V, THE
CD Set _____ JWD 102301
JWD / Nov '94 / Target/BMG.

DIVINE ONE, THE
CD _____ CDCD 1082
Charly / Apr '93 / Charly / THE / Cadillac.

DIVINE SARAH VAUGHAN, THE (2CD Set/The CBS Years 1949-1953)
CD _____ 4655972
Sony Jazz / Jan '95 / Sony.

DUKE ELLINGTON SONG BOOK, VOL. 1
In a sentimental mood / I'm just a lucky so and so / Solitude / I let a song go out of my heart / I didn't know about you / All too soon / Lush life / In a mellow tone / So-phisticated lady / Daydream
CD _____ PACD 2312111
Pablo / Oct '93 / Jazz Music / Cadillac / Complete/Pinnacle.

DUKE ELLINGTON SONG BOOK, VOL. 2
I ain't got nothin' but the blues / Black butterfly / Chelsea Bridge / What am I here for / Tonight I shall sleep / Rocks in my bed / I got it bad and that ain't good / Everything but you / Mood indigo / It don't mean a thing if it ain't that swing / Prelude to a kiss
CD _____ CD 2312116
Pablo / Oct '93 / Jazz Music / Cadillac / Complete/Pinnacle.

EASY LIVING (Vaughan, Sarah & Oscar Peterson)
CD _____ JWD 102219
JWD / Jul '95 / Target/BMG.

ELLINGTON SONGBOOK
In a sentimental mood / I'm just a lucky so and so / Solitude / I let a song go out of my heart / I didn't know about you / All too soon / Lush life / In a mellow tone / So-phisticated lady / Daydream
CD _____ CD 2312111
Pablo / Apr '94 / Jazz Music / Cadillac / Complete/Pinnacle.

ESSENTIAL SARAH VAUGHAN, THE
CD _____ 4671522
Columbia / Oct '93 / Sony.

GERSHWIN SONGBOOK VOL. 1
CD _____ PRS 23021
Personality / Jan '95 / Target/BMG.

GERSHWIN SONGBOOK VOL. 2
CD _____ PRS 23022
Personality / Jan '95 / Target/BMG.

GOLDEN HITS
CD _____ 8248912
Mercury / Apr '91 / PolyGram.

HOW LONG HAS THIS BEEN GOING ON
I've got the world on a string / Midnight sun / How long has this been going on / You're blase / Easy living / More than you know / My old flame / Teach me tonight / Body and soul / When your lover has gone
CD _____ CD 2310821
Pablo / Oct '92 / Jazz Music / Cadillac / Complete/Pinnacle.

I'VE GOT IT GOOD
CD _____ LDJ 274918
Radio Nights / Nov '91 / Harmonia Mundi / Cadillac.

IN THE LAND OF HI-FI
CD _____ 8264542
Emarcy / Mar '94 / PolyGram.

IRVING BERLIN SONGBOOK
CD _____ PRS 23023
Personality / Jan '95 / Target/BMG.

IT'S YOU OR NO ONE
CD _____ 1046700552
Discovery / May '95 / Warner Music.

JAZZ 'ROUND MIDNIGHT
CD _____ 5100862
Verve / Apr '91 / PolyGram.

JAZZ MASTERS
CD _____ 518199-2
Verve / May '94 / PolyGram.

LIVE IN CHICAGO
CD _____ JHR 73580
Jazz Hour / Jun '94 / Target/BMG / Jazz Music / Cadillac.

LIVE IN JAPAN
CD _____ 557304
Accord / Dec '89 / Discovery / Harmonia Mundi / Cadillac.

MEMORIAL ALBUM
CD _____ VJC 1015-2
Victorious Discs / Feb '91 / Jazz Music.

MY FUNNY VALENTINE AND OTHER LOVE SONGS
My funny valentine / I'm in the mood for love / Touch of your lips / All the things you are / That old black magic / Lover man / Misty / It's magic / All of me / They say it's wonderful / Prelude to a kiss / Man I love / Cheek to cheek / My romance / Love walked in / Body and soul / Just one of those things / Bewitched / Thou swell / S'wonderful
CD _____ PRS 23020
Personality / Nov '95 / Target/BMG

PERDIDO (Vaughan, Sarah & Dizzy Gillespie)
CD _____ NI 4004
Natasha / Jun '93 / Jazz Music / ADA / CM / Direct / Cadillac.

SARAH & CLIFFORD
Lullaby of Birdland / April in Paris / He's my guy / Jim / You're not the kind / Embrace-able you / I'm glad there is you / September song / It's crazy
CD _____ JHR 73581
Jazz Hour / Jun '94 / Target/BMG / Jazz Music / Cadillac.

SARAH SLIGHTLY CLASSICAL
Be my love / Intermezzo / I give to you / Because / Full moon and empty arms / My reverie / Moonlight love / Ah sweet mystery of life / Till the end of time / None but the lonely heart / Night / If you are but a dream / Only / Experience unnecessary
CD _____ CDROU 1029
Roulette / Mar '91 / EMI.

SARAH VAUGHAN
Timeless Treasures / Oct '94 / THE.
CD _____ CD 107

SARAH VAUGHAN (1944-50)
CD _____ CD 14568
Jazz Portraits / May '95 / Jazz Music.

SARAH VAUGHAN COLLECTOR'S EDITION
Deja Vu / Apr '95 / THE.
CD _____ DVAD 6012

SASSY 1944-1950
CD _____ CD 53162
Giants Of Jazz / Nov '95 / Target/BMG / Cadillac.

SASSY 1950-1954
CD _____ CD 53165
Giants Of Jazz / Jan '95 / Target/BMG / Cadillac.

SASSY AT RONNIE'S
Here's that rainy day / Like someone in love / I'll remember April / Sophisticated lady / If you could see me now / Foggy day / I cried for you / But not for me/Embraceable you (CD only) / Man I love / My funny valentine / Passing strangers / Blue skies / More I see you / Early Autumn / Tenderly
CD _____ JHCD 015
Ronnie Scott's Jazz House / Jan '94 / Jazz Music / Magnum Music Group / Cadillac.

SASSY SWINGS THE TIVOLI
CD Set _____ 8327882
Emarcy / Jul '90 / PolyGram.

SEND IN THE CLOWNS (Vaughan, Sarah & Count Basie)
I gotta right to sing the blues / Just friends / Ill wind / If you could see me now / I hadn't anyone till you / Send in the clowns / When your lover has gone / Indian Summer / When your lover has gone / From this moment on
CD _____ PACD 23121302
Pablo / Jan '94 / Jazz Music / Cadillac / Complete/Pinnacle.

SEND IN THE CLOWNS
CD _____ 4806822
Sony Jazz / Jan '95 / Sony.

SIDE BY SIDE (Vaughan, Sarah & Billy Eckstine)
CD _____ CDCD 1113
Charly / Jul '93 / Charly / THE / Cadillac.

SOFT & SASSY
CD _____ HCD 601
Hindsight / Apr '94 / Target/BMG / Jazz Music.

SONGS OF THE BEATLES
CD _____ 756781483-2
Atlantic / Jun '93 / Warner Music.

SPOTLIGHT ON SARAH VAUGHAN
That old black magic / Careless / Separate ways / Are you certain / Mary contrary / Broken hearted melody / I've got the world on a string / Friendly enemies / What's so bad about it / Sweet affection / Misty / Send in the clowns / If you could see me now
CD _____ HADCD 108
Javelin / Feb '94 / THE / Henry Hadaway Organisation.

SWINGIN' EASY
CD _____ 5140722
Verve / Feb '93 / PolyGram.

TENDERLY
It's you or no one / Tenderly / Lord's Prayer / What a difference a day makes / Gentleman friend / East of the sun and west of the moon / Motherless child / One I love (belongs to somebody else) / September song / Time after time / Hundred years from today / Signing off
CD _____ 1046700572
Discovery / May '95 / Warner Music.

TIME AND AGAIN
CD _____ 1046700612
Discovery / May '95 / Warner Music.

Vaughan, Stevie Ray

COULDN'T STAND THE WEATHER (Vaughan, Stevie Ray & Double Trouble)
Scuttle buttin' / Couldn't stand the weather / Things that I used to do / Voodoo chile / Cold shot / Tin Pan Alley / Honey bee / Stang's swang
CD _____ 4655712
Epic / Apr '91 / Sony.
CD _____ EK 64425
Epic / Feb '95 / Sony.

COULDN'T STAND THE WEATHER/ SOUL TO SOUL/TEXAS FLOOD (3CD Set)
CD Set _____ 4683362
Epic / Jan '94 / Sony.

FAMILY STYLE, THE (Vaughan Brothers)
Hard to be / White boots / D/FW / Good Texan / Hillbillies from outerspace / Long way from home / Tick tock / Telephone song / Baboom/Mama said / Brothers
CD _____ 4670142
Epic / Oct '90 / Sony.

GREATEST HITS (Vaughan, Stevie Ray & Double Trouble)
Taxman / Texas flood / House is rockin' / Pride & joy / Tightrope / Little wing / Crossfire / Sky is crying / Cold shot / Couldn't stand the weather / Life without you
CD _____ 4810232
Epic / Nov '95 / Sony.

IN STEP
House is rockin' / Tightrope / Leave my girl alone / Wall of denial / Love me darlin' / Crossfire / Let me love you baby / Travis walk / Scratch 'n' sniff / Riviera paradise
CD _____ 4633952
Epic / Jul '89 / Sony.

IN THE BEGINNING (Vaughan, Stevie Ray & Double Trouble)
In the open / Slide thing / They call me guitar hurricane / All your love / I miss loving / Tin Pan alley / Love struck baby / Tell me / Shake for me / Live another day
CD _____ 472624-2
Epic / Sep '94 / Sony.

SKY IS CRYING, THE (Vaughan, Stevie Ray & Double Trouble)
Boot Hill / Sky is crying / Empty arms / Little wing / Wham / May I have a talk with you / Close to you / Chitlins con carne / So excited / Life by the drop
CD _____ 4686402
Epic / Nov '91 / Sony.

SOUL TO SOUL
Say what / Looking out the window / Look at little sister / Ain't gonna give up on love / Gone home / Change it / You'll be mine / Empty arms / Come on / Life without you
CD _____ 4663302
Epic / Apr '91 / Sony.

TEXAS FLOOD (Vaughan, Stevie Ray & Double Trouble)
Lovestruck baby / Pride and joy / Texas flood / Tell me / Testify / Rude mood / Mary had a little lamb / Dirty pool / I'm cryin' / Lenny
CD _____ CD 460951
Epic / Jul '89 / Sony.

Vaughn, Ben

DRESSED IN BLACK
Big drum solo / Man who has everything / Dressed in black / Doormat / Long black hair / New wave dancing / Cashier girl / Words can't say what I want to say / Hey Romeo / Too sensitive for this world / Growin' a beard / Don't say you don't wanna / Poor Jimmy Gordon
CD _____ FIENDCD 166
Demon / Feb '90 / Pinnacle / ADA.

MONO

Daddy rollin' in your arms / Cross ties / Goin' down the road / Sundown sundown / Our favourite martian / Strange desire / Jailbait / Exploration in fear / Just a little bit of you / Dark glasses / Magdalena / I waited too long too late / Out of control / Skip a rope / I'll come runnin' / That's how I got to Memphis / Sheba / We belong together
CD _____ 882772
Sky Ranch / Oct '93 / New Note.

MOOD SWINGS
CD _____ FIENDCD 724
Demon / Nov '92 / Pinnacle / ADA.

RAMBLER 65
CD _____ MRCD 066
Rubble / Jun '95 / Plastic Head.

Vaughn, Billy

22 OF HIS GREATEST HITS
CD _____ RCD 7025
Ranwood / May '89 / Jazz Music.

Vaughn, Maurice John

GENERIC BLUES ALBUM
CD _____ ALCD 4763
Alligator / Apr '93 / Direct / ADA.

IN THE SHADOW OF THE CITY
CD _____ ALCD 4813
Alligator / May '94 / Direct / ADA.

Veasley, Gerald

LOOK AHEAD
CD _____ 101S 8771312
101 South / Aug '94 / New Note.

SIGNS
Marvin's mood / Lasting moment / Highway home / Exit to the street / Signs / Salamanca / Imani (faith) / Soul seduction / What are you doing for the rest of your life / Walking through walls / Tranquility
CD _____ 101S 8770522
101 South / Oct '94 / New Note.

Ved Buens Ende

WRITTEN IN WATERS
CD _____ AMAZON 006CD
Misanthropy / Nov '95 / Plastic Head.

Vee, Bobby

EP COLLECTION: BOBBY VEE
CD _____ SEECD 297
See For Miles/C5 / Mar '95 / Pinnacle.

I REMEMBER BUDDY HOLLY
That'll be the day / It doesn't matter anymore / Peggy Sue (CD only) / True love ways / It's so easy / Heartbeat / Oh boy / Raining in my heart / Think it over / Maybe baby / Early in the morning / Buddy's song / Wishing (CD only) / Measure my love (CD only) / Everyday (CD only) / Love's made a fool of you / Mr. and Mrs. (CD only) / Forget me not (CD only) / White silver sands (CD only) / Well alright (CD only)
CD _____ CZ 498
EMI / May '92 / EMI.

TAKE GOOD CARE OF MY BABY - 22 GREATEST HITS
Remember / Sep '94 / Total/BMG. _____ RMB 75075

Vega, Alan

DEUCE AVENUE
CD _____ 105582
Musidisc / Jun '90 / Vital / Harmonia Mundi / ADA / Cadillac / Discovery.

NEW RACEION
Pleaser / Christ dice / Gamma pop / Viva the legs / Do the job / Junior's little sister dropped ta cheap / How many lifetimes / Holy skips / Keep it alive / Go trane go
CD _____ 110122
Musidisc / May '93 / Vital / Harmonia Mundi / ADA / Cadillac / Discovery.

Vega, Louie

LOUIE VEGA AT THE UNDERGROUND
CD _____ REACTCD 024
React / Sep '93 / Vital.

Vega, Suzanne

99.9 F
Rock in this pocket (Song of David) / Blood makes noise / In Liverpool / 99.9 F / Blood sings / Fat man and dancing girl / (If you were) in my movie / As a child / Bad wisdom / When heroes go down / As girls go / Song of sand / Private goes public
CD _____ 540012-2
A&M / Sep '92 / PolyGram.

DAYS OF OPEN HAND
CD _____ 3952932
A&M / Apr '95 / PolyGram.

SOLITUDE STANDING
Tom's diner / Luka / Ironbound / Fancy poultry / In the eye / Night vision / Solitude standing / Calypso / Language / Gypsy / Wooden horse

CD _____ SUZCD 2
A&M / May '87 / PolyGram.

SUZANNE VEGA
Cracking / Freeze tag / Marlene on the wall / Small blue thing / Straight lines / Undertow / Some journey / Queen and the soldier / Night movies / Neighbourhood girls
CD _____ CDMID 177
A&M / Mar '93 / PolyGram.

TOM'S ALBUM (Various Artists)
CD _____ 395363 2
A&M / Oct '91 / PolyGram.

Vega, Tony

APARENTEMENTE
Aparentemente / Donde estas / En resumen / Esposa / Me gusta que seas celosa / No me liames amor / Deja / Con su mejor amiga / Por fin
CD _____ 66058017
RMM / Jun '93 / New Note.

Vegas

VEGAS
Possessed / Walk into the wind / She's alright / Take me for what i am / Trouble with lovers / Nothing alas alack / Thought of you / Anthem / Wise guy / Day it rained forever / She
CD _____ 74321110442
RCA / Oct '92 / BMG.

Veillon, Jean-Michel

E KOAD NIZAN
CD _____ GWP 004CD
Gwerz Productions / Aug '93 / ADA.

JEAN-MICHEL VEILLON
CD _____ GWP 009CD
Gwerz Productions / Aug '95 / ADA.

Vela, Rosie

ZAZU
Fool's paradise / Magic smile / Interlude / Tonto / Sunday / Taxi / Second emotion / Boxes / Zazu
CD _____ 3950162
A&M / Apr '95 / PolyGram.

Velez, Glen

DOCTRINE OF SIGNATURES
CD _____ CMPCD 54
CMP / Jun '92 / Vital/SAM.

PAN EROS
Pan eros / Inner smile / Madrepora / Souk / Different world / Urban medicine / Gemini rising / Blue herons
CD _____ CMPCD 63
CMP / Oct '93 / Vital/SAM.

RAMANA
CD _____ CDH 307
Topic / Apr '93 / Direct / ADA.

SEVEN HEAVEN
CD _____ CMPCD 30
CMP / Jan '88 / Vital/SAM.

Velo Deluxe

SUPERELASTIC
Superelastic / Velo deluxe / Simple / Dirtass / Alibi / Desiree / Angels / Skin and bones / Saturday / Eleven / Said / Miracle
CD _____ DEDCD 020
Dedicated / Feb '95 / Vital.

Velocity Girl

6 SONG CD
I don't care if you go / Always / Forgotten favorite / Why should I be nice to you / Not at all / I don't care if you go (accoustic)
CD _____ SLUM 023
Slumberland / Feb '93 / Vital.

COPACETIC
CD _____ SPCD 75242
Sub Pop / Apr '93 / Disc.

GILDED STARS AND ZEALOUS HEARTS
CD _____ SPCD 340
Sub Pop / Mar '96 / Disc.

SIMPATICO
CD _____ SPCD 122/303
Sub Pop / Jul '94 / Disc.

Veloso, Caetano

CIRCULADO
CD _____ 5106392
Philips / Feb '94 / PolyGram.

Velvet Cactus Society

26 SONGS
When I sleep naked / With utmost apologies / Some of my best friends / Lydia mench / Dogma / All decked out / Beautiful people / Necrophilia / Soggy biscuit / Last stride of Loma the pig woman / Death by steamboat / Brush with life / Can I borrow your baby / Euthanasia / Last Sunday / Royal blood / Cruel and usual punishment / Abusive spouse / On six legs / Universe is expanding / Morning sickness / Flowers in my bed / Pink umbrella is a lyrical genius / Hear and

now / Always greener / Peace and love anyone
CD _____ SHIMMYBOOT 001
Shimmy Disc / Jan '94 / Vital.

Velvet Color

NOW IS THE TIME
CD _____ EFA 128192
Hot Wire / Dec '95 / SRD.

Velvet Crush

TEENAGE SYMPHONIES TO GOD
Hold me up / My blank pages / Why not your baby / Time wraps around you / Atmosphere / Ten / Faster days / Something's gotta give / This life is killing me / Weird summer / Star trip / Keep on lingerin'
CD _____ CRECD 130
Creation / Jun '94 / 3MV / Vital.

Velvet Monkeys

RAKE
CD _____ DANCD 061
Danceteria / Feb '95 / Plastic Head / ADA.

ROTTING CORPSE AUGOGO
CD _____ SDE 8905CD
Shimmy Disc / May '89 / Vital.

Velvet Underground

15 MINUTES (A Tribute To The Velvet Underground) (Various Artists)
Here she comes now / Jesus / Stephanie says / All tomorrow's parties / I'm free / Lady Godiva's operation / Sunday morning / Ocean / Foggy notion / What goes on / She's my best friend / I heard her call my name / Pale blue eyes / European son
CD P.Disc _____ ILLCD 047P
Imaginary / Jan '94 / Vital.

1969 VOL. 1
Waiting for my man / Lisa says / What goes on / Sweet Jane / We're gonna have a real good time together / Femme fatale / New age / Rock 'n' roll / Beginning to see the light / Heroin
CD _____ 834823-2
Mercury / '88 / PolyGram.

1969 VOL. 2
Ocean / Pale blue eyes / Heroin / Some kinda love / Over you / Sweet Bonnie Brown / It's just too much / White light / White heat / I can't stand it / I'll be your mirror
CD _____ 834824-2
Mercury / '88 / PolyGram.

ANOTHER VIEW
We're gonna have a real good time together / I'm gonna move right in / Hey Mr. Rain (versions 1 & 2) / Ride into the sun / Coney Island steeplechase / Guess I'm falling in love (instrumental) / Ferryboat Bill / Rock 'n' roll (original)
CD _____ 8294052
Polydor / Jan '94 / PolyGram.

BEST OF THE VELVET UNDERGROUND
I'm waiting for the man / Femme fatale / Run run run / Heroin / All tomorrow's parties / I'll be your mirror / White light, white heat / Stephanie says / What goes on / Beginning to see the light / Pale blue eyes / I can't stand it / Lisa says / Sweet Jane / Rock 'n' roll
CD _____ 8411642
Polydor / Oct '89 / PolyGram.

LIVE AT MAX'S KANSAS CITY
I'm waiting for the man / Sweet Jane / Lonesome Cowboy Bill / Beginning to see the light / I'll be your mirror / Pale blue eyes / Sunday morning / New age / Femme fatale / After hours
CD _____ 756790370-2
Atlantic / May '93 / Warner Music.

LIVE MCMXCIII
We're gonna have a real good time together (CD/MC set only) / Venus in furs / Guess I'm falling in love (CD/MC set only) / Afterhours / All tomorrow's parties / Some kinda love / I'll be your mirror (CD/MC set only) / Beginning to see the light (CD/MC set only) / Gift / I heard her call my name (CD/MC set only) / Femme fatale (CD/MC set only) / Hey Mr. Rain (CD/MC set only) / Sweet Jane / Velvet nursery rhyme (CD/MC set only) / White light, white heat (CD/MC set only) / I'm sticking with you (CD/MC set only) / Black angel's death song (CD/MC set only) / Rock 'n' roll / I can't stand it (CD/MC set only) / I'm waiting for the man / Heroin / Pale blue eyes / Coyote (CD/MC set only)
CD _____ 936245465-2
CD Set _____ 936245464-2
WEA / Oct '93 / Warner Music.

LOADED
Who loves the sun / Sweet Jane / Rock 'n' roll / Cool it down / New age / Head held high / Lonesome Cowboy Bill / I found a reason / Train round the bend / Oh sweet nuthin'
CD _____ 756790367-2
Atlantic / May '93 / Warner Music.

PEEL SLOWLY AND SEE (4CD Set)
CD _____ 5278872
Polydor / Sep '95 / PolyGram.

VELVET DOWN UNDERGROUND, THE (Various Artists)
Sunday morning / I'm waiting for the man / Femme fatale / Venus in furs / Run run run / All tomorrow's parties / Heroin / There she goes again / I'll be your mirror / Black angel's death song / European son
CD _____ SUR 529CD
Survival / Jun '93 / Pinnacle.

VELVET UNDERGROUND
Candy says / What goes on / Some kinda love / Pale blue eyes / Jesus / Beginning to see the light / I'm set free / Murder mystery / After hours / Story of my life
CD _____ 815 454-2
Polydor / May '86 / PolyGram.

VELVET UNDERGROUND AND NICO (Velvet Underground & Nico)
Sunday morning / I'm waiting for the man / Femme fatale / Venus in furs / Run run run / All tomorrow's parties / Heroin / There she goes again / I'll be your mirror / Black angel's death song / European son
CD _____ 823 290-2
Polydor / '86 / PolyGram.

VU
I can't stand it / Stephanie says / She's my best friend / Lisa says / Ocean / Foggy notion / Temptation inside your heart / One of these days / Andy's chest / I'm sticking with you
CD _____ 8237212
Polydor / Jul '89 / PolyGram.

Velvett Fogg

VELVETT FOGG...PLUS
Yellow cave woman / New York mining disaster 1941 / Wizard of Gobsolod / Once among the trees / Lady Caroline / Come away Melinda / Owed to the dip / Within the night / Plastic man / Telstar '69
CD _____ SEECD 259
See For Miles/C5 / Sep '89 / Pinnacle.

Vendemian

BETWEEN TWO WORLDS
CD _____ ABCD 1
Resurrection / May '94 / Plastic Head.

THROUGH THE DEPTHS
CD _____ ABCD 002
Gothic / Jan '96 / Plastic Head.

TREACHEROUS
CD _____ ABCD 003
Resurrection / Jan '96 / Plastic Head.

Vendetta

SOMEWHERE IN THE NIGHT
Somewhere in the night / So do I / 1-2-3 / I've got you in my heart / Could have done without it / Don't let the world drag you under / I've got you in my sight tonight / Living day at a time / Gotta see Jane / Somewhere in the night (2) / So do I (AOR) / In and out of love / Stay tonight / Only you can save my life / If you want my love / One step at a time / Larsen effect / Somewhere in the night (Reprise)
CD _____ PZA 006CD
Plaza / Mar '94 / Pinnacle.

Veni Domine

MATERIAL SANCTUARY
CD _____ MASSCD 074
Massacre / Oct '95 / Plastic Head.

Venom

AT WAR WITH SATAN
At war with satan / Rip ride / Genocide / Cry wolf / Stand up (and be counted) / Women, leather and hell / Aaaaarrghh
CD _____ CLACD 256
Castle / '91 / BMG.

BLACK METAL
Black metal / To hell and back / Buried alive / Raise the dead / Teacher's pet / Leave me in hell / Sacrifice / Heaven's on fire / Countess Bathory / Don't burn the witch / At war with Satan (Intro)
CD _____ CLACD 254
Castle / '91 / BMG.

COLLECTION
Welcome to hell / Dead on arrival / Snots shit / Black metal / Hounds of hell / At war with Satan (TV Adverts) / At war with Satan (Full re-edited version) / Bitch witch / Intro tapes / Possessed / Sadist (Mistress of the whip) / Manitou / Angel dust / Raise the dead / Red light fever / Venom station ids for America and Spain
CD _____ CCSCD 367
Castle / Mar '93 / BMG.

EINE KLEINE NACHTMUSIK
Too loud for the croed / Seven gates of hell / Leave me in hell / Nightmare / Countess Bathory / Die hard / Schizo / Guitar solo by Mantas / In nomine Satanus / Witching hour / Black metal / Chanting of the priest / Satanchrist / Fly trap / Warhead / Alive / Love amongst / Bass solo Cronos / Welcome to hell / Bloodlust
CD _____ NEATXSO 132
Neat / Nov '87 / Plastic Head.

IN MEMORIUM - BEST OF VENOM
Angel dust / Raise the dead / Red light fever / Buried alive / Witching hour / At war with satan / Warhead / Manitou / Under a spell / Nothing sacred / Dead love / Welcome to hell / Black metal / Countess bathory / 1000 Days in sodom / Prime evil / If you wanna war / Surgery
CD _____ MCCD 097
Music Club / Mar '93 / Disc / THE / CM.

LIVE OFFICIAL BOOTLEG
Leave me in hell / Countess bathory / Die hard / Seven gates of hell / Buried alive / Don't burn the witch / In nomine satanus / Welcome to hell / Warhead / Stand up and be counted / Bloodlust
CD _____ CDTB 110
Thunderbolt / '91 / Magnum Music Group.

OLD, NEW, BORROWED AND BLUE
CD _____ CDBLEED 7
Bleeding Hearts / Oct '93 / Pinnacle.

POSSESSED
Powerdrive / Flytrap / Satanchist / Burn this place (to the ground) / Harmony dies / Possessed / Hellchild / Moonshine / Wing and a prayer / Suffer not the children / Voyeur / Mystique / Too loud for the croed
CD _____ CLACD 402
Castle / Jun '94 / BMG.

PRIME EVIL
CD _____ CDFLAG 38
Under One Flag / Oct '89 / Pinnacle.

SINGLES 1980-1986
In league with Satan / Live like an angel / Blood lust / In nomine satanus / Dio hard / Acid queen / Bustin' out / Warhead / Lady lust / Seven gates of hell / Manitou / Dead of the nite
CD _____ CLACD 246
Castle / '92 / BMG.

TEAR YOUR SOUL APART
CD _____ CDFLAG 50
Under One Flag / Sep '90 / Pinnacle.

TEMPLES OF ICE
CD _____ CDFLAG 56
Music For Nations / Jun '91 / Pinnacle.

WASTELAND, THE
Cursed / I'm paralysed / Back legions / Riddle of steel / Need to kill / Kissing the beast / Crucified / Shadow king / Wolverine / Clarisse
CD _____ CDFLAG 72
Under One Flag / Nov '92 / Pinnacle.

WELCOME TO HELL
Sons of Satan / Welcome to hell / Schizo / Mayhem with mercy / Poison / Live like an angel / Witching hour / 1000 days in Sodom / Angel dust / In league with Satan / Red light fever
CD _____ CLACD 255
Castle / '91 / BMG.

Ventilators

VENTILATORS, THE
CD _____ EFA 046222
Pork Pie / Sep '95 / SRD.

Ventura, Charlie

JACKIE & ROY (Ventura, Charlie Band)
Euphoria / F Y I / Lady be good / If I had you / Deed I do / I'm forever blowing bubbles / Pina colada / Gone with the wind / Once in a while / Lonely tonight
CD _____ SV 0218
Savoy Jazz / May '93 / Conifer / ADA.

LIVE 1947 (Ventura, Charlie & Bill Harris)
CD _____ EBCD 2122-2
Jazzband / Oct '94 / Jazz Music / Wellard.

Ventures

ANOTHER SMASH/THE COLOURFUL VENTURES
Riders in the sky / Wheels / Lonely heart / Bulldog / Lullaby of the leaves / Beyond the reef / Rawhide / Meet Mister Callaghan / Trombone / Last date / Ginchy / Josie / Blue moon / Yellow jacket / Bluer than blue / Cherry pink and apple blossom white / Green leaves of summer / Blue skies / Green fields / Red top / White silver sands / Yellow bird / Orange fire / Silver city
CD _____ C5HCD 619
See For Miles/C5 / Aug '94 / Pinnacle.

DON'T WALK RUN VOL.2/KNOCK ME OUT
House of the rising sun / Diamond head / Night train / Peach fuzz / Rap city / Blue star / Walk don't run '64 / Night walk / One mint julep / Pedal pusher / Creeper / Stranger on the shore / I feel fine / Love potion no.9 / Tomorrow's love / Oh pretty woman / Mariner no.4 / When you walk in the room / Gone gone gone / Slaughter on 10th avenue / She's not there / Lonely girl / Bird rockers / Sha la la
CD _____ C5HCD 630
See For Miles/C5 / Aug '95 / Pinnacle.

EP COLLECTION: VENTURES
No trespassing / Night train / Ram bunk shush / Lonely heart / Ups 'n' downs / Torquay / Bulldog / Meet Mr. Callaghan / Trombone / Josie / Yellow jacket / Bluer than blue / Gringo / Moon dawg / Sunny river /

Guitar twist / Telstar / Percolator / Silver city / Wildwood flower / Wabash cannonball / Secret agent man / Man from U.N.C.L.E. / Hot line
CD _____ SEECD 292
See For Miles/C5 / Jan '90 / Pinnacle.

EP COLLECTION: VENTURES VOL. 2
Walk don't run / Last night / Red river rock / You are my sunshine / Scratch / Action / No matter what / Wild thing / Wild cat / Walk don't run '64 / Running wild / Memphis / El cumbanchero / McCoy / Green onions / Lovesick blues / Penetration / Pipeline / Stop action / Little bit of action / Woolly and wild / Wild child / Cruel sea / Tall cool one / Tarantella / Skip to m'limbo
CD _____ SEECD 363
See For Miles/C5 / Jan '93 / Pinnacle.

GREATEST HITS: VENTURES
CD _____ MATCD 284
Castle / Jan '95 / BMG.

GUITAR FREAKOUT/SUPER PSYCHEDELICS
Good thing / High and dry / Standing in the shadow of love / Off in the 93rds / Cookout freakout on lookout mountain / Wack wack / Mod east / I'm a believer / Guitar freakout / Snoopy Vs. the Red Baron / Paper airline / Theme from the wild angels / Strawberry fields forever / Psychedelic venture / Western Union / Guitar psychedelics / Kandy koncoction / Reflections / Little bit me, a little bit you / Endless dream / Vibrations / Psyched out / 1999 A.D. / Happy together
CD _____ C5MCD 627
See For Miles/C5 / Jul '95 / Pinnacle.

MASHED POTATOES AND GRAVY/ GOING TO THE VENTURES DANCE PARTY
Lucille / Gravy (for mashed potatoes) / Hernando's hideaway / Mashed potato time / Summertime / Hot summer (Asian mashed) / Poison ivy / Wah-watusi / Instant mashed / Scratch / Hully gully (baby) / Spudnik / Mr Moto / Theme from come September / Gully-ver / Loco-motion / Lolita ya ya / Limbo rock / Sweet and lovely / Gandy dancer / Intruder / Venus / Night drive / Ya ya wobble
CD _____ C5CHD 635
See For Miles/C5 / Jan '96 / Pinnacle.

PLAY THE CARPENTERS/THE JIM CROCE SONGBOOK
We've only just begun / Yesterday once more / It's going to take some time / Bless the beasts and children / Top of the world / Sing / Superstar / Close to you / Hurting each other / Rainy days and Mondays / Jambalaya / Goodbye to love / I got a name / Bad, Bad Leroy Brown / I'll have to say I love you in a song / Lover's cross / It doesn't have to be that way / Age / Time in a bottle / Don't mess around with Jim / One less set of footsteps / Operator / Five short minutes / Speedball Tucker
CD _____ C5HCD 620
See For Miles/C5 / Oct '94 / Pinnacle.

TWIST WITH THE VENTURES/TWIST PARTY VOL.2
Driving guitars / Twist / Roadrunner / Gringo / Moon dawg / Guitar twist / Opus twist / Movin' and groovin' / Sunny river / Let's twist again / Shanghai'd / Bumble bee twist / My bonnie lies / Twisted / Twomp / Besame mucho / Blue tailed fly / Swanee River twist / Instant guitars / Dark eyes twist / Counterpoint / Kicking around / Bluebird / Red winn twist
CD _____ C5HCD 621
See For Miles/C5 / Oct '94 / Pinnacle.

VENTURES A GO-GO/WHERE THE ACTION IS
Satisfaction / Go go slow / Louie Louie / Night stick / La bamba / In crowd / Woolly bully / Go go guitar / Go go dancer / Swingin' creeper / Whittier boulevard / I like it like that / Action / Lies / Fever / Stop action / Three's a crowd / Taste of honey / No matter what shape / Action plus / Hang on sloopy (my girl sloopy) / Nutty / Little bit of action / She's just my style
CD _____ C5HCD 622
See For Miles/C5 / Aug '94 / Pinnacle.

VENTURES, THE
Driving guitars (Ventures twist) / Ups 'n' downs / Wailin' / Lonely heart / Perfidia / McCoy / Better than blue / Ram-bunk-shush / No trespassing / Lullaby of the leaves / Bulldog / Silver City / Lolita ya ya / 2000 pound bee (pts 1 & 2) / Ninth wave / Journey to the stars / Torquay / Walk don't run / Slaughter on 10th avenue / Diamonds head / Ten seconds to heaven / Secret agent man / Blue star / Rap city / Walk don't run/Land of a 1000 dances / Hawaii Five-O
CD _____ CDSL 8257
EMI / Jul '95 / EMI.

WALK DON'T RUN/THE VENTURES
Morgen / Raunchy / Home / My own true love (Tara's theme) / Switch / Walk don't run / Night train / No trespassing / Caravan / Sleep walk / McCoy / Honky tonk / Shuck / Detour / Ram-bunk-shush / Hawaiian war chant / Perfidia / Harlem nocturne / Blue tango / Up's and downs / Lonesome tonight / Torquay / Wailin' / Moon of manakoora

CD _____ C5HCD 618
See For Miles/C5 / Aug '94 / Pinnacle.

Venus

MISS PARIS
No.1 fan / Peter Pan man / John and Yoko / I am the son / Boy 4 girl 4 ever / Sweetest dream / Us against the world / Million dollar ass / Miss Paris / In season / Share a bid / Pretty when you're down / I always did / No.1 fan reprise
CD _____ PVCCD 002
PVC / Feb '94 / Vital.

Venus Beads

BLACK ASPIRIN
CD _____ EM 9264 2
Roadrunner / Sep '91 / Pinnacle.

INCISION
CD _____ EM 93242
Roadrunner / Mar '91 / Pinnacle.

Venus Fly Trap

TOTEM
CD _____ DANCD 024
Danceteria / Jan '90 / Plastic Head / ADA.

Venuti, Joe

GEMS (Venuti, Joe & George Barnes)
I want to be happy / I'm coming Virginia / Almost like being in love / I'll never be the same / Oh, baby / Hindustan / Lover / Humoresque / Poor butterfly / Uh lady be good
CD _____ CCD 6014
Concord Jazz / Nov '94 / New Note.

JAZZ PORTRAITS (Venuti, Joe & Eddie Lang)
Dinah / Wild dog / Sweet Sue, just you / I've found a new baby / Stringin' the blues / Black and blue bottom / Wild cat / Beatin' the dog / Sunshine / Goin' places / Doin' things / Cheese and crackers / Little girl / Wolf wobble / Penn beach blues / I'll never be the same / Raggin' the scale
CD _____ CD 14515
Jazz Portraits / May '91 / Jazz Music.

JOE VENUTI AND EDDIE LANG, VOL.1 (Venuti, Joe & Eddie Lang)
CD _____ JSPCD 309
JSP / Aug '89 / ADA / Target/BMG / Direct / Cadillac / Complete/Pinnacle.

JOE VENUTI AND EDDIE LANG, VOL.2 (Venuti, Joe & Eddie Lang)
CD _____ JSPCD 310
JSP / Aug '89 / ADA / Target/BMG / Direct / Cadillac / Complete/Pinnacle.

PRETTY TRIX
CD _____ IAJRCCD 1003
IAJRC / Jun '94 / Jazz Music.

STRINGIN' THE BLUES
CD _____ TPZ 1015
Topaz Jazz / Apr '95 / Pinnacle / Cadillac.

Vera, Joey

THOUSAND FACES
CD _____ CDZORRO 81
Metal Blade / Sep '94 / Pinnacle.

Verbal Abuse

RED, WHITE AND VIOLENT
CD _____ CM 77005CD
Century Media / Aug '95 / Plastic Head.

Verbal Assault

LIVE
CD _____ YCLS 004
Your Choice / May '94 / Plastic Head.

Verdell, Jackie

LAY MY BURDEN DOWN
Lay my burden down / Praise him / Can I get a witness / Storm is passing over / Walk all over God's heaven / Whon the saints go marching in / Let it be / I want Jesus to walk with me
CD _____ CDCH 375
Ace / Jun '93 / Pinnacle / Cadillac / Complete/Pinnacle.

Veritas

MO SMO SOKEI
CD _____ EUCD 1078
ARC / '89 / ARC Music / ADA.

Verity, John

HOLD YOUR HEAD UP
CD _____ SPRAYCD 305
Making Waves / Dec '94 / CM.

Verlaine, Tom

COVER
Five miles of you / Let go the mansion / Travelling / O foolish heart / Miss Emily / Rotation / Swim
CD _____ CDV 2314
Virgin / Jun '89 / EMI.

FLASH LIGHT
Cry mercy Judge / Say a prayer / Town called Walker / Song / Scientist / Bomb / 4 a.m. / Funniest thing / Annie's telling me / Sundown
CD _____ 8308612
Fontana / Jan '96 / PolyGram.

WARM AND COOL
CD _____ R 2882
Rough Trade / Apr '92 / Pinnacle.

WONDER, THE
Kaleidescopin' / August / Ancient Egypt / Shimmer / Stalingrad / Pillow / Storm / Five hours from Calais / Cooleridge / Prayer
CD _____ 8424202
Fontana / Jan '96 / PolyGram.

WORDS FROM THE FRONT
Present arrived / Postcard from Waterloo / True story / Clear it away / Words from the front / Coming apart / Days on the mountain
CD _____ CDV 2227
Virgin / Jun '89 / EMI.

Verlaines

BIRD DOG
CD _____ HMS 095 CD
Flying Nun / Nov '88 / Disc.

WAY OUT WHERE
Mission of love / I stare out... / This valentine / Blanket over the sky / Cathedrals under the sea / Aches in whisper / Way out where / Lucky in my dreams / Black wings / Stay gone / Incarceration / Dirge
CD _____ 828388-2
Slash / Apr '94 / PolyGram.

Vermenton Plage

J'SUIS CONTENT D'ETRE UN CAJUN
CD _____ VP 03CD
Weaving / Jun '94 / Koch / Direct / ADA.

Vermin

OBEDIENCE TO INSANITY
CD _____ CHAOSCD 01
Chaos / Oct '94 / Plastic Head.

Vernon, Nan

MANTA RAY
Motorcycle / Tattoo tears / Elvis waits / No more lullabyes / Big picture / Lay down Joe / While my guitar gently weeps / Iron John / Treasure / Fisherman / Johnny's birthday / Manta ray
CD _____ 4509939432
WEA / May '94 / Warner Music.

Vernons Girls

VERY BEST OF THE VERNONS GIRLS, THE
Hey lover boy / We love the Beatles / Don't wanna go / Dat's love / Funny all over / Do the bird / Mama doesn't know / Stay at home / Why why why / Stupid little girl / Just another girl / You know what I mean / Lover please / Locomotion / Be nice to him Mama / See for yourself / I'm gonna let my hair down / He'll never come again / Tomorrow is another day / Only you can do it / Do you know what I mean
CD _____ C5CD 616
See For Miles/C5 / Aug '94 / Pinnacle.

Veronica

V...AS IN VERONICA
Without love / What I wanna do / Unnecessary trip / Lockdown / Can't stop loving you / Sista / Love to come home to / Really don't miss you / House party / Trippin' / Ova & ova / 4 U
CD _____ 5285482
Mercury / Oct '95 / PolyGram.

VerPlanck, Billy

DANCING JAZZ
Summer evening / On top of mountie / I'll keep loving you / Day by day / Oh gee, oh me, oh my / Make up your mind / Embraceable you
CD _____ SV 0235
Savoy Jazz / Nov '93 / Conifer / ADA.

JAZZ FOR PLAYGIRLS
Senor blues / Playgirl stroll / Aw c'mon sugah / Whoo-ee / Miss spring blues / Winds / Duh-udah-udah
CD _____ SV 0209
Savoy Jazz / Apr '93 / Conifer / ADA.

VerPlanck, Marlene

BREATH OF FRESH AIR, A
CD _____ ACD 109
Audiophile / Apr '93 / Jazz Music / Swift.

EVERY BREATH I TAKE
With every breath I take / Accent on youth / Snuggled on your shoulder / Some other time / If I sing again / We could make such beautiful music together / Deep in a dream / Two cigarettes in the dark / Without a word of warning / You leave me breathless
CD _____ SV 0233
Savoy Jazz / Nov '93 / Conifer / ADA.

LIVE! IN LONDON
CD _____ ACD 280
Audiophile / Jan '94 / Jazz Music / Swift.

LOVES JOHNNY MERCER
CD _____ APCD 138
Audiophile / Apr '89 / Jazz Music / Swift.

MARLENE VERPLANCK MEETS SAXOMANIA IN PARIS
CD _____ ACD 288
Audiophile / Apr '95 / Jazz Music / Swift.

PURE AND NATURAL
CD _____ ACD 235
Audiophile / May '95 / Jazz Music / Swift.

QUIET STORM, A
CD _____ ACD 256
Audiophile / Feb '91 / Jazz Music / Swift.

SINGS ALEC WILDER
CD _____ ACD 218
Audiophile / Apr '93 / Jazz Music / Swift.

Versus

DEAD LEAVES
CD _____ RAIN 015CD
Cloudland / May '95 / Plastic Head / SRD.

STARS ARE INSANE, THE
CD _____ RAIN 011CD
Cloudland / Feb '95 / Plastic Head / SRD.

Vertical Hold

HEAD FIRST
Head first / Now that it's over / Let me break it down / Love today / Spend some time / You keep giving me / Sounds of New York / Well I guess you / Crash course to heartbreak / Morning after / Blue skies / Pray
CD _____ 5403332
A&M / Jun '95 / PolyGram.

Vertigo

NAIL HOLE
CD _____ ARRCD 46/297
Amphetamine Reptile / Sep '93 / SRD.

Vertinsky, Alexander

ALEXANDER VERTINSKY
CD _____ LDX 274939/40
La Chant Du Monde / Jan '93 / Harmonia Mundi / ADA.

Veruca Salt

AMERICAN THIGHS
Get back / All hail me / Seether / Spiderman '79 / Forsythia / Wolf / Celebrate you / Fly / Number one blind / Victrola / Twinstar / Twenty five / Sleeping where I want (On CD/LP only)
CD _____ FLATCD 9
Rise / Oct '94 / Pinnacle.

Verve

NO COME DOWN
No come down / Blue (USA Mix) / Make it till Monday (Acoustic) / Butterfly (Acoustic) / Where the geese go / Six o'clock / One way to go / Gravity grave (Live Glastonbury 93) / Twilight
CD _____ CDHUT 18
Hut / May '94 / EMI.

NORTHERN SOUL, A
New decade / This is music / On your own / So it goes / Northern soul / Brainstorm interlude / Drive you home / History / No knock on my door / Life's an ocean / Stormy clouds / Reprise
CD _____ DGHUT 27
CD _____ CDHUT 27
Hut / Jul '95 / EMI.

STORM IN HEAVEN, A
Star sail / Slide away / Already there / Beautiful mind / Sun the sea / Virtual world / Make it 'til Monday / Blue / Butterfly / See you in the next one (have a good time)
CD _____ CDHUT 10
Hut / Jun '93 / EMI.

Very Things

BUSHES SCREAM WHILE MY DADDY PRUNES, THE
CD _____ REFIRECD 12
Fire / Feb '94 / Disc.

IT'S A DRAG, IT'S A DRUG
CD _____ REFIRECD 13
Fire / Feb '94 / Disc.

MOTORTOWN
CD _____ REFIRECD 14
Fire / Feb '94 / Disc.

Vesala, Edward

INVISIBLE STORM (Vesala, Edward's Sound & Fury)
Sheets and shrouds / Murming morning / Gordion's flashes / Shadows on the frontier / In the gate of another gate / Somnambules / Sarastus / Wedding of all essential parts / Invisible storm / Haze of the frost / Caccaroo boohoo
CD _____ 5119282
ECM / Mar '92 / New Note.

LUMI (Vesala, Edward's Sound & Fury)
Wind / Frozen melody / Calypso bulbosa / Third moon / Lumi / Camel walk / Fingo / Early messenger / Together
CD _____ 8315172
ECM / Jul '87 / New Note.

NORDIC GALLERY (Vesala, Edward's Sound & Fury)
Bird in the high room / Fulflandia / Quay of meditative / Hadendas / Unexpected guest / Bluego / Lavender lass blossom / Steaming below the time / 1-2-3 or 4-5-6 / Significant look of birch grove / On the shady side of forty / Flavor lust
CD _____ 5232942
ECM / Nov '94 / New Note.

ODE TO THE DEATH OF JAZZ
Sylvan swizzle / Infinite express / Time to think / Winds of Sahara / Watching for the signal / Glimmer of sepal / Mop mop / What? Where? Hum hum
CD _____ 8431962
ECM / Jun '90 / New Note.

Vesga, Jose Luis

EL TIPLE - MUSICA COLUMBIANA
CD _____ 15354
Laserlight / '91 / Target/BMG.

Vetta, Patty

WILL (Vetta, Patty & Alan Franks)
CD _____ RGFCD 023
Road Goes On Forever / May '95 / Direct.

Vetter, Michael

OVERTONES - INSTRUMENTAL: FLOWERS
CD _____ JD 6372
Jecklin Disco / Sep '90 / Pinnacle.

Vexed

GOOD FIGHT
CD _____ CZ 021CD
C/Z / Dec '91 / Plastic Head.

Vibert & Simmons

WIERS
CD _____ CAT 016CD
Rephlex / Oct '94 / Disc.

Vibraphonic

VIBRAPHONIC
Trust me / I see you / Meter's runner / Lonnie's legacy / Bounce / Believe in me / Fall for you / So what / Tell me / Evidence (Features on CD only.)
CD _____ JAZIDCD 063
Acid Jazz / Apr '94 / Pinnacle.

VIBRAPHONIC 2
Heavy vibes / Buck the system / Down home / Can't get enough / Strolling / To know you is to love you / Light and shade / True life / Funkly / Watch out for this one
CD _____ JAZIDCD 118
Acid Jazz / Mar '95 / Pinnacle.

Vibrasonic

VIBRASONIC
CD _____ YEPCD 01
Yep / Mar '95 / SRD.

Vibrations

SOMBRAS
CD _____ CDART 101
Arc / Jul '95 / Total/BMG.

Vibrators

BBC LIVE IN CONCERT (Vibrators/Boys)
CD _____ WINCD 036
Windsong / Jul '93 / Pinnacle.

BEST OF THE VIBRATORS
Guilty: Wolfman howl / Rocket to the moon / Sleeping / Parties / Jumpin' Jack Flash / Watch out baby / Do a runner / We name the guilty / Baby baby / Fighter pilot / Day they caught the killer / Kick it / Dot ain't a lot / Claws in my brain / Amphetamine blue / Somnambulist / Baby blue eyes / Peepshow / 4875 / 3-D Jesus / Jesus always lets you down / Flying home / Shadow love / M.X. America / Flash flash flash / Punish me with kisses
CD _____ CDPUNK 43
Anagram / Jan '95 / Pinnacle.

FIFTH AMENDMENT/RECHARGED
Blown away by love / Rip up the city / Tomorrow is today / Wipe away / Too late for love / Demolishers / Running right into your heart / Frankenstein stomp / Crazy dream / Criminal / String him along / Hay little doll / I don't trust you / Go go go / Hey nonny no (Instrumental) / Picture of you / Every day I die a little / Too dumb / Rip it up tear it up / Someone stole my heart / Electricity / Tight black jeans / Reach for that star
CD _____ CDPUNK 34
Anagram / May '94 / Pinnacle.

GUILTY & ALASKA 127
Wolfman howl / Rocket to the moon / Sleeping / Parties / Jumpin' jack flash / Watch out baby / Do a runner / We name

the guilty / Baby baby / Fighter pilot / Day they caught the killer / Kick it / Dot ain't a lot / Claws in my brain / Amphetamine blue / Somnambulist / Baby blue eyes / Peepshow / 4875 / 3-D Jesus / Jesus always lets you down / Flying home / Shadow love / M.X. America / Flash flash flash / Punish me with kisses
CD _____ CDPUNK 16
Anagram / Sep '93 / Pinnacle.

HUNTING FOR YOU
CD _____ DOJOCD 179
Dojo / Nov '94 / BMG.

MELTDOWN/VICIOUS CIRCLE
Office girls / Don't cha lean on me / So young / Speed trap / Other side of midnight / Cruel to you / U2 38 / Dynamite / Letting you go / Danger streets / Let's go / Baby / Sally gardens / No getting over you / Poll tax blues / I don't wanna fall / Rocket ride to heaven / Count on me / Slow death / Fire / Halfway to paradise / Ruby's got a heart / Don't trust anyone / No mercy / Work
CD _____ CDPUNK 58
Anagram / Jun '95 / Pinnacle.

Vicari, Andreas

LUNAR SPELL
You're reported / Blue, green and space / Chequemate / Bedsprings / Way you treat people / Lunar spell / Birthday song / Voy a lomar / Last chair blues
CD _____ 33 JAZZ 026
33 Jazz / Nov '95 / Cadillac / New Note.

SUBURBAN GORILLAS
Pegasus / Fly so high / Awakening / In Africa Maibouye / Pin stripe woman / Southern comfort / Danse vendange / L'orchestre de fous / Sverr / Whispering whales
CD _____ 33JAZZ 016CD
33 Jazz / May '95 / Cadillac / New Note.

Vice Squad

LAST ROCKERS
CD _____ AABCD 805
Abstract / Oct '91 / Pinnacle / Total/BMG.

LAST ROCKERS/SINGLES
CD _____ AABT 805CD
Abstract / Sep '94 / Pinnacle / Total/BMG.

NO CAUSE FOR CONCERN
Summer fashion / 1981 / Saturday night special / Offering / Times they are a changing / Evil / Angry youth / It's a sell-out / Still dying / Last rockers
CD _____ DOJOCD 167
Dojo / Feb '94 / BMG.

SHOT AWAY
New blood / Take it or leave it / Out in the cold / Nowhere to hide / You'll never know / Rebels and kings / Playground / Rest of your life / What's going on / Killing time / Teenage rampage / Black sheep / Times they are a changin' / High spirits / New bond (Version) / Pledge / Nothing
CD _____ CDPUNK 28
Anagram / Dec '93 / Pinnacle.

STAND STRONG STAND PROUD
Stand strong, stand proud / Humane / Cheap / Gutterchild / Rock 'n' roll massacre / Fist full of dollars / Freedom begins at home / Out of reach / Saviour machine / No right of reply / Deathwish / Propaganda
CD _____ DOJOCD 170
Dojo / Nov '93 / BMG.

Viceroys

AT STUDIO ONE: YA HO
CD _____ CDHB 133
Heartbeat / Jun '95 / Greensleeves / Jetstar / Direct / ADA.

Vicious Circle

BARBED WIRE SLIDE
CD _____ CDSA 54027
Semantic / Feb '94 / Plastic Head.

Vicious Rumors

ANYTIME DAY OR NIGHT
CD _____ AHOY 20
Captain Oi / Nov '94 / Plastic Head.

DIGITAL DICTATOR
Replicant / Digital dictator / Minute to kill / Lady took a chance / Towns on fire / Out of sounds / Worlds and machines / Crest / Condemned / R.L.H. / Out of the shadows
CD _____ RR 9571 2
Roadrunner / Feb '88 / Pinnacle.

SOLDIER OF THE NIGHT
CD _____ RO 97342
Roadrunner / Feb '88 / Pinnacle.

VICIOUS RUMOURS
Don't wait for me / World church / On the edge / Ship of fools / Can you hear it / Down to the temple / Hellraiser / Electric twilight / Thrill of the hunt / Axe and smash
CD _____ 7567820752
Geffen / Feb '90 / BMG.

WORD OF MOUTH
CD _____ SPV 084-62232
Rising Sun / Jun '94 / Plastic Head.

Vicious, Sid

SID SINGS
Born to lose / I wanna be your dog / Take a chance on me / Stepping stone / My way / Belsen was a gas / Something else / Chatterbox / Search and destroy / Chinese rocks / I killed the cat
CD _____ CDV 2144
Virgin / Feb '89 / EMI.

Victim's Family

4 GREAT THRASH SONGS
CD _____ K 161C
Konkurrel / Jun '95 / SRD.

GERM, THE
CD _____ VIRUS 108CD
Alternative Tentacles / '92 / Pinnacle.

HEADACHE REMEDY
CD _____ K 151CD
Konkurrel / Mar '94 / Pinnacle.

Victoria Kings

MIGHTY KINGS OF BENGA, THE
V.B. Pod Warnol / Dick Ooro / Jack jack 2 / Jessica adhiambo / Akinyi / Eddo #1 / Eddo #2 / Yworo law kwach / Marine atiesh / Oluoch odalo / Wee juok / Yukabeth / Musa aloo / Ojowi telo
CD _____ CDORBD 079
Globestyle / Jun '93 / Pinnacle.

Victoria Police Pipe Band

VICTORIA POLICE PIPE BAND LIVE IN IRELAND
CD _____ MON 819CD
Monarch / Dec '93 / CM / ADA / Duncans / Direct.

Victoria, Irma

PHANTASMAGORIA
CD _____ MM 3000CD
Pingo / Dec '94 / Plastic Head.

Victory

DON'T GET MAD GET EVEN
CD _____ MERD 2105
Mercenary / Dec '93 / CM.

EARLY SINGLES, THE
CD _____ VE 18CD
Victory / Mar '95 / Plastic Head.

Victory Of The Better Man

WEGEN BROT
CD _____ CMPCD 69
CMP / Sep '95 / Vital/SAM.

Vidal, Lluis

MILIKITULI (Vidal, Lluis Trio)
CD _____ FSNT 009 CD
Fresh Sound / Nov '95 / Jazz Music / Discovery.

Vidalias

MELODYLAND
CD _____ UPSTART 014
Upstart / Feb '95 / Direct / ADA.

Vienna Art Orchestra

A NOTION IN PERPETUAL MOTION
CD _____ ARTCD 6096
Hat Art / Sep '90 / Harmonia Mundi / ADA / Cadillac.

FROM NO TIME TO RAG TIME
CD _____ ARTCD 6073
Hat Art / Nov '93 / Harmonia Mundi / ADA / Cadillac.

LIVE IN VIENNA
CD _____ 5133252
Verve / Apr '92 / PolyGram.

ORIGINAL CHARTS, THE
CD _____ 521998-2
Verve / Nov '94 / PolyGram.

Vienna Boys Choir

CHRISTMAS CAROLS
CD _____ 10594
Total / Oct '95 / Total/BMG.

Vienna Symphony Orchestra

ORCHESTRAL ROCK
Sledgehammer / I wanna dance with somebody (who loves me) / They dance alone / Man in the mirror / Against all odds / Nothing's gonna stop us now / Prelude / V.S.O.P. / Mull of Kintyre / Groovy kind of love / One moment in time / Orinoco flow / First time / Looking for freedom / Phantom of the opera / Living years / Hand in hand / Beatles medley
CD _____ MCCD 031
Music Club / Oct '91 / Disc / THE / CM.

ORCHESTRAL ROCK II
Private dancer / Bohemian rhapsody / Radio ga ga / Power of love / St. Elmo's fire / Space oddity / Satisfaction / Brothers in arms / Bridge over trouble water / Kyrie /

Rock me Amadeus / Heart on fire / Dreamer / Sailing / Stairway to heaven
CD _____ MCCD 065
Music Club / '92 / Disc / THE. CM.

Vierny, Dina

CHANTS DU GOULAG
CD _____ LDX 274933
La Chant Du Monde / Mar '92 / Harmonia Mundi / ADA.

Vigilantes Of Love

KILLING FLOOR
CD _____ SKY 75020CD
Sky / Sep '94 / Koch.

Vignola, Frank

APPEL DIRECT
Appel direct / Play fiddle play / Ready'n able / Indian love call / Jeannine / Whirly twirly / Jitterbug waltz / Love for sale / Again / I'll never smile again / It might as well be spring
CD _____ CCD 4576
Concord Jazz / Nov '93 / New Note.

LET IT HAPPEN
Let it happen / Tico tico / Diminishing blackness / String of pearls / Ligia / Spanish eyes / Quizas quizas quizas / Felche d'or / Seven minds / Unit seven / Lu Lu's trip / Ah so
CD _____ CCD 4625
Concord Jazz / Nov '94 / New Note.

Vilas, Ricardos

BRASILIAN KALEIDOSCOPE
CD _____ HOCD 001
Turpin / Nov '94 / Grapevine.

Villa, Beto

FATHER OF THE TEJANO ORQUESTA
CD _____ ARHCD 364
Arhoolie / Apr '95 / ADA / Direct / Cadillac.

Village People

GREATEST HITS
Y.M.C.A. / In the navy / Can't stop the music / San Francisco / Macho man / Go west / Fire island / Ready for the 80's / Sex over the phone / New York City / Just a gigolo/I ain't got nobody / Five o'clock in the morning / In Hollywood / YMCA (remix)
CD _____ 7432117831-2
Arista / Nov '93 / BMG.

VILLAGE PEOPLE: THE HITS
Y.M.C.A. / Macho man / San Francisco (you've got me) / Can't stop the music / Megamix / In the navy / In Hollywood / Fire island / Go West / Village people / Ready for the 80's / Do you wanna spend the night
CD _____ MCCD 004
Music Club / Feb '91 / Disc / THE / CM.

Villalona, Angel

HECHO CON FERNANDO
Solo tu / La esquinita / Colegiala / Vivir sin ti / Maldito ron / Mil lagrimas / Corazon / Rubia del alma (mi hembra) / Como baila / Me dejaste solo
CD _____ 66058059
RMM / Dec '95 / New Note.

Vincent, Gene

AM I THAT EASY TO FORGET
CD _____ CDCD 1017
Charly / Mar '93 / Charly / THE / Cadillac.

EP COLLECTION: GENE VINCENT
Race with the devil / Crazy legs / Hold me, hug me, rock me / Wayward wind / Somebody help me / Five feet of lovin' / Peace of mind / Look what you gone and done to me / Summertime / Keep it a secret / Rocky road blues / Dance to the bop / Baby blue / Dance in the street / Lovely Loretta / I'm important words / Gone gone gone / She she little Sheila / Weeping willow / Crazy beat / I'm gonna catch me a rat / If you want my lovin'
CD _____ SEECD 253
See For Miles/C5 / Jan '96 / Pinnacle.

GENE VINCENT
Say mama / Blue jean bop / Wild cat / Right here on earth / Who slapped John / Walkin' home from school / Five feet of lovin' / She-she little Sheila / Be bop a lula / Jump back / Dance in the street / Pistol packin' mama / Crazy beat / High blood pressure / Five days, five days / Bi bickey bi bo bo boo
CD _____ LECD 038
Dynamite / May '94 / THE.

GENE VINCENT CD BOX SET (Complete Capitol & Columbia Recordings 1956-64)
CD Set _____ CDGV 1
EMI / Aug '90 / EMI.

HIS 30 ORIGINAL HITS
CD _____ ENTCD 260
Entertainers / Mar '92 / Target/BMG.

I'M BACK AND I'M PROUD
Rockin' Robin / In the pines / Be bop a lula / Rainbow at midnight / Black letter / White

lightning / Sexy ways / Ruby baby / Lotta lovin' / Circle never broken / (I heard that) lonesome whistle / Scarlet ribbons
CD _____ SEECD 415
See For Miles/C5 / Oct '94 / Pinnacle.

Into The Seventies

Sunshine / I need woman's love / 500 miles away from home / Slow time's coming / Listen to the music / If only you could see me today / Million shades of blue / Tush hog / How I love them old songs / High on life / North Carolina line / There is something on your mind / Day the world turned blue / Boppin' the blues / Looking back / Oh lonesome me / Woman in black / Danse colinda (CD only) / Geese (CD only) / You can make it if you try (CD only) / Our souls (CD only)
CD _____ SEECD 233
See For Miles/C5 / Sep '88 / Pinnacle.

REBEL HEART
Hound dog / Be bop a lula / Blue jean bop / Last word in lonesome / Pretty girls everywhere / Dance to the bop / Lonely street / Rainy day sunshine / Green grass / Mr. love / Roll over Beethoven / Rocky road blues / Say Mama / Pistol packin' Mama / (I heard that) Lonesome whistle / Maybellene / Whole lotta shakin' goin' on
CD _____ CDMF 087
Magnum Force / Nov '92 / Magnum Music Group.

REBEL HEART VOL. 2
Who slapped John / Dance to the bop / In my dreams / Lotta lovin' / Nervous / Ramble / Mr. Loneliness / Say Mama / Frankie and Johnny / Where have you been all my life / Come on in / Downtown / Girl from Ipanema (Inst.) / Mean (Inst.) / Story of the rockers / Pickin' poppies / Whole lotta shakin' goin' on / Day the world turned blue / Say Mama (2) / Rocky road blues / I'm movin' on / Say Mama (3)
CD _____ CDMF 093
Magnum Force / Apr '95 / Magnum Music Group.

Vincent, Rick

WANTED MAN, A
CD _____ 474749-2
Curb / Jan '94 / PolyGram.

Vingerhoeds, Vera

LIVE (Vingerhoeds, Vera & Lazybones)
CD _____ BVHAASTCD 9208
Bvhaast / Jan '92 / Cadillac.

WALL WORKS
CD _____ BVHAASTCD 9405
Bvhaast / Oct '94 / Cadillac.

Vinnegar, Leroy

WALKIN' THE BASSES
CD _____ CCD 14068
Pablo / Jun '95 / Jazz Music / Cadillac / Complete/Pinnacle.

Vinson, Eddie

BATTLE OF THE BLUES VOL. 3 (Vinson, Eddie & Jimmy Witherspoon)
CD _____ KCD 000634
King/Paddle Wheel / Sep '92 / New Note.

BATTLE OF THE BLUES VOL. 4 (Vinson, Eddie, Roy Brown & Wynomie Harris)
Big mouth gal / Bring it back / If you don't think I'm sinking / Trouble at midnight / Hard luck blues / Mama's boy / Long about sundown / Bloodshot eyes / Freight train / Old age boogie / Bald headed blues / Grandma plays the numbers / Good bread alley / Queen of diamonds
CD _____ KCD 668
King/Paddle Wheel / Mar '90 / New Note.

CLEANHEAD AND CANNONBALL (Vinson, Eddie & Cannonball Adderley)
CD _____ LCD 13092
Landmark / Oct '88 / New Note.

EDDIE 'CLEANHEAD' VINSON (Vinson, Eddie 'Cleanhead')
CD _____ SCD 029
Southland / Oct '93 / Jazz Music.

FUN IN LONDON
CD _____ JSPCD 204
JSP / Nov '87 / ADA / Target/BMG / Direct / Cadillac / Complete/Pinnacle.

JAMMING THE BLUES
Black Lion / Jul '93 / Jazz Music / Cadillac / Wellard / Koch.
CD _____ BLCD 760188

MEAT'S TOO HIGH
CD _____ JSPCD 253
JSP / Aug '94 / ADA / Target/BMG / Direct / Cadillac / Complete/Pinnacle.

ROOMFUL OF BLUES
CD _____ MCD 5282
Muse / Sep '92 / New Note / CM.

Vinton, Bobby

16 MOST REQUESTED SONGS
Blue velvet / Tell me why / To know you is to love you / Take good care of my baby / There, I've said it again / Coming home soldier / Over the mountain across the sea /

Halfway to paradise / Please love me forever / Blue on blue / L.O.N.E.L.Y. / Just as much as ever / I love how you love me / My heart belongs to only you / Mr. lonely / Roses are red
CD _____ 469091 2
Columbia / Nov '92 / Sony.

Vinx

STORYTELLER, THE
Forever yours / Moondance / Just one dance / Armida prelude / Armida / Living in the Metro / Grits and pate / Please come back / When I cover me / I will always care / East of away / Dial it / I know the way / Letter to the killer / I feel incredible
CD _____ 540195-2
A&M / Jan '94 / PolyGram.

Vinyas, Layas

TRICHY SANKARENT
CD _____ CDT 120
Topic / Apr '93 / Direct / ADA.

Vio-Lence

NOTHING TO GAIN
Atrocity / Twelve gauge justice / Ageless eyes / Pain of pleasure / Virtues of vice / Killing my words / Psychotic memories / No chains / Welcoming party / This is system / Color of life
CD _____ CD BLEED 4
Bleeding Hearts / Mar '93 / Pinnacle.

Viola, Al

MELLO AS A CELLO
CD _____ SLCD 9010
Starline / Dec '94 / Jazz Music.

Violent Children

SPLIT SCENE
CD _____ LF 108CD
Lost & Found / Jan '95 / Plastic Head.

Violent Femmes

'3'
Nightmares / Just like my father / Dating days / Fat / Fool in the full moon / Nothing worth living for / World we're living in / Outside the palace / Telephone book / Mother of a girl / See my ships
CD _____ 828 130-2
Slash / Jan '89 / PolyGram.

BLIND LEADING THE NAKED, THE
Old Mother Reagan / No killing / Love and make me three / Faith / Breakin' hearts / Special / I held her in my arms / Children of the revolution / Good friends / Heartaches / Cold canyon / Two people / Candlelight song / Country death song / Black girls / World without mercy
CD _____ 828 006-2
Slash / Apr '86 / PolyGram.

NEW TIMES
Don't start me on the liquor / Breakin' up / Key of 2 / Four Seasons / Machine / I'm nothing / When everybody's happy / Agamemmon / Island life / I saw you in the crowd / Mirror mirror (I see a damsel) / Jesus of Rio
CD _____ 755961553-2
Warner Bros. / May '94 / Warner Music.

GONE DADDY GONE
Gone daddy gone / Add it up / To the hill / Kiss off / Good feeling / Confessions / Promises
CD _____ 828 0352
Slash / Aug '91 / PolyGram.

WHY DO BIRDS SING
American music / Out the window / Do you really want to hurt me / Hey nonny nonny / Used to be / Girl trouble / He likes me / Life is a scream / Flamingo baby / Lack of knowledge / More money tonight / I'm free
CD _____ 8282392
Slash / Apr '91 / PolyGram.

Violet Arcana

IN THE SCENE OF MIND
CD _____ CDZOT 112
Zoth Ommog / Jun '94 / Plastic Head.

Violets

WILD PLACE
CD _____ SZ 216
Blue Rose / Dec '95 / 3MV.

Viper

LIVE MANIACS
CD _____ MASSCD 046
Massacre / Feb '95 / Plastic Head.

Virgin Prunes

ARTFUCK
CD _____ NR 422476
New Rose / Jan '94 / Direct / ADA.

HERESIE
CD _____ NR 422475
New Rose / Jan '94 / Direct / ADA.

VIRGIN PRUNES

HIDDEN LIE (Live In Paris)
Sweet hymn / Lady Day / God bless the child / Never ending story / Pagan love song / Love is danger / Moon looked down and laughed / Caucasian walk / Blues song
CD _____ NR 422473
New Rose / Jan '94 / Direct / ADA.

IF I DIE I DIE
CD _____ 452043
New Rose / May '94 / Direct / ADA.

MOON LOOKED DOWN AND LAUGHED, THE
CD _____ NR 422474
New Rose / Jan '94 / Direct / ADA.

NEW FORM OF BEAUTY, A
CD _____ NR 452042
New Rose / Jan '94 / Direct / ADA.

PAGAN LOVE SONG
CD _____ NR 453041
New Rose / Jan '94 / Direct / ADA.

Virgin Steele

AGE OF CONSENT
CD _____ 854 605
Maze / May '89 / Plastic Head.

MARRIAGE OF HEAVEN AND HELL, THE
CD _____ TT 00192
T&T / Jan '96 / Pinnacle / Koch.

NOBEL SAVAGE
CD _____ 857531
Steamhammer / '90 / Pinnacle / Plastic Head.

Virus

WARMONGER
CD _____ MIA 001CD
MIA / Sep '94 / Plastic Head.

Visage

FADE TO GREY - BEST OF VISAGE
Anvil / Night train / Pleasure boys / Damned to cry / Love glove / Fade to grey / Mind of a toy / Visage / We move / Tar / In the year 2525
CD _____ 521 053-2
Polydor / Jan '94 / PolyGram.

VISAGE
CD _____ 800 029-2
Polydor / May '91 / PolyGram.

Visby Big Band

FINE TOGETHER
CD _____ DRCD 210
Dragon / Feb '87 / Roots / Cadillac / Wellard / CM / ADA.

Visceral Evisceration

INCESSANT DESIRE
CD _____ SPV 08407922
Napalm / Sep '94 / Plastic Head.

Viscount Oliver

JUST ONE MOMENT
CD _____ FECD 13
First Edition / Apr '93 / Jetstar.

Viseur, Gus

COMPOSITIONS 1934-42
CD _____ FA 010CD
Fremeaux / Nov '95 / Discovery / ADA.

Vision

INSTRUMENTAL HEALING
CD _____ INDIGO 45792
Funfundvierzig / Dec '94 / SRD.

MENTAL HEALING
CD _____ INDIGO 45772
Funfundvierzig / Dec '94 / SRD.

Vision

WAVEFORM TRANSMISSION 2
CD _____ EFA 1750D
Tresor / Jun '93 / SRD.

Visitors

IN MY YOUTH
In my youth / Juggler / Visit / Mood seekers / Giant steps
CD _____ MCD 5024
Muse / May '95 / New Note / CM.

Vital Remains

INTO COLD DARKNESS
Immortal crusade / Under the moons fog / Crown of the black hearts / Scrolls / Into cold darkness / Descent into hell / Angels / Dethroned emperor
CD _____ CDVILE 48
Peaceville / Nov '95 / Pinnacle.

LET US PRAY
CD _____ CDVILE 58
Peaceville / Mar '95 / Pinnacle.

Vitale, Lito

CUARTETO
CD _____ MES 159952
Messidor / Jun '93 / Koch / ADA.

Vitale, Richie

DREAMSVILLE (Vitale, Richie Quintet)
My turn / Bibbo's suite / Saudade / Eclypso / Namely you / When I last saw you / Dreamsville / Sound for sore ears / Asiatic races
CD _____ TCB 93302
TCB / Nov '93 / New Note.

Vitous, Miroslav

ATMOS (Vitous, Miroslav & Jan Garbarek)
Pegasos / Goddess / Forthcoming / Atmos / Time out part I / Direvision / Time out part II / Helikon / Hippukrene
CD _____ 5133732
ECM / Jun '93 / New Note.

EMERGENCE
Epilogue / Transformation / Atlantis suite / Atlantis suite: Emergence of the spirit / Atlantis suite: Matter and spirit / Atlantis suite: Choice / Atlantis suite: Destruction into energy / Wheel of fortune / Regards to Gershwin's honeymar / Alice in Wonderland / Morning lake for ever / Variations on Spanish themes
CD _____ 8278552
ECM / Dec '86 / New Note.

FIRST MEETING
Silver lake / Beautiful place to / Trees / Recycle / First meeting / Concert in three parts / You make me so happy
CD _____ 5192802
ECM / Mar '94 / New Note.

GUARDIAN ANGELS
His meaning/Rising resolution / Inner peace / Guardian angels / Off to buffalo / Eating it raw / Shinkansen
CD _____ ECD 22055
Evidence / Jul '93 / Harmonia Mundi / ADA / Cadillac.

JOURNEY'S END
U dunaje u prespurka / Tess / Carry on No. 1 / Paragraph Jay / Only one / Windfall
CD _____ 8431712
ECM / May '91 / New Note.

MIROSLAV
CD _____ FCD 741040
Freedom / Sep '88 / Jazz Music / Swift / Wellard / Cadillac.

Vitro, Roseanna

SOFTLY
Falling in love with love / In summer (Estate) / Song for all ages / Softly as in a morning sunrise / Moon and sand / So many stars / I'm through with love / Wild is the wind / Life I choose / Our love rolls on / Nothing like you / Why try to change me now / I ain't got nothin' but the blues
CD _____ CCD 4587
Concord Jazz / Feb '94 / New Note.

Viva Saturn

BRIGHTSIDE
Send a message / Black cloud / Brightside / Here comes April / Abandoned car string me out a line / Mourn the light / Distracted / Nothing helps / Heart of you / One for my baby
CD _____ 729092
Restless / Jul '95 / Vital.

SOUNDMIND
CD _____ NORMAL 139
Normal/Okra / May '94 / Direct / ADA.

Vivid

SHINING
CD _____ TIN 41602
Tin Can Discs / Jan '96 / EWM / Total/BMG.

Vixen

REV IT UP
Rev it up / How much love / Love is a killer / Not a minute too soon / Streets in paradise / Hard 16 / Bad reputation / Fallen hero / Only a heartbeat away / It wouldn't be love / Wrecking ball
CD _____ CDMTL 1054
EMI Manhattan / Aug '90 / EMI.

VIXEN
Edge of a broken heart / I want you to rock me / Crying / American dream / Desperate / One night alone / Hellraisers / Love made me / Waiting / Cruisin' / Charmed life (CD only.)
CD _____ CDFA 3256
Fame / Aug '91 / EMI.

Vloeimans, Eric

FIRST FLOOR
CD _____ CHR 70011
Challenge / Aug '95 / Direct / Jazz Music / Cadillac / ADA.

Voeks, Erik

SANDBOX
CD _____ ROCK 6130-2
Rockville / Feb '94 / SRD.

Vogel, Christian

ABSOLUTE TIME
CD _____ EFA 017832
BMG / Jul '95 / BMG.

BEGINNING TO UNDERSTAND
CD _____ EFA 006582
Mille Plateau / Nov '94 / SRD.

Vogel, Karsten

SINDBILLEDE
CD _____ MECCACD 1011
Music Mecca / Nov '94 / Jazz Music / Cadillac / Wellard.

Voice Of Authority

AMERICA RIGHT NOW
CD _____ CDBRED 62
Cherry Red / Sep '91 / Pinnacle.

Voice Of Destruction

RING OF DEATH
CD _____ CDSATE 013
Talitha / Jul '94 / Plastic Head.

SOULS OF THE DAMNED
CD _____ CDSATE 04
Talitha / Aug '93 / Plastic Head.

Voice Of The Beehive

HONEY LINGERS
Monsters and angels / Adonis Blue / I think I love you / Look at me / Beauty to my eyes / Just like you / Little gods / I'm shooting Cupid / Say it / Perfect place
CD _____ 8282592
London / Jul '91 / PolyGram.

LET IT BEE
Beat of love / Sorrow floats / Don't call me baby / Man in the moon / What you have is enough / Oh love / I walk the earth / Trust me / I say nothing / There's a barbarian in the back of my car / Just a city
CD _____ 828 100-2
London / May '92 / PolyGram.

SEX AND MISERY
CD _____ 0630110042
East West / Feb '96 / Warner Music.

Voice Squad

HOLLYWOOD
CD _____ HB 0002CD
Hummingbird / Oct '93 / ADA / Direct.

MANY'S THE FOOLISH YOUTH
When a man's in love / Bonny Irish maid / Willie Taylor / Banks of the Bann / Holly she bears a berry / Parting glass / Kilmore Carol / Annan waters / Shepherds arise / Ode to autumn / Oh good ale
CD _____ TARACD 4004
Tara / Nov '95 / CM / ADA / Direct / Conifer.

Voices Of East Harlem

CAN YOU FEEL IT
CD _____ UFOXY 6CD
Vexfilms / May '95 / Pinnacle.

VOICES OF EAST HARLEM
CD _____ UFOXY 5CD
Vexfilms / May '95 / Pinnacle.

Voices Of Silence

VOICES OF SILENCE
CD _____ 74321236092
Arista / Apr '95 / BMG.

Void

CONDENSED FLESH
CD _____ LF 92CD
Lost & Found / Nov '94 / Plastic Head.

VoiVod

NEGATRON
Insect / Project X / Nanoman / Reality / Negatron / Planet hell / Meteor / Cosmic conspiracy / Bio TV / Drift / D.N.A. (Don't no anything)
CD _____ HYP 001CD
Play It Again Sam / Oct '95 / Vital.

WAR AND PAIN
Voi void / Suck your bone / War and pain / Live for violence / Nuclear war / Warriors of ice / Iron gang / Blower / Black city
CD _____ CDMZORRO 75
Metal Blade / May '94 / Pinnacle.

Volcano

RAT RACE
CD _____ CORECD 2
Metalcore / Sep '91 / Plastic Head.

Volcano Suns

FARCED
CD _____ SST 210 CD
SST / Sep '88 / Plastic Head.

THINGS OF BEAUTY
CD _____ SST 257 CD
SST / Nov '89 / Plastic Head.

Vollenweider, Andreas

BOOK OF ROSES
La Strega (Her journey to the grand ball) / Grand ball of the Duljas / Morning at Boma Park / Five curtains / Book of roses / In the woods of Kroandal / Jugglers in Obsidian / Chanson de L'Heure Bleue / Czippa and the Ursanian girl / Birds of Tilmun / Hirzel / Jours d'amour / Manto's arrow and the sphinx / Letters to a young rose
CD _____ 4688272
Columbia / Jan '92 / Sony.

EOLIAN MINSTREL
Song of Isolde / Across the iron river (the return) / Reason enough (all the king's men) / Eolian minstrel / Jaden maiden / Secret shrine of Icarus / Harvest / Years in the forest / Desert of rain / Private fires / Five sisters / Painter's waltz / Leaves of the great tree / Lake of time
CD _____ 474784 2
Columbia / Jan '94 / Sony.

Volz, Greg

COME OUT FIGHTING
CD _____ MYRCD 6865
Myrrh / '89 / Nelson Word.

RIVER IS RISING, THE
CD _____ MYRCD 6846
Myrrh / Nov '86 / Nelson Word.

Vomacka, Sammy

EASY RIDER
CD _____ BLR 84 019
L&R / May '91 / New Note.

Vomiting Corpses

SPHERES, THE
CD _____ IR 013CD
Invasion / Jun '95 / Plastic Head.

Vomito Negro

DARE
CD _____ KK 009 CD
KK / '89 / Plastic Head.

HUMAN
CD _____ KK 050 CD
KK / Sep '90 / Plastic Head.

SAVE THE WORLD
CD _____ KKUK 002CD
KK / '90 / Plastic Head.

SHOCK
CD _____ KK 023 CD
KK / '89 / Plastic Head.

Vomiturition

LEFTOVER AGE, A
CD _____ IR 014CD
Invasion / Jun '95 / Plastic Head.

Von Daniken

NEW WORLDS
CD _____ CYCL 028
Cyclops / Nov '95 / Pinnacle.

Von Groove

RAINMAKER
CD _____ 342122
No Bull / Oct '95 / Koch.

Von Magnet

COMPUTADOR
CD _____ HYPE 06CD
Roughneck / Nov '92 / Disc.

Von Schlippenbach, Alex

MORLOCKS AND OTHER PIECES, THE
CD _____ FMPCD 61
FMP / Oct '94 / Cadillac.

SMOKE (Von Schlippenbach, Alex & Sunny Murray)
CD _____ FMPCD 23
FMP / May '87 / Cadillac.

Von Trapp Family

SOUND OF CHRISTMAS, THE
CD _____ 15466
Laserlight / Nov '95 / Target/BMG.

Von Westernhagen, Thilo

FORGOTTEN GARDENS (Von Westernhagen, Thilo & Charlie Mariano/Peter Weihe)
CD _____ BEST 1011CD
Acoustic Music / Nov '93 / ADA.

Von Zamla

ZAMLARANAMMA
CD _____ RES 511CD
Resource / Dec '94 / ADA.

Vond

SELUMORD
CD _____ MR 004CD
Malicious / Oct '95 / Plastic Head.

Voodoo Gearshift

GLUE GOAT
CD _____ CZ 052CD
C/Z / Dec '92 / Plastic Head.

Voodoo Glow Skulls

FIRME
CD _____ 864542
Epitaph / Oct '95 / Plastic Head / Pinnacle.

WHO IS, THIS IS
CD _____ DSR 018CD
Dr. Strange / Jan '96 / Plastic Head.

Voodoo Queens

CHOCOLATE REVENGE
CD _____ PURECD 030
Too Pure / Dec '93 / Vital.

PEEL SESSIONS
CD _____ SFRCD 125
Strange Fruit / May '94 / Pinnacle.

Voodoo Sioux

S.K.R.A.P.E.
Jesus Christ / Misty / That's for me to know / In through the out door / Witness tree /

Backwards / Something you said / Every mother's son / Catching flies / Can't stand to see you cry
CD _____ CDBLEED 14
Bleeding Hearts / Jul '95 / Pinnacle.

Voodoo X

AWAKENING, THE (vol.1)
CD _____ NTHEN 16
Now & Then / Apr '95 / Plastic Head.

Voros, Kalman

EVERGREENS (Voros, Kalman & His Gypsy Band)
CD _____ HCD 101 852
Conifer / '88 / Conifer.

Voss, Jochen

ALTERATIONS
CD _____ BEST 1029CD
Acoustic Music / Nov '93 / ADA.

Vowel Movement

VOWEL MOVEMENT
Dinosaur / Hitch hiker / Frank / When we collide / I don't wanna / Las Vegas / Death of a surfer / Vowel movement (A-E-I-O-U) / Ohohoh / Jackie baby / Gecko / Jesus / Tiny music
CD _____ MR 106-2
Mammoth / May '95 / Vital.

Vox Humana

UNSAMPLED
CD _____ ALIGCD 1
Alligator / Jan '95 / Direct / ADA.

Voyager

TRANSMISSION
Underworld theme / In unity / Suck acid / Suck acid (mix) / Underworld theme (Jetslags version) / In unity (irdial 7:35 version) / Arrival
CD _____ UCRCD 22
Union City / Jul '93 / EMI.

Vranican, Mick

CLOAK OF SKIN
CD _____ NAR 092CD
SST / Feb '94 / Plastic Head.

Vranich, Mick

IDOLS OF FEAR
CD _____ NAR 098CD
SST / Sep '94 / Plastic Head.

Vriends, Peter

EMOTIONAL TRAVELLOG
Serenity / Joy / Fear / Anger / Envy / Lust / Jealousy / Security / Greed / Love
CD _____ SMCCD 8002
Smile Communications / Aug '94 / Vital.

Vrod, Jean-Francois

VOYAGE
CD _____ Y 225036CD
Silex / Oct '94 / ADA.

Vujicsics

VUJICSICS
CD _____ HNCD 1310
Hannibal / May '89 / Vital / ADA.

Vulgar Boatmen

OPPOSITE SEX
CD _____ 0630109412
East West / Jun '95 / Warner Music.

Vulgar Unicorn

UNDER THE UMBRELLA
House at fudge corner / By post-chaise to the prim rose legue / Waiting under the umbrella / Thief of clubs
CD _____ CYCL 018
Cyclops / Apr '95 / Pinnacle.

Vulva

FROM THE COCKPIT
CD _____ CAT 021CD
Rephlex / Mar '95 / Disc.

Vybe

VYBE
CD _____ BRCD 618
4th & Broadway / Oct '95 / PolyGram.

Vylinda

KISS, THE
CD _____ CHM 6001
Chimera / Oct '94 / Grapevine.

Vysniauskas, Petras

LITHUANIA
CD _____ ITM 1449
ITM / Jan '91 / Tradelink / Koch.

W.A.S.P.

FIRST BLOOD...LAST CUTS
Animal (fuck like a beast) / L.O.V.E. machine (remix) / I wanna be somebody (remix) / On your knees / Blind in Texas / Wild child (remix) / I don't need no doctor (remix) / Real me / Headless children / Mean man / Forever free / Chainsaw Charlie / Idol / Sunset and Babylon / Hold on to my heart / Rock 'n' roll to death
CD _____ CDESTG 2217
Capitol / Nov '93 / EMI.

HEADLESS CHILDREN, THE
Heretic (the lost child) / Real me / Headless children / Thunderhead / Mean man / Neutron bomber / Mephisto waltz / Forever free / Maneater / Rebel in the F.D.G.
CD _____ CDEST 2087
Capitol / Jul '94 / EMI.

INSIDE THE ELECTRIC CIRCUS
Big welcome / I don't need no doctor / 95 nasty / Shoot from the hip / I'm alive / Easy livin' / Sweet cheetah / Mantronic / King of Sodom and Gomorrah / Rock rolls on / Restless gypsy
CD _____ CDEST 2025
Capitol / Jul '94 / EMI.

LIVE IN THE RAW
Inside the electric circus / I don't need no doctor / L.O.V.E. machine / Wild child / 95 nasty / Sleeping (in the fire) / Manimal / I wanna be somebody / Harder faster / Blind in Texas / Scream until you like it
CD _____ CDEST 2040
Capitol / Jul '94 / EMI.

Waby Spider

SIDA
CD _____ ADC 1001
PAM / Feb '94 / Direct / ADA.

Wackerman, Chad

FORTY REASONS
Holiday insane / You came along / Forty reasons / Fearless / Quite life / Waltzing on jupiter / Tell me / House on fire / Hidden places / Go / Schemes
CD _____ CMPCD 48
CMP / Jun '93 / Vital/SAM.

VIEW, THE
Close to home / Across the bridge / Black coffee / Empty suitcase / Introduction / Starry nights / All sevens / On the edge / Just a moment / View / Flares / Bash / Days away
CD _____ CMPCD 64
CMP / Oct '93 / Vital/SAM.

Waddell, Steve

EGYPTIAN ELLA (Waddell, Steve & His Creole Bells)
CD _____ SOSCD 1230
Stomp Off / Oct '92 / Jazz Music / Wellard.

Wades

TOUCH OF HEAVEN, A
CD _____ KMCD 822
Kingsway / Mar '95 / Total/BMG / Complete/Pinnacle.

Wagner, Robert

TO CATCH A CHRISTMAS STAR
CD _____ DE 3072
Delos / Dec '89 / Conifer.

Wagon Christ

PHAT LAB NIGHTMARE
CD _____ RSNCD 18
Rising High / Jul '94 / Disc.

THROBBING POUCH
CD _____ RSNCD 30
Rising High / Mar '95 / Disc.

Wagoner, Porter

THIN MAN FROM WEST PLAINS
Settin' the woods on fire / Headin' for a weddin' / Lovin' letters / I can't live with you (I can't live without you) / Bringing home the bacon / Angel made of ice / Takin' chances / All roads lead to love / That's it / Beggar for love / Trademark / Don't play that song (You lied) / Flame of love / Dig that crazy moon / Trinidad / Bad news travels fast / Get out of here / My bonfire / Town crier / Love at first sight / Be glad you ain't me / Our shivaree / Company's coming / Tricks of the trade / Satisfied mind / Good time was had by all / Hey maw / You quick / I like girls / Itchin' for my baby / Eat, drink and be merry / I'm stepping out tonight / Let's squiggle / Living in the past / What would you do (if Jesus came to your house)

Wah

WORD TO THE WISE GUY, A (Mighty Wah)
Yuh learn I / Weekends / Lost generation / Yuh learn II / Know there was something / Yuh learn III / In the bleak (body and soul) mid winter / What's happening here / Papa crack - God's lonely man / Yuh learn IV / Come back
CD _____ BBL 54CD
Lowdown/Beggars Banquet / Jan '89 / Warner Music / Disc.

Waikikis

HAWAIIAN FAVOURITES (Waikiki Beach Boys)
Hawaiian wedding song / Hawaiian march / Analani E / Ports of paradise / Shimmering sands / My little grass shack in Kealakekua, Hawaii / Kono koni / Mamoola moon / Kahola march / Hawaii calls / Hawaii tattoo / Sweet Leilani / Flower of the islands / Honi kaua / Garlands for your hair / Song of the Islands / Tiny bubbles / Beautiful Moorea / Hawaiian honeymoon / March to Diamond Head
CD _____ CC 254
Music For Pleasure / May '90 / EMI.

Wailer, Bunny

BLACKHEART MAN
Blackheart man / Fighting against conviction / Oppressed song / Fig tree / Dreamland / Rastaman / Reincarnated soul / Amagideon / Bide up / This train
CD _____ RRCD 6
Reggae Refreshers / Jun '90 / PolyGram / Vital.

BUNNY WAILER SINGS THE WAILERS
Dancing shoes / Mellow mood / Dreamland / Keep on moving / Hypocrite / I'm the toughest / Rule this land / Burial / I stand predominate / Walk the proud land
CD _____ RRCD 8
Reggae Refreshers / Jun '90 / PolyGram / Vital.

CRUCIAL ROOTS CLASSICS
CD _____ SHCD 45014
Shanachie / Apr '94 / Koch / ADA / Greensleeves.

GUMPTION
CD _____ SMCD 014
Solomonic / Jul '91 / Jetstar / Pinnacle.

HALL OF FAME
CD _____ RASCD 3502
Ras / Jan '96 / Jetstar / Greensleeves / SRD / Direct.

JUST BE NICE
CD _____ RASCD 3121
Ras / Jul '93 / Jetstar / Greensleeves / SRD / Direct.

Liberation

LIBERATION
CD _____ SHANCD 43059
Shanachie / Feb '89 / Koch / ADA / Greensleeves.

MARKETPLACE
CD _____ SHCD 43071
Shanachie / Jun '91 / Koch / ADA / Greensleeves.

PROTEST
Moses children / Get up stand up / Scheme of things / Quit trying, follow fashion monkey / Wanted children / Who feels it / Johnny too bad
CD _____ RRCD 7
Reggae Refreshers / Jun '90 / PolyGram / Vital.

RETROSPECTIVE
CD _____ SHCD 45021
Shanachie / Mar '95 / Koch / ADA / Greensleeves.

ROOTS MAN SKANKING
CD _____ SHANCD 43043
Shanachie / Sep '87 / Koch / ADA / Greensleeves.

ROOTS RADICS ROCKERS REGGAE
CD _____ SHANCD 43013
Shanachie / Jan '84 / Koch / ADA / Greensleeves.

RULE DANCE HALL
CD _____ SHANCD 43050
Shanachie / Jun '88 / Koch / ADA / Greensleeves.

Wailers

JAH JAH MESSAGE
CD _____ SPVCD 08455242
Red Arrow / Apr '95 / SRD / Jetstar.

MAJESTIC WARRIORS
CD _____ 364002 2
A&M / Oct '91 / PolyGram.

NEVER ENDING WAILERS, THE
CD _____ RASCD 3501
Ras / Feb '94 / Jetstar / Greensleeves / SRD / Direct.

WAILING WAILERS, THE
CD _____ SOCD 1001
Studio One / Aug '94 / Jetstar.

Wailing Roots

FEELINGS AND DUB
CD _____ ACPCG 014
Melodie / Oct '95 / Triple Earth / Discovery / ADA / Jetstar.

Wailing Souls

FACE THE DEVIL
Trojan / Jun '95 / Jetstar / Total/BMG.
CD _____ CDTRL 360

INCHPINCHERS
Inchpinchers / Things and time / Baby come rock / Mass charley ground / Oh what a lie / Ghetto of Kingston Town / Tom sprang / Don't get lost / Modern slavery / Infidels
CD _____ GRELCD 47
Greensleeves / Sep '92 / Total/BMG / Jetstar / SRD.

KINGSTON 14
Kingston 14 / Dem coming / Front door / Ring my bell / Don't run / Full moon / Yet the world waits / Pity the poor / Real rock
CD _____ LLCD 28
Live & Love / May '88 / Jetstar.

LAY IT ON THE LINE
CD _____ LLCD 024
Live & Love / '88 / Jetstar.

STRANDED
Stranded in L. A. / File for your machete / Thinking / Peace and love shall reign / Helmet of salvation / War deh round a John shop / Eyes of love / Divided and rule / Sunrise till sunset / Best is yet to come
CD _____ GRELCD 73
Greensleeves / Aug '95 / Total/BMG / Jetstar / SRD.

VERY BEST OF THE WAILING SOULS
War / Jah give us life / Bredda / Old broom / Kingdom rise, kingdom fall / Firehouse rock / Who no waan come / Things and time / Stop red eye / Sticky stay / They don't know Jah / War deh round a John shop
CD _____ GRELCD 99
Greensleeves / Oct '95 / Total/BMG / Jetstar / SRD.

WILD SUSPENSE
Row fisherman / Slow coach / We got to be together / Feel the spirit / Bredda Gravilicious / Wild suspense / They never knew / Black rose / Something funny / Very well / Walk but mind you don't fall (CD only) / Row fisherman (dub) (CD only) / Bredda Gravilicious (dub) (CD only) / Slow coach (dub) (CD only) / Something funny (dub) (CD only) / We've got to be together (dub) (CD only) / Very well (dub) (CD only)
CD _____ RRCD 53
Reggae Refreshers / Apr '95 / PolyGram / Vital.

Wainwright III, Loudon

ALBUM III
Dead skunk / Red guitar / East Indian princess / Muse blues / Hometeam crown / B side / Needless to say / Smoky Joe's cafe / New paint / Trilogy (circa 1967) / Drinking song / Say that you love me
CD _____ EDCD 168
Edsel / Feb '91 / Pinnacle / ADA.

ATTEMPTED MOUSTACHE
Swimming song / A.M. world / Bell bottom pants / Liza / I am the way / Clockwork chartreuse / Down drinking at the bar / Man who couldn't cry / Come a long way / Nocturnal stumblebutt / Dilated to meet you / Lullaby
CD _____ ED CD 269
Edsel / May '88 / Pinnacle / ADA.

CAREER MOVES
Road ode / I'm alright / Five years old / Your mother and I / Westchester county / He said, she said / Christmas rap / Suddenly it's Christmas / Thanksgiving / Fine Celtic name / T.S.M.N.W.A. / Some balding guys / Swimming song / Absence makes the heart grow fonder / Happy birthday Elvis / Fabulous songs / Unhappy anniversary / I'd rather be lonely / Just say no / April fool's day morn / Man who couldn't cry / Acid song / Tip that waitress / Career moves
CD _____ CDV 2718
Virgin / Jul '93 / EMI.

FAME AND WEALTH
Reader and advisor / Grammy song / Dump the dog / Five years old / Westchester county / Saturday morning fever / April fools day morn / Fame and wealth / Thick and thin / Revenge / Ingenue / IDTTYWLM
CD _____ CD 3076
Rounder / Aug '88 / CM / Direct / ADA / Cadillac.

FAME AND WEALTH/I'M ALRIGHT
CD _____ FIENDCD 711
Demon / Nov '91 / Pinnacle / ADA.

GROWN MAN
Birthday present / Grown man / That hospital / Housework / Cobwebs / Year / Father/Daughter dialogue / 1994 / Iwiwal / Just a john / I suppose / Dreaming / End has begun / Human cannonball / Dreaming untold
CD _____ CDV 2789
Virgin / Oct '95 / EMI.

HISTORY
People in love / Men / Picture / When I'm At Your House / Doctor / Hitting You / I'd rather be lonely / Between / Talking New Bob Dylan / So many songs / Four times ten / Father And A Son / Sometimes I forget / Handful Of Dust
CD _____ CDV 2703
Virgin / Sep '92 / EMI.

I'M ALRIGHT
One man guy / Lost love / I'm alright / Not John / Cardboard boxes / Screaming issue / How old are you / Animal song / Out of this world / Daddy take a nap / Ready or not / Career moves
CD _____ CD 3096
Rounder / Aug '88 / CM / Direct / ADA / Cadillac.

LIVE ONE, A
Motel blues / Hollywood hopeful / Whatever happened to us / Natural disaster / Suicide song / School days / Kings and queens / Down drinking at the bar / B side / Nocturnal stumblebutt / Red guitar / Clockwork chartreuse / Lullaby
CD _____ ROUNDERCD 3050
Rounder / Aug '88 / CM / Direct / ADA / Cadillac.

MORE LOVE SONGS
Hard day on the planet / Synchronicity / Your mother and I / I eat out / No / Home stretch / Unhappy anniversary / Man's world / Vampire blues / Overseas calls / Expatriot / Back nine
CD _____ CD 3106
Rounder / '88 / CM / Direct / ADA / Cadillac.

ONE MAN GUY (The Best Of Loudon Wainwright III 1984-1989)
CD _____ MCCD 166
MCI / Jul '94 / Disc / THE.

UNREQUITED
Sweet nothin's / Lowly trust / Kings and queens / Kick in the head / Whatever happened to us / Crime of passion / Absence

makes the heart grow fonder / On the rocks / Mr. Guilty / Guru / Hardy Boys at the Y / Unrequited to the ninth degree / Rufus is a tit man
CD ______ **EDCD 273**
Edsel / Apr '91 / Pinnacle / ADA.

Waite, John

ESSENTIAL JOHN WAITE
Head above the waves / Piece of action / Broken heart / Love don't prove I'm right / Love is a rose to me / White lightning / Run to Mexico / World in a bottle / Union Jack / Jesus are you there / Darker side of town / Rock 'n' roll is alive and well / Gonna be somebody / White heat / Make it happen / Change / Mr. Wonderful / If anybody had a heart / Missing you
CD ______ **CDCHR 1864**
Chrysalis / Oct '92 / EMI.

NO BRAKES
Saturday night / Missing you / Dark side of the sun / Restless heart / Tears / Euroshima / Dreamtime - shake it up / For your love / Love collision
CD ______ **NSPCD 514**
Connoisseur / Jun '95 / Pinnacle.

Waits, Tom

ASYLUM YEARS
Diamonds on my windshield / Looking for the heart of Saturday night / Martha / Ghosts of Saturday night / Grapefruit moon / Small change / Burma shave / I never talk to strangers / Tom Traubert's blues / Blue valentines / Potter's field / Kentucky Avenue / Somewhere / Ruby's arms
CD ______ **960 494-2**
Asylum / Oct '86 / Warner Music.

BIG TIME
CD ______ **ITWCD 4**
Island / Sep '88 / PolyGram.

BLACK RIDER
CD ______ **CID 8021**
Island / Nov '93 / PolyGram.

BLUE VALENTINE
Red shoes by the drugstore / Christmas card from a hooker in Minneapolis / Romeo is bleeding / Twenty nine dollars / Wrong side of the road / Whistlin' past the graveyard / Kentucky Avenue / Sweet little bullet from a pretty blue gun / Title track
CD ______ **7559605332**
WEA / Oct '94 / Warner Music.

BONE MACHINE
Earth died screaming / Dirt in the ground / Such a scream / All stripped down / Who are you this time / Ocean / Jesus gonna be here / Little rain / In the colosseum / Going out West / Murder in the red barn / Black wings / Whistle down the wind / I don't wanna grow up / Let me get up on it / That feel
CD ______ **CID 9993**
Island / Aug '92 / PolyGram.

CLOSING TIME
Ol' 55 / Hope that I don't fall in love with you / Virginia Avenue / Old shoes / Midnight lullaby / Martha / Rosie / Ice cream man / Little trip to heaven / Grapefruit moon / Closing time
CD ______ **9608362**
WEA / Feb '93 / Warner Music.

EARLY YEARS VOL. 1
CD ______ **EDCD 332**
Edsel / Jul '91 / Pinnacle / ADA.

EARLY YEARS VOL. 2
Hope I don't fall in love / Ol 55 / Mockingbird / In between love / Blue skies / Nobody / I want you / Shiver me timbers / Grapefruit moon / Diamonds on my windshield / Please call me, baby / So it goes / Old shoes
CD ______ **EDCD 371**
Edsel / Feb '93 / Pinnacle / ADA.

FOREIGN AFFAIRS
Cinny's waltz / Muriel / I never talk to strangers / Sight for sore eyes / Potter's field / Burma shave / Barber shop / Foreign affair
CD ______ **7559606182**
WEA / Feb '95 / Warner Music.

FRANKS WILD YEARS
Hang on St. Christopher / Straight to the top (Rhumba) / Blow wind blow / Temptation / I'll be gone / Yesterday is here / Please wake me up / Franks theme / More than rain / Way down in the hole / Straight to the top / I'll take New York / Telephone call from Istanbul / Cold cold ground / Train song / Innocent when you dream
CD ______ **IMCD 50**
Island / Jun '89 / PolyGram.

HEART ATTACK AND VINE
In shades / Saving all my love for you / Downtown / Jersey girl / Till the money runs out / On the nickel / Mr. Seigal / Ruby's arms / Heart attack and vine
CD ______ **755960547-2**
Elektra / May '93 / Warner Music.

HEART OF SATURDAY NIGHT, THE
New coat of paint / San Diego serenade / Semi suite / Shiver me timbers / Diamonds on my windshield / Looking for the heart of Saturday night / Fumblin' with the blues / Please call me, baby / Depot depot / Drunk on the moon / Ghosts of Saturday night
CD ______ **755960597-2**
WEA / Jan '89 / Warner Music.

NIGHTHAWKS AT THE DINER
Emotional weather report / On a foggy night / Eggs and sausages / Better off without a wife / Nighthawk postcards / Warm beer and cold women / Putnam county / Spare parts 1 / Nobody / Big Joe and Phantom 309
CD ______ **960620 2**
WEA / '89 / Warner Music.

RAIN DOGS
Singapore / Clap hands / Cemetery polka / Jockey full of Bourbon / Tango till they're sore / Big black Maria / Diamonds and gold / Hang down your head / Time / Rain dogs / Midtown / Ninth and headpin / Gun Street girl / Union Square / Blind love / Walking Spanish / Downtown train / Bride of raindog / Anywhere I lay my head
CD ______ **IMCD 49**
Island / Aug '89 / PolyGram.

RAINDOGS/ SWORDFISHTROMBONES
CD Set ______ **ITSCD 5**
Island / Nov '92 / PolyGram.

SMALL CHANGE
Tom Traubert's blues / Step right up / Jitterbug boy / I wish I was in New Orleans / Piano has been drinking / Invitation to the blues / Pasties and a G string / Bad liver and a broken heart / One that got away / Small change / I can't wait to get off work
CD ______ **960612 2**
WEA / '89 / Warner Music.

STEP RIGHT UP (The Songs Of Tom Waits) (Various Artists)
Old shoes / Mockin' bird / Better off without a wife / Red shoes by the drugstore / Step right up / Downtown / Big Joe & the Phantom 309 / You can't unring a bell / Pasties & a G-string / Christmas card from a hooker in Minneapolis / Ol' 55 / Jersey girl / Martha / Ruby's arms / I hope that I don't fall in love with you
CD ______ **CARCD 30**
Caroline / Nov '95 / EMI.

SWORDFISHTROMBONES
Underground / Shore leave / Dave the butcher / Johnsburg, Illinois / Sixteen shells from A 30.6 / Town with no cheer / In the neighbourhood / Just another sucker on the vine / Frank's wild years / Swordfishtrombones / Down down down / Soldier's things / Gin soaked boy / Trouble's braids / Rainbirds
CD ______ **IMCD 48**
Island / Jun '89 / PolyGram.

Wake

MASKED
CD ______ **CLEO 9187-2**
Cleopatra / Mar '94 / Disc.

TIDAL WAVE OF HYPE
Shallow end / Obnoxious Kevin / Crasher / Selfish / Provincial disco / I told you so / Britain / Back of beyond / Solo project / Down on your knees / Britain (remix) / Big nose big deal
CD ______ **SARAH 618CD**
Sarah / Mar '95 / Vital.

Wake RSV

PRAYERS TO A BROKEN STONE
CD ______ **PLASCD 025**
Plastic Head / Mar '90 / Plastic Head.

Wakely, Graham

MANHATTAN SKYLINE
Winter games / Fascination / Solitaire / Orange coloured sky / Girl from Corsica / Devil's gallop / You make me feel brand new / Skylark / Mornings at seven / Blaze away / Missing / Love theme from St. Elmo's Fire / Manhattan skyline
CD ______ **MSKY 001**
Wakely Graham / Apr '94 / Wakely Graham.

Wakeman, Adam

100 YEARS OVERTIME
See what you see / Too late to cry / Take my hand / 100 Years overtime / Hold on / Here with me / More to say / Too long dead / Only me missing / Someone / Sound of a broken heart / Lonely heart tonight
CD ______ **RWCD 26**
President / Nov '94 / Grapevine / Target/ BMG / Jazz Music / President.

SOLILOQUY
Words of love / Don't say goodbye / There go the angels / One way down / Soliloquy / Little justice / Edge of my heart / Soliloquy part II: The act is over / No time for your love no more / Something strange / Save a tear for me
CD ______ **RWCD 15**
President / Nov '93 / Grapevine / Target/ BMG / Jazz Music / President.

Wakeman, Rick

2000 AD INTO THE FUTURE
Into the future / Toward peace / 2000 AD / A.D.Rock / Time tunnel / Robot dance / New beginning / Forward past / Seventh dimension
CD ______ **RWCD 21**
President / Nov '93 / Grapevine / Target/ BMG / Jazz Music / President.

AFRICAN BACH
African Bach / Message of mine / My homeland / Liberty / Anthem / Brainstorm / Face in the crowd / Just a game / Africa east / Don't touch the merchandise
CD ______ **RWCD 20**
President / Nov '93 / Grapevine / Target/ BMG / Jazz Music / President.

ASPIRANT SUNRISE
Thoughts of love / Gentle breezes / Whispering cornfields / Peaceful beginnings / Dewy morn / Musical dreams / Distant thoughts / Dove / When time stood still / Secret moments / Peaceful
CD ______ **RWCD 17**
President / Nov '93 / Grapevine / Target/ BMG / Jazz Music / President.

ASPIRANT SUNSET
Floating clouds / Still waters / Dream / Sleeping village / Sea of tranquility / Peace / Sunset / Dying embers / Dusk / Evening moods
CD ______ **RWCD 18**
President / Nov '93 / Grapevine / Target/ BMG / Jazz Music / President.

ASPIRANT SUNSHADOWS
Nightwind / Churchyard / Tall shadows / Shadowlove / Melancholy mood / Mount Fuji by night / Hidden reflections / Evening harp / Moonraker pond / Last lamplight / Japanese sunshadows
CD ______ **RWCD 19**
President / Nov '93 / Grapevine / Target/ BMG / Jazz Music / President.

BLACK KNIGHT AT THE COURT OF FERDINAND
CD ______ **WCPCD 1009**
President / Jun '94 / Grapevine / Target/ BMG / Jazz Music / President.

CLASSIC, THE
CD ______ **CDSGP 115**
Prestige / Apr '94 / Total/BMG.

CLASSICAL CONNECTION I, THE
Gone but not forgotten / After the ball / Elgin mansions / Sea horses / Merlin the magician / Catherine of Aragon / Catherine Howard / 1984 Overture / Hymn / Finale incorporating Julia
CD ______ **RWCD 13**
President / Nov '93 / Grapevine / Target/ BMG / Jazz Music / President.

CLASSICAL CONNECTION II, THE
Eleanor Rigby / Birdman of Alcatraz / Day after the fair / Opus 1 / Painter / Summertime / Dancing in heaven / A garden of music / Mackintosh / Farandol / Pont Street / Art and soul
CD ______ **RWCD 14**
President / May '93 / Grapevine / Target/ BMG / Jazz Music / President.

COUNTRY AIRS
Lakeland walks / Wild moors / Harvest festival / Glade / Dandelion dreams / Ducks and drinks / Green to gold / Stepping stones / Morning haze / Waterfalls / Spring / Quiet valleys / Nature trails / Heather carpets
CD ______ **NAGE 10CD**
Art Of Landscape / Apr '86 / Sony.

COUNTRY AIRS (1992 version)
CD ______ **RWCD 10**
President / Nov '93 / Grapevine / Target/ BMG / Jazz Music / President.

FAMILY ALBUM, THE
Adam (Rick's second son) / Black beauty (black rabbit) / Jemma (Rick and Nina's daughter) / Benjamin (Rick's third son) / Oscar (Rick and Nina's son) / Oliver (Rick's eldest son) / Nina (Rick's wife) / Wiggles (black and white rabbit) (Only on cassette and CD.) / Chloe / Kookie / Tilly / Mum / Dad / Day after the fair / MacKintosh
CD ______ **RWCD 4**
President / Nov '93 / Grapevine / Target/ BMG / Jazz Music / President.

GREATEST HITS
CD Set ______ **CDFRL 001**
Fragile / Nov '93 / Grapevine.

HERITAGE SUITE
Chasms / Thorwald's cross / St. Michael's isle / Spanish head / Ayres / Mona's isle / Dhoon / Bee orchid / Chapel hill / Curraghs / Painted lady / Peregrine falcon
CD ______ **RWCD 16**
President / Nov '93 / Grapevine / Target/ BMG / Jazz Music / President.

JOURNEY TO THE CENTRE OF THE EARTH
Journey / Battle
CD ______ **5500614**
Spectrum/Karussell / May '93 / PolyGram / THE.

LIVE AT HAMMERSMITH
Arthur / Three wives / Journey / Merlin
CD ______ **RWCD 2**
President / Nov '93 / Grapevine / Target/ BMG / Jazz Music / President.

LIVE ON THE TEST
Recollection / Part IV, the realisation / Sir Lancelot and the black knight / Part III, the spaceman / Catherine Parr / Prisoner / Merlin the magician
CD ______ **WHISCD 007**
Windsong / Oct '94 / Pinnacle.

MYTHS AND LEGENDS OF KING ARTHUR, THE
Arthur / Lady of the lake / Guinevere / Sir Lancelot and the black knight / Merlin the magician / Sir Galahad / Last battle
CD ______ **CDMID 135**
A&M / Oct '92 / PolyGram.

NEW GOSPELS, THE (2CD Set)
CD Set ______ **HRHCD 001**
OTL Music / Jan '96 / Grapevine.

NIGHT AIRS
CD ______ **RWCD 9**
President / Nov '93 / Grapevine / Target/ BMG / Jazz Music / President.

NO EXPENSE SPARED (Wakeman, Rick & Adam)
No expense spared / Dylic / It's your move / No one cares / Luck of the draw / Dream the world away / Is it the spring / Nothing ever changes / Number 10 / Jungle / Children of Chernobyl / Find the time
CD ______ **RWCD 22**
President / Nov '93 / Grapevine / Target/ BMG / Jazz Music / President.

OFFICIAL LIVE ALBUM (Wakeman, Rick & Adam)
Lure of the wild / Catherine Howard / Eleanor Rigby / Past and present / Myths and legends of King Arthur / Catherine Parr / Journey to the centre of the Earth / Paint it black
CD ______ **CYCL 006**
Cyclops / May '94 / Pinnacle.

PHANTOM POWER
CD ______ **RIOCD 1003**
Rio Digital / Nov '92 / Grapevine.

PIANO ALBUM, THE
CD ______ **ESSCD 322**
Essential / Nov '95 / Total/BMG.

PRIVATE COLLECTION
Battle / Penny's piece / Pearl and dean piano concerto / Piece for granny / Steamhole dance (parts 1 and 2) / Mountain / Warmongers / Aberlady / Now a word from our sponsor
CD ______ **RWCD 23**
President / Apr '94 / Grapevine / Target/ BMG / Jazz Music / President.

ROCK 'N' ROLL PROPHET...PLUS
Return of the prophet / I'm so straight I'm a weirdo / Dragon / Dark / Alpha sleep / Maybe '80 / March of the child soldiers / Early warning / Spy of '55 / Stalemate / Do you believe in fairies / Rock 'n' roll prophet
CD ______ **RWCD 12**
President / Nov '93 / Grapevine / Target/ BMG / Jazz Music / President.

ROMANCE OF THE VICTORIAN AGE (Wakeman, Rick & Adam)
Burlington Arcade / If only / Last teardrop / Still dreaming / Memories of the Victorian age / Lost in words / Tale of love / Mysteries unfold / Forever in my heart / Days of wonder / Swans / Another mellow day / Dance of the elves
CD ______ **RWCD 25**
President / Nov '94 / Grapevine / Target/ BMG / Jazz Music / President.

SEA AIRS
Harbour lights / Pirate / Storm clouds / Lost at sea / Mermaid / Waves / Fisherman / Flying fish / Marie Celeste / Time and tide / Lone sailor / Sailor's lament
CD ______ **RWCD 8**
President / Nov '93 / Grapevine / Target/ BMG / Jazz Music / President.

SEVEN WONDERS OF THE WORLD, THE
Pharos of Alexandra / Colossus of Rhodes / Pyramids of Eygpt / Hanging gardens of Babylon / Temple of Artemis / Statue of Zeus / Mausoleum at Halicarnassus
CD ______ **RWCD 27**
President / Jun '95 / Grapevine / Target/ BMG / Jazz Music / President.

SILENT NIGHTS
Tell 'em all you know / Opening line / Opera / Man's best friend / Glory boys / Silent nights / Ghost of a rock 'n' roll star / Dancer / Elgin mansions / That's who I am
CD ______ **RWCD 1**
President / Nov '93 / Grapevine / Target/ BMG / Jazz Music / President.

SIX WIVES OF HENRY VIII, THE
Catherine of Aragon / Ann of Cleves / Catherine Howard / Jane Seymour / Anne Boleyn / Catherine Parr
CD ______ **CDMID 136**
A&M / Oct '92 / PolyGram.

SOFTSWORD (KING JOHN AND THE MAGNA CHARTER)
Magna charter / After prayers / Battle sonata / Siege / Rochester collage / Story of love (King John) / March of time / Don't fly away / Isabella / Softsword / Hymn of hope
CD _____ RWCD 24
President / Apr '94 / Grapevine / Target/ BMG / Jazz Music / President.

SUITE OF GODS (Wakeman, Rick & Ramon Ramedios)
CD _____ RWCD 5
President / Nov '93 / Grapevine / Target/ BMG / Jazz Music / President.

SURREAL STATE CIRCUS OF IMAGINATION
CD _____ DSHLCD 7018
D-Sharp / Jun '95 / Pinnacle.

TIME MACHINE
Custer's last stand / Ocean city / Angel of time (Extended version CD only) / Slaveman (Extended version on CD only) / Ice / Open up your eyes / Elizabethan rock / Make me a woman (Extended version on CD only) / Rock age (Extended version on CD only)
CD _____ RWCD 7
President / Nov '93 / Grapevine / Target/ BMG / Jazz Music / President.

VISIONS
Fantasy / Peace of mind / Innermost thoughts / Vision of light / Higher planes / Astral traveller / Dream on / Thought waves / Drifting patterns / Future memories / Levitation / Moondreams
CD _____ RWCD 28
President / Oct '95 / Grapevine / Target/ BMG / Jazz Music / President.

WAKEMAN WITH WAKEMAN (Wakeman, Rick & Adam)
Lure of the wild / Beach comber / Meglomania / Rage and rhyme / Sync or swim / Jiggaig / Caesarea / After the atom / Suicide shuffle / Past and present / Paint it black
CD _____ RWCD 11
President / Feb '93 / Grapevine / Target/ BMG / Jazz Music / President.

ZODIAQUE (Wakeman, Rick & Tony Fernandez)
CD _____ RWCD 6
President / Nov '93 / Grapevine / Target/ BMG / Jazz Music / President.

Wakenins, Ulf

HEART OF MINE
CD _____ DRGCD 91416
DRG / Jul '94 / New Note.

NEW YORK MEETING
Bernie's tune / Way you look tonight / Crazy he calls me / Nature of business / Spartacus / New York meeting / Jet lag / Angel eyes / Georgia on my mind
CD _____ CDLR 45082
L&R / Jul '94 / New Note.

Wakeooloo

HEAR NO EVIL
CD _____ EFA 262072
Pravda / Dec '94 / SRD.

WHAT ABOUT IT
CD _____ EFA 061972
House In Motion / Jul '95 / SRD.

Walcott, Collin

GRAZING DREAMS
Song of the morrow / Gold sun / Swarm / Mountain morning / Jewel ornament / Grazing dreams / Samba tala / Moon lake
CD _____ 8278662
ECM / Jun '86 / New Note.

WORKS: COLLIN WALCOTT
Scimitar / Song of the morrow / Like that of sky / Travel by night / Godumada / Hey da boom lullaby / Prancing / Cadona / Awakening / Padma / Travel by day
CD _____ 8372762
ECM / Jun '89 / New Note.

Waldo, Elisabeth

SACRED RITES
Serpent and the eagle / Within the temple of macuilzochitl / Papaganga lament / Ritual of the human scarifice / Festival of Texcatlipoca / Song for the mountain spirits / Penitente procession / Land of the sun kings / Song of the chasqui / Incan festival dance / Making chica / Balsa boat / Swinging the quipu / Saycuscui (weary stones) / Dance of the nustas
CD _____ GNPD 2225
GNP Crescendo / Oct '95 / Silva Screen.

Waldo, Terry

TERRY WALDO AND THE GOTHAM CITY BAND, VOL. 2 (Waldo, Terry & The Gotham City Band)
CD _____ SOSCD 1201
Stomp Off / Oct '92 / Jazz Music / Wellard.

Waldron, Mal

BLUES FOR LADY DAY (Personal Tribute To Billie Holiday)
Blues for Lady Day / Just friends / Don't blame me / You don't know what love is / Man I love / You're my thrill / Strange fruit / Easy living / Mean to me
CD _____ BLC 760193
Black Lion / Jun '94 / Jazz Music / Cadillac / Wellard / Koch.

CROWD SCENE (Waldron, Mal Quintet)
CD _____ 121218-2
Soul Note / Nov '92 / Harmonia Mundi / Wellard / Cadillac.

FREE AT LAST (Waldron, Mal Trio)
Rat now / 1-3-234 / Willow weep for me / Balladina / Rock my soul / Boo
CD _____ 8313322
ECM / Aug '89 / New Note.

LEFT ALONE '86 (Waldron, Mal & Jackie McLean)
CD _____ K32Y 6167
King/Paddle Wheel / Oct '88 / New Note.

LIVE AT DE KAVE
CD _____ SER 01
Serene / Mar '90 / Cadillac.

MUCH MORE (Waldron, Mal & Marion Brown)
CD _____ FRLCD 010
Freelance / Oct '92 / Harmonia Mundi / Cadillac / Koch.

NO MORE TEARS (FOR LADY DAY)
Yesterdays / No more tears / Melancholy waltz / Solitude / Love me or leave me / All night through / As time goes by / Smoke gets in your eyes / Alone together
CD _____ CDSJP 328
Timeless Jazz / Aug '90 / New Note.

OUR COLLINE'S A TREASURE
CD _____ 121198-2
Soul Note / May '91 / Harmonia Mundi / Wellard / Cadillac.

QUADROLOGUE AT UTOPIA, VOL. 1 (Waldron, Mal Quartet & Jim Pepper)
CD _____ 888118
Tutu / Mar '91 / Vital/SAM.

SONGS OF LOVE AND REGRET (Waldron, Mal & Marion Brown)
CD _____ FRLCD 006
Freelance / Oct '92 / Harmonia Mundi / Cadillac / Koch.

SUPER QUARTET - LIVE AT SWEET BASIL, THE
CD _____ K32Y 6208
King/Paddle Wheel / Feb '89 / New Note.

WALDRON-HASLAM (Waldron, Mal & George Haslam)
CD _____ SLAMCD 305
Slam / Oct '94 / Cadillac.

WHERE ARE YOU (Waldron, Mal Quintet)
CD _____ 121248-2
Soul Note / May '94 / Harmonia Mundi / Wellard / Cadillac.

Walk Away

SATURATION
Saturation / Many kochanas / For you / Bobok / Softly / Sheet / She's like a sexmachine / Joy is better / Sambula
CD _____ IOR 770242
In & Out / Sep '95 / Vital/SAM.

Walkabouts

JACK CANDY
CD _____ SPCD 251
Sub Pop / Jan '93 / Disc.

NEW WEST HOTEL
CD _____ SPCD 81 252
Sub Pop / Feb '93 / Disc.

SATISFIED MIND
CD _____ SPCD 116-294
Sub Pop / Nov '93 / Disc.

SEE BEAUTIFUL RATTLESNAKE GARDENS
CD _____ GRCD 335
Glitterhouse / May '95 / Direct / ADA.

SETTING THE WOODS ON FIRE
CD _____ SP 128 319-2
Sub Pop / May '94 / Disc.

Walker

STRIKE WHILE THE IRON'S HOT
Strike while the iron's hot / Mon ami / Don't look over your shoulder / It all takes time / Ships that pass in the night / Everyone was a baby / Curacao - blue sky / Tender zone / Looking for an answer / Belong / Month of Sundays / Tudor sweet
CD _____ ZYZ 077CD
Zyzzle / Jan '94 / Zyzzle Records.

Walker Brothers

AFTER THE LIGHTS GO OUT (The Best Of The Walker Brothers 1965-1967)
Love her / Make it easy on yourself / First love never dies / My ship is coming in /

Deadlier than the male / Another tear falls / Baby you don't have to tell me / After the lights go out / Mrs. Murphy / In my room / Arcangel / Sun ain't gonna shine anymore / Saddest night in the world / Young man cried / Livin' above your head / Stay with me baby / Walking in the rain / Orpheus / I can't let it happen to you / Just say goodbye / Disc and Music Interview / Japanese Interview
CD _____ 8428312
Fontana / May '90 / PolyGram.

GALA
Make it easy on yourself / Summertime / My ship is coming in / Lonely winds / There goes my baby / Livin' above your head / Here comes the night / Stay with me baby / No sad songs for me / Sun ain't gonna shine anymore / Land of 1000 dances / (Baby) You don't have to tell me / Dancing in the street / In my rain / Walking in the rain / Just say goodbye
CD _____ 830 212-2
Phonogram / Feb '89 / PolyGram.

NO REGRETS
No regrets / Hold an old friend's hand / Boulder to Birmingham / Walkin' in the sun / Lover's lullaby / I've got to have you / He'll break your heart / Everything that touches you / Lovers / Burn our bridges
CD _____ 983276-2
Pickwick/Sony Collector's Choice / Apr '94 / Carlton Home Entertainment / Pinnacle / Sony.
CD _____ 477354-2
GT / Aug '94 / Sony.

Walker, Big Moose

LIVE AT THE RISING SUN
CD _____ RS 0008CD
Rising Sun / Jul '95 / ADA.

Walker, Billy

CROSS THE BRAZOS AT WACO
Headin' for heartaches / I'm gonna take my heart away from you / You're gonna pay with a broken heart / You didn't try and didn't care / Too many times / Dirt 'neath your feet / I guess I'll have to die / Anything your heart desires / Last kiss is the sweetest / Alcohol love / I ain't got no roses / Beautiful brown eyes / Don't tell a soul / She's got honky tonk blood in her veins / What would you do / Always think of you / Ting a ling a school pickney sing ting / Fifteen hugs past midnight / Millie darling / Anything your heart desires (2) / What makes me love you (like I do) / One heart's beatin', one heart's cheatin' / If I should live that long / Stolen love / Who took my ring from your finger / True love's so hard to find / You have my heart now / You know what did / One you hurt / I can tell / I didn't have the nerve it took to leave / Don't let your pride break your heart / Mexican Joe / Time will tell / Headin' for heartaches (2) / It hurts too much to laugh (and I'm too big) / I got lost along the way / I can't keep the girls away / Thank you for calling / Candlelight / Pretend you just don't know me / I'm a fool to care / Going going gone / Kissing you / You're the only good thing that's happened to me / Let me hear from you / Let me hear from you (2) / Hey / Fool that I am / Record / Which one of us is to blame / Let's make memories tonight / Whirlpool / Go ahead and make me cry / Most important thing / Can't you love me just a little / Blue mountain waltz / Why does it have to be / So far / Little baggy britches / Leavin' on my mind / I'll never stand in your way / Untamed heart / Especially for fools / If you were happy (then I'm satisfied) / Headin' down the wrong highway / On my mind again / Viva la Matador / I care no more / Image of me / I need it / Where my baby goes she goes with me / Put your hand in mine / It'll take a while / It's doggone tough on me / Ghost of a promise / Love's got a hold on me / I dreamed of an old love affair / Mr. Heartache / I thought about you / Storm within my heart / One way give and take / Woman like you / I call it heaven / Forever / Farewell party / Changed my mind / Gotta find a way / I'll be true to you / Little lover / I wish you love / Yes, I've made it / Faded lights and lonesome people / Just call me lonesome / Let's think about living / Alone with you / They'll never take love from me / I take the chance / Guess things happen that way / Remember me, I'm the one who loves you / Molly darling (2) / Rockin' alone in an old rocking chair / Gonna find me a bluebird / There stands the glass / Jambalaya / Charlie's shoes / Funny how time slips away / Joey's back in town / Charlie's shoes (2) / Wild colonial boy / I know I'm lying / Next voice you hear / Willie the weeper / It's me not them / Lovely hula hands / Beggin' for trouble / Plaything / I've got a new heartache / Give me back my heart / Ancient history / Man who had everything / These arms of mine / Throw me out / Storm of love / That would sure go good / Heart be careful / Circumstances / It's lonesome / Morning paper / Coming back for more / Cross the brazos at Waco / Down to my last cigarette / It it pleases you / I'm so miserable without you / Matamoros / Samuel Colt / Blue moonlight / Come a little bit closer / Gun, the gold, the

girl / Blizzard / Pancho villa / Cattle call / Amigo's guitar / Lawman / Buy Juanita some flowers / I'm nothin' to you / Smoky memories / Nobody but a fool / Pretend you don't see me / Don't change
CD Set _____ BCD 15657
Bear Family / Oct '93 / Rollercoaster / Direct / CM / Swift / ADA.

Walker, Billy Jr.

BILLY WALKER JR.
Under the stars / 5th of July / Ballerina dance / Marotta / Hot steel / China girl / Night rider / Add two / Perfect love / Water bells
CD _____ GEFD 24469
Geffen / Mar '92 / BMG.

WALK, THE
Walk / Hourglass / Dream on / Mystery man / Street dancin' / Illusions / Free flight / Fields of stone / Crystal speak to me / Breezes
CD _____ GEFD 24315
Geffen / May '91 / BMG.

Walker, Clay

CLAY WALKER
Dreaming with my eyes open / What's it to you / Silence speaks for itself / How to make a man lonesome / Next step in love / White palace / Money can't buy (the love we had) / Things I should have said / Where do I fit in the picture / Live until I die / I don't know how love starts
CD _____ 74321166762
Giant / Aug '94 / BMG.

IF I COULD MAKE A LIVING
If I could make a living / Melrose Avenue cinema / My heart will never know / What do you want for nothin' / This woman and this man / Boogie till the cows come home / Heartache highway / You make it look so easy / Lose your memory / Money ain't everything / Down by the river
CD _____ 74321250172
Giant / Apr '95 / BMG.

Walker, Dee

JUMP BACK
CD _____ TANGCD 6
Tangerine / Aug '92 / Disc.

Walker, Gordon

PIPE BANDS OF DISTINCTION (Walker, Corporal Gordon)
CD _____ CDMON 804
Monarch / Dec '89 / CM / ADA / Duncans / Direct.

Walker, Ian

CROSSING THE BORDERLINES (Walker, Ian & Setanta)
CD _____ FE 088CD
Fellside / Apr '93 / Target/BMG / Direct / ADA.

Walker Jazz Band

BIG BAND STORY VOLUME 2
CD _____ PV 785093
Disques Pierre Verany / Feb '86 / —

Walker, Jerry Jeff

CHRISTMAS GONZO STYLE
I'll be home for Christmas / White Christmas / Santa Claus is coming to town / Christmas song / Here comes Santa Claus (medley - Up on the housetop) / Rudolph the red nosed reindeer / Jingle bells / Walking in a winter wonderland / Frosty the snowman / Jingle bell rock / Twelve days of Christmas / We wish you a Merry Christmas
CD _____ RCD 10312
Rykodisc / Nov '94 / Vital / ADA.

DRIFTIN' WAY OF LIFE
Driftin' way of life / Morning song to Sally / Shell game / Ramblin' scramblin' / No roots in ramblin' / Old road / North Cumberland blues / Let it ride / Fading lady / Gertrude / Dust on my boots
CD _____ VND 73124
Vanguard / Complete/Pinnacle / Discovery.

GYPSY SONGMAN
Gypsy songman / David and me / Mr. Bojangles / Hands on the wheel / Ramblin' hearts / Then came the children / She knows her daddy sings / Long afternoons / Borderline / Driftin' way of life / Hard livin' / Railroad lady / Jaded lover / Rain just falls / Night rider's lament / We were kind of crazy then / Cadillac cowboy / Pass it on / Charlie Dunn / Hill country rain
CD _____ RCD 20071
Rykodisc / May '92 / Vital / ADA.

HILL COUNTRY RAIN
CD _____ RCD 10241
Rykodisc / Jun '94 / Vital / ADA.

LIVE AT GRUENE HALL
Lovin' makes livin' worthwhile / Pickup truck song / Long long time / I feel like Hank Williams tonight / Man with the big hat / Quiet faith of man / Little bird / Woman in Texas / Rodeo wind / Trashy wind

CD _____ **RCD 10123**
Rykodisc / May '92 / Vital / ADA.

MR. BOJANGLES
Gypsy songman / Mr. Bojangles / Little bird / I makes money (money don't make me) / Round and round / My old man / Ballad of the hulk / Broken toys / Mexico Mexico / I keep changin' / I makes money (money makes me change)

CD _____ **8122715182**
East West / Oct '93 / Warner Music.

NAVAJO RUG
Navajo rug / Just to celebrate / Blue mood / Lucky man / Detour / I'm all through throwing good love after bad / Rockin' on the river / Nolan Ryan (a hero to us all) / Flowers in the snow / If I'd loved you then

CD _____ **RCD 10175**
Rykodisc / Jul '91 / Vital / ADA.

VIVA LUCKENBACH
Gettin' by / Viva Luckenbach / Learning to p'like and Luckenbach women's lib / Keep Texas beautiful / What I like about Texas / I'll be here in the morning / Gift / Little man / Some phone numbers / I makes money (money don't make me) / Gonzo compadres / Movin' on

CD _____ **RCD 10268**
Rykodisc / Mar '94 / Vital / ADA.

ROUGH AND READY BOOGIE WOOGIE FOR 4 HANDS (Walker, Jimmy & Erwin Helfer)

CD _____ **TCD 5011**
Testament / Dec '94 / Complete/Pinnacle / ADA / Koch.

I'M IN THE DOG HOUSE
I'm in the dog house / Couche couche and ky-yay / Bullet through my heart / Give me what I want / I left my home / Watch that black cat / Tante Sarah / I screwed up / I'd like to put my hand on that / Seen it for myself / Keep on pushing / Mom and pop waltz

CD _____ **ZNCD 1006**
Zane / Oct '95 / Pinnacle.

ZYDECO FEVER
CD _____ **ZNCD 1004**
Zane / Oct '95 / Pinnacle.

BLUE SOUL
Prove your love / Ain't nothin' goin' on / T.L.C. / Personal baby / Since you've been gone / Alligator / Dead sea / City of angels / I'll get to Heaven on my own

CD _____ **FIENDCD 159**
Demon / Oct '89 / Pinnacle / ADA.

GIFT, THE
One time around / Thin line / 747 / Gift / What about you / Shade tree mechanic / Quarter to three / Mama didn't raise no fools / Everybody's had the blues / Main goal

CD _____ **HCD 8012**
Sound / Jan '89 / Direct / ADA.

LIVE AT SLIM'S
CD _____ **FIENDCD 212**
Demon / Apr '91 / Pinnacle / ADA.

LIVE AT SLIM'S VOL.2
Don't you know / Thin line / One woman / Blue guitar / Shade tree mechanic / 747 / Just a little bit / Brother go ahead and take her / Love at first sight

CD _____ **FIENDCD 716**
Demon / Apr '92 / Pinnacle / ADA.

MY FAVOURITE LENNON/MCCARTNEY (Walker, John & The Digital Sunset)
CD _____ **C5MCD 565**
See For Miles/C5 / Jun '91 / Pinnacle.

MY FAVOURITE SINATRA (Walker, John & The Digital Sunset)
New York, New York / Something stupid / Strangers in the night / It's been a long, long time / Five minutes more / Saturday night is the loneliest night of the week / Love and marriage / Three coins in the fountain / It's nice to go travellin' / I'll be seeing you / Nancy with the laughing face / I'm a fool to want you / Come fly with me / Witchcraft / Nice 'n' easy / London by night / Tender trap / Begin the beguine / I've got you under my skin / Night and day / All the way / High hopes / If you never come to me / Hey jealous lover / Lady is a tramp / My kind of town / Young at heart / My way

CD _____ **C5CD-530**
See For Miles/C5 / May '89 / Pinnacle.

PLAYS MY FAVOURITE JOHN WALKER ORIGINALS (Walker, John & The Digital Sunset)
CD _____ **C5MCD 575**
See For Miles/C5 / '91 / Pinnacle.

SUMMER SONG/BY SPECIAL REQUEST
Water babies / I got rhythm / S'wonderful / On the street where you live / Tritsch-tratsch polka / Island in the sun / Jamaica farewell / Mon amour / Jive alive / Forgotten

dreams / Theme from "New York, New York" / Lonely shepherd / John & Julie / Chanson de matin / My favourite things / Ave Maria / Caribbean melody / In the mood / Little brown jug / American patrol / Chattanooga choo choo / Lambada / We'll be together again / Amor / If (they made me a king) / Weep they will / I left my heart in San Francisco

CD _____ **C5CD 629**
See For Miles/C5 / Oct '95 / Pinnacle.

TIME TO RELAX/LIVE AT TURNER'S
Atlantis / Seasons / Elizabethan serenade / Thousand and one nights / Fleur de Paris / Pastoral symphony / Jesu joy of my soul / Minuet in G / Morning / Skater's waltz / Valse des fleurs / Morgenblaetter / Wiener blut / I know not where / Stars fell on Alabama / People on the hills / Hooked in space / 2001 / Close encounters of the third kind / Star Wars / Cair paravel / Blue danube / Liebestraum / Artist's life / Cuckoo waltz / Voices of spring / Nocturne in E flat / Wine, women and song / Coppelia valse / Tales from the Vienna Woods / March of the toys / Yellow bird / Stranger in paradise / Evening clam ski Sunday / Love changes everything / Till / Jesu joy of man's desiring / Village parade / Valentino / Classical romance / Aces high / Meditation / Tico tico / Valse romantique / Sunrise / In a monastery garden / May you always

CD _____ **C5CD 626**
See For Miles/C5 / Jul '95 / Pinnacle.

UNCHAINED MELODIES
Unchained melody / Any dream will do / Wooden heart / Forever and ever / One day in your life / Ferry across the Mersey / Nothings gonna change my love for you / Annie's song / Clair / House of the rising sun / Puppet on a string / Take my breath away / Summer holiday / I just called to say I love you / Lady in red / Sacrifice / Those were the days / In the summertime / Hello / Dancing queen / Uptown girl / Wombling song

CD _____ **C5JCD 615**
See For Miles/C5 / Apr '95 / Pinnacle.

SWEAR TO TELL THE TRUTH (Walker, Johnny 'Big Moose')
CD _____ **JSPCD 242**
JSP / Oct '91 / ADA / Target/BMG / Direct / Cadillac / Complete/Pinnacle.

19 GREATEST HITS: JUNIOR WALKER
CD _____ **530033-2**
Motown / Jan '93 / PolyGram.

BEST OF JUNIOR WALKER & THE ALL STARS, THE (Walker, Junior & The All Stars)
CD Set _____ **530293-2**
Motown / Apr '94 / PolyGram.

SHAKE AND FINGERPOP
Shotgun / How sweet it is (to be loved by you) / Home cooking / Money / Pucker up buttercup / What does it take (to win your love) / Come see about me / Hip city / Cleo's mood / Shake and fingerpop / Shoot your shot

CD _____ **CDBM 072**
Blue Moon / Apr '89 / Magnum Music Group / Greensleeves / Hot Shot / ADA / Cadillac / Discovery.

DANCING ON THE EDGE OF THE WORLD
CD _____ **WD 0109**
Windham Hill Jazz / Mar '92 / New Note.

FIRE IN THE LAKE
CD _____ **WD 0117**
Windham Hill Jazz / Mar '92 / New Note.

WHATEVER MOOD YOU'RE IN
Whatever mood you're in / Jemima surrender / Dying to live / Come on down / Roadmaster / Give it everything you got / All about you / Behind closed doors / Chop no wood / Freedom for the stallion

CD _____ **RTCD 901178**
Line / Apr '92 / CM / Grapevine / ADA / Conifer / Direct.

BIG BLUES FROM TEXAS (Walker, Philip & Otis Grand)
CD _____ **JSPCD 248**
JSP / Nov '92 / ADA / Target/BMG / Direct / Cadillac / Complete/Pinnacle.

BLUES
How many more years / 90 proof / What'd you hope to gain / Don't be afraid of the dark / Big rear window / Her own keys / Talk to that man / Sometime girl / I had a dream

CD _____ **FIENDCD 128**
Demon / Oct '88 / Pinnacle / ADA.

BOTTOM OF THE TOP, THE
I can't lose (with the stuff I use) / Tin Pan Alley / Hello central / Hello my darling / Laughin' and clownin' / Crazy girl / It's all

in your mind / Bottom of the top / Hey hey baby's gone / Crying time

CD _____ **FIENDCD 158**
Demon / Feb '90 / Pinnacle / ADA.

SOMEDAY YOU'LL HAVE THESE BLUES
CD _____ **HCD 8032**
Hightone / Sep '94 / ADA / Koch.

WORKING GIRL BLUES
CD _____ **CDBT 117**
Rounder / Aug '95 / CM / Direct / ADA / Cadillac.

IN CONCERT
CD _____ **BRAM 199016-2**
Brambus / Nov '93 / ADA / Direct.

BOY CHILD
Plague / Such a small love / Plastic palace people / Big Louis / Seventh seal / Old man's back again / Little things (that keep us together) / Girls from the streets / Copenhagen / War is over / Montague Terrace (in blue) / Amorous Humphrey Plugg / Bridge / We came through / Boy child / Prologue / Time operator / It's raining today / On your own again / Rope and the colt

CD _____ **8428322**
Fontana / May '90 / PolyGram.

CLIMATE OF HUNTER, THE
Rawhide / Dealer / Sleepwalkers woman / Blanket roll blues

CD _____ **CDV 2303**
Virgin / Nov '89 / EMI.

NO REGRETS - THE BEST OF SCOTT WALKER (Walker, Scott & The Walker Brothers)
No regrets / Make it easy on yourself / Sun ain't gonna shine anymore / My ship is comin' in / Joanna / Lights of Cincinatti / Another tear falls / Boy child / Montague Terrace in blue / Jackie / Stay with me baby / If you go away / First love never dies / Love her / Walking in the rain / Baby you don't have to tell me / Deadlier than the male / We're all alone

CD _____ **5108312**
Fontana / Jan '92 / PolyGram.

SCOTT
CD _____ **510879-2**
Fontana / Feb '92 / PolyGram.

SCOTT 2
CD _____ **510880-2**
Fontana / Feb '92 / PolyGram.

SCOTT 3
CD _____ **510881-2**
Fontana / Aug '92 / PolyGram.

SCOTT 4
Seventh seal / On your own again / World's strongest man / Angels of ashes / Boy child / Hero of the war / Old mans back again / Duchess / Get behind me / Rhymes of goodbye

CD _____ **510882-2**
Fontana / Aug '92 / PolyGram.

SINGS JACQUES BREL
Mathilde / Amsterdam / Jackie / My death / Next / Girl and the dogs / If you go away / Funeral tango / Sons of

CD _____ **838212-2**
Fontana / Sep '92 / PolyGram.

TILT
Farmer in the city / Quadfighter / Deaths: see bouncer / Manhattan / Face on breast / Bolivia '95 / Patriot / Tilt / Rosary

CD _____ **5268592**
Fontana / May '95 / PolyGram.

VERY SPECIAL COLLECTION, A (Walker, Scott & The Walker Brothers)
No regrets / Nite flights / We're all alone / Boulder to Birmingham / Ride me down easy / Lines / I'll be home / Brand new Tennesse waltz / Sundown / Many rivers to cross / No easy way down / Just one smile / Delta dawn / We had it all / Burn our bridges / Shut out

CD _____ **PWKS 4165**
Carlton Home Entertainment / Sep '93 / Carlton Home Entertainment.

LAMB'S BREAD
CD _____ **GRELCD 119**
Greensleeves / May '90 / Total/BMG / Jetstar / SRD.

COMPLETE CAPITOL BLACK & WHITE RECORDINGS, THE
T-Bone blues / I got a break baby / Mean old world / No worry blues (Alt) / No worry blues / Don't leave me baby / Bobby sox baby (Alt) / Bobby sox baby / I'm gonna find my baby / I'm in an awful mood / Don't give me the runaround / Hard pain blues / I know your wig is gone / T-bone jumps again / Call it stormy Monday / She had to let me down / She's my old time used to be / Dream girl blues (Alt) / Dream girl blues / Midnight blues (Alt) / Midnight blues / Long lust lover blues / Long lust lover blues (Alt) / Trifflin /

Woman blues / Long skirt baby blues (Alt) / Long skirt baby blues / Goodbye blues / Too much trouble blues (Alt) / Too much trouble blues / I'm waiting for a call / Hypin' woman blues (Alt) / Hypin' woman blues / So blue blues / On your way blues / Natural blues / That's better for me / First love blues (Alt) / First love blues / Lonesome woman blues (Alt.1) / Lonesome woman blues (Alt.2) / Lonesome woman blues / Vacation blues / Inspiration blues / Description blues (Alt) / Description blues / T-Bone shuffle (Alt) / T-Bone shuffle / That old feelin' is gone / Time seems so long / Prison blues / Hometown blues / Wise man blues (Alt) / Wise man blues / Misfortune blues (Alt) / Misfortune blues / I wish you were mine (Alt) / I wish you were mine / I'm gonna move you out and get somebody else / She's the no sleepin 'est woman (Alt) / She's the no sleepin 'est woman / Plain old down home blues / Born to be no good / Go back to the one you love / I want a little girl / I'm still in love with you / You're my best poker hand / West Side story

CD Set _____ **CDEM 1552**
Capitol Jazz / Jul '95 / EMI.

FUNKY TOWN
Goin' to funky town / Party girl / Why my baby (keep on bothering me) / Jealous woman / Going to build me a playhouse / Long skirt baby blues / Struggling blues / I'm in an awful mood / I wish my baby (would come home at night)

CD _____ **BGOCD 116**
Beat Goes On / Sep '91 / Pinnacle.

GOOD FEELIN'
CD _____ **5197232**
Verve / Feb '94 / PolyGram.

HUSTLE IS ON, THE
CD _____ **NEXCD 124**
Sequel / Jun '90 / BMG.

I WANT A LITTLE GIRL
CD _____ **DD 633**
Delmark / Nov '92 / Hot Shot / ADA / CM / Direct / Cadillac.

LOW DOWN BLUES
Don't leave me baby / I'm gonna find my baby / It's a lowdown dirty deal / I know your wig has gone / T-Bone jumps again / Call it stormy Monday / She's my old time used to be / Midnight blues / Long skirt baby blues / Too much trouble blues / Hypin' woman blues / Natural blues / That's better for me / Lonesome woman blues / Inspiration blues / I wish you were mine / She's the no sleepin 'est woman / Plain old down home blues / Go back to the one you love / You're my best poker hand

CD _____ **CDCHARLY 7**
Charly / Dec '86 / Charly / THE / Cadillac.

STORMY MONDAY
Stormy Monday blues / All night long / My patience keeps running out / Glamour girl / T-Bone's way / That evening train / Louisiana bayou drive / When we were schoolmates / Don't go back to New Orleans / Got to cross the deep blue sea / You'll never find anyone to be a slave like me / Left home / When I was a kid / When I grow up / Long lost lover / Shake it baby

CD _____ **CDINS 5022**
Instant / Feb '90 / Charly.

STORMY MONDAY (2)
Every day I have the blues / I woke up this morning / Stormy Monday blues / Why my baby (keep on bothering me) / Late blues / Sail on / T-Bone blues special / Treat me so slow down / When I grow up / Long lost lover / Shake it baby

CD _____ **CDC 9051**
LRC / Nov '92 / New Note / Harmonia Mundi.

T-BONE BLUES
CD _____ **RSACD 811**
Sequel / Oct '94 / BMG.

T-BONE SHUFFLE (Charly Blues - Masterworks Vol. 14)
I got a break baby / No worry blues / Bobby Sox blues / I'm in an awful mood / Don't give me the runaround / Hard pain blues / Goodbye blues / I'm waiting for your call / First love blues / Born to be no good / Inspiration blues / Description blues / T-Bone shuffle / I want a little girl / I'm still in love with you / West side baby

CD _____ **CDBM 14**
Charly / Apr '92 / Charly / THE / Cadillac.

T-BONE'S THAT WAY
Stormy Monday blues / All night long / My patience keeps running out / Glamor girl / T-Bone's that way / That evening train / Louisiana Bayou drive / When we were schoolmates / Don't go back to New Orleans / You'll never find anyone to be a slave like me / Left home

CD _____ **CDCD 1058**
Charly / Mar '93 / Charly / THE / Cadillac.

WELL DONE
Back on the scene / Good boy / No ball / Please come back to me / Natural ball / Baby / She's a hit / Treat your Daddy well / Further on / Up the road / Why don't my baby treat me right / Afraid to close my eyes

/ She's my old time used to be / I used to be a good boy
CD _____ CDBM 096
Blue Moon / Apr '94 / Magnum Music Group / Greensleeves / Hot Shot / ADA / Cadillac / Discovery.

Walker, Wailin'

WAILIN' WALKER
CD _____ CD 3030
Double Trouble / Oct '92 / CM / Hot Shot.

Walking On Ice

NO MARGIN FOR ERROR
Jealous hearts / Set me free / Today, tomorrow / Thinking man's friend / End of an era / Walk in the rain / What you see, what you hear / Footpump / Loser's waltz / Everyman / Rock
CD _____ CYCL 009
Cyclops / Sep '94 / Pinnacle.

Walking Seeds

BAD ORB...WHIRLING BALL
CD _____ PAPCD 001
Paperhouse / Apr '90 / Disc.

Walking Wounded

HARD TIMES
CD _____ TX 2005CD
Taxim / Jan '94 / ADA.

Wall

JAZZ IN SWEDEN 1985
CD _____ 1312
Caprice / Dec '90 / CM / Complete / Pinnacle / Cadillac / ADA.

Wall, Chris

HONKY TONK HEART
CD _____ RCD 10179
Hannibal / Jul '92 / Vital / ADA.

NO SWEAT
CD _____ RCD 10219
Rykodisc / Mar '92 / Vital / ADA.

Wall Of Sleep

WALL OF SLEEP
CD _____ WO 24CD
Woronzow / Jun '95 / Pinnacle.

Wall Of Voodoo

INDEX MASTERS
Longarm / Passenger / Can't make love / Struggle / Ring of fire / Granma's house / End of an era / Tomorrow / Animal day / Invisible man / Red light / Good, the bad and the ugly / Hang 'em high / Back in flesh / Call box
CD _____ MAUCD 619
Mau Mau / Apr '92 / Pinnacle.

Wallace Brothers

LOVER'S PRAYER (Classic Southern Soul)
Lover's prayer / Love me like I love you / Faith / I'll let nothing seperate me / Who's fooling who / I'll still love you / Precious words / You're mine / One way affair / Bye bye bye / Go on girl / She loves me not / I'll step aside / Hold my hurt for awhile / No more / Darlin' I love you so / Stepping stone / Girl's alright with me / These arms of mine / Talking about my baby / Thanks a lot / Line between love and hate
CD _____ CDKEND 128
Kent / Nov '95 / Pinnacle.

Wallace, Bennie

ART OF THE SAXOPHONE, THE
Edith Head / You go to my head / Rhythm head / Monroe County moon / Thangs / All too soon / Chester leaps in / Prelude to a kiss / Prince Charles
CD _____ CY 1648
Denon / Oct '88 / Conifer.

BIG JIM'S TANGO
CD _____ ENJA 40462
Enja / May '95 / New Note / Vital/SAM.

BRILLIANT CORNERS (Wallace, Bennie & Yosuke Yamashita)
It don't mean a thing if it ain't got that wing / Light blue / P.S. I love you / Night in Tunisia / Brilliant corners / Blues Yamashita / My ideal / Rhythm-a-ning / Another beauty
CD _____ CY 30003
Denon / Sep '88 / Conifer.

PLAYS MONK
Skippy / Ask me now / Evidence / Round Midnight / Straight no chaser / Prelude / Ugly beauty / Variation on a theme (tinkle tinkle)
CD _____ ENJ 30912
Enja / Nov '94 / New Note / Vital/SAM.

Wallace, Ian

MY MUSIC
Roses of Picardy / Limehouse reach / O mistress mine / Long ago in Alcala / Rose of Tralee / Elephant song / Welcome home

/ Margate / When a woman smiles / Laird of Cockpen / Silent worship / Sweethearts and wives / Love is a very light thing / Lazin' / Lookin' river / Armadillo / Very thought of you / Tit willow / For you alone / Ill wind / Who is Sylvia / I'll walk beside you / Mud (the hippopotamus song) / Bonnie Mary of Argyle / Cobbler's song / September song / Spanish lady / This is my lovely day / Reverie
CD _____ PWK 089
Carlton Home Entertainment / Feb '89 / Carlton Home Entertainment.

Wallace, Sippie

WOMEN BE WISE
Women be wise / Trouble everywhere / I roam / Lonesome hours blues / Special delivery blues / Murder gonna be my crime / Gambler's dream / Caldonia blues / You got to know how / Shorty George blues / I'm a mighty tight woman / Bedroom blues / Up the country blues / Suitcase blues
CD _____ ALCD 4810
Alligator / May '93 / Direct / ADA.
CD _____ STCD 8024
Storyville / Dec '94 / Jazz Music / Wellard / CM / Cadillac.

Wallen, Byron

SOUND ADVICE
Time and space / Rhythms of vision / Moonchild / Crazy black / Ngoba (army) / Paradox / Let go and embrace / Sesame Street / Stay open / Sunday calling / Time and space (reprise)
CD _____ BW 063
B&W / Apr '95 / New Note.

Waller, Fats

12TH STREET RAG (Waller, Fats & His Rhythm)
CD _____ MU 5014
Musketeer / Oct '92 / Koch.

AIN'T MISBEHAVIN'
CD _____ GOJCD 53078
Giants of Jazz / Mar '92 / Target/BMG / Cadillac.

AIN'T MISBEHAVIN'
Ain't misbehavin' / Flat foot floogie / Tisket-a-tasket / All God's chillun got wings / Deep river / Go down Moses / Waterboy / Lonesome road / That old feeling / Pent-up in a penthouse / Music, maestro, please / Don't try your jive on me / You can't have your cake and eat it / I can't give you anything but love / Not there, right there / Cottage in the rain / London suite - Piccadilly / London suite - Chelsea / London suite - Soho / London suite - Bond Street / London suite - Limehouse / London suite - Whitechapel / Smoke dreams of you / You can't have your cake and eat it (2)
CD _____ CDGRF 095
Tring / '93 / Tring / Prism.

AIN'T MISBEHAVIN'
CD _____ 17011
Laserlight / Jan '95 / Target/BMG.

AIN'T MISBEHAVIN'
CD _____ CDCD 1268
Charly / Oct '95 / Charly / THE / Cadillac.

CLASSIC JAZZ FROM RARE PIANO ROLLS
18th street strut / If I could be with you one hour tonight / I'm coming Virginia / T'aint nobody's business if I do / Clearing house blues / Squeeze me / Snake hips / Laughin' cryin' blues / You can't do what my last man did / New kind of man with a new kind of love / Nobody but my baby / Got to cool my doggies now / Ain't misbehavin'
CD _____ BCD 104
Biograph / Jul '91 / Wellard / ADA / Hot Shot / Jazz Music / Cadillac / Direct.

CLASSICS 1926-27
CD _____ CLASSICS 674
Classics / Nov '92 / Discovery / Jazz Music.

CLASSICS 1929-34
CD _____ OJCCD 720
Original Jazz Classics / Dec '93 / Wellard / Jazz Music / Cadillac / Complete/Pinnacle.

CLASSICS 1935
CD _____ CLASSICS 746
Classics / Aug '94 / Discovery / Jazz Music.

CLASSICS 1935 VOL. 2
CD _____ CLASSICS 760
Classics / Jun '94 / Discovery / Jazz Music.

CLASSICS 1936-37
CD _____ CLASSICS 816
Classics / May '95 / Discovery / Jazz Music.

CLASSICS 1937
CD _____ CLASSICS 838
Classics / Sep '95 / Discovery / Jazz Music.

COMPLETE EARLY BAND WORKS (1927-9)
Fats Waller stomp / Savannah blues / Won't you take me home / He's gone away / Red

hot Dan / Geechee / Please take me out of jail / Minor drag / Harlem fuss / Lookin' good but feelin' bad / I need someone like you / Lookin' for another sweetie / Ridin' but walkin' / Won't you get off it / When I'm alone
CD _____ DHDL 115
Halcyon / Sep '93 / Jazz Music / Wellard / Swift / Harmonia Mundi / Cadillac.

CREAM SERIES VOL.2
CD _____ PASTCD 7020
Flapper / Sep '93 / Pinnacle.

DEFINITIVE FATS WALLER
CD _____ STCD 528
Stash / Jan '93 / Jazz Music / CM / Cadillac / Direct / ADA.

DOESN'T SING - GREAT ORIGINAL PERFORMANCES 1927 - 1941
Clarinet marmalade / Chant the groove / Pantin' in the panther room / Sippi / I'm 100% for you / Baby brown / I ain't got nobody / Whose honey are you / Honeysuckle rose / Functionizin' / Scram / Rosetta / I've got a new lease of love / Swinga-dilla street / Sweet heartache / Blue turning grey over you / In the gloaming / Buck jumpin' / Moon is low
CD _____ RPCD 635
Robert Parker Jazz / Nov '93 / Conifer.

DUST OFF THAT OLD PIANNA (Waller, Fats & His Rhythm)
I'm 100% for you / Baby brown / Night wind / Because of once upon a time / I believe in miracles / You fit into the picture / Louisiana fairy tale / I ain't got nobody / Whose honey are you / Rosetta / Pardon my love / What's the reason I'm not pleasin' you / Cinders / (Oh Suzanna) dust off that old pianna / Lulu's back in town / Sweet and slow / You've been taking lessons in love (from somebody new) / You're the cutest one / I'm gonna sit right down and write myself a letter / Hate to talk about myself
CD _____ CDSVL 189
Saville / Mar '93 / Conifer.

EARLY YEARS PART 1, THE (Breaking The Ice 1934-1935/2CD Set)
Porter's love song / I wish I were twins / Armful o'sweetness / De me a favor / Georgia May / Then I'll be tired of you / Don't let it bother you / Have a little dream on me / Serenade for a wealthy widow / How can you face me / Sweetie pie / Mandy / Let's pretend there's a moon / You're not the only oyster in the stew / Honeysuckle rose / Belive it, beloved / Dream man (make me dream some more) / I'm growing fonder of you / If it isn't love / Breakin' the ice / I'm 100% for you / Baby brown / Night wind / Because of once upon a time / I believe in miracles / You fit into the picture / Louisiana fairy tale / I ain't got nobody (and nobody cares for me) / Who's honey are you / Rosetta / Pardon my love / What's the reason / Cinders / Oh Suzannah / Dust off that old pianna / Lulu's back in town / Sweet and slow / You've been taking lessons in love (from somebody new) / You're the cutest one
CD _____ 7863666182
Bluebird / Aug '95 / BMG.

ESSENTIAL COLLECTION
CD Set _____ LECD 616
Wisepack / Apr '95 / THE / Conifer.

FASCINATIN' FATS
CD _____ CDSG 401
Starline / Aug '89 / Jazz Music.

FATS AND HIS BUDDIES (1927-29)
Minor drag / Harlem fuss / Lookin' good but feelin' bad / I need someone like you / Lookin' for another sweetie / Ridin' but walkin' / Won't you get up off it, please / When I'm alone / Willow tree / Sippi / Thou swell (Takes 2 and 3) / Persian rug / Fats Waller stomp / Savannah blues / Won't you take me away / Red hot Dan / Geechee stomp / Please take me out of jail
CD _____ ND 90649
Bluebird / May '92 / BMG.

FATS AT HIS FINEST (Waller, Fats & His Rhythm)
I'm gonna sit right down and write myself a letter / Dinah / My very good friend the milkman / Baby Brown / Whose honey are you / Blue because of you / 12th Street rag / You've been taking lessons in love (from somebody new) / Somebody stole my gal / Breakin' the ice / I ain't got nobody / Just as long as the world goes round and round / I'm on a see-saw / I got rhythm / Sweet Sue, just you / Rhythm and romance / Sweet thing / Serenade for a wealthy widow
CD _____ PAR 2003
Parade / May '90 / Koch / Cadillac.

FATS AT THE ORGAN
Eighteenth Street strut / If I'm coming Virginia / If I could be with you one hour tonight / Laughin' cryin' blues / Midnight blues / Papa better watch your step / T'ain't nobody's business if I do / Time time now will be mine after a while / Nobody but my baby is getting my love / Do it Mr So-and-so / Clearing house blues / You can't do what my last man did / Don't try to take my loving man away / Squeeze me

CD _____ CD AJA 5007
Living Era / Oct '88 / Koch.

FATS SINGS WALLER
CD _____ JZCD 348
Suisa / Jan '93 / Jazz Music / THE.

FATS WALLER
CD _____ LECD 051
Dynamite / May '94 / THE.

FATS WALLER
CD _____ 887858
Milan / Jul '94 / BMG / Silva Screen.

FATS WALLER (1935-36)
CD _____ CD 14569
Jazz Portraits / May '95 / Jazz Music.

FATS WALLER
CD _____ DVX 08102
Deja Vu / May '95 / THE.

FATS WALLER
CD _____ 22712
Music / Nov '95 / Target/BMG.

FATS WALLER 1927-1929
CD _____ CLASSICS 689
Charly / Mar '93 / Charly / THE / Cadillac.

FATS WALLER 1929
CD _____ CLASSICS 702
Classics / Jul '93 / Discovery / Jazz Music.

FATS WALLER 1934-35
CD _____ CLASSICS 732
Classics / Jan '94 / Discovery / Jazz Music.

FATS WALLER 1935-36
CD _____ CLASSICS 776
Classics / Mar '95 / Discovery / Jazz Music.

FATS WALLER 1936
CD _____ CLASSICS 797
Classics / May '95 / Discovery / Jazz Music.

FATS WALLER IN LONDON
London suite / Don't try your jive on me / Ain't misbehavin' / Flat foot Floogie / Pent-up in a penthouse / Music maestro please / Tisket-a-tasket / That old feeling / I can't give you anything but love / Smoke dreams of you / You can't have your cake and eat it
CD _____ CDXP 8442
DRG / '88 / New Note.

FATS WALLER VOL.13
CD _____ K 133FS
King Jazz / Nov '93 / Jazz Music / Cadillac / Discovery.

FATS WALLER VOL.14
CD _____ KJ 134FS
King Jazz / Nov '93 / Jazz Music / Cadillac / Discovery.

FUN WITH FATS
Handful of keys / You're not the only oyster in the stew / Lulu's back in town / I'm gonna sit right down and write myself a letter / Sweet Sue, just you / Just you / It's a sin to tell a lie / Meanest thing you ever did was kiss me / Honeysuckle rose / Keepin' out of mischief now / Joint is jumpin' / Two sleepy people / Hold tight, hold tight / Spider and the fly / Your feet's too big / Hey stop kissin' my sister / All that meat and no potatoes
CD _____ CDCD 1004
Charly / Mar '93 / Charly / THE / Cadillac.

GREAT ORIGINAL PERFORMANCES
CD _____ RPCD 629
Robert Parker Jazz / Sep '93 / Conifer.

HALLELUJAH
CD _____ STCD 539
Stash / Sep '92 / Jazz Music / CM / Cadillac / Direct / ADA.

HANDFUL OF KEYS 1929-1934
CD _____ CD 56049
Jazz Roots / Nov '94 / Target/BMG.

HERE 'TIS
CD _____ 3801072
Jazz Archives / Jun '92 / Jazz Music / Discovery / Cadillac.

HONEYSUCKLE ROSE
CD _____ CDHD 184
Happy Days / Sep '92 / Conifer.

HONEYSUCKLE ROSE
CD _____ JHR 73503
Jazz Hour / '91 / Target/BMG / Jazz Music / Cadillac.

I'M 100% FOR YOU
My very good friend the milkman / Come down to Earth my angel / You must be losing your mind / Stop pretending / Shortnin' bread / Pantin' in the panther room / Twelfth street rag / Old grandad / I'm gonna salt away some sugar / Your socks don't match / Too tired / Your feet's too big / By the light of the silvery moon / Twenty four robbers / Bless you / Romance a la mode / Us on a bus / Pan pan / Sugar rose / I'm 100% for you / Imagine my surprise / Truckin' / Music maestro please / Ain't misbehavin'
CD _____ RAJCD 824
Empress / Mar '94 / THE.

INTRODUCTION TO FATS WALLER 1928-1942
CD _____ 4006
Best Of Jazz / Mar / '94 / Discovery.

IT'S A SIN TO TELL A LIE (Waller, Fats & His Rhythm)
CD _____ CDSGP 0168
Prestige / Nov / '95 / Total/BMG.

JAZZ PORTRAITS
You're not the only oyster in the stew / African ripples / Honeysuckle rose / Alligator crawl / If it isn't love / Viper's drag / I'm growing fonder of you / Do me a favour / Handful of keys / Mandy / Let's pretend there's a moon / Dream man / Have a little dream on me / Smashing thirds / I wish I were twins / Armful o'sweetness
CD _____ CD 14516
Jazz Portraits / May / '94 / Jazz Music.

JAZZ SINGER
CD _____ JZCD 350
Suisa / Jan / '93 / Jazz Music / THE.

JOINT IS JUMPIN'
Handful of keys / Minor drag / Numb fumblin' / Ain't misbehavin' / Smashing thirds / African ripples / Alligator crawl / Viper's drag / Lulu's back in town / Crazy about my baby / S'posin' / Blues / Tea for two / I ain't got nobody / Joint is jumpin' / Sheikh of Araby / Yacht club swing / Squeeze me / Your feet's too big / Carolina shout / Honeysuckle rose
CD _____ ND 86288
Bluebird / Apr / '88 / BMG.

JUGGLING JIVE OF FATS WALLER (LIVE)
CD _____ CDSH 2097
Derann Trax / Nov / '91 / Pinnacle.

LOW DOWN PAPA
I'm crazy 'bout my baby / Wild cat blues / Jailhouse blues / Do it Mr So-and-So / Don't try to take my man away / Your time now / Papa better watch your step / Haitian blues / Mama's got the blues / Midnight blues / Last go round blues / Cryin' for my used to be / Low down papa
CD _____ BCD 114
Biograph / Jul / '91 / Wellard / ADA / Hot Shot / Jazz Music / Cadillac / Direct.

LULU'S BACK IN STORE
CD _____ HADCD 189
Javelin / Nov / '95 / THE / Henry Hadaway Organisation.

MASTERPIECES 1929-41
CD _____ 158152
Masterpieces / Mar / '94 / BMG.

MIDDLE YEARS, PART 1 (1936-38) (Waller, Fats & His Rhythm)
Havin' a ball / I'm sorry I made you cry / Who's afraid of love / Please keep me in your dreams / One in a million / Nero / You're laughing at me / I can't break the habit of you / Did anyone tell you / When love is young / Meanest thing you ever did was kiss me / Cryin' mood / Where is the sun / Old plantation / To a sweet pretty thing / You've been reading my mail / Spring cleaning / You showed me the way / Boo-hoo (Instrumental) / Love bug will bite you (Instrumental track) / San Anton, San Anton (Instrumental) / I've got a new lease of love / I've got a new lease on love / Sweet heartache / Sweet heartache (Instrumental) / Honeysuckle rose (Instrumental) / Smarty (you know it all) / Don't you know or don't you care / Just like the gipsy told me / You put you in your place / Blue turning grey over you / You've got me under your thumb / Beat it out / Our love was meant to be / I'd rather call you baby / I'm always in the mood for you / She's tall, she's terrific / You're my dish / More power to you / How can I (with you in my heart) / Joint is jumpin' / Hopeless love affair / What will I do in the morning / How ya baby / Jealous of me / Everyday's a holiday / Neglected / My window faces the south / I'm in another world / Why do Hawaiians sing aloha / My first impression of you / On the sunny side of the street / Georgia on my mind / Something tells me / I love to whistle / You went to my head / Florida Flo / Lost and found / Don't try to cry your way back to me / Marie / In the gloaming (Instrumental) / You had an evi'ning to spare / Let's break the good news / Skronitch / I simply adore you / Sheikh of Araby / Hold my hand / Inside
CD Set _____ 7863660832
RCA / Dec / '92 / BMG.

MIDDLE YEARS, PART 2 (1935 - 1940) (A Good Man Is Hard To Find - 3CD Set)
In the gloaming / I simply adore you / Sheikh of araby / Hold my hand / Inside / There's honey on the moon tonight / If I were you / Wide open spaces / On the bumpy road to love / Fair and square / We the people / Two sleepy people / Shame shame (Everybody knows your game) / I'll never forgive myself (For not forgiving you) / You look good to me / Tell me with your kisses / I wish I had you / I'll dance at your wedding / Imagine my surprise / Yacht club swing / Love / I'll give my life for you / I won't believe it (Till I hear from you) / Spider and the fly / Patty cake, patty cake / Good man is hard to find / You outsmarted your-

self / Last night a miracle happened / Good for nothin' but love / Hold tight, hold tight (Want some sea food, Mama) / Kiss me with your eyes / You asked for it - you got it / Some rainy day / T'ain't what you do (it's the way that you do it) / Got no time / Step up and shake my hand / Undecided / Remember who you're promised to / Honey hush / I used to love you (But it's all over now) / Wait and see / You meet the nicest people in your dreams / Anita / What a pretty Miss / Squeeze me / Bless you / It's the tune that counts / Abdullah / Who'll take my place / Bond Street / It's you who taught me / Suitcase Susie / Your feet's too big / You're lettin' the grass grow under your feet / Darktown strutter's ball / I can't give you anything but love / Swinga-dilla street / At twilight / Oh frenchy / Cheatin' on me / Black Maria / Mighty fine / Moon is low
CD Set _____ 7863665522
Bluebird / Jun / '95 / BMG.

MISBEHAVIN'
I can't give you anything but love / Your feet's too big / Let's swing again / Viper's drag / Joint is jumpin' / Ain't misbehavin'
CD _____ BSTCD 9105
Best Compact Discs / May / '92 / Complete/ Pinnacle.

OUR VERY GOOD FRIEND, FATS (Waller, Fats & His Rhythm)
12th street rag / I ain't got nobody / Dinah / My very good friend the milkman / I'm on a see-saw / I'm gonna sit right down and write myself a letter / Basin Street blues / Why do hawaiians sing aloha / Paswonky / Lost love / Don't you know or don't you care / She's tall, she's tan, she's terrific / I'm always in the mood for you / St. Louis blues / Shortnin' bread / Sugar rose / That never to be forgotten night / After you've gone / Old plantation / Dinah
CD _____ DBCD 16
Dance Band Days / Jul / '89 / Prism.

PEARL SERIES: FATS WALLER
It's a sin to tell a lie / Your feet's too big / I'm crazy 'bout my baby / Draggin' my heart around / Music, maestro, please / Flat foot floogie / You're not the only oyster in the stew / T'ain't nobody's business if I do / Viper's drag / My very good friend the milkman / Write myself a letter / Truckin' / I'm on a see-saw / Handful of keys / Joint is jumpin' / I wish I were twins / Minor drag / Sweet Sue, just you / Black raspberry jam / Tisket-a-tasket / Dinah / Clothes line ballet / Nagasaki / Ain't misbehavin'
CD _____ PASTCD 9742
Flapper / Mar / '91 / Pinnacle.

PHENOMENAL FATS
I'm gonna put you in your place / Patty cake, patty cake / Good for nothing (but love) / Last night a miracle happened / Twelfth street rag / Paswonky / Neglected / How ya baby / Lost love / She's tall, she's terrific / Why do Hawaiians sing Aloha / Spider and the fly / Old plantation / I love to Whistle / That never to be forgotten night
CD _____ PAR 2011
Parade / Jul / '94 / Koch / Cadillac.

PIANO SOLOS (1929-1941)
Blue black bottom / Handful of keys / Numb fumblin' / Ain't misbehavin' / Sweet savannah Sue / I've got a feeling I'm falling in love / Love me or leave me / Gladyse / Valentine stomp / Waiting at the end of the road / Baby, oh where can you be / Goin' about / My feelin's are hurt / Smashing thirds / My fate is in your hands / Turn on the heat / St. Louis blues / After you've gone / African ripples / Clothes line ballet / Alligator crawl / Viper's drag / Down home blues / E flat blues / Zonky / Keepin' out of mischief now / Stardust / Basin Street blues / Tea for two / I ain't got nobody / Georgia on my mind / Rockin' chair / Carolina shout / Honeysuckle rose / Ring dem bells
CD Set _____ ND 89741
Jazz Tribune / May / '94 / BMG.

POP SINGER
CD _____ JZCD 349
Suisa / Jan / '93 / Jazz Music / THE.

PRIVATE ACETATES & FILM SOUNDTRACKS 1939-1940
Ain't misbehavin' / Sweet Sue, just you / Nagasaki / Lonesome me / Hallelujah / Handful of keys / Then you'll remember / Sextet from Lucia Di Lammermoor / My heart at thy sweet voice / Joint is jumpin' / Your feet's too big / Honeysuckle rose / I've got my fingers crossed / I'm livin' in a great big way
CD _____ 550222
Jazz Anthology / Feb / '94 / Harmonia Mundi / Cadillac.

YOU LOOK GOOD TO ME (Waller, Fats & His Rhythm)
CD _____ CDSGP 089
Prestige / Oct / '93 / Total/BMG.

YOU RASCAL, YOU
Georgia May / I'm crazy 'bout my baby / Breakin' the ice / Baby, oh where can you be / If it isn't love / Won't you get up off it, please / I wish I were twins / Numb fumblin' / (I'll be glad when you're dead) you rascal you / Ain't misbehavin' / Porter's love song / Draggin' my heart around / Minor drag /

My fate is in your hands / That's what I like about you / Harlem fuss / Believe it, beloved / Honeysuckle rose
CD _____ CD AJA 5040
Living Era / Oct / '88 / Koch.

Wallgren, Jan Edvard

STANDARDS AND BLUEPRINTS
CD _____ DRCD 246
Dragon / Oct / '94 / Roots / Cadillac / Wellard / CM / ADA.

Wallin, Per Henrik

DOLPHINS, DOLPHINS, DOLPHINS
CD _____ DRCD 215
Dragon / Sep / '89 / Roots / Cadillac / Wellard / CM / ADA.

ONE KNIFE IS ENOUGH
CD _____ 1273
Caprice / Feb / '90 / CM / Complete/ Pinnacle / Cadillac / ADA.

TRIO
CD _____ 1185
Caprice / May / '89 / CM / Complete/ Pinnacle / Cadillac / ADA.

Wallington, George

GEORGE WALLINGTON TRIO, THE (Wallington, George Trio)
Twins / Polka dot / I'll remember April / High score / Hyacinth / Joy bell / I didn't know what time it was / Fine and dandy / Knockout / Igloo / Fairyland / Racing
CD _____ SV 0136
Savoy Jazz / Jan / '94 / Conifer / ADA.

JAZZ AT HOTCHKISS (Wallington, George Quintet)
Before the infidels / Strange music / Before dawn / Ow / S make T
CD _____ CY 78994
Savoy Jazz / Nov / '95 / Conifer / ADA.

LIVE AT CAFE BOHEMIA (Wallington, George Quintet)
Johnny one note / Sweet blanche / Monor march / Snakes / Jay Mac's crib / Bohemia after dark / Minor march (alternate)
CD _____ OJCCD 1813
Original Jazz Classics / Apr / '93 / Wellard / Jazz Music / Cadillac / Complete/Pinnacle.

TRIOS (Wallington, George & Jimmy Jones)
Fairyland / Woody 'n' you / Just one of these things / Honeysuckle rose / Star eyes / Day in Paris / These foolish things / Easy to love / Little girl blue / Lush life / Just squeeze me / My funny valentine / Good morning heartache
CD _____ 74321115042
Vogue / Jul / '93 / BMG.

Wallochmore Ceilidh Band

HIGHLANDERS COMPANION, THE (Dr Walloch's Fifth Prescription)
Paddy's potion / Canadian barn dance / St. Bernard's waltz / Broon's reel / Eva three step / Jack Tarr two step / Gay gordons / Corn rigs / Welcome Christmas morning / Wee Todd / Polka / Retreat marches / Pride of North / Hornpipe and reel / Final dose
CD _____ LAPCD 111
Lapwing / Dec / '88 / CM.

LOOKING FOR A PARTNER
LP _____ LAP 8B 101
Lapwing / Dec / '88 / CM.

Wallowitch, John

MY MANHATTAN
My Manhattan / Cosmic surgery / Come a little closer / Oh wow / Bruce / I live alone again / None of your business / Florida / It's come true at last / Threepenny things / Tony and I / Cheap decadent drivel / This most / Beekman place elegy / Night train to Chicago / Oy vey / Time to come home again / Old friends
CD _____ DRGCD 91414
DRG / Sep / '93 / New Note.

Walrath, Jack

HI JINX
CD _____ STCD 576
Stash / Feb / '94 / Jazz Music / CM / Cadillac/ Direct / ADA.

HIPGNOSIS (Walrath, Jack & The Masters Of Suspense)
Sweet hip gnosis / Hip gnosis / Trane trip / Philosopher stone / Mingus piano / Blue sinistra / Games / Baby fat / Premature optomism / Eclipse / Love enough for everybody
CD _____ TCB 01062
TCB / Feb / '96 / New Note.

OUT OF THE TRADITION
Clear out this world / So long Eric / Stardust / Wake up and wash it off / Come Sunday / Brother can you spare a dime / Cabin in the sky / I'm getting sentimental over you
CD _____ MCD 5403
Muse / Sep / '92 / New Note / CM.

SERIOUS HANG (Walrath, Jack & The Masters Of Suspense)
Anya and Liz on the veranda / Get on the good foot / Better git it in your soul / Izlyal e delyo haidoutin / Monk's feet / Decisions / Gloomy Sunday / Weird and wonderful
CD _____ MCD 5475
Muse / Mar / '94 / New Note / CM.

Walser, Don

ARCHIVES VOL.1 (Walser, Don & The Pure Texas Band)
CD _____ WM 1041CD
Watermelon / Nov / '95 / ADA / Direct.

ARCHIVES VOL.2 (Walser, Don & The Pure Texas Band)
CD _____ WM 1042CD
Watermelon / Nov / '95 / ADA / Direct.

ROLLING STONE FROM TEXAS
CD _____ WMCD 1028
Watermelon / Oct / '94 / ADA / Direct.

Walsh, Colin

ENGLISH ORGAN MUSIC FROM LINCOLN CATHEDRAL
CD _____ PRCD 379
Priory / Jul / '92 / Priory.

Walsh, Joe

BUT SERIOUSLY FOLKS
Over and over / Second hand store / Indian Summer / At the station / Tomorrow / Inner tube / Boat Weirdos (Theme) / Life's been good
CD _____ 7559605272
WEA / Oct / '93 / Warner Music.

GOT ANY GUM
Radio song / Fun / In my car / Malibu / Half of the time / Got any gum / Up to me / No peace in the jungle / Memory lane / Time
CD _____ 7599256062
WEA / Jan / '96 / Warner Music.

LOOK WHAT I DID
Tuning, part 1 / Take a look around / Funk # 48 / Bomber / Tend my garden / Funk # 49 / Ashes the rain and I / Walk away / It's all the same / Midnight man / Here we go / Midnight visitor / Mother says / Turn to stone / Comin' down / Meadows / Rocky mountain way / Welcome to the club / All night laundry mat blues / Country fair / Help me thru the night / Life's been good / Over and over / All night long / Life of illusion / Theme from the island weirdos / I can play that rock and roll / I.L.B.T.'S / Space age whizz kids / Rosewood bitters / Shut up / Decades / Song for a dying planet / Ordinary average guy
CD _____ MCD 11233
MCA / Oct / '95 / BMG.

SMOKER YOU DRINK, THE PLAYER YOU GET, THE
Rocky mountain way / Bookends / Wolf / Midnight moodies / Happy ways / Meadows / Dreams / Days gone by / (Daydream) prayer
CD _____ MCLD 19020
MCA / Apr / '92 / BMG.

Walsh, John

TIME TO SPARE
CD _____ LCOM 5204
Lismor / Nov / '91 / Lismor / Direct / Duncans / ADA.

Walsh, Seán

HAYMAKER, THE
CD _____ GTDCD 001
GTD / Jan / '95 / Else / ADA.

WILL THE CIRCLE BE UNBROKEN
CD _____ GTD 008
GTD / Feb / '95 / Else / ADA.

Walt Mink

BAREBACK RIDE
Subway / Shine / Zero day / Disappear / Sunnymeade / Frail / Turn / Fragile / What a day / Tree in orange / Miss happiness / Chowdertown / Love you better / Showers down / Quiet time / Pink moon / Smoothing the ride / Croton-harmon (Local) / Twinkle and shine / Factory
CD _____ QUIGD 3
Quigley / Sep / '93 / EMI.

MISS HAPPINESS
Miss Happiness / Chowdertown / Love You Better / Showers down / Quiet Time / Pink Moon / Smoothing the ride / Crowton-Harmon (Local) / Twinkle And Shine / Factory
CD _____ QUIGD 1
Quigley / Oct / '92 / EMI.

Waltari

TORCHA
CD _____ EM 91292
Roadrunner / Aug / '92 / Pinnacle.

Walter Elf

HOMO SAPIENS
CD _____ XM 027 CD
X-Mist / Apr / '92 / SRD.

Waltham Forest Pipe Band

TRADITIONAL SCOTTISH PIPES AND DRUMS
CD _____ EUCD 1171
ARC / '91 / ARC Music / ADA.

Walton, Bill

MEN ARE MADE IN PAINT
CD _____ ISS 002CD
SST / Jan '94 / Plastic Head.

Walton, Brenda

MORTGAGED HEART, THE
CD _____ HARTCD 002
Heartsongs / Apr '94 / CM.

Walton, Cedar

AMONG FRIENDS (Walton, Cedar Trio)
For all we know / Without a song / Off minor / My foolish heart / Midnight waltz / Ruby my dear / My old flame / I've grown accustomed to her face
CD _____ ECD 220232
Evidence / Aug '92 / Harmonia Mundi / ADA / Cadillac.

AS LONG AS THERE'S MUSIC
Young and foolish / Newest blues / Meaning of the blues / Pannonica / I'm not so sure / As long as there's music / Ground work / Voices deep within
CD _____ MCD 5405
Muse / Nov '93 / New Note / CM.

BLUES FOR MYSELF
CD _____ RED 1232052
Red / Aug '95 / Harmonia Mundi / Jazz Horizons / Cadillac / ADA.

CEDAR WALTON PLAYS (Walton, Cedar, Ron Carter & Billy Higgins)
CD _____ DCD 4008
Delos / '88 / Conifer.

CEDAR'S BLUES (Walton, Cedar Quintet)
CD _____ 1231792
Red / Apr '95 / Harmonia Mundi / Jazz Horizons / Cadillac / ADA.

EASTERN REBELLION (Walton, Cedar Quartet)
Bolivia / 5/4 thing / Mode for Joe / Naima / Bittersweet
CD _____ CDSJP 101
Timeless Jazz / Jun '89 / New Note.

FIRST SET
CD _____ SCCD 31085
Steeplechase / Jul '88 / Impetus.

MANHATTAN AFTERNOON (Walton, Cedar Trio)
CD _____ CRISS 1082CD
Criss Cross / May '94 / Cadillac / Harmonia Mundi.

OFF MINOR (Walton, Cedar, David Williams, Billy Higgins)
CD _____ 1232422
Red / Mar '92 / Harmonia Mundi / Jazz Horizons / Cadillac / ADA.

SOUL CYCLE
CD _____ OJCCD 847
Original Jazz Classics / Nov '95 / Wellard / Jazz Music / Cadillac / Complete/Pinnacle.

Walton, Frank

REALITY
CD _____ DD 436
Delmark / Aug '94 / Hot Shot / ADA / CM / Direct / Cadillac.

Walton, Joice

DOWNSVILLE GIRL
First train / Funkey blues / Blacktop baby / Life's revolving door / Make yourself at home / When Daddy sang / Come as you are / One way street / Blessed with the blues
CD _____ 901303
Line / Jan '95 / CM / Grapevine / ADA / Conifer / Direct.

Walton, Mercy Dee

ONE ROOM COUNTRY SHACK
One room country shack / My woman knows the score / Misery blues / Great mistake / Save me some / Strugglin' with the blues / Lonesome cabin blues / Rent man blues / Fall guy / Drifter / Hear me shout / Love is a mystery / Winter blues / Pauline / Get to gettin' / Dark muddy bottom / What'cha gonna do / My woman and the devil / Big minded daddy / Perfect health / Problem child / Pull 'em and pop 'em / Eighth wonder of the world / Rock 'n' roll fever
CD _____ CDCHD 475
Ace / Jun '93 / Pinnacle / Cadillac / Complete/Pinnacle.

PITY AND SHAME
CD _____ OBCCD 552
Original Blues Classics / Jan '94 / Complete/Pinnacle / Wellard / Cadillac.

TROUBLESOME MIND
CD _____ ARHCD 369
Arhoolie / Apr '95 / ADA / Direct / Cadillac.

Walton, Peter

DANCE GUITAR
CD _____ DLD 1019
Dance & Listen / '92 / Savoy.

Waltons

COCK'S CROW
CD _____ 4509994352
Warner Bros. / Jun '95 / Warner Music.

ESSENTIAL COUNTRY BULLSHIT
CD _____ SPV 08476802
Steamhammer / Jun '94 / Pinnacle / Plastic Head.

LIK MY TRAKTER
Colder than you / Sunshine / Water well and the farmer's hand / In the meantime / I could care less / Truth and beauty / Living room / Look at me / Naked rain / (Don't let it) Slide / Fine line / Like my tractor
CD _____ 450991951-2
WEA / Mar '94 / Warner Music.

LOCK UP YER LIVESTOCK
CD _____ RAUCD 007
Raucous / Aug '93 / Nervous / Disc.

Wamma Jamma

SIX BY FOUR
Wotcha gonna tell me / Hanging on a string / Fairer slink / Slow walk / Down the track / Six-one-two
CD _____ WAMMA 003CD
Dr. Woolybach / Dec '94 / Dr. Woolybach.

Wammack, Travis

THAT SCRATCHY GUITAR FROM MEMPHIS
Night train / Fire fly / It's karate time / Scratchy / Flip flop and bop / Your love / Louie Louie / Tech-nically speaking / Hallelujah, I love her so / Thunder road / I ain't lyin' / Upset / Super soul beat / Distortion part 2 / There's a UFO up there / Umm how sweet it is / Hideaway / Find another man / Fannie Mae / You are my sunshine / Memphis, Tennessee
CD _____ BCD 15415
Bear Family / Nov '87 / Rollercoaster / Direct / CM / Swift / ADA.

Wampas

CHAUDS SALES ET HUMIDES
CD _____ ROSE 161CD
New Rose / Mar '89 / Direct / ADA.

Wanamaker, Lisa

SHIRIM
CD _____ SYNCOOP 5754CD
Syncoop / Feb '95 / ADA / Direct.

Wanderley, Walter

BRAZIL'S GREATEST HITS
A felicidade / Wave / Tristeza / Meditation / Recado / Feelings / Baia / Carnaval / Mas que nade / Girl from Ipanema / Canta de Ossanha / Triste / One note Samba / Quiet nights / Berimbau / Desfinado / Summer samba / How insensitive / Samba d'Orpheus / Brazil
CD _____ GNPD 2137
GNP Crescendo / Dec '91 / Silva Screen.

Wangford, Hank

COWBOYS STAY ON LONGER (Wangford, Hank Band)
Cowboys stay on longer / You turned me on / Jenny / Running backwards fast / Chico / Stranded / Whiskey on my guitar / Wild thing / She don't wanna be / All I want / Big G / D.F.W. / Suppin' whiskey / Two time polka / Hymn / Joggin' with Jesus
CD _____ CDSD 070
Magnum Music / '89 / Magnum Music Group.

HARD SHOULDER TO CRY ON (Wangford, Hank & The Lost Cowboys)
Dim lights / You're still on my mind / Jealousy / My lips want to stay (but my heart wants to go) / Birmingham hotel / Stormy horizons / My baby's gone / Gonna paint this town / Jalisco / What happens / Get rhythm / Prisoner song / Lay down my old guitar / I'm coming home / End of the road
CD _____ HANKCD 001
Sincere Sounds / Mar '93 / Vital / Direct.

Wanna-Bees

VIOLENT VIBRATIONS
CD _____ RA 91772
Roadrunner / Apr '92 / Pinnacle.

Wannabes

MOD FLOWER CAKE
CD _____ DJD 3211
Dejadisc / Dec '94 / Direct / ADA.

POPSUCKER
CD _____ DJD 3222
Dejadisc / Nov '95 / Direct / ADA.

Wannadies

AQUANAUTIC
Everything's true / Cherry man / Things that I would love to have undone / Love is dead / So happy now / Lucky you / 1.07 / December days / Something to tell / Suddenly I missed her / God knows / Never killed anyone / I love you love me love
CD _____ SNAP 005
Soap / Jan '93 / Vital.

Waorani Indians

WAORANI WAAPONI
CD _____ TUMICD 043
Tumi / '94 / Sterns / Discovery.

War

ALL DAY MUSIC
All day music / Get down / That's what love will do / There must be a reason / Nappy head / Slippin' into darkness / Baby brother
CD _____ 74321305202
Avenue / Sep '95 / BMG.

DELIVER THE WORLD
H2Overture / In your eyes / Gypsy man / Me and baby brother / Deliver the word / Southern part of Texas / Blisters
CD _____ 74321305222
Avenue / Sep '95 / BMG.

PEACE SIGN
CD _____ 74321297662
BMG / Jun '95 / BMG.

PLATINUM JAZZ
War is coming / Slowly we walk together / Platinum jazz / I got you / LA sunshine / River Niger / H2Overture / City, country, city / Smile happy / Deliver the word / Nappy head / Four cornered room
CD _____ 74321305242
Avenue / Sep '95 / BMG.

WHY CAN'T WE BE FRIENDS
Don't let no-one get you down / Lotus blossom / Heartbeat / Leroy's Latin lament / Smile happy / So / Low rider / In Mazatian / Why can't we be friends
CD _____ 74321305232
Avenue / Sep '95 / BMG.

WORLD IS A GHETTO
Cisco kid / City, country, city / Beetles in a bog / Four cornered room / Where was you at / World is a ghetto
CD _____ 74321305212
Avenue / Sep '95 / BMG.

War Collapse

ROLLED OVER BY TANKS
CD _____ DISTCD 018
Distortion / Nov '95 / Plastic Head.

War Pipes

WAR PIPES
CD _____ BRGCD 20
Bridge / Jul '95 / Grapevine.

Ward, Anita

RING MY BELL
I'm ready for your love / Curtains go up / This must be love / Ring my bell / Sweet splendour / There's no doubt about it / You lied / Make believe in lovers / If I could feel that old feeling again / Spoiled by your love / I won't stop loving you
CD _____ MSCD 17
Music De-Luxe / Apr '95 / Magnum Music Group.

Ward, Billy

BILLY WARD & HIS DOMINOES (Ward, Billy & His Dominoes)
Sixty minute man / Do something for me / That's what you're doing to me / Deep sea blues / Pedal pushin' papa / Don't leave me this way / Have mercy baby / I am with you / Chicken blues / Weeping willow blues / Love love love / Bells
CD _____ KCD 559
King/Paddle Wheel / Mar '90 / New Note.

FEAT (Ward, Billy & His Dominoes)
Tenderly / Over the rainbow / Learnin' the blues / When the swallows come back to Capistrano / Harbour lights / These foolish things / Three coins in the fountain / Little things mean a lot / Rags to riches / May I never love again / Lonesome road / Until the real thing comes along
CD _____ KCD 733
King/Paddle Wheel / Mar '90 / New Note.

SIXTY MINUTE MAN (Ward, Billy & The Dominoes)
Sixty minute man / Chicken blues / Don't leave me this way / Do something for me / That's what you're doing to me / Weeping willow blues / How long blues / I am with you / Have mercy baby / If I ever get to heaven / Pedal pushin' papa / I'd be satisfied / Deed I do / Bells / My baby's 3-D / Tenderly / I ain't gonna cry for you / You can't keep a good man down / I really don't want to know / I'm gonna move to the outskirts of town
CD _____ CDCHARLY 242
Charly / Oct '90 / Charly / THE / Cadillac.

Ward Brothers

WAVE GOODBYE TO GRANDMA
CD _____ SRC 2
Serious / Aug '95 / Else.

Ward, Clifford T.

GAYE - AND OTHER STORIES
Gaye / Wherewithal / Cellophane / Dubious circus company / Not waving, drowning / Time the magician / Home thoughts from abroad / Way of love / Open university / Jigsaw girl / Day to myself / Nightingale / We could be talking / Where's it going to end / Crisis / Scullery / Where would that leave me / To an air hostess / Sad affair
CD _____ CDVM 9009
Virgin / Jun '92 / EMI.

JULIA & OTHER NEW STORIES
CD _____ GRADCD 4
Graduate / Sep '94 / Graduate.

SINGER SONGWRITER PLUS
Coathanger / Leader / Anticipation / Session singer / God help me / Sympathy / You knock when you should come in / Sam / Dream / Rayne / Carrie / Cause is good / Circus girl / Sidetrack
CD _____ SEECD 418
See For Miles/C5 / May '95 / Pinnacle.

Ward, John

WATER ON THE STONE
Water on the stone / Free world market place / Paper chase / Stoney ground / Heart of the town / Status / I want to see your face / Leakin' minister / Rural vandals / Must I go bound / Way of the world / Only treasure / Binding light
CD _____ IONGF 5
Green Fingers / Jun '92 / Green Fingers Music.

Ward, Paul

FOR A KNAVE
Flying South / First home / Love, lies and magic / Borderline / Interleave / Last stand / Cetacean / Glidepath / Alchemist / Twelve towers
CD _____ REAL 097
Surreal / Aug '91 / Surreal To Real / C & D Compact Disc Services.

Ward, Robert

BLACK BOTTOM
CD _____ BT 1123CD
Black Top / Nov '95 / CM / Direct / ADA.

FEAR NO EVIL (Ward, Robert & The Black Top All Stars)
CD _____ ORECD 520
Silvertone / Mar '94 / Pinnacle.

RHYTHM OF THE PEOPLE
CD _____ BT 1088CD
Black Top / May '93 / CM / Direct / ADA.

Warden, Monte

HERE I AM
CD _____ WMCD 1037
Watermelon / Aug '95 / ADA / Direct.

MONTE WARDEN
CD _____ WMCD 1015
Watermelon / May '94 / ADA / Direct.

Ware, Bill

LONG & SKINNY (Ware, Bill & The Club Bird Allstars)
CD _____ KFWCD 131
Knitting Factory / Feb '95 / Grapevine.

Ware, David S.

CRYPTOLOGY (Ware, David S. Quartet)
CD _____ HMS 2202
Homestead / Mar '95 / SRD.

EARTHQUATION
CD _____ DIW 892
DIW / Jan '95 / Harmonia Mundi / Cadillac.

FLIGHT OF I
CD _____ DIW 856
DIW / May '92 / Harmonia Mundi / Cadillac.

Ware, Leon

TASTE THE LOVE
CD _____ XECD 5
Expansion / Aug '95 / Pinnacle / Sony / 3MV.

Warfare

CONFLICT OF HATRED
Waxworks / Revolution / Dancing in the flames of insanity / Evolution / Fatal vision / Death charge / Order of the dragons / Elite forces / Rejoice the feast of quarantine / Noise filth and fury

CD _____ NEATCD 1044
Neat / Mar '88 / Plastic Head.

DECADE OF DECIBELS
CD _____ CDBLEED 8
Bleeding Hearts / Oct '93 / Pinnacle.

Warfield, Justin

JUSTIN WARFIELD SUPERNAUT, THE
CD _____ 9362458712
Qwest / May '95 / Warner Music.

MY FIELD TRIP TO PLANET 9
Tequila flats / Introduction / Dip dip divin' /
K sera sera / Fisherman's grotto / Live from
the opium den / Glass tangerine / Guavafish
centipede / Teenage caligula / Cool like the
blues / Drug store cowboy / Pick it up y'all
/ B boys on acid / Stormclouds left of
heaven / Thoughts in the buttermilk / Tequila flats (ghosts of Laurel Canyon)
CD _____ 936245085-2
Qwest / Jan '94 / Warner Music.

Warfield, Tim

COOL BLUE, A
CD _____ CRISS 1102
Criss Cross / Oct '95 / Cadillac /
Harmonia Mundi.

Wargasm

FIREBALL
CD _____ MASSCD 036
Massacre / Jul '94 / Plastic Head.

UGLY
CD _____ MASSCD 020
Massacre / Nov '93 / Plastic Head.

Warhead

WARHEAD
CD _____ CMGCD 011
Communique / Nov '95 / Plastic Head.

Warhorse

OUTBREAK OF HOSTILITIES
Vulture blood / No chance / Burning / St.
Louis / Ritual / Solitude / Woman of the
devil / Red Sea / Back in time / Confident
but wrong / Feeling better / Sybilla / Mouth-
piece / I who have nothing
CD _____ CDTB 104
Magnum Music / May '91 / Magnum Music
Group.

RED SEA
Red sea / Back in time / Confident but
wrong / Feeling better / Sybilla / Mouth
piece / I who have nothing
CD _____ REP 4056-WP
Repertoire / Aug '91 / Pinnacle / Cadillac.

WARHORSE
CD _____ REP 4055-WP
Repertoire / Aug '91 / Pinnacle / Cadillac.

Waring, Steve

**GUITAR PICKING (Waring, Steve &
Roger Mason)**
CD _____ LDX 274969
La Chant Du Monde / Oct '94 / Harmonia
Mundi / ADA.

Warlow, Anthony

CENTRE STAGE
Music of the night / Easy to love / Luck be
a lady / Somewhere / This nearly was mine
/ I am what I am / Anthem / Bring him home
/ You're nothing without me / Impossible
dream / Johanna / Colours of my life /
Soliloquy
CD _____ 5112232
London / Nov '91 / PolyGram.

Warner, Tom

LONG NIGHT BIG DAY
CD _____ 804102
New World / Jun '91 / Harmonia Mundi /
ADA / Cadillac.

Warnes, Jennifer

FAMOUS BLUE RAINCOAT
First we take Manhattan / Bird on the wire
/ Famous blue raincoat / Joan of Arc / Ain't
no cure for love / Coming back to you /
Song of Bernadette / Singer must die /
Came so far for beauty
CD _____ PD 90048
RCA / Jun '87 / BMG.

HUNTER, THE
Rock you gently / Somewhere, somebody /
Big noise, New York / True emotion / Pre-
tending to care / Whole of the moon / Light
of Louisanne / Way down deep / Hunter / I
can't hide
CD _____ 261974
Private Music / Jun '92 / BMG.

Warp Drive

GIMME GIMME
Bang the drum / I 4 U / Words / Take take
me now / Stay on stay on / Moments away
/ Crying girl / Eyes on you / Rockin' the boat
/ Making time stand still

CD _____ CDMFN 99
Music For Nations / May '90 / Pinnacle.

Warrant

ULTRAPHOBIC
CD _____ CDMFN 183
Music For Nations / Feb '95 / Pinnacle.

Warren G.

REGULATE G FUNK ERA
Regulate / Do you see / Gangsta sermon /
Recognize / Super soul sis / '94 Ho draft /
So many ways / This DJ / This is the Shack
/ What's next / And ya don't stop / Runnin'
wit no breaks
CD _____ 523 335-2
Island Red / Jul '94 / PolyGram / Vital.

Warrior

LET BATTLE COMMENCE
Let battle commence / Long stretch Broad-
moor blues / Night time girl / Memories /
Yesterday's hero / Invaders / Ulster bloody
Ulster / Warrior
CD _____ ETHEL 2
Vinyl Tap / Dec '94 / Vinyl Tap.

Warrior River Boys

SOUNDS LIKE HOME
CD _____ ROU 310CD
Rounder / Jan '94 / CM / Direct / ADA /
Cadillac.

Warrior Soul

**DRUGS, GOD AND THE NEW
REPUBLIC**
CD _____ DGCD 24389
Geffen / May '91 / BMG.

LAST DECADE, DEAD CENTURY
I see the ruins / We cry out / Losers / Downtown / Trippin' on ecstasy / One minute
years / Super power dreamland / Charlie's
out of prison / Blown away / Lullaby / In
conclusion / Four more years
CD _____ DGCD 24285
Geffen / Aug '91 / BMG.

SPACE AGE PLAYBOYS
CD _____ CDMFN 172
Music For Nations / Oct '94 / Pinnacle.

Warsaw

WARSAW
CD _____ MPG 74034
Movieplay Gold / Feb '95 / Target/BMG.

Wartime

FAST FOOD FOR THOUGHT
Mindfield / Wartime / Right to life / Whole
truth / Franklin's tower
CD _____ MPCD 1753
Chrysalis / Aug '94 / EMI.

Warwick, Dionne

20 GREATEST HITS: DIONNE WARWICK
Walk on by / I say a little prayer / Valley of
the dolls / I'll never fall in love again / Anyone who had a heart / Message to Michael
/ Do you know the way to San Jose / Are
you there (with another girl) / Who can I turn
to / House is not a home / Don't make me
over / You'll never get to heaven (if you
break my heart) / Make it easy on yourself
/ Reach out for me / Alfie / You've lost that
lovin' feelin' / Trains and boats and planes
/ I just don't know what to do with myself /
Window of the world / Promises, promises
CD _____ CD 36
Bescol / May '87 / CM / Target/BMG.

25TH ANNIVERSARY COLLECTION
Walk On By / Close to you / Always some-
thing there to remind me / Wishin' and
hopin' / Look of love / Message To Michael
/ I Just Don't Know What To Do With Myself
/ Wives and lovers / Reach Out For Me /
Are you there (with another girl) / Do you
know the way to San Jose / I say a little
prayer
CD _____ PWKS 512
Carlton Home Entertainment / Sep '88 /
Carlton Home Entertainment.

AQUARELA DO BRASIL
Jobim medley / Virou areia / Oh Bahia / Pi-
ano na manquiera / Captives of the heart /
Samba dobrado / Heart of Brasil / N'kosi
sikeleli's - Afrika / So bashiya bahlala ekhaya
/ Brasil / Caravan / Flower of Bahia / 10,000
words
CD _____ 07822187772
Arista / Jan '95 / BMG.

DIONNE
Who, what, when, where and why / After
you / Letter / I'll never love this way again /
Deja vu / Feeling old feelings / In your eyes
/ My everlasting love / Out of my hands /
All the time
CD _____ MCCD 169
MCI / Sep '94 / Disc / THE.

DIONNE WARWICK COLLECTION
Walk on by / Close to you / (There's) Always
something there to remind me / Wishin' and
hopin' / Look of love / Message to Michael
/ I just don't know what to do with myself /

Wives and lovers / Reach out for me / Are
you there with another girl / Anyone who
had a heart / You'll never get to heaven /
Alfie / I say a little prayer / Do you know the
way to San Jose / Make it easy on yourself
/ Another night / Don't make me over /
Trains boats and planes / House is not a
home / I'll never fall in love again / Let it be
/ Here where there is love / I love Paris /
C'est si bon / Hurt so bad / As long as he
needs me / Blowing in the wind / Valley of
dolls / Unchained melody / Somewhere /
It's the good life / People got to be free /
Who can I turn to / Gettin' ready for the
heartbreak / Baubles, bangles and beads /
Your all I need to get by / This girls in love
with you / People / You can have him / One
hand, one heart / With these hands / What
the world needs now / Yesterday / Raindrops keep falling on my head / Promises,
promises / You've lost that lovin' feeling /
I'm your puppet / Something / We've only
just begun / Macarthur Park / My way / Up,
up and away / Going out of my head / People get ready / You're my world / Loving you
is sweeter than ever / Window of the world
/ Games people play / I've been loving you
too long / Someday we'll be together / Put
yourself in my place
CD Set _____ BOXD 48T
Carlton Home Entertainment / Oct '95 /
Carlton Home Entertainment.

**DIONNE WARWICK SINGS COLE
PORTER**
Night and day / I love Paris / I get a kick out
of you / What is this thing called love / So
in love / You're the top / I've got you under
my skin / Begin the beguine / It's all right
with me / Anything goes / You'd be so nice
to come home to / All of you / I concentrate
on you / Night and day (jazz version) (Only
on CD and Cassette.) / Just one of those
things
CD _____ 260918
Arista / Oct '90 / BMG.

FRIENDS CAN BE LOVERS
Where my lips have been / Sunny weather
lover / Age of miracles / Love will find a way
/ Much to much / Till the end of time /
Woman that I am / Fragile / Can't break this
heart / Superwoman
CD _____ 07822186822
Arista / Mar '93 / BMG.

GREAT SONGS OF THE SIXTIES
CD _____ PWKS 4191
Carlton Home Entertainment / Mar '94 /
Carlton Home Entertainment.

GREATEST HITS: DIONNE WARWICK
CD _____ 259279
Arista / Aug '91 / BMG.

HEARTBREAKER
All the love in the world / I can't see any-
thing but you / You are my love / Just one
more night / Our day will come / Heart-
breaker / Yours / Take the short way home
/ It makes no difference / Misunderstood
CD _____ 258719
Arista / Oct '87 / BMG.

**HERE I AM/HERE WHERE THERE IS
LOVE**
In between the heartaches / Here I am / If I
ever make you cry / Lookin' with my eyes /
Once in a lifetime / This little light / Don't go
breaking my heart / Window wishing / Long
day, short night / Are you there (with another girl) / How can I hurt you / I love you
Porgy / Go with love / What the world needs
now to know / I just don't know what to do
with myself / Here where there is love /
Trains and boats and planes / Alfie / As long
as he needs me / I wish you love / I never
knew what you were up to / Blowin' in the
wind
CD _____ NEMCD 762
Sequel / Oct '95 / BMG.

LOVE SONGS COLLECTION
I'll never fall in love again / Let it be me /
Here where there is love / I love Paris / Hurt
so bad / As long as he needs me / Blowin'
in the wind / One hand, one heart / You can
have him / People / This girl's in love with
you / You're all I need to get by / Baubles,
bangles and beads / Getting ready for the
heartbreak / Who can I turn to / People got
to be free / It's the good life / Valley of the
dolls / Unchained melody / Valley of the dolls
CD _____ PWKS 525
Carlton Home Entertainment / Feb '96 /
Carlton Home Entertainment.

**MAKE WAY FOR DIONNE WARWICK/
THE SENSITIVE SOUND OF DIONNE**
House is not a home / People / (They want
to be) Close to me / Last one to be loved /
Land of make believe / Reach out for me /
You'll never get to heaven (if you break my
heart) / Walk on by / Wishin' & hopin' / I
smiled yesterday / Get rid of him / Make the
night a little longer / Unchained melody /
Who can I turn to / How many days of sad-
ness / Is there another way to love him /
Where can I go without you / You can have
him / Wives & lovers / Don't say I didn't tell
you so / Only the strong, only the brave /
Forever my love
CD _____ NEMCD 761
Sequel / Oct '95 / BMG.

ORIGINAL HITS 1962-1972, THE
CD _____ DCD 5366
Disky / Apr '94 / THE / BMG / Discovery /
Pinnacle.

**PRESENTING DIONNE WARWICK/
ANYONE WHO HAD A HEART**
This empty place / Wishin' & hopin' / I cry
alone / Zip-a-dee-doo-dah / Make the music play / If you see Bill / Don't make me
over / It's love that really counts (in the long
run) / Inlucky / I smiled yesterday / Make it
easy on yourself / Love of a boy / Anyone
who had a heart / Shall I tell her / Gettin'
ready for the heartbreak / Oh Lord what are
you doing to me / Any old time of day / Mr.
Heartbreak / Put yourself in my place / I
could make you mine / Please make him
love me
CD _____ NEMCD 760
Sequel / Oct '95 / BMG.

SINGS BURT BACHARACH
CD _____ ENTCD 268
Entertainers / Mar '92 / Target/BMG.

SOULFUL
You've lost that lovin' feelin' / I'm your pup-
pet / People got to be free / You're all I need
to get by / We can work it out / Silent voices
(Not on Pye LP) / Hard day's night / Do right
woman, do right man / I've been loving you
too long / People get ready / Hey Jude /
What's good about goodbye (Not on Pye
LP)
CD _____ DCD 5401
Disky / Oct '94 / THE / BMG / Discovery /
Pinnacle.

**WALK ON BY AND OTHER
FAVOURITES**
Don't make me over / This empty place /
Wishin' and hopin' / Anyone who had a
heart / Make it easy on yourself / It's love
that really counts / Walk on by / You'll never
get to heaven (if you break my heart) /
Reach out for me / I just don't know what
to do with myself / I say a little prayer / Do
you know the way to San Jose / I'm your
puppet / Trains and boats and planes / Here
where there is love / Are you there (with another girl) / Wives and lovers / Valley of the
dolls / I'll never fall in love again / Make the
music play
CD _____ CDCHARLY 101
Charly / Oct '87 / Charly / THE / Cadillac.

Warzone

**OPEN YOUR EYES, DON'T FORGET
THE STRUGGLE**
Into bust / It's your choice / Crazy but not
insane / Fuck your attitude / As one / We're
the crew / Don't forget the struggle / In the
mirror / Skinhead youth / Growing up - the
next step / Judgement day / Fight for our
country / Open up your eyes / Dance hard
or die / Face up to it / Always - a friend for
life / Racism - World history part 1 / Back
to school again / American movement /
Fight the oppressoh / Deceive us - no more
/ Striving for a better life
CD _____ LF 109CD
Lost & Found / Oct '94 / Plastic Head.

Was Not Was

HELLO DAD... I'M IN JAIL
Listen like thieves / Shake your head / Tell
me that I'm dreaming / Papa was a rollin'
stone / Are you okay / Spy in the house of
love / I feel better than James Brown /
Somewhere in America / There's a street
named after my dad / Out come the freaks
/ How the heart behaves / Walk the dinosaur / Hello dad... I'm in jail
CD _____ 512 464-2
Fontana / Jun '92 / PolyGram.

Washboard Rhythm Kings

**WASHBOARD RHYTHM KINGS VOL. 3
(1931-32)**
CD _____ COCD 25
Collector's Classics / '95 / Cadillac /
Complete/Pinnacle.

**WASHBOARD RHYTHM KINGS
VOLUME 1 - 1931**
Please don't talk about me / Minnie the
moocher / One more time / Walkin' my baby
back home / Porter's love song / Everyman
for himself / Blues in my heart / Just one
more chance / Many happy returns of the
day / Shoot 'em / Wake 'em up / Georgia
on my mind / Pepper steak / If you don't
love me / Please tell me / (I'll be glad when
you're dead) you rascal you / Crooked
world blues / Call of the freaks / It's crazy
'bout my baby / Because I'm yours
sincerely / Star dust / You can't stop me
from lovin' you / Boola boo / Who stole the
lock
CD _____ COCD 17
Collector's Classics / Feb '95 / Cadillac /
Complete/Pinnacle.

Washboard Sam

ROCKIN' MY BLUES AWAY
My feet jumped salty / Flying crow blues /
Levee camp blues / I'm feeling low down /
She belongs to the devil / I've been treated
wrong / Evil blues / Get down brother / Lover's lane blues / River hip mama / The dust
shake dance / How can you love me / Red

river dam blues / Down South woman blues / Ain't that a shame / I get the blues at bedtime / You can't make the grade / You can't have none of that / I just can't help it / Soap and water blues
CD _____ ND 90652
Bluebird / May '92 / BMG.

WASHBOARD SAM VOL.1 - 1935-36
CD _____ DOCD 5171
Blues Document / Oct '93 / Swift / Jazz Music / Hot Shot.

WASHBOARD SAM VOL.2 - 1937-38
CD _____ DOCD 5172
Blues Document / Oct '93 / Swift / Jazz Music / Hot Shot.

WASHBOARD SAM VOL.3 - 1938
CD _____ DOCD 5173
Blues Document / Oct '93 / Swift / Jazz Music / Hot Shot.

WASHBOARD SAM VOL.4 - 1939-40
CD _____ DOCD 5174
Blues Document / Oct '93 / Swift / Jazz Music / Hot Shot.

WASHBOARD SAM VOL.5 - 1940-41
CD _____ DOCD 5175
Blues Document / Oct '93 / Swift / Jazz Music / Hot Shot.

WASHBOARD SAM VOL.6 - 1941-42
CD _____ DOCD 5176
Blues Document / Oct '93 / Swift / Jazz Music / Hot Shot.

WASHBOARD SAM VOL.7 - 1942-49
CD _____ DOCD 5177
Blues Document / Oct '93 / Swift / Jazz Music / Hot Shot.

Washer, Bill

A.S.A.P. (Washer, Bill & Danny Gottlieb)
CD _____ ITMP 970054
ITM / Jan '91 / Tradelink / Koch.

Washingmachine, George

SWEET ATMOSPHERE
(Washingmachine, George & Ian Date)
CD _____ JH 2008
Jazz Hour / Oct '93 / Target/BMG / Jazz Music / Cadillac.

Washington, Dinah

1954
CD _____ CD 53146
Giants Of Jazz / Nov '95 / Target/BMG / Cadillac.

50 GREATEST HITS
CD _____ DBP 102004
Double Platinum / Nov '93 / Target/BMG.

BEST OF DINAH WASHINGTON
CD Set _____ ATJCD 8006
All That's Jazz / Aug '94 / THE / Jazz Music.

BEST OF DINAH WASHINGTON - ROULETTE YEARS
You're nobody 'til somebody loves you / Take you shoes off baby / Call me irresponsible / You've been a good ole wagon / He's my guy / Where are you / For all we know / Red sails in the sunset / Me and my gin / It's a mean old man's world / Is you is or is you ain't my baby / That Sunday that summer / Something's gotta give / Let me be the first to know / You're a sweetheart / Fly me to the moon / I'll close my eyes / Why was I born / Baby, won't you please come home / Drinking again / Romance in the dark / Destination moon / Nobody knows the way I feel this morning
CD _____ CDROU 1054
Roulette / Apr '92 / EMI.

COLLECTION
CD _____ COL 057
Collection / Jun '95 / Target/BMG.

DINAH & CLIFFORD
CD _____ JHR 73583
Jazz Hour / Dec '94 / Target/BMG / Jazz Music / Cadillac.

DINAH STORY, THE
CD _____ 5148412
Verve / Dec '93 / PolyGram.

DINAH WASHINGTON SINGS STANDARDS
CD _____ 5220552
Verve / Apr '94 / PolyGram.

FATS WALLER SONGBOOK, THE
Christopher Columbus / T'ain't nobody's business if I do / Jitterbug waltz / Someone's rocking my dreamboat / Ain't cha glad / Squeeze me / Ain't misbehavin' / Black and blue / Everybody loves my baby / I've got a feeling I'm falling in love / Honeysuckle rose / Keepin' out of mischief now
CD _____ 8189302
Emarcy / Apr '85 / PolyGram.

FOR THOSE IN LOVE
CD _____ 5140732
Verve / Feb '93 / PolyGram.

HER GREATEST HITS
Am I asking too much / It's too soon to know / Baby get lost / Long John blues / I

only know / I wanna be loved / I'll never be free / Cold cold heart / Wheel of fortune / T.V. is the thing (this year) / I don't hurt anymore / Teach me tonight / What a difference a day makes / Unforgettable / Baby (you've got what it takes) / Rockin' good way / This bitter earth / Love walked in / September in the rain / Mad about the boy
CD _____ CPCD 8008
Charly / Oct '93 / Charly / THE / Cadillac.

IN THE LAND OF HI-FI
CD _____ 8264532
Emarcy / Mar '91 / PolyGram.

JAZZ 'ROUND MIDNIGHT
CD _____ 5100872
Verve / Apr '91 / PolyGram.

JAZZ MASTERS
CD _____ 518200-2
Verve / May '94 / PolyGram.

JAZZ SIDES OF MISS D, THE
CD Set _____ JWD 102312
JWD / Nov '94 / Target/BMG.

MAD ABOUT THE BOY
Mad about the boy / What a difference a day makes / Unforgettable / Baby, you got what it takes / Rockin' good way / September in the rain / Love for sale / Every time we say goodbye / Makin' whoopee / All of me / Let's do it / If I were a bell / Teach me tonight / Manhattan / Everybody loves somebody / Our love is here to stay / Cry me a river
CD _____ 512214-2
Mercury / Apr '92 / PolyGram.

MAD ABOUT THE BOY
CD _____ MPV 5522
Movieplay / May '92 / Target/BMG.

MELLOW MAMA
CD _____ DD 451
Delmark / Dec '87 / Hot Shot / ADA / CM / Direct / Cadillac.

ROULETTE SESSIONS - IN LOVE
Fly me to the moon / You're a sweetheart / Our love / Love is the sweetest thing / I'll close my eyes / I didn't know about you / If it's the last thing I do / Do nothin' 'til you hear from me / My devotion / That's my desire / Was it like that / Me and the one that I love / What's new / I used to love you / Somebody else is taking my place / That old feeling / He's gone again / These foolish things
CD _____ CDROU 1038
Roulette / Aug '91 / EMI.

TEACH ME TONIGHT
CD _____ JHR 73565
Jazz Hour / Oct '92 / Target/BMG / Jazz Music / Cadillac.

TWO ON ONE: DINAH WASHINGTON & SARAH VAUGHAN (Washington, Dinah & Sarah Vaughan)
CD _____ CDTT 4
Charly / Apr '94 / Charly / THE / Cadillac.

UNFORGETTABLE
CD _____ 5106022
Mercury / Apr '93 / PolyGram.

WHAT A DIFFERENCE A DAY MADE
I remember you / I thought about you / That's all there is to that / I'm through with love / Cry me a river / What a difference a day makes / Nothing in the world (could make me love you more than I do) / Manhattan / Time after time / It's magic / Sunday kind of love / I won't cry anymore
CD _____ 818 815 2
Mercury / Oct '84 / PolyGram.

WHAT A DIFFERENCE A DAY MAKES
CD _____ CDCD 1127
Charly / Mar '93 / Charly / THE / Cadillac.

WITH QUINCY JONES
CD _____ CD 53152
Giants Of Jazz / May '95 / Target/BMG / Cadillac.

Washington, Geno

GENO
I can't turn you loose (live) / You left the water running (live) / In the midnight hour (live) / Gimme a little sign/Raise your hand/ I get so excited / Knock on wood / Dirty, dirty / Bring it to me baby / Alison please / I can't let you go / Michael the lover / Hold on I'm comin' (live) / Don't fight it (live) / Land of 1000 dances (live) / You don't know (like I know) (live) / Tell it like it is / Put out the fire / All I need / Water / Whatever will be will be (Que sera sera) / Hi hi Hazel
CD _____ 5507692
Spectrum/Karussell / Mar '95 / PolyGram / THE.

HAND CLAPPIN'-FOOT STOMPIN'-FUNKY BUTT-LIVE (Washington, Geno & The Ram Jam Band)
Philly dog / Ride your pony / Up tight / Roadrunner / Hold on / Don't fight it / Land of 1000 dances / Respect / Willy nilly / Get down with it / Michael / Whatever will be will be (Que sera sera) / You don't know
CD _____ REP 4189-WZ
Repertoire / Aug '91 / Pinnacle / Cadillac.

HANDCLAPPIN'-FOOTSTOMPIN'-FUNKYBUTT-LIVE/HIPSTERS, FLIPSTERS (Washington, Geno & The Ram Jam Band)
Philly dog / Up tight (everything's alright) / Hold on I'm comin' / Land of 1000 dances / Willy nilly / Michael / You don't know (like I know) / Day tripper / You left the water running / Hi-heel sneakers / Raise your hand / Things get better / She shot a hole in my soul / Ride your pony / Roadrunner / Don't fight it / Respect / Get down with it / Whatever will be will be (Que sera sera) / Herk's works / I can't turn you loose / In the midnight hour / Shotgun / Who's foolin' who / It's a wonder / Wild thing
CD _____ C5CD 581
See For Miles/C5 / Mar '92 / Pinnacle.

HIPSTERS, FLIPSTERS AND FINGER POPPIN' DADDIES
CD _____ REP 4190-WZ
Repertoire / Aug '91 / Pinnacle / Cadillac.

LOOSE LIPS
CD _____ RRCD 011
Blue Rose / Oct '95 / 3MV.

Washington, Grover Jr.

ALL MY TOMORROWS
CD _____ 4745532
Sony Jazz / Jan '95 / Sony.

ANTHOLOGY (1) : GROVER WASHINGTON JR.
Best is yet to come / East River drive / Be mine tonight / Can you dig it / In the name of love / Just the two of us / Jamming / Little black samba / Jetstream / Let it flow
CD _____ 9604152
Elektra / '89 / Warner Music.

BEST IS YET TO COME
Can you dig it / Best is yet to come / More than meets the eye / Things are getting better / Mixed emotions / Brazilian memories / I'll be with you / Cassie's theme
CD _____ 9602152
Elektra / Feb '87 / Warner Music.

COME MORNING
East River drive / Come morning / Be mine tonight / Reaching out / Jamming / Little black samba / Making love to you / I'm all yours
CD _____ 252337
Elektra / Apr '84 / Warner Music.

INSIDE MOVES
Inside moves / Dawn song / Watching you watching me / Secret sounds / Jetstream / When I look at you / Sassy stew
CD _____ 7559603182
Pickwick/Warner / Oct '94 / Pinnacle / Warner Music / Carlton Home Entertainment.

MISTER MAGIC
Earth tones / Passion flower / Mr. Magic / Black frost
CD _____ 530103-2
Motown / Jan '93 / PolyGram.

NEXT EXIT
Take five / Your love / Only for you (siempre para d'sers) / Greene street / Next exit / I miss home / Love like this / Summer chill / Till you return to me / Get on up / Check out Grover
CD _____ 4690882
Columbia / Jul '92 / Sony.

STRAWBERRY MOON
Strawberry moon / Look of love / Shivaree Ride / Caught a touch of your love / Maddie's Blues / I will be here for you / Keep in touch / Summer nights
CD _____ 4504642
Sony Jazz / Jan '95 / Sony.

TIME OUT OF MIND
Jamaica / Gramercy Park / Sacred kind of love / Brand new age / Fly away / Don't take your love from me / Time out of mind / Spilt second (Act II, The Bar Scene) / Nice'n'easy / Unspoken love / Protect the dream
CD _____ 4655262
Sony Jazz / Jan '95 / Sony.

WINELIGHT
Winelight / Let it flow / In the name of love / Take me there / Just the two of us / Make a memory
CD _____ 252 262
Asylum / Nov '83 / Warner Music.

Washington, Keith

MAKE TIME FOR LOVE
All night / Make time for love / Kissing you / Are you still in love with me / When you love somebody / Ready, willing and able / I'll be there / When it comes to you / Lovers after all / Closer
CD _____ 759926528-2
Warner Bros. / Mar '91 / Warner Music.

YOU MAKE IT EASY
Let me make love to you / Stay in my corner / Don't leave me in the dark / You always gotta go / What it takes / We need to talk / Before I let go / trippin' / Do what you like / Believe that / No one / You make it easy
CD _____ 9362453362
Warner Bros. / Sep '93 / Warner Music.

Washington, Peter

WHAT'S NEW
CD _____ DIW 605
DIW / Jun '91 / Harmonia Mundi / Cadillac.

Washington, Toni Lynn

BLUES AT MIDNIGHT
CD _____ CDTC 1152
Tonecool / Apr '95 / Direct / ADA.

Washington, Tuts

NEW ORLEANS PIANO (The Larry Borenstein Collection vol.3)
On the sunny side of the street / Muskrat ramble / Fast blues no.1 / Blue moon / Basin Street blues / Some of these days / Yancey special no.1 / After you've gone / Early one morning / Cow cow blues / Pinetop's boogie / Trouble trouble / Tack head blues / Yancey special no.2 / (Back home again in) Indiana / St. Louis blues
CD _____ 504CD 32
504 / Aug '94 / Wellard / Jazz Music / Target/BMG / Cadillac.

NEW ORLEANS PIANO PROFESSOR
CD _____ CD 11501
Rounder / '88 / CM / Direct / ADA / Cadillac.

Washington, Walter

BEST OF NEW ORLEANS RHYTHM & BLUES VOL. 2 (Washington, Walter 'Wolfman')
CD _____ MG 9008
Mardi Gras / Feb '95 / Jazz Music.

BLUE MOON RISIN' (Washington, Walter 'Wolfman' & The JB Horns)
CD _____ 4TR 95112
Go Jazz / Dec '95 / Vital/SAM.

GET ON UP (Charly Blues - Masterworks Volume 9) (Washington, Walter 'Wolfman')
It's raining in my life / Good and juicy / Girl, don't ever leave me / Nobody's fault but mine / Honky tonk / Get on up (The Wolfman's song) / You got me worried / Sure enough it's you / Lovely day
CD _____ CD BM 9
Charly / Apr '92 / Charly / THE / Cadillac.

OUT OF THE DARK (Washington, Walter 'Wolfman')
CD _____ CD 2068
Rounder / '88 / CM / Direct / ADA / Cadillac.

SADA (Washington, Walter 'Wolfman')
I'll be good / Skin tight / Ain't no love in the heart of the city / Girl I wanna dance with you / Share your love / Chockin' kind / Southern comfort / I got a woman / Sada / Nothing left to be desired / What's it gonna take
CD _____ VPBCD 5
Pointblank / Jun '91 / EMI.

WOLF TRACKS (Washington, Walter 'Wolfman')
CD _____ CD 2048
Rounder / '88 / CM / Direct / ADA / Cadillac.

Wasserman, Rob

SOLO
CD _____ ROU 0179CD
Rounder / Apr '94 / CM / Direct / ADA / Cadillac.

TRIOS
Fantasy is reality/Bells of madness / Put your big toe in the milk of human kindness / White wheeled limousine / Country / Zillionaire / Dustin' off the bass / Easy answers / Satisfaction / Home is where you get across / Spike's bulls (Bass trilogy: Part 3) / Gypsy one / Gypsy two / American popsicle / Three guys named Schmoo
CD _____ GRM 40222
GRP / Feb '94 / BMG / New Note.

Wasteland

DAYS OF THE APOCALYPSE
CD _____ WASTE 003CD
Nightbreed / Jun '95 / Plastic Head.

Wat Tyler

TUMMY
Justify your book / Poems on the underground / It makes me belch / My dead relation / Hops and barley / Coming home / Perry Groves / You've stolen my heart / Definitive love song / How does Ed cope / Dodgepotterydo / Billy Bond's clarinet and blue army / Discipline / Not superstitious / James Whale / My dead relation 2 / Rude girl / Rude girl / Operation Ivy and Don Brennan / If the kids are united / Real shocks / Smells like dog poo / Our wedding / 100% top quality / God rest ye merry gentlemen / Song for Guy Fawkes / Masters of the universe / Fat wa / Four minute puzzle / Eternal triangle / Prophecy / Somewhere Too young, too bitter / Played for and got / Big girl's blouse / Wet, wet, wet (the fucking bed) / Rude girl (2) / Little people make lurve

/ Fuck pimp / We curse you a wicked satan / Steven do / Crappy song for a crappy compilation
CD _____ SEEP 014CD
Rugger Bugger / Oct '95 / Vital.

Watanabe, Kazumi

DOGATANA
Nuevo espresso / Loosey goosey / Ti-fa-let / Island / Diana / Waterfall - Autumn / Please don't bundle me / Haru no Tsurara
CD _____ CY 72374
Denon / Mar '90 / Conifer.

KILOWATT
100 mega / Capri / No one / Jive / Papyrus / Sunspin / Pretty soon / Bernard / Dolphin dance / Goodnight machines
CD _____ 794 152
Gramavision / Mar '90 / Vital/SAM / ADA.

MOBO 2
Voyage / Yatokesa / Alicia / Shang hi / All beets are coming
CD _____ GRCD 8406
Gramavision / May '85 / Vital/SAM / ADA.

MOBO CLUB
CD _____ 1885062
Gaia / May '89 / New Note.

MOBO SPLASH
CD _____ 1886022
Gaia / May '89 / New Note.

PANDORA
Pandora / Peaking doll / Vega / Ashita tenki ni / Passy home / Dr. Manmbo X. / Firecracker / Kumpoo manman / Arahi no yoru kimi ni tsugu / Django 1953 / Winter swallow / Satisfaction / We got lost / Memories of Phonecia / Lady Jane / I mean you / Angie / Slippin' into the river / Continental dirth
CD _____ R2 79473
Gramavision / Nov '92 / Vital/SAM / ADA.

SPICE OF LIFE TOO
Andre / Fu bu ki / Small wonder / Kaimon / We planet / Rain / Concrete cows / Men and angels
CD _____ 1888102
Gramavision / Dec '88 / Vital/SAM / ADA.

TO CHI KA
Liquid fingers / Black canal / To chi ka / Cokumo island / Unicorn / Don't be silly / Sayonara / Manhattan flu dance
CD _____ DC 8568
Denon / Oct '90 / Conifer.

Watanabe, Sadao

BOSSA NOVA CONCERT
Felicidade / Meditation / Song of Jet / Bonita / Train samba / Doralice / O grande amor / You and I / Girl from Ipanema / Agua de beber / Raza / Corcovado felicidade / Music break / Mais que nada / I might as well as Spring / Samba de Orfeu / So dance samba / Falicidade
CD _____ DC 8556
Denon / Oct '89 / Conifer.

CALIFORNIA SHOWER
California shower / Duo-creatics / Desert ride / Seventh high / Turning pages of wind / Ngoma party / My country
CD _____ JMI 20122
JVC / Apr '94 / New Note.

DEDICATED TO CHARLIE PARKER
Parker's mood / Song for Bird / Everything happens to me / I can't get started (with you) / Au privave / If I should lose you
CD _____ DC 8558
Denon / Oct '89 / Conifer.

IN TEMPO
CD _____ 5272212
PolyGram Jazz / Feb '95 / PolyGram.

MODERN JAZZ ALBUM
Going home / My favourite things / From Russia with love / And I love / There's no business like show business / Days of wine and roses / Emily / Shadow of your smile / I feel pretty / I could have danced all night
CD _____ CY 1386
Denon / '88 / Conifer.

PLAYS BALLADS
Here's that rainy day / My foolish heart / I thought about you / Old folks / Spring is here / Little girl blue / That's all / They say it's wonderful / My romance / nightingale sang in berkeley square / It's easy to remember
CD _____ DC 8555
Denon / Oct '89 / Conifer.

SADAO MEETS BRAZILIAN FRIENDS
Bim bom / E nada mais / Jequibau / Eu e a brisa / Barquinho diferente / Ritmo / Tristeza / Carolina / Bossa na praia / Mostra morena / Muito a vontade
CD _____ DC 8557
Denon / Oct '89 / Conifer.

Watchman

WATCHMAN, THE
Laundry days / Summer at the empty playground II / Captain's tune / Freddy's race / Considering the lowlands of Holland / Lowland tune / Darling angel / I wanna be with you / Wiener cowboy / After the night shift / Letter to your wedding / Farewell baby

CD _____ HNCD 1362
Hannibal / Jun '91 / Vital / ADA.

Watchman

PEACEFUL ARTILLERY
CD _____ INTREPID 4202
Intrepid / Nov '95 / Direct.

Watchtower

CONTROL AND RESISTANCE
Instruments of random murder / Eldritch / Mayday in Kiev / Fall of reason / Control and resistance / Hidden instincts / Life cycles / Dangerous toy
CD _____ N 0140 2
Noise/Modern Music / Feb '90 / Pinnacle / Plastic Head.

Waterboys

BEST OF THE WATERBOYS, THE (1981 - 1990)
Girl called Johnny / Big music / All the things she gave me / Whole of the moon / Spirit / Don't bang the drum / Fisherman's blues / Killing my heart / Strange boat / And a bang on the ear / Old England / Man is in love
CD _____ CAD 1845
Ensign / Apr '91 / EMI.

DREAM HARDER
CD _____ GED 24476
Geffen / May '93 / BMG.

FISHERMAN'S BLUES
Fisherman's blues / Strange boat / Sweet thing / Has anybody seen Hank / When ye go away / We will not be lovers / World party / And a bang on the ear / When will we be married / Stolen child
CD _____ CCD 1589
Chrysalis / Oct '88 / EMI.

PAGAN PLACE, A
Church not made with hands / All the things she gave me / Thrill is gone / Rags / Somebody might wave back / Big music / Red army blues / Pagan place
CD _____ CCD 1542
Ensign / Jul '94 / EMI.

ROOM TO ROAM
In search of a rose / Song from the end of the world / Man is in love / Kaliope House / Bigger picture / Natural bridge blues / Something that is gone / Star and the sea / Life of Sundays / Island man / Raggle taggle gipsies / How long will I love you / Upon the wind and waves / Spring comes to Spiddal / Trip to Broadford / Further up, further in / Room to roam
CD _____ CCD 1768
Ensign / Sep '90 / EMI.

SECRET LIFE OF THE WATERBOYS ('81-'85), THE
Medicine bow / That was the river / Pagan place / Billy Sparks / Savage earth heart / Don't bang the drum / Ways of men / Rags (Second amendment) / Earth only endures / Somebody might wave back / Going to Paris / Three day man / Bury my heart / Out of control / Love that kills
CD _____ CDCHEN 35
Ensign / Oct '94 / EMI.

THIS IS THE SEA
Don't bang the drum / Whole of the moon / Pan within / Medicine bow / Old England / Be my enemy / Trumpets / This is the sea
CD _____ CD25CR 23
Chrysalis / Mar '94 / EMI.

Waterlillies

ENVOLUPTUOUSITY
Sunshine like you / Hip to my way / Lie with you / Tired of you / Only one (I could stand) / Girl's affair / Nether nether / Day and age / Mermaid song
CD _____ 7599267292
Sire / Oct '92 / Warner Music.

TEMPTED
Tempted / I wanna be there / Never get enough / Free / I don't want your love / No-lion doll / Take my breath away / Supersonic / She must be in love / How does it feel / Work it out / Close to you
CD _____ 936245539-2
Warner Bros. / Aug '94 / Warner Music.

Waterman, Steve

DESTINATION UNKOWN
Changing places (prelude) / Mute retrieval / Long forgotten dreams / Ella's waltz / Changing places / Song for Annie / Changing places (interlude) / Reservations / Destination unkown / Changing places (epilogue)
CD _____ ASCCD 4
ASC / Oct '95 / New Note / Cadillac.

Waters, Benny

(SMALL'S) TO SHANGRI-LA
CD _____ MCD 5340
Muse / Sep '92 / New Note / CM.

PLAYS SONGS OF LOVE
CD _____ CDJP 1039
Jazz Point / May '94 / Harmonia Mundi / Cadillac.

SWINGING AGAIN (Waters, Benny Quartet)
CD _____ CDJP 1037
Jazz Point / Jan '94 / Harmonia Mundi / Cadillac.

TAKE IT HOME
CD _____ BMSTRCD 001
Blues Master / Jun '94 / Direct / ADA.

Waters, Crystal

STORYTELLER
100% pure love / Ghetto day / Regardless / I believe I love you / Relax / What I need / Storyteller / Is it for me / Listen for my beep / Daddy do / Lover lay low / Piece of lonely
CD _____ 5223372
Manifesto / Nov '95 / PolyGram.

Waters, Ethel

1931-34
CD _____ CLASSICS 735
Classics / Feb '94 / Discovery / Jazz Music.

CABIN IN THE SKY
CD _____ 239772
Milan / Mar '95 / BMG / Silva Screen.

CLASSICS 1925-26
CD _____ CLASSICS 672
Classics / Nov '92 / Discovery / Jazz Music.

CLASSICS 1929-31
CD _____ OJCCD 721
Original Jazz Classics / Dec '93 / Wellard / Jazz Music / Cadillac / Complete/Pinnacle.

CLASSICS 1935-40
CD _____ CLASSICS 755
Classics / Aug '94 / Discovery / Jazz Music.

ETHEL WATERS 1921-23
CD _____ CLASSICS 796
Classics / Mar '95 / Discovery / Jazz Music.

ETHEL WATERS 1923-1925
CD _____ CLASSICS 775
Classics / Feb '95 / Discovery / Jazz Music.

ETHEL WATERS 1926-1927
CD _____ CLASSICS 688
Charly / Mar '93 / Charly / THE / Cadillac.

Waters, Kim

IT'S TIME FOR LOVE
CD _____ RIPEXD 215
Ripe / Nov '94 / Total/BMG.

Waters, Muddy

BLUE SKY
Jealous hearted man / I can't be satisfied / Cross-eyed cat / Who do you trust / Mamie / Screamin' and cryin' / Streamline woman / Deep down in Florida / Too young to know / Foreer lonely / I feel like going home / (My eyes) keep me in trouble
CD _____ 4678922
Columbia / Jul '92 / Sony.

BLUES ANTHOLOGY
CD _____ 13118
Laserlight / Jan '95 / Target/BMG.

CHESS BOX SET
CD Set _____ CHD 680002
Chess/MCA / Jul '90 / BMG / New Note.

CHICAGO BLUES
Rollin' stone / Louisiana blues / Long distance call / Honey bee / I want you to love me / I just want to make love to you / Hoochie coochie man / Mannish boy / I'm ready / Forty days and forty nights / She's alright / Walkin' blues / She moves me / Still a fool
CD _____ CDINS 5003
Instant / Jul '89 / Charly.

CHICAGO BLUES MASTERS VOL.1 (Waters, Muddy/Memphis Slim)
Hoochie coochie man / Walkin' thru the park / Boogie woogie Memphis / Rollin' and tumblin' / How long (live) / Rock me / Blow wind blow / John Henry / Stagger Lee / How long / All this piano boogie / Bye bye baby / Love my baby / When the sun goes down / Someday baby / Slim's slow blues / Gee ain't it hard to find somebody
CD _____ CZ 547
Capitol Jazz / Jul '95 / EMI.

CHICAGO BLUESV BAND
CD _____ LS 2908
Landscape / Nov '92 / THE.

COLLECTION, THE
CD _____ COL 034
Collection / Feb '95 / Target/BMG.

COMPLETE MUDDY WATERS, THE (9CD Set/1947-1967)
Gypsy woman / Little Anna Mae / Good looking woman / Mean disposition / I can't be satisfied / I feel like going home / Train

fare home blues / Down south blues / Kind hearted woman blues / Sittin' here drinkin' / You're gonna miss me / Mean red spider / Stand here tremblin' / Streamline woman / Hard days / Muddy jumps one / Little Geneva / Canary bird / Burying ground / Screamin' and cryin' / Where's my woman been / Last time I fool around with you / Rollin' and tumblin' / Rollin' stone / Walkin' blues / You're gonna need my help I said / Sad letter blues / Early morning blues / Appealing blues / Louisiana blues / Evan's shuffle / Long distance call / Too young to know / Honey bee / Howling wolf / Country boy / She moves me / My fault / Still a fool / They call me Muddy Waters / All night long / Stuff you gotta watch / Lonesome day / Please have mercy / Who's gonna be your sweet man when I'm gone / Standing around crying / Gone to the main street / Iodine in my coffee / My life is ruined / She's alright / Sad, sad day / Turn the lamp down low (baby please don't go) / Loving man / Blow wind blow / Mad love (I want you to love me) / Hoochie coochie man / She's so pretty / I just want to make love to you / Oh yeh / I'm ready / Smokestack lightnin' / I don't know why / I'm a natural born lover / Ooh wee / This pain / Young fashioned ways / I want to be loved / My eyes (keep me in trouble) / Sugar sweet / Trouble no more / Clouds in my heart / Forty days and forty nights / All aboard / Just to be with you / Don't go with you / Don't go no further / Diamonds at your feet / I love the life I live, I live the life I love / Rock me / Look what you've done / Got my mojo working / Good news / Evil / Come home baby / I wish you would / Let me hang around / I won't go on / She's got it / Born lover / She's 19 years old / Close to you / Walkin' thru the park / Blues before sunrise / Mean mistreater / Crawlin' kingsnake / Lonesome road blues / Moppers blues / Take the bitter with the sweet / She's into something / Southbound train / Just a dream / I feel so good / Hey hey / Love affair / Recipe for love / Baby I done got wise / Tell me baby / When I get to thinking / Double trouble / Woman wanted / Read way back / I'm your doctor / Deep down in my heart / Tiger in your tank / Soon forgotten / Meanest woman / I got my brand on you / Baby, please don't go / Goodbye Newport blues / Real love / Lonesome room blues / Messin' with the man / Going home / Down by the deep blue sea / Muddy Waters twist / Tough times / You shook me / You need love / Little brown bird / Five long years / Brown skin woman / Twenty four hours / Coming round the mountain / Elevate me mama / So glad I'm living / My love strikes like lightning / Early in the morning / One more mile / 13 highway / You don't have to go / Things I used to do / Wee wee baby / Sittin' and thinkin' / My home is in the delta / Long distance / My captain / Good morning little school girl / Got my mojo working / Cold weather blues / Big leg woman / Feel like going home / Same thing / You can't lose what you ain't never had / My John the conquer root / Short dress woman / Put me in your lay away / My dog can't bark / I got a rich man's woman / Making friends / Betty and Dupree / Trouble / Black night / Trouble in mind / Take my advice / Hard loser / Going back to Memphis / Piney brown blues / Sweet little angel / Corine Corina / It's all over / County jail / Two steps forward / Blind man / Find yourself another fool / Kinfolk's blues / Bird nest on the ground / When the eagle flies / Baby, please don't go (2) / Ready way back
CD Set _____ CUREDBOX 3
Chess/Charly / Nov '92 / Charly.

ELECTRIC MUD AND MORE (Charly R&B Masters Vol. 15)
I just want to make love to you / Hoochie coochie man / Let's spend the night together / She's alright / Herbert Harper's free press / Tom cat / Same thing / Mannish boy / Got my mojo working / I can't be satisfied / Rollin' stone
CD _____ CDRB 15
Charly / Mar '95 / Charly / THE / Cadillac.

EP COLLECTION: MUDDY WATERS & HOWLIN' WOLF (Waters, Muddy & Howlin' Wolf)
Howlin' for my baby / Tell me / Back door man / My country sugar Mama / Evil / Louise / You'll be mine / You gonna wreck my life / Going down slow / 300 pounds of joy / Spoonful / Smokestack lightnin' / Louisiana blues / Little brown bird / I'm ready / I just want to make love to you / Messin' with the man / Got my mojo working (Live) / Still a fool / You need love / She moves on / I can't be satisfied / Hoochie Coochie man / Wee wee baby
CD _____ SEECD 379
See For Miles/C5 / Oct '93 / Pinnacle.

ESSENTIAL RECORDINGS, THE
CD _____ QSCD 6004
Quality (Charly) / Feb '92 / Charly.

FATHER OF CHICAGO BLUES, THE
Sugar sweet / Twenty four hours / All abroad / Hoochie coochie man / I'm ready / Long distance call / I want you to love me / Honey bee / Gone to main street / She moves me / I can't call her sugar / I can't be satisfied / Rollin' stone / You gonna miss

me / Baby, please don't go / Standing around crying / Got my mojo working / Still a fool / Louisiana blues / I just want to make love to you / You can't lose what you ain't never had / Blow wind blow / Forty days and forty night / Walkin' thru the park
CD _____ CD 52001
Blues Encore / '92 / Target/BMG.

FATHERS AND SONS (Waters, Muddy & Michael Bloomfield)
All aboard / Mean disposition / Blow wind blow / Can't lose what you ain't never had / Walkin' through the park / Forty days and forty nights / Standing around crying / I'm ready / Twenty four hours / Sugar sweet / Long distance call / Baby, please don't go / Honey bee / Same thing / Got my mojo working (part 1) / Got my mojo working (part 2)
CD _____ CDRED 8
Charly / Sep '88 / Charly / THE / Cadillac.

FUNKY BUTT (Charly Blues - Masterworks Vol. 39)
Can't get no grindin' (what's the matter with the mill) / Mother's bad luck child / Funky butt / Sad letter / Someday I'm gonna ketch you / Love weapon / Garbage man / After hours / Whiskey ain't no good / Muddy Waters' shuffle / Rollin' and tumblin' / Just to be with you / Electric man / Trouble no more / Link in funk / Drive my blues away / Katy / Waterboy, waterboy / Everything gonna be alright
CD _____ CDBM 39
Charly / Jan '93 / Charly / THE / Cadillac.

GOODBYE NEWPORT BLUES
I got my brand on you / Hoochie coochie man / Baby, please don't go / Soon forgotten / Tiger in your tank / I feel so good / I've got my mojo working pt.1 / I've got my mojo working pt.2 / Goodbye Newport blues / Wee wee baby / Sittin' and thinkin' / Cousins in my heart / Nineteen years old / Long distance call / Same thing
CD _____ CDBM 101
Blue Moon / May '93 / Magnum Music Group / Greensleeves / Hot Shot / ADA / Cadillac / Discovery.

GOT MY MOJO WORKING
I just want to make love to you / When the eagle flies / Rollin' and tumblin' / Crawlin' kingsnake / Rollin' stone / Whiskey ain't no good / Still a fool / Good morning little school girl / Feel like going home / Find yourself another fool / Can't get no gridin' (What's the matter with the mill) / Got my mojo working / Mannish boy / Young fashioned ways / Hoochie coochie man / You need love
CD _____ CDCD 1039
Charly / Mar '93 / Charly / THE / Cadillac.

HARD AGAIN
Mannish boy / Bus driver / I want to be loved / Jealous hearted man / I can't be satisfied / Blues had a baby and they named it rock 'n' roll / Deep down in Florida / Cross-eyed cat / Little girl
CD _____ CD 32357
Columbia / Mar '94 / Sony.

HOOCHIE COOCHIE MAN
CD _____ CDC 9050
LRC / Jun '93 / New Note / Harmonia Mundi.

HOOCHIE COOCHIE MAN
CD _____ CDCD 1100
Charly / Jun '93 / Charly / THE / Cadillac.

HOOCHIE COOCHIE MAN
Mannish boy / I'm ready / Champagne and reefer / I want to be loved / Baby, please don't go / Sad, sad day / I'm a king bee / Blues had a baby and they named it rock and roll / Screamin' and cryin' / I can't be satisfied / She's nineteen years old / Hoochie coochie man
CD _____ 4611862
Epic / Aug '88 / Sony.

HOOCHIE COOCHIE MAN
CD _____ 3001082
Scratch / Jul '95 / BMG.

I'M READY
I'm ready / Thirty three years / Who do you trust / Copper brown / Hoochie coochie man / Mamie / Rock me / Screamin' and cryin' / Good morning little school girl
CD _____ BGOCD 108
Beat Goes On / Aug '91 / Pinnacle.

IN CONCERT
CD _____ CDCD 1257
Charly / Jun '95 / Charly / THE / Cadillac.

KINGS OF CHICAGO
CD Set _____ CDDIG 9
Charly / Feb '95 / Charly / THE / Cadillac.

LEGENDARY HITS
CD _____ 90153-2
Jazz Archives / Oct '92 / Jazz Music / Discovery / Cadillac.

LIVE IN 1958
CD _____ MW 261058
Muddy Waters / Feb '94 / Jazz Music.

LIVE IN ANTIBES 1974
Honky tonk women / Blow wind blow / Off the wall / Can't get no grindin' (What's the matter with the mill) / Trouble no more /

Garbage man / Hoochie coochie man / Baby, please don't go / Mannish boy / Everything gonna be alright / Got my mojo working
CD _____ FCD 116
France's Concert / Jun '88 / Jazz Music / BMG.

LIVE IN PARIS 1968
CD _____ FCD 121
France's Concert / Jun '89 / Jazz Music / BMG.

LIVE IN SWITZERLAND
CD _____ 449082
Landscape / Aug '93 / THE.

LIVE IN SWITZERLAND 1976 (Waters, Muddy & Chicago Blues Band)
CD _____ JH 02
Jazz Helvet / Dec '90 / Magnum Music Group.

LIVE IN SWITZERLAND 1976 VOL.2
CD _____ LS 2921
Landscape / Sep '93 / THE.

MISSISSIPPI ROLLIN' STONE
I can't call her sugar / You can't lose what you ain't never had / Sad letter / I can't be satisfied / Baby, please don't go / Walkin' thru the park / Train fare blues / Sittin' here drinkin' / I got a rich man's woman / Mean mistreater
CD _____ CDBM 014
Blue Moon / Jul '89 / Magnum Music Group / Greensleeves / Hot Shot / ADA / Cadillac / Discovery.

MUD IN YOUR EAR
Diggin' my potatoes / Watchdog / Sting it / Why d'you do me / Natural wig / Mud in your ear / Excuse me baby / Sad day up-town / Top of the boogaloo / Long distance call / Mini dress / Remember me / Snake / Comin' home baby / Blues for hippies / Chicken shack / Love u trouble / I'm so glad / Love without jealousy / Evil
Muse / Feb '91 / New Note / CM. _____ 600630

MUDDY WATERS
Stuff you gotta watch / Iodine in my coffee / Close to you / You gonna miss me / Mean red spider / Diamonds at your feet / You gonna need my help / She's alright / So glad I'm living / One more mile / I can't call her sugar / You can't lose what you ain't never had / Sad letter / I can't be satisfied / Baby, please don't go / Walkin' through the park / Trainfare blues / Sittin' here drinkin' / I got a rich man's woman / Mean mistreater / Forty days and forty nights / Rollin' and tumblin' / All aboard / Rock me / Rollin' stone / I'm ready
CD _____ CDGRF 025
Tring / '93 / Tring / Prism.

MUDDY WATERS & HOWLIN' WOLF GOLD (2CD Set) (Waters, Muddy & Howlin' Wolf)
CD Set _____ D2CD 4015
Deja Vu / Jan '96 / THE.

MUDDY WATERS (2)
Can't get no grindin' (What's the matter with the mill) / Trouble no more / Everything gonna be alright / Hoochie coochie man / Blues straight ahead / Rollin' and tumblin'
CD _____ BSTCD 9104
Best Compact Discs / May '92 / Complete/ Pinnacle.

MUDDY WATERS 1941-46
CD _____ DOCD 5146
Blues Document / Mar '95 / Swift / Jazz Music / Hot Shot.

MUDDY WATERS ANTHOLOGY (The Finest Recordings)
You shook me / I feel so good / Mannish boy / Rollin' stone / You need love / Stuff you gotta watch / Baby, please don't go / Still a fool / Evan's shuffle / Rollin' and tumblin' / Hoochie coochie man / She's into something / My home is in the Delta / I just want to make love to you / Gypsy woman / Elevate me mama / Got my mojo working / Twenty four hours / Honey Bee / Forty days and forty nights / I feel so go
CD _____ PLATCD 3911
Platinum Music / May '91 / Prism / Ross.

MUDDY WATERS BLUE BAND, THE
CD _____ MCD 6004
Muse / Sep '92 / New Note / CM.

MUDDY WATERS COLLECTOR'S EDITION
CD _____ DVBC 9042
Deja Vu / Apr '95 / THE.

MUDDY WATERS IN CONCERT
CD _____ CDSGP 0150
Prestige / Mar '95 / Total/BMG.

MUDDY WATERS LIVE
Mannish boy / She's nineteen years old / Nine below zero / Streamline woman / Howling wolf / Baby, please don't go / Deep down in Florida
CD _____ BGOCD 109
Beat Goes On / Sep '91 / Pinnacle.

MY HOME IS IN THE DELTA
CD _____ CD 52021
Blues Encore / Nov '92 / Target/BMG.

ROCK ME (Charly Blues - Masterworks Volume 10)
Sugar sweet / Trouble no more / All aboard / Don't go no further / I love the life I love, I live the life I love / Rock me / Got my mojo working / She's got it / Close to you / Walking through the park / Mean mistreater / Lonesome road blues / Mopper's blues / Southbound train / Take the bitter with the sweet / She's into something
CD _____ CD BM 10
Charly / Apr '92 / Charly / THE / Cadillac.

ROLLIN' AND TUMBLIN'
Gypsy woman / I feel like going home / Train fare home / Down South blues / Sittin' here drinkin' / Mean red spider / Streamline woman / Little Geneva / Canary bird / Rollin' and tumblin' / You're gonna need my help / Sad letter blues / Early morning blues / Too young to know / Howling Wolf / Flood / My life is ruined / Baby, please don't go / Blow wind blow / Smokestack lightnin' / Young fashioned ways / Just to be with you / Don't go no further / I love the life I love, I live the life I love
CD _____ CDRED 17
Charly / Jun '90 / Charly / THE / Cadillac.

ROLLIN' STONE
Forty days and forty nights / Rollin' and tumblin' / All aboard / Rock me / Rollin' stone / I'm ready / Standing around crying / She moves me / I feel so good / Going home
CD _____ CDBM 006
Blue Moon / Jan '89 / Magnum Music Group / Greensleeves / Hot Shot / ADA / Cadillac / Discovery.

ROLLIN' STONE
I can't be satisfied / Kind hearted woman blues / Screamin and cryin / Rollin' stone / Walkin' blues / Appealing blues / Louisiana blues / Long distace call / Honey bee / She moves me / Still a fool / They call me Muddy Waters / Standing around crying / She's alright / I want you to love me / Hoochie coochie man / I just want to make love to you / I'm ready / Mannish boy / Forty days and forty nights / Crawlin' kingsnake / Just a dream / I feel good
CD _____ CDRED 1
Charly / Oct '88 / Charly / THE / Cadillac.

VERY BEST OF MUDDY WATERS, THE (& Roots Of the Blues #2 Compilation/ 3CD Set)
CD _____ VBCD 302
Charly / Jul '95 / Charly / THE / Cadillac.

Waters, Patty

COLLEGE TOUR
CD _____ ESP 1055-2
ESP / Jan '93 / Jazz Horizons / Jazz Music.

Waters, Roger

AMUSED TO DEATH
Ballad of Bill Hubbard / What God wants (pt 1) / Perfect sense (pts 1 & 2) / Bravery of being out of range / Late home tonight (pts 1 & 2) / Too much rope / What God wants (pt 2) / What God wants (pt 3) / Watching TV / Three wishes / It's a miracle / Amused to death
CD _____ 4687612
Columbia / Sep '92 / Sony.

PROS AND CONS OF HITCH HIKING, THE
Apparently they were travelling abroad / Running shoes / Arabs with knives and West German skies / For the first time today (part 2) / Sexual revolution / Remains of our being out of range / For the first time today (part 1) / Dunroamin' duncarin' dunlivin' / Pros and cons of hitch hiking / Every stranger's eyes / Moment of clarity
CD _____ CDP 746 029 2
Harvest / May '84 / EMI.

RADIO K.A.O.S.
Radio waves / Who needs information / Me or him / Powers that be / Sunset strip / Home / Four minutes / Tide is turning
CD _____ CDKAOS 1
Harvest / Jun '87 / EMI.

WALL, THE (Live in Berlin) (Various Artists)
In the flesh / Thin ice / Another brick in the wall pt 1 / Happiest days of our lives / Another brick in the wall pt 2 / Mother / Goodbye blue sky / Empty spaces / What shall we do now / One of my turns / Don't leave me now / Another brick in the wall pt 3 / Goodbye cruel world / Hey you / Is there anybody out there / Nobody home / Vera / Bring the boys back home / Comfortably numb / In the flesh (2) / Run like hell / Waiting for the worms / Trial / Tide is turning
CD Set _____ 846 911 2
Mercury / Aug '90 / PolyGram.

Waterson, Norma

WATERSON:CARTHY (Waterson, Norma & Martin/Eliza Carthy)
CD _____ TSCD 475
Topic / Oct '94 / Direct / ADA.

Watersons

EARLY DAYS
CD _____ TSCD 472
Topic / Jul '94 / Direct / ADA.

FOR PENCE & SPICY ALE
Country life / Swarthfell rocks / Barney / Swinton May song / Bellman / Adieu adieu / Apple tree / Wassailing song / Sheep shearing / Three day millionaire / King Pharin / T stands for Thomas / Malpas wassail song / Chickens in the garden / Good old way
CD _____ TSCD 462
Topic / May '93 / Direct / ADA.

Watford, Michael

MICHAEL WATFORD
Luv 4-2 / Love me tonight / First mistake / Holdin' on / Happy man / Interlude / So into you / Love to the world / Yesterday love / Michael's prayer
CD _____ 756792323-2
East West / Jan '94 / Warner Music.

Watkins, Mitch

HUMHEAD
CD _____ DOS 7501
Dos / Oct '95 / CM / Direct / ADA.

STRINGS WITH WINGS
Zephyr / One lost love / Oh how we danced / May your sorrows pass / Map of the dark / Suspicion / October 7 / Cry / Wildest flame / Only one moment
CD _____ TIP 8888142
Tiptoe / Nov '92 / New Note.

Watrous, Bill

BONE-IFIED
CD _____ GNPD 2211
GNP Crescendo / Jan '92 / Silva Screen.

LIVE AT THE PIZZA EXPRESS 1982
Straight no chaser / When your lover has gone / Diane / Falling in love with love / There is no greater love / Dearly beloved / I should care
CD _____ MOLECD 7
Mole Jazz / Jul '83 / Jazz Horizons / Jazz Music / Cadillac / Wellard / Impetus.

TIME FOR LOVE, A
Low life / Shadow of your smile / Time for love / Close enough for love / Emily / Where do you start / Shining sea / Zoot / Not really the blues
CD _____ GNPD 2222
GNP Crescendo / Jun '95 / Silva Screen.

Watson, Bobby

GUMBO
Unit seven / Point the finger / Luqman's dream / From east to west / Gumbo / Wheel within a wheel / Premonition
CD _____ ECD 220782
Evidence / Feb '94 / Harmonia Mundi / ADA / Cadillac.

INVENTOR, THE
Heckle and jeckle / Inventor / P.D. in concert / Jones Street / Sun / For children of all ages / Dreams so real / Shaw of Newark / Homemade blues (CD only.) / Long way home
CD _____ CDB1 91915
Blue Note / Feb '90 / EMI.

MIDWEST SHUFFLE
Blues of hope / Time will tell / Cats / Welcome / Complex dialogue / Mirrors (We all need) / Ladies / Midwest shuffle / I'll love you always / He's more good than bad / Finger games / Mable is able / Simon says
CD _____ 475925 2
Columbia / Apr '94 / Sony.

TAILOR MADE
CD _____ 4737662
Sony / Jan '95 / Sony.

URBAN RENEWAL
Lou B / Agaya / Hi-tech trap / If / Love/hate / Beattitudes / Here's to you babe / Back in the day / P D On Great Jones Street / Reachin' and searchin' / Welcome to my world
CD _____ KOKO 1209
Kokopelli / Feb '96 / New Note.

Watson, Chris

STEPPING INTO THE DARK
CD _____ TO 27
Touch / Oct '95 / These / Kudos.

Watson, Dale

CHEATIN' HEART ATTACK
CD _____ H 8061CD
Hightone / Jul '95 / ADA / Koch.

Watson, Doc

BALLADS FROM DEEP (Watson, Doc & Merle)
Rollin' in my sweet baby's arms / Wreck / Cuckoo / My rough and rowdy ways / Gambler's yodel
CD _____ VND 6576
Vanguard / Mar '90 / Complete/Pinnacle / Discovery.

DOC WATSON
CD _____ VND 79152
Vanguard / Oct '95 / Complete/Pinnacle / Discovery.

DOC WATSON FAMILY TRADITION, THE
CD _____ ROUCD 0129
Rounder / Aug '95 / CM / Direct / ADA / Cadillac.

DOCABILLY
CD _____ SHCD 3836
Sugarhill / May '95 / Roots / CM / ADA / Direct.

DOWN SOUTH
Solid gone / Bright sunny south / Slidin' delta / Coal miner's blues / Hesitation blues / What a friend we have in Jesus / Fifteen cents / Twin sisters / Hobo / Cotton eyed Joe / Hello stranger / Down south
CD _____ SHCD 3742
Sugarhill / Mar '85 / Roots / CM / ADA / Direct.

ELEMENTARY DOC WATSON
CD _____ SH 3812CD
Sugarhill / Jan '94 / Roots / CM / ADA / Direct.

ESSENTIAL DOC WATSON VOL.1
Tom Dooley / Alberta / Froggie went a-courtin' / Beaumont rag / St. James hospital / Muskrat / Down in the valley to pray / Blue railroad train / Rising sun blues / Shady grove / My rough and rowdy ways / Train that carried my girl from town
CD _____ VMCD 7308
Vanguard / Oct '89 / Complete/Pinnacle / Discovery.

GUITAR ALBUM, THE (Watson, Doc & Merle)
Sheeps in the meadow / Stoney fork / Talking to Casey / Liza / Lady be good / Black pine waltz / Guitar polka / Going to Chicago blues / Black mountain rag / Cotton row / John Henry / Worried blues / Twinkle twinkle / Take me out to the ball game / Gonna lay down my old guitar
CD _____ FF 301CD
Flying Fish / Jul '92 / Roots / CM / Direct / ADA.

MEMORIES
CD _____ SHCD 2204
Sugarhill / Apr '95 / Roots / CM / ADA / Direct.

MY DEAR SOUTHERN HOME
My dear old southern home / Ship that never returned / Your lone journey / My friend Jim / No telephone in heaven / Dream of the miner's child / Wreck of old no.9 / Grandfather's clock / Don't say goodbye if you love me / Sleep, baby, sleep / Signal light / That silver haired Daddy of mine / Life is like a river
CD _____ SHCD 3795
Sugarhill / '91 / Roots / CM / ADA / Direct.

OLD TIMEY CONCERT
New river train / What does the deep sea blues / Sunny Tennessee / Walkin' in Jerusalem / Sittin' on top of the world / Pretty little pink / My home's across the Blue Ridge Mountains / Slewfoot / Little orphan girl / Long journey home / Rank stranger / Crawdad / Fire on the mountain / Eastbound train / On the old banks of the old Tennessee / Mountain dew / Corine Corina / Footprints in the snow / I saw a man (at the close of day) / Cacklin' hen / Wanted man / Way down town / Will the circle be unbroken
CD Set _____ VCD 107/8
Vanguard / Dec '92 / Complete/Pinnacle / Discovery.

ON PRAYING GROUND
You must come in at the door / Precious Lord / On praying ground / I'll live on / Gathering buds / Beautiful golden somewhere / We'll work 'til Jesus comes / Ninety and nine / Farther along / Christmas lullaby / Did Christ o'er sinners weep / Uncloudy day
CD _____ SHCD 3779
Sugarhill / '90 / Roots / CM / ADA / Direct.

ORIGINAL FOLKWAYS RECORDINGS 1960-62 (Watson, Doc & Clarence Ashley)
CD _____ SFWCD 40029
Smithsonian Folkways / Jun '94 / ADA / Direct / Koch / CM / Cadillac.

PICKIN' THE BLUES (Watson, Doc & Merle Watson)
Mississipppi heavy water blues / Sittin' hear pickin' the blues / Stormy weather / Windy and warm / St. Louis blues / Jailhouse blues / Freight train blues / Hobo Bill's last ride / Carroll county blues / Blue ridge mountain blues / I'm a stranger here / Honey babe blues
CD _____ FF 352CD
Flying Fish / Jul '92 / Roots / CM / Direct / ADA.

RED ROCKING CHAIR (Watson, Doc & Merle)
Sadie / Fisher's hornpipe / Devil's dream / Along the road / Smoke, smoke, smoke / Below freezing / California blues / John Hurt / Mole in the ground / Any old time / Red

rocking chair / How long blues / Down yonder
CD _____ FF 252CD
Flying Fish / Jul '92 / Roots / CM / Direct / ADA.

RIDIN' THE MIDNIGHT TRAIN
I'm going back to the old home / Greenville high trestle / Highway of sorrow / Fill my way with love / We'll meet again sweetheart / Ridin' that midnight train / Stone's rag / Ramshackle shack / Midnight on the stormy deep / Blue baby eyes / What does the deep sea say / Let the church roll on / Sweet heaven when I die
CD _____ SHCD 3752
Sugarhill / Dec '88 / Roots / CM / ADA / Direct.

SONGS FOR LITTLE PICKERS
Talkin' guitar / Mole in the ground / Mama blues / Froggie went a-courtin' / Shady grove / Riddle song / Crying baby kitty / John Henry / Sally Goodin / Crawdad song / Grass grew all around / Liza Jane / Tennessee stud
CD _____ SHCD 3786
Sugarhill / '90 / Roots / CM / ADA / Direct.

SONGS FROM THE SOUTHERN MOUNTAINS (Watson, Doc & Family)
CD _____ SHCD 3829
Sugarhill / Oct '94 / Roots / CM / ADA / Direct.

SOUTHBOUND
CD _____ VND 79213
Vanguard / Oct '95 / Complete/Pinnacle / Discovery.

THEN AND NOW/TWO DAYS IN NOVEMBER (Watson, Doc & Merle)
Bonaparte's retreat / Milkcow blues / Bottle of wine / Matchbox blues / Freight train boogie / If I needed you / Frankie & Johnny / Summertime / That's all / Corrina, Corrina / Meet me somewhere in your dreams / Old camp meetin' time / Rain crow Bill / Walk on boy / Poor boy blues / I'm going out of my mind / Lonesome moan / Little beggar man / Old Joe Clark / Kaw Liga / Three times seven / Train that carried my girl from town / Snow bird / Doc's rag
CD _____ BGOCD 297
Beat Goes On / Nov '95 / Pinnacle.

TREASURES UNTOLD (Watson, Doc & Family)
Intro / Lights in the valley / Beaumont rag / I heard my mother weeping / Billy in the lowground / Omie wise / Rueben's train / Hick's farewell / Ramblin' hobo / White House blues / Jimmy Sutton / The old buck ram / I want him to love me more / Grandfather's clock / Chinese breakdown / Handsome Molly / Beaumont rag (2) / Farewell blues / Lonesome road blues / Footprints in the snow
CD _____ VCD 77001
Vanguard / '91 / Complete/Pinnacle / Discovery.

Watson, Eric
BROADWAY BY TWILIGHT
CD _____ 500482
Musidisc / May '94 / Vital / Harmonia Mundi / ADA / Cadillac / Discovery.

MEMORY OF WATER, THE (Watson, Eric & John Lindberg)
CD _____ LBLC 6535
Label Bleu / Jun '91 / New Note.

Watson Family
WATSON FAMILY, THE
CD _____ CDSF 40012
Smithsonian Folkways / Aug '94 / ADA / Direct / Koch / CM / Cadillac.

Watson, James
JAMES WATSON SOLO
Concert scherzo / Trumpet concerto (Goedicke) / Albumblat / June from The Seasons / Trumpet concerto (Arutiunian) / Vocalise / Valse sentimentale / Concert etude
CD _____ DOYCD 036
Doyen / Oct '94 / Conifer.

Watson, Johnny 'Guitar'
AIN'T THAT A BITCH
I need it / I want to ta ta you baby / Superman lover / Ain't that a bitch / Since I met you baby / We're no exception / Won't you forgive me baby
CD _____ NEM 774
Sequel / Jan '96 / BMG.

FUNK BEYOND THE CALL OF DUTY
Funk beyond the call of duty / It's all about the dollar bill / Give me my love / It's a damn shame / I'm gonna get you baby / Barn door / Love that will not die
CD _____ NEM 776
Sequel / Jan '96 / BMG.

GANGSTER OF LOVE
I got eyes / Motorhead baby / Gettin' drunk / Walkin' to my baby / Highway 60 / Space guitar / Sad fool / Half pint of whiskey / No I can't / Thinking / Broke and lonely / Cuttin' in / What you do to me / Those lonely,

lonely nights / You can't take it with you / I just wants me some love / Gangster of love / Sweet lovin' mama
CD _____ CDCHARLY 267
Charly / Feb '91 / Charly / THE / Cadillac.

GANGSTER OF LOVE
CD _____ CCSCD 802
Castle / Aug '95 / BMG.

LISTEN
If I had the power / You've got a hard head / Loving you / It's all about you / You're the sweetest thing I've ever had / I get a feeling / Like I'm not your man / You bring love / You stole my heart / I don't want to be a lone ranger / Your new love is a player / Tripping / Lonely man's prayer / You make my heart want to sing / It's way too late / Love is sweet misery / You can stay but the noise must go / Strong vibrations
CD _____ CDCHD 408
Ace / Sep '92 / Pinnacle / Cadillac / Complete/Pinnacle.

REAL MOTHER FOR YA, A
Real Mother for you / Nothing left to be desired / Your love is my love / Real deal / Tarzan / I wanna thank you / Lover Jones
CD _____ NEM 775
Sequel / Jan '96 / BMG.

STRIKE ON COMPUTERS
You do me bad so good / Boogie down party down / Scratching / Let's get together / Strike on computers / Byrd ball train / Statue of Liberty / Please send me someone to love
CD _____ SOSCD 2001
PolyGram TV / Jul '87 / PolyGram.

Watson, Junior
LONG OVERDUE
CD _____ BMCD 9021
Black Magic / Apr '93 / Hot Shot / Swift / CM / Direct / Cadillac / ADA.

Watson, Robert
JEWEL (Watson, Robert Sextet)
To see her face / Orange blossom / Jewel / Karita / You're lucky to me / And then again
CD _____ ECD 22043
Evidence / Mar '93 / Harmonia Mundi / ADA / Cadillac.

Watt, Ben
NORTH MARINE DRIVE
On Box Hill / Some things don't matter / Lucky one / Empty bottles / North Marine Drive / Waiting like mad / Thirst for knowledge / Long time no see / You're gonna make me lonesome when you go / Walter and John / Aquamarine / Slipping slowly / Another conversation with myself / Girl in winter
CD _____ CDBRED 40
Cherry Red / Jun '87 / Pinnacle.

Watt, Mike
BALL-HOG OR TUGBOAT
Big train / Against the 70's / Drove up from Pedro / Piss bottle man / Chinese firedrill / Intense song for Madonna to sing / Tuff gnarl / Sexual military dynamics / Max and wells / E-ticket ride / Forever-one reporters opinion / Song for Igor / Tell' em boy / Sidemouse advice / Heartbeat / Maggot brain / Coincidence is either hit of miss
CD _____ 4780750
Columbia / Feb '95 / Sony.

Watters, Lu
COMPLETE GOOD TIME JAZZ RECORDINGS, THE (Watters, Lu & The Yerba Buena Jazz Band)
CD Set _____ 4GTJCD 4409-2
Good Time Jazz / Oct '93 / Jazz Music / Wellard / Pinnacle / Cadillac.

DAWN CLUB FAVOURITES (Watters, Lu & The Yerba Buena Jazz Band)
CD _____ GTCD 12001
Good Time Jazz / Nov '95 / Jazz Music / Wellard / Pinnacle / Cadillac.

HAMBONE KELLY (Watters, Lu & The Yerba Buena Jazz Band)
CD _____ MMRCD 10
Merry Makers / Aug '95 / Jazz Music.

TOGETHER AGAIN (Watters, Lu & Turk Murphy)
CD _____ MMRCD 8
Merry Makers / Mar '95 / Jazz Music.

YERBA BUENA JAZZ BAND VOL. 12
CD _____ BCD 97
GHB / Mar '95 / Jazz Music.

Watts, Charlie
FROM ONE CHARLIE (Watts, Charlie Quintet)
CD _____ UFO 002 CD
UFO Jazz / May '91 / Pinnacle.

MY SHIP
CD _____ CDCTUM 103
Continuum / Dec '93 / Pinnacle.

WARM AND TENDER
My ship / Bewitched, bothered and bewildered / My foolish heart / Someone to watch over me / I'll be around / Love walked in / It never entered my mind / My one and only love / If I should lose you / Ill wind / Time after time / Where are you / For all we know / They didn't believe me / You go to my head
CD _____ CDCTUM 4
Continuum / Oct '93 / Pinnacle.

Watts, Ernie
ERNIE WATTS QUARTET (Watts, Ernie Quartet)
CD _____ JD 3309
JVC / Sep '88 / New Note.

REACHING UP
Reaching up / Mr. Sums / I hear a rhapsody / Transparent sea / High road / Inward glance / You leave me breathless / Juice Lucy / Angels flight / Sweet solitude
CD _____ JVC 20312
JVC / Feb '94 / New Note.

UNITY
You say you care / In your own sweet way / Tricotism / Unity / Silver hollow / Some kind a blue / Don't look now / Joyous reunion / Lonely hearts / Sticky kisses / Soul eyes
CD _____ JVC 20462
JVC / Apr '95 / New Note.

Watts, Jeff
MEGAWATTS (Watts, Jeff 'Tain')
CD _____ 500552
Sunnyside / Aug '93 / Pinnacle.

Watts, Marzette
MARZETTE WATTS
CD _____ ESP 1044-2
ESP / Jan '93 / Jazz Horizons / Jazz Music.

Watts, Noble
RETURN OF THE THIN MAN
CD _____ ALCD 4785
Alligator / May '93 / Direct / ADA.

Watts, Trevor
MOIRE MUSIC (Watts, Trevor Moire Music)
Egungi / Ahoom mbram / Tetegramatan / Free flow / Tetegramatan reprise / Opening gambit / Otublohu / Bomsu / Hunter's song: Ibrumankuman / Rocky road to Dublin / Brekete takai / Southern memories / We are
CD _____ 5213512
ECM / Feb '94 / New Note.

WIDER EMBRACE, A
CD _____ ECM 1449
ECM / May '94 / New Note.

Waulk Elektrik
UPROOTED
West wind / Ud Nameh / Lendrick Hill / Green fingers / List / Breakout / Dreampad / Punch it / Stumpie/Madam Frederick's/Hunter's purse
CD _____ DREXCD 102
Dangerous / Apr '94 / Pinnacle / ADA.

Wavestar
MOONWIND
Voyager / Edge of morning / Cabala / Troll valley / Moonwind / Chase the evening / For the whales
CD _____ REAL 100
Surreal / Apr '90 / Surreal To Real / C & D Compact Disc Services.

Wax
HUNDRED THOUSAND IN FRESH NOTES, A
Anchors aweigh / Wherever you are / Railroad to heaven / He said she said / Spell on you / Don't play that song (You lied) / Pictures of Paris / Maybe / Madelaine / Credit where credit's due
CD _____ PD 74182
RCA / Nov '89 / BMG.

Waxworth Industries
ALIEN DISCO
CD _____ WAX 100CD
Abstract / Aug '94 / Pinnacle / Total/BMG.

Way, Anthony
CHOIRBOY, THE
CD _____ PERMCD 41
Permanent / Nov '95 / Total/BMG.

Way We Live
CANDLE FOR JUDITH/TRACTOR (Way We Live/Tractor)
Kick Dick II / Squares / Siderial / Angle / Storm / Willow / Madrigal / Way ahead / All ends up / Little girl in yellow / Watcher / Reavenscroft / Bar boogie / Shubunkin' / Hope in favour / Everytime it happens / Make the journey

CD _____ SEECD 409
See For Miles/C5 / Sep '94 / Pinnacle.

WAY WE LIVE, THE
CD _____ REP 4204-WP
Repertoire / Aug '91 / Pinnacle / Cadillac.

Waybill, Fee

READ MY LIPS
You're still laughing / Nobody's perfect / Who loves you baby / I don't even know your name (passion play) / Who said life would be pretty / Thrill of the kill / Saved my life / Caribbean sunsets / Star of the show / I could've been somebody
CD _____ BGOCD 283
Beat Goes On / Aug '95 / Pinnacle.

Wayland

ON BREAD ALONE
CD _____ FWCDS 001
Figurehead / Aug '95 / Total/BMG.

STICKED AND STONED
CD _____ FWCDA 001
Figurehead / Oct '95 / Total/BMG.

Wayne, Chuck

JAZZ GUITARIST
Taking a chance on love / Sirod / Uncus / Stella by starlight / Prospecting / Tasty pudding / While my lady sleeps / Sidewalks of Cuba / Butterfingers / S.S. cool / Mary Ann / You brought a new kind of love
CD _____ SV 0189
Savoy Jazz / Oct '92 / Conifer / ADA.

TASTY PUDDING (Wayne, Chuck/Brew Moore/Zoot Sims)
You brought a new kind of love to me / S Cool / Mary Ann / Butterfingers / Taking a chance on love / Sirod / While my lady sleeps / Tasty pudding / Prospecting / Sidewalks of Cuba / Uncas / Stella by starlight
CD _____ SV 0253
Savoy Jazz / Nov '94 / Conifer / ADA.

Wayne, Jeff

WAR OF THE WORLDS
Coming of the Martians / Eve of the war / Horsell Common and the heat ray / Artilleryman and the fighting machine / Forever autumn / Thunder child / Earth under the Martians / Red weed #2 / Red weed #3 / Spirit of man / Brave new world / Dead London / Epilogue (part 1) / Epilogue (part 2)
CD _____ CDX 96000
Columbia / Aug '95 / Sony.

WAR OF THE WORLDS (Highlights)
Eve of the war / Horsell Common and the heat ray / Forever autumn / Fighting machine / Thunderchild / Red weed / Spirit of man / Dead London / Brave new world
CD _____ CD 32356
Columbia / Feb '91 / Sony.

Wayra, Pukaj

BOLIVIA
CD _____ LYRCD 7361
Lyrichord / '91 / Roots / ADA / CM.

MUSICA ANDINA
CD _____ CD 12511
Music Of The World / Nov '92 / Target/ BMG / ADA.

Waysted

GOOD, THE BAD AND THE WAYSTED, THE
Hang 'em high / Hi ho my baby / Heaven tonight / Manuel / Dead on my legs / Rolling out the pie / Land that's lost the love / Crazy about the stuff / Around and around / Won't get out alive / Price you pay / Rock steady / Hurt so good / Cinderella boys / Ball and chain
CD _____ CDMFN 43
Music For Nations / Dec '92 / Pinnacle.

WC & The Maad Circle

CURB SERVIN'
Intro / West up / Granny nuttin' up / One / Crazy break pt.2 / Put on the set / In a twist / Homesick / Feel me / Curb servin' / Stuckie mack / Taking ova / Kill a habit / Reality check / Creator
CD _____ 8286502
Payday / Sep '95 / PolyGram / Vital.

We All Together

WE ALL TOGETHER
CD _____ HBG 122/8
Background / Apr '94 / Background.

We Are Going To Eat You

EVERYWHEN
If I could / Heart in hand / This conspiracy / Each life a mystery / Glory / Ride upon the tide / Eye to eye / On a day like this / Just another one / Here always / If you believe / Her dreamworld
CD _____ ABBCD 014
Big Cat / Jan '90 / SRD / Pinnacle.

We Are The

FUTURE 3
CD _____ APR 010
April / Nov '95 / Plastic Head.

We The People

DECLARATION OF INDEPENDENCE
CD _____ EVA 842144
EVA / Nov '94 / Direct / ADA.

Weapon Of Choice

NUT MEG SEZ "BOZO THE TOWN"
Nutty nutmeg phantasy / Uppity yuppity doolittle / Icy cold / Cat a chronick / Inhale the earth / Slave driver / Mark of the feast / Life of da dotty contest (live intro) / U owe it to U / Gee ga ga / Iz funk aroma thera'd / I / Gutterball
CD _____ 4783782
Epic / Jul '95 / Sony.

Weather Girls

DOUBLE TONS OF FUN
We're gonna party / Sweet thang / Can U feel it (dee ooh la la la) / We shall all be free / Sexy ghost / Still I'm free / Here goes my heart / Love somebody tonite / Happy, happy / I want to take you higher / Can't let you go / It's raining men
CD _____ 450994018-2
WEA / Mar '94 / Warner Music.

WEATHER GIRLS
Land of the believer / Love's on the way / Why can't we show our love / Opposite directions / Love you like a train / Worth my weight in love / Burn me / Something for love
CD _____ 983315-2
Pickwick/Sony Collector's Choice / Apr '94 / Carlton Home Entertainment / Pinnacle / Sony.

Weather Prophets

JUDGES, JURIES AND HORSEMEN
CD _____ CRECD 033
Creation / May '94 / 3MV / Vital.

TEMPERANCE HOTEL
CD _____ CRECD 50
Creation / May '94 / 3MV / Vital.

WEATHER PROPHETS LIVE
CD _____ CRECD 085
Creation / May '94 / 3MV / Vital.

Weather Report

8.30 (2CD Set)
Black market / Scarlet woman / Teen town / Remark you made / Slang / In a silent way / Birdland / Thanks for the memory / Badia / Boogie woogie waltz medley / 8.30 / Brown Street / Orphan / Sightseeing
CD Set _____ 4769082
Sony Jazz / Jan '95 / Sony.

BLACK MARKET
CD _____ 4682102
Sony Jazz / Jan '95 / Sony.

COLLECTION: WEATHER REPORT
Birdland / Teen town / Juggler / Pursuit of the woman in the feathered hat / Elders / Punk jazz / And then / Black market / Night passage / Rockin' in rhythm / Fast city / Madagascar / Remark you made (live)
CD _____ CCSCD 244
Castle / Aug '90 / BMG.

DOMINO THEORY
Can it be done / D flat waltz / Peasant / Predator / Blue sound-note / Swamp cabbage / Domino theory
CD _____ CD 25839
CBS / Feb '84 / Sony.

HEAVY WEATHER
Birdland / Remark you made / Teen town / Harlequin / Rumba mama / Palladium / Juggler / Havona
CD _____ CK 64427
Columbia / Feb '95 / Sony.

I SING THE BODY ELECTRIC
CD _____ 4682072
Sony Jazz / Jan '95 / Sony.

MR. GONE
Pursuit of the woman in the feathered hat / River people / Young and fine / Elders / Mr. Gone / Punk jazz / Pinocchio / And then
CD _____ 4682082
Sony Jazz / Jan '95 / Sony.

MYSTERIOUS TRAVELLER
CD _____ 4718602
Sony Jazz / Jan '95 / Sony.

NIGHT PASSAGE
Dream clock / Port of entry / Forlorn / Rockin' in rhythm / Fast city / Night passage / Three views of a secret / Madagascar
CD _____ 4682112
Sony Jazz / Jan '95 / Sony.

TALE SPINNIN'
CD _____ 4769072
Sony Jazz / Jan '95 / Sony.

THIS IS THIS
This is this / Face the fire / I'll never forget you / Jungle stuff (part 1) / Man with the

copper fingers / Consequently / Update / China blues
CD _____ CD 57052
Sony Jazz / Jan '95 / Sony.

WEATHER REPORT
Volcano for hire / Current affairs / N.Y.C. / Dara factor one / When it was now / Speechless
CD _____ 983339 2
Pickwick/Sony Collector's Choice / Mar '94 / Carlton Home Entertainment / Pinnacle / Sony.

WEATHER REPORT
Milky way / Umbrellas / Seventh arrow / Orange lady / Morning lake / Waterfall / Tears / Eurydice
CD _____ 4682122
Columbia / Jan '95 / Sony.

Weaver, Curley

COMPLETE RECORDED WORKS 1933-35
CD _____ DOCD 5111
Blues Document / Nov '92 / Swift / Jazz Music / Hot Shot.

Weaver, Sylvester

COMPLETE RECORDED WORKS VOL. 1
CD _____ DOCD 5112
Blues Document / Nov '92 / Swift / Jazz Music / Hot Shot.

COMPLETE RECORDED WORKS VOL. 2
CD _____ DOCD 5113
Blues Document / Nov '92 / Swift / Jazz Music / Hot Shot.

Weavers

AIMANIAC
CD _____ VND 79100
Vanguard / Oct '95 / Complete/Pinnacle / Discovery.

TOGETHER AGAIN
CD _____ CD 1681
Rounder / '88 / CM / Direct / ADA / Cadillac.

Webb, Cassell

HOUSE OF DREAMS
CD _____ WOLCD 1025
China / May '92 / Pinnacle.

Webb, Chick

'TAIN'T WHAT YOU DO, IT'S THE WAY THAT YOU DO IT (Webb, Chick & Ella Fitzgerald)
Strictly jive / If you can't sing it, you'll have to swing it (Mr. Paganini) / Gee boy you're swell / Liza / Moonlight and magnolias / Facts and figures / T'aint what you do, it's the way that you do it / Love you're just a laugh / Wacky dust / Midnight in Harlem / Dipsy doodle / Congo / Rusty hinge / I've got a guy / Down home rag / Tisket-a-tasket / Take another guess / Sweet Sue, just you / Rock it for me / Go Harlem / Holiday in Harlem / Azure
CD _____ RAJCD 836
Empress / Oct '94 / THE.

CHICK WEBB WITH GUESTS
CD _____ CD 14548
Jazz Portraits / Jan '94 / Jazz Music.

FOR RADIO ONLY RECORDINGS 1939
CD _____ TAXCD 3706
Tax / Aug '89 / Jazz Music / Wellard / Cadillac.

INTRODUCTION TO CHICK WEBB 1929-39
CD _____ 4015
Best Of Jazz / Nov '94 / Discovery.

ON THE AIR 1939
CD _____ TAX 37062
Tax / Aug '94 / Jazz Music / Wellard / Cadillac.

RHYTHM MAN (1931-1934) (Webb, Chick Orchestra)
Heebie jeebies / Blues in my heart / Soft and sweet / On the sunnyside of the street / At the Darktown strutter's ball / If dreams come true / Let's get together / I can't dance / Imagination / Why should I beg / Stompin' at the Savoy / Blue minor / True / Lonesome moments / If it ain't love / That rhythm man / On the sunnyside of the street (2) / Lona / It's over because we're through / What a shuffle / Blue Lou
CD _____ HEPCD 1023
Hep / May '92 / Cadillac / Jazz Music / New Note / Weilard.

Webb, Jimmy

ARCHIVE
P.F. Sloan / Love song / Three songs (Including: Let it be me/Never my love/I wanna be free.) / Met her on a plane / All my love's laughter / One lady / If ships were made to sail / Galveston / Once in the morning / When can Brown begin / Piano / Highwayman / Christian no / Where the universes are / Moon is a harsh mistress / Feet in the sunshine / Lady fits her blue jeans / Just this one time / Crying in my sleep / Land's end/Asleep on the wind
CD _____ 954832063-2
WEA / Jun '93 / Warner Music.

SUSPENDING DISBELIEF
Too young to die / I don't know how to love you anymore / Elvis and me / It won't bring her back / Sandy cove / Friends to burn / What does a woman see in a man / Postcard from Paris / Just like always / Adios / I will arise
CD _____ 7559615062
WEA / Oct '93 / Warner Music.

Webb, Marti

ALWAYS THERE
Always there / Onedin line / Reilly, ace of spies / Moonlighting / To have and to hold / I could be so good for you (Theme from Minder) / To serve them all my days / EastEnders
CD _____ PWKS 647
Carlton Home Entertainment / Apr '88 / Carlton Home Entertainment.

MARTI WEBB SINGS GERSHWIN
Fascinating rhythm / I got rhythm / Rhapsody in blue / Porgy, I's your woman now / Love walked in / I love's here to stay / Somebody loves me / How long has this been going on / Someone to watch over me / Do it again / Summertime / But not for me / Man I love / Embraceable you / He loves and she loves
CD _____ PWKS 657
Carlton Home Entertainment / Oct '89 / Carlton Home Entertainment.

Webb, Natalie

TAKE ME TO PARADISE
CD _____ NATCD 1
Nation / Jun '95 / Disc.

Webb, Stan

40 BLUE FINGERS FRESHLY PACKED (Chicken Shack)
Letter / Lonesome whistle blues / When the train comes back / San-Ho-Zay / King of the world / See see baby / First time I met the blues / Webbed feet / You ain't no good / What you did last night
CD _____ 477357-2
Columbia / Aug '94 / Sony.

CHANGES (Chicken Shack)
CD _____ INAK 19008
In Akustik / Jul '95 / Magnum Music Group.

CHICKEN SHACK ON AIR (Chicken Shack)
Tired eyes / I'd rather go blind / Tears in the wind / Night is when it matters / Telling your fortune / You knew you did / Midnight hour / Hey baby / Things you put me through / Get like you used to be / You done lost that good thing now / Look ma I'm crying
CD _____ BOJ CD002
Band Of Joy / Nov '91 / ADA.

COLLECTION: CHICKEN SHACK (Chicken Shack)
Letter / When the train comes back / Lonesome whistle blues / You ain't no good / Baby's got me crying / Right way is my way / Get like you used to be / Woman is blues / I wanna see my baby / Remmington ride / Mean old world / San-Ho-Zay / Way it is / Tears in the wind / Maudie / Some other time / Andalucian blues / Crazy about you baby / Close to me / I'd rather go blind
CD _____ CCSCD 179
Castle / Jan '94 / BMG.

IMAGINATION LADY (Chicken Shack)
Crying won't help you now / Daughter of the hillside / If I were a carpenter / Going down / Poor boy / Telling your fortune / Loser
CD _____ 8441692
Deram / Dec '94 / PolyGram.

OK KEN (Chicken Shack)
Baby's got me crying / Right way is my way / Get like you used to be / Pony and trap / Tell me / Woman is the blues / I wanna see my baby / Remington ride / Fishing in your river / Mean old world / Sweet sixteen
CD _____ BGOCD 186
Beat Goes On / Jun '93 / Pinnacle.

SIMPLY LIVE
CD _____ 848492
SPV / Jan '90 / Plastic Head.

STAN THE MAN LIVE
CD _____ IGOCD 2053
Indigo / Nov '95 / Direct / ADA.

WEBB'S BLUES (Webb, Stan's Chicken Shack)
CD _____ IGOCD 2013
Indigo / Dec '94 / Direct / ADA.

Webber, A.J.

RUNNING OUT OF SKY
Somewhere in the darkness / Hello old friend hello / Reservation blues / Decision / Running out of sky / Sebastapol bay / Eye of the wind / Barry's song / Chosen one / That old road back home / Seeing you again

Webber, Dave

CD _____ AJWCD 1
Smart / Sep '93 / Sony.

TOGETHER SOLO (Webber, Dave &
Anni Fentiman)
CD _____ DRGNCD 931
Dragon / Mar '94 / Roots / Cadillac /
Wellard / CM / ADA.

Webber, Garth

ON THE EDGE (Webber, Garth & Mark
Ford)
CD _____ CCD 11045
Crosscut / Nov '94 / ADA / CM / Direct.

Weber, Eberhard

COLOURS OF CHLOE, THE
CD _____ 8333312
ECM / Jul '88 / New Note.

FOLLOWING MORNING, THE
T on a white horse / Moana I / Following
morning / Moana II
CD _____ 8291162
ECM / Jun '86 / New Note.

ORCHESTRA SOLO BASS (Weber,
Eberhard Orchestra)
CD _____ 8373432
ECM / Feb '89 / New Note.

PENDULUM
Bird out of a cage / Notes after an evening
/ Delirium / Children's song no.1 / Street
scenes / Silent for a while / Pendulum / Un-
finished self - portrait / Closing scene
CD _____ 5197072
ECM / Oct '93 / New Note.

SILENT FEET (Weber, Eberhard Colours)
CD _____ 8350172
ECM / Sep '88 / New Note.

WORKS: EBERHARD WEBER
Sand / Dark spell / More colours / Touch /
Eyes that can see in the dark / Moana II
CD _____ 8254292
ECM / Jun '89 / New Note.

YELLOW FIELDS
Touch / Sand glass / Yellow fields / Left
lane
CD _____ 8432052
ECM / May '91 / New Note.

Webster, Ben

AUTUMN LEAVES
CD _____ 152162
EPM / Mar '94 / Discovery / ADA.

BEN AND 'SWEETS' (Webster, Ben &
Harry 'Sweets' Edison)
Better go / How long has this been going
on / Kitty / My Romance / Did you call her
today / Embraceable you
CD _____ 4606132
Sony Jazz / Jan '95 / Sony.

BEN WEBSTER
Round horn / Moonglow / Satin doll / For
Max / But not for me / For all we know /
Sunday
CD _____ BLCD 760141
Black Lion / Apr '90 / Jazz Music / Cadillac
/ Wellard / Koch.

BEN WEBSTER (2)
Perdido / Yesterday / I'm gonna sit right
down and write myself a letter / Set call /
That's all / Gone with the wind / Over the
rainbow / (Back home again in) Indiana /
Misty
CD _____ BLCD 760125
Black Lion / May '90 / Jazz Music / Cadillac
/ Wellard / Koch.

BEN WEBSTER MEETS DON BYAS
(Webster, Ben & Don Byas)
Blues for Dottie Mae / Lullaby for Dottie
Mae / Sundae / Perdido / When Ash meets
Henry / Caravan
CD _____ 8279202
ECM / Jun '86 / New Note.

BEN WEBSTER MEETS OSCAR
PETERSON
Touch of your lips / When your lover has
gone / Bye bye blackbird / How deep is the
ocean / In the wee small hours of the morn-
ing / Sunday / This can't be love
CD _____ 8291672
Verve / Feb '93 / PolyGram.

BIG BEN TIME
Just a sittin' and a rockin' / Exactly like you
/ How deep is the ocean / My one and only
love / Honeysuckle rose / Jeep is jumpin' /
Where or when / Wrap your troubles in
dreams (and dream your troubles away) /
Solitude / Remember
CD _____ 814 410-2
Verve / Sep '84 / PolyGram.

DIFFERENT PATHS (Webster, Ben &
Buck Clayton)
CD _____ SKCD 2-2037
Sackville / Oct '94 / Swift / Jazz Music /
Jazz Horizons / Cadillac / CM.

EVOLUTION
CD _____ TPZ 1014
Topaz Jazz / Feb '95 / Pinnacle / Cadillac.

FOR THE GUV'NOR
I got it bad and that ain't good / Drop me
off in Harlem / One for the guv'nor / Prelude
to a kiss / In a sentimental mood / John
Brown's body / Work song / Preacher /
Straight no chaser / Rockin' in rhythm
CD _____ LEJAZZCD 8
Le Jazz / Mar '93 / Charly / Cadillac.

FROG 1956-62, THE
CD _____ CD 53167
Giants Of Jazz / Jan '94 / Target/BMG /
Cadillac.

GONE WITH THE WIND
CD _____ BLC 760125
Black Lion / Apr '91 / Jazz Music /
Cadillac / Wellard / Koch.

HORN, THE
CD _____ PCD 7001
Progressive / Jun '93 / Jazz Music.

IN A MELLOW TONE (Archive Series -
Live At Ronnie Scott's)
In a mellow tone / Over the rainbow / Gone
with the wind / Someone to watch over me
/ C jam blues / Perdido / Stardust / Ben's
blues / My romance / Ben's theme tune
CD _____ JHAS 601
Ronnie Scott's Jazz House / Jun '95 / Jazz
Music / Magnum Music Group / Cadillac.

JEEP IS JUMPING, THE
CD _____ BLC 760147
Black Lion / Oct '90 / Jazz Music /
Cadillac / Wellard / Koch.

LIVE IN PARIS
CD _____ LEJAZZCD 29
Le Jazz / Aug '94 / Charly / Cadillac.

LIVE IN PARIS - 1972
CD _____ FCD 131
France's Concert / '89 / Jazz Music /
BMG.

LIVE IN VIENNA - 1972
CD _____ RST 91529
RST / '91 / Jazz Music / Hot Shot.

MASTERS OF JAZZ VOL 5
CD _____ STCD 4105
Storyville / Feb '89 / Jazz Music / Wellard
/ CM / Cadillac.

MY ROMANCE
CD _____ JHR 73513
Jazz Hour / '91 / Target/BMG / Jazz
Music / Cadillac.

PROVIDENCE, RHODE ISLAND 1963
Perdido / Danny boy / On green dolphin
street / Go home / Bye bye blackbird /
Lover come back to me / My romance /
Wee dot / Tenderly / Sometimes I'm happy
/ How long has this been going on /
Embraceable you / Theme
CD _____ STCD 8237
Storyville / Dec '94 / Jazz Music / Wellard
/ CM / Cadillac.

SOULVILLE
CD _____ 8335512
Verve / Oct '93 / PolyGram.

STORMY WEATHER
CD _____ BLCD 760108
Black Lion / Dec '88 / Jazz Music /
Cadillac / Wellard / Koch.

THERE IS NO GREATER LOVE
CD _____ BLCD 760151
Black Lion / Apr '91 / Jazz Music /
Cadillac / Wellard / Koch.

TRIBUTE TO A GREAT JAZZMAN, A
CD _____ 3801152
Jazz Archives / Feb '93 / Jazz Music /
Discovery / Cadillac.

Webster, E.T.

CHANGES
CD _____ NGCD 527
Twinkle / Apr '92 / SRD / Jetstar /
Kingdom.

LAMENT OF A DREAD
Reggae symphony / Cold sweat / Loner /
Same, same, same / Dom say / Lament of
a dread / Experience / What about I /
Deeper love / Cry cry cry
CD _____ NGCD 539
Twinkle / Apr '94 / SRD / Jetstar / Kingdom.

Webster, Joe

I'M IN THE MOOD FOR BIG BAND
MUSIC (Webster, Joe & Swing Fever
Band)
CD _____ LPCD 1025
Disky / Apr '94 / THE / BMG / Discovery /
Pinnacle.

I'M IN THE MOOD FOR DIXIE MUSIC
(Webster, Joe & His River City Jazzmen)
CD _____ LPCD 1026
Disky / Apr '94 / THE / BMG / Discovery /
Pinnacle.

Webster, Katie

I KNOW THAT'S RIGHT
CD _____ ARHCD 393
Arhoolie / Apr '95 / ADA / Direct /
Cadillac.

NO FOOLIN'
Little man on the side / I'm bad / No de-
posit, no return / Zydeco shoes and Cali-
fornia blues / Too much sugar for a dime /
Hard lovin' mama / It's might hard / Tangled
in your web / Those lonely, lonely nights /
Mama cat cuttin' no slack
CD _____ ALCD 4803
Alligator / May '93 / Direct / ADA.

SWAMP BOOGIE QUEEN
CD _____ ALCD 4766
Alligator / Aug '93 / Direct / ADA.

TWO FISTED MAMA
CD _____ ALCD 4777
Alligator / Mar '93 / Direct / ADA.

Webster, Roger

PIECES
Four variations on a theme of Domenico
Scarlatti / Aria & Scherzo / Prelude op.8
no.11 / Allegro from Toot Suite / Sicilienne
/ Slavish fantasie / Nightsongs / Concerto
scherzo / Reflections / Concerto
(Arutiunian)
CD _____ QPRZ 018D
Polyphonic / Nov '95 / Conifer.

TWILIGHT DREAMS
Jubilance / I'd rather have Jesus / Russian
dance / Twilight dreams / Concert study /
Heavenly gales / Someone cares / Concerto
for cornet and brass bands
CD _____ QPRL 066D
Polyphonic / Jul '94 / Conifer.

Weckl, Dave

HARD WIRED
Hard wired / Afrique / Dis' place this / In
flight / Crazy horse / Just an illusion / Whe-
re's Tom / In the pocket / Tribute
CD _____ GRP 97602
GRP / Mar '94 / BMG / New Note.

HEADS UP
CD _____ GRP 96732
GRP / '92 / BMG / New Note.

MASTER PLAN
Tower of inspiration / Here and there / Fes-
tival de Ritmo / In common / Garden wall /
Auratune / Softly as in a morning sunrise /
Masterplan / Island magic
CD _____ GRP 96192
GRP / Aug '90 / BMG / New Note.

Wedding Anniversary

WEDDING ANNIVERSARY, THE
CD _____ DANCD 010
Danceteria / May '89 / Plastic Head /
ADA.

Wedding Present

BIZARRO
Brassneck / Crushed / No / Thanks / Ken-
nedy / What have I said now / Granadaland
/ Bewitched / Take me / Be honest
CD _____ PD 74302
RCA / Oct '89 / BMG.

GEORGE BEST
Everyone thinks he looks daft / What did
your last servant die of / Don't be so hard
/ Million miles / All this and more / My favourite dress / Something and nothing / It's
what you want that matters / Give my love
to Kevin / Anyone can make a mistake / You
can't moan can you
CD _____ LEEDS 001CD
Reception / Oct '87 / Vital.

HIT PARADE 1
CD _____ PD 75343
RCA / Jun '92 / BMG.

PEEL SESSIONS
CD _____ SFRCD 122
Strange Fruit / Oct '93 / Pinnacle.

SEAMONSTERS
Dalliance / Dare / Suck / Blonde / Rotter-
dam / Lovenest / Corduroy / Carolyn /
Heather / Octopussy
CD _____ PD 75012
RCA / Jun '91 / BMG.

TOMMY
Go out and get 'em boy / Everything's
spoiled again / Once more / At the edge of
the sea / Living and learning / This boy can
wait / You should always keep in touch with
your friends / Felicity / What becomes of the
broken hearted / Never said / Every mother's son / My favourite dress
CD _____ LEEDS 002CD
Reception / Jul '88 / Vital.

UKRAINSKI VISTUPI V JOHNA PEELA
Davni chasy / Yikhav khozak za dunai / Tiu-
tiunyk / Zadumay didochok / Svitit misyats
/ Katrusya / Vasya vasyl'ok / Hude dnipro
hude / Verhovyno
CD _____ PD 74104
RCA / May '89 / BMG.

WATUSI
So long baby / Click click / Yeah yeah yeah
yeah yeah / Let him have it / Gazebo /
Shake it / Spangle / It's a gas / Swimming
pools, movie stars / Big rat / Catwoman /
Hot pants
CD _____ CID 8014
Island / Aug '94 / PolyGram.

Weddings, Parties &...

DIFFICULT LOVES (Weddings, Parties &
Anything)
Father's day / Taylor Square / Difficult loves
/ Old Ronny / Telephone in her car / Nothin'
but time / Alone amongst savages / Ram-
bling girl / Step in, step out / Four corners
of the earth / For your ears only / Do not go
gently
CD _____ COOKCD 059
Cooking Vinyl / Feb '95 / Vital.

KING TIDE (Weddings, Parties &
Anything)
Monday's experts / Live it everyday /
Money cuts you out / Rain in my heart / It
wasn't easy / Keep talking to me / Island of
humour / Easy money / In my lifetime / Al-
ways leave something behind / If you were
a cloud / Year she spent in England /
Stalactites
CD _____ 450993773-2
WEA / Mar '94 / Warner Music.

NO SHOW WITHOUT PUNCH
(Weddings, Parties & Anything)
CD _____ UTICD 4
Utility / Mar '93 / Grapevine.

ROARING DAYS (Weddings, Parties &
Anything)
Industrial town / Under the clocks / Gun /
Brunswick / Tilting at windmills / Sergeant
Small / Sisters of mercy / Roaring days /
Say the word / Missing in action / Laughing
boy / Big river / Summons in the morning /
Morton (Song for Tex)
CD _____ COOKCD 026
Cooking Vinyl / Nov '89 / Vital.

Wedgwood, Michael

PLACES LIKE THESE
Lifeline / Places like these / Act like a dog /
Loving and leaving / New man coming /
Piece / Searching for a fantasy / Funda-
mental fool / Indigo / Cry nightly / Take me
away / Looking forward to missing you /
Take it as it comes / You and I combine
CD _____ VP 143CD
Voice Print / Mar '93 / Voice Print.

Weedon, Bert

ENCORE
First man you remember / I dreamed a
dream / Bali Ha'i / Losing my mind / Can't
help lovin' dat man / 42nd street / True love
/ Song on the sand / I've grown accustomed to her face / True love ways / Last
night of the world / Bewitched, bothered
and bewildered / I won't send roses / Anything goes / Heather on the hill / What I
did for love / How to handle a woman / All
I ask of you
CD _____ PWKS 4025
Carlton Home Entertainment / Sep '90 /
Carlton Home Entertainment.

GUITAR FAVOURITES
CD _____ PWK 093
Carlton Home Entertainment / '88 /
Carlton Home Entertainment.

KING SIZE GUITAR/HONKY TONK
GUITAR
Guitar boogie shuffle / Nashville boogie /
King size guitar / Apache / Teenage guitar
/ Querida / I wonder where my baby is to-
night / Pretty baby / Elmer's tune / Charles-
ton / Chicago / Sweet georgia Brown / Big
hoot hoogin / I only guitar / Bronco rock /
Blue guitar / Bert's boogie / Summer place
(theme) / Bye bye blackbird / Varsity drag /
Ma, he's making eyes at me / Carolina in
the morning / Jealous / (In) a shanty in old
Shanty Town
CD _____ C5HCD 617
See For Miles/C5 / Aug '94 / Pinnacle.

ONCE MORE WITH FEELING (16 Great
love songs)
Love letters / Three times a lady / Music of
the night / Always on my mind / I just called
to say I love you
CD _____ PWKS 517
Carlton Home Entertainment / Nov '88 /
Carlton Home Entertainment.

Weems, Ted

1940-41 BROADCAST RECORDINGS
(Weems, Ted & His Orchestra)
CD _____ JH 1032
Jazz Hour / Jul '93 / Target/BMG / Jazz
Music / Cadillac.

MARVELLOUS (Weems, Ted & His
Orchestra)
Marvellous / Oh if I only had you / From
Saturday night to Sunday morning / She'll
never find a fellow like me / Chick, chick,
chick, chick, chicken / Cobblestones /
You're the cream in my coffee / My troubles
are over / Piccolo Pete / Man from the south
/ Come on baby / Harmonica Harry / Mysterious Mose / Slappin' the bass / Washing
dishes with my sweetie / Egyptian Ella / Jig
time / Play that hot guitar / Oh Mo'nah / My
favourite band
CD _____ CD AJA 5029
Living Era / May '84 / Koch.

Ween

CHOCOLATE AND CHEESE
CD _____ FNCD 314
Flying Nun / Jan '95 / Disc.

GOD WEEN SATAN
CD _____ TTR 891862
Twin Tone / Feb '91 / Pinnacle.

POD, THE
CD _____ FNCD 322
Flying Nun / Mar '95 / Disc.

PURE GUAVA
Little birdy / Tender situation / Stallim / Big
Jim / Push little daisey's / Goin' gets tough
/ Reggae junkie jew / Play it off legit / Pum-
pin for the man / Sarah / Sprim theme / Flies
on my dick / I saw Gene crying in her sleep
/ Touch my tooter smoocher / Morning glory
/ Lovin' you through it all / Her fatboy (As-
shole) / Don't get to close to my fantasy /
Poor ship destroyer
CD _____ RUST 002 CD
Creation / Dec '92 / 3MV / Vital.

Weezer

WEEZER
My name is Jonas / On one else / World
has turned and left me here / Buddy Holly
/ Undone / Sweater song / Surf wax Amer-
ica / Say it ain't so / In the garage / Holiday
/ Only in dreams
CD _____ GED 24629
Geffen / Feb '95 / BMG.

Wehrmacht

BIERMACHT
You broke my heart / Gore fix / Beer is here
/ Drink beer be free / Everb / Micro E / Bal-
ance of opinion / Suck / Drink Jack / Rad-
ical dissection / Beermacht / Outro
CD _____ SHARK 009CD
Shark / Apr '92 / Plastic Head.

BIERMACHT/SHARK ATTACK
CD _____ SHARK 9CD
Shark / May '89 / Plastic Head.

Wein, George

**MAGIC HORN, THE (Wein, George &
The Dixie Victors)**
Magic horn / Sugar / I ain't gonna give nobody none o'
this jelly roll / Monday date / Squeeze me /
On the sunny side of the street / Loveless
love / Dippermouth blues
CD _____ 74321 13038-2
RCA / Sep '93 / BMG.

**SWING THAT MUSIC (Wein, George &
The Newport Allstars)**
Swing that music / T'ain't what you do (It's
the way thatcha do it) / If I had you / Open
wider please / Tears/Nuages / Just you, just
me / What's new / Clark bars / Sleep / What
am I here for / George's jacquet / Marie's
den part II
CD _____ 474048 2
Columbia / Apr '94 / Sony.

Weinert, Susan

CRUNCH TIME (Weinert, Susan Band)
Don't try that again, M.F. / Hopeless case /
Don't you guys know any nice songs / One
for George / Member of the Syndicate /
Crown / He knows / Pacific Palisades /
Maybe / Guess who called
CD _____ VBR 21442
Vera Bra / Aug '94 / New Note.

Weir, Bob

ACE
Greatest story ever told / Walk in the sunshine / Looks like rain / One more saturday
night / Black throated wind / Playing in the
band / Mexicali blues / Cassidy
CD _____ GDCD 4004
Grateful Dead / Feb '89 / Pinnacle.

KINGFISH
Lazy lightnin' / Supplication / Wild northland
/ Asia minor / Home to Dixie / Jump for joy
/ Goodbye yer honer / Big iron / This time /
Hypnotize / Bye and bye
CD _____ GDCD 4012
Grateful Dead / Oct '89 / Pinnacle.

Weiskopf, Walt

SIMPLICITY (Weiskopf, Walt Sextet)
CD _____ CRISS 1075CD
Criss Cross / Nov '93 / Cadillac /
Harmonia Mundi.

Weiss, Harald

OTHER PARADISE, THE
CD _____ SM 18112
Wergo / Sep '95 / Harmonia Mundi / ADA
/ Cadillac.

TROMMELGEFLUSTER
Trommelgefluster (pts 1 & 2)
CD _____ 8492852
ECM / May '91 / New Note.

Weiss, Klaus

L.A. CALLING
Other side / L.A. calling / Spring passed /
I've heard this before / Four four / Bad girl
/ I'll take it / All night through
CD _____ CDLR 45033
L&R / Jun '91 / New Note.

MESSAGE FROM SANTA CLAUS, A
CD _____ MM 801053
Minor Music / Dec '95 / Vital/SAM.

Weiss, Michael

**MICHAEL WEISS QUINTET
FEATURING... (Tom Kirkpatrick/R.
Lalama/R. Drummond)**
CD _____ CRISS 1022CD
Criss Cross / May '91 / Cadillac /
Harmonia Mundi.

Weisser, Michael

PHANCYFUL FIRE
CD _____ 710 053
Innovative Communication / Apr '90 /
Magnum Music Group.

**SOFTWARE VISIONS (Weisser, Michael
& Peter Mergener)**
CD _____ PALM 729013
Magnum Music / Nov '89 / Magnum
Music Group.

Weissman, Dick

NEW TRADITIONS
CD _____ FE 1400CD
Folk Era / Dec '94 / CM / ADA.

Weizmann, Danny

WET DOG SHAKES, THE
CD _____ NAR 065 CD
New Alliance / May '93 / Pinnacle.

Welch, Elisabeth

ELISABETH WELCH LIVE IN NEW YORK
CD _____ CDVIR 8313
TER / Sep '91 / Koch.

SOFT LIGHTS AND SWEET MUSIC
CD _____ PASTCD 7060
Flapper / Nov '95 / Pinnacle.

THIS THING CALLED LOVE
What is this thing called love / Hello my
lover, goodbye / Porgy / When your lover
has gone / Yesterday / Boy what love has
done to me / If I ever fall in love again / Long
before I knew you / I love you truly / True
love / How do you do it / I'll follow my secret
heart / Losing my mind / One life to live /
Moon river / Give me something to remember you by
CD _____ CDVIR 8309
Ter / Sep '89 / Koch.

ULTIMATE ELISABETH WELCH, THE
CD _____ 313752
Koch / Nov '92 / Koch.

WHERE HAVE YOU BEEN
It was worth it / I got it bad and that ain't
good / My love is a wanderer / I always say
hello (to a flower) / How little it matters, how
little we know / Where have you been /
Manhattan madness / He was too good to
me / Little girl blue / You were there / Dancing in the dark / Mean to me / As long as I
live / Come rain or come shine / Remember
you
CD _____ CDSL 5202
DRG / Jun '91 / New Note.

Welch, Kevin

LIFE DOWN HERE ON EARTH
CD _____ DR 003
Dead Reckoning / Aug '95 / Direct.

Weldon, Casey Bill

**CASEY BILL WELDON VOLS. 1-3 -
1935-38**
CD Set _____ DOCD 5217/8/9
Blues Document / Jan '94 / Swift / Jazz
Music / Hot Shot.

**HAWAIIAN GUITAR WIZARD 1935-38,
THE**
CD _____ 158292
Blues Collection / Jan '95 / Discovery.

Welk, Lawrence

22 ALL TIME BIG BAND FAVOURITES
CD _____ RCD 7023
Ranwood / May '89 / Jazz Music.

22 ALL TIME FAVOURITE WALTZES
CD _____ RCD 7028
Ranwood / May '89 / Jazz Music.

22 GREAT SONGS FOR DANCING
CD _____ RCD 7009
Ranwood / May '89 / Jazz Music.

22 OF THE GREATEST WALTZES
CD _____ RCD 7004
Ranwood / May '89 / Jazz Music.

BEST OF LAWRENCE WELK, THE
CD _____ RCD 8226
Ranwood / May '89 / Jazz Music.

DANCE TO THE BIG BAND SOUNDS
CD _____ RCD 8228
Ranwood / May '89 / Jazz Music.

Well Oiled Sisters

ALCOHOL & TEARS
CD _____ CYCLECD 001
Cycle / Apr '94 / Direct / ADA.

Weller, Paul

LIVE WOOD
CD _____ 8285612
Go Discs / Sep '94 / PolyGram.

PAUL WELLER
Uh huh oh yeh / Bullrush / Remember how
we started / Clues / Amongst butterflies /
Into tomorrow / Strange museum / Above
the clouds / Bitterness rising
CD _____ 828343-2
Go Discs / Sep '92 / PolyGram.

STANLEY ROAD
Changing man / Porcelein Gods / Walk on
gilded splinters / You do something to me
/ Woodcutter's son / Time passes / Stanley
Road / Broken stones / Out of the sinking /
Pink on white walls / Whirlpool's end /
Wings of speed
CD _____ 8286192
CD Set _____ 8286202
Go Discs / May '95 / PolyGram.

WILD WOOD
Sunflower / Can you heal us (holy man) /
Wild wood / Instrumental (pt. 1) / All the pic-
tures on the wall / Has my fire really gone
out / Country / Fifth Season / Weaver / In-
strumental (pt. 2) / Foot of the mountain /
Shadow of the sun / Holy man (reprise) /
Moon on your pyjamas
CD _____ 828435 2
Go Discs / Sep '93 / PolyGram.

Wellington, Sheena

CLEARSONG
CD _____ DUNCD 012
Dunkeld / Jun '87 / Direct / ADA / CM.

STRONG WOMEN
Strong women rule us with their tears / Dark
eyed Molly / Address the haggis / Mill
O'Tifty's Annie / Tryst / False bride / Glas-
gow councillor / Slaves lament / Seattle /
Great Silkie O'Sule Skerrie / Shearin' /
Waulkrife Minnie / Silver tassie / My luv's
like a red red rose / Little Sunday school
CD _____ CDTRAX 094
Greentrax / Oct '95 / Conifer / Duncans /
ADA / Direct.

Wellington, Valerie

LIFE IN THE BIG CITY
CD _____ GBW 002
GBW / Feb '92 / Harmonia Mundi.

MILLION DOLLAR SECRET
CD _____ R 2619
Rooster / Apr '95 / Direct.

Wellins, Bobby

NOMAD
CD _____ HHCD 1008
Hot House / May '95 / Cadillac / Wellard /
Harmonia Mundi.

Wells, Dicky

DICKY'S DELIGHT
CD _____ TPZ 1023
Topaz Jazz / Jul '95 / Pinnacle / Cadillac.

**SWINGIN' IN PARIS (Wells, Dicky & Bill
Coleman)**
CD _____ LEJAZZCD 20
Le Jazz / Jun '93 / Charly / Cadillac.

Wells, Jean

SOUL ON SOUL
Have a little mercy / I'll drown in my own
tears / After loving you / Sit down and cry /
Ease away a little bit at a time / Our sweet
love turned bitter / Somebody's been loving
you (but it ain't been me) / Keep your mouth
shut and your eyes open / If you've ever
loved someone / Broomstick horse cowboy
/ I couldn't love you (more than I do now) /
I feel good / With my love and what you've
got / Keep on doin' it / Take time to make
time for me / Try me and see / Roll up your
sleeves, come out lovin' (winner takes all) /
What have I got to lose / Puttin' the best on
the outside / He ain't doin' bad / Hello baby,
goodbye too
CD _____ CDKEND 113
Kent / Jun '94 / Pinnacle.

Wells, Junior

**BETTER OFF WITH THE BLUES (Wells,
Junior & Buddy Guy)**
CD _____ CD 83354
Telarc / Aug '93 / Conifer / ADA.

COMING AT YOU
CD _____ VMD 79262
Vanguard / Jan '96 / Complete/Pinnacle /
Discovery.

EVERYBODY'S GETTIN' SOME
Sweet sixteen / Everybody's gettin' them
some / I can't stand no signifyin' shaky
ground / Trying to get over you / Use me /
You're tough enough / Get down / That's
what love will make you do / Don't you lie
to me / Last hand of the night / Back into
the fold / Keep on steppin'
CD _____ CD 83360
Telarc / May '95 / Conifer / ADA.

IT'S MY LIFE BABY
It's my life baby / Country girl / Stormy
Monday blues / Checking on my baby / I
got a stomach ache / Slow, slow / It's so
sad to be lonely / You lied to me / Shake it
baby / Early in the morning / Look how baby
/ Everything's gonna be alright
CD _____ VND 73120
Vanguard / Oct '95 / Complete/Pinnacle /
Discovery.

MESSIN' WITH THE KID
Messin' with the kid / I'm a stranger / Come
on in this house / Little by little / Cha cha
cha in blues / Prison bars all round me /
Love me / It hurts me too / Things I'd do
for you / I could cry / So tired / Lovey dovey
lovely one / I need me a car / You sure look
good to me / You don't care / Two headed
woman
CD _____ CDCHARLY 219
Charly / May '90 / Charly / THE / Cadillac.

ON TOP
CD _____ DD 635
Delmark / Oct '86 / Hot Shot / ADA / CM /
Direct / Cadillac.

**PLEADING THE BLUES (Wells, Junior &
Buddy Guy)**
Pleading the blues / It hurts me too / Cut
out the lights / Quit teasing my baby / I'll
take care of you / Take your time baby / I
smell something
CD _____ BLE 599012
Black & Blue / Dec '90 / Wellard / Koch.
CD _____ ECD 260352
Evidence / Sep '93 / Harmonia Mundi / ADA
/ Cadillac.

SOUTHSIDE BLUES JAM
CD _____ DD 628
Delmark / Jan '93 / Hot Shot / ADA / CM /
Direct / Cadillac.

Wells, Kitty

GREATEST HITS VOLUME 1
It wasn't God who made honky tonk angels
/ Left to right / I don't claim to be an angel
/ Password / Wedding ring ago / Dust on
the bible / Thank you for the roses / Whose
shoulder will you cry on / Lonely street /
Love makes the world go round / Loving
you was all I ever needed / Amigo's guitar
CD _____ SORCD 0046
D-Sharp / Oct '94 / Pinnacle.

QUEEN OF COUNTRY MUSIC
CD _____ 15484
Laserlight / Dec '94 / Target/BMG.

**QUEEN OF COUNTRY MUSIC (1949-58),
THE**
Death at the bar / Love or hate / Gathering
flowers for the master's bouquet / Don't
wait til the last minute to pray / How far is
heaven / My mother / Make up your mind /
I'll be all smiles tonight / I'm too lonely to
smile / Things I might've been / I heard the
jukebox playing / Wedding ring ago / Divided by two / Crying steel guitar waltz /
Paying for that back street affair / Icicles
hanging from your heart / I don't claim to
be an angel / Honky tonk waltz / Life they
live in songs / You said you could do without / Whose shoulder will you cry on /
Hey Joe / My cold cold heart is melting now
/ I'll love you 'til the day I die / I've kissed
you my last time / I'm a stranger in my
home / I gave my wedding dress away /
Cheatin's a sin / You're not easy to forget /
Satisfied, so satisfied / One by one / Release me / After dark / (Honky tharg around)
he's married to me / Thou shalt not steal /
Lonely side of town / I hope my divorce is
never granted / I'm in love with you / Make
believe / You and me / As long as I live /
No one but you / Making believe / I'd rather
stay home / I was wrong / There's passion
in your heart / Goodbye Mr. Brown / Mother
hold me tight / Searching / Dust on the bible
/ Beside you / I'm counting on you / They
can't take your love / I'm tired of pretending
/ Oh so many years / One week later / When
I'm with you / Can I find it in your heart /
Repenting / I guess I'll go on dreaming /
Each day / Pace that kills / Change of heart
/ Stubborn heart / Standing room only /
Mansion on the hill / Your wild life's gonna
get you down / Right or wrong / Winner of
your heart / Dancing with a stranger / Three
ways (to love you) / She's no angel / Broken
marriage vows / What about you / Sweeter
than the flowers / You can't conceal a broken heart / Just when I needed you / Lonely
street / That's me without you / Cheated out
of the angels / May you never
be alone / If teardrops were pennies / Touch
and go heart / My ued to be darling /
Fraulein / Love me to pieces / What I believe
dear (is all up to you) / I can't stop loving
you / Slowly dying / I can't help wondering
/ He's lost his love for me / Jealousy /
Mommy for a day / Hands you're holding

now / Let me help you forget / All the time / (I've got my) one way ticket to the sky / I heard my saviour call / I dreamed I searched heaven for you / Great speckled bird / Matthew 24 / I need the prayers / My loved ones are waiting for me / Lord I'm coming home / He will set your fields on fire / Lonesome valley / We buried her beneath the willows
CD _____ BCD 15638
Bear Family / Jul '93 / Rollercoaster / Direct / CM / Swift / ADA.

Wells, Mary

22 GREATEST HITS
My guy / Bye bye baby / I don't want to take a chance / Only one who really loves you / You beat me to the punch / Two lovers / Your old standby / Old Joe (let's try again) / Oh little boy (what you did to me) / What love has joined together / You lost the sweetness / What's easy for two is so hard for one / Two wrongs don't make a right / Everybody needs love / I'll be available / One block from heaven / When I'm gone / He's the one I love / Whisper you love me boy / Does he love me / Was it worth it
CD _____ 5301042
Polydor / '95 / PolyGram.

AIN'T IT THE TRUTH (THE BEST OF MARY WELLS)
CD _____ VSD 5514
Varese Sarabande/Colosseum / Apr '95 / Pinnacle / Silva Screen.

COMPLETE JUBILEE SESSIONS, THE
Soul train / Apples, peaches, pumpkin pie / Stagger Lee / Make me yours / Two lovers history / Can't get away from your love / Doctor / Don't look back / Sunny / Woman in love / 500 Miles / Bye bye baby / Love shooting bandit / Mind reader / Sometimes I wonder / Dig the way I feel / Brand new me / Hold on / Leaving on a jet plane / Come together / Sweet love / Mr. Touch / Never give a man the world / Raindrops keep falling on my head / It must be me / Love and tranquility
CD _____ NEXCD 257
Sequel / Nov '93 / BMG.

DEAR LOVER (The Atco Years)
CD _____ SCLCD 2059
Ichiban Soul Classics / Mar '95 / Koch.

MY GUY
He's the one I love / Whisper you love me boy / My guy / Does he love me / How / When my heart belongs to you / He holds his own / My baby just cares for me / I only have eyes for you / You do something to me / It had to be you / If you love me (really love me) / At last
CD _____ CDCD 1146
Charly / Feb '94 / Charly / THE / Cadillac.

MY GUY - THE BEST OF MARY WELLS
CD _____ CDSGP 057
Prestige / May '93 / Total/BMG.

SISTERS OF SOUL
CD _____ RSACD 806
Sequel / Oct '94 / BMG.

VERY BEST OF THE MOTORCITY RECORDINGS, THE
My guy / Hold on a little longer / Walk on the city streets / Don't burn your bridges / What's easy for two is so hard for one / Keeping my mind on love / Stop before it's too late / You're the answer to my dreams / You beat me to the punch / Once upon a time
CD _____ 30359 90122
Motor City / Feb '96 / Carlton Home Entertainment.

Wellstood, Dick

STRETCHING OUT (Wellstood, Dick & Kenny Davern Quartet)
CD _____ JCD 187
Jazzology / Feb '91 / Swift / Jazz Music.

THIS IS THE ONE...DIG
CD _____ SACD 119
Solo Art / Dec '95 / Jazz Music.

Welsh, Alex

CLASSIC CONCERT (Britain's Jazz Heritage)
CD _____ BLCD 760503
Black Lion / Oct '90 / Jazz Music / Cadillac / Wellard / Koch.

DOGGIN' AROUND
CD _____ BLCD 760510
Black Lion / May '93 / Jazz Music / Cadillac / Wellard / Koch.

LOUIS ARMSTRONG MEMORIAL CONCERT
CD _____ BLCD 760515
Black Lion / Nov '95 / Jazz Music / Cadillac / Wellard / Koch.

Welsh Guards Band

BAND OF THE WELSH GUARDS, THE (Directed by Captain Andrew Harris)
Under the double eagle / The merry peal / Floradora / Cupid's army / Serenadeno / Voyage in a troopship / Rusticanella / London Scottish / Turkish patrol / Cavalcade of

martial songs / Jungle drums / On the quarterdeck / Baby's sweetheart / Knightsbridge march / Silver stars / Children of the regiment / Bells of Somerset / Maid of the mountains
CD _____ PASTCD 9726
Flapper / Mar '91 / Pinnacle.

GILBERT AND SULLIVAN
Overture- The yeoman of the guard / Take a pair of sparkling eyes / Regular royal queen / When a wooer goes a wooing / Cheerily carols the lark / I am a courtier grave and serious / When the night wind howls / Hornpipe from Ruddigore / Man who would woo a fair maid / Refrain audacious tar / I hear the soft note / Long years ago / If you're anxious for to shine / Minerva / When the buds are blossoming / Strange adventure / Once more gondolieri
CD _____ BNA 5022
Bandleader / Jul '88 / Conifer.

HOUR OF THE GUARDS, AN (Welsh Guards & Grenadier Guards)
Nimrod / Children's patrol / Norwegian carnival / Hoch heidecksburg / I hope I get better / At the ballet / I can do that / Nothing / One / What I did for love / Entry of The Boyards / Cardiff arms / Bilitis / Abide with me / In the Dolomites / In storm and sunshine / Kennebec / True comrades in arms / Washington Grays / Bridge too far / Robinson's grand entree / Birdcage walk / Army and Marine / Children of the regiment / Piper in the meadow / Man o'brass / Always Vienna (CD only.) / Raiders of the Lost Ark (CD only.)
CD _____ CDB 792 180 2
Music For Pleasure / Sep '89 / EMI.

LAND OF MY FATHERS (H.M. Welsh Guards)
CD _____ EMPRCD 572
Emporio / May '95 / THE / Disc / CM.

MUSIC FROM THE CHANGING OF THE GUARD (Band Of The Welsh Guards)
To your guard / Empire / Birdcage walk / Guardsman / Long live Elizabeth / Royal review / Oxford street / Music of the night / Waterloo march / Welsh airs and fancies / Children's patrol / Gold and silver waltz / Spirit of pageantry / Welsh rhapsody / Great and glorious / Guard's parade / Lord Rothermere's march / Guards armoured division / King's guard / Welshman
CD _____ BNA 5045
Bandleader / '91 / Conifer.

ROYAL SALUTE
CD _____ SRCD 319
Souvenir / Jul '94 / Target/BMG.

Welt

PARANOID DELUSION
CD _____ PCD 14
Progress / May '95 / Plastic Head.

Welti, Stephen

TAKE OFF
Take off / Ocean dream / Alpine adventure / Riviera / Olympic arena / Another love / Russian vine / Stampede / Satellite / Chopper chase / Caribbean can can / Pacific paradise / Cochabamba / Return to mijas / Santa Monica freeway / Lights of Lugano / Hawaiian cocktail / Continental express
CD _____ DLCD 107
Dulcima / Jan '90 / Savoy / THE.

Wemba, Papa

EMOTION
Yolele / Mandola / Show me the way / Fa fa fa fa fa (Sad song) / Rail on / Shofele / Image / Sala keba (Be careful) / Away y' okeyi (If you go away) / Epelo / Ah ouais (Oh yes)
CD _____ CDRW 52
Realworld / Mar '95 / EMI / Sterns.

KERSHAW SESSIONS
M'fond yami / Hambaye Ede / Bokulaka / Le voyageur / Lingo lingo / Matinda / Annah
CD _____ ROOTCD 003
Strange Fruit / Jun '94 / Pinnacle.

LE VIE EST BELLE
CD _____ TUGCD 001
Sterns / Nov '89 / Sterns / CM.

LE VOYAGEUR
Maria Valencia / Lingo lingo / Le voyageur / Ombela / Jamais kolonga / Matinda / Yoko / Madilamba / Zero
CD _____ CDRW 20
Realworld / Apr '92 / EMI / Sterns.

PAPA WEMBA
CD _____ STCD 1026
Sterns / Mar '89 / Sterns / CM.

Wench

TIDY SIZE CHUNK OF SOMETHING, A
CD _____ CORECD 5
Abstract / Apr '91 / Pinnacle / Total/BMG.

Wendholt, Scott

SCHEME OF THINGS, THE (Wendholt, Scott Quintet)
CD _____ CRISS 1078CD

Criss Cross / Nov '93 / Cadillac / Harmonia Mundi.

Wendy & Lisa

FRUIT AT THE BOTTOM
Lolly lolly / Satisfaction / Everyday / Tears of joy / Fruit at the bottom / Are you my baby / Always in my dreams / From now on / I think it was December / Someday
CD _____ CDV 2580
Virgin / Apr '92 / EMI.

RE-MIX-IN-A-CARNATION
Lolly Lolly / Waterfall / Are you my baby / Staring at the sun / Satisfaction / Sideshow
CD _____ CDV 2676
Virgin / '91 / EMI.

Wentzel, Magni

ALL OR NOTHING AT ALL
CD _____ GMCD 150
Gemini / Oct '90 / Cadillac.

MY WONDERFUL ONE
CD _____ GMCD 157
Gemini / Oct '89 / Cadillac.

NEW YORK NIGHTS
CD _____ GMCD 174
Gemini / Oct '90 / Cadillac.

Werdell, Leonard

MYSTO'S HOT LIPS
CD _____ BCD 306
GHB / Jul '93 / Jazz Music.

Werefrogs

SWING
CD _____ TOPPCD 3
Ultimate / Jul '94 / 3MV / Vital.

Werner, Kenny

GU-RU
Little blue man / Trio for Bill / Shivaya / Have you met Miss Jones / Dolphin dance / Playground / Gu-ru / Georgia James/Black well
CD _____ TCB 94502
TCB / Jun '94 / New Note.

LIVE AT MAYBECK RECITAL HALL, VOL. 34
Roberta moon / Someday my prince will come / In your own sweet way / Naima / Autumn leaves / Try to remember / Guru / Child is born
CD _____ CCD 4622
Concord Jazz / Nov '94 / New Note.

LIVE AT VISIONES
Stella by starlight / Fall / All the things you are / Blue in green / There will never be another you / Blue train / Windows / Soul eyes / I hear a rhapsody
CD _____ CCD 4675
Concord Jazz / Dec '95 / New Note.

PRESS ENTER
CD _____ SSC 1056D
Sunnyside / May '92 / Pinnacle.

Wernick, Pete

ON A ROLL
CD _____ SH 3815CD
Sugarhill / Mar '94 / Roots / CM / ADA / Direct.

Werth, Howard

KING BRILLIANT (Werth, Howard & The Moonbeams)
Cocktail shake / Got to unwind / Embezzler / Human note / Ugly water / Midnight flyher / Fading star / Dear Joan / Roulette / Aleph / Lucinda
CD _____ CASCD 1104
Charisma / Jun '92 / EMI.

SEVEN OF ONE AND HALF A DOZEN OF THE OTHER
CD _____ MAUCD 620
Mau Mau / Aug '92 / Pinnacle.

Wertico, Paul

YIN & THE YOUT
CD _____ VBR 21502
Vera Bra / Jun '93 / Pinnacle / New Note.

Werup, Jacques

PROVINSENS LJUS
CD _____ DRCD 208
Dragon / Jul '87 / Roots / Cadillac / Wellard / CM / ADA.

Wesley, Fred

AMALGAMATION
CD _____ MM 801045
Minor Music / Jan '95 / Vital/SAM.

BLOW FOR ME AND A TOOT TO YOU, A (Wesley, Fred & The Horny Horns)
CD _____ NEDCD 268
Sequel / May '94 / BMG.

FINAL BLOW, THE (Wesley, Fred & The Horny Horns)
CD _____ NEDCD 270
Sequel / May '94 / BMG.

New Friends

Rockin' in rhythm / Blue monk / Plenty plenty soul / Birk's works / Peace fugue / Eyes to beautiful / Bright Mississippi
CD _____ ANCD 8758
Antilles/New Directions / Jun '91 / PolyGram.

SAY BLOW BY BLOW BACKWARDS (Wesley, Fred & The Horny Horns)
CD _____ NEXCD 269
Sequel / May '94 / BMG.

Wess, Frank

DEAR MR. BASIE (Wess, Frank & Harry Edison Orchestra)
Jumpin' at the woodside / Very thought of you / Blue on blue / All riled up / This is all I ask / I wish I knew / Whirly bird / Li'l darlin' / Dejection blues / Battle royal / One o'clock jump
CD _____ CCD 4420
Concord Jazz / Jul '90 / New Note.

JAZZ FOR PLAYBOYS
Playboy / Miss Blues / Baubles, bangles and beads / Low life / Pin up / Blues for a playmate
CD _____ SV 0191
Savoy Jazz / Nov '92 / Conifer / ADA.

JAZZ IS BUSTING OUT ALL OVER
Walkin' / Monday stroll / Stroll / M.C. / June is bustin' out all over / Stomp / Sugar dugar / Jan Cee Brown
CD _____ SV 0178
Savoy Jazz / Jan '94 / Conifer / ADA.

NORTH, SOUTH, EAST...WESS
What'd ya say / Dill pickles / Dancing on the ceiling / Hard sock dance / Salvation / Lazy Sal
CD _____ SV 0139
Savoy Jazz / Jun '94 / Conifer / ADA.

OPUS DE BLUES
I hear ya talkin' / Liz / Boop-pe-doop / Opus de blues / Struttin' down blues
CD _____ SV 0137
Savoy Jazz / Jan '94 / Conifer / ADA.

OPUS IN SWING
Kansas City slide / Southern exposure / Over the rainbow / Wess side / East wind
CD _____ SV 0144
Savoy Jazz / Apr '92 / Conifer / ADA.

TROMBONES & FLUTE
You'll do / wanting you / Lo-fi / Don't blame me / Crackerjack
CD _____ SV 0190
Savoy Jazz / Oct '92 / Conifer / ADA.

TRYIN' TO MAKE MY BLUES TURN GREEN
Come back to me / Tryin' to make my blues turn green / Listen to the dawn / So it is / Short circuit / Little Esther / Stray horn / Night lights / Surprise surprise / Blues in the car / Small talk / Afie
CD _____ CCD 4592
Concord Jazz / Apr '94 / New Note.

West Bam

BAM BAM BAM
Acid sausage from Salzburgo / Wizards of the sonic / Celebration generation / Raving society / Strictly bam / Club canossa / Escapist / Track / Bam bam bam / After hours
CD _____ 5271122
Low Spirit/Polydor / Jun '95 / PolyGram.

West Coast All Stars

CELEBRATION OF WEST COAST JAZZ, A
CD Set _____ CCD 79711/12
Candid / Nov '95 / Cadillac / Jazz Music / Wellard / Koch.

West, David

ARCANE
CD _____ TX 3003CD
Taxim / Jan '94 / ADA.

West, Gordie

GORDIE WEST
CD _____ 833 433-2
Polydor / May '88 / PolyGram.

West Indies Jazz Band

MEDLEY FOR MARIUS
CD _____ LBLC 6542
Label Bleu / Oct '91 / New Note.

West, Keith

EXCERPTS FROM GROUPS AND SESSIONS 6
Time is on my side / Don't lie to me / That's how strong my love is / Things she says / You're on your own / I don't mind / Am I glad to see you / Blow up / Three jolly little dwarfs / Revolution / Excerpt from a teenage opera / Sam / Shy boy / Colonel Brown / On a Staurday / Kid was a killer / Visit / She / Little understanding / Power and the glory / West country / Riding for a fall / Having someone
CD _____ RPM 141
RPM / Jun '95 / Pinnacle.

West, Leslie

DODGIN' THE DIRT
CD _____ RR 90262
Roadrunner / Nov '93 / Pinnacle.

West, Mick

FINE FLOWERS & FOOLISH GLANCES
CD _____ CDLDL 1229
Lochshore / Jul '95 / ADA / Direct /
Duncans.

West, Mike

INTERSTATE 10
Levee song / This song / Never resist /
Wedding song / Burn to drive / Buddy Holly
/ Don't move back / Dinosaur / Barefoot
boy / 6th Street Austin / Fishin' / Blues on
a C Harp / Barefoot / Not angry, tired
CD _____ QCD 010
Quark / Sep '95 / Vital.

West, Sonny

RELENTLESS
Come on everybody / Come on let's go /
Guitar attack / Relentless / Think it over
baby / Almost grown / Jasmine / Icehouse
/ Take and give / Wyle E. Coyote / Blue fire
/ I'm a man / So long baby / Doin' the boo-
gie / Darlene / Hot choc / Runaway girl / I'll
be there
CD _____ NERCD 067
Nervous / Apr '92 / Nervous / Magnum Mu-
sic Group.

Westbrook, Mike

BRIGHT AS FIRE (The Westbrook Blake)
CD _____ IMPCD 18013
Impetus / Mar '92 / CM / Wellard /
Impetus / Cadillac.

**ON DUKE'S BIRTHDAY (Westbrook,
Mike Orchestra)**
CD _____ ARTCD 6021
Hat Art / Apr '94 / Harmonia Mundi / ADA
/ Cadillac.

PIERIDES (Westbrook, Mike & Kate)
Parade of the Pierides / Terpsichore: dance
/ Calliope: epic (Amazon girl) / Polyhymnis:
sacred sons / Euterte: erotic music (Song
for a stripper) / Thalia: Lindy Hop (Air mail
special) / Thalia: pastoral festival / Melpom-
ene: tragedy (Land thieves) / Erato: love (Erato: boogie) / Uranis: astronomy / Clio: history (Clio's cosmetics)
CD _____ 900377
Line / Jul '95 / CM / Grapevine / ADA / Conifer / Direct.

ROSSINI (Studio)
CD _____ ARTCD 6002
Hat Art / Jul '88 / Harmonia Mundi / ADA /
Cadillac.

ROSSINI - ZURICH LIVE 1986
CD Set _____ ARTCD 2-6152
Hat Art / May '94 / Harmonia Mundi / ADA /
Cadillac.

Westen, Eric

WORKING DREAMER
CD _____ BVHAASTCD 9212
Bvhaast / Dec '89 / Cadillac.

Westerberg, Paul

14 SONGS
Knockin' on mine / First glimmer / World
class fad / Runaway wind / Dice behind
your shades / Even here we are / Silver naked ladies / Few minutes of silence / Someone I once knew / Black eyed Susan /
Things / Something is me / Mannequin
shop / Down love
CD _____ 936245255-2
Sire / Jun '93 / Warner Music.

Westerman, Floyd

CUSTER DIED/THIS LAND
CD _____ TRIK 017
Trikont / Oct '94 / ADA / Direct.

Western, Johnny

GUNFIGHT AT OK CORRAL
Ghost riders in the sky / Gunfight at the
O.K. Corral / Gunfighter / Don't take your
guns to town / Ringo / Hangin' tree / Cross
the Brazos at Waco / Johnny Yuma / Bo-
nanza / Ballad of Paladin / Rawhide /
Searchers / High noon / Song of the bandit
/ Hannah Lee / Lillies grow high / Ballad of
Boot Hill / Cheyenne / Wyatt Earp / Bat
Masterson
CD _____ BCD 15429
Bear Family / Jun '89 / Rollercoaster / Direct
/ CM / Swift / ADA.

HEROES AND COWBOYS
Ballad of Paladin (2) / Guns of the Rio
Muerto (and Richard Boone) / Gunfighter/
Geronimo / Lonely man / Hannah Lee /
Streets of Laredo / Cowpoke / Lillies grow
high / Cotton wood tree / Rollin' dust /
Searchers / Nineteen men / Long trail
shadow / Last round-up / Streets of old
dodge city / Mr. Rodeo cowboy / Singin'
man / Big battle / Forty shades of green /

Violet and a rose / Give me more, more,
more (of your kisses) / Let old mother nature
have her way / Little buffalo Bill / Love me
love me love me / Honey, how sweet can
you be / Echo of your voice / Ten years /
Uh huh / Delia's gone / Time has run out on
me / Willowgreen / Don't cry little girl /
Darling Corey / Stranger drive away / I love
you more / All by my lonesome / Just for
the record / Kathy come home / Only the
lonely / Light the fuse / Tender years / Turn
around and look at me / Sincerely your
friend / Don't take your love to town /
Used to / I'll try hard to forget you if I can
/ Whoever finds this, I love you / Last time
I saw phoenix / Hustler / You wouldn't know
love / Arizona morning / Stay a little longer,
stay all night (theme) / Lonely street / You
weren't ashamed to kiss me last night /
John Henry / Remember me / Wayward
wind / Gotta travel on / Ghost riders in the
sky / I still miss someone / I take a country
girl for mine (Texas Bill strength) / I walk the
line / Ballad of Paladin / Guns of Rio Muerto
CD Set _____ BCD 15552
Bear Family / May '93 / Rollercoaster /
Direct / CM / Swift / ADA.

Westlake, David

WESTLAKE
Word around town / Dream come true /
Rings on her fingers / Everlasting / She
grew and she grew / Talk like that
CD _____ CRECD 019
Creation / Jul '93 /3MV / Vital.

Westminster Cathedral...

**FESTIVAL OF CAROLS, A (Westminster
Cathedral Choir)**
O come all ye faithful / Ding dong merrily
on high / In the bleak midwinter / I saw three
ships / Silent night / Once in Royal David's
city / In Dulci Jubilo / Sussex Carol / Bethlehem down / First nowell / I sing of a
maiden / Good king Wenceslas / Coventry
carol / Holly and the ivy / Rocking / Hark
the herald angels sing / Carillon de
Westminster
CD _____ PCD 2033
Carlton Home Entertainment / Oct '95 /
Carlton Home Entertainment.

Weston, Calvin

DANCE ROMANCE
Chocolate rock / I can tell / Planetarian Lis-
izen / Preview / Dance romance / House
blues
CD _____ IOR 7002
In & Out / Sep '95 / Vital/SAM.

Weston, John

SO DOGGONE BLUE
CD _____ FIENDCD 743
Demon / Nov '93 / Pinnacle / ADA.

Weston, Kim

KIM, KIM, KIM
You just don't know / Love I've been looking for / What could be better / When something is wrong with my baby / Love vibrations / Buy myself a man / Got to get you
off my mind / Soul on fire / Brothers and
sisters (get together) / Penny blues / Choice
is up to you (Walk with me Jesus)
CD _____ CDSXE 063
Stax / Jul '92 / Pinnacle.

VERY BEST OF KIM WESTON, THE
Somebody's eyes / Helpless / You hit me
where it hurt me / Signal your intention / My
heart's not made of stone / Doin' it for myself / Investigate / It's too late / Case of too
much loves making / Talkin' loud / It should
have been me / After the rain / Just one
man for me / Riding on the crest of a wave
/ Restless feet / Oh no not my baby /
Springtime in my heart / Baby I'm yours
CD _____ 30359 90012
Carlton Home Entertainment / Oct '95 /
Carlton Home Entertainment.

Weston, Randy

BLUES TO AFRICA
African village / Bedford stuyvesant / Tan-
gier Bay / Blues to Africa / Kasbah kids /
Uhuru Kwanza / Call / Kucheza blues /
Sahel
CD _____ FCD 41014
Freedom / Sep '87 / Jazz Music / Swift /
Wellard / Cadillac.

CARNIVAL
Carnival / Tribute to Duke Ellington / Mys-
tery of love
CD _____ FCD 41004
Freedom / Sep '87 / Jazz Music / Swift /
Wellard / Cadillac.

**MARRAKESH IN THE COOL OF THE
EVENING**
CD _____ 521588-2
Verve / May '94 / PolyGram.

MONTEREY 1966
CD _____ 519698-2
Verve / May '94 / PolyGram.

PERSPECTIVE (Weston, Randy & Vishnu
Wood Duo)

Blues to be there / Body and soul / Hi fly /
Khadesha / African cookbook
CD _____ DC 8554
Denon / Jun '89 / Conifer.

SPIRITS OF ANCESTORS
CD _____ 5118572
Verve / Feb '92 / PolyGram.

UHURU AFRICA/HIGHLIFE
Uhuru kwanza (part one) (Introduction) /
Uhuru kwanza (part two) (1st movement.) /
African lady (2nd movement.) / Kucheza
blues (4th movement.) / Caban bamboo
highlife / Niger mambo / Zulu / In memory
of / Congolese children / Blues of Africa /
Mystery of love
CD _____ CDP 794 510 2
Roulette / Jun '90 / EMI.

Wet Wet Wet

END OF PART ONE - GREATEST HITS
Wishing I was lucky / Sweet little mystery /
Temptation / Angel eyes / With a little help
from my friends / Sweet surrender / Bro-
keaway / Stay with me heartache / Hold
back the river / This time / Make it tonight
/ More than love / Put the light on / Good-
night girl / Lip service / Blue for you (Live) /
Shed a tear / Cold cold heart
CD _____ 5184772
Precious / Nov '93 / PolyGram.

HIGH ON THE HAPPY SIDE
More than love / Lip service / Put the light
on / High on the happy side / Maybe to-
morrow / Goodnight girl / Celebration /
Make it tonight / How long / Brand new
sunrise / Two days after midnite
CD _____ 510 427 2
Precious / Jan '92 / PolyGram.

HOLDING BACK THE RIVER
Sweet surrender / Can't stand the night /
Blue for you / Brokeaway / You've had it /
I wish / Keys to your heart / Maggie May /
Hold back the river
CD _____ 842 011 2
Precious / Mar '92 / PolyGram.

**LIVE AT THE ROYAL ALBERT HALL
(Wet Wet Wet & The Wren Orchestra)**
CD _____ 5147742
Precious / May '93 / PolyGram.

MEMPHIS SESSIONS, THE
I don't believe / Sweet little mystery / East
of the river / This time / Temptation / I re-
member / For you are / Heaven help us all
CD _____ 836 603-2
Precious / Nov '88 / PolyGram.

PICTURE THIS
Julia says / After the love goes / Some-
where, somehow / Gypsy girl / Don't want
to forgive me now / She might never know
/ Someone like you / Love is my shepherd
/ She's on my mind / Morning / Home to-
night / Love is all around
CD _____ 5268512
Precious / Apr '95 / PolyGram.

POPPED IN SOULED OUT
Wishing I was lucky / East of the river / I
remember / Angel eyes / Sweet little mys-
tery / Temptation / I can give you everything
/.Moment you left me
CD _____ 832 726-2
Precious / Sep '87 / PolyGram.

Wetton, John

CHASING THE DRAGON
CD _____ HTDCD 37
HTD / Jul '95 / Pinnacle.

KING'S ROAD 1972-1980
Nothing to lose / In the dead of night / Baby
come back / Caught in the crossfire / Night
after night / Turn on the radio / Rendezvous
602 / Book of Saturday / Paper talk / As
long as you want me here / Cold is the night
/ Eyesight to the blind (CD only) / Starless
(CD only)
CD _____ EGCD 70
EG / Oct '87 / EMI.

Whale

PAY FOR ME
Pay for me / I think no / Darling Nikki / Buzz-
box babe / Trying
CD _____ DGHUTM 24
Hut / May '95 / EMI.

WE CARE
Kickin' / That's where it's at / Pay for me /
Eurodog / I'll do ya / Electricity / Hobo hum-
pin' slobo babe / Tryzasnice / Happy in you
/ I miss me / Young, dumb and full of cum
/ I'm cold / Born to raise hell
CD _____ CDHUT 25
CD _____ DGHUT 25
Hut / Jul '95 / EMI.

Whalum, Kirk

CACHE
CD _____ 4726792
Sony Jazz / Jan '95 / Sony.

FLOPPY DISC
CD _____ CK 40221
Pickwick/Sony Collector's Choice / Jun
'88 / Carlton Home Entertainment /
Pinnacle / Sony.

IN THIS LIFE
Is this life / Till I get it right / Drowning in
the sea of love / Peaceful hideway / I
wouldn't be a man / Livin' for the city / My
Father's hope / When the night rolls in / I
turn to you / Reck'n so / Way I need you
now / Dans cette vie (in this life)
CD _____ 4804912
Sony Jazz / Jul '95 / Sony.

Wham

FANTASTIC
Bad boys / Ray of sunshine / Love machine
/ Wham rap / Club Tropicana / Nothing
looks the same in the light / Come on /
Young guns (go for it)
CD _____ 4500902
Epic / '91 / Sony.

FINAL, THE
Wham rap / Young guns go for it / Bad boys
/ Club Tropicana / Wake me up before you
go go / Careless whisper / Freedom / Last
Christmas / Everything she wants / I'm your
man / Blue (armed with love) / Different cor-
ner / Battlestations / Where did your heart
go / Edge of heaven
CD _____ CD 88681
Epic / '86 / Sony.

MAKE IT BIG
Wake me up before you go go / Everything
she wants / Heartbeat / Like a baby / Free-
dom / If you were there / Credit card baby
/ Careless whisper
CD _____ CD 86311
Epic / Nov '84 / Sony.

TWELVE INCH MIXES
Wham rap / Careless whisper / Freedom
(long mix) / Everything she wants / I'm your
man (extended stimulation)
CD _____ 450125-2
Epic / Nov '92 / Sony.

Wharton, Bill

SOUTH OF THE BLUES
CD _____ KS 023
Flying Fish / Nov '94 / Roots / CM / Direct
/ ADA.

What Noise

FAT
CD _____ BND 8 CD
One Little Indian / Feb '90 / Pinnacle.

Wheater, Paul

SOUVENIRS
CD _____ LCYCD 109
Paul Wheater / Jul '92 / Pinnacle /
Pinnacle / THE.

TWENTY GOOD YEARS
CD _____ CLCD 01
Rio Digital / Feb '91 / Grapevine.

Wheatstraw, Peetie

DEVIL'S SON-IN-LAW, THE
CD _____ SOB 035412
Story Of The Blues / Apr '93 / Koch /
ADA.

**PEETIE WHEATSTRAW VOL. 1 1930-
1941**
CD _____ DOCD 5241
Blues Document / May '94 / Swift / Jazz
Music / Hot Shot.

**PEETIE WHEATSTRAW VOL. 2 1930-
1941**
CD _____ DOCD 5242
Blues Document / May '94 / Swift / Jazz
Music / Hot Shot.

**PEETIE WHEATSTRAW VOL. 3 1930-
1941**
CD _____ DOCD 5243
Blues Document / May '94 / Swift / Jazz
Music / Hot Shot.

**PEETIE WHEATSTRAW VOL. 4 1930-
1941**
CD _____ DOCD 5244
Blues Document / May '94 / Swift / Jazz
Music / Hot Shot.

**PEETIE WHEATSTRAW VOL. 5 1930-
1941**
CD _____ DOCD 5245
Blues Document / May '94 / Swift / Jazz
Music / Hot Shot.

PEETIE WHEATSTRAW VOL. 6 1930-1941
CD _____ DOCD 5246
Blues Document / May '94 / Swift / Jazz Music / Hot Shot.

PEETIE WHEATSTRAW VOL. 7 1930-1941
CD _____ DOCD 5247
Blues Document / May '94 / Swift / Jazz Music / Hot Shot.

Wheeler, Cheryl

CIRCLES AND ARROWS
I know this town / Hard line to draw / Aces / Estate sale / Don't wanna / Northern girl / Soon as I find my voice / Miss you more than I'm mad / Moonlight and roses / When you're gone / Arrow
CD _____ CDPH 1162
Philo / May '95 / Direct / CM / ADA.

DRIVING HOME
CD _____ PH 1152CD
Philo / Jan '94 / Direct / CM / ADA.

MRS PINOCCI'S GUITAR
CD _____ CDPH 1192
Philo / Nov '95 / Direct / CM / ADA.

Wheeler, Ian

IAN WHEELER AT FARNHAM MALTINGS
CD _____ LACD 32
Lake / Nov '94 / Target/BMG / Jazz Music / Direct / Cadillac / ADA.

Wheeler, Kenny

CALIFORNIA DAYDREAM (Wheeler, Kenny & Gardner/Van De Geyn/Ceccarelli)
CD _____ 500292
Musidisc / Nov '93 / Vital / Harmonia Mundi / ADA / Cadillac / Discovery.

DOUBLE YOU
Foxy trot / Ma bel / W. W. / Three for D'reen / Blue for Lou / Mark time
CD _____ 8156752
ECM / Jan '90 / New Note.

GNU HIGH
CD _____ 8255912
ECM / Aug '85 / New Note.

KAYAK
CD _____ AHUM 012
Ah-Um / Jul '92 / New Note / Cadillac.

MUSIC FOR LARGE AND SMALL ENSEMBLES
Part I (opening) / Part II (For H) / Part III (for Jan) / Part IV (for P.A.) / Part V (know where you are) / Part VI (consolation) / Part VII (Freddy C) / Part VIII (closing) / Sophie / Sea lady / Gentle piece / Trio / Duet I / Duet II / Duet III / By myself
CD Set _____ 8431522
ECM / Nov '90 / New Note.

WALK SOFTLY (Wheeler, Kenny & Guildhall Jazz Band)
CD _____ WAVE CD 32
Wave / Apr '90 / Wellard / These.

WIDOW IN THE WINDOW (Wheeler, Kenny Trio)
Aspire / Ma balle Helene / Widow in the window / Ana / Hotel le hot / Now, and now again
CD _____ 8431982
ECM / Jan '88 / New Note.

Wheeler, Onie

ONIE'S BOP
Jump right out of this jukebox / Tell em off / I wanna hold my baby / Onie's bop / Booger gonna getcha / Going back to the city / Long gone / Steppin' out / I'll love you for a lifetime / Beggar for your love / Walkin' shoes / That's all / Cut it out / That's what I like / She wiggled and giggled / I'm satisfied with my dreams / No, I don't guess i will / Would you like to wear a crown / I saw mother with God last night / My home is not a home at all / Little mama / Hazel / Closing time / Tried and tried, I / I'll swear you don't love me / Love me like you used to do / When we all fet there / Mother prays loud in her sleep / Million years in glory / Run 'em off / Bonaparte's retreat
CD _____ BCD 15542
Bear Family / May '91 / Rollercoaster / Direct / CM / Swift / ADA.

Whelan, Bill

RIVERDANCE
CD _____ 7567806112
Warner Bros. / Mar '95 / Warner Music.

RIVERDANCE (New Version)
CD _____ 7567828162
Atlantic / Nov '95 / Warner Music.

Whelan, John

FRESH TAKES (Whelan, John & Eileen Ivers)
CD _____ GLCD 1075
Green Linnet / Feb '93 / Roots / CM / Direct / ADA.

Whellans, Mike

SWING TIME JOHNNY RED
CD _____ COMD 2036
Temple / Feb '94 / CM / Duncans / ADA / Direct.

When

DROWNING BUT LEARNING
CD _____ TAT 024CD
Tatra / Aug '95 / Plastic Head.

SLACK, WHITE AND GREY
CD _____ RERWHCD
ReR Megacorp / Jan '94 / These / ReR Megacorp.

SVARTEDAVEN
CD _____ TATCD 008
Tatra / Aug '95 / Plastic Head.

When People Were Shorter.

BILL KENNEDY'S SHOWTIME (When People Were Shorter & Lived Near The Water)
Catfish / Just like an Aborigine / East side story / I who have nothing / Shoe salesman / Old time shimmy / Creepin' / Sock it to me baby / Story of my life / What'cha see is what'cha get / End of the line (Part 1) / End of the line (Part 2) / I don't need love / Up all night / Open up your door / Feelin' lost / What a way to die / Rock 'n' roll music
CD _____ SHIMMY 064CD
Shimmy Disc / Aug '93 / Vital.

BOBBY (When People Were Shorter & Lived Near The Water)
Muddy Mississippi line / Broomstick cowboy / Watching Scotty crow / Straight life / If you've got a heart / See the funny little clown / Can you feel it / Honey / Little things / Autumn of my life / Voodoo woman / With pen in hand / It's too late / My Japanese boy / I'm a drifter
CD _____ SDE 8913CD
Shimmy Disc / Oct '89 / Vital.

Where Eagles Fly

SCOTTISH FANTASIA
CD _____ WEF 3
Glencoe / May '95 / Duncans.

Whigfield

WHIGFIELD
Think of you / Another day / Don't walk away / Big time / Out of sight / Close to you / Sexy eyes / Ain't it blue / I want to love / Saturday night
CD _____ 8286272
Systematic / Jun '95 / PolyGram.

While, Chris

LOOK AT ME NOW
CD _____ FAT 003CD
Fat Cat / Aug '94 / Direct / ADA / CM.

Whiplash

TICKET TO MAYHEM
CD _____ RO 95962
Roadrunner / Apr '89 / Pinnacle.

Whipped Cream

...& OTHER DELIGHTS
Explosion / Remember / Silver 1 / Let us try it out / Wishing / This time next time / Theodora while / I know your mine / Whatever / Together / Come together / Explosion '93
CD _____ RESNAP 001
Soap / Jan '94 / Vital.

TUNE IN THE CENTURY
Yes / Tune in the century / Wait for a minute / Lay down beside / Give away / Sensational / Virtuosly / Observatory crest / Up the country / Come and find / Beyond the sun
CD _____ SNAP 003
Soap / Sep '92 / Vital.

Whipping Boy

HEARTWORM
Blinded / Personality / Users / Fiction / Morning rise / Twinkle / When we were young / Tripped / Honeymoon is over / We don't need nobody else
CD _____ 4802812
Columbia / Oct '95 / Sony.

Whirligig

CELTIC DAWN
CD _____ CDLDL 1227
Lochshore / Mar '95 / ADA / Direct / Duncans.

Whirling Pope Joan

SPIN
CD _____ TAT 294CD
Panic ATC / Aug '94 / ADA / Direct.

Whirlpool Productions

BRIAN DE PALMA
CD _____ LAD 0201612
Ladomat / May '95 / Plastic Head.

Whirlwind

IN THE STUDIO
Hang loose (I've gotta rock) / Boppin' high school baby / My bucket's got a hole in it / My advice / Thousand stars / One more chance / Don't be crazy / Rockin' Daddy / Slow down / Blue moon of Kentucky / Together forever / Who's that knocking / Tore apart / Do what I do / Duck tail / I only wish (That I'd been told) / Midnight blue / Teenage cutie / You got class / Honey hush / Cruisin' around / Stay cool / Running wild / Okie's in the pokie / Heaven knows / Big Sandy / Such a fool / Nightmares / If it's all the same to you / Stayin' out all night
CD _____ CDWIKD 147
Chiswick / Jun '95 / Pinnacle.

Whisky Priests

BLEEDING SKETCHES
CD _____ WPTCD 13
Whippet / Oct '95 / CM / Pinnacle / ADA.

BLOODY WELL LIVE
CD _____ WPT CD7
Whippet / May '93 / CM / Pinnacle / ADA.

FIRST FEW DROPS, THE
CD _____ WPTCD 10
Whippet / Oct '94 / CM / Pinnacle / ADA.

NEE GUD LUCK
CD _____ WPTCD 11
Whippet / Oct '94 / CM / Pinnacle / ADA.

POWER & THE GLORY, THE
CD _____ WPT 008CD
Whippet / Apr '94 / CM / Pinnacle / ADA.

TIMELESS STREET
CD _____ WPTCD 12
Whippet / Oct '94 / CM / Pinnacle / ADA.

Whispers

30TH ANNIVERSARY ANTHOLOGY
Seems like I gotta do wrong / There's a love for everyone / Can't help but love you / I only meant to wet my feet / Somebody loves you / Mother for my children / Bingo / One for the money / Living together (In sin) / Make it with you / (Let's go) All the way / Lost and turned out / Can't do without love / Song for Donny / And the beat goes on / Lady my girl / It's a love thing / I'm the one for you / I can make it better / This kind of lovin' / In the raw / Emergency / Tonight / Keep on loving me / Contagious / Some kinda lover / Rock steady / Just gets better with time / In the mood / No pain no gain / Say yes / Special F/X
CD Set _____ NEDCD 257
Sequel / Aug '94 / BMG.

BEST OF THE WHISPERS, THE
and the beat goes on / My girl / Headlights / One for the money / I can make it better / It's a love thing / In the raw / Tonight / Some kinda lover / Contagious / Rock steady / Special FX / Lady / No pain, no gain / Make it with you / Let's go all the way / Out the box / Living together
CD _____ CCSCD 804
Renaissance Collector Series / Sep '95 / BMG.

LOVE THING
It's a love thing / And the beat goes on / My girl / Can't do without your love / Cruisin' in / Welcome into my dreams / Only you / Rock steady / Lady / Emergency / Keep on lovin' me / Tonight / Imagination / I want to make it with you
CD _____ 5507562
Spectrum/Karussell / Mar '95 / PolyGram THE.

SLOW GROOVES VOL. 2
CD _____ DGPCD 727
Deep Beats / May '95 / BMG.

Whistlebinkies

ANNIVERSARY
Farewell to Nigg / Piper, the harper, the fiddler / Fiddle Strathspey and Reel / MacBeth / Island jigs / Whistlebinkies' reel / Ane ground / Sir John Fenwick / Ailein Duinn / MacDonald of the Isles / Dominic McGowan / Fiddlers' farewell / Winter it is past / Dogs among the bushes / Rattlin' roarin' Willie / Barlinnie Highlander / Change of tune
CD _____ CC 54CD
Claddagh / Nov '92 / ADA / Direct.

INNER SOUND
CD _____ CDLOC 1063
Lochshore / Feb '95 / ADA / Direct / Duncans.

Whitcomb, Ian

HAPPY DAYS ARE HERE AGAIN (Whitcomb, Ian Dance Band)
CD Set _____ DAPCD 242
Audiophile / Apr '89 / Jazz Music / Swift.

IAN WHITCOMB & MERRY BAND 1967-93 - RAGTIME
CD _____ SOSCD 1276
Stomp Off / Apr '94 / Jazz Music / Wellard.

LOTUS LAND

CD _____ ACD 283
Audiophile / Jun '95 / Jazz Music / Swift.

RAGTIME AMERICA

CD _____ ACD 277
Audiophile / Aug '94 / Jazz Music / Swift.

THIS SPORTING LIFE

This sporting life / Soho / Boney Maronie / Dance again / Turn a song (Test pressing version) / You turn me on (Turn a song) / Be my baby / That is rock 'n' roll / N-n-nervous / Good hard rock / Where did Robinson Crusoe go with Friday on Saturday night / Poor little bird / Your baby has gone down the plughole / Louie Louie / Lover's prayer / Naked ape / Kingfisher of the loving pack / Life has no reason / Sally sails the sky / Notable yacht club of staines / Star / When rock 'n' roll was young / Oh pretty woman / Rolling with the quake / Rocking the baby to sleep
CD _____ CREV 032CD
Rev-Ola / Jul '94 / 3MV / Vital.

White, Alan

RAMSHACKLED
CD _____ 7567803962
Atlantic / Jan '96 / Warner Music.

White, Aline

JUST A LITTLE WHILE
CD _____ BCD 292
GHB / Oct '93 / Jazz Music.

White, Andy

DESTINATION BEAUTIFUL
Street scenes from my heart / Thinking of change / John / Mary's the time / Punk outside the secret police / She doesen't want to cry any more / Learning to cry / He's out there / Ciao baby / Looking into friends / I couldn't leave you / Government of love
CD _____ COOKCD 072
Cooking Vinyl / Aug '94 / Vital.

HIMSELF
In a groovy kinda way / 1,000,000 miles / Six string street / Freeze out / Just jumped out of a tree / Twenty years / Guildford four / Pale moonlight / Bird of passage / St. Patrick's good luck / Coup I / Whole love story / Six strings street (30 mph) (CD only) / Travelling circus (CD only)
CD _____ COOKCD 029
Cooking Vinyl / Feb '95 / Vital.

OUT THERE
Palaceful of noise / Where's my home / Colour of love / Waiting for the 39 / La Rue Beaurepaire / Speechless / Berlin 6 a.m / James Joyce's grave / One last kiss / Na na na na / Placeful of noise
CD _____ 9031770122
East West / Jun '92 / Warner Music.

White, Artie

BEST OF ARTIE WHITE, THE
Today I started loving you again / Nothing takes the place of you / Tore up / Tired of sneaking around / Jody / Dark end of the street / That's where it's at / Nobody wants you when you're old and grey / Funny how time slips away / Hattie Mae / Thangs got to change / I need someone
CD _____ CDICH 1131
Ichiban / Oct '93 / Koch.

THINGS GOT TO CHANGE
Things got to change / Rainy day / I ain't taking no prisoners / You upset me baby / Thank you pretty baby / Hattie Mae / I wonder why / Reconsider baby / Somebody's on my case
CD _____ CDICH 1044
Ichiban / Oct '93 / Koch.

TIRED OF SNEAKIN' AROUND
Today I started loving you / Thinking about making a change / Jody / Peeping Tom / Tired of sneaking around / Don't pet my dog / Can't get you off my mind / I can't seem to please you / Turn about is fair play / Nose to the grindstone
CD _____ CDICH 1061
Ichiban / Oct '93 / Koch.

WHERE IT'S AT
CD _____ CDICH 1026
Ichiban / Oct '93 / Koch.

White, Barry

BARRY AND GLODEAN (White, Barry & Glodean)
Our theme / I want you / You're the only one for me / This love / Better love is you / We can't let go of love / You make my life easy livin' / Didn't we make it happy baby
CD _____ CDSEWM 073
Southbound / Mar '93 / Pinnacle.

BEWARE
Beware / Relax to the max / Let me in and let's begin with love / Your love, your love / Hio de janeiro / You're my high / Ooooo...ahhh / I won't settle for less than the best (you baby) / Louie Louie
CD _____ CDSEWM 074
Southbound / Mar '93 / Pinnacle.

CHANGE
Change / Turnin' on, tunin' in / Don't tell me about heartaches / Passion / I've got that love fever / I like you, you like me / It's all about love / Let's make tonight an evening to remember / I've got that love fever #2
CD _____ CDSEWM 075
Southbound / Apr '93 / Pinnacle.

COLLECTION: BARRY WHITE
You're the first, the last, my everything / You see the trouble with me / Can't get enough of your love babe / I'll do for you anything you want me to / Just the way you are / Walking in the rain with the one I love / It may be Winter outside / Love's theme / Sho' you right / What am I gonna do with you / Never, never gonna give you up / Baby we better try and get it together / Let the music play / Don't make me wait too long / I'm gonna love you just a little more babe / Right night
CD _____ 8347902
PolyGram TV / Feb '94 / PolyGram.

COME IN LOVE
CD _____ CDCD 1188
Charly / Sep '94 / Charly / THE / Cadillac.

DEDICATED
America / Free / Don't forget... remember / Life / Love song / All in the run of a day / Don't let 'em blow your mind / Dreams
CD _____ CDSEWM 076
Southbound / Apr '93 / Pinnacle.

I'M GONNA LOVE YOU
CD _____ MPG 74030
Movieplay Gold / Nov '94 / Target/BMG.

ICON IS LOVE, THE
Practice what you preach / There it is / I only want to be with you / Time is right / Baby's home / Come on / Love is the icon / Sexy undercover / Don't you want to know / Whatever we had, we had
CD _____ 540280-2
A&M / Oct '94 / PolyGram.

JUST FOR YOU (2CD Set)
CD Set _____ 5141432
Phonogram / Jan '93 / PolyGram.

LET THE MUSIC PLAY
You're the first, the last, my everything / Your sweetness is my weakness / I feel love coming on / Midnight and you / Barry's theme / Oh love, well we finally made it / I'm qualified to satisfy you / Oh what a night for dancing / You see the trouble with me / Sha la la means I love you / It's ecstasy when you lay next to me / Standing in the shadows of love / What a groove / Honey please can't you see / Rhapsody in white / Let the music play on
CD _____ PWKS 4128P
Carlton Home Entertainment / Oct '92 / Carlton Home Entertainment.

LET THE MUSIC PLAY
CD _____ MPG 74032
Movieplay Gold / Nov '94 / Target/BMG.

LET THE MUSIC PLAY
Let the music play / I can't get enough of your love, babe / I love you more than anything (In this world girl) / Love serenade I / Hard to believe that I found you / September when I first met you / Don't make me wait too long / Look at her / I'm gonna love you just a little more, baby / Oh love, well we finally made it / Let me live my life lovin' you babe / Love serenade II
CD _____ 5515152
Spectrum/Karussell / Oct '95 / PolyGram / THE.

MAN IS BACK, THE
Responsible / Super lover / L.A. my kinda place / Follow that and see (where it leads y'all) / When will I see you again / I wanna do it good to ya / It's getting harder all the time / Don't let go / Love's interlude / Goodnight my love
CD _____ CDA 5256
A&M / Aug '89 / PolyGram.

MESSAGE IS LOVE, THE
It ain't love baby / Hung up in your love / You're the one I need / Any fool could see / Love ain't easy / I'm on fire / I found love
CD _____ CDSEWM 071
Southbound / Feb '93 / Pinnacle.

PUT ME IN YOUR MIX
Let's get busy / Love is good for you / For real chill / Break it down with you / Volare / Put me in your mix / Who you giving your love to / Love will find us / We're gonna have it all / Dark and lovely (you over there) / Sho' you right
CD _____ 394377 2
A&M / Oct '91 / PolyGram.

RIGHT NIGHT AND BARRY WHITE, THE
Sho' you right / For your love / There is a place / Love is in your eyes / Right night / I'm ready for love / Share / Who's the fool
CD _____ CDMID 155
A&M / Oct '92 / PolyGram.

SHEET MUSIC
Sheet music / Sheet music (part 2) / Lady sweet lady / Ghetto letto / Rum and coca cola / She's everything to me / Love makin' music / I believe in love
CD _____ CDSEWM 072
Southbound / Feb '93 / Pinnacle.

SOUL SEDUCTION
Never never gonna give ya up / Standing in the shadows of love / What am I gonna do with you / Honey please can't you see / Your sweetness is my weakness / I love to sing the songs I sing / It's only love doing it's thing / Bring back my yesterday / I've got so much to give / You see the trouble with me / Playing your game baby / You're so good, you're so bad / Oh me oh my (I'm such a lucky guy)
CD _____ 5500902
Spectrum/Karussell / Oct '93 / PolyGram / THE.

SPOTLIGHT ON BARRY WHITE
My buddy / Long black veil / Where can I turn to / I've got the world to hold me up / Your heart and soul / Out of the shadows of love / Under the influence of love / Fragile hadnle with care / All in the run of love / Come on in love / I owe it all to you
CD _____ HADCD 142
Javelin / Feb '94 / THE / Henry Hadaway Organisation.

WITH LOVE UNLIMITED
Walking in the rain with the one I love / Don't make me wait too long / Don't tell me about heartaches / I won't settle for less than the best (You baby) / Didn't we make it happy baby / Let me in, let's begin with love / Let the music play / Lady sweet lady / I like you, you like me / Change / Gotta be where you are / What am I gonna do with you / You're the one I need / Life / Any fool could see / I found love / Our theme (part 2) / Baby we better try and get it together / She's everything to me / Let's make tonight an evening to remember / I can't let him down / You're the only one for me
CD Set _____ DVSOPCD 154
Connoisseur / Dec '90 / Pinnacle.

YOU'RE THE FIRST, THE LAST, MY EVERYTHING
CD _____ MPG 74031
Movieplay Gold / Nov '94 / Target/BMG.

White, Brian

C'EST MAGNAFIQUE (White, Brian & His Magna Jazz Band)
CD _____ JCD 248
Jazzology / Jun '95 / Swift / Jazz Music.

MUGGSY REMEMBERED
CD _____ JCD 200
Jazzology / Oct '92 / Swift / Jazz Music.

PLEASURE MAD (White, Brian & His Magna Jazz Band)
CD _____ JCD 178
Jazzology / Oct '92 / Swift / Jazz Music.

RAGTIMERS VOL.1 (White, Brian & Alan Gretsy)
CD _____ JCD 116
Jazzology / Aug '94 / Swift / Jazz Music.

White, Bukka

1963 NOT 1962
CD _____ EDCD 382
Edsel / Oct '94 / Pinnacle / ADA.

COMPLETE RECORDINGS, THE
Pine bluff / Arkansas / Shake'em on down / Black train blues / Strange place blues / When can I change my clothes / Sleepy man blues / Parchman farm blues / Good gin blues / High fever blues / District attorney blues / Fixin' to die blues / Aberdeen / Mississippi / Bukka's jitterbug swing / Special stream line
CD _____ 475704 2
Columbia / May '94 / Sony.

COMPLETE SESSIONS (1930-1940)
New Frisco train / Panama limited / I am in the heavenly way / Pine bluff Arkansas / Where can I change my clothes / Sleepy man blues / Parchman farm / Good gin blues / Special line
CD _____ TMCD 03
Travellin' Man / Apr '90 / Wellard / CM / Jazz Music.

MEMPHIS HOT SHOTS
Bed spring blues / Aberdeen / Mississippi blues / Driftin' blues / (Brand new) Decoration blues / Baby, please don't go / Give me an old, old lady / Got sick and tired / World boogie / School of learning / Old man Tom / Gibson town
CD _____ 4759702
Blue Horizon / Feb '95 / Sony.

SKY SONGS VOLS. 1 & 2
CD _____ ARHCD 323
Arhoolie / Apr '95 / ADA / Direct / Cadillac.

White, Carla

LISTEN HERE
Devil may care / Harlem nocturne / Dreamsville / It's you or no one / Lotus blossom / It's only a paper moon / Darn that dream / I've got your number / Listen here / Feelin' / Dream
CD _____ ECD 221092
Evidence / Jan '95 / Harmonia Mundi / ADA / Cadillac.

White, Chris

CHRIS WHITE PROJECT, THE
Might love / My life / Want to be loved / Saturday afternoon / I'm just a lucky so and so / In a sentimental mood / Satin doll / One for the woofer
CD _____ MCD 5494
Muse / Feb '94 / New Note / CM.

SHADOWDANCE
Control / Mr. Fats / New day / Shadowdance / Don't take no / Jericho walls / Eve's song / You will / Dreamtime / Brilliant silence / Way of life
CD _____ 29007162
Bellaphon / May '91 / New Note.

White, Clifford

LIFESPRING, THE
Last snows of winter / Voyage voyage / In the beginning / Lost at shore / Rain trek / Hym-Malaya / Water garden / Lifestream / Plateau / Shimmering gold / First to love
CD _____ SCD 213
Start / May '89 / Koch.

White Devil

REINCARNATION
CD _____ LF 210CD
Lost & Found / Jan '96 / Plastic Head.

White, Frank

DOG IT
CD _____ KFCD 2
JVO / Apr '95 / Pinnacle.

White, George

GEORGE WHITE AT THE MIGHTY WURLITZER
CD _____ CD 407
Bescol / Aug '94 / CM / Target/BMG.

White, Georgia

1930-1936 VOL.1
CD _____ DOCD 5301
Blues Document / May '95 / Swift / Jazz Music / Hot Shot.

1936-1937 VOL.2
CD _____ DOCD 5302
Blues Document / May '95 / Swift / Jazz Music / Hot Shot.

1937-1939 VOL.3
CD _____ DOCD 5303
Blues Document / May '95 / Swift / Jazz Music / Hot Shot.

1939-1941 VOL.4
CD _____ DOCD 5304
Blues Document / May '95 / Swift / Jazz Music / Hot Shot.

TROUBLE IN MIND 1935-41
CD _____ 158322
Blues Collection / Apr '95 / Discovery.

White Heaven

OUT
CD _____ PSFD 11
PSF / Sep '95 / Harmonia Mundi.

White, Howard

NASHVILLE SIDEMAN WITH FRIENDS
Jealous heart / Blue eyes cryin' in the rain / Roly poly / Deep water / Rose of ol' Pawnee / San Antonio rose / Faded love / Midnight / Columbus stockade blues / Before I met you / Steel guitar dowve / Ensonata / Rosette / Steel guitar swallow
CD _____ BCD 15575
Bear Family / Apr '92 / Rollercoaster / Direct / CM / Swift / ADA.

WESTERN SWING & STEEL INSTRUMENTALS
Jealous heart / Blue eyes cryin' in the rain / Roly poly / Deep water / Rose of ol' Pawnee / San Antonio rose / Faded love / Midnight / Columbus stockade blues / Before I met you / Steel guitar dove / Ensonata / Rosette / Steel guitar swallow
CD _____ BCD 15575
Bear Family / Apr '93 / Rollercoaster / Direct / CM / Swift / ADA.

White, James

BUY THE CONTORTIONS
CD _____ 74321327572
Infinite Zero / Oct '95 / BMG.

OFF WHITE
CD _____ 74321318792
Infinite Zero / Oct '95 / BMG.

White, Joe Lynn

WILD LOVE
Tonight the heartache's on me / Bad lose / Too gone to care / Why can't I stop loving you / Whiskey, lies and tears / Wild love / Burning memories / On and on and on / You were right from your side / I am just a rebel
CD _____ 474802 2
Columbia / Sep '94 / Sony.

White, Joshua

JOSH WHITE VOL.1 - 1929-1933
CD _____ DOCD 5194
Blues Document / Oct '93 / Swift / Jazz Music / Hot Shot.

JOSH WHITE VOL.2 - 1933-1935
CD _____ DOCD 5195
Blues Document / Oct '93 / Swift / Jazz Music / Hot Shot.

JOSH WHITE VOL.3 - 1935-1940
CD _____ DOCD 5196
Blues Document / Oct '93 / Swift / Jazz Music / Hot Shot.

ROOTS OF THE BLUES (White, Joshua & Big Bill Broonzy)
CD _____ CD 406
Bescol / Aug '94 / CM / Target/BMG.

White, Karyn

KARYN WHITE
Way you love me / Secret rendezvous / Slow down / Superwoman / Family man / Love saw it / Don't mess with me / Tell me tomorrow / One wish
CD _____ K 9256372
WEA / Mar '94 / Warner Music.

MAKE HIM DO RIGHT
Hungah / Nobody but my baby / I'm your woman / Weakness / One minute / Simple Pleasure / I'd rather be alone / Thinkin' bout love / Make him do right / Can I stay / With you / Here comes the pain again
CD _____ 936245400-2
Warner Bros. / Sep '94 / Warner Music.

RITUAL OF LOVE
Romantic / Ritual of love / Way I feel about you / Hooked on you / Walking the dog / Love that's mine / How I want you / One heart / Tears of joy / Beside you / Do unto me / Hard to say goodbye
CD _____ 7599263202
WEA / Sep '91 / Warner Music.

White, Lari

WISHES
That's my baby / Somebody's fool / Wishes / Now I know / If I'm not already crazy / That's how you don't know / When it rains / Go on / It's love / If you only knew
CD _____ 7863663952
RCA / Apr '95 / BMG.

White, Lavelle

MISS LAVELLE
CD _____ ANT 0031CD
Antones / Sep '94 / Hot Shot / Direct / ADA.

White, Lenny

PRESENT TENSE
CD _____ HIBD 8004
Hip Bop / Apr '95 / Conifer / Total/BMG / Silva Screen.

White Lion

BEST OF WHITE LION
Wait / Radar love / Broken heart / Hungry / Little fighter / Lights and thunder / All you need is rock 'n' roll (live) / When the children cry / Love don't come easy / Cry for freedom / Lady of the valley (live) / Tell me / Farewell to you
CD _____ 7567824252
Atlantic / Oct '92 / Warner Music.

FIGHT TO SURVIVE
CD _____ CDMFN 130
Music For Nations / Jul '92 / Pinnacle.

MANE ATTRACTION
Lights and thunder / Leave me alone / Love don't come easy / You're all I need / Broken heart / Warsong / It's over / Till death do us part / Out with the boys / Farewell to you / She's got everything (Not available on CD)
CD _____ 756782193-2
Atlantic / Apr '91 / Warner Music.

PRIDE
Hungry / Lonely nights / Don't give up / Sweet little loving / Lady of the valley / Wait / All you need is rock 'n' roll / Tell me / All join our hands / When the children cry
CD _____ 781 768-2
Atlantic / Jul '87 / Warner Music.

White, Lily

SOMEWHERE BETWEEN TRUTH AND FICTION
CD _____ KFWCD 153
Knitting Factory / Feb '95 / Grapevine.

White, Michael

HOW STRONG WE BELIEVE
You are the one / One more time / So far away / Fe-fe / How strong we believe / Song for Rachel / I want you
CD _____ K32Y 6279
King/Paddle Wheel / Aug '91 / New Note.

White Moon

TRADITIONAL MUSIC FROM MONGOLIA
CD _____ PANCD 2010
Pan / May '93 / ADA / Direct / CM.

White Noise

ELECTRIC STORM, AN
Love without sound / My game of loving / Here comes the fleas / Firebird / Your hidden dreams / Visitation / Black mass / Electric storm in hell
CD _____ 3D CID1001
Island / '94 / PolyGram.

White Orange

WHITE ORANGE
CD _____ 1215
Caprice / Dec '91 / CM / Complete / Pinnacle / Cadillac / ADA.

White, Peter

EXCUSEZ MOI
Excusez moi / Smooth sailin' / Dreamwalk / All I want / Drive-by night / My girl Madge / Juggler / In the rain / Lost in your eyes / Mr. Caribbean / Don't wait for me
CD _____ 101S8770722
101 South / Jul '94 / New Note.

REVEILLEZ-VOUS
Reveillez-vous / Moonlight Montreal / Play your guitar for me / Romance dance / Everyday / Festival / Crazy feeling / Song for Robin / Danny Bianco / If only for you
CD _____ 101S 8770582
101 South / Aug '94 / New Note.

White Plains

MY BABY LOVES LOVIN'
I've got you on my mind / When tomorrow comes tomorrow / Taffeta rose / Taffeta rose (I remember) / (I remember) Summer morning / Ecstasy / Julie Anne / Does anybody know where my baby is / Step into a dream / Dad you saved the world / I can't stop / Carolina's coming home / I gonna miss her mississippi / When you are a king / Every little move she makes / Julie do ya love me / Lovin' you baby / Honey girl / Young birds fly / Show me your hand / You've got your troubles / Today I killed a man I didn't know / My baby loves lovin' / In a moment of madness / To love you
CD _____ 820 622-2
London / May '93 / PolyGram.

White, Roland

TRYING TO GET TO YOU
CD _____ SH 3826CD
Sugarhill / May '95 / Roots / CM / ADA / Direct.

White, Saylor

THAT'S JUST THE WAY IT GOES
CD _____ 422491
New Rose / Nov '94 / Direct / ADA.

White, Sheila G.

50 MOODS IN COUNTRY
CD _____ SOW 502
Sound Waves / Aug '92 / Target/BMG.

50 SHADES OF COUNTRY
CD _____ SOW 501
Sound Waves / Jun '92 / Target/BMG.

LOVE SONG, A
CD _____ SOW 503
Soundsrite / Jun '93 / THE / Target/BMG.

White, Snowy

CHANGE MY LIFE
CD _____ RDCD 1203
Rio Digital / Feb '91 / Grapevine.

GOLDTOP (The Definitive Collection)
Carol / Modern times / Pigs on the wing / Drop in from the top / Renegade / Memory pain / Slaybo day / In the skies / Answer / Bird of paradise / Tailfeathers / Someone else is gonna love me / That certain thing / Out of order / Open for business / Highway to the sun / Time has come / Judgement day
CD _____ RPM 154
RPM / Nov '95 / Pinnacle.

HIGHWAY TO THE SUN
Highway to the sun / Can't find love / Burning love / Loving man / Time has come / Heartful of love / Love, pain, and sorrow / Hot Saturday night / Keep on working / I loved another woman / I can't get enough of the blues
CD _____ 29007205
Bellaphon / Sep '95 / New Note.

White Stains

WHY NOT FOREVER
CD _____ EFA 11230-2
Danse Macabre / Feb '94 / SRD.

White, Tam

KEEP IT UNDER YOUR HAT (White, Tam & The Band)
More / Dream / Coupe de Ville / Mad Sam / Good morning heartache (CD only) / Street people / Stone mason's blues / Sleep-late Louie's / Woman in love / Nature of the beast / 36th Street mission blues (CD only)
CD _____ JHCD 018
Ronnie Scott's Jazz House / Jan '94 / Jazz Music / Magnum Music Group / Cadillac.

White, Tony Joe

BEST OF TONY JOE WHITE
Polk salad Annie / Willie and Laura Mae Jones / Soul Francisco / Don't steal my love / Roosevelt and Ira Lee / For Lee Ann / Elements and things / Rainy night in Georgia / High sheriff of Calhoun Parrish / Widow Wimberly / Stud spider / Old man Willis / Save your sugar for me / Polka salad Annie
CD _____ 9362453052
Warner Bros. / Sep '93 / Warner Music.

BEST OF TONY JOE WHITE, THE
Roosevelt and Ira Lee / Stockholm blues / High sheriff of Calhoun Parrish / Old man Willis / Train I'm on / If I ever saw a good thing / As the crow flies / Even trolls love to rock and roll / Backwood preacher man / Takin' the midnight train / Did somebody make a fool out of you / Caught the Devil and put him in jail in Eudor, Arkansas / Saturday night in Oak Grove, Louisiana / I've got a thing about you baby / For ol' time sake / Ol' Mother earth
CD Set _____ MPG 74177
Movieplay Gold / Nov '94 / Target/BMG.

CLOSER TO THE TRUTH
CD _____ 511386-2
Polydor / Nov '91 / PolyGram.

GROUPIE GIRL
CD _____ MPG 74023
Movieplay Gold / Nov '93 / Target/BMG.

LIVE
CD _____ DFG 8407
Dixie Frog / Sep '90 / Magnum Music Group.

PATH OF A DECENT GROOVE, THE
CD _____ 519938-2
Polydor / Nov '93 / PolyGram.

POLKA SALAD ANNIE
CD _____ MPG 74021
Movieplay Gold / Nov '93 / Target/BMG.

ROOSEVELT AND IRA LEE
CD _____ MPG 74022
Movieplay Gold / Nov '93 / Target/BMG.

White Zombie

ASTRO CREEP
Electric head pt.1 (The agony) / Supercharger heaven / Real solution # 9 / Creature of the wheel / Electric head pt.2 (The ecstasy) / Grease paint and monkey brains / I zombie / More human than human / El phantasmo and the chicken run blast-o-rama / Blur the technicolor / Blood milk and sky
CD _____ GED 24806
Geffen / May '95 / BMG.

LA SEXORCISTO: DEVIL MUSIC VOL. 1
Welcome to planet motherfucker/Psychoholic slag / Knuckle duster (Radio 1-A) / Thunder kiss / Black sunshine / Soul crusher / Cosmic monsters inc. / Spiderbaby (yeah yeah yeah) / I am legend / Knuckle duster (Radio 2-B) / Thrust / One big crunch / Grindhouse (A go-go) / Starface / Warp asylum
CD _____ GEFD 24460
Geffen / Mar '92 / BMG.

Whitehead Brothers

SERIOUS
Forget I was a G / Your love is a 187 / Shaniqua / Change / Interlude / Late nite tip / Just a touch of love / Where ya at / Serious / Beautiful black princess / Sex on the beach / Turn U out / She needed me / Love goes on / Beautiful black princess (reprise)
CD _____ 5303462
Motown / Jan '95 / PolyGram.

Whitehead, Tim

AUTHENTIC
Falling grace / No more war / All I ever wanted / Neighbourly complaint (CD only) / Aspiration / One view of Annet / Come on home / Gypsy (CD only)
CD _____ JHCD 017
Ronnie Scott's Jazz House / Jan '94 / Jazz Music / Magnum Music Group / Cadillac.

SILENCE BETWEEN WAVES
Southend / Sky seas / Return / Third exposure / One view of Annet / Secret talks / Warners well / True to your word / 34 Cambrian road / These tears / Come on home
CD _____ JHCD 038
Ronnie Scott's Jazz House / Nov '94 / Jazz Music / Magnum Music Group / Cadillac.

Whitehorn, Geoff

BIG IN GRAVESEND
CD _____ OMMR 941
Music Maker / Nov '94 / Grapevine / ADA.

GEOFF WHO?
CD _____ CMMR 902
Music Maker / Jun '92 / Grapevine / ADA.

Whitekaps

CANNONBALL
CD _____ HR 604CD
Hopeless / Nov '95 / Plastic Head.

Whiteley, John Scott

GREAT ROMANTIC ORGAN MUSIC
Improvisation sur le te deum (tournemire) / Menuet-Scherzo / Tu es petra / Trois preludes et fugues / Hochzeitspraludium (wedding prelude) / Three pastels / Eleven chorale preludes / Prelude and fugue on Bach
CD _____ YORKCD 101
York Ambisonic / Sep '90 / Target/BMG.

Whiteman, Paul

BIRTH OF RHAPSODY IN BLUE, THE
CD Set _____ MMD 60113 T
Music Masters / Jan '89 / Nimbus.

COMPLETE CAPITOL RECORDINGS
I've found a new baby / Serenade in blue / General jumped at dawn / I've got a gal in Kalamazoo / Trav'lin' light / Old music master / I'm old fashioned / You were never lovelier / San / Wang wang blues / American in Paris / Rhapsody in blue
CD _____ CDP 8301032
Capitol / Mar '95 / EMI.

GREAT COMBINATION, A
This can't be love / Simple and sweet / Mexican jumpin' bean / My melancholy baby / Cuckoo in the clock / Sing for your supper / Kiss your hand Madam
CD _____ DAWE 45
Magic / Sep '93 / Jazz Music / Swift / Wellard / Cadillac / Harmonia Mundi.

JAZZ PORTRAITS
You took advantage of me / Mississippi mud / I'm coming Virginia / Whispering / Side by side / Milenberg joys / St. Louis blues / Whiteman stomp / Changes / Five step / Sensation stomp / Magnolia / Wang wang blues / Everybody step / Hot lips (He's got hot lips when he plays jazz) / Red hot Henry Brown / Charlestonette / Bell hoppin' blues
CD _____ CD 14521
Jazz Portraits / May '94 / Jazz Music.

PAUL WHITEMAN AND HIS ORCHESTRA (1921-1934 recordings) (Whiteman, Paul & His Orchestra)
Southern Rose / Merry widow waltz (Indigo, Alice blue and helitrope) / I'm a dreamer / Nola / Carioca / Caprice futuristic / South Sea isles / Suite of serenades (Spanish, Chinese, Cuban, Oriental.) / It all depends on you / Parade of the tin soldiers / Liebestraum / Park Avenue fantasy / When you're in love / Night with Paul Whiteman at The Biltmore / Signature tune
CD _____ PASTCD 9718
Flapper / '90 / Pinnacle.

WHEN DAY IS DONE
CD _____ CDHD 171
Conifer / Jul '93 / Conifer.

Whiteout

BITE IT
CD _____ ORECD 536
Silvertone / Jun '95 / Pinnacle.

Whiteouts

WHITEOUTS
CD _____ E 11919.2
Vince Lombard / Dec '93 / SRD.

Whiteside, Taylor

NEW ENGLAND FAVOURITES
CD _____ FE 1406
Folk Era / Nov '94 / CM / ADA.

Whitesnake

1987
Still of the night / Bad boys / Give me all your love / Looking for love / Crying in the rain / Is this love / Straight for the heart / Don't turn away / Children of the night / Here I go again (1987) / You're gonna break my heart again (CD only)
CD _____ CDEMS 1531
EMI / Jul '94 / EMI.

COME AN' GET IT
Come an' get it / Hot stuff / Don't break my heart again / Lonely days, lonely nights / Wine, women and song / Child of Babylon / Would I lie to you / Girl / Hit and run / Till the day I die
CD _____ CDEMS 1528
EMI / Jul '94 / EMI.

FORKED TONGUE THE INTERVIEW
CD P.Disc _____ CBAK 4064
Baktabak / Feb '94 / Baktabak.

GREATEST HITS

Still of the night / Here I go again / Is this love / Love ain't no stranger / Looking for love / Now you're gone / Slide it in / Slow an' easy / Judgement day / You're gonna break my heart again / Deeper the love / Crying in the rain / Fool for your loving / Sweet lady luck
CD _____ CDEMD 1065
EMI / Jan '94 / EMI.

LIVE IN THE HEART OF THE CITY
Come on / Sweet talker / Walking in the shadow of the blues / Love hunter / Fool for your loving / Ain't gonna cry no more / Ready an' willing / Take me with you / Might just take your life / Lie down / Ain't no love in the heart of the city / Trouble / Mistreated
CD _____ CDEMS 1525
EMI / Jul '94 / EMI.

LOVEHUNTER
Long way from home / Walking in the shadow of the blues / Help me thro' the day / Medicine man / You 'n' me / Mean business / Love hunter / Outlaw / Rock 'n' roll women / We wish you well
CD _____ CDEMS 1529
EMI / Jul '94 / EMI.

READY AN' WILLING
Fool for your loving / Sweet talker / Ready an' willing / Carry your load / Blindman / Ain't gonna cry no more / Love man / Black and blue / She's a woman
CD _____ CDEMS 1526
EMI / Jul '94 / EMI.

SAINTS 'N' SINNERS
Young blood / Rough and ready / Bloody luxury / Victim of love / Crying in the rain / Here I go again / Love and affection / Rock 'n' roll angels / Dancing girls / Saints and sinners
CD _____ CDEMS 1521
EMI / Jul '94 / EMI.

SLIDE IT IN
Gambler / Slide it in / Standing in the shadow / Give me more time / Love ain't no stranger / Slow an' easy / Spit it out / All or nothing / Hungry for love / Guilty of love / Need your love so bad (MC only)
CD _____ CZ 88
EMI / Apr '88 / EMI.

SLIDE IT IN/1987/SLIP OF THE TONGUE
CD Set _____ CDOMB 016
EMI / Oct '95 / EMI.

SLIP OF THE TONGUE
Slip of the tongue / Cheap an' nasty / Fool for your loving / Now you're gone / Kitten's got claws / Wings of the storm / Deeper the love / Judgement day / Slow poke music / Sailing ships
CD _____ CDEMS 1527
EMI / Jul '94 / EMI.

TROUBLE
Take me with you / Love to keep you warm / Lie down / Day tripper / Nighthawk (vampire blues) / Time is right for love / Trouble / Belgian Tom's hat trick / Free flight / Don't mess with me
CD _____ CDFA 3234
Fame / May '90 / EMI.

Whitfield, Barrence

BARRENCE WHITFIELD & THE SAVAGES (Whitfield, Barrence & The Savages)
CD _____ 4ZL050 I 6050
Fan Club / Jan '95 / Direct.

COWBOY MAMBO (Whitfield, Barrence & Tom Russell)
CD _____ RTMCD 64
Round Tower / Apr '94 / Pinnacle / ADA / Direct / BMG / CM.

FIRST LP (Whitfield, Barrence & The Savages)
CD _____ FC 058CD
Fan Club / '90 / Direct.

HILLBILLY VOO DOO
CD _____ RTMCD 55
Round Tower / Sep '93 / Pinnacle / ADA / Direct / BMG / CM.

LET'S LOSE IT
CD _____ 422391
New Rose / May '94 / Direct / ADA.

LIVE EMULSIFIED (Whitfield, Barrence & The Savages)
CD _____ 422392
New Rose / Jan '95 / Direct / ADA.

OW! OW! OW! (Whitfield, Barrence & The Savages)
CD _____ CD 9011
Rounder / '88 / CM / Direct / ADA / Cadillac.

RITUAL OF THE SAVAGES
CD _____ FIEND 760
Demon / Oct '94 / Pinnacle / ADA.

SAVAGE TRACKS (Whitfield, Barrence & The Savages)
CD _____ 422402
New Rose / May '94 / Direct / ADA.

Whitfield, David

DAVID WHITFIELD SINGS STAGE & SCREEN FAVOURITES
CD _____ PWK 096
Carlton Home Entertainment / '89 / Carlton Home Entertainment.

FROM DAVID WITH LOVE
CD _____ 8209482
Deram / Jan / '96 / PolyGram.

GREATEST HITS: DAVID WHITFIELD
Cara mia / Santo natale / Book / Mama / Everywhere / Rags to riches / When you lose the one you love / My son John / Bridge of sighs / My September love / Answer me / Beyond the stars / Adoration waltz / On the Street where you live / Willingly / I'll find you / Right to love / Cry my heart / My unfinished symphony / I believe
CD _____ 8206432
Eclipse / Nov / '90 / PolyGram.

Whitfield, Weslia

LUCKY TO BE ME
Lucky to be me / Something to remember you by / Do I love you / Glad to be unhappy / Moments like this / My buddy / This funny world / He was too good to me / By myself / Be careful it's my heart / For all we know / Face like yours / Rhode Island is famous for you / Don't you know I care (or don't you care to) / Two for the road
CD _____ LCD 15242
Landmark / Aug / '90 / New Note.

NICE WORK
Nice work if you can get it / How deep is the ocean / I'm crazy 'bout my baby / I'm gonna laugh you right out of my life / Bewitched, bothered and bewildered / This can't be love / Where's that rainbow / Thou swell / Kiss to build a dream on / I concentrate on you / I'm confessin' that I love you / Of my life / I'm an errand girl for rhythm / Golden earrings / Nevertheless
CD _____ LCD 15442
Landmark / Aug / '95 / New Note.

Whiting, Margaret

GREAT LADIES OF SONG, THE
Day in day out / But not for me / Gypsy in my soul / Like someone in love / He's funny that way / Time after time / My heart stood still / Nobody but you / I hadn't anyone till now / I've never been in love before / But beautiful / My foolish heart / I get a kick out of you / Let's fall in love / Someone to watch over me / I could write a book / Back in your own backyard
CD _____ CDP 8303952
Capitol Jazz / Aug / '95 / EMI.

LADY'S IN LOVE WITH YOU, THE
CD _____ ACD 207
Audiophile / Feb / '91 / Jazz Music / Swift.

MARGARET WHITING
CD _____ ACD 173
Audiophile / Aug / '94 / Jazz Music / Swift.

THEN AND NOW
I fought every step of the way / Moonlight in Vermont / That old black magic / It might as well be Spring / Lies of handsome men / Coffee shoppe / Hell of a way to run a love affair / I got lost in his arms / Best thing for you / Our little day / Blame it on my youth / Young and foolish / Can't teach my old heart new tricks / My best friend / What is a man / Bewitched, bothered and bewildered / Old devil moon / Now that I have everything
CD _____ DRGCD 91403
DRG / Mar / '92 / New Note.

TOO MARVELLOUS FOR WORDS
CD _____ ACD 152
Audiophile / Jun / '95 / Jazz Music / Swift.

Whitley, Chris

DIN OF ECSTACY
Narcotic prayer / Know / O God my heart is ready / Can't get off / God thing / Din / New machine / Guns and dolls / WPL / Ultraglide
CD _____ 4777572
Columbia / Mar / '95 / Sony.

LIVING WITH THE LAW
Excerpt / Living with the law / Big sky country / Kick the stones / Make the dirt stick / Poison girl / Dust radio / Phone call from Leavenworth / I forget you every day / Long way around / Look what love has done / Bordertown
CD _____ 4685682
Columbia / Sep / '94 / Sony.

Whitley, Keith

DON'T CLOSE YOUR EYES
Flying colours / It's all coming back to me now / Lucky dog / Don't close your eyes / Birmingham turnaround / Some old side road / Would these arms be in your way / I'm no stranger to the rain / I never go around mirrors / When you say nothing at all / Day in the life of a fool / Honky tonk heart
CD _____ PD 90313
RCA / Apr / '89 / BMG.

Whitman, Slim

COUNTRY STYLE
Rhinestone cowboy / Red river valley / Tumbling tumbleweeds / Kentucky waltz / Home on the range / I can't stop loving you / Cattle call / Rose Marie / Riders in the sky / From a jack to a king / Broken wings / Paper roses / It keeps right on a-hurtin' / Wayward wind / Top of the world / Cool water
CD _____ CDMFP 6035
Music For Pleasure / Nov / '88 / EMI.

LOVE SONGS
Rose Marie / Indian love call / Let me call you sweetheart / Somewhere my love / My elusive dreams / When you were sweet sixteen / Love song of the waterfall / I'll take you home again Kathleen / HAve I told you lately that I love you / Happy Anniversary / Beautiful dreamer / When you wore a tulip / Serenade / Roses are red / Girl of my dreams / Edelweiss / Oh my darlin' (I love you) / Twelfth of never / Can't help falling in love / You are my sunshine
CD _____ CDMFP 6113
Music For Pleasure / Mar / '94 / EMI.

SLIM WHITMAN VOL. 1
I'm casting my lasso towards the sky / Indian love call / Love song of the waterfall / Rose Marie / I leave the Milky Way / Tumbling tumbleweeds / Danny boy / You have my heart / I must have been blind / Lord help me be as thou / China doll / When it's springtime in the Rockies / Love knot in my lariat / Riding the range for Jesus / Poor little Angeline / Cryin' for the moon / Serenade / Many times / I'll take you home again Kathleen / First one to find the rainbow / Secret love / Stairway to heaven / I'm a fool / Heartbreak hill / Too late now / My wild Irish rose / You're the only one / Just call me lonesome / Annie Laurie / Bells that broke my heart / Sweeter than the flowers / Happy Street / Eileen / When I grow too old to dream / Tomorrow never comes / I wanna go to heaven / Blue Canadian Rockies / Yesterday's roses / I climbed the mountain / I'll see you when / Stranger on the shore / What's this world a-comin' to / Rockin' alone in an old rocking chair / Little drops of silver / Another tomorrow / Twelfth of never / It's a small world / Mr. Ting-a-Ling / It's a sin to tell a lie / As you take a walk through my mind / Happy Anniversary
CD Set _____ CDEM 1482
EMI / Mar / '93 / EMI.

UNDER HIS WINGS
CD _____ CDC 5383
Disky / May / '94 / THE / BMG / Discovery / Pinnacle.

Whitstein Brothers

OLD TIME DUETS
Mansion on the hill / We parted by the riverside / There's an open door waiting / Sinner you'd better get ready / We met in the saddle / I'm troubled / That silver haired daddy / Seven year blues / Weary lonesome blues / Somewhere in Tennessee / Maple on the hill / If I could hear my mother pray again / Pitfall / Beautiful lost river valley
CD _____ ROUNDERCD 0264
Rounder / '89 / CM / Direct / ADA / Cadillac.

ROSE OF MY HEART
Rose of my heart / Highway headin' South / Kentucky / My curly headed baby / Weary days / Weary blues from waiting / Arkansas / Bridge over troubled water / Eighth wonder of the world / Scared of the blues / Where the old river flows / Smoky mountain memories
CD _____ ROUCD 0206
Rounder / Oct / '94 / CM / Direct / ADA / Cadillac.

WHITSTEIN BROTHERS SING GOSPEL SONGS OF THE LOUVINS
CD _____ ROUCD 0308
Rounder / Nov / '94 / CM / Direct / ADA / Cadillac.

Whittaker, Roger

BEST OF ROGER WHITTAKER, THE
CD _____ MATCD 326
Castle / Feb / '95 / BMG.

BUTTERFLY
Butterfly / Settle down / After the laughter came tears / Santa Anna / Steel men / Mud puddle / You've got a friend / Handful of dreams / Sinner / Sunrise sunset / Acre of wheat / Impossible dream / Jenny's gone (And I don't care)
CD _____ PWK 133
Carlton Home Entertainment / May / '90 / Carlton Home Entertainment.

DANNY BOY
When Irish eyes are smiling / Down by the Sally gardens / Forty shades of green / Rose of Tralee / Giant land / Star of the county down / Irish whistler / Unicorn / Minstrel boy / I'll tell me Ma / Rooney / Rising of the lark / Believe me, if all those endearing young charms / Uncle Benny / Danny boy / Kilgarry mountain
CD _____ 09026619722
RCA / Jun / '94 / BMG.

DURHAM TOWN
Durham town / Morning has broken / Dirty old town / Impossible dream / San Miguel / I don't believe in it anymore / Many times / Taste of honey / Why / Those were the days / Scarborough Fair / By the time I get to Phoenix
CD _____ PWK 129
Carlton Home Entertainment / Apr / '90 / Carlton Home Entertainment.

EIN GLUCK, DAS ES DICH GIBT
CD _____ INT 861 552
Interchord / '88 / CM.

EVENING WITH ROGER WHITTAKER, AN
CD _____ PLATCD 3929
Prism / May / '94 / Prism.

FEELINGS
Feelings / Time in a bottle / Harbour lights / For I loved you / Love me tender / Leavin' on a jet plane / Everytime is gonna be the last time / Send in the clowns / Honey / Gentle on my mind / Unchained melody / When I need you / Miss you nights / Before she breaks my heart / Have I told you lately that I love you
CD _____ 74321 18330-2
RCA / Jun / '94 / BMG.

HIS FINEST COLLECTION
Durham Town / Streets of London / Leaving on a jet plane / New world in the morning / Harbour lights / I don't believe in if anymore / Stranger on the shore / Feelings / Last farewell / Skye boat song / Annie's song / Gentle on my mind / Make the world go away / You were always on my mind / Twelfth of never / For the good times / Shenandoah / Amazing grace
CD _____ 7432113463-2
RCA / Apr / '93 / BMG.

I DON'T BELIEVE IN IF ANYMORE
CD _____ RMB 75077
Remember / Sep / '94 / Total/BMG.

I WILL ALWAYS LOVE YOU
CD _____ 09026626822
RCA / Sep / '94 / BMG.

LEGENDS IN MUSIC - ROGER WHITTAKER
CD _____ LECD 061
Wisepack / Jul / '94 / THE / Conifer.

LIVE
CD _____ 15089
Laserlight / Aug / '91 / Target/BMG.
CD _____ MU 5062
Musketeer / Oct / '94 / Koch.

NEW WORLD IN THE MORNING
New world in the morning / Streets of London / Early one morning / Lemon tree / Morning please don't come / Last farewell / From both sides now / Waterboy / Special kind of man / Leaving of Liverpool / Mexican whistler
CD _____ PWK 092
Carlton Home Entertainment / Mar / '89 / Carlton Home Entertainment.
CD _____ WMCD 5697
Disky / Oct / '94 / THE / BMG / Discovery / Pinnacle.

ROGER WHITTAKER COLLECTION
New world in the morning / Sunrise, sunset / Imagine both sides now / Love lasts forever / Send in the clowns / Wind beneath my wings / I can see clearly now / She / What a wonderful world / Evergreen / Last farewell
CD _____ 74321339392
Camden / Jan / '96 / BMG.

ROGER WHITTAKER IN CONCERT (Live From The Tivoli)
New world in the morning / I love you / My land in Kenya / What a wonderful world / Mexican whistler / Wimoweh / I'll tell me ma / Skye boat song / I don't believe in if anymore / Russellin' along / Rocky top / Willkommen / Cabaret / Oh mein papa / Send in the clowns / If I were a rich man / Thank you love / Make the world go away / Durham Town / Last farewell / Kilgarry mountain
CD _____ PD 74854
RCA / Jan / '91 / BMG.

ROGER WHITTAKER LIVE
CD _____ EMPRCD 522
Empress / Sep / '94 / THE.

ROMANTIC SIDE OF ROGER WHITTAKER (MFP)
It's your love / One other / Love will / New love / Man without love / I would if I could / See you shine / Tall dark stranger / Goodbye / My world / Don't fight / Before she breaks my heart / Time / Summer days / Pretty bird of love / Let me be your sun / Indian lady (CD only.) / New we stand (CD only.) / Newport Belle (CD only.) / For I loved you (CD only.)
CD _____ CDMFP 5882
Music For Pleasure / Apr / '90 / EMI.

SINCERELY YOURS
New world in the morning / Before she breaks my heart / Say my goodbyes to the world / What a wonderful world (with you) / All the way to Richmond / Summer days / Imagine / Love will / My son / Feelings / I would if I could / Man without love

It's your love / Time / Weekend in New England / Pretty bird of love / Let me be your sun / New love / Here we stand / Don't fight / One another / For I loved you / Shoe you shine / What a wonderful world
CD _____ VSOPCD 129
Connoisseur / Nov / '88 / Pinnacle.

SONGS OF LOVE AND LIFE
Flip flap / Sugar in my tea / Halfway up the mountain / Berceuse pour mon amour / Book / I believe / Finnish whistler / Emily / I should have taken my time / Festival / Swaggy / Mistral
CD _____ PWK 4044P
Carlton Home Entertainment / Apr / '91 / Carlton Home Entertainment.

STEEL MAN
Steel man / After the laughter (came tears) / You've got a friend / Impossible dream / Sinner / Charge of the light brigade / Sunrise sunset / Mud puddle / Settle down / Butterfly / Jenny's gone (and I don't care) / Handful of dreams / Acre of wheat / Santa Anna
CD _____ 5501222
Spectrum/Karussell / Oct / '93 / PolyGram / THE.

TYPISCH ROGER WHITTAKER
CD _____ INT 861 548
Interchord / '88 / CM.

WIND BENEATH MY WINGS
Wind beneath my wings / Annie's song / Always on my mind / I can see clearly now / Most beautiful girl / She believes in me / You needed me / Evergreen / Try to remember / For the good times / Still the sea / Weekend in New England / One another / Sailing / Candle in the night / Image to my mind
CD _____ 71321 18331-27
RCA / Jun / '94 / BMG.

YOU DESERVE THE BEST
Good old love / You deserve the best / Just across the Rio Grande / Early morning memories / Take away my pain / One song / Keep on chasing rainbows / I have you / But she loves me / Little love can go a long, long way / Only real hero / I'd fall in love tonight
CD _____ PD 74817
RCA / Oct / '90 / BMG.

Whittaker, Sebastian

ONE FOR BU
CD _____ JR 02032
Justice / Apr / '94 / Koch.

SEARCHIN' FOR THE TRUTH (Whittaker, Sebastian & The Creators)
CD _____ JR 002022
Justice / Nov / '94 / Koch.

Whittle, Tommy

WARM GLOW (Whittle, Tommy Quartet)
CD _____ TEEJAY 103
Teejay / Nov / '92 / THE / Cadillac.

Who

30 YEARS OF MAXIMUM R'N'B
I'm the face / Here 'tis / Zoot suit / Leaving here / I can't explain / Anyway anyhow anywhere / Daddy rollin' stone / My generation / Kids are alright / Ov / Legal matter / Substitute / I'm a boy / Disguises / Happy Jack / Boris the spider / So sad about us / Quick one / Pictures of Lily / Early morning cold taxi / last time / I can't reach you / Girl's eyes / Bag o' nails / Call me lightning / I can see for miles / Mary Anne with the shaky hand / Armenia city in the sky / Tattoo / Our love was / Rael 1 / Rael 2 / Sunrise / Jaguar / Melancholia / Fortune teller / Magic bus / Little Billy / Dogs / Overture / Acid queen / Underture (live) / Pinball wizard / I'm free / See me, feel me (live) / Heaven and hell / Young man blues (live) / Summertime blues (live) / Shakin' all over / Baba O'Riley / Bargain / Pure and easy / Song is over / Behind blue eyes / Won't get fooled again / Seeker / Bony Moronie (live) / Let's see action / Join together / Replay / Real me / 5.15 / Bell boy / Love reign o'er me / Long live rock / Naked eye (live) / Slip kid / Dreaming from the waist (Live) / Blue, red and grey / Squeeze box / My wife (Live) / Who are you / Music must change / Sister disco / Guitar and pen / You better you bet / Eminence front / Twist and shout (Live) / I'm a man (Live) / Saturday night's alright for fighting
CD Set _____ 521751-2
Polydor / Feb / '94 / PolyGram.

JOIN TOGETHER
Overture / 1921 / Amazing journey / Sparks / Hawker (eyesight to the blind) / Christmas / Cousin Kevin / Acid queen / Pinball wizard / Do you think it's alright / Fiddle about / There's a doctor / Go to the mirror / Smash the mirror / Tommy can you hear me / I'm free / Miracle cure / Sally Simpson / Sensation / Tommy's holiday camp / We're not gonna take it / Eminence front / Face the face / Dig / I can see for miles / Little is enough / 5.15 / Love reign o'er me / Trick of the light / Rough boys / Join together / You better you bet / Behind blue eyes / Won't get fooled again

CD _____ **CDVDT 102**
Virgin / Mar '90 / EMI.

KIDS ARE ALRIGHT, THE (Film Soundtrack)
My generation / I can't explain / Happy Jack / I can see for miles / Magic bus / Long live rock / Anyway anyhow anywhere / Young man blue / Baba O'Riley / My wife / Quick one / Tommy can you hear me / Sparks / Pinball wizard / See me, feel me / Join together / Roadrunner / My generation blues / Won't get fooled again
CD _____ **517 947-2**
Polydor / Jun '93 / PolyGram.

LIVE AT LEEDS - 25TH ANNIVERSARY EDITION
Heaven and hell / I can't explain / Fortune teller / Tattoo / Young man blues / Substitute / Happy Jack / I'm a boy / Quick one / Amazing journey / Summertime blues / Shakin' all over / My generation / Magic bus / Sparks
CD _____ **5271692**
Polydor / Feb '95 / PolyGram.

ODDS AND SODS
Postcard / Now I'm a farmer / Put the money down / Little Billy / Too much of anything / Glow girl / Pure and easy / Faith in something bigger / I'm the face / Naked / Long live rock
CD _____ **517 946-2**
Polydor / Jun '93 / PolyGram.

QUADROPHENIA
I am the sea / Real me / Cut my hair / Punk and the godfather / I'm one / Dirty jobs / Helpless dancer / Is it in my head / I've had enough / 5.15 / Sea and sand / Drowned / Bell boy / Dr. Jimmy / Rock / Love reign o'er me
CD Set _____ **831 074-2**
Polydor / '88 / PolyGram.

QUICK ONE, A
Run run run / Boris the spider / I need you / Whiskey man / Heatwave / Cobwebs and strange / Don't look away / See my way / Quick one / I've been away (On CD) / So sad about us / Doctor doctor (On CD) / Bucket T (On CD) / Barbara Ann (On CD) / Batman (On CD) / Disguises (On CD) / In the city (On CD) / Man with money (On CD) / Happy Jack (On CD) / My generation/Land of hope and glory (On CD)
CD _____ **5277582**
Polydor / Jun '93 / PolyGram.

RARITIES VOLUMES 1 AND 2
CD _____ **847 670-2**
Polydor / Jan '91 / PolyGram.

SINGLES, THE
Substitute / I'm a boy / Happy Jack / Pictures of lily / I can see for miles / Magic bus / Pinball wizard / Summertime blues / Won't get fooled again / Let's see action / Join together / Squeeze box / Who are you / You better you bet
CD _____ **815 965-2**
Polydor / Nov '84 / PolyGram.

TALKIN' BOUT THEIR GENERATION
CD P.Disc _____ **CBAK 4067**
Baktabak / Feb '94 / Baktabak.

TOMMY
Overture / It's a boy / 1921 / Amazing journey / Sparks / Eyesight to the blind / Miracle cure / Sally Simpson / I'm free / Welcome / Tommy's holiday camp / We're not gonna take it / Christmas / Cousin Kevin / Acid queen / Underture / Do you think it's alright / Fiddle about / Pinball wizard / There's a doctor / Go to the mirror / Tommy can you hear me / Smash the mirror / Sensation
CD Set _____ **800 077-2**
Polydor / Apr '89 / PolyGram.

WHO ARE YOU
New song / Had enough / 905 / Music must change / Trick of the light / Guitar and pen / Love is coming down / Who are you
CD _____ **831 557-2**
Polydor / Jul '89 / PolyGram.

WHO BY NUMBERS, THE
Slip kid / However much I booze / Squeeze box / Dreaming from the waist / Imagine a man / Success story / They are all in love / Blue, red and grey / How many friends / In a hand or a face
CD _____ **831 552-2**
Polydor / Jul '89 / PolyGram.

WHO SELL OUT, THE
Armenia city in the sky / Heinz baked beans / Mary Anne with the shaky hand / Odorono / Tattoo / Our love was / I can see for miles / Medac / Relax / Rael #1/#2 / Glittering girl (On CD) / Melancholia (On CD) / Someone's coming (On CD) / Jaguar (On CD) / Early morning cold taxi (On CD) / Hall of the mountain King (On CD) / Girls eyes (On CD) / Mary Anne with the shaky hand (2) (On CD) / Glow girl (On CD)
CD _____ **5277592**
Polydor / Jun '95 / PolyGram.

WHO'S BETTER WHO'S BEST (Very Best Of The Who)
My generation / Anyway anyhow anywhere / Kids are alright / Substitute / I'm a boy / Happy Jack / Pictures of lily / I can see for miles / Who are you / Won't get fooled

again / Magic bus / I can't explain / Pinball wizard / I'm free / See me, feel me / Squeeze box / Join together / You better you bet / Baba O'Riley (CD only)
CD _____ **835 389-2**
Polydor / Mar '88 / PolyGram.

WHO'S LAST
My generation / I can't explain / Substitute / Behind blue eyes / Baba O'Riley / Boris the spider / Who are you / Pinball wizard / See me, feel me / Love reign o'er me / Long live rock / Long live rock (reprise) / Won't get fooled again / Dr. Jimmy / Magic bus / Summertime blues / Twist and shout
CD _____ **MCLD 19005**
MCA / Apr '92 / BMG.

WHO'S NEXT
Baba O'Riley / Getting in tune / Love ain't for keeping / My wife / Song is over / Bargain / Going mobile / Behind blue eyes / Won't get fooled again / Pure and easy (On CD) / Baby don't you do it (On CD) / Naked eye (On CD) / When I was a boy (On CD) / Too much of anything (On CD) / I don't even know myself (On CD) / Let's see action (On CD)
CD _____ **5277602**
Polydor / Jun '95 / PolyGram.

Who By Fire

ROAD MOVIE
Madchen Amick / Wrong planet / Summer honey fades / Fire my love / Gravitate / My Niagara / Caught in time / Hippy hurricane / Horse, sex and radio / Third wave
CD _____ **ILLCD 040**
Imaginary / Nov '93 / Vital.

Whole Thing

WHOLE THING, THE
Another time / It's all in / Natural feeling / Missing you already / Who's got the makings / Rubberneckin' / Peer pressure / Rope walks
CD _____ **JAZIDCD 088**
Acid Jazz / Sep '93 / Pinnacle.

Whores Of Babylon

METROPOLIS
CD _____ **CANDLE 006CD**
Candlelight / Aug '94 / Plastic Head.

Whyte, Ronny

ALL IN A NIGHT'S WORK
Audiophile / '89 / Jazz Music / Swift.
CD _____ **ACD 247**

SOFT WHYTE
CD _____ **ACD 204**
Audiophile / Apr '94 / Jazz Music / Swift.

Wicked Maraya

CYCLES
CD _____ **9040212**
Mausoleum / Feb '95 / Grapevine.

Wickman, Putte

BEWITCHED (Wickman, Putte & Trio)
CD _____ **ABCD 051**
Bluebell / Mar '94 / Cadillac / Jazz Music.

IN SILHOUETTE (Wickman, Putte Quintet)
CD _____ **NCD 8848**
Phontastic / Aug '95 / Wellard / Jazz Music / Cadillac.

IN TROMBONES
CD _____ **NCD 8826**
Phontastic / Aug '94 / Wellard / Jazz Music / Cadillac.

SEARCHING & SWINGING 1945-1955
CD _____ **PHONTCD 9304**
Phontastic / Aug '94 / Wellard / Jazz Music / Cadillac.

SOME OF THIS AND SOME OF THAT (Wickman/Kellaway/Mitchell)
CD _____ **DRCD 187**
Dragon / Jun '88 / Roots / Cadillac / Wellard / CM / ADA.

VERY THOUGHT OF YOU, THE (Wickman, Putte & Red Mitchell)
CD _____ **DRCD 161**
Dragon / Oct '88 / Roots / Cadillac / Wellard / CM / ADA.

Widespread Depression...

DOWNTOWN UPROAR (Widespread Depression Orchestra)
CD _____ **STCD 540**
Stash / '91 / Jazz Music / CM / Cadillac / Direct / ADA.

Widowmaker

BLOOD & BULLETS
CD _____ **CDMFN 161**
Music For Nations / Apr '94 / Pinnacle.

STAND BY FOR PAIN
CD _____ **CDMFN 175**
Music For Nations / Oct '94 / Pinnacle.

Wiggins, Gary

TIME FOR SAXIN'
CD _____ **BEST 1012CD**
Acoustic Music / Nov '93 / ADA.

Wiggins, Gerald

WIG IS HERE
You are the sunshine of my life / Edith is the sweetest / Lover / Oh give me something to remember you by / Lady is a tramp / On a clear day / Stolen sweets / This is the end of a beautiful friendship
CD _____ **BLE 590692**
Black & Blue / Dec '90 / Wellard / Koch.

Wigham, Jiggs

JIGGS UP, THE
My romance / Pound cake / For someone never known / Haram / Milt / nightingale sang in berkeley square / Doctor is in
CD _____ **CAP 74024-2**
Capri / Oct '90 / Wellard / Cadillac.

Wights, Jamie

SPREADING JOY
CD _____ **JCD 232**
Jazzology / Apr '94 / Swift / Jazz Music.

Wigwam

LIGHT AGES
CD _____ **WISHCD 46**
Digelius / Jun '93 / Direct.

LIVE MUSIC FROM THE TWILIGHT ZONE, THE
CD _____ **LXCD 517**
Love / Dec '95 / Direct / ADA.

NUCLEAR NIGHTCLUB
CD _____ **CDOVD 466**
Virgin / Jan '96 / EMI.

Wiklund/Svensson/Ekblad

SURGE
CD _____ **DRCD 216**
Dragon / Jun '88 / Roots / Cadillac / Wellard / CM / ADA.

Wilber, Bob

BOB WILBER AND THE BECHET LEGACY
Down in honky Tonk Town / Si tu vois ma mere / Stop shimmying sister / Lazy blues / If I let you get away with it / Roses of Picardy / Petite fleur / Rue des Champes Elysees / Chant in the night / I'm a little blackbird looking for a bluebird / Kansas City man blues / China boy
CD _____ **CHR 70018**
Challenge / Jun '95 / Direct / Jazz Music / Cadillac / ADA.

BOB WILBER/DICK WELLSTOOD DUET (Wilber, Bob & Dick Wellstood)
CD _____ **PCD 7080**
Progressive / Mar '95 / Jazz Music.

HORNS A-PLENTY
CD _____ **ARCD 19135**
Arbors Jazz / Nov '94 / Cadillac.

IN THE MOOD FOR SWING
I'm in the mood for swing / Talk of the town / Dinah / I'm confessin' that I love you / When lights are low / Ring dem bells / Memories of you / Bei mir bist du schon / Yours and mine / Chinatown
CD _____ **PHONTCD 7526**
Phontastic / Apr '88 / Wellard / Jazz Music / Cadillac.

MAN AND HIS MUSIC, A (Wilber, Bob Quintet)
World is waiting for the sunrise / Stalkin' the Bean / Do I love you / That old gang of mine / Django / I want to be happy / Chu / Freeman's way / Lazy afternoon / J.J. Jump / Accent on youth / Lullaby in rhythm / Smoke rings / Bossa losada
CD _____ **J&MCD 503**
J&M / Aug '94 / Jazz Music / Wellard / Cadillac / Discovery.

MOMENTS LIKE THIS (Wilber, Bob & Antti Sarpila)
Rent party blues / See see rider / Estrellita / Lester's bounce / Snake charmer / I want a little girl / Moments like this
CD _____ **NCD 8811**
Phontastic / '93 / Wellard / Jazz Music / Cadillac.

RAPTUROUS REEDS
Jumpin' at the woodside / Chloe / Sherman shuffle / Sultry summer day / Rhythm at the Savoy / You are my lucky star / I've loved you all my life / I double dare you / Alone together / Linger awhile / Yours is my heart alone
CD _____ **PHONTCD 7517**
Phontastic / Apr '94 / Wellard / Jazz Music / Cadillac.

SOPRANO SUMMIT - LIVE AT CONCORD '77 (Wilber, Bob & Kenny Davern)
Strike up the band / Pubbles / Elsa's dream / How can you face me / Dreaming butterfly

/ Tracks in the snow / Lament / Panic is on / Panama rag
CD _____ **CCD 4052**
Concord Jazz / May '91 / New Note.

SOPRANO SUMMIT CONCERTO (Wilber, Bob & Kenny Davern)
CD _____ **CCD 4029**
Concord Jazz / Dec '90 / New Note.

Wilburn Brothers

WONDERFUL WILBURN BROTHERS
CD _____ **KCD 746**
King/Paddle Wheel / Nov '92 / New Note.

Wilce, Malcolm

BEST OF FAMILY FAVOURITES (Wilce, Malcolm Duo)
CD _____ **CDTS 004**
Maestro / Aug '93 / Savoy.

DANCE GOES ON (Wilce, Malcolm Duo)
CD _____ **CDTS 039**
Maestro / Nov '93 / Savoy.

DANCING ALL OVER THE WORLD (Wilce, Malcolm Duo)
CD _____ **CDTS 051**
Maestro / Nov '93 / Savoy.

Wilcox, Spiegle

JAZZ KEEPS YOU YOUNG
CD _____ **CHR 70015**
Challenge / Aug '95 / Direct / Jazz Music / Cadillac / ADA.

Wild Angels

ROCKIN' ON THE RAILROAD
Rockin' on the railroad / Don't leave me now / Miss Froggie / Weekend (time to rock) / Boogie woogie country boy / I'll be me / Old Jack Joe/Carry me back to Old Virginny / Lights out / Blue Monday / Moonshine boogie / Ballad of a teenage queen / There's a fight goin' on / Little GTO / Break up / Lucille / Sledgehammer strikes back
CD _____ **VALD 8060**
Valentine / Jul '88 / Conifer.

Wild Canyon

18 GUITAR TRACKS
Enchanted canyon / Raunchy / Teen scene / Trambone / Strollin' / Mexican lady / Corn pickin' / My memories / We were born with the music of rock / Dobro / Buffalo skip / Sunny river / Skip along / Poor boy jamboree / Flamingo shuffle / Snail pace / Take me back home / Blue steel blues
CD _____ **BCD 15538**
Bear Family / Nov '90 / Rollercoaster / Direct / CM / Swift / ADA.

Wild Ones

WRITING ON THE WALL
CD _____ **HMRXD 171**
Heavy Metal / Apr '91 / Sony.

Wild Planet

BLUEPRINTS
CD _____ **WARPCD 11**
Warp / Jun '93 / Disc.

Wild Tchoupitoulas

WILD TCHOUPITOULAS, THE
Brother John / Meet de boys on de battlefront / Here dey come / Hey pocky away / Indian red / Big chief got a golden crown / Hey mama / Hey hey
CD _____ **IMCD 89**
Island / Feb '90 / PolyGram.

Wild Turkey

BATTLE HYMN
CD _____ **EDCD 333**
Edsel / Sep '91 / Pinnacle / ADA.

TURKEY
Good old days / Tomorrow's friend / Universal man / Eternal mother - the return / Ballad of Chuck Stallion and the Mustangs / Street / See you next Tuesday / Changes
CD _____ **EDCD 424**
Edsel / May '93 / Pinnacle / ADA.

Wildchild Experience...

BEST OF WILDTRAX, THE (Wildchild Experience vol.2)
CD _____ **LOADW 1CD**
Loaded / Jun '93 / 3MV.

Wilde, Eugene

I CHOOSE YOU TONIGHT
CD _____ **MCAD 42282**
MCA / Jul '89 / BMG.

Wilde Flowers

WILDE FLOWERS, THE
Impotence / Those words they say / Memories / Don't try to change me / Parchman farm / Almost grown / She's gone / Slow walkin' talk / He's bad for me / It's what I feel (A certain kind) / Memories (instrumental) / Never leave me

CD _____ VP 123CD
Voice Print / Nov '94 / Voice Print.

Wilde, Kim

KIM WILDE
Water on glass / Our town / Everything we know / Young heroes / Kids in America / Chequered love / 2-6-5-8-0 / You'll never be so wrong / Falling out / Tuning in, turning on
CD _____ CDFA 3214
Fame / Nov '88 / EMI.

KIM WILDE/SELECT/CATCH AS CATCH CAN
Water on glass / Our town / Everything we know / Young heroes / Kids in America / Chequered love / 2-6-5-8-0 / You'll never be so wrong / Falling out / Tuning in turning out / Ego / Words fell down / Action City / View from a bridge / Just a feeling / Chaos at the airport / Take me tonight / Can you come over / Wendy Sadd / Cambodia / House of Salome / Back street Joe / Stay awhile / Love blonde / Dream sequence / Dancing in the dark / Shoot to disable / Can you hear it / Sparks / Sing it out for love
CD Set _____ CDOMB 012
EMI / Oct '95 / EMI.

NOW AND FOREVER
Breakin' away / High on you / This I swear / C'mon love me / True to you / Hypnotise / Heaven / Sweet inspiration / Where do you go from here / Hold on / You're all I wanna do / Life and soul / Now and forever / Back to heaven
CD _____ MCD 60002
MCA / Nov '95 / BMG.

SINGLES 1981-1993, THE
Kids in America / Chequered love / Water on glass / Cambodia / View from bridge / Child come away / Love blonde / Second time / Rage to love / You keep me hangin' on / Another step (Closer to you) / You came / Never trust a stranger / Four letter word / Love is holy / If I can't have you / In my life
CD _____ MCD 10921
MCA / Sep '93 / BMG.

VERY BEST OF KIM WILDE, THE
Kids in America / Chequered love / Water on glass / 2-6-5-8-0 / Boys / Our town / Everything we know / You'll never be so wrong / Cambodia / View from a bridge / Love blonde / House of Salome / Dancing in the dark / Child come away / Take me tonight / Stay awhile
CD _____ CDFA 3275
Fame / Oct '92 / EMI.

Wilde, Marty

BEST OF MARTY WILDE, THE
Teenager in love / Donna / Sea of love / Endless sleep / Bad boy / Rubber ball / Put me down / Danny / Johnny Rocco / Ever since you said goodbye / Don't pity me / Splish splash / High school confidential / Wild cat / Blue moon of Kentucky / Teenage tears / Tomorrow's clown / Little girl / Are you sincere / Flight / Hide and seek / Jezebel / Honeycomb / Dream lover
CD _____ 5517942
Spectrum/Karussell / Nov '95 / PolyGram / THE.

TEENAGER IN LOVE
Teenager in love / Donna / Tomorrows clown / Jezebel / Sea of love / Little girl / Rubber ball / Bad boy / Johnny rocco / Fight / Hide and seek / Ever since you said goodbye / Endless sleep / Abergavenny
CD _____ 5500852
Spectrum/Karussell / Oct '93 / PolyGram / THE.

Wilder, Joe

WILDER 'N' WILDER
Cherokee / Prelude to a kiss / My heart stood stil / Six bit blues / Mad about the boy / Darn that dream
CD _____ CY 78988
Savoy Jazz / Nov '95 / Conifer / ADA.

Wilder, Webb

IT CAME FROM NASHVILLE (Wilder, Webb & The Beatnicks)
How long can she last / Horror hayride / I'm burning / Is this all there is / Devil's right hand / Move on down the line / One taste of the bait / I'm wise to you / It gets in your blood / Poolside / Ruff rider / Keep it on your mind
CD _____ WM 1018CD
Watermelon / Feb '94 / ADA / Direct.

TOWN & COUNTRY (Wilder, Webb & Nashvegas)
CD _____ WMCD 1032
Watermelon / Apr '95 / ADA / Direct.

Wildhearts

DON'T BE HAPPY...JUST WORRY
CD _____ 450996067-2
Bronze / Apr '94 / Warner Music.

EARTH VS THE WILDHEARTS
Greetings from Shitsville / TV tan / Everlone / Shame on me / Loveshit / Miles away

baby / My baby is a headfuck / Suckerpunch / News of the world / Drinking about life (Not on LP) / Love you till I don't
CD _____ 4509932012
Bronze / Feb '94 / Warner Music.

P.H.U.Q.
I wanna go where the people go / V Day / Just in lust / Baby strange / Nita nitro / Jonesing for Jones / Woah shit you got through / Cold patootie tango / Caprice / Be my drug / Naivety play / In Lilly's garden / Getting it / Don't worry 'bout me
CD _____ 0630104372
CD _____ 0630104042
East West / May '95 / Warner Music.

Wilen, Barney

BARNEY WILEN
CD _____ FSCD 48
Fresh Sound / Oct '90 / Jazz Music / Discovery.

MOVIE THEMES FROM FRANCE (Wilen, Barney & Mal Waldron Trio)
Un homme et une femme / Julien dans l'ascenseur / Florence sur les Champs Elysees / Les parapluies de Cherbourg / No problem / Manha de Carnaval / Generique / Les feuilles mortes / Quiet temple
CD _____ CDSJP 335
Timeless Jazz / Aug '90 / New Note.

Wiley, Fletch

NIGHTWATCH
Fiesta / I am what I am / People get ready / Started right / Are you ready / Nightwatch / Joy dance
CD _____ CDPM 6000
Prestige / Mar '90 / Total/BMG.

Wiley, Lee

ART VOCAL 1931-40
CD _____ AV 015
Art Vocal / Sep '95 / Discovery.

BACK HOME AGAIN
CD _____ ACD 300
Audiophile / May '95 / Jazz Music / Swift.

DUOLOGUE (1954) (Wiley, Lee & Ellis Larkins)
CD _____ BLCD 760911
Black Lion / Jun '88 / Jazz Music / Cadillac / Wellard / Koch.

LEE WILEY 1931-37
CD _____ VJC 1023 2
Vintage Jazz Classics / Oct '91 / Direct / ADA / CM / Cadillac.

LEE WILEY RARITIES
CD _____ JASSCD 15
Jass / Oct '91 / CM / Jazz Music / ADA / Cadillac / Direct.

LEE WILEY SINGS RODGERS AND HART AND HAROLD ARLE
CD _____ ACD 10
Audiophile / Feb '91 / Jazz Music / Swift.

SINGS THE SONGS OF GEORGE & IRA GERSHWIN & COLE
CD _____ ACD 1
Audiophile / Feb '91 / Jazz Music / Swift.

Wilhelm, Mick

WOOD AND FIRE
CD _____ NR 422457
New Rose / Mar '94 / Direct / ADA.

Wilkins, Ernie

K.A.L.E.I.D.O.D.U.K.E.
CD _____ 519346-2
Birdology / Oct '94 / PolyGram.

Wilkins, Jack

ALIEN ARMY (Wilkins, Jack Trio)
CD _____ MM 5049
Music Masters / Oct '94 / Nimbus.

CALL HIM RECKLESS (Wilkins, Jack Trio)
CD _____ MM 5019
Music Masters / Oct '94 / Nimbus.

Wilkins, Robert

WILKINS, DICKSON AND ALLEN 1928-35 (Wilkins, Robert, Tom Dickson & Allen Shaw)
CD _____ DOCD 5014
Blues Document / Dec '81 / Swift / Jazz Music / Hot Shot.

Wilkinson, Jeff

BALLADS IN PLAIN TALK
CD _____ BRAM 199010-2
Brambus / Nov '93 / ADA / Direct.

BRAVE & TRUE
CD _____ BRAM 199121-2
Brambus / Nov '93 / ADA / Direct.

Willemark, Lena

NORDAN (Willemark, Lena & Ale Moller)
CD _____ 5231612
ECM / Sep '94 / New Note.

SECRETS OF LIVING (Willemark, Lena & Elise Einarsdotter)
CD _____ 21377
Caprice / Jun '85 / CM / Complete/ Pinnacle / Cadillac / ADA.

Willetts, Dave

STAGES OF LOVE
Stages of love / Almost like being in love / Impossible dream (The quest) / You'd be so nice to come home to / Baby mine / I love you Samantha / Love is here to stay / Come rain or come shine / My funny valentine / Somewhere out there / If I loved you / Soliloquy / Our song / Show's at an end
CD _____ PWKS 4130P
Carlton Home Entertainment / Feb '96 / Carlton Home Entertainment.

William Davis...

TOUCH MORE SPICE, A (William Davis Construction Group Band)
America/Love on the rocks / Overture from 'Phantom of the opera' / Bring him home / Invictus / Party piece / Men of Harlech / Pie Jesu / Fidgety feet / Skye boat song / Rhapsody in blue
CD _____ QPRL 042D
Polyphonic / Jun '90 / Conifer.

Williams Holdings Band

DOUBLE CHAMPIONS
Land of the long white cloud / Masquerade / Devil and the deep blue sea / Rhapsody for euphonium / Capriccio / Dance sequence / Variations on a welsh theme
CD _____ QPRL 065D
Polyphonic / Jan '94 / Conifer.

MIDNIGHT EUPHONIUM
Midnight euphonium / Euphonism / Arioso / How soon / On my own / Concerto No. 1 / nessun dorma / Deep inside the sacred temple / Somewhere / Jeanie with the light brown hair / Your tiny hands are frozen / Carnival cocktail / Love is forever / Hail acient walls / Allegro / Ina / Pokarekareana
CD _____ QPRL 064D
Polyphonic / Jan '94 / Conifer.

Williams, Alyson

RAW
Just call my name / We're gonna make it / I looked into your eyes / Not on the outside / Masquerade / I'm so glad / My love is so raw / On the rocks / Still my No.1 / I need your lovin' / Sleep talk
CD _____ 5274362
Def Jam / Jan '96 / PolyGram.

RAW
CD _____ 9833142
Pickwick/Sony Collector's Choice / Oct '93 / Carlton Home Entertainment / Pinnacle / Sony.

Williams, Andy

16 MOST REQUESTED SONGS
Canadian sunset / Hawaiian wedding song / Can't get used to losing you / Red roses for a blue lady / Dear heart / Born free / Danny Boy / Days of wine and roses / Emily / Sweet memories / More / Maria / What now my love / Romeo and Juliet / Impossible dream (The quest)
CD _____ 4720502
Columbia / Jul '92 / Sony.

16 MOST REQUESTED SONGS
Butterfly / Are you sincere / Lonely street / Village of St. Bernadette / Sweetest sounds / Charade / Stranger on the shore / On the street where you live / Quiet nights / Speak softly love / Music from across the way / Happy heart / Where do I begin / Michelle / In the arms of love / Music to watch girls by
CD _____ 4805152
Columbia / May '95 / Sony.

ANDY WILLIAMS CHRISTMAS ALBUM, THE
CD _____ 12326
Laserlight / Nov '95 / Target/BMG.

BEST OF ANDY WILLIAMS, THE
Moon river / Days of wine and roses / More I see you / Hawaiian wedding song / It's a most unusual day / Look of love / Music to watch the girls go by / I can't take my eyes off you / Solitaire / Happy heart / Can't get used to losing you / You lay so easy on my mind / Time for us / In the arms of love / Danny boy / May each day
CD _____ 4810372
Columbia / Dec '95 / Sony.

CAN'T GET USED TO LOSING YOU/ LOVE ANDY
Falling in love with love / I left my heart in San Francisco / You are my sunshine / What kind of fool am I / When you're smiling / Days of wine and roses / It's a most unusual day / My colouring book / Can't get used to losing you / I really don't want to know / Exactly like you / May each day / Somethin' stupid / Watch what happens / Look of love / What now my love / Can't take my eyes off you / Kisses sweeter than wine / Holly / When I look in your eyes /

More I see you / There will never be another you / God only knows
CD _____ 477591 2
Columbia / Oct '94 / Sony.

FEELINGS - A PRIVATE COLLECTION
CD _____ RLBTC 007
Realisation / Oct '93 / Prism.

GREAT PERFORMANCES
CD _____ DBP 102009
Double Platinum / Oct '95 / Target/BMG.

GREATEST HITS
CD _____ 12351
Laserlight / Aug '94 / Target/BMG.

GREATEST LOVE CLASSICS (Williams, Andy & The Royal Philharmonic Orchestra)
Romeo and Juliet / Love made me a fool / Vino de amor / Different light / Another Winter's day / Vision / Journey's end / Twist of fate / Home / Brave new world / She'll never know / In my world of illusion / Words
CD _____ CDMFP 6173
Music For Pleasure / Sep '95 / EMI.

PERSONAL CHRISTMAS COLLECTION
It's the most wonderful time of the year / My favourite things / Christmas song / Bells of St. Mary's / Christmas present / Winter wonderland / First Noel / O come all ye faithful (Adeste Fidelis) / Sleigh ride / Silver bells / Hark the herald angels sing / Christmas bells / Silent night / White Christmas / Happy holiday/The holiday season
CD _____ CK 64155
Columbia / Nov '95 / Sony.

PORTRAIT OF A SONG STYLIST
Somewhere / Days of wine and roses / What kind of fool am I / Misty / Summertime / Blue Hawaii / Impossible dream / Falling in love with you / Spanish eyes / Twelfth of never / Love is a many splendoured thing / I want to be wanted / Moon river / Mona Lisa / More I see you / Kisses sweeter than wine / Taste of honey
CD _____ HARCD 104
Masterpiece / Apr '89 / BMG.

REFLECTIONS
Moon river / Both sides now / Home loving man / Seasons in the sun / Days of wine and roses / Happy heart / Born free / Love story / Almost there / Can't help falling in love / Can't get used to losing you / God only knows / Solitaire / Your song / Way we were / Can't take my eyes off you / My way / May each day of the year be a good one
CD _____ 4687812
Columbia / Jun '91 / Sony.

VERY BEST OF ANDY WILLIAMS, THE
Moon river / Way we were / Home loving man / Can't take my eyes off you / God only knows / Can't get used to losing you / It's so easy / Last tango in Paris / Almost there / In the Summertime / Born free / Can't help falling in love / Watch what happens / More / Solitaire / Danny boy
CD _____ PWKS 505
Carlton Home Entertainment / Aug '88 / Carlton Home Entertainment.

WEDDING AND ANNIVERSARY ALBUM
Hawaiian wedding song / Very thought of you / When I look in your eyes / Close to you / I'll never stop loving you / Embraceable you / Touch me in the morning / Anniversary song / Where do I begin / We've only just begun / Man and a woman / Touch of your lips / You are the sunshine of my life / Moon river / Since I fell for you / I wish you love / What are you doing the rest of your life
CD _____ 983402-2
Pickwick/Sony Collector's Choice / Apr '94 / Carlton Home Entertainment / Pinnacle / Sony.

WORLD OF LOVE, A
CD _____ MCCD 218
Music Club / Oct '95 / Disc / THE / CM.

Williams, Beau

STAY WITH ME
CD _____ MAUCD 636
Mau Mau / Apr '93 / Pinnacle.

Williams, Big Joe

1935-41, VOL. 1
CD _____ BDCD 6003
Blues Document / '91 / Swift / Jazz Music / Hot Shot.

9 STRING BLUES
CD _____ DD 627
Delmark / Oct '86 / Hot Shot / ADA / CM / Direct / Cadillac.

BABY PLEASE DON'T GO
CD _____ CD 52035
Blues Encore / May '94 / Target/BMG.

BIG JOE WILLIAMS & SONNY BOY WILLIAMSON 1945-49, VOL. 2 (Williams, Big Joe & Sonny Boy Williamson)
CD _____ BDCD 6004
Blues Document / '91 / Swift / Jazz Music / Hot Shot.

BIG JOE WILLIAMS AT FOLK CITY
CD _____ OBCCD 580
Original Blues Classics / Jan '96 /
Complete/Pinnacle / Wellard / Cadillac.

BLUES ON HIGHWAY 49
CD _____ DD 604
Delmark / Jul '93 / Hot Shot / ADA / CM /
Direct / Cadillac.

CLASSIC DELTA BLUES
CD _____ OBCCD 545
Original Blues Classics / Nov '92 /
Complete/Pinnacle / Wellard / Cadillac.

**DELTA BLUES (1951) (Williams, Big Joe
& Willie Love, Luther Huff)**
CD _____ ALCD 2702
Alligator / Oct '93 / Direct / ADA.

**MISSISSIPPI'S BIG JOE WILLIAMS AND
HIS NINE STRING GUITAR**
CD _____ SFWCD 40052
Smithsonian Folkways / Nov '95 / ADA /
Direct / Koch / CM / Cadillac.

SHAKE YOUR BOOGIE
CD _____ ARHCD 315
Arhoolie / Apr '95 / ADA / Direct /
Cadillac.

STARVIN' CHAIN BLUES
CD _____ DD 609
Delmark / May '87 / Hot Shot / ADA / CM
/ Direct / Cadillac.

Williams, Blind Connie

PHILADELPHIA STREET SINGER
CD _____ TCD 5024
Testament / Jul '95 / Complete/Pinnacle /
ADA / Koch.

Williams, Brooks

INLAND SAILOR
CD _____ GLCD 2114
Green Linnet / Apr '94 / Roots / CM /
Direct / ADA.

KNIFE EDGE
CD _____ GLCD 2121
Green Linnet / Aug '95 / Roots / CM /
Direct / ADA.

Williams, Buster

SOMETHING MORE
Air dancing / Christina / Fortunes dance /
Ballade / Deception / Sophisticated lady / I
didn't know what time it was
CD _____ IOR 70042
In & Out / Sep '95 / Vital/SAM.

TOKUDO
Tokudo / This time the dream's on me /
Guego / This is the end of a beautiful friend-
ship / Someday my Prince will come
CD _____ DC 8549
Denon / Jun '89 / Conifer.

Williams, Carol

HAMMOND TODAY
Tico-tico / Fancy pants / Dizzy fingers / Un-
forgettable / What now my love / May you
always / Jumpin' Jupiter / Rhapsody rag /
Fools rush in / Red roses for a blue lady /
We'll meet again / It's today / Kitchen rag /
March: City of Chester / Bess, you is my
woman now / Promette / Brazil / White cliffs
of Dover / Russian rag / In the news / You
and the night and the music
CD _____ MCTCD 002
Melcot / Feb '93 / Melcot Music.

JUST RAGS
Leicester Square rag / Tiger rag / Black and
white rag / Brittania rag / Maple leaf rag /
12th Street rag / Barrel house rag / Root
beer rag / Pineapple rag / Chatterbox rag /
Tin Pan Alley rag / Spaghetti rag / Ivory rag
/ Entertainer / Fiddlesticks rag / Coronation
rag / Jingles / Kitchen rag / Zig zag rag /
Temptation rag / Bugle call rag / Rhapsody
rag / Peanuts rag / Russian rag (Rockies
rag) / Alexander's ragtime band
CD _____ MCTCD 007
Melcot / Aug '93 / Melcot Music.

Williams, Christopher

NOT A PERFECT MAN
CD _____ 74321254552
RCA / Jun '95 / BMG.

Williams, Clarence

CLARENCE WILLIAMS 1924-1926
CD _____ CLASSICS 695
Classics / Jul '93 / Discovery / Jazz
Music.

CLARENCE WILLIAMS 1926-27
CD _____ CLASSICS 718
Classics / Jul '93 / Discovery / Jazz
Music.

CLARENCE WILLIAMS 1927
CD _____ CLASSICS 736
Classics / Feb '94 / Discovery / Jazz
Music.

**CLARENCE WILLIAMS COLLECTION,
THE (Volume 1, 1927-28)**
CD _____ COCD 19
Collector's Classics / Nov '94 / Cadillac /
Complete/Pinnacle.

CLARENCE WILLIAMS, VOL. 2 (1924-30)
CD _____ VILCD 0222
Village Jazz / Sep '92 / Target/BMG / Jazz
Music.

CLASSICS 1927-28
CD _____ CLASSICS 752
Classics / May '94 / Discovery / Jazz
Music.

CLASSICS 1928-9
CD _____ CLASSICS 771
Classics / Aug '94 / Discovery / Jazz
Music.

CLASSICS 1929
CD _____ CLASSICS 791
Classics / Jan '95 / Discovery / Jazz
Music.

CLASSICS 1929-1930
CD _____ CLASSICS 810
Classics / May '95 / Discovery / Jazz
Music.

CLASSICS 1930-31
CD _____ CLASSICS 832
Classics / Sep '95 / Discovery / Jazz
Music.

Williams, Claude

LIVE AT J'S VOL.1
CD _____ ARHCD 405
Arhoolie / Apr '95 / ADA / Direct /
Cadillac.

LIVE AT J'S VOL.2
CD _____ ARHCD 406
Arhoolie / Apr '95 / ADA / Direct /
Cadillac.

Williams, Cootie

CLASSICS 1941-44
CD _____ CLASSICS 827
Classics / Sep '95 / Discovery / Jazz
Music.

**COOTIE WILLIAMS IN HI-FI (Williams,
Cootie & His Orchestra)**
Just in time / Summit Ridge Drive / Nevertheless / I'm in love with you / On the street
where you live / I'll see you in my dreams /
Contrasts / Caravan / If I could be with you
one hour tonight / Air mail special / My old
flame / Swingin' down the lane / New concerto for Cootie
CD _____ 74321218262
RCA Victor / Nov '94 / BMG.

**INTRODUCTION TO COOTIE WILLIAMS
1930-43**
CD _____ BEST 4018
Best Of Jazz / Apr '95 / Discovery.

SEXTER AND BIG BAND 1941-44
CD _____ 158382
Jazz Archives / Sep '95 / Jazz Music /
Discovery / Cadillac.

Williams, Danny

BEST OF DANNY WILLIAMS, THE
CD _____ CDSGP 006
Prestige / Aug '91 / Total/BMG.

Williams, Deniece

GREATEST GOSPEL HITS
Fire inside my soul / So glad I know / My
soul desire / His eye is on the sparrow /
Healing / God made you special / Special
love / They say / I surrender all / Every mo-
ment / God is amazing / We sing praises
CD _____ SPD 1461
Alliance Music / May '95 / EMI.

LET'S HEAR IT FOR THE BOY
Let's hear it for the boy / I want you / Pick-
ing up the pieces / Black butterfly / Next
love / Haunting me / Don't tell me we have
nothing / Blind dating / Wrapped up / Whiter
than snow
CD _____ 982981 2
Pickwick/Sony Collector's Choice / Jun '95
/ Carlton Home Entertainment / Pinnacle /
Sony.

THIS IS NIECY
It's important to me / That's what friends
are for / How'd I know that love would slip
away / 'Cause you love me baby / Free /
Watching over / If you don't believe
CD _____ 983396-2
Pickwick/Sony Collector's Choice / Mar '94
/ Carlton Home Entertainment / Pinnacle /
Sony.

Williams, Dicky

FULL GROWN MAN
CD _____ ICH 1186
Ichiban / Dec '95 / Koch.

I WANT YOU FOR BREAKFAST
Weekend playboy / You hurt the wrong man
/ I've been loving you too long / Letter from
a soldier / Need your love / Lost my woman
to a woman / Good used man / I'm in love

with two women / I want you for breakfast
/ Let me love you before we make love /
Don't give your love to anyone but me / Lit-
tle closer
CD _____ CDICH 1115
Ichiban / Oct '93 / Koch.

IN YOUR FACE
Same motel / I didn't do nothin' / Come
back pussy / Laughin' and grinnin' / I
wanna know why / Ugly men / Fat girls / Do
you know (where your woman is tonight) /
Bad luck and hard times
CD _____ CMCCD 4012
CMC / Oct '89 / Ichiban Records.

Williams, Don

BEST OF LIVE
CD _____ COLORSCD 1
Colors Music / Mar '94 / Total/BMG.

BORROWED TALES
Fever / Crying in the rain / Lay down Sally
/ My rifle, my pony & me / I'll be there if you
ever want me / Reason to believe / Games
people play / If you could read my mind /
Peace train / Long black veil / Letter /
You've got a friend / Pretend
CD _____ 30363 00012
Carlton Home Entertainment / Oct '95 /
Carlton Home Entertainment.

CURRENTS
Only water (shining in the air) / Too much
love / That song about the river / Catfish
bates / Back on the street again / So far,
so good / Gettin' back together tonight / In
the family / Standing knee deep in a river
(dying of thirst) / Lone star state of mind /
Old trail / It's who you love
CD _____ PD 90645
RCA / Mar '92 / BMG.

**GREATEST HITS: DON WILLIAMS,
VOL.1**
Amanda / Come early morning / Shelter of
your eyes / What a way to go / She's in love
with a rodeo man / Down the road I go / I
wouldn't want to live if you didn't love me /
We should be together / Ties that bind /
Ghost story / Don't you believe / I recall a
gypsy woman
CD _____ PWKS 503
Carlton Home Entertainment / Jan '89 /
Carlton Home Entertainment.

IT'S GOTTA BE MAGIC
It's gotta be magic / I would like to see you
again / Lay down beside me / Tears of the
lonely / You've got a hold on me / Fallin' in
love again / I need someone to hold me
when I cry / Turn out the lights and love me
tonight / Lovin' understandin' man / Fly
away / Your sweet love / Tempted / No use
running / Oh misery / Sweet fever / Missing
you, missing me
CD _____ PWKS 535
Carlton Home Entertainment / Feb '90 /
Carlton Home Entertainment.

LOVE SONGS
I'll never be in love again / Desparately /
Heartbeat in the darkness / Jamaica farewell / Lone star state of mind / Looking
back / Another place another time / Come
a little closer / I've been loved by the best
/ Shot full of love / Come from the heart /
Lovin' you's like coming home / We got love
/ It's who you love / Flowers won't grow (in
the gardens of stone) / We've got a good
fire going / Easy touch / Senorita / You love
me through it all / Running out of reasons
to run
CD _____ CDMFP 6100
Music For Pleasure / Dec '93 / EMI.

RUBY TUESDAY
Where do we go from here / Ruby Tuesday
/ There's never been a time / Always something there to remind me / Strawberry fields
/ Tears / Take my hand for a while / Coming
apart / Apartment no. 9 / In my life / Long
walk from childhood / On her way to be a
woman / Storybook children / Follow me back
to Louisville / There's no angel on my
shoulder
CD _____ 16218 CD
Success / Sep '94 / Carlton Home
Entertainment.

RUBY TUESDAY
CD _____ HADCD 185
Javelin / Nov '95 / THE / Henry Hadaway
Organisation.

SHELTER OF YOUR EYES, THE
Shelter of your eyes / Come early morning
/ Amanda / Atta way to go / We should be
together / Down the road I go / I wouldn't
want to live if you didn't love me / I recall a
gypsy woman / Playing around / Miller's
cafe / She's in love with a rodeo man / He's
a friend of mine / Bringing it down to you /
There's never been a time / Coming apart /
Follow me back to Louisville / (There's) Always something there to remind me
CD _____ CTS 55435
Country Stars / Jan '96 / Target/BMG.

SOME BROKEN HEARTS
Stay young / You're my best friend / I'm just
a country boy / Listen to the radio / All I'm
missing is you / Some broken hearts never
mend / I believe in you / Turn out the lights

(love me tonight) / Tulsa time / Years from
now / Say it again / Till the rivers all run dry
/ Amanda / I wouldn't want to live if you
didn't love me / We should be together /
Come early morning
CD _____ PLATCD 301
Prism / Oct '92 / Prism.

YOU'RE MY BEST FRIEND
You're my best friend / Help yourselves to
each other / I don't wanna let go / Sweet
fever / Someone like you / Love me tonight
/ Where are you / You're the only one /
Reason to be / Tempted
CD _____ CTS 55436
Country Stars / Oct '95 / Target/BMG.

YOU'RE MY BEST FRIEND
CD _____ PWKS 438
Carlton Home Entertainment / Sep '89 /
Carlton Home Entertainment.

Williams, George

SHADES
CD _____ CDSGP 0113
Prestige / Mar '94 / Total/BMG.

Williams, Hank

24 GREATEST HITS VOL.2
My buckets got a hole in it / Crazy heart /
I'll never get out of this world alive / Moanin'
the blues / I could never be ashamed of you
/ Lost highway / You're gonna change (or
I'm gonna leave) / House without love / I'd
still want you / Dear John / Let's turn back
the years / Howlin' at the moon / Mansion
on the hill / I saw the light / I'm a long gone Daddy
/ lonesome whistle / I'm a long gone Daddy
/ Why should we try anymore / Long gone
lonesome blues / Nobody's lonesome for
me / My sweet love ain't around / I just
don't like this kind of livin' / I won't be home
no more / I'm sorry for you my friend
CD _____ 823 294-2
Polydor / Jul '94 / PolyGram.

**24 OF HANK WILLIAMS GREATEST
HITS**
Your cheatin' heart / Move it on over / I'm
so lonesome I could cry / Ramblin' man /
My heart would know / Kaw-liga / Cold cold
heart / Lovesick blues / Honky tonk blues /
Honky tonkin' / Mind your own business /
Jambalaya / Wedding bells / Hey good
lookin' / Window shopping / Setting the
woods on fire / I can't help it (if I'm still in
love with you) / Half as much / Why don't
you love me / You win again / May you
never be alone / Baby we're really in love /
Take these chains from my heart / There'll
be no teardrops tonight
CD _____ 823 293-2
Polydor / Jul '94 / PolyGram.

40 GREATEST HITS
Move it on over / Mansion on the hill / Lovesick blues / Wedding bells / Mind your own
business / You're gonna change (or I'm
gonna leave) / Lost highway / My buckets
got a hole in it / I'm so lonesome I could cry
/ I just don't like this kind of livin' / Long
gone lonesome blues / My son calls another
man Daddy / Why don't you leave me / Why
should we try anymore / They'll never take
her love from me / Moanin' the blues / Nobody's lonesome for me / Cold cold heart /
Dear John / Howlin' at the moon / I can't
help it (if I'm still in love with you) / Hey good
lookin' / Crazy heart / (I heard that) Lonesome whistle / Half as much / Weary blues
from waiting / I won't be home no more /
Take these chains from my heart / Your
cheatin' heart / Kaw-liga / I'll never get out
of this world alive / You win again / Settin'
the woods on fire / Window shopping /
Jambalaya / Half as much / I'm sorry for
my friend / Honky tonk blues / Ramblin'
man / Baby we're really in love
CD _____ 821 233-23
Polydor / Apr '89 / PolyGram.

CHEATING HEARTS
Take these chains from my heart / Long
gone lonesome blues / You win again / My
son calls another man Daddy / With tears
in my eyes / Cold cold heart / I've become / I could cry / Your cheatin' heart /
Ramblin' man / Hey good lookin' / Settin'
the woods on fire / Kaw-liga / Fool about
you / Jambalaya
CD _____ 5500992
Spectrum/Karussell / Oct '93 / PolyGram /
THE.

GREAT HITS OF HANK WILLIAMS SNR
Hey good lookin' / Lovesick blues / My son
calls another man daddy / You win again /
Take these chains from my heart / Your
cheatin' heart / Jambalaya / I'm so lone-
some I could cry / Settin' the woods on fire
/ Kaw-liga / My bucket's got a hole in it /
Cold cold heart
CD _____ PWK 114
Carlton Home Entertainment / Jun '89 /
Carlton Home Entertainment.

I SAW THE LIGHT
I saw the light / Calling you / Dear brother
/ Wealth won't say your soul / I'm gonna
sing / Message to my mother / How can
you refuse him now / When God comes and
gathers his jewels / Jesus remembered me
/ House of gold / Thank God / Angel of
death

CD _____ 811 900-2
Polydor / Jul '94 / PolyGram.

RARE DEMOS: FIRST TO LAST
Won't you sometimes think of me / Why should I cry / Calling you / You break your own heart / Pan American / Mother is gone / I watched my dreamworld crumble like clay / In my dreams you still belong to me / Wealth won't save your soul / I told a lie to my heart / Singing waterfall / I'm goin' home / Jambalaya / Heaven holds all my treasures / You better keep it in your mind / Lost on the river / Your cheatin' heart / House of gold / Honky tonk blues / Help me understand / 'Neath a cold grey tomb of stone / There's nothing as sweet as my baby / Fool about you / Log train
CD _____ CMFCD 067
Country Music Foundation / Jan '93 / Direct / ADA.

VERY BEST OF HANK WILLIAMS VOL.1, THE
Lovesick blues / Crazy heart / I'm sorry for you my friend / Wedding bells / Window shopping / Honky tonk blues / (I heard that) lonesome whistle / Half as much / Jambalaya / Dear John / Prodigal son / I saw the light / I won't be home no more / There's room in my heart (for the blues) / We live in two different worlds / Long gone lonesome blues
CD _____ PWK 138
Carlton Home Entertainment / Jun '90 / Carlton Home Entertainment.

Williams, Harvey

REBELLION
Song for a weekend / Gidea Park / Day the stuntman died / Song for close friends / Girl from the East tower / Don't shout at me / She sleeps around
CD _____ SARAH 406CD
Sarah / Mar '94 / Vital.

Williams, Huw

NEXT EXIT, THE (Williams, Huw & Tony)
CD _____ TCS 1001CD
TCS Productions / Oct '94 / ADA.

PARADISE CIRCUS (Williams, Huw & Tony)
CD _____ TCS 1002C
TCS Productions / Oct '94 / ADA.

ROSEMARY'S SISTER (Williams, Huw & Tony)
CD _____ TCS 1003CD
TSC Productions / Jul '95 / ADA.

Williams, James

JAMES WILLIAMS MEETS THE SAXOPHONE MASTERS
CD _____ 4729732
Sony Jazz / Jan '95 / Sony.

PROGRESS REPORT (Williams, James Sextet)
Progress report / Episode from a village dance / Affaire d'amour / Mr. Day's dream / Unconscious behaviour / Renaissance lovers
CD _____ SSC 1012D
Sunnyside / Feb '86 / Pinnacle.

UP TO THE MINUTE BLUES
CD _____ DIW 882CD
DIW / Apr '94 / Harmonia Mundi / Cadillac.

Williams, Jerry

PARTY TONITE/CUFFED COLLARED AND TAGGED (Swamp Dogg)
CD _____ EDCD 338
Edsel / Sep '91 / Pinnacle / ADA.

Williams, Jessica

AND THEN, THERE'S THIS
Bemsha swing / And then, there's this / All alone / Nichol's bag / Child within / Elaine / House that Rouse, built / Newk's fluke / Swanee / I mean you
CD _____ CDSJP 345
Timeless Jazz / Feb '91 / New Note.

ARRIVAL
CD _____ JFCD 001
Jazz Focus / Nov '94 / Cadillac.

IN THE POCKET
Weirdo / Gal in calico / I really love you / Driftin' / For you again / Cheek to cheek / I remember Bill / Ghost of a chance / Pfrancing
CD _____ HEPCD 2055
Hep / Jun '94 / Cadillac / Jazz Music / New Note / Wellard.

MOMENTUM
CD _____ JFCD 003
Jazz Focus / Nov '94 / Cadillac.

NEXT STEP, THE
Taking a chance on love / Stonewall blues / Easter parade / Bongo's waltz / I didn't know until you told me / Quilt / Clear blue Lou / I should care / Theme for Lester Young / Like someone in love / I'll always be in love with you / I got it bad / Little waltz
CD _____ HEPCD 2054

Hep / Sep '93 / Cadillac / Jazz Music / New Note / Wellard.

SONG THAT I HEARD, A
Make it so / Burning castle / I wish I knew / (Beautiful girl of my dreams) I love you / Geronimo / Kristen / Alone together / Blues mont / Say not / Say it / Song that I heard somewhere / Blues for Mandela / I'll remember April
CD _____ HEPCD 2061
Hep / May '95 / Cadillac / Jazz Music / New Note / Wellard.

Williams, Joe

AT NEWPORT '63
Without a song / Gravy waltz / She's warm, she's willing, she's wonderful / Come back baby / All God's chillun got rhythm / Do you wanna jump children / Wayfaring stranger / Every day / Anytime anyday anywhere / April in Paris / In the evening (when the sun goes down) / Some of this 'n' some of that / Roll 'em Pete
CD _____ 74321218312
RCA Victor / Nov '94 / BMG.

BALLAD AND BLUES MASTER
CD _____ 5113542
Verve / Mar '92 / PolyGram.

BEST OF THE VERVE YEARS, THE
CD Set _____ 519813-2
Verve / Mar '92 / PolyGram.

CHAINS OF LOVE
CD _____ NI 4019
Natasha / Jul '93 / Jazz Music / ADA / CM / Direct / Cadillac.

COME BACK
Come back / Hold it right there / Sent for you yesterday / Yesterday / Who she do
CD _____ D/PC 2102
Delos / '88 / Conifer.

HAVING THE BLUES UNDER EUROPEAN SKIES
Don't get around much anymore / Satin doll / Experiment / Gee baby ain't I good to you / Early in the morning / Nobody know the way I feel this morning / What a difference a day makes / Goin' to Chicago blues / Everyday I have the blues / Alright O.K. you win / Evening / Roll 'em Pete / One o'clock jump
CD _____ DC 7684
Denon / Apr '89 / Conifer.

HERE'S TO LIFE
What a wonderful world / Save that time / I found a million dollar baby / When I fall in love / If I had you / Little Sir Echo / Young and foolish / I didn't know about you / Maybe September / Time for love / Here's to life
CD _____ CD 83357
Telarc / Jan '94 / Conifer / ADA.

I JUST WANT TO SING (Williams, Joe & Friends)
CD _____ DCD 4004
Delos / May '94 / Conifer.

JOE WILLIAMS SINGS
It's raining again / Detour ahead / Every day / They didn't believe me / Blow Mr. Low / Time for moving / When the sun goes down / Kansas city blues / Always on the blue side / Safe sane and single
CD _____ SV 0199
Savoy Jazz / Nov '92 / Conifer / ADA.

JUMP FOR JOY
CD _____ 07863527132
Novus / Jul '93 / BMG.

LIVE AT ORCHESTRA HALL (Williams, Joe & The Count Basie Orchestra)
CD _____ CD 83329
Telarc / Mar '93 / Conifer / ADA.

ME AND THE BLUES
I'm sticking with you baby / Me and the blues / Every night rocks in my bed / Come on blues / Workin' (work song) / Soothe me / Early in the morning / Good morning heartache / Kansas city / Woman / Hobo flats
CD _____ 74321218232
RCA / Jan '95 / BMG.

NOTHIN' BUT THE BLUES
Who she do / Just a dream / Please send me someone to love / Alright O.K. you win / Hold it right there / In the evening / Rocks in my bed / Sent for you yesterday / Goin' to Chicago blues / Ray Brown's in town
CD _____ DCD 4001
Delos / May '94 / Conifer.

WAR NO MORE
War no more / What a difference a day makes / After you're gone / All the things you are
CD _____ D/PC 2103
Delos / '88 / Conifer.

Williams, John

500 YEARS OF THE GUITAR
CD _____ CD 414
Bescol / May '95 / CM / Target/BMG.

BEST OF JOHN WILLIAMS, THE
Cavatina / Horizon / Raga vilasakhani todi / Sarabande / Deer may safely graze / River God / Z, Theme from / All at sea minor /

Bach changes / Dance of the emperor's clothes / Dance of the living / El tuno / Good morning freedom / J.S.B. / Lisa Larne / Lorelei / Spanish trip
CD _____ MCCD 007
Music Club / Feb '91 / Disc / THE / CM.

COLLECTION: JOHN WILLIAMS
Air on a G string / Good morning freedom / Woodstock / House of the rising sun / Height below / Sambalaya / Cavatina / Bach changes / J.S.B. / All at sea minor / Spanish trip / Dance of the emperor's clouds / Dance of the living Lorelei / El tuno / Rasa vilaskhani todi / Nuages / Nadia's theme / Lisa Larne / Lorelei / Sans souci
CD _____ CCSCD 190
Castle / Nov '88 / BMG.

MAGIC GUITAR OF JOHN WILLIAMS, THE
CD _____ PWKS 504
Carlton Home Entertainment / '90 / Carlton Home Entertainment.

Williams, John

JOHN WILLIAMS
CD _____ GLCD 1157
Green Linnet / Dec '95 / Roots / CM / Direct / ADA.

Williams, Juanita

INTRODUCING
CD _____ BIGMO 1024
Big Mo / Jul '94 / Direct / ADA.

Williams, Larry

BEST OF LARRY WILLIAMS
Short fat Fannie / Baby's crazy / Dizzy Miss Lizzy / Lawdy Miss Clawdy / Slow down / I was a fool to let you go / You bug me baby / Rockin' pneumonia and the boogie woogie flu / She said "yeah" / Hootchy-koo / Bony moronie / Little school girl / Just because / Hocus pocus / Took a trip / Jelly belly Nellie / Peaches and cream / Oh babe / Zing zing / Dummy / Bad boy
CD _____ CDCH 917
Ace / May '88 / Pinnacle / Cadillac / Complete/Pinnacle.

CAUSE I LOVE YOU - THE BEST OF LARRY WILLIAMS
CD _____ SCL 2107
Ichiban Soul Classics / Dec '95 / Koch.

FABULOUS LARRY WILLIAMS
Short fat Fannie / Bony Moronie / Dizzy Miss Lizzy / Lawdy Miss Clawdy / Baby's crazy / Just because / Slow down / You dug me baby / Rockin' pneumonia and the boogie woogie flu / Little school girl / Hocus pocus / Peaches and cream
CD _____ CDFAB 012
Ace / Oct '91 / Pinnacle / Cadillac / Complete/Pinnacle.

LARRY WILLIAMS SHOW, THE
Slow down / Louisiana Hannah / Two hours past midnight / Baby / Out of tears / For your love / Whole lotta shakin' goin' on / Hoochie coo / Sweet little baby / Looking back / Stormsville groove / Trust in me
CD _____ EDCD 119
Edsel / Jan '92 / Pinnacle / Cadillac / ADA.

Williams, Lester

I CAN'T LOSE WITH THE STUFF I USE
I can't lose with the stuff I use / My home ain't here / Crawlin' blues / Lonely heart blues / When I miss her most / Trying to forget / Let me tell you a thing or two / Lost gal / Sweet lovin' daddy / Disgusted blues / Don't leave me baby / Brand new baby / If you knew how much I loved you / Balling blues / When you're tired of running / Crazy about a woman / You're the sweetest thing / 'Bout to put you down / Going away baby / Foolin' with my heart / My time is running out / Life's no bed of roses / Waking up baby
CD _____ CDCHD 476
Ace / Jun '93 / Pinnacle / Cadillac / Complete/Pinnacle.

Williams, Lucinda

HAPPY WOMAN BLUES
Lafayette / Lost it / Maria / Happy woman blues / King of hearts / Rolling along / One night stand / Howlin' at midnight / Hard road / Louisiana man / Sharp cutting wings (song to a poet)
CD _____ NETCD 12
Network / '90 / Direct / ADA.
CD _____ MRCD 149
Munich / '90 / CM / ADA / Greensleeves / Direct.
CD _____ SFWCD 40003
Smithsonian Folkways / Dec '94 / ADA / Direct / Koch / CM / Cadillac.

RAMBLIN'
CD _____ SFWCD 40042
Smithsonian Folkways / Oct '94 / ADA / Direct / Koch / CM / Cadillac.

SWEET OLD WORLD
Six blocks away / Something about what happens when we talk / He never got enough love / Sweet old world / Little angel /

little brother / Pineola / Lines around your eyes / Prove my love / Sidewalks of the city / Memphis pearl / Hot blood / Which will
CD _____ 3705613512
WEA / Jan '93 / Warner Music.

Williams, Marion

BORN TO SING GOSPEL
CD _____ SHCD 6009
Shanachie / Mar '95 / Koch / ADA / Greensleeves.

CAN'T KEEP IT TO MYSELF
CD _____ SHCD 6007
Shanachie / Dec '93 / Koch / ADA / Greensleeves.

MY SOUL LOOKS BACK/THE GENIUS OF MARION WILLIAMS 1962-1992
CD _____ SHCD 6011
Shanachie / Dec '94 / Koch / ADA / Greensleeves.

STRONG AGAIN
CD _____ SFCD 1013
Spirit Feel / Jun '91 / Koch.

Williams, Mary Lou

CLASSICS 1944
CD _____ CLASSICS 814
Classics / May '95 / Discovery / Jazz Music.

FIRST LADY OF THE PIANO 1952-71
CD _____ CD 53180
Giants Of Jazz / Jan '94 / Target/BMG / Cadillac.

FREE SPIRITS
CD _____ SCCD 31043
Steeplechase / Jul '88 / Impetus.

GREATEST LADY JAZZ PIANIST, THE (1936-44)
CD _____ JZCD 357
Suisa / Feb '92 / Jazz Music / THE.

KEY MOMENTS
CD _____ TPZ 1016
Topaz Jazz / Apr '95 / Pinnacle / Cadillac.

LONDON SESSIONS, THE
Perdido / Ladybird / Don't blame me / Ti-toros / For you / They can't take that away from me / Kool bongo / Round Midnight / Azure te / Flying home / Nickels / Man I love / Twilight / Just one of those things / Why / Yesterdays
CD _____ 74321115162
Vogue / Sep '93 / BMG.

MARY LOU WILLIAMS - 1927-40
CD _____ CLASSICS 630
Classics / '92 / Discovery / Jazz Music.

ON VOGUE (Williams, Mary Lou & Gerry Wiggins)
Mary waltz / Just you, just me / Lullaby of the leaves / Moonglow / Why / N.M.E. / Blues / Too marvellous for words / Wiggin' wit / Have you met Miss Jones / Three little words / Why was I born / Coffee time / I get a kick out of you / All the things you are
CD _____ 74321115052
Vogue / Jul '93 / BMG.

TOWN HALL 1945
CD _____ VJC 1035-2
Vintage Jazz Classics / Oct '92 / Direct / ADA / CM / Cadillac.

ZODIAC SUITE
CD _____ SFWCD 40810
Smithsonian Folkways / Nov '95 / ADA / Direct / Koch / CM / Cadillac.

ZONING
CD _____ SFWCD 40811
Smithsonian Folkways / Nov '95 / ADA / Direct / Koch / CM / Cadillac.

Williams, Mason

CLASSICAL GAS (Williams, Mason & Mannheim Steamroller)
CD _____ AGCD 800
American Gramophone / Oct '88 / New Note.

Williams, Maurice

SPOTLIGHT ON MAURICE WILLIAMS
High heeled sneakers / Bare footin' / Spanish harlem / Up on the roof / On broadway / Corine Corina / Drift away / Save the last dance for me / Raindrops keep falling on my head / Mustang Sally / Running around / Little darlin' / This feeling / Stay
CD _____ HADCD 120
Javelin / Feb '94 / THE / Henry Hadaway Organisation.

Williams, Melanie

HUMAN CRADLE
Everyday thang / Not enough / You are everything / Walk along side / Terrified / Keep it in the family / All cried out / Fair-weather / Building up love / Crave it / How d'you make love stay
CD _____ 476579 2
Columbia / Mar '95 / Sony.

Williams, Midge

CLASSICS 1937-1938
CD _____ CLASSICS 745
Classics / Aug '94 / Discovery / Jazz
Music.

Williams, Otis

OTIS WILLIAMS & THE CHARMS (The Original Rockin' And Chart Masters) (Williams, Otis & His Charms)
Love love stick stov / Love's our inspiration / Heart of a rose / I offer you / Fifty five seconds / My baby dearest darling / Bye bye baby / Please believe in me / When we get together / Mambo sh-mambo / Heaven only knows / Happy are we / Come to me baby / Loving baby / Let the happening happen / Quiet please / This love of mine / It's you, you, you / One fine day / What do you know about that / First time we met / Boom diddy boom boom / I'll be true / Crazy crazy love / Hearts of stone / Two hearts
CD _____ CDCHD 531
Ace / Mar '94 / Pinnacle / Cadillac / Complete/Pinnacle.

SING THEIR ALL-TIME HITS (Williams, Otis & His Charms)
Hearts of stone / Bazoom (I need your loving) / Ivory tower / Kokomo / Friends call me a fool / Gum drop / Ling ting tong / Walkin' after midnight / Creation of love / That's your mistake / Pardon me / Two hearts
CD _____ KCD 570
King/Paddle Wheel / Mar '90 / New Note.

Williams, Richard

NEW HORN IN TOWN
CD _____ CCD 79003
Candid / Jul '87 / Cadillac / Jazz Music / Wellard / Koch.

Williams, Robert Pete

FREE AGAIN
CD _____ OBCCD 553
Original Blues Classics / Jan '94 / Complete/Pinnacle / Wellard / Cadillac.

I'M AS BLUE AS A MAN CAN BE
CD _____ ARHCD 394
Arhoolie / Apr '95 / ADA / Direct / Cadillac.

WHEN A MAN TAKES THE BLUES
CD _____ ARHCD 395
Arhoolie / Apr '95 / ADA / Direct / Cadillac.

Williams, Robin

CLOSE AS WE CAN GET/9 TILL MIDNIGHT (Williams, Robin & Linda)
CD _____ FF 359CD
Flying Fish / May '93 / Roots / CM / Direct / ADA.

GOOD NEWS (Williams, Robin & Linda)
CD _____ SHCD 3832
Sugarhill / Apr '95 / Roots / CM / ADA / Direct.

RHYTHM OF LOVE, THE (Williams, Robin & Linda)
Rhythm of love / When I hear that whistle blow / House of gold / I'll remember you love in my prayers / Gone to the West / Hired gun / They all faded away / Six o'clock / All along / Dancin' / Devil in a mighty wind / Poor wayfaring stranger / You done me wrong
CD _____ SHCD 1027
Sugarhill / '90 / Roots / CM / ADA / Direct.

ROBIN & LINDA WILLIAMS LIVE (Williams, Robin & Linda)
CD _____ SHCD 1043
Sugarhill / Nov '94 / Roots / CM / ADA / Direct.

TURN TOWARD TOMORROW (Williams, Robin & Linda)
CD _____ SH 1040CD
Sugarhill / Jan '94 / Roots / CM / ADA / Direct.

Williams, Rod

DESTINY EXPRESS
Closet romantics / Middle way / Edge / False face / Blanche's wedding / Far west woman / Mama Laura / Destiny express
CD _____ MCD 5412
Muse / Nov '93 / New Note / CM.

HANGING IN THE BALANCE
CD _____ MCD 5380
Muse / Sep '92 / New Note / CM.

Williams, Roy

GRUESOME TWOSOME (Williams, Roy & John Barnes)
CD _____ BLCD 760507
Black Lion / Oct '93 / Jazz Music / Cadillac / Wellard / Koch.

ROYAL TROMBO
CD _____ PHONTCD 7556
Phontastic / '93 / Wellard / Jazz Music / Cadillac.

Williams, Rozz

DREAM HOME HEARTACHE (Williams, Rozz & Gitane Demone)
CD _____ TX 51026CD
Triple X / Sep '95 / Plastic Head.

Williams, Sylvia

FROM NEW ORLEANS
CD _____ BCD 319
GHB / Jan '94 / Jazz Music.

Williams, Tom

INTRODUCING TOM WILLIAMS (Williams, Tom Quintet)
CD _____ CRISS 1064CD
Criss Cross / Oct '92 / Cadillac / Harmonia Mundi.

STRAIGHT STREET
CD _____ 1091CD
Criss Cross / Jan '95 / Cadillac / Harmonia Mundi.

Williams, Tony

LIFETIME: THE COLLECTION
CD _____ 4689242
Sony Jazz / Jan '95 / Sony.

Williams, Valdo

NEW ADVANCED JAZZ
Desert fox / Bad manners / Move faster / Conqueror
CD _____ SV 0238
Savoy Jazz / Nov '93 / Conifer / ADA.

Williams, Vanessa

IN THE COMFORT ZONE
Comfort zone / Running back to you / Work to do / You gotta go / Still in love / Save the best for last / What will I tell my heart / Stranger's eyes / Two of a kind / Freedom dance (get free) / Just for tonight / One reason / Better off now / Goodbye / Right stuff
CD _____ 5112672
Wing / Oct '91 / PolyGram.

RIGHT STUFF, THE
Right stuff / Be a man / Dreamin' / If you really love him / (He's got) That look / I'll be the one / Security / Darlin' I / Am I too much / Can this be real / Whatever happens
CD _____ 835 694-2
Wing / Sep '88 / PolyGram.

SWEETEST DAYS
Intro-lude / Way that you love / Betcha never / Sweetest days / Higher ground / You don't have to say you're sorry / Ella-mental / Sister moon / You can't run / Long way home / Constantly / Moonlight over Paris
CD _____ 5261722
Mercury / Feb '95 / PolyGram.

Williams, Victoria

HAPPY, COME HOME
Shoes / Frying pan / Merry go round / Happy / TC / I'll do his will / Big fish / Main road / Lights / Opalousas / Statue of a bum / Poetry / Animal world
CD _____ GFLD 19239
Geffen / Jan '94 / BMG.

LIVE
CD _____ 7667926422
Atlantic / Jan '96 / Warner Music.

LOOSE
CD _____ 7567924302 CD
Mammoth / Jan '95 / Vital.

SWING THE STATUE
Why look at the moon / Boogieman / Clothes line / Tarbelly and featherfoot / On time / Holy spirit / Summer of drugs / I can't cry hard / Enough / Wobbling / Vieux amis / Weeds / Lift him up
CD _____ MR 0752
Mammoth / Apr '94 / Vital.

Williams, Willie

ARMAGIDEON TIME
Masterplan / See you when I get there / People / Armagideon time / All the way / Turn on the power / Easy / Burn
CD _____ CDHB 3509
Heartbeat / '90 / Greensleeves / Jetstar / Direct / ADA.

JAH WILL
CD _____ DS 007
Drumstreet / Jun '95 / Jetstar.

MESSENGER MAN
CD _____ CRCD 022
Charm / Sep '95 / Jetstar.

NATTY WITH A CAUSE
CD _____ SHAKACD 922
Jah Shaka / Nov '92 / Jetstar / SRD / Greensleeves.

SEE ME
CD _____ SHAKACD 949
Jah Shaka / Jul '93 / Jetstar / SRD / Greensleeves.

WW3

Out for a walk / Frozen sun / Third time is a charm / Takin' it with me / La mesha / Dr. Jackie / You can if you try / WW3 / Thousand years of peace
CD _____ ENJ 80602
Enja / Jun '94 / New Note / Vital/SAM.

Williams-Fairey...

FREEDOM (Williams-Fairey Engineering Band)
Silkstream / Scheherazade / Laughter in the rain / Brassmens holiday / Disney fantasy / Swiss air / Lass of Richmond Hill / Thoughts of love / Freedom
CD _____ QPRL 038D
Polyphonic / Sep '88 / Conifer.

GOLDEN JUBILEE (Williams-Fairey Engineering Band)
Tritsch Tratsch Polka / Swing low, sweet chariot / Kirn / Piper in the meadow / Pie Jesu / Marching with Sousa / Carnival for brass / Scarecrow and Mrs. King / Serenade / Bohemian rhapsody / Folk festival of love / Freedom
CD _____ GRACC 17
Grasmere / May '94 / Target/BMG / Savoy.

HYMNS ANCIENT AND MODERN (Williams-Fairey Engineering Band)
CD _____ QPRL 054D
Polyphonic / Mar '93 / Conifer.

PROCESSION TO THE MINSTER (Williams-Fairey Engineering Band)
Boys in blue / Tuesday blues / Concertino classico / Autumn leaves / Land of the mountain and the flood / Gladiator's farewell / Batman / Festival music / Caprice / Procession to the minster
CD _____ GRCD 42
Grasmere / Nov '90 / Target/BMG / Savoy.

TOURNAMENT FOR BRASS (Williams-Fairey Engineering Band)
President / Over the rainbow / Tournament for brass / Trouble with the tuba is... / Blenheim flourishes / Fest musik der stadt wien / Military overture / Ballycastle bay / Twin Peaks / Neapolitan scenes
CD _____ GRCD 35
Grasmere / May '94 / Target/BMG / Savoy.

Williamson, Ann

AMAZING GRACE
CD _____ CDITV 600
Scotdisc / Mar '95 / Duncans / Ross / Conifer.

COUNT YOUR BLESSINGS
Morning has broken / By cool Siloam's shady rill / O love that wilt not let me go / Safe in the arms of Jesus / Mine eyes have seen the glory / How sweet the name of Jesus sounds / All things bright and beautiful / Whispering hope / When I survey the wondrous cross / O perfect love / All people that on earth do dwell / Count your blessings / I need thee every hour / In the sweet bye and bye
CD _____ ERTVCD 2
Emerald / Nov '87 / Direct.

FLOWER OF SCOTLAND
Water is wide / Forty shades of green / Flower of Scotland / Rose / Beyond the sunset / Crying time / Bluebells of Scotland / Wild mountain thyme / Mountains of mourne / Rowan tree / Picture of me / Star O'Rabbie Burns / Dark island / Bonnie Mary Of Argyll / Battle's o'er / Farewell my love
CD _____ CDITV 590
Scotdisc / Aug '94 / Duncans / Ross / Conifer.

Williamson, Bruce

BIG CITY MAGIC
You say you care / View from the east / Arts and leisure / Growing concern / Sima / Missing rose / Freddie's night out / Moonwatch / Open wings / Slice
CD _____ CDSJP 413
Timeless Jazz / Feb '94 / New Note.

Williamson, Claude

BLUES IN FRONT/ NEW DEPARTURE (Williamson, Claude & 7 Others)
CD _____ STCD4163
Storyville / Feb '90 / Jazz Music / Wellard / CM / Cadillac.

MULLS THE MULLIGAN SCENE
CD _____ FSCD 54
Fresh Sound / Oct '90 / Jazz Music / Discovery.

Williamson, Robin

AMERICAN STONEHENGE (Williamson, Robin & His Merry Band)
Port London early / Pacheco / Keepsake / Zoo blues / These Islands green / Man in the van / Sands and the glass / Her scattered gold / When evening shadows / Rab's last woollen testament
CD _____ EDCD 389
Edsel / Jun '94 / Pinnacle / ADA.

GLINT OF THE KINDLING, A (Williamson, Robin & His Merry Band)
Road to the gypsies / Me and the mad girl / Lough foyle / Woodcutter's song / By

weary well / Boyhood of Henry Morgan / Poachers song / Five denials
CD _____ TMC 9201
Eclectic / Jan '96 / Pinnacle.

ISLAND OF THE STRONG DOOR
CD _____ TMC 9504
Eclectic / Feb '96 / Pinnacle.

JOURNEY'S EDGE
Border tango / Tune I hear so well / Red eye blues / Tomorrow / Mythic times / Lullaby for a rainy night / Rap city rhapsody / Maharajah of Mogador / Bells / Voices of the Barbary coast / Out on the water
CD _____ EDCD 374
Edsel / Jun '93 / Pinnacle / ADA.

LEGACY OF THE SCOTTISH HARPERS
Scotch cap/Leonard / Flowers of the forest/Cromlet's lilt/Chevy chase / Weel hoddled Lucky/Lochmaben harper / Gilderoy/ Cow the Gowan / MacGregor's lament/ MacGregor's search / Kilt thy coat Maggie/ Three sheepskins / Lord Dundee's lamentation/Brae's o'Killiecrankie / I'll mek ye fain to follow me / Lady Cassilis' lilt/Auld jew/ Broom o'Cowdenknowes / MacDonald of the Isles salutation / Rushes/Birk and green hollin / Soor plooms / Jockey went to the wood / Banks of Helicon/Deil tak the wars
CD _____ CCF 12CD
Claddagh / Nov '84 / ADA / Direct.

SONGS OF LOVE & PARTING/5 BARDIC MYSTERIES
CD _____ TMC 9403
Eclectic / Jan '96 / Pinnacle.

TEN OF SONGS, THE
CD _____ PLCD 081
Plant Life / '88 / Soundalive / ADA / Symposium.
CD _____ FF 448CD
Flying Fish / Dec '94 / Roots / CM / Direct / ADA.

WINTER'S TURNING
CD _____ FF 407CD
Flying Fish / Dec '94 / Roots / CM / Direct / ADA.

Williamson, Roy

LONG JOURNEY SOUTH, THE
Long journey South / Laggan love / Skye boat song / Donald Og / Peggy Gordon / Nicky's theme / Number one / Tuscan / Long journey South (reprise)
CD _____ MOICD 001
Moidart / Oct '91 / Conifer / ADA.

Williamson, Sonny Boy

ANTHOLOGY 1937-44
CD _____ EN 519
Encyclopaedia / Sep '95 / Discovery.

KING OF BLUES HARMONICA 1938-1940
CD _____ BLE 592512
Black & Blue / Dec '92 / Wellard / Koch.

SONNY BOY WILLIAMSON 1940-42
CD _____ 158102
Blues Collection / Dec '93 / Discovery.

SONNY BOY WILLIAMSON VOL.1 1937-1939
CD _____ 157602
Blues Collection / Feb '93 / Discovery.

Williamson, Sonny Boy

BEST OF SONNY BOY WILLIAMSON
Don't start me talkin' / All my love in vain / Let me explain / Keep it to yourself / Key / Fattenin' frogs for snakes / Cross my heart / Born blind / Ninety nine / Your funeral and my trial / Let your conscience be your guide / Goat / It's sad to be alone / Checkin' up on my baby / Lonesome cabin / Trust my baby / Too close together / Nine below zero / Help me / Bring it on home / Decoration day / One way out
CD _____ CDRED 2
Charly / Sep '91 / Charly / THE / Cadillac.

BLUES OF SONNY BOY WILLIAMSON, THE
CD _____ STCD 4062
Storyville / Jun '87 / Jazz Music / Wellard / CM / Cadillac.

BOPPIN' WITH SONNY
Shuckin' woman / I'm not beggin nobody / Boppin' with Sonny / Empty bedroom / From the bottom / No nights by myself / Red hot kisses / Keep it to yourself / Going in your direction / Gettin' out of town / Sonny's rhythm / She's crazy / City of New Orleans / 309 Cat / Cat hop / Clownin' with the world
CD _____ CDBM 088
Blue Moon / '90 / Magnum Music Group / Greensleeves / Hot Shot / ADA / Cadillac / Discovery.

CHESS YEARS, THE (4CD Set)
Good evening everybody / All my love in vain / Don't start me talkin' / You killing me / Work with me / Let me explain / I know what love is all about / Your imagination / I wonder why / Don't lose your way / Keep it to yourself / Key / Have you ever been in love / Please forgive / Fattenin' frogs for snakes / Hurts me so much / I don't know

/ This is my apartment / Like wolf / Cross my heart / Unseen eye / Ninety nine / Dissatisfied / Born blind / Little village / Wake up baby / She got next to me / Your funeral and my trial / Let your conscience be your guide / Unseeing eye / Keep your hand out of my pocket / Cool disposition / Goat / I never do wrong / Santa Claus / It's sad to be alone / I can't do without you / Open road / Checkin' up on my baby / Peach tree / Lonesome cabin / Temperature 110 / Down child / Trust my baby / Somebody help me / This old life / Too young to die / She's my baby / Stop right now / That's all I want / Too close together / Hunt / Too old to think / Nine below zero / One way out / Bye bye bird / Got to move / Help me / Bring it on home / My younger days / Stop cryin' / Trying to get back on my feet / Understand my life / Decoration day / Close to me (I want you) / Don't make a mistake / Find another woman / I can't be alone / Nine is Sonny Boy / Cool disposition / Ninetynine
CD Set _____ CDREDBOX 1
Chess/Charly / Jan '91 / Charly.

CLOWNIN' WITH THE WORLD
CD _____ ALCD 2700
Alligator / Oct '93 / Direct / ADA.

COLLECTION, THE
CD _____ COL 044
Collection / Feb '95 / Target/BMG.

DON'T SEND ME NO FLOWERS
Don't send me no flowers / I see a man downstairs / She was so dumb / Goat / Walkin' / Little girl how old are you / It's a bloody life / Getting out of town / Slow walk / Pontiac blues / Lonesome cabin / Bye bye bird
CD _____ CDLIK 80
Charly / Jan '93 / Charly / THE / Cadillac.

DOWN AND OUT BLUES
Don't start me talkin' / I don't know / All my love in vain / Key / Keep it to yourself / Dissatisfied / Fattenin' frogs for snakes / Wake up baby / Your funeral and my trial / Ninety nine / Cross my heart / Let me explain
CD _____ CHLD 19106
Chess/MCA / Oct '92 / BMG / New Note.

E.P. COLLECTION PLUS, THE
Help me / Bring it on home / Checkin' up on my baby / Don't start me talkin' / Your funeral and my trial / Keep it to yourself / Cross my heart / Too old to think / One way out / Let your conscience be your guide / Temperature 110 / Tryin' to get back on my feet / You killing me / Ninety nine / I don't know / Too young to die / Dissatisfied / It's sad to be alone / Key / Trust my baby / Wake up baby / Bye bye bird / Hurts me so much / That's all I want / (I want you) close to me
CD _____ SEECD 395
See For Miles/C5 / Feb '94 / Pinnacle.

GOIN' IN YOUR DIRECTION
CD _____ AL 2803
Alligator / Jul '94 / Direct / ADA.

HARP FROM DEEP SOUTH, THE
Your funeral and my trial / Wake up baby / Checkin' up on my baby / Down child / Too young to die / Fattenin' frogs for snakes / Don't start me talkin' / Sky is crying / Got to move / Help me / Bring it on home / Story of Sonny Boy Williamson / When the light went out / Keep it to yourself / Sonny's rhythm / Bye bye bird / Work with me / Movin' down the river Rhine / I wonder do I have a friend / Eyesight to the blind / Mighty long time / Nine below zero
Blues Encore / Apr '92 / Target/BMG.
CD _____ CD 52018

KEEP IT TO OURSELVES
CD _____ ALCD 4787
Alligator / Aug '92 / Direct / ADA.

KING BISCUIT TIME
CD _____ ARHCD 310
Arhoolie / Apr '95 / ADA / Direct / Cadillac.

LIVE IN ENGLAND
Bye bye bird / Mr. downchild / River Rhine / Twenty three hours too long / Lost care / Take it easy / Out of the water closet / Western Arizona / Slow walk / Highway 69 / My little cabin / Sonny's slow walk / Pontiac blues / My babe / I don't care no more / Baby don't you worry / Night time is the right time / I'm gonna put you down / Fattenin' frogs for snakes / Nobody but you
CD _____ CDRB 21
Charly / Apr '95 / Charly / THE / Cadillac.

NINE BELOW ZERO (Charly Blues - Masterworks Vol. 22)
Work with me / Don't start me talkin' / Let me explain / Keep it yourself / Have you ever been in love / Fattenin' frogs for snakes / Born blind / Ninety nine / Your funeral and my trial / Wake up baby / Let your conscience be your guide / Unseeing eye / Open road / Lonesome cabin / Nine below zero / Help me / Bring it on home / One way out
CD _____ CDBM 22
Charly / Apr '92 / Charly / THE / Cadillac.

ONE WAY OUT
Born blind / Work with me / You killing me / Keep it to yourself / Don't lose your eye /

This is my apartment / Like wolf / Cross my heart / Unseen eye / Ninety nine / Dissatisfied / Born blind / Little village / Wake up baby / She got next to you / Your funeral and my trial / Let your conscience be your guide / Unseeing eye / Keep your hand out of my pocket / Cool disposition / Goat / I never do wrong / Santa Claus / It's sad to be alone / I can't do without you / Open road / Checkin' up on my baby
Charly / Mar '93 / Charly / THE / Cadillac.

SONNY BOY WILLIAMSON & YARDBIRDS 1963 (with Eric Clapton) (Williamson, Sonny Boy & The Yardbirds)
CD _____ CDLR 42.020
L&R / Aug '87 / New Note.

SUGAR MAMA
CD _____ IGOCD 2014
Indigo / Feb '95 / Direct / ADA.

VERY BEST OF SONNY BOY WILLIAMSON, THE (& Roots Of The Blues No.4 Compilation/3CD Set)
Work with me / Don't start me talkin' / All my love in vein / Don't lose your eye / Keep it to yourself / Key (to your door) / Have you ever been in love / Fattening frogs for snakes / I don't know / Cross my heart / Born blind / Ninety nine / Dissatisfied / Your funeral and my trial / Wake up baby / Let your conscience be your guide / Unseeing eye / Goat / It's sad to be alone / Checkin' up on my baby / Temperature 110 / Somebody help me / Down child / Trust my baby / Too close together / Too young to die / Hunt / Nine below zero / Got to move / Bye bye bird / Help me, bring it on home / One way out / Trying to get back on my feet / Decoration / Day / Mister downchild / 23 Hours too long / Take it easy, baby / Highway 69 / My little cabin / Cool drink of water / Statesboro blues / Candy man blues / Nobody knows you when you're down and out / That's no way to get along / Broken hearted / Kingfisher blues / Walking blues / Sugar Mama blues / Roll 'em Pete / New 'shake 'em on down / Rockin' chair / Take a little walk with me / I be's troubled / Rock island line / Ramblin' mind blues
CD Set _____ VBCD 304
Charly / Jul '95 / Charly / THE / Cadillac.

WORK WITH ME
Good evening everybody / You killing me / Work with me / I wonder why / Don't lose your eye / This is my apartment / Like Wolf / Dissatisfied / Ninety nine / She got next to me / Keep your hand out of my pocket / Open road / I can't do without you / Down child / Too young to die / She's my baby / Stop right now / Hunt / Too old to think / That's all I want / Got to move / My younger days / Stop crying / Close to me (I want you)
CD _____ CDRED 14
Charly / Sep '89 / Charly / THE / Cadillac.

Willie & The Poor Boys

WILLIE AND THE POOR BOYS
Baby, please don't go / Can you hear me / These arms of mine / Revenue man / You never can tell / Slippin' and slidin' / Saturday night / Let's talk it over / All night long / Chicken shack boogie / Sugar bee / Poor boy boogie
CD _____ NEMCD 688
Sequel / Apr '94 / BMG.

WILLIE AND THE POOR BOYS LIVE
High school confidential / Baby, please don't go / Mystery train / Chicken shack boogie / stagger lee / Red hot / Poor boy boogie medley / Land of the 1000 dances / Tear it up / OOh pah pah doo / Rockin' pneumonia and the boogie woogie flu / What'd I say / Lovin' up a storm / Hound dog / Shake, rattle and roll / Looking for someone to love
CD _____ NEMCD 689
Sequel / Apr '94 / BMG.

Willimas, Derede

WHY NOT TONIGHT
CD _____ FECD 11
First Edition / Apr '93 / Jetstar.

Willis, Butch

REPEATS (Willis, Butch & The Rocks)
CD _____ TB 134CD
Teenbeat / May '94 / SRD.

Willis, Chick

BACK TO THE BLUES
Don't let success (turn our love around) / Goin' to the dogs / Bow legged woman / I ain't superstitious / Tell papa / Story of my life / My adorable one / I ain't jivin' baby / Strange things happening
CD _____ CDICH 1106
Ichiban / Oct '93 / Koch.

FOOTPRINTS ON MY BED
Love crazy / Use what you got / What's to become of the world / Roll the dice / Footprints in my bed / Big red caboose / Hello central / Jack you up / Voodoo woman / Nuts for sale
CD _____ CDICH 1054
Ichiban / Oct '93 / Koch.

I GOT A BIG FAT WOMAN
CD _____ ICH 1171CD
Ichiban / May '94 / Koch.

NOW

I want a big fat woman / What have you got on me / I want to play with your poodle / I can't stop loving you / For your precious love / Stoop down '88 / It's all over / Garbage man
CD _____ CDICH 1029
Ichiban / Feb '89 / Koch.

Willis, Ike

SHOULD' A GONE BEFORE I LEFT
CD _____ EFA 034062
Muffin / Jul '94 / SRD.

Willis, Kelly

BANG BANG
CD _____ MCLD 19245
MCA / Mar '94 / BMG.

Willis, Larry

HEAVY BLUE (Willis, Larry Quartet)
CD _____ SCCD 31269
Steeplechase / Oct '90 / Impetus.

MY FUNNY VALENTINE
For openers / It could happen to you / Blues for Wynton Kelly / Who's kidding who / Rhythm-a-ning / Blood count / My shining hour / Lazy afternoon / Ethiopia / My funny Valentine
CD _____ 66053005
Jazz City / Dec '90 / New Note.

SERENADE
CD _____ SSCD 8063
Sound Hills / Jan '96 / Harmonia Mundi / Cadillac.

TRIBUTE TO SOMEONE, A
King cobra / Wayman's way / Sensei / Tribute to someone / Maiden voyage / For Jean / Teasdale place
CD _____ AQCD 1022
Audioquest / Jul '95 / New Note.

Willis, Ralph

RALPH WILLIS VOL. 1 1944-1950
CD _____ DOCD 5256
Blues Document / May '94 / Swift / Jazz Music / Hot Shot.

RALPH WILLIS VOL. 2 1950-1953
CD _____ DOCD 5257
Blues Document / May '94 / Swift / Jazz Music / Hot Shot.

Willson, Christian

BLUES ON THE WORLD
Little angel / Blues on the world / Diddlin' / Tin pan alley / See see rider / Sykesism / Let them talk / Mystery train / How long / Baby what you want me to do / I'd rather go blind
CD _____ BLU 10252
Blues Beacon / Dec '95 / New Note.

BOOGIE WOOGIE AND SOME BLUES
CD _____ 1007-2
Blues Beacon / Apr '91 / New Note.

Wills, Bob

LONGHORN RECORDINGS, THE
Sooner or later / Buffalo twist / All night long / You can't break a broken heart / If he's movin' in / Let's get it over and done with / Big tater in the sandy land / Mayflower waltz / Billy in the lowground / Beaumont rag / Faded love / Dian waltz / Done gone / Put your little foot / Bob's first fiddle tune / Bob's schottische / Gone indian / No disappointments in heaven / Will's junction / You'll never walk out of my heart / Betty's waltz / San Antonio rose
CD _____ BCD 15689
Bear Family / Aug '93 / Rollercoaster / Direct / CM / Swift / ADA.

TIFFANY TRANSCRIPTIONS VOL.9
Texas playboy rag / My life's been a pleasure / Elmer's tune / G.I. wish / Milk cow blues / Shame on you / 12th street rag / In the mood / You don't care what happens / St. Louis blues / St. Louis blues pt.2 / What is this thing called love / Sentimental journey / Back home in Indiana
CD _____ EDCD 329
Edsel / Sep '91 / Pinnacle / ADA.

YOUR FRIENDLY KING OF WESTERN SWING (Selections From The Tiffany Transcriptions) (Wills, Bob & His Texas Playboys)
Texas playboy theme / Lone star rag / Cotton patch blues / Jumpin' at the woodside / Cotton eyed Joe / Take me back to Tulsa / Corine Corina / San Antonio rose / I'm a ding dong daddy from Dumas / Please don't talk about me when I'm gone / take the 'a' train / New Spanish two-step / Home in San Antone / Across the valley from the alamo / My brown eyed-Texas rose / My window faces south / Sweet Georgia Brown / Oklahoma Hills / Keep a knockin' / Tea for two / Big beaver / Get along home Cindy

CD _____ NESTCD 905
Demon / May '95 / Pinnacle / ADA.

Willson, Michelle

EVIL GAL BLUES
CD _____ BB 9550CD
Bullseye Blues / Aug '94 / Direct.

Willson-Piper, Marty

ART ATTACK
CD _____ RCD 20042
Rykodisc / Jun '92 / Vital / ADA.

I CAN'T CRY
CD _____ RCD 51025
Rykodisc / Jul '92 / Vital / ADA.

SPIRIT LEVEL
CD _____ RCD 10197
Rykodisc / Jul '92 / Vital / ADA.

Wilmot, Gary

LOVE SITUATION
CD _____ DSHCD 7007
D-Sharp / Mar '93 / Pinnacle.

Wilson, Al

SHOW AND TELL
CD _____ CDSGP 0160
Prestige / Nov '95 / Total/BMG.

Wilson, Bobby

I'LL BE YOUR RAINBOW
Deeper and deeper / Hey girl (Tell me) / Let me (Put love back in your life) / I'll be your rainbow / Here is where the love is / Don't shut me out / You make me feel good all over / I'll take good care of you / All I need (I've got) / When I don't see a smile on your face
CD _____ NEMCD 635
Sequel / Mar '93 / BMG.

Wilson, Brian

AMERICAN SPRING... PLUS (American Spring)
Tennessee waltz / Thinkin' 'bout you baby / Mama said / Superstar / Awake / Sweet mountain / Everybody / This whole world / Forever / Good time / Now that everything's been said / Down home / Shyin' away / Fallin' in love / It's like Heaven / Had to phone ya
CD _____ SEECD 269
See For Miles/C5 / Dec '89 / Pinnacle.

BRIAN WILSON
Love and mercy / Walkin' the line / Melt away / Baby let your hair grow long / Little children / One for the boys / There's so many / Night time / Let it shine / Rio Grande / Meet me in my dreams tonight
CD _____ 7599256692
WEA / Nov '95 / Warner Music.

I JUST WASN'T MADE FOR THESE TIMES
Meant for you / This whole world / Caroline, no / Let the wind blow / Love and mercy / Do it again / Warmth of the sun / Wonderful / Still I dream of it / Melt away / 'Til I die
CD _____ MCD 11270
MCA / Aug '95 / BMG.

ORANGE CRATE ART (Wilson, Brian & Van Dyke Parks)
CD _____ 9362454272
WEA / Nov '95 / Warner Music.

Wilson, Cassandra

BLUE LIGHT 'TIL DAWN
You don't know what love is / Come on in my kitchen / Tell me you'll wait for me / Children of the night / Hellhound on my trail / Black crow / Sankofa / Estrellas / Redbone / Tupelo honey / Blue light 'til dawn / I can't stand the rain
CD _____ CDP 7813572
Blue Note / Jan '94 / EMI.

DANCE TO THE DRUMS AGAIN
CD _____ 4729722
Sony Jazz / Jan '95 / Sony.

DAYS AWEIGH
Electromagnolia / Let's face the music and dance / Days aweigh / Subatomic blues / Apricots on their wings / If you only know how / You belong to you / Some other time / Black and yellow
CD _____ JMT 872012
Watt / Oct '87 / New Note.

Wilson, Charles

BLUES IN THE KEY OF C
Who it's going to be / Is it over / Leaning tree / You cut off my love supply / Let's have a good time / Selfish lover / It's a crying shame / I've got a good woman
CD _____ CDICH 1120
Ichiban / Oct '93 / Koch.

Wilson, Chris

RANDOM CENTURIES
CD _____ FM 1007CD
Marilyn / Jul '92 / Pinnacle.

Wilson, Delroy

22 MAGNIFICENT HITS
CD _____ BLCD 017
Graylan / Jan '96 / Jetstar / Grapevine /
THE.

GOLDEN MEMORIES OF DELROY WILSON, THE
CD _____ RNCD 2111
Rhino / Jul '95 / Jetstar / Magnum Music
Group / THE.

GREATEST HITS
CD _____ JMC 200102
Jamaica Gold / Dec '92 / THE / Magnum
Music Group / Jetstar.

MY SPECIAL LADY
CD _____ CDSGP 069
Prestige / Oct '94 / Total/BMG.

SARGE
CD _____ CD 1
Chambers / May '95 / Jetstar.

SPECIAL
CD _____ RASCD 3119
Ras / Sep '93 / Jetstar / SRD.

TUNE INTO REGGAE MUSIC
CD _____ RNCD 2061
Rhino / Jun '94 / Jetstar / Magnum Music
Group / THE.

WHAT'S GOING ON
CD _____ CDSGP 0147
Prestige / Jul '95 / Total/BMG.

Wilson, Eddie

DANKESCHON, BITTESCHON, WIEDERSEHEN
Wabash cannonball / Strictly nothin' /
Streets of Laredo / Mid the green fields of
Virginia / It's OK / I wish I could / Johnny
Reb / I found my girl in the USA / Show her
lots of gold / Long time to forget
CD Set _____ BCD 15615
Bear Family / Mar '93 / Rollercoaster
Direct / CM / Swift / ADA.

Wilson, Edith

HE MAY BE YOUR MAN
CD _____ DD 637
Delmark / Nov '93 / Hot Shot / ADA / CM
/ Direct / Cadillac.

Wilson, Elder Roma

THIS TRAIN
CD _____ ARHCD 429
Arhoolie / Sep '95 / ADA / Direct /
Cadillac.

Wilson, Garland

CLASSICS 1931-38
CD _____ CLASSICS 808
Classics / Apr '95 / Discovery / Jazz
Music.

Wilson, Gerald

PORTRAITS
So what / Round Midnight / Paco / Ravi /
Aram / Eric / Caprichos
CD _____ CZ 490
Pacific Jazz / Feb '92 / EMI.

Wilson, Glenn

BITTER SWEET (Wilson, Glenn & Stuart, Rory)
CD _____ SSC 1057D
Sunnyside / Aug '92 / Pinnacle.

BITTERSWEET
CD _____ 500572
Sunnyside / Nov '92 / Pinnacle.

Wilson, Greg

PIPER OF DISTINCTION
CD _____ CDMON 822
Monarch / Oct '04 / CM / ADA / Duncans
/ Direct.

Wilson, Hop

HOUSTON GHETTO BLUES
CD _____ BB 9538CD
Bullseye Blues / Jan '94 / Direct.

STEEL GUITAR FLASH (Wilson, Hop & His Two Buddies)
My woman has a black cat bone / I'm a
stranger / I ain't got a woman / Merry christmas darling / Rockin' in the coconuts / Why
do you twist / You don't move me anymore
/ You don't love me anymore / Feel so glad
/ Be careful with the blues / My woman
done quit me / Dance to it / Fuss too much
/ Good woman is hard to find / Need your
love to keep me warm / I done got over /
Toot toot Tootsie goobye / Your Daddy
wants to rock / Broke and hungry / Always
be in love with you / I met a strange woman
/ Love's got me all fenced in / Chicken stuff
/ Rockin' with Hop / That wouldn't satisfy
CD _____ CDCHD 240
Ace / Jan '94 / Pinnacle / Cadillac / Com-
plete/Pinnacle.

Wilson, Jack

IN NEW YORK
CD _____ DIW 615
DIW / Jan '94 / Harmonia Mundi /
Cadillac.

RAMBLIN'
CD _____ FSRCD 152
Fresh Sound / Dec '90 / Jazz Music /
Discovery.

Wilson, Jackie

CHICAGO YEARS VOL. 1, THE
Beautiful day / Pretty little angel eyes / I still
love you / To change my love / I've learned
about life / Just as soon as the feeling's
over / Just got me walking / Tears will tell it all /
That lucky old sun (Just rolls around heaven
all day) / Love is funny that way / Since you
showed me how to be happy / My heart is
calling / Higher and higher / I don't need
you / A round of need your loving / Let this be
a letter (To my baby) / Hard to get a thing
called love / Fountain / Don't you know I
love you / Didn't I
CD _____ CPCD 8052
Charly / Mar '95 / Charly / THE / Cadillac.

DYNAMIC JACKIE WILSON
Higher and higher / I get the sweetest feeling / Squeeze her, tease her (but love her)
/ She's alright / Think twice (Duet with
LaVern Baker) / I've got to get back (Country boy) / Whispers (gettin' louder) / Just be
sincere / Since you showed me how to be
happy / I don't want to lose you / I've lost
you / Stop lying / When you cry (With Count Basie) / I can feel
those vibrations) This love is real / You got
me walking / No more goodbyes / Don't
burn no bridges (With the Chi-Lites) / Open
the door to your heart
CD _____ CPCD 8018
Charly / Feb '94 / Charly / THE / Cadillac.

HIGHER AND HIGHER
Soul galore / I've lost you / I don't want to
lose you / Who who song / Nothing but blue
skies / I get the sweetest feeling / You
brought about a change in me / I'm the one
to do it / Nobody but you / Higher and
higher / Uptight / Whispers (gettin' louder) /
You got me walking / Let this be a letter (to
my baby) / Because of you / What'cha
gonna do about love / (I can feel those vibrations) This love is real / Since you
showed me how to be happy
CD _____ CDKEN 901
Kent / May '86 / Pinnacle.

HIGHER AND HIGHER
Reet petite / Lonely teardrops / Come back
to me / Danny boy / Why can't you be mine
/ If I can't have you / That's why (I love you
so) / I'll be satisfied / You better know it /
Talk that talk / I know I'll always be in love
with you / Doggin' around / Woman / Lover,
a friend / Am I the man / Tear of the year /
Please tell me why / I'm comin' on back to
you / You don't know what it means / I just
can't help it / Baby workout / Shake, shake,
shake / No pity (in the naked city) / Whispers (gettin' louder) / Higher and higher / I
get the sweetest feeling
CD _____ CPCD 8005
Charly / Oct '93 / Charly / THE / Cadillac.

JACKIE WILSON STORY - THE CHICAGO YEARS VOL.1
Beautiful day / Pretty little angel eyes / I still
love you / To change my love / I've learned
about life / Just as soon as the feeling's
over / Just be sincere / Tears will tell it all /
That lucky old sun (just rolls around heaven
all day) / Love is funny that way / Since you
showed me how to be happy / My heart is
calling / (Your love keeps lifting me) Higher
and higher / I don't need you around / I
need your loving / Let this be a letter (to my
baby) / Hard to get a thing called love /
Fountain / Don't you know I love you /
Didn't I
CD _____ JWCD 6
Charly / Oct '95 / Charly / THE / Cadillac.

JACKIE WILSON STORY - THE CHICAGO YEARS VOL.2
I get lonely sometimes / Love changed her
face / (I can feel those vibrations) This love
is real / Because of you / Go away / Who
am I / Whispers (gettin' louder) / Hum de
dum de do / Somebody up there likes you
/ You left the fire burning / Think about the
good times / Woman needs to be loved /
Growin' tall / Light my fire / Try it again /
Those heartaches / With these hands /
Where is love / You got me wlaking / Don't
burn no bridges
CD _____ JWCD 1
Charly / Oct '95 / Charly / THE / Cadillac.

JACKIE WILSON STORY - THE NEW YORK YEARS
Etcetera / You better know it / Sazzle dazzle
/ Try a little tenderness / (You were made
for) All my love / I'm wanderin' / I'll be satisfied / So much / Years from now / I apol-
ogize / Please tell me why / Crazy she calls
me / To be loved / I'm comin' on back to
you / Lonely teardrops / It's been a long
time / My heart belongs to only you / Love
is all / Keep smiling at trouble (trouble's a
bubble) / Night
CD _____ JWCD 1
Charly / Oct '95 / Charly / THE / Cadillac.

NEW YORK YEARS VOL.2
CD _____ JWCD 2
Charly / Jan '96 / Charly / THE / Cadillac.

PORTRAIT OF JACKIE WILSON, A
CD _____ PWKS 4238
Carlton Home Entertainment / Feb '95 /
Carlton Home Entertainment.

REET PETITE
Shake, shake, shake / Why can't you be
mine / I'm wanderin' / Lonely teardrops /
Yeah yeah / It's so fine / Come back to me
/ Shake a hand / Reet petite / If I can't have
you / All my love / So much / I know I'll
always be in love with you / Danny boy /
Doggin' around / Do Lord
CD _____ CDCH 902
Ace / May '86 / Pinnacle / Cadillac / Com-
plete/Pinnacle.

REET PETITE AND OTHER CLASSICS
Reet petite / That's why I love you so /
Lonely teardrops / Night / I'm wanderin' /
Singing a song / We have love / It's so fine
/ By the light of the silvery moon / Come
back to me / To be loved / Only you, only
me / Stormy weather / Lonely life / Ask /
Magic of love / Happiness / Never go away
CD _____ CDCD 1142
Charly / Nov '93 / Charly / THE / Cadillac.

VERY BEST OF JACKIE WILSON, THE
Reet petite / Lonely teardrops / To be loved
/ That's why / I'll be satisfied / Doggin'
around / Lonely life / Night / You better
know it / Talk talk talk / Am I the man / I'm
comin' on back to you / Woman, a love, a
friend / Baby workout / Squeeze her, tease
her (but love her) / No pity (in the naked city)
/ Whispers (gettin' louder) / I get the
sweetest feeling / Since you showed me
how to be happy / Love is funny that way /
Just be sincere / Higher and higher / You
got me walking / (I can feel those vibrations)
this love is real
CD _____ CDCHK 913
Ace / Nov '94 / Pinnacle / Cadillac / Com-
plete/Pinnacle.

VERY BEST OF JACKIE WILSON, THE (2)
Reet petite / Lonely teardrops / That's why
I love you so / Night / You better know it /
Talk that talk / To be loved / I'll be satisfied
/ Whispers (gettin' louder) / Higher and
higher / I get the sweetest feeling / Doggin'
around / Am I the man / I'm comin' on back
to you / Woman, a lover, a friend / No pity
(in the naked city)
CD _____ MCCD 017
Music Club / Feb '91 / Disc / THE / CM.

Wilson, Joe Lee

ACID RAIN
CD _____ BL 012
Bloomdido / Oct '93 / Cadillac.

Wilson, Joemy

TURLOUGH O'CAROLAN
CD _____ DMCD 102
Dargason Music / Jun '93 / ADA.

Wilson, John

TELL ME SOMETHING NEW
River of love / Rainbows and you / Jump
back / We all wanna be in love / Jump / Tell
me something new / Is this love / Everything
I need / 24 Reasons / Little Mis-treater /
Buddy doing the blues
CD _____ 30360 00182
Carlton Home Entertainment / Feb '96 /
Carlton Home Entertainment.

Wilson, Kim

THAT'S LIFE
CD _____ ANTCD 0034
Antones / Jul '95 / Hot Shot / Direct /
ADA.

TIGERMAN
CD _____ ANTCD 0023
Antones / Nov '03 / Hot Shot / Direct /
ADA.

Wilson, Mari

RHYTHM ROMANCE, THE
CD _____ DINCD 31
Dino / Sep '91 / Pinnacle / 3MV.

Wilson, Marty

RHYME
CD _____ RCD 10114
Rykodisc / Sep '91 / Vital / ADA.

Wilson, Nancy

FORBIDDEN LOVER
Forbidden lover / I was telling him about
you / If you only knew / Deeper / Puttin' my
trust / You know / Too good to be true / I
never held your heart / What will it take this
time / Song for you
CD _____ 983326 2
Pickwick/Sony Collector's Choice / Oct '93
/ Carlton Home Entertainment / Pinnacle /
Sony.

Wilson, Smokey

LUSH LIFE
Free again / Midnight sun / Only the young
/ When the world was young / Right to love
/ Lush life / Over the weekend / You've
changed / River shallow / Sunny / I stayed
too long at the fair
CD _____ CDP 8327452
Capitol Jazz / Aug '95 / EMI.

SPOTLIGHT ON NANCY WILSON
What a little moonlight can do / Little girl
blue / My one and only love / Best is yet to
come / Midnight sun / Good life / You'd be
so nice to come home to / Time after time
/ All of you / Very thought of you / Back in
your own back yard / When the sun comes
out / At long last love / You've changed /
Someone to watch over me / I wish you
love / Angel eyes / Here's that rainy day /
Song is you / Miss Otis regrets
CD _____ CDP 8285152
Capitol / Jul '95 / EMI.

Wilson Phillips

SHADOWS AND LIGHT
I hear you (prelude) / It's only life / You
won't see me cry / Give it up / This doesn't
have to be love / Where are you / Flesh and
blood / Don't take me down / All the way
from New York / Fueled for Houston /
Goodbye Carmen / Alone / I hear you
(reprise)
CD _____ SBKCD 13
SBK / Jun '92 / EMI.

WILSON PHILLIPS
Hold on / Release me / Impulsive / Next to
you (someday I'll be) / You're in love / Over
and over / Reason to believe / Ooh you're
gold / Eyes like twins / Dream is still alive
CD _____ SBKCD 5
SBK / Jun '90 / EMI.

Wilson, Robert

VERY BEST OF ROBERT WILSON, THE
Road to the isles / Bonnie Mary of Argyle /
Eriskay love lilt / Uist tramping song / My
love is like a red red rose / Westering home
/ Maid of Kenmore / Bonnie Strathyre /
Lewis bridal song / Down the glen / Bonnie
Scots lassie / Gordon for me / Scotland the
brave / Northern lights of Aberdeen / To-
bermory Bay / Marching through the
heather / Rothesay Bay / Soft lowland
tongue of the south / Song of the Clyde /
Haste ye back
CD _____ CDSL 8268
Music For Pleasure / Sep '95 / EMI.

Wilson, Roger

STARK NAKED
CD _____ WH 001CD
Whiff / Apr '94 / ADA.

Wilson, Sean

50 GREAT SONGS (King & Queen Of Irish Country) (Wilson, Sean & Susan McCann)
CD _____ PLATCD 3927
Prism / May '94 / Prism.

50 SUPER SONGS
CD _____ SWCD 1010
TC Records / Apr '92 / Pinnacle / Prism.

ANOTHER 50 FAVOURITE SONGS
CD _____ SWCD 1003
TC Records / Aug '92 / Pinnacle / Prism.

COUNTRY AND IRISH
CD _____ SWCD 1002
TC Records / Jun '92 / Pinnacle / Prism.

FOREVER AND EVER
CD _____ SWCD 1004
TC Records / Jun '92 / Pinnacle / Prism.

GREAT PARTY SINGALONG-50 SONGS
CD _____ SWCD 1001
TC Records / Nov '92 / Pinnacle / Prism.

HAPPY CHRISTMAS SINGALONG
Jingle bells / Santa and the kids / Mary's
boy child / White Christmas / Rudolph the
red nosed reindeer / Blue Christmas / Away
in a manger / Christmas in Innisfree / Silver
bells / Santa claus is coming to town /
Christmas time in Ireland / Santa looks a lot
like Daddy / Winter wonderland / Silent
night / Auld lang syne
CD _____ SWCD 1013
Prism / Oct '93 / Prism.

SINGALONG WITH SEAN WILSON
CD _____ SWCD 1009
TC Records / Jul '92 / Pinnacle / Prism.

TURN BACK THE YEARS
CD _____ PLATCD 911
Prism / Apr '93 / Prism.

WORKING MAN
CD _____ SWCD 1007
TC Records / Jun '92 / Pinnacle / Prism.

Wilson, Smokey

88TH STREET BLUES
CD _____ BPCD 5026
Blind Pig / Dec '95 / Hot Shot / Swift /
CM / Roots / Direct / ADA.

REAL DEAL, THE
CD _____ CDBB 9559
Rounder / Aug '95 / CM / Direct / ADA / Cadillac.

SMOKE 'N' FIREFIRE
CD _____ BB 9534CD
Bullseye Blues / Jan '94 / Direct.

SMOKEY WILSON WITH THE WILLIAM CLARKE BAND
CD _____ BMCD 9013
Black Magic / Nov '93 / Hot Shot / Swift / CM / Direct / Cadillac / ADA.

Wilson, Spanky

SINGIN' AND SWINGIN'
CD _____ BBRC 9104
Big Blue / Nov '92 / Harmonia Mundi.

Wilson, Steve

BLUES FOR MARCUS (Wilson, Steve Quintet)
CD _____ CRISS 1073CD
Criss Cross / Nov '93 / Cadillac / Harmonia Mundi.

NEW YORK SUMMIT (Wilson, Steve Quintet)
CD _____ CRISS 1062CD
Criss Cross / Oct '92 / Cadillac / Harmonia Mundi.

STEP LIVELY
CD _____ CRISS 1096
Criss Cross / Apr '95 / Cadillac / Harmonia Mundi.

Wilson, Teddy

AIR MAIL SPECIAL
CD _____ BLCD 760115
Black Lion / Oct '90 / Jazz Music / Cadillac / Wellard / Koch.

ALONE
Tea for two / Body and soul / After you've gone / I can't get started (with you) / Moonglow / Sweet Georgia Brown / Shiny stockings / Li'l darlin' / One o'clock jump / Medley / But not for me / Sophisticated Lady / Medley #3 / Medley #2
CD _____ STCD 8211
Storyville / Mar '95 / Jazz Music / Wellard / CM / Cadillac.

AND THEN THEY WROTE...
CD _____ 4765242
Sony Jazz / May '94 / Sony.

B FLAT SWING 1944 (Wilson, Teddy Sextet)
CD _____ 3801282
Jazz Archives / Oct '92 / Jazz Music / Discovery / Cadillac.

BLUES FOR THOMAS WALLER
Honeysuckle rose / My fate is in your hands / Ain't cha glad / I've got a feeling I'm falling in love / Stealin' apples / Blues for Thomas Waller / Handful of keys / Striding after Fats / Squeeze me / Zonky / Blue turning grey over you / Ain't misbehavin' / Black and blue
CD _____ BLCD 760131
Black Lion / Apr '90 / Jazz Music / Cadillac / Wellard / Koch.

COLE PORTER CLASSICS
Get out of town / Just one of those things / I get a kick out of you / It's all right with me / Why shouldn't I / Love for sale
CD _____ BLC 760164
Black Lion / '92 / Jazz Music / Cadillac / Wellard / Koch.

COMPLETE ALL STAR AND V-DISCS SESSIONS
CD _____ VJC 1013-2
Victorious Discs / Feb '91 / Jazz Music.

EARLY YEARS, THE (Wilson, Teddy & His Piano Band)
CD _____ CDSGP 0159
Prestige / Sep '95 / Total/BMG.

FINE AND DANDY (Wilson, Teddy Orchestra & Billie Holiday)
Sentimental and melancholy / This is my last affair / Carelessly / Moanin' low / Fine and dandy / There's a lull in my life / It's swell of you / How am I to know / I'm comin' Virginia / Sun flowers / Yours and mine / I'll get by / Mean to me / Foolin' myself / Easy living / I'll never be the same / I've found a new baby / You're my desire / Remember me / Hour of parting / Coquette
CD _____ HEPCD 1029
Hep / Oct '91 / Cadillac / Jazz Music / New Note / Wellard.

GENTLEMEN OF THE KEYBOARD
Somebody loves me / Sailin' / I've found a new baby / Just a mood / I got rhythm / Wham / Liza / 71 / China boy / (Back home again in) Indiana / I want to be happy / Rose room / Just like a butterfly / Fine and dandy / Under a blanket of blue / Airmail special
CD _____ GOJCD 53059
Giants Of Jazz / Mar '92 / Target/BMG / Cadillac.

GOLDEN DAYS, THE
My melancholy baby / Rosetta / Mean to me / Now it can be told / China boy / Tisket-

---

a-tasket / Them there eyes / If I were you / Jungle love / On treasure Island / Sugar plum / I know that you know / You let me down / Mary had a little lamb / If you were mine / All my life / Sailin' / Breakin' in a pair of shoes / Hour of parting / Coquette / My last affair / You brought a new kind of love
CD _____ PASTCD 7025
Flapper / Oct '93 / Pinnacle.

JUMPIN' FOR JOY (Wilson, Teddy Orchestra & Billie Holiday)
Somebody loves me / Blues in C sharp minor / Why do I lie to myself about you / Way you look tonight / Sailin' / Why was I born / I've found a new baby / You can't stop me from dreaming / Just a mood / Don't blame me / More than you know / Jumpin' for joy / Jumpin' on the blacks and whites / Wham (re-bop-boom-bam) / 711 / China boy / Fine and dandy
CD _____ CDCD 1122
Charly / Jul '93 / Charly / THE / Cadillac.

MEETS E.KITAMURA
CD _____ STCD 4152
Storyville / Feb '90 / Jazz Music / Wellard / CM / Cadillac.

MOMENTS LIKE THIS
Alone with you / Moments like this / I can't face the music / Don't be that way / If I were you / You go to my head / I'll dream tonight / Jungle love / Now it can be told / Laugh and call it love / Tisket-a-tasket / Everybody's laughing / Here is tomorrow again / Say it with a kiss / April in my heart / I'll never fail you / They say / You're so desirable / You're gonna see a lot of me / Hello my darling / Let's dream in the moonlight / What shall I say / It's easy to blame the weather / Sugar / More than you know
CD _____ HEPCD 1043
Hep / May '95 / Cadillac / Jazz Music / New Note / Wellard.

OF THEE I SWING (Wilson, Teddy & Billie Holiday)
You turned the tables on me / Sing baby sing / Easy to love / With thee I swing / Way you look tonight / Who loves you / Pennies from Heaven / That's life / Sailin' / I can't give you anything but love / Warmin' up (with right or wrong) / Where the lazy river goes by / Tea for two / I'll see you in my dreams / He ain't got rhythm / This year's kisses
CD _____ HEPCD 1020
Hep / Jun '90 / Cadillac / Jazz Music / New Note / Wellard.

PIANO SOLOS
Somebody loves me / Sweet and simple / Liza / Rosetta / Every now and then / It never dawned on me / I found a dream / On a treasure island / I feel like a feather in the breeze / Breakin' in a pair of shoes / Don't blame me / Between the devil and the deep blue sea / Sweat and simple
CD _____ CDAFS 1016
Affinity / Sep '91 / Charly / Cadillac / Jazz Music.

REVISITS THE GOODMAN YEARS (1980 - Copenhagen) (Wilson, Teddy Trio)
CD _____ STCD 4046
Storyville / Feb '89 / Jazz Music / Wellard / CM / Cadillac.

RUNNIN' WILD
One o'clock jump / Mood indigo / Take the 'A' train / Satin doll / Smoke gets in your eyes / Running wild / St James infirmary blues / After you've gone
CD _____ BLCD 760184
Black Lion / Apr '93 / Jazz Music / Cadillac / Wellard / Koch.

STOMPING AT THE SAVOY
I can't get started (with you) / Sometimes I'm happy / Body and soul / I'll never be the same / Easy living
CD _____ BLCD 760152
Black Lion / Apr '91 / Jazz Music / Cadillac / Wellard / Koch.

TEDDY WILSON & HIS ORCHESTRA VOL. 5 (Wilson, Teddy & His Orchestra)
CD _____ HEPCD 1035
Hep / May '94 / Cadillac / Jazz Music / New Note / Wellard.

TEDDY WILSON (2)
CD _____ CDC 9003
LRC / Oct '90 / New Note / Harmonia Mundi.

TEDDY WILSON 1937-1938
CD _____ CLASSICS 548
Classics / Dec '90 / Discovery / Jazz Music.

TEDDY WILSON 1939-41 (Wilson, Teddy & His Orchestra)
CD _____ CLASSICS 620
Classics / '92 / Discovery / Jazz Music.

TEDDY WILSON WITH BILLIE HOLIDAY (Wilson, Teddy & Billie Holiday)
Nice work if you can get it / Where the lazy river goes by / If you were mine / My last love affair / Why do I lie to myself about you / Mood that I'm in / I'm coming Virginia / Easy living / How am I to know / Hour of parting / Coquette / You let me down / I've found a new baby / All my life / Mary had a little lamb / Miss Brown to you / What a little moonlight can do / I wished on the moon

---

CD _____ CD AJA 5053
Living Era / Jun '88 / Koch.

THREE LITTLE WORDS
CD _____ BLE 233094
Black & Blue / Apr '91 / Wellard / Koch.

TOO HOT FOR WORDS (Wilson, Teddy Orchestra & Billie Holiday)
I wished on the moon / What a little moonlight can do / Miss Brown to you / Sun bonnet blue / It never dawned on me / Spreadin' rhythm round the world / You let me down / Sugar plum / Rosetta / Liza / Sweet Lorraine
CD _____ HEPCD 1012
Hep / Mar '90 / Cadillac / Jazz Music / New Note / Wellard.

WARMIN' UP
Life begins when you're in love / Rhythm in my nursery rhymes / Christopher Columbus / My melancholy baby / All my life / I found a dream / On treasure island / Mary had a little lamb / Too good to be true / Warmin up / Blues in C sharp minor / It's like reaching for the moon / These foolish things / Why do I lie to myself about you / I cried for you / Guess who / I feel like a feather in the breeze / Breakin' in a pair of shoes / You came to my rescue / Here's love in your eyes
CD _____ HEPCD 1014
Hep / Oct '92 / Cadillac / Jazz Music / New Note / Wellard.

Wilson, Tom

TOM WILSON'S BOUNCIN' BEATS
CD _____ BNCCD 1
Rumour / Oct '94 / Pinnacle / 3MV / Sony.

Wilson, Tony

BEST OF TONY WILSON, THE
Give your lady what she wants / Lay next to you / Africa / New Orleans music / Love I thought I would never find love / I like your style / New York City life / Politician (A man of many words) / What does it take / Gotta make love to you / Loving you ain't the same / Better off just loving you / Legal paper / Just when I need you most / Try love / Forever young / Anything that keeps you satisfied / I can't leave it alone
CD _____ SEECD 323
See For Miles/C5 / May '93 / Pinnacle.

DO YOUR OWN THING
Do your own thing / Can't waste a good thing / Gotta get a good thing goin' / Good lovin' never hurt / Let me love you / We got love / Sweet kinda lovin' / I feel fine / Do it / Goodbye baby goodbye / What did I do / You're too somebody / Baby you touch my soul / Karen won't you smile / You're everything I need / Time / Now that I'm loving you / Do your own talk / Kis on the radio
CD _____ 901183
Line / Aug '95 / CM / Grapevine / ADA / Conifer / Direct.

I LIKE YOUR STYLE
CD _____ REP 4076-WZ
Repertoire / Aug '91 / Pinnacle / Cadillac.

WALKING THE HIGHWIRE
CD _____ LICD 901222
Line / Nov '92 / CM / Grapevine / ADA / Conifer / Direct.

Wilson, U.P.

BOOGIE BOY
CD _____ JSPCD 255
JSP / Jan '95 / ADA / Target/BMG / Direct / Cadillac / Complete/Pinnacle.

THIS IS U.P. WILSON
Hold on baby / Boots and shades / Bad luck and trouble / You're one woman / Changes / Go home with me / Hold me / Peaches / Used to be mine / Fool for you
CD _____ JSPCD 266
JSP / Jan '96 / ADA / Target/BMG / Direct / Cadillac / Complete/Pinnacle.

Wimme

WIMME
CD _____ ZENCD 2043
Rockadillo / May '95 / Direct / ADA.

Winans

ALL OUT
Payday / It's not heaven if you're not there / If he doesn't come tonight / That extra mile / Tradewinds / All you ever been was good / Money motive / Love will never die / Heaven belongs to you / He said go
CD _____ 9362452132
Qwest / Aug '93 / Warner Music.

Winans, Bebe & Cece

RELATIONSHIPS
Count it all joy / Love of my life / Don't let me walk down this road alone / Both day and night / Stay with me / He's always there / Right away / If anything ever happened to you / These what about's / (If I was only) Welcomed in / We can make a difference
CD _____ CDEST 2237
Capitol / Sep '94 / EMI.

Winans, Vickie

VICKIE WINANS
We work it out / We shall overcome / Precious Lord (tribute to Martin Luther King) / Stand up and praise him / We shall behold Him / Only one / Suddenly / I remember when / You never left me / Believing is seeing / Mary, did you know
CD _____ CDK 9127
Alliance Music / Sep '95 / EMI.

Winbush, Angela

ANGELA WINBUSH
Treat U rite / Keep turnin' me on / Too good to let you go / Baby hold on / You're my everything / Dream lover / Inner city blues / I'm the kind of woman / Sensitive heart / Hot summer love
CD _____ 755961591-2
Elektra / Apr '94 / Warner Music.

Winchester Cathedral...

CAROLS FOR CHRISTMAS (Winchester Cathedral Choir)
O come all ye faithful (Adeste Fidelis) / Unto us a boy is born / Rocking / God rest ye merry gentlemen / Away in a manger / First Noel / Once in Royal David's city / Silent night / In dulci jubilo / While shepherds watched their flocks by night / Coventry carol / O little town of Bethlehem / In the bleak midwinter / Hark the herald angels sing
CD _____ 261 279
Arista / Oct '94 / BMG.

Winchester, Jesse

BEST OF JESSE WINCHESTER
Payday / Biloxi / Snow / Brand new Tennessee waltz / Yankee lady / Midnight bus / Do it / All your own stories / Mississippi, you're on my mind / Third rate romance / End is not in sight / Defying gravity / Let the rough side drag / Blow on, chilly wind / Nothing but a breeze / Seems like only yesterday / Touch on the rainy side / I'm looking for a miracle / Say what / Talk Memphis
CD _____ SEECD 231
See For Miles/C5 / Feb '91 / Pinnacle.

JESSE WINCHESTER
CD _____ SPCD 1198
Stony Plain / Dec '94 / ADA / CM / Direct.

LEARN TO LOVE IT
CD _____ SPCD 1205
Stony Plain / May '95 / ADA / CM / Direct.

LET THE ROUGH SIDE DRAG
CD _____ SPCD 1206
Stony Plain / May '95 / ADA / CM / Direct.

THIRD DOWN 10 TO GO
CD _____ SPCD 1199
Stony Plain / Dec '94 / ADA / CM / Direct.

Wind In The Willows

WIND IN THE WILLOWS
Moments spent / Uptown girl / So sad (to watch good love go bad) / My uncle used to love me but she died / There is but one truth / Daddy / Friendly lion / Park Avenue blues / Djini Judy / Little people / She's fantastic and she's yours / Wheel of changes
CD _____ DOCD 1985
Drop Out / Aug '93 / Pinnacle.

Wind Machine

PORTRAITS OF CHRISTMAS
CD _____ SD 606
Silver Wave / Jan '93 / New Note / Jazzizit Organisation.

RAIN MAIDEN
CD _____ SD 508
Silver Wave / Jan '93 / New Note / Jazzizit Organisation.

ROAD TO FREEDOM
CD _____ SD 602
Silver Wave / Jan '93 / New Note / Jazzizit Organisation.

UNPLUGGED
CD _____ SD 152
Silver Wave / Jan '93 / New Note / Jazzizit Organisation.

VOICES IN THE WIND
CD _____ SD 701
Silver Wave / Jan '93 / New Note / Jazzizit Organisation.

WIND MACHINE
CD _____ SD 151
Silver Wave / Jan '93 / New Note / Jazzizit Organisation.

Winding, Kai

BOB CITY (Small Groups 1949-1951)
CD _____ C&BCD 110
Cool 'n' Blue / Oct '93 / Jazz Music / Discovery.

CLEVELAND 1957 (Winding, Kai Septet)
CD _____ DSTS 1012
Status / '94 / Jazz Music / Wellard / Harmonia Mundi.

FEATURING BILL EVANS
CD _____ CD 53150
Giants Of Jazz / May '95 / Target/BMG / Cadillac.

JAI AND KAI + 6 (Winding, Kai & Jay Jay Johnson)
Night in Tunisia / Piece for two trombon-iums / Rise 'n' shine / All at once you love her / No moon at all / Surrey with the fringe on top / Peanut vendor / You're my thrill / Jeanne / Four plus four / You don't know what love is / Continental (you kiss while you're dancing)
CD _____ 4809902
Sony Jazz / Dec '95 / Sony.

Windows

BLUE SEPTMBER
CD _____ 101 SS 7088 2
101 South / Nov '92 / New Note.

Windracht Acht

OP DE WILDE VAART
CD _____ PAN 148CD
Pan / Aug '94 / ADA / Direct / CM.

Winfield, Roger

WINDSONGS - THE SOUND OF THE AEOLIAN HARP
CD _____ CDSDL 394
Saydisc / Mar '94 / Harmonia Mundi / ADA / Direct.

Winger

PULL
Blind revolution mad / Down incognito / Spell I'm under / In my veins / Junkyard dog (tears on stone) / Lucky one / In for the kill / No man's land / Like a ritual / Who's the one
CD _____ 756782485-2
Atlantic / May '93 / Warner Music.

Wings

BACK TO THE EGG
Reception / Getting closer / We're open to-night / Spin it on / Again and again and again / Old Siam sir / Arrow through me / Rockestra theme / To you / After the ball / Million miles / Winter rose / Love awake / Broadcast / So glad to see you here / Ba-by's request / Daytime nightime suffering (CD only) / Wonderful Christmas time (CD only) / Rudolph the red nosed reggae (CD only)
CD _____ CDPMCOL 10
EMI / Jun '93 / EMI.

BAND ON THE RUN
Band on the run / Jet / Bluebird / Mrs. Van-derbilt / Let me roll it / Marmunia / No words / Picasso's last words / 1985
CD _____ CDPMCOL 5
Parlophone / Apr '93 / EMI.

LONDON TOWN
London town / Gate on the left bank / I'm carrying / Backwards traveller / Cuff link / Chicken children / I've had enough / With a little luck / Famous groupies / Deliver your children / Name and address / Don't let it bring you down / Morse moose and the grey goose / Girlfriend / Girls school
CD _____ CDPMCOL 8
Parlophone / Apr '93 / EMI.

VENUS AND MARS
Venus and Mars / Rock show / Love in song / You gave me the answer / Magneto and Titanium man / Letting go / Venus and Mars reprise / Spirits of ancient egypt / Medicine jar / Call me back again / Listen to what the man said / Treat her gently - lonely old peo-ple / Crossroads
CD _____ CDPMCOL 6
Parlophone / Apr '93 / EMI.

WILD LIFE
Mumbo / Bip bop / Love is strange / Wild life / Some people never know / I am your singer / Bip bop link (CD only) / Tomorrow / Dear friend / Mumbo link (CD only) / Oh woman, oh why (CD only) / Mary had a little lamb (CD only) / Little woman love (CD only)
CD _____ CDPMCOL 3
Parlophone / Apr '93 / EMI.

WINGS AT THE SPEED OF SOUND
Let 'em in / Note you never wrote / She's my baby / Beware my love / Wino junko / Silly love songs / Cook of the house / Time to hide / Must do something about it / San Ferry Anne / Warm and beautiful
CD _____ CDPMCOL 7
Parlophone / Apr '93 / EMI.

WINGS GREATEST
Another day / Silly love songs / Live and let die / Junior's farm / With a little luck / Band on the run / Uncle Albert / Admiral Halsey / Hi hi hi / Let 'em in / My love / Jet / Mull of Kintyre
CD _____ CDPMCOL 9
EMI / Jun '93 / EMI.

Winkler, Harold

BORN WITH A KISS (Winkler, Harold & Norman Candler Orchestra)

CD _____ ISCD 156
Intersound / Jun '95 / Jazz Music.

Winkler, Mark

HOTTEST NIGHT OF THE YEAR
Dancin' in the sunshine / Stain doll / Hottest night of the year / Tropical breezes / Beauty and the beast / Forward motion / Moon made me do it / Takin' chances / In a minor key
CD _____ CDLR 45015
L&R / Apr '90 / New Note.

Winski, Colin

HELLDORADO
CD _____ FCD 3027
Fury / Sep '93 / Magnum Music Group / Nervous.

Winsome

STORY OF A BLACK WOMAN
CD _____ SGCD 019
Sir George / Oct '94 / Jetstar / Pinnacle.

Winston, George

AUTUMN
Colors/dance / Woods / Longing/love / Road / Moon / Sea / Stars
CD _____ WD 1012
Windham Hill / May '91 / Pinnacle / BMG / ADA.

BALLADS AND BLUES
CD _____ 08022340022
RCA / Jun '94 / BMG.

DECEMBER
Thanksgiving / Jesus Jesus rest your head / Joy / Prelude / Carol of the bells / Night / Midnight (part 2) / Minstrels (part 3) / Vari-ations on the kanon / Holly and the ivy / Some children see him / Peace / Snow
CD _____ WD 1025
Windham Hill / May '91 / Pinnacle / BMG / ADA.

FOREST
CD _____ 01934111572
Windham Hill / Oct '94 / Pinnacle / BMG / ADA.

SUMMER
CD _____ 111072
Windham Hill / May '91 / Pinnacle / BMG / ADA.

WINTER INTO SPRING
January stars / February sea / Ocean waves (o mar) / Reflection / Raindance / Blossom meadow / Venice dreamer / Introduction (part 1) / Part 2
CD _____ WD 1019
Windham Hill / May '91 / Pinnacle / BMG / ADA.

Winstone, Eric

REMINISCING WITH ERIKA & LISA (Winstone, Eric & His Band)
Stage coach / Swing bugler / Isn't that just like love / Out every Friday / Night flight / Whispering grass / Atmosphere / Bitin' the dust / Dolores / How did he look / Safari / Boa note / Shepherd serenade / Evening / Cornsilk / Oasis / I know why / Mirage / There's a land of begin again / My devotion / Promenade
CD _____ PLCD 536
President / May '93 / Grapevine / Target/ BMG / Jazz Music / President.

TEACH ME TO DANCE (Winstone, Eric & His Band)
Happy feet / You've got your troubles / Somewhere my love / From a window / Bye bye blues / I'll just close my eyes / Bonnie and Clyde / Pepito's tune / Green eyes / Cuban nights / Darling / Last waltz / Co-pacabana / Tico tico / Games that lovers play / Teach me to dance / International waltz / Rebecca / Thourghly modern Millie / Goodbye blues / (We're gonna) Rock around the clock / Can't buy me love / Con-gratulations / Girl about town
CD _____ DNSN 903
President / Apr '94 / Grapevine / Target/ BMG / Jazz Music / President.

Winstone, Norma

WELL KEPT SECRET (Winstone, Norma & Jimmy Rowles)
Where or when / Timeless place / I dream too much / It amazes me / Prelude to a kiss / Joy spring / Remind me / Flower is a lov-esome thing / Dream of you / Morning star
CD _____ HHCD 1015
Hot House / May '95 / Cadillac / Wellard / Harmonia Mundi.

Winter

ETERNAL FROST
CD _____ NB 107
Nuclear Blast / Sep '94 / Plastic Head.

INTO DARKNESS
CD _____ NB 064CD
Nuclear Blast / Nov '92 / Plastic Head.

Winter, Cathy

NEXT SWEET TIME
CD _____ FF 598CD
Flying Fish / Feb '93 / Roots / CM / Direct / ADA.

Winter, Edgar

BEST OF EDGAR WINTER, THE
CD _____ 4675072
CBS / Apr '91 / Sony.

COLLECTION
CD _____ 8122708952
Rhino / Jun '95 / Warner Music.

HARLEM NOCTURNE
Searching / Tingo tango / Cry me a river / Save your love for me / Quiet gas / Satin doll / Jordu / Girl from Ipanema / Harlem nocturne / Come back baby / Before the sunset / Who dunnit / Please come home for Christmas
CD _____ CDTB 089
Thunderbolt / Dec '90 / Magnum Music Group.

I'M NOT A KID ANYMORE
Way down south / I'm not a kid anymore / Against the law / Brothers keeper / I wanta rock / Crazy / Just like you / Big city woman / Innocent lust / Frankenstein
CD _____ CDTB 152
Thunderbolt / Jan '94 / Magnum Music Group.

MISSION EARTH
CD _____ 8122707092
WEA / Jul '93 / Warner Music.

Winter, Johnny

1ST LP
I'm yours and I'm hers / Be careful with a fool / Dallas / Mean mistreater / Leland Mis-sissipi / When you got a good friend / I'll drown my tears / Back door friend
CD _____ ED CD 163
Edsel / Nov '85 / Pinnacle / ADA.

AND
CD _____ BGOCD 105
Beat Goes On / Sep '91 / Pinnacle.

BACK IN BEAUMONT (Winter, Johnny & Uncle John Turner)
Made in the shade / They call my lazy / Family rules / Ooh pooh pah do / Drivin' wheel / Allons dancez / Struggle in Houston / You're humbuggin' me / Just a little bit / Rainin' breakdown
CD _____ CDTB 077
Thunderbolt / Apr '90 / Magnum Music Group.

BLUE SUEDE SHOES
Don't drink whiskey / Hook you / Blue suede shoes / Ronettes / Voodoo twist / How do you live a lie / Lost without you / Jolie blon / Bring it on home / Hello my lover / Rockin' pneumonia and the boogie woo-gie flu / Ice cube / Gangster of love / Parch-man farm / Bad news / Roadrunner
CD _____ CDTB 078
Thunderbolt / Feb '92 / Magnum Music Group.

BROTHERS IN ROCK 'N' ROLL (Winter, Johnny & Edgar)
Frankenstein / Johnny B. Goode / Let it bleed / Tobacco Road / I can't turn you loose / Jumpin' Jack Flash / Back in the U.S.A / Good morning little school girl / Like a rolling stone / Tony Marania / Highway 61 revisited / It's all over now
CD _____ ELITE 012CD
Elite/Old Gold / Aug '93 / Carlton Home Entertainment.

EARLY WINTER
Ease my pain / That's what love does / Cry-ing in my heart / Guy you left behind / Shed so many tears / Creepy / Gangster of love / Roadrunner / Leave my woman alone / I can't believe you want to leave / Broke and lonely / Oh my darling / By the light of the silvery moon / Five after four A.M.
CD _____ PRCD 116
Sound / Jan '87 / Direct / ADA.

FIVE AFTER FOUR AM
Oh my darling / Five after four A.M. / That's what love does / Shed so many tears / Roadrunner / Guy you left behind / Gang-ster of love / By the light of the silvery moon / Leave my woman alone / I can't believe you want to leave
CD _____ CDTB 073
Thunderbolt / Nov '89 / Magnum Music Group.

GUITAR SLINGER
It's my life baby / Iodine in my coffee / Trick bag / Mad dog / Boot Hill / I smell trouble / Lights out / Kiss tomorrow goodbye / My soul / Don't take advantage of me
CD _____ ALCD 4735
Alligator / May '93 / Direct / ADA.

HEY, WHERE'S YOUR BROTHER
Johnny Guitar / She likes to boogie real low / White line blues / Please Come Home For Christmas / Hard Way / You keep sayin' that you're leavin' / Treat Me Like You Wanta / Sick and tired / Blues This Bad / No More Doggin' / Check

out her mama / Got my brand on you / One step forward
CD _____ VPBCD 11
Pointblank / Sep '92 / EMI.

JACK DANIELS KIND OF DAY
Sloppy drunk / Mistress / Careful with a fool / Shed so many tears / Eternally / Raining teardrops / Jack Daniels kind of a day / Go-ing down slow / Stay by my side / We go back quite a ways / Low down gal of mine / Thirty two twenty blues / Silvery moon / I had to cry / Gonna miss me when I'm gone / Crazy baby
CD _____ CDTB 142
Magnum Music / Dec '92 / Magnum Music Group.

JOHNNY WINTER AND LIVE
Good morning little school girl / It's my own fault / Jumpin' Jack Flash / Great balls of fire / Long tall Sally / Whole lotta shakin' goin' on / Mean town blues / Johnny B. Goode
CD _____ BGOCD 29
Beat Goes On / Jun '92 / Pinnacle.

LET ME IN
CD _____ VPBCD 5
Pointblank / Sep '91 / EMI.

LIVE IN HOUSTON, BUSTED IN AUSTIN
E.Z. rider / Walking by myself / Mother earth / Boney Maronie / Busted in Austin / Mes-sin' with the kid / I can't make it by myself / Johnny B. Goode / It's all over now / Jum-pin' Jack flash
CD _____ CDTB 083
Thunderbolt / '91 / Magnum Music Group.

LIVING IN THE BLUES
Goin' down slow / Kind hearted woman blues / 38-20-30 blues / Low down gal of mine / Avocado green / My world turns around her / Coming up fast / Living in the blues / Bad news / I had to cry / Kiss to-morrow goodbye / parchman farm / Tramp / Harlem nocturne
CD _____ CDTB 083
Thunderbolt / '91 / Magnum Music Group.

NO TIME TO LIVE
Ain't that kindness / Stranger / Am I here / Self destructive blues / Golden days of rock and roll / Rock 'n' roll hoochie coo / Guess I'll go away / Rock 'n' roll people / Lay down your sorrows / Raised on rock / Let the mu-sic play / Prodigal son / Mind over matter / Pick up on my mojo / No time to live / On the limb
CD _____ CDTB 136
Thunderbolt / Mar '92 / Magnum Music Group.

NOTHING BUT THE BLUES
Tired of tryin' / TV Mama / Sweet love and evil women / Everybody's blues / Drinkin' blues / Mad blues / It was rainin' / Bladie Mae / Walking through the park
CD _____ BGOCD 104
Beat Goes On / Aug '91 / Pinnacle.

PROGRESSIVE BLUES EXPERIMENT
Rollin' and tumblin' / Tribute to Muddy / Got love if you want it / Bad luck and trouble / Help me / Mean town blues / Broke down engine / Black cat bone / It's my own fault / Forty four
CD _____ CDLL 57350
One Way / Jul '94 / Direct / ADA.

RAW TO THE BONE (Winter, Johnny & Calvin Johnson)
Late on blues / They call me loudmouth / Take my choice / Unwelcome in your home / Going down slow / Alone in my bedroom / hoochie coochie man / Moth balls / She's mine / Unsatisfied mind / Rock me baby
CD _____ CDTB 126
Magnum Music / Feb '92 / Magnum Music Group.

SEARCHIN' BLUES
Walking by myself / Diving duck / One step at a time / Bladie Mae / Mad blues / It was rainin' / Man mistreater / Mother-in-law blues / Dallas / Mean town blues
CD _____ 4716612
Columbia / Jul '92 / Sony.

SECOND WINTER
Memory pain / Good love / Miss Ann / High-way 61 revisited / Hustled down in Texas / Fast life rider / I'm not sure / Slippin' and slidin' / Johnny B. Goode / I love everybody
CD _____ EDCD 312
Edsel / Apr '89 / Pinnacle / ADA.

SERIOUS BUSINESS
Master mechanic / Sound the bell / Mur-dering the blues / It ain't your business / Good time woman / Unseen eye / My time after awhile / Serious as a heart attack / Give it back / Route 90
CD _____ ALCD 4742
Alligator / Oct '93 / Direct / ADA.

TEXAS TORNADO, THE
Roadrunner / Gangster of love / Leave my woman alone / I can't believe you want to leave / That's what love does / Five after four A.M. / Out of sight / Parchman farm / Low down gal of mine / Goin' down slow / Leavin' blues / Kind hearted woman blues
CD _____ CDCD 1033
Charly / Mar '93 / Charly / THE / Cadillac.

THIRD DEGREE
Mojo boogie / Love life and money / Evil on my mind / See see baby / Tin Pan Alley / I'm good / Third degree / Shake your moneymaker / Bad girl blues / Broke and lonely
CD _____ ALCD 4748
Alligator / May '93 / Direct / ADA.

WHITE LIGHTNING
Mean town blues / Black cat bone / Mean mistreater / Talk to your daughter / Look up / I can love you baby
CD _____ CDTB 149
Magnum Music / Oct '93 / Magnum Music Group.

Winter, Paul

CALLINGS
Lullaby from the great mother whale / Magdelena / Love swim / Blues' cathedral / Sea Wolf / Sea joy / Dance of the silkies / Seal eyes
CD _____ LD 0001
Living Music / Jul '95 / New Note.

EARTHBEAT
CD _____ LD 0015
Living Music / Aug '88 / New Note.

PRAYER FOR THE WILD THINGS
Eagle mountain / Round dance / On the river / Buffalo prairie / Osprey / Grizzly bear cubs / Tritones in the canyon / Moose walk / Gates of the mountain / Cougar bassoon / Antelope dreams / Afternoon's end / Sunset on eagle mountain / White goat of the rockies / Loon on mud pond / Night voices / Elk horns / North fork wolves / Night into dawn / Dance of all beings
CD _____ LD 0028
Living Music / Nov '94 / New Note.

SUN SINGER
Sun singer theme / Hymn to the sun / Dolphin morning / Reflections in a summer pond / Dancing particles / Winter's dream / Heaven within / Big Ben's bolero / Sun singer
CD _____ LD 0003
Living Music / Jul '95 / New Note.

WHALES ALIVE (Narration By Leonard Nimoy) (Winter, Paul & Paul Halley)
Whales weep not / Dawnwatch / George and Gracie / Turning / Concerto for whale and organ / Humphrey's blues / Queenqueg and I the water is wide / Ocean dream / Voyage home
CD _____ LD 0013
Living Music / Feb '94 / New Note.

Winters, Ruby

RUBY WINTERS
CD _____ RNCD 1008
Rhino / Jan '93 / Jetstar / Magnum Music Group / THE.

Winther, Jens

LOOKING THROUGH (Winther, Jens Quintet)
CD _____ STCD 4127
Storyville / Feb '90 / Jazz Music / Wellard / CM / Cadillac.

Winwood, Steve

ARC OF A DIVER
While you see a chance / Second hand woman / Slowdown sundown / Spanish dancer / Night train / Dust / Arc of a diver
CD _____ CID 9576
Island / Jan '87 / PolyGram.

BACK IN THE HIGH LIFE
Higher love / Take it as it comes / Freedom overspill / Back in the high life / Finer things / Wake me up on judgement day / Split decision / My love's leavin'
CD _____ CID 9844
Island / Jul '86 / PolyGram.

CHRONICLES
Wake me up on judgement day / While you see a chance / Vacant chair / Help me angel / My love's leavin' / Valerie / Arc of a diver / Higher love / Spanish dancer / Talking back to the night
CD _____ SSWCD 1
Island / Nov '87 / PolyGram.

FINER THINGS, THE (4 CDs)
Dimples / I Can't stand it / Every little bit hurts / Strong love / Keep on running / Somebody help me / When I come home / I want to know / Crossroads / Gimme some lovin' / I'm a man / Paper sun / Dealer / Coloured rain / No face, no name, no number / Heaven is in your mind / Smiling phases / Dear Mr. Fantasy / Pearly Queen / Forty thousand headmen / No time to live / Shanghai noodle factory / Medicated goo / Withering tree / Had to cry today / Can't find my way home / Sea of joy / Sleeping in the ground / Under my thumb (Live) / Stranger to himself / John Barleycorn / Glad / Freedom rider / Empty pages / Low spark of high heeled boys / Rainmaker / Shoot out at the fantasy factory / (Sometimes I feel so) Uninspired / Happy vibes / Something new / Dream Gerrard / Walking in the wind / When the eagle flies / Winner/Loser / Crossing the line (Live) / Hold on / Time is running out / Vacant chair / While you see

a chance / Arc of a diver / Spanish dancer / Night train / Dust / Valerie / Talking back to the night / Your silence is your song / Higher love / Freedom overspill / Back in the high life / Finer things / Roll with it / Don't you know what the night can do / One and only man
CD Set _____ IBXCD 2
Island / Mar '95 / PolyGram.

KEEP ON RUNNING
CD _____ IMCD 224
Island / Mar '96 / PolyGram.

REFUGEES OF THE HEART
You'll keep on searching / Every day (oh Lord) / One and only man / I will be here / Another deal goes down / Running on / Come out and dance / In the light of day
CD _____ CDV 2650
Virgin / Nov '90 / EMI.

ROLL WITH IT
Roll with it / Holding on / Morning side / Put on your dancing shoes / Don't you know what the night can do / Hearts on fire / One more morning / Shining song
CD _____ CDV 2532
Virgin / Jun '88 / EMI.

STEVE WINWOOD
Hold on / Time is running out / Let me make something in your life / Luck's in / Vacant chair / Midland maniac
CD _____ IMCD 161
Island / Mar '93 / PolyGram.

TALKING BACK TO THE NIGHT
Valerie / Big girls walk away / I go / While there's a candle burning / Still in the game / It was happening / Help me angel / Talking back to the night / There's a river
CD _____ CID 9777
Island / Feb '87 / PolyGram.

Wipers

IS THIS REAL
CD _____ SPOD 82/253
Sub Pop / Mar '93 / Disc.

SILVER SAIL
Y I came / Back to basics / Warning / Mars / Prisoner / Standing there / Sign of the times / Line / On a roll / Never win / Silver sail
CD _____ TK 92CD031
T/K / Jun '94 / Pinnacle.

Wire

154
I should have known better / Two people in a room / 15th / Other window / Single K.O. / Touching display / On returning / Mutual friend / Blessed state / Once is enough / Map ref. 41 degrees N. 93 degrees W. / Indirect enquiries / Forty versions
CD _____ CDGO 2064
EMI / Jul '94 / EMI.

BEHIND THE CURTAIN
Mary is a dyke / Too true / Just don't care / TV / New York city / After midnight / Pink flag / Love ain't polite / Oh no not so / It's the motive / Practice makes perfect / Sand in my joints / Stablemates / I feel mysterious today / Underwater experience / Dot dash / Options R / From the nursery / Finistaire / No romans / Another the letter / Forty Versions / Blessed state / Touching display / Once is enough / Stepping off too quick / Indirect enquiries / Map ref. 41 degrees N. 93 degrees W. / Question of degree / Two people in a room / Former airline
CD _____ CDGO 2066
EMI / May '96 / EMI.

BELL IS A CUP UNTIL IT IS STRUCK, A
Silk skin paws / Finest drops / Queen's of Ur and The King of Urn / Free falling divisions / It's a Bob / Boiling boy / Kidney bongos / Come back in two halves / Follow the locust / Public place
CD _____ CDSTUMM 54
Mute / Jun '88 / Disc.

CHAIRS MISSING
Practice makes perfect / French film blurred / Another the letter / Men 2nd / Marooned / Sand in my joints / Being sucked in again / Heartbeat / Mercy / Outdoor miner / I am the fly / I feel mysterious today / From the nursery / Used to / Too late
CD _____ CDGO 2065
EMI / Jul '94 / EMI.

EXPLODED VIEWS
CD _____ SCONC 25
Audioglobe / Sep '94 / Plastic Head.

FIRST LETTER, THE
CD _____ CDSTUMM 87
Mute / Oct '91 / Disc.

IDEAL COPY, THE
Point of collapse / Ahead / Madman's honey / Feed me / Ambitious / Cheeking tongues / Still shows / Over theirs / Ahead (II) (CD only) / Serious of snakes (CD only) / Drill (CD only) / Advantage in height (CD only) / Up to the sun (CD only) / Ambulance chasers (CD only) / Feed me (II) (CD only) / Vivid riot of red (CD only)
CD _____ CDSTUMM 42
Mute / Apr '87 / Disc.

IT'S BEGINNING TO AND BACK AGAIN
Finest drops / Eardrum buzz (Original & 12" versions) / German shepherds / Public place / It's a boy / Illuminated / Boiling boy / Over theirs / Offer / In vivo
CD _____ CDSTUMM 66
Mute / Apr '89 / Disc.

MANSCAPE
CD _____ CDSTUMM 80
Mute / Apr '90 / Disc.

PEEL SESSIONS: WIRE VOL.2
Practice makes perfect / I am the fly / Culture vultures / 106 beats that / Other window / Mutual friend / On retujrning / Indirect enquiries / Crazy about love
CD _____ SFRCD 108
Strange Fruit / Jan '90 / Pinnacle.

PINK FLAG
Reuters / Field day for the Sundays / Three girl rhumba / Ex lion tamer / Lowdown / Start to move / Brazil / It's so obvious / Surgeon's girl / Pink flag / Commercial / Straight line / 106 Beats that / Mr. Suit / Strange / Fragile / Mannequin / Different to me / Champs / Feeling called love / 12XU / Dot dash / Options R
CD _____ CDGO 2063
EMI / Jul '94 / EMI.

WHORE (Various Artists Play Wire) (Various Artists)
40 Versions / Mannequin / It's a boy / Series of snakes / Question of degree / Ahead / Three girl rhumba / On returning / 12XU / Lowdown / German shephers / Mutual friend / Eastern standards / Our swimmer / Eardrum buzz / Being sucked in again / Fragile / Map ref 41N 93W / Outdoor miner / Used to / 15th
CD _____ WMO 002CD
WMO / Feb '96 / Vital.

WIRE 1985 - 1990
CD _____ CDSTUMM 116
Mute / Jun '93 / Disc.

Wiregrass Sacred Harp...

COLORED SACRED HARP (Wiregrass Sacred Harp Singers)
CD _____ 804332
New World / Feb '94 / Harmonia Mundi / ADA / Cadillac.

Wisdom

SIGNS OF THE TIME
CD _____ WBM 2002
Wisdom Wise / Sep '93 / Jetstar.

Wisdom, Norman

MUSICAL WORLD OF NORMAN WISDOM
CD _____ DSHCD 70013
D-Sharp / Mar '94 / Pinnacle.

Wiseblood

PEDAL TO THE METAL
CD _____ ABB 030CD
Big Cat / Nov '91 / SRD / Pinnacle.

Wiseman, Bob

CITY OF WOOD
CD _____ GRCD 324
Glitterhouse / Sep '94 / Direct / ADA.

Wiseman, Mac

TEENAGE HANGOUT
Teenage hangout / Step it up and go / Sundown / I hear you knocking / Meanest blues in the world / Hey Mr. Bluesman / One mint julep / I'm waiting for the ships that never come in / Fool / I like this kind of music / Now that you have me / Talk of the town / Glad rags / I'm eatin' high on a hog / I sent someone / Camptown races / I'll still write your name in the sand / Promise of things to come / Thinkin' about you / Because we are young / Be good baby / 'Tis sweet to be remembered / Running bear / Ballad of Davy Crockett / Tom Dooley / Sixteen tons / El Paso / Old lamplighter / Three bells / I'm movin' on
CD _____ BCD 15694
Bear Family / Jul '93 / Rollercoaster / Direct / CM / Swift / ADA.

Wiseman, Val

LADY SINGS THE BLUES
CD _____ ESSCD 248
Essential / Feb '95 / Total/BMG.

Wishbone Ash

ARGUS
Time was / Sometime world / Blowin' free / King will come / Leaf and stream / Warrior / Throw down the sword
CD _____ MCLD 19085
MCA / Nov '92 / BMG.

BLOWIN' FREE
Blind eye / Phoenix / Persephone / Outward bound / Pilgrim / You rescue me / Time was / Blowin' free / Lady whiskey / Rock 'n' roll widow / Ballad of the beacon / Jailbait / Everybody needs a friend / Mother of pearl

CD _____ NTRCD 014
Nectar / Feb '94 / Pinnacle.

IN CONCERT
CD _____ HP 93452
Start / Nov '94 / Koch.

LIVE DATES
King will come / Warrior / Throw down the sword / Lady whiskey / Phoenix / Rock 'n' roll widow / Ballad of the beacon / Baby, what you want me to do / Pilgrim / Blowin' free / Jailbait
CD _____ BGOCD 293
Beat Goes On / Sep '95 / Pinnacle.

PILGRIMAGE
Vas dis / Pilgrim / Jailbait / Alone / Lullaby / Valediction / Where were you tomorrow
CD _____ MCLD 19084
MCA / Nov '92 / BMG.

RAW TO THE BONE
Cell of fame / People in motion / Don't cry / Love is blue / Long live the night / Rocket in my pocket / It's only love / Don't you mess / Dreams (searching for an answer) / Perfect timing
CD _____ CLACD 390
Castle / Aug '93 / BMG.

THERE'S THE RUB
Silver shoes / Don't come back / Persephone / Hometown / Lady Jay / F.U.B.B.
CD _____ MCLD 19249
MCA / Oct '94 / BMG.

TWIN BARRELS BURNING
Engine overheat / Can't fight love / Genevieve / Me and my guitar / Hold on / Streets of shame / No more lonely nights / Angels have mercy / Wind up
CD _____ CLACD 389
Castle / Aug '93 / BMG.

WISHBONE ASH
Blind eye / Lady whisky / Errors of my ways / Queen of torture / Handy / Phoenix
CD _____ BGOCD 234
Beat Goes On / Oct '94 / Pinnacle.

WISHBONE ASH IN CONCERT
CD _____ WINCCD 4
Windsong / Sep '91 / Pinnacle.

WISHBONE FOUR
So many things to say / Ballad of the beacon / No easy road / Everybody needs a friend / Doctor / Sorrel / Sing out the song / Rock 'n' roll widow
CD _____ MCLD 19149
MCA / Aug '94 / BMG.

Wishdokta

POST MODERN BREAKS (Wishdokta & James Hyman)
CD _____ KICKCD 2
Kickin' / Apr '93 / SRD.

Wishing Stones

WILDWOOD
CD _____ HVNCD 004
Creation / Nov '91 / 3MV / Vital.

Wishplants

COMA
CD _____ WOLCD 1033
China / Oct '93 / Pinnacle.

Witch Hazel

LANDLOCKED
CD _____ FLY 014
Blue Rose / Dec '95 / 3MV.

Witchkiller

DAY OF THE SAXONS
CD _____ 047554
Steamhammer / '89 / Pinnacle / Plastic Head.

Withers, Bill

LEAN ON ME (The Best Of Bill Withers)
Ain't no sunshine / Grandma's hands / Lean on me / Use me / Kissing my love / Who is he and what is he to you / I don't want you on my mind / Same love that made me laugh / Hello, like before / Lovely day / Let me be the one you need / I want to spend the night / Stepping right along / Whatever happens / Watching you watching me / Heart is your life / You try to find a love / Just the two of uus
CD _____ 4805062
Columbia / May '95 / Sony.

Witherspoon, Jimmy

AIN'T NOBODY'S BUSINESS
Ain't nobody's business / In the evening / Froggie Moore rag / McShann bounce / How long blues / Money's getting cheaper / Skid Row blues / Spoon calls Hootie / Backwater blues / Jumpin' with Louis / Destruction blues
CD _____ JHR 73563
Jazz Hour / Oct '92 / Target/BMG / Jazz Music / Cadillac.

AIN'T NOTHIN' NEW ABOUT THE BLUES (Witherspoon, Jimmy & Robben Ford)
CD _____ AIM 1050
Aim / Apr '95 / Direct / ADA / Jazz Music.

BABY-BABY-BABY
CD _____ OBCCD 527
Original Blues Classics / Nov '92 / Complete/Pinnacle / Wellard / Cadillac.

BIG BLUES
CD _____ JSPCD 205
JSP / Sep '87 / ADA / Target/BMG / Direct / Cadillac / Complete/Pinnacle.

BLOWIN' IN FROM KANSAS CITY
Love my baby / There ain't nothing better / Love and frendship / T.B. blues / Goin' around in circles / She's evil / I'm just a country boy / Good jumping aka jump children / Blowing the blues / It's raining outside / I'm just a lady's man / I'm just wandering (pts 1 & 2) / Who's been jivin' you / Sweet lovin' baby / Thelma Lee blues / Slow your speed (CD only) / Dr. Knows His Business aka Dr. Blues (CD only) / Rain rain rain (CD only) / Baby baby (CD only)
CD _____ CDCHD 279
Ace / Feb '91 / Pinnacle / Cadillac / Complete/Pinnacle.

BLUES AROUND THE CLOCK
CD _____ OBCCD 576
Original Blues Classics / Jan '96 / Complete/Pinnacle / Wellard / Cadillac.

BLUES THE WHOLE BLUES AND NOTHING BUT THE BLUES
You got a hold of my heart / It never rains but it pours / Real bad day / Sooner or later / Killing time / Blues the whole blues and nothing but the blues / Help me operator / Would man be satisfied / Two sides to every story / Wake up call / Think / You ain't foolin' me
CD _____ IGOCD 2001
Indigo / Jul '95 / Direct / ADA.

CRY THE BLUES
CD _____ TKOCD 004
TKO / '92 / TKO.

EVENIN' BLUES
Money's gettin' cheaper / Grab me a freight / Don't let go / I've been treated wrong / Evening / Cane River / Baby how long / Good rockin' man / Kansas city / Drinking beer
CD _____ OBCCD 511
Original Blues Classics / Apr '94 / Complete/Pinnacle / Wellard / Cadillac.

GOIN' TO KANSAS CITY BLUES (Witherspoon, Jimmy & Jay McShann Band)
Jumpin' the blues / Until the real thing comes along / Hootie blues / Rain is such a lonesome sound / Confessin' the blues / Piney Brown blues / Froggy bottom / Gee baby ain't I good to you / Blue Monday blues / Ooo-wee then the lights go out
CD _____ 74321 13027-2
RCA / Sep '93 / BMG.

JAY'S BLUES
Foolish prayer / Lucille / One fine gal / Blues in trouble / Two little girls / Corn whiskey / Don't tell me now / Last mile / Day is dawning / Back door blues / Fast woman, slow gin / Twenty four sad hours / Just for you / Sad life / Move me baby / I'm not so young / Highway to happiness / I done told you / Oh boy / Jay's blues (pts 1 & 2) / Back home / Miss, Miss Mistreater
CD _____ CDCHARLY 270
Charly / Sep '91 / Charly / THE / Cadillac.

JIMMY WITHERSPOON & JAY MCSHANN (Witherspoon, Jimmy & Jay McShann)
CD _____ BLCD 760173
Black Lion / Mar '93 / Jazz Music / Cadillac / Wellard / Koch.

JIMMY WITHERSPOON SINGS THE BLUES
CD _____ AIM 1005CD
Aim / Oct '93 / Direct / ADA / Jazz Music

LIVE AT CONDON'S, NEW YORK
Goin' to Chicago / Gee baby ain't I good to you / You got me runnin' / Big boss man / Sweet lotus blossom / I'm gonna move to the outskirts of town (CD only) / If I didn't get well no more / Money's getting cheaper (CD only) / In the dark / I'm knocking out your teeth tonite / Ain't nobody's business (CD only) / Trouble in mind (CD only) / Don't you miss your baby
CD _____ CDGATE 7023
Kingdom Jazz / Nov '90 / Kingdom.

LIVE AT MONTEREY
CD _____ M&MJ 421
Fresh Sound / Feb '88 / Jazz Music / Discovery.

MASTER OF BLUES
CD _____ 722017
Scorpio / May '92 / Complete/Pinnacle.

MIDNIGHT LADY CALLED THE BLUES
New York City blues / Barber / Blinded by love / Happy hard times / Something rotten in East St Louis / Midnight lady called the blues / Blues hall of fame

CD _____ MCD 5327
Muse / Sep '92 / New Note / CM.

ROCKIN' WITH SPOON (Charly Blues - Masterworks Vol. 25)
Good rockin' tonight / When I been drinkin' / Big fine girl / No rollin' blues / Ain't nobody's business / Times gettin' tougher than tough / How long / Corine / C.C. rider / Roll 'em Pete / Everyday / Outskirts of town / Kansas city / Trouble in mind / St. Louis blues
CD _____ CDBM 25
Charly / Apr '92 / Charly / THE / Cadillac.

SPOON'S LIFE
Night life / Help me / Big boss man / Cold cold feeling / Worried life blues / Did you ever / Blues with a feeling / Big leg woman
CD _____ ECD 260442
Evidence / Mar '94 / Harmonia Mundi / ADA / Cadillac.

Withschinsky, Hill

LATIN MOODS (2CD/MC Set)
Girl from Ipanema / One note samba / Meditation / Volare / Spanish eyes / Quiet nights of quiet stars / Begin the beguine / How insensitive / Latin nights / Guantamera / Desafinado / Cubana / Wave / Agua de beber / Kiss of fire / Gift / Once I loved / Night and day / Lambada / Summer samba / Spanish harlem / Dindi / La cumparsita / Amor / On a clear day / Evergreen / La bamba / Tango / Light my fire / Peal of bells / Killing me softly / Brasilia / Copacabana / Breeze from Rio / Tico tico / Perfidia
CD Set _____ 30360 00122
Carlton Home Entertainment / Oct '95 / Carlton Home Entertainment.

Wizards Of Twiddly

MAN MADE SELF
CD _____ FFPCD 2
Fracture For Pleasure / Jan '94 / SRD.

Wizo

UUAARRGH
CD _____ FAT 527CD
Fat Wreck Chords / Jun '95 / Plastic Head.

Wob

I CAN'T STAY LONG
CD _____ CYCLECD 002
Cycle / Jan '96 / Direct / ADA.

Wobbling Woodwinds

SOLO FLIGHT (Wobbling Woodwinds & Ulf Johansson)
Phontastic / Mar '94 / Wellard / Jazz Music / Cadillac.
_____ NCD 8829

Wofford, Mike

LIVE AT MAYBECK RECITAL HALL, VOL. 18
CD _____ CCD 4514
Concord Jazz / Jul '92 / New Note.

Wolf, Kate

BACKROADS (Wolf, Kate & Wildwood Flower)
Lately / Emma Rose / Sitting on the porch / Tequila and me / Legget serenade / It ain't in the wine / Tequila and me / Legend in his time / Riding in the country / Oklahoma going home / Back roads
CD _____ R 2714
Rhino / Oct '94 / ADA.

CLOSE TO YOU
Across the great divide / Legget serenade / Like a river / Unfinished life / Friend of mine / Love still remains / Eyes of a painter / Here in California / Stone in the water / Close to you
CD _____ R 271482
Rhino / Oct '94 / ADA.

EVENING IN AUSTIN, AN
Eyes of a painter / Green eyes / Carolina pines / Give yourself to love / Let's get together / Friend of mine
CD _____ R 271487
Rhino / Oct '94 / ADA.

GIVE YOURSELF TO LOVE 1 & 2
CD _____ R 271483
Rhino / Oct '94 / ADA.

LOOKING BACK AT YOU
CD _____ RH 71613CD
Rhino / Jul '94 / Warner Music.

Wolf Spider

DRIFTEN IN THE SULLEN SEA
CD _____ CDFLAG 63
Under One Flag / Sep '91 / Pinnacle.

KINGDOM OF PARANOIA
Manifestants / Pain / Black'n'white / Foxes / Nightmare for sense / Desert / Sickened nation / Nasty-ment / Survive / Weakness
CD _____ CDFLAG 49
Under One Flag / Nov '90 / Pinnacle.

Wolfe, Robert

ANY DREAM WILL DO
It's the natural thing to do / Gal in Calico / It only happens when I dance with you / Take these chains from my heart / Nobody's child / Your cheatin' heart / Crystal chandeliers / Jardin secret / Dolannes melodie / Oh lady be good / Love is here to stay / Liza / Embraceable you / Fascinating rhythm / They can't take that away from me / Somebody loves me / Someone to watch over me / Golden wedding day (La Cinquantaine) / From a distance / Mr. Mistofelees / Tell me on a Sunday / Close every door / Any dream will do / Chanson de Matin / I'm beginning to see the light / I've got a gal in Kalamazoo / It don't mean a thing if it ain't got that swing / Romantica / At the Cafe Continental / Serenade in the night / Florentiner march
CD _____ GRCD 51
Grasmere / '92 / Target/BMG / Savoy.

BLACKPOOL REVISITED
High school cadets march / Wind beneath my wings / Meditation / South American Joe / Tequila / As I love you / Once in a while / Sentimental journey / She didn't say 'yes' / I'm old fashioned / Make believe / Smoke gets in your eyes / Song is you / Somewhere out there / Spanish fies / Wedding samba / Cumana / Unchained melody / True love ways / Money is the root of all evil / We're in the money / At the end of the day / Castle on a cloud / I dreamed a dream / Master of the house / Empty chairs at empty tables / On my own / Do you hear the people sing
CD _____ CDGRS 1238
Grosvenor / '91 / Target/BMG.

EVERYTHING'S IN RHYTHM
Household Brigade / If you love me / Vilia / All I do is dream of you / Hold me / Have you ever been lonely / Summer of '42 / Happy whistler / Stumbling / Nearness of you / Under the double eagle / Head over heels in love / When you've got a little springtime in your heart / Everything's in rhythm / Over my shoulder / When the midnight choo choo leaves for Alabama / Blackfoot walk / Crazy words crazy tune / Can you feel the love tonight / Oliver selection / You've got to pick a pocket or two / I'd do anything / Oom-pah-pah / As long as he needs me / Nights of gladness / Gimme dat ding / Bare necessities / Bring me sunshine / One moment in time
CD _____ GRCD 69
Grasmere / Nov '95 / Target/BMG / Savoy.

FRIENDS FOR LIFE
Royal Air Force march past / Silver threads among the gold / When your old wedding ring was new / Till we meet again / Parade of the tin soldiers / Songs my mother taught me / My fair lady / Gymnopedie No.1 / Mona Lisa / Orange coloured sky / Those lazy-hazy-crazy days of summer / Aces high / Gold and silver waltz / I've got a pocketful of dreams / Zing went the strings of my heart / Painting the clouds with sunshine / Sanctuary of the heart / Friends for life (Amigos para siempre) / Mairzy doats and dozy doats / We're gonna hang out the washing on the siegfried line / Don't fence me in / When you tell me that you love me / Me and my girl
CD _____ GRCD 56
Grasmere / Mar '93 / Target/BMG / Savoy.

SPREAD A LITTLE HAPPINESS
CD _____ GRCD 61
Grasmere / May '94 / Target/BMG /
Savoy.

Wolfetones

25TH ANNIVERSARY : WOLFETONES (2)
CD Set _____ SHCD 52024/5
Shanachie / Jul '91 / Koch / ADA / Greensleeves.

BELT OF THE CELTS
CD _____ SHAN 52035CD
Shanachie / Aug '93 / Koch / ADA / Greensleeves.

IRISH TO THE CORE
CD _____ SHAN 52033CD
Shanachie / Aug '93 / Koch / ADA / Greensleeves.

SING OUT FOR IRELAND
CD _____ TRCD 1015
Triskel / '88 / I&B / CM / Roots.

Wolff, Henry

TIBETAN BELLS II (Wolff, Henry & Nancy Hennings)
CD _____ CDCEL 005
Celestial Harmonies / Jul '88 / ADA / Select.

TIBETAN BELLS III
CD _____ CDCEL 027
Celestial Harmonies / Feb '89 / ADA / Select.

Wolff, Michael

MICHAEL WOLFF
CD _____ 4743412
Sony Jazz / Jan '95 / Sony.

Wolfgamme, Nani

20 GOLDEN HITS OF HAWAII
CD _____ MCD 71804
Monitor / Jun '93 / CM.

Wolfgang Press

BIRD WOOD CAGE
King of soul / Raintime / Bottom drawer / Kansas / Swing like a baby / See my wife / Holy man / Hang on me / Shut that door
CD _____ CAD 810CD
4AD / Oct '88 / Disc.

FUNKY LITTLE DEMONS
CD _____ CAD 4016CD
4AD / Sep '94 / Disc.

LEGENDARY WOLFGANG PRESS AND OTHER TALL STORIES
CD _____ CAD 514 CD
4AD / Feb '87 / Disc.

MAMA TOLD ME NOT TO COME
CD _____ BAD 1007 CD
4AD / May '91 / Disc.

QUEER
CD _____ CADCD 1011
4AD / Aug '91 / Disc.

STANDING UP STRAIGHT
Dig a hole / My life / Hammer the halo / Bless my brother / Fire-fly / Rotten fodder / Forty days, thirty nights / I am the crime
CD _____ CAD 606 CD
4AD / Feb '87 / Disc.

Wolfhound

HALLELUJA
CD _____ BLR 84 024
L&R / May '91 / New Note.

NEVER ENDING STORY, THE (Wolfhound & Anne Haigis)
CD _____ BLR 84 025
L&R / May '91 / New Note.

Wolfsbane

WOLFSBANE
CD _____ ESSCD 211
Essential / Feb '94 / Total/BMG.

Wolfstone

CHASE, THE
Tinnie Run / Glass And The Can / Prophet / Appropriate Dipstick / Flames And Hearts / Ten pound float / Close it down / Jake's Tune / Early Mist / Cannot Lay Me Down
CD _____ IRCD 018
Iona / Aug '92 / ADA / Direct / Duncans.

UNLEASHED
Cleveland park / Song for yesterday / Silver spear / Sleepy toon / Hector the hero / Howl / Here is where the heart is / Hard heart / Erin
CD _____ IR 014 CD
Iona / Nov '91 / ADA / Direct / Duncans.

WOLFSTONE
CD _____ CMCD 072
Celtic Music / Apr '94 / CM / Roots.

YEAR OF THE DOG
Green Linnet / Jul '94 / Roots / CM / Direct / ADA.
_____ GL 1145CD

Wolstenholme, Woolly

SONGS FROM THE BLACK BOX
Has to be a reason / Down the line / All get burned / Too much, too loud, too late / Even the night / Deceivers all / Will to fly / Sunday bells / Open / Sail away / Quiet island / Prospect of Whitby / Lives on the line / Paratriots / Gates of heaven (14/18) / American excess / Maestoso a hymn in the roof of the worl
CD _____ VP 174CD
Voice Print / Aug '94 / Voice Print.

Wolverton Brothers

SUCKING HIND TIT
CD _____ OK 33012CD
Normal/Okra / Sep '90 / Direct / ADA.

Wolz, Christian

COR
CD _____ EFA 11234-2
Danse Macabre / Nov '94 / SRD.

INTUS MESTRA DE LA FORE
CD _____ EFA 11228-2
Danse Macabre / Jan '94 / SRD.

Womack & Womack

CONSCIENCE
Conscious of my conscience / M.P.B. / Friends / Slave / Teardrops / Good man monologue / Life's just a ball game / I am love / Celebrate the world
CD _____ IMCD 213
Island / Mar '96 / PolyGram.

LOVE WARS
Love wars / Express myself / Baby I'm scared of you / T.K.O.A.P.B. / Catch and

don't look back / Woman / Angie / Good
times
CD _____ 7559602932
Carlton Home Entertainment / Jan '93 /
Carlton Home Entertainment.

TEARDROPS
Teardrops / Celebrate the world / Slave /
Conscious of my conscience / Good man
monologue / M.P.B. / Life's just a ball game
/ Friends (so called) / I am love / Love wars
/ Take me home country roads / Family /
Rejoice
CD _____ 5500672
Spectrum/Karussell / May '93 / PolyGram.
THE.

**TRANSFORMATION TO THE HOUSE OF
ZEKKARIYAS**
Drive (first gear) / Fiesta / Understanding /
Passion and pain / Long time / Second gear
/ Candy world / Land of odd / Pie in the sky
/ Star / Focus
CD _____ 936245075-2
Warner Bros. / May '93 / Warner Music.

Womack, Bobby

COLLECTION
CD _____ CCSCD 404
Castle / Apr '94 / BMG.

FACTS OF LIFE
Nobody wants you when you're down and
out / I'm through trying to prove my love to
you / If you can't give her love, give her up
/ That's heaven to me / Holdin' on to my
baby's love / Nobody / Fact of life / He'll be
there when the sun goes down / Can't stop
a man in love / Look of love / Natural man
/ All along the watchtower / Interlude 1 (I
don't know) / Superstar / If you want my
love, put something down on it / Git it /
What's your world / Check it out / Interlude
2 / Jealous love / It's all over now / Yes
Jesus loves me
CD _____ CDCHARLY 157
Charly / Mar '89 / Charly / THE / Cadillac.

HOME IS WHERE THE HEART IS
Home is where the heart is / Little bit salty
/ Standing in the safety zone / How long has
this been going on / I could never be sat-
isfied / Something for my head / Change is
gonna come / We've only just begun
CD _____ EDCD 172
Edsel / Feb '91 / Pinnacle / ADA.

I FEEL A GROOVE COMIN' ON
Let's get together / Broadway walk / What
is this / I'm a midnight mover / Communication / I can understand it / Hang on in
there / Can't stop a man in love / Let it hang
out / Check it out / Daylight / I feel a groove
comin' on / So many sides of you / Secrets
/ Stand up / Tryin' to get over you / Tell me
why / Falling in love again
CD _____ CPCD 8083
Charly / Mar '95 / Charly / THE / Cadillac.

LOOKIN' FOR A LOVE AGAIN
Looking for a love / I don't wanna be hurt
by ya love again / Doing it my way / Let it
hang out / Point of no return / You're welcome, stop on by / You're messing up a
good thing / Don't let me down / Copper
kettle / There's one thing that beats failing
CD _____ CDCHARLY 153
Charly / Jan '89 / Charly / THE / Cadillac.

**MIDNIGHT MOVER (The Bobby Womack
Story)**
I'm a midnight mover / Broadway walk /
What is this / I'm in love / Somebody spe-
cial / What you gonna do when your love
is gone / How I miss you baby / More than
I can stand / I can't take it like a man /
Laughing and clowning (live) / It's gonna
rain / Fly me to the moon / I left my heart
in San Francisco / Arkansas State Prison /
Come l'amore / (If you don't want my love)
give it back / That's the way I feel about
cha / Communication / I can understand it /
Woman's gotta have it / Sweet Caroline /
Harry hippie / Preacher/More than I can
stand (live) / Nobody wants you when
you're down and out / Across 110th street /
Fact of life/He'll be there when the sun
goes down / I'm through trying to prove my
love to you / If you can't give her love, give
her up / Holdin' on to my baby's love /
That's heaven to me / Looking for a love / I
don't wanna be hurt by ya love again /
You're welcome, stop on by / Interlude 1 (I
don't know) / If you want my love, put
something down on it / Check it out / It's
all over now / Tarnished rings / Trust in me
/ Everything's gonna be alright / Where there's a will / Love ain't something you can
get for free / Daylight / Jealous love
CD Set _____ CDEM 1514
EMI / Mar '94 / EMI.

MIDNIGHT MOVER, THE
I can understand it / Looking for a love / It's
all over now / I'm a midnight mover / I'm in
love / Arkansas state prison / That's heaven
to me / Harry hippie / Tried and convicted
/ Don't look back / Fly me to the moon /
California dreamin' / Woman's gotta have it
/ Behind closed doors
CD _____ CDINS 5000
Instant / Jul '89 / Charly.

POET II, THE
Love has finally come at last / It takes a lot
of strength to say goodbye / Through the

eyes of a child / Surprise surprise / Tryin' to
get over you / Tell me why / Who's foolin'
who / I wish I had someone to go home to
/ American dream
CD _____ MUSCD 506
MCI / Sep '94 / Disc / THE.

POET, THE
So many sides of you / Lay your lovin' on
me / Secrets / Just my imagination / Stand
up / Games / If you think you're lonely now
/ Where do we go from here
CD _____ MUSCD 505
MCI / Sep '94 / Disc / THE.

RESURRECTION
Good ole days / You made me love again /
So high on your love / Don't break your
promise (too soon) / Forever love / Please
change your mind / Trying not to break
down / Cousin Henry / Centerfield / Goin'
home / Walking on the wildside / Cry myself
to sleep / Wish / Color him father
CD _____ CDCTUM 8
Continuum / Sep '94 / Pinnacle.

SAFETY ZONE/B.W. GOES C & W
Everything's gonna be alright / I wish it
would rain / Trust me / Where there's a will
/ Love ain't something you can get for free
/ Something you got / Daylight / I feel a
groove comin' on / Don't make this the last
date for you and me / Behind closed doors
/ Bouquet of roses / Tired of living in the
country / Tarnished rings / Big bayou / Song
of the mockingbird / I'd be ahead if I could
quit while I'm behind / You / I take it on
home
CD _____ CDCHARLY 199
Charly / Nov '89 / Charly / THE / Cadillac.

UNDERSTANDING - COMMUNICATION
I can understand it / Woman's gotta have it
/ And I love her / Got to get you back /
Simple man / Ruby Dean / Thing called love
/ Sweet Caroline / Harry hippie / Com-
munication / Come l'amore / Fire and rain /
If you don't want my love, give it back /
Close to you / Everything is beautiful /
That's the way I feel about cha / Yield not
to temptation
CD _____ CDCHARLY 152
Charly / Jan '89 / Charly / THE / Cadillac.

VERY BEST OF BOBBY WOMACK, THE
I can understand it / Harry hippie / I'm a
midnight mover / What is this / Somebody
special / That's the way I feel about cha /
Communication / California dreamin' / If you
don't want my love, give it back / I wish it
would rain / Nobody wants you when you're
down and out / Across 110th street / If you
want my love, put something down on it /
Lookin' for love / I don't wanna be hurt by
ya love again / Got to get you back / Woman's gotta have it / There's one thing that
beats failing / You're messing up a good
thing / Love ain't something you can get for
free
CD _____ MCCD 014
Music Club / May '91 / Disc / THE / CM.

WOMACK IN MEMPHIS
Fly me to the moon / Baby you oughta think
it over / I'm a midnight mover / What is this
/ Somebody special / Take me / Moonlight
in Vermont / Love the time is now / I'm in
love / California dreamin' / No money in my
pocket / Little Mae / How I miss you baby
/ More than I can stand / It's gonna rain /
Everyone's gone to the moon / I can't take
it like a man / I left my heart in San Francisco / Arkansas State Prison / I'm gonna
forget about you / Don't look back / Tried
and convicted / Thank you
CD _____ CDCHARLY 198
Charly / Sep '89 / Charly / THE / Cadillac.

WOMACK LIVE
Let it out / Intro / Oh how I miss you baby
/ California dreamin' / Something / Every-
body's talkin' / Laughin' and clownin' / To
live the past / I'm a midnight mover / More
than I can stand
CD _____ CDCHARLY 155
Charly / Feb '89 / Charly / THE / Cadillac.

WOMACK WINNERS
Broadway walk / Somebody special / I'm a
midnight mover / What is this / How I miss
you baby / More than I can stand / Communication / That's the way I feel about cha
/ If you don't want my love, give it back / I
can understand it / Woman's gotta have it /
Harry Hippie / Across 110th street / Nobody wants you when you're down and out
/ I'm through trying to prove my love to you
/ Looking for a love / You're welcome, stop
on by / I don't know (what the world is coming to) / If you want my love, put something
down on it / Check it out / It's all over now
/ Where there's a will / Daylight
CD _____ CDINS 5074
Charly / Jun '93 / Charly / THE / Cadillac.

Women's Choir Of Sofia

LE MYTHE DES VOIX BULGARES
CD _____ 15344
Laserlight / '91 / Target/BMG.

Wonder Stuff

**CONSTRUCTION FOR THE MODERN
IDIOT**
Change every light bulb / I wish them all
dead / Cabin fever / Hot love now / Full of

life (happy now) / Storm drain / On the
ropes / Your big assed Mother / Swell / Sing
the absurd / Hush / Great drinker
CD _____ 519 894-2
Polydor / Oct '93 / PolyGram.

**IF THE BEATLES HAD READ HUNTER -
THE SINGLES**
Welcome to the cheap seats / Wish away /
Caught in my shadow / Don't let me down
gently / Size of a cow / Hot love now / Dizzy
/ Unbearable / Circlesquare / Who wants to
be the Disco King / Golden green / Give
give give me more more more / Coz I luv
you / Sleep alone / Full of life (happy now)
/ It's yer money I'm after baby / On the
ropes / It's not true
CD _____ 5213972
PolyGram / Sep '94 / PolyGram.

LIVE IN MANCHESTER
CD _____ WINCD 074
Windsong / Jun '95 / Pinnacle.

Wonder, Stevie

CONVERSATION PEACE
Rain your love down / Edge of eternity / Ta-
boo to love / Take the time out / I'm new /
My love is with you / Treat myself / Tomor-
row Robins will sing / Sensuous whisper /
For your love / Cold chill / Sorry / Conver-
sation peace
CD _____ 5302382
Motown / Mar '95 / PolyGram.

ESSENTIAL STEVIE WONDER
Yester-me, yester-you, yesterday / My
cherie amour / If you really love me / We
can work it out / Signed, sealed, delivered
(I'm yours) / Never had a dream come true
/ Something out of the blue / Heaven help
us all / Do yourself a favour / I was made
to love her / Thank you love / Until you
come back to me / I'm wondering / Shoo-
be-doo-be-doo-da-day / Angie girl / More
than a dream / For once in my life / You met
your match / Don't know why I love you /
Uptight / Music talk / Ain't that asking for
trouble / Love a-go-go / Nothing's too good
for my baby / Be cool be calm (and keep
yourself together) / I'd cry / Travellin' man /
Place in the sun / Ribbon in the wind / Fingertips / Workout Stevie,workout / Hey harmonica man / Kiss me baby / Hi-heel
sneakers / Happy Street / Don't you feel it
/ Castles in the sand / Contract on love / I
call it pretty music, but the old folks call it
the blues
CD _____ 530047-2
Motown / Jan '93 / PolyGram.

FULFILLINGNESS FIRST FINALE
Smile please / Heaven is ten zillion light
years away / Too shy to say / Boogie on
reggae woman / Creepin' / You haven't
done nothin' / It ain't no use / They won't
go when I go / Bird of beauty / Please don't
go
CD _____ 530105-2
Motown / Jan '93 / PolyGram.

GREATEST HITS VOLUME 1
Shoo be doo be doo da day / Place in the
sun / Uptight (everything's alright) / Travelin'
man / Hi-heel sneakers / Sad boy / Kiss me
baby / Workout Stevie workout / Fingertips
/ Hey harmonica man / Contract on love /
Castles in the sand / Nothing's too good for
my baby / I was made to love her / Blown
in the wind / I'm wondering
CD _____ 5302122
Motown / Nov '93 / PolyGram.

**GREATEST HITS: STEVIE WONDER,
VOL.2**
Signed, sealed, delivered (I'm yours) / We
can work it out / For once in my life / If you
really love me / Shoo-be-doo-be-doo-da-
day / You met your match / My Cherie
amour / Yester-me, yester-you, yesterday /
Never had a dream come true / Heaven
help us all / Don't know why I love you /
Never dreamed you'd leave in summer
CD _____ 5302132
Motown / Nov '93 / PolyGram.

HOTTER THAN JULY
Did I hear you say you love me / All I do /
Rocket love / I ain't gonna stand for it / As
if you read my mind / Masterblaster / Do
like you / Cash in your face / Lately / Happy
birthday
CD _____ 530044-2
Motown / Jan '93 / PolyGram.

IN SQUARE CIRCLE
Part time lover / I love you too much /
Whereabouts / Stranger on the shore of
love / Never in your sun / Spiritual walkers
/ Land of la la / Go home / Overjoyed / It's
wrong (la la) / I wish he didn't trust me so
much / Baby don't leave home without it /
So many rivers / Got to be with you tonight
/ Whatever happened to these times / Let
me kiss it where it hurts / Only survivor /
That's where it's at / Check it out
CD _____ 530046-2
Motown / Jan '93 / PolyGram.

INNERVISIONS
Too high / Visions / Living for the city /
Golden lady / Higher ground / Jesus children of America / All in love is fair / Don't
you worry about a thing / He's misstra know
it all

CD _____ 530035-2
Motown / Jan '93 / PolyGram.

**JOURNEY THROUGH THE SECRET LIFE
OF PLANTS**
Earth's creation / First garden / Voyage to
India / Same old story / Venus flytrap and
the bug / Ai no, sono / Seed's a star and
treed medley / Secret life of plants / Finale
/ Seasons / Power flower / Send one your
love (instrumental) / Race babbling / Outside my window / Black orchid / Ecclesi-
astes / Kesse ye lolo de ye / Come back as
a flower / Send one your love
CD Set _____ 530106-2
Motown / Jan '93 / PolyGram.

LOVE SONGS - 20 CLASSIC HITS
Contract on love / My cherie amour / Until
you come back to me / Yester-me, yester-
you, yesterday / Never had a dream come
true / If you really love me / Heaven help us
all / If you really love me / Heaven help us
all / Place in the sun / Alfie / Hey love / For
once in my life / We can work it out / I was
made to love her / Don't know why I love
you / Blowin' in the wind / Shoo-be-doo-
be-doo-da-day / I'm wondering / Nothing's
too good for my baby / Signed, sealed,
delivered (I'm yours)
CD _____ 530037-2
Motown / Jan '93 / PolyGram.

MUSIC OF MY MIND
Love having you around / Superwoman / I
love every little thing about you / Sweet little
girl / Happier than the morning sun / Girl
blue / Seems so long / Keep on running /
Evil
CD _____ 530028-2
Motown / Jan '93 / PolyGram.

**NATURAL WONDER - LIVE IN
CONCERT (2CD/MC Set)**
Love's in need of love today / Master
blaster (Jammin') / Higher ground / Rocket
love / Ribbon in the sky / Pastime paradise
/ If it's magic / Village ghetto land / Tomor-
row Robins will sing / Overjoyed / My cherie
amour / Signed, sealed, delivered I'm yours
/ Living for the city / Sir Duke / I wish / You
are the sunshine of my life / Superstition / I
just called to say I love you / For your love
/ Another star / Stevie Ray blues / Ms. and
Mr. Little Ones / Stay gold
CD _____ 5305462
Motown / Oct '95 / PolyGram.

ORIGINAL MUSIQUARIUM
Isn't she lovely / You are the sunshine of
my life / Higher ground / Superwoman /
Send me your love / Do I do / Superstition
/ Living for the city / Front line / You haven't
done nothin' / Sir Duke / Ribbon in the sky
/ Masterblaster / That girl / I wish / Boogie
on reggae woman
CD Set _____ 530029-2
Motown / Jan '93 / PolyGram.

SONGS IN THE KEY OF LIFE
Love's in need of love today / Have a talk
with God / Village ghetto land / Confusion /
I am singing / If it's magic / As / Another
star / I wish / Knocks me off my feet / Pas-
time paradise / Summer soft / Ordinary pain
/ Isn't she lovely / Joy inside my tears /
Black man / Sir Duke / Ngiculela es una
historia
CD Set _____ 530034-2
Motown / Jan '93 / PolyGram.

**STEVIE WONDER SONGBOOK (Various
Artists)**
I was made to love you / It's a shame / Until
you come back to me / Heaven is ten zillion
light years away / Try Jah love / Buttercup
/ Creepin' / You are the sunshine of my life
/ Pastime paradise / Perfect angel / Too shy
to say / Never said / I've changed / bone
nothin' / Do I do / Girl blue / Don't you worry
about a thing / Tell me something good
CD _____ VSOPCD 216
Connoisseur / Apr '95 / Pinnacle.

TALKING BOOK
You are the sunshine of my life / Maybe
your baby / You and I / Tuesday heartbreak
/ You've got it bad, girl / Superstition / Big
Brother / Blame it on the sun / Lookin' for
another pure love / I believe
CD _____ 530036-2
Motown / Jan '93 / PolyGram.

WHERE I'M COMING FROM
Look around / Do yourself a favour / Think
of me as your soldier / Something out of the
blue / If you really love me / I wanna talk to
you / Take up a course in happiness / Sunshine
in their eyes
CD _____ 5302232
Polydor / Sep '93 / PolyGram.

Wonder, Wayne

ALL ORIGINAL BOMBSHELL
CD _____ PHRICD 27
Penthouse / Jan '96 / Jetstar.

DON'T HAVE TO
CD _____ PHCD 24
Penthouse / Oct '93 / Jetstar.

Wongraven

HELLTRONEN
CD _____ FOG 006CD
Moonfog / Jun '95 / Plastic Head.

Wonky Alice

ATOMIC RAINDANCE
Linar Adam / Radius / Sirius / Son of the sun / Guidance / Captain paranoia / Astro nauts / Moon / Atomic raindance
CD _____ ONA 001 CD
Pomona / Jan '93 / Vital.

Woob

WOOB
CD _____ EMIT 1194
Time Recordings / Aug '94 / Pinnacle.

Wood Brothers

HOOKED ON COUNTRY (Wood Brothers & The Nashville Greats)
Hooked on country love / Hooked on Randy Travis / Hooked on Willie Nelson / Hooked on trains / Hooked on Merle Haggard / Hooked on George Strait / Hooked on Marty Robbins / Hooked on a waltz / Hooked on Johnny Cash / Hooked on a country party
CD _____ ECD 3072
K-Tel / Jan '95 / K-Tel.

I'M IN THE MOOD FOR COUNTRY MUSIC
CD _____ LPCD 1027
Disky / Apr '94 / THE / BMG / Discovery / Pinnacle.

Wood, Chris

LISA (Wood, Chris & Andy Cutting)
CD _____ RUF 002
Ruf / '92 / Pinnacle / ADA.

LIVE AT SIDMOUTH (Wood, Chris & Andy Cutting)
CD _____ RUF 003CD
Ruf / Feb '95 / Pinnacle / ADA.

LUSIGNAC (Wood, Chris & Andy Cutting)
CD _____ RUFCD 04
Ruf / Nov '95 / Pinnacle / ADA.

Wood, Clynt

TEARS OF SUCCESS
CD _____ WINK 1994
Wink / Oct '94 / Jetstar.

Wood, Lauren

CAT TRICK
CD _____ 7599268722
WEA / Jan '96 / Warner Music.

LAUREN WOOD
CD _____ 7599268712
WEA / Jan '96 / Warner Music.

Wood, Ronnie

I'VE GOT MY OWN ALBUM TO DO
CD _____ 936245692-2
Warner Bros. / Oct '94 / Warner Music.

MAHONEY'S LAST STAND (Wood, Ronnie & Ronnie Lane)
Tonight's number / From the late to the early / Chicken wire / Chicken wired / I'll fly away / Title one / Just for a moment / Mona the blues / Car radio / Hay tumble / Woody's thing / Rooster funeral
CD _____ CDTB 067
Thunderbolt / '88 / Magnum Music Group.

NOW LOOK
I got lost when I found you / Big bayou / Breathe on me / If you don't want my love for you / I can say she's alright / Caribbean boogie / Now look / Sweet baby of mine / I can stand the rain / It's unholy / I got a feeling
CD _____ 9362456932
Warner Bros. / Sep '94 / Warner Music.

SLIDE ON LIVE, PLUGGED IN AND STANDING
CD _____ CDCTUM 3
Continuum / Oct '93 / Pinnacle.

Wood, Roy

BOULDERS
Songs of praise / Wake up / Rock down low / Nancy sing me a song / Dear Elaine / All the way over the hill / Irish loafer (and his hen) / Miss Clarke and the computer / When Gran'ma plays the banjo / Rockin' shoes / She's too good for me / Locomotive
CD _____ BGOCD 219
Beat Goes On / Mar '94 / Pinnacle.

DEFINITIVE ALBUM, THE
CD _____ BRCD 50
BR Music / May '94 / Target/BMG.

ROY WOOD & WIZZARD (16 Greats) (Wood, Roy & Wizzard)
CD _____ EMPRCD 573
Emporio / Jul '95 / THE / Disc / CM.

ROY WOOD SINGLES ALBUM
Night of fear / I can hear the grass grow / Flowers in the rain / Fire brigade / Black-berry way / Curly / Brontosaurus / Tonight / Chinatown / California man / Ball park in-cident / See my baby jive / Dear Elaine / Angel fingers / Forever / I wish it could be Christmas every day / Rock 'n' roll winter / Going down the road / This is the story of my love / Are you ready to rock
CD _____ VSOPCD 189
Connoisseur / Aug '93 / Pinnacle.

STARTING UP
Red cars are after me / Raining in the city / Under fire / Turn your body to the light / Hot cars / Starting up / Keep it steady / On top of the world / Ships in the night
CD _____ CLACD 387
Castle / May '93 / BMG.

Woodard, Rickey

TOKYO EXPRESS, THE
CD _____ CCD 79527
Candid / Apr '93 / Cadillac / Jazz Music / Wellard / Koch.

YAZOO
Icicle / Fried bananas / Abell / Turbulence / Portrait of Jennie / Holy land / 14th and Jef-ferson / Tadd's delight / September in the rain / Yazoo City blues
CD _____ CCD 4629
Concord Jazz / Jan '95 / New Note.

Woodentops

HYPNOBEAT LIVE
Well well well / Love train / Travelling man / Get it on / Plenty / Why / Everyday living / Good thing / Everything breaks / Move me
CD _____ ROUGHCD 117
Rough Trade / May '87 / Pinnacle.

Woods

IT'S LIKE THIS
Sign of the times / Next rain / Girlfriends / Chain my heart / Some other world / I don't want her (anymore) / Battleship chains / Sand / What about me / Close as you get / Why / Come off with your lies
CD _____ DECD 900318
Demon / '89 / Pinnacle / ADA.

Woods, Chris

SOMEBODY DONE STOLE MY BLUES
CD _____ DD 434
Delmark / Sep '87 / Hot Shot / ADA / CM / Direct / Cadillac.

Woods, Gay

LIVE IN CONCERT (Woods, Gay & Terry)
CD _____ WINCD 071
Windsong / Apr '95 / Pinnacle.

Woods, Mitch

SHAKIN' THE SHACK (Woods, Mitch & His Rocket 88s)
CD _____ BP 5008CD
Blind Pig / Mar '94 / Hot Shot / Swift / CM / Roots / Direct / ADA.

STEADY DATE (Woods, Mitch & His Rocket 88s)
CD _____ BP 1784CD
Blind Pig / Mar '94 / Hot Shot / Swift / CM / Roots / Direct / ADA.

Woods, Phil

BOP STEW (Woods, Phil Quintet)
Dreamsville / Bop stew / Poor Butterfly / Yes there is a Coya
CD _____ CCD 4345
Concord Jazz / Jul '88 / New Note.

ELSA (Woods, Phil & Pieranunzi, Enrico)
CD _____ W 206-2
Philology / Aug '92 / Harmonia Mundi / Cadillac.

EUROPEAN TOUR
CD _____ 1231632
Red / Apr '95 / Harmonia Mundi / Jazz Horizons / Cadillac / ADA.

EVOLUTION (Woods, Phil Little Big Band)
Alvin G / Black flag / Hal mallet / Miles ahead (CD only) / Rain go away (CD only) / Song for Sisyphus / Thaddeus / Which way is uptown
CD _____ CCD 4361
Concord Jazz / Nov '88 / New Note.

FLOWERS FOR HODGES (Woods, Phil & Jim McNeely)
CD _____ CCD 4485
Concord Jazz / Nov '91 / New Note.

FULL HOUSE
CD _____ MCD 9196
Milestone / Oct '93 / Jazz Music / Pinnacle / Wellard / Cadillac.

GRATITUDE (Woods, Phil Quartet)
111-444 / Another Jones / Gratitude / My azure / Serenade in blue / Tenor of the times / Times mirror / Ya know
CD _____ CY 1316
Denon / Oct '88 / Conifer.

HARD SOCK DANCE
CD _____ ATJCD 5964
All That's Jazz / Jul '92 / THE / Jazz Music.

JAZZ 1968 (Woods, Phil & Slide Hampton)
CD _____ 7812532
Jazztime / Aug '93 / Discovery / BMG.

JAZZ LIFE, A
CD _____ W 74 Ω
Philology / Sep '92 / Harmonia Mundi / Cadillac.

LIVE AT THE CORRIDONIA JAZZ FESTIVAL (Woods, Phil & Space Jazz Trio)
CD _____ W 211-2
Philology / Aug '92 / Harmonia Mundi / Cadillac.

MUSIQUE DU BOIS
CD _____ MCD 5037
Muse / Sep '92 / New Note / CM.

ORNITHOLOGY
CD _____ PHIL 69-2
Philology / Oct '94 / Harmonia Mundi / Cadillac.

PIPER AT THE GATES OF DAWN (Woods, Phil & Chris Swansen)
CD _____ RCD 10007
Rykodisc / Mar '92 / Vital / ADA.

RIGHTS OF SWING (1960-1961)
Prelude and part 1 / Part 2 (ballad) / Part 2 (waltz) / Part 4 (scherzo) / Part 5 (presto)
CD _____ CD 53142
Giants Of Jazz / Sep '94 / Target/BMG / Cadillac.

STOLEN MOMENTS (Woods, Phil Quartet)
CD _____ JMY 1012-2
JMY / Aug '91 / Harmonia Mundi.

WOODLORE (Woods, Phil Quartet)
CD _____ OJCCD 052
Original Jazz Classics / '92 / Wellard / Jazz Music / Cadillac / Complete/Pinnacle.

Woods, Rosemary

WALKING TOGETHER
CD _____ SP 1027CD
Spring / Feb '93 / Direct / ADA.

Woods, Terry

GAY AND TERRY WOODS IN CONCERT (Woods, Terry & Gay)
CD _____ WIN 071CD
Windsong / Jul '95 / Pinnacle.

Woodshed

40 MILES OF ROUGH ROAD
Cropduster / Holloway to Memphis / Shoo-tin cactus / Return of yet I / Tale from the woodshed past return of two / Tales from the wood-shed part one / Change / Scuffle town shuffle / 40 Miles of rough road / No
CD _____ NLX 5008CD
Cloak & Dagger / Oct '95 / Vital.

Woodward, Edward

FEELINGS
Morning has broken / I need you to turn to / It had to be you / They didn't believe me / You are beautiful / September song / My foolish heart / Yesterday when I was young / When I fell in love / Can't smile without you / Way you look tonight / Send in the clowns / First time ever I saw your face / Didn't we / Evergreen / Feelings
CD _____ PWKS 4102P
Carlton Home Entertainment / Mar '92 / Carlton Home Entertainment.

Woodward, Ricky

CALIFORNIA COOKING
CD _____ CCD 79509
Candid / Nov '93 / Cadillac / Jazz Music / Wellard / Koch.

Wool

BOX SET
Eden / Kill the crow / Eat some ziti / Su-perman is dead / B-350 / Chances are / Coalinga / Speak / God rest his soul / Blackeye / Take a look
CD _____ 8284982
London / Feb '95 / PolyGram.

BUDSPAWN
CD _____ ALLCD 1
Parallel / May '93 / PolyGram.

Wooley, Sheb

RAWHIDE/HOW THE WEST WAS WON
Rawhide / Goodnight loving trail / Shifting whispering sands / Indian maiden / Story of Billy Bardell / Enchantment of the prairie / Lonley man / Wayward wind / Bars across the widow / Cattle call / How the west was won / Gotta pull up stakes (and move on west) / High lonesome / Wagonmaster's di-ary / Buffalo stampede / Rosie the queen of California / Building a railroad / Plowin' in

new ground / Papa's old fiddle / Silver tar-get / I belong / Big land
CD _____ BCDAH 15899
Bear Family / Nov '95 / Rollercoaster / Direct / CM / Swift / ADA.

Woosey, Dominic

STRAYLIGHT
Stay down, first light / Uncubation / Oceans of infinity / Straylightsong
CD _____ 450995343-2
Warner Bros. / Mar '94 / Warner Music.

Work

RUBBER CAGE
CD _____ WOOF 012 CD
Woof / '90 / Grapevine.

Work, Jimmy

MAKING BELIEVE
That's the way it's gonna be / Rock Island line / Puttin' on the dog / When she said you all / Digging my own grave / Don't give me a reason to wonder why / Blind heart(1) / You've got a heart like a merry-go-round / That cold, cold look in your eyes / Hands away from my heart / That's the way the juke box plays / There's only one you / Making believe / Blind heart(2) / Let 'em talk / Just like downtown / My old stomping ground / Don't knock just come on in / Those Kentucky bluegrass hills / You're gone, I won't forget / Rainy rainy blues / Hear that steamboat whistle blow / Tennes-see border / Your jealous heart is broken now / Bluegrass ticklin' my feet / Please don't let me love you / I would send you roses (but they cost too much) / Sur-rounded by water and bars / Smoky moun-tain moon / Who's been here since I've been gone / Mr. and Mrs. Cloud / Hospi-tality / Pickup truck / Do your honky tonkin' at home / Southern fried chicken / Let's live you (when you're not around) / Out of my mind / That's what makes the jukebox play / Don't knock, just come in / Blind heart / Let me be alone / I never thought I'd have the blues / I dreamed last night
CD _____ BCD 15651
Bear Family / Aug '93 / Rollercoaster / Direct / CM / Swift / ADA.

Working Week

PAYDAY (Collection)
Soul train / Venceremos / South Africa / King of the night / Touching heaven / Doc-tor / Friend / Largo / Knocking on your door / Strut / Apocalypse / I thought I'd never see you again / Storm of light / Sweet nothin's / Who's foolin' who / We will win
CD _____ CDVE 19
Venture / Jul '88 / EMI.

Workman, Reggie

SYNTHESIS (Workman, Reggie Ensemble)
CD _____ CDLR 131
Leo / Feb '89 / Wellard / Cadillac / Impetus.

Workshop

TALENT
CD _____ LADO 17030
Ladomat / Jan '95 / Plastic Head.

World Of Leather

JESUS CHRIST SUPERSTORE
CD _____ CAKECD 17
Soundcakes / Sep '95 / 3MV / Sony.

World Of Twist

QUALITY STREET
CD _____ CIRCD 17
Circa / Nov '91 / EMI.

World Party

BANG
Kingdom come / Is it like today / What is love all about / And God said.... / Give it all away / Sooner or later / Hollywood / Radio-days / Rescue me / Sunshine / All I gave / Give it all away (Reprise)
CD _____ CDCHEN 33
Ensign / Apr '93 / EMI.

GOODBYE JUMBO
Is it too late / Way down now / When the rainbow comes / Put the message in the box / Ain't gonna come til I'm ready / And I fell back alone / Take it up / God on my side / Show me to the top / Love street / Sweet soul dream / Thank you world
CD _____ CCD 1654
Ensign / Apr '90 / EMI.

PRIVATE REVOLUTION
Private revolution / Making love (to the world) / Ship of fools / All come true / Dance of the happy lads / It can be beautiful (sometimes) / Ballad of the little man / Ha-

waiian island world / All I really want to do / World party / It's all mine
CD _____ CCD 1552
Ensign / Apr '87 / EMI.

World Sax Orchestra

WORLD SAX ORCHESTRA
CD _____ BVHAASTCD 8902
Bvhaast / Oct '85 / Cadillac.

World Saxophone Quartet

BREATH OF LIFE (World Saxophone Quartet & Fontella Bass)
CD _____ 755979309-2
Elektra Nonesuch / Nov '94 / Warner Music.

DANCES AND BALLADS
CD _____ 979164 2
Elektra Nonesuch / Jun '88 / Warner Music.

LIVE IN ZURICH
Funny paper / Touchic / My first winter / Bordertown / Steppin' / Stick / Hattie wall
CD _____ BSR 0077
Black Saint / '86 / Harmonia Mundi / Cadillac.

METAMORPHOSIS (World Saxophone Quartet & African Drums)
CD _____ 7559792582
Elektra Nonesuch / Jul '94 / Warner Music.

MOVING RIGHT ALONG
CD _____ 120127-2
Black Saint / May '94 / Harmonia Mundi / Cadillac.

PLAYS DUKE ELLINGTON
CD _____ 7559791372
Elektra Nonesuch / Jul '94 / Warner Music.

STEPPIN'
CD _____ BSR 0027
Black Saint / '86 / Harmonia Mundi / Cadillac.

WORLD SAXOPHONE QUARTET
CD _____ 979 137 2
Elektra Nonesuch / Oct '87 / Warner Music.

World Trio

WORLD TRIO
Palantir / Whirling dervish / Over there / Will o' the wisp / Dr. Do-Right / Arch mage / Billy Jean / Seven rings / Eulogy
CD _____ VBR 21522
Vera Bra / Aug '95 / Pinnacle / New Note.

World Without Walls

MOTHERGROOVE
Mother groove / Mama's warning / No-one's slave / Aluna / Dreams of the great mother / Big wave / Black to black / Wake up / Mama's in the mix / One human family
CD _____ WWW 001CD
X-Static / Jun '94 / Vital.

Worlds Apart

TOGETHER
Could it be I'm falling in love / Papa wouldn't understand / Beggin' to be written / Everlasting love / Come back and stay / Arnold Schwarzenegger / Heaven must be missing an angel / Same old promises / Experienced / Wonderful world / September / Like it was, like it is
CD _____ 74321198122
Arista / Apr '94 / BMG.

Worlds Collide

ALL HOPE ABANDON
CD _____ LF 120
Lost & Found / Mar '95 / Plastic Head.

Worms, Marcel

JAZZ IN 20TH CENTURY PIANO MUSIC
CD _____ BVHCD 9403
Bvhaast / Oct '94 / Cadillac.

Worrell, Bernie

BLACKTRONIC SCIENCE
CD _____ GCD 79474
Gramavision / Sep '95 / Vital/SAM / ADA.

FUNK OF AGES
CD _____ GCD 79460
Gramavision / Sep '95 / Vital/SAM / ADA.

Wraith

DANGER CALLING
CD _____ WARCD 7
Warhammer / Sep '92 / Grapevine.

RIOT
CD _____ WARCD 9
Warhammer / May '93 / Grapevine.

Wray, Link

APACHE AND WILD SIDE OF THE CITY LIGHTS
Wild one / Dallas blues / Big boss man / Shawnee / Joker / Apache / Beautiful brown eyes / Stars and stripes forever / Green hornet / Dick Tracy / Private eye / Hotel Loneliness / Raunchy / Flying wedge / Don't leave me / American sunset / Little sister / Love me tender / Wild side of the city lights / Viva zapata / As long as I have you / Street beat
CD _____ CDCHD 931
Ace / Jun '90 / Pinnacle / Cadillac / Complete/Pinnacle.

INDIAN CHILD
CD _____ SHED 001CD
Creation / Jun '93 / 3MV / Vital.

LIVE AT THE PARADISO
Blue suede shoes / Ace of spades / Walk away from love / I saw her standing there / Run chicken run / She's no good / Rumble / Rawhide / Subway blues / Money / Shake, rattle and roll / Be bop a lula
CD _____ CDMF 008
Magnum Force / Apr '91 / Magnum Music Group.

LIVE IN 85/GROWLING GUITAR
Rumble / It's only words / Fire / Mystery train / I got a woman / Baby let's play house / Jack the ripper / Love me / King Creole / I'm counting on you / Rawhide / Born to be wild
CD _____ CDWIK 972
Big Beat / Apr '91 / Pinnacle.

ORIGINAL RUMBLE, THE
Rumble / Swag / Batman / Ace of spades / Jack the ripper / I'm branded / Fat back / Run chicken run / Turnpike U.S.A. / Dueces wild / Mustang / Blueberry Hill / Run boy run / Sweeper / Hound dog / That'll be the day / Fuzz / Rawhide / Draggin' / Aces wild / Bull dawg / Rumble man / Copenhagen boogie
CD _____ CDCH 924
Ace / Nov '89 / Pinnacle / Cadillac / Complete/Pinnacle.

POLYGRAM YEARS, THE
CD _____ 5277172
Polydor / Aug '95 / PolyGram.

RUMBLE PLUS
CD _____ CDWIK 924
Big Beat / Feb '89 / Pinnacle.

WALKIN' WITH LINK
Slinky / Ramble / Hand clapper / Rawhide / Dixie doodle / Studio blues / Comanche / Right turn / Radar / Lillian / Deuce central / Guitar cha cha / Rumble mambo / Ain't that lovin' you baby / New studio blues / Walkin' with Link
CD _____ 472866 2
Columbia / May '93 / Sony.

Wreckery

LAYING DOWN THE LAW
CD _____ CGAS 809 CD
Citadel / Jun '89 / ADA.

Wreckless Eric

AT THE SHOP
Big old world / Waiting for the shit (to hit the fan) / Bony Moronie / Our neck of the woods / If it makes you happy / Depression / Semaphore signals / You're the girl for me
CD _____ 422395
New Rose / Jun '94 / Direct / ADA.

BIG SMASH
Pop song / Tonight / Too busy / Broken doll / Can I be your hero / Back in my hometown / Whole wide world / Take the cash / Let's go to the pictures / Walking on the surface of the moon / Hit and miss Judy / I wish it would rain / It'll soon be the weekend / Strange towns / Excuse me / Break my mind / Good conversation / Out of the blue / Reconnez cherie / Veronica / Brain thieves / Semaphore signals / I need a situation / Final taxi / There isn't anything else
CD _____ STIFFCD 13
Disky / Jan '94 / THE / BMG / Discovery / Pinnacle.

LE BEAT GROUP ELECTRIQUE
Tell me I'm the only one / Wishing my life away / Depression / It's a sick sick world / Just for you / Sarah / Sun is pouring down / I'm not going to cry / You sweet big thing / Fuck by fuck / Parallel beds / True happiness
CD _____ 422396
New Rose / Jun '94 / Direct / ADA.

WRECKLESS ERIC
Reconnez cherie / Rags 'n' tatters / Waxworks / Grown ups / Telephone home / Whole wide world / Rough kids / Personal hygiene / Brain thieves / There isn't anything
CD _____ REP 4217-WY
Repertoire / Aug '91 / Pinnacle / Cadillac.

Wreckx N Effect

HARD OR SMOOTH
New jack swing II (Hard version) / Wreckx shop / Rump shaker / Knock-n-boots / Tell me how you feel / Wreckx-N-Effect / Here we come / Ez come ez go (what goes up must come down) / Hard (short) / Smooth (Short) / My cute (CD & cassette only.)

CD _____ MCD 10566
MCA / Nov '92 / BMG.

Wrecks 'N' Effect

Go for what you know / We be Mafia / I need money / Let's do it again / Wreckx-n-effect
CD _____ K 781 860 2
Atlantic / Jul '94 / Warner Music.

Wrekking Machine

MECHANISTIC TERMINATION
CD _____ 9040182
Mausoleum / Apr '95 / Grapevine.

Wrens

SILVER
CD _____ GROW 010-2
Grass / Apr '94 / SRD.

Wretched

LIFE OUT THERE
CD _____ HELL 024
Hellhound / Sep '93 / Plastic Head.

PSYCHOSMATIC MEDICINE
CD _____ H 0031-2
Hellhound / May '94 / Plastic Head.

Wright, Andrew

PIPERS OF DISTINCTION
CD _____ CDMON 802
Monarch / Dec '89 / CM / ADA / Duncans / Direct.

Wright, Betty

4U2 NJOY
4 U 2 NJOY / It's been real / Quiet storm / Keep love new / From pain to joy / Valley of lonely / Lightning / We "down" / Won't be long now
CD _____ SDCD 2
Sure Delight / Jul '89 / Jetstar.

BEST OF BETTY WRIGHT
Shoorah shoorah / Tonight is the night pts 1 and 2 / Where is the love / That's when I'll stop loving you / Ooh la la / Slip and do it / If I ever do you wrong / Life / Do right girl / I think I'd better think about it / Smother me / You can't see for looking / Loving is really my game / That man of mine / If you abuse my love / Sometime kind of thing / Room at the top / My love is
CD _____ NEMCD 671
Sequel / May '94 / BMG.

MOTHER WIT
CD _____ MSBCD 3301
MS. B. / Oct '89 / Jetstar.

Wright, Billy

GOIN' DOWN SLOW
If I didn't love you so / Sad hour blues / Goin down slow / After a while / Four cold cold wails / Live the life / I remember / Will you need me / Billy's boogie blues / This love of mine / If I had my life to live over / Every evenin' / Drinkin' and thinkin' / Restless blues
CD _____ SV 0257
Savoy Jazz / Nov '94 / Conifer / ADA.

Wright, Chely

RIGHT IN THE MIDDLE OF IT
CD _____ 5295532
Polydor / Jan '96 / PolyGram.

Wright, David

DISSIMILAR VIEWS
CD _____ AD9 CD
AD Music / Mar '95 / Select.

Wright, Frank

YOUR PRAYER
CD _____ ESP 1053-2
ESP / Jan '94 / Jazz Horizons / Jazz Music.

Wright, John

RIDE THE ROLLING SKY
CD _____ FE 097CD
Fellside / Jan '94 / Target/BMG / Direct / ADA.

Wright, Marva

I STILL HAVEN'T FOUND WHAT I'M LOOKING FOR
CD _____ AIMA 2CD
Aim / Oct '95 / Direct / ADA / Jazz Music.

Wright, O.V.

O.V. WRIGHT 45'S
CD _____ HILOCD 2
Hi / Nov '93 / Pinnacle.

O.V. WRIGHT LIVE
I'd rather be blind, crippled and crazy / Eight men, four women / Love and happiness / When a man loves a woman / You're gonna make me cry / Ace of spades / Precious, precious / God blessed of our love /

That's how strong my love is / Into something (can't shake loose)
CD _____ HIUKCD 426
Hi / Jul '89 / Pinnacle.

THAT'S HOW STRONG MY LOVE IS
Live my life without you / God blessed our love / When a man loves a woman / That's how strong my love is / Bottom line / I don't do windows / That's the way I feel about cha / Your good thing is about to end / Let's straighten it out / I don't know why / No easy way to say goodbye / Little more time / Since you left (these arms of mine) / Long road / Rhymes / Fool can't see the light / I'm gonna be a big man
CD _____ HIUKCD 108
Hi / Dec '89 / Pinnacle.

WRIGHT STUFF, THE
Into something (can't shake loose) / I feel love growin' / Precious, precious / Trying to live my life without you / Your good thing is about to end / Bottom line / I don't do windows / I don't know why / Time we have / You gotta have love / Rhymes / Without you
CD _____ HIUKCD 414
Hi / May '87 / Pinnacle.

WRIGHT STUFF, THE/LIVE
Into something (can't shake loose) / I feel love growin' / Precious, precious / Trying to live my life without you / Your good thing is about to end / Bottom line / I don't do windows / I don't know why / Time we have / You gotta have love / Rhymes / Without you / I'd rather be blind, crippled and crazy / Ace of spades / Eight men, four women / Love and happiness / God blessed our love / When a man loves a woman / That's how strong my love is / You're gonna make me cry
CD _____ HIUKCD 103
Hi / Dec '89 / Pinnacle.

Wright, Rev. Robert

REMEMBER ME
CD _____ EDCD 380
Edsel / Dec '93 / Pinnacle / ADA.

Wright, Sandra

WOUNDED WOMAN
Wounded woman / Sha-la bandit / I'm not strong enough to love you again / I come running back / Lovin' you, lovin' me / Man can't be a man (without a woman) / Midnight affair / I'll see you through / Please don't say goodbye
CD _____ VEXCD 11
Demon / Jun '92 / Pinnacle / ADA.

Wright, Stephen

INTERNATIONAL CHANGE
CD _____ ROTCD 003
Reggae On Top / Nov '94 / Jetstar / SRD.

Wright, Tim

SURVIVAL
CD _____ LICD 901221
Line / Nov '92 / CM / Grapevine / ADA / Conifer / Direct.

Wrigley, Jennifer

WATCH STONE, THE (Wrigley, Jennifer & Hazel)
CD _____ AT 038CD
Attic / Jan '95 / CM / ADA.

Wu Man

CHINESE MUSIC FOR THE PIPA
CD _____ NI 5368CD
Nimbus / Oct '93 / Nimbus.

Wu Tang Clan

ENTER THE WU TANG (36 CHAMBERS)
Shaolin sword / Bring da ruckus / Shame on a nigga / Clan in da front / Wu-tang / Seventh Chamber / Can it be so simple / Wu-tang sword / da mystery of chessboxin' / Wu-tang: ain't nuthing ta taf' wit / C.R.E.A.M. / Method man / Protect ya neck / Tearz / Seventh Chamber pt 2
CD _____ 74321203672
RCA / Apr '94 / BMG.

Wubble-U

WHERE'S WUBBLE-U
Theme from Wubble-U / Jellied eels / Petal / I like the future / Wow man / Name Czech / Europhobix / Realitea break / Down / Theme reprisal / Giantkillaz / Kazum / Ambient bingo nuns / Time / Stanley clears the throakus (featuring Stanley Unwin) / Angel in Bermondsey (pt 1)
CD _____ 8286662
Go Discs / Oct '95 / PolyGram.

Wunderlich, Klaus

IN A ROMANTIC MOOD (28 Romantic Melodies)
Limelight / Breeze and I / More / I could have danced all night / Love story / Feelings / Don't cry for me Argentina / Un homme et une femme / I love Paris / Our love is here to stay / La vie en rose / Over the rainbow / Lara's theme / This is my song / Twilight

time / They can't take that away from me / C'est si bon / I kiss your hand, Madame / If you could read my mind / Massachusetts / Something stupid / Greensleeves / Parlez-moi d'amour / Song of the Indian guest / Killing me softly / Ave Maria / Deine spuren im sand / Strangers in the night / This guy's in love with you
CD _____ **CD MFP 6011**
Music For Pleasure / Oct '87 / EMI.

KEYS FOR LOVERS
CD _____ **NSPCD 507**
Connoisseur / Mar '95 / Pinnacle.

PLAYS ABBA - THE WINNER TAKES IT ALL
CD _____ **NSPCD 506**
Connoisseur / Jan '94 / Pinnacle.

SAMBA SOUTH AMERICA (Samba Sudamerika)
Amor amor amor / Cu-cu-rru-cu-cu-paloma / Summer samba / Besame mucho / Mas que nada / One note samba / La felicidad / Desafinado / Brazil / Amorada / Amapola / El cumbanchero
CD _____ **8.27419**
Crystal Clear / Oct '88 / Pinnacle.

TRIBUTE TO FRANK SINATRA, A
Lady is a tramp / Strangers in the night / I only have eyes for you / Something / From here to eternity / I've got you under my skin / My way / Downtown / New York, New York / Something stupid / Someone to watch over me / What now my love / Autumn in New York / Night and day / I'm gettin' sentimental over you / Just one of those things
CD _____ **NSPCD 502**
Connoisseur / Apr '91 / Pinnacle.

VERY BEST OF KLAUS WUNDERLICH, THE
Ballade pour Adeline / Yesterday / My way / I just called to say I love you / New York, New York / Tico-tico / Strangers in the night / Whiter shade of pale / What a wonderful world / Last waltz / Raindrops keep falling on my head / In the mood / I left my heart in San Francisco / Something stupid / Brazil / Wonderful by night
CD _____ **PWKS 4082**
Carlton Home Entertainment / Aug '91 / Carlton Home Entertainment.

Wushcatte

THIS THIRD ANIMAL
Deserted / Rudy Vallee / Joe / White horses / It's not Herne Bay / Down in the marigolds / Wushcatte / Latimer's phrasing / Hey crazy
CD _____ **KWCD 026**
Kitchenware / Oct '93 / Sony / PolyGram / BMG.

Wyands, Richard

ARRIVAL, THE (Wyands, Richard Trio)
CD _____ **DIW 611**
DIW / Nov '92 / Harmonia Mundi / Cadillac.

REUNITED
CD _____ **CRISS 1105**
Criss Cross / Oct '95 / Cadillac / Harmonia Mundi.

Wyatt, Robert

DONESTAN
CD _____ **R AY IA**
Rough Trade / Sep '91 / Pinnacle.

FLOTSAM AND JETSAM
CD _____ **R 3112**
Rough Trade / Aug '94 / Pinnacle.

GOING BACK A BIT (A little history of Robert Wyatt)
Moon in June / Alifib / Alifie / Soup song / Calyx / Sonia / All she wanted / I'm a believer / Yesterday man
CD _____ **CDVM 9031**
Virgin / Jul '94 / EMI.

MID EIGHTIES
CD _____ **R 2952**
Rough Trade / Jan '93 / Pinnacle.

NOTHING CAN STOP US
CD _____ **ROUGHCD 35**
Rough Trade / May '87 / Pinnacle.

OLD ROTTEN HAT
CD _____ **ROUGHCD 69**
Rough Trade / Nov '86 / Pinnacle.

ROCK BOTTOM
Sea song / Last straw / Little Red Riding Hood hit the road / Alifib / Little Red Robin Hood hit the road
CD _____ **CDV 2017**
Virgin / Feb '89 / EMI.

RUTH IS STRANGER THAN RICHARD
Soup song / Sonia / Team spirit / Song for Che / Muddy mouse (A) / Solar flares / Muddy mouse (B) / Five black notes and one white note / Muddy mouse (C) / Muddy mouth
CD _____ **CDV 2034**
Virgin / Feb '89 / EMI.

SHORT BREAK, A
Short break / Tubab / Kutcha / Ventilatir / Unmasked
CD _____ **VP 108 CD**
Voice Print / Oct '92 / Voice Print.

Wycherley, Ellen

SCOTTISH CANTICLE, A
CD _____ **EWCD 004**
Auldgate / Jul '94 / CM.

Wygals

HONEYOCKS IN THE WHITHERSOEVER
CD _____ **ROUGHCD 134**
Rough Trade / Jun '89 / Pinnacle.

Wylie-Hubbard, Ray

LOCO GRINGO'S LAMENT
CD _____ **DJD 3213**
Dejadisc / Dec '94 / Direct / ADA.

LOST TRAIN OF THOUGHT
CD _____ **DJD 3223**
Dejadisc / Nov '95 / Direct / ADA.

Wynberg, Simon

SIMON WYNBERG
Opal moon / Enriquito / Night sail / Bert's cafe / Amathunzi - shadows / Idler / No para vender / Cancao do amor / My gemini / Medicine man / Sanctuary
CD _____ **ND 61039**
Narada / Nov '93 / New Note / BMG.

Wyndham-Read, Martyn

MUSSELS ON A TREE
Bold Reynolds / Hills are clad / Irish lords / Reunion / Flash stockman / Bunch of red roses / Valley of todd / Brokenback land / Jim Jones / 'ard tack / Cockleshells /

Springtime it brings on the shearing / Ginny on the moor / Van dieman's land / Shelter
CD _____ **FE 084CD**
Fellside / '92 / Target/BMG / Direct / ADA.

SUNLIT PLAINS
CD _____ **FECD 102**
Fellside / Jan '95 / Target/BMG / Direct / ADA.

Wynette, Tammy

BEST OF TAMMY WYNETTE
Stand by your man / Lonely street / D.I.V.O.R.C.E. / Gentle on my mind / Take me to your world / Almost persuaded / Your good girl's gonna go bad / Apartment no. 9 / Hey good lookin' / It don't wanna play house / My arms stay open late / There goes my everything
CD _____ **CD 32015**
CBS / Jun '91 / Sony.

BIGGEST HITS
I don't wanna play house / Take me to your world / D.I.V.O.R.C.E. / Stand by your man / Ways to love a man / When he loves me (he loves me all the way) / Run woman run / Bedtime story / My man (mon homme) / Till I get it right / Kids say the darndest things / Till I can make it on my own / You and me / Starting over / Cowboys don't shoot straight (like they used to) / Crying in the rain
CD _____ **983320 2**
Pickwick/Sony Collector's Choice / Nov '93 / Carlton Home Entertainment / Pinnacle / Sony.

COUNTRY STARS (Wynette, Tammy & George Jones)
No show jones / Race is on / Bartender blues / I always get lucky with you / She's my rock / Chicken reel (Instr.) / He stopped loving her today / Who's gonna fill their shoes / One I loved back then / Welcome to my world / Another chance / You good girl's gonna go bad / Ode to Billy Joe / Singing my song / Till I can make it on my own / Womanhood / Fairy tales / When the grass grows over me / Amazing grace / I'll fly away / Will the circle be unbroken / I saw the light / Stand by your man / Crying in the rain
CD _____ **PLATCD 351**
Platinum Music / May '91 / Prism / Ross.

FIRST LADY OF COUNTRY
Stand by your man / There goes my everything / Gentle on my mind / Honey / Almost persuaded / I can still believe in you / Your good girl's gonna go bad / Ode to Billy Joe / No charge / If we never love again / Crying in the chapel / Cry / Heaven's just a sin away / D.I.V.O.R.C.E.
CD _____ **PWKS 4047**
Carlton Home Entertainment / Apr '91 / Carlton Home Entertainment.

GREATEST HITS: TAMMY WYNETTE
I don't wanna play house / D.I.V.O.R.C.E. / Kids / Cowboys don't shoot straight (like they used to) / Starting over / Run woman run / Take me to your world / Ways to love a man / Till I can make it on my own / Crying in the rain / Bedtime story
CD _____ **902122-2**
Pickwick/Sony Collector's Choice / Mar '94 / Carlton Home Entertainment / Pinnacle / Sony.

I'LL FLY AWAY (Wynette, Tammy & George Jones)
CD _____ **MU 6048**
Musketeer / Oct '92 / Koch.

IN CONCERT
CD _____ **CDCD 1259**
Charly / Jun '95 / Charly / THE / Cadillac.

SOMETIMES WHEN WE TOUCH
Sometimes when we touch / You can lead a heart to love (but you can't make it fall) / Breaking away / Everytime you touch her / Between twenty-nine and danger / It's only over for you / Part of the first part / It's hard to be the dreamer (When I used to be the dream) / If it ain't love / He talks to me
CD _____ **983398-2**
Pickwick/Sony Collector's Choice / Mar '94 / Carlton Home Entertainment / Pinnacle / Sony.

STAND BY YOUR MAN
You make me want to be a mother / Another lonely song / Kids say the darndest things / Love's the answer / Woman to woman / Bedside story / Stand by your man / Good lovin' / Reach out your hand / Please come to Boston / Till I get it right / My man (understands) / There goes that old steel guitar / Help me make it through the night
CD _____ **983283 2**
Pickwick/Sony Collector's Choice / Oct '93 / Carlton Home Entertainment / Pinnacle / Sony.

WITHOUT WALLS
It's the last thing I do / Woman's needs / Every breath you take / If you were to wake up / Glasshouses / What do they know / All I am to you / I second that emotion / This love / Girl thang
CD _____ **4748002**
Epic / Apr '95 / Sony.

Wynn, Steve

DAZZLING DISPLAY
CD _____ **812202832-2**
WEA / Mar '93 / Warner Music.

FLOURESCENT
CD _____ **OUT 116-2**
Brake Out / Nov '94 / Vital.

TAKE YOUR FLUNKY AND DANGLE
CD _____ **RTS 13**
Return To Sender / Dec '94 / Direct / ADA.

Wynne, Philippe

PHILIPPE WYNNE
Sexy girl / You ain't going anywhere but gone / Help us to stand / You made me love you (why did you do it) / Let me go, lover / All the way / Did I jump / He don't love you / Lovin' you is killing me / America we're still No. 1 / Whip it
CD _____ **NEMCD 625**
Sequel / Jun '92 / BMG.

Wynona Riders

J.D. SALINGER
CD _____ **LOOKOUT 104CD**
Lookout / Sep '95 / SRD.

Wynter, Mark

RECOLLECTED
CD _____ **NEXCD 162**
Sequel / Apr '91 / BMG.

X

X Marks The Pedwalk

AIR BACK TRAX
CD _____ CDZOT 118
Zoth Ommog / Aug '94 / Plastic Head.

KILLING HAD BEGUN
CD _____ CDZOT 107
Zoth Ommog / Mar '94 / Plastic Head.

PARANOID ILLUSIONS
CD _____ CDZOT 29
Talitha / Aug '93 / Plastic Head.

X-103

ATLANTIS
CD _____ E 01740CD
Tresor / Mar '93 / SRD.

X-CNN

X-CNN 4
CD _____ XCNN 4CD
Transglobal / May '94 / Vital.

X-Cops

YOU HAVE THE RIGHT TO REMAIN SILENT
CD _____ 14080-2
Metal Blade / Oct '95 / Plastic Head.

X-Mal Deutschland

FETISCH
Qual / Geheimnis / Young man / In der nacht / Orient / Hand in hand / Kaempfen / Danghem / Boomerang / Stummes kind / Qual (remix) (CD only) / Sehnsucht (CD only) / Zeit (CD only)
4AD / '87 / Disc.
CD _____ CAD 302CD

TOCSIN
Mondicht / Eiland / Reigen / Tag fur tag (day by day) / Augen blich / Begrab / Mein herz / Nacht schatten / Christmas in Australia / Der wisch / Incubus succubus II (CD only) / ViFo (CD only)
CD _____ CAD 407CD
4AD / Jun '87 / Disc.

X-Rated

TIGHT PUM PUM
CD _____ LG 21077
Lagoon / May '93 / Magnum Music Group / THE.

X-Ray Spex

GERM FREE ADOLESCENTS
CD _____ CDVM 9001
Virgin / Jun '92 / EMI.

X-Specials

COZ I LUV YOU
CD _____ RRSCD 1010
Receiver / Feb '94 / Grapevine.

X-Tal

DIE MONSTER DIE
CD _____ A 012D
Alias / Jul '92 / Vital.

GOOD LUCK
Stating the obvious again / Smells like smoke / Good shepherd / Cat box / I know that / Good luck
CD _____ A 036D
Alias / Jul '93 / Vital.

MAYDAY
Union sunrise / Apocalypservice / Basics 101 / Airy toy / Frightened / Five legged spider / Soul politics / Blotterdammerung / Diet of worms / Studpuppet / Offhand / Never been young / Look of love / Best sellers
CD _____ RTD 15718642
World Service / Sep '94 / Vital.

Xalam

APARTHEID
CD _____ ENC 134C
Encore / '88 / EMI.

Xenakis Ensemble

REBONDS/AKEA/EPICYLES
CD _____ BVHAASTCD 9219
Bvhaast / Jun '89 / Cadillac.

Xentrix

SCOURGE
CD _____ HMRXD 198
Heavy Metal / Nov '95 / Sony.

Xerxes

BEYOND MY IMAGINATION
CD _____ GIT 001
General Inquisitor Torquemado's / Oct '93 / Plastic Head.

Xiame

PENSA
Pensa / Tokyoto / Arastape pe / Falando / Anduva / Kleiner bar / Carioca / Nossa doce lia / Hickyoung / Dois berlinese in Rio / Goodbye, pork pie hat / Dor da floresta
CD _____ VBR 21072
Vera Bra / Aug '92 / Pinnacle / New Note.

XIAME (OUR EARTH)
Xiame / Nosso destino / Minha rua / Guar-atiba / Rio De Janeiro / Um brasileiro em Berlin / Mutio swer / Gone but still here / Round Midnight / Choro de crainza / I can't stand the pain / Flor da terra
CD _____ VRB 20362
Vera Bra / Jul '90 / Pinnacle / New Note.

Xid

XID
CD _____ RTD 19519182
Our Choice / Nov '94 / Pinnacle.

XIII

SALT
CD _____ 342712
No Bull / Nov '95 / Koch.

Xingu Hill

MAPS OF THE IMPOSSIBLE
CD _____ NZ 035CD
Nova Zembla / May '95 / Plastic Head.

XL

XLENT
CD _____ OCTO 4042
Ondine / Aug '95 / Koch / ADA.

XLNC

R U READY
CD _____ DMUT 1254
Multitone / Aug '93 / BMG.

Xolton, Blake

COOL ON MY SKIN
CD _____ ROSE 166CD
New Rose / Mar '89 / Direct / ADA.

Xscape

HUMMIN' COMIN' AT 'CHA
Hummin' comin' at 'cha (intro) / Just kickin' it / Pumpin' / Let me know / W.S.S. Deez nuts / With you / Is my living in vain / Love on my mind / Tonight / Just kickin' it (remix) / Understanding (Not on original LP)
CD _____ 474344 2
Columbia / Nov '94 / Sony.

OFF THE HOOK
Do your thang / Feels so good / Hard to say goodbye / Can't hang / Who can I run to / Hip hop barber shop request line / Do you want to / What can I do / Do like lovers do / Work me slow / Love's a funny thing / Keep it on the real
CD _____ 4896442
Columbia / Jul '95 / Sony.

XTC

BIG EXPRESS, THE
Wake up / All you pretty girls / Shake you donkey up / Seagulls screaming kiss her kiss her / This world over / Everyday story of smalltown / I bought myself a liarbird /

Reign of blows / You're the wish (you are) I had / I remember the sun / Train running low on soul coal / Red brick dream (CD & MC only) / Washaway (CD & MC only) / Blue overall (CD & MC only)
CD _____ CDV 2325
Virgin / '84 / EMI.

BLACK SEA
Respectable street / Generals and majors / Living through another Cuba / Love at first sight / Rocket from a bottle / No language in our lungs / Towers of London / Paper and iron (notes and coins) / Burning with optim-ism's flame / Sgt. Rock (is going to help me) / Travels in nihilon / Smokeless zone (CD only) / Don't lose your temper (CD only) / Somnambulist (CD only)
CD _____ CDV 2173
Virgin / Jun '88 / EMI.

COMPACT XTC, THE (The Singles 1978-1985)
Science friction / Making plans for Nigel / Sgt. Rock (is going to help me) / Senses working overtime / Love on a famboy's wages / Wake up / Statue of Liberty / This is pop / Are you receiving me / Life begins at the hop / Wait till your boat goes down / Generals and majors / Towers of London / Ball and chain / Great fire / Wonderland / All you pretty girls / This world over
CD _____ CDV 2251
Virgin / '86 / EMI.

DRUMS AND WIRES
Making plans for Nigel / Helicopter / Day in, day out / When you're near me I have diffi-culty / Ten feet tall / Roads girdle the globe / Real by reel / Millions / That is the way / Outside world / Scissor man / Complicated game
CD _____ CDV 2129
Virgin / Jun '88 / EMI.

ENGLISH SETTLEMENT
Runaways / Ball and chain / Senses work-ing overtime / Jason and the Argonauts / No thugs in our house / Yacht dance / All of a sudden (it's too late) / Melt the guns / Leisure (LP & MC only) / It's nearly Africa / Knuckle down / Fly on the wall / Down in the cockpit (LP & MC only) / English round-about / Snowman
CD _____ CDV 2223
Virgin / Dec '81 / EMI.

EXPLODE TOGETHER (The Dub Experiments 1978-1980)
Part 1 (go) / Dance with me Germany / Beat the bible / Dictionary of modern marriage / Clap clap clap / We kill the beast / Part II (take away) / Commerciality / Day they pulled the North Pole down / Forgotten language of light / Steam fist futurist / Shore leave ornithology (another 1950) / Cairo / Part III (the lure of the salvage) / Rotary / Madhattan / I sit in the snow / Work away / Tokyo day / New broom
CD _____ CDOVD 308
Virgin / Jul '93 / EMI.

GO 2
Meccanik dancing / Crowded room / Bat-tery brides (Andy paints Brian) / Buzzcity talking / Rhythm / Beattown / Life is good in the greenhouse / I am the audience / Ted / My weapon / Jumping in Gomorrah / Su-per tuff / Are you receiving me (CD only)
CD _____ CDV 2108
Virgin / Jul '87 / EMI.

MUMMER
Beating of hearts / Wonderland / Love on a famboy's wages / Great fire / Deliver us from the elements / Human alchemy / La-dybird / In loving memory of a name / Me and the wind / Funk pop a roll
CD _____ CDV 2264
Virgin / Jun '88 / EMI.

NONSUCH
Ballad of Peter Pumpkinhead / My bird per-forms / Dear Madam Barnum / Humble daisy / Smartest monkeys / Disappointed / Holly up on poppy / Crocodile / Rook / Om-nibus / That wave / She appeared / War dance / Wrapped in grey / Ugly underneath / Bungalow / Books are burning
CD _____ CDV 2699
Virgin / Apr '92 / EMI.

ORANGES AND LEMONS
Garden of earthly delights / King for a day / Loving / Across the antheap / Pink thing /

Chalkhills and children / Mayor of Simpleton / Here comes President kill again / Poor skeleton steps out / Hold me daddy / Min-ature sun / One of the millions / Scarecrow people / Merely a man / Cynical days
CD _____ CDV 2581
Virgin / Apr '92 / EMI.

RADIO 1 SESSIONS
Opening speech / No thugs in our house / Runaways / You're the wish (you are) I had / Poor skeleton steps out / Crosswires / Seagulls screaming kiss her kiss her / Real by reel / Into the atom age / Meccanik dancing / Ten feet tall / Scarecrow people / I'm bugged / Dance band / Jason and the argonauts / One of the millions / Roads gir-dle the globe
CD _____ CDNT 008
Strange Fruit / Oct '94 / Pinnacle.

RAG 'N' BONE BUFFET (Rarities & Out-Takes)
Extrovert / Ten feet tall / Mermaid smiled / Too many cooks in the kitchen (the colonel) / Respectable street / Looking for footprints / Over rusty water / Heaven is paved with broken glass / World is full of angry young men / Punch and Judy / Thanks for Christ-mas (the three wise men) / Tissue tigers / I need protection (the colonel) / Another sat-ellite / Strange tales / Officer blue / Scissor man / Cockpit dance minute / Pulsing puls-ing / Happy families / Countdown to Christ-mas party time / Blame the weather / Take this town / History of rock 'n' roll
CD _____ CDOVD 311
Virgin / Jul '93 / EMI.

SKYLARKING
Summer's cauldron / Grass / Meeting place / That's really super, supergirl / Ballet for a rainy day / 1000 umbrellas / Season cycle / Earn enough for us / Big day / Another satellite / Mermaid smiled / Man who sailed around his soul / Dying / Sacrificial bonfire
CD _____ CDV 2399
Virgin / Jul '93 / EMI.

WHITE MUSIC
Radios in motion / Crosswires / This is pop / Do what you do / Statue of Liberty / All along the watchtower / Into the atom age / I'll set myself on fire / I'm bugged / Spinning top / Neon shuffle / New town animal in a furnished cage / Science friction (CD only) / She's so square (CD only) / Dance band (CD only) / Hang on to the night (CD only) / Heatwave (CD only) / Traffic light rock (CD only) / Instant tunes (CD only)
CD _____ CDV 2095
Virgin / Jun '88 / EMI.

Xymox

CLAN OF XYMOX
CD _____ CAD 503CD
4AD / '85 / Disc.

HEADCLOUDS
Spiritual high / It's your life / Prophecy / Wild is the wind / Single day / Love thrills / Beginning / Reaching out / Headclouds / January
CD _____ ZCTMT 4
Zok / May '93 / Grapevine / PolyGram / Pin-nacle / Koch.

MEDUSA
CD _____ CAD 613CD
4AD / Nov '86 / Disc.

METAMORPHOSIS
CD _____ ZCDXY 005
Zok / Oct '94 / Grapevine / PolyGram / Pinnacle / Koch.

REMIX ALBUM
CD _____ 340372
Koch / Dec '94 / Koch.

Xysma

DELUXE
CD _____ SP 1020
Spinefarm / Jul '94 / Plastic Head.

XYZ

COMPAS-ZOUK
CD _____ CD 1379
Sterns / Jan '91 / Sterns / CM.

Y & T

MUSICALLY INCORRECT
Long way down / I've got my own / 21st Century / Fly away / Nowhere land / I'm lost / Quicksand / Pretty prison / Confusion / Cold day in hell / Don't know what to do / No regrets
CD _____ CDMFN 191
Music For Nations / Sep '95 / Pinnacle.

YESTERDAY AND TODAY LIVE
CD _____ CDZORRO 21
Metal Blade / Mar '91 / Pinnacle.

Y Cyrff

MAE DDOE YN DDOE
CD _____ ANKCD 30
Ankst / Oct '92 / SRD.

MUE DDOE VW DDOE
CD _____ ANECD 30
Ankst / Nov '92 / SRD.

Y Live

Y ON EARTH
Humanity takes over / Who owns your soul / I want you all / Vortex vision / Don't buy it / Killing the innocents / Earthquake at Sel-lafield / Death of a nation / Logo of love / Humanity (reprise)
CD _____ ICACD 001
CyberArts / Dec '93 / Electronic Synthesiser Sound Projects.

Y.L.D.

FOOL'S PARADISE
CD _____ CDMFN 113
Music For Nations / Mar '91 / Pinnacle.

Yacoub, Gabriel

BEL
CD _____ KMCD 15
Red Sky / '91 / CM / ADA / Direct.

QUATRE
CD _____ BP 3182CD
Chantons Sous La True / Apr '95 / ADA.

Yaffayo

OVERTIME
CD _____ INTER 0001
Interaction / Sep '95 / Grapevine.

Yah Congo

YAH CONGO MEETES KING TUBBY & PROFESSOR AT DUB TABLE (Yah Congo & King Tubby/Mad Professor)
CD _____ RUSCD 8217
Roir USA / Oct '95 / Plastic Head.

Yakutia

EPICS AND IMPROVISATIONS
CD _____ 925652
Buda / Aug '93 / Discovery / ADA.

Yamaguchi, Takeshi

ALONE TOGETHER
I hear a rhapsody / Soloar / Spring time / Summertime / Alone together / Body and soul / Squirrel / Y Song / Nardis / Greensleeves
CD _____ KICJ 214
King/Paddle Wheel / Feb '95 / New Note.

Yamashita, Yosuke

DAZZLING DAYS
CD _____ 521303-2
Verve / May '94 / PolyGram.

KODO VERSUS YOSUKE YAMASHITA LIVE (Yamashita, Yosuke & Kodo)
Bolero / Monochrome / Secret of the base-ment room / Sing, sing, sing / Gezan Beyashi
CD _____ C 387900
Denon / '88 / Conifer.

WAYS OF TIME
CD _____ 5328412
Verve / Jun '95 / PolyGram.

Yamashta, Stomu

SEA AND SKY
Photon / Appeared / And / Touched / Ah / Time / To see / To know
CD _____ CDKUCK 072
Kuckuck / Jun '87 / CM / ADA.

Yamato Ensemble

ART OF THE JAPANESE BAMBOOFLUTE AND KOTO
CD _____ EUCD 1248
ARC / Nov '93 / ARC Music / ADA.

Yanagisawa, Rie

KUROKAMI - THE MUSIC OF JAPAN (Yanagisawa, Rie & Clive Bell)
Hari no umi (Sea in spring) / Kurokami / Dis-guised as a silverer of mirrors / Midare rin-zetsu / Yugao (The moon-flower) / Esashi Oiwake / Aki no shirabe (Tune of Autumn)
CD _____ CDSDL 367
Saydisc / Mar '94 / Harmonia Mundi / ADA / Direct.

Yancey, Jimmy

ETERNAL BLUES
CD _____ CD 52031
Blues Encore / May '94 / Target/BMG.

IN THE BEGINNING
CD _____ SACD 1
Solo Art / Jul '93 / Jazz Music.

JIMMY YANCEY, VOL. 1 (1939-40)
CD _____ DOCD 5041
Blues Document / Feb '92 / Swift / Jazz Music / Hot Shot.

JIMMY YANCEY, VOL. 2 (1940-43)
CD _____ DOCD 5042
Blues Document / Feb '92 / Swift / Jazz Music / Hot Shot.

JIMMY YANCEY, VOL. 3 (1943-50)
CD _____ DOCD 5043
Blues Document / Feb '92 / Swift / Jazz Music / Hot Shot.

Yankee Brass Band

YANKEE BRASS BAND, THE
Arizona quickstep / Bond's serenade / No one to love / Blondinette polka / Mabel waltz / Helene Schottisch / American hymn / Red stocking quickstep / Mockingbird quickstep / Memories of home-waltz / Schottische / Moon is above us / Brin d'amour polka / Goodnight my angel / Fi-remen's polka
CD _____ NW 312
New World / Aug '92 / Harmonia Mundi / ADA / Cadillac.

Yankovic, Weird Al

OFF AT THE DEEP END
CD _____ 5125062
Polydor / Jan '94 / PolyGram.

Yanni

CHAMELEON DAYS
Swept away / Marching season / Chasing shadows / Rain must fall / Days of summer / Reflections of passion / Walkabout / Ev-erglade run / Word in private
CD _____ 259644
Private Music / May '89 / BMG.

DARE TO DREAM
CD _____ 262667
Private Music / Aug '95 / BMG.

IN CELEBRATION OF LIFE
Santorini / Song for Antarctica / Marching season / Walkabout / Keys to imagination / Looking glass / Someday / Within attraction / Standing in motion / Sand dance
CD _____ 262342
Private Music / Jan '92 / BMG.

KEYS TO IMAGINATION
North shore of Matsushima / Looking glass / Nostalgia / Santorini / Port of mystery / Keys to imagination / Forgotten yesterdays / Forbidden dreams
CD _____ 259.960
Private Music / Nov '89 / BMG.

LIVE AT THE ACROPOLIS
Santorini / Keys to imagination / Until the last moment / Rain must fall / Acroyali/ Standing in motion (medley) / One man's dream / Within attraction / Nostalgia / Swept away / Reflections of passion / Aria (reissue only)
CD _____ 01005821222
Private Music / Jul '95 / BMG.

NIKI NANA
Niki nana (We're one) / Dance with a stranger / Running time / Someday / Human condition / First touch / Nightbird / Quiet man
CD _____ 260208
Private Music / Oct '89 / BMG.

OUT OF SILENCE
Sand dance / Standing in motion / Mermaid / With attraction / Street level / Secret vows / Point or origin / Acroyali / Paths on water
CD _____ 25 9965
Private Music / Nov '89 / BMG.

REFLECTIONS OF PASSION
After the sunrise / Mermaid / Quiet man / Nostalgia / Almost a whisper / Acrorali / Rain must fall / Swept away / Farewell / Se-cret vow / Flight of fantasy / Word in private / First touch / Reflections
CD _____ 260652
Private Music / May '90 / BMG.

Yano, Akiko

LOVE LIFE
CD _____ 7559792792
Elektra Nonesuch / Jan '95 / Warner Music.

Yarborough, Glenn

FAMILY PORTRAIT (Yarborough, Glenn & Holly)
Folk Era / Dec '94 / CM / ADA.
_____ FE 1416

LIVE AT THE TROUBADOUR
_____ FE 1704
Folk Era / Dec '94 / CM / ADA.

Yardbirds

COLLECTION: YARDBIRDS
I wish you would / Good morning little school girl / I ain't got you / Boom boom / Good morning little school girl (instr.) / Got to hurry / For your love / Too much monkey business / Got love if you want it / Here 'tis / Pontiac blues / Twenty three hours too long / Let it rock / Smokestack lightnin' / Honey in your hips / Heart full of soul / Evil hearted you / Still I'm sad / I'm a man / Jeff's blues / You're a better man than I / Shapes of things / Stroll on
CD _____ CCSCD 141
Castle / '88 / BMG.

HEART FULL OF SOUL
CD _____ 12206
Laserlight / May '94 / Target/BMG.

HONEY IN YOUR HIPS
CD _____ CDRB 4
Charly / Apr '94 / Charly / THE / Cadillac.

ON AIR
I ain't got you / For your love / I'm not talk-ing / I wish you would / Heart full of soul / I've been wrong / Too much monkey busi-ness / Love me like I love you / I'm a man / Evil hearted you / Still I'm sad / Hang on sloopy / Smokestack lightnin' / Mister, you're a better man than I / Train kept a rollin' / Shapes of things / Dust my blues / Scratch my back / Over under sideways down / Sun is shining / Most likely you'll go your way / Little games / Drinking muddy water / Thnik about it / Goodnight sweet Josephine / My baby
CD _____ BOJCD 20
Band Of Joy / May '91 / ADA.

OVER UNDER SIDEWAYS DOWN
CD _____ RVCD 12
Raven / May '91 / Direct / ADA.

RARITIES
CD _____ PRCDSP 501
Prestige / Aug '92 / Total/BMG.

ROGER THE ENGINEER
Happenings ten years time ago / Psycho daisies / Over under sideways down / Nazz are blue / Rack my mind / Lost women / I can't make your way / Farewell / Jeff's boo-gie / Hot house of Omagararshid / He's al-ways there / Turn into earth / What do you want / Ever since the world began
CD _____ EDCD 116
Edsel / Feb '83 / Pinnacle / ADA.

TRAIN KEPT A ROLLIN' (The Complete Georgio Gomelsky Productions/4CD Set)
CD Set _____ CDLIKBOX 3
Decal / Nov '95 / Charly / Swift.

VERY BEST OF THE YARDBIRDS, THE
For your love / Heart full of soul / Good morning little school girl / Still I'm sad / Evil hearted you / Certain girl / Jeff's blues / I wish you would / New York City / I'm not talking / You're a better man than I / Shapes of things / I'm a man / Boom boom / Smokestack lightnin' (live) / Let it rock (live) / You can't judge a book by the cover / Who do you love / Too much monkey business / Pretty girl / Stroll on / Respectable
CD _____ MCCD 023
Music Club / May '91 / Disc / THE / CM.

YARDBIRDS AVEC ERIC CLAPTON
CD _____ 842148
EVA / May '94 / Direct / ADA.

YARDBIRDS REUNION CONCERT (McCarty, Jim/Chris Deja & Band)
CD _____ CD 202020
Promised Land / Sep '92 / Kingdom / Direct.

Yared, Gabriel

MAP OF THE HUMAN HEART
CD _____ 5149002
Polydor / Jan '94 / PolyGram.

SHAMROCK
CD _____ TWI 854CD
Les Disques Du Crepuscule / Jun '88 / Discovery / ADA.

Yasar, Necdet

MUSIC OF TURKEY (Yasar, Necdet Ensemble)
CD _____ CDT 128
Topic / Apr '93 / Direct / ADA.

Yasus Afari

MENTAL ASSASSIN
CD _____ CDTZ 015
Tappa / Aug '93 / Jetstar.

Yawp

EXCUSES FOR HATE
CD _____ KANG 005CD
Kangaroo / Aug '95 / Plastic Head.

Yazbek, David

LAUGHING MAN
CD _____ BAH 22
Humbug / Mar '95 / Pinnacle.

Yazoo

UPSTAIRS AT ERIC'S
CD _____ CDSTUMM 7
Mute / May '95 / Disc.

YOU AND ME BOTH
CD _____ CDSTUMM 12
Mute / May '95 / Disc.

Yazz

ONE ON ONE
Have mercy / Calling 2 U / Child / One on one / How long / Back in love again / Baby talk / Everybody's gotta learn sometime / Look of love / Live your life / That's just the way that it is
CD _____ 521989-2
Polydor / Aug '94 / PolyGram.

Ybarra, Eva

A MI SAN ANTONIO (Ybarra, Eva Y Su Conjunto)
CD _____ ROU 6056CD
Rounder / Apr '94 / CM / Direct / ADA / Cadillac.

Year Zero

CREATION
CD _____ HOO 382
Noise/Modern Music / Jul '95 / Pinnacle / Plastic Head.

NIHIL'S FLAME
Prefall (Intro) / Planetfall / Headache station / Turish bolloring / Brilliantion draaming / Wishing horse / Year zero / Evergreen / Shining violet / Invention of God / Eternal dawn
CD _____ H 0027-2
Hellhound / Aug '94 / Plastic Head.

Yearwood, Trisha

HEARTS IN ARMOUR
Wrong side of Memphis / Nearest distance shore / You say you will / Walkaway Joe / Woman walk the line / Oh lonesome you / Down on my knees / For reasons I've for-gotten / You don't have to move the moun-tain / Hearts in armour
CD _____ MCD 10730
MCA / Apr '95 / BMG.

SONG REMEMBERS WHEN, THE
Song remembers when / Better your heart than mine / I don't fall in love so easy / Hard promises to keep / Mr. Radio / Nightingale / If I ain't got you / One in a row / Here comes temptation / Lying to the moon
CD _____ MCD 11024
MCA / Feb '94 / BMG.

THINKIN' ABOUT YOU
CD _____ MCD 11226
MCA / Feb '95 / BMG.

TRISHA YEARWOOD
CD _____ MCAD 10297
MCA / Nov '91 / BMG.

Yeats, Gráinne

BELFAST HARP FESTIVAL, THE
CD _____ CEFCD 156
Gael Linn / Jan '94 / Roots / CM / Direct / ADA.

Yello

1980-1985 - THE NEW MIX IN ONE GO
Daily disco / Swing / Evening's young / Pin-ball cha cha / I love you / Sometimes (Dr. Hirsch) / Base for Alec / Oh yeah / Lost again / Tub dub / Angel no / Desire / Ba-nanas to the beat / Koladiola / Domingo / Bostich / Live at the Roxy
CD _____ 826 773-2
Mercury / Jun '89 / PolyGram.

BABY
Intro / Rubber band man / Sticky jungle / Ocean club / Who's groove / Capri calling / Lazy / On the run / Blender / Sweet thunder
CD _____ 8487912
Mercury / Jun '91 / PolyGram.

CLARO QUE SI
Daily disco / No more Roger / Take it all / Evening's young / She's got a gun / Ballet mechanique / Quad el habib / Lorry / Homer hossa / Pinball cha cha
CD _____ 818 340 2
Mercury / Mar '88 / PolyGram.

FLAG
Tied up / Of course I'm lying / 3rd of June / Blazing saddles / Race / Alhambra / Tied up in gear / Otto di catania
CD _____ 8367782
Mercury / Aug '90 / PolyGram.

HANDS ON YELLO
Lost again / Excess / La habanera / L'hotel / I love you / Live at the Roxy / Oh yeah / Vicious circle / Crash dance / Dr. Van Steiner / Bostich / Ciel Ouvert / You gotta say yes to another excess / Great mission
CD _____ 5273832
Urban / Mar '95 / PolyGram.

ONE SECOND
Habanera / Moon on ice / Call it love / Le secret farida / Hawaiian chance / Rhythm divine / Santiago / Gold rush / Dr. Van Steiner / Si senor and the hairy grill
CD _____ 830 956-2
Mercury / Jun '89 / PolyGram.

SOLID PLEASURE
Bimbo / Night flanger / Reverse lion / Down-down samba / Magneto / Massage / Assis-tant's cry / Bostich / Rock stop / Coast to polka / Blue green / Eternal legs / Stanz-trigge / Bananas to the beat
CD _____ 818 339 2
Mercury / Mar '88 / PolyGram.

STELLA
Desire / Vicious games / Oh yeah / Desert inn / Stalakdrama / Koladiola / Domingo / Memories (Dr. Hirsch) / Let me cry / Ciel ouvert / Angel no
CD _____ 8228202
Mercury / Mar '88 / PolyGram.

YOU GOTTA SAY YES TO ANOTHER EXCESS
I love you / Look again / No more words / Crash dance / Great mission / You gotta say yes to another excess / Swing / Heavy whispers / Smile on you / Pumping velvet / Salut mayoumba
CD _____ 812 166-2
Mercury / Mar '88 / PolyGram.

ZEBRA
CD _____ 5224962
Mercury / Nov '94 / PolyGram.

Yellow Jackets

COLLECTION
Wildlife / Spin / Oz / Man facing north / Rev-elation / Freedomland / Jacket town / Dream / Foreign correspondent / You know that / Dewey
CD _____ GRP 98092
GRP / Mar '95 / BMG / New Note.

LIKE A RIVER
Men facing North / My old school / River waltz / Dewey (for miles) / Memoirs / Azure moon / Suenos / 1998 / Sandstone / Soli-tude / Man facing north / Dewey
CD _____ GRP 96892
GRP / Jan '93 / BMG / New Note.

LIVE WIRES
Homecoming / Bright lights / Dream / Free-domland / Downtown / Clair's song / Ger-aldine / Spin / Wildlife / Revelation
CD _____ GRP 96672
GRP / Mar '92 / BMG / New Note.

RUN FOR YOUR LIFE
Jacket town / Even song / Runferyerlife / Red sea / Muhammed / City of lights / Sage / Ancestors / Wisdom
CD _____ GRP 97542
GRP / Feb '94 / BMG / New Note.

Yellow Magic Orchestra

HI TECH-NO CRIME
CD _____ TRUCD 1
Internal / Nov '92 / PolyGram / Pinnacle.

MULTIPLIES
Technopolis / Absolute ego dance / Behind the mask / Computer game / Firecracker / Snakeman show / Nice age / Multiplies / Citizens of science / Tighten up
CD _____ L91492
Roadrunner / Sep '92 / Pinnacle.

SERVICE
CD _____ LS 91512
Roadrunner / Aug '92 / Pinnacle.

SOLID STATE SURVIVOR
Technopolis / Absolute ego dance / Rydeen / Castalia / Behind the mask / Day tripper / Insomnia / Solid state survivor
CD _____ LS 91552
Roadrunner / Jul '92 / Pinnacle.

Yellowman

20 SUPER HITS
CD _____ SONCD 0006
Sonic Sounds / Oct '90 / Jetstar.

BADNESS
CD _____ LACD 005
La / May '94 / Plastic Head.

BEST OF YELLOWMAN
Melodie / Dec '95 / Triple Earth / 794502
Discovery / ADA / Jetstar.
CD _____ 794502

BEST OF YELLOWMAN LIVE IN PARIS
CD _____ 503552
CD _____ 503562
Blue Silver / Apr '95 / Jetstar.

BLUEBERRY HILL
Blueberry Hill / Letter to Rosey / Jean a miss follow fashion / Who say yellow don't go hotel / Nah pay no tax / Anything me say / Young girl be wise / Another Saturday night
CD _____ GRELCD 107
Greensleeves / Sep '92 / Total/BMG / Jets-tar / SRD.

DON'T BURN IT DOWN
CD _____ GRELCD 110
Greensleeves / May '88 / Total/BMG / Jetstar / SRD.

FANTASTIC YELLOWMAN
CD _____ LG 21091
Lagoon / Nov '93 / Magnum Music Group / THE.

GALONG GALONG GALONG
Galong galong galong / Beat it / Under mi fat thing / Cus cus / Reggae get the grammy / Throw me corn / Skank quadrille / Blow saxophone / Money make friend / Bubble with mi ting
CD _____ GRELCD 87
Greensleeves / Nov '87 / Total/BMG / Jets-tar / SRD.

GOOD SEX GUIDE
CD _____ GRELCD 217
Greensleeves / Oct '95 / Total/BMG / Jetstar / SRD.

KING OF THE DANCE HALL
CD _____ RRTGCD 7717
Rohit / '88 / Jetstar.

KISS ME
Kiss me / Dicky / Hot again / Jordan river / Thanks and praise / Murderer / Hek she gwan / Love is a splendid thing / Woman / Slow motion
CD _____ 113862
Musidisc / Jul '95 / Vital / Harmonia Mundi / ADA / Cadillac / Discovery.

LIVE IN ENGLAND
CD _____ SON 0024
Greensleeves / Apr '92 / Total/BMG / Jetstar / SRD.

MAN YOU WANT, A
CD _____ SHCD 45011
Shanachie / Mar '94 / Koch / ADA / Greensleeves.

MESSAGE TO THE WORLD
CD _____ RASCD 3185
Ras / Jan '96 / Jetstar / Greensleeves / SRD / Direct.

MISTER YELLOWMAN
Natty sat upon the rock / Lost mi love / Mr. Chin / Two to six super mix / Morning ride / How you keep a dance / Jamaica a little Miami / Yellowman get's married / Duppy or gunman / Cocky did a hurt me
CD _____ GRELCD 35
Greensleeves / '87 / Total/BMG / Jetstar / SRD.

NEGRIL CHILL (Yellowman & Charlie Chaplin)
Arrival / Feeling sexy / Don't sell yourself / Nuff punany / Naw breed again / Undergal frock / Blueberry Hill / Reason with enter-tainers / Gone a South Africa / Jah mi fear / Trouble Rosie / Old lady / Listen Charlie / Same way it taste / Calypso jam / Don't drop yu pants / Rent a dread
CD _____ RE 155CD
Reach Out International / Nov '94 / Jetstar.

NOBODY MOVE - NOBODY GET HURT
Nobody move nobody get hurt / Strictly mi belly / Bedroom mazurka / Body move / Good lovin' / Wreck a pum pum / Hill and gully rider / Yellowman a lover boy / Watch your words / Why you bad so
CD _____ GRELCD 71
Greensleeves / Jul '89 / Total/BMG / Jetstar / SRD.

REGGAE CALYPSO ENCOUNTER
CD _____ RMJLCD 0101
Rohit / '88 / Jetstar.

REGGAE ON THE MOVE
CD _____ RASCD 3094
Greensleeves / Sep '93 / Total/BMG / Jetstar / SRD.

SATURDAY NIGHT
CD _____ RB 3009
Reggae Best / Jul '94 / Magnum Music Group / THE.

THEM A MAD OVER ME
CD _____ 78249700060
Channel One / Apr '95 / Jetstar.

THIEF
CD _____ MLCD 004
Mixing Lab / Jul '90 / Jetstar.

TWO GIANTS CLASH (Yellowman & Josey Wales)
Society party / Strictly bubbling / Mr. Big shot / King of the crop / Wrong girl to play with / Bobo dread / Mi have Fi get you / Cure for the fever / Jah a mi guiding star / Sorry to say
CD _____ GRELCD 63
Greensleeves / '89 / Total/BMG / Jetstar / SRD.

YELLOW LIKE CHEESE
Budget / Easy me ting / Gaze / Want a woman / To touch ya so / Yellow like cheese / No get nuthin' / Ain't no meaning / Na no lyrics / Mi mother love, my father love
CD _____ RASCD 3019
Ras / Jun '87 / Jetstar / Greensleeves / SRD / Direct.

YELLOWMAN GOING TO THE CHAPEL
Look in a me eye / Rub-a-dub / Going to the chapel / Hunnu fi move / Come back to Jamaica / No lucky in gambling / Ready fe them / Amen / To the bump
CD _____ GRELCD 97
Greensleeves / '86 / Total/BMG / Jetstar / SRD.

YELLOWMAN RIDES AGAIN
CD _____ RASCD 3034
Ras / Sep '88 / Jetstar / Greensleeves / SRD / Direct.

YELLOWMAN STRIKES AGAIN
CD _____ CY 78936
Nyam Up / Apr '95 / Conifer.

Yelworc

COLLECTION 1988-94
CD _____ EFA 125252
Celtic Circle / Apr '95 / SRD.

Yes

90125
Owner of a lonely heart / Hold on / It can happen / Changes / Cinema / Leave it / Our song / City of love / Hearts
CD _____ 790 125-2
Atlantic / Nov '83 / Warner Music.

AFFIRMATIVE (The Yes Family Album)
CD _____ VSOPCD 190
Connoisseur / Sep '93 / Pinnacle.

BIG GENERATOR
Rhythm of love / Big generator / Shoot high aim low / Almost like love / Love will find a way / Final eyes / I'm running / Holy lamb
CD _____ 790 522-2
Atlantic / Aug '87 / Warner Music.

CLASSIC YES
Heart of the sunrise / Wonderous stories / Yours is no disgrace / Starship trooper / Long distance runaround / Fish / And you and I
CD _____ 756782687-2
Atlantic / Sep '94 / Warner Music.

CLOSE TO THE EDGE
Solid time of change / Total mass retain / I get up, I get down / Seasons of man / And you and I / Cord of life / Eclipse / Preacher / Teacher / Siberian Khatru
CD _____ 756782666-2
Atlantic / Aug '94 / Warner Music.

DRAMA
Machine messiah / White car / Does it really happen / Into the lens / Run through the light / Tempus fugit
CD _____ 756782685-2
Atlantic / Sep '94 / Warner Music.

FRAGILE
Roundabout / Cans and Brahms / We have heaven / South side of the sky / Five per cent of nothing / Long distance runaround / Fish / Mood for a day / Heart of the sunrise
CD _____ 756782667-2
Atlantic / Aug '94 / Warner Music.

GOING FOR THE ONE
Going for the one / Turn of the century / Parallels / Wonderous stories / Awaken
CD _____ 756782670-2
Atlantic / Aug '94 / Warner Music.

RELAYER
Gates of delirium / Sound chaser / To be over

CD _____ 756782664-2
Atlantic / Sep '94 / Warner Music.

TALES FROM TOPOGRAPHIC OCEANS
Revealing science of God / Remembering / Ancient / Ritual
CD _____ 756782683-2
Atlantic / Sep '94 / Warner Music.

TALK
Calling / I am waiting / Real love / State of play / Walls / Where will you be / Endless dream (Silent spring/Talk/Endless dream)
CD _____ 828489-2
London / Mar '94 / PolyGram.

TIME AND A WORD
No opportunity necessary / No experience needed / Then / Everdays / Sweet dreams / Prophet / Clear days / Astral traveller / Time and a word
CD _____ 756782681-2
Atlantic / Sep '94 / Warner Music.

TORMATO
Future times / Rejoice / Don't kill the whale / Madrigal / Release release / Arriving UFO / Circus of heaven / Onward / On the silent wings of freedom
CD _____ 756782671-2
Atlantic / Aug '94 / Warner Music.

UNION
I would have waited forever / Shock to the system / Masquerade / Lift me up / Without hope you cannot start the day / Saving my heart / Miracle of life / Silent talking / More we live-let go / Angkor Wat (Not on LP) / Dangerous / Holding on / Evensong / Take the water to the mountain / Give and take (Not on LP)
CD _____ 261558
Arista / Apr '94 / BMG.

VERY BEST OF YES (Highlights)
Survival / Time and a word / Starship trooper / Life seeker / Disillusion / Wurm / I've seen all good people / Your move / All good people / Roundabout / Long distance runaround / Soon / Wonderous stories / Going for the one / Owner of a lonely heart / Leave it / Rhythm of love
CD _____ 7567825172
Atlantic / Sep '93 / Warner Music.

YES
Beyond and before / I see you / Yesterday and today / Looking around / Harold land / Every little thing / Sweetness / Survival
CD _____ 756782680-2
Atlantic / Aug '94 / Warner Music.

YES ALBUM, THE
Yours is no disgrace / Clap / Starship trooper / Life seeker / Disillusion / Wurm / I've seen all good people / Your move / All good people / Venture / Perpetual change
CD _____ 7567826652
Atlantic / Sep '94 / Warner Music.

YES YEARS, THE, (4CD Set)
Something's coming / Survival / Every little thing / Then / Everydays / Sweet dreams / No opportunity necessary, no experience needed / Time and a word / Starship trooper / Yours is no disgrace / I've seen all good people / Long distance runaround / Fish (schindleria praematurus) / Roundabout / Heart of the sunrise / America / Close to the edge (medley) / Ritual / Sound chaser / Soon / Amazing grace / Vevey (part 1) / Wonderous stories / Awaken / Mon-treux's theme / Vevey (part 2) / Going for the one / Money / Abilene / Don't kill the whale / On the silent wings of freedom / Does it really happen / Tempus fugit / Run with the fox / I'm down / Make it easy / It can happen / Owner of a lonely heart / Hold on / Shoot high aim low / Rhythm of love / Love will find a way / Changes / And you and I (medley) / Love conquers all
CD _____ 7567916442
Atlantic / Aug '91 / Warner Music.

YESSHOWS
Parallels / Time and a word / Going for the one / Gates of Delirium
CD _____ 756782686-2
Atlantic / Sep '94 / Warner Music.

YESSONGS (2CD Set)
Opening: Excerpt from the firebird suite / Siberian Khatru / Heart of the sunrise / Per-petual change / And you and I / Cord of life / Eclipse / Preacher and the teacher / Apocalypse / Mood for a day / Excerpts from the six wives of Henry VIII / Round-about / Long distance runaround / Fish / Close to the edge / Solid time of change / Total mass retain / I get up, I get down / Seasons of man / Yours is no disgrace / Starship trooper / Life seeker / Disillusion / Wurm
CD Set _____ 756782682-2
Atlantic / Sep '94 / Warner Music.

YESSTORY (2CD Set)
Survival / No opportunity necessary, no experience needed / Time and a word / Starship trooper / I've seen all good people / Roundabout / Heart of the sunrise / Close to the edge / Ritual / Soon / Wonderous stories / Going for the one / Don't kill the whale / Does it really happen / Make it easy / Owner of a lonely heart / Rhythm of love / Changes
CD _____ 7567917472
Atlantic / Sep '91 / Warner Music.

YESTERDAYS

America / Looking around / Time and a word / Sweet dreams / Then / Survival / Astral traveller / Dear father
CD _____ 756782684-2
Atlantic / Sep '94 / Warner Music.

Yetties

COME TO THE YETTIES BARN DANCE

Gay Gordons / Hello / Family waltz / Clopton bridge / Swanee river / Strip the willow / Cumberland square eight / Barn dance / Timber salvage reel / Swedish masquerade / Tom Pate / Devil's dream / Circassian circle
CD _____ GRCD 53
Grasmere / May '92 / Target/BMG / Savoy.

FIDDLER KNOWS, THE

CD _____ CD ALA 3010
ASV / '89 / Koch.

MUSICAL HERITAGE OF THOMAS HARDY

CD Set _____ CD ALD 4010
ASV / Feb '88 / Koch.

SINGALONG PARTY

CD _____ GRCD 72
Grasmere / Oct '95 / Target/BMG / Savoy.

SINGING ALL THE WAY

Over the hills and far away / Ball of yarn / Grey hawk / Polka medley / Rabbit / John Barleycorn / Winter / Poor, poor farmer / Ee weren't all bad / Man at the nore / Bread and cheese and kisses / We've got oil / Beggar's song / Beaumont rag / Back 'n' back yer you / Scarlet and the blue / Carolina moon / Beautiful dreamer / Early one evening / Linden lea / Bell ringing / Levi Jackson's rag / Wave over wave / Last rose of Summer / Praise o'Dorset
CD _____ CD ALA 3009
ASV / Jul '89 / Koch.

TOP OF THE CROPS

CD _____ GRCD 68
Grasmere / Oct '95 / Target/BMG / Savoy.

Yiladi Trio

SONGS IN YIDDISH & LADINO 3

CD _____ YILADI 9103
Yiladi / Sep '94 / Direct.

YN-Vee

YN-VEE

Even when U sleep / All I wanna do / 4 play / I'm goin' down / Sceamin' / Sonshine's groove / Chocolate / Stra8 hustler / Tricks-n-trainin' / YN-Vee / Real G / Gangsta's prayer / We got a good thing
CD _____ 523 585 2
Island / Oct '94 / PolyGram.

YO 3

BITTER SWEET

CD Set _____ GPRCD 5
General Production Recordings / Jun '94 / Pinnacle.

Yo La Tengo

MAY I SING WITH ME

CD _____ A 021CD
Alias / Jun '92 / Vital.

PAINFUL

CD _____ EFA 049272
Olly Olung / Gop '80 / Dloo.

Yo Yo

YOU BETTER ASK SOMEBODY

IBWin' wit my crewin' / Can you handle it / Westside story / Mackstress / Twenty Sack / You better ask somebody / They shit don't stink / Letter to the pen / Givin' it up / Pass it on / Girl's got a gun / Bonnie and Clyde theme
CD _____ 756792252-2
East West / Jun '93 / Warner Music.

Yoakam, Dwight

BUENOS NOCHES FROM A LONELY ROOM

I got you / One more name / What I don't know / Home of the blues / Buenos noches from a lonely room / She wore red dresses / I hear you knocking / I sang Dixie / Streets of Bakersfield / Floyd county / Send me the pillow that you dream on / Hold onto God
CD _____ 925749-2
Reprise / Jan '89 / Warner Music.

DWIGHT LIVE

CD _____ 9362459072
Reprise / May '95 / Warner Music.

GONE

CD _____ 9362460512
Reprise / Nov '95 / Warner Music.

GUITARS CADILLACS ETC ETC

Honky tonk man / It won't hurt / I'll be gone / South of cincinnati / Bury me / Guitars and cadilacs / Twenty years / Ring of fire / Miner's prayer / Heartache by the number
CD _____ 9253722
Reprise / Feb '93 / Warner Music.

HILLBILLY DELUXE

Little ways / Smoke along the track / Johnson's love / Please please baby / Readin', ritin' RT.23 / Always late (with your kisses) / 1000 miles from nowhere / Throughout all times / Little sister / This drinking will kill me
CD _____ 9255672
Reprise / Jun '87 / Warner Music.

IF THERE WAS A WAY

Distance between you and me / Heart that you own / Takes a lot to rock you / Nothing's changed here / Sad, sad music / Since I started drinkin' again / If there was a way / Turn it on, turn it up, turn me loose / It only hurts when I cry / Send a message to my heart / I don't need it done / You're the one
CD _____ 7599263342
Reprise / Nov '90 / Warner Music.

LA CROIX D'AMOUR

Things we said today / Truckin' / If there was a way / Hey little girl / What I don't know / Here comes the night / Dangerous man / Let's work together / Doin' what I did / Takes a lot to rock you / Suspicious minds / Long white cadillac
CD _____ 9362451362
Reprise / Nov '92 / Warner Music.

THIS TIME

Pocket of a clown / 1000 miles from nowhere / Home for sale / This time / Two doors down / Ain't that lonely yet / King of fools / Fast of you / Try not to look so pretty / Wild ride / Lonesome roads
CD _____ 936245241-2
Reprise / Apr '93 / Warner Music.

Yobs

XMAS II

CD _____ RRCD 153
Receiver / Oct '91 / Grapevine.

Yodellers In Gold

BEST YODELLERS, THE

CD _____ 323010
Koch / Sep '93 / Koch.

Yokota

FRANKFURT-TOKYO CONNECTION

CD _____ HHCD 3
Harthouse / Apr '94 / Disc / Warner Music.

Yole

A LA SOURCE

CD _____ SCD 711
Several / Nov '95 / ADA.

L'AMOUR D'ELOISE

CD _____ SCD 709
Several / Nov '95 / ADA.

Yona Kit

YONA KIT

CD _____ GR 20CD
Skingraft / Sep '95 / SRD.

Yoni

MY LITTLE YONI

Creepy bitch / Spirit of adventure / Black forest / Aquasonics / Beanz meanz jazz / P-yonic / Beach bun / Funk star (Classic mix)
CD _____ 940815CD
Source / Jun '95 / Vital.

York, Nora

TO DREAM THE WORLD

Driftin' on a dream / Vishnu's dream / Out of this world / Beirut / Pilgrim/When did you leave heaven / If I fell / War anthems/Is it the end of the world / Denial / You go to my head/Manic depression / Somebody else / Nobody else but me / Love for sale / Pursuit of happiness / You must believe in spring
CD _____ TCB 94602
TCB / Oct '94 / New Note.

York, Pete

STRING TIME IN NEW YORK

CD _____ BLR 84 015
L&R / May '91 / New Note.

SWINGING LONDON

CD _____ 341172
Koch / Apr '94 / Koch.

York Waits

CITY MUSICKE, THE

CD _____ BH 9409CD
Brewhouse / Jul '94 / Complete/Pinnacle.

MUSIC FROM THE TIME OF RICHARD III

CD _____ CDSDL 364
Saydisc / Oct '87 / Harmonia Mundi / ADA / Direct.

MUSIC FROM THE TIME OF THE SPANISH ARMADA

Queene's visiting of the campe at Tilsburie / Spanish pavan / Galliard (la gamba) / Crimson velvet / La doune cella / La shy myze / La bransle / Obtaining of the great galleazzo / Browninge my dere / Browninge fantasy / Les bransles gays / Delight pavan

/ Galliard to delight pavan / Staines morris / Quarter brawles / Pavana / Galiarda / Coranto / Watkin's ale / Robin is to the greenwood gone / Wilson's fantasie / Spanish lady / Cushion dance / Dulcina / All you that love good fellowes / Eighty eight or Sir Francis drake / Les bransles de Champagne / Carman's whistle / Under and over / Pepper is black / Millfield / Roowe well ye marynors
CD _____ CDSDL 373
Saydisc / Jul '88 / Harmonia Mundi / ADA / Direct.

OLD CHRISTMAS RETURN'D

CD _____ CDSDL 398
Saydisc / Oct '92 / Harmonia Mundi / ADA / Direct.

Yorkshire Imperial Band

PAGEANTRY

Strike up the band / Chelsea bridge / Homage march (from Sigurd Jorsalfar) / On the way home / Can can / Girl with the flaxen hair / March: Le coq d'or / Pageantry / Arnhem / Toccata from 'Organ symphony No. 5' / Drink to me only with thine eyes / Entry of the huntresses from 'Sylvia' / Country scene / Sandpaper ballet / Norwegian wood / Downfall of lucifer
CD _____ QPRL 040D
Polyphonic / Jun '88 / Conifer.

Yosefa

DESERT SPEAKS, THE

Hatizmoret onah / Gluya me' Morocco / Shafshaf's song / Desert speaks / Kav Hachof / Rachamim / Taj Mahal / Double life / Zahav (Gold) / longings (Kisoofim) / Place with no name / Before the night is gone
CD _____ CDEMC 3721
Hemisphere / Oct '95 / EMI.

YOSEFA

Love can burn / Forbidden love / Green eyed lady / Yaraya / If your heart is pure / Waiting for you / Sidi hbibi / My beautiful one / Love bird / Outro - "Yaraya"
CD _____ 3202012
Triloka / Nov '93 / New Note.

Yoshizawa, Hajime

HAJIME

Bless me with your breath / Beyond twilight / Yesterdays / Snake dance / Stardust / Love letters / September air / Tropic of Cancer / Voyage / Peatan's blues / Autumn in New York and Spring Cadenza
CD _____ AHUM 008
Ah-Um / Nov '91 / New Note / Cadillac.

Yothu Yindi

FREEDOM

CD _____ TVD 93380
Mushroom / Mar '94 / BMG / 3MV.

Youmans, Vincent

VINCENT YOUMANS

CD _____ ACD 089
Audiophile / Oct '93 / Jazz Music / Swift.

Young Black Teenagers

DEAD END KIDZ DOIN' LIFETIME BIDS

CD _____ MCLD 19256
MCA / Jun '94 / BMG.

Young Canadians

NO ESCAPE

CD _____ ZULU 014CD
Zulu / Oct '95 / Plastic Head.

Young, Dave

FABLES AND DREAMS (Young, Dave & Phil Dwyer Quartet)

CD _____ JUST 53-2
Justin Time / Nov '93 / Harmonia Mundi / Cadillac.

TWO BY TWO

CD _____ JUST 76-2
Justin Time / Sep '95 / Harmonia Mundi / Cadillac.

Young Disciples

ROAD TO FREEDOM

Get yourself together (pts 1 & 2) / Apparently nothin' (Soul River) / Move right on / No more / As we come (to be) / Step right on (Dub) / Freedom / Wanting / To be free / Young Disciples theme
CD _____ 5100972
Talkin' Loud / Aug '91 / PolyGram.

Young, Dougie

SONGS OF DOUGIE YOUNG, THE

CD _____ AIAS 19CD
Larrikin / Nov '94 / Roots / Direct / ADA / CM.

Young, Dr. Noah

FREAKS NO FEAR OF CONTAGION

CD _____ NAR 117CD
SST / Jan '95 / Plastic Head.

Young, Faron

CAPITOL YEARS: FARON YOUNG (5CD Set)

If you ain't lovin' (you ain't livin') / I've got five dollars and it's Saturday night / Place for girls like you / I can't tell my heart that / In the chapel in the moonlight / If that's the fashion / Forgive me, Dear / Just married / Baby my heart / What's the use to love you / That's what I do for you / I'm gonna tell Santa Claus on you / You're the angel on my christmas tree / I hardly knew it was you / That's what it's like to be lonesome / You're right (but I wish you were wrong) / Down Lover's Lane alone / So I'm in love with you / Goin' steady / Just out of reach / I can't wait (for the sun to go down) / Have I waited too long / Tattle tale tears / What can I do with my sorrow / Good Lord must have sent you / I knew you when / Saving my tears for tomorrow / Foolish pride / Live fast, love hard, die young / Go back, you fool / All right / For the love of a woman like you / It's a great life / Better things than these / Turn her down / You're still mine / Sweet dreams / Till I met you / I'm gonna live some before I die / Candy kisses / Have I told you lately that I love you / I'll be satisfied with love / I can't help it / Your cheatin' heart / I'll be yours / Sweethearts or strangers / Shame on you / Worried mind / I miss you already / I'm a poor boy / You call everybody darlin' / You are my sunshine / Moonlight mountain / Anything your heart desires / Vacation's over / Shrine of St. Cecilia / Love has finally come my way / Face of love / That's the way it's gotta be / We're talking it over / I made a fool of myself / I'll be all right / You old used to be / Out of my heart / Every time I'm kissing you / Alone with you / That's the way I feel / I hate myself / Last night at the party / Long time ago / Hey good lookin' / Tennessee waltz / Let old Mother Nature have her way / Making believe / Almost / Mom and Dad's waltz / Don't let the stars get in your eyes / Bouquet of roses / Slowly / Bimbo / Chattanooga shoe shine boy / I don't hurt anymore / I'll go on alone / Honey stop / Locket / Snowball / When it rains it pours / Rosalie (is gonna get married) / I can't dance / Once in a while / Riverboat / Country girl / Face to the wall / There's not any like you left / Forget the past / World so full of love / Hello walls / Is she all you thought she'd be / Congratulations / Three days / Safely in love again / Down by the river / Part where I cry / I hear you talkin' / Big shoes / Believing it yourself / Come back / Overlonely and underkissed / Things to remember / I fall to pieces / Moment isn't very long / Moments to remember / Lifetime isn't long enough / I can't find the time / Trail of tears / I let it slip away / Let's pretend we're lovers again / Backtrack / How can I forget you / I'll fly away / Mansion over the hilltop / He was there / How long has it been / Beautiful garden of prayer / My home sweet home / Suppertime / May the good Lord bless and keep you / What can he do / He knows just what I need / When I've learned enough to live / Now I belong to Jesus / I won't have to cross Jordan alone / Travelling on / My wonderful Lord / I know who holds tomorrow / Where could I go but to the Lord / God bless God / Don't take your love from me / If I had you / Stay as sweet as you are / My darling, my darling / Who wouldn't love you / I can't believe that you're in love with me / Object of my affection / It all depends on you / Thank you for a lovely evening / Everything I have is yours / Nearness of you / Sweet and lovely
CD Set _____ BCD 15493
Bear Family / Mar '92 / Rollercoaster / Direct / CM / Swift / ADA.

FOUR IN THE MORNING

If you ain't lovin' (you ain't livin') / All right / Three days / Sweet dreams / Going steady / Hello walls / Backtrack / Wine me up / Your times comin' / I miss you already / This little girl of mine / Four in the morning / Seasons come, seasons go / Alone with you / Heartache for a keepsake / Apartment no. 9 / Live fast, love hard, die young / Your cheatin' heart / Satisfied mind / As far as I'm concerned / Is it really over / Chapel in the moonlight / Some of those memories / There goes my everything / Crying time / Swingin' doors / Tiger by the tail / Here comes my baby back again / Once a day / Sweet thang / I could never be ashamed of you / Are you sincere / Memphis
CD _____ CDGRF 073
Tring / Feb '93 / Tring / Prism.

GREATEST HITS

CD _____ PWKS 4221
Carlton Home Entertainment / Nov '94 / Carlton Home Entertainment.

HELLO WALLS

CD _____ CDSGP 0166
Prestige / Oct '95 / Total/BMG.

MEMORIES THAT LAST (Young, Faron & Ray Price)

Memories that last / Everybody loves somebody / Too big to fight / Take a chance on

745

me / Cold cold heart / Side by side / Somewhere along the way / Walking my baby back home / Whole lot of you / Mansion on the hill / When I fall in love / Funny how time slips away
CD _____ SORCD 0068
D-Sharp / Oct '94 / Pinnacle.

Young Fresh Fellows

INCLUDES A HELMET
CD _____ UTIL 010 CD
Utility / Jun '90 / Grapevine.

IT'S LOW BEAT TIME
Low beat jingle / Right here / Snow White / Mr. Anthony's last / Whatever you are / Two headed flight / Minor bird / Faultess / Crafty clerk / Low beat / Love is a beautiful thing / She sees color / Monkey says / Ninety nine girls / She won't budge / Green green
CD _____ 346432
Frontier / Jan '93 / Vital.

MEN WHO LOVED MUSIC
CD _____ 461112
Frontier / Jul '91 / Vital.

SOMOS LOS MEJORES
CD _____ MR 015CD
Munster / Apr '92 / Plastic Head.

TOPSY TURVY THE FABULOUS SOUNDS OF THE NORTHWEST
CD _____ PLCD 101
Pop Llama / May '95 / 3MV.

TOTALLY LOST
CD _____ FCD 1028
Frontier / Jul '91 / Vital.

Young, Gary

HOSPITAL
Plant man / First Impression / Mitchell / Foothill blud / Real crill (no video) / Warren / Hospital for the chemically insane / Birds in traffic / Where you are at / Ralph the vegetarian robot / Missing in action / Wipeout / Twentieth day / Geri / Hooks of the highway
CD _____ ABB74CD
Big Cat / Aug '95 / SRD / Pinnacle.

Young, George

OLEO
CD _____ K32Y 6221
King/Paddle Wheel / Sep '88 / New Note.

SPRING FEVER
It might as well be Spring / All of me / Imagination / Bernie's tune / Mysticized / Garden of desire / Kid stuff / Little O's / Domingo en la tarde / Don't stay away / Spring fever
CD _____ 66055009
Sweet Basil / Nov '91 / New Note.

YESTERDAY AND TODAY
CD _____ 292E6028
King/Paddle Wheel / Nov '89 / New Note.

Young Gods

LIVE SKY TOUR
Intro / TV sky / Jimmy / Envoye/chanson rouge / L'eau rouge / Skinflowers / She rains / Summer eyes / Pas mal / Longue route / September song / Seerauber Jenny
CD _____ BIAS 241CD
Play It Again Sam / Jul '93 / Vital.

ONLY HEAVEN
Outside / Strangel / Speed of night / Donnez les esprits / Moon revolutions / Kissing the sun / Dreamhouse / Lointaine / Grdez les esprits / Child in the tree
CD _____ BIAS 301CD
Play It Again Sam / Jun '95 / Vital.

RED WATER, THE
CD _____ BIAS 130CD
Play It Again Sam / Aug '89 / Vital.

T.V. SKY
Our house / Gasoline man / T.V. sky / Skinflowers / Dame chance / Night dance / She rains / Summer eyes
CD _____ BIAS 201CD
Play It Again Sam / Feb '92 / Vital.

YOUNG GODS
Nous de la lune / Jusqu'au bout / Ciel ouvert / Jimmy / Fai la mouette / Percussions / Feu / Did you miss me / Si tu gardes
CD _____ LDCD 8821
Play It Again Sam / Aug '89 / Vital.

YOUNG GODS PLAY KURT WEILL, THE
CD _____ BIAS 188CD
Play It Again Sam / Apr '91 / Vital.

Young, James

FOREVER YOUNG
James 'Foo' Young / Lord Mayor speaks / Crabbed old woman / Ulster's spaceman / Our wee boy / James joins up / Hilda / O come ye to Ulster / What's on tonight / Wife (Big Aggie) / American view of Ulster / School days / My old slum clearance home / PM speaks
CD _____ ERTVCD 3
Emerald / Nov '88 / Direct.

Young, James

SONGS THEY NEVER PLAY ON THE RADIO
Mystery of love / Long wooden box / For the sunrise / Mr. Misterioso / Listen to the rain / Aphro gypsia / Curious / Tall tales / Der leiermann / Planet pussy / Silver sweet siren / Songs they never play on the radio
CD _____ CREDCD 158
Creation / Dec '93 / 3MV / Vital.

Young Jessie

I'M GONE
Mary Lou / Lonesome desert / Rabbit on a log / Don't think I will / Well baby / Nothing seems right / Down at Hayden's / I smell a rat / Why do I love you / Pretty soon / Oochie coochie / Don't happen no more / Hit, git and split / Here comes Henry / Hot dog / Do you love me / This is young Jessie / Maybelline - Fragment / I hear you knocking - Fragment
CD _____ CDCHD 607
Ace / Nov '95 / Pinnacle / Cadillac / Complete/Pinnacle.

Young, John Paul

LOVE IS IN THE AIR
CD _____ 12212
Laserlight / '93 / Target/BMG.

Young, Johnny

CHICAGO BLUES
CD _____ ARHCD 325
Arhoolie / Apr '95 / ADA / Direct / Cadillac.

JOHNNY YOUNG AND HIS FRIENDS
CD _____ TCD 5003
Testament / Aug '94 / Complete/Pinnacle / ADA / Koch.

Young, La Monte

JUST STOMPIN'
Stompin' / Young Dorian's blues in G
CD _____ R2 71262
Gramavision / Aug '93 / Vital/SAM / ADA.

SECOND DREAM OF...
CD _____ GRV 74672
Gramavision / Oct '91 / Vital/SAM / ADA.

WELL TUNED PIANO, THE
CD Set _____ 1887012
Gramavision / Jul '90 / Vital/SAM / ADA.

Young, Lester

1936-44
CD _____ CD 14551
Jazz Portraits / Jul '94 / Jazz Music.

ALTERNATIVE LESTER, THE
Way down yonder in New Orleans / Countless blues / I want a little girl / Pagin' the devil
CD _____ TAXCD S 62
Tax / Apr '91 / Jazz Music / Wellard / Cadillac.

BLUE LESTER
Ghost of a chance / Crazy over jazz / Ding dong / Back home in Indiana / These foolish things / Exercise in swing / Blues 'n' bells / Salute to Fats / June bug / Blue Lester / Jump Lester jump / Basie English / Circus in rhythm / Poor little plaything / Tush
CD _____ SV 0112
Savoy Jazz / Apr '92 / Conifer / ADA.

COMPLETE ALADDIN RECORDINGS, THE (2CD Set)
Indiana / I can't get started / Tea for two / Body and soul / D.B. blues / Lester blows again / These foolish things / Jumpin' at Mesner's / It's only a paper moon / After you've gone / Lover come back to me / Jammin' with Lester / You're driving me crazy / New Lester leaps in / Lester's be bop boogie / She's funny that way / Sunday / S.M. blues / Jumpin' with my symphony Sid / Yo yes blues / Sax-o-be-bop / On the sunny side of the street / Easy does it / Easy does it (2) / Movin' with Lester / One o'clock jump / Jumpin' at the Woodside / I'm confessin' / Lester smooths it out / Just cooling / East of the sun / Sheik of Araby / Something to remember you by / Untitled / Please let me forget / He don't love me anymore / Pleasing man blues / See See rider / It's better to give than receive
CD Set _____ CDP 8327872
Blue Note / Oct '95 / EMI.

IN WASHINGTON D.C. - VOL.1
Foggy day / When you're smiling / I can't get started (with you) / Fast Bob blues / D.B. blues / Tea for two / Jeepers creepers
CD _____ OJCCD 782-2
Original Jazz Classics / Apr '94 / Wellard / Jazz Music / Cadillac / Complete/Pinnacle.

JAMMIN' WITH LESTER
CD _____ 3801182
Jazz Archives / Feb '93 / Jazz Music / Discovery / Cadillac.

JAZZ ARCHIVES 1941-44
CD _____ 158352
Jazz Archives / May '95 / Jazz Music / Discovery / Cadillac.

JAZZ MASTERS
CD _____ 5218592
Verve / Feb '94 / PolyGram.

LADY BE GOOD
CD _____ ATJCD 5968
All That's Jazz / Aug '92 / THE / Jazz Music.

LESTER LEAPS AGAIN
Up 'n' at 'em / (Back home again in) Indiana / Too marvellous for words / Mean to me / Sweet Georgia Brown / I'm confessin' that I love you / Neenah / I cover the waterfront / Lester leaps in / I don't stand a ghost of a chance with you / How high the moon / Be bop boogie / D.B. blues / Lavender blues / These foolish things / Just you, just me / Lester leaps again
CD _____ LEJAZZCD 4
Le Jazz / Mar '93 / Charly / Cadillac.

LESTER LEAPS IN
CD _____ JHR 73571
Jazz Hour / Nov '93 / Target/BMG / Jazz Music / Cadillac.

LESTER YOUNG 1943-47
CD _____ GOJCD 53073
Giants Of Jazz / Mar '92 / Target/BMG / Cadillac.

LESTER YOUNG 1950-1958
CD _____ CD 53193
Giants Of Jazz / Sep '94 / Target/BMG / Cadillac.

LIVE AT THE ROYAL ROOST 1948
Lester leaps in / Ghost of a chance / Just you, just me / How high the moon / Be bop boogie / These foolish things / D.B. Blues / Lavender blue / Lester leaps again / Sweet Georgia Brown
CD _____ 550092
Jazz Anthology / Jan '94 / Harmonia Mundi / Cadillac.

MASTER TAKES WITH COUNT BASIE (Young, Lester & Earle Warren/Johnny Guarnieri)
Circus in rhythm / Poor little plaything / Tush / These foolish things / Exercise in swing / Salute to Fats / Basie English / Blue Lester / Ghost of a chance / (Back home again in) Indiana / Jump Lester jump / Crazy over jazz / Ding dong / Blues 'n' bells / June bug
CD _____ SV 0250
Savoy Jazz / Oct '94 / Conifer / ADA.

MASTER'S TOUCH
Crazy over jazz / Ghost of a chance / Ding dong / Blues 'n' bells / (Back home again in) Indiana / Basie English / Salute to Fats / Exercise in swing / Circus in rhythm / Tush / Poor little plaything
CD _____ SV 0113
Savoy Jazz / Apr '92 / Conifer / ADA.

MASTERPIECES OF LESTER YOUNG, THE
CD _____ 393462
Music Memoria / Aug '94 / Discovery / ADA.

PRES, THE (Jazz Immortal Series Vol. 2)
Lester warms up / I can't get started (with you) / Lester's blues #1 and 2 / Body and soul / Up and atom / How high the moon / Pennies from Heaven / One o'clock jump / Jumpin' with Symphony Sid
CD _____ SV 0180
Savoy Jazz / Jan '94 / Conifer / ADA.

PRESIDENT VOL.2, THE
CD _____ COD 039
Jazz View / Jul '92 / Harmonia Mundi.

PRESIDENT VOL.4, THE
CD _____ COD 038
Jazz View / Jun '92 / Harmonia Mundi.

PRESIDENT VOL.6, THE
CD _____ COD 040
Jazz View / Aug '92 / Harmonia Mundi.

PRESIDENT, THE
CD _____ COD 029
Jazz View / Mar '92 / Harmonia Mundi.

PREZ CONFERENCES
CD _____ JASSCD 18
Jass / Oct '91 / CM / Jazz Music / ADA / Cadillac / Direct.

RARITIES
CD _____ MCD 0482
Moon / Nov '93 / Harmonia Mundi / Cadillac.

RARITIES AND JAM SESSIONS (The Golden Age of Jazz)
CD _____ JZCD 365
Suisa / May '92 / Jazz Music / THE.

SUPER SESSIONS, THE
(Back home again in) Indiana / I can't get started (with you) / Tea for two / Body and soul / Just you / Just you, just me / I never knew / Afternoon of Basie-ite / Sometimes I'm happy / After theatre jump / Six cats and a prince / Lester leaps again / Destination K.C.
CD _____ LEJAZZCD 36
Le Jazz / May '95 / Charly / Cadillac.

Young MC

STONE COLD RHYMIN'
Come off / Bust a move / Name is Young / Roll with the punches / Stone cold buggin' / Principal's office / Fastest rhyme / Know how / I let 'em know / Just say no
CD _____ IMCD 122
4th & Broadway / Apr '91 / PolyGram.

Young, Mighty Joe

BLUESY JOSEPHINE
CD _____ BLE 595212
Black & Blue / Oct '94 / Wellard / Koch.

LIVE AT THE WISE FOOLS PUB
CD _____ AIM 1052CD
Aim / Oct '95 / Direct / ADA / Jazz Music.

Young, Neil

AFTER THE GOLDRUSH (Young, Neil & Crazy Horse)
Tell me why / After the goldrush / Only love can break your heart / Southern man / Till the morning comes / Oh, lonesome me / Don't let it bring you down / Birds / When you dance I can really love / I believe in you / Cripple Creek ferry / Tell me why (2)
CD _____ 244088
Reprise / Mar '93 / Warner Music.

AMERICAN STARS AND BARS
Old country waltz / Saddle up the palomino / Hey babe / Hold back the tears / Bite the bullet / Star of Bethlehem / Will to live / Like a hurricane / Homegrown
CD _____ 759927234-2
Reprise / Jun '94 / Warner Music.

COMES A TIME
Goin' back / Comes a-time / Look out for my love / Peace of mind / Lotta love / Human highway / Already one / Field of opportunity / Motorcycle mama / Four strong winds
CD _____ 759927235-2
Reprise / Jun '93 / Warner Music.

DECADE (2CD Set)
Down to the wire / Burned / Mr. Soul / Broken arrow / Expecting to fly / Sugar mountain / I am a child / Loner / Old laughing lady / Cinnamon girl / Down by the river / Cowgirl in the sand / I believe in you / After the goldrush / Cinnamon girl / Helpless / Ohio / Soldier / Old man / Man needs a maid / Heart of gold / Star of Bethlehem / Needle and the damage done / Tonight's the night (pt 1) / Turnstiles / Winterlong / Deep forbidden lake / Like a hurricane / Love is a rose / Cortez the killer / Campaigner / Long may you run / Harvest
CD _____ 759927233-2
Reprise / Jun '93 / Warner Music.

EVERYBODY KNOWS THIS IS NOWHERE (Young, Neil & Crazy Horse)
Cinnamon girl / Everybody knows this is nowhere / Round and round / Down by the river / Losing end / Running dry (Requiem for the rockets) / Cowgirl in the sand
CD _____ 244073
Reprise / Jun '89 / Warner Music.

FREEDOM (Young, Neil & The Restless)
Rockin' in the free world / Crime in the city / Don't cry / Hangin' on a limb / Eldorado / Ways of love / Someday / On Broadway / Wrecking ball / No more / Too far gone
CD _____ 9258992
Reprise / Feb '95 / Warner Music.

HARVEST
Out on the weekend / Harvest / Man needs a maid / Heart of gold / Are you ready for the country / Old man / There's a world / Alabama / Needle and the damage done / Words (between the lines of age)
CD _____ 244131
Reprise / '92 / Warner Music.

HARVEST MOON
Unknown legend / From Hank to Hendrix / You and me / Harvest moon / War of man / One of these days / Such a woman / Old king / Dreamin' man / Natural beauty
CD _____ 9362450572
Reprise / Nov '92 / Warner Music.

HAWKS & DOVES
Little wing / Homestead / Lost in space / Captain Kennedy / Staying power / Coastline / Union man / Comin' apart at every nail / Hawks and doves
CD _____ 759925868-2
Reprise / Jun '94 / Warner Music.

JOURNEY THROUGH THE PAST
For what it's worth / Mr. Soul / Rock 'n' roll woman / Find the cost of freedom / Ohio / Southern man / Alabama / Are you ready for the country / Words / Soldier
CD _____ 7599261232
Reprise / Jun '94 / Warner Music.

LANDING ON WATER
Weight of the world / Violent side / Hippie dream / Bad news beat / Touch the night / People on the street / Hard luck stories / I got a problem / Pressure / Drifter
CD _____ GFLD 19130
Geffen / Jun '92 / BMG.

LIVE RUST (Young, Neil & Crazy Horse)
Sugar mountain / I am a child / Comes a-time / After the goldrush / My my, hey hey

(out of the blue) / When you dance I can really love / Loner / Needle and the damage done / Lotta love / Sedan delivery / Powder finger / Cortez the killer / Cinnamon girl / Like a hurricane / Hey hey, my my (into the black) / Tonight's the night
CD _____ 759927250-2
Reprise / Jun '93 / Warner Music.

LUCKY THIRTEEN
Sample and hold / Transformer man / Depression blues / Get gone / Don't take your love away from me / Once an angel / Where is the highway tonight / Hippie dream / Pressure / Around the world / Mid East vacation / Ain't it the truth / This note's for you
CD _____ GED 24452
Geffen / Jan '93 / BMG.

MIRROR BALL
Song X / Act of love / I'm the ocean / Big green country / Truth be known / Downtown / What happened yesterday / Peace and love / Throw your hatred down / Scenery / Fallen angel
CD _____ 9362459342
Reprise / Jun '95 / Warner Music.

NEIL YOUNG
Emperor of Wyoming / Loner / If I could have her tonight / I've been waiting for you / Old laughing lady / String quartet from whiskey boot hill / Here we are in the years / What did you do to my life / I've loved her so long / Last trip to Tulsa
CD _____ 244059
Reprise / Mar '93 / Warner Music.

ON THE BEACH
Walk on / See the sky about to rain / Revolution blues / For the turnstiles / Vampire blues / On the beach / Motion pictures / Ambulance blues
CD _____ 759927213-2
Reprise / Jun '94 / Warner Music.

RAGGED GLORY (Young, Neil & Crazy Horse)
Country home / White line / Fuckin' up / Over and over / Love to burn / Farmer John / Mansion on the hill / Days that used to be / Love and only love / Mother Earth (natural anthem)
CD _____ 7599263152
Reprise / Feb '95 / Warner Music.

RE-AC-TOR
Opera star / Surfer Joe and Moe the sleaze / T-Bone / Get back on it / Southern Pacific / Motor city / Rapid transit / Shots
CD _____ 759925869-2
Reprise / Jun '94 / Warner Music.

RUST NEVER SLEEPS (Young, Neil & Crazy Horse)
My my, hey hey (out of the blue) / Thrasher / Ride my llama / Pocohontas / Sail away / Powder finger / Welfare mothers / Sedan delivery / Hey hey, my my (into the black)
CD _____ 759927249-2
Reprise / Jun '93 / Warner Music.

SLEEPS WITH ANGELS
My heart / Prime of life / Drive-by / Sleeps with angels / Western hero / Change your mind / Blue Eden / Safeway cart / Train of love / Trans Am / Piece of crap / Dream that can last
CD _____ 936245749-2
Reprise / Aug '94 / Warner Music.

THIS NOTE'S FOR YOU (Young, Neil & The Blue Notes)
Ten men workin' / This note's for you / Coupe de ville / Life in the city / Twilight / Married man / Sunny inside / Can't believe your lyin' / Hey hey / One thing
CD _____ 9257192
Reprise / Feb '95 / Warner Music.

TIME FADES AWAY
Time fades away / L.A. / Journey through the past / Bridge / Love in mind / Don't be denied / Last dance / Yonder stands the sinner
CD _____ 759925934-2
Reprise / Jun '94 / Warner Music.

TONIGHT'S THE NIGHT
Tonight's the night / Speakin' out / World on a string / Borrowed tune / Come on baby / Let's go down-town / Mellow my mind / Roll another number (for the road) / Albequerque / New mama / Look out, Joe / Tired eyes / Tonight's the night pt 2
CD _____ 759927221-2
Reprise / Jun '93 / Warner Music.

UNPLUGGED
Old laughing lady / Mr. Soul / World on a string / Pocahontas / Stringman / Like a hurricane / Needle and the damage done / Helpless / Harvest moon / Transformer man / Unknown legend / Look out for my love / Long may you run / From Hank to Hendrix

CD _____ 936245310-2
Reprise / Jun '93 / Warner Music.

WELD (2CD/LP/MC Set) (Young, Neil & Crazy Horse)
Hey, hey, my my (into the black) / Crime in the city / Blowin' in the wind / Welfare mothers / Love to burn / Cinnamon girl / Mansion on the hill / Fuckin' up / Cortez the killer / Powder finger / Love and only love / Rockin' in the free world / Like a hurricane / Farmer John / Tonight's the night / Roll another number (for the road) / Arc (On ltd ed triple CD set 7599267462 only)
CD Set _____ 7599266712
Reprise / Nov '91 / Warner Music.

ZUMA
Don't cry no tears / Danger bird / Pardon my heart / Looking for a love / Barstool blues / Stupid girl / Drive back / Cortez the killer / Through my sails
CD _____ 759927226-2
Reprise / Jun '93 / Warner Music.

CROSSING
Hope in a hopeless world / Now I know what made Otis blue / Bring me home / Heart is a lonely hunter / Won't look back / Only game in town / Love has no pride / Down in Chinatown / Half a step away / Follow on / It will be you
CD _____ 473928 2
Columbia / Oct '93 / Sony.

FROM TIME TO TIME (The Singles Collection)
Every time you go away / Come back and stay / I'm only foolin' myself / Senza una Donna / I'm gonna tear your playhouse down / Broken man / Everything must change / Wonderland / Don't dream it's over / Love of the common people / Wherever I lay my hat / Both sides now / Oh Girl / Softly whispering I love you / Some people (CD/MC only)
CD _____ 4688252
Columbia / Aug '91 / Sony.

NO PARLEZ
Come back and stay / Love will tear us apart / Wherever I lay my hat / Ku-ku kurama / No parlez / Love of the common people / Oh women / Iron out the rough spots / Broken man / Tender trap / Sex
CD _____ 4609092
CBS / Jul '91 / Sony.

NO PARLEZ/THE SECRET OF ASSOCIATION (2CD Set)
Come back and stay / Love will tear us apart / Wherever I lay my hat / Ku-ku kurama / No parlez / Love of the common people / Oh women / Iron out the rough spots / Broken man / Tender trap / Sex / Bite the hand that feeds / Everytime you go away / I'm gonna tear your playhouse down / Standing on the edge / Soldier's things / Everything must change / Tomb of memories / One step forward / This means anything / I was in chains / Man in the iron mask
CD Set _____ 4784812
Columbia / Mar '95 / Sony.

OTHER VOICES
Heaven can wait / Little bit of love / Softly whispering I love you / Together / Stop on by / Our time has come / Oh girl / Right about now / It's what she didn't say / Calling you
CD _____ 4669172
CBS / Jun '90 / Sony.

REFLECTIONS
CD _____ VISCD 1
Vision / Oct '94 / Pinnacle.

SECRET OF ASSOCIATION, THE
Bite the hand that feeds / Everytime you go away / I'm gonna tear your playhouse down / Standing on the edge / Soldier's things / Everything must change / Tomb of memories / One step forward / Hot fun / This means anything / I was in chains
CD _____ CD 26234
CBS / Mar '85 / Sony.

1ST VIRGINIA VOLUNTEERS
CD _____ VMFM 21CD
Lookout / Jul '95 / SRD.

FIRST VIRGINIA VOLUNTEERS
CD _____ VMFM 212
Vermiform / May '95 / Plastic Head.

ANTHOLOGY (2CD Set) (Rascals/Young Rascals)

I ain't gonna eat out my heart anymore / Good lovin' / Do you feel it / Mustang Sally / Baby let's wait / In the midnight hour / You better run / Lonely to long / Come on up / Too many fish in the sea / Love is a beautiful thing / Groovin' / Find somebody / How can I be sure / If you knew / I'm so happy now / Easy rollin' / Rainy day / It's wonderful (to be loved by you) / Silly girl / Once got to be free / Island of love / Look around / Ray of hope / Heaven / See / I'd like to take you home / Temptation's bout to get me / Nubia / Real thing / Carry me back / Right on / Ready for love / I believe / Glory glory / Girl like you
CD _____ 8122710772
Atlantic / Jul '93 / Warner Music.

TIME PEACE - GREATEST HITS (Rascals/Young Rascals)
CD _____ 7567814412
Atlantic / Jun '95 / Warner Music.

ROCK, SALT & NAILS
That's how strong my love is / Rock, salt and nails / In a one woman man / Coyote / Gonna find me a bluebird / Love in my time / Seven Bridges Road / Kenny's song / Holler in the swamp / Hoboin' / My sweet love ain't around
CD _____ EDCD 193
Edsel / Feb '91 / Pinnacle / ADA.

SOLO/LIVE
CD _____ WM 1004
Watermelon / Jun '93 / ADA / Direct.

SWITCHBLADES OF LOVE
CD _____ RTMCD 63
Round Tower / Apr '94 / Pinnacle / ADA / Direct / BMG / CM.

HOLLY BEARS THE CROWN, THE
CD _____ FLED 3006
Fledg'ling / Nov '95 / CM / ADA / Direct.

TRAVELIN' LIGHT
Travelin light / Queen bee / Football widow / Mama jama / Key to the highway / Daughter of a son-of-a-gun / Stumbling blocks and stepping stones / Girlfriend / Brain damage / Can't take nothin out
CD _____ DEL 3003
Deluge / Dec '95 / Direct / ADA.

FEELING FREE
Feelin' free / If only I could / I'd rather go blind / Sit and wait / Kiss and say goodbye / Ain't no sunshine / Your lover / Not just a lover but a friend / Congratulations / Could it me (I'm in love) / That was yesterday / Good times, bad times
CD _____ CIRCD 9
Circa / Apr '92 / EMI.

HOOKED ON YOU - THE BEST OF SYDNEY YOUNGBLOOD
If only I could / Spookey (Instrumental) / Sit and wait / Feeling free (Duet with Elaine Hudson) / Hooked on you / Body and soul / Wherever you go / Feels like forever (Featuring Elaine Hudson) / I'm your lover / I'd rather go blind / Could it be (I'm in love) / Ain't no sunshine
CD _____ CDVIP 129
Virgin / Apr '95 / EMI.

EARTH MUSIC
Euphoria / All my dreams blue / Monkey Business / Dreamer's dream / Sugar Babe / Long and tall / I Can Tell / Don't Play Games / Wine song / Fool me / Reason to believe
CD _____ EDCD 274
Edsel / Apr '91 / Pinnacle / ADA.

ELEPHANT MOUNTAIN
Darkness darkness / Smug / On Sir Frances Drake / Sunlight / Double sunlight / Beautiful / Turn it over / Rainsong / Trillium / Quicksand / Black mountain breakdown / Sham / Ride the wind
CD _____ EDCD 276
Edsel / Apr '91 / Pinnacle / ADA.

RIDE THE WIND
Ride the wind / Sugar babe / Sunlight / Dolphin / Get together / Beautiful
CD _____ 901021
Line / Oct '94 / CM / Grapevine / ADA / Conifer / Direct.

YOUNGBLOODS
Grizzly bear / All over the world / Statesboro Blues / Get Together / One note man / Other side of this life / Tears Are Falling / Four In The Morning / Foolin' Around / Ain't that lovin' you / C.C. rider
CD _____ EDCD 271
Edsel / Jul '91 / Pinnacle / ADA.

COME AGAIN
CD _____ BY 0025CD
Better Youth Organisation / Nov '93 / SRD.

HAPPY HOUR
CD _____ EFA 200272
Better Youth Organisation / Mar '94 / SRD.

SINK WITH KALIFORNIJA
CD _____ BYO 2CD
Better Youth Organisation / Feb '91 / SRD.

TAKE A STAND
CD _____ LF 044CD
Lost & Found / Sep '95 / Plastic Head.

CLASSICAL CHINESE PIPA
CD _____ EUCD 1176
ARC / '91 / ARC Music / ADA.

HOMELAND
CD _____ EUCD 1260
ARC / Mar '94 / ARC Music / ADA.

ANCIENT ART MUSIC OF CHINA
CD _____ LYRCD 7409
Lyrichord / '91 / Roots / ADA / CM.

RUSSIAN ROMANTIC SONGS
CD _____ MCD 71597
Monitor / Jun '93 / CM.

L'INTEGRALE
CD _____ LDX 274948/52
La Chant Du Monde / Jan '93 / Harmonia Mundi / ADA.

18 HEARTBREAKING SONGS
CD _____ RMB 75061
Remember / Oct '95 / Total/BMG.

HURT
CD _____ WMCD 5668
Disky / May '94 / THE / BMG / Discovery / Pinnacle.

LEGENDS IN MUSIC - TIMI YURO
CD _____ LECD 066
Wisepack / Jul '94 / THE / Conifer.

LOST VOICE OF SOUL, THE
Hurt / Just say I love him / Trying / Smile / Let me call you sweetheart / Count everything / I know (I love you) / What's the matter baby / Only love me / That's right, walk on by / Should I ever love again / Love in a boy / I ain't gonna cry no more / Insult to injury / Make the world go away / Leavin' on your mind / She's got you / Are you sure / I'd fight the world / Gotta travel on / Down in the valley / Permanently lonely / Legend in my time / Call me / Something bad on my mind / It'll never be over for me
CD _____ RPM 117
RPM / Oct '93 / Pinnacle.

FUNAMBULES (Yvert, Oller & Trio)
CD _____ ARN 64235
Arion / Jun '93 / Discovery / ADA.

BY PRESCRIPTION ONLY
Rush hour / After the rain / Rocky Road / D B / By prescription only / Mad about town / Far side / Follow me to the edge / Bianca / Morocco junction
CD _____ 103 254
Musidisc / Mar '90 / Vital / Harmonia Mundi / ADA / Cadillac / Discovery.

Z

Z, Rachel

TRUST THE UNIVERSE
CD _____ 4730582
Sony Jazz / Jan '95 / Sony.

Zabaleta

NEW AGE HARP, OLD AGE MUSIC
CD _____ CD 404
Bescol / Aug '94 / CM / Target/BMG.

Zabrina

Z = MC2
Take a minute / Nu sound / Sunsister / Philosophy of fiction / Tell me something good / Irresistible / Housework / Keystone groove / This gun's for hire / Killer is with me / Chosen one / Godmother / Fellas from the Southside / You can make it / Sucker for a man with a body
CD _____ CDICH 1122
Ichiban / Oct '93 / Koch.

Zacharias, Helmut

SWING PARTY
Ich kusse ihre hand, Madame / Dark eyes / Those white little lies / Swing '48 / Kosaken patrouille / Man I love / You made me love you / Mob mob / Embraceable you / What is this thing called love / Presto / How high the moon / Tigerjagd (tiger rag) / Blue moon / C jam blues / Swing party / Schwips boogie / Ich habe rhythmus (I got rhythm) / Mr. Callahan / Carioca / Sabeltanz boogie (sabre dance) / Boogie tur Geige / Fiddler's boogie / Blue blues / China boogie / Smoky / Minne minne ha ha
CD _____ BCD 15642
Bear Family / Jun '92 / Rollercoaster / Direct / CM / Swift / ADA.

Zachrisson, Johan

RITMO DE ESTORNINHOS
CD _____ XOUCD 102
Xource / Oct '93 / ADA / Cadillac.

Zachze

HIMMEL, ARSCH & ZWIRN
CD _____ BEST 1008CD
Acoustic Music / Nov '93 / ADA.

Zadeh, Aziza Mustafa

ALWAYS
CD _____ 4738852
Sony Jazz / Jan '95 / Sony.

AZIZA MUSTAFA ZADEH
Quiet alone / Tea on the carpet / Cemetry / Inspiration / Reflection / Oriental fantasy / Blue day / Character / Aziza's dream / Chargah / My ballad / I cannot sleep / Moment / Exprompt / Two candles
CD _____ 468286 2
Columbia / Apr '94 / Sony.

DANCE OF FIRE
Boomerang / Dance of fire / Sheherezadeh / Aspiration / Bana bana gel (Bad girl) / Shadow / Carnival / Passion / Spanish picture / To be continued / Father
CD _____ 4803522
Sony Jazz / Jun '95 / Sony.

Zahar

LIVE AT THE KNITTING FACTORY
CD _____ KFWCD 112
Knitting Factory / Oct '92 / Grapevine.

Zamagni, Tony

GET DOWN WITH THE BLUES
CD _____ CDTC 1153
Tonecool / Jul '95 / Direct / ADA.

Zamfir, Gheorghe

CHRISTMAS AT NOTRE DAME
CD _____ 5174532
Phonogram / Mar '91 / PolyGram.

FOLKSONGS FROM RUMANIA (Zamfir, Gheorghe & The Ciocirlia Orchestra)
CD _____ 15208
Laserlight / '91 / Target/BMG.

HEART OF ROMANIA, THE (Zamfir, Gheorghe & Marcel Cellier)
Inima ci venin muit / Doina din banat / Ca din banat / Cintec muntenesc / Ciorcilia / Doina Sus pe cilmea dealului / Joc dins oas / Joc de dai din banat / In memoriam Maria Lataretu / Geampara "Lelita I Oana" / Doina Gheoghe mina boll bine / Doina Lui efta botoca / Balada sarpelui / Doina da jale
CD _____ PV 750002
Disques Pierre Verany / Jul '94 / Kingdom.

KING OF THE PAN FLUTE AND OTHER FAVOURITES
CD _____ CD 45
Bescol / '87 / CM / Target/BMG.

LIVE IN CONCERT FROM THEIR AMERICAN TOUR (Zamfir, Gheorghe & Marcel Cellier)
Balada sarpelui / Doina de la domasnea / Doina din jebel / Joc dins oas / Doina Sus pe culmea dealului / Doina oltului / Doina lui petru unc / Doina Rugulet cu negra mure / Doina da jale
CD _____ PV 750001
Disques Pierre Verany / Jul '94 / Kingdom.

LOVE SONGS
CD _____ 5102122
Phonogram / Mar '91 / PolyGram.

MAGIC OF THE MOMENTS
CD _____ DCD 5358
Disky / Apr '94 / THE / BMG / Discovery / Pinnacle.

MASTER OF THE PAN PIPES
CD _____ 11016
Laserlight / '86 / Target/BMG.

MELODIES OF THE HEART
CD _____ DCD 5327
Disky / Apr '94 / THE / BMG / Discovery / Pinnacle.

MOMENTS OF MY DREAMS
CD _____ DCD 5356
Disky / Apr '94 / THE / BMG / Discovery / Pinnacle.

NAMES IN MY LIFE
CD _____ DCD 5352
Disky / May '94 / THE / BMG / Discovery / Pinnacle.

PAN FLUTES & ORGAN
CD _____ 323123
Koch / Feb '94 / Koch.

PANPIPE DREAMS
Love changes everything / Unchained melody / Somewhere / Theme from 'Limelight' / Chariots of fire / Just the way you are / Don't cry for me Argentina / Black rose / Memory / Beautiful dream / Endless dream / Your song / Bilitis / Chanson d'amour / Rose / Run to me / Serenade / Only love
CD _____ 5518212
Spectrum/Karussell / Nov '95 / PolyGram / THE.

PIPE DREAMS
Chariots of fire / Aranjuez mon amour / Yesterday / Your song / Run to me / I know him so well / Andrew's theme / Annie's song / What now my love / Plasir d'amour / Rose / Lonely shepherd / Rescuerdos / Gymnopedie No.1
CD _____ 5501202
Spectrum/Karussell / Oct '93 / PolyGram / THE.

SPOTLIGHT ON GHEORGHE ZAMFIR
Stranger on the shore / Don't cry for me Argentina / Chanson d'amour / Rose / She / Yesterday / Just the way you are / Annie's song / Tema du un'estate del '42 (the summer knows) / Till / Run to me / I know him so well / If you go away / Sleepy shores / Memory / Lonely shepherd / Sleepy shores (tema da luci della rabalta) (limelight) / What now my love
CD _____ 8483732
Phonogram / Mar '91 / PolyGram.

WONDERFUL WORLD OF PANPIPES
CD _____ MCCD 202
Music Club / May '95 / Disc / THE / CM.

Zander, Robin

ROBIN ZANDER
Reactionary girl / I've always got you / Show me heaven / Jump into the fire / Time will let you know / Boy (I'm so in love with you) / Tell it to the world / Emily / I believe in you / Secret / Everlasting love / Walkin' shoes
CD _____ 6544922042
Interscope / Sep '93 / Warner Music.

Zanki, Edo

WACHE NACHT
CD _____ INT 845 081
Interchord / '88 / CM.

Zap Mama

SABSYLMA
Fusahi / Sabsylma / Mais qu'est ce / India / De la via a la most / Citoyen 120 / Locklat Africa / Mr. Brown / Reveil en Australie / Fidunia / Mamadit / For no one / Mamas of the Mamas / Adjosio omonie
CD _____ CRAW 12
Crammed Discs / Aug '95 / Grapevine / New Note.

ZAP MAMA
Mupepe / Ndje mukanie / Abadou / Marie Josee / Etupe / Nabambeli yo / Take me coco / Son Cubano / Guzophela / Plekete / Bottom / I ne suhe / Mizike / Babanzele / Din din / Brrlak
CD _____ CRAW 3CD
Crammed Discs / Aug '95 / Grapevine / New Note.

Zapp

ALL THE GREATEST HITS (Zapp & Roger)
More bounce to the ounce / Be alright / I heard it through the grapevine / So ruff, so tuff / Do it Roger / Dance floor / Doo wa ditty (Blow that thing) / I can make you dance / Heartbreaker (pts 1 & 2) / In the mix / Midnight hour / Computer love / Night and day / I want to be your man / Curiosity / Slow and easy / Mega medley
CD _____ 936245143-2
Reprise / Dec '93 / Warner Music.

ZAPP 3
CD _____ 7599238752
Reprise / Jan '96 / Warner Music.

Zappa, Dweezil

CONFESSIONS
Food For Thought / Mar '91 / Pinnacle. CDGRUB 19

HAVIN' A BAD DAY
CD _____ RCD 10057
Rykodisc / May '92 / Vital / ADA.

SHAMPOOHORN (Z (2))
CD _____ CDGRUB 25
Food For Thought / May '93 / Pinnacle.

Zappa, Frank

ABSOLUTELY FREE (Zappa, Frank & The Mothers Of Invention)
Plastic people / Uncle Bernie's farm / Brown shoes don't make it / Status back baby / America drinks and goes home / Invocation and ritual dance of the young pumpkin / Call any vegetable / Big Leg Emma (Reissues only) / Why don'tcha do me right (Reissues only) / Son of Suzy Creamcheese / Duke of prunes / Amnesia vivace / Duke regains his chops / Soft sell conclusion
CD _____ RCD 10502
Rykodisc / May '95 / Vital / ADA.

AHEAD OF THEIR TIME (Zappa, Frank & The Mothers Of Invention)
CD _____ RCD 10559
Rykodisc / May '95 / Vital / ADA.

APOSTROPHE
Don't eat the yellow snow / Nanook rubs it / St. Alfonzo's pancake breakfast / Father O'Blivion / Cosmik debris / Excentrifugal forz / Apostrophe / Uncle Remus / Stinkfoot
CD _____ RCD 10519
Rykodisc / Apr '95 / Vital / ADA.

ARK, THE
CD _____ ESMCD 957
Essential / Aug '91 / Total/BMG.

BABY SNAKES
CD P.Disc _____ RCD 10539
Rykodisc / May '95 / Vital / ADA.

BEST BAND YOU NEVER HEARD IN YOUR LIFE, THE (2CD Set)
CD Set _____ RCD 10553/54
Rykodisc / May '95 / Vital / ADA.

BONGO FURY
Debra Kadabra / Carolina hard-core ecstasy / Sam with the showing scalp flat top / Poofter's Froth Wyoming plans ahead / 200 years old / Cucamonga / Advance romance / Man with the woman head / Muffin man
CD _____ RCD 10522
Rykodisc / May '95 / Vital / ADA.

BROADWAY THE HARD WAY
CD _____ RCD 10552
Rykodisc / May '95 / Vital / ADA.

BURNT WEENY SANDWICH (Zappa, Frank & The Mothers Of Invention)
WPLJ / Igor's boogie, phase one / Overture to A Holiday In Berlin / Theme from Burnt Weeny Sandwich / Igor's boogie, phase two / Holiday in Berlin, full-blown / Aybe sea / Little house I used to live in / Valarie
CD _____ RCD 10509
Rykodisc / May '95 / Vital / ADA.

CHUNGA'S REVENGE
Transylvania boogie / Road ladies / Twenty small cigars / Nancy and Mary music (1-3) / Tell me you love me / Would you go all the way / Chunga's revenge / Clap / Rudy wants to buy yez drink / Sharleena
CD _____ RCD 10511
Rykodisc / May '95 / Vital / ADA.

CIVILIZATION PHAZE III (2CD Set)
CD Set _____ CDDZAP 56
Zappa / Oct '94 / Pinnacle.

CRUISING WITH RUBEN & THE JETS (Zappa, Frank & The Mothers Of Invention)
CD _____ RCD 10505
Rykodisc / May '95 / Vital / ADA.

DOES HUMOR BELONG IN MUSIC
Zoot allures / Tinsel Town rebellion / Trouble every day / Penguin in bondage / Hotplate heaven at the green hotel / What's new in Baltimore / Cocksuckers' ball / WPLJ / Let's move to Cleveland / Whipping post
CD _____ RCD 10548
Rykodisc / Apr '95 / Vital / ADA.

FILLMORE EAST - JUNE 1971 (Zappa, Frank & The Mothers Of Invention)
Little house I used to live in / Mud shark / What kind of girl do you think we are / Bwana dik / Latex solar beef / Willie the pimp (pts 1 & 2) / Do you like my new car / Happy together / Lonesome electric turkey / Peaches en regalia / Tears begin to fall
CD _____ RCD 10512
Rykodisc / May '95 / Vital / ADA.

FRANCESCO ZAPPA (Barking Pumpkin Digital Gratification Consort)
CD _____ RCD 10546
Rykodisc / May '95 / Vital / ADA.

FRANK ZAPPA MEETS THE MOTHERS OF PREVENTION
We're turning again / Alien orifice / Yo cats / What's new in Baltimore / I don't even care / One man, one vote / H.R. 2911 / Little beige sambo / Aerobics in bondage
CD _____ RCD 10547
Rykodisc / May '95 / Vital / ADA.

FRANK ZAPPA: INTERVIEW PICTURE DISC
CD P.Disc _____ CBAK 4012
Baktabak / Apr '88 / Baktabak.

FREAK OUT (Zappa, Frank & The Mothers Of Invention)
CD _____ RCD 10501
Rykodisc / May '95 / Vital / ADA.

GRAND WAZOO, THE
For Calvin (and his next two hitch-hikers) / Grand wazoo / Gletus awreetus-awrightus / Eat that question / Blessed relief
CD _____ RCD 10517
Rykodisc / May '95 / Vital / ADA.

GUITAR (2CD Set)
Sexual harassment in the workplace / Republicans / That's not really reggae / When no one was no one / Once again, without the net / Outside Now / Jim and Tammy's upper room / Were we ever really safe / That ol' G minor thing again / Move it or park it / Sunrise redeemer / But who was Fulcanneli / Winos do not match / Systems of edges / Things that look like meat / Watermelon in Easter hay
CD Set _____ RCD 10550/51
Rykodisc / May '95 / Vital / ADA.

HOT RATS
Peaches en regalia / Willie the pimp / Son of Mr. Green Genes / Little umbrellas / Gumbo variations / It must be a camel
CD _____ RCD 10508
Rykodisc / May '95 / Vital / ADA.

JAZZ FROM HELL
Night school / Beltway bandits / While you were out / Jazz from hell / G spot tornado / Damp ankles / St. Etienne / Massaggio galore
CD _____ RCD 10549
Rykodisc / May '95 / Vital / ADA.

JOE'S GARAGE ACTS I, II & III (2CD Set)
Central scrutinizer / Joe's garage / Catholic girls / Crew slut / Wet t-shirt nite / Toad-O-Line / Why does it hurt when I pee / Lucille has messed my mind up / Token of his extreme / Stick it out / Sy Borg / Dong work for Yuda / Keep it greasy / Outside now / He used to cut the grass / Packard goose / Watermelon in Easter hay / Little green rosetta
CD Set _____ RCD 10530/31
Rykodisc / May '95 / Vital / ADA.

JUST ANOTHER BAND FROM L.A. (Zappa, Frank & The Mothers Of Invention)
Billy the mountain / Call any vegetable / Eddie, are you kidding / Magdalena / Dog breath
CD _____ RCD 10515
Rykodisc / May '95 / Vital / ADA.

LONDON SYMPHONY ORCHESTRA I & II (2CD Set) (London Symphony Orchestra)
CD Set _____ RCD 10540/41
Rykodisc / Apr '95 / Vital / ADA.

LOST EPISODES, THE
Blackouts / Lost ina whirlpool / Ronnie sings / Kenny's booger story / Mount St. Mary's concert excerpt / Take your clothes off when you dance / Tiger roach / Run home slow theme / Fountain of love / Run home cues #2 / Any way the wind blows / Run homes cues #3 / Charva / Dick Kunc story / Wedding dress song / Handsome cabin boy / Cops and buns / Big Squeeze / I'm a band leader / Alley cat / Grand wazoo / Wonderful wino / Kung fu / RDNZL / Basement music #1 / Inca roads / Lil' Clanton shuffle / I don't wanna get drafted / Sharleena
CD _____ RCD 40573
Rykodisc / Feb '96 / Vital / ADA.

LUMPY GRAVY
Lumpy gravy (pts I & II)
CD _____ RCD 10504
Rykodisc / Apr '95 / Vital / ADA.

MAKE A JAZZ NOISE HERE (2CD Set)
Stinkfoot / When yuppies go to hell / Fire and chains / Let's make the water turn black / Harry, you're a beast / Orange county lumber truck / Oh no / Lumpy gravy / Eat that question / Black napkins / Big swifty / King Kong / Star Wars won't work / Black page / T'mershi duween / Dupree's paradise / City of tiny lites / Royal March (L'Histoire du Soldat)/Theme from Bartok's 3rd / Sinister footwear / Stevie's spanking / Alien orifice / Cruisin' for burgers / Advance romance / Strictly genteel
CD Set _____ RCD 10555/56
Rykodisc / May '95 / Vital / ADA.

MAN FROM UTOPIA, THE
Cocaine decisions / Dangerous kitchen / Tink walks amok / Radio is broken / Moggio / Man from Utopia meets Mary Lou / Stick together / Sex / Jazz discharge party hats / We are not alone
CD _____ RCD 10538
Rykodisc / May '95 / Vital / ADA.

ONE SIZE FITS ALL (Zappa, Frank & The Mothers Of Invention)
Inca roads / Can't afford no shoes / Sofa No. 1 / Po-jama people / Florentine / Pogen / Evelyn, a modified dog / San Ber'dino / Andy / Sofa No. 2
CD _____ RCD 10521
Rykodisc / May '95 / Vital / ADA.

ORCHESTRAL FAVORITES
Strictly genteel / Pedro's dowry / Naval aviation in art / Duke of prunes / Bogus pomp
CD _____ RCD 10529
Rykodisc / May '95 / Vital / ADA.

OVERNITE SENSATION
Camarillo brillo / I'm the slime / Dirty love / 50/50 / Zomby woof / Dinah-Moe-Humm / Montana
CD _____ RCD 10518
Rykodisc / Apr '95 / Vital / ADA.

PERFECT STRANGER, THE (Boulez Conducts Zappa) (Barking Pumpkin Digital Gratification Consort)
Dupree's paradise / Jazz in the magnesium dress / Jonestown / Love story / Naval aviation in art / Outside now, again / Perfect stranger
CD _____ RCD 10542
Rykodisc / May '95 / Vital / ADA.

PLAYGROUND PSYCHOTICS (2CD Set) (Zappa, Frank & The Mothers Of Invention)
CD Set _____ RCD 10557/58
Rykodisc / May '95 / Vital / ADA.

ROXY AND ELSEWHERE (Zappa, Frank & The Mothers Of Invention)
Preamble / Penguin in bondage / Pygmy twylyte / Dummy up / Village of the sun / Echidna's arf (of you) / Don't you ever wash that thing / Cheepnis / Son of Orange County / More trouble every day / Be bop tango (of the old jazzmen's church)
CD _____ RCD 10520
Rykodisc / May '95 / Vital / ADA.

SHEIK YERBOUTI
I have been in you / Flakes / Broken hearts are for assholes / I'm so cute / Jones crusher / Whatever happened to all the fun in the world / Rat tomago / We gotta get into something real / Bobby Brown / Rubber shirt / Sheik Yerbouti tango / Baby snakes / Tryin' to grow a chin / City of tiny lites / Dancin' fool / Jewish princess / Wild love / Yo mama
CD _____ RCD 10528
Rykodisc / May '95 / Vital / ADA.

SHIP ARRIVING TOO LATE TO SAVE A DROWNING WITCH
No not now / Valley girl / I come from nowhere / Drowning witch / Envelopes / Teenage prostitute
CD _____ RCD 10537
Rykodisc / May '95 / Vital / ADA.

SHUT UP 'N PLAY YER GUITAR (3CD Set)
Five, five, five / Hog Heaven / Shut up 'n play yer guitar / While you were out / Treacherous cretins / Heavy duty Judy / Soup 'n old clothes / Variations on the Carlos Santana / Can't you hear your pants / Canarsie / Ship ahoy / Deathless horsie / Pink napkins / Beat it with your fist / Return of

the son of shut up 'n play / Pinocchio's furniture / Why Johnny can't read / Stucco Homes / Canard du Jour
CD Set _____ RCD 10533/34/35
Rykodisc / May '95 / Vital / ADA.

SLEEP DIRT
Filthy habits / Flambay / Spider of destiny / Regyption strut / Time is money / Sleep dirt / Ocean is the ultimate solution
CD _____ RCD 10527
Rykodisc / May '95 / Vital / ADA.

STRICTLY COMMERCIAL (The Best Of Frank Zappa)
Peaches en regalia / Don't eat the yellow snow / Dancin' fool / San Ber'dino / Dirty love / My guitar wants to kill your Mother / Cosmik debris / Trouble every day / Disco boy / Fine girl / Sexual harassment in the workplace / Let's make the water turn black / I'm the slime / Joe's garage / Bobby Brown goes down / Montana / Valley girl / Be in my video / Muffin man / Tell me you love me (LP only) / Planet of the baritone women (LP only)
CD _____ RCD 40600
Rykodisc / Aug '95 / Vital / ADA.

STUDIO TAN
CD _____ RCD 10526
Rykodisc / May '95 / Vital / ADA.

THEM OR US
Closer you are / In France / Ya hozna / Sinister footwear II / Truck driver divorce / Stevie's spanking / Baby take your teeth out / Marque - son's chicken / Planet of my dreams / Be in my video / Them or us / Frogs with dirty little lips / Whipping post
CD _____ RCD 10543
Rykodisc / May '95 / Vital / ADA.

THING FISH (2CD Set)
Prologue / Mammy nuns / Harry and Rhonda / Galoot up-date / Torchum never stops / That evil prince / You are what you are / Mud club / Meek shall inherit nothing / Clowns on velvet / Harry as a boy / He's so gay / Massive improve'lence / Artificial Rhonda / Crabbgrass baby / White boy troubles / No no no / Brief case boogie / Brown Moses / Wistful wit a fist-full / Drop dead
CD Set _____ RCD 10544/45
Rykodisc / May '95 / Vital / ADA.

TINSELTOWN REBELLION
Fine girl / Easy meat / For the young sophisticate / Love of my life / I ain't got no heart / Panty rap / Tell me you love me / Now you see it, now you don't / Dance contest / Blue light / Tinseltown rebellion / Pick me, I'm clean / Bamboozled by love / Brown shoes don't make it / Peaches III
CD _____ RCD 10532
Rykodisc / May '95 / Vital / ADA.

TRIBUTE TO THE MUSIC OF FRANK ZAPPA (Various Artists)
CD _____ EFA 034202
Muffin / Jul '95 / SRD.

UNCLE MEAT (2CD Set) (Zappa, Frank & The Mothers Of Invention)
CD Set _____ RCD 10506/7
Rykodisc / May '95 / Vital / ADA.

WAKA/JAWAKA
Big Swifty / Your mouth / It might just be a one-shot deal / Waka / Jawaka
CD _____ RCD 10516
Rykodisc / Apr '95 / Vital / ADA.

WE'RE ONLY IN IT FOR THE MONEY (Zappa, Frank & The Mothers Of Invention)
Are you hung up / Who needs the peace corps / Concentration moon / Mom and Dad / Bow tie Daddy / Harry, you're a beast / What's the ugliest part of your body / Absolutely free / Flower punk / Hot poop / Nasal retentive caliope music / Mother people
CD _____ RCD 10503
Rykodisc / Apr '95 / Vital / ADA.

WEASELS RIPPED MY FLESH (Zappa, Frank & The Mothers Of Invention)
Didja get any onya / Directly from my heart to you / Prelude to the afternoon of a sexually aroused gas mask / Toads of the short forest / Get a little / Eric Dolphy memorial barbecue / Dwarf Nebula processional march / Oh no / Orange county lumber truck / Weasels ripped my flesh / Charles Ives (CD only)
CD _____ RCD 10510
Rykodisc / May '95 / Vital / ADA.

YELLOW SHARK (Ensemble Modern)
CD _____ RCD 40560
Rykodisc / May '95 / Vital / ADA.

YOU ARE WHAT YOU IS
Teenage wind / Harder than your husband / Doreen / Goblin girl / Third movement of sinister footwear, Theme from / Society pages / I'm a beautiful guy / Beauty knows no pain / Charlie's enormous mouth / Any downers / Conehead / You are what you is / Mudd club / Meek shall inherit nothing / Dumb all over / Heavenly bank account / Suicide chump / Jumbo go away / If only she woulda / Drafter again
CD _____ RCD 10536
Rykodisc / May '95 / Vital / ADA.

YOU CAN'T DO THAT ON STAGE ANYMORE VOL.1 (2CD Set) (Zappa, Frank & The Mothers Of Invention)
CD Set _____ RCD 10561/62
Rykodisc / Jul '95 / Vital / ADA.

YOU CAN'T DO THAT ON STAGE ANYMORE VOL.2 (The Helsinki Tapes/2CD)
Tush tush tush / Stinkfoot / Inca roads / R.D.N.Z.L. / Village of the sun / Echidna's arf (of you) / Don't you ever wash that thing / Pygmy twylyte / Room service / Idiot bastard son / Cheepnis / Approximate / Dupree's paradise / Satumaa / T'mershi duween / Dog breath variations / Uncle meat / Building a girl / Montana (whipping floss) / Big swifty
CD Set _____ RCD 10563/64
Rykodisc / Jul '95 / Vital / ADA.

YOU CAN'T DO THAT ON STAGE ANYMORE VOL.3 (2CD Set)
Sharleena / Bamboozled by love / Lucille has messed my mind up / Advance romance / Bobby Brown / Keep it greasy / Honey don't you want a man like me / In France / Drowning witch / Ride my face to Chicago / Carol you fool / Chana in the Bushwah / Joe's garage / Why does it hurt when I pee / Dicky's such an asshole / Hands with a hammer / Zoot allures / Society pages / Beautiful guy / Beauty knows no pain / Charlie's enormous mouth / Cocaine decisions / Nigger biznis / King Kong / Cosmik debris
CD Set _____ RCD 10565/66
Rykodisc / Jul '95 / Vital / ADA.

YOU CAN'T DO THAT ON STAGE ANYMORE VOL.4 (2CD Set)
Little rubber girl / Stick together / My guitar / Willie the pimp / Montana / Brown Moses / Evil prince / Approximate / Love of my life / Let's move to Cleveland / You call that music / Pound for a brown on the bus / Black page 2 / Take me out to the ball game / Filthy habits / Torture never stops / Church chat / Stevie's spanking / Outside now / Disco boy / Teenage wind / Truck driver divorce / Florentine pogen / Tiny sick tears / Smell my beard / Booger man / Carolina hard-core ecstasy / Are you upset / Little girl of mine / Closer you are / Johnny darling / No no cherry / Man from Utopia meets Mary Lou
CD Set _____ RCD 10567/68
Rykodisc / Jul '95 / Vital / ADA.

YOU CAN'T DO THAT ON STAGE ANYMORE VOL.5 (2CD Set)
CD Set _____ RCD 10569/70
Rykodisc / Jul '95 / Vital / ADA.

YOU CAN'T DO THAT ON STAGE ANYMORE VOL.6 (2CD Set)
CD Set _____ RCD 10571/72
Rykodisc / Jul '95 / Vital / ADA.

ZAPPA IN NEW YORK
CD _____ RCD 10524/25
Rykodisc / May '95 / Vital / ADA.

ZAPPA'S UNIVERSE (Various Artists)
CD _____ 5135752
Verve / Apr '93 / PolyGram.

ZOOT ALLURES
Wind up workin' in a gas station / Black napkins / Torture never stops / Ms. Pinky / Find her finer / Friendly little finger / Wonderful wino / Zoot allures / Disco boy
CD _____ RCD 10523
Rykodisc / May '95 / Vital / ADA.

ZAWINUL
Dr. Honoris Causa / In a silent way / His last journey / Double image / Arrival in New York
CD _____ 7567813752
Atlantic / Apr '95 / Warner Music.

Zayas, Edwin Colon

Y SU TALLER CAMPESINO BIEN JIBARO
CD _____ ROU 5056CD
Rounder / May '94 / CM / Direct / ADA / Cadillac.

Zazou, Hector

GEOGRAPHIES
CD _____ MTM 5CD
Made To Measure / May '93 / Grapevine.

I'LL STRANGLE YOU (Zazou, Hector & Depardieu)
CD Set _____ CRAM 80
Crammed Discs / Oct '92 / Grapevine / New Note.

SAHARA BLUE
CD _____ MTM 32
Made To Measure / Nov '92 / Grapevine.

Ze, Tom

BRAZIL 5 (The hips of tradition)
Ogodo, ano 2000 / Sem a letra / Fiera de santana / Sofro de juventude / Cortina 1 / Tai / Iracema / Fliperama / O amor e velho-menina / Cortina 2 / Taturamba / Jingle do disco / Lua-gira-sol / Cortina 3 / Multiplicarse unica / Cortina 4 / O pao nosso de cada mes / Amor
CD _____ 9362-45118-2
Luaka Bop / Feb '93 / Warner Music.

BRAZIL CLASSICS 4
Ma / O riso e a faca / Toc / To / Um "oh" e um "ah', ui! (voce inventa) / Cademar / So (solidao) / Hein / Augusta / Doi / Complexo de epico / A felicidade / Vai (menina, amanha de manha)
CD _____ 7599263962
Sire / Dec '90 / Warner Music.

Zebra

3V
CD _____ 7567816922
Atlantic / Jan '96 / Warner Music.

NO TELLIN' LIES
Wait until the summer's gone / I don't like it / Bears / I don't care / Lullaby / No tellin' lies / Takin' a stance / But no more / Little things / Drive me crazy
CD _____ 7567801592
Atlantic / Jan '96 / Warner Music.

Zeigler, Diane

STING OF THE HONEYBEE
CD _____ CDPH 1174
Philo / Apr '95 / Direct / CM / ADA.

Zein Musical Party

STYLE OF MOMBASA
Mtindo wa mombasa / Maneno tisiya / Wanawake wa kiamu / Taksim bayati / Baina macho na moyo / Mwiba wa kujitoma / Binti mombasa / Nataka rafiki / Mwana hasahau mana / Taksim jirka
CD _____ CDORBD 066
Globestyle / Nov '90 / Pinnacle.

Zariz, Jose

EL CONDOR PASA
CD _____ 12411
Laserlight / Jul '95 / Target/BMG.

Zawinul, Joe

BEGINNING, THE (Zawinul, Joe Trio)
CD _____ FSRCD 142
Fresh Sound / Dec '90 / Jazz Music / Discovery.

BLACK WATER (Zawinul Syndicate)
Carnavalito / Familial / In the same boat / Little rootie tootie / Black water / Medicine man / Monk's mood / They had a dream
CD _____ 4653442
Sony Jazz / Jan '95 / Sony.

JOE ZAWINUL & AUSTRIAN ALLSTARS/ SWINGING NEPHEWS 1954-57
CD _____ RST 91549
RST / Mar '95 / Jazz Music / Hot Shot.

LOST TRIBES (Zawinul Syndicate)
CD _____ 4689002
Sony Jazz / Jan '95 / Sony.

RISE AND FALL OF THE THIRD STREAM/MONEY IN POCKET
Baptismal / Soul of a village (part 1) / Soul of a village (part 2) / Fifth canto / From Vienna with love / Lord, lord, lord / Concerto retitled / Money in the pocket / If / My one and only love / Midnight mood / Some more of dat / Sharon's waltz / Riverbend / Del sasser
CD _____ 812271675-2
Atlantic / Jul '94 / Warner Music.

Zeke

SUPER SOUND RACING
CD _____ IFACD 001
IFA / Oct '95 / Plastic Head.

Zayas

(continued in body)

Zeitlin, Denny

CONCORD DUE SERIES VOL.8 (Zeitlin, Denny & David Friesen)
All of you / Echo of a kiss / Night has a thousand eyes / Old folks / Oleo / Turn around / Island / Signs and wonders
CD _____ CCD 4639
Concord Jazz / Apr '95 / New Note.

IN CONCERT (Zeitlin, Denny & David Friesen)
CD _____ ITM 970068
ITM / Nov '92 / Tradelink / Koch.

IN THE MOMENT
CD _____ WD 0121
Windham Hill Jazz / Mar '92 / New Note.

LIVE AT MAYBECK RECITAL HALL, VOL. 27
Blues on the side / Girl next door / My man's gone now / Lazy bird / Round Midnight / Love for sale / And then I wondered if you knew / Country fair / Sophisticated lady / End of a love affair / Just passing by / What is this thing called love / Fifth house
CD _____ CCD 4572
Concord Jazz / Sep '93 / New Note.

TRIO
CD _____ WD 0112
Windham Hill Jazz / Mar '92 / New Note.

Zeke

SUPER SOUND RACING
CD _____ IFACD 001
IFA / Oct '95 / Plastic Head.

Zellar, Martin

BORN UNDER
Lie to me / Something's gotta happen / East side boys / Falling sky / Problem solved / Cross my heart / Lay this down gently / Summer kind of sad / Force a smile / Let's go
CD _____ RCD 10318
Rykodisc / Mar '95 / Vital / ADA.

Zen Guerrilla

ZEN GUERRILLA
CD _____ OPS 8
Compulsive / Mar '93 / SRD.

Zen Paradox

FROM THE SHORE OF A DISTANT LAND
Nova Zembla / Oct '94 / Plastic Head. NZCD 014

INTO THE ABYSS
CD _____ NZCD 011
Nova Zembla / Jun '94 / Plastic Head.

VOYAGE, THE
CD _____ NZCD 041
Nova Zembla / Oct '95 / Plastic Head.

Zeni Geva

DESIRE FOR AGONY
CD _____ VIRUS 135CD
Alternative Tentacles / Feb '94 / Pinnacle.

Zenith Brass Band

ECLIPSE ALLEY
CD _____ AMCD 75
American Music / Aug '94 / Jazz Music.

Zenith Hot Stompers

SILVER JUBILEE
CD _____ SOSCD 1191
Stomp Off / Aug '90 / Jazz Music / Wellard.

ZENITH HOT STOMPERS PLAYS JELLY ROLL MORTON
CD _____ BCD 012
GHB / Oct '93 / Jazz Music.

Zeno

ZENOLOGY
CD _____ A2Z 0023CD
A2Z / Jan '96 / Plastic Head.

Zentner, Michael

PRESENT TIME
CD _____ EFA 132472
Ozone / May '94 / SRD.

Zepf, Manfred

PAINTINGS (Zepf, Manfred & Andrew Cyrille)
CD _____ WWCD 003
West Wind / Jul '88 / Swift / Charly / CM / ADA.

Zephaniah, Benjamin

BACK TO ROOTS
CD _____ DUBI 01CD
Acid Jazz / Jun '95 / Pinnacle.

Zephyr

ZEPHYR
CD _____ BGOCD 41
Beat Goes On / '89 / Pinnacle.

Zerbe-Blech, Hannez

RANDO A LA FRIED (Zerbe-Blech, Hannez Band)
CD _____ BVHAASTCD 9207
Bvhaast / Mar '86 / Cadillac.

Zeros

4-3-2-1
CD _____ LS 92422
Roadrunner / Nov '91 / Pinnacle.

Zerouki, Charef

GHOZALI - MY GAZELLE
Ma andaklah tgoulili kalma / Al wa'ad armm-ani / Al 'achaq / Ghozali / Al 'adra / Yamra
CD _____ CDORB 047
Globestyle / Aug '89 / Pinnacle.

Zerra One

DOMINO EFFECT
Rescue me / Domino effect / I know I feel I stand / Hands up / Forever and ever / Cry for you / All forgiven / Guardian angel / Heaven
CD _____ 8300352
Mercury / Jan '87 / PolyGram.

Z'Ev

ONE FOOT IN THE GRAVE (1968-1990/ 2CD Set)
CD Set _____ TO 13
Touch / Mar '91 / These / Kudos.

Zevon, Warren

BAD LUCK STREAK IN DANCING SCHOOL
CD _____ 7559605612
Carlton Home Entertainment / Oct '94 / Carlton Home Entertainment.

EXCITABLE BOY
Johnny strikes up the road / Roland the headless thompson gunner / Excitable boy / Werewolves of London / Accidentally like a martyr / Nighttime in the switching yard / Vera Cruz / Tenderness on the block / Law-yers, guns and money
CD _____ 7559 605212
Carlton Home Entertainment / Jan '93 / Carlton Home Entertainment.

MUTINEER
CD _____ 74321276852
RCA / Jun '95 / BMG.

QUIET NORMAL LIFE, A (The Best Of Warren Zevon)
Werewolves of London / Play it all night long / Roland the headless Thompson gun-ner / Envoy / Mohammed's radio / Desper-ados under the eaves / I'll sleep when I'm dead / Lawyers, guns and money / Ain't that pretty at all / Poor, poor pitiful me / Accidentally like a martyr / Looking for the next best thing
CD _____ 960 503-2
Asylum / Nov '86 / Warner Music.

SENTIMENTAL HYGIENE
Sentimental hygiene / Boom boom Mancini / Factory / Trouble waiting to happen / Re-consider me / Detox mansion / Bad karma / Even a dog can shake hands / Heartache / Leave my monkey alone
CD _____ CDV 2433
Virgin / Jul '93 / EMI.

TRANSVERSE CITY
Transverse city / Run straight down / Long arm of the law / Turbulence / They moved the moon / Splendid isolation / Networking / Gridlock / Down in the mall / Nobody's in this year
CD _____ CDVUS 9
Virgin / Jan '90 / EMI.

ZGA

ZGANONIUMS
CD _____ ZGACD 1
RER / Jan '93 / Grapevine.

Zhane

PRONOUNCED JAH-NAY
CD _____ 530283-2
Motown / Mar '94 / PolyGram.

Ziegler, Anne

LOVE'S OLD SWEET SONG (Ziegler, Anne & Webster Booth)
CD _____ PASTCD 7034
Flapper / Aug '94 / Pinnacle.
CD _____ CDGO 2057
EMI / May '95 / EMI.

Ziegler, Finn

ANDERSEN, NIELSEN OG DEN UKENDTE
CD _____ MECCACD 1044
Music Mecca / Nov '94 / Jazz Music / Cadillac / Wellard.

Zig Zag

ZIG ZAG'S FAMILY FUN ALBUM (Memorable Tunes For Everyone)
CD _____ DUOCD 89025
Meridian / Dec '93 / Nimbus.

Zil

ZIL
CD _____ 841 929-2
Polydor / Aug '90 / PolyGram.

Zimbo Trio

AQUARELA DO BRASIL
CD _____ JHR 73567
Jazz Hour / Nov '93 / Target/BMG / Jazz Music / Cadillac.

Zimmerman, Richard

ROOTS OF RAGTIME, THE
CD _____ CD 409
Bescol / Aug '94 / CM / Target/BMG.

Zimmermann, Tabea

CREAM OF VICTOR SYLVESTER, THE (Zimmerman, Tabea & Thomas Zehetmair)
You're dancing on my heart (#) / Give a little whistle (#) / So deep is the night / I shall be waiting / Love bells / Fragrant flowers / It's a hap-hap-happy day / When you wish upon a star / I'm in love for the last time / Love everlasting / Blue orchids / Mist is over the moon / If I were sure of you / In the middle of a dream / Lonely sweetheart /

Love never grows old / Little rain must fall / Summer sweetheart / Summer evening in Santa Cruz / Dear Madam / Where of when / Don't say goodbye
CD _____ PASTCD 9786
Flapper / Apr '92 / Pinnacle.

Zion Train

GREAT SPORTING MOMENTS IN DUB
CD _____ WWCD 3
Wibbly Wobbly / Dec '93 / SRD.

HOMEGROWN FANTASY
Dance of life / Free the bass / Healing of the nation / Universal celebration / Venceremos / Get ready / For the revolution / Why do we have to fight / Live goes (IV) / Better day / Love the earth / One world, one heart, one conscience
CD _____ WOLCD 1060
China / Jun '95 / Pinnacle.

NATURAL WONDERS OF THE WORLD IN DUB
CD _____ WOLCD 1055
China / Jan '95 / Pinnacle.

PASSAGE TO INDICA
CD _____ WOLCD 1054
China / Jan '95 / Pinnacle.

SIREN
CD _____ WOLCD 1056
China / Jan '95 / Pinnacle.

Zior

ZIOR... PLUS
I really do / Za za za Zilda / Love's desire / New land / Now I'm sad / Give me love / Quabala / Oh Mariya / Your life will burn / I was fooling / Before my eyes go blind / Roll-ing thunder / Dudi Judy / Evolution / Cat's eyes / Strange kind of magic / Ride me baby / Entrance of the devil (the Chicago spine) (CD only) / Every inch a man (CD only) / Angel of the highway (CD only)
CD _____ SEECD 276
See For Miles/C5 / Oct '89 / Pinnacle.

Zitro, James

JAMES ZITRO
CD _____ ESP 1052-2
ESP / Jan '93 / Jazz Horizons / Jazz Music.

Zlatne Uste Blakan Brass.

NO STRINGS ATTACHED (Zlatne Uste Blakan Brass Band)
CD _____ ROU 6054CD
Rounder / Aug '93 / CM / Direct / ADA / Cadillac.

Znowhite

ACT OF GOD
Last breath / Baptised by fire / Pure blood / Thunderdome / War machine / Disease bigotry / Something wicked / Rest in peace / Soldier's greed
CD _____ RR 95872
Roadrunner / May '88 / Pinnacle.

ZNR

BARRICADE 3
CD _____ ZNR 1CD
ReR Megacorp / Feb '94 / These / ReR Megacorp.

Zodiac Mindwarp

HOODLUM THUNDER (Zodiac Mindwarp & The Love Reaction)
CD _____ 108642
Musidisc / Jan '92 / Vital / Harmonia Mundi / ADA / Cadillac / Discovery.

LIVE AT READING '87
CD _____ FRSCD 011
Raw Fruit / Aug '93 / Pinnacle.

MY LIFE STORY
CD _____ 109832
Musidisc / Nov '92 / Vital / Harmonia Mundi / ADA / Cadillac / Discovery.

Zoller, Attila

WHEN IT'S TIME
Joy for hoy / Lu and Shu / After the morning / Song is you / When it's time / Homage to OP / Voyage / Meant to be
CD _____ ENJ 90312
Enja / Aug '95 / New Note / Vital/SAM.

Zombies

BEST OF THE ZOMBIES
She's not there / Time of the season / I must move / I got my mojo working / I re-member how I loved her / Summertime / What more can I do / Can't nobody love you / Can't make up my mind / Tell her no / I don't want to know / I love you / You really got a hold on me / Whenever you're ready / You make me feel good / Roadrunner
CD _____ MCCD 002
Music Club / Feb '91 / Disc / THE / CM.

COLLECTION: ZOMBIES
Goin' out of my head / Leave me be / Gotta get a hold on myself / I can't make up my

mind / Kind of girl / Sticks and stones / Summertime / Woman / I got my mojo working / Roadrunner / You really got a hold on me / Nothing's changed / You make me feel good / She's not there / Don't go away / How we were before / Tell her no / When-ever you're ready / Just out of reach / Re-member you / Indication / She does every-thing for me / Time of the season / I love you
CD _____ CCSCD 196
Castle / Aug '88 / BMG.

NEW WORLD
New world (my America) / Love breaks down / I can't be wrong / Lula Lula / Heav-en's gate / Time of the season / Moonday morning dance / Blue / Losing you / Alone in paradise / Knowing you / Love conquers all / Nights on fire
CD _____ CLACD 348
Castle / Jun '94 / BMG.

SINGLES A'S & B'S
She's not there / Leave me be / Tell her no / She's coming home / I want her back / Whenever you're ready / Is this the dream / Remember you / Indication / Gotta get a hold on myself / Goin' out of my head / You make me feel good / Woman / What more can I do / I must move / I remember when I loved her / I love you / Don't go away / Just out of reach / How we were before / Way I feel inside / She does everything for me
CD _____ SEECD 30
See For Miles/C5 / Sep '88 / Pinnacle.

ZOMBIES 1964-67, THE
She's not there / Rose for Emily / I can't make up my mind / You make me feel good / Tell her no / Kind of girl / Leave me be / Sometimes / It's all right with me / I don't want to know / I love you / Indication / Nothing's changes / Hung up on a dream / Whenever you're ready / Hold your head up (live) / She's not there (live) / Time of the season (Live) (Mixes) / I'm in the mood (live)
CD _____ MOCD 3009
More Music / Feb '95 / Sound & Media.

Zoo

ZOO PRESENTS CHOCOLATE MOOSE, THE
Chocolate moose / Written on the wind / I've been waiting too long / Soul drippin's / Get some beads / Ain't nobody / Try me / Love machine / Have you been sleepin' / From a camel's hump
CD _____ CDWIKM 123
Big Beat / Oct '93 / Pinnacle.

Zoo

SHAKIN' THE CAGE
CD _____ 9362420042
WEA / Jun '92 / Warner Music.

Zoogz Rift

MURDERING HELL'S HAPPY CRETINS
CD _____ SST 211 CD
SST / Feb '89 / Plastic Head.

NONENTITY WATER 3 (FAN BLACK DADA)
CD _____ SST 184 CD
SST / May '93 / Plastic Head.

TORMENT
CD _____ SST 251 CD
SST / May '93 / Plastic Head.

VILLAGERS
CD _____ EFA 11372 CD
Musical Tragedies / May '93 / SRD.

WATER : AT A SAFE DISTANCE
CD _____ SST 137 CD
SST / May '93 / Plastic Head.

Zoom

HELIUM OCTIPEDE
Balboa's kitchen / Can fighting / Five fingers and a thumb / Ephedrine breakfast / Ex-trano / Letter from Allan / Bottle king / Mynr / Cycle of fifths
CD _____ TK 93CD053
T/K / Aug '94 / Pinnacle.

Zorn, John

COBRA
CD Set _____ ARTCD 26040
Hat Art / '91 / Harmonia Mundi / ADA / Cadillac.

HARRAS (Zorn, John & Derek Bailey/ William Parker)
CD _____ AVAN 056
Avant / Jan '96 / Harmonia Mundi / Cadillac.

JOHN ZORN'S COBRA LIVE AT THE KNITTING FACTORY
CD _____ KFWCD 124
Knitting Factory / Feb '95 / Grapevine.

MASADA
CD _____ DIW 888
DIW / Mar '95 / Harmonia Mundi / Cadillac.

MASADA 5
CD _____ DIW 899
DIW / Dec '95 / Harmonia Mundi /
Cadillac.

**MORE NEWS FOR LULU (Zorn, John/
Bill Frisell/George Lewis)**
CD _____ ARTCD 6055
Hat Art / Feb '92 / Harmonia Mundi / ADA
/ Cadillac.

NAKED CITY
CD _____ 7559792382
Elektra Nonesuch / Jan '94 / Warner
Music.

**NEWS FOR LULU (Zorn, John/Bill
Frisell/George Lewis)**
CD _____ ARTCD 6005
Hat Art / Jul '88 / Harmonia Mundi / ADA /
Cadillac.

SPILLANE
CD _____ K 979172 2
Elektra Nonesuch / Mar '88 / Warner
Music.

**SPY VS SPY - THE MUSIC OF
ORNETTE COLEMAN**
CD _____ K 960 844 2
Elektra Nonesuch / Aug '89 / Warner
Music.

**TORTURE GARDEN (Zorn, John &
Naked City)**
CD _____ MOSH 028CD
Earache / Sep '90 / Vital.

Zounds

CURSE OF ZOUNDS
Fear / Did he jump / My Mummy's gone /
Little bit more / This land / New band / Dirty
squatters / Loads of noise / Target / Mr.
Disney / War goes on / Can't cheat karma
/ War / Subvert / Demystification / Great
white hunter / Dancing / True love / More
trouble coming every day / Knife / Not me
/ Biafra / Wolves
CD _____ SEEP 006
Rugger Bugger / Jan '94 / Vital.

Zubop

CYCLE CITY
CD _____ 33JAZZ 006CD
33 Jazz / Jun '93 / Cadillac / New Note.

FREEWHEELING
CD _____ 33JAZZ 015CD
33 Jazz / Oct '94 / Cadillac / New Note.

Zucchero

MISERERE
CD _____ 5170972
London / Jan '93 / PolyGram.

SPIRITO DI VINO
CD _____ 5277852
London / Aug '95 / PolyGram.

ZUCCHERO
Diamante / Wonderful world / Il mare /
Mama / Dunes of mercy / Senza una Donna
/ You're losing me / Solo una sana / You've
chosen me / Diavolo in me (Only on CD and
cassette) / Overdose (d'amore) (Only on CD
and cassette) / Nice (nietzsche) che dice
(Only on CD and cassette)
CD _____ 849 063 2
London / May '91 / PolyGram.

Zukie, Tappa

FROM THE ARCHIVES
CD _____ RASCD 3135
Ras / Jun '95 / Jetstar / Greensleeves /
SRD / Direct.

TAPPA ZUKIE IN DUB
CD _____ BAFCD 8
Blood & Fire / Sep '95 / Grapevine /
PolyGram.

Zulu, Philomon

HOW LONG
CD _____ SHCD 434048
Shanachie / Apr '92 / Koch / ADA /
Greensleeves.

Zumaque, Francisco

**VOICES CARIBES (Zumaque, Francisco,
& Super Macumbia)**
CD _____ SH 64051
Shanachie / Doo '94 / Koch / ADA /
Greensleeves.

Zumi-Kai

KOTO MUSIC OF JAPAN
CD _____ 12184
Laserlight / Aug '95 / Target/BMG.

Zumpano

LOOK WHAT THE ROOKIE DID
CD _____ SPCD 140344
Sub Pop / Jan '95 / Disc.

Zuvuya

**SHAMANIA (Zuvuya & Terence
McKenna)**
Shaman I am (Mixes) / FX return / Black sun
yadaki / Whisper in trees / Into the future /
Shamania
CD _____ DELECCD 021
Delerium / Sep '94 / Vital.

Zyklon B

ZYKLON B
CD _____ MR 005CD
Malicious / Nov '95 / Plastic Head.

ZZ Top

AFTERBURNER
Sleeping bag / Stages / Woke up with wood
/ Rough boy / Can't stop rockin' / Planet of
women / I got the message / Velcro fly /
Dipping low / Delirious
CD _____ 925342-2
WEA / Mar '94 / Warner Music.

ANTENNA
Pincushion / PCH / Breakaway / Lizard life
/ Cover your rig / Antenna head / Fuzzbox
voodoo / World of swirl / T-shirt / Deal goin'
down / Cherry red / Everything
CD _____ 74321 18260-2
RCA / Mar '94 / BMG.

DEGUELLO
I thank you / She loves my automobile / I'm
bad I'm nationwide / Fool for your stockings
/ Manic mechanic / Dust my broom / Low-
down in the street / Hi-fi mama / Cheap
sunglasses / Esther be the one
CD _____ K 256701
WEA / Mar '94 / Warner Music.

EL LOCO
Tube snake boogie / I wanna drive you
home / Ten foot pole / Leila / Don't tease
me / It's so hard / Pearl necklace / Groove
little hippie pad / Heaven, Hell or Houston /
Party on the patio
CD _____ 759923593-2
WEA / Mar '94 / Warner Music.

ELIMINATOR
Gimme all your lovin' / Got me under
pressure / Sharp dressed man / I need you
tonight / I got the six / Legs / Thug / T.V.
dinners / Dirty dog / If I could only flag her
down / Bad girl
CD _____ W 37742
WEA / Mar '94 / Warner Music.

FANDANGO
Thunderbird / Jailhouse rock / Backdoor
medley / Backdoor love affair / Mellow
down easy / Backdoor love affair no.2 /
Long distance boogie / Nasty dogs and
funky kings / Blue jean blues / Balinese /
Mexican blackbird / Heard it on the X / Tush
CD _____ K 256604
WEA / Mar '94 / Warner Music.

GREATEST HITS
Gimme all your lovin' / Sharp dressed man
/ Rough boy / Tush / My head's in Missis-
sippi / Viva Las Vegas / Legs / Doubleback
/ Gun love / Got me under pressure / Give
it up / Sleeping bag / La grange / Tube
snake boogie
CD _____ 7599268462
WEA / Apr '92 / Warner Music.

ONE FOOT IN THE BLUES
CD _____ 9362458152
WEA / Nov '94 / Warner Music.

RECYCLER
Concrete and steel / Love thing / Penthouse
eyes / Tell it / My head's in Mississippi /

Decision or collision / Give it up / 2000
blues / Burger man / Doubleback
CD _____ 759926265-2
WEA / Mar '94 / Warner Music.

RIO GRANDE MUD
Francine / Just got paid / Mushmouth shoutin' / Koko blue / Chevrolet / Apologies to
pearly / Bar B Q / Sure got cold after the
rain fell / Whisky 'n' mama / Down brownie
CD _____ 759927380-2
WEA / Mar '94 / Warner Music.

**RIO GRANDE MUD/TRES HOMBRES/
FANDANGO/TEJAS/EL LOCO/FIRST LP
(ZZ Top's Sixpack/3CD Set)**
(Somebody else been) shaking your tree /
Brown sugar / Squank / Goin' down to
Mexico / Old man / Neighbour, neighbour /
Certified blues / Bedroom thang / Just got
back from baby's / Backdoor love affair /
Francine / Just got paid / Mushmouth shou-
tin' / Koko blue / Chevrolet / Apologies to
Pearly / Bar B Q / Sure got cold after the
rain fell / Whisky 'n' mama / Down brownie
/ Waitin' for the bus / Jesus just left Chicago
/ Beer drinkers and hell raisers / Master of
sparks / Hot, blue and righteous / Move me
on down the line / Precious and grace / La
grange / Sheik / Have you heard / Thunderbird / Jailhouse rock / Mellow down easy
/ Back door love affair No.2 / Long distance
boogie / Nasty dogs and funky kings / Blue
jean blues / Balinese / Mexican blackbird /
Heard it on the X / Tush / It's only love /
Arrested for driving while blind / El diablo /
Snappy kakkie / Enjoy and get it on / Ten
dollar man / Pan am highway blues / Avalon
hideaway / She's a heartbreaker / Asleep in
the desert / Tube snake boogie / I wanna
drive you home / Ten foot pole / Leila /
Don't tease me / It's so hard / Pearl necklace / Groovy little hippy pad / Heaven, hell
or Houston / Party on the patio
CD Set _____ 925661 2
WEA / Dec '87 / Warner Music.

TEJAS
It's only love / Arrested for driving while
blind / El diablo / Snappy kakkie / Enjoy and
get it on / Ten dollar man / Pan Am highway
blues / Avalon hideaway / She's a heartbreaker / Asleep in the desert
CD _____ 759927383-2
WEA / Mar '94 / Warner Music.

TRES HOMBRES
Waitin' for the bus / Jesus just left Chicago
/ Beer drinkers and hell raisers / Master of
sparks / Hot, blue and righteous / Move me
on down the line / Precious and grace / La
grange / Sheik / Have you heard
CD _____ K 256603
WEA / Mar '94 / Warner Music.

ZZ TOP'S FIRST ALBUM
(Somebody else been) shaking your tree /
Brown sugar / Squank / Goin' down to
Mexico / Old man / Neighbour, neighbour /
Certified blues / Bedroom thang / Just got
back from baby's / Backdoor love affair
CD _____ K 256601
WEA / Mar '94 / Warner Music.

Compilations

1-800 NEW FUNK
Minneapolis: *MPLS* / Hollywood: *Clinton, George* / Love sign: *Gaye, Nona & Prince* / If I love U 2 nite: *Mayte* / Colour: *Steeles* / 2gether: *N.P.G.* / Standing at the altar: *Cox, Margie* / You will be moved: *Staples, Mavis* / Seventeen: *Madhouse* / Woman's gotta have it: *Gaye, Nona* / Minneapolis reprise: *MPLS*
CD _____ NPG 60512
New Power Generation / Aug '94 / Grapevine / THE.

3 BEAT HIGH & RISING
CD _____ 3BTTCD 1
3 Beat / Jun '93 / PolyGram.

3 VOCAL GREATS OF THE 50'S
(Lita Roza/Petula Clark/Marion Ryan) (3 CD Set)
That's the beginning of the end: *Roza, Lita* / I've got my eyes on you: *Roza, Lita* / Oh dear what can the matter be: *Roza, Lita* / I'll never say Never Again again: *Roza, Lita* / End of a love affair: *Roza, Lita* / Not mine: *Roza, Lita* / As children do: *Roza, Lita* / There's nothing rougher than love: *Roza, Lita* / Somewhere, somehow, someday: *Roza, Lita* / Allentown jail: *Roza, Lita* / Once in a while: *Roza, Lita* / Nel blu dipinto di blu: *Roza, Lita* / This is my town: *Roza, Lita* / Maybe you'll be there: *Roza, Lita* / Sorry, sorry, sorry: *Roza, Lita* / I could have danced all night: *Roza, Lita* / All alone (by a telephone): *Roza, Lita* / Other woman: *Roza, Lita* / Love can change the stars: *Roza, Lita* / I, Yi, Yi, Yi.: *Clark, Petula* / You are my lucky star: *Clark, Petula* / Afraid to dream: *Clark, Petula* / It's the natural thing to do: *Clark, Petula* / As tiem goes by: *Clark, Petula* / Slumming on Park Avenue: *Clark, Petula* / I wish I knew: *Clark, Petula* / Goodnight my love: *Clark, Petula* / Alone: *Clark, Petula* / Zing went the strings of my heart: *Clark, Petula* / Sonny boy: *Clark, Petula* / Love me forever: *Ryan, Marion* / Stairway of love: *Ryan, Marion* / Hit the road to dreamland: *Ryan, Marion* / Jeepers creepers: *Ryan, Marion* / Mr. Wonderful: *Ryan, Marion* / I'm beginning to see the light: *Ryan, Marion* / Cry me a river: *Ryan, Marion* / That's happiness: *Ryan, Marion* / There will never be another you: *Ryan, Marion* / Oh oh, I'm falling in love again: *Ryan, Marion* / I'll take romance: *Ryan, Marion* / World goes round and round: *Ryan, Marion* / If I can't take it with me: *Ryan, Marion* / My heart belongs to Daddy: *Ryan, Marion* / I might as well be spring: *Ryan, Marion* / I need you: *Ryan, Marion* / Make the man love me: *Ryan, Marion* / Always and forever: *Ryan, Marion* / High life: *Ryan, Marion* / Why do fools fall in love: *Ryan, Marion* / Wait for me: *Ryan, Marion* / Hot diggidy (dog diggity boom): *Ryan, Marion* / Chantez chantez: *Ryan, Marion* / Please don't say goodnight: *Ryan, Marion* / Sailor boy: *Ryan, Marion*
CD Set _____ MAGPIE 7
See For Miles/C5 / Sep '95 / Pinnacle.

3RD ST. PATRICK'S DAY FESTIVAL
CD _____ MAG 201
Magnetic / Mar '95 / Magnum Music Group.

4 ON 1
CD _____ DBMTRCD 19
Rogue Trooper / Sep '95 / SRD.

4-2-4
(The El Football Scrapbook)
Nice one Cyril / I'm forever blowing bubbles / Onward Sexton soldiers / Canaries / Football football / World Cup Willie / Good old Arsenal / Back home / We are Wimbledon / Belfast boy / We are the owls / Hibernian / Going back to Derby / Boys in blue / Viva el Fulham / Sunderland
CD _____ MONDE 15CD
Cherry Red / Aug '93 / Pinnacle.

5 YEARS OF NUCLEAR BLAST
CD _____ NB 083CD
Nuclear Blast / Dec '93 / Plastic Head.

5TH ST.PATRICK'S DAY FESTIVAL
In these fields / Matt peoples / Used to / Donegal lass / Flower of Magherally / Paddy's in Japan / Newry highwayman / Terry Crehan's / Hard times / Dezi's tune / Kid on the mountain / Rocky road to dublin / B'fheidir / Four ages of man / Leslie's tune / Saratoga set / While they're all talking / Guns of the magnificent seven set / Kerry polkas / Rocks of bawn / Mountain road reels
CD _____ MAG 601
Magnetic / Mar '95 / Magnum Music Group.

7" WONDERS OF THE WORLD
CD _____ SST 070 CD
SST / May '93 / Plastic Head.

10 GLAM STARS VOLUME 1
CD _____ STACD 077
Wisepack / Nov '93 / THE / Conifer.

10 GLAM STARS VOLUME 2
CD _____ STACD 078
Wisepack / Nov '93 / THE / Conifer.

10 HIT STARS VOLUME 1
CD _____ STACD 071
Wisepack / Nov '93 / THE / Conifer.

10 HIT STARS VOLUME 2
CD _____ STACD 072
Wisepack / Nov '93 / THE / Conifer.

10 HIT STARS VOLUME 3
CD _____ STACD 073
Wisepack / Nov '93 / THE / Conifer.

10 HIT STARS VOLUME 4
Walking on sunshine: *Katrina & The Waves* / Sun street: *Katrina & The Waves* / Living in a box: *Living In A Box* / Room in your heart: *Living In A Box* / Too shy: *Kajagoogoo* / Big apple: *Kajagoogoo* / Cap in hand: *Proclaimers* / If this is it: *Lewis, Huey & The News* / Stuck with you: *Lewis, Huey & The News* / Smile: *Pussycat* / Mississippi: *Pussycat* / Turning Japanese: *Vapors* / News at ten: *Vapors* / Fade to grey: *Visage* / Mind of a toy: *Visage* / Living on the ceiling: *Blancmange* / Day before you came: *Blancmange* / Stand up for your love rights: *Yazz* / Fine time: *Yazz*
CD _____ STACD 074
Wisepack / Nov '93 / THE / Conifer.

10 LOVE STARS VOLUME 1
CD _____ STACD 059
Wisepack / Nov '93 / THE / Conifer.

10 LOVE STARS VOLUME 2
CD _____ STACD 060
Wisepack / Nov '93 / THE / Conifer.

10 LOVE STARS VOLUME 3
CD _____ STACD 061
Wisepack / Nov '93 / THE / Conifer.

10 LOVE STARS VOLUME 4
CD _____ STACD 062
Wisepack / Nov '93 / THE / Conifer.

10 METAL STARS VOLUME 1
CD _____ STACD 075
Wisepack / Nov '93 / THE / Conifer.

10 METAL STARS VOLUME 2
CD _____ STACD 076
Wisepack / Nov '93 / THE / Conifer.

10 METER OHNE KOPF
Fishcore / Sep '92 / SRD.

CD _____ EFA 15179CD

10 ROCK STARS VOLUME 1
CD _____ STACD 067
Wisepack / Nov '93 / THE / Conifer.

10 ROCK STARS VOLUME 2
CD _____ STACD 068
Wisepack / Nov '93 / THE / Conifer.

10 ROCK STARS VOLUME 3
No particular place to go: *Berry, Chuck* / Route 66: *Berry, Chuck* / Life is for living: *Barclay James Harvest* / Just a day away: *Barclay James Harvest* / Be good to yourself: *Journey* / Who's crying now: *Journey* / San Francisco nights: *Burdon, Eric* / Ring of fire: *Burdon, Eric* / Heat is on: *Frey, Glenn* / You belong to the city: *Frey, Glenn* / After midnight: *Cale, J.J.* / Cocaine: *Cale, J.J.* / Dust my broom: *Fleetwood Mac* / Need your love so bad: *Fleetwood Mac* / Radar love: *Golden Earring* / Back home: *Golden Earring* / Woodstock: *Matthew's Southern Comfort* / Music: *Miles, John*
CD _____ STACD 069
Wisepack / Nov '93 / THE / Conifer.

10 ROCK STARS VOLUME 4
CD _____ STACD 070
Wisepack / Nov '93 / THE / Conifer.

10 SOUL STARS VOLUME 1
CD _____ STACD 063
Wisepack / Nov '93 / THE / Conifer.

10 SOUL STARS VOLUME 2
CD _____ STACD 064
Wisepack / Nov '93 / THE / Conifer.

10 SOUL STARS VOLUME 3
CD _____ STACD 065
Wisepack / Nov '93 / THE / Conifer.

10 SOUL STARS VOLUME 4
Sanctified lady: *Gaye, Marvin* / My love is waiting: *Gaye, Marvin* / Always and forever: *Isley Brothers/Jellybuggin': Heatwave* / That lady: *Isley Brothers* / Harvest for the world: *Isley Brothers* / Cuba: *Gibson Brothers* / Ooh what a life: *Gibson Brothers* / If you asked me to: *Labelle, Patti* / Oh people: *Labelle, Patti* / Please don't go: *K.C. & The Sunshine Band* / That's the way I like it: *K.C. & The Sunshine Band* / Dominoes: *Nevil, Robbie* / C'est la vie: *Nevil, Robbie* / Slowhand: *Pointer Sisters* / Jump: *Pointer Sisters* / Heaven must be missing an angel: *Tavares* / Don't take away the music: *Tavares* / Ain't

no sunshine: *Withers, Bill* / Lean on me: *Withers, Bill*
CD _____ STACD 066
Wisepack / Nov '93 / THE / Conifer.

10TH NEW ORLEANS JAZZ FESTIVAL
CD _____ FF 099CD
Flying Fish / May '93 / Roots / CM / Direct / ADA.

NOW 1983 - 10TH ANNIVERSARY
You can't hurry love: *Collins, Phil* / Red red wine: *UB40* / Dont under: *Men At Work* / Is there something I should know: *Duran Duran* / I'm still standing: *John, Elton* / Bad boys: *Wham* / Wings of a dove: *Madness* / Don't talk to me about love: *Altered Images* / Speak like a child: *Style Council* / True: *Spandau Ballet* / Only you: *Flying Pickets* / Every breath you take: *Police* / Sweet dreams (are made of this): *Eurythmics* / Let's stay together: *Turner, Tina* / New Year's Day: *U2* / Mama: *Genesis* / Moonlight shadow: *Oldfield, Mike* / Africa: *Toto* / Up where we belong: *Cocker, Joe & Jennifer Warnes* / Total eclipse of the heart: *Tyler, Bonnie* / Karma chameleon: *Culture Club* / Give it up: *K.C. & The Sunshine Band* / Temptation: *Heaven 17* / I.O.U.: *Freeze* / Sun goes down (Living it up): *Level 42* / Love town: *Newberry, Booker III* / Candy girl: *New Edition* / Too shy: *Kajagoogoo* / New song: *Jones, Howard* / They don't know: *Ullman, Tracey* / (Keep feeling) Fascination: *Human League* / Nobody's diary: *Yazoo* / Steppin' out: *Jackson, Joe* / Waterfront: *Simple Minds* / Beat surrender: *Jam* / Walk: *Cure* / Dear Prudence: *Siouxsie & The Banshees* / Everything counts: *Depeche Mode* / Never never: *Assembly* / Hold me now: *Thompson Twins*
CD _____ CDNOW 1983
EMI / Aug '93 / EMI.

NOW 1984 - 10TH ANNIVERSARY
I want to break free: *Queen* / Careless whisper: *Michael, George* / What's love got to do with it: *Turner, Tina* / No more lonely nights: *McCartney, Paul* / Missing you: *Waite, John* / Shout: *Tears For Fears* / I should have known better: *Diamond, Jim* / Against all odds: *Collins, Phil* / Time after time: *Lauper, Cyndi* / Your love is king: *Sade* / Pride (in the name of love): *U2* / Gimme all your lovin': *ZZ Top* / Young at heart: *Bluebells* / Michael Caine: *Madness* / Nelson Mandela: *Special AKA* / Master and servant: *Depeche Mode* / Killing moon: *Echo & The Bunnymen* / You're the best thing: *Style Council* / Heaven knows I'm miserable now: *Smiths* / Do they know it's Christmas: *Band Aid* / Reflex: *Duran Duran* / Wake me up before you go go: *Wham* / I won't let the sun go down on me: *Kershaw, Nik* / Dancing with tears in my eyes: *Ultravox* / Together in electric dreams: *Oakey, Philip & Giorgio Moroder* / Locomotion: *O.M.D.* / Smalltown boy: *Bronski Beat* / Here comes the rain again: *Eurythmics* / Wood beez (pray like Aretha Franklin): *Scritti Politti* / Too late for goodbyes: *Lennon, Julian* / I feel for you: *Khan, Chaka* / It's raining men: *Weather Girls* / Automatic: *Pointer Sisters* / Let's hear it for the boy: *Williams, Deniece* / Caribbean queen (no more love on the run): *Ocean, Billy* / White lines (don't don't do it): *Grandmaster Flash & Melle Mel* / Thinking of you: *Sister Sledge* / Joanna: *Kool & The Gang* / Dr. Beat: *Miami Sound Machine* / Self control: *Branigan, Laura*
CD _____ CDNOW 1984
EMI / Aug '93 / EMI.

NOW 1985 - 10TH ANNIVERSARY
Money for nothing: *Dire Straits* / Good heart: *Sharkey, Feargal* / There must be an angel (playing with my heart): *Eurythmics* / 1999: *Prince* / Road to nowhere: *Talking Heads* / Running up that hill: *Bush, Kate* / Johnny come home: *Fine Young Cannibals* / I got you babe: *UB40 & Chrissie Hynde* / Slave to love: *Ferry, Bryan* / One more night: *Collins, Phil* / Nikita: *John, Elton* / Drive: *Cars* / Kayleigh: *Marillion* / St. Elmo's fire: *Parr, John* / We built this city: *Starship* / Power of love: *Lewis, Huey & The News* / Walking on sunshine: *K.C. & The Sunshine Band* / Out in the fields: *Moore, Gary & Phil Lynott* / New England: *MacColl, Kirsty* / Everybody wants to rule the world: *Tears For Fears* / Take on me: *A-Ha* / View to a kill: *Duran Duran* / Kiss me: *Duffy, Stephen 'Tin Tin'* / West End girls: *Pet Shop Boys* / We close our eyes: *Go West* / Nineteen: *Hardcastle, Paul* / If I was: *Ure, Midge* / Alive and kicking: *Simple Minds* / Word girl: *Scritti Politti* / Love don't live here anymore: *Nail, Jimmy* / I want to know what love is: *Foreigner* / Move closer: *Nelson, Phyllis* / Saving all my love for you: *Houston, Whitney* / Solid: *Ashford & Simpson* / Money's too tight to mention: *Simply Red* / Sisters are doin' it for themselves: *Eurythmics & Aretha Franklin* / Yah mo be there: *Ingram, James & Michael McDonald* / Trapped:

Abrams, Colonel / Something about you: *Level 42* / Everything she wants: *Wham*
CD _____ CDNOW 1985
EMI / Aug '93 / EMI.

NOW 1986 - 10TH ANNIVERSARY
Kind of magic: *Queen* / Walk of life: *Dire Straits* / Sledgehammer: *Gabriel, Peter* / Manic Monday: *Bangles* / Thorn in my side: *Eurythmics* / Invisible touch: *Genesis* / You can call me Al: *Simon, Paul* / Don't get me wrong: *Pretenders* / Happy hour: *Housemartins* / Panic: *Smiths* / Rise: *Public Image Ltd* / Absolute beginners: *Bowie, David* / Addicted to love: *Palmer, Robert* / Final countdown: *Europe* / My favourite waste of time: *Paul, Owen* / (I just) died in your arms: *Cutting Crew* / In the army now: *Status Quo* / Stuck with you: *Lewis, Huey & The News* / Broken wings: *Mr. Mister* / Lady in red: *De Burgh, Chris* / When the going gets tough (the tough get going): *Ocean, Billy* / Don't leave me this way: *Communards* / Edge of heaven: *Wham* / Venus: *Bananarama* / Sometimes: *Erasure* / You keep me hangin' on: *Wilde, Kim* / We don't have to take our clothes off: *Stewart, Jermaine* / Let's go all the way: *Sly Fox* / Showing out (get fresh at the weekend): *Mel & Kim* / Rain or shine: *Five Star* / Kiss: *Prince & The Revolution* / Reet petite: *Wilson, Jackie* / Livin' in America: *Brown, James* / Ain't nothin' goin' on but the rent: *Guthrie, Gwen* / Word up: *Cameo* / Lessons in love: *Level 42* / Higher love: *Winwood, Steve* / Breakout: *Swing Out Sister* / Holding back the years: *Simply Red* / Different corner: *Michael, George*
CD _____ CDNOW 1986
EMI / Aug '93 / EMI.

NOW 1987 - 10TH ANNIVERSARY
I wanna dance with somebody (who loves me): *Houston, Whitney* / Wishing I was lucky: *Wet Wet Wet* / I knew you were waiting (for me): *Franklin, Aretha & George Michael* / Living in a box: *Living In A Box* / If you let me stay: *D'Arby, Terence Trent* / Running in the family: *Level 42* / Right thing: *Simply Red* / When Smokey sings: *ABC* / Stand by me: *King, Ben E.* / When a man loves a woman: *Sledge, Percy* / Pump up the volume: *M/A/R/R/S* / It's a sin: *Pet Shop Boys* / Respectable: *Mel & Kim* / Never gonna give you up: *Astley, Rick* / Love in the first degree: *Bananarama* / Down to earth: *Curiosity Killed The Cat* / Walk the dinosaur: *Was Not Was* / Labour of love: *Hue & Cry* / I need love: *L.L. Cool J* / Faith: *Michael, George* / La Bamba: *Los Lobos* / Heaven is a place on earth: *Carlisle, Belinda* / Crazy crazy nights: *Kiss* / You're the voice: *Farnham, John* / Hourglass: *Squeeze* / Valerie: *Winwood, Steve* / Alone: *Heart* / Is this love: *Whitesnake* / I still haven't found what I'm looking for: *U2* / Letter from America: *Proclaimers* / China in your hand: *T'Pau* / Nothing's gonna stop us now: *Starship* / Little lies: *Fleetwood Mac* / You win again: *Bee Gees* / My baby just cares for me: *Simone, Nina* / Everything I own: *Boy George* / (Something inside) so strong: *Siffre, Labi* / Wonderful life: *Black* / Crockett's theme: *Hammer, Jan*
CD _____ CDNOW 1987
EMI / Aug '93 / EMI.

NOW 1988 - 10TH ANNIVERSARY
With a little help from my friends: *Wet Wet Wet* / Little respect: *Erasure* / Always on my mind: *Pet Shop Boys* / Only way is up: *Yazz* / Theme from S'Express: *S'Express* / Race: *Yellow* / Fine cadillac: *Cole, Natalie* / Get outta my dreams, get into my car: *Ocean, Billy* / Tell it to my heart: *Dayne, Taylor* / Twist (yo, twist): *Fat Boys & Chubby Checker* / I should be so lucky: *Minogue, Kylie* / I want you back: *Bananarama* / I think we're alone now: *Tiffany* / You came: *Wilde, Kim* / Nathan Jones: *Bananarama* / Inner City* / Tribute (right on): *Pasadenas* / Teardrops: *Womack & Womack* / Come into my life: *Sims, Joyce* / Kiss: *Art Of Noise & Tom Jones* / Groovy kind of love: *Collins, Phil* / Perfect: *Fairground Attraction* / Mary's prayer: *Danny Wilson* / Everywhere: *Fleetwood Mac* / Love changes everything: *Climie Fisher* / Gimme hope Jo'anna: *Grant, Eddy* / Don't turn around: *Aswad* / Don't worry be happy: *McFerrin, Bobby* / Orinoco flow: *Enya* / He ain't heavy, he's my brother: *Hollies* / King of rock 'n' roll: *Prefab Sprout* / Somewhere in my heart: *Aztec Camera* / Real gone kid: *Deacon Blue* / Desire: *U2* / Don't go: *Hothouse Flowers* / You have placed a chill in my heart: *Eurythmics* / These dreams: *Heart* / Sign your name: *D'Arby, Terence Trent* / Oh Patti (don't feel sorry for loverboy): *Scritti Politti* / I don't want to talk about it: *Everything But The Girl*
CD _____ CDNOW 1988
EMI / Nov '93 / EMI.

NOW 1989 - 10TH ANNIVERSARY
If you don't know me by now: *Simply Red* / All around the world: *Stansfield, Lisa* / She

752

drives me crazy: *Fine Young Cannibals* / Best: *Turner, Tina* / Loco in Acapulco: *Four Tops* / This time I know it's for real: *Summer, Donna* / Sweet surrender: *Wet Wet Wet* / Stop: *Brown, Sam* / Miss you like crazy: *Cole, Natalie* / Don't know much: *Ronstadt, Linda & Aaron Neville* / Back to life: *Soul II Soul* / I'm every woman: *Khan, Chaka* / Ride on time: *Black Box* / Pump up the jam: *Technotronic & Felly* / My perogative: *Brown, Bobby* / Buffalo stance: *Cherry, Neneh* / Good life: *Inner City* / Straight up: *Abdul, Paula* / Waiting for a star to fall: *Boy Meets Girl* / If only I could: *Youngblood, Sydney* / Another day in paradise: *Collins, Phil* / Eternal flame: *Bangles* / Living years: *Mike & The Mechanics* / Sowing the seeds of love: *Tears For Fears* / Getting away with it: *Electronic* / Song for whoever: *Beautiful South* / I don't want a lover: *Texas* / You got it: *Orbison, Roy* / Road to hell: *Rea, Chris* / Right here waiting: *Marx, Richard* / Need you tonight: *INXS* / Leave a light on for me: *Carlisle, Belinda* / I want that man: *Harry, Deborah* / Baby I don't care: *Transvision Vamp* / Look: *Roxette* / You're history: *Shakespears Sister* / Hand on your heart: *Minogue, Kylie* / I may have broken hearts: *Donovan, Jason* / Especially for you: *Minogue, Kylie & Jason Donovan*
CD _____ CDNOW 1989
EMI / Nov '93 / EMI.

NOW 1990 - 10TH ANNIVERSARY
Little time: *Beautiful South* / It must have been love: *Roxette* / Nothing compares 2 U: *O'Connor, Sinead* / I'll never fall in love again: *Deacon Blue* / Sacrifice: *John, Elton* / I wish it would rain down: *Collins, Phil* / Unchained melody: *Righteous Brothers* / Kingston Town: *UB40* / Lily was here: *Stewart, David A. & Candy Dulfer* / Hold on: *Wilson Phillips* / Same thing: *Carlisle, Belinda* / Love shack: *B-52's* / Suicide blonde: *INXS* / Anniversary waltz: *Status Quo* / This is how it feels: *Inspiral Carpets* / There she goes: *La's* / I've been thinking about you: *London Beat* / Birdhouse in your soul: *They Might Be Giants* / Black velvet: *Myles, Alannah* / Nothing ever happens: *Del Amitri* / Killer: *Adamski* / What time is love: *K.L.F. & Children Of The Revolution* / Power: *Snap* / Get up (before the night is over): *Technotronic & Ya Kid K* / U can't touch this: *M.C. Hammer* / Dirty cash (money talks): *Stevie V* / Fascinating rhythm: *Bass-O-Matic* / Got to have your love: *Mantronix* / Fantasy: *Black Box* / I still haven't found what I'm looking for: *Chimes* / Tom's diner: *DNA* / Blue savannah: *Erasure* / Enjoy the silence: *Depeche Mode* / Unbelievable: *EMF* / Groovy train: *Farm* / Naked in the rain: *Blue Pearl* / Better the devil you know: *Minogue, Kylie* / Don't worry: *Appleby, Kim* / Opposites attract: *Abdul, Paula* / Dub be good to me: *Beats International*
CD _____ CDNOW 1990
EMI / Nov '93 / EMI.

NOW 1991 - 10TH ANNIVERSARY
Bohemian rhapsody: *Queen* / Whole of the moon: *Waterboys* / Sit down: *James* / Should I stay or should I go: *Clash* / Love rears its ugly head: *Living Colour* / Winds of change: *Scorpions* / Word of mouth: *Mike & The Mechanics* / Joyride: *Roxette* / Size of a cow: *Wonder Stuff* / Something got me started: *Simply Red* / I ain't over 'til it's over: *Kravitz, Lenny* / Set adrift on memory bliss: *PM Dawn* / Gypsy woman: *Waters, Crystal* / Baby baby: *Grant, Amy* / You got the love: *Source & Candi Staton* / Senza una Donna: *Zucchero & Paul Young* / Get here: *Adams, Oleta* / Saltwater: *Lennon, Julian* / Promise me: *Craven, Beverley* / I'm too sexy: *Right Said Fred* / Let's talk about sex: *Salt 'N' Pepa* / Everybody's free: *Rozalla* / Insanity: *Oceanic* / Get ready for this: *2 Unlimited* / Any more than this (Pro-gen '91): *Shamen* / 3 a.m. Eternal: *K.L.F. & Children Of The Revolution* / Now that we've found love: *Heavy D & The Boyz* / Things that make you go hmmmm: *C & C Music Factory* / Summertime: *D.J. Jazzy Jeff & The Fresh Prince* / Sadness: *Enigma* / Sunshine on a rainy day: *Zoe* / Crazy: *Seal* / Thinking about your love: *Thomas, Kenny* / Any dream will do: *Donovan, Jason* / Love to hate you: *Erasure* / Shocked: *Minogue, Kylie* / Sailing on the seven seas: *O.M.D.* / Dizzy: *Reeves, Vic & Wonder Stuff* / Always look on the bright side of life: *Monty Python*
CD _____ CDNOW 1991
EMI / Nov '93 / EMI.

NOW 1992 - 10TH ANNIVERSARY
Would I lie to you: *Charles & Eddie* / Piece of my heart: *Franklin, Erma* / My girl: *Temptations* / Walking on broken glass: *Lennox, Annie* / Sleeping satellite: *Archer, Tasmin* / Just another day: *Secada, Jon* / For your babies: *Simply Red* / I wonder why: *Stigers, Curtis* / Goodnight girl: *Wet Wet Wet* / Stay: *Shakespears Sister* / Don't let the sun go down on me: *Michael, George & Elton John* / I can't dance: *Genesis* / Always the last to know: *Del Amitri* / Everything about you: *Ugly Kid Joe* / It must be love: *Madness* / Weather with you: *Crowded House* / To be with you: *Mr. Big* / Radioactive: *Firm* / Barcelona: *Mercury, Freddie & Montserrat Caballe* / Rhythm is a dancer: *Snap* / Could it be magic: *Take That* / Take a chance on me: *Erasure* / Ebeneezer Goode: *Shamen* / Justified and ancient: *K.L.F. & Children Of*

The Revolution / Shake your head: *Was Not Was* / Ain't no doubt: *Nail, Jimmy* / Achy breaky heart: *Cyrus, Billy Ray* / Be my baby: *Paradis, Vanessa* / I love your smile: *Shanice* / Deeply dippy: *Right Said Fred* / People everyday: *Arrested Development* / Jump: *Kriss Kross* / Finally: *Peniston, Ce Ce* / I'm good you: *Bizarre Inc.* / On a ragga tip: *SL2* / Twilight zone: *2 Unlimited* / Something good: *Utah Saints* / It's my life: *Dr. Alban* / Please don't go: *KWS* / Baker Street: *Undercover*
CD _____ CDNOW 1992
EMI / Nov '93 / EMI.

NOW 1993 - 10TH ANNIVERSARY
Living on my own: *Mercury, Freddie* / Mr. Vain: *Culture Beat* / No limit: *2 Unlimited* / Key, the secret: *Urban Cookie Collective* / Ain't no love (ain't no use): *Sub Sub* / Mr. Melanie Williams* / All that she wants: *Ace Of Base* / Informer: *Snow* / Sweat (a la la la la long): *Inner Circle* / It keeps rainin' (tears from my eyes): *McLean, Bitty* / Oh Carolina: *Shaggy* / Dreams: *Gabrielle* / Deep: *East 17* / Why can't I wake up with you: *Take That* / Show me love: *Robin S* / Slave to the vibe: *Aftershock* / We are family: *Sister Sledge* / I will survive (remix): *Gaynor, Gloria* / Love I lost: *Sybil* / U got 2 know: *Cappella* / Do you see the light: *Snap* / Love song for a vampire: *Lennox, Annie* / I don't wanna fight: *Turner, Tina* / Constant craving: *Lang, k.d.* / Ordinary world: *Duran Duran* / What's up: *4 Non Blondes* / Cats in the cradle: *Ugly Kid Joe* / Are you gonna go my way: *Kravitz, Lenny* / Animal nitrate: *Suede* / Young at heart: *Bluebells* / Shout (it out): *Louchie Lou & Michie One* / Phorever people: *Shamen* / Believe in me: *Utah Saints* / Temptation (Remix): *Heaven 17* / Step it up: *Stereo MC's* / Sweet harmony: *Beloved* / No ordinary love: *Sade* / In all the right places: *Stansfield, Lisa*
CD _____ CDNOW 1993
EMI / Nov '93 / EMI.

12 SMOKIN' REGGAE HITS
CD _____ TBCD 1077
Tommy Boy / Jan '94 / Disc.

**12 X 12 - VOLUME 1
(The First Bite)**
Never can say goodbye: *Communards* / Venus: *Bananaman* / Push it: *Salt 'N' Pepa* / Big area: *Then Jerico* / This is your life (Less stress mix): *Banderas* / Smalltown boy: *Bronski Beat* / Living on the ceiling: *Blancmange* / I feel love: *Bronski Beat & Marc Almond* / Bass (How low can you go): *Harris, Simon* / It is time to get funky: *D-Mob* / Gun law (Full version): *Kane Gang* / I'm falling: *Bluebells*
CD _____ 5500912
Spectrum/Karussell / Oct '93 / PolyGram / THE.

**12 X 12 - VOLUME 2
(The Second Assortment)**
Night man: *Visage* / Living in America: *Brown, James* / Obsession (Dance): *Animotion* / Poison arrow: *ABC* / Talking with myself: *Electribe 101* / Say hello, wave goodbye: *Soft Cell* / Back and forth: *Cameo* / Breakout: *Swing Out Sister* / Hot water: *Level 42* / Promised land: *Style Council* / Big decision: *That Petrol Emotion* / Wipe-out: *Fat Boys*
CD _____ 5500892
Spectrum/Karussell / Oct '93 / PolyGram / THE.

**12 X 12 - VOLUME 3
(The Third Impression)**
Can I kick it: *Tribe Called Quest* / Blame it on the bassline: *Cook, Norman* / Road-block: *Stock/Aitken/Waterman* / Get busy: *Mr. Lee* / Touch me (Sexual version): *49ers* / Wee rule: *Wee Papa Girl Rappers* / I'm a wonderful thing, baby: *Kid Creole & The Coconuts* / Can I get a witness: *Brown, Sam* / Too good to be forgotten: *Amazulu* / Love's crashing waves: *Difford & Tilbrook* / Sweetest smile: *Black* / Lies: *Butler, Jonathan*
CD _____ 5501252
Spectrum/Karussell / Oct '93 / PolyGram / THE.

12" CLUB CLASSICS
CD _____ NTRCD 021
Nectar / Jun '94 / Pinnacle.

12" OF PLEASURE
CD _____ ALMYCD 10
Almighty / Nov '94 / Total/BMG.

14 SONGS FOR GREG SAGE & THE WIPERS
CD _____ TK 91CD010
T/K / May '94 / Pinnacle.

15 KILLERS VOLUME 2
CD _____ SZ 205
Blue Rose / Jun '95 / 3MV.

15 KILLERS VOLUME 3
CD _____ SZ 213
Blue Rose / Jun '95 / 3MV.

16 ORIGINAL ONE HIT WONDERS
CD _____ CDCD 1269
Charly / Oct '95 / Charly / THE / Cadillac.

17 DUB SHOTS FROM STUDIO ONE
CD _____ CDBH 142
Heartbeat / Aug '95 / Greensleeves / Jetstar / Direct / ADA.

18 BLUES MASTERPIECES
CD _____ CD 52000
Blues Encore / May '94 / Target/BMG.

**18 CHART HITS VOL.1
(1968-1973)**
All the young dudes: *Mott The Hoople* / In the summertime: *Mungo Jerry* / Lola: *Kinks* / Yellow river: *Christie* / Albatross: *Fleetwood Mac* / One and one is one: *Medicine Head* / Neanderthal man: *Hotlegs* / You wear it well: *Stewart, Rod* / Free electric band: *Hammond, Albert* / Down the dust-pipe: *Status Quo* / Never ending song of love: *New Seekers* / Ruby Tuesday: *Melanie* / Rose garden: *Anderson, Lynn* / Call me number one: *Tremeloes* / Family affair: *Sly & The Family Stone* / Giving it all away: *Daltrey, Roger* / Broken down angel: *Nazareth* / Isn't life strange: *Moody Blues*
CD _____ PMP 108
Carlton Home Entertainment / May '93 / Carlton Home Entertainment.

**18 CHART HITS VOL.2
(1974-1977)**
Let your love flow: *Bellamy Brothers* / Girls, girls, girls: *Sailor* / Shame, shame, shame: *Shirley & Company* / Night Chicago died: *Paper Lace* / I'm on fire: *5000 Volts* / Kung fu fighting: *Douglas, Carl* / Jukebox jive: *Rubettes* / Gonna make you a star: *Essex, David* / I love to love (but my baby loves to dance): *Charles, Tina* / Shanghai'd in Shanghai: *Nazareth* / You to me are everything: *Real Thing* / Sing baby sing: *Stylistics* / Arms of Mary: *Sutherland Brothers & Quiver* / red light spells danger: *Ocean, Billy* / Most beautiful girl in the world: *Rich, Charlie* / Lost in France: *Tyler, Bonnie* / Delilah: *Harvey, Alex Sensational Band* / Bangin' man: *Slade*
CD _____ PMP 109
Carlton Home Entertainment / May '93 / Carlton Home Entertainment.

**18 CHART HITS VOL.3
(1977-1981)**
Don't bring me down: *E.L.O.* / Dreadlock holiday: *10cc* / Stand and deliver: *Adam Ant* / Mind of a toy: *Visage* / Can you feel the force: *Real Thing* / September: *Earth, Wind & Fire* / Come back and finish what you started: *Knight, Gladys & The Pips* / Funky town: *Lipps Inc.* / I will survive: *Gaynor, Gloria* / Hersham boys: *Sham 69* / Married men: *Tyler, Bonnie* / Under your thumb: *Godley & Creme* / Dead ringer for love: *Meat Loaf* / Hold the line: *Toto* / Midnite groovies: *Matchbox* / Can can: *Bad Manners* / Matchstalk men and matchstalk cats and dogs: *Brian & Michael* / Keep on loving you: *REO Speedwagon*
CD _____ PMP 110
Carlton Home Entertainment / May '93 / Carlton Home Entertainment.

**18 CHART HITS VOL.4
(1982-1985)**
Young guns go for it: *Wham* / Down under: *Men At Work* / manic monday: *Bangles* / Self control: *Branigan, Laura* / (Feels like) heaven: *Fiction Factory* / Hit that perfect beat: *Bronski Beat* / Na na hey hey kiss him goodbye: *Bananarama* / Something about you: *Level 42* / Midnight at the lost and found: *Meat Loaf* / Poison arrow: *ABC* / Look mama: *Jones, Howard* / Riddle: *Kershaw, Nik* / Lion sleeps tonight: *Tight Fit* / Fields of fire: *Big Country* / Life in a life: *Opus* / Pass the dutchie: *Musical Youth* / Axel F: *Faltermeyer, Harold* / Dance hall days: *Wang Chung*
CD _____ PMP 111
Carlton Home Entertainment / May '93 / Carlton Home Entertainment.

18 GEMS OF THE GIANTS OF JAZZ CD COLLECTION
CD _____ CD 53000
Giants Of Jazz / May '92 / Target/BMG / Cadillac.

**18 LOVE CLASSICS VOL.1
(It's over)**
I won't let the sun go down on me: *Kershaw, Nik* / Love really hurts without you: *Ocean, Billy* / What's another year: *Logan, Johnny* / Way we were/Try to remember: *Knight, Gladys & The Pips* / Cry: *Godley & Creme* / Piano in the dark: *Russell, Brenda* / You'll never get to heaven (if you break my heart): *Stylistics* / January February: *Dickson, Barbara* / I can dream about you: *Hartman, Dan* / Could've been: *Tiffany* / Harvest for the world: *Isley Brothers* / Stay with me 'til dawn: *Tzuke, Judie* / Leaving me now: *Level 42* / Every little bit hurts: *Turner, Ruby* / If she knew what she wants: *Bangles* / Cry me a river: *Wilson, Mari* / Real love: *Watley, Jody* / Our last song together: *Sedaka, Neil*
CD _____ PMP 112
Carlton Home Entertainment / May '93 / Carlton Home Entertainment.

**18 LOVE CLASSICS VOL.2
(Two Hearts)**
It's my party: *Stewart, Dave & Barbara Gaskin* / Little piece of heaven: *Godley & Creme* / Loving you's a dirty job but somebody's got to do it: *Tyler, Bonnie & Todd Rundgren* / Heartache: *Pepsi & Shirlie* / There's nothing better than love: *Vandross, Luther & Gregory Hines* / Loving arms: *Kristofferson, Kris & Rita Coolidge* / Heart on my sleeve: *Gallagher & Lyle* / Last time I made love:

Kennedy, Joyce & Jeffery Osborne* / Never again: *Ledin, Tomas & Agnetha* / We do it: *Stone, R & J* / If you're ready (come go with me): *Turner, Ruby & Jonathan Butler* / Betcha by golly wow: *Henderson, Michael & Phyllis Hyman* / What becomes of the broken hearted: *Stewart, Dave & Colin Blunstone* / Unchained melody: *Righteous Brothers* / Love will keep us together: *Captain & Tennille* / Day by Day: *Shakatak & Al Jarreau* / It this world were mine: *Vandross, Luther & Cheryl Lynn* / Two hearts: *Mills, Stephanie & Teddy Pendergrass*
CD _____ PMP 113
Carlton Home Entertainment / May '93 / Carlton Home Entertainment.

**18 LOVE CLASSICS VOL.3
(Shades Of Love)**
Hold me now: *Logan, Johnny* / I think we're alone now: *Tiffany* / She drives me crazy: *Fine Young Cannibals* / Hazy shade of winter: *Bangles* / I should have known better: *Diamond, Jim* / Never can say goodbye: *Communards* / Wouldn't it be good: *Kershaw, Nik* / Signed, sealed, delivered (I'm yours): *Turner, Ruby* / First time: *Beck, Robin* / I only wanna be with you: *Fox, Samantha* / Together we're beautiful: *Kinney, Fern* / Wind beneath my wings: *Greenwood, Lee* / Have you ever seen the rain: *Tyler, Bonnie* / I hear you now: *Jon & Vangelis* / Amoureuse: *Dee, Kiki* / On the wings of a nightingale: *Everly Brothers* / Nothing's gonna change my love for you: *Medeiros, Glenn* / Will you: *O'Connor, Hazel*
CD _____ PMP 114
Carlton Home Entertainment / May '93 / Carlton Home Entertainment.

**18 LOVE CLASSICS VOL.4
(Loving Feelings)**
No regrets: *Walker Brothers* / If you think you know to love me: *Smokie* / I can help: *Swan, Billy* / Without you: *Nilsson, Harry* / Ms. Grace: *Tymes* / You don't have to say you love me: *Springfield, Dusty* / Music: *Miles, John* / Young girl: *Puckett, Gary & The Union Gap* / Kiss and say goodbye: *Manhattans* / Seasons in the sun: *Jacks, Terry* / You've lost that lovin' feelin': *Righteous Brothers* / If I said you had a beautiful body: *Bellamy Brothers* / If I can't have you: *Elliman, Yvonne* / La la means I love you: *Delfonics* / Love me tonight: *Jones, Tom* / Answer me: *Dickson, Barbara* / Tears on my pillow: *Nash, Johnny* / Torn between two lovers: *MacGregor, Mary*
CD _____ PMP 115
Carlton Home Entertainment / May '93 / Carlton Home Entertainment.

**18 LOVE CLASSICS VOLS.1-4
(The Love Experience/4CD Set)**
CD Set _____ BOXD 30
Carlton Home Entertainment / Nov '92 / Carlton Home Entertainment.

**18 ROCK CLASSICS VOL.1
(Rock Dreams)**
Heat is on: *Frey, Glenn* / Fade to grey: *Visage* / More than a feeling: *Boston* / Wishing (If I had a photograph of you): *Flock Of Seagulls* / Sweetest taboo: *Sade* / Secrets: *Sutherland Brothers* / Oh Sherrie: *Perry, Steve* / Loving You Is Sweeter Than Ever: *Kamen, Nick* / Dark Lady: *Cher* / Heartbeat: *Johnson, Don* / Rosanna: *Toto* / You are the girl: *Cars* / What is love: *Jones, Howard* / Lessons In Love: *Level 42* / Carrie: *Europe* / Wide boy: *Kershaw, Nik* / You send me: *Stewart, Rod* / Life is for living: *Barclay James Harvest*
CD _____ PMP 100
Carlton Home Entertainment / May '93 / Carlton Home Entertainment.

**18 ROCK CLASSICS VOL.2
(Born To Be Wild)**
Hold on tight: *E.L.O.* / Can't fight this feeling: *REO Speedwagon* / Come on Eileen: *Dexy's Midnight Runners* / Roll on down the highway: *Bachman-Turner Overdrive* / Gypsies, tramps and thieves: *Cher* / All day and all of the night: *Stranglers* / Lucky man: *Emerson, Lake & Palmer* / Morning Dance: *Spyro Gyra* / Boy from New York City: *Darts* / I'm not in love: *10cc* / Look away: *Big Country* / Africa: *Toto* / Cutter: *Echo & The Bunnymen* / Hold you head up: *Argent* / Spooky: *Atlanta Rhythm Section* / Born to be wild: *Steppenwolf* / Ramblin' man: *Allman Brothers* / Let's groove: *Earth, Wind & Fire*
CD _____ PMP 101
Carlton Home Entertainment / May '93 / Carlton Home Entertainment.

**18 ROCK CLASSICS VOL.3
(Danger Zone)**
St. Elmo's fire: *Parr, John* / Stop loving you: *Toto* / 99 Red balloons: *Nena* / Total eclipse of the heart: *Tyler, Bonnie* / Parisienne walkways: *Moore, Gary* / Gloria: *Branigan, Laura* / Cum on feel the noize: *Slade* / Bat out of hell: *Meat Loaf* / Silver dagger: *Oldfield, Sally* / Like to get to know you well: *Jones, Howard* / Eloise: *Damned* / Oh no, not my baby: *Newman, Randy* / Start: *Jam* / Hold me close: *Essex, David* / Take it on the run: *REO Speedwagon* / Goody two shoes: *Adam Ant* / God gave rock 'n' roll to you: *Argent* / Sun goes down (Living it up): *Level 42*
CD _____ PMP 102

Carlton Home Entertainment / May '93 / Carlton Home Entertainment.

**18 ROCK CLASSICS VOL.4
(Rock Power)**
This fight tonight: *Nazareth* / Who do you love: *Juicy Lucy* / Iron fist: *Motorhead* / Paranoid: *Black Sabbath* / Start talking love: *Magnum* / Please don't touch: *Headgirl* / (Don't fear) the reaper: *Blue Oyster Cult* / Roll away the stone: *Mott The Hoople* / I want you to want me: *Cheap Trick* / Free me: *Uriah Heep* / Night games: *Bonnet, Graham* / Rock the night: *Europe* / Shot in the dark: *Osbourne, Ozzy* / Whiskey in the jar: *Thin Lizzy* / Holding out for a hero: *Tyler, Bonnie* / Walking on sunshine: *Rockers Revenge* / You took the words right out of my mouth: *Meat Loaf*
CD _____ **PMP 103**
Carlton Home Entertainment / May '93 / Carlton Home Entertainment.

**18 SOUL CLASSICS VOL.1
(Disco Nights)**
Just an illusion: *Imagination* / I'm so excited: *Pointer Sisters* / System addict: *Five Star* / Going back to my roots: *Odyssey* / (You said) You'd gimme more time: *K.C. & The Sunshine Band* / She's strange: *Cameo* / Rock the boat: *Hues Corporation* / Jumpin' Jack flash: *Franklin, Aretha* / Let the music play: *White, Barry* / Fantasy: *Earth, Wind & Fire* / Can you feel it: *Jacksons* / Burn rubber on me: *Gap Band* / Love come down: *King, Evelyn 'Champagne'* / Mama used to say: *Giscombe, Junior* / Rockit: *Hancock, Herbie* / Fight the power: *Isley Brothers* / Livin' in America: *Brown, James*
CD _____ **PMP 104**
Carlton Home Entertainment / May '93 / Carlton Home Entertainment.

**18 SOUL CLASSICS VOL.2
(Stay With Me)**
Do what you do: *Jackson, Jermaine* / All the love in the world: *Warwick, Dionne* / Joanna: *Kool & The Gang* / Night to remember: *Shalamar* / Your love is king: *Sade* / Never knew love like this before: *Mills, Stephanie* / Secret lovers: *Atlantic Starr* / Stay with me tonight: *Osborne, Jeffrey* / There goes my first love: *Drifters* / Reach out, I'll be there: *Gaynor, Gloria* / A hundred ways: *Jones, Quincy & James Ingram* / You make me feel brand new: *Stylistics* / Never, never gonna give you up: *White, Barry* / Woman in love: *Three Degrees* / Summer breeze: *Isley Brothers* / My love is waiting: *Gaye, Marvin* / Lovely day (remix): *Withers, Bill* / What a fool believes: *Franklin, Aretha*
CD _____ **PMP 105**
Carlton Home Entertainment / May '93 / Carlton Home Entertainment.

**18 SOUL CLASSICS VOL.3
(Heart & Soul)**
Letter: *Box Tops* / Kissin' in the back row of the movies: *Drifters* / Hang on in there baby: *Bristol, Johnny* / Reunited: *Peaches & Herb* / Best thing that ever happened to me: *Knight, Gladys & The Pips* / Didn't I blow your mind this time: *Delfonics* / Me and Mrs. Jones: *Paul, Billy* / Running away: *Sly & The Family Stone* / Love Train: *O'Jays* / What a difference a day makes: *Phillips, Esther* / Betcha by golly wow: *Stylistics* / I'm your puppet: *Purify, James & Bobby* / That lady: *Isley Brothers* / I can see clearly now: *Nash, Johnny* / L.O.D. (love on delivery): *Ocean, Billy* / Can't get enough of your love babe: *White, Barry* / Where did our love go: *Elbert, Donnie* / Get up offa that thing: *Brown, James*
CD _____ **PMP 106**
Carlton Home Entertainment / May '93 / Carlton Home Entertainment.

**18 SOUL CLASSICS VOL.4
(Rhythm Of The Night)**
Loco in acapulco: *Four Tops* / Wishing well: *D'Arby, Terence Trent* / Jump: *Pointer Sisters* / Who's zoomin' who: *Franklin, Aretha* / Get outta my dreams, get into my car: *Ocean, Billy* / Star: *Earth, Wind & Fire* / Can't wait another minute: *Five Star* / Best of my love: *Emotions* / Always and forever: *Heatwave* / Lies: *Butler, Jonathan* / Caravan of love: *Isley-Jasper-Isley* / Why can't we live together: *Sade* / I won't cry: *Goldsmith, Glen* / I'd rather go blind: *Turner, Ruby* / On the wings of love: *Osborne, Jeffrey* / Sweetest sweetest: *Jackson, Jermaine* / Hurt: *Manhattans* / Never too much: *Vandross, Luther*
CD _____ **PMP 107**
Carlton Home Entertainment / May '93 / Carlton Home Entertainment.

**20 ALL TIME GREATS
(Coasters And More)**
Charlie Brown: *Coasters* / Little Egypt: *Coasters* / Why do fools fall in love: *Diamonds* / Poetry in motion: *Tillotson, Johnny* / Rubber ball: *Vee, Bobby* / Smoke gets in your eyes: *Platters* / Rock 'n' roll: *Coasters* / Hats off to Larry: *Shannon, Del* / Sealed with a kiss: *Hyland, Brian* / Night has a 1000 eyes: *Vee, Bobby* / Lion sleeps tonight: *Tokens* / Yakety yak: *Coasters* / Will you still love me tomorrow: *Shirelles* / Peggy Sue: *Crickets* / La Bamba: *Tokens* / Poison Ivy: *Coasters* / Tell Laura I love her: *Peterson, Ray* / Party doll: *Knox, Buddy* / At the hop: *Original Juniors* / Young blood: *Coasters*
CD _____ **HADCD 155**

Javelin / May '94 / THE / Henry Hadaway Organisation.

20 AMERICAN ROCK 'N' ROLL GREATS
Why do fools fall in love: *Lymon, Frankie & The Teenagers* / Barbara Ann: *Regents* / Honeycomb: *Rodgers, Jimmie* / I'm stickin' with you: *Bowen, Jimmy* / Tears on my pillow: *Imperials* / Peppermint twist: *Dee, Joey & The Starlighters* / I'm confessin' that I love you: *Chantels* / I only have eyes for you: *Flamingos* / Forty days: *Hawkins, Ronnie* / Woo hoo: *Rock A Teens* / Walkin' miracle: *Essex* / Girl of my best friend: *Donner, Ral* / Heart and soul: *Cleftones* / Party doll: *Knox, Buddy* / Don't ask me to be lonely: *Dubs* / Gypsy cried: *Christie, Lou* / Hey lover: *Dovale, Debbie* / Darling how long: *Heartbeats* / Beep beep: *Playmates* / Cry like I cried: *Harptones*
CD _____ **CDMFP 6132**
Music For Pleasure / Sep '94 / EMI.

20 BEST LOVED HYMNS
Music Club / Oct '95 / Disc / THE / CM.
CD _____ **MCCD 214**

20 BEST OF TODAYS FOLK AND WORLD MUSIC, VOL. 2
ARC / '91 / ARC Music / ADA.
CD _____ **EUCD 1141**

20 BIG BAND CLASSICS
Avid / Dec '92 / Avid/BMG / Koch.
CD _____ **AVC 503**

20 BOOGIE WOOGIE MASTERPIECES
Charly / Oct '95 / Charly / THE / Cadillac.
CD _____ **CDCD 1272**

20 CLASSIC IRISH LOVE BALLADS
Outlet / Oct '95 / ADA / Duncans / CM / Ross / Direct / Koch.
CD _____ **CDIRISH 006**

20 CLASSIC SONGS OF LOVE
True: *Spandau Ballet* / Room in your heart: *Living In A Box* / Man with the child in his eyes: *Bush, Kate* / Dreamin': *Burnette, John* / Rock 'N' Roll Trio / Missing you: *Waite, John* / Tonight I celebrate my love for you: *Flack, Roberta & Peabo Bryson* / More than I can say: *Vee, Bobby* / Why do fools fall in love: *Lymon, Frankie & The Teenagers* / Tears on my pillow: *Imperials* / God only knows: *Beach Boys* / Air that I breathe: *Hollies* / Love changes everything: *Climie Fisher* / Is there something I should know: *Duran Duran* / I apologise: *Proby, P.J.* / I only have eyes for you: *Flamingos* / I honestly love you: *Newton-John, Olivia* / When you're in love with a beautiful woman: *Dr. Hook* / Honey: *Goldsboro, Bobby* / Tell Laura I love her: *Valance, Ricky* / Crying: *McLean, Don*
CD _____ **CDMFP 5974**
Music For Pleasure / Dec '92 / EMI.

20 COUNTRY LOVE SONGS
It's only make believe: *Campbell, Glen* / When I dream: *Gayle, Crystal* / There'll be no teardrops tonight: *Nelson, Willie* / July you're a woman: *Stewart, John* / Come to me: *Newton, Juice* / Summer wind: *Newton, Wayne* / Will you still love me tomorrow: *Darin, Bobby* / Misty blue: *Spears, Billie Jo* / For the people: *Ford, Tennessee Ernie* / Sharing the night together: *Dr. Hook* / Let it be me: *Campbell, Glen & Bobbie Gentry* / I'll take you home: *Campbell, Glen* / Whitman, Slim* / Stand by your man: *Jackson, Wanda* / It doesn't matter anymore: *Anka, Paul* / Give me your word: *Ford, Tennessee Ernie* / Everything a man could ever need: *Campbell, Glen* / Think I'll go somewhere and cry myself to sleep: *Shepard, Jean* / Minute you're gone: *James, Sonny* / We must believe in magic: *Gayle, Crystal* / Don't it make my brown eyes blue: *Gayle, Crystal*
CD _____ **CDMFP 6036**
Music For Pleasure / Oct '87 / EMI.

20 EXPLOSIVE DYNAMIC SUPER SMASH HIT EXPLOSIONS
CD _____ **EFA 201152**
Pravda / May '95 / SRD.

20 FAVOURITE IRISH PUB SONGS VOL.1
CD _____ **DOCD 2024**
Koch / Oct '93 / Koch.

20 FAVOURITE IRISH PUB SONGS VOL.2
CD _____ **DOCD 2029**
Koch / Oct '93 / Koch.

20 FILM AND STAGE CLASSICS JAMAICAN STYLE
People will say we're in love: *Spence, Tremor* / Orchestra / Summertime: *Clarke, Lloyd* / Guns of Navarone: *Skatalites* / Bonanza ska: *Malcolm, Carlos & Afro Caribs* / Shot in the dark: *Soul Brothers* / From Russia with love: *Alphonso, Roland* / Dr. Zhivago: *McCook, Tommy & The Supersonics* / To sir with love: *Tait, Lynn & the Jets* / Ol' man river: *Silvertones* / Get me to the church on time: *McCook, Tommy & The Supersonics* / Jesse me high: *Ace, Richard* / Zip a dee doo dah: *Smith, Slim* / Magnificent seven: *Wright, Winston* / Hello Dolly: *Pat Satchmo* / Summer place: *Charmers, Lloyd* / Try to remember: *Kelly, Pat* / Shaft: *Chosen Few* / I'm in the mood for love: *Chosen Few*

Moon river: *Ellis, Alton* / There's no business like show business: *Ellis, Alton*
CD _____ **CDTRL 319**
Trojan / Mar '94 / Jetstar / Total/BMG.

20 GERMAN FOLK SONGS
Monitor / Jun '93 / CM.
CD _____ **MCD 71398**

20 GIRL VOCAL BIG BAND CLASSICS
Charly / Nov '95 / Charly / THE / Cadillac.
CD _____ **CDCD 1273**

20 GOLDEN GREATS FROM THE BIG BAND ERA
Trumpet blues and cantabile / One o'clock jump / Yes indeed / Intermission riff / You made me love you / Four brothers / Artistry in rhythm / I've got a gal in Kalamazoo / I'll never smile again / Jeeps blues / Solitude / Don't be that way / Midnight sun / Red bank boogie / La paloma / Stardust / Skyliner / Goosey gander / Well, get it
CD _____ **HRM 7005**
Hermes / Jun '87 / Nimbus.

20 GOLDEN NO.1'S
Nut rocker: *B. Bumble & The Stingers* / I'm alive: *Hollies* / Bad to me: *Kramer, Billy J. & The Dakotas* / Poor me: *Faith, Adam* / Johnny remember me: *Leyton, Johnny* / Do wah diddy diddy: *Manfred Mann* / Kon-Tiki: *Shadows* / January: *Pilot* / See my baby jive: *Wizzard* / Anyone who had a heart: *Black, Cilla* / You're my world: *Black, Cilla* / I'll never find another you: *Seekers* / Tell Laura I love her: *Valence, Ricky* / You'll never walk alone: *Gerry & The Pacemakers* / World without love: *Peter & Gordon* / Lily the pink: *Scaffold* / Only sixteen: *Douglas, Craig* / Little children: *Kramer, Billy J. & The Dakotas* / What do you want: *Faith, Adam* / Pretty flamingo: *Manfred Mann*
CD _____ **CDMFP 50491**
Music For Pleasure / Oct '90 / EMI.

20 GOLDEN NO.1'S VOL.2
Whiter shade of pale: *Procul Harum* / This is my song: *Clark, Petula* / Sweets for my sweet: *Searchers* / Have I the right: *Honeycombs* / Always something there to remind me: *Shaw, Sandie* / Sunny afternoon: *Kinks* / Michelle: *Overlanders* / Let the heartaches begin: *Baldry, Long John* / Blackberry Way: *Move* / (If paradise is) half as nice: *Amen Corner* / In the Summertime: *Mungo Jerry* / Baby, now that I've found you: *Foundations* / Kung fu fighting: *Douglas, Carl* / Matchstalk men and matchstalk cats and dogs: *Brian & Michael* / Sad sweet dreamer: *Sweet Sensation* / Out of time: *Farlowe, Chris* / Israelites: *Dekker, Desmond* / Mouldy old dough: *Lieutenant Pigeon* / Double barrel: *Collins, Dave & Ansil* / Everything I own: *Boothe, Ken*
CD _____ **CDMFP 5898**
Music For Pleasure / May '90 / EMI.

20 GOSPEL GREATS
Love of God: *Taylor, Johnnie* / Trouble in my way: *Swan Silvertones* / My rock: *Swan Silvertones* / Get away Jordan: *Love Coates, Dorothy* / You better run: *Love Coates, Dorothy* / Ninety nine and a half (won't do): *Love Coates, Dorothy* / Straight Street: *Pilgrim Travelers* / Jesus hits like the atom bomb: *Pilgrim Travelers* / I'm determined to run this race: *Cleveland, James* / Living for my Jesus: *Five Blind Boys Of Alabama* / Alone and motherless: *Five Blind Boys Of Alabama* / This may be the last time: *Five Blind Boys Of Alabama* / Ball game: *Carr, Sister Wynona* / Touch the hem of his garment: *Cooke, Sam & The Soul Stirrers* / Prayer for the doomed: *Chosen Gospel Singers* / Holy ghost: *Bradford, Alex* / Lifeboat: *Bradford, Alex* / Whosoever will: *Griffin, Bessie* / Wade in the water: *Original Gospel Harmonettes*
CD _____ **CDROP 1017**
Cascade / May '90 / Pinnacle.

20 GREAT BLUES RECORDINGS OF THE 50'S AND 60'S
Rolling and rolling: *Hopkins, Lightnin'* / Drifting blind: *Bobby* / Gone with the wind: *Sykes, Roosevelt* / Me and my chauffeur: *Thornton, Willie Mae* / No rollin' blues: *Witherspoon, Jimmy* / No nights by myself: *Williamson, Sonny Boy* / Cool little car: *Hooker, John Lee* / Dark and dreary: *James, Elmore* / Ain't drunk: *Turner, Ike's Rhythm Kings* / Crying at daybreak: *Howlin' Wolf* / Three hours past midnight: *Watson, Johnny 'Guitar'* / Talking woman: *Fulson, Lowell* / Moon is rising: *Littlefield, Little Willie* / Tease me baby: *Hooker, John Lee* / Dedicating the blues: *Crayton, Pee Wee* / Ten years long: *King, B.B.* / Beer drinking woman: *McCracklin, Jimmy* / Sunnyland: *James, Elmore* / Cow town: *Dixon, Floyd* / Heartache baby: *Louis, Joe Hill*
CD _____ **CDROP 1005**
Cascade / Jan '90 / Pinnacle.

20 GREAT CRUISING FAVOURITES OF THE 50'S AND 60'S
Wanderer: *Dion* / Party girl: *Carroll, Bernadette* / Chattanooga choo choo: *Fields, Ernie Orchestra* / Dizzy Miss Lizzy: *Williams, Larry* / Rockin' robin: *Day, Bobby* / Angel baby: *Rose & The Originals* / Sunday kind of love: *Mystics* / Will you still love me tomorrow: *Shirelles* / Bandit of my dreams: *Hodges, Eddie* / Baby face: *Little Richard* / Denise: *Randy & The Rainbows* / Chantilly lace: *Big Bopper* / Pretty girls everywhere:

Church, Eugene / No wheels: *Chordettes* / Problems: *Everly Brothers* / Way you look tonight: *Jarmels* / It's my party: *Gore, Lesley* / Heart: *Chandler, Kenny* / Rockin' pneumonia and the boogie woogie flu: *Neville, Art* / I got a feeling: *Tillotson, Johnny*
CD _____ **CDROP 1015**
Cascade / Jan '90 / Pinnacle.

20 GREAT CRUISING FAVOURITES OF THE 50'S AND 60'S
Lovers who wander / Rock everybody / When will I be loved / She said "yeah" / Hickory dickory dock / Little star / My boyfriend's back / One fine day / I cried a tear / Lawdy Miss Clawdy / Mary Lou / Lucille / Hey doll baby / Forever / My block / Please don't tell me know / Little bitty pretty one / Buzz buzz buzz / Hey boy, hey girl / Bama lama bama loo
CD _____ **CDROP 1016**
Cascade / Oct '88 / Pinnacle.

20 GREAT CRUISING FAVOURITES OF THE 50'S AND 60'S
Wake up little Susie / Nut rocker / Lonely teenager / Over and over / Church bells may ring / In the mood / Short fat Fanny / Tall Paul / Poetry in motion / Runaround Sue / I'll come back to you / I cried a tear / Tick tock / Girl of my dreams / Take a message to Mary / She say / He's so fine / Pink shoe laces / Tra la la la Suzy
CD _____ **CDROP 1014**
Cascade / Jan '90 / Pinnacle.

20 GREAT DOOWOP RECORDINGS
Pennies from Heaven: *Skyliners* / Hush-a-bye: *Mystics* / Automobile: *Stickshifts* / Over my head: *Gordon* / Only sixteen: *Douglas, Craig* / Let the good times roll: *Flairs* / Way you look tonight: *Lonely Guys* / Under stars of love: *Carlos Brothers* / Stay where you are: *Olympics* / Saturday night fish fry: *Blue dots* / These golden rings: *Strangers* / Just for you and I: *Supremes* / Why don't you write me: *Jacks* / I love you: *Meadowlarks* / All I do is rock: *Robins* / I believe: *Twilighters* / Please understand: *Milton, Buddy & Twilighters* / Please don't tell 'em: *Blue dots* / Cold chills: *Sounds* / When I fall in love: *Skyliners*
CD _____ **CDROP 1008**
Cascade / Jan '92 / Pinnacle.

20 GREAT LOVE SONGS OF THE ROCK 'N' ROLL ERA
CD _____ **CDROP 1018**
Cascade / Apr '92 / Pinnacle.

20 GREAT RHYTHM & BLUES OF THE 50'S
Rockin' pneumonia and the boogie woogie flu: *Smith, Huey 'Piano' & The Clowns* / Ain't a better story told: *Littlefield, Little Willie* / B.B. boogie: *King, B.B.* / Good rockin' daddy: *James, Etta* / Rock house boogie: *Hooker, John Lee* / Got the good times roll: *Shirley & Lee* / Bop hop: *Crayton, Pee Wee* / Don't you know Yockomo: *Smith, Huey & The Clowns* / Oop shoop: *Queens* / reelin' and rockin': *McCracklin, Jimmy* / Who's been jivin' with you: *Witherspoon, Jimmy* / Road I travel: *Turner, Ike's Rhythm Kings* / Morning at midnight: *Howlin' Wolf* / Is everything alright: *King, Earl* / Love bandit: *Cadets* / Goodbye baby: *James, Elmore* / No more doggin': *Gordon, Roscoe* / Early times: *Turner, Ike's Rhythm Kings* / Gee baby: *Joe & Ann* / Kansas City blues: *Turner, Big Joe*
CD _____ **CDROP 1001**
Cascade / Oct '88 / Pinnacle.

20 MORE EXPLOSIVE DYNAMIC SUPER SMASH HIT EXPLOSIONS
CD _____ **EFA 201162**
Pravda / May '95 / SRD.

20 MORE GOSPEL GREATS
I'm climbing higher mountains: *Echoes Of Zion* / New walk: *Swanee Quintet* / Tell the angels: *Angelic Gospel Singers* / Let the church roll on: *Barbee, Lucille* / Building a home: *Radio Four* / Go devil, go: *Littlejohn, Madame Ira Mae* / Wake me, shake me: *May, Brother Joe* / Yea Lord: *Trumpet Kings* / Lord bring me down: *Consolers* / Earnest prayer: *Radio Four* / I want to see Jesus: *Littlejohn, Madame Ira Mae* / Fadeless days: *Smith Jubilee Singers* / How I got over: *Swanee Quintet* / Bible is right: *Gospel Songbirds* / Dark hours of distress: *Littlefield, Sister Lillie Mae* / In the sun: *Fairfield Four* / On my way (part one): *Chapman, Rev CC* / You got to be born again: *Christland singers* / Mother's advice: *Taylor Brothers* / Father I stretch my arms to thee: *Killens, Rev GW*
CD _____ **CDROP 1019**
Cascade / Oct '93 / Pinnacle.

20 NO.1'S OF THE 70'S
In the summertime: *Mungo Jerry* / Sad sweet dreamer: *Sweet Sensation* / Matchstalk men and matchstalk cats and dogs: *Brian & Michael* / Heart of glass: *Blondie* / Love grows (Where my Rosemary goes): *Edison Lighthouse* / When you're in love with a beautiful woman: *Dr. Hook* / When I need you: *Sayer, Leo* / Kung fu fighting: *Douglas, Carl* / Woodstock: *Nilsson, Harry* / Oh Boy: *Mud* / Bye bye baby: *Bay City Rollers* / Blockbuster: *Sweet* / So you win again: *Hot Chocolate* / Yes sir, I can boogie: *Baccara* / I love you love me love: *Glitter, Gary* / See my baby jive: *Wizzard* / Make me

smile (come up and see me): Harley, Steve & Cockney Rebel / Can the can: Quatro, Suzi / Seasons in the sun: Jacks, Terry / Ms. Grace: Tymes
CD _____ CDMFP 5985
Music For Pleasure / Apr '93 / EMI.

20 NO.2'S OF THE 70'S
Air that I breathe: Hollies / American pie: McLean, Don / Kissin' in the back row of the movies: Drifters / Do you wanna touch me (Oh yeah): Glitter, Gary / Don't let it die: Smith, Hurricane / Denis: Blondie / Moonlighting: Sayer, Leo / Lola: Kinks / Let's work together: Canned Heat / When I'm dead and gone: McGuinness Flint / Cat crept in: Mud / Shang-a-lang: Bay City Rollers / Goodbye my love: Glitter Band / Hellraiser: Sweet / Little bit more: Dr. Hook / You sexy thing: Hot Chocolate / Some girls: Racey / Loving you: Riperton, Minnie / Rock me gently: Kim, Andy / Can't get by without you: Real Thing
CD _____ CDMFP 5986
Music For Pleasure / Apr '93 / EMI.

20 ONE HIT WONDERS
So much in love: Mighty Avengers / Birds and the bees: Warm Sounds / I can't let Maggie go: Honey Bus / She's not there: MacArthur, Neil / Can't you hear my heartbeat: Goldie & The Gingerbreads / I keep ringing my baby: Soul Brothers / Beggin': Timebox / Leaving here: Birds / Can you hear my heart: Rivers, Danny / I was Kaiser Bill's batman: Smith, Jack 'Whispering' / Can can: Jay, Peter & The Jaywalkers / Now we're through: Poets / That's what I want: Marauders / Girl: St. Louis Union / Please stay: Crying Shames / Walk with me my angel: Charles, Don / Not too little not too much: Sanford, Chris / More I see you: Marshall, Joy / Goin' out of my head: West, Dodie / House of the rising sun: Frijid Pink
CD _____ C5CD 607
See For Miles/C5 / Oct '93 / Pinnacle.

20 ORIGINAL COUNTRY GREATS
Southern nights: Campbell, Glen / Wichita lineman: Campbell, Glen / Don't it make my brown eyes blue: Gayle, Crystal / Talking in your sleep: Gayle, Crystal / When you're in love with a beautiful woman: Dr. Hook / Sexy eyes: Dr. Hook / Ode to Billy Joe: Gentry, Bobbie / I'll never fall in love again: Gentry, Bobbie / Blanket on the ground: Spears, Billie Jo / Sing me an old fashioned song: Spears, Billie Jo / Lucille: Rogers, Kenny / Coward of the county: Rogers, Kenny / Snowbird: Murray, Anne / You needed me: Murray, Anne / Games people play: South, Joe / Hello walls: Nelson, Willie / There'll be no teardrops tonight: Nelson, Willie / It keeps right on a-hurtin': Shepard, Jean / Angel of the morning: Newton, Juice / July you're a woman: Stewart, John
CD _____ CDMFP 6084
Music For Pleasure / Jun '90 / EMI.

20 ORIGINAL DOO WOP CLASSICS
Daddy's home: Shep & The Limelites / Sunday kind of love: Harptones / Pretty little angel eyes: Lee, Curtis / I'm not a juvenile delinquent: Lymon, Frankie & The Teenagers / I only have eyes for you: Flamingoes / Maybe: Chantels / Heart and soul: Cleftones / Blue moon: Marcels / Chains: Cookies / Little star: Elegants / Thousand miles away: Heartbeats / Barbara Ann: Regents / Priscilla: Cooley, Eddie / Don't ask me to be lonely: Dubs / Tears on my pillow: Little Anthony & The Imperials / Why do fools fall in love: Lymon, Frankie & The Teenagers / Teenager in love: Dion & The Belmonts / Gee: Crows / Just to be with you: Passion / My melancholy baby: Marcels / Two people in the world: Little Anthony & The Imperials
CD _____ CDMFP 6207
Music For Pleasure / Nov '95 / EMI.

20 ORIGINAL RADIO STARS
CD _____ 399236
Koch / Feb '94 / Koch.

20 R&B DANCE FLOOR FILLERS
Harlem shuffle: Traits / Show me: Tex, Joe / Higher and higher: Wilson, Jackie / Don't mess up a good thing: Fontella Bass & Bobby McClure / Gonna send you back to Georgia: Shaw, Timmy / Hi-heel sneakers: Tucker, Tommy / Shame, shame, shame: Reed, Jimmy / Soulful dress: Desanto, Sugar Pie / Put on your tight pants: Turner, Ike & Tina / Boom boom: Hooker, John Lee / Barefootin': Parker, Robert / We're gonna make it: Little Milton / Holy cow: Dorsey, Lee / Something's got a hold on me: James, Etta / You left the water running: Maurice & Mac / Gettin' mighty crowded: Everett, Betty / Everybody come clap your hands: Moody & The Deltas / (Down at) Papa Joe's: Dixiebells / Ain't love good: Clarke, Tony / Land of 1000 dances: Cannibal & The Head Hunters
CD _____ CDRB 23
Charly / May '95 / Charly / THE / Cadillac.

20 R&B DIVAS
My baby just cares for me: Simone, Nina / It's in his kiss (Shoop shoop song): Everett, Betty / Hello stranger: Lewis, Barbara / Oh no not my baby: Brown, Maxine / I didn't mean to hurt you: Shirelles / Do right woman, do right man: James, Etta / Woman will do wrong: Thomas, Irma / You don't know: Greenwich, Ellie / No stranger to love: Foxx, Inez / Take me for a little while:

Sands, Evie / There's gonna be trouble: DeSanto, Sugar Pie / Selfish one: Ross, Jackie / Recovery: Fontella Bass / I don't want to cry: Big Maybelle / Love of my man: Kilgore, Theola / Let me down easy: Lavette, Bettye / Sit down and cry: Washington, Ella / You're gonna miss me: Sexton, Ann / Do I make myself clear: James, Etta & Sugar Pie DeSanto / Shame, shame, shame: Shirley & Company
CD _____ CDRB 20
Charly / Apr '95 / Charly / THE / Cadillac.

20 REGGAE BLOCKBUSTERS
CD _____ CDTRL 176
Trojan / Mar '94 / Jetstar / Total/BMG.

20 REGGAE CLASSICS
Red red wine: Tribe, Tony / Sweet sensation: Melodians / Love of the common people: Thomas, Nicky / Johnny too bad: Slickers / Pressure drop: Toots & The Maytals / Liquidator: Harry J All Stars / Skinhead moonstomp: Simaryp / Longshot kick de bucket: Pioneers / Please don't make me cry: Groovy, Winston / Many rivers to cross: Cliff, Jimmy / 007: Dekker, Desmond & The Aces / Rudie, a message to you: Livingstone, Dandy / Version girl: Friday, Boy / Cherry on baby: Donaldson, Eric / Fattie fattie: Eccles, Clancy / Keep on moving: Marley, Bob / Rivers of Babylon: Melodians / Train to Skaville: Ethiopians
CD _____ CDTRL 224
Trojan / Mar '94 / Jetstar / Total/BMG.

20 REGGAE CLASSICS VOL.2
54-46 (was my number): Toots & The Maytals / Phoenix city: Alphonso, Roland / Love I can feel: Holt, John / Java: Pablo, Augustus / Reggae in your jeggae: Groovy, Winston / Pop a top: Capp, Andy / Double barrel: Collins, Dave & Ansil / Wear you to the ball: U-Roy & John Holt / Herbsman shuffle: King Stitt & The Dynamites / Small axe: Marley, Bob / Battle axe: Upsetters / Israelites: Dekker, Desmond & The Aces / Law: Capp, Andy / Fat man: Morgan, Derrick / So easy: Groovy, Winston / Whip: Ethiopians / Pomp and pride: Toots & The Maytals / Further you look: Holt, John / Return of Django: Upsetters / Soul shakedown party: Marley, Bob & The Wailers / Cool me down: Holt, John / Casino ner: King Stitt / Next corner: Dynamites
CD _____ CDTRL 256
Trojan / Mar '94 / Jetstar / Total/BMG.

20 REGGAE CLASSICS VOL.3
CD _____ PWKS 4226
Carlton Home Entertainment / Nov '94 / Carlton Home Entertainment.

20 ROCK 'N' ROLL GREATS
Summertime blues: Cochran, Eddie / Blueberry Hill: Domino, Fats / Rubber ball: Vee, Bobby / Say mama: Vincent, Gene / You're sixteen: Burnette, Johnny Rock 'N' Roll Trio / Ma, he's making eyes at me: Otis, Johnny Show / Why do fools fall in love: Lymon, Frankie & The Teenagers / Perfidia: Ventures / Mother-in-law: Doe, Ernie K. / Bony Moronie: Williams, Larry / Stay: Williams, Maurice & The Zodiacs / Piltdown rides again: Piltdown Men / Walk don't run: Ventures / I'm not a juvenile delinquent: Lymon, Frankie & The Teenagers / Willie and the hand jive: Otis, Johnny Show / Dreamin': Burnette, Johnny Rock 'N' Roll Trio / Be bop a lula: Vincent, Gene / Take good care of my baby: Vee, Bobby / Ain't that a shame: Domino, Fats / C'mon everybody: Cochran, Eddie
CD _____ CDMFP 6007
Music For Pleasure / Nov '88 / EMI.

20 ROCK 'N' ROLL GREATS VOL.2
Rock 'n' roll music: Berry, Chuck / See you later alligator: Haley, Bill / Rave on: Holly, Buddy / Hello Mary Lou: Nelson, Rick / Hey little girl: Shannon, Del / Run to him: Vee, Bobby / I'm in love again: Domino, Fats / Move it: Richard, Cliff / Only sixteen: Douglas, Craig / Shakin' all over: Kidd, Johnny & The Pirates / Wild cat: Vincent, Gene / Say man: Diddley, Bo / Sweetie pie: Cochran, Eddie / Don't ever change: Crickets / Night has a thousand eyes: Vee, Bobby / Little town flirt: Shannon, Del / It's late: Nelson, Rick / It doesn't matter anymore: Holly, Buddy / Shake, rattle and roll: Haley, Bill / No particular place to go: Berry, Chuck
CD _____ CDMFP 6006
Music For Pleasure / Oct '89 / EMI.

20 SONGS OF LOVE FROM THE 70'S
All by myself: Carmen, Eric / Living next door to Alice: Smokie / Daytime friends: Rogers, Kenny / Emma: Hot Chocolate / There goes my first love: Drifters / Torn between two lovers: McGregor, Mary / Love is in the air: Young, John Paul / I can't stop loving you (Though I try): Sayer, Leo / I don't want to put a hold on you: Flint, Bernie / Romeo: Mr. Big / Give a little love: Bay City Rollers / Heaven must be missing an angel: Tavares / Where do I begin: Bassey, Shirley / And I love you so: Como, Perry / It's only make believe: Child / You're my everything: Garrett, Lee / I don't wanna lose you: Karandidate / I not you: Dr. Hook / If you go away: Jacks, Terry / Softly whispering I love you: Congregation

CD _____ CDMFP 5987
Music For Pleasure / Apr '93 / EMI.

20 SUPERSONIC MEGA HITS
CD _____ RUNT 04CD
Runt / Aug '95 / Plastic Head.

20 WELSH FOLK DANCES
CD _____ SCD 2094
Sain / Mar '95 / Direct / ADA.

20TH ANNIVERSARY COLLECTION
Give me back my wig / No cuttin' loose / Black cat bone / Big chief / That's why I'm crying / Double eyed whammy / I'm free / These blues is killing me / Rain / Look but don't touch / Fannie Mae / Serves me right to suffer / Leaving / Born in Louisiana / Leaving your town / Drowning on dry land / If I hadn't been high / Trouble in mind / Brick / Pussy cat moan / You don't exist anymore / Second hand man / I've got dreams to remember / Going down to Big Mary's / 300 pounds of heavenly joy / Going back home / Strike like lightning / Middle aged blues boogie / Eyeballin' / Full moon on Main Street / Crow Jane blues / I'm the Zydeco Man / You don't know what love is / Blues after hours / Boot Hill
CD Set _____ ALCD 1056
Alligator / May '93 / Direct / ADA.

20TH ANNIVERSARY OF THE NEW YORK SALSA FESTIVAL, THE (2CD Set)
Por eso yo canto salsa / Pedro navaja / Azucar negra / El cantante / Sonora pa'l balladore / Dejame sonar / Mi primera rumba / Mentiras / Salsa caliente / Los tenis / Sonambulo / Si tu no te fueras / Experto en ti / Otra noche caliente / Que monora de quererte / Salsumba / Una adventura / Torero / Sisculpeme senora / Puerto rico
CD Set _____ 6758001
Bellaphon / Jan '96 / New Note.

20TH ANNIVERSARY OF THE SUMMER OF LOVE
CD _____ SDE 9024CD
Shimmy Disc / Nov '90 / Vital.

20TH ANNIVERSARY TOUR
CD _____ ALCD 1078
Alligator / May '93 / Direct / ADA.

20TH CONCORD FESTIVAL ALL STARS
Blues for Sam Nassi / Time after time / I wish I knew / Just a closer walk with thee / Sophisticated lady / Bye bye blackbird / I got it bad and that ain't good
CD _____ CCD 366
Concord Jazz / Jan '89 / New Note.

21 SWING BAND ALL-TIME GREATS
Cherokee: Barnet, Charlie / One o'clock jump: Basie, Count / I can't get started (with you): Berigan, Bunny / Honky tonk train blues: Crosby, Bob & Bob Cats / Amapola: Dorsey, Jimmy / Besame mucho: Dorsey, Jimmy / Boogie woogie: Dorsey, Tommy / I'm gettin' sentimental over you: Dorsey, Tommy / Don't get around much anymore: Ellington, Duke / Take the 'A' train: Ellington, Duke / Sing, sing, sing: Goodman, Benny / Why don't you do right: Goodman, Benny & Peggy Lee / Flying home: Hampton, Lionel & Illinois Jacquet / Body and soul: Hawkins, Coleman / At the woodchoppers' ball: Herman, Woody / All or nothing at all: James, Harry & Frank Sinatra / Ciribiribin: James, Harry & Frank Sinatra / Chattanooga choo choo: Miller, Glenn / In the mood: Miller, Glenn / Back bay shuffle: Shaw, Artie / Begin the beguine: Shaw, Artie
CD _____ CDAJA 5141
Living Era / Sep '94 / Koch.

21 YEARS OF ALTERNATIVE RADIO 1
Hey Joe: Hendrix, Jimi / Whiter shade of pale: Procul Harum / Delta lady: Cocker, Joe / My father's gun: John, Elton / So man: Jethro Tull / Mandolin king: Lindisfarne / Keep yourself alive: Queen / No love for free: Armatrading, Joan / New rose: Damned / Dancing in the moonlight: Thin Lizzy / Overground: Siouxsie & The Banshees / Read it in books: Echo & The Bunnymen / Can't stand losing you: Police / It's better this way: Associates / 5-8-6: New Order / What difference does it make: Smiths / Sally MacLennane: Pogues / Inside me: Jesus & Mary Chain / My favourite dress: Wedding Present / Ruby red lips: Gaye Bykers On Acid / Strong enough to change: Unseen Terror
CD Set _____ SFRCD 200
Strange Fruit / Oct '88 / Pinnacle.

21ST CENTURY DUB
CD _____ RE 147CD
Reach Out International / Nov '94 / Jetstar.

24 ALL TIME VOCAL GREATS
Zing went the strings of my heart: Garland, Judy / Last time I saw Paris: Martin, Tony / Pennsylvania 6-5000: Andrews Sisters / Begin the beguine: Hutch / Amapola: Durbin, Deanna / Wanderer: Tracy, Arthur / Atumn nocturne: Carless, Dorothy / Can't get Indiana out of my mind: Crosby, Bing / I yi yi yi yi (I like you very much): Miranda, Carmen / Autumn nocturne: Carless, Dorothy / Can't get Indiana off my mind: Crosby, Bing / You are too beautiful: Jolson, Al / I'll be with you in apple blossom time: Lynn, Vera / I'm so used to you now: Bowlly, Al / Boulevard of

broken dreams: Langford, Frances / You were never lovelier: Astaire, Fred / Jim: Fitzgerald, Ella / In a moment of weakness: Powell, Dick / Let's call it a day: Martin, Mary / Do I worry: Ink Spots / Wrap yourself in cotton wool: Shelton, Anne / That lovely week end: Brown, Issy / Room 504: Hall, Adelaide / Nagasaki: Mills Brothers / I got rhythm: Merry Macs / Sweethearts: Jones, Alan
CD _____ RAJCD 831
Empress / Jul '94 / THE.

24 BELLES CHANSONS DE PARIS
CD _____ 995102
EPM / Jun '93 / Discovery / ADA.

24 CARAT VOL.1
CD _____ AGCD 1
Q / Aug '95 / Warner Music.

24 NUMBER ONES OF THE 60'S
I like it: Gerry & The Pacemakers / Bad to me: Kramer, Billy J. & The Dakotas / Young ones: Richard, Cliff / You're my world: Black, Cilla / Pretty flamingo: Manfred Mann / Apache: Shadows / Shakin' all over: Kidd, Johnny & The Pirates / Poor me: Faith, Adam / World without love: Peter & Gordon / How do you do it: Gerry & The Pacemakers / Bachelor boy: Richard, Cliff / House of the rising sun: Animals / Do wah diddy diddy: Manfred Mann / Lily the pink: Scaffold / I remember you: Ifield, Frank / Anyone who had a heart: Black, Cilla / I'm alive: Hollies / Where do you go to my lovey: Sarstedt, Peter / Needles and pins: Searchers / Little children: Kramer, Billy J. & The Dakotas / Summer holiday: Richard, Cliff / I'm into something good: Herman's Hermits / Walkin' back to happiness: Shapiro, Helen / You'll never walk alone: Gerry & The Pacemakers
CD _____ CDMFP 6006
Music For Pleasure / Oct '87 / EMI.

25 ALL THE BEST IRISH PUB SONGS
CD _____ CDIRISH 004
Outlet / Jan '95 / ADA / Duncans / CM / Ross / Direct / Koch.

25 CONTINENTAL ALL-TIME GREATS
Lili Marlene: Andersen, Lale / Voulez vous de la canne a sucre: Baker, Josephine & Adrien Lamy / Due chitarre: Buti, Carlo / Maria La-O: Celis, Elyane & Lecuona Cuban Boys / Louise: Chevalier, Maurice / Night and day: Comedy Harmonisters / Ich bin vom kopf bis fuss (Falling in love again): Dietrich, Marlene / Mama: Gigli, Beniamino / Like Nina: Hendrik, John / Darling je vous aime beaucoup: Hildegarde / Es liebte einst in Hamburg: Igelhoff, Peter / Von der puszta will ich Traumen: Leander, Zarah / Bir mir bist du schoen: Marjane, Leo / La partie de bridge: Mireille, Pills et Tabet & Jean Sablon / Au fond de tes yeux: Mistinguett / Rosa da Madrid: Piquer, Concha / Nuages: Reinhardt, Django / Guitare d'amour: Rossi, Tino / J'attendrai and Je sais que vous etes jolie: Sablon, Jean & Django Reinhardt / Andiamo a Napoli: Serra, Daniele / Guter mann im mond: Serrano, Rosita / La canzone del domani: Del Signore, Gino / Lamento Borinqueno: Supervia, Conchita / J'ai ta main: Trenet, Charles
CD _____ CDAJA 5129
Living Era / May '94 / Koch.

25 FAVOURITE IRISH DRINKING SONGS
CD _____ CDIRISH 003
Outlet / Jan '95 / ADA / Duncans / CM / Ross / Direct / Koch.

25 GREATEST HITS VOL.1
CD _____ SPCD 355
Disky / Nov '93 / THE / BMG / Discovery / Pinnacle.

25 GREATEST HITS VOL.2
CD _____ SPCD 356
Disky / Nov '93 / THE / BMG / Discovery / Pinnacle.

25 GREATEST HITS VOL.3
CD _____ SPCD 357
Disky / Nov '93 / THE / BMG / Discovery / Pinnacle.

25 GREATEST HITS VOL.4
CD _____ SPCD 358
Disky / Nov '93 / THE / BMG / Discovery / Pinnacle.

25 GREATEST HITS VOL.5
CD _____ SPCD 359
Disky / Nov '93 / THE / BMG / Discovery / Pinnacle.

25 IRISH REBEL SONGS
CD _____ KOL 600CD
Outlet / Jul '95 / ADA / Duncans / CM / Ross / Direct / Koch.

25 IRISH REPUBLICAN SONGS
Ireland's 32 / Gra mo chroi / Take me home to Mayo / Lonely woods of Upton / They were soldiers everyone / Four green fields / Fields of Athenry / Dying rebel / Lid of me granny's bin / I.R.E.L.A.N.D. / Sean South / Ireland united / West awake / Shall my soul pass through old Ireland / Boys of the old brigade / Off to Dublin in the green / Lough Sheelin eviction / Little armalite / James Connolly / Broad black brimmer / Kevin Barry / Sniper's promise / Patriot game / Only our rivers run free / Nation once again
CD _____ KOL 602CD

755

Outlet / Jul '95 / ADA / Duncans / CM / Ross / Direct / Koch.

25 USA NO.1 HITS FROM 25 YEARS
Please Mr. Postman: *Marvelettes* / My girl: *Temptations* / You can't hurry love: *Ross, Diana & The Supremes* / I heard it through the grapevine: *Gaye, Marvin* / ABC: *Jackson Five* / Just my imagination: *Temptations* / Let's get it on: *Gaye, Marvin* / Baby love: *Ross, Diana & The Supremes* / I can't help myself: *Four Tops* / Reach out, I'll be there: *Four Tops* / I want you back: *Jackson Five* / Ain't no mountain high enough: *Ross, Diana* / Tears of a clown: *Robinson, Smokey* / What's going on: *Gaye, Marvin* / You are the sunshine of my life: *Wonder, Stevie* / Keep on truckin': *Kendricks, Eddie* / Don't leave me this way: *Houston, Thelma* / Three times a lady: *Commodores* / Give it to me baby: *James, Rick* / Superstition: *Wonder, Stevie* / Got to give it up: *Gaye, Marvin* / Still: *Commodores* / Endless love: *Ross, Diana & Lionel Richie*
CD _____ 5300322
Motown / Jan '93 / PolyGram.

25 YEARS OF ROCK 'N' ROLL VOLUME 1, 1959
Oh carol: *Sedaka, Neil* / Way down yonder in New Orleans: *Cannon, Freddy* / It's late: *Nelson, Rick* / Someone: *Mathis, Johnny* / Day the rains came: *Morgan, Jane* / Reveille rock: *Johnny & The Hurricanes* / Among my souvenirs: *Francis, Connie* / Seven little girls sitting in the back seat: *Avons* / Wonder of you: *Peterson, Ray* / Cathy's clown: *Everly Brothers* / Donna: *Wilde, Marty* / Stagger lee: *Price, Lloyd* / Poor me: *Faith, Adam* / Very precious love: *Day, Doris* / Sleep walk: *Santo & Johnny* / Why: *Newley, Anthony* / Maybe tomorrow: *Fury, Billy* / Dance with me: *Drifters* / Lovin' up a storm: *Lewis, Jerry Lee* / Charlie Brown: *Coasters*
CD _____ RRTCD 59
Connoisseur / Apr '92 / Pinnacle.

25 YEARS OF ROCK 'N' ROLL VOLUME 1, 1960
Apache: *Shadows* / Good timin': *Jones, Jimmy* / I'm sorry: *Lee, Brenda* / You'll never know what you're missing: *Ford, Emile & The Checkmates* / Pistol packin' mama: *Vincent, Gene* / How about that: *Faith, Adam* / Misty: *Mathis, Johnny* / Mama: *Francis, Connie* / Angela Jones: *Cox, Michael* / Tell Laura I love her: *Valance, Ricky* / Red river rock: *Johnny & The Hurricanes* / So sad (to watch good love go bad): *Everly Brothers* / As long as he needs me: *Bassey, Shirley* / Stairway to heaven: *Sedaka, Neil* / Please help me, I'm falling: *Locklin, Hank* / Heart of a teenage girl: *Douglas, Craig* / What in the world's come over you: *Scott, Jack* / Be mine: *Fortune, Lance* / He'll have to go: *Reeves, Jim* / Save the last dance for me: *Drifters*
CD _____
Connoisseur / Apr '92 / Pinnacle.

25 YEARS OF ROCK 'N' ROLL VOLUME 1, 1961
Runaway: *Shannon, Del* / Rubber ball: *Vee, Bobby* / Little devil: *Sedaka, Neil* / Walkin' back to happiness: *Shapiro, Helen* / Running scared: *Orbison, Roy* / Where the boys are: *Francis, Connie* / Portrait of my love: *Monro, Matt* / Big bad john: *Dean, Jimmy* / Lion sleeps tonight: *Tokens* / Stand by me: *King, Ben E.* / Walk right back: *Everly Brothers* / You always hurt the one you love: *Henry, Clarence 'Frogman'* / Take five: *Brubeck, Dave* / North to Alaska: *Horton, Johnny* / Tribute to Buddy Holly: *Berry, Mike & The Outlaws* / Michael: *Highwaymen* / Halfway to paradise: *Fury, Billy* / You don't know: *Shapiro, Helen* / Well I ask you: *Kane, Eden* / Will you still love me tomorrow: *Shirelles*
CD _____ RRTCD 61
Connoisseur / Apr '92 / Pinnacle.

25 YEARS OF ROCK 'N' ROLL VOLUME 1, 1962
Wanderer: *Dion* / Crying in the rain: *Everly Brothers* / Dream baby: *Orbison, Roy* / Ain't that funny: *Justice, Jimmy* / Nut rocker: *B. Bumble & The Stingers* / Swiss maid: *Shannon, Del* / Love me warm and tender: *Anka, Paul* / Deep in the heart of Texas: *Eddy, Duane* / Take good care of my baby: *Vee, Bobby* / Happy birthday sweet sixteen: *Sedaka, Neil* / Sheila: *Roe, Tommy* / Devil woman: *Robbins, Marty* / Wimoweh: *Denver, Karl* / Walk on by: *Van Dyke, Leroy* / There comes that feeling: *Lee, Brenda* / Let there be drums: *Nelson, Sandy* / Let there be love: *Cole, Nat King* / Ginny come lately: *Hyland, Brian* / Town without pity: *Pitney, Gene* / When my little girl is smiling: *Drifters*
CD _____ RRTCD 62
Connoisseur / Apr '92 / Pinnacle.

25 YEARS OF ROCK 'N' ROLL VOLUME 1, 1963
If I had a hammer: *Lopez, Trini* / Sweets for my sweet: *Searchers* / Wishing: *Holly, Buddy* / Island of dreams: *Springfields* / Good life: *Bennett, Tony* / It's almost tomorrow: *Wynter, Mark* / He's so fine: *Chiffons* / Twist and shout: *Poole, Brian & The Tremeloes* / Just like Eddie: *Heinz* / I'll keep you satisfied: *Kramer, Billy J.* / From a jack to a king: *Miller, Ned* / Scarlett O'Hara: *Har-*

ris, Jet & Tony Meehan / Deep purple: *Tempo, Nino & April Stevens* / Can't get used to losing you: *Williams, Andy* / Casanova: *Clark, Petula* / That's what love will do: *Brown, Joe & The Bruvvers* / Don't you think it's time: *Berry, Mike & The Outlaws* / In dreams: *Orbison, Roy*
CD _____ RRTCD 63
Connoisseur / Apr '92 / Pinnacle.

25 YEARS OF ROCK 'N' ROLL VOLUME 2, 1964
All day and all the night: *Kinks* / Don't bring me down: *Pretty Things* / Over you: *Freddie & The Dreamers* / I think of you: *Merseybeats* / Anyone who had a heart: *Black, Cilla* / Swinging on a star: *Irwin, Big Dee* / Someone, someone: *Poole, Brian & The Tremeloes* / I'm into something good: *Herman's Hermits* / Can't you hear my heartbeat: *Goldie & The Gingerbreads* / No particular place to go: *Berry, Chuck* / 5-4-3-2-1: *Manfred Mann* / Little children: *Shaw, Sandie* / Everything's alright: *Mojos* / Boys cry: *Kane, Eden* / Um um um um um um: *Fontana, Wayne* / Move over darling: *Day, Doris* / Don't throw your love away: *Searchers* / She's not there: *Zombies* / Losing you: *Springfield, Dusty* / Good golly miss molly: *Swinging Blue Jeans*
CD _____ RRTCD 64
Connoisseur / Apr '92 / Pinnacle.

25 YEARS OF ROCK 'N' ROLL VOLUME 2, 1965
Price of love: *Everly Brothers* / Unchained melody: *Righteous Brothers* / Mr. Tambourine Man: *Byrds* / World of our own: *Seekers* / Hang on sloopy: *McCoys* / King of the road: *Miller, Roger* / Some of your lovin': *Springfield, Dusty* / Almost there: *Williams, Andy* / Colours: *Donovan* / In the midnight hour: *Pickett, Wilson* / Leader of the pack: *Shangri-Las* / Yesterday man: *Andrews, Chris* / Funny how love can be: *Ivy League* / Looking through the eyes of love: *Pitney, Gene* / Here it comes again: *Fortunes* / I left my heart in San Francisco: *Bennett, Tony* / Trains and boats and planes: *Kramer, Billy J. & The Dakotas* / In thoughts of you: *Fury, Billy* / We gotta get out of this place: *Animals* / Go now: *Moody Blues*
CD _____ RRTCD 65
Connoisseur / Apr '92 / Pinnacle.

25 YEARS OF ROCK 'N' ROLL VOLUME 2, 1966
Good vibrations: *Beach Boys* / Daydream: *Lovin' Spoonful* / Rescue me: *Fontella Bass* / My mind's eye: *Small Faces* / Green green grass of home: *Jones, Tom* / Bus stop: *Hollies* / My girl: *Redding, Otis* / Tomorrow: *Shaw, Sandie* / With a girl like you: *Troggs* / Eight miles high: *Byrds* / Holy cow: *Dorsey, Lee* / Happy together: *Turtles* / Just one smile: *Pitney, Gene* / Little man: *Sonny & Cher* / Dead end street: *Kinks* / Get away: *Fame, Georgie & The Blue Flames* / My love: *Clark, Petula* / Hold tight: *Dave Dee, Dozy, Beaky, Mick & Tich* / Out of time: *Farlowe, Chris* / When a man loves a woman: *Sledge, Percy*
CD _____ RRTCD 66
Connoisseur / Apr '92 / Pinnacle.

25 YEARS OF ROCK 'N' ROLL VOLUME 2, 1967
Respect: *Franklin, Aretha* / Knock on wood: *Floyd, Eddie* / First cut is the deepest: *Arnold, P.P.* / Flowers in the rain: *Move* / Boat that I row: *Lulu* / Itchycoo Park: *Small Faces* / Release me: *Humperdinck, Engelbert* / From the underworld: *Herd* / House that Jack built: *Price, Alan* / Groovin': *Rascals* / San Francisco: *McKenzie, Scott* / On a carousel: *Hollies* / Ode to Billy Joe: *Gentry, Bobbie* / I'll never fall in love again: *Jones, Tom* / Ballad of Bonnie and Clyde: *Fame, Georgie* / Something's gotten hold of my heart: *Pitney, Gene* / Silence is golden: *Tremeloes* / Homburg: *Procul Harum* / Sweet soul music: *Conley, Arthur* / 007: *Dekker, Desmond*
CD _____ RRTCD 67
Connoisseur / Apr '92 / Pinnacle.

25 YEARS OF ROCK 'N' ROLL VOLUME 2, 1968
Young girl: *Puckett, Gary* / I say a little prayer: *Franklin, Aretha* / Joanna: *Walker, Scott* / Hurdy gurdy man: *Donovan* / Everlasting love: *Love Affair* / Step inside love: *Black, Cilla* / Delilah: *Jones, Tom* / Albatross: *Fleetwood Mac* / Eloise: *Ryan, Barry* / Mony mony: *James, Tommy & The Shondells* / (Sittin' on) the dock of the bay: *Redding, Otis* / Son of Hickory Holler's tramp: *Smith, O.C.* / What a wonderful world: *Armstrong, Louis* / Dream a little dream of me: *Mama Cass* / Can't take my eyes off you: *Williams, Andy* / Classical gas: *Williams, Mason* / Only one woman: *Marbles* / I don't want no loving to die: *Herd* / I close my eyes and count to ten: *Springfield, Dusty* / Dance to the music: *Sly & The Family Stone*
CD _____ RRTCD 68
Connoisseur / Apr '92 / Pinnacle.

25 YEARS OF ROCK 'N' ROLL VOLUME 2, 1969
I can hear music: *Beach Boys* / Son of a preacher man: *Springfield, Dusty* / Hey Jude: *Pickett, Wilson* / Oh happy day: *Hawkins, Edwin Singers* / Man of the world: *Fleetwood Mac* / Natural born boogie: *Humble Pie* / Fox on the run: *Manfred Mann*

/ (If paradise is) Half as nice: *Amen Corner* / Time is tight: *Booker T & The MG's* / I'd rather go blind: *Chicken Shack* / Private number: *Bell, William & Judy Clay* / One road: *Love Affair* / You've made me so very happy: *Blood, Sweat & Tears* / Minute of your time: *Jones, Tom* / Sorry Suzanne: *Hollies* / In the bad bad old days: *Foundations* / First of May: *Bee Gees* / My sentimental friend: *Herman's Hermits* / Call me number one: *Tremeloes* / Boy named Sue: *Cash, Johnny*
CD _____ RRTCD 69
Connoisseur / Jul '92 / Pinnacle.

25 YEARS OF ROCK 'N' ROLL VOLUME 2, 1970
Victoria: *Kinks* / Rag mama rag: *Band* / Gasoline Alley bred: *Hollies* / Spirit in the sky: *Greenbaum, Norman* / Yellow river: *Christie* / Patches: *Carter, Clarence* / Both sides now: *Collins, Judy* / Love is life: *Hot Chocolate* / My baby loves lovin': *White Plains* / In my chair: *Status Quo* / Who do you love: *Juicy Lucy* / Ruby Tuesday: *Melanie* / Make it with you: *Bread* / Cotton fields: *Beach Boys* / Venus: *Shocking Blue* / Me and my life: *Tremeloes* / Don't play that song (You lied): *Franklin, Aretha* / Can't help falling in love: *Williams, Andy* / Montego Bay: *Bloom, Bobby* / Paranoid: *Black Sabbath*
CD _____ RRTCD 70
Connoisseur / Jul '92 / Pinnacle.

25 YEARS OF ROCK 'N' ROLL VOLUME 2, 1971
Strange kind of woman: *Deep Purple* / Back street luv: *Curved Air* / Malt and barley blues: *McGuinness Flint* / Reason to believe: *Stewart, Rod* / Spanish harlem: *Franklin, Aretha* / I believe (in love): *Hot Chocolate* / Tonight: *Move* / Get down and get with it: *Slade* / Witch Queen of New Orleans: *Redbone* / Baby jump: *Mungo Jerry* / When you are a king: *White Plains* / Chestnut mare: *Byrds* / Shaft: *Hayes, Isaac* / Pied piper: *Bob & Marcia* / Walkin': *CCS* / Rose garden: *Anderson, Lynn* / I will return: *Springwater* / What have they done to my song Ma: *Melanie* / Sultana: *Titanic* / Amazing grace: *Collins, Judy*
CD _____ RRTCD 71
Connoisseur / Aug '92 / Pinnacle.

25 YEARS OF ROCK 'N' ROLL VOLUME 2, 1972
American pie: *McLean, Don* / Isn't life strange: *Moody Blues* / Baby I'm a want you: *Bread* / All I ever need is you: *Sonny & Cher* / I don't believe in miracles: *Blunstone, Colin* / Look wot you dun: *Slade* / Donna: *10cc* / California man: *Move* / Open up: *Mungo Jerry* / Lovin' you ain't easy: *Pagliaro* / I can see clearly now: *Nash, Johnny* / Where did our love go: *Elbert, Donnie* / Walkin' in the rain with the one I love: *Love Unlimited Orchestra* / Sister Jane: *New World* / Thing called love: *Cash, Johnny* / I'm stone in love with you: *Stylistics* / Running away: *Sly & The Family Stone* / Storm in a teacup: *Fortunes* / Brand new key: *Melanie* / My ding a ling: *Berry, Chuck*
CD _____ RRTCD 72
Connoisseur / Jul '92 / Pinnacle.

25 YEARS OF ROCK 'N' ROLL VOLUME 2, 1973
Paper plane: *Status Quo* / God gave rock 'n' roll to you: *Argent* / You're so vain: *Simon, Carly* / Stuck in the middle with you: *Stealer's Wheel* / If you don't know me by now: *Melvin, Harold & The Bluenotes* / Amoureuse: *Dee, Kiki* / Showdown: *E.L.O.* / Lamplight: *Essex, David* / Angel fingers: *Wizzard* / Dynamite: *Mud* / Cum on feel the noize: *Slade* / 48 crash: *Quatro, Suzi* / Part of the union: *Strawbs* / One and one is one: *Medicine Head* / Alright alright alright: *Mungo Jerry* / Pick up the pieces: *Hudson - Ford* / Free electric band: *Hammond, Albert* / Radar love: *Golden Earring* / Could it be I'm falling in love: *Detroit Spinners* / That lady: *Isley Brothers*
CD _____ RRTCD 73
Connoisseur / Jul '92 / Pinnacle.

25 YEARS OF ROCK 'N' ROLL VOLUME 2, 1974
I've got the music in me: *Dee, Kiki* / Rock your baby: *McCrae, George* / Queen of clubs: *K.C. & The Sunshine Band* / Love's theme: *Love Unlimited Orchestra* / Magic: *Pilot* / Touch too much: *Arrows* / Stardust: *Essex, David* / Golden age of rock 'n' roll: *Mott The Hoople* / My coo ca choo: *Stardust, Alvin* / Air that I breathe: *Hollies* / Zing went the strings of my heart: *Trammps* / Walkin' miracle: *Limmie & Family Cooking* / Never, never gonna give you up: *White, Barry* / Hang on in there baby: *Bristol, Johnny* / Most beautiful girl in the world: *Rich, Charlie* / Jukebox jive: *Rubettes* / Cat crept in: *Mud* / Na na na: *Powell, Cozy* / Stop and slide: *Medicine Head* / Pool Hall Richard: *Faces*
CD _____ RRTCD 74
Connoisseur / Aug '92 / Pinnacle.

25 YEARS OF ROCK 'N' ROLL VOLUME 2, 1975
That's the way I like it: *K.C. & The Sunshine Band* / Right back where we started from: *Nightingale, Maxine* / Best thing that ever happened to me: *Knight, Gladys & The Pips* / Mr. Raffles: *Harley, Steve* / Rock me gently: *Kim, Andy* / Motor bikin': *Spedding, Chris* / My white bicycle: *Nazareth* / Art for

art's sake: *10cc* / Roll over lay down: *Status Quo* / I can do it: *Rubettes* / Good love can never die: *Stardust, Alvin* / Send in the clowns: *Collins, Judy* / Rhinestone cowboy: *Campbell, Glen* / Stand by your man: *Wynette, Tammy* / This will be: *Cole, Natalie* / Take good care of yourself: *Three Degrees* / Let me try again: *Jones, Tammy* / It's been so long: *McRae, Gordon* / Dolly my love: *Moments* / Blue guitar: *Hayward, Justin & John Lodge*
CD _____ RRTCD 75
Connoisseur / Jul '92 / Pinnacle.

25 YEARS OF ROCK 'N' ROLL VOLUME 2, 1976
Harvest for the world: *Isley Brothers* / I love music: *O'Jays* / Don't make me wait too long: *White, Barry* / You are my love: *Liverpool Express* / Livin' thing: *E.L.O.* / I'm Mandy fly me: *10cc* / What I've got in mind: *Spears, Billie Jo* / Heaven must be missing an angel: *Tavares* / More, more, more: *Andrea True Connection* / Love me: *Elliman, Yvonne* / Get up offa that thing: *Brown, James* / Dr. Love: *Charles, Tina* / Kiss and say goodbye: *Manhattans* / Young hearts run free: *Staton, Candi* / Rubberband man: *Detroit Spinners* / Wonderful world: *Nash, Johnny* / It not you: *Dr. Hook* / Mississippi: *Pussycat* / Ships in the night: *Be-Bop Deluxe* / Girls, girls, girls: *Sailor*
CD _____ RRTCD 76
Connoisseur / Jul '92 / Pinnacle.

25 YEARS OF ROCK 'N' ROLL VOLUME 2, 1977
More than a feeling: *Boston* / Show you the way to go: *Jacksons* / Whodunit: *Tavares* / Telephone line: *E.L.O.* / Best of my love: *Emotions* / Dance, dance, dance: *Chic* / Home is where the heart is: *Knight, Gladys & The Pips* / Daddy cool: *Darts* / Girl can't help it: *Darts* / Lonely boy: *Gold, Andrew* / Lucille: *Rogers, Kenny* / Southern nights: *Campbell, Glen* / Slow down: *Miles, John* / Shuffle: *McCoy, Van* / Stop me: *Ocean, Billy* / Hurt: *Manhattans* / Ain't gonna bump no more (With no big fat woman): *Tex, Joe* / Too hot to handle: *Heatwave* / Saturday nite: *Earth, Wind & Fire* / She's a wind up: *Dr. Feelgood* / Modern world: *Jam*
CD _____ RRTCD 77
Connoisseur / Jul '92 / Pinnacle.

25 YEARS OF ROCK 'N' ROLL VOLUME 2, 1978
Le freak: *Chic* / September: *Earth, Wind & Fire* / Boogie shoes: *K.C. & The Sunshine Band* / Wishing on a star: *Rose Royce* / If I can't have you: *Elliman, Yvonne* / Just the way you are: *White, Barry* / Talking in your sleep: *Gayle, Crystal* / Boogie oogie oogie: *Taste Of Honey* / Use ta be my girl: *O'Jays* / Blame it on the boogie: *Jacksons* / Always and forever: *Heatwave* / It's raining: *Darts* / Lovely day: *Withers, Bill* / If I had words: *Fitzgerald, Scott & Yvonne Keeley* / Mr. blue sky: *E.L.O.* / Never let her slip away: *Gold, Andrew* / Jilted John: *Jilted John* / Don't take no for an answer: *Robinson, Tom* / Ever fallen in love: *Buzzcocks* / Don't look back: *Tosh, Peter*
CD _____ RRTCD 78
Connoisseur / Jul '92 / Pinnacle.

25 YEARS OF ROCK 'N' ROLL VOLUME 2, 1979
I want you to want me: *Cheap Trick* / Brass in pocket: *Pretenders* / He's the greatest dancer: *Sister Sledge* / Reunited: *Peaches & Herb* / Just what I needed: *Cars* / She's in love with you: *Quatro, Suzi* / Get it right next time: *Rafferty, Gerry* / Devil went down to Georgia: *Daniels, Charlie* / Hersham Boys: *Sham 69* / Deer hunter: *Shadows* / Is it love you're after: *Rose Royce* / Get down: *Chandler, Gene* / My love is your love: *Positive Force* / I love America: *Juvet, Patrick* / Haven't stopped dancing yet: *Gonzalez* / Shake your body: *Jacksons* / Star: *Earth, Wind & Fire* / Please don't go: *K.C. & The Sunshine Band* / I want your love: *Chic* / Ladies night: *Kool & The Gang*
CD _____ RRTCD 79
Connoisseur / Jul '92 / Pinnacle.

25 YEARS OF ROCK 'N' ROLL VOLUME 2, 1980
Talk of the town: *Pretenders* / Start: *Jam* / Working my way back to you: *Detroit Spinners* / Jump to the beat: *Lattisaw, Stacy* / Nine to Five: *Easton, Sheena* / Don't stop the music: *Yarbrough & Peoples* / To be or not to be: *Robertson, B.A.* / Silver dream machine: *Essex, David* / We are glass: *Numan, Gary* / Special brew: *Bad Manners* / There there my dear: *Dexy's Midnight Runners* / Feels like I'm in love: *Marie, Kelly* / What's another year: *Logan, Johnny* / Coward of the county: *Rogers, Kenny* / Better love next time: *Dr. Hook* / Hold on to my love: *Ruffin, Jimmy* / Don't push it, don't force it: *Haywood, Leon* / Crying: *McLean, Don* / Southern freeze: *Freeze* / Dog eat dog: *Adam Ant*
CD _____ RRTCD 80
Connoisseur / Jul '92 / Pinnacle.

25 YEARS OF ROCK 'N' ROLL VOLUME 2, 1981
Tainted love: *Soft Cell* / My own way: *Duran Duran* / I could be happy: *Altered Images* / Prince Charming: *Adam Ant* / Cambodia: *Wilde, Kim* / Show me: *Dexy's Midnight Runners* / Only crying: *Marshall, Keith* / Hold on tight: *E.L.O.* / Night games: *Bonnet, Gra-*

ham / And the bands played on: Saxon / Do the hucklebuck: Coast To Coast / Can't get enough of you: Grant, Eddy / Everybody salsa: Modern Romance / When he shines: Easton, Sheena / Can you feel it: Jacksons / I've had enough: Earth, Wind & Fire / When she was my girl: Four Tops / Under your thumb: Godley & Creme / Funeral pyre: Jam / She's got claws: Numan, Gary
CD _____ RRTCD 81
Connoisseur / Jul '92 / Pinnacle.

25 YEARS OF ROCK 'N' ROLL VOLUME 2, 1982
Come on Eileen: Dexy's Midnight Runners / Freeze frame: Geils, J. Band / Strange little girl: Stranglers / Look of love: ABC / Living on the ceiling: Blancmange / Is it a dream: Classix Nouveaux / I don't wanna dance: Grant, Eddy / Love's comin' at ya: Moore, Melba / Suspicious minds: Station, Candi / Really saying something: Bananarama / Don't walk away: Four Tops / Night birds: Shakatak / Lover in you: Sugarhill Gang / Classic: Gurvitz, Adrian / Brave new world: Toyah / Girl crazy: Hot Chocolate / Ooh la la la (let's go dancin'): Kool & The Gang / Love makes the world go round: Jets / Beat surrender: Jam / Talk talk: Talk Talk
CD _____ RRTCD 82
Connoisseur / Jul '92 / Pinnacle.

25 YEARS OF ROCK 'N' ROLL VOLUME 2, 1983
Club Tropicana: Wham / Joanna: Kool & The Gang / What is love: Jones, Howard / It's raining men: Weather Girls / I gave you my heart (didn't I): Hot Chocolate / Candy girl: New Edition / Na na hey hey kiss him goodbye: Bananarama / Soul inside: Soft Cell / Blind vision: Blancmange / Cry me a river: Wilson, Mari / Blue world: Moody Blues / Oblivious: Aztec Camera / Speak like a child: Style Council / Love blonde: Wilde, Kim / Dark is the night: Shakatak / Ooh to be ah: Kajagoogoo / He knows you know: Marillion / Chance: Big Country / Bad day: Carmel
CD _____ RRTCD 83
Connoisseur / Jul '92 / Pinnacle.

25 YEARS OF TROJAN
CD Set _____ CDTRD 413
Trojan / Mar '94 / Jetstar / Total/BMG.

25TH FUJITSU CONCORD JAZZ FESTIVAL
You're lucky to me: Alden, Howard Trio / Very thought of you: Alden, Howard Trio / Nobody else but me: Alden, Howard Trio / Crazy she calls me: Alden, Howard Trio / All alone/Tango el bongo: Alden, Howard Trio / Kung fu willie: Harris, Gene Quartet / Grass is greener: Harris, Gene Quartet / Sweet Georgia Brown: Harris, Gene Quartet / Just a closer walk with thee: Harris, Gene Quartet / Robbin's nest: Harris, Gene Quartet / Tenderly: Harris, Gene Quartet / This one's for Scott: Harris, Gene Quartet / There is no greater love: McPartland, Marian Trio / Prelude to a kiss: McPartland, Marian Trio / There will never be another you: McPartland, Marian Trio / Gone with the wind: McPartland, Marian Trio / My foolish heart: McPartland, Marian Trio / I'll remember April: McPartland, Marian Trio
CD _____ CCD 7002
Concord Jazz / Mar '94 / New Note.

26 HAPPY HONKY TONK MEMORIES
CD _____ MICH 4529
Hindsight / Sep '92 / Target/BMG / Jazz Music.

26TH FUJITSU CONCORD JAZZ FESTIVAL
CD _____ CCD 7003
Concord Jazz / Apr '95 / New Note.

30 TOP TEN HITS OF THE 60'S
CD _____ MATCD 201
Castle / Nov '93 / BMG.

30 YEARS OF DUB MUSIC
CD _____ RNCD 2046
Rhino / Mar '94 / Jetstar / Magnum Music Group / THE.

30 YEARS OF DUB MUSIC ON THE GO
CD _____ RNCD 2094
Rhino / Mar '95 / Jetstar / Magnum Music Group / THE.

30 YEARS OF JAMAICAN MUSIC ON THE GO
CD Set _____ RNCD 2034
Rhino / Jan '94 / Jetstar / Magnum Music Group / THE.

30 YEARS OF JAMAICAN MUSIC VOL.2
CD _____ RNCD 87
Rhino / Feb '95 / Jetstar / Magnum Music Group / THE.

30 YEARS OF NO.1'S VOL.1 (1956-1958)
(We're gonna) Rock around the clock: Haley, Bill & The Comets / Memories are made of this: Martin, Dean / Why do fools fall in love: Lymon, Frankie / Singin' the blues: Steele, Tommy / Cumberland Gap: Donegan, Lonnie / All shook up: Presley, Elvis / That'll be the day: Holly, Buddy / Great balls of fire: Belafonte, Harry / Whole lotta woman: Holliday, Michael / Sixteen tons: Ford, Tennessee Ernie / Rock 'n' roll waltz: Starr, Kay / Lay down your arms: Shelton, Anne / Garden of Eden: Vaughan, Frankie / Diana: Anka, Paul / Gamblin' man: Donegan, Lonnie / Mary's boy child: Belafonte, Harry / Jailhouse rock: Presley, Elvis / Magic moments: Como, Perry
CD _____ TYNOCD 100
Connoisseur / Nov '88 / Pinnacle.

30 YEARS OF NO.1'S VOL.10 (1980-1983)
I lisa it up and wear it out (Not on CD): Odyssey / Start: Jam / Feels like I'm in love: Marie, Kelly / Tide is high: Blondie / Green door: Stevens, Shakin' / Japanese boy (Not on CD): Aneka / Tainted love: Soft Cell / Prince Charming: Adam & The Ants / Land of make believe (Not on CD): Bucks Fizz / Model: Kraftwerk / Seven tears: Goombay Dance Band / My camera never lies (Not on CD): Bucks Fizz / House of fun: Madness / Goody two shoes: Adam & The Ants / Happy Talk: Captain Sensible / Fame: Cara, Irene / Come on Eileen: Dexy's Midnight Runners & Emerald Express / Do you realy want to hurt me: Culture Club / I don't wanna dance: Grant, Eddy / Down under: Men At Work / Too shy: Kajagoogoo / Total eclipse of the heart: Tyler, Bonnie / Is there something I should know: Duran Duran / True: Spandau Ballet
CD _____ TYNOCD 109
Connoisseur / Apr '90 / Pinnacle.

30 YEARS OF NO.1'S VOL.11 (1983-1986)
Give it up: K.C. & The Sunshine Band / Karma Chameleon: Culture Club / Only You: Flying Pickets / 99 red balloons: Nena / Wake me up before you go go: Wham / I feel for you: Khan, Chaka / I should have known better: Diamond, Jim / I want to know what love is: Foreigner / Nineteen: Hardcastle, Paul / Frankie: Sister Sledge / Good heart: Sharkey, Feargal / Sun always shines on TV: A-Ha / Rock me Amadeus: Falco / Spirit in the sky (Not on CD): Dr. & The Medics / Every loser wins (Not on CD): Berry, Nick / Final countdown: Europe / Reet petite (Not on CD): Wilson, Jackie / Stand by me: King, Ben E. / Nothing's gonna stop us now: Starship / Never gonna give you up: Astley, Rick / You win again: Bee Gees / I think we're alone now (Not on CD): Tiffany / Perfect: Fairground Attraction / Orinoco flow: Enya
CD _____ TYNOCD 110
Connoisseur / Jun '90 / Pinnacle.

30 YEARS OF NO.1'S VOL.2 (1958-1961)
It's all in the game: Edwards, Tommy / It's only make believe: Twitty, Conway / Smoke gets in your eyes: Platters / Fool such as I: Presley, Elvis / Only sixteen: Douglas, Craig / Why: Newley, Anthony / Running bear: Preston, Johnny / Three steps to heaven: Cochran, Eddie / Please don't tease: Richard, Cliff / Apache: Shadows / Hoots mon: Lord Rockingham's XI / As I love you: Bassey, Shirley / Side saddle: Conway, Russ / Living doll: Richard, Cliff / What do you want: Ford, Emile / Poor me: Faith, Adam / Do you mind: Newley, Anthony / Good timin': Jones, Jimmy / Shakin' all over: Kidd, Johnny & The Pirates
CD _____ TYNOCD 101
Connoisseur / Nov '88 / Pinnacle.

30 YEARS OF NO.1'S VOL.3 (1961-1963)
Sailor: Clark, Petula / You're driving me: Temperance Seven / You don't know: Shapiro, Helen / Kon-Tiki: Shadows / Tower of strength: Vaughan, Frankie / Young ones: Richard, Cliff / Not rocker: B. Bumble & The Stingers / Telstar: Tornados / Next time: Richard, Cliff / Diamonds: Harris, Jet & Tony Meehan / How do you do it: Gerry & The Pacemakers / Sweets for my sweet: Searchers / Blue moon: Marcels / Runaway: Shannon, Del / Johnny remember me: Leyton, Johnny / Walkin' back to happiness: Shapiro, Helen / Moon river: Williams, Danny / Wonderful land: Shadows / I remember you: Ifield, Frank / Lovesick blues: Ifield, Frank / Dance on: Shadows / Summer holiday: Richard, Cliff / I like it: Gerry & The Pacemakers / Do you love me: Poole, Brian & The Tremeloes
CD _____ TYNOCD 102
Connoisseur / May '89 / Pinnacle.

30 YEARS OF NO.1'S VOL.4 (1963-1965)
You'll never walk alone: Gerry & The Pacemakers / Diane: Bachelors / Little children: Kramer, Billy J. & The Dakotas / Don't throw your love away: Searchers / House of the rising sun: Animals / Have I the right: Honeycombs / Always something there to remind me: Shaw, Sandie / Go now: Moody Blues / Tired of waiting for you: Kinks / It's not unusual: Jones, Tom / Minute you're gone: Richard, Cliff / I'm alive: Hollies / Needles and pins: Searchers / Anyone who had a heart: Black, Cilla / World without love: Peter & Gordon / Juliet: Four Pennies / Do wah diddy diddy: Manfred Mann / You really got me: Kinks / Yeh yeh: Fame, Georgie & The Blue Flames / You've lost that lovin' feelin': Righteous Brothers / I'll never find another you: Seekers / Concrete and clay: Unit 4+2 / Long live love: Shaw, Sandie
CD _____ TYNOCD 103
Connoisseur / Jul '89 / Pinnacle.

30 YEARS OF NO.1'S VOL.6 (1969-1972)
Blackberry way: Move / (If paradise is) half as nice: Amen Corner / Where do you go to my lovely: Sarstedt, Peter / Israelites: Dekker, Desmond & The Aces / Dizzy: Roe, Tommy / In the year 2525: Zager & Evans / I'll never fall in love again: Gentry, Bobbie / Sugar sugar: Archies / Love grows (Where my Rosemary grows): Edison Lighthouse / Wandering star: Marvin, Lee / In the Summertime: Mungo Jerry / Woodstock: Matthew's Southern Comfort / I hear you knocking: Edmunds, Dave / Baby jump: Mungo Jerry / Hot love: T. Rex / Double barrel: Collins, Dave & Ansil / Knock three times: Dawn / Chirpy chirpy cheep cheep: Middle Of The Road / Get it on: T. Rex / Hey girl don't bother me: Tams / Coz I luv you: Slade / Without you: Nilsson, Harry / Metal guru: T. Rex / Vincent: McLean, Don
CD _____ TYNOCD 105
Connoisseur / Jun '88 / Pinnacle.

30 YEARS OF NO.1'S VOL.7 (1972-1975)
You wear it well: Stewart, Rod / Mouldy old dough: Lieutenant Pigeon / Clair: O'Sullivan, Gilbert / Blockbuster: Sweet / See my baby jive: Wizzard / Can the can: Quatro, Suzi / Rubber bullets: 10cc / Welcome home: Peters & Lee / I'm the leader of the gang (I am): Glitter, Gary / Angel fingers: Wizzard / Daydreamer: Cassidy, David / You won't find another fool like me: New Seekers / Tiger feet: Mud / Devil gate drive: Quatro, Suzi / Seasons in the sun: Jacks, Terry / Sugar baby love: Rubettes / Streak: Stevens, Ray / Always yours: Glitter, Gary / Kung fu fighting: Douglas, Carl / Sad sweet dreamer: Sweet Sensation / Everything I own: Boothe, Ken / You're the first, the last, my everything: White, Barry / Down down: Status Quo / Ms. Grace: Tymes
CD _____ TYNOCD 106
Connoisseur / Dec '89 / Pinnacle.

30 YEARS OF NO.1'S VOL.8 (1975-1977)
January: Pilot / Make me smile (come up and see me): Harley, Steve & Cockney Rebel / Bye bye baby: Bay City Rollers / Oh boy: Mud / Stand by your man: Wynette, Tammy / I'm not in love: 10cc / Tears on my pillow: Nash, Johnny / Give a little love: Bay City Rollers / Barbados: Typically Tropical / Can't give you anything (but my love): Stylistics / Hold me close: Essex, David / Mamma mia: Abba / December 1963 (Oh what a night): Four Seasons / I love to love (but my baby loves to dance): Charles, Tina / Forever and ever: Roussos, Demis / Dancing queen: Abba / Mississippi: Pussycat / Don't give up on us: Soul, David / Free: Williams, Deniece / Lucille: Rogers, Kenny / Show you the way to go: Jacksons / So you win again: Hot Chocolate / Silver lady: Soul, David / Yes sir, I can boogie: Baccara
CD _____ TYNOCD 107
Connoisseur / Jan '90 / Pinnacle.

30 YEARS OF NO.1'S VOL.9 (1977-1980)
Name of the game: Abba / Up town top ranking (Not on CD): Althia & Donna / Figaro (Not on CD): Brotherhood Of Man / Take a chance on me: Abba / Wuthering Heights: Bush, Kate / Dreadlock holiday: 10cc / Rat trap: Boomtown Rats / Hit me with your rhythm stick: Dury, Ian / I will survive: Gaynor, Gloria / Ring my bell (Not on CD): Ward, Anita / Are friends electric: Tubeway Army / I don't like Mondays: Boomtown Rats / Cars: Numan, Gary / Video killed the radio star: Buggles / Mary's boy child / oh my what a beautiful woman: Dr. Hook / Too much too young: Specials / Coward of the county: Rogers, Kenny / Together we're beautiful (Not on CD): Kinney, Fern / Going underground: Jam / Dream of children: Jam / Call me: Blondie / Geno: Dexy's Midnight Runners / Crying: McLean, Don / Sunday girl: Blondie
CD _____ TYNOCD 108
Connoisseur / Mar '90 / Pinnacle.

30'S GIRLS
Second hand man / Rhythm for sale / Doin' the Suzie Q / All God's chillun got rhythm / Summertime / My castles rockin'
CD _____ CBC 1026
Timeless Jazz / Sep '95 / New Note.

32 COUNTRY SUPER HITS
CD Set _____ 24002
Laserlight / Jan '95 / Target/BMG.

32 SUPERHITS
CD _____ 24020
Laserlight / Mar '94 / Target/BMG.

36 IRISH LOVE BALLADS
CD _____ CHCD 3202
Chyme / Oct '95 / CM / ADA / Direct.

39 SHADES OF REGGAE
CD _____ RIPEXD 193
Ripe / Aug '94 / Total/BMG.

39 STEPS TO SEATTLE
You are my friend: Rain Parade / Mountain of love: Giant Sand / Everyone to go: American Music Club / It's OK: Thin White Rope / Ron Klaus wrecked his house: Big Dipper / When you smile: Dream Syndicate / I had a dream: Long Ryders / Speak the same to everyone: Non Fiction / Crazy girl: Casuals / Inside: Sidewinder / She's alright: Downsiders / Drifter: Green On Red / Wild dog waltz: Band Of Blacky Ranchette / Everything you need and everything you want: Tolman, Russ
CD _____ DIAB 809
Diabolo / Apr '94 / Pinnacle.

40 COMPLETE FAVOURITE IRISH BALLADS
CD _____ CDBALLAD 002
Outlet / Jan '95 / ADA / Duncans / CM / Russ / Direct / Koch.

40 COMPLETE IRISH PUB SONGS
CD _____ CDBALLAD 001
Outlet / Jan '95 / ADA / Duncans / CM / Ross / Direct / Koch.

40 FOLK BALLADS OF IRELAND
CD _____ CHCD 1042
Chyme / Jan '95 / CM / ADA / Direct.

40 IRISH LOVE SONGS
CD _____ CHCD 1069
Chyme / Oct '95 / CM / ADA / Direct.

40 YEARS OF ACAPELLA GOSPEL SINGING
CD _____ JASSCD 637
Jass / Jul '93 / CM / Jazz Music / ADA / Cadillac / Direct.

50 BEST IRISH REBEL BALLADS VOL.1
CD _____ IRB 1798CD
Outlet / Oct '95 / ADA / Duncans / CM / Ross / Direct / Koch.

50 CLASSIC PUB SONGS
CD _____ PUBCD 01
Primetime / Nov '94 / Silva Screen.

50 COMPLETE REBEL SONGS
CD _____ IRBCD 1916
Outlet / Jul '94 / ADA / Duncans / CM / Ross / Direct / Koch.

50 COUNTRY NO.1'S
CD Set _____ DBG 53033
Double Gold / Jun '94 / Target/BMG.

50 NO.1 HITS OF THE 60'S
CD _____ RADCD 08
Global / Apr '95 / BMG.

50 ORIGINAL DANCE GOLDEN OLDIES
CD Set _____ 55525
Laserlight / Nov '94 / Target/BMG.

50'S - JUKE JOINT BLUES, THE
Three o'clock blues: King, B.B. / Long tall woman: James, Elmore / Ramblin' on my mind: Gilmore, Boyd / Gonna let you go: Turner, Babyface / Love my baby: Bland, Bobby & Junior Parker / Riding in the moonlight: Howlin' Wolf / 44 blues: Curtis, James Peck / Step back baby: Blair, Sunny / This is the end: Reed, James / Juke head boogie: Hopkins, Lightnin' / Down in New Orleans: Smith, Little George / Monte Carlo: Dixie Blues Boys / Doin' the town: Dixon, Floyd / Just got in from Texas: Gordon, Roscoe / Big mouth: Nelson, Jimmy 'T-99' / Have you ever: Watson, Mercy Dee / Sputnit blues: Robertson, Walter / Prowling blues: Fuller, Johnny / Going to New Orleans: Tanner, Kid / Good morning little angel: Louis, Joe Hill / Panic's on (Available on CD only): McCracklin, Jimmy / What's the matter with you (Available on CD only): Horton, Big Walter
CD _____ CDCH 216
Ace / Jul '87 / Pinnacle / Cadillac / Complete/Pinnacle.

50'S - R & B VOCAL GROUPS, THE
Rock bottom: Rams / Hold me, thrill me, chill me: Flairs / My darling, my sweet: Flairs / I made a vow: Robins / Please remember my heart: Five Bells / My cutie pie: Five Bells / Girl in my dreams: Cliques / Even since your sweet going gone: Hawks / It's all over: Hawks / Please don't go: Chanters / Tick tock: Marvin & Johnny / Why did I fall in love: Jacks / Sweet thing: Maye, Arthur Lee & The Crowns / Hands across the table: Cadets / Hey Rube: Rocketeers / It won't take long/Native girl: Native Boys / Farewell: Relf, Bobby & The Laurels / At last: Berry, Richard & the Dreamers / Please please baby: Five Hearts / Love me love me love me (Available on CD only): Chimes / I love you, yes I do (Available on CD only): Marvin,
CD _____ CDCH 212
Ace / Jul '87 / Pinnacle / Cadillac / Complete/Pinnacle.

50'S - ROCKABILLY FEVER, THE
I guess it's meant that way: Cupp, Pat / Long gone daddy: Cupp, Pat / Don't do me no wrong: Cupp, Pat / Everybody's movin': Glenn, Glen / If I had me a woman: Glenn, Glen / I don't know when: Harris, Hal / True affection: Johnson, Byron / Be boppin' daddy: Cole, Les & The Echoes / Rock little baby: Cole, Les & The Echoes / My big fat baby: Hall, Sonny & The Echoes / Rock my wigwam mama: Cole, Don / Nuthin' but a nuthin': Stewart, Jimmy & His Nighthawks / Wild wild party: Feathers, Charlie / Pink cadillac: Todd, Johnny / Slippin' and slidin': Davis, Link / All the time: Le Beef, Sleepy / Go home letter: Barber, Glen / Boppin' wigwam Willie: Scott, Ray / I can't find the doorknob: Jimmy & Johnny / Jitterbop baby (Available

on CD only): Harris, Hal / Little bit more (Available on CD only): La Beef, Sleepy
CD _____ CDCH 218
Ace / Jul '87 / Pinnacle / Cadillac / Complete/Pinnacle.

50'S NO.1'S VOL.1
(Ballads)
Magic moments: Como, Perry / Whatever will be will be (Que sera sera): Day, Doris / It's almost tomorrow: Dream Weavers / Cherry pink and apple blossom white: Prado, Perez / On the street where you live: Damone, Vic / Little things mean a lot: Kallen, Kitty / Cara mia: Whitfield, David / Answer me: Laine, Frankie / Hold my hand: Cornell, Don / Mambo Italiano: Clooney, Rosemary / Unchained melody: Young, Jimmy / It's all in the game: Edwards, Tommy / Carolina moon: Francis, Connie / Rock 'n' roll waltz: Starr, Kay
CD _____ OG 3501
Old Gold / May '88 / Carlton Home Entertainment.

50'S REVISITED, THE
Yellow rose of Texas: Miller, Mitch / Rawhide: Laine, Frankie / I'll never stop loving you: Day, Doris / Mangoes: Clooney, Rosemary / If you believe: Ray, Johnnie / Stranger in paradise: Bennett, Tony / Hawkye: Laine, Frankie / Somebody stole my gal: Ray, Johnnie / Secret love: Day, Doris / Chicka boom: Mitchell, Guy / Hey there: Ray, Johnnie / Strange lady in town: Laine, Frankie / Butterfly: Williams, Andy / Affair to remember: Damone, Vic / Where the wind blows: Laine, Frankie / Feet up: Mitchell, Guy
CD _____ PWKS 4152
Carlton Home Entertainment / Aug '94 / Carlton Home Entertainment.

50TH ANNIVERSARY SALUTE
CD _____ AVC 544
Avid / Jun '94 / Avid/BMG / Koch.

55 MILES FROM TEXACO
CD _____ EFA 06187CD
House In Motion / Jul '93 / SRD.

60 FAVOURITE HYMNS
(3CD Set)
Soldiers of Christ arise: Massed Male Voice Choirs Of Honley, Skelmanthorpe & Gledholt / O worship the king: Brighouse & Rastrick Band / All creatures of our God and King: Brighouse & Rastrick Band / Sun of my soul: Brighouse & Rastrick Band / Leads us Heavenly Father lead us: Brighouse & Rastrick Band / O love that wilt not let me go: Brighouse & Rastrick Band / Come ye thankful people come: Brighouse & Rastrick Band / Love divine: Brighouse & Rastrick Band / Crown him with many crowns: Brighouse & Rastrick Band / How sweet the name of Jesus sounds: Brighouse & Rastrick Band / Jesus keeps me near the cross: Brighouse & Rastrick Band / Now thank we all our God: Brighouse & Rastrick Band / All glory laud and honour: Brighouse & Rastrick Band / Were you there when they crucified my Lord: Wallace, Ian / How great thou art: Wallace, Ian / I will sing the wondrous story: Wallace, Ian / Behold me standing at the door: Wallace, Ian / He hideth my soul: Wallace, Ian / When I survey the wondrous cross: Wallace, Ian / Swing low sweet chariot: Wallace, Ian / In the sweet by and by: Wallace, Ian / Steal away: Wallace, Ian / In heavenly love abiding: Wallace, Ian / For all the saints: Wallace, Ian / Deep river: Wallace, Ian / There is a greenhill far away: Massed Choirs / Rock of ages: Massed Choirs / Lord's my shepherd: Massed Choirs / Who is on the Lord's side: Massed Choirs / To God be the glory: Massed Choirs / Onward Christian soldiers: Massed Choirs / All hail the power of Jesus' name: Massed Choirs / O for a thousand tongues to sing: Massed Choirs / All in the April evening: Massed Choirs / Let all the world in every corner sing: Massed Choirs / He lives: Massed Choirs / Praise my soul: Massed Choirs / Jesus shall reign where'er the sun: Massed Choirs / O Jesus I have promised: Carousel Children / Lord of the dance: Carousel Children / Jesu lover of my soul: Monese, Valerie / Sweet hour of prayer: Monese, Valerie / My Jesus I love thee: Monese, Valerie / Amazing grace: Monese, Valerie / King of love my shepherd is: Monese, Valerie / Lord of all hopefulness: Monese, Valerie / I am so glad: Heatherbell Children
CD Set _____ CDTRBOX 204
Trio / Oct '95 / EMI.

60 GREAT BLUES RECORDINGS
Jealous woman: Walker, T-Bone / I'm sinking: Fulson, Lowell / Same old lonesome day: Fulson, Lowell / Rocks in my pillow: Brown, Roy / We can't make it: King, B.B. / Time to say goodbye: King, B.B. / Please love me: King, B.B. / Past day: King, B.B. / My own fault darlin': King, B.B. / T.B. blues: Witherspoon, Jimmy / I'm going around in circles: Witherspoon, Jimmy / Telephone blues: Smith, George / Women in my life: Hooker, John Lee / Boogie chillun: Hooker, John Lee / Crawlin' kingsnake: Hooker, John Lee / Heartache baby: Louis, Joe Hill

/ Walkin' talkin' blues: Louis, Joe Hill / Going down slow: Louis, Joe Hill / When night falls: Carter, Goree / Sinful woman: James, Elmore / I believe: James, Elmore / Dust my blues: James, Elmore / Sho' nuff I do: James, Elmore / That's all I care: Dixon, Floyd / Houston jump: Dixon, Floyd / Draftin' blues: Dixon, Floyd / Hey Mr. Porter: Smith, George / Good lovin': Bland, Bobby / Summertime: King, Saunders / Everything about midnight: King, Saunders / I'm so worried: King, Saunders / I ain't in the mood: Humes, Helen / Central Avenue blues: Crayton, Pee Wee / If that's the way you feel: Champion, Mickey / Best friend: Champion, Mickey / Gene's guitar blues: Phillips, Gene / Gene jumps the blues: Phillips, Gene / Jockey blues: Turner, Big Joe / Playful baby: Turner, Big Joe / Johnny's lowdown blues: Fuller, Johnny / Riding in the moonlight: Howlin' Wolf / How many more times: Wilson, Smokey / Straighten up baby: Wilson, Smokey / Standing in the backdoor crying: Thomas, Lafayette / Tired of everybody: Parker, Johnny / Dr. Brown: Reed, James / Lonesome dog blues: Hopkins, Lightnin' / Jake head boogie: Hopkins, Lightnin' / Mississippi blues: Dixon, Floyd Trio / John Henry: Pinetop Slim / Thrill is gone: Hawkins, Roy / Tennessee woman: Robinson, Fenton / Applejack boogie: Pinetop Slim / Hardhearted woman: Horton, Big Walter / Black gal: Horton, Big Walter / Big chested mama: Cotton, Sylvester / Love me baby: Bland, Bobby & Junior Parker / I may be crazy baby but (I ain't no fool): Smith, Geechie / Cold blooded woman: Great Gates / I cried: Ace, Johnny
CD Set _____ CBOXCD 3
Cascade / Jan '92 / Hot Shot.

60 MORE CLASSIC DANCE HITS OF THE 70'S
Rock your baby: McCrae, George / Shake your body: Jacksons / Car wash: Rose Royce / You see the trouble with me: White, Barry / Boogie oogie oogie: Taste Of Honey / Yum yum (gimme some): Fatback Band / Blame it on the boogie: Jacksons / We are family: Sister Sledge / Good times: Chic / Young hearts run free: Staton, Candi / Take that to the bank: Shalamar / Do what you wanna do: T-Connection / No that we've found love: Third World / Can you feel the force: Real Thing / Hi-Tension: Hi-Tension / Dancing in the city: Marshall Hain / Silly games: Kay, Janet / Up town top ranking: Althia & Donna / British hustle: Hi-Tension / Reach out, I'll be there: Gaynor, Gloria / Footsee: Wigan's Chosen Few / Reaching for the best: Exciters / That's the way I like it: K.C. & The Sunshine Band / Funky Nassau: Beginning Of The End / Play that funky music: Wild Cherry / Disco stomp: Bohannon, Hamilton / I love music: O'Jays / Best of my love: Emotions / This will be: Cole, Natalie / Right back where we started from: Nightingale, Maxine
CD Set _____ TCD 70
Connoisseur / Sep '91 / Pinnacle.

60'S BOX SET, THE
CD Set _____ SETCD 002
Stardust / Jan '94 / Carlton Home Entertainment.

60'S CLASSICS
CD Set _____ DCDCD 205
Castle / Jun '95 / BMG.

60'S DANCE PARTY: LET'S DANCE
CD _____ MU 5002
Musketeer / Oct '92 / Koch.

60'S HITS COLLECTION: AT THE HOP
Leader of the pack: Shangri-Las / Let's twist again: Checker, Chubby / Then he kissed me: Crystals / Runaround Sue: Dion / Good golly Miss Molly: Little Richard / Blueberry Hill: Domino, Fats
CD _____ MU 8006
Musketeer / Nov '93 / Koch.

60'S HITS COLLECTION: DA DOO RON RON
Sweet talking guy: Chiffons / Tell Laura I love her: Valance, Ricky / Rhythm of the rain: Cascades / Will you still love me tomorrow: Shirelles / Chapel of love: Dixie Cups / Surfin' safari: Beach Boys
CD _____ MU 8005
Musketeer / Dec '93 / Koch.

60'S HITS COLLECTION: DOWNTOWN
Downtown: Clark, Petula / Ferry 'cross the mersey: Gerry & The Pacemakers / Happy together: Turtles / Young girl: Puckett, Gary / Calender girl: Sedaka, Neil / Hold me: Proby, P.J.
CD _____ MU 8002
Musketeer / Nov '93 / Koch.

60'S HITS COLLECTION: EVERLASTING LOVE
Wild thing: Troggs / Breaking up is hard to do: Sedaka, Neil / Everlasting love: Love Affair / Walkin' back to happiness: Shapiro, Helen / Crying game: Berry, Dave / California dreamin': Mamas & Papas
CD _____ MU 8001
Musketeer / Nov '93 / Koch.

60'S HITS COLLECTION: SILENCE IS GOLDEN
Don't take your love to town: Rogers, Kenny / Silence is golden: Tremeloes / Save the last dance for me: Drifters / No milk today:

Herman's Hermits / Wishin' and hopin': Merseybeats / Bobby's girl: Maughan, Susan
CD _____ MU 8004
Musketeer / Nov '93 / Koch.

60'S HITS COLLECTION: UP ON THE ROOF
I'm into something good: Herman's Hermits / Do you love me: Poole, Brian / Sugar sugar: Archies / Hello Mary Lou: Nelson, Rick / Night has a thousand eyes: Vee, Bobby / Moon river: Williams, Danny
CD _____ MU 8003
CD _____ MU 7003
Musketeer / Nov '93 / Koch.

60'S LOVE SONGS
When a man loves a woman: Sledge, Percy / Crying game: Berry, Dave / Just a matter of time: Benton, Brook / Don't let the sun catch you crying: Gerry & The Pacemakers / Maria: Proby, P.J. / No greater love: Dove, Ronnie / So much in love: Tymes / You don't have to be a baby to cry: Caravelles / Beautiful you: Sedaka, Neil / Wishing and hopin': Merseybeats / Hello little girl: Fourmost / Heartaches: Marcels / Day without you: Love Affair / Chapel of love: Dixie Cups / Tell him: Davis, Billie / Softly whispering I love you: New Congregation / Rhythm of the rain: Cascades / Girl's in love with you: Warwick, Dionne
CD _____ WPCD 012
Stardust / Oct '90 / Carlton Home Entertainment.

60'S LOVE SONGS: DRIFT AWAY
CD _____ MU 5001
Musketeer / Oct '92 / Koch.

60'S MANIA
CD _____ WPCD 014
Stardust / Oct '90 / Carlton Home Entertainment.

60'S NO.1'S VOL.1
(Pop Hits)
Are you lonesome tonight: Presley, Elvis / Johnny remember me: Leyton, Johnny / Good timin': Jones, Jimmy / Poetry in motion: Tillotson, Johnny / Blue moon: Marcels / Running bear: Preston, Johnny / Runaway: Shannon, Del / Wooden heart: Presley, Elvis / Not rocker: B. Bumble & The Stingers / Sailor: Clark, Petula / On the rebound: Cramer, Floyd / Why: Newley, Anthony / Sweets for my sweet: Searchers / My old man's a dustman: Donegan, Lonnie
CD _____ OG 3512
Old Gold / Jul '89 / Carlton Home Entertainment.

60'S NO.1'S VOL.2
(Pop Hits)
You've lost that lovin' feelin': Righteous Brothers / Always something there to remind me: Shaw, Sandie / Tired of waiting for you: Kinks / Make it easy on yourself: Walker Brothers / I've gotta get a message to you: Bee Gees / All or nothing: Small Faces / I'm alive: Hollies / Yeh yeh: Fame, Georgie / It's not unusual: Jones, Tom / With a girl like you: Troggs / Whiter shade of pale: Procul Harum / Do it again: Beach Boys / Good, the bad and the ugly: Montenegro, Hugo / In the year 2525: Zager & Evans
CD _____ OG 3513
Old Gold / Jun '89 / Carlton Home Entertainment.

60'S NO.1'S VOL.4
Only the lonely: Orbison, Roy / Tower of strength: Vaughan, Frankie / Do you mind: Newley, Anthony / Diamonds: Harris, Jet & Tony Meehan / Go now: Moody Blues / Have I the right: Honeycombs / You don't have to say you love me: Springfield, Dusty / Do you love me: Poole, Brian & The Tremeloes / Don't throw your love away: Searchers / Long live love: Shaw, Sandie / Oh pretty woman: Orbison, Roy / Concrete and clay: Unit 4+2 / Ballad of Bonnie and Clyde: Fame, Georgie / Sugar sugar: Archies
CD _____ OG 3517
Old Gold / Sep '89 / Carlton Home Entertainment.

60'S PARTY HITS
CD _____ MATCD 222
Castle / Nov '93 / BMG.

60'S POP CLASSICS VOL.1
Itchycoop park: Small Faces / Cry like a baby: Box Tops / 24 Hours from Tulsa: Box Tops / Silence is golden: Tremeloes / Ob-la-di, ob-la-da: Marmalade / Hello Susie: Amen Corner / Runaway: Shannon, Del / Only you: Platters / Love letters: Lester, Ketty / Stand by me: King, Ben E. / He's so fine: Chiffons / Ferry cross the mersey: Gerry & The Pacemakers
CD _____ 74321339242
Camden / Jan '96 / BMG.

60'S POP CLASSICS VOL.2
Go now: Moody Blues / Man of the world: Fleetwood Mac / In the year 2525: Zager & Evans / Captain of your ship: Zager & Evans / Yeah yeah: Fame, Georgie / Out of time: Farlowe, Chris / I'm a believer: Monkees / If paradise is half as nice: Amen Corner / Light my fire: Feliciano, Jose / Harlem shuffle: Bob & Earl / Leader of the pack: Shangri-Las / I'm believer: Monkees

60'S POP CLASSICS VOL.3
Good bad and the ugly: Montenegro, Hugo / Ain't got no - I got life: Simone, Nina / Eve of destruction: McGuire, Barry / I'm your puppet: Purify, James & Bobby / Simon says: 1910 Fruitgum Company / Waterloo sunset: Kinks / Catch the wind: Donovan / Needles and pions: Searchers / Yummy yummy yummy: Ohio Express / First cut is the deepest: Arnold, P.P. / Let the heartache begin: Baldry, Long John / Aquarius/ Let the sun shine: Fifth Dimension
CD _____ 74321339262
Camden / Jan '96 / BMG.

60'S ROCK
CD _____ WPCD 015
Stardust / Oct '90 / Carlton Home Entertainment.

60'S SENSATIONS
CD _____ WPCD 013
Stardust / Oct '90 / Carlton Home Entertainment.

60'S SMASH HITS
Let's twist again: Checker, Chubby / Speedy Gonzalez: Boone, Pat / Chapel of love: Dixie Cups / Wooly bully: Sam The Sham / Night has a thousand eyes: Vee, Bobby / Sheila: Roe, Tommy / Remember (walkin' in the sand): Shangri-Las / Judy in disguise: Fred, John / Deep purple: Tempo, Nino & April Stevens / Hitchin' a ride: Vanity Fair / Surfer girl: Beach Boys / Somewhere: Proby, P.J. / Save the last dance for me: Drifters / Help me Rhonda: Jan & Dean
CD _____ WPCD 007
Stardust / Aug '93 / Carlton Home Entertainment.

60'S SOUL
CD _____ WPCD 009
Stardust / Oct '90 / Carlton Home Entertainment.

60'S SOUL CLASSICS
Rescue me: Fontella Bass / Hi-heel sneakers: Tucker, Tommy / Clapping song: Ellis, Shirley / Holy cow: Dorsey, Lee / In crowd: Gray, Dobie / Private number: Clay, Judy & William Bell / Heat and shout: Isley Brothers / Wade in the water: Lewis, Ramsey / I can't believe what you say: Turner, Ike & Tina / Hey girl don't bother me: Tams / It's all right: Impressions / Knock on wood: Floyd, Eddie / Working in a coalmine: Dorsey, Lee / Peaches 'n' cream: Ikettes / But I do: Henry, Clarence 'Frogman' / Barefootin': Parker, Robert / Tell it like it is: Neville, Aaron / Shoop shoop song (It's in his kiss): Everett, Betty / Time is tight: Booker T & The MG's / Keep on pushing: Impressions
CD _____ PWKS 4196
Carlton Home Entertainment / Oct '94 / Carlton Home Entertainment.

60'S SOUL CLUB
Summertime: Stewart, Billy / Farther on up the road: Simon, Joe / Show me: Tex, Joe / How I miss you baby: Womack, Bobby / Barefootin': Parker, Robert / Getting mighty crowded: Everett, Betty / Get on up: Esquires / Rescue me: Bass, Fontella / Come on sock it to me: Johnson, Syl / Land of 1000 dances: Kenner, Chris / Ride your pony: Dorsey, Lee / Selfish one: Ross, Jackie / Lover's holiday: Scott, Peggy & Jo Jo Benson / Nothing can stop me: Chandler, Gene
CD _____ CDINS 5005
Instant / Jul '89 / Charly.

60'S SUPER GROUPS
Surfer girl: Beach Boys / In the one: Gerry & The Pacemakers / Tobacco Road: Nashville Teens / That same old feeling: Pickettywitch / I think of you: Merseybeats / Here it comes again: Fortunes / If you gotta make a fool of somebody: Freddie & The Dreamers / Can't take my eyes off you: Jay & The Americans / Hippy hippy shake: Swinging Blue Jeans / How do you do it: Gerry & The Pacemakers / Sorrow: Merseys / I'm telling you now: Freddie & The Dreamers / Girl like you: Troggs / Crying in the chapel: Platters / You've got your troubles: Fortunes / To know him is to love him: Teddy Bears / Saturday night at the movies: Drifters / Silence is golden: Tremeloes
CD _____ WPCD 010
Stardust / Oct '90 / Carlton Home Entertainment.

60'S SUPER STARS
CD _____ WPCD 016
Stardust / Oct '90 / Carlton Home Entertainment.

60'S THE HITS GO ON: LOVE IS ALL AROUND
CD _____ MU 5050
Musketeer / Oct '92 / Koch.

60'S UK HITS COLLECTION: TWIST AND SHOUT
CD _____ MU 5053
Musketeer / Oct '92 / Koch.

60'S USA HITS COLLECTION: SWEET TALKIN' GUY
CD _____ MU 5052
Musketeer / Oct '92 / Koch.

60S COLLECTION
(3CD/MC Set)
CD Set _____ TBXCD 501
TrueTrax / Jan '96 / THE.

70'S BLOCKBUSTERS
Blockbuster: Sweet / Tiger feet: Mud / Devil gate drive: Quatro, Suzi / Rasputin: Boney M / Under the moon of love: Showaddywaddy / I think I love you: Partridge Family / Walk on the wild side: Reed, Lou / Seasons in the sun: Jacks, Terry / You to me are everything: Real Thing / So you win again: Hot Chocolate / Rock the boat: Hues Corporation / It's in his kiss: Lewis, Linda
CD _____ 74321339332
Camden / Jan '96 / BMG.

70'S COLLECTION
(3CD/MC Set)
CD Set _____ TBXCD 502
TrueTrax / Jan '96 / THE.

70'S GLAM ROCK BLITZ
CD _____ PWKS 4198
Carlton Home Entertainment / Nov '94 / Carlton Home Entertainment.

70'S NO.1'S VOL.3
Can't give you anything (but my love): Stylistics / You won't find another fool like me: New Seekers / Gonna make you a star: Essex, David / Love grows (where my Rosemary goes): Edison Lighthouse / Don't go breaking my heart: John, Elton & Kiki Dee / How can I be sure: Cassidy, David / Yellow river: Christie / Tie a yellow ribbon round the old oak tree: Dawn / I love you because: Glitter, Gary / Sunday girl: Blondie / Bye bye baby: Bay City Rollers / When a child is born: Mathis, Johnny / Mamma mia: Abba / Ms. Grace: Tymes
CD _____ OG 3518
Old Gold / Sep '89 / Carlton Home Entertainment.

70'S NO.1'S VOL.4
Spirit in the sky: Greenbaum, Norman / Telegram Sam: T. Rex / Baby jump: Mungo Jerry / I hear you knocking: Edmunds, Dave / Maggie May: Stewart, Rod / Voodoo chile: Hendrix, Jimi Experience / Hot love: T. Rex / Woodstock: Matthew's Southern Comfort / Rubber bullets: 10cc / I'm the leader of the gang (I am): Glitter, Gary / Down down: Status Quo / Heart of glass: Blondie / I don't like Mondays: Boomtown Rats
CD _____ OG 3519
Old Gold / Sep '89 / Carlton Home Entertainment.

70'S SENSATIONS
Roll away the stone: Mott The Hoople / God gave rock 'n' roll to you: Argent / Mind blowing decisions: Heatwave / Year of decision: Three Degrees / Lamplight: Essex, David / Summer of '42: Biddu Orchestra / D.I.V.O.R.C.E.: Wynette, Tammy / Chosen few: Dooleys / When will I see you again: Quatro, Suzi / Groovie line: Heatwave / Wake up everybody: Melvin, Harold & The Bluenotes / Sylvia's mother: Dr. Hook / There are more questions than answers: Nash, Johnny / Anthem: New Seekers / Wanted: Dooleys / Stop me: Ocean, Billy / All the way from Memphis: Mott The Hoople
CD _____ PWKS 4158
Carlton Home Entertainment / Aug '94 / Carlton Home Entertainment.

70'S SOUL HOT WAX VOL.2
Don't hurt me no more: Woods, Wendy / All I want from you is your love: Neal, C.C. / Come and ask me: 5 Wagers / Something I gotta am: Universal Mind / What's bothering me: Thomas, Timmy / You can win: Bileo / Heartaches and pain: Pages / Some kind of man: Pride, Passion & Pain / From the top of my heart: Wells, Wes & the Steelers / Wrong crowd: Prince George / You're mine: Veroneeca / Lord what's happening to your people: Smith, Kenny / Come back: Fantastic Puzzles / He's always somewhere around: Gerrard, Donny / I can make it on my own: Simmons, Vessie / Bet you if you ask around: Velvet / Strange Travelwinds / I want to be loved: Stevens & Foster / Let's spend some time together: Houston, Larry / Love built on a strong foundation: Big Jim's Border Crossing / Oh happy day: Flame 'n' King / Turning point: Simmons, Mack / Have love will travel: James, Rosey / Let's get nasty: Stephens, Chuck / Honey vision: Innervision / Alone with no love: Rock Candy
CD _____ GSCD 035
Goldmine / Apr '94 / Vital.

70'S SOUL HOT WAX VOL.3
I've got to have your love: hunt, Pierre / I'm your pimp: Skull Snaps / Man of money: Barkley, Tyrone / I can make him loving you: Anderson Brothers / Your smallest wish: 21st Century Ltd / Dancing on a daydream: Soulvation Army / Time passed by: Bynum, James / You only live once: Imperial Wonders / Happy: Velvet Hammer / It's not where you start: Davis, Luckey / Sweet love: Cody, Black / Like taking candy from a baby: Brown, J.T. / Mama I wish I stayed at home: Chaplin, Denice / Take me as I am: Hughes, Freddie / When you see what you want: Weathers, Oscar / Operataor operator: Baker, Johnny / I'm gonna get you: Floyd, Frankie / World wide: Drinkyard, Kevin / Paradise: Neo Experience / Love will

turn around: Entertains / My baby's gone: Blade Family / I'm a winner: Just Bobby / I won't be completely happy: Cantera / Don't waste your time girl: Miller, Catherine
CD _____ GSCD 037
Goldmine / Aug '94 / Vital.

70'S SOUL SEARCHERS
It really hurts me girl: Carstairs / Ain't nothin' wrong makin' love: Jones, Jimmy / Economy: Mitchell, Lee / Shady lady: Newton, Bobby / Spellbound: Everett, Frank / You better keep her: Holmes, Marvin & Justice / When the fuel runs out: Ambitions / I can't let you walk away: Caress / I've got to start my life over: Houston, Larry / You're my main squeeze: Crystal Motion / Loneliness: Will, David / Shy guy: Baker, Johnny / Baby hard times: Love, Dave / Dance all nite: Master Plan / If it wasn't for my baby: Four Sonics / Secret place: Brothers / In a world so cold: St. Germain, Tyrone / I hope you really love me: Family Circle / Give in to the power of love: Committee / Over the top: Dawson, Roy
CD _____ GSCD 024
Goldmine / Nov '93 / Vital.

72 TRAD JAZZ CLASSICS
CD Set _____ MBSCD 413
Castle / Jul '95 / BMG.

80 SUPER BACKTRACKS
(Hits Of The 60's & 70's)
Itsy bitsy teeny weeny yellow polka dot bikini: Hyland, Brian / Calendar girl: Sedaka, Neil / Michael, row the boat ashore: Highwayman / Runaround Sue: Dion / Lion sleeps tonight: Tokens / Quarter to three: Bonds, Gary U.S. / Hello Mary Lou: Nelson, Rick / Vacation: Francis, Connie / Don't treat me like a child: Shapiro, Helen / Where have all the flowers gone: Kingston Trio / Locomotion: Little Eva / Sherry: Four Seasons / I will follow him: March, Little Peggy / Surfin' USA: Beach Boys / Pretty little baby: Francis, Connie / Surf city: Jan & Dean / Mr. Bassman: Cymbal, Johnny / Walk right in: Rooftop Singers / Hello Dolly: Armstrong, Louis / World without love: Peter & Gordon / Oh pretty woman: Orbison, Roy / House of the rising sun: Animals / Do wah diddy diddy: Manfred Mann / You really love me: Kinks / Mr. Lonely: Vinton, Bobby / Love potion no.9: Searchers / You've lost that lovin' feelin': Righteous Brothers / Mrs. Brown you've got a lovely daughter: Herman's Hermits / Do you believe in magic: Lovin' Spoonful / Don't let me be misunderstood: Animals / Bus stop: Hollies / Good vibrations: Beach Boys / Last train to Clarksville: Monkees / Sunshine superman: Donovan / Summer in the city: Lovin' Spoonful / Monday, Monday: Mamas & Papas / You don't have to say you love me: Springfield, Dusty / Sunny: Hebb, Bobby / I love you: Zombies / Happy together: Turtles / Somebody to love: Jefferson Airplane / San Francisco: McKenzie, Scott / Whiter shade of pale: Procul Harum / Daydream believer: Monkees / To sir with love: Lulu / I say a little prayer: Warwick, Dionne / Let's live for today: Grassroots / Georgy girl: Seekers / Can't take my eyes off you: Valli, Frankie / By the time I get to Phoenix: Campbell, Glen / Simon says: 1910 Fruitgum Company / Born to be wild: Steppenwolf / White room: Cream / Honey: Goldsboro, Bobby / Lady Willpower: Puckett, Gary / Yummy yummy yummy: Ohio Express / Wasn't born to follow: Byrds / Weight: Band / Love me tonight: Jones, Tom / Release me: Humperdinck, Engelbert / Time of the season: Zombies / Aquarius: 5th Dimension / In the year 2525: Zager & Evans / Spinning wheel: Blood, Sweat & Tears / Sugar sugar: Archies / Get together: Youngbloods / Venus: Shocking Blue / Black magic woman: Santana / Raindrops keep falling on my head: Thomas, B.J. / Layla: Derek & The Dominoes / Rose garden: Anderson, Lynn / Joy to the world: Three Dog Night / Maggie May: Stewart, Rod / Metal guru: T. Rex / American pie: McLean, Don / Without you: Nilsson, Harry / It never rains in Southern California: Harmond, Albert / Gypsies, tramps and thieves: Cher / Alone again (naturally): O'Sullivan, Gilbert / Your song: John, Elton
CD Set _____ SBTCD 801
Connoisseur / Oct '89 / Pinnacle.

80'S ALBUM
CD _____ RADCD 09
Global / Apr '95 / BMG.

80'S REVISITED VOL.2, THE
(Hit City)
Total eclipse of the heart: Tyler, Bonnie / Goody two shoes: Adam Ant / Love and pride: King / Pretty in pink: Psychedelic Furs / (Feels like) Heaven: Friction Factory / Don't talk to me about love: Altered Images / Take it on the run: REO Speedwagon / One rule for you: After The Fire / Down under: Men At Work / Kings of the wild frontier: Adam & The Ants / Dog eat dog: Adam & The Ants / I could be happy: Altered Images / Who can it be now: Men At Work / Alone without you: King / January February: Dickson, Barbara / Keep on loving you: REO Speedwagon / Susanna: Art Company / Holding out for a hero: Tyler, Bonnie
CD _____ PWKS 4063
Carlton Home Entertainment / Jul '91 / Carlton Home Entertainment.

94 & 10TH - A DECADE OF 4TH & BROADWAY
Somebody else's guy: Brown, Jocelyn / Thinking about your love: Skipworth & Turner / Seventh heaven: Guthrie, Gwen / Gotta get you home tonight: Wilde, Eugene / I surrender to your love: By All Means / Let's start over: Jaye, Miles / My one temptation: Paris, Mica / Love supreme: Downing, Will / Teardrops: Womack & Womack / Love makes the world go round: Don-E / Where is the love: Paris, Mica & Will Downing / Real love: Divza Bone / Try my love: Washburn, Lalomie / Way we are: Affair / Lite up your life: Act Of Faith / King of rock: Run DMC / Drop the bomb: Trouble Funk / Boops (here to go): Sly & Robbie / Chief Inspector: Badarou, Wally / Paid in full: Eric B & Rakim / Friends and countrymen: Wild Bunch / Straight outta Compton: N.W.A. / Television, the drug of the nation: Disposable Heroes Of Hiphoprisy / Wash your face in my sink: Dream Warriors / Turn on, tune in, cop out: Freakpower / Connected: Stereo MC's / It was a good day: Ice Cube / Aftermath: Tricky / Braindead: Bomb The Bass / Beat at slavery: Silent Eclipse
CD Set _____ BRCDD 614
4th & Broadway / Aug '94 / PolyGram.

100 BLUES AND SOUL GREATS
Dimples: Hooker, John Lee / You'll be mine: Howlin' Wolf / My babe: Little Walter / I got it bad and that ain't good: Holiday, Billie / Stuff you gonna watch: Waters, Muddy / Born blind: Williamson, Sonny Boy / Boogie chillun: Williamson, Sonny Boy / Catfish blues: King, B.B. / Who's been talkin': Howlin' Wolf / Early in the morning: Milton, Roy / Please don't talk about me when I'm gone: Holiday, Billie / Poor Howard Green corn: Holiday, Billie / Sad hours: Little Walter / Dust my broom: James, Elmore / Iodine in my coffee: Waters, Muddy / Tupelo: Hooker, John Lee / Nice work if you can get it: Holiday, Billie / Wang dang doodle: Howlin' Wolf / Sixty minute man: Little Walter / Little baby: Howlin' Wolf / Drug store woman: Hooker, John Lee / B.B. boogie: King, B.B. / Work with me: Williamson, Sonny Boy / Close to you: Waters, Muddy / Red rooster: Howlin' Wolf / Boom boom: King, B.B. / You gonna miss me: Waters, Muddy / Last night: Little Walter / You will bring me: Williamson, Sonny Boy / Walkin' and cryin': King, B.B. / Boll weevil blues: Leadbelly / Shake for me: Howlin' Wolf / Frisco blues: Howlin' Wolf / Don't explain: Holiday, Billie / Look on yonder wall: James, Elmore / Mean red spider: Waters, Muddy / Blues with a feeling: Little Walter / Spoonful: Howlin' Wolf / Please love me: King, B.B. / No shoes: Hooker, John Lee / I loves you Porgy: Holiday, Billie / Gallis pole: Leadbelly / Keep it to yourself: Leadbelly / Diamonds at your feet: Waters, Muddy / Can't hold out much longer: Little Walter / I'm in the mood: Hooker, John Lee / Goin' down slow: Howlin' Wolf / Little rain: Reed, Jimmy / Baby please don't go: Waters, Muddy / Hobo blues: Hooker, John Lee / Down in the bottom: Howlin' Wolf / Fine and mellow: Holiday, Billie / Don't lose your eye: Williamson, Sonny Boy / Joke: Little Walter / Blue tail fly: Leadbelly / Walkin' and talkin': Charles, Ray / Baby Lee: Hooker, John Lee / Trainfare blues: Waters, Muddy / Back door man: Howlin' Wolf / It hurts me too: James, Elmore / Fooling myself: Holiday, Billie / Everyday I have the blues: King, B.B. / Mean old world: Little Walter / Trouble blues: Hooker, John Lee / Howlin' for my baby: Howlin' Wolf / Where can you be: Reed, Jimmy / One way out: Williamson, Sonny Boy / Hey now: Charles, Ray / Easy to remember: Holiday, Billie / Old settin' here drinkin': Holiday, Billie / One time shimmy: Hooker, John Lee / Tell me: Howlin' Wolf / How long: Leadbelly / I got a rich man's woman: Waters, Muddy / When your lover has gone: Holiday, Billie / My baby has walked off: Howlin' Wolf / Little wheel: Hooker, John Lee / How blue can you get: King, B.B. / Off the wall: Little Walter / Cool disposition: Williamson, Sonny Boy / I'm wonderin' and wonderin': Charles, Ray / Big fat woman: Charles, Ray / Whiskey and women: Hooker, John Lee / Killing floor: Howlin' Wolf / Easy to remember (2): Holiday, Billie / Mean mistreater: Waters, Muddy / Coming home: James, Elmore / You better watch yourself: Little Walter / Moanin' at midnight: Little Walter / Process: Hooker, John Lee / In New Orleans: Leadbelly / Commit a crime: Howlin' Wolf / Dusty road: Hooker, John Lee / Last letter: Waters, Muddy / I ain't nobody's business: Holiday, Billie / I wonder who's kissing her now: Charles, Ray / What do you say: Hooker, John Lee / Hand in hand: James, Elmore
CD Set _____ TFP 006
Tring / Nov '92 / Tring / Prism.

100 COUNTRY CLASSICS
Reuben James: Rogers, Kenny / I believe: Laine, Frankie / You'll always have someone: Nelson, Willie / Wasted days and wasted nights: Fender, Freddy / Burning memories: Jennings, Waylon / Daddy: Fargo, Donna / Your tender years: Jones, George / Come on in: Cline, Patsy / Take these chains from my heart: Jones, George / Slippin' away: Fairchild, Barbara / Shine on Ruby Mountain: Rogers, Kenny / Ol' blue: Jackson, Stonewall / Ragged but right: Jones, George / Sticks and stones: Fargo, Donna / High noon: Laine, Frankie / Last letter: Drusky, Roy / Wild side of life: Fender, Freddy / Should I go home: Jackson, Stonewall / Dream baby: Jennings, Waylon / Crazy love: Fairchild, Barbara / Cry not for me: Cline, Patsy / Ruby, don't take your love to town: Rogers, Kenny / Luckenbach, Texas (Back to the basics of love): Drusky, Roy / Wishful thinking: Fargo, Donna / Money: Jennings, Waylon / Singin' the blues: Mitchell, Guy / Hello walls: Drusky, Roy / I've lost at love again: Cline, Patsy / Rain: Laine, Frankie / Home sweet home: Mandrell, Barbara / Wedding bells: Jones, George / Four in the morning: Young, Faron / Blue eyes cryin' in the rain: Drusky, Roy / Sally was a good old girl: Jennings, Waylon / It wasn't God who made honky tonk angels: Parton, Dolly / Touch me: Nelson, Willie / Release me: Mandrell, Barbara / Heartaches by the number: Mitchell, Guy / Shake 'em up roll 'em: Jackson, Stonewall / Sunshine: Rogers, Kenny / Things have gone to pieces: Jones, George / 9,999,999 Tears: Bailey, Razzy / I let my mind wander: Nelson, Willie / Crying: Jennings, Waylon / Honky tonk merry go round: Cline, Patsy / Ticket to nowhere: Rogers, Kenny / Keep off the grass: Jackson, Stonewall / Daddy sang bass: Perkins, Carl / Ghost: Nelson, Willie / If you ain't lovin' (you ain't livin'): Young, Faron / Kentucky means paradise: Mandrell, Barbara / Stop, look and listen: Cline, Patsy / I can't escape from you: Jones, George / Making believe: Wells, Kitty / Honky tonk angels: Parton, Dolly / Abilene: Jennings, Waylon / Ruby Tuesday: Williams, Don / Elvira: Rogers, Kenny / Maybellene: Robbins, Marty / Dream baby (2): Jennings, Waylon / Good rockin' tonight: Cline, Patsy / Jerry Lee / Little blossom: Parton, Dolly / From a Jack to a King: Miller, Ned / I can't find the time: Nelson, Willie / Love's gonna live here: Jennings, Waylon / Jambalaya: Jones, George / Where do we go from here: Williams, Don / Homemade lies: Rogers, Kenny / Turn the cards slowly: Cline, Patsy / Things to talk about: Jackson, Stonewall / Your song: Lee, Johnny / I didn't sleep a wink: Nelson, Willie / Cold coat heart: Jones, George / Town without pity: Pitney, Gene / Send me the pillow that you dream on: Locklin, Hank / Six days on the road: Dudley, Dave / Rose garden: Anderson, Lynn / Rawhide: Laine, Frankie / Walkin' after midnight: Cline, Patsy / Rhythm and booze: Owens, Buck / Wings of a dove: Husky, Ferlin / Always leaving, always gone: Rogers, Kenny / Ramblin' rose: Lee, Johnny / I feel sorry for him: Nelson, Willie / In care of the blues: Cline, Patsy / Have I stayed away too long: Ritter, Tex / I'll repossess my heart: Wells, Kitty / Waterloo: Jackson, Stonewall / Last day in the mines: Dudley, Dave / Moonlight gambler: Laine, Frankie / This ole house: Perkins, Carl / Candy store: Lee, Johnny / Don't think twice, it's alright: Jennings, Waylon / I can't get enough of you: Jackson, Stonewall / The heart you break may be your own: Cline, Patsy / I have good looking': Cash, Johnny / Open pit mine: Jones, George / If I don't understand: Nelson, Willie / Please don't let that woman get me: Jones, George
CD Set _____ TFP 003
Tring / Nov '88 / Tring / Prism.

100 CRUISIN' GREATS
CD Set _____ TFP 018
Tring / Nov '92 / Tring / Prism.

100 DANCE HITS OF THE 80'S
(5 CD Set)
Ride on time: Black Box / Pump up the jam: Technotronic / Only way is up: Yazz & The Plastic Population / Doctorin' the house: Coldcut & Yazz/The Plastic Population / People hold on: Coldcut & Lisa Stansfield / Numero uno (radio edit): Starlight / Lambada: Kaoma / Don't make me over: Sybil / Fake ('88): O'Neal, Alexander / Who found who: Jellybean & Elisa Fiorillo / Lovely day (sunshine mix): Withers, Bill / I really didn't mean it: Vandross, Luther / Tribute (right on): Pasadenas / Hustle (to the music): Funky Worm / Roadblock: Stock/Aitken/Waterman / Respectable: Mel & Kim / Loco in Acapulco: Four Tops / Shake your body: Abbott, Gregory / Real thing: Jellybean & Steven Dante / Automatic: Pointer Sisters / Midas touch: Midnight Star / In the name of love ('88): Thompson Twins / Let's hear it for the boy: Williams, Deniece / Now that we've found love: Third World / Lost in music: Sister Sledge / Ghostbusters: Parker, Ray / Lost in music: Five Star / Wap bam boogie: Matt Bianco / Dance sucker: Set The Tone / Dr. Beat: Estefan, Gloria & Miami Sound Machine / Takes a little time: Total Contrast / Let the music play: Shannon / Gotta get you home tonight: Wilde, Eugene / I wonder if I take you home: Lisa Lisa & Cult Jam & Full Force / She's strange: Cameo / Money's too tight to mention: Simply Red / I found lovin': Fatback Band / Finest: S.O.S. Band / I can't wait: Nu Shooz / Going to the bank: Commodores / Jump: Pointer Sisters / Dancin' in the key of life (remix): Arrington, Steve / Showing out (get fresh at the weekend): Mel & Kim / Rapper's delight: Sugarhill Gang / Breaks: Blow, Kurtis / Message: Grandmaster Flash / Get on the dancefloor: Base, Rob & D.J. E-Z Rock / I know you got soul: Eric B & Rakim / White lines (don't don't do it):

Grandmaster Flash & Melle Mel / (Nothing serious) just buggin': *Whistle* / Break 4 love: *Raze* / Alice I want you just for me: *Full Force* / Bang zoom (let's go go): *Real Roxanne* / Let's get brutal: *Nitro Deluxe* / Jack the groove: *Raze* / Jack le freak: *Chic* / Jack to the sound of the underground: *Hithouse* / Don't stop the music: *Yarbrough & Peoples* / Jump to the beat: *Lattisaw, Stacy* / Get down on it: *Kool & The Gang* / Jump to it: *Franklin, Aretha* / Stomp: *Brothers Johnson* / Love come down: *Nu, Evelyn 'Champagne'* / Funkin' for Jamaica: *Browne, Tom* / Searching: *Change* / I'll be good: *Rene & Angela* / Razzamatazz: *Jones, Quincy* / She's a bad mama jama: *Carlton, Carl* / Once bitten twice shy: *Williams, Vesta* / Back and forth: *Cameo* / Groove: *Franklin, Rodney* / Who's zoomin' who: *Franklin, Aretha* / I'm in love: *King, Evelyn 'Champagne'* / Walking on sunshine: *Rockers Revenge* / Juicy fruit: *Mtume* / Silver shadow: *Atlantic Starr* / Keepin' love new: *Johnson, Howard* / Save your love (for number one): *Rene & Angela* / Night to remember: *Shalamar* / Love town: *Newberry, Booker III* / We got the funk: *Positive Force* / Let's groove: *Earth, Wind & Fire* / Inside out: *Odyssey* / Going back to my roots: *Odyssey* / Rock!: *Hancock, Herbie* / Celebration: *Kool & The Gang* / Mama used to say: *Giscombe, Junior* / Sexual healing: *Gaye, Marvin* / Make that move: *Shalamar* / There it is: *Shalamar* / Candy girl: *New Edition* / I.O.U.: *Freeez* / Nineteen: *Hardcastle, Paul* / Funky town: *Lipps Inc.* / Walking into sunshine: *Central Line* / Southern Freeez: *Freeez* / Ai no corrida: *Jones, Quincy* / Everybody salsa: *Modern Romance* / Flashback: *Imagination* / And the beat goes on: *Whispers*

CD Set _____ **DBOXCD 101**
Connoisseur / Sep '90 / Pinnacle.

100 GREATEST JAZZ & SWING HITS 1917-1942
(4CD Set)
CD _____ **CDAFS 1036-4**
Affinity / Jun '93 / Charly / Cadillac / Jazz Music.

100 HITS OF THE 1950'S
CD Set _____ **SETCD 022**
Stardust / Jan '94 / Carlton Home Entertainment.

100 HITS OF THE 1960'S
CD Set _____ **SETCD 023**
Stardust / Jan '94 / Carlton Home Entertainment.

100 HITS OF THE FIFTIES
CD Set _____ **TFP 015**
Tring / Nov '92 / Tring / Prism.

100 HITS OF THE SEVENTIES
CD Set _____ **TFP 021**
Tring / Nov '92 / Tring / Prism.

100 HITS OF THE SIXTIES
Save the last dance for me: *Drifters* / Sweet talking guy: *Chiffons* / Let's twist again: *Checker, Chubby* / It's in his kiss (Shoop shoop song): *Everett, Betty* / Let it rock: *Berry, Chuck* / Surfin' safari: *Beach Boys* / Blueberry hill: *Domino, Fats* / Ride the wild surf: *Jan & Dean* / Every beat of my heart: *Knight, Gladys* / Hats off to Larry: *Shannon, Del* / When a man loves a woman: *Sledge, Percy* / Venus: *Avalon, Frankie* / Limbo rock: *Checker, Chubby* / Then he kissed me: *Crystals* / Leader of the pack: *Shangri-Las* / Venus in blue jeans: *Clanton, Jimmy* / Hold on I'm comin': *Sam & Dave* / On Broadway: *Drifters* / Sixteen candles: *Crests* / Rubber ball: *Vee, Bobby* / Sugar sugar: *Archies* / My guy: *Wells, Mary* / There's a kind of hush: *Herman's Hermits* / So sad the song: *Knight, Gladys* / Runaway: *Shannon, Del* / Judy in disguise: *Fred, John & His Playboy Band* / Up on the roof: *Drifters* / Surfin': *Beach Boys* / No particular place to go: *Berry, Chuck* / Letter full of tears: *Knight, Gladys* / Soul man: *Sam & Dave* / He's so fine: *Chiffons* / Devil or angel: *Vee, Bobby* / Twist: *Checker, Chubby* / You beat me to the punch: *Wells, Mary* / Da doo ron ron: *Crystals* / Tequila: *Champs* / Drag City: *Jan & Dean* / Chapel of love: *Dixie Cups* / No milk today: *Herman's Hermits* / Duke of Earl: *Chandler, Gene* / Groovy kind of love: *Fontana, Wayne* / Under the boardwalk: *Drifters* / Behind closed doors: *Sledge, Percy* / Night has a thousand eyes: *Vee, Bobby* / Pony time: *Checker, Chubby* / Bobby sox to stockings: *Avalon, Frankie* / Ain't that a shame: *Domino, Fats* / Little old lady from Pasadena: *Jan & Dean* / Build me up buttercup: *Foundations* / There goes my baby: *Drifters* / Operator: *Knight, Gladys* / My boyfriend's back: *Angels* / Little town flirt: *Shannon, Del* / Johnny B. Goode: *Berry, Chuck* / I thank you: *Sam & Dave* / Oh no: *Floyd, Eddie* / Run to him: *Vee, Bobby* / Surfer girl: *Beach Boys* / Give him a great big kiss: *Shangri-Las* / Rockin' Robin: *Day, Bobby* / Corine Corina: *Peterson, Ray* / Promised land: *Berry, Chuck* / G.T.O.: *Regents* / Hucklebuck: *Checker, Chubby* / Rescue me: *Bass, Fontella* / Dead man's curve: *Jan & Dean* / He's a rebel: *Crystals* / Backfield in motion: *Mel & Tim* / Why do fools fall in love: *Diamonds* / Memphis: *Berry, Chuck* / Can't you hear my heartbeat: *Herman's Hermits* / Some kind of

wonderful: *Drifters* / Soul sister brown sugar: *Sam & Dave* / Drift away: *Gray, Dobie* / Remember (walkin' in the sand): *Shangri-Las* / Rhythm of the rain: *Cascades* / Itchycoo Park: *Small Faces* / Dance with me: *Drifters* / Barefootin': *Parker, Robert* / Cry baby cry: *Angels* / It's my party: *Gore, Lesley* / Letter: *Box Tops* / Wooly bully: *Sam The Sham & The Pharaohs* / Yakety yak: *Coasters* / Little darlin': *Diamonds* / In crowd: *Gray, Dobie* / Ferry 'cross the Mersey: *Gerry & The Pacemakers* / Tell Laura I love her: *Peterson, Ray* / Barbara Ann: *Regents* / Maybellene: *Berry, Chuck* / Deep purple: *Tempo, Nino & April Stevens* / I don't know why (I just do): *Henry, Clarence 'Frogman'* / Wild thing: *Troggs* / Mrs. Brown you've got a lovely daughter: *Herman's Hermits* / Surf city: *Jan & Dean* / Don't let the sun catch you crying: *Gerry & The Pacemakers* / Nadine: *Berry, Chuck*

CD Set _____ **TFP 004**
Tring / Nov '92 / Tring / Prism.

100 HITS OF THE SIXTIES VOLUME 2
CD Set _____ **TFP 016**
Tring / Nov '92 / Tring / Prism.

100 OF THE GREATEST LOVE SONGS
Then he kissed me: *Crystals* / It's in his kiss (Shoop shoop song): *Everett, Betty* / Girls: *Moments* / Remember (walkin' in the sand): *Shangri-Las* / Let there be love: *Lee, Peggy* / I'm in the mood for love: *Day, Doris* / My boyfriend's back: *Angels* / Every beat of my heart: *Knight, Gladys & The Pips* / Venus in blue jeans: *Clanton, Jimmy* / Groovy kind of love: *Fontana, Wayne* / I can't find the time: *Nelson, Willie* / Don't let the sun catch you crying: *Gerry & The Pacemakers* / Sixteen candles: *Crests* / Warm and tender love: *Sledge, Percy* / Ain't no sunshine: *Jarreau, Al* / I'm so lonesome I could cry: *Spears, Billie Jo* / Night has a thousand eyes: *Vee, Bobby* / Love walked in: *Benson, George* / Embraceable you: *Day, Doris* / Where were you on our wedding day: *Price, Lloyd* / Release me: *Mandrell, Barbara* / Shelter of my arms: *Nelson, Willie* / Ruby, don't take your love to town: *Rogers, Kenny* / Portrait of my love: *Clark, Dee* / What is this thing called love: *Lee, Peggy* / Behind closed doors: *Sledge, Percy* / Lean on me: *Jarreau, Al* / Run to him: *Vee, Bobby* / Singin' in the rain: *Day, Doris* / Oh no not my baby: *Bass, Fontella* / There goes my baby: *Drifters* / He's a rebel: *Crystals* / Letter full of tears: *Knight, Gladys* / But I do: *Henry, Clarence 'Frogman'* / My guy: *Wells, Mary* / 'S wonderful: *Day, Doris* / I've loved and lost again: *Cline, Patsy* / Save the last dance for me: *Drifters* / Home is where you're happy: *Nelson, Willie* / Kisses sweeter than wine: *Rodgers, Jimmie* / Leader of the pack: *Shangri-Las* / Just a dream: *Clanton, Jimmy* / Best thing that ever happened to me: *Knight, Gladys* / Uptown: *Crystals* / Come what may: *Crosby, Bing* / Do I love you: *Garland, Judy* / Chapel of love: *Dixie Cups* / Runaway: *Shannon, Del* / Young and in love: *Dick & Deedee* / Just one of those things: *Lee, Peggy* / Rock your baby: *McCrae, George* / When a man loves a woman: *Sledge, Percy* / Dream baby: *Shannon, Del* / Stardust: *Day, Doris* / Do it love you: *Garland, Judy* / Give him a great big kiss: *Shangri-Las* / While I dream: *Sedaka, Neil* / High noon: *Laine, Frankie* / Let your love flow: *Burke, Solomon* / So sad the song: *Knight, Gladys & The Pips* / Why do fools fall in love: *Diamonds* / Rainy night in Georgia: *Benton, Brook* / World without you: *Shannon, Del* / Rhythm of the rain: *Cascades* / I can't give you anything but love: *Garland, Judy* / Love we had: *Dells* / Make it easy on yourself: *Butler, Jerry* / Just you, just me: *Day, Doris* / So many ways: *Benton, Brook* / It coulda been me: *Spears, Billie Jo* / Sh-boom: *Crew Cuts* / Tender years: *Jones, George* / Build me up buttercup: *Foundations* / Girls (2): *Moments* / Stormy weather: *Horne, Lena* / I ever I should fall in love: *Knight, Gladys & The Pips* / Deep purple: *Tempo, Nino & April Stevens* / Crying my heart out for you: *Day, Doris* / When my little girl is smiling: *Drifters* / Spanish Harlem: *King, B.B.* / Lyin' eyes: *Jones, Jack* / Single girl: *Posey, Sandy* / Tell Laura I love her: *Peterson, Ray* / Under the moon of love: *Lee, Curtis* / Everything I have is yours: *Crosby, Bing* / Little darlin': *Diamonds* / You and me against the world: *Knight, Gladys & The Pips* / One who really loves you: *Wells, Mary* / Why do fools fall in love (2): *Diamonds* / Closer you are: *Channel* / Just the two of us: *Jones, Jack* / What a man in love won't do: *Posey, Sandy* / Because you're mine: *Day, Doris* / Young and in love #2: *Dick & Deedee* / Up on the roof: *Drifters* / Please love me forever: *Edwards, Tommy* / When the red roses grow: *Crosby, Bing* / Earth angel: *Penguins* / Fools rush in: *Benton, Brook*

CD Set _____ **TFP 008**
Tring / Nov '92 / Tring / Prism.

100 ROCK 'N' ROLL ERA HITS
CD Set _____ **SETCD 028**
Stardust / Jan '94 / Carlton Home Entertainment.

100 ROCK 'N' ROLL HITS
Roll over Beethoven: *Berry, Chuck* / Blueberry Hill: *Domino, Fats* / Yakety yak: *Coasters* / (We're gonna) Rock around the clock: *Haley, Bill & The Comets* / Venus: *Av-*

alon, Frankie* / Reelin' and rockin': *Berry, Chuck* / Let's twist again: *Checker, Chubby* / My boyfriend's back: *Angels* / Keep a knockin': *Little Richard* / Sweet talking guy: *Chiffons* / Personality: *Price, Lloyd* / Hats off to Larry: *Shannon, Del* / Blue Monday: *Domino, Fats* / Sweet little rock 'n' roller: *Berry, Chuck* / Tequila: *Champs* / Tutti frutti: *Little Richard* / Rock 'n' roll is here to stay: *Danny & The Juniors* / Rockin' pneumonia and the boogie woogie flu: *Smith, Huey 'Piano'* / Crossfire: *Johnny & The Hurricanes* / Then he kissed me: *Crystals* / Rubber ball: *Vee, Bobby* / Be bop a lula: *Vincent, Gene* / Runaround Sue: *Shannon, Del* / Promised land: *Berry, Chuck* / Good golly Miss Molly: *Little Richard* / Twist: *Checker, Chubby* / Duke of Earl: *Chandler, Gene* / No particular place to go: *Berry, Chuck* / Ain't that a shame: *Domino, Fats* / Da doo ron ron: *Crystals* / At the hop: *Danny & The Juniors* / Shake, rattle and roll: *Haley, Bill* / School day: *Berry, Chuck* / Long tall Sally: *Little Richard* / Stagger Lee: *Price, Lloyd* / Charlie Brown: *Coasters* / Runaway: *Shannon, Del* / Book of love: *Monotones* / Beatnik fly: *Johnny & The Hurricanes* / Night has a thousand eyes: *Vee, Bobby* / Great balls of fire: *Lewis, Jerry Lee* / Too much monkey business: *Berry, Chuck* / Little Egypt: *Coasters* / Cry baby cry: *Angels* / Rockin' Robin: *Day, Bobby* / Rip it up: *Little Richard* / I go to pieces: *Shannon, Del* / Back in the U.S.A.: *Berry, Chuck* / Cool jerk: *Capitols* / Nadine: *Berry, Chuck* / See you later alligator: *Haley, Bill & The Comets* / Red river rock: *Johnny & The Hurricanes* / Huckle-buck: *Checker, Chubby* / Johnny B. Goode: *Berry, Chuck* / Ooh my soul: *Little Richard* / Whole lotta shakin' goin' on: *Lewis, Jerry Lee* / Chapel of love: *Dixie Cups* / Little town flirt: *Shannon, Del* / Sweet little sixteen: *Berry, Chuck* / Jambalaya: *Domino, Fats* / Sea cruise: *Ford, Frankie* / He's a rebel: *Crystals* / Leader of the pack: *Shangri-Las* / Poison ivy: *Coasters* / Because they're young: *Eddy, Duane* / Whole lotta shakin' goin' on (2): *Little Richard* / Angels listened in: *Crests* / Let it rock: *Berry, Chuck* / Matchbox: *Perkins, Carl* / Kansas City: *Harrison, Wilbert* / Brown eyed handsome man: *Lewis, Jerry Lee* / Little bitty pretty one: *Day, Bobby* / I'm walkin': *Domino, Fats* / Short fat Fanny: *Little Richard* / Almost grown: *Berry, Chuck* / Maybellene: *Berry, Chuck* / Lucille: *Little Richard* / Shout: *Dee, Joey* / Limbo rock: *Checker, Chubby* / Reveille rock: *Johnny & The Hurricanes* / Why do fools fall in love: *Diamonds* / Brown eyed handsome man (2): *Berry, Chuck* / Baby blue: *Vincent, Gene* / Hello Josephine: *Domino, Fats* / She's got it: *Little Richard* / Mr. bass Man: *Cymbal, Johnny* / Say man: *Diddley, Bo* / Rock 'n' roll music: *Berry, Chuck* / Handyman: *Shannon, Del* / He's so fine: *Chiffons* / This ole house: *Perkins, Carl* / Wooly bully: *Sam The Sham & The Pharaohs* / Pony time: *Checker, Chubby* / Girl can't help it: *Little Richard* / Rebel rouser: *Eddy, Duane* / Stroll: *Diamonds* / Under the moon of love: *Lee, Curtis* / Domino twist: *Domino, Fats* / Memphis: *Berry, Chuck* / Guitar man: *Eddy, Duane*

CD Set _____ **TFP 002**
Tring / Nov '92 / Tring / Prism.

100 SOUL HITS
Soul man: *Sam & Dave* / Papa's got a brand new bag: *Brown, James* / Knock on wood: *Floyd, Eddie* / Under the boardwalk: *Drifters* / Rescue me: *Bass, Fontella* / It's just a matter of time: *Benton, Brook* / In crowd: *Gray, Dobie* / Oh no not my baby: *Brown, Maxine* / Every beat of my heart: *Knight, Gladys* / Rock your baby: *McCrae, George* / Barefootin': *Parker, Robert* / When a man loves a woman: *Sledge, Percy* / Backfield in motion: *Mel & Tim* / You don't know what you mean to me: *Sam & Dave* / Expressway to your heart: *Soul Survivors* / Save the last dance for me: *Drifters* / When something is wrong with my baby: *Sam & Dave* / If you need me: *Pickett, Wilson* / Do the funky chicken: *Thomas, Rufus* / Please please please: *Brown, James* / Rainy night in Georgia: *Benton, Brook* / Hold on I'm comin': *Burke, Solomon* / Bring it on home to me: *Floyd, Eddie* / Stand by me: *King, Ben E.* / I got the feelin': *Brown, James* / On broadway: *Drifters* / Hold on I'm comin' (2): *Sam & Dave* / It's a man's man's man's world: *Brown, James* / Oh what a night: *Dells* / California girl: *Floyd, Eddie* / Spanish Harlem: *King, Ben E.* / True love: *Drifters* / Soul man (2): *Lewis, Ramsey* / So many ways: *Benton, Brook* / Letter full of tears: *Knight, Gladys* / Walking the dog: *Thomas, Rufus* / Hi-heel sneakers: *Lewis, Ramsey* / All in my mind: *Brown, Maxine* / Best thing that ever happened to me: *Knight, Gladys* / Turn it loose: *Brown, James* / Said I wasn't gonna tell nobody: *Sam & Dave* / I wha home nothing: *King, Ben E.* / My guy: *Wells, Mary* / Sweets for my sweet: *Drifters* / Georgia on my mind: *Knight, Gladys* / Both weevil song: *Benton, Brook* / You don't know like I know: *Sam & Dave* / Get up offa that thing: *Brown, James* / Warm and tender love: *Sledge, Percy* / Challenge: *Butler, Jerry* / It's too funky here: *Brown, James* / Tighten up: *Bell, Archie & The Drells* / I thank you: *Sam & Dave* / Lovin' arms: *Gray, Dobie* / Supernatural thing: *King, Ben E.* / Dancing in the street: *Lewis, Ramsey* / There goes my baby: *Drifters* / Operator:*

Knight, Gladys & The Pips* / I wanna go home: *Drells* / Try me: *Brown, James* / Uptight: *Lewis, Ramsey* / So sad the song: *Knight, Gladys & The Pips* / Fools rush in: *Benton, Brook* / Girls: *Moments* / This magic moment: *Drifters* / Behind closed doors: *Sledge, Percy* / Listen: *Impressions* / Hard day's night: *Lewis, Ramsey* / Duke of Earl: *Chandler, Gene* / You got the hummin': *Sam & Dave* / Think twice: *Benton, Brook* / Since you've been gone: *Lewis, Ramsey* / Cold sweat/I can't stand myself (medley): *Brown, James* / I who have nothing (2): *King, Ben E.* / Soul sister brown sugar: *Sam & Dave* / Get up I feel like being a sex machine: *Brown, James* / Love me again: *Knight, Gladys & The Pips* / Up on the roof: *Drifters* / Look at me (I'm in love): *Moments* / Drift away: *Gray, Dobie* / It's too late: *Pickett, Wilson* / She does it right: *King, Ben E.* / Hotel happiness: *Benton, Brook* / Louie Louie: *Kingsmen* / Get on the good foot: *Brown, James* / Soul twist: *King Curtis* / Never found a girl: *Floyd, Eddie* / Don't pull your love out on me baby: *Sam & Dave* / Dance with me: *Drifters* / If ever I should fall in love: *Knight, Gladys & The Pips* / In crowd (2): *Lewis, Ramsey* / Love on a two way street: *Moments* / Take time to know her: *Sledge, Percy* / I need your love: *Impressions* / Can't you find another way: *Sam & Dave* / Some kind of wonderful: *Drifters* / Thank you pretty baby: *Benton, Brook* / What shall I do: *Knight, Gladys & The Pips* / I feel good: *Brown, James*

CD Set _____ **TFP 001**
Tring / Nov '92 / Tring / Prism.

100% ACID JAZZ
CD _____ **TCD 2733**
Telstar / Sep '94 / BMG.

100% ACID JAZZ VOLUME 2
CD _____ **TCD 2767**
Telstar / Jun '95 / BMG.

100% CARNIVAL
CD _____ **TCD 2782**
Telstar / Nov '94 / BMG.

100% CHRISTMAS
CD Set _____ **TCD 2754**
Telstar / Nov '94 / BMG.

100% DETROIT WORKOUT
CD Set _____ **CDFIT 5**
Music For Pleasure / Nov '95 / EMI.

100% HOUSE CLASSICS
CD Set _____ **TCD 2759**
Telstar / Feb '95 / BMG.

100% PURE LOVE
CD _____ **TCD 2737**
Telstar / Oct '94 / BMG.

100% PURE UNDERGROUND DANCE
CD Set _____ **XCLU 001CDC**
X-Clusive / Sep '94 / Pinnacle.

100% REGGAE
CD _____ **TCD 2695**
Telstar / Nov '93 / BMG.

100% REGGAE ORIGINALS
CD _____ **TCD 2775**
Telstar / Jul '95 / BMG.

100% REGGAE VOLUME 2
CD _____ **TCD 2716**
Telstar / Apr '94 / BMG.

100% SUMMER
CD _____ **TCD 2730**
Telstar / Jul '94 / BMG.

100% SUMMER '95
CD _____ **TCD 2777**
Telstar / Jun '95 / BMG.

100% SUMMER JAZZ
CD _____ **TCD 2781**
Telstar / Jul '95 / BMG.

101 + 303 + 808 = NOW FORM A BAND
Metamorphic structures: *Turbulent Force* / Alpha acid: *Point Alpha* / Steel mill: *T.H.D.* / Spalding: *T.H.D.* / Molluak: *POD* / Untitled: *Turbulent Force* / Data blast: *Point Alpha* / Street stomper: *Psyche* / Geodesic dome: *POD* / Untitled (2): *Lords Of Afford* / Adrenalin rush: *Psyche*

CD _____ **SBR 004CD**
Sabrettes Of Paradise / Oct '95 / Vital.

101% REGGAE
Sing a little song: *Dekker, Desmond* / We play record: *In Crowd* / Work all day: *Biggs, Barry* / Mad about you: *Ruffin, Bruce* / Island music: *Calendar, Phil* / Girlie girlie: *George, Sophia* / Do you really want to hurt me: *Heptones* / Sweet cherrie: *Honey Boy* / Keep on riding: *Donaldson, Eric* / Side show: *Biggs, Barry* / Take care of my heart: *Gardiner, Boris* / Blue moon: *Francis, Winston* / Come back Charlie: *Chaplin, Charlie* / Rock my soul: *Pioneers* / It hurt me bad: *George, Sophia* / Happy anniversary: *Schloss, Cynthia* / Busted land: *Dekker, Desmond* / Kool and deadly: *Eastwood, Clint & General Saint*

CD _____ **ECD 3074**
K-Tel / Jan '95 / K-Tel.

104.9
CD _____ **XFMCD 2**
XFM / Oct '95 / Pinnacle.

300 YEARS OF SCOTLAND'S MUSIC
CD _____ MMSCD 951
Scott Music / Apr '95 / Select.

313 DETROIT
War of the worlds: *Dark Comedy* / Distance: *Reel By Reel* / Baby can: *K.E.L.S.E.Y.* / Unconscious world: *Subterfuge* / Electricity: *Santonio* / Warwick: *Fowlkes, Eddie* / Desire: *69* / Free Your Mind: *Piece*
CD _____ INFO 1CD
Infonet / Nov '92 / Pinnacle / Vital.

1000 VOLTS OF STAX
Hideaway: *Booker T & The MG's* / (Sittin' on) the dock of the bay: *Booker T & The MG's* / Don't you lie to me: *King, Albert* / Cupid: *Redding, Otis* / I've got dreams to remember: *Redding, Otis* / Don't worry about tomorrow: *Marchan, Bobby* / Walking the dog: *Thomas, Rufus* / Runaround: *Thomas, Carla* / Floyd's beat: *Newman, Floyd* / When my love comes down: *Johnson, Ruby* / She won't be like you: *Bell, William* / Never let me go: *Bell, William* / Sweet devil: *John, Mable* / Cloudburst: *Mad Lads* / Hippy dippy: *Mar-Keys* / Don't mess up a good thing: *Thomas, Rufus & Carla* / Just enough to hurt me: *Astors* / Knock on wood: *Floyd, Eddie*
CD _____ CDSXD 042
Stax / Sep '91 / Pinnacle.

1327 TAGE
CD _____ EYEUKCD 007
Harthouse / Nov '95 / Disc / Warner Music.

1943-47
CD _____ 22026
Caprice / Feb '89 / CM / Complete / Pinnacle / Cadillac / ADA.

1991 TRIANGLE JAZZ PARTYBOYS
CD _____ FINCD 101
Arbors Jazz / Nov '94 / Cadillac.

2000 VOLTS OF STAX
Kinda easy like: *Booker T & The MG's* / Ride your pony: *Thomas, Rufus* / You don't know like I know: *Taylor, Johnnie* / Pain in my heart: *Redding, Otis* / It's not that easy: *Johnson, Ruby* / How about you: *Parker, Deanie* / Hotshot: *Bar-Kays* / Come out tonight: *Astors* / Bark at the moon: *Floyd, Eddie* / I found a brand new love: *Kirk, Eddie* / Please don't go: *Tonettes* / Try me: *Thomas, Carla* / Slinky: *Mar-Keys* / Crosscut saw: *King, Albert* / She's the one: *Mad Lads* / You don't miss your water: *Bell, William* / I say a little prayer: *Booker T & The MG's* / Try a little tenderness: *Redding, Otis*
CD _____ CDSXD 074
Stax / Oct '92 / Pinnacle.

2001: A GRASS ODYSSEY
CD _____ GROW 0272
Grass / May '95 / SRD.

3000 VOLTS OF STAX
Spoonful: *Booker T & The MG's* / Come to me: *Redding, Otis* / I'd rather fight than switch: *Johnson, Ruby* / Sixty minutes of your time: *Taylor, Johnnie* / Quittin' time: *Bell, William* / Good good lovin': *Thomas, Carla* / I got everything I need: *Floyd, Eddie* / Count your many blessings: *Stars Of Virginia* / Big bad wolf: *Jenkins, Johnny* / Rotation: *Tonettes* / Wee little bit: *Marchan, Bobby* / Juanita: *Prince Conley* / Win you over: *Porter, David* / Hunter: *King, Albert* / Per-culating: *Mar-Keys* / Patch my heart: *Mad Lads* / Remember me: *Redding, Otis* / Water: *Taylor, Johnnie* / Sock soul: *Bar-Kays* / Big bird: *Floyd, Eddie* / All I need is some sunshine in my life: *Dixie Nightingales*
CD _____ CDSXD 102
Stax / Mar '94 / Pinnacle.

4000 VOLTS OF STAX AND SATELLITE
Home grown: *Booker T & The MG's* / Woman who needs the love of a man: *Astors* / Just to hold your hand: *Marchan, Bobby* / Ain't that good: *Prince Conley* / All that I am: *Prince Conley* / As you can see: *Chips* / Shake up: *Cobras* / I'll never give her up (My friend): *Canes* / Somewhere along the line: *Canes* / Popeye the sailor man: *Del Rios* / Any other way: *Bell, William* / Strut this Sally: *Astors* / Uncle Willie good time: *Astors* / I wish I were that girl: *Rene Wendy* / Hawg (pt 2): *Kirk, Eddie* / I see my baby coming: *Mack, Oscar* / Please don't leave: *Drapels* / Someday: *Veltones* / All the way: *Prince Conley* / Hard times (Every dog's got his day): *Prince Conley* / About noon: *Mar-Keys* / Something is worrying me: *Redding, Otis*
CD _____ CDSXD 107
Stax / May '95 / Pinnacle.

5000 OHM
CD Set _____ IRCD 03
Influence / Jun '94 / Plastic Head.

6000 OHM
No good (Start the dance) (Edit): *Prodigy* / I need your love: *Microwave Prince* / Signs of life: *Meteor Seven* / Feel the melodee (Mix): *Komakino* / Sacred cycles: *Lazonby* / Cybertrance: *Blue Alphabet* / My: *Van Dyke, Paul* / Bagdad: *Paragliders* / Perpetuum noble: *Luxor* / Filterside: *Dimitri* / Phraser: *Bionic Boom* / Self immolation: *Hiroshima* / Forwart: *Deep Piece* / Mono 1: *Nervous Project* / Amphetamine: *Drax* / Drag: *Titan* / Red Acid: *Mongolian ride: *Phoenixx* / sita (Remix): *Source T-10* / Let there by

rhythm: *Mason, Steve* / Two full moons (Original Version): *Union Jack*
CD Set _____ SUCK CD6
Suck Me Plasma / Oct '94 / Plastic Head.

$10,000 WORTH OF DOO WOP
Pretty, pretty girl: *Timetones* / Where are you: *Bel Aires* / Why be a fool: *Nobles* / My life's desire: *Verdicts* / Ride away: *Revalons* / Tight skirt and sweater: *Versatones* / Tell me: *Mastertones* / Bang bang shoot 'em Daddy: *Emblems* / Crying for you: *Centuries* / My love: *Timetones* / Fool rock and roll: *Nobles* / Can I come over tonight: *Velours* / Tomorrow: *Decoys* / Sindy: *Squires* / Rita: *Versatones* / Oh darling: *Jaytones* / My love (2): *Revalons* / I love you: *4 Mosts* / Jerry: *Minors* / In my heart: *Timetones*
CD _____ FICD 1
Finbarr International / Dec '93 / Finbarr International.

A IS FOR ACTIVE
CD _____ ACTIVCD 4
Activ / Sep '95 / Total/BMG.

A TODA CUBA LE GUSTA
CD _____ CCD 505
Caney / Nov '95 / ADA / Discovery.

A-SIDES
CD _____ CATNO 8CD
Crass / Nov '92 / SRD.

A-SIDES VOL.2
CD _____ CATNO 9CD
Crass / May '93 / SRD.

ABBASALUTELY
CD _____ FNCD 315
Flying Nun / Jan '96 / Disc.

ABRACADABRA
CD _____ 1212012
Soul Note / Nov '90 / Harmonia Mundi / Wellard / Cadillac.

ABSOLUTE COLLECTION - FEELINGS
CD _____ LECD 425
Wisepack / Jul '93 / THE / Conifer.

ABSOLUTE COLLECTION - GOLDEN INSTRUMENTALS
CD _____ LECD 424
Wisepack / Jul '93 / THE / Conifer.

ABSOLUTE COLLECTION - THEMES & DREAMS
CD _____ LECD 426
Wisepack / Jul '93 / THE / Conifer.

ABSOLUTE COUNTRY
Chattahoochee: *Jackson, Alan* / Rock my world: *Brooks & Dunn* / Desperado: *Black, Clint* / Every little thing: *Carter, Carlene* / My baby loves me: *McBride, Martina* / Fine line: *Foster, Radney* / He would be sixteen: *Wright, Michelle* / When you walk in the room: *Tillis, Pam* / Lying to the moon: *Berg, Matraca* / When she cries: *Restless Heart* / On the road: *Parnell, Lee Roy* / Dreaming with my eyes open: *Walker, Clay*
CD _____ 74321219002
RCA / Oct '94 / BMG.

ABSOLUTE COUNTRY 2
CD _____ 74321279242
RCA / Apr '95 / BMG.

ABSOLUTE REGGAE
Everything I own: *Boothe, Ken* / Let your yeah be yeah: *Pioneers* / You make me feel: *Gardiner, Boris* / Eighteen with a bullet: *Harriott, Derrick* / Return of Django: *Upsetters* / Love of the common people: *Thomas, Nicky* / Cherry oh baby: *Donaldson, Eric* / Black and white: *Greyhound* / Reggae man: *Dekker, George* / Walk away: *Pierre, Marie* / Rain: *Ruffin, Bruce* / Young, gifted and black: *Bob & Marcia* / Suzanne beware of the devil #2: *Livingstone, Dandy* / Lively up yourself: *Marley, Bob* / Then he kissed me: *Marvels* / Heart made of stone: *Hall, Audrey* / Johnny too bad: *Slickers* / Many rivers to cross: *Cliff, Jimmy* / Israelites: *Dekker, Desmond & The Aces* / Oh what a feeling: *Simon, Tito* / Hurt so good: *Cadogan, Susan* / Rivers of Babylon: *Melodians* / First time ever I saw your face: *Griffiths, Marcia* / Help me make it through the night: *Holt, John* / Suzanne beware of the devil: *Livingstone, Dandy*
CD _____ VSOPCD 104
Connoisseur / Nov '87 / Pinnacle.

ABSOLUTION
Spellbound: *Siouxsie & The Banshees* / Don't let me down gently: *Wonder Stuff* / Deliverance: *Mission* / Eloise: *Damned* / Never enough: *Cure* / Ziggy Stardust: *Bauhaus* / Love like blood: *Killing Joke* / European female: *Stranglers* / Some candy talking: *Jesus & Mary Chain* / Cutter: *Echo & The Bunnymen* / Love my way: *Psychedelic Furs* / Enjoy the silence: *Depeche Mode* / Martha's harbour: *All About Eve* / Baby I love you: *Ramones* / Miss the girl: *Creatures*

/ No rest: *New Model Army* / Heartache: *Gene Loves Jezebel* / Moonchild (first seal): *Fields Of The Nephilim*
CD _____ 8457472
Polydor / Sep '91 / PolyGram.

ABSTRACT EXPRESSION CHAPTER 1
CD _____ FLAGCD 107
Flag Bearer / Jun '95 / SRD.

ABSTRACT PUNK SINGLES COLLECTION
48 Crash: *Gymslips* / Big sister: *Gymslips* / Robot man: *Gymslips* / Self destruct: *UK Subs* / Police state: *UK Subs* / War of the roses: *UK Subs* / Vengence: *New Model Army* / Nowhere to run: *Outcasts* / Denise: *Joolz* / Three Johns: *AWOL* / Great expectations: *New Model Army* / Price: *New Model Army* / Armchair: *Hagar The Womb* / Evil eye: *Gymslips* / Drink problem: *Gymslips* / Daddy's been working: *Downbeats* / Lean on me: *Redskins* / Unionise: *Redskins* / Kick out the tories: *Newtown Neurotics* / Mindless violence: *Newtown Neurotics*
CD _____ CDPUNK 52
Anagram / Apr '95 / Pinnacle.

ACCESS ALL AREAS
CD _____ BW 033
B&W / Oct '93 / New Note.

ACCORDEON JAZZ 1911-44
(2 CD)
CD Set _____ FA 038
Fremeaux / Nov '95 / Discovery / ADA.

ACCORDEON VOL.1 1913-41
(2CD Set)
CD Set _____ DH 002CD
Fremeaux / Nov '95 / Discovery / AUA.

ACCORDEON VOL.2 1952-42
(2CD Set)
CD Set _____ FA 005CD
Fremeaux / Nov '95 / Discovery / ADA.

ACCOUSTIC SAMPLER 5
Secret garden: *Kostia* / Enzian: *Gratz, Wayne* / Merced: *Tingstad, Eric* / Briarcombe: *Stein, Ira* / Opal moon: *Wynberg, Simon* / Peru: *Tingstad, Eric* / La couronne: *Kolbe, Martin* / Imaginary friend: *Gratz, Wayne* / Windance: *Andrew / Dream of the forgotten child: *Lanz, David* / Touchstone: *Ellwood, William* / Magical child: *Jones, Michael*
CD _____ ND 61041
Narada / Jul '94 / New Note / ADA.

ACID FLASH
(2CD Set)
CD Set _____ SPV 08938422
Subterranean / Jan '96 / Plastic Head.

ACID FLASHBACK
CD _____ TRIPCD 1
Rumour / Mar '95 / Pinnacle / 3MV / Sony.

ACID HOUSE CLASSICS
CD _____ CCSCD 377
Castle / Sep '93 / BMG.

ACID JAZZ AND OTHER ILLICIT GROOVES
Introduction: *Ace Of Clubs* / Ace of clubs: *Ace Of Clubs* / Jalal: *Jalal* / Push: *Traffic* / Shaft in action: *Acid Jazz* / Galliano: *Six Sharp Fists* / And now we have rhythm: *Night Trains* / Doin' it naturally: *Rhythm Blades* / Jazz renegades
CD _____ 8373472
Urban / Sep '88 / PolyGram.

ACID JAZZ JAZZ
CD _____ JAZIDCD 038
Acid Jazz / Jul '91 / Pinnacle.

ACID JAZZ MO' JAZZ
CD _____ JAZIDCD 051
Acid Jazz / Jun '92 / Pinnacle.

ACID JAZZ VOL.1
Better half: *Funk Inc.* / Got myself a good man: *Pucho* / Houston Express: *Person, Houston* / Grits and gravy: *Kloss, Eric* / Hoochie coo chickie: *Jones, Ivan 'Boogaloo Joe'* / Lady Mama: *Ammons, Gene* / Hip shaker: *Spencer, Leon* / Psychedelic Sally
CD _____ CDBGP 1015
BGP / Oct '91 / Pinnacle.

ACID JAZZ VOL.2
Super bad: *Muhammad, Idris* / Cold sweat: *Purdie, Bernard* / Wildfire: *Bryant, Rusty* / Hot barbecue: *McDuff, Jack* / Reelin' with the feelin': *Kynard, Charles* / Spinky: *Earland, Charles* / Who's gonna take the weight: *Sparks, Melvin*
CD _____ CDBGP 1017
BGP / Oct '91 / Pinnacle.

ACID JAZZ VOL.3
I want you back: *Mabern, Harold* / Psychedelic Pucho: *Pucho* / Zebra walk: *Kynard, Charles* / Akiah: *Sparks, Melvin* / What it is: *Jones, Ivan 'Boogaloo Joe'* / Bad Montana: *Parker, Maynard* / Dig on it: *Smith, Johnny 'Hammond'* / Bowlegs: *Funk Inc.*
CD _____ CDBGP 1025
BGP / Oct '91 / Pinnacle.

ACID JAZZ VOL.4
Soul dance: *Person, Houston* / Sing a simple song: *Earland, Charles* / Twang thang: *Butler, Billy* / Shaft: *Purdie, Bernard* / Sure nuff sure nuff: *Phillips, Sonny* / Mambluees: *Tjader, Cal & Bernard Purdie* / Haw right

now: *Rushen, Patrice* / Life is funky: *Round Robin Monopoly*
CD _____ CDBGP 1029
BGP / Oct '91 / Pinnacle.

ACID RESISTANT
CD _____ EFA 262332
Smile / May '95 / SRD.

ACOUSTIC FREEWAY
CD _____ 5257352
PolyGram TV / Aug '95 / PolyGram.

ACOUSTIC MOODS
Lady Eleanor: *Lindisfarne* / Stuck in the middle with you: *Stealer's Wheel* / Baker Street: *Rafferty, Gerry* / Year of the cat: *Stewart, Al* / They shoot horses don't they: *Racing Cars* / Arms of Mary: *Sutherland Brothers & Quiver* / Chestnut mare: *Byrds* / Castles in the air: *McLean, Don* / Blue guitar: *Hayward, Justin & John Lodge* / Moonlight shadow: *Oldfield, Mike* / Lay down: *Strawbs* / How come: *Lane, Ronnie & Slim Chance* / Reason to believe: *Stewart, Rod* / Journey: *Browne, Duncan* / I don't mind at all: *Bourgeois Tagg* / Pinball: *Protheroe, Brian* / Streets of London: *McTell, Ralph* / Time in a bottle: *Croce, Jim* / Morning has broken: *Stevens, Cat* / After the goldrush: *Prelude*
CD _____ 5166592
PolyGram TV / Apr '94 / PolyGram.

ACOUSTIC MOODS
CD _____ RADCD 13
Global / Jun '95 / BMG.

ACOUSTIC MUSIC PROJECT
Step right this way: *Prophet, Chuck & Stephanie Finch* / Trying: *Prophet, Chuck & Stephanie Finch* / On borrowed time: *Houston, Penelope* / Looking for a reason: *DeRoss, Nancie* / Say please: *Sorentino, Danny* / Such a fine line: *Shelfer, Jerry* / Hootenanny: *Muskrats* / Love's not lost: *Segal, Jonathan* / Guantanamerika: *Chilton, Alex* / Everywhere that I'm not: *Barton, Darlington & Dekker* / Words: *Movie Stars* / Penny in the sky: *Winningham, patrick* / Paint: *Hunter, Sonya* / Dreamers of the dream: *American Music Club* / Don't rewind: *Manning, Barbara* / Rude: *Haynes, Ed* / More than I will: *Champagne, Connie* / When the morning falls: *Porter, Eddie Ray*
CD _____ A009 D
Alias / Mar '93 / Vital.

ACOUSTIC ROCK
Wild wood: *Weller, Paul* / Weather with you: *Crowded House* / Heal the pain: *Michael, George* / Prettiest eyes: *Beautiful South* / 74-75: *Connells* / Mmm mmm mmm mmm: *Crash Test Dummies* / Driving with the brakes on: *Del Amitri* / How men are: *Aztec Camera* / Is it like today: *World Party* / You & me song: *Wannadies* / Run baby run: *Crow, Sheryl* / Linger: *Cranberries* / Jennifer she said: *Cole, Lloyd* / Julie: *Levellers* / High and dry: *Radiohead* / Only living boy in New York: *Everything But The Girl* / It's about time: *Lemonheads* / You have place a chill in my heart: *Eurythmics* / Walk this world: *Nova, Heather* / Let it grow: *Clapton, Eric*
CD _____ 5258962
PolyGram TV / Sep '95 / PolyGram.

ACOUSTIC ROUTES
CD _____ NINETY 7
Demon / Oct '93 / Pinnacle / ADA.

ACROBATES ET MUSICIENS
CD _____ SHAN 21009CD
Shanachie / Nov '95 / Koch / ADA / Greensleeves.

ACROSS THE GREAT DIVIDE
CD _____ DJD 3203
Dejadisc / May '94 / Direct / ADA.

ACROSS THE WATERS
(Irish Traditional Music From England)
CD _____ NI 541CD
Nimbus / Oct '94 / Nimbus.

ACT BLUE ACT
Before birth: *Krantz, Wayne* / Cortesanos: *Paxarino, Javier* / Is anybody listening: *Bazillus* / Love for all: *Lateef, Yusef & Eternal Wind* / Captain Captain: *Waters, Muddy* / White blues: *Brookmeyer, Bob* / Summertime: *Evans, Gil* / Ayamina (Pour une infante defunte): *Mendoza, Vince* / Nuages: *Coryell, Larry & Philip Catherine* / Sweet Stan: *Fagano, Tony* / Regulator: *Bazillus* / La cigarras: *Pardo, Jorge* / Tangos: *Mendoza, Vince*
CD _____ 892182
Act / Jul '94 / New Note.

ACTION
CD _____ BB 2812
Blue Beat / Oct '95 / Magnum Music Group / THE.

ADULTS ONLY
(The Filthiest Party Album In The World)
CD _____ PLATCD 4910
Prism / Dec '95 / Prism.

ADULTS ONLY VOL 2
Rub up, push up: *Hinds, Justin* / Want me cock: *Owen & Leon* / Pussy cat: *Stranger Cole* / Dr. Dick: *Perry, Lee 'Scratch'* / Push it up: *Termites* / Adults only: *Calypso Joe* / Pussy catch a fire: *Soulmates* / Big boy and teacher: *U-Roy* / Rough rider: *U-Roy* / Play with your

pussy: *Romeo, Max* / Papa do it sweet: *Lloyd & Patsy* / In a de pum pum: *Flowers & Alvin* / Mr. Whittaker: *Charlie Ace & Fay* / Hole under crutches: *Homeo, Max* / Yum yum pussy: *Lloydie & Lowbites*
CD _____ CDTRL 308
Trojan / Mar '94 / Jetstar / Total/BMG.

ADVENTURES IN AFROPEA #3: AFRO PORTO
CD _____ 9362456692
WEA / Feb '96 / Warner Music.

AFRICA - NEVER STAND STILL
CD Set _____ CT 3300
Ellipsis Arts / Aug '94 / Direct / ADA.

AFRICA CALLING
CD _____ RRTGCD 7734
Rohit / Mar '89 / Jetstar.

AFRICA DANCE
CD _____ CDCH 366
Milan / Apr '90 / BMG / Silva Screen.

AFRICA IN AMERICA
CD Set _____ MT 115/7
Corason / Jan '94 / CM / Direct / ADA.

AFRICA ON THE MOVE
CD _____ CDC 210
Music Of The World / Jun '93 / Target/BMG / ADA.

AFRICA: THE MUSIC OF A CONTINENT
CD _____ PS 66006
Playasound / Oct '95 / Harmonia Mundi / ADA.

AFRICAN DUB SERIES CHAPTERS 3 & 4
CD _____ RGCD 024
Rocky One / Jan '95 / Jetstar.

AFRICAN HORNS
Next stop Soweto / Tshona / Black and brown cherries / Tegeni / Msunduza / Mafuta
CD _____ KAZCD 8
Kaz / Aug '89 / BMG.

AFRICAN MELODICA DUB
CD _____ ROTCD 008
Reggae On Top / Jan '96 / Jetstar / SRD.

AFRICAN MOVES
CD _____ CD 11513
Rounder / Jan '88 / CM / Direct / ADA / Cadillac.

AFRICAN MOVES VOL.2
Pole mama: *Somo Somo* / Amilo: *Ley, Tabu* / Boya ye: *M'Bilia Bell* / Sanza Misato: *Orchestra Africa* / Mon couer balance: *Daouda* / Gbebe mi: *Obey, Ebenezer* / Segun Adewale: *Adewale, Segun* / Yreme breeo: *African Brothers*
CD _____ STCD 1029
Sterns / Nov '89 / Sterns / CM.

AFRICAN MUSEUM SELECTION
CD _____ HBCD 19
Heartbeat / May '90 / Greensleeves / Jetstar / Direct / ADA.

AFRICAN RHYTHMS AND INSTRUMENTS, VOL. 1
(Mali, Niger, Ghana, Nigeria, Upper Volta, Senegal)
CD _____ LYRCD 7328
Lyrichord / '91 / Roots / ADA / CM.

AFRICAN RUBBER DUB VOL.2
CD _____ CEND 1400
Century / Aug '95 / Total/BMG / Jetstar.

AFRICAN RUBBER DUB VOL.3
CD _____ CEND 1200
Century / Sep '94 / Total/BMG / Jetstar.

AFRICAN SUMMIT
CD _____ KAZCD 16
Kaz / Apr '95 / BMG.

AFRICAN TRIBAL MUSIC AND DANCES
CD _____ 12179
Laserlight / Aug '95 / Target/BMG.

AFRICOLOR
CD _____ 795242
Melodie / Nov '90 / Triple Earth / Discovery / ADA / Jetstar.

AFRIQUE PARADE VOL. 3
CD _____ 829042CD
Buda / Jul '95 / Discovery / ADA.

AFRIQUE PARADE-TOP DU SOUKOUS
CD _____ 828672
Buda / Jun '93 / Discovery / ADA.

AFRO BLUE
Afro blue: *Reeves, Dianne* / Capoeira: *Pullen, Don* / Home is Africa: *Parlan, Horace* / Mystery of love: *Blakey, Art* / Tin tin deo: *Moody, James* / Night in Tunisia: *Powell, Bud* / O'tinde: *Blakey, Art* / Man from Tanganyika: *Tyner, McCoy* / Experiment in Ghana, McLean, Jackie / Feast: *Blakey, Art* / Mr. Kenyatta: *Martinez, Sabu* / Message from Kenya: *Silver, Horace* / Rhapsodia del marisillio: *Martinez, Sabu*
CD _____ BNZ 304
Blue Note / Nov '92 / EMI.

AFRO CUBA
Cuban lullaby: *Bauza, Mario* / Mambo: *Bauza, Mario* / Yo siempre odiara: *Bunnett, Jane* / Despojo: *D'Rivera, Paquito* / Relax: *Sandoval, Arturo* / El montuno de patatp:

Patato / Guaguanjira: *D'Rivera, Paquito* / La comparsa: *D'Rivera, Paquito* / Come fue: *D'Rivera, Paquito* / El mansiero: *Bauza, Mario* / Comelon: *Patato* / Adios pampa mia: *Patato* / GMS: *Bunnett, Jane*
CD _____ NSCD 007
Nascente / Oct '95 / Disc / THE.

AFRO CUBA: MUSICAL ANTHOLOGY
CD _____ ROU 1068CD
Rounder / Feb '94 / CM / Direct / ADA / Cadillac.

AFRO LIMONESE: MUSIC FROM COSTA RICA
CD _____ LYRCD 7412
Lyrichord / '91 / Roots / ADA / CM.

AFTER DARK
Where do broken hearts go: *Houston, Whitney* / Just another day: *Secada, Jon* / She's gone: *Hall & Oates* / House is not a home: *Vandross, Luther* / Tired of being alone: *Green, Al* / If you're looking for a way out: *Odyssey* / I keep forgettin': *McDonald, Michael* / Wishing on a star: *Rose Royce* / Different corner: *Michael, George* / Why: *Lennox, Annie* / Just my imagination: *Temptations* / Let the music play: *White, Barry* / Oh girl: *Young, Paul* / Don't leave me this way: *Melvin, Harold & The Bluenotes* / Teardrops: *Womack & Womack* / Heartbreaker: *Warwick, Dionne* / What's love got to do with it: *Turner, Tina* / I wonder why: *Stigers, Curtis*
CD _____ SETVCD 5
Epic / Aug '93 / Sony.

AFTER HOURS
Music Unites / Jan '96 / Sony / 3MV / SRD.
_____ JDJAH 1CD

AFTER MIDNIGHT
Midnight at the Oasis: *Muldaur, Maria* / Sweet love: *Baker, Anita* / Feeling good: *Simone, Nina* / Nature boy: *Cole, Nat King* / Let's face the music and dance: *Fitzgerald, Ella* / Dream a little dream of me: *Fygi, Laura* / Rockin' good way: *Washington, Dinah* / Mack the knife: *Darin, Bobby* / Cry me a river: *London, Julie* / Good morning heartache: *Holiday, Billie* / Tenderly: *Vaughan, Sarah* / Look of love: *Washington, Grover Jr.* / Like dreamers do: *Paris, Mica* / Razzamatazz: *Jones, Quincy* / Running away: *Ayers, Roy* / Cantaloop (Flip fantasia): *US 3* / Love supreme: *Downing, Will* / Time after time: *Davis, Miles* / Children of the ghetto: *Pine, Courtney* / Wrong side of town: *BBM*
CD _____ 5168712
PolyGram / Sep '94 / PolyGram.

AFTER THE ANARCHY
Rich kids: *Rich Kids* / Marching men: *Rich Kids* / Ghosts of princes in towers: *Rich Kids* / Justifiable homicide: *Goodman, Dave & Friends* / Public image: *Public Image Ltd* / London boys: *Thunders, Johnny* / 1-2-3: *Professionals* / Stones: *Spectres* / Join the professionals: *Professionals* / This is not a love song: *Public Image Ltd* / Street full of soul: *London Cowboys* / Let's get crazy: *London Cowboys* / It ain't me girl: *Holi Club* / World gone wild: *Chequered Past* / Only the strong survive: *Chequered Past* / Animal speaks: *Golden Palaminos* / World destruction: *Time Zone* / Mercy: *Jones, Steve*
CD _____ VSOPCD 188
Connoisseur / Jun '93 / Pinnacle.

AFTER THE SEPULTURE
CD _____ RAD 003CD
Radiation / Nov '95 / Plastic Head.

AGE OF ENLIGHTENMENT, THE - PROG ROCK VOL.1
Master of the universe: *Hawkwind* / See my way: *Blodwyn Pig* / Baby lemonade: *Barrett, Syd* / Flower king of flies: *Nice* / I keep singing that same old song: *Heavy Jelly* / Shield: *Deep Purple* / Notting Hill Gate: *Quintessence* / Killer: *Van Der Graaf Generator* / Song for Jeffrey: *Jethro Tull* / Cherry red: *Groundhogs* / I never did believe: *Gong* / Bad scene: *Ten Years After* / Many are called but few get up: *Man*
CD _____ CDCHR 6097
Chrysalis / Feb '95 / EMI.

AGE OF SWING, THE
In the mood / Very thought of you / Let's dance / Americarpatrol / Artistry in rhythm / Begin the beguine / Big John special / Skyliner / What is this thing called love / Hamp's boogie woogie / I've got a gal in Kalamazoo / Cherokee / Opus in pastels / Pinetop's boogie / Snowfall / One o'clock jump / Song of India / Perdido / Sing, sing, sing / King Porter stomp / Little brown jug / Solitude / Eager beaver / Serenade in blue / I know why / On the Alamo / Hornet / Listen to my music / Wrappin' it up on the Lindy slide / Chatanooga choo choo / Apple honey / I'm getting sentimental over you / Harlem nocturne / Leave us leap / You made me love you / Boogie woogie Maxine / Moonlight sonata / South Rampart Street parade / St. Louis blues march / Mood indigo / Intermission riff / Jersey bounce / Hot toddy / 'S Wonderful / Oh lady be good / Chloe / Leapfrog / Pennsylvania 6-5000 / Opus / I got it bad and that ain't good / String of pearls / Sweet Georgia Brown / I'll never smile again / Stardreams / I get a kick out of you / Long John Silver / Down South camp meeting / Don't be that way / Anvil

---

chorus / Moonlight serenade / After you've gone / Pompton turnpike / On the sunny side of the street / Do nothin' 'til you hear from me / At last / Flying home / Cotton tail / Body and soul / Painted rhythm / Tuxedo junction / Take the 'A' train / Swanee river / Don't sit under the apple tree / Sophisticated lady / Swingin' the blues / Memories of you / I can't get started (with you) / Poor butterfly / Song of the Volga boatmen / At the woodchoppers' ball
CD Set _____ TFP 002
Tring / Nov '92 / Tring / Prism.

AGE OF SWING, THE
CD _____ EMPRCD 507
Emporio / Apr '94 / THE / Disc / CM.

AGENDA 22
CD _____ ELEC 14CD
New Electronica / Oct '94 / Pinnacle / Plastic Head.

AI CONFINI/INTERZONE
CD _____ NT 6714
Robi Droli / Jan '94 / Direct / ADA.

AIN'T NOTHIN' BUT A HOUSE PARTY
Bless your soul: *Dreamlovers* / You gave me somebody to love: *Dreamlovers* / You ain't sayin' nothin' new: *Virgil, Henry* / You fooled me: *Virgil, Henry* / Ain't nothing but a house party: *Showstoppers* / Eeeny meeny: *Showstoppers* / How easy your heart forgets me: *Showstoppers* / Suddenly: *Cherry People* / Father's angels: *Cherry People* / Bok to bak: *Cherry People* / I've been hurt: *Deal, Bill & The Rhondells* / Baby show it: *Festival* / Green grow the lilacs: *Festival* / You're gonna make it: *Devonnes* / Mob: *Devonnes* / I dig everything about you: *Devonnes* / Loan shark: *Chapter One* / Money won't do it, love will: *Chapter One* / I'll get by without you: *Gamble, Kenny & Tommy Bell* / Someday you'll be my love: *Gamble, Kenny & Tommy Bell*
CD _____ NEMCD 678
Sequel / Apr '94 / BMG.

AIN'T NUTHIN' BUT A SHE THING
Ain't nuthin' but a she thing: *Salt 'N' Pepa* / Mama: *Lennox, Annie* / 69 anee erotique: *Luscious Jackson* / Weakness in me: *Etheridge, Melissa* / Woman of the ghetto: *Oliver, Andi* / Open your eyes, you can fly: *Williams, Vanessa* / Hard times: *Queen Latifah* / Cimarron: *Come* / Don't smoke in bed: *Smith, Patti* / Women of Ireland: *O'Connor, Sinead*
CD _____ 8286742
London / Oct '95 / PolyGram.

AIN'T TIMES HARD
CD Set _____ CDDIG 3
Charly / Feb '95 / Charly / THE / Cadillac.

ALABADOS Y BAILES
CD _____ 80292
New World / Sep '95 / Harmonia Mundi / ADA / Cadillac.

ALABAMA: BLACK COUNTRY DANCE BANDS 1924-49
CD _____ DOCD 5166
Blues Document / May '93 / Swift / Jazz Music / Hot Shot.

ALABAMA: SECULAR & RELIGIOUS MUSIC
CD _____ DOCD 5165
Blues Document / May '93 / Swift / Jazz Music / Hot Shot.

ALADDIN RECORDS STORY, THE
Flying home: *Jacquet, Illinois & His Orchestra* / Be baba leba: *Humes, Helen* / Driftin' blues: *Moore, Johnny B. & Three Blazers* / When I'm in my tea: *Davis, Maxwell* / I don't stand a ghost of a chance with you: *Harris, Wynonie* / Mother Fuyer: *Dirty Red* / He may be your man: *Humes, Helen* / Milky white way: *Trumpeteers* / Guitar in my hand: *Brown, Clarence 'Gatemouth'* / Too late: *Five Keys* / Chicken shack boogie: *Milburn, Amos* / Loch Lomond: *Rockets* / Shotgun blues: *Hopkins, Lightnin'* / Round Midnight: *Robins* / Glory of love: *Five Keys* / Safronia B: *Bose, Calvin* / Trouble blues: *Brown, Charles* / I got loaded: *Harris, Peppermint* / Sad journey blues: *Dixon, Floyd Orchestra* / Dad gum ya hide boy: *Dixon, Louis* / Hucklebuck with jimmy: *Five Keys* / Wigg fromt boogie: *Burrage, Harold* / Blue turning grey over you: *Holiday, Billie* / Feels so good: *Shirley & Lee* / Telephone blues: *Dixon, Floyd* / Kokomo: *Gene & Eunice* / Let me good times roll: *Shirley & Lee* / How long: *Five Keys* / I need you, I want you: *Parker, Jack* / Don't let go (hold me, hold me): *Cookies* / Messy Bessy: *Jordan, Louis & His Tympany Five* / This is my story: *Gene & Eunice* / Don't leave me baby: *Fulson, Lowell* / Call operator 210: *Dixon, Floyd* / Ding dong ding: *Bip & Bop* / Remember: *Aladdins* / Rockin' with the clock: *Shirley & Lee* / Honest I do: *Foster, Cell* / Rockin' at Cosmo's: *Allen, Lee* / Be cool my heart: *Allen, Lee* / I'm so high: *Five Keys* / I'm in the mood for love: *King Pleasure* / Ray Pearl: *Jivers* / Dreamy eyes: *Squires* / Yak, yak: *Marvin & Johnny* / Darling it's wonderful: *Lovers* / Our love is here to stay: *Sharps* / King Kong: *Tyler, Big T* / Smack, smack: *Marvin & Johnny* / Little girl in the cabin: *Sloan, Flip* / Sugar doll: *Belvin, Jesse* / Little bitty pretty one: *Harris, Thurston*

CD Set _____ ALADDIN 1
EMI / Jan '95 / EMI.

ALAN FREED'S ROCK & ROLL DANCE PARTY
Pretzel / Rock rock rock / Maybellene / Ruby baby / Tear it up / (We're gonna) Rock around the clock / My prayer speedo / Be bop a lula / Why don't you write me / Little girl of mine / Rip it up
CD _____ CDMF 075
Magnum Force / '91 / Magnum Music Group.

ALANTE DI MUSICA TRADIZIONALE
CD _____ NT 6736CD
Robi Droli / Apr '95 / Direct / ADA.

ALBANIA: SONGS AS OLD AS THE EARTH
CD _____ T 33.12
Touch / Mar '91 / These / Kudos.

ALCHEMY OF SCOTT LA FARO, THE
Too close for comfort / I've never been in love before / Time remembered / Jade vision / Variants on a theme of Thelenious Monk (criss cross) / C & D / First take / Alchemy of Scott La Faro
CD _____ CD 53213
Giants Of Jazz / Jan '96 / Target/BMG / Cadillac.

ALEXIS KORNER MEMORIAL CONCERT VOL. 1
CD _____ IGOCD 2060
Indigo / Dec '95 / Direct / ADA.

ALEXIS KORNER MEMORIAL CONCERT VOL. 2
CD _____ IGOCD 2051
Indigo / Dec '95 / Direct / ADA.

ALIVE IN THE LIVING ROOM
CD _____ CRECD 01
Creation / May '94 / 3MV / Vital.

ALL ABOUT SOUL
Divine emotions: *Narada* / Love supreme: *Downing, Will* / There's nothing like this: *Omar* / Sexual healing: *Gaye, Marvin* / How do you stop: *Brown, James* / Sha la la (means my baby): *Green, Al* / Wishing on a star: *Rose Royce* / Rainy night in Georgia: *Crawford, Randy* / Always: *Atlantic Starr* / That lady: *Isley Brothers* / Shake you down: *Abbott, Gregory* / Me and Mrs Jones: *Jackson, Freddie* / Love I lost: *Melvin, Harold* / Ain't no sunshine: *Withers, Bill* / You'll never know: *Hi-Gloss* / Cherish: *Kool & The Gang* / Softly whispering I love you: *Congregation* / I'm doing fine now: *New York City*
CD _____ RENCD 108
Renaissance Collector Series / Oct '95 / Pinnacle.

ALL AMERICAN ROCK 'N' ROLL FROM FRATERNITY RECORDS
Rock-a-bop: *Moore, Sparkle* / Flower of my heart: *Moore, Sparkle* / Killer: *Moore, Sparkle* / She's neat: *Wright, Dale* / Take hold of my hand: *Dobkins, Carl Jr.* / That's why I'm asking: *Dobkins, Carl Jr.* / Makin' love with my baby: *Turley, Richard* / That's my girl: *Turner, Jesse Lee* / Absolutely nothin': *Parsons, Bill* / Dance, dance, dance: *Parsons, Bill* / Hand me down my rockin' shoes: *Parsons, Bill* / Jungle bandstand: *Parsons, Bill* / Try it no more: *Marcum, Gene* / That's showbiz: *Wright, Dale & The Wright Guys* / You're the answer: *Wright, Dale & The Wright Guys* / Buddies with the blues: *Bare, Bobby & The All American Boys' Orchestra* / Teardrops from the eyes: *Jeffers, Jimmy & The Jokers* / Rubber dolly: *Bare, Bobby* / All American boy: *Bare, Bobby*
CD _____ CDCHD 316
Ace / Jul '91 / Pinnacle / Cadillac / Complete/Pinnacle.

ALL FRUITS RIPE VOL.1
CD _____ VPCD 1242
Shocking Vibes / Jul '92 / Jetstar.

ALL MY LOVE
CD _____ NTRCD 001
Nectar / May '93 / Pinnacle.

ALL NIGHT LONG
(Dave Cash Presents The Best Of The 60's)
I can't equalize: *Who* / For your love: *Yardbirds* / Daydream: *Lovin' Spoonful* / Sha la la la lee: *Small Faces* / Keep on running: *Davis, Spencer Group* / Wild thing: *Troggs* / This wheel's on fire: *Driscoll, Julie* / I'm alive: *Hollies* / Bring it on home to me: *Animals* / Concrete and clay: *Unit 4+2* / Sorrow: *Merseys* / Out of time: *Farlowe, Chris* / Let's hang on: *Four Seasons* / Days of Pearly Spencer: *McWilliams, David* / Whiter shade of pale: *Procul Harum* / Nights in white satin: *Moody Blues* / Sunny afternoon: *Kinks* / Reflections of my life: *Marmalade* / Make it easy on yourself: *Walker Brothers* / Unchained melody: *Righteous Brothers* / Groovy kind of love: *Mindbenders* / Some of your lovin': *Springfield, Dusty* / Getaway: *Fame, Georgie* / Oh not my baby: *Manfred Mann* / Hold tight: *Dave Dee, Dozy, Beaky, Mick & Tich* / Something in the air: *Thunderclap Newman*
CD _____ 5163752
PolyGram TV / Aug '93 / PolyGram.

ALL NIGHT LONG THEY PLAY THE BLUES
Part time love / Country boy / I know you hear me calling / Little green house / Hey my baby's gone / I'm serving time / Life goes on / Mama Rufus
CD _____ CDCHD 440
Ace / Jan '93 / Pinnacle / Cadillac / Complete/Pinnacle.

ALL OF MY APPOINTED TIME
CD _____ JCD 640
Jass / Aug '93 / CM / Jazz Music / ADA / Cadillac / Direct.

ALL PLATINUM FUNK
You got it (talkin' bout my love): Youngblood, Lonnie / I got a suspicion: Patterson, Bobby / This is it: First Class / In the bottle: Brother To Brother / Funk you: B.B.P. / Stay: Moments / Let your mind be free: Brother To Brother / Thump and bump: Fisher, Eddie / (I'm in) The prime of love: B.B.P. / On top: Youngblood, Lonnie / I'm gonna take your love: Brother To Brother / Is it funky enough: Communications & Black Experiences Band / Cosmic blues: Fisher, Eddie / Chance with you: Brother To Brother / Walter's inspiration: Rimshots / Music makes me feel good: Fisher, Eddie / I may be right, I may be wrong: Mill Street Depo / Gotta get it back: Mother Freedom Band / Give me, lend me, loan me (let me have): Fisher, Eddie / 7-6-5-4-3-2-1 Blow your whistle: Rimshots
CD _____ CPCD 8082
Charly / Mar '95 / Charly / THE / Cadillac.

ALL RAVE ULTRA
CD _____ PC 002CD
Public Propaganda / Jan '95 / Plastic Head.

ALL SPICE
Never like this: Two Tons Of Fun / I think I love you: Shock / Slipped away: Allspice / Give it up (don't make me wait): Sylvester / Rainy day stormy nights: Impact / Hungry for your love: Allspice / Keep it up: Everett, Betty / Lovin': Hurtt, Phil / Just us: Two Tons Of Fun / I want this that: Rappin' Reverend / S.O.S.: Side Effect / Feel good all over: McWilliams, Paulette / For you: Reason, Johnny / I believe in you: Muhammad, Idris / Love's such a wonderful sound: Reason, Johnny / Finally found someone: Side Effect / Never been here before: McWilliams, Paulette
CD _____ CDBGPD 074
BGP / Oct '93 / Pinnacle.

ALL STAR CHICAGO BLUES SESSION
CD _____ JSPCD 214
JSP / '88 / ADA / Target/BMG / Direct / Cadillac / Complete/Pinnacle.

ALL STAR COUNTRY CHRISTMAS
We wish you a Merry Christmas / Silver bells / Winter wonderland / Jingle bells / Christmas in Virginia / Chrsitmas song / White Christmas / Sleigh ride / I'll be home for Christmas / With Christmas near / My favourite time of the year / Christmas song / Lighten up for Christmas / Blue christmas / Merry Christmas baby / Have yourself a merry little Christmas
CD _____ CDSOR 0072
D-Sharp / Nov '95 / Pinnacle.

ALL SUMMER LONG
CD _____ CDCD 1126
Charly / Mar '93 / Charly / THE / Cadillac.

ALL THAT BLUES
CD _____ OBCCD 5001
Original Blues Classics / Nov '88 / Complete/Pinnacle / Wellard / Cadillac.

ALL THAT COUNTRY
CD _____ LECD 418
Wisepack / Nov '92 / THE / Conifer.

ALL THAT JAZZ
CD _____ SETCD 086
Stardust / Sep '94 / Carlton Home Entertainment.

ALL THAT JAZZ
CD _____ 290432
Ariola / Jul '95 / BMG.

ALL THAT JAZZ IS BACK
Things are getting better: Adderley, Cannonball / How high the moon: Baker, Chet / Jumpin' at the Woodside: Basie, Count / Afro jaws: Davis, Eddie 'Lockjaw' / There is no greater love: Davis, Miles New Quintet / Latin American sunshine: Ellington, Duke Orchestra / Waltz for Debbie: Evans, Bill Trio / I ain't got nothin' but the blues: Fitzgerald, Ella & Tommy Flanagan Trio / Foggy day: Garland, Red / Birk's works: Gillespie, Dizzy / My funny valentine: Jackson, Milt Quartet / Bearcat: Jordan, Clifford Quartet / Spring is here: Kessel, Barney/Ron Brown/Shelly Manne
CD _____ OJCCD 1001
Original Jazz Classics / Oct '93 / Wellard / Jazz Music / Cadillac / Complete/Pinnacle.

ALL THAT SWING
CD _____ SETCD 087
Stardust / Sep '94 / Carlton Home Entertainment.

ALL THAT TRAD
Kansas city stomp: Welsh, Alex / Mama don't allow it: Kelly, George & Mick Mulligan / Sweet Georgia Brown: Barber, Chris / Lazy river: Ball, Kenny
CD _____ PWK 054
Carlton Home Entertainment / Mar '88 / Carlton Home Entertainment.

ALL THE BEST FROM SCOTLAND
CD _____ TREB 3033
Scratch / Mar '95 / BMG.

ALL THE BEST FROM SCOTLAND VOL.1
Rowan tree / Scotland again / Dark Lochnagar / Aye ready / Ae fond kiss / Work o' the weavers / Caledonia / Skye boat song / Amazing grace / Contentment / Lord's my shepherd / Man'a man / Ye banks and braes o' bonnie Doon / Massacre of Glencoe / Auld lang syne
CD _____ LBP 2018CD
Klub / Oct '94 / CM / Ross / Duncans / ADA / Direct.

ALL THE BEST FROM SCOTLAND VOL.2
Bonnie Aberdeen / Highland bridge depot / Major J. McGillvary / My ain folk / Loch Lomond / Dark island / Sweet afton / Bonnie lass o'Fyvie / Jessie's hornpipe / Kirk's hornpipe / Drumlees / Island spinning song / Banjo breakdown / Fiddlers choice / Scotland your a lady / Flowers of Edinburgh / Wee dug Tim / Lucky Scaup / Rose of Allendale / Skye boat song / Morag of Dunvegan / When you and I were young Maggie / Twa recruiting sergeants
CD _____ LBP 2019CD
Klub / Oct '94 / CM / Ross / Duncans / ADA / Direct.

ALL THE PRESIDENT'S MEN
CD _____ CRECD 140
Creation / Jul '92 / 3MV / Vital.

ALL THE WORLD NEEDS IS A LITTLE LOVE, PEACE AND UNDERSTANDIN
CD _____ SCL 2511
Ichiban Soul Classics / Nov '95 / Koch.

ALL THESE THINGS
(The Sound of New Orleans)
Barefootin': Parker, Robert / Tell it like it is: Neville, Aaron / Mother in law: Doe, Ernie K. / Working in a coalmine: Dorsey, Lee / I take it like that: Kenner, Chris / Ooh poo pah doo: Hill, Jessie / It will stand: Showman / You always hurt the one you love: Henry, Clarence 'Frogman' / Fortune teller: Spellman, Benny / All these things: Neville, Art / Iko iko: Dixie Cups / Ruler of my heart: Thomas, Irma / Rockin' pneumonia and the boogie woogie flu: Smith, Huey 'Piano' / Chicken strut: Meters / Release me: Adams, Johnny / Something you got: George, Barbara
CD _____ CDINS 5024
Instant / Feb '90 / Charly.

ALL THROUGH THE YEAR
CD _____ HPRCD 2002
Hokey Pokey / Oct '93 / ADA / Direct.

ALL TIME COUNTRY & WESTERN HITS
CD _____ KCD 000710
King/Paddle Wheel / Dec '92 / New Note.

ALL TIME COUNTRY AND WESTERN HITS
CD _____ KCD 537
King/Paddle Wheel / Nov '92 / New Note.

ALL TIME COUNTRY GREATS
Streets of Baltimore: Pride, Charley / Welcome to my world: Reeves, Jim / I'm movin' on: Snow, Hank / I'm a ramblin man: Jennings, Waylon / Funny how time slips away: Nelson, Willie / I will always love you: Parton, Dolly / Send me the pillow you dream on: Locklin, Hank / Yakety axe: Atkins, Chet / Sea of heartbreak: Gibson, Don / End of the world: Davis, Skeeter / Once a day: Smith, Connie / She's a little bit country: Hamilton, George IV / Is anybody going to San Antone: Pride, Charley
CD _____ 74321339342
Camden / Jan '96 / BMG.

ALL TIME REGGAE HITS
CD _____ CPCD 8028
Charly / Feb '94 / Charly / THE / Cadillac.

ALL WOMAN 3
CD _____ ALLWOCD 3
Quality / Feb '94 / Pinnacle.

ALL WOMAN 4
CD _____ ALLWOCD 4
Quality / Oct '94 / Pinnacle.

ALL YOU NEED IS LOVE
CD _____ MPV 5532
Movieplay / Sep '93 / Target/BMG.

ALLIGATOR MAKES THE BLUES COME ALIVE
CD _____ ALCD 0007
Alligator / Jan '93 / Direct / ADA.

ALLIGATOR RECORDS CHRISTMAS COLLECTION, THE
Christmas song: Bishop, Elvin / Christmas on the bayou: Brooks, Lonnie / Let me be your Santa Claus: Clarke, William / Santa Claus wants some lovin': Ellis, Shanley / Santa Claus Boogie: Brown, Charles / Christmas: Brown, Clarence 'Gatemouth' / I'm your santa: Lil' Ed & The Blues Imperials / Santa Claus: Little Charlie & The Nightcats / Silent night: Musselwhite, Charlie / Christmas in the country: Neal, Kenny / One parent christmas: Saffire / Lonesome christmas: Seals, Son / Merry merry Christmas: Taylor, Koko / Deck the halls boogie: Webster, Katie
CD _____ ALCDXMAS 9201
Alligator / Oct '93 / Direct / ADA.

ALLIGATOR SAMPLER
CD _____ ACDS 3657
Alligator / Aug '90 / Direct / ADA.

ALLONS CAJUN ROCK 'N' ROLL
Lafayette two-step: Roger, Aldus / Lacassine special: Roger, Aldus / Mardi gras dance: Roger, Aldus / La valse d'ennui: Roger, Aldus / Diga ding ding dong: Roger, Aldus / Allons rock 'n' roll: Roger, Aldus / Allons cush cush: Forester, Blackie / Just because: Forester, Blackie / Hang your hat: Forester, Blackie / La fille de la ville: Bruce, Vin / Le sud de la Louisianne: Bruce, Vin / Lake Arthur stomp: Thibodeaux, Rufus / Les veuves de la coulee: Happy Fats / Married life: Cormier, Louis / Rock the water: Forester, Blackie / Ooo / Grand mamou: Newman, Jimmy C. / Creole stomp: Breaux, Jimmy / Bosco stomp: Breaux, Jimmy / La valse de KLFY: Doucet, Michael / Ma belle Evangeline: Doucet, Michael / La maison a deux portes: Doucet, Michael
CD _____ CDCHD 367
Ace / Apr '91 / Pinnacle / Cadillac / Complete/Pinnacle.

ALMANAC
_____ 1238512
IAI / May '94 / Harmonia Mundi / Cadillac.

ALMIGHTY 12" VOL.1, THE
CD _____ ALMYCD 01
Almighty / Jan '93 / Total/BMG.

ALMIGHTY 12" VOL.2, THE
CD _____ ALMYCD 02
Almighty / Jan '93 / Total/BMG.

ALMIGHTY 12" VOL.3, THE
CD _____ ALMYCD 05
Almighty / Dec '93 / Total/BMG.

ALMIGHTY 12" VOL.5, THE
CD _____ ALMYCD 08
Almighty / Feb '94 / Total/BMG.

ALMIGHTY 12" VOL.6, THE
CD _____ ALMYCD 09
Almighty / Feb '94 / Total/BMG.

ALMIGHTY 12" VOL.7, THE
CD _____ ALMYCD 12
Almighty / May '95 / Total/BMG.

ALMIGHTY DEFINITIVE '95
CD _____ ALMYCD 15
Almighty / Oct '95 / Total/BMG.

ALTERNATIVE CURRENT
CD _____ CDACV 2002
ACV / Nov '94 / Plastic Head / SRD.

ALTERNATIVE CURRENT VOL.2
CD _____ CDACV 2008
ACV / Jan '96 / Plastic Head / SRD.

ALTERNATIVE NRG
Drive: R.E.M. / Ring the bells: James / Until the end of the world: U2 / Tell me the truth: Midnight Oil / Everyday life has become a health risk: Disposable Heroes Of Hiphoprisy / New damage: Soundgarden / New kind of kick: Jesus & Mary Chain / Sing our own song: UB40 / Cold: Lennox, Annie / Looking through patient eyes: PM Dawn / ... .: ... . / ... Scorch and destroy: EMF / Yolngu boy: Yothu Yindi / J.C.: Sonic Youth / Fam bam: Boo-Yaa T.R.I.B.E. / Shitlist: L7
CD _____ 74321180912
Arista / Jan '94 / BMG.

ALWAYS AND FOREVER
(Love Songs Of The 70's)
Always and forever: Heatwave / Every night: Snow, Phoebe / Free: Williams, Deniece / Summer breeze: Isley Brothers / I don't believe in miracles: Blunstone, Colin / When will I see you again: Three Degrees / I can see clearly now: Nash, Johnny / Most beautiful girl: Rich, Charlie / Me and Mrs. Jones: Paul, Billy / Lovely day: Withers, Bill / Hurt: Manhattans / Highways of my life: Isley Brothers / More than a feeling: Boston / That's what friends are for: Williams, Deniece / Love train: O'Jays / Say you don't mind: Blunstone, Colin / Arms of Mary: Hook
CD _____ PWKS 4064
Carlton Home Entertainment / Jul '91 / Carlton Home Entertainment.

AM I BLACK ENOUGH FOR YOU
Am I black enough for you: Paul, Billy / Thank you for talkin' to me Africa: Sly & The Family Stone / Freedom: Isley Brothers / Big gangster: O'Jays / Freddie's dead: MFSB / Brother brother: O'Jays / Don't call me brother: O'Jays / Ebony woman: Melvin, Harold & The Bluenotes / Keep smilin': Sigler, Bunny / Where are all my friends: Melvin, Harold & The Bluenotes / Save the children: Intruders / Go for your guns: Isley Brothers / Man of war: Jacksons
CD _____ 4808862
Columbia / Jan '96 / Sony.

AM I DREAMING
They talk about us: Williams, Cindy / I deserve it: Jones, Samantha / Town I live in: Lee, Jackie / You've got that hold on me: Hillery, Jane / I can't stop thinking about you: Kaye, Linda / Baby let me be your baby: Deano / You'd think he didn't know me: Browne, Sandra / Sour grapes: Noble, Patsy Ann / Am I dreaming: Tiffany / Softly in the night: Three Bells / Snakes and snails: Cogan, Alma / Wait 'til my Bobby gets home: Jones, Beverley / Breakaway: Marsden, Beryl / You don't love me no more: Bell, Madeline / Don't come any closer: Jones, Samantha / Cry to me: Track / Be his girl: Sloan, Sam / Too young to go steady: Siver, Andee / You kissed me boy: Duncan, Lesley / Biggity big: Cope, Suzie / Some people: Deene, Carol / I gotta be with you: Rede, Emma / Once more with feeling: Wonder, Alison / I didn't love him anyway: Peanut
CD _____ RPM 137
RPM / Aug '94 / Pinnacle.

AM-REP SAMPLER
CD _____ ARR 279CD
Amphetamine Reptile / '94 / SRD.

AMAZING GRACE
CD _____ MU 3012
Musketeer / Oct '92 / Koch.

AMAZING GRACE AND OTHER SCOTTISH FAVOURITES
CD _____ CC 266
Music For Pleasure / May '91 / EMI.

AMAZONIA
CD _____ LYRCD 7300
Lyrichord / Feb '94 / Roots / ADA / CM.

AMBIENCE
CD _____ 5259522
PolyGram TV / Sep '95 / PolyGram.

AMBIENT
CD _____ EMIT 0094
Time Recordings / Apr '94 / Pinnacle.

AMBIENT AMAZON
CD _____ TMCD 1
Tumi Dance / Nov '95 / SRD.

AMBIENT AURAS
CD _____ CDRAID 519
Rumour / Sep '94 / Pinnacle / 3MV / Sony.

AMBIENT COMPILATION VOL.4
CD _____ SR 9753
Silent / Mar '95 / Plastic Head.

AMBIENT DUB VOL. 4
Oracle: Space Time Continuum / Solar prophet: Insanity Sect / Callacop: Deep Space Networks / Regina from the future: Starseeds / Step: Coldcut / In 7: Another Fine Day / Warehouse 5AM: Positive Life / White darkness: Sandoz / Triangle: Sounds From The Ground
CD _____ RBADCD 11
Beyond / Jun '95 / Kudos / Pinnacle.

AMBIENT GROOVE VOL.3
CD _____ SUN 49952
Mumbo / Mar '95 / Pinnacle.

AMBIENT NORTHERN LIGHTS VOL. 1
CD _____ JCRCD 005
Just Create / Jun '95 / Total/BMG.

AMBIENT RITUALS
CD _____ CLEO 9516CD
Cleopatra / Jun '95 / Disc.

AMBIENT SENSES
(The Mating)
Towers of club: Orb / Papua New Guinea: Future Sound Of London / Joyrex J9 ii: Caustic Window / Dreams of children: Slater, Luke / Earthdance: Mandragora / Ageispolis: Aphex Twin / Ready for dead: Ready For Dead / Minky starshine: Seefeel / O Locco: Sun Electric / Alqa: Alien Mutation / Galapagos: Sunkings
CD _____ CDTOT 12
Jumpin' & Pumpin' / Jun '94 / 3MV / Sony.

AMBIENT SENSES 2
(The Feeling)
Underground (Ambient mix): Irresistable Force / My travels: Larkin, Kenny / Naiad: Ishi, Ken / Lean on me: Moby / Listening (Aural sculpture): Optic Eye / Path: El Mal / Moist mass: Locust / Stoned: Golden Claw Music / A.M.: Wagon Christ / Manuel versus the apaches: Deep Secret
CD _____ CDTOT 16
Jumpin' & Pumpin' / Oct '94 / 3MV / Sony.

AMBIENT SENSES 3
CD _____ CDTOT 23
Jumpin' & Pumpin' / Mar '95 / 3MV / Sony.

AMEN
Curtain: Marden Hill / I bloodbrother be: Shock Headed Peters / Vallari: King Of Luxembourg / Nice on the ice (#): King Of Luxembourg / You Mary you: Phillipe, Louis / Nicky: Momus / O come all ye faithful (Aceste fidelis): Monochrome Set / Cecil beaton's scrapbook: Would-Be-Goods / Blue shinin' quick star: Flippers Guitar / Curry crazy: Bad Dream Fancy Dress / It's love: Hunki-Dori / Andy Warhol: Fisher-Turner, Simon / Mystery stone: Fisher-Turner, Simon / Maria Celesta: Adverse, Anthony /

Whoops what a palaver: *Bid* / Belfast boy: *Fardon, Don* / Fruit paradise: *Would-Be-Goods* / My cheri amour: *Phillipe, Louis* / Trial of Dr. Fancy: *King Of Luxembourg* / Diary of a narcissist: *Momus* / Temptation of the angel: *Amen: Great Chefs Of Europe*
CD _____ MONDE 1CD
Richmond / Feb '92 / Pinnacle.

AMERICAN & EUROPEAN TECHNOLOGICAL INNOVATIONS
CD _____ ELEC 1CD
New Electronica / Jun '93 / Pinnacle / Plastic Head.

AMERICAN BANJO: THREE FINGER & SCRUGGS STYLE
CD _____ SFWCD 40037
Smithsonian Folkways / Nov '94 / ADA / Direct / Koch / CM / Cadillac.

AMERICAN BIG BANDS
You're driving me crazy: *May, Billy* / Little brown jug: *May, Billy* / I guess I'll have to change my plan: *May, Billy* / Rose Marie: *May, Billy* / Tenderly: *May, Billy* / When I take my sugar to tea: *May, Billy* / Diane: *May, Billy* / Do you ever think of me: *May, Billy* / Unforgettable: *May, Billy* / Cocktails for two: *May, Billy* / Charmaine: *May, Billy* / Artistry in rhythm: *Kenton, Stan* / Printed rhythm: *Kenton, Stan* / I told ya I love ya, now get out: *Kenton, Stan* / Eager beaver: *Kenton, Stan* / Artistry in percussion: *Kenton, Stan* / Lover: *Kenton, Stan* / Spider and the fly: *Kenton, Stan* / Laura: *Kenton, Stan* / How high the moon: *Kenton, Stan* / How am I to know: *Kenton, Stan* / Harlem nocturne: *Brown, Les & His Band Of Renown* / Continental: *Brown, Les & His Band Of Renown* / Riding high: *Brown, Les & His Band Of Renown* / On a little street in Singapore: *Brown, Les & His Band Of Renown* / Hit the road to dreamland: *Brown, Les & His Band Of Renown* / Lover's leap: *Brown, Les & His Band Of Renown* / Johnson rag: *Brown, Les & His Band Of Renown* / Leapfrog: *Brown, Les & His Band Of Renown* / That certain feeling: *Brown, Les & His Band Of Renown* / Sentimental journey: *Brown, Les & His Band Of Renown* / I've got my love to keep me warm: *Brown, Les & His Band Of Renown* / I wonder what's become of Sally: *Anthony, Ray & His Orchestra* / Rockin' through Dixie: *Anthony, Ray & His Orchestra* / Skip to my Lou: *Anthony, Ray & His Orchestra* / Did he do right by you: *Anthony, Ray & His Orchestra* / Wanted: *Anthony, Ray & His Orchestra* / Tuxedo junction: *Anthony, Ray & His Orchestra* / It's de-lovely: *Anthony, Ray & His Orchestra* / Mr. Anthony's boogie: *Anthony, Ray & His Orchestra* / When the saints go marching in: *Anthony, Ray & His Orchestra*
CD _____ CDDL 1284
EMI / Nov '94 / EMI.

AMERICAN CLAVE - AN ANTHOLOGY
CD Set _____ AMCL 1020/26
American Clave / Jan '94 / New Note / ADA / Direct.

AMERICAN DREAMS
CD _____ 24094
Laserlight / Mar '95 / Target/BMG.

AMERICAN DREAMS 50'S VOL.1
My heart cries for you: *Shore, Dinah* / Be my love: *Lanza, Mario* / Slow poke: *King, Pee Wee* / C'est si bon: *Kitt, Eartha* / Cherry pink and apple blossom white: *Prado, Perez* / Cattle call: *Arnold, Eddy* / Rock 'n' roll waltz: *Starr, Kay* / Heartbreak hotel: *Presley, Elvis* / Banana boat song (Day O): *Belafonte, Harry* / Melodie d'amour: *Ames Brothers* / Lazy man: *Monte, Lou* / Oh lonesome me: *Gibson, Don* / Send me the pillow that you dream on: *Locklin, Hank* / Guess who: *Belvin, Jesse* / Making love: *Robinson, Floyd* / Three bells: *Browns* / Oh Carol: *Sedaka, Neil* / He'll have to go: *Reeves, Jim*
CD _____ ND 90370
RCA / Sep '89 / BMG.

AMERICAN DREAMS 50'S VOL.2
I'm movin' on: *Snow, Hank* / Thing: *Harris, Phil* / I get ideas: *Martin, Tony* / Because you're mine: *Lanza, Mario* / On my papa: *Fisher, Eddie* / Crying in the chapel: *Valli, June* / Naughty lady of Shady Lane: *Ames Brothers* / Hot diggity (dog ziggity boom): *Como, Perry* / Canadian sunset: *Winterhalter, Hugo* / Don't be cruel: *Presley, Elvis* / Love is strange: *Mickey & Sylvia* / Mama look a boo boo: *Belafonte, Harry* / Four walls: *Reeves, Jim* / Patricia: *Prado, Perez* / Diary: *Sedaka, Neil* / Wonder of you: *Peterson, Ray* / Battle of Kookamonga: *Homer & Jethro* / Don't know you: *Reese, Della* / Shout: *Isley Brothers*
CD _____ ND 90371
RCA / Sep '89 / BMG.

AMERICAN DREAMS 60'S VOL.1
Tell Laura I love her: *Peterson, Ray* / It's now or never: *Presley, Elvis* / Chain gang: *Cooke, Sam* / Last date: *Cramer, Floyd* / I just don't understand: *Ann-Margaret* / Lion sleeps tonight: *Tokens* / Love me warm and tender: *Anka, Paul* / Breaking up is hard to do: *Sedaka, Neil* / End of the world: *Davis, Skeeter* / I will follow him: *March, Little Peggy* / Maria Elena: *Los Indios Tabajaros* / 500 miles away from home: *Bare, Bobby* / Java: *Hirt, Al* / Baby the rain must fall: *Yarborough, Glenn* / Make the world go away: *Arnold, Eddy* / Somebody to love: *Jefferson*

Airplane / Light my fire: *Feliciano, Jose* / These eyes: *Guess Who* / Grazing in the grass: *Friends Of Distinction* / Romeo and Juliet: *Mancini, Henry*
CD _____ ND 90372
RCA / Sep '89 / BMG.

AMERICAN DREAMS 60'S VOL.2
Old lamplighter: *Browns* / Please help me, I'm falling: *Locklin, Hank* / On the rebound: *Cramer, Floyd* / Funny how time slips away: *Elledge, Jimmy* / Twistin' the night away: *Cooke, Sam* / Steel guitar and a glass of wine: *Anka, Paul* / Guitar man: *Eddy, Duane* / Detroit city: *Bare, Bobby* / Abilene: *Hamilton, George IV* / Hello heartache, goodbye love: *March, Little Peggy* / I can't stay mad at you: *Davis, Skeeter* / We'll sing in the sunshine: *Garnett, Gale* / Ringo: *Greene, Lorne* / Ballad of the Green Berets: *Sadler, Sgt. Barry* / My cup runneth over: *Ames, Ed* / Good, the bad and the ugly: *Montenegro, Hugo* / In the year 2525: *Zager & Evans* / Let's get together: *Youngbloods* / Everybody's talkin': *Nilsson, Harry* / Suspicious minds: *Presley, Elvis*
CD _____ ND 90373
RCA / Sep '89 / BMG.

AMERICAN DREAMS 70'S VOL.1
Love or let me be lonely: *Friends Of Distinction* / American woman: *Guess Who* / Amos Moses: *Reed, Jerry* / It's impossible: *Como, Perry* / Without you: *Nilsson, Harry* / Troglodyte (caveman): *Castor, Jimmy* / Bunch / Everybody plays the fool: *Main Ingredient* / Burning love: *Presley, Elvis* / My Maria: *Stevenson, B.W.* / Rock the boat: *Hues Corporation* / You little trustmaker: *Tymes* / Life is a rock (but the radio rolled me): *Reunion* / Lady: *Styx* / Miracles: *Jefferson Starship* / Turn the beat around: *Robinson, Vickie Sue* / Rich girl: *Hall & Oates* / Here you come again: *Parton, Dolly* / Shame: *King, Evelyn 'Champagne'*
CD _____ ND 90374
RCA / Sep '89 / BMG.

AMERICAN FM
CD _____ NTRCD 018
Nectar / Jun '94 / Pinnacle.

AMERICAN FM VOL.2
CD _____ NTRCD 029
Nectar / Sep '94 / Pinnacle.

AMERICAN FOLK BLUES FESTIVAL 1970
Introduction / Hard hearted woman / That ain't it / Maggie Lee / World boogie / Old lady / Going to Louisiana / Blues before sunrise / Hootin' the blues / Back water blues / Walk on / When I was drinking / Juanita / After hours / Crazy for my baby / Sittin' and cryin' the blues
CD _____ CDLR 42021
L&R / Jul '91 / New Note.

AMERICAN FOLK BLUES FESTIVAL 1972
CD _____ CDLS 42018
L&R / Jul '92 / New Note.

AMERICAN HEARTBEAT
Night train: *Brown, James* / What made Milwaukee famous (has made a loser out of me): *Lewis, Jerry Lee* / Do you know the way to San Jose: *Warwick, Dionne* / In a station: *Band* / Chattanooga choo choo: *Miller, Glenn* / City of New Orleans: *Guthrie, Arlo* / Promised land: *Allan, Johnnie* / California girls: *Beach Boys* / Woodstock: *Matthew's Southern Comfort* / Spanish harlem: *Franklin, Aretha* / Deep in the heart of Texas: *Eddy, Duane* / El paso: *Robbins* / Route 66: *Troup* / Twenty four hours from Tulsa: *Pitney, Gene* / By the time I get to Phoenix: *Campbell, Glen* / Walking to New Orleans: *Domino, Fats* / Memphis, Tennessee: *Berry, Chuck* / Nashville cats: *Lovin' Spoonful* / Meet me in St. Louis: *Garland, Judy* / Baltimore: *Newman, Randy*
CD _____ CDV 2728
Virgin / Apr '94 / EMI.

AMERICAN INDIAN - WOUNDED KNEE
CD _____ SM 10882CD
Wergo / Nov '95 / Harmonia Mundi / ADA / Cadillac.

AMERICAN INDIAN DANCE THEATRE
CD _____ 824312
Buda / Jan '90 / Discovery / ADA.

AMERICAN INDIAN DANCES
CD _____ EUCD 1317
ARC / Jul '95 / ARC Music / ADA.

AMERICAN JAZZ FESTIVAL IN LATIN AMERICA
CD _____ WWCD 2025
West Wind / May '89 / Swift / Charly / CM / ADA.

AMERICAN LIVIN' BLUES FESTIVAL 1982
CD _____ 157742
Blues Collection / Feb '93 / Discovery.

AMERICAN PENSIONERS ON ECSTASY
CD _____ CRECD 095
Creation / Apr '91 / 3MV / Vital.

AMERICAN RHYTHM & BLUES
CD _____ CDRB 27
Charly / Aug '95 / Charly / THE / Cadillac.

AMERICAN ROCKABILLY
CD _____ NERCD 048
Nervous / Sep '95 / Nervous / Magnum Music Group.

AMERICAN WILDS
CD _____ 12148
Laserlight / May '94 / Target/BMG.

AMERICANISM
CD _____ NTMCD 509
Nectar / Jan '96 / Pinnacle.

AMERICANS IN PARIS VOL.2
CD _____ 2512772
Jazztime / Mar '90 / Discovery / BMG.

AMERICANS IN PARIS VOL.7 (1946-50)
CD _____ 8274142
Jazztime / Jan '95 / Discovery / BMG.

AMERICA'S ROCK
Burning heart: *Survivor* / Travellin' shoes: *Bishop, Elvin* / Ramblin' man: *Allman Brothers* / Take me home: *Cher* / Spooky: *Atlanta Rhythm Section* / Sweet dreams: *Buchanan, Roy* / Do you like it: *Kingdom Come* / Run run run: *Velvet Underground* / Gypsy road: *Cinderella* / Tom Sawyer: *Rush* / Midnight rider: *Allman, Greg* / Na na hey hey kiss him goodbye: *Steam* / Rock 'n' roll children: *Dio* / House of the rising sun: *Frijid Pink*
CD _____ 5506402
Spectrum/Karussell / Aug '94 / PolyGram / THE.

AMONG MY SOUVENIRS: THOSE ROMANTIC 20'S
Eclipse / Mar '92 / PolyGram.
CD _____ 8440832

AMONG MY SOUVENIRS: THOSE ROMANTIC 30'S
Eclipse / Mar '92 / PolyGram.
CD _____ 8440842

AMOREUSE - THE FEMININE TOUCH
How can I be sure: *Springfield, Dusty* / Loving and free: *Dee, Kiki* / Answer me: *Dickson, Barbara* / I can't get you out of my mind: *Elliman, Yvonne* / September in the rain: *Washington, Dinah* / I put a spell on you: *Simone, Nina* / Je t'aime: *Birkin, Jane & Serge Gainsbourgh* / Amoreuse: *Dee, Kiki* / It may be Winter outside: *Love Unlimited Orchestra* / Some of your lovin': *Springfield, Dusty* / Love me: *Elliman, Yvonne* / Here I go again: *Twiggy* / Stay with me 'til dawn: *Tzuke, Judie*
CD _____ PWKS 539
Carlton Home Entertainment / Oct '89 / Carlton Home Entertainment.

AMPHETAMINE REPTILE 1993 SAMPLER
CD _____ ARRCD 42/279
Amphetamine Reptile / Jul '93 / SRD.

AMPHETAMINE REPTILE MOTORS 1995 MODELS
CD _____ ARRCD 62005
Amphetamine Reptile / May '95 / SRD.

AMPLIFIED VOL.1
CD _____ AABT 807CD
Abstract / Apr '95 / Pinnacle / Total/BMG.

ASSORTMENT, AN
Surfer Baby: *Blind Mr. Jones* / Hey: *Blind Mr. Jones* / Brad: *Tse Tse Fly* / On purpose: *Tse Tse Fly* / PDF: *Prolapse* / Screws: *Prolapse* / Jack: *Monochrome Set* / House of God: *Monochrome Set* / Humtone 4: *Fisher, Morgan* / Humtone 4 (remix): *Fisher, Morgan*
CD _____ CDMRED 107
Cherry Red / Feb '94 / Pinnacle.

AN CEOL AGAINN FHEIN
CD _____ DUAL 3CD
Macmeanma / Aug '95 / Duncans / CM / ADA.

ANAGRAM PUNK SINGLES COLLECTION
Give us a future / Just another hero / You talk we talk / Woman in disguise / Lust for glory / Baby baby / Dragnet / Jerusalem / Pressure / Solidarity / Five flew over the cuckoo's nest / Guilty / Hang ten / Cum on feel the noize / Breakin' in / Nowhere left to run / Not just a name / This is the age / Black sheep / Children of the night / You'll never know / Legacy / Teenage rampage
CD _____ CDPUNK 37
Anagram / Sep '94 / Pinnacle.

ANALOGUE ELEMENTS VOL 2
CD _____ NEUCD 2
Neuton / Oct '94 / Plastic Head.

ANALOGUE ELEMENTS VOL.1
CD _____ NEUCD 1
Neuton / May '94 / Plastic Head.

ANARCHY IN THE UK
Anarchy in the U.K.: *Sex Pistols* / Pretty vacant: *Sex Pistols* / God save the queen: *Sex Pistols* / Modern world: *Jam* / Down in the tube station at midnight: *Jam* / (Get a) Grip (on yourself): *Stranglers* / Duchess: *Stranglers* / Like clockwork: *Boomtown Rats* / She's so modern: *Boomtown Rats* / Everybody's happy nowadays: *Buzzcocks* / Harmony in my head: *Buzzcocks* / Hurry up Harry: *Sham 69* / Wednesday week: *Un-*

dertones / Hanging on the telephone: *Blondie*
CD _____ CDFA 3263
Fame / Oct '91 / EMI.

ANCIENT EGYPT
CD _____ LYRCD 7347
Lyrichord / '91 / Roots / ADA / CM.

ANCIENT HEART - MANDINKA & FULANI MUSIC
CD _____ 5101482
Axiom / Oct '92 / PolyGram / Vital.

AND THE ANGELS SING
CD _____ AVC 527
Avid / Nov '93 / Avid/BMG / Koch.

AND THE ANGELS SING OVER THE RAINBOW - 1939
Jeepers creepers: *Armstrong, Louis* / Jive at five: *Basie, Count* / Undecided: *Webb, Chick* / Zigeuner: *Shaw, Artie* / Moonlight serenade: *Miller, Glenn* / When lights are low: *Hampton, Lionel* / Ain't she sweet: *Lunceford, Jimmie* / At the woodchoppers' ball: *Herman, Woody* / I'm checkin' out (goodbye): *Ellington, Duke* / Body and soul: *Hawkins, Coleman* / And the angels sing: *Goodman, Benny* / I wish I could shimmy like my sister Kate: *Spanier, Muggsy* / Lady's in love with you: *Miller, Glenn* / Over the rainbow: *Garland, Judy* / Sugar: *Wilson, Teddy* / Lester leaps in: *Basie, Count* / I've got my eyes on you: *Dorsey, Tommy* / Opus 5: *Kirby, John* / Flyin' home: *Goodman, Benny* / 'T ain't what you do: *Lunceford, Jimmie* / I'm coming Virginia: *Shaw, Artie*
CD _____ PHONTCD 7667
Phontastic / Apr '90 / Wellard / Jazz Music / Cadillac.

AND THE FUN JUST NEVER ENDS
CD _____ LF 071
Lost & Found / Jan '94 / Plastic Head.

ANDALUSIAN FLAMENCO SONG AND DANCE
CD _____ LYRCD 7388
Lyrichord / '91 / Roots / ADA / CM.

ANGEL OF THE MORNING (Rock & Pop Ballads)
CD _____ CD 12202
Laserlight / Aug '93 / Target/BMG.

ANGER, FEAR, SEX AND DEATH
CD _____ E 86402CD
Epitaph / Nov '92 / Plastic Head / Pinnacle.

ANOTHER SATURDAY NIGHT
Before I grow too old: *McLain, Tommy* / Cajun fugitive: *Belton, Richard* / Try to find another man: *McLain, Tommy & Clint West* / Jolie blon: *Bruce, Vin* / I cried: *Cookie & The Cupcakes* / Oh Lucille: *Belton, Richard* / Who needs you so bad: *Walker, Gary* / Don't mess with my man: *White, Margo* / Another Saturday night: *White, Margo* / Un auter soir d'ennui: *Belton, Richard* / Promised land: *Allan, Johnnie* / Two steps de bayou teche: *Pitre, Austin* / Sweet dreams: *McLain, Tommy* / Breaking up is hard to do: *Cookie & The Cupcakes* / Laisser les cajun danser: *Belton, Richard* / Down home music: *Jangeaux, Rufus*
CD _____ CDCH 288
Ace / Feb '90 / Pinnacle / Cadillac / Complete/Pinnacle.

ANOTHER SENTIMENTAL JOURNEY THROUGH THE 50'S
Nina never knew: *Brent, Tony* / Undecided: *Beverley Sisters* / When you lose the one you love: *Martin, Ray* / Finger of suspicion points at you: *Jupp, Eric Orchestra* / Only yesterday: *Campbell, Jean* / How wonderful to know: *Carr, Pearl* / Roulette: *Conway, Russ* / Moon is blue: *Cogan, Alma* / I'm yours: *Hughes, David* / Now and forever: *Hughes, David* / How well I may: *Harris, Ronnie* / Sing little birdie: *Carr, Pearl* / Gypsy in my soul: *Boswell, Eve* / So deep my love: *Dean, Alan* / Holiday affair: *Day, Jill* / Hey there: *Hockridge, Edmund* / Donna: *Calvert, Eddie* / It's not for me to say: *Cordell, Frank* / Cinco Robles (Five oaks): *Day, Jill* / Just say I love her: *Hockridge, Edmund* / Long long ago: *Buxton, Sheila & Ronnie Harris/Ray Martin Orchestra* / I really feel: *Brent, Tony* / If you love me: *Brennan, Rose* / I may never pass this way again: *Lotis, Dennis* / Give her my love when you meet her: *Day, Jill* / Tammy: *Brown, Jackie* / Meet me on the corner: *Jupp, Eric Orchestra* / Charm: *Buxton, Sheila & Ronnie Harris/Ray Martin Orchestra* / I ever you heard: *Brent, Tony* / No one will ever know: *Campbell, Jean* / Surprisingly: *Harris, Ronnie* / How wonderful to know: *Beverley Sisters* / Tear fell: *Day, Jill* / Royal event: *Conway, Russ* / From the time you say goodbye: *Miller, Gary* / My lucky number: *Coronets* / Lonely ballerina: *Lawrence, Lee* / How lucky you are: *Carr, Pearl* / Give me the right to be wrong: *Brent, Tony* / In-between age: *Buxton, Sheila & Ronnie Harris/Ray Martin Orchestra* / Erica: *Calvert, Eddie* / Where can I go without you: *Campbell, Jean* / No one could love you (more than I do): *Carr, Pearl* / Birds and the bees: *Lyon, Barbara* / Make me love you: *Hughes, David* / Unsuspecting heart: *Brown, Fay* / My darling, my darling: *Miller, Gary* / I'd rather take my time: *Anthony, Billie* / Waltzing the blues: *Brent, Tony* / Take me in your arms and hold me: *Carr, Pearl*

CD Set _____ CDDL 1296
EMI / Jun '95 / EMI.

ANOTHER SHADE OF LOVERS
CD _____ RNCD 2109
Rhino / Jun '95 / Jetstar / Magnum Music Group / THE.

ANOTHER WORLD DOMINATION SAMPLER
Soft focus a.m.: Lizard Music / Carolida: I atimer / Life and death: Low Pop Suicide / Deal: Psyclone Rangers / Scapegoat: Sky Cries Mary / Supermonkey: Stanford Prison Experiment / Caxton Vs the fourth estate: Elastic Purejoy / Drug groove: Crack Babies
CD _____ WDOM 018CD
World Domination / Jul '95 / Pinnacle.

ANSWER IS - GREAT ANSWER SONGS OF THE 50'S
Wild side of life: Thompson, Hank / It wasn't God who made honky tonk angels: Wells, Kitty / Back street affair: Pierce, Webb / Paying for that back street affair: Wells, Kitty / There stands the glass: Pierce, Webb / Please throw away the glass: Cody, Betty / Yesterday's girl: Thompson, Hank / I'm yesterday's girl: Hill, Goldie / I forgot more than you'll ever know: Davis Sisters / I found out more than you'll ever know: Cody, Betty / I really want you to know: Cody, Betty / I really don't want to know: Arnold, Eddy / Don't let the stars get in your eyes: Mc-Donald, Skeets / I let the stars get in my eyes: Hill, Goldie / Long black veil: Frizzell, Lefty / My long black veil: Wilkin, Marijohn / I fall to pieces: Cline, Patsy / Mexican Joe: Reeves, Jim / Marriage of Mexican Joe: Bradshaw, Carolyn / Jambalaya: Williams, Hank / I'm Yvonne (from the bayou): Hill, Goldie / Dear John letter: Husky, Ferlin / Forgive me, John: Husky, Ferlin / Geisha girl: Locklin, Hank / Lost to a geisha girl: Davis, Skeeter / Fraulein: Helms, Bobby / I'll always be your fraulein: Wells, Kitty
CD _____ BCD 15791
Bear Family / Nov '94 / Rollercoaster / Direct / CM / Swift / ADA.

ANSWER IS - GREAT ANSWER SONGS OF THE 60'S
Ballad of a teenage queen: Cash, Johnny / Return of the teenage queen: Tucker, Tommy / Charlie's shoes: Walker, Billy / Answer to Charlie's Shoes: Mosby, Johnny & Jonie / He'll have to go: Reeves, Jim / He'll have to stay: Black, Jeanne / She's got you: Cline, Patsy / She has a way to love you: Judy / Almost persuaded: Houston, David / Almost persuaded #2: Harris, Donna / Detroit city: Bare, Bobby / Why don'cha come home: Ray, Shirley / Wolverton mountain: King, Claude / I'm the girl from Wolverton: Campbell, Jo Ann / Walk on by: Van Dyke, Leroy / I'll just walk on: Singleton, Margie / Ruby, don't take your love to town: Rogers, Kenny / Billy, I've got to go to town: Stevens, Geraldine / King of the road: Miller, Roger / Queen of the house: Miller, Jody / 5000 Miles away from home: Bare, Bobby / He's coming home: Taylor, Mary / Evil on your mind: Howard, Jan / Evil off my mind: Ives, Burl / Please help me, I'm falling: Locklin, Hank / (I can't help you) I'm fallin' too: Davis, Skeeter / Good hearted woman: Nelson, Willie / Good hearted man: Cato, Connie / Only Daddy that'll walk the line: Shepard, Jean / Only Mama that'll walk the line: Shepard, Jean
CD _____ BCD 15793
Bear Family / Nov '94 / Rollercoaster / Direct / CM / Swift / ADA.

ANSWER IS - VOL.2
Burning bridges: Scott, Kjack / You burned the bridges: Jean, Bobbie / Bobby's girl: Blane, Marcie / Stay away from Bobbie: Sherry's Sisters / Diana: Anka, Paul / Remember Diana: Anka, Paul / Roses are red: Vinton, Bobby / As long as the rose is red: Darlin, Florraine / Tell Laura I love her: Peterson, Ray / Tell Tommy I need him: Michaels, Marilyn / Who's sorry now: Francis, Connie / I'm sorry now: Shields / Wooden heart: Dowell, Joe / You know your hearts not made of wood: Marie Ann / Take good care of my baby: Vee, Bobby / I'll take good care of you: Emery, Ralph / Mr. Lonely: Vinton, Bobby / Little Miss Lonely: Harris, Mike / Is it true what they say about Barbara: Regal, Mike / Honey: Goldsboro, Bobby / Honey (I miss you too): Lewis, Margaret / Are you lonesome tonight: Boone, Pat / Yes I am lonesome tonight: Carpenter, Thelma / Fool # 1: Lee, Brenda / No you're the fool: Stewart, Mark / Who put the bomp: Mann, Barry / I put the bomp: Lymon, Frankie
CD _____ BCDAH 15792
Bear Family / Jun '95 / Rollercoaster / Direct / CM / Swift / ADA.

ANTHEMS VOL.2
Running away: Ayers, Roy / Expansions: Smith, Lonnie Liston / Champagne: Earland, Charles / Six million steps: Harris, Rahni / Shame: King, Evelyn 'Champagne' / You can do it: Hudson, Al & The Partners / Which way is up: Starguard / Don't stop the music: Yarbrough & Peoples / You know how to love me: Hyman, Phyllis / Risin' to the top: Burke, Keni
CD _____ SOUNDSCD 5
Street Sounds / May '95 / BMG.

ANTHOLOGY OF ARAB-ADALUSIAN MUSIC OF ALGERIA VOL. 3
CD _____ C 560004
Ocora / Jan '94 / Harmonia Mundi / ADA.

ANTHOLOGY OF BRETON TRADITIONS - ACCORDIAN
CD _____ SCM 034CD
Diffusion Breizh / Apr '95 / ADA.

ANTHOLOGY OF BRETON TRADITIONS - BOMBARDE & BINIOU
CD _____ SCM 032CD
Diffusion Breizh / Apr '95 / ADA.

ANTHOLOGY OF BULGARIAN FOLK MUSIC VOL. 2
(Music From Rhodope/Dobroudja)
CD _____ LDX 274975
La Chant Du Monde / Jun '94 / Harmonia Mundi / ADA.

ANTHOLOGY OF COLUMBIANA
CD _____ 7992342
Hispavox / Jan '95 / ADA.

ANTHOLOGY OF CUBAN MUSIC
Mi son, mi son, mi son: Miguelito Cuni Con Chappottin / Trae rumbavana: Conjunto Rumbavana / Bacalao con pan: Irakere / Unicornio: Rodriguez, Silvio / Cantido Celina: Gonzalez, Celina / Ese sentimiento que se llama amor: Alonso, Pacho Y Su Orquestra / La chica mamey: Orquesta Ritmo Oriental / El diapason: Orquesta Original De Manzanillo / Que es lo que hace ud: Gomez, Tito Con Su Conjunto / De mis recuerdos: Burke, Elena / A bayomo en coche: Son 14 / Por encima del nivel: Los Van Van
CD _____ PSCCD 1010
Pure Sounds From Cuba / Feb '95 / Henry Hadaway Organisation / THE.

ANTHOLOGY OF FLAMENCO
CD _____ 7992362
Hispavox / Jan '95 / ADA.

ANTHOLOGY OF FLAMENCO SONGS
CD Set _____ 7914562
Hispavox / Jan '95 / ADA.

ANTHOLOGY OF HOT R&B FROM BATON ROUGE
CD _____ FLYCD 41
Flyright / Oct '91 / Hot Shot / Wellard / Jazz Music / CM.

ANTHOLOGY OF MEXICAN SONES VOL. 1
(Tierra Caliente, Jalisco Y Rio Verde)
CD _____ CO 101
Corason / Jan '94 / CM / Direct / ADA.

ANTHOLOGY OF MEXICAN SONES VOL. 2
(Tixtla, Costa Chica, Istmo Y Veracruz)
CD _____ CO 102
Corason / Jan '94 / CM / Direct / ADA.

ANTHOLOGY OF MEXICAN SONES VOL. 3
(Huasteca)
CD _____ CO 103
Corason / Jan '94 / CM / Direct / ADA.

ANTHOLOGY OF MEXICAN SONES VOLS. 1 - 3
CD Set _____ MT 01/03
Corason / Jan '94 / CM / Direct / ADA.

ANTHOLOGY OF NEGRO WORKSONGS, A
(Compiled By Alan Lomax)
Road song / No more, my lawd / Katy left memphis / Old Alabama / Black woman / Jumpin' Judy / Whoa back / Prettiest train / Old cuban mamie / It makes a long time man feel bad / Rosie / Long comp holler / Early in the morning / Tangle eye blues / Stagger Lee / Prison blues / Sometimes I wonder / Bye bye baby
CD _____ NEXCD 121
Sequel / Apr '90 / BMG.

ANTHOLOGY OF RUMBA
CD _____ 7992642
Hispavox / Jan '95 / ADA.

ANTHOLOGY OF SOLEA
CD _____ 7995412
Hispavox / Feb '95 / ADA.

ANTHOLOGY OF TARANTA
CD _____ 7992662
Hispavox / Jan '95 / ADA.

ANTONES ANNIVERSARY ANTHOLOGY VOL. II
Chicago bound / Trouble blues / Shake for me / Everything is going to be alright / Natural ball / Sloppy drunk / Moanin' at midnight / Evan's shuffle / Black cat bone / Same thing could happen to you / High Jack
CD _____ ANTCD 0016
Antones / Mar '92 / Hot Shot / Direct / ADA.

ANTWERPEN 93
CD _____ KK 087CD
KK / Oct '93 / Plastic Head.

ANYTHING FOR YOU
CD _____ 295729
Ariola Express / Dec '92 / BMG.

APOLLO
Kinetic: Golden Girls / Passage: Model 500 / Evolution: Morley, David / Cloudwalker: Biosphere / X-Tal: Aphex Twin / Paradise (Part 1): Atlantis / I love you: Electrotete

Calibration: Morley, David / Intelligent universe: Love Craft / Mama: Neuro
CD _____ AMB 926CD
Apollo / Mar '94 / Vital.

APOLLO 2
Number readers: Subsurfing / Seal and the hydrophone: Biosphere / Skank: Manna / Too good to be strange: Two Sandwiches Sort Of A Lunchbox / Incidental harmony: Global Communication / Sick porter: u-Ziq / Agraphobia: L.A. Synthesis / First floor: Morley, David / Epique: Felman, Thomas / Blue orgasmic light: Tournesol / Like old movies: Word Up / Patashnik: Biosphere / Autophia: Leiner, Robert / Nine to five: Global Communication / Aural grey: Meditation Y.S. / I feel cold inside because of the things you say: Locust / Stampede: Andie / Stardance: Morley, David / Traveller's dream: Aedena Cycle
CD Set _____ AMB 5933CD
Apollo / May '95 / Vital.

APPALOOSA ALL STARS
CD _____ APP 6114CD
Appaloosa / Jun '94 / ADA / Magnum Music Group.

APPALOOSA ALL STARS
CD _____ AP 095
Appaloosa / Nov '95 / ADA / Magnum Music Group.

APPALOOSA COMPILATION
CD _____ AP 1994
Appaloosa / Jun '95 / ADA / Magnum Music Group.

APPOINTMENT WITH FEAR
CD _____ CYBERCD 11
Cyber / Aug '94 / Plastic Head.

APPROACHIMG INCANDESCENCE
CD _____ CANDRCD 8010
Candor / Oct '94 / Else.

ARAB-ANDUKUSIAN ANTHOLOGY
CD _____ C 560055
Ocora / Jan '94 / Harmonia Mundi / ADA.

ARABIAN JAM
CD _____ MHCD 0005
Madhouse / Apr '95 / Nervous.

ARCANE
My mother is not the white dove: Gifford, Alex / Ginger: Kennedy, Nigel / Chinese canon: Gifford, Alex & Simon Jeffes / Yodel 3: Gifford, Alex & Simon Jeffes / Youth and age: Gifford, Alex / Which way out/Esmerelda Pia Fini: Sheppard, Andy & Nana Vasconcelos / Thoughts on the departure of a lifelong friend: Gifford, Alex / Cage dead (Word version): Gifford, Alex & Simon Jeffes / Morecambe Bay: Gifford, Alex
CD _____ CDRW 40
Virgin / Oct '94 / EMI.

ARCHIVES OF TURKISH MUSIC VOL.1
CD _____ C 560081CD
Ocora / Jul '95 / Harmonia Mundi / ADA.

ARCHIVES OF TURKISH MUSIC VOL.2
(Historic Recordings 1903-1935)
CD _____ C 560082
Ocora / Jan '96 / Harmonia Mundi / ADA.

ARE
(Panpipe Ensembles From The Solomon Islands)
CD Set _____ LDX 274961/62
La Chant Du Monde / Feb '94 / Harmonia Mundi / ADA.

ARE
CD _____ GR 4100CD
Ozapp / Nov '95 / ADA.

AREA CODE 212
CD _____ CRECD 114
Creation / Nov '91 / 3MV / Vital.

ARIWA 12TH ANNIVERSARY ALBUM, THE
Together we're beautiful: Cadogan, Susan / Country living: Cross, Sandra / If I gave my heart to you: McLean, John / Proud of Man-dela: Macka B / Daydreaming: Brown, Jocelyn & Robotiks / True born african: U-Roy & Sister Audrey / Show some love: Thompson, Carroll / Runaround girl: Mclean, John & Dego Ranks / Don't drink too much: Macka B / Creator: Aisha / Lonely/Love on a mountain top: Stone, Davina & Ranking Ann / True true loving: Aquizm / Stylers: Delena / Ganga smuggling: Mother Nature / Six million dub: Mad Professor/Mafia/Fluxy
CD _____ ARICD 067
Ariwa Sounds / Nov '92 / Jetstar / SRD.

ARIWA HITS '89
I'm in love with a dreadlock: Kofi / At the dance: Simmonds, Leroy / Don't sell your body: Macka B / You'll never get to heaven (If you break my heart): Annette B / Let's make a tape: Tajah, Paulette / Midnight train to Georgia: McLean, John / Stop chat: Lorna G. / On my mind: Intense / Best friend's man: Cross, Sandra / Sheba's verandah: King, Allan
CD _____ ARICD 050
Ariwa Sounds / Oct '89 / Jetstar / SRD.

ARMENIAN FOLK MUSIC
CD _____ SOW 90126
Sounds Of The World / Sep '94 / Target/ BMG.

ARMY, THE NAVY & THE AIR FORCE, THE
Army, Navy and Airforce: Central Band of The Royal Air Force / Royal Air Force march past: Central Band of The Royal Air Force / Aces high: Central Band of The Royal Air Force / Battle of Britain: Central Band of The Royal Air Force / Evening hymn: Central Band of The Royal Air Force / Last post: Central Band of The Royal Air Force / Sunset: Central Band of The Royal Air Force / British Grenadiers: Band Of The Grenadier Guards / Old comrades: Band Of The Grenadier Guards / Liberty bell: Band Of The Grenadier Guards / Scipio march: Band Of The Grenadier Guards / Life on the ocean wave: Royal Marines / National emblem: Royal Marines / Sailing: Royal Marines / Heart of oak: Royal Marines / Les Huguenots: Bandsmen From Grenadier Guards / Radetsky march: Bandsmen From Grenadier Guards / Trumpet tunes: Bandsmen From Grenadier Guards / Amazing grace: Regimental Band, Pipes & Drums of Royal Scots Dragoon Band / Holyrood: Regimental Band, Pipes & Drums of Royal Scots Dragoon Band / Flower of Scotland: Regimental Band, Pipes & Drums of Royal Scots Dragoon Band / Flower of the forest: Regimental Band, Pipes & Drums of Royal Scots Dragoon Band
CD _____ CDPMFP 6131
Music For Pleasure / Sep '94 / EMI.

ARNHEM
(A Musical Tribute)
CD _____ ODFRS 1002
Fragile / Sep '94 / Grapevine.

AROUND THE DAY IN 80 WORLDS
CD _____ SSR 130
SSR / Feb '95 / Grapevine.

AROUND THE WORLD (FOR A SONG)
CD _____ RCD 00217
Rykodisc / Sep '91 / Vital / ADA.

ART OF FLAMENCO, THE
Jaleo / Solea / Tanguillo / Solo guitarra / Tangos / Nuevo flamenco / Alegrias / Bulerias / Siguiriyas / Buleria rancheros / Fandango de huelva / Cantinas / Martinetes / Sevillana
CD _____ 893002
Emocion / May '94 / New Note.

ART OF LANDSCAPE VOL.1
CD _____ ALC 11CD
Art Of Landscape / Aug '92 / Sony.

ART OF LANDSCAPE VOL.2
CD _____ ALC 12CD
Art Of Landscape / Aug '92 / Sony.

ART OF TATUM
(25 Great Solo Performances 1932-1944)
Tiger rag / Sophisticated lady / (I would do) anything for you / After you've gone / Stardust / Shout / Liza / Gone with the wind / Stormy weather / Chloe / Sheikh of araby / Teas for two / Deep purple / Elegie / Humoresque / Get happy / Lullaby of the leaves / Moonglow / Love me / Cocktails for two / St. Louis blues / Begin the beguine / Rosetta / Sweet Lorraine
CD _____ AIA 5164
ASV / Apr '95 / Koch.

ART OF THE SOUL BALLAD, THE
You send me: Cooke, Sam / At last: James, Etta / Warm and tender love: Sledge, Percy / Sittin' in the park: Stewart, Billy / Hello stranger: Lewis, Barbara / Hey there lonely girl: Holman, Eddie / Let me down easy: Lavette, Bettye / Misty blue: Simon, Joe / Rainy night in Georgia: Benton, Brook / Every little bit hurts: Scott, Peggy / Tell it like it is: Neville, Aaron / (If loving you is wrong) I don't want to be right: Ingram, Luther / Giving up: Ad Libs / Make it easy on yourself: Butler, Jerry / Reconsider me: Adams, Johnny / I've been loving you too long: Thomas, Irma / That's the way I feel about cha: Womack, Bobby / Either way I lose: Knight, Gladys & The Pips / Anyday now: Jackson, Chuck / Stand by me: Little Milton
CD _____ CDCD 1096
Charly / Jun '93 / Charly / THE / Cadillac.

ARTCORE - AMBIENT JUNGLE
Greater love: Soundman & Don Lloydie / Living for the future: Omni Trio / We enter: Alladin / Tranquility: Reynolds, Austin / Jazz note: D.J. Krust / Jazz juice: Jazz Juice / Currents: Sounds Of Life / Sweet dreams: D.J. Crysti / Soothe my soul: Justice / Dance of the saroes: Rogue Unit / Atmosphere: D.J. Phantasy / Sparkling: Little Matt / Amenity: Link / Phat and phuturistic: Little Matt / Inhabitants of pandemonium: Spirits From An Urban Jungle / Deep in the jungle: Amazon II / Second heaven: Atlas / Angels in dub: Code Blue / Natural high: Chaos & Julia Set
CD _____ REACTCD 059
React / Apr '95 / Vital.

ARTE FLAMENCO VOL.1
CD _____ MAN 4828
Mandala / May '94 / Mandala / Harmonia Mundi.

ARTE FLAMENCO VOL.2
CD _____ MAN 4829
Mandala / May '94 / Mandala / Harmonia Mundi.

ARTE FLAMENCO VOL.3
CD _____ MAN 4832
Mandala / May '94 / Mandala / Harmonia Mundi.

ARTISTRY IN JAZZ
(Black Lion Jazz sampler)
CD _____ BLCD 760100
Black Lion / '88 / Jazz Music / Cadillac / Wellard / Koch.

ARTISTS FOR THE ENVIRONMENT
CD _____ 0029292
Edel / Oct '95 / Pinnacle.

AS TIME GOES BY
CD _____ DINCD 77
Dino / Nov '93 / Pinnacle / 3MV.

AS TIME GOES BY
Lili Marlene: Anderson, Lale / Moonlight serenade: Miller, Glenn / As time goes by: Vallee, Rudy / At the woodchopper's ball: Herman, Woody / Swinging on a star: Crosby, Bing / I've heard that song before: James, Harry / You'll never know: Haymes, Dick / Don't fence me in: Andrews Sisters & Bing Crosby / It's a lovely day tomorrow: Lynn, Vera / For me and my gal: Garland, Judy & Gene Kelly / I don't want to set the world on fire: Geraldo / Paper doll: Mills Brothers / Don't get around much anymore: Ellington, Duke / All or nothing at all: Sinatra, Frank / Tangerine: Dorsey, Jimmy / I don't want to walk without you: Rhodes, Betty Jane / Whispering grass: Ink Spots / Blues in the night: Shore, Dinah / Star dust: Shaw, Artie / Over the rainbow: Garland, Judy / You made me love you: James, Harry / Last time I saw Paris: Martin, Tony / In the mood: Miller, Glenn / Why don't you do right: Lee, Peggy / White cliffs of Dover: Lynn, Vera / Rum and coca cola: Andrews Sisters / Chattanooga choo choo: Miller, Glenn / I'll walk alone: Shore, Dinah / Waiter and the porter and the upstairs maid: Martin, Mary & Jack Teagarden / Yours: Lynn, Vera / Night and day: Sinatra, Frank / Begin the beguine: Shaw, Artie / Nightingale sang in Berkeley Square: Shelton, Anne / You are my sunshine: Roy, Harry / If I didn't care: Ink Spots / I know why: Miller, Glenn / Boogie woogie bugle boy: Andrews Sisters / I'll be seeing you: Shelton, Anne / Frenesi: Shaw, Artie / Moonlight becomes you: Crosby, Bing / Little on the lonely side: Geraldo / Long ago and far away: Haymes, Dick & Helen Forrest / Take the 'A' train: Ellington, Duke / You always hurt the one you love: Mills Brothers / Cow cow boogie: Fitzgerald, Ella & Ink Spots / I'll never smile again: Sinatra, Frank / When the lights go on again: Monroe, Vaughan / If I had my way: Crosby, Bing / I've got a gal in Kalamazoo: Miller, Glenn / We'll meet again: Lynn, Vera
CD Set _____ CPCD 8105
Charly / Jun '95 / Charly / THE / Cadillac.

ASCENSION COLLECTION, THE
It's all we know: OBX / Another kind of find: Red Red Groovy / That's how my heart sings: Dial 4 FX / Freak you: Euphonia / Nebula: Positive Science / Soul feel free: Positive Science / Caspar ound: House / Eternal prayer: OBX / Tangled in my thoughts: R.H.C. & Plavka / Maximum motion: Plavka
CD _____ ASCCD 1
Ascension / Apr '95 / 3MV / Sony.

ASIA CLASSICS 1 - DANCE RAJA DANCE
Aatavu chanda / Naane maharaja / Aase hechchagide / Prema rudaayade / Neeva nana / ellellu preethi / Ba ennalu / I love you, Yenthare / Dheem thana thana nana / Naleya savimathe / Yerida gunginalli
CD _____ 7599268472
Luaka Bop / Jun '92 / Warner Music.

ASSEMBLAGE
CD _____ XVA 001
Extreme / Feb '95 / Vital/SAM.

ASSUMPTION OF DABRA GANNAT, THE
(Ethiopian Orthodox Church of Jerusalem)
CD Set _____ C 560027/28
Ocora / Mar '92 / Harmonia Mundi / ADA.

ASURINI
(Music From Brazil)
CD _____ C 560084
Ocora / Dec '95 / Harmonia Mundi / ADA.

AT DEATH'S DOOR 2
Martyr: Fear Factory / Stench of paradise burning: Disincarnate / Prelude to repulsion: Suffocation / Uriboric tomes: Cynic / Hideous infirmity: Gorguts / Illusion of freedom: Sorrow / God of thunder: Death / Piece by piece: Malevolent Creation / Unspoken names: Atrocity / Padre nuestro: Brujeria / No forgiveness: Immolation / Sucked inside: Skin Chamber
CD _____ RR 91052
Roadrunner / Jan '94 / Pinnacle.

AT THE COURT OF CHERA KING
CD _____ WLACS 34CD
Waterlilly Acoustics / Nov '95 / ADA.

AT THE DARKTOWN STRUTTER'S BALL
CD Set _____ DCD 8004
Disky / Jan '95 / THE / BMG / Discovery / Pinnacle.

AT THE HOP
(15 Rockin' Million Sellers Of The 50's)
At the hop: Danny & The Juniors / Peggy Sue: Holly, Buddy & The Crickets / See you later alligator: Haley, Bill & The Comets / When: Kalin Twins / Stagger Lee: Price, Lloyd / Come go with me: Del-Vikings / That'll be the day: Holly, Buddy & The Crickets / Here comes summer: Keller, Jerry / I hear you knocking: Storm, Gale / Shake, rattle and roll: Haley, Bill & The Comets / Green door: Lowe, Jim / Jingle bell rock: Helms, Bobby / I'm gonna get married: Price, Lloyd / Maybe baby: Holly, Buddy & The Crickets / (We're gonna) Rock around the clock: Haley, Bill & The Comets
CD _____ PWKS 511
Carlton Home Entertainment / Jan '89 / Carlton Home Entertainment.

AT THE JAZZ BAND BALL
I'm gonna stomp Mr. Henry Lee: Condon, Eddie / That's serious thing: Condon, Eddie / Big butter and egg man: Spanier, Muggsy & His Ragtime Band / Someday, sweetheart: Spanier, Muggsy & His Ragtime Band / Eccentric (that eccentric rag): Spanier, Muggsy & His Ragtime Band / That old da strain: Spanier, Muggsy & His Ragtime Band / At the Jazz Band Ball: Spanier, Muggsy & His Ragtimers / I wish I could shimmy like my sister Kate: Spanier, Muggsy & His Ragtime Band / Dippermouth blues: Spanier, Muggsy & His Ragtime Band / Livery stable blues: Spanier, Muggsy & His Ragtime Band / Riverboat shuffle: Spanier, Muggsy & His Ragtime Band / Relaxin' at the Touro: Spanier, Muggsy & His Ragtime Band / At sundown: Spanier, Muggsy & His Ragtime Band / Bluin' the blues: Spanier, Muggsy & His Ragtime Band / Lonesome road: Spanier, Muggsy & His Ragtime Band / Dinah: Spanier, Muggsy & His Ragtime Band / What did I do to be so black and blue: Spanier, Muggsy & His Ragtime Band / Mandy, make up your mind: Spanier, Muggsy & His Ragtime Band / I've found a new baby: Freeman, Bud / Easy to get: Freeman, Bud / China boy: Freeman, Bud / Eel: Freeman, Bud
CD _____ ND 86752
Bluebird / Apr '89 / BMG.

ATHLETICO COMPILATION VOL.1
CD _____ JAZIDCD 131
Acid Jazz / Nov '95 / Pinnacle.

ATLANTIC 252 HIT LIST
If you love me: Brownstone / Sweet dreams (are made of this): Eurythmics / Girl like you: Collins, Edwyn / Can't stay away from you: Estefan, Gloria / Dreams: Gabrielle / Sing hallelujah: Dr. Alban / Little time: Beautiful South / I can see clearly now: Cliff, Jimmy / You gotta be: Des'ree / Stay: Eternal / Sadness: Enigma / Open your heart: M People / Why: Lennox, Annie / It must have been love: Roxette / Thinking about your love: Thomas, Kenny / Things can only get better: D Ream / I want to know what love is: Foreigner / Another night: Real McCoy / Don't be a stranger: Carroll, Dina / Sweat (a la la la la la): Inner Circle
CD _____ SONYTV 4CD
Sony Music / Aug '95 / Sony.

ATLANTIC GROOVES - THE FUNK 'N' JAZZ EXPERIENCE VOL.1
Rock steady / Captain Buckles / Drum man / But I was cool / Bishop school / Wild man on the loose / Little ghetto boy / Dealing with hard times / No more / Behold the day / Groovin' time / Right on / Jive Samba / Backlash / Can't git enough / Motherless child / Well I'll be white black / Funky how time can change the meaning of a word
CD _____ 9548327712
Atlantic / Aug '94 / Warner Music.

ATLANTIC JAZZ - AVANT GARDE
Black mystery has been revealed / Wednesday night prayer meeting / Eventually / Lonely woman / Cherryco / Countdown / Inflated tear / Nonaah
CD _____ 7817092
Atlantic / Dec '87 / Warner Music.

ATLANTIC JAZZ - BEBOP
Love is here to stay / Evidence / Bebop / Koko / Salt peanuts / Almost like me / Allen's alley (be bop tune)
CD _____ 7817022
Atlantic / Dec '87 / Warner Music.

ATLANTIC JAZZ - FUSION
Freedom jazz dance / Beaux J.Pooboo / Quadrant four / Beneath the earth / Homunculus / Egocentric molecules
CD _____ 7817112
Atlantic / Dec '87 / Warner Music.

ATLANTIC JAZZ - INTROSPECTION
Yoruba / Tones for Joan's bones / Forest flower-sunrise / In a silent way / Standing outside / Chega de saudade (no more blues) / Fortune smiles
CD _____ 7817102
Atlantic / Dec '87 / Warner Music.

ATLANTIC JAZZ - KANSAS CITY
You're driving me crazy / Lamp is low / Hootie blues / E flat boogie / Confessin' the blues / Jumpin' at the woodside / Until the real thing comes along / Undecided / Evening / Buster's tune / Piney brown blues
CD _____ 7817012
Atlantic / '88 / Warner Music.

ATLANTIC JAZZ - MAINSTREAM
I'll be seeing you / Ain't misbehavin' / Stuffy / Django / Daphne / Perdido / Embraceable you / Four brothers / Everything happens to me / Speedy reeds
CD _____ 7817042
Atlantic / '87 / Warner Music.

ATLANTIC JAZZ - NEW ORLEANS
Bourbon street parade / Burgundy St. Blues / My bucket's got a hole in it / Cielito lindo / Salty dog / Eh la bas / Maple leaf rag / Joe Avery's blues / Nobody knows the way I feel this morning / Shreveport stomp / Sing on / Shake it and break it / Tiger rag
CD _____ 7817002
Atlantic / '88 / Warner Music.

ATLANTIC JAZZ - POST BOP
Lydian M-1 / I can't get started (with you) / Bag's groove / This 'n' that / Giant steps / Sister salvation / White sand / Misty (instrumental version) / Thoroughbred
CD _____ 7817052
Atlantic / Dec '87 / Warner Music.

ATLANTIC JAZZ - SOUL
Think / Twist city / How long blues / Comin' home baby / Russell and Eliot / Listen here / With these hands / Compared to what / You're the one / Jive samba / Money in the pocket
CD _____ 7567817082
Atlantic / '88 / Warner Music.

ATLANTIC JAZZ - WEST COAST
Sa-frantic / Not really / Paradox / Chermoya / Martians go home / You name it / Tripin' awhile / Topsy / Song is you
CD _____ 7567817032
Atlantic / Feb '94 / Warner Music.

ATLANTIC JAZZ GALLERY - FLUTES
Ain't no sunshine / Laugh for Rory / Night of Nisan / Thirteenth floor / Memphis underground / Little girl of mine / Nubian lady / Stay with me / All soul / If you knew / Sombrero Sam / Journey within
CD _____ 8122716372
Atlantic / May '94 / Warner Music.

ATLANTIC JAZZ GALLERY - KEYBOARDS
How long blues / Way you look tonight / Evidence / Little girl blue / C minor complex / Genius after hours / Rockin' chair / Sweet Georgia Brown / Catbird seat / Doin' that thing / My one and only love / Everything I love / Straight up and down
CD _____ 8122715962
Atlantic / Feb '94 / Warner Music.

ATLANTIC JAZZ GALLERY - LEGENDS VOL.1
Hard times / Compared to what / Whispering grass / Golden striker / Inflated tear / Comin' home baby / Ramblin' / Your mind is on vacation / Sweet sixteen bars / Nubian Lady / Wednesday night prayer meeting
CD _____ 8122712572
Atlantic / Jun '93 / Warner Music.

ATLANTIC JAZZ GALLERY - SAXOPHONES
If I loved you / Freedom jazz dance / Willow weep for me / Russell and Eliot / Lonely lament / Confirmation / Giant steps / Lonely woman / Forest flower-sunrise / Forest flower-sunset
CD _____ 8122712562
Atlantic / Jun '93 / Warner Music.

ATLANTIC JAZZ GALLERY - SAXOPHONES VOL.2
Blues shout / I wish you love / Old rugged cross / Don't get around much anymore / Topsy / Love theme from the Sandpiper (Shadow of your smile) / Down in Atlanta / September song / Senor blues / Parker's mood / Mr. P.C. / Embraceable you
CD _____ 81227177262
Atlantic / Aug '94 / Warner Music.

ATLANTIC JAZZ GALLERY - THE BEST OF THE 50'S
Django / All about Ronnie / Martians go home / Evidence / Backwater blues / Cousin Mary / Train and the river / Wee baby blues / Come rain or come shine / You go to my head / Fathead / Pithecanthropus erectus
CD _____ 8122712822
Atlantic / Feb '94 / Warner Music.

ATLANTIC JAZZ GALLERY - THE BEST OF THE 60'S VOL.1
Comin' home baby / Equinox / Una muy bonita / Volunteered slavery / In the evening / Stop this world / Groovin' / Summertime / Yesterday / With these hands / Listen here / Ecclusiastics / Sombrero Sam
CD _____ 8122715542
Atlantic / Feb '94 / Warner Music.

ATLANTIC JAZZ GALLERY - THE BEST OF THE 60'S VOL.2
Creole love call / Silver cycles / Chained no more / Soul of the village part II / Hey Jude / One note samba / You can count on me to do my part / Devil's dance / Dream weaver / Stardust / Buddy and Lou / Dick's Holler / Eat that chicken / When I fall in love / Bagpipe blues
CD _____ 8122717272
Atlantic / Aug '94 / Warner Music.

ATLANTIC JAZZ GALLERY - THE BEST OF THE 70'S
Samia / Come Sunday / Freaks for the festival / Ladies man / Missy / Dedicated to you / Moonchild / In your quiet place / Blues in A minor / Birdland (Vocal) / Yoruba / Egocentric molecules / Funky thide of sings
CD _____ 8122716102
Atlantic / Feb '94 / Warner Music.

ATLANTIC JAZZ VOCALS VOL.1
(Voices Cool)
CD _____ 8122717482
Atlantic / Aug '94 / Warner Music.

ATLANTIC JAZZ VOCALS VOL.2
(Voices Cool)
CD _____ 8122717842
Atlantic / Oct '94 / Warner Music.

ATLANTIC R & B VOL.1
(1947-1952)
Lovesick blues: Morris, Joe / That old black magic: Grimes, Tiny / Annie Laurie: Grimes, Tiny / Midnight special: Grimes, Tiny / Applejack: Morris, Joe / Drinkin' wine spo-dee-o-dee: McGhee, Stick / Coleslaw: Culley, Frank / So long: Brown, Ruth / I'll get along somehow (pts 1 & 2): Brown, Ruth / Hey little girl: Professor Longhair / Mardi Gras in New Orleans: Professor Longhair / Tee nah nah: Van Walls, Harry / Anytime anyplace anywhere: Morris, Joe / Teardrops from my eyes: Brown, Ruth / One monkey don't stop no show: McGhee, Stick / Don't you know I love you: Clovers / Shouldn't I know: Cardinals / Chill is on: Turner, Big Joe / Chains of love: Turner, Big Joe / Fool, fool, fool: Clovers / One mint julep: Clovers / Wheel of fortune: Cardinals / Sweet sixteen: Turner, Big Joe / 5-10-15 hours: Brown, Ruth / Ting a ling: Clovers / Gator's groove: Jackson, Willis / Daddy Daddy: Brown, Ruth / Midnight hour: Charles, Ray
CD _____ 7812932
Atlantic / Feb '95 / Warner Music.

ATLANTIC R & B VOL.2
(1952-1955)
Beggar for your kisses: Diamonds / Mama he treats your daughter mean: Brown, Ruth / Good lovin': Clovers / Wild wild young men: Brown, Ruth / Mess around: Charles, Ray / Hush hush: Turner, Big Joe / Soul on fire / Money honey: McPhatter, Clyde & Drifters / Such a night: McPhatter, Clyde & Drifters / Tipitina: Professor Longhair / White Christmas: McPhatter, Clyde & Drifters / Honey love: McPhatter, Clyde / What'cha gonna do: McPhatter, Clyde / Shake, rattle and roll: Turner, Big Joe / Sh-boom: Chords / Jam up: Ridgley, Tommy / Tomorrow night / Tweedlee dee / I got a woman: Charles, Ray / Door is still open: Cardinals / Flip flop and fly: Turner, Big Joe / Fool for you: Charles, Ray / This little girl of mine: Charles, Ray / Play it fair / Adorable: Drifters / Smoky Joe's cafe: Robins
CD _____ 7812942
Atlantic / Feb '95 / Warner Music.

ATLANTIC R & B VOL.3
(1955-1958)
Ruby baby: Drifters / In paradise: Cookies / Chicken and the hawk: Turner, Big Joe / Devil or angel: Clovers / Drown in my own tears: Charles, Ray / Hallelujah, I love her so: Charles, Ray / Jim Dandy: Baker, LaVern / Down in Mexico: Coasters / Corine Corina: Turner, Big Joe / Treasure of love: McPhatter, Clyde / Lucky lips: Baker, LaVern / It's too late: Willis, Chuck / Lonely avenue: Charles, Ray / Since I met you baby: Hunter, Lloyd Serenaders / Lucky lips: Brown, Ruth / Without love: McPhatter, Clyde / Fools fall in love: Drifters / Midnight special train: Turner, Big Joe / Empty arms: Hunter, Ivory Joe / C.C. rider: Willis, Chuck / Betty and Dupree: Bobbettes / What am I living for: Willis, Chuck / Hang up my rock 'n' roll shoes: Willis, Chuck / Yakety yak: Coasters / Lover's question: McPhatter, Clyde / I cried a tear: Charles, Ray / Right time: Charles, Ray / What'd I say (parts 1 and 2): Charles, Ray / There goes my baby: Drifters
CD _____ 7812952
Atlantic / Feb '95 / Warner Music.

ATLANTIC R & B VOL.4
(1958-1962)
Along came Jones: Coasters / Let the good times roll: Charles, Ray / Poison ivy: Coasters / Dance with me: Drifters / Just for a thrill: Charles, Ray / This magic moment: Charles, Ray / Save the last dance for me: Drifters / Spanish Harlem: King, Ben E. / Young boy blues: King, Ben E. / Stand by me: King, Ben E. / Gee whiz: Thomas, Carla / Saved / Just out of reach: Burke, Solomon / Little Egypt: Coasters / Amor: King, Ben E. / Last night: Mar-Keys / I'm blue (the gong-gong song): Ikettes / You don't miss your water: Bell, William / I found a love: Falcons / Cry to me: Burke, Solomon / Don't play that song (You lied): King, Ben E. / Green onions: Booker T & The MG's
CD _____ 7812962
Atlantic / Feb '95 / Warner Music.

ATLANTIC R & B VOL.5
(1962-1966)
Up on the roof: Drifters / C.C. rider / I who have nothing: King, Ben E. / If you need me: Burke, Solomon / These arms of mine: Redding, Otis / Hello stranger: Lewis, Barbara / On Broadway: Drifters / Just one look: Troy,

Doris / Do the mashed potato: Kindricks, Nat & The Swans / Land of 1000 dances: Kenner, Chris / Walking the dog: Kenner, Chris / Release me: Phillips, Esther / Mercy mercy: Covay, Don / Under the boardwalk: Drifters / And I love him: Phillips, Esther / Hold what you've got: Tex, Joe / Mr. Pitiful: Redding, Otis / Baby, I'm yours: Lewis, Barbara / Teasin' you: Tee, Willie / I've been loving you too long: Redding, Otis / In the midnight hour: Pickett, Wilson / See saw: Covay, Don / Respect: Redding, Otis / You don't know like I know: Sam & Dave / When a man loves a woman: Sledge, Percy / Hold on I'm comin': Sam & Dave / Cool jerk: Capitols / Neighbour, neighbour: Hughes, Jimmy
CD ___ 7812972
Atlantic / Feb '95 / Warner Music.

ATLANTIC R & B VOL.6
(1966-1969)
Land of 1000 dances: Pickett, Wilson / Knock on wood: Floyd, Eddie / Try a little tenderness: Redding, Otis / Mustang Sally: Pickett, Wilson / When something is wrong with my baby: Sam & Dave / Sweet soul music: Conley, Arthur / Soul man: Sam & Dave / I never loved a man (the way I love you): Franklin, Aretha / Do right woman, do right man: Franklin, Aretha / Show me: Tex, Joe / Tramp: Redding, Otis & Carla Thomas / Funky Broadway: Pickett, Wilson / Hip hug-her: Booker T & The MG's / Respect: Franklin, Aretha / (You make me feel like) a natural woman: Franklin, Aretha / Soul finger: Bar-Kays / Baby I love you: Franklin, Aretha / Skinny legs and all: Tex, Joe / Chain of fools: Franklin, Aretha / I'm in love: Pickett, Wilson / Memphis soul stew: King Diamond / (Sittin' on) the dock of the bay: Redding, Otis / Tighten up: Redding, Otis / Slip away: Carter, Clarence / Think: Franklin, Aretha / First time ever I saw your face: Flack, Roberta / Take a letter, Maria: Greaves, R.B. / Rainy night in Georgia: Charles, Ray / Ghetto: Hathaway, Donny
CD ___ 7812982
Atlantic / Feb '95 / Warner Music.

ATLANTIC R & B VOL.7
(1969-1974)
Turn back the hands of time: Davis, Walter / Compared to what: McCann, Les / Don't play that song (You lied): Franklin, Aretha / Groove me: Floyd, King / Patches: Carter, Clarence / Funky Nassau (parts 1and2): Beginning Of The End / Thin line between love and hate: Persuaders / Rock steady: Franklin, Aretha / You've got a friend: Flack, Roberta & Donny Hathaway / Clean up woman: Wright, Betty / Could it be I'm falling in love: Spinners / Killing me softly: Flack, Roberta / Where is the love: Flack, Roberta & Donny Hathaway / I'll be around: Spinners / Feel like makin' love: Flack, Roberta / Mighty love: Spinners / Love won't let me wait: Major Harris
CD ___ 7812992
Atlantic / Feb '95 / Warner Music.

ATLANTIC SOUL BALLADS
Try a little tenderness: Redding, Otis / I say a little prayer: Franklin, Aretha / Save the last dance for me: Drifters / I'm in love: Pickett, Wilson / Warm and tender love: Sledge, Percy / Patches: Carter, Clarence / Thin line between love and hate: Persuaders / Spanish Harlem: King, Ben E. / When something is wrong with my baby: Sam & Dave / My girl: Redding, Otis / Love won't let me wait: Harris, Major / On Broadway: Drifters / Baby, I'm yours: Lewis, Barbara / Rainy night In Georgia: Benton, Brook / Hey Jude: Pickett, Wilson
CD ___ 2411362
Atlantic / Jun '88 / Warner Music.

ATLANTIC SOUL CLASSICS
Sweet soul music: Conley, Arthur / In the midnight hour: Pickett, Wilson / Knock on wood: Floyd, Eddie / Soul man: Sam & Dave / Respect: Franklin, Aretha / See saw: Covay, Don / Everybody needs somebody to love: Burke, Solomon / Soul finger: Bar-Kays / Stand by me: King, Ben E. / B-A-B-Y: Thomas, Carla / Under the boardwalk: Drifters / Tramp: Redding, Otis & Carla Thomas / Green onions: Booker T & The MG's / When a man loves a woman: Sledge, Percy / Tribute to a king: Bell, William / (Sittin' on) the dock of the bay: Redding, Otis
CD ___ 2411382
Atlantic / May '87 / Warner Music.

ATLANTIC STORY, THE
Drinkin' wine spo-dee-o-dee: McGhee, Stick / 5-10-15 hours: Brown, Ruth / One mint julep: Clovers / Shake, rattle and roll: Turner, Big Joe / Jim Dandy: Baker, LaVern / Lover's question: McPhatter, Clyde / What'd I say: Charles, Ray / Mack the knife: Darin, Bobby / Giant steps: Coltrane, John / Poison ivy: Coasters / Save the last dance for me: Drifters / Stand by me: King, Ben E. / Deep purple: Tempo, Nino & April Stevens / I got you babe: Sonny & Cher / Green onions: Booker T & The MG's / Hold on I'm comin': Sam & Dave / Knock on wood: Floyd, Eddie / When a man loves a woman: Sledge, Percy / Got to get you off my mind: Burke, Solomon / In the midnight hour: Pickett, Wilson / I say a little prayer: Franklin, Aretha / Sweet soul music: Conley, Arthur / (Sittin' on) the dock of the bay: Redding, Otis / Groovin': Young Rascals / You keep me hangin' on: Vanilla Fudge / In-A-Gadda-Da-Vida: Iron Butterfly / For what it's worth: Buffalo Springfield / Sweet Jane: Velvet Underground / Rock and roll: Led Zeppelin / Can't get enough: Bad Company / Could it be I'm falling in love: Detroit Spinners / Such a night: Dr. John / Chanson d'amour: Manhattan Transfer / Soul man: Blues Brothers / Good times: Chic / We are family: Sister Sledge / Gloria: Branigan, Laura / I want to know what love is: Foreigner / Casanova: Levert / From a distance: Levert / Black velvet: Myles, Alannah / Walking in Memphis: Cohn, Marc / It's a shame about Ray: Lemonheads / Silent all these years: Amos, Tori / Hold on: En Vogue
CD Set ___ 9548324242
Atlantic / Dec '92 / Warner Music.

ATMOSPHERIC SYNTHESIZER SPECTACULAR
CD Set ___ TFP 012
Tring / Nov '92 / Tring / Prism.

AU BAL ANTILLAIS
CD ___ FL 7013
Folklyric / Apr '95 / Direct / Cadillac.

AUDIOPHILE SAMPLER
CD ___ ASCD 1
Audiophile / May '95 / Jazz Music / Swift.

AUF ZUM OKTOBERFEST
(Songs & Music From The Bavarian Beer Festival)
CD ___ 15181
Laserlight / '91 / Target/BMG.

AURA SURROUND SOUNDBITES VOL.2
(Access All Areas)
CD ___ SUSCD 3
Aura Surround Sounds / Sep '95 / Grapevine / PolyGram.

AUSTIN COUNTRY NIGHTS
CD ___ WMCD 1039
Watermelon / Dec '95 / ADA / Direct.

AUSTRALIAN STARS OF THE INTERNATIONAL MUSIC HALL VOL. 1
(Boiled Beef & Cabbage)
CD ___ LARRCD 325
Larrikin / Nov '94 / Roots / Direct / ADA / CM.

AUSTRALIAN STARS OF THE INTERNATIONAL MUSIC HALL VOL. 2
(Is 'E An Aussie, Is 'E Lizzie)
CD ___ LARRCD 324
Larrikin / Nov '94 / Roots / Direct / ADA / CM.

AUSTRIA FOLKLORE
CD ___ 399426
Koch / Jul '91 / Koch.

AUSTRIAN TECHNOLOGIES 1
CD ___ GELB 01CD
Gelb / Jul '94 / Plastic Head.

AUTHENTIC EXCELLO RHYTHM & BLUES
I'm evil: Lightnin' Slim / You're gonna ruin me baby: Lazy Lester / Got love if you want it: Harpo, Slim / Going through the park: Anderson, Jimmy / I'm warning you baby: Lightnin' Slim / Lonesome lonely blues: Lonesome Sundown / Wild cherry: Washington, Leroy / You're too late baby: Hogan, Silas / I'm a lover not a fighter: Lazy Lester / I love the life I'm livin': Harpo, Slim / Naggin': Anderson, Jimmy / I'm gonna quit you pretty baby: Hogan, Silas / I'm glad she's mine: Lonesome Sundown / I'm a king bee: Harpo, Slim / Mean woman blues: Smith Whispering / Loving around the clock: Lightnin' Slim / Tell me pretty baby: Lazy Lester / Hoodoo party: Thomas, Tabby / Lonesome la la: Hogan, Silas / Wake up old maid: Smith, Whispering / I'm tired waitin' baby: Lightnin' Slim / Gonna stick to you baby: Lonesome Sundown / No naggin' no draggin': Gunter, Arthur / I'm doin' alright: Shy Guy Douglas
CD ___ CDCHD 492
Ace / Oct '93 / Pinnacle / Cadillac / Complete/Pinnacle.

AUTHENTIC JAMAICA SKA
CD ___ AJSCD 001
K&K / Jul '93 / Jetstar.

AUTHENTIC NATIVE AMERICAN MUSIC
CD ___ 12551
Laserlight / Nov '95 / Target/BMG.

AUTUMN RECORDS STORY, THE
C'mon and swim pt.1: Freeman, Bobby / S-W-I-M: Freeman, Bobby / Scat swim: Stewart, Sly / Buttermilk: Stewart, Sly / Somebody to love: Great Society / Free advice: Great Society / She's my baby: Mojo Men / Jerk: Beau Brummels & B.Freeman Band / Sad little girl: Beau Brummels / No 1: Charlatans / Anything: Vejtables / Pay attention to me: Tikis
CD ___ EDCD 145
Edsel / May '86 / Pinnacle / ADA.

AVANT KNITTING TOUR
CD ___ KFWCD 142
Knitting Factory / Nov '94 / Grapevine.

AVANTI
CD ___ FILERCD 424
Profile / May '92 / Pinnacle.

AVANTI VOL.2
CD ___ FILERCD 432
Profile / Jul '92 / Pinnacle.

AVE MARIA
(Hearts Of Gold)
CD ___ TCD 2708
Telstar / Dec '93 / BMG.

AXE BRAZIL
(Afro-Brazilian Music Of Brazil)
CD ___ CDP 7950572
World Pacific / Jul '91 / EMI.

AXIOM COLLECTION 2
Mantra: Material / Animal behaviour: Praxis / Capitao do asfalto: Bahia Black / Reality: Material / Tarab dub: Skopelitis, Nicky / A habibi oujee t'allei allaila: Master Musicians Of Jajouka / Better wrapped: Threadgill, Henry / Lanmbasy: Mandingo / Baniya: Gnawa music of Marakesh / Dead man walking: Praxis / Playin' with fire: Praxis / Feridem: Ozkan, Talip
CD ___ 5144532
Axiom / Nov '93 / PolyGram / Vital.

B

B IS FOR BROCCOLI
CD ___ KUDCD 007
Kudos / Jan '96 / Kudos / Pinnacle.

B9 RECORDS THE EXTREME COLLECTION VOL.2
CD ___ CDB 9007
B9 / Jun '95 / Total/BMG / Plastic Head.

BABY BOOMERS
CD Set ___ MBSCD 418
Castle / Nov '93 / BMG.

BABYLON A FALL DOWN
CD ___ CDTRL 290
Trojan / Apr '91 / Jetstar / Total/BMG.

BACHOLOGY
Blow: Zolothukin, Adrian / Sidelines: McSween / B-bopper: Eleggua / Bachone: Mrs. Wood & Mr. McGee / Brazilian reverie: Sutherland, Rowland / Suburban picture: Sound Barrier / Sebastian: Trio South / Cubano dip: Donlon, Mark / Toccata salata: Glamorre & Kaczor / Poeme: Jones, Ed / Sexto sentido: Sentido / Cartwheel: Beesley Jnr., Maxston G. / Thirteen things to do: Lindt, Virna
CD ___ CDEMC 3715
EMI / Jul '95 / EMI.

BACK FROM THE GRAVE
(Rockin' Sixties Punkers)
CD ___ E 11566 CD
Crypt / Mar '93 / SRD.

BACK FROM THE GRAVE VOL.3
(Mid-60's Garage Punkers)
CD ___ EFA 115202
Crypt / Mar '94 / SRD.

BACK FROM THE GRAVE VOL.4
(Mid-60's Garage Punk Screamers)
CD ___ EFA 115252
Crypt / Sep '95 / SRD.

BACK IN THE SADDLE AGAIN
Old Chisholm trail: McClintock, Harry'Haywire Mac' / Pot wrassler: Jackson, Harry / Gol-durned wheel: Holyoak, Van / When the work's all done this fall: Sprague, Carl T. / Streets of Laredo: Prude, John G. / Sioux Indians: Williams, Marc / Dying cowboy: Allen, Jules Verne / Tyin' knots in the devil's tail: Jack, Powder River & Kitty Lee / Strawberry Road: Arizona Wranglers / Lone star trail: Maynard, Ken / Ridge runnin' road: Rice, Glen & His Beverly Hill Billies / Whoopie ti yi yo: White, John / Cowhand's last ride / Little old log shack I always call my home: Carter, Wilf / A-ridin' old paint: Ritter, Tex / I want to be a cowboy's sweetheart: Montana, Patsy / Cattle call: Owens, Tex / One more ride: Sons Of The Pioneers / Dim narrow trail: Ruby, Texas / I want to be a real cowboy girl: Girls Of The Golden West / Back in the saddle again: Autry, Gene / My dear old Arizona home: Allen, Rex / Cowboy stomp / D-Bar-2 horse wrangler: Critchlow, Slim / City boarders: Agins, Sam / Cowboys: Ohrlin, Glenn / Rusty spurs: Doux, Chris Le / Cowboy song: Riders In The Sky
CD ___ NW 314/315
New World / Aug '92 / Harmonia Mundi / ADA / Cadillac.

BACK TO MONO
CD ___ WALLCD 002
Wall Of Sound / Sep '95 / Disc / Soul Trader.

BACK TO THE 50'S
Whatever will be will be (Que sera sera): Day, Doris / Walkin' my baby back home: Ray, Johnnie / Mambo Italiano: Clooney, Rosemary / Look homeward angel: Ray, Johnnie / Kid's last fight: Laine, Frankie / Pretty little black eyed Susie: Mitchell, Guy / Blowin' wind (the ballad of black gold): Laine, Frankie / Affair to remember: Damone, Vic / This ole house: Clooney, Rosemary / On the street where you live: Damone, Vic / Half as much: Clooney, Rosemary / Hernando's hideaway: Ray, Johnnie / Sippin' soda: Mitchell, Guy / Cool water: Laine, Frankie / If I give my heart to you: Day, Doris / Look at that girl: Mitchell, Guy / Close your eyes: Bennett, Tony / Where will the baby's dimple be: Clooney, Rosemary
CD ___ PWKS 4151
Carlton Home Entertainment / Aug '94 / Carlton Home Entertainment.

BACK TO THE 60'S VOL.1
Love grows (Where my rosemary goes): Edison Lighthouse / With a girl like you: Troggs / Lightning strikes: Christie, Lou / Build me up buttercup: Foundations / How do you do it: Gerry & The Pacemakers / Love on a mountain top: Knight, Robert / Little arrows: Lee, Leapy / Yellow river: Christie / She's not there: Zombies / Dizzy: Roe, Tommy / Happy together: Turtles / It's my party: Gore, Lesley / Da doo ron ron: Crystals / Gimme little sign: Wood, Brenton / Letter: Box Tops / You've got your troubles (I've got mine): Fortunes / Groovy kind of love: Fontana, Wayne / Young girl: Puckett, Gary & The Union Gap
CD ___ ECD 3046
K-Tel / Jan '95 / K-Tel.

BACK TO THE 70'S
(40 Chart Busting Seventies Hits)
Killer queen: Queen / Make me smile (come up and see me): Harley, Steve & Cockney Rebel / Maggie May: Stewart, Rod / Band on the run: McCartney, Paul & Wings / Lola: Kinks / American pie: McLean, Don / You're so vain: Simon, Carly / Never let her slip away: Gold, Andrew / Goodbye to love: Carpenters / Without you: Nilsson, Harry / Baker Street: Rafferty, Gerry / Rocket man: John, Elton / I don't like Mondays: Boomtown Rats / Hit me with your rhythm stick: Dury, Ian & The Blockheads / Oliver's army: Costello, Elvis & The Attractions / You ain't seen nothin' yet: Bachman-Turner Overdrive / All right now: Free / Wuthering Heights: Bush, Kate / I'm not in love: 10cc / I want you back: Jackson Five / Rock your baby: McCrae, George / That's the way (I like it): K.C. & The Sunshine Band / Nutbush City Limits: Turner, Ike & Tina / You to me are everything: Real Thing / You're the first, the last, my everything: White, Barry / Y.M.C.A.: Village People / Rivers of Babylon: Boney M / So you win again: Hot Chocolate / Let's stay together: Green, Al / Love don't live here anymore: Rose Royce / December 1963 (Oh what a night): Valli, Frankie & Four Seasons / We don't talk anymore: Richard, Cliff / When you're in love with a beautiful woman: Dr. Hook / In the summertime: Mungo Jerry / Ride a white swan: T. Rex / Coz I luv you: Slade / I'm the leader of the gang (I am): Slade / Ballroom blitz: Sweet / Tiger feet: Mud / Heart of glass: Blondie
CD Set ___ CDEMTV 77
EMI / Sep '93 / EMI.

BACK TO THE 70'S
CD Set ___ MBSCD 432
Castle / Jan '95 / BMG.

BACK TO THE BEEHIVE
CD ___ KLMCD 053
Scratch / Jun '95 / BMG.

BACK TO THE BLUES
CD ___ 157152
Blues Collection / Feb '93 / Discovery.

BACK TO THE STREETS
CD ___ SHACD 9006
Shanachie / Nov '93 / Koch / ADA / Greensleeves.

BACKLOG
CD ___ VOW 050CD
Voices Of Wonder / Jun '95 / Plastic Head.

BACKTRACKIN' TO THE 70'S
(4CD Set)
CD Set ___ MBSCD 437
Castle / Nov '95 / BMG.

BACKWATER 2
CD ___ NBX 004
Noisebox / Jun '94 / Disc.

BAD, BAD WHISKEY
(The Galaxy Masters)
She's looking good: Collins, Rodger / Rufus Jr: Merced Blue Notes / I got to tell somebody: Everett, Betty / Chicken heads: Rush, Bobby / Get your lie straight: Coday, Bill / Why do you have to lie: Right Kind / You better stop: Rhodes, Sonny / Nightingale melody: Taylor, Little Johnny / I pity the fool: Saunders, Merl / It's a shame: Malone, J.J. / Rainbow 71: Holloway, Loleatta / Foxy girls in Oakland: Collins, Rodger / When you find a fool bump his head: Coday, Bill / Mama Rufus: Merced Blue Notes / For your precious love: Taylor, Little Johnny / Abraham, Martin and John: Brown, Charles / Bad bad whiskey: Merced Blue Notes / How can I forget you: Williams, Lenny / Ain't nothing gonna change me: Everett, Betty / Woman rules the world: Coday, Bill / Why did our love go: Huey, Claude 'Baby' / Let me be your handy man: Coday, Bill / Fever

fever fever: *Eaton, Bobby* / Lisa's gone: *Williams, Lenny* / Don't want to be a lone ranger: *Watson, Johnny 'Guitar'*
CD ____ **CDCHD 516**
Ace / Jan '94 / Pinnacle / Cadillac / Complete/Pinnacle.

BAD BOY
Screamin' Mimi Jeanie: *Hawks, Mickey* / Bip bop boom: *Hawks, Mickey* / Rock 'n' roll rhythm: *Hawks, Mickey* / Hidi hidi hidi: *Hawks, Mickey* / I'm lost: *Hawks, Mickey* / Cotton pickin': *Night Raiders* / Bad boy: *France, Steve* / Born to lose: *Deckelman, Sonny* / Don't hang around me anymore: *Ford, Jimmy* / You're gonna be sorry: *Ford, Jimmy* / Bad bad boy: *Lollar, Bobby* / Red hot Mama: *Williams, Wayne* / Okie's in the pokie: *Patton, Jimmy* / Yah, I'm movin': *Patton, Jimmy* / Willie was a bad boy: *Gentry, Ray* / Bad bad way: *Rodger & Tempests* / Missed the workhouse: *Watkins, Bill* / Look what I found: *Hubbar, Orangie* / Curfew: *Chuck & Gene* / Bad: *Amory, John* / Big Sandy: *Roberts, Bobby* / Hop, skip and jump: *Roberts, Bobby* / She's my woman: *Roberts, Bobby* / Go boy: *Lee, Floyd* / Take it easy, Greasy: *Lehmann, Bill* / Is there no woman for my love: *McAdams, Johnny* / All night in jail: *Bernard, Rod* / Meaner than an alligator: *Ty B & Johnny* / I've been a bad bad boy: *Kingbeats* / Teenage riot: *Portuguese Joe*
CD ____ **CDBB 55003**
Buffalo Bop / Apr '94 / Rollercoaster.

BADAKHSHAN: MUSIC FROM THE TAJIK PAMIR MOUNTAINS
CD ____ **PAN 2024CD**
Pan / Mar '94 / ADA / Direct / CM.

BAGPIPE, THE
CD ____ **LYRCD 7327**
Lyrichord / Dec '94 / Roots / ADA / CM.

BAILA MI AMOR
CD ____ **DCD 5392**
Disky / Jul '94 / THE / BMG / Discovery / Pinnacle.

BALI - COURT MUSIC AND BANJAR MUSIC
CD ____ **BCD 8059**
Auvidis/Ethnic / Jan '95 / Harmonia Mundi.

BALI - GAMELAN & KECAK
CD ____ **7559792042**
Elektra Nonesuch / Jan '95 / Warner Music.

BALI - MUSIC FROM THE MORNING OF THE WORLD
CD ____ **7559791962**
Elektra Nonesuch / Jan '95 / Warner Music.

BALI - THE CLASH OF THE GONGS
CD ____ **122119**
Long Distance / Jul '95 / ADA / Discovery.

BALI - THE GREAT GONG KEBYAR
CD ____ **C 560057**
Ocora / Aug '94 / Harmonia Mundi / ADA.

BALL TONIGHT, A
That's what I call a ball: *Donn, Larry* / Honey bun: *Donn, Larry* / Girl next door: *Donn, Larry* / Wild wild party: *Vincent, Darrly* / Ball tonight: *Campbell, Ray* / Rockin' spot: *Coldiron, Curley* / I've got love: *Deckleman, Sonny* / Forty nine women: *Irby, Jerry* / There'll be a rockin' party tonight: *Volk, Val* / I fell for your line baby: *Faire, Johnny* / Bertha Lou: *Faire, Johnny* / Hot dog: *Curtin, Lee* / Is this the place: *Royal Lancers* / Long pony tail: *Tom & Tornados* / Saturday night party: *Perkins, Reggie* / Pretty Kitty: *Perkins, Reggie* / Party time: *Noris, Bob* / Stop at the hop: *Eee, Don* / My queen and me: *Lenny & The Star Chiefs* / Rockin' bones: *Dietzel, Elroy* / Teenage ball: *Dietzel, Elroy* / Pretty baby rock: *Mayo, Danny* / Chicken walk: *Adkins, Hasil* / She's mine: *Adkins, Hasil* / Betcha I getcha: *Faire, Johnny* / Bo peep rock: *Vinyard, Eddie* / Wildwood fun: *Lefty & Leadsmen* / There's gonna be a party: *Gray, Bobby* / Dream night: *Houle Brothers* / Teen age ball: *White, Buddy*
CD ____ **CDBB 55007**
Buffalo Bop / Apr '94 / Rollercoaster.

BALLAD NO.1'S OF THE 70'S VOL.2
CD ____ **OG 3514**
Old Gold / Jun '89 / Carlton Home Entertainment.

BALLADEERS, THE
CD ____ **SETCD 081**
Stardust / Sep '94 / Carlton Home Entertainment.

BALLADS IN BLUE
(Big Sounds For The Small Hours)
Child is born: *Turrentine, Stanley* / Since I fell for you: *Morgan, Lee* / Guess I'll hang my tears out to dry: *Gordon, Dexter* / Autumn leaves: *Adderley, Cannonball Quintet* / I'm old fashioned: *Coltrane, John* / Cry me not: *Hubbard, Freddie* / Bouquet: *Hutcherson, Bobby* / Lazy afternoon: *La Roca, Pete* / Easy living: *Brown, Clifford* / Nature boy: *Quebec, Ike* / You taught my heart to sing: *Tyner, McCoy*
CD ____ **BNZ 266**
Blue Note / May '91 / EMI.

BALLROOM DANCING FAVOURITES
(3CD Set)
I don't care if I never dream: *Loss, Joe & His Orchestra* / You moved right in: *Roy, Harry & His Band* / I'll never say Never Again again: *Smith, Bryan & His Festival Orchestra* / That's a plenty: *Smith, Bryan & His Festival Orchestra* / Waltz of my heart: *Silvester, Victor* / Whisper while you waltz: *Silvester, Victor* / In the mood: *Power Pack Orchestra* / Opus 1: *Power Pack Orchestra* / Don't get around much anymore: *Power Pack Orchestra* / American patrol: *Power Pack Orchestra* / Tango Hacienda: *Smith, Bryan & His Festival Orchestra* / Tango sombrero: *Smith, Bryan & His Festival Orchestra* / I'll buy that dream: *Preager, Lou & His Orchestra* / I'm so all alone: *Fenoulhet, Paul & the Skyrockets Dance Orchestra* / Never on a Sunday: *Power Pack Orchestra* / Spanish flee: *Power Pack Orchestra* / Monday, Tuesday, Wednesday: *Dean, Syd & His Orchestra* / I should care: *Winstone, Eric & His Band* / Once in a while: *Smith, Bryan & His Festival Orchestra* / April in Paris: *Silvester, Victor* / You red head: *Dean, Syd & his Band* / Gotta be this or that: *Loss, Joe & His Orchestra* / Edwardians: *Smith, Bryan & His Festival Orchestra* / Blue Tahitian moon: *Smith, Bryan & His Festival Orchestra* / Moonlight serenade: *Power Pack Orchestra* / Mood indigo: *Silvester, Victor* / Tuxedo Junction: *Power Pack Orchestra* / It happened in Monterey: *Power Pack Orchestra* / String of pearls: *Power Pack Orchestra* / I wonder where my baby is tonight: *Silvester, Victor* / Just for a while: *Smith, Bryan & His Festival Orchestra* / Suzy: *Smith, Bryan & His Festival Orchestra* / You can't be true dear: *Rabin, Oscar & His Band with Harry Davis* / I'll be your sweetheart: *Loss, Joe & His Orchestra* / Echo told me a lie: *Adam, Paul & His Mayfair Music* / Guantanamera: *Love, Geoff & His Orchestra* / Make believe: *Smith, Bryan & His Festival Orchestra* / It looks like rain in cherry blossom: *Smith, Bryan & His Festival Orchestra* / Sobre Las Olas: *Smith, Bryan & His Festival Orchestra* / How little we know: *Winstone, Eric & His Band* / Red roses for a blue lady: *Adam, Paul & His Mayfair Music* / Rags and tatters: *Smith, Bryan & His Festival Orchestra* / Stumbling: *Smith, Bryan & His Festival Orchestra* / By candlelight: *Silvester, Victor* / Unforgettable: *Silvester, Victor* / Tango 65: *Smith, Bryan & His Festival Orchestra* / I can dream can't I: *Silvester, Victor* / Come dance with me: *Silvester, Victor* / C'est si bon: *Silvester, Victor* / Always true to you in my fashion: *Silvester, Victor* / Out of the night: *Roy, Harry & His Band* / Lipstick on your collar: *Power Pack Orchestra* / Let there be drums: *Power Pack Orchestra* / One note samba: *Love, Geoff & His Orchestra* / Sucu sucu: *Love, Geoff & His Orchestra* / Egerland march: *Smith, Bryan & His Festival Orchestra* / Bandstand march: *Smith, Bryan & His Festival Orchestra* / Turn over a new leaf: *Benson, Ivy & Her Girls Band* / Last waltz: *Power Pack Orchestra*
CD Set ____ **CDTRBOX 200**
Trio / Sep '95 / EMI.

BAM BAM
CD ____ **VPCD 1237**
VP / Jul '92 / Jetstar.

BANDA RIO-COPA
CD ____ **SOW 90125**
Sounds Of The World / Sep '94 / Target/BMG.

BANDLEADER DIGITAL SPECTACULAR
(Various Military & Brass Bands)
Berne patrol / Thunderbird / Royal salute / Regimental slow march / Motorcycle display / Chocolate dancing / Shepherd's song / Music box dancer / Canter / St. Louis blues march / Caesar's romp / Concerto for clarinet in A / Mount Longden / Drumbeatings / Rule Britannia / Jerusalem / Last post / Auld lang syne / Colonel Bogey / Artillery salvo and opening fanfare / Fanfare / God save the Queen / Bugle flute and drum calls / Precision in percussion / Tornado
CD ____ **BNA 5000**
Bandleader / Feb '85 / Conifer.

BANDOLAS DE VENEZUELA
CD ____ **DIS 80114**
Dorian Discovery / Jan '94 / Conifer.

BANDONEON PURE - DANCES OF URUGUAY
CD ____ **SF 40431CD**
Smithsonian Folkways / Jan '94 / ADA / Direct / Koch / CM / Cadillac.

BANKLANDS
CD ____ **FECB 100**
Fellside / Jan '95 / Target/BMG / Direct / ADA.

BAR RAM TOP 20 HITS
CD ____ **SONCD 0071**
Sonic Sounds / Sep '94 / Jetstar.

BARCELONA GOLD
Barcelona: *Mercury, Freddie & Montserrat Caballe* / One song: *Campbell, Tevin* / How fast now: *Baker, Anita* / Higher baby: *D.J. Jazzy Jeff & The Fresh Prince* / Keep it comin': *Sweat, Keith* / Free your mind: *En Vogue* / Don't tread on me: *Damn Yankees* / Go out dancing: *Stewart, Rod* / Texas flyer: *Tritt, Travis* / Heart to climb the mountain: *Travis, Randy* / Old soldier: *Cohn, Marc* / This used to be my playground: *Madonna* / No se tu: *Miguel, Luis* / Wonderful tonight: *Clapton, Eric* / Love is here to stay: *Cole, Natalie* / Friends for life: *Carreras, Jose & Sarah Brightman*
CD ____ **9362450462**
Warner Bros. / Aug '92 / Warner Music.

BARNBRACK: 22 IRISH FOLK PUB SONGS
CD ____ **HRL 199CD**
Outlet / Aug '94 / ADA / Duncans / CM / Ross / Direct / Koch.

BARRELHOUSE BOOGIE
Honky tonk train blues: *Lewis, Meade Lux* / Whistlin' blues: *Lewis, Meade Lux* / Yancy stomp: *Yancy, Jimmy* / State Street special: *Yancy, Jimmy* / Tell 'em about me: *Yancy, Jimmy* / Five o'clock blues: *Yancy, Jimmy* / Slow and easy blues: *Yancy, Jimmy* / Mellow blues: *Yancy, Jimmy* / Crying in my sleep: *Yancy, Jimmy* / Death letter: *Yancy, Jimmy* / Yancy's bugle call: *Yancy, Jimmy* / 35th and dearborn: *Yancy, Jimmy* / Boogie woogie man: *Johnson, Pete & Albert Ammons* / Boogie woogie jump: *Johnson, Pete & Albert Ammons* / Barrelhouse boogie: *Johnson, Pete & Albert Ammons* / Cuttin' the boogie: *Johnson, Pete & Albert Ammons* / Walkin' the boogie: *Johnson, Pete & Albert Ammons* / Foot pedal boogie: *Johnson, Pete & Albert Ammons* / Sixth Avenue express: *Johnson, Pete & Albert Ammons* / Pine Creek: *Johnson, Pete & Albert Ammons* / Movin' the boogie: *Johnson, Pete & Albert Ammons*
CD ____ **ND 88334**
Bluebird / Mar '90 / BMG.

BARRELHOUSE PIANO BLUES
CD ____ **DOCD 5193**
Blues Document / Oct '93 / Swift / Jazz Music / Hot Shot.

BASS-IC ELEMENTS
CD ____ **CDTOT 33**
Jumpin' & Pumpin' / Sep '95 / 3MV / Sony.

BASSA MUSICA
CD ____ **CT 0001CD**
Robi Droli / Apr '95 / Direct / ADA.

BATAK OF NORTH SUMATRA
CD ____ **NA 046 CD**
New Albion / Oct '92 / Harmonia Mundi / Cadillac.

BATTERY POINT
Dirty mags: *Blueboy* / He gets me so hard: *Boyracer* / Autobiography: *Hit Parade* / Fran: *Aberdeen* / River: *Blueboy* / Last September's farewell kiss: *Northern Picture Library* / Wish you would: *Ivy* / Reproduction is pollution: *Shelley* / Mustard gas: *Action Painting* / Avenge: *Ivy* / Deep thinker: *Secret Shine* / Top 40 sculpture: *Sugargliders* / Paris: *Northern Picture Library* / Fireworks: *Aberdeen* / Toulouse: *Blueboy* / Hero: *Shelley*
CD ____ **SARAH 359CD**
Sarah / Jul '95 / Vital.

BATTLE OF THE BIG BANDS
Blue juice: *Barnet, Charlie* / Topsy: *Basie, Count* / I can't get started (with you): *Berigan, Bunny* / Lightly and politely: *Brown, Les* / Are you allreet: *Calloway, Cab* / Smoke rings: *Casa Loma Orchestra* / Smoky Mary: *Crosby, Bob* / Tangerine: *Dorsey, Jimmy* / Song of India: *Dorsey, Tommy* / Take the 'A' train: *Ellington, Duke* / I'm gonna meet my sweetie now: *Goldkette, Jean & His Orchestra* / Let's dance: *Goodman, Benny* / Rug cutter's swing: *Henderson, Fletcher* / At the woodchoppers' ball: *Herman, Woody* / Strictly instrumental: *James, Harry* / What's your story Morning Glory: *Kirk, Andy* / Rhythm is our business: *Lunceford, Jimmie* / In the mood: *Miller, Glenn* / Save it pretty Mama: *Redman, Don* / Frenesie: *Shaw, Artie* / Tisket-a-tasket: *Webb, Chick* / Darktown strutter's ball: *Whiteman, Paul*
CD ____ **RPCD 611**
Robert Parker Jazz / Jul '94 / Conifer.

BATTLE OF THE GARAGES PART 1
CD ____ **VOXXCD 2067**
Voxx / Oct '93 / Else / Disc.

BATTLE OF THE GARAGES PART 2
CD ____ **VOXXCD 2068**
Voxx / Oct '93 / Else / Disc.

BAULE VOCAL MUSIC FROM THE IVORY COAST
CD ____ **AUD 008048**
Auvidis/Ethnic / Nov '93 / Harmonia Mundi.

BAWDY BLUES
CD ____ **OBCCD 544**
Original Blues Classics / Nov '92 / Complete/Pinnacle / Wellard / Cadillac.

BAYERN: VOLKSMUSIK 1906-1941
CD ____ **US 0196**
Trikont / Jul '95 / ADA / Direct.

BAYOU BLUES MASTERS - GOLDBAND BLUES
I'm a country boy / Purty little dolly / Going crazy baby / Broke and hungry / Make up my mind / Need shorter hours / It ain't right / Just got to (take a) ride / Wanna do me wrong / Tin pan alley / I got fever / Life's journey / Honey bee / Sunday morning / Trouble in my home / Oh Ramona / Highway back home / I'm going / Please stand by me / Too tired / Let me hold your hand / What in the world are you gonna do / Something working baby / Pretty little red dress / C-Key blues / Catch that morning train
CD ____ **CDCHD 427**
Ace / Aug '93 / Pinnacle / Cadillac / Complete/Pinnacle.

BAZOOKA EXPLOSION, THE
CD ____ **SONCD 0061**
Sonic Sounds / Mar '94 / Jetstar.

BBC SONGS OF PRAISE FROM OLD TRAFFORD
All people that on earth do dwell / Guide me o thou great redeemer / Amazing Grace / Thorns in the straw / Rejoice rejoice / When the saints go marching in / Mine eyes have seen the glory / Oh happy day / Shine, Jesus, shine / Alleluia / Sing to Jesus / Abide with me / You'll never walk alone
CD ____ **ALD 026**
Alliance Music / Jun '95 / EMI.

BE BOP 1945-1953
CD ____ **CD 53029**
Giants Of Jazz / Mar '90 / Target/BMG / Cadillac.

BE THANKFUL - AN ATTACK SAMPLER
CD ____ **CDAT 115**
Attack / Jun '94 / Jetstar / Total/BMG.

BE-BOP IN PARIS VOL.1
CD ____ **2512882**
Jazztime / Mar '90 / Discovery / BMG.

BEACH, SUN AND SURFIN'
CD ____ **12541**
Laserlight / Jul '95 / Target/BMG.

BEALE STREET GET-DOWN
CD ____ **PRCD 9907**
Prestige / Feb '96 / Complete/Pinnacle / Cadillac.

BEAT MERCHANTS
Man of the moment: *Clayson, Alan & The Argonauts* / Call of the wild: *Overlanders* / Pigtails in Paris: *MacBeth, David* / P.F.B.: *Flee-Rekkers* / Come on baby (to the floral dance): *Eagles* / I could write a book: *Chants* / If you don't come back: *Takers* / Lies: *Sandon, Johnny & The Remo Four* / Show you mean it too: *Me & Them* / He's telling you lies: *Kingpin* / Think it over: *Hellions* / Funny how love can be: *Rockin' Berries* / Bags groove: *Sheffields* / Stage door: *Jackson, Tony* / Harry rag: *Kinks* / Lady Jane: *Garrick, David* / What a world: *Hill, Benny* / End of the season: *Uglys* / Popcorn double feature: *Searchers* / Everything's funny: *Troggs* / Born to be wild: *Nashville Teens* / Break up: *Downliners* / I'm still raving: *Sutch, Screaming Lord* / Heavy weather: *British Invasion* / Moonlight skater: *Berry, Dave*
CD ____ **SEECD 430**
See For Miles/C5 / Sep '95 / Pinnacle.

BEAT THE BHANGRA VOL.1
CD ____ **DMUT 1234**
Multitone / Aug '93 / BMG.

BEAT THE BHANGRA VOL.2
CD ____ **DMUT 1235**
Multitone / Aug '93 / BMG.

BEAT THE SYSTEM PUNK SINGLES COLLECTION
Stab the judge: *One Way System* / Riot torn city: *One Way System* / Youth of today: *External Menace* / Someday: *External Menace* / Die for me: *Uproar* / Better off dead: *Uproar* / Sad society: *Chaotic Youth* / No future UK: *Chaotic Youth* / I hate: *Fits* / Time is right: *Fits* / Official hooligan: *Anti Social* / No views: *External Menace* / Poor excuse: *External Menace* / Backstreet boys: *Anti Social* / Death and pure destruction: *Death Sentence* / Death sentence: *Death Sentence* / Too many people: *Anti Social* / Rebel youth: *Uproar* / Victims: *Uproar* / IRA: *Post Mortem* / Day by day: *Post Mortem* / Me and you: *One Way System* / Arms race: *Chaotic Youth* / Victims of war: *Death Sentence* / Listen to me: *Fits*
CD ____ **CDPUNK 61**
Anagram / Aug '95 / Pinnacle.

BEATING PUNK, PAST
CD ____ **REM 20**
Released Emotions / May '93 / Pinnacle.

BEATLES COVERS VOLUME 3
CD ____ **CDTRL 365**
Trojan / Jan '96 / Jetstar / Total/BMG.

BEATS BY DOPE DEMAND
CD ____ **KICKCD 28**
Kickin' / Sep '95 / SRD.

BEATS RHYMES AND BASSLINES
(The Best Of Rap)
Set adrift on memory bliss: *PM Dawn* / Paid in full: *Eric B & Rakim* / Say no go: *De La Soul* / Mama gave birth to the soul children: *Queen Latifah & De La Soul* / My definition of a boombastic jazz style: *Dream Warriors* / It's a shame (my sister): *Monie Love & True Image* / Summertime: *D.J. Jazzy Jeff & The Fresh Prince* / Now that we've found love: *Heavy D & The Boyz* / Rebel without a pause: *Public Enemy* / (You gotta) Fight for your right (to party): *Beastie Boys* / Express

yourself: *N.W.A.* / U can't touch this: *M.C. Hammer* / Push it: *Salt 'N' Pepa* / Street tuff: *Rebel MC & Double Trouble* / Funky cold medina: *Tone Loc* / Got to keep on: *Cookie Crew*
CD _____ 5153842
4th & Broadway / May '92 / PolyGram.

BEAUTY AN OILEAN
Seainin Mhicil O Suilleabhain / *Muiris O Dalaigh* / *Sean O Dunnshleibhe* / *Sean O Cearnaigh* / *Padraig O Cearnaigh* / *Eibhlin Ni Chearna* / *Thomas O Dalaigh* / *Peaiti O Duinnshleibhe* / *Sean Cheaist O Cathain* / *Aine Ui Laoithe* / *Breanndan O Beaglaoich*
CD _____ CC 56 CD
Claddagh / Oct '92 / ADA / Direct.

BEAUTY OF THE BLUES
(Roots 'n' Blues Sampler)
Travelling riverside blues: *Johnson, Robert* / Southern can is mine: *McTell, Blind Willie* / Vas y carrement: *Breaux, Amedee* / Don't sell it (don't give it away): *Woods, Buddy* / Homeless blues: *Smith, Willie* / Signifying monkey: *Big Three Trio* / No more troubles now: *Johnson, Lonnie* / Horny frog: *Broonzy, Big Bill* / Lollypop: *Hunter & Jenkins* / Hot fingers: *Johnson, Lonnie* / You've got something there: *Fuller, Blind Boy* / I hate to see the sun go down: *Memphis Minnie* / God's got a crown: *Arizona Dranes* / T'aint nobody's business if I do: *Smith, Bessie* / If you take me back: *Big Joe* / You don't know my mind: *Leadbelly* / Is that a monkey you got: *Gillum, Bill 'Jazz'* / St. Louis blues: *Smith, Bessie*
CD _____ 4687682
Columbia / Nov '91 / Sony.

BEAVIS AND BUTTHEAD EXPERIENCE, THE
I hate myself and want to die: *Nirvana* / Looking down the barrel of a gun: *Anthrax* / Come to Butthead: *Beavis & Butthead* / Ninety nine ways to die: *Megadeth* / Bounce: *Run DMC* / Deuces wild: *Aerosmith* / I am hell: *White Zombie* / Poetry and prose: *Primus* / Monsta Mack: *Sir Mix-a-Lot* / Search and destroy: *Red Hot Chili Peppers* / Mental motherfuckers: *Jackyl* / I got you babe: *Cher, Beavis & Butthead* / Come to Butthead (Positive K Version): *Beavis & Butthead*
CD _____ GFLD 19283
Geffen / Oct '95 / BMG.

BEFORE THE FALL
CD _____ SFRCD 203
Strange Fruit / Sep '91 / Pinnacle.

BEGGARS OPERA
CD _____ 8283822
London / Jan '93 / PolyGram.

BEGIN THE BEGUINE - 1938
Begin the beguine: *Shaw, Artie* / Tisket-a-tasket: *Webb, Chick* / Ring dem bells: *Hampton, Lionel* / Sweet Georgia Brown: *Goodman, Benny Quartet* / I can't give you anything but love: *Armstrong, Louis* / Flat foot floogie: *Gaillard, Slim & Slam Stewart* / Music maestro please: *Dorsey, Tommy* / March of the bob cats: *Crosby, Bob* / When you're smiling: *Wilson, Teddy* / Swingin' the blues: *Basie, Count* / Louise: *Goodman, Benny* / Margie: *Lunceford, Jimmie* / Really the blues: *Ladnier, Tommy* / Little Joe from Chicago: *Kirk, Andy* / Back in your own backyard: *Holiday, Billie* / Back bay shuffle: *Shaw, Artie* / I let a song go out of my heart: *Ellington, Duke* / Jeepers creepers: *Kaye, Gene* / You must have been a beautiful baby: *Crosby, Bing* / Lullaby in rhythm: *James, Harry*
CD _____ PHONTCD 7665
Phontastic / Apr '90 / Wellard / Jazz Music / Cadillac.

BEGINNERS GUIDE TO TRADITIONAL SCOTTISH MUSIC
My fair young love/Father John MacMillan's farewell to Barra: *MacKay, Rhona* / Lude's supper: *Ossian* / Flame of wrath for squinting Patrick: *Livingstone, Pipe Major Bill* / Ewe wi'the crooked horn/Mrs. Mcpherson of Inveran: *Strathclyde Police Pipe Band* / Cradle song: *Gonnella, Ron* / Little pickle/Hare among the corn/Money in both pockets: *Glasgow Caledonian Strathspey & Reel Society* / Duke of Perth/Hunter's hill/Rakes of Mallow: *Ellis, John & His Highland Country Band* / Island of heather/Ciaro (Oran na Ciaoro): *Ellis, John & His Highland Country Band* / Puirt a beul: *MacInnes, Mairi* / Dh'theidhinn a dh'uibhist: *MacDonald Sisters* / Renfrewshire Militia/Tenpenny bit: *Stewart, Bella* / Dh'ni m geamhradh: *Runrig* / Battle of Harlaw: *Hunter, Andy* / Nicky Tams: *Stewart, Andy* / Flower o'the Quern: *Redpath, Jean* / Skye boat song: *McKellar, Kenneth* / Tartan: *Alexander Brothers* / Freedom come all ye: *Johnstone, Arthur* / Flying haggis/Peacock/MacArthur Road/Kiss the train goodbye: *Mathieson, Pipe Major Robert* / Journey to Skye: *Mathieson, Pipe Major Robert* / Ca' the yowes: *Gaelforce Orchestra* / Boys of Ballymoat: *Wolfstone*
CD _____ LCOM 5227
Lismor / Mar '94 / Lismor / Direct / Duncans / ADA.

BEGINNING, THE
(Jazz At The Philharmonic)
Lester leaps in / Tea for two / Blues / Body and soul / I've found a new baby / Rosetta / Bugle call rag / How high the music
CD _____ LEJAZZCD 41
Le Jazz / Jun '95 / Charly / Cadillac.

BEHIND THE EYE
(Eye Q Compilation Vol.1)
Cafe del mar: *Energy 52* / Magnifica: *Sonic Infusion* / Wonderer: *Vernon* / No fate: *Zyon* / See you virtual symmetry: *Odysee Of Noises* / Freebeach: *Goahead* / Airborn: *Mirage* / Sundown: *Volunteers* / Cosmos: *Java* / Synfonica: *Brainchild*
CD _____ 4509962162
Eye Q / Feb '94 / Disc / Warner Music.

BEHIND THE EYE VOL.2
CD _____ 4509990922
Eye Q / Feb '95 / Disc / Warner Music.

BELIEVE IN THE FREQUENCY POWER
Eternal: *Organisation* / Gotham City: *Animism* / Day of return (with dolphins): *Drawing Future Life* / Vermillion: *Suzukiski* / Colona: *Solaire* / Prussian blue smog: *Ultra AA* / Deep inside of me: *Ken Inaoka* / Halo: *Palomatic* / Dawn in the rainland: *Hazemato, Kiyoshi* / Phonetic: *Mind Design*
CD _____ JAP 100CD
North South / May '94 / Pinnacle.

BELLEVUE
CD _____ MFCD 004
Mafia/Fluxy / Jan '94 / Jetstar / SRD.

BELLISSIMO - EL RECORDS STORY PART 1
La pluie fait des claquettes: *Philippe, Louis* / Ruling class: *Adverse, Anthony* / Straits of Malacca: *King Of Luxembourg* / St. Lucy: *Gol Gappas* / Nicky: *Momus* / Reach for your gun: *Bid* / It's a beautiful game: *Cavaliers* / Southern fields: *Rosemary's Children* / Our fairy tale: *Adverse, Anthony* / Valleri: *King Of Luxembourg* / Like nobody do: *Philippe, Louis* / Dreams of leaving: *Always* / Fire: *Underneath* / Curtain: *Marden Hill* / Montague terrace (In blue): *Mayfair Charm School* / Never underestimate the ignorance of the rich: *Klaxon 5* / West 14: *Gol Gappas* / Libera me: *Cagliostra* / You Mary you: *Philippe, Louis* / Picture of Dorian Gray: *King Of Luxembourg*
CD _____ MONDE 11CD
Richmond / Apr '93 / Pinnacle.

BELLISSIMO - EL RECORDS STORY PART 2
Man of mine: *Florentines* / Whoops what a palaver: *Raj Quartet* / Metroland: *Always* / Fruit paradise: *Would-Be-Goods* / Imperial violets: *Adverse, Anthony* / Rose: *Marden Hill* / Anthony bay: *Philippe, Louis* / Trial of Dr. Fancy: *King Of Luxembourg* / Curry crazy: *Bad Dream Fancy Dress* / Thames Valley leather club: *Always* / Red shoes waltz: *Adverse, Anthony* / Oh Constance: *Marden Hill* / Pop up man: *Ambassador 277* / Flirt bliss love kiss: *King Of Luxembourg* / Camera loves me: *Would-Be-Goods* / Guess I'm dumb: *Philippe, Louis* / Supremes: *Bad Dream Fancy Dress* / Flair: *Bad Dream Fancy Dress* / Paradise lost: *Adverse, Anthony* / Sean Connery: *James Dean Driving Experience*
CD _____ MONDE 12CD
Richmond / Apr '93 / Pinnacle.

BELLY DANCE IN CAIRO
CD _____ PS 65141CD
Playasound / Apr '95 / Harmonia Mundi / ADA.

BEN & JERRY'S NEWPORT FESTIVAL
CD _____ RHR 36CD
Red House / Jul '95 / Koch / ADA.

BEND IT '91
CD _____ PELE 001CD
Exotica / Dec '91 / Vital.

BEND IT '92
Football Football I Like Football / Luton v Bristol City: *Morecambe, Eric* / Dreamhome: *Best, George* / Fore Grooming Aids: *Best, George* / Ryan Giggs We Love You / Manchester United football double / I've Got You Under My Skin: *Venables, Terry* / Brian Clough Shredded Wheat / Gary Goals / Ooh Gary Gary / Linekers In Barcelona / Le Match Du Jour / Leeds United Calypso / Rock 'n' roll with a ball / Give The Ball To Uwe Seeler / Alfredo Di Stefano Film Theme / Rancho D'Alfredo / Disco Johan Cryff / Sampdoria Formazione / Sampdoria Samba De Toninho / Roberto Baggio - Menajugo Milan / Love In A Porto Fino: *Charles, John* / I do like to see a game of football - 1932 / Zanzibar: *Matthews, Stan* / Blackpool: *Nolan Sisters* / Ipswich Football Calypso: *Nolan Sisters* / She Loves You: *Alfield Ray* / Vernon's Football Pools Girls / Kevin Keegan / World Cup Waltz / Pele's Injury / Eusebio Blues / Dateline Mexico '70 / Hugh McIlvanney Brazil '70 / I Like To Be The Best: *Pele* / Falling In Love With Brazil / Back home: *Stewart, Ed* / Goal Theme End
CD _____ PELE 002CD
Exotica / Sep '92 / Vital.

BEND IT '93
It only takes a second to score a goal: *Lira* / Hotspurs boogie: *Glitterbeat* / My ideal woman: *Best, George* / George (you've broken my heart): *Her* / Rah rah rah for Man

Utd.: *Dollies* / 1-0 for your love: *Beckenbauer, Franz* / Julie Brown loves Captain Cook: *Barrett, Les* / Le match de football: *Antoine* / Funky Manchester City: *Antoine* / Pele at Aston Villa: *Antoine* / Canoca: *Philippe, Louis* / World Cup doo wop: *Rosettes* / Don't shoot the ref: *McLeod, John X1* / Brian talk: *McLeod, John X1* / I'm football crazy: *Chinaglia, Giorgio* / Diego Armando Maradona: *Baccini, Francesco* / Fiorentina canzone viola: *Poti, Otello* / Genoa red and blue: *Baccini, Francesco & Fabrizio De Andre* / Cantona superstar: *Her* / J League freakout: *Rainbow Choir*
CD _____ PELE 005CD
Exotica / Sep '93 / Vital.

BEND IT '94
Goal - world cup 1966: *Sound Of Johnny Hawksworth* / Pele: *Cornelius* / Sampdoria formazione: *Cornelius* / Brazil Brazil: *Narraga O De Waldir Amaral* / World Cup football jazz: *Kane, Kahimi* / World Cup chacha: *Silvester, Victor* / Roberto Baggio - Non e un miraggio: *Il General & Ludus Pinski* / George Best - Belfast boy: *Romaine* / Georgie you've broken my heart: *Her* / George Best: *El Beatle* / World Cup chitchat: *Magnificent Andersons* / Carioca maracana: *Dreamers* / Tip top Tottenham Hotspurs: *Tottenham* / Roger Milla - My number 9 dream: *Rainbow Choir* / Ryan Giggs we love you: *Rainbow Choir* / Diego Armando Maradona: *Baggini, Francesco* / 1-0 For your love: *Bekenbaur, Franz* / Eusebio: *Phillipe, Louise* / Johan Cruyff - Flying Dutchman: *Bridge* / Pele - El Rey: *Alberto, Luis* / Manchester United calypso: *Connor, Edric & Ken Jones* / Blackpool Blackpool: *Nolans* / World Cup doo wop: *Rosettes* / Back home - England 1970: *Stewart, Ed* / Soccer boppers: *Posh*
CD _____ HARP 013
Exotica / Aug '94 / Vital.

BEND IT '94 VOLUME 2
Sunshine of your smile: *Light Billy Wright* / Nice one Cyril: *Stewart, Ed Stewpot & Junior Choice* / Come on The Fish: *Fisher Athletic* / Up The Shakers: *Bury* / Sunderland are back in the First Division: *Fine Art* / We'll be with you: *Stoke City* / Oh oh oh oh oh: *West Bromwich Albion* / Georgie: *Lucy* / George Best - Belfast Boy: *Chocolate Barry* / Glory glory Man United: *Rainbow Choir* / Love only me: *Grainger, Colin* / Red red robin: *Cotton, Billy & Charlton Athletic* / We want Rodney Marsh: *Cotton, Billy & Charlton Athletic* / Good morning Mexico: *Cotton, Billy & Charlton Athletic* / My Christmas song (Cancao de natal): *Pele* / Pele: *Marsh, Peggy* / Popstyle of a Brazilian footballer: *Cezar, Paolo* / Dedicated to Giancarlo Antognoni: *Cezar, Paolo* / Roberto Mancini: *De Scalzi Brothers* / Song of the Clyde: *Rochetaeu, Dominique* / Simple little things: *Charlton, Jack*
CD _____ PELE 008CD
Exotica / Jan '94 / Vital.

BERKELEY EP'S
Bass strings: *Country Joe & The Fish* / Thing called love: *Country Joe & The Fish* / Section 43: *Country Joe & The Fish* / Hearts to cry: *Fruminous Bandersnatch* / Misty cloud: *Fruminous Bandersnatch* / Cheshire: *Fruminous Bandersnatch* / Gazelle: *Mad River* / Grange fire: *Mad River* / Windchimes: *Mad River* / Where does love go: *Notes From The Underground* / Down in the basement: *Notes From The Underground* / What am I doing here: *Notes From The Underground* / Got to get out of this dream: *Notes From The Underground* / You don't love me: *Notes From The Underground* / Let yourself fly: *Notes From The Underground* / Where I'm at today: *Notes From The Underground*
CD _____ CDWIKD 153
Big Beat / Jun '95 / Pinnacle.

BERLIN ALWAYS
Cheek to cheek: *Astaire, Fred* / This year's kisses: *Faye, Alice* / Alexander's ragtime band: *Goodman, Benny Orchestra* / Slumming on Park Avenue: *Lunceford, Jimmie & Orchestra* / I'm putting all my eggs in one basket: *Armstrong, Louis* / Waiting on the edge of the road: *Waters, Ethel* / Isn't this a lovely day (to be caught in the rain): *Ambrose & His Orchestra* / Shakin' the blues away: *Etting, Ruth* / When I lost you: *Crosby, Bing* / Always: *Goodman, Benny Orchestra* / He ain't got rhythm: *Holiday, Billie* / I've got my love to keep me warm: *Tatum, Art* / Blue skies: *Dorsey, Tommy Orchestra* / I want to be in Dixie: *American Ragtime Octette* / Let yourself go: *Astaire, Fred* / How's chances: *Hall, Henry & The BBC Dance Orchestra* / Harlem on my mind: *Waters, Ethel* / Russian lullaby: *Berigan, Bunny & His Orchestra* / How deep is the ocean: *Crosby, Bing* / When the midnight choo choo leaves for Alabam': *Dorsey, Tommy Orchestra* / Now it can be told: *Bowlly, Al*
CD _____ AVC 517
Avid / Apr '93 / Avid/BMG / Koch.

BERLIN BY NIGHT
Ungarwein (gipsy wine): *Von Geczy, Barnabas & His Orchestra* / Ich tanze mit dir in den himmel hinein: *Harvey, Lilian & Willi Fritsch* / Gruss und kuss Veronika (Vocal: Eva Bloch): *Die Weintraubs* / Regentropfen: *Ruth, Ludwig Orchestra & Metropol Vocal-*

ists / Musik Musik (Vocal: Wilfried Sommer.): *Stenzel, Otto Dance Orchestra* / Arpanetta: *Gaden, Robert Orchestra* / Abends in der taverne: *Strienz, Wilhelm* / Du hast gluck bei dem frau'n bei mir: *Waldmuller, Lizzi* / Wochenend und sonnenschein: *Comedy Harmonists* / Liebling mein herz lasst dich grussen: *Harvey, Lilian & Willi Fritsch* / Rosamunde: *Glahe, Will Orchestra* / Liebe is ein geheimnis: *Hildebrand, Hilde & Orchestra* / O mia bella Napoli: *Schuricke, Rudi* / Lili Marlene: *Andersen, Lale* / Schones wetter heute: *Zacharias, Helmut* / Sing: *Kuhombe, Evelyn* / Liebe, kleine schaffnerin: *Carl, Rudolf* / Es geht alles voruber, es geht alles vorbei: *Andersen, Lale* / Das alte spinnrad: *Groh, Herbert Ernst & Odeon-Kunstler Orchester* / Sag' beim abschied leise "servus": *Forst, Willi*
CD _____ CDEMS 1395
EMI / May '91 / EMI.

BERLIN UNWRAPPED
(2CD/2MC/6LP)
CD Set _____ DVNT 006CD
Deviant / Jan '96 / Vital.

BERSERKLEY
CD _____ CREV 010CD
Rev-Ola / Mar '93 / 3MV / Vital.

BEST 80'S ALBUM IN THE WORLD...EVER, THE
(2CD/MC Set)
Don't you want me: *Human League* / There must be an angel (playing with my heart): *Eurythmics* / Sledgehammer: *Gabriel, Peter* / Don't you forget about me: *Simple Minds* / Money for nothing: *Dire Straits* / Gimme all your lovin': *77 Top* / Dead ringer for love: *Meat Loaf* / Good heart: *Sharkey, Feargal* / Every breath you take: *Police* / Faith: *Michael, George* / If I could turn back time: *Cher* / Girls just wanna have fun: *Lauper, Cyndi* / Relax: *Frankie Goes To Hollywood* / House of fun: *Madness* / Going underground: *77* / She drives me crazy: *Fine Young Cannibals* / Golden brown: *Stranglers* / What's love got to do with it: *Turner, Tina* / I can't go for that (no can do): *Hall & Oates* / Wherever I lay my hat (that's my home): *Young, Paul* / Take on me: *A-Ha* / Freedom: *Wham* / Only way is up: *Yazz* / Ride on time: *Black Box* / Temptation: *Heaven 17* / Ain't nobody: *Rufus & Chaka Khan* / Back to life: *Soul II Soul* / All around the world: *Stansfield, Lisa* / Look of love: *ABC* / Stop: *Erasure* / Only you: *Yazoo* / Song for whoever: *Beautiful South* / You got it: *Orbison, Roy* / Heaven is a place on earth: *Carlisle, Belinda* / Alone: *Heart* / Moonlight shadow: *Oldfield, Mike* / China in your hand: *T'Pau* / Drive: *Cars* / Vienna: *Ultravox* / Enola Gay: *O.M.D.*
CD Set _____ VTDCD 68
Virgin / Oct '95 / EMI.

BEST ALBUM IN THE WORLD...EVER, THE
(2CD/MC Set)
Alright: *Supergrass* / Girls and boys: *Blur* / Waking up: *Elastica* / Girls from mars: *Ash* / Whatever: *Oasis* / Girl like you: *Collins, Edwyn* / Only one I know: *Charlatans* / Do you remember the first time: *Pulp* / Yes: *McAlmont & Butler* / Everyday is like Sunday: *Morrissey* / High and dry: *Radiohead* / Zombie: *Cranberries* / Today: *Smashing Pumpkins* / La tristesse durera (Scream to a sigh): *Manic Street Preachers* / Sit down: *James* / Wake up boo: *Boo Radleys* / Animal nitrate: *Suede* / This is music: *Verve* / I want you: *Inspiral Carpets* / Screamager: *Therapy?* / This charming man: *Smiths* / April skies: *Jesus & Mary Chain* / Supersonic: *Oasis* / Fools gold: *Stone Roses* / Connection: *Stereo MC's* / Out of space: *Prodigy* / Destination eschaton: *Shamen* / True faith '94: *New Order* / Leave home: *Chemical Brothers* / Bullet: *Fluke* / Loaded: *Primal Scream* / Unbelievable: *EMF* / Real real real: *Jesus Jones* / Personal Jesus: *Depeche Mode* / Chemical world: *Blur* / Fifteen years: *Levellers* / Lenny Valentino: *Auteurs* / I can dream: *Skunk Anansie* / Captain Dread: *Dreadzone* / Lifeforms: *Future Sound Of London*
CD Set _____ VTDCD 58
Virgin / Sep '95 / EMI.

BEST ALBUM IN THE WORLD...EVER, THE
(2CD/MC Set)
Wonderwall (2): *Oasis* / Wild wood: *Weller, Paul* / Creep: *Radiohead* / Finetime: *Cast* / Commom people: *Pulp* / Life of riley: *Lightning Seeds* / Parklife: *Lightning Seeds* / He's on the phone: *St. Etienne* / What do I do now: *Sleeper* / Hope street: *Levellers* / Caught by the fuzz: *Supergrass* / Hobo humpin' slobo babe: *Whale* / Angel interceptor: *Ash* / Single girl: *Lush* / Connection: *Elastica* / Queer: *Garbage* / She bangs the drum: *Stone Roses* / Blue Monday: *Charlatans* / Far gone and out: *Jesus & Mary Chain* / Great things: *Echobelly* / Might be stars: *Wannadies* / Weak: *Skunk Anansie* / Life is

sweet: *Chemical Brothers* / Tosh: *Fluke* / Protection: *Massive Attack* / You do: *Mc-Almont & Butler*
CD Set _____ **VTDCD 76**
Virgin / Jan '96 / EMI.

BEST BLUES, THE
CD _____ **CD 904**
Sound / Jun '89 / Direct / ADA.

BEST CHOICE
CD _____ **DCD 5388**
Disky / Jul '94 / THE / BMG / Discovery / Pinnacle.

BEST CHRISTMAS ALBUM...EVER, THE (2CD/MC Set)
Do they know it's Christmas: *Band Aid* / Last Christmas: *Wham* / Step into Christmas: *John, Elton* / Santa Claus is coming to town: *Jackson Five* / Merry Christmas everybody: *Slade* / In dulci jubilo: *Oldfield, Mike* / Stop the cavalry: *Lewie, Jona* / Rockin' around the Christmas tree: *Wilde, Kim* / Another rock and roll Christmas: *Glitter, Gary* / Mary had a little boy: *Snap* / Ring out, solstice bells: *Jethro Tull* / Saviour's day: *Richard, Cliff* / Mull of Kintyre: *Wings* / Spaceman came travelling: *De Burgh, Chris* / Winter's tale: *Essex, David* / Keeping the dream alive: *Freiheit* / Peace on earth - little drummer boy: *Bowie, David & Bing Crosby* / White Christmas: *Crosby, Bing* / Let it snow, let it snow, let it snow: *Martin, Dean* / Christmas song: *Fitzgerald, Ella* / Winter wonderland: *Day, Doris* / Warm December: *London, Julie* / Merry Christmas darling: *Carpenters* / Santa baby: *Kitt, Eartha* / Happy holiday: *Williams, Andy* / Lonely pup (in a Christmas shop): *Faith, Adam* / Blue Christmas: *Nelson, Willie* / Silver bells: *Reeves, Jim* / Mary's boy child: *Belafonte, Harry* / Twelve days of Christmas: *Daugherty, Jack* / Gaudete: *Steeleye Span* / Silent night: *Temptations* / Only you: *Flying Pickets* / Walking in the air: *Jones, Aled* / Christmas wrapping: *Waitresses* / Sadness part 1: *Enigma* / Merry Christmas everyone: *Stevens, Shakin'*
CD Set _____ **VTDCD 23**
Virgin / Oct '95 / EMI.

BEST COUNTRY ALBUM IN THE WORLD...EVER, THE
Rhinestone cowboy: *Campbell, Glen* / Jolene: *Parton, Dolly* / When you're in love with a beautiful woman: *Dr. Hook* / Rose garden: *Anderson, Lynn* / Blanket on the ground: *Spears, Billie Jo* / Coward of the county: *Rogers, Kenny* / I recall a gypsy woman: *Williams, Don* / Most beautiful girl in the world: *Rich, Charlie* / Ode to Billy Joe: *Gentry, Bobbie* / Stand by your man: *Wynette, Tammy* / Crazy: *Cline, Patsy* / I love you because: *Reeves, Jim* / Don't it make my brown eyes blue: *Gayle, Crystal* / All I have to do is dream: *Gentry, Bobbie & Glen Campbell* / Wind beneath my wings: *Greenwood, Lee* / Angel of the morning: *Newton, Juice* / Banks of the Ohio: *Newton-John, Olivia* / We're all alone: *Coolidge, Rita* / Crying: *McLean, Don* / End of the world: *Davis, Skeeter* / Achy breaky heart: *Cyrus, Billy Ray* / Devil went down to Georgia: *Daniels, Charlie Band* / Promised land: *Allan, Johnnie* / I can help: *Swan, Billy* / Ring of fire: *Cash, Johnny* / I'll never fall in love again: *Gentry, Bobbie* / King of the road: *Miller, Paulette* / Games people play: *South, Joe* / Margaritaville: *Buffett, Jimmy* / Wichita lineman: *Campbell, Glen* / I will always love you: *Parton, Dolly* / From a distance: *Griffith, Nanci* / I fall to pieces: *Cline, Patsy* / Little bit more: *Dr. Hook* / Lucille: *Rogers, Kenny* / What I've got in mind: *Spears, Billie Jo* / It's here: *Orbison, Roy* / Me and Bobby McGee: *Kristofferson, Kris* / Funny how time slips away: *Nelson, Willie* / Night they drove old dixie down: *Band*
CD Set _____ **CDEMTV 87**
EMI / Nov '94 / EMI.

BEST DANCE ALBUM IN THE WORLD...EVER, THE
Ride on time: *Black Box* / No limit: *2 Unlimited* / What is love: *Haddaway* / It's my life: *Dr. Alban* / Power: *Snap* / Pump up the jam: *Technotronic & Felly* / All that she wants: *Ace Of Base* / Ride like the wind: *East Side Beat* / Take a chance on me: *Erasure* / Everybody's free: *Rozalla* / Pump up the volume: *M/A/R/R/S* / Theme from S'Express: *S'Express* / Temptation: *Heaven 17* / Ain't no love (ain't no use): *Sub Sub & Melanie Williams* / How can I love you more: *M People* / Phorever people: *Shamen* / I am eternal: *K.L.F.* / I'm gonna get you: *Bizarre Inc.* / Something good: *Utah Saints* / Run to you: *Rage* / Groove is in the heart (Peanut butter mix): *Deee-Lite* / We are family: *Sister Sledge* / I'm every woman: *Khan, Chaka* / Finally: *Peniston, Ce Ce* / Big fun: *Inner City* / Got to have your love: *Mantronix* / You got the love: *Source & Candi Staton* / People everyday: *Arrested Development* / Jump: *Kriss Kross* / Gonna make you sweat: *C & C Music Factory* / Back to life: *Soul II Soul* / Dirty cash (money talks): *Adventures Of Stevie V* / Love lost: *West End & Sybil* / Always there: *Incognito & Jocelyn Brown* / On a ragga tip: *SL2* / On Carolina: *Shaggy* / Mr. Loverman: *Shabba Ranks* / Thinking about your love: *Thomas, Kenny* / If only I could: *Youngblood, Sydney* / Joy: *Soul II Soul*

CD _____ **VTDCD 17**
Virgin / Jul '93 / EMI.

BEST DANCE ALBUM IN THE WORLD...EVER (PART 2)
Rhythm is a dancer: *Snap* / Get up (before the night is over): *Technotronic* / Tribal dance: *2 Unlimited* / U got 2 know: *Cappella* / Boom shake the room: *D.J. Jazzy Jeff & The Fresh Prince* / Boom shak-a-lak: *Apache Indian* / Jump around: *House Of Pain* / Hey, the secret: *Urban Cookie Collective* / Last train to Transcentral: *K.L.F.* / L.S.I: Love Sex Intelligence: *Shamen* / Out of space: *Prodigy* / It keeps rainin' (tears from my eyes): *McLean, Bitty* / Sweat (a la la la long): *Inner Circle* / Please don't go: *KWS* / Right here: *S.W.V.* / I love your smile: *Shanice* / Keep on movin': *Soul II Soul* / My lovin': *En Vogue* / Gypsy woman: *Waters, Crystal* / Dreams: *Gabrielle* / Set adrift on memory bliss: *PM Dawn* / Killer: *Seal* / Only way is up: *Yazz* / Peace: *Johnston, Sabrina* / When I'm good and ready: *Sybil* / I will survive: *Gaynor, Gloria* / People hold on: *Coldcut* / Slave to the vibe: *Aftershock* / Too blind to see it: *Sims, Kym* / Good life: *Inner City* / Fascinating rhythm: *Bass-O-Matic* / Open your mind: *Usura* / Don't you want me: *Felix* / Insanity: *Oceanic* / House of love: *Slawn* / It shout (it out): *Louchie Lou & Michie One* / Dub be good to me: *Beats International* / Step it up: *Stereo MC's* / Magic number: *De La Soul* / Buffalo stance: *Cherry, Neneh* / Beat dis: *Bomb The Bass* / Regret: *New Order*
CD _____ **VTDCD 22**
Virgin / Oct '93 / EMI.

BEST DANCE ALBUM IN THE WORLD...EVER (PART 3)
Let the beat control your body: *2 Unlimited* / Get a life: *Soul II Soul* / Straight up: *Abdul, Paula* / Things can only get better: *D Ream* / You got 2 let the music: *Cappella* / It's alright: *East 17* / I like to move it: *Reel 2 Real* / Sweets for my sweet: *Lewis, C.J.* / Real thing: *Di Bart, Tony* / Get-a-way: *Maxx* / Get ready for this: *2 Unlimited* / Moving on up: *M People* / Exterminate: *Snap* / Rock my heart: *Haddaway* / Swamp thing: *Grid* / Informer: *Snow* / Living train runnin': *Doobie Brothers* / Love it up: *Glowworm* / Touch me: *49ers* / Carry me home: *Glowworm* / Let's talk about sex: *Glowworm* / Blue Monday (Remix): *New Order* / We got a love thang: *Peniston, Ce Ce* / U can't touch this: *M.C. Hammer* / Stay: *Eternal* / Flintstones: *BC 52s* / Come baby come: *K7* / Naked in the rain: *Blue Pearl* / Doop: *Doop* / Always: *Erasure* / Feels like heaven: *Urban Cookie Collective* / (I wanna give you) Devotion: *Nomad* / Dedicated to the one I love: *McLean, Bitty* / Light my fire: *Club House* / Ebeneezer goode: *Shamen* / Caught in the middle (Remix): *Roberts, Juliet* / Shine: *Aswad* / It's too late: *Quartz & Dina Carroll* / Show me love: *Robin S* / Real love: *Time Frequency*
CD _____ **VTDCD 32**
Virgin / Jul '94 / EMI.

BEST DANCE ALBUM IN THE WORLD...EVER (PART 4)
Confide in me: *Minogue, Kylie* / Real thing: *2 Unlimited* / Dream's a dream: *Soul II Soul* / Don't turn around: *Ace Of Base* / One night in heaven: *M People* / Relight my fire: *Take That* / Ooops up: *Snap* / Word up: *Cameo* / Too funky: *Michael, George* / Move on baby: *Cappella* / U R the best thing: *D Ream* / Just a step from heaven: *Eternal* / Mr. Vain: *Culture Beat* / Rhythm is a mystery: *K-Klass* / Chain reaction: *Ross, Diana* / No good (start the dance): *Prodigy* / No more (I can't stand it): *Maxx* / Total mix: *Black Box* / Tease me: *Demus, Chaka & Pliers* / Searching: *China Black* / Hangin' on a string: *Loose Ends* / Let's get ready to rhumble: *PJ & Duncan* / We don't have to...: *Stewart, Jermaine* / Don't worry: *Appleby, Kim* / Relax: *Frankie Goes To Hollywood* / You don't love me (no no): *Penn, Dawn* / Rhythm of the night: *Corona* / Incredible: *M-Beat & General Levy* / Human nature: *Clail, Gary* / Ain't nothin' goin' on but the rent: *Guthrie, Gwen* / Compliments on your kiss: *Red Dragon* / Things that make you go hmmmm: *C & C Music Factory* / Go on move: *Reel 2 Real* / Baby come back: *Banton, Pato* / She's got that vibe: *R. Kelly* / Unfinished sympathy: *Massive Attack* / No more tears (enough is enough): *Mazelle, Kym & Jocelyn Brown* / Turn up the power: *N-Trance* / Everything is alright (Uptight): *Lewis, C.J.* / What's going on: *Music Relief*
CD Set _____ **VTDCD 40**
Virgin / Nov '94 / EMI.

BEST DANCE ALBUM IN THE WORLD...EVER (PART 5)
Right in the night: *Jam & Spoon* / Excited: *M People* / Dreamer: *Livin' Joy* / Don't give me your life: *Alex Party* / Scatman: *Scatman John* / Don't stop (Wiggle wiggle): *Outhere Brothers* / Bomb: *Bucketheads* / Humpin' around: *Brown, Bobby* / Push the feeling on: *Nightcrawlers* / Another night: *Real McCoy* / Zombie: *A.D.A.M. & Amy* / Whoomph (there it is): *Clock* / Cotton eye Joe: *Rednex* / Got to get it: *Culture Beat* / Baby baby: *Corona* / What's up: *D.J. Miko* / Call it love: *Deuce* / Set you free: *N-Trance* / Reach up: *Perfecto All Stars*
CD _____ **VIDCD 55**
Virgin / Jul '95 / EMI.

BEST DANCE ALBUM IN THE WORLD...EVER 1995, THE (2CD/MC Set)
Boombastic: *Shaggy* / Stayin' alive: *N-Trance* / La la la hey hey: *Outhere Brothers* / I luv U baby: *Original* / Two can play at that game: *Brown, Bobby* / Hideaway: *De-'Lacy* / Bomb (these sounds fall into my mind): *Bucketheads* / Open your heart: *M People* / Surrender your love: *Nightcrawlers* / Dreamer: *Livin' Joy* / 3 is family: *Dawson, Dana* / Love enuff: *Soul II Soul* / Flavour of the old school: *Knight, Beverley* / Here comes the hotstepper: *Kamoze, Ini* / Turn on, tune in, cop out: *Freak Power* / Baby come back: *Banton, Pato* / Right in the night (fall in love with music): *Jam & Spoon* / Run away: *Real McCoy* / Whoomph (there it is): *Clock* / Cotton eye Joe: *Rednex* / Don't you want me: *Human League* / Baby baby: *Corona* / Reach up (Papa's got a brand new big bag): *Perfecto All Stars* / Cory India: *Umboza* / Fee fi fo fum: *Candy Girls* / Sweet harmony: *Liquid* / U sure do: *Strike* / Not over yet: *Grace* / Your loving arms: *Martin, Billie Ray* / Set you free: *N-Trance* / Axel F: *Clock* / Keep warm: *Jinny* / Shoot me with your love: *D Ream* / Say it: *Deuce* / Freedom: *Gayle, Michelle* / Mary Jane (all night long): *Blige, Mary J.* / My prerogative: *Brown, Bobby* / La luna (to the beat of the drum): *Ethics* / I'm ready: *Size 9*
CD Set _____ **VTDCD 67**
Virgin / Oct '95 / EMI.

BEST DANCE HALL
CD _____ **RNCD 2053**
Rhino / Mar '94 / Jetstar / Magnum Music Group / THE.

BEST FOLK, THE
CD _____ **CD 902**
Sound / Jun '89 / Direct / ADA.

BEST FOOT FORWARD
CD _____ **PUSSYCD 001**
Pussy Foot / Jul '95 / Disc.

BEST FUNK ALBUM IN THE WORLD...EVER, THE
(Get up / feel like being a) Sex machine: *Brown, James* / Funky stuff: *Kool & The Gang* / Oops upside your head: *Gap Band* / She's strange: *Cameo* / My lovin': *En Vogue* / If you're ready (come go with me): *Staple Singers* / Family affair: *Sly & The Family Stone* / Inner city blues (make me wanna holler): *Gaye, Marvin* / Green onions: *Booker T & The MG's* / Papa was a rollin' stone: *Was Not Was* / Cloud 9: *Temptations* / Yum yum (gimme some): *Fatback Band* / Give up the funk (Tear the roof off the sucker): *Parliament* / Which way is up: *Starguard* / Ain't nothin' goin' on but the rent: *Guthrie, Gwen* / I gotcha: *Tex, Joe* / Got to get you into my life: *Earth, Wind & Fire* / Fire: *Ohio Players* / Use me: *Withers, Bill* / Good times: *Chic* / Strut your stuff: *Frantique* / Get down tonight: *K.C. & The Sunshine Band* / Pick up the pieces: *Average White Band* / Papa's got a brand new pig-bag: *Pigbag* / Higher ground: *Red Hot Chili Peppers* / Rockit: *Hancock, Herbie* / Theme from S'Express: *S'Express* / Something got me started: *Simply Red* / Once you get started: *Rufus* / Atomic dog: *Clinton, George* / I feel sanctified: *Commodores* / Sunshine day: *Osibisa* / Hard work: *Handy, John* / Never, never gonna give you up: *White, Barry* / Mr. Big Stuff: *Knight, Jean* / Ain't gonna bump no more (with no big fat woman): *Tex, Joe* / Where is the love: *Wright, Betty* / Right place, wrong time: *Dr. John*
CD Set _____ **VTDCD 44**
Virgin / Feb '95 / EMI.

BEST IRISH REQUESTS
CD _____ **DH 002**
Outlet / Jul '94 / ADA / Duncans / CM / Ross / Direct / Koch.

BEST JAZZ, THE
CD _____ **CD 906**
Sound / Jun '89 / Direct / ADA.

BEST JOVENES FLAMENCOS, THE
El vito cante / Jaleo pa las flamencas / Vengo del mora / Mi fe ni min miguel / El reloj del carino / Lo bueno y lo malo / Vuela, vuela pajarito / Chana / Venta zoraida / Chi-cuelina / Nubes de colores / De perdidos al rio / Anonimo jerezano / Que no quiero dinero / Piel de habichuela / Refrito
CD _____ **93042**
Emocion / Feb '95 / New Note.

BEST OF 100% DANCE, THE
CD Set _____ **TCD 2752**
Telstar / Nov '94 / BMG.

BEST OF 12" GOLD VOL.1
Boogie wonderland: *Earth, Wind & Fire* / Disco nights: *G.Q.* / You can do it: *Hudson, Al & The Partners* / I thought it was you: *Hancock, Herbie* / Street life: *Crusaders* / You know how to love me: *Hyman, Phyllis* / It's a disco night (rock don't stop): *Isley Brothers* / Stuff like that: *Jones, Quincy*
CD _____ **OG 3401**
Old Gold / Oct '88 / Carlton Home Entertainment.

BEST OF 12" GOLD VOL.10
Let the music play: *Shannon* / Hip hop be bop (Don't stop): *Man Parrish* / Alice, I want you just for me: *Full Force* / Haunted house

of rock: *Whodini* / Body work: *Hot Streak* / Street dance: *Break Machine* / Sexomatic: *Bar-Kays* / Rockit: *Hancock, Herbie*
CD _____ **OG 3410**
Old Gold / Nov '89 / Carlton Home Entertainment.

BEST OF 12" GOLD VOL.11
Ain't no stoppin' us now: *McFadden & Whitehead* / Ring my bell: *Ward, Anita* / This time baby: *Moore, Jackie* / Can you feel the force: *Real Thing* / Shake your body: *Jacksons* / Time: *Light Of The World* / Turn the music up: *Players Association* / We got the funk: *Positive Force*
CD _____ **OG 3411**
Old Gold / Feb '90 / Carlton Home Entertainment.

BEST OF 12" GOLD VOL.12
High energy: *Thomas, Evelyn* / Where is my man: *Kitt, Eartha* / You think you're a man: *Divine* / On a crowded street: *Pennington, Barbara* / Light my fire (1985 remix): *Stewart, Amii* / So many men, so little time: *Brown, Miquel* / Can't take my eyes off you: *Boystown Gang* / Y.M.C.A.: *Village People*
CD _____ **OG 3412**
Old Gold / Feb '90 / Carlton Home Entertainment.

BEST OF 12" GOLD VOL.13
Dancing tight: *Galaxy & Phil Fearon* / I am somebody: *Jones, Glenn* / Your personal touch: *King, Evelyn 'Champagne'* / Emergency (dial 999): *Loose Ends* / Encore: *Lynn, Cheryl* / You can't have my love: *Jones Girls* / Tossing and turning: *Windjammer* / You get the best from me (say say): *Myers, Alicia*
CD _____ **OG 3413**
Old Gold / Feb '90 / Carlton Home Entertainment.

BEST OF 12" GOLD VOL.14
Love me like this: *Real To Reel* / My love is waiting: *Gaye, Marvin* / Risin' to the top: *Burke, Keni* / Can't from Ipanema: *Gilberto, Astrud* / Does she have a friend: *Chandler, Gene* / Mind blowin' decisions: *Heatwave* / Mellow mellow right on: *Lowrell* / Pillow talk: *Sylvia*
CD _____ **OG 3414**
Old Gold / Jul '90 / Carlton Home Entertainment.

BEST OF 12" GOLD VOL.15
You gave me love: *Crown Heights Affair* / Casanova: *Coffee* / Never knew love like this before: *Mills, Stephanie* / She's a bad mama jama: *Carlton, Carl* / Burn rubber on me: *Gap Band* / Celebration: *Kool & The Gang* / Southern Freeez: *Freeez* / Walking into sunshine: *Central Line*
CD _____ **OG 3415**
Old Gold / Jul '90 / Carlton Home Entertainment.

BEST OF 12" GOLD VOL.16
Somebody's else's guy: *Brown, Jocelyn* / Thinking of you: *Sister Sledge* / Change of heart: *Change* / Touch me: *Rae, Fonda* / Who do you love: *Intruders* / You're the one for me (medley): *Hardcastle, Paul* / Feel so real: *Arrington, Steve* / Say I'm your number one: *Princess*
CD _____ **OG 3416**
Old Gold / Jun '91 / Carlton Home Entertainment.

BEST OF 12" GOLD VOL.18
Forget me nots: *Rushen, Patrice* / I wish you would: *Brown, Jocelyn* / Love wars: *Womack & Womack* / Dancin' in the key of life: *Arrington, Steve* / You are my melody: *Change* / In your car: *Cool Notes* / After the love has gone: *Princess* / Rainforest: *Hardcastle, Paul*
CD _____ **OG 3418**
Old Gold / '92 / Carlton Home Entertainment.

BEST OF 12" GOLD VOL.19
Best disco in town: *Ritchie Family* / Shame: *King, Evelyn 'Champagne'* / Don't leave me this way: *Melvin, Harold & The Bluenotes* / You to me are everything: *Real Thing* / Native New Yorker: *Odyssey* / Take that to the bank: *Shalamar* / Groove line: *Heatwave* / Galaxy of love: *Crown Heights Affair*
CD _____ **OG 3419**
Old Gold / Apr '92 / Carlton Home Entertainment.

BEST OF 12" GOLD VOL.2
And the beat goes on: *Whispers* / Check out the groove: *Thurston, Bobby* / Music: *Miles, John* / You're lying: *Linx* / Stomp: *Brothers Johnson* / Star: *Earth, Wind & Fire* / You bet you're free: *Hancock, Herbie* / I don't want to be a freak (but I can't help myself): *Dynasty*
CD _____ **OG 3402**
Old Gold / Oct '88 / Carlton Home Entertainment.

BEST OF 12" GOLD VOL.20
Get down on it: *Kool & The Gang* / Just an illusion: *Imagination* / Inside out: *Odyssey* / Walking on sunshine: *Rockers Revenge* / Massage: *Grandmaster Flash & The Furious Five* / Automatic: *Pointer Sisters* / Try jah love: *Third World* / Night to remember: *Shalamar*
CD _____ **OG 3420**

Old Gold / Apr '92 / Carlton Home Entertainment.

BEST OF 12" GOLD VOL.21
Word up: Cameo / Spend the night: Cool Notes / Fresh: Kool & The Gang / Sleeptalk: Williams, Alyson / All and all: Sims, Joyce / Never too much: Vandross, Luther / Tribute: Pasadenas / Midas touch: Midnight Star
CD _____ CD 3421
Carlton Home Entertainment / Sep '92 / Carlton Home Entertainment.

BEST OF 12" GOLD VOL.3
Let's groove: Earth, Wind & Fire / I'm in love: King, Evelyn 'Champagne' / Ai no corrida: Jones, Quincy / Groove: Franklin, Rodney / Funkin' for Jamaica: Browne, Tom / Don't stop the music: Yarbrough & Peoples / Strut your funky stuff: Frantique / Don't push it, don't force it: Haywood, Leon
CD _____ OG 3403
Old Gold / Oct '88 / Carlton Home Entertainment.

BEST OF 12" GOLD VOL.4
Jump to it: Franklin, Aretha / I can make you feel good: Shalamar / Put our heads together: O'Jays / I've had enough: Earth, Wind & Fire / Love come down: King, Evelyn 'Champagne' / Get down Saturday night: Cheatham, Oliver / Crazy: Manhattans / It's a love thing: Whispers
CD _____ OG 3404
Old Gold / Oct '88 / Carlton Home Entertainment.

BEST OF 12" GOLD VOL.5
Love town: Newbury, Booker / Joy: Band AKA / Get it right: Franklin, Aretha / Stay with me tonight: Osborne, Jeffrey / Hi, how ya doin': Kenny G. / I'll be around: Wells, Terri / Extraordinary girl: O'Jays / Silver shadow: Atlantic Starr
CD _____ OG 3405
Old Gold / Jan '89 / Carlton Home Entertainment.

BEST OF 12" GOLD VOL.6
Close to you: Guthrie, Gwen / You make it heaven: Wells, Terri / Serious: Griffin, Billy / On the wings of love: Osborne, Jeffrey / After the love has gone: Earth, Wind & Fire / Secret lovers: Atlantic Starr / How 'bout us: Champaign / Weekend girl: S.O.S. Band
CD _____ OG 3406
Old Gold / Jan '89 / Carlton Home Entertainment.

BEST OF 12" GOLD VOL.7
History: Mai Tai / Hangin' on a string: Loose Ends / Tell me how it feels: 52nd Street / Mine all mine: Cashflow / Ain't nothin' goin' on but the rent: Guthrie, Gwen / Takes a little time: Total Contrast / I'll be good: Rene & Angela / You and me tonight: Aurra
CD _____ OG 3407
Old Gold / Jul '89 / Carlton Home Entertainment.

BEST OF 12" GOLD VOL.8
Grace: Band AKA / Can't keep holding on: Second Image / Hold me tighter in the rain: Griffin, Billy / Nightbirds: Shakatak / I specialise in love: Brown, Sharon / This beat is mine: Vicky D. / So fine: Johnson, Howard / Nights over Egypt: Jones Girls
CD _____ OG 3408
Old Gold / Jul '89 / Carlton Home Entertainment.

BEST OF 12" GOLD VOL.9
Caravan of love: Isley-Jasper-Isley / Always and forever: Heatwave / Juicy fruit: Mtume / Sexual healing: Gaye, Marvin / Let's make a baby: Paul, Billy / Outrageous: Anderson, Carl / New York eyes: Nicole & Timmy Thomas / Just be good to me: S.O.S. Band
CD _____ OG 3409
Old Gold / Nov '89 / Carlton Home Entertainment.

BEST OF 12" SYNTH
Love on your side: Thompson Twins / Living on the ceiling: Blancmange / Play to win: Heaven 17 / Mind of a toy: Visage / Life in Tokyo: Japan / Dancing with tears in my eyes: Ultravox / Einstein a go go: Landscape / Souvenir: O.M.D.
CD _____ OG 3802
Old Gold / Jun '90 / Carlton Home Entertainment.

BEST OF 2-TONE, THE
Ghost town: Specials / On my radio: Selecter / Too much too young: Special AKA / Do nothing: Specials / People do rock steady: Bodysnatchers / Stereotype: Specials / Prince: Madness / Rat race: Specials / Boiler: Rhoda & Special A.K.A. / I can't stand up for falling down: Costello, Elvis / Nelson Mandela: Special AKA / Missing words: Selecter / Message to you Rudy: Specials / Selecter: Selecter
CD _____ CDCHRTT 5012
Chrysalis / Nov '93 / EMI.

BEST OF 90'S COUNTRY
If tomorrow never comes: Brooks, Garth / Shotgun: Tucker, Tanya / Never ending song of love: Gayle, Crystal / On a good night: Campbell, Glen / I'm a survivor: Dalton, Lacy / My side of the story: Bogguss, Suzy / Race is on: Brown, Sawyer / On the bayou: Wild Rose / Moonshadow Road: Brown, T. Graham / Other side of love: Davies, Gail / Do you know where your man is:

Mandrell, Barbara / Good times: Seals, Dan / Everything: Chapman, Cee Cee / What would you do about you (if you were me): Osmond, Marie / Country girl heart: Gatlin, Larry & The Gatlin Brothers / Tear it up: Harms, Jonie
CD _____ CDMFP 5912
Music For Pleasure / Apr '91 / EMI.

BEST OF ACID
(4 CD)
Get the hole: Townsell / Got the bug: Phuture Fantasy Club / Shout: Frost, Jack & The Circle Jerks / Act of acid: Jerks / Slam: Phuture Fantasy Club / That shits wild: Dr. Derelict / Box energy: D.J. Pierre / Feels good: Mr. Lee / Never gonna change: Mr. Lee / Bango acid: Wilson, Mike 'Hitman' / I got a big dick: Joshua, Maurice / Feel the mood: Joshua, Maurice / I'll make you dance: Townsell, Lidell / Acid man: Frost, Jack & The Circle Jerks / Desire: Scappy & The Box Boyz / Ecstasy: Love Story / Drug store: Professor Of Acid / Battery acid: Six Brown Brothers / Stomach acid: Overdose / City hall: Six Brown Brothers / Jackin' tall: Townsell, Lidell / Hello lover: VL & The Porch Monkeys / In the brain: Kool, Domo / Hot hands: Hot Hanas Hula / 70th and king drive: Hot Hanas Hula / Revenge of the bass: Acid Gang / Acid out: Frost, Jack & The Circle Jerks / Let the music pump you up: Irving, Kevin / Living in a land: Owens, Robert / Acid trax: Phuture / House this house: Mr. Lee / Downfall: Armando / Cool and dry: Frost, Jack & The Circle Jerks / Tom Tom: Frost, Jack & The Circle Jerks / Two the max: Frost, Jack & The Circle Jerks / Ghetto ratz: Acid Gang / Seventeen days of acid rain: Nouveau Nation / This isn't acid: Fangdanz & Domo
CD Set _____ LOWBOXCD 5
Low Price Music / Sep '94 / Total/BMG.

BEST OF ACID HOUSE VOLUME 1
CD _____ LOWCDX 17
Low Price Music / Mar '95 / Total/BMG.

BEST OF ACID JAZZ
Chicken lickin': Funk Inc. / Zebra walk: Kynard, Charles / Reelin' with the feelin': Kynard, Charles / Dig on it: Smith, Johnny 'Hammond' / Get myself a good man: Pucho / Super bad: Muhammad, Idris / Who's gonna take the weight: Sparks, Melvin / Sure nuff sure nuff: Phillips, Sonny / Cold sweet: Purdie, Bernard / Psychedelic Sally: Jefferson, Eddie / Soul dance: Person, Houston / Houston Express: Person, Houston / Smokin' at Tiffany's: Funk Inc.
CD _____ CDBGP 921
BGP / Jun '89 / Pinnacle.

BEST OF ACID JAZZ
CD _____ JAZIDCD 029
Acid Jazz / Jan '91 / Pinnacle.

BEST OF ACID JAZZ VOL.2
Don't let it go to your head: Brand New Heavies / Masterplan: Brown, Diana & Barrie K Sharpe / Peace and love: Sewell, Janette / Watch my garden grow: Humble Souls / Jazz Jupiter: A-Zel / Hope you're feeling better: Mother Earth / E-type: Corduroy / Lucky fellow: Snowboy / Girl overboard: Snowboy / Living life your own way (CD only): Windross, Rose
CD _____ JAZIDCD 066
Acid Jazz / May '93 / Pinnacle.

BEST OF ACID VOL.2
CD _____ LOWCDX 18
Low Price Music / Aug '95 / Total/BMG.

BEST OF AIM, THE
CD _____ AIM 005CD
Aim / Oct '95 / Direct / ADA / Jazz Music.

BEST OF ALL WOMAN
Show me heaven: McKee, Maria / From a distance: Griffith, Nanci / If I could hold back time: Cher / Sweet love: Baker, Anita / I say a little prayer: Franklin, Aretha / You're so vain: Simon, Carly / Stay with me baby: Ellison, Lorraine / Piano in the dark: Russell, Brenda / Stay: Shakespears Sister / Stop: Brown, Sam / Get here: Adams, Oleta / Mad about the boy: Washington, Dinah / So close: Carroll, Dina / Love and affection: Armatrading, Joan / First time: Beck, Robin / Remember me: Ross, Diana / I close my eyes and count to ten: Springfield, Dusty / Promise me: Craven, Beverley / Damn, I wish I was your lover: Hawkins, Sophie B. / Free: Williams, Deniece / Piece of my heart: Franklin, Erma / Eternal flame: Bangles / Anything for you: Estefan, Gloria / That old black magic: Moyet, Alison / Smooth operator: Sade / You gotta be: Des'ree / I feel the earth move: Martika / I'll be there: Carey, Mariah / See the day: Lee, Dee C. / True colors: Lauper, Cyndi / Think twice: Dion, Celine / Why are you being: Diana / Nothing compares 2 U: O'Connor, Sinead / All woman: Stansfield, Lisa / Why: Lennox, Annie / Move closer: Nelson, Phyllis / My one temptation: Paris, Mica / Another sad love song: Braxton, Toni / Oh baby, I: Eternal / Heaven is a place on earth: Carlisle, Belinda / Man with the child in his eyes: Bush, Kate
CD _____ BOWOCD 001
Dino / Sep '95 / Pinnacle / 3MV.

BEST OF BALLET MUSIC
CD _____ DCD 5329
Disky / Dec '93 / THE / BMG / Discovery / Pinnacle.

BEST OF BELLYDANCE FROM EGYPT AND LEBANON
CD _____ EUCD 1320
ARC / Nov '95 / ARC Music / ADA.

BEST OF BELLYDANCE, THE
CD _____ EUCD 1211
ARC / Sep '93 / ARC Music / ADA.

BEST OF BGP
Always there: Side Effect / Got myself a good man: Pucho / Black whip: Jones, Ivan 'Boogaloo Joe' / So what: Jefferson, Eddie / Sister Janie: Funk Inc. / Nuther'n like thuther'n: Jackson, Willis / Rock Creek Park: Blackbyrds / Ban montana: Parker, Maynard / O baby I believe I'm losing you: Hawks, Billy / Ping pong: Blakey, Art & The Jazz Messengers / Selim (Available on CD format only.): Lytle, Johnny / Milestones (Available on CD format only.): Murphy, Mark / Jungle strut (Available on CD format only.): Ammons, Gene / Jazz carnival (Available on CD format only.): Azymuth
CD _____ CDBGP 1030
BGP / Oct '90 / Pinnacle.

BEST OF BLUE NOTE
(A Selection From 25 Albums)
Moanin': Blakey, Art / Midnight blue: Burrell, Kenny / Caravan: Ellington, Duke / Atomic Mr. Basie: Basie, Count / Un poco loco: Powell, Bud / Ornithology: Parker, Charlie / Rocker: Davis, Miles / I guess I'll hang my tears out to dry: Gordon, Dexter / Let's get lost: Baker, Chet / Tune up: Hollins, Sonny / Criss cross: Monk, Thelonious / Blue train: Coltrane, John / Maiden voyage: Hancock, Herbie / Song for my father: Silver, Horace
CD _____ CDP 8299642
Blue Note / Mar '95 / EMI.

BEST OF BLUE NOTE
(Sampler)
Tropical legs: Klugh, Earl / Back at the chicken shack: Smith, Jimmy / Soy Califa: Gordon, Dexter / Miss Ann's tempo: Green, Grant / Moanin': Blakey, Art / Move: Davis, Miles / Eleanor Rigby: Jordan, Stanley / Louie: Burrell, Kenny / Jody Grind: Green, Horace / My funny valentine: Baker, Chet
CD _____ CDP 8349572
Blue Note / Oct '91 / EMI.

BEST OF BLUE NOTE VOL.1
Blue train: Coltrane, John / Maiden voyage: Hancock, Herbie / Christo redemptor: Byrd, Donald / Moanin': Blakey, Art / Blues walk: Donaldson, Lou / Song for my father: Silver, Horace / Back to the chicken shack: Smith, Jimmy / Chitlins com carne: Burrell, Kenny / Sidewinder: Morgan, Lee
CD _____ CDP 7961102
Blue Note / Oct '91 / EMI.

BEST OF BLUE NOTE VOL.2
Senor blues: Silver, Horace / Decision: Rollins, Sonny / Three o'clock in the morning: Gordon, Dexter / Blues march: Blakey, Art / Wadin': Parlan, Horace / Rumproller: Morgan, Lee / Something else: Adderley, Cannonball / Blue bossa: Henderson, Joe / Watermelon man: Hancock, Herbie
CD _____ CDP 7979602
Blue Note / Feb '93 / EMI.

BEST OF BOTH WORLDS
CD _____ HNCD 8304
Hannibal / Oct '94 / Vital / ADA.

BEST OF BRITISH BLUES, THE
CD _____ CD IMB 502
Charly / Mar '93 / Charly / THE / Cadillac.

BEST OF BRITISH FOLK
CD _____ TRTCD 156
TrueTrax / Oct '94 / THE.

BEST OF BRITISH FOLK
CD Set _____ DCDCD 215
Castle / Nov '95 / BMG.

BEST OF BRITISH FOLK, THE
Streets of London: McTell, Ralph / Net hauling song: Campbell, Ian Folk Group / Drag queen blues: Digance, Richard / Join us in our game: Mr. Fox / Day at the seaside: Renbourn, John / Market song: Pentangle / Judy: Renbourn, John / Roisin dubh: Dubliners / Reed's favourite: Renbourn, John & Bert Jansch / Light flight: Pentangle / Spiral staircase: McTell, Ralph / Carolan's concerto: Billy / Pavanna (Anna Banana): Renbourn, John / Off to Dublin in the green: Dubliners / Hermit: Renbourn, John / Dear river thames: McTell, Ralph / Young love: Giltrap, Gordon / So what: Renbourn, John & Bert Jansch / Shoe shine boy: Humblebums / Willoughby's farm: McTell, Ralph
CD _____ MATCD 218
Qastle / May '93 / BMG.

BEST OF BRITISH FOLK.
Light flight: Pentangle / Travel away: Humblebums / My friend up the road: Digance, Richard / Byker Hill: Swarbrick, Dave & Martin Carthy / Spiral staircase: McTell, Ralph / Continental trailways bus: Johnstons / Streets of London: McTell, Ralph / Mary Skeffington: Rafferty, Gerry / Rosemary Lane: Jansch, Bert / White House blues: Renbourn, John / If it wasnae for your weel lies: Connolly, Billy / Up to now: Dransfields

/ Join us in our game: Mr. Fox / Easy street: James, John & Pete Berryman / All in a dream: Tilston, Steve / Sir Gavin Grimbold: Gryphon / Ungodly: Decameron / Gingerbread man: Story Teller / Lover for all seasons: Sallyangie / Boxing match: Black Country Three / Mouse and crow: Pegg, Carole / Dear River Thames: Digance, Richard / After the dance: Jansch, Bert & John Renbourn / Maid that's deep in love: Pentangle
CD _____ CCSCD 222
Castle / Jun '89 / BMG.

BEST OF BRITISH JAZZ
CD _____ CDSR 056
Telstar / Feb '95 / BMG.

BEST OF BRITISH JAZZ
(3CD Set)
Crazy rhythm: Daniel, Joe Jazz Group / St. Louis blues: Daniel, Joe Jazz Group / Jazz me blues: Daniel, Joe Jazz Group / Chicago: Daniel, Joe Jazz Group / Little brown jug: Daniel, Joe Jazz Group / I wish I could shimmy like my sister Katie: Daniel, Joe Jazz Group / Avalon: Daniel, Joe Jazz Group / Rosetta: Daniel, Joe Jazz Group / Susie: Daniel, Joe Jazz Group / Bad penny blues: Lyttelton, Humphrey & His Band / Heatwave: Lyttelton, Humphrey & His Band / Slippery horn: Lyttelton, Humphrey & His Band / Early call: Lyttelton, Humphrey & His Band / That's my home: Lyttelton, Humphrey & His Band / P.T.Q. rag: Lyttelton, Humphrey & His Band / March hare: Lyttelton, Humphrey & His Band / Hoppin'mad: Lyttelton, Humphrey & His Band / Careless love: Lyttelton, Humphrey & His Band / Panama rag: Lyttelton, Humphrey & His Band / Maple leaf rag: Lyttelton, Humphrey & His Band / Alexander's ragtime band: Phillips, Sid & His Band / You've got to see mama ev'ry night: Phillips, Sid & His Band / Pasadena: Phillips, Sid & His Band / Disillusioned: Phillips, Sid & His Band / Muskrat ramble: Phillips, Sid & His Band / Mama don't allow it: Phillips, Sid & His Band / Forty cups of coffee: Phillips, Sid & His Band / Pete Kelly's blues: Phillips, Sid & His Band / Clarinet marmalade: Phillips, Sid & His Band / Tiger rag: Phillips, Sid & His Band / Sensation rag: Randall, Freddy & His Band / Black & blue: Randall, Freddy & His Band / Hotter than that: Randall, Freddy & His Band / Sunday: Randall, Freddy & His Band / Farewell blues: Randall, Freddy & His Band / Someday sweetheart: Randall, Freddy & His Band / Won't you come home Bill Bailey: Randall, Freddy & His Band / On Sunday I go sailing: Richford, Doug & The London Jazzmen / Yip-I-addy-l-ay: Richford, Doug & The London Jazzmen / Twelve over the eight: Richford, Doug & The London Jazzmen / Nagasaki: Gonella, Nat & His Georgians / Jubilee: Gonella, Nat & His Georgians / Swingin' the jinx away: Gonella, Nat & His Georgians / I can't dance I got ants in my pants: Gonella, Nat & His Georgians / Lily of the valley: Crane River Jazz Band / Who walks in when I walk out: Saints Jazz Band / Hey lawdy Papa: Saints Jazz Band
CD Set _____ CDTRBOX 208
Music For Pleasure / Mar '95 / EMI.

BEST OF BRITISH JAZZ
CD _____ URCD 118
Upbeat / Oct '95 / Target/BMG / Cadillac.

BEST OF BRITISH MILITARY MUSIC
CD _____ CDSR 043
Telstar / May '94 / BMG.

BEST OF BRITISH VOL. 1
CD _____ CDSIV 6146
Horatio Nelson / May '95 / THE / BMG / Avid/BMG / Koch.

BEST OF BRITISH, THE
CD _____ DINCD 92
Dino / Jun '94 / Pinnacle / 3MV.

BEST OF CAPITAL GOLD, THE
Something in the air: Thunderclap Newman / Waterloo sunset: Kinks / Out of time: Farlowe, Chris / Daydream: Lovin' Spoonful / Son of a preacher man: Springfield, Dusty / I don't want our love to die: Herd / I hear you knocking: Edmunds, Dave / Green tambourine: Lemon Pipers / (If paradise is) Half as nice: Amen Corner / This wheel's on fire: Driscoll, Julie & The Brian Auger Trinity / Concrete and clay: Unit 4+2 / Jesamine: Casuals / Israelites: Dekker, Desmond / In the summertime: Mungo Jerry / With a little help from my friends: Cocker, Joe / White shade of pale: Procul Harum / Get it on: T. Rex / Sweets for my sweet: Searchers / First cut is the deepest: Arnold, P.P. / Will you still love me tomorrow: Shirelles / Only one woman: Marbles / Rescue me: Bass, Fontella / Judy in disguise: Freud, John & His Playboy Band / Itchycoo Park: Small Faces
CD _____ AHLCD 2
Hit / Oct '92 / PolyGram.

BEST OF CAPITOL CLASSICS VOL.1 & 2
Key to the world: Reynolds, L.J. / On the beat: B B & Q Band / Prance on: Henderson, Eddie / Love on a summer night: McCrarys / It's a pleasure: Brown, Sheree / Sound of music: Dayton / Doin' alright: O'Bryan / Music is my sanctuary: Bartz, Gary / Be thankful for what you've got / Hard to get around: B B & Q Band / Before

you break my heart: *Dunlap, Gene* / Really, really love you: *Parker, Cecil* / There ain't nothin' (like your lovin'): *Laurence, Paul* / It's just the way I feel: *Dunlap, Gene & The Ridgeways*
CD __________ **CZ 208**
Capitol / Jun '89 / EMI.

BEST OF CARNIVAL IN RIO
CD __________ **EUCD 1097**
ARC / '91 / ARC Music / ADA.

BEST OF CARNIVAL IN RIO VOL.2
CD __________ **EUCD 1136**
ARC / '91 / ARC Music / ADA.

BEST OF CHARLY BLUES MASTERWORKS, THE
Downhearted blues: *Smith, Bessie* / Crossroads blues: *Johnson, Robert* / Bobby sox blues: *Walker, T-Bone* / Wolf is at your door (Howlin' for my baby): *Howlin' Wolf* / Easy: *Horton, Big Walter* / Got my mojo working: *Waters, Muddy* / Blues leave me alone: *Rogers, Jimmy* / Juke: *Little Walter* / I got it made (when I marry Shirley Mae): *Guitar Junior* / Gotta find my baby: *Memphis Slim* / Dimples: *Hooker, John Lee* / Baby, what you want me to do: *Reed, Jimmy* / Big car blues: *Hopkins, Lightnin'* / Searchin' for a woman: *King, Albert* / Don't start me talkin': *Williamson, Sonny Boy* / First time I met the blues: *Guy, Buddy* / Rollin' and tumblin': *James, Elmore* / Goin' down slow: *Super Super Blues Band* / Nobody's fault but mine: *Washington, Walter 'Wolfman'* / I ain't got you: *Mayall, John & The Bluesbreakers* / I wish you would: *Arnold, Billy Boy* / Everybody rockin': *Hooker, John Lee* / Bad boy: *Taylor, Eddie* / Everyday I have the blues: *Witherspoon, Jimmy* / Smokestack lightnin': *Howlin' Wolf* / One way out: *James, Elmore* / I can't quit you baby: *Rush, Otis* / Jelly roll king: *Frost, Frank* / All your love: *Magic Sam* / Sweet home Chicago: *Allison, Luther* / Wee wee baby: *Waters, Muddy* / My love is real: *Guy, Buddy* / One bourbon, one scotch, one beer: *Hooker, John Lee* / Can't get no grindin' (what's the matter with the mill): *Waters, Muddy* / Morning blues: *Hopkins, Lightnin'* / Gate's salty blues: *Brown, Clarence 'Gatemouth'* / Highway: *Howlin' Wolf & Eric Clapton* / Don't burn down the bridge: *King, Albert* / Who's been talkin': *Cray, Robert* / My baby's coming home: *Dupree, Champion Jack*
CD Set __________ **CDBMS 102**
Charly / Jun '93 / Charly / THE / Cadillac.

BEST OF CHARLY GROOVE, THE
Little soul party: *Ohio Players* / If she won't (find someone who will): *Dorsey, Lee* / Big legged woman: *Hobbs, Willie* / Good old funky music: *Meters* / Working in a coal mine: *Dorsey, Lee* / Give the baby anything the baby wants: *Tex, Joe* / Chokin' kind: *Toussaint, Allen* / It takes two to do wrong: *Patterson, Bobby* / Is it funky enough: *Communications & Black Experiences Band* / Thank you for letting me be myself again: *Maceo & All The King's Men* / All I do everyday: *Meters* / Full speed ahead: *Jungle Band* / Gone too far: *Toussaint, Allen* / Move on up: *Mayfield, Curtis* / Medley (Live): *Brown, James* / It's too funky in here: *Payback* / (I got) so much trouble in my mind (pts 1 & 2): *Quarterman, Sir Joe & Free Soul* / Ain't gonna bump no more (with big fat women): *Tex, Joe* / Soul music: *Mayfield, Curtis* / Tell me why: *Womack, Bobby* / Shine it on: *Sly & The Family Stone* / Cholly (funk getting ready to roll): *Funkadelic* / Mother's son: *Mayfield, Curtis* / Oh I: *Funkadelic* / Thump and bump: *Fisher, Eddie* / If it's not addin' up: *Sly & The Family Stone* / Tripping out (Album version): *Mayfield, Curtis* / One nation under a groove: *Funkadelic* / (Get up I feel like being a) sex machine (Live): *Brown, James* / 7-6-5-4-3-2-1 Blow your whistle: *Rimshots* / Mambo mongo: *Santamaria, Mongo*
CD Set __________ **CPCD 8085**
Charly / Jun '95 / Charly / THE / Cadillac.

BEST OF CHESS 2, THE
Happy, happy birthday baby: *Tune Weavers* / I'm so young: *Students* / Book of love: *Monotones* / Teardrops: *Andrew, Lee & The Hearts* / Ten commandments of love: *Harvey & The Moonglows* / Let me in: *Sensations* / Over the mountain across the sea: *Johnnie & Joe* / Hi-heel sneakers: *Tucker, Tommy* / Rinky dink: *Cortez, Dave 'Baby'* / Sally go round the roses: *Jaynetts* / No particular place to go: *Berry, Chuck* / Roadrunner: *Diddley, Bo*
CD __________ **CHLD 19222**
Chess/MCA / Jul '93 / BMG / New Note.

BEST OF CHESS BLUES VOL.1, THE
CD __________ **CHLD 19093**
Chess/MCA / Oct '92 / BMG / New Note.

BEST OF CHESS BLUES VOL.2, THE
CD __________ **CHLD 19094**
Chess/MCA / Oct '92 / BMG / New Note.

BEST OF CHESS BLUES, THE
(First Time I Met the Blues)
Don't start me talkin': *Williamson, Sonny Boy* / Key to the highway: *Little Walter* / Hoochie coochie man: *Waters, Muddy* / Walkin' the boogie: *Hooker, John Lee* / Smokestack lightnin': *Howlin' Wolf* / So many roads, so many trains: *Rush, Otis* / When the lights go out: *Witherspoon, Jimmy* / Worried life blues: *Berry, Chuck* / First time I met the blues: *Guy, Buddy* / Off the wall: *Little Walter* / Third degree: *Boyd, Eddie* / I'm leaving you: *Spann, Otis* / Sun is shining: *James, Elmore* / Reconsider baby: *Fulson, Lowell* / I don't know: *Mabon, Willie* / Red rooster: *Howlin' Wolf* / Fattenin' frogs for snakes: *Williamson, Sonny Boy* / Sugar mama: *Hooker, John Lee* / Be careful: *Brim, John* / Wee wee hours: *Berry, Chuck* / Walking the blues: *Dixon, Willie* / Howlin' for my darling: *King, Albert* / Guess I'm a fool: *Memphis Slim* / Got my mojo working: *Waters, Muddy*
CD __________ **CDRED 11**
Charly / Jun '89 / Charly / THE / Cadillac.

BEST OF CHESS R & B VOL.1
CD __________ **CHLD 19160**
Chess/MCA / Nov '91 / BMG / New Note.

BEST OF CHESS R & B VOL.2
CD __________ **CHLD 19161**
Chess/MCA / Nov '91 / BMG / New Note.

BEST OF CHESS, THE
Maybellene: *Berry, Chuck* / Bo Diddley: *Diddley, Bo* / Rocket 88: *Brenston, Jackie & The Delta Cats* / See you later alligator: *Charles, Bobby* / Suzie Q: *Hawkins, Dale* / Oh oh: *Bo, Eddie* / Johnny B. Goode: *Berry, Chuck* / Sincerely: *Moonglows* / Ain't got no home: *Henry, Clarence 'Frogman'* / Most of all: *Moonglows* / I'll be home: *Flamingos* / Who do you love: *Diddley, Bo*
CD __________ **CHLD 19221**
Chess/MCA / Jul '93 / BMG / New Note.

BEST OF CHURCH STREET STATION VOL.1
(Country Stars Live)
D.I.V.O.R.C.E.: *Wynette, Tammy* / Four in the morning: *Young, Faron* / Behind closed doors: *Rich, Charlie* / Mamas don't let your babies grow up to be cowboys: *Bruce, Ed* / This land is your land: *Allen, Rex Snr & Rex Allen Jnr* / Duellin' banjos: *Devol, Skip* / Texas when I die: *Tucker, Tanya* / Before the next teardrop falls: *Fender, Freddy* / He stopped loving her today: *Jones, George* / Love in the hot afternoon: *Watson, Gene* / Detroit city: *Tillis, Mel* / He ain't heavy, he's my brother: *Osmond Brothers* / Cheating situation: *Bandy, Moe* / Wabash cannonball: *Boxcar Willie* / Big bad John: *Dean, Jimmy* / Teddy bear: *Fairchild, Barbara* / Tequila sunrise: *Bare, Bobby*
CD __________ **PLATCD 359**
Prism / '91 / Prism.

BEST OF CHURCH STREET STATION VOL.2
(Country Stars Live)
Delta town: *Tucker, Tanya* / Mr. Bojangles: *Nitty Gritty Dirt Band* / Heart of the country: *Mattea, Kathy* / Let your love flow: *Bellamy Brothers* / Mexico rose: *Fender, Freddy* / Secret love: *Fender, Freddy* / Who's gonna fill their shoes: *Jones, George* / Door is always open: *Dave & Sugar* / Lonely days, lonely nights: *Loveless, Patty* / Key Largo: *Higgins, Bertie* / Carmen: *Watson, Gene* / Chains of gold: *Sweethearts Of The Rodeo* / Auctioneer: *Van Dyke, Leroy* / I like beer: *Hall, Tom T.* / Love don't care: *Conley, Earl Thomas* / Please Mr. Please / God bless America: *Greenwood, Lee* / Harper Valley PTA: *Riley, Jeannie C.* / Okie from Muskogee: *Haggard, Merle*
CD __________ **PLATCD 360**
Platinum Music / May '91 / Prism / Ross.

BEST OF COUNTRY
CD __________ **LOXCD 1**
Low Price Music / Nov '94 / Total/BMG.

BEST OF COUNTRY & IRISH, THE
Lovely Leitrim: *Cunningham, Larry* / There's been a change in you: *Cunningham, Larry* / I used to be a railroad bum: *Cunningham, Larry* / Blue side of lonesome: *Cunningham, Larry* / I love you because: *Cunningham, Larry* / Night coach to Dallas: *Cunningham, Larry* / They wouldn't do it now: *Cunningham, Larry* / Good old country music: *Cunningham, Larry* / Annaghdown: *Cunningham, Larry* / Forty shades of green: *Cunningham, Larry* / Seems like I'm always leaving: *Cunningham, Larry* / Emerald Isle express: *Cunningham, Larry* / When my blue moon turns to gold again: *Coll, Brian* / Mail call: *Coll, Brian* / These are my mountains: *Coll, Brian* / Fool's castle: *Coll, Brian* / Cover Mama's flowers: *Coll, Brian* / Back to Birmingham: *Coll, Brian* / Cattle call: *Coll, Brian* / Tears of St. Anne: *Coll, Brian* / Asthoreen bawn: *Coll, Brian* / China doll: *Coll, Brian* / Petal from a faded rose: *Coll, Brian* / Sing me back home: *Coll, Brian* / Made for each other: *Two's Company* / Red river valley: *Two's Company* / If teardrops were pennies: *Two's Company* / Before I'm fool enough: *Two's Company* / Best love I've ever had: *Two's Company* / Dear John: *Two's Company* / Gonna lay me down (Beside a memory): *Two's Company* / Pride and dignity: *Two's Company* / Sing me an old fashioned song: *Two's Company* / My heart cries for you: *Two's Company* / You're the highlight of my life: *Two's Company* / Love drives out the cold: *Two's Company* / It must be you: *Two's Company* / Sweet dreams: *Two's Company* / Coming closer: *Two's Company* / Let's start all over again: *Two's Company*
CD Set __________ **HBOXCD 75**
Carlton Home Entertainment / Jul '94 / Carlton Home Entertainment.

BEST OF COUNTRY & WESTERN
CD Set __________ **4417272**
Pilz / Oct '92 / BMG.

BEST OF COUNTRY AND IRISH
CD __________ **RITZCD 0072**
Ritz / Apr '94 / Pinnacle.

BEST OF COUNTRY, THE
CD __________ **SETCD 077**
Stardust / Sep '94 / Carlton Home Entertainment.

BEST OF DANCE '92
CD __________ **TCD 2610**
Telstar / Oct '92 / BMG.

BEST OF DANCE BAND DAYS VOL. 1
Moonlight serenade / Clarinade / Jumpin' at the woodside / Sweet Georgia Brown / Stars fell on Alabama / Angry / Stardust / Song of India / Caldonia / Airmail stomp / Rockin' in rhythm / Bei mir bist du schon / Little brown jug / Don't be that way / Tweet tweet / Button up your overcoat / Some people / 'S wonderful / Opus one / At the woodchoppers' ball / Blue moon / I got a girl named Netty
CD __________ **DBCD 20**
Dance Band Days / Oct '87 / Prism.

BEST OF DANCE BAND DAYS VOL. 2
Symphony / King Porter stomp / Rockin' in rhythm / I'll be seeing you / Down the road apiece / Man with a horn / Begin the beguine / Cheek to cheek / There, I've said it again / Everybody eats when they come to my house / Newport up / Lullaby of Broadway / Seven-o-five / All the cats join in / King size blues / Fare thee well to Harlem / Bedford drive / Blue skies / Goosey gander / Cruisin' with cab / St. Louis blues / Rum and coca cola
CD __________ **DBCD 21**
Dance Band Days / Oct '87 / Prism.

BEST OF DANCE MANIA
CD Set __________ **PMCD 7026**
Pure Music / Oct '95 / BMG.

BEST OF DISCO
CD Set __________ **LOWBOXCD 15**
Low Price Music / Jun '95 / Total/BMG.

BEST OF DJ MIXES
CD Set __________ **LOWBOXCD 20**
Low Price Music / Jul '95 / Total/BMG.

BEST OF EAST EUROPEAN SONGS AND DANCES
CD __________ **EUCD 1148**
ARC / '91 / ARC Music / ADA.

BEST OF ELECTRO 1
CD __________ **SOUNDSCD 8**
Street Sounds / Oct '95 / BMG.

BEST OF FLAMENCO
CD __________ **EUCD 1158**
ARC / Jun '91 / ARC Music / ADA.

BEST OF FRANCE'S CONCERT COMPILATION
CD __________ **FCD 130**
France's Concert / '89 / Jazz Music / BMG.

BEST OF GARAGE
CD Set __________ **LOWBOXCD 17**
Low Price Music / Jul '95 / Total/BMG.

BEST OF GOSPEL, THE
CD __________ **DSHCD 7015**
D-Sharp / Jun '94 / Pinnacle.

BEST OF GOTHAM RHYTHM AND BLUES
CD __________ **KKCD 04**
Krazy Kat / Oct '90 / Hot Shot / CM.

BEST OF GREECE VOL.2
CD __________ **EUCD 1159**
ARC / Jun '91 / ARC Music / ADA.

BEST OF H.T.D., THE
Down in the bottom: *Terraplane* / Shake for me: *Terraplane* / We lie: *Albion Band* / Thank Christ for the bomb/Soldier: *Groundhogs* / Land of my fathers (Hen wlad fy nhadau): *Caravan* / Foolish pride: *McPhee, Tony* / Railway station: *Tylor* / Children of the stones: *Rose Among Thorns* / Fogbound: *Banks, Peter* / Why: *Sister Mary Elephant*
CD __________ **HTDCD 20**
HTD / Apr '94 / Pinnacle.

BEST OF HAPPY HARD CORE
CD Set __________ **LOWBOXCD 17**
Low Price Music / Nov '95 / Total/BMG.

BEST OF HAPPY HOUSE
CD Set __________ **LOWBOXCD 19**
Low Price Music / Jul '95 / Total/BMG.

BEST OF HARDCORE
CD Set __________ **LOWBOXCD 12**
Low Price Music / May '95 / Total/BMG.

BEST OF HARDCORE VOL. 1
CD __________ **LOWCDX 45**
Low Price Music / Dec '95 / Total/BMG.

BEST OF HOUSE
(4 CD)
Brutal house: *Nitro Deluxe* / LFO: *LFO* / Love can't turn around: *Farley Jackmaster Funk* / Jack to the sound: *D.J. Fast Eddie* / Don't make me jack: *Grey, Paris* / Free at last: *Reese Project* / Poke: *Adonis* / I know you like it: *React 2 Rhythm* / What can I do for you: *Gardner, Taanya* / I can't forget: *Mr. Lee* / Move your body: *Jefferson, Marshall* / Please don't go: *KWS* / Super real: *Body Medusa* / Can U feel it: *Fingers Inc.* / House master: *Baldwin, Terry* / Aftermath: *Nightmares On Wax* / Pump up Chicago: *Mr. Lee* / Get out on this dancefloor: *D.O.P.* / Give me back the love: *On The House* / No way back: *Adonis* / House nation: *Adonis* / Running away: *Rasario, Ralphi* / Yo yo get funky: *D.J. Fast Eddie* / Bounce your body: *Saunderson, Kevin* / What is house: *LFO* / Intoxication: *React 2 Rhythm* / Don't need your love: *Irving, Kevin* / Jack your body: *Hurley, Steve 'Silk'* / Free: *Kate B* / Mystery: *Phase II* / Groovy beat: *D.O.P.* / So deep: *Reese Project* / Promised land: *Smooth, Joe* / Hip house: *D.J. Fast Eddie* / Let's get busy: *Mr. Lee* / Baby wants to ride: *Knuckles, Frankie* / On and on: *Saunders, Jesse* / Nightmare: *Kid Unknown* / Magic: *Khan, Bou* / Let the music use you: *Night Riders*
CD Set __________ **LOWBOXCD 2**
Low Price Music / Dec '93 / Total/BMG.

BEST OF HOUSE VOL.2
CD __________ **LOWCDX 06**
Low Price Music / Aug '95 / Total/BMG.

BEST OF INDIE METAL, THE
CD __________ **EMPRCD 552**
Emporio / Nov '94 / THE / Disc / CM.

BEST OF INDIE TOP 20
CD __________ **BOTT 1CD**
Beechwood / May '91 / BMG / Pinnacle.

BEST OF INDIE TOP 20.
CD __________ **CD 88**
Beechwood / Jun '93 / BMG / Pinnacle.

BEST OF IRELAND
(3 CD/MCs)
Let him go, let him tarry: *Murray, Ruby* / Teddy O'Neil: *Murray, Ruby* / Delaney's donkey: *Murray, Ruby* / Dear old Donegal: *Murray, Ruby* / McNamara's band: *Murray, Ruby* / When Irish eyes are smiling: *Murray, Ruby* / Danny boy: *Murray, Ruby* / Cockles and mussels: *Murray, Ruby* / Trottin' to the fair: *Murray, Ruby* / It's a great day for the Irish: *Murray, Ruby* / Believe me if all those endearing young charms: *Murray, Ruby* / Mush, mush, mush: *O'Dowda, Brendan* / Ballymaquilty band: *O'Dowda, Brendan* / Dear little shamrock: *O'Dowda, Brendan* / On the one road: *O'Dowda, Brendan* / Paddy McGinty's goat: *O'Dowda, Brendan* / Come back to Erin: *O'Dowda, Brendan* / Phil the fluter's ball: *O'Dowda, Brendan* / Mountains of Mourne: *O'Dowda, Brendan* / Come back Paddy Reilly: *O'Dowda, Brendan* / Are you right there Michael: *O'Dowda, Brendan* / Si do Mhaimeo/Peter Street: *O'Duill, Brendan* / Doonaree: *Murray, Ruby & Brendan O'Dowda* / Eileen O'Grady: *Murray, Ruby & Brendan O'Dowda* / Three tunes (A haste to the wedding/Leslie's horn pipe/The German bean): *Gallowglass Ceili Band* / Reel (Paddy on the railroad/Miss McLeod): *Gallowglass Ceili Band* / I'll take you home again Kathleen: *Locke, Josef* / When you were sixteen: *Locke, Josef* / Galway Bay: *Locke, Josef* / Macushla: *Locke, Josef* / Rose of Tralee: *Locke, Josef* / Isle of Innisfree: *Locke, Josef* / Maire my girl: *Locke, Josef* / How can you buy Killarney: *Locke, Josef* / My heart's in the heart of Killarney: *Cunningham, Larry* / Vely Leitrim: *Cunningham, Larry* / Moonshiner: *Murphy, Delia* / Spinning wheel: *Murphy, Delia* / Courtin' in the kitchen: *Murphy, Delia* / Three drunken maidens: *Planxty* / Whiskey in the jar: *Dubliners* / Galway races: *Dubliners* / Kelly, the boy from Killan: *Dubliners* / Limerick rake: *Dubliners* / Bantry Bay: *O'Shea, Sean* / Banks of my own lovely Lee: *O'Shea, Sean* / Star of the County Down: *McCormack, John* / Jeannie with the light brown hair: *McCormack, John* / Down by the Sally Gardens: *McCormack, John* / Queen of Connemera (featuring John Bennett): *Ardellis Ceili Band* / Jigs (Eavesdropper/Donnybrook boys/A visit to Ireland): *Ardellis Ceili Band* / Old Skibbereen: *Gallagher, Bridie* / Castlebar Fair: *Gallagher, Bridie* / Flower of sweet Strabane: *Gallagher, Bridie* / Where the River Shannon flows: *Gallagher, Bridie* / Wearin' of the green: *Henry, Dermot* / Ireland my home: *MacEwan, Father Sydney* / Mother MacHree: *MacEwan, Father Sydney* / Rose of Killarney: *MacEwan, Father Sydney* / Irish lullaby: *Shannonside Ceili Band* / Old bog road: *Drennan, Tommy* / Claddagh ring: *Tulla Céili Band* / Three reels (Sheehans/Merry blacksmith/Music in the glen): *Kilfernora Ceili Band* / Kitty of Coleraine: *Bunratty Singers* / Coulin: *O'Grady, Geraldine* / My lagan love: *O'Duffy, Michael* / Irish salute (Galway Bay/With my shillelagh under my arm/Dear old Donegal): *Band of the Irish Guards*
CD Set __________ **CDTRBOX 164**
Trio / Sep '95 / EMI.

BEST OF IRELAND, A
(Celtic Graces)
Midnight walker: *Spillane, Davy* / Ballymun regatta: *Whelan, Bill* / Plains of Kildare: *Brady, Paul* / Maids of Mitchelstown: *Bothy Band* / Wee weaver: *Keane, Dolores & John Faulkner* / Aaron's key: *Stockton's Wing* / Arthur McBride: *Brady, Paul* / Eigigh suas a stoirin: *Clannad* / Rip the calico: *Bothy Band* / Mr. O'Connor: *De Dannan* / Scar an nollaig

sinn/It takes two: *King, Philip & Peter Browne* / Pursuit of Farmer Michael Hayes: *Planxty & Christy Moore* / Maid of Coolmore: *Bothy Band* / Declan: *Lunny, Donal* / Lord Franklin: *Burke, Kevin & Michael O'Dohmnhaill*
CD _____ **CDEMC 3693**
EMI / Nov '94 / EMI.

BEST OF IRISH FOLK FEST
CD _____ **CDTUT 727478**
Wundertute / '89 / CM / Duncans / ADA.

BEST OF IRISH FOLK, THE
CD _____ **HMCD 064**
Harmac / Aug '90 / I&B.

BEST OF IRISH FOLK.
Rocky road to Dublin: *Dubliners* / Curragh of Kildare: *Furey, Finbar & Eddie* / Glenside polka: *Glenside Ceilidh Band* / Henry joy: *Grehan Sisters* / Handsome cabin boy: *Sweeney's Men* / Frog's wedding: *Johnstons* / Exile's jig: *Sweeney's Men* / Lambs on the green hills: *Johnstons* / Spanish cloak: *Furey, Finbar & Eddie* / Golden jubilee: *Glenside Ceilidh Band* / Cook in the kitchen: *Dubliners* / Orange and the green: *Grehan Sisters* / St. Patrick's breastplate: *Wood, Royston & Heather* / Inis dhun ramha: *Na Fili* / Foggy dew: *Imlach, Hamish* / Three pieces by O'Carolan: *Renbourn, John* / Madame Bonaparte: *Furey, Finbar* / Rakish Paddy: *Furey, Finbar* / Roisin dubh: *Dubliners* / Chanters tune: *Na Fili* / Spanish lady: *Johnstons* / Killarney boys of pleasure: *Swarbrick, Dave*
CD _____ **CCSCD 221**
Castle / Jun '89 / BMG.

BEST OF IRISH SHOWBANDS
CD _____ **MATCD 231**
Castle / Dec '92 / BMG.

BEST OF IRISH TRADITIONAL MUSIC (2CD/MC Set)
CD Set _____ **2CHDHX 807**
Outlet / May '95 / ADA / Duncans / CM / Ross / Direct / Koch.

BEST OF ITALIAN HOUSE
Shock the beat: *Electric Choc* / Moment in time: *4 For Money* / Loving you: *Hi-Liner* / Rave is your party: *Prophetia* / Don't stop: *System* / Apollonia: *Indie* / Over me: *M.C.P.* / Move your body: *Selector* / Friends: *Fluid* / Shake it: *Extraordinary* / Get up: *50 HTZ* / I gonna get the boy: *G & V Jay* / Everybody: *Jam Jam* / Anmesia: *Double FM* / Soul groove: *Father Funking* / Read my lips: *People In Town* / Chica boom: *S-Bam* / Take me away now: *S-Bam* / House music lover: *S-Bam* / Hallelujah: *Interceptor* / Take me to the top: *Kristaal* / Coming now: *II Examples* / Temptation: *M.C. Fear* / Moving now: *Feroldi, Pierre* / Everyday: *D.J. Pierre* / Come on come on: *Aysha* / Just can't get enough: *S-Bam* / Moving up and down: *Adams, Anita* / What time is it: *Dirty Mind* / Mover your body: *D.J. Pierre* / Keep warm: *Jinny* / Get on the floor: *D.J. Pierre* / I need your love: *Jinny* / Dirty love: *Infinity* / Killer: *Dirty Mind* / For your love: *Maya* / Tribute: *Piranoman* / Heart: *Karma* / Move your body raun: *Electric Choc* / Show me: *Ga Ga Ga* / Action: *Alfredo* / Electric choc: *Arkanoid* / Let's go: *Future Tense*
CD Set _____ **LOWBOXCD 10**
Low Price Music / Dec '94 / Total/BMG.

BEST OF ITALIAN HOUSE
CD _____ **LOWCDX 37**
Low Price Music / Aug '95 / Total/BMG.

BEST OF JAMAICA GOLD 1
CD _____ **JMC 200219**
Jamaica Gold / May '94 / THE / Magnum Music Group / Jetstar.

BEST OF JAMAICA GOLD 2
CD _____ **JMC 200220**
Jamaica Gold / May '94 / THE / Magnum Music Group / Jetstar.

BEST OF JAZZ
CD _____ **YDG 74602**
Yesterday's Gold / Feb '93 / Target/BMG.

BEST OF JAZZ FUSION
CD _____ **NTRCD 022**
Nectar / Sep '94 / Pinnacle.

BEST OF JAZZ FUSION 2
Strawberry moon: *Washington, Grover Jr.* / I wanna play for you: *Clarke, Stanley* / Give it all you've got: *Mangione, Chuck* / Ginseng woman: *Gale, Eric* / Throw down: *Browne, Tom* / Birdland: *Weather Report* / Grandma's hands: *Scott-Heron, Gil* / Jazz carnival: *Azymuth* / Liquid groove: *Maria, Tania* / Modern time blues: *Ponty, Jean-Luc* / Running away: *Ayers, Roy* / East River: *Brecker Brothers* / Sudden samba: *Larsen, Neil* / By all means: *Mouzon, Alphonse* / Spiral: *Crusaders*
CD _____ **NTRCD 042**
Nectar / Jan '96 / Pinnacle.

BEST OF JAZZ ORGANS
CD _____ **CDC 9006**
LRC / Oct '90 / New Note / Harmonia Mundi.

BEST OF JAZZ SAXOPHONES VOL.3
CD _____ **CDC 9009**
LRC / Oct '90 / New Note / Harmonia Mundi.

BEST OF JAZZ SINGERS VOL.2
CD _____ **CDC 9008**
LRC / Oct '90 / New Note / Harmonia Mundi.

BEST OF JUNGLE
Calling the people: *A-Zone* / Above the clouds (Mix): *Sunshine* / Digable bass: *D.J. Rap* / You can: *Quarterback* / Jungle warriors: *Bay B Kane* / Deal wid it: *D.J. Solo* / Positive (Future Assassins remix): *Love Nation* / Warning: *Darkenator* / King of the swingers: *Cheetah* / Licked: *D.J. NKS* / Retreat: *Dodson* / Super hero (my knight): *House Crew* / Wheel up: *D.J. Gunshot* / Libetan jungle: *D.J. Rap* / Thunder: *Rood Project* / Flute fx: *Nut Ei & Technarchy* / Shadowlands: *Flytronix* / Untitled: *House Crew* / Lost: *D.J. Kane* / Good good sensi: *Bay B Kane* / Jungle jazz: *Money & Dubtronics* / Sound murderer: *Remarc* / Spirtual aura: *D.J. Rap* / United: *D.J. SS* / Life is a circle: *Boneman X* / Tuneful: *Nut Ei & Technarchy* / Speared: *D.J. NKS* / What you gonna do: *Intellect* / Jungle juice: *D.J. Trace* / Triple on sunshine: *N-ZO & D.J. Invincible* / Barehedd one: *Code K* / Smokin' a blunt: *Chuckie* / Darkage (Original): *D.J. Solo* / Creation: *Phrenetic* / Altored ego: *Mainline* / Casanova (Down to earth remix): *Baby D* / Rhythm: *Just Another Artist* / Bludclot artattack: *D.J. Ed Rush* / Dream sequence: *Mental Power* / Good love: *Just Another Artist* / Roll it: *Funky T* / Double barrel: *Intelligent Jungalist*
CD Set _____ **LOWBOXCD 8**
Low Price Music / Nov '94 / Total/BMG.

BEST OF JUNGLE 1
CD _____ **LOWCDX 29**
Low Price Music / Mar '95 / Total/BMG.

BEST OF JUNGLE 2
CD Set _____ **LOWBOXCD 14**
Low Price Music / Jan '96 / Total/BMG.

BEST OF JUNGLE 2
CD _____ **LOWCDX 30**
Low Price Music / Aug '95 / Total/BMG.

BEST OF JUNGLE VOL.1
CD _____ **PNCCA 2**
Production House / Aug '94 / Jetstar / Total/BMG.

BEST OF JUNGLE VOL.3
CD _____ **PNCCA 4**
Production House / Jan '95 / Jetstar / Total/BMG.

BEST OF JUNGLE VOL.4
CD _____ **PNCCA 6**
Production House / May '95 / Jetstar / Total/BMG.

BEST OF LATIN AMERICA - EL CONDOR PASA
El condor pasa / Tres bailecitos / Mburucya nostalgia Colombiana / Frederico / Recuerdo del puno / Que nadie sepa mi sufrir / Noche del Paraquay despedida / Burrerita / Estampa Panamena / Adie viejo companario / La tropilla / Pastor de nubes Asuncion del Paraguay
CD _____ **PV 793093**
Disques Pierre Verany / Oct '93 / Kingdom.

BEST OF LATIN AMERICA - LA COLEGIALA
La colegiala / La Peregrinacion / Palmeras / Concierto en la llanura / Sueno de angelita / Cascada la baguala / El arriero / Porque / Cruzando el nalca / Zamponas / Reservista purajhei / Villa guillermina / Paraguay pe el Indio muerte / Misionera / La danza del colibri
CD _____ **PV 793094**
Disques Pierre Verany / Oct '93 / Kingdom.

BEST OF LATIN AMERICA - MOLIENDO CAFE
Moliendo cafe / Pajaro campana / Madrecita / Indiecita Linda / Cerro cora / Che picazu mi / Kantu / Itagua poti / Guesta de pampa azui / Virginia / Sanz del destino / Estancia ava ne-e / Genoveva / Recuerdos de ipacarari / Angela Rosa / Esperanza mia
CD _____ **PV 793095**
Disques Pierre Verany / Oct '93 / Kingdom.

BEST OF LATIN AMERICA VOL.1
CD _____ **EUCD 1115**
ARC / '91 / ARC Music / ADA.

BEST OF LATIN AMERICA VOL.2
CD _____ **EUCD 1147**
ARC / '91 / ARC Music / ADA.

BEST OF LATIN JAZZ
Nica's dream: *Burrell, Kenny* / Sambop: *Adderley, Cannonball* / Gunky: *Lytle, Johnny* / Baion baby: *Stitt, Sonny* / Mambo inn: *Taylor, Billy* / Caravan: *Pucho & His Latin Soul Brothers* / Montuneando: *Santamaria, Mongo & La Lupe* / Ping pong: *Blakey, Art & The Jazz Messengers* / Mau mau: *Farmer, Art Septet* / Manteca: *Garland, Red Trio* / Seafood Wally: *Rodriguez, Willie* /

Screamin': *McDuff, Brother Jack* / Fatman: *Montego Joe* / Mambo ricci: *Dolphy, Eric & Latin Jazz 5*
CD _____ **CDBGP 1034**
BGP / Mar '92 / Pinnacle.

BEST OF LEGGO
CD _____ **504012**
Declic / Nov '95 / Jetstar.

BEST OF LISTEN TO THE BAND VOL.1
Mephistopheles / Carmen suite / Laura / Batman (theme) / Molly on the shore / Bolero / Overture 'Tancredi' / Over the rainbow / Rhythm and blues / Festive prelude / Pastime with good company / Music from 'Ballet Russe' / March 'Le Reve Passe' / Cappriccio Espagnol / Skye boat song / Fiorentiner march / Soldiers in the park
CD _____ **DOYCD 016**
Doyen / Oct '92 / Conifer.

BEST OF LOADING BAY VOL.1
CD _____ **LBAYCD 1**
Loading Bay / Jan '93 / Loading Bay Records.

BEST OF LOMA RECORDS, THE
CD Set _____ **9362457112**
WEA / Jan '96 / Warner Music.

BEST OF LOUISIANA MUSIC, THE
CD _____ **ROUANCD 08**
Rounder / Jun '93 / CM / Direct / ADA / Cadillac.

BEST OF LOVERS ROCK VOL.1
CD _____ **RNCD 2018**
Rhino / Feb '94 / Jetstar / Magnum Music Group / THE.

BEST OF LOVERS ROCK VOL.2
CD _____ **RNCD 2039**
Rhino / Jan '94 / Jetstar / Magnum Music Group / THE.

BEST OF LOVERS ROCK VOL.3
CD _____ **RNCD 2062**
Rhino / Jun '94 / Jetstar / Magnum Music Group / THE.

BEST OF MEMPHIS ROOTS
CD _____ **RITZRCD 537**
Ritz / Dec '93 / Pinnacle.

BEST OF MISSING YOU
Missing you: *De Burgh, Chris* / It must have been love: *Roxette* / Just another day: *Secada, Jon* / I don't wanna lose you: *Turner, Tina* / Power of love: *Rush, Jennifer* / Come in out of the rain: *Moten, Wendy* / Get here: *Adams, Oleta* / Wishing on a star: *Rose Royce* / Everytime you go away: *Young, Paul* / Missing you (2): *Waite, John* / Fool (if you think it's over): *Rea, Chris* / She's gone: *Hall & Oates* / Different corner: *Michael, George* / After the love has gone: *Earth, Wind & Fire* / This time: *Carroll, Dina* / Move closer: *Nelson, Phyllis* / Please don't go: *K.C. & The Sunshine Band* / Unchained melody: *Righteous Brothers* / I miss you: *Haddaway* / Someday I'm coming back: *Stansfield, Lisa* / Stay: *Eternal* / Teardrops: *Womack & Womack* / Don't turn around: *Ace Of Base* / Dedicated to the one I love: *McLean, Bitty* / Can't stay away from you: *Estefan, Gloria* / When you tell me that you love me: *Ross, Diana* / Up where we belong: *Cocker, Joe & Jennifer Warnes* / Nothing compares 2 U: *O'Connor, Sinead* / Crazy: *Cline, Patsy* / Without you: *Nelson, Harry* / Your song: *John, Elton* / Good inky release: *Beach Boys* / Now and forever: *Marx, Richard* / Promise me: *Craven, Beverley* / Don't know much: *Ronstadt, Linda & Aaron Neville* / All by myself: *Carmen, Eric* / Loving you: *Riperton, Minnie*
CD Set _____ **CDEMTVD 86**
EMI / Oct '94 / EMI.

BEST OF MUSIC OF LIFE, THE
CD _____ **MOLCD 029**
Music Of Life / Apr '93 / Grapevine.

BEST OF MUSICRAFT JAZZ
Salt peanuts: *Gillespie, Dizzy* / How high the moon: *Wilson, Teddy* / Mo mo: *Auld, Georgie* / What a difference a day makes: *Vaughan, Sarah* / Jam-a-ditty: *Ellington, Duke* / Handsome Harry the hipster: *Gillespie, Dizzy* / Night and day: *Torme, Mel* / I'll always be in love with you: *Chittison, Herman* / Boyd's nest: *Raeburn, Boyd* / Just you, just me: *Wilson, Teddy* / Three little words: *Torme, Mel* / Button up your overcoat: *Vaughan, Sarah*
CD _____ **70002**
Discovery / Nov '93 / Warner Music.

BEST OF NASHBORO GOSPEL
Touch me Lord Jesus: *Angelic Gospel Singers* / I've fixed it with Jesus: *Boggs, Professor Harold* / Family prayer: *Bright Stars* / Milky white way: *CBS Trumpeteers* / Give me my flowers: *Consolers* / Stop gambler: *Cook, Madame Edna Gallmon* / Bible is right: *Gospel Songbirds* / Wake me, shake me: *May, Brother Joe* / Roll Jordan roll: *Famous Skylarks* / How I got over: *Angelic Gospel Singers* / Mother's advice: *Taylor Brothers* / Step by step: *Boyer Brothers* / In my saviours care: *Sons of the south* / Jesus be my keeper: *Silvertone singers* / I'm a soldier: *Jordan River Singers* / If you miss me from praying: *Radio Four* / Sell out to the master: *Christland singers* / Since Jesus came into my heart: *Silvertone singers* / Didn't it rain

children: *Sons of the south* / My life is in his hands: *Jordan River Singers* / Let the church roll on: *Barbee, Lucille* / You got to be born again: *Christland singers* / Earnest prayer: *Radio Four* / Don't drive your children away: *Fairfield Four* / I want to be just like him: *Supreme Angels* / No cross no crown: *Brooklyn Allstars* / Step by step (#2): *Swanee Quintet*
CD _____ **CDCHD 373**
Ace / Jan '93 / Pinnacle / Cadillac / Complete/Pinnacle.

BEST OF NEWPORT IN NEW YORK '72 VOL.1 - JAM SESSIONS
Lo-slo blue / Night in Tunisia / Perdido / Misty / Now's the time
CD _____ **NEMCD 632**
Sequel / Feb '93 / BMG.

BEST OF NEWPORT IN NEW YORK '72 VOL.2 - MORE JAM SESSIONS
Blues 'n' boogie no.1 / So what / Blues 'n' boogie no.2 / Medley: What's new/Since I fell for you/Man I love
CD _____ **NEMCD 633**
Sequel / Feb '93 / BMG.

BEST OF NEWPORT IN NEW YORK '72 VOL.3 - THE SOUL SESSIONS
Medley: Ode to Billy Joe/Please send me someone to love / I apologise / Jelly jelly / Stone junkie / Pusherman / I need you baby / Hold on I'm comin' / Price you got to pay to be free / Ain't no mountain high enough / Somewhere
CD _____ **NEMCD 634**
Sequel / Feb '93 / BMG.

BEST OF NOW DANCE '94, THE
Another night (Radio Mix): *Real McCoy* / Rhythm of the night (Rapino Brothers Radio Mix): *Corona* / Baby come back: *Banton, Pato* / I like to move it (Radio Edit): *Reel 2 Real* / Incredible (Radio Edit): *M-Beat & General Levy* / She's got that vibe: *R. Kelly* / Carry me home (Radio Mix): *Gloworm* / Just a step from heaven (Remix): *Eternal* / Things can only get better: *D Ream* / Renaissance (Radio Mix): *M People* / Light my fire (Cappella RAF Zone Remix): *Club House* / Anything: *Culture Beat* / Get-a-way (Airplay Mix): *Maxx* / Real thing: *2 Unlimited* / Sweat (Radio Mix): *Grid* / A, B, C and D: *Blue Bamboo* / Waterfall: *Atlantic Ocean* / Move on baby (Definitive Edit): *Cappella* / Sweets for my sweet: *Lewis, C.J.* / Don't turn around: *Ace Of Base* / Shine: *Aswad* / Compliments on your kiss: *Red Dragon* / Can you feel it (Erik More Radio Edit): *Reel 2 Real & The Mad Stuntman* / No good (start the dance): *Prodigy* / Dreamer (Radio Mix): *Livin' Joy* / Can't get a man, can't get a job (Radio Mix): *Sister Bliss* / Let the music (lift you up): *Loveland* / I can get lifted (Loveland's High On Life Radio Edit): *Tucker, Barbara* / Caught in the middle (Remix): *Roberts, Juliet* / No more tears (enough is enough) (Radio Edit): *Mazelle, Kym & Jocelyn Brown* / Let the beat control your body (Airplay Edit): *2 Unlimited* / Doop: *Doop* / Rock my heart (Radio Mix): *Haddaway* / No more (I can't stand it): *Maxx* / Come baby come (Radio Edit): *K7* / Shoop: *Salt 'N' Pepa* / Best of my love (Radio Mix): *Lewis, C.J.* / Dedicated to the one I love: *McLean, Bitty* / Searching (Mykael S. Riley Mix): *China Black* / Sweet lullaby (Radio Version): *Deep Forest*
CD Set _____ **CDNOD 14**
Virgin / Nov '94 / EMI.

BEST OF OI
Suburban rebels: *Business* / Barmy army: I'm gonna die: *Blitz* / George Davis is innocent: *Sham 69* / G.L.C.: *Menace* / Police oppression: *Angelic Upstarts* / England belongs to me: *Cock Sparrer* / One law for them: *4 Skins* / King of the jungle: *Last Resort* / S.P.G: *Red Alert* / Summer of '81: *Violators* / Police story: *Partizan* / Smash the discos: *Business* / Runnin' riot (Live): *Cock Sparrer* / Right to choose: *Combat 84* / Working class kids: *Last Resort* / Yesterday's heroes: *4 Skins* / Police car: *Cockney Rejects* / Razors in the night: *Blitz* / Maniac: *Blood* / Maniac: *Peter & The Test Tube Babies* / Tuckers ruckers ain't no suckers: *Gonads* / Two pints of lager: *Splodge* / Kids of the 80's: *Infa Riot* / They don't understand: *Sham 69* / England (Live): *Angelic Upstarts*
CD _____ **DOJOCD 94**
Dojo / Apr '93 / BMG.

BEST OF OI VOL 2
Harry May: *Business* / Nation on fire: *Blitz* / Evil: *4 Skins* / Johnny Barden: *Last Resort* / Chip on my shoulder (live): *Cock Sparrer* / I'm civilised: *Menace* / Such fun: *Blood* / I wanna be a star: *Cockney Rejects* / Transvestite: *Peter & The Test Tube Babies* / I lost my love to a U.K. sub: *Gonads* / What am I gonna do: *Ejected* / For the love of oi: *Section 5* / Real enemy: *Business* / Rapist: *Combat 84* / Each dawn I die: *Infa Riot* / Skinhead: *Blitz* / Police 5: *Cock Sparrer* / Take the blame: *Vicious Rumors* / Arms race: *Partizan* / Don't you ever let me down: *Crack* / Violence in our minds: *Last Resort* / On the streets: *4 Skins* / Action man: *Strike* / Emergency: *Infa Riot* / Kids on the streets (live): *Angelic Upstarts*
CD _____ **LINK CD 158**
Street Link / Oct '92 / BMG.

BEST OF OI VOL. 3
CD _____ DOJOCD 207
Dojo / Mar '95 / BMG.

BEST OF PIANO JAZZ
Sept a dire / Force tranquille / Agripaume III / Bouillie bordelaise / Adi / Valse no.2 / Sep petits jeux / Beeing sincere / Leila / E si...si...si / Voice of Zak / Trio du porto / E H F T B
CD _____ TCB 01042
TCB / Sep '95 / New Note.

BEST OF RAP
(4 CD)
Bang zoom (let's go go): Real Roxanne & Hitman Howie Tee / It takes two: Base, Rob & D.J. E-Z Rock / Can I get soul clap: Grand Wizard Theodore / 900 Number: 45 King / For the lover in you: True Mathematics / I'm all shook up: Spoonie Gee / Time zone: Bambaataa, Afrika / Split personality: U.T.F.O / I'm ready: Caveman / Friday night, Saturday morning: Einstein / Godfather: Spoonie Gee / Ya bad chubbs: Chubb Rock / Heartbreak: Little Shawn / It's tricky: Run DMC / Do this my way: Kid 'N' Play / Ya cold wanna be with me: U.T.F.O / Fingertips (clap your hands): E.S.P. / Give it a rest: She Rockers / Roxanne Roxanne: Roxanne / Brooklyn banditts: Black Madness / Last night: Kid 'N' Play / Get on the dancefloor: Base, Rob & D.J. E-Z Rock / What's next: Run DMC / Recognition: Demon Boyz / Raggamuffin hip hop: Asher D & Daddy Freddy / Not U again: Brothers Uv Da Blackmarket / Down with the king: Run DMC / Whose the captain: Microphone Prince / Miracles: M.C. Duke / Untitled: Hard Noise / (Nothing serious) just buggin': Whistle / King of rock: Run DMC / Roxanne's on a roll: Real Roxanne / I'm riffin': M.C. Duke / You ain't just a fool: Spoonie Gee / Yabba dabba doo: Chubb Rock / It's like that ya'll: Sweet Tee / Hip hop regae: Longsy D / Get ya self together: Kash Da Masta / This is ska: Longsy D
CD Set _____ LOWBOXCD 4
Low Price Music / Jul '94 / Total/BMG.

BEST OF RAP VOL.1
CD _____ LOWCDX 13
Low Price Music / Mar '95 / Total/BMG.

BEST OF RAP VOL.2
CD Set _____ LOWBOXCD 18
Low Price Music / Jul '95 / Total/BMG.

BEST OF RAP VOL.2
CD _____ LOWCDX 14
Low Price Music / Aug '95 / Total/BMG.

BEST OF RAVE
(4 CD)
Everybody in the place: Prodigy / All we wanna do is dance: House Crew / Activ 8 (Come with me): Altern 8 / Playing with knives: Bizarre Inc. / Rave alert: Khan, Praga & Jade 4 U / Mr. Kirk's nightmare: 4 Hero / Ebeneezer Goode: Shamen / Criminal: Criminal Minds / Oblivion: Manix / Vengeance: DMS / D.J.'s take control: SL2 / Music takes you: Blame / Trip II the moon: Acen / Roughneck: Project One / We are hardcore: House Crew / Phorever people: Shamen / Injected with a poison: Khan, Praga & Jade 4 U / As nasty as you wanna be: Nasty Habits / One drop of rain: Sure Is Pure / Jump: Funkatarium / Out of space: Prodigy / Sesame's treet: Smart E's / Somebody scream: Prophet Of Rage / Evapor 8: Altern 8 / Let me be your fantasy: Baby D / I'm gonna get you: Bizarre Inc. / Charly: Prodigy / Original man: Angel, Dave / Live in Berlin: Hypnotist / Peacemakers: Nebula II / I need someone: Groove Committee / Hypnotic st8: Altern 8 / Hold it down: 2 Bad Mice / Baptized by dub: Criminal Minds / Far out: Sonz Of A Loop Da Loop Era / Hardcore will never die: Q-Bass / On a ragga tip: SL2 / Phantasia forever: Khan, Praga & Jade 4 U / Keep the fire burning: House Crew / Cooking up ya brain: 4 Hero / Took my love: Bizarre Inc. / High on love: Hypnotyz / Church of extacy: Church Of Extacy / Brutal 8: Altern 8 / Joy rider: Criminal Minds / Fires burning: Run Tings / Start da panic: Homeboy, A Hippy & A Funki-Dred / Journey from the light: 4 Hero
CD Set _____ LOWBOXCD 1
Low Price Music / Dec '93 / Total/BMG.

BEST OF RAVE 2 VOL. 1
CD _____ LOWCDX 33
Low Price Music / Dec '95 / Total/BMG.

BEST OF RAVE 2 VOL. 2
CD _____ LOWCDX 34
Low Price Music / Dec '95 / Total/BMG.

BEST OF RAVE VOL.1
CD _____ LOWCDX 1
Low Price Music / Mar '95 / Total/BMG.

BEST OF RAVE VOL.2
CD Set _____ LOWBOXCD 9
Low Price Music / Feb '95 / Total/BMG.

BEST OF RAVE VOL.2
CD _____ LOWCDX 2
Low Price Music / Aug '95 / Total/BMG.

BEST OF REGGAE SUNSPLASH
Ital love: Chalice / Revival time: Chalice / Calling you: Sandi & The Sunsetz / Do you feel like dancing: Bloodfire Posse / Can't stop rocking tonight: Bloodfire Posse / It's

---

magic: Brown, Dennis / Wild fire: Brown, Dennis & John Holt / Botha: Cocoa T / Medley: Charlie Chaplin & Yellowman / Oh what a feeling: Isaacs, Gregory / Let off: Wales, Josey / Ram jam dance: Wailer, Bunny / Jolly session: Wailer, Bunny / Sabotage: Wailer, Bunny
CD _____ CDCHARLY 235
Charly / Sep '90 / Charly / THE / Cadillac.

BEST OF REGGAE VOL.1
CD Set _____ LOWBOXCD 11
Low Price Music / May '95 / Total/BMG.

BEST OF REGGAE VOL.2
CD _____ LOWCDX 42
Low Price Music / Aug '95 / Total/BMG.

BEST OF RIO CARNIVAL
CD _____ CDEB 2224
Earthbeat / May '93 / Direct / ADA.

BEST OF ROCK 'N' ROLL LOVE SONGS, THE
CD _____ DINCD 91
Dino / Jun '94 / Pinnacle / 3MV.

BEST OF ROCK LIVE
Come together: MC5 / What goes on: Velvet Underground / Somebody to love: Jefferson Airplane / Shape I'm in: Band / Sweet Jane: Reed, Lou / Only women bleed: Cooper, Alice / It's all over now: Faces / Highway star: Deep Purple / Boys are back in town: Thin Lizzy / I want to go to the sun: Frampton, Peter / Peter Gunn: Pirates / All through the city: Dr. Feelgood / Junior's wailing: Status Quo / Long train runnin': Doobie Brothers / In trance: Scorpions
CD _____ VSOPCD 202
Connoisseur / Aug '94 / Pinnacle.

BEST OF ROCK ON STAGE VOL.2, THE
Pinball wizard: Who / Kill the king: Rainbow / Paranoid: Black Sabbath / Stealin': Uriah Heep / Too old to rock 'n' roll: Jethro Tull / I'm going home: Ten Years After / Woke up this morning: Hendrix, Jimi / Voodoo chile: Vaughan, Stevie Ray / Black magic woman: Santana / Full moon boogie: Beck, Jeff / Born to be wild: Blue Oyster Cult / Do the strand: Roxy Music / This flight tonight: Nazareth / Breaking the law: Judas Priest / Ace of spades: Motorhead
CD _____ VSOPCD 208
Connoisseur / Nov '94 / Pinnacle.

BEST OF ROTTERDAM RECORDS
CD _____ ROF CD1
Rotterdam records / Mar '93 / SRD.

BEST OF SALSA
CD _____ EUCD 1319
ARC / Nov '95 / ARC Music / ADA.

BEST OF SAXON VOL.1
CD _____ SAXCD 002
Saxon Studio / Oct '95 / Jetstar.

BEST OF SAXON VOL.2
CD _____ SAXCD 0032
Saxon Studio / Oct '95 / Jetstar.

BEST OF SCOTLAND
Donald, where's yer troosers: Stewart, Andy / Road to the isles: Stewart, Andy / Scottish soldier: Stewart, Andy / Campbell Town Loch: Stewart, Andy / Drunken piper / Highland laddie / Black bear: Pipes & Drums, 1st Bat Blackwatch / Auld Scotch sangs: Anderson, Moira / Rowan tree: Anderson, Moira / My ain house: Anderson, Moira / My ain folk: Anderson, Moira / Wild rover: Tartan Lads / Sky is bluer in Scotland: Tartan Lads / West's awake hornpipe/ Robertson hornpipe: Johnstone, Jim & His Band / Castles in the air: Johnstone, Jim & His Band / Bonnie lass o'Bon Accord: Johnstone, Jim & His Band / I love a lassie: Logan, Jimmy / Roamin' in the gloamin': Logan, Jimmy / My home/ Sky boat song: Royal Scots Dragoon Guards / Flower of Scotland: Royal Scots Dragoon Guards / Mull of Kintyre: Royal Scots Dragoon Guards / Amazing Grace: Royal Scots Dragoon Guards / Hiking group: Gay Gordons / Bonnie Dundee: Corries / Isle of Skye: Corries / Black Douglas: Corries / Scottish waltz selection: Wick Scottish Dance Band / Cock o' the North: Scots Guards / Garb of old cat: Scots Guards / Wee MacGregor: Scots Guards / Gathering of the clans: Scots Guards / Northern lights of old Aberdeen: Shand, Jimmy / Linton Ploughman's jig/ Muckin O'Geordies Byre: Shand, Jimmy / Lady Nellie Wemyss/ Braidley's house/ Major Mackie: Shand, Jimmy / Circle waltz/ Queen Mary Queen Mary/ If you will marry me: Glen Lomond Scottish Band / Kate Barber/ My wee Lauds a sojer: Glen Lomond Scottish Band / Middleton medley/ Craighall/ Lady Carmichael: Glen Lomond Scottish Band / auld Inn/ Fill your glasses/ Lively Tim: Glen Lomond Scottish Band / I belong to Glasgow: Fyffe, Will / Para handy: Houliston, Max & his Scottish Band / Holy rood: Gordon Highlanders / National emblem: Gordon Highlanders / Steadfast and true: Gordon Highlanders / Ye banks and braes o' bonnie Doon: MacEwan, Father Sydney / Toronto Scottish Regiment/ Durrator Bridge/ Duntroon: Black Watch Band / Caledonian bay: MacLeod, Jim / Scotland the brave: Wilson, Robert / Down in the glen: Wilson, Robert / March selection/ O'Donnel ABU/ Dawning of the day:

Holmes, Ian / Who fears to speak of the '98: Holmes, Ian / With a hundred pipers/ Finglas weeping: 2nd Battalion Scots Guards
CD Set _____ CDTRBOX 120
Trio / Oct '94 / EMI.

BEST OF SCOTTISH DANCE BANDS, THE
CD _____ CC 264
Music For Pleasure / May '91 / EMI.

BEST OF SCOTTISH PIPES AND DRUMS
CD _____ EUCD 1306
ARC / Jul '95 / ARC Music / ADA.

BEST OF SIOUX VOL.1, THE
Wave of war: Higgs, Joe / Pharoah's walk: Exodus & Jam Rock / Funny man: King Reggie / In the ghetto: Dillon, Phillis / With these hands: Wayne, Mark / African people (Indian Reservation): Brown, Funky / Super bad: J.D. / I stand on: Smith, Junior / Train (Engine 54): Lloyd The Matador / Lay a foundation: Higgs, Joe / You just gotta get ready: Jackson, Pooch / Cool girl: King Reggie / Mammy blue: Circles / Julia sees me: Exodus / I'm in a dancing mood: Smith, Junior / World is spinning around: Higgs, Joe / Happy song: Twinkle Brothers / To be young, gifted and black: King Reggie / Vietnam: Smith, Sammi / Heavy reggae: Roosevelt Singers
CD _____ PRCD 602
President / Jun '95 / Grapevine / Target/ BMG / Jazz Music / President.

BEST OF SKA LIVE
CD _____ EMPRCD 579
Emporio / Jul '95 / THE / Disc / CM.

BEST OF SOLAR, THE
I can make you feel good: Shalamar / And the beat goes on: Whispers / Midas touch: Midnight Star / I don't wanna be a freak: Dynasty / Fantastic voyage: Lakeside / Dance with you: Lucas, Carrie / Romeo, where's Juliet: Collage / Take that to the bank: Shalamar / Come back lover: Sylvers / Body talk: Deele / It's a love thing: Whispers / Headlines: Midnight Star / I wanna be rich: Calloway / I gotta keep dancin': Lucas, Carrie / Make that move: Shalamar / Rock steady: Whispers
CD _____ RENCD 106
Renaissance Collector Series / Sep '95 / BMG.

BEST OF SOUL
CD Set _____ LOWBOXCD 13
Low Price Music / May '95 / Total/BMG.

BEST OF SOUNDTRACKS
CD Set _____ 4417222
Pilz / Oct '92 / BMG.

BEST OF SUN ROCKABILLY VOL.1
Ten cats down / Jump right out of this jukebox / Gonna romp and stomp / Domino / Rakin' and scrapin' / Slow down / Red cadillac and a black moustache / Break up / Greenback dollar / Red headed woman / Flyin' saucer rock 'n' roll / Crawdad hole / Love my baby / Red hot / We wanna boogie / Come on little mama / Right behind you baby / Ubangi stomp / Let's bop / Rabbit action / Put your cat clothes on / Rockin' with my baby
CD _____ CDSUN 16
Sun / Apr '86 / Charly.

BEST OF SUN ROCKABILLY VOL.2
Got love if you want it: Smith, Warren / That don't move me: Perkins, Carl / Itchy: Burgess, Sonny / Drinkin' wine: Simmons, Gene / How come you do me: Thompson, Junior / Gimme some lovin': Jenkins, Harold / Johnny Valentine: Anderson, Andy / Baby, please don't go: Riley, Billy Lee / Sentimental fool: Pittman, Barbara / Rebound: Rich, Charlie / Miss Froggie: Smith, Warren / Rock around the town: Beard, Dean / Wild one: Lewis, Jerry Lee / My baby don't rock: McDaniel, Luke / Find my baby for me: Burgess, Sonny / My gal Mary Ann: Earls, Jack / Me and my rhythm guitar: Powers, Johnny / All night rock: Honeycutt, Glenn / Your loving man: Taylor, Vernon / Madman / Wages, Jimmy / Fairlane rock: Thompson, Hayden / I need your loving kiss: Jenkins, Harold / Perkin's wiggle: Perkins, Carl / Ain't got a thing: Burgess, Sonny
CD _____ CDCHARLY 36
Charly / Nov '86 / Charly / THE / Cadillac.

BEST OF SWING '95
CD Set _____ TCD 2789
Telstar / Oct '95 / BMG.

BEST OF SWING BANDS, THE
CD _____ HCD 311
Hindsight / Sep '92 / Target/BMG / Jazz Music.

BEST OF SYNTHESIZER HITS, THE
CD _____ EMPRCD 506
Emporio / Apr '94 / THE / Disc / CM.

BEST OF TECHNO
(4 CD)
Love: Greed / Rainbows in the sky: Hypnotist / Circular motion: Dark LLama / Pure: G.T.O. / Off to battle: Model 500 / Quarter pounder: Angel, Dave / Jet star: Tekno 2 / High on hope: Hardcore Uproar / Tricky disco: Tricky Disco / Set up 707: Edge Of Motion / Bee: Scientist / Chaotic state: Dearborn, Mike / Complex: Voorn, Orlando

---

/ Out of it: Spirit Level / Evolution: BFC / Church of extacy: Church Of Extacy / Total techno: Audio Assault / Gangster hood coruption: Chant / Toytown: Interface / Phobia: Phobia / Hardcore (U know the score): Hypnotist / Exorcist: Science / 3181: Acid Junkies / Illusion: Rtyme / Beyond the dance: Rhythim Is Rhythim / Quadrophinia: Quadrophonia / Infinity: Guru Josh / It's just a feeling: Terrorize / Give me: Greed / Psycho: Tekno 2 / Strings of life: Rhythim Is Rhythim / Temple of acid: Rhythim Is Rhythim / Bug: Bug / Revenge of Betty Bleep: Bleeps Anonymous / Themes: NRG / James brown is still alive: Holy Noise / Nature: Nature / Wave of the future: Quadrophonia / Art of stalking: Suburban Knight / Interference: Model 500
CD _____ LOWBOXCD 3
Low Price Music / Apr '94 / Total/BMG.

BEST OF TECHNO VOL.1
CD _____ LOWCDX 9
Low Price Music / Mar '95 / Total/BMG.

BEST OF THE 1960'S GOLDEN OLDIES VOL.1, THE
Monday Monday: Mamas & Papas / Eve of destruction: McGuire, Barry / Honey: Goldsboro, Bobby / Tracy: Cuff Links / Hush, not a word to Mary: Rowles, John / Magic carpet ride: Steppenwolf / Bend me, shape me: American Breed / Summertime: Stewart, Billy / Mama told me not to come: Three Dog Night / Dizzy: Roe, Tommy / Livin' next door to Alice: Smokie / I'm a believer: Monkees / White rabbit: Jefferson Airplane / Letter: Box Tops / Deep water: Grapefruit / Lion sleeps tonight: Tokens
CD _____ MCD 30204
Ariola Express / Mar '94 / BMG.

BEST OF THE 90'S, THE
CD Set _____ TCD 2749
Telstar / Nov '94 / BMG.

BEST OF THE BEAT
CD _____ PERMCD 18
Permanent / May '95 / Total/BMG.

BEST OF THE BEST
Memories are made of this: Martin, Dean / Story of my life: Holliday, Michael / Cry me a river: London, Julie / Stranger in paradise: MacRae, Gordon / It must be him: Carr, Vikki / Buttons and bows: Shore, Dinah / Softly, softly: Murray, Ruby / Shrimp boats: Stafford, Jo / Dreamboat: Cogan, Alma / Yellow rose of Texas: Freberg, Stan / Born free: Monro, Matt / Fever: Lee, Peggy / On the street where you live: Damone, Vic / Sugarbush: Boswell, Eve / No other love: Hilton, Ronnie / Over the rainbow: Garland, Judy / Vaya con dios: Paul, Les & Mary Ford / How high the moon: Christy, June / Istanbul: Vaughan, Frankie / My thanks to you: Conway, Steve
CD _____ CDEMS 1391
Capitol / Jan '91 / EMI.

BEST OF THE BEST VOL.2
CD _____ RASCD 3133
Ras / Feb '94 / Jetstar / Greensleeves / SRD / Direct.

BEST OF THE BEST VOL.3
CD _____ RASCD 3149
Ras / Jun '95 / Jetstar / Greensleeves / SRD / Direct.

BEST OF THE BEST VOL.4
CD _____ RASCD 3153
Ras / Jun '95 / Jetstar / Greensleeves / SRD / Direct.

BEST OF THE BIG BANDS
CD _____ DCD 5337
Disky / Dec '93 / THE / BMG / Discovery / Pinnacle.

BEST OF THE BIG DANCE BANDS
CD _____ CDC 9010
LRC / Oct '90 / New Note / Harmonia Mundi.

BEST OF THE BLUES SINGERS VOL.2
CD _____ CDC 9007
LRC / Oct '90 / New Note / Harmonia Mundi.

BEST OF THE BOOGIE WOOGIE VOL. 2
CD _____ 158022
Jazz Archives / Jun '93 / Jazz Music / Discovery / Cadillac.

BEST OF THE DJ'S BOUT YA!, THE
CD _____ SONCD 0048
Sonic Sounds / Jul '93 / Jetstar.

BEST OF THE JAMESON COLLECTION, THE
CD _____ PWKS 663
Carlton Home Entertainment / Jul '91 / Carlton Home Entertainment.

BEST OF THE OLD GREY WHISTLE TEST
CD Set _____ OGWTCD 1
Windsong / Aug '91 / Pinnacle.

BEST OF TODAY'S BLACK AFRICAN FOLK MUSIC, THE
CD _____ EUCD 1205
ARC / Sep '93 / ARC Music / ADA.

BEST OF TOMMY QUICKLY, JOHNNY SANDON, GREGORY PHILLIPS...
Tip of my tongue: Quickly, Tommy & The Remo Four / Heaven only knows: Quickly,

---

Tommy & The Remo Four / Lies: Sandon, Johnny & The Remo Four / On the horizon: Sandon, Johnny & The Remo Four / Yes: Sandon, Johnny & The Remo Four / Magic potion: Sandon, Johnny & The Remo Four / Kiss me now: Quickly, Tommy & The Remo Four / No other love: Quickly, Tommy & The Remo Four / Prove it: Quickly, Tommy & The Remo Four / Haven't you noticed: Quickly, Tommy & The Remo Four / I wish I could shimmy like my sister Kate: Remo Four / Peter Gunn: Remo Four / You might as well forget him: Quickly, Tommy & The Remo Four / It's simple as that: Quickly, Tommy & The Remo Four / Sally go round the roses: Remo Four / I know a girl: Remo Four / Wild side of life: Quickly, Tommy & The Remo Four / Forget the other guy: Quickly, Tommy & The Remo Four / Humpty dumpty: Quickly, Tommy & The Remo Four / I go crazy: Quickly, Tommy & The Remo Four / Everybody knows: Phillips, Gregory & The Remo Four / Closer to me: Phillips, Gregory & The Remo Four / Angie: Phillips, Gregory / Please believe me: Phillips, Gregory / Don't bother me: Phillips, Gregory / Make sure that you're mine: Phillips, Gregory / Sixteen tons: Sandon, Johnny / Donna means heartbreak: Sandon, Johnny / Legend in my time: Sandon, Johnny

CD _____ SEECD 349
See For Miles/C5 / Apr '92 / Pinnacle.

BEST OF TRANCE
CD Set _____ LOWBOXCD 16
Low Price Music / Jun '95 / Total/BMG.

BEST OF UK DANCE
CD _____ LOWBOXCD 19
Low Price Music / Jan '96 / Total/BMG.

BEST OF UNDERGROUND DANCE VOL.1
CD _____ LOWCDX 25
Low Price Music / May '95 / Total/BMG.

BEST OF UNDERGROUND DANCE, THE
Calling the people (Remix): A-Zone / Sound murderer: Remarc / Jungle warrior: Bay B Kane / Smokin' a blunt: Chuck E / Creation: Phrenetic / Barehedd one: Intelligent Jungalist / Shadowlandz: Flytronix / Thunder: Rood Project / Warning: Darkenator / Good good sensi: Bay B Kane / Power: Warped Kore / Double barrel: Intelligent Jungalist / Trance dance: Njoko / To amora: Mamba / Funkaturism (Steve Proctor remix): Jump / NRG (Bootleg mix): Floor / Kinky people (Nombes des pisies mix): Pyjama Party / Pick ups (House of house mix): Sound Generation / Clandestine: Mamba / No rich fat Daddy (Fat mix): Jump / Dance 2 house: Floor / Ibiza (Mix mas elecante): Denia / Luv it up (Original mix): Jump / Chant (4 the floor remix): Jump / Chant: Gangster Hood Corp / Dig deep: Blokka / Goosebump: Loco / Ice station zebra: Temple Of Acid / Trancition: Choci & Freedom Of Sound / Ghost: Dark LLama / Visions of the oracle: Eniola / Meaning (Fat club mix): Sound Gathering / Keep on pushing: Big Noise / Release your mind: Naughty But Nice / (Luv is) what we need (Club edit): Intergrated Society / It's over: Circle Line / Party children: Upgrade Massive / You make me feel so: Slice Of Life / Way down inside: Fat Tulips / I'll nostra tempo de la vita: Torfinn / Hold on: Rhythm Inc. / Come together: Bass Construction / Wanna be free: 2 High

CD Set _____ LOWBOXCD 7
Low Price Music / Nov '94 / Total/BMG.

BEST OF WALES (3CD Set)
God bless the Prince of Wales: Morriston Orpheus Choir / How great thou art: Morriston Orpheus Choir / Hiraeth (longing) (with Ken Williams): Morriston Orpheus Choir / Love, could I only tell thee: Morriston Orpheus Choir / Tros y gareg: Morriston Orpheus Choir / Swansea Town: Morriston Orpheus Choir / Land of song: Morriston Orpheus Choir / For king and country: Morriston Orpheus Choir / Steal away: Morriston Orpheus Choir / Old rugged cross: Morriston Orpheus Choir / Amazing grace: Morriston Orpheus Choir / David of the White Rock (Dafydd y Garreg Wen): Morriston Orpheus Choir / Comrades in arms: Morriston Orpheus Choir / Silver birch: Morriston Orpheus Choir / Lord's prayers: Morriston Orpheus Choir / Unwaith etton nghymru anwyl: Morriston Orpheus Choir / Cartef (featuring Nancy Richards): Morriston Orpheus Choir / Morte Christe (when I survey the wondrous cross): Treorchy Male Choir / Easter hymn: Treorchy Male Choir / All through the night (Ar hyd y nos): Treorchy Male Choir / Llef (Deus salutis): Treorchy Male Choir / Tydi a roddaist (Thou gavest): Treorchy Male Choir / We'll keep a welcome: Treorchy Male Choir / Valley called the Rhondda: Treorchy Male Choir / Jimmy Brown song (Les trois cloches): Treorchy Male Choir / Dolch I'r lor: Treorchy Male Choir / Speed your journey: Treorchy Male Choir / Counting the goats: Treorchy Male Choir / Gwahoddiad: Treorchy Male Choir / Easter hymn: Treorchy Male Choir / Eli Jenkins' prayer: Dunvant Male Choir / Llanfair: Dunvant Male Choir / With a voice of singing: Dunvant Male Choir / Dashenka

(Y Sipsiwn): Dunvant Male Choir / Calon lan: Treorchy Male Choir & The Cory Band / Roman war song: Treorchy Male Choir & The Cory Band / Laudamus (Bryn Calfaria): Monmouthshire Massed Choir / Lily of the valley: Monmouthshire Massed Choir / Kalinka: Orpheus Male Choir, Rhos / Bugeilio'r Gwenith Gwyn: Orpheus Male Choir, Rhos / En route: Morriston Orpheus Choir & The Band of the Welsh Guards / March of the men of Harlech: Morriston Orpheus Choir & The Band of the Welsh Guards / Pilgrims' chorus: Morriston Orpheus Choir & Gus Footwear Band / Cavalry of the Steppes: Morriston Orpheus Choir & Gus Footwear Band / Goin' home: Dowlais Male Choir / Medley (Myfanwy/Cwm Rhondda (Guide me, oh thou great Jehovah)/Hen wlad fy Nhadau (Land of my fathers)): Second Festival Of One Thousand Welsh Male Voices
Trio / Sep '95 / EMI.

BEST OF WASHINGTON D.C. R & B
Duet trumpet blues / Bow wow wow / That's alright with me / Herbert's jump / Hurricane lover / Movin' man / Fat man / Groove / Good mama / Half a pint of whiskey / Oh babe / Red hot boogie / Long gone / Annie's boogie
CD _____ FLYCD 32
Flyright / Apr '91 / Hot Shot / Wellard / Jazz Music / CM.

BEST OF WOODSTOCK, THE
CD _____ 7567826182
Warner Bros. / Jun '94 / Warner Music.

BEST OF ZOTH OMMOG
CD _____ CLEO 94712
Cleopatra / Jul '94 / Disc.

BEST OF ZOUK, THE
Exile one medley / En peke ponile / L'hivernagea 39-45 / Carniva animal / Musique la / Ban danq / Immigrant / More power / I'm in love with you / Now thats its Benn Schattered
CD _____ 908322
PMF / Jul '94 / Kingdom / Cadillac.

BEST PARTY ALBUM IN THE WORLD...EVER, THE (2CD/MC Set)
Wake me up before you go go: Wham / Good times: Chic / Staying alive: N-Trance / Y.M.C.A.: Village People / Stars on 45 Abba medley: Star Sounds Orchestra / Saturday night: Whigfield / What is love: Haddaway / Rhythm of the night: Corona / It's my life: Dr. Alban / Relight my fire: Take That / Hey now (girls just wanna have fun): Lauper, Cyndi / All that she wants: Ace Of Base / Here comes the hotstepper: Kamoze, Ini / Boombastic: Shaggy / One step beyond: Madness / Baby come back: Banton, Pato / Twist and shout: Demus, Chaka / Give it up: Goodmen / Moving on up: M People / Ride on time: Black Box / Come on Eileen: Dexy's Midnight Runners / Young at heart: Bluebells / Love shack: B-52's / Shoop shoop song (it's in his kiss): Cher / Crocodile rock: John, Elton / La bamba: Los Lobos / Reet petite: Wilson, Jackie / Baby love: Supremes / I will survive: Gaynor, Gloria / I'm in the mood for dancing: Nolan Sisters / Locomotion: Minogue, Kylie / Only way is up: Yazz & The Plastic Population / Stars on 45 disco medley: Starsound / Groove is in the heart: Deee-Lite / December '63: Four Seasons / Let's dance: Monterez, Chris / Shout: Lulu & The Luvvers / D.I.S.C.O.: Ottawan / I'm too sexy: Right Said Fred / Can can: Bad Manners / Time warp: Damian / Cotton eye Joe: Rednex / Always look on the bright side of life: Monty Python
CD Set _____ VTDCD 71
Virgin / Nov '95 / EMI.

BEST PUNK ALBUM IN THE WORLD...EVER, THE
Anarchy in the U.K.: Sex Pistols / Ever fallen in love: Buzzcocks / Teenage kicks: Undertones / Into the valley: Skids / New rose: Damned / Babylon's burning: Ruts / Sheena is a punk rocker: Ramones / Sound of the suburbs: Members / All around the world: Jam / Another girl another planet: Only Ones / Passenger: Iggy Pop / Making plans for Nigel: XTC / Peaches: Stranglers / Sex and drugs and rock 'n' roll: Dury, Ian & The Blockheads / (I don't want to go to) Chelsea: Chelsea / Denis: Blondie / 2-4-6-8 motorway: Robinson, Tom Band / Milk and alcohol: Dr. Feelgood / Looking after no.1: Boomtown Rats / Deutscher girls: Adam & The Ants / Christine: Siouxsie & The Banshees / Identity: X-Ray Spex / C30 C60 C90 Go: Bow Wow Wow / Public Image Ltd / My way: Vicious, Sid / God save the queen: Sex Pistols / Neat neat neat: Damned / Gary Gilmore's eyes: Adverts / Dancing the night away: Motors / What do I get: Buzzcocks / Jilted John: Jilted John / I am the fly: Wire / Mongoloid: Devo / Roadrunner: Richman, Jonathan & Modern Lovers / White punks on dope: Tubes / Blank generation: Hell, Richard & The Voidoids / Marquee moon: Television / Psycho killer: Talking Heads / Stop your sobbing: Pretenders / Is she really going out with him: Jackson, Joe / Ready steady go: Generation X / (Get a) grip (on yourself): Stranglers / Shot by both sides: Magazine / Alternative

Ulster: Stiff Little Fingers / Eighties: Killing Joke / Money: Flying Lizards / Kung fu international: Cooper Clarke, John
CD Set _____ VTDCD 42
Virgin / Jan '95 / EMI.

BEST REGGAE ALBUM IN THE WORLD...EVER 2, THE
Baby come back: Banton, Pato / Compliments on your kiss: Red Dragon / Higher ground: UB40 / Searching: China Black / Wild world: Priest, Maxi / You don't love me (no no no): Penn, Dawn / Shine: Aswad / Everything is alright (Uptight): Lewis, C.J. / I like to move it: Reel 2 Real & The Mad Stuntman / Incredible: M-Beat & General Levy / Arranged marriage: Apache Indian / Oh Carol: General Saint & Don Campbell / You can get it if you really want: Dekker, Desmond / I shot the sheriff: Inner Circle / No woman no cry: Boothe, Ken / Pressure drop: Toots & The Maytals / Hurt so good: Cadogan, Susan / Help me make it through the night: Holt, John / Kingston town: Lord Creator / Many rivers to cross: Cliff, Jimmy / Silly games: Kay, Janet / Girlie girlie: George, Sophia / Living on the frontline: Grant, Eddy / Don't turn around: Ace Of Base / Yummy yummy: Summit / Here I stand: McLean, Bitty / Rudi's in love: Locomotive / Message to you Rudy: Specials / Prince: Madness / Tears of a clown: Beat / Walking on the moon: Police / Tide is high: Blondie / Games people play: South, Joe / Sugar sugar: Baysee, Duke / Pass the dutchie: Musical Youth / Cupid: JC 001 / Midnight rider: Davidson, Paul / Walking in the sunshine: Bad Manners / Liquidator: Harry J All Stars / Everything I own: Boy George
CD Set _____ VIDCD 39
Virgin / Dec '94 / EMI.

BEST REGGAE ALBUM IN THE WORLD...EVER, THE
Mr. Loverman: Shabba Ranks / Sweat (A la la la la loop): Inner Circle / Sweets for my sweet: Lewis, C.J. / Dedicated to the one I love: McLean, Bitty / Informer: Snow / Close to you: Priest, Maxi / Oh Carolina: Shaggy / Riddim: US 3 / Love you like crazy / Dance hall mood: Aswad / Dancing on the floor: Third World / Wonderful world, beautiful people: Cliff, Jimmy / Love of the common people: Thomas, Nicky / Young, gifted and black: Bob & Marcia / Small axe: Marley, Bob / Israelites: Dekker, Desmond / Double barrel: Collins, Dave & Ansil / Red red wine: Tribe, Tony / Return of Django: Upsetters / I'm in the mood for ska: Lord Tanamo / Money in my pocket: Brown, Dennis / Everything I own: Boothe, Ken / Rivers of Babylon: Melodians / It keeps rainin' (Tears from my eyes): McLean, Bitty / All that she wants: Ace Of Base / Dub be good to me: Beats International / On a ragga tip: SL2 / Too much too young: Specials / One step beyond: Madness / Shout (It out): Louchie Lou & Michie One / Lip up fatty: Bad Manners / On my radio: Selector / Bed's too big without you: Hylton, Sheila / Silly games: Kay, Janet / Good thing going: Minott, Sugar / I don't wanna dance: Grant, Eddy / Just don't want to be lonely: McGregor, Freddie / I can see clearly now: Nash, Johnny / Uptown top ranking: Alfred & Donald / Amigo: Black Slate / Don't look back: Tosh, Peter / Tomorrow people: Marley, Ziggy / Jamaican in New York: Shinehead / I want to wake up with you: Gardiner, Boris
CD _____ VIDCD 27
Virgin / May '94 / EMI.

BEST REGGAE, THE
CD _____ CD 903
Sound / Jun '89 / Direct / ADA.

BEST ROCK 'N' ROLL
CD _____ CD 901
Sound / Jun '89 / Direct / ADA.

BEST ROCK 'N' ROLL ALBUM IN THE WORLD...EVER, THE
(We're gonna) Rock around the clock: Haley, Bill & The Comets / Ain't that a shame: Domino, Fats / Sweet little sixteen: Berry, Chuck / Bye bye love: Everly Brothers / La bamba: Valens, Ritchie / Peggy Sue: Holly, Buddy / That'll be the day: Crickets / Tutti frutti: Little Richard / Be bop a lula: Vincent, Gene / At the hop: Danny & The Juniors / Reet petite: Wilson, Jackie / Let's twist again: Checker, Chubby / Runaway: Shannon, Del / Summertime blues: Cochran, Eddie / Move it: Richard, Cliff / Locomotion: Little Eva / Why do fools fall in love: Lymon, Frankie & The Teenagers / Lipstick on your collar: Francis, Connie / Sealed with a kiss: Hyland, Brian / Teenager in love: Wilde, Marty / Rubber ball: Vee, Bobby / Wanderer: Dion / You're 16: Burnette, Johnny / Oh Carol: Sedaka, Neil / Chantilly lace: Big Bopper / Little darlin': Diamonds / Halfway to paradise: Fury, Billy / Let's dance: Montez, Chris / Red hot rock: Johnny & The Hurricanes / Nutrocker: B. Bumble & The Stingers / Will you still love me tomorrow: Shirelles / Poetry in motion: Tillotson, Johnny / Do you love me: Poole, Brian & The Tremeloes / Little bitty pretty one: Harris, Thurston / Bad to me: Henry, Clarence 'Frogman' / Bony moronie: Williams, Larry / That's all right Mama: Crudup, Arthur / Get a job: Silhouettes / Teach your children: Isleys / Shake, rattle and roll: Haley, Bill & The Comets / Wake up little Susie: Everly Broth-

ers / Golly Miss Molly: Little Richard / C'mon everybody: Cochran, Eddie / Happy birthday sweet sixteen: Sedaka, Neil / Blueberry Hill: Domino, Fats
CD Set _____ VTDCD 37
Virgin / Oct '94 / EMI.

BEST ROCK ALBUM IN THE WORLD...EVER 2, THE
Seven seas of Rhye: Queen / Desire: U2 / Why can't this be love: Van Halen / Bad love: Clapton, Eric / All night long: Rainbow / Here I go again: Whitesnake / Two princes: Spin Doctors / Viva Las Vegas: ZZ Top / Stay with me: Faces & Rod Stewart / Elected: Cooper, Alice / Rock 'n' roll dreams come through: Meat Loaf / Turn it on again: Genesis / Waterfront: Simple Minds / Rocks: Primal Scream / Wishing well: Free / Crossroads: Cream / Join together: Who / Rocky Mountain way: Walsh, Joe / Let love rule: Kravitz, Lenny / Losing my religion: R.E.M. / Solsbury Hill: Gabriel, Peter / Whole of the moon: Waterboys / Street life: Roxy Music / We gotta get out of this place: Animals / Cum on feel the noize: Slade / Pretty vacant: Sex Pistols / Blockbuster: Sweet / Telegram Sam: T. Rex / Cigarettes and alcohol: Oasis / Wild thing: Troggs / You really got me: Kinks / No more heroes: Stranglers / Down down: Status Quo / Don't believe a word: Thin Lizzy / Out in the fields: Moore, Gary & Phil Lynott / Black night: Deep Purple / She's not there: Santana / Feel like makin' love: Bad Company / All the young dudes: Mott The Hoople / Walk on the wild side: Reed, Lou
CD _____ VTDCD 47
Virgin / Mar '95 / EMI.

BEST ROCK ALBUM IN THE WORLD...EVER, THE
We will rock you: Queen / Inside: Stiltskin / Are you gonna go my way: Kravitz, Lenny / I'd do anything for love (But I won't do that): Meat Loaf / Smoke on the water: Deep Purple / Pride (In the name of love): U2 / Born to be wild: Steppenwolf / Free bird: Lynyrd Skynyrd / All right now: Free / (Don't fear) The reaper: Blue Oyster Cult / Can't get enough: Bad Company / School's out: Cooper, Alice / More than a feeling: Boston / Boys are back in town: Thin Lizzy / Since you've been gone: Rainbow / Walk this way: Run DMC & Aerosmith / Twentieth century boy: T. Rex / Silver machine: Hawkwind / Mama: Genesis / Sledgehammer: Gabriel, Peter / In the air tonight: Collins, Phil / Paranoid: Black Sabbath / Ace of spades: Motorhead / All day and all of the night: Kinks / Gimme all your lovin': ZZ Top / She sells sanctuary: Cult / Owner of a lonely heart: Yes / Do the strand: Roxy Music / Passenger: Iggy Pop / Sunshine of your love: Cream / Mannish boy: Waters, Muddy / Life's been good: Walsh, Joe / Won't get fooled again: Who / Crazy crazy nights: Kiss / Eye of the tiger: Survivor / Caroline: Status Quo / Money for nothing: Dire Straits / In a broken dream: Python Lee Jackson
CD _____ VTDCD 35
Virgin / Aug '94 / EMI.

BEST ROCK BALLADS IN THE WORLD...EVER, THE (2CD/MC Set)
Kind of magic: Queen / Girl like you: Collins, Edwyn / Over my shoulder: Mike & The Mechanics / Stuck in the middle with you: Stealer's Wheel / Don't stop: Fleetwood Mac / Heaven is a place on earth: Carlisle, Belinda / Dignity: Deacon Blue / Road to hell #2: Rea, Chris / I wish it would rain down: Collins, Phil / Romeo and Juliet: Dire Straits / Don't dream it's over: Crowded House / Waiting for a girl like you: Foreigner / I'll stand by you: Pretenders / Show me heaven: McKee, Maria / Eternal flame: Bangles / Oh yeah (on the radio): Roxy Music / Drive: Cars / Wind of change: Scorpions / To be with you: Mr. Big / Heaven help: Kravitz, Lenny / I'd do anything for love (but I won't do that): Meat Loaf / If I could turn back time: Cher / Is this love: Whitesnake / Black velvet: Myles, Alannah / Days: MacColl, Kirsty / Pure: Lightning Seeds / Mary's prayer: Danny Wilson / Valerie: Winwood, Steve / Every little thing she does is magic: Police / Roxanne: Toto / Keep on loving you: REO Speedwagon / Hard to say I'm sorry: Chicago / Follow you follow me: Genesis / Walking in Memphis: Cohen, Marc / Missing you: Waite, John / (I just) died in your arms: Cutting Crew / Kayleigh: Marillion / Babe: Styx / Listen to your heart: Roxette / Right here waiting: Marx, Richard
CD Set _____ VTDCD 60
Virgin / Aug '95 / EMI.

BEST SCOTLAND IN MUSIC AND SONG, THE
CD _____ CD 415
Bescol / May '95 / CM / Target/BMG.

BEST SELLERS 1
CD _____ DCD 5354
Disky / Apr '94 / THE / BMG / Discovery / Pinnacle.

BEST SELLERS 2
CD _____ DCD 5355
Disky / Apr '94 / THE / BMG / Discovery / Pinnacle.

BEST SELLERS 3
CD _____ DCD 5379
Disky / Apr '94 / THE / BMG / Discovery / Pinnacle.

BEST SIXTIES ALBUM IN THE WORLD...EVER, THE
(2CD/MC Set)
I'm a believer: Monkees / I got you babe: Sonny & Cher / It might as well rain until September: King, Carole / Young ones: Richard, Cliff & The Shadows / Runaway: Shannon, Del / Let's hang on: Four Seasons / I only want to be with you: Springfield, Dusty / Price of love: Everly Brothers / Mony mony: James, Tommy & The Shondells / Hi ho silver lining: Beck, Jeff / Flowers in the rain: Move / Waterloo sunset: Kinks / Good vibrations: Beach Boys / She's not there: Zombies / Pretty flamingo: Manfred Mann / Love is all around: Troggs / Unchained melody: Righteous Brothers / Ferry cross the Mersey: Gerry & The Pacemakers / Winter shade of pale: Procul Harum / Wichita lineman: Campbell, Glen / He ain't heavy, he's my brother: Hollies / Sun ain't gonna shine anymore: Walker Brothers / Downtown: Clark, Petula / Can't get used to losing you: Williams, Andy / Silence is golden: Tremeloes / I heard it through the grapevine: Gaye, Marvin / (Sittin' on) The dock of the bay: Redding, Otis / I say a little prayer: Franklin, Aretha / Do you know the way to San Jose: Warwick, Dionne / You can't hurry love: Supremes / Reach out, I'll be there: Four Tops / Dancing in the street: Reeves, Martha & The Vandellas / Uptight (everything's alright): Wonder, Stevie / Soul man: Sam & Dave / It's not unusual: Jones, Tom / Yeh yeh: Fame, Georgie & The Blue Flames / Sha la la la lee: Small Faces / Got to get you into my life: Bennett, Cliff & The Rebel Rousers / In the midnight hour: Pickett, Wilson / Knock on wood: Floyd, Eddie / I got you (I feel good): Brown, James / Rescue me: Fontella Bass / Go now: Moody Blues / Brown eyed girl: Morrison, Van / Mr. Tambourine Man: Byrds / House of the rising sun: Animals / When a man loves a woman: Sledge, Percy / Crazy: Cline, Patsy / We have all the time in the world: Armstrong, Louis / Stand by me: King, Ben E.
CD Set _____ VTDCD 66
Virgin / Nov '95 / EMI.

BEST SOUL, THE
CD _____ CD 905
Sound / Jun '89 / Direct / ADA.

BEST SUMMER...EVER, THE
In the summertime: Shaggy / Compliments on your kiss: Red Dragon / Boom boom boom: Outhere Brothers / Wipeout: Fat Boys & The Beach Boys / Hot hot hot: Arrow / Saturday night: Whigfield / Dreamer: Livin' Joy / Sweets for my sweet: Lewis, C.J. / Don't turn around: Aswad / You don't love me (no no no): Penn, Dawn / Sweat (A la la la la long): Inner Circle / Humpin' around: Brown, Bobby / Love city groove: Love City Groove / Grease megamix: Travolta, John & Olivia Newton John / Give it up: K.C. & The Sunshine Band / Wake up Boo: Boo Radleys / Walking on sunshine: Katrina & The Waves / Beach baby: First Class / Barbados: Typically Tropical / Y viva Espana: Sylvia / Days: MacColl, Kirsty / Long hot summer: Style Council / Summer breeze: Isley Brothers / Back to life: Soul II Soul & Caron Wheeler / Lovely day: Withers, Bill / Summertime: D.J. Jazzy Jeff & The Fresh Prince / I'll be around: Rappin' 4-Tay / Searching: China Black / Now that we've found love: Third World / Club Tropicana: Wham / Do it again: Beach Boys / Echo beach: Martha & The Muffins / Summertime in my heart: Aztec Camera / Summertime blues: Cochran, Eddie / Summer rain: Carlisle, Belinda / On the beach: Rea, Chris / Under the boardwalk: Drifters / Summertime (2): Gerry & The Pacemakers / Summer (The first time): Goldsboro, Bobby / Spanish wine: White, Chris
CD Set _____ VTDCD 57
Virgin / Jul '95 / EMI.

BEST SWING '96
CD _____ TCD 2805
Telstar / Jan '96 / BMG.

BETWEEN FATHER SKY AND MOTHER EARTH
Ancient ground: Nakai, R.Carlos / Amazing grace: Nakai, R.Carlos / Wind spirit: Miller, Bill / Moonlit Stallions: Native Flute Ensemble / Riding with thunder: Native Flute Ensemble / Holy people: Douglas Spottedd Eagle / Snow geese: Douglas Spottedd Eagle / Ashne ate: Silverbird, Perry / Happy shepherd: Silverbird, Perry / Zuni friendship song: Manhooby, Chester / 500 Drums: Adams, Mel / Enchanted forest: Tsa'ne Dos'e / Kiowa hymn (II): Pewewardy, Cornel / Healing song: Primeaux, Mike & Attson
CD _____ ND 63915
Narada / Aug '95 / New Note / ADA.

BEVERLEY HILLS - WILD YOUNG & RICH VOL. 1
CD _____ DCD 5287
Disky / Feb '93 / THE / BMG / Discovery / Pinnacle.

BEVERLEY HILLS - WILD YOUNG & RICH VOL. 2
CD _____ DCD 5288
Disky / Feb '93 / THE / BMG / Discovery / Pinnacle.

BEWARE OF THE TEXAS BLUES
I'm a stepper: Fritz, Joe 'Papoose' / Can't sleep tonight: Moore, Henry & Guitar Slim / Workin' man blues: Copeland, Johnny / Life's highway: Big Walter / Empty house of so many tears: Green, Clarence / Drowning on dry land: Eastwood Revue / Rock of Gibraltar / Farther on up the road / Line your body / Freeze / That's fat / Rock me baby / It's alright / Good as old time religion
CD _____ CDBM 064
Blue Moon / Apr '91 / Magnum Music Group / Greensleeves / Hot Shot / ADA / Cadillac / Discovery.

BEWARE OF THE TEXAS BLUES VOL. 2
CD _____ CDBM 085
Blue Moon / May '92 / Magnum Music Group / Greensleeves / Hot Shot / ADA / Cadillac / Discovery.

BEYOND BOUNDARIES
CD _____ CDEB 2552
Earthbeat / May '93 / Direct / ADA.

BEYOND THE BEACH
CD _____ UPSTARTCD 12
Upstart / Jan '95 / Direct / ADA.

BEYOND THE CALICO WALL
CD _____ VOXXCD 2051
Voxx / Feb '94 / Else / Disc.

BEYOND THE FRONTLINE
Looks is deceiving: Gladiators / Message from the king: Prince Far-I / Right time: Mighty Diamonds / Wear you to the ball: U-Roy / If I don't have you: Isaacs, Gregory / Lightning flash weak heart: Drop Big Youth / Behold: Culture / Great psalms: U-Roy / Never get burn: Twinkle Brothers / Declaration of rights: Clarke, Johnny / Universal tribulation: Isaacs, Gregory / Natty rebel: U-Roy / Civilisation: Hudson, Keith / Freedom fighters: Washington, Delroy
CD _____ FRONT 1
Frontline / Jul '90 / EMI / Jetstar.

BEYOND THE SUN
CD _____ DAPCD 001
Dance Arena / Sep '95 / Disc.

BGP PRESENTS: BACK TO FUNK
(Selection Of Killer Cuts From East/Westbound Collective)
Back to funk: Lowe, Robert / Hicky burr: Frazier, Caesar / Monkey hips 'n' rice: 19th Whole / Pain: Person, Houston / Rainy day fun: Austin, Donald / Stone thing: Cash, Alvin / Gettin' off: Mason, Bill / Slippin' into darkness: 19th Whole / Whip whop (CD only): Sparks, Melvin / Kaleidoscope (CD only): Chandler, Gary / Stone thing (2): Cash, Alvin
CD _____ CDBGPD 096
BGP / Sep '95 / Pinnacle.

BHANGRA - EAST 2 WEST
CD _____ MCCD 121
Music Club / Aug '93 / Disc / THE / CM.

BHANGRA HOT CUTS VOL.1
CD _____ DMUT 1258
Multitone / Aug '93 / BMG.

BHANGRA HOT CUTS VOL.3
CD _____ DMUT 1297
Multitone / Jul '94 / BMG.

BHANGRA NOW
Soniyae ni Soniaye: Shoring / Gurdh nalo ishq mitah: Azaad / Rail Gaddi / Jago aye: Premi / Ik pathi jehi mutyaar: Sahotas / Saun Rabdi Maug Lag Javey: Kapoor, Mahendra / Paliey Punjean Waliey: Premi / Sanu Roki Na Kar: Sidhu, Amarjit / Giddh wich nachdi de: Manak, Kuldip / Kar Gai Jat Sharabi: Azaad / Giddha Penda / Bhangra rap: Sidhu, Amarjit
CD _____ BHANGRA 2CD
Multitone / Apr '88 / BMG.

BHANGRA POWER
Bhangra Paa Ni...: Sidhu, Amarjit / Bhabi gal na kari: Kapoor, Mahendra / Sachi Muchi: Sachi Muchi / Ek Sohni Jahe Mutiyear: Paaras / Aa Kudiye: D.C.S. / Yaar pooch de yaaran nu / Nachdi di gooth khulgaye: Premi / Tere husan di gall baat: / Akh mar ghide vich: Sahotas / O mere yaaro: Paaras / Giddhe Wich Nach Patia: Sachi Muchi / Nachdi pitho da: Premi
CD _____ BHANGRA 1CD
Multitone / Apr '88 / BMG.

BHANGRA TOP TEN
CD _____ DMUT 1279
Multitone / Jul '94 / BMG.

BHANGRA TOP TEN VOL.12
CD _____ CDSR 016
Star / Aug '90 / Pinnacle / Sterns.

BHANGRA WEDDING SONGS
CD _____ BHANGRA 3CD
Multitone / Aug '88 / BMG.

BIG ALBUM NO.1, THE
CD _____ BISWMMCD 001
Big Issue / Jul '95 / Total/BMG.

BIG BAD BLUES
(25 Sun Blues Classics)
Before long: Jimmy & Walter / We all gotta go sometime: Louis, Joe Hill / Bear cat: Thomas, Rufus / Carry my business on: Bolnes, Houston / Baby I'm coming home: Booker, Charlie / Juiced: Love, Billy / My real gone rocket: Brenston, Jackie / Greyhound blues: Hunt, D.A. / Wolf call boogie: Hot Shot Love / Prison bound blues: Nix, Willie / Blues train: Randolph, Tot / Mystery train: Parker, Junior & The Blue Flames / Beggin' my baby: Little Milton / Red hot: Emerson, Billy 'The Kid' / Cotton crop blues: Cotton, James / I'm gonna murder my baby: Hare, Pat / Rattlesnakin' mama: Stewart, William / Tiger man: Vinson, Mose / Gonna leave you baby: Lewis, Sammy & Willie Johnson / Cool down mama: Hunter, Long John / Come back home: Howlin' Wolf / Come back baby: Dr. Ross / I feel so worried: Lewis, Sammy & Willie Johnson / Let's get high: Gordon, Roscoe / Ain't that right: Snow, Eddie
CD _____ CPCD 8100
Charly / Jun '95 / Charly / THE / Cadillac.

BIG BAND BALLADS
CD _____ CDCD 1271
Charly / Oct '95 / Charly / THE / Cadillac.

BIG BAND BASH
CD Set _____ CDB 1209
Giants Of Jazz / Apr '92 / Target/BMG / Cadillac.

BIG BAND BLAST
CD _____ CDCD 1243
Charly / Jun '95 / Charly / THE / Cadillac.

BIG BAND BOX
(3CD/MC Set)
TrueTrax / Jan '96 / THE.
CD Set _____ TBXCD 512

BIG BAND CLASSICS
In the mood: Miller, Glenn / Little brown jug: Miller, Glenn / American patrol: Miller, Glenn / Moonlight serenade: Miller, Glenn / Tuxedo junction: Miller, Glenn / Pennsylvania 6-5000: Miller, Glenn / String of pearls: Miller, Glenn / Take the 'A' train: Ellington, Duke / Perdido: Ellington, Duke / Creole love call: Ellington, Duke / Black and tan fantasy: Ellington, Duke / Mood indigo: Ellington, Duke / Caravan: Ellington, Duke / Solitude: Ellington, Duke / Stompin' at the Savoy: Goodman, Benny / One o'clock jump: Goodman, Benny / And the angels sing: Goodman, Benny / Sing, sing, sing: Goodman, Benny / Pinetop's boogie: Dorsey, Tommy / Night and day: Dorsey, Tommy / After you've gone: Dorsey, Tommy / Song of India: Dorsey, Tommy / Blue skies: Dorsey, Tommy / I'm getting sentimental over you: Dorsey, Tommy / Marie: Dorsey, Tommy
CD _____ KAZCD 106
Kaz / Nov '89 / BMG.

BIG BAND CLASSICS
CD Set _____ DCDCD 212
Castle / Jan '96 / BMG.

BIG BAND CLASSICS VOL.2
CD _____ KAZCD 107
Kaz / Feb '92 / BMG.

BIG BAND COMPILATION
CD _____ 905112
Jazz Archives / Aug '91 / Jazz Music / Discovery / Cadillac.

BIG BAND ERA
(4CD Set)
CD Set _____ CDDIG 15
Charly / Jun '95 / Charly / THE / Cadillac.

BIG BAND ERA VOL.1
CD _____ MICH 5601 CD
Hindsight / Sep '92 / Target/BMG / Jazz Music.

BIG BAND ERA VOL.10
CD _____ MICH 5610 CD
Hindsight / Sep '92 / Target/BMG / Jazz Music.

BIG BAND ERA VOL.2
CD _____ MICH 5602 CD
Hindsight / Sep '92 / Target/BMG / Jazz Music.
CD _____ CDB 103
Giants Of Jazz / Jan '96 / Target/BMG / Cadillac.

BIG BAND ERA VOL.3
CD _____ MICH 5603 CD
Hindsight / Sep '92 / Target/BMG / Jazz Music.

BIG BAND ERA VOL.4
CD _____ MICH 5604 CD
Hindsight / Sep '92 / Target/BMG / Jazz Music.

BIG BAND ERA VOL.5
CD _____ MICH 5605 CD
Hindsight / Sep '92 / Target/BMG / Jazz Music.

BIG BAND ERA VOL.6
CD _____ MICH 5606 CD
Hindsight / Sep '92 / Target/BMG / Jazz Music.

BIG BAND ERA VOL.7
CD _____ MICH 5607 CD
Hindsight / Sep '92 / Target/BMG / Jazz Music.

BIG BAND ERA VOL.8
CD _____ MICH 5608 CD
Hindsight / Sep '92 / Target/BMG / Jazz Music.

BIG BAND ERA VOL.9
CD _____ MICH 5609 CD
Hindsight / Sep '92 / Target/BMG / Jazz Music.

BIG BAND FAVOURITES
(3CD Set)
Kick off: Parnell, Jack / Skin deep: Parnell, Jack / Champ: Parnell, Jack / When Yuba plays the rumba: Parnell, Jack / Love and marriage: Parnell, Jack / Tender trap: teacher: Watt, Tommy & Orchestra / Crumpets for the Count: Watt, Tommy & Orchestra / Overdrive: Watt, Tommy & Orchestra / Sugar: Watt, Tommy & Orchestra / Won't you come home Bill Bailey: Watt, Tommy & Orchestra / Easy Street: Watt, Tommy & Orchestra / Goin' to the County Fair: Watt, Tommy & Orchestra / Charmaine: May, Billy / Mad about the boy: May, Billy / Always: May, Billy / Air express: MacKintosh, Ken / Crew cut: MacKintosh, Ken / Creepin' Tom: MacKintosh, Ken / Riot in Cell Block II: MacKintosh, Ken / Monster: MacKintosh, Ken / Wembley Stadium: MacKintosh, Ken / Hampden Park: MacKintosh, Ken / Misty: MacKintosh, Ken / Black velvet: MacKintosh, Ken / Woodchoppers ball: Watt, Tommy & The Forty Two Big Band / Tuxedo Junction: Watt, Tommy & The Forty Two Big Band / Cobblers song: Ainsworth, Alyn / Bedtime for drums: Ainsworth, Alyn / When the guards are on parade: Ainsworth, Alyn / Intermission riff: Kenton, Stan / Fascinating rhythm: Kenton, Stan / How high the moon: Kenton, Stan / Comin' thro' the Rye: Geraldo / I only have eyes for you: Geraldo / One o'clock jump: Loss, Joe / Skyliner: Loss, Joe / Take the 'A' train: Loss, Joe / I wonder what's become of Sally: Anthony, Ray / Columbia, the gem of the ocean: Anthony, Ray / Rockin' through Dixie: Anthony, Ray / Washington whirligig: Rabin, Oscar & His Band with Harry Davis / Painted rhythm: Rabin, Oscar & His Band with Harry Davis / Basin Street blues: Rabin, Oscar & His Band with Harry Davis / Crazy bear: Squadronaires
CD Set _____ CDTRBOX 160
Music For Pleasure / Sep '95 / EMI.

BIG BAND JAZZ - TULSA TO HARLEM
CD _____ DD 439
Delmark / Mar '89 / Hot Shot / ADA / CM / Direct / Cadillac.

BIG BAND SAMPLER
Minne the moocher: Calloway, Cab / I gotta go places and do things baby to forget you: Calloway, Cab / Under a blanket of blue: Gray, Glen / Limehouse blues: Gray, Glen / Sentimental journey: Brown, Les / On the beach at Wikiki: Brown, Les / Taking a chance on love: Goodman, Benny / Something new: Goodman, Benny / Everybody knew but me: Herman, Woody / Apple honey: Herman, Woody / Daddy: Kaye, Sammy / Harbour lights: Kaye, Sammy / Leap frog: Brown, Les / Caldonia: Herman, Woody / At the woodchoppers' ball: Elgart, Les & Larry / Skyliner: Elgart, Les & Larry
CD _____ 4666172
Columbia / Jan '91 / Sony.

BIG BAND SELECTION, THE
In the mood: Miller, Glenn / Temptation: Shaw, Artie / Tea for two: Armstrong, Louis / September song: Brown, Les / Blowing up a storm: Herman, Woody / One o'clock jump: Goodman, Benny / Take the 'A' train: Ellington, Duke / Basie boogie: Basie, Count / Imagination: Dorsey, Jimmy / Cherokee: Barnet, Charlie / Single in India: Dorsey, Tommy / Little brown jug: Dorsey, Tommy / Moon glow: Dorsey, Tommy / Stompin' at the Savoy: Armstrong, Louis / Love me or leave me: Brown, Les / Caldonia: Herman, Woody / Sing, sing, sing: Goodman, Benny / Mooche: Ellington, Duke / April in Paris: Ellington, Duke / Nightmare: Shaw, Artie / Lover: Armstrong, Louis / Nutcracker suite: Brown, Les / Jersey bounce: Goodman, Benny / Caravan: Ellington, Duke / Lester leaps in: Basie, Count / Nearness of you: Dorsey, Jimmy / Skyliner: Barnet, Charlie / On the sunny side of the street: Dorsey, Tommy / Chattanooga choo choo: Miller, Glenn / Donkey serenade: Shaw, Artie / Jeepers creepers: Armstrong, Louis / How about you: Brown, Les / Northwest passage: Herman, Woody / Frankie and Johnny: Goodman, Benny / Pretty woman: Ellington, Duke / Moonlight serenade: Miller, Glenn / Stardust: Shaw, Artie / C'est si bon: Armstrong, Louis / It's all right with me: Brown, Les / Early autumn: Herman, Woody / There's a small hotel: Herman, Woody / I'll never be the same: Krupa, Gene / Goin' to Chicago: Krupa, Gene / Just you, just me: Krupa, Gene / Boogie for nothin' Joe: Barnet, Charlie / This love of mine: Dorsey, Tommy / Pennsylvania 6-5000: Miller, Glenn / Fre-

nesi: *Shaw, Artie* / Tiger rag: *Armstrong, Louis* / Cabin in the sky: *Brown, Les* / After glow: *Herman, Woody* / Get happy: *Goodman, Benny* / Uptown blues: *Barnet, Charlie* / All the things you are: *Barnet, Charlie* / Blue and sentimental: *Basie, Count* / It started all over again: *Dorsey, Tommy* / Sleepy lagoon: *Dorsey, Tommy* / That old black magic: *Miller, Glenn* / Blues in the night: *Shaw, Artie* / When the saints go marching in: *Armstrong, Louis* / Sentimental journey: *Brown, Les* / Bijou: *Herman, Woody* / Stompin' at the Savoy (2): *Goodman, Benny* / Do nothin' 'til you hear from me: *Ellington, Duke* / Red bank boogie: *Basie, Count* / Fools rush in: *Dorsey, Jimmy* / East side, West side: *Barnet, Charlie* / Marie: *Dorsey, Tommy* / Tuxedo junction: *Miller, Glenn* / I can't get started (with you): *Miller, Glenn* / Ain't misbehavin': *Miller, Glenn* / I'm forever blowing bubbles: *Brown, Les* / At the woodchoppers' ball: *Herman, Woody* / Down south camp meeting: *Goodman, Benny* / Perdido: *Ellington, Duke* / I've got rhythm: *Dorsey, Jimmy* / Jumpin' at the woodside: *Basie, Count* / Taking a chance on love: *Dorsey, Tommy* / Trumpet blues: *James, Harry*
CD Set ______________ **TFP 007**
Tring / Nov '92 / Tring / Prism.

BIG BAND SOUND VOL.1, THE
Jeepers creepers: *Armstrong, Louis* / Does your heart beat for me: *Morgan, Russ* / Tiger rag: *Dorsey, Jimmy* / Cherokee: *Barnet, Charlie* / Magenta haze: *Ellington, Duke* / (In) a shanty in old Shanty Town: *Long, Johnny* / Sophisticated lady: *Ellington, Duke* / Harlem nocturne: *Barnet, Charlie* / Northwest passage: *Herman, Woody* / Let's dance: *Goodman, Benny* / Begin the beguine: *Shaw, Artie* / So rare: *Dorsey, Jimmy* / Night and day: *Shaw, Artie* / Oh Johnny: *Fitzgerald, Ella & Chick Webb* / Opus one: *Dorsey, Tommy* / One o'clock jump: *Basie, Count* / C'est si bon: *Armstrong, Louis* / (Back home again in) Indiana: *Ellington, Duke* / When the saints go marching in: *Armstrong, Louis* / Woodchopper's ball: *Herman, Woody* / Summit ridge drive: *Pastor, Tony* / They can't take that...: *Basie, Count*
CD ______________ **CDGRF 012**
Tring / '93 / Tring / Prism.

BIG BAND SOUND VOL.2, THE
Pompton turnpike: *Barnet, Charlie* / What is this thing called love: *Shaw, Artie* / Ain't misbehavin': *Ellington, Duke* / Take the 'A' train: *Ellington, Duke* / Frenesi: *Pastor, Tony* / My heart belongs to dad: *Shaw, Artie* / Count steps in: *Basie, Count* / Sultry sunset: *Ellington, Duke* / Dipsy doodle: *Clinton, Larry* / I want the waiter (with the water): *Webb, Chick* / Flat foot floogie: *Basie, Count* / St. Louis blues: *Dorsey, Jimmy* / Skyliner: *Barnet, Charlie* / Bijou: *Herman, Woody* / Mame: *Armstrong, Louis* / Tip toe topic: *Ellington, Duke* / Old rocking chair: *Armstrong, Louis* / Caldonia: *Herman, Woody* / Margie: *Lunceford, Jimmie* / I'm just wild about Harry: *Dorsey, Jimmy* / Just a gigolo: *Armstrong, Louis* / Body and soul: *Armstrong, Louis* / Linger awhile: *Morgan, Russ*
CD ______________ **CDGRF 013**
Tring / '93 / Tring / Prism.

BIG BAND VOL.1
(The RCA Jazz Collection)
CD Set ______________ **74321248172**
RCA / Dec '94 / BMG.

BIG BAND'S GREATEST HITS
Stompin' at the Savoy: *Goodman, Benny* / Fidgety feet: *Henderson, Fletcher* / Rockin' in rhythm: *Ellington, Duke* / One O'clock jump: *Basie, Count* / I can't get started (with you): *Berigan, Bunny* / Begin the beguine: *Shaw, Artie* / Undecided: *Webb, Chick* / I'm getting sentimental over you: *Dorsey, Tommy* / For dancers only: *Lunceford, Jimmie* / Until the real thing comes along: *Kirk, Andy* / In the mood: *Miller, Glenn* / Skyliner: *Barnet, Charlie* / Let me off uptown: *Krupa, Gene* / At the woodchoppers' ball: *Herman, Woody* / Flying home: *Hampton, Lionel* / Snowfall: *Thornhill, Claude*
CD ______________ **CDCD 1002**
Charly / Mar '93 / Charly / THE / Cadillac.

BIG BAND, THE
CD ______________ **CD 56032**
Jazz Roots / Nov '94 / Target/BMG.

BIG BANDS
Dragnet: *Anthony, Ray* / Early autumn: *Herman, Woody* / Satin doll: *Ellington, Duke* / Creep: *MacKintosh, Ken* / Brother John: *Riddle, Nelson* / September song: *Kenton, Stan* / Man with golden arm: *May, Billy* / Don't be that way: *Goodman, Benny* / All the things you are: *Barnet, Charlie* / No name jive: *Gray, Glen & The Casa Loma Orchestra* / Staccato's theme: *Bernstein, Elmer* / Sleepy lagoon: *James, Harry* / Younger than springtime: *Brown, Les* / Up a lazy river: *Zentner, Si* / Experiments with mice: *Dankworth, John* / Mama's talking soft: *Basie, Count* / Once around: *Jones, Thad & Mel Lewis* / Nightmare: *Shaw, Artie* / Midnight sleighride: *Sauter-Finegan Orchestra* / Diabolus: *Rich, Buddy*
CD ______________ **CDMFP 6164**
Music For Pleasure / May '95 / EMI.

BIG BANDS 1945
CD ______________ **JZCD 355**
Suisa / Oct '93 / Jazz Music / THE.

BIG BANDS IN HI-FI VOL.1 - LET'S DANCE
Let's dance: *Goodman, Benny* / Moonglow: *Goodman, Benny* / And the angels sing: *Goodman, Benny* / Don't be that way: *Goodman, Benny* / Stompin' at the Savoy: *Goodman, Benny* / Jersey bounce: *Goodman, Benny* / Satin doll: *Ellington, Duke* / Flying home: *Ellington, Duke* / Rockin' in rhythm: *Ellington, Duke* / Don't get around much anymore: *Ellington, Duke* / It's been a long, long time: *James, Harry* / Sleepy lagoon: *James, Harry* / You made me love you: *James, Harry* / Two o'clock jump: *James, Harry* / I can't get started (with you): *Gray, Glen* / No name jive: *Gray, Glen* / String of pearls: *Gray, Glen* / Tuxedo Junction: *Gray, Glen* / Moonlight serenade: *Gray, Glen* / Traffic jam: *Shaw, Artie* / It had to be you: *Shaw, Artie* / Softly as in a morning sunrise: *Shaw, Artie* / Octaroon: *Shaw, Artie* / What is this thing called love: *Shaw, Artie* / Serenade in blue: *Anthony, Ray* / Harlem nocturne: *Anthony, Ray* / Stardust: *Anthony, Ray* / Topsy: *Basie, Count* / Cute: *Basie, Count* / Jumpin' at the woodside: *Basie, Count* / Blue and sentimental: *Basie, Count* / Artistry jumps: *Kenton, Stan* / Peanut vendor: *Kenton, Stan* / Leapfrog: *Brown, Les* / Twilight time: *Brown, Les* / Why don't we do this more often: *Kyser, Kay* / Jingle jangle jingle: *Kyser, Kay* / Cherokee/Redskin rhumba: *Barnet, Charlie* / Skyliner: *Barnet, Charlie* / Memories of you: *Gray, Glen & Orchestra* / Smoke rings: *Gray, Glen & Orchestra* / Bumble boogie: *Martin, Freddy* / Blue champagne: *Martin, Freddy* / Caldonia: *Herman, Woody* / There are such things: *Modernaires* / Auld Lang Syne: *Lombardo, Guy*
CD Set ______________ **CDP 8278132**
Capitol / Mar '95 / EMI.

BIG BANDS IN HI-FI VOL.2 - IN THE MOOD
In the mood: *Gray, Glen* / Song of India: *Gray, Glen* / I'm getting sentimental over you: *Gray, Glen* / Opus one: *Gray, Glen* / Casa Loma stomp: *Gray, Glen* / I'm beginning to see the light: *James, Harry* / Cherry: *James, Harry* / Avalon: *Goodman, Benny* / Down south camp meeting: *Goodman, Benny* / King Porter stomp: *Goodman, Benny* / Sing, sing, sing: *Goodman, Benny* / Goodbye: *Goodman, Benny* / Bizet has his day: *Brown, Les* / Mexican hat dance: *Brown, Les* / Sentimental journey: *Brown, Les* / I've got my love: *Brown, Les* / Canto Karaball (Jungle drums): *Shaw, Artie* / Lover come back to me: *Shaw, Artie* / Back Bay shuffle: *Shaw, Artie* / Begin the beguine: *Shaw, Artie* / Nightmare: *Shaw, Artie* / Who wouldn't love you: *Kyser, Kay* / Pushin' sand: *Kyser, Kay* / Warsaw concerto: *Martin, Freddy* / Tonight we love: *Martin, Freddy* / Down for double: *Basie, Count* / Taps Miller: *Basie, Count* / Lullaby of Birdland: *Basie, Count* / Broadway: *Basie, Count* / Pompton Turnpike: *Barnet, Charlie* / Song of the Islands: *Crosby, Bob & His Bobcats* / Once in a while: *Crosby, Bob & His Bobcats* / Big noise from Winnetka: *Crosby, Bob & His Bobcats* / Apple honey: *Herman, Woody* / Woodchopper's ball: *Herman, Woody* / Early Autumn: *Herman, Woody* / Sleepy time gal: *Gray, Glen & Orchestra* / Sunrise serenade: *Gray, Glen & Orchestra* / At last: *Anthony, Ray* / Dancing in the dark: *Anthony, Ray* / Take the 'A' train: *Ellington, Duke* / Sophisticated lady: *Ellington, Duke* / Perdido: *Ellington, Duke* / Eager beaver: *Kenton, Stan* / Ciribiribin: *James, Harry & His Music Makers* / I've heard that song before: *James, Harry & His Music Makers* / Jukebox Saturday night: *Beneke, Tex & the Modernaires*
CD Set ______________ **CDP 8278162**
Capitol / Mar '95 / EMI.

BIG BANDS OF THE SWINGING YEARS
CD ______________ **CD 104**
Timeless Treasures / Oct '94 / THE.

BIG BLUES HONKS & WAILS
CD ______________ **PRCD 9905**
Prestige / Feb '96 / Complete/Pinnacle / Cadillac.

BIG BREAKFAST ALBUM, THE
CD ______________ **ARC 3100082**
Arcade / Aug '93 / Sony / Grapevine.

BIG CITY SOUL VOL.1
Looking for you: *Mimms, Garnet* / Love is not a game: *Soul, Sam E* / My Dear heart: *Robinson, Shawn* / Mend my broken heart: *St. John, Rose & The Wonderettes* / Hold on: *O'Jays* / Ready, willing and able: *Holiday, Jimmy & Clydie King* / Lot of love: *Banks, Homer* / Hooked by love: *Banks, Homer* / I lost a true love: *Wagner, Danny & The Kindred Soul* / Then came heart break: *Jive Five* / Strange neighbourhood: *McDaniels, Gene* / Stick close: *Brown, Estelle* / Be careful girl: *Turner, Betty* / I'll never forget you: *O'Jays* / It's what's underneath that counts: *Jackson, June* / Working on your case: *O'Jays* / My heart is in danger: *Ray, Alder* / Honest to goodness: *Diplomats* / Are you trying to get rid of me baby: *Crystals* / Breakaway (part 1): *Karman, Steve* / I only get this feeling: *Irwin, Dee* / Livin' above your head: *Jay & The Americans* / Don't: *Josie, Marva* / It's a sad thing: *Pollard, Ray* / Walk with a winner: *McDaniels, Gene* / Drifter: *Pollard, Ray* / It'll never be over for me: *Yuro, Timi*
CD ______________ **GSCD 042**
Goldmine / Jul '94 / Vital.

BIG CITY SOUL VOL.2
Stop and think it over: *Mimms, Garnet* / I love you baby: *Ambers* / Pretty little face: *Four Hi's* / You can split: *Youngblood Smith* / What would I do: *Superiors* / Living a lie: *High Keys* / Stop and take a look at yourself: *Shalimars* / Take a step in my direction: *Little Eva* / Real jive guy: *Ahres, Dajh* / Walkin' the duck: *Triumphs* / I can't make it without you baby: *Banks, Bessie* / Just a fool: *Gainey, Jerry* / I watched you slowly slip away: *Guyton, Howard* / Mighty good way: *Banks, Robert* / Right direction: *Ward, Clara* / My heart belongs to you: *Pickett, Wilson* / I don't want to lose your love: *Woods, Billy* / Love I give: *Murray, Louise* / (You'd better) Straighten up and fly right: *Bryant, Terry* / Born to please: *Prince Harold* / Baby I love you: *Tate, Howard* / I'm a practical guy: *Gardner, Don* / Backfield in motion: *Poindexter Brothers* / I don't need no doctor: *Ashford, Nick* / Can't deny the hurt: *Rakes, Pal & The Prophets* / Picture me gone: *Brooks, Diane* / Let's take a chance: *High Keys* / Let me be your boy: *Pickett, Wilson*
CD ______________ **GSCD 044**
Goldmine / Sep '94 / Vital.

BIG CITY SOUL VOL.3
I'm alive with the love feeling: *Turner, Spyder* / Street talk: *Tymes* / To the ends of the earth: *Middleton, Tony* / I'm gonna change: *Velours* / (Love) You can't just walk away: *Courtney, Dean* / I can't make it anymore: *Turner, Spyder* / Key to my happiness: *Charades* / I got what you need: *Weston, Kim* / My heart took a licking: *Jackson, Millie* / Everything you always wanted to know about love: *Roberts, Lou* / I'm gonna hold on (to your love): *Mars, Marlina* / Can't make it without you: *Superiors* / At the top of the stairs: *Formations* / Watch out girl: *Embers* / You fooled me: *Roberts, Lou & The Marks* / You're just the kind of guy: *Weston, Kim* / We got togetherness: *Jewels* / What would I do: *Tymes* / Cry your eyes out: *Cambridge, Dottie* / Wanting you: *Stevens, April* / You just don't know: *Broadways* / Weeping cup: *Charades* / Betcha can't change my mind: *Courtney, Dean* / You never know: *Nash, Johnny* / Fool that I am: *Solitaires* / You can count on me: *Hamilton, Roy* / Panic is on: *Hamilton, Roy*
CD ______________ **GSCD 047**
Goldmine / Jan '95 / Vital.

BIG CITY SOUL VOL.4
(2CD Set)
Fell in love with you baby: *Charts* / Wait til I give the signal: *Shirelles* / When it comes to my baby: *Mislap, Ronnie* / Not my girl: *Platters* / You can't fight love: *Shirley & Jessie* / Call on Billy: *Soul, Billy T.* / I feel better: *Bruce, Alan* / To get your love back: *Dodds, Nella* / Bricks, broken bottles and sticks: *Parish, Dean* / Never in a million years: *Honey Bees* / Glamour girls: *Hopkins, Harold* / How much pressure (do you think I can stand): *Robinson, Roscoe* / Mr Creator: *Candy & The Kisses* / Change: *Eady, Ernestine* / Think twice before you walk away: *Porgy & The Monarchs* / Never love a robin: *Inez & Charlie Foxx* / Tonight I'm gonna see my baby: *Hughes, Freddie* / I've got to be strong: *Jackson, Chuck* / Three rooms: *Freeman, Audrey* / Jerkin' time: *Diplomats* / Ain't that the truth: *Troy, J B* / If I'm hurt you'll feel the pain: *Barbara & Brenda* / You lie so well: *Knight, Marie* / I've got love for you: *Intruders* / First date: *Dodds, Nella* / Woman: *Esquires* / Hey girl: *Porgy & The Monarchs* / You've got my love: *Wells, Donnie* / Upset my heart (got me upset): *Clay, Judy* / Lover: *Hunt, Tommy* / Tonight's the night: *Candy & The Kisses* / Since you've been gone: *Anglos* / Magic touch: *Moore, Melba* / Try some soul: *Crossen, Ray* / You could be my remedy: *Shirelles* / No stranger to love: *Inez & Charlie Foxx* / In the long run: *Blandon, Curtis* / Live on: *Troy, J B* / Hand it over: *Wand Orchestra* / I've got to find someone to love: *Fisher, Jerry & The Night beats* / Honey boy: *Dodds, Nella* / There goes a forgotten man: *Radcliffe, Jimmy* / That's no way to treat a girl: *Knight, Marie* / Fear of losing you: *Platters* / Just one more time: *Barnes, J.J.* / Silencer: *Jackson, Chuck* / There's still a tomorrow: *Diplomats* / Are you trying to get rid of me baby: *Candy & The Kisses* / Words can never tell it: *Hunt, Tommy* / Nobody made you love me: *Charts* / Keep a hold on me: *Porgy & The Monarchs* / Doesn't it ring a bell: *Platters* / Way to a woman's heart: *Soul, Billy T.* / All the way from heaven: *Chancellors* / Nobody knows: *Williams, Maurice* / Anything you do is right: *Brown, Maxine* / No doubt about it: *Shirelles* / Your kind of lovin: *Clay, Judy* / My little plaything: *Watts, Glen* / If I had you: *Big Maybelle*
CD Set ______________ **GSCD 065**
Goldmine / Oct '95 / Vital.

BIG DANCE HITS 1992
Ebeneezer Goode: *Shamen* / Rhythm is a dancer: *Snap* / Jump: *Kriss Kross* / Rock your baby: *KWS* / Don't talk just kiss: *Right Said Fred* / Are you ready to fly: *Rozalla* / I don't care: *Shakespears Sister* / Baker Street: *Undercover* / Expression: *Salt 'N' Pepa* / I feel love: *Messiah* / Too funky: *Michael, George* / Twilight zone: *2 Unlimited* / M.A.S.H. (Suicide is painless): *Manic Street Preachers* / Blue room: *Orb* / Reality used to be a friend of mine: *PM Dawn* / I'm doing fine now: *Pasadenas* / It only takes a minute: *Take That* / Humpin' around: *Brown, Bobby* / Mutations (Chime): *Orbital* / Love makes the world go round: *Don-E* / I'm gonna get you: *Bizarre Inc.* / It's a fine day: *Opus III* / Hypnotic st8 (St8 of Art edit): *Altern 8* / Dream come true: *Brand New Heavies* / Make it on my own: *Limerick, Alison* / Love U more: *Sunscreen* / Everybody in the place: *Prodigy* / Crucified: *Army Of Lovers* / Kings of the ring: *Du Berry, Steve & Born 2 B* / Different strokes: *Isotonik*
CD ______________ **AHLCD 4**
Hit / Nov '92 / PolyGram.

BIG NOISE: A MAMBO INN COMPILATION
Dub lion (remake): *D.J. Food* / Kinna sohna: *Khan, Nusrat Fateh Ali* / Did-funk club: *Khaled* / Angelina: *Sweet Talks* / Zing zong: *Kanda Bongo Man* / Ussak ndja: *Tchando* / Mango mango mangue: *Mambomania* / El swing: *Montanez, Andy* / Elena Elena: *Libre* / Samba de flora: *Airto* / Wack wack: *Young-Holt Trio* / Do what you wanna: *Lewis, Ramsey* / You're the one: *McGriff, Jimmy* / My God can do anything: *Barnes, Luther & The Red Budd Gospel Choir*
CD ______________ **HNCD 1382**
Hannibal / Nov '94 / Vital / ADA.

BIG ONE, THE
CD ______________ **FLIP 30CD**
Burning Heart / Sep '95 / Plastic Head.

BIG SQUEEZE, THE
Johnny Allen's reel/Sporting Nell: *McComiskey, Billy & Sean McGlynn* / Miller of Draughin/Humours of Castlefin: *O'Brien, Paddy* / High reel/Geoghegan's reel: *Burke, Joe* / Maids of Selma/Larry Redican's/Dancing tables: *Keane, James* / Crossing the Sahannon/Lad O'Beirne's reel/Rough road: *Keane, James* / Andy Stewart's reel/Harsh February: *Cunningham, Phil* / Desaunay/Petticoat I bought in Mullingar: *Cunningham, Phil* / Sweeney's reel: *Daly, Jackie* / Bucks of Oranmore: *Burke, Joe* / Spike Island lassies/Humours of Tulla: *McComiskey, Billy* / Strathspey and reel: *O'Brien, Paddy* / La Bastringue: *Daly, Jackie* / Connaught man's rambles/Cat in the corner: *Burke, Joe* / Master Crowley's reels: *Keane, James* / Lament from Eoin Rhua/March of the Gaelic order: *O'Brien, Paddy* / Yellow tinker/Sally Gardens: *McComiskey, Billy* / Tom Fleming's reel/Kitty's wedding/Sean McGuire's reel: *Whelan, John* / Jackson's reel/Jean's reel/Moving cloud: *Cunningham, Phil*
CD ______________ **GLCD 1093**
Green Linnet / Nov '90 / Roots / CM / Direct / ADA.

BIG SURF
Pipeline: *Lively Ones* / Scratch: *Lively Ones* / Misirlou: *Lively Ones* / Surfbeat: *Lively Ones* / High tide: *Lively Ones* / Baja: *Lively Ones* / Torquay: *Lively Ones* / Soul surfer: *Lively Ones* / Rik-a-tik: *Lively Ones* / Church key: *Myers, Dave & The Surftones* / Moment of truth: *Myers, Dave & The Surftones* / Bullwinkle (part 2): *Centurions* / Sano: *Centurions* / Surfin' at Mazatland: *Centurions* / Body surfin': *Centurions* / Vesuvius: *Centurions* / Latin'ia: *Centurions* / Intoxica: *Centurions* / Steel pier: *Impacts* / Impact: *Impacts* / Blue surf: *Impacts* / Wipeout: *Impacts* / Fort Lauderdale: *Impacts* / Exotic: *Sentinals* / Pipe: *Sentinals* / Latin soul: *Sentinals* / Tor chula: *Sentinals* / Big surf: *Sentinals*
CD ______________ **CDCHD 319**
Ace / Aug '91 / Pinnacle / Cadillac / Complete/Pinnacle.

BIG TIMES IN A SMALL TOWN
CD ______________ **PH 1155CD**
Philo / Oct '93 / Direct / CM / ADA.

BIG UP JAZZ VOL.2
CD ______________ **CUTUPCD 007**
Jump Cut / Sep '94 / Total/BMG / Vital/ SAM.

BIG WHEELS OF AZULI
(1991-1995)
Bring me love: *Mendez, Andrea* / R U sleeping: *Indo* / Ministry of love: *Romanthony* / Anthem: *Black Shells* / Feeling: *Jasper Street Co* / Place called Heaven: *Tension* / In a fantasy: *Chocolate Fantasy* / Running: *Disco Elements* / Heaven: *KCC & Emile* / Falling from grace: *Romanthony* / Summer groove: *Sensory Elements*
CD ______________ **AZNYCD 1**
Azuli / Nov '95 / Azuli / Empire.

BIGGEST BAND SPECTACULAR IN THE WORLD
(1985 Military Musical Pageant Wembley Stadium)
General salute and opening fanfare / By beat of drum / Light of foot / Pipes and drums / Queen's guards / Massed bands / Royal military band of The Netherlands / War and peace / Finale
CD Set ______________ **BNW 9002**
Bandleader / '89 / Conifer.

BIGSHOT MIXES
CD _____ DBCD 506
Debut / May '90 / Pinnacle / 3MV / Sony.

BIONIC DUB
CD _____ LG 21114
Lagoon / Aug '95 / Magnum Music Group / THE.

BIORHYTHM
Take me back (bass head mix): Rhythmatic / Mood (optimystic mix): Symbols & Instruments / Free: Kate B / Emanon: Rhythm Is Rhythm / Fall into a trance: Critical Rhythm / Self hypnosis: Nexus 21 / Somebody new: MK / Bio rhythms: C & M Connection / Indulge: Howard, Neal / Don't lead me: Grey, Paris
CD _____ BIOCD 1
Network / Jul '90 / Sony / 3MV.

BIORHYTHM 2
CD _____ BIOCD 2
Network / '92 / Sony / 3MV.

BIRD LIVES
Yardbird suite: Pepper, Art / Confirmation: Ammons, Gene / Ornithology: Evans, Bill / Parker's mood (bless my soul): Jefferson, Eddie / Scrapple from the apple: Mitchell, Blue / I au revoir: Moody, James / Repitition: Montgomery, Wes / Billie's bounce: Griffin, Johnny / Steeplechase: Hawes, Hampton / Now's the time: Morgan, Frank / Relaxin' at Camarillo: Henderson, Joe
CD _____ MCD 91662
Milestone / Apr '94 / Jazz Music / Pinnacle / Wellard / Cadillac.

BIRD'S NIGHT
(A Celebration Of The Music Of Charlie Parker)
Parker's mood / Steeplechase / Buzzy / Scrapple from the apple
CD _____ SV 0143
Savoy Jazz / Jan '94 / Conifer / ADA.

BIRKS' WORKS
(The Music Of Dizzy Gillespie)
Birk's works: Burrell, Kenny / Groovin' high: Fuller, Gil & The Monterey Jazz orchestra / Be bop: Clark, Sonny / I waited for you: Davis, Miles / Manteca: Evans, Gil / Champ: Smith, Jimmy / Groovin high: Parker, Charlie / Night in Tunisia: Rollins, Sonny / Anthropology: Jordan, Clifford / Leap here: Metronome All Stars
CD _____ BNZ 310
Blue Note / Mar '93 / EMI.

BIRTH OF SKA, THE
Carry go bring home: Hinds, Justin & The Dominoes / River bank: Brooks, Baba / Musical communion: Brooks, Baba / Feeling fine: Alphonso, Roland / Strongarm Specimen: Hinds, Justin & The Dominoes / Over the river: Hinds, Justin & The Dominoes / Next door neighbour: Silvera, Owen & Leon & The Skatalite Band / When I call your name: Brooks, Baba / Yeah yeah baby: Stranger & Patsy/Baba Brooks/Skatalite Band / Hop in a cocoa: Skatalite Band / Musical storeroom: Anderson, Frank & Skatalite Band / Corner stone: Hinds, Justin & The Dominoes
CD _____ CDTRL 274
Trojan / Mar '94 / Jetstar / Total/BMG.

BITING BACK
CD _____ WOWCD 35
Words Of Warning / Jan '94 / SRD.

BITTER FRUITS
CD _____ IUKCD 002
Harthouse / Apr '95 / Disc / Warner Music.

BIWA & SHAKUHACHI
CD _____ C 580059
Ocora / Jan '95 / Harmonia Mundi / ADA.

BIX BEIDERBECKE LEGEND, THE
Clementine: Goldkette, Jean & His Orchestra / I didn't know: Goldkette, Jean & His Orchestra / Sunday: Goldkette, Jean & His Orchestra / Changes: Whiteman, Paul / Lonely melody: Whiteman, Paul / There ain't no sweet man that's worth the salt of my tears: Whiteman, Paul / San Dardanella: Whiteman, Paul / You took advantage of me: Whiteman, Paul / Barnacle Bill, the sailor: Carmichael, Hoagy & His Orchestra / I'll be a friend with pleasure: Beiderbecke, Bix
CD _____ 74321130372
RCA / Sep '93 / BMG.

BLACK & BLUES
CD _____ VGCD 660510
Vogue / Oct '93 / BMG.

BLACK & BLUES - SWEET LITTLE ANGEL
CD _____ 12207
Laserlight / Jul '93 / Target/BMG.

BLACK & SOUL
CD _____ 12403
Laserlight / Feb '95 / Target/BMG.

BLACK & WHITE BLUES
CD Set _____ MBSCD 431
Castle / Oct '94 / BMG.

BLACK AND BLUE
CD _____ TJ 050
That's Jazz / Mar '94 / BMG.

BLACK AND TAN CLUB, THE
CD _____ NAR 060 CD
New Alliance / May '93 / Pinnacle.

BLACK BOX OF JAZZ
(4CD Set)
CD Set _____ MBSCD 450
Castle / Nov '95 / BMG.

BLACK CALIFORNIA
Blow blow blow / Blues a la Russ / What is this thing called love / Wake up old maid / Sad feeling / Rock me to sleep / This love of mine / He may be yours / Jam man / Slim's riff / I'm confessin' / Oxydol highball / Strollin' / Sonor / Blues mood / Skoot / I've lost your love
CD _____ SVOCD 274
Savoy Jazz / Nov '95 / Conifer / ADA.

BLACK GOLD
CD _____ HRCD 8047
Disky / Jul '94 / THE / BMG / Discovery / Pinnacle.

BLACK MAGIC
Maybellene: Berry, Chuck / Keep a knockin': Little Richard / Rockin' Robin: Day, Bobby / Lover's question: McPhatter, Clyde / Dedicated to the one I love: Shirelles / Girl I love: Benton, Brook / Tears on my pillow: Imperials / You're got too marvellous: Holiday, Billie / Please love me forever: Edwards, Tommy / All in my mind: Brown, Maxine / Sixteen candles: Crests / Unforgettable: Washington, Dinah / Let the good times roll: Shirley & Lee / Misty: Vaughan, Sarah / C.C. rider: Charles, Ray / Dance with me Henry: James, Etta / Chains of love: Phillips, Esther / My way: Simone, Nina / Alley oop: Hollywood Argyles / Earth angel: Penguins / Baby, it's you: Labelle, Patti / Duke of Earl: Chandler, Gene
CD _____ C5LCD 586
See For Miles/C5 / Apr '92 / Pinnacle.

BLACK METAL COMPILATION, THE
CD Set _____ BLACK 001DCD
Blackend / Mar '95 / Plastic Head.

BLACK MUSIC
CD _____ SETCD 082
Stardust / Sep '94 / Carlton Home Entertainment.

BLACK OR WHITE
(Music Of Michael Jackson - 16 Instrumental Hits)
CD _____ 5708574338103
Carlton Home Entertainment / Sep '94 / Carlton Home Entertainment.

BLACK ROCK/CYBERFUNK/FUTURE BLUES
CD _____ RCD 10313
Rykodisc / Oct '94 / Vital / ADA.

BLACK SCORPIO ALL STARS
CD _____ 794522
Melodie / Dec '95 / Triple Earth / Discovery / ADA / Jetstar.

BLACK TO THE FUTURE VOL.1
CD _____ DIVCD 02
Diverse / May '94 / Grapevine.

BLACK TOP BLUES COSTUME PARTY
CD _____ BT 1116CD
Black Top / Jun '95 / CM / Direct / ADA.

BLACK TOP BLUES VOCAL DYNAMITE
CD _____ BT 1124CD
Black Top / Nov '95 / CM / Direct / ADA.

BLACK TOP BLUES-A-RAMA
(Budget Sampler)
CD _____ BT 002CD
Black Top / Dec '90 / CM / Direct / ADA.

BLACK TOP BLUES-A-RAMA VOL.2
CD _____ BT 1045CD
Black Top / '92 / CM / Direct / ADA.

BLACK TOP BLUES-A-RAMA VOL.3
(Live From Tipitinas)
CD _____ BT 1056CD
Black Top / '92 / CM / Direct / ADA.

BLACK TOP BLUES-A-RAMA VOL.4
(Down And Dirty)
CD _____ BT 1057CD
Black Top / '92 / CM / Direct / ADA.

BLACK TOP BLUES-A-RAMA VOL.5
CD _____ BT 1058CD
Black Top / '92 / CM / Direct / ADA.

BLACK TOP BLUES-A-RAMA VOL.6
CD _____ BT 1073CD
Black Top / May '92 / CM / Direct / ADA.

BLACK TOP BLUES-A-RAMA VOL.7
CD _____ BT 1089CD
Black Top / May '92 / CM / Direct / ADA.

BLACK VOCAL GROUPS 1935-44
CD _____ RFDCD 10
Country Routes / Feb '92 / Jazz Music / Hot Shot.

BLACK VOCAL GROUPS VOL.1
CD _____ DOCD 5340
Blues Document / May '95 / Swift / Jazz Music / Hot Shot.

BLACK VOCAL GROUPS VOL.2
CD _____ DOCD 5347
Blues Document / May '95 / Swift / Jazz Music / Hot Shot.

BLACKPOOL MECCA STORY, THE
Love factory: Laws, Eloise / Seven day lover: Fountain, James / Bet if you ask around: Velvet / Get all of my conscience: Lovelites / I need you: Jenkins, Dianne / Time passes by: Bynum, James / Make up your mind: Connelly, Earl / Payback's a drag: Smith Bros / Destination unkown: Delrey's Incorporated / Ladies choice (part 1): Franklin, Boby / Wash and wear love: Varnado, Lynn / Cashing in: Voices Of East Harlem / Woman is hard to understand: Mack, Jimmy / Alone with no love: Rock Candy / I don't know what foot to dance on: Tolliver, Kim / Tow-a-way love: Jenkins, Dianne / Lord what's happening to your people: Smith, Kenny / You made me this way: Vann, Ila / Don't care anymore: Mathis, Jodi / I can see him loving you: Anderson Brothers / Let our love grow higher: Cooper, Eula / You've been gone too long: Sexton, Ann
CD _____ GSCD 068
Goldmine / Oct '95 / Vital.

BLACKPOOL TOWER CENTENARY, THE
Tiger rag: Dixon, Reginald / Little girl: Dixon, Reginald / As time goes by: Dixon, Reginald / When I take my sugar to tea: Dixon, Reginald / Happy feat: Dixon, Reginald / Sabre dance: Dixon, Reginald / Symphonic poem: Dixon, Reginald / Samurin: Dixon, Reginald / I love the sunshine of your smile: Dixon, Reginald / When I grow too old to dream: Dixon, Reginald / Let's have another one: Dixon, Reginald / Oh you beautiful doll: Dixon, Reginald / Have you ever been lonely: Dixon, Reginald / Happy wanderer: Dixon, Reginald / Over the waves: Dixon, Reginald / Ma, he's making eyes at me: Dixon, Reginald / Maybe it's because I'm a Londoner: Dixon, Reginald / Blaydon races: Dixon, Reginald / Maybe it's because I'm a Londoner: Dixon, Reginald / I belong to Glasgow: Dixon, Reginald / I do like to be beside the seaside: Dixon, Reginald / Quicksteps: Kelsall, Phil / Mr. Sandman: Kelsall, Phil / Avalon: Kelsall, Phil / Crazy rhythm: Kelsall, Phil / Viennese waltz: Kelsall, Phil / Skater's waltz: Kelsall, Phil / Bossa novas: Kelsall, Phil / Girl from Ipanema: Kelsall, Phil / Destination unkown: Kelsall, Phil / Barn dance: Kelsall, Phil / Tip toe through the tulips: Kelsall, Phil / I don't know why (I just do): Kelsall, Phil / My mammy: Kelsall, Phil / Cha cha cha: Kelsall, Phil / Cherry pink and apple blossom white: Kelsall, Phil / For favor: Kelsall, Phil / Slow mumbas: Kelsall, Phil / He-ne's that rainy day: Kelsall, Phil / La Golondrina: Kelsall, Phil / St. Bernard's waltz: Kelsall, Phil / Bless 'em all: Kelsall, Phil / Band played on: Kelsall, Phil / Ash grove: Kelsall, Phil / Daisy bell: Kelsall, Phil / Mayfair quicksteps: Kelsall, Phil / Little white lies: Kelsall, Phil / Happy feet: Kelsall, Phil / It's just the time for dancing: Kelsall, Phil / Tango: Kelsall, Phil / La Comparsita: Kelsall, Phil / Jealousy: Kelsall, Phil / Nagasaki: Kelsall, Phil / Sweet Georgia Brown: Kelsall, Phil / Gay Gordons: Kelsall, Phil / Scotch mist: Kelsall, Phil / Rosetta: Barlow, Charles & His Orchestra / Apple for the teacher: Barlow, Charles & His Orchestra / Waltzes: Barlow, Charles & His Orchestra / Maria Elena: Barlow, Charles & His Orchestra / Sambas: Barlow, Charles & His Orchestra / Ei cumbanchero: Barlow, Charles & His Orchestra / Hawaiian samba: Barlow, Charles & His Orchestra / Cha chas: Barlow, Charles & His Orchestra / Something stupid: Barlow, Charles & His Orchestra / Swingin' shepherd blues: Barlow, Charles & His Orchestra / Paso dobles: Barlow, Charles & His Orchestra / For you, Rio Rita: Barlow, Charles & His Orchestra / March of the matadors: Barlow, Charles & His Orchestra / Annientamento: Barlow, Charles & His Orchestra / Foxtrots: Barlow, Charles & His Orchestra / Vilia: Barlow, Charles & His Orchestra / Red roses for a blue lady: Barlow, Charles & His Orchestra / Quaker girl: Turner, Ken & His Orchestra / Dollar princess: Turner, Ken & His Orchestra / Two-steps: Turner, Ken & His Orchestra / Semper fidelis: Turner, Ken & His Orchestra / Namur: Turner, Ken & His Orchestra / Saunters: Turner, Ken & His Orchestra / On my papa: Turner, Ken & His Orchestra / Trust in me: Turner, Ken & His Orchestra / Biberacher-valtzer: Turner, Ken & His Orchestra / Gavottes: Turner, Ken & His Orchestra / Country gardens: Turner, Ken & His Orchestra / I leave my heart in an English garden: Turner, Ken & His Orchestra / Way to the heart: Turner, Ken & His Orchestra / Tangos: Turner, Ken & His Orchestra / Midnight in Malaga: Turner, Ken & His Orchestra / Madame: Turner, Ken & His Orchestra / Modern waltz: Turner, Ken & His Orchestra / Peyton Place theme: Turner, Ken & His Orchestra / Manhattan: Turner, Ken & His Orchestra / Boo hoo: Dixon, Reginald
CD _____ CDDL 1272
Music For Pleasure / Mar '94 / EMI.

BLACKTHORN
CD _____ CDBALLAD 007
Outlet / Jan '95 / ADA / Duncans / CM / Ross / Direct / Koch.

BLAME IT ON THE BOOGIE
Blame it on the boogie: Jacksons / Boogie nights: Heatwave / Dance, dance, dance: Chic / He's the greatest dancer: Sister Sledge / Get down on it: Kool & The Gang

/ Oops upside your head: Gap Band / Play that funky music: Wild Cherry / Let's groove: Earth, Wind & Fire / Use it up and wear it out: Odyssey / Never can say goodbye: Gaynor, Gloria / That's the way (I like it): K.C. & The Sunshine Band / Lady Marmalade: Labelle, Patti / Night to remember: Shalamar / Hot stuff: Summer, Donna / Rock the boat: Hues Corporation / Funky town: Lipps Inc. / Boogie oogie oogie: Taste Of Honey / More, more, more: Andrea True Connection / Disco inferno: Trammps / I haven't stopped dancing yet: Gonzales
CD _____ 5155172
PolyGram TV / Jul '92 / PolyGram.

BLANK GENERATION
(4 CD)
CD _____ OG 333
Old Gold / Jun '92 / Carlton Home Entertainment.

BLANKET ON THE GROUND
CD _____ MU 5056
Musketeer / Oct '92 / Koch.

BLAS
CD _____ RTE 161CD
RTE / May '93 / ADA / Koch.

BLASTING CONCEPT VOL 1
CD _____ SST 013 CD
SST / May '93 / Plastic Head.

BLESS MY BONES
(Memphis Gospel Radio: The Fifties)
CD _____ CD 2063
Rounder / '88 / CM / Direct / ADA / Cadillac.

BLIND/FRAGMENT
CD _____ ASH 1.4
Ash International / Jan '95 / These / Kudos.

BLITZ 1
Shout: Tears For Fears / Lady writer: Dire Straits / Hot water: Level 42 / Come to Milton Keynes: Style Council / Now those days are gone: Bucks Fizz / Robin (The hooded man): Clannad / I will be your friend: Sade / I'm your man: Wham / Mad world: Tears For Fears / Twisting by the pool: Dire Straits / Sun goes down (living it up): Level 42 / Have you ever had it blue: Style Council / Land of make believe: Bucks Fizz / Harry's Game: Clannad / Hang on to your love: Sade / Different corner: Michael, George
CD _____ PWKS 530
Carlton Home Entertainment / Jul '89 / Carlton Home Entertainment.

BLITZ 2
CD _____ PWKS 519
Carlton Home Entertainment / Dec '88 / Carlton Home Entertainment.

BLOODSTAINS ON THE WALL
Bloodstains on the wall: Honey Boy / You better move on away from here: Honey Boy / Have you a match: Honey Boy / Uncle Sam blues: Pine Blues Pete / Woman acts funny: Pine Blues Pete / Going back to Mama: Pine Blues Pete / Got a letter this morning: Pine Blues Pete / Want to boogie woogie: Pine Blues Pete / Ride my new car with me: Williams, Big Joe / Dial 110 blues: Bledsoe, Country Jim / Hollywood boogie: Bledsoe, Country Jim / One thing my baby likes: Bledsoe, Country Jim / Stormin' and rainin': Bledsoe, Country Jim / I ate the wrong part: Little Temple / What a mistake: Little Temple / Mean and evil: Little Temple / Cool love: Little Temple / Black snake blues: McKinley, Pete / Cryin' for my baby: McKinley, Pete / Look-a-here boy: McKinley, Pete / Whistlin' blues: McKinley, Pete / Don't want me blues: McKinley, Pete / David's boogie: McKinley, Pete / Sail on little girl, sail on: McKinley, Pete
CD _____ CDCHD 576
Ace / Jul '94 / Pinnacle / Cadillac / Complete/Pinnacle.

BLOODY FUCKING HARDCORE
CD _____ MOK 97CD
Mokum / Mar '94 / Pinnacle.

BLOW BROTHER BLOW - 18 BLUES HARMONICA CLASSICS
(Charly Blues - Masterworks Vol. 32)
Good morning little school girl: Williamson, Sonny Boy / Sugar mama blues: Williamson, Sonny Boy / Juke: Little Walter / Blue light: Little Walter / Back track: Little Walter / Little Walter's boogie: Little Walter / Easy: Little Walter / Tiger man: Little Walter / Baker shop boogie: Little Walter / Take the life I live, I live the life I love: Little Walter / Wolf call boogie: Little Walter / Jukebox boogie: Little Walter / You tried to ruin me: Little Walter / Kissing at midnight: Little Walter / I ain't got your love: Little Walter / Signals of love: Little Walter / Ninety nine: Little Walter / Trust my baby: Little Walter
CD _____ CDBM 32
Charly / Jan '93 / Charly / THE / Cadillac.

BLOW MR. HORNSMAN
Jumpin' Jack / Super Special / Death rides / Run for your life / On the moon / Undertaker's burial / Roll On / Franco Nero / Leaving Rome / Ghost capturer / Nightmare / Judgement warrant / East of the River Nile / Harvest in the East / Va Va Voom / Broken Contract / Butter sefish / If you're ready

CD _____ CDTRL 257
Trojan / Mar '94 / Jetstar / Total/BMG.

BLOW MY BLUES AWAY VOL.1
CD _____ ARHCD 401
Arhoolie / Apr '95 / ADA / Direct /
Cadillac.

BLOW MY BLUES AWAY VOL.2
CD _____ ARHCD 402
Arhoolie / Apr '95 / ADA / Direct /
Cadillac.

BLOW THE MAN DOWN: SEA SONGS &
SHANTIES
Wild goose: *Killen, Louis* / Lovely Nancy:
Campbell, Ian / Black ball line: *MacColl,*
Ewan / Nightingale: *Tawney, Cyril* / Blow the
man down: *Corbett, Harry H.* / Heave away,
my Johnny: *Killen, Louis* / Lofty tall ship:
Larner, Sam / Row bullies row: *Campbell,*
Ian / Flying cloud: *Killen, Louis* / Fireship:
Tawney, Cyril / Tom's gone to Hilo: *Tawney,*
Cyril / General whale fishery: *Watersons*
/ Ship in distress: *Killen, Louis* / Lowlands
low: *Campbell, Ian* / Bold bandging: *Hart, Bob*
/ Hilo Johnny Brown: *Killen, Louis* / Bonny
ship the Diamond: *Lloyd, A.L.* / Bold Prin-
cess Royal: *Killen, Louis* / Billy boy: *Dav-*
enport, Bob / Windy old weather: *Roberts,*
A.V. 'Bob' / Bold Benjamin: *Tawney, Cyril* /
Hog eye man: *Campbell, Ian* / Goodbye fare
thee well: *Killen, Louis*
CD _____ TSCD 464
Topic / May '93 / Direct / ADA.

BLUE
CD _____ CDSTUMM 49
Mute / Oct '93 / Disc.

BLUE & SENTIMENTAL
CD _____ AVM 531
Avid / May '94 / Avid/BMG / Koch.

BLUE BOOGIE
(Boogie Woogie Stride & The Piano
Blues)
Boogie woogie stomp: *Ammons, Albert* /
Boogie woogie blues: *Ammons, Albert* /
Chicago in mind: *Ammons, Albert* / Bass
goin' crazy: *Ammons, Albert* / Blues part 1:
Lewis, Meade Lux / Honky tonk train blues:
Lewis, Meade Lux / Variations on a theme
(Part 1): *Lewis, Meade Lux* / Nineteen ways
of playing a chorus: *Lewis, Meade Lux* /
Bass on top: *Lewis, Meade Lux* / Two's and
fews: *Lewis, Meade Lux/Albert Ammons &*
Pete Johnson / Vine Street boogie: *Johnson,*
Pete / Barrelhouse breakdown: *Johnson,*
Pete / Mule walk (stomp): *Johnson, James*
P. / Blue note boogie: *Johnson, James P.* /
Call of the blues: *Johnson, James P.* /
World is waiting for the sunrise: *Benskin,*
Sammy / Jug head boogie: *Hodes, Art* /
Funny feathers: *Hodes, Art* / Father's gate-
way: *Hines, Earl* / Aunt Hagar's blues: *Ta-*
tum, Art
CD _____ BNZ 292
Blue Note / Apr '92 / EMI.

BLUE BRAZIL
(Blue Note In A Latin Groove)
Upa neguinho: *Paez, Luiz Arrunda* / Catav-
ento: *Costa, Alaide* / Berimbau: *Som, Man-*
drake / Vim de santana: *Quarteto Novo* /
Deus Brasileiro: *Ribiero, Perry & Bossa 3* /
Primitivo: *Milton Banana Trio* / Noa noa: *Mil-*
ton Banana Trio / Viola fora de moda: *Lobo,*
Edo / Nao me diga adeus: *Bossa 3* / Batu-
cada Sergiu: *Valle, Marcus* / Aldeia de
ogum: *Joyce* / Tudo que voce podia ser: *Lo*
Borges / Homenagem a mongo: *Som Tres*
/ Deixa isso pra la: *Soares, Elza* / Misturada:
Quarteto Novo / Rebe: *Deodato, Eumir* / Um
tema p'ro Simon: *Alf, Johnny* / Cala boca
menino: *Benatu, Joao* / Na dulce: *Brasil,*
Joao / Night and day: *Brasil, Victor Assis*
CD _____ CDP 8291962
Blue Note / Jun '94 / EMI.

BLUE BREAK BEATS
(You Gotta Hear Blue Note To Dig Def
Jam)
Grooving with Mr G: *Holmes, Richard*
'Groove' / Sookie sookie: *Green, Grant* /
Who's making love: *Donaldson, Lou* /
Weasil: *Byrd, Donald* / Kudu: *Henderson,*
Eddie / Harlem river drive: *Humphrey, Bobbi*
/ Blue juice: *McGriff, Jimmy* / Final come-
down: *Green, Grant* / Turtle walk: *Donald-*
son, Lou / Your love is too much: *Three*
Sounds / Black Jack: *Byrd, Donald* / Olillo-
qui Valley: *Hancock, Herbie*
CD _____ BNZ 288
Blue Note / Apr '92 / EMI.

BLUE BREAK BEATS VOL.2
Street lady: *Byrd, Donald* / Jasper country
man: *Humphrey, Bobbi* / Kumquat kids:
Henderson, Eddie / Higga boom: *Harris,*
Gene / Orange peel: *Wilson, Reuben* /
Worm: *McGriff, Jimmy* / Caterpillar: *Donald-*
son, Lou / Ain't it funky now: *Green, Grant*
/ Ummh: *Hutcherson, Bobby* / Good hu-
mour man: *Mitchell, Blue* / Beale Street:
Byrd, Donald / Viva Tirado: *Wilson, Gerald* /
Pot belly (Available on LP only): *Donaldson,*
Lou / Spinning wheel (Available on LP only):
Smith, Lonnie Liston / Phantom (Available
on LP only): *Pearson, Duke*
CD _____ BNZ 311
Blue Note / Jul '93 / EMI.

BLUE EYED BLUES
(Charly Blues - Masterworks Vol. 20)
Twenty three hours too long / Out on the
Water Coast / Five long years / I ain't got

you / Good morning little school girl / Little
red rooster (rehearsal) / Little red rooster /
Highway 49 / Wang dang doodle / I'm a
man / Train kept a rollin' / Jeff's blues /
Steeled blues / New york City blues / It's a
bloody life / I see a man downstairs
CD _____ CDBM 20
Charly / Apr '92 / Charly / THE / Cadillac.

BLUE EYES
(Music Of Elton John - 16 Instrumental
Hits)
CD _____ 5708574338165
Carlton Home Entertainment / Sep '94 /
Carlton Home Entertainment.

BLUE EYES CRYING IN THE RAIN
Blue eyes cryin' in the rain: *Drusky, Roy* /
Shine on Ruby mountain: *Rogers, Kenny* / I
didn't sleep a wink: *Nelson, Willie* / Daddy:
Fargo, Donna / Your song: *Lee, Johnny* /
Stop, look and listen: *Cline, Patsy* / Making
believe: *Wells, Kitty* / Slippin' away: *Fair-*
child, Barbara / Aberline: *Jennings, Waylon* /
Ruby, don't take your love to town: *Rogers,*
Kenny / I feel sorry for him: *Nelson, Willie* /
Where do we go from here: *Williams, Don* /
Turn the cards slowly: *Cline, Patsy* / Moon-
light gondolier: *Laine, Frankie* / From a jack
to a king: *Miller, Ned* / Elvira: *Rogers, Kenny*
/ Have I stayed away too long: *Ritter, Tex* /
Ghost: *Nelson, Willie* / 9,999,999 tears:
Baily, Razzy / Sticks and stones: *Fargo,*
Donna / Shake 'em up roll 'em: *Jackson,*
Stonewall / Heartaches by the number:
Mitchell, Guy / Homemade lies: *Rogers,*
Kenny / Hello walls: *Drusky, Roy* / I let my
mind wander: *Nelson, Willie*
CD _____ CDGRF 121
I ring / Feb '93 / Tring / Prism.

BLUE FOR YOU
CD _____ STACD 047
Stardust / Sep '94 / Carlton Home
Entertainment.

BLUE GRASS MUSIC
CD _____ 12181
Laserlight / May '94 / Target/BMG.

BLUE HAWAII
(A Vintage Anthology)
Little heaven of the seven seas: *Coral Is-*
landers / Moon of Manakoora: *Coral Island-*
ers / Blue Hawaii: *Crosby, Bing & Lani Mc-*
Intire & Hawaiians / Palace in paradise:
Crosby, Bing & Lani McIntire & Hawaiians /
Sweet Leilani: *Crosby, Bing & Lani McIntire*
& Hawaiians / Love dreams of Lula Lu: *Fer-*
era, Frank / For you: *Fillis, Len* / Goodbye
Hawaii: *Hall, Henry & The BBC Dance Or-*
chestra / Pua Kealoha: *Hoopii, Sol & Nov-*
elty Trio/Quartet / Weave a lei: *Hoopii, Sol*
& Novelty Trio/Quartet / Hawaiian paradise:
Iona, Andy & Islanders / Night is young:
Iona, Andy & Islanders/Cliff Edwards / St.
Louis blues: *Jim & Bob, the genial Hawai-*
ians / Tom, Tom: *Kanui & Lula* / Makalapua
O Kamakeaha: *Klein, Manny & Hawaiians* /
Hawaiian oaths (When you dream about
Hawaii/Drifting and dreaming/Aloma): *Men-*
delssohn, Felix & His Hawaiian Serenaders
/ I got rhythm: *Mendelssohn, Felix & His*
Hawaiian Serenaders / Sing me a song of
the Islands: *Mendelssohn, Felix & His Ha-*
waiian Serenaders / Song of the rose: *Men-*
delssohn, Felix & His Hawaiian Serenaders
/ Where the waters are blue: *Mendelssohn,*
Felix & His Hawaiian Serenaders / Palms of
paradise: *Johnny Kaonohi Pineapple & Na-*
tive Islanders / On the beach at Waikiki:
Sharpe, A.P. & Honolulu Hawaiians / O
muki, muki O: *Shaw, Al & Hawaiian Beach-*
combers / Lullaby of the leaves: *Smeck,*
Roy & Vita Trio / Paradise beside the sea:
Tabuer, Richard
CD _____ CDAJA 5121
Living Era / Feb '94 / Koch.

BLUE HIGHWAY
CD _____ BT 003CD
Black Top / Aug '94 / CM / Direct / ADA.

BLUE JAZZ
CD _____ AVM 530
Avid / Feb '94 / Avid/BMG / Koch.

BLUE JAZZ - LIVE IN MONTREUX
C.C. rider: *Thomas, Leon Band* / East St.
Louis blues: *Thomas, Leon Band* / Awak-
ening the leaves: *Lasser, Max Ark* / Where's
the mouse: *Lasser, Max Ark* / Turtle back
hill: *Lasser, Max Ark* / Morning breeze:
Doran, Christy / Integration: *Leimgruber,*
Urs & Dave Brennan / Baby, please don't
go: *Rogers, Roy* / Down in Mississippi: *Rog-*
ers, Roy
CD _____ BW 015
B&W / Oct '93 / New Note.

BLUE LADIES 1934-41
CD _____ DOCD 5327
Blues Document / Mar '95 / Swift / Jazz
Music / Hot Shot.

BLUE MONK
(Blue Note Plays Monk's Music)
Bemsha swing: *Peterson, Ralph Trio* /
Rocky mount: *Tracey, Stan Octet* / Monk's
dream: *Young, Larry* / Monk in wonderland:
Moncur, Grachan III / Blue Monk: *Tyner,*
McCoy & Bobby Hutcherson / Round mid-
night: *Evans, Gil* / Round about midnight:
Gonzales, Baba & Jimmy Smith / Epistro-
phy: *Taylor, Art* / Straight no chaser: *Three*
Sounds / Well you needn't: *Rubalcaba,*
Gonzalo / Hat & beard: *Dolphy, Eric*

CD _____ CDP 8354712
Blue Note / Oct '95 / EMI.

BLUE MOON
(20 Great Hits Of The Sixties)
What do you want to make those eyes at
me for: *Ford, Emile & The Checkmates* / Venus in blue jeans: *Wynter, Mark* / There
days that song again: *Miller, Gary* / Midnight in Moscow: *Ball, Kenny & His Jazzmen*
/ My old man's a dustman: *Donegan, Lon-*
nie / Warpaint: *Brook Brothers* / Ain't that
funny: *Justice, Jimmy* / Little bitty tear: *Miki*
& Griff / Be mine: *Fortune, Lance* / What a
crazy world we're living in: *Brown, Joe* / My
friend the sea: *Clark, Petula* / Charmaine:
Bachelors / Blue moon: *Marcels* / Them
there eyes: *Ford, Emile & The Checkmates*
/ Go away little girl: *Wynter, Mark* / All my
love: *Wilson, Jackie* / It only took a minute:
Brown, Joe / Have a drink on me: *Donegan,*
Lonnie / Romeo: *Clark, Petula* / Green
leaves of summer: *Ball, Kenny*
CD _____ TRTCD 101
TrueTrax / Oct '94 / THE.

BLUE 'N' GROOVY
(Blue Note Connects With The Good
Vibes)
Chili peppers: *Pearson, Duke* / On children:
Wilson, Jack / Hi-heel sneakers: *Mitchell,*
Blue / Senor blues: *Silver, Horace* / Meat
wave: *Turrentine, Stanley* / One ton tambou-
rines: *Wilkerson, Don* / Sidewinder: *Morgan,*
Lee / Cantaloupe island: *Hancock, Herbie* /
Ping pong: *Blakey, Art* / True blue: *Brooks,*
Tina / Jeannine: *Byrd, Donald* / My favourite
things: *Green, Grant* / 8/4 Beat: *Hutcher-*
son, Bobby / Tom Thumb: *Shorter, Wayne*
CD _____ BN7 300
Blue Note / Oct '92 / EMI.

BLUE NOTE BOX, THE
(4CD Set)
Blue train: *Coltrane, John* / Maiden voyage:
Hancock, Herbie / Cristo redentor: *Byrd,*
Donald / Moanin': *Blakey, Art & The Jazz*
Messengers / Blues walk: *Donaldson, Lou* /
Song for my father: *Silver, Horace* / Back at
the Chicken Shack: *Smith, Jimmy* / Chitlins
con carne: *Burrell, Kenny* / Sidewinder:
Morgan, Lee / Senor blues: *Silver, Horace* /
Decision: *Rollins, Sonny* / Three o'clock in
the morning: *Gordon, Dexter* / Blues march:
Blakey, Art / Wadin': *Parlan, Horace* / Rum-
proller: *Morgan, Lee* / Somethin' else: *Ad-*
derley, Cannonball / Blue bossa: *Hender-*
son, Joe / Watermelon man: *Hancock,*
Herbie / Hold on, I'm comin': *Wilson, Reu-*
ben / It's your thing: *Green, Grant* / Scorpion: *Donaldson, Lou* / Village lee: *Patton,*
John / Spooky: *Turrentine, Stanley* / Dancin'
in an easy groove: *Smith, Lonnie Liston* /
You want me to stop loving you: *Turrentine,*
Stanley / Do like Eddie: *Scofield, John* /
Blue monk: *Tyner, McCoy & Bobby Hutch-*
erson / Immediate no telling: *Kiane, Tim* / I
waited for you: *Jackson, Javon* / Take the
D flat train: *Hays, Kevin* / One of another
kind: *Green, Benny* / Reflections: *Fortune,*
Sonny / Donna Lee: *Rubalcaba, Gonzalo* /
Rounders mood: *Lovano, Joe* / I love Paris:
Terrasson, Jacky
CD Set _____ CDP 8360542
Blue Note / Nov '95 / EMI.

BLUE RIBBON BLUEGRASS
CD _____ AN 11CD
Rounder / Jan '94 / CM / Direct / ADA /
Cadillac.

BLUE-EYED RHYTHM AND BLUES
CD _____ CDRB 25
Charly / Aug '95 / Charly / THE / Cadillac.

BLUEBEAT, SKA & REGGAE
REVOLUTION
CD _____ SEECD 319
See For Miles/C5 / May '91 / Pinnacle.

BLUEBEAT, SKA & REGGAE
REVOLUTION VOL.2
CD _____ SEECD 353
See For Miles/C5 / Sep '92 / Pinnacle.

BLUEBELLS
CD _____ CMPCD 76
CMP / Nov '92 / Vital/SAM.

BLUEBERRY HILL - 40 COUNTRY &
LIVERPOOL FAVOURITES
CD _____ SOW 505
Soundsrite / Jun '93 / THE / Target/BMG.

BLUEFUNKERS CHAPTER 1
(Pitchers, Leftfielders & Flipsiders)
CD _____ ZEN 002CD
Indochina / Jan '95 / Pinnacle.

BLUEGRASS ALBUM VOL.4
Age / Cheyenne / Cora is gone / Old home
town / Talk it all over with him / Head over
heels / Nobody loves me / When you are
lonely / I might take you back again / Lonesome wind blues
CD _____ ROUCD 0210
Rounder / Feb '95 / CM / Direct / ADA /
Cadillac.

BLUEGRASS ALBUM VOL.5
(Sweet Sunny South)
Rock hearts / Big black train / Thinking
about you / Out in the cold war / On the old
Kentucky shore / Preaching, praying, singing / Someone took my place with you /
Foggy mountain rock / My home's across
the Blue Ridge Mountains / Along about
daybreak / Sweet sunny South

CD _____ ROUNDER 0240CD
Rounder / '89 / CM / Direct / ADA / Cadillac.

BLUEGRASS AT NEWPORT
CD _____ VCD 121
Vanguard / Oct '95 / Complete/Pinnacle /
Discovery.

BLUEGRASS BREAKDOWN
CD _____ VCD 77006
Vanguard / Oct '95 / Complete/Pinnacle /
Discovery.

BLUEGRASS COMPACT DISC
CD _____ CD 11502
Rounder / '88 / CM / Direct / ADA /
Cadillac.

BLUEGRASS COMPACT DISC VOL.2
CD _____ CD 11516
Rounder / '88 / CM / Direct / ADA /
Cadillac.

BLUEGRASS SPECTACULAR
CD _____ CTS 55424
Country Stars / Sep '94 / Target/BMG.

BLUEGRASS: THE WORLD'S GREATEST
SHOW
When somebody wants to leave: *Seldom*
Scene / House of the rising sun: *Seldom*
Scene / Hickory wind: *Seldom Scene* / Wild
Kentucky road: *Seldom Scene* / Alabama
jubilee: *Seldom Scene* / Old train: *Seldom*
Scene / Through the bottom of the glass:
Seldom Scene / Out among the stars: *Sel-*
dom Scene / Two little boys: *Country Gen-*
tlemen / Today has been a lonesome day:
Country Gentlemen / Bringing Mary home:
Country Gentlemen / I'll stay around: *Orig-*
inal New South / I'm not broke, but I'm
badly bent: *Original New South* / Fireball:
Original New South / Why don't you tell me
so: *Original New South* / Freeborn man:
Original New South / Train 45: *Original New*
South / Fox on the run: *Country Gentlemen*
/ Waiting for the boys to come home: *Coun-*
try Gentlemen / Ages and ages ago: *Coun-*
try Gentlemen / Saturday night at the Opry:
Country Gentlemen / Feel like my time ain't
long: *Country Gentlemen*
CD _____ SH CD 2201
Sugarhill / Mar '89 / Roots / CM / ADA /
Direct.

BLUES & SOUL COLLECTION: MY GUY
CD _____ MU 5054
Musketeer / Oct '92 / Koch.

BLUES 60'S
I have a dream: *Hancock, Herbie* / Cease
the bombing: *Green, Grant* / Acid, pot &
pills: *Silver, Horace* / Psychedelic: *Morgan,*
Lee / Black heroes: *Hutcherson, Bobby* /
There is the bomb: *Cherry, Don* / Black
rhythm happening: *Gale, Eddie* / Watts
happening: *Jazz Crusaders* / Blowing in the
wind: *Turrentine, Stanley* / I wish I knew
the world I'd feel to be free: *Taylor, Billy* / Say it
loud (I'm black and I'm proud): *Donaldson,*
Lou
CD _____ CDP 8354720
Blue Note / Oct '95 / EMI.

BLUES ALBUM, THE
Mannish boy: *Waters, Muddy* / Boom
boom: *Hooker, John Lee* / Crossroads:
Cream / When love comes to town: *U2 &*
B.B. King / Mustang Sally: *Guy, Buddy* /
Born under a bad sign: *King, Albert* / Need
your love so bad: *Fleetwood Mac* / Some-
where down the crazy river: *Robertson,*
Robbie / Black magic woman: *Santana* /
Piece of my heart: *Franklin, Erma* / Dixie
chicken: *Little Feat* / On the road again:
Canned Heat / Smokestack lightnin': *How-*
lin' Wolf / I'd rather go blind: *James, Etta* /
Try a little tenderness: *Commitments* / Right
next door (because of me): *Cray, Robert*
Band / Fade to black: *Dire Straits* / Nineties
blues: *Rea, Chris* / Bell bottom blues: *Derek*
& The Dominoes / Cocaine: *Cale, J.J.* / Still
got the blues: *Moore, Gary* / Hunter: *Free* /
Thrill is gone: *King, B.B.* / Hoochie coochie
man: *Waters, Muddy* / Muddy waters blues
(acoustic version): *Rodgers, Paul* / I'm a
king bee: *Harpo, Slim* / I'm in the mood:
Hooker, John Lee / Dust my broom: *James,*
Elmore / Help me: *Williamson, Sonny Boy* /
Love in vain: *Johnson, Robert* / I'm a man:
Diddley, Bo / My head's in Mississippi: *ZZ*
Top / Shake your moneymaker: *Fleetwood*
Mac / Shame, shame, shame: *Winter,*
Johnny / I'm leaving you (commit a crime):
Vaughan, Stevie Ray / Sloop blues: *Berry,*
Chuck / My baby: *Fabulous Thunderbirds* /
All your love: *Mayall, John & The Bluesbreakers* / You shook
me: *Beck, Jeff* / Greeny: *Blues Breakers* /
Little red rooster: *Howlin' Wolf*
CD Set _____ VTDCD 54
Virgin / Jun '95 / EMI.

BLUES AND BOOGIE - EXPLOSION
CD _____ BLR 84003
L&R / May '91 / New Note.

BLUES ANYTIME VOL.1
(An Anthology Of British Blues)
I'm your witch doctor / Snake drive / Ain't
gonna cry no more / I tried / Tribute to El-
more / I feel so good / Telephone blues /
You don't love me / West coast idea / Ain't
seen no whisky / Flapjacks / Cold blooded
woman
CD _____ CDIMM 008
Immediate / Nov '93 / Charly / Target/BMG.

BLUES AT NEWPORT 1959-64
CD _____ VCD 115
Vanguard / Oct '95 / Complete/Pinnacle / Discovery.

BLUES AT NEWPORT 1963
CD _____ 662248
Vanguard / Jan '94 / Complete/Pinnacle / Discovery.

BLUES AT NEWPORT 1964
CD Set _____ 662247
Vanguard / Jan '94 / Complete/Pinnacle / Discovery.

BLUES AT XMAS VOL.3
CD _____ ICHCD 1173
Ichiban / Oct '94 / Koch.

BLUES BALLADS VOL.2
CD _____ 01434161
Arcade / May '90 / Sony / Grapevine.

BLUES BRITANNIA
CD _____ BRGCD 07CD
Music Maker / Jul '94 / Grapevine / ADA.

BLUES BROTHER, SOUL SISTER - BEST OF
(2CD/MC Set)
Boom boom: Hooker, John Lee / Take a little pie: Franklin, Erma / Soul man: Sam & Dave / I'd rather go blind: James, Etta / Green onions: Booker T & The MG's / Think: Franklin, Aretha / Harlem shuffle: Bob & Earl / Take me to the river: Green, Al / Mannish boy: Waters, Muddy / Rescue me: Fontella Bass / In the midnight hour: Pickett, Wilson / Knock on wood: Floyd, Eddie / Stormy monday: Little Milton / Drift away: Gray, Dobie / Need your love so bad: Fleetwood Mac / I'm in the mood: Hooker, John Lee / It's a man's man's man's world: Brown, James / Born under a bad sign: King, Albert / Tired of being alone: Green, Al / Night time is the right time: Turner, Ike & Tina / I'm a roadrunner: Walker, Junior & The All Stars / I just want to make love to you: James, Etta / Tell it like it is: Neville, Aaron / High heeled sneakers: Tucker, Tommy / I'll take you there: Staple Singers / Private number: Bell, William / Little red rooster: Howlin' Wolf / Oh no not my baby: Brown, Maxine / I put a spell on you: Simone, Nina / When a man loves a woman: Sledge, Percy / Respect: Franklin, Aretha / Thrill has gone: King, B.B. / Sweet soul music: Conley, Arthur / What'd I say: Charles, Ray / Stay with me baby: Ellison, Lorraine / Who's that lady: Isley Brothers / Got my mojo working: Waters, Muddy / (Sittin' on) The dock of the bay: Redding, Otis / B.A.B.Y: Thomas, Carla / My guy: Wells, Mary / Misty blue: Moore, Misty / How sweet it is: Gaye, Marvin / Dancing in the street: Martha & The Vandellas / Going to a go go: Robinson, Smokey & The Miracles / Uptight: Wonder, Stevie / Midnight train to Georgia: Knight, Gladys
CD Set _____ DINCD 115
Dino / Nov '95 / Pinnacle / 3MV.

BLUES BROTHER, SOUL SISTER VOL.3
I got you (I feel good): Brown, James / Respect: Franklin, Aretha / Ain't nobody home: King, B.B. / Sweet soul music: Conley, Arthur / Midnight train to Georgia: Knight, Gladys / Mustang Sally: Pickett, Wilson / Warm and tender love: Sledge, Percy / Smokestack lightnin': Howlin' Wolf / What'd I say: Charles, Ray / Nutbush city limits: Turner, Ike & Tina / That lady: Isley Brothers / Got my mojo working: Waters, Muddy / I'm still in love with you: Green, Al / B-A-B-Y: Thomas, Carla / My girl: Temptations / My guy: Wells, Mary / Serves you right to suffer: Hooker, John Lee / (Sittin' on) the dock of the bay: Moore, Dorothy
CD _____ DINCD 85
Dino / Apr '94 / Pinnacle / 3MV.

BLUES BUSTERS VOL.1
CD _____ MSA 4
Munich / Oct '93 / CM / ADA / Greensleeves / Direct.

BLUES BUSTERS VOL.2
CD _____ MSA 008CD
Munich / Apr '94 / CM / ADA / Greensleeves / Direct.

BLUES COCKTAIL PARTY
CD _____ BT 1066CD
Black Top / Mar '92 / CM / Direct / ADA.

BLUES COLLECTION
(3CD/MC Set)
CD Set _____ TBXCD 508
TrueTrax / Jan '96 / THE.

BLUES DELUXE
Clouds in my heart: Blues Deluxe / Hey bartender: Taylor, Koko / Wang dang doodle: Dixon, Willie / Sweet home Chicago: Brooks, Lonnie / Don't throw your love on me so strong: Seals, Son / You big ugly, need a friend: Young, Mighty Joe
CD _____ XRTCD 9301
Alligator / Oct '93 / Direct / ADA.

BLUES EXPERIENCE
When love comes to town: U2 / Still got the blues (for you): Moore, Gary / Somewhere down the crazy river: Robertson, Robbie / Black magic woman: Fleetwood Mac / I'd rather go blind: Chicken Shack / Crossroads: Cream / Cocaine: Cale, J.J. / Please don't let me be misunderstood: Cocker, Joe

---

/ Ronettes: Cray, Robert Band / Try a little tenderness: Commitments / She's not there: Santana / On the road again: Canned Heat / Nineties blues: Rea, Chris / Fade to black: Dire Straits / Stormy windows: White, Tony Joe / Walking the dog: Thomas, Rufus / Who do you love: Thorogood, George / Red house: Hendrix, Jimi
CD _____ 5162282
PolyGram TV / Jun '93 / PolyGram.

BLUES EXPERIENCE VOL.1
CD _____ CDRR 301
Request / May '92 / Jazz Music.

BLUES FIREWORKS
CD _____ CAD 465
Blues Collection / Apr '95 / Discovery.

BLUES FOR LOVERS
CD _____ DCD 5272
Kenwest / Nov '92 / THE.

BLUES FOR YOU
CD _____ ALSCD 7958
Alligator / Jul '89 / Direct / ADA.

BLUES FROM DOLPHIN'S OF HOLLYWOOD
Darkest hour: Crayton, Pee Wee / Forgive me: Crayton, Pee Wee / Crying and walking: Crayton, Pee Wee / Pappy's blues: Crayton, Pee Wee / Baby, pat the floor: Crayton, Pee Wee / I'm your prisoner: Crayton, Pee Wee / Lovin' John: Crayton, Pee Wee / Fillmore Street blues: Crayton, Pee Wee / Boogie bop: Crayton, Pee Wee / You can't bring me down: Little Caesar / Cadillac baby: Little Caesar / WDIA station ID: Mayfield, Percy / Look the whole world over: Mayfield, Percy / Monkey song: Mayfield, Percy / Treat me like I treat you: Mayfield, Percy / My country girl: Mayfield, Percy / Worried life blues: Mayfield, Percy / Pete's boogie: Mayfield, Percy / Big family blues: Witherspoon, Jimmy / Cain River blues: Witherspoon, Jimmy / Teenage party: Witherspoon, Jimmy / S.K. blues: Witherspoon, Jimmy / Never know when a woman changes her mind: Dixon, Floyd / Oh baby: Dixon, Floyd / Cadillac funeral: Harris, Peppermint
CD _____ CDCHD 357
Ace / Nov '91 / Pinnacle / Cadillac / Complete/Pinnacle.

BLUES GIANTS
CD _____ MATCD 272
Castle / Apr '93 / BMG.

BLUES GIANTS IN CONCERT
Blues everywhere: Memphis Slim / John Henry: Memphis Slim & Willie Dixon / Captain captain: Waters, Muddy / Catfish blues: Waters, Muddy / In the city: Waters, Muddy / I feel like cryin': Waters, Muddy / Your love for me is true: Williamson, Sonny Boy / Don't misuse me: Williamson, Sonny Boy / I'm getting tired: Williamson, Sonny Boy / Getting down slow: Spann, Otis / Careless love: Johnson, Lonnie / C.C. rider: Johnson, Lonnie / T.B. blues: Spivey, Victoria / Big roll blues: Williams, Big Joe / Back in the bottom: Williams, Big Joe / Baby, please don't go: Williams, Big Joe
CD _____ 92052
Act / Aug '94 / New Note.

BLUES GOLD COLLECTION
(2CD Set)
CD Set _____ D2CD 4008
Deja Vu / Jun '95 / THE.

BLUES GUITAR
CD _____ MATCD 271
Castle / Apr '93 / BMG.

BLUES GUITAR BLASTERS
After hours: Nolan, Jimmy / Killing floor: King, Albert / You threw your love on me too strong: King, Albert / Talkin' woman: Fulson, Lowell / Everytime it rains: Fulson, Lowell / Early in the morning: King, B.B. / Talkin' the blues: King, B.B. / Dust my blues: James, Elmore / Elmo's shuffle: James, Elmore / Jumpin' in the heart of town: Thomas, Lafayette / Certainly all: Guitar Slim / Things that I used to do: Guitar Slim / Twistin' the strings: Turner, Ike / Three hours past midnight: Watson, Johnny 'Guitar' / Twinky: Crayton, Pee Wee / Mistreated so bad: Crayton, Pee Wee / Hey hey baby: Walker, T-Bone / I had a good girl: Hooker, John Lee
CD _____ CDCH 232
Ace / Jan '88 / Pinnacle / Cadillac / Complete/Pinnacle.

BLUES GUITAR HEROES
CD _____ TRTCD 154
TrueTrax / Dec '94 / THE.

BLUES HARMONICA SPOTLIGHT
CD _____ BT 1083CD
Black Top / Jan '93 / CM / Direct / ADA.

BLUES HARP BOOGIE
CD _____ MCCD 124
Music Club / Jan '92 / Disc / THE / CM.

BLUES HOLLERIN' BOOGIE
Help: Scott, Isaac / Hoochie coochie man: Waters, Muddy / I wouldn't treat a dog (the way you treated me): Big Twist & The Mellow Fellows / Just a dream: Arnold, Billy Boy & Tony McPhee / Never let me go: Tucker, Tommy / Wandering blues: Hooker, John Lee / Lowdown and funky: Gaines,

---

Ropy & The Crusaders / Sorry: Benton, Buster & Carey Bell / Oh what a feeling: Ricks, Jimmy & The Ravens / War is starting: Hopkins, Lightnin' / That's all right: Turner, Titus / Cut you loose: Smith, Byther / Whammy: Hawkins, Screamin' Jay / Don't you feel my leg: Muldaur, Maria / Hey hey: Turner, Ike & Jimmy Thomas / Insane asylum: Baldry, Long John & Kathi McDonald / Trouble all my days: Red, Louisiana / Touch of your love: Sharpville, Todd / Mayor Daley's blues: Clearwater, Eddy / Walk right in: Musselwhite, Charlie
CD _____ MCCD 173
MCI / Sep '94 / Disc / THE.

BLUES IN JAZZ, THE
CD _____ CD 56002
Jazz Roots / Aug '94 / Target/BMG.

BLUES IN THE MISSISSIPPI NIGHT
Life is like that / Pitied every groan / My black name / Ratty ratty section / Have you ever been Nashville / Stagger Lee / Berta / I ain't got long / Don't you hear your poor Mother calling / Piano blues / Another man done gone / Piano blues (no 2)
CD _____ NEXCD 122
Sequel / Apr '90 / BMG.

BLUES IN THE MISSISSIPPI NIGHT.
CD _____ RCD 10206
Rykodisc / Feb '92 / Vital / ADA.

BLUES IN THE NIGHT
CD _____ 79779
Laserlight / Jan '93 / Target/BMG.

BLUES IN THE NIGHT NO.1
(Newport Jazz Festival 1958 July 3rd-6th)
CD _____ NCD 8815
Phontastic / '93 / Wellard / Jazz Music / Cadillac.

BLUES IN THE NIGHT NO.2
(Newport Jazz Festival 1958 July 3rd-6th)
CD _____ NCD 8816
Phontastic / '93 / Wellard / Jazz Music / Cadillac.

BLUES IS A TRAMP - LIVE PARADISO
CD Set _____ TRCD 99122
Tramp / Nov '93 / Direct / ADA / CM.

BLUES JAM IN CHICAGO
Watch out / Ooh baby / South Indiana / Last night / Red hot jam / I'm worried / I held my baby last night / Madison blues / I can't hold out / I need your love / I got the blues / World's in a tangle / Talk with you / Like it this way / Someday soon baby / Hungry country girl / Black Jack blues / Rockin' boogie / Sugar mama / Homework
CD _____ 4805272
Columbia / May '95 / Sony.

BLUES LEGENDS
CD Set _____ MBSCD 015
Castle / Mar '93 / BMG.

BLUES LEGENDS
Baby, won't you please come home: Smith, Bessie / Milkcow's calf blues: Johnson, Robert / Matchbox blues: Jefferson, Blind Lemon / Ain't no tellin': Hurt, Mississippi John / Lord I just can't keep from crying: Nelson, Willie / Low down St. Louis blues: Johnson, Lonnie / Stormy night blues: Carr, Leroy / I believe I'll make a change: White, Joshua / C.C. rider: Leadbelly / Truckin my blues away: Fuller, Blind Boy / Spreadin snake blues: Broonzy, Big Bill / Nothin in ramblin: Memphis Minnie / You can't get that stuff no more: Tampa Red
CD _____ CDCD 1028
Charly / Mar '93 / Charly / THE / Cadillac.

BLUES LEGENDS
CD Set _____ MCBX 009
Music Club / Apr '94 / Disc / THE / CM.

BLUES LEGENDS VOL. 1
CD _____ 901592
FM / May '91 / Sony.

BLUES LEGENDS VOL. 2
CD _____ 901602
FM / May '91 / Sony.

BLUES LEGENDS VOL. 3
CD _____ 901612
FM / May '91 / Sony.

BLUES MASTERS
Ain't nobody's business: Witherspoon, Jimmy / T-bone blues: Walker, T-Bone / Laundromat blues: King, Albert / Rollin' and tumblin': Leroy, Baby Face / All your love (I miss loving): Rush, Otis / Little by little: Wells, Junior / Evening son: Shines, Johnny / Short haired woman: Hopkins, Lightnin' / Freeze: Collins, Albert / Stumble: King, Freddie / Flood down in Texas: Vaughan, Stevie Ray / Sugar coated love: Lazy Lester / Steady: McCain, Jerry / Got love if you want it: Harpo, Slim / Shake, rattle and roll: Turner, Big Joe / Hoy hoy: Jones, Little Johnny / Hello little boy: Brown, Ruth / I'm a woman: Taylor, Koko / Master change: Collins, Albert / Mojo boogie: Winter, Johnny / Blue Flames / Bear cat: Thomas, Rufus
CD _____ 8122713682
Atlantic / Mar '94 / Warner Music.

BLUES MASTERS
Can't get you off my mind: Jones, Lloyd / Kansas city monarch: Earl, Ronnie / Too proud: Mighty Sam / Bring it on home: MacLeod, Doug / Feel like going home: Lucas, Robert / Down in Mississippi: Evans, Terry / Feets out in the hallway: Beard, Joe / I'm so lonely: Mighty Sam / Moonshine 2: Lucas, Robert
CD _____ AQCD 1034
Audioquest / Feb '96 / New Note.

BLUES MISTLETOE & SANTA'S LITTLE HELPER
CD _____ BT 1122CD
Black Top / Oct '95 / CM / Direct / ADA.

BLUES NOTES - AND BLACK
(A Blues Survey From 1920-1960)
CD _____ PHONTNCD 8827
Phontastic / '93 / Wellard / Jazz Music / Cadillac.

BLUES ROOTS
CD _____ 269 618 2
Tomato / Feb '89 / Vital.

BLUES ROUND MIDNIGHT
Three o'clock blues: Davis, Larry / Old man blues: Copeland, Johnny / Something about you: Davis, Larry / Blues around midnight: Fulson, Lowell / Love will lead you right: Walker, T-Bone / You're breaking my heart: King, B.B. / You're mine: King, B.B. / Shattered dreams: Fulson, Lowell / T-99 Blues (Available on CD and cassette only): Nelson, Jimmy 'T-99' / I'm wonderin' and wonderin' (Available on CD and cassette only): Charles, Ray / Second hand fool: Nelson, Jimmy 'T-99' / Quit hanging around: King, Saunders / Dragnet blues: Ervin, Frankie / Crazy with the blues: Jones, Marti / Love is here to stay: Holden, Lorenzo / I need somebody: Witherspoon, Jimmy / Gee baby ain't I good to you: Witherspoon, Jimmy / Picture of you: Green, Vivianne / Playing the numbers: Ervin, Frankie / It just wasn't true: Jones, Marl
CD _____ CDCH 235
Ace / Apr '88 / Pinnacle / Cadillac / Complete/Pinnacle.

BLUES, THE
Give me a break: Cox, Ida / Nothin' but blues: Gibson, Cleo & Her Hot Three / Barrel house blues: Henderson, Rosa / Midnight Mama: Hereford, Frances & The Levee Senders / Kansas city blues: Memphis Jug Band / Prove it on me blues: Rainey, Ma / Be on your merry way: Ringgold, Issie / Blue yodel no. 9: Rodgers, Jimmie & Louis & Lil Armstrong / Nobody knows you when you're down and out: Smith, Bessie / Jenny's ball: Smith, Mamie / Moaning the blues: Spivey, Victoria / Organ grinder: Taylor, Eva / Get up off your knees: Waters, Ethel & Clarence Williams / I've got what it takes: Webster, Margaret & Clarence Williams / That thing's done been put on me: Whitmire, Margaret / He used to be your man: Wilson, Lena & The Nubian Five
CD _____ RPCD 630
Robert Parker Jazz / Jan '94 / Conifer.

BLUES, THE
(2CD Set)
CD Set _____ R2CD 4008
Deja Vu / Jan '96 / THE.

BLUES VOL.1
(3CD Set)
CD _____ CPSC 303
Charly / May '95 / Charly / THE / Cadillac.

BLUES VOL.2
(3CD Set)
CD _____ CPSC 304
Charly / May '95 / Charly / THE / Cadillac.

BLUES VOLUME 1
CD _____ 74321244592
RCA / Dec '94 / BMG.

BLUES WITH A DIFFERENCE
CD _____ CDS 4
Rounder / '88 / CM / Direct / ADA / Cadillac.

BLUES WITH A FEELING
CD Set _____ VCD 277005
Vanguard / Oct '95 / Complete/Pinnacle / Discovery.

BLUES WITH THE GIRLS
CD _____ 157582
Blues Collection / Feb '93 / Discovery.

BLUESIANA HOT SAUCE
CD _____ SHCD 5009
Shanachie / Apr '94 / Koch / ADA / Greensleeves.

BLUESIANA HURRICANE
CD _____ SHCD 5014
Shanachie / Oct '95 / Koch / ADA / Greensleeves.

BLUESVILLE VOL. 1
Judge Boushay blues: Lewis, Furry / Country girl blues: Memphis Willie B / Big road blues: Douglas, K.C. / Levee camp blues: Williams, Big Joe / Catfish: Smith, Robert Curtis / San Quentin blues: Maiden, Sidney / Big fat mama: Walton, Wade / Grievin' me: Franklin, Pete / Dyin' crapshooters blues: McTell, Blind Willie / Fine booze and heavy dues: Johnson, Lonnie / Blues before sunrise: Blackwell, Scrapper / You got to move:

Davis, Rev. Gary / Brown skin woman: *Eaglin, Snooks* / Pawn shop: *McGhee, Brownie & Sonny Terry* / T-model blues: *Hopkins, Lightnin'* / You is one black rat: *Quattlebaum, Doug* / Highway 61 (Available on CD and cassette only): *Lewis, Furry* / Hand me down baby (Available on CD and cassette only): *Maiden, Sidney* / Alberta (Available on CD and cassette only): *Eaglin, Snooks* / See what you have done (Available on CD and cassette only): *Tate, Baby* / Goin' where the moon crosses the yellow dog (Available on CD and cassette only): *Blackwell, Scrapper*
CD _____ **CDCH 247**
Ace / Jun '88 / Pinnacle / Cadillac / Complete/Pinnacle.

BLUESVILLE VOL. 2
Train done gone: *Kirkland, Eddie* / Down on my knees: *Kirkland, Eddie* / Homesick's blues: *Homesick James* / Stones in my passway: *Homesick James* / Rack 'em back Jack: *Memphis Slim* / Happy blues for John Glenn: *Hopkins, Lightnin'* / Devil jumped the black man: *Hopkins, Lightnin'* / My baby done gone: *Terry, Sonny* / School time: *Arnold, Billy Boy* / Big legged woman: *Johnson, Lonnie* / I have to worry: *King Curtis* / Calcutta: *Lewis, Roosevelt* / Show down: *Lucas, Buddy* / How long, how long blues: *Witherspoon, Jimmy* / You better cut that out (Available on CD and cassette only): *Arnold, Billy Boy* / Drivin' wheel (Available on CD and cassette only): *Witherspoon, Jimmy* / It's a lonesome old world (Available on CD and cassette only): *Witherspoon, Jimmy* / Jolly roll baker (Available on CD and cassette only): *Johnson, Lonnie*
CD _____ **CDCH 250**
Ace / Oct '88 / Pinnacle / Cadillac / Complete/Pinnacle.

BOAT TO PROGRESS
CD _____ **GRELCD 602**
Greensleeves / May '90 / Total/BMG / Jetstar / SRD.

BOB MARLEY 50TH ANNIVERSARY
CD Set _____ **CDTAL 800**
Trojan / Jan '96 / Jetstar / Total/BMG.

BODY AND SOUL
CD _____ **YDG 74611**
Yesterday's Gold / Feb '93 / Target/BMG.

BODY BEATS
CD _____ **DCD 5414**
Disky / Oct '94 / THE / BMG / Discovery / Pinnacle.

BODY RAPTURES VOL.3
CD _____ **CDZOT 110**
Zoth Ommog / Sep '94 / Plastic Head.

BOGLE AT LARGE
CD _____ **EWCD 01**
Teams / Oct '92 / Jetstar.

BOGLE FEVER
CD _____ **WRCD 003**
World / Sep '94 / Jetstar / Total/BMG.

BOLERO - THE COOL COMPILATION
Popurri de boleros - si mi comprendieras: *Faz, Roberto Conjunto* / Como pienso en ti: *Alonso Y Los Bocucos* / Amor fugaz: *More, Benny Y Su Orquesta* / A mi manera (Comme d'habitude): *Alvarez, Adalberto & Su Son* / Si me pudieras querer: *Faz, Roberto Con Conjunto Casino* / Frenesi: *Gomez, Tito Con Su Conjunto* / Tu mi adoracion: *Faz, Roberto Con Conjunto Casino* / Me falabas tu: *Alonso, Pacho Y Su Orquestra* / Popurri de boleros - irremodulablemente solo: *Faz, Roberto Conjunto*
CD _____ **PSCCD 1008**
Pure Sounds From Cuba / Feb '95 / Henry Hadaway Organisation / THE.

BOLLOCKS TO CHRISTMAS
Christmas time again: *Bad Manners* / Christmas is really fantastic: *Sidebottom, Frank* / Step into Christmas: *Business* / Snowman: *Anti Nowhere League* / Blue Christmas: *Frantic Flintstones* / Merry Christmas everybody: *4 Skins* / Oh come all ye faithful: *Sidebottom, Frank* / Jingle bells: *Judge Dread* / Hey Santa: *UK Subs* / Twelve days of Christmas: *Splodge* / Stuff the turkey: *Alien Sex Fiend* / Another Christmas: *Yobs* / I wish it could be Christmas: *Sidebottom, Frank* / Jingle bells (2): *Mauc Lads* / Christmas in Dreadland: *Judge Dread* / Turkey stomp: *Hotknives* / Santa bring my baby back: *Frantic Flintstones* / Auld Lang Syne: *UK Subs* / Ch-ri-s-t-m-a-s: *Yobs* / White Christmas: *Gonads* / Drinking and driving: *Business* / Christmas medley: *Sidebottom, Frank* / White Christmas (live): *Stiff Little Fingers*
CD _____ **DOJOCD 204**
Dojo / Dec '94 / BMG.

BOMBA
CD _____ **MCD 71355**
Monitor / Jun '93 / CM.

BOMBARDES ET BINIOUS DE BRETAGNE
CD _____ **ARN 64243**
Arion / Aug '93 / Discovery / ADA.

BONANZA SKA
CD _____ **CDTRL 309**
Trojan / Mar '94 / Jetstar / Total/BMG.

BONNIE SCOTLAND
CD _____ **PASTCD 9800**
Flapper / Nov '92 / Pinnacle.

BOO!
Mountaineering in Belgium: *Attila The Stockbroker* / Charm: *Shoulders* / Oh Marie: *Tender Trap* / Music down: *Tansads* / Carry me: *Levellers* / She drives my train: *Resque* / Shotgun: *Bleach* / Turpentine: *Newcranes* / On Sunday: *Shoulders* / Polishing your hate: *Stranglmartin* / Eye of the average: *Tansads* / Love comes through: *Tender Trap* / Trash Madonna: *Zodiac Mindwarp & The Love Reaction* / Nature's love: *Newcranes*
CD _____ **10062**
Musidisc / Jan '93 / Vital / Harmonia Mundi / ADA / Cadillac / Discovery.

BOOGALUSA
CD _____ **CDLDL 1223**
Klub / Feb '95 / CM / Ross / Duncans / ADA / Direct.

BOOGIE WOOGIE
CD _____ **CD 14552**
Jazz Portraits / Jul '94 / Jazz Music.

BOOGIE WOOGIE & BARRELHOUSE PIANO VOL. 1
CD _____ **DOCD 5102**
Blues Document / Nov '92 / Swift / Jazz Music / Hot Shot.

BOOGIE WOOGIE & BARRELHOUSE PIANO VOL. 2
CD _____ **DOCD 5103**
Blues Document / Nov '92 / Swift / Jazz Music / Hot Shot.

BOOGIE WOOGIE BEAT
CD _____ **CWNCD 2008**
Javelin / Jun '95 / THE / Henry Hadaway Organisation.

BOOGIE WOOGIE BLUES
Cow cow blues: *Davenport, Cow Cow* / 5th street blues: *Davenport, Cow Cow* / Hurry and bring it home blues: *Davenport, Cow Cow* / Harlem choc'late babies on parade: *Johnson, James P.* / Birmingham blues: *Johnson, James P.* / Sugar blues: *Williams, Clarence* / Papa de da da: *Williams, Clarence* / Gulf coast blues: *Johnson, Clarence* / You're always messin' 'round with my man: *Johnson, Clarence* / Low down papa: *Johnson, Clarence* / Chicago stomp: *Blythe, Jimmy* / Society blues: *Blythe, Jimmy* / Boogie woogie blues: *Blythe, Jimmy* / Hard luck blues: *Robbins, Everett* / Fives: *Thomas, Hersal* / Down and out blues: *Fowler, Lemuel*
CD _____ **BCD 115**
Biograph / Jul '91 / Wellard / ADA / Hot Shot / Jazz Music / Cadillac / Direct.

BOOGIE WOOGIE GIANTS, THE
CD _____ **JHR 73533**
Jazz Hour / May '93 / Target/BMG / Jazz Music / Cadillac.

BOOGIE WOOGIE MASTERS
Cow cow blues: *Davenport, Cow Cow* / State street jive: *Davenport, Cow Cow* / Pinetop's boogie woogie: *Smith, Pine Top* / Pinetop's boogie woogie: *Smith, Pine Top* / Jump steady blues: *Smith, Pine Top* / Detroit rocks: *Taylor, Montana* / Dirty dozen: *Perryman, Rufus* / Right string baby, but the wrong yo-yo: *Perryman, Rufus* / Honky tonk train blues: *Lewis, Meade Lux* / Yancey special: *Lewis, Meade Lux* / Celeste blues: *Lewis, Meade Lux* / Boogie woogie stomp: *Ammons, Albert* / Mr. Freddie blues: *Williams, Mary Lou* / Boogie woogie: *Basie, Count* / Basement boogie: *Johnson, Pete* / Death ray boogie: *Johnson, Pete*
CD _____ **CDCD 1007**
Charly / Mar '93 / Charly / THE / Cadillac.

BOOGIE WOOGIE PIANO
CD _____ **CD 14525**
Jazz Portraits / Jan '94 / Jazz Music.

BOOGIE WOOGIE PIANO
CD _____ **CD 56001**
Jazz Roots / Aug '94 / Target/BMG.

BOOGIE WOOGIE RIOT
(Piano & Guitar Boogie Blues)
Tribute / Rocket 88 / Wine-o baby boogie / Rattler / Earl's boogie woogie / Cows / Lightnin's boogie / Atlanta bounce / Rock 'n' roll bed / Three boogie woogie / Boogie down the road apiece / Fast Santa Fe / Boogie all the time / Right string baby, but the wrong yo-yo / Half tight boogie / Hammond boogie / Red light / Walter's boogie / Houston boogie / Pine top's boogie woogie / I know that's right / Fillmore street boogie / Skid row boogie
CD _____ **CDCHD 526**
Ace / Feb '95 / Pinnacle / Cadillac / Complete/Pinnacle.

BOOGIE WOOGIE SPECIAL
CD _____ **TPZ 1025**
Topaz Jazz / Aug '95 / Pinnacle / Cadillac.

BOOGIE WOOGIE STOMP
Boogie woogie stomp: *Ammons, Albert* / Foot pedal boogie: *Ammons, Albert & Pete Johnson* / Boogie woogie prayer: *Ammons, Albert/Pete Johnson/Meade Lux Lewis* / Boogie woogie: *Basie, Count* / Boogie woogie (2): *Brown, Cleo* / Fat fanny stomp: *Clarke, Jim* / Yancey special: *Crosby, Bob*

& Bob Zurke / Rocks: *Custer, Clay* / Boogie woogie (3): *Dorsey, Tommy & Howard Smith* / Chain 'em down: *Garnett, Blind Leroy* / Roll 'em: *Goodman, Benny & Jess Stacy* / After hours: *Hawkins, Erskine & Avery Parrish* / Chip's boogie woogie: *Herman, Woody & Tommy Linehan* / Indian boogie woogie: *Herman, Woody & Tommy Linehan* / Boogie woogie on St. Louis blues: *Hines, Earl* / Boo-woo: *James, Harry & Pete Johnson* / Bear cat crawl: *Lewis, Meade Lux* / Honky tonk train blues: *Lewis, Meade Lux* / Vine Street boogie: *McShann, Jay* / No special rider: *Montgomery, Little Brother* / Pinetop's boogie woogie: *Smith, Pine Top* / Wilkins Street stomp: *Speckled Red* / Roll 'em: *Pete Turner, Big Joe & Pete Johnson* / Crying in my sleep: *Yancey, Jimmy* / Slow and easy blues: *Yancey, Jimmy*
CD _____ **CDAJA 5101**
Living Era / Feb '93 / Koch.

BOOGIE WOOGIE STORY
(3CD Set)
CD Set _____ **CDB 1207**
Giants Of Jazz / Apr '92 / Target/BMG / Cadillac.

BOOGIE WOOGIE VOCALISTS
CD _____ **CD 14541**
Jazz Portraits / Jan '94 / Jazz Music.

BOOGIE WOOGIE VOL.1
(Piano Soloists)
Pinetop's boogie woogie: *Smith, Clarence 'Pinetop'* / Jump steady blues: *Smith, Clarence 'Pinetop'* / Detroit rocks: *Taylor, Montana* / Indiana Avenue stomp: *Taylor, Montana* / Dirty dozens: *Speckled Red* / Wilkins Street stomp: *Speckled Red* / Head rag hop: *Nelson, Romeo* / Cow cow blues: *Davenport, Cow Cow* / State Street jive: *Davenport, Cow Cow* / Yancey special: *Yancey, Jimmy* / Midnight stomp: *Yancey, Jimmy* / Streamline train: *Loften, Cripple Clarence* / I don't know: *Loften, Cripple Clarence* / Shout for joy: *Ammons, Albert* / Bass goin' crazy: *Ammons, Albert* / Yancey special (2): *Lewis, Meade Lux* / Honky tonk train blues: *Lewis, Meade Lux* / Blues on the downbeat: *Johnson, Pete* / Kaycee on my mind: *Johnson, Pete* / Ross Tavern boogie: *Hodes, Art*
CD _____ **JASMCD 2538**
Jasmine / Feb '95 / Wellard / Swift / Conifer / Cadillac / Magnum Music Group.

BOOGIE WOOGIE VOL.2
(The Small Groups)
Boogie woogie stomp: *Ammons, Albert & His Rhythm Kings* / Boogie woogie: *Basie, Count* / Down the road apiece: *Bradley, Will / Basin Street boogie: *Bradley, Will* / St. Louis blues: *Butterfield, Erskine* / Grand slam: *Goodman, Benny Sextet* / Munson Street breakdown: *Hampton, Lionel & His Orchestra* / Bouncing at the beacon: *Hampton, Lionel & His Orchestra* / We're gonna pitch a boogie woogie: *Harlem Hamfats* / Chip's boogie woogie: *Herman, Woody* / Boo woo: *James, Harry* / Boogie woogie's mother-in-law: *Johnson, Buddy Orchestra* / Cherry red: *Johnson, Pete & Joe Turner* / Baby look at you: *Johnson, Pete & Joe Turner* / Far away blues: *Johnson, Pete & Joe Turner* / Bye bye baby: *Big Maceo* / Anytime for you: *Big Maceo* / Dirty dozen: *Price, Sammy* / Lead me Daddy: *Price, Sammy* / Straight to the bar: *Price, Sammy* / Rock it in rhythm: *Tampa Red* / She's love crazy: *Tampa Red*
CD _____ **JASMCD 2539**
Jasmine / Apr '95 / Wellard / Swift / Conifer / Cadillac / Magnum Music Group.

BOOGIE WOOGIE VOL.3
(The Big Bands)
Scrub me Mama with a boogie beat / Basie boogie / Beat me, Daddy, eight to the bar / Rock-a-bye boogie / Back to boogie / Yancey special / Honky tonk train blues / Boogie woogie / Roll 'em / Indian boogie woogie / Boogie woogie baby boy / Boogie woogie on St. Louis blues / Back beat boogie / Little Joe from Chicago / Drum boogie / Teddy bear boogie / Bluebird boogie woogie / Meade lux special / Cuban boogie woogie / Rum boogie
CD _____ **JASMCD 2540**
Jasmine / Jun '95 / Wellard / Swift / Conifer / Cadillac / Magnum Music Group.

BOOGIE WOOGIE, THE
In the mood: *Miller, Glenn* / Red bank boogie: *Basie, Count* / Beulah's sister's boogie: *Hampton, Lionel* / Honky tonk train blues: *Crosby, Bob* / Jammin' the boogie: *Lewis, Meade Lux* / Jammin' the boogie: *Ammons, Albert* / Hamp's boogie woogie: *Hampton, Lionel* / Pinetop's boogie woogie: *Price, Sammy* / Jimmy's boogie woogie: *Basie, Count & Jimmy Rushing* / Boogie woogie on St. Louis blues: *Hines, Earl* / Hamp's walkin' boogie: *Hampton, Lionel* / Chip's boogie woogie: *Herman, Woody* / Calloway boogie: *Calloway, Cab* / Boo woo: *James, Harry & Pete Johnson* / Central Avenue breakdown: *Cole, Nat King & Lionel Hampton* / Roll 'em: *Goodman, Benny* / Cow cow blues: *Zurke, Bob* / Tatum-pole boogie: *Tatum, Art* / Oscar's boogie: *Peterson, Oscar* / Just jazz boogie: *Johnson, Pete*
CD _____ **CD 53003**
Giants Of Jazz / Mar '92 / Target/BMG / Cadillac.

BOOM BOOM
CD _____ **MPV 5531**
Movieplay / '93 / Target/BMG.

BOOM REGGAE HITS VOL.5
CD _____ **VPCD 1449**
VP / Nov '95 / Jetstar.

BOPPIN' THE BLUES
CD _____ **CPCD 8139**
Charly / Nov '95 / Charly / THE / Cadillac.

BOPPIN' TONIGHT
Let's go boppin' tonight: *Ferrier, Al* / Honey baby: *Ferrier, Al* / No no baby: *Ferrier, Al* / What is that thing called love: *Ferrier, Al* / My baby done gone away: *Ferrier, Al* / Couple in the car: *Earl, Little Billy* / Who's baby are you: *Earl, Little Billy* / Go dan tucker: *Earl, Little Billy* / I never had the blues: *Earl, Little Billy* / Honey baby: *Earl, Little Billy* / Freight train: *Hart, Larry* / Oh Nellie: *Hart, Larry* / I'm just a member: *Hart, Larry* / Coffins have no pockets: *Hart, Larry* / Come on baby: *Hart, Larry* / Flashiest classiest: *Hart, Larry* / Never run out of love: *Hart, Larry* / Hold me baby: *Bill & Carroll* / Bluff city rock: *Bill & Carroll* / Bop stop rock: *Victorian, Ray* / Oh baby: *Jano, Johnny* / Mabel's gone: *Jano, Johnny* / High voltage: *Jano, Johnny* / Castro rock: *Chevalier, Jay*
CD _____ **CDCHD 442**
Ace / Feb '93 / Pinnacle / Cadillac / Complete/Pinnacle.

BORDER MUSIC
Laissez-faire: *Daigrepont, Bruce* / Kolinda: *Beausoleil* / La Viejito: *Jimenez, Flaco* / Allons a Lafayette: *Sonnier, Jo El* / This little girl: *Menard, D.L* / Big chief: *Richard, Zachary* / Hundred Ladrones: *Los Jaimes* / Corrido el aceite: *Jordan, Steve* / J'etais au bal: *Doucet, David* / Someone else is steppin' in: *Buckwheat Zydeco* / High point two step: *Riley, Steve* / La otra modesta: *Jimenez, Santiago* / Cuando me miraste: *Salvidar, Mingo* / Tennis shoes: *Newman, Jimmy C.* / Aquella noche: *Hinojosa, Tish*
CD _____ **NETCD 1004**
Network / '92 / Direct / ADA.

BORDERLANDS - FROM CONJUNTO TO CHICKEN SCRATCH
CD _____ **SF 40418CD**
Smithsonian Folkways / Jan '94 / ADA / Direct / Koch / CM / Cadillac.

BOREDOM IS DEEP AND MYSTERIOUS
CD _____ **APR 001CD**
April / Feb '95 / Plastic Head.

BORN TO BE WILD
Born to be wild: *Steppenwolf* / All right now: *Free* / Keep on running: *Davis, Spencer Group* / Green onions: *Booker T & The MG's* / That's all right (mama): *Stewart, Rod* / Need your love so bad: *Fleetwood Mac* / Got my mojo working: *Manfred Mann* / We gotta get out of this place: *Animals* / 20th Century boy: *T. Rex* / Let's work together: *Canned Heat* / Whatever you want: *Status Quo* / Cocaine: *Cale, J.J.* / Don't mess up a good thing: *Cooder, Ry & Chaka Khan* / Smokin' gun: *Cray, Robert* / Love and marriage: *Third Man* / I'd rather go blind: *Chicken Shack* / Texas flood: *Vaughan, Stevie Ray* / Baby please don't go: *Them*
CD _____ **TCD 2524**
Telstar / Sep '91 / BMG.

BORN TO CHOOSE
Photograph: *R.E.M. & Natalie Merchant* / She said she said: *Sweet, Matthew* / Running out of time (live): *Sugar* / Born to choose: *Mekons* / Rant 'n' roll: *Trudell, John* / Box spring hog: *Waits, Tom* / Pancakes: *Williams, Lucinda* / Crackrobot: *Pavement* / Don't talk about my music: *New Rhythm & Blues Quartet* / Lost my driving wheel: *Cowboy Junkies* / H.I.V. Baby: *Soundgarden* / Distracted: *Helmet*
CD _____ **RCD 10256**
Rykodisc / Nov '93 / Vital / ADA.

BORN UNDER A BAD SIGN
CD _____ **VSOPCD 205**
Connoisseur / Oct '94 / Pinnacle.

BORN WITH THE BLUES
CD _____ **EMPRCD 525**
Empress / Sep '94 / THE.

BORN WITH THE BLUES II
CD _____ **EMPRCD 526**
Empress / Sep '94 / THE.

BOSNIA - ECHOES FROM AN ENDANGERED WORLD
CD _____ **SF 40407CD**
Smithsonian Folkways / Nov '94 / ADA / Direct / Koch / CM / Cadillac.

BOSSA NOVA
CD _____ **CD 62029**
Saludos Amigos / Oct '93 / Target/BMG.

BOSSA NOVA
Embala a bola: *Djavan* / Samba de bencao: *De Moraes, Vinicus* / Tempo de saudade: *Creuza, Maria* / Mais um adeus: *Toquinho & Marilia Medalha* / A felicidade: *Dos Santos, Agostinho* / Para viver um grande amor: *De Moraes, Vinicus* / Para que digladiar: *Ben, Jorge* / Desencontro: *Buarque, Chico & Toquinho* / Samba de verao: *Zimbo Trio* / Sao demais os perigos desta vida: *Vinicius & Toquinho* / Apelo: *Bethania, Maria & Vinicius* / Canto de ossanha: *Creuza, Maria &*

Vinicius & Toquinho / Na boca de beco: *Djavan* / Voce abusu: *Creuza, Maria* / Carolina: *Buarque, Chico* / Garota de ipanema: *De Moraes, Vincius* / Corcovado: *Creuza, Maria* / Morena de flor: *De Moraes, Vincius* / Marina: *Creuza, Maria* / Paiol de polvora: *De Moraes, Vincius* / Trocando em miudo: *Hime, Francis* / Katarina, Katarina: *Ben, Jorge*
CD _____ NSCD 003
Nascente / Jul '91 / Disc / THE.

BOSSA NOVA & SAMBA IN CONCERTO
CD _____ CD 62011
Saludos Amigos / Oct '93 / Target/BMG.

BOSSA NOVA VOL.2
CD _____ GLO 143
RGE / Aug '93 / Discovery.

BOSTON BLUES BLAST VOL. 1
CD _____ TONECOOLCD 1146
Tonecool / May '94 / Direct / ADA.

BOTTLENECK BLUES
CD _____ TCD 5021
Testament / Oct '95 / Complete/Pinnacle / ADA / Koch.

BOTTOM LINE
CD _____ NTMCD 501
Nectar / Jun '95 / Pinnacle.

BOUNCY TECHNO ANTHEMS
CD _____ DBMTRCD 21
Rogue Trooper / Dec '95 / SRD.

BOUZOUKIS & SIRTAKIS
CD _____ 995142
EPM / Jun '93 / Discovery / ADA.

BOXING CLEVER
CD _____ DRGNCD 943
Dragon / May '94 / Roots / Cadillac / Wellard / CM / ADA.

BOYS ARE BACK IN TOWN, THE
Boys are back in town: *Thin Lizzy* / School's out: *Cooper, Alice* / Cum on feel the noize: *Slade* / Saturday night's alright for fighting: *John, Elton* / Blockbuster: *Sweet* / You ain't seen nothin' yet: *Bachman-Turner Overdrive* / I didn't know I loved you (till I saw you rock 'n' roll): *Glitter, Gary* / This town ain't big enough for the both of us: *Sparks* / Street life: *Roxy Music* / Twentieth century boy: *Bolan, Marc & T.Rex* / Let's stick together: *Ferry, Bryan* / Run run run: *Jo Jo Gunne* / Maggie May: *Stewart, Rod* / Wishing well: *Free* / Once bitten twice shy: *Hunter, Ian* / Make me smile (come up and see me): *Harley, Steve & Cockney Rebel* / Walk on the wild side: *Reed, Lou* / All the young dudes: *Mott The Hoople*
CD _____ MOODCD 23
Columbia / Jun '92 / Sony.

BOYZ WHO SOULED THE WORLD, THE
CD _____ AHLCD 18
Hit / Feb '94 / PolyGram.

BRAIN TICKET - ADRENALIN TRIP
CD Set _____ SPV 08992302
Subterranean / Jul '95 / Plastic Head.

BRAINDEAD 3
(Hardcore Cyberspace)
CD _____ EFA 008752
Shockwave / Jan '96 / SRD.

BRAND NEW SECONDHAND
D'yer mak'er: *Eek-A-Mouse* / Bed's too big without you: *Hylton, Sheila* / On and on: *Aswad* / Hey Joe: *Black Uhuru* / Around the world: *Krystal* / Everday people: *Brown, Rula* / Best of my love: *Aswad* / Walk on by: *I Tones & Ram* / Just my imagination: *Murvin, Junior* / Some guys have all the luck: *Tucker, Junior* / Groovin' (with Cyril Neville.): *Killer Bees* / Take me home country roads: *Toots & The Maytals*
CD _____ RCD 10247
Rykodisc / Feb '93 / Vital / ADA.

BRASIL
Batucada 1 / Zanzibar / Amazon river / Berimbau / Capoeira / Magika / Forro / Misturada / Batucada 2
CD _____ SJRCD 022
Soul Jazz / Nov '94 / New Note / Vital.

BRASILEIRO
CD _____ CD 62038
Saludos Amigos / Nov '93 / Target/BMG.

BRASILICA
After sunrise: *Mendes, Sergio* / Barumba: *Tamba Trio* / Birimbau: *Dom Um Romao* / Vera Cruz: *Nascimento, Milton* / Roda: *Gil, Gilberto* / Solo: *Meirelles E Os Copa 5* / Crickets song for Anamaria: *Valle, Marcus* / Blues Avoirdre: *Powell, Baden* / Adam Adam: *Joyce* / Tereza Sabe Sambar: *Regina, Elis* / Tamba: *Tamba Trio* / Zanzibar: *Mendes, Sergio √* / Uga neguinho: *Mendes, Sergio* / Mas que nada: *Jorge, Ben* / Tudo Tom: *Donato, Joao* / Vig = digal: *Resende, Marcos*
CD _____ 516853-2
Talkin' Loud / Aug '94 / PolyGram.

BRASS BAND FAVOURITES
Guns of Navarone / Magnificent seven / Over the rainbow / Trouble with the tuba is / Headless horseman / Men of Harlech / Marche militaire / Death of glass / Tea for two / Puttin' on the Ritz / Coronation Street / March of the cobblers / My way / Ein

schnapps / Swan / Sailing by / Tango taquin / Can can / Semper sousa / Colonel Bogey
CD _____ CC 257
Music For Pleasure / Oct '90 / EMI.

BRASS BAND SPECTACULAR
CD _____ MATCD 235
Castle / Dec '92 / BMG.

BRASS BAND WALTZES AND POLKAS
CD _____ PS 65154
Playasound / Sep '95 / Harmonia Mundi / ADA.

BRAZIL
CD _____ CD 62031
Saludos Amigos / Oct '93 / Target/BMG.

BRAZIL BLUE
Regra tres: *Monteiro, Doris* / Nereci (A name): *Djavan* / Cidade vazia (Empty city): *Milton Banana Trio* / Sarau para radames: *Da Viola, Paulinho* / O cantador (The street singer): *Brasil, Victor Assis* / Comecar de novo: *Lins, Ivan* / Sao Tome (St Thomas): *Venturini, Flavio* / Vento de maio: *Regina, Elis* / Bate-papo (Shoot the breeze): *Os Chorees & Radames Gnattali* / Chorando baixinho (Crying low): *Ferreira, Abel* / Copacabana: *Sete, Bola* / Samba de uma nota so: *Joyce* / Corcovado: *Gilberto, Joao* / Emotiva no.1: *Delmiro, Helio* / Ecos (Echoes): *Nascimento, Joel* / Fica mal com deus (Be bad with God): *Quarteto Novo & Hermento Pascoal* / Milage dos peixes (Miracle of the fishes): *Nascimento, Milton* / Cantareiro (Dish rack): *Mariano, Cesar Camargo* / Choro de Mae (Mother's choro): *Tiso, Wagner* / Nem uma lagrima (Not one tear): *Caymmi, Nana*
CD _____ CDEMC 3676
EMI / May '94 / EMI.

BRAZIL CLASSICS
(Beleza Tropical)
CD _____ K 9260192
WEA / Oct '89 / Warner Music.

BRAZIL CLASSICS 1
(Beleza tropical)
Ponta de lanca Africano: *Ben, Jorge* / Sonho meu: *Bethania, Maria e Gal Costa* / So quero um xodo: *Gil, Gilberto* / Um canto de afoxe para o bloco do ile / Leaozinho: *Veloso, Caetano* / Cacada: *Buarque, Chico & Milton Nascimento* / Equatorial (Not on cassette.): *Borges Lo* / San Vincente / Quilombo, O el dorado negro: *Gil, Gilberto* / Caramba...galileu de galileia (Not on cassette.): *Ben, Jorge* / Caixa de sol: *Pereira, Nazare* / Maculele (Not on cassette.): *Pereira, Nazare* / Queixa: *Veloso, Caetano* / Andar com fe: *Gil, Gilberto* / Fio maravilha: *Ben, Jorge* / Anima: *Nascimento, Milton* / Terra: *Veloso, Caetano*
CD _____ CDEMC 3551
EMI / Feb '89 / EMI.

BRAZIL CLASSICS 2
Deusa dos orixas / Ijexa (filhos de gandhy) / S.P.C. / Sufoco / Formosa / Olere camara / O encanto de gantois / Aldeia de okarimbe / E preciso muito amor / Caxambu / Quem me guia / Ela nao gosta de mim / Claustofobia / Batuca no chao / Sarau para radames
CD _____ 926019-2
WEA / '90 / Warner Music.

BRAZILIAN NIGHTS
CD _____ CDCH 539
Milan / Sep '91 / BMG / Silva Screen.

BREAD AND ROSES
(Festival of Acoustic Music, Greek Theatre)
CD _____ CDWIK 103
Big Beat / Mar '92 / Pinnacle.

BREAK BEATS 1 & 2
(Various Unknown D.J.'s)
CD _____ WRCD 001
Warrior / '91 / Pinnacle.

BREAK BEATS 3 & 4
(Various Unknown D.J.'s)
CD _____ WRCD 002
Warrior / Oct '92 / Pinnacle.

BREAKING HEARTS
CD _____ DINCD 34
Dino / Feb '92 / Pinnacle / 3MV.

BREAKING THE BARRIERS WITH SOUND
(Captured By The Vibes)
Captured by the vibes: *Robotiks* / Didn't I: *Kofi* / I just want to love you: *Simmonds, Leroy* / Dancing time: *Aisha* / Roots and culture: *Macka B* / Let's make it work: *Cross, Sandra* / And now you're gone: *McLean, John* / Baby, baby, my love's all for you: *Tajah, Paulette* / Mellow: *Intense* / Daylight and darkness: *Sister Audrey* / Captured by the dub: *Mad Professor*
CD _____ ARICD 040
Ariwa Sounds / Sep '88 / Jetstar / SRD.

BREAKS, BASS AND BLEEPS
Exorcist: *Scientist* / Q: *Mental Cube* / Dance tones (stoned mix): *Hypersonic* / Jokers: *Jokers* / Brainstorm (part 1): *LFO* / Evolution: *Candy Flip* / It's a moment in time (#): *Candy Flip* / T.T.O. (O.T.T. mad bastard mix): *Turntable Overload* / Deja vu: *Brothers Grimm* / Scheme: *F.X.U* / Ital's anthem: *Ital Rockers* / Themes: *N-R-Gee Posse* / Teknologi: *Urban Hype*

CD _____ CDRAID 502
Rumour / Nov '90 / Pinnacle / 3MV / Sony.

BREAKS, BASS AND BLEEPS 2
CD _____ CDRAID 504
Rumour / Jul '91 / Pinnacle / 3MV / Sony.

BREAKS, BASS AND BLEEPS 3
CD _____ CDRAID 506
Rumour / Nov '91 / Pinnacle / 3MV / Sony.

BREAKS, BASS AND BLEEPS 4
CD _____ CDRAID 507
Rumour / Feb '92 / Pinnacle / 3MV / Sony.

BREEZIN'
Summer breeze: *Isley Brothers* / Lovely day: *Withers, Bill* / Drift away: *Bolton, Michael* / California here I come: *Hawkins, Sophie B.* / Steady on: *Colvin, Shawn* / Quittin' time: *Carpenter, Mary-Chapin* / Living with the law: *Whitley, Chris* / Poor boy blues: *Atkins, Chet & Mark Knopfler* / I can help: *Swan, Billy* / Fraction too much friction: *Finn, Tim* / Love thy will be done: *Martika* / Carnival 2000: *Prefab Sprout* / Can't get it out of my head: *E.L.O.* / Going down to Liverpool: *Bangles* / Don't wanna lose you: *Estefan, Gloria*
CD _____ 4803352
Columbia / May '95 / Sony.

BRESIL '90
CD _____ 824882
Buda / Nov '90 / Discovery / ADA.

BRESIL EN FETE: BRAZILIAN FOLK FESTIVITIES
CD _____ PS 65096
Playasound / Nov '92 / Harmonia Mundi / ADA.

BRIEF HISTORY OF AMBIENT VOL.1, A
(152 Minutes 33 Seconds)
Flowered knife shadows: *Budd, Harold* / Thru metamorphic rock (edit): *Tangerine Dream* / Evening star: *Fripp, Robert & Brian Eno* / Mountain goat: *Amorphous Androgynous* / Sea of vapours: *Khan, Nusrat Fateh Ali* / Forge of volcan: *Hawkwind* / Requiem: *Killing Joke* / Ending (ascent): *Eno, Brian* / Marnia's tent: *Horowitz, Richard* / Rapido de noir: *Schmidt, Irmin & Bruno Spoerri* / Kazoo: *Ahsra* / Their memories: *Budd, Harold & Brian Eno* / Leave your body: *Orbit* / Electric becomes eclectic: *Franke, Christopher* / Phaedra (edit): *Tangerine Dream* / Delta rain dream: *Eno, Brian & Jon Hassell* / Monkey king: *Orbit, William* / Castle in the clouds: *Gong* / Life form: *Hawkwind* / Dance #2: *Laraaji* / Sacred stones: *Chandra, Sheila* / Earth floor: *Earth Floor* / Gift of fire: *Hassell, Jon* / End of words: *Material* / Panorphelia: *Froese, Edgar* / Voices: *Eno, Roger* / Traum mal wieder: *Czukay, Holger* / Home: *Sylvian, David*
CD _____ AMBT 1
Virgin / Aug '93 / EMI.

BRIEF HISTORY OF AMBIENT VOL.2, A
(Imaginary Landscapes/2CD Set)
Call to prayer: *Maal, Baaba* / Tal coat: *Eno, Brian* / In mind: *Amorphous Androgynous* / Rubicon pt.2: *Tangerine Dream* / Healing colour (part 3): *Orbit* / Crystal clear (Orb remix): *Grid* / Nuages: *Sakamoto, Ryuichi* / Wind on water: *Fripp, Robert & Brian Eno* / Wildlife: *Penguin Cafe Orchestra* / When things dream: *Jansen, Steve & Richard Barbieri* / Magick mother invocation: *Gong* / Bringing down the light: *Sylvian, David & Robert Fripp* / Not another: *Jah Wobble* / One flower: *Goo Brothers* / Black Jesus: *God* / Mountain of needles: *Eno, Brian & David Byrne* / You are here: *Manzanera, Phil* / Bendel dub: *Prince Far-I* / Slow kaliuki (edit): *Pokrovsky, Dmitri Ensemble* / Euterpe gratitude piece: *Allen, Daevid* / Water music: *Fripp, Robert* / New moon at red deer wallow: *Rain Tree Crow* / Attack of the 50 foot drum demon: *Bass-O-Matic* / Mekong: *Jam Nation* / Endless life: *Verve* / Nachtmusik schattenhaft: *Schulze, Klaus* / Arrival: *Voyager* / Specific gravity of smile: *Froese, Edgar* / Orovela: *Tsinandali Choir* / Dance no. 3: *Laraaji* / Premonition: *Sylvian, David & Holger Czukay* / Island: *Grid*
CD Set _____ AMBT 2
Virgin / Dec '93 / EMI.

BRIEF HISTORY OF AMBIENT VOL.3, A
(The Music Of Changes)
Sygyt khoomei kargyraa: *Shu-De* / When the waters came to life: *Schmidt, Irmin* / Gringatcho demento: *Orbit, William* / Red earth (As summertime ends): *Rain Tree Crow* / Last emperor (Theme variation 1): *Sakamoto, Ryuichi* / 1988: *Fripp, Robert* / Epiphany: *Sylvian, David* / Study of six guitars: *Amorphous Androgynous* / Amy yo t: *Trisan* / Kingdom come: *Laswell, Bill* / You will be all right: *Ono, Seigen* / Meditation #2: *Laraaji* / Pendulum man: *Bark Psychosis* / Distant village: *Brook, Michael* / Mystery R.P.S. (No.8): *Jah Wobble* / Throw away your gun (Dub): *Prince Far-I* / Wind and lonely fences: *Fripp, Robert & Brian Eno* / Nuages (That which passes awakes like clouds): *King Crimson* / Musitt musitt: *Khan, Nusrat Fateh Ali* / Concert for gender: *Shakuhachi & Zither* / Healthy colours (#II): *Fripp, Robert & Brian Eno* / Cascade parts 2 and 3: *Tangerine Dream* / Sound Of London / Summer storm: *Quine, Robert & Fred Maher* / Rising thermal: *Hassell, Jon & Brian Eno* / Muta-

bility (A new begining is in the offing): *Sylvian, David*
CD _____ AMBT 3
Virgin / May '94 / EMI.

BRIEF HISTORY OF AMBIENT VOL.4, A
(Isolationism/2CD Set)
Lost: *KK Null* / Null without a back: *O'Rourke, Jim* / Dredger: *Ice* / Strangers: *Bjorkenheim, Raoul* / Daisy gun: *Soviet France* / Air lubricated free axis trainer: *Labradford* / Self strangulation: *Techno Animal* / Hallucinations (In memory of Reinaldo Arenas): *Schutze, Paul* / Silver rain fell: *Scorn* / Lost in fog: *Disco Inferno* / Six: *Total* / Once again I cast myself into the flames of atonement: *Nijumu* / Aphex airlines: *Aphrodisiac* / Vandoevre: *A.M.M.* / Lief: *Seefeel* / O'rang: *Little Sister* / Hydroponic: *E.A.R.* / Desert flower: *Sufi* / Burial rites: *Toop, David & Max Eastley* / Crater scar (Adrenchrome): *Main* / Hide: *Final* / Thoughts: *Lull* / Kamom (Part one: Brohuk): *Koner, Thomas*
CD Set _____ AMBT 4
Virgin / Aug '94 / EMI.

BRILLIANCE FOR A BETTER FUTURE
CD _____ SR 9455
Silent / Nov '94 / Plastic Head.

BRINGING IT ALL BACK HOME
(2CD Set)
CD Set _____ BBC 844CD
Hummingbird / Apr '95 / ADA / Direct.

BRINGING IT ALL BACK HOME - GUINNESS TOUR '92
CD _____ HB 0001CD
Hummingbird / Oct '93 / ADA / Direct.

BRISTOL SESSIONS, THE
Skip to my Lou: *Dunford, Uncle Eck* / O Molly dear: *Shelton, B.F.* / Walking in the way of Jesus: *Shelton, B.F.* / Newmarket wreck: *Barker, J.W.* / Soldier's sweetheart: *West Virginia Coon Hunters* / Greasy string: *West Virginia Coon Hunters* / Are you washed in the blood: *Stoneman, Ernest V.* / Henry Whitter's fox chase: *Whitter, Henry* / Bury me beneath the willow: *Carter Family* / Jealous sweetheart: *Johnson Brothers* / Will they ring the golden bells: *Karnes, Alfred G.* / Sandy river belle: *Dad Blackard's Moonshiners* / Sleep: *Rodgers, Jimmie* / Johnny Goodwin: *Bull Mountain Moonshiners* / I'm redeemed: *Alcoa Quartet* / Little log cabin by the sea: *Carter Family* / Old time corn shuckin': *Blue Ridge Corn Shuckers* / I want to go where Jesus is: *Phipps, Ernest* / Midnight on the stormy deep: *Stoneman, Ernest* / Irma Frost & Erk Dunford* / Wandering boy: *Carter Family* / To the work: *Karnes, Alfred G.* / Blackeyed Susie: *Nestor, J.P.* / Passing Policeman: *Johnson Brothers* / Tell mother I will meet her: *Stoneman, Ernest V.* / Single girl, married girl: *Carter Family* / Potlicker blues: *Watson, El* / Longest train I ever saw: *Tenneva Ramblers* / Resurrection: *Stoneman, Ernest V.* / Storms are on the ocean: *Carter Family* / Wreck of the Virginian: *Reed, Blind Alfred* / Billy Grimes, the Rover: *Shellor family* / Standing on promises: *Tennessee mountaineers* / Mountaineer's courtship: *Stoneman, Ernest* / Irma Frost & Erk Dunford* / Poor orphan child: *Carter Family* / I am bound for the promised land: *Karnes, Alfred G.*
CD Set _____ CMFCD 011
Country Music Foundation / Jan '93 / Direct / ADA.

BRIT HOP AND AMYL HOUSE
CD _____ 74321339832
De-Construction / Jan '96 / BMG.

BRITISH BEAT BEFORE THE BEATLES - VOL. 1 (1955-6)
Tweedle dee: *Miller, Suzi* / Dance with me Henry: *Miller, Suzi* / Earth angel: *Southlanders* / Ain't that a shame: *Southlanders* / (We're gonna) rock around the clock: *Deep River Boys* / Rock island line: *Donegan, Lonnie* / My boy flat top: *Vaughan, Frankie* / Dungaree doll: *Bennett, Dickie* / Tutti frutti: *Four Jones Boys* / Why do fools fall in love: *Cogan, Alma* / I'm in love again: *Cogan, Alma* / Bad penny blues: *Lyttelton, Humphrey* / Rock 'n' roll blues: *Lang, Don* / Left hand boogie: *Ellington, Ray* / Giddy up a ding dong: *Ellington, Ray* / Teach you to rock: *Crombie, Tony & His Rockets* / Let's you and I rock: *Crombie, Tony & His Rockets* / Rock with the caveman: *Steele, Tommy* / Singin' the blues: *Steele, Tommy* / Don't nobody move: *Lawrence, Lee*
CD _____ CDGO 2046
EMI / Jul '93 / EMI.

BRITISH BEAT BEFORE THE BEATLES - VOL. 2 (1957)
Don't knock me: *Baxter, Art & His Rock 'N' Roll Sinners* / White sports coat and a pink carnation: *King Brothers* / Don't you rock me Daddy-o: *Vipers Skiffle Group* / Party doll: *James, Ricky* / School day: *Lang, Don & His Frantic 5* / Red planet rock: *Lang, Don & His Frantic 5* / Bye bye love: *Blackwell, Rory* / Start movin': *Page, Larry* / That'll be the day: *Page, Larry* / Fabulous: *Cogan, Alma* / Butterfly: *Steele, Tommy* / Matchbox: *Wayne, Terry* / Your true love: *Wayne, Terry* / Wanderin' eyes: *Vaughan, Frankie* / Be my girl: *Dale, Jim* / He's got the whole world in his hands: *London, Laurie* / Trying to get to you: *Castle, Joey* / I'm left, you're right, she's gone: *Castle, Joey* / Baby

she's gone: Dene, Terry / Empty arms blues: Hicks, Colin & The Cabin Boys
CD _____ CDGO 2047
EMI / Jul '93 / EMI.

BRITISH BEAT BEFORE THE BEATLES - VOL. 3 (1958)
Slim Jim tie: Wayne, Terry / Raunchy: MacKintosh, Ken / Under control: Page, Larry / Riot in cell block 9: Harris, Wee Willie / Whole lotta woman: Most Brothers / Yea yea: Eager, Vince & The Vagabonds / Book of love: Mudlarks / Endless sleep: Wilde, Marty & his Wildcats / Mercy mercy Percy: Taylor, Neville / Teenage love: Five Chesternuts / Nothin' shakin': Douglas, Craig / Move it: Richard, Cliff & Drifters / hoots mon: Lord Rockingham's XI / Come on let's go: Steele, Tommy / Tears on my pillow: Taylor, Neville & The Cutters / Pretty little Pearly: Dene, Terry / No more: Eager, Vince / This little girl's gone rockin': Peters, Janice & Frank Barber Band / Queen of the hop: Lang, Don / High School confidential: Faith, Adam
CD _____ CDGO 2048
EMI / Jul '93 / EMI.

BRITISH BEAT BEFORE THE BEATLES - VOL. 4 (1959)
Maybe tomorrow: Fury, Billy / Brand new Cadillac: Taylor, Vince & Playboys / Once more: Forbes, Bill / Girl likes: Peters, Janice / Slippin' and slidin': Pride, Dickie / Frantic: Pride, Dickie / Hey Miss Fannie: Webb, Dean / This should go on forever: Eager, Vince / Please don't touch: Kidd, Johnny & The Pirates / Teenager in love: Wilde, Marty / Dream lover: Power, Duffy / Ah poor little baby: Faith, Adam / She's mine: Wayne, Terry / Apron strings: Richard, Cliff & Drifters / Only sixteen: Douglas, Craig / Tallahassie lassie: Steele, Tommy / Jet black: Drifters / I don't know: Lesley, Lorne / Little cutie: Kelly, Sally / What do you want to make those eyes at me for: Ford, Emile & The Checkmates
CD _____ CDGO 2049
EMI / Aug '93 / EMI.

BRITISH BEAT BEFORE THE BEATLES - VOL. 5 (1960)
Saturday dance: Shadows / Betty Betty (Go steady with me): Pride, Dickie / Lonely blue boy: Eager, Vince / Amapola: Jones, Davy / If you don't know: Gibson, Jody & The Muleskinners / (Must you always) Tease me: Kelly, Keith / Sweet dreams: Sampson, Dave & The Hunter / Sixteen reason: Ryan, Marion / I mistehavin': Bruce, Tommy & The Bruisers / You'll never know what you miss: Ford, Emile & The Checkmates / That's love: Fury, Billy / Shakin' all over: Kidd, Johnny & The Pirates / Made you: Faith, Adam / Apache: Weedon, Bert / Angry: Wilde, Marty / Tell Laura I love her: Valance, Ricky / Walk don't run: Barry, John Seven / Nine times out of ten: Richard, Cliff & The Shadows / Teen scene: Hunters
CD _____ CDGO 2050
EMI / Aug '93 / EMI.

BRITISH BEAT BEFORE THE BEATLES - VOL. 6 (1961)
Music: Storme, Robb & Whispers / Teenage love: Cox, Michael / High class feeling: MacRae, Josh / Are you sure: Allisons / Don't treat me like a child: Shapiro, Helen / Gee whiz it's you: Richard, Cliff / Halfway to paradise: Fury, Billy / Trombone: Krew Kats / I'll step down: Diamond, Lee / You've got what I like: Bennett, Cliff & The Rebel Rousers / Sweet little sixteen: Cox, Michael / Baby sittin': Angelo, Bobby & The Tuxedos / All grown up: Raven, Paul / I'm a moody guy: Fenton, Shane & The Fentones / Please don't bring me down: Kidd, Johnny & The Pirates / When I get paid: Bennett, Cliff / Tomorrows clown: Wilde, Marty / Savage: Shadows / Till the following night: Screaming Lord Sutch / Your Ma said you cried in your sleep last night: Sheldon, Doug
CD _____ CDGO 2051
EMI / Sep '93 / EMI.

BRITISH BEAT BEFORE THE BEATLES - VOL. 7 (1962)
Someone to love: Newman, Brad / True fine mama: Casey, Howie & the Seniors / Lessons in love: Allisons / Honey 'cause I love you: Cox, Michael / Stand up: Cox, Michael / Wonderful land: Shadows / Dance on: Shadows / Sugar babe: Powell, Jimmy / Mexican: Fentones / Picture of you: Brown, Joe & The Bruvvers / I sold my heart to the junkman: Cornell, Lynn / I shoulda listened to mama: Crawford, Jimmy / Johnny get angry: Deene, Carol / It'll be me: Richard, Cliff & The Shadows / Why little girl: Fenton, Shane & The Fentones / Ever since you said goodbye: Wilde, Marty / All of me: Lynton, Jackie / Ubangi stomp: Shannon, Dean / I can tell: Kidd, Johnny & The Pirates / Shot of rhythm and blues: Kidd, Johnny & The Pirates
CD _____ CDP 7892262
EMI / Oct '93 / EMI.

BRITISH BLUEGRASS VOL.1
CD _____ BBMA 1001CD
British Bluegrass / Nov '95 / Direct / ADA.

BRITISH BLUES HEROES
CD _____ MCCD 194
Music Club / Mar '95 / Disc / THE / CM.

BRITISH DANCE BANDS
CD _____ AVC 539
Avid / May '94 / Avid/BMG / Koch.

BRITISH DANCE BANDS (3CD Set)
Sioux Sue: Loss, Joe / Deep in the heart of Texas: Loss, Joe / You again: Loss, Joe / That lovely weekend: Loss, Joe / How green was my valley: Loss, Joe / Oasis: Loss, Joe / What more can I say: Loss, Joe / Hazy lazy lane: Loss, Joe / Concerto for two: Loss, Joe / Fur trappers ball: Loss, Joe / Baby mine: Loss, Joe / Soft shoe shuffle: Loss, Joe / When I see an elephant fly: Loss, Joe / Daddy: Loss, Joe / You say the sweetest things: Loss, Joe / I don't want to set the world on fire: Loss, Joe / There's a land of begin again: Loss, Joe / Johnny Pedler: Loss, Joe / Cornsilk: Loss, Joe / Bounce me brother with a solid four: Loss, Joe / Rancho pillow: Loss, Joe / Don't cry cherie: Loss, Joe / Georgia on my mind: Gonella, Nat / Tuxedo junction: Gonella, Nat / Big noises from Winnekta: Gonella, Nat / I understand: Gonella, Nat / Nat at the woodchoppers ball: Gonella, Nat / South of the boarder: Gonella, Nat / Hep hep the jumpin' jive: Gonella, Nat / Johnson rag: Gonella, Nat / If you were the only girl in the world: Gonella, Nat / Beat me Daddy eight to a bar: Gonella, Nat / In the mood: Gonella, Nat / Ay ay ay: Gonella, Nat / No Mama no: Gonella, Nat / I haven't time to be a millionaire: Gonella, Nat / Vox poppin': Gonella, Nat / Oh Buddy in my love: Gonella, Nat / It's a pair of wings for me: Gonella, Nat / Eep ipe wanna piece of pie: Gonella, Nat / Sunrise serenade: Gonolla, Nat / Yes my darling daughter: Gonella, Nat / Plucking on the golden harp: Gonella, Nat / That's my home: Gonella, Nat / Tangerine: Roy, Harry / Hold your hats on: Roy, Harry / Oh the pity of it all: Roy, Harry / Humpt dumpty heart: Gonella, Nat / When I love I love: Roy, Harry / Was it love: Roy, Harry / Sentimental interlude: Roy, Harry / You bring the boogie woogie out in me: Roy, Harry / Greetings from you: Roy, Harry / Zoot suit: Roy, Harry / Do you care: Roy, Harry / When Daddy comes home: Roy, Harry / Darling Daisy: Roy, Harry / Elmer's tune: Roy, Harry / Madelaine: Roy, Harry / Chattanooga choo choo: Roy, Harry / Tica ti tica ta: Roy, Harry / It's funny to everyone but me: Roy, Harry / In the middle of a dance: Roy, Harry / Blues in the night: Roy, Harry / Green eyes: Roy, Harry / Shrine of St. Cecilia: Roy, Harry
CD Set _____ EMPRESS 1001
Empress / Oct '95 / THE.

BRITISH DANCE BANDS OF THE FORTIES
If I had my way / More and more / Cook house serenade / Better not roll those blue blues eyes / Hour never passes, An / I threw a kiss in the ocean / Shrine of St. Cecilia / My wubba dolly (#) / Coming in on a wing and a prayer / It's a blue world: Stone, Lew & His Band / In a little rocky valley: Stone, Lew & His Band / There's nothing new to tell you: Stone, Lew & His Band / Sing a round up song: Stone, Lew & His Band / Too romantic: Stone, Lew & His Band / Hut sut song: Stone, Lew & His Band / Mother's prayer at twilight: Stone, Lew & His Band / And so do I: Stone, Lew & His Band / We'll meet again: Stone, Lew & His Band / Keep an eye on your heart: Royal Air Force Dance Orchestra / Blue champagne: Royal Air Force Dance Orchestra / It's foolish but it's fun: Royal Air Force Dance Orchestra / Out of nowhere: Royal Air Force Dance Orchestra / There I go: Royal Air Force Dance Orchestra / Cinema / Whichever way the wind is blowing: Royal Air Force Dance Orchestra / Lover's lullaby: Royal Air Force Dance Orchestra / All our tomorrows: Royal Air Force Dance Orchestra / You started something: Royal Air Force Dance Orchestra / Apple for the teacher: Rabin, Oscar & His Band / You're mine: Rabin, Oscar & His Band / When the night is thru': Rabin, Oscar & His Band / Sometimes: Rabin, Oscar & His Band / Man and his dream: Rabin, Oscar & His Band / Moonlight avenue: Rabin, Oscar & His Band / When the rose of Tralee met Danny boy: Rabin, Oscar & His Band / Basin Street ball: Rabin, Oscar & His Band / Sing,everybody,sing: Rabin, Oscar & His Band
CD _____ CDSVL 217
Saville / Oct '91 / Conifer.

BRITISH FOLK COLLECTION
CD _____ CDSR 048
Telstar / May '94 / BMG.

BRITISH INVASION, THE
CD _____ TFP 025
Tring / Nov '92 / Tring / Prism.

BRITISH POP HISTORY
CD _____ 16103
Laserlight / Nov '94 / Target/BMG.

BRITISH POP HISTORY - THE 60'S
CD _____ 16081
Laserlight / Nov '94 / Target/BMG.

BRITISH ROCK GIANTS
CD _____ NTRCD 004
Nectar / May '93 / Pinnacle.

BRITISH SOUL VOLUME 1
This beautiful day: Jackson, Levi / Serving a sentence of life: Douglas, Carl / Beautiful night: Thomas, Jimmy / What love brings: Bernard, Kenny / I'll hold you: Frankie & Johnny / Don't make me: Lynn, Sue / Lost summer love: Silva, Lorraine / Our love is getting stronger: Night, Jason / Love is wonderful: Parfit, Paula / Stop and you'll become aware: Shapiro, Helen / Nobody knows: St. John, Tammy / Everything's gonna be alright: Arnold, P.P. / Invitation: Band Of Angels / If you knew me: Keyes, Johnny / Number one in your heart: Goins, Herbie / Need your love: Notations / Nothin' away: Lynch, Kenny / Baby I don't need your love: Chants / Stand accused: Colton, Tony / Never ever: Clements, Soul Joe / Tears of joy: Merrell, Ray
CD _____ GSCD 049
Goldmine / Feb '95 / Vital.

BRITISH TRADITIONAL JAZZ COLLECTIONS VOL.2
CD _____ 830 788-2
Philips / Mar '93 / PolyGram.

BRITS - THE AWARDS 1990
All around the world: Stansfield, Lisa / Fine time: Yazz / My prerogative: Brown, Bobby / Sowing the seeds of love: Tears For Fears / Best: Turner, Tina / My one temptation: Paris, Mica / Eye know: De La Soul / Sensual world: Bush, Kate / Girl I'm gonna miss you: Milli Vanilli / Bamboleo: Gipsy Kings / Best of me: Richard, Cliff
CD Set _____ TCD 2386
Telstar / Feb '90 / BMG.

BRITS - THE AWARDS 1992
Innuendo: Queen / Calling Elvis: Dire Straits / Mysterious ways: U2 / Cream: Prince / Rescue me (remix): Madonna / Stars: Simply Red / Can't stop this thing we started: Adams, Bryan / Don't let the sun go down on me: Michael, George & Elton John / When a man loves a woman: Bolton, Michael / All woman: Stansfield, Lisa / Promise me: Craven, Beverley / Hole hearted: Extreme / Shiny happy people: R.E.M. / Love is a stranger: Eurythmics / Sit down: James / Mystify (Live): Inxs / Love to hate you: Erasure / Killer Seal / Justified and ancient: K.L.F. / Unbelievable: EMF / Just another dream: Dennis, Cathy / Set adrift on memory bliss: PM Dawn / Thinking about your love: Thomas, Kenny / All I love: Color Me Badd / Sunshine on a rainy day: Zoe / Unfinished sympathy: Massive Attack / King is half undressed: Jellyfish / Mustang Sally: Commitments / Blue hotel: Isaak, Chris / It had to be you: Connick, Harry Jr. / Caribbean blue: Enya / Inspector Morse (main theme): Pheloung, Barrington
CD Set _____ 5152072
PolyGram TV / Feb '92 / PolyGram.

BRITS - THE AWARDS 1993
Bohemian rhapsody: Queen / Who's gonna ride your wild horses: U2 / Drowning in my own tears: Simply Red / Rhythm of my heart: Stewart, Rod / Drive: R.E.M. / Walking on broken glass: Lennox, Annie / Feels like forever: Cocker, Joe / Bad love: Clapton, Eric / One: John, Elton / No regrets: Bush, Kate / End of the road: Boyz II Men / Stay: Shakespars Sister / Too funky: Michael, George / Sleeping satellite: Archer, Tasmin / Your town: Deacon Blue / Digging in the dirt: Gabriel, Peter / Sexy M.F.: Prince / People everyday: Arrested Development / Lay all your love on me: Erasure / Boss drum: Shamen / Blue room: Orb / Please don't go: KWS / Baker Street: Undercover / Ain't no man: Carroll, Dina / Free your mind: En Vogue / Friday I'm in love: Cure / Weather with you: Crowded House / Million love songs: Take That / Time to make you mine: Morgan, Lisa / I wonder why: Shoers, Curtis / Crucify: Amos, Tori / Deeply dippy: Right Said Fred / Constant craving: Lang, k.d. / Celts: Enya
CD _____ 5160752
PolyGram TV / Feb '93 / PolyGram.

BRITS - THE AWARDS 1995
What's the frequency, Kenneth: R.E.M. / My heart: Young, Neil & Crazy Horse / Patience of angels: Reader, Eddi / Mmm mmm mmm mmm: Crash Test Dummies / Red shoes: Bush, Kate / Kiss from a rose: Seal / Cornflake girl: Amos, Tori / Sulky girl: Costello, Elvis / Run to you: Adams, Bryan / Hung up: Weller, Paul / You gotta be: Des'ree / Love town: Gabriel, Peter / More you ignore me, the closer I get: Morrissey / Thank you for hearing me: O'Connor, Sinead / Zombie: Cranberries / Motherless child: Clapton, Eric / I believe: Detroit, Marcella / Circle of life: John, Elton / Seven seconds: N'Dour, Youssou / Searching: China Black / Sweetness: Gayle, Michelle / Half the man: Jamiroquai / Just a step from heaven: Eternal / Midnight at the oasis: Brand New Heavies / Love the one you're with: Vandross, Luther / Sight for sore eyes: M People / Mama said: Anderson, Carleen / If I only knew: Jones, Tom / So natural: Stansfield, Lisa / Sly: Massive Attack / Stay another day: East 17 / Things can only get better: D Ream / Girls and boys: Blur / Insomnia: Echobelly / Wild ones: Suede / Numb: Portishead / Live forever: Oasis
CD Set _____ MOODCD 39
Columbia / Feb '95 / Sony.

BROKEN DOWN ANGELS
CD _____ PWKS 4156
Carlton Home Entertainment / Nov '94 / Carlton Home Entertainment.

BROTHER, CAN YOU SPARE A DIME
Were you there / Maledetto / Lungi da te / Bist du bei mir / Hear de lambs/Plenty good room / Go down Moses / Bye and bye / Steal away / Crucifixion / Roun' about de mountain / Standin' in the need of prayer / Negro spiritual medley / Heav'n heav'n / Waterboy / Go down Moses/Deep river / Couldn't hear nobody pray / Every time I feel the spirit / Swing low, sweet chariot / Goin' to shoot all over God's heaven / Ol' man river / Street cries of New Orleans / Cobbler's song / Brother can you spare a dime
CD _____ GEMM CD 9484
Pearl / Mar '91 / Harmonia Mundi.

BROWNSWOOD WORKSHOP
CD _____ 518960-2
Talkin' Loud / Mar '94 / PolyGram.

BROWNSWOOD WORKSHOP MULTI-DIRECTION 2
Spontaneity: Jazz Brothers / April in Tokyo: Pronoia / Hug: Tiny Voice Production / La tune: Naoyuki Honzawa / Return of the space age: Audio Active / Seasons change: Sylk 130 / Deep water: Trio Da Lata / Por El Diet Music / Tune for us: Kruder & Dorfmeister / Rock 'n' roll philosophy: Love T.K.O. / Is it worth it: D.J. Milo
CD _____ 5286792
Talkin' Loud / Sep '93 / PolyGram.

BRUMBEAT - MOTORCITY MUSIC
What's the matter baby: Wayne, Carl & The Vikings / This is love: Wayne, Carl & The Vikings / My girl: Wayne, Carl & The Vikings / Flashback: Rockin' Berries / Walk baby walk: Neal, Johnny & The Starliners / Some people only: Powell, Keith / It keeps rainin': Powell, Keith / My colour is blue: James, Nicky / Wake up my mind: Uglys / Halleiujah: Revolution / Daydreaming of you / Go now / Night of fear / Stephanie knows who / Your lovin' ways: Wayne, Carl & The Vikings / You could be fun (at the end of a party): Wayne, Carl & The Vikings / Shimmy shammy jingle: Wayne, Carl & The Vikings / Let's try again: Rockin' Berries / Goodbye girl: Powell, Keith / Two little people: Powell, Keith & Billie Davis / Swingin' tight: Powell, Keith & Billie Davis / Take me back: James, Nicky / That's alright: Powell, Jimmy & The Dimensions / Green light / Lose your money / I don't want to go on without you / Sunshine help me / Something else
CD _____ NEXCD 251
Sequel / Sep '93 / BMG.

BUDAL LARDIL
CD _____ LARRCD 285
Larrikin / Jun '94 / Roots / Direct / ADA / CM.

BUDDHIST CHANT 1/MAHA PIRIT - THE GREAT CHANT
Jecklin Disco / Nov '90 / Pinnacle.
CD _____ JD 6512

BUENOS AIRES 30'S TANGOS
CD _____ 995222
EPM / Jun '93 / Discovery / ADA.

BUENOS AIRES BANONEON ORCHESTRA
CD _____ CDCH 702
Milan / Feb '91 / BMG / Silva Screen.

BUENOS AIRES BY NIGHT
La cumparsita: Basso, Jose / El firulete: Basso, Jose / El choclo: Sexeto Mayor / Adios nonino: Sexeto Mayor / De vuelta y media: Varela, Hector / Paloma blanca: Varela, Hector / Quejas de bandoneon: Troilo, Anibal / Danzarin: Trojilo, Anibal / Verano porteno: Garello, Paul / Margarita de agosto: Garello, Paul / La Cachila: Pugliese, Osvaldo / La Yumba: Pugliese, Osvaldo / El dia que me quieras: Gardel, Carlos / Mi buenos aires querido: Gardel, Carlos / Grisel: Mores, Mariano / Taquito militar: Mores, Mariano / La puñalada: Canaro, Francisco / La tablada: Canaro, Francisco / Yira yira: Sassone, Florindo / Adios muchachos: Sassone, Florindo
CD _____ CDEMS 1487
EMI / May '93 / EMI.

BULGARIA - MUSIC OF SHOPE COUNTY
CD _____ LDX 274970
La Chant Du Monde / Apr '94 / Harmonia Mundi / ADA.

BULGARIAN BRASS
CD _____ PAN 153CD
Pan / Mar '95 / ADA / Direct / CM.

BULGARIAN FOLK MUSIC
CD _____ SOW 90115
Sounds Of The World / Sep '93 / Target/BMG.

BULLSEYE BLUES CHRISTMAS
CD _____ CDBB 9567
Bullseye Blues / Oct '95 / Direct.

BURIED ALIVE
CD _____ BCD 4052
Backs / Feb '96 / Disc.

BURLESQUE IN JAZZ (20 Songs)
CD _____ GOJCD 53080
Giants Of Jazz / Mar '92 / Target/BMG / Cadillac.

BURNING AMBITIONS
(History of punk)
Boredom: *Buzzcocks* / Bingo masters breakout: *Fall* / 12XU: *Wire* / Life: *Alternative TV* / Keys to your heart: *101'ers* / I'm alive: *999* / Gary Gilmore's eyes: *Adverts* / (Get a) grip (on yourself): *Stranglers* / Baby baby: *Vibrators* / Oh bondage up yours: *X-Ray Spex* / I'm stranded: *Saints* / Chinese rocks: *Thunders, Johnny & The Heartbreakers* / Love song: *Damned* / In a rut: *Ruts* / Stranglehold: *UK Subs* / Flares and slippers: *Cockney Rejects* / Wait: *Killing Joke* / Holiday in Cambodia: *Dead Kennedys* / Last rockers: *Vice Squad* / Someone's gonna die: *Anti Pasti* / City baby attacked by rats: *G.B.H.* / Russians in the DHSS: *Attila The Stockbroker* / Lust for glory: *Angelic Upstarts*
CD _____ CDBRED 3
Cherry Red / Oct '88 / Pinnacle.

BURNING AMBITIONS VOL.2
Then he kissed me: *Hollywood Brats* / I don't care: *Boys* / Thinkin' of the USA: *Eater* / Safety pin stuck in my heart: *Fitzgerald, Patrick* / Automatic lover: *Vibrators* / Action time vision: *Alternative TV* / Murder of Liddle Towers: *Angelic Upstarts* / C.I.D.: *UK Subs* / Police car: *Cockney Rejects* / Teenage kicks: *Undertones* / Totally wired: *Fall* / Kill the Poor: *Dead Kennedys* / Exploited barmy army: *Exploited* / So what: *Anti Nowhere League* / Seventeen years of hell: *Partizan* / Stab the Judge: *One Way System* / Run like hell: *Peter & The Test Tube Babies* / Smash the discos: *Business* / Warriors: *Blitz* / Dozen girls: *Damned* / Summer of '81: *Violators* / Megalomania: *Blood* / vengeance: *New Model Army* / You'll never know: *New Model Army*
CD _____ CDGRAM 64
Cherry Red / Jun '93 / Pinnacle.

BURNING LOVE
CD _____ HRCD 8045
Disky / Dec '93 / THE / BMG / Discovery / Pinnacle.

BURNING UP
CD _____ CDTRL 336
Trojan / Mar '94 / Jetstar / Total/BMG.

BURNLEY BLUES FESTIVAL '89
CD _____ JSPCD 228
JSP / Jun '89 / ADA / Target/BMG / Direct / Cadillac / Complete/Pinnacle.

BUSTIN' OUT
CD _____ VPRC 1046
Steely & Cleevie / May '89 / Jetstar.

BUSTIN' SURFBOARDS
Surf jam: *Beach Boys* / Out of limits: *Marketts* / Fast freight: *Valens, Ritchie* / Our man Flint: *Challengers* / Curl rider: *Surf Raiders* / Our favorite Martian: *Fuller, Bobby* / Perfect wave: *Norman, Neil* / Wild weekend: *Rockin' Rebels* / Victor: *Dale, Dick & His Del-Tones* / Bustin' surfboards: *Tornadoes* / Yang bu: *Messina, Jim* / Surf rider: *Lively Ones* / Lonely surfer: *Nitzsche, Jack*
CD _____ GNPD 2152
GNP Crescendo / Jul '95 / Silva Screen.

BUY THIS USED CD
CD _____ DE 12064-2
Homestead / Oct '93 / SRD.

BUYAKA
(The Ultimate Dancehall Collection)
CD _____ 923722
Big Beat / Mar '94 / Pinnacle.

BY ANY MEANS NECESSARY
CD _____ YRECD 001
YRE / Nov '93 / Grapevine.

BY REQUEST
CD _____ GSCD 041
Goldmine / Aug '94 / Vital.

C

CABARET CHRISTMAS, A
Winter wonderland: *Hampton Callaway, Ann & Billy Stritch* / Christmas love song: *Hampton Callaway, Ann* / I'll be home for Christmas: *Stritch, Billy* / Merry Christmas to me/Hard candy Christmas: *Sullivan, K.T.* / Let it snow, let it snow, let it snow: *Carroll, Barbara* / It must be Christmas: *Mulligan, Gerry* / After the holiday: *Marcovicci, Andrea* / Silent night: *Akers, Karen & Andrea Marcovicci* / I don't remember Christmas: *Akers, Karen* / Christmas waltz: *Whiting, Margaret* / What are you doing New Year's Eve: *Haran, Mary Cleere* / Christmas in the city: *Leonhart, Jay* / Have yourself a merry little Christmas: *Loudon, Dorothy* / White Christmas: *Cook, Barbara*
CD _____ DRGCD 91415
DRG / Nov '93 / New Note.

CABARET'S GOLDEN AGE VOL.1
Lili Marlene: *Andersen, Lale* / Suppose: *Baker, Josephine* / Just once for all time: *Garat, Henri* / La cucaracha: *Niessen, Gertrude* / Solomon: *Welch, Elisabeth* / Luxury cruise: *Andersen, Inga* / I'm one of the queens of England: *Byng, Douglas* / Il m'a vue nue: *Mistinguett* / I want yer, ma honey: *Guilbert, Yvette* / I should like to be really in love: *Ahlers, Anny* / 2-2-22 Timbuctoo: *Blaney, Norah* / Pretty little baby: *Baker, Josephine* / I'm just a poor little woman: *Leander, Zarah* / Folies musicales: *Betove* / Under the red lamps: *Andersen, Lale* / Je voudrais vous dire en Francais: *Serrano, Rosita* / Is your heart still free: *Ahlers, Anny* / Nymph errant: *Lawrence, Gertrude* / Hollyholly/hollyhollywood: *Hansen, Max* / Ca c'est Paris: *Mistinguett* / Symphonie: *Dietrich, Marlene* / Spring: *Byng, Douglas* / When lights are low: *Welch, Elisabeth* / La Conga: *Niessen, Gertrude* / Falling in love again: *Dietrich, Marlene*
CD _____ PASTCD 9727
Flapper / '90 / Pinnacle.

CABARET'S GOLDEN AGE VOL.2
Night and day: *Hutch* / Darling je vous aime beaucoup: *Hildegarde* / Button up your shoes and dance: *Wall, Max* / Wistaria: *Mayerl, Billy* / Stately homes of England: *Coward, Sir Noel* / La paloma: *Serrano, Rosita* / Dre rote rosen: *Andersen, Lale* / You've got to pay for everything you get: *Frankau, Ronald* / Hold 'em Joe: *Lili-Verona* / Je ne dis pas non: *Chevalier, Maurice* / Come and join the no-shirt party: *Long, Norman* / Am I blue: *Anona Winn* / Le chanson des rues: *Sablon, Jean* / Thank you so much, Mrs Lowsborough-Goodby: *Porter, Cole* / Where are the songs: *Coward, Sir Noel* / Sombreros et mantillas: *Ketty, Rina* / Paddlin' Madelin' home: *Layton & Johnstone* / Room with a view: *Hildegarde* / Mon coeur: *Chevalier, Maurice* / Two little babes in the wood: *Porter, Cole* / I'm shooting high: *Marsh, Carolyn* / Her mother came too: *Buchanan, Jack* / Le potpourri d'Alain Gerbault: *Printemps, Yvonne*
CD _____ PASTCD 9737
Flapper / Mar '91 / Pinnacle.

CADENCE STORY, THE
Butterfly / All I have to do is dream / Poetry in motion / Lollipop / I'm gonna knock on your door / Rumble / Forty five men in a telephone booth / Dead Don / Bye bye love / Ballad of Davy Crockett / Mr. Sandman / Hernando's hideaway / I like your kind of love / Born to be with you / Lighthouse / Message from James Dean / Wake up little Susie / Baby doll / I love my girl / Swag / IT keeps right on a-hurtin' since I left / Ain't gonna wash for a week / Ebb Tide / Eh, cumpari
CD _____ CDCHD 550
Ace / Aug '95 / Pinnacle / Cadillac / Complete/Pinnacle.

CAFE CLASSICS
CD _____ 74321263432
RCA / Mar '95 / BMG.

CAFE DE PARIS 1930-41
(24 Accordian Classics From The Boulevards of Paris)
Falmbee montalbanaise / L'accordeoniste / El ferrero / Enivrante / Strange harmony / Mado / Matelotte / Quand on se promene / Sporting java / Pepee / La guinguette a ferme ses volets / Swing valse / Brise napolitaine / Soir de dispute / Le charmeur de serpents / Les triolets / Gallito / Swing '39 / Pinsonnette / Rosetta / Melancolie / Jeanette
CD _____ MCCD 096
Music Club / Mar '93 / Disc / THE / CM.

CAFE DEL MAR
CD _____ REACTCD 041
React / Jun '94 / Vital.

CAFE DEL MAR IBIZA VOLUMEN DOS
Haunted dancehall: *Sabres Of Paradise* / Making of Jill: *Mark & Henry's* / Tarenah: *Lab* / Moment scale: *Silent Poets* / Entre dos aguas: *Lucia, Paco De* / Sunset: *T.B.M.P.* / Eugene: *Salt Tank* / Devotion: *D-Note* / Blue eyes sunrise: *Woodshed* / Easter song: *Man Called Adam* / Unity: *Antoine, Marc* / Everybody loves the sunshine: *Ramp* / La mar: *Atlas*
CD _____ REACTCD 062
React / Jul '95 / Vital.

CAJUAL RELIEF
CD _____ SOMCD 3
Ministry Of Sound / Jul '95 / 3MV / Warner Music.

CAJUN CLASSICS
Back door: *Louisiana aces* / Pine grove blues: *Abshire, Nathan* / Saturday night special: *Cormier, Lesa & The Sundown Playboys* / Jolie blon: *Bruce, Vin* / Sugar bee: *Cleveland Crochet* / Lafayette two-step: *Roger, Aldus* / Cher cherie: *Guidry, Doc* / Flames d'enfer: *Pitre, Austin* / Step it fast: *Bonsall, Joe & the orange playboys* / Parlez vous francais: *Matte, Bill* / I'll take you home: *Bertrand, Robert* / Equand j'etais pauvre: *Balfa, Dewey* / Lemonade song: *Broussard, Leroy* / Grande bosco: *Lejeune, Iry* / Mamou two step: *Walker, Lawrence* / Hippy ti yo: *Newman, Jimmy C.* / Sha ba ba: *Brown, Sidney* / Cajun stripper: *Richard, Belton* / J'ai fait mon idee: *Bergeron, Shirley* / Choupique two step: *Greely, David* / La pointe aux pins: *Jambalaya Cajun Band & Reggie Matte* / Creole stomp: *Breaux,*

CAJUN DANCE HALL SPECIAL
CD _____ ROU 11570CD
Rounder / Feb '93 / CM / Direct / ADA / Cadillac.

CAJUN FAIS DO-DO
CD _____ ARHCD 416
Arhoolie / Jan '96 / ADA / Direct / Cadillac.

CAJUN HONKY TONK
CD _____ ARHCD 427
Arhoolie / Apr '95 / ADA / Direct / Cadillac.

CAJUN HOT SAUCE
CD _____ CDCHD 591
Ace / Feb '96 / Pinnacle / Cadillac / Complete/Pinnacle.

CAJUN LOUISIANE 1928-39
CD Set _____ FA 019CD
Fremeaux / Nov '95 / Discovery / ADA.

CAJUN SATURDAY NIGHT
CD _____ CD 102
Swallow / '88 / ADA.

CAJUN SOCIAL MUSIC
CD _____ SFCD 40046
Smithsonian Folkways / Sep '94 / ADA / Direct / Koch / CM / Cadillac.

CAJUN SPICE
CD _____ CD 11550
Rounder / Oct '93 / CM / Direct / ADA / Cadillac.

CAJUN VOL.1
(Abbeville Breakdown 1929-1937)
CD _____ 4672502
Columbia / Apr '91 / Sony.

CAJUN VOL.2
(Fais Do Do)
Ma blonde est partie: *Breaux, Amedee* / Les tracas du hobo: *Breaux, Amedee* / Two step de Mama: *Ardoin, Amade* / Two step de eunice: *Ardoin, Amade* / Rasalia: *Segura, Dewey* / You're small and sweet: *Segura, Dewey* / Far away from home blues: *Segura, Dewey* / Fais do-do negre: *Freres, Breaux* / Tiger rag blues: *Freres, Breaux* / One step a Marie: *Freres, Breaux* / Mazurka de la louisiane: *Freres, Breaux* / Le vieux soulard et sa femme: *Breaux, Cleoma* / Madam atchen: *Ardoin, Amade* / Taunt aline: *Ardoin, Amade* / Le blues du petit chien: *Freres, Breaux* / La valse d'auguste: *Freres, Breaux* / La valse d'utah: *Freres, Breaux*
CD _____ 4757032
Columbia / May '94 / Sony.

CALANAIS
An Lanntair / May '95 / Duncans / ADA.

CD _____ CD 001

CALBMELAN
Dat / Nov '95 / Pinnacle.

CD _____ DATCD 22

CALENDAR MUSIC IN THE CENTRAL VALLEYS
La Chant Du Monde / Sep '92 / Harmonia Mundi / ADA.

CD _____ LDX 274938

CALIENTE - HOT
CD _____ NW 244
New World / '88 / Harmonia Mundi / ADA / Cadillac.
CD _____ NW 244
New World / Aug '92 / Harmonia Mundi / ADA / Cadillac.

CALIENTE GOLD COLLECTION
(2CD Set)
CD Set _____ D2CD 4021
Deja Vu / Jun '95 / THE.

CALIFORNIA COOL
(Hip Sounds Of The West Coast)
This could be the start of something: *Murphy, Mark* / Man with the golden arm (main title): *May, Billy & His Orchestra* / Black nightgown: *Mulligan, Gerry & Shelly Manne* / Squimp: *Hamilton, Chico* / But not for me: *Baker, Chet Quartet* / Ironic: *Guiffre, Jimmy & Jack Sheldon Quartet* / I hear music: *Hawes, Hampton Trio* / Lover man: *Konitz, Lee & Gerry Mulligan Quartet* / Hey Bellboy: *Woods, Gloria & Peter Candoli* / Diablo's dance: *Pepper, Art & Shorty Rogers* / Our love is here to stay: *Edwards, Teddy & Les McCann Ltd* / Route 66: *Troup, Bobby* / Two can play: *Gordon, Bob & Jack Montrose Quintet* / Take five: *Shank, Bud* / Jimmy's theme: *Baker, Chet & Bud Shank Orchestra* / Something cool: *Christy, June* / Mambo de la pinta: *Pepper, Art Quartet* / Don't worry you: *Lee, Peggy & George Shearing* / Katanga: *Amy, Curtis & Dupree Bolton* / Handful of stars: *Chaloff, Serge* / West coast blues: *Criss, Sonny*
CD _____ BNZ 303
Blue Note / Feb '93 / EMI.

CALIFORNIA DREAMIN'
CD _____ MPV 5515
Movieplay / Jun '95 / Target/BMG.

CALIFORNIA DREAMING
Cantamilla: *Tranquility Bass* / Three nudes: *Hawke* / Energize: *Island Universe* / Reality of nature: *Young American Primitive* / Funk you very much: *Ultraviolet Catastrophe* / Taste of your own medicine: *Elements of Trance* / Feelin' real good (Not on LP): *Aquatherium* / Transmit liberation (Not on LP): *Single Cell Orchestra* / Straight up caffeine: *Up Above The World* / Theme from Daisy Glow (Not on LP): *Daisy Glow*
CD _____ TRUCD 3
Internal / Jan '94 / PolyGram / Pinnacle.

CALL OF THE BANSHEE
CD _____ SPV 08438932
SPV / Feb '95 / Plastic Head.

CALLING ALL WORKERS
F.D.R. Jones / Bandwagon / Mrs. Bagwash / Ernie Bagwash / Bell / It's that man again / Lambeth walk / Calling all workers / I'm one of the Whitehall warriors / It's foolish but it's fun / All over the place / Chattanooga choo choo / I-love-you so / Out in Indiah / Blues in the night / Take the world exactly as you find it / Why don't you do it right / Warsaw concerto / People will say we're in love / My heart and I / This is the army / Dark music / I couldn't sleep a wink last night
CD _____ CDCHD 302
Happy Days / Aug '94 / Conifer.

CALYPSO CALALOO
(Early Carnival Music From Trinidad 1914-50)
CD _____ ROU 1105CD
Rounder / Apr '94 / CM / Direct / ADA / Cadillac.

CALYPSO CARNIVAL
CD _____ ROU 1077CD
Rounder / Feb '93 / CM / Direct / ADA / Cadillac.

CALYPSO LADIES - 1926-41
CD _____ HTCD 06
Heritage / Feb '91 / Swift / Roots / Wellard / Direct / Hot Shot / Jazz Music / ADA.

CALYPSO WAR
Women police in England: *Mighty Terror & His Calypsonians* / Brown skin gal: *Mighty Terror & His Calypsonians* / Kitch cavalcade: *Mighty Terror & His Calypsonians* / Little Jeannie: *Mighty Terror & His Calypsonians* / Patricia gone with Millicent: *Mighty Terror & His Calypsonians* / Heading north: *Mighty Terror & His Calypsonians* / Calypso war: *Mighty Terror & His Calypsonians* / Jamaica girl: *Mighty Terror & His Calypsonians* / T.V. calypso: *Mighty Terror & His Calypsonians* / Prince Rainer: *Lord Invader & His Calypso Quintet* / Mahalia, I want back my dollar: *Lord Invader & His Calypso Quintet* / Donkey City: *Bowers, Ben & Bertie King's Royal Jamaicans* / Not me: *Bowers, Ben & Bertie King's Royal Jamaicans* / Naughty little flea: *Bowers, Ben & Bertie King's Royal Jamaicans* / Belinda: *Lord Ivanhoe & His Caribbean Knights* / Water gobbler: *Lord Ivanhoe & His Caribbean Knights* / Africa, here I come: *Lord Ivanhoe & His Caribbean Knights* / Life the iron curtain: *Lord Ivanhoe & His Caribbean Knights* / You don't need glasses to see: *Lord Invader & His Calypso Rhythm Boys* / New York subway: *Lord Invader & His Calypso Rhythm Boys* / I'm going back to Africa: *Lord Invader & His Calypso Rhythm Boys* / Me one alone: *Lord Invader & His Calypso Rhythm Boys* / Reincarnation: *Lord Invader & His Calypso Rhythm Boys* / Teddy boy calypso (Bring back the old cat-o-nine): *Lord Invader & His Calypso Rhythm Boys* / My experience on the Rieperbahn: *Lord Invader & His Calypso Rhythm Band*
CD _____ NEXCD 232
Sequel / Aug '93 / BMG.

CALYPSOS - 1930'S
CD _____ FL 7004
Folklyric / Apr '95 / Direct / Cadillac.

CAMBODIA - MUSIC OF THE ROYAL PALACES
CD _____ C 5560034CD
Ocora / Jul '94 / Harmonia Mundi / ADA.

CAMDEN CRAWL, THE
CD _____ PUBE 07CD
Love Train / Nov '95 / SRD.

CAME FROM OUTER SPACE
CD _____ OUTERSPACE 23
Neuton / Jun '94 / Plastic Head.

CAMINO AL SOL
CD _____ TUMICD 044
Tumi / Apr '95 / Sterns / Discovery.

CAN YOU HANDLE IT
Zoom: *Fat Larry's Band* / Purely by coincidence: *Sweet Sensation* / Jack in the box: *Moments* / No one can say no to you: *Hyman, Phyllis* / Midas touch: *Midnight Star* / Friends: *Shalamar* / You to me are everything: *Real Thing* / Part time love: *Knight, Gladys & The Pips* / My girl: *Whispers* / Where did our love go: *Elbert, Donnie* / Lean on me: *Moore, Melba* / Can you handle it: *Redd, Sharon* / Best thing that ever*

happened to me: *Knight, Gladys & The Pips* / You'll never know what you're missing: *Real Thing* / Still in love: *Lucas, Carrie* / Homely girl: *Chi-Lites* / Casanova: *Coffee* / You are my starship: *Connors, Norman*
CD _____ TRTCD 141
TrueTrax / Oct '94 / THE.

CAN YOU SEE IT 1988-93
CD _____ INVCD 023
Invisible / Feb '94 / Plastic Head.

CANDID JAZZ SAMPLER
CD _____ CCD 79000
Candid / Nov '93 / Cadillac / Jazz Music / Wellard / Direct.

CANDLELIGHT
CD _____ CANDLE 011CD
Candlelight / Sep '95 / Plastic Head.

CANNABIS WEEKEND
CD _____ EFA 127022
Dope / Mar '95 / SRD.

CANNED BLUES
CD _____ HRCD 8036
Disky / Jul '94 / THE / BMG / Discovery / Pinnacle.

CANNED HEAT BLUES
(Masters Of The Delta Blues)
Furry's blues: *Lewis, Furry* / I will turn your money green: *Lewis, Furry* / Mistreatin' mama: *Lewis, Furry* / Dry land blues: *Lewis, Furry* / Cannonball blues: *Lewis, Furry* / Kassie Jones (pts 1 & 2): *Lewis, Furry* / Judge harsh blues: *Lewis, Furry* / Cool drink of water blues: *Johnson, Tommy* / Big road blues: *Johnson, Tommy* / Bye bye blues: *Johnson, Tommy* / Maggie Campbell blues: *Johnson, Tommy* / Canned heat blues: *Johnson, Tommy* / Lonesome home blues: *Johnson, Tommy* / Big fat mama blues: *Johnson, Tommy* / Saturday blues: *Bracey, Ishman* / Left alone blues: *Bracey, Ishman* / Leavin' town blues: *Bracey, Ishman* / Brown mama blues: *Bracey, Ishman* / Trouble hearted blues: *Bracey, Ishman* / Four day blues: *Bracey, Ishman*
CD _____ ND 90648
Bluebird / May '92 / BMG.

CAN'T KEEP FROM CRYING
(Blues From The Death Of President Kennedy)
CD _____ TCD 5007
Testament / Oct '94 / Complete/Pinnacle / ADA / Koch.

CAN'T LIVE WITHOUT IT
Can't live without it: *Tucker, Luther* / Voodoo man: *White, Lavelle* / Why'd you have to say that I word: *Kane, Candye* / Bird nest on the ground: *Bramhall, Doyle* / Baby please don't lie to me: *Wilson, Kim* / Give me time: *Foley, Sue* / Slow down baby: *Pryor, Snooky* / She put the hurt on me: *Sahm, Doug* / It won't be long: *Kane, Candye* / Itchy and scratchy: *Cowdrey, Lewis* / Keep on drinking: *Tucker, Luther* / Stop these teardrops: *White, Lavelle*
CD _____ ANTCD 9905
Antones / Jul '95 / Hot Shot / Direct / ADA.

CANTE FLAMENCO
CD _____ NI 5251
Nimbus / Sep '94 / Nimbus.

CANTONA - THE ALBUM
Eric Cantona: *Ratmond Bizarre* / Have you heard about Eric: *Captain Sensible* / Cantona Superstar: *Her* / Ooh ah Cantona: *Boyle, Pete & The K-Stand* / Monsieur Genius: *Boyle, Pete & The K-Stand* / Grand old Cantona: *Boyle, Pete & The K-Stand* / Eric the King: *Boyle, Pete & The K-Stand* / 12 days of Cantona: *Boyle, Pete & The K-Stand* / Do the frog: *Phillipe, Louis* / Eric (please don't go): *Half Time Oranges* / Eric Cantona what a bloody star: *Red Deville*
CD _____ PELE 010CD
Exotica / Oct '95 / Vital.

CAPE BRETON ISLAND
CD _____ NI 5383
Nimbus / Sep '94 / Nimbus.

CAPE-VERDE ISLANDS (THE ROOTS)
CD _____ PS 65061
Playasound / Nov '90 / Harmonia Mundi / ADA.

CAPITOL RARE
(Funky Notes From The West Coast)
Music is my sanctuary: *Bartz, Gary* / Sky islands: *Caldera* / Annie Mae: *Cole, Natalie* / Sunshine: *Wilson, Nancy* / As: *Harris, Gene* / Genie: *Lyle, Bobby* / I love you: Taste Of Honey / While I'm alone: *Mabu* / Peace of mind: *Allen, Rance Group* / Inside you: *Henderson, Eddie* / Every generation: *Laws, Ronnie* / She's my summer breeze: *Reflections* / Losalamitos (Latinfunklovesong): *Harris, Gene* / About love: *Sidran, Ben* / Dindi: *Lawson, Janet* / Woman of the ghetto: *Shaw, Marlena* / Cheshire cat: *Foster, Ronnie*
CD _____ CDP 8298652
Capitol / Jun '94 / EMI.

CAPITOL RARE 2
It's a pleasure: *Brown, Sheree* / Before you break my heart: *Dunlap, Gene* / La Costa: *Cole, Natalie* / Carnival de L'esprit: *Bartz, Gary* / Sunshower: *Mouzon, Alphonse* / Abdullah & Abraham: *Hamilton, Chico* / Tidal wave: *Laws, Ronnie* / It's a plea-

McRae, Carmen / Space spiritual: *Adderley, Nat Sextet* / Expressway to your heart: *Thunder, Margo* / Beggar for the blues: *Drew, Patti* / Windy C: 100% Pure Poison / Theme for Relana: *Harris, Gene* / Inside my love: *Riperton, Minnie* / Nightfall: *Stratavarious*
CD _____ CDP 8356072
Capitol / Oct '95 / EMI.

CAPTAIN OF YOUR SHIP
(New Dancehall Shots)
CD _____ SHCD 45006
Shanachie / Sep '93 / Koch / ADA / Greensleeves.

CARAMBOLAGE
CD _____ CMPCD 58
CMP / Nov '92 / Vital/SAM.

CARIB SOUL
CD _____ RASCD 3089
Ras / Apr '92 / Jetstar / Greensleeves / SRD / Direct.

CARIBBEAN BEAT
La ki ni nano: *Dixie Band* / No dji m'en nouille: *Caribbean Combo* / Sally Brown: *Aitken, Laurel* / Bailando: *Orlando, Ramon* / Sans cesse di nouille: *Cabrimol, Jean Michel* / No dance: *Imagination Brass* / Argent: *Amoro, Rene Paul* / Sabor y pena: *Roque, Victor* / Pa kita' m: *Vega Band* / La jan mwe: *Reasons Orchestra* / Gozolinn: *Rosier, Piar* / Wasmashin: *Prudencia, Macorio* / Agua: *Vargas, Wilfred*
CD _____ INT 31122
Intuition / Aug '92 / New Note.

CARIBBEAN BEAT VOL.2
Bayoe: *Imagination Brass* / On et yo: *Toumpak* / El emneito: *La Fuerza Mayor* / Sinking ship: *Gypsy* / Bayo bayo: *Dixie Band* / Doux doux cherne: *Heartbeat* / Enojado: *Huracan* / Which one is me home: *Exile One* / Sa ki di sa: *Dede Saint Prix* / Guns of Navarone: *Skatalites* / Party feeling: *Massive Chandelier* / Musica latina: *Fernadito Villalona* / Hot hot hot: *Arrow*
CD _____ INT 31262
Intuition / Nov '93 / New Note.

CARIBBEAN BEAT VOL.3
El bailabien / La pachanga del futbol / Pimpele / Tafia / Mata shimaraya / Hickee / La pachanga / Pitaste / Pajaro loco / La negra quiere / No le crea / Zap zap / Laissez passer
CD _____ INT 31472
Intuition / Oct '94 / New Note.

CARIBBEAN BEAT VOL.4
Baila / Quien ha visto por ahi mi sombrero de yarey / Moon hop / El baile del perrito / Que seria de cali / Tipico caliente / El merengue / Karayib leve / Echao pa 'lante / Para que aprendan / SOS Maya / Beberte / Losd sitio entera
CD _____ INT 31532
Intuition / Oct '95 / New Note.

CARIBBEAN COCKTAIL
CD _____ EMPRCD 580
Emporio / Jul '95 / THE / Disc / CM.

CARIBBEAN TROPICAL DANCE PARTY - 20 HOT CARIBBEAN RHYTHMS
Marinero: *Los Latinos* / Quiero un sombrero: *Carcamo, Pablo* / Consigueme eso: *Musica Latina* / O cana sordi: *Tumbao* / Chapa'lante Catalina: *Carcamo, Pablo* / El pescador: *Carcamo, Pablo* / Un, dos, tres: *Musica Latina* / Mensaje de mi Colombia: *Carcamo, Pablo* / Villa carino: *Carcamo, Pablo* / Candela y tumbao: *Tumbao* / Fantasia caliente: *Carcamo, Pablo* / Los plru-los: *Musica Latina* / Mi alegre serenata: *Carcamo, Pablo* / Vuela paloma: *Tumbao* / Solo quedo: *Carcamo, Pablo* / Suave: *Carcamo, Pablo* / El africano: *Musica Latina* / Ojala que llueva cafe: *Carcamo, Pablo* / Sol y arena: *Carcamo, Pablo*
CD _____ EUCD 1209
ARC / Sep '93 / ARC Music / Direct.

CARIBEAN STEEL DRUMS
CD _____ GRF 201
Tring / Jan '93 / Tring / Prism.

CARNEGIE HALL SALUTES THE JAZZ MASTERS
CD _____ 523150-2
Verve / Oct '94 / PolyGram.

CARNIVAL IN RIO
Bescol / Aug '94 / CM / Target/BMG. _____ CD 399

CARNIVAL JUMP-UP
CD _____ DE 4014
Delos / Feb '94 / Conifer.

CARNIVAL OF SOUL VOLUME 1: WISHES
Wishes: *Metrics* / She's so fine: *Topics* / All I need is your love: *Manhattans* / Me, myself and I: *Jenkins, Norma* / I need a guy: *Lovettes* / Forget him: *Brown, Barbara* / Nobody loves me (like my baby): *Caldwell, Harry* / I love you more: *Williams, Lee & The Cymbals* / I'll keep holding on: *Ruffin, Kenneth* / Nothing will ever change (this love of mine): *Jules, Jimmy* / My love is yours to-night: *Turner Brothers* / It's everything about you (that I love): *Williams, Lee & The Cymbals* / I wanna be (your everything): *Pretenders* / Love has passed me by: *Terrell, Phil* / I say yeah: *Pets* / I'll catch you on

the rebound: *Leon & The Metronomes* / Can I come in: *Terrell, Phil* / Come home to Daddy: *Goggins, Curby* / I can tell: *Little Royal* / I'm gonna be missing you: *Bailey, Rene* / My baby's gone: *Tren-Teens* / I call it love: *Pretenders* / Until you come back to me: *Manhattans* / Go right on: *Three Reasons*
CD _____ CDKEND 108
Kent / Oct '91 / Pinnacle.

CARNIVAL OF SOUL VOLUME 2: FEELIN' GOOD
I'm just a young boy: *Terrell, Phil* / So in love: *Brown, Barbara* / Hey girl (where are you going): *Topics* / There goes a fool: *Manhattans* / Please come back: *Caldwell, Harry* / Peeping through the window: *Williams, Lee & The Cymbals* / I found you: *Metrics* / That's what love will do: *Symphonies* / I'm love one forgot: *Pretenders* / Some-times I wonder: *Brown, Barbara* / Don't let yourself go: *Jules, Jimmy* / Boogaloo party: *Harold & Connie* / Little Miss Soul: *Lovettes* / Love is breaking out all over: *Manhattans* / Broken heart: *Pretenders* / Warm and tender love: *Bailey, Rene* / Don't you run away: *Terrell, Phil* / I need someone to love: *Jenkins, Norma* / I don't have to cry: *Topics* / I'm afraid (to say I love you): *Lovettes* / New world (is just beginning): *Caldwell, Harry* / Lost love: *Williams, Lee & The Cymbals* / Leave me if you want to: *Goggins, Curby* / Feelin' good: *Carnival Kings*
CD _____ CDKEND 118
Kent / Mar '95 / Pinnacle.

CARNIVAL OF SOUL VOLUME 3: I WANNA BE
I need you baby: *Williams, Lee & The Cymbals* / I'll be gone: *Williams, Lee & The Cymbals* / I'll leave you: *Terrell, Phil* / I wanna be (your everything): *Manhattans* / I call it love: *Pretenders* / If love comes knockin': *Topics* / Send him to me: *Brown, Barbara* / I'm the man for you baby: *Turner Brothers* / Just one more time: *Jules, Jimmy* / What kind of man are you: *Johnson, Dolores* / Try me one time: *Johnson, Dolores* / Oh why: *Mays, Curly* / You made me love you: *Little Royal* / Git go: *Simon, Maurice & The Pie Men* / Just be yourself: *Pretenders* / April lady: *Perry, James* / Take me back: *Three Reasons* / Lonely girl: *Lovettes* / Cry, cry, cry: *Ruffin, Kenneth* / Buy this record for me: *Leon & The Metronomes* / Your yah-yah is gone: *Trenteens* / It's too late for tears: *Bailey, Rene* / I don't wanna go: *Manhattans* / Groove in G: *Bascomb, Wilbur & The Blue Zodiact* / Love don't come easy: *New Jersey Connection*
CD _____ CDKEND 124
Kent / Oct '95 / Pinnacle.

CARNIVAL TIME: THE BEST OF RIC RECORDS
(Vol. 1)
CD _____ CD 2075
Rounder / '88 / CM / Direct / ADA / Cadillac.

CAROLINA BLUES 1926-29
CD _____ DOCD 5168
Blues Document / May '93 / Swift / Jazz Music / Hot Shot.

CAROLINA MY DARLING
CD _____ VPCD 1290
VP / May '93 / Jetstar.

CASA DE LA TROVA: SANTIAGO DE CUBA
CD _____ COCD 120
Corason / Oct '94 / CM / Direct / ADA.

CASTLE IN THE AIR
(Scottish Country Dancing)
CD _____ MU 3005
Musketeer / Oct '92 / Koch.

CATALOGUE NO. 1
(Hypertension Sampler)
CD _____ HYCD 200153
Hypertension / Jun '95 / Total/BMG / Direct.

CATFISH BLUES
CD _____ CDBM 090
Blue Moon / Jun '93 / Magnum Music Group / Greensleeves / Hot Shot / ADA / Cadillac / Discovery.

CAVA SESSIONS
CD _____ TLV 003 CD
Tennants Live Vinyl / May '90 / Pinnacle.

CD '88
CD _____ CD 88CD
Band Of Joy / Oct '88 / ADA.

CEILIDH HOUSE SESSIONS
(From The Tron Tavern Edinburgh)
Maggie Lauder / Full rigged ship / Turnpike / Trowie burn / Shady grove / Reel of tulla / Tron blues / Pottinger's reel / Mountain road / Lark in the morning
CD _____ CDTRAX 5002
Greentrax / May '94 / Conifer / Duncans / ADA / Direct.

CELEBRATE THIS LOVE
CD Set _____ NSCD 006
Newsound / Feb '95 / THE.

CELEBRATION
(25 Years Of The Organist Entertains)
CD _____ CDGRS 1273
Grosvenor / Feb '95 / Target/BMG.

CELEBRATION - THE BEST OF REGGAE
(2CD/MC/LP Set)
I'm in the mood for ska: *Lord Tanamo* / 007: *Dekker, Desmond* / Train to skaville: *Ethiopians* / Israelites: *Dekker, Desmond* / It meke: *Dekker, Desmond* / Red red wine: *Tribe, Tony* / Wonderful world, beautiful people: *Cliff, Jimmy* / Liquidator: *Harry J All Stars* / Return of Django: *Upsetters* / Dollar in the teeth: *Upsetters* / Longshot kick de bucket: *Pioneers* / Sweet sensation: *Melodians* / Vietnam: *Cliff, Jimmy* / Young, gifted and black: *Bob & Marcia* / Monkey man: *Toots & The Maytals* / You can get it if you really want: *Dekker, Desmond* / Love of the common people: *Thomas, Nicky* / Black pearl: *Faith, Horace* / Montego Bay: *Notes, Freddie & The Rudies* / Rivers of Babylon: *Melodians* / Skinhead moonstomp: *Symarip* / Double barrel: *Collins, Dave & Ansil* / Rain: *Ruffin, Bruce* / Pied piper: *Bob & Marcia* / Black and white: *Greyhound* / Small axe: *Marley, Bob* / Monkey spanner: *Collins, Dave & Ansil* / Let your yeah be yeah: *Pioneers* / Moon river: *Greyhound* / Suzanne beware of the devil: *Livingstone, Dandy* / Big 7: *Judge Dread* / I am what I am: *Greyhound* / Everything I own: *Boothe, Ken* / Irie feelings (skanga): *Edwards, Rupie* / Help me make it through the night: *Holt, John* / Crying over you: *Boothe, Ken* / Hurt so good: *Cadogan, Susan* / Eighteen with a bullet: *Harriott, Derrick* / You make me feel brand new: *Gardner, Boris* / Money in my pocket: *Brown, Dennis*
CD Set _____ QTVCD 010
Quality / Jun '92 / Pinnacle.

CELEBRATION OF SCOTTISH MUSIC, A
CD _____ COMD 2003
Temple / Feb '94 / CM / Duncans / ADA / Direct.

CELEBRATION OF SOUL
CD _____ VSD 5488
Varese Sarabande/Colosseum / Oct '94 / Pinnacle / Silva Screen.

CELEBRATION OF SOUL 2
CD _____ VSD 5494
Varese Sarabande/Colosseum / Jan '95 / Pinnacle / Silva Screen.

CELLO SOLO - ALL DIGITAL
CD _____ CDLR 301
Leo / Apr '89 / Wellard / Cadillac / Impetus.

CELTIC CIRCLE SAMPLER VOL.3
CD _____ EFA 125322
Celtic Circle / Oct '95 / SRD.

CELTIC CONNECTIONS
CD _____ LTCD 001
Living Tradition / Jan '95 / Direct / Duncans.

CELTIC DAWN
CD _____ HCD 003
GTD / Apr '91 / Else / ADA.

CELTIC HEART
Fergus sings the blues: *Deacon Blue* / Don't go: *Hothouse Flowers* / My special child: *O'Connor, Sinead* / In a lifetime: *Bono & Clannad* / Pair of brown eyes: *Pogues* / Fisherman's blues: *Waterboys* / Letter from America: *Proclaimers* / Abhainn an t-aluaigh: *Runrig* / Perfect: *Fairground Attraction* / Voyage: *Moore, Christy* / Harry's Game: *Clannad* / Island: *Brady, Paul* / N17: *Saw Doctors* / Captured: *Kennedy, Brian* / Against the wind: *Brennan, Maire* / Man is alive: *Bloom, Luka* / Coisich a ruin (walk my beloved): *Capercaillie* / Golden mile: *Black, Mary*
CD _____ 7432113166-2
RCA / Feb '93 / BMG.

CELTIC HEARTBEAT COLLECTION
CD _____ 7567827322
Warner Bros. / Apr '95 / Warner Music.

CELTIC INSPIRATION
CD _____ NTRCD 031
Nectar / Mar '95 / Pinnacle.

CELTIC INSPIRATION 2
He aint' give you none: *Morrison, Van* / Man is in love: *Waterboys* / Pair of brown eyes: *Moore, Christy* / My old friend the blues: *Proclaimers* / All or nothing: *Reader, Eddi* / Mandinka: *O'Connor, Sinead* / Flower of the west: *Runrig* / Spanish horses: *Runrig* / I need love: *Bloom, Luka* / Great song of indifference: *Geldof, Bob* / Cath: *Bluebells* / In a big country: *Big Country* / Moon over bourbon street: *Coughlan, Mary* / You will rise again: *Capercaillie* / Railway hotel: *Fureys* / Fairytale of New York: *Pogues & Kirsty MacColl*
CD _____ NTRCD 043
Nectar / Jan '96 / Pinnacle.

CELTIC LEGACY
Elnini: *Coulter, William* / Douce mousito-manie: *Oisin* / Lone harper: *Barra MacNeils* / Dacw 'nghariad: 4 Yn Y Bar / If ever you were mine: *MacMaster, Natalie* / Invernia: *Milladoiro* / Dheanainn sugradh: *Poozies* / Swans at Coole: *Breathnach, Maire* / Cailin gaelach: *Maighread Ni Dhomhnaill* / An cailin gaelach: *Maighread Ni Dhomhnaill* / Lorraine's waltz: *Whelan, John* / Dulaman: *Altan* / Culloden's harvest: *Deanta* / Si beag si mor: *Deiseal* / Une chanson a la mariee:

Bouchard, Dominic / Theid mi mhachaigh: MacKenzie, Talitha
CD _____ ND 63916
Narada / Mar '95 / New Note / ADA.

CELTIC MOODS
(Musical Reflections Of Ireland)
CD _____ DOCD 105
Dolphin / Apr '94 / CM / Koch / Grapevine.

CELTIC MOODS
Riverdance: Whelan, Bill / Only a woman's heart: McEvoy, Eleanor / New grange: Clannad / She moved through the fair: Sharkey, Feargal / Strange boat: Waterboys / Sarah: Thin Lizzy / abhainn an 't-aluaigh (The crowded river): Runrig / Grace and pride: Capercaillie / Three babies: O'Connor, Sinead / Ride on: Moore, Christy / Pair of brown eyes: Pogues / Blackbird: Shannon, Sharon / Against the wind: Brennan, Maire / Heroine: Edge & Sinead O'Connor / Invisible to you: Coughlan, Mary / Can't help falling in love: Bloom, Luka / Always travelling: Spillane, Davy / Island: Brady, Paul / Woodbrook: O Suilleabhain, Micheal
CD _____ VTCD 537
Virgin / Jun '95 / EMI.

CELTIC ODYSSEY
Carolan's ramble to Chashel: Coulter, Steve & Harris Moore / Butterfly: Orison / Donal Agus Morag/the new rigged ship: Altan / Calliope house/the cowboy jig: Fraser, Alasdair & Paul Machlis / Chuaigh me 'na Rosann: Scartaglen / Trip to Skye: Whelan, John & Eileen Ivers / Are ye sleeping Maggie: Fraser, Alasdair / Tribute to Peadar O'Donnell: Moving Hearts / Siun ni phuibhir: Relativity / Alasdair Mhic cholla ghasda: Capercaillie / Purt a buel: Sileas / York reel, The/dancing feet: Trimble, Gerald / Morghan meaghan: Riley, Laurie & Bob McNally / Strathgarry: Wynberg, Simon
CD _____ ND 63912
Narada / Jul '93 / New Note / ADA.

CELTIC SEASON, A
CD _____ 01934111782
Windham Hill / Nov '95 / Pinnacle / BMG / ADA.

CELTIC VOICES: WOMEN OF GAEL
Sealwoman: McLaughlin, Mary / Yundah: McLaughlin, Mary / Bring the peace: McLaughlin, Mary / You saw his eyes: McLaughlin, Mary / Little red bird: Christian, Emma / Birth in Bethlehem: Christian, Emma / O Kirre, thou wilt leave me: Christian, Emma / Cantus: Dover, Connie / Wishing well: Dover, Connie / In aimsir bhaint an fhei: Dover, Connie / Siuil a ruin: Dover, Connie / Colour me: Sullivan, Maireid / She moved through the fair: Sullivan, Maireid / Waly waly: Sullivan, Maireid
CD _____ ND 63921
Narada / Oct '95 / New Note / ADA.

CELTS RISE AGAIN, THE
CD _____ GLCD 0104
Green Linnet / Nov '87 / Roots / CM / Direct / ADA.

CENTRAL AFRICAN REPUBLIC: MUSIQUE GBAYA/CHANTS A PENSER
CD _____ C 580008
Ocora / Nov '92 / Harmonia Mundi / ADA.

CEOL TIGH NEACHTAIN
(Music From Galway)
CD _____ CEFCD 172
Gael Linn / Jan '94 / Roots / CM / Direct / ADA.

CEREMONIAL AND WAR DANCES
(Native American Music)
Navahoe boy (Navahoe) / Prisoner song (Tewa) / Girl and many boys (Apache) / Mountain by the sea / Mescalero trail (Apache) / Montana grass-song (Sioux) / Mountain spirit song (Apache) / Lightning song (Apache) / Song of the Black Mountain (Papago) / Song of the Green Rainbow (Papago) / Yei-be-chai chant (Navahoe) / Our father's thoughts (Paiute) / War dance (Ponca) / War dance (2) (Taos) / War dance (slow/fast) (Kiowa) / Warrior song (Arikara) / Honoring song (Sioux) / Glory song (Navahoe) / Memorial song (Sioux)
CD _____ 12552
Laserlight / Nov '95 / Target/BMG.

CERTIFIED DOPE VOL.1
CD _____ EFA 012932
Word Sound Recordings / Nov '95 / SRD.

C'EST FUN: CAJUN CLASSICS
C'est fun: Jambalaya / Louisiana two step: Cajun Tradition Band / L'anse aux pailles: Balfa Toujours / Fool's waltz: Thibodeaux, Jimmy / T-bec do: Warren Cormier, Joe / Jolie blon: Tasso Cajun Band / Chank-achank two step: Passe Partout Cajun Band / Pauvre hobo: Mamou Cajun Band / Makes me feel like movin': Cormier, Sheryl / Faire whiskey: Castille, Hadley J. / Cajun saints go marching in: Fontenet, Harry & Friends / Comme un cadjin: Olivier, Jim / Danse Marie danse: Cajun Gold / Scott playboys special: Greely, David / Little petite: Sonnier, Jo El / La valse de misere: Kershaw Brothers / Diga ding ding dong: Roger, Aldus / Donnes moi mon chapeau: Lejeune, Iry
CD _____ PWKS 4212

Carlton Home Entertainment / Oct '94 / Carlton Home Entertainment.

CHA-CHA-CHA
CD _____ CD 62030
Saludos Amigos / Oct '93 / Target/BMG.

CHAKRA JOURNEY, THE
(2CD/MC/LP Set)
Base: Medicine Drum / Sex: Mammal / Solar plexus: Prana / Crown: Mindfield / Third eye: Third Eye / Throat: Cosmosis / Heart: Transwave
CD Set _____ RTTSCD 002
Volume / Feb '96 / Vital.

CHAMAME - MUSIC OF THE PARANA
CD _____ C 560052CD
Ocora / Jul '94 / Harmonia Mundi / ADA.

CHAMPAGNE COUNTRY
Stardust: Nelson, Willie / Miss the Mississippi and you: Gayle, Crystal / For the good times: Kristofferson, Kris / Sweet music man: Wynette, Tammy / Always: Nelson, Willie & Leon Russell / Most beautiful girl: Rich, Charlie / Here we are: Jones, George & Emmylou Harris / Thing called love: Cash, Johnny / Things I might've been: Kristofferson, Kris & Rita Coolidge / Best of my love: Tucker, Tanya / Faded love: Nelson, Willie & Ray Price / Very special love song: Rich, Charlie / Near you: Jones, George & Tammy Wynette / Me and the elephant: Goldsboro, Bobby / Please help me, I'm falling: Frickie, Janie / I don't know why: Robbins, Marty
CD _____ PWKS 566
Carlton Home Entertainment / Feb '90 / Carlton Home Entertainment.

CHAMPION BRASS
CD _____ EMPRCD 568
Emporio / May '95 / THE / Disc / CM.

CHANSONS INTROUVABLES,
CHANSONS RETROUVEES VOL.3
CD _____ 171272
Musidisc / Jul '95 / Vital / Harmonia Mundi / ADA / Cadillac / Discovery.

CHANTS AND MUSIQUES DE PROVENCE
CD _____ PV 782 112
Disques Pierre Verany / '88 / Kingdom.

CHANTS ET DANSES
CD _____ ARN 64244
Arion / Aug '93 / Discovery / ADA.

CHANTS ET TAMBOURS
(Music From Venezuela)
CD _____ C 560085
Ocora / Dec '95 / Harmonia Mundi / ADA.

CHANTS TZIGANES
CD _____ QUI 903028
Quintana / Nov '91 / Harmonia Mundi.

CHARLESTON DAYS, THE
Let's all go to Mary's house: Whidden, Jay & His New Midnight Follies Band / After I say I'm sorry: Mackey, Percival & His Band / Laugh clown laugh: Schubert, Adrian Dance Orchestra / Charleston: Bell, Edison & His Dance Orchestra / I've never seen a straight banana: Happiness Boys / What did I tell ya: Savoy Orpheans / Where's that rainbow: Baker, Edythe Piano / How could Red Riding Hood: Royal Automobile Club Orchestra / Chinese moon: Douglas, Fred / High up in the sky: Maddison, Bert & Dance Orchestra / Under the moon: Radio Imps / Latest dance hits of 1926: Coliseum Dance Orchestra / Julian: Denza Dance Band / Thanks for the buggy ride: Mackey, Percival & His Band / Breezin' along with the breeze: Revelers / Hitch up the horses: Savoy Orpheans / If I had a talking picture of you: Alfredo & His Band / Russian lullaby: Bidgood, Harry & His Broadcasters / Seven and eleven: Corona Dance Orchestra / Dainty Miss: Da Costa, Raie / Molly: Hylton, Jack & His Orchestra / My wife is on a diet: Hudson, Harry Melody Men / Barcelona: Savoy Orpheans / Electric flashes of 1926: Munro, Ronnie & His Dance Orchestra
CD _____ PASTCD 9706
Flapper / '90 / Pinnacle.

CHARLESTON OF THE TWENTIES
CD _____ 995362
EPM / Dec '93 / Discovery / ADA.

CHARM RAGGA SAMPLER VOL.1
CD _____ MPCCD 1
Charm / Jul '94 / Jetstar.

CHART ATTACK
(3CD Set)
All the young dudes: Mott The Hoople / In the summertime: Mungo Jerry / Lola: Kinks / Yellow river: Christie / Albatross: Fleetwood Mac / One and one is one: Medicine Head / Neanderthal man: Hotlegs / You wear it well: Stewart, Rod / Free electric band: Hammond, Albert / Down the drain: Status Quo / Never ending story of love: New Seekers / Ruby Tuesday: Melanie / Rose garden: Anderson, Lynn / Can't number one: Tremeloes / Family affair: Sly & The Family Stone / Giving it all away: Daltrey, Roger / Broken down angel: Nazareth / Isn't life strange: Moody Blues / Let your love flow: Bellamy Brothers / Girls, girls, girls: Sailor / Shame, shame, shame: Shirley & Company / Night Chicago died: Paper Lace / I'm on fire: 5000 Volts / Kung fu fighting: Douglas, Carl / Jukebox jive: Rubettes

---

/ Gonna make you a star: Essex, David / I love to love (but my baby loves to dance): Charles, Tina / Shanghai'd in Shanghai: Nazareth / You to me are everything: Real Thing / Sing baby sing: Stylistics / Arms of Mary: Sutherland Brothers & Quiver / red light spells danger: Ocean, Billy / Most beautiful girl in the world: Rich, Charlie / Lost in France: Tyler, Bonnie / Delilah: Harvey, Alex Sensational Band / Bangin' man: Slade / Don't bring me down: E.L.O. / Dreadlock holiday: 10cc / Stand and deliver: Adam & The Ants / Mind of a toy: Visage / Can you feel the force: Real Thing / September: Earth, Wind & Fire / Come back and finish what you started: Knight, Gladys & The Pips / Funky town: Lipps Inc. / I will survive: Gaynor, Gloria / Hersham boys: Sham 69 / Married men: Tyler, Bonnie / Under your thumb: Godley & Creme / Dead ringer for love: Meat Loaf / Hold the line: Toto / Midnite dynamos: Matchbox / Can can: Bad Manners / Matchstalk men and matchstalk cats and dogs: Brian & Michael / Keep on loving you: REO Speedwagon
CD Set _____ BOXD 41
Carlton Home Entertainment / Nov '93 / Carlton Home Entertainment.

CHART MACHINE
Dreamer: Livin' Joy / Love city groove: Love City Groove / Not over yet: Grace / Your body's calling: R. Kelly / I'm going down: Blige, Mary J. / Don't stop (wiggle wiggle): Outhere Brothers / Two can play that game: Brown, Bobby / Turn on, tune in, cop out: Freak Power / One night stand: Let Loose / Baby baby: Corona / Love me for a reason: Boyzone / Whatever: Oasis / Stay another day: East 17 / Don't give me your life: Alex Party / Call it love: Deuce / Another day: Whigfield / Crazy: Morrison, Mark / Hoochie booty: Ultimate Kaos / Axel F: Ace Of Base / Living in danger: Ace Of Base
CD _____ 525039-2
PolyGram / May '95 / PolyGram.

CHART SHOW DANCE ALBUM 2
CD _____ 5352412
PolyGram TV / Feb '96 / PolyGram.

CHART SHOW DANCE ALBUM, THE
CD _____ 5257682
PolyGram TV / Jul '95 / PolyGram.

CHART SHOW ULTIMATE BLUES ALBUM
CD _____ AHLCD 19
Hit / Jun '94 / PolyGram.

CHARTBUSTERS
CD Set _____ RADCD 15
Global / Jun '95 / BMG.

CHARTBUSTERS VOL 1
Tokyo blues / No room for squares / If ever I would leave you / So tired / Blues in a jiff / Una mas / Down under / Blues on the corner
CD _____ NYC 60172
NYC / Jul '95 / New Note.

CHARTBUSTERS VOL. 1
(4CD Set)
CD Set _____ MBSCD 422
Castle / Nov '93 / BMG.

CHARTBUSTERS VOL. 2
(4CD Set)
CD Set _____ MBSCD 423
Castle / Nov '93 / BMG.

CHEAP SHOTS
CD _____ BHR 022CD
Burning Heart / Mar '95 / Plastic Head.

CHEATIN' FROM A MAN'S POINT OF VIEW
CD _____ SCLCD 2508
Ichiban Soul Classics / Mar '95 / Koch.

CHEATIN' FROM A WOMAN'S POINT OF VIEW
CD _____ SCLCD 2507
Ichiban Soul Classics / Mar '95 / Koch.

CHECK OUT THE FLAVOUR
CD _____ RAPTURE 6001CD
Rapture / Sep '93 / Plastic Head.

CHECK OUT THE GROOVE
CD _____ MCCD 203
Music Club / May '95 / Disc / THE / CM.

CHEGA DE SAUDADE
(No More Blues)
CD _____ CD 53139
Giants Of Jazz / Jan '94 / Target/BMG / Cadillac.

CHEMICAL DUB
CD _____ RSNCD 36
Rising Sun / Jun '95 / Disc.

CHERRY RED PUNK SINGLES COLLECTION
Bad hearts / It / Cracked / Howard Hughes / China's eternal / Bored / You're gonna die / Then he kissed me / Sick on you / November 22nd 1963 / Meet the creeper / Right now / Black leather / No body knows / What do I get / Holiday in Cambodia / Police truck / Kill the poor / In sight / Too drunk to fuck / Prey
CD _____ CDPUNK 51
Anagram / Apr '95 / Pinnacle.

CHESS BLUES
(4CD Set)
CD Set _____ CHD 49340
Chess/MCA / Mar '93 / BMG / New Note.

CHESS EP COLLECTION, THE
Long tall shorty: Tucker, Tommy / Suzie Q: Hawkins, Dale / Ain't got no home: Henry, Clarence 'Frogman' / Rescue: Fontella Bass / You all green: Diddley, Bo / I got to find my baby: Little Walter / Good morning little school girl: Don & Bob / Oh baby: Williams, Larry / Walk: McCracklin, Jimmy / I don't want 'cha: Tucker, Tommy / When the lights go out: Witherspoon, Jimmy / Entertainer: Clarke, Tony / Summertime: Stewart, Billy / I had a talk with my man: Collier, Mitty / Sitting in the park: Stewart, Billy / Who's cheating who: Little Milton / In crowd: Lewis, Ramsey Trio / Leave my baby alone: Guy, Buddy / Hi-heel sneakers: Tucker, Tommy / Soulful dress: Desanto, Sugar Pie / Crazy for my baby: Dixon, Willie / I can tell: Diddley, Bo / You gonna wreck my life: Howlin' Wolf / Messin' with the man: Waters, Muddy / Promised land: Berry, Chuck
CD _____ SEECD 380
See For Miles/C5 / Oct '93 / Pinnacle.

CHESS R&B LEGENDS IN LONDON
After it's over: Berry, Chuck / St. Louis blues: Berry, Chuck / Why should we end this way: Berry, Chuck / Let's boogie: Berry, Chuck / Mean old world: Berry, Chuck / Red rooster: Howlin' Wolf / Rehearsal: Howlin' Wolf / Finished take: Howlin' Wolf / I ain't superstitious: Howlin' Wolf / Who's been talkin': Howlin' Wolf / Poor boy: Howlin' Wolf / Rockin' daddy: Howlin' Wolf / Key to the highway: Waters, Muddy / Who's gonna be your sweet man when I'm gone: Waters, Muddy / Man when I come: Waters, Muddy / I'm ready: Waters, Muddy / Blind man blues: Waters, Muddy / Walkin' blues: Waters, Muddy / Don't want no lyin' woman: Diddley, Bo / Bo Diddley: Diddley, Bo / Make a hit record: Diddley, Bo / Do the robot: Diddley, Bo / Get out of my life: Diddley, Bo
CD _____ CDRB 22
Charly / Apr '95 / Charly / THE / Cadillac.

CHESS STORY VOL.1, THE
(From Blues To Doo Wop)
CD _____ CDCD 1123
Charly / Oct '93 / Charly / THE / Cadillac.

CHESS STORY VOL.2, THE
(From Doo Wop To R&B)
CD _____ CDCD 1124
Charly / Oct '93 / Charly / THE / Cadillac.

CHESS STORY VOL.3, THE
(From R&B To Soul)
CD _____ CDCD 1125
Charly / Oct '93 / Charly / THE / Cadillac.

CHIARASCURO CHRISTMAS, A
CD _____ CRD 332
Chiara Scuro / Nov '95 / Jazz Music / Kudos.

CHICAGO - THAT TOODLIN' TOWN
CD Set _____ DCD 8002
Disky / Jan '95 / THE / BMG / Discovery / Pinnacle.

CHICAGO 1935
CD _____ CJR 1001
Gannet / Nov '95 / Jazz Music / Cadillac.

CHICAGO ALL STARS, THE
(2CD/LP Set)
Reach out: Yesterday Dreamers / Welcome to the storm: Outerrealm / Operation sneak: D.J. Sneak / Migraine headache: Fade 2 / Tha Future / Submarine: Felix Da Housecat / It's time to excel: MD Connection / Radikal bitch: Armando / Move traxx: Professor Traxx / Trickster: Fiasco, Johnny / I just need: K Hand / My my my: Alexi, Kaay / Can u dance: Crump, Harrison / Metropolis: Felix Da Housecat / Daybreak: Aphrohead / Tunnel vision: Armando / Footsteps of rage: Felix Da Housecat / Spiritual drum II: Professor Traxx / Ruhrschellweg: Broccoli Bothers & Righteous Men / Wicked city: Righteous Men / Diafana: Random Logic
CD Set _____ FEAR 025CDLTD
Radikal Fear / Jan '96 / Vital.

CHICAGO BLUES
(4CD Set)
CD Set _____ CDDIG 4
Chess/Charly / Feb '95 / Charly.

CHICAGO BLUES AT BURNLEY
CD _____ JSPCD 247
JSP / '91 / ADA / Target/BMG / Direct / Cadillac / Complete/Pinnacle.

CHICAGO BLUES AT HOME
CD _____ TCD 5028
Testament / Oct '95 / Complete/Pinnacle / ADA / Koch.

CHICAGO BLUES BASH
CD _____ 77001
Laserlight / Jan '93 / Target/BMG.

CHICAGO BLUES NIGHT
CD _____ GBW 001
GBW / Feb '92 / Harmonia Mundi.

CHICAGO BLUES TODAY VOL.1
CD _____ VND 79216
Vanguard / Oct '95 / Complete/Pinnacle / Discovery.

CHICAGO BLUES TODAY VOL.2
CD _____ VMD 79217
Vanguard / Oct '95 / Complete/Pinnacle /
Discovery.

CHICAGO BLUES TODAY VOL.3
CD _____ VND 79218
Vanguard / Oct '95 / Complete/Pinnacle /
Discovery.

CHICAGO GARAGE BAND GREATS
(The Best Of Rembrandt Records 1966-
1968)
Hassle: Nite Owls / Boots are made for talk-
ing: Nite Owls / Open up your mind: Nuchez
/ No reservations: Circus / Come on back:
Nickel Bag / Woods: Nickel Bag / Games
we play: Circus / Sands of mind: Circus /
Long lost friend: Monday's Child / It's a
hassle: Nickel Bag / I live in the springtime:
Lemon Drops / Listen girl: Lemon Drops /
Nobody for me: Lemon Drops / Flowers on
the hillside: Lemon Drops / Trilogy: Water-
melon / Ocean song: Watermelon / I can
make you happy: Buzzsaw / Nowhere to go:
Buzzsaw / Roll on angeline: Buzzsaw /
Walking through a rainbow: Buzzsaw
CD _____ CDTB 164
Thunderbolt / Mar '95 / Magnum Music
Group.

CHICAGO GOSPEL
CD _____ HTCD 08
Heritage / '92 / Swift / Roots / Wellard /
Direct / Hot Shot / Jazz Music / ADA.

CHICAGO JUMP BANDS 1945-1953
CD _____ RST 91577-2
RST / Jun '94 / Jazz Music / Hot Shot.

CHICAGO SOUNDS
CD _____ CSCD 001
ACV / Dec '94 / Plastic Head / SRD.

CHICAGO SOUTH SIDE JAZZ 1927-1931
I'm goin' huntin' / If you want to be my
sugar papa / My baby / Pleasure mad /
Some do and some don't / Tack it down /
Endurance stomp / Bull fiddle rag / Shake
your shimmy / Shake that jelly roll / Don't
cry honey / Shanghai honeymoon / Good
feelin' blues / Wild man stomp / Stomp your
stuff
CD _____ NEOVOX 868
Neovox / Mar '94 / Wellard.

CHICAGO STYLE
CD _____ 3801012
Jazz Archives / Jun '92 / Jazz Music /
Discovery / Cadillac.

CHILDREN - 100% KIDS
CD _____ TCD 2798
Telstar / Nov '95 / BMG.

CHILDREN - A FAMILY CHRISTMAS
Here comes Santa Claus / Rudolph the red
nosed reindeer / Joy to the world / Frosty
the snowman / Sleigh ride / Away in a manger / Winter wonderland / We wish you a
Merry Christmas / Jingle bells / Twelve days
of Christmas / Silver bells / First Noel / Deck
the halls with boughs of holly / O Christmas
tree / Here we come a-caroling / Jolly old
St. Nicholas / Silent night / From all of us
to all of you
CD _____ DSBCD 469
Disney / Oct '95 / Carlton Home
Entertainment.

CHILDREN - A TRADITIONAL
CHRISTMAS
CD _____ CD 251
CYP Children's Audio / Jul '94 / Total/
BMG.

CHILDREN - ALL ABOARD
(All Time Children's Favourites)
Laughing policeman: Penrose, Charles /
Ugly duckling: Kaye, Danny / Robin Hood:
James, Dick / Right said Fred: Cribbins,
Bernard / Hippopotamus song: Wallace, Ian
/ Banana boat song (Day O): Freberg, Stan
/ Goodness gracious me: Sellers, Peter &
Sophia Loren / Bee song: Askey, Arthur /
Who's afraid of the big bad wolf: Pinky &
Perky / I know an old lady: Ives, Burl / My
boomerang won't come back: Drake, Char-
lie / Teddy bears' picnic: Hall, Henry / Nellie
the elephant: Miller, Mandy / Sparky's
magic piano: Blair, Henry & Ray Turner /
Owl and the pussycat: Hayes, Elton / Ernie
(the fastest milkman in the West): Hill,
Benny / Buckingham Palace: Stephens,
Anne / Morningtown ride: Seekers /
Gnu song: Flanders, Michael & Donald
Swann / Two little boys: Harris, Rolf / Run-
away train: Holliday, Michael
CD _____ CDEMS 1479
EMI / Mar '93 / EMI.

CHILDREN - CHANTEFABLES,
CHANTEFLEURS
(French Children's Songs, Poems &
Music)
Desnos/Tardieu/Mechin
CD _____ LDX 200314
La Chant Du Monde / Jan '93 / Harmonia
Mundi / ADA.

CHILDREN - CHRISTMAS PARTY POPS
CD _____ CD 250
CYP Children's Audio / Oct '93 / Total/
BMG.

CHILDREN - EURODISNEY
(Feel The Magic)
Feel the magic / Supercalifragil Eurodisney
vacation / Thank god I'm a country bear /
Night life/Macho duck / Main street U.S.A.
/ Frontierland / Lucky nugget / Grim griming
ghosts, are you from Dixie / Adventureland
/ I wanna be like you / Pirates / Discovery-
land / Fantasyland / Medley/finale
CD _____ DSTCD 460
Disney / Jul '92 / Carlton Home
Entertainment.

CHILDREN - JUNIOR CHOICE VOL.1
Nellie the elephant: Miller, Mandy / Runa-
way train: Dalhart, Vernon / Gilly gilly os-
senfeffer katzenellenbogen by the sea: By-
graves, Max / You're a pink toothbrush:
Bygraves, Max / Robin Hood: James, Dick /
I taut I taw a puddy tat: Blanc, Mel / Woody
Woodpecker: Blanc, Mel / Ernie (the fastest
milkman in the West): Hill, Benny / I've lost
my mummy: Harris, Rolf / Jake the peg:
Harris, Rolf / My boomerang won't come
back: Drake, Charlie / Mr. Custer: Drake,
Charlie / Little boy fishin': Abicair, Shirley /
Laughing policeman: Penrose, Charles /
Ragtime Cowboy Joe: Chipmunks / Buck-
ingham Palace: Stephens, Anne / Hippo-
potamus song: Flanders & Swann / Ballad
of Davy Crockett: Ford, Tennessee Ernie /
Grandad: Dunn, Clive
CD _____ CDMFP 5890
Music For Pleasure / Oct '90 / EMI.

CHILDREN - JUNIOR CHOICE VOL.2
Ugly ducking: Kaye, Danny / King's new
clothes: Kaye, Danny / Little white duck:
Kaye, Danny / Tubby the tuba: Kaye, Danny
/ Little red monkey: Nicols/ Edwards/ Bentley / Grandfather's clock: Radio Revellers /
Kitty in the basket: Dekker, Diana / I know
an old lady: Ives, Burl / Big Rock Candy
Mountain: Ives, Burl / There's a friend for
little children: Uncle Mac / All things bright
and beautiful: Uncle Mac / Three billy goat
gruff: Luther, Frank / Owl and the pussycat:
Hayes, Elton / Puffin' Billy: Melodi Light Orchestra / (How much is that) doggie in the
window: Roza, Lita / Mr. Cuckoo (sing your
song): Ross, Edmundo / Typewriter: Anderson, Leroy / Little shoemaker: Michael
Twins / Bimbo: Miller, Suzi / Swedish rhapsody: Mantovani
CD _____ CDMFP 5891
Music For Pleasure / Oct '90 / EMI.

CHILDREN - JUNIOR PARTY POPS
CD _____ CD 249
CYP Children's Audio / May '93 / Total/
BMG.

CHILDREN - JUNIOR PARTY POPS 2
CD _____ PT 247CD
CYP Children's Audio / Mar '93 / Total/
BMG.

CHILDREN - JUNIOR PARTY POPS
VOL.2
CD _____ PT 249CD
CYP Children's Audio / Mar '93 / Total/
BMG.

CHILDREN - MR. BOOM IS OVER THE
MOON
CD _____ MB 007CD
Moonbeam Music / Nov '95 / Duncans.

CHILDREN - MUSICAL FUN AND
GAMES
Children's games / Sorcerer's apprentice /
Dolly Suite: Academy Of St. Martin in the
Fields/Neville Marriner / Knightsbridge
March / Royal Philharmonic Orchestra /
Pied piper: MacDonald, George &
Narnia: Robles, Marisa Ensemble & Chris-
topher Hyde-Smith / Scaramouche-Brazili-
era: Johnson, Emma & Gordon Back
CD _____ CD DCA 673
ASV / Oct '89 / Koch.

CHILDREN - WILD WORLD OF ANIMAL
SONGS
CD _____ JJCD 477
Jumping Jack / Jul '95 / THE.

CHILDREN - YOUNG AT HEART
Christopher Robin: Lee, Mary / Animal
crackers: BBC Dance Orchestra / Little man
you've had a busy day: Rosing, Val & Jay
Wilbur Band / Horsey horsey: Campbell, Big
Bill & His Rocky Mountain Rhythm / Mickey
Mouse's birthday party: Marcellinon, Muzzy
& Ted Fiorito Band / Little drummer boy:
Robins, Phyllis & Jay Wilbur Band / On the
good ship Lollipop: Geraldo & His Orchestra
/ Mommy I don't want to go to bed: Gio-
nella, Nat & His Georgians / Wedding of
Jack and Jill: Wilbur, Jay & his band / Run-
away train: Dalhart, Vernon / Trains: Gardi-
ner, Reginald / Bee song: Askey, Arthur /
Teddy bears' picnic: Hall, Henry Orchestra
/ It's my mother's birthday today: Yates, Hal
& His Orchestra / Three little fishes: Gonella,
Nat & His Georgians / When the circus
comes to town: Kyser, Kay Orchestra /
Hush hush hush, here comes the bogey-
man: Hall, Henry Orchestra / Laughing
policeman: Penrose, Charles / Lion and Al-
bert: Holloway, Stanley / Buckingham Palace: Stephens, Anne
CD _____ PASTCD 9769
Flapper / Oct '93 / Pinnacle.

CHILDREN - YOUR FAVOURITE
CHRISTMAS PARTY SONGS AND
CAROLS
CD _____ CDMFP 5955
Music For Pleasure / Dec '94 / EMI.

CHILDREN'S SING-A-LONG
CD _____ CDSR 025
Telstar / Sep '93 / BMG.

CHILDREN'S SONGS FROM SOUTH
INDIA
CD _____ ARN 6428
Arion / Oct '94 / Discovery / ADA.

CHILIK: SONGS & MELODIES OF THE
NAGAYBAKS
(Recordings From Russian Tartar
Province Of Chelyabinsk)
CD _____ PAN 7003CD
Pan / Feb '95 / ADA / Direct / CM.

CHILL OUT OR DIE
CD _____ RSNCD 8
Rising High / Jul '93 / Disc.

CHILL OUT OR DIE II
(2CD/4LP Set)
CD Set _____ RSNCD 17
Rising High / May '94 / Disc.

CHILL OUT OR DIE III
CD _____ RSNCD 25
Rising High / Oct '94 / Disc.

CHILL OUT OR DIE IV
(2CD/4LP Set)
CD Set _____ RSNCD 33
Rising High / Jun '95 / Disc.

CHILLIN'
(The Best Of Jazz Funk)
Sun goddess: Lewis, Ramsey / Expansions:
Smith, Lonnie Liston / Keep that same old
feeling: Crusaders / Morning dance: Spyro
Gyra / Always and forever: Jordan, Stanley
/ School days: Clarke, Stanley / Mystic voy-
age: Ayers, Roy / Mr. Magic: Washington,
Grover Jr. / Feels so good: Mangione,
Chuck / Sneakin' up behind you: Brecker
Brothers / Funkin' for Jamaica: Browne,
Tom / Action speaks louder than words:
Chocolate Milk / Jaws: Schifrin, Lalo / Black
cow: Connors, Norman
CD _____ 74321288852
Ariola / Jun '95 / BMG.

CHILLOUT CLASSICS VOLUME 1
CD _____ CHILLCD 1
Chillout / May '94 / Disc / Kudos.

CHINESE BAMBOO FLUTE MUSIC
CD _____ 12183
Laserlight / Aug '94 / Target/BMG.

CHISWICK SAMPLER, THE
(Good Clean Fun)
Beautiful Delilah / Sweet revenge / Gate-
crasher / Groovy Ruby / Enemies / Tear it
up / Train kept a rollin' / I want candy / Ra-
dio stars / Smash it up / Romford girls /
Dead vandals / Teenage cutie / Come on
let's go / Driver's seat / Let's talk about the
weather / There's a boy on our street / Buy
Chiswick records
CD _____ CDWIKX 162
Chiswick / Oct '95 / Pinnacle.

CHISWICK STORY, THE
(2CD Set)
Route 66: Count Bishops / Teenage letter:
Count Bishops / Train train: Count Bishops
/ Keys to your heart: 101'ers / She's my gal:
Gorillas / Gorilla got me: Gorillas / Drip drop:
Sharpe, Rocky & The Razors / I'm jumping
Story, Little Bob / Dirty pictures: Radio Stars
/ No Russians in Russia: Radio Stars / Nerv-
ous wreck: Radio Stars / Real me: Radio
Stars / Television screen: Radiators From
Space / Motorhead: Motorhead / I wanna
be free: Rings / No one: Moped, Johnny /
Darling let's have another baby: Moped,
Johnny / Little queenie: Moped, Johnny / I
want you to dance with me: Hill, Jeff / Common truth: Amazorblades / Saints and sinners: Johnny & The Self Abusers / Hang
loose (I've gotta rock): Whirlwind / I only
wish that I'd been told): Whirlwind / Heaven
knows: Whirlwind / Million dollar hero: Radiators / Dancing years: Radiators / Cosmonaut: Riff Raff / I want candy: Bishops /
Gay boys in bondage: Drug Addix / Rama
lama ding dong: Sharpe, Rocky & The Replays / Imagination: Sharpe, Rocky & The
Replays / Shout shout (knock yourself out):
Sharpe, Rocky & The Replays / Heart:
Sharpe, Rocky & The Replays / Driver's
seat: Sniff 'N' The Tears / Hey baby: Disguise / I couldn't help but cry: Kelleher, Dan
/ Automobile: Stickshifts / Love song:
Damned / Smash it up: Damned / Gabrielle:
Nips / That driving beat: Red Beans & Rice
/ I can't fight it: Textones / Albania (are you
all mine): Albania / So go all: Albania / Tomahawk cruise: Smith, TV's Explorers / Tennessee stud: Woods, Terry / Radioactive
kid: Meteors / Insufficient data: 2-2 / Kwa-
gayo: 2-2 / Desire: Radiation, Roddy & Tear-
jerkers / Grab what you can (biez co moz-
esz): Jakko
CD Set _____ CDWIK2 100
Chiswick / Mar '92 / Pinnacle.

CHOMP
CD _____ TKCD 6
2 Kool / Apr '95 / SRD.

CHOROS FROM BAHAI
CD _____ NI 5404
Nimbus / Feb '95 / Nimbus.

CHRISTMAS BLUES
White Christmas / Far away Christmas
blues / Love for Christmas / Trim your tree
/ Wonderful Christmas night / Rudolph the
red nosed reindeer / Silent night / Mr. San-
ta's boogie / Christmas blues / Frosty the
snowman / I want to spend Christmas with
Elvis / Santa's secret
CD _____ SV 0241
Savoy Jazz / Oct '94 / Conifer / ADA.

CHRISTMAS CAROLS
God rest ye merry gentlemen / While shep-
herds watched their flocks by night / See
amid the winter's snow / Silent night / Good
King Wenceslas / O little town of Bethle-
hem: Guildford Cathedral Choir / Unto us is
born a son / Away in a manger / Rocking /
In dulci jubilo: Westminster Abbey Choir /
Ding dong merrily on high / Coventry carol
/ I saw three ships: St. Paul's Cathedral
Choir / Holly and the ivy / Angels from the
realms of glory: St. Paul's Cathedral Choir /
First Noel / O come all ye faithful (Adeste
Fidelis) / Once in Royal David's City: Exeter
Cathedral Choir / Hark the herald angels
sing: Exeter Cathedral Choir
CD _____ CC 224
Music For Pleasure / Dec '94 / EMI.

CHRISTMAS COLLECTION
Il est ne (He is born): Gettel, Michael / From
heaven above: Illenberger, Ralf / Gloria:
Lauria, Nando / Lo how a rose e'er bloom-
ing: Mirowitz, Sheldon / Christmas song
(Chestnuts roasting on an open fire): Cam-
eron, Doug & Kostia / Rock the herald an-
gels: Lanz, David & Paul Speer / Coventry
carol/noel nouvelet: Reed, Bob / First Noel:
Brewer, Spencer / Joseph dearest Joseph
mine: Wynberg, Simon / Christmas eve:
Stein, Ira / Unto us a boy is born: Jones,
Michael / O come, o come, Emmanuel:
Gratz, Wayne / We three kings: Arkenstone,
David / O holy night: Buffett, Peter
CD _____ ND 63909
Narada / Nov '92 / New Note / ADA.

CHRISTMAS COLLECTION, A
Christmas song: Cole, Nat King / O come
all ye faithful (Adeste fidelis): Cole, Nat King
/ Walking in the air: Jones, Aled / Santa
Claus is coming to town: Lee, Peggy /
Christmas waltz: Lee, Peggy / Rudolph the
red nosed reindeer: Martin, Dean / White
Christmas: Martin, Dean / Jingle bells: Paul,
Les & Mary Ford / Silent night: Paul, Les &
Mary Ford / When a child is born: Rogers,
Kenny / Christmas is my favourite time of
year: Rogers, Kenny / Little drummer boy:
Lynn, Vera / Mary's boy child: Lynn, Vera /
Have yourself a merry little Christmas:
Campbell, Glen / Christmas is for children:
Campbell, Glen / O holy night: Rodgers,
Jimmie / I'll be home for Christmas: Beach
Boys / Winter wonderland: Mercer, Johnny
/ What child is this (CD only.): Rodgers, Jim-
mie / We three kings of Orient are (CD
only.): Beach Boys
CD _____ CDMFP 5903
Music For Pleasure / Dec '94 / EMI.

CHRISTMAS COUNTRY COLLECTION
CD _____ MCCDX 004
Music Club / Nov '94 / Disc / THE / CM.

CHRISTMAS CROONERS
CD _____ MCCDX 003
Music Club / Nov '93 / Disc / THE / CM.

CHRISTMAS FAVOURITES
CD _____ 15463
Laserlight / Nov '95 / Target/BMG.

CHRISTMAS JUBILEE
CD _____ VJC 1016 2
Vintage Jazz Classics / Oct '91 / Direct /
ADA / Cadillac.

CHRISTMAS LOVE SONGS
(2CD/MC/LP Set)
CD Set _____ ARC 948202
Arcade / Dec '91 / Sony / Grapevine.

CHRISTMAS PARTY SING-A-LONG
First Noel / Have yourself a merry little
Christmas / Silent night / Santa Claus is
coming to town / Away in a manger / Winter
wonderland / Mary's boy child / God rest
ye merry gentlemen / Little drummer boy /
O come all ye faithful (Adeste Fidelis) / Jin-
gle bells / Little donkey / White Christmas /
Christmas song / Good king Wenceslas /
While shepherds watched their flocks by
night / Hark the herald angels sing / Let it
snow, let it snow, let it snow / Rudolph the
red nosed reindeer
CD _____ PWK 035
Carlton Home Entertainment / Oct '95 /
Carlton Home Entertainment.

CHRISTMAS REFLECTIONS
CD _____ MCCDX 005
Music Club / Nov '94 / Disc / THE / CM.

CHRISTMAS SOUL SPECIAL
Jingle bells / Silent night / Drummer boy /
Oh holy night / Jingle bell rock / Christmas
song / Santa Claus is coming to town / Noel
/ Winter wonderland / O come all ye faithful
(Adeste Fidelis) / Frosty the snowman / Sil-
ver bells
CD _____ CDVR 015
Varrick / '88 / Roots / CM / Direct / ADA.

CHRISTMAS SPECTACULAR OF CAROLS & SONGS, A
Away in a manger: Nicholas, Paul / Winter boy: Wilkinson, Colm / When a child is born: Ball, Michael & Claire Moore / In the bleak midwinter: Brightman, Sarah / Silent night: McKenzie, Julia / Let's pretend: Crawford, Michael / Ave Maria: Paige, Elaine / Most wonderful birthday of all: Lawrence, Stephanie / I watch you sleeping: Ruffelle, Frances / Winter wonderland: Willetts, Dave / In dulci jubilo: Romano, Dave / Silver bells: Me & My girl Co. New York / Have yourself a merry little christmas: Cats Co. London / Joy to the world: Les Miserables Company / White Christmas: Me & My girl Co. New York / While shepherds watched their flocks by night: 42nd street Co / First Noel, The/ Hark the Herald Angels sing: Into the woods Co, New York / We wish you a merry Christmas: South Pacific Co / Ding dong merrily on high: Les Miserables Company / God rest ye merry gentlemen: Chess / Save the children: All companies, London & New York
CD _____ PWKS 4135
Carlton Home Entertainment / Oct '95 / Carlton Home Entertainment.

CHRISTMAS TIME WITH THE STARS
White Christmas / Jingle Bells / Santa Claus is coming to town / Siberian sleigh ride / Snow White and the seven dwarfs / Christmas bells at eventide / Sitting on the ice at the ice rink / Say it with carols / Kiddies go carolling / Christmas day in the cookhouse / Hansel and Gretel dance duet / Christmas dinner / Christmas swing / March of the toys / Christmas night in Harlem / It happened in sun valley / O little town of Bethlehem / Christmas song / Ghost of the turkey / Snowman / Fairy on the Christmas tree / I'm going home for Christmas / Don't wait till the night before Christmas
CD _____ CDYULE 300
Happy Days / Oct '94 / Conifer.

CHRISTMAS WITH THE STARS
Silent night: Belafonte, Harry / Santa baby: Kitt, Eartha / Winter wonderland: Air Supply / Silver bells: Hirt, Al / E natale: D'Angelo, Nino / Mary's boy child: Boney M / Feliz Navidad: Feliciano, Jose / Miracolo a goyania: Branduardi, Angelo / Homecoming Christmas: Alabama / Christmas in my home town: Pride, Charley / Have yourself a merry little Christmas: Mancini, Henry / Son of Mary (Available on CD only): Belafonte, Harry / Rudolph the red nosed reindeer (Available on CD only): Emery, Ralph / I hear the bells on Christmas day (Available on CD only): Arnold, Eddy / O holy night (Available on CD only): Milsap, Ronnie
CD _____ 290 399
Ariola Express / Jan '94 / BMG.

CHRISTMAS WITH THE STARS, A
CD _____ MCCDX 008
Music Club / Nov '94 / Disc / THE / CM.

CHRONOLOGICAL HARMONISATIONS
CD _____ ELEC 3CD
New Electronica / '94 / Pinnacle / Plastic Head.

CHRYSALIS 25TH ANNIVERSARY - EDITED HIGHLIGHTS
People everyday: Arrested Development / Love is a battlefield: Arrested Development / Heart of glass: Blondie / Only living boy in New Cross: Carter U.S.M. / We close our eyes: Go West / White wedding: Idol, Billy / Living in the past: Jethro Tull / Ten years asleep: Kingmaker / Power of love: Lewis, Huey & The News / Down that road: Nelson, Shara / Nothing compares 2 U: O'Connor, Sinead / Letter from America: Proclaimers / True: Spandau Ballet / Ghost train: Specials / Love like a man: Ten Years After / Thinking about your love: Thomas, Kenny / Vienna: Ultravox / Whole of the moon: Waterboys / Is it like today: World Party
CD _____ CD25CR 26
Chrysalis / Mar '94 / EMI.

CHUNKS
CD _____ SST 069 CD
SST / May '93 / Plastic Head.

CHUNKS OF THE CHOCOLATE FACTORY
(Best Of Choc's Chewns Vol.1/2CD Set)
CD Set _____ SUSCD 2
Aura Surround Sounds / Jan '95 / Grapevine / PolyGram.

CIELITO LINDO
CD _____ CD 62021
Saludos Amigos / Jan '93 / Target/BMG.

CINCOS ANOS
CD _____ TR 38CD
Trance / Oct '95 / SRD.

CINEMA ORGAN
CD _____ EMPRCD 560
Emporio / Mar '95 / THE / Disc / CM.

CINEMA ORGAN, VOL.1
CD _____ PASTCD 9722
Flapper / Jul '91 / Pinnacle.

CINEMA ORGAN, VOL.2
CD _____ PASTCD 7052
Flapper / Oct '94 / Pinnacle.

CIRCLE DANCE
(Hokey Pokey Charity Compilation)
CD _____ CONED 1
Hokey Pokey / Oct '90 / ADA / Direct.

CITY LIMITS
CD _____ TMPMC 016
Telstar / Oct '95 / BMG.

CITY SPACE VOL. 2
CD _____ E 3759CD
Atatak / Nov '93 / SRD.

CLAMCHOWDER & ICE
CD _____ EFA 11374
Musical Tragedies / Apr '93 / SRD.

CLARE TRADITION, THE
CD _____ GTDHCD 082
GTD / Jul '93 / Else / ADA.

CLARINET MARMALADE
Dizzy debutante: Bailey, Buster & Rhythm Busters / Blues in thirds: Bechet, Sidney Trio / Barney's concerto: Bigard, Barney & Duke Ellington / Dee blues: Carter, Benny & Chocolate Dandies / Too tight: Dodds, Johnny / Praying the blues: Dorsey, Jimmy / My inspiration: Fazola, Irving & Bob Crosby / Sweet Georgia Brown: Goodman, Benny Quartet / Sheikh of araby: Hamilton, Jimmy & Teddy Wilson / Woodsheddin' with Woody: Herman, Woody / Climax rag: Lewis, George & New Orleans Stompers / Reunion in Harlem: Marsala, Joe & Delta Four / Can't we be friends: Matlock, Matty & Bob Crosby/Bobcats / Everybody loves my baby: Mezzrow, Mezz & Mezzrow-Ladnier Quartet / High society: Miller, Eddie & Mound City Blues Blowers / Chinatown, my Chinatown: Mince, Johnny & Tommy Dorsey/Clambake Seven / Monday date: Noone, Jimmie Apex Club Orchestra / Stratton Street strut: Polo, Danny & Swing Stars / She's crying for me blues: Roppolo, Leon & Original New Orleans Rhythm Kings / Friars Point Shuffle: Russell, Pee-Wee & Eddie Condon/Chicagoans / Summit Ridge Drive: Shaw, Artie & His Gramercy Five / Clarinet marmalade: Shields, Larry / Beau Koo Jack: Simeon, Omer / (Back home again in) Indiana: Teschemacher, Frank & Eddie Condon / Pagin' the devil: Young, Lester & The Kansas City Six
CD _____ CDAJA 5132
Living Era / May '94 / Koch.

CLASH OF THE IRIES
CD _____ VPCD 1235
VP / Jul '92 / Jetstar.

CLASS & RENDEZVOUS STORY, THE
Rockin' Robin: Day, Bobby / Nut rocker: B. Bumble & The Stingers / Miami: Church, Eugene / In the mood: Fields, Ernie Orchestra / Little bitty pretty one: Day, Bobby & The Satellites / Hey girl, hey boy: McLollie, Oscar & Jeanette Baker / Bear: Watson, Johnny 'Guitar' / That's my desire: Bob & Earl / Pretty girls everywhere: Church, Eugene & the Fellows / Texas twister: Fields, Ernie Orchestra / I'm confessin' that I love you: Belvin, Jesse / Bluebird, the buzzard and the oriole: Day, Bobby / No time: Titans / Ez: Rene, Googie / You made a boo boo: Bob & Earl / One more kiss: Watson, Johnny 'Guitar' / Wow wow baby: Searchers / Good news: Church, Eugene / Alley oop: Dynasores / Let me know, let me know: McLollie, Oscar & Jeanette Baker / Mama Julie: Terry & Gerry / I ain't goin' for that: Church, Eugene / Chattanooga choo choo: Fields, Ernie Orchestra / Over and over: Day, Bobby
CD _____ CDCHD 461
Ace / Jun '93 / Pinnacle / Cadillac / Complete/Pinnacle.

CLASSIC 80'S GROOVE MASTERCUTS VOL.1
Do it to the music: Raw Silk / So fine: Johnson, Howard / After the dance is through: Krystol / I'll be a freak for you: Royalle Delite / Main thing: Shot / You used to hold me so tight: Houston, Thelma / Fool's paradise: Morgan, Meli'sa / Who do you love: Wright, Bernard / Hangin' on a string: Loose Ends / Change of heart: Change / Settle down: Thomas, Lillo / Encore: Lynn, Cheryl
CD _____ CUTSCD 15
Beechwood / Nov '93 / BMG / Pinnacle.

CLASSIC 80'S GROOVE MASTERCUTS VOL.2
I am somebody: Jones, Glenn / Serious: Serious Intention / She's strange: Cameo / You aint' really down: Status IV / I'm in love: Thomas, Lillo / Twilight: Maze / Let's groove: Earth, Wind & Fire / I wonder if I take you home: Lisa Lisa & Cult Jam & Full Force / Thinking about your love: Skipworth & Turner / Stomp: Brothers Johnson / Breakin' down: Julia & Co. / Act like you know: Fat Larry's Band
CD _____ CUTSCD 26
Beechwood / Mar '95 / BMG / Pinnacle.

CLASSIC BANDS OF THE THIRTIES
Song of India: Dorsey, Tommy Orchestra / South Rampart street parade: Crosby, Bob & His Orchestra / Begin the beguine: Shaw, Artie & His Orchestra / I let a song go out of my heart: Ellington, Duke Orchestra / One o'clock jump: Goodman, Benny Orchestra / Sunrise serenade: Kemp, Hal Orchestra / At the woodchoppers ball: Herman, Woody & His Orchestra / It's only a paper moon: Whiteman, Paul & His Orchestra / Stop, look

and listen: Dorsey Brothers Orchestra / Minnie the moocher: Calloway, Cab & His Orchestra / My prayer: Dorsey, Jimmy Orchestra / Don't be that way: Wilson, Teddy & His Orchestra / All God's chillun got rhythm: Berigan, Bunny & His Orchestra / In the mood: Miller, Glenn Orchestra / St. Louis blues: Lombardo, Guy & His Royal Canadians / Jumpin' at the woodside: Basie, Count Orchestra
CD _____ HADCD 160
Javelin / May '94 / THE / Henry Hadawy Organisation.

CLASSIC BIG BAND JAZZ
CD _____ AVC 540
Avid / May '94 / Avid/BMG / Koch.

CLASSIC CHRISTMAS, A
CD _____ DCD 5311
Disky / Dec '93 / THE / BMG / Discovery / Pinnacle.

CLASSIC CLUB COLLECTIVE
(A Classic Collection Of Club Anthems)
Got to have your love: Mantronix / Let the beat hit 'em: Lisa Lisa & Cult Jam / Optimistic: Sounds Of Blackness / Love under moonlight: Graham, Jaki / Twilight: Maze & Frankie Beverly / Secret rendezvous: Rene & Angela / Laughin' at you: Dazz Band / Come into my life: Sims, Joyce / Got to be real: Lynn, Cheryl / Sleep talk: Williams, Alyson / You and me tonight: Aurra / Good lovin': Belle, Regina / Heaven: Chimes / Can't stop: After 7
CD _____ CDUBC 01
Debut / Jan '94 / Pinnacle / 3MV / Sony.

CLASSIC COUNTRY
CD _____ 9548330072
WEA / Nov '95 / Warner Music.

CLASSIC CROONERS
Anything goes: Bennett, Tony / Granada: Laine, Frankie / Love letters: Como, Perry / Blue skies: Haymes, Dick / So many ways: Benton, Brook / Hello Dolly: Armstrong, Louis / Come fly with me: Sinatra, Frank / My heart is taking lessons: Crosby, Bing / Mona Lisa: Cole, Nat King / Cry: Ray, Johnnie / Life is a song: Bennett, Tony / Woman in love: Laine, Frankie / Song of songs: Como, Perry / Night and day: Haymes, Dick / Kiddio: Benton, Brook / Cabaret: Armstrong, Louis / East side of heaven: Crosby, Bing / Hernando's hideaway: Ray, Johnnie / Unforgettable: Cole, Nat King / I've got you under my skin: Sinatra, Frank
CD _____ MUCD 9012
Start / Apr '95 / Koch.

CLASSIC CROONERS
CD _____ CDCD 1246
Charly / Jun '95 / Charly / THE / Cadillac.

CLASSIC DISCO MASTERCUTS VOLUME.1
Vertigo/Relight my fire: Hartman, Dan / Can't live without your love: Jones, Tamiko / I need you: Sylvester / This time baby: Moore, Jackie / Disco nights: G.Q. / Sure shot: Weber, Tracy / Music music: Strikers / Delirium: McGee, Francine / Casanova: Coffee / Shame: King, Evelyn 'Champagne' / Do what you wanna do: T-Connection / I hear music in the street: Unlimited Touch
CD _____ CUTSCD 25
Beechwood / Feb '95 / BMG / Pinnacle.

CLASSIC DOO WOP
You promise me love: Lewis, Earl & The Channels / Come back to me: Sylvia, Margo & The Tune Weavers / Sweetest one: Joel & The Dymensions / At the altar: Staton, Johnny & The Feathers / Miracle moment of love: West, Rudy & The Five Keys / My angel lover: Cox, Herb & The Cleftones / Heaven and Cindy: Five Boroughs & Brian Daly / Wherever you are: Blandon, Richard & The Dubs / One little teardrop: Grant, George & The Castelles / Heaven's for real / Alice from above: Peels, Leon & The Bluejays / Whispering bells: Joel & The Dymensions / I've tried: Sylvia, Margo & The Tune Weavers / Play a love song: Jaguars / You lost the game of love: Cox, Herb & The Cleftones / One too many tears: Five Boroughs & Siobhan Daly / That's the way it goes: Joel & The Dymensions / Why can't you: Wrens / Surrender to love: Grant, George & The Castelles / Moonlight: Maye, Arthur Lee / Our love: Julian, Don & The Meadowlarks / Accept me for what I am: Green, Vernon & the Medallions / My junaita: Joel & The Dymensions / This time: Blandon, Richard & The Dubs
CD _____ CDCHD 417
Ace / Sep '92 / Pinnacle / Cadillac / Complete/Pinnacle.

CLASSIC ELECTRO MASTERCUTS VOLUME 1
Walking on sunshine: Rockers Revenge & Donnie Calvin / Don't make me wait: Peech Boys / White lines (don't don't do it): Grandmaster Flash & Melle Mel / Hip hop be bop (Don't stop): Man Parrish / Rockit: Hancock, Herbie / Smurf: Brunson, Tyrone / In the bottle: C.O.D. / London bridge is falling down: Newtrament / Al-Naafiysh (The soul): Hashim / Magic's wand: Whodini / Wildstyle: Time Zone / Adventures of Grandmaster Flash on the wheels of steel: Grandmaster Flash & The Furious Five
CD _____ CUTSCD 19
Beechwood / May '94 / BMG / Pinnacle.

CLASSIC FUNK
CD _____ MCCD 200
Music Club / May '95 / Disc / THE / CM.

CLASSIC FUNK MASTERCUTS VOL. 1
Who is he and what is he to you: Creative Source / Wicky wacky: Fatback Band / Gimme some more: J.B.'s / For the love of money: O'Jays / Fire: Ohio Players / Pusherman: Mayfield, Curtis / Blow your head: Wesley, Fred & The J.B.'s / Fencewalk: Mandrill / Pick up the pieces: Average White Band / Rock creek park: Blackbyrds / N.T. Pts 1 and 2: Kool & The Gang / Stone to the bone: Brown, James
CD _____ CUTSCD 6
Beechwood / May '92 / BMG / Pinnacle.

CLASSIC FUNK MASTERCUTS VOL.2
Movin': Brass Construction / Express yourself Pt.1: Wright, Charles & The Watts 103rd St.Rhythm Band / You can have your Watergate: J.B.'s / It's alright now: Harris, Eddie / Funky stuff/More funky stuff: Kool & The Gang / Keep on steppin': Fatback Band / It's just begun: J.B.'s / Ghetto: Hathaway, Donny / Baby let me take you (in my arms): Detroit Emeralds / Boss: Brown, James / Do it fluid: Blackbyrds / Stomp and buck dance: Crusaders
CD _____ CUTSCD 14
Beechwood / Sep '93 / BMG / Pinnacle.

CLASSIC FUNK MASTERCUTS VOL.3
Just kissed my baby: Meters / Goin' to see my baby: Fatback Band / Turn off the light: Young, Larry / Hands of time: Perfect Circle / Let a man come in and do the popcorn: Brown, James / (I've got) So much trouble in my mind: Quarterman, Sir Joe & Free Soul / Sideway shuffle: Lewis, Linda / Miss Fatback: Philips, Saundra / This is it: Davis, Betty / Stop the rain: Average White Band / Can you get it: Mandrill / Who's in town: Nature Boys
CD _____ CUTSCD 24
Beechwood / Jan '95 / BMG / Pinnacle.

CLASSIC HIGHLIFE
CD _____ AIM 1053
Aim / Oct '95 / Direct / ADA / Jazz Music.

CLASSIC HIP HOP MASTERCUTS VOL. 1
My philosophy: Boogie Down Productions / It's my beat: Sweet Tee & Jazzy Joyce / Peter Piper: Run DMC / Strong island: J.V.C.F.O.R.C.E. / Eric B for president: Eric B & Rakim / Have a nice day: Shante, Roxanne / Serious: Steady B / Jimbrowski: Jungle Brothers / Description of a fool: Tribe Called Quest / Talkin' all that jazz: Stetsasonic / King of the beats: Mantronix
CD _____ CUTSCD 29
Beechwood / Jul '95 / BMG / Pinnacle.

CLASSIC HOUSE MASTERCUTS VOLUME 1
Someday: Rogers, Cece / Tears: Knuckles, Frankie / Let the music (use you): Night Writers / Give it to me: Bam Bam / Big fun: Inner City / You used to hold me: Rosario, Ralph / Baby wants to ride: Principle, Jamie & Frankie / Devotion: Ten City / It's alright: Sterling Void / Promised land: Smooth, Joe
CD _____ CUTSCD 20
Beechwood / Jun '94 / BMG / Pinnacle.

CLASSIC HOUSE MASTERCUTS VOLUME 2
Music is the key: Silk, J.M. / Strings of life: Rythim Is Rythim / Open our eyes: Jefferson, Marshall / I'm in love: Sha-Lor / Love will find a way: Romeo, Victor / Morning after: Fallout / Let's get busy: McClaine, Curtis & On The House / Make my body rock: Jomanda / Take some time out: Jarvis, Arnold / If you should need a friend: Blaze / Definition of a track: Back Room / Musical freedom: Simpson, Paul
CD _____ CUTSCD 22
Beechwood / Oct '94 / BMG / Pinnacle.

CLASSIC HOUSE MASTERCUTS VOLUME 3
Ma boom bey: Cultural Vibe / Give me back the love: On The House / Can U dance: Jason, Kenny 'Jammin' & Fast Eddie / Night moves: Rickster / Forever together: Raven Maize / String free: Phortune / Can you party: Royal House / Who's gonna ease the pressure: Thornhill, Mac / Sound: Reese & Santonio / Release your party: Bang The Party / Can you feel it: Mr. Fingers
CD _____ CUTSCD 28
Beechwood / Jun '95 / BMG / Pinnacle.

CLASSIC JAZZ PIANO (1927-1957)
Mr. Jelly Lord: Morton, Jelly Roll / Glad rag doll: Hines, Earl / State Street special: Yancey, Jimmy / Honky tonk train blues: Lewis, Meade Lux / Thou swell: Johnson, James P / Rompin': Johnson, James P / Smashing thirds: Waller, Fats / Contrary motions: Smith, Willie 'The Lion' / Out of nowhere: Tatum, Art / Where or when: Wilson, Teddy / Daybreak serenade: Stacy, Jess / Rosetta: Hines, Earl / Honeysuckle rose: Waller, Fats / Solitude: Ellington, Duke / Tonk: Ellington, Duke & Billy Strayhorn / Shine on harvest moon: Basie, Count / All God's chillun got rhythm: Williams, Mary Lou / Erroll's bounce: Garner, Erroll / Poor butterfly: Peterson, Oscar / I don't stand a ghost of a chance with you: Tristano, Lennie / Shaw

'nuff: Powell, Bud / Concerto for Billy the Kid: Evans, Bill
CD _____ ND 86754
Bluebird / Apr '89 / BMG.

CLASSIC JAZZ-FUNK MASTERCUTS
Expansions: Smith, Lonnie Liston / Always there: Laws, Ronnie / Bottle: Scott-Heron, Gil / Change (makes you want to hustle): Byrd, Donald / Inherit the wind: Felder, Wilton / Shaker song: Spyro Gyra / Jazz carnival: Azymuth / Los conquistadores chocolates: Smith, Johnny 'Hammond' / Say you will: Henderson, Eddie / Brasilia: Klemmer, John / Till you take my love: Mason, Harvey / Unicorn: Gillespie, Dizzy
CD _____ CUTSCD 2
Beechwood / Sep '91 / BMG / Pinnacle.

CLASSIC JAZZ-FUNK MASTERCUTS 2
Could heaven ever be like this: Muhammad, Idris / Brazilian love affair: Duke, George / Easy: Jarreau, Al / Dominoes: Byrd, Donald / To prove my love: Doheny, Ned / Snowblower: Baker, B / Poo poo la la: Ayers, Roy / Come with me: Maria, Tania / Rotation: Alpert, Herb / Chicago song: Sanborn, David / New killer Joe: Golson, Benny / Keep that same old feeling: Crusaders
CD _____ CUTSCD 4
Beechwood / Nov '91 / BMG / Pinnacle.

CLASSIC JAZZ-FUNK MASTERCUTS 3
Feel the real: Bendeth, David / Roller jubilee: Di Meola, Al / Saturday night: Hancock, Herbie / Love has come around: Byrd, Donald / Spring high: Lewis, Ramsey / Love will bring us back together: Ayers, Roy / Westchester lady: James, Bob / Summer madness: Kool & The Gang / Sun goddess: Lewis, Ramsey & Earth, Wind & Fire / Darlin' darlin' baby: Khan, Steve / You're a star: Aquarian Dream / Best of friends: White, Lenny
CD _____ CUTSCD 7
Beechwood / Jun '92 / BMG / Pinnacle.

CLASSIC JAZZ-FUNK MASTERCUTS 4
Birdland: Weather Report / I thought it was you: Hancock, Herbie / Can't you see me: Ayers, Roy / Dancing in outer space: Atmosfear / You got the floor: Adams, Arthur / Whistle bump: Deodato, Eumir / Real thing: Mendes, Sergio / Magic fingers: Hamilton, Chico / Strawberry letter 23: Brothers Johnson / Chief inspector: Badarou, Wally / Funkin' for Jamaica: Browne, Tom / Street life: Crusaders
CD _____ CUTSCD 16
Beechwood / Jan '94 / BMG / Pinnacle.

CLASSIC JAZZ-FUNK MASTERCUTS 5
Countdown (Captain Fingers): Ritenour, Lee / Grand prix: Fuse One / Freeze thaw: Basia / Sausalito: Washington, Grover Jr. / Intro (The River Niger): Ayers, Roy / Dreamin': Heath Brothers / Keep smiling: Szabo, Gabor / Watching life: L.A. Boppers / Boulevard: White, Peter / La Cuna: Barretto, Ray / African bird: OPA
CD _____ CUTSCD 23
Beechwood / Nov '94 / BMG / Pinnacle.

CLASSIC JAZZ-FUNK MASTERCUTS 6
CD _____ CUTSCD 31
Beechwood / Jan '96 / BMG / Pinnacle.

CLASSIC LOVE DUETS
CD _____ CDMOIR 430
Memoir / Jul '95 / Target/BMG.

CLASSIC MELLOW MASTERCUTS VOL.
She's so good to me: Vandross, Luther / Risin' to the top: Burke, Keni / Outstanding: Gap Band / Joy and pain: Maze / Give me the sunshine: Leo's Sunshine / Hold me tighter in the rain: Griffin, Billy / I'm out of your life: Arnie's Love / You'll never know: Hi-Gloss / What you won't do for love: Caldwell, Bobby / I'm back for more: Johnson, Al & Jean Carn / Fruit song: Reynolds, Jeannie / Mellow mellow right on: Lowrell
CD _____ CUTSCD 3
Beechwood / Sep '91 / BMG / Pinnacle.

CLASSIC MELLOW MASTERCUTS VOL. 2
Don't look any further: Edwards, Dennis / Baby I'm scared of you: Womack & Womack / Mind blowing decisions: Heatwave / I don't think that man should sleep alone: Parker, Ray Jnr. / All night long: Mary Jane Girls / Sweet sticky thing: Ohio Players / It's ecstasy when you lay down next to me: White, Barry / Juicy fruit: Mtume / What'cha see is what'cha get: Dramatics / Yu-ma/Go away little boy: Shaw, Marlena / I choose you: Paris / So delicious: Fatback Band
CD _____ CUTSCD 8
Beechwood / Jul '92 / BMG / Pinnacle.

CLASSIC MELLOW MASTERCUTS VOL. 3
Never too much: Vandross, Luther / You're gonna get next to me: Kirkland, Bo & Ruth Davis / Nights over Egypt: Jones Girls / Now that we've found love: O'Jays / Don't let it go to your head: Carne, Jean / Do you get enough love: Jones, Shirley / You are the one: Emotions / Reasons (Live): Earth, Wind & Fire / Rock me tonight: Jackson, Freddie / Gotta get you home tonight: Jackson, Freddie / Wilde, Eugene: Jackson, Freddie / Sweet love: Baker, Anita / We're in this love together: Jarreau, Al

---

CD _____ CUTSCD 17
Beechwood / Feb '94 / BMG / Pinnacle.

CLASSIC MIX MASTERCUTS VOL.1
Yah me be there: Ingram, James / Medicine song: Mills, Stephanie / You're the one for me: D-Train / Seventh heaven: Guthrie, Gwen / You don't know: Serious Intention / Searchin' to find the one: Unlimited Touch / Beat the street: Redd, Sharon / You can't hide your love: Joseph, David / Ain't nothin' goin' on but the rent: Guthrie, Gwen / Thinking of you: Sister Sledge / Searching: Change / Running away: Ayers, Roy
CD _____ CUTSCD 1
Beechwood / Sep '91 / BMG / Pinnacle.

CLASSIC NEW JACK SWING MASTERCUTS VOL.1
Rub you the right way: Gill, Johnny / Her: Guy / I got the feelin': Today / New Jack swing: Wreckx N Effect / She's got that vibe: R. Kelly / Do me right: Guy / Sensitivity: Tresvant, Ralph / So you like what you see: Samuelle / Poison: Bell Biv Devoe / Treat them like they want to be treated: Father MC / Another like my lover: Guy, Jasmine / Mama told me: Jackson, Keisha
CD _____ CUTSCD 5
Beechwood / Mar '92 / BMG / Pinnacle.

CLASSIC NEW JACK SWING MASTERCUTS VOL.2
Is it good to you: Lucas, Tammy & Teddy Riley / Don't be afraid: Hall, Aaron / Yo that's a lot of body: Ready For The World / I like your style: Bubba / Whatever it takes: Basic Black / Swinging single: Groove B Chill / Just got paid: Kemp, Johnny / My fantasy: Guy / Why you get funky on me: Today / Coool and express card: Nation Funktasia / Serious: La Rue / My prerogative: Brown, Bobby
CD _____ CUTSCD 9
Beechwood / Oct '92 / BMG / Pinnacle.

CLASSIC NEW JACK SWING MASTERCUTS VOL.3
Ain't too proud to beg: TLC / I want her: Sweat, Keith / I just can't handle it: Hi-Five / Judy had a boyfriend: Riff / Somebody for me: Heavy D & The Boyz / I'm dreaming: Williams, Christopher / D.O.G. me out: Guy / Rump shaker: Wreckx N Effect / 69: Father MC / I'm so into you: S.W.V. / Real love: Blige, Mary J. / Love thang: Intro
CD _____ CUTSCD 18
Beechwood / Mar '94 / BMG / Pinnacle.

CLASSIC NEW JACK SWING MASTERCUTS VOL.4
CD _____ CUTSCD 27
Beechwood / Apr '95 / BMG / Pinnacle.

CLASSIC P-FUNK MASTERCUTS VOL.1
CD _____ CUTSCD 12
Beechwood / Jan '93 / BMG / Pinnacle.

CLASSIC PERFORMERS
When the saints go marching in: Armstrong, Louis / Shall we dance: Astaire, Fred / One o'clock jump: Basie, Count / Where the blue of the night meets the gold of the day: Crosby, Bing / Boogie woogie: Dorsey, Tommy / It don't mean a thing if it ain't got that swing: Ellington, Duke / Tisket-a-tasket: Fitzgerald, Ella / Stompin' at the savoy: Goodman, Benny / Easy living: Holiday, Billie / Moonlight serenade: Miller, Glenn / Begin the beguine: Shaw, Artie / Honeysuckle Rose: Waller, Fats / Boogie woogie bugle boy: Andrews Sisters / I've got the world on a string: Sinatra, Frank / Woodchopper's ball: Herman, Woody / Over the rainbow: Garland, Judy / March of the bob cats: Crosby, Bob & His Bobcats / There's a small hotel: Baker, Josephine / April showers: Jolson, Al / Thanks for the memory: Hope, Bob & Shirley Ross / Swingin' with Django: Quintette Du Hot Club De France / Rose Marie: Eddy, Nelson / Time on my hands: Bowly, Al
CD _____ HADCD 170
Javelin / May '94 / THE / Henry Hadaway Organisation.

CLASSIC RARE GROOVE MASTERCUTS VOL.1
Turned on you: 80's Ladies / Riding high: Faze-O / Why I came to California: Ware, Leon / Say you love me girl: Break Water / Movin' in the right direction: Parks, Steve / Number one: Rushen, Patrice / Good love: Jeffries, Rome / So different: Kinky Foxx / Much too much: Sass / All I want is my baby: Gilliam, Roberta / Moonshadow: LaBelle, Patti / It's your love: Beatty, Ethel
CD _____ CUTSCD 15
Beechwood / Apr '93 / BMG / Pinnacle.

CLASSIC RARE GROOVE MASTERCUTS VOL.2
Caveman boogie: Wilson, Lesette / L.A. nights: Agawa, Yasuko / No.1 girl: Light Of The World / You need a change of mind: Brooklyn Express / There's a reason: High Tension / Work it out: Break Water / Barely breaking even: Universal Robot Band / I'd like to get into you: Kelly, Denise & Fame / Windy city theme: Davis, Carl / Bump and hustle music: Stewart, Tommy / God made me funky: Head Hunters / Give me some: L.A. Boppers
CD _____ CUTSMC 21
CD _____ CUTSCD 21
Beechwood / Sep '94 / BMG / Pinnacle.

CLASSIC REGGAE IN 90'S STYLE
CD _____ RASCD 3104
Ras / Jan '95 / Jetstar / Greensleeves / SRD / Direct.

CLASSIC REGGAE MASTERCUTS
CD _____ CUTSCD 30
Beechwood / Oct '95 / BMG / Pinnacle.

CLASSIC REGGAE VOL.1
We've got a good thing going: Minott, Sugar / Agony: Pinchers / One draw: Marley, Rita / Buddy bye: Osbourne, Johnny / Murderer: Levy, Barrington / Cocaine in my brain: Dillinger / Cottage in negril: Taylor, Tyrone / What one dance can do: Hammond, Beres / Baltimore: Tamlins / Greetings: Half Pint / Sitting and watching: Brown, Dennis / Soon forward: Isaacs, Gregory
CD _____ PCD 1434
Profile / Jan '93 / Pinnacle.

CLASSIC REGGAE VOL.1
CD _____ RNCD 2096
Rhino / Mar '95 / Jetstar / Magnum Music Group / THE.

CLASSIC ROCK
All or nothing: Small Faces / Giving it all away: Small Faces / Daltrey, roger: Small Faces / Something in the air: Thunderclap Newman / fire: Crazy World Of Arthur Brown / This wheel's on fire: Driscoll, Julie & The Brian Auger Trinity / Cry to me: Pretty Things / Mighty Quinn: Manfred Mann / Buddy Joe: Golden Earring / From the underworld: Herd / Gin house blues: Amen Corner / One and one is one: Medicine Head / Everything's alright: Mojos / With a girl like you: Troggs / You ain't seen nothin' yet: Bachman-Turner Overdrive
CD _____ 5506452
Spectrum/Karussell / Aug '94 / PolyGram / THE.

CLASSIC ROCK 'N' ROLL
CD _____ 66450172
In Toto / Dec '92 / Target/BMG.

CLASSIC ROCKERS
Baby, I love you so: Miller, Jacob / King Tubby meets the rockers uptown: Pablo, Augustus / Isn't it time to see / Jah in the hills: Pablo, Augustus / Can't keep a good man down: Immortals / Earth, wind and fire: Blackman, Paul / Love won't be so easy: Sibbles, Leroy / Changing world: Earl 16 / Blackman's heart: Delgado, Junior / Jah says the time has now come: Mundell, Hugh / You never know: Williams, Delroy / Stop the fighting: Rockers All Stars / Stop the fighting dub: Rockers All Stars / Sukiyaki: Pablo, Augustus / Eastern promise: Pablo, Augustus
CD _____ RRCD 52
Reggae Refreshers / Apr '95 / PolyGram / Vital.

CLASSIC SALSOUL MASTERCUTS VOL.1
CD _____ CUTSCD 10
Beechwood / Feb '93 / BMG / Pinnacle.

CLASSIC SALSOUL MASTERCUTS VOL.2
First choice: Dr. Love / My love is free: Double Exposure / Ain't no mountain high enough: Inner Life / This will be a night to remember: Holman, Eddie / Just as long as I got you: Love Committee / Helplessly: Moment Of Truth / Spring rain: Silvetti / Moment of my life: Inner Life / Sing, sing: Gaz / Hit and run: Holloway, Loleatta / Ooh, I love it (love break): Salsoul Orchestra / Dancin' and prancin': Candido
CD _____ CUTSCD 13
Beechwood / Jun '93 / BMG / Pinnacle.

CLASSIC SOUL
CD _____ STACD 057
Stardust / Aug '93 / Carlton Home Entertainment.

CLASSIC TO THE CORE VOL.1
(2CD/MC/3LP Set)
Hypnosis: Psychotropic / Let's do it: Cox, Carl / Feel the rhythm (comin' on strong): Rhythm Section / Take no chance: Xray Xperiments / Some justice ('91): Urban Shakedown & Mickey Finn / 40 miles: Congress / Narra mine: Genaside II / What have you done: One Tribe & Gem / Vamp: Outlander / Energy flash: Beltram, Joey / Feel real good: Manix / Take me away: True Faith & Final Cut
CD Set _____ BSECD 1
Bass Section / Dec '95 / Grapevine.

CLASSICAL TRADITIONS (Music From Central Asia/2CD Set)
CD Set _____ C 56003536
Ocora / Nov '93 / Harmonia Mundi / ADA.

CLASSICAL TURKISH MUSIC
CD _____ CMT 2741013
La Chant Du Monde / Sep '95 / Harmonia Mundi / ADA.

CLASSICS OF 1975
CD _____ RNCD 2048
Rhino / Apr '94 / Jetstar / Magnum Music Group / THE.

CLASSICS SAMPLER
CD _____ CLASS 99
Classics / Apr '95 / Discovery / Jazz Music.

CLOCKWORK ORANGE (Ibiza Experience)
CD _____ HF 48CD
PWL / Nov '95 / Warner Music / 3MV.

CLOSE TO THE HEART
Through Bucky's eyes: Gettel, Michael / Gabriel's dream: Mann, Brian / Portraits: Brewer, Spencer / Gemina: Illenberger, Ralf / Summer's lullaby: Stein, Ira / Summer's child: Lanz, David / Back home: Lauria, Nando / Je t'aime: Mann, Brian / Old house is silent: Gettel, Michael / Memory: Rumbel, Nancy / Another star in the sky: Arkenstone, David / Return to the heart: Lanz, David / Shape of her face: Whalen, Michael
CD _____ ND 63918
Narada / Apr '95 / New Note / ADA.

CLOSE TO THE HEART
CD _____ NSCD 019
Newsound / May '95 / THE.

CLUB BUZZ
CD _____ CUTZCD 1
Rumour / Feb '95 / Pinnacle / 3MV / Sony.

CLUB BUZZ '95
CD _____ CUTZCD 50
CD _____ CUTZBX 95
Rumour / Nov '95 / Pinnacle / 3MV / Sony.

CLUB BUZZ 2
CD _____ CUTZCD 2
Rumour / Aug '95 / Pinnacle / 3MV / Sony.

CLUB CLASS
CD _____ RADCD 10
Global / Apr '95 / BMG.

CLUB CLASSICS 95 (Volume 1)
Passion: Jon Of The Pleased Wimmin / Another star: Sledge, Kathy / Feel it: Hi Lux / Message of love: Lovehappy / Reach up: Perfecto All Stars / Feel it (1): Bailey, Carol / Control: Time Of The Mumph / I luv you baby: Original / Everything: Hysterix / Come together: Watford, Michael & Robert Owens / Let me hear music: Ramjack / Love so strong: Secret Life
CD _____ RCRCD 001
Recurrent / Mar '95 / Pinnacle.

CLUB CLASSICS 95 (Volume 2)
U sure do: Strike / Not over yet: Grace / Always something there to remind me: Tin Tin Out & Espiritu / Respect: Cheeks, Judy / Burning up: De Vit, Tony / Baby: Rozalla / Conway: Reel 2 Real / Let love shine: Amos / You sexy dancer: Rockford Files / Embracing the sunshine: Embracing The Sunshine / Spirit inside: Spirits / Love come rescue me: Love Station
CD _____ RCRCD 002
Recurrent / May '95 / Pinnacle.

CLUB CULTURE
CD _____ STRSCD 3
CD Set _____ STRSCDDJ 3
Stress / May '94 / Pinnacle.

CLUB GROOVES VOL. 1
Death Becomes Me / Apr '94 / Pinnacle / Vital.
CD _____ DCOMPCD 2

CLUB IBIZA
CD _____ OBMCD 1
Beechwood / Oct '95 / BMG / Pinnacle.

CLUB MEETS DUB VOL.1
CD _____ ZD 5CD
Zip Dog / Oct '95 / Grapevine.

CLUB SKA 67
Guns of Navarone: Skatalites / Phoenix city: Alphonso, Roland / Shanty town: Dekker, Desmond / Broadway jungle: Flames / Contact: Richards, Roy / Guns fever: Brooks, Baba / Rub up, push up: Hinds, Justin / Dancing mood: Wilson, Delroy / Stop making love: Gaylads / Pied piper: Marley, Rita / Lawless Street: Soul Brothers / Skaing West: Sir Lord Comic / Copasetic: Rulers
CD _____ IMCD 53
Mango / Jul '89 / Vital / PolyGram.

CLUB TOGETHER
U girls: Nush / I got a feeling: Tin Tin Out & Sweet Tee / Two faft guitars: Direckt / For the love of you: Elevator / Help my friend: Slo Moshun / Time 2 stop: Sanchez, Roger / Bits 'n' pieces: Artemisia / Satisfy my love: Johnston, Sabrina / That's where my love goes (Luv dup 1): Slamm / Dreamer: Livin' Joy / Secret life (mega mix): Blur / I want you: Secret Life / On ya way: Helicopter / Calm down: Chris & James / Congo: Boss, The / Trippin' on sunshine: Pizzaman
CD _____ CDEMC 3692
EMI / Sep '94 / EMI.

CLUB TOGETHER 2
Love so strong: Secret Life / Real: Allen, Donna / Burning up: De Vit, Tony / To the beat: Rave Bass / Apparently nothin': Anderson, Carleen / Embracing the future: B.T. / Yeke yeke: Kante, Mory / Color of my skin: Swing 52 / I need somebody: Loveland /

Your loving arms: *Martin, Billie Ray* / Reach up: *Perfecto All Stars* / Bomb: *Bucketheads* / Accens: *D.J. Misjah* / Always something there to remind me: *Tin Tin Out & Espiritu* / Look ahead: *Tenaglia, Danny* / If you should need a friend: *Tenaglia, Danny*
CD _____ CDEMC 3704
EMI / Mar '95 / EMI.

CLUB X:PRESS
CD _____ XPS 1CDU
X:Press / May '95 / SRD.

CLUB ZONE
CD _____ TCD 2779
Telstar / Jul '95 / BMG.

CLUB ZONE VOL.2
CD _____ TCD 2787
Telstar / Oct '95 / BMG.

CLUBBED TO DEATH
CD _____ RDCD 001
RDR / Feb '95 / Disc.

C'MON & DANCE
CD _____ GSCD 008
Goldmine / Nov '92 / Vital.

C'MON & DANCE TOO
I'm comin' home in the mornin': *Pride, Lou* / R 'n' B time: *Jones, E. Rodney* / Airplane song: *Jenkins, Norma & The Dolls* / Fine, fine, fine: *Hughes, Judy* / Wee oo, I'll let it be your babe: *Hughes, Judy* / Stronger than love: *Flirtations* / Love you baby: *Parker, Eddie* / My terms: *Ferguson, Helena* / I gotta know: *Tonnettes* / You'll never make the grade: *Sunlovers* / Where can my baby be: *Martells* / We must be doing something right: *Moody, Joan* / Goose pimples: *Scott, Shirley J.* / You've got to love your baby: *Millionaires* / Walkin' by: *Boss Four* / You gotta do what you gotta do: *Contenders* / Can't get over these memories: *John & The Weirdest* / Baby I dig you: *Anderson, Gene* / Ever again: *Woodberry, Gene* / It's all gone: *Magicians* / You won't say nothing: *Lewis, Tamala* / We've got a love that's out of sight: *Spencer* / I can't change: *Baker, Yvonne* / Poor unfortunate me: *Taylor, Gloria*
CD _____ GSCD 017
Goldmine / Jul '93 / Vital.

C'MON & DANCE VOL.3
Black power: *Coit, James* / Cool aid: *Humphrey, Paul & his Cool Aid Chemists* / Dancin' a hole in the world: *Esquires* / Come go with me: *Paramounts* / Easy baby: *Adventures* / Just as much: *Peterson, Kris* / Prepared to love you: *Lindsay, Thelma* / How good can it get: *Lyle, Jay* / Babysitter: *Turner, Duke & Chitowns* / Running wild: *Ex Saveyons* / What have I got now: *Fletcher, Darrow* / I can't give up on losing you: *Remarkables* / Feel good all over: *Huey, Claude 'Baby'* / Dancin' everywhere: *Bob & Earl* / I wouldn't come: *Mask Man & the Agents* / My heart is calling: *Magnificents* / Mine exclusively: *Olympics* / Ain't nobody's business: *Marbray, Ernie* / Just a little while: *Jackson, Ollie* / Love bandit: *Lang, Don* / I'm looking for my baby: *Suil, Eddie* / I'm gonna love you: *Hamilton, Edward & Arabians* / You got me where you want me: *Santos, Larry* / Personally: *Paris, Bobby* / Hold on: *Generation* / Build your house on a strong foundation: *Given & Rae* / Job opening (Part 1): *Del-Larks* / What good am I: *Champion, Mickey* / Don't make you feel funky: *Hicks, Joe* / I've got something good: *Sam & Kitty*
CD _____ GSCD 033
Goldmine / Apr '94 / Vital.

COCKNEY KINGS OF THE MUSIC HALL
CD _____ CDSDL 413
Saydisc / Oct '95 / Harmonia Mundi / ADA / Direct.

COFFEE BAR DAYS
(2CD/MC Set)
All I have to do is dream: *Everly Brothers* / Claudette: *Everly Brothers* / Something else: *Cochran, Eddie* / Three steps to heaven: *Cochran, Eddie* / I'm not a juvenile delinquent: *Lymon, Frankie & The Teenagers* / Why do fools fall in love: *Lymon, Frankie & The Teenagers* / Pretty little angel eyes: *Lee, Curtis* / Wanderer: *Dion* / He's so fine: *Chiffons* / More than I can say: *Vee, Bobby* / Baby sittin': *Angelo, Bobby & The Tuxedos* / I'm walkin': *Domino, Fats* / Ma, he's making eyes at me: *Otis, Johnny* / Sea cruise: *Ford, Frankie* / Mother-in-law: *Dose, Ernie K.* / Blue jean bop: *Vincent, Gene* / I'm a moody guy: *Fenton, Shane & The Fentones* / Ain't misbehavin': *Bruce, Tommy & The Bruisers* / Witch doctor: *Lang, Don* / Cloudburst: *Lang, Don* / Lollipop: *Mudlarks* / Don't you rock me daddy-o: *Vipers Skiffle Group* / Cumberland gap: *Vipers Skiffle Group* / It takes a worried man (to sing a worried song): *Vipers Skiffle Group* / Runaway: *Shannon, Del* / Teenager in love: *Dion & The Belmonts* / Shakin' all over: *Kidd, Johnny & The Pirates* / Cindy oh Cindy: *Brent, Tony* / Girl of my dreams: *Brent, Tony* / Someday (you'll want me to want you): *Nelson, Rick* / You're sixteen: *Burnette, Johnny Rock 'N' Roll Trio* / Tell Laura I love her: *Valance, Ricky* / Fever: *Lee, Peggy* / Send me the pillow that you dream on: *Tillotson, Johnny* / Kisses sweeter than wine: *Rodgers, Jimmie* / Volare: *Martin, Dean* / Only sixteen: *Douglas, Craig* / Be my girl:

Dale, Jim / Big man: *Four Preps* / Love letters: *Lester, Ketty*
CD Set _____ CDDL 1254
Music For Pleasure / Jan '94 / EMI.

COLLABORATIONS LO RE
CD _____ LCD 02
Beechwood / Nov '95 / BMG / Pinnacle.

COLLECTED WORKS - 15 YEARS OF MUSIC
CD _____ SP 116CD
Stony Plain / Oct '93 / ADA / CM / Direct.

COLLECTION OF MODERN SOUL CLASSICS, A
Just loving you: *Andrews, Ruby* / Come back baby: *Justice Department* / I'm so glad you're mine: *Perkins, George* / Lonely girl: *Side Show* / Talkin': *Vee Gees* / Making new friends: *Tracy, Jeanie* / Girl, you're my kind of wonderful: *Relf, Bobby* / Girl I've been trying to tell you: *Ultimates* / Lightin' up: *Karim, Ty* / Teasin you again: *Tee, Willie* / Let's go fishing: *Turner Bros* / Dream: *Creations* / I need your love: *Woods, Ella* / Here stands a man who needs you: *Wilson, George* / Given up on love: *Thompson, Johnny* / If it's not love don't waste my time: *Johnson, Dorothy* / Have I really loved you: *Smoke* / Footsteps across your mind: *Shock* / Girl I love you: *Fisher, Shelley* / You're gone: *Hardin, Celest* / Better to bend than break: *Simmons, Cissie* / Colour him father: *Winstons* / Wash and wear love: *Vernado, Lynne*
CD _____ GSCD 009
Goldmine / Jan '93 / Vital.

COLLECTION, THE
Out of this world: *Taylor, Livingston* / Caribbean sunrise: *Santamaria, Mongo* / Wanna spend more time: *Sara K* / Jesus is mine: *Cephas, John & Phil Wiggins* / Num pagode em planaltina: *Solo* / Wings beat time: *Dunlap, Bruce* / Isn't it a pity: *Butler, Laverne* / Caminho de casa: *Mann, Herbie* / Haven't we met: *Rankin, Kenny* / Meditation: *Caram, Ana* / Manancia: *Lubambo & Rabello* / O magnum mysterium: *Westminster Choir* / Samba de Orfeu: *Bonfa, Luiz* / My blue heaven: *Pizzarelli, John* / White water: *Chesky, David* / Songs without words: *Salon New York*
CD _____ PJD 1000
Chesky / Nov '93 / Complete/Pinnacle.

COLLECTORS JACKPOT
CD _____ 3801212
Jazz Archives / Oct '92 / Jazz Music / Discovery / Cadillac.

COLOMBIA TE CANTA
Mi negrita: *Grupo Caneo* / Soy tu amigo: *La Misma Gente* / Caliche: *La Misma Gente* / La gota fria: *Pancho Gomez Y Sus Acordeones* / Gracias amor: *Orq Matecana* / Torero: *Orq Guayaean* / Come te quiero: *Orq Matecana* / Alabio, alabao: *Orq Guayaean* / Kaquiry kaquiry: *Orq Guayaean* / Linda mujer: *Aleman, Cali* / Amor sin control: *Aleman, Cali* / Que vas a hacer conmigo: *Santana, Kike* / Maldita duda: *Barros, Alberto* / Dejala: *Grupo Caneo*
CD _____ 66058082
RMM / Nov '95 / New Note.

COLORS OF ZOTH OMMOG, THE
CD Set _____ CDZOT 121
Zoth Ommog / Nov '94 / Plastic Head.

COLOURS
Understand this groove: *U.F.I.* / Metropolis: *Metropolis* / Cry freedom (Malawi Mix): *Mombassa* / Burning: *MK* / I'm comin' hardcore (Original Mix): *M.A.N.I.C.* / Berry: *TC 1991* / Bad man: *Urban Jungle* / Funky guitar (Remix): *TC 1992* / Hyporeel: *Metropolis* / Appolonia (Quatmix): *B.M.EX* / Always: *MK* / Unity / Hold your head up high (CJ's Master Remix) / Is this love really real (Yowzah Vocal): *Sure Is Pure & Aphrique*
CD _____ CDUCR1
Union City / Jan '93 / EMI.

COLOURS
(20 Great Hits Of The Sixties)
Needles and pins: *Searchers* / All day and all of the night: *Kinks* / I couldn't live without your love: *Clark, Petula* / Silence is golden: *Tremeloes* / Build me up buttercup: *Foundations* / Mockingbird Hill: *Migil 5* / Colours: *Donovan* / Itchycoo Park: *Small Faces* / Girl don't come: *Shaw, Sandie* / I'm gonna be strong: *Pitney, Gene* / Suddenly you love me: *Tremeloes* / First cut is the deepest: *Arnold, P.P.* / Daydream: *Lovin' Spoonful* / Funny how love can be: *Ivy League* / Ice in the sun: *Status Quo* / Something here in my heart: *Paper Dolls* / Don't sleep in the subway: *Clark, Petula* / She'd rather be with me: *Turtles* / Only love can break a heart: *Pitney, Gene* / Hello Susie: *Amen Corner*
CD _____ TRTCD 104
TrueTrax / Oct '94 / THE.

COME ON PEEL THE NOISE
CD _____ TANGCD 11
Tangerine / Jul '95 / Disc.

COME TOGETHER UK
CD _____ COTINDCD 6
Cottage Industry / Nov '95 / Total/BMG.

COMEDIENS 1930-39
CD Set _____ 982742
EPM / Jun '93 / Discovery / ADA.

COMEDIES/OPERAS FROM SRI LANKA
CD _____ CMT 2741006CD
La Chant Du Monde / Jul '95 / Harmonia Mundi / ADA.

COMIN' HOME TO THE BLUES
She's into something: *Cray, Robert* / You can't judge a book by the cover: *Buchanan, Roy* / Two fisted mama: *Webster, Katie* / Blues overtook me: *Musselwhite, Charlie* / Don't you call that boogie: *Hopkins, Lightnin'* / That woman is poison: *Thomas, Rufus* / Everyday I have the blues: *Memphis Slim* / Sonny's whoopin' the doop: *Terry, Sonny* / I think I got the blues: *Dixon, Willie* / What am I living for: *Brown, Clarence 'Gatemouth'* / Don't take advantage of me: *Winter, Johnny* / Who's lovin' you tonite: *Eaglin, Snooks* / Moon is full: *Collins, Albert* / Long for joy: *Taylor, Koko* / Whole lotta lovin': *Professor Longhair* / Drinkin' wine spo-dee-o-dee: *Otis, Johnny*
CD _____ MCCD 016
Music Club / Feb '91 / Disc / THE / CM.

COMIN' HOME TO THE BLUES VOL.2
Red rooster: *Howlin' Wolf* / I'm a man: *Diddley, Bo* / Your funeral and my trial: *Williamson, Sonny Boy* / Wee wee hours: *Berry, Chuck* / First time I met the blues: *Guy, Buddy* / Mannish boy: *Waters, Muddy* / Dust my broom: *James, Elmore* / Juke: *Little Walter* / So many roads, so many trains: *Rush, Otis* / Tell mama: *James, Etta* / Walking the blues: *Dixon, Willie* / Sugar mama: *Hooker, John Lee* / I asked for water (she gave me gasoline): *Howlin' Wolf* / Bring it to Jerome: *Diddley, Bo* / Worried life blues: *Berry, Chuck* / Got my mojo working: *Waters, Muddy* / Don't start me talkin': *Williamson, Sonny Boy* / In the mood: *Hooker, John Lee* / Chicago bound: *Rogers, Jimmy* / Wang dang doodle: *Taylor, Koko* / I'd rather go blind: *James, Etta* / Diggin' my potatoes: *Washboard Sam* / Reconsider baby: *Fulson, Lowell* / My baby: *Little Walter*
CD _____ MCCD 026
Music Club / May '91 / Disc / THE / CM.

COMIN' HOME TO THE BLUES VOL.3
When you see the tears from my eyes: *Guy, Buddy* / Goin' mad blues: *Hooker, John Lee* / All my love in vain: *Williamson, Sonny Boy* / Standing at the burial ground (live): *McDowell, 'Mississippi' Fred* / His heel taps and lowers: *Tucker, Tommy* / She's 19 years old (live): *Waters, Muddy* / How blue can you get (live): *Collins, Albert* / Hoodoo man (live): *Wells, Junior* / No friend around: *Hooker, John Lee* / Don't know where I've been: *Diddley, Bo* / Christo redemptor (live): *Musselwhite, Charlie* / Blue and lonesome: *McPhee, Tony & Billy Boy Arnold* / Hoochie coochie man (live): *Waters, Muddy* / Baptize me in wine: *Hawkins, Screamin' Jay* / Sad hours: *Little Walter* / One room country shack: *Butterfield, Paul*
CD _____ MCCD 044
Music Club / Sep '91 / Disc / THE / CM.

COMIN' HOME TO THE BLUES VOLS. 1-3
(3CD Set)
CD Set _____ MCBX 002
Music Club / Jan '93 / Disc / THE / CM.

COMING DOWN
CD _____ CRECD 135
Creation / Feb '95 / 3MV / Vital.

COMING ON STRONG
CD Set _____ NSCD 004
Newsound / Feb '95 / THE.

COMMERCIAL BREAKS
Only you: *Praise* / Lovely day: *Withers, Bill* / Summer breeze: *Isley Brothers* / Love train: *O'Jays* / How 'bout us: *Champaign* / Turn turn turn: *Byrds* / It's over: *Orbison, Roy* / Move over darling: *Day, Doris* / I can see clearly now (remix): *Nash, Johnny* / Stand by your man: *Wynette, Tammy* / Always on my mind: *Nelson, Willie* / Blue velvet: *Vinton, Bobby* / I can help: *Swan, Billy* / Take five: *Brubeck, Dave* / Summertime: *Vaughan, Sarah* / Mannish boy: *Waters, Muddy* / Should I stay or should I go: *Clash*
CD _____ 4690482
Columbia / Nov '91 / Sony.

COMMITTED TO JUNGLE
CD _____ VZS 16CD
Vizion Sound / Apr '95 / Jetstar.

COMMITTED TO SOUL
CD _____ ARC 3100142
Arcade / Jul '94 / Sony / Grapevine.

COMPACT 2-TONE STORY, THE
(4CD Set)
Gangsters: *Special AKA* / Selector: *Selector* / Prince: *Madness* / On my radio: *Selector* / Message to you Rudy: *Specials & Rico* / Tears of a clown: *Beat* / I can't stand up for falling down: *Costello, Elvis* / Too much too young: *Special AKA* / Three minute hero: *Selecter* / People do rock steady: *Bodysnatchers* / Missing words: *Selecter* / Rat race: *Specials* / Stereotype: *Specials* / Easy life: *Bodysnatchers* / Mantovani: *Swinging Cats* / Sea cruise: *Rico* / Do nothing: *Specials & Rico* / Ghost town: *Specials* / Boiler: *Rhoda & Special A.K.A.* / Jungle music: *Special AKA & Rico* / Feeling's gone and the feeling's back: *Apollinaires* / Tear the whole thing down: *Higsons* / Envy the lone: *Apollinaires* / War crimes: *Special AKA* /

Run me down: *Higsons* / Racist friend: *Special AKA* / Nelson Mandela: *Special AKA* / Window shopping: *Friday Club* / Alphabet army: *J.B's Allstars* / Madness: *Madness* / Too much pressure: *Selecter* / Nite klub: *Specials & Rico* / Ranking full stop: *Beat* / Girls talk: *Costello, Elvis* / Guns of Navarone: *Special AKA* / Skinhead symphony: *Special AKA* / James Bond: *Selecter* / Ruder than you: *Bodysnatchers* / Carry go bring come: *Selecter* / Rude boys outa jail: *Specials* / Too experienced: *Bodysnatchers* / International jet set: *Specials* / Away: *Swinging Cats* / Carolina: *Rico* / Maggie's farm: *Specials* / Why: *Specials* / Friday night, Saturday morning: *Specials* / Theme from the boiler: *Rhoda & Special A.K.A.* / Rasta call you: *Rico & Special A.K.A.* / Easter Island: *Rico & Special A.K.A.* / Feeling's gone: *Apollinaires* / Bongo medley: *Apollinaires* / Ylang Ylang: *Higsons* / Give it up: *Apollinaires* / War crimes (2): *Special AKA* / Put the punk back into funk: *Higsons* / Bright lights (Instrumental): *Special AKA* / Break down the door: *Special AKA* / Can't get a break: *Special AKA* / Window shopping (Instrumental): *Special AKA* / Alarm: *J.B's Allstars* / Braggin' and tryin' not to lie: *Radiation, Roddy & Specials* / Rude boys outa jail (Version): *Staples, Neville A.K.A.* / Judge Roughneck / Racquel: *Special AKA* / 007: *Bodysnatchers*
CD Set _____ CDCHRTT 5013
Chrysalis / Nov '93 / EMI.

COMPACT D'AFRIQUE
Adjani Muana Kini: *Mabele, Aurlus* / Voici: *Kanda Bongo Man* / Masquereau: *Les Quatre Etoiles* / Sane-mamadou: *Tchico & Les Officers Of African Music* / Sazsa Ta Kapi: *Choc Stars* / Izia: *Wemba, Papa et Mavuela* / Le bon samaritain: *Sukami, Teddy*
CD _____ CDORB 907
Globestyle / Aug '86 / Pinnacle.

COMPAGNU TI MANNU
CD _____ TA 012CD
Robi Droli / Apr '95 / Direct / ADA.

COMPETING HIGHLAND DANCER, THE
(Highland & National Dances From Beginners To Open Dancers)
CD _____ CDITV 516
Scotdisc / Jul '90 / Duncans / Ross / Conifer.

COMPILATIONS
CD _____ NATCD 50
Nation / Feb '95 / Disc.

COMPLETE 'D' SINGLES COLLECTION VOL.1, THE
(4CD Set)
Can't play hookey: *Noack, Eddie* / My steady dream: *Noack, Eddie* / Mom and Dad I love you too: *Travis, Al* / He brough us together: *Travis, Al* / Cotton picker: *Watts, Wortham* / Lonesome: *Watts, Wortham* / Never meant for me: *Carl, Utah* / Treasured memories: *Carl, Utah* / I can't find the doorknob: *Jimmy & Johnny* / Keep telling me: *Jimmy & Johnny* / Baby, when the sun goes down: *Douglas, Tony* / World in my arms: *Douglas, Tony* / Talk to me lonesome heart: *O'Gwynn, James* / Changeable: *O'Gwynn, James* / I want to be where you're gonna be: *Singleton, Margie* / Shattered kingdom: *Singleton, Margie* / Chantilly lace: *Big Bopper* / Purple people eater meets the witch doctor: *Big Bopper* / Gonna pack up my toubles: *Hall, Sonny & The Echoes* / My big fat baby: *Hall, Sonny & The Echoes* / Walking away: *Dollar, Johnny* / No memories: *Dollar, Johnny* / Texas Alaska: *Jackson, Ray* / Alaska: *Jackson, Ray* / I played the fool: *Four B's* / Love eternal: *Four B's* / Don't hold me to a vow: *Moncrief, Bobby* / Here is my heart: *Moncrief, Bobby* / Dreaming in vain: *Sheets, Sonny* / Wheels: *Terry & The Pirates* / Blues gone and the feeling: *Bond, Eddie* / Standing in your window: *Bond, Eddie* / Same old fool: *Barber, Glen* / Tomorrow: *Barber, Glen* / Hello sadness: *Barber, Glen* / Daydreaming again: *Bragg, Doug* / I'll find my dreamgirl: *Bragg, Doug* / Have blues, will travel: *Noack, Eddie* / Price of love: *Noack, Eddie* / Ohh wow: *Dee & Patty* / Sweet lovin' baby: *Dee & Patty* / Understand: *Forrer, Johnnie* / Fools paradise: *Forrer, Johnnie* / Blue memories: *O'Gwynn, James* / You don't want to hold me: *O'Gwynn, James* / Draggin' the fiddle: *Choates, Harry* / Allons a lafayette: *Choates, Harry* / Jole Blon: *Choates, Harry* / Corpus Christie waltz: *Choates, Harry* / Echo mountain: *Jackson, Ray* / Tears of tomorrow: *Jackson, Ray* / Lookin: *Porter, Royce* / I still belong to you: *Porter, Royce* / Lonely night: *Mathis, James* / Seablin' sugar: *Lindsay, Merle* / Hoy rag: *Lindsay, Merle* / I'm all wrapped up: *Doyle, Ted* / He made you mine: *Doyle, Ted* / Mean autry: *Thibodeaux, Rufus* / Cameron memorial waltz: *Thibodeaux, Rufus* / True affection: *Johnson, Byron* / You were only fooling: *Johnson, Byron* / I need someone: *Mac, Johnny* / That's all I can do: *Mac, Johnny* / Step aside old heart: *Timmons, Patsy* / I understand him: *Timmons, Patsy* / Won't you tell me: *Stanford, Doug* / Sady: *Stanford, Doug* / Men do cry: *Hall, Sonny* / Day you walked away: *Hall, Sonny* / I kept it a secret: *Edge, Dave* / I didn't think of you: *Edge, Dave* / I don't live there any more: *Noack, Eddie* / Walk em off: *Noack, Eddie* / Reprieve of Tom

Dooley: *Johnson, Rick* / Barbara Allen: *Johnson, Rick* / Maple sugar: *Allen, Ward* / Back up and punch: *Allen, Ward* / Bugger burns: *Lynn, Jerry* / Queen of the moon: *Lynn, Jerry* / It'll be my first time: *Kilgore, Merle* / I take a trip to the moon: *Kilgore, Merle* / Opelousas waltz: *Choates, Harry* / Poor Hobo: *Choates, Harry* / Honky tonk boogie: *Choates, Harry* / Port arthur waltz: *Choates, Harry* / I'm all alone: *Bragg, Doug* / Calling me back: *Bragg, Doug* / Whirlwind: *Bragg, Doug* / Man I met: *Campz, Ray* / Ballad of Donna and Peggy Sue: *Campz, Ray* / Dottie: *McCoy, Doyle* / Some how I don't mind: *McCoy, Doyle* / Justice of love: *Bowman, Cecil* / Man awaitin': *Bowman, Cecil* / Penalty of love: *Velvetones* / Come back: *Velvetones* / Born to love you: *Heap, Jimmy* / Some one else is filling my shoes: *Heap, Jimmy* / I love only you: *Heap, Jimmy* / I Like it: *Heap, Jimmy* / Cold records in the snow: *Heap, Jimmy* / Happy little bluebird: *Barnes, Benny* / Chantilly lace cha cha: *Kimbrough, Bill* / Egg head: *Kimbrough, Bill* / From a kiss to the blues: *Mathis, Johnny* / Since I said goodbye to love: *Mathis, Johnny* / What makes you cry: *Jackson, Ray* / Tea leaves don't cry: *Jackson, Ray* / Trumpets and clarinets: *Kucera, Ernie* / Annie waltz: *Kucera, Ernie* / One more heartache: *Doyle, Ted* / Just for the thrill: *Doyle, Ted* / It's wrong for me to love you: *Johnson, Byron* / Our love is not worth living for: *Johnson, Byron* / Letter overdue: *Gray, Claude* / I'm not supposed: *Gray, Claude* / Don't look behind: *Noack, Eddie* / Thinking man's woman: *Noack, Eddie* / Baby don't go: *Charles, Andy & The Blues Kings* / Love come back: *Charles, Andy & The Blues Kings*
CD   **BCD 15832**
Bear Family / Nov '95 / Rollercoaster / Direct / CM / Swift / ADA.

COMPLETE IRISH DANCING SET
(2CD/MC Set)
CD Set   **CDH 1050CD**
Outlet / Jul '95 / ADA / Duncans / CM / Ross / Direct / Koch.

COMPLETE IRISH NATIONAL ANTHEM, THE
CD   **IRBCD 1937**
Outlet / Jul '94 / ADA / Duncans / CM / Ross / Direct / Koch.

COMPLETE STAX/VOLT SINGLES, THE
(1959-1968/9CD Set)
Fool in love: *Veltones* / Because I love you: *Carla & Rufus* / Gee whiz: *Thomas, Carla* / You make me feel so good: *Chips* / Love of my own: *Thomas, Carla* / Last night: *Mar-Keys* / I didn't believe: *Rufus & Friend* / I'm going home: *Prince Conley* (Mama, mama) Wish me good luck: *Thomas, Carla* / Morning after: *Mar-Keys* / Life I live: *Stephens, Barbara* / About noon: *Mar-Keys* / Burnt biscuits: *Triumphs* / I kinda think he does: *Thomas, Carla* / Foxy: *Mar-Keys* / You don't miss your water/Formula of love: *Bell, William* / Goofin' off: *Skipper, Macy* / Wait a minute: *Stephens, Barbara* / Sunday jealous: *Charles, Nick* / That's the way it is with me: *Stephens, Barbara* / Pop-eye stroll: *Mar-Keys* / Three dogwoods: *Charles, Nick* / No tears: *Tonettes* / Why should I suffer: *Canes* / What's happenin': *Mar-Keys* / Just across the street/There's a love: *Del Rios* / Can't ever let go: *Thomas, Rufus* / Green onions/Behave yourself: *Booker T & The MG's* / Any other way: *Bell, William* / I'll bring it home to you: *Thomas, Carla* / Sack o' woe: *Mar-Keys* / These arms of mine: *Redding, Otis* / Teardrop sea: *Tonettes* / Dog: *Thomas, Rufus* / Jelly bread: *Booker T & The MG's* / I told you so: *Bell, William* / Bo-time: *Mar-Keys* / Home grown: *Booker T & The MG's* / My imaginary guy: *Parker, Deanie* / Just as I thought: *Bell, William* / What a fool I've been: *Thomas, Carla* / Hawg (pt 1): *Kirk, Eddie* / Don't be afraid of love: *Mack, Oscar* / That's my guy: *Johnson, Cheryl & Pam* / Chinese checkers: *Booker T & The MG's* / Somebody mentioned your name: *Bell, William* / What can I do: *Marchan, Bobby* / That's what my heart needs: *Redding, Otis* / What can it be: *Astors* / Bango: *Billy & The King Bees* / Them bones: *Kirk, Eddie* / Walking the dog: *Thomas, Rufus* / I'll show you: *Bell, William* / Pain in my heart: *Redding, Otis* / Gee whiz it's Christmas: *Thomas, Carla* / Mo' onions: *Booker T & The MG's* / Frog stomp: *Newman, Floyd* / Can your monkey do the dog: *Thomas, Rufus* / You won't do right: *Marchan, Bobby* / Wondering: *Drapels* / Each step I take: *Parker, Deanie* / Honeydripper: *Van-Dells* / Who will it be tomorrow: *Bell, William* / Come to me/Don't leave me this way: *Redding, Otis* / I don't want you anymore: *Jefferson, Eddie* / Restless: *Cobras* / Somebody stole my dog: *Thomas, Rufus* / Big party: *Barbara & The Browns* / That's really some good/Night time is the right time: *Rufus* / Security: *Redding, Otis* / Dream girl: *Mack, Oscar* / Closer to my baby: *Williams, Dorothy* / I've got no time to lose: *Thomas, Carla* / Young man: *Drapels* / Soul dressing: *Booker T & The MG's* / Affer laughter (comes tears): *Rene, Wendy* / Can't explain how it happened: *Hunter, Ivory Joe* / Boot pain: *Mar-Keys* / Please return to me: *Fleets* / Jump back: *Thomas, Rufus* / Chained and bound: *Redding, Otis* / In my heart: *Barbara & The Browns* /

Spunky: *Jenkins, Johnny* / Bar B Q: *Rene, Wendy* / Sidewalk surf: *Mad Lads* / Can't be still: *Booker T & The MG's* / Woman's love: *Thomas, Carla* / Yank me (doodle): *Baraculas* / That's how strong my love is: *Mr. Pitiful*: *Redding, Otis* / Don't let her be your baby: *Del Rays* / Can't see you when I want you: *Porter, David* / My lover: *Barbara & The Browns* / Got you on my mind: *Barbara & The Browns* / How do you quit (someone you love): *Thomas, Carla* / Biggest fool in town: *Gorgeous George* / Banana juice: *Mar-Keys* / Little Sally Walker: *Thomas, Rufus* / Goodnight baby: *Sam & Dave* / Boot-leg/Outrage: *Booker T & The MG's* / I've been loving you too long: *Redding, Otis* / Candy: *Astors* / Give you what I got/Reap what you sow: *Rene, Wendy* / Stop look what you're doin': *Thomas, Carla* / Willy willy: *Thomas, Rufus* / Don't have to shop around: *Mad Lads* / Crying all by myself: *Bell, William* / I take what I want: *Sam & Dave* / When you move to lose: *Thomas, Rufus & Carla* / Respect: *Redding, Otis* / Make it me: *Premiers* / World is round: *Thomas, Rufus* / In the twilight zone: *Astors* / Blue groove: *Sir Isaac & The Dodads* / You don't know like I know: *Sam & Dave* / Grab this thing: *Mar-Keys* / Be my lady: *Booker T & The MG's* / Comfort me: *Thomas, Carla* / I can't turn you loose/Just one more day: *Redding, Otis* / I want someone: *Mad Lads* / Birds and the bees: *Thomas, Rufus & Carla* / Philly dog: *Mar-Keys* / I had a dream: *Taylor, Johnnie* / Satisfaction: *Redding, Otis* / Things get better: *Floyd, Eddie* / I'll run your hurt away: *Johnson, Ruby* / Hot dog: *Four Shells* / Let me be good to you: *Thomas, Carla* / Hold on I'm comin': *Sam & Dave* / Laundromat blues: *King, Albert* / Sugar sugar: *Mad Lads* / Share what you got/Marching off to war: *Bell, William* / My lover's prayer: *Redding, Otis* / Your good thing is about to end: *John, Mable* / I got to love somebody's baby: *Taylor, Johnnie* / What will love tend to make: *Mad Lads* / Knock on wood: *Floyd, Eddie* / B-A-B-Y: *Thomas, Carla* / My sweet potato/Booker-loo: *Booker T & The MG's* / Oh pretty woman: *King, Albert* / Said I wasn't gonna tell nobody: *Sam & Dave* / Never like this before: *Bell, William* / Fa fa fa fa (Sad song): *Redding, Otis* / Patch my heart: *Mad Lads* / Let's get a boyfriend: *Thomas, Rufus* / Come to me my darling/When love comes down: *Johnson, Ruby* / Try a little tenderness: *Redding, Otis* / Crosscut saw: *King, Albert* / Little bluebird/Toe hold: *Taylor, Johnnie* / Jingle bells: *Booker T & The MG's* / You got me hummin': *Sam & Dave* / You're taking up another: *John, Mable* / All I want for Christmas is you: *Thomas, Carla* / Please uncle Sam: *Charmels* / Something good: *Thomas, Carla* / Raise your head: *Floyd, Eddie* / Ain't that love: *Taylor, Johnnie* / I don't want to lose: *Mad Lads* / When something is wrong: *Sam & Dave* / Let me down slow: *Wilson, Bobby* / Hip hug-her: *Booker T & The MG's* / Everybody loves a winner: *Bell, William* / Minnie skirt Minnie: *Rice, Sir Mack* / When tomorrow comes: *Thomas, Carla* / Spoiler: *Purrell, Eddie* / I love you more than words can say: *Redding, Otis* / If ever I needed love: *Johnson, Ruby* / Same time, same place: *John, Mable* / Tramp: *Redding, Otis & Carla Thomas* / Soul finger/Knucklehead: *Bar-Kays* / Shake: *Redding, Otis* / Born under a bad sign: *King, Albert* / Soothe me/I can't stand up: *Sam & Dave* / Don't rock the boat: *Floyd, Eddie* / My inspiration: *Mad Lads* / Love sickness: *Rice, Sir Mack* / How can you: *Jeanne & The Darlings* / Sophisticated sissy: *Thomas, Rufus* / I'll always hang faith in you: *Thomas, Carla* / Love is a doggone good thing: *Floyd, Eddie* / Groovin'/Slim Jenkins place: *Booker T & The MG's* / Glory of love: *Redding, Otis* / I'm a big girl now/Wait you dog: *John, Mable* / You can't get away from it: *Taylor, Johnnie* / Eloise: *Bell, William* / Knock on wood (1): *Redding, Otis & Carla Thomas* / I'm glad to do it: *Blast, C.L.* / You can't run away from your heart: *Clay, Judy* / I'll gladly take you back: *Charmels* / Soul man: *Sam & Dave* / Daddy didn't tell me: *Astors* / Give everybody some: *Bar-Kays* / On a Saturday night: *Floyd, Eddie* / Don't hit me no more: *John, Mable* / Somebody's sleeping: *Taylor, Johnnie* / Winter snow: *Booker T & The MG's* / Every day: *Bell, William* / Home grown: *Booker T & The MG's* / Frog stomp: *New—* (cut off) to satisfaction: *Daye, Johnny* / Pick up the pieces: *Thomas, Carla* / Down ta my house: *Charmels* / Soul girl: *Jeanne & The Darlings* / Cold feet: *King, Albert* / I thank you/Wrap it up: *Sam & Dave* / (Sittin' on) the dock of the bay: *Redding, Otis* / Don't pass your judgement: *Memphis Nomads* / Lovey dovey: *Redding, Otis & Carla Thomas* / I got a sure thing: *Nightingales* / Big bird: *Floyd, Eddie* / Hard day's night: *Bar-Kays* / Next time: *Taylor, Johnnie* / Tribute to a king/Every man: *Bell, William* / Memphis train/I think I made a boo boo: *Thomas, Rufus* / What will later on be like/Hang me now: *Jeanne & The Darlings* / Soul power: *Martin, Derek* / Bring your love back to me: *Lyndell, Linda* / Dime a dozen: *Thomas, Carla* / Whatever hurts you: *Mad Lads* / Happy song: *Redding, Otis* / Lucy: *King, Albert* / I ain't particular: *Taylor, Johnnie* / Oh oh oh oh baby: *Eddie, Floyd*
CD Set   **7567822182**
Atlantic / May '91 / Warner Music.

COMPLETE STAX/VOLT SOUL SINGLES VOL.2, THE
(1968-1971/9CD Set)
I was born to love you: *Walton, Shirley* / Precious, precious: *Hayes, Isaac* / Send peace and harmony home: *Walton, Shirley* / Soul limbo: *Booker T & The MG's* / I've never found a girl: *Floyd, Eddie* / It's been a long time coming: *Delaney & Bonnie* / What a man: *Lyndell, Linda* / I like everything about you: *Hughes, Jimmy* / Stay baby stay: *Daye, Johnny* / Private number: *Clay, Judy & William Bell* / So nice: *Mad Lads* / Long walk to D.C.: *Staple Singers* / Give 'em love: *Soul Children* / Funky Mississippi: *Thomas, Rufus* / Lovin' feeling: *Charmels* / Where do I go: *Thomas, Carla* / Bed of roses: *Clay, Judy* / Bring it on home to me: *Floyd, Eddie* / It's unbelievable (how you control my soul): *Jeanne & The Darlings* / Who's making love: *Taylor, Johnnie* / Mighty cold Winter: *Dino & Doc* / Hang 'em high: *Booker T & The MG's* / You're leaving me: *Ollie & The Nightingales* / Copy kat: *Bar-Kays* / I forgot to be your lover: *Bell, William* / Running out: *John, Mable* / My baby specializes: *Bell, William & Judy Clay* / I'll understand: *Soul Children* / Ghetto: *Staple Singers* / Blues power: *King, Albert* / Eccie Epsilons / Funky way: *Thomas, Rufus* / Take care of your homework: *Taylor, Johnnie* / I like what you're doing (to me): *Thomas, Carla* / I've got to have your love: *Floyd, Eddie* / Let 'em down baby: *Hughes, Jimmy* / Love is here today and gone tomorrow: *Mad Lads* / It ain't long enough: *Clay, Judy* / Mellow way you treat your man: *Ollie & The Nightingales* / Private number (2): *Still, Sunny* / Time is tight: *Booker T & (Sittin' on) the dock of the bay: *Staple Singers* / So I can love you: *Emotions* / Don't stop dancing (to the music): *Bar-Kays* / One more chance: *Joseph, Margie* / I wanna be good (to you): *Dotson, Jimmy* / Finger lickin' good: *Miller, Art Jerry* / Tighten up my thang: *Soul Children* / Whole world is falling down: *Bell, William* / Testify (I wonna): *Taylor, Johnnie* / Drowning on dry land: *King, Albert* / Do the sissy: *Stingers* / Don't fall in love: *Marvel, Eddie* / Mrs. Robinson: *Booker T & The MG's* / Love's sweet sensation: *Bell, William & Mavis Staples* / Just because your love has gone: *Banks, Darrell* / Chains of love: *Hughes, Jimmy* / Happy: *Bell, William* / Challenge: *Staple Singers* / Soul-a-lujah: *Taylor, Johnnie/Eddie Floyd/William Bell* / Never, never let you go: *Floyd, Eddie & Mavis Staples* / Just keep on loving me: *Taylor, Johnnie & Carla Thomas* / I need you woman: *Bell, William & Carla Thomas* / I've got a feeling: *Ollie & The Nightingales* / It's time to pay for the fun (we've had): *Jeanne & The Darlings* / I could never be to Phoenix: *Mad Lads* / Slum baby: *Booker T & The MG's* / Best part of a love affair: *Emotions* / By the time I get to Phoenix (2): *Hayes, Isaac* / Walk on by: *Hayes, Isaac* / Tupelo Part 1: *Staples, Pops/ Steve Cropper/ Albert King* / Water: *Staples, Pops/ Steve Cropper/ Albert King* / Sweeter he is: *Soul Children* / You're driving me (To the arms of a stranger): *Staples, Mavis* / Open up your heart: *Newcomers* / Why is the wine sweeter (on the other side): *Floyd, Eddie* / When will we be paid: *Staple Singers* / Grinder man: *Hooker, John Lee* / Born under a bad sign: *Bell, William* / What you gonna do: *Joseph, Margie* / I'm so glad: *Hunter, Jimmy* / Beautiful feelings: *Banks, Darrell* / Your love was strange: *Dramatics* / Love bones: *Taylor, Johnnie* / Hard to say goodbye: *Delaney & Bonnie* / Got to get rid of you: *Barnes, J.J.* / Habit forming love: *Milner, Reggie* / My thing is a moving thing: *T S U Tornadoes* / Stealing love: *Emotions* / Wrapped up in love again: *King, Albert* / Do the funky chicken: *Thomas, Rufus* / California girl: *Floyd, Eddie* / Tribute to a black woman, Part 1: *Hayes, Isaac* / Song and dance: *Bar-Kays* / Hold on I'm comin': *Soul Children* / Love's gonna tear your playhouse down Part 1: *Brooks, Chuck* / Help me put out the flame (in my heart): *Hines, Ernie* / Black buy: *Staples, Pops* / Bracing myself for a fall: *Ollie & The Nightingales* / All I have to do is dream: *Bell, William & Carla Thomas* / Singing about love: *Jeanne & The Darlings* / Goodies: *Chris & Shack* / Just the way you are today: *Lewis, Barbara* / Creeper returns: *Little Sonny* / Guide me well: *Thomas, Carla* / Give a damn: *Staple Singers* / Steal away: *Taylor, Johnnie* / Your sweet lovin': *Joseph, Margie* / I forgot to remember: *Jones & Blumenburg* / Can't see you when I want you: *Porter, David* / Never be true: *Thomas, Carla* / Can't you see what you're doing to me: *King, Albert* / Sixty minute man: *Thomas, Rufus* / Preacher and the bear: *Thomas, Rufus* / Something: *Booker T & The MG's* / Seeing is believing: *Mad Lads* / You're my only temptation: *Ryan, Roz* / What I don't know won't hurt me: *Thompson, Paul* / Right, tight and out of sight: *Branding Iron* / (What's under) The natural do: *Kasandra, John* / My girl: *Floyd, Eddie* / I have learned to do without you: *T S U Tornadoes* / Lonely soldier: *Bell, William* / Heart association: *Emotions* / I stand accused: *Hayes, Isaac* / Brand new day:

Staple Singers / Sweeter tomorrow: *Joseph, Margie* / Cool strut: *Hayes, Bernie* / You put the sunshine back in my world: *Newcomers* / Montego Bay: *Bar-Kays* / Got it together parts I and II: *Robinson, Rudy & The Hungry Five* / Wade in the water: *Little Sonny* / You're movin' much too fast: *Nightingales* / Best year of my life: *Floyd, Eddie* / I am somebody (pt 2): *Taylor, Johnnie* / I loved you like I love my very life: *Thomas, Carla* / Soul machine: *Milner, Reggie* / (Follow her) Rules and regulations: *Temprees* / Do the Push and pull (part 1): *Thomas, Rufus* / Love changes: *Charlene & The Soul Serenaders* / Put your world in my world (Best of two worlds): *Soul Children* / Love is plentiful: *Staple Singers* / Heavy makes you happy: *Staple Singers* / Who took the merry out of christmas: *Staple Singers* / Too many years: *Shack* / Black christmas: *Emotions* / Mistletoe and me: *Hayes, Isaac* / Ask the lonely: *Lewis, Barbara* / Jody's got your girl and gone: *Taylor, Johnnie* / Finish me off: *Soul Children* / Oh how it rained: *Floyd, Eddie* / Look of love: *Hayes, Isaac* / Electrified love: *Hines, Ernie* / Melting pot: *Booker T & The MG's* / That's the way I like it (I like it that way): *Lewis, Barbara* / Mr. Big Stuff: *Knight, Jean* / You make me want to love you: *Emotions* / Stop, In the name of love: *Joseph, Margie* / I don't wanna lose you: *Taylor, Johnnie* / Girl I love you: *Temprees* / World is round: *Thomas, Rufus* / Penny for your thoughts: *Bell, William* / Never can say goodbye: *Hayes, Isaac* / I don't want to be like my daddy: *Nightingales* / You've got to earn it: *Staple Singers* / Hold on to it: *Limitations* / What'cha see is what'cha get: *Dramatics* / Born too late: *Branding Iron* / Just ain't as strong as I used to be: *Hughes, Jimmy* / That other woman got my man and gone: *Joseph, Margie* / If you think it (You may as well do it): *Emotions* / Shame on the family name: *Scott, Calvin* / Blood is thicker than water: *Floyd, Eddie* / Hijackin' love: *Taylor, Johnnie* / Sweetback's theme: *Van Peebles, Melvin* / Breakdown (part 1): *Thomas, Rufus* / Pin the tail on the donkey: *Newcomers* / Them hot pants: *Sain, Lee* / If that ain't a reason (for your woman to leave you): *Little Milton* / It's good to be careful (But it's better to be loved): *Shack* / Where would you be today: *Ilana* / Everybody wants to go to heaven: *King, Albert* / Got to get away from it all: *Soul Children* / Love's creepin' up on me: *United Image* / Show me how: *Emotions* / If I gave you, I want it back: *Porter, David* / Woman named trouble: *Little Sonny* / Losing you: *Giles, Eddie* / Respect yourself: *Staple Singers* / I'll kill a brick (About my man): *Hot Sauce* / You think you're hot stuff: *Knight, Jean* / All for the love of a woman: *Bell, William* / Shaft: *Hayes, Isaac* / Jamaica this morning: *MG's* / Promises of yesterday: *Mad Lads* / Girl, come on home: *Lance, Major* / Let hurt put you in (the Loser's seat): *Wilson, Joni* / My baby loves: *Temprees* / How do you move a mountain: *Leaders* / Black nasty boogie: *Black Nasty* / Do the funky penguin (part 1): *Thomas, Rufus* / You've got a cushion to fall on: *Thomas, Carla* / Get up and get down: *Dramatics* / Son of Shaft: *Bar-Kays* / Don't you mess with my money, my honey or my woman: *Johnson, L.V.* / I can smell that funky music: *Mercury, Eric* / Sadness for things: *Scott, Calvin* / That's what love will make you do: *Little Milton* / Standing in for Jody: *Taylor, Johnnie*
CD Set   **9SCD 4411**
Stax / Sep '93 / Pinnacle.

COMPLETE STAX/VOLT SOUL SINGLES VOL.3, THE
(1972-1975/10CD Set)
Yum yum yum (I want some): *Floyd, Eddie* / Carry on: *Knight, Jean* / Do your thing: *Hayes, Isaac* / I've been lonely for so long: *Knight, Frederick* / Nothing is everlasting: *Thomas, Annette* / Hearsay: *Soul Children* / Angel of mercy: *King, Albert* / In the rain: *Dramatics* / She's my old lady too: *Sain, Lee* / Explain it to her Mama: *Temprees* / Right on: *Sons Of Slum* / Doing my own thing: *Taylor, Johnnie* / My honey and me: *Emotions* / Let's stay together: *Hayes, Isaac* / Bring it home (and give it to me): *Hot Sauce* / Look around you: *Black Society* / Don't do it: *Nightingales* / I'm with you: *Nightingales* / I'll take you there: *Staple Singers* / Which way: *Leaders* / Living a life without you: *Brown, Veda* / What's good for you (don't have to be good to you): *Scales, Harvey* / Let me repair your heart: *Mad Lads* / What's usual seems natur'l: *Mercury, Eric* / I wanna make up (before we break up): *Lance, Major* / ain't that lovin' you: *Hayes, Isaac & David Porter* / Walking the back streets and crying: *Little Milton* / Save us: *Bell, William* / 6-3-8 (that's the number to play): *Thomas, Rufus* / Starting all over again: *Me & Tim* / Keep on loving me: *Stefan* / (I'm afraid) the masquerade is over: *Porter, David* / Going down slow (parts 1 and 2): *Little Sonny* / I could never be happy: *Emotions* / Don't take my kindness for weakness: *Soul Children* / I'll play the blues for you (pt 1): *King, Albert* / I dedicate my life for you: *Hatcher, Roger* / Do the sweetback: *March Wind* / Getting funky round here: *Black Nasty* / When the chips are down: *Porter, David* / Sugar: *Thomas, Carla* / You're good enough (to be my baby): *Floyd, Eddie* / This world: *Staple Singers* / Helping man: *Knight, Jean* / Ain't I good: *Kasandra, John* / Dance,

791

dance, dance: Bar-Kays / Dedicated to the one I love: Temprees / Toast to the fool: Dramatics / Stop doggin' me: Taylor, Johnnie / Trouble: Knight, Frederick / I'm gonna cry a river: Little Milton / Itch and scratch (part 1): Thomas, Rufus / What would I do: Hines, Ernie / I know it's not right (to be in love with a married man): Brown, Veda / Holy cow: Stefan / What goes around (must come around): Sons Of Slum / men: Hayes, Isaac / Endlessly: Staples, Mavis / You hurt me for the last time: Foxx, Inez / My sweet Lord: Williams, John Gary / Breaking up somebody's home: King, Albert / How can you mistreat the one you love: Love, Kate / From toys to boys: Emotions / Dryer: Johnson, Roy Lee & The Villagers / I may not be all you want (but I'm all you got): Thomas, Carla / Ain't no sweat: Lance, Major / Do me: Knight, Jean / Rainy day: Little Milton / It ain't always what you do (it's who you let see you do it): Soul Children / I may not be what you want: Mel & Tim / Funky robot (part 1): Thomas, Rufus / Don't you fool with my soul (part 1): Taylor, Johnnie / Oh la de da: Staple Singers / What do you see in her: Hot Sauce / Thousand miles away: Temprees / Hey you get off my mountain: Dramatics / Rolling down a mountainside: Hayes, Isaac / You're still my brother: Bar-Kays / Stop half loving these women: Lewis, Jimmy / Lovin' on borrowed time: Bell, William / Lay your loving on me: Floyd, Eddie / Time: Foxx, Inez / Heaven knows: Mel & Tim / I believe in you (you believe in me): Taylor, Johnnie / Short stopping: Brown, Veda / Be what you are: Staple Singers / I've got to love somebody's baby: Stefan / Playing on me: King, Albert / Long as you're the one somebody in the world: you: Knight, Frederick / Sugarcane: MG's / Love is a hurtin' thing: Soul Children / Baby, lay your head down: Floyd, Eddie / Check me out: Floyd, Eddie / Running (back and forth): Emotions / Crossing over the bridge: Foxx, Inez / Love's maze: Temprees / It ain't easy: Bar-Kays / Love another day: Thomas, Carla / What is it: Little Milton / I've got to go without you: Bell, William / Love is taking over: Mercury, Eric / Ruby Dean: Hicks, Joe / I'm so glad I fell in love with you: Mad Lads / Fell for you: Dramatics / Cheaper to keep her: Taylor, Johnnie / I know you don't want me no more: Thomas, Rufus / If you're ready (come go with me): Staple Singers / Slipped and tripped: Sweet Inspirations / Peace, be still: Emotions / I'll be the other woman: Soul Children / Martin hop: Newcomers / I had a talk with my man: Foxx, Inez / At last: Temprees / Joy: Hayes, Isaac / Good woman turning bad: Hot Sauce / Mose (part 3): Kasandra, John / I'll be your Santa baby: Thomas, Rufus / I wanna do things for you: Floyd, Eddie / That's what the blues is all about: King, Albert / One way love affair: Hutson, Carolyn / Tin pan alley: Little Milton / Funky bird: Thomas, Rufus / We're getting careless with our love: Taylor, Johnnie / What do the lonely get at Christmas: Emotions / Season's greetings: Cix Bits / Don't lose faith in me Lord: Mercury, Eric / Don't start lovin' me (If you're gonna stop): Brown, Veda / Touch a hand, make a friend: Staple Singers / I am kicked: Dramatics / Change it all: Flemming, Joy / Gettin' what you want (losin' what you get): Bell, William / He's mine: Verdell, Jackie / My woman is good to me: Little Sonny / I got you and I'm glad: Porter, David / Put a little love away: Emotions / Suzy: Knight, Frederick / Same folks: Mel & Tim / You make the sunshine: Temprees / Whole damn world is going crazy: Williams, John Gary / Circuits overloaded: Foxx, Inez / Wonderful: Hayes, Isaac / Behind closed doors: Little Milton / Guess who: Floyd, Eddie / Sweet inspiration: Dirty Tricks / Which way did it go: Pop Staples / Talking to the people: Black Nasty / I've been born again: Taylor, Johnnie / Neckbone: MG's / Wounded woman: Wright, Sandra / Stop dogging me: Hot Sauce / Goodness gracious: Weston, Kim / City in the sky: Staple Singers / Title theme: Hayes, Isaac / Soul street: Floyd, Eddie / Flat tire: King, Albert / Love makes it right: Soul Children / Mr. Cool that ain't cool: Temprees / Boogie ain't nuttin' (but gettin' down) (Part 1): Thomas, Rufus / Highway to heaven: Banks, Ron & The Dramatics / Get it while it's hot: Bell, William / Passing thru: Knight, Frederick / Keep an eye on your close friends: Newcomers / My main man: Staple Singers / There is a God: Staple Singers / That's the way I want to live my life: Mel & Tim / Forever and a day: Mel & Tim / Baby, I'm through: Emotions / It's September: Taylor, Johnnie / Woman to woman: Brown, Shirley / Did you hear yourself: Brown, Randy / You need a friend like mine: Thomas, Annette / Love, I love: Temprees / Let me back in: Little Milton / Crossing over: King, Albert / Coldblooded: Bar-Kays / Bump meat: Rice, Sir Mack / Too little in common to be lovers) Too much going to say go: Newcomers / Bump and boogie (part 1): Wrecking Crew / What's happening baby (part 1): Soul Children / Who made the man: Staple Singers / I keep thinking to myself: Benton, Brook / I got a reason to smile (cause I got you): Floyd, Eddie / Try to leave me if you can (i bet you can't do it): Banks, Bessie / Burning on both ends: Singleton, Willie / There are more questions than answers: Emotions / Santa

Claus wants some lovin': King, Albert / I can't let you go: Hot Sauce / I betcha didn't know that: Knight, Frederick / Lovin' you, lovin' me: Wright, Sandra / Do the double bump: Thomas, Rufus / Come and get your love: Temprees / Dark skin woman: Rice, Sir Mack / It ain't no fun: Brown, Shirley / If you talk in your sleep: Little Milton / Talk to the man: Floyd, Eddie / You're astounding: Barbara & Joe / Dy-no-mite (Did you say my love): Green Brothers / Boom-a-rang: Dynamic Soul Machine / Come what may: Williams, John Gary / Try me tonight: Taylor, Johnnie / Groovin' on my baby's love: Hunters, Freddie / I can't shake your love (can't shake you lose): Fiestas / I wanna play with you: Knight, Frederick / I'm doing fine: King, Albert / No way: Davis, Theresa / Back road into town: Staple Singers / I'm so glad I met you: Floyd, Eddie / Packed up and took my mind: Little Milton / Just wanna hold on to you: Taylor, Johnnie / How can I be a witness: Hudmon, R.B. / Jump back '75 (part 1): Thomas, Rufus / I got to be myself: Staple Singers / It's worth a whipping: Brown, Shirley / Holy ghost (pt 1): Bar-Kays

CD Set _____ 10SCD 4415
Stax / Oct '94 / Pinnacle.

COMPLETE SUN SINGLES VOL.1, THE
CD Set _____ BCD 15801
Bear Family / Feb '95 / Rollercoaster / Direct / CM / Swift / ADA.

CONCENTRATED UNDERGROUND VOL 1
Peechi: Reload / Emotional experience: Amorph / Crying is devine: 4D / Jacob's ladder: A-Sides / Deliverer: Pergon / Dark matter: Subject vs. Jeff Mill / Memory of God: CYM Dimensions / Part 5: Hedgehog Affair / Atmosphere: Chaos & Julia Set / Captain's log: Teckno Bros / First rebirth: Jones & Stephenson / Two full moons and a trout: Union Jack / Mad cap laughs: Drax
CD _____ DC0MPCD 1
Death Becomes Me / Mar '94 / Pinnacle / SRD.

CONCENTRATED UNDERGROUND VOL 2
CD _____ FLAG 103CD
Flag Bearer / Nov '94 / SRD.

CONCEPTION
CD _____ OJCCD 1726
Original Jazz Classics / Feb '93 / Wellard / Jazz Music / Cadillac / Complete/Pinnacle.

CONCORD JAZZ CHRISTMAS, A
Christmas time is here: Clooney, Rosemary / Have yourself a merry little Christmas: Peplowski, Ken / I'll be home for Christmas: Harris, Gene / Apple, an orange and a little stick doll: Cheatham, Jeannie & Jimmy / Angels we have heard on high: Scaggian Trio / Carol of the bells: Byrd, Charlie / Secret of Christmas: McCorkle, Susannah / God rest ye merry gentlemen: McPartland, Marian / Jingle bells: Vignola, Frank / Coventry carol: Allyson, Karrin / Christmas love song: Hamilton, Scott / Santa Claus is coming to town: Bruno, Jimmy / Christmas waltz: McConnell, Rob / Let it snow, let it snow, let it snow: Atwood, Eden / Little town of Bethlehem: McKenna, Dave / Winter wonderland: Alden, Howard & Ken Peplowski / What are you doing New Year's Eve: Sloane, Carol
CD _____ CCD 4613
Concord Jazz / Oct '94 / New Note.

CONCORD JAZZ COLLECTOR'S SERIES SAMPLER
Sweetback / Benny's bugle / Spring is here / I'm on my way / Look for the silver lining / Summertime, bidin' my time / After you've gone / Seven come eleven / Soft shoe / Carioca hills / Embraceable you / Smooth one / I wish I were in love again / I've found a new baby
CD _____ CCD 6013
Concord Jazz / Nov '93 / New Note.

CONCORD JAZZ GUITAR COLLECTION VOL 1 & 2
La petite mambo / Isn't this a lovely place / Dolphin dance / Zigeuner / Prelude to a kiss / I'm on my way / I can't get started (with you) / Side track / Georgia on my mind / You don't know what love is / Claire de Lune / Seven come eleven / When Sunny gets blue / Orange, brown and green / Don't cry for me Argentina
CD _____ CCD 4160
Concord Jazz / Mar '90 / New Note.

CONCORD JAZZ GUITAR COLLECTION VOL 3
Band call / Ecaroh / Joy spring / Avalon / Count down / Ain't misbehavin' / Too marvellous for words / East to West / Beija flor / There will never be another you / Song is you / Reflections in d / Skye boat song
CD _____ CCD 4507
Concord Jazz / May '92 / New Note.

CONFERENCE OF THE BIRDS - LIVE AT WILLISAU
CD _____ ITM 970070
ITM / Sep '92 / Tradelink / Koch.

CONFESSIN' THE BLUES
CD _____ IGOCD 2020
Indigo / Jun '95 / Direct / ADA.

CONJUNTO VOL.1 (Tex Mex Border Music)
CD _____ ROUCD 6023
Rounder / '88 / CM / Direct / ADA / Cadillac.

CONJUNTO VOL.2
CD _____ ROUCD 6024
Rounder / '88 / CM / Direct / ADA / Cadillac.

CONJUNTO VOL.3
CD _____ ROUCD 6030
Rounder / CM / Direct / ADA / Cadillac.

CONJUNTO VOL.4
CD _____ ROUCD 6034
Rounder / CM / Direct / ADA / Cadillac.

CONJUNTO VOL.5 (Polkas De Oro)
CD _____ ROU 6051CD
Rounder / Feb '94 / CM / Direct / ADA / Cadillac.

CONJUNTO VOL.6 (Contrabando)
CD _____ ROU 6052CD
Rounder / Apr '94 / CM / Direct / ADA / Cadillac.

CONQUEST OF DANCE VOL 1
CD _____ SCRCD 003
Scratch / Oct '94 / BMG.

CONSCIOUS RAGGA VOLUME 1
Greensleeves / Oct '95 / Total/BMG / Jetstar / SRD.
CD _____ GRELCD 220

CONSTANT SOURCE OF INTERRUPTION, A
CD _____ LCP 6004
Rough Trade / Jun '90 / Pinnacle.

CONTEMPORARY FLUTE
CD _____ BVHAASTCD 9211
Bvhaast / Dec '91 / Cadillac.

CONTEMPORARY JAZZ MASTERS SAMPLER
Frelun brun (Brown hornet) / Moors / Two to tango / Pieces of dreams / Wings of change / Chicago theme (Love loop) / Gotcha / Medieval overture / Velvet darkness / Delzura / Phenomenon / Compulsion / Skylark / Fatback / Chameleon / Such a night
CD _____ 4670862
Columbia / Jan '92 / Sony.

CONTROVERSY OF PIPERS, A
CD _____ COMD 1008
Temple / Apr '95 / CM / Duncans / ADA / Direct.

COOKING VINYL SAMPLER
CD _____ GRILLCD 006
Cooking Vinyl / Oct '94 / Vital.

COOKING VINYL SAMPLER VOL.4
Ontario, quebec and me: Bragg, Billy / Levens lament: Leven, Jackie / Jam tomorrow: Oyster Band / Memphis: Pere Ubu / Sunmer heat: Jansch, Bert / Cachapaya shuffle: Incantation / All our trades: Tabor, June / How can you keep on moving: McLeod, Rory / Not on forever: Rockingbirds / Let it snow: Goats Don't Shave / No dancing: Immaculate Fools / You gotta survive: TRB / Persons unknown: Poison Girls / Liberty: Barely Works / Blackberry blossom: Barely Works / Cuckoo's nest: Barely Works / Rumbidzai: Four Brothers
CD _____ GRILLCD 008
Cooking Vinyl / Aug '95 / Vital.

COOL & CRAZY
Kool kat: Sherrell, Bill / Rock on baby: Sherrell, Bill / Rock 'n' roll teenager: Sherrell, Bill / Yes, no, or maybe: Sherrell, Bill / Rock crazy baby: Adams, Art / Dancing doll: Adams, Art / Ingemar: Ray, Don / Those rock 'n' roll blues: Ray, Don / Cool cat: Montgomery, Joe / Woodpecker rock: Couty, Nat / Wont' you come along with me: Couty, Nat / Bon bon baby: Coulston, Jerry / Little rocker: Stuart, Scottie / Marlene: Sonics / Minus one: Sonics / Blast off: Sonics / Cool cool baby: Yarborough, Lafayette / Livin' doll: Yarborough, Lafayette / Rock 'n' roll fever: Graham B / Cool baby: Cole, Lee / Short fat Ben: Barclay, Phil / I love me all: Barclay, Phil / Come along with me: Parker, Malcom / Servant of love: Van Bros / Cool cats: Huften, Jim / Get hot or go home: Kerby, John / Pizza pie: Irwin, Phil / Little bitty boy: Hulin, T.K. / Cool baby cool: Hulin, T.K. / Ricky Tic: Davis, Al / She's cool: Vikings
CD _____ CDBB 55006
Buffalo Bop / Apr '94 / Rollercoaster.

COOL BEAT
CD _____ RENCD 101
Castle / Jul '95 / BMG.

COOL CHRISTMAS
Please come home for Christmas: Eagles / Blanche comme la neige: McGarrigle, Kate & Anna / Lights of the stable: Harris, Emmylou / Soon after Christmas: Nordenstam, Stina / White Christmas: Redding, Otis / Winter: Amos, Tori / Fairytale of New York: Pogues / Silent night: Enya / Coventry carol: Page, Elaine / 2000 miles: Pretenders / Driving home for Christmas: Rea, Chris / Power of love: Frankie Goes To Hollywood

/ Walk out to winter: Aztec Camera / Winter wonderland: Booker T & The MG's / Christmas in February: Reed, Lou / Santa's beard: They Might Be Giants / Little boy that Santa Claus forgot: Associates / Christmas card from a hooker in Minneapolis: Waits, Tom
CD _____ 954832485-2
WEA / Dec '93 / Warner Music.

COOL SOUNDS FOR WARM NIGHT
CD _____ MCCD 195
Music Club / Mar '95 / Disc / THE / CM.

COOL STRUTTIN' VOL.2
CD _____ AM 00512
Amber / Aug '94 / Pinnacle.

COOLTEMPO REMIXED
I thank you: Adeva / Alright: Urban Soul / Love and happiness (Yemaya y ochun): River Ocean & India / Give you: Djamin / Trippin' on your love: Thomas, Kenny / Power: Love, Monie / I want you: Roberts, Juliet / Mr. Wendal: Arrested Development / Follow me: Aly-us / Six o'clock: Tyrrel Corporation
CD _____ CTCD 49
Cooltempo / Sep '95 / EMI.

COPULATIN' BLUES
CD _____ JCD 1
Jass / Oct '91 / CM / Jazz Music / Cadillac / Direct.

COPULATIN' COLLECTION VOL.1
CD _____ VN 168
Viper's Nest / Aug '95 / Direct / Cadillac / ADA.

CORNEMUSE ECOSSAISE
Massed pipes and drums / Country dance / Grand march / Set dance / Pipe major march / Quick march / Piper dance / Pipes and drums in Kathmandou / Scottish dance / Royal Scots polka / Drummer's call / Hills of Glenorchy / Greenwood side / Slow march / Banks of Allan / Amazing grace / Auld Lang Syne / Military fanfare / Black bear / Fanfare Drawbridge
CD _____ ARN 64030
Arion / '87 / Discovery / ADA.

CORNERSTONE CONNECTION
CD _____ SONCD 0069
Sonic Sounds / Oct '94 / Jetstar.

CORPORATE DEATH
CD _____ NB 095
Nuclear Blast / Apr '94 / Plastic Head.

CORPORATE ROCK WARS
Strike it: Dub War / My mind still speaks: Misery Loves Co / Lighter form of killing: Pitch Shifter / Exodus: Scorn / Joy of irony: Fudge Tunnel / Freak wow: Old / Touch my soul: Godflesh / North Korea goes bang: Violent, Johnny / Honour code loyalty: Misery Loves Co / Mental: Dub War / NCM: Pitch Shifter / Sex mammoth: Fudge Tunnel / Glitch: Old / Electric chair: Ultraviolence / New spite: Godflesh / Ind: Scorn
CD _____ MOSH 136CD
Earache / May '95 / Vital.

CORRIB FOLK, THE
CD _____ CDBALLAD 006
Outlet / Jan '95 / ADA / Duncans / CM / Ross / Direct / Koch.

CORRIDINHOS
CD _____ PS 65093
Playasound / Aug '92 / Harmonia Mundi / ADA.

COSMIC CUBES (2CD Set)
CD Set _____ SPV 08938252
SPV / Feb '95 / Plastic Head.

COSMIC CUBES II (2CD Set)
CD Set _____ SPV 08938342
SPV / Jun '95 / Plastic Head.

COSMIC ENERGY VOL.1 (2CD/LP Set)
CD Set _____ IR 002CD
Independence / Jan '96 / Plastic Head.

COSMIC TRANCE
CD _____ DI 242
Distance / Dec '95 / 3MV.

COTTON CLUB - ORIGINAL MUSIC (Featuring Ellington, Calloway, Horne & Waters)
CD _____ CD 53022
Giants Of Jazz / Mar '90 / Target/BMG / Cadillac.

COTTON CLUB, THE
Cotton Club stomp: Ellington, Duke & His Cotton Club Orchestra / Just a crazy song: Robinson, Bill 'Bojangles' / Am I blue: Waters, Ethel / Heebie jeebies: Webb, Chick & His Orchestra / I must have that man: Hall, Adelaide / Stormy weather: Arlen, Harold / When you're smiling: Armstrong, Louis Orchestra / Lazybones: Williams, Midge / Old yazoo: Calloway, Cab & His Orchestra / Honey just for you: Kirk, Andy & His Twelve Clouds of Joy / Between the devil and the deep blue sea: Armstrong, Louis Orchestra / Sweet rhythm: Lunceford, Jimmie & his Chickasaw Syncopators / Blues I love to sing: Hall, Adelaide / Kicking the gong around: Calloway, Cab & His Orchestra / Serenade to a wealthy widow: Foresythe,

Reginald / Jubilee stomp: Ellington, Duke & His Cotton Club Orchestra / I can't give you anything but love: Mills, Irving / Doin' the new low down: Mills, Irving
CD _____ **CD AJA 5031**
Living Era / Oct '88 / Koch.

COUNTERFORCE
Better place (mixes): D.J. Tasmin & The Monk / Carrie: Inna Rhythm / Disturbance: Hyper On Experience / Let it roll: D.J. Crystal / Deep space (I see sunshine): Lemon D / Warpdrive: D.J. Crystal / Lock up: Zero B / Deep: Koda / Dream of you: D.J. Flynn & Flora / Dance of the sarooees: Rogue Unit
CD _____ **TRUCD 6**
Internal / Oct '94 / PolyGram / Pinnacle.

COUNTERFORCE
Better place (Mixes): D.J. Tasmin & The Monk / Disturbance: Hyper On Experience / Inner city life: Goldie & The Metalheadz / Let it roll: D.J. Crystal / Warpdrive: D.J. Crystal / Lock up: Zero B / Deep space (I see sunshine): Lemon D / Dream of you: Flynn & Flora / Carrie: Inna Rhythm / Deep: Koda / Dance of the darooees: Rogue Unit / Are we here: Orbital
CD _____ **TRUCD 7**
Internal / Jul '95 / PolyGram / Pinnacle.

COUNTRY & WESTERN FAVOURITES
(4CD Set)
CD Set _____ **MBSCD 410**
Castle / Jan '95 / BMG.

COUNTRY AND WESTERN GREATS
(Sea Of Heartbreak)
I can't stop loving you: Gibson, Don / Almost persuaded: Jones, George / Ruby, don't take your love to him: Rogers, Kenny / Where do I go from here: Williams, Don / Shelter of my arms: Nelson, Willie / For the good times: Husky, Ferlin / Four in the morning: Young, Faron / But I do: Fender, Freddy / Daddy sang bass: Perkins, Carl / Catfish John: Russell, Johnny / Love's gonna live here: Jennings, Waylon / There goes everything: Greene, Jack / Things to talk about: Jackson, Stonewall / Send me the pillow that you dream on: Locklin, Hank / Son of Hickory Holler's tramp: Darrell, Johnny / Sea of heartbreak: Gibson, Don / Talk back trembling lips: Jones, George / Rueben James: Rogers, Kenny / Tears: Williams, Don / Broken promises: Nelson, Willie
CD _____ **MUCD 9013**
Start / Apr '95 / Koch.

COUNTRY BALLADS
(3 CD/MCs)
Somebody loves you: Gayle, Crystal / Country Willie: Nelson, Willie / Take me in your arms and hold me: Whitman, Slim / All I have to do is dream: Nelson, Willie / Better love next time: Dr. Hook / Love lifted me: Rogers, Kenny / Jambalaya (on the Bayou): Nitty Gritty Dirt Band / Country girl: Newton-John, Olivia / Another place, another time: Williams, Don / Son of a preacher man: Gentry, Bobbie / Games people play: South, Joe / Rose garden: Spears, Billie Jo / By the time I get to Phoenix: Campbell, Glen / Among my souvenirs: Whitman, Slim / Wayward wind: Gayle, Crystal / If we only have love: Newton-John, Olivia / Funny how time slips away: Nelson, Willie / Misty blue: Spears, Billie Jo / Little bit more: Dr. Hook / Love me like you used to: Tucker, Tanya / Reason to believe: Campbell, Glen / Give me your word: Ford, Tennessee Ernie / Am I blue: Nelson, Willie / Dreaming my dreams with you: Gayle, Crystal / She believes in me: Rogers, Kenny / Sweet dreams: Young, Faron / Reuben James: Jackson, Wanda / My blue heaven: Whitman, Slim / Angel of the morning: Newton, Juice / Let it be me: Gentry, Bobbie / Country girl heart: Gatlin, Larry & The Gatlin Brothers / There'll be no teardrops tonight: Nelson, Willie / All I wanna do in life: Gayle, Crystal / I'm walking behind you: Newton-John, Olivia / Silver threads and golden needles: Whitman, Slim / It's only make believe: Campbell, Glen / You've made me so very happy: Gentry, Bobbie / You love me through it all: Williams, Don / I just had you on my mind: Craddock, Billy Crash / Love is love: Spears, Billie Jo / We've got tonight: Rogers, Kenny / Hey Mr. Dream Maker: West, Dottie / Crying: McLean, Don / My arms stay open all night: Tucker, Tanya
CD Set _____ **CDTRBOX 172**
Trio / Sep '95 / EMI.

COUNTRY BLUES COLLECTORS ITEMS
1924-28
CD _____ **DOCD 5169**
Blues Document / May '93 / Swift / Jazz Music / Hot Shot.

COUNTRY BLUES COLLECTORS ITEMS
VOL.2
CD _____ **SOB 035402**
Story Of The Blues / Apr '93 / Koch / ADA.

COUNTRY BLUES VOL. 1
(The Best Of Kicking Mule)
CD _____ **12353CD**
Kicking Mule / Jul '95 / Swift / CM.

COUNTRY BOX
(CD/MC Set)
CD Set _____ **TBXD 505**
BlueTrax / Jan '96 / THE.

COUNTRY BOX SET
CD _____ **KWCD 804**
Disky / Jul '94 / THE / BMG / Discovery / Pinnacle.

COUNTRY BOYS
Country boy: Campbell, Glen / Amazing grace: Campbell, Glen / Reuben James: Rogers, Kenny / Son of Hickory Holler's tramp: Rogers, Kenny / Crazy: Nelson, Willie / Night life: Nelson, Willie / Rose Marie: Whitman, Slim / Red River valley: Whitman, Slim / Folsom Prison blues: Haggard, Merle / San Antonio rose: Haggard, Merle / Desperately: Williams, Don / Another place another time: Williams, Don / I heard you crying in your sleep: Jones, George / I get lonely in a hurry: Jones, George / Jambalaya: Nitty Gritty Dirt Band / Sweet dreams: Young, Faron / Baby's got her blue jeans on (CD only): McDaniel, Mel / I just had you on my mind (CD only): Craddock, Billy Crash / I've got a tiger by the tail (CD only): Owens, Buck / Wings of a dove (CD only): Husky, Ferlin
Music For Pleasure / May '91 / EMI.

COUNTRY CHARTBUSTERS
Devil went down to Georgia: Daniels, Charlie Band / Rose garden: Anderson, Lynn / Stand by your man: Wynette, Tammy / Always on my mind: Nelson, Willie / El Paso: Robbins, Marty / Me and Bobby McGee: Kristofferson, Kris / River unbroken: Parton, Dolly / Ring of fire: Cash, Johnny / Seven year ache: Cash, Rosanne / North to Alaska: Horton, Johnny / Take this job and shove it: Paycheck, Johnny / Banjo man: Scruggs, Earl / Kern river: Haggard, Merle / Most beautiful girl: Rich, Charlie / Would you lay with me: Tucker, Tanya
CD _____ **4771202**
Embassy / Oct '95 / Sony.

COUNTRY CHRISTMAS
CD _____ **DCD 5353**
Disky / Dec '93 / THE / BMG / Discovery / Pinnacle.

COUNTRY CLASSICS
CD _____ **LECD 044**
Wisepack / Jul '94 / THE / Conifer.

COUNTRY CLASSICS
Rose garden: Anderson, Lynn / Big bad John: Dean, Jimmy / No charge: Montgomery, Melba / Harper Valley PTA: Riley, Jeannie C. / Four in the morning: Young, Faron / Abilene: Hamilton, George IV / Please help me, I'm falling: Locklin, Hank / Wolverton mountain: King, Claude / From a jack to a king: Miller, Ned / One day at a time: Seely, Jeannie / Mr. Walker, it's all over: Spears, Billie Jo / Satisfied mind: Wagoner, Porter / It wasn't God who made honky tonk angels: Wells, Kitty / Take this job and shove it: Paycheck, Johnny / Waterloo: Jackson, Stonewall / Misty blue: Burgess, Wilma / Ruby, don't take your love to town: Darrell, Johnny / End of the world: Davis, Skeeter
CD _____ **ECD 3057**
K-Tel / Jan '95 / K-Tel.

COUNTRY COLLECTION
(3CD/MC Set)
Take me make it through the night: Nelson, Willie / Singin' the blues: Robbins, Marty / There goes my everything: Wynette, Tammy / Outlaw's prayer: Paycheck, Johnny / I just started lovin' today: Frickie, Janie / Still doin' time: Jones, George / I've been to Georgia on a fast train: Cash, Johnny / Blue eyes cryin' in the rain: Nelson, Willie / All around cowboy: Robbins, Marty / Cowboys don't shoot straight (like they used to): Wynette, Tammy / Very special love song: Rich, Charlie / Easy on the eye: Gatlin, Larry & The Gatlin Brothers / To all the girls I've loved before: Haggard, Merle / Miss the Mississippi and you: Gayle, Crystal / Jackson: Cash, Johnny & June Carter / Ain't gonna hobo no more: Cash, Johnny / Sure feels like love: Gatlin, Larry & The Gatlin Brothers / Sleeping with your memory: Frickie, Janie / Fool inside of me: Coe, David Allen & Eve Shapiro / Teddy bear song: Fairchild, Barbara / What a man my man is: Anderson, Lynn / Don't be a stranger: Coe, David Allen & Eve Shapiro / Tennessee whiskey: Jones, George / Only the strong survive: Wynette, Tammy / Some memories just won't die: Robbins, Marty / My elusive dreams: Miller, Roger & Willie Nelson / Michigan City howdy do: Cash, Johnny / Nobody's darlin' but mine: Haggard, Merle / Woman in me: Gayle, Crystal / Mamas don't let your babies grow up to be cowboys: Nelson, Willie / Country girl: Anderson, Lynn / I forgot more than you'll ever know: Cash, Johnny / Mississippi: Fairchild, Barbara / Barstool Mountain: Paycheck, Johnny / Come a little bit closer: Frickie, Janie / Janie Fricke / Kiss it all goodbye: Gatlin, Larry / Almost persuaded: Tucker, Tanya / Man in black: Cash, Johnny / You are so beautiful: Tucker, Tanya / Cowboy and the lady: Duncan, Johnny / For all the right reasons: Fairchild, Barbara / Gambler: Bare, Bobby / Alive and well: Bandy, Moe & Joe Stampley / This country girl is woman wise: Anderson, Lynn / Time of the preacher: Nelson, Willie
CD Set _____ **BOX 5T**

Carlton Home Entertainment / Oct '94 / Carlton Home Entertainment.

COUNTRY COLLECTION
(3CD Set)
Rose Marie: Whitman, Slim / Indian love call: Whitman, Slim / You are my sunshine: Whitman, Slim / Riders in the sky: Whitman, Slim / Have I told you lately that I love you: Nelson, Willie / Crazy: Nelson, Willie / Country Willie: Nelson, Willie / Gentle on my mind: Campbell, Glen / Reason to believe: Campbell, Glen / Amazing Grace: Campbell, Glen / Rhinestone Cowboy: Campbell, Glen / Southern nights: Campbell, Glen / Today I started loving you again: Spears, Billie Jo / What I've got in mind: Spears, Billie Jo / Blanket on the ground: Spears, Billie Jo / '57 Chevrolet: Spears, Billie Jo / Ode to Billy Joe: Spears, Billie Jo / Don't it make my brown eyes blue: Gayle, Crystal / Cry me a river: Gayle, Crystal / Wrong road again: Gayle, Crystal / Wayward wind: Gayle, Crystal / When I dream: Gayle, Crystal / You've lost that lovin' feelin': Rogers, Kenny & Dottie West / Lady: Rogers, Kenny / Lucille: Rogers, Kenny / Ruby, don't take your love to town: Rogers, Kenny / Stand by your man: Jackson, Wanda / When you're in love with a beautiful woman: Dr. Hook / Sexy eyes: Dr. Hook / I just had you on my mind: Craddock, Billy Crash / I wish that I could sit in love today: Montgomery, Barbara / Wings of a dove: Husky, Ferlin / Oki from Muskogee: Haggard, Merle / Legend of Bonnie and Clyde: Haggard, Merle / Desperately: Williams, Don / Sweet dreams: Young, Faron / King of the road: Ford, Tennessee Ernie / Baby's got her blue jeans on: McDaniel, Mel / Raindrops keep falling on my head: Gentry, Bobbie / I'll never fall in love again: Gentry, Bobbie / All I have to do is dream: Newton, Juice / Hey Mr. Dream Maker: West, Dottie / Sing me an old fashioned song: Shepard, Jean / It keeps right on a-hurtin': Shepard, Jean / Daddy and home: Tucker, Tanya / What would you do about you (if you were me): Osmond, Marie / Still crazy after all these years: Dalton, Lacy J
CD Set _____ **CDTRBOX 124**
Trio / Oct '94 / EMI.

COUNTRY COLLECTION VOL.1
Help me make it through the night / Singin' the blues / There goes my everything / Outlaws prayer / I just started livin' today / Love is worth it all / Still doin' time / I've been to Georgia on a fast train / Blue eyes cryin' in the rain / All around cowboy / Cowboys don't shoot straight (like they used to) / Very special love song / Easy on the eye / To all the girls / Miss the Mississippi / Jackson
CD _____ **PWKS 567**
Carlton Home Entertainment / '89 / Carlton Home Entertainment.

COUNTRY COLLECTION VOL.2
Four in the morning: Young, Faron / Harper Valley PTA: Riley, Jeannie C. / Luckenbach, Texas (Back to the basics of love): Russell, Johnny / Blue eyes cryin' in the rain: Paycheck, Johnny / No charge: Montgomery, Melba / From a jack to a king: Miller, Ned / Please help me, I'm falling: Locklin, Hank / Wolverton mountain: King, Claude / I love you because: Jackson, Stonewall / Big bad John: Dean, Jimmy / Rose garden: Anderson, Lynn / Everything is beautiful: Felts, Narvel / Good hearted woman: Russell, Johnny
CD _____ **PWKS 568**
Carlton Home Entertainment / Aug '87 / Carlton Home Entertainment.

COUNTRY COLLECTION VOL.3
Blue eyes cryin' in the rain / Country girl: Anderson, Lynn / I forgot more than you'll ever know / Mississippi / Barstool Mountain / Come a little bit closer / Kiss it all goodbye / Almost persuaded / Man in black: Cash, Johnny
CD _____ **PWKS 569**
Carlton Home Entertainment / '89 / Carlton Home Entertainment.

COUNTRY COLLECTION VOL.4
Stand by your man: Wynette, Tammy / She thinks I still care: Jones, George / I still sing the old songs: Tucker, Tanya / From cotton to satin: Paycheck, Johnny / Everyday I have to cry some: Stampley, Joe / Fireball snow: Bare, Bobby / Love is just a game: Gatlin, Larry / Tall handsome stranger: Robbins, Marty / What're you doing tonight: Frickie, Janie / I don't know why (I just do): Robbins, Marty / In melancholie now: Cash, Johnny / Red red wine: Duncan, Johnny
CD _____ **PWK 091**
Carlton Home Entertainment / Feb '89 / Carlton Home Entertainment.

COUNTRY COOKING
(26 Bluegrass Originals)
CD _____ **ROU 11551**
Rounder / '88 / CM / Direct / ADA / Cadillac.

COUNTRY CREAM VOL.1
(2CD Set)
CD Set _____ **CDSGP 0100**
Prestige / Aug '94 / Total/BMG.

COUNTRY CROSSOVER
It's only make believe: Twitty, Conway / As usual: Young, Faron / Pretend: Smith, Margo / Little things mean a lot: Kendalls / Love me tender: Haggard, Merle / You don't have to say you love me: Tucker, Tanya / Crying: Thomas, B.J. / Crazy: Lynn, Loretta / Everlasting love: Hamilton, George IV / Tear fell: Craddock, Billy Crash / True love: Cline, Patsy
CD _____ **PWKS 570**
Carlton Home Entertainment / Feb '90 / Carlton Home Entertainment.

COUNTRY DYNASTY
Sylvia's mother: Dr. Hook / Me and Bobby McGee: Kristofferson, Kris / Crying: Orbison, Roy / Walkin' after midnight: Cline, Patsy / Golden ring: Jones, George & Tammy Wynette / Jackson: Cash, Johnny & June Carter / Thing called love: Cash, Johnny / Help me make it through the night: Kristofferson, Kris & Brenda Lee / What will baby be: Parton, Dolly / Always on my mind: Nelson, Willie / To all the girls I've loved before: Haggard, Merle / Behind closed doors: Rich, Charlie / Seven year ache: Cash, Johnny / Downtown train: Carpenter, Mary-Chapin / You're gonna love yourself in the morning: Nelson, Willie & Brenda Lee / Honey come back: Anderson, Lynn / There goes my everything: Wynette, Tammy
CD _____ **474791 2**
Columbia / Nov '93 / Sony.

COUNTRY GEMS
Honey come back: Campbell, Glen / Cry me a river: Gayle, Crystal / Daytime friends: Rogers, Kenny / Wayward wind: Ritter, Tex / Raindrops keep falling on my head: Gentry, Bobbie / Duellin' banjos: Jackson, Carl / Race is on: Jones, George / Angel of the morning: Newton, Juice / Life gits tee-jus don't it: Williams, Tex / Tumbling tumbleweeds: Husky, Ferlin / Lesson in leavin': West, Dottie / Sing me an old fashioned song: Spears, Billie Jo / Hello walls: Nelson, Willie / Country girl: Young, Faron / Home on the range: Whitman, Slim / Destiny: Murray, Anne / I got a new field to plough: McDonald, Skeets / Take me home country roads: Newton-John, Olivia / Loving him was easier: Carter, Anita / Jambalaya: Axton, Hoyt / Stand by your man: Jackson, Wanda / Mercy: Shepard, Jean / Mule train (CD only): Ford, Tennessee Ernie / Young love (CD only): James, Sonny
CD _____ **CC 243**
Music For Pleasure / Sep '89 / EMI.

COUNTRY GIANTS VOL.1
Reuben James: Rogers, Kenny / Honky tonk angels: Rogers, Kenny / Sweet dreams: Young, Faron / You'll know: Young, Faron / I'm so lonesome I could cry: Spears, Billie Jo / I can't find the time: Nelson, Willie / Ruby, don't take your love to town: Rogers, Kenny / Things to talk about: Jackson, Stonewall / Talk about me: Paycheck, Johnny / I didn't sleep a wink: Nelson, Willie / From a Jack to a King: Miller, Ned / While it waiting: Jennings, Waylon / Look what they've done to my song ma: Spears, Billie Jo / Making believe: Parton, Dolly / Home is where you're happy: Nelson, Willie / Wings of a dove: Husky, Ferlin / Shine on Ruby mountain: Rogers, Kenny / Sticks and stones: Fargo, Donna / Rose garden: Anderson, Lynn / Turn the cards slowly: Cline, Patsy / Ramblin' rose: Lee, Johnny / Country girl: Young, Faron / Dear heart: Miller, Roger / Heart you made may be your own: Cline, Patsy / Little green apples: Miller, Roger
CD _____ **CDGER 003**
Tring / Jun '92 / Tring / Prism.

COUNTRY GIANTS VOL.2
Is there something on your mind: Nelson, Willie / Rhythm 'n' booze: Owens, Buck / Candy store: Lee, Johnny / stop, look and listen: Cline, Patsy / Four in the morning: Young, Faron / Hello walls: Young, Faron / Wishful thinking: Fargo, Donna / Reuben James: Rogers, Kenny / Both sides now: Murray, Anne / Billy Jack Washburn: Paycheck, Johnny / Shelter of my arms: Williams, Don / This ole house: Perkins, Carl / Then you'll know: Cline, Patsy / Letter to heaven: Parton, Dolly / Ol' blue: Jackson, Stonewall / Sally was a good old girl: Jennings, Waylon / Honky tonk merry go round: Laine, Frankie / Moonlight gambler: Laine, Frankie / Wine me up: Young, Faron / Send me the pillow that you dream on: Locklin, Hank / Building heartaches: Nelson, Willie / Ease the pain: Nelson, Willie / Billie Jo: Sad and lonely days: Dudley, Dave / Heartaches by the number: Mitchell, Guy / Blue is the way I feel: Twitty, Conway
CD _____ **CDGFR 004**
Tring / Jun '92 / Tring / Prism.

COUNTRY GIRLS
Wrong road again: Gayle, Crystal / Somebody loves you: Gayle, Crystal / What I've got in mind: Spears, Billie Jo / '57 Chevrolet: Spears, Billie Jo / Daddy and home: Tucker, Tanya / All I have to do is dream: Newton, Juice / Sweetest thing (I've ever known): Newton, Juice / I wish that I could fall in love today: Mandrell, Barbara / It all came true: Mandrell, Barbara / Pinkertons flowers: Montgomery, Melba / Hey Mr. Dream Maker: West, Dottie / Still crazy after

793

all these years: Dalton, Lacy J / Reuben James: Jackson, Wanda / Mississippi delta: Gentry, Bobbie / Under the sun: Bogguss, Suzy / Slippin' away (CD only): Shepard, Jean / Coat of many colours (CD only): Peppers, Nancy / It's morning (and I still love you) (CD only): Colter, Jessi / Simple little words (CD only): Lane, Christy
CD _____ CDMFP 5911
Music For Pleasure / Apr '91 / EMI.

COUNTRY GOLD
CD _____ 15042
Laserlight / Aug '91 / Target/BMG.

COUNTRY GOLD
Sweet dreams: Cline, Patsy / You're my best friend: Williams, Don / Dream lover: Campbell, Glen & Tanya Tucker / I've cried the blue right out of my eyes: Gayle, Crystal / Coal miner's daughter: Lynn, Loretta / Ramblin' fever: Haggard, Merle / Big four poster bed: Lee, Brenda / Sail away: Oak Ridge Boys / You've never been this far before: Twitty, Conway / Hand that rocks the cradle: Campbell, Glen / Texas (When I die): Tucker, Tanya / I was country when country wasn't cool: Mandrell, Barbara / Somebody's knockin': Gibbs, Terri / There goes my everything: Greene, Jack / Satin sheets: Pruett, Jeanne / Still: Anderson, Bill / Busted: Conlee, John / Country bumpkin: Smith, Carl / My special angel: Helms, Bobby / Hello darlin': Twitty, Conway
CD _____ MCCD 080
Music Club / Jun '92 / Disc / THE / CM.

COUNTRY GOLD
CD _____ LECD 42
Wisepack / Jul '94 / THE / Conifer.

COUNTRY GOLD
(It's Only Make Believe)
CD _____ MU 5055CD
Musketeer / Oct '92 / Koch.

COUNTRY GOLD
CD _____ RADCD 25
Global / Nov '95 / BMG.

COUNTRY GOLD VOL.2
CD _____ MCCD 053
Music Club / '93 / Disc / THE / CM.

COUNTRY GOLD VOL.3
CD _____ MCCD 132
Music Club / Sep '93 / Disc / THE / CM.

COUNTRY GOLDEN HITS
CD _____ DCD 5309
Disky / Dec '93 / THE / BMG / Discovery / Pinnacle.

COUNTRY GOSPEL 1946-53
CD _____ DOCD 5221
Blues Document / Apr '94 / Swift / Jazz Music / Hot Shot.

COUNTRY GREATS
CD _____ PWK 044
Carlton Home Entertainment / Dec '87 / Carlton Home Entertainment.

COUNTRY GREATS
(4CD Set)
CD Set _____ MBSCD 429
Castle / Sep '94 / BMG.

COUNTRY GREATS
(4CD Set)
CD Set _____ SETCD 079
Stardust / Sep '94 / Carlton Home Entertainment.

COUNTRY GREATS
CD _____ CPMV 023
Cromwell / Sep '94 / THE / BMG.

COUNTRY GREATS VOL. 1
CD _____ TRTCD 174
TrueTrax / Jun '95 / THE.

COUNTRY GREATS VOL.2
(4CD Set)
CD Set _____ CDPK 408
Charly / Feb '95 / Charly / THE / Cadillac.

COUNTRY GREATS VOL.2
CD _____ TRTCD 189
TrueTrax / Feb '96 / THE.

COUNTRY HALL OF FAME
CD _____ LECD 045
Wisepack / Jul '94 / THE / Conifer.

COUNTRY HEARTBREAKERS
Heartaches: Cline, Patsy / She's got you: Cline, Patsy / It hurts so much (to see you go): Reeves, Jim / When something is wrong with my baby: Rich, Charlie / I'll always love you: Parton, Dolly / Daddy come and get me: Parton, Dolly / Don't fall in love with a dreamer: Rogers, Kenny / Till I can make it on my own: Rogers, Kenny / Cry me a river: Gayle, Crystal / I still miss someone: Gayle, Crystal / Your cheatin' heart: Lynn, Loretta / Please Mr. Please: Newton-John, Olivia / I honestly love you: Newton-John, Olivia / Honey come back: Campbell, Glen / Hey won't you play another somebody done somebody wrong song: Spears, Billie Jo / Misty blue: Spears, Billie Jo / I'll never fall in love again: Gentry, Bobbie / There'll be no teardrops tonight: Nelson, Willie / It keeps right on a-hurtin': Shepard, Jean
CD _____ CDMFP 6116
Music For Pleasure / Mar '94 / EMI.

COUNTRY HEROES LIVE
CD _____ 15402
Laserlight / Aug '91 / Target/BMG.

COUNTRY HICKS VOL.1
CD _____ BARKLOG 1CD
No Hit / Sep '95 / SRD.

COUNTRY HIGHWAY - 100 HITS
CD Set _____ SETCD 030
Stardust / Jan '94 / Carlton Home Entertainment.

COUNTRY HITS
(2CD Set)
CD Set _____ 24001
Delta Doubles / Jan '95 / Target/BMG.

COUNTRY JUNCTION
(2CD/MC Set)
Country junction: Ford, Tennessee Ernie / Goin' steady: Young, Faron / Satisfied mind: Shepard, Jean / My home town: Husky, Ferlin / High noon: Ritter, Tex / There my future goes: Thompson, Hank / Smoke, smoke, smoke: Williams, Tex / I don't hurt anymore: Ford, Tennessee Ernie / Could cold heart: Jackson, Wanda / Ain't it funny what heart: Jackson, Wanda / Ain't it funny what a fool will do: Jones, George / What's bad for you is good for me: Montgomery, Melba / I'm wasting my tears on you: Ritter, Tex / You're calling me sweetheart again: Shepard, Jean / Sixteen tons: Ford, Tennessee Ernie / Sioux City Sue: Husky, Ferlin / That's what I like about the West: Williams, Tex / Sweet dreams: Young, Faron / Streets of Laredo: Ritter, Tex / Tears on my pillow: Ford, Tennessee Ernie / Left my gal in the mountains: Thompson, Hank / Forget the past: Young, Faron / Wild side of life: Thompson, Hank / Funny how time slips away: Ford, Tennessee Ernie / My wedding ring: Shepard, Jean / Billy the kid: Ritter, Tex / My home in San Antone: Husky, Ferlin / Shot gun boogie: Williams, Tex / Silver threads and golden needles: Jackson, Wanda / There'll be no teardrops tonight: Ford, Tennessee Ernie / I can still see him in your eyes: Mack, Billy / You'd better go: Shepard, Jean / If I could keep you off my mind: Mathis, Johnny / We must have been out of our minds: Jones, George & Melba Montgomery / Alabama Jubilee: Husky, Ferlin / Don't let the stars get in your eyes: McDonald, Skeets / Mule train: Ford, Tennessee Ernie / I've got five dollars and it's Saturday night: Young, Faron / Crying steel guitar waltz: Shepard, Jean / Rye whiskey: Husky, Ferlin / Rye whiskey: Ritter, Tex
CD Set _____ CDDL 1215
Music For Pleasure / Nov '91 / EMI.

COUNTRY LADIES LIVE
CD _____ 15404
Laserlight / Aug '91 / Target/BMG.

COUNTRY LEGENDS
CD Set _____ DCDCD 201
Castle / Jun '95 / BMG.

COUNTRY LEGENDS
Talking in your sleep: Gayle, Crystal / By the time I get to Phoenix: Campbell, Glen / Better love next time: Dr. Hook / Queen of the house: Miller, Jody / Funny how time slips away: Nelson, Willie / If you could read my mind: Newton-John, Olivia / Wichita lineman: Campbell, Glen / I love you because: Spears, Billie Jo / Gambler: Rogers, Kenny / Give me your word: Ford, Tennessee Ernie / Hey Mr. Dream maker: West, Dottie / All I have to do is dream: Campbell, Glen & Bobbie Gentry / Don't it make my brown eyes blue: Gayle, Crystal / Games people play: South, Joe / When you're in love with a beautiful woman: Dr. Hook / She believes in me: Rogers, Kenny / Ode to Billie Joe: Gentry, Bobbie / Crazy: Nelson, Willie / I honestly love you: Newton-John, Olivia / '57 Chevrolet: Spears, Billie Jo
CD _____ CDSL 8259
EMI / Jul '95 / EMI.

COUNTRY LOVE
CD _____ MCLD 19175
MCA / Oct '92 / BMG.

COUNTRY MEETS SOUL
I'm so lonesome I could cry: Green, Al / Rainin' love: Wood, Brenton / No easy way to say goodbye: Wright, O.V. / Funny how time slips away: Green, Al / You win again: Rich, Charlie / I die a little each day: Clay, Otis / Say yes to love: Clayton, Willie / It was jealousy: Peebles, Ann / When something is wrong with my baby: Rich, Charlie / I'm gone: Clayton, Willie / Hurry up freight train: Rich, Charlie / You don't know me: Johnson, Syl / One woman: Green, Al / To fool a fool: Rich, Charlie / Time we have: Wright, O.V. / Since I met you baby: Felts, Narvel / I'll be standing by: Green, Al / Wedding bells: Rich, Charlie
CD _____ HILOCD 14
Hi / Jul '95 / Pinnacle.

COUNTRY MOODS
When you're in love with a beautiful woman: Dr. Hook / Let your love flow: Bellamy Brothers / Ruby, don't take your love to town: Rogers, Kenny / Good year for the roses: Costello, Elvis & The Attractions / Jolene: Parton, Dolly / Wichita lineman: Campbell, Glen / Don't it make my brown eyes blue: Gayle, Crystal / Thing called love:

Cash, Johnny / ode to billy joe: Gentry, Bobbie / We're all alone: Coolidge, Rita / Blue bayou: Ronstadt, Linda / Horse with no name: America / Crazy: Cline, Patsy / Help me make it through the night: Kristofferson, Kris / Behind closed doors: Rich, Charlie / D.I.V.O.R.C.E.: Wynette, Tammy / You're my best friend: Williams, Don / Four in the morning: Young, Faron / Here, there and everywhere: Harris, Emmylou / Me and Bobby McGee: Nelson, Willie / Angel of the morning: Newton, Juice / Harper Valley PTA: Riley, Jeannie C. / King of the road: Miller, Roger
CD _____ 515 299 2
PolyGram TV / Apr '92 / PolyGram.

COUNTRY MUSIC INTERNATIONAL
CD _____ CMID 001
MCA / Sep '95 / BMG.

COUNTRY MUSIC: CAT'N AROUND
CD _____ KKCD 07
Krazy Kat / Feb '93 / Hot Shot / CM.

COUNTRY NEGRO JAM SESSIONS
CD _____ ARHCD 372
Arhoolie / Apr '95 / ADA / Direct / Cadillac.

COUNTRY NO.1'S VOL 1
Jambalaya: Williams, Hank / Fraulein: Helms, Bobby / He'll have to go: Reeves, Jim / El paso: Robbins, Marty / Three bells: Browns / Please help me, I'm falling: Locklin, Hank / Make the world go away: Arnold, Eddy / She called me baby: Rich, Charlie / Walk on by: Van Dyke, Leroy / I fall to pieces: Cline, Patsy / Big bad John: Dean, Jimmy / My elusive dreams: Houston, David & Tammy Wynette / Still: Anderson, Bill / Ring of fire: Cash, Johnny / King of the road: Miller, Roger / Stand by your man: Wynette, Tammy
CD _____ OG 3508
Old Gold / Mar '89 / Carlton Home Entertainment.

COUNTRY NO.1'S VOL 2
Is it really over: Reeves, Jim / There goes my everything: Greene, Jack / Almost persuaded: Houston, David / Harper Valley PTA: Riley, Jeannie C. / D.I.V.O.R.C.E.: Wynette, Tammy / Oh lonesome me: Gibson, Don / North to Alaska: Horton, Johnny / Boy named Sue: Cash, Johnny / All I have to offer you is me: Pride, Charley / Next in line: Twitty, Conway / Coal miner's daughter: Lynn, Loretta / Rose garden: Anderson, Lynn / When you're hot you're hot: Reed, Jerry / Four in the morning: Young, Faron / Year that Clayton Delaney died: Hall, Tom T.
CD _____ OG 3509
Old Gold / Mar '89 / Carlton Home Entertainment.

COUNTRY NO.1'S VOL 3
Then you can tell me goodbye: Arnold, Eddy / Distant drums: Reeves, Jim / Folsom Prison blues: Cash, Johnny / Hello darlin': Twitty, Conway / Happiest girl in the whole USA: Fargo, Donna / Chantilly Lace: Lewis, Jerry Lee / Is anybody going to San Antone: Pride, Charley / Good hearted woman: Waylon & Willie / Behind closed doors: Rich, Charlie / Satin sheets: Pruett, Jeannie / Teddy bear song: Fairchild, Barbara / Eleven roses: Williams, Hank Jr. / Keep me in mind: Anderson, Lynn / I will always love you: Parton, Dolly / Convoy: McCall, C.W. / Before the next teardrop falls: Fender, Freddy
CD _____ OG 3510
Old Gold / Mar '89 / Carlton Home Entertainment.

COUNTRY NO.1'S VOL 4
Jolene: Parton, Dolly / I can help: Swan, Billy / Legend in my time: Milsap, Ronnie / Would you lay with me (in a field of stone): Tucker, Tanya / Hello love: Snow, Hank / Wasted days and wasted nights: Fender, Freddy / Are you sure Hank done it this way: Jennings, Waylon / One piece at a time: Cash, Johnny / You're my best friend: Williams, Don / Blue eyes cryin' in the rain: Nelson, Willie / She's got you: Lynn, Loretta / You've never been this far before: Twitty, Conway / We're gonna hold on: Jones, George & Tammy Wynette / Abilene: Hamilton, George IV / For the good times: Price, Ray / I'll be leaving alone: Pride, Charley
CD _____ OG 3511
Old Gold / Mar '89 / Carlton Home Entertainment.

COUNTRY NUMBER ONES
Dukes Of Hazzard: Jennings, Waylon / Crazy: Cline, Patsy / I fall to pieces: Cline, Patsy / Lucille: Rogers, Kenny / Coward of the county: Rogers, Kenny / Nine to five: Parton, Dolly / Here you come again: Parton, Dolly / Distant drums: Reeves, Jim / Rhinestone cowboy: Campbell, Glen / Southern nights: Campbell, Glen / Blanket on the ground: Spears, Billie Jo / Love in the first degree: Alabama / Coal miner's daughter: Lynn, Loretta / Kiss an angel good morning: Pride, Charley / Make the world go away: Arnold, Eddy / Abilene: Hamilton, George IV / I was country when country wasn't cool: Mandrell, Barbara / Rose Marie: Whitman, Slim / Hello walls: Nelson, Willie / You're the best break this heart ever had: Bruce, Ed

CD _____ CDMFP 6108
EMI / Jan '94 / EMI.

COUNTRY ORIGINALS
I will always love you: Parton, Dolly / Love of the common people: Jennings, Waylon / Guitar man: Reed, Jerry / I can't stop loving you: Gibson, Don / Tabacco road: Loudermilk, John D. / Gentle on my mind: Harford, John / Green grass of home: Waggoner, Porter / In the ghetto: Davis, Mac / Help me make it through the night: Kristofferson, Kris / Singing the blues: Robbins, Marty / For the good times: Price, Ray / Crazy: Nelson, Willie / Everybody's talkin': Neil, Fred / Rose garden: South, Joe / Sweet dreams: Young, Faron / Good year for the roses: Jones, George / Always on my mind: Lee, Brenda / From a distance: Griffith, Nanci / Wind beneath my wings: Greenwood, Lee / Misty blue: Burgess, Wilma
CD _____ VSOPCD 204
Connoisseur / Nov '95 / Pinnacle.

COUNTRY ROCKERS LIVE
CD _____ 15403
Laserlight / Mar '95 / Target/BMG.

COUNTRY SPECIAL
CD _____ LECD 041
Wisepack / Jul '94 / THE / Conifer.

COUNTRY STARS
Rhinestone cowboy: Campbell, Glen / Talking in your sleep: Gayle, Crystal / Riders in the sky: Whitman, Slim / If you ain't lovin' (you ain't livin'): Young, Faron / Wabash cannonball: Jackson, Wanda / Country Willie: Nelson, Willie / United we stand: Murray, Anne & Glen Campbell / I still miss someone: Ronstadt, Linda / Orange blossom special: Jackson, Carl / Gambler's guitar: Travis, Merle / One woman man: Colter, Jessi / Every time two fools collide: Rodgers, Kenny & Dottie West / Sing me an old fashioned song: Shepard, Jean / Wild side of life: Thompson, Hank / Tip of my fingers: Clark, Roy / Harper Valley PTA: Spears, Billie Jo / High noon: Ritter, Tex / Angel of the morning: Newton, Juice / King of the road: Ford, Tennessee Ernie / Ode to billie joe: Gentry, Bobbie
CD _____ CC 208
Music For Pleasure / May '88 / EMI.

COUNTRY STARS
I recall a gypsy woman: Williams, Don / Always: Cline, Patsy / I'm knee deep in loving you: Tucker, Tanya / Most beautiful girl: Stampley, Joe / Sweet dreams: Lynn, Loretta / Burning memories: Jennings, Waylon / Remember me, I'm the one who loves you: Haggard, Merle / Forever young: Hamilton, George IV / I believe you: Mandrell, Barbara / I'm wanting you: Robbins, Marty / Too far: Gayle, Crystal / Dream on: Oak Ridge Boys / We had it all: Twitty, Conway
CD _____ PWKS 599
Carlton Home Entertainment / '91 / Carlton Home Entertainment.

COUNTRY STARS
(2CD Set)
CD Set _____ 24078
Delta Doubles / Mar '95 / Target/BMG.

COUNTRY STARS OF THE 80'S - LIVE
CD _____ 15405
Laserlight / Aug '91 / Target/BMG.

COUNTRY SUPERSTARS
CD _____ CDCD 1248
Charly / Jun '95 / Charly / THE / Cadillac.

COUNTRY WOMEN
CD _____ DINCD 72
Dino / Oct '93 / Pinnacle / 3MV.

COUNTRY'S GOLDEN GREATS
CD Set _____ TREB 3020
Scratch / Nov '95 / BMG.

COVER ME SOUL
CD _____ HIUKCD 140
Hi / May '93 / Pinnacle.

COVERED AND REDISCOVERED
September: Undercover / Never let her slip away: Undercover / Love I lost: West End & Sybil / Celebration: Kool & The Gang / Locomotion: Minogue, Kylie / Virginia plain: Slamm / Dancing queen: Abbacadabra / Let's all chant: Pat 'n' Mick / Rhythm of the rain: Donovan, Jason / Fool such as I: Donovan, Jason / It's a fine day: Opus III / New York afternoon: Kane, Mondo / Love pains: Dean, Hazell / Higher and higher: Davis, Nancy / Don't you want me baby: Mandy / Who's gonna love me: 1 On One
CD _____ CDFA 3300
Fame / Sep '94 / EMI.

COW COW BOOGIE 1943
CD _____ PHONTCD 7670
Phontastic / Apr '94 / Wellard / Jazz Music / Cadillac.

COWBOY RECORDS COMPILATION VOL.2
2 Damned free: Perks Of Living Society / want you: Secret Life / Timetravellers: Love / echild & Rolfe / All over me: Carr, Suzi / Peace, love, harmony: Re-Joice / How sweet the sound: Forthright / Why why why / Deja Vu / Only you: Talisman / Trippin' on sunshine: Pizzaman / Rock the discotheque: Ramp / It this is love: Tracey, Jason / All I do: Voodoo Blue

CD Set _____ RODEO 2CD
Cowboy / Nov '94 / Pinnacle.

COWBOYS SONGS ON FOLKWAYS
CD _____ CDSF 40043
Smithsonian Folkways / Aug '94 / ADA /
Direct / Koch / CM / Cadillac.

CRACKS IN THE SIDEWALK
CD _____ SST 092 CD
SST / May '93 / Plastic Head.

CREAM - ANTHEMS
Bomb: _Bucketheads_ / Let me show you
how: _K-Klass_ / Get your hands off my man:
Vasquez, Junior / Caught in the middle:
Roberts, Juliet / Love and happiness: _India_
/ Love: _Roberts, Joe_ / Saturday night, Sun-
day morning: _T-Empo_ / Lemon: _U2_ / Girls &
boys: _Hed Boys_ / Hideaway: _De'Lacy_ /
Where love lies: _Limerick, Alison_ / Musik: _X-
Press 2_ / Bells of NY: _Slo Moshun_ / Plastic
dreams: _Jaydee_ / Question: _Seven Grand
Housing Authority_ / Is there anybody out
there: _Bassheads_ / Eighteen strings: _Tin
Man_ / Yeka yeke: _Kante, Mory_ / Chemical
beats: _Chemical Brothers_ / My mercury
mouth: _Chemical Brothers_ / On ya way: _Hel-
icopter_ / Funkaterium: _Jump_ / All funked up:
Mother / Passion: _Gat Decor_ / One: _Mind-
warp_ / Acperience: _Hardfloor_ / Waterfall: _At-
lantic Ocean_ / Positive education: _Soma_ / In
the dark we live: _Aphrohead_ / Into your
heart: _Rozzo_
CD _____ 74321326152
De-Construction / Oct '95 / BMG.

CREAM - LIVE
(DJs Paul Oakenfold/Pete Tong/Justin
Robertson/Graeme Park)
Club lonely: _Ellis, Sam_ / Keeping the jam
going: _Ill Disco_ / Feel it: _Bailey, Carol_ / Sex-
ual (Parkside mix): _Rowe, Maria_ / Love's got
me (on a trip so high) (Parkside mix): _Clark,
Loni_ / Drunk on love (roger's ultimate an-
them): _Basia_ / True faith (Tall Paul mix): _New
Order_ / Train of thought (Freedom mix): _Ex-
crima_ / Sight for sore eyes (Hed Boys mix):
M People / Always: _Tin Tin Out_ / Only me
(Systematic mix): _Hyper Logic_ / Sound of
Eden (Development Corp mix): _Shades Of
Rhythm_ / Things can only get better: _D
Ream_ / Witch doktor: _Van Helden, Armand_
/ Witch doktor (remix): _Van Helden, Armand_
/ Boys revenge: _Original Creators_ / Wild
pitch: _Music Freaks_ / Yes it is (I love Mark
mix): _Lady D_ / Voodoo ray: _Guy Called Ger-
ald_ / Let's get ready to rhumble (Make up
mix): _D.J. Fiovanni_ / So get up (Junior fac-
tory mix): _Underground Sound Of Lisbon_ / I
luv you baby (Dancin divas mix): _D.J. Pipi_ /
Ajare: _Way Out West_ / Your loving arms
(Disscuss mix): _Martin, Billie Ray_ / Save the
day: _Disscuss_ / Odyssey to Anyoena (Odyssey mix): _Jam & Spoon_ / Let me be your
fantasy (Trance mix): _Baby D_ / Le voie: _Sub-
liminal Cuts_ / Vernon's wonderland: _Vernon_
/ How can I love you more: _M People_ / Kut
it: _Reo Eye_
CD _____ 74321272192
De-Construction / Apr '95 / BMG.

CREAM OF AMBIENT VISIONS, THE
Chase the Manhattan: _Black Dog_ / Dark and
long: _Underworld_ / My beautiful blue sky:
Moby / Dr. Peter: _Rejuvination_ / Wilmot: _Sa-
bres Of Paradise_ / Dolce vita: _Optica_ / Lost
continent: _Inner Circle_ / Wave form: _Mono
Now_ / Mission impossible: _Naturists_ /
Dream: _Evolve Now_ / Total toxic tranquility:
Holmes & McMillan
CD _____ KOLDCD 008
Arctic / Apr '95 / Pinnacle.

CREAM OF IRISH FOLK
CD _____ CHCD 1040
Chyme / May '95 / CM / ADA / Direct.

CREAM NEW COUNTRY, THE
CD _____ MCCD 137
Music Club / Jan '95 / Disc / THE / CM.

CREAM OF TRIP HOP
Cosmic trigger happy: _Glamorous Hooligan_
/ Small world: _Small World_ / Shaolin Buddha
finger: _Depth Charge_ / Electric lazyland: 9
Lazy 9 / Move ya: _Rising High Collective &
Plavka_ / Santa Cruz: _Fatboy Slim_ / Know
kname (Down): _Juryman_ / Anafey: _Hip Op-
timist_ / Showdown at Voodoo Creek: _Deep
Freeze Production_ / Onamission: _Coldcut_ /
Shadiest breaks: _Dark Globe_
CD _____ KOLDCD 009
Equator / Jun '95 / Pinnacle.

**CREAM OF UNDERGROUND HOUSE
VOL.1, THE**
De Niro: _Disco Evangelists_ / Ethnic Prayer:
Havanna / Percussion obsession: _Okatu_ /
Devo: _Crunch_ / Buruchacca: _Mukka_ / Slum-
berland: _Solitaire Gee_ / Skelph: _Harri_ / Givin'
you no rest: _E-Lustrious_ / Le Noir: _Diceman_
/ Two fatt Guitars: _Direckt_ / Jump to my
beat: _Wildchild Experience vol.2_ / Te Qui-
ero: _La Camorra_
CD _____ KOLDCD 001
Arctic / May '93 / Pinnacle.

**CREAM OF UNDERGROUND HOUSE
VOL.2, THE**
Skinnybumblebee: _Gipsy_ / London x-press
(the journey continues): _Xpress 2_ / Tonight
(club mix): _108 Grand_ / Paranoid part 1: _Re-
jvination_ / I've got it: _Rolling Gear_ / Journey: _Rolling Gear_ / Rez: _Underworld_ / Positive education: _Slam_ / Babyloop: _Pizzaman_

/ Funk and drive: _K & M_ / Trumpet release
(no mercy mix): _Funky Punch_
CD _____ KOLDCD 003
Arctic / Sep '93 / Pinnacle.

**CREAM OF UNDERGROUND HOUSE
VOL.3, THE**
Open up: _Leftfield & John Lydon_ / Texas
cowboys: _Grid_ / Say what: _X-Press 2_ /
Good time: _Luvdup_ / Saturday night party:
Alex Party / Back stab: _Direct 2 Disc_ /
Theme from outrage: _Outrage_ / Transmes-
potter: _Vinyl Blair_ / Dubious kettle: _Channel
/ Musik: Technicality_ / Mandala:
Monumental
CD _____ KOLDCD 004
Arctic / Jan '94 / Pinnacle.

**CREAM OF UNDERGROUND HOUSE
VOL.4, THE**
On ya way: _Helicopter_ / Who runs the show:
Question / In your dance: _E-Lustrious_ / It's
gonna be alright: _Ill Disco_ / Make it funky:
Rebound / Feeling: _Tin Tin Out_ / Echo drop:
Taiko / Choir boys and kinky girls: _Social
Outrage Choir_ / Psychotherapy: _Rejuvina-
tion_ / Dope: _Vinyl Blair_ / Blinder: _Mukkaa_
CD Set _____ KOLDCD 005
Equator / Sep '94 / Pinnacle.

**CREAM OF UNDERGROUND HOUSE
VOL.5, THE**
You and me: _Rhyme Time Productions_ / Do
what U like: _Goodfellos_ / Partners: _Move
Inc._ / No pain: _Dark Star_ / 4 you: _4th
Measure Men_ / Beat beat: _Nostalgia Freaks_
/ Keep the jam going: _Ill Disco_ / Cognoman:
Clubland Refugees / So damn tuff: _Boo-
merang_ / Retro Euro vibe piece: _Woomera_ /
Spirit: _Eskubar_
CD _____ KOLDCD 006
Arctic / Jan '95 / Pinnacle.

CREATION REBEL
CD _____ LG2 1110
Lagoon / Jul '95 / Magnum Music Group /
THE.

CREATION ROCKERS 1 & 2
Guns fever: _Brooks, Baba_ / Message from
a black man: _Harriott, Derrick_ / I've got soul:
Carlton & His Shoes / Flashing my whip: _U-
Roy_ / Blood and fire: _Niney The Observer_ /
Little way different: _Dunkley, Errol_ / Reggae
phenomenom: _Big Youth_ / Financial
endorsement: _Isaacs, Gregory_ / Enter into
his gates with praise: _Clarke, Johnny_ / Big
rip off: _Pablo, Augustus_ / Man hungry: _Min-
ott, Sugar_ / I and I are the chosen one:
Prince Far-I / Dance crasher: _Ellis, Alton_ /
My conversation: _Smith, Slim_ / Caution:
Wailers / My satisfaction: _Holt, John_ / Feel-
ing soul: _Andy, Bob_ / More music: _McCook,
Tommy_ / Beat new second hand: _Tosh,
Peter_ / Glitter not gold: _Big Joe_ / Pretty girl:
Wilson, Delroy / Conquerer: _Brown, Dennis_
/ Step by step: _Dread, Mikey_ / You're no
good: _Boothe, Ken_
CD _____ CDTRL 180
Trojan / Jun '94 / Jetstar / Total/BMG.

CREATION SOUP VOL 1
CD _____ CRECD 101
Creation / May '94 / 3MV / Vital.

CREATION SOUP VOL 2
CD _____ CRECD 102
Creation / May '94 / 3MV / Vital.

CREATION SOUP VOL 3
CD _____ CRECD 103
Creation / May '94 / 3MV / Vital.

CREATION SOUP VOL 4
CD _____ CRECD 104
Creation / May '94 / 3MV / Vital.

CREATION SOUP VOL 5
CD _____ CRECD 105
Creation / May '94 / 3MV / Vital.

**CREATION'S JOURNEY
(Native American Music)**
CD _____ SFWCD 40410
Smithsonian Folkways / May '95 / ADA /
Direct / Koch / CM / Cadillac.

CREOLE KINGS OF NEW ORLEANS
Going back to New Orleans: _Liggins, Joe &
His Honey Drippers_ / Louisiana: _Mayfield,
Percy_ / River's invitation: _Mayfield, Percy_ /
Lawdy Miss Clawdy: _Price, Lloyd_ / Where
you at: _Price, Lloyd_ / Frog legs: _Price, Lloyd_
/ Teachin' and preachin': _Royal Kings_ /
Things that I used to do: _Guitar Slim_ / Till I
say well done: _Kings_ / Ay tete fee: _Chenier,
Clifton_ / Oh how I need your love: _Hall, Al-
berta_ / Send me some lovin': _Price, Leon-
tyne_ / Do baby do: _Kador, Ernest_ / Who's
been foolin' you: _Myles, Big Boy & Sha-
Weez_ / Rich woman: _Millet, Lil_ / Whistlin'
Joe: _Lambert, Lloyd_ / No buts, no maybes:
Professor Longhair / Baby, let me hold your
hand: _Professor Longhair_ / Everytime I hear
that mellow saxophone: _Montrell, Roy_ / Bop
sitin blues: _Blanchard, Edgar_ / Just to hold
my hand: _Myles, Big Boy_ / Lights out:
Byrne, Jerry / Cha dooky-doo: _Neville, Art_ /
I'm a fool to care: _Neville, Art_ / Jockomo:
Williams, Larry / Bad boy: _Williams, Larry_
CD _____ CDCHD 393
Ace / Mar '92 / Pinnacle / Cadillac / Com-
plete/Pinnacle.

**CREOLE KINGS OF NEW ORLEANS
VOL.2**
Bouncin' the boogie: _Royal Kings_ / Got a
brand new baby: _Little Mr. Midnight & Paul

Gayten Band_ / Four o'clock blues: _Little Mr.
Midnight & Paul Gayten Band_ / Restless
heart: _Price, Lloyd_ / Ain't it a shame: _Price,
Lloyd_ / Say baby: _Johnson, Willie_ / That
night: _Johnson, Willie_ / Eating and sleeping:
King, Earl / Heavy sugar: _Lambert. Lloyd_ /
Think it over: _Guitar Slim_ / So glad you're
mine: _Kador, Ernest_ / That girl I married:
Myles, Big Boy & Sha-Weez / Squeeze box
boogie: _Chenier, Clifton_ / Good golly Miss
Molly: _Blackwell, Bumps_ / Oooh wow: _Mon-
trell, Roy_ / Stepping high: _Blanchard, Edgar_
/ All around the world: _Millet, Lil_ / Oooh-wee
baby: _Neville, Art_ / Just because: _Williams,
Larry_ / Cry pretty baby: _Professor Longhair_
/ Look what you're doing to me: _Professor
Longhair_ / Misery: _Professor Longhair_ /
Look no hair: _Professor Longhair_ / Rock 'n'
roll fever: _Monitors_ / Carry on: _Byrne, Jerry_
CD _____ CDCHD 477
Ace / Jun '93 / Pinnacle / Cadillac / Com-
plete/Pinnacle.

CREOLE MUSIC OF PERU
CD _____ X 55520
Aspic / Sep '95 / Harmonia Mundi.

CRIMINAL JUSTICE
Banana co: _Radiohead_ / 911 is a joke:
Duran Duran / Ground level: _Stereo MC's_ /
Impact: _Orbital_ / Kids: _Jamiroquai_ / Lay my
troubles down: _Aswad_ / Moment in dark-
ness: _Shamen_ / Perfect day: _EMF_ / Revo-
lution: _Dodgy_ / Practice what you preach:
Corduroy / Paranoid: _Inspiral Carpets_
CD _____ CDCRIM 001
Ultimate / Jul '94 / 3MV / Vital.

CRITIC'S CHOICE
Me and my baby: _Green, Benny_ / Fort
Worth: _Lovano, Joe_ / Man talk: _Osby, Greg_
/ On golden beams: _De Johnette, Jack_ / To
know one: _Calderazzo, Joey_ / Body and
soul: _Margitza, Rick_ / Substance of things
hoped for: _Peterson, Ralph_ / Capoeira: _Pul-
len, Don_ / Twang: _Scofield, John_ / Our
gang: _Allen, Geri_ / Airegin: _Rubalcaba, Gon-
zalo_ / Beija eu: _Monte, Marisa_
CD _____ BNZ 293
Blue Note / Jul '92 / EMI.

CROONERS
CD _____ MCCD 104
Music Club / May '93 / Disc / THE / CM.

CROSSING BORDERS
CD _____ CBM 010CD
Cross Border Media / Mar '94 / Direct /
ADA.

CRUISIN'.
Boom boom: _Hooker, John Lee_ / No parti-
cular place to go: _Berry, Chuck_ / Got my
mojo working: _Waters, Muddy_ / Working in
the coalmine: _Dorsey, Lee_ / Bandstop:
Parker, Robert / Reet petite: _Parker, Robert_
/ It's in his kiss (Shoop shoop song): _Every-
ett, Betty_ / Wonderful world: _Cooke, Sam_ /
When a man loves a woman: _Sledge, Percy_
/ Will you still love me tomorrow: _Shirelles_ /
Twenty four hours from Tulsa: _Pitney, Gene_
/ Leader of the pack: _Shangri-Las_ / You
can't judge a book by the cover: _Diddley,
Bo_ / But I do: _Henry, Clarence_ / Chapel of
love: _Dixie Cups_ / Oh what a night: _Dells_ /
Harlem shuffle: _Bob & Earl_ / Smokestack
lightnin': _Howlin' Wolf_ / Walking through the
park: _Waters, Muddy_ / You can't catch me:
Berry, Chuck
CD _____ CPCD 8056
Charly / Feb '95 / Charly / THE / Cadillac.

CRUSADE FROM THE NORTH
CD _____ FOG 010CD
Haunfog / Jan '96 / Plastic Head.

CRYING SCENE
CD _____ NSCD 017
Newsound / May '95 / THE.

CRYPT CHEAPO SAMPLER
CD _____ EFA 11567-2
Crypt / Apr '94 / SRD.

CRYSTALIZE YOUR MIND
Crystalize your mind: _Living Children_ / Now
it's over: _Living Children_ / I'll be around:
Poor Souls / Shadows: _Vejtables_ / Feel the
music: _Vejtables_ / Excitation: _Rear Exit_ /
Miles beyond: _Rear Exit_ / Train: _Transatlan-
tic Train_ / You're bringing me down: _Trans-
atlantic Train_ / She was a lady: _Transatlantic
Train_ / I'm going: _Flying Circus_ / Midnight
highway: _Flying Circus_ / Green eyes green
world: _Flying Circus_ / Swallow the sun (dark
on you now): _Love Exchange_ / Light switch:
Mourning Reign / Cut back: _Mourning Reign_
/ Kissy face: _Maze_ / Dejected soul: _Maze_ /
Napoleon: _Staff_ / Would you take me for a
ride: _Staff_ / Morning: _Afterglow_ / Susie's
gone: _Afterglow_
CD _____ CDWIKD 131
Big Beat / Aug '94 / Pinnacle.

CUBAN BOXSET
CD Set _____ 320302
Total / Jan '96 / Total/BMG.

CUBAN CLASSICS
Taka taka-ta: _Irakere_ / El coco: _Irakere_ / Locas por el mambo: _More, Benny_ / Mi chiquita: _More, Benny_ / El bobo de la yuca:
More, Benny / Lo que me pasa en la guagua: _Alvarez, Alberto_ / Longina: _Burke, Mal-
ena_ / Santa Barbara: _Gonzalez, Celina_ /
Pare cochero: _Orquesta Aragon_ / Yo no quiero que seas celosa: _Reve Y Su Charangon_
/ Los sitios entero: _NG La Banda_ / La pro-

testa de los chivos: _NG La Banda_ / Coge el
Camaron: _Origina De Manzanillo_ / Se muere
la tia: _Los Van Van_ / Eso que anda: _Los Van
Van_
CD _____ HADCD 169
Javelin / May '94 / THE / Henry Hadaway
Organisation.

CUBAN FANTASY
CD _____ CD 62023
Saludos Amigos / Apr '94 / Target/BMG.

CUBAN RHYTHMS
CD _____ CCD 504
Caney / Nov '95 / ADA / Discovery.

CUBAN SANTERIA
CD _____ SFWCD 40419
Smithsonian Folkways / Oct '95 / ADA /
Direct / Koch / CM / Cadillac.

CULTURE TRAIN
CD _____ MRCD 005
Metronome / May '94 / Jetstar.

CUMBIA CUMBIA 2
CD _____ WCD 033
World Circuit / Apr '93 / New Note / Direct
/ Cadillac / ADA.

CUMBIAS, BABUCOS & PASILOS
CD _____ PS 65123
Playasound / Apr '94 / Harmonia Mundi /
ADA.

CUTTING IT TO THE X-TREME
CD _____ XTR 11CD
Cutting / Jun '91 / Pinnacle.

CYBERNETIC BIOREAD TRANSMISSION
CD _____ BIOCD 01
Messerschmitt / Mar '94 / Plastic Head.

CYCLOPS SAMPLER
Future: _Abfinoosty_ / Kindness: _Credo_ /
Swords and knives: _Epilogue_ / Fool: _Grace
/ 12.02: Grey Lady Down_ / Another country:
Haze / Into the blue: _Hillman, Steve_ /
Creation: _Mann, Geoff_ / Circus: _Mr. So & So_
/ Slaves: _Primitive Instinct_ / Set me free:
Grace
CD _____ CYCL 007
Cyclops / Jul '94 / Pinnacle.

CYCLOPS SAMPLER 2
CD _____ CYCL 023
Cyclops / Nov '95 / Pinnacle.

CYLINDER JAZZ 1913-1927
Hungarian rag / Clarinet squawk: _Louisiana
Five_ / Dardanella: _Raderman, Harry's Jazz
Orchestra_ / Meadow lark: _Yellman, Duke &
his orchestra_ / Where's my sweetie hiding:
Merry Sparklers / Blue eyed sally / Ain't she
sweet / She's a cornfed Indiana gal: _Oliver,
Earl's Jazz Babies_ / Make that trombone
laugh: _Raderman, Harry's Jazz Orchestra_ /
Night time in little Italy: _Frisco Jazz Band_ /
I'm going to park myself in your arms: _Yell-
man, Duke & his orchestra_ / That certain
feeling: _Tennessee Happy Boys_ / Do it again
(intro, drifting along with the tide): _Louis-
ville Lou_
CD _____ CDSDL 334
Saydisc / Mar '94 / Harmonia Mundi / ADA
/ Direct.

D&D PROJECT, THE
One-two pass it: _D&D All Stars_ / Look alive:
Big C / Act up: _Ill Breed_ / Da good die
young: _N-Tyse_ / Stone to the bone: _Big
Jaz_ / From within out: _Fabidden Frut_ / Get
up: _Maniac Mob_ / Just a little flava: _Ill Un-
orthodox_ / Blowin' up the spot: _Ill Will_ /
Rude boy: _Night Dwellers_ / Nine inches
hard: _Juice_ / Mental illness: 2 _Mental_
CD _____ 07822187802
Arista / Jun '95 / BMG.

**D-DAY
(20 Big Band Tracks)**
Skyliner: _Big Eighteen_ / There'll be a hot
time in the town of Berlin: _Miller, Glenn &
The Army Airforce Orchestra_ / East of the
sun and west of the moon: _Dorsey, Tommy
& Frank Sinatra_ / Take the 'A' train: _Elling-
ton, Duke_ / Blitzkrieg baby (You can't bomb
me): _Carlisle, Una Mae_ / Flying home: _Bar-
net, Charlie_ / Thanks for the memory: _Good-
man, Benny_ / Summit ridge drive: _Shaw, Ar-
tie_ / Skylark: _Barnet, Charlie_ / Blackout:
Hawkins, Erskine / As time goes by: _Wiley,
Lee_ / Robbin's nest: _Basie, Count_ / Oh what
a beautiful morning: _Miller, Glenn & The
Army Airforce Orchestra_ / Ain't misbehavin':
Waller, Fats / Swing out to victory: _Waller,
Fats_ / Sunny side of the street: _Dorsey,
Tommy_ / Slip of the lip (Can sink a ship):
Ellington, Duke / Bugle call rag: _Goodman,
Benny_ / St James' infirmary: _Armstrong,
Louis_ / Lady be good: _Bechet, Sidney_
CD _____ 74321209522
Bluebird / May '94 / BMG.

D-DAY 50TH ANNIVERSARY - A MUSICAL TRIBUTE
CD _____ DDAY 50
Start / May '94 / Koch.

D-DAY: A COMMEMORATION IN SOUND
CD Set _____ DDCD 6644
Conifer / May '94 / Conifer.

D-DAY: THE 50TH ANNIVERSARY
(Marches From The Second World War)
CD _____ SRCD 321
Music Masters / Mar '94 / Target/BMG.

D.J. ERICK MORILLO LIVE AND MORE
CD _____ SR 323CD
Strictly Rhythm / Nov '95 / SRD / Vital.

D.J. IN THE BOX VOL.1
Get your hands off my man (Nush mix): Vasquez, Junior / Play this house: BB Club / Key: Goss, Matt / U girls (Junior Vasquez mix): Nush / Ultra flavour: Farley & Heller / Bash 2: Passion / Spread love: Blu Room / It's what's upfront that counts: D.J. Yosh / Let's whip it up: Sleaze Sisters / Reach: Party Pumpers / That sound: Musaphia, Joey / Feel: Zone 1 / I believe: Happy Clappers / There must be music (Emissary remix): Garrett, Justin / There must be music (Phil Jubb remix): Garrett, Justin / Remember me (Koolworld remix): Jubb, Phil
CD _____ UCCD 001
Urban Collective / Oct '95 / Vital.

D.J. IN THE BOX VOL.2
Positive vibration: Black Box / There must be music: Jubb, Phil / Remember me: Koolworld Productions / Heritage rap: Emissary / Untitled: Jubb, Phil / Pressor: Force Mass Motion / Ispirazione: XVX6 / Build it with love: London Beat / Perfect lover: Jennifer C / Vangroovey EP: Modifiers / Best thing: Miss Bliss
CD _____ UCCD 002
Urban Collective / Feb '96 / Vital.

D.J. JUNGLE FEVER UK COMPILATION
CD _____ RSNCD 35
Rising High / Jun '95 / Disc.

D.J. POWER
CD _____ POWCD 1
Escapade / Aug '94 / 3MV / Sony.

D.J. POWER VOL. 2
CD _____ POWCD 2
Escapade / Nov '94 / 3MV / Sony.

D.J. REMIX CULTURE
CD _____ STRSCD 5
CD _____ STRSCDDJ 5
Stress / Nov '94 / Pinnacle.

D.J. SY
CD Set _____ SDIMCD 2
Sound Dimension / Jun '95 / Total/BMG.

D.J.'S DELIGHT VOL.3
CD _____ DBMTR CD22
Rogue Trooper / Nov '95 / SRD.

D.J.'S DELITE VOLUME 1
CD _____ TROOPCD 5
Rogue Trooper / Jun '95 / SRD.

D.J.'S DELITE VOLUME 2
CD _____ DBMTROOPCD 9
Rogue Trooper / Nov '95 / SRD.

D.J.'S MEET THE SINGERS VOL. 2
CD _____ SONCD 0049
Sonic Sounds / Jul '93 / Jetstar.

D.J.'S UNITE VOL. 2
CD _____ TROOPCD 10
Rogue Trooper / May '95 / SRD.

D.J.'S UNITE VOL.3
CD _____ DBMTRCD 20
Rogue Trooper / Oct '95 / SRD.

D.J'S UNITE VOL.1
CD _____ TROOPCD 2
Rogue Trooper / Oct '94 / SRD.

DAFFAN SINGLES
These hands: Jericho, Jerry / Walk my way: Jericho, Jerry / Tangled mind: Irby, Jerry / Bottom of the list: Irby, Jerry / Heartaches for gold: Tillman, Floyd / Running away: Tillman, Floyd / Always lend a helping hand: Jericho, Jerry / I'm getting more than my share: Jericho, Jerry / Our daily bread: McBride, Dickie / Silent partners: McBride, Dickie / Call for me Darling: Irby, Jerry / It's time you started looking: Irby, Jerry / How foolish can woman be: McBride, Laura Lee / I want my man: McBride, Laura Lee / Clickety clack: Irby, Jerry / Man is a slave: Irby, Jerry / Rich and the poor: Jericho, Jerry / Which way are you going: Jericho, Jerry / Be kind to a man: Jericho, Jerry / I'm ashamed: Jericho, Jerry / That's too bad: Irby, Jerry / I'd give you anything in this world: Irby, Jerry / Waltz you saved for me: Jericho, Jerry / Floyd's song: Tillman, Floyd / Cold, cold beer: Tillman, Floyd / Hopeless: Fidlo / Triflin' heart: Fidlo / Who's getting your love: Lee, Ted / Blues that way: Lee, Ted / Dig that crazy driver: Pennix, William / How old do you get: Pennix, William / Teach 'em how to swim: Pennix, William / Them old blues got me: Pennix, William / Ride the waves of love: Elliott, Margaret / Last call: Elliott, Margaret / Strange love: Bundrick, John / Made in Japan: Bundrick, John / This wallflower's gonna bloom: Elliott, Margaret / What's her name: Elliott,

---

Margaret / Cold grey walls of yesterday: Pickering Bros / Please (come back to me): Pickering Bros / Surviving half of a love affair: Pickering Bros / Lady luck my love: Pickering Bros / Letter from nashville: Pickering Bros
CD Set _____ BCDBH 15878
Bear Family / Jun '95 / Rollercoaster / Direct / CM / Swift / ADA.

DAN MASKS
CD _____ C 580048
Ocora / Nov '93 / Harmonia Mundi / ADA.

DANCA
Roda: Gil, Gilberto / Besta e tu: Baianos, Novos / Fato consumado: Djavan / Te futaco: Guerreiro, Cid / Taj Mahal/Filhomaravilha/Pais Tropical: Ben, Jorge / Chove da mironga do kabulete: Toquinho & Vinicius / Rei no bagaco coisas do vida: De Belem, Fafa / Salve simpatia: Ben, Jorge / Tiro de misericordia: Bosco, Joao & Chico Batera / Adeita: Ben, Jorge / A banda do ze pretinho: Ben, Jorge / Nem ouro nem prata: Maurity, Roy / Ague negra da lagoa: Toquinho / Africaner brother bound: Shock, Obina & Gilberto Gil / Gabriel Guerreiro galactico: Ben, Jorge / Mambembe: De Belem, Fafa / Perfume de cebola (Fragance of onion): Filo / Da cor do pecado: Creuza, Maria / Em matogrosso fronteira com: Ben, Jorge
CD _____ NSCD 006
Nascente / Jul '91 / Disc / THE.

DANCE '95
Cotton eye Joe: Rednex / Set you free: N-Trance / Total eclipse of the heart: French, Nicki / Another night: M.C. Sar & The Real McCoy / Saturday night: Whigfield / Let me be your fantasy: Baby D / Sweet love: M-Beat & Nazlyn / Can you feel it: Reel 2 Real / Baby come back: Banton, Pato / Baby, I love your way: Big Mountain / Love so strong: Secret Life / Don't leave me this way: Houston, Thelma / Apparently nothin': Anderson, Carleen / Sweetness: Gayle, Michelle / Midnight at the oasis: Brand New Heavies / Welcome to tomorrow (are you ready): Snap / Texas cowboys: Grid / Eighteen strings: Tinman / What's up: D.J. Miko / Sign: Ace Of Base
CD _____ VTCD 43
Virgin / Feb '95 / EMI.

DANCE BAND HITS
CD _____ CDCD 1201
Charly / Sep '94 / Charly / THE / Cadillac.

DANCE BAND HITS OF THE BLITZ
(2CD/MC Set)
It can't be wrong: Geraldo & His Orchestra / Long ago and far away: Geraldo & His Orchestra / Humpty Dumpty heart: Geraldo & His Orchestra / Every night about this time: Geraldo & His Orchestra / I don't want to set the world on fire: Geraldo & His Orchestra / Anywhere on earth is heaven: Geraldo & His Orchestra / I'm nobody's baby: Gonella, Nat & His New Georgians / Aurora: Gonella, Nat & His New Georgians / I can't get Indiana off my mind: Gonella, Nat & His New Georgians / Be careful it's my heart: Roy, Harry & His Band / Daddy: Roy, Harry & His Band / Sand in my shoes: Roy, Harry & His Band / Pennsylvania polka: Roy, Harry & His Band / Five o'clock whistle: Roy, Harry & His Band / White Christmas: Roy, Harry & His Band / Down Forget-me-Not Lane: Loss, Joe & His Orchestra / I'll never smile again: Loss, Joe & His Orchestra / You made me care: Loss, Joe & His Orchestra / How sweet you are: Benson, Ivy & Her Girls Band / If I had my way: Benson, Ivy & Her Girls Band / I'm sending my blessing: Benson, Ivy & Her Girls Band / Rome coming waltz: Benson, Ivy & Her Girls Band / Does she love me: Leader, Harry & His Band
CD Set _____ CDDL 1185
Music For Pleasure / Aug '93 / EMI.

DANCE BOOM
CD _____ TCD 2763
Telstar / Apr '95 / BMG.

DANCE BOOM 2
CD _____ TCD 2783
Telstar / Aug '95 / BMG.

DANCE BUZZ
CD _____ RADCD 17
Global / Jan '95 / BMG.

DANCE CLASSICS
CD _____ DSPCD 106
Disky / Sep '93 / THE / BMG / Discovery / Pinnacle.

DANCE COLLECTION
(3CD/MC Set)
CD Set _____ TBXCD 504
TrueTrax / Jan '96 / THE.

DANCE CRASHER
(Ska To Rock Steady)
Big bamboo: Lord Creator / Latin goes ska: Skatalites / Garden of love: Drummond, Don / Rough and tough: Cole, Stranger / Beardman ska: Skatalites / Shame and scandal: Tosh, Peter & The Wailers / Street corner: Skatalites / Bonanza ska: Malcolm, Carlos & Afro Cambs / Dance crasher: Ellis, Alton & The Flames / Let George do it: Drummond, Don / Rudie bam bam: Clarendonians / Dr. Dick: Perry, Lee 'Scratch' & The Soulettes / Ball o' fire: Skatalites / Independence ska:

Brooks, Baba & Band / Don't be a rude boy: Rulers / Ska jam: McCook, Tommy & The Soulettes / Hallelujah: Toots & The Maytals / Owe me no pay me: Ethiopians
CD _____ CDTRL 260
Trojan / Mar '94 / Jetstar / Total/BMG.

DANCE CRAZY
(From The Charleston To The Jive)
Charleston: Savoy Orpheans / Blue room: Savoy Orpheans / Black bottom: Johnny Hamp's Kentucky Serenaders / That's you, baby: Hylton, Jack / Walking with Susie: Hylton, Jack / Happy feet: Whiteman, Paul / Rockin' in rhythm: Ellington, Duke / Put on your old grey bonnet: Casa Loma Orchestra / Boogie woogie man: Casa Loma Orchestra / Man from Harlem: Calloway, Cab / Tiger rag: Payne, Jack / Tailspin: Dorsey Brothers / Clap hands, here comes Charlie: Webb, Chick / For dancers only: Lunceford, Jimmie / Just you, just me: Norvo, Red / At the swing cats' ball: Jordan, Louis / Deep night: Dorsey, Tommy / Boulder buff: Miller, Glenn / Jitney man: Hines, Earl / King Porter stomp: Crosby, Bob / Hep hep - the jumpin' jive: Gonella, Nat
CD _____ PPCD 78104
Past Perfect / Feb '95 / THE.

DANCE, DANCE, DANCE
CD _____ CDCD 1117
Charly / Jul '93 / Charly / THE / Cadillac.

DANCE DECADE
(Dance Hits Of The 80's)
Don't leave me this way: Communards / Relax: Frankie Goes To Hollywood / Good thing: Fine Young Cannibals / Tainted love: Soft Cell / Breakout: Swing Out Sister / Love in the first degree: Bananarama / Oh l'amour: Dollar / Kiss: Art Of Noise & Tom Jones / Only way is up: Yazz / Push it: Salt 'N' Pepa / Got to keep on: Cookie Crew / People hold on: Coldcut & Lisa Stansfield / House arrest: Krush / Jack your body: Hurley, Steve 'Silk' / Wipeout: Fat Boys / Walk this way: Run DMC & Aerosmith / She works hard for the money: Summer, Donna / Livin' in America: Brown, James / Word up: Cameo / Get down on it: Kool & The Gang / Oops upside your head: Gap Band / Ain't nothin' goin' on but the rent: Guthrie, Gwen / Walk the dinosaur: Was Not Was / Mama used to say: Glasgow, Junior / Smalltown boy: Bronski Beat / Poison arrow: ABC / Let the music play: Shannon / Funky town: Lipps Inc. / Obsession: Animotion / Night train: Visage / Maniac: Sembello, Michael / Fame: Cara, Irene
CD _____ 8406212
Polystar / Oct '89 / PolyGram.

DANCE DIVAS
Express: Carroll, Dina / U: Clark, Loni / Big time sensuality: Bjork / Give it up, turn it loose: En Vogue / Don't walk away: Jade / So natural: Stansfield, Lisa / I wish: Gabrielle / You and me: Lisa B / Gotta get it right: Fiagbe, Lena / Everybody's free: Rozalla / My love is guaranteed: Sybil / Luv 4 luv: Robin S / Little bit more: Jones, Kym / Can't get enough of your love: Dayne, Taylor / Lost in music: Sister Sledge / Free love: Roberts, Juliet / I will always love you: Washington, Sarah / Born to B.R.E.E.D.: Love, Monie / Respect: Adeva / Alex Party: Alex Party
CD _____ 516652-2
PolyGram TV / Jan '94 / PolyGram.

DANCE FEVER
CD _____ MPV 5551
Movieplay / May '94 / Target/BMG.

DANCE FLOOR HEAVEN
Do you wanna funk: Sylvester / Menergy: Cowley, Patrick / Somebody else's guy: Brown, Jocelyn / You think you're a man: Divine / Last night a DJ saved my life: Indeep / Feels like I'm in love: Marie, Kelly / Downtown: Clark, Petula / Let the music play: Shannon / Can you feel the force: Real Thing / Can you handle it: Redd, Sharon / Night to remember: Shalamar / What's your name what's your number: Andrea True Connection / Pump up the jam: Technotronic / Hip hop be bop (Don't stop) (Don't stop): Man Parrish / Foot on the rock: Cherry, Neneh & GMC
CD _____ TRTCD 119
TrueTrax / Oct '94 / THE.

DANCE FLOOR HEAVEN VOL.2
Walk like a man: Divine / Die hard lover: Cowley, Patrick & Linda Imperial / I wish you would: Brown, Jocelyn / Band of gold: Sylvester / When boys talk: Indeep / Hot love: Marie, Kelly / I can make you feel good: Shalamar / More, more, more: Andrea True Connection / This is it: Moore, Melba / Dance with you: Lucas, Carrie / Get up (Before the night is over): Technotronic / On the dance floor: New Guys On The Block / Highwire: Carr, Linda & The Love Squad / Sending out an S.O.S.: Young, Retta / Soul je t'aime: Sylvia & Ralfi Pagan
CD _____ TRTCD 143
TrueTrax / Dec '94 / THE.

DANCE HEAT '95
Scatman: Scatman John / Dreamer: Livin' Joy / Your loving arms: Martin, Billie Ray / Don't make me wait: Loveland / Not over yet: Grace / Don't stop (wiggle wiggle): Outhere Brothers / Reach up (Papa's got a brand new pigbag): Perfecto All Stars /

Guaglione: Prado, Perez 'Prez' / Bubbling hot: Banton, Pato & Ranking Roger / Love city groove: Love City Groove / Crazy: Morrison, Mark / Two can play that game: Brown, Bobby / U sure do: Strike / Axel F: Clock / Max don't have sex with your ex: E-Rotic / Baby baby: Corona / Conway: Reel 2 Real / Always something there to remind me: Tin Tin Out & Espiritu / Take you there: Simon, Ronni / Too many fish: Knuckles, Frankie / I believe: Happy Clappers / Sex on the streets: Pizzaman
CD _____ VTCD 50
Virgin / May '95 / EMI.

DANCE HITS
Ebeneezer Goode: Shamen / Sesame Street: Smarties / Bee: Scientist / Move your body: Jefferson, Marshall / It's just a feeling: Terrorize / It takes two: Base, Rob & D.J. E-Z Rock / On a ragga tip: SL2 / Aris 8 (Come with me): Altern 8 / Sweet harmony: Liquid / This brutal house: Nitro Deluxe / Please don't go: KWS / Move any mountain: Shamen / Hardcore (I should know the score): Hypnotist / Infinity: Guru Josh / So real: Love Decade / Casanova: Baby D / Injected with a poison: Khan, Praga & Jade 4 U / 900 Number: 45 King / Last night: Kid 'N' Play / I'm gonna get you: Bizarre Inc. / Boss drum: Shamen / Love can't turn around: Farley Jackmaster Funk / Bang zoom let's go go: Real Roxanne & Hitman Howie Tee / House nation: House Master Boyz / Hypnotise: Altern 8 / You used to hold me: Rasario, Ralphi / Godfather: Spoonie Gee / Strings of life: Rhythim Is Rhythim / Trip II the moon: Acen / Pure: G.T.O. / King of rock: Run DMC / All we wanna do is dance: House Crew / Tricky disco: Tricky Disco / Phorever people: Shamen / Is this the dream: Love Decade / Quadrasophonia / Nothing serious just buggin: Whistle / Brutal 8: Altern 8 / Evapor-8: Altern 8
CD Set _____ LOWBOXCD 6
Low Price Music / Sep '94 / Total/BMG.

DANCE HITS '94
CD _____ DINCD 95
Dino / Jul '94 / Pinnacle / 3MV.

DANCE HITS OF THE 80'S
Let's groove: Earth, Wind & Fire / Ooh la la: Marie, Teena / Jump: Pointer Sisters / She wants to dance with me: Astley, Rick / Alice, I want you just for me: Full Force / Rockit: Hancock, Herbie / My love is so raw: Williams, Alyson / I'm that type of guy: L.L. Cool J / Going back to my roots: Odyssey / Encore: Lynn, Cheryl / I wonder if I take you home: Lisa Lisa & Cult Jam & Full Force / Roses: Haywoode / Love come down: King, Evelyn / System addict: Five Star / Call me: Spagna / My toot toot: Lasalle, Denise
CD _____ PWKS 4199
Carlton Home Entertainment / Aug '94 / Carlton Home Entertainment.

DANCE HITS VOL.1
CD _____ LOWCDX 21
Low Price Music / Mar '95 / Total/BMG.

DANCE HITS VOL.2
CD _____ LOWCDX 22
Low Price Music / Aug '95 / Total/BMG.

DANCE LIKE THE DEVIL
(22 Northern Soul Favourites From Pye Records)
Thought of mine: James, Jimmy / Love is getting stronger: Knight, Jason / If you knew: Ebony Eyes / What love brings: Bernard, Kenny / Ain't no soul (left in these ole shoes): Bernard, Kenny / Come home baby: Powell, Keith / As long as I live: Roberts, Kenny / Gonna fix you good (everytime you're bad): Bovin, Alan Set / Step out of line: Cotton, Mike Sound / (Just like) Romeo and Juliet: Peter's Faces / Black is black: Sounds Orchestral / You baby: Trent, Jackie / Something to give: Rossi, Mila / Lost Summer love: Silver, Lorraine / Happy faces: Silver, Lorraine / Bring him back: Starr, Stella / Nobody knows what's goin' on: St. John, Tammy / Real thing: Kim D / Number one guy: Ferris Wheel / Take me for a while: Shapiro, Helen / Just walk in my shoes: Davis, Billie
CD _____ NEXCD 194
Sequel / Mar '92 / BMG.

DANCE MANIA '95
CD _____ PMCD 7008
Pure Music / Jan '95 / BMG.

DANCE MANIA '95 VOL.2
CD _____ PMCD 7010
Pure Music / Mar '95 / BMG.

DANCE MANIA '95 VOL.3
CD _____ PMCD 7013
Pure Music / Jul '95 / BMG.

DANCE MANIA '95 VOL.4
CD _____ PMCD 7015
Pure Music / Oct '95 / BMG.

DANCE MASSIVE '94
(2CD/MC/LP Set)
CD Set _____ DINCD 94
Dino / Aug '94 / Pinnacle / 3MV.

DANCE MASSIVE '94 VOL.2
(2CD/MC Set)
CD Set _____ DINCD 103
Dino / Nov '94 / Pinnacle / 3MV.

DANCE MASSIVE '95
(2CD/MC Set)
Dreamer: Livin' Joy / Let love shine: Amos
/ Crazy: Eternal / Raise your hands: Reel By
Reel / Sex on the streets: Pizzaman / Two
can play that game: Brown, Bobby / Tune
in turn up cop out: Freak Power / Yeke
yeke: Kante, Mory / Push the feeling on:
Nightcrawlers / Don't give me your life: Alex
Party / Always something there to remind
me: Tin Tin Out / Reach up: Perfecto All
Stars / Baby baby: Corona / Don't stop
(Wiggle wiggle): Outhere Brothers / Don't
need your love: Motiv 8 / Your loving arms:
Martin, Billie Ray / Baby: Rozalla / I'm going
down: Blige, Mary J. / Lift me up: M-Five /
Bomb: Nightcrawlers / You can have it all:
Gallagher, Eve / Max don't have sex with
your ex: E-Rotic / Magic on you: Sugar Ba-
bies / Cotton eye Joe: Rednex / Bump 'N'
Grind: R. Kelly / Down with the clique: Aa-
liyah / U sure do: Strike / Set you free: N-
Trance / Pump up the volume: Greed / I be-
lieve: Happy Clappers / I need somebody:
Loveland / You: Staxx / Everyday of the
week: Jade / Runaway: M.C. Sar / Not over
yet: Grace / Love city groove: Love City
Groove / Lone ranger: Swagman / Scatman:
Scatman John
CD Set _____ DINCD 87
Dino / May '95 / Pinnacle / 3MV.

DANCE PARTY
CD _____ BLS 1015 CD
BLS / Jul '92 / Jetstar.

DANCE PARTY
Choice: Blow Monkeys / Never gonna give
you up: Astley, Rick / Indestructible: Four
Tops / Love take over: Five Star / I'm so
excited: Pointer Sisters / Flashback: Imagination / Going back to my roots: Odyssey /
Love come down: King, Evelyn / Runner:
Three Degrees / Gonna get along without
you know: Wills, Viola / Armed and
extremely dangerous: First Choice / (We've
got a) Good thing going: Minott, Sugar
CD _____ 74321339232
Camden / Jan '96 / BMG.

DANCE PARTY: THE ROARING 60S
(2CD Set)
CD Set _____ 24036
Delta Doubles / Sep '92 / Target/BMG.

DANCE PARTY: THE ROCKING 50S
(2CD Set)
CD Set _____ 24035
Delta Doubles / Sep '92 / Target/BMG.

**DANCE PLANET - SOUNDS OF THE
DETONATOR**
CD _____ DPRCD 1
Dance Planet / Sep '95 / SRD.

DANCE POWER
(Club Classics Vol.1)
Car wash: Jiani, Carol / I'm not in love:
Payne, Scherrie / Starman: Free Style / One
night only: Payne, Scherrie / Up the ladder
to the roof: Kydd, John & The Supreme
Event / My guy: Angie / Knowing me, know-
ing you: Springate, John / Born to be alive:
Meantime / Guilty: Alexander, Ross / Can't
help falling in love: Absolutely / Pick up the
pieces: Enterprise 7 / Can you feel the
force: Prime DC / Queen of clubs: Sprin-
gate, John / Shame, shame, shame: Linda
& The Funky Boys / Love machine: Blood
/ Come together Free Style / Magic fly: Raw
Recruits / Uptown top ranking: Tight N Up
/ Future brain: Huntington, Eddie / Mickey:
XYZ
CD _____ PWKM 4073
Carlton Home Entertainment / Aug '91 /
Carlton Home Entertainment.

DANCE SOUNDS OF DETROIT
(2CD/MC Set)
Memories & souveniers: Payne, Freda / I
want to be loved: Supremes / Fear: Starr,
Edwin / Two way street: Jacas, Jake / Don't
wait around: Elgins / Sitting in the park: Lovetones / Right direction: Littles, Hattie /
Fresh out of tears: Laurence, Lynda / One
shot at happiness: Demps, Louvain / Wake
me up when it's over: Ruffin, Jimmy / Which
way do I turn: Crawford, Carolyn / Send
some love: Barnes, Ortheia / Lost: Randolph, Barbara / I'm dedicating to you:
McNeir, Ronnie / Weak hearted: Taylor,
Sherri / Hotter than the summer days: Ed-
wards, Sandra / See this man in love: Wylie,
Richard 'Popcorn' / Look into the future:
Leverette, Chico / Look into the eyes of a
fool: Bristol, Johnny / Better love next time:
Johnson, Marv / City lights: Lewis, Pat /
Grazing in the grass: Monitors / Timeless:
Crawford, Carolyn / I've fallen and can't get
up: Fantastic Four / Come back and start
again: Nero, Frances / Six by six: Van Dyke,
Earl / Sister Lee: Ward, Sammy / Fire alarm:
Lovetones / One and one makes two: Starr,
Edwin / That girl is dangerous: Jacas, Jake
/ Lovestruck: Edwards, Sandra / All around
the motorcity: Andantes / Just us: Royster,
Vermettya / Half hearted: Gordon, Billy /
Bad case of nerves: Marvelettes / Breaking
into my heart: Randolph, Barbara
CD _____ 3035990077
Old Gold / Oct '95 / Carlton Home
Entertainment.

DANCE SOUNDS OF HI
CD _____ HILOCD 3
Hi / Nov '93 / Pinnacle.

DANCE SOUNDS OF THE 70'S
Tring / Aug '93 / Tring / Prism.

DANCE TO THE MAX
Living on my own: Mercury, Freddie /
Things can only get better (Mixes): D Ream
/ Relight my fire: Take That & Lulu / Moving
on up: M People / Boom shake the room:
D.J. Jazzy Jeff & The Fresh Prince / Come
baby come: K7 / Rhythm is a dancer: Snap
/ Ride on time: Black Box / Got to get it:
Culture Beat / U got 2 let the music: Cap-
pella / Long train runnin': Doobie Brothers /
Give it up: Goodmen / No limit: 2 Unlimited
/ Relax: Frankie Goes To Hollywood / It's my
life: Dr. Alban / I want to stand: McLean, Bitty
/ Respect: Sub Sub / No matter what you
do: Flavour / Things that make you go
hmmmm: C & C Music Factory
CD _____ VTCD 24
Virgin / Mar '94 / EMI.

DANCE TO THE MAX 2
Real thing: 2 Unlimited / Move on baby (De-
finitive edit): Cappella / Light my fire (RAF
zone remix): Club House / I like to move it:
Reel 2 Real / Sweets for my sweet: Lewis,
C.J. / Dedicated to the one I love: McLean,
C.J. / Dedicated to the one I love: McLean,
M People / Real thing (2): Di Bart, Tony / U R
the best thing (Perfecto radio mix): D Ream
/ Shine on: Degrees Of Motion / Move me:
Black Machine / Life: Haddaway / Son of a
gun (Hooj edit): JX / Rockin' for myself (Ra-
dio edit): Motiv 8 / Funky love: Time Fre-
quency / Hold that sucker down: OT Quar-
tet / Exterminate: Snap / It's alright: East 17
CD _____ VTCD 29
Virgin / May '94 / EMI.

DANCE TO THE MAX 3
Shine: Aswad / You don't love me (no no
no): Penn, Dawn / Swamp thing: Grid /
What goes around: McLean, Bitty / Just a
step from heaven: Eternal / Key, the secret:
Urban Cookie Collective / One night in
heaven: M People / Take me away: D Ream
/ No good (Start the dance): Prodigy / Go
on move: Reel 2 Real / U and me: Cappella
/ No more (I can't stand it): Maxx / Every-
body don't jam: Two Cowboys / Think
about the way: Ice M.C. / Run to the sun:
Erasure / Let the beat control your body: 2
Unlimited / Mr. Vain: Culture Beat / Power:
Snap / Whammer slammer: Warp 9 / Sum-
mertime: D.J. Jazzy Jeff & The Fresh Prince
CD _____ VTCD 33
Virgin / Aug '94 / EMI.

**DANCE WITH ME - THE AUTUMN TEEN
SOUND**
Dance with me: Mojo Men / She goes with
me: Mojo Men / Off the hook: Mojo Men /
Draggin' the main: Upsetters / Little one:
Spearmints / Anything: Vejtables / I still love
you: Vejtables / Where did I fail: Knight Rid-
ers / I: Knight Riders / Torture and pain:
Knight Riders / Won't you be my baby:
Knight Riders / I should be glad: Gear One
/ Hello little girl: Gear One / I think it's time:
Chosen Few / Nothing but me: Chosen Few
/ Pay attention to me: Tikis / I'll never forget
about you: Tikis / Darkest night of my mind:
Tikis / Blue eyes: Tikis / Just me: Us / How
can I tell her: Us / Mark my words: Bundles
/ Watch me get: Bundles / Something bad:
Mojo Men / My woman's head: Mojo Men /
Can't you see me: Mojo Men / Not too long:
Why: Mojo Men / As I get older: Mojo Men
/ All over town: Au Go Go's / I still love you
(version): Vejtables
CD _____ CDWIKD 128
Big Beat / Mar '94 / Pinnacle.

DANCE ZONE '94
(2CD/MC Set)
Let me be your fantasy: Baby D / Another
night: Real McCoy / Saturday night: Whigfield / She's got that vibe: R. Kelly / Best of
my love: Lewis, C.J. / Confide in me:
Minogue, Kylie / Compliments on your kiss:
Red Dragon / Twist and shout: Demus,
Chaka & Pliers / Rhythm of the night: Co-
rona / Move on baby: Cappella / What's up:
D.J. Miko / Incredible: M-Beat & General
Levy / Go on move: Reel 2 Real / Carry me
home: Gloworm / Swamp thing: Grid /
Everybody gonfti gon: Two Cowboys / Eight-
een strings: Tinman / No good (Start the
dance): Prodigy / 100% pure love: Waters,
Crystal / Midnight at the oasis: Brand New
Heavies / Whatta man: Salt 'N' Pepa & En
Vogue / Doop: Doop / Shine on: Degrees Of
Motion / Son of a gun: JX / Anything: Cul-
ture Beat / U and me: Cappella / Rock my
heart: Haddaway / Real thing: 2 Unlimited /
Get-a-way: Maxx / Sweets for my sweet:
Lewis, C.J. / Sign: Ace Of Base / It's alright:
East 17 / Things can only get better: D
Ream / Renaissance: M People / Searching:
China Black / Sweet Lullaby: Deep Forest /
Save our love: Eternal / Shine: Aswad / You
don't love me (no no no): Penn, Dawn /
Dedicated to the one I love: McLean, Bitty
/ How gee: Black Machine / Light my fire:
Clubhouse & Carl / Rockin' for myself: Motiv
8 / Whistle your whistle: D.J. Duke
CD Set _____ 5251302
PolyGram TV / Nov '94 / PolyGram.

DANCE ZONE '95
(2CD/MC Set)
CD Set _____ 5350452
PolyGram TV / Oct '95 / PolyGram.

DANCE ZONE LEVEL 5
I need your loving (everybody's gotta love
sometime): Baby D / Scatman: Scatman
John / Boom boom boom: Outhere Broth-
ers / Your loving arms: Martin, Billie Ray /
Hold my body tight: East 17 / Dreamer:
Livin' Joy / Love and devotion: Real McCoy
/ Not anyone: Black Box / Eternity: Snap / I
need you: Deuce / Two can play that game:
Brown, Bobby / Not over yet: Grace / Raise
your hands: Reel 2 Real / Respect: Cheeks,
Judy / Open your heart: M People / Love
city groove: Love City Groove / Swing low,
sweet chariot: Ladysmith Black Mambazo &
China Black / Turn on, tune in, cop out:
Freak Power / Let it rain: East 17 / Tears
don't lie: Mark Oh / Guaglione: Prado, Perez
/ 'Prez' / Think of you: Whigfield / Sex on the
streets: Pizzaman / I believe: Happy Clappers / J. tribute: A.S.H.A. / Direct me:
Reese Project / Take you there: Simon,
Ronni / Work it out: Shiva / Everybody in
the world: Ashah / Access: D.J. Misjah /
Move your body: Eurogroove / High as a
kite: One Tribe / Love love love: Rollo Goes
/ Always something there to remind
me: Tin Tin Out & Espiritu / Wizards of the
sonic: West Bam / Invader: Koolworld Pro-
ductions / Gudvibe: Tinman / Spirit inside:
Spirits / Bomb, The (These sounds fall into
my mind): Bucketheads / Lifting me higher:
Gems For Jem
CD _____ 5256332
PolyGram TV / Jul '05 / PolyGram.

DANCEHALL CONNECTION VOL.1 & 2
CD _____ MFCD 006
Mafia/Fluxy / Dec '92 / Jetstar / SRD.

DANCEHALL DAYS
CD _____ FILECD 458
Profile / Jan '91 / Pinnacle.

DANCEHALL HITS VOL 1
CD _____ VPCD 1335
Digital B / Oct '93 / Jetstar.

DANCEHALL HITS VOL 2
CD _____ VPCD 1321
Digital B / Sep '93 / Jetstar.

DANCEHALL HITS VOL 3
CD _____ VPCD 1344
John John / Dec '93 / Jetstar.

DANCEHALL HITS VOL 4
CD _____ PHCD 2015
Penthouse / Aug '94 / Jetstar.

DANCEHALL KILLERS
CD _____ 792092
Jammy's / Jun '93 / Jetstar.

DANCEHALL KILLERS VOL 3
CD _____ SHCD 45018
Shanachie / Dec '94 / Koch / ADA /
Greensleeves.

DANCEHALL ROUGHNECK
CD _____ HBCD 148
Greensleeves / Aug '93 / Total/BMG /
Jetstar / SRD.

DANCEHALL STYLEE VOL 2
Here I come (Broader than Broadway):
Levy, Barrington / Burrup: Nardo Ranks /
Murder dem: Ninja Man / Ring the alarm:
Tenor Saw / Drum pan sound: Stepper,
Reggie / Stop loving you: McGregor, Fred-
die / Roots and culture: Shabba Ranks /
Cabin stabhin': Super Cat/Nina Roy /
Junior Demus / Wicked in bed: Shabba
Ranks / D.J. in my country: Irie, Clement /
Proud to be black: Crucial Robbie / Golden
touch: Brown, Rula & Commander Shad
CD _____ FILECD 291
Profile / Feb '91 / Pinnacle.

DANCEHALL STYLEE VOL 3
Stopper: Cutty Ranks / Dance hall rock:
Levy, Barrington / Ambition: Lady Patra /
Maddy maddy cry: Papa San / Cassandra:
Home Hammond, Beres / Gold spoon: Dean,
Paul, Frankie / Manhunt: Shabba Ranks &
Lovindeer / Typewriter: Rankin, Louie /
Press up: Poison Chang / No. 1 Upon the
look good chart: Capleton / Bandelero:
Pinchers / Zig it up: Ninja Man & Flourgon /
Tune in: Cocoa T
CD _____ PCD 1433
Profile / Jan '91 / Pinnacle.

DANCEHALL STYLEE VOL 4
Hustle hustle: Cutty Ranks / Come back
home: Frankie, Paul / Gold spoon: Banton, Buju / Jah Jah is the ruler: Garnet Silk
/ Bed work sensation: Bajja Jedd / Don't
expect me to be your friend: Wade, Wayne
/ You don't love me: Penn, Dawn / Copper
shot: Bounty Killer / Second class love:
Banton, Buju & Carol Gonzales / Whosoever
will may come: Capleton, Terry / Guns 'n' ammunition: Tony Rebel / Rude boy remember: Jender, Jessie
CD _____ FILECD 447
Profile / Jan '94 / Pinnacle.

DANCEHALL STYLEE VOL.5
CD _____ FILECD 456
Profile / Jan '94 / Pinnacle.

DANCES OF THE GODS
CD _____ C 559 051
Ocora / Apr '89 / Harmonia Mundi / ADA.

DANCES OF THE WORLD
(Music From Elektra Nonesuch
'Explorer' Series)
CD _____ 7559791672
Elektra Nonesuch / Jan '95 / Warner
Music.

DANCING 'TIL DAWN
Last minute miracle: Shirelles / Help me:
Wilson, Al / This man (CD only) / Woman
lover thief: Stemmons Express / One in a
million (CD only) / Come back baby: Dodds,
Nella / Everything is everything (CD only) /
Marching (CD only) / Out on the street
again: Candy & The Kisses / Love it's get-
ting better (CD only) / Get on up (CD only)
/ Desiree (CD only) / Do you believe it (CD
only) / I'm your yes man: Reid, Clarence /
Work song (CD only) / These chains of love
(are breaking me down): Jackson, Chuck /
Ain't that peculiar: Tindley, George / Stop
sign (CD only) / Ain't no soul (CD only) /
Name it and claim it: Stewart, Darryl / Tight-
rope (CD only) / You busted my mind: Clay,
Judy / Love is a good foundation (CD only)
/ There comes a time (CD only) / I don't
have a mind of my own (CD only) / Lost love
(LP only): Irma & The Fascinations / Please
stay (LP only): Ivorys / Show me a man (LP
only): Bradshaw, Bobby / Livin' the nightlife
(LP only): Charts / Let me give you my lovin'
(LP only): Brown, Maxine / Black eyed girl
(LP only): Thompson, Billy
CD _____ CDKEND 106
Kent / Feb '94 / Pinnacle.

DANCING BRAZIL
CD _____ 15343
Laserlight / May '94 / Target/BMG.

DANCING ON SUNSHINE
I got you babe: UB40 & Chrissie Hynde /
Wild world: Priest, Maxi / I can see clearly
now: Nash, Johnny / Now that we've found
love: Third World / Don't turn around: Aswad / Dub be good to me: Beats International / Word girl: Scritti Politti / To love
somebody: Somerville, Jimmy / Everything
I own: Boy George / Love of the common
people: Thomas, Nicky / Dreadlock holiday:
10cc / Israelites: Dekker, Desmond / Double
barrel: Collins, Dave & Ansil / Uptown top
ranking: Althia & Donna / Tomorrow people:
Marley, Ziggy & The Melody Makers / Silly
games: Kay, Janet / Help me make it
through the night: Holt, John / Just don't
want to be lonely: McGregor, Freddie /
Wonderful world, beautiful people: Cliff,
Jimmy / I don't wanna dance: Grant, Eddy
/ Sing our own song: UB40
CD _____ 5155192
PolyGram TV / Jul '92 / PolyGram.

**DANCING ON THE ROOF RAGGA
PARTY PART 1**
CD _____ RN 0016 CD
Runn / Jul '92 / Jetstar / SRD.

DANCING THROUGH THE 70'S
Relight my fire: Hartman, Dan / Lady Marmalade: Labelle, Patti / Blame it on the boogie: Jacksons / Dance to the music: Sly &
The Family Stone / Play that funky music:
Wild Cherry / Baby love (live): Mother's Finest / Boogie wonderland: Earth, Wind & Fire
& The Emotions / Dirty ol' man: Three Degrees / Rockin' after midnight: Gaye, Marvin
/ I love to love: Charles, Tina / You bet your
love: Hancock, Herbie / Don't leave me this
way: Melvin, Harold & The Bluenotes / I'm
on fire: 5000 Volts / Best of my love: Emotions / Yellow river: Christie
CD _____ 4803672
Embassy / Oct '95 / Sony.

DANCING THROUGH THE 80'S
Girls just want to have fun: Lauper, Cyndi /
Young guns (Go for it): Wham / It's raining
men: Weather Girls / Reggae night: Cliff,
Jimmy / Jeans on: Mysterious Art / Walk
like an egyptian: Bangles / You spin me
round (like a record): Dead Or Alive / Step
by step: New Kids On The Block / 1-2-3:
Chimes / Let's groove: Earth, Wind & Fire /
Riding on a train: Pasadenas / When will I
be famous: Bros / Can you feel the beat:
Lisa Lisa & Cult Jam
CD _____ 4803682
Columbia / Dec '95 / Sony.

DANCING TO THE BANDS AGAIN
(2CD/MC Set)
Say it everyday: Skyrockets Orchestra /
That's my desire: Rabin, Oscar & His Band
/ I'll do it all over again: Roy, Harry / Another
day: Roy, Harry / It's all over now: Preager,
Lou & His Band / I'm always chasing rain-
bows: Fenoulhet, Paul / I walked in with my
eyes open: Fenoulhet, Paul / Little on the
lonely side: Fenoulhet, Paul / I wonder
who's kissing her now: Rabin, Oscar & His
Band / You can't be true dear: Rabin, Oscar
& His Band / I'm not in love: Rabin, Oscar
& His Band / June night: Rabin, Oscar & His
Band / Far away place: Rabin, Oscar & His
Band / You're still the only girl in the world:
Rabin, Oscar & His Band / Turn over a new
leaf: Benson, Ivy / Tree in the meadow:
Benson, Ivy / I'm in the mood for love: Ben-
son, Ivy / I cover the waterfront: Benson, Ivy
/ I'll buy that dream: Preager, Lou & His Or-
chestra / I want to learn to dance: Preager,
Lou & His Orchestra / When the red, red
robin goes bob, bobbin' along:
Preager, Lou & His Orchestra / I'm so alone:
Fenoulhet, Paul & Skyrockets Dance Or-
chestra / I'll close my eyes: Fenoulhet, Paul

& Skyrockets Dance Orchestra / In Pinetop's footsteps: Fenhoulet, Paul & Skyrockets Dance Orchestra / Please don't say no: Fenhoulet, Paul & Skyrockets Dance Orchestra / It's dreamtime: Fenhoulet, Paul & Skyrockets Dance Orchestra / I don't care if I never dream again: Loss, Joe & His band / Gotta be this or that: Loss, Joe & His band / I'll be your sweetheart: Loss, Joe & His band / Lavender blue: Geraldo & His Dance Orchestra / Maria from Bahia: Geraldo & His Dance Orchestra / On a slow boat to China: Geraldo & His Dance Orchestra / After all: Geraldo & His Mayfair Music / You moved right in: Roy, Harry & His Orchestra / Cynthia's in love: Roy, Harry & His Orchestra / Out of the night: Roy, Harry & His Orchestra / Last waltz of the evening: Roy, Harry & His Orchestra / You red head: Dean, Syd & his Band / Dreamer's holiday: Dean, Syd & his Band / Monday, Tuesday, Wednesday: Dean, Syd & his Band / Red roses: Adam, Paul & His Mayfair Music / Put your shoes on Lucy: Adam, Paul & His Mayfair Music / Echo told me a lie: Adam, Paul & His Mayfair Music / Two lips: Adam, Paul & His Mayfair Music / How little it matters, how little we know: Winstone, Eric / I should care: Winstone, Eric / There must be a way: Foster, Teddy & The Band / I'm in love with two sweethearts: Foster, Teddy & The Band
CD Set _____ CDDL 1260
Music For Pleasure / May '94 / EMI.

DANGERHOUSE VOL.2
CD _____ 346402
Frontier / Aug '92 / Vital.

DANIEL POOLE - WORLD SOUND SYSTEMS
CD _____ TLCDPCD 001
TLC / Jan '96 / SRD.

DANISH TRAD JAZZ
CD _____ MECCACD 1006
Music Mecca / Aug '90 / Jazz Music / Cadillac / Wellard.

DANISH TRAD JAZZ VOLUME 2
CD _____ MECCACD 1031
Music Mecca / Nov '94 / Jazz Music / Cadillac / Wellard.

DANSE MACABRE SAMPLER
CD _____ EFA 11213
Danse Macabre / Apr '93 / SRD.

DARK EMPIRE STRIKES BACK
CD _____ DARK 005-2
Dark Empire / Apr '94 / SRD.

DARK HEARTS
CD _____ HHSP 006CD
Harthouse / Feb '95 / Disc / Warner Music.

DARK HEARTS II
CD _____ HHSP 009CD
Harthouse / Nov '95 / Disc / Warner Music.

DARK SIDE VOL 2
CD _____ REACTCD 032
React / Dec '93 / Vital.

DARN IT - POEMS BY PAUL HAINES/MUSIC BY MANY
CD _____ AMCL 1014
Normal/Okra / May '94 / Direct / ADA.

DAS MACH ICH MIT MUSIK
Das mach ich mit musik: Johns, Bibi / Die gipsy band: Johns, Bibi / Bimbo: Johns, Bibi / Billy boy: Sauer, Wolfgang & Angele Durand / Das klavier uber mir: Kuhn, Paul / Swing hei: Kuhn, Paul / Federball: Kuhn, Paul / Chanson d'amour: Durand, Angele / Sailor's boogie: Durand, Angele / Warum strahlen heut' nacht di sterne so hell: Sauer, Wolfgang / Liebe im april: Sauer, Wolfgang / Little rock: Durand, Angele & Bibi Johns / Bye bye baby: Durand, Angele & Bibi Johns / Ich mocht auf deiner hochzeit tanzen: Kuhn, Paul & Bibi Johns / Lillie boogie: Sauer, Rosita / Mitternachts blues: Schachtner, Heinz / Dein herz aus stein: De Vale, Mariette / Willy lilly rock a billy: Boswell, Eve / Paris dixie: Cordy, Annie / Ma belle mademoiselle: Constantine, Eddie
CD _____ BCD 15413
Bear Family / Dec '87 / Rollercoaster / Direct / CM / Swift / ADA.

DAUGHTERS OF TEXAS
Young and dumb / Breaking up somebody's home / In the mood / Say the wrong thing / Rock 'n' roll fever / Horny old buzzard, dirty old man / Your magic touch (quit working on me) / Nobody knows you (when you're down and out) / Walk rightin / I can tell I'm losing you / Stepping up in class / Breaking mama's rule / Ain't nobody gonna take my man
CD _____ CDTB 080
Thunderbolt / Jan '92 / Magnum Music Group.

DAYDREAM
(Summer Chart Party)
Build me up buttercup: Foundations / I'm gonna make you mine: Christie, Lou / Popcorn: Hot Butter / Daydream: Lovin' Spoonful / Waterloo sunset: Kinks / Yummy yummy yummy: Ohio Express / Mirrors: Oldfield, Sally / Isn't she lovely: Parton, David / Dancing on a Saturday night: Blue, Barry / Lady rose: Mungo Jerry / Ain't nothing but a house party: Showstoppers / Lazy

Sunday: Small Faces / Down the dustpipe: Status Quo / That same old feeling: Pickettywitch / Roadrunner: Richman, Jonathan & Modern Lovers / What have they done to my song Ma: Melanie / Who were you with in the moonlight: Dollar / Surfin' safari: Beach Boys / Mexico: Baldry, Long John
CD _____ TRTCD 144
TrueTrax / Oct '94 / THE.

DEAR OLD ERIN'S ISLE
CD _____ NI 5350
Nimbus / Sep '94 / Nimbus.

DEATH IS JUST THE BEGINNING III
(2CD & Video/2CD Sets)
CD Set _____ NB 1112
CD Set _____ NB 1119
Nuclear Blast / Jan '95 / Plastic Head.

DECADE OF CALLIGRAPH, A
Lady Jekyll and Mistress Hyde: Lyttelton, Humphrey / Black butterfly: Lyttelton, Humphrey / Caribana Queen: Lyttelton, Humphrey / Strange Mr Peter Charles: Lyttelton, Humphrey / My funny valentine: Lyttelton, Humphrey / Bad penny blues: Lyttelton, Humphrey / Happy go lucky local: Lyttelton, Humphrey / Jack the bear: Lyttelton, Humphrey / Madly: Lyttelton, Humphrey / Drop me off in Harlem: Shapiro, Helen / When a woman loves a man: Shapiro, Helen / Turner minor: Turner, Bruce / Buddy Tate from Texas State: Lyttelton, Humphrey & Buddy Tate / I got a pocket of dreams: Daniels, Maxine & Brian Lemon / Fascinating rhythm: Barnes, John / Down in honky tonk town: Lyttelton, Humphrey & Lillian Boutte / My Mama socks me: Davern, Kenny / Summertime: Lyttelton, Humphrey & Acker Bilk
CD _____ CLGCD 031
Calligraph / Oct '95 / Cadillac / Wellard / Jazz Music.

DECADE OF INSTRUMENTALS, 1959-1967
Entry of the gladiators: Nero & The Gladiators / Bongo rock: Jetstreams / Chariot: Stoller, Rhet / Taboo: Sounds Incorporated / Eclipse: Greenslade, Arthur & The Gee-men / Paella: Sunspots / Grumbling guitar: Other Two / Surfside: Revell, Digger & The Denver Men / Saturday jump: Midnight Shift / Stand up and say that: Nashville Five / Night train: Fifty Fingers Give Guitars / Stand and deliver: Snobs / Bogey man: Moontrekkers / I didn't know the gun was loaded: Cannons / Fugitive: Thunderbolts / Song of Mexico / Treck to Rome: Nero & The Gladiators / More like Nashville: Nashville Five / Savage (part 2): Sneaky Petes / Pop the whip: Dynamic Sounds / Mind reader: Howard, Johnny, Group / Curly: Bluesbreakers / Feeling in the mood (Only available on CD.): Thunderbolts / Hall of the mountain king (Only available on CD.): Nero & The Gladiators / Savage (Only available on CD.): Sneaky Petes / Sounds like locomotion (Only available on CD.): Sounds Incorporated
CD _____ SEECD 204
See For Miles/C5 / May '92 / Pinnacle.

DECK THE HALLS
CD _____ 15304
Laserlight / Nov '95 / Target/BMG.

DECONSTRUCTION CLASSICS
Ride on time: Black Box / Rhythm is a mystery: K-Klass / Anthem: N-Joi / Dream 17: Annette / Higher ground: Sasha / Confide in me: Minogue, Kylie / Sight for sore eyes: M People / Don't you want me: Felix / Open your mind: Usura / Texas cowboys: Grid / High: Hyper Go Go / Cantino: T-Coy / Movin' on up: M People / Infinity: Guru Josh / How can I love you more: M People / Packet of peace: Lion Rock / Love thing: Evolution / I'm in love: Sha-Lor / Everybody everybody: Black Box / Don't come to stay: Hot House / Sly one: Van-Rooy, Marina / Is there anybody out there: Bassheads / Future F.J.P.: Liaison D / Ajare: Way Out West / Girls and boys: Hed Boys / Swamp thing: Grid
CD _____ 74321299002
De-Construction / Aug '95 / BMG.

DEDICATED TO ANTONIO CARLOS JOBIM VOL.1
Samba de uma nota so (one note samba) / Desafinado / Chega de saudade (no more blues) / Corcovado (quiet nights) / Meditacao / O amor em paz / Insensatez (how insentative) / Outra vez (once again) / Dis scissao / O Grand amor / Vivo sonhando (dreamer) / Brigas, nunca maiss / So em tues bracos / So danca samba (I only dance samba) / Este seu olhar / A felicidade
CD _____ CD 62083
Saludos Amigos / Jun '96 / Target/BMG.

DEDICATED TO PLEASURE
Unchained melody: Righteous Brothers / After the love has gone: Earth, Wind & Fire / Between the sheets: Isley Brothers / Eternal flame: Bangles / Time to make you mine: Stansfield, Lisa / Show and tell: Pointer Sisters / Show me heaven: McKee, Maria / She makes my day: Palmer, Robert / Make yourself comfortable: Vaughan, Sarah / Lovin' you: Riperton, Minnie / Moments of pleasure: Bush, Kate / Love don't live here anymore: Nail, Jimmy / Sexual healing: Gaye, Marvin / We have all the time in the world: Armstrong, Louis / Get here: Adams, Oleta / Save the best for last: Williams, Vanessa / Tracks of my tears: Go West / Move closer:

Nelson, Phyllis / Every breath you take: Police / Slave to love: Ferry, Bryan / I want your sex: Michael, George / Crazy: Seal / You gotta be: Des'ree / Close to you: Priest, Maxi / Two can play that game: Brown, Bobby / Midnight at the Oasis: Brand New Heavies / Fever: Lee, Peggy / Thinking about your love: Thomas, Kenny / Oh, baby I: Eternal / Listen to your heart: Roxette / Why can't I wake up with you: Take That / Independent love song: Scarlet / I get weak: Carlisle, Belinda / Fool (If you think it's over): Rea, Chris / All of my heart: ABC / You're all that matters to me: Stigers, Curtis / Age of loneliness (Carly's song): Enigma / Do you really want to hurt me: Culture Club / Life on your own: Human League / It must be love: Madness
CD _____ CDEMTV 91
EMI / Jul '95 / EMI.

DEDICATED TO THE ONE I LOVE
CD _____ MCCD 087
Music Club / Dec '92 / Disc / THE / CM.

DEDICATED TO YOU
(18 More Songs From The Heart)
Coward of the county: Rogers, Kenny / I will always love you: Parton, Dolly / Have I told you lately that I love you: Reeves, Jim / Roses are red: O'Donnell, Daniel / Who's sorry now: Francis, Connie / Years from now / I don't know why I love you: Rose Marie / Blanket on the ground: Spears, Billie Jo / Honey: Goldsboro, Bobby / Crystal chandeliers: Price, Charley / Sunshine of your smile: Berry, Mike / You are my sunshine: Boxcar Willie / Love is like a butterfly: Parton, Dolly / I need you: O'Donnell, Daniel / Green apples: Miller, Roger / Single girl: Posey, Sandy / Last farewell: Whittaker, Roger
CD _____ PLATCD 3901
Platinum Music / Oct '88 / Prism / Ross.

DEEJAY'S DELITE
CD _____ 504582
Declic / Nov '95 / Jetstar.

DEEP BLUE
(Rounder 25th Anniversary Blues Anthology)
CD _____ ROUCDAN 20
Rounder / Nov '95 / CM / Direct / ADA / Cadillac.

DEEP BLUES
Jumper on the line: Burnside, R.L. / Jr. Blues: Jr. Kimborough / Catfish blues: Johnson, Big Jack / Daddy, when is Momma coming home: Johnson, Big Jack / Big boy now: Johnson, Big Jack / Midnight prowler: Frost, Frank / You can talk about me: Hemphill, Jessie Mae / Shame on you: Hemphill, Jessie Mae / Long haired doney: Burnside, R.L. / Heartbroken man: Barnes, Roosevelt / Ain't gonna worry about tomorrow: Barnes, Roosevelt / Love like I wanna: Barnes, Roosevelt / Terraplane blues: Pitchford, Lonnie / If I had possessed over judgement day: Pitchford, Lonnie / Devil blues: Owens, Jack & Bud Spires
CD _____ 450991981-2
WEA / Mar '93 / Warner Music.

DEEP DISTRAXION
Geera: Monumental / Not gonna do it: S1000 / Do one more: Spoonio / Mandala: Monumental / Stoneage: Floorjam / Who's in the house: S1000 / Viewfinder: Back II Front / Deep distraxion: Floorjam / I'm gonna get you: Hook Line & Sinker / Ibiza: Back II Front / By dawn's early light: Thee Madkatt Courtship / Lego beat: Happy Larry
CD _____ SLIKCD 002
Deep Distraxion/Profile / Jul '94 / Pinnacle.

DEEP DOWN IN FLORIDA
(TK Deep Soul)
All because of your love: Clay, Otis / Honey honey: Hudson, David / Sometimes: Facts Of Life / If he hadn't slipped up and got caught: Patterson, Bobby / Sweet woman's love: Clay, Otis / God blessed our love: Allen, Charles / All I need is you: Clay, Otis / I've tried it all: Meadows Bros. / Baby I cried cried cried: Johnson, Charles / Today my whole world felt: Clay, Otis / It's never too late: Willie & Anthony / Let me in: Clay, Otis / Love on the phone: Mitchell, John / Caught in the act: Facts Of Life / Love you save: Williams, Lee Shot / When I'm loving you: Hudson, David / Special kind of love: Clay, Otis
CD _____ NEMCD 721
Sequel / Mar '95 / BMG.

DEEP DOWN SOUTH
CD _____ CDRB 29
Charly / Nov '95 / Charly / THE / Cadillac.

DEEP GREEN
Save a place for me / Deep green: Carlin how / Old man of the ocean: Skinningrove bay / North country girl / Kilten castle / Abbess St. Hilda
CD _____ FG 2803
Frog / Dec '95 / Total/BMG.

DEEP IN JUNGLE TERRITORY
CD _____ DMUT 1317
Multitone / Mar '95 / BMG.

DEEP IN THE HEART OF TEXAS
Deep in the heart of Texas: Kevin & The Blacktears / Let somebody else drive: Kevin & The Blacktears / Will you love me manana: Saldana, Sir Doug / Whiter shade of pale:

Saldana, Sir Doug / Black cat: Beall, Charlie / Take a walk in the rain: Kosub, Kevin / Loco vaquero: Jimenez, Flaco / Joint is jumpin': Meyers, Augie / I don't get the blues when I'm stoned: Dogman & The Shepherds / Mexico: Torres, Toby / I got it: Mike The Leadsinger
CD _____ CDZ 2016
Zu Zazz / Apr '94 / Rollercoaster.

DEEP IN THE PHILLY GROOVE
La la means I love you / I need your love so bad / So long, goodbye, it's over / When times are bad / Goodbye pain / Face the future / Didn't I / One and one is five / When the bottom falls out / Follow the lamb / Not goin' to let you (Talk to me that way) / Didn't we make it / Puff puff, you're gone / Ruby Lee / You are my sun sign part 1 / Handle with care / I want to be your lover / Player / Armed and extremely dangerous / Smarty pants / Delfonics theme / Can't go on living
CD _____ CDKEND 115
Kent / May '94 / Pinnacle.

DEEP JAZZ TRIP
Night tripper (CD only.): Donato, Joao / Soul village (CD only.): Bishop, Walter Jr. / Rafiki (CD only.): Creque, Neal / Swamp demon: Barron, Kenny / Murilley: Earland, Charles / Freedom jazz dance: Jefferson, Eddie / Good shepherd: Garnett, Carlos / Taurus woman: Garnett, Carlos / Banks of the nile (CD only.): Garnett, Carlos / Old man Moses: Green, Grant
CD _____ PHOCD 8002
Muse / Sep '95 / New Note / CM.

DEEP SOUTH BLUES PIANO 1935-1937
CD _____ DOCD 5233
Blues Document / May '94 / Swift / Jazz Music / Hot Shot.

DEEPER INTO THE VAULT
CD _____ CDMFN 124
Music For Nations / Nov '91 / Pinnacle.

DEEPEST SHADE OF TECHNO VOL. 1
CD _____ REFCD 001
Reflective / Apr '94 / SRD.

DEEPEST SOUL
I'm lonely: Sanders, Nelson / You got me on a string: Freeman Brothers / You should have told me: New Yorkers / I'll be gone: Turner, Tommy / Just a little more love: Soul Commanders / Love as true as mine: Rockers Band / I've learned my lesson: Richardson, Donald Lee / Don't waste my time: Sinceres / Ain't gonna do you no good: Willis, Betty / These feelings: Phil & Del / Helpless girl: Staten, Little Mary / Whole lot of tears: Stuart, Jeb / Pick yourself up: Taylor, E.G. & The Sound of Soul / I'm still hurt: Little Tom / Human: Ad Libs / I worship the ground you walk on: Ad Libs / Teach me to love again: Scott, Kurtis / It won't hurt: Bogen, Richard / I'll be there: Tenderonies / Please come back: Tate, Jimmy / Make the best of what you've got: Patton, Alexander / I'm beggin' you baby: Vibra-Tones & George Johnson / Never let me go: Vibra-Tones & George Johnson
CD _____ GSCD 016
Goldmine / Jul '93 / Vital.

DEEPEST SOUL VOLUME 2
This beautiful day: Jackson, Levi / Serving a sentence of life: Douglas, Carl / Beautiful night: Thomas, Jimmy / What love brings: Bernard, Kenny / I'll hold you: Frankie & Johnny / Don't pity me: Lynn, Sue / Lost summer love: Silva, Lorraine / Our love is wonderful: Parfit, Paula / Stop and you'll become aware: Shapiro, Helen / Nobody knows: St. John, Tammy / Everything's gonna be alright: Arnold, P.P. / Invitation: Band Of Angels / If you knew me: Keyes, Ebony / Number one in your heart: Goins, Herbie / Need your love: Notations / Movin away: Lynch, Kenny / Baby I don't need your love: Chants / Stand accused: Colton, Tony / Never ever: Clements, Soul Joe / Tears of joy: Merrell, Ray
CD _____ GSCD 041
Goldmine / Jan '95 / Vital.

DEF JAM 10TH ANNIVERSARY BOX SET
(4CD Set)
CD Set _____ 5238482
Def Jam / Nov '95 / PolyGram.

DEFINITION OF HARDCORE
CD _____ RIVCD 3
Reinforced / Sep '93 / SRD.

DEFINITIVE AMBIENT COLLECTION VOL 1
(Featuring Pete Namlook)
CD _____ RSNCD 13
Rising High / Feb '94 / Disc.

DEFINITIVE COLLECTION OF IRISH BALLADS VOL. 1
(2CD/MC Set)
CD Set _____ BALLAD 001CD
Outlet / Aug '94 / ADA / Duncans / CM / Ross / Direct / Koch.

DEFINITIVE COLLECTION OF IRISH BALLADS VOL. 2
(2CD/MC Set)
CD Set _____ BALLAD 002CD
Outlet / Aug '94 / ADA / Duncans / CM / Ross / Direct / Koch.

DEFINITIVE HOUSE FOR ALL
CD _____ XTR 16CD
X:Treme / Jul '95 / Pinnacle / SRD.

DEL-FI AND DONNA STORY, THE
Hippy hippy shake: Romero, Chan / I don't care now more: Romero, Chan / I want some more: Romero, Chan / My little Ruby: Romero. Chan / That's my little Suzie: Valens, Ritchie / La Bamba: Valens, Ritchie / My babe: Holden, Ron / Love you so: Holden, Ron / Jungle fever: Shadows / Under stars of love: Shadows / Humours: Crawford, Johnny / Proud: Crawford, Johnny / Little cupid: Carlos Brothers / Gonna see my baby: Addrisi Brothers / Cherrystone: Addrisi Brothers / Back to the old salt mine: Addrisi Brothers / Marie: Dale, Dick / Untouchables: Hall, Rene / Fast freight: Valens, Ritchie / Blabbermouth: Fantastics / Is it a dream: Flamingo, Johnny / When I do the mashed potato: Bright, Larry / Little more wine my dear: Hawks / To be loved (forever): Pentagons / Everything's gonna be alright: Holden, Ron / Please please please: Ronnie & The Pomona Casuals / Misirlou: Lively Ones / Big surf: Sentinals / Okie surfer: Gates, David / Original surferstomp: Johnstone, Bruce / KRLA jingle: Surfettes
CD _____ CDCHD 313
Ace / Jul '91 / Pinnacle / Cadillac / Complete/Pinnacle.

DELICIOUS TOGETHER
CD _____ CDCD 1270
Charly / Oct '95 / Charly / THE / Cadillac.

DELIRIUM PRESENTS AFTER 6AM
CD _____ DELACD 02
Delirium / Jan '94 / Plastic Head.

DELIRIUM PRESENTS AFTER 6AM VOL.2
CD _____ DELACD 03
Delirium / May '95 / Plastic Head.

DELMARK 40TH ANNIVERSARY - BLUES
CD _____ DXCD 2
Delmark / Aug '93 / Hot Shot / ADA / CM / Direct / Cadillac.

DEMAGNETIZED
CD _____ MAGNETCD 13
Magnetic North / Nov '95 / SRD / ADA.

DER KLANG DER FAMILLE
CD _____ NOMU 4CD
Nova Mute / Jul '92 / Disc.

DEREK LAWRENCE SESSIONS, THE (TAKE 1)
CD _____ LICD 901118
Line / Aug '95 / CM / Grapevine / ADA / Conifer / Direct.

DEREK LAWRENCE SESSIONS, THE (TAKE 2)
CD _____ 901119
Line / Aug '95 / CM / Grapevine / ADA / Conifer / Direct.

DESPERATE ROCK'N'ROLL VOL.1
CD _____ FLAMECD 001
Flame / Jul '95 / SRD.

DESPERATE ROCK'N'ROLL VOL.2
CD _____ FLAMECD 002
Flame / Jul '95 / SRD.

DESPERATE ROCK'N'ROLL VOL.3
CD _____ FLAMECD 003
Flame / Jul '95 / SRD.

DESPERATE ROCK'N'ROLL VOL.4
CD _____ FLAMECD 004
Flame / Jul '95 / SRD.

DESPERATE ROCK'N'ROLL VOL.5
CD _____ FLAMECD 005
Flame / Sep '95 / SRD.

DESTINATION BOMP
CD Set _____ BCD 40482
Bomp / Jan '95 / Pinnacle.

DETROIT SOUL FROM THE VAULTS VOL.1
Soul sloopy: Dynamics / Yes I love you baby (Inst.): Dynamics / Head and shoulders: Young, Patti / Love keeps falling away: Williams, Lloyd & Highlights / It won't matter at all: Williams, Lloyd & Highlights / Arabia (Inst.): Royal Playboys / What's wrong with your love (#2): Metros / Don't let her give you some of her love: Metros / It's real: Sanders, Nelson / Music in my soul: Milner, Reggie / Make a change: Rogers, Johnny / Soul food (Inst.): Rogers, Johnny / Open the door to your heart: Burdick, Doni / I have faith in you: Burdick, Doni / Give my heart a break: Turner, Sammy / Fascinating girl (Inst.): Lemons, George / We go to pieces (Inst.): Hairston, Forest / Love to a guy: Dynamics / Keep a hold on me: Lewis, Diane / Kangaroo dance: Williams, Lloyd & Highlights / Opposites attract: Swingers / I'll be on my way: Bob & Ford
CD _____ GSCD 019
Goldmine / Aug '93 / Vital.

DETROIT SOUL FROM THE VAULTS VOL.2
Yes I love you baby: Dynamics / Head and shoulders: Young, Patti / I've got that feelin': Garcia, Frankie / Lovin' touch: Satin Dolls / First degree love: Vaughan, Lafayette / Arabia: Royal Playboys / What's wrong with your love (#1): Metros / We still have

time: Metros / Candle: Burdick, Doni / What'cha gonna do: Burdick, Doni / Make a change (inst): Rogers, Johnny / Soul food: Rogers, Johnny / If you walk out of my life: Burdick, Doni / Heart break: Burdick, Doni / Merry go round: Frontera, Tommy / Fascinating girl: Lemons, George / We go to pieces: Hairston, Forest / Whenever I'm without you: Dynamics / Nobody likes me: White, Willie / Go down: Highlights / Lookin' for a woman: Brooks Brothers / I'll be on my way: Bob & Ford
CD _____ GSCD 020
Goldmine / Aug '93 / Vital.

DETROIT SOUL OF POPCORN WYLIE, THE
Sweet darlin': Clark, Joe / Going to a deal: Neal, Tommy / Quit twistin' my arm: Mitchell, Stanley / It's OK with me: Wright, Larry / Just can't leave you: Hester, Tony / Save my lovin' for you: People's Choice / Stone broke: Ward, Sam / With a lonely heart: 4 Voices / Such a soul stays: Third Party / Cool off: Detroit Executives / Rosemary: Wylie, Richard 'Popcorn' / My baby ain't no plaything: New Holidays / You better go go: Lucas, Matt / Say it isn't so: Boo, Betty / Down in the dumps: Hester, Tony / Hold your horses: Clarke, Jimmy / I'll make you mine: Valiant Trio / Spaceland: Hester, Tony / Spellbound: Boo, Betty / Angelina, Angelina: Ames, Stuart / Hanky panky: Wylie, Richard 'Popcorn' / I'll be your champion: Hester, Tony / Hurting: Eric & The Vikings / Stop that boy: Boo, Betty / King for a day: Ames, Stuart
CD _____ GSCD 030
Goldmine / Mar '94 / Vital.

DEUTSCHES JAZZ FESTIVAL 1954-1955 (8CD Set)
Jennie's ball: 2 Beat Stompers / Flamingo: Strasser, Hugo / Fine and dandy: Koller, Hans New Jazz Stars / Just you, just me: Edelhagen All Stars / Is you is or is you ain't my baby: Valente, Caterina / I never knew: Hipp, Jutta Combo / Creole love call: Bunge, Fred Star Band / September song: Kuhn, Rolf All Stars / Jazz time net: Edelhagen, Kurt / Paul's festival blues: Kuhn, Paul Quartet / Lullaby of Birdland: Rediske, Johannes Quintet / Klagita: Schonberger, Heinz / Festival jump: Valente, Caterina / Get out of here: Spree City Stompers / Just a blues: Spree City Stompers / Just a closer walk with thee: Spree City Stompers / St. James infirmary: Spree City Stompers / Eight bar blues: Spree City Stompers / That da da strain: Spree City Stompers / Mississippi mud: 2 Beat Stompers / Got no blues: 2 Beat Stompers / Panama: 2 Beat Stompers / Black bottom blues: 2 Beat Stompers / I'm confessin' that I love you: 2 Beat Stompers / Music goes round and round: 2 Beat Stompers / Manuskript blues: Haensch, Delle Jump Combo / Blue moon: Haensch, Delle Jump Combo / There's no one but you: Haensch, Delle Jump Combo / Hey good lookin': Haensch, Delle Jump Combo / Flamingo special: Haensch, Delle Jump Combo / There's no blue: Haensch, Delle Jump Combo / You go to my head: Edelhagen, Kurt / Jazz 55: Edelhagen, Kurt / Nancy and the colonel: Edelhagen, Kurt / Light stuff: Edelhagen, Kurt / Stuff lover: Edelhagen, Kurt / Flying home: Edelhagen, Kurt / My funny valentine: Edelhagen, Kurt / I ain't gonna tell you: Edelhagen, Kurt / Don't blame me: Edelhagen, Kurt / Time: Edelhagen, Kurt / Purple hyazinth: Edelhagen, Kurt / All the things you are: Francesco, Silvio Quartet / Long journey: Francesco, Silvio Quartet / Ain't misbehavin': Francesco, Silvio Quartet / Lagwood walk: Buschmann, Glen Quartet / All of me: Buschmann, Glen Quartet / Farewell blues: Buschmann, Glen Quartet / St. Louis blues: Buschmann, Glen Quartet / Blue prelude: Buschmann, Glen Quartet / For you my love: Buschmann, Glen Quartet / Just one of those things: Buschmann, Glen Quartet / Shine: Buschmann, Glen Quartet / Embraceable you: Buschmann, Glen Quartet / Berlin blues: Buschmann, Glen Quartet / Too marvellous for words: Kuhn, Rolf Quartet / Frankfurt blues (now's the time): Kuhn, Rolf Quartet / Hipp noses: Hipp, Jutta Quartet / Song is you: Hipp, Jutta Quartet / Indian Summer: Hipp, Jutta Quartet / Cool talk: Hipp, Jutta Quartet / These foolish things: Hipp, Jutta Quartet / Gone with the wind: Hipp, Jutta Quartet / Jutta: Koller, Hans New Jazz Stars / Iris: Koller, Hans New Jazz Stars / When your lover has gone: Koller, Hans New Jazz Stars / Porsche: Koller, Hans New Jazz Stars / Squeeze me: Brandt, Helmut Combo / Sum: Brandt, Helmut Combo / Breeze and I: Brandt, Helmut Combo / I can't believe that you're in love with me: Brandt, Helmut Combo / Out of nowhere: Wenig, Erhard Quartet / Tenor jump: Wenig, Erhard Quartet / September riff: Wenig, Erhard Quartet / Cynthia's in love: Christmann, Freddy Quartet / As long as there's music: Christmann, Freddy Quartet / Passe: Christmann, Freddy Quartet / Theme in B: Lauth, Wolfgang Quartet / Tomorrow: Lauth, Wolfgang Quartet / Cool march: Lauth, Wolfgang Quartet / Cave souvenir: Lauth, Wolfgang Quartet / Jumpin' with Symphony Sid: Lehn, Erwin / Blues intermezzo: Lehn, Erwin / Gerry walks: Lehn, Erwin / Cool Street: Lehn, Erwin / Autumn nocturne: Lehn, Erwin /

Conference mit mosch: Lehn, Erwin / What is this thing called love: Lehn, Erwin / Blues for Tenorsaxophon: Lehn, Erwin / Lester leaps in: Lehn, Erwin / E.V.G.: Lehn, Erwin / Indikativ: Banter, Harald Ensemble / Moon over Miami: Banter, Harald Ensemble / Autumn in New York: Banter, Harald Ensemble / Tabu jump: Banter, Harald Ensemble / Polyphonia: Banter, Harald Ensemble / Nature boy: Banter, Harald Ensemble / Happy days are here again: Banter, Harald Ensemble / To dance or not to dance: New Jazz Group Hannover / I only have eyes for you: New Jazz Group Hannover / Continuation: New Jazz Group Hannover / Cloe: Rediske, Johannes Quintet / Boptical illusion: Rediske, Johannes Quintet / Sweet Georgia Brown: Rediske, Johannes Quintet / Thou swell: Kuhn, Paul Quintet / Dancing in the dark: Kuhn, Paul Quintet / Delaunay's dilemma: Rediske, Johannes Quintet / Jumpin' at the rosengarten: Rediske, Johannes Quintet / Flip: Rediske, Johannes Quintet / Ghost of a chance: Rediske, Johannes Quintet / Crazy rhythm: Rediske, Johannes Quintet
CD Set _____ BCD 15430
Bear Family / Oct '90 / Rollercoaster / Direct / CM / Swift / ADA.

DEVOLUTION ALTERNATIVE ROCK CLASS
CD _____ DEVOCD 1
Big Life / Mar '95 / Pinnacle.

DEVOTED TO YOU (16 Songs From The Heart)
Crazy: Cline, Patsy / Some broken hearts never mend: Williams, Don / Happy anniversary: Whitman, Slim / Wheel of fortune: Rose Marie / She wears my ring: King, Solomon / Your, Tony, Timi / With pen in hand: Carr, Vikki / Devoted to you: Everly Brothers / Sing me an old fashioned song: Spears, Billie Jo / Have I got some blues for you: Pride, Charley / I will love you all my life: Foster & Allen / Pal of my cradle days: Breen, Ann / When I leave the world behind: Rose Marie / I fall to pieces: Cline, Patsy / All I'm missing is you: Williams, Don / So sad no watch good love go bad: Everly Brothers / Ebony eyes: Everly Brothers / Love hurts: Everly Brothers
CD _____ PLATCD 21
Platinum Music / Apr '88 / Prism / Ross.

DEWAR'S BAGPIPE FESTIVAL
CD _____ KFWCD 133
Knitting Factory / Nov '94 / Grapevine.

DIALOGUES
Frissell frazzle / Calypso Joe / Uncle Ed / Snowbound / Dream steps / Bon Ami / Stern stuff / Skylark / Simple things / Dialogue
CD _____ CD 83369
Telarc / Nov '95 / Conifer / ADA.

DIAMOND JUBILEE PIPE BAND CHAMPIONSHIPS
CD _____ CDMON 809
Monarch / Sep '90 / CM / ADA / Duncans / Direct.

DIE NOW (Engine/Blackout Sampler)
Not waving, drowning: Sheer Terror / Booze cabana: Goops / Running with scissors: Deadguy / Morning breath: Sweet Diesel / Faith healer: Outpour / Grounded ex-patriot: New Bomb Turks / I got your numbers: Cringing I titmon / Wait till the brute Killin' Time / Temple body: Crawlpappy / Hard way: Outburst / Harsh truth: Icemen
CD _____ EB 024ECD
Engine / Aug '95 / Vital.

DIGGIN' IN THE CRATES (Profile Rap Classics Volume 1)
Sucker MC's (Krush-groove 1): Run DMC / King MC: Word Of Mouth & DJ Cheese / Genius rap: Dr. Jekyll & Mr. Hyde / Drag rap: Showboys / Fly guy: Pebblee-Poo / I can't wait (To rock the mike): Spyder D & DJ Doc / Beat bop: Rammelzee Vs.K-Rob / Here comes that beat: Pumpkin & The Profile All Stars / Rock box: Run DMC / Lifestyles Of The Fresh And Fly: MC. Dollar Bill / Fresh: Fresh 3 MC's / Nightmares: Dane, Dana
CD _____ FILERCD 449
Profile / Jun '94 / Pinnacle.

DIGITAL SHOWCASE
Musket volley / Fanfare- the 300th / Victory drums / In the hall of the mountain king / King cotton / A-Team / I got rhythm / Hornucopia / Two little finches / Lucy Long / Early one morning / Drumsticks for two / Nobilmente / March: 1st suite for military band / To seek and strike / Last starfighter / Stars and stripes forever / Finlandia / Mars god of war / Artillery salvoes
CD _____ BNA 5005
Bandleader / Nov '86 / Conifer.

DIGNITY OF HUMAN BEING IS VULNERABLE
CD _____ AWA 1993CD
Konkurrel / May '93 / SRD.

DIMENSION 2
CD _____ EFA 200872
Trip Trap / Jul '95 / SRD.

DINNER AT EIGHT (The Great London Dance Bands)
Dancing in the dark / Without rhythm / This'll make you whistle / Honey coloured moon / Star fell out of heaven / You turned the tables on me / You / I won't dance / It's easy to remember / Dinner at eight / My romance / Zing, went the strings of my heart / One, two, button your shoe / Toy trumpet / Soft lights and sweet music / Alone / Nice work if you can get it / When you've got a little springtime in your heart / Tinkle, tinkle, tinkle / Over my shoulder / Not bad / Here's to the next time / Auf wiedersehen, my dear / Smoke gets in your eyes / Keep a twinkle in your eye
CD _____ PLCD 539
President / Oct '95 / Grapevine / Target/ BMG / Jazz Music / President.

DINNER JAZZ
CD _____ MUSCD 024
MCI / Nov '94 / Disc / THE.

DIRECT HITS FROM BULLSEYE
CD _____ BB 9001CD
Bullseye / May '93 / Bullseye / ADA.

DIRTY HOUSE
CD _____ CDHIGH 2
Passion / Nov '95 / Pinnacle / 3MV.

DIRTY ROCK VOL 1
CD _____ KNEWCD 736
Kenwest / Apr '94 / THE.

DIRTY ROCK VOL 2
CD _____ KNEWCD 737
Kenwest / Apr '94 / THE.

DISAGREEMENT OF THE PEOPLE, THE
Ain't but just one way: Cope, Julian / Justice/injustice: Chumbawamba / Guildford Four: White, Andy / Won't get fooled away: McNabb, Ian / Birmingham six: Pogues / All our trades: Tabor, June / How can you keep moving on: McLeod, Rory / Electro Ray's: Back To The Planet / Hobo: Reservoir Frogs / Men of England: New Model Army & Joolz / One green hill: Oyster Band / Babylon: Det-Ri-Mental / Clay jugg: Leven, Jackie & Mike Scott / Stonehenge: Poison Girls / Pastor Niemoler's lament (Never Again): Kitchens Of Distinction / Come dancing: Credit To The Nation / This land: Bragg, Billy
CD _____ COOKCD 088
Cooking Vinyl / Jun '95 / Vital.

DISAPPEARING WORLD, THE
CD _____ CDSDL 376
Saydisc / Mar '94 / Harmonia Mundi / ADA / Direct.

DISCLOSURE - VOICES OF WOMEN
CD _____ NAR 067 CD
New Alliance / May '93 / Pinnacle.

DISCO DANCE CATS
CD _____ 12547
Laserlight / Jul '95 / Target/BMG.

DISCO DAZE
CD _____ MATCD 261
Castle / May '93 / BMG.

DISCO DYNAMITE
CD _____ CDCD 1219
Charly / Jun '95 / Charly / THE / Cadillac.

DISCO EXPLOSION
CD _____ GRF 211
Tring / Apr '93 / Tring / Prism.

DISCO FEVER
Get up offa that thing: Brown, James / I love the nightlife (Disco round): Bridges, Alicia / Rock the boat: Hues Corporation / That's the way I like it: K.C. & The Sunshine Band / Ladies night: Kool & The Gang / Right back where we started from: Nightingale, Maxine / Hustle: McCoy, Van / I'm on fire: 5000 Volts / Yes sir, I can boogie: Baccara / Best disco in town's: Ritchie Family / I was made for dancin': Garrett, Leif / Do what you wanna do: Elliman, Yvonne / Don't push it, don't force it: Haywood, Leon / Hang on in there baby: Bristol, Johnny / Ms. Grace: Tymes / Rock your baby: McCrae, George / Disco queen: Hot Chocolate / More than a woman: Tavares / You're the first, the last, my everything: White, Barry
CD _____ CDPR 110
Music For Pleasure / Jun '93 / EMI.

DISCO HEAT
Use it up and wear it out: Odyssey / Car wash: Rose Royce / More, more, more: Andrea True Connection / You can do it: Hudson, Al & The Partners / Do the Spanish hustle: Fatback Band / Shame, shame, shame: Shirley & Company / Higher and higher: Wilson, Jackie / Sending out an S.O.S.: Wilson, Jackie / You make me feel (Mighty real): Sylvester / Shaft: Hayes, Isaac / I'll take you there: Staple Singers / My man, a sweet man: Jackson, Millie / Shame: King, Evelyn 'Champagne' / Rock the boat: Hues Corporation / Disco stomp: Bohannon, Hamilton / Walking in rhythm: Blackbyrds
CD _____ PWKS 4148
Carlton Home Entertainment / Oct '94 / Carlton Home Entertainment.

DISCO INFERNO
CD _____ GRF 212
Tring / Mar '93 / Tring / Prism.

DISCO INFERNO
Lost in music: *Sister Sledge* / Le Freak: *Chic* / You make me feel (mighty real): *Sylvester* / I'm every woman: *Khan, Chaka* / Young hearts run free: *Staton, Candi* / Is it love you're after: *Rose Royce* / Jump to the beat: *Lattisaw, Stacy* / Working my way back to you: *Detroit Spinners* / Here I go again: *Bell, Archie* / Supernature: *Cerrone* / Disco Inferno: *Trammps* / dance, dance, dance: *Chic* / Nights on Broadway: *Staton, Candi* / Lover's holiday: *Change* / I shoulda loved ya: *Walden, Narada Michael* / Then came you: *Warwick, Dionne & The Detroit Spinners* / Spacer: *Devotion, Sheila B.* / Searching: *Change* / We are family: *Sister Sledge* / Shaft: *Hayes, Isaac*
CD _____ 9548319632
East West / Jul '95 / Warner Music.

DISCO INFERNO 2
Shame: *King, Evelyn 'Champagne'* / Funkin' for Jamaica: *Browne, Tom* / Thinking of you: *Sister Sledge* / Native New Yorker: *Odyssey* / I'll be around: *Detroit Spinners* / Keep the fire burning: *McCrae, Gwen* / Love has come around: *Byrd, Donald* / You're a star: *Aquarian Dream* / Southern Freeez: *Freeez* / He's the greatest dancer: *Sister Sledge* / Everybody dance: *Chic* / It makes you feel like dancin': *Rose Royce* / Just a touch of love: *Slave* / Glow of love: *Change* / Ghetto child: *Detroit Spinners* / Funky nassau: *Beginning Of The End* / Get up and boogie: *Silver Convention* / Funky sensation: *McCrae, Gwen* / Forget me nots: *Rushen, Patrice*
CD _____ 954832423-2
East West / Dec '93 / Warner Music.

DISCO MIXES
CD _____ JHD 087
Tring / Mar '93 / Tring / Prism.

DISCO NIGHTS
Disco nights: *G.Q.* / Car wash: *Rose Royce* / Boogie wonderland: *Earth, Wind & Fire* / Rock the boat: *Hues Corporation* / Use it up wear it out: *Odyssey* / Turn the beat around: *Robinson, Vickie Sue* / Ms. Grace: *Tymes* / Which way is up: *Starguard* / Shame: *King, Evelyn* / Instant replay: *Hartman, Dan* / Hi fidelity: *Kids from Fame* / Daddy cool: *Boney M* / One way ticket: *Eruption* / Givin' up givin' in: *Three Degrees* / You're more than a number in my little red book: *Drifters* / Disco lady: *Taylor, Johnny* / Everybody up: *Ohio Players* / Y.M.C.A.: *Village People*
CD _____ 74321290382
Ariola / Jun '97 / BMG.

DISCO TECH
Papillon: *Vandross, Luther & Cissy Houston* / More, more, more (parts 1 & 2): *Andrea True Connection & Samantha Fox* / Paradise diamond: *Vandross, Luther & Cissy Houston* / Chain diamonds: *Vandross, Luther & Cissy Houston* / Cream always rises to the top diamond: *Vandross, Luther & Cissy Houston* / More, more more (part 3): *Bananarama* / Hot butterfly: *Khan, Chaka* / Risky diamond: *Bionic Boogie* / Starcruiser diamond: *Starcruiser Band* / Fancy dancer diamond: *Starcruiser Band* / Tiger, tiger: *Vandross, Luther & Cissy Houston* / Crazy luck diamond: *Vandross, Luther* / Most of all diamond: *Gaynor, Gloria*
CD _____ CDPS 001
Pulsar / Sep '95 / Magnum Music Group.

DISCOVER NARADA
From the forge to the field: *Arkenstone, David, Kostia & David Lanz* / Day by day by day: *Mann, Brian* / Americana: *Rubaja, Bernardo* / Behind the waterfall/Desert rain: *Lanz, David* / Rug merchant: *Arkenstone, David* / Millennium theme: *Zimmer, Hans* / Seven days: *Koble, Martin* / Parterre: *Tingstad, Eric & Nancy Rumbel* / Simple joys: *Souther, Richard* / Overture: *Miorowitz, Sheldon* / Lament for Hetch Hetchy: *Fraser, Alasdair* / New amazon: *Junior Homrich* / Stand and water: *Kostia* / Nebraska: *Buffett, Peter* / Hawk: *Trapezoid* / Endings: *Jones, Michael*
CD _____ CD 9002
Narada / Jun '92 / New Note / ADA.

DISCOVER NARADA 2
CD _____ ND 69008
Narada / Nov '93 / New Note / ADA.

DISCOVER SCOTLAND VOL.1
Original: *Carmichael, John & His Band* / Kathleen's reel: *Carmichael, John & His Band* / Bauaria: *Carmichael, John & His Band* / Dixie: *Carmichael, John & His Band* / Do you think you could love me again: *MacLeod, Jim & His Band* / Skye boat song: *Scott, Tommy Strings of Scot* / Richmora: *Oakbank Sound* / Pomander jig: *Oakbank Sound* / Wee sergeant: *Oakbank Sound* / Rab Smillies J.G: *Oakbank Sound* / Maggie: *Gillies, Alasdair* / Silver darlin': *Marlettes* / Marie's wedding: *Garden, Bill & His Highland Fiddle Orchestra* / Vist tramping songs: *Garden, Bill & His Highland Fiddle Orchestra* / Marquis of inverity: *Garden, Bill & His Highland Fiddle Orchestra* / Roxburgh Castle: *Garden, Bill & His Highland Fiddle Orchestra* / Scotland the brave: *Garden, Bill & His Highland Fiddle Orchestra* / From Scotland with love: *Scott, Tommy Strings of Scot* / Wild mountain thyme: *Marlettes* / Marching through the heather: *Frazer, Grant* / Johnny lad: *Frazer, Grant* / Flower of Scotland: *Frazer, Grant* / Jig time: *Garden, Bill &*

His Highland Fiddle Orchestra / McFlannels. Garden, Bill & His Highland Fiddle Orchestra / Para Handy: *Garden, Bill & His Highland Fiddle Orchestra* / Man's a man for a' that: *Harper, Addie & The Wick Trio* / Scots wha hae: *Harper, Addie & The Wick Trio* / Auld lang syne: *Harper, Addie & The Wick Trio* / I love a lassie: *Anderson, Stuart* / Roamin' in the gloamin': *Anderson, Stuart* / Wee Deoch an' Doris: *Anderson, Stuart* / Stop your ticklin' Jock: *Anderson, Stuart* / Keep right on to the end of the road: *Anderson, Stuart* / Denny and Dunipace Pipe Band: *Denny & Dunipace Pipe Band* / Major Bobby: *Denny & Dunipace Pipe Band* / Muckin' o' Geordie's byre: *Denny & Dunipace Pipe Band* / Glendaurel highlanders: *Denny & Dunipace Pipe Band* / Bonnie Dundee: *Denny & Dunipace Pipe Band*
CD _____ CDITV 428
Scotdisc / Aug '88 / Duncans / Ross / Conifer.

DISTANCE TO ACID TRANCE VOL.1
CD _____ DI 192
Distance / Dec '95 / 3MV.

DISTANCE TO GOA 1
CD _____ DI 152
Distance / Dec '95 / 3MV.

DISTANCE TO GOA 2
CD _____ DI 172
Distance / Dec '95 / 3MV.

DISTANCE TO HAPPY TRANCE - THE ENERGISER
CD _____ DI 232
Distance / Dec '95 / 3MV.

DISTORTION TO HELL
CD _____ DISTCD 5
Distortion / Oct '94 / Plastic Head.

DISTURB MY SOUL
(Gospel From Stax Records' Chalice Label)
Assassination: *Dixie Nightingales* / Nail print: *Dixie Nightingales* / Hush hush: *Dixie Nightingales* / He's a friend of mine: *Jubilee Hummingbirds* / Our freedom song: *Jubilee Hummingbirds* / All I need is some sunshine in my life: *Dixie Nightingales* / I don't know: *Dixie Nightingales* / All these things to me: *Stars Of Virginia* / Wade in the water: *Stars Of Virginia* / God's promise: *Pattersonaires* / I learned to pray: *Pattersonaires* / Stop laughing at your fellow man: *Jubilee Hummingbirds* / Jesus will fix it: *Jubilee Hummingbirds* / This is our prayer: *Dixie Nightingales* / It comes at the end of the race: *Dixie Nightingales* / He's worthy: *Pattersonaires* / Child of God: *Pattersonaires* / Till Jesus comes: *Pattersonaires* / Give me one more chance: *Jubilee Hummingbirds* / Press my dying pillow: *Jubilee Hummingbirds* / There's not a friend: *Dixie Nightingales* / Forgive these fools: *Dixie Nightingales* / Son of God: *Stars Of Virginia* / Even me: *Stars Of Virginia*
CD _____ CDSXD 086
Stax / Feb '94 / Pinnacle.

DIVAS
CD _____ MOTCCD 67
Motor City / Oct '92 / Total/BMG.

DIX IMPROVISATIONS - VICTORIAVILLE 1989
CD _____ VICTOCD 09
Victo / Nov '94 / These / ReR Megacorp / Cadillac.

DIXIE BOPPIN' COUNTRY BILLIES VOL. 1
Big big man: *Brockman, Danny* / Yodlin chime bells: *Mills, Gene* / Devil's heart: *Weller, Bob* / Gertie's garter: *Bryant, Elmer* / Lonesome guitar: *Walker, Missouri* / I'm going to heaven when I die: *Stamper, Dallas* / True loving woman: *King Brothers* / Country jitterbug: *Goodwin, Horave* / Don't wake me: *Webb, Hoyt & Jo* / Red wing: *Peters, Pete* / Got it made: *Waldroop, Les* / Doin' my time: *Bill & Paul* / Blue grass hop: *Bill & Paul* / Dang you pride: *Miller, Ronnie* / I've got my brand on you: *Daniels, Little Chuck* / Red rover: *Bragg, Doug* / Lovin' on my mind: *Bragg, Doug* / Just like it: *Beck Bros* / Big rocker: *Beck Bros* / Gee whiz: *Pat & Dee* / It must be me: *Ontario, Art* / Last goodbye: *Ontario, Art* / Just look, don't touch: *Johnson, Dee* / Blue guitar jump: *Hammock, Ken* / Weekend boogie: *Croock, Tom* / Feelin' blue: *Skelton, Eddie* / Meanest blues: *Thomas, Jake* / Poor boy blues: *Thomas, Jake* / Blue suede shoes: *Various Narrators*
CD _____ CDDIXIE 3333
White Label/Bear Family / Apr '94 / Bear Family / Rollercoaster.

DIXIE BOPPIN' COUNTRY BILLIES VOL. 2
Brady and Dunky: *Hanna, Jack* / Way you want it: *Meers, Arvil* / Handful of love: *Keefer, Lyle* / Long time ago: *Dunn, J.P.* / Kentucky fandango: *Dunn, J.P.* / Lying all the time: *Dycus, Connie* / I could shoot myself: *Dycus, Connie* / Blue news: *Swan, Dottie* / Purty lil't: *Veluzat, Renaud* / Change of heart: *Bill & Paul* / More in the man: *Davis Brothers* / Alone with you: *Harden, Charlotte* / Your number one: *Johnson, Dee* / Never again: *Clayron, Johnny* / You're gonna pay: *Ridings, Jim* / My baby don't want me no

more : *Ridings, Jim* / Wrangler: *Reynolds, Eddy* / Nobody cares: *Pearson, Jimmie* / I guess I'm wise: *Nash, Malcolm* / Going down to Sal's house: *Willis, Bill* / Your lying ways: *Goodwin, Bill* / I've got a bead on you baby: *Williams Brothers* / This little girl of mine: *Half Brothers* / You're so easy to love: *La Beef, Sleepy* / Holiday for love: *Blakely, Jimmy* / Until: *Price, Mel* / Like let's get out: *Nelson, Tommy* / Old blue: *Hanna, Jack* / I walk the line: *Various Narrators*
CD _____ CDDIXIE 4444
White Label/Bear Family / Apr '94 / Bear Family / Rollercoaster.

DIXIELAND
(Featuring Eddie Condon/George Wetting)
CD _____ GOJCD 53041
Giants Of Jazz / Mar '90 / Target/BMG / Cadillac.

DIXIELAND
CD _____ 490311
RCA / Jul '95 / BMG.

DIXIELAND
Midnight in Moscow: *Ball, Kenny* / Riverboat shuffle: *Dukes Of Dixieland* / Winin' boy blues: *Dukes of Dixieland feat. Danny Barker* / Eh, la bas: *Original Dixieland Stompers* / My bonnie is over the ocean: *Original Dixieland Stompers* / Black roses blues: *Original Dixieland Stompers* / It's a plenty: *Brixie Dixie Jazz Band* / Somebody loves me: *Brixie Dixie Jazz Band* / March of the Siamese children: *Ball, Kenny* / Alexander's ragtime band: *Dukes Of Dixieland* / Bugle call blues: *Original Dixieland Stompers* / C.C. rider: *Original Dixieland Stompers* / Basin Street blues: *Brixie Dixie Jazz Band* / Raggie time: *Original Dixieland Stompers* / Casey Jones: *Station Hall Jazz Band* / Over in the Gloryland: *Original Dixieland Stompers*
CD _____ 12461
Laserlight / Nov '95 / Target/BMG.

DIXIELAND
Joshua fit the Battle of Jericho: *Original Dixieland Stompers* / When the saints: *Original Dixieland Stompers* / Buddy Bolden blues: *Original Dixieland Stompers* / Sweet Georgia Brown: *Brixie Dixie Jazz Band* / There you're smiling: *Brixie Dixie Jazz Band* / Handeysuckle rose: *Brixie Dixie Jazz Band* / Down by the riverside: *Original Dixieland Stompers* / Go tell it to the mountains: *Original Dixieland Stompers* / Lizzy's rag: *Original Dixieland Stompers* / I want a little girl: *Brixie Dixie Jazz Band* / When my sugar walks down the street: *Brixie Dixie Jazz Band* / Georgia: *Dutch Swing College Band* / Bad, bad Leroy Brown: *Dutch Swing College Band* / Play it to me: *Original Dixieland Stompers* / Champs Elysses: *Dutch Swing College Band* / Ice cream: *Brixie Dixie Jazz Band*
CD _____ 12460
Laserlight / Nov '95 / Target/BMG.

DIXIELAND FAVOURITES
CD _____ EMPRCD 521
Emporio / Oct '94 / THE / Disc / CM.

DIXIELAND JAZZ - THE COLLECTION
Tiger rag: *Original Dixieland Jazz Band* / Look at 'em doing it now: *Original Dixieland Jazz Band* / Copenhagen: *Original New Orleans Rhythm Kings* / That's no bargain: *Nichols, Red & His Five Pennies* / Way down yonder in New Orleans: *Trumbauer, Frank & His Orchestra* / I'm more than satisfied: *Chicago Loopers* / Royal goden blues: *Beiderbecke, Bix & His Gang* / Nobody's sweetheart: *McKenzie & Condon's Chicagoans* / Coquette: *Whiteman, Paul & His Orchestra* / I found a new baby: *Chicago Rhythm Kings* / There'll be some changes made: *Chicago Rhythm Kings* / Shake your can: *Dodds, Johnny* / Moanin' low: *Mole, Miff, Molers* / Strut Miss Lizzie: *Mills, Irving & His Hotsy Totsy Gang* / Georgia on my mind: *Carmichael, Hoagy & His Orchestra* / What you've gone: *Venuti-Lang All Stars* / Spider crawl: *Banks, Billy & His Orchestra* / Eel: *Condon, Eddie & His Orchestra* / When the saints go marching in: *Armstrong, Louis* / At the jazz band ball: *Rhythm Cats* / Relaxin' at the touro: *Spanier, Muggsy* / Muskrat ramble: *Armstrong, Louis*
CD _____ CDGRF 078
Tring / '93 / Tring / Prism.

DIXIELAND JUBILEE
(2CD Set)
CD Set _____ DBG 53030
Double Gold / Jan '94 / Target/BMG.

DIXIELAND TO SWING
(2CD Set)
CD Set _____ R2CD 4009
Deja Vu / Jan '96 / THE.

DIXIELAND TO SWING GOLD
(2CD Set)
CD Set _____ D2CD 4009
Deja Vu / Jun '95 / THE.

DO IT FLUID/B&G PARTY
(14 Rare Grooves)
Fantasy: *Smith, Johnny 'Hammond'* / Shifting gears: *Smith, Johnny 'Hammond'* / Joyous: *Pleasure* / Hump: *Rushen, Patrice* / Al-

ways there: *Side Effect* / Keep that same old feeling: *Side Effect* / Do it fluid: *Blackbyrds* / Rock creek park: *Blackbyrds* / Concrete jungle: *Three Pieces* / Glide: *Pleasure* / Ghettos of the mind: *Pleasure* / Straight to the bank: *Summers, Bill* / I've learned from my bums: *Spyder's Webb* / Sister Jane: *Funk Inc.*
CD _____ CDBGPD 035
BGP / Apr '92 / Pinnacle.

DO THE CROSSOVER BABY
I'll never stop loving you: *Thomas, Carla* / I got the vibes: *Armstead, Jo* / Stars: *Lewis, Barbara* / I'm the one who loves you: *Banks, Darrell* / I may not be what you want: *Mel & Tim* / Whole damned world gone crazy: *Williams, John Gary* / Be my lady: *Astors* / Since I lost my baby's love: *Lance, Major* / Bark at the moon: *Floyd, Eddie* / Catch that man: *John, Mable* / Little by little and bit by bit: *Weston, Kim* / You're my only temptation: *Ryan, Roz* / Whole world's a picture show: *Newcomers* / Special kind of woman: *Thompson, Paul* / I play for keeps: *Thomas, Carla* / Sweet sherry: *Barnes, J.J.* / Sacrifice: *Bell, William* / Loving by the pound: *Redding, Otis* / Just keep on loving me: *Mancha, Steve* / Man in the street: *Bell, William* / Trippin' on your love: *Staple Singers* / Did my baby call: *Mad Lads* / Where would you be today: *Ilana* / One more chance: *Joseph, Margie*
CD _____ CDKEND 105
Kent / Aug '93 / Pinnacle.

DO THE NUCLEAR TESTS IN PARIS AND BEIJING
Queenie: *Pimlico* / 911 KGGI: *Citrus* / Face on the bar room floor: *Flaming Stars* / Spineless little shit: *Thee Headcoatees* / GLC: *Armitage Shanks* / I'm afraid they're all talking about me: *Mickey & Ludella* / Shit parade: *Tokyo Skunx* / Jet love boogie: *Rockings* / I wanna go to Coney Island: *Jet Boys* / Hells three: *Gigantor* / Scuba scuba: *Revillos* / Little terrors: *Revolta* / Hangover head: *Diaboliks* / He used to paint in colours: *TV Personalities* / Mud: *Grape* / My boy and his motorbike: *Carousel* / Nostalgia: *Weekend* / New crush: *Bugbear* / Winona, I'll be up my Nan's: *Parker, Pop* / Clearly: *McTells* / Open to persuasion: *Chesterfields* / I wanna bang on the drum: *Dee, Johnny* / Cars in the grass: *Moxham, Stuart & The Original Artists* / Good enough: *Holly Golightly* / Cheat: *Earls Of Suave*
CD _____ MASKCD 058
Vinyl Japan / Feb '96 / Vital.

DO YOU BELIEVE IN LOVE
CD _____ CRECD 063
Creation / May '94 / 3MV / Vital.

DO YOU BELIEVE IN LOVE
CD Set _____ NSCD 007
Newsound / Feb '95 / THE.

DO YOU WANNA DANCE
(Hits Of The 70's)
Flight tonight: *Nazareth* / Brand new key: *Melanie* / Baby jump: *Mungo Jerry* / That same old feeling: *Pickettywitch* / In my chair: *Status Quo* / Part time love: *Knight, Gladys & The Pips* / Do you wanna dance: *Blue, Barry* / After the goldrush: *Prelude* / Bad, Bad Leroy Brown: *Croce, Jim* / Lola: *Kinks* / Kung fu fighting: *Douglas, Carl* / Sad sweet dreamer: *Sweet Sensation* / What have they done to my song Ma: *Melanie* / Medley: *Knight, Gladys & The Pips* / Alright alright alright: *Mungo Jerry* / Black superman (Muhammed Ali): *Wakelin, Johnny* / Time in a bottle: *Croce, Jim* / Shame, shame, shame: *Shirley & Company* / Swing your daddy: *Gilstrap, Jim* / Have you seen her: *Chi-Lites*
CD _____ TRTCD 108
TrueTrax / Dec '94 / THE.

DO YOUR DUTY
CD _____ IMP 940
Iris Music / Jul '95 / Discovery.

DO Y'SELF A FAVOUR - THE COUNTDOWN YEARS 1975-79
CD _____ RVCD 35
Raven / Jan '94 / Direct / ADA.

DOBRO
CD _____ SH 2206CD
Sugarhill / Oct '94 / Roots / CM / ADA / Direct.

DOCTOR LOVE
CD _____ DCD 5397
Disky / Oct '94 / THE / BMG / Discovery / Pinnacle.

DOCUMENT 01
CD _____ DOROB 001CD
Dorobo / Sep '95 / Plastic Head.

DOES THE WORD 'DUH' MEAN ANYTHING TO YOU
CD _____ CHE 40CD
Che / Sep '95 / SRD.

DOIN' IT
Zaius: *Russ, Eddie* / Groove: *Franklin, Rodney* / Always there: *Bobo, Willie* / That's the way of the world: *Lewis, Ramsey* / Reach out: *Duke, George* / Doin' it: *Hancock, Herbie* / Sneaking up behind you: *Brecker Brothers* / Funkin' for America: *Browne, Tom* / Get down everybody (it's time for world peace): *Smith, Lonnie Liston* / Johannesburg: *Scott-Heron, Gil* / Hooked on

young stuff: Tempo, Nino & 5th Avenue Sax / Street wave: Brothers Johnson
CD _____ RNBCD 104
Connoisseur / Aug '93 / Pinnacle.

DOING GOD'S WORK
(A Creation Compilation)
Ten miles: Wilson, Phil / In a mourning town: Biff Bang Pow / Murderers, the hope of women: Momus / Shine on: House Of Love / Cut me deep: Jasmine Minks / Word around town: Westlake / Kiss at dawn: Sudden, Nikki / Catch me: Blow Up
CD _____ CRECD 024
Creation / May '94 / 3MV / Vital.

DOING IT FOR THE KIDS
Cut me deep: Jasmine Minks / Ballad of the band: Felt / Christine: House Of Love / Well done sonny: Weather Prophets / All fall down: Primal Scream / She paints: Biff Bang Pow / Loft 49: Jazz Butcher / North shore train: Berry, Heidi / Death is hanging over me: Sudden, Nikki / Cigarette in my bed: My Bloody Valentine / Jetstream: Pacific / Godevil: Times / Complete history of sexual jealousy Parts 17 - 24: Momus / Reflects of rye: Emily / Brighter now: Razorcuts
CD _____ CRECD 037
Creation / Aug '88 / 3MV / Vital.

DON'T ASK FOR THE MOON, WE HAVE THE STARS
Way you look tonight: Astaire, Fred / Let there be love: Hutch / Boy next door: Garland, Judy / September song: Huston, Walter / She's funny that way: Sinatra, Frank / You're a sweetheart: Bowlly, Al / I'm made believe: Ink Spots & Ella Fitzgerald / Amor amor: Rey, Monte / I'm knee deep in daisies: Smith, Whispering / How do I know it's real: Sullivan, Maxine / That old feeling: Lee, Peggy & Capitol Jazzmen / Too marvelous for words: Stafford, Jo / That old black magic: Whiting, Margaret & Freddie Slack / Sweet Lorraine: Cole, Nat King Trio / It can't be wrong: Carlisle, Dorothy / Let's do it: Martin, Mary / Never took a lesson in my life: Carlisle, Elsie / Let's get away from it all: Lane, Muriel & Woody Herman / Long ago and far away: Forrest, Helen & Dick Haymes / Only forever: Crosby, Bing / Divi-sion Cantor, Eddie / I've got a heart filled with love: Desmond, Johnny & Glenn Miller / Very thought of you: Holiday, Billie / Boy what love has done to me: Froman, Jane / I remember you: Forrest, Helen & Harry James / Now voyager: Davis, Bette & Paul Henreid
CD _____ UCD 400
Conifer / Jan '95 / Conifer.

DON'T SHOOT
Bend in the road: Danny & Dusty / Hello walls: Jimmy & The Rhythm Pigs / I'll get out somehow: McCarthy, Steve / Wreckin' ball: Doe, John / Almost persuaded: Christensen, Julie / Tears fall away: Divine Horsemen / Tear it down: Gilkyson, Terry / Never get out of this world alive: Waterson, Jack / Blind justice: Band Of Blacky Ranchette / Freight train: Allison, Clay / Tear it all to pieces: Romans
CD _____ MAUCD 606
Mau Mau / Jul '91 / Pinnacle.

DON'T STOP THE MUSIC
Don't stop the music: Yarbrough & Peoples / Get down: Chandler, Gene / Ladies night: Kool & The Gang / Never can say goodbye: Gaynor, Gloria / Shake your groove thing: Peaches & Herb / You're my first my last: White, Barry / Candy girl: New Edition / Get on up, get on down: Ayers, Roy / She's a bad mama jama: Carltoit, Carl / Happy radio: Starr, Edwin / Love come down: King, Evelyn 'Champagne' / Ms. Grace: Tymes / Rock the boat: Hues Corporation / Jump: Pointer Sisters / Just an illusion: Imagination / Going back to my roots: Odyssey / Stomp: Brothers Johnson / Razzamatazz: Jones, Quincy / Be thankful for what you've got: DeVaughan, William / I'm doing fine now: New York City / Swing your daddy: Gilstrap, Jim / Sending out an S.O.S.: Young, Retta / Zing went the strings of my heart: Trammps / You to me are everything: Real Thing
CD _____ OG 3218
Old Gold / Sep '92 / Carlton Home Entertainment.

DON'T TALK JUST KISS
CD _____ UPCD 05
Nitro / Sep '95 / Plastic Head.

DON'T TOUCH THAT DIAL
(The History Of Music Radio)
Because they're young: Eddy, Duane / Judy in disguise: John Fred & Playboy Band / Rescue me: Fontella Bass / She'd rather be with me: Turtles / Spooky: Classics IV / Days of Pearly Spencer: McWilliams, David / Harlem shuffle: Bob & Earl / B-A-B-Y: Thomas, Carla / Soul man: Sam & Dave / Knock on wood: Floyd, Eddie / Stand by me: King, Ben E. / All my loving: Martin, George Orchestra / Warm and tender love: Sledge, Percy / For your love: Yardbirds / Livin' above your head: Jay & The Americans
CD _____ TJLCD 1068
Start / Dec '94 / Koch.

DOO WOP CLASSICS
Book of love: Monotones / Over and over again: Harvey & The Moonglows / Please come back come: Flamingos / Heart and

soul: Cleftones / Baby, please don't go: Orioles / Tell it to the judge: Monotones / Real gone Mama: Harvey & The Moonglows / Chica boom (that's my baby): Flamingos / Little girl of mine: Cleftones / Crying in the chapel: Orioles / Look in my eyes: Chantels / Secret love: Harvey & The Moonglows / I found a new baby: Flamingos / Maybe: Chantels / Sixteen candles: Crests / Blue moon: Marcels / Just for a trick: Flamingos / Blue velvet: Harvey & The Moonglows / Legend of sleepy hollow: Monotones
CD _____ GRF 196
Tring / Jan '93 / Tring / Prism.

DOO WOP DYNAMITE
CD _____ CDCD 1059
Charly / Mar '93 / Charly THE / Cadillac.

DOO WOP DYNAMITE VOL. 2
In the still of the nite: Five Satins / Clock: Andrews, Lee & The Hearts / Most of all: Moonglows / Kiss from your lips: Flamingos / Twilight time: Platters / Over the mountain across the sea: Johnny & Joe / Smoky places: Corsairs / Been so long: Pastels / I'm so young: Students / This broken heart: Sonics / False alarm: Re-Vels / Darling I know: El Fays / For your precious love: Impressions / M.T.Y.L.T.T.: Dreamkings / Red sails in the sunset: Spaniels / Those oldies but goodies (Remind me of you): Little Caesar & The Romans / Time after time: Isley Brothers / Needles and pins: Clovers / I can sing a rainbow/Love is blue: Dells / Diamonds and pearls: Paradons
CD _____ CDCD 1132
Charly / May '94 / Charly THE / Cadillac.

DOO WOP FROM DOLPHIN'S OF HOLLYWOOD VOL.1
Goose is gone aka the nest is warm: Turbans / Tick tock a woo: Turbans / No no cherry: Turbans / When I return: Turbans / Two things I love: Voices / Why: Voices / Crazy: Voices / Takes two to make a home: Voices / Hunter Hancock radio ad: Voices / My aching feet: Gassers / Why did you leave me: Gassers / Tell me: Gassers / Beloved: Gassers / Hum-de-hum: Gassers / Untitled blues: Relf, Bobby & The Laurels / Our love: Relf, Bobby & The Laurels / Honey bun: Turks / It can't be true: Turks / How to be a lover: Hodge, Gaynell & The Blue Aires / Love you night: Hodge, Gaynell & The Blue Aires / One time is enough: Byrd, Bobby / Hold me baby: Byrd, Bobby / Girl named Joe: Miracles / My angel: Miracles / Nine Boogie: Miracles / Let us be as one (aka Sweet thing): Miracles
CD _____ CDCHD 364
Ace / Jan '92 / Pinnacle / Cadillac / Complete/Pinnacle.

DOOTONE STORY VOL.1, THE
Ding a ling: Crescendos / Baby doll: Crescendos / I can't go on: Milton, Roy & his Orchestra / You got me reelin' and rockin': Milton, Roy & his Orchestra / My girl: McCullough, Charles & the Silks / I got tore up: Julian, Don & The Meadowlarks / This must be paradise: Julian, Don & The Meadowlarks / Please Mr. Jordan: Duncan, Cleve & the Penguins / Flee oo wee: Calvanes / Wet back hop: Higgins, Chuck / Don't you know I love you: Higgins, Chuck / Boogie woogie teenage: Meadowlarks / Be fair: Pipes / Buck '59: Green, Vernon & the Medallions / Magic mountain: Green, Vernon & the Medallions / Jump and hop: Romancers
CD _____ CDCHD 579
Ace / Jan '96 / Pinnacle / Cadillac / Complete/Pinnacle.

DOPE ON PLASTIC
Ode to a blunt: Men With Sticks / Dubble agent (Spying On-u): Strange Brew / Is a wizard or a blizzard: Mighty Truth / Reefer man cometh: Woodshed / Conversations with Julian Dexter: Grassy Knoll / Snapper: Red Snapper / Cities: A.P.E. / Steppin': Box Saga / Inner spaces: Digi Alliance / Black jesus: 9 Lazy 9 / Tempest dub: Edge Test 2 / Seashell: Skylab
CD _____ REACTCD 055
React / Jan '95 / Vital.

DOPE ON PLASTIC 2
Radio Woodside: Woodshed / Jailbird: Primal Scream / Spirit: Kitachi / To the hip: Bootman / Striplight: A.P.E. / Tribhuwan: Purple Penguin / Sinsemilia: Dillinjah / Massive Dub Beats / Wildfire: Disciples / Now or never: Crustation / Acoustic blues: Cool Breeze / It's not a man's world: Strata 3
CD _____ REACTCD 065
React / Jul '95 / Vital.

DOPE ON PLASTIC 3
Worlds: Midfield General / Go off (cut le roc goes off): Midfield General / Mountain: Purple Penguin / D.D. Luxe: Clutch Deluxe / Livin free: Small World / GBH Dub: Death In Vegas / Scratch: Kitachi / Wallop: D.J. Food / Just a lil dope: Masters At Work / 29: Turntable TEchnova / Bobimore dub: Henry & Louis / We wanna go back: Word Up / Images: Aquasky / 89: Funky Fresh News / Shine the light: Wood, Matt / Bean to the world: Cabbage Boy
CD _____ REACTCDX 073
CD _____ REACTCD 073
React / Feb '96 / Vital.

DORADO COMPILATION 1
Scheme of things: D-Note / Impressions: Giant Steps NYC / Sally's knocking: Jhelisa

/ Thirteenth key: Sunship / Rain: D-Note / Ain't no fun: Monkey Business / Circle of cruelty: Circle in the sun
CD _____ DOR 008 CD
Dorado / Sep '92 / Disc.

DORADO COMPILATION 2
CD _____ DOR 016CD
Dorado / Oct '93 / Disc.

DORADO COMPILATION 3
CD _____ DORO 20CD
Dorado / Mar '94 / Disc.

DORKCRUSHER
CD _____ TUPEPCD 031
Tupelo / Jul '91 / Disc.

DOT'S COVER TO COVER
(Hit Upon Hit)
Hearts of stone: Fontane Sisters / Two hearts: Boone, Pat / Maybellene: Lowe, Jim / Why don't you write me: Lanson, Snooky / Ain't that a shame: Boone, Pat / Only you (and you alone): Hilltoppers / Rollin' stone: Fontane Sisters / At my front door: Boone, Pat / Blue suede shoes: Lowe, Jim / Eddie my love: Fontane Sisters / Ka-ding-dong: Hilltoppers / I hear you knocking: Storm, Gale / Seventeen: Fontane Sisters / I'll be home: Boone, Pat / Why do fools fall in love: Storm, Gale / Seven days: Lanson, Snooky / Long tall Sally: Boone, Pat / Ivory tower: Storm, Gale / I'm in love again: Fontane Sisters / I almost lost my mind: Boone, Pat / Please don't leave me: Fontane Sisters / Chains of love: Boone, Pat / Lucky lips: Storm, Gale / Young love: Hunter, Tab / Marianne: Hilltoppers / Plaything: Todd, Nick / Raunchy: Vaughn, Billy / Get a job: Mills Brothers / Joker: Hilltoppers / At the hop: Todd, Nick
CD _____ CDCHD 609
Ace / May '95 / Pinnacle / Cadillac / Complete/Pinnacle.

DOUBLE ECLIPSE - TRIBUTE TO NEDLY ELSTAK
CD _____ BVHAASTCD 9210
Bvhaast / Dec '89 / Cadillac.

DOWN AND OUT BLUES
(4CD Set)
CD Set _____ MBSCD 434
Castle / Nov '95 / BMG.

DOWN TO THE ROACH
CD _____ CDTEP 9
Debut / Sep '95 / Pinnacle / 3MV / Sony.

DOWNTOWN
(20 Great Hits Of The Sixties)
You really got me: Kinks / Sweets for my sweet: Searchers / Always something there to remind me: Shaw, Sandie / Here comes my baby: Tremeloes / Catch the wind: Donovan / Downtown: Clark, Petula / Twenty four hours from Tulsa: Pitney, Gene / Go now: Moody Blues / Baby, now that I've found you: Foundations / Sugar and spice: Searchers / Cast your fate to the wind: Sounds Orchestral / Elenore: Turtles / Tossin' and turnin': Lee, Leapy / Here comes the nice: Small Faces / Out of time: Farlowe, Chris / Louie Louie: Kingsmen / That girl belongs to yesterday: Pitney, Gene / Michelle: Overlanders / This is my song: Clark, Petula / Don't throw your love away: Searchers
CD _____ TRTCD 103
TrueTrax / Oct '94 / THE.

DR. JAZZ SAMPLER
CD _____ STCD 6040
Storyville / Aug '94 / Jazz Music / Wellard / CM / Cadillac.

DR. MARTENS - UNLACED
True faith '94: New Order / Girls and boys: Blur / Babies: Pulp / Come home: James / Great big no: Lemonheads / Two princes: Spin Doctors / Low: Cracker / From despair to where: Manic Street Preachers / Shame: SMASH / Creep: Radiohead / Loaded: Primal Scream / Higher ground: Red Hot Chili Peppers / One way: Levellers / Unbelievable: EMF / Fool's gold: Stone Roses / Only one I know: Charlatans / Snakedriver: Jesus & Mary Chain / Flawed is beautiful: These Animal Men / Lenny Valentino: Auteurs / Stay together: Suede
CD _____ CDEMTV 90
EMI / Feb '95 / EMI.

DRAUMKVEDET
CD _____ HCD 7098CD
Musikk Distribusjon / Apr '95 / ADA.

DREAD POETS SOCIETY
CD _____ EFA 11665CD
T'Bwana / Apr '93 / SRD.

DREAM IN COLOUR
CD _____ NTHEN 9
Now & Then / Sep '95 / Plastic Head.

DREAM TOPPING
Hangover square: Always / Ulysses and the siren: Adverse, Anthony / Tidal wave: Apples / Discotheque: Bad Dream Fancy Dress / Pele: Cornelius / 6 A.M.: Daily Planet / Mike alway's diary: Karie, Kahimi / Zoom up: Karie, Kahimi / Where have all the school-boys gone: King Of Luxembourg / Martine: Philippe, Louis / Hot cherry love bombs: Magnificent Andersons / Toffee spot: Magnificent Andersons / Grant me the day: Marbles / Our man in: Marden Hill / You're

an angel: Mr. Martini / Sadness of things: Momus / Jackie Onassis: Milky / Noise: Monochrome Set / Big beat Jesus cheat: Pink Kross / Pure: Pulling Jessica's Hair / When I think: Romaine / Sit down I think I love you: Turner, Simon / Ecuador days: Would-Be-Goods / Camera loves me: Would-Be-Goods
CD _____ MONDE 21CD
Richmond / Sep '95 / Pinnacle.

DRINK ME SAMPLER '96
CD _____ DRINK 1
Echo / Jan '96 / Pinnacle / EMI.

DRIVE TIME
(2CD/MC Set)
CD Set _____ DINCD 96
Dino / Mar '95 / Pinnacle / 3MV.

DRIVE TIME VOL.2
(2CD/MC Set)
Weather with you: Crowded House / Valerie: Winwood, Steve / Addicted to love: Palmer, Robert / Everybody's talkin': Beautiful South / Brown eyed girl: Morrison, Van / American pie: McLean, Don / Heat is on: Frey, Glenn / Walking in Memphis: Cohn, Marc / How soon is now: Smiths / Black velvet: Myles, Alannah / Right beside you: Hawkins, Sophie B. / Walking on sunshine: Katrina & The Waves / Calling all the heroes: It Bites / Living in America: Brown, James / Imagination: Belouis Some / The needle and the damage done: Young, Neil / Belfast child: Simple Minds / Is it like today: World Party / Brass in pocket: Pretenders / Show me heaven: McKee, Maria / Wake up Boo: Boo Radleys / Love shack: B-52's / Sit down: James / Independent love song: Scarlet / Crazy for you: Let Loose / Suspicious minds: Fine Young Cannibals / Thorn in my side: Eurythmics / Road to hell: Rea, Chris / Bridge to your heart: Wax / Summer in the city: Lovin' Spoonful / Come undone: Duran Duran / Stay: Shakespears Sister / Waiting for a star to fall: Boy Meets Girl / Kyrie: Mr. Mister / Glory of love: Cetera, Peter / Driver's seat: Sniff 'N' The Tears / Everybody's gotta learn sometime: Korgis / (Feels like) Heaven: Fiction Factory / Sailing on the seven seas: O.M.D. / Race: Yello
CD Set _____ DINCD 99
Dino / Jul '95 / Pinnacle / 3MV.

DRIVE TIME VOL.3
(40 Of The Greatest Radio Anthems Of All Time - 2CD/MC Set)
74-75: Connells / Shoop shoop song: Cher / Here I stand: Milltown Brothers / There she goes: La's / Flashdance what a feeling: Cara, Irene / She drives me crazy: Fine Young Cannibals / Don't look back: Mock Turtles / Different for girls: Jackson, Joe / Lost weekend: Cole, Lloyd / Stir it up: Labelle, Patti / Maniac: Sembello, Michael / Olivers army: Costello, Elvis / Moon light shadow: Oldfield, Mike / Girl like you: Collins, Edwyn / Sleeping satellite: Archer, Tasmin / Will you: O'Connor, Hazel / Walk of life: Dire Straits / I could be so good to you: Waterman, Dennis / Lessons in love: Level 42 / Once in a lifetime: Talking Heads / Baker Street: Rafferty, Gerry / Betty Davis eyes: Carnes, Kim / Fall at your feet: Crowded House / Airport: Motors / Everybody wants to rule: Tears For Fears / I don't want a lover: Texas / Letter from America: Proclaimers / Missing you: Waite, John / Blinded by the light: Manfred Mann / Mustang Sally: Commitments / Eloise: Damned / I want your love: Transvision Vamp / Good tradition: Tikaram, Tanita / Your so vain: Simon, Carly / Owner of a lonely heart: Yes / Constant craving: Lang, k.d. / Somewhere in my heart: Aztec Camera / Life in a northern town: Dream Academy / Kiss from a rose: Seal / I got my mind set on you: Harrison, George
CD Set _____ DINCD 119
Dino / Dec '95 / Pinnacle / 3MV.

DRIVIN' ROCK VOL 1
CD _____ KNEWCD 729
Kenwest / Feb '94 / THE.

DRIVIN' ROCK VOL 2
CD _____ KNEWCD 730
Kenwest / Feb '94 / THE.

DRIVIN' ROCK VOL 3
CD _____ KNEWCD 731
Kenwest / Feb '94 / THE.

DRIVIN' ROCK VOL 4
CD _____ KNEWCD 732
Kenwest / Feb '94 / THE.

DRIVING ROCK
CD _____ RADCD 03
Global / Mar '95 / BMG.

DRONES AND THE CHANTERS, THE
CD _____ CC 61CD
Claddagh / Mar '95 / ADA / Direct.

DROP IN THE OCEAN, A
CD _____ ETCD 10
Semantic / Feb '94 / Plastic Head.

DROP OF THE IRISH, A
CD _____ PASTCD 9799
Flapper / Sep '92 / Pinnacle.

DROP THE BOX
CD _____ CDLDL 1234
Lochshore / Oct '95 / ADA / Direct / Duncans.

DROS BIANT Y BYD
CD _____ SCD 2113
Sain / Aug '95 / Direct / ADA.

DRUM AND BASS COLLECTION 1
CD _____ BDRBOX 1
Breakdown / Nov '95 / SRD.

DRUM AND BASS COLLECTION 2
(Drum & Bass Selection Vols. 3 & 4 and Telepathy) (5 CD Set)
CD Set _____ BDRBOX 2
Breakdown / Nov '95 / SRD.

DRUM AND BASS SELECTION 1
CD _____ BDRCD 1
Breakdown / Apr '94 / SRD.

DRUM AND BASS SELECTION 2
(2CD Set)
Rrroll da bbeats: D.J. Hype / Maximum style: Tom & Jerry / Hello lover: Fallen Angel / Sweet vibrations: DMS & Boneman X / Maniac music: Lick Back Organisation / Johnny 94: Johnny quaytle / It's a jazz thing: Roni Size / No musik: D.J. Ron / Stand easy: J.B. / Callin' all the people: A-Zone / Terrorist: Renegade / You must think first: Dope Style / Predator: Shimon / Heavy revival: Run Tings / Droppin' science vol.1: Droppin' Science / Screw face: Brain Killers / Time to move: D.J. Dextrous / Kall da kops: Sacred / What kind of world: Send / Burial: Leviticus
CD Set _____ BDRCD 3
Breakdown / Sep '94 / SRD.

DRUM AND BASS SELECTION 3
(2CD Set)
Cool down: Andy C / Lionheart: Bert & Dillinger / King of the jungle: King Of The Jungle / Feel the magic: Sophisticated Bad Boyz / War in '94: Badman / Dead bass: Dead Dred / Air freshener: Tom & Jerry Vol 9 / Booyaaa: Amazon II / Rude boy: Flex / Hitman (VIP mix): Marvellous Caine / Ganja man: Krome & Time / Little roller Vol 1: L Double / Sound murderer: Remarc / Heavenly body: Dextrous / Firing line: Droppin' Science / Mash up da place: Ganga Vol 4 / Ali Baba: Hopa & Bones / Yeah man: Dream Team / Alive and kicking (origin unknown mix): Red One / Selectors roll: Rus De Tox & Teebone
CD Set _____ BDRCD 5
Breakdown / Nov '94 / SRD.

DRUM AND BASS SELECTION 4
(2CD Set)
CD _____ BDRCD 6
Breakdown / Apr '95 / SRD.

DRUM AND BASS SELECTION 5
CD _____ BDRCD 9
Breakdown / Sep '95 / SRD.

DRUM, CHANT & INSTRUMENTAL MUSIC OF NIGER, MALI & UPPER VOLT
CD _____ 7559720732
Elektra Nonesuch / Jan '95 / Warner Music.

DRUMS OF THE EARTH
CD _____ AUB 6773
Auvidis/Ethnic / Mar '93 / Harmonia Mundi.

DRUMS OF THE EARTH 2
(Asia)
CD _____ AUB 006774
Auvidis/Ethnic / Apr '93 / Harmonia Mundi.

DRY LUNGS
(2CD Set)
CD Set _____ DVLR 1DCD
Dark Vinyl / Aug '93 / Plastic Head.

DUB EXPLOSION
CD _____ CDTRL 366
Trojan / Jan '96 / Jetstar / Total/BMG.

DUB HOUSE DISCO
CD _____ GRCD 004
Guerilla / Aug '92 / Pinnacle.

DUB HOUSE DISCO 2000
Land of Oz: Spooky / I still want ya: Outer Mind / Feel: Chameleon Project / Schudelfloss: Dr. Atomic / Product: 10th Chapter / Alchemy: Drum Club / Oh yeah: D.O.P. / Dub house disco: 2 Shiny Heads / Feeling warm: Eagles Prey / Supereal: One Nation / Intoxication: React 2 Rhythm / Schmoo: Spooky
CD _____ GRCD 007
Guerilla / Jul '94 / Pinnacle.

DUB HOUSE DISCO THE THIRD
Little bullet: Spooky / Here I go: D.O.P. / Underground: Matter / Aquamarine: Lemon Sol / Blue beyond: Supereal / Persuasion: Martin, Billie Ray & Spooky / Come into my life: Abfahrt / Higher: Code MD / Columbia: Chameleon Project / Prologue: 10th Chapter / Solar: Shape Navigator / Persuasion (mix): Martin, Billie Ray & Spooky
CD _____ GRCD 012
Guerilla / Jul '94 / Pinnacle.

DUB OR DIE VOL.1
CD _____ RE 099CD
Reach Out International / Nov '94 / Jetstar.

DUB OR DIE VOL.2
CD _____ RE 098CD
Reach Out International / Nov '94 / Jetstar.

DUB PLATE SELECTION
CD _____ STHCCD 15
Strictly Hardcore / Sep '95 / SRD.

DUB REVOLUTION
CD _____ RUSCD 8207
Roir USA / Jul '95 / Plastic Head.

DUB, TRIP AND HOP
CD _____ FRCD 5
Flex / Jun '95 / Jetstar.

DUBBLE ATTACK - DEE-JAY COLLECTION 1972-74
No. 1 in the world: U-Roy / Opportunity rock: Big Youth / Meaning of one: Prince Jazzbo / Rasta on a Sunday: I-Roy / Father's call: Beckford, Dean / This is a year for rebels: Godsons / Spider to the fly: Big Youth / Brother Toby is a movie from London: I-Roy / Mr. Harry Skank: Prince Jazzbo / Dubble attack: Big Youth / Whole lot of sugar: Prince Hammer / Festive season: I-Roy / Mr. Want All: Prince Jazzbo / Butter bread: Young, Lloyd
CD _____ GRELCD 601
Greensleeves / May '90 / Total/BMG / Jetstar / SRD.

DUBHEAD - THE 90'S DUB SAMPLER
CD _____ IVECD 2
Shiver / Oct '95 / SRD.

DUBLIN SONGS
Molly Malone: Band Of Dubs / Rocky road to Dublin: Dubliners / Spanish lady: Reilly, Paddy / Biddy Mulligan: Grace, Brendan / Dublin saunter: Dubliners / St. Laurence O'Toole: Fureys & Davey Arthur / Dublin, my Dublin: Reilly, Paddy / Ringsend rose: Grace, Brendan / Raglan Road: McCann, Jim / Dublin saunter: Reilly, Paddy / Night ferry: Fureys & Davey Arthur / Dublin town: Grace, Brendan / Foggy dew: McCann, Jim / Auld triangle: Dubliners / Summer in Dublin: McCann, Jim / Anna Liffey: Dubliners / Dublin in my tears: Fureys & Davey Arthur / Jem: Drew, Ronnie / Dublin - take me: Fureys & Davey Arthur
CD _____ MCCD 042
Music Club / Sep '91 / Disc / THE / CM.

DUBNOLOGY
CD _____ MIDDL 4CD
Middle Earth / Nov '95 / Disc.

DUCK AND COVER
CD _____ SST 263 CD
SST / Aug '90 / Plastic Head.

DUENDE
CD _____ ELLICD 3350
Ellipsis Arts / Oct '94 / Direct / ADA.

DUETS
CD _____ CWNCD 2004
Javelin / Jun '95 / THE / Henry Hadaway Organisation.

DUETS - DITHYRAMBISCH
CD _____ FMPCD 19-20
FMP / Nov '87 / Cadillac.

DULCE & FORTISSIMAE
CD _____ NT 6733CD
Robi Droli / Apr '95 / Direct / ADA.

DUM TRAX
CD _____ DUM 100
Dum / Mar '95 / Plastic Head.

DUNGEON OF DELIGHT
(2CD Set)
CD Set _____ NZ 010CD
Nova Zembla / Jun '94 / Plastic Head.

DUSTY AND FORGOTTEN
(1950's Vocal Groups)
CD _____ FLYCD 54
Flyright / Feb '94 / Hot Shot / Wellard / Jazz Music / CM.

DYNAMO OPEN AIR 10TH ANNIVERSARY
Self-abuse resistor: Fear Factory / Once solemn: Paradise Lost / Blood and fire: Type O Negative / Ball of destruction: Madball / Gorrit: Dub War / No fronts: Dog Eat Dog / Paint it black: Grip Inc. / Old: Machine Head / Till the end of time: Trouble / Proof: Eleven Pictures / Still pounds: Mental Hippie Blood / Systems failing: Nevermore / On the toad again: Motorpsycho / Pump it up: Warrior Soul / Liefe: Waving Corn / Whatever that hurts: Tiamat / Body cry: Downset / Falling: Biohazard
CD _____ RR 89272
Roadrunner / May '95 / Pinnacle.

EARLY CANTE FLAMENCO VOL.1
(The Early 1930's)
CD _____ ARHCD 326
Arhoolie / Apr '95 / ADA / Direct / Cadillac.

EARLY NEGRO VOCAL GROUPS VOL.3
(1921-24)
CD _____ DOCD 5355

Blues Document / Jun '95 / Swift / Jazz Music / Hot Shot.

EARLY NEGRO VOCAL QUARTETS 1893-1922 VOL. 2
CD _____ DOCD 5288
Blues Document / Dec '94 / Swift / Jazz Music / Hot Shot.

EARLY YEARS VOL 2
CD _____ WBRCD 802
Business / Nov '92 / Jetstar.

EARLY YEARS VOL 3
CD _____ WBRCD 803
Business / Mar '94 / Jetstar.

EARPLUGGED
CD _____ MOSH 115CD
Earache / Sep '94 / Vital.

EARTH BEAT
Mental cube-Q: Mental Cube / Quazi: Yage / You took my love: Candese / Papua New Guinea: Future Sound Of London / So this is love: Mental Cube / Child of the bass generation: Mental Cube / Tingler: Smart Systems / Coda coma: Yage / Owl: Indo Tribe / People livin' for today: Semi Real / Theme from Hot Burst: Yage / Shrink: Indo Tribe / Stakker humanoid: Humanoid / In the mind of a child: Indo Tribe / Creator: Smart Systems / Bite the bullet baby: Indo Tribe
CD _____ CDTOT 7
Jumpin' & Pumpin' / Nov '91 / 3MV / Sony.

EARTH SONGS
(12 Original Songs Honouring The Earth)
My heart sears: Friedmann / Out of the earth: Wynberg, Simon / Desert song: Stein, Ira / Thousand small gold bells: Arkenstone, David / Earth cry mercy: Gettel, Michael / In return: Tingstad, Eric & Nancy Rumbel / Calling: Jones, Michael / Universal garden: Kostia / Remember remember: Mirowitz, Sheldon / Forgotten places: Illenberger, Ralf / Which is yes: Brewer, Spencer / Earth tribe: Lauria, Nando
CD _____ ND 63913
Narada / Oct '93 / New Note / ADA.

EARTHRISE
(The Rainforest Album)
I still haven't found what I'm looking for: U2 / Here comes the rain again: Eurythmics / Don't give up: Gabriel, Peter & Kate Bush / Saltwater: Lennon, Julian / How many people: McCartney, Paul / Is this the world we created: Queen / Walk of life: Dire Straits / Brazilian: Genesis / Yes we can: Artists United For Nature / Spirit of the forest: Spirit Of The Forest / Fragile: Sting / Crazy: Seal / Under African skies: Simon, Paul / Learning to fly: Pink Floyd / Wake me up on judgement day: Winwood, Steve / It's the end of the world as we know it (and I feel fine): R.E.M. / I'm still standing: John, Elton
CD _____ 5154192
Polystar / Jun '92 / PolyGram.

EARTH'S ANSWER
CD _____ CDCEL 016
Celestial Harmonies / Aug '88 / ADA / Select.

EAST COAST ASSAULT
CD _____ TOODAMNHY 22
Too Damn Hype / Jul '93 / SRD.

EAST COAST BLUES
CD _____ FLYCD 45
Flyright / Nov '92 / Hot Shot / Wellard / Jazz Music / CM.

EAST COAST BLUES IN THE THIRTIES
CD _____ SOB 035282
Story Of The Blues / Feb '93 / Koch / ADA.

EAST COAST JIVE
(Apollo Theatre Recordings)
CD _____ DD 669
Delmark / Dec '94 / Hot Shot / ADA / CM / Direct / Cadillac.

EAST COAST PROJECT
CD _____ 74321307152
Arista / Aug '95 / BMG.

EASY AND SLOW
CD _____ HCD 127
GTD / Apr '95 / Else / ADA.

EASY LISTENING - 40 GEMS OF THE GENRE
Mas que nada: Mendes, Sergio & Brazil 66 / Man & a woman: Longet, Claudine / I'll never fall in love again: Bacharach, Burt / Look around: Mendes, Sergio & Brazil 66 / Happy Brazilia: Last, James / Everyday people: Last, James / Baby elephant walker: Stevens, Carl / Venus: Denjean, Claudine / Spanish flea: Barber, Frank / Walk in the forest: Barber, Frank / Drum diddley: Moorhouse, Alan / Funky fever: Moorhouse, Alan / Picasso summer: Legrand, Michel / Jungle juice: Elektrik Cokernut / Chirpy chirpy chirpy: Elektrik Cokernut / Live & let die: Papetti, Fausto / (This is Chico) Wout it: Arnez, Chico / Good, the bad & the ugly: Timoney, Mike / Theme from 'The Fox': Montenegro, Hugo / Peter Gunn: Mancini, Henry / House of the Rising Sun: Mancini, Henry / Pink Panther: Mancini, Henry / Great egg race: Denton, Richard & Martin Cook / Quiller: Denton, Richard & Martin Cook / My name is nobody: Morri-

cone, Ennio / Tomatoes: Hot Butter / Popcorn: Hot Butter / Spooky: Williams, Andy / Downtown: Barry, John / Love, love drags the down: Crewe, Bob Generation / I love all the love in you: Crewe, Bob Generation / Florida fantasy: Barry, John / Aquarius/Let the sun shine: Age Of Aquarius / Superfly: Holmes, Cecil / Mission Impossible: Schifrin, Lalo / Third Man theme: Enoch Light & Orchestra / Wipe out: Eliminators / Liquidator: Schifrin, Lalo / Journey: Gentle People / Wonderwall: Flowers, Mike
CD _____ FIRMCD 2
Firm / Feb '96 / Pinnacle.

EASY LISTENING 3
CD _____ NORMAL 192CD
Normal/Okra / Aug '95 / Direct / ADA.

EASY LISTENING MOODS
CD _____ 5404142
A&M / Sep '95 / PolyGram.

EASY PROJECT, THE
(20 Lounge Favourites)
Shake: Johnston, Laurie Orchestra / Kinda kinky: McVay, Ray Orchestra / Mas que nada: Sounds Orchestral / Lunar walk: Hawksworth, Johnny Orchestra / Walk on the wild side: Tew, Alan Orchestra / It's murder: Hawksworth, Johnny Orchestra / Theme from San Benedict: Keating, Johnny Orchestra / House of the rising sun: Synthesonic Sound / Blue 'n' groovy: Paraffin Jack Flash Ltd / Clown: Keating, Johnny Orchestra / Echo four two: Johnson, Laurie Orchestra / Mucho Mexico Seven-O: Shakespeare, John Orchestra / High society: Reed, Les Piano / Staccato: Eliminators / Ironside: Tew, Alan Orchestra / Getaway: Keating, Johnny & The Z Men / Superfly: Synthesonic Sound / Revenge: McVay, Ray Orchestra / But she ran the other way: Schroeder, John Orchestra / Spiral: Roache, Harry Constellation
CD _____ NEMCD 772
Sequel / Oct '95 / BMG.

EBB STORY, THE
I've got a feeling / What is life without a home / If you please / Time brings about a change / Look what you're doing to me / True lips / Buzz buzz buzz / Way you carry on / Love like a fool / Look no hair / I wanna know / Darkness / Keep walkin' on / Good mornin' baby / Sure nuff / You fascinate me / Mine all mine / Voodoo love / Never let me go / Wrapped up in a dream / She's my witch / Oh Linda / Lucky Johnny / Need your lovin' / Much too much / Come on / My silent prayer / Run run run / Kiss me squeeze me / Hali-lou
CD _____ CDCHD 524
Ace / Feb '95 / Pinnacle / Cadillac / Complete/Pinnacle.

EDISON DIAMOND DISC HOT DANCE BANDS 1927-1929
CD _____ NEOVOX 969
Neovox / Oct '93 / Wellard.

EIGHT BALL - THE SOUND OF NEW YORK
CD _____ XTR 13CD
X:Treme / Sep '94 / Pinnacle / SRD.

EIGHT OVER THE EIGHT BALL
CD _____ EBALL 2CD
Produce / Feb '95 / 3MV / Sony.

EIN SCHIFFWIRD KOMMEN
Komm wir machen eine kleine reise: Lind, Gitta & Christa Williams / Vaya con dios: Lind, Gitta & Christa Williams / Kein auto: Lind, Gitta & Christa Williams / Denn sie fahren hinaus auf das meer: Brown, Peggy / Musik von zuckerhut: Club Jamaika / Augen has du wie kakao: Club Jamaika / Adieu lebewohl goodbye (Tonight is so right for love): Bottcher, Gerd / Ich komm wieder: Bottcher, Gerd / Abends in Ahlen: Andersen, Lale / En schiff wird kommen: Andersen, Lale / Ein fremder mann: Andersen, Lale / Bahama melodie: Bertelmann, Fred / Das blaue meer und du: Bertelmann, Fred / Einen ring it zwei blutroten steinen: Valente, Caterina / Wos ist das land: Valente, Caterina / Schick mie einen gruss: Valente, Caterina / Weisse mowe flieg in die ferm: Valente, Caterina / Wenn die sonne scheint in Portugal: Assia, Lys / Zeig mir bei nacht die sterne: Engel, Detlef / Mr. Blue: Engel, Detlef / Komm zu mir wenn du einsam bist: Torriani, Vico / Sweet Hawaii: Gitte & Rex Gildo / Fern von de Heimat: Lind, Gitta / Wo die sonne in das meer versinkt: Durand, Andre / Heim, heim mocht ich zienn: Bottcher, Gerd & Detlef Engel
CD _____ BCD 15414
Bear Family / Dec '87 / Rollercoaster / Direct / CM / Swift / ADA.

EITHER SIDE OF MIDNIGHT
(2CD Set)
I'm a fool to want you: Morgan, Lee / All blues: Bridgewater, Dee Dee / But not for me: Jamal, Ahmad / I don't know what time it was: Shorter, Wayne / Willow weep for me: Edison, Harry / Here's the rainy day: Bridgewater, Dee Dee / Make the man love me: Kelly, Wynton / I got it bad (and that ain't good): Webster, Ben / Loverman: McRae, Carmen / Round midnight: Ellington, Duke / Little girl blue: Simone, Nina / Tenderly: Byas, Don / I loves you porgy: Simone, Nina / My one and only love: Grappelli, Stephane / Mellow mood: Marmarosa,

Dodo / Star eyes: *Kral, Irene* / Pleasingly plump: *Basie, Count* / Turn out the stars: *Evans, Bill* / Blue gardenia: *Washington, Dinah* / Come rain or come shine: *Kelly, Wynton* / Why try to change me now: *Foster, Frank* / What are you doing the rest of your life: *Evans, Bill* / Indian summer: *Hawkins, Coleman* / Darn that dream: *Washington, Dinah* / Mr. Lucky: *Byrd, Donald* / Moonlight in Vermont: *McRae, Carmen* / Waltz Latino: *Feidman, Victor* / In a sentimental mood: *Stitt, Sonny*
CD Set _____ **CPCD 80582**
Charly / Feb '95 / Charly / THE / Cadillac.

EITHER SIDE OF MIDNIGHT VOL.2
(2CD Set)
Blue room: *Sims, Zoot* / More I see you: *Vaughan, Sarah* / Detour ahead: *Evans, Bill* / Just in time: *Morgan, Lee* / Girl talk: *Burrell, Kenny* / Misty: *Bridgewater, Dee Dee* / All or nothing at all: *Shorter, Wayne* / Everything happens to me: *Marmarosa, Dodo* / Crazy he calls me: *Washington, Dinah* / In a mellow tone: *Ellington, Duke* / Lonely melody: *Ashby, Dorothy* / My funny Valentine: *Farmer, Art* / Lullaby of Birdland: *Torme, Mel* / You've changed: *Weller, Don* / Theodora: *Taylor, Billy* / Playtime: *Rich, Buddy* / I could write a book: *McRae, Carmen* / In a sentimental mood: *Webster, Ben* / It's wonderful: *Braff, Ruby* / All the things you are: *Jamal, Ahmad* / Lulu's back in town: *Torme, Mel* / Here's that rainy day: *Montgomery, Wes* / Prelude to a kiss: *Stitt, Sonny* / Autumn leaves: *Kelly, Wynton* / How long has this been goin' on: *Connor, Chris* / Confessin': *Norvo, Red* / Hey there: *Gray, Wardell* / When the world was young: *Bryant, Ray* / Love me or leave me: *Simone, Nina*
CD Set _____ **CDPCD 81402**
Charly / Oct '95 / Charly / THE / Cadillac.

EL CHA CHA CHA DE CU
CD _____ **283382**
Total / Jan '96 / Total/BMG.

EL CONDOR PASA
(South American Indian Harp & Flute Music)
CD _____ **15163**
Laserlight / May '94 / Target/BMG.

EL CONDOR PASA
CD _____ **CD 62042**
Saludos Amigos / Nov '93 / Target/BMG.

EL PRIMITIVO
(American rock 'n' roll & rockabilly)
Save it: *Robbins, Mel* / Oh yeah: *Jeffrey, Wally* / I wanna dance all night: *Wiley, Chuck* / It's love: *Wiley, Chuck* / Bandstand: *Nash, Cliff* / Times is tough: *Wiley, Chuck* / Are you with me: *Robbins, Mel* / I wanna shake it: *Hobock, Curtis* / I love you dearly: *Hurt, Jimmy & the Del Rio's* / Thump: *Embers* / Baby moon: *Smith, Herbie* / Best dressed beggar in town: *Turner, Buck* / Door to door: *Wiley, Chuck* / Uh oh: *Imps* / I walked all night: *Embers* / Explosion: *Nash, Cliff* / Out of gas: *Howard, Chuck* / Tell me baby: *Nash, Cliff* / Why worry about me: *Wiley, Chuck* / That'll get it: *Imps* / No time for sister: *Nash, Cliff* / I love you so much: *Wiley, Chuck* / Jenny Lou: *Nash, Cliff*
CD _____ **CDCHD 473**
Ace / Aug '93 / Pinnacle / Cadillac / Complete/Pinnacle.

EL RITMO LATINO
(18 Classic Latin Grooves)
Hit the bongo: *Puente, Tito* / Muneca: *Palmieri, Eddie* / El escencia del guaguanco: *Pacheco, Johnny* / Belen Barunto: Miranda, Ismael* / Jave samba: *Constanzo, Jack & Gerry Woo* / La verdad: *Palmieri, Eddie* / El malecon: *Orchestra Harlow* / Nanteca: *Alegre All Stars* / Aguzate: *Ray, Ricardo* / Mambo tipico: *Puente, Tito & His Orchestra* / Fever: *La Lupe* / Wipeout: *Barretto, Ray* / La jicota: *Ruiz, Rosendo Jr* / Work song: *Puente, Tito* / Mambo Manila: *Rodriguez, Tito & His Orchestra* / Carmelina: *Valdes, Alfredito* / Song for my father: *Valentin, Bobby* / Arsenio: *Harlow, Larry*
CD _____ **MCCD 025**
Music Club / May '91 / Disc / THE.

EL SALAO
CD _____ **TUMICD 012**
Tumi / '92 / Sterns / Discovery.

EL SON DE CUBA
CD _____ **283432**
Total / Jan '96 / Total/BMG.

ELECTRIC DREAMS
CD _____ **NTRCD 033**
Nectar / Mar '95 / Pinnacle.

ELECTRIC DREAMS
Blue Monday: *New Order* / Love is a stranger: *Eurythmics* / Mirror man: *Human League* / Tainted love: *Soft Cell* / Victim of love: *Erasure* / If I was: *Ure, Midge* / Heart of glass: *Blondie* / Mad world: *Tears For Fears* / Come live with me: *Heaven 17* / Wood beez (pray like Aretha Franklin): *Scritti Politti* / Living on the ceiling: *Blancmange* / Situation: *Yazoo* / Careless memories: *Duran Duran* / Quiet life: *Japan* / All stood still: *Ultravox* / Chant no.1 (I don't need this pressure on): *Spandau Ballet* / Talk Talk: *Talk Talk* / We close our eyes: *Go West* / Politics of dancing: *Re-Flex* / Together in electric dreams: *Moroder, Giorgio*

& *Philip Oakey* / Enola Gay: *O.M.D.* / Change: *Tears For Fears* / Fade to grey: *Visage* / Never never: *Assembly* / Are friends electric: *Tubeway Army* / Wishing (If I had a photograph of you): *Flock Of Seagulls* / Wishful thinking: *China Crisis* / I'm in love with a German film star: *Passions* / Don't go: *Yazoo* / Torch: *Soft Cell* / Is it a dream: *Classix Nouveaux* / Treason: *Teardrop Explodes* / Love on your side: *Thompson Twins* / Change your mind: *Sharpe & Numan* / Sgt. Rock (is going to help me): *XTC* / Wouldn't it be good: *Kershaw, Nik* / Love shadow: *Fashion* / Vienna: *Ultravox*
CD Set _____ **5254352**
PolyGram TV / Feb '95 / PolyGram.

ELECTRIC LADYLAND
CD _____ **EFA 006692**
Mille Plateau / Nov '95 / SRD.

ELECTRIC RADIO SAMPLER MUSIC TEST
CD _____ **TEST 001CD**
Haven/Backs / Sep '93 / Disc / Pinnacle.

ELECTRIC SUGAR CUBE FLASHBACKS
CD _____ **AIPCD 1054**
AIP / Mar '93 / Disc.

ELECTRICITY
(18 Synth Pop Hits)
CD _____ **MUSCD 008**
MCI / Sep '93 / Disc / THE.

ELECTROCITY VOL.4
CD _____ **E 06321-2**
Ausfahrt / Dec '93 / SRD.

ELECTROCITY VOL.5
CD _____ **EFA 05323 2**
Ausfahrt / Aug '94 / SRD.

ELECTROCITY VOL.6
CD _____ **EFA 063262**
Ausfahrt / Apr '95 / SRD.

ELECTRONIC FRANKFURT
(2CD Set)
CD Set _____ **PODDCD 023**
Pod / Sep '94 / Total/BMG.

ELECTRONIC GENERATORS
CD _____ **GR 009**
No CD / Dec '95 / Vital/SAM.

ELECTRONIC YOUTH
CD _____ **MRSP 001**
Music Research / Feb '94 / Plastic Head.

ELEMENTAL FORCE OF PHUNKEE NOIZE
Rising High / May '95 / Disc. _____ **RSNCD 35**

ELEMENTS
Stratus: *Cobham, Billy* / BAck together again: *Mouzon, Alphonse & Larry Coryell* / Oceanliner: *Passport* / Black market: *Weather Report* / Birds of fire: *McLaughlin, John* / Hello JEff: *Clarke, Stanley* / Dinner music of the gods: *Di Meola, Al* / Romantic warrior: Return To Forever* / Nuclear burn: *Brand X* / War dance: *Colosseum II*
CD _____ **VSOPCD 218**
Connoisseur / Aug '95 / Pinnacle.

ELEPHANT TABLE ALBUM
Xtract / Oct '89 / Disc. _____ **XXCD 001**

ELEVEN YEARS FROM YESTERDAY
CD _____ **FMRCD 02**
Future / Feb '88 / Harmonia Mundi / ADA.

EMERALD ROCK
Where the streets have no name: *U2* / Linger: *Cranberries* / Whole of the moon: *Waterboys* / Small bit of love: *Saw Doctors* / Real real gone: *Morrison, Van* / I don't like Mondays: *Boomtown Rats* / Dancing in the moonlight: *Thin Lizzy* / Nowhere: *Therapy* / Teenage kicks: *Undertones* / Somebody to love: *In Tua Nua* / Don't go: *Hothouse Flowers* / Mandinka: *O'Connor, Sinead* / Nobody knows: *Brady, Paul* / Parisienne walkways: *Moore, Gary & Phil Lynott* / Good heart: *Sharkey, Feargal* / After all: *Frank & Walters* / In the midnight hour: *Commitments* / She's the one that I adore: *Energy Orchard* / Big decision: *That Petrol Emotion* / In the name of the father: *Bono & Gavin Friday*
CD _____ **5149442**
PolyGram / Mar '95 / PolyGram.

EMOTIONS FOR THE WEISHUI RIVER
CD _____ **PAN 149CD**
Pan / Aug '94 / ADA / Direct / CM.

EMPORIUM OF DANCE
CD Set _____ **CATCD 001**
BMG / Nov '95 / BMG.

EMPTY SAMPLER
CD _____ **MT 273CD**
Empty / Jun '94 / Plastic Head / SRD.

EN-TRANCE
CD _____ **ENTCD 1**
Abstract / Sep '93 / Pinnacle / Vital.

EN-TRANCE 2
CD _____ **ENT 2CD**
Abstract / Apr '94 / Pinnacle / Total/BMG.

ENCHANTED CAROLS
Church bells: *Townsend, Dave & Nick Hooper* / Hark the herald angels sing (Barrel organ, musical boxes, roller barrel organ & Orpheus disc player.) / Virgin most pure:

Dartington Handbell Choir / Jingle bells: *Penny piano* / Star of Bethlehem / Angels from the realms of glory (Medley, 4 items) from the mists of time: *Grosmont Handbell Ringers* / Away in a manger: *Grosmont Handbell Ringers* / O little town of Bethlehem: *Grosmont Handbell Ringers* / First Noel (end of medley): *Grosmont Handbell Ringers* / As, with gladness, men of old: *Sun Life Stanshawe Band* / Glory to God in the highest: *Sun Life Stanshawe Band* / See amid the winter's snow: *Sun Life Stanshawe Band* / O come all ye faithful (Adeste Fidelis) (Barrel organ, musical box, disc player. End s1) / Silent Night / Down in yon forest: *Dartington Handbell Choir* / Good King Wenceslas (Musical boxes, barrel organ) / Little Jesus sweetly sleep: *Launton Handbell Ringers* / Little drummer boy: *Launton Handbell Ringers* / Deck the halls with boughs of holly: *Launton Handbell Ringers* / Little donkey: *Launton Handbell Ringers* / While shepherds watched their flocks by night: *Barrel Organ* / Auld lang syne
CD _____ **CDSDL 327**
Saydisc / '85 / Harmonia Mundi / ADA / Direct.

ENCHANTING MONGOLIA
CD _____ **EFA 11949-2**
Nebelhorn / Feb '94 / SRD.

ENCHANTMENTS
CD _____ **CLEO 95202**
Cleopatra / Aug '95 / Disc.

ENCOUNTER
CD _____ **EFA 11606CD**
Planet / Apr '93 / Grapevine / ADA / CM.

END OF MUSIC
CD _____ **DANCD 078**
Danceteria / Nov '94 / Plastic Head / ADA.

ENDLESS LOVE
(2CD Set)
One last love song: *Beautiful South* / Bump 'n' grind: *R. Kelly* / Crazy for you: *Madonna* / Around the world: *East 17* / I'll stand by you: *Pretenders* / Crash boom bang: *Roxette* / Kiss from a rose: *Seal* / Stay: *Eternal Basement* / Stars: *China Black* / Don't be a stranger: *Carroll, Dina* / Can't stay away from you: *Estefan, Gloria* / Love ain't here anymore: *Take That* / Now and forever: *Marx, Richard* / I'll never fall in love again: *Deacon Blue* / When love breaks down: *Prefab Sprout* / Ordinary world: *Duran Duran* / La la (means I love you): *Swing Out Sister* / Nothing compares 2 U: *O'Connor, Sinead* / Love me for a reason: *As We Speak* / Endless love: *Ross, Diana & Lionel Richie* / Love don't live here anymore: *Nail, Jimmy* / Jealous guy: *Roxy Music* / Every breath you take: *Police* / I don't want to talk about it: *Everything But The Girl* / Don't let the sun go down on me: *John, Elton* / Unchained melody: *Righteous Brothers* / Without you: *Nilsson, Harry* / If you leave me now: *Chicago* / My love: *McCartney, Paul* / Man with the child in his eyes: *Bush, Kate* / On the wings of love: *Osborne, Jeffrey* / Secret lovers: *Atlantic Starr* / Love and affection: *Armatrading, Joan* / Babe: *Styx* / I wanna stay with you: *Gallagher & Lyle* / Love is all around: *Troggs* / Nights in white satin: *Moody Blues* / I'm not in love: *10cc*
CD Set _____ **5253412**
PolyGram / Jan '95 / PolyGram.

ENERGY '94 & STREETPARADE
Milky way (Lunatic Asylum Acid Mix): *Borealis, Aurora* / Bagdad: *Paragliders* / Spoon nord la weelu title feli 8 Bungee Park: D.J. Yves De Ruyther & D.J. Franky* / Orient: *Luke Slaters 7th Pain* / Ambulance two (Bonzai remix): *Armani, Robert* / Primitive passion: *Dee, Alici & Alphia* / Boo ya (Live): *Jens / Symphony: *Gangsta* / We don't care: *T-Bass & O. Kunzer* / Fairz 721: *Hood, Robert* / Helix: *Synetics* / M 3 of canes venatici: *Direct Force* / Kneels before me: *Agent Loft*
CD Set _____ **SUPER 2022CD**
Superstition / Aug '94 / Vital / SRD.

ENERGY TRANCE
(The Ultimate Trance Collection)
CD _____ **341642**
Koch / Dec '94 / Koch.

ENFORCERS 4
CD _____ **RIV 490**
Reinforced / Sep '93 / SRD.

ENFORCERS 5
CD _____ **RIVET 52CD**
Reinforced / Oct '93 / SRD.

ENGINE COMMON
In Gunnersbury park: *Hit Parade* / Letter from a lifeboat: *Sugargliders* / Thaumaturgy: *Orchids* / You do my world the world of good: *Harvest Ministers* / Clearer: *Blueboy* / Half hearted: *Brighter* / What we had hoped: *Sugargliders* / Leaving: *Rosaries* / Missing the moon: *Field Mice* / I was just dreaming: *Orchids* / Fruitloopin': *Sugargliders* / Popkiss: *Blueboy* / Honey sweet: *Secret Shine* / Six o'clock is rosary: *Harvest Ministers* / End: *Brighter* / I don't suppose I'll get a second chance: *Another Sunny Day*
CD _____ **SARAH 628CD**
Sarah / Mar '95 / Vital.

ENGLISH FOLK SONGS
(A Selection From The Penguin Book)
When I was young / Gaol song / Whale catchers / Young and single sailor / False bride / Ratcliffe highway / Grey cock / Basket of eggs / One night as I lay on my bed / Banks of Green Willow / All things are quite silent / Banks of Newfoundland
CD _____ **FECD 47**
Fellside / Nov '95 / Target/BMG / Direct / ADA.

ENGLISH FREAKBEAT VOL.1
CD _____ **AIPCD 1039**
AIP / May '95 / Disc.

ENGLISH FREAKBEAT VOL.2
CD _____ **APICD 1047**
Backs / Feb '96 / Disc.

ENJA - 20TH ANNIVERSARY
Dance Benita dance: *Blythe, Arthur* / Maybe September: *Flanagan, Tommy* / Sossity; you're a woman: *Krantz, Wayne* / Wow: *Dennerlein, Barbara* / Green chimneys: *Reedus, Tony* / Time until: *Degen, Bob* / Storyteller: *Abou-Khalil, Rabih* / Giant steps: *Tyner, McCoy* / Phantoms: *Barron, Kenny* / You and I: *Lincoln, Abbey* / Lakutshon ilanga: *Ibrahim, Abdullah* / Straight no chaser: *Wallace, Bennie* / Yawn: *Scofield, John* / Ballad to Mahalia: *Tsilis, Gust William* / Edge to edge: *Formanek, Michael* / My funny valentine: *Baker, Chet*
CD _____ **ENJACD 80602**
Enja / Jun '94 / New Note / Vital/SAM.

ENTER THE HARDBAG
Fee fi fo fum: *Candy Girls & Sweet Pussy Pauline* / Something about you. Mr. Roy / Move your body: *Xpansions* / Son of a gun: *JX* / It's what's upfront that counts: *Yosh* / Diablo: *Grid* / Conway: *Reel 2 Real* / I'm rushin': *Bump* / Bullet: *Fluke* / Deeper: *Funky See Funky Do* / Happiness (is just around the bend): *Brooklyn's Poor & Needy* / Joanna: *Mrs. Woods* / Sweet harmony: *Liquid* / Don't you want me: *Felix* / Blue Monday: *New Order* / Club America: *Club America* / All night: *Tocayo* / Housework: *Rizzo* / Burning up: *De Vit, Tony* / Magic: *Blu Peter* / Hooked: *99th Floor Elevators* / Only me: *Hyperlogic* / I need a man: *Li Kwan* / Stomp: *Ramp* / Let the rhythm flow: *Diva Rhythms* / Want me love me: *Justine*
CD _____ **5404572**
A&M / Dec '95 / PolyGram.

ENTRANCE
CD Set _____ **ENT 12CD**
Entrance / Mar '95 / Plastic Head.

EPIDEMIC
CD _____ **SABOTAGE 01CD**
Sabotage / May '95 / Plastic Head.

EPITONE
CD _____ **BTR 002CD**
Bad Taste / Nov '95 / Plastic Head.

EQUINOX SAMPLER ONE
CD _____ **CD 30041**
Lotus / Feb '93 / Jazz Horizons / Impetus.

EQUINOX SAMPLER TWO
CD _____ **ND 63016**
Lotus / Feb '93 / Jazz Horizons / Impetus.

ERC MUSIC INC.
CD _____ **ERCMCD 63602**
ERC / Aug '93 / Jetstar.

ESCAPE TO TRANSCYBERIA
CD _____ **K 7036CD**
Studio K7 / Oct '95 / Disc.

ESP
Smiling faces / Little girl / Straight from a dream / This place we call home / Always / Sly / Soul urge / Nothing else is better / Tuesday AM / Vigilance
CD _____ **101S 877082**
101 South / Jan '96 / New Note.

ESQUIRE ALL AMERICAN JAZZ CONCERT 1944
Jazz Archives / Jan '95 / Jazz Music / Discovery / Cadillac. _____ **158262**

ESQUIRE JAZZ CONCERT, METROPOLITAN OPERA HOUSE
CD _____ **CD 53035**
Giants Of Jazz / Jan '89 / Target/BMG / Cadillac.

ESSENCE OF FUNK
Cornbread / Loose change / Slow drag / Eternal flame / Freedom jazz dance / Jive samba / Comin' home baby
CD _____ **HIBD 8007**
Hip Bop / Oct '95 / Conifer / Total/BMG / Silva Screen.

ESSENCE OF THE BLUES, THE
(3CD Set)
CD Set _____ **MCBX 015**
Music Club / Dec '94 / Disc / THE / CM.

ESSENTIAL 60'S NORTHERN SOUL DANCEFLOOR CLASSICS #2
This is the house where love died: *First Choice* / Turning my heartbeat up: *MVP's* / Help me: *Wilson, Al* / Glad all over: *Young, Leon Strings* / Sally saying something: *Harner, Billy* / Don't just look at me: *Farlowe, Chris* / Good things come to those who wait: *Jackson, Chuck* / Don't take it out of this world: *Adam's Apples* / Under my

thumb: Gibson, Wayne / Livin' the nightlife: Charts / I'm so glad I found you: Jones, Linda & The Whatnauts / I don't want to lose you: Wilson, Jackie / Last minute miracle: Shirelles / One in a million: Brown, Maxine / Black eyed girl: Thompson, Billy / I'm gonna pick up my toys: Devonnes / You're puttin' me on: Taylor, Carmen / Have more time: Smith, Marvin / In the long run: Blandon, Curtis / Just in the nick of time: Lamarr, Tony / California montage: Young Holt Unlimited

CD _____ **DGPCD 728**

Deep Beats / Jun '95 / BMG.

ESSENTIAL 60'S NORTHERN SOUL DANCEFLOOR CLASSICS VOL.1
Purple haze: Jones, Johnny & The King Casuals / Baby boy: Hughes, Freddie / Tryin to find my woman: Courtney, Lou / There was a time: Chandler, Gene / Who who song: Wilson, Jackie / Marble and iron: Douglas, Carl / Our love is getting stonger: Knight, Jason / What about the music: Harner, Billy / Boc to bach: Father's Angels / What love brings: Bernard, Kenny / Everything's gonna be alright: Arnold, P.P. / Scrub board: Trammps / Ton of dynamite: Crocker, Frankie 'Loveman' / Soul improvisations: McCoy, Van / Goodbye nothing to say: Javells / Bring him back: Starr, Stella / Stop what you're doing to me: Playthings / I get the sweetest feeling: Wilson, Jackie / Love makes a woman: Acklin, Barbara / I'm gonna miss you: Artistics / Stay close to me: Five Stairsteps / Hold back the night: Trammps

CD _____ **DGPCD 704**

Deep Beats / Sep '94 / BMG.

ESSENTIAL ARGO/CADET GROOVES (Off The Wall)
Off the wall: Johnson, Buddy / Milestones: Three Souls / Wailer: Cox, Sonny / Feel: Clarke, Buck / Slick Eddie: Stitt, Sonny / Hanky panky: Scott, Shirley / Fourth dimension: McDuff, Jack / Daylie's double: Nelson, Oliver / Black foot: Jacquet, Illinois / Acquarian: Land, Harold

CD _____ **CDARC 507**

Charly / Jan '93 / Charly / THE / Cadillac.

ESSENTIAL ARGO/CADET GROOVES VOL.2 (The Heatin' System)
Heatin' system: McDuff, Jack / Liberation conversation: Shaw, Marlena / Scootin': Lazar, Sam / Samba blues: Foster, Frank / Please don't leave me: Shihab, Sahib / Passing zone: Donaldson, Lou / Blue bongo: Lewis, Ramsey / Favourite things: Holt, Red

CD _____ **CDARC 508**

Charly / Sep '91 / Charly / THE / Cadillac.

ESSENTIAL ARGO/CADET GROOVES VOL.3 (Free Soul)
Straussmania: Salinas, Daniel / Ju ju: McDuff, Brother Jack / Woman of the ghetto: Shaw, Marlena / Tight money: Wilson, Reuben / Moondance: Tate, Grady / Little sunflower: Ashby, Dorothy / Ordinary Joe: Callier, Terry / Free soul: Klemmer, John / Pressure gauge: McDuff, Brother Jack / Can't catch the 'trane: Callier, Terry

CD _____ **CDARC 510**

Charly / Jun '93 / Charly / THE / Cadillac.

ESSENTIAL BIG BANDS
CD _____ **4671502**

Sony Jazz / Jan '95 / Sony.

ESSENTIAL CHILL, THE
CD _____ **948902**

Arcade / Apr '92 / Sony / Grapevine.

ESSENTIAL COLLECTION FROM SCOTLAND
CD _____ **RECD 496**

REL / May '95 / THE / Gold / Duncans.

ESSENTIAL DANCEFLOOR CLASSICS VOL. 1
Somebody else's guy: Brown, Jocelyn / Love fever: Adams, Gayle / Last night a DJ saved my life: Indeep / Can you handle it: Redd, Sharon / And the beat goes on: Whispers / Take that to the bank: Shalamar / Giving it back: Hurtt, Phil / Nice and soft: Wish / Romeo where's Juliet: Collage / I like (what you're doing to me): Young & Co. / Dancin': Crown Heights Affair / Let's start the dance: Bohannon, Hamilton

CD _____ **DGPCD 668**

Deep Beats / Mar '94 / BMG.

ESSENTIAL DANCEFLOOR CLASSICS VOL. 2
Go deh yaka (Go to the top): Monyaka / Share the night: World Premiere / There it is: Shalamar / I don't want to be a freak (but I can't help myself): Dynasty / Check out the groove: Thurston, Bobby / Rock steady: Whispers / Beat the street: Redd, Sharon / Operator: Midnight Star / Body work: Hot Streak / Casanova: Coffee / Use your body and soul: Crown Heights Affair / Do you wanna funk: Sylvester

CD _____ **DGPCD 709**

Deep Beats / Feb '95 / BMG.

ESSENTIAL DETROIT SOUL COLLECTION
CD _____ **GSCD 003**

Goldmine / Mar '92 / Vital.

ESSENTIAL DISCO DANCEFLOOR CLASSICS VOL. 1
Penguin at the big apple/Zing went the strings of my heart: Trammps / Uptown festival: Shalamar / Come to me: Joli, France / Dance with you: Lucas, Carrie / Phoenix: Aquarian Dream / There but for the grace of God go I: Machine / In the bush: Musique / Feed the flame: Johnson, Lorraine / Afreak-a: Lemon / This is it: Moore, Melba / Baby don't change your mind: Knight, Gladys & The Pips / Loving you - losing you: Hyman, Phyllis

CD _____ **DGPCD 703**

Deep Beats / Sep '94 / BMG.

ESSENTIAL DRUM AND BASS
CD _____ **DBMEM 1**

Essential Dance Music / Dec '95 / Disc.

ESSENTIAL ELECTRO DANCEFLOOR CLASSICS VOL.1
Let the music play: Shannon / Body work: Hot / Hip hop be bop (Don't stop) (Don't stop): Man Parrish / Feel the force: G-Force / Boogie down: Man Parrish / Mosquito aka Hobo scratch: West Street Mob / Papa was a rollin' stone: Wolfer, Bill / Girl you need a change of mind: Fowler, Fred / In the bottle: C.O.D. / Give me tonight: Shannon

CD _____ **DGPCD 685**

Deep Beats / Jun '94 / BMG.

ESSENTIAL ELECTRO DANCEFLOOR CLASSICS VOL.2
Your life: Konk / Out of sight: Lefturno / Soul makossa: Nairobi / Sunshine, partytime: Rockers Revenge & Donnie Calvin / On the upside: Xena / Nunk: Warp 9 / Whip it: Treacherous Three & Philippe Wynne / Message II (survival): Melle Mel & Duke Bootee / Hobo rock: Griffin, Reggie & Technofunk / Uphill (peace of mind): C.O.D.

CD _____ **DGPCD 742**

Deep Beats / Nov '95 / BMG.

ESSENTIAL ELEMENTS VOL.6
CD _____ **703011**
CD _____ **703011X**

Essential Dance Music / Feb '96 / Disc.

ESSENTIAL ELLA, BILLIE, SARAH, ARETHA, MAHALIA
CD _____ **4737332**

Sony Jazz / Jan '95 / Sony.

ESSENTIAL FOLK
CD _____ **NTRCD 030**

Nectar / Mar '95 / Pinnacle.

ESSENTIAL FUNK CLASSICS VOL.1
Everyway but loose: Phunky / Hypertension: Calender / Hustle bus stop: Mastermind / Water bed parts 1 and 2: LTG Exchange / Zone: Rhythm Makers / Who's got the monster: Rimshots / Boogie woogie: Sound Experience / Monster from the black tongs: Calender / Back it up parts 1 and 2: Lanlords & Tenants / Message: Cymande / Chance with you: Brother To Brother / Give me your love: Mason, Barbara

CD _____ **DGPCD 684**

Deep Beats / Jun '94 / BMG.

ESSENTIAL GARAGE DANCEFLOOR CLASSICS VOL.1
In and out of my life: Adeva / You don't know: Serious Intention / Ma foom bey: Cultural Vibe / Jazzy rhythm: Wallace, Michelle / Tee's happy: Northend / You're all played out: Life / Touch me: Rae, Fonda / Standing right there: Moore, Melba / I'm caught up (in a one night love affair): Inner Life / What I got is what you need: Unique

CD _____ **DGPCD 686**

Deep Beats / Jun '94 / BMG.

ESSENTIAL GARAGE DANCEFLOOR CLASSICS VOL.2
Music is the answer: Abrams, Colonel / You can't run from me: Singleton, Maxine / Who's gonna ease the pressure: Thornhill, Mac / Touch me the love tonight: Keith, Brian / I can't wait too long: Church, Joe / Music's got me: Visual / One hot night: Pure Energy & Lisa Stevens / Love itch: Flemming, Rochelle / You are the one: Pilot / I'd like to: Feel / I need you now: Sinnamon

CD _____ **DGPCD 739**

Deep Beats / Nov '95 / BMG.

ESSENTIAL GROOVE
This DJ: Warren G. / Bump 'n' grind: R. Kelly / Cry for you: Jodeci / Your love is a 187: Whitehead Brothers / Midnight at the oasis: Brand New Heavies / Everything's gonna be alright: Sounds Of Blackness / Blow your mind: Jamiroquai / Ease my mind: Arrested Development / Anything: S.W.V. / True spirit: Anderson, Carleen / Looking through patient eyes: PM Dawn / Sly: Massive Attack / All about Eve: Marx-man / Spiritual love: Urban Species / Twyford Down: Galliano / You know how we do it: Ice Cube / Outside: Omar / Love makes the world go round: Don-E / Get in touch: Freak Power / Don't you worry about a thing: Incognito

CD _____ **5254382**

PolyGram / Mar '95 / PolyGram.

ESSENTIAL HI-NRG DANCEFLOOR CLASSICS VOL.1
Hit and run lover: Jiani, Carol / Harmony: Suzy Q / Last call: Jolo / Computer music: Suzy Q / I've got it: Payne, Scherrie / Pushin' too hard: Parker, Paul / Cuba libra: Modern Rocketry / Don't leave me this way:

Tracy, Jeanie / One look: Moore, Jackson / Menergy: Cowley, Patrick / Homosexuality: Modern Rocketry

CD _____ **DGPCD 664**

Deep Beats / Mar '94 / BMG.

ESSENTIAL HIGHLIGHTS FROM THE SERIES
CD _____ **4736862**

Sony Jazz / Jan '95 / Sony.

ESSENTIAL HOLLYWOOD JAZZ
CD _____ **4743732**

Sony Jazz / Jan '95 / Sony.

ESSENTIAL JAZZ
Take five: Brubeck, Dave / Girl from Ipanema: Getz, Stan & Astrud Gilberto / One note samba: Gillespie, Dizzy / I've got you under my skin: Washington, Dinah / Summertime: Vaughan, Sarah / Foggy day: Marsalis, Wynton / Take the 'A' train: Marsalis, Wynton / Love for sale: Davis, Miles / God bless the child: Holiday, Billie / Laird baird: Parker, Charlie / Polka dots and moonbeams: Peterson, Oscar / Autumn leaves: Evans, Bill / Goodbye pork pie hat: Mingus, Charles / Soul eyes: Coltrane, John

CD _____ **MUSCD 005**

MCI / Nov '92 / Disc / THE.

ESSENTIAL JAZZ CONCERTS
CD _____ **4685742**

Sony Jazz / Jan '95 / Sony.

ESSENTIAL JAZZ DRUMMERS
Sing, sing, sing: Woody, Sam / Hi fi fo fum: Bellson, Louie & Duke Ellington / Skin Deep: Roach, Max / Drum suite (pts 1-5): Rich, Buddy / Sugarfoot stomp: Morello, Joe / Flash: Morello, Joe / C jam blues: Blakey, Art / Sacrifict: Woodyard, Sam / Duel fuel (pts 1-3): Woodyard, Sam

CD _____ **468573 2**

Columbia / Jul '93 / Sony.

ESSENTIAL JAZZ LEGENDS
CD _____ **4716842**

Sony Jazz / Jan '95 / Sony.

ESSENTIAL JAZZ PIANO
CD _____ **4685722**

Sony Jazz / Jan '95 / Sony.

ESSENTIAL JAZZ SAX
CD _____ **4741862**

Sony Jazz / Jan '95 / Sony.

ESSENTIAL LATIN JAZZ
CD _____ **4716832**

Sony Jazz / Jan '95 / Sony.

ESSENTIAL MELLOW GROOVE
CD _____ **GSCD 005**

Goldmine / Sep '92 / Vital.

ESSENTIAL MERENGUE - STRIPPING THE PARROTS
CD _____ **CORACD 122**

Corason / Feb '95 / CM / Direct / ADA.

ESSENTIAL MIX (Tong/Cox/Sasha/Oakenfold/2CD/MC Set)
Hide-a-way: Rich, Kelli / Over and over: Plux & Georgia Jones / Nakasaki: Kendoh / Tempo fiesta: Itty Bitty Boozy Woozy / Dancing daffodils: Beat Syndicate / Are you the cost: Crescendo / I need you: Pendulum / Access: D.J. Misjah & Tim / Are you ready to fly: Dune / Neurodancer: Wippenberg / Harmonio groove: Garnier, Laurent / Outrage: D.J. Powerout / Dance 2 the music: Men With Rhythm / Education: Pox And Cowell / Mantra to the Buddha: Hyperspace / Cut for life: Leftfield / Static: Markey / Step back: Slam / Thunder: Clarke, Dave / Lets turn it on: Doof / Paradise regime: Blue Amazon / Save me: Beat Foundation / Wired: Tenth Chapter / Rays of the rising sun: Mozalo / Runaway: Evoke / Coma aroma: In Aura / Survive: Brothers Grimm / Skylined: Prodigy / Floor essence: Man With No Name / Down to earth: Grace / Star: Utah Saints / Sun: Virus

CD _____ **8287012**

FFRR / Nov '95 / PolyGram.

ESSENTIAL MODERN SOUL DANCEFLOOR CLASSICS VOL.1
It really hurts me girl: Carstairs / Nine times: Moments / On the real side: Saunders, Larry / You're my one weakness, girl: Street People / Sorry, that number's been disconnected: Green, Marie / I wanna give you tomorrow: Troy, Benny / You beat me to the punch: Young, Retta / Never get enough of your love: Street People / Keep on trying: LTG Exchange / Sweet sweet lady: Moments / Reach out for me: Universal Mind / I've got the need: Moments / Do what you feel: Rimshots / Party music: Lundi, Part / Something fishy going on: Universal Mind / Don't send me away: Fleming, Garfield

CD _____ **DGPCD 710**

Deep Beats / Feb '95 / BMG.

ESSENTIAL MODERN SOUL SELECTION VOL.3, THE
For real: Flowers / Alone again: Baker, Ernest / Da da da da da (I love you): Naturals / I think I've got a good chance: Barnes, J.J. / Can this be real: Perfections / He's a better liar than me: Lampkin, Tony / I just want to do my own thing: Reachers / That's the way the world should be: Up From The Bottom / At work and no play: Jordan, Vivalore / Put your lovin' on me: Fisher, Willie / Since you said you'd be mine: Ragland, Lou /

Can't nobody love me like you do: Storm / I gotta make you believe in me: BJB / I'll do anything for you: McDonald, Lee / Doin' it cause it feels good: Strong, Chuck / All of a sudden: Moore, Melvin / Ain't nothing like the love: Simmons, John / Hungry: Sandy's Gang / What does the future hold: 24 Karat Gold

CD _____ **GSCD 040**

Goldmine / Jun '94 / Vital.

ESSENTIAL NORTHERN SOUL STORY
CD _____ **GSCD 001 X**

Goldmine / Sep '91 / Vital.

ESSENTIAL OLD SCHOOL RAP DANCEFLOOR CLASSICS VOL.1
Funky sound (Tear the roof off): Sequence / Do you want to rock (before I let go): Funky Four / King tim theory: Funky Four / Showdown: Furious Five & Sugarhill Gang / Pump me up: Trouble Funk / Birthday party: Grandmaster Flash & The Furious Five / Apache: Sugarhill Gang / Feel it (The Mexican): Funky Four / Eighth wonder: Sugarhill Gang / Ice cream dreams: Lady L / Mosquito: West Street Mob / Message: Grandmaster Flash & The Furious Five

CD _____ **DGPCD 708**

Deep Beats / Mar '95 / BMG.

ESSENTIAL ORGAN/PIANO BOOGIE WOOGIE
CD _____ **4716902**

Sony Jazz / Jan '95 / Sony.

ESSENTIAL PARTY MEGAMIX
CD _____ **SOW 715**

Sound Waves / Dec '94 / Target/BMG.

ESSENTIAL SLOW GROOVE DANCEFLOOR CLASSICS 1
Making love: Todd, Pam & Love Exchange / All I want is my baby: Gilliam, Roberta / In the night time: Henderson, Michael / Sexy Mama: Moments / I want you: Jones, Tamiko / Love talk: Gilstrap, Jim / You are my starship: Connors, Norman / Valentine love: Connors, Norman / We both need each other: Connors, Norman / Be thankful for what you've got: DeVaughan, William / You'll never know: Hi-Gloss / Curious: Midnight Star

CD _____ **DGPCD 706**

Deep Beats / Sep '94 / BMG.

ESSENTIAL SLOW GROOVE DANCEFLOOR CLASSICS 2
I'm the one for you: Whispers / Over and over: Shalamar / Show me what you're coming from: Lucas, Carrie / Window on a dream: Wolfer, Bill / Curious: Midnight Star / Winners and losers: Collage / Two occasions: Deele / Don't keep me waiting: Whispers / Hello stranger: Lucas, Carrie / Feels so good: Midnight Star / One girl: Dynasty / No pain, no gain: Whispers / This is for the lover in you: Shalamar

CD _____ **DGPCD 711**

Deep Beats / Feb '95 / BMG.

ESSENTIAL SOUL COLLECTION
Native New Yorker: Odyssey / Rock the boat: Hues Corporation / Ms Grace: Tymes / Shame: King, Evelyn / Automatic: Pointer Sisters / Kissing in the back row of the movies: Drifters / Who's zoomin' who: Franklin, Aretha / Torg vu: Warwick, Dionne / Didn't I blow your mind: Delfonics / I'm your puppet: Purify, James & Bobby / Shoop shoop song (it's in his kiss): Everett, Betty

CD _____ **74321339302**

Camden / Jan '96 / BMG.

ESSENTIAL SUN ROCKABILLIES VOL.1
Put your cat clothes on: Perkins, Carl / Red hot: Riley, Billy Lee / We wanna boogie: Burgess, Sonny / Tennessee zip: Parchman, Kenny / Rabbit action: Haggett, Jimmy / Come on little mama: Harris, Ray / Madman: Wages, Jimmy / Red cadillac and a black moustache: Smith, Warren / Mama mama mama: Thompson, Hayden / Flat foot Sam: Blake, Tommy / Crowdad hole: Earls, Jack / Goin' crazy: Self, Mack / Crazy woman: Simmons, Gene / Tough tough tough: Anderson, Andy / Huh babe: Mc-Danie, Luke / Ten cats down: Miller Sisters / Rakin' and scrapin': Beard, Dean / Rockin' with my baby: Yelvington, Malcolm / Bottle to the baby: Feathers, Jerry Lee / Your love is the heart of mine: Bond, Eddie / Milkshake mademoiselle: Lewis, Jerry Lee / Your lovin' man: Taylor, Vernon / Me and my rhythm guitar: Powers, Johnny / Just in time: Jenkins, Harold / Ooby dooby: Orbison, Roy

CD _____ **CPCD 8099**

Charly / Jun '95 / Charly / THE / Cadillac.

ESSENTIAL SUN ROCKABILLIES VOL.2
CD _____ **CPCD 8118**

Charly / Aug '95 / Charly / THE / Cadillac.

ESSENTIAL UNDERGROUND DANCEFLOOR CLASSICS VOL.1
Once I've been there: Connors, Norman / Mainline: Black Ivory / Show you my love: Alexander, Goldie / Feel my love: Hudson, Laurice / I really love you: Heaven & Earth / Don't send me away: Fleming, Garfield / We rap more mellow: Younger Generation / Key: Wuf Ticket / Bad times it can't stand my tip: Captain Rapo / On a journey (I sing the funk electric): Electric Funk / (I'm just a sucker for a pretty face: Phillips, West / Thanks to you: Sinnamon

CD _____ DGPCD 667
Deep Beats / Mar '94 / BMG.

ESSENTIAL UNDERGROUND DANCEFLOOR CLASSICS VOL. 2
Go with the flow: Weeks & Co / Don't you love it: Singleton, Maxine / No news is news: Kreamcicle / You've reached the bottom line: Williams, Carol / All I need is you: Starshine / Your love: Satin, Silk & Lace / I'll do anything for your love: Morgan, Denroy / I hear music in the street: Unlimited Touch / Fantastic voyage: Lakeside / Sweeter as the days goes by: Shalamar / Must be the music: Secret Weapon / Can't fake the feeling: Hunt, Geraldine
CD _____ DGPCD 705
Deep Beats / Sep '94 / BMG.

ETERNAL FLAME
(Baltimore Jam)
CD _____ STBCD 2504
Stash / Sep '95 / Jazz Music / CM / Cadillac / Direct / ADA.

ETERNAL LOVE
CD _____ WBRCD 1001
Business / Aug '94 / Jetstar.

ETERNAL VOICES
(2CD Set)
CD Set _____ NAR 053
New Alliance / May '94 / Pinnacle.

ETERNALLY
CD _____ STACD 052
Wisepack / Sep '93 / THE / Conifer.

ETERNALLY ALIVE VOL.II
CD _____ MILL 017CD
Millenium / Nov '95 / Plastic Head.

EUPHORIA
Rumour / Mar '94 / Pinnacle / 3MV / Sony.

EUPHORIA
CD Set _____ SPV 085-38892
SPV / Jul '94 / Plastic Head.

EURO DANCE HITS
Dino / Feb '94 / Pinnacle / 3MV.

EUROBEAT 2000
CD _____ KICKCD 32
Slip 'n' Slide / Jan '96 / Vital / Disc.

EUROBEAT 2000 - CLUB CLASSICS VOLUME 1
CD _____ KICKCD 13
Kickin' / Oct '94 / SRD.

EUROBEAT 2000 - CLUB CLASSICS VOLUME 2
CD _____ KICKCD 19
Kickin' / Mar '95 / SRD.

EUROCLUB 1
Get up: Technotronic / Jack to the sound of the underground: Hithouse / Don't let me be misunderstood: Santa Esmerelda / James Brown in still alive: Holy Noise / Quadraphonia: Quadrophonia / Sonar system: Meng Syndicate / To piano: Clarke, Rozline / Dancing is like making love: Mainx / Can this be love: Eden / Make my day: Grace Under Pressure / Move: Guaranteed Raw / Feel the groove: Cartouche / I won't let you down: Two Boys / Nightlife: T.P.F.F / Feel good: Chique / Keep the fire burning: Bass X / Let your love flow: Melissa / Down on the street: Glow / This beat is technotronic: Technotronic
CD _____ EUROCD 1
Charly / Jul '95 / Charly / THE / Cadillac.

EUROCLUB 2
Pump up the jam: Technotronic / Voices: K.C. Flightt / Good love: Xaviera Gold / Alice (who the fuck is Alice): Steppers / Wave of the future: Quadrophonia / Love with love: Black Diamond / I can handle it: M.S.D. / 99 Luftballons: Donn-Ah / Fue amor: Jazzy Mel / Glow of love: Grace Under Pressure / Hot (wonderful world): Reggie / Touch the sky: Cartouche / Just the two of us: 2 Boy's / Just a little pain: Laurenz / Rage: Twins / Night is mine (x-tra compact mix): MC-X / Give me your love: Boogie / Gonna move your body: Voice Over
CD _____ EUROCD 2
Charly / Jul '95 / Charly / THE / Cadillac.

EUROPEAN BRASS BAND CHAMPIONSHIP 1993
CD _____ QPRL 059D
Polyphonic / Aug '93 / Conifer.

EUROPEAN POLKA HITS
Trumpet echo / Cross polka / Polka from Tegernsee / Fast polka
CD _____ 15282
Laserlight / '91 / Target/BMG.

EUROPEAN TRUMPET SUMMIT
CD _____ EFA 084282
Konnex / Apr '95 / SRD.

EVE COMPILATION
CD _____ EVRCD 19
Eve / Mar '93 / Grapevine.

EVEN SANTA GETS THE BLUES
Christmas celebration: King, B.B. / I'll be coming home for Christmas: Brooks, Hadda / Merry Christmas baby: Brown, Charles / I want you with me at Christmas: Belvin, Jesse / White Christmas: Brooks, Hadda /

La Christmas blue: Brooks, Hadda / Please come home for Christmas: Winter, Johnny / I wanna spend Christmas with you: Fulson, Lowell / Only if you were here: Hayes, Isaac / So glad you were born: Hayes, Isaac
CD _____ VPBCD 28
Virgin / Nov '95 / EMI.

EVERY SONG TELLS A STORY
Boxer: Simon & Garfunkel / Candle in the wind: John, Elton / Praying for time: Michael, George / Little time: Beautiful South / Alison: Costello, Elvis / Hazard: Marx, Richard / Romeo and Juliet: Dire Straits / Living years: Mike & The Mechanics / Dignity: Deacon Blue / Up the junction: Squeeze / You're so vain: Simon, Carly / W.O.L.D.: Chapin, Harry / Ode to Billy Joe: Gentry, Bobbie / Ruby, don't take your love to town: Rogers, Kenny / Babooshka: Bush, Kate / Vincent: McLean, Don / Uptown, uptempo woman: Edelman, Randy / Waterloo sunset: Kinks / Classic: Gurvitz, Adrian
CD _____ 5251702
PolyGram TV / Apr '95 / PolyGram.

EVERYONE'S A WINNER
Twilight cafe: Fassbender, Susan / Keeping the dream alive: Freiheit / It's raining men: Weather Girls / Satellite: Hooters / Thank you: Pale Fountains / Town to town: Microdisney / Last film: Kissing The Pink / See that glow: This Island Earth / Walk: Inmates / Funky town: Pseudo Echo / Flaming sword: Care / Brilliant mind: Furniture / Dam-ger game: Pinkees / Waiting for a star: Boys Meets Girl / Riders on the storm: Lamb, Annabel / Magic smilo: Vola, Rosie
CD _____ OG 3305
Old Gold / Oct '92 / Carlton Home Entertainment.

EVIDENCE BLUES SAMPLER
CD _____ ECD 260002
Evidence / Jan '92 / Harmonia Mundi / ADA / Cadillac.

EVIDENCE BLUES SAMPLER THE THIRD
House cat blues: Linkchain, Hip / Don't throw your love on me so strong: Campbell, Eddie C. / Boxcar shorty: Cousin Joe / Giving up on love: Davis, Larry / Little red rooster: Peterson, Lucky / Night life: Witherspoon, Jimmy / That's alright: Rogers, Jimmy / Cold cold feeling: Taylor, Melvin / You've got me running: Johnson, Luther 'Georgia Snake Boy' / Don't you lie to me: Edwards, Honeyboy / It hurts me too: Wells, Junior / You just a baby child: Dawkins, Jimmy / Broke and hungry: Sumlin, Hubert / I can't quit you baby: Rush, Otis
CD _____ ECD 260482
Evidence / Mar '94 / Harmonia Mundi / ADA / Cadillac.

EVIDENCE BLUES SAMPLER TOO
Johnnie's boogie: Johnson, Johnnie / Ramblin' on my mind: Lockwood, Robert Jnr. / Worried about the blues: Fulson, Lowell / You say that you love me honey: Odom, Andrew / Giving up on love: Davis, Larry / Choo choo ch' boogie: Brown, Clarence 'Gatemouth' / Trouble in mind: Smith, Carrie / Blues is alright: Little Milton / Orange driver: Burns, Eddie Band / My baby and me: Shaw, Eddie / Talking to anna man, part 1: Taylor, Melvin / Takes money: Young, Joe / Special road: Robinson, Fenton / Young man young woman blues: Robinson, Fenton / That's your thing: Benton, Buster / All for business: Dawkins, Jimmy
CD _____ ECD 260402
Evidence / Sep '93 / Harmonia Mundi / ADA / Cadillac.

EVOLUTION'S CHRISTMAS
CD _____ EVCD 3
Evolution / Dec '95 / Total/BMG.

EVOLVING TRADITION
CD _____ MCRCD 5991
Mrs. Casey / Apr '95 / Direct / ADA.

EXCELLO HITS
Little darlin': Gladiolas / Raining in my heart: Harpo, Slim / Oh Julie: Crescendos / Prisoners song: Storm, Warren / Rollin' stone: Marigolds / Pleadin' for love: Birdsong, Larry / Congo mombo: Guitar Gable / Hey baby: Ferrier, Al / Emmitt Lee: Fran, Carol / Shoop shoop: Gladiolas / I'm a mojo man: Lonesome Sundown / This should go on forever: King Karl / I'm a lover not a fighter: Lazy Lester / Now that she's gone: King Crooners / Doin' the hoose: Brooks, Skippy / Rooster blues: Lightnin' Slim / Please think it over: Shelton, Roscoe / School daze: Little Rico & The King Crooners / Hello Mary Lee: Lightnin' Slim / You know baby: Meloaires / Baby scratch my back: Harpo, Slim / Snake out of the grass: Anderson, Roshell
CD _____ CDCHD 400
Ace / Jan '94 / Pinnacle / Cadillac / Complete/Pinnacle.

EXIST DANCE
CD _____ HHCD 11
Harthouse / Jan '96 / Disc / Warner Music.

EXOTIC VOICES & RHYTHMS OF BLACK AFRICA
CD _____ EUCD 1204
ARC / Sep '93 / ARC Music / ADA.

EXOTIC VOICES & RHYTHMS OF THE SOUTH SEAS
CD _____ EUCD 1254
ARC / Mar '94 / ARC Music / ADA.

EXPANSION PHAT JAMS
Just let me be close to you: Valentine Brothers / No more tears: Jeter, Genobia / Beverly: Jamariah / You know what it's like: Brooks, Calvin / Callin' up (Old memories): Haynes, Victor / Shoulda been you: Ware, Leon / Didn't mean to hurt you: Valentine, Billy / Starlite: Ballin, Chris / Victory: Baylor, Helen / Kissing in the dark: Rodni / Miss you: Fresh Air / Love hurts: Glaze / Show your love: Hutson, Leroy / I can't stand the pain: Lorenzo / If you don't want my love (soul mix): Williams, Lewis
CD _____ EXCDP 3
Expansion / Jun '94 / Pinnacle / Sony / 3MV.

EXPANSION SOUL SAUCE VOL.1
My favourite thing: Brooks, Calvin & Hari Paris / Share your love: Hutson, Leroy / Oasis: Baylor, Helen / I found someone: Gaines, Billy & Sarah / Shine: Aja / Heartbeat: Ware, Leon / Win your love: James, Josie / Everybody's in a hurry: McNeir, Ronnie / Main squeeze: Crook, General / Hang on: Robbins, Rockie / Love is the magic: Blu, Peggi / We got one: Covington, Matt / Power to the people: Linsey / Friends or lovers: Burke, Keni / Promises: Glaze
CD _____ CDEXP 1
Expansion / Jul '93 / Pinnacle / Sony / 3MV.

EXPANSION SOUL SAUCE VOL.2
Late night hour: Waters, Kim / Surrender (my soul): Skinner, Belinda A. / Paradise: Tankard, Ben / Give me all your love: Ballin, Chris / You are my star: Reeves, Paulette / Forever: Felder, Wilton / I can only think of you: McCrae, Gwen / Love for love: Warren, Tony / It's up to me: James, Josie / One step back for love: El Coco / Stay with me: Clear, Crystal / Shame on you: Lovesmith, Michael / Goodbye song: Vanesse & Carolyn / Look of love: Hutson, Leroy / After affect: Taylor, Gary
CD _____ CDEXP 3
Expansion / May '93 / Pinnacle / Sony / 3MV.

EXPANSION SOUL SAUCE VOL.3
Think about it: Webb, Rick / Ja miss me: Valentine, Billy / I don't know why: White, Lynn / One and only: Rodni / Take a little time: James, Josie / Just to be happy: Haynes, Victor / Blind to it all: Taylor, Gary / Love's gonna bring you home: RockmeIons / All my love: Carmichael, James / This kind of love (so special): Valentine Brothers / I'd like to into you: Kelly, Denise & Fame / Get into your life: Beloyd / Losers weepers: Blackfoot, J. / If you don't want my love: Williams, Lewis
CD _____ CDEXP 6
Expansion / Nov '93 / Pinnacle / Sony / 3MV.

EXPANSION SOUL SAUCE VOL.4
CD _____ CDEXP 9
Expansion / Feb '95 / Pinnacle / Sony / 3MV.

EXPERIENCE IN KOOL
CD _____ TKCD 14
2 Kool / Oct '95 / SRD.

EXPERIMENTA
Middle earth: Drax Two / Amecia: Connective Zone / Intervalid: Terrace / Letter: Tura / Clank: Stassis / Gaspar: Kape III Musier / Formation: Plasma / Arfecth: Angel, Dave / Another acid: Mono Junk / Soft key: Tura / Speng II: Kinesthesia / Memories of the future: Edge Of Motion
CD _____ AA 001CD
A13 Productions / Sep '94 / Vital.

EXTRA HOT 8
CD _____ DMUT 1246
Multitone / Aug '93 / BMG.

EXTRA HOT 9
CD _____ DMUT 1271
Multitone / Jan '94 / BMG.

EXTRA SENSUAL PERCEPTION VOLUME 1
CD _____ SUN 49972
Mokum / Mar '95 / Pinnacle.

EXTRA SENSUAL PERCEPTION VOLUME 2
CD _____ SUN 49962
Mokum / Mar '95 / Pinnacle.

EYE ON THE PRIZE
Together forever: Exodus / Keep in touch: Montana, Vince Jr. / Get down: Aleem & Leroy Burgess / Long enough: Last Poets / Barely breaking even: Universal Robot Band / Weekend: Class Action / What happend to the music: Trammps
CD _____ SURCD 02
Grapevine / Jun '94 / Grapevine.

FABULOUS 30'S, THE
CD _____ DCD 5335
Disky / Dec '93 / THE / BMG / Discovery / Pinnacle.

FABULOUS 40'S, THE
CD _____ CDSR 058
Telstar / Nov '94 / BMG.

FABULOUS FIFTIES ROCK 'N' ROLL
Great balls of fire: Lewis, Jerry Lee / Shake, rattle and roll: Haley, Bill & The Comets / Bony moronie: Williams, Larry / Raunchy: Justis, Bill / Lucille: Little Richard / Tiger: Fabian / Claudette: Everly Brothers / Leroy: Scott, Jack / Rave on: Holly, Buddy & The Crickets / Johnny B. Goode: Berry, Chuck / (We're gonna) Rock around the clock: Haley, Bill & The Comets / Blue suede shoes: Perkins, Bill / When: Kalin Twins / Tallahassie lassie: Cannon, Freddy / Good golly Miss Miss: Little Richard / Wake up little Susie: Everly Brothers / Lawdy Miss Clawdy: Price, Lloyd / Whole lotta shakin' goin' on: Lewis, Jerry Lee
CD _____ PWKS 4180
Carlton Home Entertainment / Oct '94 / Carlton Home Entertainment.

FABULOUS FLIPS
Slow down: Williams, Larry / Give me love: Rosie & The Originals / Leroy: Scott, Jack / I wonder if I care as much: Everly Brothers / Sweetheart please don't go: Gladiolas / Miss Ann: Little Richard / Crazy: Hollywood Flames / Tram to nowhere: Champs / My little girl: Crescendos / What'cha gonna do: Kuf Linx / Did you cry: Dicky Doo & Don'ts / Can it be: Titans / Swag: Wray, Link & His Raymen / She's the one for me: Aquatones / Flippin': Hall, Rene / Gotta getta date: Jan & Arnie / Over and over: Day, Bobby / One night, one night: Skyliners / Beside you: Crests / Crazy baby: Rockin' R's / Rock 'n' roll cha cha: Matys Bros / This is love you: Cortez, Dave 'Baby' / Taking care of business: Turner, Titus / Last night I dreamed: Fiestas / Sweet thing: Bland, Billy / My babe: Holden, Ron
CD _____ CDCHD 444
Ace / Oct '93 / Pinnacle / Cadillac / Complete/Pinnacle.

FABULOUS FLIPS VOLUME 2
Little Billy boy / Lonesome for a letter / Trouble, is it's really you / Why / Well / Little Queenie / Ch-kow-ski / I could hold out any longer / Don't start cryin' now / Red sails in the sunset / Rubber dolly / Living's loving you / Sweet was the wine / Tight capris / Girl of my dreams / Love is a swingin' thing / Gunshot / Chicken necks / Havin' so much fun / Back shack track / Monster
CD _____ CDCHD 560
Ace / Apr '95 / Pinnacle / Cadillac / Complete/Pinnacle.

FACE OF THE FUTURE
CD _____ BDRCD 4
Breakdown / Nov '94 / SRD.

FACE THE CHALLENGE IN MUSIC VOL.1
CD _____ CHR 70020
Challenge / Sep '95 / Direct / Jazz Music / Cadillac / ADA.

FACE THE MUSIC - TORVILL & DEAN
Mack and Mabel / Summertime / Barnum / Bolero / Capriccio / Song of India / Venus / Love duet from Fire and Ice / Oscar tango - the Procession of the Tsar Berendey / Incantation / Oscar tango / Iceworks / Skaters' waltz / Let's face the music and dance / History of love / Medley
CD _____ 8450652
PolyGram TV / Feb '94 / PolyGram.

FACING THE WRONG WAY
CD _____ FTWW 1
4AD / Sep '95 / Disc.

FADO DE LISBOA
CD _____ HTCD 14
Heritage / Jan '93 / Swift / Roots / Wellard / Direct / Hot Shot / Jazz Music / ADA.

FAIKAVA: THE TONGAN KAVA CIRCLE
CD _____ PAN 2022CD
Pan / Oct '93 / ADA / Direct / CM.

FALLING IN LOVE AGAIN
CD _____ CDHD 188
Happy Days / Oct '92 / Conifer.

FALLOUT PUNK SINGLES COLLECTION, THE
Fallen hero: Enemy / Viva la revolution: Acts / Suicide bag: Action Pact / Punks alive: Enemy / Jubilee: Rabid / New barbarians: Urban Dogs / People: Action Pact / Limo life: Urban Dogs / First class: Enemy / London bouncers: Action Pact / Another typical city: UK Subs / Question of choice: Action Pact / Decapitated: Broken Bones / Am-

phetamine blues: *Fallen Angels* / Private army: *UK Subs* / Cruxifix: *Broken Bones* / Yet another dole queue song: *Action Pact* / Inner planet love: *Fallen Angels* / Cocktail credibility: *Action Pact* / Seeing through my eyes: *Broken Bones* / This gun says: *UK Subs* / Champs Elysees: *Adicts* / Never say die: *Broken Bones* / Hey Santa: *UK Subs* / Jodie Foster: *UK Subs*
CD _____ CDPUNK 30
Anagram / Mar '94 / Pinnacle.

FAMILIA RMM EN VIVO
Oiga, mire, vea: *Orquesta Guayacan* / Overture: *Orchestra RMM* / Apaga la luz: *Cartagena, Antonio* / Para que: *Pena, Miles* / Por eso esta conmigo: *Rivera, Johnny* / Mi primera rumba: *India* / Hasta que te conoci: *Anthony, Marc* / Aparentemente: *Vega, Tony* / Amores como tu: *Nieves, Tito* / Otra noche caliente: *De La Paz, Ray* / Disculpame senora: *Alberto, Jose* / Azucar negra: *Cruz, Celia*
CD _____ 66058067
RMM / Dec '95 / New Note.

FAMILY CIRCLE FAMILY TREE
Off with the old: *Chamaeleon Church* / Ina kindly way: *Chamaeleon Church* / Here's a song: *Chamaeleon Church* / Ready Eddie: *Chamaeleon Church* / Camellia is changing: *Chamaeleon Church* / Your golden love: *Chamaeleon Church* / Remembering's all I can do: *Chamaeleon Church* / Blueberry pie (Mixes): *Chamaeleon Church* / Tompkins square park: *Chamaeleon Church* / Spring this year: *Chamaeleon Church* / Maybe more than you: *Lost* / Back door blues: *Lost* / I want to know: *Lost* / Here she comes: *Lost* / Everybody knows: *Lost* / Violet gown: *Lost* / Mystic (Mixes): *Lost* / Kaleidoscope: *Lost* / Ultimate spinach III: *Lost* / Happiness child: *Lost*
CD _____ CDWIKD 146
Chiswick / Jan '96 / Pinnacle.

FAMOUS BIG BANDS, THE
(2CD Set)
CD Set _____ 24044
Delta Doubles / Sep '92 / Target/BMG.

FAMOUS CHARISMA BOX, THE
(4CD Set)
Hoopoe's tales: *Stanshall, Vivian* / Sympathy: *Rare Bird* / Refugees: *Van Der Graaf Generator* / Lady Eleanor: *Lindisfarne* / Knife: *Genesis* / Indian summer: *Audience* / Witchi-tai-to: *Topo D Bil* / Terry keeps his clips on: *Stanshall, Vivian* / Hungarian peasant girl: *Biltmuss, Trevor* / Regent street incident: *String Driven Thing* / Gaye: *Ward, Clifford T.* / Imperial zeppelin: *Hammill, Peter* / Painted ladies: *Moore, G T* / Money game: *Hull, Alan* / Ooh mother: *Unicorn* / Liar: *Brown, Capability* / Intermezzo from Karelia suite: *Nice* / Quark, strangeness and charm: *Hawkwind* / Sulishury Hill: *Gabriel, Peter* / Lucinda: *Werth, Howard* / Why can't I be satisfied: *Jack The Lad* / Doubting Thomas: *Heights, Jackson* / Fog on the Tyne: *Lindisfarne* / I get a kick out of you: *Shearston, Gary* / Ritt Mickley: *Refugee* / Disco suicide: *Brand X* / Working in line: *Rutherford, Mike* / Go placidly: *Every Which Way* / Robot man: *Wakeman, Rick* / And the wheels keep turning: *Banks, Tony* / Out in the sun: *Moraz, Patrick* / How can I: *Hackett, Steve* / Too many people: *Bell & Arc* / Happy the man: *Genesis* / She belongs to me: *Bell & Arc* / Window city: *Stanshall, Vivian* / Travel agent sketch (Live at Drury Lane): *Monty Python* / Cultural attache: *Humphries, Barry* / Talks turf: *O'Sullevan, Peter* / Three fold attunement: *Turner, Gordon* / Talks cricket: *Arlott, John* / One and tow: *Lang, R D* / Sir Henry at Rawlinson End: *Stanshall, Vivian* / Theme of Monty Python / Varsity students rag: *Betjeman, Sir John* / I bet you they won't play this song on the radio: *Monty Python* / Theme one: *Van Der Graaf Generator* / Window city (Fade): *Stanshall, Vivian* / Chasing sheep is best left to shepherds: *Nyman, Michael* / Front door: *Isaacs, Gregory* / Cloudy day: *Congo Ashanti Roy* / Put it out: *Prince Far-I* / Don't leave me this way: *Desperadoes* / Move it on up: *Moore, G T* / (Hey you) the Rocksteady crew: *Rocksteady Crew* / Hey DJ: *World's Famous Supreme Team* / Paperheart: *King, Robert* / Anticipation: *Delta 5* / All about you: *Scars* / Ten inch for honeymooners: *Monochrome Set* / Making time: *Creation* / Freedom dance jazz: *Emerson, Keith* / It's all over now baby blue: *Wray, Link* / Embezzler: *Werth, Howard & The Moonbeams* / Kittiwake: *Jansch, Bert* / Too late for goodbyes: *Lennon, Julian* / God rock: *Turner, Nik*
CD Set _____ CASBOX 7
Charisma / Nov '93 / EMI.

FAMOUS SPIRITUAL & GOSPEL FESTIVAL 1965
Jesus said if you go / Lord send the rain / Travelling shoes / Preaching/Exodus, 3rd / Tell me how long the train been gone / It's a needed time / It's in my heart / What low / Good somewhere / John saw the number / O why / Lord you have been good to me
CD _____ CDLR 44005
L&R / Feb '92 / New Note.

FANFARE
(20 Brass Band Classics)
Fanfare: *G.U.S. Footwear Band Quartet* / Elegy from a 'Downland suite': *Cory Band* / Snowy polka: *Royal Doulton Band* / Austria:

Wingates Temperance Band / Pixies parade: *Foden Motor Works Band* / Eye level: *Hendon Brass Band* / Prelude for an occasion: *Black Dyke Mills Band* / El matador: *Cambridge Band* / Slavonic dance no.8: *Carlton Main Colliery Band* / Waltz from memories of Schubert: *Cambridge Band* / Top o' the morning: *Wingates Temperance Band* / Comedians gallop: *Hammonds Sauce Works Band* / Pineapple poll: *Black Dyke Mills Band* / Zorba's dance: *Hammonds Sauce Works Band* / Promenade: *Cory Band* / Contestor: *Black Dyke Mills Band* / Entertainer: *Royal Doulton Band* / Shepherd's song: *G.U.S. Footwear Band Quartet* / Streets of Paris: *C.W.S. Band* / Entry of the gladiators: *Cambridge Band*
CD _____ TRTCD 127
TrueTrax / Oct '94 / THE.

FANTASTIC 40'S, THE
CD _____ DCD 5336
Disky / Dec '93 / THE / BMG / Discovery / Pinnacle.

FANTAZIA
(The First Taste)
I got the real feel: *Sunset Regime* / Operation acid: *New Age* / Rock to the max: *Dee, Ellis* / Worldwide regime: *Top Buzz* / CFU play DAT: *Cybertronic* / Sonar: *Orca* / Looking out my window: *Ratpack* / E.B.E. 1: *P.S.I.* / Good for me: *4 Real* / Feel my love: *Mac, Nikky* / P.S.I.: *Fantazia* / Aquabatics (Available on CD only.): *Orca* / Give me a rush (Available on CD only.): *New Age*
CD _____ FANTA 1CD
Fantazia Music / Nov '92 / 3MV / Sony.

FANTAZIA I/II
(3CD Set)
Lords of the dance: *Ratpack* / Live 4 the feeling: *D.J. Vibes* / Desire: *Dee, Ellis* / Psikop: *PSI* / Don't hold back: *Mac, Nikky* / Forever (free your mind): *PSI* / Pulse: *St. Ives* / You gotta believe: *Sunset Regime* / Your love is taking me: *St. Ives* / Free: *Shake Ya Bones* / Baby: *Transhuman* / Inerunderstanding: *PSI* / Indonesia: *Transhuman* / Astral: *Orca* / Raja: *Orca* / What is art: *Orca* / Substance: *Orca* / Love makes it easy: *Orca* / I got the real feel: *Sunset Regime* / Operation Acid: *New Age* / Rock to the max: *Dee, Ellis* / Worldwide regime: *Top Buzz* / CFU play DAT: *Cybertronic* / Sonar: *Orca* / Looking out my window: *PSI* / E.B.E. 1: *Ratpack* / Good for me: *4 Real* / Feel my love: *Mac, Nikky* / Fantazia: *PSI* / Aquabatics: *Orca* / Give me a rush: *New Age*
CD Set _____ FANTA 001/2CD
Fantazia Music / Dec '94 / 3MV / Sony

FANTAZIA II
(Twice as nice)
Lords of the dance: *Ratpack* / Live 4 the feeling: *D.J. Vibes* / Desire: *Dee, Ellis* / Psiko: *PSI* / Don't hold back: *Mac, Nikky* / Forever (Free your mind): *PSI* / Pulse: *St. Ives* / You've gotta believe: *Sunset Regime* / Your love is taking me: *St. Ives* / Free: *Shake Ya Bones* / Baby: *Transhuman* / Inerunderstanding: *PSI* / Indonesia: *Transhuman* / Astral: *Orca* / Rajah: *Orca* / What is art: *Orca* / Substance: *Orca* / Love makes it easy: *Orca*
CD _____ FANTA 002CD
Fantazia Music / Jul '93 / 3MV / Sony.

FANTAZIA III
(Made In Heaven)
Montana: *Way Out West* / Natural high: *Q-Tex* / Majorca: *Nevins, Jason* / Move on: *Secret Society* / Space: *Omer & Crooks* / Musika: *Lost Tribe* / We gonna funk: *D.J. Pierre* / Megwana: *Moon* / Big bang: *Luxor* / You got me: *NRG* / Free the feeling: *D.J. Pierre* / Looking into the light: *D.J. Slam* / What a dream (Available on LP only): *True Life* / No way: *PSI* / Power of love: *Q-Tex* / How can I become (Available on CD only): *Shake Ya Bones* / Bring it down (Available on LP only): *Wild Child Experience* / Time to let go (Available on LP only): *K.O.T.T.*
CD _____ FANTA 5CD
Fantazia Music / Apr '94 / 3MV / Sony.

FANTAZIA IV
(The Fourth Dimension)
Let's groove: *Morel's Grooves* / Feels good: *Osibisa* / Everybody get up: *Two Amigos* / Rock to the beat: *RM Project* / Short dick man: *20 Fingers* / Take over: *Reznor, Bridget* / Plastic dreams: *Jaydee* / Sensation of the mind: *Elysian* / Treaty: *Yothu Yindi* / Tribal love: *Ramone'll Ropiak* / Makes me feel like: *Capital Underground* / Cosmic love: *V Tracks* / Dosh: *Netherland Power* / My dreams: *Transfiguartion* / Mistral: *Gad* / Laika: *In Foundation* / Black dragon: *Van Basten* / Mesquite: *Hyperspectres* / June project: *Berra* / Move your tables: *Outdance* / Ohm: *Shafty*
CD _____ FANTA 8CD
Fantazia Music / Jun '95 / 3MV / Sony.

FANTAZIA PRESENT THE DJ COLLECTION VOLUME 1
Deep in Milan: *Hyper Space Europa* / Sun dreams: *Wax* / Infanta-ci: *Baby Doc & The Dentist* / Midi function: *System* / In the dark we live: *Aphrohead Aka Felix Da Housecat* / Mania: *Rainforest* / Shivaratri: *Fosim* / Mr. Peacock goes to Boscaland: *White Label* / Moonflux: *Black & Brown* / Nervous distortion: *Judge Dread* / Second rebirth: *Jones*

& Stephenson* / Killer: *Buzz & Ace* / Odyhand trance: *Osysee* / Ride: *English Muffin* / Do you wanna party: *D.J. Scott* / Infiltrator: *Technosis* / Mad one: *Smith, Marc* / Varispeed: *D.J. Edge* / On the groove: *Interstate* / Point break: *Sulfurex* / Storm: *Speed Jack*
CD _____ FANTA 7CD
Fantazia Music / Oct '94 / 3MV / Sony.

FANTAZIA TAKES YOU INTO THE JUNGLE VOL.2
(3CD/MC Set)
Awareness: *Interrogater* / London something (Remix): *Tek 9* / Unkown: *Mental Power* / Touch my toes: *Dr. S. Gachet* / Lipsing jam ring: *T Power* / Sovereign melody: *Dillinja* / Half step: *Photek* / Sound murderer: *Remark* / Driftin' thru the galaxy: *White Label* / Tiger style: *D.J. Hype* / Flavour of a sound: *Photek* / Lionheart: *Berty B & Dillinja* / Alive and kickin: *Red 1* / Can U feel it: *School Of Hard Knocks* / Hitman: *Marvellous Caine* / Relics of pressure: *Studio Pressure* / Still lets me down: *Tom & Jerry* / World of confusion: *D.J. Rap* / Wheel and deal (Remix): *D.J. Gunshot* / Calling the people: *A-Zone* / Spiritual aura (Remix): *D.J. Rap* / Safety zone: *A-Zone* / Big band: *Flatliner* / Just play music: *4th Dimension* / Switch: *D.J. Rap* / Digable bass: *D.J. Rap* / Gimp: *D.J. Rap* / Intelligent w'man: *D.J. Rap* / License: *Krome & Time* / World of music: *Peshay* / Yeah man: *Dream Team* / Tibetan jungle: *D.J. Rap* / Shadow: *Dream Team* / Universal: *4 Hero* / Release the bells: *Sounds Of Life* / Dope: *Good Looking* / All around the world: *Grooverider* / Plasmic life volume 1: *Water BaBy* / Voyager 2: *Lucky Spin* / Force 10: *White Label* / Journies: *FBD Project* / Intense: *Genesis Project* / Cold fresh air: *Higher Sense* / Photek 2: *Photek* / Only you: *Nookie* / Sound control: *Andy C* / Champion sound (Remix): *Q-Project* / Thunder: *Rood Project*
CD Set _____ FADJ 002CD
Fantazia Music / Nov '94 / 3MV / Sony.

FAREWELL TO LISSY CASEY
CD _____ OSS 79CD
Ossian / Aug '95 / ADA / Direct / CM.

FARMER'S WEDDING IN JOURE
CD _____ PAN 2004CD
Pan / Aug '94 / ADA / Direct / CM.

FASCINATION
(2CD Set)
CD Set _____ 24021
Delta Doubles / Mar '95 / Target/BMG.

FAST FALLS THE RAIN
(A Compilation Of Moravian Folk Music)
CD _____ LT 0014
Lotos / Nov '95 / Czech Music Enterprises.

FATHER'S FAVOURITES
CD _____ CDC 5388
Disky / May '94 / THE / BMG / Discovery / Pinnacle.

FAVOURITE CHRISTMAS CAROLS
Hark the herald angels sing / I saw three ships / in the bleak midwinter / We've been awhile a-wandering / Past three o'clock / Up good Christian folk, and listen / I sing of a maiden / Tomorrow shall be my dancing day / It came upon a midnight clear / Sussex carol / Ding dong merrily on high / God rest ye merry gentlemen / Away in a manger / O little one sweet / Unto us is born a son / Wassail / When Christ was born / Infant holy / When an angel host entuned / Born in a manger / Patapan / Carol with lullaby / Christmas carol / Masters in this hall / Gabriel's message / See amid the winter's snow / Child is born / Rocking / Coventry carol / While shepherds watched their flocks by night
CD _____ CDCFP 4629
Classics For Pleasure / Dec '94 / EMI.

FAVOURITE IRISH DRINKING SONGS
CD _____ EMPRCD 520
Emporio / Jul '94 / THE / Disc / CM.

FAVOURITE IRISH SONGS VOL.1
(3CD/MC Set)
Pretty little girl from Omagh: *Cunningham, Larry* / Old Bog Road: *Cunningham, Larry* / Ballybanion by the sea: *Cunningham, Larry* / Forty shades of green: *Cunningham, Larry* / Lough Gowna: *Cunningham, Larry* / My Kathleen: *Cunningham, Larry* / Me ould tambourine: *Cunningham, Larry* / Is his love better than mine: *Cunningham, Larry* / 50 years on: *Cunningham, Larry* / Come back to Erin: *Cunningham, Larry* / Slaney Valley / Galway Shawl / Village in County Tyrone / Sing Irishmen sing / Rose of Tralee / I'll take you home again Kathleen / Where the three counties meet / Far from Erne's shore / Balck Velvet Band / Green Hills of Kerry / Beautiful city / Give an Irish girl to me / Galway Shawl (2): *O'Brien, Dermot* / Three leaf shamrock: *O'Brien, Dermot* / Sleive Gallion braes: *O'Brien, Dermot* / Farewell to Galway: *O'Brien, Dermot* / Connemara Rose: *O'Brien, Dermot* / Gypsy Boy: *O'Brien, Dermot* / Sailing home: *O'Brien, Dermot* / Co. Leitrim Queen: *O'Brien, Dermot* / My Eileen: *O'Brien, Dermot* / World goes round: *O'Brien, Dermot* / My ould tambourine: *O'Brien, Dermot* / I'm goin' home: *O'Brien, Dermot*
CD Set _____ HBOXCD 71

Carlton Home Entertainment / Jul '94 / Carlton Home Entertainment.

FAVOURITE IRISH SONGS VOL.2
(3CD/MC Set)
West of the old River Shannon: *Margo* / Roads and the miles to Dundee: *Margo* / Red is the rose: *Margo* / Sing my song: *Margo* / Hills above Drumquin: *Margo* / Boys from County Armagh: *Margo* / Glen of Ahelow: *Margo* / Mommy don't I have a daddy: *Margo* / Kingassalagh I love you: *Margo* / Jimmy Stowaway: *Margo* / Danny Farrell: *Hegarty, Dermot* / James Connely: *Hegarty, Dermot* / Sleive no mbam: *Hegarty, Dermot* / Avondale: *Hegarty, Dermot* / Hi for the beggarman: *Hegarty, Dermot* / Town I love so well: *Hegarty, Dermot* / Scorn not his simplicity: *Hegarty, Dermot* / Red is the rose (2): *Hegarty, Dermot* / Sweet Alice Ben Bolt: *Hegarty, Dermot* / Maid of Fyfe: *Hegarty, Dermot* / Lakes of Coolfin: *Hegarty, Dermot* / Shores of Lough Bran: *Hegarty, Dermot* / Sound the Piobrach: *Hegarty, Dermot* / Come back to Erin: *Cunningham, Larry* / Cottage on the Borderline: *Cunningham, Larry* / Among the Wicklow Hills: *Cunningham, Larry* / Lovely Leitrim: *Cunningham, Larry* / Men behind the wire: *Cunningham, Larry* / Slaney Valley: *Cunningham, Larry* / Pretty little girl from Omagh: *Cunningham, Larry* / Freedom walk: *Cunningham, Larry* / Ballad of James Connelly: *Cunningham, Larry* / They wouldn't do it now: *Cunningham, Larry* / 90 years old: *Cunningham, Larry*
CD Set _____ HBOXCD 76
Carlton Home Entertainment / Jul '94 / Carlton Home Entertainment.

FAVOURITE IRISH SONGS VOL.3
(3CD/MC Set)
Rosie: *Dunphy, Sean* / Paddy McGinty's goat: *Dunphy, Sean* / Eugene: *Dunphy, Sean* / Shanagolden: *Dunphy, Sean* / Mountains of Mourne: *Dunphy, Sean* / I'll remember you love in my prayers: *Dunphy, Sean* / Danny Farrell: *Dunphy, Sean* / Star of the Co. Down: *Dunphy, Sean* / Delaney's Donkey: *Dunphy, Sean* / Boolavogue: *Dunphy, Sean* / Little mountain: *Dunphy, Sean* / Flower of Sweet Strabane: *Dunphy, Sean* / Juice of the Barley: *Dunphy, Sean* / Golden jubilee: *Dunphy, Sean* / Ould Claddagh Ring: *O'Brien, Dermot* / Connemara rose: *O'Brien, Dermot* / Road to Malinmore: *O'Brien, Dermot* / Where the three counties meet: *O'Brien, Dermot* / Nora: *O'Brien, Dermot* / Song of an Irish husband: *O'Brien, Dermot* / Boys of Killybegs: *O'Brien, Dermot* / Home boys home: *O'Brien, Dermot* / Come to the bower: *O'Brien, Dermot* / Jimmie Brown the newsboy: *Hegarty, Dermot* / Whistling thief: *Hegarty, Dermot* / Boys of Barna Straide: *Hegarty, Dermot* / Dear old Donegal: *Hegarty, Dermot* / Ballad of Patrick Furey: *Hegarty, Dermot* / Song to remember: *Hegarty, Dermot* / Paddy's Navy: *Hegarty, Dermot* / After 21 years: *Hegarty, Dermot* / Love is teasin': *Hegarty, Dermot* / Connemara by the lake: *Hegarty, Dermot* / If those lips could only speak: *Hegarty, Dermot* / I've been everywhere: *Hegarty, Dermot*
CD Set _____ HBOXCD 73
Carlton Home Entertainment / Jul '94 / Carlton Home Entertainment.

FAX IT, CHARGE IT, DON'T ASK ME WHAT'S FOR DINNER
CD _____ SHCD 8018
Shanachie / Oct '95 / Koch / ADA / Greensleeves.

FEDERATION OF TECHNO HOUSE CHAPTER 1
(2CD Set)
CD Set _____ LD 9455CD
LD / Feb '95 / Vital.

FEED YOUR HEAD
CD _____ BARKCD 2
Planet Dog / Oct '93 / 3MV / Vital.

FEEL LIKE MAKING LOVE
CD _____ AHLCD 25
Hit / Feb '95 / PolyGram.

FEEL THE FIRE DUETS
CD _____ 12544
Laserlight / May '95 / Target/BMG.

FEEL THE FORCE
(20 Smash Hits Of The Seventies)
I wanna hold your hand: *Dollar* / Long legged woman dressed in black: *Mungo Jerry* / L-L-Lucy: *Mud* / Man who sold the world: *Lulu* / Love hurts: *Nazareth* / Roadrunner twice: *Richman, Jonathan & Modern Lovers* / Come back and finish what you started: *Knight, Gladys & The Pips* / Burlesque: *Family* / Lost in France: *Tyler, Bonnie* / You don't have to go: *Chi-Lites* / Dance the body music: *Osibisa* / Lean on me: *Mud* / Make it with you: *Bread* / Baby don't change your mind: *Knight, Gladys & The Pips* / Mirrors: *Oldfield, Sally* / My white bicycle: *Nazareth* / Love's gotta hold on me: *Dollar* / Can you feel the force: *Real Thing*
CD _____ TRTCD 110
TrueTrax / Oct '94 / THE.

FEELIN' DOWN ON THE SOUTH SIDE
CD _____ PRCD 9906
Prestige / Feb '96 / Complete/Pinnacle / Cadillac.

FEELIN' GOOD - AMERICAN R&B HITS VOLUME 1
CD _____ CDRB 11
Charly / Nov '94 / Charly / THE / Cadillac.

FEELING THE BLUES
Poor boy blues: Atkins, Chet & Mark Knopfler / I'd rather go blind: Chicken Shack / I'm your hoochie coochie man: Waters, Muddy / Ain't gone 'n' give up on love: Vaughan, Stevie Ray & Double Trouble / Cheap tequila: Winter, Johnny / Tabacco road: Winter, Edgar / Gamblers roll: Allman Brothers / Need your love tonight: Fleetwood Mac / Tuff enuff: Fabulous Thunderbirds / Season of the witch: Bloomfield, Mike & Al Cooper / Skyscraper blues: Derringer, Rick / Down in Mississippi: Omar & The Howlers / Boogie my way back home: Moore, Gary / Brothers: Vaughan Brothers / Schoolgirl: Argent / Killing floor: Electric Flag
CD _____ 4758282
Columbia / Oct '95 / Sony.

FEELINGS NOT FREQUENCIES
CD _____ ABCD 001
Holistic / Feb '95 / Plastic Head.

FEELS SO GOOD
Free as the wind: Crusaders / Burnin' up the carnival: Sample, Joe / Young child: Laws, Ronnie / Heart work: Handy, Captain John / Intergalactic lovo song: Earland, Charles / Running away: Ayers, Roy / Feels so good: Mangione, Chuck / Ghetto: Hathaway, Donny / Night crusader: Deodato, Eumir / Toda menina bina: Gil, Gilberto / Wind parade: Byrd, Donald / Fantasy: Smith, Johnny 'Hammond'
CD _____ RNBCD 106
Connoisseur / Jan '94 / Pinnacle.

FEMALE COUNTRY BLUES VOL.1 - THE TWENTIES
CD _____ SOB 035292
Story Of The Blues / Dec '92 / Koch / ADA.

FEMALE VOCALISTS
(3CD Set)
While the mucic plays on: Shelton, Anne / Daddy: Shelton, Anne / Better not roll those blue blue eyes: Shelton, Anne / Minnie from Trinidad: Shelton, Anne / Russian rose: Shelton, Anne / St. Louis blues: Shelton, Anne / Yes my darling daughter: Shelton, Anne / Until you fall in love: Shelton, Anne / Little steeple pointing to a star: Shelton, Anne / Let there be love: Shelton, Anne / Amapola: Shelton, Anne / Tomorrow's sunrise: Shelton, Anne / Always in my heart: Shelton, Anne / How about you: Shelton, Anne / How green was my valley: Shelton, Anne / I don't want to walk without you: Shelton, Anne / My devotion: Shelton, Anne / Taxi driver's serenade: Shelton, Anne / South wind: Shelton, Anne / Only you: Shelton, Anne / My yiddish Momme: Shelton, Anne / Daddy (2): Carless, Dorothy / It can't be wrong: Carless, Dorothy / My sister and I: Carless, Dorothy / Room 504: Carless, Dorothy / That lovely weekend: Carless, Dorothy / You too can have a lovely romance: Carless, Dorothy / Love stay in my heart: Carless, Dorothy / We three: Carless, Dorothy / Where's my love: Carless, Dorothy / I want to be in Dixie: Carless, Dorothy / This is no laughing matter: Carless, Dorothy / When the sun comes out: Carless, Dorothy / Our love affair: Carless, Dorothy / I'll always love you: Carless, Dorothy / I'd know you anywhere: Carless, Dorothy / I guess I'll have to dream the rest: Carless, Dorothy / I'm sending my blessing: Carless, Dorothy / Ragtime cowboy Joe: Carless, Dorothy / Never a day goes by: Carless, Dorothy / Walkin' by the river: Carless, Dorothy / Deep purple: Daniels, Bebe / Stop it's wonderful: Daniels, Bebe / As round and round we go: Daniels, Bebe / Start the day right: Daniels, Bebe / Your company's requested: Daniels, Bebe / It's a small world: Daniels, Bebe / Give me a little whistle: Daniels, Bebe / I'm singing to a million: Daniels, Bebe / There I go: Daniels, Bebe / Rio Rita: Daniels, Bebe / Little Swiss whistling song: Daniels, Bebe / Imagination: Daniels, Bebe / Nursie nursie: Daniels, Bebe / Somewhere in France with you: Daniels, Bebe / Mother's prayer at twilight: Daniels, Bebe / Our love: Daniels, Bebe / Three little fishes: Carless, Dorothy / With the wind and rain in your hair: Carless, Dorothy / Little Sir Echo: Carless, Dorothy / Masquerade is over: Daniels, Bebe / Little ring on your doorstep: Daniels, Bebe / Little boy who never told a lie: Daniels, Bebe
CD Set _____ EMPRESS 1002
Empress / Oct '95 / THE.

FEMO JAZZ FESTIVAL - 25TH ANNIVERSARY
CD _____ MECCACD 1038
Music Mecca / Nov '94 / Jazz Music / Cadillac / Wellard.

FEST NOZ DE KLEG
CD _____ GLEG 001CD
Diffusion Breizh / Aug '95 / ADA.

FEST-DEIZ ACCORDEONS
CD _____ CD 427
Diffusion Breizh / Jul '94 / ADA.

FESTIVAL FLAMENCO
CD _____ EUCD 1210
ARC / Sep '93 / ARC Music / ADA.

FESTIVAL FLAMENCO GITANO VOL.3
CD _____ CDLR 44.015
L&R / New Note.

FESTIVAL OF BRASS
CD _____ DOYCD 008
Doyen / Oct '92 / Conifer.

FESTIVAL OF CAROLS
Once in royal David's city: Guildford Cathedral Choir / While shepherds watched their flocks by night: Sunbury Junior Singers Of The Salvation Army / Holly and the ivy: St. Paul's Cathedral Choir / God rest ye merry gentlemen: Guildford Cathedral Choir / Unto us is born a son: Westminster Abbey Choir / As with gladness men of old: Guildford Cathedral Choir / O little town of Bethlehem: St. Paul's Cathedral Choir / Hark the herald angels sing: Guildford Cathedral Choir / I saw three ships: St. Paul's Cathedral Choir / Silent night: Sunbury Junior Singers Of The Salvation Army / In dulci jubilo: Westminster Abbey Choir / First Noel: Guildford Cathedral Choir / In the bleak midwinter: St. Paul's Cathedral Choir / Good King Wenceslas: Guildford Cathedral Choir / Rocking: Sunbury Junior Singers Of The Salvation Army / Coventry carol: St. Paul's Cathedral Choir / It came upon a midnight clear: Guildford Cathedral Choir / Away in a manger: Westminster Abbey Choir / Ding dong merrily on high: Sunbury Junior Singers Of The Salvation Army / O come all ye faithful (Adeste Fidelis): Guildford Cathedral Choir
CD _____ CDMFP 6088
Music For Pleasure / Dec '94 / EMI.

FESTIVAL OF GOSPEL AND NEGRO SPIRITUAL
(2CD Set)
CD Set _____ FA 403
Fremeaux / Nov '95 / Discovery / ADA.

FESTIVAL OF IRISH FOLK MUSIC 1
(2CD/3MC Set)
Cliffs of Dooneen: Dublin City Ramblers / Slievenamon: Dublin City Ramblers / Finnegan's wake: Dublin City Ramblers / Town I loved so well: Dublin City Ramblers / Sea around us: Dublin City Ramblers / Four green fields: Dublin City Ramblers / My lovely rose of Clare: Reilly, Paddy / Snowy breasted pearl: Reilly, Paddy / Rose of Allendale: Reilly, Paddy / Come back Paddy Reilly: Reilly, Paddy / Down by the Sally gardens: Reilly, Paddy / Black velvet band: Dubliners / McAlpine's fusiliers: Dubliners / Fairmoye lasses/Sporting Paddy: Dubliners / Seven drunken nights: Dubliners / Home boys home: Dubliners / Blue mountain rag: Dubliners / Raglan road: Reilly, Paddy / Steal away: Furey Brothers & Davy Arthur / Now is the hour: Furey Brothers & Davy Arthur / Silver threads among the gold: Furey Brothers & Davy Arthur / When you were sweet sixteen: Furey Brothers & Davy Arthur / My love is like a red real rose: Furey Brothers & Davy Arthur / Song for Ireland: Furey Brothers & Davy Arthur / Dirty old town: Dubliners / Farewell to Carlingford: Dubliners / Foggy dew: Dubliners / Parcel o' rogues: Dubliners / Rare auld times: Dubliners / Man you don't meet every day: Barleycorn / Donegal Danny: Barleycorn / Only our river run free: Barleycorn / Lakes of Coolfin: Barleycorn / Buachaill an Eirne: Barleycorn
CD Set _____ CHCD 1013
Chyme / Oct '90 / CM / ADA / Direct.

FESTIVAL OF IRISH FOLK MUSIC 2
(2CD/3MC Set)
Butterfly: Bothy Band / Kesh jig: Bothy Band / Sixteen come next Sunday: Bothy Band / Rip the calico: Bothy Band / Strayaway child: Bothy Band / Death of Queen Jane: Bothy Band / Dheanainn sugradh: Clannad / By chance it was: Clannad / Rince Briotanach: Clannad / Dulaman: Clannad / No mhaire: Clannad / Cumha eoghain rue ui neill: Clannad / Teddy bears head: Wolfetones / Ode to Biddy Magee: Wolfetones / Foggy dew: Wolfetones / Ti-coloured ribbon: Wolfetones / Banks of the Ohio: Wolfetones / Black Ribbon Band: Wolfetones / Whiskey in the jar: Dubliners / Town I loved so well: Dubliners / Free the people: Dubliners / Lord of the dance: Dubliners / Musical priest/Blackthorn stick: Dubliners / Finnegan's wake: Dubliners / Green fields of France: Furey Brothers & Davy Arthur / Garrett Barry's jig: Furey Brothers & Davy Arthur / Reason I left Mullingar: Furey Brothers & Davy Arthur / Morning les heavy: Furey Brothers & Davy Arthur / Ted Furey's selection: Furey Brothers & Davy Arthur / Lament: Furey Brothers & Davy Arthur / Ril gan ainm/Cinnte le dia/The union reel: Bergin, Mary / Garrai na bhfeileoig/Miss Galvin: Bergin, Mary / Step it out Mary: Doyle, Danny / Irish soldier laddie: Doyle, Danny / Red haired Mary: Doyle, Danny / Whiskey on a Sunday: Doyle...
CD Set _____ CHCD 1035
Outlet / Sep '93 / ADA / Duncans / CM / Ross / Direct / Koch.

FESTIVAL OF IRISH MUSIC
CD _____ EUCD 1156
ARC / Jun '91 / ARC Music / ADA.

FESTIVAL OF IRISH MUSIC
CD _____ EUCD 1323
ARC / Nov '95 / ARC Music / ADA.

FESTIVAL OF IRISH MUSIC VOL.2
CD _____ EUCD 1160
ARC / '91 / ARC Music / ADA.

FESTIVAL OF IRISH MUSIC VOL.3
Summer in Ireland: Oisin / Mungo Kelly's: Oisin / Winds of change: Oisin / Blantyre explosion: Dubliners / Botany Bay: McLoughlin, Noel / Baloo baleenie: Dubliners / Hal on the mountain: Pied Pipers / Leithrim fancy: Pied Pipers / Cold blow and the rainy night: McLoughlin, Noel / Star of the county down: Golden Bough / Hare's paw and Jackie Coleman's No 2: Golden Bough / Carrickfergus: McLoughlin, Noel / Samhradh samradh: Tara / Chief O'Neill's favourite: Pied Pipers / Nine points of roughery: Pied Pipers / Faral O'Gara: Pied Pipers / Spancil hill: McLoughlin, Noel / Maids of the barrel: Golden Bough / Lea Rig: Butler, Margie / Kind Robin: Butler, Margie / Foggy dew: Dubliners / Jeannie C: Oisin
CD _____ EUCD 1212
ARC / Sep '93 / ARC Music / ADA.

FESTIVAL OF TRADITIONAL IRISH MUSIC
(2CD/3MC Set)
CD Set _____ CHCD 1037
Chyme / Aug '94 / CM / ADA / Direct.

FESTIVAL OF YORKSHIRE VOICES, A
(With the Brighouse & Rastrick Band)
March of the peers / Let there be peace on earth / Song of the jolly Roger / Valse / Funiculi, funicula / Softly as I leave you / Finlandia / On Ilkley moor baht'at / Lost chord / When the saints go marching in / Sound an alarm / Morte Criste / Gwahoddiad / Ouverture solenelle (1812) / Pomp and circumstance No.1
CD _____ QPRZ 008D
Polyphonic / Mar '92 / Conifer.

FESTIVAL TROPICAL
CD _____ EUCD 1250
ARC / Mar '94 / ARC Music / ADA.

FEVER IN THE JUNGLE
CD _____ F2FFCD 1
Fist 2 Fist / Oct '94 / Jetstar.

FEVER IN THE JUNGLE VOLUME 2
CD _____ F2FCD 2
Fist 2 Fist / Apr '95 / Jetstar.

FEVER PITCH
CD _____ FADCD 028
Fashion / Aug '93 / Jetstar / Grapevine.

FIAFIA
(Dances From The South Pacific)
CD _____ PAN 150CD
Pan / Dec '94 / ADA / Direct / CM.

FIDDLE STICKS
CD _____ NI 5320
Nimbus / Sep '94 / Nimbus.

FIDJERI - SONGS OF THE PEARL DIVERS
(Music from Bahrain)
CD _____ AUD 08046
Auvidis/Ethnic / Feb '93 / Harmonia Mundi.

FIFTY YEARS OF SUNSHINE
CD _____ PS 9333
Pulse Sonic / Jul '95 / Plastic Head.

FILL YOUR HEAD WITH PHANTASM
CD _____ PTM 131
Phantasm / May '95 / Vital/SAM / Plastic Head.

FILTERLESS COLLECTIVE VOL.1, THE
CD _____ 5FKFCD
Filterless / Jul '95 / Kudos.

FINE AS WINE
CD _____ FLYCD 30
Flyright / Apr '91 / Hot Shot / Wellard / Jazz Music / CM.

FINEST VINTAGE JAZZ
(Greatest Jazz 1918-1940)
Savoy blues: Armstrong, Louis / When it's sleepy time down South: Armstrong, Louis / Jumpin' at the woodside: Basie, Count / Blues in thirds: Becher, Sidney & Earl Hines / Singin' the blues: Beiderbecke, Bix / Symphony in riffs: Carter, Benny / Big noise from Winnetka: Crosby, Bob Orchestra / Marie: Dorsey, Tommy / East St. Louis toodle-oo: Ellington, Duke / Sing me a swing song: Fitzgerald, Ella / Roll 'em: Goodman, Benny / Cloud nine call: Hall, Adelaide / Running wild: Hampton, Lionel / Crazy rhythm: Hawkins, Coleman / Easy living: Wilson, Teddy & Rillie Holiday / Walkin' and swingin': Kirk, Andy & His Clouds Of Joy / Handful of riffs: Lang, Eddie & Lonnie Johnson / Honky tonk train blues: Lewis, Meade Lux / Feelin' no pain: Nichols, Red & His Five Pennies / Livery stable blues: Original Dixieland Jazz Band / I got rhythm: Reinhardt, Django & Stephane Grappelli / St. Louis blues: Smith, Bessie & Louis Armstrong / Relaxin' at the Touro: Spanier, Muggsy / I gotta right to sing the blues: Teagarden, Jack & Benny Goodman / Honeysuckle rose: Waller, Fats

CD _____ CD AJA 5117
Living Era / Oct '93 / Koch.

FINGERPRINTS
CD _____ 02602
Glitterhouse / May '95 / Direct / ADA.

FIRE DOWN BELOW
Fire down below: Burning Spear / African skank: Prince Francis / Love and peace: Marshall, Larry / No happiness: Webber, Marlene / What does it take: Francis, Winston & Alton Ellis / Nite ride: 'Im & Dave / Up park camp: Jarrett, Winston / Reggae children: Richards, Roy / What is love: Brown, Errol / Midnight soul: 'Im & The Invaders / Sweet talking: Heptones / Love again: Jackie & The Invaders / Rainy night in Georgia: Parker, Ken / Mission impossible: Mittoo, Jackie
CD _____ CDHB 81
Heartbeat / Sep '90 / Greensleeves / Jetstar / Direct / ADA.

FIREPOINT
See me running: Cooper, Mike / I wouldn't mind: Moore, Gerald / No whiskey: Robinson, Tom / Here's to the future kid: Cooper, Mike / No more doggin': Kelly, Dave / City woman: Power, Duffy / Oh really: Cooper, Mike / Leaf without a tree: Mitchell, Sam / Big boss man: Robinson, Tom / Sunflower: Robinson, Tom / Halfway: Power, Duffy
CD _____ C5CD 593
See For Miles/C5 / Oct '92 / Pinnacle.

FIRST COMETH, THE
(A Collection Of Guitarists)
CD _____ RLBTC 006
Realisation / Oct '93 / Prism.

FIRST LADIES OF COUNTRY
Don't it make my brown eyes blue: Gayle, Crystal / Snowbird: Anderson, Lynn / Ode to Billy Joe: Wynette, Tammy / Dumb blonde: Parton, Dolly / Delta dawn: Tucker, Tanya / '57 chevrolet: Spears, Billie Jo / No charge: Wynette, Tammy / It's only make believe: Anderson, Lynn / Fuel to the flame: Parton, Dolly / Stand by your man: Wynette, Tammy / Blanket on the ground: Spears, Billie Jo / D.I.V.O.R.C.E: Wynette, Tammy / Wrong road again: Gayle, Crystal / Honey come back: Anderson, Lynn / You are so beautiful: Tucker, Tanya / Your ole handy man: Parton, Dolly / Little bit more: Anderson, Lynn / Let me be there: Tucker, Tanya / Rose garden: Anderson, Lynn
CD _____ CD 32235
Columbia / Mar '91 / Sony.

FISHTANK UNDERWATER CONSPIRACY
CD _____ FTANKCD 1
Hos Wasp / Nov '95 / Total/BMG.

FISTFUL OF PUSSIES/FOR A FEW PUSSIES MORE, A
Repo man: Meteors / Mystery street: Batmobile / Alley cat king: Frantic Flintstones / Spy catcher: Guana Batz / Brand new Cadillac: Milkshakes / No dog: Turnpike Cruisers / Hangman's Caesars: Quakes / Cyclonic: Quakes / I knew sky: Golden Horde / My brain is in the cupboard: Alien Sex Fiend / Surf city: Meteors / I get so exited: Dexter, Levi & The Ripchords / Rumble in the jungle: Rochee & The Sarnos / Holy hack Jack: Demented Are Go / Thirteen times: Wigs / Boneshaker baby: Alien Sex Fiend / She's gone: Riverside Trio / Thee holy jukebox: Raymen
CD _____ CDMGRAM 36
Anagram / May '93 / Pinnacle.

FLAMENCO INOLVIDABLE FROM SPAIN
CD _____ 15162
Laserlight / '91 / Target/BMG.

FLAMENCO RUMBA GITANA
CD _____ EUCD 1208
ARC / Sep '93 / ARC Music / ADA.

FLAMENCO VIVO
CD _____ B 6824
Auvidis/Ethnic / Oct '95 / Harmonia Mundi.

FLAMES OF HELL - SWAMP MUSIC VOLUME 1
CD _____ TRIKONT 0156
Trikont / Jan '95 / ADA / Direct.

FLAPPER BOX, THE
(5 CDs)
Begin the beguine: Shaw, Artie / Drum stomp: Hampton, Lionel / Bugle call rag: Roy, Harry / Georgia on my mind: Gonella, Nat / Stompin' at the Savoy: Goodman, Benny / Love is the sweetest thing: Bowlly, Al / Save it pretty Mama: Armstrong, Louis / World is waiting for the sunrise: Geraldo & His Orchestra / Continental: Stone, Lew / One o'clock jump: Basie, Count / On the air: Gibbons, Carroll / Say it with music: Payne, Jack / Whispering: Fox, Roy / Take the 'A' train: Ellington, Duke / Sweetest music this side of Heaven: Winnick, Maurice / Somebody stole my gal: Cotton, Billy / In the mood: Loss, Joe / Here's to the next time: Hall, Henry / At the woodchoppers' ball: Herman, Woody / I used to be colour blind: Hylton, Jack / Trumpet blues and cantabile: James, Harry / Hors d'oeuvres: Ambrose & His Orchestra / Donkey serenade: Jones, Allan / You've done something to my heart: Laye, Evelyn / Night and day: Astaire, Fred / Indian love call: Eddy, Nelson & Jeanette MacDonald / My heart belongs to Daddy:

Martin, Mary / Louise: Chevalier, Maurice / Amapola: Durbin, Deanna / Goodnight Vienna: Buchanan, Jack / Let yourself go: Rogers, Ginger / One night of love: Moore, Grace / Little white room: Day, Frances & John Mills / Inka dinka doo: Durante, Jimmy / Lovely to look at: Dunn, Irene / I'll see you again: Coward, Sir Noel / Falling in love again: Dietrich, Marlene / I'll get by: Haymes, Dick / I can give you the starlight: Ellis, Mary / Experiment: Lawrence, Gertrude / Thanks for the memory: Hope, Bob & Shirley Ross / Dancing on the ceiling: Matthews, Jessie / I get a kick out of you: Merman, Ethel / We're gonna hang out the washing on the Siegfried line: Flanagan & Allen / Yours: Lynn, Vera / Nearness of you: Hutch / I'm stepping out with a memory tonight: Bowlly, Al & Jim Mesene / I have to be a millionaire: Bowlly, Al & Jim Mesene / Wings over the Navy: Stone, Lew / Our Sergeant Major: Formby, George / American patrol: Miller, Glenn / It's a hap-hap-happy day: Roy, Harry / Run rabbit run: Flanagan & Allen / It's a pair of wings for me: Gonella, Nat / Bless 'em all: Cotton, Billy / Turn the money in your pocket: Bowlly, Al & Jim Mesene / I'll never smile again: Bowlly, Al & Jim Mesene / We'll go smiling along: Bowlly, Al & Jim Mesene / We must all stick together: Geraldo & Cyril Grantham / White cliffs of Dover: Lynn, Vera / My prayer: Henderson, Chick / Oh buddy I'm in love: Gonella, Nat / Oh Johnny oh: Roy, Harry & His Tiger Ragamuffins / Kiss me goodnight, Sergeant Major: Cotton, Billy / Jukebox Saturday night: Cotton, Billy / All over the place: Thorburn, Billy / Moonlight serenade: Miller, Glenn / Wish me luck as you wave me goodbye: Fields, Gracie / If you were the only girl in the world: Ziegler, Anne & Webster Booth / Be careful it's my heart: Sinatra, Frank / Bless you: Ink Spots / Little white gardenia: Brisson, Carl / Very thought of you: Bowlly, Al / J'Attendrai: Rossi, Tino / Stop beatin' around the mulberry bush: Merry Macs / What do you know Joe: Stafford, Jo & The Pied Pipers / Great mistake of my life: Henderson, Chick / Body and soul: Boswell, Connie / Sonny boy: Jolson, Al / Tisket-a-tasket: Fitzgerald, Ella / Without a song: Dennis, Denny / How about you: Carless, Dorothy / Where the blue of the night meets the gold of the day: Crosby, Bing / Trans-Atlantic lullaby: Hall, Adelaide / Last time I saw Paris: Martin, Tony / Fools rush in: Shelton, Anne / My very good friend the milkman: Waller, Fats / Pennsylvania 6-5000: Andrews Sisters / These foolish things: Layton, Turner / Someone to watch over me: Langford, Frances / Ma, I miss your apple pie: Ambrose & His Orchestra / There's a land of Begin Again: Loss, Joe / Don't sit under the apple tree: Andrews Sisters / I'll never smile again (2): Sinatra, Frank / You are my sunshine: Roy, Harry / I don't want to walk without you: Lipton, Celia / String of pearls: Miller, Glenn / When I see an elephant fly: Lea, Jimmy / That lovely weekend: Carless, Dorothy & Geraldo / Moonlight becomes you: Crosby, Bing / Someone's rocking my dreamboat: Crosby, Bing / Drummin' man: Squadronaires / Who wouldn't love you: Ink Spots / Elmer's tune: Miller, Glenn / Kiss the boys goodbye: Martin, Mary / My devotion: Winstone, Eric & His Band / Rancho pillow: Martin, Freddy / Beat me Daddy, eight to the bar: Shearing, George / Daybreak: Sinatra, Frank / I've got a gal in Kalamazoo: Andrews Sisters / Nightingale sang in Berkeley Square: Shelton, Anne / White Christmas: Crosby, Bing
CD Set _____ PASTCDS 7010
Flapper / Jun '93 / Pinnacle.

FLARED HITS AND PLATFORM SOUL
CD _____ VISCD 7
Vision / Feb '95 / Pinnacle.

FLASH OF '29
(Portrait of music in 1929)
Some of these days / If I had a talking picture of you / Mess-a-stomp / Louise / Dinah / Button up your overcoat / Honey / Won't you get up off it, please / Muskrat ramble / After you've gone / Black and blue / When I'm a dreamer (aren't we all) / Everybody loves my baby / Bashful baby
CD _____ PHONTCD 7608
Phontastic / '93 / Wellard / Jazz Music / Cadillac.

FLASHBACK
Flashback: Imagination / Let's groove: Earth, Wind & Fire / Celebration: Kool & The Gang / Contact: Starr, Edwin / Love come down: King, Evelyn 'Champagne' / Gangsters of the groove: Heatwave / Cuba: Gibson Brothers / Going back to my roots: Odyssey / Don't stop the music: Yarbrough & Peoples / Oops upside your head: Gap Band / Funky town: Lipps Inc. / I will survive: Gaynor, Gloria / D.I.S.C.O.: Ottawan / Y.M.C.A.: Village People / Car wash: Rose Royce / Hustle: McCoy, Van / I love to love (but my baby loves to dance): Charles, Tina / You're the first, the last, my everything: Charles, Tina
CD _____ MUSCD 004
MCI / Nov '92 / Disc / THE.

FLASHBACK TO THE 50'S
(2CD Set)
Wanted: Martino, Al / Comes a-long-a-love: Starr, Kay / That's how a love song was

born: Burns, Ray / Fever: Lee, Peggy / Story of my life: Holliday, Michael / Undecided: Radio Revellers & Geraldo/Orchestra / I'll be around: Boswell, Eve & Chorus/Orchestra / True love: Crosby, Bing & Grace Kelly/Johnny Green / Volare: Martin, Dean / Pretend: Dawn, Julie & Norrie Paramor/Orchestra / Bewitched, bothered and bewildered: Torme, Mel / Cry me a river: London, Julie / Young and foolish: Lawrence, Lee & Ray Martin Orchestra / Happy days and lonely nights: Murray, Ruby / When I fall in love: Cole, Nat King / No other love: Hilton, Ronnie / I'll be hanging around: MacKintosh, Ken / It breaks my heart: Carr, Carole & Frank Cordell Orchestra / Eternally: Campbell, Jean & Philip Green Orchestra / Keep me in mind: Buxton, Sheila & Ronnie Harris/Ray Martin Orchestra / Holiday affair: Day, Jill & Frank Cordell Orchestra / Blacksmith blues (Vocal: Pattie Forbes): Rabin, Oscar & His Band / Story of Tina: Beeton, Gerry & Philip Green Orchestra / Ciao ciao Bambina: Cardinali, Roberto & the Rita Williams singers / Stealin': Warren, Alma & Ron Goodwin Chorus/Orchestra / Ferryboat Inn: Cogan, Alma & Frank Cordell Chorus/Orchestra / Lucky lips: Cogan, Alma & Frank Cordell Chorus/Orchestra / Me and my imagination: Peers, Donald & Sydney Torch/Orchestra / Poor little fool: Nelson, Rick / My love and devotion: Johnson, Teddy / Met me on the corner (CD only): Coronets / Every day of my life (CD only): Vaughan, Malcolm / Oh oh I'm falling in love again (CD only): Rodgers, Jimmie & Hugo Peretti Orchestra / Jezebel (Vocals: Howard Jones & The Low Chords. CD only): Loss, Joe & His Orchestra / He's got the whole world in his hands (CD only): London, Laurie & Geoff Love Orchestra / Oh! my papa (O mein Papa) (CD only): Klooger, Annette & Teddy Foster Orchestra / I will never change (CD only): James, Dick & Ron Goodwin Orchestra / Small talk (CD only): Small, Joan & Peter Knight Orchestra / My heart belongs to only you (CD only): Morton, Peter & Ray Martub Orchestra / Buona Sera (CD only): Prima, Louis & Sam Butera/Witnesses / Band of gold (Cd only): Lyon, Barbara & Ray Martin Orchestra / Vaughan, Frankie & Ken MacKintosh Orchestra / With these hands (CD only): Hughes, David & Frank Cordell Orchestra / Get with it (CD only): Kentones & Ron Goodwin Orchestra / Zambezi (CD only): Bousch, Lou & His Orchestra / Dance with me Henry (Vocals : Jean Campbell. CD only): Kirchin Band / If you go (CD only): Dean, Alan / Things go wrong (CD only): Anthony, Billie / Seven little girls sitting in the back seat (CD only): Avons / Chances are (CD only): Desmond, Michael & Bill Shepherd Orchestra
CD Set _____ CDDL 1236
Music For Pleasure / Nov '92 / EMI.

FLASHBACK TO THE 60'S
(2CD Set)
I like it: Gerry & The Pacemakers / World without love: Peter & Gordon / Walkin' back to happiness: Shapiro, Helen / One way love: Bennett, Cliff & The Rebel Rousers / Kites: Dupree, Simon & The Big Sound / Anyone who had a heart: Black, Cilla / Bad to me: Kramer, Billy J. & The Dakotas / Look through my window: Hollies / I'm telling you now: Freddie & The Dreamers / Kon-Tiki: Shadows / You're driving me crazy: Temperance Seven / Pretty flamingo: Manfred Mann / little lovin': Fourmost / I'm the urban spaceman: Bonzo Dog Band / What do you want: Faith, Adam / Surfin' USA: Beach Boys / I remember you: Ifield, Frank / House of the rising sun: Animals / I'm into something good: Herman's Hermits / Up on the roof: Lynch, Kenny / Lily the pink: Scaffold / I'm a tiger: Lulu / I'll never fall in love again: Gentry, Bobbie / I've been a bad bad boy: Jones, Paul
CD Set _____ CDDL 1112
Music For Pleasure / Jun '91 / EMI.

FLASHBACK TO THE 70'S
(2CD Set)
I hear you knocking: Edmunds, Dave / When I'm dead and gone: McGuinness Flint / Strange kind of woman: Deep Purple / Don't let it die: Smith, Hurricane / California man: Move / Crash: Quatro, Suzi / See my baby jive: Wizzard / Cat crept in: Mud / Bump: Kenny / Rock your baby: McCrae, George / You sexy thing: Hot Chocolate / That's the way I like it: K.C. & The Sunshine Band / Motor bikin': Spedding, Chris / Moonlighting: Sayer, Leo / Little bit more: Dr. Hook / They shoot horses don't they: Racing Cars / Spanish stroll: Mink Deville / Peaches: Stranglers / Dancing in the dark: Marshall Hain / More than a woman: Tavares / Wuthering Heights: Bush, Kate / Ever fallen in love: Buzzcocks / Hanging on the telephone: Blondie / Darlin': Miller, Frankie / My Sharona: Knack / Tears of a clown: Beat / Message to rudy: Specials / On my radio: Selecter / American pie (CD only): McLean, Don / Roll over Beethoven (CD only): E.L.O. / Nutbush City Limits (CD only): Turner, Ike & Tina / Dance with the devil (CD only): Powell, Cozy / Right back where we started from (CD only): Nightingale, Maxine / Make me smile (come up and see me) (CD only): Harley, Steve & Cockney Rebel / Loving you (CD only): Reddy, Helen / Angie baby (CD only): Robinson, Tom / 2-4-6-8 Motorway (CD only): Robinson, Tom / Baker Street (CD only): Rafferty, Gerry / Rich kids (CD

only): Rich Kids / Milk and alcohol (CD only): Dr. Feelgood
CD Set _____ CDDL 1233
Music For Pleasure / Nov '92 / EMI.

FLICKNIFE PUNK SINGLES COLLECTION
Shake some action / Total control / Shell shock / Waiting for the man / Teenage in love / Do the geek / Thatcher / Follow the leader / Fight to win / Let's get crazy / Werewolf / We don't care / Wanna world / No romance / No sign of life / Leaders of tomorrow / Respectable / Playing cards with dead men / Summertime now / Nicely does it
CD _____ CDPUNK 42
Anagram / Feb '95 / Pinnacle.

FLIGHT OF THE CONDOR
CD _____ CDSR 065
Telstar / May '95 / BMG.

FLIGHT OF THE GREEN LINNET
CD _____ GLCD 0103
Green Linnet / Nov '88 / Roots / CM / Direct / ADA.

FLIGHTS OF FANCY
(Beautiful Sound of the Panpipes)
Light of experience / El condor pasa / Picnic at hanging rock (theme) / Cacharpaya / First time ever I saw your face / Godfather / Endless love / True / Bluebird / Do you know where you're going to / And I love her / Tara's theme / Once upon a time in the west / Flame Trees of Thika / Feelings / True love ways (CD only.) / Why can't it wait till morning (CD only.)
CD _____ CDMFP 5896
Music For Pleasure / Sep '90 / EMI.

FLOWER POWER
CD _____ HRCD 8041
Disky / May '94 / THE / BMG / Discovery / Pinnacle.

FLOWER POWER DAZE
CD _____ DCD 5297
Disky / Sep '93 / THE / BMG / Discovery / Pinnacle.

FLOWER POWER DAZE 2
CD _____ DCD 5359
Disky / Apr '94 / THE / BMG / Discovery / Pinnacle.

FLOYD'S CAJUN FAIS DO DO
Wafus two step: Sundown Playboys / Valse de soleil coucher: Cormier, Lesa & The Sundown Playboys / Back home again in Louisiana: Cormier, Lesa & The Sundown Playboys / La valse san espoir: Cormier, Lesa & The Sundown Playboys / Step it fast: Bonsall, Joe / La pointe au pain: Hebert, Adam / I can't sleep at night: Hebert, Adam / Posalie: Hebert, Adam / Valse de toute le monde: Prejean, Lezman / Teardrop special: Hebert, Adam & The Teardrops / 73 special: Lejeune, Rodney / Flumes d'enfer: Pitre, Austin / Fee Fee can't dance: Cajun Trio + 1 / One step de duson: Cormier, Louis / Ville platte widow: Fontenot, Allen / Bachelor's life: Badeaux & The Louisiana Aces / Valse de meche: Barzas, Maurice & The Mamau Playboys / Rodare special: Thibodeaux, Eugene / Webb Pierce blues (Not available on LP.): Fontenot, Allen / Si tu m'aimes (Not available on LP.): Bruce, Vin / Bo Sparkle waltz (Not available on LP.): Broussard, August / Calcasieu rambler's special (Not available on LP.): Broussard, August
CD _____ CDCH 304
Ace / Oct '90 / Pinnacle / Cadillac / Complete/Pinnacle.

FLUTE & SITAR MUSIC OF INDIA
CD _____ 12178
Laserlight / Aug '95 / Target/BMG.

FLUTE AND GAMELAN MUSIC OF WEST JAVA
CD _____ TSCD 913
Topic / Apr '95 / Direct / ADA.

FLUXTRAX
(2CD Set)
CD Set _____ EXPCD 001
Exp / Aug '95 / Disc.

FLY DE GATE
CD _____ VPCD 1285
VP / May '93 / Jetstar.

FLY, FRESH & PHAT
Feel it: A Level / Lonliness Avenue: Phipps, Stacey / We're on our way: Deneshae / Fly away: Silver / Star: Marx, Sira / Be there for you: Vann, Yvonne / Lean on me: Deneshae & Stacey Phipps / Night and day: Prime, Nathan / I endeavour: Clarke, Garlene / Love train: C 223 / Dawn: Powell, Bryan
CD _____ CDEMC 3719
EMI / Oct '95 / EMI.

FLYIN' HIGH
CD _____ RNBCD 107
Connoisseur / Jan '94 / Pinnacle.

FLYING HIGH
CD _____ CDTOT 25
Jumpin' & Pumpin' / Apr '95 / 3MV / Sony.

FLYING NUN SAMPLER
CD _____ NUN 1CD
Flying Nun / Sep '93 / Disc.

FOLK BOX
(2CD/MC Set)
CD Set _____ TBXCD 513
TrueTrax / Jan '96 / THE.

FOLK COLLECTION, THE
Another Irish rover: Four Men & A Dog / Carthy's reel/The return to Camden Town: Carthy, Martin & Dave Swarbrick / Almost every circumstance: Prior, Maddy & June Tabor / Oh I swear: Thompson, Richard / Company policy: Carthy, Martin / I specialise: Gregson & Collister / Party's over: Albion Band / Brighton camp/March past: Kirkpatrick, John / Good old way: Watersons / Johnny Cope: MacColl, Ewan / Battle of Falkirk Muir: Battlefield Band / Reaper: Tabor, June / Farewll to the gold: Jones, Nic / Reconciliation: Kavana, Ron / Watch's polkas: Patrick Street / Lakes of ponchartrain: Simpson, Martin / Mariano: Keen, Robert Earl / Through moorfields: Cronshaw, Andrew / Now westlin' winds: Gaughan, Dick
CD _____ TSCD 470
Topic / Oct '93 / Direct / ADA.

FOLK COLLECTION, THE VOL.2
CD _____ TSCD 481
Topic / Oct '95 / Direct / ADA.

FOLK HERITAGE
Fiddle diddle: Chilli Willi & Red Hot Peppers / Dalesman's litany: Hart, Tim & Maddy Prior / Calling on song: Steeleye Span / Handsome Polly-O: Carthy, Martin / Copshawholme Fair: Steeleye Span / Sing me back home: Matthews, Iain / My ramblin' boy: Denny, Sandy / Fool like you: Moore, Tim / Famous flower of serving men: Carthy, Martin / Adieu sweet lovely Nancy: Hart, Tim & Maddy Prior / Blacksmith: Steeleye Span / Just as the tide was flowing: Collins, Shirley / Rock 'n' roll love letter: Moore, Tim / Last thing on my mind: Denny, Sandy / Lark in the morning: Steeleye Span / Wager a wager: Hart, Tim & Maddy Prior
CD _____ MCCD 043
Music Club / Sep '91 / Disc / THE / CM.

FOLK HERITAGE 2
Time to ring some changes: Thompson, Richard / Not a day passes: Gregson & Collister / Ramble away: Albion Band / Music for a found harmonium: Patrick Street / Song of the iron road: MacColl, Ewan / Band played waltzing Matilda: Tabor, June / Handsome Molly: Simpson, Martin / World turned upside down: Gaughan, Dick / So vay: Carthy, Martin & Dave Swarbrick / All things are quite silent: Collins, Shirley / Spaghetti panic: Blowzabella / Hidden love/Sheila Coyles: Four Men & A Dog / Fine horsemen: Silly Sisters / Lovely cottage/Gold ochra at Killarney point to points: Alias Ron Kavana / Canadee-I-O: Jones, Nic / Country life: Watersons
CD _____ MCCD 049
Music Club / Mar '92 / Disc / THE / CM.

FOLK HERITAGE 3
Granite years: Oyster Band / Who cares: Shocked, Michelle / First time ever I saw your face: MacColl, Ewan / Mississippi summer: Tabor, June & The Oyster Band / Hush little baby: Horseflies / Breaths: Sweet Honey In The Rock / I still saw Louisiana: Silver wheels: Cockburn, Bruce / Byker hill: Barely Works / Angry love: McLeod, Rory / Six string street: White, Andy / Sea never dry: God's Little Monkeys / Turn things upside down: Happy End / That's entertainment: Colorblind James Experience / Free Mexican airforce: Jimenez, Flaco / Raining: Ancient Beatbox
CD _____ MCCD 076
Music Club / Jun '92 / Disc / THE / CM.

FOLK HERITAGE VOLS. 1 - 3
CD Set _____ MCBX 004
Music Club / Jan '93 / Disc / THE / CM.

FOLK MASTERS
CD _____ SF 40047CD
Smithsonian Folkways / Dec '94 / Direct / Koch / CM / Cadillac.

FOLK MASTERS
CD _____ CDAR 1017
Action Replay / Oct '94 / Tring.

FOLK MUSIC (1)
CD _____ D8005
Auvidis/Ethnic / Jun '89 / Harmonia Mundi.

FOLK MUSIC (2)
CD _____ D8003
Auvidis/Ethnic / Jun '89 / Harmonia Mundi.

FOLK MUSIC FROM NORTHERN SPAIN
CD _____ CMT 2741003CD
La Chant Du Monde / Jul '95 / Harmonia Mundi / ADA.

FOLK MUSIC FROM SCOTLAND
CD _____ 12250
Laserlight / Apr '94 / Target/BMG.

FOLK MUSIC IN SWEDEN VOL.5
CD _____ CAP 21476CD
Caprice / Nov '95 / CM / Complete/ Pinnacle / Cadillac / ADA.

FOLK MUSIC OF ALBANIA
CD _____ TSCD 904
Topic / Oct '94 / Direct / ADA.

FOLK MUSIC OF BULGARIA
CD _____ TSCD 905
Topic / Sep '94 / Direct / ADA.

FOLK MUSIC OF CUBA
CD _____ D 8064
Unesco / Oct '95 / Harmonia Mundi.

FOLK MUSIC OF GREECE
CD _____ TSCD 907
Topic / Sep '94 / Direct / ADA.

FOLK MUSIC OF NORTHERN SPAIN
CD _____ CMT 2741003
La Chant Du Monde / Apr '95 / Harmonia
Mundi / ADA.

FOLK MUSIC OF TURKEY
CD _____ TSCD 908
Topic / Sep '94 / Direct / ADA.

FOLK MUSIC OF YUGOSLAVIA
CD _____ TSCD 906
Topic / Sep '94 / Direct / ADA.

FOLK ROUTES
Siege of Yaddlethorpe: *Amazing Blondel* /
Matty Groves: *Fairport Convention* / John
Barleycorn: *Traffic* / Seven black roses:
Martyn, John / It suits me well: *Denny,
Sandy* / Road: *Drake, Nick* / When I get to
the border: *Thompson, Richard & Linda* /
Strangely strange but oddly normal: *Dr.
Strangely Strange* / Black Jack David: *In-
credible String Band* / Nutting girl: *Hutch-
ings, Ashley* / She moved through the fair:
Fairport Convention / I was a young man:
Albion Country Band / Peace in the end:
Fotheringay / Long odds/Mr. Cosgill's
delight: *Hutchings, Ashley & John Kirkpa
trick* / Audrey: *Heron, Mike* / Man of iron:
Denny, Sandy / Girl in the month of May:
Bunch / Honeypie: *Locke, John*
CD _____ IMCD 197
Island / Jul '94 / PolyGram.

FOLK SONGS FROM NAPLES
CD _____ 15369
Laserlight / '91 / Target/BMG.

**FOLK SONGS FROM NORTH EAST
SCOTLAND**
CD _____ CDTRAX 5003
Greentrax / Nov '95 / Conifer / Duncans /
ADA / Direct.

FOLKLORE FROM VENEZUELA
CD _____ EUCD 1237
ARC / Nov '93 / ARC Music / ADA.

**FOLKSONGS OF THE LOUISIANA
ARCADIANS VOL. 1**
CD _____ ARHCD 359
Arhoolie / Apr '95 / ADA / Direct /
Cadillac.

FOLLOW THAT ROAD
(2nd Annual Vineyard Retreat - 2CD/MC
Set)
CD Set _____ PH 1165/66CD
Philo / Sep '94 / Direct / CM / ADA.

FOOM FOOM
CD _____ BFCD 05
Bruce's Fingers / Oct '93 / Cadillac.

**FOOTBALL CLASSICS - MANCHESTER
UNITED**
Manchester United calypso / Red Devils /
Ryan Giggs we love you / George Best -
Belfast boy / I love George Best / Echoes
of the chaers / Manchester United football
double / United, Manchester United / Look
around / Yellow submarine / Oh what a
lovely morning / Storm in a teacup / Precious memories / Congratulations / Never
be alone / Glory glory shoop shoop /
Love again, live again / Saturday afternoon
at the football / Raindrops keep falling on
my head / Munich air disaster - Flowers of
Manchester
CD _____ MONDE 16CD
Cherry Red / Apr '95 / Pinnacle.

FOR A LOVELY MOTHER
CD _____ DCD 5382LM
Disky / May '94 / THE / BMG / Discovery /
Pinnacle.

**FOR A LOVELY MOTHER
(Instrumental)**
CD _____ CNCD 5994LM
Disky / May '94 / THE / BMG / Discovery /
Pinnacle.

FOR COLLECTORS ONLY
(Kent/Modern's Serious Shades Of Soul)
You brought it all on yourself: *Hammond,
Clay* / Burning out: *Garrett, Vernon* / Long
as I've got my baby: *Day, Jackie* / I've been
done wrong: *Holiday, Jimmy* / Nobody but
me: *Other Brothers* / I'm coming home:
John, Bobby / Remove my doubts: *Johnson, Stacey* / You make me feel like someone: *Gilliam, Johnny* / You are my sunshine:
Shane, Jackie / Baby I'm sorry: *Hill, Z.Z.* /
Them love blues: *Wright, Earl* / Beauty is
just skin deep: *Sweethearts* / You are my
first love: *Hunt, Tommy* / I'm lonely for you: *Adams, Arthur* / All that shines isn't gold:
Windjammers / One more chance: *Four
Tees* / My love, she's gone: *Intentions* / I'm
in love: *Sanders, Larry* / Would you like to
believe in love: *Lovett, Lyndell* / You're the
one: *Holiday, Jimmy* / Like it stands:
Ramsey, Robert / You make me cry: *Adams, Arthur* / I was born to love you: *Copeland, Johnny* / I need money: *Davis, Ruth*
/ It's been a long time baby: *Other Brothers*
/ Think it over baby: *Love, Mary*

CD _____ CDKEND 119
Kent / Sep '95 / Pinnacle.

FOR DANCERS FOREVER
(25 Storming 60's Soul Sounds)
You turned my bitter into sweet: *Love, Mary* /
Baby, without you: *Monday, Danny* / Before it's too late: *Day, Jackie* / Your love has
made me a man: *Hutch, Willie* / You just
cheat and lie: *Hill, Z.Z.* / This man wants
you: *Cox, Wally* / Three lonely guys: *Brilliant
Corners* / My baby needs me: *Baker,
Yvonne* / I don't need: *Turner, Ike & Tina* /
You better be good: *Woods, Peggy* / Lay
this burden down: *Love, Mary* / If I could
turn back the hands of time: *Garrett, Vernon*
/ Can it be me: *Williams, Mel* / Dancing fast,
dancing slow: *Intentions* / My jealous girl:
Hammond, Clay / My aching back: *Fulson,
Lowell* / I can't believe what you say:
Turner, Ike & Tina / This couldn't be me:
Sweethearts / Love is gonna get you:
Woods, Peggy / I can feel your love: *Taylor,
Felice* / Oh what heartaches: *Day, Jackie* /
No puppy love: *Copeland, Johnny* / What
more: *Hill, Z.Z.* / I'm so thankful: *Ikettes* /
I'm in your hands: *Love, Mary*
CD _____ CDKEND 100
Kent / Sep '92 / Pinnacle.

FOR MY VALENTINE
CD _____ WMCD 5677VT
Disky / Feb '94 / THE / BMG / Discovery /
Pinnacle.

FOR ONE AND ALL
CD _____ 9425742
Music For Little People / Jan '96 / Direct.

FOR SENTIMENTAL REASONS
Mountain greenery: *Torme, Mel* / Blueberry
Hill: *Armstrong, Louis* / Tammy: *Reynolds,
Debbie* / Too close for comfort: *Gorme,
Eydie* / (I love you) for sentimental reasons:
Fitzgerald, Ella / Standing on a corner: *Mills
Brothers* / True love ways: *Holly, Buddy* /
Dream a little dream of me: *Mama Cass* /
Friendly persuasion: *Boone, Pat* / Pretty
blue eyes: *Lawrence, Steve* / Love me or
leave me: *Davis, Sammy Jnr.* / Unchained
melody: *Hibbler, Al* / Lollipops and roses:
Jones, Jack / Sweet old fashioned girl:
Brewer, Teresa / Around the world: *Crosby,
Bing* / Mr. Wonderful: *Lee, Peggy* / Love is
a many splendoured thing: *Four Aces* /
Moonglow and theme from picnic: *Stoloff,
Morris*
CD _____ 3035900032
Carlton Home Entertainment / Oct '95 /
Carlton Home Entertainment.

FOR YOUR PRECIOUS LOVE
(2CD Set)
CD Set _____ DBG 53040
Double Gold / Jun '95 / Target/BMG.

FORCE 1 - THE CLUB IS HERE
CD _____ 343322
Koch Dance Force / Nov '95 / Koch.

FOREGANGARE
CD _____ MNW 240/2
MNW / Jan '94 / Vital / ADA.

FOREVER AND EVER
(18 Songs from the heart)
Gambler: *Rogers, Kenny* / True love ways:
Holly, Buddy / You're breaking my heart:
Rose Marie / What a wonderful world:
Armstrong, Louis / When your old wedding
ring was new: *Longthorne, Joe* / Love letters: *Lester, Ketty* / Something's gotten
hold of my heart: *Pitney, Gene* / It's only
make believe: *Twitty, Conway* / Wind beneath my wings: *Greenwood, Lee* / Long
arm of the law: *Rogers, Kenny* / Sweet
dreams: *Cline, Patsy* / You're my best
friend: *Williams, Don* / It's wrong: *Long* /
Someone loves you honey: *Pride, Charley*
/ Jackson: *Sinatra, Nancy & Lee Hazelwood*
/ Just beyond the moon: *Ritter, Tex* / Dedicated to the one I love: *Mamas & Papas* /
Moonlight and roses: *Reeves, Jim*
CD _____ PLATCD 3906
Platinum Music / Jun '89 / Prism / Ross.

FOREVER DOO WOP VOL.1
(2CD Set)
CD Set _____ KNEWCD 738
Kenwest / Apr '94 / THE.

FOREVER DOO WOP VOL.2
(2CD Set)
CD Set _____ KNEWCD 739
Kenwest / Apr '94 / THE.

FOREVER GRATEFUL
Shine down / Oh Lord, our Love / Forever
grateful / Faithful and just / I hear angels /
Lord of my heart
CD _____ HMD 517
Myrrh / '88 / Nelson Word.

FORTIES DANCE BAND HITS
There's a harbour of dreamboats / I'm
gonna get lit up (when the lights go on in
London) / Baby please stop and think about
me / As time goes by / Coming in on a wing
and a prayer / Why don't you fall in love with
me / Ragtime cowboy Joe / I left my heart
at the stage door canteen / Lady who didn't
believe in love / Lover lullaby / Don't get
around much anymore / It can't be wrong /
Pistol packin' Mama / Sunday, Monday or
always / Walkin' by the river / Mr. Five by
five / If I had my way / In the blue of evening
/ Johnny Zero / What's the good word Mr

Bluebird / Tell me the truth / Where's my
love / So long Sarah Jane
CD _____ RAJCD 818
Empress / Jul '94 / THE.

FORTY YEARS OF WOMEN IN JAZZ
CD Set _____ JCD 09/10
Jass / Oct '91 / CM / Jazz Music / ADA /
Cadillac / Direct.

FORWARD
(Selection Of Top Greensleeves Singles
1977-82)
Another one bites the dust: *Eastwood, Clint
& General Saint* / Wa-do-dem: *Eek-A-
Mouse* / Diseases: *Michigan & Smiley* / Gun
man: *Prophet, Michael* / Fattie boom boom:
Ranking Dread / Born for a purpose: *Dr. Al-
imantado* / Bathroom sex: *General Echo* /
War: *Wailing Souls* / Yellowman get's mar-
ried: *Yellowman* / Fat she fat: *Holt, John*
CD _____ GRELCD 60
Greensleeves / Mar '94 / Total/BMG / Jets-
tar / SRD.

FOUND IN THE FLURRY
CD _____ BEST 1073CD
Acoustic Music / Nov '95 / ADA.

FOUNDATION OF ROOTS VOL.1
CD _____ RRCD 016
Roots / Jan '96 / SRD.

FOUNDATION OF ROOTS VOL.1 IN DUB
CD _____ RRCD 018
Roots Collective / Dec '95 / SRD / Jetstar
/ Roots Collective.

FOUR BITCHIN' BABES
CD _____ SH 8018CD
Shanachie / Nov '95 / Koch / ADA /
Greensleeves.

FOUR DECADES OF POP
CD Set _____ MBSCD 433
Castle / Feb '95 / BMG.

FOUR FRENCH HORNS
Four men on a horn / Come rain or come
shine / On the Alamo / Blues for Milt / Lobo
nocho / Mood in motion / I want to be
happy / Wilhemine Worthington Valley
CD _____ SV 0214
Savoy Jazz / Jun '93 / Conifer / ADA.

**FOUR TRUMPET STARS: LOUIS, DIZZY,
MILES & CHET**
CD _____ 4749242
Sony Jazz / Jan '95 / Sony.

FRANCOPHONIX
CD _____ CPCD 8132
Sony / Oct '95 / Charly / THE / Cadillac.

FRANKLINTON MUSCATEL SOCIETY
CD _____ CDBM 091
Blue Moon / Apr '93 / Magnum Music
Group / Greensleeves / Hot Shot / ADA /
Cadillac / Discovery.

**FREDDIE MCGREGOR PRESENTS THE
BEST OF BIG SHIP**
CD _____ RASCD 3162
Ras / Dec '95 / Jetstar / Greensleeves /
SRD / Direct.

FREE AT LAST
Hungry on arrival / Giya kasiamore / Sani-
bonani / Ningakhali / Don't cry / Long walk
to freedom / Bongani's theme
CD _____ BW 076
B&W / Oct '95 / New Note.

FREE SPIRIT
I want it all: *Queen* / If I could turn back
time: *Cher* / Poison: *Cooper, Alice* / Talking
to myself: *Terraplane* / It must have been
love: *Roxette* / Need you tonight: *INXS* /
Touch: *Noiseworks* / Best: *Tyler, Bonnie* /
You took the words right out of my mouth:
Meat Loaf / You give love a bad name: *Bon
Jovi* / How can we be lovers: *Bolton, Mi-
chael* / I don't love you anymore: *Quireboys*
/ Carrie: *Europe* / Black velvet: *Myles, Alan-
nah* / (I just) died in your arms: *Cutting Crew*
/ Flame: *Cheap Trick* / Living years: *Mike &
The Mechanics*
CD _____ MOODCD 16
Columbia / Apr '91 / Sony.

FREE THE FUNK 1
Philip Marlow: *Word Up* / Where I'm going:
Fried Funk Food / Punks not dead: *Dadamo*
/ Sundown: *Koh Tao* / Step into Eden: *Bal-
listic Brothers* / Dark jazz: *Daphreephunka-
teeaz* / Drakes equation: *Spacer* / On da
rocks: *Bangalter, Thomas* / Sporfit: *Heights
Of Abraham* / Hot flush: *Red Snapper* /
Flow: *Model 500* / What I'm feelin' (good):
Nightmares on Wax
CD _____ RS 95085CD
R & S / Jan '96 / Vital.

FREE ZONE 1
(The Phenomenology Of Ambient - 2CD/
4LP Set)
CD Set _____ SSR 129
SSR / May '94 / Grapevine.

FRENCH COLLECTION
CD _____ LECD 121
Wisepack / Nov '94 / THE / Conifer.

FRENCH COLLECTION
CD _____ CDWNCD 2009
Javelin / Jun '95 / THE / Henry Hadaway
Organisation.

FRENCH COLLECTION 2
CD _____ LECDD 635
Wisepack / Aug '95 / THE / Conifer.

FRENCH COLLECTION VOL 1, THE
CD _____ CD 352070
Duchesse / May '93 / Pinnacle.

FRENCH COLLECTION VOL 2, THE
CD _____ CD 352133
Duchesse / Jul '93 / Pinnacle.

FRENCH COLLECTION VOL 3, THE
CD _____ CD 352134
Duchesse / Jul '93 / Pinnacle.

FRENCH COLLECTION, THE
(3 CDs)
CD Set _____ CD 333503
Duchesse / Nov '93 / Pinnacle.

FRENCH-BELGIAN INDUSTRIES
CD _____ MA 43-2
Machinery / Apr '94 / Plastic Head.

FRENESI - 1940
Frenesi: *Shaw, Artie* / Koko: *Ellington, Duke*
/ Sweet Lorraine: *Cole, Nat King* / Gilly:
Goodman, Benny / Laughin': *Holiday, Billie*
/ Boo wah, boo wah: *Calloway, Cab* / Fats
Waller's original E-flat blues: *Waller, Fats* /
Swingtime up in Harlem: *Dorsey, Tommy* /
When day is done: *Hawkins, Coleman* / Just
like taking candy from a baby: *Astaire, Fred*
/ Boogie woogie on St. Louis blues: *Hines,
Earl* / Jack hits the road: *Freeman, Bud* /
Louisiana: *Basie, Count* / I'll never smile
again: *Dorsey, Tommy* / Boog it: *Miller,
Glenn* / Singin' the blues: *Hackett, Bobby* /
Okay for baby: *Lunceford, Jimmie* / 2.19
blues: *Armstrong, Louis* / Jazz me blues:
Bobcats / King Porter stomp: *Metronome
All Star Band*
CD _____ PHONTCD 7668
Phontastic / Apr '90 / Wellard / Jazz Music
/ Cadillac.

FRESH BLUES
CD _____ INAK 19001
In Akustik / Sep '95 / Magnum Music
Group.

FRESH EMISSIONS
Frust: *Being* / Try: *Being* / Anackrohn: *Ver-
min* / Afflicted: *Vermin* / Pedal bin liner boy
melts the bag: *Bishop* / Charic roots: *Herb*
/ Splinter group: *Conemelt* / Hats off to
tracksuit: *Conemelt* / Funny five minutes:
Panash / Lemmy parts 1 and 2: *Panash* /
Space is forever: *Uriel* / Andromeda ses-
sion: *Uriel* / Through mist at one hundred:
Two Lone Swordsman / Midnight auto-
matic: *Day, Deanne* / No-fi: *Corridor* / 1:
Bios / 2: *Bios*
CD Set _____ SOP 005CD
Emissions / Nov '95 / Vital.

**FRESH RECORDS PUNK SINGLES
COLLECTION**
My minors: *Dark* / John Wayne: *Dark* / Ein-
stein's brain: *Dark* / On the wires: *Dark* /
Masque: *Dark* / Punk rock stars: *Art Attacks*
/ Rat city: *Art Attacks* / Madman: *Cuddly
Toys* / Astral Joe: *Cuddly Toys* / Someone's
crying: *Cuddly Toys* / That's a shame: *Cuddly
Toys* / Hawaii Five-O: *Dark* / Young one's:
Menace / Debbie Harry: *Family Fodder* / I've
had the time of my life: *Manufactured Ro-
mance* / Hobby for a day: *Wall* / Earbending:
J.C.'S Mainmen / Poison takes hold: *Play
Dead* / Rebecca's room: *Wasted Youth* /
Puppets of war: *Chron Gen* / T.V. Eye: *Play
Dead*
CD _____ CDPUNK 32
Anagram / May '94 / Pinnacle.

FRESHEN UP VOL.1
CD _____ FRSHCD 1
Fresh / May '95 / 3MV.

FRESKA
CD _____ REACTCD 039
React / Jun '94 / Vital.

FRESKA 2
Dreamer (Rollo mix): *Livin' Joy* / Don't wait
for me: *Loveland* / I believe: *Happy Clappers*
/ Taking me higher: *Gems For Jem* / In-
vader: *Kool World* / Horny as funk: *Soapy* /
Love and sex: *Boyfriend* / Ooh baby: *Raw
Tunes* / Hot (CD & MC only.): *Majik Village*
/ It's alright: *S.A.I.N.* / Dance MF: *Nelson,
Grant* / Latinos on parade: *Franco, Chico*
/ Let the rhythm flow (CD & MC only.): *Diva
Rhythms* / You can have it (CD & MC.): *Ca-
sanova, Charlie* / Fe fi fo fum: *Raw* / Do you
wanna party (CD & MC only.): *Wand &
Storm HQ* / Sex on the streets (CD & MC.):
Pizzaman / Krazy noise (CD & MC.):
Numerical Value
CD _____ REACTCD 061
React / Jun '95 / Vital.
CD _____ REACTCDX 061
React / Jun '95 / Vital.

FRIED TO PERFECTION BY EXPERTS
Mary Queen of Scots: *Eugenius* / Pillow
fight: *18 Wheeler* / Wet dream: *18 Wheeler*
/ Butterfly boy: *Shonen Knife* / Get the wow:
Shonen Knife / Apple: *Boyfriend* / Summer
thing: *Boyfriend* / Don't get 2 close 2 my
fantasy: *Ween* / Sarah: *Ween* / She must be
Spanish: *Autohaze* / Ween feels so good /
Plant me: *Suddenly Tammy*
CD _____ RUST 011CD
August / Sep '93 / Vital.

FRIENDS IN HIGH PLACES
More than a friend: Baylor, Helen / Out front: Angel / You changed my life: Marquis Ubu / Thank you Jesus: Jasper, Chris / Call me: Smith, Kenny / Step by step: Hammond, Fred / One love one people: Taylor, Gary / I'll shine for you: Austin, Dennis / Empty promises: Futrel / God in you: Dawkins & Dawkins / Will you be ready: Redeemed / It's only natural: Thomas, Keith / Be for real: Mitchell, Vernessa / Love's the key: Gaines, Billy & Sarah
CD _____ CDEXP 5
Expansion / Dec '93 / Pinnacle / Sony / 3MV.

FRIFOT
CD _____ CAP 2138CD
Caprice / Nov '95 / CM / Complete / Pinnacle / Cadillac / ADA.

FROM ACOUSTIC TO ELECTRIC BLUES
CD _____ D2CD08
Recording Arts / Dec '92 / THE / Disc.

FROM BAM BAM TO CHERRY OH BABY
Bam bam: Toots & The Maytals / Ba ba boom: Jamaicans / Intensified: Dekker, Desmond / Sweet and dandy: Toots & The Maytals / Boom shacka lacka: Lewis, Hopeton / Unity is love: Dice, Billy / Da da: Byles, Junior / Pomp and pride: Toots & The Maytals / Festival 10: Morgan, Derrick / Cherry oh baby: Donaldson, Eric
CD _____ JMC 200101
Jamaica Gold / Nov '92 / THE / Magnum Music Group / Jetstar.

FROM DIXIELAND TO SWING
CD _____ D2CD09
Recording Arts / Dec '92 / THE / Disc.

FROM GALWAY TO DUBLIN
CD _____ ROU 1087CD
Rounder / Feb '93 / CM / Direct / ADA / Cadillac.

FROM HERE TO TRANQUILITY
CD _____ PS 9336
Silent / Nov '93 / Plastic Head.

FROM HERE TO TRANQUILITY II
CD _____ SR 9343
Silent / May '94 / Plastic Head.

FROM HERE TO TRANQUILITY III
CD _____ SR 9460
Silent / Feb '95 / Plastic Head.

FROM IRELAND - WHISKEY IN THE JAR
CD _____ 15160
Laserlight / '91 / Target/BMG.

FROM MOUNTAIN AND VALLEY
CD _____ QPRZ 006D
Polyphonic / Jun '91 / Conifer.

FROM OUT OF NOWHERE
Shove: Cosmic Psychos / Modern girl: Dubrovniks / Heading right back to you: Dubrovniks / Build it up: Nursery Crimes / Eleanor Rigby: Nursery Crimes / Fatal fascination: Screaming Tribesmen / Bugging: Screemfeeder / End of this day: Screemfeeder / Dreaming: Chevelles / Run and hide: Chevelles / Degenerate boy: Bored / Rain: Bored / Shame: You Am I / Snake tide: You Am I / Cheers: Front & Loader / Me to know: Front & Loader / Chrysalidz: Massappeal
CD _____ SUR 525CD
Survival / Jun '93 / Pinnacle.

FROM RIPLEY TO CHICAGO
(26 Original Cuts That Inspired Eric Clapton)
Let it rock: Berry, Chuck / Certain girl: Doe, Ernie K. / Good morning little school girl: Don & Bob / I ain't got you: Arnold, Billy Boy / Too much monkey business: Berry, Chuck / Here 'tis: Diddley, Bo / Crossroads: Johnson, Robert / Steppin' out: Memphis Slim / All your love: Rush, Otis / Ramblin' on my mind: Johnson, Robert / Spoonful: Howlin' Wolf / Key to the highway: Little Walter / Evil: Howlin' Wolf / Mean ol' Frisco: Crudup, Arthur 'Big Boy' / I can't hold out: James, Elmore / Steady rollin' man: Johnson, Robert / Ain't that lovin' you baby: Reed, Jimmy / It hurts me too: James, Elmore / Driftin' blues: Berry, Chuck / Double trouble: Rush, Otis / Worried life blues: Berry, Chuck / Before you accuse me: Diddley, Bo / Watch yourself: Guy, Buddy / Rollin' and tumblin': Waters, Muddy
CD _____ CDINS 5071
Instant / Jan '93 / Charly.

FROM THE DANUBE TO THE BALKAN
(Music From Bulgaria)
CD _____ CMT 274981
La Chant Du Monde / Dec '95 / Harmonia Mundi / ADA.

FROM THE HEART
CD _____ STACD 051
Wisepack / Sep '94 / THE / Conifer.

FROM THE HEART
(Corason Sampler)
CD _____ CORACD 701
Corason / Feb '95 / CM / Direct / ADA.

FROM THE IRISH TRADITION: VOL 3
CD _____ CDTCD 003
Gael Linn / Dec '94 / Roots / CM / Direct / ADA.

FRONTLINE REGGAE
CD _____ CONQ 998CD
Conqueror / May '95 / Jetstar / SRD.

FROZEN BRASS: AFRICA & LATIN AMERICA
CD _____ PAN 2026CD
Pan / Oct '93 / ADA / Direct / CM.

FUCKING HARDCORE
CD _____ MOK 99CD
Mokum / Sep '93 / Pinnacle.

FUCKING HARDCORE PART 3
Fucking hardcore: Chosen Few / I wanna be a hippy: Technohead / Freak tonight: Speedfreak / Edge of panic: Cyanide / Realm of darkness: Annihilator / Abba gabba: Riot Nation / Toxic waste 396: High Energy / Headsex: Technohead / Don't fuck with me: Original Gabber / To da rhythm: Dee, Lenny / Voodoo vibe: Tellurian / Happe-people: Search & Destroy / We keep going on: Riot Nation / This is not the end: One, Walter / Energy boost: D.J. Dano & Liza N Eliaz
CD _____ DB 47932
Deep Blue / Jul '95 / Pinnacle.

FUCKING HARDFLOOR VOL.1 & 2
CD Set _____ 005DCD
Atomic Fate Inc / Oct '95 / Plastic Head.

FULL METAL - THE ALBUM
CD _____ 0086372 CTR
Edel / Jan '96 / Pinnacle.

FULL ON - VOL.1
(A Year In The Life Of House Music)
Open your mind: Usura / Shift: Havana / Hablando: Ramirez / Lionrock: Lionrock / Movin' to the beat: Little Rascal / Tonight: Orson Kart / Mind odyssey: Eternal / It will make me crazy: Felix / Belgium: Megatonk / Don't stop: Frendzy / Nush: Nush / I'm stronger now: Definitive Two / Perfect day: Visions Of Shiva / Yerba del diablo: Datura / Givin' you no rest: E-Lustrious / France: THK
CD _____ 7432112803-2
De-Construction / Feb '93 / BMG.

FULL-E RECORDS VOL.1
CD _____ FUE C1
Full-E / Nov '95 / Plastic Head.

FUN OF THE FAIR
Cabaret / Me and my shadow / Ciribiribin / Stripper / Can can / My blue heaven / Viva Espana / Twelfth street rag / I do like to be beside the seaside / At the Darktown strutter's ball / King cotton / Waiting for the Robert E. Lee / Carolina in the morning / Pretty baby / Toot toot tootsie goodbye / I'm sitting on top of the world / I'm looking over a four leaf clover / Chinatown, my Chinatown / Baby face / California here I come / Avalon / Little boogie / Skokiaan / Annen polka / Day trip to Bangor / Roses from the South / Eleanor waltz / Dinah / Alexander's ragtime band
CD _____ SOV 007CD
Sovereign / Jun '92 / Target/BMG.

FUN WHILE IT LASTED
CD _____ ONLYCD 006
Avalanche / Nov '90 / Disc.

FUN WITH MUSHROOMS
Toadstool soup (slight send slight return): Boris & His Bolshie Balalaika / Night descent: Bazaar, Saddar / Electric sensation: Praise Space Electric / Yuppi deadhead party: 14th Wray / Government splus 3am: Carter, Dean & The High Commission / Awakened: Omnia Opera / Who's my name: Iron / Uncle Sam: Juana, Harold / Chocolate staircase: Dead Flowers / Half moon flower: Tangle Edge / Did you feed the fish: Watch children / Thoughts of the sky: Wobble jaggle jiggle / Thought dial: Mooseheart Faith / Ritual people (Features on CD only.): Cosmic kangaroos / Mr. and Mrs. Creature (Features on CD only.): Reefus moons / Thirteen ghosts (Features on CD only.): Marshmallow Overcoat / Freakbeat (Features on CD only.): Dr. Brown / River (Features on CD only.): Jasmine Love Bomb
CD _____ DELECCD 009
Delerium / Jun '93 / Vital.

FUNK 7
Super cool: Hunt, Pat / Branded: Leach, C.J. / Funky strut: Fabulous Soul Eruption / Hook and boogie pt.1: Abraham / It's your love: Theron & Darrell / Dap walk: Ernie & The Top Notes / Gimme some: General Crook / Boilin' water: Soul Stoppers Band / Bad luck: Carbo, Hank / Fresh head: Slim & Soulful Saints / Green power: Wallace, Sir Sidney / Slow down: Elliott, Don / Is your own thing: Moultrie, Sam / Soul chicken: Allen, Bobby / Soul power: Willis, Jamie / Whip: Brown, Al / Hook and boogie pt.2: Abraham / Gimme some (pt.2): General Crook / Slow down (2): Elliott, Don
CD _____ GSCD 060
Goldmine / Dec '94 / Vital.

FUNK 8
Ain't no other way: Hitson, Herman / Baby don't cry: Third Guitar / Do the Bobby

Dunn: Dunn, Bobby / Popcorn baby: Hench, Freddy / Check your battery: Talbot, Johny / Baby I've got it: Fabulous Souls / You lost your thing: Johnson, Hank / Sagittarius: Landlord & Tennants / Ain't that fun: Harris, Tyrone / Movin' and groovin': Volcanos / Lady: Superiors Band & Their Soul Singers / Funky donkey: Illusions / Groove penguin: Wonsley, Excell / Soul encyclopedia: Jones, Geraldine / Get off your butt (CD only.): Hines, Debbie / Jungle (CD only.): Young Senators / Funky jive (CD only.): Soul Crusaders / Village sound (CD only): Village Sound
CD _____ GSCD 064
Goldmine / Jun '95 / Vital.

FUNK 9
Free and easy: Apples & The Oranges / Take it and get: Zere & The Soul Sisters / I don't want to hear it now: Brinson, Jimmy / Cool it: Morris, Guy / To the brain: Thrillers / Number one prize: Bare Faxx / Cookies: Brother Soul / What it is: Apollis / Funky wah wah: La Mar, Tony / Tormented: Holliday, Johnny / What you do do it good: Williams, Gene / Sound success: Wallis, Joe / Funky mule Pt.1: Holmes, Martin & The Uptights / Times are bad: Barnes, Bobby / I got a new thing: Smith, Willie / Akiwawa: Village Crusaders / Nabbit juice pt.1: Eastwind / Happy fool: Belva / Sock it to me: Moore, Henry / Do it good: Brother Soul
CD _____ GSCD 067
Goldmine / Jan '96 / Vital.

FUNKY ALTERNATIVES VOL.7
CD _____ CPRODCD 25
Concrete Productions / Feb '94 / Plastic Head.

FUNKY ALTERNATIVES VOL.8
Menofearthe reaper: Pop Will Eat Itself / Pure spite: Godflesh / Crackin' up: Revolting Cocks / You coma: Optimum Wound Profile / Bombs in my head: Ultraviolence / Momentous lamentous: Pig / Mind razor: Gunshot / Untitled: Surfers for Satan / Obsession: Shining / We know who you are: Judda / Compassion: Mussolini Headkick
CD _____ CPRODCD 026
Concrete Productions / Mar '95 / Plastic Head.

FUNKY GOOD TIME
Come get it, I got it: Ousley, Harold / Kid (CD Only.): Ousley, Harold / Little virgo (CD only.): Ousley, Harold / Peoples groove (CD Only.): Ousley, Harold / Opus for OP (CD Only.): Pleasant, Bu / Put on your high heel sneakers: Green, Grant / Gator's groove: Jackson, Willis / Hello, good luck: Jackson, Willis / Ode to Larry Young: Groove Holmes
CD _____ PHOCD 8001
Muse / Sep '95 / New Note / CM.

FUNKY JAMS VOL.1
CD _____ HUBCD 1
Hubbub / Aug '95 / SRD / BMG.

FUNKY JAMS VOL.2
CD _____ HUBCD 2
Hubbub / Sep '95 / SRD / BMG.

FUNKY JAMS VOL.3
Cornbread and beans: Brodie, Hugh / Can you feel it: S.O.U.L. / Stand up and be counted: Getto Kitty / Untouchable machine shop #2: Machine Shop / My friend: Marrero, Ricardo & The Group / Freakin' time: Asphalt Jungle / Ain't it good enough: Nu Sound Express Ltd. / Funky way: Dynamics / Funky four corners: Marks, Richard / She's a love maker: Fields, Lee / Time to love: Candy Coated People / Boots grove: Soul Tornadoes
CD _____ HUBCD 4
Hubbub / Nov '95 / SRD / BMG.

FURTHER SELF EVIDENT TRUTHS
CD _____ RSNCD 31
Rising High / Apr '95 / Disc.

FURTHER SELF EVIDENT TRUTHS 2
CD _____ RSNCD 39
Rising High / Aug '95 / Disc.

FUSE I & II
CD _____ NATCD 35
Nation / Jul '94 / Disc.

FUSION OF CLASSICAL AND POP STYLES, A
CD _____ SPOTS 13
Intersound / Oct '91 / Jazz Music.

FUSION OF CLASSICAL AND POP STYLES, A VOL. 2
CD _____ SPOTS 14
Intersound / Oct '91 / Jazz Music.

FUSION PHEW
Sudden samba: Larson, Neil / Latin America: Walton, Cedar / Hip skip: Williams, Tony / El bobo: Lewis, Webster / Hump: Rushen, Patrice / Rio: Glenn, Roger / Caveman boogie: Wilson, Lesette / Harlem boys: Rollins, Sonny / Walk tall: Soskin, Mark / Do it to it: Owens, Jimmy / Little sunflower: Hubbard, Freddie / On the path: Franklin, Rodney
CD _____ CDELV 10
Elevate / Dec '93 / 3MV / Sony.

Baby don't you know: Humphrey, Bobbi / I'm staying forever: Henderson, Wayne / Life is like a samba: Benoit, David / There are many stops along the way: Sample, Joe / Scapegoat: Johnson, Al / Slick Eddie: Stitt, Sonny
CD _____ CDELV 15
Elevate / Jan '94 / 3MV / Sony.

FUTILITY OF A WELL-ORDERED LIFE
CD _____ VIRUS 147CD
Alternative Tentacles / May '95 / Pinnacle.

FUTURE PERFECT
Domus in nebulae: Eno, Roger / Saint columbas walk: Eno, Roger / Western island of apples: Partridge, Andy / Bruegel: Partridge, Andy / Stravinsky: Eno, Brian / Distant hill: Eno, Brian / Radiothesia III: Eno, Brian / Testify: Channel Light Vessel / Faint aroma of snow: Channel Light Vessel / For the love of you: St. John, Kate / Your promised land: St. John, Kate / Big noise in Twangtown: Nelson, Bill / Her presence in flowers: Nelson, Bill
CD _____ ASCD 024
All Saints / Mar '95 / Vital / Discovery.

FUTURE SHOCK
CD _____ CDTB 012
Magnum Music / Oct '94 / Magnum Music Group.

FUTURE SOUND OF HARDCORE, THE
CD _____ KFCD 002
Knite Force / Jan '96 / Jumpstart / Mo's Music Machine.

G.I. JUKEBOX
(100 Original Hits From The Swing Era 1936-46 - 5CD/MC Set)
CD Set _____ H5CD 3345
Hindsight / Sep '93 / Target/BMG / Jazz Music.

G.I. JUKEBOX VOL.1
CD _____ HCD 2001
Hindsight / Sep '93 / Target/BMG / Jazz Music.

G.I. JUKEBOX VOL.2
CD _____ HCD 2002
Hindsight / Sep '93 / Target/BMG / Jazz Music.

G.I. JUKEBOX VOL.3
CD _____ HCD 2003
Hindsight / Sep '93 / Target/BMG / Jazz Music.

G.I. JUKEBOX VOL.4
CD _____ HCD 2004
Hindsight / Sep '93 / Target/BMG / Jazz Music.

G.I. JUKEBOX VOL.5
CD _____ HCD 2005
Hindsight / Sep '93 / Target/BMG / Jazz Music.

GAGAKU
CD _____ LYRCD 7126
Lyrichord / Aug '94 / Roots / ADA / CM.

GAL YU GOOD
CD _____ VPCD 1123
VP / Oct '90 / Jetstar.

GAMELAN ENSEMBLE OF BATUR
CD _____ C559 002
Ocora / '88 / Harmonia Mundi / ADA.

GAOL FERRY BRIDGE
Air: Even As We Speak / Try happiness: Blueboy / Reinventing penicillin: Sugargliders / Atta girl: Heavenly / Classic music: Action Painting / My life is wrong: East River Pipe / Ahprahran: Sugargliders / I've got it and it's not worth having: Boyracer / P.U.N.K. Girl: Heavenly / Getting faster: Even As We Speak / Coup: Boyracer / Happy town: East River Pipe / Blueboy: Air France / Loveblind: Secret Shine / Helmet on: East River Pipe / Theme from Boxville: Sugargliders
CD _____ SARAH 530CD
Sarah / Nov '94 / Vital.

GARAGE MIX VOL.1
(Roger Sanchez)
CD _____ GMCD 001
Dance Mix / Jul '94 / Vital.

GARAGE MIX VOL.2
(David Morales)
CD _____ GMCD 002
Dance Mix / Jul '94 / Vital.

GARAGE PUNK UNKNOWNS PART 2
CD _____ EFA 115802
Crypt / Jun '95 / SRD.

GARGULA MECANICA
CD _____ BIOCD 03
Messerschmitt / Mar '94 / Plastic Head.

GARNI: ARMENIAN DANCES
CD _____ VANGEEL 9404
Van Geel / Aug '95 / ADA. Direct.

GARO OF THE MUDHUPAR FOREST, THE
CD _____ C 580054
Ocora / May '94 / Harmonia Mundi / ADA.

GATHERING OF THE ELDERS, THE
CD _____ WLAAS 25CD
Waterlilly Acoustics / Nov '95 / ADA.

GAY 90'S, THE
(Musical Boxes/Pianolas)
Runaway girl / Robin Hood / Florodora / Belle of New York / Geisha / Greek slave and San toy / Dozen discs / Canary and nightingale warble / Evergreens / Stephen Foster favourites / Gay 90's favourites / Miscellany
CD _____ CDSDL 273
Saydisc / Jun '92 / Harmonia Mundi / ADA / Direct.

GAY ANTHEMS
CD _____ ALMYCD 11
Almighty / Feb '95 / Total/BMG.

GAY ANTHEMS II
CD _____ ALMYCD 16
Almighty / Nov '95 / Total/BMG.

GBG HARDCORE 81-85
CD _____ DOLCD 9
Distortion / Sep '93 / Plastic Head.

GEE WIZZ - THE BEST IN THE HOUSE
(2LP/CD/MC Set)
CD Set _____ WIZZD 23
Wizz / Oct '95 / Grapevine.

GEMS OF THE MUSIC HALL
I love a lassie: Lauder, Sir Harry / Every little movement: Lloyd, Marie / Lily of Laguna: Stratton, Eugene / Gas inspector: Little Tich / 'E can't take a roise out of oi: Chevalier, Albert / Put on your slippers: Lloyd, Marie / Burlington Bertie from Bow: Shields, Ella / Little idea of my own: Robey, George / Little Dolly daydream: Elliot, G.H. / When I took my morning parade: Lloyd, Marie / Has anyone here seen Kelly: Forde, Florrie / Whistling bowery boy: Whelan, Albert / Same as his father did before him: Lauder, Sir Harry / Archibald certainly not: Robey, George / Going to the races: Leno, Dan / When father papered the parlour: Williams, Billy / Old bull and bush: Forde, Florrie / Preacher and the bear: Whelan, Albert / Hold your hand out, naughty boy: Forde, Florrie / Fill 'Em Up: King, Hetty / 'E dunno where 'E are: Elen, Gus / Three trees: Whelan, Albert
CD _____ PASTCD 7005
Flapper / Mar '93 / Pinnacle.

GENERAL MEETS THREE BLIND MICE
CD _____ 790092
King Dragon / Jun '93 / Jetstar / Greensleeves.

GENERICS
Cakewalk of crime: Jonathan Fire Eater / Something for nothing: Spoiler / Black eyed girl: Speedball Baby / Sun to sun: Spitters / Milky white entropy: Poem Rocket / Aurora F: Slug / Welcome to my head: Noisext / Boppin high school baby: 68 Comeback / Drag house: Chrome Cranks / Brad Mayor PhD: Slowworm / Pro choice: Fuse / Ordinary nights: Railroad Jerk
CD _____ PCP 0222
PCP / Nov '95 / Vital.

GENIUS OF BOOGIE-WOOGIE
CD _____ CD 53053
Giants Of Jazz / Mar '90 / Target/BMG / Cadillac.

GENTLEMEN OF THE COUNTRY
CD _____ HADCD 177
Javelin / Nov '95 / THE / Henry Hadaway Organisation.

GENTLEMEN PIPERS, THE
(Classic Recordings Of Irish Traditional Piping)
Banks of the Suir: Walsh, Liam / Portlaw reel: Walsh, Liam / Ask my father/The mountain lark: Andrews, William / May day/ The Cuckoo's nest: Andrews, William / Lass of the Cork road/The Irish washerwoman: Rowsome, Leo / Kiss the maid behind the barrel/Touch me if you dare: Rowsome, Leo / Snowy breasted pearl: Rowsome, Leo / Langstern pony: Clancy, Willie / Dear Irish boy: Clancy, Willie / Flogging reel: Clancy, Willie / Boys of Bluehill/Dunphy's hornpipe: Ennis, Seamus / Flags of Dublin/Wind that shakes the barley: Ennis, Seamus / Wandering minstrel/Jackson's morning brush: Ennis, Seamus / Blackbird: Ennis, Seamus / First house in Connaught/The copperplate: McAloon, Sean & John Rea / An buachaill caol dubh/Drops of brandy: McAloon, Sean / Ash plant: Doran, Felix / Late in the morning: Doran, Felix / Mary of Murroe/The green gates: Doran, Felix / Boys of the lough: Doran, Felix / Frieze breeches: Mitchell, Pat / Mairseail alasdruim: Mitchell, Pat / Garrett Barry's/The Virginia reel: Mitchell, Pat / Ballyoran: O'Brien, Michael / Rakish Paddy/Castle Kelly: O'Brien, Michael
CD _____ CDORBD 084
Globestyle / Mar '94 / Pinnacle.

GENUINE HOUSEROCKIN' VOL.1
CD _____ ALCD 101
Alligator / Oct '93 / Direct / ADA.

GENUINE HOUSEROCKIN' VOL.2
CD _____ ALCD 102
Alligator / Oct '93 / Direct / ADA.

GENUINE HOUSEROCKIN' VOL.3
CD _____ ALCD 103
Alligator / Oct '93 / Direct / ADA.

GENUINE HOUSEROCKIN' VOL.4
CD _____ ALCD 109
Alligator / Nov '93 / Direct / ADA.

GENUINE HOUSEROCKIN' VOL.5
CD _____ ALCD 109
Alligator / Nov '93 / Direct / ADA.

GEORGE PHANG PRESENTS POWERHOUSE VOL.1
CD _____ SONCD 0007
Sonic Sounds / Feb '91 / Jetstar.

GEORGIA BLUES & GOSPEL 1927-31
CD _____ DOCD 5160
Blues Document / May '93 / Swift / Jazz Music / Hot Shot.

GEORGIA SEA ISLAND SONGS
Moses: Davis, John / Kneebone: Armstrong, Joe / Sheep, sheep, don't you know the road: Jones, Bessie / Live humble: Davis, John / Daniel: Proctor, Willis / O Death: Jones, Bessie / Read 'em John: Davis, John / Beulah land: Davis, John / Buzzard lope: Jones, Bessie / Raggy Levi: Davis, John / Ain't I right: Morrison, Henry / See Aunt Dinah: Jones, Bessie / Walk, Billy Abbul. Proctor, Willis / Reg'lar reg'lar rollin' under: Jones, Bessie / Pay me: Armstrong, Joe / Carrie Belle: Davis, John / Laz'rus: Morrison, Henry / Titanic: Jones, Bessie
CD _____ 802782
New World / Aug '92 / Harmonia Mundi / ADA / Cadillac.

GEORGIA STRING BANDS 1928-30
CD _____ SOB 035162
Story Of The Blues / Feb '93 / Koch / ADA.

GERMAN DRINKING SONGS
CD _____ MCD 71419
Monitor / Jun '93 / CM.

GERMAN MYSTIC SOUND SAMPLER
CD _____ EFA 910102
Zillo / Dec '95 / SRD.

GET DANCIN'
(16 Original Soul Hits)
CD _____ 12214
Laserlight / Jan '94 / Target/BMG.

GET DANCING
(Disco Classics)
Get dancing: Disco Tex & The Sexolettes / 7-6-5-4-3-2-1 Blow your whistle: Rimshots / Shame, shame, shame: Shirley & Company / Disco stomp: Bohannon, Hamilton / Swing your daddy: Gilstrap, Jim / I get the sweetest feeling: Wilson, Jackie / Take that to the bank: Shalamar / This is it: Moore, Melba / Rapper's delight: Sugarhill Gang / Sunshine day: Osibisa / Now is the time: James, Jimmy & The Vagabonds / Boogie down (Get funky now): Real Thing / What's your name what's your number: Andrea True Connection / White lines (don't don't do it): Grandmaster Flash & Melle Mel / Disappearing act: Shalamar / You don't have to go: Chi-Lites
CD _____ TRTCD 118
TrueTrax / Dec '94 / THE

GET DANCING
CD _____ MU 5044
Musketeer / Oct '92 / Koch.

GET HOT OR GO HOME
(Vintage RCA Rockabillies 1956-59)
Duck tail: Clay, Joe / Sixteen chicks: Clay, Joe / Doggone it: Clay, Joe / Goodbye goodbye: Clay, Joe / Slipping out and sneaking in: Clay, Joe / Get on the right track baby: Clay, Joe / You look that good to me: Clay, Joe / Crackerjack: Clay, Joe / Did you mean jelly bean (what you said cabbage head): Clay, Joe / Ooh-eee: Cartey, Ric / Heart throb: Cartey, Ric / I wancha to know: Cartey, Ric / Mellow down easy: Cartey, Ric / My babe: Cartey, Ric / Two tone shoes: Homer & Jethro / Catty Town: King, Pee Wee / Sugar sweet: Houston, David / Honky tonk mind: Blake, Tommy & the rhythm rebels / All night long: Blake, Tommy & the rhythm rebels / Now stop: Carson, Martha / Love me to pieces: Martin, Janis / Two long years: Martin, Janis / All right baby: Martin, Janis / Chicken house: Rich, Dave / Teen Billy Baby: Sprouts / Don't bug me baby: Allen, Milt / Rainbow Doll: Dell, Jimmy / It ain't right: Terry, Gordon / Let's get goin': Morgan Twins / Almost eighteen: Osborne, Roy / Little boy blue: Johnson, Hoyt
CD _____ CMFCD 014
Country Music Foundation / Jan '93 / Direct / ADA.

GET INTO JAZZ
CD _____ 525030-2
PolyGram / Nov '94 / PolyGram.

GET INTO THE GROOVE
Keep that same old feeling: Side Effect / Jazz carnival: Azymuth / Rock Creek Park: Blackbyrds / Do it fluid: Blackbyrds / Walking in rhythm: Blackbyrds / Joyous: Pleasure / Beale Street: Adams, Arthur / Dancin': McWilliams, Paulette / Midnight and you: Turrentine, Stanley / Giving it back: Hunt, Phil / I don't know what's on your mind: Spider's Webb / Will they miss me: Simmons, David / Ghettos of the mind: Pleasure / Space bass: Slick / I don't want to be alone ranger: Watson, Johnny 'Guitar' / Sweet Dan: Everett, Betty / Let your heart be free: Rushen, Patrice
CD _____ CDSEWD 034
Southbound / Jan '91 / Pinnacle.

GET ME JESUS ON THE LINE
Good news: Staple Singers / He has a way: Greatest Harvest Choir / See how he kept me: Argo Singers / It's Jesus in me: Caravans / This may be the last time: Staple Singers / Will the circle be unbroken: Staple Singers / Working on the building: Highway QC's / I'm going through: Caravans / Please hear my call: Bells Of Joy / One talk with Jesus: Five Blind Boys Of Mississippi / Where there's a will: Five Blind Boys Of Mississippi / Father I stretch my hand to thee: Harmonizing Four / I can see everybody's Mother: Five Blind Boys Of Alabama / He saved my soul: Swan Silvertones / Oh Mary don't you weep: Swan Silvertones / Get your soul right: Swan Silvertones / What about you: Swan Silvertones / God is standing by: Soul Stirrers / Wade in the water: Harmonizing Four
CD _____ NTMCD 519
Nectar / Oct '95 / Pinnacle.

GET ON BOARD LITTLE CHILDREN
Get on board little children / Climbing Jacob's ladder / Go devil / Satisfied / Steal away to Jesus / Brother Noah / Charge to keep I have / Just a little talk with Jesus / Who should I worry / Jesus said if you go / In my saviour's care / Heavenly highway / Those chiming bells / Sun will never go down / Dig a little deeper / I took my master's hand / God rode into the windstorm / Take your burdens to the Lord / I John Saw / King Jesus is listening / I wanna see Jesus / Daniel / I'll rest after a while / Lord remember me / On the battlefield for the Lord / Father I Stretch my arms to thee / On my way (got my travelin' shoes)
CD _____ CDCHD 537
Ace / Feb '95 / Pinnacle / Cadillac / Complete/Pinnacle.

GET REAL
Mansize rooster: Supergrass / Find the answer within: Boo Radleys / Marvellous: Lightning Seeds / Girl like your: Collins, Edwyn / Steel guitars: 18 Wheeler / Waking up: Elastica / Breaking the ice: Molly Half Head / New generation: Suede / Sleep freak: Heavy Stereo / To the end: Blur / High and dry: Radiohead / Daffodil lament: Cranberries / Sparky's dream: Teenage Fanclub / Inbetweener: Sleeper / Last day on Earth: Swervedriver / Tom Driver: King L / Birthday wish: Mother May I / Summertime: Buffalo Tom / Now they'll sleep: Belly
CD _____ CDGET 1
EMI / Sep '95 / EMI.

GET RIGHT WITH GOD
(Hot Gospel 1947-53)
Tree of life: Powers, Prophet / Blood done signed my name: Radio Four / I got good religion: National Independent Gospel Singers / Tell me why you like Roosevelt: Jackson, Otis
CD _____ HTCD 01
Heritage / Jan '89 / Swift / Roots / Wellard / Direct / Hot Shot / Jazz Music / ADA.

GET THE RHYTHM
(2CD Set)
CD Set _____ 24302
Dadella Doubles / May '94 / Target/BMG.

GET WEAVING VOL. 1
CD _____ GWCD 001
Weaving / Jun '92 / Koch / Direct / ADA.

GET WEAVING VOL. 2
(The Cajun/Zydeco Collection)
CD _____ GWD 02CD
Weaving / Aug '93 / Koch / Direct / ADA.

GET WITH THE BEAT - THE MAR-VEL MASTERS
(A Lost Decade of American Rock & Roll)
Get with the beat: Nix, Billy / Honky tonkin' rhythm: Sisco, Bobby / Come on let's go: Dallis, Chuck / Jump baby jump: Carter, Harry / My friend: Dallis, Chuck / Seven lonely days: Carter, Ginny / Out of the picture: Bradshaw, Jack / I'm settin' you free: Allen, Harold & J T Watts / I need some lovin': Allen, Harold / Heartsick and blue: Wall, Rem / Count down: Smith, Lorenzo / Hot lips baby: Duncan, Herbie / Ha ha hey hey: Kimbrough, Mel / Would it matter at all: Durbin, Ronnie / A-sleepin' at the foot: Ashford, Shorty / Let me love you: Hall, Billy / Ronnie's boogie: Durbin, Ronnie / Tired of

rocking: Burton, Bob / Itchy feet: Jennings, Rex / Sweet Lucy: Ashford, Shorty
CD _____ RCD 20126
Rykodisc / Feb '93 / Vital / ADA.

GETTIN' IT OFF - WESTBOUND FUNK
Gettin' it off (Instrumental): Haskins, Fuzzy / Just us: Crowd Pleasers / Thinking single: Counts / Funk it down: Frazier, Ceasar / Super funk: Hall, Erasmus / In the pocket: Boots & His Buddies / Walt's first trip: Ohio Players / Funky world part 1 and 2: Silky Vincent / Get down with the get down: Sparks, Melvin / Sugar: Morrison, Junie / Which way do I disco: Haskins, Fuzzy / Be what you is: US Music & Funkadelic / Funky Beethoven: Anderson, Gene / Crazy legs: Austin, Donald / What's up front that counts: Counts / Loose booty: Funkadelic / Satan's boogie: Ohio Players / Sweet thing: Houston outlaws / Hit it and quit it: Bobby Franklin's insanity / Hicky Burr: Frazier, Ceasar
CD _____ CDSEWD 061
Westbound / Apr '93 / Pinnacle.

GHAFRAN
CD _____ MFTEQ 931
Trident / Jun '93 / Pinnacle.

GHANA - ANCIENT CEREMONIES/ DANCE MUSIC & SONGS
CD _____ 7559720822
Elektra Nonesuch / Jan '95 / Warner Music.

GHANA - THE NORTHERN TRIBES
CD _____ LYRCD 7321
Lyrichord / '91 / Roots / ADA / CM.

GHETTO CELEBRITY
CD _____ BB 2811
Blue Beat / Apr '95 / Magnum Music Group / THE.

GHETTO FEEL
Part time lover: Yinka / Bustin' outta play pen: Da Bigg Kidz / Get with you tonight: Montage / Friend not a lover: Serenade / You make me feel: Rhythm Within / Don't lead me on: Serenade / Blast from the past: Da Bigg Kidz / Come correct: Yinka / Tell me: Da Fellas / You're the one for me: Montage
CD _____ CDMISH 1
Mission / Dec '93 / 3MV / Sony.

GHOSTS OF CHRISTMAS PAST
CD _____ TWI 0582
Les Disques Du Crepuscule / Jan '91 / Discovery / ADA.

GIANT JINGLES - 60 OF THE BEST FROM THE 70'S
CD _____ GJ 001CD
Giant Jingles / Nov '93 / THE.

GIANT JINGLES - 99 ORIGINAL CUTS
CD _____ GJ 003CD
Giant Jingles / Nov '93 / THE.

GIANTS IN ROCK 'N' ROLL
CD _____ LECD 053
Wisepack / Jul '94 / THE / Conifer.

GIANTS OF BOOGIE WOOGIE, THE
CD _____ CD 53083
Giants Of Jazz / Mar '92 / Target/BMG / Cadillac.

GIANTS OF JAZZ
Ain't misbehavin': Hampton, Lionel / When it's sleepy time down South: Hampton, Lionel / Hampton, Rich / Dido blues: Rich, Buddy / Limelight: Mulligan, Gerry / Buddy's Idea (Drum solo): My living / intermission: Mulligan, Gerry / Walkin' shoes: Mulligan, Gerry / Volare: Hampton, Lionel / Fatha meets Gates: Hines, Earl & Lionel Hampton / Lullaby of the leaves: Hampton, Lionel / So long Eric: Mingus, Charles / Blues for Hamp: Hampton, Lionel
CD _____ AAOHP 93322
Start / Dec '94 / Koch.

GIANTS OF JAZZ COLLECTION, THE
(2CD Sampler)
CD Set _____ CDB 912
Giants Of Jazz / Jan '93 / Target/BMG / Cadillac.

GIANTS OF JAZZ, THE
CD _____ APRCD 002
Apricot / Aug '95 / Target/BMG.

GIANTS OF JAZZ, THE
CD _____ 4716822
Sony Jazz / Jan '95 / Sony.

GIANTS OF ROCK 'N' ROLL ESSENTIALS
CD _____ LECDD 627
Wisepack / Aug '95 / THE / Conifer.

GIBSON GUITAR GREATS
CD _____ MCD 33016
MCA / Sep '95 / BMG.

GIFT OF SONG, THE
Breaking hearts (ain't what it used to be): John, Elton / I found someone: Cher / Goodnight girl: Wet Wet Wet / Throwing it all away: Genesis / One more night: Collins, Phil / Bad love: Clapton, Eric / Time to make you mine: Stansfield, Lisa / Precious: Level 42 / Some people: Richard, Cliff / Heaven: Adams, Bryan / I can't stand the rain: Turner, Tina / This woman's work: Bush, Kate / Little time: Beautiful South /

811

Living years: Mike & The Mechanics / Violet:
Seal / Missing you: De Burgh, Chris / Yes-
terday's men: Madness / Winter in July:
Bomb The Bass
CD _____ 5160582
Polystar / Jun '93 / PolyGram.

GIN HOUSE BLUES
What have you done to make me feel this
way: Smith, Mamie / Graysom Street blues:
Johnson, Margaret / Gin house blues:
Smith, Bessie / Sweet Virginia blues: Smith,
Mamie / Low down dirty: McGraw, Lether /
When a 'gator hollers, folk say its a sign of
rain: Johnson, Margaret / After you've gone:
Smith, Bessie / Way after one and my
daddy ain't come home yet: Winston, Edna
/ Rent man blues: Winston, Edna / Goin'
crazy with the blues: Smith, Mamie / Hard
driving papa: Smith, Bessie / If you're a viper: Howard, Rosetta / Do your duty: Mc-
Graw, Lether / My daddy rocks me (Parts 1
and 2): Smith, Trixie / I've lost my head over
you: Hines, Babe / I'm tired of fattenin' frogs
for snakes: Crawford, Rossetta / Young
woman's blues: Smith, Bessie / Double
crossin' papa: Crawford, Rossetta / This is
the end: Hines, Babe / What's the matter
now: Smith, Bessie
CD _____ PASTCD 9788
Flapper / Jun '92 / Pinnacle.

GIPSY JAZZ
CD _____ JHR 73588
Jazz Hour / Oct '95 / Target/BMG / Jazz
Music / Cadillac.

GIRL FROM IPANEMA, THE
CD _____ CD 53124
Giants Of Jazz / Nov '92 / Target/BMG /
Cadillac.

GIRL FROM IPANEMA, THE
(Samba & Bossa Nova)
CD _____ CD 56046
Jazz Roots / Nov '94 / Target/BMG.

GIRL FROM IPANEMA, THE
CD _____ CD 62022
Saludos Amigos / Jan '93 / Target/BMG.

GIRLS AND GUITARS
CD _____ RADCD 6
Global / Feb '95 / BMG.

GIRLS GIRLS GIRLS
CD _____ TMPCD 009
Telstar / Jan '95 / BMG.

GIRLS GIRLS GIRLS
CD _____ 12522
Laserlight / May '95 / Target/BMG.

GIRLS GIRLS GIRLS
CD _____ RNCD 2112
Rhino / Jul '95 / Jetstar / Magnum Music
Group / THE.

GIRLS GIRLS GIRLS
CD _____ CDCD 1233
Charly / Jun '95 / Charly / THE / Cadillac.

GIRLS' SOUND 1957-1966, THE
(2CD Set)
CD Set _____ DBG 53032
Double Gold / Jun '94 / Target/BMG.

GIVE 'EM ENOUGH BEATS
CD _____ WALLCD 4
Wall Of Sound / May '95 / Disc / Soul
Trader.

GIVE 'EM ENOUGH DOPE VOL.1
CD _____ WALLCD 001
Wall Of Sound / Feb '95 / Disc / Soul
Trader.

GIVE 'EM HELL
Don't take mothing: Tygers Of Pan Tang /
Backs to the grind: White Spirit / Don't need
your money: Raven / Name rank and serial
number: Fist / To hell and back: Venom /
Buried alive: Quartz / Backstreet woman:
Jaguar / Music: Witchfinder General / I sur-
vive: Terraplane / Take it all away: Girls-
chool / All the time: Spider / All around the
world: Torme, Bernie / Give 'em hell: Witch-
fynde / One of these days: Trespass /
Straight from hell: Angel Witch / Am I evil:
Diamond Head
CD _____ NTMCD 513
Nectar / Sep '95 / Pinnacle.

GIVE ME A HOME AMONG THE GUM
TREES
CD _____ LARRCD 232
Larrikin / Nov '94 / Roots / Direct / ADA /
CM.

GIVING PEOPLE CHOICES
Actionaid / Nov '93 / ADA.
CD _____ AA 1001CD

GLAD I'M A GIRL
CD _____ EFA 061942
House In Motion / Aug '95 / SRD.

GLAM ROCK SPECIAL
CD _____ 12539
Laserlight / May '95 / Target/BMG.

GLASS ARCADE
CD _____ SARAH 501CD
Sarah / Mar '95 / Vital.

GLASTONBURY 25TH ANNIVERSARY -
A CELEBRATION
Solsbury Hill: Gabriel, Peter / Live forever:
Oasis / Sit down: James / Fire on Babylon:
O'Connor, Sinead / Wild wood: Weller, Paul

/ Shellshock: New Order / Higher than the
sun: Primal Scream / Put the message in
the box: World Party / Advert: Blur / Sunshine on Leith: Proclaimers / Becoming
more like God: Jah Wobble's Invaders Of
The Heart / My iron lung: Radiohead / New
England: Bragg, Billy / Sinsemilla: Black
Uhuru / Sheep: Housemartins / Goin' back
to Glasters: Scott, Mike
CD _____ CHR 6107
Chrysalis / Jun '95 / EMI.

GLENFIDDICH PIPING CHAMPIONSHIP
(Ceol Mor Piobaireachd)
CD _____ CDMON 811
Monarch / Jul '94 / CM / ADA / Duncans /
Direct.

GLENFIDDICH PIPING CHAMPIONSHIP
(Ceol Beag - March, Strathspey & Reel)
CD _____ CDMON 812
Monarch / Jul '94 / CM / ADA / Duncans /
Direct.

GLOBAL BRAZILIANS
CD _____ EFA 064622
Metalimbo / Aug '95 / SRD.

GLOBAL CELEBRATION
(4CD/MC Set)
CD Set _____ ELLICD 3230
Ellipsis Arts / Apr '94 / Direct / ADA.

GLOBAL CUTS
Piano power: Remy & Sven / 20 Hz: Capri-
corn / Hectic boogie: X-Tatic / Hammond
groove: Mr. Marvin / Monkey forest: X-Tatic
/ Cool lemon: Cool Lemon / Tsjika boem
tsjak: Remy & Sven / Ride the wave: Man-
power / Warwick: Fowlkes, Eddie 'Flashin' /
L.F.Ohhh: Remy & Sven / Tribal zone:
OHM / Crystal clear: Soul Searchers
CD _____ RSGC 012CD
Global Cuts / Jul '93 / Vital.

GLOBAL CUTS 2
In thee garden: Aphrohead / Soul glow:
Soap Factory / Planet jupiter 6: Van Hees,
Sven / Saints go marching on: K.Hand /
Smoke: Dynetic / Inside your mind: God /
One dance: Fowlkes, Eddie 'Flashin' / Psy-
chedelic bellydance: Van Hees, Sven /
Harder: FRS / Drop (take off): Symmetrics /
Lush: Orbital / Dynetic: Smoke
CD _____ GCO 26CD
R & S / Nov '95 / Vital.

GLOBAL DIVAS
(3CD/MC Set)
CD Set _____ ROUCD 5062/3/4
Rounder / Dec '95 / CM / Direct / ADA /
Cadillac.

GLOBAL HOUSE CULTURE
CONTINUOUS MUSIC
CD _____ SUN 49892
Mokum / Nov '95 / Pinnacle.

GLOBAL HOUSE GROOVES
CD _____ BDRCD 2
Breakdown / Jul '94 / SRD.

GLOBAL HOUSE GROOVES 2
CD _____ BDRCD 7
Breakdown / Apr '95 / SRD.

GLOBAL MEDITATION
(4CD Set)
CD Set _____ ELL 3210
Ellipsis Arts / Oct '93 / Direct / ADA.

GLOBAL PARTNERSHIP VOL.1
CD _____ GP 001CD
Labarynth / Nov '94 / Pinnacle.

GLOBAL PARTNERSHIP VOL.2
CD _____ RGNET 1003CD
World Music Network / Oct '95 / New
Note.

GLOBAL PSYCHEDELIC TRANCE
COMPILATION VOL.1
Zoa: K.U.R.O. / Solar energy: Electric Uni-
verse / Telepathy: Infinity Project / Seventh
L: Crossbreed / Harddome 140: Adrenalin
Drum / Neutron dance: Electric Universe /
Binary neuronaut: Infinity Project / Hypno-
tiser: Adrenalin Drum / Brix: Crossbreed
CD _____ SPIRIT 4006
Spiritzone / May '95 / Vital.

GLOBESTYLE WORLDWIDE - YOUR
GUIDE
Saludando / Yachilvi veyachail / Kesetse
Mahiomolenu / Chorepste / Raha manina /
Sirvientas / El anillo / Le Brijano / Iyole / El
Beso / Ah laa jarah / Knowale / Chedh Hime
Dh'Louyeare / Fuego Lento / Les Dorla-
nes / Feam Baliha
CD _____ CDORB 018
Globestyle / Mar '88 / Pinnacle.

GLORIOUS VICTORY
CD _____ PWK 099
Carlton Home Entertainment / Oct '89 /
Carlton Home Entertainment.

GLORY GLORY TOTTENHAM HOTSPUR
Glory glory Tottenham / Ossie's dream /
Hot shot Tottenham / Tottenham Totten-
ham / It's a grand old team to play for /
When the year ends in one / We're all for
Wembley / Nice one Cyril / One team in
London / Tottenham win away / We are Tot-
tenham / Tribute to Ardiles and villa / Tip
top Tottenham Hotspurs / Spurs go Spurs
boogie / Up the Spurs / Spurs go marching
on / Cry Gazza cry / Gascoigne please /
Nice one Gazza / New cockeral chorus /

Ooh Gary / Gary Lineker a young girls
dream / Diamond lights / It's goodbye / Fog
on the Tyne / All you need is love / Happy
Christmas (war is over)
CD _____ CDGAFFER 2
Cherry Red / Nov '95 / Pinnacle.

GLORY OF LOVE
CD _____ 12204
Laserlight / Dec '94 / Target/BMG.

GLORY OF SPAIN
CD _____ CDMOIR 416
Memoir / Oct '92 / Target/BMG.

GLORY OF THE MUSIC HALL, THE VOL
1
Let's have a song upon the gramophone:
Williams, Billy / Seaside holiday at home:
Campbell, Herbert / Man who broke the
bank at Monte Carlo: Coborn, Charles / Two
lovely black eyes: Coborn, Charles / Topsy
turvy: Roberts, Arthur / Fishing club: Anderson, Harry / I wouldn't leave my little
wooden hut for you: Shepard, Burt / Something tickled her fancy: Randall, Harry / Our
little nipper: Chevalier, Albert / Adam
missed it: Knowles, R.G. / Girl, the woman
and the widow: Knowles, R.G. / Little Dolly
Daydream: Stratton, Eugene / Wait 'til I'm
his father: Leno, Dan / Wait 'til the work
comes round: Elen, Gus / Never introduce
yer Donah to a pal: Elen, Gus / There's another fellow looks like me: Lashwood,
George / Piccaninny: Hurley, Alec / What a
nut: Tilley, Vesta / There's a good time coming for the ladies: Tilley, Vesta / You can't
help laughing can yer: Champion, Harry /
Wotcher, my old brown son: Champion,
Harry / Paperbag cookery: Fragson, Harry /
Goodbye Dolly Gray: Stormont, Leo / Belgium put the kibosh on the Kaiser: Sheridan,
Mark / Here we are again: Sheridan,
Mark
CD _____ GEMM CD 9475
Pearl / Feb '91 / Harmonia Mundi.

GLORY OF THE MUSIC HALL, THE VOL
2
Poor, proud and particular: Ford, Harry /
Tally ho: Little Tich / Best man: Little Tich /
Editress: Robey, George / Servants' registry
office: Robey, George / Something on his
mind: Lloyd, Marie / Wee Jean McGregor:
Lauder, Sir Harry / Rob Roy-Tam-O-
Chanter O'Brian: Lauder, Sir Harry /
Cuckoo: Wallace, Nellie / Mother's pie
crust: Wallace, Nellie / Honeysuckle and the
bee: Davies, Belle / While you wait: Albert,
Ben / I'll be your sweetheart: Hawthorne, Lil
/ Fishing: Tate, Harry / I was having my
breakfast in bed: Mayo, Sam / Put that
gramophone record on again: Mayo, Sam /
I shall sulk: Pleasants, Jack / I'm shy, Mary
Ellen, I'm shy: Pleasants, Jack / Give a little
smile: Whelan, Albert / Everybody loves me:
Terriss, Ellaline / I can say 'truly rural': Bard,
Wilkie / It's nice to have a friend: Forde,
Florrie / Old Bull and Bush: Forde, Florrie /
Come into the garden John: Williams, Billy /
We go again: Williams, Billy
CD _____ GEMM CD 9476
Pearl / Feb '91 / Harmonia Mundi.

GLORY OF THE MUSIC HALL, THE VOL
3
If you knew Susie like I know Susie: Shields,
Ella / Ours is a nice 'ouse, ours is: Lester,
Alfred / Germs: Lester, Alfred / Odds and
ends, or Sunday mornings: Formby, George
/ I kept on waving my flag: Formby, George
/ If the wind had only blown the other way:
Scott, Maidie / Spaniard who blighted my
life: Merson, Billy / I've had my future told:
Elliott, G.H. / I can't do my bally bottom button up: Mayne, Ernie / Moonlight bay: Connolly, Dolly / Agatha Green: Cooper, Mar-
garet / So long Sally: Weldon, Harry / What
do you want to make (parody): Weldon,
Harry / Gretchen: Moore Duprez, May / And
it was: Laurier, Jay / Anna Gray: Gitana,
Gertie / Never mind: Gitana, Gertie / Rickety
stairs: Latona, Jen / Come over the garden
wall: Mayne, Clarice & That / Don't have
any more, Mrs. Moore: Morris, Lily / I want
a girl - just like the girl that married dear old
Dad: Ward, Dorothy / Oh Mr. Porter: Blaney,
Norah / 'E can't take a roise out of oi:
Chevalier, Albert
CD _____ GEMM CD 9477
Pearl / Feb '91 / Harmonia Mundi.

GO GO POWER
Go go power: Desanto, Sugar Pie / Let's
wade in the water: Shaw, Marlena / Jerk
and twine: Ross, Jackie / Love ain't nothin':
Nash, Johnny / Secret love: Stewart, Billy /
In the basement: Desanto, Sugar Pie & Etta
James / Something's got a hold of me: Etta
James / Little Milton / Ain't love
good, ain't love proud: Clarke, Tony / Look
at me now: Callier, Terry / Peak of love: Mc-
Clure, Bobby / Do I make myself clear: De-
santo, Sugar Pie & Etta James / Seven day
fool: James, Etta / That'll get it: Knight
Brothers / I don't wanna fuss: Desanto,
Sugar Pie / Strange feeling: Nash, Johnny /
Take me for a little while: Ross, Jackie /
Love is a five letter word: Phelps, James /
Ain't no big deal: Little Milton
CD _____ CDARC 512
Charly / Jan '93 / Charly / THE / Cadillac.

GO JAZZ ALL-STARS/LIVE IN JAPAN
CD _____ VBR 20862
Go Jazz / Oct '92 / Vital/SAM.

GO SKA GO
CD _____ CDHB 199
Heartbeat / Nov '95 / Greensleeves /
Jetstar / Direct / ADA.

GOA TRANCE
CD _____ TRIPCD 2
Rumour / Oct '95 / Pinnacle / 3MV / Sony.

GOA TRANCE VOLUME 2
CD _____ TRIPCD 3
Rumour / Jan '96 / Pinnacle / 3MV / Sony.

GOD IS THE OWNER OF THEE WORLD
CD _____ ALCHECD 001
Spinefarm / Feb '94 / Plastic Head.

GOD LESS AMERICA
CD _____ EFA 115952
Crypt / Nov '95 / SRD.

GODFATHERS OF BRITPOP, THE
CD _____ 5352572
PolyGram TV / Jan '96 / PolyGram.

GODFATHERS OF GERMAN GOTH
VOL.2
CD _____ SPV 08438372
SPV / Jul '95 / Plastic Head.

GODS OF GRIND
Stranger aeons: Entombed / Incarnated sol-
vent abuse: Carcass / Soul sacrafice: Ca-
thedral / Condemned: Confessor / Tools of
the trade: Carcass / Dusk: Entombed /
Golden blood (flooding): Cathedral / Pyos-
isified (Still rotten to the gore): Carcass /
Shreds of flesh: Entombed / Autumn twi-
light: Cathedral / Last judgement: Confessor
/ Hepatic tissue fermentation: Carcass /
Frozen rapture: Cathedral / Endtime:
Confessor
CD _____ MOSH 063CD
Earache / Mar '92 / Vital.

GOING BACK IN TIME
CD _____ KWCD 807
Disky / Jul '94 / THE / BMG / Discovery /
Pinnacle.

GOLD HEART LOVE SONGS
CD _____ FEBCD 14
Connoisseur / Jan '94 / Pinnacle.

GOLDEN AGE OF AMERICAN ROCK 'N'
ROLL
Denise: Randy & The Rainbows / Sally go
round the roses: Jaynetts / Mule skinner
blues: Fendermen / Sixteen candles: Crests
/ Pretty little angel eyes: Lee, Curtis / Love
how you love me: Paris Sisters / Big hurt:
Fisher, Miss Toni / Thousand stars: Young,
Kathy / Rockin' robin: Day, Bobby / Earth
angel: Penguins / Bongo rock: Epps, Pres-
ton / Tossin' and turnin': Lewis, Bobby / My
true story: Jive Five / Stranded in the jungle:
Cadets / Angel baby: Rosie & The Originals
/ Party lights: Clark, Claudine / When we get
married: Dreamlovers / Cindy's birthday:
Crawford, Johnny / Let's dance: Montez,
Chris / Who's that knocking: Genies / Love
you so: Holden, Ron / Cherry pie: Skip & Fly
/ Since I don't have you: Skyliners / Louie
Louie: Kingsmen / Since I fell for you:
Welch, Lenny / Image of a girl: Safaris /
Smoky places: Corsairs / Gee whiz: Inno-
cents / Little bit of soap: Jarmels / Eddie my
love: Teen Queens
CD _____ CDCHD 289
Ace / Oct '91 / Pinnacle / Cadillac / Com-
plete/Pinnacle.

GOLDEN AGE OF AMERICAN ROCK 'N'
ROLL VOL. 2
Memphis: Mack, Lonnie / I sold my heart to
the junkman: Blue Belles / You belong to
me: Duprees / Your Ma said you cried in
your sleep last night: Dino, Kenny / Million
to one: Charles, Jimmy / Rockin' in the jungle: Eternals / Wild weekend: Rockin' Rebels / Stay: Williams, Maurice & the zodiacs
/ Down the aisle of love: Quintones / Mountain of love: Dorman, Harold / Nag: Halos /
Let the little girl dance: Bland, Billy / There's
no doubt about tonight: Capris / Get a job: Silhouettes / You: Aquatones / Buzz buzz
buzz: Hollywood Flames / I've had it: Bell
Notes / I know (you don't love me no more):
George, Barbara / Mr. Lonely: Videls / In the
still of the nite: Five Satins / Church bells
may ring: Willows / That's life (that's tough):
Gabriel & the angels / Rumble: Wray, Link /
Let's dance: Comstock, Bobby / Oh Julie:
Crescendos / Little darlin': Gladiolas / Teen
beat: Nelson, Sandy / Diamonds and pearls:
Paradons / Alley oop: Hollywood Argyles /
California sun: Rivieras
CD _____ CDCHD 445
Ace / May '93 / Pinnacle / Cadillac / Com-
plete/Pinnacle.

GOLDEN AGE OF AMERICAN ROCK 'N'
ROLL VOL. 3
All American boy: Parsons, Bill / Kansas
city: Harrison, Wilbert / My true love: Scott,
Jack / Jennie Lee: Jan & Arnie / Joker: My-
les, Billy / Beat: Rockin R's / To know him
is to love him: Teddy Bears / When you
dance: Turbans / Love letters: Lester, Ketty
/ So tough: Kuf Linx / To the aisle: Five Sat-
ins / La dee dah: Billy & Lillie / Endless
sleep: Reynolds, Jody / Chicken baby
chicken: Harris, Tony / Lover's island: Blue
Jays / No chemise please: Granahan, Gerry
/ It was I: Skip & Flip / Tonight I fell in love:
Tokens / Happy birthday blues: Young,
Karen & The Innocents / Rockin' little angel:
Smith, Ray / Tonite tonite: Mello Kings / Cha

hua hua: *Pets* / Western movies: *Olympics* / Girl in my dreams: *Cliques* / Sugar shack: *Fireballs* / There is something on your mind: *McNeely, Big Jay* / Womans a mans best friend: *Teddy & The Twilights* / Sacred: *Castells* / Freeze: *Tony & Joe* / Click clack: *Dicky Doo & Don'ts*
CD _____ CDCHD 497
Ace / Jan '94 / Pinnacle / Cadillac / Complete/Pinnacle.

GOLDEN AGE OF AMERICAN ROCK 'N' ROLL VOL. 4
Linda Lou: *Sharpe, Ray* / Little by little: *Brown, Nappy* / Rama lama ding dong: *Edsels* / Flamingo express: *Royaltones* / New Orleans: *Bonds* / Maybe: *Chantels* / Drip drop: *Dion* / Start movin' (in my direction): *Mined, Sal* / Lonely Saturday night: *French, Don* / Don't let go: *Hamilton, Roy* / Pop pop pop-pie: *Sherry's* / Life's too short: *Harris, Lafayette Jr* / High school USA: *Facenda, Tommy* / Glory of love: *Roomates* / Peanuts: *Little Joe & The Thrillers* / Need you: *Owens, Donnie* / Party doll: *Knox, Buddy* / Could this be magic: *Dubs* / Killer Joe: *Rocky Fellers* / Barbara: *Temptations* / Peek-a-boo: *Cadillacs* / You'll lose a good thing: *Lynn, Barbara* / Lucky ladybug: *Billie & Lillie* / Tears on my pillow: *Imperials* / Baby talk: *Jan & Dean* / Here I stand: *Rip Chords* / Do the mashed potato: *Kendrick, Nat* / Why don't you write me: *Jacks* / Barbara Ann: *Regents* / Those oldies but goodies (remind me of you): *Little Caesar & The Romans*
CD _____ CDCHD 500
Ace / Oct '94 / Pinnacle / Cadillac / Complete/Pinnacle.

GOLDEN AGE OF AMERICAN ROCK 'N' ROLL VOL. 5
Wiggle wobble: *Accents* / Love potion no. 9: *Clovers* / I'm leaving it up to you: *Dale & Grace* / You cheated: *Shields* / It will stand: *Showmen* / Sleepwalk: *Santo & Johnny* / Nothin' shakin': *Fontane, Eddie* / Happy, happy birthday baby: *Tune Weavers* / Heart and soul: *Jan & Dean* / What's your name: *Don & Juan* / Little bitty pretty one: *Harris, Thurston & The Sharps* / Darling Lorraine: *Knockouts* / Tallahassee lassie: *Cannon, Freddy* / Tell me why: *Belmonts* / Over the mountain, across the sea: *Johnnie & Joe* / Ka-ding dong: *G-Clefs* / Underwater: *Frogmen* / She cried: *Jay & The Americans* / Just a little bit: *Gordon, Roscoe* / Sometime: *Thomas, Gene* / Ain't gonna kiss ya: *Ribbons* / Midnight stroll: *Revels* / Walk: *McCracklin, Jimmy* / Hey little girl: *Clark, Dee* / This is the nitie: *Valiants* / Tell him no: *Travis & Bob* / Bad boy: *Jive Bombers* / Stranded in the jungle: *Jayhawks* / Duke of Earl: *Chandler, Gene* / Goodnight sweetheart goodnight: *Spaniels*
CD _____ CDCHD 600
Ace / Sep '95 / Pinnacle / Cadillac / Complete/Pinnacle.

GOLDEN AGE OF SWING 1929-39, THE (Big Band Legends Vol.1)
CD _____ 158452
Jazz Archives / Nov '93 / Jazz Music / Discovery / Cadillac.

GOLDEN COUNTRY VOL.1 (Let Your Love Flow)
CD _____ MU 5029
Musketeer / Oct '92 / Koch.

GOLDEN COUNTRY VOL.2 (From A Jack To A King)
CD _____ MU 5030
Musketeer / Oct '92 / Koch.

GOLDEN COUNTRY VOL.3 (Love Hurts)
CD _____ MU 5031
Musketeer / Oct '92 / Koch.

GOLDEN COUNTRY VOL.4 (Love Me Tender)
CD _____ MU 5032
Musketeer / Oct '92 / Koch.

GOLDEN COUNTRY VOL.5 (Games People Play)
CD _____ MU 5033
Musketeer / Oct '92 / Koch.

GOLDEN FLUTE
CD _____ GRF 238
Tring / Aug '93 / Tring / Prism.

GOLDEN GIRLS OF THE 60'S
CD _____ PLATCD 344
Platinum Music / Oct '90 / Prism / Ross.

GOLDEN GROUPS
Tears on my pillow: *Chimes* / I'll find her: *Dukes* / Don't you know (I love you so): *Maye, Arthur Lee & The Crowns* / Nite owl: *Allen, Tony & The Champs* / Love you so: *Crystals* / Chimes ring out: *Chimes* / Foolish fool: *Zeppa, Ben Joe & The Zephyrs* / So long love: *Dukes* / Cool loving: *Maye, Arthur Lee & The Crowns* / She's gone: *Metronomes* / Sweet sixteen: *Tropicals* / My little girl: *Pharoahs* / It's true: *Twilighters* / Chop chop: *Chimes* / Gloria: *Maye, Arthur Lee & The Crowns* / I want that baby: *Gipson, Byron 'Slick' & The Sliders* / Our romance: *King, Clydie* / Over the rainbow: *Echoes* / It's spring again: *Pentagons* / Silly dilly: *Pentagons* / Arlene: *Titans* / What have I done: *Titans* / Our school days: *Monitors* /

Closer to heaven: *Monitors* / Miracle: *Five Knights*
CD _____ CDCHD 515
Ace / Jan '94 / Pinnacle / Cadillac / Complete/Pinnacle.

GOLDEN HYMNS
CD _____ CDSR 040
Telstar / May '94 / BMG.

GOLDEN MILES
CD _____ RVCD 39
Raven / Dec '94 / Direct / ADA.

GOLDEN PAN FLUTES
CD _____ TREB 3001
Scratch / Mar '95 / BMG.

GOLDEN SAXOPHONE
CD _____ GRF 239
Tring / Aug '93 / Tring / Prism.

GOLDEN SHOWER OF 73 HITS
CD _____ LF 200DCD
Lost & Found / Aug '95 / Plastic Head.

GOLDEN SOUNDS OF HOME
CD _____ 321062
Koch / Sep '92 / Koch.

GOLDEN TORCH STORY, THE
Just like the weather: *Chance, Nolan* / I've got something: *Sam & Kitty* / Sliced tomatoes: *Just Brothers* / Sweet darlin': *Clarke, Jimmy* / Our love: *Barnes, J.J.* / Honey bee: *Johnson, Johnny* / I can't get away: *Garrett, Bobby* / I still love you: *Superlatives* / Crackin' up over you: *Hamilton, Roy* / Love you baby: *Parker, Eddie* / Personally: *Paris, Bobby* / One in a million: *Brown, Maxine* / Thumb a ride: *Wright, Earl* / I'm standing: *Lumley, Rufus* / I feel an urge: *Armstead, Jo* / I don't want to cry: *Gray, Pearlean & The Passengers* / Exus trek: *Ingram, Luther* / Keep on keeping on: *Porter, N.F.* / I'm so glad: *Johnson, Herb* / Quick change artist: *Soul Twins* / One wonderful moment: *Shakers* / Hit and run: *Shakers* / Soul self satisfaction: *Jackson, Earl* / That's alright: *Crook, Ed* / Compared to what: *Mr. Floods Party* / Blowing up my mind: *Exciters* / Please let me in: *Barnes, J.J.* / I love you baby: *Scott, Cindy* / Queen of the Go-Go: *Garvin, Rex* / Angel baby: *Banks, Darrell*
CD _____ GSCD 061
Goldmine / May '95 / Vital.

GOLDEN TREASURY OF ELIZABETHAN MUSIC
Sellengers round: *Broadside Band* / This is the record of John: *Red Byrd & The Rose Consort Of Viols* / Bergamasca: *Broadside Band* / In nomine a 5: *Fretwork Consort Of Viols* / Coventry carol: *Sneak's Noyse* / Passamezzo pavan: *Weigand, George* / Sing unto God: *Red Byrd & The Rose Consort Of Viols* / Spanish pavan/Galliard la gamba: *York Waits* / Go cristall tears: *Trevor, Caroline & The Rose Consort Of Viols* / A toye: *Burnett, Richard* / La doune cella: *York Waits* / Pavan - Lachrimae coactae: *Rose Consort Of Viols* / Greensleeves: *Potter, John & The Broadside Band* / Crimson velvet: *York Waits* / There dwelt a man in Babylon: *Roberts, Deborah & The Broadside Band* / Almain – The Night watch: *York Waits* / Come let me live: *Potter, John & The Broadside Band* / Bonny sweet Robin: *Weigand, George* / Pavan - Heigh ho Hollyday: *York Waits* / Sweet was the song the virgin sung: *Red Byrd & The Rose Consort Of Viols* / Staines Morris: *York Waits* / Libera nos - salva nos a 5: *Fretwork Consort Of Viols* / Fortune my foe: *Roberts, Deborah & The Broadside Band* / Dulcina/All you that love good fellowes: *York Waits* / Poor soul sat sighing: *Roberts, Deborah & The Broadside Band* / Fantasy a 5: Browning: *Rose Consort Of Viols* / Pavan - The cradle: *York Waits* / Farewell dear love: *Potter, John & The Broadside Band* / La bounette: *York Waits*
CD _____ CDSAR 62
Amon Ra / Feb '96 / Harmonia Mundi.

GOLDEN YEARS OF MUSIC HALL, THE
CD _____ CDSDL 380
Saydisc / Mar '94 / Harmonia Mundi / ADA / Direct.

GOOD MORNIN' BLUES
Went out on the mountain: *Leadbelly* / Whoa back: *Leadbelly* / Worried blues: *Leadbelly* / Good morning blues: *Leadbelly* / You can't lose me Charlie: *Leadbelly* / Boll weevil song: *Leadbelly* / Babylon is falling down: *Smith, Dan* / Where shall I be: *Smith, Dan* / Lining the track: *Smith, Dan* / Cotton needs pickin': *Smith, Dan* / Candy man: *Davis, Rev. Gary* / Hesitation blues: *Davis, Rev. Gary* / Whistlin' blues: *Davis, Rev. Gary* / How happy I am: *Davis, Rev. Gary* / Soon my work will all be done: *Davis, Rev. Gary*
CD _____ BCD 113
Biograph / Jul '91 / Analed / AD A / Hot Shot / Jazz Music / Cadillac / Direct.

GOOD MORNING BLUES (4CD Set)
CD Set _____ CDDIG 14
Charly / Jun '95 / Charly / THE / Cadillac.

GOOD MORNING VIETNAM
CD _____ LB 8049
Disky / Dec '93 / THE / BMG / Discovery / Pinnacle.

GOOD NEWS
I'm going through: *Caravan* / It's Jesus in me: *Caravan* / I'm a rollin': *Five Blind Boys Of Mississippi* / Where there's a will: *Five Blind Boys Of Mississippi* / Wade in the water: *Harmonizing Four* / Father I stretch my arms to thee: *Harmonizing Four* / Nobody knows: *Highway QC's* / Working on the building: *Highway QC's* / Uncloudy day: *Staple Singers* / This may be the last time: *Staple Singers* / Going away: *Staple Singers* / Good news: *Staple Singers* / Don't drive me away: *Staple Singers* / Will the circle be unbroken: *Staple Singers* / Too close: *Staple Singers* / Great day in December: *Swan Silvertones* / Oh Mary don't you weep: *Swan Silvertones* / How I got over: *Swan Silvertones* / What about you: *Swan Silvertones* / Brighter day ahead: *Swan Silvertones* / Seek, seek: *Swan Silvertones* / I'll search heaven: *Swan Silvertones*
CD _____ CDCHARLY 98
Charly / Dec '87 / Charly / THE / Cadillac.

GOOD OLD ARSENAL
Good old Arsenal / Boys from Highbury / Come on you gunners / Arsenal / Arsenal we're on your side / Here we go again / Arsenal rap / Highbury sunshine / Goonerroonie / Ooh ooh Tony Adams / Charlie George Calypso / Fever pitch / Arriverdici Liam / Gus Caesar rap / One night at Anfield / Roll out the red carpet / Kings of London / Victory song 1993 / Highbury heartbeat / Ian Wright Wright Wright / I wish I could play like Charlie George
CD _____ CDGAFFER 1
Cherry Red / Nov '95 / Pinnacle.

GOOD THINGS ARE HAPPENING
Hide yourself: *Vejtables* / Better rearrange: *Vejtables* / Good things are happening: *Vejtables* / Good times: *Vejtables* / Time and place: *Vejtables* / I can't do it: *E-Type* / Long before: *E-Type* / I'm over you: *Shillings* / Part time man: *Shillings* / Going home: *Engle, Butch & The Styx* / Hey I'm lost: *Engle, Butch & The Styx* / If you believe: *Engle, Butch & The Styx* / I call her name: *Engle, Butch & The Styx* / I can't hide: *Soul Owners* / I'll cry: *Soul Owners* / In my way: *Dutch Masters* / Revenge: *Others* / I'm in need: *Others* / Satisfaction guaranteed: *Mourning Reign* / Our fate: *Mourning Reign* / I'm a lover not a fighter: *Pullice* / Little girl: *Pullice* / Tomorrow is another day: *Navarros* / Sad man: *Navarros* / My chance will come: *Original Wild Oats* / I'll get my way: *Chimney Sweeps* / Knock knock: *Innocents*
CD _____ CDWIKD 133
Big Beat / Oct '94 / Pinnacle.

GOOD TIME BLUES - HARMONICAS, KAZOOS, WASHBOARDS & COW BELLS
Hittin' the bottle stomp: *Mississippi Jook Band* / Skippy whippy: *Mississippi Jook Band* / Mary Anna cut off: *Memphis Jug Band* / Gator wobble: *Memphis Jug Band* / Barbecue: *Memphis Jug Band* / Son Becky / Baby you win: *Burse, Charlie & His Memphis Mudcats* / Tampa strut: *Browns, Georgia* / Diddle-da-diddle: *Georgia Cotton Pickers* / If you take me back: *Big Joe & His Washboard Band* / I'm through with you: *Big Joe & His Washboard Band* / I love you baby: *Big Joe & His Washboard Band* / Struggle buggy: *Moss, Buddy* / I'm sittin' here tonight: *Moss, Buddy* / Dangerous woman: *Mississippi Jook Band* / Barbecue bust: *Mississippi Jook Band* / Diggin' my potatoes: *Chatman, Peter* / Touch it up and go: *Terry, Sonny & Jordan Webb* / Ninth Street stomp: *Edwards, Bernice* _____ 4010812
Columbia / Nov '91 / Sony.

GOOD VIBRATIONS PUNK
Big time / Strange things by night / Love is for sops / Emergency cases / Dance away love / Don't ring me up / Listening in / Parents / Dancing in the street / Cops are comin' / Overcome by fumes / Cross the line / Love affair / Ya don't do ya / I spy / Airline disaster / Self concious over you / Love you for never / On my mind / Decisions / Original terminal / Belfast telegraph / I don't want you / Bondage in Belfast / Laugh at me
CD _____ CDPUNK 36
Anagram / Sep '94 / Pinnacle.

GOOD VIBRATIONS STORY, THE
CD _____ DOJOCD 180
Dojo / Jun '94 / BMG.

GOOD WHISKEY BLUES (Collection Of Contemporary Blues Songs From Tennessee)
CD _____ TX 1004CD
Taxim / Jan '94 / ADA.

GORAU GWERIN CYFROL (The Best of Welsh Folk Music)
Torth of fara / Y gwr a'i farch / Mi gysgi di' maban / Cerrig yr afon / Mor o gariad / Mae 'nghariad i'n fenws / Llancesau trefaldwyn / Bachgen bach o dincer / Y g'lomen / Ymryson canu / Ar gyfer heddiw'r bore / Clychau Aberdyfi / Ymdaith milwr mwnc / Cyfri' geifr / Machynlleth / Cwm rhymni / Ffidl ffadl / Ffarwel i blwyf llangower / Wyres Megan / Gwrachod Llanddona / Mil hardach wyt / Yma o hyd
CD _____ SCD 2006
Sain / Oct '88 / Direct / ADA.

GOSPEL CHRISTMAS
Hark the herald angels sing: *Hutchins, Norman* / O holy night: *Smallwood, Richard* / Away in a manger/Silent night: *West Angeles C.O.G.I.C. Angelic & Mass Choir* / Angels we have heard on high: *Crouch, Sandra* / Joy to the world: *West Angeles C.O.G.I.C. Angelic & Mass Choir* / First Noel: *Grundy, Rickey Chorale* / Go tell it on the mountain: *Winans, Mom & Pop* / O come, o come: *Coley, Daryl* / Hallelujah chorus: *Alford, Pastor Donald & The Progressive Radio Chorus*
CD _____ CDMFP 6196
Music For Pleasure / Nov '95 / EMI.

GOSPEL CLASSICS
CD _____ DOCD 5190
Blues Document / Mar '95 / Swift / Jazz Music / Hot Shot.

GOSPEL CLASSICS VOL. 2 1927-35
CD _____ DOCD 5313
Blues Document / Dec '94 / Swift / Jazz Music / Hot Shot.

GOSPEL CLASSICS VOL.3
CD _____ DOCD 5350
Blues Document / May '95 / Swift / Jazz Music / Hot Shot.

GOSPEL COLLECTION, THE
CD _____ DCD 5271
Disky / Aug '92 / THE / BMG / Discovery / Pinnacle.

GOSPEL COUNTRY
CD _____ DCD 5314
Dicky / Nov '93 / THE / BMG / Discovery / Pinnacle.

GOSPEL EVANGELISTS
CD _____ HTCD 09
Heritage / '92 / Swift / Roots / Wellard / Direct / Hot Shot / Jazz Music / ADA.

GOSPEL SHIP, THE
CD _____ 802942
New World / Oct '94 / Harmonia Mundi / ADA / Cadillac.

GOSPEL SINGERS AND CHOIRS
CD _____ TPZ 1011
Topaz Jazz / Jun '95 / Pinnacle / Cadillac.

GOSPEL SOUND OF CHICAGO
CD _____ SHAN 6008CD
Shanachie / Dec '93 / Koch / ADA / Greensleeves.

GOSPEL TRAIN
Lift up your hands / Constant love / Potter's house / Somebody somewhere / It's mighty nice to be on the Lord's side / He's got up / What shall I do / Give me Jesus / Want to get to know you / Holy is your name / Lord's prayer / Joyful, joyful
CD _____ ALD 027
Alliance Music / Jan '96 / EMI.

GOSPEL VOL.3 1927-44 (2 CD)
CD Set _____ FA 044
Fremeaux / Nov '95 / Discovery / ADA.

GOSPELS & SPIRITUALS GOLD (2CD Set)
CD Set _____ D2CD 4026
Deja Vu / Jun '95 / THE.

GOSPELS AND SPIRITUALS
CD _____ CD 50002
Lotus / Dec '88 / Jazz Horizons / Impetus.

GOSPELS AND SPIRITUALS (2CD Set)
CD Set _____ R2CD 4026
Deja Vu / Jun '96 / THE.

GOT HARP IF YOU WANT IT
CD _____ CCD 11030
Crosscut / '92 / ADA / CM / Direct.

GOT TO DANCE
CD _____ CDSVL 205
Saville / '89 / Conifer.

GOT TO GET YOUR OWN (Some Rare Grooves, Vol 1)
Got to get your own: *Wilson, Reuben* / Black water gold: *African Music Machine* / Goo bah: *Continental Showstoppers* / Funky song: *Ripple* / Moon walk: *Ellis, Pee Wee* / Tropical: *African Music Machine* / You're losing me: *Sexton, Ann* / I don't know what it is but it sure is funky: *Ripple* / (I've got) so much trouble in my mind: *Quatermain, Joe* / That thang: *Ellis, Pee Wee* / Daup: *African Music Machine* / I don't dig no phony, part 2: *Scott, Moody* / Brother man, sister Ann: *Smith, Clemon*
CD _____ CDINS 5050
Charly / Sep '91 / Charly / THE / Cadillac.

GOTHAM BEAT
CD _____ HCD 258
Hindsight / Aug '95 / Target/BMG / Jazz Music.

GOTHIC ROCK
CD _____ FREUDCD 38
Jungle / Nov '91 / Disc.

GOTHIC ROCK VOL.2 (2CD Set)
CD Set _____ FREUD 051CD
Jungle / Jul '95 / Disc.

GOTHIC SPIRIT VOL. 1
CD   SPV 07625242
SPV / Oct '94 / Plastic Head.

GRAMAVISION'S 10TH ANNIVERSARY
CD   GV 794612
Gramavision / Dec '90 / Vital/SAM / ADA.

GRAMMY NOMINEES 1995, THE
I'll make love to you: Boyz II Men / He thinks he'll keep her: Carpenter, Mary-Chapin / All I wanna do: Crow, Sheryl / Love sneakin' up on you: Raitt, Bonnie / Streets of Philadelphia: Springsteen, Bruce / Said I loved you but I lied: Bolton, Michael / Can you feel the love tonight: John, Elton / Prayer for the dying: Seal / I live my life for you: Van-dross, Luther / Hero: Carey, Mariah / Power of love: Dion, Celine / Longing in their hearts: Raitt, Bonnie / Ordinary miracles: Streisand, Barbra
CD   4785372
Columbia / Mar '95 / Sony.

GRAMMY'S GREATEST MOMENTS (2CD Set)
What's love got to do with it: Turner, Tina / Sweet dreams: Eurythmics / She works hard for the money: Summer, Donna / Thing called love: Raitt, Bonnie / Don't wanna lose you: Collins, Phil / Unforgettable: Cole, Natalie & Nat King Cole / Cradle of love: Idol, Billy / Sexual healing: Gaye, Marvin / Russians: Sting / You don't bring me flowers: Streisand, Barbra & Neil Diamond / We didn't start the fire: Joel, Billy / Heart of rock 'n' roll: Lewis, Huey & The News / Come together: Aerosmith / Vision of love: Carey, Mariah / What a fool believes: Doobie Brothers / Save the best for last: Williams, Vanessa / Respect: Franklin, Aretha / How am I supposed to live without you: Bolton, Michael & Kenny G / If you let me stay: D'Arby, Terence Trent / Constant craving: Lang, k.d. / One moment in time: Houston, Whitney / Tears in heaven: Clapton, Eric
CD Set   7567805822
Atlantic / Apr '94 / Warner Music.

GRAN PRAIRIE (Cajun Music Vol.3: Victor Bluebird Sessions 1935-40)
One step de morse: Abshire, Nathan & The Rayn-Bo Ramblers / Noveau grand guey-dan: Rayne-Bo Ramblers / It la bas: Hack-berry Ramblers / Les blues de bosco: Rayne-Bo Ramblers / Two step du la teill: Fuselier, J.B. & His Merrymakers / Jolie pe-tite fille: Hackberry Ramblers / Rayne break-down: Rayne-Bo Ramblers / Ta oblis de nernier: Happy Fats & His Rayne-Bo Ramblers / Pine island: Miller's Merrymakers / Las vas de la prison: Hackberry Ramblers / Les escrivas dan shatten: Rayne-Bo Ramblers / Crap shooters hop: Werner, Joe & Ramblers / Ma chere bouclett: Fuselier, J.B. & His Merrymakers / Tickle her: Hackberry Ramblers / La response de blues de bosco: Happy Fats & His Rayne-Bo Ramblers / Hackberry hop: Soileau, Leo / La place mon coeur desire: Rayne-Bo Ramblers / La breakdown a prie: Hackberry Ramblers
CD   CMF 018D
Country Music Foundation / Aug '93 / Direct / ADA.

GRAND AIRS OF CONNEMARA (Various Traditional Irish Songs)
Mainistir na buille: MacDonnchadha, Séan / An Caisdeach ban: Ó Cathain, Padraic / Piopa Andy mhoir: Ó Neachtain, Tomas / Una bhan: Ó Connluain, Feichin / Bean on thir rua: Ó Cathain, Padraic / Stor mo chroi: MacDonnchadha, Séan / Noirin mo mhian: MacDonnchadha, Séan / Cailin schoth na luachra: Ó Cathain, Padraic / Peigi Misteal: O Neachtain, Feichin / An goirtin eornan: Ó Connluain, Feichin / Cuaichin Ghleann Nei-fin: Ó Cathain, Padraic / An spailpin fanach: MacDonnchadha, Séan
CD   OSS 28CD
Ossian / Dec '93 / ADA / Direct / CM.

GRAND HIT PACK, THE
CD   HRCD 8044
Disky / Jul '94 / THE / BMG / Discovery / Pinnacle.

GRASS ROOTS VOL. 9
CD   LACD 9
La / Sep '94 / Plastic Head.

GREAT 1955 SHRINE CONCERT, THE
Spoken introduction: Pilgrim Travelers / All the way: Pilgrim Travelers / Straight Street: Pilgrim Travelers / Since I met Jesus: Car-avans / What kind of man is this: Caravans / It's a long, long way: May, Brother Joe / I'm happy working for the Lord: May, Brother Joe / Consider me: May, Annette / I have a friend above all others: Soul Stirrers / Be with me, Jesus: Soul Stirrers / Nearer to thee: Soul Stirrers / My troubles are so hard to bear: Davenport, Ethel / Medley: Love Coates, Dorothy
CD   CDCHD 483
Ace / Jul '93 / Pinnacle / Cadillac / Complete/Pinnacle.

GREAT ACOUSTICS
CD   CIC 067CD
Clo lar-Chonnachta / Nov '93 / CM.

GREAT AMERICAN BIG BANDS
Sent for you yesterday: Basie, Count / Chicks is wonderful: Teagarden, Jack /

These foolish things: Carter, Benny / When I get low I get high: Webb, Chick / Chris-topher Columbus: Goodman, Benny / I never knew: Armstrong, Louis / Flop: Ven-uti, Joe / Take the 'A' train: Ellington, Duke / Strictly instrumental: James, Harry / All of me: Dorsey, Jimmy / Prisoner's song: Beri-gan, Bunny / Barrelhouse Bessie from Basin Street: Crosby, Bob / My blue heaven: Lun-ceford, Jimmie / String of pearls: Miller, Glenn / Run little rabbit: Calloway, Cab / Twin City blues: Herman, Woody / I wonder who's kissing her now: Weems, Ted / Stop, look and listen: Dorsey, Tommy / I hope Ga-briel likes my music: Trumbauer, Frankie / Study in brown: Casa Loma Orchestra / Deep purple: Shaw, Artie / Drummin' man: Krupa, Gene / Nola: Hampton, Lionel
CD   PPCD 78101
Past Perfect / Feb '95 / THE.

GREAT AMERICAN COMPOSERS
CD   CD 112
New Note / Jul '94 / New Note / Cadillac.

GREAT AMERICAN SONGWRITERS, THE (5CD Set)
CD Set   15991
Laserlight / Oct '95 / Target/BMG.

GREAT BERLIN BAND SHOW, THE
National anthems / Fanfare - Union Jack / Jupiter / Posthorn galop / Crown of state / Per mare per terram / Globe and lauret / Rule Britannia / Pipes and drums / Glen-daurel highlanders / Skye boat song / Ca-ledonian canal / Lexy border / Bugler's delight / Light infantry / Londonderry air / St. Patrick's Day / Caubeen trimmed with blue / Irish washerwoman / Flight of the bumble bee / Brandenburg concerto / Da-vid of the White Rock / Men of Harlech / All through the night / God bless the Prince of Wales / Radetzky march / Prussia's glory / Drum display / British Grenadiers / York-shire march / Muss I dehn / Royal standard / Zadok the priest / Water music / Music from the Royal fireworks / Lament / Salute to Berlin / Berliner luft / Auld lang syne
CD   BNA 5047
Bandleader / '91 / Conifer.

GREAT BIG BAND SINGERS
CD   HCD 326
Hindsight / Jun '95 / Target/BMG / Jazz Music.

GREAT BIG BAND THEMES
CD   HCD 321
Hindsight / Mar '95 / Target/BMG / Jazz Music.

GREAT BIG BANDS OF THE '50S
Fanfare boogie: Winstone, Eric / Drum crazy: Johnson, Laurie / Rhythm and blues: Winstone, Eric / Anticipation: Winstone, Eric / Nexy train out of town: Miller, Betty / Cob-bler's song: Winstone, Eric / Heatwave: Johnson, Laurie / In a Persian market: Johnson, Laurie / Fascinating rhythm: Clark, Petula / Hallelujah: Johnson, Laurie / Frustration: Winstone, Eric / Treasure of love: Shepherd, Pauline / Jamboree: John-son, Laurie / Slow train blues: Winstone, Eric / Cat walk: Winstone, Eric / Georgia's got a moon: Miller, Betty / Opus one mambo: Winstone, Eric / Heartbreak: Win-stone, Eric / It might as well be spring: Johnson, Laurie / Robber's march: Win-stone, Eric / Majorca: Clark, Petula / Stick or twist: Johnson, Laurie / Things we did last summer: Johnson, Laurie
CD   C5LCD 601
See For Miles/C5 / May '94 / Pinnacle.

GREAT BLUES GUITAR LEGENDS, THE (4CD Set)
CD Set   HRCD 8030
Disky / May '93 / THE / BMG / Discovery / Pinnacle.

GREAT BLUES GUITARISTS - STRING DAZZLERS
Hot fingers: Johnson, Lonnie & Eddie Lang / Handful of riffs: Johnson, Lonnie & Eddie Lang / Work on blues: Johnson, Lonnie & Eddie Lang / I'm busy and you can't come in: Weaver, Sylvester / Georga rag: McTell, Blind Willie / Warm it up for me: McTell, Blind Willie / Untitled: Weaver, Sylvester / When the war was on: Johnson, Blind Willie / It's nobody's fault but mine: Johnson, Blind Willie / How you want it done: Broonzy, Big Bill / Getting older every day: Broonzy, Big Bill / Guitar swing: Weldon, Casey Bill / Bullfrog moan: Johnson, Lonnie & Eddie Lang / Black snake moan: Jeffer-son, Blind Lemon / Little brother blues: White, Joshua / Prodigal son: White, Joshua / Denver blues: Tampa Red / Away down in the alley blues: Johnson, Lonnie / I love you Mary Lou: Johnson, Lonnie
CD   4678942
Columbia / May '91 / Sony.

GREAT BLUESMEN (Newport 1959, 1960 & 1963)
Midnight boogie: Williams, Robert Pete / Levee camp blues: Williams, Robert Pete / My baby done changed the lock on the door: Terry, Sonny & Brownie McGhee / Tu-pelo: Hooker, John Lee / Bus station blues: Hooker, John Lee / Son's blues: House, Son / Death letter: House, Son / Pony blues: House, Son / Mailman blues: Estes, Sleepy John / Clean up at home: Estes, Sleepy

---

John / Hey rattler: Reese, Dock / Oh my Lord: Reese, Dock / Sliding Delta: Hurt, Mississippi John / Trouble, I've had it all day: Hurt, Mississippi John / Hard times: James, Skip / Killing floor blues: James, Skip / Cherry ball blues: James, Skip / Illi-nois blues: James, Skip / Death don't have no mercy: Davis, Rev. Gary / Catfish blues: Doss, Willie / I had a woman: Doss, Willie / I'm going down south: McDowell, 'Missis-sippi' Fred / If the river was whisky: Mc-Dowell, 'Mississippi' Fred / Cotton field blues: Hopkins, Lightnin' / Shake that thing: Hopkins, Lightnin'
CD   VCD 77
Vanguard / Oct '95 / Complete/Pinnacle / Discovery.

GREAT BRASS BANDS
633 squadron: Grand Massed Bands / Tricky trombones (Trombone trio): Grand Massed Bands / Colditz march: Grand Massed Bands / Three trumpeters: Grand Massed Bands / H.M.S. Pinafore (overture): Grand Massed Bands / Thunderbirds march: Grand Massed Bands / Can can (From 'Orpheus In The Underworld'): Grand Massed Bands / Rover's return: Grand Massed Bands / New world fantasy: Grand Massed Bands / Beau ideal: Grand Massed Bands / Fireman's galop: Grand Massed Bands / Out of the blues: G.U.S. Footwear Band / Samum: G.U.S. Footwear Band / Es-pana: G.U.S. Footwear Band / Royal Air Force march past: G.U.S. Footwear Band / Spanish gypsy dance: G.U.S. Footwear Band / Estudiantina: G.U.S. Footwear Band / Sons of the brave: G.U.S. Footwear Band / Bells across the meadow: G.U.S. Footwear Band / Seventy six trombones: G.U.S. Footwear Band / Tango taquin: G.U.S. Footwear Band / Lisbon carnival: G.U.S. Footwear Band / London Bridge march: G.U.S. Footwear Band
CD   CDEMS 1394
EMI / Mar '91 / EMI.

GREAT BRITISH BANDS (4CD Set)
CD Set   HRCD 8026
Disky / May '93 / THE / BMG / Discovery / Pinnacle.

GREAT BRITISH DANCE BANDS, THE
Did you mean it: Hylton, Jack / I guess I'll have to change my mind: Ambrose / Got to dance my way to heaven: Hall, Henry / You go to my head: Loss, Joe / One in a million: Lawrence, Brian / I've got beginner's luck: Fox, Roy / From the top of your head: Gib-bons, Carroll / Eyes of the world are on you: Levy, Louis / My heart belongs to Daddy: Cotton, Billy / Just as long as the world goes round and around: Wilbur, Jay / Mr. Rhythm Man: Gonella, Nat / You turned your head: Jackson, Jack / Let's fall in love for the last time: Mantovani / Temptation rag: Roy, Harry / Walkin' by the river: Ger-aldo / Crazy rhythm: Silvester, Victor / Or-gan grinder swing: Payne, Jack / Plain Mary Jane: Hylton, Mrs Jack / Stars fell on Ala-bama: Stone, Lew / My pet: Firman, Bert / Palais de Danse: Phillips, Sid / Shout for happiness: Noble, Ray
CD   PPCD 78112
Past Perfect / Feb '95 / THE.

GREAT BRITISH PSYCHEDELIC TRIP VOL. 1 (1966-1969)
Tales of Flossie Fillett: Turquoise / Baked jam roll in your eye: Timebox / In your tower: Poets / Leave me here: 23rd Turnoff / Muffin man: World of Oz / anniversary of love: Ice / Shades of orange: End / Ice man: Ice / Come on back: Paul & Ritchie & The Cryin' Shames / Vacuum cleaner: Tintern Abbey / Love: Virgin Sleep / Saving your love: Ro-meo and Juliet: Toby Twirl / Magician: Amazingly Friendly Apple / Beeside: Tintern Abbey / Stepping stone: Flies / Red sky at night: Accent / Renaissance fair: Human In-stinct / Miss Pinkerton: Cuppa T / Toffee apple Sunday: Toby Twirl / Green plant: Cherry Smash / Follow me: California / Just one more chance: Outer Limits / Heav-enly club: Sauterelles / Deep inside your mind: Shields, Keith / Elf: Stewart, Al
CD   SEECD 225
See For Miles/C5 / May '88 / Pinnacle.

GREAT BRITISH PSYCHEDELIC TRIP VOL. 2 (1965-1970)
That's the way it's got to be: Poets / I lied to Auntie May: Neat Change / Movin' in: Toby Twirl / Glasshouse green, splinter red: Kinsmen / Lazy day: Tinkerbell's Fairydust / Water woman: Pacific Drift / Paper chase: Love Children / Whisper her name: Mania Laine: Ice / Peacefully asleep: Life 'n' Soul / Turn into earth: Stewart, Al / Baby get your head screwed on: Double Feature / Eighty hours of paradise: Elastic Band / Fade away: Maureen: Cherry Smash / Gotta wait: Game / 8.35 on the dot: Stirling, Peter Lee / All our Christmases: Majority / Requiem: Chocolate Watch Band / I'll be home (in a day or so): Dream Police / Walking through the streets of my mind: Timebox / Happy castle: Cro-cheted Doughnut Ring / Death at the sea-side: Human Instinct / Secret: Virgin Sleep / In my magic garden: Tinkerbell's Fairydust / Woodstock: Turquoise

---

CD   SEECD 226
See For Miles/C5 / May '88 / Pinnacle.

GREAT BRITISH PSYCHEDELIC TRIP VOL. 3
My white bicycle: Tomorrow / Skeleton and the roundabout: Idle Race / In the land of the few: Idle Race / Kites: Dupree, Simon & The Big Sound / Mr. Armageddon: Loco-motive / You've got a habit of leaving: Jones, Davy & The Lower Third / Excerpt from a teenage opera: West, Keith / Ru-mours: Kippington Lodge / It's so nice to come home: Lemon Trees / Real love guar-anteed: Gods / We are the moles (part one): Moles / Friendly man: July / S.F. Sorrow is born: Pretty Things / I see: July / Lady on a bicycle: Kippington Lodge / On a saturday: West, Keith / Worn red carpet: Idle Race / Strawberry fields forever: Tomorrow / She says good morning: Pretty Things / Hey bulldog: Gods / William Chalker's time ma-chine: Lemon Trees / Little games: Yard-birds / Puzzles: Yardbirds / First cut is the deepest: Koobas / Sabre dance: Love Sculpture
CD   SEECD 76
See For Miles/C5 / Jan '90 / Pinnacle.

GREAT BRITISH PUNK ROCK EXPLOSION
Anarchy in the U.K.: Sex Pistols / No time to be 21: Adverts / First time: Boys / New rose (Live): Damned / I hate people: Anti Nowhere League / Homicide (live): 999 / I live in a car: UK Subs / Blind ambition: Par-tizan / Dogs of war: Exploited / Flares and slippers: Cockney Rejects / Murder of liddle towers: Angelic Upstarts / Harry May: Busi-ness / I wanna be me: Sex Pistols / Let's break the law: Anti Nowhere League / Disco demand: Damned / One chord wonders: Ad-verts / Ain't got a clue (Live): Lurkers / Tin soldier (live): Stiff Little Fingers / Borstal breakout: Sham 69 / C.I.D.: UK Subs / Baby baby: Vibrators
CD   DOJOCD 122
Dojo / Feb '94 / BMG.

GREAT BRITISH PUNK ROCK EXPLOSION VOL.2, THE
Safety in numbers: Adverts / Woman in dis-guise: Angelic Upstarts / Pretty vacant: Sex Pistols / Brickfield nights: Sex Pistols / Ev-erybody's happy nowadays: Buzzcocks / B.I.C.: UK Subs / Nobody's heroes (Live): Stiff Little Fingers / Feelin' alright with the crew (Live): 999 / Ignite: Damned / Streets of London: Anti Nowhere League / Bored teenagers: Adverts / I don't need to tell her (Live): Lurkers / National insurance blacklist: Business / Viv la revolution: Adicts / Punk's not dead: Exploited / You'll never know: Vice Squad / Judy says: Vibrators / Warri-ors: Blitz / Something that I said: Ruts / I think I'm wonderful: Damned / For you: Anti Nowhere League / Jinx: Peter & The Test Tube Babies / Alternative: Exploited / An-gels with dirty faces (Live): Sham 69
CD   DOJOCD 131
Dojo / May '93 / BMG.

GREAT CLASSIC BLUES SINGERS
CD   158092
Blues Collection / Oct '93 / Discovery.

GREAT COMPOSERS, THE
Free-thee-well to Harlem: Mercer, Johnny / Someone to watch over me: Gershwin, George / Anything goes: Porter, Cole / Room with a view: Coward, Sir Noel / How can you face me: Waller, Fats & His Rhythm / Hong kong blues: Carmichael, Hoagy / Caravan: Ellington, Duke Orchestra / Hand-writing on the wall: Fain, Sammy / Very thought of you: Noble, Ray & His Orchestra / Yes indeed: Oliver, Sy / Mr. Meadowlark (With Bing Crosby): Mercer, Johnny / I'll see you again: Coward, Sir Noel / Fine and mellow: Holiday, Billie / Gal from Joe's: El-lington, Duke / You're the top: Porter, Cole / Touch of your lips: Noble, Ray / Judy: Car-michael, Hoagy / My one and only: Gersh-win, George / Solitude: Ellington, Duke / Mad dogs and Englishmen: Coward, Sir Noel / If you don't want to be sweethearts: Fain, Sammy
CD   AVC 521
Avid / Apr '93 / Avid/BMG / Koch.

GREAT DANCE FAVOURITES
CD   HCD 328
Hindsight / Jun '95 / Target/BMG / Jazz Music.

GREAT DAY IN HARLEM, A
Late show: Blakey, Art / No name jive: Krupa, Gene / U.M.M.G.: Ellington, Duke / Utter chaos: Mulligan, Gerry / Taxi war dance: Basie, Count / Goodbye pork pie hat: Mingus, Charles / Back room romp: Stewart, Rex / Prelude to a kiss: Hinton, Milt / Silver's blues: Silver, Horace / Oh, lady be good: Jones-Smith INC / In a mellow tone: Monk, Thelonious
CD   4605002
Sony Jazz / Oct '95 / Sony.

GREAT DAYS OF MUSIC HALL
Jolly good luck to the girl who loves a sol-dier: Tilley, Vesta / When father papered the parlour: Williams, Billy / Gas Inspector: Little Tich / I may be crazy: Stratton, Eugene / Has anybody here seen Kelly: Forde, Florrie / Archibald certainly not: Robey, George / Burlington Bertie from Bow: Shields, Ella /

Lily of Laguna: *Stratton, Eugene* / Every little movement: *Lloyd, Marie* / My old Dutch: *Chevalier, Albert* / Naughty Victorian days: *Byng, Douglas* / Mocking bird: *Leno, Dan* / It's a big shame: *Ellen, Gus* / Art a pint of ale: *Ellen, Gus* / Three trees: *Whelan, Albert* / Preacher and the bear: *Whelan, Albert* / Don't send my boy to prison: *Williams, Billy* / Music Hall medley: *Retford, Ella* / PC 49: *Fay, Harry* / Two lovely black eyes: *Coburn, Charles* / Three times a day: *Wallace, Nellie*
CD _____ **RAJCD 834**
Empress / Oct '94 / THE.

GREAT DAYS OF THE ACCORDION BANDS
Old timer: *Geraldo & His Orchestra* / Sleepy time in sleepy hollow: *Geraldo & His Orchestra* / Marching along together: *Geraldo & His Orchestra* / At eventide: *Geraldo & His Orchestra* / Song of the bells: *Geraldo & His Orchestra* / Silver hair and heart of gold: *Geraldo & His Orchestra* / Sing a new song: *Geraldo & His Orchestra* / Clouds will soon roll by: *Geraldo & His Orchestra* / Marta: *Geraldo & His Orchestra* / Sweetest song in the world: *Reid, Billy & His Orchestra* / First time I saw you: *Reid, Billy & His Orchestra* / Blossoms on broadway: *Reid, Billy & His Orchestra* / Little drummer boy: *Reid, Billy & His Orchestra* / Moonlight on the waterfall: *Reid, Billy & His Orchestra* / So many memories: *Reid, Billy & His Orchestra* / My heaven in the pines: *Reid, Billy & His Orchestra* / Are you sincere: *Reid, Billy & His Orchestra* / Rose covered shack: *Reid, Billy & His Orchestra* / Chocolate soldier's daughter: *Reid, Billy & His Orchestra* / Apple blossom time: *London Piano Accordion Band* / South of the border: *London Piano Accordion Band* / All alone with my shadow: *London Piano Accordion Band* / Whose little what's it are you: *London Piano Accordion Band* / For all that I care: *Scala, Primo & His Accordion Band* / Down forget-me-not lane: *Scala, Primo & His Accordion Band* / I yi yi yi yi (I like you very much): *Scala, Primo & His Accordion Band* / There goes that song again: *Scala, Primo & His Accordion Band* / Hey little hen: *Scala, Primo & His Accordion Band*
CD _____ **RAJCD 828**
Empress / Jul '94 / THE.

GREAT DIXIE ROCK & ROLL
This just can't be puppy love: *Mayberry, Howard* / Corner of love: *Lightner, Ken* / Hangover blues: *Floyd, Jessie* / Darling on my mind: *Nelson, Tommy* / Swanky: *Gentry Bros* / If you keep doing: *Take, Thomas* / Blues walked away: *Hudson, Ray* / Teen lover: *Reynolds, Eddy* / Good lovin' / Let's go, let's go: *Swoony: Gentry Bros* / Poor man: *Wills, Bob* / Three little wishes: *Lee, Jimmy* / Little things you do: *Lee, Jimmy* / Blues ganging roud: *Kelley, Cathy* / Oh my love: *Howard & The Darts* / Curley: *Skelton, Eddie* / Gee whiz: *Pat & Dee* / Ten long fingers: *Poovey, Joe* / Tea leaf lie: *Mishoe, Watson* / Future I hold: *Meers, Arvil* / Ali-baba: *Williams Brothers* / Crazy legs: *Gallegher, Jay* / Hi-yo silver: *Buchanan, Art* / Telephone boogie: *Waynick, Don* / Wheepers: *Felts, Derrell* / Move around: *Poovey, Groovey Joe* / I'm your guy: *Johnson, Dee* / High society: *Gardner, Guy* / Steady: *Gallegher, Jay*
CD _____ **CDDIXIE 2222**
White Label/Bear Family / Apr '94 / Bear Family / Rollercoaster.

GREAT FRENCH STARS OF THE 30'S
Paris je t'aime d'amour: *Chevalier, Maurice* / C'est si facile de vous aimer: *Baker, Josephine* / Boum: *Trenet, Charles* / Il n'est pas distingue: *Piaf, Edith* / Ignace: *Fernandel* / C'est vrai: *Mistinguett* / Si tu m'aimes: *Sablon, Jean* / En Septembre sous la pluie: *Marjane, Leo* / Amapola: *Rossi, Tino* / Quand un vicomte: *Hildegarde* / Swing quand: *Reinhardt, Django & Stephane Grapelli* / Melancolie: *Sablon, Jean* / Et voila, voila les hommes: *mirielle* / Vous valez mieux qu'un sourire: *Chevalier, Maurice* / La musique vient par ici: *Ventura, Ray & His Collegians* / Chez moi: *Boyer, Lucienne* / Je chante: *Trenet, Charles* / C'est un nid charmant: *Baker, Josephine* / Berceuse de Jocelyn: *Rossi, Tino* / La java de cezique: *Piaf, Edith* / Oh que j'aime Paris: *Mistinguett*
CD _____ **CDHD 157**
Happy Days / '89 / Conifer.

GREAT GENTLEMEN OF SONG VOL.1 (Hooray For Love)
In the wee small hours of the morning: *Sinatra, Frank* / Imagination: *Martin, Dean* / My buddy: *Torme, Mel* / There, I've said it again: *Damone, Vic* / P.S. I love you: *Manning, Bob* / Cuddle up a little closer: *MacRae, Gordon* / I'm beginning to see the light: *Monro, Matt* / I get along without you very well: *Monro, Matt* / So marvelous for words: *Russell, Andy* / I guess I'll have to change my plan: *Bennett, Tony* / When I fall in love: *Haymes, Dick* / That's all: *Haymes, Dick* / My funny valentine: *Baker, Chet* / Just squeeze me: *Armstrong, Louis* / Affair to remember: *Martino, Al* / Hooray for love: *Mercer, Johnny* / Stardust: *Ifield, Frank* / Stormy weather: *Rawls, Lou* / Impossible: *Jones, Jack* / You are my lucky star: *Davis, Sammy Jnr.*

GREAT GENTLEMEN OF SONG VOL.2 (Pennies From Heaven)
Now you has jazz: *Crosby, Bing* / I've got the world on a string: *Sinatra, Frank* / Until the real thing comes along: *Martin, Dean* / Let's face the music and dance: *Monro, Matt* / Always: *Darin, Bobby* / I want a little girl: *Eckstine, Billy* / I cried for you: *Russell, Andy* / But not for me: *Baker, Chet* / Goodbye: *Torme, Mel* / Just a giguolo: *Prima, Louis* / Every day I have the blues: *Williams, Joe* / There will never be another you: *Cole, Nat King* / That old black magic: *Murphy, Mark* / I'm nobody's baby: *Damone, Vic* / Love walked in: *Haymes, Dick* / Moon faced starry eyed: *Mercer, Johnny* / Don't take your love from me: *Martino, Al* / Pennies from heaven: *MacRae, Gordon* / With plenty of money and you: *Bennett, Tony* / It don't mean a thing if it ain't got that swing: *Armstrong, Louis*
CD _____ **CDP 8317752**
Capitol / Apr '95 / EMI.

GREAT GIRL SINGERS
It's been so long: *Forrest, Helen* / If that's the way you want it baby: *Forrest, Helen* / I couldn't sleep a wink last night: *Forrest, Helen* / At least you could say hello: *O'Connell, Helen* / I'm steppin' out with a memory tonight: *O'Connell, Helen* / Just for a thrill: *O'Connell, Helen* / Them there eyes: *Starr, Kay* / It's a good day: *Starr, Kay* / I only have eyes for you: *Starr, Kay* / I'll never forget you: *Clooney, Rosemary* / You make me feel so young: *Clooney, Rosemary* / Don't worry 'bout me: *Clooney, Rosemary*
CD _____ **HCD 320**
Hindsight / Apr '95 / Target/BMG / Jazz Music.

GREAT GIRL SINGERS
CD _____ **HCD 414**
Hindsight / Sep '92 / Target/BMG / Jazz Music.

GREAT GOSPEL CHOIRS
CD _____ **HRCD 8054**
Disky / Apr '94 / THE / BMG / Discovery / Pinnacle.

GREAT GOSPEL MEN
CD _____ **SHAN 06005CD**
Shanachie / Aug '93 / Koch / ADA / Greensleeves.

GREAT GOSPEL WOMEN
CD _____ **SHAN 06004CD**
Shanachie / Aug '93 / Koch / ADA / Greensleeves.

GREAT GUITARS
CD _____ **GC 6004**
Concord Jazz / Jul '88 / New Note.

GREAT HARP PLAYERS
CD _____ **DOCD 5100**
Blues Document / Nov '92 / Swift / Jazz Music.

GREAT HITS FROM THE GIRL GROUPS
CD _____ **CDCD 1094**
Charly / May '93 / Charly / THE / Cadillac.

GREAT HORNS, THE (5CD Set)
CD Set _____ **JWD 2518**
JWD / Nov '92 / Target/BMG.

GREAT INSTRUMENTAL FAVOURITES
CD _____ **HCD 325**
Hindsight / May '95 / Target/BMG / Jazz Music.

GREAT JAZZ BANDS
Rock-a-bye Basie: *Basie, Count* / Baby, won't you please come home: *Basie, Count* / Jumpin' at the woodside: *Basie, Count* / Someone: *Ellington, Duke* / Suddenly it jumped: *Ellington, Duke* / Perdido: *Ellington, Duke* / Jeep is jumpin': *Ellington, Duke* / To gether: *Kirk, Andy* / 9.20 Special: *Kirk, Andy* / For dancers only: *Lunceford, Jimmie* / Holiday for strings: *Lunceford, Jimmie* / Wham: *Lunceford, Jimmie*
CD _____ **HCD 413**
Hindsight / Sep '92 / Target/BMG / Jazz Music.

GREAT JAZZ BANDS
CD _____ **HCD 323**
Hindsight / Apr '95 / Target/BMG / Jazz Music.

GREAT JAZZ PIANISTS, THE
Carolina shout: *Waller, Fats* / Ain't misbehavin': *Waller, Fats* / Fifty seven varieties: *Hines, Earl* / My melancholy baby: *Hines, Earl* / Snowy morning blues: *Johnson, James P.* / You've got to be modernistic: *Johnson, James P.* / King Porter stomp: *Morton, Jelly Roll* / Original rags: *Morton, Jelly Roll* / Swampy river: *Ellington, Duke* / Passionette: *Smith, Willie 'The Lion'* / Morning air: *Smith, Willie 'The Lion'* / Humoresque: *Tatum, Art* / Begin the beguine: *Tatum, Art* / Tiger rag: *Wilson, Teddy* / When you and I were young: *Wilson, Teddy* / Maggie: *Wilson, Teddy* / Finishing up a date: *Kyle, Billy* / My blue heaven: *Weatherford, Teddy* / Pilgrim's chorus: *Lambert, Donald* / Rockin' chair: *Wilson, Garland* / Swingin' for joy: *Williams, Mary Lou* / Ladder: *Turner, Big Joe* / Little Rock getaway: *Sullivan, Joe*

CD _____ **PPCD 78107**
Past Perfect / Feb '95 / THE.

GREAT JAZZ VOCALISTS, THE
Now you has jazz: *Crosby, Bing & Louis Armstrong* / Late late show: *Staton, Dakota* / Pete Kelly's blues: *Fitzgerald, Ella* / I know that you know: *Cole, Nat King* / Midnight sun: *Christy, June* / Satin doll: *Wilson, Nancy* / Dinah: *Williams, Joe* / Call me irresponsible: *Washington, Dinah* / Honeysuckle rose: *Dankworth, John Seven & Cleo Laine* / Lulu's back in town: *Hi-Lo's* / I got rhythm: *Vaughan, Sarah* / Star eyes: *McCrae, Carmen & Dave Brubeck* / Got the gate on the golden gate: *Torme, Mel* / Things are swinging: *Lee, Peggy* / Her tears flowed like wine: *O'Day, Anita* / Love is just around the corner: *Four Freshmen* / Walk in the Black Forest: *Jones, Salena* / Lil' Darlin: *Lambert, Hendricks & Ross* / Jon Hendricks: *Four Brothers* / God bless the child: *Holiday, Billie*
CD _____ **CDMFP 6162**
Music For Pleasure / May '95 / EMI.

GREAT MARCHES VOL 1, THE
Colonel Bogey / Blaze away / On the quarterdeck / Liberty bell / Washington greys / Army of the Nile / Berliner luft / Great little army / Radetzky march / With sword and lance / National emblem / Holyrood / Semper fidelis / Boots and saddles / La reve passe / Scarlet and gold / Thunderer / Fehrbelliner reitermarsch / Thin red line / Anchors aweigh / Old comrades / Standard of St. George
CD _____ **BNA 5006**
Bandleader / Apr '87 / Conifer.

GREAT MARCHES VOL 2, THE
Hands across the sea / Fame and glory / March Lorriane / General Mitchell / Children of the regiment / High school cadets / Through bolts and bars / Sons of the brave / Preobrajensky march / Sarafand / Invincible eagle / Staffordshire knot / To your guard / Le pere la victoire / Skywrite / Waldmere / Triumph of right / Arromanches / Ridgewood / Steadfast and true / Glorious victory / El Abanico / Marche militaire
CD _____ **BNA 5018**
Bandleader / Jul '88 / Conifer.

GREAT MARCHES VOL 3, THE
Voice of the guns / Golden spurs / Wings / Royal Air Force march past / Black horse troop / Gunners / Barvada / Officer of the day / Mad major / Red cloak / Down the Mall / Iron regiment / Trombone king / Cavalry of the clouds / Imperial Life Guards / Trumpet major / Grid iron club / My congratulations / Royal standard / Purple pageant / Marche des parachutistes belges / Chief of staff / Inkerman / Pentland hills / Imperial march
CD _____ **BNA 5029**
Bandleader / Aug '89 / Conifer.

GREAT MARCHES VOL 4, THE
CD _____ **BNA 5053**
Bandleader / Feb '92 / Conifer.

GREAT MARCHES VOL 5, THE
Contemptibles / On the square / Aces high / King's guard / Hoch und deutschmeister / Vedette / Cavalry walk / Carmen march / H. M. Jollies / Alma / Sounding brass / B.B. and C.F. / March of the Royal British Legion / British Eighth / Barnum and Bailey's favourite / Guard's parade / Old gray mare / Grandioso / Flying eagle / Cavalry of the steppes / Through night to light / Blue devils / Marcha Amalurena / My regiment
CD _____ **BNA 5060**
Bandleader / Apr '92 / Conifer.

GREAT MARCHES VOL. 7, THE
Stars and stripes forever / Imperial echoes / Army and marine / Father Rhine / Wait for the wagon / Sarie Marais / Grenadier Mars / Gladiator's farewell / Thundering guns / Quality plus / Under freedom's banner / Royal buglers
CD _____ **BNA 5112**
Bandleader / Nov '94 / Conifer.

GREAT MOMENTS IN JAZZ
CD _____ **74321218292**
Arista / Nov '94 / BMG.

GREAT MUSICAL MEMORIES
CD _____ **HCD 322**
Hindsight / Jul '95 / Target/BMG / Jazz Music.

GREAT NEW YORK SINGLES
CD _____ **RE 116CD**
Reach Out International / Nov '94 / Jetstar.

GREAT ORIGINAL PERFORMANCES 1926-1934
Side walk blues / Someday, sweetheart / Savoyager's stomp / African hunch / Singin' the blues / Nobody's sweetheart / Walking the dog / What do I care what somebody said / Milenberg joy / Yellow fire / Shake that jelly roll / My oh my / That's a plenty / Get 'em again blues / Stomp your stuff / Hear me talkin' to ya / Beau Koo Jack / Maple leaf rag / Jump steady blues / Memphis shake
CD _____ **RPCD 614**
Robert Parker Jazz / Apr '94 / Conifer.

GREAT RADIO STARS OF THE 30'S VOL.1
It's that man again: *Handley, Tommy* / Mermaid: *Fletcher, Cyril* / Down upon the farm: *Sarony, Leslie & Leslie Holmes* / On the telephone: *Mrs. Feather* / Goes naughty: *Oliver, Vic* / Gert, Daisy and a piano: *Waters, Elsie & Doris* / Play the game, you cads: *Western Brothers* / Police station: *Wilton, Robb* / Kiss me goodnight, Sergeant Major: *Carlisle, Elsie* / Last year's calendar: *Stainless Stephen* / Buggines at the seaside: *Constanducos, Mabel/Michael Hogan & Company* / We must all stick together: *Murgatroyd & Winterbottom* / Tomsky, the great counter-spy: *Handley, Tommy* / It's an overrated pastime: *Frankau, Ronald* / I taught her to play br-oop, br-oop: *Fields, Gracie* / Joe Ramsbottom at the dentist: *Evans, Norman* / Woodland romance: *Gourley, Ronald* / Play up and pay the dame: *Wakefield, Oliver* / Why should the dustman get it all: *Miller, Max* / Good old General Guiness: *Handley, Tommy*
CD _____ **PASTCD 9721**
Flapper / '90 / Pinnacle.

GREAT RADIO STARS VOL 2
Bee song / I didn't ofter a'ett it: *Warner, Jack* / Laughing bachelor: *Penrose, Charles* / Trains: *Gardner, Reginald* / Rachmaninov's prelude: *Henson, Leslie* / Annual dinner of the state club secretaries: *Johnson, Cecil* / Chin chin cheerio: *Frankau, Ronald* / Stanelli and his hornchestra: *Stanelli* / Much ado about little or nothing: *Wakefield, Oliver* / More chestnut corner: *Askey/Murdoch* / Pussy cat news: *Flotsam & Jetsam* / Splitting up: *Flanagan & Allen* / Teasing tongue twisters: *Comber, Bobbie* / Fiddling and fooling: *Ray, Ted* / I must have one of those: *Henry, Leonard* / Lion and ALbert: *Holloway, Stanley* / Jolly old ma, jolly old Pa: *Sarony, Leslie* / Truth about society: *Potter, Gillie*
CD _____ **PASTCD 9728**
Flapper / '90 / Pinnacle.

GREAT SEX
CD _____ **RADCD 16**
Global / Jun '95 / BMG.

GREAT SOUL BALLADS
CD Set _____ **CDPK 401**
Charly / Feb '95 / Charly / THE / Cadillac.

GREAT SOUND OF COUNTRY VOL.1, THE
CD _____ **EMPRCD 541**
Emporio / Sep '94 / THE / Disc / CM.

GREAT SOUND OF COUNTRY VOL.2, THE
CD _____ **EMPRCD 542**
Emporio / Sep '94 / THE / Disc / CM.

GREAT SOUND OF COUNTRY VOL.3, THE
CD _____ **EMPRCD 543**
Emporio / Sep '94 / THE / Disc / CM.

GREAT SOUND OF COUNTRY VOL.4, THE
CD _____ **EMPRCD 544**
Emporio / Sep '94 / THE / Disc / CM.

GREAT SOUND OF COUNTRY, THE (4CD Set)
CD _____ **EMPRBX 006**
Emporio / Sep '94 / THE / Disc / CM.

GREAT STARS OF COUNTRY (2CD Set)
CD _____ **24060**
Delta Doubles / Sep '92 / Target/BMG.

GREAT SWEET BANDS
CD _____ **HCD 324**
Hindsight / Jul '95 / Target/BMG / Jazz Music.

GREAT SWING JAM SESSIONS 1938-1939
Keep smilin' at trouble / Just the blues / China boy / Someday sweetheart / Sugar / St. Louis blues / You took advantage of me / Someday sweetheart (2) / Basin Street blues / Honeysuckle rose / (I would do) anything for you / Boogie woogie blues / I'm coming Virginia
CD _____ **JUCD 2029**
Storyville / Mar '95 / Jazz Music / Wellard / CM / Cadillac.

GREAT VOCALS OF THE FIFTIES
Wait for me: *Ryan, Marion* / Bell bottom blues: *Radio Revellers* / No not much: *Shepherd, Pauline* / Answer me: *Goff, Reggie* / Broken heart: *Young, Jimmy & Petula Clark* / Allentown jail: *Roza, Lita* / Sixteen tons: *Hockridge, Edmund* / Love me forever: *Ryan, Marion* / Tomorrow: *Brandon, Johnny* / Bridge of sighs: *Goff, Reggie* / So many times I have cried over you: *Young, Jimmy* / Maybe you'll be there: *Roza, Lita* / Wisdom of a fool: *Shepherd, Pauline* / Arrivederci darling: *Radio Revellers* / That's how a love song was born: *Clark, Petula* / Moon above Malaya: *Goff, Reggie* / Maryandle: *Young, Jimmy & Petula Clark* / Hot diggitty (dog digster): *Ryan, Marion* / Rags to riches: *Goff, Reggie* / Who are we: *Miller, Betty* / Memories are made of this: *Clark, Petula* / Young and foolish: *Hockridge, Edmund* / Once in a while: *Roza, Lita* / You young: *Young, Jimmy*
CD _____ **C5LCD 599**
See For Miles/C5 / May '94 / Pinnacle.

GREAT XPECTATIONS - LIVE
(X-rated vol.1)
Colour me grey: Family Cat / Armchair anarchist: Kingmaker / Queen Jane: Kingmaker / Chrome: Catherine Wheel / I want to touch you: Catherine Wheel / Keepsake: Senseless Things / Walter's trip: Frank & Walters / Full moon: Belly / Empty heart: Belly / Dusted: Belly / Cheer up, it might never happen: Carter U.S.M. / Bloodsports for all: Carter U.S.M. / Just like heaven: Cure / Disintegration: Cure / For tomorrow (Not on LP): Blur

CD _____ XFMCD 1
XFM / Jul '93 / Pinnacle.

GREATER LONDON GROOVES
CD _____ THE 33332
Three / Sep '95 / EWM.

GREATEST ARTISTES OF THE 30'S & 40'S
Lili Marlene: Dietrich, Marlene / Such trying times: Dietrich, Marlene / Kisses sweeter than wine: Dietrich, Marlene / Near you: Dietrich, Marlene / Black market: Dietrich, Marlene / Illusions: Dietrich, Marlene / Another spring: Dietrich, Marlene / Candles glowing: Dietrich, Marlene / I may never go home anymore: Dietrich, Marlene / Boys in the backroom: Dietrich, Marlene / You go to my head if he swings by the string: Dietrich, Marlene / This world of ours: Dietrich, Marlene / Near you (2): Dietrich, Marlene / La petite tonkinoise: Baker, Josephine / Pretty little baby: Baker, Josephine / J'au deux amours: Baker, Josephine / Dis-moi Josephine: Baker, Josephine / Si j'etais Blanche: Baker, Josephine / Ram-pam pam: Baker, Josephine / C'est lui: Baker, Josephine / Haiti: Baker, Josephine / Sous le ciel d'Afrique: Baker, Josephine / Espabitae: Baker, Josephine / Partir sur un bateuau tout blanc: Baker, Josephine / Nuit d'Alger: Baker, Josephine / La conga blicoti: Baker, Josephine / Vous faites partie de moi: Baker, Josephine / J'ai peur de rever: Baker, Josephine / Honeysuckle rose: Reinhardt, Django / Sapne: Reinhardt, Django / My sweet: Reinhardt, Django / Undecided: Reinhardt, Django / Don't worry 'bout me: Reinhardt, Django / Sweet Georgia Brown: Reinhardt, Django / Lambeth walk: Reinhardt, Django / H.C.Q. strut: Reinhardt, Django / Man I love: Reinhardt, Django / Improvisation sur le ler MVT de J.S. Bach: Reinhardt, Django / Echoes of Spain: Reinhardt, Django / Improvisation no.2: Reinhardt, Django / Minor swing: Reinhardt, Django

CD Set _____ 90836-2
PMF / May '94 / Kingdom / Cadillac.

GREATEST COUNTRY SHOW, THE
CD _____ HRCD 8020
Disky / Jul '93 / THE / BMG / Discovery / Pinnacle.

GREATEST DANCE ALBUM IN THE WORLD, THE
CD _____ VTCD 13
Virgin / Jul '92 / EMI.

GREATEST DANCE ALBUM OF ALL TIME, THE
Rhythm of the night: Corona / Back to life: Soul II Soul / Opps up side your head: Gap Band / You're the one for me: D-Train / No limit: 2 Unlimited / I feel for you: Khan, Chaka / Pump up the volume: M.A.R.S. / Connected: Stereo MC's / Play that funky music: Wild Cherry / Le freak: Chic / Out of space: Prodigy / Push it: Salt 'N' Pepa / I will survive: Gaynor, Gloria / Blame it on the boogie: Jacksons / Things can only get better: D Ream / We are family: Sister Sledge / You make me feel: Sylvester / Young hearts run free: Staton, Candi / Dance to the music: Sly & The Family Stone / One nation under a groove: Funkadelic / Grooves is in the heart: Deee-Lite / Let the music play: Shannon / I found lovin: Fatback Band / I like to move it: Reel 2 Real & The Mad Stuntman / Ebenezer good: Shamen / Contact: Starr, Edwin / Jump to the beat: Lattisaw, Stacy / Message: Grandmaster Flash / Word up: Cameo / Move on up: Mayfield, Curtis / Y M C A: Village People / Come in to my life: Sims, Joyce / Don't stop (Wiggle wiggle): Outhere Brothers / Night to remember: Shalamar / Power: Snap / Just be good to me: S.O.S. Band / Ride on time: Black Box / Celebration: Kool & The Gang / Car wash: Rose Royce

CD _____ DINCD 108
Dino / Oct '95 / Pinnacle / 3MV.

GREATEST FOLK SINGERS OF THE SIXTIES
You were on my mind: Ian & Sylvia / Now that the buffalo's gone: Sainte-Marie, Buffy / Walk right in: Rooftop Singers / East Virginia: Baez, Joan / Old Blue: Houston, Cisco / I feel like I'm fixin' to die rag: Country Joe & The Fish / John Henry: Odetta / Pack up your sorrows: Farina, Richard / Greenland whale fisheries: Collins, Judy & Theodore Bikel / Well, well, well: Gibson, Bob & Hamilton Camp / Ramblin' boy: Paxton, Tom / La Bamba: Feliciano, Jose / Virgin Mary had one son: Baez, Joan & Bob Gibson / Salty dog blues: Flatt, Lester & Earl Scruggs / Blowin' in the wind: Dylan, Bob / There but for: Ochs, Phil / Violets of the dawn: Anderson, Eric / Sittin' on top of the world: Watson, Doc / Travelling riverside: Ham-

mond, John / Crazy words crazy tune: Kweskin, Jim & The Jug Band / Candy man: Hurt, Mississippi John / Erie canal: Weavers / Wish I had answered: Staple Singers / Ballad of Springhill: Seeger, Peggy & Ewan MacColl / Mellow down easy: Butterfield, Paul / I got it: Chambers Brothers / Whistling gypsy: Makem, Tommy / Paper of pins: Brand, Oscar & Jean Ritchie / East Virginia blues: Seeger, Pete

CD _____ VCD 17
Vanguard / Oct '95 / Complete/Pinnacle / Discovery.

GREATEST GOSPEL GEMS VOLS 1 AND 2
Last mile of the way: Cooke, Sam & The Soul Stirrers / Touch the hem of his garment: Cooke, Sam & The Soul Stirrers / Search me, Lord: May, Brother Joe / Do you know him: May, Brother Joe / Mother bowed: Pilgrim Travelers / Straight street: Pilgrim Travelers / Jesus met the woman at the well: Pilgrim Travelers / Oh Lord, stand by me: Five Blind Boys Of Alabama / I'll fly away: Five Blind Boys Of Alabama / Too close to heaven: Bradford, Alex / Lord, Lord, Lord: Bradford, Alex / Get away Jordan: Love Coates, Dorothy / He's calling me: Love Coates, Dorothy / I'm sealed: Love Coates, Dorothy / My rock: Swan Silvertones / Jesus is a friend: Swan Silvertones / Let god abide: Anderson, Robert / Prayer for the doomed: Chosen Gospel Singers / Ball game: Carr, Sister Wynona / By and by: Soul Stirrers / Love of God: Taylor, Johnnie / I'm determined to run this race: Meditation Singers / Lead me, guide me: May, Brother Joe / Now the day is over: Cleveland, James

CD _____ CDCHD 344
Ace / May '91 / Pinnacle / Cadillac / Complete/Pinnacle.

GREATEST GUITAR HITS VOL. 1
Apache / Foottapper / Time is tight / memphis / Raunchy / Walk don't run / Shazam / Wipeout / Chariot / Pipeline / Red river rock / Telstar / Man of mystery / Perfidia

CD _____ 901018-2
PMF / May '94 / Kingdom / Cadillac.

GREATEST GUITAR HITS VOL. 2
Cavatina (Deerhunter) / Sleepwalk / Green onions / Let there be drums / Cruel sea / In dreams / Peter Gunn / Albatross / Riders in the sky / Diamonds / Scarlett O'Hara / F.B.I. / Sylvia / Samba pa ti

CD _____ 90102-2
PMF / May '94 / Kingdom / Cadillac.

GREATEST HITS 1990
CD _____ TCD 2439
Telstar / Nov '90 / BMG.

GREATEST HITS OF 1970, THE
In the summertime: Mungo Jerry / Rag mama rag: Band / Lola. Kinks / Down the dustpipe: Status Quo / Brontosaurus: Move / Whole lotta love: CCS / Black night: Deep Purple / Let's work together: Canned Heat / Voodoo chile: Hendrix, Jimi / Question: Moody Blues / Ride a white swan: T. Rex / I hear you knocking: Edmunds, Dave / When I'm dead and gone: McGuinness Flint / Neanderthal man: Hotlegs / I can't tell the bottom from the top: Hollies / Blame it on the Pony Express: Johnson, Johnny & Bandwagon / Love grows (where my Rosemary goes): Edison Lighthouse / Ruby Tuesday: Melanie

CD _____ CDGH 1970
Premier/MFP / Jul '91 / EMI.

GREATEST HITS OF 1971, THE
Maggie May: Stewart, Rod / Get it on: T. Rex / Malt and barley blues: McGuinness Flint / Strange kind of woman: Deep Purple / Tonight: Move / Tap turns on the water: CCS / Coz I luv you: Slade / Witch Queen of New Orleans: Redbone / Your song: John, Elton / Hot love: T. Rex / Double barrel: Collins, Dave & Ansil / Banner man: Blue Mink / Pushbike song: Mixtures / Something old, something new: Fantastics / I believe (in love): Hot Chocolate / If not for you: Newton-John, Olivia / Rose garden: Anderson, Lynn / Chestnut mare: Byrds

CD _____ CDGH 1971
Premier/MFP / Jul '91 / EMI.

GREATEST HITS OF 1972, THE
Rocket man: John, Elton / You wear it well: Stewart, Rod / Rock 'n' roll (part 2): Glitter, Gary / Metal guru: T. Rex / Ball park incident: Wizzard / Gudbuy t' Jane: Slade / Hold your head up: Argent / Family affair: Sly & The Family Stone / All the young dudes: Mott The Hoople / American pie: McLean, Don / 10538 overture: E.L.O. / Telegram Sam: T. Rex / Mama weer all craxee now: Slade / California man: Move / I didn't know I loved you (till I saw you rock 'n' roll): Glitter, Gary / Brand new key: Melanie / Say you don't mind: Blunstone, Colin / Sylvia's mother: Dr. Hook

CD _____ CDGH 1972
Premier/MFP / Jul '91 / EMI.

GREATEST HITS OF 1973, THE
Caroline: Status Quo / Roll over Beethoven: E.L.O. / Whiskey in the jar: Thin Lizzy / Do you wanna touch me (oh yeah): Glitter, Gary / Dance with the devil: Roussel, Cozy / The can: Quatro, Suzi / Cum on feel the noize: Slade / All the way from Memphis: Mott The Hoople / Twentieth century boy: T. Rex

/ I'm the leader of the gang (I am): Glitter, Gary / Nutbush City Limits: Turner, Ike & Tina / See my baby jive: Wizzard / Rubber bullets: 10cc / One and one is one: Medicine Head / Rock on: Essex, David / If you don't know me by now: Melvin, Harold & The Bluenotes / Me and Mrs. Jones: Paul, Billy / Daniel: John, Elton

CD _____ CDGH 1973
Premier/MFP / Jul '91 / EMI.

GREATEST HITS OF 1974, THE
You ain't seen nothin' yet: Bachman-Turner Overdrive / Down down: Status Quo / Always yours: Glitter, Gary / Tiger feet: Mud / Sugar baby love: Rubettes / Wall Street shuffle: 10cc / Waterloo: Abba / Far far away: Slade / Gonna make you a star: Essex, David / You're the first, the last, my everything: White, Barry / Never can say goodbye: Gaynor, Gloria / Summer breeze: Isley Brothers / Most beautiful girl: Rich, Charlie / Candle in the wind: John, Elton / You make me feel brand new: Stylistics / Rock your baby: McCrae, George / Judy Teen: Harley, Steve & Cockney Rebel / I can help: Swan, Billy

CD _____ CDGH 1974
Premier/MFP / Jul '91 / EMI.

GREATEST HITS OF 1975, THE
Jive talkin': Bee Gees / Lady Marmalade: Labelle, Patti / Hold back the night: Trammps / Can't give you anything (but my love): Stylistics / Take good care of yourself: Three Degrees / You sexy thing: Hot Chocolate / I can do it: Rubettes / Best thing that ever happened to me: Knight, Gladys & The Pips / Loving you: Riperton, Minnie / I'm not in love: 10cc / Tears on my pillow: Nash, Johnny / Hold me close: Essex, David / I'm stone in love with you: Mathis, Johnny / Make me smile (come up and see me): Harley, Steve & Cockney Rebel / Mamma mia: Abba / Doing alright with the boys: Glitter, Gary / Thanks for the memory (wham bam thank you man): Slade / Oh boy: Mud / Goodbye my love: Glitter Band / Moonlighting: Sayer, Leo

CD _____ CDGH 1975
Premier/MFP / Nov '91 / EMI.

GREATEST HITS OF 1976, THE
Pinball wizard: John, Elton / Boys are back in town: Thin Lizzy / Here comes the sun: Harley, Steve & Cockney Rebel / Devil woman: Richard, Cliff / Boston tea party: Harvey, Alex Band / You make me feel like dancing: Sayer, Leo / Little bit more: Dr. Hook / Things we do for love: 10cc / Harvest for the world: Isley Brothers / You should be dancing: Bee Gees / Don't go breaking my heart: John, Elton & Kiki Dee / Dr. Kiss Kiss: 5000 Volts / Dancing queen: Abba / I love to love (but my baby loves to dance): Charles, Tina / I love music: O'Jays / More, more, more: Andrea True Connection / Love really hurts without you: Ocean, Billy / Music: Miles, John / You to me are everything: Real Thing / Miss you nights: Richard, Cliff

CD _____ CDGH 1976
Premier/MFP / Nov '91 / EMI.

GREATEST HITS OF 1977, THE
Rockin' all over the world: Status Quo / Dancing in the moonlight: Thin Lizzy / She's not there: Santana / Spanish stroll: Mink Deville / Peaches: Stranglers / All around the world: Jam / Lido shuffle: Scaggs, Boz / Whodunit: Tavares / Ain't gonna bump no more (with no big fat woman): Tex, Joe / Don't leave me this way: Melvin, Harold & The Bluenotes / Jack in the box: Moments / shuffle: McCoy, Van / How deep is your love: Bee Gees / When I need you: Sayer, Leo / They shoot horses don't they: Racing Cars / It's a heartache: Tyler, Bonnie / Knowing me, knowing you: Abba / So you win again: Hot Chocolate / 2 4-6-8 motorway: Robinson, Tom / No more heroes: Stranglers

CD _____ CDGH 1977
Premier/MFP / Nov '91 / EMI.

GREATEST HITS OF 1978, THE
Night fever: Bee Gees / September: Earth, Wind & Fire / If I can't have you: Elliman, Yvonne / Dancing in the city: Marshall Hain / Every 1's a winner: Hot Chocolate / Stayin' alive: Bee Gees / Take a chance on me: Abba / Dreadlock holiday: 10cc / Lovely day: Withers, Bill / Song for Guy: John, Elton / Wuthering Heights: Bush, Kate / Darlin': Miller, Frankie / You took the words right out of my mouth: Meat Loaf / Don't fear the reaper: Blue Oyster Cult / Denis: Blondie / If the kids are united: Sham 69 / Down in the tube station at midnight: Jam / Rat trap: Boomtown Rats / Hanging on the telephone: Blondie / Baker Street: Rafferty, Gerry

CD _____ CDGH 1978
Premier/MFP / Jul '91 / EMI.

GREATEST HITS OF 1979, THE
Eton rifles: Jam / I don't like Mondays: Boomtown Rats / Hersham boys: Sham 69 / Duchess: Stranglers / Heart of glass: Blondie / Gangster: Special AKA / Tears of a clown: Beat / On my radio: Selecter / Milk and alcohol: Dr. Feelgood / Waiting for an alibi: Thin Lizzy / Whatever you want: Knack / When you fall in love with a beautiful woman: Dr. Hook / I have a dream: Abba / I will survive: Gaynor, Gloria / Tragedy: Bee

Gees / Ring my bell: Ward, Anita / Sunday girl: Blondie

CD _____ CDGH 1979
Premier/MFP / Nov '91 / EMI.

GREATEST HITS OF 1980
Call me: Blondie / Going underground: Jam / Someone's looking at you: Boomtown Rats / My best cousin: Undertones / Poison ivy: Lambrettas / Ant music: Adam Ant / What you're proposing: Status Quo / Killer on the loose: Thin Lizzy / Fool for loving you: Whitesnake / All over the world: E.L.O. / Geno: Dexy's Midnight Runners / Celebration: Kool & The Gang / Oops upside your head: Gap Band / Babooshka: Bush, Kate / Sexy eyes: Dr. Hook / What's another year: Logan, Johnny / Dreamin': Richard, Cliff / Fade to grey: Visage

CD _____ CDGH 1980
Premier/MFP / Aug '92 / EMI.

GREATEST HITS OF 1981
Dead ringer for love: Meat Loaf / Stand and deliver: Adam Ant / Girls on film: Duran Duran / Kids in America: Wilde, Kim / Funeral pyre: Jam / Happy birthday: Altered Images / Reward: Teardrop Explodes / Model: Kraftwerk / Ghost town: Specials / Lunatics (have taken over the asylum): Fun Boy Three / There's a guy works down the chip shop swears he's Elvis: MacColl, Kirsty / Bette Davis eyes: Carnes, Kim / Keep on loving you: REO Speedwagon / Why do fools fall in love: Ross, Diana / Easier said than done: Shakatak / Let's groove: Earth, Wind & Fire / Get down on it: Kool & The Gang / Intuition: Linx

CD _____ CDGH 1981
Premier/MFP / Aug '92 / EMI.

GREATEST HITS OF 1982
Eye of the tiger: Survivor / Town called Malice: Jam / Come on Eileen: Dexy's Midnight Runners & Emerald Express / Hungry like the wolf: Duran Duran / Centrefold: Jets, J. Band / Goody two shoes: Adam Ant / Young guns (go for it): Wham / Work that body: Ross, Diana / Golden brown: Stranglers / Look of love: ABC / Today: Talk Talk / Living on the ceiling: Blancmange / It ain't what you do it's the way that you do it: Fun Boy Three & Bananarama / I don't wanna dance: Grant, Eddy / It started with a kiss: Hot Chocolate / Night birds: Shakatak / Sexual healing: Gaye, Marvin / Blue eyes: John, Elton

CD _____ CDGH 1982
Premier/MFP / Aug '92 / EMI.

GREATEST HITS OF 1983
I'm still standing: John, Elton / I guess that's why they call it the blues: John, Elton / Bad boys: Wham / Is there something I should know: Duran Duran / Too shy: Kajagoogoo / Down under: Men At Work / Fields of fire: Big Country / Marguerita time: Status Quo / Garden party: Marillion / True: Spandau Ballet / Let's stay together: Turner, Tina / Long hot summer: Style Council / Our lips are sealed: Fun Boy Three / True love ways: Richard, Cliff / Tonight I celebrate my love: Bryson, Peabo & Roberta Flack / What kinda boy you looking for (girl): Hot Chocolate / Electric avenue: Grant, Eddy / Rockit: Hancock, Herbie

CD _____ CDGH 1983
Premier/MFP / Aug '92 / EMI.

GREATEST HITS OF 1984
Private dancer: Turner, Tina / What's love got to do with it: Turner, Tina / Your love is king: Sade / Sad songs (say so much): John, Elton / Missing you: Waite, John / Feels like) heaven: Fiction Factory / Joanna: Kool & The Gang / Robert De Niro's waiting: Bananarama / Only when you leave: Spandau Ballet / Whatever I do (wherever I go): Dean, Hazell / Reflex: Duran Duran / Politics of dancing: Re-Flex / Hyperactive: Dolby, Thomas / Smalltown boy: Bronski Beat / Shout to the top: Style Council / Electric avenue: Grant, Eddy / Dr. Beat: Miami Sound Machine / Wake me up before you go go: Wham

CD _____ CDGH 1984
Premier/MFP / Nov '91 / EMI.

GREATEST HITS OF 1985
CD _____ CDGH 1985
Premier/MFP / Oct '92 / EMI.

GREATEST HITS OF 1986
CD _____ CDGH 1986
Premier/MFP / Oct '92 / EMI.

GREATEST HITS OF 1987
CD _____ CDGH 1987
Premier/MFP / Oct '92 / EMI.

GREATEST HITS OF 1988
CD _____ CDGH 1988
Premier/MFP / Oct '92 / EMI.

GREATEST HITS OF 1989
CD _____ CDGH 1989
Premier/MFP / Oct '92 / EMI.

GREATEST HITS OF 1994
CD _____ TCD 2744
Telstar / Oct '94 / BMG.

GREATEST HITS OF 1995, THE
CD Set _____ TCD 2792
Telstar / Oct '95 / BMG.

GREATEST HITS OF THE 60'S/70'S
CD _____ HRCD 8046
Disky / Dec '93 / THE / BMG / Discovery / Pinnacle.

GREATEST HITS OF THE 80'S
Love is a stranger: Eurythmics / Who's zommin' who: Franklin, Aretha / Never gonna give you up: Astley, Rick / Perfect: Fairground Attraction / Slow hand: Pointer Sisters / Funkin' for Jamaica: Browne, Sandra / Ride on time: Black Box / I can't go for that (no can do): Hall & Oates / Human boys: Stray Cats / Broken wings: Mr. Mister / Every day hurts: Sad Cafe / Love plus one: Haircut 100
CD _____ 74321339312
Camden / Jan '96 / BMG.

GREATEST HITS OF THE SIXTIES
CD Set _____ 4417232
Pilz / Oct '92 / BMG.

GREATEST HITS: ONE LITTLE INDIAN
CD _____ TPCD 7
One Little Indian / Dec '88 / Pinnacle.

GREATEST HITS: ONE LITTLE INDIAN VOL 2
CD _____ TP CD 17
One Little Indian / Apr '90 / Pinnacle.

GREATEST IN COUNTRY BLUES VOLUME 1, THE
CD _____ SOB 35212
Story Of The Blues / Dec '92 / Koch / ADA.

GREATEST IN COUNTRY BLUES VOLUME 2, THE
CD _____ SOB 35222
Story Of The Blues / Dec '92 / Koch / ADA.

GREATEST IN COUNTRY BLUES VOLUME 3, THE
CD _____ SOB 35232
Story Of The Blues / Dec '92 / Koch / ADA.

GREATEST JAZZ, BLUES AND RAGTIME OF THE CENTURY
Squeeze me: Waller, Fats / I'm crazy 'bout my baby: Waller, Fats / Ivy: Johnson, James P. & J. Russell Robinson / Charleston: Johnson, James P. / Daddy blues: Jones, Clarence / Doggone blues: Jones, Clarence / Fast stuff blues: Blythe, Jimmy / Alley rat blues: Blythe, Jimmy / Charleston blues: Blake, Eubie / Maple leaf rag: Joplin, Scott / Gin mill blues: Fowler, Lemuel / Fowler's hot strut: Fowler, Lemuel / King Porter stomp: Morton, Jelly Roll / Bucksnort stomp: Tichenor, Trebor
CD _____ BCD 116
Biograph / Jul '91 / Wellard / ADA / Hot Shot / Jazz Music / Cadillac / Direct.

GREATEST LOVE
CD Set _____ DCDCD 202
Castle / Jun '95 / BMG.

GREATEST LOVE 1
CD _____ TMPCD 004
Telstar / Jan '95 / BMG.

GREATEST LOVE 2
CD _____ TMPCD 005
Telstar / Jan '95 / BMG.

GREATEST LOVE 3
CD _____ TMPCD 006
Telstar / Jan '95 / BMG.

GREATEST LOVE SONGS
Honey: Goldsboro, Bobby / Seasons in the sun: Jacks, Terry / Without you: Nilsson, Harry / Torn between two lovers: McGregor, Mary / Dedicated to the one I love: Mamas & Papas / Sealed with a kiss: Hyland, Brian / Drift away: Gray, Dobie / I am sorry: Lee, Brenda / I got you babe: Sonny & Cher / If I only had time: Rowles, John / Somebody to love: Jefferson Airplane / Escape (Pina colada song): Holmes, Rupert / Fire: Pointer Sisters / Lady: Styx / Love story: Lai, Francis / Thrill is gone: King, B.B.
CD _____ MCD 30201
Ariola Express / Mar '94 / BMG.

GREATEST LOVE SONGS, THE
(3CD Set)
Just one look: Hollies / Bus stop: Hollies / I can't let go: Hollies / I'm in the mood for love: Cogan, Alma / You're nobody 'til somebody loves you: Martin, Dean / That's amore (That's love): Martin, Dean / True love (all over the world): Martin, Dean / Zing went the strings of my heart: Garland, Judy / Let's do it (Let's fall in love): Hutch / What now my love: Bassey, Shirley / Something: Bassey, Shirley / Love story: Bassey, Shirley / My funny valentine: MacRae, Gordon / Begin the beguine: MacRae, Gordon / What I've got in mind: Spears, Billie Jo / Blanket on the ground: Spears, Billie Jo / Stand by your man: Spears, Billie Jo / All my loving: Monro, Matt / With these hands: Monro, Matt / Speak softly love: Monro, Matt / There's a kind of hush (all over the world): Herman's Hermits / Moon river: Williams, Danny / You're so good to me: Beach Boys / Wouldn't it be nice: Beach Boys / Then I kissed her: Beach Boys / You are so beautiful: Rogers, Kenny / Lady: Rogers, Kenny / Love changes everything: Keel, Howard / Wind beneath my wings: Keel, Howard / I

love you because: Martino, Al / Can't help falling in love: Martino, Al / Don't it make my brown eyes blue: Gayle, Crystal / Cry me a river: London, Julie / Fly me to the moon: London, Julie / Rose Marie: Whitman, Slim / For all we know: Cole, Nat King / Let's fall in love: Cole, Nat King / To know you is to love you: Peter & Gordon / And I love you so: Reddy, Helen / I didn't mean to love you: Reddy, Helen / Spanish eyes: Martino, Al / I'll be with you in apple blossom time: Stafford, Jo & Nat King Cole / Honey: Goldsboro, Bobby / By the time I get to Phoenix: Campbell, Glen / I love you bit: Cogan, Alma & Lionel Bart / All I have to do is dream: Campbell, Glen & Bobbie Gentry / I am in love: Damone, Vic / You belong to me: Stafford, Jo
CD Set _____ CDTRBOX 112
Trio / Oct '94 / EMI.

GREATEST PARTY ALBUM UNDER THE SUN, THE
(2 CD/MCs)
C'mon everybody: Cochran, Eddie / La bamba: Valens, Ritchie / Rock around the clock: Haley, Bill & The Comets / Let's twist again: Checker, Chubby / Hippy hippy shake: Swinging Blue Jeans / Shout: Lulu & The Luvvers / Fleet petite: Wilson, Jackie / Locomotion: Little Eva / Do wah diddy diddy: Manfred Mann / Mony Mony: James, Tommy & The Shondells / Let's dance: Montez, Chris / Hi ho silver lining: Beck, Jeff / Leader of the gang: Glitter, Gary / Tiger feet: Mud / See my baby jive: Wizzard / Rockin' all over the world: Status Quo / 2-4-6-8 motorway: Robinson, Tom Band / That's the way I like it: K.C. & The Sunshine Band / Celebration: Kool & The Gang / I will survive: Gaynor, Gloria / Y.M.C.A.: Village People / Never can say goodbye: Communards / Move closer: Nelson, Phyllis / True: Spandau Ballet / Shoop shoop song (It's in his kiss): Cher / Grease megamix: Travolta, John & Olivia Newton John / Mustang Sally: Commitments / I'm a believer: EMF/Reeves & Mortimer / Young at heart: Bluebells / Come on Eileen: Dexy's Midnight Runners / One step beyond: Madness / Can can: Bad Manners / O Carolina: Shaggy / Twist and shout: Demus, Chaka & Pliers / Here comes the hotstepper: Kamoze, Ini / I'm too sexy: Right Said Fred / Ride on time: Black Box / Only way is up: Yazz / Saturday night: Whigfield / Things can only get better: D Ream / Relight my fire: Take That & Lulu / Best: Turner, Tina / Unchained melody: Robson & Jerome / You'll never walk alone: Gerry & The Pacemakers
CD Set _____ CDEMTVD 107
EMI / Oct '95 / EMI.

GREATEST RAGTIME OF THE CENTURY
Shreveport stomp: Morton, Jelly Roll / Sweet man: Morton, Jelly Roll / Tom cat blues: Morton, Jelly Roll / New kind of man: Waller, Fats / Nobody but my baby: Waller, Fats / Got to cool my doggies now: Waller, Fats / Maple leaf rag: Joplin, Scott / Weeping willow rag: Joplin, Scott / Something doing: Joplin, Scott / Steeplechase rag: Johnson, James P. / Twilight rag: Johnson, James P. / Charleston rag: Blake, Eubie / It's right here for you: Blake, Eubie / Fare thee honey blues: Blake, Eubie / Mr. Freddie blues: Blythe, Jimmy / Regal stomp: Blythe, Jimmy
CD _____ BCD 103
Biograph / Jul '91 / Wellard / ADA / Hot Shot / Jazz Music / Cadillac / Direct.

GREATEST ROCK 'N' ROLL SHOW
CD _____ HRCD 8021
Disky / Jul '93 / THE / BMG / Discovery / Pinnacle.

GREATEST SINGERS, GREATEST SONGS
(3CD Set)
Over the rainbow: Garland, Judy / Zing went the strings of my heart: Garland, Judy / Little children: Kramer, Billy J. & The Dakotas / Dance, ballerina, dance: Cole, Nat King / Smile: Cole, Nat King / Let there be love: Cole, Nat King / It must be him: Carr, Vikki / When you're in love with a beautiful woman: Dr. Hook / Climb every mountain: Bassey, Shirley / On the street where you live: Damone, Vic / Dreamboat: Cogan, Alma / Lady: Rogers, Kenny / Lucille: Rogers, Kenny / Shrimp boats: Stafford, Jo / Portrait of my love: Monro, Matt / Softly as I leave you: Monro, Matt / Walk away: Monro, Matt / Folks who live on the hill: Lee, Peggy / Story of my life: Holliday, Michael / Starry eyed: Holliday, Michael / Talking in your sleep: Gayle, Crystal / Don't it make my brown eyes blue: Gayle, Crystal / Volare: Martin, Dean / Memories are made of this: Martin, Dean / That's amore (That's love): Martin, Dean / Come along a love: Starr, Kay / Still: Dodd, Ken & Geoff Love Orchestra / He was beautiful: Williams, Iris / Honey: Goldsboro, Bobby / Air that I breathe: Hollies / Cry me a river: London, Julie / Dreams of an everyday housewife: Campbell, Glen / To sir with love: Lulu / Sing me an old fashioned song: Spears, Billie Jo / What I've got in mind: Spears, Billie Jo / O what a beautiful morning: Keel, Howard / Walkin' back to happiness: Shapiro, Helen / And I love you so: Reddy, Helen / And I love you so (2): McLean, Don / Loving you: Riperton, Minnie / Spanish eyes: Martino, Al

/ Carnival is over: Seekers / Call me irresponsible: Washington, Dinah / Edelweiss: Hill, Vince / Good vibrations: Beach Boys
CD Set _____ CDTRBOX 136
Trio / Oct '94 / EMI.

GREATEST SONGS OF WOODY GUTHRIE #1
CD _____ VMD 73105
Vanguard / Jan '96 / Complete/Pinnacle / Discovery.

GREATEST SOUL ALBUM OF ALL TIME, THE
(2CD/MC Set)
You are everything: Ross, Diana & Marvin Gaye / Rock me tonight: Jackson, Freddie / Ain't no sunshine: Withers, Bill / How bout us: Champaign / Me & Mrs. Jones: Paul, Billy / Cherish: Kool & The Gang / Gotta get you home: Wilde, Eugene / Juicy fruit: Mtume / You body's callin': R. Kelly / Bootylak: Imagination / Always: Atlantic Starr / Shake you down: Abbott, Gregory / Streetlife: Crusaders / Rock wit'cha: Brown, Bobby / I wanna get next to you: Royce, Rose / Do you wanna make love: Jackson, Michael & Isaac Hayes / Let's stay together: Green, Al / Midnight train to Georgia: Knight, Gladys & The Pips / Be thankful for what you: De Vaughn, William / It's a man's man's world: Brown, James / Don't leave me this way: Melvin, Harold / Do what you do: Jackson, Jermaine / Sexual healing: Gaye, Marvin / There's nothing like this: Omar / Love supreme: Downing, Will / Joy and pain: Maze / Strawberry letter 23: Johnson, Bros / I found lovin': Fatback Band / If loving you is wrong: Jackson, Millie / Hold back the night: Trammps / It's a love thang: Whispers / Love come down: King, Evelyn 'Champagne' / Stay with me tonight: Osborne, Jeffrey / Misty blue: Moore, Dorothy / You're the first the last my everything: White, Barry / Lovin' you: Riperton, Minnie / Dolly my love: Moments / This is it: Moore, Melba / Now is the time: James, Jimmy / Rescue me: Fontella Bass
CD _____ DINCD 113
Dino / Nov '95 / Pinnacle / 3MV.

GREATEST TROUSERS
CD _____ EYEUKCD 003
Harthouse / Jun '95 / Disc / Warner Music.

GREECE - BYZANTINE MUSIC
CD _____ LDX 274971
La Chant Du Monde / Apr '94 / Harmonia Mundi / ADA.

GREEK-ORIENTAL REBETICA
CD _____ FL 7005
Folklyric / Apr '95 / Direct / Cadillac.

GREEN VELVET
(4CD Set)
CD Set _____ MBSCD 436
Castle / Nov '95 / BMG.

GREEN VELVET - THE IRISH FOLK COLLECTION
She moved through the fair: Shades of McMurrough / From Clare to here: Fureys & Davey Arthur / Shaney boy: Bards / Cliffs of Dooneen: Dublin City Ramblers / Emigrant: Fureys & Davey Arthur / Shores of Lough Bran: De Dannan / Follow me up to Carlo: Shades of McMurrough / Lonesome boatman: Fureys & Davey Arthur / Sligo Fair: Fergia / Ramblin' Irishman: De Dannan / Wind in the willows: Spud / Slipside: Shockton's Wing / Tabhair dom do lamh: Shades of McMurrough / Silver in the stubble: Dublin City Ramblers
CD _____ 5501842
Spectrum/Karussell / Mar '94 / PolyGram / THE.

GREENBELT FRINGE '95
Defiled: Fresh Claim / Magnum mysterium: Eve & The Garden / Paper chain: 3rd Day / Who you really are: Before & Beyond / Take me: Rumours are True / Wake me when the madness ends: Full Circle / Isn't he: Catley, Marc / Thank God for car stockers: Catley, Marc / Set the moose loose: about Machine / Bold love: Red Delivery Animal / It's like everything else: Worner-Phillips, Nigel / Never mind: Bernards's Dog / Calling: Skellig / Watching the war: Ryder, Pete / Children: Mudhead's Monkey / Really me: Obviously 5 Believers / Flawed: Days, Jonathan Earthhouse / Just one minute: Bickley, Jon & Angel Train / Rain people: Hunt / Art of the artsong song: Paley's Watch / Dreamscape: Asylum
CD _____ PCDN 147
Plankton / Nov '95 / Plankton.

GREENSLEEVES SAMPLER
Crazy list: Brown, Dennis / Feel the rydim: Minott, Sugar / Zungguzungguguzungguzeng: Yellowman / Pass the Tu-Sheng-Peng: Paul, Frankie / Let off supm: Isaacs, Gregory / Africa must be free by 1983: Mundell, Hugh / I love King Selassie: Black Uhuru / They don't know Jah: Wailing Souls / Dematerialise: Scientist / Ganja smuggling: Eek-A-Mouse / Stop that train: Eastwood & Saint / We are going: Burning Spear / Winnie Mandela (CD only): Davis, Carlene / Real enemy (CD only): Mighty Diamonds
CD _____ GREZCD 1
Greensleeves / Jun '87 / Total/BMG / Jetstar / SRD.

GREENSLEEVES SAMPLER 2
Telephone love: Lodge, J.C. / She loves me now: Hammond, Beres / Rock me: Mowatt, Judy / Man is a man: Boothe, Ken / Knight in shining armour: Glasgow, Deborahe / Fly away: Burning Spear / Rumours: Isaacs, Gregory / Tonight I'm going to take it easy: Mighty Diamonds / Girl E: Kamoze, Ini / Magnet and steel: Fraser, Dean / Miserable woman: McGregor, Freddie / Blueberry Hill: Yellowman / More them chat: Cocoa T & Krystal / Golden touch: Shabba Ranks
CD _____ GREZCD 2
Greensleeves / Sep '88 / Total/BMG / Jetstar / SRD.

GREENSLEEVES SAMPLER 3
CD _____ GREZCD 3
Greensleeves / Oct '89 / Total/BMG / Jetstar / SRD.

GREENSLEEVES SAMPLER 4
Twice my age: Shabba Ranks & Krystal / Report to me: Isaacs, Gregory / Love me baby: Tiger / Pirate's anthem: Home T, Coco Tea & Shabba Ranks / No more walls: Brown, Dennis / Wicked and wild: Little Lenny / Mr. Loverman: Glasgow, Deborahe & Shabba Ranks / Blinking something: Pinchers / Round table talk: Papa San / Why turn down the sound: Cocoa T / Make up your mind: Brown, Dennis & Tiger / Tell me which one: Admiral Tibet
CD _____ GREZCD 4
Greensleeves / Apr '90 / Total/BMG / Jetstar / SRD.

GREENSLEEVES SAMPLER 5
Your body's here with me: Home T, Coco Tea & Shabba Ranks / It's not enough: Papa San & Fabian / Ruling cowboy: Cocoa T / Home boy: Brown, Dennis / Gun talk: Redrose & Tony Rebel / Roughneck sound: Robinson, Ed 'Roughneck' / Going is rough: Home T, Coco Tea & Shabba Ranks / Monday morning blues: Melody, Mikey / Shepherd be careful: Cocoa T & Dennis Brown / Guilty: Mowatt, Judy / More them chat: Cocoa T & Krystal / Golden touch: Shabba Ranks
CD _____ GREZCD 5
Greensleeves / Nov '90 / Total/BMG / Jetstar / SRD.

GREENSLEEVES SAMPLER 6
Fanciness: Shabba Ranks & Lady G / One way woman: Cocoa T / John Law: Isaacs, Gregory, Freddie McGregor & Ninjaman / Mr. Bodyguard: Mighty Diamonds / Something in my heart: Levy, Barrington & Reggie Stepper / Mixed feelings: Brown, Dennis & Fabiana / Another one for the road: Home T, Coco Tea & Shabba Ranks / Midnight rock: Mawga / Freddie / Looking for love: Cutty Ranks & Barrington Levy / Fancy girl: Fabiana & Shabba Ranks / I'm your man: Brown, Dennis & Reggie Stepper / Stallion: Demus, Chaka
CD _____ GREZCD 6
Greensleeves / Apr '92 / Total/BMG / Jetstar / SRD.

GREENSLEEVES SAMPLER 7
Oh Carolina: Shaggy / Bed work sensation: Baja Jedd / I Spy: General TK / Getting closer: Cocoa T / Yardie: Banton, Buju / Don man girl: Isaacs, Gregory / Ting a ling a ling a school pickney sing ting: Ninjaman / Tender loving: Cocoa T & Shaka Shamba / Wealth: Cutty Ranks / Playing hard to get: McGregor, Freddie / After dark: Capleton / I need a roof: Mighty Diamonds / Screwface: General TK / Bedroom eyes: Yellowman / Certain friends: Lady G / Dance hall queen: Lloyd, Peter
CD _____ GREZCD 7
Greensleeves / May '93 / Total/BMG / Jetstar / SRD.

GREENSLEEVES SAMPLER 8
CD _____ GREZCD 8
Greensleeves / Nov '93 / Total/BMG / Jetstar / SRD.

GREENSLEEVES SAMPLER 9
Two woman: Levy, Barrington & Beenie Man / Gimme little sign: Harvey, Maxine / Tune in: Cocoa T / Statement: Bounty Killer / One way ticket: Luciano / I will furever love you: Sanchez / More than loving: Capleton & Nadine Sutherland / Love and devotion: Hammond, Beres / Nice and lovely: Shaggy & Rayvon / Not because I smile: Isaacs, Gregory / He will see you through: Griffiths, Marcia / Inna de dance: Reid, Junior / More love: French, Robert & Heavy D / Punk boys ride again: Cutty Ranks / There's nothing like this: Brown, Dennis
CD _____ GREZCD 9
Greensleeves / Apr '94 / Total/BMG / Jetstar / SRD.

GREENSLEEVES SAMPLER VOL 10
Under mi sensi: Levy, Barrington & Beenie Man / Gangster: Lieutenant Stitchie / No no no (World a respect mix): Penn, Dawn / Can't stop the dance: Yardcore Collective / Down in the ghetto: Bounty Killer / Bumptious girl: Sanchez & Stingerman / Press button (Remix): Beenie Man / Fowl affair: Silver Cat / All over you: Roach, Colin / Shoo-be-doo: Papa San / Firehouse: Redrose & Spragga Benz / One love: Cocoa T & Shaka Shamba / Bad publicity: Ninja Man

GREENSLEEVES SAMPLER VOL 10
/ One good turn: Isaacs, Gregory & Beres Hammond / Runaround girl: Bounty Killer & Chuck Turner / You don't love me (no no no): Penn, Dawn
CD _____ GREZCD 10
Greensleeves / Sep '94 / Total/BMG / Jetstar / SRD.

GREENSLEEVES SAMPLER VOL 11
CD _____ GREZCD 11
Greensleeves / Dec '94 / Total/BMG / Jetstar / SRD.

GREENSLEEVES SAMPLER VOL 12
CD _____ GREZCD 12
Greensleeves / Jun '95 / Total/BMG / Jetstar / SRD.

GREETINGS FROM HAWAII
_____ 15184
Laserlight / '91 / Target/BMG.

GREETINGS FROM LUGANO
Amapola / Marina / Amore a Rivabella / Limon Limonero
CD _____ 15447
Laserlight / Jun '92 / Target/BMG.

GRETSCH DRUM NIGHT AT BIRDLAND
Wee dot / Now's the time / Tune up / El Sino / Night in Tunisia
CD _____ CDROU 1057
Roulette / Feb '94 / EMI.

GRINDCORE
CD _____ NB 064CD
Nuclear Blast / Dec '93 / Plastic Head.

GROOVESVILLE COLLECTION
No-one to love: Lewis, Pat / Stone broke: Ward, Sam / Keep a hold on me: Barnes, J.J. / Warning: Inst / Lovin' you all of my time: Debonaires / Watch out: Holidays / Monday to Thursday: Mancha, Steve / Never alone: Ward, Robert / That's why I love you: Inst / Hit and run: Batiste, Rose / Don't be sore at me: Parliaments / That's why I love you (2): Professionals / Did my baby call: Inst / Still in my heart: Mancha, Steve / I've been searchin': Hatchen, Will / Pay back (vocal): Goode, Johnny / I love you forever: Inst
CD _____ GSCD 056
Goldmine / Oct '94 / Vital.

GROOVIN'
(20 soulful summer grooves)
Regulate: Warren G. & Nate Dogg / Summertime: D.J. Jazzy Jeff & The Fresh Prince / Breakadawn: De La Soul / Set adrift on memory bliss: PM Dawn / Back and forth: Aaliyah / Lover: Roberts, Joe / Your body's calling: R. Kelly / I'm in luv: Joe / Long time gone: Galliano / Joy: Soul II Soul / Connected: Stereo MC's / People everyday: Arrested Development / It was a good day: Ice Cube / Brother: Urban Species / Turn on, tune in, cop out: Freak Power / Be thankful for what you've got: Massive Attack / Apparently nothin': Young Disciples / Still a friend of mine: Incognito / There's nothing like this: Omar / Groovin': Tyson
CD _____ 5169682
PolyGram / Aug '94 / PolyGram.

GROOVIN' AT THE GO-GO
Not only the girl knows: Victors / Hurt: Victors / Stay mine for heaven's sake: Holman, Eddie / Eddie's my name: Holman, Eddie / I'll cry 1000 tears: Holman, Eddie / I can't break the habit: Garrett, Lee / One more year: United 4 / It's gonna be a false alarm: Volcanos / Deeper than that: Preludes / Shiggy diggy: Preludes / Groovin' at the Go-Go: 4 larks / She's puttin' you on: United 4 / I still love you: 4 larks / Another chance: 4 larks / Without you baby: Larks / For the love of money: Larks / I surrender: Holman, Eddie / Where I'm not wanted: Holman, Eddie / Hurt (2): Holman, Eddie / She's wanted: Clinton, Larry / Focused on you: Williams, B. / It's needless to say: Williams, B.
CD _____ GSCD 026
Goldmine / Nov '93 / Vital.

GROOVY GHETTO
CD _____ ARC 925602
Arcade / Sep '91 / Sony / Grapevine.

GROOVY GHETTO 2
CD _____ ARC 948102
Arcade / Feb '92 / Sony / Grapevine.

GROOVY REGGAE STARS
(2CD Set)
CD Set _____ 24314
Delta Doubles / Oct '95 / Target/BMG.

GROOVY SHUFFLE
CD _____ CHILLCD 005
Chillout / Nov '95 / Disc / Kudos.

GROOVY SITUATION
CD _____ SLCD 013
Seven Leaves / Mar '94 / Roots Collective / SRD / Greensleeves.

GROUPS OF WRATH, THE
(Songs of the Naked City)
CD _____ DANCD 080
Danceteria / Feb '95 / Plastic Head / ADA.

GRP LIVE AT THE NORTH SEA JAZZ FESTIVAL
Searching, finding: Patitucci, John / When love come to town: King, B.B. / Nothing to lose: Spyro Gyra / Chasin' the trane: Corea, Chick / Real man: Ford, Ron / Curves ahead: Rippingtons / Going home: Burton, Gary
CD _____ GRP 88792
GRP / Aug '95 / BMG / New Note.

GUADELOUPE VOL.1
CD _____ C 560030
Ocora / Jan '93 / Harmonia Mundi / ADA.

GUADELOUPE VOL.2
CD _____ C 560031
Ocora / Jan '93 / Harmonia Mundi / ADA.

GUERILLA IN DUB
Rhythm is life: Lemon Sol / Schmooo/aqualung: Spooky / Alchemy: Drum Club / Oh no: D.O.P. / Dub house disco: 2 Shiny Heads / Intoxication: React 2 Rhythm / Schudefloss: Dr. Atomic / Higher: Code MD / Dub house disco (reprise): 2 Shiny Heads
CD _____ GRCD 011
Guerilla / Jul '94 / Pinnacle.
Pow Wow / May '94 / Jetstar.

GUINEA: RECITS ET EPOPEES
CD _____ C 560009
Ocora / Nov '92 / Harmonia Mundi / ADA.

GUITAR BLUES
CD _____ 12336
Laserlight / May '94 / Target/BMG.

GUITAR EVANGELIST
CD _____ DOCD 5101
Blues Document / Nov '92 / Swift / Jazz Music / Hot Shot.

GUITAR EXPLORATION
CD _____ WKFMXXD 169
FM / Apr '91 / Sony.

GUITAR HEROES
CD Set _____ KBOX 350
Collection / Oct '95 / Target/BMG.

GUITAR MAN
CD _____ NSCD 022
Newsound / May '95 / THE.

GUITAR PARADISE OF EAST AFRICA
Sukuma songa: Sukuma Bin Ongaro / Achi Maria / Mumbi ni wakwa: Kamau, Daniel / Odesia: Les Mangelpa / Wana wanyika: Wanyika, Simba / Mama kamale: Sukuma Bin Ongaro / Shauri yako: Orchestra Super Mazembe / Ndia: Mwambi, Peter / Harare: Les Mangelpa / Ndiretikia ni nii: Famous Nyahururu Boys / Mwendwa Jane: Kilimambogo Brothers
CD _____ CDEWV 21
Earthworks / Oct '90 / EMI / Sterns.

GUITAR ROCK
CD _____ STACD 045
Wisepack / Sep '94 / THE / Conifer.

GUITAR SAMPLER VOL. 2
Momentary change of heart: De Grassi, Alex / Deep at night: De Grassi, Alex / Sunday on the violet sea: Torn, David / Lion of Boaz: Torn, David / Ritual dance: Hedges, Michael / If I needed someone: Hedges, Michael / Selene: Manring, Michael / Red right returning: Manring, Michael / Sweet pea: Andress, Tuck / Betcha by golly wow: Andress, Tuck
CD _____ WD 1106
Windham Hill / Jun '94 / Pinnacle / BMG / ADA.

GUITAR WORKS
Monoghahela: Tingstad, Eric / Barcelona: White, Andy / Hexagram of the heavens: Kolbe, Martin / Light a candle: Ellwood, William / Inner movement: Illenberger, Ralf / Leaving home: Mirowitz, Sheldon / Nocturne: Wynberg, Simon / Maria's watermill: Wynberg, Simon / Sonho (Dream): Lauria, Nando / Since you asked: Mirowitz, Sheldon / Amber: Montfort, Matthew / Remembering greensleeves: Doan, John / By bye lullaby: Kolbe, Martin
CD _____ ND 31032
Narada / Nov '92 / New Note / ADA.

GUITAR WORKSHOP IN L.A.
Take it all / Bawls / Donna / Bull funk / Blues for Ronnie / Skunk blues / Hyper stork / Vicky's song / Beverly Hill / Roppongi
CD _____ JD 3314
JVC / May '89 / New Note.

GUITARES CELTIQUES
CD _____ GR 1190602
Griffe / Nov '95 / Discovery / ADA.

GUITARIST COLLECTION VOL 1, THE
CD _____ BRGCD 011
Music Maker / Aug '94 / Grapevine / ADA.

GUITARIST OF THE YEAR '94
CD _____ CMMR 951
Music Maker / Apr '95 / Grapevine / ADA.

GUITARS THAT RULED THE WORLD
CD _____ CDZORRO 40
Metal Blade / Jul '90 / Pinnacle.

GULF COAST BLUES
Everyday is not the same / Emmitt Lee / Miss too fine / Apron strings / Lonesome saxophone part I / Lonesome saxophone part II / Young girl's got a lot of patience / I work five days a week / I don't want your money / Texas son
CD _____ BT 1055CD
Black Top / Sep '94 / CM / Direct / ADA.

GUMBO STEW
(New Orleans R&B)
Olde wine: Afo executives / I know (You don't love me no more): George, Barbara / Mojo hanna: Lynn, Tammi / Things have changed: Prince La La / Tee na na na na: Bo, Eddie / My key don't fit: Dr. John & Ronnie Barron / Mary: Tick tocks / All for one: Tee, Willie / Private eye: Johnson, Wallace / Pot: Dr. John / Keep on lovin' you: Pistol / Time has expired: Carson, Charles / I'll make a bet: Nookie boy / True love: Lee, Robbie / I found out (You are my cousin): Tee, Willie / Is it too late: Tick tocks / Tell me the truth: Turquinettes / Tuned in, turned on: Robinson, Alvin / Give her up: Robinson, Alvin / Ignat: Lastie, Melvin & Harold Battiste/Cornell Dupree / Empty talk: Robinson, Alvin / I shall not be moved: Pastor
CD _____ CDCHD 450
Ace / Apr '93 / Pinnacle / Cadillac / Complete/Pinnacle.

GUN COURT DUB VOL.1
CD _____ SBCD 002
Soul Beat / Aug '94 / Jetstar.

GUN COURT DUB VOL.2
CD _____ SBCD 008
Soul Beat / May '95 / Jetstar.

GUN SHOT LICKS
CD _____ RNCD 2069
Rhino / Jul '94 / Jetstar / Magnum Music Group / THE.

GUTBUCKET
Gimme dat harp boy: Captain Beefheart & His Magic Band / The wall: Hapshash & The Coloured Coat / You're gonna miss me: Hopkins, Lightnin' / I'm tore down: Korner, Alexis / Still a fool: Groundhogs / Dismal swamp: Nitty Gritty Dirt Band / Wine, women and whiskey: Lightfoot, Papa George / Pony blues: Canned Heat / Down in Texas: Hour Glass, The / No more dogin': McPhee, Tony / Can blue men sing the whites: Bonzo Dog Band / Mama don't like me runnin' round: Williams, Big Joe / Rollin' and tumblin': Kelly, Jo Ann / Got love if you want it: Winter, Johnny / Preparation G: T.I.M.E. / Walking down their outlook: High Tide / Oh death: Kelly, Jo Ann & Tony McPhee / Don't mean a thing: Kelly, Jo Ann & Tony McPhee / Mistreated: Groundhogs / Sic 'em pigs: Canned Heat / Hard headed woman: Fernbach, Andy / T.B. blues: McKenna Mendelson Mainline / Hurry up John: Idle Race / To need: Marvin, Brett & The Thunderbolts / Leavin' my home: T.I.M.E.
CD _____ CZ 540
EMI / Sep '94 / EMI.

GYPSY PASSIONS: THE FLAMENCO GUITAR
CD _____ LYRCD 7399
Lyrichord / '91 / Roots / ADA / CM.

GYPSY SONGS AND MUSIC
CD _____ CDCH 295
Milan / Feb '91 / BMG / Silva Screen.

H

H.I.M. DUB CHAPTER 1
CD _____ SZCD 002
Surr Zema Musik / Mar '94 / Jetstar.

HACIENDA COLLECTION, THE
(2CD/MC/3LP Set)
Voices inside my head: Police / Satisfied: H2O & Billie / Love come rescue me: Lovestation / Freedom: Shiva / About you: Loose & Yolanda Reynolds / Feel the spirit: Giant City / Love shine: Rhythm Source / Sweetest day of May: Vannelli, Joe T. Project / My love: Kellee / Renegade master: Wildchild / Stand up: Love Tribe / Color of my skin: Swing 52 / Weekend: Terry, Todd Project / We can make it: Mone / There will come a day: Absolute Us / I believe in you: Yojo Working / Feel like singing: Taktix / I know a place: English, Kim / I can't get no sleep: Masters At Work / Forever: Key To Life / Happy days: Sweet Mercy / Look ahead: Tenaglia, Danny / Serious situation: Nuff Sisters / 1963: New Order / Hideaway: De'Lacy / This time baby: Pandella
CD _____ 5404412
A&M / Oct '95 / PolyGram.

HADRA OF THE GNAWA OF ESSAOUIRA
CD _____ C 560006
Ocora / Mar '93 / Harmonia Mundi / ADA.

HAILE SELASSIE CENTENARY DUB 2
CD _____ S 200002
Surr Zema Musik / Apr '94 / Jetstar.

HAITI RAP & RAGGA
CD _____ 3192
Declic / Apr '95 / Jetstar.

HALF CENTURY OF RCA
CD Set _____ 07863660642
RCA / Dec '92 / BMG.

HALLELUJAH
CD _____ AVC 528
Avid / Nov '93 / Avid/BMG / Koch.

HAMBURG STRIKES BACK
CD _____ HY 21034CD
Hypertension / Nov '92 / Total/BMG / Direct / ADA.

HAMMER DOWN
(20 Driving Classics)
Workin' at the car wash blues: Croce, Jim / Long legged woman dressed in black: Mungo Jerry / Roadrunner: Diddley, Bo / All day and all of the night: Kinks / Kentucky sundown: Tennessee / Why do you love: Juicy Lucy / Mean girl: Status Quo / You don't mess around with Jim: Croce, Jim / Freightloader: Clapton, Eric & Jimmy Page / Bad, Bad Leroy Brown: Croce, Jim / This flight tonight: Nazareth / It's a heartache: Tyler, Bonnie / Car 67: Driver 67 / Race with the devil: Girlschool / Born to be wild: Blue Oyster Cult / Roadrunner twice: Richman, Jonathan / Spinning wheel blues: Status Quo / Snake drive: Clapton, Eric & The Immediate All-Stars / Eye of the tiger: Nighthawks / Blues for dancers: Hooker, Earl
CD _____ TRTCD 123
TrueTrax / Oct '94 / THE.

HAMMOND STYLE SINGALONG
CD _____ SWBCD 206
Sound Waves / Oct '95 / Target/BMG.

HAND PICKED
(25 Years Of Rounder Bluegrass)
CD _____ ROUCDAN 22
Rounder / Nov '95 / CM / Direct / ADA / Cadillac.

HANDFUL OF KEYS
(13 Great Jazz Pianists)
Monday date: Hines, Earl / I ain't got nobody: Hines, Earl / Black beauty: Ellington, Duke / Swampy river: Ellington, Duke / Don't blame me: Wilson, Teddy / Every now and then: Wilson, Teddy / Honky tonk train blues: Lewis, Meade Lux / Shout for joy: Ammons, Albert / How long blues: Basie, Count / Dirty dozens: Basie, Count / Between sets: Kyle, Billy / Finishing up a date: Kyle, Billy / Handful of keys: Waller, Fats / Numb fumblin': Waller, Fats / Overland: Williams, Mary Lou / Pearls: Williams, Mary Lou / Gin mill blues: Sullivan, Joe / Onyx bringdown: Sullivan, Joe / In a mist: Beiderbecke, Bix / In the dark: Stacy, Jess / Flashes barrelhouse: Stacy, Jess / World is waiting for the sunrise: Stacy, Jess / Gone with the wind: Tatum, Art / Stormy weather: Tatum, Art
CD _____ CDAJA 5073
Living Era / Sep '90 / Koch.

HANG ELEVEN (MUTANT SURF PUNKS)
I want my woody back: Barracudas / Who stole the summer: Surfin' Lungs / 308: Malibooz / Herman's new woody: Palominos / Fun at the beach: B Girls / Gas money: Lloyd, Bobby & The Windfall Prophets / Pipeline: Agent Orange / Tuff little surfer boy: Trash & Beauty / Girls cars girls sun girls surf girls fun girls: Corvettes / Automobile: Sticks'n'fits / Day they raised the Thames barrier: Beach Bums / Shotgun: Beach Coma / Surfin' CIA: Buzz & The B-Days / Mighty morris ten: Episode Six / Depth charge: Jon & The Nightriders
CD _____ CDGRAM 23
Cherry Red / May '95 / Pinnacle.

HAPPY ALBUM 2
CD _____ CDTOT 34
Jumpin' & Pumpin' / Oct '95 / 3MV / Sony.

HAPPY ANTHEMS VOL.1
CD _____ CDRAID 520
Rumour / Oct '94 / Pinnacle / 3MV / Sony.

HAPPY ANTHEMS VOL.2
CD _____ CDRAID 522
Rumour / Mar '95 / Pinnacle / 3MV / Sony.

HAPPY ANTHEMS VOL.3
CD _____ CDRAID 526
Rumour / Oct '95 / Pinnacle / 3MV / Sony.

HAPPY BIRTHDAY BABY JESUS
(2CD Set)
CD Set _____ SFTRI 1396CD
Sympathy For The Record Industry / Nov '95 / Plastic Head.

HAPPY BIRTHDAY ROCK'N'ROLL
Shake, rattle and roll: Haley, Bill & The Comets / That'll be the day: Holly, Buddy & The Crickets / Maybellene: Berry, Chuck / At the hop: Danny & The Juniors / Bo Diddley: Diddley, Bo / Stagger Lee: Price, Lloyd / When: Kalin Twins / Nothing shaking (but the leaves on the trees): Fontaine, Eddie / Rock 'n' roll music: Berry, Chuck / Sheila: Roe, Tommy / Book of love: Monotones / Wander: Keller, Jerry / Sum dum: Lee, Brenda / Young love: Hunter, Tab / (We're gonna) rock around the clock: Haley, Bill & The Comets / Wipeout: Surfaris / I'm gonna sit right down and write myself a letter: Williams, Billy / Personality: Price, Lloyd / Sealed with a kiss: Hyland, Brian / Peggy Sue: Holly, Buddy / Suzie Q: Hawkins, Dale / Come go with me: Del-Vikings / Rock 'n' roll is here to stay: Danny & The Juniors / No particular place to go: Berry, Chuck /

Let's jump the broomstick: *Lee, Brenda* / See you later alligator: *Haley, Bill & The Comets* / Peggy Sue got married: *Crickets*
CD _____ MCLD 19261
MCA / Nov '94 / BMG.

HAPPY DAYS
CD _____ DSPCD 112
Disky / Sep '94 / THE / BMG / Discovery / Pinnacle.

HAPPY DAZE VOL.2
There she goes: *La's* / Box set go: *High* / All on you (perfume): *Paris Angels* / Wonderment / Wagon: *Dinosaur Jnr* / Godlike / Falling on a bruise: *Carter U.S.M.* / Sweetness and light: *Lush* / Something's got to give: *Spooky* / She's all the world: *Top* / Window pane: *Real People* / Pearl / Close to me: *Cure*
CD _____ CIDTV 3
Island / Apr '91 / PolyGram.

HAPPY HARDCORE FEVER
CD _____ TROOPHTCD 16
Happy Trax / Jul '95 / SRD.

HAPPY HARDCORE VOL.1
Breakin' free: *Slipmatt* / Visions of light: *Higher Level* / Don't beg 4 love: *Jack 'n' Phil* / Ronnie's revenge (remix): *Citadel of Kaos* / Kounter attack: *Druid & Vinyl Groover* / Rhythm: *Just Another Artist* / Drop the bass: *D.J. Seduction* / Positive: *Love Nation* / Piano progression (mix): *Luna-C* / In complete darkness: *Fat Controller* / Take me away (Remix): *Jimmy J & Cru-L-T* / Let's do it: *D.J. Red Alert & Mike Slammer*
CD _____ CDTOT 18
Jumpin' & Pumpin' / Oct '94 / 3MV / Sony.

HAPPY HARDCORE VOL.2
Make it ruff: *D.J. Brisk* / Play the theme: *Sy & Unknown* / Feel so real: *D.J. Red Alert & Mike Slammer* / Better day: *D.J. Seduction & Dougal* / Hold me in your arms: *Storm* / Feels good: *Urban Shakedown* / Movin': *Justin Time* / Burn baby burn: *Sensitize* / Summer vibe: *D.E.A.* / Lust: *Just Another Artist* / Slave to the rave: *Love Nation* / Lift me up: *Future Primitive*
CD _____ CDTOT 22
Jumpin' & Pumpin' / Jan '95 / 3MV / Sony.

HAPPY HARDCORE VOL.3
Jumpin' & Pumpin' / Jun '95 / 3MV / Sony.
CD _____ CDTOT 30

HAPPY MAIO FAMILY, A
(Dance & Song From SW China)
CD _____ PANCD 2023
Pan / Aug '94 / ADA / Direct / CM.

HAPPY TOGETHER
CD _____ TRTCD 158
TrueTrax / Feb '96 / THE.

HARD & HEAVY
CD _____ CDSR 054
Telstar / Feb '95 / BMG.

HARD AS HELL 3
CD _____ MODEF 3CD
Music Of Life / May '88 / Grapevine.

HARD AS HELL VOL 4
CD _____ MODEF 4CD
Music Of Life / Dec '90 / Grapevine.

HARD CELL
CD _____ MAUCD 622
Mau Mau / Aug '92 / Pinnacle.

HARD HOP AND TRYPNO
██ _____ MM 999110
Moonshine / Feb '96 / Disc.

HARD LEADERS 3
CD _____ KICKCD 7
Kickin' / Oct '93 / SRD.

HARD LEADERS 7: JUNGLE DUB 3
CD Set _____ KICKCD 23
Kickin' / May '95 / SRD.

HARD LEADERS VOL IV
CD _____ KICKCD 8
Kickin' / Apr '94 / SRD.

HARD ROCK
Spirit of radio: *Rush* / You ain't seen nothin' yet: *Bachman-Turner Overdrive* / Come on Eileen: *Dexy's Midnight Runners & Emerald Express* / Final countdown: *Europe* / Living after midnight: *Judas Priest* / Pretty in pink: *Psychedelic Furs* / Paranoid: *Black Sabbath* / Bat out of hell: *Meat Loaf* / Down your Status Quo / Bark at the moon: *Osbourne, Ozzy* / Cum on feel the noize: *Quiet Riot* / Skin deep: *Stranglers* / Ace of spades: *Motorhead* / Gypsy: *Uriah Heep* / Start talking love: *Magnum* / St. Elmo's fire: *Parr, John* / Rock 'n' roll children: *Dio* / Silver machine: *Hawkwind*
CD _____ STACD 003
Wisepack / Oct '91 / THE / Conifer.

HARD ROCK
Tower of strength: *Mission* / St. Elmo's fire: *Parr, John* / Eye of the tiger: *Survivor* / Stone cold: *Rainbow* / Losing my grip: *Samson* / I didn't know I loved you (till I saw you rock 'n' roll): *Rock Goddess* / Whatever you want: *Status Quo* / Epic: *Faith No More* / Bastille day: *Rush* / Mystery: *Dio* / It's all over now baby blue: *Bonnet, Graham* / Perfect strangers: *Deep Purple* / Central park

arrest: *Thunderthighs* / Get it on: *Kingdom Come*
CD _____ 5506492
Spectrum/Karussell / Aug '94 / PolyGram / THE.

HARD STEP DRUM AND BASS VOL.1
Regulators remix: *Marvellous Caine* / International: *Eskubar* / Boogie down: *Marvellous Caine* / Heroes welcome: *Dextrous & T-Bone* / Bump 'n' bounce: *T.Bones* / Da bass 11 dark: *Asylum* / This is L.A: *Lemon D* / Sample and hold: *Pyskus* / Get on the mike: *Eskubar* / Beyond all reasonable doubt: *Keith, Ray* / Jazz and all dat: *Eskubar* / Lighter: *Keith, Ray* / Babylon remix 2 (CD/MC): *D.J. Trace* / Selectors roll V.I.P. (CD/MC): *Tom & Jerry* / Step pon dub (CD/MC): *Faze 1 FM* / She's so revisited: *Neal Trix & D.J. Apollo* / Jungle blanca (CD/MC): *Faze 1 FM* / So this is love (CD/MC): *Essence Of Aura*
CD _____ STORM 1 CD
Desert Storm / Jan '96 / Sony.

HARD TECHNO CLASSIC FROM DEEPEST GERMANY
Phasematic: *Colone* / Disturancing: *X-Ray* / Nervous acid: *Nervous Project* / Hidden: *4D* / Crush: *Colone* / Jumping golliwogs: *Integrated Circuits* / Moby tits: *Cellblock X* / Art mechanique: *Sectral Emotions* / Yip: *Integrated Circuits* / Foible: *4D* / Caffeine rush: *S.D.L.* / God assists: *Integrated Circuits*
CD _____ LABUKCD 1
Labworks / Mar '94 / SRD / Disc.

HARD TECHNO CLASSICS VOL.2
CD _____ UNDLAB 24CD
Labworks / May '95 / SRD / Disc.

HARD TIMES AND HEARTACHES
Preachin' blues: *Johnson, Robert* / Long tall Mama: *Broonzy, Big Bill* / Ain't it a cryin' shame: *Fuller, Blind Boy* / Packin' trunk: *Leadbelly* / Dark was the night: *Johnson, Blind Willie* / Denver blues: *Tampa Red* / Bukka's jitterbug swing: *White, Bukka* / Southern can is mine: *McTell, Blind Willie* / Steppin' on the blues: *Johnson, Lonnie* / Goodbye now: *McGhee, Brownie* / St. Louis blues: *Smith, Bessie* / Hurry down sunshine: *Dupree, Champion Jack* / Death letter: *House, Son* / I can't be satisfied: *Waters, Muddy* / Dust my broom: *Taj Mahal* / Stateboro blues: *Rising Sons*
CD _____ 476683 2
Columbia / May '94 / Sony.

HARD TRANCE AND PSYCHEDELIC TECHNO
CD _____ PTM 129
Phantasm / Feb '95 / Vital/SAM / Plastic Head.

HARD TRANCE AND PSYCHEDELIC TECHNO VOL II
CD _____ PTM 130CD
Phantasm / Feb '95 / Vital/SAM / Plastic Head.

HARD TRANCE CLASSICS FROM DEEPEST GERMANY VOL 1
CD _____ LABUKCD 2
Labworks / Apr '94 / SRD / Disc.

HARD TRANCE CLASSICS FROM DEEPEST GERMANY VOL.2
CD _____ UNDLABCD 025
Labworks / May '95 / SRD / Disc.

HARD TRANCE CLASSICS FROM DEEPEST GERMANY VOL.3
CD _____ UBMLABCD 12
Labworks / Dec '95 / SRD / Disc.

HARDBEATS AND SOFT DRINKS
CD _____ OZONCD 25
Ozone / Apr '92 / SRD.

HARDCORE - LEADERS OF THE NEW SCHOOL
CD _____ KICKCD 4
Kickin' / Nov '92 / SRD.

HARDCORE - LEADERS VOL 2
CD _____ KICKCD 5
Kickin' / Mar '93 / SRD.

HARDCORE - LEADERS VOL 5
(Jungle dub)
CD _____ KICKCD 12
Kickin' / Aug '94 / SRD.

HARDCORE ALLIANCE
CD _____ STAGE 1CD
Stage One / Nov '95 / Pinnacle.

HARDCORE CHEDDAR
(Dutch Masters)
CD _____ CDRAID 527
Rumour / Oct '95 / Pinnacle / 3MV / Sony.

HARDCORE CLASSICS
CD _____ CCSCD 378
Castle / Sep '93 / BMG.

HARDCORE DOO-WOP
(In The Hallway - Under The Street Lamp)
Wheel of fortune: *Four Flames* / Dream girl: *Jesse & Marvin* / Nite owl: *Allen, Tony & The Champs* / Oooh-Rooba-Lee: *Maye, Arthur Lee & The Crowns* / Where's my girl: *Belvin, Jesse / I: Allen, Tony & The Champs* / Sweet breeze: *Green, Vernon & The Phantoms* / Check yourself baby: *Allen, Tony & The Chimes* / Foot loose and fancy free: *Gipson, Byron 'Slick' & The Sliders* / Gloria: *Maye, Arthur Lee & The Crowns* / Especially: *Allen, Tony & The Chimes* / Baby need (ting-a-ling): *Zeppa, Ben Joe & The Zephyrs* / Old willow tree: *Green, Vernon & The Phantoms* / Cool loving: *Maye, Arthur Lee & The Crowns* / Pretty little girl: *Chimes* / How long: *Church, Eugene* / Malinda: *Mandolph, Bobby* / Hold me tight: *Jaguars* / Don't you know: *Maye, Arthur Lee & The Crowns* / Never let you go: *Ambers & Ralph Mathis* / Open up your heart: *Church, Eugene* / Mine all mine: *Jaguars* / Guardian angel: *Selections* / Soft and sweet: *Selections*
CD _____ CDCHD 514
Ace / Jan '94 / Pinnacle / Cadillac / Complete/Pinnacle.

HARDCORE ECSTASY
CD _____ DINCD 29
Dino / Nov '91 / Pinnacle / 3MV.

HARDCORE FOR THE MASSES VOL.2
CD _____ BHR 101
Burning Heart / Oct '94 / Plastic Head.

HARDCORE HAPPINESS
CD _____ J4U 001CD
Just 4 U / Mar '95 / SRD.

HARDCORE HOLOCAUST 2
CD _____ SFRCD 113
Strange Fruit / '90 / Pinnacle.

HARDCORE JUNGLIST FEVER VOL. 1
CD _____ STHCCD 6
Strictly Underground / Aug '94 / SRD.

HARDCORE JUNGLIST FEVER VOL. 2
CD _____ STHCCD 7
Strictly Underground / Aug '94 / SRD.

HARDCORE MASSIVE 1
CD _____ TROOPCD 14
Rogue Trooper / Jul '95 / SRD.

HARDCORE RAGGAMUFFIN
CD _____ GRELCD 151
Greensleeves / Nov '90 / Total/BMG / Jetstar / SRD.

HARDCORE UPROAR
CD _____ DINCD 20
Dino / Mar '91 / Pinnacle / 3MV.

HARDCORE VOL.2
CD _____ LOWCDX 46
Low Price Music / Aug '95 / Total/BMG.

HARDER THAN THE REST
Signe says: *Killout Trash* / Deutschland: *ATR* / We need a chance: *EC8TOR* / Suicide: *Empire, Alec* / Sweat shizuo: *Shizuo* / Turntable terrorist: *Sonic Subjunkies* / Nizza: *Hanin* / Deaf dumb and blind: *D.J. Bleed* / Into the death: *Atari Teenage Riot* / Straight outta Berlin: *Killout Trash* / Discriminate: *ES8TOR* / Central industrial: *Sonic Subjunkies* / Smash him to grapoon: *EC8TOR & Moonraker* / Anarchy: *Shizuo* / Destroyer pt.2: *Empire, Alec*
CD _____ DHRCD 002
Digital Hardcore / Oct '95 / Vital.

HARDWARE 2
CD _____ HARD 2
PSY Harmonics / Sep '95 / Plastic Head.

HARLEM BIG BANDS 1925-31
Don't forget you'll regret day by day: *Johnson, Charlie & His Paradise Orchestra* / Meddlin' with the blues: *Johnson, Charlie & His Paradise Orchestra* / Paradise wobble: *Johnson, Charlie Paradise Ten* / Birmingham black bottom: *Johnson, Charlie Paradise Ten* / Don't leave me here: *Johnson, Charlie Paradise Ten* / Charleston is the best dance of all: *Johnson, Charlie Paradise Ten* / Hot tempered blues: *Johnson, Charlie Paradise Ten* / Boy in the boat: *Johnson, Charlie Paradise Ten* / Walk that thing: *Johnson, Charlie & His Paradise Orchestra* / Hot bones and rice: *Johnson, Charlie & His Paradise Orchestra* / Harlem shuffle: *Scott, Lloyd & his orchestra* / Symphonic screech: *Scott, Lloyd & his orchestra* / Happy hour blues: *Scott, Lloyd & his orchestra* / Lawd, lawd: *Scott, Cecil & his Bright Boys* / In a corner: *Scott, Cecil & his Bright Boys* / Bright boy blues: *Scott, Cecil & his Bright Boys* / Springfield stomp: *Scott, Cecil & his Bright Boys* (I'll be glad when you're dead) you rascal you: *Russell, Luis & His Orchestra* / Goin' to town: *Russell, Luis & His Orchestra* / Say the word: *Russell, Luis & His Orchestra* / Freakish blues: *Russell, Luis & His Orchestra* / I've found a new baby: *Preer, Andy & The Cotton Club Orchestra*
CD _____ CBC 1010

Timeless Historical / Aug '94 / New Note / Pinnacle.

HARLEM COMES TO LONDON
Silver rose: *Plantation Orchestra* / Arabella's wedding day: *Plantation Orchestra* / Smilin' Joe: *Plantation Orchestra* / For baby and me: *Plantation Orchestra* / Camp meeting day: *Sissle Noble & his Orchestra* / Sophisticated lady: *Ellington, Duke Orchestra* / Ike: *Ellington, Duke Orchestra* / Dinah: *Hatch & his Harlem Stompers* / Some of these days: *Hatch & his Harlem Stompers* / I can't dance / A must have that man: *Valaida* / Keep a twinkle in your eye: *Nicholas Brothers* / Your heart and mine: *Nicholas Brothers* / Dixie isn't Dixie any more: *Carter, Lavaida* / Jo Jo the cannibal kid: *Carter, Lavaida* / Breakfast in Harlem: *Buck & Bubbles* / I ain't got nobody: *Buck & Bubbles* / Sweet Georgia Brown: *Buck & Bubbles* / Harlem in my heart: *Welch, Elisabeth* / Ain't misbehavin': *Waller, Fats & His Continental Rhythm* / I can't give you anything but love
CD _____ DRGCD 8444
DRG / Sep '93 / New Note.

HARLEM JOYS
Riffs: *Johnson, James P.* / Handful of keys: *Waller, Fats* / Ain't misbehavin': *Armstrong, Louis* / New call of the freaks: *Russell, Luis* / Horse feathers: *Jackson, Cliff* / Jungle nights in Harlem: *Ellington, Duke* / Stop crying: *Oliver, King* / Sugarfoot stomp: *Henderson, Fletcher* / Trickeration: *Calloway, Cab* / Hot and anxious: *Redman, Don* / Strange as it seems: *Hall, Adelaide* / Swing it: *Carter, Benny* / Harlem joys: *Smith, Willie 'The Lion'* / I cried for you: *Holiday, Billie* / Brittwood stomp: *Newton, Frankie* / Church street sobbin' blues: *Hopkins, Claude* / King Porter stomp: *Hill, Teddy* / Jammin' for the jackpot: *Milinder, Lucky & Mills Blue Rhythm Band* / Time out: *Basie, Count* / Harlem congo: *Webb, Chick* / In the mood: *Hayes, Edgar* / Miss Annabella Brown: *Hawkins, Erskine* / Honey in the bee ball: *Jordan, Louis* / Tea for two: *Profit, Clarence* / Uptown blues: *Lunceford, Jimmie*
CD _____ CDMOIR 507
Memoir / Apr '94 / Target/BMG.

HARLEM SHUFFLE
(Charly R&B Masters Vol. 18)
Gimme little star: *Wood, Brenton* / Dancin' holiday: *Olympics* / Love makes the world go round: *Jackson, Deon* / Spring: *Birdlegs & Pauline* / Expressway to your heart: *Soul Survivors* / Ooh wee baby: *Hughes, Freddie* / Baby, I'm yours: *Lewis, Barbara* / Count Harlem: *Capitols* / Get on up: *Esquires* / And get away: *Esquires* / Duck: *Lee, Jackie* / I know: *George, Barbara* / Snake: *Wilson, Al* / Harlem shuffle: *Bob & Earl* / Hello stranger: *Lewis, Barbara* / Oh how happy: *Shades Of Blue* / Oogum boogum song: *Wood, Brenton* / Bounce: *Olympics* / Backfield in motion: *Mel & Tim* / Make me your baby / You can make it if you try
CD _____ CDRB 18
Charly / Mar '95 / Charly / THE / Cadillac.

HARLEMANIA
CD _____ AVM 532
Avid / May '94 / Avid/BMG / Koch.

HARMONICA BLUES 1927-1941
(2CD Set)
CD Set _____ FA 040
Fremeaux / Nov '95 / Discovery / ADA.

HARMONICA BLUES OF THE 1920S AND 1930S
CD _____ YAZCD 1053
Yazoo / Apr '91 / GM / ADA / Roots / Koch.

HARMONY AND INTERPLAY
CD _____ ELL 3210B
Ellipsis Arts / Oct '93 / Direct / ADA.

HARP BLOWERS 1926-29
CD _____ DOCD 5164
Blues Document / May '93 / Swift / Jazz Music / Hot Shot.

HARPS OF THE WORLD
CD _____ PS 66004CD
Playasound / Jul '95 / Harmonia Mundi / ADA.

HARTHOUSE COMPILATION CHAPTER 1
(The Point Of No Return)
Quicksand: *Spice Lab* / Spectrum: *Metal Master* / M.Z. 5: *Zaffarano, Marco* / Acperience 1: *Hardfloor* / Tribal groovy heartbeat: *Overboust* / Freedom of expression: *Arpeggiators* / Spicecowboy: *Spice Lab* / It's so simple to do: *Pulsation* / Butch: *Futurhythm* / Amorph: *Spice Lab* / Xenophobe: *Arpeggiators* / M.Z. 2: *Zaffarano, Marco* / Pulsar: *Pulsation*
CD _____ 4509918902
Harthouse / Jun '93 / Disc / Warner Music.

HARTHOUSE COMPILATION CHAPTER 2
(Dedicated To The Omen)
Clapconfusion: *Zaffarano, Marco* / Spirit of fear: *Spice Lab* / Astralis: *Frankfurt/Tokyo Connection* / Adventure of dama: *Cyberdelics* / Mikado: *Pulse* / X-plain the unexplained: *Arpeggiators* / Human: Resistance D / Mecon: *Aurin* / Multiplex: *Aurin* / Secrets of love: *Progressive Attack* / Schneller pfeil: *Curare*

CD _____ 4500942612
Harthouse / Dec '93 / Disc / Warner Music.

HARTHOUSE COMPILATION CHAPTER 3
(Axis Of Vision)
CD _____ 4509963292
Harthouse / Jun '94 / Disc / Warner Music.

HARTHOUSE COMPILATION CHAPTER 4
(Global Virus)
CD _____ 4509982572
Harthouse / Nov '94 / Disc / Warner Music.

HARVEST STORM
CD _____ TUT 727493
Wundertute / Jan '94 / CM / Duncans / ADA.

HAUNTED HOUSE PARTY
CD _____ JCD 623
Jass / Dec '87 / CM / Jazz Music / ADA / Cadillac / Direct.

HAVANA CUBA BOYS VOL. 1
CD _____ HQCD 48
Harlequin / Jan '95 / Swift / Jazz Music / Wellard / Hot Shot / Cadillac.

HAVE A WONDERFUL CHRISTMAS
CD _____ CNCD 5955
Disky / Dec '93 / THE / BMG / Discovery / Pinnacle.

HAVE I TOLD YOU LATELY THAT I LOVE YOU
CD _____ 295732
Ariola Express / May '92 / BMG.

HAVE YOURSELF A SOULFUL CHRISTMAS
CD _____ CPCD 8145
Charly / Nov '95 / Charly / THE / Cadillac.

HAVIN' IT IN IBIZA
CD _____ HAVINCD 001
21st Century Opera / Dec '94 / Total/‑ BMG.

HAVIN' IT IN IBIZA VOL.2
CD _____ HAVINCD 002
21st Century Opera / Oct '95 / Total/BMG.

HAVIN' IT IN THE UK
CD _____ HAVINCD 002
21st Century Opera / Mar '95 / Total/ BMG.

HAVIN' IT IN THE UK VOL.2
CD _____ HAVINCD 005
21st Century Opera / Sep '95 / Total/ BMG.

HAVIN' IT STATESIDE VOL.1
CD _____ HAVINCD 004
21st Century Opera / Jun '95 / Total/BMG.

HAVIN' IT STATESIDE VOL.2
CD _____ HAVINCD 006
21st Century Opera / Jan '96 / Total/BMG.

HAVIN' IT... DANCE FLOOR CLASSICS VOL.1
(Judge Jules Remixes)
CD _____ HAVINCD 003
21st Century Opera / May '95 / Total/ BMG.

HAVIN' IT... DANCE FLOOR CLASSICS VOL.2
CD _____ HAVINCD 007
21st Century Opera / Dec '95 / Total/ BMG.

HAWAIIAN DRUM DANCE CHANTS
(Sounds Of Power In Time)
CD _____ SFWCD 40015
Smithsonian Folkways / May '95 / ADA / Direct / Koch / CM / Cadillac.

HAWAIIAN STEEL GUITAR CLASSICS
CD _____ FL 7027
Folklyric / Apr '95 / Direct / Cadillac.

HEADZ
(2CD/3LP Set)
Freedom now: _Patterson_ / Contemplating jazz: _Attica Blues_ / Symmetrical jazz: _Awunsound_ / Stars: _Nightmares On Wax_ / Ravers suck our sound: _Le Funk Mob_ / Miles out of time: _M.F. Outa National_ / Inside: _R.P.M._ / Lowride: _Autochre_ / Wildstyle - The krush handshake: _Olde Scottish_ / Lost and found (S.F.L.): _D.J. Shadow_ / Destroy all monsters: _Skull_ / Don't take it: _Sallahr, Deflon_ / 2000: _R.P.M._ / Slipper suite: _Palm Skin Productions_ / Jeremy's velvet slippers: _Palm Skin Productions_ / Moonraker: _Palm Skin Productions_ / Unspeakeable acts: _Palm Skin Productions_ / Time has come: _U.N.K.L.E. Vs The Major Force Ems Orchestra_ / Head west - gun fight at O.K. Corral: _Howie B_ / They come in peace: _Tranquility Bass_ / In flux: _D.J. Shadow_
CD Set _____ MW 026CD
Mo Wax / Oct '94 / Vital.

HEALER'S BREW
Blessing ceremony / Marimba song / Mamgobhozi - a woman's name / Healers brew / Amen / Bazophumula abangkwele / Mangibe nawe baba / Djembe amam / Togetherness
CD _____ BW 077
B&W / Oct '95 / New Note.

HEART & SOUL OF ROCK & ROLL, THE
CD _____ TCD 2351
Telstar / Oct '88 / BMG.

HEART AND SOUL III
(Heart Full Of Soul)
Sign your name: _D'Arby, Terence Trent_ / Easy: _Commodores_ / Love don't live here anymore: _Rose Royce_ / Private dancer: _Turner, Tina_ / I live for your love: _Cole, Natalie_ / Tracks of my tears: _Robinson, Smokey & The Miracles_ / Respect: _Franklin, Aretha_ / Lovers: _O'Neal, Alexander_ / Come into my life: _Sims, Joyce_ / Papa was a rollin' stone: _Temptations_ / My girl: _Redding, Otis_ / When a man loves a woman: _Sledge, Percy_ / Tired of being alone: _Green, Al_ / Touch me in the morning: _Ross, Diana_ / My cherie amour: _Wonder, Stevie_ / Farewell my summer love: _Jackson, Michael_ / Way we were: _Knight, Gladys_ / Loving you: _Riperton, Minnie_
CD _____ 8450092
Polystar / Jul '90 / PolyGram.

HEART OF AMERICA
CD _____ RENCD 105
Castle / Jul '95 / BMG.

HEART OF ARGENTINIAN TANGO, THE
Taquito militar / Romance de barrio / Los mareados / El dia que me quieras / Corrientera / Caseron de tejas / Niebla de reachuelo / Fuimos / Elegie / El portenito / La cumparsita
CD _____ PV 795052
Disques Pierre Verany / Jul '95 / Kingdom.

HEART OF ROCK
Brilliant disguise: _Springsteen, Bruce_ / C'est la vie: _Nevil, Robbie_ / I didn't mean to turn you on: _Palmer, Robert_ / Touch of grey: _Grateful Dead_ / Solitude standing: _Vega, Suzanne_ / Way it is: _Hornsby, Bruce_ / Should've known better: _Marx, Richard_ / Modern woman: _Joel, Billy_ / Nothing's gonna stop us now: _Starship_ / Final countdown: _Europe_
CD _____ NTRCD 002
Nectar / Jun '93 / Pinnacle.

HEART OF ROCK 'N' ROLL, THE
Born to be wild: _Steppenwolf_ / All night long: _Rainbow_ / Ace of spades: _Rainbow_ / Boys are back in town: _Thin Lizzy_ / Spirit of radio: _Rush_ / Milk and alcohol: _Dr. Feelgood_ / Something better change: _Stranglers_ / Who do you love: _Thorogood, George & The Destroyers_ / Mony Mony: _James, Tommy & The Shondells_ / Rebel yell: _Idol, Billy_ / Heart of rock and roll: _Lewis, Huey & The News_ / Natural born boogie: _Humble Pie_ / Down down: _Status Quo_ / I hear you knocking: _Edmunds, Dave_ / Wild thing: _Troggs_ / Free me: _Daltrey, Roger_ / You ain't seen nothin' yet: _Bachman-Turner Overdrive_ / Out demons out: _Broughton, Edgar Band_ / Smoke on the water: _Deep Purple_ / Freebird (Live): _Lynyrd Skynyrd_
CD _____ CDPR 109
Premier/MFP / May '93 / EMI.

HEART OF SOUTHERN SOUL, THE
Falling in love again: _Kelly Brothers_ / You're that great big feelin': _Kelly Brothers_ / That's all I can do: _Anderson, Kip_ / Snake out of the grass (part 1): _Anderson, Roshell_ / Snake out of the grass (part 2): _Anderson, Roshell_ / Soldier's sad story: _Watkins, Tiny_ / Pretty little thing: _Anderson, Roshell_ / Johnny / Talk to me: _Avons_ / Your love's so good: _Webber, Lee_ / Somewhere out there: _Matthis, Lucille_ / Mr. Fortune teller: _Dee & Don_ / Midnight tears: _Watkins, Tiny_ / Woman in me: _Mariann_ / Steppin' stone: _Wallace Brothers_ / Gonna need somebody: _Lane, Stacy_ / I went off and cried: _Anderson, Kip_ / You'll never know: _Brown, Shirley_ / C.C. rider: _Powell, Bobby_ / Price is too high: _Harpo, Slim_ / There goes a girl: _Truitt, Johnny_ / Do your thing: _Whitney, Marva_ / Power is good: _Kemp, Eugene_
CD _____ CDCHD 568
Ace / Sep '94 / Pinnacle / Cadillac / Complete/Pinnacle.

HEART OF THE ARK II
CD _____ RRCD 003
Roots Collective / Jun '93 / SRD / Jetstar / Roots Collective.

HEART OF THE GAELS
CD _____ GLCD 0105
Green Linnet / Jun '88 / Roots / CM / Direct / ADA.

HEART OF THE LION
CD _____ IR 022CD
Iona / Mar '94 / ADA / Direct / Duncans.

HEARTACHES
(20 Songs Of Love)
No more the fool: _Brooks, Elkie_ / Let the heartaches begin: _Baldry, Long John_ / I don't believe in miracles: _Blunstone, Colin_ / Angel of the morning: _Arnold, P.P._ / Red red wine: _James, Jimmy_ / It's a heartache: _Tyler, Bonnie_ / You to me are everything: _Real Thing_ / I'll have to say I love you in a song: _Croce, Jim_ / Mirrors: _Oldfield, Sally_ / Just one smile: _Pitney, Gene_ / Sorry doesn't always make it right: _Knight, Gladys & The Pips_ / Handbags and gladrags: _Farlowe, Chris_ / Ruby Tuesday: _Melanie_ / Darling be home soon: _Lovin' Spoonful_ / Man of the world: _Fleetwood Mac_ / Kiss me for the last time: _Brooks, Elkie_ / Love's gotta hold on

me: _Dollar_ / Oh girl: _Chi-Lites_ / Days: _Kinks_ / One less set of footsteps: _Croce, Jim_
CD _____ TRTCD 113
TrueTrax / Feb '96 / THE.

HEARTBEAT OF CALIFORNIA
All this love: _Johnson, Henry_ / Never be lonely: _McBride, Joe_ / Slippin' and slidin': _Latcoriel, Abraham_ / Pescaderp Pointe: _Dickerson, Stefan_ / Signs: _Veasley, Gerald_ / Bus song: _Gable, Tony_ / Just one step away: _Cobham, Billy_ / Armed response: _Porcupine_ / Dreamwalk: _White, Peter_ / Back on the beat: _Navarro, Ken_ / Autobahn: _Kraukas, Gregg_ / What can I say: _Blake, Kenny_ / Sun city at night: _Townes, Billy_ / Take me there: _Navarro, Ken_ / Sound of emotion: _Kraukas, Gregg_ / Now and forever: _Bernsen, Randy_
CD _____ 101S8770682
101 South / Apr '95 / New Note.

HEARTBEAT OF SOWETO
Nwana wamina: _Chauke, Thomas_ / Thathezakho: _Miokothwa_ / Jabula mfana: _Emvelo, Amaswazi_ / Nsati wa wina: _Shirinda, M.D. & Family_ / Siyoklishaya kusasa: _Elimnyama, Kati_ / Waqala Ngowendlala: _Usuthu_ / Mashama: _ChiJumane, Arando Bila_ / Xumaxilovile: _Chauke, Thomas & Shinyori_ / Yithinamhlaje: _Miokothwa_ / Bumnandi utshwala bakho: _Elimnyama, Kati_ / Kamakhalawana: _ChiJumane, Arando Bila_ / Ndzi Hkensa: _Shirinda, M.D. & Family_
CD _____ SHANCD 43051
Shanachie / Mar '89 / Koch / ADA / Greensleeves.

HEARTBEAT REGGAE NOW
CD _____ HBCDAN 9
Greensleeves / Jun '93 / Total/BMG / Jetstar / SRD.

HEARTBREAKERS
CD Set _____ 353697
RCA / May '90 / BMG.

HEARTBREAKERS
CD _____ STACD 053
Wisepack / Sep '93 / THE / Conifer.

HEARTBREAKERS
Power of love: _Rush, Jennifer_ / Afer the love has gone: _Earth, Wind & Fire_ / I love you too much: _Santana_ / Do I love you too much: _Lake_ / Do I love you: _Blunstone, Colin_ / Me and Mrs Jones: _Paul, Billy_ / Kiss and say goodbye: _Manhattans_ / In my dreams: _REO Speedwagon_ / Most beautiful girl in the world: _Rich, Charlie_ / You made me so very happy: _Blood, Sweat & Tears_ / When your heart is weak: _Cock Robin_ / Longer: _Fogelberg, Dan_ / Something's gotten hold of my heart: _Window Speaks_ / Long distance love: _Bailey, Philip_ / Only one woman: _Belcanto_ / How 'bout us: _Champaign_
CD _____ 4804442
Columbia / Oct '95 / Sony.

HEARTBREAKERS OF THE 60'S
Let the heartaches begin: _Baldry, Long John_ / I just don't know what to do with myself: _Springfield, Dusty_ / Sun ain't gonna shine anymore: _Walker Brothers_ / First cut is the deepest: _Arnold, P.P._ / Halfway to paradise: _Fury, Billy_ / Don't let the sun catch you crying: _Gerry & The Pacemakers_ / See my friends: _Kinks_ / Every time we say goodbye: _Fitzgerald, Ella_ / Crying game: _Berry, Dave_ / It might as well rain until September: _King, Carole_ / Take good care of my baby: _Vee, Bobby_ / Juliet: _Four Pennies_ / No milk today: _Herman's Hermits_ / I'll never get over you: _Kidd, Johnny & The Pirates_ / Sorry Suzanne: _Hollies_ / Always something there to remind me: _Shaw, Sandie_ / You've got your troubles: _Fortunes_ / I'll never fall in love again: _Gentry, Bobbie_ / Joanna: _Walker, Scott_ / You've lost that lovin' feelin': _Righteous Brothers_
CD _____ CDPR 118
Premier/MFP / Nov '93 / EMI.

HEARTBREAKERS OF THE 70'S
Without you: _Nilsson, Harry_ / All by myself: _Carmen, Eric_ / Reason to believe: _Stewart, Rod_ / It's a heartache: _Tyler, Bonnie_ / If you can't give me love: _Quatro, Suzi_ / Hold back the night: _Trammps_ / Tears of a clown: _Beat_ / Break up to make up: _Stylistics_ / There goes my first love: _Drifters_ / Every day hurts: _Sad Cafe_ / I'm not in love: _10cc_ / Sylvia's mother: _Dr. Hook_ / Say you don't mind: _Blunstone, Colin_ / Most beautiful girl: _Rich, Charlie_ / Tears on my pillow: _Nash, Johnny_ / Love really hurts without you: _Ocean, Billy_ / Darlin': _Miller, Frankie_ / Raining in my heart: _Sayer, Leo_ / Don't let the sun go down on me: _John, Elton_ / Miss you nights: _Richard, Cliff_
CD _____ CDPR 119
Premier/MFP / Nov '93 / EMI.

HEARTBREAKERS OF THE 80'S
Heartbreaker: _Warwick, Dionne_ / Missing you: _Waite, John_ / Suspicious minds: _Fine Young Cannibals_ / Brand new friend: _Cole, Lloyd & The Commotions_ / Love on your side: _Thompson Twins_ / Heartbeat: _Wham_ / All of my heart: _ABC_ / Wishing: _Dean, Hazell_ / Heartache: _Pepsi & Shirlie_ / Dancing with tears in my eyes: _Ultravox_ / Broken wings: _Mr. Mister_ / Total eclipse of the heart: _Tyler, Bonnie_ / Only when you leave: _Spandau Ballet_ / Rise to the occasion: _Climie Fisher_ / It's over: _Level 42_ / Kayleigh: _Marillion_ / What's another year:

Logan, Johnny / Teardrops: _Stevens, Shakin'_ / I really didn't mean it: _Vandross, Luther_ / My arms keep missing you: _Astley, Rick_
CD _____ CDPR 120
Premier/MFP / Nov '93 / EMI.

HEARTCORE DEMOS, THE
CD _____ PACEMAKER 001CD
Burning Heart / Sep '95 / Plastic Head.

HEARTS DESIRE
CD _____ RENCD 103
Castle / Jul '95 / BMG.

HEAT
CD _____ FADCD 026
Fashion / Nov '92 / Jetstar / Grapevine.

HEAT IS ON, THE
CD Set _____ NSCD 002
Newsound / Feb '95 / THE.

HEAVEN
Stop: _Brown, Sam_ / Come into my life: _Sims, Joyce_ / Poison arrow: _ABC_ / Message is love: _Baker, Arthur & The Backbeat Disciples_ / Have you ever had it blue: _Style Council_ / Cry: _Godley & Creme_ / I'll find my way home: _Jon & Vangelis_ / Suspicious minds: _Fine Young Cannibals_ / Your history: _Shakespears Sister_ / Running in the family: _Level 42_ / Closest thing to Heaven: _Kane Gang_ / If I can't have you: _Elliman, Yvonne_ / You make me feel brand new: _Stylistics_ / Oh what a circus: _Essex, David_
CD _____ 5501492
Spectrum/Karussell / Jan '94 / PolyGram / THE.

HEAVENLY HARDCORE
CD _____ DINCD 35
Dino / Mar '92 / Pinnacle / 3MV.

HEAVENLY VOICES
CD Set _____ HY 39100852
Hyperium / Feb '94 / Plastic Head.

HEAVY GUITAR
(2CD Set)
CD Set _____ 24079
Delta Doubles / Mar '95 / Target/BMG.

HEAVY METAL RECORDS COMPILATION
CD _____ HMRXD 143
Heavy Metal / Jul '90 / Sony.

HECTIC - CHAPTER ONE
CD _____ HECTCD 001
Hectic / Oct '95 / Disc / Jumpstart / Mo's Music Machine.

HEIVA I TAHITI - FESTIVAL OF LIFE
CD _____ EUCD 1238
ARC / Nov '93 / ARC Music / ADA.

HELLS BENT ON ROCKIN'
CD _____ NERCD 017
Nervous / Nov '91 / Nervous / Magnum Music Group.

HELP
Fade away: _Oasis_ / Oh brother: _Boo Radleys_ / Love speaads: _Stone Roses_ / Lucky: _Radiohead_ / Adrian: _Orbital_ / Mourning air (war child): _Portishead_ / Fake the aroma: _Massive Attack_ / Shipbuilding: _Suede_ / Time for loving: _Charlatans & The Chemical Brothers_ / Sweetest truth: _Stereo MC's_ / Ode to Billy Joe: _O'Connor, Sinead_ / Search light: _Levellers_ / Raindrops keep falling on my head: _Manic Street Preachers_ / Tom Petty loves Venuca Salt: _Terrorvision_ / Magnificent: _One World Orchestra_ / Message to crommie: _Planet 4 Folk Quartet_ / Dream a little dream: _Hall, Terry & Salad_ / 1,2,3,4,5: _Cherry, Neneh & Trout_ / Eine kleine lift muzik: _Blur_ / Come together: _Smokin' Mojo Filters_
CD _____ 8286822
Go Discs / Sep '95 / PolyGram.

HELTER SHELTER BOX
(Elastica/Gene/Supergrass/S*M*A*S*H)
CD Set _____ SP 1776
Sub Pop / Jul '95 / Disc.

HEMISPHERE NO MORE
(A Listener Friendly Guide To Music Of The World)
Sango ya mawa: _Dabany, Patience_ / La Cosecha De Mujeres: _Tribu Band_ / Nereci (A name): _Djavan_ / Konifale: _Tangara, Kadja_ / Cortina: _Vasconcelos, Nana_ / Midnight walker: _Sjolline, Davy_ / Khaeft dharram: _Fouad, Mohamed_ / Sweet reggae: _Harley & The Rasta Family_ / Yele congo: _Ketu, Ara_ / Africa: _Depeu, Dave_ / Madambadamba: _Tshola, Tsepo_ / Koufenko: _Manfila, Kante_ / E dai (A waiat): _Nascimento, Milton_ / Huajira: _Inti-Illimani_ / Rag Pahadi: _Sharma, Shivkumar_
CD _____ CDHEMI 2
Hemisphere / Jun '95 / EMI.

HENT SANT JAKEZ
CD _____ SHAM 1018CD
Shamrock / Aug '93 /.Wellard / ADA.

HEP CATS FROM BIG SPRING
Move mama: _Hall, Ben_ / Be bop ball: _Hall, Ben_ / Blue days black nights: _Hall, Ben_ / Honey you talk too much: _Fox, Orville & The Harmony Masters_ / Silly Sally: _Lara, Sammy_ / Tell me: _Regals_ / Waitin' (on the steps at school): _Regals_ / Lover's regret: _Classics_ / Hep cat: _Teen Kings_ / Some day sweet day: _Box, David & The Ravens_ / That's all I want

from you: Box, David & The Ravens / I do the best I can: Box, David & The Ravens / Waitin' (don't wait too long): Box, David & The Ravens / Guitar hop: Welborn, Larry / It's gonna happpen: Osburn, Bob / Heart theif: Osburn, Bob / Goin' back to Louisiana: Osburn, Bob / Too young to love to old to cry: Nicholas, Don & The Four Teens / Bark like a dog: Allison, Bobby
CD _____ RCCD 3003
Rollercoaster / Oct '91 / CM / Swift.

HERBS, THE
CD _____ EBCD 001
Early Bird / Feb '95 / Jetstar.

HERE COME THE GIRLS
(British Girl Singers Of The Sixties)
That's how it goes: Breakaways / We were lovers (when the party began): Barry, Sandra / There he goes (the boy I love): Antoinette / He knows I love him too much: Macari, Glo / As long as you're happy baby: Shaw, Sandie / Song without end: Ruskin, Barbara / Tell me what to do: Jackson, Simone / Put yourself in my place: Panter, Jan / It's hard to believe it: Collins, Glenda / So much in love: Brown, Polly / Very first day I met you: Cannon, Judy / How can I hide from my heart: Darren, Maxine / No other baby: Davis, Billie / Listen people: Lane, Sarah / Come to me: Grant, Julie / Dark shadows and empty hallways: St. John, Tammy / Happy faces (CD only.): Silver, Lorraine / Something must be done (CD only.): Harris, Anita / You'd better come home (CD only.): Clark, Petula / When my baby cries (CD only.): Prenosilova, Yvonne / Something I've got to tell you (CD only.): Honeycombs / I want you (CD only.): Jeannie & The Big Guys / I can't believe what you say (CD only.): McKenna, Val / If you love me (really love me) (CD only.): Trent, Jackie
CD _____ NEXCD 111
Sequel / Mar '90 / BMG.

HERE COME THE GIRLS VOL.3
(Run Mascara)
Easier said than done: Essex / Walkin' miracle: Essex / She's got everything: Essex / Run mascara: Exciters / I want you to be my boy: Exciters / There they go: Exciters / Kind of boy you can't forget: Raindrops / What a guy: Raindrops / That boy is messing up my mind: Raindrops / My one and only Jimmy boy: Girlfriends / For my sake: Girlfriends / Lover's concerto: Toys / What's wrong with me baby: Toys / Can't stop lovin' the boy: Carolines / Evening time: Elena / Girl is not a girl: Wine, Toni / Johnny Angel: Fabares, Shelly / He don't love me: Fabares, Shelly / I'm into something good: Earl Jean
CD _____ NEXCD 193
Sequel / Mar '92 / BMG.

HERE COME THE GIRLS VOL.4
(You Can Be Wrong About Boys)
He doesn't love me: Breakaways / I've found love: Tandy, Sharon / Pay you back with interest: Gillespie, Dana / Thank goodness for the rain: Peanut / It's so fine: King, Dee / Where am I going: Clark, Petula / You can be wrong about boys: Page, Mally / He's the one for me: St. John, Tammy / Don't you know: Darren, Maxine / Thinking of you: West, Dodie / Well how does it feel: Ruskin, Barbara / You can't take it away: Reed, Tawney / When love slips away: Margo & The Marvettes / There he goes: Plainghtgwitoh / London life: Harris, Anita / As I watch you walk away: Smith, Martha / Lonely without you: Grant, Julie / You really have started something: Britt / Someone has to cry (Why must I): Kay, Barbara / My life (is in your hands): Paper Dolls / Untrue unfaithful (That was you): Rossi, Nita / Scratch my back: Panter, Jan / Love ya Ilya: Angela & The Fans
CD _____ NEXCD 238
Sequel / Jun '93 / BMG.

HERE COME THE GIRLS VOL.5
(Sisters From The City)
CD _____ NEMCD 675
Sequel / Sep '94 / BMG.

HERE COME THE GIRLS VOL.6
Question: Barry, Sandra / I'm tired just lookin' at you: St. John, Tammy / Life and soul of the party: St. John, Tammy / Take me away: Trent, Jackie / Reach out, I'll be there: Clark, Petula / Thank you for loving me: Antoinette / Here she comes: Breakaways / Donna Star: Douglas, Donna / Love / Please don't talk about me when I'm gone: Stern, Nina / Halfway to paradise: Ruskin, Barbara / Come on baby: Kim D / He don't want your love anymore: Doll, Linda & the Sundowners / Something I've got to tell you: Collins, Glenda / Da-di-da-da: Satin Bells / So goes love: Abicair, Shirley / Thank you boy: Gillespie, Dana / I know you'll be & The Fans / He's no good: Baker Twins / Heaven is being with you: Brook, Patti / Long after tonight is all over: Rogers, Julie / In the deep of the night: West, Dodie / You make my head spin: Lee, Jackie
CD _____ NEMCD 718
Sequel / Feb '95 / BMG.

HERE COME THE GIRLS VOL.7
(The Trouble With Boys)
Baby baby (I still love you): Cinderellas / Please don't wake me: Cinderellas / Baby toys: Toys / See how they run: Toys / May my heart be cast in stone: Toys / Curfew lover: Essex / What did I do: Essex / Are you going my way: Essex / Moon of love: Bobbettes / Will you love me in heaven: Del Vetts / Send him to me: Uniques / Breaking up is hard to do: Fabares, Shelly / Toom Toom (is a little boy): Applebee, Marie / Down by the sea (end of summer): Applebee, Marie / Hey lover: Dovale, Debbie / Opportunity: Jewels / I never wonder where my baby goes: Elaine / There's danger ahead: Elaine / It should'a been me (instead of company): Elaine / Get him: Little Eva / Trouble with boys: Little Eva
CD _____ NEMCD 752
Sequel / Aug '95 / BMG.

HERE COMES THE SUMMER
Hooray hooray it's a holi holiday: Boney M / Summer love sensation: Bay City Rollers / Down on the beach tonight: Drifters / Farewell my summer love: Kaos / Surfin' U.S.A. / golt summer: Atlantic Starr / Gimme the sunshine: Curiosity / Loco in Acapulco: Four Tops / Fantastic day: Haircut 100 / Surfin' USA: Astronauts / Surfin' in the summertime: Ronnie & The Daytonas / Summer (the first time): Goldsboro, Bobby / Aquarius (let the sunshine in): Fifth Dimension / Seasons in the sun: Jacks, Terry / Good thing going: Minott, Sugar / Montego bay: Sugar Cane / Sunshine reggae: Laid Back / Sun will shine: Feliciano, Jose / Island in the sun: Belafonte, Harry / Santa Monica sunshine: Sweet / Current of love: Hasselhoff, David
CD _____ 74321286102
Ariola / May '95 / BMG.

HERITAGE 14-HIP HOP
We got our own thing: Heavy D & The Boyz / Hip hop junkies: Nice 'n Smoothe / Mama said knock you out: L.L. Cool J / I come off: Young MC / It takes two: Base, Rob & D.J. E-Z Rock / Make it happen: Ultra Magnetic MC's / Flavor of the month: Black Sheep / O.P.P.: Naughty By Nature / Jump: Kriss Kross / Express yourself: N.W.A. / Fuck Compton: Dog, Tim / I'm ready: Caveman
CD _____ CDELV 08
Debut / Jul '93 / Pinnacle / 3MV / Sony.

HERITAGE-COLOSSUS STORY, THE
When we get married: Dreamlovers / Ain't nothing but a house party: Showstoppers / May I: Deal, Bill & The Rhondells / And suddenly: Cherry People / Ma belle Amie: Tee Set / Venus: Shocking Blue / Check yourself: Italian Asphalt & Paving Co / Little green bag: Baker, George Selection / Sooner I get to you: Biddu / Carolina on my mind: Crystal Mansion / Don't hang me up girl: Cherry People / I've been hurt: Deal, Bill & The Rhondells / Everything is beautiful: Ross, Jerry / You're gonna make it: Festivals / Give it to me: Mob / Venus (2): Ross, Jerry / Pick up my toys: Devonnes / What kind of fool do you think I am: Deal, Bill & The Rhondells / I dig everything about you: Mob / Goodnight my love: Duprees
CD _____ NEMCD 677
Sequel / Nov '94 / BMG.

HEXENTEXT
CD _____ CODE 1
Overground / Oct '94 / SRD.

HEY DRAG CITY
CD _____ WIGCD 16
Domino / Oct '94 / Pinnacle.

HEY GUITAR
CD Set _____ ECMBOX 02
ECM / Nov '92 / New Note.

HI ENERGY
CD _____ NTRCD 019
Nectar / Jun '94 / Pinnacle.

HI GIRLS
You gotta take the bitter with the sweet: Starks, Veniece / What more do you want from me: Starks, Veniece / Step child: Starks, Veniece / Eighteen days: Starks, Veniece / Every now and then: Starks, Veniece / Trying to live my life without you: Starks, Veniece / I still love you: Starks, Veniece / Without a reason: Janet & The Jays / Hurting over you boy: Janet & The Jays / Love what you're doing to me: Janet & The Jays / Pleading for your love: Janet & The Jays / When the battle is over: Joint Venture / I'd rather hurt you now: Joint Venture / Quiet elegence: Joint Venture / Mama said: Joint Venture / I need love: Joint Venture / Love will make you feel better: Joint Venture / Your love is strange: Joint Venture / Roots of love: Joint Venture / Look at the boy: Plum, Jean / Here's to you again: Plum, Jean / Pour the lovin': Plum, Jean / You ask me: Plum, Jean / It's you that I need (Part 1): Duncan Sisters / Anyway the wind blows: Coffee, Erma / You made me what I am: Coffee, Erma / He's got it: Known Facts / How can I believe you: Known Facts
CD _____ HILOCD 7
Hi / Mar '94 / Pinnacle.

HI LIFE COMPILATION
Time for love: English, Kim / Joy and happiness: Stabbs / I see only you: Nootropic / Fantasy: Angel Heart / Pleasure: Medium High / Oohhh baby: Simpson, Vida / I know

a place: English, Kim / Lost in love: Up Yer Ronson / Renegade master: Wildchild / Bailando con lobos: Cabana / Nite life: English, Kim / Another night: Kitsch In Synch / Prayer to the music: Polo, Marco / Manifest your love: D.O.P. / Raise: Boston Bees / Manifest your love #2: D.O.P.
CD _____ 5294002
Hi Life / Jan '96 / PolyGram.

HI RECORDS STORY, THE
CD _____ HIUKCD 101
Hi / Jul '89 / Pinnacle.

HI RECORDS: THE EARLY YEARS VOL.1
Tootsie: McVoy, Carl / You are my sunshine / Little John's gone / Daydreaming / Skating in the blue light: Charmettes / You made a hit: Fuller, Joe / Please please: Coburn, Kimball / Teenage love / I'm so lonely: Loyd, Jay B / Going back to Memphis: Simmons, Gene / Lovin' Lil: Tucker, Tommy / Man in love: Tucker, Tommy / Millers cave: Tucker, Tommy / Stranger: Tucker, Tommy / Pipliner: Reddell, Teddy / Want to hold you: Reddell, Teddy / There was a time: Reeder, Bill / Till I Waltz again with you: Reeder, Bill / Judy: Reeder, Bill / Secret love: Reeder, Bill / Twenty six miles to Joliet: Wallace, Darlen / Smokie: Black, Bill Combo
CD _____ HIUKCD 127
Hi / Apr '92 / Pinnacle.

HI RECORDS: THE EARLY YEARS VOL.2
My girl Josephine: Jayes, Jerry / Five miles from home: Jayes, Jerry / Middle of nowhere: Jayes, Jerry / Long black veil: Jayes, Jerry / Sugar bee: Jayes, Jerry / I'm in love again: Jayes, Jerry / I washed my hands in muddy water: Jayes, Jerry / Shackles and chains: Tucker, Tommy / I'm in love with a shadow: Tucker, Tommy / Wild side of life: Tucker, Tommy / Since I met you baby: Felts, Narvel / Dee Dee: Felts, Narvel / Eighty six miles: Felts, Narvel / Little bit of soap: Felts, Narvel / Dark shaded glasses: Eldred, Charles / Long tall texan: Kellum, Murray & Rhythm Four / I gotta leave this town: Sutton, Glenn / Shame, shame, shame: Tucker, Tommy / Listen to me lie: Simmons, Gene / Wedding bells: Simmons, Gene / Invitation to the blues: Simmons, Gene / Time is right: Lloyd, Jay B. / Honey babe: Arnold, Jerry / Son of Smokie: Black, Bill Combo / Crank case: Black, Bill Combo / TD's boogie woogie: Black, Bill Combo / Deep elem blues: Cannon, Ace & Bill Black's combo / Sittin' tight: Cannon, Ace
CD _____ HIUKCD 128
Hi / Apr '92 / Pinnacle.

HI-BOP SKA
CD _____ 45019
Shanachie / Dec '94 / Koch / ADA / Greensleeves.

HI-FI ROCK 'N' ROLL PARTY
Lights out: Byrne, Jerry / Roll hot rod roll: McLollie, Oscar / Runaround sue: Dion / Sea cruise: Ford, Frankie / Little bit of soap: Jarmels / Thinking of you: Beasley, Jimmy / Maybellene: Walton, Mercy Dee / Poetry in motion: Tillotson, Johnny / Tutti frutti: Little Richard / Wake up little Susie: Everly Brothers / Peanut butter: Marathons / Promised land: Allan, Johnnie / Wanderer: Dion / Deuces wild: Wray, Link / Hush-a-bye: Mystics / Teenager in love: Dion & The Belmonts / Lollipop: Chordettes / My true story: Jive Five / Goodnight my love: Belvin, Jesse / He's so fine: Chiffons / Way I like it: Gunter, Shirley / Reet petite: Wilson, Jackie
CD _____ CDCH 904
Ace / May '86 / Pinnacle / Cadillac / Complete/Pinnacle.

HIATUS - THE PEACEVILLE SAMPLER
CD _____ VILECD 006
Peaceville / Apr '89 / Pinnacle.

HIDDEN ENGLISH
CD _____ TSCD 600
Topic / Oct '94 / Direct / ADA.

HIGH ATMOSPHERE
CD _____ ROUCD 0028
Rounder / Apr '95 / CM / Direct / ADA / Cadillac.

HIGH ENERGY
CD _____ JHD 042
Tring / Jun '92 / Tring / Prism.

HIGH ON DANCE
Baby, I love your way: Big Mountain / Twist and shout: Demus, Chaka & Pliers / Sweets for my sweet: Lewis, C.J. / Sign: Ace Of Base / What is love: Haddaway / Moving on up: M People / Mr. vain: Culture Beat / It's my life: Dr. Alban / Real thing: Di Bart, Tony / Move on baby: Cappella / Here we go: Stakka Bo / Connected: Stereo MC's / Anything: S.W.V. / Dreams: Gabrielle / Return to innocence: Enigma / Incredible: M-Beat & General Levy / Set the world on fire: E-Type / Penso positivo (Molella remix): Jovanotti / Got to give it up: Masterboy / Somewhere over the rainbow: Marusha
CD _____ 525143-2
PolyGram TV / Oct '94 / PolyGram.

HIGH PLATEAUX SONGS
(Music From Madagascar)
CD _____ PS 65096

Playasound / Oct '92 / Harmonia Mundi / ADA.

HIGH VOLTAGE VOLUME 1
CD _____ RNCD 2091
Rhino / Mar '95 / Jetstar / Magnum Music Group / THE.

HIGHLIGHTS FROM EDINBURGH TATTOO 1965-79
Fanfare: Royal Marines School Of Music / My love she's but a lassie yet: Massed Pipes & Drums / Heughs o' Cromdale: Massed Pipes & Drums / Mrs. MacDougall: Massed Pipes & Drums / Angus McKinnon: Massed Pipes & Drums / Thunderbirds: Massed Military Bands / 633 squadron: Massed Military Bands / Burns on the march: Massed Military Bands / Scotland the brave: Massed Military Bands / Athol Highlanders: Brigade Of Gurkhas / Dear old donegal: Brigade Of Gurkhas / Lutzow's wild hunt: Brigade Of Gurkhas / Sirmoor rifles: Brigade Of Gurkhas / Barren rocks Aden: Brigade Of Gurkhas / Dundee city: Brigade Of Gurkhas / Get me to the church on time: Corps Of Drums / Wonderful Copenhagen: Corps Of Drums / Cock o' the North: Massed Military Bands / British Grenadiers: Massed Military Bands / Soldiers in the park: Massed Military Bands / Dovecote park: Scots College Sydney / Road to the isles: Scots College Sydney / Meetings of the waters: Scots College Sydney / Old rustic bridge: Scots College Sydney / Highland cradle song: Scots College Sydney / Whistle o'er the lave o't: Scots College Sydney / Earl of Mansfield: Scots College Sydney / H.M. Jollies: Massed Bands Of The Hoyal Marines / Blaze of brass: Massed Bands Of The Royal Marines / Edinburgh castle: Massed Bands Of The Royal Marines / Life on the ocean wave: Massed Bands Of The Royal Marines / Prinz Carlmarsch: Massed Pipes, Drums & Military Bands / Caubeen trimmed with blue: Massed Pipes, Drums & Military Bands / Heart of oak: Massed Pipes, Drums & Military Bands / Royal artillery slow march: Massed Pipes, Drums & Military Bands / Abide with me: Massed Pipes, Drums & Military Bands / Royal artillery slow match: Massed Pipes, Drums & Military Bands / Royal artillery last post: Massed Pipes, Drums & Military Bands / Lament for Red Hector of the Battles lone piper: Massed Pipes, Drums & Military Bands / Zum staedtli hinaus: Massed Pipes, Drums & Military Bands / We're no awa' tae bide awa': Massed Pipes, Drums & Military Bands / Loch Lomond: Massed Pipes, Drums & Military Bands
CD _____ CDMFP 5993
Music For Pleasure / Jun '93 / EMI.

HIGHLIGHTS FROM WEMBLEY COUNTRY MUSIC FESTIVAL
CD _____ PWK 049
Carlton Home Entertainment / Jan '88 / Carlton Home Entertainment.

HIGHLY RECOMMENDED
CD _____ FORM CD3
Formation / Nov '95 / SRD.

HIGHTONE RECORDS FIRST TEN YEARS (SAMPLER), THE
CD _____ HCD 2002
Hightone / Jul '94 / ADA / Koch.

HILLBILLY ROCK
Watchdog / Everybody's rockin' but me / Oh yeah / Roughneck blues / Red hen boogie / Too many / Get me on your mind / Hey, heavy / Stepped out a runnin' hey Mae / Good deal Lucille / Looking for love / What's the use (I still love you) / I ain't gonna waste my time / Billy goat boogie / I've got a brand new baby / Start all over / Lonesome journey / Hey you there / No help wanted
CD _____ CDMF 034
Magnum Force / '91 / Magnum Music Group.

HILLS OF HOME: 25 YEARS OF FOLK MUSIC ON ROUNDER
(2CD/MC Set)
CD _____ ROUCDAN 16/17
Rounder / Jul '95 / CM / Direct / ADA / Cadillac.

HIP HOP 18
(Various artists)
We'll make your body move: Devastation / Devastator / Force desire: Keith, Jazzy / Take a walk: Seville & Jazzy J / Go southside: Frick'n'Frack / Who's on mine: Frick'n'Frack / You know how to reach us: Kings of Pressure / She's a dog: Kay Gee The All & D.J.Drew / Cotton Club: Jury / Opesta now: Royal Ron / We have risen: Almighty El-Cee
CD _____ CDELC 18
Street Sounds / Oct '87 / BMG.

HIP HOP 21
Feel the tones: Cold Crush Brothers / You know what time: Spicy Ham / Sir Vere: Sir Fresh & D J Critical / Listen to my turbo: Jungle Brothers / Damn I'm good: King Tree / Let me love you: 5 Star Motet / Funky bass: M.C. Rajah
CD _____ CDELC 21
Street Sounds / Jun '88 / BMG.

HIP HOP 23
CD _____ CDELC 23
Street Sounds / Dec '88 / BMG.

HIP HOP AND MORE
CD _____ 12610
Laserlight / Oct '95 / Target/BMG.

**HIPPY HIPPY SHAKE
(The Beat Era Vol.2)**
Hully gully slip and slide: Roulettes / La Bamba: Roulettes / Hippy hippy shake: Harris, Pat & The Blackjacks / Is it right: Monotones / Tomorrow: Comanches / Kelly: Gibson, Wayne & The Dynamic Sounds / I keep forgettin': Hi-Fi's / She's the one: Hi-Fi's / I don't care: Peter's Faces / Since you've gone: Britten, Buddy & The Regents / See if I care: Diamond, Brian & The Cutters / Let's lock the door (And throw away the key): Lancastrians / I go to sleep: Truth / Girl: Truth / Where has your smile gone: Shelley, Percy Bysshe / Love is strange: Storme, Robb & Whispers / But I do: Game / I could have danced all night: Cop's 'N' Robbers / I tried: Paddy, Klaus & Gibson / Michelle: Overlanders / Blue turns to grey: Epics / Norwegian wood: Frugal Sound / Nowhere man: Settlers
CD _____ NEXCD 218
Sequel / Mar '93 / BMG.

HIPPY HOUSE & HAPPY HOP 2
To the rhythm: Dayglo, Johnny / Manifesto: Extasis / Mainstream: Sons of be-bop / Aftertouch: Prophet Five / Let the good times roll: Quiet Boys & Galliano / Drop it: M.C. Sleaze & Solid gone / Jack to this: A Silent way
CD _____ JAZIDCD 054
Acid Jazz / Oct '92 / Pinnacle.

HISTORY OF CARNIVAL 1929-1939
CD _____ MBCD 301-2
Matchbox / Feb '93 / Roots / CM / Jazz Music / Cadillac.

**HISTORY OF CHERRY RED
"AMBITION", VOL. 1**
Bored / Right now / Holiday in Cambodia / Too drunk to fuck / What Stanley saw / You scare me to death / History of rock 'n' roll / Rangers in the night / D'ya think I'm sexy / Contract buster / Hungry so angry / Four corners of the earth / It's a fine day / Sun bursts in / Chenko / Jonny Dulump / Die liebe / Girl / This brilliant evening / Primitive painters / Look of love / Psych out / World / What's in your mind
CD _____ CDBRED 95
Cherry Red / Oct '91 / Pinnacle.

**HISTORY OF CHERRY RED
"AMBITION", VOL. 2**
Jest set junta / Night and day / From a to b / Something sends me to sleep / Plain sailing / if she doesn't smile (It'll rain) / Letter from America / Xoyo / Walter and John / Your holiness / On my mind / Mating game / Spain / Talking glamour / Foreign correspondent / Penelope tree / Taboos / Simply couldn't care / You frighten / Paraffin brain / Departure / How to die with style / English rose
CD _____ CDBRED 96
Cherry Red / Oct '91 / Pinnacle.

**HISTORY OF CHESS JAZZ, THE
(2CD Set)**
Poinciana: Jamal, Ahmad / My main man: Stitt, Sonny & Benny Green / Shaw' nuff: Rodney, Red / Killer Joe: Jazztet / Man I love: Sims, Zoot / Soul station: Kirk, Roland / Parker's mood: Moody, James / Keep on keepin' on: Herman, Woody / Gotta travel on: Bryant, Ray / Benny rides again: Goodman, Benny / My love has butterfly wings: Klemmer, John / At last: James, Etta / "In" crowd: Lewis, Ramsey / Windjammer: Harris, Barry / Last train from Overbrook: Moody, James / My foolish heart: Ammons, Gene / Baltimore oriole: Alexandria, Lorez / Bientot: Nelson, Oliver / Morning (excerpt): Lateef, Yusef / Mellow yello: Brown, Odell & The Organizers / Tonk: Farmer, Art / You're my thrill: Jacquet, Illinois / House warmin': McGhee, Howard / Tiny's blues: Jackson, Chubby / Candy: Terry, Clark / Touch: Golson, Benny / Silent night: Burrell, Kenny
CD Set _____ GRP 28122
GRP / Jan '96 / BMG / New Note.

**HISTORY OF COUNTRY MUSIC: THE
1940S VOL. 1**
Bouquet of roses: Arnold, Eddy / When it's lamplighting time in the valley: Ritter, Tex / Guitar polka: Dexter, Al / Smoke on the water: Foley, Red / I'm biting my fingernails and thinking of you: Dexter, Al / At mail call today: Autry, Gene / Detour: Willing, Foy / Prodigal son: Acuff, Roy / Lovesick blues: Williams, Hank / No letter today: Daffan, Ted & The Texans / Each night at nine: Tillman, Floyd / I'll hold you in my heart: Arnold, Eddy / I want to be a cowboy's sweetheart: Allen, Rosalie / Soldier's last letter: Tubb, Ernest / Shame on you: Cooley, Spade / Pistol packin' mama: Dexter, Al / New Spanish two-step: Wills, Bob & His Texas Playboys / Riders in the sky: Monroe, Vaughan / New San Antonio rose: Wills, Bob & His Texas Playboys / It's been so long darling: Tubb, Ernest / Waltz of the wind: Acuff, Roy / It's a sin: Arnold, Eddy / Cool water: Sons Of The Pioneers / They took the stars out of heaven: Tillman, Floyd / New Jole blonde: Foley, Red / There's a

new moon over my shoulder: Javis, Jimmie / Someday you'll want me to want you: Britt, Elton / Candy kisses: Morgan, George / I'll forgive you, but I can't forget: Acuff, Roy / Sugar moon: Wills, Bob & His Texas Playboys / Rainbow at midnight: Tubb, Ernest / Deep in the heart of Texas: Autry, Gene / Wedding bells: Williams, Hank / Tennessee saturday night: Foley, Red / Don't rob another man's castle: Arnold, Eddy / Pistol packin' mama (2): Crosby, Bing
CD Set _____ KNEWCD 715
Disky / Mar '93 / THE / BMG / Discovery / Pinnacle.

**HISTORY OF COUNTRY MUSIC: THE
1940S VOL. 2**
CD Set _____ KNEWCD 716
Kenwest / Jan '93 / THE.

**HISTORY OF COUNTRY MUSIC: THE
1950S VOL. 1**
Crazy arms: Price, Ray / Rumba boogie: Snow, Hank / Let old mother nature have her way: Smith, Carl / Jambalaya: Williams, Hank / Always late (With your kisses): Frizell, Lefty / Gambler's guitar: Draper, Rusty / Chattanooga shoe shine boy: Foley, Red / I take the chance: Browns / In the jailhouse now: Pierce, Webb / Cattle call: Arnold, Eddy / White lightning: Jones, George / It wasn't God who made honky tonk angels: Wells, Kitty / Slow poke: King, Pee Wee / Mexican Joe: Reeves, Jim / So many times: Acuff, Roy / Singin' the blues: Robbins, Marty / Golden rocket: Snow, Hank / Blue suede shoes: Perkins, Carl / Story of my life: Robbins, Marty / I let the stars get in my eyes: Hill, Goldie / Let me go, lover: Snow, Hank / Four walls: Reeves, Jim / I wanna play house with you: Arnold, Eddy / Don't just stand there: Smith, Carl / I want to be with you always: Frizzell, Lefty / Birmingham bounce: Foley, Red / I forgot more than you'll ever know: Davis Sisters / There you go: Cash, Johnny / Hey Sheriff: Rusty & Doug / Your cheatin' heart: Williams, Hank / When it's springtime in Alaska: Horton, Johnny / City light: Price, Ray / Why baby why: Pierce, Webb & Red Sovine / Blue blue day: Gibson, Don / I walk the line: Cash, Johnny / One by one: Wells, Kitty & Red Foley
CD Set _____ KNEWCD 717
Disky / Mar '93 / THE / BMG / Discovery / Pinnacle.

**HISTORY OF COUNTRY MUSIC: THE
1950S VOL. 2**
CD Set _____ KNEWCD 718
Kenwest / Jan '93 / THE.

**HISTORY OF COUNTRY MUSIC: THE
1960S VOL. 1**
CD Set _____ KNEWCD 719
Disky / Mar '93 / THE / BMG / Discovery / Pinnacle.

**HISTORY OF COUNTRY MUSIC: THE
1960S VOL. 2**
CD Set _____ KNEWCD 720
Kenwest / Jan '93 / THE.

**HISTORY OF COUNTRY MUSIC: THE
1970S VOL. 1**
Kiss an angel good morning: Pride, Charley / Hello darlin': Twitty, Conway / I ain't never: Tillis, Mel / Happiest girl in the whole USA: Fargo, Donna / All for the love of sunshine: Williams, Hank Jr. / Chantilly lace: Lewis, Jerry Lee / Country bumpkin: Smith, Cal / Wasted days and wasted nights: Fender, Freddy / Riding my thumb to Mexico: Rodriguez, Johnny / Year that Clayton Delaney died: Hall, Tom T. / Only one love in my life: Milsap, Ronnie / On my knees: Rich, Charlie & Janie Frickie / Luckenbach, Texas (Back to the basics of love): Jennings, Waylon / Lizzie and the rainman: Tucker, Tanya / She never knew me: Williams, Don / Hey won't you play another somebody done somebody wrong song: Thomas, B.J. / Georgia on my mind: Nelson, Willie / Here you come again: Parton, Dolly / Rose garden: Anderson, Lynn / watermelon wine: Hall, Tom T. / Linda on my mind: Twitty, Conway / There must be more to love than this: Lewis, Jerry Lee / Most beautiful girls: Rich, Charlie / Coca cola cowboy: Tillis, Mel / Teddy bear song: Fairchild, Barbara / I'm a ramblin' man: Jennings, Waylon / Eleven roses: Williams, Hank Jr. / Rub it in: Craddock, Billy Crash / Golden tears: Dave & Sugar / You're my best friend: Nelson, Don / Sunday morning coming down: Cash, Johnny / El paso city: Robbins, Marty / Coal miner's daughter: Lynn, Loretta / Blue eyes cryin' in the rain: Nelson, Willie / You can't be a beacon (If your lights don't shine): Fargo, Donna / Secret love: Fender, Freddy
CD Set _____ KNEWCD 721
Disky / Mar '93 / THE / BMG / Discovery / Pinnacle.

**HISTORY OF COUNTRY MUSIC: THE
1970S VOL. 2**
CD Set _____ KNEWCD 722
Kenwest / Jan '93 / THE.

**HISTORY OF COUNTRY MUSIC: THE
1980S VOL. 1**
Nine to Five: Parton, Dolly / City of New Orleans: Nelson, Willie / Love in the first degree: Alabama / Dukes of Hazzard: Jennings, Waylon / Thank god for the radio: Kendalls / My favorite: Milsap, Ronnie / She got the goldmine (I got the shaft): Reed,

Jerry / True love ways: Gilley, Mickey / Seven year ache: Cash, Rosanne / I believe in you: Williams, Don / Give me wings: Johnson, Michael / You look so good in love: Strait, George / He's back and I'm blue: Desert Rose Band / Goin' gone: Mattea, Kathy / Whatever happened to old fashioned love: Thomas, B.J. / Fire I can't put out: Strait, George / I wouldn't change you if I could: Skaggs, Ricky / Can't stop my heart from loving you: O'Kanes / Have mercy: Judds / Lost in the fifties tonight: Milsap, Ronnie / My heroes have always been cowboys: Nelson, Willie / Somebody lied: Shelton, Ricky Van / Cajun moon: Skaggs, Ricky / He stopped loving her today: Jones, George / Bobbie Sue: Oak Ridge Boys / Fourteen carat mind: Watson, Gene / Never been so loved (In all my life): Pride, Charley / Older women: McDowell, Ronnie / Drifter: Sylvia / Wanderer: Rabbitt, Eddie / I'll still be loving you: Restless Heart / I think I'll just stay here and drink: Haggard, Merle / Radio heart: McClain, Charly / Common man: Conlee, John / Take me down: Alabama / Elizabeth: Statler Brothers
CD Set _____ KNEWCD 723
Disky / Mar '93 / THE / BMG / Discovery / Pinnacle.

**HISTORY OF COUNTRY MUSIC: THE
1980S VOL. 2**
CD Set _____ KNEWCD 724
Kenwest / Jan '93 / THE.

**HISTORY OF DANCE 1
(1959 - 1979)**
Shout: Isley Brothers / Green onions: Booker T & The MG's / Walking the dog: Thomas, Rufus / Knock on wood: Floyd, Eddie / Soul finger: Bar-Kays / Sweet soul music: Conley, Arthur / Chain of fools: Franklin, Aretha / Do the funky chicken: Thomas, Rufus / Family affair: Sly & The Family Stone / Could it be I'm falling in love: Detroit Spinners / Sound your funky horn: K.C. & The Sunshine Band / Satisfaction guaranteed: Melvin, Harold & The Bluenotes / Walking in rhythm: Blackbyrds / Get up offa that thing: Brown, James / Funky weekend: Stylistics / Movin': Brass Construction / Can't get by without you: Real Thing / Car wash: Royce, Rose / Do what you wanna do: T-Connection / Darlin' darlin' baby: O'Jays / Free: Williams, Deniece / If I can't have you: Elliman, Yvonne / I love the nightlife: Bridges, Alicia / Take that to the bank: Shalamar / September: Earth, Wind & Fire / Groove line: Heatwave / I want your love: Chic / Backstrokin': Fatback Band
CD Set _____ DBOX 001
Connoisseur / Oct '93 / Pinnacle.

**HISTORY OF DANCE 2
(1980 - 1992)**
Check out the groove: Thurston, Bobby / Brazilian love: Duke, George / Can you handle it: Redd, Sharon / Risin' to the top: Burke, Keni / You're the one for me: D-Train / Zoom: Fat Larry's Band / Last night a DJ saved my life: Indeep / Hold me tighter in the rain: Griffin, Billy / Let the music play: Shannon / Trapped: Abrams, Colonel / Solid: Ashford & Simpson / Tossing and turning: Windjammer / Finest: S.O.S. Band / Love supreme: Downing, Will / Don't be cruel: Brown, Bobby / Going back to my roots: FPI Project / Heaven: Chimes / Wash your face in my sink: Dream Warriors / Don't go messin' with my heart: Mantronix / Power: Snap / Finally: Peniston, Ce Ce / How can I love you more: M People / Love power: Vandross, Luther / Sensitivity: Tresvant, Ralph / Key, the secret: Urban Cookie Collective
CD Set _____ DBOX 002
Connoisseur / Oct '93 / Pinnacle.

HISTORY OF DUB: THE GOLDEN AGE
CD _____ MRMCD 10
Munich / Sep '95 / CM / ADA / Greensleeves / Direct.

HISTORY OF HARDCORE, A
CD _____ JOINT 3 CD
Suburban Base/Moving Shadow / Nov '95 / SRD.

HISTORY OF POP (1958-1965)
CD Set _____ MBSCD 424
Castle / Nov '93 / BMG.

HISTORY OF POP (1966-1973)
CD Set _____ MBSCD 425
Castle / Nov '93 / BMG.

HISTORY OF POP (1974-1982)
CD Set _____ MBSCD 426
Castle / Nov '93 / BMG.

HISTORY OF POP MUSIC
CD _____ HRCD 8019
Disky / Mar '93 / THE / BMG / Discovery / Pinnacle.

**HISTORY OF SKA, BLUEBEAT &
REGGAE**
CD _____ LG 21060
Lagoon / Mar '93 / Magnum Music Group / THE.

HISTORY OF SKA, THE VOL. 2
CD _____ LG 21097
Lagoon / May '94 / Magnum Music Group / THE.

HISTORY OF TAMOKI WAMBESI
CD _____ TWCD 1002
Tamoki Wambesi / Jul '94 / Jetstar / SRD / Roots Collective / Greensleeves.

HISTORY OF THE TANGO
CD _____ 10498
Laserlight / May '95 / Target/BMG.

**HISTORY OF TROJAN RECORDS 1968-
1971**
CD _____ CDTAL 700
Trojan / Feb '95 / Jetstar / Total/BMG.

HISTORY OF TROJAN VOL.2
CD _____ CDTAL 900
Trojan / Feb '96 / Jetstar / Total/BMG.

**HIT BOUND
(The Revolutionary Sound Of Studio 1)**
CD _____ CDHB 43
Heartbeat / Jan '91 / Greensleeves / Jetstar / Direct / ADA.

HIT LOVE SONGS OF THE 60'S
Michelle: Overlanders / Don't sleep in the subway: Petula / Don't throw your love away: Searchers / Girl don't come: Shaw, Sandie / Days: Kinks / Catch the wind: Donovan / He's in town: Rockin' Berries / When my little girl is smiling: Justice, Jimmy / Somewhere in my heart: Paper Dolls / Build me up buttercup: Foundations / Waterloo sunset: Kinks / Colours: Donovan / Let the heartaches begin: Baldry, Long John / Goodbye love: Searchers / Where are you now my love: Trent, Jackie / This is my song: Clark, Petula / Spanish harlem: Justice, Jimmy / Always something there to remind me: Shaw, Sandie
CD _____ PWK 116
Carlton Home Entertainment / Jul '89 / Carlton Home Entertainment.

**HIT ME WITH A FLOWER
(The New Sounds Of San Francisco)**
CD _____ SPEXCD 5901
Normal/Okra / Mar '94 / Direct / ADA.

HIT PARADE ITALIA
CD _____ 290056
RCA / Dec '92 / BMG.

HIT PARADE ITALIA VOL. 2
CD _____ 290055
RCA / Dec '92 / BMG.

HIT SOUND OF NEW ORLEANS
CD _____ CDRB 24
Charly / Aug '95 / Charly / THE / Cadillac.

HIT THE DECKS II
CD _____ QTVCD 008
Quality / Jul '92 / Pinnacle.

HIT THE DECKS III
Ultimation: Megabass / Learn to love: Marveline / Sesame's treet: Smart E's / Rumbletism: Serotonin / Protein: Sonic Experience 3 / Come on: D.J. Seduction / Manic stampede: Krome & Time / Voice of Buddha: Aurora / On a ragga tip: SL2 / Sound is for the underground: Krome & Time / Trip II the moon: Acen / Bad boy: Bad Boy / Hypnosis: Psychotropic / D.J.'s unite: D.J. 's Unite / Does it feel good to you: Cox, Carl / Temple of dreams: Messiah / Feel the rhythm: Terrorize / Peace and loveism: Sonz Of A Loop Da Loop Era / Keep you movin': Nu Matic / Bass shake: Urban Shakedown / Eliminator: Radioactive / Mother Dawn: Blue Pearl / Moog eruption: Digital Orgasm / 2 B Reel: Zone Ranger / Mind on the beat: Groove Technology / Jimi Hendrix was deaf: Two Little Boys / Revelations: H.H.F.D. / Million colours: Channel X / Sunshine: Aurora / Spectral bass: Aurora / Obumbratta: Apotheosis / Rave alert: Khan, Praga / Can we do it: General Max
CD _____ QTVCD 017
Quality / Oct '92 / Pinnacle.

HIT THE FLOOR VOL 1
CD _____ CDMUT 1123
Multitone / Apr '90 / BMG.

HIT THE FLOOR VOL 2
CD _____ CDMUT 1124
Multitone / Apr '90 / BMG.

HITRIDERS VOL. 1
CD _____ 290312
RCA / Dec '92 / BMG.

HITRIDERS VOL. 2
CD _____ 290313
RCA / Dec '92 / BMG.

HITS '96
CD Set _____ RADCD 30
Global / Dec '95 / BMG.

**HITS FROM THE 40'S
(3CD Set)**
That lovely weekend: Roy, Harry & His Band / Madelaine: Roy, Harry & His Band / Put your arms around me honey: Loss, Joe & His Orchestra / I've got the sun in the morning: Loss, Joe & His Orchestra / Jenny: Loss, Joe & His Orchestra / Gal in Calico: Loss, Joe & His Orchestra / I'll string along with you: Peers, Donald / When you wish upon a star: Bowlly, Al / Who's taking you home tonight: Bowlly, Al / Blow, blow thou winter wind: Bowlly, Al / It was a lover and his lass: Bowlly, Al / Oh Buddy I'm in love: Gonella, Nat / What'll I do: Lewis, Archie / I dream of you: Lewis, Archie / In the land of

beginning again: Lewis, Archie / Promenade: Winstone, Eric & His Band / Dreams of yesterday: Winstone, Eric & His Band / I'll buy that dream: Preager, Lou & His Orchestra / Was it love: Roy, Harry & His Band / Gettin' nowhere: Geraldo & His Dance Orchestra / Hey little hen: Gonella, Nat & His Georgians / That's my home: Gonella, Nat & His Georgians / I haven't time to be a millionaire: Gonella, Nat & His Georgians / I'd rather be me: Roy, Harry & His Band / Safari: Winstone, Eric & His Band / Bitin' the dust: Winstone, Eric & His Band / My sister and I: Loss, Joe & His Orchestra / They say it's wonderful: Hutchinson, Leslie / Five o'clock whistle: Roy, Harry & His Orchestra / Sentimental interlude: Roy, Harry & His Orchestra / Whispering grass: Winstone, Eric & His Band / I know why: Winstone, Eric & His Band / Dreamer's holiday: Winstone, Eric & His Band / When that man is dead and gone: Bowlly, Al / Can't get Indiana off my mind: Gonella, Nat & His Georgians / Aurora: Gonella, Nat & His Georgians / Vox: Gonella, Nat & His Georgians / Tiggerty boo: Warner, Jack / Long ago and far away: Geraldo & His Orchestra / I'm not in love: Rabin, Oscar & His Band / You made me care: Loss, Joe & His Orchestra / I'm gonna love that guy (like he's never been loved before): Green, Paula & Her Orchestra / Candy: Roy, Harry & His Band / I fell in love with an airman: Roy, Harry & His Band / I understand: Gonella, Nat & His Georgians / No orchids for my lady: Gonella, Nat & His Georgians / Takin' the trains out (chasin' after you): Foster, Teddy & The Band

CD Set _____ CDTRBOX 176
Trio / Oct '95 / EMI.

HITS FROM THE 50'S
(3CD Set)

Twenty tiny fingers: Cogan, Alma / Love and marriage: Cogan, Alma / You belong to me: Cogan, Alma / Ricochet: Cogan, Alma / Wake up little Susie: King Brothers / In the middle of the island: King Brothers / Stairway of love: Holliday, Michael / I saw Esau: Holliday, Michael / My house is your house: Holliday, Michael / Treasure of love: Anthony, Billie / This ole house: Anthony, Billie / Tammy: Lotis, Dennis / Idle gossip: Campbell, Jean / Answer me: Campbell, Jean / Istanbul: Vaughan, Frankie / Look at that girl: Vaughan, Frankie / Don't let the stars get in your eyes: MacKenzie, Giselle / Slow coach: Radio Revellers / Wake the town and tell the people: Brennan, Rose / Heartbeat: Murray, Ruby / Softly, softly: Murray, Ruby / Mule train: Ford, Tennessee Ernie / At last at last: Hughes, David / Mangoes: Day, Jill / Happiness Street: Day, Jill / Sincerely: Day, Jill / Day that the rains came: Jones Boys / Somewhere along the way: Cole, Nat King / Mona Lisa: Cole, Nat King / Orange coloured sky: Cole, Nat King / If I give my heart to you: Shelton, Anne / Story of Tina: Harris, Ronnie / Man from Laramie: Hockridge, Edmund / Hey there: Hockridge, Edmund / Have I told you lately that I love you: Tanners Sisters / Bewitched, bothered and bewildered: Boswell, Eve / I'd love to fall asleep: Nichols, Penny / My foolish heart: Conway, Steve / Mr. Wonderful: Yana / Suddenly there's a valley: Lawrence, Lee / I talk to the trees: Nicholls, Joy / Green door: Ellington, Ray / We're gonna) Rock around the clock: Deep River Boys / Wanted: Brent, Tony / Wheel of fortune: Starr, Kay

CD Set _____ CDTRBOX 144
Trio / Oct '94 / EMI.

HITS FROM THE 60'S
(3CD Set)

Surfin' USA: Beach Boys / Without you: Monro, Matt / Let true love begin: Cole, Nat King / Pasadena: Temperance Seven / Just one look: Hollies / From a window: Kramer, Billy J. / Who could be bluer: Lordan, Jerry / Rubber ball: Avons / Pistol packin' mama: Vincent, Gene / She wears my ring: King, Solomon / Little lovin': Fourmost / Thank U very much: Scaffold / Lucky five: Conway, Russ / As you like it: Faith, Adam / Games people play: South, Joe / Goldfinger: Bassey, Shirley / Don't let me be misunderstood: Animals / I'm a tiger: Lulu / Happiness: Dodd, Ken / It's all in the game: Richard, Cliff / Don't let the sun catch you crying: Gerry & The Pacemakers / Hanky panky: James, Tommy & The Shondells / Got to get you into my life: Bennett, Cliff / Wild cat: Vincent, Gene / Fever: Shapiro, Helen / Lucky devil: Ifield, Frank / Hippy hippy shake: Swinging Blue Jeans / One fine day: Chiffons / Moon river: Williams, Danny / My boy lollipop: Lettermen / Poison ivy: Paramounts / 5-4-3-2-1: Manfred Mann / Bang bang (my baby shot me down): Cher / Oh no not me: Manfred Mann / James Bond: Barry, John / Apache: Shadows / Seventy six trombones: King Brothers / Tell Laura I love her: Valance, Ricky / Royal event: Conway, Russ / There's a kind of hush: Herman's Hermits / Do you want to know a secret: Kramer, Billy J. & The Dakotas / I'm crying: Animals / It must be him: Carr, Vikki / Morningtown ride: Seekers / Poor me: Faith, Adam / I'm telling you now: Freddie & The Dreamers / Sabre dance: Love Sculpture / Bus stop: Hollies

CD Set _____ CDTRBOX 104
Trio / Oct '94 / EMI.

HITS FROM THE 70'S
(3CD Set)

48 crash: Quatro, Suzi / If you can't give me love: Quatro, Suzi / It's the same old song: K.C. & The Sunshine Band / How much love: Sayer, Leo / Let's work together: Canned Heat / Dynamite: Mud / I don't wanna lose you: Kandidate / Magic: Pilot / Down at the doctors: Dr. Feelgood / Spanish stroll: Mink Deville / Heart of stone: Kenny / Fancy pants: Kenny / Touch too much: Arrows / Judy Teen: Harley, Steve & Cockney Rebel / Here comes the sun: Harley, Steve & Cockney Rebel / Ships in the night: Be-Bop Deluxe / Ranking full stop: Beat / Heaven is in the back seat of my cadillac: Hot Chocolate / Every 1's a winner: Hot Chocolate / On my radio: Selecter / Cotton fields: Beach Boys / Gertcha: Chas & Dave / Freedom come freedom go: Fortunes / Better use your head: Imperials / 10538 overture: E.L.O. / My Sharona: Knack / Malt and barley blues: McGuinness Flint / Journey: Browne, Duncan / Rich kids: Rich Kids / Right back where we started from: Nightingale, Maxine / Rag mama rag: Band / Tonight: Move / You're my everything: Garrett, Lee / Peaches: Stranglers / Darlin': Miller, Frankie / Ball park incident: Wizzard / Movin': Brass Construction / This will be: Cole, Natalie / Softly whispering I love you: Congregation / Oh you pretty thing: Noone, Peter / Whole lot of love: CCS / Dancing in the city: Marshall Hain / Na na na: Powell, Cozy / Motor bikin': Spedding, Chris / Boogie oogie oogie: Taste Of Honey / Crazy: Mud / More like the movies: Dr. Hook / Prince: Madness

CD Set _____ CDTRBOX 108
Trio / Oct '94 / EMI.

HITS FROM THE 80'S
(3CD Set)

Freeze: Spandau Ballet / Wizard: Hardcastle, Paul / Classic: Gurvitz, Adrian / What's wrong with dreaming: River City People / Mony mony: Amazulu / Lawn chairs: Our Daughters Wedding / People do rock steady: Bodysnatchers / Modern girl: Easton, Sheena / Missing you: Waite, John / It started with a kiss: Hot Chocolate / You're lying: Linx / Plan B: Dexy's Midnight Runners / This little girl: Bonds, Gary U.S. / View from a bridge: Wilde, Kim / Respect: Adeva / Girl crazy: Hot Chocolate / Talk talk: Talk Talk / Bette Davis eyes: Carnes, Kim / Tarzan boy: Baltimore / Crying: McLean, Don / Searchin' (I gotta find a man): Dean, Hazell / Missing words: Selecter / Deep walk: Ultravox / Politics of dancing: Re-Flex / C30 C60 C90 Go: Bow Wow Wow / Summertime: Fun Boy Three / Oh well: Oh Well / I could be so good for you: Waterman, Dennis / Goodbye girl: Go West / Can you keep a secret: Brother Beyond / Rise to the occasion: Climie Fisher / Strange little girl: Stranglers / There there my dear: Dexy's Midnight Runners / Comin' on strong: Broken English / C'est la vie: Nevil, Robbie / I'm forever blowing bubbles: Cockney Rejects / Somebody let me out: Beggar & Co / Freeze frame: Geils, J. Band / That certain smile: Ure, Midge / Summer fun: Barracudas / Dancing with myself: Generation X / Round and round: Graham, Jaki / Turning Japanese: Vapors / I shot the sheriff: Light Of The World / Love missile F-11: Sigue Sigue Sputnik / Big apple: Kajagoogoo / Is it a dream: Classix Nouveaux

CD Set _____ CDTRBOX 152
Trio / Oct '94 / EMI.

HITS, HITS AND MORE HITS
CD _____ RADCD 2
Global / Nov '94 / BMG.

HITS IN THE FIRST DEGREE
CD Set _____ NSCD 013
Newsound / Feb '95 / THE.

HITS OF '37
Bei mir bist du schon: Andrews Sisters / On the sunny side of the street: Armstrong, Louis / Rockin' chair: Bailey, Mildred / That old feeling: Boswell, Connie / Will you remember: Costa, Sam / Bob White: Crosby, Bing & Connie Boswell / Moon got in my eyes: Crosby, Bing / Sweet Leilani: Crosby, Bing / I've got you under my skin: Day, Frances / Marie: Dorsey, Tommy / Moon at sea: Fields, Shep / Leaning on a lamp-post: Formby, George / All God's chillun got rhythm: Garland, Judy / To Mary with love: Geraldo / Oh they're tough, mighty tough in the West: Gonella, Nat / Pennies from heaven: Gonella, Nat / Nice work if you can get it: Holiday, Billie / Slap that bass: Ink Spots / Was it rain: Langford, Frances / Greatest mistake of my life: Mesene, Jimmy / I've got my love to keep me warm: Powell, Dick / Broken hearted clown: Roy, Harry / Can I forget you: Sablon, Jean / September in the rain: Tracy, Arthur / Where is the sun: Valaida

CD _____ CD AJA 5116
Living Era / Nov '93 / Koch.

HITS OF '38
Oh ma-ma: Andrews Sisters / Ti-pi-tin: Andrews Sisters / Change partners: Astaire, Fred / I used to be colour blind: Astaire, Fred / Nice work if you can get it: Astaire, Fred / Bei mir bist du schon: Bowlly, Al / You couldn't be cuter: Bowlly, Al / Somebody's thinking of you tonight: Browne, Sam / Me and my girl: Cooper, Jack / Big

noise from Winnetka: Crosby, Bob / My heart is taking lessons in love: Crosby, Bing / On the sentimental side: Crosby, Bing / Boogie woogie: Dorsey, Tommy / Donkey serenade: Fields, Gracie / Whistle while you work: Fields, Shep / Tisket-a-tasket: Fitzgerald, Ella / Just let me look at you: Geraldo / Dipsy doodle: Gonella, Nat / Flat foot floogie: Gonella, Nat / Two sleepy people: Lynn, Vera & Denny Dennis / I hadn't anyone till you: Martin, Tony / Down and out blues: Mesene, Jimmy / Begin the beguine: Shaw, Artie / Music maestro please: Waller, Fats

CD _____ CD AJA 5104
Living Era / May '93 / Koch.

HITS OF '39
Small town: Bowlly, Al / What do you know about love: Bowlly, Al / Oh you crazy moon: Clare, Wendy / I cried for you: Crosby, Bing / My melancholy baby: Crosby, Bing / I'm falling in love with someone: Crosby, Bing & Frances Langford / On the outside looking in: Currie, Bill / (I'm afraid) the masquerade is over: Dennis, Denny / F.D.R. Jones: Fitzgerald, Ella / Over the rainbow: Garland, Judy / Blue orchids: Grantham, Cyril / Wish me luck as you wave me goodbye: Grantham, Cyril / I get along without you very well: Hall, Adelaide / Transatlantic lullaby: Hall, Adelaide / At the woodchoppers' ball: Herman, Woody / My prayer: Ink Spots / Deep purple: Layton, Turner / And the angels sing: Lenner, Anne / We'll meet again: Lynn, Vera / Wishing: Lynn, Vera / They say: Melachrino, George / In the mood: Miller, Glenn / Goodnight children everywhere: Hoy, Harry / Indian summer: Simms, Ginny

CD _____ CDAJA 5086
Living Era / Mar '92 / Koch.

HITS OF '40
Beat me daddy, eight to the bar: Andrews Sisters / Woodpecker song: Andrews Sisters / If I had my way: Crosby, Bing / I haven't time to be a millionaire: Crosby, Bing / Only forever: Crosby, Bing / I can't love you anymore: Daniels, Bebe / Amapola: Durbin, Deanna / Love is all: Durbin, Deanna / Shake down the stars: Hall, Adelaide / Begin the beguine: Henderson, Chick & Joe Loss / Maybe: Ink Spots / Whispering grass: Ink Spots / It's a hap-hap-happy day: Lipton, Celia / Faithful forever: Carmen & Guy Lombardo / I'm in love for the last time: Lynn, Vera / It's a lovely day tomorrow: Lynn, Vera / Nearness of you: Miller, Glenn / Pennsylvania 6-5000: Miller, Glenn / Tuxedo junction: Miller, Glenn / Comes love: O'Connell, Helen & Jimmy Dorsey / Vagabond song: O'Connor, Cavan / I'm stepping out with a memory tonight: Shelton, Anne & Ambrose / Fools rush in: Sinatra, Frank & Tommy Dorsey / I'll never smile again: Sinatra, Frank & Tommy Dorsey

CD _____ CD AJA 5087
Living Era / Oct '92 / Koch.

HITS OF '41
When that man is dead and gone: Bowlly, Al / I'd know you anywhere: Crosby, Bing / San Antonio rose: Crosby, Bing / You are my sunshine: Crosby, Bing / Six lessons from Madame La Zonga: Dorsey, Jimmy / Beneath the lights of home: Durbin, Deanna / It's foolish but it's fun: Durbin, Deanna / Down Forget-Me-Not Lane: Flanagan & Allen / I Daddy: Geraldo / Hey little hen: Gonella, Nat / Hut sut song: Gonella, Nat / Five o'clock whistle: Herman, Woody / Yesterday's dreams: Hutch / Ring, telephone, ring: Ink Spots / We three: Ink Spots / Amapola: Loss, Joe / Yours: Lynn, Vera / Last time I saw Paris: Martin, Tony / Johnson rag: Miller, Glenn / Yes my darling daughter: Miller, Glenn / Frenesi: Shaw, Artie / There goes that song again: Shelton, Anne

CD _____ CD AJA 5100
Living Era / Feb '93 / Koch.

HITS OF '42
Don't sit under the apple tree: Andrews Sisters / Pennsylvania polka: Andrews Sisters / Green eyes: Barreto, Don / Deep in the heart of Texas: Crosby, Bing & Woody Herman / Moonlight becomes you: Crosby, Bing / White Christmas: Crosby, Bing / Zoot suit: Crosby, Bob / Skylark: Eckstine, Billy & Earl Hines / Always in my heart: Geraldo / Lamplighter's serenade: Geraldo / Jingle jangle jingle: Gonella, Nat / That lovely weekend: Henderson, Chick & Joe Loss / Anywhere on Earth is heaven: Hutch / Who wouldn't love you: Ink Spots / You made me love you: James, Harry / Where in the world: Martin, Tony / Chattanooga choo choo: Miller, Glenn / I know why: Miller, Glenn / Miss you: Roy, Harry / Sailor with the navy blue eyes: Roy, Harry / Three little sisters: Shore, Dinah / How about you: Sinatra, Frank & Tommy Dorsey / Without a song: Sinatra, Frank & Tommy Dorsey / Someone's rocking my dreamboat: Winstone, Eric

CD _____ CD AJA 5103
Living Era / Mar '93 / Koch.

HITS OF '45
One meat ball: Andrews Sisters / More I see you: Cavallaro, Carmen / Tampico: Christy, June & Stan Kenton / Temptation: Como, Perry / Till the end of time: Como, Perry / Nina: Coward, Sir Noel / Ac-cent-tchu-ate the positive: Crosby, Bing / Baia: Crosby, Bing / I can't begin to tell you: Crosby, Bing

/ Sentimental journey: Day, Doris & Les Brown / Opus No.1: Dorsey, Tommy / There's no you: Dorsey, Tommy / I'm beginning to see the light: Fitzgerald, Ella & Ink Spots / Together: Haymes, Dick & Helen Forrest / Laura: Herman, Woody / Estrellita: James, Harry / Cocktails for two: Jones, Spike / Caldonia: Jordan, Louis / Little on the lonely side: Lombardo, Guy / Juke box Saturday night: Miller, Glenn / Cool water: Monroe, Vaughan / Cow cow boogie: Morse, Ella Mae / Conversation while dancing: Stafford, Jo & Johnny Mercer / We'll gather lilacs: Tauber, Richard / Moonlight in Vermont: Whiting, Margaret

CD _____ CDAJA 5186
Living Era / Jan '96 / Koch.

HITS OF '93
CD _____ PHCD 001
Penthouse / Apr '94 / Jetstar.

HITS OF 1943
He's my guy: Fitzgerald, Ella / I'm thinking tonight of my blue eyes: Crosby, Bing / I left my heart at the stage door canteen: Winstone, Eric / Johnny Zero: Song Spinners / Murder he says: Dorsey, Jimmy / What's the good word Mr Bluebird: Roy, Harry / Mr. Five by five: Andrews Sisters / Dearly beloved: Astaire, Fred / Every night about this time: Geraldo / G'bye now: Tilton, Martha / Let's get lost: Winstone, Eric / Coming in on a wing and a prayer: Song Spinners / That old black magic: Barnet, Charlie / Ain't got a time to my name: Crosby, Bing / In the blue of evening: Geraldo / I'm gonna get lit up (when the lights go on in London): Loss, Joe / When Johnny comes marching home: Miller, Glenn / Don't get around much anymore: Ink Spots / Hit the road to dreamland: Roy, Harry / I had the craziest dream: Lynn, Vera / Better not roll those blye blue eyes: Ambrose / Be honest with me: Heist, Horace / Really and truly: Lynn, Vera

CD _____ RAJCD 829
Empress / Jul '94 / THE.

HITS OF 1960-64, THE
How do you do it: Gerry & The Pacemakers / Love of the loved: Black, Cilla / Nobody I know: Peter & Gordon / Somewhere: Proby, P.J. / How about that: Faith, Adam / Tell me what he said: Shapiro, Helen / Time: Douglas, Craig / Sun arise: Harris, Rolf / Little children: Kramer, Billy J. & The Dakotas / Little loving: Fourmost / Hungry for love: Kidd, Johnny & The Pirates / Wonderful world of the young: Williams, Danny / Legion's Last Patrol (theme from the film): Thorne, Ken / You can never stop me loving you: Lynch, Kenny / Sharing you: Vee, Bobby / You're no good: Swinging Blue Jeans / I understand: Freddie & The Dreamers / From a Jack to a King: Miller, Ned / Beatnik fly: Johnny & The Hurricanes / Unchained melody: Young, Jimmy

CD _____ CDSL 8270
Music For Pleasure / Sep '95 / EMI.

HITS OF 1965-69, THE
Sloop John B: Beach Boys / Jennifer juniper: Donovan / Supergirl: Bonney, Graham / I've been wrong before: Black, Cilla / Elusive butterfly: Doonican, Val / Lover's concerto: Toys / Trains and boats and planes: Kramer, Billy J. / Ode to Billy Joe: Gentry, Bobbie / Come tomorrow: Manfred Mann / Got to get you into my life: Bennett, Cliff / On the road again: Canned Heat / Sunny: Hebb, Bobby / Kites: Dupree, Simon & The Big Sound / Wichita lineman: Campbell, Glen / Me the peaceful heart: Lulu / Mockingbird: Foxx, Inez & Charlie / Georgy girl: Seekers / Quelle e bella sunonymin / It's gotta get out of this place: Animals / He ain't heavy, he's my brother: Hollies

CD _____ CDSL 8271
Music For Pleasure / Sep '95 / EMI.

HITS OF INVICTUS & HOT WAX, THE
You've got me: Chairmen Of The Board / Crumbs off the table: Glass House / Give me just a little more time: Chairmen Of The Board / Somebody's been sleeping in my bed: 100 Proof (Aged In Soul) / Band of gold: Payne, Freda / She's not just another: Eighth Wonder / Finders keepers: Chairmen Of The Board / While you're out: Honey Cone / Westbound no.9: Flaming Ember / Chairman of the board: Chairmen Of The Board / One monkey: Chairmen Of The Board / Want ads: Honey Cone / Stick up: Honey Cone / Girls it ain't easy: Honey Cone / Everything's Tuesday: Chairmen Of The Board / Women's love rights: Lee, Laura / If you can beat me rockin': Lee, Laura / Mind, body and soul: Flaming Ember / Bring the boys home: Payne, Freda / Deeper and deeper: Payne, Freda / I'm on my way: Chairmen Of The Board

CD _____ HDH CD 501
HDH / Jul '89 / Pinnacle.

HITS OF THE 50'S
CD _____ MATCD 208
Castle / Dec '92 / BMG.

HITS OF THE 50'S VOLUME 2
(We're gonna) Rock around the clock: Haley, Bill & The Comets / April love: Boone, Pat / Great pretender: Platters / Sleep walk: Santo & Johnny / Rockabilly: Mitchell, Guy / It's only make believe: Twitty, Conway / It's only make believe: Twitty, Conway / Stagger Lee: Price, Lloyd / Tennesse waltz:

Page, Patti / Party doll: Knox, Buddy / Love is a many splendoured thing: Four Aces / Just walking in the rain: Ray, Johnnie / Twilight time: Platters / Come softly to me: Fleetwoods / I'll be home: Boone, Pat / I went to our wedding: Page, Patti
CD _____ MUCD 9006
Start / Apr '95 / Koch.

HITS OF THE 50S - VOLUME 1
Singin' the blues: Mitchell, Guy / Smoke gets in your eyes: Platters / All my love: Page, Patti / At the top: Danny & The Juniors / Love letters in the sand: Boone, Pat / Cry: Ray, Johnnie / Mr. Blue: Fleetwoods / Three coins in the fountain: Four Aces / This ole house: Clooney, Rosemary / Ain't that a shame: Boone, Pat / Tom Dooley: Kingston Trio / Answer me: Lane, Frankie / Great balls of fire: Lewis, Jerry Lee / Tequila: Champs / Heartache by the number: Mitchell, Guy / My prayer: Platters / (How much is that) doggie in the window: Page, Patti
CD _____ MUCD 9005
Start / Apr '95 / Koch.

HITS OF THE 60'S
Needles and pins / Always something there to remind me / Have I the right / Downtown / Catch the wind / Tossing and turning / Hang on Sloopy / Michelle / Out of time / Sunny afternoon / Summer in the city / Itchycoo Park / Let the heartaches begin / Silence is golden / First cut is the deepest / Build me up buttercup / Pictures of matchstick men / (If paradise is) Half as nice
CD _____ MCCD 028
Music Club / Sep '91 / Disc / THE / CM.

HITS OF THE 60'S
You've made me so very happy: Blood, Sweat & Tears / Mercy, mercy, mercy: Buckinghams / Mr. Tambourine Man: Byrds / Hang on Sloopy: McCoys / Just like me: Revere, Paul & The Raiders / Flowers on the wall: Statler Brothers / Young girl: Puckett, Gary & The Union Gap / Somebody to love: Great Society & Grace Slick / So you want to be a rock and roll star: Byrds / Evil ways: Santana / Weight: Kooper, Al & Mike Bloomfield / Down in the boondocks: Royal, Billy Joe / Time has come today: Chambers Brothers / Groovin' is easy: Electric Flag / More today than yesterday: Spiral Staircase
CD _____ 4804482
Embassy / Oct '95 / Sony.

HITS OF THE 60'S AND 70'S
CD Set _____ SBTCD 80
Connoisseur / Oct '89 / Pinnacle.

HITS OF THE 60'S VOL 2
CD Set _____ MBSCD 427
Castle / Nov '93 / BMG.

**HITS OF THE 60'S VOL.1
(4CD/MC Set)**
CD Set _____ MBSCD 401
Castle / Nov '95 / BMG.

HITS OF THE 60'S VOLUME 2
Runaway: Shannon, Del / Bachelors: Diane / Bad to me: Kramer, Billy J. / Ob la di ob la da: Marmalade / It's my party: Gore, Lesley / Do you love me: Poole, Brian / I like it: Gerry & The Pacemakers / Leader of the pack: Shangri-Las / Telstar: Tornados / When a man loves a woman: Sledge, Percy / Baby, now that I've found you: Foundations / Moody river: Boone, Pat / Alley oop: Hollywood Argyles / Big bad John: Dean, Jimmy / Deep purple: Tempo, Nino & April Stevens / Stranger on the shore: Bilk, Acker / Blue moon: Marcels / Those were the days: Hopkin, Mary
CD _____ MUCD 9008
Start / Apr '95 / Koch.

HITS OF THE 60'S VOLUME ONE
Chapel of love: Dixie Cups / Will you still love me tomorrow: Shirelles / I'm into something good: Herman's Hermits / I'm telling you now: Freddie & The Dreamers / Nut rocker: B Bumble & The Stingers / Young girl: Puckett, Gary / King of the road: Miller, Roger / Sheila: Roe, Tommy / Hey Paula: Paul & Paula / Save the last dance for me: Drifters / I'm sorry: Lee, Brenda / My old man's a dustman: Donegan, Lonnie / Little children: Kramer, Billy J. / Harper Valley PTA: Riley, Jeannie C. / Everlasting love: Love Affair / Baby come back: Equals / Sugar sugar: Archies / You'll never walk alone: Gerry & The Pacemakers
CD _____ MUCD 9007
Start / Apr '95 / Koch.

HITS OF THE 70'S
CD _____ CDSR 057
Telstar / Feb '95 / BMG.

HITS OF THE 80'S
Love action (I believe in love): Human League / Church of the poison mind: Culture Club / Temptation: Heaven 17 / Echo beach: Martha & The Muffins / Black Man Ray: China Crisis / Love don't live here anymore: Nail, Jimmy / You little thief: Sharkey, Feargal / Driving away from home: It's Immaterial / We don't have to take our clothes off: Stewart, Jermaine / (I just) died in your arms: Cutting Crew / Shattered dreams: Johnny Hates Jazz / China in your hand: T'Pau / Stutti: Wylie, Pete / Dream kitchen: Frazier Chorus / Straight up: Abdul, Paula / Mary's prayer: Danny Wilson / If only I could: Youngblood, Sydney

CD _____ CDVIP 126
Virgin / Jul '94 / EMI.

HITS OF THE 80'S
Centrefold: Geils, J. Band / Road to nowhere: Talking Heads / French kissin' in the USA: Harry, Deborah / Nineteen: Hardcastle, Paul / Wishful thinking: China Crisis / Running up that hill: Bush, Kate / If I was: Ure, Midge / She makes my day: Palmer, Robert / Heart and soul: T'Pau / True: Spandau Ballet / Cushed by the wheels of industry: Heaven 17 / Dancing with tears in my eyes: Ultravox / Don't worry be happy: McFerrin, Bobby / We close our eyes: Go West / Letter from America: Proclaimers / More than I can say: Sayer, Leo
CD _____ CDMFP 6136
Music For Pleasure / Feb '95 / EMI.

HITS OF THE 80'S VOL.2
Days: MacColl, Kirsty / Do you really want to hurt me: Culture Club / Christian: China Crisis / Life's what you make it: Talk Talk / Looking for Linda: Hue & Cry / Turning Japanese: Vapors / This is not a love song: Public Image Ltd / Sit and wait: Youngblood, Sydney / Come live with me: Heaven 17 / Calling all the heroes: It Bites / Big fun: Inner City / Wild world: Priest, Maxi / Night boat to Cairo: Madness / Moonlight shadow: Oldfield, Mike / Too late for goodbyes: Lennon, Julian / Turn back the clock: Johnny Hates Jazz / Heart and soul: T'Pau / Bette Davis eyes: Carnes, Kim / Enola Gay: O.M.D.
CD _____ CDVIP 136
Virgin / Sep '95 / EMI.

HITS OF THE 90'S
Baker Street: Undercover / Lovesick: Undercover / Happenin' all over again: Gordon, Lonnie / Beyond your wildest dreams: Gordon, Lonnie / Better the devil you know: Minogue, Kylie / Give me just a little more time: Minogue, Kylie / Shocked: Minogue, Kylie / Happy together: Donovan, Jason / I'm doing fine: Donovan, Jason / R.S.V.P.: Donovan, Jason / It's a fine day: Opus III / We got the love: Layton, Lindy / Energize: Slamm / Never gonna give you up: FKW / If you were with me now: Minogue, Kylie & Keith Washington / Nothing is forever: Ultracynic
CD _____ CDFA 3305
Fame / Sep '94 / EMI.

HITS OF THE 90'S
Whole of the moon: Waterboys / Thinking about your love: Thomas, Kenny / King of the road: Proclaimers / Ring my bell: Adeva & Monie Love / Is it like today: World Party / Got to have your love: Mantronix / Love and anger: Bush, Kate / Hold on: Wilson Phillips / I believe: EMF / Faithful: Go West / One and only: Hawkes, Chesney / Don't worry: Appleby, Kim / U can't touch this: M.C. Hammer / Ice ice baby: Vanilla Ice / Turtle power: Partners In Kryme / Counting every minute: Sonia
CD _____ CDMFP 6139
Music For Pleasure / Feb '95 / EMI.

HITS OF THE BLITZ
If a grey-haired lady says How's yer father: Wilbur, Jay & his band / We'll meet again: Petersen, Joe / It's a hap-hap-happy day: Roy, Harry & His Orchestra / We must all stick together: Geraldo & His Orchestra / Mem'ry of a rose: Loss, Joe & His band / Man who comes around: Connelly, Campbell & Co. Ltd / Oh Johnny oh Johnny: Young, Arthur / Run rabbit run: Ambrose & His Orchestra / Careless: White, Jack & His Collegians / Memories live longer than dreams: Dash, Irwin & Monte Ray / I haven't time to be a millionaire: Gonella, Nat & His New Georgians / It's a lovely day tomorrow: Hutch / nightingale sang in berkeley square: Layton, Turner / I hear bluebirds: Organ Dance Band & Me / Tiggerty boo: Geraldo & His Orchestra / We're gonna hang out the) washing on the Siegfried Line: Ambrose & His Orchestra / Make believe island: Bowlly, Al & Jim Mesene / I shall be waiting: Lipton, Sydney & His Grosvenor House Orchestra / Arm in arm: Lipton, Sydney & His Grosvenor House Orchestra / F.D.R. Jones: Askey, Arthur & Jack Hylton / Crash bang I want to go home: Robins, Phyllis / In the mood: Philips, Sid Trio
CD _____ PASTCD 9754
Flapper / Mar '92 / Pinnacle.

HITS OF THE SIXTIES
CD _____ EMPRCD 574
Emporio / Jul '95 / THE / Disc / CM.

HITS OF THE WAR YEARS
CD _____ CWNCD 2003
Javelin / Jun '95 / THE / Henry Hadaway Organisation.

**HITSVILLE USA
(The Tamla Motown Singles Collection 1959-1971/4CD Set)**
Money (That's what I want): Strong, Barrett / Shop around: Miracles / Please Mr. Postman: Marvelettes / Jamie: Holland, Eddie / One who really loves you: Wells, Mary / Do you love me: Contours / Beechwood 4-5789: Marvelettes / You beat me to the punch: Wells, Mary / Stubborn kind of fellow: Gaye, Marvin / Two lovers: Wells, Mary / You really got a hold on me: Miracles / Come and get these memories: Reeves, Martha & The Vandellas / Pride and joy:

Gaye, Marvin / Fingertips-Part 2: Wonder, Stevie / Heatwave: Reeves, Martha & The Vandellas / Mickey's monkey: Miracles / Leaving here: Holland, Eddie / Way you do the things you do: Temptations / My guy: Wells, Mary / Devil with the blue dress: Shorty Long / Every little bit hurts: Holloway, Brenda / Baby I need your loving: Four Tops / Dancing in the street: Reeves, Martha & The Vandellas / My smile is just a frown (turned upside down): Crawford, Carolyn / Needle in a haystack: Velvelettes / Baby love: Supremes / Come see about me: Supremes / How sweet it is (to be loved by you): Gaye, Marvin / My Girl (2): Temptations / My girl: Temptations / Really saying something: Velvelettes / Ask the lonely: Four Tops / Shotgun: Walker, Junior & The All Stars / Nowhere to run: Reeves, Martha & The Vandellas / When I'm gone: Holloway, Brenda / Ooo baby baby: Miracles / I can't help myself: Four Tops / First I look at the purse: Contours / Tracks of my tears: Miracles / It's the same old song: Four Tops / Love (makes me do foolish things): Reeves, Martha & The Vandellas / Take me in your arms: Weston, Kim / Uptight: Wonder, Stevie / Don't mess with Bill: Marvelettes / Darling baby: Elgins / This old heart of mine (is weak for you): Isley Brothers / Greetings (this is Uncle Sam): Monitors / Function at the junction: Shorty Long / Roadrunner: Walker, Junior & The All Stars / Ain't too proud to beg: Temptations / What becomes of the broken hearted: Ruffin, Jimmy / How sweet it is (to be loved by you) (2): Walker, Junior & The All Stars / Love's gone bad: Clark, Chris / You can't hurry love: Supremes / Beauty is only skin deep: Temptations / Heaven must have sent you: Elgins / Reach out, I'll be free: Four Tops / I'm losing you: Temptations / Standing in the shadows of love: Four Tops / It takes two: Gaye, Marvin & Kim Weston / Hunter gets captured by the game: Marvelettes / Jimmy Mack: Reeves, Martha & The Vandellas / Bernadette: Four Tops / Ain't no mountain high enough: Gaye, Marvin & Tammi Terrell / More love: Robinson, Smokey & The Miracles / I heard it through the grapevine: Knight, Gladys & The Pips / I second that emotion: Robinson, Smokey & The Miracles / I wish it would rain: Temptations / I can't give back the love I feel for you: Wright, Rita / Does your mama know about me: Taylor, Bobby & The Vancouvers / Ain't nothing like the real thing: Gaye, Marvin & Tammi Terrell / Love child: Ross, Diana & The Supremes / For once in my life: Wonder, Stevie / Cloud 9: Temptations / I heard it through the grapevine (2): Gaye, Marvin / Baby, baby, don't cry: Robinson, Smokey & The Miracles / Twenty five miles: Starr, Edwin / My whole world ended (the moment you left me): Starr, Edwin / What does it take (to win your love): Walker, Junior & The All Stars / I can't get next to you: Temptations / Baby I'm for real: Originals / Up the ladder to the roof: Supremes / I want you back: Jackson Five / Bells: Originals / Get ready: Rare Earth / ABC: Jackson Five / Ball of confusion: Temptations / Love you save: Jackson Five / Signed, sealed, delivered (I'm yours): Wonder, Stevie / War: Starr, Edwin / It's a shame: Spinners / Ain't no mountain high enough (2): Temptations / Still water (love): Four Tops / I'll be there: Jackson Five / Stoned love: Supremes / If I were your woman: Knight, Gladys & The Pips / Just my imagination: Temptations / What's going on: Gaye, Marvin / Never can say goodbye: Jackson Five / Nathan Jones: Supremes / I don't want to do wrong: Knight, Gladys & The Pips / Smiling faces sometimes: Undisputed Truth / Mercy mercy me: Gaye, Marvin / I just want to celebrate: Rare Earth
CD Set _____ 5301292
Motown / Jan '93 / PolyGram.

HITZ BLITZ
CD _____ RADCD 23
Global / Aug '91 / BMG.

HMV SAMPLER
Sleepy lagoon: Coates, Eric / Springtime suite fresh morning: Coates, Eric / Springtime suite noonday song: Coates, Eric / London suite (part 2): Coates, Eric / Saxorhapsody: Coates, Eric / Calling all workers: Coates, Eric / Coronation Scot: Torch, Sidney / Jumping bean: Torch, Sidney / Dambusters march: Torch, Sidney / Horse guards, Whitehall: Torch, Sidney / Barwick Green: Torch, Sidney / Smilin' through: Booth, Webster / Roses of Picardy: Oldham, Derek / I'll walk beside you: McCormack, John / Perfect day: Robeson, Paul / Bless this house: Midgley, Walter / Kashmiri love song: Dawson, Peter / Over the gate: Miles, Bernard / Me an' old Charlie: Miles, Bernard / Mind your heads please: Miles, Bernard / Danny Deever: Miles, Bernard
CD _____ CDHRS 1
HMV / Mar '92 / EMI.

HOAGY CARMICHAEL SONGBOOK
Stardust: Cole, Nat King / Washboard blues: Dorsey, Tommy / Rockin' chair: Armstrong, Louis / Little old lady: Hutch / Lamplighter's serenade: Miller, Glenn Orchestra / Lazybones: Carmichael, Hoagy / Georgia on my mind: Jones, Tom / Skylark: Shore, Dinah / Old music master: Mercer, Johnny / Nearness of you: Fitzgerald, Ella / Old buttermilk sky: Four Freshmen / I should have known you years ago: Davis,

Beryl / One morning in May: Monro, Matt / Blue orchids: Vaughan, Sarah / I get along without you very well: Newley, Anthony / In the cool, cool, cool of the evening: Mancini, Henry / Doctor, lawyer, indian chief: Hutton, Betty / Judy: Laine, Frankie / My resistance is low: Sarstedt, Robin / When love goes wrong: Whiting, Margaret & Jimmy Wakely / Memphis in June: Skellern, Peter / Ivy: Stafford, Jo / How little it matters, how little we know: Monro, Matt
CD _____ VSOPCD 123
Connoisseur / Oct '88 / Pinnacle.

HOBO BOP
Hobo bop: Nelson, Tommy / That long black train: Franklin, Stewart / Hey Mr. Porter: Pruitt, Ralph / I'm so lonely: Flagg, Bill / Goodbye train: Foley, Jim / Mystery train: Taylor, Vernon / Ho bo: Money, Curley / Midnight line: Riley, Bob / Long gone night train: Norman, Gene / One way track: Davis, Hank / Boxcar blues: Spurling, Hank / I'm a hobo: Reevers, Danny / Loco choo choo: Miller Bros. / Ride that train: James, Leon / Midnite express: Treadway / Back road to Dixie: Busbice, Wayne / Big black train: Johnston, Stan / Midnight train: Newman, Wayne / Train wistle boogie: Dean, Charles / Big train: Law, Art / Lonely lonely train: Anderson, Sonny / Folsom prison blues: Tidwell, Billy / Train: Runabouts / Haunted train: Millionaires / Woman train: Davis, Hank / Miami road: Phillipson, Larry Lee / Kansas city train: Lowery, Frankie / Long black train: Farmer, Larry / Train rock: Boni, Johnny
CD _____ CDBB 55012
Buffalo Bop / Apr '94 / Rollercoaster.

HOKUM BLUES 1924-29
CD _____ DOCD 5370
Document / Jul '95 / Jazz Music / Hot Shot / ADA.

HOLD BACK THE NIGHT
CD _____ DCD 5396
Scratch / Oct '94 / BMG.

HOLD YOUR GROUND
CD _____ LF 131CD
Lost & Found / Jan '95 / Plastic Head.

HOLDING ON
CD _____ SHCD 6015
Shanachie / Oct '95 / Koch / ADA / Greensleeves.

HOLDING ON TO LOVE
CD _____ STACD 048
Stardust / Aug '93 / Carlton Home Entertainment.

HOLIDAY GREETINGS
CD _____ SOW 90142
Sounds Of The World / Oct '95 / Target/ BMG.

HOLIDAY TRAILS FROM ROUMANIA
CD _____ CNCD 5983
Disky / Apr '94 / THE / BMG / Discovery / Pinnacle.

HOLLANDBILLY
CD _____ ROCKCD 9005
Charly / May '90 / Charly / THE / Cadillac.

HOLLERIN'
CD _____ ROUCD 0071
Rounder / Jul '95 / CM / Direct / ADA / Cadillac.

HOLLYWOOD LEGENDS
CD _____ LECDD 634
Wisepack / Aug '95 / THE / Conifer.

**HOLLYWOOD ROCK'N'ROLL
(12 Rare Rockabilly Tracks)**
Blue jeans: Glenn, Glen / Everybody's movin': Glenn, Glen / Would you: Rock 'n' Roll / Goofin' around: Glenn, Glen / I'm glad my baby's gone away: Glenn, Glen / One cup of coffee: Glenn, Glen / Don't push: Deal, Don / Topsy turvy: Zeppa, Ben Joe / Great shakin' fever: Burnette, Dorsey / Ezactly: Busch, Dick / Hollywood party: Busch, Dick / He will come back to me: Leslie, Alis
CD _____ CDCHM 1
Ace / Oct '89 / Pinnacle / Cadillac / Complete/Pinnacle.

HOMAGE TO NEW ORLEANS
CD _____ GOJCD 53087
Giants Of Jazz / Mar '92 / Target/BMG / Cadillac.

HOME ON THE RANGE
No one to call me darling: Autry, Gene / When the moon hangs high: Hillbillies / Any old time: Rodgers, Jimmie / Old trail: Autry, Gene / Why there's a tear in my eye: Rodgers, Jimmie & Sara Carter / Sunset trail: Hillbillies / Wonderful city: Rodgers, Jimmie / Dying cowboy: Hillbillies / Round up time out west: Rodgers, Jimmie / Blue yodel No. 5: Autry, Gene / Colorado sunset: Rogers, Roy / There's a bridle hangin' on the wall: Robison, Carson & His Pioneers / I've got the jailhouse blues: Autry, Gene / Whisper your mother's name: Autry, Gene / There's a ranch in the rockies: Rogers, Roy / Pistol packin' papa: Autry, Gene / Blue river train: Robison, Carson & His Pioneers / I'll always be a rambler: Autry, Gene

CD _____ PASTCD 7028
Flapper / Jan '94 / Pinnacle.

HOMELAND
(Collection of Black South African Music)
Ngayishela / Ea nyoloha khanyapa / Maraba start 500 / Ntlela a tingangeni / Nginbonile ubaba / Sayishayinduku / Khutsana / Umuntu / Mti wa wangeka / Ntate bereng / Yashimizi / Nayintombi ibaleka
CD _____ ROU 11549
Rounder / '91 / CM / Direct / ADA / Cadillac.

HONKY TONK FAVOURITES
CD _____ SWBCD 205
Sound Waves / Sep '94 / Target/BMG.

HONKY TONK JUMP PARTY
Honky tonk (pt 1) / Jump children (vooit vooit) / House party / Strato cruiser / Breaking up the house / Good morning judge / Special delivery stomp / Club Savoy / Hucklebuck with Jimmy / Flying home / Joe Joe jump / Mighty mighty man / Deacon moves in / I want you to be my baby / Joops jump / Train kept a rollin' / Have mercy baby / Harlem nocturne / Kidney stew / Bloodshot eyes / Love don't love nobody
CD _____ CDCHARLY 22
Charly / Aug '86 / Charly / THE / Cadillac.

HOOKED ON BIG BANDS
CD _____ EMPRCD 540
Emporio / Sep '94 / THE / Disc / CM.

HOOKED ON COUNTRY
CD Set _____ TREB 3011
Scratch / Mar '95 / BMG.

HOOKED ON DIXIE
CD _____ EMPRCD 517
Emporio / Jul '94 / THE / Disc / CM.

HOOKED ON MELODIES & MEMORIES
(4CD: Hooked On 40's, Dixie & Big Bands + Switched On Swing)
CD Set _____ EMPRBX 001
Emporio / Sep '94 / THE / Disc / CM.

HOOKED ON NUMBER ONES
CD _____ 74321101122
RCA / Aug '92 / BMG.

HOOTENANNY
Raining: _Ancient Beatbox_ / Just as the ...: _Edward II & The Red Hot Polkas_ / Valentine's: _Tabor, June & The Oyster Band_ / Wind and the ...: _Weddings, Parties & Anything_ / Vimbayi: _Four Brothers_ / Frontera del ensueno: _Rey De Copas_ / See how I miss you: _Cockburn, Bruce_ / Liberty: _Barely Works_ / Gastown: _God's Little Monkeys_ / Travelling circus: _White, Andy_ / Pigeon on the gate: _Spillane, Davy_ / Tape decks all over hell: _Boiled In Lead_ / Rumba for Nicaragua: _Happy End_ / Collectorman: _McLeod, Rory_ / Back to back: _Jolly Boys_
CD _____ GRILLCD 003
Cooking Vinyl / May '90 / Vital.

HORN, THE
(The Tenor Sax In Jazz)
Bird of Prey blues: _Hawkins, Coleman_ / Newport men (Not on CD.): _Freeman, Bud_ / Prelude to a kiss: _Webster, Ben_ / Neenah (Not on CD.) / No dues: _Cobb, Arnett_ / You are too beautiful: _Davis, Eddie 'Lockjaw'_ / Hey there: _Gray, Wardell_ / Darn that dream: _Gordon, Dexter_ / Going South (Not on CD.): _Ammons, Gene_ / Jive at five: _Chase is on: Rouse/Quinchette_ / Way you look tonight: _Stitt/Holloway_ / A la carte / I didn't know what time it was: _Shorter, Wayne_ / I want to talk about you: _Coltrane, John_ / Big George (Not on CD.): _Coleman, George_
CD _____ CDCHARLY 114
Charly / Apr '88 / Charly / THE / Cadillac.

HOT AIRE
(American Hot Bands Of The Twenties)
Hot aire: _Olsen, George & His Music_ / If I had a girl like you: _Seattle Harmony Kings_ / Darktown shuffle: _Seattle Harmony Kings_ / I'm goin' out if Lizzie comes in: _Romano, Phil & His Orchestra_ / Keep on croonin' a tune: _Romano, Phil & His Orchestra_ / Melancholy Lou: _Lanin, Howard & His Ben Franklin Dance Orchestra_ / Don't wake me up, let me dream: _Lanin, Howard & His Ben Franklin Dance Orchestra_ / Paddlin' Madelin' home: _White Kaufman & His Orchestra_ / Breezin' along with the breeze: _Seattle Harmony Kings_ / How many times: _Seattle Harmony Kings_ / Tiger rag: _Dornberger, Charles & His Orchestra_ / Does she love me positively, absolutely: _Garber, Jan & His Orchestra_ / What do I care what somebody said: _Garber, Jan & His Orchestra_ / You don't like it, not much: _Garber, Jan & His Orchestra_ / Swanee shore: _Crawford, Jack & His Ochestra_ / Sugar babe I'm leavin': _Blue Steele & His Orchestra_ / When the morning Glories wake up in the morning / Full title: When the morning glories wake up in the morning (Them I'll k): _Renard, Jacques & His Cocoanut Grove Orchestra_ / Baltimore: _Crawford, Jack & His Ochestra_
CD _____ DHAL 16
Halcyon / Sep '93 / Jazz Music / Cadillac.

HOT BRITISH DANCE BANDS 1925-1937
Riverboat shuffle: _Kit Kat Band_ / Sugarfoot stomp: _Devonshire Restaurant Dance Band_ / Stomp your feet: _Elizalde, Fred_ / Buffalo

---

rhythm: _Piccadilly Revels Band_ / That's a plenty: _Rhythm Maniacs_ / Tiger rag: _Hylton, Jack_ / 11.30 Saturday night: _Arcadian Dance Orchestra_ / Kalua: _Hughes, Spike_ / Choo choo: _Payne, Jack_ / Bessie couldn't help it: _Cotton, Billy_ / Stomping: _Wornell, Jimmy Hot Blue-Bottles_ / Nobody's sweetheart: _Fox, Roy_ / White jazz: _Stone, Lew_ / Sentimental gentleman from Georgia: _Loss, Joe_ / Rockin' in rhythm: _Madame Tussaud's Dance Orchestra_ / Your mother's son-in-law: _Six Swingers_ / Shine: _Lawrence, Brian_ / China boy: _Bond Street Swingers_ / Milenberg joys: _Roy, Harry_ / Cotton pickers' congregation: _Ambrose_ / What a perfect combination: _Noble, Ray_
CD _____ CBC 1005
Timeless Historical / Jan '92 / New Note / Pinnacle.

HOT CITY NIGHTS
(16 Classic Rock Tracks)
I want to break free: _Queen_ / Alone: _Heart_ / New sensation: _INXS_ / Crazy crazy nights: _Kiss_ / Summer of '69: _Adams, Bryan_ / Big log: _Plant, Robert_ / I want to know what love is: _Foreigner_ / Wonderful tonight: _Clapton, Eric_ / Livin' on a prayer: _Bon Jovi_ / Hot in the city: _Idol, Billy_ / Start talking love: _Magnum_ / Here I go again: _Whitesnake_ / Lavender: _Marillion_ / We belong: _Benatar, Pat_ / Look away: _Big Country_ / Spirit of radio: _Rush_
CD _____ 836 057-2
Vertigo / Aug '88 / PolyGram.

HOT GYPSY SUMMER
CD _____ HRCD 8058
Disky / Jul '94 / THE / BMG / Discovery / Pinnacle.

HOT HATS INCLUDING FATS
CD _____ NCD 8812
Phontastic / Dec '94 / Wellard / Jazz Music / Cadillac.

HOT HOT REGGAE, VOLS 1 & 2
CD _____ 840602
FM / '91 / Sony.

HOT HOT SOCA
CD _____ RRTGCD 7706
Rohit / '88 / Jetstar.

HOT JAZZ 1928-30
CD _____ HRM 6004
Hermes / Jan '89 / Nimbus.

HOT MUSIC FROM CUBA 1907-1936
CD _____ HQCD 23
Harlequin / Oct '93 / Swift / Jazz Music / Wellard / Hot Shot / Cadillac.

HOT REGGAE FEVER
CD _____ 12232
Laserlight / Sep '93 / Target/BMG.

HOT RHYTHM AND COOL BLUES - TEXAS STYLE
CD _____ IMP 702
Iris Music / Jul '95 / Discovery.

HOT ROD GANG
Big wheel: _Benton, Walt_ / This old bomb of mine: _Stange, Howie_ / Hot rod: _Berry Brothers_ / Spinning my wheels: _Brooks, Chuck_ / Spanner hub caps: _Davis, Pat_ / Full racing cam: _Ringo, Eddie_ / Girl and a hot rod: _Dean, Richie_ / Big green car: _Carroll, Jimmy_ / Gas money: _Carroll, Jimmy_ / Hot rod baby: _Davis, Rocky_ / Long John's flagpole rock: _Roller, Long John_ / Hot rod boogie: _Brady, Ronny_? / Pump I hood of hot rod / '56 Ford: _Ball, Woody_ / Shot rod: _Conny & Bellhops_ / Fred and shaker: _Gallagher, James_ / Hot-rodders dream: _Burden, Ray_ / Hot rod race: _Williams, Rob_ / Daddy Joe: _Ciolino, Pete_ / Sidewalk rock 'n' roll: _Warden, J.W._ / I'll be leavin' you: _Moore, Turner_ / Brake Jake: _Fern, Mike_ / Cruisin': _Bucky & Premiers_ / Red hot car: _Verne, Bobby_ / Lorene: _Lemons, Bill_ / Speedway rocker: _Woodard, Jerry_ / Stop jivin' start drivin': _Reyes, Burt_ / Dig that crazy driver: _Penix, William_ / Car hop: _Export_ / High way robbery: _Fry, Bobby_ / Cop car: _West, Rick_
CD _____ CBBB 55005
Buffalo Bop / Apr '94 / Rollercoaster.

HOT ROD HITS
Double a fueler: _Deuce Coupes_ / Nite prowler: _Deuce Coupes_ / Road rattler: _Deuce Coupes_ / Tijuana gasser: _Deuce Coupes_ / Gear masher: _Deuce Coupes_ / Candy apple blues: _Deuce Coupes_ / Satan's chariot: _Deuce Coupes_ / Monkey see: _Deuce Coupes_ / Top eliminator: _Darts_ / Street machine: _Darts_ / Corn pone: _Darts_ / Hollywood drag: _Darts_ / Alky burner: _Darts_ / Slauson and soto: _Darts_ / Detroit iron: _Darts_ / Cruisin': _Darts_ / Four banger: _De-Fenders_ / Deuces wild: _De-Fenders_ / Taco wagon: _De-Fenders_ / Movin' and groovin': _De-Fenders_ / Skin diver: _De-Fenders_ / Loose nuts: _De-Fenders_ / Little Deuce Coupe: _De-Fenders_ / Drag beat: _De-Fenders_ / Wheelin' home: _De-Fenders_ / Tequila Joe: _De-Fenders_ / Rum runner: _De-Fenders_ / Roadrunner: _De-Fenders_
CD _____ CDCHD 303
Ace / Feb '91 / Pinnacle / Cadillac / Complete/Pinnacle.

HOT SOUL MUSIC VOL.1
CD _____ 377161
Arcade / Aug '89 / Sony / Grapevine.

HOT WIRED MONSTERTRUX
Intro / Wish: _Nine Inch Nails_ / Finger on the trigger: _Excessive Force_ / Tool and die: _Consolidated_ / Godlike: _K.M.F.D.M._ / Jesus built my hotrod: _Ministry_ / Kooler than Jesus: _My Life With The Thrill Kill Kult_ / Provision: _Frontline Assembly_ / Looking forward: _CNN_ / Murder Inc: _Murder Inc._ / Edge of no control: _Meat Beat Manifesto_ / Skinflower: _Young Gods_ / Motorbike: _Sheep On Drugs_ / Headhunter: _Front 242_ / Family man: _Nitzer Ebb_
East West / Feb '93 / Warner Music.

HOTDOGS, HITS & HAPPY DAYS 1
CD _____ LPCD 1011
Disky / May '94 / THE / BMG / Discovery / Pinnacle.

HOTDOGS, HITS & HAPPY DAYS 10
CD _____ LPCD 1020
Disky / May '94 / THE / BMG / Discovery / Pinnacle.

HOTDOGS, HITS & HAPPY DAYS 2
CD _____ LPCD 1012
Disky / May '94 / THE / BMG / Discovery / Pinnacle.

HOTDOGS, HITS & HAPPY DAYS 3
CD _____ LPCD 1013
Disky / May '94 / THE / BMG / Discovery / Pinnacle.

HOTDOGS, HITS & HAPPY DAYS 4
CD _____ LPCD 1014
Disky / May '94 / THE / BMG / Discovery / Pinnacle.

HOTDOGS, HITS & HAPPY DAYS 5
CD _____ LPCD 1015
Disky / May '94 / THE / BMG / Discovery / Pinnacle.

HOTDOGS, HITS & HAPPY DAYS 6
CD _____ LPCD 1016
Disky / May '94 / THE / BMG / Discovery / Pinnacle.

HOTDOGS, HITS & HAPPY DAYS 7
CD _____ LPCD 1017
Disky / May '94 / THE / BMG / Discovery / Pinnacle.

HOTDOGS, HITS & HAPPY DAYS 8
CD _____ LPCD 1018
Disky / May '94 / THE / BMG / Discovery / Pinnacle.

HOTDOGS, HITS & HAPPY DAYS 9
CD _____ LPCD 1019
Disky / May '94 / THE / BMG / Discovery / Pinnacle.

HOTTER THAN HELL
CD _____ BMCD 50
Black Mark / Mar '94 / Plastic Head.

HOUSE 2 HOUSE MEGA RAVE 1
CD _____ DCD 5317
Disky / Nov '93 / THE / BMG / Discovery / Pinnacle.

HOUSE COLLECTION
Lifting me higher: _Gems For Jem_ / Sexy movemaker: _Fifth Circuit_ / Anthem: _Black Shells_ / Choose me: _Cookie_ / Angel: _Sub Sub_ / I'm in love: _Summers, Kathy_ / Make my love: _Christopher, Shawn_ / All over me: _Carr, Suzi_ / Get down to love: _Music Choir_ / You don't turn around: _Bottom Dollar_ / Trouble: _Cardwell, Joi_ / Time to stop: _Sanchez, Roger_ / House luck: _Jump Cutz_ / 2 Fatt guitars: _Delorme_ / Le voie le soleil: _Subliminal Cuts_ / Action: _Alfredo_ / I've got the freedom: _Tin Tin Out_ / Retro Euro vibe peace: _Woomera_ / Callin': _Callin_ / Foreplay EP: _UK Movin_ / Ibiza go wild: _Pedro & Raoul_ / Into your heart: _Rozzo_ / Calm down: _Chris & James_ / Voices inside my handbag: _Paterson & Price_ / So damn hot: _Boomerand_ / Hot dog: _Key Aura_ / Better with Gee: _Thermo Statik_ / Time travellers: _Love Child & Rolfe_ / Never gonna give you up: _Turner, Ruby_ / Ay ninos: _Amnesia_ / 2 Fatt guitars (mix): _Delorme_ / Trippin on sunshine: _Pizzaman_ / Echo drop: _Taiko_ / You and me: _Rhyme Time Productions_ / Testiment one: _Chubby Chunks_ / Beatniks: _Delorme_ / Shake your body: _L.W.S._ / Better vibes: _Funky Monkey_ / Acid folk: _Perplexer_
CD Set _____ FHC 1CD
Fantazia Music / Nov '94 / 3MV / Sony.

HOUSE COLLECTION VOL.3
(3LP/2MC/2CD Set)
CD Set _____ FHC 3CD
Fantazia Music / Sep '95 / 3MV / Sony.

HOUSE COLLECTION VOLUME 2
Useless man: _Minty_ / House fever: _Burger_ / G marks the spot: _Rozzo_ / Throw: _Paperclip People_ / Sweet attitude: _Sophie's Boys_ / Lazy swing is: _Sound Crowd_ / Throw reprise: _Paperclip People_ / Liberation: _Lippy_ / You / Love Vs. Hate: _League Of Sinners_ / Nu energy: _Hard 2 Dance_ / Why are your feet stompin': _Hard 2 Dance_ / Cool n' chips E.P.: _Hard 2 Dance_ / Pitch 'n' drop: _Cakebread, Lee_ / Where's the party: _D.J. Saab_ / It's alright: _Sain II_ / Manhattan anthem: _East Village Loft Society_ / It: _Creation_ / Juds submarine: _Submarine_ / In T house: _Johans_ /

You took my lovin': _Total Control_ / Basement in sound: _More & Groove_ / Feel the music: _BBR Street Gang_ / Stomp: _Shimmon_ / Funky thing: _Indigo_ / Everybody is somebody: _Flipped Out_ / Tall and handsome: _Outrage_ / Hey man: _Antyma_ / Son of Eilmot: _Mighty Dubaiks_ / Strong: _Phorce_ / Cry boy: _Cosmopolitan_ / Krazy noise: _Numerical Value_ / Driftwood: _Tom Tom_ / Mooncat: _Shaker_ / Good times: _Funkydory_ / Hooked: _99th Floor Elevators_ / Bits and pieces: _Artomesia_ / Burning up: _De Vit, Tony_ / Gotta get: _Must_ / Keep ya head on: _Rizzo_ / Organgrinder: _Deeper Cut_ / Rock express: _Wizzard_
CD Set _____ FHC 2CD
Fantazia Music / Apr '95 / 3MV / Sony.

HOUSE FUNKIN'
CD _____ JAPECD 102
Escapade / Sep '94 / 3MV / Sony.

HOUSE FUNKIN' 3
CD _____ JAPECD 104
Escapade / Jun '95 / 3MV / Sony.

HOUSE FUNKIN'2
CD _____ JAPECD 103
Escapade / Feb '95 / 3MV / Sony.

HOUSE NATION VOL. 1
CD _____ REACTCD 047
React / Sep '94 / Vital.

HOUSE OF HANDBAG AUTUMN WINTER COLLECTION, THE
CD Set _____ USCD 4
Ultrasound / Oct '95 / Grapevine.

HOUSE OF HANDBAG, THE
CD Set _____ USCD 3
Ultrasound / Jul '95 / Grapevine.

HOUSE OF HITS
CD _____ CDHI 88
Needle / Apr '88 / Pinnacle.

HOUSE OF LIMBO
CD _____ LIMB 18CD
Limbo / Jul '93 / Pinnacle.

HOUSE OF LONDON
CD _____ OCEAN 1CD
Ocean / Apr '95 / Else.

HOUSE OF LONDON VOL.2
CD _____ OCEANCD 002
Ocean / Sep '95 / Else.

HOUSE OF LOVERS VOL. 1
CD _____ RECD 01
Rupie Edwards / Apr '93 / Jetstar.

HOUSE ON FIRE
CD _____ RHRCD 58
Red House / Oct '95 / Koch / ADA.

HOUSE PARTY
(20 Great Hits Of The Sixties)
Ain't nothing but a house party: _Showstoppers_ / When you walk in the room: _Searchers_ / Summer in the city: _Lovin' Spoonful_ / Colour my world: _Clark, Petula_ / Even the bad times are good: _Tremeloes_ / Sunny afternoon: _Kinks_ / Nobody needs your love: _Pitney, Gene_ / Massage understood: _Shaw, Sandie_ / Lazy Sunday: _Small Faces_ / Universal soldier: _Donovan_ / Pictures of matchstick men: _Status Quo_ / Angel of the morning: _Arnold, P.P._ / Judy in disguise: _Fred, John & His Playboy Band_ / Let the heartaches begin: _Baldry, Long John_ / Long live love: _Shaw, Sandie_ / My love: _Clark, Petula_ / Love potion no.9: _Searchers_ / Death of a clown: _Davies, Dave_ / Looking through the eyes of love: _Pitney, Gene_ / Happy together: _Turtles_
CD _____ TRTCD 105
TrueTrax / Dec '94 / THE.

HOUSE RARITIES
CD _____ XTR 17CDM
CD _____ XTR 17CDU
X:Treme / Oct '95 / Pinnacle / SRD.

HOUSE ROCKIN' BLUES
I got to go: _Little Walter_ / Mama talk to your daughter: _Lenoir, J.B._ / Young fashioned ways: _Waters, Muddy_ / I have a little girl: _Howlin' Wolf_ / You don't love me (you don't care): _Diddley, Bo_ / Tired of crying: _Hope, Morris_ / I'm leaving you: _Spann, Otis_ / Rattlesnake: _Brim, John_ / Poison Ivy: _Mabon, Willie_ / You got to love me: _Arnold, Billy Boy_ / Mellow down easy: _Little Walter_ / Little girl: _Diddley, Bo_ / Date bait: _Blue Smitty_ / I would hate to see you go (Be careful): _Brim, John_ / If it ain't me: _Rogers, Jimmy_ / Who will be next: _Howlin' Wolf_ / Close to you: _Waters, Muddy_ / Sweet on you baby: _Arnold, Billy Boy_ / Goat: _Williamson, Sonny Boy_ / He knows the rules: _McCracklin, Jimmy_ / I'm satisfied: _Rush, Otis_ / Let me love you baby: _Guy, Buddy_ / Madison blues: _James, Elmore_ / Look out Mabel: _Crockett, G.L._ / Twirl: _Little Luther_ / Someday: _Nighthawk, Robert_ / Let's go out tonight: _Hooker, John Lee_
CD _____ CDCHD 610
Ace / Mar '95 / Pinnacle / Cadillac / Complete/Pinnacle.

HOUSETRAX 2
Can you party: _Royal House_ / Day in the life: _Black Riot_ / Don't turn your love: _Park Avenue_ / And the break goes on: _Break Boys_ / Jealousy and lies: _Jonah, Julian_ / Number nine: _Dereck_ / Magic: _Kahn, Bon_

CD _____ CDTRAX 2
Street Sounds / Jun '88 / BMG.

HOW DOES IT FEEL
CD _____ 8283832
London / Jan '93 / PolyGram.

HOW LONG HAS THIS BEEN GOING ON ?
CD _____ CD 20044
Pablo / May '86 / Jazz Music / Cadillac / Complete/Pinnacle.

HOW TO USE MACHINERY
CD _____ MA33-2
Machinery / Nov '93 / Plastic Head.

HOW YOU FE SEY DAT PRESENTS "HOT"
CD _____ SONCD 0052
Sonic Sounds / Jul '93 / Jetstar.

HOWDY
(25 Hillbilly All Time Greats)
Goin' to the barn-dance tonight: Robinson, Carson & His Pioneers / It ain't gonna rain no mo': Hall, Wendell / Wreck of the old '97: Dalhart, Vernon / Runaway train: Dalhart, Vernon / Red wing: Puckett, Riley / Blue yodel: Rodgers, Jimmie / Brakeman's blues: Rodgers, Jimmie / My clinch mountain home: Carter Family / Foggy mountain top: Carter Family / Little Bessie: Alabama Barnstormers / She's too good for me: Cole, Rex Mountaineers / In the Cumberland mountains: Robinson, Carson / When the curtains of the night are pinned back by the stars: Layman, Zora & The Hometowners / Atlanta bound: Autry, Gene / She came rollin' down the mountain: Aarons Sisters / Little old sod shanty on my claim: Williams, Marc / Ragtime Cowboy Joe: Hilbillies / I want to be a cowboy's sweetheart: Montana, Patsy & The Prairie Ramblers / Meet me by the icehouse, Lizzie: Original Hoosier Hotshots / Wabash cannonball: Acuff, Roy & His Crazy Tennesseans / Golden lariat: Montana Slim / New San Antonio Rose: Wills, Bob & His Texas Playboys / Walkin' the floor over you: Tubb, Ernest / Born to lose: Daffan, Ted & The Texans / West ain't what it used to be: Robinson, Carson & His Pioneers
CD _____ CDAJA 5140
ASV / May '95 / Koch.

HOWL - A FAREWELL COMPILATION OF UNRELEASED SONGS
CD _____ GRCD 352
Glitterhouse / Dec '94 / Direct / ADA.

HUAYNO MUSIC OF PERU VOL.1 1949-89
CD _____ ARHCD 320
Arhoolie / Apr '95 / ADA / Direct / Cadillac.

HUAYNO MUSIC OF PERU VOL.2 1960-70
CD _____ ARHCD 338
Arhoolie / Apr '95 / ADA / Direct / Cadillac.

HUBERT GREGG SAYS THANKS FOR THE MEMORY
China stomp: Hampton, Lionel & His Orchestra / Transatlantic lullaby: Layton, Turner / There's a small hotel: Daniels, Bebe / Scatterbrain: Brisson, Carl / Thanks for the memory: Hope, Bob & Shirley Ross / Baby face: Jolson, Al / Too romantic: Dorsey, Tommy Orchestra / Wind in the willows: Hutch / Physician: Lawrence, Gertrude / You're driving me crazy: Reinhardt, Django & Stephane Grappelli / After you've gone: Venuti, Joe & Eddie Lang / Sugarfoot stomp: Goodman, Benny Orchestra / Super special picture of the year: Yacht Club Jazz Band / Let's put out the lights and go to sleep: Howes, Bobby / Dinah: Crosby, Bing / Tea for two: Tatum, Art / One I'm looking for: Buchanan, Jack / I'm gonna get lit up (when the lights go on in London): Gregg, Hubert / Si tu m'aimes: Sablon, Jean / At the Darktown strutter's ball: Dorsey, Jimmy Orchestra / Jealous of me: Waller, Fats / Begin the beguine: Shaw, Artie / Princess is awakening: Laye, Evelyn / Maybe it's because I'm a Londoner: Gregg, Hubert
CD _____ PASTCD 7024
Flapper / Sep '93 / Pinnacle.

HUGE COMPILATION
CD _____ ORBITCD 4
Orbital / Aug '92 / BMG.

HUMAN MUSIC
CD _____ HMS 100CD
Homestead / Sep '88 / SRD.

HUMBUGGARY
CD _____ BAH 13
Humbug / May '95 / Pinnacle.

HUNGARIAN TRADITIONAL MUSIC
CD _____ PS 65117
Playasound / Nov '93 / Harmonia Mundi / ADA.

HUNGARY - THE LAST PASSAGE
CD _____ C 580031
Ocora / Oct '94 / Harmonia Mundi / ADA.

HURDY GURDY IN FRANCE, THE
CD _____ Y 225109CD
Silex / Feb '95 / ADA.

HUT PEEL SESSIONS, THE
Siva: Smashing Pumpkins / Girl named Sandoz: Smashing Pumpkins / Smiley:

Smashing Pumpkins / Wave: Revolver / John's not mad: Revolver / Already there: Verve / Je reve: Moose
CD _____ SFMCD 214
Strange Fruit / Nov '92 / Pinnacle.

HYMNE AN DIE POSIE
CD _____ EFA 127142
Weisser Herbst / Apr '95 / SRD.

HYPERTENSION SAMPLER
CD _____ HY 153CD
Hypertension / Apr '95 / Total/BMG / Direct / ADA.

HYPNOTRANCE - INTERGALACTIC HARD TRANCE
CD Set _____ AR 9902206
Arcade / Aug '94 / Sony / Grapevine.

I ASKED FOR WHISKEY
CD _____ IGOCD 2028
Indigo / Aug '95 / Direct / ADA.

I BELIEVE
CD _____ TCD 2811
Telstar / Dec '95 / BMG.

I CAN'T BELIEVE IT'S NOT TRIP HOP
CD _____ NOR 001CD
North South / Oct '95 / Pinnacle.

I FALL TO PIECES
(20 Country Classics)
Charly / Mar '93 / Charly / THE / Cadillac.
CD _____ CDCD 1073

I GOT IT BAD AND THAT AIN'T GOOD
I got it bad and that ain't good: Holiday, Billie / Sad letter: Waters, Muddy / Dusty road: Hooker, John Lee / Commit a crime: Howlin' Wolf / Cool disposition: Williamson, Sonny Boy / Little rain: Reed, Jimmy / Blues with a feeling: Little Walter / Please don't talk about me when I'm gone: Holiday, Billie / Mean mistreater: Waters, Muddy / Process: Hooker, John Lee / Moanin' at midnight: Howlin' Wolf / Blue tail fly: Leadbelly / Dust my broom: James, Elmore / Nice work if you can get it: Holiday, Billie / Whiskey and wimmen: Hooker, John Lee / Diamonds at your feet: Waters, Muddy / I'm in the mood: Hooker, John Lee / In New Orleans: Leadbelly / Killing floor: Howlin' Wolf / Fine and mellow: Holiday, Billie / How blue can you get: King, B.B. / Off the wall: Little Walter / Mean red spider: Waters, Muddy / Goin' down slow: Howlin' Wolf / Frisco blues: Hooker, John Lee
CD _____ CDGRF 127
Tring / '93 / Tring / Prism.

(I GOT NO KICK AGAINST) MODERN JAZZ
Long and winding road: Benson, George / She's leaving home: Tyner, McCoy / She's so heavy: Groove Collective / And I love her: Krall, Diana / Fool on the hill: Scott, Tom / Michelle: Lewis, Ramsey / Day in the life: Ritenour, Lee / Let it be: Rangel, Nelson / Eleanor Rigby: Corea, Chick / While my guitar gently weeps: Freeman, Russ & The Rippingtons / In my life: Spyro Gyra / Here there and everywhere: Benoit, David / Blackbird: Sandoval, Arturo / Yesterday: Grusin, Dave / Imagine: Kishino, Yoshiko
CD _____ GRP 98322
GRP / Oct '95 / BMG / New Note.

I HAVE TO PAINT MY FACE
CD _____ ARHCD 432
Arhoolie / Jan '96 / ADA / Direct / Cadillac.

I JUST LOVE JAZZ PIANO
Jumpin' Jacques / Thou swell / It's you or no one / 'S Wonderful / Nichols and dimes / Who's blues / Cherokee / Blues too much / Thou swell #2 / Together / How about you / Apart
CD _____ SV 0117
Savoy Jazz / Apr '92 / Conifer / ADA.

I LOVE FUSE
CD _____ FUSE 001CD
Fuse / Jan '96 / Plastic Head.

I ONLY WROTE THIS SONG
CD _____ ESSCD 223
Essential / Oct '94 / Total/BMG.

I SHALL SING
CD _____ CDTRL 289
Trojan / Mar '94 / Jetstar / Total/BMG.

I SHALL SING! VOL 2
Best thing for me: Powell, June / I see you my love: Griffiths, Marcia / Silly wasn't it: Forrester, Sharon / Love that a woman should give a man: Dillon, Phyllis / She said on talking: Mowatt, Judy / Please Mr. Please: Powell, June / Mother nature: Sweet, Roslyn / Heart made of stone (Vocal): Hall, Audrey / Heart made of stone (Version): Hit Squad / You can wake up with me: Powell, June / Love the one you're with: Dillon, Phyllis / Promises: Richard,

Cynthia / You're not my kind: Naomi / I can't help it darling: Jones, Barbara / Put a little love away: Forrester, Sharon / Something about you: Jordon, Sidonie / I'll be everything to you (Vocal): Naomi / I'll be everything to you (Version): Hit Squad
CD _____ CDTRL 316
Trojan / Mar '94 / Jetstar / Total/BMG.

I TURNED INTO A HELIUM BALLOON
Mirror of your mind: We The People / Color of love: We The People / You burn me up and down: We The People / St. John's shop: We The People / I'm gonna be: We The People / Half of wednesday: We The People / My brother, the man: We The People / Free information: We The People / Too much noise: We The People / By the rule: We The People / Alfred, what kind of man are you: We The People / Beginning of the end: We The People / I ain't no miracle worker: Brogues / Don't shoot me down: Brogues / Let it be: Blaskey, Lindy & The Lavelles / You ain't tuff: Blaskey, Lindy & The Lavelles / Spinach: Boston Tea Party / Words: Boston Tea Party / I'm spinning: Fenwyck / Mindrocker: Fenwyck / State of mind: Fenwyck / Away: Fenwyck / I wanna die: Fenwyck / Iye: Fenwyck / Show me the way: Free For All / Psychedelic siren: Daybreakers / Somebody's son: Tikis / Thoughts: Front Page News / Lies: Knickerbockers / My feet are off the ground: Knickerbockers
CD _____ CDWIKD 130
Big Beat / Jun '94 / Pinnacle.

I WILL ALWAYS LOVE YOU
All the love in the world: Warwick, Dionne / Do what you do: Jackson, Jermaine / As time goes by: Nilsson, Harry / One to one: Hall & Oates / Help me make it through the night: Nelson, Willie / Love me warm and tender: Anka, Paul / Hurry home: Wavelength / Love is the sweetest thing: Skellern, Peter / Never gonna let you go: Mendes, Sergio / Fool (if you think it's over): Brooks, Elkie / On the wings of love: Osborne, Jeffrey / I wanna stay with you: Gallagher & Lyle / I will: Fury, Billy / Answer me: Dickson, Barbara / Losing you: Springfield, Dusty / Love me: Elliman, Yvonne / Nothing's gonna change my love for you: Medeiros, Glenn / You don't know how glad I am: Dee, Kiki / I just wanna be your everything: Gibb, Andy / Love her: Walker Brothers / Darling be home soon: Lovin' Spoonful / Baby don't change your mind: Knight, Gladys / True love ways: Holly, Buddy / Wind beneath my wings: Greenwood, Lee
CD _____ CD 3219
Carlton Home Entertainment / Sep '92 / Carlton Home Entertainment.

I-5 KILLERS VOL.3
What used to be: Gift / Blondes: Everclear / Crash: Kpants / Punch: Thirty Ought Six / Lines: Kaia / Simeon flick: Skiploader / Edward Hopper song: Whirlees / Jake's dream: Tree Killing Isabel / Never win: Wipers / It's a lie: Gravel Pit / Ugly stick: Ice Cream Headache / Get outta my way: Starlite Trio / Rock your baby: Oblivion Seekers / Evil style: Anal Solvent / Josh has a crush: New Bad Things / Metropolis 2664: Caveman Shoestore / Aloha Steve and Dan-O: Oswald 5-0 / Your Mom rules: Supersuckers
CD _____ SZ 0213
T/K / Jun '94 / Pinnacle.

I.A.I. FESTIVAL
CD _____ 123859-2
IAI / Nov '93 / Harmonia Mundi / Cadillac.

IBIZA '95
CD _____ 21 CCCD 001
21st Century Opera / Nov '95 / Total/BMG.

ICHIBAN BLUES AT CHRISTMAS
(All I want for Christmas is to) lay around: Willis, Chuck / Absent minded Santa: McCain, Jerry / Lonesome Christmas: Blues Boy Willie / Santa Claus is back in town: Brown, Nappy / Christmas is here again: Taylor, Johnny / Christmas time (comes but once a year): Lynn, Trudy / I didn't get nothin' for Christmas: Garrett, Vernon / Christmas tears: Dee, David / Christmas, don't forget about me: Drink Small / Please come home for Christmas: Willis, Chuck
CD _____ ICH 1126 CD
Ichiban / Nov '91 / Koch.

ICHIBAN SAMPLER
CD _____ ICH 7802-2
Ichiban / Jan '94 / Koch.

IF IT AIN'T A HIT I'LL EAT MY....BABY
Think twice: Wilson, Jackie & Laverne Baker / Two time Slim/Hey, shine: Snatch & The Poontangs / Somebody else was suckin' my dick last night: Wolff, Fred Combo / Meat man: Vickery, Mack / Stoop down baby: Willis, Chuck / Deacon Jones/L.A. women love Uncle Bud: Chavis, Boozoo / Don't fuck around with love: Blenders / Long John/Short John: Washington, Dinah / Rotten cocksuckers' ball: Clovers / Hard driving blues: Milburn, Amos / Stackers feet: Brown, Roy / Joe's joint: Ferre, Cliff / Fuck off (You dirty rooster): Gaillard, Slim
CD _____ CDZ 2009
Zu Zazz / Apr '94 / Rollercoaster.

IF YOU JUST TUNED IN
(Live From The Mean Fiddler's Acoustic Room)
Dollar tree: Hawkins, Ted / When we were young: Orchard, Pat / Love your shoes: Cunningham, Andrew / Rover: Sons Of The Desert / Down the wine garden: Little Big Band / It's not that bad anymore: Barely Works / White cloud: To Hell With Burgundy / Spitting: And All Because The Lady Loves / Three legged men: Harding, John Wesley / Tree to breathe: Dinner Ladies / Partisan: Keineg, Katell / I ain't got nothin' yet: Hawkins, Ted
CD _____ AWCD 1017
Awareness / Apr '90 / ADA.

IFACH VOL. 1
CD _____ IFACHCD 1
Ifach / Jun '95 / Kudos.

IFI PALASA - TONGAN BRASS
CD _____ PANCD 2044
Pan / May '94 / ADA / Direct / CM.

IL SUONO DI ROMA
CD _____ ACVCD 2001
ACV / Oct '94 / Plastic Head / SRD.

I'LL BE SEEING YOU
CD _____ CECD 002
Collector's Edition / Jan '96 / Magnum Music Group.

I'LL BE SEEING YOU: THOSE ROMANTIC 40'S
(Nice 'n' Easy Series)
CD _____ 8440581
Eclipse / Mar '92 / PolyGram.

I'LL DANCE TILL DE SUN BREAKS THROUGH
(Ragtime, Cakewalks & Stomps 1898-1923)
That moaning saxophones rag: Six Brown Brothers / Florida rag: Van Eps Trio / Bacchanal rag: Peerless Orchestra / Alabama skedaddle: Mitcham, William / Castle walk: Europe's Society Orchestra / From soup to nuts: Arndt, Felix / Smoky mokes: Metropolitan Orchestra / Eli Green's cake walk: Cullen & Collins / Cake walk: Victor Minstrels / I'll dance till de sun breaks through: Joyce, Archibald & His Orchestra / T'ain't nobody's business if I do: Matson, Charles Creole Serenaders / Whistling Rufus: Oakley, Olly / Wild cherries rag: Victor Orchestra / Won't you come home, Bill Bailey: Collins, Arthur / Stomp dance: Victor Military Band / Calico rag: Banta, Frank & Howard Kopp / Smiles and chuckles - A jazz rag: Six Brown Brothers / On the Levee: Victor Minstrels / Trombone sneeze - a humoresque cakewalk: Sousa's Band / Two key rag: Conway's Band
CD _____ CDSDL 336
Saydisc / Mar '94 / Harmonia Mundi / Direct.

ILLEGAL JUNGLE VOL.2
Lovin' you: Suburban Soul / Worries 'n' trouble: Stache & Michael X / Little star: Elegant Posse / Keep risin': Stache & Roger Payne / Coming from behind: Dubologist & MCG / I Runnin': Mix Factory / Nex'st Ardsteppa: D.J. Nexus Scott Potential / Hi-ya: Twilight Dawn / Smells like lithium: Cartell & D-Tone / Something's gotta hold: Scott Potential / Lighter: Co-Accused / Shadow: Dubscientist / Jack's back: Hyper X / Prophecy: Ridley E / Just walk: Rosencrantz, Phillistine & Jake / Wake: Killer M
CD _____ JARCD 17
Cookie Jar / Jun '95 / SRD.

ILLEGAL PIRATE RADIO
CD _____ STHCD 3
Strictly Underground / Aug '93 / SRD.

ILLEGAL PIRATE RADIO VOL.2
CD _____ STHCD 4
Strictly Underground / Apr '94 / SRD.

ILLEGAL PIRATE RADIO VOL.3
CD _____ STHCD 9
Strictly Hardcore / May '95 / SRD.

ILLEGAL RAVE VOL.2
CD _____ STHCCD 2
Strictly Underground / Jun '94 / SRD.

ILLEGAL RAVE VOL.3
CD _____ STHCCD 5
Strictly Underground / Jun '94 / SRD.

ILLICIT LATIN
Jammin' with Joey: Pastrana, Joey / Fuerza y cara: Rivera, Ismael / Jumpy: Colon, Johnny / Joe Cuba's madness: Cuba, Joe / Mama guela: Fania Allstars / Abran paso el sabo: Palmieri, Charlie / Ya llego descarga: Rodriguez, Pete / Rush hour in Hong Kong: Ramirez, Louie / Pa lante: Puente, Tito / Oakan puerto final: Pacheco, Johnny / El carbonera: La Lupe / Nick's dream: Martinez, Sabu / Malambo: Sabater, Jimmy / No hay manteca: Cruz, Celia / Mambito: Vladimir / Confusion: Tico Allstars
CD _____ CDCHARLY 228
Charly / Aug '90 / Charly / THE / Cadillac.

I'M BEGINNING TO SEE THE LIGHT
Opus one: Dorsey, Tommy / Saturday night: Sinatra, Frank / I only have eyes for you: Hawkins, Coleman / As time goes by: Holiday, Billie / Lady Day: Shaw, Artie / Somebody loves me: Condon, Eddie / Blue Lester: Young, Lester / GI jive: Jordan, Louis

Red cross: *Parker, Charlie* / I'm beginning to see the light: *Ellington, Duke* / Night and day: *Hall, Edmond* / Down by the riverside: *Johnson, Bunk* / I confessin' that I love you: *Guarnieri, Johnny & Lester Young* / Someone to watch over me: *Wiley, Lee* / All the cats join in: *Goodman, Benny* / Jack Armstrong blues: *Teagarden, Jack & Louis Armstrong* / Sentimental journey: *Day, Doris & Les Brown* / Skyliner: *Barnet, Charlie* / Don't fence me in: *Bailey, Mildred* / Woody 'n' you: *Hawkins, Coleman & Dizzy Gillespie* / There'll be a hot time in the town of Berlin: *Miller, Glenn*
CD _____ PHONTCD 7672
Phontastic / Jun '94 / Weilard / Jazz Music / Cadillac.

I'M IN THE MOOD FOR BLUES
CD _____ DCD 5322
Disky / Dec '93 / THE / BMG / Discovery / Pinnacle.

I'M LEAVING TIPPERARY - CLASSIC IRISH TRADITIONAL MUSIC
(Recorded In America In The 1920's & 1930's)
Lord Gordon's reel: *Hanafin, Michael* / I'm leaving Tipperary: *Sullivan, Dan & Shamrock Band* / My darling asleep/Maids on the green: *McGettigan, John* / Martha, the flower of sweet Strabane: *McGettigan, John* / Curlew hills/Peach Blossoms: *Morrison, James* / Frieze breeches: *Ennis, Tom* / Auld blackthorn: *Flanagan Brothers* / My Irish Molly-O: *Flanagan Brothers* / Irish mazurka: *Gillespie, Hugh* / Jenny's welcome to Charlie: *Gillespie, Hugh* / Stone outside Dan Murphy's door: *McGettigan, John* / Tailor's twist/Flower of Spring: *Morrison, James* / Billy Hanafin's reel: *Hanafin, Michael* / Green grow the rushes-o: *Sullivan, Dan & Shamrock Band* / Beggarman song: *Flanagan Brothers* / Tickling Mary Jane: *Rabbet, Murty & Gaelic Band* / Miller's reel/Duffy the dancer: *Nolan, Neil* / Moneymusk/Johnny will you marry me/Keel row: *Morrison, James* / Kildare rakes/Stack of wheat: *Ennis, Tom* / New steamboat/Bucks of Oranmore/Gardeners daughter: *Morrison, James & Tom Ennis* / Erin's lovely lea: *McGettigan, John* / Dowd's No. 9/Jackson's: *Gillespie, Hugh* / Versevanna: *Gillespie, Hugh* / Irish delight: *Flanagan Brothers*
CD _____ CDORBD 082
Globestyle / Jan '94 / Pinnacle.

I'M SO LONESOME I COULD CRY
CD _____ MU 5057
Musketeer / Oct '92 / Koch.

IMMACULATE MIXES
CD _____ JHD 084
Tring / Mar '93 / Tring / Prism.

IMMEDIATE HIT SINGLES
CD _____ CSL 6039
Immediate / Apr '94 / Charly / Target / BMG.

IMMEDIATE RECORD COMPANY ANTHOLOGY, THE
(3CD Set)
CD Set _____ DO BOX 1
Dojo / Aug '92 / BMG.

IMMEDIATE SINGLES COLLECTION, THE
Little Miss Understood: *Stewart, Rod* / So much to say (so little time): *Stewart, Rod* / I'm not saying: *Nico* / Last mile: *Nico* / Someone's gonna get their head kicked in tonite: *Vince, Earl & The Valients* / Man of the world: *Fleetwood Mac* / Out of time: *Farlowe, Chris* / Itchycoo Park: *Small Faces* / As Much / I'm your witch doctor: *Mayall, John* / Itchycoo Park: *Small Faces* / Lazy Sunday: *Small Faces* / Hang on Sloopy: *McCoys* / Natural born boogie: *Humble Pie* / Angel of the morning: *Arnold, P.P.* / First cut is the deepest: *Arnold, P.P.* / America: *Nice* / Second amendment: *Nice* / Ars longa vita brevis: *Nice* / Acceptance brandenburger: *Nice* / (If paradise is) half as nice: *Amen Corner* / Bend me, shape me: *Amen Corner*
CD _____ CLACD 353
Castle / Aug '93 / BMG.

IMMORTAL INSTRUMENTALS
CD _____ KLMCD 051
Scratch / Jan '95 / BMG.

IMMORTAL LOVE SONGS
CD _____ KLMCD 040
Scratch / May '95 / BMG.

IMMORTAL US NO. 1 HITS
CD _____ KLMCD 044
Scratch / Jan '95 / BMG.

IN CASE YOU MISSED IT
Schafe mein prinzchen: *Bue, Papa Viking Jazz Band* / Muskrat ramble: *Collie, Max & his Rhythm Aces* / Mood indigo: *Ball, Kenny* / Bourbon street parade: *Dutch Swing College Band* / Flyin' house: *Dr. Dixie Jazz Band* / That's a plenty: *Prowizorka Dzezz Bed* / Stranger on the shore: *Bilk, Acker* / Struttin' with some barbecue: *Down Town Jazzband* / Ice cream: *Sunshine, Monty Jazz Band* / Basin Street blues: *Sunshine, Monty Jazz Band* / Jumpin' at the woodside: *Huub Janssen's Amazing Jazz Band* / World is waiting for the sunrise: *Huub Janssen's Amazing Jazz Band* / Bye and bye: *Bouble, Lillian* / Petite fleur: *Lightfoot, Terry* / West End blues: *Mason, Rod Five* / At the

jazz band ball: *World's Greatest Jazz Band* / Jambalaya: *Barber, Chris & His Jazz Band* / As I go to the quick river: *Uralski All Stars*
CD _____ CDTTD 522
Timeless Jazz / Feb '95 / New Note.

IN CRUST WE TRUST
CD _____ LF 050CD
Lost & Found / Aug '93 / Plastic Head.

IN DEFENSE OF ANIMALS
Porch: *Pearl Jam* / Arms of love: *Stipe, Michael* / Too many puppies: *Primus* / Ode to groovy: *Skinny Puppy* / Crystal blue persuasion: *Concrete Blonde* / Velvet dog: *Sister Psychic* / Untold stories: *Meat Beat Manifesto* / For love: *Lush* / Praxis 'Bold as love': *Consolidated* / Beef: *Boogie Down Productions* / Shelter: *McLachlan, Sarah* / Hyperreal selector: *Shamen* / Language of violence: *Disposable Heroes Of Hiphoprisy* / You borrowed: *Helmet* / Clean: *Grotus* / Desert Star: *Material* / Hey hey high class butcher: *Cope, Julian*
CD _____ 72747-2
Restless / Nov '93 / Vital.

IN FROM THE STORM
And the gods made love / Have you ever been (to Electric Ladyland) / Rainy day, dream away / Wind cries Mary / Spanish castle magic / Little wing / In from the storm / Drifting / Bold as love / Burning of the midnight lamp / Purple haze / One rainy wish
CD _____ 74321315502
RCA / Nov '95 / BMG.

IN FULL SWING
Don't keep me waiting: *Rhythm Within* / Fine sexy thing: *In 2 U* / I'll be good to you: *Lace* / I like: *Serenade* / Lovin's got me crazy: *Ruff House Crew* / Freak in me: *M.C. Juice* / Wanna make U jack: *Weird M.C.* / Do you wanna do me: *J.J.* / Hot lover: *Lace* / Surrender: *Silance* / Ready for your love: *Laverne, Elisha* / Your love my love: *Nazlyn* / All I do: *Roman-A-Clef* / Satisfaction: *M.C. Juice*
CD _____ RULCD 303
Rumour / Sep '93 / Pinnacle / 3MV / Sony.

IN GOTH DAZE
Hex: *Specimen* / Vegas: *Nico* / I walk the line: *Alien Sex Fiend* / Psychotic Louie Louie: *Alien Sex Fiend* / Kicking up the sawdust: *Bone Orchard* / Can't stop smoking: *Alien Sex Fiend* / Sharp teeth pretty teeth: *Specimen* / Last year's wife: *Zero Lacreche* / Carnivale of the gullible: *In Excelsis* / Tenant: *Play Dead* / Beating my head: *Red Lorry Yellow Lorry* / Mind disease: *Ritual* / Creatures of the night: *Screaming Dead* / Hole: *Specimen* / Alone she cries: *Skeletal Family* / Legacy: *Furyo* / Boys 18: *Bauhaus* / Caged 19: 1919 / Hollow eyes: *Red Lorry Yellow Lorry* / So sure: *Skeletal Family*
CD _____ CDMGRAM 89
Anagram / Oct '94 / Pinnacle.

IN HOUSE WE TRUST
Voices kill: *Hani* / Better love: *Deep Sensation* / Satori: *Satori* / Phantasy: *XS* / Give me love: *Alcatrazz* / Submarine: *Submarine* / Iriestomp: *Hani* / Unplugged: *Dished Out Bums* / Reelin' with the feelin': *Deep Sensation* / Nada mas: *XS* / Come back: *DC Depressed* / Deeper: *XS* / Glass of Chianti: *Dished Out Bums*
CD _____ TRIUKCD 011
Tribal UK / Jan '96 / Vital.

IN LOVE WITH THESE TIMES
CD _____ FNE 28CD
Normal/Okra / Mar '94 / Direct / ADA.

IN ORDER TO DANCE 5
(2CD Sets)
CD Set _____ RS 94036CDXX
CD Set _____ RS 94036CD
R & S / Sep '94 / Vital.

IN PRAISE OF GOD
CD _____ CD DCA 573
ASV / Dec '88 / Koch.

IN SEARCH OF THE FREEDOM
CD _____ CDMF 090
Magnum Force / Nov '93 / Magnum Music Group.

IN THE BELLY OF THE WHALE
CD _____ HCD 7005
Hightone / Aug '94 / ADA / Koch.

IN THE CEILIDH AND DANCE TRADITION
CD _____ LC 5246CD
Lismor / Nov '95 / Lismor / Direct / Duncans / ADA.

IN THE CELTIC TRADITION
CD _____ LC 5245CD
Lismor / Nov '95 / Lismor / Direct / Duncans / ADA.

IN THE GROOVES
Dixie frenzy / Pain killer / Voice in the wind / Burn up / Shakin' all over / Good times / Everyday / Don't you lie to me / Got to hurry / Boll Weevil song / You might have Jesus / Too much monkey business
CD _____ CDTB 053
Thunderbolt / '91 / Magnum Music Group.

IN THE KEY OF BLUES
Prestige / Feb '96 / Complete/Pinnacle / Cadillac.

IN THE LAND OF BEGINNING AGAIN - NOW THE WAR IS OVER
(2CD/MC Set)
In the land of beginning again: *Layton, Turner* / How lucky you are: *Layton, Turner* / Primrose Hill: *Layton, Turner* / I'll always love you: *Clark, Petula* / Put your shoes on Lucy: *Clark, Petula* / House in the sky: *Clark, Petula* / On the 5.45: *Peers, Donald* / Strawberry moon (in a blueberry sky): *Peers, Donald* / Oh my darling: *Shelton, Anne* / You've changed: *Shelton, Anne* / I keep forgetting to remember: *Shelton, Anne* / If you ever fail in love again: *Shelton, Anne* / You're my thrill: *Campbell, Bruce & his band* / I never lived until I met you: *Campbell, Bruce & his band* / Once upon a wintertime: *Lynn, Vera* / You're the one I care for: *Lynn, Vera* / Again: *Lynn, Vera* / You keep coming back like a song: *Hutch* / Till then: *Hutch* / Dream: *Green, Paula & Her Orchestra* / Let's keep it that way: *Green, Paula & Her Orchestra* / Be true: *Goff, Reggie* / Crystal gazer: *Goff, Reggie* / I love you so much it hurts: *Goff, Reggie* / Olwen: *Goff, Reggie* / My bolero: *Goff, Reggie* / Am I wasting my time on you: *Goff, Reggie* / I'm gonna let you cry for a change: *Goff, Reggie* / Time may change: *Williams, Rita* / My happiness: *Williams, Rita* / Take me to your heart again: *Williams, Rita* / My lovely world and you: *Lewis, Archie* / Bless you: *Lewis, Archie* / Maybe you'll be there: *Conway, Steve* / In all the world: *Conway, Steve* / Sweetheart we'll never grow old: *Harris, Doreen* / When you're in love: *Harris, Doreen*
CD Set _____ CDDL 1263
Music For Pleasure / May '94 / EMI.

IN THE PIPING TRADITION
CD _____ LC 5243CD
Lismor / Nov '95 / Lismor / Direct / Duncans / ADA.

IN THE POPULAR SONG TRADITION
CD _____ LC 5244CD
Lismor / Nov '95 / Lismor / Direct / Duncans / ADA.

IN THE SPIRIT
CD _____ AL 2801
Alligator / Jul '94 / Direct / ADA.

IN THE STILL OF THE NIGHT
There's a moon out tonight: *Capris* / Goodnight sweetheart, goodnight: *Spaniels* / Tonite, tonite: *Mello Kings* / Earth angel: *Penguins* / Thousand miles away: *Shep & The Limelites* / Daddy's home: *Shep & The Limelites* / To the aisle: *Five Satins* / In the still of the nite: *Five Satins* / I'll be seeing you: *Five Satins* / New Orleans: *Bonds, Gary U.S.* / Quarter to three: *Bonds, Gary U.S.* / Rip it up: *Haley, Bill & The Comets* / (We're gonna) rock around the clock: *Haley, Bill & The Comets*
CD _____ NEBCD 651
Sequel / Jun '93 / BMG.

IN THE SWISS MOUNTAINS
CD _____ 399408
Koch / Jul '91 / Koch.

INCANDESCENCE
CD _____ CDREP 8013
Elusive / Sep '94 / Disc.

INDIA O FAST DHRUPAD
CD _____ SM 1517CD
Wergo / Oct '94 / Harmonia Mundi / ADA / Cadillac.

INDIAN FLUTES OF SOUTH AMERICA
CD _____ PS 65060
Playasound / Nov '90 / Harmonia Mundi / ADA.

INDIAN FLUTES OF SOUTH AMERICA VOL.2
CD _____ PS 65090
Playasound / Jul '92 / Harmonia Mundi / ADA.

INDIE TOP 20 (VOL.19)
In your room: *Depeche Mode* / Saturn 5: *Inspiral Carpets* / Play dead: *Bjork* / Linger: *Cranberries* / Creep: *Radiohead* / V.H.F. 855V: *Tiny Monroe* / Slowly slowly: *Magnapop* / My dark star: *Suede* / Razor: *Shark-cops* / Carter U.S.M. / Can't get out of bed: *Charlatans* / Plan B: *Rancho Diablo* / Sunday Sunday: *Blur* / Ich bin ein auslander: *Pop Will Eat Itself* / Barney (and me): *Boo Radleys* / Broken and mended: *Blue Aeroplanes* / French disco: *Stereolab* / Diminished clothes: *Salad* / Where I find my heaven: *Gigolo Aunts*
CD _____ TT 019CD
Beechwood / Apr '94 / BMG / Pinnacle.

INDIE TOP 20 (VOL.20)
CD _____ TT 020CD
Beechwood / Oct '94 / BMG / Pinnacle.

INDIE TOP 20 (VOL.21)
CD _____ TT 021CD
Beechwood / Mar '95 / BMG / Pinnacle.

INDIGO BLUES COLLECTION VOL.1
(Budget Sampler)
CD _____ IGOCD 2033
Indigo / Sep '95 / Direct / ADA.

INDUSTRIAL CHRISTMAS CAROL
CD _____ INV 053CD
Invisible / Jan '96 / Plastic Head.

INDUSTRIAL REVOLUTION 2ND EDITION
CD _____ CLEO 77712
Cleopatra / May '94 / Disc.

INFINITE SUMMER OF LOVE
CD _____ TX 2016CD
Taxim / Jul '94 / ADA.

INFLUENCE: HARD TRANCE
CD _____ CLEO 94762
Cleopatra / Jun '94 / Disc.

INNER SECRETS
Deer Hunter theme: *Williams, John* / Chariots Of Fire theme: *Hawk & Co* / Marta's song: *Deep Forest* / Only you: *Praise* / Albatross: *Fleetwood Mac* / Sunrise: *Atkins, Chet & George Benson* / Midnight Cowboy: *Barry, John* / Ave mundi: *Rodriguez* / Dances With Wolves (John Dunbar's theme): *Barry, John* / Trois gymnopedies: *Blood, Sweat & Tears* / Samba pa ti: *Santana* / Time after time: *Davis, Miles* / Hill Street Blues theme: *Franklin, Rodney* / Misty: *Getz, Stan* / M.A.S.H. theme: *M.A.S.H.* / Why worry: *Knopfler, Mark & Chet Atkins* / Year Of Living Dangerously theme (L'enfant): *Boyd, Liona* / Belladonna: *Vollenweider, Andreas* / Facades: *Glass, Philip* / Mission theme (Gabriel's oboe): *Morricone, Ennio*
CD _____ 4814532
Columbia / Oct '95 / Sony.

INNERNATION
(Nation Records Compilation)
CD _____ SFRCD 131
Strange Fruit / Mar '95 / Pinnacle.

INNINGS AND QUARTERS
CD _____ NAR 069 CD
New Alliance / May '93 / Pinnacle.

INNOVATIVE/INTELLIGENT DRUM AND BASS VOL.1
Horizons: *Bukem, L.T.J.* / Rain: *Photek* / High flyers: *Area 39* / Heavy vibes: *Origination* / Jazzmin (Tango remix): *Cloud 9* / Western: *P.F.M.* / Into the 90's: *Photek* / Sunshine: *Eugenix & Corelle* / Universal horn: *JMJ & Richie* / Maracas beach: *Origination* / Projection: *Timeline* / Jazz and all dat: *Eskubar* / Rhys project (CD/MC): *James, Mikey* / Come to me (CD/MC): *Street Science* / Wired (CD/MC): *Fokus* / Part of life (CD/MC): *Timeline* / Are we in (CD/MC): *D'Cruze* / Searchin' (CD/MC): *Dead Calm*
CD _____ STORM 2 CD
Desert Storm / Jan '96 / Sony.

INNOVATOR
CD _____ NWKCD 21
Network / '92 / Sony / 3MV.

INNSBRUCK, THE BEAUTIFUL ALPINE CITY
CD _____ 399425
Koch / Jul '91 / Koch.

INSIDE
(The Best Of British)
When we're making love: *Opaz* / Be still: *French, Michelle* / We in my: *Mid 8 Production* / Been fooled: *Caitaine, Ria* / Fight: *McKoy* / Whole thing: *Act Of Faith* / Even when you're gone: *Green, Tee* / Mystery girl: *Green, Tee* / If I knew: *D-Swing* / Hold me closer: *Circle Of Life* / Love away: *Pearce, Mary* / Coming closer: *Feel* / Simple solution: *Dee, Jay* / Running to my baby's arms: *Ipso Facto* / Slow down: *Metropolis* / Through all times: *Perfect Taste*
CD _____ CDTEP 1
Debut / Nov '93 / Pinnacle / 3MV / Sony.

INSIDE 2
Greater love: *Nu Colours* / Reach out: *Perception* / Take me: *D-Swing* / Just don't care: *Funhill* / Visions: *Julianne* / I'll be good to you: *Gems For Jem* / Doing it for love: *Act Of Faith* / Get it on: *Solid State Sound* / Sunday morning blue: *Mapp, Chantel* / I know how: *Stevens, Kenni* / Calling her name: *Ipso Facto* / 2 be a friend: *Pearce, Mary* / Love when it's like this: *Antony, Joseph* / Your love my love: *Nazlyn* / Give it (this love song): *Caitaine, Ria*
CD _____ CDTEP 2
Debut / Jul '93 / Pinnacle / 3MV / Sony.

INSIDE 3
Movin' in the right direction: *FM Inc* / Fever (rider): *D-Swing* / So much feeling: *Closer Than Close* / Gotta get it: *Index* / Deeper: *Uschi* / Fallin': *Tyson* / Heaven: *Menzies, Steve* / I Luv U: *Sovereign* / I like the way: *Evens* / Hurt so bad (till U like it): *Marshall, Wayne* / Learned my lesson: *Smith, Charlene* / There ain't enough love: *Zushii* / You belong to me: *Fyza* / Searching: *Robyn*
CD _____ CDTEP 3
Debut / Mar '94 / Pinnacle / 3MV / Sony.

INSIDE 4
CD _____ CDTEP 5
Debut / Oct '94 / Pinnacle / 3MV / Sony.

INSIDE OUT
Inside out / California soul / Liberation song / Eternal journey / Chocolate candy / Blue monsoon / Long goodie / I am the blackgold of the sun / Dancing girl / Prayer for peace
CD _____ CDARC 513
Charly / Jan '93 / Charly / THE / Cadillac.

INSPIRATIONAL SAX
Will you still love me tomorrow / I can't stop loving you / Holding back the years / To all the girls I've loved before / Against all odds / Moonlight shadow / I guess why they call it the blues / How deep is your love
CD _____ GRF 193
Tring / Jun '92 / Tring / Prism.

INSTRUMENTAL CLASSICS VOL.1
CD _____ MODUB 2CD
Music Of Life / Aug '92 / Grapevine.

INSTRUMENTAL DIAMONDS VOL.2 - HIGHLY STRUNG
(British 60's Instrumentals)
Music train: Honeycombs / Cleopatra's needle: Ahab & The Wailers / Red dragon: Black Jacks / Ghoul friend: Ravens / Jump Jeremiah: Ford, Mike & The Consuls / Ten swinging bottles: Chester, Peter & The Consulate / Pompeii: Checkmates / Husky: Nicol, Jimmy / Packabeat: Packabeats / First love: Clark, Dave Five / Man in space: Vigilantes / Organiser: Organisers & Harold Smart / Mad goose: Sons Of The Piltdown Men / Eliminator: Eliminators / Switch: Brown, Joe / Neb's tune: Ahab & The Wailers / Traitors: Packabeats / Caroline: Jay, Peter & The Jaywalkers / Husky team: Saints / Dream lover: Packabeats / Highly strung: Rustlers / Pigtails: Saints / Evening in Paris: Packabeats / Thunderbirds theme: Eliminators / Hurricane: Honeycombs
CD _____ NEXCD 150
Sequel / Feb '91 / BMG.

INSTRUMENTAL DIAMONDS VOL.3 - OUT OF THIS WORLD
Before the beginning: Jay, Peter & The Jaywalkers / Red cabbage: Jay, Peter & The Jaywalkers / Out of this world: Hatch, Tony / Bullfight: Rowena, Jeff Group / Peanut vendor: Rowena, Jeff Group / Caravan: Checkmates / Honky tonk: Checkmates / Land of 1000 dances: Eliminators / Eleanor Rigby: Eliminators / Comin' home baby: Cymbaline / Big beat: Delaney, Eric & His Band / Ding dong John: Ede, David / Baja: Jones, John Paul / Gospel train: Soul Agents / Green man: Ford, Mike & The Consuls / Completely: Kinks / Revenge: Kinks / Explosive corrosive oxygen: Schroeder, John Orchestra / Mad goose: Sons Of The Piltdown Men / Be a party: Sons Of The Piltdown Men / Eclipse: Vigilantes / I walk the line: Clark, Dave Five / Exodus: Eagles / Telstar '69: Velvett Fogg / Happy talk: Saints / Parade of the tin soldiers: Saints
CD _____ NEXCD 244
Sequel / Jun '93 / BMG.

INSTRUMENTAL MOODS
Riverdance: Anderson, John Concert Orchestra / Cacharpaya: Incantation / Return to innocence: Enigma / Yeha noha: Sacred Spirit / Celts: Enya / Sentinel: Oldfield, Mike / Samba pa ti: Santana / Albatross: Fleetwood Mac / Love's theme from Midnight Express: Moroder, Giorgio / Adiemus: Adiemus / Songbird: Kenny G. / Cavatina: Williams, John / Don't cry for me Argentina: Shadows / Inspector Morse theme: Pheloung, Barrington / Brideshead revisited: Burgon, Geoffrey / Theme from Soldier Soldier: Parker, Jim / Chi mai: Morricone, Ennio / Stranger on the shore: Bilk, Acker / People's Century (theme): People's Century Orchestra / Panis Angelicus: Way, Anthony
CD _____ VTCD 65
Virgin / Nov '95 / EMI.

INSTRUMENTALLY YOURS
Blue roofs of Ispahan: Phillipe, Louis / March of the eligible bachelors: Monochrome Set / Constance from Cadaquez: Marden Hill / Another conversation with myself: Watt, Ben / 1000 guitars of St. Dominiques: Fantastic Something / Hasta pronto: King Of Luxembourg / All day and all of the night: Page, Larry Orchestra / Maestroso con anima: Deebank, Maurice / You're the queer one, Les Mun: Hepburns / Aperitivo: Phillipe, Louis / Star trek for jazz guitar: Posh / West End: Leer, Thomas / Through Eastfields: Eyeless In Gaza / Zophia: Underneath / Falling: Beech, Isadora / Ballet of the red shoes: Adverse, Anthony / Execution of Emperor Maximillian: Marden Hill / Fantasia, childhood memories: Fisher-Turner, Simon / Twangy twangy: Phillipe, Louis / Park row: Always / Flying with lux: Blind Mr. Jones / Tender bruises and scars: Hewick, Kevin / Geneve: Fisher, Morgan / Yo ho ho (and three bottles of wine): Monochrome Set / Cavaliere servente: Phillipe, Louis
CD _____ MONDE 18CD
Cherry Red / Oct '93 / Pinnacle.

INSTRUMENTOS MUSICAIS POPULARES GALEGOS
CD _____ H 026CD
Sonifolk / Jun '94 / ADA / CM.

INSTRUMENTS
(Hannibal Sampler)
CD _____ HNCD 8302
Hannibal / May '93 / Vital / ADA.

INTELLIGENT DRUM & BASS VOL.1
CD _____ STHCCD 2
Strictly Hardcore / Jun '95 / SRD.

INTELLIGENT DRUM & BASS VOL.2
CD _____ STHCCD 13
Strictly Hardcore / Jul '95 / SRD.

INTELLIGENT SELECTA
CD _____ PNCCA 5
Production House / Apr '95 / Jetstar / Total/BMG.

INTERFERENCE LIVE AT LOVE PARADE 94
CD _____ EFA 001452
Interference / Aug '95 / SRD.

INTERNAL JOURNAL 2
CD _____ NAR 115CD
SST / Nov '94 / Plastic Head.

INTERNATIONAL CEILIDH BAND CHAMPIONSHIP, THE
Strip the willow / Songs and reels / Songs (Keltie Clippie) / Reels / Highland Schottische / Song / Dashing white sergeant / Boston two step / Song (Sound of Pibroch) / Selection / Dance 13, Jig
CD _____ LCOM 5218
Lismor / Jan '93 / Lismor / Direct / Duncans / ADA.

INTERNATIONAL FESTIVAL OF COUNTRY MUSIC, FRUTIGEN
(Live May 1987)
I'm goin', I'm leaving: Hollow, Traver / Lonesome, on'y and mean: Young, Steven & Tom Russell Band / Mezcal: Russell, Tom / Alkali: Russell, Tom / Walkin' after midnight: Moffatt, Katy & Tom Russell Band / First taste of Texas: Bruce, Ed / Man who turned my mama on: Bruce, Ed / Summer wages: Tyson, Ian & Andrew Hardin / Someday soon: Tyson, Ian & Andrew Hardin / Navajo rug: Russell, Tom / Edge of a heartbreak: Moeller, Dee / Where is the magic: Moeller, Dee / Mamas don't let your babies grow up to be cowboys: Bruce, Ed
CD _____ BCD 15466
Bear Family / Jun '89 / Rollercoaster / Direct / CM / Swift / ADA.

INTERNATIONAL GUITAR FESTIVAL
CD _____ BEST 1051CD
Acoustic Music / Jul '94 / ADA.

INTIMATE LOVERS VOLUME 1
CD _____ VGCD 015
Virgo / Dec '94 / Jetstar.

INTIMATE SOUND VOL. 1, THE
(1989-1993)
Please come back: Edwards, Dean / Way we are: Affair / There is no way: Sound Principle / Bring me back: Davis, Richard Anthony / Welcome to yesterday: Sound Principle / Keep it comin': Julianne / I'm back for more: Lulu & Bobby Womack / Getting on with my own life: Jones Girls / Lovers for life: Davis, Richard Anthony / Is it true: Drakes, Anthony
CD _____ EMHCD 1
Intimate / Mar '94 / Jetstar / Total/BMG.

INTO THE MYSTIC
Jali: Diop, Vieux / Lullaby: Kahn, Ali Akbar / Contemplation: Beal, Jeff / Himene tatou: Tahitian Choir / Raghupati: Uttal, Jai / Flight of the dove: Nichols, Roger Project / Prayer song: Little Wolf Band / Puja-celebration, light of love: Dissidenten / Aboriginal dream: Perry, Foster / Twilight: Perry, Foster / Prayer of hanuman: Dass, Ram & Amazing Grace
CD _____ 3202132
Triloka / Oct '95 / New Note.

INTO THE NIGHT
Roll on down the highway: Bachman-Turner Overdrive / Highway blues: Savoy Brown / Mustang Sally: Sam & Dave / I got you (I feel good): Brown, James / Standing at the crossroads again: Dr. Feelgood / This wheel's on fire: Driscoll, Julie / Heart attack and vine: Hawkins, Screamin' Jay / Route 66: Berry, Chuck / Davy's on the road again: Manfred Mann's Earthband / Loud music in cars: Bremner, Billy / Driver's seat: Sniff 'N' The Tears / Sure feels good: Blues Band / Pontiac blues: Chicago / Bat out of hell: Meat Loaf / Ramblin' man: Allman Brothers / Promised land: Allen, Johnny / Forty miles of bad road: Eddy, Duane / Roadrunner: Diddley, Bo
CD _____ NTRCD 011
Nectar / Mar '94 / Pinnacle.

INTRODUCING
CD _____ 101 S 7777 2
101 South / Jun '93 / New Note.

INUIT GAMES AND SONGS
CD _____ AUD 8032
Auvidis/Ethnic / Mar '93 / Harmonia Mundi.

INVISIBLE ROUTE 666
CD _____ INV 666
Invisible / Nov '95 / Plastic Head.

IRAN: MASTERS OF TRADITIONAL MUSIC, VOL. 1
CD _____ C 560024
Ocora / Aug '91 / Harmonia Mundi / ADA.

IRAN: MASTERS OF TRADITIONAL MUSIC, VOL. 2
CD _____ C 560025
Ocora / Aug '91 / Harmonia Mundi / ADA.

IRAN: MASTERS OF TRADITIONAL MUSIC, VOL. 3
CD _____ C 560026
Ocora / Nov '92 / Harmonia Mundi / ADA.

IRELAND - IN MUSIC
CD _____ CD 394
Bescol / Aug '94 / CM / Target/BMG.

IRELAND A SONG FOR EVERY COUNTY
CD _____ CHCD 3201
Chyme / Oct '95 / CM / ADA / Direct.

IRELAND'S GREATEST LOVE SONGS
CD _____ TCD 2753
Telstar / Nov '94 / BMG.

IRIE IRIE
(A Ragamuffin Showcase)
CD _____ MSACD 003
Munich / Nov '94 / CM / ADA / Greensleeves / Direct.

IRISH COLLECTION
CD _____ RITZRCD 553
Ritz / Oct '95 / Pinnacle.

IRISH CREAM
My lagan love: O'Duffy, Michael / Dawning of the day: O'Duffy, Michael / Lark in the clear air: O'Duffy, Michael / Old refrain: O'Duffy, Michael / Spinning wheel: Murphy, Delia / Bantry girl's lament: Murphy, Delia / Down by the Glenside: Murphy, Delia / If I were a blackbird: Murphy, Delia / Sittin' on the bridge down below: O'Donovan, Frank / Road by the river: O'Donovan, Frank / Garden where the praties grow: Irwin, Robert / When he who adores thee: Burke-Sheridan, Margaret / Danny boy: Burke-Sheridan, Margaret / Believe me, if all those endearing young charms: Burke-Sheridan, Margaret / Down by the Sally gardens: Burke-Sheridan, Margaret / Terence's farewell to kathleen: McCormack, John / Where the River Shannon flows: McCormack, John / Kerry dance: McCormack, John / Green bushes: McCormack, John / Decent Irish boy: Murphy, Angela / Melodies from four provinces: Healy, Albert / Three flowers: Hayward, Richard / Bare brown bog: O'Higgins, Michael / Kitty my love will you marry me: O'Higgins, Michael / Ballynore ballad: O'Higgins, Michael / Streams of Bunclody: O'Higgins, Michael / MOlly Brannigan: MacCafferty, James / Open the door softly: MacCafferty, James / Donovans: MacCafferty, James / Enniskillen dragoons: Murphy, Delia / Little Mary Cassidy: Irwin, Robert / Sea fever: Irwin, Robert / She moved through the fair: Irwin, Robert / Gartan mothers lullaby: Mullen, Barbara / My curly headed baby: Mullen, Barbara / Are you there moriarty: Mooney, Sean / I know of two bright eyes: Valentine, Hubert / Macushla: Valentine, Hubert / Limerick is beautiful: O'Doherty, Seamus / Savoureen deelish: Rowsome, Leo / Clare's dragoons: Rowsome, Leo / What will you do love: Murphy, Delia / Green Isle of Erin: Ryan, Frank / Bright silvery light of the moon: Hayward, Richard / Meeting of the waters: McEwan, Sydney / Banks of the Suir: O'Cronin, Nelius
CD _____ CDGO 2067
EMI / Apr '95 / EMI.

IRISH DANCE MUSIC
CD _____ TSCD 602
Topic / Oct '95 / Direct / ADA.

IRISH FAVOURITES
CD _____ MATCD 216
Castle / Dec '92 / BMG.

IRISH FAVOURITES
CD _____ CPMV 028
Cromwell / Sep '94 / THE / BMG.

IRISH FAVOURITES VOL.1
CD _____ DMC 4370
Disky / May '94 / THE / BMG / Discovery / Pinnacle.

IRISH FAVOURITES VOL.2
CD _____ DMC 4371
Disky / May '94 / THE / BMG / Discovery / Pinnacle.

IRISH FOLK COLLECTION
(3CD/MC Set)
CD Set _____ TBXCD 509
TrueTrax / Jan '96 / THE.

IRISH FOLK COLLECTION VOL.2
CD _____ CCSCD 312
Castle / Feb '93 / BMG.

IRISH FOLK FAVOURITES
(4CD Set)
CD Set _____ MBSCD 404
Castle / Nov '94 / BMG.

IRISH FOLK FAVOURITES
(3CD/MC Set)
Roddy McCorley: Dubliners / Both sides now: Johnstons / I know my love: Crowley, Jimmy / Girl: Moore, Barry / Curragh of kildare: Furey, Finbar & Eddie / Bunch of thyme: Shaskeen / Farewell to Erin: Bothy Band / Wild rover: Dubliners / Dainty Davie: Na Fili / Sweet Williams town: Na Fili / Off to Dublin in the Green: Dubliners / I'll tell me ma: Dubliners / Patriot game: Dubliners / McAlpine's Fusiliers: Dubliners / Donegal Reel: Dubliners / Longford collector: Dubliners / Leaving of Liverpool: Dubliners / Home boys home: Dubliners / Mason's apron: Dubliners / Will you come to the bower: Dubliners / Old orange flute: Dubliners / Wild rover (2): Dubliners / Mr. McGrath: Dubliners / Pipe on the hob: Bothy Band / Nightingale: Dubliners / Arthur

McBRIDE: Brady, Paul / Town is not your
own: Furey, Finbar & Eddie / Maid at the spinningwheel: Na Fili / Dicey Riley: Sweeney's Men / Streets of London: Johnstons / Crosses of Annagh: Brady, Paul & Matt Malloy / Love is pleasing: Dubliners / Kiss in the morning early: Hanly, Mick / Ceol an phiobaire: Na Fili
CD Set _____ HBOX CD74
Carlton Home Entertainment / Jul '94 / Carlton Home Entertainment.

IRISH FOLK FAVOURITES VOL.1
CD _____ HCD 1001
Carlton Home Entertainment / Nov '92 / Carlton Home Entertainment.

IRISH FOLK FAVOURITES VOL.2
CD _____ HCD 1006
Carlton Home Entertainment / Nov '92 / Carlton Home Entertainment.

IRISH FOLK FEST - BACK TO THE FUTURE
CD _____ CDTUT 727490
Wundertute / '89 / CM / Duncans / ADA.

IRISH FOLK FEST - JUBILEE
CD _____ CDTUT 727491
Wundertute / '89 / CM / Duncans / ADA.

IRISH MELODIES
Darlin' girl from Clare: O'Dowda, Brendan / Molly Brannigan: O'Dowda, Brendan / Tootin' to the fair: O'Dowda, Brendan / La galondrina (The Swallow): O'Dowda, Brendan / Believe me, if all those endearing young charms: Murray, Ruby / Meeting of the waters: Murray, Ruby / Little bit of heaven: Murray, Ruby / Marie my girl: Locke, Josef / Macushla: Locke, Josef / When it's moonlight in Mayo: Locke, Josef / Rose of Tralee: Locke, Josef / Star of the County Down: MacEwan, Father Sydney / Killarney in the spring: MacEwan, Father Sydney / Connemara: O'Dowda, Brendan & Ruby Murray / Pretty Irish girl: O'Dowda, Brendan & Ruby Murray / Dan O'Hara: Gallagher, Bridie / Old Skibbereen: Gallagher, Bridie / Jaunting car: Nelson, Havelock & Orchestra / Minstrel boy: Nelson, Havelock & Orchestra / Old turf fire: Hinds, Eric / Bonny wee lass: Hinds, Eric / My singing bird: Dunne, Veronica / I have a bonnet trimmed with blue: Dunne, Veronica / Wearing of the green: Henry, Dermot / My lagan love: O'Duffy, Michael / Scorn not his simplicity: Carroll, Alma
CD _____ CC 291
Music For Pleasure / Dec '92 / EMI.

IRISH ROCK
(Ireland's Beat Groups 1964-1969)
6.10 Special: Hootenannys / You must be the one: Greenbeats / Dreamworld: Boomerangs / Upgraded: Boomerangs / Look out (Here comes tomorrow): Strangers / Mary Mary: Strangers / Tell her: Movement / Something you got: Movement / Do you wanna dance: Vampires / My girl: Vampires / Three jolly little dwarfs: Orange Machine / Real life permanent dream: Orange Machine / That's the way life goes: Deep Set / Dr. Crippen's waiting room: Orange Machine / Money and love: Pan Pipers / Run baby run: Bye-Laws / Hi ho silver lining: Hughes, Danny / I washed my hands in muddy water: Hughes, Danny / You got what I need: Mahon, Mitch & The Editions / Counting time my way: Taxi / Deep water: Bye-Laws / You've made me so very happy: Purple Pussycat / Choo choo Charlie: Jacobites / Lovely Loretta: Others
CD _____ NEXCD 262
Sequel / Feb '94 / BMG.

IRISH SHOW BAND YEARS
CD _____ CHCD 1060
Chyme / Oct '95 / CM / ADA / Direct.

IRISH SHOWBAND STARS
(3CD/MC Set - We Love To Sing/Till/Sincerely)
You and me, her and him: Lynam, Ray & Philomena Begley / All these little things: Lynam, Ray & Philomena Begley / We've run out of tomorrows: Lynam, Ray & Philomena Begley / We go together: Lynam, Ray & Philomena Begley / Seeing eye to eye: Lynam, Ray & Philomena Begley / That's when my baby sings his song: Lynam, Ray & Philomena Begley / Mr. and Mrs. used to be: Lynam, Ray & Philomena Begley / Daddy was an accordian man: Lark in the morning: Lynam, Ray & Philomena Begley / Anything's better than nothing: Lynam, Ray & Philomena Begley / We love to sing about Jesus: Lynam, Ray & Philomena Begley / Silver sandles: Lynam, Ray & Philomena Begley / Till: Rock, Dickie / From a jack to a king: Rock, Dickie / Hazel: Rock, Dickie / My girl Emily: Rock, Dickie / Tears on my pillow: Rock, Dickie / When will I see you again: Rock, Dickie / Without you: Rock, Dickie / My Eileen: Rock, Dickie / So many ways: Rock, Dickie / Let me try again: Rock, Dickie / When: Hurley, Red / Isadora: Hurley, Red / Hold me just one more time: Hurley, Red / Bring back the good times: Hurley, Red / Sometimes: Hurley, Red / Poor man's roses: Hurley, Red / Arkansas: Hurley, Red / Don't say goodnight tonight: Hurley, Red / Rosetta on the phone: Hurley, Red / Prelude: Hurley, Red
CD Set _____ HBOX CD72
Carlton Home Entertainment / Jul '94 / Carlton Home Entertainment.

IRISH SHOWBANDS - GET DOWN WITH IT
Boys: *Rock, Dickie & The Miami Showband* / Foolin' time: *Moore, Butch & The Capitol Showband* / Land of love: *Blue Aces* / Chapel of love: *Cadets* / Round and round: *Rock, Dickie & The Miami Showband* / Do what I want you to do: *Fagan, Sean & The Pacific Showband* / Jealous heart: *Cadets* / There's nothing to it: *Dee, Alan & The Chessman* / I'll always love you: *Dolan, Joe & The Drifters* / Honey and wine: *Capitols* / My heartache's got heartaches: *Ruane, Jack Band* / Among the Wicklow hills: *Gerry & The Ohio* / Love of our own: *Debonaires* / Don't let the stars get in your eyes: *O'Brien, Brendan & The Dixies* / Holiday romance: *Carousels* / Love and the country: *Cribben, Shea & The Riviera* / Love of the common people: *Dolan, Joe & The Drifters* / Goodbye baby: *Gentiles* / Go granny go (The little old lady from Pasadena): *Freshmen* / Look at the sunshine: *Freshmen* / Morning papers and margarine: *Derrick & The Sounds* / Make it with you: *Freshmen* / Piccolo man: *Airchords* / Get down with it: *Collins, Donie Showband* / I can't help myself: *Collins, Donie Showband*
CD _____ NEXCD 261
Sequel / Feb '94 / BMG.

IRISH SONGBOOK, THE
Killarney: *McCormack, John* / Last rose of summer: *Araniel, Florence* / Father O'Flynn: *Santley, Charles* / Kathleen Mavoureen: *Butt, Clara* / Trottin' to the fair: *Greene, Harry Plunket* / Garden where the praties grow: *Greene, Harry Plunket* / Minstrel boy: *Burko, Tom* / I know where I'm going: *Sheridan, Margaret* / Next market day: *McCormack, John* / Boat song: *Kirkby-Lunn, Louise* / Believe me, if all those endearing young charms: *Tibbett, Lawrence* / Kitty of Coleraine: *O'Doherty, Seamus* / Danny Boy: *Labette, Dora* / Kitty my love will you marry me: *McCafferty, James* / Open the door softly: *McCafferty, James* / Love at my heart: *Robeson, Paul* / Lover's curse: *Hill, Carmen* / Mother Machree: *Crooks, Richard* / She moved through the fair: *MacEwan, Sydney* / Come back to Erin: *Sheridan, Margaret* / Phil the fluter's ball: *Dawson, Peter*
CD _____ MIDCD 006
Moidart / Apr '95 / Conifer / ADA.

IRISH TIMES
CD _____ TUT 494
Wundertute / Oct '94 / CM / Duncans / ADA.

IRISH TIN WHISTLES
CD _____ TRADHCD 007
GTD / Jul '93 / Else / ADA.

IRISH WHISTLES
CD _____ HCD 007
GTD / Apr '94 / Else / ADA.

IRON MUSE, THE
(A Panorama Of Industrial Folk Music)
Sangate girl's lament/Elsie Marley: *High Level Ranters* / Doon the waggonway: *High Level Ranters* / Miner's life: *Gilfellon, Tom* / Coal-owner and the pitman's wife: *MacColl, Ewan & Peggy Seeger* / Trimdon Grange explosion: *Killen, Louis* / Blackleg miner: *Killen, Louis* / Auchengeich disaster: *Gaughan, Dick & Alisdair Anderson* / Fra aye, aa cud hew: *Pickford, Ed* / Durham lockout: *Craik, Maureen* / Aa'm glad the strike's done: *High Level Ranters* / Weaver's march: *Celebrated working man's band* / Spinner's song: *Fisher, Ray* / Oh, dear me: *MacColl, Ewan & Peggy Seeger* / Doffin mistress: *Briggs, Anne* / Little piecer: *Brooks, Dave* / Hand loom weaver's lament: *Boardman, Harry* / Dundee lassie: *Fisher, Ray* / Success to the weavers: *Oldham Tinkers* / Fourpence a day: *MacColl, Ewan & Peggy Seeger* / Up the raw: *Killen, Louis* / Row between the cages: *Davenport, Bob* / Aw wish pay Friday would come: *Killen, Louis & Colin Ross* / Keep your feet still Geordie Hinny: *Killen, Louis & Colin Ross* / Farewell to the Monty: *Killen, Louis*
CD _____ TSCD 465
Topic / May '93 / Direct / ADA.

IS IT COOL
Linda who: *Crothers, Scott* / Blitz: *Three Blue Teardrops* / Red hot and ready: *Memphis Mafia* / Rockabilly baby: *Erik & The Dragtones* / Tear it up: *High Noon* / Push-rod: *Potter, Jeff* / Bad cat: *Scoffed* / Hillibilly hell: *Wreckin' Ball* / Chicken walk: *Mustang Lightning* / What'd I do now: *Whole Lotsa Papa* / Naked cowboy: *Rotgut* / Rockabilly not fade away: *LeVey, Larry* / Long hard night: *Three Blue Teardrops* / Hey baby: *Wreckin' Ball* / Itchen fever: *Scoffed* / Blackjack county chains: *Whole Lotsa Papa* / Wild wild women: *Mustang Lightning* / Sun #209: *Thompson, Danny* / Lonesome road: *Rockabilly 88* / Buzz and the flyers: *Is It Cool*
CD _____ NERCD 081
Nervous / Jun '95 / Nervous / Magnum Music Group.

IS IT LOVE
(Music From The Lovers' Guide)
Theme for lovers / Tender invitation / Touch me / Secret whispers / Echoes of love / I need your love / Toledo / Making love in the rain / Love ocean / Now that you're a part of me / Hold me close

IS THIS LOVE
CD Set _____ NSCD 008
Newsound / Feb '95 / THE.

ISLAND MUSIC
CD _____ RNCD 2077
Rhino / Oct '94 / Jetstar / Magnum Music Group / THE.

ISLAND OF ST. HYLARION, THE
CD _____ NA 038 CD
New Albion / Apr '91 / Harmonia Mundi / Cadillac.

ISLE OF WIGHT FESTIVAL 1970, THE
CD _____ EDFCD 327
Essential / Dec '95 / Total/BMG.

ISTANBUL 1925
CD _____ CD 4266
Traditional Crossroads / Dec '94 / CM / Direct.

IT CAME FROM BENEATH LA
CD _____ TX 51213CD
Triple X / Jan '96 / Plastic Head.

IT CAME FROM MEMPHIS
CD _____ UPSTART 022
Upstart / Nov '95 / Direct / ADA.

IT CAME FROM OUTER SPACE
CD _____ OUTERSPACE 11CD
Neuton / Jan '95 / Plastic Head.

IT CAME FROM OUTER SPACE VOL.3
CD _____ OUTERSPACE 2CD
Uptown / Sep '95 / Plastic Head.

IT DON'T MEAN A THING IF IT AIN'T GOT THAT SWING
Moonlight serenade: *Miller, Glenn* / Taking a chance on love: *Dorsey, Tommy* / Jumpin' at the woodside: *Basie, Count* / Take the 'A' train: *Ellington, Duke* / September song: *Brown, Les* / Blowin' up a storm: *Herman, Woody* / Jersey bounce: *Goodman, Benny* / Pennsylvania 6-5000: *Miller, Glenn* / Red bank boogie: *Basie, Count* / Marie: *Dorsey, Tommy* / Love me or leave me: *Brown, Les* / Lester leaps in: *Basie, Count* / Caledonia: *Herman, Woody* / Little brown jug: *Miller, Glenn* / Skyliner: *Barnet, Charlie* / I'll never be the same: *Krupa, Gene* / On the sunny side of the street: *Dorsey, Tommy* / Perdido: *Ellington, Duke* / I'm forever blowing bubbles: *Brown, Les* / Blue and sentimental: *Basie, Count*
CD _____ CDGRF 128
Tring / '93 / Tring / Prism.

IT STARTED WITH A KISS
CD _____ ARC 910302
Arcade / Jun '91 / Sony / Grapevine.

ITALIAN HOUSE VOL.2
CD _____ LOWCDX 38
Low Price Music / Aug '95 / Total/BMG.

ITALIAN MANDOLINE
CD _____ 15441
Laserlight / Nov '91 / Target/BMG.

ITALIAN STRING VIRTUOSI
CD _____ ROUCD 1095
Rounder / Mar '95 / CM / Direct / ADA / Cadillac.

ITALY AFTER DARK - ITALIA NOSTALGICA
Vivere: *Buti, Carlo* / Amami se vuoi: *Fiordaliso, Marisa* / Venezia la luna e tu: *Virgili, Luciano / Volare: Arigliano, Nicola* / Bella ragazza dalle trecce bionde: *Buti, Carlo* / Capriccio mazurka: *Gargano, Guiseppe* / Santa Lucia: *De Muro Lomanto, Enzo* / Come prima: *Eigs, Franco* / Sul Lungarno: *Buti, Carlo* / Papavari e papere: *Barimar e La Sua Orchestra* / Reginella: *Buti, Carlo* / Whatever will be will be (Que sera sera): *Power, Romina* / Luna rossa: *Ricci, Franco* / Guaglione: *Carosone, Renato* / Mama: *Gigli, Beniamino* / Anema e core: *De Palma, Jula* / Violino tzigano: *Virgili, Luciano* / Piano fortissimo: *Carosone, Renato* / Stornellando alla toscana: *Villa, Claudio* / Arrivederci Roma: *Gilardini, Renzo*
CD _____ CDEMS 1458
EMI / Sep '92 / EMI.

IT'S A LOVE THING VOLUME 1
CD _____ DTCD 18
Discotex / Nov '93 / Jetstar.

IT'S A LOVE THING VOLUME 2
CD _____ DTCD 22
Discotex / Apr '94 / Jetstar.

IT'S A TRIPLE EARTH
CD _____ TRECD 114
Triple Earth / Oct '95 / Sterns / Grapevine.

IT'S CEILI TIME
(3CD/MC Set)
Green groves of Erin: *Shaskeen* / Cherish the ladies: *Shannon, Seamus* / Music in the glen: *Owenmore Ceili Band* / Reels: *Gardiner, Bobby* / New broom: *Bushwackers* / Shaskeen: *Shaskeen* / Loughmanes: *Shannon, Seamus* / Theme from Ben Hall: *Bushwackers* / Pride of Sligo: *Owenmore Ceili Band* / Hornpipes: *Gardiner, Bobby* / Tony Mulhaire's jig: *Shaskeen* / Chanters tune an samhradh crua: *Na Fili* / Ash plant: *Shaskeen* / Shaskeen (2): *O'Brien, Dermot* / Ma-

son's apron: *Gallowglass Ceili Band* / March of the high kings: *Shannon, Seamus* / Hornpipe selection: *Shaskeen* / Set dance: *Mulhaire Ceili Band* / Reel set: *Kilfenora Ceili Band* / Jig set: *Owenmore Ceili Band* / March set: *Gallowglass Ceili Band* / Jig set (2): *Gardiner, Bobby* / Polka set: *Na Fili* / Cait ni dhuir: *Na Fili* / My love in America: *Dubliners* / Pride of Sligo/Tommy Flynn's / Owenmore jig / Hungry rock / Coleman's / Humours of lisadel / Rising sun / Bucks of Oranmore / Down the broom / Barton's reel / Music in the glen (2) / Coolata jig/Innesfree jig / Salamanca/Ned Killen's reels / Boyne hunt / Come West along the road / Holy well/Ballisodare / Around Lough Gill / Queen of the fair / Is art Eirenin / Ni ene osfainn ce hi / Molloy's favourite/Fox hunter / Michael Anderson's jig / Burke's fancy / Maloney's favourite / Rambling through Erin / Union hornpipe / Plains of Boyle / Trim the velvet/Shaskeen / Duke of Leinster
CD _____ HCD 1003
Carlton Home Entertainment / Nov '92 / Carlton Home Entertainment.

IT'S CEILI TIME VOL.2
CD _____ HCD 1004
Carlton Home Entertainment / Nov '92 / Carlton Home Entertainment.

IT'S CHRISTMAS TIME
CD _____ 15152
Laserlight / Nov '95 / Target/RMG

IT'S CHRISTMAS TIME AGAIN
It's Christmas time again: *Lee, Peggy* / It's beginning to look like Christmas: *Crosby, Bing* / Winter wonderland: *Andrews Sisters* / Sleigh ride: *Andrews Sisters* / White Christmas: *Crosby, Bing*
CD _____ PWKS 597
Carlton Home Entertainment / Oct '95 / Carlton Home Entertainment.

IT'S COUNTRY TIME
(2CD Set)
CD Set _____ 24033
Delta Doubles / Apr '93 / Target/BMG.

IT'S DOUBLE JAZZ TIME
(2CD Set)
CD Set _____ ATJCD 5974
Disky / May '93 / THE / BMG / Discovery / Pinnacle.

IT'S DOUBLE SWING TIME
(2CD Set)
CD Set _____ ATJCD 5973
Disky / May '93 / THE / BMG / Discovery / Pinnacle.

IT'S ELECTRIC
Sometimes: *Erasure* / Enola Gay: *O.M.D.* / Temptation: *Heaven 17* / Are friends electric: *Tubeway Army* / Reward: *Teardrop Explodes* / Smalltown boy: *Bronski Beat* / Mad world: *Tears For Fears* / Tainted love: *Soft Cell* / Fade to grey: *Visage* / Cars: *Numan, Gary* / Vienna: *Ultravox* / To cut a long story short: *Spandau Ballet* / Wishing: *Flock Of Seagulls* / It's my life: *Talk Talk* / Model: *Kraftwerk* / Blue monday: *New Order* / Girls on film: *Duran Duran* / Sweet dreams (are made of this): *Eurythmics* / Quiet life: *Japan*
CD _____ DINCD 73
Dino / Feb '96 / Pinnacle / 3MV.

IT'S GOT TO BE LOVE
It's got to be love: *Fox, Roy & His Orchestra/* tra/Mary Lee / Embraceable you: *Sinatra, Frank* / Cheek to cheek: *Astaire, Fred* / Life begins when you're in love: *Hildegarde* / Love is the sweetest thing: *Noble, Ray & His Orchestra & Al Bowlly* / I've got my love to keep me warm: *Powell, Dick* / With all my heart: *Boswell, Connie* / There isn't any limit to my love: *Ambrose & His Orchestra/Jack Cooper* / Dearest love: *Coward, Sir Noel* / That sentimental sandwich: *Lamour, Dorothy* / Until today: *Weems, Ted & His Orchestra/Perry Como* / Goodnight my love: *Hylton, Jack & His Orchestra/Bert Yarlett* / Trusting my love: *Matthews, Jessie* / When did you leave Heaven: *Martin, Tony* / You made me love you: *Crosby, Bing & The Merry Macs* / It had to be you: *Gibbons, Carroll & Savoy Hotel Orpheans/Julie Dawn* / You are my love song: *Hutch* / Sweet someone: *Fox, Roy & His Orchestra/Denny Dennis* / Nearness of you: *Shore, Dinah* / P.S. I love you: *Geraldo & His Sweet Music/Cyril Graham* / Man I love: *Langford, Frances* / Long ago and far away: *Haymes, Dick & Helen Forrest*
CD _____ PPCD 78119
Past Perfect / Mar '95 / THE.

IT'S HARD BUT IT'S FAIR
(The Blues Today)
CD _____ MCCD 147
Music Club / Nov '93 / Disc / THE / CM.

IT'S JESUS Y'ALL
Jesus you've been good to me: *Gospel Keynotes* / Hungry child: *Salem travellers* / Thankyou Lord: *Salem travellers* / I can't stop holding on: *Ramey, Troy* / I know a man from Galilee: *Ramey, Troy* / It's Jesus y'all: *Ramey, Troy* / Borrowed time: *Swanee Quintet* / Oh yes he did: *Swanee Quintet* /

I've got that feeling: *Swanee Quintet* / I want to be loved: *Ellison, Tommy* / Grandma's hands: *Robinson, Cleophus* / Gamblin' man: *Angelic Gospel Stars* / I'm going to serve Jesus: *Supreme Angels* / Crown of life: *Supreme Angels* / I stood on the banks of Jordan: *Brooklyn Allstars* / People get ready: *Brooklyn Allstars* / That's my son: *Gospel Keynotes* / Won't it be grand: *Consolers* / Lord give me strength: *Boggs, Harold*
CD _____ CDCHM 381
Ace / Apr '94 / Pinnacle / Cadillac / Complete/Pinnacle.

IT'S JUST BEGUN
Put your brain in gear: *S.L. Troopers* / Cool sailing: *Rude Boy Business* / Two and a half years: *Katch 22* / Greed is the system: *Super Cee* / I'm a warrior: *F9's* / You need discipline: *Prime Rhyme Masters* / Cynical world: *Katch 22* / Microphone nutter: *Korperayshun* / Milk in the chocolate: *Son Of Noise* / I'm not a weakling: *Dynametrix* / Planting semtex: *Pointblank* / Cinderella: *Moving In The Right Direction* / Put the brakes on: *F9's*
CD _____ KSCD 5
Kold Sweat / Jan '94 / 3MV.

IT'S MUSICAL TIME
CD _____ 12358
Laserlight / May '94 / Target/BMG.

IT'S MY PARTY
CD _____ 12168
Laserlight / Jul '93 / Target/BMG.

IT'S ONLY ROCK & ROLL
(Album Tracks & New Music From Virgin 1215 - 2CD/MC Set)
CD Set _____ CDFRL 1004
Fragile / Oct '94 / Grapevine.

IT'S SWING TIME
(3CD Set)
CD _____ 55144
Laserlight / Oct '95 / Target/BMG.

IT'S THE SENSATIONAL 70'S
Sugar baby love: *Rubettes* / I'm the leader of the gang (I am): *Glitter, Gary* / Easy kisses for me: *Brotherhood Of Man* / Beach baby: *First Class* / Sugar candy kisses: *Kissoon, Mac & Katie* / You won't find another fool like me: *New Seekers* / Doctor's orders: *Sunny* / Boogie on up: *Rokotto* / Where is the love: *Delegation* / Don't throw it all away: *Benson, Gary* / I love you love me love: *Glitter, Gary* / Jukebox jive: *Rubettes* / Love grows (where my Rosemary goes): *Edison Lighthouse* / Falling apart at the seams: *Marmalade* / Paper documents: *Brotherhood Of Man* / Don't do it baby: *Kissoon, Mac & Katie* / You've been doing me wrong: *Delegation* / Something old, something new: *Fantastics* / Daddy don't you walk so fast: *Boone, Daniel* / Sweet inspiration: *Johnson, Johnny & Bandwagon*
CD _____ MCCD 051
Music Club / Mar '92 / Disc / THE / CM.

IT'S THE TALK OF THE TOWN
Marie: *Dorsey, Tommy* / It's the talk of the town: *Henderson, Fletcher* / Lonesome nights: *Carter, Benny* / My fine feathered friend: *Miller, Glenn* / Song of India: *Dorsey, Tommy* / Devil's holiday: *Carter, Benny* / Silhoutted in the moonlight: *Miller, Glenn* / Down a Carolina Lane: *Ellington, Duke* / Queer notions: *Henderson, Fletcher* / Stardust: *Dorsey, Tommy* / Blue Lou: *Carter, Benny* / Everyday's a holiday: *Miller, Glenn* / Nagasaki: *Henderson, Fletcher* / Six bells stampede: *Carter, Benny* / Music maestro please: *Dorsey, Tommy* / Don't wake up my heart: *Miller, Glenn* / Night life: *Henderson, Fletcher* / Who: *Dorsey, Tommy* / Sophisticated lady: *Ellington, Duke*
CD _____ MUCD 9027
Start / Apr '95 / Koch.

I'VE LOVED AND LOST AGAIN
CD _____ MU 5059
Musketeer / Oct '92 / Koch.

IVOR NOVELLO - CENTENARY CELEBRATION
Pearl / Nov '93 / Harmonia Mundi.

IVORS - THE WINNERS, THE
(40th Anniversary Album - 2CD/MC Set)
Everywhere: *Whitfield, David* / By the fountains of Rome: *Hockridge, Edmund* / Handful of songs: *Steele, Tommy* / Trudie: *Henderson, Joe* / Side saddle: *Conway, Russ* / As long as he needs me: *Bassey, Shirley* / Walkin' back to happiness: *Shapiro, Helen* / Summer holiday: *Richard, Cliff* / She loves you: *Beatles* / Downtown: *Clark, Petula* / Yesterday: *Beatles* / Winchester Cathedral: *New Vaudeville Band* / Puppet on a string: *Shaw, Sandie* / Urban spaceman: *Innes, Neil* / Where do you go to my lovely: *Sarstedt, Peter* / In the summertime: *Mungo Jerry* / My sweet Lord: *Harrison, George* / Without you: *Nelson, Harry* / Daniel: *John, Elton* / Streets of London: *McTell, Ralph* / Bohemian rhapsody: *Queen* / Save all you kisses for me: *Brotherhood Of Man* / Don't cry for me Argentina: *Covington, Julie* / Baker Street: *Rafferty, Gerry* / I don't like Mondays: *Boomtown Rats* / Stop the cavalry: *Lewie, Jona* / Stand and deliver: *Adam & The Ants* / Private investigations: *Dire Straits* / Every breath you take: *Police* /

Against all odds: Collins, Phil / We don't need another hero: Turner, Tina / Don't give up: Gabriel, Peter & Kate Bush / (Something inside) so strong: Siffre, Labi / Love changes everything: Climie Fisher / All around the world: Stansfield, Lisa / Killer: Adamski / Whole of the moon: Waterboys / Why: Lennox, Annie / Pray: Take That
CD Set _____ CDBASCA 1
EMI / May / '95 / EMI.

J

JABBERJAW GOOD TO THE LAST DROP
Mogattraction: Girls Against Boys / Broken E strings: Unwound / Rock star (Alternate version): Hole / Cleaning woman: Hammerhead / In a cold ass fashion: Beck / Total weirdness: Teenage Fanclub / Boxar: Slug / Narrow: Chokebore / Charger: Mule / Turned out (Live): Helmet / Jabberjammin': Southern Culture On The Skids / Rocky mountain rescue: Karp / Chump II: Jawbox / Little girl: Surgery / Blew: Unsane / My letters: Seaweed / Buzzers and bells: Inch / Explain: That Dog / Rich kids: Further
CD _____ MR 081-2
Mammoth / Jul / '94 / Vital.

JACKSON BLUES (1928-38)
CD _____ YAZCD 1007
Yazoo / Jul / '91 / CM / ADA / Roots / Koch.

JAH LOVE INA WI
CD _____ SKYHIGHCD 2002
Sky High / Oct / '95 / Jetstar.

JAH SCREW PRESENTS - DANCEHALL GLAMITY
CD _____ RASCD 3117
Greensleeves / Sep / '93 / Total/BMG / Jetstar / SRD.

JAH WISDOM
CD _____ 86102
Greensleeves / Jun / '93 / Total/BMG / Jetstar / SRD.

JAHMENTO RECS
CD _____ HCD 7006
Hightone / Aug / '94 / ADA / Koch.

J'AI ETE AU BAL
(Cajun & Zydeco Music Of Louisiana Vol.1)
CD _____ ARHCD 331
Arhoolie / Apr / '95 / ADA / Direct / Cadillac.

J'AI ETE AU BAL VOL.2
(Cajun & Zydeco Music of Louisiana)
CD _____ ARHCD 332
Arhoolie / Apr / '95 / ADA / Direct / Cadillac.

JAILHOUSE ROCK
CD _____ BFMSD 5019
Rogue / Oct / '89 / Sterns.

JAKE LEG BLUES
CD _____ JCD 642
Jass / Jun / '94 / CM / Jazz Music / ADA / Cadillac / Direct.

JAKIE JAZZ 'EM 'UP
(Old Time Klezmer Music 1912-26)
CD _____ GV 101CD
Global Village / Nov / '93 / ADA / Direct.

JAM JAM JAM
(Original Full Length Sugarhill 12" Mixes)
Rapper's delight: Sugarhill Gang / That's the joint: Funky 4 Plus 1 / Adventures of Grandmaster Flash on the wheels of steel: Grandmaster Flash / Rapper's reprise: Sugarhill Gang & Sequence / Message II (Survival): Melle Mel & Duke Bootee / White lines (Don't don't do it): Grandmaster Flash & Melle Mel / Pump me up: Trouble Funk
CD _____ MUSCD 016
MCI / May / '94 / Disc / THE.

JAM SESSION
CD _____ 86102
Giants Of Jazz / May / '93 / Target/BMG / Cadillac.

JAM SESSIONS MONTREUX '77
CD _____ OJCCD 385-2
Original Jazz Classics / Feb / '92 / Wellard / Jazz Music / Cadillac / Complete/Pinnacle.

JAMIE/GUYDEN STORY, THE
(2CD Set)
Rebel rouser: Eddy, Duane / You'll lose a good thing: Lynn, Barbara / Quarter to four stomp: Stompers / Pink chiffon: Torok, Mitchell / One million years: Heartbeats / Maybe you'll be there: Billy & The Essentials / Pop pop pop pie: Sherry's / Unchained melody: Blackwells / Mother nature: Robinson, Floyd / Girl from the mountain: Ernie & Halos / Sound off: Turner, Titus / Sweet dreams: McLain, Tommy / Yes I'm ready:

Mason, Barbara / Going back to Louisiana: Channel, Bruce / I wonder: Pentagons / Sea of love: Kit Kat's / Dry your eyes: Brenda & Tabulations / I really love you: Ambrassadors / Won't find better than me: New Hope Singers / Horse: Nobles, Cliff / Let me be your man: Ashley, Tyrone / Ain't nothin' but a house party: Show Stoppers / Storm warning: Volcanoes / Tell me: Ethics / Here am I broken hearted: Four J'S / Oh la la limbo: Danny & The Juniors / Hole in the ground: Rivers, Johnny / I'm a poor loser: Davis, Mac / Time out for tears: Churchill, Savannah / Linda Lu: Sharpe, Ray / Because they're young: Eddy, Duane / Dancing the strand: Gray, Maureen / Ring a rockin': Sedaka, Neil / Dry your eyes (2): Inspirations / Words mean nothing: Hazlewood, Lee / Jam: Gregg, Bobby / Need you: Owens, Donnie / Have love, will travel: Sharps / Dance is over: Billy & The Essentials / Never never: Jordan Brothers / Darling I want to get married: Heartbeats / Come on in: Alden, Craig / Forty miles of bad road: Eddy, Duane / Son of a gun: Clark, Sanford / I'm in love: Pentagons / (I cried at) Laura's wedding: Lynn, Barbara / Caribbean: Torok, Mitchell / Strollin' after school: Fields, Ernie / Get out: Melvin, Harold & The Bluenotes / Slop time: Sherry's / Love (can make you happy): Merci / Living doll: Bond, Bobby / Oh how it hurts: Mason, Barbara / For your precious love: Davis, Geater / Boogaloo down broadway: Fantastic Johnny C / Don't make the good girls go bad: Humphries, Della / Love addict: Honey & The Bees / Right on the tip of my tongue: Brenda & Tabulations / Goodbye: Temptones
CD Set _____ BCD 15874 BH
Bear Family / Oct '95 / Rollercoaster / Direct / CM / Swift / ADA.

JAMMIN'
Jamming: Marley, Bob & The Wailers / 54-46 (was my number): Toots & The Maytals / You can get if you really want: Cliff, Jimmy / Johnny too bad: Slickers / Israelites: Dekker, Desmond / Somebody's watching you: Black Uhuru / Now that we've found love: Third World / Don't turn around: Aswad / Wonderful world: Kotch / Electric boogie: Griffiths, Marcia / Baltimore: Tamlins / Long-shot kick de bucket: Pioneers / Bed's too big without you: Hylton, Sheila / All night till daylight: Miller, Jacob / Easy: Lindsay, Jimmy / Breakfast in bed: Bennett, Lorna / Guava jelly: Gray, Owen / Book of rules: Heptones / Sitting and watching: Brown, Dennis / Some guys have all the luck: Tucker, Junior / Silly games: Kay, Janet / Pass the kouchie: Mighty Diamonds / Police and thieves: Murvin, Junior
CD _____ CIDM 1010
Mango / Jun / '89 / Vital / PolyGram.

JAMMIN' THE BOOGIE WOOGIE
CD _____ CD 56025
Jazz Roots / Nov / '94 / Target/BMG.

JAPAN - KABUKI MUSIC
CD _____ BCD 6809
Auvidis/Ethnic / Jan / '95 / Harmonia Mundi.

JAPANESE HARDCORE 3
CD _____ DISCCD 013
Voices Of Wonder / Jun / '95 / Plastic Head.

JAPANESE KOTO ORCHESTRA
CD _____ LYRCD 7167
Lyrichord / '91 / Roots / ADA / CM.

JAPANESE MASTERPIECES FOR THE SHAKUHACHI
CD _____ LYRCD 7176
Lyrichord / '91 / Roots / ADA / CM.

JAVANESE COURT GAMELAN
CD _____ 7559720442
Elektra Nonesuch / Jan / '95 / Warner Music.

JAZZ - SACRED AND SECULAR
CD _____ DM 25CD
Dormouse / Jun / '92 / Jazz Music / Target/ BMG.

JAZZ AFTER HOURS
CD _____ EMPRCD 571
Emporio / May / '95 / THE / Disc / CM.

JAZZ ALBUM, THE
Leroy Brown: Kidd, Carol / Eye witness: Newton, David / Moon ray: Martin, Claire / Ally: Smith, Tommy / Partners in crime: Martin, Claire / Gentle rain: Taylor, Martin / Don't take your love: Kidd, Carol / It's only a paper moon: Grappelli, Stephane & Martin Taylor / Lean baby: Kidd, Carol / Home from home: Newton, David / Old boyfriends: Martin, Claire / Angel's camp: Taylor, Martin / Please don't talk about me: Kidd, Carol
CD _____ AKD 032
Linn / Sep / '94 / PolyGram.

JAZZ ANTHOLOGY 1942
CD Set _____ 152052
EPM / Apr / '94 / Discovery / ADA.

JAZZ ANTHOLOGY 1943-44
CD _____ 152302
EPM / Apr / '95 / Discovery / ADA.

JAZZ ARCHIVES SAMPLER
CD _____ CAD 466
Jazz Archives / Mar / '94 / Jazz Music / Discovery / Cadillac.

JAZZ AT THE PHILHARMONIC - LONDON 1969
(2CD Set)
Ow / Stardust / Yesterdays / You go to my head / Tin tin deo / Champ / Woman you must be crazy / Goin' to Chicago / Stormy Monday / Shiny stockings / Undecided / I've got the world on a string / L.O.V.E. / Blue Lou / I can't get started (with you) / September song / Body and soul / Bean stalkin' / What is this thing called love /
CD Set _____ 2PACD 26201192
Pablo / Apr / '94 / Jazz Music / Cadillac / Complete/Pinnacle.

JAZZ AT THE PHILHARMONIC - STOCKHOLM '55
(The Exciting Battle)
Little David / Ow / Sticks / Man I love / I'll never be the same / Skylark / My old flame
CD _____ PACD 23107132
Pablo / Apr / '94 / Jazz Music / Cadillac / Complete/Pinnacle.

JAZZ AT THE PHILHARMONIC: HARTFORD 1953
Cotton tail / Airmail special / Swinging on a star / Man I love / Seven come eleven / D.B. blues / I cover the waterfront / Up-'n'-Adam
CD _____ CD 2308240
Pablo / Apr / '94 / Jazz Music / Cadillac / Complete/Pinnacle.

JAZZ BLUES RARITIES 1924 - 1939
CD _____ 99736
Laserlight / Jan / '93 / Target/BMG.

JAZZ, BLUE & SENTIMENTAL
CD _____ DCD 5310
Disky / Dec / '93 / THE / BMG / Discovery / Pinnacle.

JAZZ CAFE VOL.1
So what: Johnson, J.J. / Lullaby: Johnson, J.J. / Watermelon man: Hendricks/Lambert / On Green Dolphin Street: Burton, Gary / Round Midnight: Rollins, Sonny / King Porter stomp: Evans, Gil / Killer Joe: Manteca / Lazy, Dizzy / Milestones: Hargrove, Roy / Every time we say goodbye: Hollyday, Christopher / Superwoman: Woods, Phil / Expansions: Woods, L.L. / Autumn leaves: Moody, James / Somewhere over the rainbow: Baker, Chet / My funny valentine: Desmond, Phil / Just a lucky so and so: Ellington, Duke / Take the 'A' train: Ellington, Duke / Love me or leave me: Horne, Lena / Creole love call: Nelson, Oliver / April in Paris: Davison, Wild Bill / Naima: Ruiz, Hilton / lady day and john coltrane: Scott-Heron, Gil
CD _____ 7432113138-2
Novus / Feb / '93 / BMG.

JAZZ CAFE: AFTERHOURS
Somewhere over the rainbow: Baker, Chet / April in Paris: Hawkins, Coleman / Yesterday: Feliciano, Jose / I'll never be the same: Reinhardt, Django
CD _____ 74321214472
Jazz Cafe / Aug / '94 / BMG.

JAZZ CAFE: AT THE MOVIES
What a wonderful world: Armstrong, Louis / Every time we say goodbye: Baker, Chet / My man: Hawkins, Coleman / Oh green Dolphin Street: Hodges, Johnny
CD _____ 74321263672
Jazz Cafe / Mar '95 / BMG.

JAZZ CAFE: FOR LOVERS
Petite fleur: Bechet, Sidney / My funny valentine: Desmond, Paul / Nearness of you: Mulligan, Gerry / Lover man: Gillespie, Dizzy
CD _____ 74321214492
Jazz Cafe / Mar '95 / BMG.

JAZZ CAFE: GUITAR
Blue Lou: Norvo, Red & Tal Farlow / Beautiful moons ago: Pizzarelli, John / Spoons: Scofield, John / For B.B. King: Walker, T-Bone
CD _____ 74321263692
Jazz Cafe / Mar '95 / BMG.

JAZZ CAFE: LATIN
Manteca: Gillespie, Dizzy / Cherry pink: Prado, Perez / Mambo Inn: Ruiz, Hilton / Manna de carnaval: Thielemans, Jean 'Toots'
CD _____ 74321263702
Jazz Cafe / Mar '95 / BMG.

JAZZ CAFE: STANDARDS
After you've gone: Basie, Count / Mood indigo: Bechet, Sidney / Georgia on my mind: Beiderbecke, Bix / Blues skies: Goodman, Benny
CD _____ 74321263722
Jazz Cafe / Mar '95 / BMG.

JAZZ CAFE: SUMMERTIME
Norwegian wood: Burton, Gary / Birdland over dark: Puente, Tito / Sidewinder: Ruiz, Hilton / Expansions: Smith, Lonnie Liston
CD _____ 74321214442
Jazz Cafe / Aug / '94 / BMG.

JAZZ CAFE: SWINGTIME
Take the 'A' train: Ellington, Duke / Flying home: Hampton, Lionel / Song of the Volga boatmen: Miller, Glenn / Creole love call: Nelson, Oliver
CD _____ 74321214482
Jazz Cafe / Aug / '94 / BMG.

JAZZ CAFE: THE BLUES
Back o' town blues: Armstrong, Louis / Stormy Monday blues: Eckstine, Billy / T'ain't nobody's business if I do: Waller, Fats / Everyday I have the blues: Williams, Joe
CD _____ 74321214452
Jazz Cafe / Aug '94 / BMG.

JAZZ CAFE: THE PIANO
Round Midnight: Monk, Thelonious / Pitter panther patter: Ellington, Duke / My blue heaven: Peterson, Oscar / Freakish: Morton, Jelly Roll
CD _____ 74321131382
Jazz Cafe / Jun / '94 / BMG.

JAZZ CAFE: THE SINGERS
I'm just a lucky so and so: Ellington, Duke / How long has this been going on: Horne, Lena / Any old time: Holiday, Billie / lady day and john coltrane: Scott-Heron, Gil
CD _____ 74321214462
Jazz Cafe / Aug / '94 / BMG.

JAZZ CAFE: TRUMPET & SAXOPHONE
Wee: Hargrove, Roy / Blue Getz blues: Herman, Woody & Stan Getz / Angel: Evans, Gil / Two of a mind: Mulligan, Gerry & Paul Desmond
CD _____ 74321263682
Jazz Cafe / Mar / '95 / BMG.

JAZZ CLASSICS
It's a sin to tell a lie / Potato head blues / Ostrich walk / Riverboat shuffle / Georgia on my mind / Struttin' with some barbecue / Creole jazz / I'm gonna sit right down and write myself a letter / Bourbon Street parade / Snag it / Sweet Georgia Brown / Sophisticated lady / This can't be love / I can't get started (with you) / After you've gone / Old grey bonnet / Old rugged cross / There will never be another you / Ain't misbehavin' / At the woodchoppers' ball
CD _____ KAZCD 11
Kaz / Feb '90 / BMG.

JAZZ CLUB - TENOR SAX
CD _____ 840 031-2
Verve / Jun / '89 / PolyGram.

JAZZ CLUB MAINSTREAM - TENOR AND BARITONE SAX
CD _____ 845 146-2
Verve / Apr '91 / PolyGram.

JAZZ COLLECTION
(3CD/MC Set)
CD Set _____ TBXCD 507
TrueTrax / Jan '96 / THE.

JAZZ COLLECTIVE
Blackbyrds' theme / E.B.F.S. / Golden wings / Mambo Inn / African bird / Casa forte / Cornbread / Reggins / Scarborough street fair / Lady smooth / You're gonna lose me / Backed up against the wall / Lifestyles / Quiet storm / Open your eyes you can fly / Ina's song
CD _____ CDBGPD 076
BGP / Feb '94 / Pinnacle.

JAZZ COMEDY CLASSICS
CD _____ JCD 20
Jass / Jan '87 / CM / Jazz Music / ADA / Cadillac / Direct.

JAZZ CONCERT LIVE - WEST COAST #1
Disorder at the border / Hunt
CD _____ SV 0164
Savoy Jazz / Jan / '94 / Conifer / ADA.

JAZZ CONCERT LIVE - WEST COAST #2
Byas a drink / Cherokee
CD _____ SV 0165
Savoy Jazz / Jan '94 / Conifer / ADA.

JAZZ CONCERT LIVE - WEST COAST #3
What is this thing called love / Backbreaker / Blow, blow, blow
CD _____ SV 0166
Savoy Jazz / Jan '94 / Conifer / ADA.

JAZZ CUTS VOL.1
CD _____ TMPCD 010
Telstar / Jun '95 / BMG.

JAZZ CUTS VOL.2
CD _____ TMPCD 011
Telstar / Jun '95 / BMG.

JAZZ CUTS VOL.3
CD _____ TMPCD 012
Telstar / Jun '95 / BMG.

JAZZ DE SCENE VOL.1
CD _____ 251 278 2
Jazztime / Mar '94 / Discovery / BMG.

JAZZ DE SCENE VOL.3
(1938-50)
CD _____ 8270962
Jazztime / Dec '93 / Discovery / BMG.

JAZZ EVENT
CD _____ MECCACD 1034
Music Mecca / Nov '94 / Jazz Music / Cadillac / Wellard.

JAZZ FESTIVALS IN LATIN AMERICA
(3CD Set)
CD Set _____ WW 2062
West Wind / Apr '91 / Swift / Charly / CM / ADA.

JAZZ FOR LOVERS
CD _____ DCD 5275
Kenwest / Nov '92 / THE.

JAZZ FOR LOVERS
CD _____ TRTCD 170
TrueTrax / Feb '96 / THE.

JAZZ FOR LOVERS
CD _____ CD 3538
Cameo / Aug '95 / Target/BMG.

JAZZ FOR SENSUAL LOVERS
CD _____ STB 2510
Stash / Sep '95 / Jazz Music / CM /
Cadillac / Direct / ADA.

**JAZZ FOR SENSUAL LOVERS:
ROMANTIC GUITARS**
CD _____ STB 2515
Stash / Sep '95 / Jazz Music / CM /
Cadillac / Direct / ADA.

**JAZZ FOR SENSUAL LOVERS:
ROMANTIC SAXOPHONES**
CD _____ STB 2512
Stash / Sep '95 / Jazz Music / CM /
Cadillac / Direct / ADA.

JAZZ FOR YOU
CD _____ NNCD 901
GRP / May '90 / BMG / New house.

JAZZ FROM THE WINDY CITY 1927-30
Sugar: McKenzie & Condon's Chicagoans / China boy: McKenzie & Condon's Chicagoans / Nobody's sweetheart: McKenzie & Condon's Chicagoans / Liza: McKenzie & Condon's Chicagoans / Jazz me blues: Pierce, Charles & his Orchestra / Jazz me blues: Pierce, Charles & his Orchestra / I wish I could shimmy like my sister Kate: Pierce, Charles & his Orchestra / There'll be some changes made: Chicago Rhythm Kings / I've found a new baby: Chicago Rhythm Kings / Friars Point Shuffle: Jungle Kings / Darktown Strutter's Ball: Jungle Kings / Jazz me blues (I): Teschemacher, Frank / Baby, won't you please come home: Louisiana Rhythm Kings / Copenhagen: Schoebel, Elmer / Prince of wails: Schoebel, Elmer / Wailing blues (I and II): Cellar Boys / House stomp (I, II and III): Cellar Boys
CD _____ CBC 1021
Timeless Historical / Aug '94 / New Note / Pinnacle.

JAZZ FUNK AND FUSION
Human spirit: Fuse One / To prove my love: Doheny, Ned / Lion dance: Hiroshima / Hunt up wind: Hiroshi Fukumura / Thighs, high, grip you hips and move: Browne, Tom / By all means: Mouzon, Alphonse & Herbie Hancock / No problem: Watanabe, Sadao / Flight by night: Ritenour, Lee / Rag bag: Grusin, Dave / Central park: Corea, Chick
CD _____ VSOPCD 219
Connoisseur / Aug '95 / Pinnacle.

JAZZ FUNK REVIVAL
Chameleon: Jefferson, Eddie / In the meantime: Barron, Kenny / Thank you talk (I can't be mice all again (CD only.): Jefferson, Eddie / Walk that funky dog: Bronstein, Stan / Philadelphia bright (CD only.): Bishop, Walter Jr. / In the middle of it all: Creque, Neal / Mean street no-bridges: Ponder, Jimmy / Black love: Garnett, Carlos / Mystery of ages (CD only.): Garnett, Carlos / Let us go (to higher heights): Garnett, Carlos
CD _____ PHOCD 8003
Muse / Sep '95 / New Note / CM.

JAZZ FUSION VOLUME 1
CD _____ FUSIONCD 1
Jazz Fusions / Jul '94 / Total/BMG.

JAZZ FUSION VOLUME 2
CD _____ FUSIONCD 2
Jazz Fusions / Jul '94 / Total/BMG.

JAZZ FUSION VOLUME 3
CD _____ FUSIONCD 3
Jazz Fusions / Jul '94 / Total/BMG.

**JAZZ FUTURES
(Live In Concert)**
Mode for John / Sterling Sylvia / Blue moon / Piccadilly square / Bewitched, bothered and bewildered / Stardust / Medgar Evers blues / You don't know what love is / Public eye
CD _____ 02141631582
Novus / Aug '93 / BMG.

JAZZ GOES TO THE MOVIES
Puttin' on the Ritz / Crazy feet / Alone with my dreams / How I'm doin'/Dinah / One little kiss from you / I like a guy what takes his time / You're hi-de-hi-ing me / Gold diggers song / Pettin' in the park / Wo ist der mann / Nasty man / My future star / Oh I didn't know (you'd get that way) / Lulu's back in town / Longo, Pat / Crickets song for amaria: Vale, Marcus / Do it fluid: Dirty Dozen Brass Band / Take five: McCrae, Carmen & Dave Brubeck / Dat dere: Brown, Oscar Jnr / Sidewinder: Herman, Woody & His Herd / Wack wack: Young Holt Trio / It's a hip: Last Poets
CD _____ SOUNDSCD 4
Street Sounds / Oct '94 / BMG.

**JAZZ GREATS
(4CD Set)**
CD Set _____ CDPK 413
Charly / Feb '95 / Charly / THE / Cadillac.

**JAZZ GREATS
(3CD Set)**
CD _____ CPSC 302
Charly / May '95 / Charly / THE / Cadillac.

JAZZ GUITAR - VOLUME 1, THE
CD _____ CD 14528
Jazz Portraits / Jan '94 / Jazz Music.

JAZZ GUITAR - VOLUME 2, THE
CD _____ CD 14535
Jazz Portraits / Jan '94 / Jazz Music.

JAZZ GUITAR - VOLUME 3, THE
CD _____ CD 14538
Jazz Portraits / Jan '94 / Jazz Music.

JAZZ GUITAR - VOLUME 4, THE
CD _____ CD 14542
Jazz Portraits / Jan '94 / Jazz Music.

JAZZ GUITAR CLASSICS
CD _____ OJCCD 6012-2
Original Jazz Classics / Apr '92 / Wellard /
Jazz Music / Cadillac / Complete/Pinnacle.

JAZZ GUITAR VOL.1, THE
CD _____ CD 56007
Jazz Roots / Aug '94 / Target/BMG.

JAZZ GUITAR VOL.3, THE
CD _____ CD 56034
Jazz Roots / Jul '95 / Target/BMG.

JAZZ HOURS, THE
CD _____ SV 0240
Savoy Jazz / Nov '93 / Conifer / ADA.

JAZZ IN AFRICA VOL 1
Delilah / Yardbird suite / Twelve times twelve / Uka-jonga phambili / Body and soul / Scullery department / Dollar's moods / Blues for Hughie / Lover come back to me / Vary-oo-voom / Carol's drive / Gafsa / Old devil moon / Cosmic ray
CD _____ KAZCD 24
Kaz / Nov '92 / BMG.

JAZZ IN AFRICA VOL 2
Tshona / Stop and start / Umgababa / Kippie's prayer / Te te mbambisa (African day) / Kalahari
CD _____ KAZCD 28
Kaz / Nov '92 / BMG.

**JAZZ IN GREAT BRITAIN - PIONEERS
(1927-1938)**
Robert Parker Jazz / Sep '93 / Conifer.

JAZZ IN JAMAICA
CD _____ LG 21093
Lagoon / Apr '94 / Magnum Music Group / THE.

JAZZ IN THE HOUSE
Our mute horn: Masters At Work / Gummed: Zig Zag / I got jazz in my soul: Just 4 Groovers / Into the kick with Tito: Deep Audio Penetration / Way i feel: Musical Expression / Sublime: Tickle / Bassline: DC Track Team / Secret code: Jazz Documents / Supreme law: Harmonious Thump / Warehouse Vs the Ritz: Battle Of The D.J's / Sax track: M & J Project / Souffle: Mondo Grosso
CD _____ SLIPCD 025
Slip 'n' Slide / Mar '95 / Vital / Disc.

JAZZ IN THE HOUSE VOL.2
Theme from change: Daphne / Buff dance: Masters At Work / My Mama said: St. Germain / Foot therapy: Damier, Chez / I'm leaving you: Ulysses / Innocence and inspiration: Elements Of Live / New Jersey deep: Black Science Orchestra / Tank: Global Logic / Moonshine: Keniou / Equinox: Code 718 / Acid ensemble: Orangtrip / Wet dreams: Mada
CD _____ SLIPCD 030
Slip 'n' Slide / Sep '95 / Vital / Disc.

**JAZZ IN THE THIRTIES
(2CD Set)**
CD Set _____ CDSW 8457/8
DRG / '88 / New Note.

JAZZ JAMAICA
CD _____ SOCD 1140
Studio One / Aug '94 / Jetstar.

JAZZ JAZZ JAZZ
CD _____ REVCC 003
REVCO / Aug '94 / Grapevine.

JAZZ JUICE 1
Miles: Davis, Miles / Jeannine: Jefferson, Eddie / Boss tres bien: Quartette Tres Bien / Cubano chant: Blakey, Art / Rhoda: Mendes, Sergio / Mas que nada: Mendes, Sergio / I'll bet you thought I'd never find you: Hendricks, Jon / It don't mean a thing if it ain't got that swing: Schurr, Diane / I believe in love: Longo, Pat
CD _____ SOUNDSCD 6
Street Sounds / Oct '94 / BMG.

JAZZ JUICE 2
CD _____ SOUNDSCD 4
Street Sounds / Mar '95 / BMG.

JAZZ JUICE 3
Hey Leroy, your Mama's callin' you: Castor, Jimmy / Shoshana: Tjader, Cal / Tema da

alma Latina: Matos, Bobby / Take five: Puente, Tito / Yumbamabe: Sanchez, Poncho / Don't be blue: Jackie & Roy / So high: Lawson, Janet / You've got to have freedom: Sanders, Pharoah / Soul bossa nova: Jones, Quincy / Triste: Shepherd, Cybill / Bossa nova ova: Mitchell, Billy / Boogaloo in room 802: Bobo, Willie / Never was love: Roberts, Judy / Who will buy: Lucien, John / Ordinary guy: Bataan, Joe
CD _____ SOUNDSCD 6
Street Sounds / Jul '95 / BMG.

JAZZ KANSAS CITY STYLEZ
CD _____ TPZ 1036
Flapper / Jan '96 / Pinnacle.

JAZZ KEYBOARDS
Supersonic / On a planet / Air pocket / Celestia / Just one of those things / But beautiful / I married an angel / I love you madly / Squeeze me / Mean to me / Indian summer / (Back home again in) Indiana
CD _____ SV 0224
Savoy Jazz / Oct '93 / Conifer / ADA.

JAZZ LIMITED VOL. 1
CD _____ DE 226
Delmark / Jun '95 / Hot Shot / ADA / CM / Direct / Cadillac.

**JAZZ MASTERS - 27 CLASSIC
PERFORMANCES**
CD _____ 4651922
CBS / '88 / Sony.

JAZZ MASTERS VOL. 1
CD _____ MATCD 333
Castle / Apr '95 / BMG.

JAZZ MASTERS VOL. 2
CD _____ MATCD 334
Castle / Apr '95 / BMG.

JAZZ MESSENGERS: PART 1, THE
CD _____ CD 53128
Giants Of Jazz / Nov '92 / Target/BMG / Cadillac.

JAZZ MESSENGERS: PART 2, THE
CD _____ CD 53129
Giants Of Jazz / Nov '92 / Target/BMG / Cadillac.

JAZZ MOODS
Let there be love: Cole, Nat King / It had to be you: Connick, Harry Jr. / Fever: Lee, Peggy / Call me irresponsible: Washington, Dinah / Love for sale: Franklin, Aretha / What a wonderful world: Armstrong, Louis / That ole devil called love: Holiday, Billie / Summertime: Vaughan, Sarah / Take five: Brubeck, Dave / Cantaloop (Flip fantasia): US 3 / Miles: Davis, Miles / So what: Jordan, Ronny / Birdland: Weather Report / Morning dance: Spyro Gyra / Breezin': Benson, George / Let it flow: Washington, Grover Jr. / Ai no corrida: Jones, Quincy / Easy: Jarreau, Al / Don't you worry about a thing: Incognito / Street life: Crusaders & Randy Crawford / Pick up the pieces: Average White Band
CD _____ TCD 2722
Telstar / Jun '94 / BMG.

JAZZ MOODS
CD _____ TRTCD 126
TrueTrax / Dec '94 / THE.

JAZZ MOODS 2
CD _____ TCD 2740
Telstar / Nov '94 / BMG.

JAZZ MOODS VOL.1
CD _____ JWD 102206
JWD / Sep '93 / Target/BMG.

JAZZ MOODS VOL.2
CD _____ JWD 102207
JWD / Sep '93 / Target/BMG.

JAZZ MOODS VOL.3
CD _____ JWD 102208
JWD / Sep '93 / Target/BMG.

JAZZ 'N' STEEL
CD _____ DE 4013
Delos / Feb '94 / Conifer.

**JAZZ NOT JAZZ VOL.2
(The New Breed)**
New jazz swing: Now School / Yeah: Jazzy Jon / Love's fantasy: Now School / Ain't really down: Shaft, Jon / Lost: Headshock / Work: Bedroom Boys / Rize: Fusion / Keep on: Jazz not Jazz
CD _____ WORLD 003CD
World Series / Aug '93 / Vital.

JAZZ ON A SUMMER'S DAY
Take five: Brubeck, Dave / Summertime: Vaughan, Sarah / Moanin': Blakey, Art & The Jazz Messengers / Take five: Lee, Peggy / Girl from Ipanema: Getz, Stan & Astrud Gilberto / So what: Davis, Miles / Mack the knife: Armstrong, Louis / Got my mojo working: Smith, Jimmy / Birdland: Weather Report / Hymn to freedom: Peterson, Oscar
CD _____ CTVCD 108
Castle / Jan '95 / BMG.

JAZZ PARADE - 1940-60'S
CD _____ CD 53025
Giants Of Jazz / Mar '92 / Target/BMG / Cadillac.

**JAZZ PIANO VOL.1
(1935-1942)**
CD _____ 251 282 2
Jazztime / Mar '90 / Discovery / BMG.

JAZZ ROMANCE, A
Speak low: Schurr, Diane / One heart call: Rangell, Nelson / Cross your mind: Howard, George / Hurricane country: Grusin, Dave / First time love: Austin, Patti / Malibu: Ritenour, Lee / Pieces of a heart: Anderson, Carl / Sarah Jane: Lewis, Ramsey / Kei's song: Benoit, David
CD _____ GRP 97902
Golden Encore / Sep '94 / BMG.

JAZZ 'ROUND MIDNIGHT - PIANO
CD _____ 8409302
Verve / Feb '91 / PolyGram.

**JAZZ 'ROUND MIDNIGHT -
SAXOPHONE**
CD _____ 8409512
Verve / Feb '91 / PolyGram.

JAZZ 'ROUND MIDNIGHT - TRUMPET
CD _____ 5110372
Verve / Apr '91 / PolyGram.

JAZZ 'ROUND MIDNIGHT - VOICES
CD _____ 8409462
Verve / Feb '91 / PolyGram.

JAZZ SAMPLER
CD _____ GMCD 6239
Gemini / Dec '89 / Cadillac.

JAZZ SAXOPHONE, THE
Autumn leaves: Getz, Stan / Limelight: Mulligan, Gerry / Walkin' shoes: Mulligan, Gerry / 500 Miles high: Farrell, Joe / Cutie: Rollins, Sonny / Every time we say goodbye: Rollins, Sonny / Mangoes: Rollins, Sonny / Apple core: Mulligan, Gerry / Song for Johnny Hodges: Mulligan, Gerry
CD _____ AAOHP 93342
Start / Dec '94 / Koch.

JAZZ SCENE, THE
CD _____ 5216612
Verve / Feb '95 / PolyGram.

JAZZ SELECTION VOL. 1, THE
T'aint what you do: Fitzgerald, Ella / When my dreamboat comes in: Rushing, Jimmy / Gusto: Lee, Peggy & Bing Crosby / St. Louis blues: Witherspoon, Jimmy / What a difference a day makes: Washington, Dinah / Me and the blues: Bailey, Mildred / My man: Holiday, Billie / I'm in the mood for love: King Pleasure / Do nothin' 'til you hear from me: Hibbler, Al / Honeysuckle rose: Charles, Ray / Our love is here to stay: Laine, Cleo & John Dankworth / Darktown strutter's ball: Lewis, Meade Lux / Bluetail fly: Leadbelly / Mean old bedbug blues: Smith, Bessie / Devil is a woman: Jeffries, Herb / Coffee house blues: Hopkins, Lightnin' / Jazz blues: Bechet, Sidney / Down by the riverside / Dippermouth blues: Oliver, King / Jazz band / Lover man: Holiday, Billie / Heebie jeebies: Armstrong, Louis / Ain't misbehavin': Waller, Fats / Guilty: Torme, Mel / Wednesday evenin' blues: Hooker, John Lee / Tenderly: Vaughan, Sarah
CD _____ CDGRF 010
Tring / '93 / Tring / Prism.

JAZZ SELECTION VOL. 2, THE
Panama rag: Ory, Kid & Jimmy Noone / Crosstown: Ellington, Duke / On the sunny side of the street: Armstrong, Louis / Ghost of a chance: Clinton, Larry / Keyhole blues: Armstrong, Louis / Meet me where they play the blues: Teagarden, Jack / South Rampart street parade: Fountain, Pete / Jelly roll blues: Morton, Jelly Roll / Tiger rag: Henderson, Fletcher / My man: Holiday, Billie / Bowing bowing: Ponty, Jean-Luc / Everything goes: Ellington, Duke / Crazeology: Parker, Charlie & Dizzy Gillespie / Guy's got to go: Christian, Charlie / Four hands: Mingus, Charles / Mame: Armstrong, Louis / Sonny moon for two: Collins, Sonny / Tune of the hickory stick: Adderley, Cannonball / Scrapple the apple: Davis, Miles / How high the moon: Wilson, Teddy / Harlem speaks: Ellington, Duke
CD _____ CDGRF 011
Tring / '93 / Tring / Prism.

JAZZ SELECTION, THE
One O'clock jump: Basie, Count / Round Midnight: Parker, Charlie / At long last love: Horne, Lena / Something new: Basie, Count / Out of nowhere: Davis, Miles / King Porter stomp: Goodman, Benny / Lover come back to me: Fitzgerald, Ella / How high the moon: Parker, Charlie / Sweet Georgia Brown: Cole, Nat King / Caravan: Ellington, Duke / Now's the time: Parker, Charlie / Air Mission to Moscow: Horne, Lena / Night in Tunisia: Davis, Miles / Basin Street blues: Fitzgerald, Ella / Crosstown: Ellington, Duke / My blue heaven: Shaw, Artie / Street beat: Parker, Charlie / All of me: Basie, Count / Black and tan fantasy: Ellington, Duke / Basin Street blues (2): Armstrong, Louis / Yardbird suite: Davis, Miles / I struck a match in the dark: Basie, Count / Rumbop concerto: Gillespie, Dizzy / Nobody knows the trouble I've seen: Horne, Lena / Starlit hour: Fitzgerald, Ella / On the sunny side of the street: Cole, Nat King / Caravan: Ellington, Duke / Fascinating rhythm: Goodman, Benny / My heart stood still: Shaw, Artie / Ornithology: Davis, Miles / Tiger rag: Armstrong, Louis / Blue juice: Barnet, Charlie /

Platterbrains: *Basie, Count* / Blue prelude: *Horne, Lena* / Stompin' at the Savoy: *Horne, Lena* / Yes sir that's my baby: *Cole, Nat King* / Move: *Parker, Charlie* / Bugle call rag: *Goodman, Benny* / Sophisticated lady: *Ellington, Duke* / Moose the mooche: *Davis, Miles* / Cannon's blues: *Adderley, Cannonball* / When the saints go marching in: *Armstrong, Louis* / Embraceable you: *Davis, Miles* / It's only a paper moon: *Cole, Nat King* / Down for double: *Basie, Count* / Little girl blue: *Basie, Count* / Bird of paradise: *Parker, Charlie* / Study in soulphony: *Gillespie, Dizzy* / Stairway to the stars: *Fitzgerald, Ella* / Ring dem bells: *Ellington, Duke* / Sugarfoot stomp: *Ellington, Duke* / Scuttlebutt: *Shaw, Artie* / Northwest passage: *Herman, Woody* / It's a rainy day: *Horne, Lena* / (Back home again in) Indiana: *Armstrong, Louis* / Feather merchant: *Basie, Count* / Riff raff: *Parker, Charlie* / Trouble with me is you: *Cole, Nat King* / Somebody stole my gal: *Goodman, Benny* / No greater love: *Adderley, Cannonball* / That old magic: *Fitzgerald, Ella* / Honeysuckle rose: *Ellington, Duke* / Yes sir that's my baby (2): *Cole, Nat King* / My old flame: *Basie, Count* / Love me or leave me: *Horne, Lena* / On the sunny side of the street (2): *Armstrong, Louis* / Parker's mood: *Parker, Charlie* / Three hearts in a tangle: *Gillespie, Dizzy* / Bijou: *Herman, Woody* / Don't be that way: *Goodman, Benny* / I can't get started (with you): *Shaw, Artie* / I can't remember to forget: *Barnet, Charlie* / Flying home: *Fitzgerald, Ella* / Ease it: *Adderley, Cannonball* / How high the moon (2): *Ellington, Duke* / Slow boat to China: *Parker, Charlie* / Don't blame me: *Parker, Charlie* / (Back home again in) Indiana (2): *Armstrong, Louis* / Fiesta in blue: *Basie, Count* / Bird of paradise (2): *Davis, Miles* / Get happy: *Goodman, Benny*
CD Set _____ TFP 005
Tring / Nov '92 / Tring / Prism.

JAZZ SHOWCASE
Basie: *Basie, Count Orchestra* / Reunion blues: *Peterson, Oscar* / So wistfully sad: *Brubeck, Dave* / Gone with the wind: *Short, Bobby* / Jo-Wes: *Pass, Joe* / Paraiso: *Mulligan, Gerry & Jane Duboc* / Little suede shoes: *Ruiz, Hilton* / Tour de force: *Hampton, Slide & The Jazz Masters* / Here's to life: *Williams, Joe & George Shearing* / Bird feathers: *Shearing, George* / I'm gonna go fishin': *Torme, Mel* / In the wee small hours of the morning: *Brown, Ray Trio* / Bittersweet: *Bryson, Jeanie* / Lullaby of Birdland: *Jamal, Ahmad*
CD _____ CD 83342
Telarc / Apr '94 / Conifer / ADA.

JAZZ SINGERS
(3CD Set)
CD _____ CPSC 301
Charly / May '95 / Charly / THE / Cadillac.

JAZZ SINGERS, THE
(5CD Set)
CD Set _____ JWD 2517
JWD / Oct '92 / Target/BMG.

JAZZ TO THE WORLD
Winter wonderland: *Alpert, Herb* / Baby it's cold outside: *Reeves, Dianne* / It came upon a midnight clear: *Fourplay* / Have yourself a merry little Christmas: *Krall, Diana* / O Tannenbaum: *Duke, George* / Let it snow, let it snow, let in snow: *Franks, Michael* / Christmas waltz: *Brecker Brothers* / Little drummer boy: *Wilson, Cassandra* / I'll be home for Christmas: *Hancock, Herbie* / O come o come Emanuel: *Hancock, Herbie* / Christmas blues: *Cole, Holly* / Angels we have heard on high: *Steps Ahead* / Christmas song: *Baker, Anita* / What child is this: *Corea, Chick* / Il est ne, le divin enfant: *Dr. John*
CD _____ CDP 8321272
Blue Note / Dec '95 / EMI.

JAZZ TODAY VOL.1
Sunday in New York: *Cole, Richie* / O.T.V.O.G.: *Rollins, Sonny* / Scrapple from the apple: *Morgan, Frank Quartet* / If dreams come true: *White, Carla* / Movin' on: *McGriff, Jimmy* / Vicki: *Crawford, Hank* / Underground express: *Campbell, Kerry* / Samba to Isabelle: *Haban, Cliff* / Toc de bola: *Azymuth* / Jacaranda: *Roditi, Claudio*
CD _____ CDBGP 1026
BGP / Oct '93 / Pinnacle.

JAZZ TREATS FOR THE HOLIDAYS
CD _____ ARCD 19122
Arbors Jazz / Nov '94 / Cadillac.

JAZZ TRIBE, THE
CD _____ 123254-2
Red / Nov '92 / Harmonia Mundi / Jazz Horizons / Cadillac / ADA.

JAZZ TRUMPET
(5CD Set)
CD Set _____ JWD 2525
JWD / Oct '94 / Target/BMG.

JAZZ VALENTINE
CD _____ MM 65091
Music Masters / Oct '94 / Nimbus.

JAZZ VIOLIN 1926-42
CD _____ 158002
Jazz Archives / Aug '93 / Jazz Music / Discovery / Cadillac.

JAZZ VOCAL GROUPS 1927-44
(2CD Set)
CD Set _____ FA 041
Fremeaux / Sep '95 / Discovery / ADA.

JAZZ VOCALISTS
On the sunny side of the street: *Hampton, Lionel* / Ain't misbehavin': *Waller, Fats* / That ain't right: *Bailey, Mildred* / St. Louis blues: *Teagarden, Jack* / Stars fell on Alabama: *Wiley, Lee* / One o'clock jump: *Lambert, Dave* / Every day I have the blues: *Williams, Joe* / My man's gone now: *Simone, Nina* / Careless love: *Turner, Big Joe* / What a wonderful world: *Armstrong, Louis* / Fine and mellow: *Rushing, Jimmy*
CD _____ 07863660722
Bluebird / Oct '92 / BMG.

JAZZ YEAR BOOK 1945
CD Set _____ 313312
Milan / Dec '95 / BMG / Silva Screen.

JAZZBOX
CD _____ ECMBOX 05
ECM / Nov '92 / New Note.

JAZZIN' AT RONNIE'S
CD _____ MCCD 212
Music Club / Oct '95 / Disc / THE / CM.

JAZZIN' BABY BLUES
Poor papa: *Jones, Clarence* / Look what a fool I've been: *Johnson, James P.* / Jazzin' baby blues: *Jones, Clarence* / Mama's gone the blues: *Waller, Fats* / Mama's gone goodbye: *Montgomery, Mike* / Goodbye: *Montgomery, Mike* / Baby, won't you please come home: *Jones, Clarence* / Play 'em for mama and sing 'em for me: *Baker, Edythe* / He's my man: *Johnson, James P.* / When you're good you're lonesome: *Baker, Edythe* / Cryin' Blues: *Randolph, Mandy* / Bloobie blooie: *Baker, Edythe* / Changes: *Lawnhurst, Vee* / Yearning (just for you): *Lawnhurst, Vee* / I'm gonna jazz my way: *Randolph, Mandy*
CD _____ BCD 117
Biograph / Jul '91 / Wellard / ADA / Hot Shot / Jazz Music / Cadillac / Direct.

JAZZIN' THE BLUES
CD _____ MCCD 186
Music Club / Nov '94 / Disc / THE / CM.

JAZZIN' THE BLUES (1936-46)
CD _____ JPCD 1515
Jazz Perspectives / May '95 / Jazz Music / Hot Shot.

JAZZIN' UNIVERSALLY
Migrant worker / Phambili / Hug courtney pine / Bo molelekwa / Dance to Africa / Nikiwe / Nobohle
CD _____ BW 078
B&W / Oct '95 / New Note.

JAZZSPEAK
CD _____ NAR 054 CD
New Alliance / May '93 / Pinnacle.

JAZZ LITTLE CHRISTMAS
CD _____ 8405012
Verve / Apr '90 / PolyGram.

JE T'AIME
Cherish: *Kool & The Gang* / Everlasting love: *Gibb, Andy* / Breaking up is hard to do: *Sedaka, Neil* / Son of a preacher man: *Springfield, Dusty* / Stuck in the middle with you: *Stealer's Wheel* / All kinds of everything: *Dana* / Je t'aime moi non plus: *Birkin, Jane & Serge Gainsbourgh* / You see the trouble with me: *White, Barry* / Love town: *Newbury, Booker* / Do that to me one more time: *Captain & Tennille* / Can't give you anything (but my love): *Stylistics* / Baby come back: *Player* / Captain of her heart: *Double* / Marguerita time: *Status Quo*
CD _____ 5501462
Spectrum/Karussell / Jan '94 / PolyGram / THE.

JEKURA - THE DEEP ETERNAL FOREST CD
CD _____ EFA 015582
Apocalyptic Vision / May '95 / Plastic Head / SRD.

JESSE DAVIS
Renon street incident / Tulsa county / Washita love child / Every night is Saturday night / You Belladonna you / Rock 'n' roll gypsies / Golden sun goddess / Crazy love
CD _____ 900943
Line / Jun '95 / CM / Grapevine / ADA / Conifer / Direct.

JEWELS OF CAJUN MUSIC
CD _____ TRIK 0157
Trikont / Oct '94 / ADA / Direct.

JIMMY JAY PRESENTS : LES COOL SESSIONS
CD _____ CDVIR 18
Virgin / Aug '93 / EMI.

JINGLE BELLS IN THE SNOW
CD _____ CNCD 5931
Hermanex / Nov '92 / THE.

JIVING JAMBOREE
Saturday night fish fry / Ain't got no home / Something's goin' on in my room / They call me big Mama / Honeydripper / Love love of my life / I want you / Buzz buzz buzz / Wet back hop / Ding dong daddy / Music goes round and round / Don't stop loving

me / Nite life boogie / Opus one / Hit, git and split / Rockin' Robin / My baby's rockin / That's all / You got me reelin' and rockin' / O sole mio boogie / Free and easy / Hey girl, hey boy / Rock that boogie / Flat foot Sam / My man
CD _____ CDCHD 561
Ace / Apr '95 / Pinnacle / Cadillac / Complete/Pinnacle.

JJ COMPILATION
CD _____ JJCD 1
JJ / Jun '95 / Plastic Head.

JOCKOMO NEW ORLEANS RHYTHM AND BLUES
CD _____ MCCD 206
Music Club / Jul '95 / Disc / THE / CM.

JOE MEEK - THE PYE YEARS VOL.2 (304 Holloway Road)
Pocket full of dreams and eyes full of tears: *Gregory, Iain* / Night you told a lie: *Gregory, Iain* / Who's the girl: *Jay, Peter* / Bittersweet love: *Riot Squad* / Try to realise: *Riot Squad* / When love was young: *Rio, Bobby & the Revelles* / Happy talk: *Saints* / Midgets: *Saints* / Parade of the tin soldiers: *Saints* / Baby I go for you: *Blue Rondos* / What can I do: *Blue Rondos* / May your hearts stay young forever: *Reader, Pat* / Goodness knows: *Wayne, Ricky & the Off-Beats* / Baby I like the look of you: *London, Peter* / Fickle heart: *Garfield, Johnny* / Stranger in paradise: *Garfield, Johnny* / As time goes by: *Dean, Alan & His Problems* / Cool water: *Cameron, Chick Ted Group & The D.J.'s* / Rescue me: *Wayne, Ricky* / It can happen to you: *Conrad, Jess* / There and Back again: *Cook, Peter* / Sing C'est la vie: *Collins, Glenda* / I'm not made of clay: *Rio, Bobby* / My saddest day: *Austin, Reg* / Two timing baby: *Carter-Lewis & The Southerners* / Tell me: *Carter-Lewis & The Southerners*
CD _____ NEXCD 216
Sequel / Feb '93 / BMG.

JOHN PEEL SUB POP SESSIONS
By her own hand: *Mudhoney* / Here comes sickness: *Mudhoney* / You make me die: *Mudhoney* / Helot: *Tad* / Sit in glass: *Seaweed* / She cracked: *Seaweed* / You pretty thins: *Pond* / Cinders: *Pond* / Here comes: *Velocity Girl* / Always: *Velocity Girl* / Crazy town: *Velocity Girl* / Broken hearted wine: *Codeine*
CD _____ SFRCD 126
Strange Fruit / Mar '94 / Pinnacle.

JOINT 2, THE
CD _____ JOINT 2 CD
Suburban Base/Moving Shadow / Oct '94 / SRD.

JOINT, THE
CD _____ JOINT 1 CD
Suburban Base/Moving Shadow / Oct '93 / SRD.

JOURNEY DOWN THE RHINE (Popular Music About The Rhine Area)
CD _____ 15371
Laserlight / '91 / Target/BMG.

JOURNEY THROUGH THE UNDERGROUND
CD _____ PLUGCD 1
Produce / Nov '94 / 3MV / Sony.

JOURNEY TO BRAZIL, A
CD _____ PS 66508
Playasound / Apr '95 / Harmonia Mundi / ADA.

JOURNEY TO LOUISISNA
CD _____ PS 66511
Playasound / Dec '95 / Harmonia Mundi / ADA.

JOURNEY TO PORTUGAL, A
CD _____ PS 66507
Playasound / Apr '95 / Harmonia Mundi / ADA.

JOURNEY TO THE EDGE (Progressive Rock Classics)
Living in the past: *Jethro Tull* / Joybringer: *Manfred Mann's Earthband* / America: *Nice* / Cirkus: *King Crimson* / In-a-gadda-da-vida: *Iron Butterfly* / Forty thousand headmen: *Traffic* / You keep me hangin' on: *Vanilla Fudge* / Child of the universe: *Barclay James Harvest* / Wishing well: *Free* / Tomorrow night: *Atomic Rooster* / Jerusalem: *Emerson, Lake & Palmer* / Freefall: *Camel* / Back street luv: *Curved Air* / Surprise surprise: *Caravan* / Natural born bugie: *Humble Pie* / Love like a man: *Ten Years After* / Burlesque: *Family* / My room (Waiting for wonderland): *Van Der Graaf Generator*
CD _____ MUSCD 018
MCI / May '94 / Disc / THE.

JOURNEY TO VIETNAM, A
CD _____ PS 66509
Playasound / Apr '95 / Harmonia Mundi / ADA.

JOURNEYS BY DJ VOL.5
CD _____ JDJCD 5
Music Unites / Jun '94 / Sony / 3MV / SRD.

JOURNEYS BY DJ VOL.6 (The ultimate house party mix)
CD _____ JDJCD 6

Music Unites / Oct '94 / Sony / 3MV / SRD.

JOURNEYS BY DJ VOL.7 (Rocky & Diesel)
CD _____ JDJCD 7
Music Unites / Jun '95 / Sony / 3MV / SRD.

JOURNEYS BY DJ VOL.9 (The Ultimate Beach Party)
CD _____ JDJCD 9
Music Unites / Dec '95 / Sony / 3MV / SRD.

JOURNEYS INTO JUNGLE
CD _____ JIJCD 001
Music Unites / Jun '95 / Sony / 3MV / SRD.

JOY OF CHRISTMAS, THE (Christmas Crooners/Christmas With Bing Crosby/Angel Voices)
CD Set _____ MCBX 012
Music Club / Apr '94 / Disc / THE / CM.

JOYEUX NOEL
CD _____ DCD 5338
Disky / Dec '93 / BMG / Discovery / Pinnacle.

JUBILEE JEZEBELS
Drive Daddy drive: *Little Sylvia* / I went to your wedding: *Little Sylvia* / Ain't gonna do it: *Little Sylvia* / Blue heaven: *Little Sylvia* / Everything I need but you: *Little Sylvia* / It must be love: *Watkins, Viola* / Really real: *Watkins, Viola* / There goes my heart: *Watkins, Viola* / I've lost: *Enchanters* / Housewife blues: *Enchanters* / How could you: *Enchanters* / Boogie woogie Daddy: *Enchanters* / Heavenly father: *McGriff, Edna* / It's raining: *McGriff, Edna* / I love you: *McGriff, Edna* / Edna's blues: *McGriff, Edna* / Why oh why: *McGriff, Edna* / I'll surender anytime: *McGriff, Edna* / It's my turn now: *Fran, Carol* / You can't stop me: *Fran, Carol* / I know: *Fran, Carol* / Any day love walks in: *Fran, Carol* / Just a letter: *Fran, Carol* / World without you: *Fran, Carol*
CD _____ NEMCD 750
Sequel / Aug '95 / BMG.

JUG AND WASHBOARD BANDS - VOL.2 (1928-1930)
CD _____ SOBCD 35142
Story Of The Blues / Mar '92 / Koch / ADA.

JUJU ROOTS 1930S-50S
CD _____ ROU 5017CD
Rounder / Feb '93 / CM / Direct / ADA / Cadillac.

JUKE BOX COLLECTION - BLUE SUEDE SHOES (Rock 'n' roll classics)
La Bamba: *Valens, Ritchie* / Wake up little Susie: *Everly Brothers* / Good golly Miss Molly: *Little Richard* / Tequila: *Champs* / Come go with me: *Del-Vikings* / Endless sleep: *Reynolds, Jody* / Great balls of fire: *Lewis, Jerry Lee* / Blue suede shoes: *Perkins, Carl* / Raunchy: *Justis, Bill* / Rockin' robin: *Day, Bobby* / Bony Moronie: *Williams, Larry*
CD _____ OG 3701
Old Gold / Jun '88 / Carlton Home Entertainment.

JUKE BOX COLLECTION - DANCING ON A SATURDAY NIGHT (Popular Hits Of The 60's & 70's)
Son of my father: *Chicory Tip* / Banner man: *Blue Mink* / Snoopy Vs. the Red Baron: *Royal Guardsmen* / Mouldy old dough: *Lieutenant Pigeon* / Beautiful Sunday: *Boone, Daniel* / Venus: *Shocking Blue* / Puppet on a string: *Shaw, Sandie* / Bridget the midget: *Stevens, Ray* / Sugar sugar: *Archies* / Beach baby: *First Class* / Dancing on a Saturday night: *Blue, Barry* / Simon says: *1910 Fruitgum Company* / Is this the way to Amarillo: *Christie, Tony* / Little arrows: *Lee, Leapy*
CD _____ OG 3713
Old Gold / Mar '90 / Carlton Home Entertainment.

JUKE BOX COLLECTION - DELILAH (Jukebox 60's Hits)
Delilah: *Jones, Tom* / Dizzy: *Roe, Tommy* / Gimmie gimmie good lovin': *Crazy Elephant* / Last train to Clarksville: *Monkees* / I've gotta get a message to you: *Bee Gees* / Looking through the eyes of love: *Pitney, Gene* / Love gives you (where my Rosemary goes): *Edison Lighthouse* / Dream a little dream on me: *Mama Cass* / Zabadak: *Dave Dee, Dozy, Beaky, Mick & Tich* / Keep on: *98.6: Keith* / Here comes my baby: *Tremeloes* / Couldn't live without your love: *Clark, Petula* / Simon Smith and the amazing dancing bear: *Price, Alan*
CD _____ OG 3726
Old Gold / Aug '91 / Carlton Home Entertainment.

JUKE BOX COLLECTION - DOWNTOWN (Sound of the 60's part 3)
Will you still love me tomorrow: *Shirelles* / Rhythm of the rain: *Cascades* / Downtown: *Clark, Petula* / He's so fine: *Chiffons* / Hey Paula: *Paul & Paula* / Swiss maid: *Shannon, Del* / When my little girl is smiling: *Justis, Jimmy* / Why: *Avalon, Frankie* / I wanna go home: *Donegan, Lonnie* / When will I be

loved: *Everly Brothers* / Too good: *Little Tony* / Beatnik fly: *Johnny & The Hurricanes*
CD _____ OG 3705
Old Gold / Jun '88 / Carlton Home Entertainment.

JUKE BOX COLLECTION - EBONY EYES
(Jukebox 60's)
Ebony eyes: *Everly Brothers* / Ginny come lately: *Hyland, Brian* / Baby blue: son: *Rockin' Berries* / Little bitty tear: *Ives, Burl* / Shy girl: *Cascades* / I understand: *G-Clefs* / Folk singer: *Roe, Tommy* / Dr. Kildare: *Chamberlain, Richard* / Angela Jones: *Ferguson, Johnny* / Pretty blue eyes: *Lawrence, Steve* / Things: *Darin, Bobby* / Kelly: *Shannon, Del* / Our day will come: *Ruby & The Romantics* / I will: *Fury, Billy*
CD _____ OG 3724
Old Gold / Jul '90 / Carlton Home Entertainment.

JUKE BOX COLLECTION - FRIDAY ON MY MIND
(Sound of the 60's part 2)
Go now: *Moody Blues* / You really got me: *Kinks* / Have I the right: *Honeycombs* / Black is black: *Los Bravos* / She'd rather be with me: *Turtles* / Death of a clown: *Davies, Dave* / Baby, now that I've found you: *Foundations* / Out of time: *Farlowe, Chris* / Red red wine: *James, Jimmy & The Vagabonds* / Friday on my mind: *Easybeats* / Delta lady: *Cocker, Joe* / To whom it concerns: *Andrews, Chris*
CD _____ OG 3704
Old Gold / Jun '88 / Carlton Home Entertainment.

JUKE BOX COLLECTION - HOT LOVE
(Sound of the 70's part 1)
Spirit in the sky: *Greenbaum, Norman* / Hot love: *T. Rex* / Devil's answer: *Atomic Rooster* / Lola: *Kinks* / In a broken dream: *Python Lee Jackson* / How long: *Ace* / Baby jump: *Mungo Jerry* / Paranoid: *Black Sabbath* / Radar love: *Golden Earring* / Conquistador: *Procul Harum* / Darlin': *Miller, Frankie* / I hear you knocking: *Edmunds, Dave*
CD _____ OG 3707
Old Gold / Jun '88 / Carlton Home Entertainment.

JUKE BOX COLLECTION - I GOT THE MUSIC IN ME
(Jukebox 70's Hits)
Candida: *Dawn* / Hitchin' a ride: *Vanity Fare* / I got the music in me: *Dee, Kiki* / Kissin' in the back row of the movies: *Drifters* / Me and you and a dog named boo: *Lobo* / My coo ca choo: *Stardust, Alvin* / Chirpy chirpy cheep cheep: *Middle Of The Road* / Take a chance on me: *Abba* / Never ending song of love: *New Seekers* / Jive talkin': *Bee Gees* / El bimbo: *Bimbo Jet* / Thank you for being a friend: *Gold, Andrew* / I wanna stay with you: *Gallagher & Lyle* / Wonderful world, beautiful people: *Cliff, Jimmy*
CD _____ OG 3729
Old Gold / '92 / Carlton Home Entertainment.

JUKE BOX COLLECTION - IN THE SUMMER TIME
(Sound of the 70's part 2)
In the Summertime: *Mungo Jerry* / Jarrow song: *Price, Alan* / Crying, laughing, loving, lying: *Siffre, Labi* / Egyptian reggae: *Richman, Jonathan* / Everything I own: *Boothe, Ken* / Barbados: *Typically Tropical* / Misty: *Stevens, Ray* / Something here in my heart: *Paper Dolls* / Popcorn: *Hot Butter* / It's a heartache: *Tyler, Bonnie* / I'll go where your music takes me: *James, Jimmy & The Vagabonds* / You to me are everything: *Real Thing* / Pepper box: *Peppers* / That same old feeling: *Pickettywitch*
CD _____ OG 3714
Old Gold / Mar '90 / Carlton Home Entertainment.

JUKE BOX COLLECTION - KING OF THE ROAD
(60's country music hits)
Four in the morning: *Young, Faron* / Make the world go away: *Arnold, Eddy* / Send me the pillow that you dream on: *Tillotson, Johnny* / Sea of heartbreak: *Gibson, Don* / I fall to pieces: *Cline, Patsy* / I won't forget you: *Reeves, Jim* / King of the road: *Miller, Roger* / Walk on by: *Van Dyke, Leroy* / There goes my everything: *Greene, Jack* / Next in line: *Twitty, Conway* / What made Milwaukee famous (has made a loser out of me): *Lewis, Jerry Lee* / Detroit city: *Bare, Bobby* / Satin sheets: *Pruett, Jeannie* / Coal miner's daughter: *Lynn, Loretta*
CD _____ OG 3718
Old Gold / Mar '90 / Carlton Home Entertainment.

JUKE BOX COLLECTION - LEADER OF THE PACK
(Sound of the 60's part 6)
Wild wind: *Leyton, Johnny* / Runaround Sue: *Dion* / Hey little girl: *Shannon, Del* / Counting teardrops: *Ford, Emile* / I'm gonna be strong: *Pitney, Gene* / Leader of the pack: *Shangri-Las* / Colours: *Donovan* / Needles and pins: *Searchers* / Everyone's gone to the moon: *King, Jonathan* / Lovers of the world unite: *David & Jonathan* / Pied piper: *St. Peters, Crispian* / Concrete and clay: *Unit 4+2*

CD _____ OG 3710
Old Gold / Jun '88 / Carlton Home Entertainment.

JUKE BOX COLLECTION - LET'S DANCE
(Sound of the 70's)
Wanderer: *Dion* / Hats off to Larry: *Shannon, Del* / Hey baby: *Channel, Bruce* / Picture of you: *Brown, Joe* / Poetry in motion: *Tillotson, Johnny* / Johnny remember me: *Leyton, Johnny* / Let's dance: *Montez, Chris* / Always something there to remind me: *Shaw, Sandie* / Twenty four hours from Tulsa: *Pitney, Gene* / Catch the wind: *Donovan* / You were on my mind: *St. Peters, Crispian* / Yesterday man: *Andrews, Chris* / Reveille rock: *Johnny & The Hurricanes*
CD _____ OG 3702
Old Gold / Jun '88 / Carlton Home Entertainment.

JUKE BOX COLLECTION - MISTY BLUE
(Love Songs Of The 70's)
Misty blue: *Moore, Dorothy* / We do it: *Stone, R & J* / Feelings: *Albert, Morris* / Have you seen her: *Chi-Lites* / Stay with me: *Blue Mink* / I will: *Winters, Ruby* / Everything is beautiful: *Stevens, Ray* / Clair: *O'Sullivan, Gilbert* / Help me make it through the night: *Holt, John* / Sad sweet dreamer: *Sweet Sensation* / Lost in France: *Tyler, Bonnie* / It must be love: *Siffre, Labi*
CD _____ OG 3706
Old Gold / Jun '88 / Carlton Home Entertainment.

JUKE BOX COLLECTION - OH BOY
(Sound of the 50's part 3)
Till I kissed you: *Everly Brothers* / Three bells: *Browns* / Making love: *Robinson, Floyd* / Mona Lisa: *Twitty, Conway* / Shape I'm in: *Restivo, Johnny* / Why baby why: *Boone, Pat* / Only sixteen: *Cooke, Sam* / Oh boy: *Holly, Buddy & The Crickets* / Last train to San Fernando: *Duncan, Johnny* / My Dixie darling: *Donegan, Lonnie* / In the mood: *Price, Lloyd* / In the mood: *Fields, Ernie* / Butterfingers: *Steele, Tommy* / Island in the sun: *Belafonte, Harry*
CD _____ OG 3720
Old Gold / Mar '90 / Carlton Home Entertainment.

JUKE BOX COLLECTION - RUBBER BULLETS
(Sound of the 70's part 3)
Stuck in the middle with you: *Stealer's Wheel* / Mama told me not to come: *Three Dog Night* / Standing in the road: *Blackfoot Sue* / Paper plane: *Status Quo* / Whiskey in the jar: *Thin Lizzy* / Rubber bullets: *10cc* / Tomorrow night: *Atomic Rooster* / Who do you love: *Juicy Lucy* / Broken down angel: *Nazareth* / One and one is one: *Medicine Head* / Show me the way: *Frampton, Peter* / Rock mountain way: *Walsh, Joe*
CD _____ OG 3717
Old Gold / Mar '90 / Carlton Home Entertainment.

JUKE BOX COLLECTION - SLEEPY SHORES
(Instrumental classics)
Il silenzio: *Rosso, Nini* / Aria: *Bilk, Acker* / Cast your fate to the wind: *Sounds Orchestral* / Cavatina: *Williams, John* / Eye level: *Park, Simon Orchestra* / Floral dance: *Petite Fleur: Barber, Chris* / Midnight in Moscow: *Ball, Kenny* / Trudie: *Henderson, Joe* / Z-cars: *Keating, Johnny* / Sleepy shores: *Pearson, Johnny* / Zorba's dance: *Minerbi, Marcello*
CD _____ OG 3703
Old Gold / Jun '88 / Carlton Home Entertainment.

JUKE BOX COLLECTION - STRANGERS ON THE SHORE
(Instrumentals Vol. 2)
Harry Lime theme: *Karas, Anton* / Ebb tide: *Bilk, Acker* / March of the Siamese children: *Ball, Kenny & His Jazzmen* / Never on a Sunday: *Chaquito* / Desafinado: *Getz, Stan & Charlie Byrd* / Love is blue: *Mauriat, Paul* / Walk in the Black Forest: *Jankowski, Horst* / Maria Elena: *Los Indios Tabajaros* / Sucu sucu: *Johnson, Laurie* / How soon: *Mancini, Henry* / Bye bye blues: *Kaempfert, Bert* / Entertainer: *Hamlisch, Marvin* / Galloping home: *London String Chorale*
CD _____ OG 3721
Old Gold / Jul '90 / Carlton Home Entertainment.

JUKE BOX COLLECTION - SUMMER IN THE CITY
(Sound of the 60's part 7)
1-2-3: *Barry, Len* / Monday, Monday: *Mamas & Papas* / Happy together: *Turtles* / Waterloo sunset: *Kinks* / Keep searchin': *Shannon, Del* / Lightning strikes: *Christie, Lou* / It's good news week: *Hedgehoppers Anonymous* / Judy in disguise: *Fred, John & The Playboys* / Wooly bully: *Sam The Sham & The Pharaohs* / Louie Louie: *Kingsmen* / I fought the law: *Fuller, Bobby Four* / Evil hearted you: *Yardbirds* / Summer in the city: *Lovin' Spoonful* / Eve of destruction: *McGuire, Barry*
CD _____ OG 3716
Old Gold / Mar '90 / Carlton Home Entertainment.

JUKE BOX COLLECTION - SUNNY AFTERNOON
(Sound Of The 60's part 5)
Sunny afternoon: *Kinks* / Flowers in the rain: *Move* / Let's go to San Francisco: *Flowerpot Men* / Eleanore: *Turtles* / Melting pot: *Blue Mink* / (If paradise is) half as nice: *Amen Corner* / Whiter shade of pale: *Procul Harum* / I put a spell on you: *Price, Alan* / Set / Man of the world: *Fleetwood Mac* / Pictures of matchstick men: *Status Quo* / Itchycoo Park: *Small Faces* / With a little help from my friends: *Cocker, Joe*
CD _____ OG 3709
Old Gold / Jun '88 / Carlton Home Entertainment.

JUKE BOX COLLECTION - SWEET TALKIN' GUY
(Greats From 60's Gals)
Soldier boy: *Shirelles* / Sweet talking guy: *Chiffons* / First cut is the deepest: *Arnold, P.P.* / Sailor: *Clark, Petula* / Long live love: *Shaw, Sandie* / Terry: *Twinkle* / It's getting better: *Mama Cass* / You don't own me: *Gore, Lesley* / Chapel of love: *Dixie Cups* / Walk on by: *Warwick, Dionne* / Big hurt: *Fisher, Toni* / Bobby's girl: *Maughan, Susan* / Born a woman: *Posey, Sandy* / You don't have to say you love me: *Springfield, Dusty*
CD _____ OG 3712
Old Gold / Mar '90 / Carlton Home Entertainment.

JUKE BOX COLLECTION - TEEN BEAT
(Sound of the 60's part 4)
What'd I say: *Lewis, Jerry Lee* / Teen beat: *Nelson, Sandy* / Lonely weekends: *Rich, Charlie* / War paint: *Brook Brothers* / Some kinda fun: *Montez, Chris* / Runaway: *Shannon, Del* / So, this is she: *Leyton, Johnny* / It only took a minute: *Brown, Joe* / Rockin' goose: *Johnny & The Hurricanes* / Be mine: *Fortune, Lance* / Blue moon: *Marcels*
CD _____ OG 3708
Old Gold / Jun '88 / Carlton Home Entertainment.

JUKE BOX COLLECTION - THIS IS MY SONG
(Popular 60's Ballad Hits)
This is my song: *Clark, Petula* / Let it be me: *Everly Brothers* / Something's gotten hold of my heart: *Pitney, Gene* / Make me an island: *Dolan, Joe* / Anyone who had a heart: *Warwick, Dionne* / Detroit city: *Jones, Tom* / Michelle: *Overlanders* / What a wonderful world: *Armstrong, Louis* / If I only had time: *Rowles, John* / And the heavens cried: *Newley, Anthony* / You'll answer to me: *Laine, Cleo* / Let the heartaches begin: *Baldry, Long John* / Mama: *Francis, Connie* / Single girl: *Posey, Sandy*
CD _____ OG 3711
Old Gold / Mar '90 / Carlton Home Entertainment.

JUKE BOX COLLECTION - WE'RE ALL ALONE
(Classic Love Songs)
I will always love you: *Parton, Dolly* / Torn between two lovers: *MacGregor, Mary* / We're all alone: *Coolidge, Rita* / Don't cry out loud: *Brooks, Elkie* / When I need you: *Sayer, Leo* / Come what may: *Leandros, Vicky* / And I love you so: *Como, Perry* / If I said you had a beautiful body: *Bellamy Brothers* / Streets of London: *McTell, Ralph* / Just when I needed you most: *Vanwarmer, Randy* / They shoot horses don't they: *Racing Cars* / All out of love: *Air Supply* / Suddenly: *Ocean, Billy* / All by myself: *Carmen, Eric*
CD _____ OG 3719
Old Gold / Mar '90 / Carlton Home Entertainment.

JUKE BOX COLLECTION - WITH A GIRL LIKE YOU
(Jukebox 60's)
Make it easy on yourself: *Stevens, Cat* / Dedicated follower of fashion: *Kinks* / Girl don't come: *Shaw, Sandie* / Bend me, shape me: *Amen Corner* / Golden lights: *Twinkle* / So much in love: *Mighty Avengers* / Groovy kind of love: *Mindbenders* / Here comes the night: *Them* / Universal soldier: *Donovan* / Goodbye my love: *Searchers* / Tell him: *Davies, Billie* / With a girl like you: *Troggs* / Sh la la la lee: *Small Faces* / You've got to hide your love away: *Silkie*
CD _____ OG 3722
Old Gold / Jul '90 / Carlton Home Entertainment.

JUKE BOX COLLECTION - YOUNG LOVE
(Sound of the 50's part 1)
To know him is to love him: *Teddy Bears* / All I have to do is dream: *Everly Brothers* / Donna: *Valens, Ritchie* / Come go with me: *Del-Vikings* / Where or when: *Dion & The Belmonts* / Lollipop: *Chordettes* / Susie darlin': *Lake, Robin* / Born too late: *Poni-Tails* / Seventeen: *Fontane Sisters* / Day that the rains came down: *Morgan, Jane* / Friendly persuasion: *Boone, Pat* / Young love: *Hunter, Tab* / No other baby: *Helms, Bobby* / Volare: *Marini, Marino*
CD _____ OG 3715
Old Gold / Mar '90 / Carlton Home Entertainment.

JUKE BOX COLLECTIONS - HANG ON IN THERE BABY
(Jukebox 70's Hits)
Saturday night at the movies: *Drifters* / Could it be I'm falling in love: *Detroit Spinners* / I'm doing fine now: *New York City* / You can do magic: *Limmie & Family Cooking* / Native New Yorker: *Odyssey* / Nights on Broadway: *Staton, Candi* / Never can say goodbye: *Gaynor, Gloria* / Hang on in there baby: *Bristol, Johnny* / Ride a wild horse: *Clark, Dee* / Montego Bay: *Bloom, Bobby* / Rock the boat: *Hues Corporation* / Turn the beat around: *Robinson, Vickie Sue* / Get dancing: *Disco Tex & The Sexolettes* / Hold back the night: *Trammps*
CD _____ OG 3725
Old Gold / '92 / Carlton Home Entertainment.

JUKE BOX GIANTS
(4CD Set)
CD Set _____ MBSCD 414
Castle / Nov '93 / BMG.

JUKE BOX R & B
I got loaded: *Cadets* / Wiggie waggie woo: *Cadets* / Sixty minute man: *Cadets* / Dance the thing: *Dixon, Floyd Orchestra* / Baby, baby every night: *James, Etta* / How big a fool: *James, Etta* / One whole year baby: *Curry, Earl* / This is the night for love: *Flairs* / She wants to rock: *Flairs* / Hit, git and split: *Young, Jessie* / Everyday I have the blues: *King, B.B.* / Don't you want a man like me: *King, B.B.* / She moves me: *Watson, Johnny 'Guitar'* / Standing at the crossroads: *James, Elmore* / Rumba rock: *Beasley, Jimmy* / I'm so blue: *Beasley, Jimmy* / Chicken shack: *Turner, Ike & Tina* / Shattered dreams: *Fulson, Lowell* / Let's make with some love: *Berry, Richard & The Flairs* / Double crossin' baby: *Robins* / My darling: *Jacks* / Rock everybody: *Teen Queens*
CD _____ CDCHD 335
Ace / Sep '91 / Pinnacle / Cadillac / Complete/Pinnacle.

JUKEBOX COLLECTION - GET IT ON
(Jukebox 70's Hits)
Get it on: *T. Rex* / He's gonna step on you again: *Kongos, John* / Apeman: *Kinks* / This flight tonight: *Nazareth* / Jig a jig: *East Of Eden* / Down the dustpipe: *Status Quo* / Coz I luv you: *Slade* / Angel face: *Glitter Band* / I'm the leader of the gang (I am): *Glitter, Gary* / Saturday night's alright for fighting: *John, Elton* / Jukebox jive: *Rubettes* / Long legged woman dressed in black: *Mungo Jerry* / This town ain't big enough for the both of us: *Sparks* / Man who sold the world: *Lulu*
CD _____ OG 3727
Old Gold / '92 / Carlton Home Entertainment.

JUKEBOX COLLECTION - WHOLE LOTTA SHAKIN' GOIN' ON
(Jukebox 50's)
Johnny B. Goode: *Berry, Chuck* / Bring a little water Sylvie: *Donegan, Lonnie* / Stagger Lee: *Price, Lloyd* / Lucille: *Little Richard* / Razzle dazzle: *Haley, Bill & The Comets* / Whole lotta shakin' goin' on: *Lewis, Jerry Lee* / Bird dog: *Everly Brothers* / Come on let's go: *Valens, Ritchie* / Pretend: *Mann, Carl* / Whispering bells: *Del-Vikings* / Reveille rock: *Johnny & The Hurricanes* / Danny: *Wilde, Marty* / Tallahassee Lassie: *Steele, Tommy*
CD _____ OG 3723
Old Gold / Jul '90 / Carlton Home Entertainment.

JUKEBOX JIVES 1936-46
Hindsight / Nov '94 / Target/BMG / Jazz Music.
CD _____ MICH 7126

JUMPIN' & PUMPIN' VS ELICIT
Papua new guinea: *Future Sound Of London* / Fire when ready: *G Double E* / Visitor: *D.J. Space* / Stakker humanoid: *Humanoid* / Dominate: *Flag* / Alchemist: *Geneside 11* / Tainted love: *Impedence* / Zum zum: *Love Men* / Check how we jam: *Bass Construction* / We can ride the boogie rock with you: *Bubbles* / Get on the move: *Psychopaths*
CD _____ CDTOT 6
Jumpin' & Pumpin' / Jul '93 / 3MV / Sony.

JUMPIN' THE BLUES
Damp rag / New kind of feelin' / Big Bob's boogie / Elephant rock / Riff / Fat man blues / There ain't enough room here to boogie / Dr. Jives / Cadillac boogie / Tra-la-la / Race horse / Pelican jump / Hi-Yo Silver / We're gonna rock this morning
CD _____ CDCHD 941
Ace / Jun '90 / Pinnacle / Cadillac / Complete/Pinnacle.

JUMPING AT JUBILEE
Hole in the ground: *Kohlman, Freddie Orchestra* / You'll never get nothing without trying: *Cousin Joe* / Ramblin' woman: *Cousin Joe* / Can't help myself (gits 1 and 2): *Powell, Jesse* / I'm all alone: *Powell, Jesse* / Don't pass me by: *Brown, Piney* / Battle with the bottle: *Brown, Piney* / 3-D Loving: *Brown, Piney* / You bring out the wolf in me: *Brown, Piney* / Ay la bah: *Cobb, Danny* / Everyday I weep and moan: *Willis, Ralph* / Somebody's got to go: *Willis, Ralph* / Blue blues blues: *Willis, Ralph* / I got a

letter: *Willis, Ralph* / Too late to scream and shout: *Willis, Ralph* / Income tax: *Willis, Ralph* / Bed tick: *Willis, Ralph* / Yes he did: *La Verne, Ray* / Rock on the top: *La Verne, Ray* / Drunk, that's all: *La Verne, Ray* / Rock 'n' roll: *La Verne, Ray*
CD _____ NEMCD 749
Sequel / Aug '95 / BMG.

JUNGLE - THE EXTREME COLLECTION
CD _____ CDB 9005
B9 / Oct '94 / Total/BMG / Plastic Head.

JUNGLE - THE EXTREME COLLECTION VOL.2
CD _____ CDB 9006
B9 / Sep '95 / Total/BMG / Plastic Head.

JUNGLE BIZZNIZZ VOLUME 2
CD _____ SCRCD 007
Scratch / Mar '95 / BMG.

JUNGLE BOOK
CD _____ RIVETCD 6
Reinforced / Aug '95 / SRD.

JUNGLE CHICH 5
CD _____ 31062
Kakchich / Dec '95 / Jetstar.

**JUNGLE DUB
(14 Jungle Tracks For The Serious Jungalist)**
Run 4 da sound clash: *Formula 7* / Dance hall massive: *D.J. Massive* / I spy: *D.J. Monk* / Phizical: *Roni Size* / Feel it: *Lemon D* / You don't know: *Dillinga* / Twisted brain: *Area 39* / Religion: *Formula 7* / Jazz note: *D.J. Krust* / Deep love: *Dillinga* / Maximum style dubplate: *Tom & Jerry & D J Stretch* / Bionic: *G. Kelly* / R 'n' B Collection: *Noodles & Wonder* / Money in your pocket: *Crown Jewels & MC Dett*
CD _____ KICKCD 17
Kickin' / Dec '94 / SRD.

**JUNGLE DUB EXPERIENCE PT. 1
(Mazaruni)**
CD _____ ARICD 09
Ariwa Sounds / Mar '95 / Jetstar / SRD.

**JUNGLE DUB EXPERIENCE PT. 2
(Rapununi Jungle)**
Perry in the dub jungle / Kunte kinte jungle / Organic pressure / Ecologically speaking / Desolate lagoon / Steamy jungle / Natural raas / Beat of the wild beast / Rapununi savannah / Juffre view / Banjui belly
CD _____ ARICD 111
Ariwa Sounds / Jun '95 / Jetstar / SRD.

JUNGLE EXOTICA
CD _____ E 11565CD
Crypt / Mar '93 / SRD.

JUNGLE FEVER
CD _____ 12606
Laserlight / Oct '95 / Target/BMG.

JUNGLE HEAT '95
Melody madness: *Coolhand Flex & Michelle Thompson* / Gangsta: *Shadow: Dynamic Duo* / Living for the night: *Stakka & K.Tee* / Bastard: *Blackman* / Bring you down: *Tek 9* / Reality: *D.J. Swift* / It's a jazz thing: *Roni Size* / Jazzmin: *Cloud 9* / I'll always be around: *Dub Hustlers* / Essences so sweet: *Jon E-2-Bad* / Silver haze: *Area 39 & Corelle*
CD _____ VTCD 51
Virgin / Jun '95 / EMI.

JUNGLE HITS VOL. 1
CD _____ STRCD 1
Street Tuff / Sep '94 / Jetstar.

JUNGLE HITS VOL. 2
CD _____ STRCD 2
Street Tuff / Dec '94 / Jetstar.

JUNGLE HITS VOL. 3
CD _____ STRCD 3
Street Tuff / Jul '95 / Jetstar.

JUNGLE MANIA
CD _____ TCD 2735
Telstar / Oct '94 / BMG.

JUNGLE MANIA 2
CD Set _____ TCD 2756
Telstar / Dec '94 / BMG.

JUNGLE MANIA 3
CD _____ TCD 2762
Telstar / Mar '95 / BMG.

JUNGLE MASSIVE
CD _____ HFCD 42
PWL / Sep '94 / Warner Music / 3MV.

JUNGLE MASSIVE 2
CD _____ HFCD 43
PWL / Nov '94 / Warner Music / 3MV.

JUNGLE MASSIVE 3
CD _____ HFCD 44
PWL / Mar '95 / Warner Music / 3MV.

JUNGLE MASSIVE 4
CD _____ HF 46CD
PWL / Jul '95 / Warner Music / 3MV.

JUNGLE ON THE STREETS
CD _____ GTOL 93
Land Of The Giants / Apr '95 / Jetstar.

JUNGLE RENEGADES VOLUME 1
CD _____ ANIMATE 3CD
Re-Animate / Mar '95 / SRD.

JUNGLE RHYTHMS VOL. 1
CD _____ SCRCD 004
Scratch / Nov '94 / BMG.

JUNGLE RHYTHMS VOL. 2
CD _____ SCRCD 006
Scratch / Mar '95 / BMG.

JUNGLE ROCK - 1ST EDITION
CD _____ SUMACD 001
Jungle Rock / Nov '92 / Jetstar.

JUNGLE SOUNDCLASH 1
CD _____ STHCD 8
Strictly Underground / '94 / SRD.

JUNGLE SOUNDCLASH 2
CD _____ STHCD 9
Strictly Underground / May '95 / SRD.

**JUNGLE SPLASH PRESENTS
JUNGLISM VOLUME 1
(No Retreat No Surrender)**
CD _____ UKBLKCD 1
UK Black / Feb '95 / SRD.

JUNGLE TEKNO - IN THE MIX
CD _____ CDTOT 28
Jumpin' & Pumpin' / Jun '95 / 3MV / Sony.

JUNGLE TEKNO 1
Music takes you: *Blame* / Ten BandH: *Freshtrax & Ace* / We can ride the boogie: *Bubbles* / Drop the bass: *Out-Phaze* / We have it: *C.M.C.* / Bomb scare: *2 Bad Mice* / Run come quick: *Audio* / Dance with the speaker: *Noise Factory* / Extreme: *Tripper* / Jungle mayhem: *Primatives* / Mind games: *Power Zone* / Sonata No.6: *D-Major* / Logical progression: *L.T.J. Bukem* / Control: *D.J. MCM & D.J. Smiley* / Junglest: *Rude-boy* / Please your soul: *Tomczak*
CD _____ CDTOT 5
Jumpin' & Pumpin' / Jun '92 / 3MV / Sony.

**JUNGLE TEKNO 2
(Happiness & darkness)**
Don't need your love: *D.J. Red Alert & Mike Slammer* / Valley of the shadows: *Origin Unknown* / Euphoria (Nino's dream): *Origin Unknown* / House Crew: *Origin Unknown* / Can you feel the rush: *Noise Factory* / Shining in da darkness: *Noise Factory* / Full logic control: *Higher Octave* / Axis: *D.J. Solo & D.J. Devine* / Who's that: *Coolhand Flex* / Touch: *Origin Unknown* / Storm trooper: *D.J. Mayhem* / Terminator: *Metal Hearts* / Whiplash: *Coolhand Flex* / Desire: *Weekend Rush* / Just a little: *M-Beat* / Girl it ever: *Kenetic*
CD _____ CDTOT 10
Jumpin' & Pumpin' / Nov '93 / 3MV / Sony.

**JUNGLE TEKNO 3
(Drum 'N' Bass A Way Of Life)**
19.5 HZT: *Bukem & the Peshay* / Tibetan jungle: *D.J. Rap* / One 2 one: *Johnson, Roger* / Skyliner: *Invisible Man* / Let the drummer go: *Invisible Man* / Gangster lean: *NW 1* / Skanka: *Hardware* / Scottie: *Sub Nation* / Stay calm: *Pulse* / Ominous clouds: *Interception* / Fallen angels: *Wax Doctor* / Champion sound: *Alliance* / Breakin' free: *Slipmatt* / Inesse (Ray Keith remix): *D.J. Mayhem*
CD _____ CDTOT 14
Jumpin' & Pumpin' / Jun '94 / 3MV / Sony.

**JUNGLE TEKNO 4
(Intelligence & Technology)**
Sound control: *Randall & Andy C.* / Attitude: *Area 39* / What kind of world: *Asend & Ultravibe* / Hit man: *Marvellous Caine* / Jungle warrior: *N-ZO & D.J. Invincible* / What the... remix: *Sonz Of A Loop Da Loop Era* / Listen up: *Higher Sense* / Calling all people (remix): *Azone* / Basher: *M6 Crew* / Stand easy: *J.B., The* / Tonight: *A-Side & Nut E-1* / Natural high: *Chaos & Julia Set*
CD _____ CDTOT 15
Jumpin' & Pumpin' / Sep '94 / 3MV / Sony.

**JUNGLE TEKNO 5
(The deep side)**
Resolution: *Photek* / Music is so special: *Brothers With Soul* / Twisted girl: *Ruff With Smooth* / Close encounter: *Jeep Head* / Peace in our time: *Van Kleef* / Rollin' intelligence: *Urban Wax* / Dub plate '94 lick: *Keith, Ray* / License: *Krome & Time* / Flying remix: *Basement Phil* / Razor's edge: *Time & S Monita* / Fall down on me: *Original Substitute* / Change: *Fast Floor*
CD _____ CDTOT 20
Jumpin' & Pumpin' / Jan '95 / 3MV / Sony.

**JUNGLE TEKNO 6
(Phat & Phuturistic)**
Phat and phuturistic: *Matt* / Champion sound: *Q-Project* / War in '94: *Badman* / I bring you the future: *Noise Factory* / Hit man: *Marvellous Caine* / Dibi DJ: *D.J. Invincible & Matticus* / Presha III: *Studio Pressure* / Drowning: *Four Horsemen Of The Apocalypse* / We enter: *Aphrodite* / See no, hear no: *Motherland* / State of mind: *Sub Sequence* / All you wanted: *Graham, John*
CD _____ CDTOT 21
Jumpin' & Pumpin' / Jan '95 / 3MV / Sony.

JUNGLE TEKNO 7
CD _____ CDTOT 27
Jumpin' & Pumpin' / Mar '95 / 3MV / Sony.

JUNGLE TEKNO 8
CD _____ CDTOT 31
Jumpin' & Pumpin' / Jul '95 / 3MV / Sony.

**JUNGLE USA
(The New Sound Of The East Coast)**
CD _____ VTX 1CD
Vortex / Jun '95 / SRD.

JUNGLE VIBES VOL.1
CD _____ SPVCD 8455362
Red Arrow / Apr '95 / SRD / Jetstar.

JUNGLE VOCAL
Vocal: *Peshay* / Heavy vibes: *Origination* / Yeamin': *Annett B. & Chuckleberry* / Int after hit: *Baby Wayne & Michael Rose* / Silver haze: *Area 39 & Corelle* / World is our future: *Origination* / Murder: *Beenie Man & Chuckleberry* / Tell me baby: *Faze 1 FM & R. Rankin* / Junglist lover: *Ron Tom & Julie* / Money money: *Andy, Horace & Ron Tom* / Talk: *Garnet Silk & Chuckleberry* / Good love: *Ron Tom & Marsha Red* / Flip flop (CD/MC): *Tenor Senior & Garnet Silk* / Sunshine (CD/MC): *Captain & Corelle* / Gal tune (ooh boy) (CD/MC): *Medoza* / Blood sweat and tears (CD/MC): *Roger Robin & Chuckleberry*
CD _____ STORM 3 CD
Desert Storm / Jan '96 / Sony.

JUNGLE WARFARE
CD Set _____ MMBK 272
Moonshine / Apr '95 / Disc.

JUNGLISM
CD _____ SOURCDLP 2
SOUR / Jul '95 / SRD.

JUNIOR BOYS OWN COLLECTION
CD _____ JBOCD 2
Junior Boys Own / Aug '94 / Disc.

**JUS' HOUSE
(14 Essential House Grooves)**
Slam me baby: *4 To The Bar* / Get huh: *Ride Committee* / Let the music set you free: *House Culture* / Sax in the ozone: *Aaron, Robert* / T.T. Lover: *Jus Us* / Way I feel: *Tears Of Velva* / I wanna be your lover: *Nuphonic* / My prayer: *Carroll, Ronnie* / Time for change: *Ulysses* / Come on baby: *Faces* / Get down: *Maxx Vibes* / Everything I got: *Faces* / Must be the music: *Serious Rope* / Friend not lover: *Serenade*
CD _____ CDELV 12
Elevate / Jul '93 / 3MV / Sony.

JUS' JEEPIN'
Deep cover: *Dr. Dre* / I made love (4 da very 1st time): *Little Shawn* / Live at the barbeque: *Main Source* / How I could just kill a man: *Cypress Hill* / You can't see what I can see: *Heavy D & The Boyz* / Fudge pudge: *Organized Konfusion* / True fuschnick: *Fu-Schnickens* / Blue cheese: *UMC's* / Lisa baby: *Father MC* / Scenario: *Tribe Called Quest* / Half time: *Nas* / Horny lil devil: *Ice Cube* / Dwyck: *Gang Starr* / Daddy: *A.D.L.*
CD _____ CDELV 09
Debut / Jun '94 / Pinnacle / 3MV / Sony.

JUS' JEEPIN' AGAIN
CD _____ CDELV 19
Elevate / Jun '95 / 3MV / Sony.

JUST A LITTLE OVERCOME - STAX VOCAL GROUPS
No strings attached: *Mad Lads* / These old memories: *Mad Lads* / I'm so glad I fell in love with you: *Mad Lads* / Highway to Heaven: *Dramatics* / Since I've been in love: *Dramatics* / Mannish boy: *Newcomers* / Girl this boy loves you: *Newcomers* / Just a little overcome: *Nightingales* / Baby, don't do it: *Nightingales* / I'm with you: *Nightingales* / Whole bit of love: *Temprees* / Your love (is all I need): *Temprees* / I refuse to be lonely: *Stingers* / Showered with love: *Ollie & The Nightingales* / Nellow way you treat your man: *Ollie & The Nightingales* / All because of you: *Limitations* / Echo: *Epsilons* / Make this young lady mine (On CD only): *Mad Lads* / Your love was strange (On CD only): *Dramatics* / Open up your heart (let me come in) (On CD only): *Newcomers* / Anyone can (On CD only): *Leaders* / Love's creepin' up on me (On CD only): *United Image*
CD _____ CDSX 019
Stax / Feb '89 / Pinnacle.

JUST IN TIME TOO LATE
CD _____ SOHO 16CD
Suburbs Of Hell / Nov '94 / Pinnacle / Plastic Head / Kudos.

JUST MY IMAGINATION
CD _____ CDTRL 286
Trojan / Mar '94 / Jetstar / Total/BMG.

JUST MY IMAGINATION - VOL. 2
CD _____ CDTRL 298
Trojan / Mar '94 / Jetstar / Total/BMG.

JUST MY IMAGINATION - VOL. 3
(Sittin' on) the dock of the bay: *Brown, Dennis* / Private number: *Honey Boy* / Forgot to be your lover: *Dennis, Denzil* / Yesterday once more: *Woung, Beverley* / Stop the war: *Parks, Lloyd* / Na na hey hey kiss him goodbye: *Pioneers* / Band of gold: *Griffiths, Marcia* / It's too late: *Now Generation* / Look what you've done for me: *Boothe, Ken* / Everybody plays the fool: *Chosen Few* / Summertime: *Johnson, Domino* / If you don't know me by now: *Zap Pow* / (If loving you is wrong) I don't want to be right: *May-*

tones / One bad people: *Briggs, Barry* / Boogie on reggae woman: *Briggs, Barry* / In my life: *Robinson, Jackie* / Blood brothers: *Boothe, Ken* / United we stand: *Wally Brothers* / Man who sold the world: *Wally Brothers*
CD _____ CDTRL 311
Trojan / Mar '94 / Jetstar / Total/BMG.

JUST MY IMAGINATION - VOL. 4
I love the way you love me: *Chosen Few* / Speak softly: *Spence, Barrington* / It's all in the game: *Gaylads* / Only you: *Gaylads* / What cha gonna do about it: *Simpson, Jeanette* / What does it take (to win your love): *Ellis, Alton* / Don't let me be lonely tonight: *Forrester, Sharon* / Crazy: *Dobson, Dobby* / California dreamin': *Francis, Winston* / What's going on: *Pat Satchmo* / Only the strong survive: *Mighty Diamonds* / Queen majesty: *Chosen Few* / Midnight train to Georgia: *Brown, Teddy* / Can't get used to losing you: *Ray, Danny* / Endlessly: *Dobson, Dobby* / Dark end of the street: *Kelly, Pat* / I second that emotion: *Chosen Few* / Lonely for your love: *Uniques* / There's no me without you: *Parks, Lloyd* / I love the way you love me (part 2): *Parks, Lloyd*
CD _____ CDTRL 328
Trojan / Mar '94 / Jetstar / Total/BMG.

JUST RAGGA
CD _____ CRCD 14
Charm / Jul '92 / Jetstar.

JUST RAGGA VOL.2
CD _____ CRCD 15
Charm / Oct '92 / Jetstar.

JUST RAGGA VOL.3
Action: *Nadine & Terror Fabulous* / Hands on lover: *Brown, Dennis & Lovindeer* / Step over: *Galaxy* / Clap dance: *Red Dragon* / Dead and bury: *Powerman* / Boom bye bye: *Ninja Kid* / Tickie: *Daddy Mite* / Butterfly: *Bailey, Admiral* / Broke wine butterfly: *Terror Fabulous & Daddy Screw* / Don't touch the coke: *Cobra* / No retreat: *Terror Fabulous* / Diseases: *Major Mackerel* / Racist: *Sweetie Irie*
CD _____ CRCD 16
Charm / Mar '93 / Jetstar.

JUST RAGGA VOL.4
CD _____ CRCD 18
Charm / Jun '93 / Jetstar.

JUST RAGGA VOL.5
CD _____ CRCD 25
Charm / Nov '93 / Jetstar.

JUST RAGGA VOL.6
CD _____ CRCD 28
Charm / Apr '94 / Jetstar.

JUST RAGGA VOL.7
CD _____ CRCD 34
Charm / Oct '94 / Jetstar.

JUST RAGGA VOL.8
CD _____ CRCD 39
Charm / Jun '95 / Jetstar.

JUST RAGGA VOL.9
CD _____ CRCD 47
Charm / Dec '95 / Jetstar.

JUST THE TWO OF US
I've had the time of my life: *Medley, Bill & Jennifer Warnes* / Don't wanna lose you: *Estefan, Gloria* / Up where you belong: *Cocker, Joe & Jennifer Warnes* / Too much, too little, too late: *Mathis, Johnny & Deniece Williams* / On the wings of love: *Osborne, Jeffrey* / Through the storm: *Franklin, Aretha* aside: *Ninja Ford* / With you I'm born again: *Preston, Billy & Syreeta* / Endless love: *Ross, Diana & Lionel Richie* / Eternal flame: *Bangles* / I know you by heart: *Parton, Dolly & Smokey Robinson* / All the love in the world: *Warwick, Dionne* / Sometimes when we touch: *Wynette, Tammy & Mark Gray* / All I want is forever: *Taylor, James 'JT' & Regina Belle* / I knew you were waiting (for me): *Franklin, Aretha & George Michael* / Wind beneath my wings: *Knight, Gladys*
CD _____ MOODCD 11
Epic / Mar '90 / Sony.

JUST THE WAY
CD _____ JERVCD 1
Street Hype / Aug '93 / Total/BMG.

JUSTICE SAMPLER #2
CD _____ JR 00052
Justice / Mar '94 / Koch.

JUSTIN TIME FOR CHRISTMAS
CD _____ JUST 75-2
Justin Time / Dec '95 / Harmonia Mundi / Cadillac.

JVC WORLD CLASS MUSIC
CD _____ JD 3307
JVC / Jul '88 / New Note.

JVC WORLD CLASS MUSIC 2
Maraculja: *Castro-Neves, Oscar* / Donna: *Guitar Workshop In LA* / Face to face: *Okoshi, Tiger* / Cool shadow: *Okoshi, Tiger* / Front runner: *Holman, Bill Band* / Beverly Hills: *Guitar Workshop In LA* / Over the rainbow: *Okoshi, Tiger* / Yamato dawn: *Neptune, John Kaizan* / The maze: *Watts, Ernie Quartet*
CD _____ JD 3319
JVC / Aug '89 / New Note.

K

KALON AR C'HAB
CD _____ CDCA 001
Diffusion Breizh / Apr '94 / ADA.

KAMIKAZE
CD _____ RRCD 192
Receiver / Sep '94 / Grapevine.

KANSAS CITY & SOUTH WEST
CD _____ DCD 8004
Disky / Jan '95 / THE / BMG / Discovery /
Pinnacle.

KANSAS CITY LEGENDS 1929-42
CD _____ 158432
Jazz Archives / Nov '95 / Jazz Music /
Discovery / Cadillac.

KAOS TOTALLY MIXED
An urban dream of America: Urban Dreams
/ Senacao: Duplex / Juice: A.Paul / So get
up: Underground Sound Of Lisbon / To-
night: Urban Dreams / Work in progress:
L.L. Project / Bottom heavy: Tenaglia,
Danny / Unreleased project: D.J. Vibes /
Blah: Algorotico / Transient sites: Ozone /
Dance with me: Underground Sound Of Lis-
bon / Free your mind: D.J. T. Ricciardi /
Don't wait for me: D.J. T. Ricciardi
CD _____ TRIUK 007CD
Tribal UK / Jul '95 / Vital.

KARAOKE - 50'S & 60'S FAVOURITES
Teddy bear / Peggy Sue / Lipstick on your
collar / Blue suede shoes / living doll /
shake, rattle and roll / Vaya con dios / Rave
on / Be bop a lula / That'll be theday / Love
me tender / (We're gonna) Rock around the
clock / Hey Jude / Da doo ron ron / Ferry
'cross the Mersey / I want to hold your hand
/ Bachelor boy / House of the Rising Sun /
Congratulations / Delilah / Wooden heart /
Return to sender / You'll never walk alone /
It's now or never
CD _____ CC 279
Music For Pleasure / Nov '91 / EMI.

KARAOKE - 70'S
Mull of Kintyre / Don't go breaking my heart
/ Hi ho silver lining / Wonder of you / Danc-
ing queen / I love you love me love / Hold
me close / Love grows (where my Rose-
mary goes) / Waterloo / In the summertime /
Knock three times / You're the one that I
want / I can't tell the bottom from the top /
American pie / Summer nights / Sailing
CD _____ CC 287
Music For Pleasure / Nov '92 / EMI.

KARAOKE - 80'S
Uptown girl / I should be so lucky / Ebony
and ivory / Karma Chameleon / Never
gonna give you up / Eye of the tiger / I just
called to say I love you / I want to break
free / Hello / Winner takes it all / Thank you
for the music / Super trouper / Chain reaction / Come on Eileen
CD _____ CC 288
Music For Pleasure / Nov '92 / EMI.

KARAOKE - 90'S
Achy breaky heart / All right now / Would I
lie to you / Should I stay or should I go / It
only takes a minute / Get here / Heartbeat
/ Baker Street / Heal the world / Tears on
my pillow / Too much love will kill you / It
must have been love / Everything I do (I do
it for you) / Itsy bitsy teeny weeny yellow
polka dot bikini
CD _____ CC 8231
Music For Pleasure / Nov '93 / EMI.

KARAOKE - CHILDREN'S KARAOKE FAVOURITES
There's no one quite like Grandma / Grandad / (How much is that) doggie in the window / Ugly duckling / Lily the pink / Teddy
bears' picnic / Hippopotamus song / Runaway train / Ten green bottles / Matchstalk
men and matchstalk cats and dogs / London Bridge is falling down / Birdie song /
My grandfather's clock / Windmill in old
Amsterdam / Three little fishes / Handful of
songs / Animals went in two by two / Simon
says / Boomps a daisy / Christopher Robin
at Buckingham Palace / If you're happy /
Hokey Cokey dance
CD _____ CC 8243
Music For Pleasure / Oct '94 / EMI.

KARAOKE - CHRISTMAS KARAOKE PARTY
Merry Christmas everybody / Mistletoe and
wine / When a child is born / Jingle bells /
Santa Claus is coming to town / Mary's boy
child / I wish it could be Christmas every
day / Silent night / We three Kings / Last
Christmas / Good King Wenceslas / Frosty
the snowman / Stop the cavalry / God rest
ye merry gentlemen / Saviour's day / Have
yourself a merry little Christmas / We wish
you a Merry Christmas / Auld lang syne
CD _____ CC 278
Music For Pleasure / Dec '94 / EMI.

KARAOKE - CHRISTMAS KARAOKE VOL.2
Sleigh ride / Let it snow, let it snow, let it
snow / Happy holiday / When Santa got
stuck up the chimney / Rudolph the red
nosed reindeer / O little town of Bethlehem
/ I saw mommy kissing Santa Claus / It
came upon a midnight clear / Little donkey
/ Rockin' around the Christmas tree / Winter
wonderland / Jolly old St. Nicholas / All I
want for Christmas (is my two front teeth) /
I saw three ships / Silver bells / Fairy on the
Christmas tree / Christmas alphabet / Good
Christian men rejoice / Little drummer boy /
Ding dong merrily on high / Deck the halls
with boughs of holly / Away in a manger /
White Christmas
CD _____ CC 8230
Music For Pleasure / Dec '94 / EMI.

KARAOKE - HIT FACTORY
Hand on your heart / Another night / Better
the devil you know / Never too late / Got to
be certain / Especially for you / When you
come back to me / I should be so lucky /
Too many broken hearts / You'll never stop
me loving you / Together forever / Never
gonna give you up / Toy boy / Wouldn't
change a thing / This time I know it's for
real / Nothing can divide us / Take me to
your heart / Nothing's gonna stop me now
CD _____ CDMFP 5968
Music For Pleasure / Oct '92 / EMI.

KARAOKE - IRISH KARAOKE
With a shillelagh under my arm / If you're
Irish come into the parlour / Galway bay /
Mountains of Mourne / Minstrel boy / Cock-
les and mussels / How are things in Glocca
Morra / Delaney's donkey / I dream of Jean-
nie with the light brown hair / When Irish
eyes are smiling / It's a long way to Tipper-
ary / Little bit of heaven / Black velvet band
/ I'll take you home again Kathleen / Believe
me, if all those endearing young charms /
Rose of Tralee / How can you buy Killarney
/ Mother Machree / It's a great day for the
Irish / Danny boy
CD _____ CC 8227
Music For Pleasure / Nov '93 / EMI.

KARAOKE - PIONEER KARAOKE VOL.1
Addicted to love / Summer nights / Killing
me softly / Candle in the wind / Crazy little
thing called love / Great balls of fire / Girls
just wanna have fun / All right now / House
of the rising sun / I will survive / I heard it
through the grapevine / Billie Jean / Locomotion / It's my party / Hey Jude / You'll
never walk alone
CD _____ CDMFP 6124
Music For Pleasure / Jul '94 / EMI.

KARAOKE - PIONEER KARAOKE VOL.2
It's not unusual / Love shack / Night fever
/ Stand by your man / He ain't heavy, he's
my brother / Let's dance / Hi ho silver lining
/ Venus / Daydream believer / If you don't
know me by now / Crazy / I wanna dance
with somebody (who loves me) / Boys are
back in town / Summer of '69 / New York,
New York / King of the road
CD _____ CDMFP 6125
Music For Pleasure / Jul '94 / EMI.

KARAOKE - PIONEER KARAOKE VOL.3
You can't hurry love / Fame / Money money /
Stop in the name of love / Super trouper /
Tainted love / Greatest love of all / Close to
you / Blues suede shoes / If I could turn
back time / Livin' on a prayer / Up where
we belong / Don't it make my brown eyes
blue / Bye bye love / Wild thing / Big
spender
CD _____ CDMFP 6126
Music For Pleasure / Jul '94 / EMI.

KARAOKE - PIONEER KARAOKE VOL.4
American pie / Like a virgin / In the summertime / Hello Dolly / Oh pretty woman /
Annie's song / Sittin' on the dock of the
bay / Daniel / Bachelor boy / Endless love
/ Help me Rhonda / Hopelessly devoted to
you / Geno / Unchain my heart / Bang a
gong (get it on) / (We're gonna) Rock
around the clock
CD _____ CDMFP 6140
Music For Pleasure / Oct '94 / EMI.

KARAOKE - PIONEER KARAOKE VOL.5
Delilah / Hello Mary Lou / Nine to Five / California dreamin' / Crocodile rock / I can see
clearly now / Eye of the tiger / Band on the
run / Every time we say goodbye / Don't go
breaking my heart / Blue moon / We are
family / Itchycoo Park / Bobby's girl / All day
and all of the night / Ferry across the
Mersey
CD _____ CDMFP 6141
Music For Pleasure / Oct '94 / EMI.

KARAOKE - PIONEER KARAOKE VOL.6
Are you lonesome tonight / Grease / I left
my heart in San Francisco / Best / I will always love you / Dizzy / Groovy kind of love
/ You're so vain / 2-4-6-8 Motorway / Power
of love / I got you babe / Tiger feet / Everybody wants to rule the world / When you're
in love with a beautiful woman / Breaking
up is hard to do / La bamba
CD _____ CDMFP 6142
Music For Pleasure / Nov '94 / EMI.

KARAOKE - PIONEER KARAOKE VOL.7
Love is all around / Centrefold / Unchained
melody / Crocodile shoes / All I have to do
is dream / Miss you nights / Angie baby /

Purple rain / Cry me a river / Knowing me,
knowing you / Nothing compares 2 U / With
or without you / Lady is a tramp / I'm still
standing / I swear / Something gotten hold
of my heart
CD _____ CDMFP 6167
Music For Pleasure / Jun '95 / EMI.

KARAOKE - PIONEER KARAOKE VOL.8
It's now or never / I'd do anything for love
(but I won't do that) / Y.M.C.A. / Careless
whisper / Take a chance on me / Sweet
dreams (are made of this) / Dizzy / Baby, I
love your way / We are family / Unbelievable / Singin' in the rain / These dreams /
Shine / Moving on up / Mmm mmm mmm
mmm / Most beautiful girl in the world
CD _____ CDMFP 6168
Music For Pleasure / Jun '95 / EMI.

KARAOKE - SCOTTISH KARAOKE
Donald, where's yer troosers / Loch Lomond / Roamin' in the gloamin' / Bluebells
of Scotland / Scotland the brave / Dancing
in Kyle / Skye boat song / Northern lights
of old Aberdeen / My ain folk / Gordon for
me / My love is like a red red rose / I love
a lassie / Amazing grace / Ye banks and
braes o' bonnie Doon / Annie Laurie / I belong to Glasgow / Charlie is my darling /
Mull of Kintyre / Westering home / Just a
wee deoch an' Doris / Comin' thro' the rye
/ Auld lang syne
CD _____ CC 8228
Music For Pleasure / Nov '93 / EMI.

KARAOKE CELEBRATION
Bells / Wedding (La novia) / She wears my
ring / Get me to the church on time / You
are my sunshine / Band of gold / If you were
the only girl in the world / Happy birthday
to you / I'm twenty-one today / When I'm
sixty four / Nobody loves a fairy when she's
forty / Anniversary waltz / My ole dutch /
Twenty tiny fingers / You must have been a
beautiful baby / When a child is born / Congratulations / It's my party / Welcome home
(Vivre) / Green green grass of home / For
he's a jolly good fellow / Bachelor boy /
From me to you / Especially for you / Auld
lang syne
CD _____ CC 8237
Music For Pleasure / May '94 / EMI.

KARAOKE COUNTRY
Rhinestone cowboy / Coalminer's daughter
/ Green green grass of home / Here you
come again / Honey come back / Nobody's
child / I walk the line / Blanket on the
ground / Last thing on my mind / Crazy /
Wayward wind / Your cheatin' heart / Welcome to my world / Distant drums / Stand
by your man / Try a little kindness / Help
me make it through the night / Take me
home country roads / Jambalaya / Harper
Valley PTA / Sixteen tons
CD _____ CC 280
Music For Pleasure / Jul '92 / EMI.

KARAOKE CROONERS
Born free / Spanish eyes / Close to you /
New York, New York / I left my heart in San
Francisco / Magic moments / Strangers in
the night / Are you lonesome tonight /
Smoke gets in your eyes / Release me /
Love is a many splendoured thing / Unfor-
gettable / What a wonderful world / I can't
stop lovin' you / Moon river / When I fall in
love / Answer me / Unchained melody /
More / That's amore / Somewhere
CD _____ CC 281
Music For Pleasure / Jul '92 / EMI.

KARAOKE DUETS
Somethin' stupid / Two sleepy people / I got
you babe / Don't go breaking my heart /
Endless love / It takes two / Cinderella
Rockefella / Tonight I celebrate my love for
you / Ebony and ivory / Something's gotten
hold of my heart / Especially for you / I'd do
anything / Who wants to be a millionaire
CD _____ CDSL 8263
Music For Pleasure / Oct '95 / EMI.

KARAOKE GLAM ROCK
I'm the leader of the gang (I am) / Hell raiser
/ Do you wanna hook me (Oh yeah) / Cat
crept in / Can the can / Doing alright with
the boys / Blockbuster / Get it on / Hello
hello I'm back again / 48 crash / Tiger feet
/ Devil gate drive / Oh boy / I love you love
me love
CD _____ CC 8242
Music For Pleasure / Oct '94 / EMI.

KARAOKE GREASE/SATURDAY NIGHT FEVER
How deep is your love / Jive talking / Night
fever / Stayin' alive / If I can't have you /
You should be dancing / Rock'n'roll is here
to stay / Grease / Hopelessly devoted to
you / You're the one that I want / Tears
on my pillow
CD _____ CDSL 8266
Virgin / Oct '95 / EMI.

KARAOKE LEGENDS - ELVIS PRESLEY
Heartbreak Hotel / Blue suede shoes /
Hound dog / Love me tender / All shook up
/ Teddy bear / Jailhouse rock / King Creole
/ One night / Girl of my best friend / It's now
or never / Are you lonesome tonight /
Wooden heart / Can't help falling in love /
Return to sender / Crying in the chapel / If
I can dream / Wonder of you / Always on
my mind / Moody blue / My way

CD _____ CC 297
Music For Pleasure / May '93 / EMI.

KARAOKE LEGENDS - LENNON & MCCARTNEY
She loves you / Sergeant Pepper's lonely
hearts club band / With a little help from my
friends / Help / Penny Lane / All my loving
is love / Can't buy me love / Love me do /
Eleanor Rigby / I want to hold your hand /
Back in the U.S.S.R / When I'm sixty four /
Please please me / Michelle / From me to
you / Let it be / Ticket to ride / Yellow sub-
marine / Hard day's night / Yesterday / Hey
Jude
CD _____ CC 8229
Music For Pleasure / Nov '93 / EMI.

KARAOKE LEGENDS - LENNON & MCCARTNEY VOL.2
Magical mystery tour / Nowhere man / Lady
Madonna / I should have known / Fool on
the hill / Paperback writer / Things we said
today / I feel fine / I wanna be your man /
Ob la di ob la da / Long and winding road
/ Drive my car / Eight days a week / And I
love her / Get back / We can work it out /
All my loving / Hello goodbye / I saw her
standing there / Day tripper / Strawberry
fields
CD _____ CC 8241
Music For Pleasure / Feb '95 / EMI.

KARAOKE LOVE SONGS
We've only just begun / Suddenly / True
love ways / Fever / Silly love songs / End-
less love / Power of love / Move closer /
When the girl in your arms (is the girl in your
heart) / It must have been love / Love letter
/ And I love you so / Always on my mind /
On the wings of love / Fool (if you think it's
over) / Three times a lady
CD _____ CC 286
Music For Pleasure / Nov '92 / EMI.

KARAOKE MILLION SELLING HITS
Roll over Beethoven / Mona Lisa / Sealed
with a kiss / Monday, Monday / Ain't that a
shame / Tears / Bright eyes / It's all in the
game / Things we do for love / Under the
moon of love / Rivers of Babylon / Wichita
lineman / He ain't heavy, he's my brother /
Anyone who had a heart / World of our own
/ There's a kind of hush (all over the world)
/ Diana / He's got the whole world in his
hands
CD _____ CC 8245
Music For Pleasure / Oct '94 / EMI.

KARAOKE NO. 1'S
Bohemian rhapsody / Everything I do (I do
it for you) / Groovy kind of love / You'll never
stop me from loving you / Singin' the blues
/ Long haired lover from Liverpool / Don't
go breaking my heart / I remember you /
Power of love / Imagine / Whatever will be
will be (Que sera sera) / House of the rising
sun / Something's gotten hold of my heart
/ Especially for you / I just called to say I
love you
CD _____ CC 8232
Music For Pleasure / Nov '93 / EMI.

KARAOKE ROCK 'N' ROLL
Chantilly lace / It's my party / Bird dog /
Locomotion / Shake, rattle and roll / Great
balls of fire / Giddy up a ding dong / Lipstick
on your collar / That'll be the day / Bye bye
love / Rubber ball / Blue suede shoes / Born
too late / Peggy Sue / Long tall Sally / Be
bop a lula / Teenager in love / Whole lotta
shakin' goin' on / Rave on / Good golly Miss
Molly / (We're gonna) Rock around the
clock / Halfway to paradise / Blueberry Hill
/ C'mon everybody
CD _____ CC 296
Music For Pleasure / Jun '93 / EMI.

KARAOKE SOUL
Save the last dance for me / (Sittin' on) the
dock of the bay / When a man loves a
woman / In the midnight hour / It takes two
/ Reach out, I'll be there / What becomes
of the broken hearted / How sweet it is (to
be loved by you) / Give me just a little more
time / Saturday night at the movies / Band
of gold / Try a little tenderness / This old
heart of mine / My guy / Stand be me / At
the club / Rescue me / My girl / Private
number
CD _____ CC 285
Music For Pleasure / Nov '92 / EMI.

KARAOKE TOP 10 HITS OF THE 60'S
Summer holiday / Tears / Speedy Gonzales
/ Anyone who had a heart / Private number
/ Whiter shade of pale / Seven little girls sit-
ting in the back seat / Do wah diddy diddy
/ Yeh yeh / What do you want / Puppet on
a string / You're sixteen / Pretty flamingo /
Boom bang a bang / Lily the pink / Where
do you go to my lovely / Tell Laura I love
her / What do you want to make those eyes
at me for / Blue moon / Three steps to
heaven
CD _____ CC 8246
Music For Pleasure / Oct '94 / EMI.

KARAOKE TOP 10 HITS OF THE 80'S
Call me / Freedom / True / House of fun /
Is there something I should know / When
the going gets tough / Wherever I lay my
hat (that's my home) / Good heart / With a
little help from my friends / Careless whisper / Only way is up / Two hearts
CD _____ CDSL 8264
Music For Pleasure / Oct '95 / EMI.

KARAOKE TOP 10 HITS OF THE 90'S
I'm too sexy / Dizzy / Million love songs / We have all the time in the world / Pray / Rhythm of my heart / Sleeping satellite / Love is all around / Crocodile shoes / Could it be magic
CD _____ CDSL 8265
Music For Pleasure / Oct '95 / EMI.

KARAOKE WARTIME FAVOURITES
There'll always be an England / Kiss me goodnight / Lili Marlene / (We're gonna hang out) The washing on the Siefried line / White cliffs of Dover / Nightingale sang in Berkeley Square / Run rabbit run / Now is the hour / Roll out the barrel / I've got six-pence / It's a long way to Tipperary / Bless 'em all / Yours / Quartermaster's stores / Coming in on a wing and a prayer / I don't want to set the world on fire / Goodnight sweetheart / I'm gonna get lit up (when the lights go on in London) / You are my sun-shine / I'll be seeing you / We'll meet again / Reprise - There'll always be an England
CD _____ CC 8236
Music For Pleasure / May '94 / EMI.

KARENNI
CD _____ PAN 2040
Pan / Oct '94 / ADA / Direct / CM.

KATZ KEEP ROCKIN' VOL.1
CD _____ LOMACD 39
Loma / Nov '94 / BMG.

KAUSTINEN FOLK MUSIC FESTIVAL 1990
CD _____ BHCD 9130
Brewhouse / Jul '91 / Complete/Pinnacle.

KAZAKH SONGS AND EPIC TRADITION OF THE WEST
CD _____ C 580051
Ocora / Nov '93 / Harmonia Mundi / ADA.

KEEP MOVIN' ON
Swingin': Light Of The World / Somebody help me out: Beggar & Co / North London boy: Incognito / You're lying: Linx / Walking into sunshine: Central Line / Southern Freeez: Freeez / Mama used to say: Gis-combe, Junior / Easier said than done: Shakatak / Wings of love: Level 42 / Danc-ing in outer space: Atmosfear / Time ma-chine: Direct Drive / Give me: I Level
CD _____ VSOPCD 185
Connoisseur / Apr '93 / Pinnacle.

KEEP ON COMING THROUGH THE DOOR
Dance beat / Jack of my trade / Sounds of Babylon / Fire corner / Heart don't leap / To the fields / Mosquito one / Mr. Harry Skank / Alpha and omega
CD _____ CDTRL 255
Trojan / Mar '94 / Jetstar / Total/BMG.

KEEP ON DANCING
CD _____ DINCD 80
Dino / Nov '93 / Pinnacle / 3MV.

KEEP ON RUNNING
CD _____ CDTRL 334
Trojan / Feb '94 / Jetstar / Total/BMG.

KEEP THE BEAT ROLLING
CD _____ DBP 102001
Double Platinum / May '93 / Target/BMG.

KEEP THE DREAM ALIVE (Now And Then Singles)
CD _____ NTHEN 19
Now & Then / May '95 / Plastic Head.

KEEP THE HOME FIRES BURNING (Songs & Music From The First World War)
Here we are, here we are (Phonograph cyl-inder): Wheeler, F. & Chorus / Goodbye-ee (Penny piano): Various Narrators / Just be-fore the battle mother (Phonograph cylin-der): Oakland, Will & Chorus / Your king and country want you (Phonograph cylinder): Clarke, Helen & Chorus / Trumpeter (78rpm record): Newell, Raymond & Ian Swinley / Deathless army (Phonograph cylinder): Kin-niburgh, T.F. / medley (Phonograph cylin-der): N.M.B. Flying squadron / Tramp, tramp, tramp (Phonograph cylinder): Harlan & Stanley/chorus / Keep the home fires burning (Penny piano): Various Narrators / Boys of the old brigade (Phonograph cyl-inder): N.M.B. Flying squadron / Boys in khaki, boys in blue (Phonograph cylinder): Wheeler, F. & Chorus / Colonel Bogey (78rpm record - Wembley Military Tattoo 1925 (medley)): Coldstream Guards Band / Pack up your troubles in your old kit bag (ditto): Coldstream Guards Band / It's a long way to Tipperary (ditto): Coldstream Guards Band / Roses of Picardy (Pianola): Murray, Templeton / Passing Review Patrol (Pho-nograph cylinder): Not Advised / What has become of hinkey-dinky-parlay-voo (Edison Diamond Disc 1924): Bernard, Al & Chorus
CD _____ CDSDL 358
Saydisc / Mar '94 / Harmonia Mundi / ADA / Direct.

KEEP YOUR SUNNY SIDE UP
CD _____ SOW 512
Sound Waves / Jul '94 / Target/BMG.

KEEPING THE FAITH
CD _____ CRECD 115
Creation / Dec '92 / 3MV / Vital.

KEEPING THE FAITH 1990
CD _____ CRECD 081
Creation / Jan '91 / 3MV / Vital.

KEF TIME
CD _____ CD 4269
Traditional Crossroads / Feb '95 / CM / Direct.

KENYA/TANZANIA - WITCHCRAFT & RITUAL MUSIC
CD _____ 7559720662
Elektra Nonesuch / Jan '95 / Warner Music.

KERRANG - THE ALBUM
Jesus Christ pose: Soundgarden / Another wordly device: Prong / Punishment: Biohaz-ard / Autosurgery: Therapy / Territory: Sep-ultura / Sweating bullets: Megadeth / Shedding skin: Pantera / Caffeine bomb: Wildhearts / My house: Terrorvision / Give it away: Red Hot Chili Peppers / Warfair: Clawfinger / Believe in me: McKagan, Duff / Ten miles high: Little Angels / Over the edge: Almighty / Down in a hole: Alice In Chains / Ace of spades (Live): Motorhead / Paranoid: Black Sabbath / Smoke on the water: Deep Purple / Victim of change (Live): Judas Priest / Stargazer: Rainbow / Bat out of hell: Meat Loaf / Cats in the cra-die: Ugly Kid Joe / In my darkest hour: Me-gadeth / Doctor doctor (live): UFO / Spirit of radio: Rush / Epic: Faith No More / Angel of death: Slayer / Youth gone wild: Skid Row / Born to be wild: Steppenwolf / Freebird: Lynyrd Skynyrd
CD _____ AHLCD 21
Hit / Jun '94 / PolyGram.

KERRANG 2 - THE KUTTING EDGE
CD _____ STVCD 27
Hit / Mar '95 / PolyGram.

KERRY FIDDLES
CD _____ OSS 10CD
Ossian / Mar '94 / ADA / Direct / CM.

KEYS OF LIFE
CD _____ CDCEL 017
Celestial Harmonies / Jun '87 / ADA / Select.

KHARTOUM HEROES
CD _____ CDLDL 1222
Klub / Feb '95 / CM / Ross / Duncans / ADA / Direct.

KICK UP THE 80'S VOL.1
Fields of fire: Big Country / Senses working overtime: XTC / Town called Malice: Jam / Our lips are sealed: Fun Boy Three / It must be love: Madness / Ghost town: Specials / Labelled with love: Squeeze / Reward: Tear-drop Explodes / Look of love: ABC / Joan of Arc: O.M.D. / Living on the ceiling: Blanc-mange / Just can't get enough: Depeche Mode / Only you: Yazoo / Fade to grey: Visage
CD _____ OG 3520
Old Gold / Oct '90 / Carlton Home Entertainment.

KICK UP THE 80'S VOL.2 (Go Wild in the Country)
Hand in glove: Smiths / Modern girl: Meat Loaf / Go wild in the country: Bow Wow Wow / Start: Jam / Come on Eileen: Dexy's Midnight Runners / First picture of you: Lo-tus Eaters / Communication: Spandau Ballet / I'm still standing: John, Elton / Reap the wild wind: Ultravox / Enola Gay: O.M.D. / Damned don't cry: Visage / Einstein a go go: Landscape / Poison arrow: ABC / Doc-tor doctor: Thompson Twins / Don't go: Ya-zoo / Christian: China Crisis
CD _____ OG 3521
Old Gold / Oct '90 / Carlton Home Entertainment.

KICK UP THE 80'S VOL.3 (Love and Pride)
Maneater: Hall & Oates / Down under: Men At Work / Break my stride: Wilder, Matthew / Human touch: Springfield, Rick / Karma chameleon: Culture Club / My oh my: Slade / 99 red balloons: Nena / Love and pride: King / Don't talk to me about love: Altered Images / Japanese boy: Aneka / Land of make believe: Bucks Fizz / Feels like I'm in love: Marie, Kelly / February again: Tight Fit / Favourite waste of time: Paul, Owen / Let's hear it for the boy: Williams, Deniece / Ghostbusters: Parker, Ray Jnr.
CD _____ OG 3522
Old Gold / Oct '90 / Carlton Home Entertainment.

KICK UP THE 80'S VOL.4
Pretty in pink: Psychedelic Furs / Heaven knows I'm miserable now: Smiths / Love on a farmboy's wages: XTC / Rip it up: Orange Juice / Walk out to winter: Aztec Camera / I'm in love with a German film star: Passions / Teen: Regents / Soul train: Swansway / New life: Depeche Mode / Black man Ray: China Crisis / Talking loud and clear: O.M.D. / Night porter: Japan / Doot doot: Freur / Da da da: Trio / (Feels like) heaven: Fiction Fac-tory / Der Kommissar: After The Fire
CD _____ OG 3523
Old Gold / Nov '90 / Carlton Home Entertainment.

KICK UP THE 80'S VOL.5
CD _____ OG 3524
Old Gold / Apr '91 / Carlton Home Entertainment.

KICK UP THE 80'S VOL.6
CD _____ OG 3525
Old Gold / Apr '91 / Carlton Home Entertainment.

KICK UP THE 80'S VOL.7
Johnny come home: Fine Young Cannibals / Graceland: Bible / Generals and majors: XTC / Walls come tumbling down: Style Council / Big decision: That Petrol Emotion / Other side of you: Mighty Lemon Drops / Ziggy Stardust: Bauhaus / Funeral pyre: Jam / In a big country: Big Country / Work-ing with fire and steel: China Crisis / Rattle-snakes: Cole, Lloyd / Staring at the rude boys: Ruts / Feel the raindrops: Adventures / Young at heart: Bluebells / There's a ghost in my house: Fall / Treason: Teardrop Explodes
CD _____ OG 3526
Old Gold / Mar '92 / Carlton Home Entertainment.

KICK UP THE 80'S VOL.8
CD _____ OG 3527
Old Gold / Jun '92 / Carlton Home Entertainment.

KICK UP THE 80'S VOL.9
Never stop: Echo & The Bunnymen / I wanna be a flintstone: Screaming Blue Messiahs / Life in a northern town: Dream Academy / She bangs the drum: Stone Roses / More you live, the more you love: Flock Of Seagulls / I'm falling: Bluebells / Disenchanted: Communards / All of my heart: ABC / Steppin' out: Jackson, Joe / Never take me alive: Spear Of Destiny / Whistle down the wind: Heyward, Nick / Ra-dio Africa: Latin Quarter / Crash: Primitives / No memory: Scarlet Fantastic / Obsession: Animotion / Honey thief: Hipsway / Big area: Then Jerico / Let my people go go: Rainmakers
CD _____ OG 3528
Carlton Home Entertainment / Nov '92 / Carlton Home Entertainment.

KINDA COUNTRY
CD _____ MATCD 221
Castle / Dec '92 / BMG.

KINDA COUNTRY VOL.2
CD _____ MATCD 265
Castle / Apr '93 / BMG.

KING KONK
CD _____ K 152C
Konkurrel / Mar '94 / SRD.

KING OF SKA
CD _____ KECD 01/02
King Edwards / Feb '93 / Jetstar.

KING OF SKA VOL.2
CD _____ KECD 03/04
King Edwards / Feb '93 / Jetstar.

KING OF THE ROAD
CD _____ MU 5058
Musketeer / Oct '92 / Koch.

KINGDOM OF THE SUN - FIESTAS OF PERU
CD _____ 7559791972
Elektra Nonesuch / Jan '95 / Warner Music.

KINGS & QUEENS OF COUNTRY
CD _____ CPMV 027
Cromwell / Sep '94 / THE / BMG.

KINGS OF BLACK MUSIC, THE
CD _____ 15169
Laserlight / Aug '91 / Target/BMG.

KINGS OF CAJUN
Les filles du Canada: Abshire, Nathan / Acadian two step: Balfa Brothers / Triangle special: Pitre, Austin / French fiddle boogie: Bonsall, Joe / Midnight special: Balfa Broth-ers / Oson two step: Roger, Aldus / La queue de torture: Abshire, Nathan / Love bridge waltz: Duhon, Bessyl / One is a lonely number: Menard, Phil / Fee fee pon-cho: Montoucet, Don / Old fashioned two step: Balfa Brothers / Zydeco hee haw: Chavis, Boozoo / That's what makes the ca-jun dance: Bearb, Ricky / Hick wagon wheel special: Montoucet, Don / Me and my cousin: Doucet, Camey / Mamou hot step: Ardoin Brothers / L'anne tu partit: Fruge, Ronnie / Jolie catin: Chavis, Boozoo / La-cassine special: Balfa Brothers / Johnny can't dance: Ardoin Family Orchestra / Sheryl's special: Cormier, Sheryl
CD _____ MCCD 066
Music Club / '92 / Disc / THE / CM.

KINGS OF CAJUN (3CD Set)
CD Set _____ MCBX 013
Music Club / Dec '94 / Disc / THE / CM.

KINGS OF CAJUN
CD _____ TRIK 0158
Trikont / Oct '94 / ADA / Direct.

KINGS OF CAJUN VOL.2
CD _____ MCCD 116
Music Club / Jun '93 / Disc / THE / CM.

KINGS OF CAJUN VOL.3
CD _____ MCCD 171
Music Club / Sep '94 / Disc / THE / CM.

KINGS OF CALYPSO
CD _____ MATCD 244
Castle / Dec '92 / BMG.

KINGS OF DUB
CD _____ RB 3019
Reggae Best / Jan '96 / Magnum Music Group / THE.

KINGS OF DUB DUB ROCK PARTS 1 & 2 (Sir Coxsone Sound)
CD _____ TMCD 3
Tribesman / Feb '95 / Jetstar / SRD.

KINGS OF THE BLUES
Sweet little angel: King, B.B. / She moves somehow: Johnny 'Guitar' / I'll get along somehow: Sims, Frankie Lee / Blues sere-nade: Turner, Babyface / On my way back home: Flash Terry / Odds against me: Hooker, John Lee / Sittin' here thinkin': Wal-ker, T-Bone / Problem child: Walton, Mercy Dee / Lonesome old feeling: Bumble Bee Slim / I tried: Young Wolf / Cotton picker: Higgins, Chuck & The Melotones / Wild hop: Crayton, Pee Wee / Worried about my baby: Howlin' Wolf / Tavern lounge boogie: Burns, Eddie 'Guitar' / Believe I'll change towns: Hogg, Smokey / Too many rivers: Fulson, Lowell / Yesterday: Chenier, Clifton / Lone-some dog blues: Hopkins, Lightnin' / Hard times: Fuller, Johnny / Riding mighty high: Dixon, Floyd / Please find my baby: James, Elmore
CD _____ CDCH 276
Ace / Jul '89 / Pinnacle / Cadillac / Com-plete/Pinnacle.

KINGS OF THE BLUES
Rollin' stone: Waters, Muddy / Dust my broom: James, Elmore / One bourbon, one scotch, one beer: Hooker, John Lee / I got the blues: King, Albert / Bring it on home: Witherspoon, Sonny Boy / Ten years ago: Guy, Buddy / Baby, what you want me to do: Reed, Jimmy / Stormy Monday blues: Walker, T-Bone / Smokestack lightnin': Howlin' Wolf / My babe: Little Walter / So many roads: Rush, Otis / Reconsider baby: Fulson, Lowell / When the lights go out: Witherspoon, Jimmy / Guess I'm a fool: Memphis Slim / I'm in love with you baby: Spann, Otis / Ludella: Rogers, Jimmy
CD _____ CDCD 1050
Charly / Mar '93 / Charly / THE / Cadillac.

KINGS OF THE BLUES GUITAR
Stormy Monday blues: Walker, T-Bone / Honey bee: Waters, Muddy / Smokestack lightnin': Clapton, Eric / First time I met the blues: Guy, Buddy / Big boss man: Reed, Jimmy / Rollin' and tumblin': James, Elmore / Shapes of things: Beck, Jeff / Gangster love: Winter, Johnny / Dimples: Hooker, John Lee / All your love: Rush, Otis / Easy baby: Magic Sam / California blues: King, Albert / Gate's salty blues: Brown, Clarence 'Gatemouth' / Walking by myself: Rogers, Jimmy / Sky is cryin': Robinson, Fenton / Back door friend: Hopkins, Lightnin'
CD _____ CDCD 1029
Charly / Mar '93 / Charly / THE / Cadillac.

KINGS OF THE BLUES GUITAR VOL.1 (4CD Set)
CD Set _____ CDPK 420
Charly / Feb '95 / Charly / THE / Cadillac.

KINGS OF THE BLUES GUITAR VOL.2
CD _____ CDCD 1092
Charly / Apr '93 / Charly / THE / Cadillac.

KINGS OF THE ROAD
King of the road: Miller, Roger / Most beautiful girl: Rich, Charlie / Devil woman: Robbins, Marty / I can help: Swan, Billy / Gambler: Bare, Bobby / Don't take your guns to town: Cash, Johnny / Heroes: Cash, Johnny & Waylon Jennings / Whiter shade of pale: Nelson, Willie / Help me make it through the night: Kristofferson, Kris / Oh pretty woman: Orbison, Roy / I'll see you in my dreams: Atkins, Chet & Mark Knopfler / Good year for the roses: Jones, George / Highwayman: Jennings, Waylon/J. Cash/K. Kristofferson/W. Nelson / Eagle: Jennings, Waylon / Devil went down to Georgia: Dan-iels, Charlie Band / Under the gun: Nelson, Willie/Kris Kristofferson/Dolly Parton
CD _____ 4680942
Columbia / Mar '91 / Sony.

KINGSTON TOWN
CD _____ HBCD 82
Heartbeat / May '93 / Greensleeves / Jetstar / Direct / ADA.

KINKY TRAX
CD _____ REACTCD 013
React / Oct '92 / Vital.

KINKY TRAX 2
CD _____ REACTCD 020
React / Jun '93 / Vital.

KINKY TRAX 3
CD _____ REACTCD 030
React / Nov '93 / Vital.

KINKY TRAX 4 (The Big Apple: Divas And Dubs)
CD _____ REACTCD 045
React / Aug '94 / Vital.

KISS IN IBIZA
CD _____ 5259112
PolyGram TV / Sep '95 / PolyGram.

KISS 'N' TELL
Celebrate your victory: *Shirelles* / Remember me: *Shirelles* / You're under arrest: *Shirelles* / Devil in his heart: *Donays* / Bad boy: *Donays* / Party lights: *Donays* / Silly little girl: *Dean & Jean* / Casanova: *Earline & her girlfriends* / Because of you: *Earline & her girlfriends* / Little girl lost: *Brown, Maxine* / Peaches 'n' cream: *Ikettes* / (He's gonna be) fine fine fine: *Ikettes* / Are you trying to get rid of me: *Candy & The Kisses* / You did the best you could: *Candy & The Kisses* / You got it baby: *Toys* / Try to get you out of my heart: *Toys* / I just couldn't say: *Lorraine & The Delights* / stop, look and listen: *Les girls* / Just wait: *Julie & The Desires* / Better be ready: *Annette* / Leave us alone: *Del-rons* / Don't hurt me: *Carroll, Bernadette* / Nicky: *Carroll, Bernadette* / Only seventeen: *Martin sisters* / Stay at home, Sue: *Linda Laurie* / Hey there, hey there: *Gypsies* / You don't love me anymore: *Dodds, Nella* / I wonder why: *Chiffons* / Foolish little girl: *Chiffons* / Three drips of ice cream: *Chiffons*
CD _____ CDCHD 330
Ace / Feb '93 / Pinnacle / Cadillac / Complete/Pinnacle.

KK COMPILATION
Fire: *2nd Communication* / Second episode: *Sloppy Wrenchbody* / Chasin' the flame: *Minister Of Noise* / Warp: *DRP* / BPM: *Storotaxic Device* / Curse: *Nimh* / Disobey: *Kode IV* / What a life: *Exquisite Corpse* / Burning bodies: *Blue Eyed Christ* / Point of no return: *Cat Rapes Dog* / Zoeloe noizz: *Insekt* / Surely get's me: *Swains* / Patience: *Psychik Warriors Ov Gaia*
CD _____ KK 088CD
KK / Dec '92 / Plastic Head.

KLEZMER 1993 - TRADITION CONTINUES ON THE LOWER EAST SIDE
CD _____ KFWCD 123
Knitting Factory / Feb '95 / Grapevine.

KLEZMER PIONEERS
CD _____ ROUCD 1089
Rounder / Jun '93 / CM / Direct / ADA / Cadillac.

KLEZMOKUM
CD _____ BVHAASTCD 9209
Bvhaast / May '89 / Cadillac.

KLONED 2
CD _____ CDKOPY 102
Klone / Dec '93 / Pinnacle / 3MV / Sony.

KLONED 3
CD Set _____ CDKOPY 103
Klone / Nov '94 / Pinnacle / 3MV / Sony.

KLONED 4
CD _____ CDKOPY 104
Klone / Jan '96 / Pinnacle / 3MV / Sony.

KNEELIN' DOWN INSIDE THE GATE
CD _____ ROUCD 5035
Rounder / Jul '95 / CM / Direct / ADA / Cadillac.

KNIGHTS OF THE TURNTABLE VOL.1
CD _____ BMRCD 01
Boomerang / Nov '94 / Jetstar.

KNITEFORCE - VINYL IS BETTER
CD _____ GUMH 010
Gumh / Nov '94 / SRD.

KNITTING FACTORY BOX SET (5CD Set)
CD Set _____ KFWCD 12345
Knitting Factory / Nov '92 / Grapevine.

KNITTING FACTORY GOES TO THE NORTH WEST
CD _____ KFWCD 101
Knitting Factory / Nov '94 / Grapevine.

KNITTING FACTORY TOURS EUROPE
CD _____ KFWCD 105
Knitting Factory / Nov '94 / Grapevine.

KNOCK OUT BLUES
CD _____ RST 91578-2
RST / Jun '94 / Jazz Music / Hot Shot.

KNOW YOUR ENEMY
CD _____ EMY 139-2
Enemy / Nov '94 / Grapevine.

KODEX VOL.4
CD _____ EFA 119152
Kodex / Nov '94 / SRD.

KONGPILATION
CD _____ BJ 999
Bananajuice / Jan '96 / Nervous.

KOOL REVOLUTION, A
CD _____ TKCD 8
2 Kool / Aug '95 / SRD.

KORA AND THE XYLOPHONE, THE
CD _____ LYRCD 7308
Lyrichord / '91 / Roots / ADA / CM.

KOREAN COURT MUSIC
CD _____ LYRCD 7206
Lyrichord / '91 / Roots / ADA / CM.

KRAZY KATS CAJUN
CD _____ TRIK 0167
Trikont / Oct '94 / ADA / Direct.

KUDOS DIGEST - ISSUE A (IS FOR APPLE), THE
Electric arc: *Nuron* / Jupiter: *Pluto* / End of an era: *Balony, B.J.* / Chevy rainbow: *Perbec* / Midst of tumult: *Roxy* / Griptape: *Spira* / Check it out: *P.V.P.* / Solitude: *Stasis* / Different emotions: in Sync Vs. *Mysteron* / Honda Suzuki's last motorcycle ride: *Le Panel De Pants* / Rustless: *Beautyon*
CD _____ KUDCD 006
Kudos / Jun '95 / Kudos / Pinnacle.

KULT DANCE KLASSIX VOL.2
CD _____ SPV 79900692
SPV / Aug '93 / Plastic Head.

KULT KLASSIX VOL. 2
CD _____ SPV 8708892
SPV / Mar '94 / Plastic Head.

KUULAS HETKI
CD _____ OMCD 46
Digelius / Jun '93 / Direct.

KWANZAA MUSIC
CD _____ ROUCD 2133
Rounder / Jan '95 / CM / Direct / ADA / Cadillac.

L.A. FREEWAY
CD _____ DINCD 25
Dino / Aug '91 / Pinnacle / 3MV.

L.A. HAPPENING (The Mid-60s Soul Sides Of Vault, Fat Fish & Autumn Records)
Nobody but you: *Wooden Nickels* / I'll never fall in love again: *Freeman, Bobby* / Baby reconsider: *Haywood, Leon* / Wishing and hoping: *Keen, Billy* / My heart's beating stronger: *Fisher, Andy* / That little old heartbreaker me: *Freeman, Bobby* / Tell me tomorrow: *Mandolph, Bobby* / Little girl: *Washington, Lee* / Tender tears: *Montgomery, Bobby* / Ain't no use: *Haywood, Leon* / Head over heels: *Bridges, Chuck & the L.A. Happening* / Going to a happening: *Neal, Tommy* / Got to get you back: *Mandolph, Bobby* / Fine, fine, fine: *Hughes, Judy* / More than a friend: *Wooden Nickels* / I've been crying: *Jones, Jesse* / Cross my heart: *Keen, Billy* / Mean old world: *Casualairs* / I have seniority over your love: *Kimball, Bobby* / I'm your stepping stone: *Montgomery, Bobby* / Wee bit longer: *Fisher, Andy* / Out of sight: *Sly* / Honey: *Averhart, Booker T. & the Mustangs* / You're flying high now baby: *Kimble, Neal* / L.A. happening: *Bridges, Chuck & the L.A. Happening* / Soul cargo: *Haywood, Leon*
CD _____ CDKEND 122
Kent / May '95 / Pinnacle.

L.A. YAYA
CD _____ HCD 8022
Hightone / Jul '94 / ADA / Koch.

LA CALLE CANTA
La chica que yo quiero: *2 To Get Funky* / Cuando pienso en ti: *3 To Get Funky* / Raga funk: *3 To Get Funky* / Si ya no estas: *3 To Get Funky* / Lo que sepa: *Tres X* / Mueve esa cosa: *Tres X* / Kid's got it going on: *Lord Ishawn & The Bronx Outlaws* / Micro-phone check: *Lord Ishawn & The Bronx Outlaws* / Condon: *MC Whiz* / Conversation: Org 7 / Jungle love: *Roc & Kato* / Flute, piano, strings: *Roc & Kato*
CD _____ 66058076
RMM / Nov '95 / New Note.

LA CHANRANGA
CD _____ 283402
Total / Jan '96 / Total/BMG.

LA FLEUR DE MON SECRET
Ay amor: *Bola De Nieve* / Tonada de luna llena: *Diaz, Simon* / En el ultimo trago: *Sandoval, Jose Alfredo Jimenez* / Titulos: *Iglesias, Alberto* / Casa con ventanas y libros: *Iglesias, Alberto* / Brevemente: *Iglesias, Alberto* / Retrato de Amanda Gris: *Iglesias, Alberto* / Tango de paria: *Iglesias, Alberto* / En Madrid nunca es tarde: *Iglesias, Alberto* / Facinacion: *Iglesias, Alberto* / Existe alguna posibilidad por pequena que sea de salvar lo n: *Iglesias, Alberto* / Interior: *Iglesias, Alberto* / Escribe compulsivamente: *Iglesias, Alberto* / Duo: *Iglesias, Alberto* / Ingenua: *Iglesias, Alberto* / Mi aldea: *Iglesias, Alberto* / Que Leo: *Iglesias, Alberto* / Vertigo: *Iglesias, Alberto* / Sola: *Iglesias, Alberto* / La flor de mi secreto: *Iglesias, Alberto* / Solea: *Iglesias, Alberto* / Poesia recitada: *Iglesias, Alberto*
CD _____ 4814442
Columbia / Jan '96 / Sony.

LA GALOUBET TAMBOURIN
CD _____ C 560073
Ocora / Nov '95 / Harmonia Mundi / ADA.

LA KORA DES GRIOTS
CD _____ PS 65079
Playasound / Nov '91 / Harmonia Mundi / ADA.

LA LEGENDE DU MUSETTE
CD Set _____ 982732
EPM / Jan '93 / Discovery / ADA.

LA RESISTANCE (Songs/Poetry Of The French Resistance)
CD _____ LDX 274734
La Chant Du Monde / Jul '94 / Harmonia Mundi / ADA.

LA RUMBA
CD _____ 283422
Total / Jan '96 / Total/BMG.

LA SONORA MANTANCERA
CD _____ CD 62033
Saludos Amigos / Apr '94 / Target/BMG.

LABELLED WITH LOVE
Magic smile: *Vela, Rosie* / On the wings of love: *Osborne, Jeffrey* / Every breath you take: *Police* / Love and affection: *Armatrading, Joan* / Stuck in the middle with you: *Stealer's Wheel* / Pearl's a singer: *Brooks, Elkie* / Steppin' out: *Jackson, Joe* / Love will keep us together: *Captain & Tennille* / Lady in red: *De Burgh, Chris* / I should have known better: *Diamond, Jim* / Heart on my sleeve: *Gallagher & Lyle* / Wonderful life: *Black* / We're all alone: *Coolidge, Rita* / Babe: *Styx* / Pick up the pieces: *Hudson - Ford* / Labelled with love: *Squeeze* / Will you: *O'Connor, Hazel* / Goodbye to love: *Carpenters* / Oh, Lori: *Alessi*
CD _____ 5518342
Spectrum/Karusseli / Nov '95 / PolyGram / THE.

LABELLO BLANCO - A DIFFERENT CLASS
CD _____ GUMH 9
Labello Blanco / Jul '94 / SRD.

LADIES OF JAZZ (5CD Set)
CD Set _____ JWD 2528
JWD / Oct '95 / Target/BMG.

LADIES OF THE 60'S
CD _____ SETCD 085
Stardust / Sep '94 / Carlton Home Entertainment.

LADIES SING JAZZ VOL. 2 1925-41
CD _____ 157762
Jazz Archives / Jun '93 / Jazz Music / Discovery / Cadillac.

LADIES SING THE BLUES
Downhearted blues: *Bailey, Mildred* / Break o'day blues: *Brown, Ada* / Evil mama blues: *Brown, Ada* / Hangover blues: *Carlisle, Una Mae* / Hard time blues: *Cox, Ida* / Take him off my mind: *Cox, Ida* / Cravin' a man blues: *Glinn, Lillian* / Blues I love to sing: *Hall, Adelaide* / Billie's blues: *Holiday, Billie* / Long gone blues: *Holiday, Billie* / Let your linen hang low: *Howard, Rosetta* / Rosetta blues: *Howard, Rosetta* / Electrician blues: *Miles, Lizzie* / My man o'war: *Miles, Lizzie* / Booze and blues: *Rainey, Ma* / Toad frog blues: *Rainey, Ma* / Empty bed blues: *Smith, Bessie* / St. Louis blues: *Smith, Bessie* / Jelly jelly look what you done done: *Smith, Clara* / Don't you leave me here: *Smith, Laura* / Goin' crazy with the blues: *Smith, Mamie* / Freight train blues: *Smith, Trixie* / Moaning the blues: *Spivey, Victoria* / I'm a mighty tight woman: *Wallace, Sippie*
CD _____ CD AJA 5092
Living Era / Jun '92 / Koch.

LADY LOVE
CD _____ DCD 5293
Disky / Feb '94 / THE / BMG / Discovery / Pinnacle.

LADY LOVE - SWEET LOVE GROOVES
CD _____ 12217
Laserlight / Jul '93 / Target/BMG.

LADY SINGS THE BLUES
CD _____ PMCD 7001
Pure Music / Oct '94 / BMG.

LAFAYETTE SATURDAY NIGHT
One scotch, one bourbon, one beer: *Roger, Aldus* / Mean woman: *Roger, Aldus* / Zydeco et pas sale: *Roger, Aldus* / Recorded in England: *Bernard, Rod* / 2 fee: *Bernard, Rod* / Kidnapper: *Jewel & The Rubies* / Allons a Lafayette: *Newman, Jimmy C.* / Hippy ti yo: *Newman, Jimmy C.* / Lena Mae: *Walker, Lawrence* / Memphis: *Shondells* / Slow down: *Shondells* / Alligator Bayou: *Raven, Eddy* / I got loaded: *Lil' Bob & The Lollipops* / Come on over: *Gee Gee Shinn* / Colinda: *Guidry, Doc* / What's her name: *Forester, Blackie* / Domino: *Miller, Rodney* / Before I grew too old: *Miller, Rodney* / Just because: *King Karl* / Everybody's feeling good: *King Karl* / I'm cajun cool: *Cajun Born* / Getting late in the evening: *Neal, Raful* / Candy Ann: *Jewel & The Rubies* / That's what's wrong with the church today: *Consoling Clouds Of Joy*
CD _____ CDCHD 371
Ace / Apr '92 / Pinnacle / Cadillac / Complete/Pinnacle.

LAMBADA
CD _____ DINCD 6
Dino / Jan '90 / Pinnacle / 3MV.

LAMBADA
Lambada / Mar de emocoes / Lambada do galo / Lambada de salvador / Maris Mariazinha / Louca Magia / Mule fubanga / Dancando lambada / Merequeza / Blanco do merengue (el organito) / Isso e bom / Forregae / Brilho Jamaica / Lambada (instrumental)
CD _____ 4660552
CBS / Nov '89 / Sony.

LAMBADA - EL RITMO DO BRASIL (17 Original Brazilian Lambadas)
Lambada: *La Banda* / Lambada de noche: *La Banda* / Lambada na mar: *La Banda* / Doida: *Vitoria* / Frecote: *Vitoria* / Pinga ne mim: *Vitoria* / A roda: *Vitoria* / Xo paturi: *Banda Marrakeche* / Sou de Bahia: *Banda Marrakeche* / Grito de Igualdade: *Banda Saliva Doce* / Coceirinha: *Banda Tiete Tips* / O fricote de galinha: *Moraes, Paulo* / A vendor de caqui: *Moraes, Paulo* / Vem pra mim: *Moraes, Paulo* / Doce multidao: *Brito, Mario* / Brilho egito: *Viera Tania & Banda Press* / Lambada (power mix): *Ipanema*
CD _____ CDINS 5025
Instant / Jan '90 / Charly.

LAMBADA BRAZIL
Lambada do remelxo: *Banda Cheiro De Amor* / Zorra: *Caldas, Luiz* / Algeria da cidade: *Menezes, Margereth* / Meia lua inteira: *Veloso, Caetano* / Ve estrelas: *Ramalho, Elba* / Roda baiana: *Banda Cheiro De Amor* / Dancando morenguao: *Banda Tomalira* / Tenda do amor (magia): *Menezes, Margereth* / La vem o trio: *Banda Tomalira* / Lambada: *Carioca* / Doida: *Ramalho, Elba* / Ode e adao: *Caldas, Luiz* / Vou te pegar: *Nonato Do Cavaquinho* / Grande Gandhi: *Caldas, Luiz* / Careou: *Caldas, Luiz*
CD _____ 841 580-2
Polydor / Nov '89 / PolyGram.

LAMBADAS OF BRAZIL
CD _____ EMPRCD 512
Emporio / Apr '94 / THE / Disc / CM.

LAMBS ON THE GREEN HILLS
CD _____ OSS 9CD
Ossian / Oct '89 / ADA / Direct / CM.

LAMENT
Lament for the dead of the north: *Spillane, Davy* / Bright lady: *Masterson, Declan* / Sean O Duibhir a Ghleanna: *Ni Dhomhnaill, Maighréad* / An droighnean donn: *Glackin, Paddy* / Plunkett: Ó Suilleabháin, *Micheal* / One breath: O'Kelly, *Alanna* / Port na buccai: *MacMahon, Tony* / Danny boy: *Moore, Christy* / Tairn-se im chodhladh: *Og Potts, Sean* / Sliabh geal gcua: *Conneff, Kevin* / Carolan's devotion: *Sheahan, John* / An bonnan buí: *Potts, Sean* / John O'Dwyer of the glen: *Martin, Neil* / O'Carolan's farewell: *Bell, Derek*
CD _____ CDRW 27
Realworld / Mar '93 / EMI / Sterns.

LAND OF HOPE AND GLORY
Rule Britannia / Strike up the band / British Grenadiers / Here's a health unto her Majesty / Royal ceremony / Marchalong / Cavalry of the clouds / Navy day / Normandy veterans march / Battle of Britain march / Drum and bugle display / Soldiers of the sea / Lionheart / Aces high / Sir John Moore concert march / Abide with me / Land of hope and glory / Life on an ocean wave / Heart of oak / Dam busters march / Bridge too far / On the march
CD _____ MUCD 9004
Start / Apr '95 / Koch.

LAND OF MY FATHERS (Welsh Choral Classics)
CD _____ MATCD 227
Castle / Dec '92 / BMG.

LAND OF MY MOTHERS
CD _____ CRAICD 048
Crai / Aug '95 / ADA / Direct.

LANOR RECORDS STORY 1960-1992, THE
J'ai fait mon idee: *Bergeron, Shirley* / Parloz vous francais: *Matte, Bill* / I love my baby: *Eltradors* / Life problem: *Anderson, Elton* / Can't stop loving you: *Little Victor* / Drifting cloud: *Drifting Charles* / Keep your arms around me: *Mann, Charles* / Your no longer mine: *Mann, Charles* / I'll be your Jim: *Malory, Willie* / Runnin' out of fools: *Bourton, Hugh* / Love don't love nobody: *Brown, Ella* / Red red wine: *Mann, Charles* / Crazy face: *Randall, Jay & The Dialtones* / Hot hot lips: *Prescott, Ralph* / I found my woman: *Carner, Roy* / Chewing gum: *Jacob, Donald* / Walk of life: *Mann, Charles* / Accordion player waltz: *Broussard, Tim* / Drop that ego: *Generation Band* / Zydeco all night: *Walker, Joe* / My music is Beau Jocque: *Jocque, Beau*
CD _____ ZNCD 1009
Zane / Jul '95 / Pinnacle.

L'APPEL DE LA MUSE VOL.2
CD _____ AJE 04CD
Vinyl Solution / Nov '92 / Disc.

LARK IN THE CLEAR AIR
CD _____ OSS 13CD
Ossian / Dec '94 / ADA / Direct / CM.

LAS VEGAS GRIND PART.2
CD _____ EFA 11512 CD
Crypt / Mar '93 / SRD.

LAST GREAT ROCKABILLY SATURDAY NIGHT, THE
CD _____ STCD 3
Stomper Time / Sep '93 / Magnum Music Group.

LAST NIGHT A DJ - SEB FONTAINE
CD _____ 21 CCCD 002
21st Century Opera / Jan '96 / Total/BMG.

LATE NIGHT SESSIONS
CD _____ SOMCD 4
Ministry Of Sound / Jan '96 / 3MV / Warner Music.

LATEX TV OBLIVION
CD _____ MHCD 008
Minus Habens / Nov '93 / Plastic Head.

LATIN AMERICAN HOLIDAYS
CD _____ CD 62019
Saludos Amigos / Jan '93 / Target/BMG.

LATIN AMERICAN MUSIC
CD _____ 301062
Musidisc / Aug '90 / Vital / Harmonia Mundi / ADA / Cadillac / Discovery.

LATIN GROOVE
Picadillo: *Fania Allstars* / Wonderful thing: *Pagan, Ralfi* / Los ejes de mi carreta: *Barretto, Ray* / Soul makossa: *Fania Allstars* / Night in Tunisia: *Barretto, Ray* / Somebody's son: *Palmieri, Eddie* / Mambo mongo: *Santamaria, Mongo* / Green onions: *Costanzo, Jack & Gerry Woo* / Change had better come: *Diamond, Mark* / Viva tirado: *Fania Allstars* / Cancion para mi viejo: *Sonora Poncena* / TP's shingaling: *Puente, Tito* / Shaft: *Bataan, Joe* / Que lindo llambu: *Palmieri, Eddie*
CD _____ CPCD 8084
Charly / Mar '95 / Charly / THE / Cadillac.

LATIN JAZZ
Cappuccino: *Sonora Poncena* / Diecisiete punto uno: *Palmieri, Eddie* / Blues a la Machito: *Machito & His Afro Cuban Salseros* / Noble cruise: *Palmieri, Eddie* / Ran kan kan: *Puente, Tito* / Manteca: *Santamaria, Mongo* / Night love: *Sonora Poncena* / Introvisate: *Impacto Crea* / Mambo jazz: *Ray, Ricardo & Bobby Cruz* / Night in Tunisia: *Barretto, Ray* / Mambo a la tito: *Puente, Tito* / New one: *Santamaria, Mongo*
CD _____ CDHOT 520
Charly / Apr '95 / Charly / THE / Cadillac.

LATIN JAZZ
Tanga: *D'Rivera, Paquito* / Snow samba: *D'Rivera, Paquito* / Lorenzo's wings: *D'Rivera, Paquito* / Bahia san juan: *Hidalgo, Giovanni* / Jazz sabor: *Seis Del Solar* / Zambia: *Bauza, Mario* / Night in Tunisia: *Bauza, Mario* / Azulito: *Bauza, Mario*
CD _____ NSCD 008
Nascente / Oct '95 / Disc / THE.

LATIN JAZZ VOL.1
Nica's dream: *Burrell, Kenny* / Gunky: *Lytle, Johnny* / Mambo inn: *Taylor, Billy Trio* / Caravan: *Pucho & His Latin Soul Brothers* / Sambop: *Adderley, Cannonball* / Baian baby: *Stitt, Sonny* / Tin tin deo: *Forrest, Jimmy* / Montuneando: *Santamaria, Mongo*
CD _____ CDBGP 1023
BGP / Mar '93 / Pinnacle.

LATIN JAZZ VOL.2
Ping pong: *Blakey, Art & The Jazz Messengers* / Mau mau: *Farmer, Art Septet* / Manteca: *Garland, Red Trio* / Sea food wally: *Rodriguez, Willie* / Screamin': *McDuff, Brother Jack* / Fat man: *Montego Joe* / Mambo ricci: *Dolphy, Eric & Latin Jazz* / Chop sticks: *Braith, George*
CD _____ CDBGP 1027
BGP / Aug '89 / Pinnacle.

LATIN PULSE
Sopa de pichon: *Machito & His Afro Cuban Salseros* / Pablo pueblo: *Blades, Ruben* / Ran kan kan: *Puente, Tito* / Kickapoo sky juice: *Fania Allstars* / Acuyuye: *Pacheco, Johnny* / Te conozco: *Lavoe, Hector* / Hard hands: *Barretto, Ray* / Quimbara: *Cruz, Celia* / La verdad: *Palmieri, Eddie* / Jive samba: *Constanzo, Jack* / Me vengare: *La Lupe* / Mambo jazz: *Ray, Ricardo & Bobby Cruz*
CD _____ CDINS 5031
Instant / Aug '90 / Charly.

LATIN VOGUE
Pete's boogaloo: *Rodriguez, Pete* / Green onions: *Constanzo, Jack & Gerry Woo* / Ran kan kan: *Puente, Tito* / El chisme: *Cruz, Celia & Ray Barretto* / Alex Mambo: *Machito* / En manicero: *Candido* / Tito on timbales: *Puente, Tito* / Descarga: *Colon, Johnny* / Bamboleo: *Fania Allstars* / Llora como voz: *Rivera, Hector* / New guaguanco: *Puente, Tito* / Y sigue: *Colon, Joe* / Yo soy latino: *Harlow, Larry* / Mani picante: *Pastrana, Joey* / Agua que va a caer: *Rivera, Ismael* / Take more candi: *Candido* / Ay que Rico: *Palmieri, Eddie* / Carnaval en campang: *Palmieri, Charlie*
CD _____ CDCHARLY 229
Charly / Aug '90 / Charly / THE / Cadillac.

LATINAS
CD _____ N 17028CD
Nimbus / Aug '95 / Nimbus.

LATINO CLUB!
Coro miyare: *Pacheco, Johnny* / Acid: *Barretto, Ray* / Ajiaco caliente: *D.R.* / Fania: *Bolanos, Reinaldo* / Ay mi cuba: *More, Benny* / Elpito (I'll never go back to Georgia): *Sabater, Cuba* / Vente conmigo: *Fania Allstars* / Taste of latin: *Merraro, R.* / Nadie se salga de la rumba: *Rodriguez, Siro* / Que sabroso
CD _____ CDCHARLY 227
Charly / Jul '90 / Charly / THE / Cadillac.

LAUGHTER ON THE HOME FRONT (Songs/Comedy That Kept A Nation Going During The Great War)
CD _____ PASTCD 7047
Flapper / Sep '94 / Pinnacle.

LAURIE VOCAL GROUPS - THE 60'S SOUND
Denise: *Randy & The Rainbows* / Little star: *Randy & The Rainbows* / Why do kids grow up: *Randy & The Rainbows* / Don't worry I'm gonna make it: *Randy & The Rainbows* / Happy teenager: *Randy & The Rainbows* / Sharin': *Randy & The Rainbows* / Bye bye: *Bon-Aires* / Jeannie baby: *Bon-Aires* / Lovely way to spend an evening: *Four Graduates* / Candy queen: *Four Graduates* / Please write: *Tokens* / Cry and be on my way: *Demilles* / In the beginning: *Illusions* / I love you Diane: *Four Epics* / Dance Joanne: *Four Epics* / July: *Rayvons* / I'll always love you: *Tokens* / Away: *Concords* / Four seasons: *Coleman, Lenny & The Ebbtides* / Let's dance close: *Curtiss, Jimmy & The Regents* / Starlit night: *Emotions* / My heart cries: *Vera, Billy* / Donna Lee: *Demilles* / Tomorrow we'll be married: *Knight, Bob* / Four / My dream: *Dino & the diplomats* / Does my love stand a chance: *Del Satins* / Love boat: *Karilions* / This whole wide world: *Ovations* / Nicky: *Bernadette* / You just you: *Criterions* / Rock 'n' roll revival: *Five Discs* / Champaign lady: *Teardrops* / Walk down the aisle: *Monte, Vinnie* / Marie: *Harps*
CD _____ CDCHD 346
Ace / Feb '92 / Pinnacle / Cadillac / Complete/Pinnacle.

LAURIE VOCAL GROUPS - THE DOO WOP SOUND
Queen of the angels: *Orients* / I shouldn't: *Orients* / Zoom, zoom, zoom: *Enchords* / I need you baby: *Enchords* / Gloria: *Passion* / Oh melancholy me: *Passion* / Just to be with you: *Passion* / This is my love: *Four Discs* / World is a beautiful place: *Five Discs* / Angel in my eyes: *Premiere, Ronnie* / Hello Dolly: *Vito & The Salutations* / Daddy's going away again: *Harps* / Shrine of St. Cecilia: *Bon-Aires* / Hush-a-bye my love: *Dino & the diplomats* / I can't believe: *Dino & the diplomats* / You, you my love: *Jo-vals* / Remain truly yours: *Criterions* / Wake up: *Elegants* / Mr. Night: *Emotions* / Falling star: *Premiers* / Karen: *Lane, Rusty & The Mystics* / Who knows, who cares: *Holidays* / Stars will remember: *Holidays* / My lullaper: *Ovations* / She's my angel: *Randy & The Rainbows* / Again: *Four Epics* / Picture an angel: *Four Graduates* / I'll never know: *Del Satins*
CD _____ CDCHD 309
Ace / Feb '91 / Pinnacle / Cadillac / Complete/Pinnacle.

LE CHANT DES ENFANTS DU MONDE
CD _____ ARN 64320
Arion / Jul '95 / Discovery / ADA.

LE GRAN MAMOU (A Cajun Music Anthology)
Basile: *Soileau, Leo & Mayuse Lafleur* / Saut' crapaud: *Fruge, Columbus* / Quelqu' un est jaloux: *Guilory, Delin T. & Lewis Lafleur* / Les blues de voyage: *Ardoin, Amedee & Dennis McGee* / Mon vieux D'Autrefois: *Falcon Trio* / Je vais jouer celea por tois: *Guidry, Bixy & Percy Babineaux* / L'abandoner: *Montet, Bethmost & Joswell Dupois* / Trois jours apres ma most: *Soileau Couzens* / O' bebe: *Doucet, Oscar & Alius Soileau* / Ma chere: *Doucet, Oscar & Alius Soileau* / La valse: *Jaime: Falcon Trio* / Grosse mama: *Soileau, Leo & Moise Robin* / Belle of Point Claire: *Mistric, Arteleus* / One stepde Lacassine: *Abshire, Nathan & The Rayn-Bo Ramblers* / Jolie bion: *Hackberry Ramblers* / Il y a pas la Claire de Lune: *Joe's Acadians* / Lake Charles waltz: *Four Aces* / Valse de maralis buleur: *Rayn-Bo Ramblers* / La two-step a Erby: *Thibodeaux Boys* / Le gran mamou: *Soileau, Leo & his three aces* / Alberta: *Walker, Lawrence* / Je va t'aimer quand meme: *Hackberry Ramblers* / Viens donc me rejoindre: *Fuselier, J.B. & His Merrymakers* / Barroom blues: *Dixie Ramblers* / La veuve da la coulee: *Happy Fats & His Rayne-Bo Ramblers*
CD _____ CMFCD 013
Country Music Foundation / Jan '93 / Pinnacle / ADA.

LE MUSETTE A PARIS
CD _____ B 6817CD
Auvidis/Ethnic / Nov '95 / Harmonia Mundi.

LE NUAGE
Breeze on the hill / Skylark poet / Clouds in the east / White light / Trip on hammock / Alone on an airship / Escalator of clouds
CD _____ C 327843
Denon / '88 / Conifer.

LE PARIS BLEU
Boom (English version): *Trenet, Charles* / Coiffeur: *Gordon, Dexter* / Afternoon in Paris: *Jackson, Milt* / Under Paris skies: *Levy, Lou* / April in Paris: *Shore, Dinah* / Rondez vous a Saint Germain: *Banneville, Annette* / Memories of Paris: *Petrucciani, Michel* / Parisian thoroughfare: *Powell, Bud* / Swing valse: *Viseur, Gus* / Made in France: *Lagrene, Birelli* / Nuages: *Reinhardt, Django* / Django: *Pass, Joe* / This little town is Paris: *Kenny, Beverley* / Paris eyes: *Young, Larry* / Evening in Paris: *Sims, Zoot* / I wish you love: *Connor, Chris* / Sous le ciel de Paris: *Torente, Emmanuelle* / Echoes of France (La Marseillaise): *Quintette Du Hot Club De France*
CD _____ BNZ 291
Blue Note / Apr '92 / EMI.

LE PLUS BELLES FRANCAIS
CD _____ DCD 5321
Disky / Dec '93 / THE / BMG / Discovery / Pinnacle.

LE TANGO A PARIS 1907-41
CD Set _____ FA0 12CD
Fremeaux / Nov '95 / Discovery / ADA.

LEAD WITH THE BASS
CD _____ WWCD 8
Wibbly Wobbly / Feb '95 / SRD.

LEADERS OF THE PACK (The Very Best Of 60's Girl Groups)
Dancing in the street: *Reeves, Martha & The Vandellas* / Baby love: *Supremes* / It's in his kiss (Shoop shoop song): *Everett, Betty* / Leader of the pack: *Shangri-Las* / Locomotion: *Little Eva* / Shout: *Lulu & The Luvvers* / Sweet talking guy: *Chiffons* / It's my party: *Gore, Lesley* / Will you still love me tomorrow: *Shirelles* / My guy: *Wells, Mary* / Needle in a haystack: *Velvelettes* / Da doo ron ron: *Crystals* / He's so fine: *Chiffons* / Where did our love go: *Supremes* / Remember (walkin' in the sand): *Shangri-Las* / Chapel of love: *Dixie Cups* / When you're young and in love: *Marvelettes* / Really saying something: *Velvelettes* / One fine day: *Chiffons* / Then he kissed me: *Crystals* / My boyfriend's back: *Angels* / Past, present and future: *Shangri-Las*
CD _____ 516 376-2
PolyGram TV / Aug '93 / PolyGram.

LEATHER AND LACE (The Men and Women of Rock)
CD _____ DINCD 9
Dino / Jun '90 / Pinnacle / 3MV.

LEATHER AND LACE - THE SECOND CHAPTER
Radio ga ga: *Queen* / Black velvet: *Myles, Alannah* / Road to hell: *Rea, Chris* / Rooms on fire: *Nicks, Stevie* / Hurting kind (I've got my eyes on you): *Palmer, Robert* / Edge of a broken heart: *Vixen* / Better days: *Gun* / I don't want a lover: *Texas* / Run to you: *Adams, Bryan* / Big love: *Fleetwood Mac* / Radar love: *Golden Earring* / Get your love: *Black Velvette* / From out of nowhere: *Faith No More* / Martha's harbour: *All About Eve* / I'm a believer: *Giant* / First time: *Beck, Robin* / Centrefold: *Geils, J. Band*
CD _____ DINCD 12
Dino / Nov '90 / Pinnacle / 3MV.

LEGACY OF GENE 'BOWLEGS' MILLER
Call of distress: *Bryant, Don* / Doin' the mustang: *Bryant, Don* / Sho is good: *Miller, Gene 'Bowlegs'* / Goodest man: *Miller, Gene 'Bowlegs'* / I was wrong: *Miller, Gene 'Bowlegs'* / What do you mean: *Miller, Gene 'Bowlegs'* / Frankenstein walk: *Miller, Gene 'Bowlegs'* / Everybody got soul: *Miller, Gene 'Bowlegs'* / Love what you're doing to me: *Janet & The Jays* / Pleading for your love: *Janet & The Jays* / Walk away: *Peebles, Ann* / I can't let you go: *Peebles, Ann* / My man: *Peebles, Ann* / Chain of fools: *Peebles, Ann* / Rescue me: *Peebles, Ann* / Won't you try me: *Peebles, Ann* / Respect: *Peebles, Ann*
CD _____ HILOCD 15
Hi / Jul '95 / Pinnacle.

LEGACY'S RHYTHM & SOUL REVUE SERIES SAMPLER
Wake up everyone: *Melvin, Harold & The Bluenotes* / Caravan of love: *Isley-Jasper-Isley* / Me and Mrs. Jones: *Paul, Billy* / Fine and say goodbye: *Manhattans* / Ain't no sunshine: *Withers, Bill* / Piece of my heart: *Franklin, Erma* / I feel so bad: *Wills, Chuck* / Backstabbers: *O'Jays* / Everyone eats when they come to my house: *Calloway, Cab* / Who loves you better: *Isley Brothers* / Hey little girl: *Lance, Major* / One girl too late: *Brenda & Tabulations* / Cowboys and girls: *Intruders* / My ship is coming in: *Jackson, Walter* / Love is the message: *MFSB* / You are my friend: *Labelle, Patti* / It rocks, it swings: *Treniers* / Lady Marmalade: *Labelle, Patti*
CD _____ 4805122
Columbia / May '95 / Sony.

LEGEND OF EL RECORDS B SIDES
Touch of evil: *Philippe, Louis* / Twangy twangy: *Philippe, Louis* / Little part: *Philippe, Louis* / What if a day: *Philippe, Louis* / Smash hit wonder: *Philippe, Louis* / T-R-O-U-B-L-E-: *Adverse, Anthony* / Eine symphonie des grauns: *Adverse, Anthony* / Fountain: *Adverse, Anthony* / Green park:

Adverse, Anthony / Good girl: *Adverse, Anthony* / How to get on in society: *King Of Luxembourg* / Sketches of Luxembourg: *King Of Luxembourg* / Espadarte: *King Of Luxembourg* / Lee Remick: *King Of Luxembourg* / Elusive pimpernel: *King Of Luxembourg* / Personality parade: *King Of Luxembourg* / Albert Parker: *Go!, Gappas* / Roman: *Go!, Gappas* / Don't leave: *Momus* / Love: *Bid* / Ian Botham the I.T. man: *Cavaliers* / Whatever happened to Alice: *Rosemary's Children* / Arcade: *Always* / Park row: *Always* / Flying dispaly: *Always* / Fire: *Underneath* / Let's make Shane and McKenzie: *Marden Hill* / Execution of Emperor Maximillian: *Marden Hill* / Hangman: *Marden Hill* / Little black dress: *Mayfair Charm School* / Great railway journeys: *Klaxon 5* / Madman and lovers: *Cagliostra* / Whisper not: *Florentines* / Invocation of filth: *Raj Quartet* / Hanging gardens of Reigate: *Would-Be-Goods* / Up the King of Luxembourg: *Bad Dream Fancy Dress* / You wind me up: *Bad Dream Fancy Dress* / Choirboys gas: *Bad Dream Fancy Dress* / Cecil Beaton's scrapbook: *Would-Be-Goods* / Valediction: *Ambassador 277*
CD _____ MONDE 20CD
Cherry Red / Apr '95 / Pinnacle.

LEGEND OF NEW ORLEANS, THE
Dr. Jazz / Sweetie dear / Alligator crawl / Too tight / That's a plenty / Pleasin' Paul / High society / Astoria strut / Weatherbird / Turtle twist / Maple leaf rag / Perdido Street blues / Clarinet marmalade / Apex blues / Ory's Creole trombone / New Orleans stomp / Sweet lovin' man / Tiger rag / Deaf stomp / Cannonball blues / Beau Koo Jack / I know that you know / Franklin Street blues / As you like it / Panama
CD _____ GOJCD 53016
Giants Of Jazz / Jul '88 / Target/BMG / Cadillac.

LEGENDARY DIG MASTERS VOL.2 (Dig These Blues)
Old folk's boogie: *Simmons, Al* / You ain't too old: *Simmons, Al* / Country home: *Sailor Boy* / What have I done wrong (parts 1 and 2): *Sailor Boy* / Hand me down baby: *Maiden, Sidney* / Going back to the plow: *Hozay* / I've got an expensive woman: *Hozay* / Wrong doin' woman: *John, Moose* / Talkin' 'bout me: *John, Moose* / Springtime blues: *Sams, TW* / Come on home: *Nolen, Jimmy* / If you ever get lonesome: *Easter, Roy* / Happy: *My woman done quit me: *Green, Slim* / Moore boogie: *Moore, Abe* / S and J: *Moore, Abe* / Singin' the blues: *Robbins, Little Bill* / Full grown woman: *Waters, Larry* / Don't tell me that you love me: *Waters, Larry* / Bring her back to me: *Robbins, Billy* / Elim stole my baby (boo hoo): *Cane, Sugar* / They say you never can miss: *Cane, Sugar*
CD _____ CDCHD 334
Ace / Jan '92 / Pinnacle / Cadillac / Complete/Pinnacle.

LEGENDARY DIG MASTERS VOL.3 (Dapper Cats, Groovy Tunes & Hot Guitars)
Telephone boogie: *Watson, Johnny & Jeannie* / I got a girl (that lives over yonder): *Watson, Johnny 'Guitar'* / My aching feet: *Strogin, Henry* / I've been blind, blind, blind: *Strogin, Henry* / Jimmy's jive: *Nolen, Jimmy* / Hey little girl: *Lewis, Richard* / Bingo: *Moore, Abe* / Talk to me baby: *Easter, Roy* / 'Happy' / Sad stories: *Waters, Larry* / Check yourself: *Allen, Tony & Barbara* / Someday: *Sams, TW* / Country boogie: *Love, Preston & Orchestra* / Get away from here: *Lewis, Pete 'Guitar'* / Ain't gonna tell: *Ray, Dessa* / Wiggle walk: *Otis, Johnny* / Things won't be right without you: *Williams, Devonia 'Lady Dee'* / Much more: *Jessie & Joyce* / Itty bitty bee: *Johnson, Ray* / Baby please come home: *Robbins, Little Billy* / Gotta have love!: *Robbins, Little Billy* / Blooper: *Otis, Johnny & The Jayos* / Bad Bad Bulldog: *Matthews, Little Arthur* / Hot diggity (dog ziggity boom): *Matthews, Little Arthur* / Dead man's shop: *Otis, Johnny & His Orchestra*
CD _____ CDCHD 351
Ace / Oct '92 / Pinnacle / Cadillac / Complete/Pinnacle.

LEGENDARY DIG MASTERS VOL.4 (Shoo-Be-Doo-Be-Ooh)
Shoobie dooby Mama: *Phantoms* / My baby doll: *Gladiators* / Girl of my heart: *Gladiators* / Another chance: *Foster, Cell* / Millie's chilli: *Foster, Cell* / Fools prayer: *Maye, Arthur Lee* / Honey honey: *Maye, Arthur Lee* / This is the night for love: *Maye, Arthur Lee* / Whispering wind: *Maye, Arthur Lee* / Crazy bells: *Stevens, Julie* / Blue mood: *Stevens, Julie* / Have a heart: *Premiers* / My darling: *Premiers* / Can it be real: *Premiers* / Take my heart: *Stevens, Julie* / You think I'm just your fool: *Stevens, Julie* / Ding a ling a ling: *Jayos* / Dying love: *Jayos* / I plead guilty: *Jayos* / Wedding ring: *Jayos* / What am I gonna do: *Jayos* / In exchange for your love: *Jayos* / Sweet thing: *Ding Dongs*
CD _____ CDCHD 569
Ace / Sep '94 / Pinnacle / Cadillac / Complete/Pinnacle.

LEGENDARY VOICES
CD _____ CWNCD 2002
Javelin / Jun '95 / THE / Henry Hadaway Organisation.

LEGENDS OF BRITISH TRADITION (Bulls Head Barns)
Sweet Georgia Brown / Of all the wrongs / Weary blues / Baby, won't you please come home / When your lover has gone
CD _____ CMJCD 014
CMJ / Oct '91 / Jazz Music / Wellard.

LEGENDS OF THE BLUES VOL.1
St. Louis blues: Smith, Bessie / Matchbox blues: Jefferson, Blind Lemon / Mississippi: Hurt, John / Ain't no tellin': Johnson, Blind Willie / Lord I just can't keep from crying: Carter, Bo / Pigmeat is what I crave: Johnson, Blind Willie / Southern can is mine: Johnson, Lonnie / Low down St. Louis blues: Patton, Charlie / Revenue man blues: Car, Leroy / Stormy night blues: White, Joshua / I believe I'll make a change: Leadbelly / Wort Worth and Dallas blues: Wheatstraw, Peetie / Stop breakin' down blues: Fuller, Blind Boy / Truckin' my blues away: Broonzy, Big Bill / Spreadin' snakes blues: Memphis Minnie / Nothing in ramblin': White, Bukka / Fixin' to die blues: Waters, Muddy / Hard day blues: Williams, Big Joe
CD _____ 4672452
CBS / Oct '90 / Sony.

LEGENDS OF THE BLUES VOL.2
Henry Ford blues: Sykes, Roosevelt / Ninety eight degree blues: Alexander, Texas / Trinity river blues: Walker, Aaron T-Bone / She shook her gin: Hicks, Robert / Turpentine blues: Tampa Red / No no blues: Weaver, Curley / Bo-easy blues: Bogan, Lucille / Schoolboy blues: Roland, Walter / Cold blooded murder: Easton, Amos / My baby won't pay me no mind: Moss, Buddy / Old Jim Canan's: Wilkins, Robert / Take it easy greasy: Wilkins, Casey / Two timin' woman: Bill, Casey / Downhill pull: Spivey, Victoria / Down in the slums: Jones, Curtis / Separation blues: Johnson, Merline / Soon this morning, no. 2: Spand, Charlie / Is that a monkey you got: Gillum, Bill 'Jazz' / Hurry down sunshine: Dupree, Champion Jack / Goodbye now: McGhee, Brownie
CD _____ 4687702
Columbia / Nov '91 / Sony.

LES ANTILLES
Ernestine attention / Ce les Antilles / Ba moin un tibo, doudou / Mr. Leonard / bande Zaoua / La ronde des cuisinieres / Serpent maigre / L'ete en pyjama / Maladie d'amour / Guitare des Antilles / Le rocher / Oh pere / Ninon, merengue, merengue / Danse de gros ca / Guyane, o Guyana / Sans chemise, sans pantalon / Maman, maman / Biguine a Henri / Aye Tumbaye / Roro / Madiana / Papillon vole / Adieu foulard / Adieu madras
CD _____ ARN 64034
Arion / May '88 / Discovery / ADA.

LES BALALAIKAS DES TZIGANES RUSSES
Les yeux verts / Boublitchki / Ne sois pas jaloux, ne sois pas Fache / Mon bohemien / Ne pars pas / Plaine, ma plaine / Le sarafan rouge / Kalinka / Tzigane et samovar / L'amour s'est enfui / Le vieux Tzigane / Vradanka / Pourquoi m'astu aime
CD _____ ARN 64019
Arion / May '88 / Discovery / ADA.

LES CHANSONS DE 1935
CD _____ UCD 19094
Forlane / Apr '95 / Target/BMG.

LES CHANSONS DE 1936
CD _____ UCD 19095
Forlane / Apr '95 / Target/BMG.

LES CHANSONS DE 1937
CD _____ UCD 19096
Forlane / Apr '95 / Target/BMG.

LES CHANSONS DE 1938
CD _____ UCD 19097
Forlane / Apr '95 / Target/BMG.

LES CHANSONS DE 1939
CD _____ UCD 19098
Forlane / Apr '95 / Target/BMG.

LES GRANDS MESSIEURS DU MUSIC HALL 1931-1943
CD _____ 983472
EPM / Apr '94 / Discovery / ADA.

LES PLUS BELLES VALSES MUSETTE
CD _____ FAO 14CD
Fremeaux / Nov '95 / Discovery / ADA.

LES PLUS GRAND ARTISTES FRANCAIS
Ma Pomme: Chevalier, Maurice / Quand un Vicomte: Chevalier, Maurice / Y'a d'la Joie: Chevalier, Maurice / Notre Espoir: Chevalier, Maurice / Dites moi ma mere: Chevalier, Maurice / Mimile: Chevalier, Maurice / Ca sent si bon la France: Chevalier, Maurice / Mon vieux Paris: Chevalier, Maurice / Partoit c'est l'amour: Chevalier, Maurice / Paris sera toujours Paris: Chevalier, Maurice / Appelez ca comme vous voulez: Chevalier, Maurice / Ca fait d'excellents Francais: Chevalier, Maurice / Fleur de Paris: Chevalier, Maurice / Mon l'egionnaire: Piaf, Edith

/ C'est lui que mon coeur a choisi: Piaf, Edith / Elle frequentait la rue Pigalle: Piaf, Edith / C'taint une histoire l'amour L'Accordeoniste: Piaf, Edith / J'ni danse avec l'amour: Piaf, Edith / J'ai danse avec amour: Piaf, Edith / Le fanion de la legion: Piaf, Edith / Lea momes de la cloche: Piaf, Edith / Le java de Cezique: Piaf, Edith / L'estranger: Piaf, Edith / Mon Apero: Piaf, Edith / Reste: Piaf, Edith / Les Hiboux: Piaf, Edith / Je Suis mordue: Piaf, Edith / Je chante: Trenet, Charles / Y's d'la Joie: Trenet, Charles / Fleur bleue: Trenet, Charles / Vous ets jolie: Trenet, Charles / J'ai ta main: Trenet, Charles / Le soleil a rendezvous avec la lune: Trenet, Charles / La oiseaux de Paris: Trenet, Charles / Menilmontant: Trenet, Charles / Boum: Trenet, Charles / La route enchantee: Trenet, Charles / La vie qui va: Trenet, Charles / Mam'zelle Clio: Trenet, Charles / Bonsoir jolie Madame: Trenet, Charles / La romance de Paris: Trenet, Charles
CD Set _____ 90835-2
PMF / May '94 / Kingdom / Cadillac.

LESSONS IN LOVE
Comment te dire adieu: Somerville, Jimmy / Obsession: Animotion / I hear you now: Jon & Vangelis / Sing baby sing: Stylistics / I know there's something going on: Frida / Giving it all away: Daltrey, Roger / Never again: Faltskog, Agnetha / Lessons in love: Level 42 / I should have known better: Diamond, Jim / I'm Mandy fly me: 10cc / On the wings of a nightingale: Everly Brothers / When Smokey sings: ABC / Just a day away (forever tomorrow): Barclay James Harvest / Lilac wine: Brooks, Elkie
CD _____ 5501472
Spectrum/Karussell / Jan '94 / PolyGram / THE.

LET 'EM IN
CD _____ 12219
Laserlight / Nov '93 / Target/BMG.

LET IT SNOW
Sleigh ride: Williams, Andy / Have yourself a merry little Christmas: Mathis, Johnny / Let it snow, let it snow, let it snow: Day, Doris / White world of winter: Crosby, Bing / Secret of Christmas: Andrews, Julie / Snowfall: Bennett, Tony / Christmas song: Torme, Mel / Joy to the world: Faith, Percy / When a child is born: Mathis, Johnny / Silver bells: Day, Doris / Do you hear what I hear: Williams, Andy / Winter wonderland: Clooney, Rosemary / Pretty paper: Orbison, Roy / Christmas eve in my hometown: Vinton, Bobby / Christmas time again: Humperdinck, Englebert / Twelve days of Christmas: Conniff, Ray
CD _____ 4746372
Columbia / Nov '95 / Sony.

LET MY HORSES RUN FREE
CD _____ APCD 001-2
Appaloosa / Apr '94 / ADA / Magnum Music Group.

LET THERE BE ROCK
CD _____ NTRCD 016
Nectar / Jun '94 / Pinnacle.

LET'S DANCE
Night fever (Megamix): UK Mixmasters / Going back to my roots: Odyssey / Everybody plays the fool: Main Ingredient / Hot hot hot: Poindexter, Buster / Knock three times: Dawn / Hooked on swing: Kings Of Swing Orchestra / Let's twist again: Checker, Chubby / He's a rebel: Crystals / Shout (Part 1): Isley Brothers / Diana: Anka, Paul / Wooly bully: Sam The Ram & The Pharaohs / Ballroom blitz: Sweet
CD _____ 74321339272
Camden / Jan '96 / BMG.

LET'S DANCE FOR LOVE '95
CD _____ FTICD 1
Freetown / Jul '95 / 3MV / Sony.

LET'S DO IT
CD _____ PHONTCD 7669
Phontastic / '93 / Wellard / Jazz Music / Cadillac.

LET'S GET IT ON
CD _____ NSCD 021
Newsound / May '95 / THE.

LET'S GO DISCO
Y.M.C.A.: Village People / That's the way i like it: K.C. & The Sunshine Band / Play that funky music: Wild Cherry / Lady marmalade: Labelle, Patti / Boogie nights: Heatwave / Shake your body: Jacksons / Love machine (part 1): Miracles / Boogie wonderland: Earth, Wind & Fire / Heaven must be missing an angel: Tavares / Let's all chant: Zager, Michael Band / Use it up and wear it out: Odyssey / Funky town: Lipps Inc. / And the beat goes on: Whispers / Oops upside your head: Gap Band / Celebration: Kool & The Gang / It's a disco night (rock don't stop): Isley Brothers / Car wash: Rose Royce / I will survive: Gaynor, Gloria / Shame, shame: King, Evelyn 'Champagne' / Turn the music up: Players Association / Shame, shame, shame: Shirley & Company / More, more, more: Andrea True Connection / Best of my love: Emotions / Hold back the night: Trammps / Love's train: Melvin, Harold & The Bluenotes / Hustle: McCoy, Van / Rock your baby: McCrae, George / Rock the boat: Hues Corporation / I love music: O'Jays /

This is it: Moore, Melba / Knock on wood: Stewart, Amii / Red light spells danger: Ocean, Billy / Ain't gonna bump no more (with no big fat woman): Tex, Joe / In the bush: Musique / Boogie oogie oogie: Taste Of Honey / September: Earth, Wind & Fire / If I can't have you: Elliman, Yvonne / Do what you wanna do: T-Connection / Disco stomp: Bohannon, Hamilton / Girls: Moments & Whatnauts
CD _____ CDEMTV 78
EMI / Oct '93 / EMI.

LET'S GO JIVIN' TO ROCK & ROLL
Say yeah: Salvo, Sammy / I've got a dollar: Dell, Jimmy / Love makes the world go round: Como, Perry / Rock-a-bye boogie: Davis Sisters / Plantation boogie: King, Pee Wee / Tennessee rock 'n' roll: Sons Of The Pioneers / Hubba hubba hubba: Como, Perry / Jackpot: Pedicin, Mike Quintet / TV hop: Morgan Twins / Shape I'm in: Restivo, Johnny / You gotta learn your rhythm and blues: Sedaka, Neil / Kewpie doll: Como, Perry / Blue suede shoes: King, Pee Wee / Fiddle diddle boogie: Davis Sisters / You gotta go: Pedicin, Mike Quintet / Jukebox baby: Como, Perry / Boom de de boom: Baker, Jane / Rock and stroll room: Mickey & Sylvia / When the cats come marching in: Pedicin, Mike Quintet / Idaho red: Ray, Wade
CD _____ BCD 15533
Bear Family / Oct '90 / Rollercoaster / Direct / CM / Swift / ADA.

LET'S GO TESKO
london x-press: X-press / Batacuda: D.J. Dero / Minge incrodiblo disco machine: Brother Love Dubs / TWA Theme: TWA Theme / Pleasure: Uncle Clio / I feel love: Additional Touch / Disco biscuit: Disko Biscuit / You can't stop the groove: Reefa / Get funky: Fierce Ruling Diva / Givin' you no rest: E-Lustrious / Funk on up: Undergraduates / Excuse me: Direct 2 Disc
CD _____ REACTCD 021
React / Sep '93 / Vital.

LET'S GO ZYDECO
Cher catin / Petite et la grosse / Used and abused / Walking down the interstate / Zydeco two step / Crying in the streets / Midland two step / Shake what you got / Lafayette special / Lonesome road / I'm coming home / I've been there / Mardi gras song / Je suis en recolteur / Check out the zydeco / Zolo go / Green's zydeco / King's zydeco / Allons a Lafayette / Moman coucrhe / Two step de grand mallet / Home sweet home
CD _____ CDCHD 543
Ace / Feb '95 / Pinnacle / Cadillac / Complete/Pinnacle.

LET'S GO, LET'S GO, LET'S GO
CD _____ 12105
Laserlight / Dec '94 / Target/BMG.

LET'S HAVE A BALL TONIGHT: THE PIONEERS OF R & B
CD _____ NI 4025
Natasha / Feb '94 / Jazz Music / ADA / CM / Direct / Cadillac.

LET'S HAVE A PARTY (36 Original Superhits - 2CD Set)
CD Set _____ 24095
Delta Doubles / Sep '92 / Target/BMG.

LET'S HEAR IT FOR THE GIRLS
All I wanna do: Crow, Sheryl / Girls just wanna have fun: Lauper, Cyndi / Ain't no man: Carroll, Dina / Every day of the week: Jade / Just a step from heaven: Eternal / Whatta man: Salt 'N' Pepa & En Vogue / Free your mind: En Vogue / Same thing: Carlisle, Belinda / Right beside you: Hawkins, Sophie B. / All I want: Those Two / Little bird: Lennox, Annie / Trouble: Shampoo / Go away: Estefan, Gloria / Jump: Pointer Sisters / It's raining men: Weather Girls / Only way is up: Yazz / I love your smile: Shanice / Gotta get it right: Fiagbe, Lena / Walk like an Egyptian: Bangles / Patience of angels: Reader, Eddi
CD _____ 5165522
PolyGram / Apr '95 / PolyGram.

LET'S PARTY (21 Favourites)
Zorba's dance / For he's a jolly good fellow / Congratulations / Hokey cokey / Conga / Superman / Birdie song / Oops upside your head / Celebration / Disco-motion / Saturday night / Y.M.C.A. / Time warp / Hot hot hot / Anniversary waltz / Lambada / Swing low sweet chariot / You'll never walk alone / Happy birthday to you / Auld lang syne / Gay Gordons
CD _____ AVC 562
Avid / Dec '94 / Avid/BMG / Koch.

LET'S ROCK TOGETHER
CD Set _____ NSCD 001
Newsound / Feb '95 / THE.

LET'S TALK ABOUT LOVE
CD _____ DINCD 39
Dino / May '92 / Pinnacle / 3MV.

LET'S TALK ABOUT SEX
CD _____ 15491
Laserlight / Aug '92 / Target/BMG.

LIFE AFTER BLOOM
CD _____ GRCD 015
Guerilla / Jun '94 / Pinnacle.

LIFE IN BLUES
CD _____ 157362
Blues Collection / Feb '93 / Discovery.

LIFE IN THE FOLK LANE II
Iron masters: Men They Couldn't Hang / Faithful departed: Chevron, Philip / Do you hear me now: Jansch, Bert / Devil's eal: Smither, Chris / Changes: Clark, Gene / Voices of the Barbary Coast: Williamson, Robin & His Merry Band / Limit: Rainer & Das Combo / Pick up your coat: Hitchcock, Nicola / Runaway train: Gutter Brothers / Caribbean wind: Revelators / Hard day on the planet: Wainwright III, Loudon / Upon a veil of midnight blue: Coughlan, Mary / My sweet potatoe: Renbourn, John / Dance to your Daddy: Sweeney's Men / That'll do baby: McTell, Ralph / Sally go round the roses: Pentangle / They watered my whiskey down: Burdett, Phil & The New World Troubadours
CD _____ DIAB 808
Diabolo / Jun '94 / Pinnacle.

LIFE IS CHANGE VOL.3
CD _____ EFA 11654 D
Beri-Beri / Jul '93 / SRD.

LIFE MADE ME BEAUTIFUL AT FORTY
CD _____ ITM 1498
ITM / Nov '95 / Tradelink / Koch.

LIFE SUCKS GET A CRASH HELMET
CD _____ RRCD 001
Retch / Oct '93 / Plastic Head.

LIFTING THE SPIRIT
CD _____ 3CL 2510
Ichiban Soul Classics / Nov '95 / Koch.

LIGHT FLIGHT (Instrumental Favourites)
Midnight in Moscow: Ball, Kenny & His Jazzmen / Aria: Bilk, Acker, His Clarinet & Strings / Floral dance: Brighouse & Rastrick Band / Walk in the Black Forest: Conway, Russ / Cast your fate to the wind: Sounds Orchestral / Popcorn: Hot Butter / Sweet Georgia Brown: Grappelli, Stephane / Somewhere my love: String Chorale / Zorba's dance: Tacticos, Manos & His Bouzouki / Girl I love: String Chorale / Moon river: String Chorale / Guantanamera: Strings Go Latin / Petite fleur: Barber, Chris Jazz Band & Monty Sunshine / Light flight: Pentangle / Hello Dolly: Ball, Kenny & His Jazzmen / Amazing grace: Royal Scots Dragoon Guards / Moonglow: Sounds Orchestral / Forsyte saga (Elizabeth Tudor): Stapleton, Cyril / Nuages: Reinhardt, Django / Sleepy shores: Sounds Orchestral
CD _____ TRTCD 121
TrueTrax / Oct '94 / THE.

LIGHTS CAN GO ON AGAIN - NOW THE WAR IS OVER, THE (2CD/MC Set)
I'll string along with you: Peers, Donald / Nice to know you care: Hutch / People will say we're in love: Hutch / Either it's love or it isn't: Hutch / I never loved anyone: Hutch / Peg O' my heart: Hutch / Far away places: Radio Revellers / Shoemaker's serenade: Radio Revellers / You're breaking my heart: Goff, Reggie / How lucky you are: Lynn, Vera / Time after time: Conway, Steve / Let bygones be bygones: Harris, Doreen / There's no one but you: Harris, Doreen / I only have eyes for you: Stapleton, Cyril / In my dreams: Goff, Reggie / All's well that ends well: Goff, Reggie / My silent love: Shelton, Anne / Love of my life: Shelton, Anne / Say something sweet to your sweetheart: Simpson, Jack / I'll give you the world (To you sweetheart): Simpson, Jack / I'll make up for everything: Conway, Steve / Moment I saw you: Conway, Steve / There, I've said it again: Green, Paula & Her Orchestra / Who do you love I hope: Stapleton, Cyril / Say that you're mine: Carr, Pearl / P.S. I love you: Carr, Pearl / Be mine beloved: Davis, Beryl / You, you, you are the one: James, Dick / When you're in love: Goff, Reggie / Blue ribbon gal: Chester, Charlie & His Gang / Clancy lowered the boom: Clark, Petula / I'll keep you in my heart: Lynn, Vera / I wonder who's kissing her now: Layton, Turner / I'd break my heart again: Conway, Steve / My love is only for you: Williams, Rita / Say it every day: Goff, Reggie / Stars will remember (So will I): Rey, Monte
CD Set _____ CDDL 1269
Music For Pleasure / May '94 / EMI.

LIKE SISTER & BROTHER
like sister and brother: Drifters / Do what you do: Jackson, Jermaine / Who's zoomin' who: Franklin, Aretha / Woman in love: Three Degrees / Jump: Pointer Sisters / We do it: Stone, R & J / Swing your daddy: Gilstrap, Jim / Body talk: Imagination / You've lost that lovin' feelin': Patti & The Lovelites / Heaven must be missing an angel: Tavares / Loving you: Riperton, Minnie / Lies: Butler, Jonathan / We've only just begun (the romance is not over): Jones, Glenn / Feelings: Gaynor, Gloria / So amazing: Vandross, Luther / Used to be my girl: O'Jays / If you let me stay: D'Arby, Terence Trent / Lady marmalade: Labelle, Patti / Free: Williams, Deniece / Signed, sealed, delivered (I'm yours): Turner, Ruby
CD _____ STAMCD 017
Stardust / Oct '92 / Carlton Home Entertainment.

839

LINN COLLECTION 1994, THE
CD _____ AKD 027
Linn / Oct '94 / PolyGram.

LION ROOTS
CD _____ CDLINC 001
Lion Kingdom / Feb '94 / Jetstar /
Pinnacle / Roots Collective.

LION ROOTS IN DUB VOLUME 1
CD _____ CDLINC 003
Lion Inc. / Feb '95 / Jetstar / SRD.

LION ROOTS JUNGLE
CD _____ CDLINC 6
Lion Inc. / Aug '95 / Jetstar / SRD.

LION ROOTS VOL.2
CD _____ CDLINC 008
Lion Inc. / Nov '95 / Jetstar / SRD.

LION TRAIN DUB VOLUME 1
CD _____ SPVCD 55342
Red Arrow / Dec '94 / SRD / Jetstar.

LIPSTICK TRACES
Boring life / It's too soon to know: Orioles /
L'amiral cherche une maison a louer: Tzara,
Tristan / Roadrunner: Richman, Jonathan /
Excerpt from "Hurlements en faveur de
Sade": Debord, Guy / Instrumentation ver-
bale: Brau, Jean-Louis / Boredom: Buzzcocks / One chord wonders: Buzzcocks /
Phoneme bbbb: Hanjaman, Raoul / At
home he's a tourist: Gang Of Four / Gary
Gilmore's eyes: Adverts / U: Kleenex / Ex-
cerpt from "Critique de la separation": De-
bord, Guy / Stage talk (Roundhouse, Sept
23, 1976): Clash / Never been in a riot: Mekons / Split: Liliput / Rohrenhose...: Ble-
gvad, Peter / Wake up: Essential Logic /
Gil / In love: Raincoats / Karawane: Osmond, Marie / I wish I was a mole in the
ground: Lunsford, Bascam Lamar / Building:
Mekons / Lipstick traces: Spellman, Benny
CD _____ R 2902
Rough Trade / Jul '93 / Pinnacle.

LIQUIDATORS
Liquidator: Harry J All Stars / Phoenix city:
Alphonso, Roland / Miss Jamaica: Cliff,
Jimmy / Pressure drop: Toots & The Maytals
/ Skinhead moonstomp: Symarip / Guns of
Navarone: Skatalites / 007: Dekker, Des-
mond / Shame and scandal: Tosh, Peter &
The Wailers / Ethiopia: Pyramids / Johnny
too bad: Slickers / Train to Skaville: Ethio-
pians / Monkey man: Toots & The Maytals /
Rudie, a message to you: Livingstone,
Dandy / It mek: Dekker, Desmond / Musical
store room: Drummond, Don / Return of
Django: Upsetters / Israelites: Dekker, Des-
mond & The Aces / Train to Rainbow City:
Pyramids / Guns never: Brooks, Baba /
Double barrel: Collins, Dave & Ansil / Dollar
in the teeth: Upsetters / Don't be a rude
boy: Rulers / Twelve minutes to go: Mc-
Cook, Tommy / Rudie's dead: Pyramids
CD _____ VSOPCD 136
Connoisseur / Jul '89 / Pinnacle.

LISMOR 21ST ANNIVERSARY ALBUM
Rolling in the high grass/Scalloway lasses/
Haint dykes o'Voe: Bain, Aly & Phil Cun-
ningham / Waulking song: MacInnes, Mairi
/ MacEwan's barn/Islay teenager/Lewis
Road dance/Horse on: So: MacDonald,
Fergie / Sonny's dream: Imlach, Hamish /
Links of Forth/Atholl Cummers/Mac-
Allister's dirk: Strathclyde Police Pipe Band
/ Wee china pig: Alexander Brothers /
Camptown races/Steamboat Bill/Oh Su-
sanna: Box & Banjo Band / Dumbarton's
drums: Gaelforce Orchestra / Murdoch /
Geordie's byre: Stewart, Andy / Gates of
Edinburgh reel: Ellis, John & His Highland
Country Band / Wiggly jig: New Celeste /
My ain folk: Anderson, Moira / Spin and
glow/McDowall's breakdown: Cowie, Char-
lie / Sonny's mazurka/Foxhunters: Mathie-
son, Pipe Major Robert / Bonnie lass
o'Ballochmyle: Morrison, Peter / Bonnie
lass o'Bon Accord: Gordon, Rob & His
Band / Lewis sailing song: Soiley, David /
West Highland way: McKellar, Kenneth /
Lord Lovat's lament: 78th Fraser Highlan-
der's Pipe Band / Barren rocks of Aden/
Duke of Atholl's Highlanders: Dancing
Strings / De niand puirt - A Beul: Runrig
CD _____ LCOM 5228
Lismor / Apr '94 / Lismor / Direct / Duncans
/ ADA.

LISTEN TO THE BANNED
(20 Risque Songs of the 20s & 30s)
I've gone and lost my little yo-yo: Cotton,
Billy / With my little ukelele in my hand:
Formby, George / Guy what takes his time:
West, Mae / You dirty old man's
daughter: Durium Dance Band / Nellie the
nudist queen: Ross & Sargent / My private
affair: Davies, Dawn / What's it: Rodgers,
Jimmie / He hadn't up 'til yesterday: Tucker,
Sophie / Winnie the worm: Frankau, Ronald
/ I'm a bear in a lady's boudoir: Edwards,
Cliff / Everyone's got sex appeal for some-
one: Frankau, Ronald & Monte Crick / All
poshed up with my daisies in my hand: Hig-
gins, Charlie / Pu-leeze Mr. Hemingway:
Carlisle, Elsie / Let's all be fairies: Durium
Dance Band / I'm going to give it to Mary
with love: Edwards, Cliff / Physician:
Lawrence, Gertrude / No wonder she's a
blushing bride: Fowler, Art / Flora Mc-
Donald: Byng, Douglas / Or anything else

I've got: Sutton, Randolph / And so does
he: Davies, Dawn
CD _____ CD AJA 5030
Living Era / Oct '88 / Koch.

LIVE
CD _____ TUT 781
Wundertute / Oct '94 / CM / Duncans /
ADA.

LIVE '55
CD _____ JCD 17
Jass / Nov '86 / CM / Jazz Music / ADA /
Cadillac / Direct.

LIVE ACTION
(Charly Blues - Masterworks Vol. 15)
Wee wee baby / Sittin' and thinkin': Waters,
Muddy / Worried blues: Guy, Buddy / Bring
it on home: Williamson, Sonny Boy / Sugar
mama: Howlin' Wolf / Clouds in my heart:
Waters, Muddy / May I have a talk with you:
Howlin' Wolf / Got my mojo working: Wa-
ters, Muddy / Don't know which way to go:
Guy, Buddy / Nineteen years old: Waters,
Muddy
CD _____ CDBM 15
Charly / Apr '92 / Charly / THE / Cadillac.

LIVE AT ANTONE'S ANNIVERSARY
ANTHOLOGY VOL.II
CD _____ ANT 00016
Antones / Sep '95 / Hot Shot / Direct /
ADA.

LIVE AT CBGB'S
For all the love of rock n roll / Operetico /
Cadilac moon / I need a million / Poe / Let
me dream if I want to / Head over heels /
Over under sideways down / Slash / It feels
alright tonight / A.V.M. / Change it comes /
We deliver / Everybody's depraved / Ro-
mance / I'm not really this way
CD _____ 756782566-2
WEA / Mar '94 / Warner Music.

LIVE AT MIDEM, 1979
CD _____ 500402
Musidisc / May '94 / Vital / Harmonia
Mundi / ADA / Cadillac / Discovery.

LIVE AT RAUL'S
CD _____ DJD 3216
Dejadisc / Sep '95 / Direct / ADA.

LIVE AT RONNIE SCOTT'S
CD _____ MATCD 256
Castle / Apr '93 / BMG.

LIVE AT ROSKILDE '94
CD _____ STOKES 001
Roskilde / Jun '95 / SRD.

LIVE AT SWEET BASIL, VOL. 2
(Eric Dolphy and Booker Little
Remembered)
CD _____ K32Y 6214
King/Paddle Wheel / Sep '88 / New Note.

LIVE AT THE BIG RUMBLE
CD _____ NERCD 066
Nervous / Nov '91 / Nervous / Magnum
Music Group.

LIVE AT THE CAVERN
Dr. Feelgood / Keep on rolling / She's sure
the girl I love / You've really got a hold on
me / Everybody loves a lover / Devoted to
you / You better move on / Somebody to
love / I got a woman / Little queenie / Diddley daddy / Bring it on home to me /
Skinny Minnie / Jezebel / I'm talking about
you / Little Egypt / What'd I say / Don't start
running away / Zip a dee doo dah / Reelin'
and rockin'
CD _____ SEECD 385
See For Miles/C5 / Dec '93 / Pinnacle.

LIVE AT THE EEL PUNK ROCK
MOUNTAIN
CD _____ FRIGHT 065CD
Fierce / Feb '92 / Disc.

LIVE AT THE GALWAY SHAWL
CD _____ CIC 065CD
Clo Iar-Chonnachta / Nov '93 / CM.

LIVE AT THE KNITTING FACTORY VOL.
1
CD _____ KFWCD 097
Knitting Factory / Nov '94 / Grapevine.

LIVE AT THE KNITTING FACTORY VOL.
2
CD _____ KFWCD 098
Knitting Factory / Nov '94 / Grapevine.

LIVE AT THE KNITTING FACTORY VOL.
3
CD _____ KFWCD 099
Knitting Factory / Nov '94 / Grapevine.

LIVE AT THE KNITTING FACTORY VOL.
4
CD _____ KFWCD 100
Knitting Factory / Nov '94 / Grapevine.

LIVE AT THE KNITTING FACTORY VOL.
5
CD _____ KFWCD 108
Knitting Factory / Nov '94 / Grapevine.

LIVE AT THE KNITTING FACTORY VOL.
6
CD _____ KFWCD 161
Knitting Factory / Feb '95 / Grapevine.

LIVE AT THE ROXY
CD _____ RRCD 132
Receiver / Jul '93 / Grapevine.

LIVE AT THE ROXY
Strange boy / Smile and wave goodbye /
Relics from the past / I live in a car / Tele-
phone numbers / Get yourself killed / Never
wanna leave / Here comes the knife / T.V.
/ Shrink / Sniper / Tough on you / Fun, fun, fun
/ Vertigo / Lullabies lie
CD _____ CDTB 011
Thunderbolt / Mar '95 / Magnum Music
Group.

LIVE AT THE VORTEX
Can't wait till '78: Wasps / Waiting for my
man: Wasps / Bunch of stiffs: Mean Street
/ Small lives: Neo / Tell me the truth: Neo /
Living for kicks: Torme, Bernie / Streetfigh-
ter: Torme, Bernie / Animal bondage: Art At-
tacks / Frankenstein's heartbeat: Art
Attacks / Nothing to declare: Suspects /
You don't break my heart: Maniacs / I ain't
gonna be history: Maniacs
CD _____ CDPUNK 68
Anagram / Nov '95 / Pinnacle.

LIVE FROM THE CHARLOTTE
CD _____ RAUCD 010
Raucous / Feb '94 / Nervous / Disc.

LIVE IN MOSCOW MCMXCII
Era so comeco nosso fim: Toninho Horta
Sextet / Eternal youth: Toninho Horta Sextet
/ No carnaval: Toninho Horta Sextet / Aqui,
Oh: Toninho Horta Sextet / Paris cafe: Ton-
inho Horta Sextet / When I fall in love: Ton-
inho Horta Sextet / Aquelas coisas todas:
Toninho Horta Sextet / I love you: Igor But-
man Quartet / Body and soul: Igor Butman
Quartet / It could be cool: Igor Butman
Quartet / Question and answer: Igor But-
man Quartet / Autumn leaves: Igor Butman
Quartet / Blue bossa: Igor Butman Quartet
/ Improvisation No.1/Sete sementes: Mor-
eira, Airto / Once I loved: Toninho Horta
Sextet / Stella by starlight: Gomez, Eddie &
Steve Amirault, Ronnie Burrage / Serenade:
Toninho Horta Sextet / Vento: Toninho
Horta Sextet / Law years: Igor Butman
Quartet / Lua floria: Fourth World
CD _____ BW 039
B&W / Mar '94 / New Note.

LIVE ROCK
Life is for living: Barclay James Harvest /
Statesboro blues: Allman Brothers / Show
me the way: Frampton, Peter / From out of
nowhere: Faith No More / Wild and won-
derful: Almighty / Delilah: Harvey, Alex Sen-
sational Band / Good morning judge: 10cc
/ Delta Lady: Cocker, Joe / Stay with me:
Faces / Spirit of radio: Rush / Roll over lay
down: Status Quo / Mama weer all crazee
now: Slade
CD _____ 5506462
Spectrum/Karussell / Aug '94 / PolyGram /
THE.

LIVE ROCK VOLUME 5
CD _____ XSRCD 3005
XS / Mar '95 / Grapevine.

LIVE ROCK VOLUME 6
CD _____ XSRCD 3006
XS / Mar '95 / Grapevine.

LIVE STIFFS
I knew the bride: Lowe, Nick / Let's eat /
Semaphore signals / Reconnez cherie / Police car: Wallis, Larry / I just don't know
what to do with myself: Costello, Elvis / Miracle man: Costello, Elvis / Wake up and
make love with me: Dury, Ian / Billericay
Dickie: Dury, Ian / Sex and drugs and rock
'n' roll / Chaos
CD _____ MAUCD 621
Mau Mau / Aug '92 / Pinnacle.

LIVE TO RIDE
(18 Rock Classics)
I want you to want me: Cheap Trick / Bar-
racuda: Heart / Carrie: Europe / She's not
there: Santana / Up around the bend: Hanoi
Rocks / Breaking the law: Judas Priest /
Ride like the wind: Saxon / Silver machine:
Saxon / Rock 'n' me: Miller, Steve / Show
me the way: Frampton, Peter / I surrender:
Rainbow / Waiting for an alibi: Thin Lizzy /
Radar love: Golden Earring / Closer to the
heart: Rush / Whatever you want: Status
Quo / Victims of circumstance: Barclay
James Harvest / Lady in black: Uriah Heep
/ This flight tonight: Nazareth
CD _____ VSOPCD 194
Connoisseur / Apr '94 / Pinnacle.

LIVERPOOL '63 -'68
Ferry 'cross the Mersey: Gerry & The Pace-
makers / Sunshine Lizzie: Gerry & The Pacemakers / Abyssinian secret: Black, Cilla / For
no one: Black, Cilla / Sandy: Swinging Blue
Jeans / It's too late now: Swinging Blue
Jeans / Everything in the garden: Fourmost
/ Breakaway: Marsden, Beryl / Whatever will
be will be (Que sera sera): Royce, Earl & The
Olympics / I really do: Royce, Earl & The
Olympics / America: Storm, Rory & The Hur-
ricanes / I got a woman: Black Knights / An-
gel of love: Black Knights / I love her: Kubas
/ Magic potion: Kubas / First cut is the
deepest: Kubas / Why don't you love me:
Blackwells / One way ticket / Don't you do
it no more: Kramer, Billy J. & The Dakotas /
How I won the war: Musketeer Gripweed &
The Third Troup
CD _____ SEECD 370
See For Miles/C5 / Aug '94 / Pinnacle.

LIVING CHICAGO BLUES, VOL.1
Your turn to cry / Serves me right to suffer
/ Ain't that just like a woman / Feel like
breaking up somebody's home / It's alright
/ Out of bad luck / Stoop down baby / Sittin'
on top of the world / My baby's so ugly /
Come home darling / Blues won't let me be
/ One room country shack / Linda Lou / Too
late / Laundromat blues / One day / Woman
in trouble
CD _____ ALCD 7701
Alligator / May '93 / Direct / ADA.

LIVING CHICAGO BLUES, VOL.2
Don't answer the door / Two headed man /
Cold lonely nights / Move over, little dog /
Would you, baby / Worry worry / Sunnyland
blues / Cry cry darlin' / Stranded on the
highway / Dirty mother for you / Spider in
my stew / Don't say that no more / Take it
easy, baby / Blues after hours / Little angel
child / How much more longer
CD _____ ALCD 7702
Alligator / May '93 / Direct / ADA.

LIVING CHICAGO BLUES, VOL.3
Hard times / She's fine / Moving out of the
ghetto / Going to New York / Big leg woman
/ Careless with our love / Roadblock / Poison ivy / I dare you / Nobody knows my
troubles / Sweet little girl / Naptown / Down
in my own tears / Crying for my baby / Feel
so bad / Wish me well / Have you ever loved
a woman / Berlin Wall / Prisoner of the blues
CD _____ ALCD 7703
Alligator / May '93 / Direct / ADA.

LIVING CHICAGO BLUES, VOL.4
Hard times: Reed, A.C. & The Spark Plugs
/ She's fine: Reed, A.C. & The Spark Plugs
/ Moving out of the ghetto: Reed, A.C. &
The Spark Plugs / Going to New York:
Reed, A.C. & The Spark Plugs / Big legged
woman: Scotty & The Rib Tips / Careless
without love: Scotty & The Rib Tips / Road-
block: Scotty & The Rib Tips / Poison ivy:
Scotty & The Rib Tips / I dare you: Lee,
Lovie & Carey Bell / Nobody knows my
troubles: Lee, Lovie & Carey Bell / Sweet
little girl: Lee, Lovie & Carey Bell / Nap town:
Lee, Lovie & Carey Bell
CD _____ ALCD 7704
Alligator / May '93 / Direct / ADA.

LIVING ON THE FRONT LINE
CD _____ CDTB 154
Magnum Music / Jul '94 / Magnum Music
Group.

LIVING THE NIGHTLIFE
Carlena: Just Brothers / Dearly beloved:
Montgomery, Jack / Black eyed girl:
Thompson, Billy / Love the nightlife: Charts
/ Groovy guy: Shirelles / It's torture: Brown,
Maxine / Gonna give her all the love I've got:
Gordon, Benny / I refuse to give up: Reid,
Clarence / Send my baby back: Hughes,
Freddie / Good things come to those who
wait: Jackson, Chuck / Do you love me
baby: Masqueraders / Please stay: Ivorys /
Pretty part of you: Hunt, Tommy / My sweet
baby: Esquires / Love ain't what it used to
be: Diplomats / Yesterday's kisses: Big
Maybelle / (Happiness will cost you) One
thin dime: Lavette, Bettye / I want you: Clay,
Judy / Since I found a love: Hadley, Sandy
/ Love keeps me crying: Johnson, Walter /
You can't keep a good man down: Gentle-
man Four / I don't want to lose you: Wynn,
Mel / Look my way: Williams, Maurice / You
must be losing your mind: Raye, Jimmy
CD _____ CDKEND 104
Kent / Jun '93 / Pinnacle.

LOCA MIA
CD _____ TUMICD 025
Tumi / '92 / Sterns / Discovery.

LOCKENHAUS 5
CD Set _____ EMBOX 06
ECM / Nov '92 / New Note.

LOGIC TRANCE 2
Stella: Jam & Spoon / Transformation:
Transform / Trans-o-phobia: Dance Trance
/ Schoneberg: Marmion / Midsummernight:
Glass Ceiling / Fragile: LSG / Brainticket 2:
Ramin / Rez: Underworld / Eternal spirit: 4
Voices / Wake up: Garnier, Laurent / Fires
of Ork II: Fires Of Ork / What is sound: Blyz
/ Little fluffy clouds: Orb / Paradise II: Atlan-
tis / Papua New Guinea: Future Sound Of
London / Silence of the water: Emo(onal / I
love you: Electrotete / How much can you
take: Visions Of Shiva / Evolution: Experi-
ence / Spacetrack: Cosmic Baby / Love
stimulation: Humate / Orbital: Lush 3.1 /
Logic trance: Microbots
CD _____ 74321212342
Logic / Jun '94 / BMG.

LOLO SY NY TARINY
(Music From Madagascar)
CD _____ PS 65121
Playasound / Feb '94 / Harmonia Mundi /
ADA.

LONDON BLUES FESTIVAL
CD Set _____ ITM 960017
ITM / Feb '94 / Tradelink / Koch.

LONDON JAZZ CLASSICS
Skindo le'le: Alive / Jump: Airto / Welcome
new warmth: Sardaby, Michel / Salsa
Mama: Richardson, Doug / Te' Caliente:
Galdari, Patsy / Searching: McClerkin, Corky
/ Atlas: Jones, Robin Seven / I feel the earth
move: First Gear & Larnelle Harris

CD _____ SJRCD 008
Soul Jazz / Jul '94 / New Note / Vital.

LONDON JAZZ CLASSICS VOL.2
Samba de flora: Moreira, Airto / Get with it:
Parker, Billy / Ain't no sunshine: Sivuca /
Cocoa funk: Franzetti, Carlos / Forty days:
Brooks, Billy / Sophie's gift: Synthesis / Feel
like makin' love: Marrero, Ricardo / Fenway
funk: Paunetto, Bobby V
CD _____ SJRCD 017
Soul Jazz / Jun '94 / New Note / Vital.

LONDON JAZZ CLASSICS VOL.3
L'eroe di plastica: Esposito, Tony / Mr.
Blindman: McGhee, Donna / Manha: Azymuth / Taz: Paunetto, Bobby V / A assim
que eu sou: Papete / Bananas: Irvine, Weldon / Bananeira: Santiago, Emilio / Mother's
land: Hannibal / Cascavel: Adolfo, Antonio
CD _____ SJCD 026
Soul Jazz / May '95 / New Note / Vital.

LONDON PAVILION VOL.3
CD _____ ACME 21CD
El / May '89 / Disc.

LONDON R & B SESSIONS, THE
You' better watch yourself: Lewis, Lew Re-
former / Shake and finger pop: Lewis, Lew
Reformer / Madison blues: Bogey Boys /
You can't catch me: Bogey Boys / Finger in
my eye: Red Beans & Rice / Pucker up but-
tercup: Red Beans & Rice / Whammy:
Johnson, Wilko & His Solid Senders / I can't
be satisfied: Untouchables / Just a little
bit: Hope & Anchor House Band / Why do
everything happen to me: American Blues /
Roostering with intent: Little Roosters /
Death letter: Blues Band / Taste and try:
Bishops / All in it together: Pirates
CD _____ 900135
Line / Aug '95 / CM / Grapevine / ADA /
Conifer / Direct.

LONELY IS AN EYESORE
Hot doggie: Colourbox / Acid bitter and sad:
This Mortal Coil / Cut the tree: Wolfgang
Press / Fish: Throwing Muses / Frontier:
Dead Can Dance / Crushed: Cocteau Twins
/ No motion: Dif Juz / Muscovite musquito:
Clan of xymox / Protagonist: Dead Can
Dance
CD _____ CAD 703CD
4AD / '88 / Disc.

LOOK OF LOVE, THE
Can't get by without you: Real Thing / Best
thing that ever happened to me: Knight,
Gladys & The Pips / Don't throw your love
away: Searchers / (If paradise is) half as
nice: Amen Corner / Always something
there to remind me: Shaw, Sandie / First cut
is the deepest: Arnold, P.P. / Just when I
needed you most: Vanwarmer, Randy /
Love hurts: Nazareth / Isn't she lovely: Parton, David / Way we were: Knight, Gladys &
The Pips / Baby, now that I've found you:
Foundations / Funny how love can be: Ivy
League / Angel of the morning: Arnold, P.P.
/ Colour of my love: Jefferson / That same
old feeling: Pickettywitch / You to me are
everything: Real Thing / Sad sweet
dreamer: Sweet Sensation / When you walk
in the room: Searchers
CD _____ MCCD 039
Music Club / Sep '91 / Disc / THE / CM.

LOOK OF LOVE, THE
Don't leave me this way: Communards /
Heartache: Pepsi & Shirlie / She ain't worth
it: Medeiros, Glenn & Bobby Brown / Look
of love: ABC / You're the best thing: Style
Council / Robert De Niro's waiting: Bana-
arama / Pale shelter: Tears For Fears / Won-
derful life: Black / Senza una Donna: Zuc-
chero & Paul Young / Never knew love like
this before: Mills, Stephanie / Look away:
Big Country / Watching you: Shakatak /
Don't walk away: Four Tops / Leaving me
now: Level 42
CD _____ 5501452
Spectrum/Karussell / Jan '94 / PolyGram /
THE.

LOOK OF LOVE, THE
CD _____ 5351902
PolyGram TV / Jan '96 / PolyGram.

LOOKEY DOOKEY
CD _____ EFA 11569CD
Crypt / Jun '93 / SRD.

LOS TIEMPOS CAMBIAN
CD _____ X 55519
Aspic / Sep '95 / Harmonia Mundi.

LOST BLUES TAPES VOLUME 1
Della bear: Hooker, John Lee / Hound dog:
Thornton, Willie Mae / Captain Captain: Wa-
ters, Muddy / I got to cut out: Williamson,
Sonny Boy / Blues harp shuffle: Horton, Big
Walter / Strong brain - broad mind: Dixon,
Willie / Big leg woman: Dixon, Willie / You
got me runnin': Desanto, Sugar Pie / South
side jump: Guy, Buddy / If I get lucky: Le-
noir, J.B. / Got a letter this morning: Mc-
Dowell, Fred / Sail on: Sykes, Roosevelt /
Memphis boogie: Memphis Slim / Your best
friend's gone: Estes, John & Hammie Nixon
/ Farewell baby: Ross, Dr. Isah / Della Mae
#2: Hooker, John Lee
CD _____ 92042
Act / Apr '94 / New Note.

LOST GROOVES, THE
Hold on I'm comin': Wilson, Reuben / It's
your thing: Green, Grant / Scorpion: Don-
aldson, Lou / Hey western union man:
Green, Grant / Brother soul: Donaldson, Lou
/ Village lee: Patton, John / Spooky: Turren-
tine, Stanley / Dancin' in a easy groove:
Smith, Lonnie Liston / You want me to stop
loving you: Turrentine, Stanley
CD _____ CDP 8318832
Blue Note / Apr '95 / EMI.

LOST MUSIC OF CELTARABIA, THE
CD _____ GRIN 942CD
Grinnigogs / Jul '95 / ADA / Harmonia
Mundi.

LOST SOUL OF DETROIT, THE VOL.1
She's not everybody's girl: Metros / That's
bad: Harris, Lafayette Jr / I hold the key:
Sanders, Nelson / I'm leaving baby: White,
Willie / Leave me alone: White, Willie / I
gotta know: Hutcher, Willie / Standing on
the sideline: Williams, Lloyd / Can't live
without you: Milner, Reggie / In the middle:
Reynolds, L.J. / Stop lost over your past:
Reynolds, L.J. / I don't mess around: Reyn-
olds, Jeannie / People make the world:
Reynolds, Jeannie / I found the right girl:
Swingers / Alone in the chapel: Doe & Joe
/ Do you want a love: Milner, Reggie / She's
alright: Milner, Reggie / Somebody help me:
Milner, Reggie / Uphill climb to the bottom:
Lemons, George / Nothing can seperate our
love: Turner, Sammy
CD _____ GSCD 021
Goldmine / Aug '93 / Vital.

LOTUS SAMPLER 3
CD _____ ND 61018
Lotus / Feb '93 / Jazz Horizons / Impetus.

LOTUS SAMPLER 4
CD _____ ND 61025
Lotus / Feb '93 / Jazz Horizons / Impetus.

LOUDEST VOLUME 1
CD _____ LOUDEST 001
Outland / Jun '94 / Vital / Plastic Head.

LOUISIANA CAJUN SPECIAL
Hee haw breakdown: Cormier, Nolan & the
LA Aces / Pine grove blues: Abshire, Nathan / Triangle club special: Prejean, Leeman / Louisiana aces special: Badeaux / Lacassine special: Balfa Brothers / Cypress
inn special: Cormier, Nolan & the LA Aces /
Zydeci Cha Cha: Mouton / Cankton two
step: Prejan / Cajun ramblers special: Der-
ouen, Wallace / Eunice two step: Barzas,
Maurice / Hippy ti yo: Bonsall, Joe / I am so
lonely: Herbert, Adam / Choupique two
step: Abshire, Nathan / Waltz of regret:
Mate, Doris / Two steps de vieux temps:
Rambling Aces
CD _____ CDCH 914
Ace / Jan '92 / Pinnacle / Cadillac / Com-
plete/Pinnacle.

LOUISIANA CHANKY-CHANK
CD _____ ZNCD 1002
Zane / Oct '95 / Pinnacle.

LOUISIANA PIANO RHYTHMS
Deep creole blues: Morton, Jelly Roll / Rum
and coca cola: Professor Longhair / So
long: Domino, Fats / You always hurt the
one you love: Henry, Clarence 'Frogman' /
Ain't misbehavin': Toussaint, Allen / Rockin'
chair blues: Charles, Ray / Who will play this
old piano: Lewis, Jerry Lee / Lucille: Little
Richard / Rockin' pneumonia and the boogie woogie flu: Smith, Huey 'Piano' / Sea
cruise: Ford, Frankie / Happiness is in your
bed: Dr. John / Send me some lovin': Little
Richard / Can't you see darling: Charles,
Ray / On the sunny side of the street: Toussaint, Allen / Big chief: Professor Longhair /
What made Milwaukee famous (has made
a loser out of me): Lewis, Jerry Lee / I'm
walkin': Domino, Fats
CD _____ 598109420
Tomato / Nov '93 / Vital.

LOUISIANA ROCKERS
Cindy Lou: Terry, Gene / Come along with
me: Perrywell, Charles / Yankee danky doodle: Wilson, Jimmy / Baby you been to
school: Page, Charles / Bye bye baby:
Gerdsen, Ray & the Yellow Jackets / Catch
that train: Anderson, Elton / Chickee town
rock: Yellow Jackets / Clemae: Morris, Jerry
/ I keep cryin': Cookie / Why did you leave
me: Lowery, Frankie / Wiggle rock: Richards, Jay / I love you: Anderson, Elton / Or-
elia: Jackson, Ivory Lee / Flim flam: Prevost,
Lionel / No mail today: Terry, Gene / Em-
magene: Stevens, Duke / Slop and stroll jolie blonde: Dean, Gabe / Fattie Hattie: Gerdsen, Ray & the Yellow Jackets / Do you take
me for a fool: Hillier, Chuck / Silly dilly: Nelson, Jimmy / Wigly roll: Parker, Bill (Part 1): Parker, Bill Showboat Band / Linda Lou: Little
Eddie / Devil made me say that: James,
Danny / Muscadine mule: Ferrier, Al
CD _____ CDCHD 491
Ace / Mar '94 / Pinnacle / Cadillac / Com-
plete/Pinnacle.

LOUISIANA SATURDAY NIGHT
Louisiana man: Kershaw, Rusty & Doug / I
cried: Allan, Johnnie / Mathilda: Cookie &
The Cupcakes / My jolie blonde: Bernard,
Rod & Clifton Chenier / She wears my ring:
Bo, Phil / Feed the farther: Broussard, Van /
Little cajun girl: King, Gene / Big boys cry:
Charles, Bobby / Sugar bee: Cleveland Cro-

chet / Jailbird: Shurley, Bob & The Vel-
Tones / Legend in my time: McLain, Tommy
/ Diggy liggy lo: Kershaw, Rusty & Doug /
You had your chance: White, Margo / You
ain't nothing but fine: Rockin' Sidney / Big
blue diamonds: West, Clint / Rubber dolly:
Allan, Johnnie / There goes that train: Mar-
tin, Lee / Let's do the cajun twist: Randy &
The Rockets / Crazy baby: Rogers, Buck /
Can't stand to see you go: Allen, Dave /
Whole lotta shakin' goin' on: Thomas, Pren-
tice / I'm not a fool anymore: Broussard,
Van / Back door: Rufus / Whiskey heaven:
Ford, Frankie / Seven letters: Storm, Warren
/ I love my Saturday night: Stutes, Herbie
CD _____ CDCHD 490
Ace / Oct '93 / Pinnacle / Cadillac / Com-
plete/Pinnacle.

LOUISIANA SCRAPBOOK
Mardi gras in New Orleans: Dirty Dozen
Brass Band / New rules: Thomas, Irma / She
said the same things to me: Adams, Johnny
/ We don't see eye to eye: Adams, Johnny
/ Wondering: Walker, Philip / Song for Re-
nee: Brown, Clarence 'Gatemouth' / It's you
I love: Beausoleil / Louisiana blues: Summer,
Jo El / Bachelor's life: Menard, D.L. & Lou-
isiana Aces / Don't you know I love you:
Ball, Marcia / Think it over one more time:
Buckwheat Zydeco / Steppin' up in class:
Lonesome Sundown & Phillip Walker / No
relations: Tyler, Alvin 'Red' / One for the
highway: Booker, James / You got me wor-
ried: Washington, Walter 'Wolfman' / Gonna
cry till my tears run dry: Thomas, Irma /
Flintstones meets the president: Dirty
Dozen Brass Band / When the saints go
marching in: Washington, Tuts
CD _____ RCD 20058
Rykodisc / Dec '92 / Vital / ADA.

LOUISIANA SPICE
(25 Years Of Louisiana Music)
CD _____ ROUCDAN 1819
Rounder / Jun '95 / CM / Direct / ADA /
Cadillac.

LOVE AFTER MIDNIGHT
We're all alone: Coolidge, Rita / Stay with
me tonight: Osborne, Jeffrey / January February: Dickson, Barbara / Arms of Mary:
Sutherland Brothers / My favourite waste of
time: Paul, Owen / Fantasy: Earth, Wind &
Fire / Mind blowing decisions: Heatwave /
Imagination / I think we're alone now: Tiffany / Captain of your heart: Double / Never knew love
like this: Mills, Stephanie / Don't stop the
music: Yarbrough & Peoples / Sorry seems
to be the hardest word: John, Elton / More
than in love: Robbins, Kate / Lay back in
the arms of someone: Smokie / I can't go
for that (no can do): Hall & Oates / Just
don't want to be lonely: Main Ingredient
CD _____ STACD 025
Stardust / Nov '92 / Carlton Home
Entertainment.

LOVE ALBUM, THE
CD _____ DSPCD 114
Disky / Feb '94 / THE / BMG / Discovery /
Pinnacle.

LOVE ALBUM, THE
(2CD/MC Set)
To be a stranger: Carroll, Dina / Yes you
don't know me by now: Simply Red / Can't
help falling in love: UB40 / Searching: China
Black / Move closer: Nelson, Phyllis / Again:
Jackson, Janet / Against all odds: Collins,
Phil / Don't let the sun go down on me: Michael, George & Elton John / It must have
been love: Roxette / Don't wanna lose you:
Estefan, Gloria / One day I'll fly away: Crawford, Randy / Sweet love: Baker, Anita /
Never too much: Vandross, Luther / Piece
of my heart: Franklin, Erma / Come in out of
the rain: Moten, Wendy / When you tell me
that you love me: Ross, Diana / Save the
best for last: Williams, Vanessa / Zoom: Fat
Larry's Band / Heartbreaker: Warwick,
Dionne / Million love songs: Take That / If
you leave me now: Chicago / I want to know
what love is: Foreigner / I'll stand by you:
Pretenders / Why: Lennox, Annie / Crazy:
Cline, Patsy / Up where we belong: Cocker,
Joe & Jennifer Warnes / Slave to love: Ferry,
Bryan / Circle in the sand: Carlisle, Belinda
/ Rush rush: Abdul, Paula / I'd do anything
for love (but I won't do that): Meat Loaf /
Good heart: Sharkey, Feargal / (I just) died
in your arms: Cutting Crew / Who's that girl:
Eurythmics / You're all that matters to me:
Stigers, Curtis / Someday (I'm coming
back): Stansfield, Lisa / Just another day:
Secada, Jon / Don't turn around: Aswad /
All that she wants: Ace Of Base / Compli-
ments on your kiss: Red Dragon
CD Set _____ VTDCD 38
Virgin / Nov '94 / EMI.

LOVE ALBUM, THE II
(2CD/MC Set)
Goodnight girl: Wet Wet Wet / One more
night: Collins, Phil / I found someone: Cher
/ Let's stay together: Turner, Tina / All
around the world: Stansfield, Lisa / Ain't no
man: Carroll, Dina / I knew you were waiting
(for me): Franklin, Aretha & George Michael
/ Sexual healing: Gaye, Marvin / Endless
love: Ross, Diana & Lionel Richie / Unchained melody: Righteous Brothers / I
When a man loves a woman: Sledge, Percy
/ My girl: Temptations / Little time: Beautiful

South / I don't want to talk about it: Everything But The Girl / Hazard: Marx, Richard /
Show me heaven: McKee, Maria / Eternal
flame: Bangles / Without you: Nilsson / Walk
on by: Warwick, Dionne / Get here: Adams,
Oleta / Power of love: Rush, Jennifer / You
don't have to say you love me: Springfield,
Dusty / Cry me a river: Welch, Denise /
Stand by me: King, Ben E. / When I fall in
love: Cole, Nat King / China girl: Bowie, David / It must be love: Madness / Every time
you go away: Young, Paul / Damn I wish I
was your lover: Hawkins, Sophie B. / Independant love song: Scarlet / China in your
hand: T'Pau / I wonder why: Stigers, Curtis
/ Pray: Take That / Love me for a reason:
Boyzone / Crazy for you: Let Loose / Love
don't live here anymore: Nail, Jimmy / Jealous guy: Roxy Music / True: Spandau Ballet
CD Set _____ VTDCD 69
Virgin / Nov '95 / EMI.

LOVE AND NAPALM
CD _____ TRA 15D
Trance / Apr '93 / SRD.

LOVE BALLADS
Letter / All by myself / Doesn't somebody
want to be wanted: Cassidy, David / Light
my fire: Feliciano, Jose / Without you: Nilsson, Harry / You were on my mind: St. Philip's Choir / There goes my first love: Drifters
/ Moments like this: Francis, Joe / Love is
the sweetest thing: Skellern, Peter / I've just
fallen in love again: Murray, Anne / Rock
wit'cha: Brown, Bobby / Your song: John,
Elton / Saved by the bell: Gibb, Robin / Rain
and tears: Aphrodite's Child / Reason to believe: Stewart, Rod / You've lost that lovin'
feelin': Righteous Brothers / Need your love
so bad: Fleetwood Mac / Kiss and say
goodbye: Manhattans / Love really hurts
without you: Ocean, Billy / Tears on my pillow: Nash, Johnny
CD _____ STACD 024
Stardust / Nov '92 / Carlton Home
Entertainment.

LOVE BALLADS
CD Set _____ LOVECD 2
Connoisseur / Oct '94 / Pinnacle.

LOVE BITES
CD _____ QTVCD 022
Quality / Apr '93 / Pinnacle.

LOVE COLLECTION
(3CD/MC Set)
CD Set _____ TBXCD 510
TrueTrax / Jan '96 / THE.

LOVE COLLECTION, THE
Let there be love: Cole, Nat King / Folks
who live on the hill: Lee, Peggy / With these
hands: Monro, Matt / True love ways: Peter
& Gordon / Tonight: Damone, Vic / Where
do you go to my lovely: Sarstedt, Peter /
Rose Marie: Whitman, Slim / I've got my
love to keep me warm: Martin, Dean / What
now my love: Bassey, Shirley / Honey:
Goldsboro, Bobby / Tears: Dodd, Ken / Let
me go, lover: Murray, Ruby / Here in my
heart: Martino, Al / Somewhere my love:
Sammes, Mike Singers / She wears my ring:
King, Solomon / Hymn a l'amour: Piaf, Edith
/ I pretend (CD only.): O'Sullivan, Gilbert / My
special angel (CD only.): Vaughan, Malcolm
/ He was beautiful (CD only.): Williams, Iris
/ Wonder of you (CD only.): Hilton, Ronnie
CD _____ CDMFP 5878
Music For Pleasure / Mar '92 / EMI.

LOVE COLLECTION, THE II
Let's fall in love: Cole, Nat King / Autumn
leaves: Cole, Nat King / True love: Bing,
Bing & Grace Kelly / Softly as I leave you:
Monro, Matt / And we were lovers: Monro,
Matt / Something: Bassey, Shirley / Where
do I begin: Bassey, Shirley / Lady: Rogers,
Kenny / Don't fall in love with a dreamer:
Rogers, Kenny / Cry me a river: London, Ju-
lie / Spanish eyes: Martino, Al / By the time
I get to Phoenix: Campbell, Glen / Don't it
make my brown eyes blue: Gayle, Crystal /
Somebody loves you: Gayle, Crystal /
That's amore (That's love): Martin, Dean /
I've got my love to keep me warm: Martin,
Dean / Till there was you: Lee, Peggy / La
vie en rose: Piaf, Edith / On the street where
you live: Damone, Vic / How deep is the
ocean: Haymes, Dick
CD _____ CDMFP 5960
Music For Pleasure / Dec '92 / EMI.

LOVE CRAZY MEETS TALAWA
CD _____ 790152
Melodie / Nov '93 / Triple Earth /
Discovery / ADA / Jetstar.

I want to stay with you: Gallagher & Lyle /
Shine silently: Lofgren, Nils / What's another year: Logan, Johnny / Uptown uptempo woman (and the downtown, downbeat guy): Edelman, Randy / Crying: Gody &
Creme / Question: Moody Blues / Someone
saved my life tonight: John, Elton / On the
wings of a nightingale: Everly Brothers / I'm
doing fine now: New York City / Last thing
on my mind: Paxton, Tom / Together we're
beautiful: Kinney, Fern / Best thing that ever
happened to me: Knight, Gladys / Tears are
not enough: ABC / Amoureuse: Dee, Kiki /
If you asked me to: Labelle, Patti / When a
heart beasts: Kershaw, Nik / Free electric
band: Hammond, Albert / Help me make it

LOVE ETERNAL

through the night: *Kristofferson, Kris* / Lady of the dawn: *Batt, Mike*

CD _____ STACD 023
Stardust / Nov '92 / Carlton Home Entertainment.

LOVE ETERNAL
(2CD/MC Set)

Goodnight girl: *Wet Wet Wet* / I want to know what love is: *Foreigner* / Power of love: *Frankie Goes To Hollywood* / Dreams: *Gabrielle* / True: *Spandau Ballet* / Unchained melody: *Righteous Brothers* / Free: *Williams, Deniece* / Don't turn around: *Aswad* / Please don't go: *KWS* / Things can only get better: *D Ream* / Lay all your love on me: *Erasure* / Stay: *Shakespears Sister* / Ain't no doubt: *Nail, Jimmy* / I should have known better: *Diamond, Neil* / First time: *Beck, Robin* / Nothing's gonna stop us now: *Starship* / Young at heart: *Bluebells* / Wake me up before you go go: *Wham* / Oh pretty woman: *Orbison, Roy* / Good vibrations: *Beach Boys* / Sun always shines on TV: *A-Ha* / Frankie: *Sister Sledge* / Band of gold: *Payne, Freda* / You're the first, the last, my everything: *White, Barry* / I got you babe: *Sonny & Cher* / I want to wake up with you: *Gardiner, Boris* / Never gonna give you up: *Astley, Rick* / When you're in love with a beautiful woman: *Dr. Hook* / Total eclipse of the heart: *Tyler, Bonnie* / Without you: *Nilsson* / Would I lie to you: *Charles & Eddie* / Pray: *Take That* / I wanna see you up: *Color Me Badd* / Move closer: *Nelson, Phyllis* / Je t'aime... moi non plus: *Birkin, Jane & Serge Gainsbourgh* / Crying: *McLean, Don* / I'm not in love: *10cc* / Eternal flame: *Bangles* / He ain't heavy, he's my brother: *Hollies* / Tainted love: *Soft Cell* / Don't stand so close to me: *Police*

CD Set _____ MIRCD 0001
Carlton Home Entertainment / Feb '96 / Carlton Home Entertainment.

LOVE HURTS

CD _____ MATCD 275
Castle / Apr '93 / BMG.

LOVE IN THE SIXTIES

CD _____ DINCD 81
Dino / Dec '93 / Pinnacle / 3MV.

LOVE IS THE SWEETEST THING

CD _____ CDHD 186
Happy Days / Oct '92 / Conifer.

LOVE LETTERS

CD _____ MPV 5534
Movieplay / Sep '93 / Target/BMG.

LOVE OVER GOLD

CD _____ TCD 2684
Telstar / Feb '94 / BMG.

LOVE PARADE '94

CD Set _____ D 945013
Bunker/D'Vision / Dec '94 / Plastic Head.

LOVE, PEACE AND HAPPINESS
(2CD Set)

CD Set _____ DBG 53037
Double Gold / Jun '95 / Target/BMG.

LOVE POWER
(Hard To Find US Hot 100 Hits Of The 60's)

I got rhythm: *Happenings* / I'm gonna love you too: *Hullabaloo* / Music to watch girls by: *Crewe, Bob Generation* / Walkin' my cat named dog: *Tenaga, Norma* / Attack: *Toys* / Her lover: *Dovale, Debbie* / Her Royal Majesty: *Darren, James* / Big wide world: *Randazzo, Teddy* / When she needs good lovin': *Chicago Loopers* / Leader of the laundromat: *Detergents* / But it's alright: *Jackson, J.J.* / That boy John: *Raindrops* / Soul heaven: *Dixie Drifter* / Opportunity: *Jewels* / Love power: *Sandpebbles* / Happy: *Blades of Grass* / You better go: *Martin, Derek* / Countdown: *Cortez, Dave* / 'Baby' / Double O seven: *Detergents*

CD _____ NEMCD 669
Sequel / Jun '94 / BMG.

LOVE SONGS

Love in the first degree: *Bananarama* / Word up: *Cameo* / You are everything: *Stylistics* / If I can't have you: *Elliman, Yvonne* / It's over: *Level 42* / Wedding bells: *Godley & Creme* / Adult education: *Hall & Oates* / Slow hand: *Pointer Sisters* / Love on your side: *Thompson Twins* / Heated: *Grant, David & Jaki Graham* / Set me free: *Graham, Jaki* / Golden brown: *Stranglers* / Tell it like it is: *Johnson, Don* / Sweetest taboo: *Sade* / Heart on my sleeve: *Gallagher & Lyle* / Take that situation: *Heyward, Nick* / If you think you know how to love me: *Smokie* / Air that I breathe: *Hollies* / Everybody needs love: *Bishop, Stephen* / Suddenly: *Ocean, Billy*

CD _____ STACD 026
Stardust / Nov '92 / Carlton Home Entertainment.

LOVE SONGS OF DETROIT
(3CD Set)

Ain't no mountain high enough: *Payne, Scherrie* / Baby I'm for real: *Originals* / Yes I'm ready: *Weston, Kim* / If this world were mine: *Lawrence, Linda* / Reach for the sky: *Jacas, Jake* / My heart won't say no: *Demps, Louvain* / Baby baby: *Lewis Sisters* / London bridge is falling down: *Cameron, G.C.* / Slow motion: *Barnes, J.J.* / Does your Mama know about me: *Taylor, Bobby & The Vancouvers* / If I were your woman: *Royster,*

Vermettya / It's impossible: *Eckstine, Billy* / Easy to love: *Griner, Linda* / Two out of three: *Stubbs, Joe* / You're love is wonderful: *Littles, Hattie* / Take me in your arms and love me: *Nero, Frances* / Give me your love: *Royster, Vermettya* / Heaven knows: *Miracles* / You'll be sorry: *Fantastic Four* / Come back to me: *Cameron, G.C.* / Special day: *Gaye, Frankie* / Soul searching: *Randolph, Barbara* / Cloudy day: *Taylor, Bobby & The Vancouvers* / Reluctant lover: *Griffin, Billy* / Hold out my hand: *Jacas, Jake* / Ain't me soul: *Littles, Hattie* / Wholeheartedly: *McNeir, Ronnie* / Smiling faces sometimes: *Vee* / Teardrops: *Starr, Edwin* / Keeping my mind on love: *Wells, Mary* / Ask the lonely: *Eckstine, Billy* / Watching the hands of time: *Preston, Billy & Syreeta* / Tracks of my tears: *Contours* / Every little bit hurts: *Holloway, Brenda* / Time is on my side: *Littles, Hattie* / Gentle lady: *Eckstine, Billy* / Free: *Greene, Susaye* / Cry to me: *Crawford, Carolyn* / Love still lives in my heart: *Originals* / Keep this thought in mind: *Bristol, Johnny* / You haven't seen my love: *Taylor, Bobby & The Vancouvers* / With you I'm born again: *Syreeta* / For old times sake: *Jacas, Jake* / Too great a price to pay: *Lavette, Betty* / Just my imagination: *Cameron, G.C.* / Let's get it on: *McNeir, Ronnie* / OOO Baby baby: *Robinson, Claudette* / Wishing on a star: *Calvin, Billie* / Save me I'm all alone: *Dixon, Hank* / Your precious love: *Parks, Fino & Frances Nero* / We're incredible: *McNeir, Ronnie* / Written in stone: *Gaye, Frankie* / No more heartaches: *Bristol, Johnny*

CD Set _____ 30359 90065
Motor City / Jan '96 / Carlton Home Entertainment.

LOVE SONGS OF THE 50'S
(3CD Set)

My special agent: *Vaughan, Malcolm* / Tammy: *Lee, Brenda* / Stairway of love: *Holliday, Michael* / It's late: *Nelson, Rick* / May you always: *Regan, Joan* / I still believe: *Hilton, Ronnie* / Somebody loves me: *Shore, Dinah* / True love: *Crosby, Bing & Grace Kelly* / Only sixteen: *Douglas, Craig* / Holiday affair: *Day, Jill* / What do you want: *Faith, Adam* / Give a fool a chance: *Cogan, Alma* / Volare: *Martin, Dean* / If I give my heart to you: *Shelton, Anne* / Forgotten dreams: *Conway, Russ* / Now and forever: *Warren, Alma* / I may never pass this way again: *Lotis, Dennis* / Bewitched: *Squires, Dorothy* / Skye boat song: *Holliday, Michael* / St Therese of the roses: *Vaughan, Malcolm* / No other love: *Hilton, Ronnie* / Do do do do it again: *Vaughan, Frankie* / Secret that's never been told: *Squires, Dorothy* / Folks who live on the hill: *Holliday, Michael* / Sugar bush: *Boswell, Eve* / More than ever: *Vaughan, Malcolm* / Garden of Eden: *James, Dick* / That's happiness: *Cogan, Alma* / Happy days and lonely nights: *Murray, Ruby* / When I fall in love: *Cole, Nat King* / Song of the valley: *Squires, Dorothy* / I'm in love again: *Domino, Fats* / Arrivederci darling: *Shelton, Anne* / Sugartime: *Dale, Jim* / If you love me: *Boswell, Eve* / Lonely ballerina: *Lawrence, Lee* / To be worthy of you: *Squires, Dorothy* / Young and foolish: *Hilton, Ronnie* / From the time you say goodbye: *Miller, Gary* / How wonderful to know: *Carr, Pearl* / Never be anyone else but you: *Nelson, Rick* / Little things mean a lot: *Cogan, Alma* / Pickin' a chicken: *Boswell, Eve* / Did you ever see a dream walking: *Holliday, Michael* / Fever: *Lee, Peggy* / Be my girl: *Dale, Jim* / Wheel of fortune: *Starr, Kay* / For all we know: *Cole, Nat King* / Around the world: *Fields, Gracie* / Heartbeat: *Murray, Ruby* / Our song: *Squires, Dorothy* / Blueberry hill: *Domino, Fats* / Till there was you: *Lee, Peggy* / Too young: *Cole, Nat King* / Nevertheless (I'm in love with you): *Murray, Ruby* / Very thought of you: *Cole, Nat King* / Gypsy in my soul: *Boswell, Eve* / My darling, my darling: *Miller, Gary* / Blue tango: *Cogan, Alma* / Wonder of you: *Hilton, Ronnie*

CD Set _____ CDTRBOX 180
Music For Pleasure / Oct '95 / EMI.

LOVE SONGS OF THE 60'S

God only knows: *Beach Boys* / Moon river: *Williams, Danny* / I'll never fall in love again: *Gentry, Bobbie* / I remember you: *Ifield, Frank* / To know you is to love you: *Peter & Gordon* / If you gotta go, go now: *Manfred Mann* / She wears my ring: *King, Solomon* / I could easily fall: *Richard, Cliff* / Step inside love: *Black, Cilla* / Softly as I leave you: *Monro, Matt* / When the girl in your arms (is the girl in your heart): *Richard, Cliff* / Here I go again: *Hollies* / Starry eyed: *Holiday, Michael* / Portrait of my love: *Monro, Matt* / Love's just a broken heart: *Black, Cilla* / I have to do is dream: *Campbell, Glen & Bobbie Gentry* / Michelle: *David & Jonathan* / Up on the roof: *Lynch, Kenny* / As long as he needs me / There's a kind of hush: *Herman's Hermits*

CD _____ CDMFP 6041
Music For Pleasure / Sep '88 / EMI.

LOVE SONGS OF THE 60'S

I only want to be with you: *Springfield, Dusty* / Little things: *Berry, Dave* / When you walk in the room: *Searchers* / Last night was made for love: *Fury, Billy* / (If paradise is) half as nice: *Amen Corner* / Game of love: *Fontana, Wayne & The Mindbenders* / It's all in the game: *Richard, Cliff* / My ship

is comin' in: *Walker Brothers* / You're my world: *Black, Cilla* / To know you is to love you: *Peter & Gordon* / God only knows: *Beach Boys* / Wishin' and hopin': *Merseybeats* / Unchained melody: *Righteous Brothers* / Tell Laura I love her: *Valance, Ricky* / You're sixteen: *Burnette, Johnny Rock 'N' Roll Trio* / There's a kind of hush: *Herman's Hermits* / Do you want to know a secret: *Kramer, Billy J. & The Dakotas* / Do you love me: *Poole, Brian & The Tremeloes* / Just one look: *Hollies* / Long live love: *Shaw, Sandie*

CD _____ CDPR 115
Premier/MFP / Nov '93 / EMI.

LOVE SONGS OF THE 60'S
(3CD Set)

I can't give you anything but love: *Cogan, Alma* / That I've found you: *Cogan, Alma* / Eight days a week: *Cogan, Alma* / Up on the roof: *Lynch, Kenny* / Ramblin' rose: *Cole, Nat King* / Look through any window: *Hollies* / We're through: *Hollies* / Yes I will: *Hollies* / I'm alive: *Hollies* / Love letters: *Black, Cilla* / I've been wrong before: *Black, Cilla* / Lover's concerto: *Black, Cilla* / One little voice: *Black, Cilla* / Poor boy: *Black, Cilla* / Don't answer me: *Black, Cilla* / Got to get you into my life: *Bennett, Cliff & The Rebel Rousers* / Something wonderful: *Shapiro, Helen* / I wish I'd never loved you: *Shapiro, Helen* / Tell me what he said: *Shapiro, Helen* / Walk on by: *Shapiro, Helen* / Boy without a girl: *Hilton, Ronnie* / It's yourself: *Bassey, Shirley* / Don't take the lovers from the world: *Bassey, Shirley* / I (who have nothing): *Bassey, Shirley* / Message to Martha: *Faith, Adam* / Cheryl's goin' home: *Faith, Adam* / We're gonna change the world: *Monro, Matt* / Yesterday: *Monro, Matt* / Portrait of my love: *Monro, Matt* / Hello young lovers: *Monro, Matt* / True love ways: *Peter & Gordon* / Woman: *Peter & Gordon* / If we only have love: *Lynn, Vera* / Somewhere: *Proby, P.J.* / I'm coming home: *Proby, P.J.* / You've come back: *Proby, P.J.* / To make a big man cry: *Proby, P.J.* / Some enchanted evening: *Proby, P.J.* / You don't know: *Shapiro, Helen* / Let's pretend: *Lulu* / Without him: *Lulu* / Best of both worlds: *Lulu* / There must be a way: *Vaughan, Frankie* / There I go: *Carr, Vikki* / Michelle: *David & Jonathan* / Someone other than me: *Squires, Dorothy* / Say it with flowers: *Squires, Dorothy* / How deep is the ocean: *Squires, Dorothy* / Do you want to know a secret: *Kramer, Billy J. & The Dakotas* / Trains and boats and planes: *Kramer, Billy J. & The Dakotas* / Edelweiss: *Hill, Vince* / Look around: *Hill, Vince* / Moon river: *Williams, Danny* / Wonderful world of the young: *Williams, Danny* / More Williams, Danny / Girl on a swing: *Gerry & The Pacemakers* / Fly me to the moon: *Cogan, Alma* / Here there and everywhere: *Kirby, Kathy* / Love is all: *Roberts, Malcolm*

CD Set _____ CDTRBOX 184
Music For Pleasure / Oct '95 / EMI.

LOVE SONGS OF THE 70'S

If I had words: *Fitzgerald, Scott & Yvonne Keeley* / Loving you: *Riperton, Minnie* / When you're in love with a beautiful woman: *Dr. Hook* / And I love you so: *McLean, Don* / I don't wanna lose your love: *Candidate* / Love hit me: *Nightingale, Maxine* / More than a woman: *Tavares* / Storm in a teacup / Turn it: *Carr, Vikki* / I can't let the bottom from the top: *Hollies* / Talking in your sleep: *Gayle, Crystal* / You'll always be a friend: *Hot Chocolate* / Softly whispering I love you: *Congregation* / Honey come back: *Campbell, Glen* / Lay your love on me: *Racey* / What I've got in mind: *Spears, Billie Jo* / Let me be the one: *Shadows* / I honestly love you (CD only.): *Newton-John, Olivia* / Summer (the first time) (CD only.): *Goldsboro, Bobby* / Oh babe what would you say (CD only.): *Smith, Hurricane* / Lucille (CD only.): *Rogers, Kenny*

CD Set _____ CDMFP 5894
Music For Pleasure / Sep '90 / EMI.

LOVE SONGS OF THE 70'S

Little bit more: *Dr. Hook* / Your song: *John, Elton* / Torn between two lovers: *MacGregor, Mary* / I believe (in love): *Hot Chocolate* / Stay with me till dawn: *Tzuke, Judie* / September: *Earth, Wind & Fire* / It not for you: *Newton-John, Olivia* / Lovely day: *Withers, Bill* / Hold me close: *Essex, David* / Who pays the ferryman: *Hart, Yannis* / Reunited: *Peaches & Herb* / You make me feel brand new: *Stylistics* / Best thing that ever happened to me: *Knight, Gladys & The Pips* / Can't get by without you: *Real Thing* / If you think you know how to love me: *Smokie* / It's in his kiss (Shoop shoop song): *Lewis, Linda* / All of me (loves all of you): *Bay City Rollers* / I'm always touched by your) presence dear: *Blondie*

CD _____ CDPR 116
Premier/MFP / Nov '93 / EMI.

LOVE SONGS OF THE 70'S
(3CD Set)

Air that I breathe: *Hollies* / When you're in love with a beautiful woman: *Dr. Hook* / Journey: *Browne, Duncan* / Storm in a teacup: *Fortunes* / Both sides now: *Laine, Cleo* / Softly whispering I love you: *Congregation* / Talking in your sleep: *Gayle, Crystal* / Put your love me: *Hot Chocolate* / Living nest

door to Alice: *Smokie* / I will survive: *Spears, Billie Jo* / Dream baby: *Campbell, Glen* / Dancing in the city: *Marshall Hain* / Right back where we started from: *Nightingale, Maxine* / Everyday: *McLean, Don* / January: *Pilot* / Where do I begin: *Bassey, Shirley* / And you smiled: *Monro, Matt* / She believes in me: *Rogers, Kenny* / This will be: *Cole, Natalie* / I don't want to put a hold on you: *Flint, Bernie* / If you can't give me love: *Quatro, Suzi* / If we only have love: *Newton-John, Olivia* / You take my heart away: *Bassey, Shirley* / Little bit more: *Dr. Hook* / He was beautiful: *Williams, Iris* / Just a smile: *Pilot* / Honey come back: *Campbell, Glen* / Somebody loves me: *Gayle, Crystal* / Darlin': *Miller, Frankie* / Love you more: *Buzzcocks* / I don't know how to love him: *Trent, Jackie* / Amourease: *Newton-John, Olivia* / If you think you know how to love me: *Smokie* / And I love you so: *McLean, Don* / Don't it make my brown eyes blue: *Gayle, Crystal* / Winterwood: *McLean, Don* / Make the world a little younger: *Bassey, Shirley* / She's in love with you: *Quatro, Suzi* / My last night with you: *Arrows* / Hi ho silver lining: *Beck, Jeff* / Freedom come, freedom go: *Fortunes* / When am I supposed to do: *Williams, Iris* / I'll put you together again: *Hot Chocolate* / Sam: *Newton-John, Olivia* / Lovin' you: *Riperton, Minnie*

CD Set _____ CDTRBOX 188
Music For Pleasure / Oct '95 / EMI.

LOVE SONGS OF THE 80'S

Missing you: *Waite, John* / Crying: *McLean, Don* / Better love next time: *Dr. Hook* / Unchain my heart: *Cocker, Joe* / Round and round: *Graham, Jaki* / It started with a kiss: *Hot Chocolate* / Classic: *Gurvitz, Adrian* / Lady: *Rogers, Kenny* / Chequered love: *Wilde, Kim* / Love changes everything: *Climie Fisher* / Tonight I celebrate my love: *Bryson, Peabo & Roberta Flack* / Rock me tonight: *Jackson, Freddie* / Let's go all the way: *Sly Fox* / Save a prayer: *Duran Duran*

CD _____ CDMFP 5927
Music For Pleasure / Oct '91 / EMI.

LOVE SONGS OF THE 80'S

Look of love: *ABC* / Hold me now: *Thompson Twins* / My favourite waste of time: *Paul, Owen* / Tell it to my heart: *Dayne, Taylor* / Can't fight this feeling: *REO Speedwagon* / I'm your man: *Wham* / (Feels like) heaven: *Fiction Factory* / Room in your heart: *Living In A Box* / Love in the first degree: *Bananarama* / Tonight I celebrate my love: *Bryson, Peabo & Roberta Flack* / Could it be I'm falling in love: *Grant, David & Jaki Graham* / Solid: *Ashford & Simpson* / Never knew love like this before: *Mills, Stephanie* / Slowhand: *Pointer Sisters* / Never too much: *Vandross, Luther* / Love changes everything *Climie Fisher* / Perfect skin: *Cole, Lloyd & The Commotions* / When I fall in love: *Astley, Rick* / Your love is king: *Sade* / She makes my day: *Palmer, Robert*

CD _____ CDPR 117
Premier/MFP / Nov '93 / EMI.

LOVE SONGS OF THE 80'S
(3CD Set)

We close our eyes: *Go West* / Sharing the night together: *Dr. Hook* / Maybe (we should call it a day): *Dean, Hazell* / Too shy: *Kajagoogoo* / One man woman: *Easton, Sheena* / Love don't live here anymore: *Nail, Jimmy* / Respect: *Adeva* / I'll fly for you: *Spandau Ballet* / Lady: *Rogers, Kenny* / Passing strangers: *Ultravox* / Tears on the telephone: *Hot Chocolate* / Chequered love: *Wilde, Kim* / Let's go all the way: *Sly Fox* / Could it be I'm falling in love: *Grant, David & Jaki Graham* / Turn back the clock: *Johnny Hates Jazz* / California dreamin': *River City People* / Love action: *Human League* / Searchin': *Dean, Hazell* / Years from now: *Dr. Hook* / Walking on sunshine: *Katrina & The Waves* / It started with a kiss: *Hot Chocolate* / Just another broken heart: *Easton, Sheena* / When he shines: *Easton, Sheena* / Castles in the air: *McLean, Don* / Have you ever been in love: *Sayer, Leo* / If I only could: *Youngblood, Sydney* / Set me free: *Graham, Jaki* / Goodbye girl: *Go West* / When will I see you again: *Brother Beyond* / Rise to the occasion: *Climie Fisher* / Love changes everything: *Climie Fisher* / New from a bridge: *Wilde, Kim* / That certain smile: *Ultravox* / We've got tonight: *Rogers, Kenny* / Harder I try: *Brother Beyond* / Who's leaving who: *Dean, Hazell* / Kayleigh: *Marillion* / Summertime: *Fun Boy Three* / Love will find a way: *Grant, David* / Crying: *McLean, Don* / Until you come back to me: *Sayer, Leo* / Shattered dreams: *Johnny Hates Jazz* / Missing you: *Waite, John* / Unchain my heart: *Cocker, Joe*

CD Set _____ CDTRBOX 192
Music For Pleasure / Oct '95 / EMI.

LOVE SONGS OF VIDYAPATI
(Traditional Indian Songs)

CD _____ C 580063CD
Ocora / Apr '95 / Harmonia Mundi / ADA.

LOVE SONGS WITH SOUL

CD _____ EMPRCD 551
Emporio / Nov '94 / THE / Disc / CM.

LOVE SUPREME

CD _____ DINCD 19
Dino / Jun '91 / Pinnacle / 3MV.

LOVE TO LOVE YOU
Daniel: *John, Elton* / Baby makes her blue jeans talk: *Dr. Hook* / Day by day: *Shakatak* / Fresh: *Kool & The Gang* / Nothing's gonna change my love for you: *Medeiros, Glenn* / Forever and ever: *Roussos, Demis* / Love me: *Elliman, Yvonne* / Reason to believe: *Stewart, Rod* / Soul and inspiration: *Walker Brothers* / I'm not in love: *10cc* / Sun ain't gonna shine anymore: *Walker Brothers* / Let's put it all together: *Stylistics* / Don't stop the music: *Yarbrough & Peoples* / Tahiti: *Essex, David*
CD _____ 5501442
Spectrum/Karussell / Jan '94 / PolyGram / THE.

LOVE WITH A REGGAE RHYTHM
CD _____ VISCD 13
Vision / Apr. '95 / Pinnacle.

LOVE...NIGHT MOODS
CD _____ STACD 049
Stardust / Sep '94 / Carlton Home Entertainment.

LOVER'S DELIGHT
Don't let me be lonely: *Kofi* / I'll never fall in love: *Klearview Harmonix* / Children of the night: *Cross, Sandra* / Give you love: *Jones, Vivian* / I'm the one who loves you: *Hartley, Trevor* / Can't hold on: *McLean, John* / Even though you're gone: *Kemi* / Hottest shot: *Kingpin* / Last night: *Tajah, Paulette* / Love in your heart: *Shaloma*
CD _____ ARICD 090
Ariwa Sounds / Oct '93 / Jetstar / SRD.

LOVERS FOR LOVERS VOL. 1
CD _____ WBRCD 901
Business / Jan '91 / Jetstar.

LOVERS FOR LOVERS VOL. 10
I miss you: *Heptones* / Just my imagination: *Mighty Diamonds* / Blackbirds singing: *Paragons* / Chuck E's in love: *Walker, Paulette* / Make up to break up: *Heptones* / Dance the reggae: *Harriott, Derrick* / Paradise: *Gayle, Erica* / Last chance: *Kelly, Pat* / Don't draw the line: *Gayle, Erica* / Golden touch* / All that glitters
CD _____ WBRCD 910
Business / Dec '95 / Jetstar.

LOVERS FOR LOVERS VOL. 2
CD _____ WBRCD 902
Business / Jan '91 / Jetstar.

LOVERS FOR LOVERS VOL. 3
CD _____ WBRCD 903
Business / Jan '91 / Jetstar.

LOVERS FOR LOVERS VOL. 4
CD _____ WBRCD 904
Business / Jan '92 / Jetstar.

LOVERS FOR LOVERS VOL. 5
CD _____ WBRCD 905
Business / Oct '95 / Jetstar.

LOVERS FOR LOVERS VOL. 5 & 6
CD _____ WBRCD 905/6
Business / Oct '95 / Jetstar.

LOVERS FOR LOVERS VOL. 6
CD _____ WBRCD 906
Business / Aug '92 / Jetstar.

LOVERS FOR LOVERS VOL. 7
CD _____ WBRCD 907
Business / Dec '93 / Jetstar.

LOVERS FOR LOVERS VOL. 8
CD _____ WBRCD 908
Business / Dec '93 / Jetstar.

LOVERS FOR LOVERS VOL. 9
CD _____ WBRCD 909
Business / Dec '94 / Jetstar.

LOVERS FOREVER VOL.3
CD _____ JFCD 0004
Joe Frazier / Jun '94 / Jetstar.

LOVERS MOODS VOL.2
CD _____ VPCD 1447
VP / Nov '95 / Jetstar.

LOVERS ROCK SERIOUS SELECTIONS VOL.1
Key to the world: *Thomas, Rudy* / Baby my love: *Callender, Fil* / After tonight: *Matumbi* / Natty dread a weh she want: *Andy, Horace & Tapper* / Wide awake in dreams: *Biggs, Barry* / Let me be your angel: *Morgan, Portia* / Ting a ling: *Tamlins* / Betcha by Golly Wow: *Dunkley, Errol* / Paradise: *Adebambo, Jean* / Lady of magic: *Maloney, Bunny* / Walk on by: *Motion* / Caught you in a lie: *Marks, Louisa*
CD _____ CDREG 1
Rewind Selecta / Feb '95 / Grapevine.

LOVERS ROCK SERIOUS SELECTIONS VOL.2
CD _____ CDREG 4
Rewind Selecta / Jan '06 / Grapevine.

LOVE'S OLD SWEET SONG
Myself when young: *Allin, Norman* / Homing: *D'Alvarez, Marguerite* / Deep river: *Anderson, Marian* / Fairytales of Ireland: *Austral, Florence* / Ciribiribin: *Bori, Lucrezia* / She wandered down the mountainside: *Buckman, Rosina* / Fairy went a-marketing: *Butt, Clara* / For you alone: *Caruso, Enrico* / Blind ploughman: *Chaliapin, Feodor* / Ich liebe dich, my dear: *Crabbe, Armand* / Song of songs: *Crooks, Richard* / Green hills of Somerset: *Dawson, Peter* / Love's old

sweet song: *Galli-Curci, Amelita* / I love you truly: *Giannini, Dusolina* / World is waiting for the sunrise: *Hackett, Charles* / Danny boy: *Labette, Dora* / Bird songs at Eventide: *McCormack, John* / By the waters of Minnetonka: *Melba, Nellie* / By the bend of the river: *Moore, Grace* / Last rose of Summer: *Patti, Adelina* / Love sends a little gift of roses: *Piccaver, Alfred* / Perfect day: *Ponsella, Rosa* / Kashmiri song: *Tauber, Richard* / I know of two bright eyes: *Widdop, Walter* / Leanin': *Williams, Harold*
CD AJA 5130
Living Era / May '94 / Koch.

LOVE'S TRAIN: THE BEST OF FUNK ESSENTIAL BALLADS
CD _____ 5260912
Mercury / Sep '95 / PolyGram.

LOVING YOU
CD Set _____ MBSCD 428
Castle / Nov '93 / BMG.

LOWLANDS
CD _____ ELEC 8CD
New Electronica / May '94 / Pinnacle / Plastic Head.

LUO ROOTS
Jadiyana: *Kapere Jazz Band* / Nath oindo: *Kapere Jazz Band* / Amagy lando: *Kapere Jazz Band* / Tum nyamwalo: *Kapere Jazz Band* / Samwel adinda: *Kapere Jazz Band* / Jacob Omolo: *Okoth, Ogwang Lelo* / Lando nyaseme: *Kapere Jazz Band* / Amisijamoko: *Kapere Jazz Band* / John Wangu: *Okoth, Ogwang Lelo* / Lynette: *Onono, Paddy J*
CD _____ CDORBD 061
Globestyle / Jun '90 / Pinnacle.

LUTZ R MASTERHAYER
CD _____ SPCD 111287
Sub Pop / Aug '93 / Disc.

LYRICS PUISSANCE 4
CD _____ 503822
Declic / Apr '95 / Jetstar.

M

M-8 EURO TECHNO HEAVEN
CD _____ CDTOT 29
Jumpin' & Pumpin' / May '95 / 3MV / Sony.

M8 DJ TECHNOTRANCE
CD _____ CDTOT 35
Jumpin' & Pumpin' / Jan '96 / 3MV / Sony.

MACEDONIAN DANCES
CD _____ PS 65076
Playasound / Jul '91 / Harmonia Mundi / ADA.

MACHINO WEIRDER
CD _____ DUKE 017CD
Hydrogen Dukebox / Jun '95 / Vital / 3MV.

MACRO DUB INFECTION VOL.1
(2CD/3LP Set)
Struggle of life: *Disciples* / Double edge: *Spring Heel Jack* / Sergio Mendez part 1: *Two Badcard* / Astral altar dub: *Automaton* / Broadway boogie woogie: *Bedouin Ascent* / Wadada: *Rootsman* / Hills are alive: *Coil* / Half cut: *Omni Trio* / If you miss: *Laika* / Crush your enemies: *New Kingdom* / Goriri: *Tortoise* / Operation mind control: *Skull Vs Ice* / Morocco: *Alzir, Bud* / Beta, seekers of smooth things: *Plutobeat* / Paranormal in four tomes: 4 *Hero* / This is how it feels: *Golden Palaminos* / Ragga doll: *Mad Professor* / Phora ride: *Wagon Christ* / End: *Scorn* / Ambient pumpkin: *Tricky* / Iration Steppas vs Dennis Rootical: *Iration Steppas* / Come forward: *Bandulu* / Nothingness: *Earthling*
CD Set _____ AMBT 7
Virgin / May '95 / EMI.

MAD ABOUT THE BOY
(Songs From The Best Known TV Commercials)
CD _____ MPV 5521
Movieplay / Jun '92 / Target/BMG.

MAD ABOUT THE GIRLS
Mad about the boy: *Washington, Dinah* / All through the night: *Lauper, Cyndi* / Dreams: *Gabrielle* / I ain't movin': *Des'ree* / Love is here to stay: *Fitzgerald, Ella* / Shadow of your smile: *Gilberto, Astrud* / Bewitched, bothered and bewildered: *Fygi, Laura* / Fever: *Lee, Peggy* / Don't let me be misunderstood: *Simone, Nina* / Gone with the wind: *Page, Patti* / Make yourself comfortable: *Vaughan, Sarah* / Some of your lovin': *Springfield, Dusty* / Use me: *Goodman, Gabrielle* / Bad day: *Carmel* / Lover man: *Holiday, Billie* / Round Midnight: *Wilson, Cassandra* / I should go home: *London, Julie* / Move over darling: *Day, Doris* / Crazy: *Cline, Patsy* / Perfect year: *Carroll, Dina*
CD _____ 5255552
PolyGram TV / Jun '95 / PolyGram.

MAD DOG
CD _____ NWSCD 5
New Sound / Apr '93 / Jetstar.

MAD LOVE
Slowly slowly: *Magnapop* / Scratch: 7 *Year Bitch* / Here comes my girl: *Throneberry* / Mokingbirds: *Grant Lee Buffalo* / Glazed: *Rocket From The Crypt* / Fallout: *Florescien* / Mona Lisa fallout: *Head Candy* / Ultra anxiety: *Madder Rose* / Icy blue: 7 *Year Bitch* / As long as you hold me: *MacColl, Kirsty*
CD _____ DEDCD 022
Dedicated / Dec '95 / Vital.

MADAGASCAR
CD _____ G 7504
Sterns / '87 / Sterns / CM.

MADAGASIKARA 1
Afindrafindraq: *Rakotoarimanana, Rakotofra & Martin* / Feam baliha: *Tombo, Daniel & Marceline Vaviroa* / Dia mahaory: *Tombo, Daniel & Marceline Vaviroa* / Bonne annee amin ny tanana: *Norbert, Georges & L. Honore Rosa* / Mamakivaky alankiminina: *Norbert, Georges & L. Honore Rosa* / Fambelo eto madagasikara: *Rabenalivo Group* / Nilentika: *Andriamamonjy, David* / Tazana kely: *Andriamamonjy, David* / Mahatsiarotsiaro fanina aeo zeho: *Volambita, Tsimialona* / Nametaa imaintso: *Volambita, Tsimialona* / King's song: *Rakotoarimanana, Martin* / Viavy rosy: *Randriamainty, Emmanuel* / Kilalao: *Ze Ze et groupe son*
CD _____ CDORBD 012
Globestyle / Oct '90 / Pinnacle.

MADAGASIKARA 2
Raha mania any / Ento rora / Madirovalo / Tsapika 2000 / Totoy tsara / Sarotra / Voromby / Ny any / Malaza avaratna / Aza mba manary toky
CD _____ CDORBD 013
Globestyle / Nov '90 / Pinnacle.

MADCHESTER
CD _____ MADCCD 1
Beechwood / Oct '95 / BMG / Pinnacle.

MADE TO MEASURE RESUME...
CD _____ MTM 16CD
Made To Measure / Mar '88 / Grapevine.

MADE TO MEASURE VOLUME 1
Pieces for nothing / A la recherche: *Lew, Benjamin* / Un chien: *Maboul, Aksak* / Scratch holiday: *Maboul, Aksak* / Verdun: *Tuxedo Moon*
CD _____ MTM 1CD
Made To Measure / '88 / Grapevine.

MADHOUSE CREW LIVE
CD _____ 793012
Jammy's / Jan '94 / Jetstar.

MADNESS INVASION VOL.1
CD _____ 842624
EVA / Jun '94 / Direct / ADA.

MAFIA & FLUXY PRESENT...
Money first (Mystery mix): *Banton, Mega* / World a girls: *Demus, Chaka & Pliers* / Looking girl: *General, Ricky* / Nah let go: *Demus, Junior* / Take a gal man: *Johnny P.* / Armed and dangerous (Remix): *Cutty Ranks* / Where did you get your looks from: *Irie, Sweetie & Debbie G* / Gun legalize: *Dirtsman* / Hugging and kissing: *Judas* / Feelings: *Jack Radics* / Money first: *Banton, Mega* / Armed and dangerous: *Cutty Ranks*
CD _____ 74321 20997-2
RCA / Oct '94 / BMG.

MAGIC CHRISTMAS
CD _____ 15148
Laserlight / Nov '91 / Target/BMG.

MAGIC MOMENTS
CD _____ CWNCD 2005
Javelin / Jun '95 / THE / Henry Hadaway Organisation.

MAGIC OF BRASS, THE
Macarthur park / Always on my mind / Don't leave me this way / Bohemian rhapsody / Tritsch tratsch polka / You can call me Al / Carnival for brass / You've lost that lovin' feelin' / Get back / All I ask of you / Shepherd's song / Hello / Pie jesu / Puttin' on the ritz
CD _____ MUCD 9003
Start / Apr '95 / Koch.

MAGIC OF IRELAND, THE
Grace: *McCann, Jim* / When you and I were young Maggie: *Doonican, Val* / My lovely rose of Clare: *Reilly, Paddy* / When you were sweet sixteen: *Fureys & Davey Arthur* / Pal of my cradle days: *Breen, Ann* / Lovely Nancy: *Dubliners* / When I leave the world behind: *Rose Marie* / Don't forget to remember: *O'Donnell, Daniel* / Daddy's hands: *Duff, Mary* / Wedding song: *Duncan, Hugo* / Village of Astee: *McCann, Susan* / Veil of white lace: *O'Brien, Michael* / I know that you know (that I love you): *Hogan, John* / Gentle Mother: *Big Tom & The Mainliners*
CD _____ ECD 3048
K-Tel / Jun '95 / K-Tel.

MAGIC OF IRELAND, THE
(4CD Set)
CD Set _____ EMPRBX 007
Emporio / Oct '95 / THE / Disc / CM.

MAGIC OF THE INDIAN FLUTE
CD _____ EUCD 1090
ARC / '89 / ARC Music / ADA.

MAGIC OF THE INDIAN FLUTE, VOL. 2
CD _____ EUCD 1129
ARC / '91 / ARC Music / ADA.

MAGIC SOUND OF THE PAN PIPES, THE
CD _____ EMPRCD 511
Emporio / Apr '94 / THE / Disc / CM.

MAGIC SOUND OF THE PAN PIPES, THE
(4CD Set)
CD Set _____ EMPRBX 005
Emporio / Sep '94 / THE / Disc / CM.

MAGIC WURLITZER, THE
CD _____ PLATCD 31
Platinum Music / Apr '92 / Prism / Ross.

MAGIC WURLITZER, THE VOL. 2
CD _____ PLATCD 34
Platinum Music / Jul '92 / Prism / Ross.

MAGICAL 50'S, THE
(3CD Set)
Fanfar boogie: *Winstone, Eric & His Orchestra* / Rhythm and blues: *Winstone, Eric & His Orchestra* / Anticipation: *Winstone, Eric & His Orchestra* / Cobblers song: *Winstone, Eric & His Orchestra* / Deep sleep: *Winstone, Eric & His Orchestra* / Frustration: *Winstone, Eric & His Orchestra* / Slow train blues: *Winstone, Eric & His Orchestra* / Cat walk: *Winstone, Eric & His Orchestra* / Opus one: *Winstone, Eric & His Orchestra* / Heartbreak: *Winstone, Eric & His Orchestra* / Don't care: *Winstone, Eric & His Orchestra* / Angelina: *Winstone, Eric & His Orchestra* / At the woodchoppers: *Winstone, Eric & His Orchestra* / Drum crazy: *Johnson, Laurie Orchestra* / Heat wave: *Johnson, Laurie Orchestra* / In a persian market: *Johnson, Laurie Orchestra* / Fascinating rhythm: *Johnson, Laurie Orchestra* / Hallelujah: *Johnson, Laurie Orchestra* / Jamboree: *Johnson, Laurie Orchestra* / It might as well be spring: *Johnson, Laurie Orchestra* / Majorca: *Johnson, Laurie Orchestra* / Stick and twist: *Johnson, Laurie Orchestra* / Things we did last summer: *Johnson, Laurie Orchestra* / Next train out of town: *Osbourne, Tony* / Treasure of love: *Osbourne, Tony* / Mad at her: *Ryan, Marion* / Bell bottom blues: *Radio Revellers* / No not much: *Shepherd, Pauline* / Answer me: *Goff, Reggie* / Allen town jail: *Roza, Lita* / Maybe you'll be there: *Roza, Lita* / Once in a while: *Roza, Lita* / Sixteen tons: *Hockridge, Edmund* / Tomorrow: *Brandon, Johnny* / Bidge of sighs: *Goff, Reggie* / So many times I cried over you: *Goff, Reggie* / Arrivederci darling: *Radio Revellers* / That's how a love song is born: *Clark, Petula* / Moon above Malaya: *Goff, Reggie* / Mariandi: *Young, Jimmy & Petula Clark* / Hot diggity: *Ryan, Marion* / Rags to riches: *Goff, Reggie* / Who are we: *Miller, Betty* / Memories are made of this: *Clark, Petula* / Young and foolish: *Hockridge, Edmund* / Too young: *Young, Jimmy* / Undecided: *Roy, Harry* / I'll make you: *Preager, Lou & His Orchestra* / Oranges and lemons: *Delaney, Eric & His Band* / Three bears: *Ellington, Ray Quartet* / Baker's boogie: *Baker, Kenny Orchestra* / Mountain greenery: *Roy, Harry & His Orchestra* / Stranger than fiction: *Geraldo & His Orchestra* / Over wyoming: *Gibbons, Carroll* / Please Mr. Sun: *Roy, Harry* / Rocking the tymps: *Delaney, Eric & His Band* / Francesca: *Gibbons, Carroll* / Egon: *Bowlly, Al* / Sydney / Our love is here to stay: *Baker, Kenny Orchestra* / Cross hands boogie: *Roy, Harry* / Piano rag: *Preager, Lou & His Orchestra* / Teddy bears picnic: *Ellington, Ray Quartet* / I'm beginning to see the light: *Delaney, Eric & His Band* / Flirtation waltz: *Roy, Harry & His Band*
CD Set _____ MAGPIE 5
See For Miles/C5 / Sep '95 / Pinnacle.

MAGICAL SOUNDS OF THE WURLITZER
CD _____ MCCD 207
Music Club / Jul '95 / Disc / THE / CM.

MAGNETIC SUBMISSION
CD _____ EFA 200792
Submission / Dec '95 / SRD.

MAGNIFICENT 14, THE
CD _____ CDTRL 283
Trojan / Mar '94 / Jetstar / Total/BMG.

MAGNUM MYSTERIUM
CD _____ CDCEL 1635188
Celestial Harmonies / Jun '87 / ADA / Select.

MAGYARPALATKA
CD _____ SYNCD 152
Syncoop / Jun '93 / ADA / Direct.

MAIN COURSE
CD _____ REDEURO 2
Red Eye / Nov '94 / Direct.

MAINSTREAM MASTERS, THE
CD _____ JHR 73529
Jazz Hour / May '93 / Target/BMG / Jazz Music / Cadillac.

MAITRES DU BOOGIE WOOGIE
CD Set _____ OJCCD 700422
Original Jazz Classics / Dec '93 / Wellard / Jazz Music / Cadillac / Complete/Pinnacle.

MAITRES DU NEW ORLEANS
CD Set _____ OJCCD 700412
Original Jazz Classics / Dec '93 / Wellard /
Jazz Music / Cadillac / Complete/Pinnacle.

MAKE IT EASY
Make it easy on yourself: Walker Brothers /
Unchained melody: Righteous Brothers /
Green grass of home: Jones, Tom / Blue
velvet: Vinton, Bobby / Need your hand in
the world: Rich, Charlie / Always on my
mind: Nelson, Willie / Lovely day: Withers,
Bill / January February: Dickson, Barbara / I
can see clearly now: Nash, Johnny / Syl-
via's mother: Dr. Hook / Release me: Hum-
perdinck, Engelbert / Nights in white satin:
Moody Blues / I just don't know what to do
with myself: Springfield, Dusty / Forever au-
tumn: Hayward, Justin / King of the road:
Miller, Roger / You're a lady: Skellern, Peter
/ Stand by your man: Wynette, Tammy /
Last farewell: Whittaker, Roger
CD _____ MUSCD 003
MCI / Nov '92 / Disc / THE.

MAKE IT FUNKY
(Connoisseur Soul Collection - Volume
5)
Movin': Brass Construction / Shack up:
Banbarra / Hustle on up: Hidden Strength /
Funky stuff: Kool & The Gang / Who'd she
coo: Ohio Players / Put your body in it: Mills,
Stephanie / Make it funky: Brown, James /
Rigamortis: Cameo / Giving up food for
funk: J.B. Allstars / Zone: Rhythm Makers /
We've got the funk: Positive Force / Hyper-
tension: Calender / Changing: Brass
Construction
CD _____ RNBCD 105
Connoisseur / Oct '93 / Pinnacle.

MAKE THE WORLD GO AWAY
(20 Classic Love Songs)
Ain't no pleasing you: Chas & Dave / Whis-
pering: Bachelors / This is my song: Clark,
Petula / Make me an island: Dolan, Joe /
Make the world go away: Rose Marie /
When my little girl is smiling: Justice, Jimmy
/ Medley: Knight, Gladys & The Pips / One
day at a time: Martell, Lena / Little bitty tear:
Miki & Griff / Story of my life: Miller, Gary /
Vaya con dios: Millican & Nesbitt / Michelle:
Overlanders / Isn't she lovely: Parton, David
/ (It's like a) Sad old kinda movie: Picketty-
witch / Something's gotten hold of my
heart: Pitney, Gene / Always something
there to remind me: Shaw, Sandie / Too
young: Young, Jimmy / Party's over: Do-
negan, Lonnie / Knock me: Butler, Jerry /
Cry me a river: Knight, Marie
CD _____ TRTCD 112
TrueTrax / Oct '94 / THE.

MAKE YOU SWEAT
CD _____ TCD 2542
Telstar / Sep '91 / BMG.

MAKING UP AGAIN
We've got tonight: Brooks, Elkie / It's too
late now: Baldry, Long John / First cut is
the deepest: Arnold, P.P. / Out of time: Farlowe, Chris / Time in a bottle: Croce, Jim /
After the goldrush: Prelude / Part time love:
Knight, Gladys / Lost in France: Tyler, Bon-
nie / Can't get by without you: Real Thing /
Love hurts: Nazareth / Second time around:
Shalamar / Go now: Moody Blues / Summer
of my life: May, Simon / Say you don't mind:
Blunstone, Colin / Shooting star: Dollar /
Love is love: Brooks, Elkie / Making up
again: Goldie / Walk on by: D-Train / Tired
of waiting for you: Kinks / It doesn't have to
be that way: Croce, Jim
CD _____ TRTCD 140
TrueTrax / Feb '96 / THE.

MALAWI - A KWELA CONCERT
CD _____ LDX 274972
La Chant Du Monde / Apr '94 / Harmonia
Mundi / ADA.

MAMADOU - THE DRUMS OF MALI
CD _____ PS 65132CD
Playasound / Jul '94 / Harmonia Mundi /
ADA.

MAMBA PERCUSSIONS VOL. 1
CD _____ PV 782 91
Disques Pierre Verany / '88 / Kingdom.

MAMBO
CD _____ CD 62020
Saludos Amigos / Oct '93 / Target/BMG.

MAN, A VAN AND A BLEEPER, THE
Hear the music: Gypsymen / Give it all (got):
Solution / Sure shot: Conway, Margaret /
What can I do for you: Gardner, Taana /
Stoppin us: Gypsymen / I wanna be free:
Luna Project / Brass disk: Dupree / Tumblin
down: Herman / Daylight: Gypsymen / Jun-
gle kisses: Roc & Kato / Feel so right: So-
lution / Riots in Brixton: Black Sunday / My
special melody (Features on CD only.): Sta-
tion Q
CD _____ SLIPCD 017
Slip 'n' Slide / Nov '94 / Vital / Disc.

MANCHESTER UNITED: THE RED ALBUM
Glory glory Man United / We are the cham-
pions / Denis the menace / Manchester
United calypso / Willie Morgan on the wing
/ Ryan Giggs we love you / Rah rah rah for
Man. Utd. / Manchester United football
double / George El Beatle / Cantona su-
perstar / Song for Matt Busby / I love
George Best / Euro Cup's all yours / Flow-

ers of Manchester / Very great Bryan Robson / George Best's dream home / Georgie
you've broken my heart / Belfast boy /
George Best's ideal woman / Always look
on the bright side of life
CD _____ PELE 006CD
Exotica / Nov '93 / Vital.

MANCHESTER VOLUME ONE
CD _____ SWDCD 001
Swamp Donkey / Nov '94 / Else.

MANCHESTER VOLUME TWO
(Streetscene)
CD _____ BOPCD 002
Boptop / Dec '95 / Else.

MANHATTAN SERENADES
(Classic Songs Of New York)
Jass / Nov '93 / CM / Jazz Music / ADA /
Cadillac / Direct.
CD _____ JCD 641

MANIFESTO
CD _____ MASO 33045CD
Materiali Sonori / Nov '88 / New Note.

MANY MOODS OF LOVE
CD _____ RN 0036
Runn / Nov '94 / Jetstar / SRD.

MARCHES OF THE WORLD - 2
CD _____ CG 1629
Denon / Jan '89 / Conifer.

MARDI GRAS - PARADE MUSIC FROM NEW ORLEANS
CD _____ BCD 107
GHB / Jul '93 / Jazz Music.

MARIJUANA'S GREATEST HITS REVISITED
CD _____ SKY 75042CD
Sky / Sep '94 / Koch.

MARK GOODIER SESSIONS
CD _____ MARK 1
Night Tracks / Mar '92 / Grapevine /
Pinnacle.

MARQUEE 30 LEGENDARY YEARS
(32 Classic Rock tracks)
Pride (in the name of love): U2 / Solid rock:
Dire Straits / Turn it on again: Genesis / Run
to you: Adams, Bryan / White wedding: Idol,
Billy / Love song: Simple Minds / Don't
stand so close to me: Police / Going underground: Jam / No more heroes: Stran-
glers / Rat trap: Boomtown Rats / Matthew
and son: Stevens, Cat / Living in the past:
Jethro Tull / Dreamer: Supertramp / Another
brick in the wall pt 2: Pink Floyd / Kayleigh:
Marillion / Killer queen: Queen / Saturday
night's alright for fighting: John, Elton / Get
it on: T. Rex / All the young dudes: Mott The
Hoople / You wear it well: Stewart, Rod /
Boys are back in town: Thin Lizzy / Caroline:
Status Quo / Layla: Derek & The Dominoes
/ Substitute: Who / All right now: Free /
Badge: Cream / Gimme some lovin': Davis,
Spencer Group / Need your love so bad:
Fleetwood Mac / For your love: Yardbirds /
Sha la la la lee: Small Faces / Purple haze:
Hendrix, Jimi / Space oddity (original ver-
sion): Bowie, David
CD _____ 840 010-2
Polydor / Jan '89 / PolyGram.

MARQUEE METAL
We will rock you: Queen / Smoke on the
water: Deep Purple / Wishing well: Free /
Voodoo chile: Hendrix, Jimi / Down down:
Status Quo / Epic: Faith No More / She's a
little angel: Little Angels / Wild in the city:
Thin Lizzy / School's out: Cooper, Alice /
Crazy crazy nights: Kiss / Can't get enough:
Bad Company / Ace of spades: Motorhead
/ Paranoid: Black Sabbath / Walk this way:
Run DMC & Aerosmith / Is there anybody
there: Scorpions / Wizard: Uriah Heep /
Days of no trust: Magnum / Living after mid-
night: Judas Priest / Free 'n' easy: Almighty
CD _____ 8454172
Polydor / Apr '91 / PolyGram.

MARSEILLE, MES AMOURS
CD _____ 878302
Music Memoria / Jun '93 / Discovery /
ADA.

MAS - A CARIBBEAN CHRISTMAS PARTY
Party for Santa Claus: Lord Nelson / Nwel
la rive: Benjamin, Lionel / Santa Claus (do
you ever come to the ghetto): Davis, Carlene / Soca santa: Machel / Noel pou you:
Claudette Et Ti Pierre / Asalto navideno: El
Gran Combo / Deck the halls with boughs
of holly: Miller, Jacob / Santa Claus is coming to town: Spence, Joseph / Quand j'entends chante Noel: Gustave, Eddy
CD _____ RCD 10150
Rykodisc / Nov '93 / Vital / ADA.

MASCULINE WOMAN AND FEMININE MEN
CD _____ PASTCD 7072
Flapper / May '95 / Pinnacle.

MASSEY HALL, TORONTO, MAY 15TH 1953.
CD _____ GOJCD 53036
Giants Of Jazz / Mar '90 / Target/BMG /
Cadillac.

MASSIVE RESISTANCE
CD _____ RASCD 3142
Ras / Jun '94 / Jetstar / Greensleeves /
SRD / Direct.

MASSIVE VOL. 4
Twice my age: Krystal & Shabba Ranks /
Worried over you: Davis, Janet & CJ Lewis
/ Poco man jam: Peck, Gregory / Shaka on
the move: Demus, Chaka / Holy water: Bai-
ley, Admiral / New talk: Sweet Irie & Joe 90
/ I know love: Priest, Maxi & Tiger / Mr. Lov-
erman: Glasgow, Deborahe & Shabba
Ranks / Good thing going: Leo, Phillip &
C.J. Lewis / One blood: Reid, Junior / Proud
of Mandela: Macka B & Kofi / Guidance:
Nerious Joseph / Dub be good to me: Beats
International & Lindy Layton / I wanna rock:
Paul, Frankie / First date: Cocoa T / Tears:
Sanchez / Glide gently: Anthony, Mike / If
you want it: Hunningale, Peter / Hurry over:
Boom, Barry / Dancing with my baby: Fos-
ter, Royden / Let's start over: Winsome &
Frankie Paul / Are you going my way:
Home-T / Baby don't go too far: Hartley,
Trevor / Paradise: Smith, Karen / You are
the one: Intense
CD Set _____ 828 2102
FFRR / Jun '90 / PolyGram.

MASTER AND DISCIPLES
CD _____ CDBM 092
Blue Moon / May '93 / Magnum Music
Group / Greensleeves / Hot Shot / ADA /
Cadillac / Discovery.

MASTER BRASS VOL. 1
(All England Masters Championship 1990)
French military march / Light cavalry overture / Miss blue bonnet / Elegy from a
'Downland Suite' / Coriolanus / Marching
through Georgia / Blitz / Someone to watch
over me / Sun has got his hat on / Three
negro spirituals / Neapolitan scenes / Blenheim flourishes / Nightfall in camp
CD _____ QPRL 046D
Polyphonic / Aug '91 / Conifer.

MASTER BRASS VOL. 2
(All England Masters Championship 1991)
Morning, Noon and night / Overture: Can-
dide / Allerseelen / Marche slave / Harmony
music / American fanfare / Jaguar / Ballet
music / Robert le diable / Cornet carillon /
Bandology / Great gate of Kiev / Witches
sabbath / Evening hymn and sunset
CD _____ QPRL 048D
Polyphonic / Aug '91 / Conifer.

MASTER BRASS VOL. 3
(All England Masters Championship 1992)
Midwest / Overture: Zampa / Summertime
/ Music from the XVI century / Cambridge
variations / Introduction act 3 / Lohengrin /
Pineapple Poll / Pantomime / Wedding pro-
cession 'Le coq d'or' / Pastime with good
company / Procession to the minster /
Finlandia
CD _____ QPRL 052D
Polyphonic / Aug '92 / Conifer.

MASTER BRASS VOL. 4
(All England Masters Championship 1993)
Overture: The marriage of Figaro / Sorcer-
er's apprentice / Pandora / Spider and the
fly / Grand march from Aida / English heri-
tage / Blue rondo a la Turk / Lost chord /
Festival overture
CD _____ QPRL 060D
Polyphonic / Sep '93 / Conifer.

MASTER BRASS VOL. 5
(All England Masters Championship 1994)
CD _____ QPRL 067D
Polyphonic / Aug '94 / Conifer.

MASTER BRASS VOL. 6
(All England Masters Championship 1995)
Victors' return / Dancing in the park / Deep
inside the sacred temple / Paganini varia-
tions / La danza / Oberon / Hoe down /
Zimba zamba / Dance of the comedians /
Bolero
CD _____ QPRL 073D
Polyphonic / Aug '95 / Conifer.

MASTERPIECE VOL.3
CD _____ LDRCD 019
Londisc / Aug '95 / Jetstar.

MASTERPIECES
Can't get enough: Bad Company / School's
out: Cooper, Alice / Listen to the music:
Doobie Brothers / Little sister: Cooder, Ry /
Running on empty: Browne, Jackson /
Raspberry beret: Prince / Rhiannon: Fleet-
wood Mac / Head of stone: Young, Neil / For
what it's worth: Buffalo Springfield / Fire
and rain: Taylor, James / She's gone: Hall &
Oates / I want to know what love is: For-
eigner / Drive: Cars / Sailing: Cross, Chris-
topher / Soul man: Blues Brothers /
Respect: Franklin, Aretha / Beast of burden:
Midler, Bette / Life's been good: Walsh, Joe
WEA / Jul '93 / Warner Music.
CD _____ 9548322972

MASTERS OF FRENCH JAZZ : 1937-44
CD _____ 2512802
Jazztime / Feb '91 / Discovery / BMG.

MASTERS OF PERCUSSION
CD _____ MRCD 1012
Moment / Jan '95 / ADA / Koch.

MASTERS OF THE FOLK VIOLIN
CD _____ ARHCD 434
Arhoolie / Apr '95 / ADA / Direct /
Cadillac.

MASTERS OF THE PANPIPES
CD _____ EUCD 1318
ARC / Nov '95 / ARC Music / ADA.

MASTERS OF ZEN
CD _____ PS 65153
Playasound / Sep '95 / Harmonia Mundi /
ADA.

MASTERS VOLUME 1
(The RCA Jazz Collection)
CD Set _____ 74321248192
RCA / Dec '94 / BMG.

MASTERWORKS
(Masters At Work - The Essential
Kenlou House Mixes)
I can't get no sleep: Masters At Work / Only
love can break your heart: St. Etienne /
Beautiful people: Tucker, Barbara / Buddy:
Cherry, Neneh / Voices in my mind: Voices
/ Photograph of Mary: Lorenz, Trey / My
love: Masters At Work / We can make it:
Sole Fusion / Moonshine: Kenlou / Can't
play around: Brown, Kathy / Souffles H:
Mondo Grosso / I like: Shanice / Bounce:
Kenlou
CD _____ HARMCD 001
Harmless / Sep '95 / Disc.

MATADOR'S ARENA VOL.1
(1968-69)
CD _____ JMC 200222
Jamaica Gold / Jun '95 / THE / Magnum
Music Group / Jetstar.

MATADOR'S ARENA VOL.2
CD _____ JMC 200223
Jamaica Gold / Aug '95 / THE / Magnum
Music Group / Jetstar.

MATADOR'S ARENA VOL.3
CD _____ JMC 200224
Jamaica Gold / Aug '95 / THE / Magnum
Music Group / Jetstar.

MATRIX DUB
CD _____ CEND 1300
Century / Aug '95 / Total/BMG / Jetstar.

MAU MAU JUNGLE
CD _____ CD 007
Sky High / Jan '93 / Jetstar.

MAURITIUS - SEGAS
CD _____ C 580060
Ocora / Oct '94 / Harmonia Mundi / ADA.

MAX THE DOG SAYS... DO THE SKA
CD _____ DOJOCD
Dojo / Dec '92 / BMG.

MAXI-MUM TENAGLIA
CD _____ XTR 18CDM
X:Treme / Nov '95 / Pinnacle / SRD.

MBUKI MVUKI
CD _____ OMCD 017
Original Music / May '93 / Direct.

MBUTI PYGMIES OF THE ITURI RAINFOREST
CD _____ SFCD 40401
Smithsonian Folkways / Sep '94 / ADA /
Direct / Koch / CM / Cadillac.

ME NAISET
CD _____ KICD 37
KICD / Nov '95 / ADA.

MECHANICAL MUSIC HALL
Burlington Bertie from Bow / After the ball /
Nellie Dean / Where did you get that hat /
K-K-K-Katy / Flanagan / Down at the old
Bull and Bush / Lily of Laguna / If it wasn't
for the 'ouses in between / Bill Bailey, won't
you please come home / Beside the sea-
side / Ask a policeman / Don't have any
more, Mrs. Moore / Any old iron / My old
dutch / Boiled beef and carrots / Ta-ra-ra-
boom-de-ay
CD _____ CDSDL 232
Saydisc / Jan '92 / Harmonia Mundi / ADA
/ Direct.

MECHANICAL PARADISE
CD _____ NBX 007
Haven/Backs / Oct '94 / Disc / Pinnacle.

MEDIEVAL CHRISTMAS, A
Ductia / Alie psallite / Angelus ad virginem
/ In seculum breve / Orientis partibus / Ecce
quod natura / Ed beo thu / This yol / Alleluia
psallat / E semine rosa / Verbum patris /
Nova, nova / Goday my lord syre christ-
masse / Danse real / Beata viscera / Virgo
/ Quene note / Solis ortus / Synge we to
thys mery cumpane / Hayl Mary / Nowel,
owt of your slepe / Nowel, synge we both
al and som / Ther ys no rose / Tardi il mio
cor / A solis ortus / Goday my lord syre
shristmasse
CD _____ PCD 844
Carlton Home Entertainment / Oct '95 /
Carlton Home Entertainment.

MEDITATION - REFLECTIONS
(2CD Set)
CD Set _____ 24059
Delta Doubles / Sep '92 / Target/BMG.

MEDITATIONS AND RELAXATION
CD _____ ACH 035 CD
Milan / Feb '89 / BMG / Silva Screen.

MEDLEY TRAIN
CD _____ CDTRL 350
Trojan / Mar '95 / Jetstar / Total/BMG.

MEET ME TONIGHT
CD _____ BB 2810
Blue Beat / Apr '95 / Magnum Music Group / THE.

MEGA VIBES
CD _____ DCD 5418
Scratch / Feb '95 / BMG.

MEGA-LO-MANIA
Ain't no love (ain't no use): Sub Sub & Melanie Williams / Beneath the sheets: Vertigo / Meglomania (Featuring Elaine Vassell): Duberry / I believe in you (Euphoric Edit): Our Tribe / Music is my life: Chase / U to 2 know (A'la Carte Paris Mix): Cappella / Do u feel 4 me: Eden / Corporation your eyes: Groove / Let freedom reign: Nu Colours / Shine on me: Lovestation / Sanctuary of love: Source / So deep: Reese Project / Appolonia (Tamazamix): B.M.EX / Devo: Crunch / Feels so good: Watchman / Love thing: Evolution / (You give me) All your love: Pro-gressive / Thankyou: Tuff Productions / Soul survivors (Original Mix): Prohibition
CD _____ 515 813-2
PolyGram TV / Apr '93 / PolyGram.

MEINE TEXTE, MEINE LIEDER
CD Set _____ BCD 15603
Bear Family / Jul '91 / Rollercoaster / Direct / CM / Swift / ADA.

MELODEON GREATS
CD _____ TSCD 601
Topic / Aug '95 / Direct / ADA.

MELODIES FROM MADAGASCAR
CD _____ PS 65124
Playasound / Apr '94 / Harmonia Mundi / ADA.

MELODIES OF LOVE
CD _____ RADCD 29
Global / Nov '95 / BMG.

MELODY RANCH/GUNHAWK CONVENTION
CD _____ CDMR 1048
Derann Trax / Aug '91 / Pinnacle.

MELTING PLOT
CD _____ SST 249 CD
SST / Jan '89 / Plastic Head.

MEMORIES DU SEGA
CD _____ PS 65139CD
Playasound / Apr '95 / Harmonia Mundi / ADA.

MEMORIES FROM RUSSIA
Moscow nights / Fisherman's dance / Katusha / Stenka rasin / He raspachol / Along the volga / Posthorn / Lonley bell / Urkranian dance / Song of the Volga boatman / Evening on the don / Cossack dance / Siberian lullaby / Twelve robbers / Maradschenka / Cossack love song / Black eyes / Katjuscha / Cossack patrol / Russian sailors dance
CD _____ SOW 90150
Sounds Of The World / Jan '96 / Target/BMG.

MEMORIES OF IRELAND
CD _____ ECD 3113
K-Tel / Jun '95 / K-Tel.

MEMORIES OF SCOTLAND
CD _____ ACD 101
Koch / Oct '93 / Koch.

MEMORIES OF THE LIGHT PROGRAMME
Housewives' choice: Williams, Charles & His Orchestra / Isn't life wonderful: Cogan, Alma / China tea: Conway, Russ / Brazil: Love, Geoff / White wedding: Southern, Sheila / Jungle fantasy: Dixon, Reginald / Music while you work: Coates, Eric / Parakeets and peacocks: Coles, Jack Orchestra / Cascade of stars: Hartley, Fred / Crazy rhythm: Geldray, Max / Good mornin' life: Lotis, Dennis / Dancer at the fair: Shadwell, Charles Orchestra / It hurts to say goodbye: Lynn, Vera / First rhapsody: Melachrino, George & His Orchestra / Laura: Inglez, Roberto Orchestra / English as she is spoken: Howard, Frankie / June is bustin' out all over: Torrent, Billy & His Orchestra / Portuguese party: Pro Arte Orchestra / You are my first love: Murray, Ruby / You're dancing on my heart: Silvester, Victor & His Ballroom Orchestra / I'm going to see you today: Grenfell, Joyce / Running on the rails: Columbia Orchestra / Skirts: Cotton, Billy Band / Cresta run: Torch, Sidney & Orchestra / Luck be a lady: Hockridge, Edmund / Anchors aweigh: Yorke, Peter / Pick of the pops: Faye, Brian Orchestra / Once in a lifetime: Spence, Johnny Orchestra / Nicola: Race, Steve / Goodness gracious me: Sellers, Peter / Paul Temple: Queen's Hall Light Orchestra / Lovely day: Chacksfield, Frank / I can dream, can't I: Boswell, Eve / Galloping comedians: Geraldo & His Orchestra / Little red monkey: Nicholls, Joy/Dick Bentley/Jimmy Edwards / Sports report: Band of the Irish Guards / Music music music: Peers, Donald / In love for the very first time: Carson, Jean / Mediterranean Concerto: Semprini / But beautiful: Cogan, Alma / How little it matters, how little we know: Monro, Matt / Mon pays: Cordell, Frank & His Orchestra / Penny serenade: Hilton, Ronnie / Radio newsreel: Band Of The RAF / Waltzing in the clouds: Jaffa, Max / Song of the trees: Shelton, Anne / Say it with music: Payne, Jack & His Orchestra / Spanish serenade: Phillips, Sid / Music for sweethearts: Jupp, Eric Orchestra / Bedtime for drums: Ainsworth, Alyn Orchestra
CD _____ CDEM 1506
EMI / Sep '93 / EMI.

MEMPHIS BLUES 1927-38
CD _____ DOCD 5159
Blues Document / May '93 / Swift / Jazz Music / Hot Shot.

MEMPHIS JAZZ MEETING
CD _____ DIW 613
DIW / Sep '93 / Harmonia Mundi / Cadillac.

MEMPHIS JAZZ MEETING : MEMPHIS CONVENTION
CD _____ DIW 874
DIW / Sep '93 / Harmonia Mundi / Cadillac.

MEMPHIS MASTERS: EARLY AMERICAN BLUES CLASSICS 1927-1934
CD _____ YAZCD 2008
Yazoo / Nov '94 / CM / ADA / Roots / Koch.

MEMPHIS SOUL GREATS
Hey little girl: West, Norm / Baby please: West, Norm / So good to me: Jackson, George / I'm gonna wait: Jackson, George / Aretha, sing one for me: Jackson, George / Patricia: Jackson, George / Let them know you care: Jackson, George / Tumbling down: Fry, James / Still around: Fry, James / Mama's boy: Fry, James / I've got enough: Fry, James / Without you: Wright, O.V. / Rhymes: Wright, O.V. / I love my baby: Hill, Lindell / Love map: Hill, Lindell / Very first time: Hill, Lindell / Be good to the one (That's good to you): Mack, Jimmy / I love her: Walker, Willie / Sweet thing: Walker, Willie / Fried chicken: Thomas, Rufus / I ain't got time: Thomas, Rufus
CD _____ HILOCD 17
Hi / Jul '95 / Pinnacle.

MEN OF HARLECH
(Welsh Choral Classics)
We'll keep a welcome: Canoldir Male Voice Choir / How great thou art: Canoldir Male Voice Choir / Lord's prayer: Canoldir Male Voice Choir / Land of my fathers (Hen wlad fy nhadau): Moriston Orpheus Choir & The Bedwas, Trethomas & Machin Band / Where shall I be: Moriston Orpheus Choir & The Bedwas, Trethomas & Machin Band / Calon lan: Moriston Orpheus Choir & The Bedwas, Trethomas & Machin Band / Rise up shepherd and follow: Moriston Orpheus Choir / Vocal chorus: Moriston Orpheus Choir / Deep harmony: Moriston Orpheus Choir / Goin' home: Moriston Orpheus Choir / Mil harddach wyt na'r rhosyn gwyn: Pontarddulais Male Choir / Christus redemptor (hyfrydol): Pontarddulais Male Choir / Jesu lover of my soul: Treorchy Male Choir / Unwaith eto'n nghymru annwyl: Treorchy Male Choir / Dove: Emanuel, Ivor & The Rhos Male Voice Choir / Star of Bethlehem: Dunvant Male Choir / Sanctus: Dunvant Male Choir / Ar hyd y nos: Dunvant Male Choir / My little Welsh home: Emanuel, Ivor & The Rhos Male Voice Choir / God bless the Prince Of Wales: Rhos Male Voice Choir / Men of Harlech: Emanuel, Ivor & The Rhos Male Voice Choir
CD _____ TRTCD 133
TrueTrax / Oct '94 / THE.

MENU, THE
On my mind: Big Cheese All Stars / Still water: Silent Majority / Eight tracks to heaven: Waik Tall / Ciscomulkr: Malka Family / Track Cheul: Ste / Le soleil brille: Schkoonk Heepooz / Mentira: Quintetto X / Netour: D.J. Gilbert / Chilling: Lionel Moyst Sextet / Lor-an's dance: Taudi Symphony / Hold it now (CD only): Batu
CD _____ 142817
Big Cheese / Nov '94 / Vital.

MERCILESS WORLD OF TRANCE II
CD _____ HOSCDX 006
Heidi Of Switzerland / Feb '95 / Pinnacle.

MERCURY MUSIC PRIZE '94
CD _____ MMPCD 3
Mercury / Aug '94 / PolyGram.

MERINGUE
CD _____ CO 107
Corason / Jan '94 / CM / Direct / ADA.

MERRY CHRISTMAS
Silent Night: Fitzgerald, Ella / O come all ye faithful (Adeste fidelis): Cole, Nat King / Let it snow, let it snow, let it snow: Martin, Dean / Have yourself a merry little Christmas: Gleason, Jackie / I like a sleighride (jingle bells): Lee, Peggy / I'll be home for Christmas: Beach Boys / Christmas dinner country style: Crosby, Bing / O holy night: Cole, Nat King / Little drummer boy: Stafford, Jo / White Christmas: Martin, Dean / O little town of Bethlehem: Fitzgerald, Ella / Do you hear what I hear: Crosby, Bing / Santa Claus is coming to town: Beach Boys / First Noel: Fitzgerald, Ella / Christmas song: Cole, Nat King / Christmas waltz: Lee, Peggy
CD _____ CD 50013
Lotus / Feb '89 / Jazz Horizons / Impetus.

MERRY CHRISTMAS
CD _____ ENTCD 200
Entertainers / '88 / Target/BMG.

MERRY CHRISTMAS
CD _____ CNCD 5969
Disky / Dec '93 / THE / BMG / Discovery / Pinnacle.

MERRY CHRISTMAS, A
CD _____ CNCD 5932
Hermanex / Nov '92 / THE.

MERSEYBEAT MEMORIES
CD _____ CDCD 1251
Charly / Jun '95 / Charly / THE / Cadillac.

MESMER VARIATIONS
(Works Inspired By Mesmer/2CD Set)
CD Set _____ ASH 1.8CD
Ash International / Oct '95 / These / Kudos.

MESSAGE - HISTORY OF RAP, THE
CD _____ NTRCD 024
Nectar / Sep '94 / Pinnacle.

MESSAGE IN THE MUSIC
CD _____ ABYSSCD 1
Total / May '90 / Total/BMG.

METAL BOX
(3CD/MC Set)
CD Set _____ TBXCD 506
TrueTrax / Jan '96 / THE.

METAL CHRISTMAS
CD _____ DCD 5419
Scratch / Nov '94 / BMG.

METAL GODS
CD _____ MATCD 321
Castle / Feb '95 / BMG.

METAL GODS 2
CD _____ MATCD 322
Castle / Feb '95 / BMG.

METAL KILLERS
White line fever: Motorhead / Blood guts and beer: Tank / Nothing to lose: Girlschool / Urban guerilla: Hawkwind / Now comes the storm: Thor / Not for sale: Girlschool / Run like hell: Tank / Beer drinkers and hell raisers: Motorhead / Start raisin' hell: Thor / Last flight: Jaguar / Bump and grind: Williams, Wendy O.
CD _____ MATCD 264
Castle / May '93 / BMG.

METAL MANIA
CD Set _____ DCDCD 206
Castle / Jun '95 / BMG.

METAL MASSACRE
CD _____ 398414082CD
Metal Blade / Nov '95 / Plastic Head.

METAL MASSACRE 10
CD _____ CD ZORRO 4
Music For Nations / May '94 / Pinnacle.

METAL MASTERS
(4CD Set)
CD Set _____ MBSCD 411
Castle / Jun '93 / BMG.

METAL PRAISE
Rock of ages? / Jehovah shreh / Holy holy holy / What a friend we have in Jesus / O come, o come Emmanuel / We exalt thee / Spirit song / I love you Lord / Life begun / He's the Lord
CD _____ 7016944611
Myrrh / Apr '92 / Nelson Word.

METALLURGY
Refuse/Resist: Sepultura / EP Two: Eleven Pictures / Drive boy, shooting: GZR / Kissing the sun: Young Gods / Second sun: Dawn / You're the vulgarian: Stanford Prison Experiment / Guarana: Faith No More / Shine: Kyuss / Street crab: Helmet / Spreader: Stanley / New breed: Fear Factory / Please don't hurt me: Skyscraper / Shovel: Quicksand / Greed killings: Napalm Death / 5 exclusive tracks: Chocolate
CD _____ VMETCD 1
Volume / Nov '95 / Total/BMG / Vital.

METEOR ROCKABILLIES
Mama's little baby: Thompson, Junior / Raw deal: Thompson, Junior / Tongue tied Jill: Feathers, Charlie / Get with it: Feathers, Charlie / Rock, roll and rhythm: McGinnis, Wayne / Lonesome rhythm blues: McGinnis, Wayne / Don't shoot me baby (I'm not ready to die): Bowen, Bill / Have myself a ball: Bowen, Bill / All messed up: Hooper, Jess / Sleepy time blues: Hooper, Jess / Latch on to your baby: Lamberth, Jimmy / Bop baby bop: Suggs, Brad / Charcoal suit: Suggs, Brad / Can't steal my way around: Burcham, Barney / Much too young for love: Burcham, Barney / Curfew: Carl, Steve & The Jags / Eighteen year old blues: Carl, Steve & The Jags / Gonna shut you off baby: Haggett, Jimmy / Women: Smith, Lendon & The Jesters / Brother that's all: Hadley, Red / Real gone baby: Velvetones / Gal named Joe: Sales, Mac / Yakety yak: Mac & Jake / Don't worry 'bout nothin': Dixon, Mason
CD _____ CDCHM 484
Ace / Jul '93 / Pinnacle / Cadillac / Complete/Pinnacle.

MEXICAN INDIAN TRADITIONS : CELEBRATIONS
CD _____ AUD 08304
Auvidis/Ethnic / Feb '93 / Harmonia Mundi.

MEXICAN LANDSCAPES VOL. 3
CD _____ PS 65903
Playasound / Mar '92 / Harmonia Mundi / ADA.

MEXICAN LANDSCAPES VOL. 4
CD _____ PS 65904
Playasound / Apr '92 / Harmonia Mundi / ADA.

MEXICAN LANDSCAPES VOL. 5
CD _____ PS 65905
Playasound / Sep '92 / Harmonia Mundi / ADA.

MEXICAN LANDSCAPES VOL. 7
CD _____ PS 65907
Playasound / Nov '93 / Harmonia Mundi / ADA.

MEXICAN LOVE SONGS VOL. 2
La numero cien: Dueto Romantico / Maria Dolores: Dueto Romantico / No te importa saber: Dueto Romantico / Ese: Dueto Romantico / Perdoname mi vida: Los Tres Agues / Los dos: Los Tres Agues / La consercuencia: Los Tres Agues / Condicion: Los Tres Agues / Besame mucho: Trio Los Duques
CD _____ 90 765-2
PMF / May '94 / Kingdom / Cadillac.

MEXICAN-AMERICAN BORDER MUSIC VOL. 1
(The Pioneer Recordings Artists 1928-1959)
CD _____ FL 7001
Folklyric / Apr '95 / Direct / Cadillac.

MEXICO
CD _____ CD 62025
Saludos Amigos / Oct '93 / Target/BMG.

MEXICO - FIESTAS OF CHIAPAS & OAXACA
CD _____ 7559720702
Elektra Nonesuch / Jan '95 / Warner Music.

MICRODELIA
Happenings ten years time ago: Yardbirds / Moonshine heather: Parliament / Candy Cane madness: George, Lowell / Faded picture: Seeds / Life is just beginning: Creation / Flowers never cry: Mystic Astrological Crystal Band / Driftin': Buckley, Tim / Country boy: HP Lovecraft / Bleeker Street: HP Lovecraft / Levity Ball: Cooper, Alice / Spinning wheel: Flaming Ember / Somebody to love: Great Society / Christopher Lucifer: Nirvana / Don't talk to strangers: Beau Brummels / Trip: Fire Escape / Revelation in slow motion: Count Five / Down on me: Big Brother & The Holding Company / Charlie: Deviants / Aton 1: Ceyleib People
CD _____ DIAB 811
Diabolo / Jun '94 / Pinnacle.

MID ATLANTIC SESSIONS
CD _____ MMB 92
Moonshine / Sep '94 / Disc.

MIDNIGHT CRUISING
You: Ten Sharp / Time after time: Lauper, Cyndi / Daniel: John, Elton / Hold on: Wilson Phillips / Higher love: Winwood, Steve / Nothing in chains: Tears For Fears / It's my life: Talk Talk / Mercy mercy me/I want you: Palmer, Robert / Feel so high: Des'ree / Listen to your heart: Roxette / Jade iid: Stray Cats / Driver's seat: Sniff 'N' The Tears / How long: Ace / Missing you: Waite, John / Africa: Toto / Sweet freedom: McDonald, Michael / Drive: Cars
CD _____ DINCD 40
Dino / Jul '92 / Pinnacle / 3MV.

MIDNIGHT GUITAR
CD _____ GRF 194
Tring / Jun '92 / Tring / Prism.

MIDNIGHT HOUR
CD _____ RNCD 2090
Rhino / Feb '95 / Jetstar / Magnum Music Group / THE.

MIDNIGHT MOODS
(The Lighter Side Of Jazz)
Unforgettable: Cole, Nat King / Fever: Lee, Peggy / Mad about the boy: Washington, Dinah / From Ipanema: Gilberto, Astrud / Smooth operator: Sade / Lily was here: Stewart, David A. & Candy Dulfer / It had to be you: Connick, Harry Jr. / Take five: Brubeck, Dave / Fine romance: Holiday, Billie / Every time we say goodbye: Fitzgerald, Ella / Misty: Garner, Erroll / Cry me a river: Wilson, Man / Goin' out of my head: Montgomery, Wes / Take the 'A' train: O'Day, Anita / Walk on the wild side: Smith, Jimmy / Shadow of your smile: Peterson, Oscar / Summertime: Vaughan, Sarah / Relax: Vaughan, Leon / Passing strangers: Vaughan,

Sarah & Billy Eckstine / What a wonderful world: *Armstrong, Louis*
CD _____ 515 816-2
PolyGram TV / Apr '93 / PolyGram.

MIDNIGHT SLOWS VOL 6
CD _____ BLE 190932
Black & Blue / Apr '91 / Wellard / Koch.

MIDNIGHT SLOWS VOL 8
CD _____ BLE 193582
Black & Blue / Apr '91 / Wellard / Koch.

MIDNIGHT SOUL
Never too much: *Vandross, Luther* / Harvest for the world: *Isley Brothers* / Street life: *Crusaders* / Higher and higher: *Wilson, Jackie* / Never knew love like this before: *Mills, Stephanie* / I'm your puppet: *Purify, James & Bobby* / Have you seen her: *Chi-Lites* / Dance to the music: *Sly & The Family Stone* / Lean on me: *Withers, Bill* / Come into my life: *Sims, Joyce* / Move on up: *Mayfield, Curtis* / I love music: *O'Jays* / It's man's world: *Brown, James* / Love I lost: *Melvin, Harold* / Reunited: *Peaches & Herb* / rescue me: *Fontella Bass* / Way we were: *Knight, Gladys & The Pips* / Soul city walk: *Bell, Archie & The Drells*
CD _____ MUSCD 006
MCI / Nov '92 / Disc / THE.

MIGHTY BOX PLAYING
CD _____ GTDCD 007
GTD / Jan '95 / Else / ADA.

MIGHTY MOON, THE
CD _____ MRSP 003
Music Research / Aug '94 / Plastic Head.

MIGHTY WURLITZER VOL. 1 - 50 ALL TIME FAVOURITES
CD _____ SWBCD 201
Sound Waves / Sep '94 / Target/BMG.

MIGHTY WURLITZER VOL. 2 - 50 ALL TIME FAVOURITES
CD _____ SWBCD 202
Sound Waves / Sep '94 / Target/BMG.

MIGHTY WURLITZER, THE
CD _____ MATCD 245
Castle / Dec '92 / BMG.

MILESTONES
(20 Rock Operas)
Bohemian rhapsody: *Queen* / I don't like Mondays: *Boomtown Rats* / Bat out of hell: *Meat Loaf* / I can't let the sun go down on me: *John, Elton* / Samba pa ti: *Santana* / Hotel California: *Eagles* / I'm not in love: *10cc* / 10538 overture: *E.L.O.* / Wuthering Heights: *Bush, Kate* / Oxygene IV: *Jarre, Jean Michel* / Vienna: *Ultravox* / Nights in white satin: *Moody Blues* / Let's work together: *Canned Heat* / Layla: *Derek & The Dominoes* / Tubular bells: *Oldfield, Mike* / Smoke on the water: *Deep Purple* / Whiter shade of pale: *Procul Harum* / Music: *Miles, John* / Albatross: *Fleetwood Mac* / Drive: *Cars*
CD _____ TCD 2379
Telstar / Dec '89 / BMG.

MILITARY BAND SPECTACULAR
CD _____ 8441742
Deram / Jan '96 / PolyGram.

MILK FOR PUSSY
CD _____ MQCD 9301
Mad Queen / Jan '94 / SRD.

MILLENNIUM: ETERNALLY ALIVE
CD _____ MILL 009CD
Millenium / Nov '94 / Plastic Head.

MILLION DOLLAR COLLECTION, THE
(20 Essential Roll Classics)
CD _____ CDCD 1097
Charly / Jun '93 / Charly / THE / Cadillac.

MILLION SELLERS - THE BEST OF THE MILLION SELLERS
CD _____ MSCD 1950
Disky / Apr '94 / THE / BMG / Discovery / Pinnacle.

MILLION SELLERS - THE EIGHTIES #1
CD _____ MSCD 1971
Disky / Apr '94 / THE / BMG / Discovery / Pinnacle.

MILLION SELLERS - THE EIGHTIES #2
CD _____ MSCD 1973
Disky / Oct '94 / THE / BMG / Discovery / Pinnacle.

MILLION SELLERS - THE EIGHTIES #3
CD _____ MSCD 1974
Disky / Oct '94 / THE / BMG / Discovery / Pinnacle.

MILLION SELLERS - THE EIGHTIES #4
CD _____ MSCD 1975
Disky / Oct '94 / THE / BMG / Discovery / Pinnacle.

MILLION SELLERS - THE EIGHTIES #5
CD _____ MSCD 1976
Disky / Apr '94 / THE / BMG / Discovery / Pinnacle.

MILLION SELLERS - THE FIFTIES #1
CD _____ MSCD 1951
Disky / Apr '94 / THE / BMG / Discovery / Pinnacle.

MILLION SELLERS - THE FIFTIES #2
CD _____ MSCD 1952
Disky / Apr '94 / THE / BMG / Discovery / Pinnacle.

MILLION SELLERS - THE FIFTIES #3
CD _____ MSCD 1953
Disky / Apr '94 / THE / BMG / Discovery / Pinnacle.

MILLION SELLERS - THE FIFTIES #4
CD _____ MSCD 1954
Disky / Apr '94 / THE / BMG / Discovery / Pinnacle.

MILLION SELLERS - THE SEVENTIES #1
CD _____ MSCD 1963
Disky / Apr '94 / THE / BMG / Discovery / Pinnacle.

MILLION SELLERS - THE SEVENTIES #2
CD _____ MSCD 1964
Disky / Apr '94 / THE / BMG / Discovery / Pinnacle.

MILLION SELLERS - THE SEVENTIES #3
CD _____ MSCD 1965
Disky / Apr '94 / THE / BMG / Discovery / Pinnacle.

MILLION SELLERS - THE SEVENTIES #4
CD _____ MSCD 1966
Disky / Apr '94 / THE / BMG / Discovery / Pinnacle.

MILLION SELLERS - THE SEVENTIES #5
CD _____ MSCD 1967
Disky / Apr '94 / THE / BMG / Discovery / Pinnacle.

MILLION SELLERS - THE SEVENTIES #6
CD _____ MSCD 1968
Disky / Apr '94 / THE / BMG / Discovery / Pinnacle.

MILLION SELLERS - THE SEVENTIES #7
CD _____ MSCD 1969
Disky / Apr '94 / THE / BMG / Discovery / Pinnacle.

MILLION SELLERS - THE SEVENTIES #8
CD _____ MSCD 1970
Disky / Apr '94 / THE / BMG / Discovery / Pinnacle.

MILLION SELLERS - THE SIXTIES #1
CD _____ MSCD 1955
Disky / Apr '94 / THE / BMG / Discovery / Pinnacle.

MILLION SELLERS - THE SIXTIES #2
CD _____ MSCD 1956
Disky / Apr '94 / THE / BMG / Discovery / Pinnacle.

MILLION SELLERS - THE SIXTIES #3
CD _____ MSCD 1957
Disky / Apr '94 / THE / BMG / Discovery / Pinnacle.

MILLION SELLERS - THE SIXTIES #4
CD _____ MSCD 1958
Disky / Apr '94 / THE / BMG / Discovery / Pinnacle.

MILLION SELLERS - THE SIXTIES #5
CD _____ MSCD 1959
Disky / Apr '94 / THE / BMG / Discovery / Pinnacle.

MILLION SELLERS - THE SIXTIES #6
CD _____ MSCD 1960
Disky / Apr '94 / THE / BMG / Discovery / Pinnacle.

MILLION SELLERS - THE SIXTIES #7
CD _____ MSCD 1961
Disky / Apr '94 / THE / BMG / Discovery / Pinnacle.

MILLION SELLERS - THE SIXTIES #8
CD _____ MSCD 1962
Disky / Apr '94 / THE / BMG / Discovery / Pinnacle.

MILLION SELLERS VOL.1, THE
CD _____ CDCD 1198
Charly / Sep '94 / Charly / THE / Cadillac.

MILLION SELLERS VOL.2, THE
CD _____ CDCD 1229
Charly / Jun '95 / Charly / THE / Cadillac.

MILLION SELLING HITS OF THE 50'S
Mona Lisa: *Cole, Nat King* / That's amore: *Martin, Dean* / Blueberry Hill: *Domino, Fats* / Rock 'n' roll waltz (CD only.): *Starr, Kay* / Shotgun boogie (CD only.): *Ford, Tennessee Ernie* / Mockin' Bird Hill: *Paul, Les & Mary Ford* / Unchained melody: *Baxter, Les* / Come softly to me: *Fleetwoods* / Shrimp boats: *Stafford, Jo* / You send me: *Cooke, Sam* / Fever: *Lee, Peggy* / Here in my heart: *Martino, Al* / On the street where you live: *Damone, Vic* / Oh mein papa: *Calvert, Eddie* / Vaya con dios: *Paul, Les & Mary Ford* / Sixteen tons: *Ford, Tennessee Ernie* / Wheel of fortune: *Starr, Kay* / Ain't that a shame: *Domino, Fats* / Return to me (CD only.): *Martin, Dean* / Blossom fell: *Cole, Nat King*
CD _____ CDMFP 6047
Music For Pleasure / Jan '89 / EMI.

MILLION SELLING HITS OF THE 60'S
Next time: *Richard, Cliff* / I'm telling you now: *Freddie & The Dreamers* / Sloop John B: *Beach Boys* / Sealed with a kiss: *Hyland, Brian* / He ain't heavy, he's my brother: *Hol-*

lies / World of our own: *Seekers* / Tracy: *Cuff Links* / Michael, row the boat ashore: *Highwaymen* / Wichita lineman: *Campbell, Glen* / Carrie Anne: *Hollies* / There's a kind of hush: *Herman's Hermits* / Don't let the sun catch you crying: *Gerry & The Pacemakers* / Little arrows: *Lee, Leapy* / Lucky lips: *Richard, Cliff* / You were made for me: *Freddie & The Dreamers* / Tears: *Dodd, Ken* / Monday: *Mamas & Papas* / Carnival is over: *Seekers* / Little children (CD only.): *Kramer, Billy J. & The Dakotas* / Anyone who had a heart (CD only.): *Black, Cilla*
CD _____ CDMFP 6063
Music For Pleasure / Aug '89 / EMI.

MIND POLLUTION
CD _____ WOWCD 11
Words Of Warning / May '93 / SRD.

MIND POLLUTION 2
CD _____ WOWCD 29
Words Of Warning / Sep '93 / SRD.

MINIATURES
CD _____ VP 159CD
Voice Print / Apr '95 / Voice Print.

MINISTRY OF SOUND - THE ANNUAL
(2CD/MC Set)
CD Set _____ ANNCD 95
Ministry Of Sound / Nov '95 / 3MV / Warner Music.

MINISTRY OF SOUND - THE SESSIONS VOL. 2
CD _____ MINSTCD 002
Ministry Of Sound / Apr '94 / 3MV / Warner Music.

MINISTRY OF SOUND - THE SESSIONS VOL. 3
CD _____ MINSTCD 003
Ministry Of Sound / Oct '94 / 3MV / Warner Music.

MINISTRY OF SOUND - THE SESSIONS VOL. 4
CD _____ MINCD 4
CD Set _____ MINCDB 4
Ministry Of Sound / Apr '95 / 3MV / Warner Music.

MINISTRY OF SOUND - THE SESSIONS VOL. 5
(4LP/2CD/2MC Set)
CD Set _____ MINCD 5
Ministry Of Sound / Sep '95 / 3MV / Warner Music.

MINISTRY OF SOUND PRESENTS AWOL - LIVE
CD _____ AWOLCD 1
Ministry Of Sound / Jul '95 / 3MV / Warner Music.

MINISTRY OF SOUND PRESENTS THE FUTURE SOUND OF NEW YORK
CD _____ SOMCD 1
Ministry Of Sound / Mar '95 / 3MV / Warner Music.

MINIT RECORDS STORY
Bad luck and trouble: *Boogie Jake* / Mother in law: *K-Doe, Ernie* / Always naggin' (grumblin' fussin' nag nag): *Del Royals* / Ooh poo pah doo: *Hill, Jessie* / Over you: *Showmen, Aaron* / I like it like that: *Kenner, Chris* / Te-ta-te-ta-ta: *K-Doe, Ernie* / Tiddle winks: *Allen & Allen* / Whip it on me: *Hill, Jessie* / I waited too long: *Reeder, Eskew* / Reality: *Neville, Aaron* / Lipstick traces: *Spellman, Benny* / Certain girl: *K-Doe, Ernie* / I cried my last tear: *K-Doe, Ernie* / Popeye Joe: *K-Doe, Ernie* / Look up: *Thomas, Irma* / Green door: *Reeder, Eskew* / Ticks of the clock: *Neville, Aaron* / 39-21-40 shape: *Showmen* / Fortune teller: *Spellman, Benny* / Miss nosey: *Orange, Allen* / I've done it again: *Neville, Aaron* / Valley of tears: *Lee, Calvin* / Never again: *Reeder, Eskew* / Ruler of the heart: *Thomas, Irma* / Power of love: *Harper, Willie* / We had love: *Reeder, Eskew* / It will stand: *Showmen* / He'll come back: *Players* / Baby I love you: *Holiday, Jimmy* / Working on your case: *O'Jays* / Dog: *McCracklin, Jimmy* / I'm glad you waited: *Players* / Baby, I can't stand it: *Womack, Bobby* / Broadway walk: *Womack, Bobby* / California dreamin': *Womack, Bobby* / I'm a midnight mover: *Womack, Bobby* / Everybody needs help: *Holiday, Jimmy* / Spread your love: *Holiday, Jimmy* / How'd to funk: *Dozier, Gene* / Get together: *McCracklin, Jimmy* / I'll never stop loving you: *King, Clydie* / I'm gonna do all I can: *Turner, Ike & Tina* / Oh I'll never be the same: *Young Hearts* / I wish it would rain: *Turner, Ike & Tina* / Am I ever gonna see my baby again: *Green, Vernon* / I've got love for my baby: *Young Hearts* / Ready, willing and able: *Holiday, Jimmy* / Clydie King / Hurry back: *Persuasions* / I wanna jump: *Turner, Ike & Tina* / Prove it: *Roberts, Lea* / Worried life blues: *Parker, Junior* / Come together: *Turner, Ike & Tina*
CD Set _____ MINIT 1
EMI / Jan '95 / EMI.

MINSTREL BANJO STYLE
CD _____ ROUCD 0321
Rounder / Dec '94 / CM / Direct / ADA / Cadillac.

MINSTREL BOY, THE
(Irish Singers Of Great Renoun)
CD _____ GEMM CD 9989
Gemm / Nov '92 / Pinnacle.

MIRKKOCALBMI
CD _____ DATCD 21
Dat / Nov '95 / ADA / Direct.

MIRWOOD STORY (THE SOUND OF SWINGIN' HOLLYWOOD)
CD _____ GSCD 010
Goldmine / Feb '93 / Vital.

MISAS Y FIESTAS MEXICANAS
Misa panamericana (messe des mariachis) / Misa tepozteca / La charreada / Sones de michoacan / El taconaso / Hymne au soleil / Danza de los negritos / Danza de los ladores / Danza de los viejitos
CD _____ ARN 64017
Arion / '88 / Discovery / ADA.

MISCELLANEOUS
Under pressure: *Bluefoot* / Unix: *Biomuse* / Lowdown: *Tranquil Elephantizer* / Lunar tunes: *Arc* / Subether: *Endermic Void* / AEA: *Circadian Rhythms* / Moonrise: *Pooley, Ian* / Jinn: *Tao* / Pentax (CD only.): *Launchdat* / Shapeshifter (CD only.): *Fantomas* / Living dust (CD only.): *Toop, David* / Sub evening lullaby (CD only.): *Takshaka*
CD _____ WORDD 1
Language / Jul '95 / Grapevine.

MISSING YOU VOL. 1
One and only: *Hawkes, Chesney* / You're in love: *Wilson Phillips* / Something's gotten hold of my heart: *Almond, Marc & Gene Pitney* / Don't you love me anymore: *Cocker, Joe* / Power of love: *Lewis, Huey & The News* / Spending my time: *Roxette* / Little bit more: *Dr. Hook* / When I need you: *Sayer, Leo* / How'm I gonna sleep: *Finn, Tim* / She makes my day: *Palmer, Robert* / Endless Summer nights: *Marx, Richard* / Some people: *Richard, Cliff* / True: *Spandau Ballet* / Fall at your feet: *Crowded House* / Way of the world
CD _____ 7986292
EMI / Feb '92 / EMI.

MISSING YOU: SENTIMENTAL SONGS OF WORLD WAR 2
CD _____ VJCD 1049
Vintage Jazz Classics / Feb '93 / Direct / ADA / CM / Cadillac.

MISSION
CD _____ TYCD 001
Jetstar / Jun '92 / Jetstar.

MISSION IMPOSSIBLE TO FINAL MISSION
CD _____ SONCD 0058
Sonic Sounds / Mar '94 / Jetstar.

MISSION INTO DRUMS, A
Closed eye view / Dimension X / Journey / Maya and Aliens / Subsonic interferences / Inner peace
CD _____ 4509962232
Harthouse / Jun '94 / Disc / Warner Music.

MISSISSIPPI BLUES
CD _____ TMCD 07
Travellin' Man / Oct '91 / Wellard / CM / Jazz Music.

MISSISSIPPI BLUES & GOSPEL
(Field Recordings 1934-42)
CD _____ DOCD 5320
Blues Document / Mar '95 / Swift / Jazz Music / Hot Shot.

MISSISSIPPI BLUES VOL.1
CD _____ DOCD 5157
Blues Document / May '93 / Swift / Jazz Music / Hot Shot.

MISSISSIPPI BLUES VOL.2
CD _____ DOCD 5158
Blues Document / May '93 / Swift / Jazz Music / Hot Shot.

MISSISSIPPI CIVIL RIGHTS MOVEMENT
CD _____ FE 1419
Folk Era / Dec '94 / CM / ADA.

MISSISSIPPI DELTA BLUES
CD _____ IGOCD 2025
Indigo / Jul '95 / Direct / ADA.

MISSISSIPPI DELTA BLUES JAM IN MEMPHIS VOL.1
CD _____ ARHCD 385
Arhoolie / Apr '95 / ADA / Direct / Cadillac.

MISSISSIPPI DELTA BLUES JAM IN MEMPHIS VOL.2
CD _____ ARHCD 386
Arhoolie / Apr '95 / ADA / Direct / Cadillac.

MISSISSIPPI GIRLS 1928-31
CD _____ SOBCD 3515
Story Of The Blues / Mar '92 / Koch / ADA.

MISSISSIPPI MASTERS: EARLY AMERICAN BLUES CLASSICS
CD _____ YAZ 2008CD
Yazoo / Nov '94 / CM / ADA / Roots / Koch.

MISSISSIPPI: FROM CANADA TO LOUISIANA
CD _____ PS 65099
Playasound / Nov '92 / Harmonia Mundi / ADA.

MIST MASTERS - FLEDGLING
Lap of God: Couch / Freud's feild day: Delgados / Absence: Supernaturals / Didn't laugh at all: Saidflorence / Spooky (Baby mix): Love Joy & Happiness / Eurostar: Margins / Bring down the sky: August / Fashion victim: Colour Wheel / Fugue: Philo / Divine in water: Fuel / Mary Jane: Limit Club / Thank funk it's Friday: Captain Shifty / Only one: Jellyhead / G 12: Microwave Babe / Make it happen: Skunk Tree / Awkward: Geiger Babies / No reason: Laughing club / Coral: Homecoming / Banging the drum: Bond
CD _____ IGCD 209
Iona / Jan '95 / ADA / Direct / Duncans.

MIX THIS PUSSY
Ragga: Jeek / Eye 2 eye: Kiwi Dreams / It all begins here: Ofunwa / In the presence of angels: Spiritual Experience / (I want to) Take you home tonight: Sextravaganza / Come drums: Sextravaganza / Some lovin': Liberty City / U gig: Eastmen / Feeling free (masters and servants): Liquid City / Mind Power: Davis, Roy Jr / Atom bomb: D.J. Pierre Pres Doomsday / X: Vasquez, Junior / Dub disco house: Two Shiny Heads / Orgasm (never get enough): Sextravaganza / I won't waste your time: Joi & Jorio / Melody and harmony: Stories In Dubh / I want your love: Adventures Of Daniel Lite Star. L. Chambers / All or nothing: R2R / Together: Interceptor / Reach for me: Funky Green Dogs From Outer Space / Pete Cochon (I like it): Pascal's Bongo Massive / What am I gonna do: Wood, Matt
CD _____ TRIUK 002CD
Tribal UK / Nov '94 / Vital.

MIX THIS PUSSY VOL.2
Give her what she wants: Jeck / Givin' my all (higher than all): Liquid City / Storm: Salt City Orchestra / Give her what she wants (Remix): Jeck / Dream: Deep Dish & Prana / Dream (Dubfire): Deep Dish & Prana / Muzik set you free: D.J. Pierre / Love to heart (too hot): Atom / If you really love someone: Liberty City / If you really love someone (Remix): Liberty City / Cassa De X: Deep Dish & Elastic Reality / Cassa De X (Remix): Deep Dish & Elastic Reality / Bottom heavy: Tenaglia, Danny / Bottom heavy (Remix): Tenaglia, Danny / So get up: Underground Sound Of Lisbon / Y: Kiwi Dreams / Y (Backside dub): Kiwi Dreams / Girlz: Namby Pamby / Theme: Electric Fro / Unreleased project: D.J. Vibes / White rain: Karnak
CD _____ TRIUK 004CD
Tribal UK / Jun '95 / Vital.

MIXIN'
CD _____ REVCC 005
REVCO / May '95 / Grapevine.

MIXING IT
CD _____ CHILLCD 004
Chillout / Nov '94 / Disc / Kudos.

MIXMAG LIVE VOL.13
(Emerson/Angel)
CD _____ MMLCD 13
Stress / Feb '95 / Pinnacle.

MIXMAG LIVE VOL.20
(Richie Hawtin)
Dry ray: Lausen / Quo vadis: G-Man / Empower: Octave One / Jump: Broom, Mark / Wiper: Teste / 5 Mouths: Fred Frash / Basic needs: Goio / Substance abuse: Fuse / Spaz: Plastikman / helicopter: Plastikman / Percussion electrique: Dwarf / Spastik: Plastikman / Eye trip: Bryant, Akilah / Boiling point: Xtrak / Electricity: Naughty & Tolls / Dollar: Schmidt, Tobias / Live wire: DBX / Venus fly trap: Too Funk / Cash machines: Synchrojack / Key follow: Hannah, Paul / Harz: Sensorama / Altes testamentn: Roman IV
CD _____ MMLCD 020
Stress / Jan '96 / Pinnacle.

MIXMAG LIVE VOL.3
(Sasha/Mackintosh)
CD _____ MMLCD 3
Stress / Feb '95 / Pinnacle.

MIXMAG LIVE VOL.4
(Rampling/Park)
CD _____ MMLCD 4
Stress / Feb '95 / Pinnacle.

MLLE. SWING ET M. ZAZOU
CD _____ DEM 017
Chansons Actualites / Nov '95 / Discovery.

MO' STEPPERS
Grazing in the grass: Wonder, Stevie / Use it or lose it: Gotham / Open your door: Guinn / Brickhouse: Commodores / Bad weather: Supremes / Too high: Brown, Norman / I can't help it: Washington, Grover Jr. / Break the ice: Lovesmith, Michael / Jones': Temptations / Can I get a witness: Randolph, Barbara / All night long: Mary Jane Girls / Tell me tomorrow (12" mix): Robinson, Smokey / T plays it cool: Gaye, Marvin / Love just wouldn't be right: Marie, Teena / World of ours: Alston, Gerald / It's a shame: Detroit Spinners
CD _____ 530233-2
Motown / Apr '94 / PolyGram.

MODERN ARCHITECTURE OF HOUSE
CD _____ D 945002
Bunker/D'Vision / Jan '95 / Plastic Head.

MODERN ART OF JAZZ, THE
CD _____ BCD 120
Biograph / '92 / Wellard / ADA / Hot Shot / Jazz Music / Cadillac / Direct.

MODERN CAJUN LOVERS
CD _____ TRIK 0166
Trikont / Oct '94 / ADA / Direct.

MODERN CHICAGO BLUES
CD _____ TCD 5008
Testament / Oct '94 / Complete/Pinnacle / ADA / Koch.

MODERN ELECTRONICS VOL.1
CD _____ SUB 2D
Subversive / Sep '95 / 3MV / SRD.

MODERN JAZZ PIANO ALBUM, THE
Be bop pastel / Seven up / Blues in be bop / Supersonic / On a planet / Air pocket / Celestia / 'S wonderful / Nichols & dimes / Who's blues / My lagging gingersnap / Night is young (and you are so beautiful) / Why was I born / My foolish heart / Twins / I'll remember April / Joy bell / I didn't know what time it was / Budo / I married an angel / Jazz message / Frissell frazzle
CD _____ SVOCD 272
Savoy Jazz / Nov '95 / Conifer / ADA.

MODERN LOVE
(17 of Today's Classic Love Songs)
Don't let the sun go down on me: Michael, George & Elton John / Save the best for last: Williams, Vanessa / Stay: Shakespears / Goodnight girl: Wet Wet Wet / You: Ten Sharp / Fall at your feet: Crowded House / I wonder why: Stigers, Curtis / Time to make you mine: Stansfield, Lisa / Everytime you go away: Young, Paul / Promise me: Craven, Beverley / Get here: Adams, Oleta / When you tell me that you love me: Ross, Diana / My girl: Temptations / Every kinda people: Palmer, Robert / Coming out of the dark: Estefan, Gloria / Unchained melody: Righteous Brothers / Valerie: Winwood, Steve
CD _____ 515 518-2
PolyGram TV / Jun '92 / PolyGram.

MODERN NEW ORLEANS MASTERS
CD _____ CD 11514
Rounder / '88 / CM / Direct / ADA / Cadillac.

MODERN ROCK
CD _____ SETCD 084
Stardust / Sep '94 / Carlton Home Entertainment.

MODERN SOUL 2 - BOSS GROOVES
Show me the way: Butler, Sam / I can't get over losing you: Butler, Sam / Take another look: Saunders, Frankie / Try love again: Pro-fascination / Let me give love: Empire, Freddie / Give me love: EKG / You keep holding back on love: Sue, Carletta / This time it's real: Nevilles, Larry / Something inside: Raj / What's the use: Troutman, Tony / I'll cry over you: Sheeler, Cynthia / You're gonna wreck my life: Guitar Ray / Where is the love: Carlton, Richard / Very special girl: White, Earl / Man in love: Wright, Bill / Sexy lady: Sideshow / I've got to have your love: Robertson, Chuck
CD _____ GSCD 015
Goldmine / May '93 / Vital.

MODERN SOUL 4
Your love's got me: Satin / Time is right for love: Reed, Bobby / My heart just can't take it: Essex IV / Beggin' for a broken heart: Jackson, Otis / Now you're gone: Smoke / I get groove from you: Shannon, Bobby / One shirt: Marshall, Gene & The Ghetto Soul / This I've gotta see: Shaw, Cecil / Love in my heart: Gunter, Cornell / I know you're leaving me: Hightower, Sy / Here we go: Spread Love / Decisions: Lowe, Freddie / Sexy lady: Giles, Eddie & The Numbers / Breaking training: Brown, Larry / Don't it: Dawson, Roy / I wish our love would last forever: Swiss Movement / You beat me at my game like a lazy: Strong, Chuck
CD _____ GSCD 057
Goldmine / Jul '95 / Vital.

MODS MAYDAY '79
Time for action: Secret Affair / Let your heart dance: Secret Affair / Don't throw your life away: Beggar / Hanging in the balance: Small Hours / Tonight's the night: Mods / Let me be the one: Mods / B-a-b-y baby love: Squire / Midnight to six: Small Hours / Broadway show: Beggar / All night / Love only me: Mods / Walking down the King's Road: Squire / Live without her love: Squire / I'm not free (But I'm cheap): Secret Affair / End of the night: Small Hours
CD _____ DOJOCD 5
Dojo / Jun '94 / BMG.

MODULATION & TRANSFORMATION
CD _____ EFA 006652
Mille Plateau / Jun '95 / SRD.

MOJO ROCKSTEADY
CD _____ HBCD 134
Heartbeat / Jun '94 / Greensleeves / Jetstar / Direct / ADA.

MOJO WORKING: THE BEST OF ACE BLUES
Dust my blues: James, Elmore / Boogie chillun: Hooker, John Lee / Little school girl: Hogg, Smokey / Happy payday: Littlefield, Little Willie / Blues after hours: Crayton, Pee Wee / Please love me: King, B.B. / Lonesome dog blues: Hopkins, Lightnin' / Riding in the moonlight: Howlin' Wolf / Things that I used to do: Guitar Slim / I miss you so: Turner, Ike / Three hours past midnight: Watson, Johnny 'Guitar' / Baby let's play house: Gunter, Arthur / I'm a mojo man: Lonesome Sundown / I'm a King Bee: Harpo, Slim / Hoodoo blues: Lightnin' Slim / I'm a lover not a fighter: Lazy Lester / Rock me baby: King, B.B. / Part time love: Taylor, Little Johnny / Black nights: Fulson, Lowell / Born under a bad sign: King, Albert
CD _____ CDCHK 964
Ace / Jan '95 / Pinnacle / Cadillac / Complete/Pinnacle.

MOMENT RECORDS COLLECTION VOL. 1
CD _____ MR 1008CD
Moment / Apr '95 / ADA / Koch.

MOMENTS IN LOVE
You've lost that lovin' feelin': Righteous Brothers / Without you: Nilsson, Harry / Cherish: Kool & The Gang / Keep on loving you: REO Speedwagon / I'm not in love: 10cc / Total eclipse of the heart: Tyler, Bonnie / Broken wings: Mr. Mister / Suddenly: Ocean, Billy / Stay with me 'til dawn: Tzuke, Judie / There's nothing better than love: Vandross, Luther / All the love in the world: Warwick, Dionne / You're the best thing: Style Council / Do what you do: Jackson, Jermaine / Just the way you are: White, Barry / Best thing that ever happened to me: Knight, Gladys & The Pips / Oh girl: Chi-Lites / All out of love: Air Supply / Every day hurts: Sad Cafe
CD _____ MUSCD 002
MCI / Nov '92 / Disc / THE.

MOMENTS OF LOVE
CD _____ DCD 5307
Disky / Dec '93 / THE / BMG / Discovery / Pinnacle.

MONEY MONEY MONEY
(Music Of Abba - 16 Instrumental Hits)
CD _____ 5708574338059
Carlton Home Entertainment / Sep '94 / Carlton Home Entertainment.

MONGOLIE
CD _____ G 7511
Sterns / '87 / Sterns / CM.

MONKEY BUSINESS
Tighten up: Untouchables / Fatty fatty: Eccles, Clancy / 54-46 (was my number): Toots & The Maytals / 007: Dekker, Desmond / Liquidator: Harry J All Stars / Fire corner: Eccles, Clancy / Double barrel: Collins, Dave & Ansil / Birth control: Lee, Byron / Herbsman: King Stitt & The Dynamites / Elizabethan reggae: Gardiner, Boris / Return of django: Upsetters / Monkey spanner: Collins, Dave & Ansil / Longshot kick de bucket: Pioneers / Young, gifted and black: Bob & Marcia / Monkey man: Toots & The Maytals / Dollar in the teeth: Upsetters / Barbwire: Dean, Nora / Shocks of mighty: Soulmates / Cherry oh baby: Donaldson, Eric
CD _____ CDTRL 188
Trojan / Jan '95 / Jetstar / Total/BMG.

MONKEY SKA
Monkey ska: Harriott, Derrick / Really now: Dreamletts / Vat seven: Drummond, Don / I don't need your love: Chuck & Dobby / Don't throw it away: Hits / Out of space: McCook, Tommy & The Supersonics / Sammy no dead: Eccles, Clancy / I'm so in love with you: Techniques / Make yourself comfortable: Los Caballeros Orchestra / Cling to me: Dawkins, Horrell / Open the door: Clive & Naomi / Live wire: Soul Brothers / Seed you sow: Bonny / True confession: Silvertones / Girl next door: Blues Blenders / Jam session: Brooks, Baba / What a good woodman: Perry, Lee 'Scratch' / Tender love prayer: Tait, Lynn / Paradise: Shirley, Roy / Third man theme: Williams, Granville Orchestra
CD _____ CDTRL 323
Trojan / Mar '94 / Jetstar / Total/BMG.

MONSTER BOP
Rockin' in the graveyard: Morningstar, Jackie / Werewolf: Bonafede, Carl / Story that's true: Bonafede, Carl / Caveman hop: Coulston, Jerry / Cat: Willis, Rod / Midnight monsters: Jack & Jim / Nightmare: Stuart, Scottie / Graveyard: Bowman, Leroy / Skeleton fight: Smith, Allen / Monster hop: Dee, Jimmy / Gorilla: Convy, Bert / Leopard man: Wallace, Joe / Nightmare hop: Patterson, Earl / Monster: Please, Bobby / Caveman: Roe, Tommy / Mad house jump: Daylighters / Jekyll and Hyde: Burgett, Jim / Haunted house: Kevin, Cris / Head hunter: Fern, Mike / I'm the wolfman: Round Robin Monopoly / Frankenstein's den: Hollywood Flames / Don't meet Mr. Frankenstein: Casal, Carlos Jnr / I was a teenage monster: Keytones / You can get him Frankenstein: Castle Kings / Gila monster: Johnson, Joe / Frankenstein: Thomas, Eddie / I was a teenage cave man: Luck, Randy / Frank Frankenstein: Ivan
CD _____ CDBB 55013
Buffalo Bop / Apr '94 / Rollercoaster.

MONSTERS OF ROCK
Stargazer: Rainbow / Another piece of meat: Scorpions / All night long: Rainbow / Don't ya know what love is: Touch / Loving you Sunday morning: Scorpions / Backs to the wall: Saxon / I like to rock: April Wine / Road racin': Riot
CD _____ 8436892
Polydor / Aug '90 / PolyGram.

MONSTERS OF ROCK
(4CD Set)
CD Set _____ MBSCD 435
Castle / Mar '95 / BMG.

MONSTERS OF ROCK II
CD _____ SMR 29
Simple Machines / Jun '94 / SRD.

MONTEREY INTERNATIONAL POP FESTIVAL
(Definitive Document Of The First Great Rock Festival)
CD Set _____ ROCCD 2
Castle / Feb '94 / BMG.

MONTREUX - A WINDHAM HILL RETROSPECTIVE
To be / Dolphins / Egrets / Let them say / October wedding / Near northern / Circular birds / Movie / Jacob do bandolim / Piacenza / Tideline / True story / Lights in the sky are stars / Free D
CD _____ 01934111222
Windham Hill / Mar '93 / Pinnacle / BMG / ADA.

MONTREUX FESTIVAL
In view: Hamilton, Chico / Let me down easy: Little Milton / We're gonna make it: Little Milton / Don't make no sense: Little Milton / Call it stormy Monday: Little Milton / For the love of a woman: King, Albert
CD _____ CDSXE 070
Stax / Nov '92 / Pinnacle.

MONTREUX SUMMIT 1
Montreux summit / Infant eyes / Blues march / Bahama Mama / Fried bananas / Andromeda
CD _____ 4786072
Sony Jazz / Dec '95 / Sony.

MOODS ORCHESTRAL
(4CD Set)
CD Set _____ MBSCD 445
Castle / Nov '95 / BMG.

MOON OF ROSES
CD _____ ITM 1487
ITM / Apr '94 / Tradelink / Koch.

MOONGLOW
Wavy gravy: Burrell, Kenny & Stanley Turrentine / Days of wine and roses: Lawson, Hugh / Made in France: Lagrene, Birelli / Summertime: Jones, Hank / My old flame: Sims, Zoot & John Eardley / Hot sauce: Hope, Elmo Trio / Moonglow: Goodman, Benny Quintet / Take the 'A' train: Newborn, Phineas Trio / Breeze and I: Pepper, Art & Carl Perkins / Lady is a tramp: Lee, Peggy / Swingin' the blues: Basie, Count Orchestra / Moonlight in Vermont: Smith, Johnny Quintet / Angelina: Klugh, Earl / Almost like being in love: Hipp, Jutta & Zoot Sims/Jerry Lloyd / Opus de funk: Silver, Horace / In a sentimental mood: Ellington, Duke
CD _____ CDJA 4
Premier/MFP / Oct '91 / EMI.

MOONLIGHTING
Divine emotions: Narada / Casanova: Levert / I want her: Sweat, Keith / Rain: Jones, Oran 'Juice' / Love is contagious: Sevelle, Taja / Gotta get you home tonight: Whole, Eugene / Nite and day: Sure, Al B. / Wishing on a star: Rose Royce / Sexual healing: Gaye, Marvin / I want to be your man: Roger / Lovers: O'Neal, Alexander / Feel so real: Arrington, Steve / Baby, come to me: Austin, Patti & James Ingram / Moonlighting: Jarreau, Al / Caught up in the rapture (remix): Baker, Anita / Tender love: Force MD's
CD _____ 2414382
WEA / Sep '88 / Warner Music.

MOONRAKER
CD _____ SPV 08538942
SPV / Sep '94 / Plastic Head.

MORE 12" OF PLEASURE
CD _____ ALMYCD 14
Almighty / Jun '95 / Total/BMG.

MORE CAJUN CLASSICS
(The Kings Of Cajun At Their Very Best)
Lacassine special / Madam boso / Sur la courtableau / La valse de reno / Les veuves de la coulee / Jolie fille / Mamou blues / Louisiana aces special / Jolie blon / Grand nuit special / I passed by your door / Cajun popo / Starvation waltz / Mowater blues / Hippy ti yo / Les traces de mon bogue / Hold my false teeth / Hey jolie / Makes me feel like dancing / Valse de cypriere / La vie de cadjin / Le ti-mouchoir / Tu peux cogner / Going back to Louisiana
CD _____ CDCHM 519
Ace / May '94 / Pinnacle / Cadillac / Complete/Pinnacle.

MORE CAJUN MUSIC AND ZYDECO
CD _____ ROUCD 11573
Rounder / Aug '95 / CM / Direct / ADA / Cadillac.

MORE GOOD WHISKEY BLUES
(Collection Of Contemporary Blues Songs From Tennessee)
CD _____ TX 1010CD
Taxim / Jan '94 / ADA.

MORE GREAT ROCKIN' GIRLS
Black cadillac: Green, Joyce / Jack pot: Fredericks, Dolores / Flipsville: Gayle, Stormy / Lou Lou knows: Wallace, Fonda / Rock-a-bop: Lynn, Dolores / Riba daba doo: Jones, Mari / Bouncing heart: Martin, Carmen / Long sideburns: Barry, Boelean / Red thunderbird: Howard, Lynn / What a man: Flowers, Vancie / Little foot: Rae, Donna / Fascinating baby: Scott, Sherree / Shaky shaky: Long, Rosalie / Gonna spend my time: Myers, Orella / Trifling man: Howard, Betty / Honky tonk top: Beaubells / Stop: Laraine, Little Rita / Scrapbook twist: Jae, Judy / Dancing teardrop: Redd, Barbara / Bald headed twister: Harding, Oneda / Baby doll: Wells, Ardis / Fish house function: Oro, Emmy / Shakin': Scott, Sherree / Jumpin' like a kangaroo: Geree / Mad Mama: Bowman, Jane / Red lite: Liz / At the end of the rainbow: Dene, Glenna / Twisteree: Jae, Judy / Crazy little baby: Gunter, Shirley / Baby, oh baby: Allen, Joyce
CD _____ CDCL 4416
White Label/Bear Family / Apr '94 / Bear Family / Rollercoaster.

MORE GUMBO STEW
Ya ya: Dorsey, Lee / Clap your hands: Johnson, Wallace / Always accused: Tee, Willie / Need you: Prince La La / You better check: Bo, Eddie / Talk that talk: Dr. John & Ronnie Barron / World of dreams: Lynn, Tammi / Gonna get you yet: Tick tocks / Peace of mind: Johnson, Wallace / Two weeks three days: Duvall, Joan / Fix (One naughty flat): Dr. John / Try me: George, Barbara / Make her you wife: Pistol / It was you: Tee, Willie / Wyld: Afo executives / Let me know: Lee, Robbie / Better be cool: Robinson, Alvin / I've never been in love: Robinson, Alvin / Light my fire: Lynn, Tammi / Johnny A's blues: Adams, Johnny
CD _____ CDCHD 462
Ace / Sep '93 / Pinnacle / Cadillac / Complete/Pinnacle.

MORE HITS OF THE 60'S
CD _____ MCCD 193
Music Club / Mar '95 / Disc / THE / CM.

MORE HOLLYWOOD ROCK'N'ROLL
She just tears me up: Stewart, Wynn / Down on the farm: Downing, Big Al / So tough: Kuf Linx / Three months to kill: Duvall, Huelyn / Kee-ro-ryin': Johnny & Jonie / Jungle hop: Tyler, Kip / Gotta lot of rhythm in my soul: Cline, Patsy / Shiver: Burgess, Dave / Uncle Tom got caught: Stewart, Wynn / Oh babe: Downing, Big Al / Come on: Stewart, Wynn / Go little go cat: Four Teens / Spark plug: Four Teens / Didn't it rock: Jim 'n' Rod / Bad Dad: Davis, Gene / Great day in the morning: Four Teens / Life begins at four o'clock: Milano, Bobby / Shiverin' and shakin': Beard, Dean / Egad, Chrome Brown: Beard, Dean / Eyeballin': Kuf Linx / You can say that again: Four Teens / Double talkin' baby: Milano, Bobby / Machine gun: Rip Tides / Hey little car hop: Weston, George / Sneakin': Weston, George / Bee-ah-ah-bee: Coburn, Kimball / Annie's not an orphan anymore: Rochell & The Candles / Rock roma rock it: Crothers, Scat Man
CD _____ CDCHD 494
Ace / Mar '94 / Pinnacle / Cadillac / Complete/Pinnacle.

MORE HOTTEST HITS FROM TREASURE ISLE
CD _____ HB 109CD
Heartbeat / Jul '94 / Greensleeves / Jetstar / Direct / ADA.

MORE, MORE, MORE
(More Classic Soul)
I wanna dance wit' choo: Disco Tex & The Sexolettes / I'm doing fine now: New York City / Dolly my love: Moments / Higher and higher: Wilson, Jackie / In Zaire: Wakelin, Johnny / More, more, more: Andrea True Connection / Hold back the night: Trammps / Dance the body music: Osibisa / Can you feel the force: Real Thing / I owe you one: Shalamar / And the beat goes on: Whispers / Check out the groove: Thurston, Bobby / Foot stompin' music: Bohannon, Hamilton / I'll go where your music takes me: James, Jimmy / Too good to be forgotten: Chi-Lites / We got the funk: Positive Force
CD _____ TRTCD 142
TrueTrax / Dec '94 / THE.

MORE RADIO FUN
Tchaikovsky: Kaye, Danny / Hit that jive Jack: Cole, Nat King Trio / Friendship: Garland, Judy & Johnny Mercer / Everthing is fresh today: Hodges, Jack / I'm the pest of Budapest: Byng, Douglas / Inka dinka doo: Durante, Jimmy / Minnie the moocher: Calloway, Cab / I can't dance, I've got ants in my pants: Valaida / You always hurt the one you love: Jones, Spike & His City Slickers / Leader of the town band: Rey, Monte & The Ovaltineys / Old school tie: Western Brothers / Percy the prawn: Alan, A.J. / King Chamcleer: International Novelty Quartet / Somebody stole my gal: Cotton, Billy / Bob White: Crosby, Bing & Connie Boswell / Wil-

liam Tell overture: Viennese Seven Singing Sisters / My canary has circles under his eyes: Harris, Marion / When you've a fella like me on the force: Frankau, Ronald / Super special picture of the year: Yacht Club Jazz Band / Oriental express: Orchestre Raymonde / Peace and quiet: Butcher, Ernest / Mary from the dairy: Miller, Max / Amy, wonderful Amy: Hylton, Jack
CD _____ CDHD 240
Happy Days / Apr '94 / Conifer.

MORE REAL JAZZ BALLADS
CD _____ MPV 5520
Movieplay / Oct '92 / Target/BMG.

MORE ROCK 'N' ROLL LOVE SONGS
Raining in my heart: Holly, Buddy / Blue moon: Marcels / Bye bye love: Everly Brothers / I only have eyes for you: Flamingos / Take good care of my baby: Vee, Bobby / You're sixteen: Burnette, Johnny Rock 'N' Roll Trio / My little girl: Crickets / I remember: Cochran, Eddie / Two people in the world: Imperials / When: Kalin Twins / Sweet nothin's: Lee, Brenda / It's late: Nelson, Rick / I want you to be my girl: Lymon, Frankie & The Teenagers / Unchained melody: Baxter, Les / She she little Sheila: Vincent, Gene / Party doll: Knox, Buddy / I'll never get over you: Kidd, Johnny & The Pirates / Only sixteen: Douglas, Craig / Ain't misbehavin': Bruce, Tommy & The Bruisers
CD _____ CDMFP 5999
Music For Pleasure / Nov '93 / EMI.

MORE STARS OF LAS VEGAS
Secret love: Doris Day / Stranger in paradise: Bennett, Tony / Almost there: Williams, Andy / Blue velvet: Vinton, Bobby / Unchained melody: Hibbler, Al / Wives and lovers: Jones, Jack / What a wonderful world: Armstrong, Louis / Fever: Lee, Peggy / It's only make believe: Campbell, Glen / When I fall in love: Cole, Nat King / Memories are made of this: Martin, Dean / I love you because: Martino, Al / And I love you so: Como, Perry / Love me warm and tender: Anka, Paul / Woman in love: Three Degrees / Welcome to my world: Reeves, Jim / Green green grass of home: Jones, Tom / Release me: Humperdinck, Engelbert / Girl from Ipanema: Getz, Stan & Astrud Gilberto / Laughter in the rain: Sedaka, Neil
CD _____ VSOPCD 201
Connoisseur / Jun '94 / Pinnacle.

MORE THAN A FEELING
You're the voice: Farnham, John / Nothing's gonna stop us now: Starship / More than a feeling: Boston / You took the words right out of my mouth: Meat Loaf / Can't fight this feeling: REO Speedwagon / Don't stop believin': Journey / Rosanna: Toto / Satellite: Hooters / Final countdown: Europe / Broken wings: Mr. Mister / When I see you smile: Bad English / (Don't fear) The reaper: Blue Oyster Cult / Flame: Cheap Trick / So tired: Osbourne, Ozzy / Rock 'n' roll dreams come through: Steinman, Jim / Stairway to heaven: Far Corporation
CD _____ 4730452
Columbia / Feb '93 / Sony.

MORE THAN JUST DANCEHALL - RAGGA PARTY PART 2
Education: Irie, Chris / Funny familiar feeling: Thriller U / Dollar bill: Demus, Nico / Girls girls: Robinson, Ed & Apache Scratchy / Last laugh: Isaacs, Gregory / Conversation: Campbell, Cornell / Billy the kid: Jigsy King / Money: Shaggy Wonder / Tek live: Professor Frisky / True love relation: Junior, John / What are girls made of: Tiger / Chicken in the corn: Robinson, Ed, Chris / Flower garden (Version): Irie, Chris / Flower garden: Irie, Chris
CD _____ RN 017CD
Runn / Nov '92 / Jetstar / SRD.

MORLEY, PARLSEY, INGLOTT
CD _____ PRCD 396
Priory / Jul '92 / Priory.

MOROCCAN TRANCE MUSIC
CD _____ SUBCD 01336
Sub Rosa / Jan '96 / Vital / These / Discovery.

MOROCCAN TRANCE MUSIC II: SUFI
CD _____ SR 97
Le Coeur Du Monde / Jan '96 / Direct.

MOROCCO/MAROC
(Berber Music From High/Anti Atlas Region)
CD _____ LDX 274991
La Chant Du Monde / Jun '94 / Harmonia Mundi / ADA.

MORTAR
CD _____ PPP 104NP
PDCD / Jan '94 / Plastic Head.

MORTUARY VOL.1
CD _____ SKELETON 93
Skeleton / Sep '94 / Plastic Head.

MOSCOW NIGHTS
CD _____ MCD 71590
Monitor / Jan '93 / CM.

MOST BEAUTIFUL SONGS OF AFRICA
CD _____ EUCD 1239
ARC / Nov '93 / ARC Music / ADA.

MOST BEAUTIFUL YODELLING FROM THE ALPS VOL.1, THE
CD _____ 321122
Koch / Sep '92 / Koch.

MOST BEAUTIFUL YODELLING FROM THE ALPS VOL.2, THE
CD _____ 330023
Koch / Sep '92 / Koch.

MOST BEAUTIFUL YODELLING FROM THE ALPS VOL.3, THE
CD _____ 330039
Koch / Sep '92 / Koch.

MOST EXCELLENT DANCE
(2CD/MC Set)
Right in the night: Jam & Spoon / Love love love here I come: Rollo Goes Mystic / Dreamer: Living Joy / Sweet harmony: Liquid / U sure do: Strike / Keep love together: Love To Infinity / Fired up: Elevator Man / Magic in U: Sugarbabees / Let love shine: Amos / Sex on the streets: Pizzaman / It's our future: Awex / Not over yet: Grace / Your loving arms: Martin, Billie Ray / Heart of glass: Blondie / Into the blue: Moby / Joanna: Mrs. Woods / I'm alive: Cut 'n' Move / Sky high: Newton / Whoomph there it is: Clock / Feel the goodtimes: Smith, Charlene / Friendly pressure: Jhelisa / Freedom: Gayle, Michelle / Three is family: Dawson, Dana / Bomb: Bucketheads / Surrender your love: Nightcrawlers / Sweetest day of May: Vannelli, Joe T. Project / As long as you're good to me: Cheeks, Judy / Saturday night party: Alex Party / I believe: Happy Clappers / Get your hands off my man: Vasquez, Junior / My love is deep: Parker, Sara / Don't make me wait: Loveland / Going around: D'Bora / Not anyone: Black Box / Work it out: Shiva / Why not believe in him: Morel Inc / Take you there: Simon, Ronni / Joy of living: Oui 3
CD Set _____ CDMXD 1
EMI / Aug '95 / EMI.

MOSTLY MILES
(Newport Jazz Festival 1958 July 3rd-6th)
CD _____ NCD 8813
Phontastic / '93 / Wellard / Jazz Music / Cadillac.

MOTHER VOLGA
(Recordings From The Banks Of The Volga River)
CD _____ PANCD 2008
Pan / May '93 / ADA / Direct / CM.

MOTOR CITY - THE MUSIC OF DETROIT
CD Set _____ TFP 014
Tring / Nov '92 / Tring / Prism.

MOTOWN CHARTBUSTERS VOL.1
Blowin' in the wind: Wonder, Stevie / I was made to love her: Wonder, Stevie / You keep me hangin' on: Supremes / Happening: Supremes / Love is here and now you're gone: Supremes / Standing in the shadows of love: Four Tops / Seven rooms of gloom: Four Tops / It takes two: Gaye, Marvin & Kim Weston / When you're young and in love: Marvelettes / I'm losing you: Temptations / What becomes of the broken hearted: Ruffin, Jimmy / Gonna give her all the love I've got: Ruffin, Jimmy / How sweet it is (to be loved by you): Walker, Junior & The All Stars / I'm ready for love: Reeves, Martha / Jimmy Mack: Reeves, Martha / Take me in your arms and love me: Knight, Gladys & The Pips
CD _____ 530066-2
Motown / Jan '93 / PolyGram.

MOTOWN CHARTBUSTERS VOL.2
Ain't nothing like the real thing: Gaye, Marvin & Tammi Terrell / If I could build my whole world around you: Gaye, Marvin & Tammi Terrell / Reflections: Ross, Diana & The Supremes / Some things you never get used to: Ross, Diana & The Supremes / If you can want / I second that emotion / You keep running away: Four Tops / If I were a carpenter: Four Tops / I could never love another (after loving you): Temptations / You're my everything: Temptations / I heard it through the grapevine: Knight, Gladys & The Pips / I'm wondering: Wonder, Stevie / Shoo-be-doo-be-doo-da-day: Wonder, Stevie / I've passed this way before: Ruffin, Jimmy / Gotta see Jane: Taylor, R. Dean / Honey chile: Reeves, Martha
CD _____ 530067-2
Motown / Jan '93 / PolyGram.

MOTOWN CHARTBUSTERS VOL.4
I want you back: Jackson Five / ABC: Jackson Five / Onion song: Gaye, Marvin & Tammi Terrell / Too busy thinking about my baby: Gaye, Marvin / I can't help myself: Four Tops / Do what you gotta do: Four Tops / Up the ladder to the roof: Supremes / Someday we'll be together: Ross, Diana & The Supremes / Cloud 9: Temptations / I can't get next to you / Temptations / Second that emotion: Temptations / Farewell is a lonely sound: Ruffin, Jimmy / What does it take (to win your love): Walker, Junior & The All Stars
CD _____ 530592
Motown / Jan '93 / PolyGram.

MOTOWN CHARTBUSTERS VOL.5
Tears of a clown: Robinson, Smokey / War: Starr, Edwin / Love you save: Jackson Five / I'll be there: Jackson Five / Ball of confusion: Temptations / It's all in the game: Four Tops / Still water (love): Four Tops / Heaven help us all: Wonder, Stevie / Signed, sealed, delivered (I'm yours): Wonder, Stevie / I'll say forever my love: Wonder, Stevie / Ain't no mountain high enough: Ross, Diana / Stoned love: Supremes / Abraham, Martin and John: Gaye, Marvin / Forget me not: Reeves, Martha / It's a shame: Motown Spinners / Never had a dream come true: Wonder, Stevie / It's wonderful (To be loved by you): Four Tops
CD _____ 5300602
Motown / Jan '93 / PolyGram.

MOTOWN CHARTBUSTERS VOL.7
Automatically sunshine: Supremes / Floy Joy: Supremes / You gotta have love in your heart: Supremes & Four Tops / Surrender: Ross, Diana / Doobedood'ndoobe, doobedood'ndoobe: Ross, Diana / Just walk in my shoes: Knight, Gladys & The Pips / Rockin' robin: Jackson, Michael / Ain't no sunshine: Jackson, Michael / Got to be there: Jackson, Michael / I want a look around: Temptations / Superstar (Remember how you got where you are): Temptations / If you really love me: Wonder, Stevie / Bless you: Reeves, Martha / Walk in the night: Walker, Junior & The All Stars / Festival time: San Remo Strings / My guy: Wells, Mary
CD _____ 5300622
Motown / Jan '93 / PolyGram.

MOTOWN CHRISTMAS
Little Christmas tree: Jackson, Michael / Christmas lullaby: Robinson, Smokey / This Christmas: Ross, Diana / This Christmas song: Gaye, Marvin / Wish you a merry Christmas: Weston, Kim / Silent night: Ross, Diana & The Supremes / Christmas in the city: Gaye, Marvin / Everyone's a kid at Christmas time: Wonder, Stevie / Winter wonderland: Funk Brothers / I want to come home for Christmas: Gaye, Marvin / Just a lonely Christmas: Ross, Diana & The Supremes / Won't be long before Christmas: Ross, Diana & The Supremes / Miracles of Christmas: Wonder, Stevie / Purple snowflake: Gaye, Marvin
CD _____ 5507192
Spectrum/Karussell / Nov '94 / PolyGram / THE.

MOTOWN HEARTBREAKERS
CD _____ TCD 2343
Telstar / Sep '89 / BMG.

MOTOWN HITS COLLECTION VOL.II
CD _____ 5306042
Polydor / Sep '95 / PolyGram.

MOTOWN HITS OF GOLD VOLS 1-8
CD Set _____ WD 724018
Motown / Feb '89 / PolyGram.

MOTOWN PRESENTS MORE CHRISTMAS CLASSICS
Santa Claus is coming to town: Ross, Diana & The Supremes / White Christmas: Temptations / One little Christmas tree: Wonder, Stevie / Christmas everyday: Robinson, Smokey & The Miracles / Rudolph the red nosed reindeer: Ross, Diana & The Supremes / Have yourself a merry little Christmas: Jackson Five / Twinkle twinkle little me: Wonder, Stevie / My Christmas tree: Temptations / Noel: Robinson, Smokey & The Miracles / Give love on Christmas day: Jackson Five / Christmas song: Temptations / Silver bells: Wonder, Stevie / Little drummer boy: Jackson Five / Joy to the world: Ross, Diana & The Supremes / Miracles of Christmas: Wonder, Stevie / Children's Christmas song: Ross, Diana & The Supremes / Someday at Christmas: Temptations / Warm little home on the hill: Wonder, Stevie / It's Christmas time: Robinson, Smokey & The Miracles / Silent night: Temptations
CD _____ 5302372
Polydor / Nov '93 / PolyGram.

MOTOWN SONGBOOK
CD _____ VSOPCD 180
Connoisseur / Jan '93 / Pinnacle.

MOUNTAIN MUSIC
CD _____ SFWCD 40038
Smithsonian Folkways / Dec '94 / ADA / Direct / Koch / CM / Cadillac.

MOUNTAIN MUSIC OF PERU VOLUME ONE
CD _____ CDS 40020
Smithsonian Folkways / Aug '94 / ADA / Direct / Koch / CM / Cadillac.

MOUNTAIN MUSIC OF PERU VOLUME TWO
CD _____ SFWCD 40406
Smithsonian Folkways / Aug '95 / ADA / Direct / Koch / CM / Cadillac.

MOUVANCES TZIGANES - NOMAD'S LAND
CD _____ PS 65134CD
Playasound / Jul '94 / Harmonia Mundi / ADA.

MOVE YOUR BODY
I'm so into you: S.W.V. / Everybody dance: Evolution / Another sleepless night: Christopher, Shawn / Where love lives: Limerick,

Alison / Love me the right way: *Rapination* / Give it to you: *Wash, Martha* / Move your body: *Expansions* / Don't you want me: *Felix* / Open your mind: *Usura* / Packet of peace: *Lion Rock* / Seven ways to love: *Cola Boy* / I don't know anything else: *Black Box* / I like it: *D.J.H.* / Got to get: *Rob 'N' Raz & Leila K*
CD _____ 74321273602
Arista / May '95 / BMG.

MOVEMENTS IN BULGARIAN FOLK MUSIC
CD _____ VGR 9405CD
Van Geel / Jul '95 / ADA / Direct.

MOVIN' ON
Introduce me to love: *Absolute* / Overjoy: S'Mone, *Guy* / It's over: *Perfect Taste* / Searching: *China Black* / Falling by candnoes: *Music & Mystery* / Keep it comin': *Julianne* / Never gonna give you up: *Watergates* / Takes time: *Funhill* / Bring me back: *Drakes, Anthony* / Pushin' against the flow: *Raw Stylus* / Mr. Magic: *Dreaming A Dream* / Reconsider: *Bell, Melissa*
CD _____ RUCD 300
Rumour / May '92 / Pinnacle / 3MV / Sony.

MOVIN' ON 2
Revival: *Girault, Martine* / Love guaranteed: *Ferrier, Robert* / Something inside: *Deep Joy* / I want you back: *Sinclair* / Got to be you: *Koo Koo* / You turn me on: *Everis* / Call me anytime: *FM Inc* / One girl too late: *Pure Silk* / 2.B.A.S.1: *Ballin, Chris* / Warm love: *Law, Joanna* / Intimate connection: *Delano, Rohan* / Yes, yes, yes: *Applemountain* / Higher love: *Naked Funk*
CD _____ RUCD 301
Rumour / Oct '92 / Pinnacle / 3MV / Sony.

MOVIN' ON 3
Don't go walking (out that door): *Watergates* / Keep on giving: *B.C.A.* / Turn me on: *A Certain Ratio* / What you won't do for love: *Nu Visions* / Girl overboard: *Snowboy* / It's not alright: *Stirling McLean* / No man the vibe: *Vibe & Delroy Pinnock* / Poetical love: *Fyza* / Slow and easy: *Moving In The Right Direction* / Coming on to me: *Mo & Beez* / No time for change: *Outside* / Joy is free: *Think 2wice* / Revelation: *Simon, Vanessa* / Oh happy day: *Beat System*
CD _____ RUCD 302
Rumour / Jun '91 / Pinnacle / 3MV / Sony.

MOVIN' ON 4
I don't want it: *Opaz* / Rebirth: *Mighty Truth* / Ain't gonna walk in your shadow no more: *Do'reen* / You can depend on me: *Clarke, Rick* / So what: *Raw Groove* / Mr. Beautiful: *Anoforo* / What's on your mind: *Rose, J.B.* / Love forever: *Deluxe* / One step (at a time): *Rose, Mary* / You bring me joy: *Miss Hailey* / Loveride: *Scott, Samantha* / Ain't no sunshine: *Fyza*
CD _____ RULCD 304
Rumour / Oct '93 / Pinnacle / 3MV / Sony.

MOVIN' ON 5
Desire: *Desire* / Chill me: *Fresh N Funky* / In the mood: *Raw To The Core* / Underhanded: *Fokus* / Last chance: *Diplomats* / Runaway love: *Serious Rope* / Highwire: *Players* / Say yeah: *Izit* / Don't rush: *Fresh Cut* / Oooh with you: *Kleeer* / Blameless: *Malaya* / You're telling me lies: *Taylor, Justine*
CD _____ RULCD 305
Rumour / Apr '94 / Pinnacle / 3MV / Sony.

MOVIN' RECORDS - THE REAL SOUND OF NEW JERSEY
CD _____ WORLD 004CD
World Series / Oct '93 / Vital.

MOZAMBIQUE 1
Magalango / Mutcico/Munguenisso / Enhipiti esquissirua / Mama na wamina anga monanga / Unabadera uhema / N'kissa / Ndiribe nyumba / Tira nikhubula monalame / Utemdene / Ntabuya mundzuku / Essifa zonhipiti / Chihire / Komvarava kovela / Saudamos o grupo ladysmith black mambazo / Nisalili aussiwanini
CD _____ CDORBD 086
Globestyle / May '94 / Pinnacle.

MOZAMBIQUE 2
Muticitco / Simbiane / Enhipiti kahi yankhani / Amiravo amutane / Amigos, somos un enxame / Onhipiti ossanta toniyo / Ngalihne ilanga / Chinhambalala / Ukapata lya, ukapela bai / Mocambicano / Maria, kwadoca / Allahi ka salauto wahi wa-salaam / Frelimo quire echemi / Arminda / Mubedo wamina ysati wana wamina / Ndjemu / Onhipiti / Amigos, somos um enxame
CD _____ CDORBD 087
Globestyle / Nov '94 / Pinnacle.

MPS PIANO HIGHLIGHTS
CD _____ 5195022
Verve / Mar '93 / PolyGram.

MRS. WOOD TEACHES TECHNO
Energy 1: *Energised* / Suck my dang a lang: *E-Rection* / Go to the moon: *DJPC* / Military City: *Mark NRG* / Get bouncy: *Pelgrim* / Driple: *Organic Substance* / No district: *Nasty Django* / Te genitro: *Instance* / Sorry: *Genlog* / Get stronger: *Hyperborea* / Nine is a classic: *Ace The Space* / N.U.F.O: *D-Shake*
CD _____ REACTCD 014
React / Mar '93 / Vital.

MTV FRESH
Alright: *Supergrass* / Just: *Radiohead* / Roll with it: *Oasis* / Girl like you: *Collins, Edwyn* / Army of you: *Björk* / Rock 'n' roll is dead: *Kravitz, Lenny* / Pay for me: *Whale* / Stories: *Therapy* / Billy Jean: *Bates* / Black steel: *Tricky* / C'mon Billy: *PJ Harvey* / Selling the dream: *Live* / Buddy Holly: *Weezer* / Ridiculous thoughts: *Cranberries* / Gotta getta way: *Offspring* / Girl you'll be a woman soon: *Urge Overkill* / This is a call: *Foo Fighters* / To the end: *Blur* / Ist es wichtig: *Selig* / Stars: *Dubstar*
CD _____ CDEMTV 111
EMI / Dec '95 / EMI.

MULL OF KINTYRE
CD Set _____ DCDCD 220
Castle / Nov '95 / BMG.

MULLIGAN IN THE MAIN
(Newport Jazz Festival 1958 July 3rd-6th)
CD _____ NCD 8814
Phontastic / '93 / Wellard / Jazz Music / Cadillac.

MUMTAZ MAHAL
CD _____ WLACS 46CD
Xenophile / Jun '95 / Direct / ADA.

MUNCHEN - VOLKSANGER 1902-1948
CD _____ US 0199
Trikont / Jul '95 / ADA / Direct.

MUNDO LATINO
Guaglione: *Prado, Perez* / La cumparsita: *Cugat, Xavier* / Oye mi canto (spanish version): *Estefan, Gloria* / Soul limbo: *Mr. Bongo* / Something in my eye: *Corduroy* / La bamba: *Los Lobos* / Oye como va: *Santana* / Liberation: *Piazzolla, Astor* / Soul sauce: *Tjader, Cal* / Soul bossa nova: *Jones, Quincy* / Mas que nada: *Mendes, Sergio* / Watermelon man: *Santamaria, Mongo* / Eso beso: *Ames, Nancy* / More, more, more: *Carmel* / Hot hot hot: *Arrow* / Cuba: *Gibson Brothers* / Got myself a good man: *Pucho* / Curveza: *Brown, Boots* / Tequila: *Champs*
CD _____ SONYTV 2CD
Columbia / Jun '95 / Sony.

MURRAY THE K'S HOLIDAY REVUE
(Live At The Brooklyn Fox - December 1964)
He's so fine: *Chiffons* / Denise: *Randy & The Rainbows* / My boyfriend's back: *Randy & The Rainbows* / Linda: *Jan & Dean* / Surf City: *Jan & Dean* / So much in love: *Tymes* / Be my baby: *Ronettes* / She cried: *Jay & The Americans* / Town without pity: *Pitney, Gene* / Shop around: *Robinson, Smokey & The Miracles* / You can't sit down: *Dovells* / Walk on by: *Warwick, Dionne* / Hang on sloopy: *Vibrations* / Thou shalt not steal: *Dick & Deedee* / Leader of the pack: *Shangri-Las* / Since I don't have you: *Jackson, Chuck* / Any day now: *Jackson, Chuck* / Stand by me: *King, Ben E.* / Under the boardwalk: *Drifters* / Saturday night at the movies: *Drifters* / Baby, it's you: *Shirelles* / Boys: *Shirelles* / Mama said: *Shirelles* / Tonight's the night: *Shirelles*
CD _____ CDMF 094
Magnum Force / Mar '95 / Magnum Music Group.

MUSCLE BUSTLE
Rendezvous stomp: *Rhythm Rockers* / Slide: *Rhythm Rockers* / Barefoot adventure: *Four Speeds* / R.P.M.: *Four Speeds* / My stingray: *Four Speeds* / Four on theefloor: *Four Speeds* / Chontar plinks: *Four Speeds* / Bite barracuda: *Knickerbockers* / Mighty barracuda: *Knickerbockers* / Midsummer night's dean: *Jan & Dean* / Heart and soul: *Jan & Dean* / Those words: *Jan & Dean* / Playmate of the year: *Sunsets* / Chug-a-lug: *Sunsets* / CC Cinder: *Sunsets* / Lonely surfer boy: *Sunsets* / Burnin' rubber: *Moles, Gene & The Softwinds* / Turn pipes: *Moles, Gene & The Softwinds* / Mag wheels: *Usher, Gary* / Power shift: *Usher, Gary* / Muscle bustle: *Loren, Donna* / Loophole: *Royal Coachmen* / Repeating: *Royal Coachmen* / Ski storm: *Snowmen* / 20,000 leagues: *Champs*
CD _____ CDCHD 533
Ace / Apr '94 / Pinnacle / Cadillac / Complete/Pinnacle.

MUSETTE DANCE, THE
(Music From Italy)
CD _____ YA 225056
Silex / Dec '95 / ADA.

MUSETTE FROM PARIS
Moulin Rouge / Milord / Souvenir de Montmartre / Marianne
CD _____ 15207
Laserlight / '91 / Target/BMG.

MUSIC AND SONG OF EDINBURGH, THE
Links of Forth / Rattlin' roarin' Willie / Capernaum / Holyrood House / Lion Wallace saw / Johnny Cope / Loose noose / Deacon Brodie / Sandy Bell's man / Festival lights / Duchess of Edinburgh / Caller oysters / Fisherman / Mallie Lee / Black swan / Roslin castle / Edinburgh town / Flowers of Edinburgh / Waly waly / Willie's gane tae Melville castle / Union canal / Burning king / Auld lang syne
CD _____ CDTRAX 090

Greentrax / Apr '95 / Conifer / Duncans / ADA / Direct.

MUSIC AND SONG OF SCOTLAND
(A Greentrax Showcase)
Scotland the brave: *Lothian & Borders Police Band* / Bonnie Galloway: *Lothian & Borders Police Band* / Rowan tree: *Lothian & Borders Police Band* / Highland laddie: *Lothian & Borders Police Band* / Dumbarton's drums: *Redpath, Jean* / Rolling hills of the borders: *McCalmans* / Burke and Hare: *Laing, Robin* / Bonnie moorhen: *Heywood, Heather* / Old bean waltz: *Hardie, Ian* / Hospital wood: *Hardie, Ian* / Auchope cairn: *Hardie, Ian* / Glasgow that I used to know: *McNaughtan, Adam* / Bleacher lass o' Kelvinhaugh: *Paterson, Rod* / If wishes were fishes: *Bogle, Eric* / Yonder banks: *Fisher, Archie* / Shipyard apprentice: *Fisher, Archie* / Carls o'Dysart: *Russell, Janet & Christine Kydd* / De'il's awa' wi' tha exciseman: *Russell, Janet & Christine Kydd* / Farm auction: *MacKintosh, Iain* / Donald MacLean's farewell to Oban: *Bain, Aly & Phil Cunningham* / Sands of Burness: *Bain, Aly & Phil Cunningham* / Miller's reel: *Bain, Aly & Phil Cunningham* / Maid of Islay: *MacDonald, Iain* / Canan nan gaidheal: *MacPhee, Catherine-Anne* / Birnie brushie: *Beck, Jack* / Fife and a' the lands about it: *Heritage* / Freedom come all ye: *Porteous, Lindsay & Friends*
CD _____ CDTRAX 030
Greentrax / Dec '89 / Conifer / Duncans / ADA / Direct.

MUSIC AT MATT MOLLOY'S
CD _____ CDRW 26
Realworld / Aug '92 / EMI / Sterns.

MUSIC AT THE EDGE
CD _____ 74321268552
RCA / Jul '95 / BMG.

MUSIC FOR A CHANGING WORLD
CD _____ XENO 401CD
Xenophile / Jun '95 / Direct / ADA.

MUSIC FOR A COUNTRY COTTAGE
Merry maker's overture / Starlings / Vanity fair / Little serenade / Woodland revel / Walk to the paradise garden / Galloping major / Watermill / Shepherd fennel's dance / A la Claire Fontaine / Waltz for string orchestra / Jenny pluck pears / Dick's maggot / Nonesuch / Woodicock / Demande et response / Patorale / Elizabethan masque / Sailing by / Dusk
CD _____ CDGO 2039
EMI / Jun '92 / EMI.

MUSIC FOR A RAINY DAY
(Romantic Piano Music)
CD _____ TQ 140
Conifer / Apr '88 / Conifer.

MUSIC FOR DREAMS
(2CD Set)
CD Set _____ FRCD 6
Flex / Jun '95 / Jetstar.

MUSIC FOR INTELLIGENT RAVERS
CD _____ IRCD 03
Influence / Jun '94 / Plastic Head.

MUSIC FOR LOVERS
CD _____ EMPRBX 002
Empress / Sep '94 / THE.

MUSIC FOR MAIDS AND TAXI DRIVERS
(Brazil Forro)
Balenco da canoa: *Toinho De Alagoas* / De pernambuico aomaranhao: *Duda Da Passira* / Eu tambem quero beijar: *Orlando, Jose* / Bicho da cara preta: *Toinho De Alagoas* / Cemaa de uaroui Helena Das Oita Baixos* / Peca licenca pra falar de alagoas: *Toinho De Alagoas* / Recorda cao da passira: *Duda Da Passira* / Agricultor p'ra frente: *Orlando, Jose* / Fenta e sai: *Heleno Dos Oito Baixos* / Linda menina: *Orlando, Jose* / Casa de tauba: *Duda Da Passira* / Morena da palmeira: *Orlando, Jose* / Caracter duro: *Toinho De Alagoas* / Minha zeze: *Orlando, Jose* / Sonho de amor: *Toinho De Alagoas* / Namoro no escuro: *Toinho De Alagoas* / Forro da minha terra: *Duda Da Passira*
CD _____ CDORB 048
Globestyle / Aug '89 / Pinnacle.

MUSIC FOR MY LOVE
CD _____ WMCD 5689VT
Disky / Feb '94 / THE / BMG / Discovery / Pinnacle.

MUSIC FOR RELAXATION
CD _____ CDCH 606
Milan / Feb '91 / BMG / Silva Screen.

MUSIC FOR STRINGS FROM TRANSYLVANIA
(Romanian Instrumental Dances)
CD _____ LDX 274937
La Chant Du Monde / Jul '92 / Harmonia Mundi / ADA.

MUSIC FOR THE GOD'S
CD _____ RYKO 10315CD
Rykodisc / Apr '95 / Vital / ADA.

MUSIC FORM THE SHRINES OF AJMER AND MUNDRA
CD _____ TSCD 911
Topic / Apr '95 / Direct / ADA.

MUSIC FROM BRAZIL
CD _____ 15497
Laserlight / Feb '94 / Target/BMG.

MUSIC FROM CAPE VERDE
CD _____ CAP 21451CD
Caprice / Nov '95 / CM / Complete/Pinnacle / Cadillac / ADA.

MUSIC FROM ECUADOR
CD _____ CAP 22031CD
Caprice / Nov '95 / CM / Complete/Pinnacle / Cadillac / ADA.

MUSIC FROM ETHIOPIA
CD _____ TSCD 910
Topic / Sep '94 / Direct / ADA.

MUSIC FROM ETHIOPIA
CD _____ CAP 21432CD
Caprice / Nov '95 / CM / Complete/Pinnacle / Cadillac / ADA.

MUSIC FROM PARAGUAY
CD _____ 15467
Laserlight / Aug '92 / Target/BMG.

MUSIC FROM PORTUGAL
CD _____ 15495
Laserlight / Jun '94 / Target/BMG.

MUSIC FROM RUSSIA
CD _____ 15186
Laserlight / '91 / Target/BMG.

MUSIC FROM SOUTH AMERICA - ARGENTINA
CD _____ 15421
Laserlight / '91 / Target/BMG.

MUSIC FROM SOUTH AMERICA - CHILE
CD _____ 15420
Laserlight / '91 / Target/BMG.

MUSIC FROM SOUTH AMERICA - VENEZUELA
CD _____ 15442
Laserlight / Nov '91 / Target/BMG.

MUSIC FROM THE 1990 ROYAL TOURNAMENT
Fanfare / Sea solider / British Grenadiers / British bulldogs too / British soldier an' soldier too / Symphonic marches of John Williams / Cockleshell heroes / Begone dull care / Heaven in my hand / Love in the first degree / Better the devil you know / I should be so lucky / Too many broken hearts / Heart of oak / HMS Pinafore / All the nice girls love a sailor / Caernarvon Castle / Sarie Marais / Blue devils / Semper fidelis / Sing, sing, sing / Apotheosis / Song of the Marines / Follow me / HM Jollies / Finalanda / Dear Lord and Father of mankind / Sunset / Britannic salute / National anthem / Life on the ocean wave
CD _____ BNA 5090
Bandleader / '91 / Conifer.

MUSIC FROM THE 1993 ROYAL TOURNAMENT
CD _____ BNA 5093
Bandleader / Aug '93 / Conifer.

MUSIC FROM THE ANDES & ARGENTINA
CD _____ CDT 112
Topic / Apr '93 / Direct / ADA.

MUSIC FROM THE HEART
CD _____ ELL 3212D
Ellipsis Arts / Oct '93 / Direct / ADA.

MUSIC FROM THE IVORY COAST & FODONON
La Chant Du Monde / Oct '94 / Harmonia Mundi / ADA. _____ LDX 274838

MUSIC FROM THE MAGIC GARDEN
Dreamed a dream: *New Troubadours* / Change can come: *New Troubadours* / In the beginning: *New Troubadours* / In my name: *New Troubadours* / Let new worlds grow: *New Troubadours* / Love one another: *New Troubadours* / Can't run out of love: *Poulson, Hans & Friends* / Can I be described in words: *Poulson, Hans & Friends* / One incredible family: *Poulson, Hans & Friends* / Universal love: *Poulson, Hans & Friends* / Rainbow song: *Cook, Joanna* / Who am I: *Campbell, Ian & Sheila* / What a way to look at life: *Poulson, Hans & Lynn Whyte* / There is more: *Campbell, Ian*
CD _____ FMCD 350
Findhorn / Aug '95 / Findhorn.

MUSIC FROM THE NIGER REGION
CD _____ D 8006
Auvidis/Ethnic / Jun '89 / Harmonia Mundi.

MUSIC FROM THE PUNJAB
CD _____ ARN 64278
Arion / Oct '94 / Discovery / ADA.

MUSIC FROM THE SILK ROADS
(Music From China, Mongolia & The C.I.S.)
CD _____ AUB 6776
Auvidis/Ethnic / Feb '93 / Harmonia Mundi.

MUSIC FROM THE TROOPNG OF THE COLOUR, THE
CD _____ CDPR 106
Premier/MFP / May '93 / EMI.

MUSIC FROM VIETNAM
CD _____ CAP 21406CD
Caprice / Nov '95 / CM / Complete /
Pinnacle / Cadillac / ADA.

**MUSIC IN THE WORLD OF ISLAM
VOL.1**
CD _____ TSCD 901
Topic / Jul '94 / Direct / ADA.

**MUSIC IN THE WORLD OF ISLAM
VOL.2**
CD _____ TSCD 902
Topic / Jul '94 / Direct / ADA.

**MUSIC IN THE WORLD OF ISLAM
VOL.3**
CD _____ TSCD 903
Topic / Jul '94 / Direct / ADA.

MUSIC IS MY OCCUPATION
(Ska Instrumentals 1962-75)
Magic: McCook, Tommy / Green island:
Drummond, Don / Musical store room:
Drummond, Don / Vitamin A: Brooks, Baba
/ Strolling in: McCook, Tommy / River bank
parts 1 and 2: Brooks, Baba / Silver dollar:
McCook, Tommy & The Skatalites / Dr.
Decker: Brooks, Baba & Don Drummond /
Eastern standard time: Drummond, Don /
Yard broom: McCook, Tommy / Music is my
occupation: McCook, Tommy & Don Drum-
mond / Apanga: McCook, Tommy / Don de
lion: McCook, Tommy & Don Drummond /
Guns fever: Brooks, Baba / Twelve minutes
to go: McCook, Tommy
CD _____ CDTRL 259
Trojan / Mar '94 / Jetstar / Total/BMG.

MUSIC LONELY PLANET
CD Set _____ KAZCD 223
Kaz / Jul '95 / BMG.

MUSIC NEVER STOPPED
CD _____ SH 8018CD
Shanachie / Nov '95 / Koch / ADA /
Greensleeves.

MUSIC NEVER STOPPED, THE
CD _____ SHCD 6014
Shanachie / Oct '95 / Koch / ADA /
Greensleeves.

MUSIC OF BALI
CD _____ LYRCD 7408
Lyrichord / '91 / Roots / ADA / CM.

MUSIC OF BRAZIL, THE
CD _____ WLD 007
Tring / Aug '93 / Tring / Prism.

MUSIC OF DON REDMAN
CD _____ NI 4027
Natasha / Feb '94 / Jazz Music / ADA /
CM / Direct / Cadillac.

MUSIC OF DREAMS
(Tony MacMahon/Noel Hill/Larla Ó
Lionáird)
CD _____ CEFCD 164
Gael Linn / Jan '94 / Roots / CM / Direct /
ADA.

MUSIC OF EGYPT
CD _____ RCD 10106
Rykodisc / Nov '91 / Vital / ADA.

MUSIC OF FRANCE, THE
CD _____ WLD 001
Tring / Aug '93 / Tring / Prism.

MUSIC OF GERMANY, THE
CD _____ WLD 003
Tring / Aug '93 / Tring / Prism.

MUSIC OF GREECE, THE
CD _____ WLD 004
Tring / Aug '93 / Tring / Prism.

MUSIC OF GUADALCANAL
(Vocal/Instrumental Music From
Solomon Islands)
CD _____ C 580049
Ocora / Feb '94 / Harmonia Mundi / ADA.

MUSIC OF HAWAII, THE
CD _____ WLD 005
Tring / Aug '93 / Tring / Prism.

MUSIC OF INDONESIA
CD _____ SFWCD 40420
Smithsonian Folkways / Dec '94 / ADA /
Direct / Koch / CM / Cadillac.

MUSIC OF INDONESIA #7
(Music From The Forests Of Riau &
Mentawai)
CD _____ SFWCD 40423
Smithsonian Folkways / Dec '95 / ADA /
Direct / Koch / CM / Cadillac.

MUSIC OF INDONESIA #8
(Vocal/Instrumental Music From East/
Central Flores)
CD _____ SFWCD 40424
Smithsonian Folkways / Dec '95 / ADA /
Direct / Koch / CM / Cadillac.

MUSIC OF INDONESIA #9
(Vocal Music From Central/West Flores)
CD _____ SFWCD 40425
Smithsonian Folkways / Dec '95 / ADA /
Direct / Koch / CM / Cadillac.

MUSIC OF IRAN
CD _____ HMA 190391CD
Musique D'Abord / Oct '94 / Harmonia
Mundi.

MUSIC OF JAPAN, THE
CD _____ WLD 006
Tring / Aug '93 / Tring / Prism.

MUSIC OF KENTUCKY VOL.1
CD _____ YAZCD 2013
Yazoo / Oct '95 / CM / ADA / Roots /
Koch.

MUSIC OF KENTUCKY VOL.2
CD _____ YAZCD 2014
Yazoo / Oct '95 / CM / ADA / Roots /
Koch.

MUSIC OF LIFE LIVE
CD _____ SPOCKCD 1
Music Of Life / Aug '89 / Grapevine.

MUSIC OF MADAGASCAR, THE
(Classic Traditional Recordings From
The 1930's)
CD _____ YAZCD 7003
Yazoo / Apr '95 / CM / ADA / Roots /
Koch.

MUSIC OF N.W. ARGENTINA
CD _____ 824992
Buda / Apr '91 / Discovery / ADA.

MUSIC OF PAPUA NEW GUINEA
CD _____ 925702
Buda / Jun '93 / Discovery / ADA.

**MUSIC OF RAHSHAAN ROLAND KIRK,
THE**
CD _____ NI 4024
Natasha / Nov '93 / Jazz Music / ADA /
CM / Direct / Cadillac.

MUSIC OF SARDINIA 1930-32
CD _____ HTCD 20
Heritage / Oct '93 / Swift / Roots / Wellard
/ Direct / Hot Shot / Jazz Music / ADA.

MUSIC OF SPAIN, THE
CD _____ WLD 008
Tring / Aug '93 / Tring / Prism.

MUSIC OF THE ANDES
Huajra: Inti-Illimani / Subida: Inti-Illimani / Fiesta panera (Festival at Punena): Inti-Illimani / Amores hallaras: Inti-Illimani / La ob-
reras (The working women): Quilapayun / Tu
(You): Quilapayun / Yarvi y Huayno de la
quebrada de humahuca (Yaravi and
Huayno: Quilapayun / Tan alta que est la
luna (How high the moon): Quilapayun / El
canto del cuculi (Song of the turtledove):
Quilapayun / Dos palomitas: Quilapayun / El
condor pasa (Flight of the condor): Conjunto Kollahuara / Cancion y huayno (Song
and huayno): Conjunto Kollahuara / Vicun-
ita: Conjunto Kollahuara / El tinku: Jara, Victor / Baila caporal (Dance master): Illapu /
Sol de maiz (Sun of corn): Illapu
CD _____ CDEMC 3680
EMI / May '94 / EMI.

**MUSIC OF THE FULANI & THE TENDA
FROM SENEGAL**
CD _____ C 560043
Ocora / May '94 / Harmonia Mundi / ADA.

MUSIC OF THE INCAS
CD _____ LYRCD 7348
Lyrichord / '91 / Roots / ADA / CM.

MUSIC OF THE MILITARY
Royal Air Force march past / Cavalry of the
Steppes / Light of foot / Blaze away / Amazing grace / Men of Harlech/God bless the
Prince Of Wales / Aces high / Anchors
aweigh / Battle of Britain / Old comrades /
Coronation march / Lochanside / Green hills
of Tyrol / Dambusters march / Washington
post / Sons of the brave / National Emblem
/ Battle of the Somme / Dagshai hills / Argyll
and Sutherland Highlanders / Under the
double eagle / Australian march / Redetzky
/ 633 Squadron / Flower of Scotland / Fa-
mous British marches / British Grenadiers /
Lilliburlero / All through the night / Highland
Laddie / Rule Britannia / Bonnie Anne /
Athol cummers / Sheepwife / Macleod of
Mull / Semper fidelis / Those magnificent
men in their flying machines
CD Set _____ CDDL 1078
Music For Pleasure / May '91 / EMI.

MUSIC OF THE NILE VALLEY
CD _____ LYRCD 7355
Lyrichord / Aug '93 / Roots / ADA / CM.

MUSIC OF THE STREETS
(Mechanical Street Entertainment)
Man who broke the bank at Monte Carlo /
I've got a lovely bunch of coconuts / Char-
maine / Oh oh Antonio / La Marseillaise /
Pomone waltz / Rule Britannia / Honey-
suckle and the bee / Just one girl / Bicycle
barn dance polka / Bells of St. Mary's / Sol-
diers of the Queen / Goodbye Dolly Gray /
Molly O'Morgan / Little Dolly Daydream /
Roamin' in the gloamin' / He had to get out
and get under / At Trinity Church / Let the
great big world keep turning
CD _____ CDSDL 340
Saydisc / Jun '87 / Harmonia Mundi / ADA
/ Direct.

MUSIC OF THE TATAR PEOPLE
CD _____ TSCD 912
Topic / Apr '95 / Direct / ADA.

MUSIC OF THE TUAREG
(Ritual Music & Dances From The
Hoggar Mountains)
CD _____ LDX 274974

La Chant Du Monde / May '94 / Harmonia
Mundi / ADA.

MUSIC OF THE WORLD
CD _____ PS 66002
Playasound / Feb '93 / Harmonia Mundi /
ADA.

MUSIC OF VENEZUELA, THE
El gavan: Armonia Y Cuerdas / Sombra en
los meadanos: Raices De Mi Pueblo / San
Rafael: Chirinos, Ali / La montuna torpe:
Trio Cabure / El grillo: Mendoza, Ricardo Y
Su Conjunto / La jurupera: Grupo Folklorico
Curigna / Entrenrao: Conjunto Piedemonte
/ Zumba que zumba: Quintana, Luis / La
guarchara: Fandino, Luis Y Conjunto Pie-
demonte / Seis por derecho: Tapia, Carlos
Y Conjunto Piedemonte / El salto: Conjunto
Montes / La culebra: Cabello, Jorge Y Su
Conjunto / Los perros: Alma Veneziolana /
La muecasa tuyera: El Periquito De Miranda
/ Barcelonesa: Grupo Crillo Universitario 'Si-
mon Bolivar'
CD _____ CDZ 2018
Zu Zazz / Apr '94 / Rollercoaster.

MUSIC OF WEST BALI
CD _____ ARN 64271
Arion / Oct '94 / Discovery / ADA.

MUSIC OF WORLD WAR 2 VOL. 1
CD _____ VJC 10362
Vintage Jazz Classics / Oct '92 / Direct /
ADA / CM / Cadillac.

**MUSIC ON A MARRAKESH MARKET
SQUARE**
CD _____ LDX 274973
La Chant Du Monde / Jun '94 / Harmonia
Mundi / ADA.

MUSIC WHILE YOU WORK
Calling all workers / National emblem / Gondoliers (Selection) / Listen to liszt / Hits of
'39 / Going Greek - selection / Mikado, The
- selection / Carefree - medley / Great waltz
(selection) / Accordion medley / Banjo on
my knee - selection / Fleet's lit up (Mixes) /
Hits of the day / Champagne waltz -
selection
CD _____ PASTCD 9791
Flapper / Jun '92 / Pinnacle.

**MUSIC WHILE YOU WORK - CALLING
ALL WORKERS**
Calling all workers: Victory Band / Love Parade selection: Victory Band / New Moon
selection: Victory Band / Dancing Years se-
lection: Fryer, Harry / White Horse Inn:
Fryer, Harry / Roberta: Simpson, Jack /
Christy Minstrels selection: Troise & His
Mandoliers / Whistling Rufus: Troise & His
Mandoliers / Sweet nothin's: Mayerl, Billy /
Canadian capers: Mayerl, Billy / Alexander's
ragtime band/Poor butterfly/Get out and get
unde: Victory Band / Flanagan and Allen se-
lection: Victory Band / Cuddle up a little
closer/Put your arms around me: Victory
Band / Wait for me Mary: Victory Band / If
I had my way: Victory Band / East side of
heaven: Simpson, Jack / Hit Parade selec-
tion: Simpson, Jack / Something in the air:
Fryer, Harry / Lisbon story: Fryer, Harry /
Sing as we go: Maciver, Percival / French
March medley: Scala, Primo
CD _____ RAJCD 819
Empress / Jul '94 / THE.

**MUSIC WHILE YOU WORK - CALLING
ALL WORKERS VOL.2**
Calling all workers: Victory Band / Dixie Lee:
Chapman, Wally & His Band / Say it with
music/Love is the sweetest thing: Simpson,
Jack & His Sextet / I'll do my best to make
you happy: Simpson, Jack & His Sextet /
Pistol packin' Mama/Pony express: Studio
Orchestra / Time on my hands: Marsh, Roy
& His Orchestra / Close your eyes: Chap-
man, Wally & His Band / But not for you/
Embraceable you/Bidin' my time: Studio
Orchestra / You are my lucky star/Broad-
way rhythm/I got a feelin': Simpson, Jack &
His Sextet / Love walked in: Marsh, Roy &
His Orchestra / Music goes round and
around: Marsh, Roy & His Orchestra / Sad-
dle your blues to a wild mustang: Atkins,
Stan & His Band / Everything I have is
yours/Coffee in the morning: Dodd, Pat &
Cecil Norman / Tea for two: Marsh, Roy &
His Orchestra / Three little words/You're
driving me crazy: Royal Navy Blue Mariners
/ My heart tells me/For the first time / I've
fallen in love: Studio Orchestra / Ain't mis-
behavin': Marsh, Roy & His Orchestra / I
double dare you/Boom: Atkins, Stan & His
Band / By a waterfall/Learn to croon: Dodd,
Pat & Cecil Norman / Dreamer/How sweet
you are: Studio Orchestra / Very thought of
you: Chapman, Wally & His Band / Bei mir
bist du schon: Marsh, Roy & His Orchestra
/ Touch of your lips/Just one more chance:
Royal Navy Blue Mariners / Who walks in
when I walk out: Chapman, Wally & His
Band / Keep an eye on your heart: Bradley,
Josephine & Her Ballroom Orchestra
CD _____ RAJCD 847
Empress / Feb '95 / THE.

**MUSIC WORKS PRESENTS TWICE MY
AGE**
CD _____ GRELCD 144
Greensleeves / Apr '90 / Total/BMG /
Jetstar / SRD.

MUSIC WORKS SHOWCASE 88
CD _____ GRELCD 117
Greensleeves / Apr '89 / Total/BMG /
Jetstar / SRD.

MUSIC WORKS SHOWCASE 89
CD _____ GRELCD 123
Greensleeves / Jun '89 / Total/BMG /
Jetstar / SRD.

MUSIC WORKS SHOWCASE 90
Too good to be true / Fatal attraction / Can't
make a slip / I.O.U. / Hard road to travel /
Big all around / Jealousy / Fall for you again
/ What's the matter / Report to me / Express
love / Break the ice / Easy life
CD _____ GRELCD 139
Greensleeves / Nov '89 / Total/BMG / Jets-
tar / SRD.

MUSICA POPULAR DO BRAZIL
CD _____ GC 900005
ITM / Dec '93 / Tradelink / Koch.

MUSICAL BANQUET, A
CD _____ CDSDLC 397
Saydisc / Feb '93 / Harmonia Mundi /
ADA / Direct.

MUSICAL BOX DANCES
CD _____ CDSDL 359
Saydisc / '88 / Harmonia Mundi / ADA /
Direct.

MUSICAL EXPLORATION, A
CD _____ 1934111732
Windham Hill / Sep '95 / Pinnacle / BMG /
ADA.

MUSICAL FEAST
CD _____ CDHB 84
Heartbeat / Apr '91 / Greensleeves /
Jetstar / Direct / ADA.

MUSICAL FEVER 1967-1968
Bad mind grudgeful: Winston & Robin /
Puppy love: Bennett & Dennis / Bad treat-
ment: Cannon & Soul Vendors / Get a lick:
Oakley, Bumps / Hip hug-her: Sultans / Let
me love you: Miller, Jacob / Rub up, push
up: Termites / Wailing time: Winston &
Robin / Venus: Frater, Eric / Norwegian
wood: Williams, Marshall / Love me girl:
Soul Vendors / You shouldn't be the one:
Holness, Winston / Ram jam: Jackie & Soul
Vendors / You gonna lose: Octaves / Get
with it: Soul Vendors / Fat fish: Viceroys /
Grooving steady: Jackie & Soul Vendors /
Bye bye baby: Sims, Zoot / Soul junction:
Soul Vendors / Mercy mercy: Slim & Free-
dom Singers / Baba boom: Jackie & Soul
Vendors / Love and unity: Viceroys / I don't
mind: Bob & Ty / Zigaloo: Sterling, Lester /
Contemplating mind: Spence, Barrington /
Good girl: Nangle, Ed / Musical fever: En-
forcers / Wiser than Solomon: Sterling,
Lester
CD _____ CDTRD 408
Trojan / Jul '89 / Jetstar / Total/BMG.

**MUSICAL FREEDOM - CLASSIC
GARAGE VOL.2**
Musical freedom: Adeva / Alright: Urban
Soul / Do you want it right now: Degrees Of
Motion / Let the rain come down: Intense /
Closer: Mr. Fingers / Follow me: Al Y Us /
Give you: Djaimin / Love's got a hold on me:
Zoo Experience / I'm the one for you: Adeva
/ Helpless: Urbanized & Silvano / Mother-
land: Tribal House / Love itch: Roche,
Sonya / One day: Tyrrel Corporation / Baby
love: Watford, Michael
CD _____ CTCD 31
Cooltempo / Nov '92 / EMI.

**MUSICAL HIGHLIGHTS OF THE BERLIN
TATTOO**
All hail to the chief - a king is crowned /
Massed pipes and drums / Prince Charles
Edward Stuart arrives / The King's troop,
royal horse / Massed bands / Kevock choir
/ Music for Scottish dancing / Gathering of
the clans (finale)
CD Set _____ LCOM 9008
Lismor / Dec '88 / Lismor / Direct / Duncans
/ ADA.

MUSICAL JOURNEY
CD _____ B 679
Auvidis/Ethnic / Oct '94 / Harmonia Mundi.

**MUSICAL ROOTS OF THE NORTH-
WEST PROVINCES**
CD _____ PS 65073
Playasound / Jun '91 / Harmonia Mundi /
ADA.

MUSICAL TRADITIONS OF PORTUGAL
CD _____ SF 40435CD
Smithsonian Folkways / Jul '95 / ADA /
Direct / Koch / CM / Cadillac.

MUSICAL TRADITIONS OF ST. LUCIA
CD _____ SF 40416CD
Smithsonian Folkways / Jan '94 / ADA /
Direct / Koch / CM / Cadillac.

MUSICAL TRAVEL 1 - CHINA
CD _____ YA 225701
Silex / Jan '95 / ADA.

MUSICAL TRAVEL 2 - MADAGASCAR
CD _____ YA 225702
Silex / Jan '95 / ADA.

MUSICAL TRAVEL 3 - PORTUGAL
CD _____ YA 225703
Silex / Jan '95 / ADA.

MUSICAL TRAVEL 4 - IRELAND
CD _____ YA 225704
Silex / Jan '95 / ADA.

MUSICAL TRAVEL 5 - QUEBEC
CD _____ YA 225705
Silex / Jan '95 / ADA.

MUSICAL TRAVEL 6 - GREECE
CD _____ YA 225706
Silex / Jan '95 / ADA.

MUSICAL TRIBUTE TO VICTORY WWII, A
CD Set _____ WARBOX 45CD
Start / Apr '95 / Koch.

MUSICAL VOYAGE TO THE AZORES
CD _____ YA 225710
Silex / Dec '95 / ADA.

MUSICS OF THE SOVIET UNION
CD _____ SFWCD 40002
Smithsonian Folkways / May '95 / ADA /
Direct / Koch / CM / Cadillac.

MUSIQUE ACTION
CD _____ VANDOUVRE 9304CD
Semantic / Feb '94 / Plastic Head.

MUSIQUE DU HAUT XINGU
(Music Of the Xingu Islands, Brazil)
CD _____ C 580022
Ocora / Jan '93 / Harmonia Mundi / ADA.

MUSIQUE QUECHUA DU LAC TITICACA
(Music From Taquile, Peru)
CD _____ C 580015
Ocora / Jan '93 / Harmonia Mundi / ADA.

MUSIQUES BRETONNES
CD _____ KMCD 01
Keltia Musique / Jul '90 / ADA / Direct /
Discovery.

MUSIQUES D'EXTASE ET DE GUERISON
(Music From The Baluchi People Of Pakistan & Iran)
CD _____ C 580017/18
Ocora / Jan '93 / Harmonia Mundi / ADA.

MUSIQUES DES BATAK
CD _____ W 260061
Inedit / Sep '95 / Harmonia Mundi / ADA /
Discovery.

MUSIQUES RITUELLES ET RELIGIEUSES
(Music From Sri Lankan Cults & Religions)
CD _____ C 580037
Ocora / Jan '93 / Harmonia Mundi / ADA.

MUSIQUES TRADITIONNELLES
(Music From Sierra Leone)
CD _____ C 580036
Ocora / Jan '93 / Harmonia Mundi / ADA.

MUSIQUES TRADITIONNELLES - BALI/JAVA
CD _____ PS 65110
Playasound / Nov '93 / Harmonia Mundi /
ADA.

MUST BE MENTAL
CD _____ PA 03
Solieimoon Recordings / Mar '95 / Plastic
Head.

MUST BE MENTAL VOL.2
CD _____ PA 001CD
Dark Vinyl / May '95 / Plastic Head.

MUST BE MUSIQUE VOL. 2
CD _____ DV 20
Dark Vinyl / Jan '94 / Plastic Head.

MUST BE SANTA
CD _____ ROUCD 3118
Rounder / Nov '95 / CM / Direct / ADA /
Cadillac.

MY BABY JUST CARES FOR ME
CD _____ YDG 74614
Yesterday's Gold / Feb '93 / Target/BMG.

MY HOUSE IS BIGGER THAN YOUR HOUSE
CD _____ BR 20142
Activ / Nov '95 / Total/BMG.

MY IRISH HOME SWEET HOME
Phil the fluter's ball / Eileon oge / Danny boy
/ Mother Machree / It takes an irish heart to
sing an irish song / My old Irish mother /
Father O'Flynn / Where the Shannon river
flows / My wild Irish rose / Down by the
glenside / Mountains of mourne / Rose of
Tralee / My Irish home sweet home / Spin-
ning wheel / That's how I spell
I.R.E.L.A.N.D. / When Irish eyes are smiling
/ If you're irish come into the parlour / Three
lovely lasses / Kathleen Mavoureen /
Laughing Irish eyes / Beautiful Eileen / Did
your mother come from Ireland
CD _____ RAJCD 809
Empress / Nov '93 / THE.

MY LOVE IS IN AMERICA
CD _____ GLCD 1110
Green Linnet / Nov '91 / Roots / CM /
Direct / ADA.

MY SPECIAL ANGEL & OTHER COUNTRY LOVE SONGS
CD _____ PRCD 202
President / Jan '88 / Grapevine / Target/
BMG / Jazz Music / President.

MY WAY
(Music Of Frank Sinatra - 16 Instrumental Hits)
CD _____ 5708574338035
Carlton Home Entertainment / Sep '94 /
Carlton Home Entertainment.

MY WILD IRISH ROSE
(22 Favourite Irish Ballads)
Black velvet band: Kelly, John / Shanagol-
den: Day, Paddy / Old maid in a garret:
Sweeneys / My auld Killarney hat: Gertrude,
Sister Mary / Enniskillen Dragoons: Ludlows
/ Flower of Macroom: Dunphy, Sean & The
Hoedowners / Lough sheelin: Nomads /
Turfman from Ardee: Gallagher, Bridie / Ar-
kle: Behan, Dominic / Nora: McEvoy,
Johnny / Beautiful city: Donal Ring Sound /
Muirsheen darkin: McEvoy, Johnny / Sea
around us: Ludlows / Leaving of Liverpool:
Lynch, Pat / My wild Irish rose: Cotton Mill
Boys / Come to the bower: Dunphy, Sean /
Slaney Valley: Kinsellas / McAlpine's Fusil-
iers: Kelly, Des / Curragh Of Kildare: John-
stons / Shores of Amerikay: Broadsiders /
Prisoner: Day, Paddy / Bold O'Donoghue:
Dragoons
CD _____ TRTCD 124
TrueTrax / Oct '94 / THE.

MYND EXCURSIONS
(A Journey Through The Vaults Of Buddah/Kama Sutra)
You're my baby (and don't you forget it):
Vacels / Can you please crawl out of your
window: Vacels / I'm just a poor boy: Vacels
/ Splendor in the grass: Boys / Mind excursion: Tradewinds / Catch me in the
meadow: Tradewinds / All I ask: Tradewinds
/ I believe in her: Tradewinds / Lifetime
lovin' you: Tradewinds / Bad misunderstanding: Tradewinds / Huggin' in the hall:
Tradewinds / There's got to be a word: Innocence / Mairzy doats and dozy doats: Innocence / Your show is over: Innocence /
Only when I'm dreamin': Innocence / Day
turns me on(The bufferin song): Innocence
/ Do you believe in magic: Innocence / Hard
life: Good Times / Yes, we have no bananas: Mulberry Fruit Band / Sunrise highway: Anders, Pete / Love don't let me
down: Bloom, Bobby / Down when it's up,
up when it's down: Ciccone, Don / Worst
that could happen: Brooklyn Bridge / She
can blow your mind: Pendulum / Rapper:
Jaggerz / Don't ask me to step so long: Myddle
Class / So much in love: (Puffins / Two is
(I'm losing you): Martin, Steve / I want your
love: Puss n' Boots
CD _____ NEXCD 237
Sequel / Jun '93 / BMG.

MYTHS COLLECTION
CD _____ SUBCD 00316
Sub Rosa / Oct '88 / Vital / These /
Discovery.

MYTHS COLLECTION VOL.2
CD _____ SUBCD 00932
Sub Rosa / Dec '90 / Vital / These /
Discovery.

N

NAIVE
CD _____ MUSH 076CD
Earache / Oct '92 / Vital.

NAME BRAND
CD _____ CRCD 30
Charm / Apr '94 / Jetstar.

NAME OF THE GAME
Ride sally ride: Green, Al / Trouble is my
name: Hines, Don / Aretha, sing one for me:
Jackson, George / Belle: Green, Al / Mack
the knife: Emmons, Buddy / Patricia: Jack-
son, George / Judy: Green, Al / Buster
Browne: Mitchell, Willie / She's Miss Won-
derful: McClure, Bobby / Jesus is waiting:
Green, Al / Teenie's dream: Mitchell, Willie
/ Sunshine (isn't that your name): Carter,
Darryl / Georgia boy: Green, Al / Please Mr.
Foreman: Joe L / Amazing grace: Green, Al
/ Mimi: Green, Al / Miss Betty Green: Big
Lucky Carter / Dr. Love power: Peebles,
Ann / Eli's game: Green, Al
CD _____ HILOCD 8
Demon / Mar '94 / Pinnacle / ADA.

NAPALM RAVE
(2CD Set)
CD Set _____ SPV 08638282
SPV / Mar '95 / Plastic Head.

NAPALM RAVE II
(2CD Set)
CD Set _____ SPV 08638332
SPV / Jun '95 / Plastic Head.

NARADA CHRISTMAS COLLECTION VOL.3
Silver bells: Arkenstone, David / God rest ye
merry gentlemen: Whalen, Michael / O holy
night: Mann, Brian / O' come all ye faithful:
Lauria, Nando / It came upon a midnight
clear: Gratz, Wayne / Ding dong merrily on

high: Rumbel, Nancy / Good King Wenceslas: Rumbel, Nancy / First Noel: Illenberger,
Ralf / Carol of the bells: Kostia / Hark, the
herald angels sing: Tingstad, Eric / Silent
night: Wynberg, Simon / We three kings:
Stein, Ira / Little drummer boy: Ellwood, William / O little town of Bethlehem: Jones, Michael / Holly and the ivy: Jones, Michael
CD _____ ND 63919
Narada / Dec '95 / New Note / ADA.

NARADA COLLECTION 5
CD _____ ND 63920
Narada / Aug '95 / New Note / ADA.

NARADA DECADE
CD _____ ND 263911
Narada / Jun '93 / New Note / ADA.

NARCOSIS
Silence of water: Emojonal / Game from
planet Onchet: Hole In One / My definition
of house music: D.J. Hell / Come into my
life: Abfahrt / New age heart core: Trance
Induction / Flash: Fix / Diamond bullet: Ef-
fective Force / In the shadow: Morganistic /
White darkness: Sandoz / Brother from jazz:
Angel, Dave / Ob-selon mi-mos: Mystic
Istitute
CD _____ GRCD 009
Guerilla / Jul '94 / Pinnacle.

NASHVILLE CLASSICS: 50'S
Take me in your arms and hold me: Arnold,
Eddy / Stampede: Rogers, Roy & Sons Of
The Pioneers / Quicksilver: Britt, Elton / I'm
movin' on: Snow, Hank / Poison love:
Johnny & Jack / Down on the trail of aching
hearts: Snow, Hank / Slow poke: King, Pee
Wee & The Golden West Cowboys / Stop
that ticklin me: Jones, Grandpa / Eddy's
song: Arnold, Eddy / (How much is that)
hound dog in the window: Homer & Jethro
/ I forgot more than you'll ever know: Davis
Sisters / I found out more than you'll ever
know: Cody, Betty / I get so lonely: Johnny
& Jack / I don't hurt anymore: Snow, Hank
/ Satisfied man: Wagoner, Porter / In the
jailhouse now No.2: Rodgers, Jimmie / Cattle call: Arnold, Eddy / Yonder comes a
sucker: Reeves, Jim / I heard the bluebirds
sing: Browns / Oh lonesome me: Gibson,
Don / Send me the pillow that you dream
on: Locklin, Hank / Blue blue day: Gibson,
Don / He'll have to go: Reeves, Jim / Five
bells: Browns / Tennessee stud: Arnold,
Eddy
CD _____ 74321280222
RCA / May '95 / BMG.

NASHVILLE CLASSICS: 60'S
Please help me: Locklin, Hank / Last dance:
Cramer, Floyd / When 2 worlds collide: Mil-
ler, Roger / Sea of heartbreak: Gibson, Don
/ I've been everywhere: Snow, Hank / End
of the world: Davis, Skeeter / Abilene: Ham-
ilton, George IV / 500 miles away from
home: Bare, Bobby / Here comes my baby:
West, Dottie / Once a day: Smith, Connie /
I wouldn't buy a used car from him: Norma
Jean / Crystal chandeliers: Belew, Carl /
Stop the world (and let me off): Jennings,
Waylon / Make the world go away: Arnold,
Eddy / Ballad of the Green Berets: Sadler,
Sgt. Barry / Distant drums: Reeves, Jim /
Just between you and me: Pride, Charley /
Mama pank: Anderson, Liz / Pop a top:
Brown, Jim Ed / Gentle on my mind: Hart-
ford, John / Last thing on my mind: Parton,
Dolly & Waylon Jennings / Caroll country
accident: Wagoner, Porter / Plastic saddle:
Stucker, Nat / Bring me sunshine: Nelson,
Willie / My blue ridge mountain boy: Parton,
Dolly
CD _____ 74321280200
RCA / May '95 / BMG.

NASHVILLE CLASSICS: 70'S
Sheriff of Boone county: Price, Kenny /
When you're hot you're hot: Reed, Jerry /
Just one time: Smith, Connie / Kiss an angel
good morning: Pride, Charley / Country
sunshine: West, Dottie / Baptism of Jesse
Taylor: Russell, Johnny / There won't be anymore: Rich, Charlie / Pure love: Milsap,
Ronnie / I will always love you: Parton, Dolly
/ This time: Jennings, Waylon / Marie Laveau: Bare, Bobby / Please don't stop loving
me: Wagoner, Porter / Out of hand: Stewart,
Gary / Storms never last: Dottsy / Shadows
of my mind: Oxford, Vernon / Door is always
open: Dave & Sugar / Suspicious minds:
Jennings, Waylon & Jessie Colter / 9999999
tears: Lee, Dickie / Luckenbach, Texas
(Back to the basics of love): Jennings, Waylon / Here you come again: Parton, Dolly /
Two doors down: Lehr, Zella / What have
you got to lose: Hall, Tom T / If love had a
face: Bailey, Razzy / I wanna come over: Alabama / How I miss you tonight: Reeves,
Jim
CD _____ 74321280242
RCA / May '95 / BMG.

NASHVILLE DREAM
CD Set _____ QTVCD 014
Quality / Oct '92 / Pinnacle.

NASTY BLUES
Strokin': Carter, Clarence / Trudy sings the
blues: Lynn, Trudy / I want to play with your
poodle: Willis, Chick / Rainy day: White, Artie / One eyed woman: Coleman, Gary B.B.
/ I want a big fat woman: Willis, Chick / Ugly
man: Taylor, Little Johnny / Watch where
you stroke: Coleman, Gary B.B. / Two
heads are better than one: Haddix, Travis /

Why do I stay here and take all this shit:
Carter, Clarence
CD _____ CDICH 1048
Ichiban / Mar '94 / Koch.

NASTY BLUES 2
Jack you up: Willis, Chick / Come back
pussy: Williams, Dicky / Cook me: Legen-
dary Blues Band / Grandpa can't fly his kite:
Blues Boy Willie / Tittie man: Drink Small /
Let me have it: Willis, Chick / Don't pet my
dog: White, Artie / Lemon squeezin' Daddy:
Brown, Nappy / Kiss you all over: Carter,
Clarence
CD _____ CDICH 1066
Ichiban / Oct '93 / Koch.

NASTY NASTY
CD _____ TRTCD 155
TrueTrax / Dec '94 / THE.

NATIONAL BRASS BAND CHAMPIONSHIP 1994
Pioneers' march / Bartered bride (overture)
/ Thoughts of love / Slaughter on 10th Av-
enue / Theme and co-operation / Dance of
the comedians / Better world / Galaxies /
Concert etude / Russian Christmas music /
Pines of Rome
CD _____ QPRL 071D
Polyphonic / Jan '95 / Conifer.

NATIONAL FOLK FESTIVAL
CD _____ CIC 068CD
Clo Iar-Chonnachta / Nov '93 / CM.

NATIVES
CD _____ 662244
FNAC / Jun '93 / Discovery.

NATTY REBEL ROOTS
Let jah be praised: Gladiators / Tune in:
Isaacs, Gregory / Cry tough: Clarke, Johnny
/ Natty rebel: U-Roy / Throw away your gun:
Prince Far-I / Declaration of rights: Clarke,
Johnny / We'll find the blessing: Gladiators
/ Do you remember: U-Roy / Jah kingdom
come: Twinkle Brothers / Slavery let I go:
Clarke, Johnny / Crazy baldheads: Clarke,
Johnny / Best things in life: Gladiators /
Praise jah: Twinkle Brothers / How love di-
vine (dub): Prince Far-I / Uptown top rank-
ing: Althia & Donna
CD _____ CDFL 9013
Frontline / Sep '90 / EMI / Jetstar.

NATURAL BORN TECHNO
CD _____ NZ 030
Nova Zembla / Feb '95 / Plastic Head.

NATURAL BORN TECHNO VOL.2
CD Set _____ NZ 042CD
Nova Zembla / Sep '95 / Plastic Head.

NATURAL BORN TECHNO VOL.3
CD _____ NZ 052CD
Nova Zembla / Jan '96 / Plastic Head.

NATURAL SELECTION
4 Better or 4 worse / Cease and seckle /
Country funkin' / Born to roll / Spirit of love
/ Dips / Hit the coast / Boom shak-a-tak /
Pork / B side / How deep is deep / Hard
rhymes
CD _____ 7567923732
East West / '93 / Warner Music.

NATURAL SELECTIONS
CD _____ 7567923732
Delicious Vinyl / May '94 / PolyGram.

NATURAL WOMAN
CD _____ RAB6D 14
Global / Jul '95 / BMG.

NAVAJO SONGS FROM CANYON DE CHELLY
CD _____ 804062
New World / Aug '92 / Harmonia Mundi /
ADA / Cadillac.

NEAT METAL
CD _____ NM 005MCD
Neat / Nov '95 / Plastic Head.

NEGRO RELIGIOUS FIELD RECORDINGS 1944-46
CD _____ DOCD 5312
Blues Document / Dec '94 / Swift / Jazz
Music / Hot Shot.

NERVOUS PSYCHOBILLY SINGLES
Rockabilly boy: Polecats / Chicken shack:
Polecats / Heart attack: Deltas / Spell
bound: Deltas / Constipation shake: Leg-
endary Lonnie / Devil's guitar: Legendary
Lonnie / City lights: Austin, Rockin' Johnny
/ Rockabilly stroll: Austin, Rockin' Johnny /
Marie celeste: Polecats / Edge you on:
Restless / Ghost town: Restless / Whistle
wiggle: Rochee & The Sarnos / Rumble in
the jungle: Rochee & The Sarnos / Shake
your hips: Scamps / Robot riot: Frenzy /
Torment: Frenzy / Cry or die: Frenzy / Vigi-
lante: Pharaohs / You're on fire: Phar-
aohs / Raid: Rapids / Silver bullet: Rapids /
Ghost train: Sharks / Mystery men: Torment
/ Rock strong: Torment / Conscription pain:
Torment
CD _____ CDMPSYCHO 5
Cherry Red / May '95 / Pinnacle.

NERVOUS SYSTEMS
CD _____ CDSTUMM 41
Mute / Sep '92 / Disc.

NERVOUS: NEW YORK
CD _____ REACTCD 011
React / Oct '92 / Vital.

NEVER AGAIN
Eighty eight seconds and still counting: Pop Will Eat Itself / Take it: Flowered Up / Make it mine: Shamen / Air you breathe: Bomb The Bass / B.M.W: Soho & Natty Sega / Magic carpet: Nutty Boys / Searchlight: Pele / We didn't know (what was going on): Robinson, Tom Band / Feel it: Sham 69 / Throw the 'R' away (live): Proclaimers / Power is yours: Redskins / Righteous preacher: Fun-Da-Mental / Celebration: Better ways / About time: Friends of Harry / Someday: Steppin' Stones / Goodbye Johnny: Pool O'Life / Badila: New Paradesi Music Machine / Communication: I'cons / Set up for the kill: Sharp teeth
CD _____ NIL 001 CD
Nil Satis / Sep '92 / Vital.

NEVER MIND THE MOLLUSCS
Sub Pop / Mar '93 / Disc.

NEW AGE MUSIC
Floating / Julia's dream / Quelle Dolce / Cloudburst flight / Just a love song / Nightmist / Astralunato / Chip meditation / Gymnopedie / Quick shot / Souvenir of China / Sunbeam / Midnight on Mars
CD Set _____ 710051/52
Magnum Music / Feb '88 / Magnum Music Group.

NEW ALTERNATIVES II
Millennium / Mar '95 / Plastic Head.
CD _____ NIGHTCD 005

NEW BEAT - EDIT 1
Move your ass and feel the beat: Erotic Dissidents / Hmm hmm: Taste Of Sugar / Don't talk about sex: Electric Shock / Secrets of China: Chinese Ways / Agreppo: Kings Of Agreppo / Beat in the street: Beat Beat Beat / Euroshima-Wardance: Snowy Red / Virgin In-D skies: In-D / D bop: Dirty Harry / S.M.: SM / Hardwax: Jade 4 U / Flesh: Split Second / Awakening (extra track on MC & CD only): Shakti / Blow up the DJ (Extra track on MC & CD only): TNT Clan
CD _____ 828 136-2
FFRR / Aug '90 / PolyGram.

NEW BLUEBLOODS
CD _____ ALCD 7707
Alligator / Aug '92 / Direct / ADA.

NEW BLUES CLASSICS
CD _____ BBAN 14CD
Bullseye Blues / Aug '94 / Direct.

NEW BORN BLUE
CD _____ 33WM 101
33 Jazz / Oct '94 / Cadillac / New Note.

NEW BREED OF RAVERS, A
CD _____ FORMCD 1
Formation / Nov '93 / SRD.

NEW COUNTRY GIRLS LIVE
CD _____ 15406
Laserlight / Aug '91 / Target/BMG.

NEW ELECTRONICA VOLUME III
Ocean reflection: Sandoz / Think quick (Maurizo mix): Infinity / Sensitive space: Planet Gong / Geep: Geep / A.H.D: Ciptalk / 6 A.M. Somewhere in Eindhoven: Max 404 / Cromen: Quadrant / Asa mia masa: As One / Moment in time: Underground Resistance / Mindpower: Underground Resistance
CD _____ ELEC 4CD
New Electronica / Mar '94 / Pinnacle / Plastic Head.

NEW ELECTRONICA VOLUME IV
CD _____ ELEC 12CD
New Electronica / Sep '94 / Pinnacle / Plastic Head.

NEW ELECTRONICA VOLUME V
Free to run: Pluto / Vibes: Graphite / Aims of me: Slater, Luke / Dimentions of dreams: Angel, Dave / Death of a disco dancer: Reload / Journey in time: Aubrey / Chrome roots: Thunderground / Peace for thought: Gabriel, Russ
CD _____ ELEC 15CD
New Electronica / Jan '95 / Pinnacle / Plastic Head.

NEW FRONTIERS
CD _____ TMPCD 017
Telstar / Oct '95 / BMG.

NEW JAZZ SPECTRUM VOL. 2
Nairod: Riverside Jazz Band / One hand: Parker, Maynard / Our generation: Hines, Ernie / Favela: Papaya / Sad song: Williams, Joe / Mucha chupar: Axelrod, David / It's about time: Callier, Terry / Death and taxes: Dickerson, Walt / Song for Pharoah: Cuber, Ronnie / Memphis: Little Sonny / Higgins holler: Walton, Cedar / Everything counts: Axelrod, David
CD _____ CDBGP 091
BGP / Oct '94 / Pinnacle.

NEW JAZZ SPECTRUM VOL. 3
Fire eater: Bryant, Rusty / Afro Texas: Mbulu, Letta / No one can love: Cosby, Bill / Shortnin' bread: Three Pieces / Shirley's guanguancho: Aguabella, Francisco / Getting funky round here: Black Nasty / Love them from Spartacus: Lateef, Yusef / Senior boogaloo: Richardson, Wally / Nana: De

Souza, Raul / Gibralter: Hubbard, Freddie / Mode: Red, Sonny / Sentido-en-seis: Bellson, Louie & Walfredo De Los Reyes / When I die: Marrow, Esther
CD _____ CDBGP 095
BGP / May '95 / Pinnacle.

NEW JAZZ SPECTRUM, THE
Rip a dip: Latin Jazz Quintet / Other side of town: Natural Essence / Things ain't right: Marrow, Esther / Cry: Dickerson, Walt / Modettle: Haynes, Roy / Web: Hawes, Hampton / Taste of honey: Andy & The Bey Sisters / Thang: Matthews, Ronnie / Eli's pork chop: Little Sonny / I've known rivers: Bartz, Gary / Alex the great (On CD only): Mabern, Harold / Letha (On CD only): Earland, Charles
CD _____ CDBGP 085
BGP / Apr '94 / Pinnacle.

NEW MUSIC FROM MALI
Ka souma man: Sekouba Bambino Diabate / Konifale: Tangra, Kadja / Tchana diani: Traore, Lobi / Ouere: Koita, Dounanke / Faso: Bougouniere Diarrah Sanogo / Sabali: Les Soeurs Sidibe / Fengue: Bagayoga, Issa / Liberia: Diakite, Djenaba / Sinsinbo: Koita, Dounanke / Kulunba: Sidibe, Kagbe / Diarabi: Wassolon Fenin (The Cream Of Wassolon) / Hampate ba: Koita, Ami / N'na djanssana: Kante, Kerfala
CD _____ CDEMC 3681
EMI / May '94 / EMI.

NEW MUSIC INDONESIA 3 - KARYA
CD _____ LYRCD 7421
Lyrichord / Feb '94 / Roots / ADA / CM.

NEW ORLEANS "WHERE JAZZ WAS BORN"
Perdido street blues / Dr. Jazz / Alligator crawl / Apex blues / That's a plenty / High society / Weatherbird / I know that you know / Ory's creole trombone / Franklin street blues / Tiger rag / Clarinet marmalade / Sweet lovin' man / New Orleans stomp / As you like it / Cannonball blues / Pleasin' Paul / Astoria strut
CD _____ 56021
Carlton Home Entertainment / Nov '92 / Carlton Home Entertainment.

NEW ORLEANS - GREAT ORIGINAL PERFORMANCES 1918 TO 1934 (Robert Parker's Jazz Classics In Digital Stereo)
Dr. Jazz: Morton, Jelly Roll & His Red Hot Peppers / Sweet lovin' man: Oliver, King Jazzband / Too tight: Dodd, Johnny Orchestra / Alligator crawl: Armstrong, Louis & His Hot Seven / Salty dog: Keppard, Freddie Jazz Cardinals / As you like it: Celestin's Original Tuxedo Orchestra / That's a plenty: New Orleans Owls / Franklin Street blues: Dumaine, Louis Jazzola Eight / Mr. Jelly Lord: New Orleans Rhythm Kings / Panama: New Orleans Rhythm Kings / Pleasin' Paul: Allen, Henry & His New York Orchestra / Astoria strut: Jones & Collins Astoria Hot Eight / Damp weather: Jones & Collins Astoria Hot Eight / Sizzling the blues: Hazel, Monk & His Bienville Roof Orchestra / High society: Hazel, Monk & His Bienville Roof Orchestra / Sweetie dear: New Orleans Feetwarmers / Weatherbird: Armstrong, Louis & Earl Hines / Blue piano blues: Dodds, Johnny Trio / Turtle twist: Morton, Jelly Roll Trio / Clarinet marmalade: Original Dixieland Jazz Band
CD _____ RPCD 613
Robert Parker Jazz / Apr '94 / Conifer.

NEW ORLEANS BLUES 1923-40
CD _____ 157612
Blues Collection / Feb '93 / Discovery.

NEW ORLEANS BRASS BANDS
CD _____ CD 11562
Rounder / Mar '90 / CM / Direct / ADA / Cadillac.

NEW ORLEANS DIXIE
CD _____ 22505
Music / Aug '95 / Target/BMG.

NEW ORLEANS FUNCTION
CD _____ CD 3560
Cameo / Jul '95 / Target/BMG.

NEW ORLEANS GOSPEL QUARTETS 1947-1956
CD _____ HTCD 12
Heritage / Feb '94 / Swift / Roots / Wellard / Direct / Hot Shot / Jazz Music / ADA.

NEW ORLEANS HIT STORY, THE (Twenty Years Of Big Easy Hits, 1950-1970)
CD Set _____ CDINSD 5073
Charly / Jun '93 / Charly / THE / Cadillac.

NEW ORLEANS IN NEW ORLEANS
CD _____ 157992
Jazz Archives / Jun '93 / Jazz Music / Discovery / Cadillac.

NEW ORLEANS IN THE TWENTIES
CD _____ CBC 1014
Bellaphon / Jun '93 / New Note.

NEW ORLEANS JAZZ
CD _____ ARHCD 346
Arhoolie / Apr '95 / ADA / Direct / Cadillac.

NEW ORLEANS JAZZ GIANTS 1936-1940
CD _____ JSPCD 336
JSP / Jul '92 / ADA / Target/BMG / Direct / Cadillac / Complete/Pinnacle.

NEW ORLEANS JAZZ HERITAGE
CD _____ 8122711112
WEA / Jul '93 / Warner Music.

NEW ORLEANS JAZZ SCENE OF THE 50'S
CD Set _____ CDB 1208
Giants Of Jazz / Apr '92 / Target/BMG / Cadillac.

NEW ORLEANS JAZZ VOL. 1
CD _____ WJS 1001CD
Wolf / Nov '93 / Jazz Music / Swift / Hot Shot.

NEW ORLEANS JAZZ VOL. 2
CD _____ WJS 1002CD
Wolf / Nov '93 / Jazz Music / Swift / Hot Shot.

NEW ORLEANS JOYS
CD Set _____ DCD 8001
Disky / Jan '95 / THE / BMG / Discovery / Pinnacle.

NEW ORLEANS LADIES
CD _____ CD 2078
Rounder / '88 / CM / Direct / ADA / Cadillac.

NEW ORLEANS RHYTHM KINGS
CD _____ VILCD 0042
Village Jazz / Sep '92 / Target/BMG / Jazz Music.

NEW ORLEANS TO CHICAGO - THE FORTIES
CD _____ CJR 1002
Gannet / Nov '95 / Jazz Music / Cadillac.

NEW ROMANTIC CLASSIC TRACKS
Tainted love: Soft Cell / Fade to grey: Visage / Chant no.1 (I don't need this pressure on): Spandau Ballet / Enola grey: O.M.D. / Play to win: Heaven 17 / I'm in love with a German film star: Passions / After a fashion: Karn, Mick & Midge Ure / Vienna: Ultravox / Quiet life: Japan / Model: Kraftwerk / Empire state human: Human League / African and white: China Crisis / Whip it: Devo / To cut a long story short: Spandau Ballet / Visage: Visage / Say hello wave goobye: Soft Cell
CD _____ CDPR 128
Premier/MFP / Nov '94 / EMI.

NEW ROMANTIC CLASSICS
Open your heart: Human League / Temptation: Heaven 17 / Chant No.1 (I don't need this pressure on): Spandau Ballet / Rio: Duran Duran / Look of love: ABC / Is it a dream: Classix Nouveaux / Together in electric dreams: Oakey, Philip & Giorgio Moroder / Dancing with tears in my eyes: Ultravox / Enola Gay: O.M.D. / Tainted love: Soft Cell / Don't go: Yazoo / Model: Kraftwerk / Wishful thinking: China Crisis / Today: Talk Talk / Cars: Numan, Gary / Fade to grey: Visage / Ghosts: Japan
CD _____ VTCD 15
Virgin Television / Oct '92 / EMI.

NEW SEASON, A
CD _____ SFRCD 205
Strange Fruit / Sep '91 / Pinnacle.

NEW SMOKING CLASSICS VOL.1
CD _____ HYPOXIA 001CD
Hypoxia / Sep '95 / Plastic Head.

NEW SOUL REBELS
CD _____ RADCD 05
Global / Feb '95 / BMG.

NEW SPIRITS IN JAZZ
CD _____ EFA 015082
World's Best / Nov '95 / SRD.

NEW STARS FROM THE HEARTLAND
Shameless: Brooks, Garth / Down at the twist and shout: Carpenter, Mary-Chapin / Here's a quarter (call someone who cares): Tritt, Travis / She's in love with the boy: Yearwood, Trisha / Don't rock the jukebox: Jackson, Alan / We both walk: Morgan, Lorrie / Forever together: Travis, Randy / Young love (strong love): Judds / Put yourself in my shoes: Black, Clint / Walk on faith: Reed, Mike / For my broken heart: McEntire, Reba / Restless: O'Connor, Mark & New Nashville Cats / Bing bang boom: Highway 101 / You know me better than that: Strait, George / Pocket full of gold: Gill, Vince / Down to my last teardrop: Tucker, Tanya / Jukebox with a country song: Stone, Doug / Someday soon: Bogguss, Suzy / Life's too long: Skaggs, Ricky / You don't count the cost: Dean, Billy
CD _____ CDESTU 2172
EMI / Apr '92 / EMI.

NEW TRAIL RIDERS: SWAMP MUSIC VOL.9
CD _____ US 0206
Trikont / Apr '95 / ADA / Direct.

NEW YORK
Burnin' the iceberg / Struggle buggy / Sugarfoot stomp / Lock and key / San / Imagination / Makin' friends / Minor drag / East St. Louis toodle-oo / Hot bones and feet / Dr. Blues / Feelin devilish / Happy hour / Casa loma stomp / Dog bottom / Minnie the

moocher / Stratosphere / Cushion foot stomp / I can't dance / Farewell blues
CD _____ RPCD 615
Robert Parker Jazz / Mar '95 / Conifer.

NEW YORK - THE JAZZ AGE
CD Set _____ DCD 8003
Disky / Jan '95 / THE / BMG / Discovery / Pinnacle.

NEW YORK IN THE TWENTIES
Davenport blues: Nichols, Red / Delirium: Nichols, Red / Slippin' around: Nichols, Red / Feelin' no pain: Nichols, Red / Harlem twist: Nichols, Red / Five pennies: Nichols, Red / Waitin': Pollack, Ben & His Orchestra / Singapore sorrows: Pollack, Ben & His Orchestra / Buy buy for baby: Pollack, Ben & His Orchestra / Wang wang blues: Pollack, Ben & His Orchestra / Yellow dog blues: Pollack, Ben & His Orchestra / My kinda love: Pollack, Ben & His Orchestra / Mean to me: Napoleon's Emperors / Getting hot: Napoleon's Emperors / Anything: Napoleon's Emperors / You can't cheat a cheater: Napoleon's Emperors / Doin' things: Venuti, Joe & Eddie Lang / Wild cats: Venuti, Joe & Eddie Lang / Wild dog: Venuti, Joe & Eddie Lang / Really blue: Venuti, Joe & Eddie Lang
CD _____ ND 83136
Bluebird / Oct '91 / BMG.

NEW YORK JAZZ 1923-31
CD _____ VILCD 0242
Village Jazz / Sep '92 / Target/BMG / Jazz Music.

NEW YORK JAZZ IN THE ROARING 20'S
CD _____ BCD 129
Biograph / Jun '94 / Wellard / ADA / Hot Shot / Jazz Music / Cadillac / Direct.

NEW YORK SCHOOL NO.3
CD _____ ARTCD 6176
Hat Art / Dec '95 / Harmonia Mundi / ADA / Cadillac.

NEW YORK THRASH
CD _____ EE 113CD
Reach Out International / Nov '94 / Jetstar.

NEW YORK UNDER COVER
CD _____ MCD 11342
MCA / Feb '96 / BMG.

NEW ZONE HISTORY VOL.1, THE
CD _____ MET 003-2
Metamatic / Jul '93 / Plastic Head.

NEWPORT
CD _____ CDVCD 78
Start / Sep '89 / Koch.

NEWPORT ALL STARS
Take the 'A' train / These foolish things / My Monday date / Body and soul / Mean to me / I surrender dear / Please don't talk about me when I'm gone / Pan Am blues
CD _____ BLCD 760138
Black Lion / Oct '90 / Jazz Music / Cadillac / Wellard / Koch.

NEWPORT BROADSINGERS
CD _____ VCD 77003
Vanguard / Oct '95 / Complete/Pinnacle / Discovery.

NEWPORT IN NEW YORK
Outside help: King, B.B. / Honky tonk train blues: Glenn, Lloyd / After hours: Glenn, Lloyd / Pinetop's boogie woogie: Glenn, Lloyd / Little red rooster: Thornton, Willie Mae / Drifter: Brown, Clarence 'Gatemouth' / Long distance call: Waters, Muddy / Where's my woman / Got my mojo working
CD _____ CDBM 071
Blue Moon / Apr '91 / Magnum Music Group / Greensleeves / Hot Shot / ADA / Cadillac / Discovery.

NEWPORT JAZZ FESTIVAL
Sweet Georgia Brown: Hall, Edmond / Tin roof blues: Kaminsky, Max / Stars fell on Alabama: McGarity, Lou / I've found a new baby: Freeman, Bud / At the jazz band ball: Chicago All Stars / Isle of Capri: Manone, Wingy / Relaxin' at the Touro: Spanier, Muggsy / I wish I could shimmy like my sister Kate: Brunis, George / Royal Garden blues: Spanier, Muggsy / I'm in the mood for love: Thomas, Joe / Big noise from Winnetka: Haggart, Bob / Stealin' apples: Hucko, Peanuts
CD _____ 74321218292
RCA Victor / Nov '94 / BMG.

NEWPORT JAZZ FESTIVAL ALL STARS
Exactly like you / Centennial blues / I didn't know about you / Nobody knows you (when you're down and out) / Rosetta / Smiles / Jeep is jumpin' / Mooche / Body and soul / Man I love / What's new / Struttin' with some barbecue / Moten swing
CD _____ CCD 4260
Concord Jazz / Dec '87 / New Note.

NEXT GENERATION
CD _____ TUT 727492
Wundertute / Jan '94 / CM / Duncans / ADA.

NICE AN' RUFF
Sun is shining: Black Uhuru / No, no, no: White, K.C. / Village of the under priviliged: Isaacs, Gregory / Things in life: Brown, Dennis / Y mas gan: Abyssinians / Bongo red: Griffiths, Albert & The Gladiators / Capture rasta: Culture / Set de prisoners free: Muta Baruka / Dub organizer: Pablo, Augustus / Maggie breast: I-Roy / Kingston town: Lord Creator / Swing and dine: Melodians / Love is overdue: Isaacs, Gregory / Woman is like a shadow: Meditations / Girl I love you: Andy, Horace / Good thing going: Minott, Sugar / Baltimore: Tamlins / Triplet: Sly & Robbie
CD _____ MCCD 092
Music Club / Dec '92 / Disc / THE / CM.

NICE ENOUGH TO EAT
CD _____ RRCD 143
Receiver / Jul '93 / Grapevine.

NICE UP DANCEE
CD _____ RCD 20202
Hannibal / Aug '91 / Vital / ADA.

NIGHT AND DAY
CD _____ CDHD 187
Happy Days / '93 / Conifer.

NIGHT AT RONNIE'S VOL.2, A
Visiting: Nazaire / Time one: Fourth World / My foolish heart: Delmar, Elaine / Coming home baby: Breaux, Zachary / Hot: Ayers, Roy / My love: Sandoval, Arturo / Lo que va a pasar: Irakere / Serenade to Sweden: Cohn, Al / Lover man: Shaw, Ian / Watching the traffic lights change: National Youth Jazz Orchestra
CD _____ NARCD 2
Ronnie Scott's Jazz House / Jan '94 / Jazz Music / Magnum Music Group / Cadillac.

NIGHT AT RONNIE'S VOL.3, A
CD _____ NARCD 3
Ronnie Scott's Jazz House / Apr '94 / Jazz Music / Magnum Music Group / Cadillac.

NIGHT AT RONNIE'S VOL.4, A
CD _____ NARCD 4
Ronnie Scott's Jazz House / Mar '95 / Jazz Music / Magnum Music Group / Cadillac.

NIGHT AT RONNIE'S VOL.5, A
CD _____ NARCD 5
Ronnie Scott's Jazz House / Oct '95 / Jazz Music / Magnum Music Group / Cadillac.

NIGHT AT RONNIE'S, A
Donna Lee: Sandoval, Arturo / White caps: Scott, Ronnie Quintet / Nice work if you can get it/Easy to love: Montgomery, Marian / Falling grace: Whitehead, Tim / La pastora: Irakere / Luminous: Freeman, Chico & Arthur Blythe / Early Autumn: Vaughan, Sarah / Spring is here: Taylor, John Trio / Sleeplate Louie's: White, Tam & The Band / Siorra: Coleman, George / You send me: Ayers, Roy / I'm beginning to see the light: Sharpe, Jack Big Band
CD _____ NARCD 1
Ronnie Scott's Jazz House / Jan '94 / Jazz Music / Magnum Music Group / Cadillac.

NIGHT AT THE EMPIRE, A
No no no: Miller, Max & His Orchestra / Littul Gel: Warner, Jack & Joan Winters / Nothin' else to do all day: Long, Norman / You gotta S-M-I-L-E to be H-A-Double-P-Y: Henderson Twins / Hawaiian gems: Mendelssohn, Felix & His Hawaiian Serenaders / When Dream about Hawaii: Mendelssohn, Felix & His Hawaiian Serenaders / Drifting and dreaming: Mendelssohn, Felix & His Hawaiian Serenaders / Aloma: Mendelssohn, Felix / After all that: Western Brothers / You must have been a beautiful baby: Costa, Sam & Dorothy Carless / When the steamboat whistle is blowing: Gonella, Nat & His Georgians / Two dresden dolls: Gonella, Nat & His Georgians / Ode of the fletcher: Fletcher, Cyril / Life begins again: Flanagan & Allen / I'm just wild about Harry: Lipton, Celia / I cried for you: Lipton, Celia / You made me love you: Lipton, Celia / Three times a day: Wallace, Nellie / To mother with love: Roy, Harry & His Orchestra / Even a crooner must eat: Bacon, Max & His Orchestra / Londone pride... and proud of it too: Waters, Elsie & Doris / Sweetest sweetheart: Mesene, Jimmy / George Elrick successes: Elrick, George & His Band / Music goes 'round and around: Elrick, George & His Band / Boo-hoo: Elrick, George & His Band / I'm nuts about nursery music: Elrick, George & His Band / He never slept a wink all night: O'Shea, Tessie / This is my day - gang show of 1939: Reader, Ralph / My honey's loving arms: Oliver, Vic / Love 'em and leave 'em alone: King, Hetty & His Orchestra
CD _____ PASTCD 9759
Flapper / May '92 / Pinnacle.

NIGHT FEVER
CD Set _____ RADCD 24
Global / Oct '95 / BMG.

NIGHT MOVES
CD _____ DBG 53036
Double Gold / Apr '95 / Target/BMG.

NIGHT MOVES IN JAZZ
Amandla: Davis, Miles / Naima: Coltrane, John / B minor waltz: Evans, Bill / Lorelei's lament: Crawford, Hank / Everything happens to me: Sullivan, Ira / Nubian lady: Lateef, Yusef / Misty: Hubbard, Freddie / Embraceable you: Farmer, Art & Jim Hall / Body and soul: Joseph, Julian / I'll be seeing you: Fruscella, Tony / You go to my head: Tristano, Lennie / Summertime: Mann, Herbie
CD _____ 9548326342
East West / Mar '94 / Warner Music.

NIGHT OF THE GUITAR
Dr. Brown, I presume: Haycock, Pete / Lucienne: Haycock, Pete / Hey Joe: California, Randy / King will come: Wishbone Ash / Never in my life: West, Leslie / Wurm: Howe, Steve / Ain't nothin' shakin': Lee, Alvin / Theme from an imaginary western: West, Leslie / Clap medley: Howe, Steve / No limit: Lee, Alvin / Whole lotta shakin' goin' on / Johnny B. Goode / Bye bye Johnny / All along the watchtower / Dizzy Miss Lizzy / Rock 'n' roll music
CD _____ EIRSACD 1005
IRS / Apr '89 / PolyGram / BMG / EMI.

NIGHT OF THE LIVING PUSSIES
Please don't touch me: Meteors / Casting my spell: Blue Cats / No more no more no more: Sergeant Fury / Street wise: Guana Batz / I go wild: Restless / Lunatics (are you insane): Frantic Flintstones / Mad mad bad bad Mama: Empress Of Fur / Charlie: Sharks / Nothing left but the bones: Long Tall Texans / Head on backwards: Thee Phantom Creeps / It's gone: Quakes / Rock on the moon: Thee Waltons / Brand new gun: Frenzy / Worms: Hangmen / Zulu Joe: King Kurt / Pink hearse: Radium Cats / Queen of disease: Demented Are Go / Throwing my baby out with the bath water: McCavity's Cat
CD _____ CDMGRAM 79
Anagram / May '94 / Pinnacle.

NIGHT SPIRIT MASTERS
(Gnawa Music Of Marrakesh)
CD _____ 5101442
Axiom / Mar '92 / PolyGram / Vital.

NIGHTIME ROUNDUP
(Collection Of Contemporary Rock Songs From Texas)
CD _____ TX 2006CD
Taxim / Jan '94 / ADA.

NIGHTS IN HEAVEN
(The Party Anthems - 2CD/MC Set)
It's raining men: Weather Girls / We are family: Sister Sledge / Your love still brings me to my knees: Hines, Marcia / Can you feel it: Jacksons / Got to be real: Lynn, Cheryl / Relight my fire: Hartman, Dan / You make me feel (mighty real): Hartman, Dan / Disco inferno: Trammps / Don't leave me this way: Houston, Thelma / Pilot error: Mills, Stephanie / This time I know it's for real: Summer, Donna / I want your sex: Michael, George / Smack my booty: Bronski Beat / Could it be magic: Take That / Take a chance on me: Erasure / Venus: Bananarama / Relax: Frankie Goes To Hollywood / Only way is up: Yazz / What do I have to do: Minogue, Kylie / Everybody's free (to feel good): Rozalla / I love the nightlife: Bridges, Alicia / Supermodel: Rupaul / Hey now (girls just want to have fun): Lauper, Cyndi / Little bird: Lennox, Annie / Losing my mind: Minnelli, Liza / Stand by your man: Wynette, Tammy
CD Set _____ JON TV 3CD
Columbia / Aug '95 / Sony.

NINETIES COLLECTION, THE
CD _____ CDTRAX 5004
Greentrax / Oct '95 / Conifer / Duncans / ADA / Direct.

NINGS OF DESIRE
(The Best Fierce Panda Album In The World Probably)
CD _____ NONGCD 01
Damaged Goods / May '95 / SRD.

NIPPON DAIKO NO MIRYKOU
CD _____ C 337030
Denon / '88 / Conifer.

NISAVA
CD _____ CDEB 2565
Earthbeat / May '93 / Direct / ADA.

NITEBEAT
CD _____ XTR 15CD
X:Treme / Apr '95 / Pinnacle / SRD.

NITEDANCIN' VOL.1
CD _____ DFDCD 017
Defender / Jun '95 / SRD.

NITTY GRITTY
This man in love: New Wanderers / I'm getting tired: Carlettes / Soeur De Lites / I need your love: Masters / I know I'm in love with you: Byrd, George Duke / That's what I want: McGowan, Syno / Oh oh oh what a love this is: Revlons / Nevertheless: Andrews, Lee & The Hearts / You're not my kind: Durante, Paula / You better think it over: Du-Shons / He's that way sometimes: Wells, Bobby / She said goodbye: Harmonic, Billy / I can't stand to lose you: Chandler, E.J. / Elijah rockin' with soul: Jacobs, Hank

/ Heartbreakin' time: Little John / You're gonna pay: Rivingtons / Lighten up baby: Karim, Ty / I'm so glad: Neal, Robert / I was born to love you: Hunter, Herbert / Love's like quicksand: Wynns, Sandy / He's a flirt: Sequins / All of my life: Detroit Soul / I need your love (2): Chaumonts / Do we let it be me babe: Evans, Karl / Cherry baby: Millionaires / I'm standing: Lumley, Rufus / Try a little harder: Fi Dels / Like a bee: Spidells / You got me in the palm of your hand: Richardson, Donald Lee / There's no you: Occasions
CD _____ GSCD 022
Goldmine / Sep '93 / Vital.

NME SINGLES OF THE WEEK 1992
Only living boy in New Cross: Carter U.S.M. / Assassins: Orbit / 100%: Sonic Youth / Sheela na gig: PJ Harvey / What you do to me: Teenage Fanclub / Changes: Sugar / Old red eyes is back: Beautiful South / Join our club: St. Etienne / California: Wedding Present / Eat yourself whole: Kingmaker / Low self opinion: Rollins, Henry / Streamroller: Family Cat / Bottle: Tyrrel Corporation / 2 Deep: Gang Starr / Bedlam: Gallon Drunk / Peep: 3 1/2 Minutes
CD _____ 74321132282
RCA / Feb '93 / BMG.

NME SINGLES OF THE WEEK 1993
Tennessee: Arrested Development / Gepetto: Belly / Key: Senser / Madder rose: Madder Rose / White love: One Dove / Marbles: Tindersticks / Call it what you want: Credit To The Nation / Believe in me: Utah Saints / Duel: Swervedriver / Venus as a boy: Bjork / Stutter: Elastica / Good times: Spiritualized / Cherub rock: Smashing Pumpkins / Movin on special: Apache Indian / Fifty foot Queenie: PJ Harvey / Tilted: Sugar / America snoring: Grant Lee Buffalo / Open up: Leftfield & John Lydon
CD _____ 74321187012
Giant / Jan '94 / BMG.

NO ALTERNATIVE
Superdeformed: Sweet, Matthew / For all to see: Buffalo Tom / Sexual healing: Soul Asylum / Take a walk: Urge Overkill / All your jeans were too tight: American Music Club / Bitch: Goo Goo Dolls / Unseen power of the picket fence: Pavement / Glynis: Smashing Pumpkins / Can't fight it: Mould, Bob / Memorial tribute: Smith, Patti / Hold on: McLachlan, Sarah / Show me: Soundgarden / Joed out: Manning, Barbara / Heavy 33: Verlaines / Effigy: Uncle Tupelo / It's the new style: Beastie Boys / Iris: Breeders / Burning spear (Available on MC only): Sonic Youth / Hot nights: Richman, Jonathan / Brittle: Straitjacket Fits
CD _____ 07822187372
Arista / Oct '93 / BMG.

NO FREE RIDES BUDGET BLUES SAMPLER
CD _____ JSPCDNFR 1
JSP / Jul '95 / ADA / Target/BMG / Direct / Cadillac / Complete/Pinnacle.

NO FUTURE - THE SINGLES COLLECTION
Someone's gonna die: Blitz / Police story: Partizan / Future must be ours: Blitzkrieg / Banned from the pubs: Peter & The Test Tube Babies / In Britain: Red Alert / Never surrender: Blitz / Today's generation: Attak / Lest we forget: Blitzkrieg / Gangland: Violators / El Salvador: Insane / I've got a guitar: Channel 3 / Seventeen years of hell: Partizan / Take no prisoners: Red Alert / Dead hero: Samples / Run like hell: Peter & The Test Tube Babies / Warriors: Blitz / Murder in the subway: Attak / Keep on running: Crux / Summer of '81: Violators / City invasion: Red Alert / Day tripper: Wall / Megalomania: Blood / Wanna riot: A.B.H. / Suffragette City: Rose Of Victory / Night creatures: Screaming Dead / Die with dignity: Violators / There's a guitar burning: Red Alert
CD _____ CDPUNK 54
Anagram / May '95 / Pinnacle.

NO LESS THAN WIRELESS
CD _____ MW 2016CD
Music & Words / Nov '95 / ADA / Direct.

NO MASTER'S VOICE
CD _____ NMV 4CD
No Master's Voice / Mar '94 / ADA.

NO MORE HEROES
(Music That Influenced A Generation)
Going underground: Jam / Promises: Buzzcocks / Rat trap: Boomtown Rats / My perfect cousin: Undertones / If the kids are united: Sham 69 / Teenage kicks (CD only): Undertones / Something better change (CD only): Stranglers / No more heroes: Stranglers / Eton rifles: Jam / Ever fallen in love: Buzzcocks / I don't like Mondays: Boomtown Rats / Jimmy Jimmy: Undertones / Hersham boys: Sham 69 / Peaches: Stranglers
CD _____ CDFA 3233
Fame / Sep '90 / EMI.

NO MORE LONELY NIGHTS
(Music Of Paul McCartney - 16 Instrumental Hits)
CD _____ 5708574338042
Carlton Home Entertainment / Sep '94 / Carlton Home Entertainment.

NO PARTICULAR PLACE TO GO
No particular place to go: Berry, Chuck / Rescue me: Bass, Fontella / Lady Luck: Price, Lloyd / Ginny come lately: Hyland, Brian / Like a baby: Barry, Len / Baby my heart: Crickets / Main attraction: Boone, Pat / Itsy bitsy teeny weeny yellow polka dot bikini: Hyland, Brian / Mr. Bass man: Cymbal, Johnny / Hi-heel sneakers: Tucker, Tommy / You never can tell: Berry, Chuck / When you ask about love: Crickets / Johnny will: Boone, Pat / Nadine: Berry, Chuck
CD _____ PWKS 574
Carlton Home Entertainment / Mar '90 / Carlton Home Entertainment.

NO REPETITIVE BEATS
CD _____ NRB 58CD
Six6 / Jan '95 / Sony / 3MV.

NO SPEAK SAMPLER
India: Currie, Billy / Arabesque: Wishbone Ash / You got me runnin': Jimmy Z / Fire and mercy: Orbit, William / Equalizer: Copeland, Stewart / Dr. Brown, I presume: Haycock, Pete / No limit: Lee, Alvin / Prisoner: Spirit / Idler: Hunter, Steve / Shotgun cha cha: Jimmy Z / Perfect flight: Currie, Billy / Glidepath: Hunter, Steve
CD _____ ILPCD 34
IRS / Jun '89 / PolyGram / BMG / EMI.

NO.1 70'S ROCK ALBUM
CD _____ 5257172
PolyGram TV / Aug '95 / PolyGram.

NO.1 ALL TIME ROCK ALBUM
CD _____ 5059542
PolyGram / Oct '95 / PolyGram.

NO.1 CHRISTMAS ALBUM
CD _____ 5259782
PolyGram TV / Nov '95 / PolyGram.

NO.1 DANCE HITS
CD Set _____ LOWBOXCD 17
Low Price Music / Mar '95 / Total/BMG.

NO.1 LOVE ALBUM, THE
CD _____ 5352622
PolyGram TV / Jan '96 / PolyGram.

NO.1'S COLLECTION
She wears red feathers: Mitchell, Guy / I believe: Laine, Frankie / Look at that girl: Mitchell, Guy / Hey Joe: Laine, Frankie / Secret love: Day, Doris / Such a night: Ray, Johnnie / This ole house #2: Clooney, Rosemary / Mambo Italiano: Clooney, Rosemary / Stranger in paradise: Bennett, Tony / Whatever will be will be (Que sera sera): Day, Doris / Woman in love: Laine, Frankie / Just walking in the rain: Ray, Johnnie / Singin' the blues: Mitchell, Guy / Butterfly: Ray, Johnnie / On the street where you live: Damone, Vic / Only the lonely: Orbison, Roy / It's over: Orbison, Roy / Oh pretty woman: Orbison, Roy / Mr. Tambourine Man: Byrds / San Francisco: McKenzie, Scott / Ballad of Bonnie and Clyde: Fame, Georgie / Everlasting love: Love Affair / Young girl: Puckett, Gary & The Union Gap / Albatross: Fleetwood Mac / When will I see you again: Three Degrees / Gonna make you a star: Essex, David / Stand by your man: Wynette, Tammy / Tears on my pillow: Nelson, Johnny / Hold me close: Essex, David / I love to love (but my baby loves to dance): Charles, Tina / Free: Williams, Deniece / Show you the way to go: Jacksons / What's another year: Logan, Johnny / M.A.S.H. (Suicide is painless): M.A.S.H. / This ole house: Stevens, Shakin' / Seventeen years of hell: Partizan / Green door: Stevens, Shakin' / Prince Charming: Adam & The Ants / Oh Julie: Stevens, Shakin' / Seven tears: Goombay Dance Band / Goody two shoes: Adam & The Ants / Total eclipse of the heart: Tyler, Bonnie / Give it up: K.C. & The Sunshine Band / Freedom: Wham / Edge of heaven: Wham / Final countdown: Europe / I owe you nothing: Bros
CD Set _____ BOXD 17T
Carlton Home Entertainment / Oct '94 / Carlton Home Entertainment.

NOBODY'S HEROES
CD _____ MATCD 270
Castle / Apr '93 / BMG.

NOCHE DE AMOUR
CD _____ TUMICD 024
Tumi / '92 / Sterns / Discovery.

NOIR
CD _____ VICTOCD 022
Victo / Nov '94 / These / ReR Megacorp / Cadillac.

NOISE 3
Bass shake: Urban Shakedown / Smoke dis one: Bass Ballistic / Caught with a spliff: Hackney Hardcore / Free your mind: Satin Storm / Don Gordon coming: Project One / Peace and sunshine: Sonz Of A Loop Da Loop Era / Now hear this: Energy Zone / Up and running: Vocation / Back again: Run Tings / Star preacher: Space Brains / Space: Dionysus / Intensity: Freshtrax & Ace / Let's go: Hardware / What the world needs: Blatant & Dangerous / Out of it: Spinal Level / Bogey man: Happy & Free
CD _____ CDTOT 8
Jumpin' & Pumpin' / Jul '93 / 3MV / Sony.

NON STOP CHRISTMAS TOP 20

Sleigh ride / Lily the pink / Have yourself a merry little Christmas / Jingle bells / White Christmas / Santa Claus is coming to town / We wish you a Merry Christmas / Little drummer boy / Rudolph the red nosed reindeer / We wish the merriest / Winter wonderland / I saw Mommy kissing Santa Claus / Do you hear what I hear / Scarlet ribbons / All I want for Christmas (is my two front teeth) / Mary's boy child / First Noel / Hark the herald angels sing / Cokey cokey / Christmas song

CD _____ SPGCD 8000
President / Nov '95 / Grapevine / Target / BMG / Jazz Music / President.

NON STOP EUROPA EXPRESS

CD _____ JAPECD 101
Escapade / May '94 / 3MV / Sony.

NON STOP-SALSA

Salsa mani / Amor can sala / El porompompero / Carnavalito gitano / Ole tus lunares / Linda malaguena / Que problema / Varnos Jose / El botelion / San Retazan / No meu pe de serra / Moliendo cafe / Granada mia / Una aventura mas

CD _____ 908042
PMF / Jul '94 / Kingdom / Cadillac.

NON-STOP CHRISTMAS PARTY

CD _____ MCCDX 009
Music Club / Nov '94 / Disc / THE / CM.

NONE OF THESE ARE LOVE SONGS VOL.1

Gonna make you move: Boomshanka / Big bud II: Tranx Project / Reach further: Progression / Ride: Boomshanka / Bug bottom hula: Big Bottom Music / Spirit: Aberration / House of dread: Dread Zone / Agent C-O: Aloof / Equatorial dawn: Mind Becomes Drum / Who killed the king: Sunz Of Ishen

CD _____ CVN 001CD
Caustic Visions / Apr '94 / Kudos / Disc.

NONE OF THESE ARE LOVE SONGS VOL.2

CD _____ CVNCD 3
Contraband / Nov '94 / Pinnacle.

NORSE TURDANSAR

CD _____ HCD 7089CD
Musikk Distribujson / Apr '95 / ADA.

NORTENO AND TEJANO ACCORDION PIONEERS

CD _____ ARHCD 7016
Arhoolie / Jan '96 / ADA / Direct / Cadillac.

NORTH - THE SOUND OF THE DANCE UNDERGROUND

Dream 17: Annette / I ain't nightclubbing: T-Coy / House tantaz-ee: D.C.B / Acid to ecstasy: ED 209 / Voodoo ray: Guy Called Gerald / Megagrip: Masters Of Acid / Carino: T-Coy / Get on one: Frequency 9

CD _____ PD 71939
RCA / Dec '88 / BMG.

NORTH INDIA-KASHMIR & GANGES PLAIN

CD _____ ARN 64227
Arion / Jun '93 / Discovery / ADA.

NORTH INDIAN VOCAL MUSIC

Khyal in raga bhairav: Khan, Hafeez Ahmed / Thumri in raga bhairavi: Bhagwat, Neela / Khyal in raga bhupali: Khan, Hafeez Ahmed / Khyal in deshkar: Bhagwat, Neela

CD _____ CDSDL 404
Saydisc / Jun '94 / Harmonia Mundi / ADA / Direct.

NORTH OF WATFORD VOLUME 1

Gimme some: Brendon / Shattered glass: Warren, Ellie / Nine times out of ten: Day, Muriel / One minute every hour: Miles, John / Run baby run: Newbeats / Sweet talking guy: Chiffons / To you me are everything: Real Thing / Gotta get along without you: Wills, Viola / Something old, something new: Fantastics / Gully: Pearls / Ski-ing in the snow: Wigan's Ovation / Touch of velvet: Mood Mosaic / Going to go go: Sharonettes / Shotgun wedding: Roy C / Long after tonight is all over: Radcliffe, Jimmy / Supergirl: Bonney, Graham / Rudi's in love: Locomotive / Man like me: James, Jimmy / Under my thumb: Gibson, Wayne / Out on the floor: Gray, Dobie / Flasher: Mistra / Hold me, thrill me, kiss me: Carter, Mel / Heartache avenue: Maisonettes / I feel love coming on: Taylor, Felice

CD _____ KRLCD 001
KRL / Apr '95 / Vital.

NORTH SEA JAZZ SESSIONS, VOL 1

CD _____ JWD 102201
JWD / Jul '93 / Target/BMG.

NORTH SEA JAZZ SESSIONS, VOL 2

CD _____ JWD 102202
JWD / Jul '93 / Target/BMG.

NORTH SEA JAZZ SESSIONS, VOL 3

CD _____ JWD 102203
JWD / Jul '93 / Target/BMG.

NORTH SEA JAZZ SESSIONS, VOL 4

CD _____ JWD 102204
JWD / Jul '93 / Target/BMG.

NORTH SEA JAZZ SESSIONS, VOL 5

CD _____ JWD 102205
JWD / Jul '93 / Target/BMG.

NORTHCORE (The Polar Scene)

CD _____ BHR 008
Burning Heart / Feb '95 / Plastic Head.

NORTHERN BEAT, THE (22 Classic Hits From The 60's)

I'm into something good: Herman's Hermits / Groovy kind of love: Mindbenders / Do you want to know a secret: Kramer, Billy J. & The Dakotas / I like it: Gerry & The Pacemakers / Just one look: Hollies / Needles and pins: Searchers / You've got your troubles: Fortunes / Little things: Berry, Dave / Juliet: Four Pennies / Hello little girl: Fourmost / Shout: Lulu & The Luvvers / Ain't she sweet: Beatles / Hippy hippy shake: Swinging Blue Jeans / House of the rising sun: Animals / If you gotta make a fool of somebody: Freddie & The Dreamers / Halfway to paradise: Fury, Billy / Game of love: Fontana, Wayne / I think of you: Merseybeats / Anyone who had a heart: Black, Cilla / Sorrow: Merseys / Everything's alright: Mojos / Varmo other guy: Big Three

CD _____ 8409682
Polydor / Jun '90 / PolyGram.

NORTHERN SOUL DANCE PARTY

That beatin' rhythm: Temple, Richard / Goose pimples: Scott, Shirley J. / My sugar baby: Clarke, Connie / Double cookin': Checkerboard Squares / Do the philly dog: Olympics / Not me baby: Silhouettes / Yes I love you baby: Dynamics / Eddie's my name: Holman, Eddie / Countdown: Temptation walk: Lee, Jackie / I'm satisfied with you: Furys / There's nothing else to say: Incredibles / My little girl: Garrett, Bobby / I got the fever: Creation / What's the matter baby: Reynolds, L.J. / Let's cop a groove: Wells, Bobby / Get on your knees: Los Canarios / I can't help myself: Ross, Johnny / Earthquake: Lynn, Bobbi / Our love is in the pocket: Banks, Darren / Blowing my mind to pieces: Relf, Bobby

CD _____ GSCD 046
Goldmine / Jul '94 / Vital.

NORTHERN SOUL FEVER

Manifesto: Case Of Tyme / My sweet baby: Puzzles / No ifs, no ands, no buts: Young, Mae / Talking eyes: Beatty, Pamela / I don't want to hear it: Exits / Very strong on you: Greer, Cortez / Girl every guy should know: Carrington, Sunny / Bring me all your heartaches: Beavers, Jackie / Don't you need a boy like me: Carlton, Carl / Broken hearted lover: Tojo / I can hear you crying: Hill, Eddie / Try my love: Toni & The Showmen / In my life: Carr, Linda / This heart these hands: Wells, Billy / Just do the best you can: Duke & Leonard / Ain't that love enough: Atkins, Larry / Bad brought the good: Turks / Standing at a standstill: Holmes, Sherlock / Someone else's turn: Clayton, Pat / I ain't got nothin' but the blues: Friendly People / Moments: Bronzettes / Sugar baby: Holland, Jimmy / Real nice: Barnes, Johnny / Beware a stranger: Jones, Bobby / I've got to face: Thunders, Johnny & The Heartbreakers / Turn to me: Chris Towns Unit / Shield all around: Holliday, Jimmy / You better check yourself: La'shell & The Shelletts / I bear witness: Apollo, Vince / No time: John & The Weirdest / I got the fever: Creation / You better believe me: Reeder, Esque / Love can't be modernised: Tripps / Take me back again: Volcanos / Why wonder: And The Echoes / Lean on me: Charles, Dave / Little things: Moore, Misty / If I only knew: Mike & Ray / Home town boy: Williams, Sebastian / Lonely lover: McFarland, Jimmy / One way lover: Volumes / Somebody help me: Jenkins, Donald & The Delighters / Let nobody love you: Blakley, Virginia / What do you think: Lamarr, Chico / If I could see you now: Sunny & The Sunliners / With these eyes: Fabulous Peps / I want to be free: Admirations / What can a man do: Showstoppers

CD Set _____ GSCD 027
Goldmine / Jan '94 / Vital.

NORTHERN SOUL FEVER VOL.2

Trouble: Agents / Deeper: Chequers / Midnight brew: Carter, Melvin / Hey girl you've changed: Vondells / No one loves you: Hot Cinnamon / You don't need my help (Part 1): Garvin, Rex / Hide out: Hideaways / Misery: Strogin, Henry / I'm where it's at: Jades / Case of love: Renfro Bros. / Love bound: Audio Arts Strings / Anyway you want it: Smith, Fred Orchestra / Lonely eyes: Elling, Melvin / I can't stop you: Performers / Sugar pie honey: Promatics / Bounce: Olympics / Gotta get you back: Mandolph, Bobby / I'd best be going: Vito & The Salutations / Permanent vacation: Sodd, Marion / Seven days of loving: Vanelli, Johnny / All that's good: Mills, Tico / Send my baby back: Hughes, Freddie / (Oh oh oh) What a love this is: King, Susan / Actions speak louder than words: Bounty, James / You took my heart: St. Clair, Kelly / Crazy little things:

Soul-Jers / Please don't go: Splenders / I'm coming apart at the seams: Kittens Three / Times gone by: Music Track / You'll have to wait: Baby Sitters / Those good times: Nicky C / Keep loving me like you do: Hargreaves, Silky / Soulful jerk: Rumblers / It was true: Big Don's Rebellion / I can take care of myself: Spyders / Dark at the top of my head: Paris, Fred / Stop along the way: Taylor, Robby / Elevator man: Nelson, Roy / Your love keeps drawing me closer: Chandlers / Baby you've got it: Dell, Frank / I didn't know how to: Constellations / I must love you: Wilson, Timothy / I'm tempted: Hollis, Sandy / Love from the Far East: Master Four / Look in the mirror: Vondors / I'll be there: Collection & The Civics / Beware, beware: Compliments / Stop (Don't give up your loving): Two Fellows / I'm losing you: New People / Don't leave me this way: Dynamites / Light drivers: Operator / Love you from the bottom of my heart: Buckner Brothers / So what: Carlton, Carl / It you don't need me: Tyrone Wonder Boy / Your money - my love: Sam & Kitty / (She keeps) Driving me out of my mind: Mighty Lovers / Open the door to your heart: Burdick, Doni / Ain't gonna do you no harm: New Wanderers / Don't give me love: Beery, Dorothy / Some good in everything bad: Fabulous Apollos

CD _____ GSCD 043
Goldmine / Aug '94 / Vital.

NORTHERN SOUL FEVER VOL.3

I'll do a little more: Olympics / (All you need is your) Good lovin': Pat & The Blenders / Got to have peace of mind: Peters, Preston / Motown: Cammotions / I love only you: Henry, Edd / We like girls: Scott Bros. / Connie: Servicemen / Gotta wipe away the teardrops: Jackson, Ollie / Poor unfortunate me (I ain't got nobody): Barnes, J.J. / What should I do: Manhattans / Just a dream: Imperial Wonders / Your love: Harrell, Vernon / My baby changes like the weather: Callender, Bobby / Here comes those heartaches: Tripps / Big search is on: Lynn, Dolores / Move it baby: Singin' Sam / It ain't no secret: Dynamic Heartbeats / Some day some way: Traits / Charge: T-K-O-S / I want the good life: Little David / Misunderstood: Kennedy, Joyce / Easily misled: Remarkables / Old days: Furys / Going going gone: Black, Cody / I'm gonna get even with you: Little Ben & The Cheers / I ain't playing baby: Taurus & Leo / Let me render my service: New Wanderers / We go together: Olympics / Just because of you: Rocky Roberts & The Airedales / Number one fool: Fabulous Emotions / You really made it good: Karim, Ty / My kind of girl: Prophets / I'm guilty: Dupree, Leontine / I'm in love with your daughter: Enchantments / Miss Heartbreaker: Ascots / We go together, yes we do: Hammond, Little Walter / I just want to satisfy: Spencer, Bobby / Joey: Petite, Jo / Jo / Sad, sad memories: Tempos / Lonely baby: Moonlighters / Blow me a kiss: Anderson, Wayne / Ain't gonna worry about you: Tinley, George / How soon: Wonderettes / Jerk it with soul: Walker, Willie / How good can it get: Lyke, Jay / Under the moon: Wonder, Rufus / Penguin breakdown: Reynolds, L.J. / Open arms - closed heart: Welsh, Janie / If I had my way: Keyes, Troy / Give me your love: Jones, A.C. / Don't you leave me baby: Founders / Giving my love to you: Apis, Fred / That's the way love goes: Disciples Of Soul / No one else can take your place: Inspirations

CD _____ GSCD 048
Goldmine / Nov '94 / Vital.

NORTHERN SOUL FEVER VOL.4

Destined to become a loser: Ellingtons / Don't forget to remember: Greater Experience / I'm satisfied just loving you: Bland, Bobbie Jean / I've got to face it: Heartbreaker / I wanna be loved to death: Moore, Bernmie / Auction on love: Boundy, James / Before 2001: Wood, Rufus / Everybody's happy but me: Williams, Cheryl / Front page love: Bee Gee Stans / Good sweet loving: Brown, Roy / Don't turn away: McDougall, Willy / Stay on the case: Innovations / New babe: Invictus / Other side: Five Of A Kind / Darling I love you: Superiors / I know what to do to satisfy you: Robert, Roy / That's not half bad: Woodbury, Gene / On a hot summer day in the big city: King, Ricardo / Sitting in my class: McNier, Ronnie / How can I forget you: Dee, Joey & The Starlighters / Especially for you baby: Four Puzzles / Don't put out the fire: Birchett, Tony / Why did you call: Wood, Eddie / Nobody loves me: Moore, Joe / I gotta have you: Brown, Bobby / You got to steal it: Flairs / I can't get away: Gantt, Bobby / We've been together too long: Antony, El / Chinatown: Knight, Victor / I need help: Detroit Land Apples / I love you just the same: Winfield, Parker / Too much for me baby: Florence, Tina / Can we talk: Allen, C / Give me love: Tootsie Love / Nervous breakdown: Forte, Ronnie / Love will conquer all: Two Plus Two / I can feel him slipping away: Brown, Tobbie / It's written all over my face: Holliday, Marva / Together forever: Pardell, Pat & The Powerdrills / Life goes on: Fabulous Sownbeats / False arm: Body Motions / Sensitive mind: General Assembly / I can't fight it: Sain, Lee / Please come back: First Grade / Give it back: Tripps / (I lost love in the) Big city: Daniels / How do you like it: Sheppards / I can't turn my back: Apollo,

Vince / Little bit of soul: Gerry & Paul & The Soul Emmissaries / You've got a good thing going: King, Jeanie / Something about you: Spoilers / Peace of mind: Spydels / I ain't got nothin' but the blues: Friendly People / Watch out Mr Lonely: Vaughn, Shirley / First time: Wills, Viola / Lucky we: Sugar & Spice / My lover: Sugar & Sweet / Set me free: Performers / Love and laughter: Anderson, Sonny & Prince Conley

CD Set _____ GSCD 074
Goldmine / May '95 / Vital.

NORTHERN SOUL GOLDEN MEMORIES VOL.1

You're everything: Lee, Jackie / (Countdown) Here I come: Tempos / You don't love me: Epitome Of Sound / Let her go: Smith, Otis / Gotta draw this line: Fletcher, Darrow / Gotta find a way: Linsey, Teresa / Quick change artist: Soul Twins / She's puttin' you on: United 4 / I'm satisfied with you: Furys / They're talking about me: Bragg, Johnny / Let's cop a groove: Wells, Bobby / They'll never know why: Chavez, Freddie / Sweet sherry: Barnes, J.J. / Put your arms around me: Sherry's / I need a helping hand: Servicemen / You won't say nothing: Lewis, Tamala / Since you left: Inticers / Head and shoulders: Young, Patti / Never too young (To fall in love): Modern Redcaps / Heartbroken memories: Ferguson, Sheila / (Come on and be my) Saturday man: Clarke, Jimmy / I never knew: Foster, Eddie / Women's liberation: Topics / This time it's love: Tymes / You don't mean me no good: Jelly Beans / New York in the dark: Ad Libs / Lady love: Vontastics

CD _____ GSCD 062
Goldmine / Aug '95 / Vital.

NORTHERN SOUL OF CHICAGO, THE

When I'm with my baby: Magnetics / Stubborn heart: Mosley, Earnest / In other words: Fascinators / Coming back girl: C.O.D.'s / No right to cry: Galore, Mamie / G.I. Joe we love you: Fantasions / Ain't no good: Copney, Bobby / You can't get away: McCall, Johnny / You've changed my whole life: Farren, Charles / It's mighty nice to know you: Wood, Bobby 'Guitar' / Your wish is my command: Inspirations / Have your fun: Topics / Lost in a city: Majors / She'll come back: Britt, Mel / Love bandit: Collins, Barnabus & Kenya / What you gonna do now: Collins, Lashdown / Two of a kind: Flemons, Wade / I'm gonna lose you: Age Of Bronze / Don't say you love me until you do: Maxwell, Holly / I'm satisfied: Gloria & The T-Arias / Cheaper than one: Hunt, Geraldine / Heart of love: Ventures / Go go gorilla: Ideals / Got to be your lover: Profiles / So much love: Taylor, Robert / Love now pay later: Williams, Lee Shot / Is this really love: Gardiner, Don

CD _____ GSCD 038
Goldmine / May '94 / Vital.

NORTHERN SOUL OF L.A. VOL.2

I thought you were: Natural Four / Rosie Brooks: Moanin / Crook his little finger: Heyward, Ann / They didn't know: Goodnight, Terri / Quicksand: Osbourne, Kell / You're welcome: Jackson, June / I'm a bashful guy: Groovers / Shy guy: Mac, Bobby / Closer together: Ster, Eddie / My faith: Dockery, James / Ain't that love enough: Karim, Ty / Ain't that right: Oldfield, Bruce / Sleepless nights: Paris / Lost: Darlettes / Love shop: Tate / Try my love: Dodds, Troy / I'm still young: Summers, Johnny / Love devotion: Abram, J.D. / Pyramid: Soul Brother Inc. / Ooh what you're doing: Capitals / I can't treat her bad: Those Two / Specially when: Rumbold, Edwick / To whom it may concern: Sands, Lola / Faith, hope and trust: Ross, Faye / Girl you're so fine: Angelle, Bobby / Strain: Little Stanley / Ain't gonna: Watson, Johnny 'Guitar'

CD _____ GSCD 039
Goldmine / Jun '94 / Vital.

NORTHERN SOUL OF SWAN, THE

And in return: Ferguson, Sheila / Are you satisfied: Ferguson, Sheila / Don't leave me lover: Ferguson, Sheila / Walking alone: Valentino, Mark / Put yourself in my place: Mortimor, Azie / Everybody crossfire: Stevens, Sammy / Watch your step: Stevens, Sammy / It will be done: Carlton, Eddie / Misery: Carlton, Eddie / I will love you: Barnet, Richie / Driving me mad: Three Degrees / Spy: Guys From Uncle / Never too young: Modern Redcaps / Empty world: Modern Redcaps / I can't be without: Anthony, Richard / Gonna find the right boy: Sio, Audrey / In love: Galla, Tony / I'm gonna get you: Harris, Leroy / Can't leave without you: Jay Walkers / Your kinda love: Renne, Betty / You're everything: Showmen / In paradise: Showmen / Take it baby: Showmen / Hey sah-lo ney: Lane, Mickey Lee / Put that woman down: Leach, John

CD _____ GSCD 063
Goldmine / Oct '95 / Vital.

NORTHERN SOUL TIME

This man in love: New Wanderers / I'm getting tired: Carlettes / Lover: Delites / That's what I want: McGowan, Syng / I know I'm in love with you: Byrd, George Duke / Nevertheless: Andrews, Lee / She said goodbye: Hambric, Billy / I can't stand to lose you: Chandler, E.J. / Elijah rockin' with soul: Jacobs, Hank / Lighten up baby:

Karim, Ty / He's a flirt: Sequins / You got me in the plam of your hands: Richardson, Donald Lee / I need your love: Chaumonts / Oo we let it be me babe: Evans, Karl / Black power: Coit, James / Easy baby: Adventures / Just a little while: Jackson, Ollie / I'm gonna love you: Hamilton, Edward / Build your house on a strong foundation: Gwen & Ray / Job opening: Del-Larks / What good am I without you: Champion, Mickey / R 'n' B time: Jones, E. Rodney / Airplay song: Jenkins, Norma & The Dolls / Oo we let it be me babe (2): Lewis, Louise / My terms: Ferguson, Helena / Where can my babe be: Martells / We must be doing something right: Moody, Joan / You got to love your babe: Millionaires / Do what you gotta do: Contenders / Baby I dig you: Anderson, Gene / Ever again: Woodbury, Gene / Is it all gone: Magicians / We got a love that's out of sight: Spencer / I can't change: Baker, Yvonne / Poor unfortunate me: Taylor, Gloria / I wouldn't come back: Mask Man & the Agents / Come on and live: Fabulous Jades / Walkin' by: Boss 4 / We got to keep on: Casanova Two / Dial L for lonely: Wilson, Madeline / Coalined baby: Love, Dave / I was born to love you: Hunter, Herbert / My heart is calling you: Manificents / Good girl: Stokes, Patti / I can't give up on losing you: Remarkables / Lies: Owen, Gwen / Can't get over these memories: John & The Weirdest / He's that way sometimes: Wells, Bobby / Lovin' you baby: Startones / Fascinating girl: Lemons, George / Come go with me: Para-Monts / Just as much: Peterson, Kris / You better think it over: Du-Shons / I love you baby: Dynamics / Ain't nobody's business: Marbray, Ernie / Just lonly: you: Andrews, Ruby / I have faith in you: Burdick, Doni / You're on my mind: Durane, Paula / Heartbreakin' time: Little John / I gotta good thing going: Executive 4
CD Set _____ GSCD 077
Goldmine / Sep '95 / Vital.

NORWEGIAN FOLK MUSIC VOLS.1-10
(10CD Set)
CD Set _____ GR 4099CD
Grappa / Jul '95 / ADA.

NOSTALGIA
(3CD Set)
CD _____ CPSC 306
Charly / May '95 / Charly / THE / Cadillac.

NOSTALGIA
Nostalgia / Barry's bop / Be bop romp / Fats blows / Dextivity / Dextrose / Dexter's mood / Index / Stealing trash / Hollerin' & screamin' / Fracture / Calling Dr. Jazz / That someone must be you
CD _____ CY 78992
Savoy Jazz / Nov '95 / Conifer / ADA.

NOT JUST RAGGA
So real: Sanchez / Thinking about you: Mc-Lean, John / Spare me: Wonder, Wayne / Rebel woman: Jones, Vivian / Do you remember # 2: Davis, Janet / Guess I know the reason why: Boom, Barry / Perfect lady: Hunningale, Peter / Jungle bungle: Banton, Starky / Run way Mr. Tickle: General Dog / Beaten: Nico Junior / Hyper: Sweetie Irie / One more request: Papa San / Gone down inna mi culture: General Levy / Dedicated to His Majesty: Jones, Vivian & Nico Junior
CD _____ FADCD 032
Jetstar / Jan '96 / Jetstar.

NOT THE SINGER BUT
CD _____ MR 012CD
Munster / Apr '92 / Plastic Head.

NOTHING BUT LOVE SONGS VOL.2
CD _____ PILCD 206
Pioneer / Dec '94 / Jetstar.

NOTHING SHORT OF TOTAL WAR
Come and smash me said the boy with the magic penis: Sonic Youth / Bugged: Head Of David / Fire in Philly: Ut / He's on fire: Sonic Youth / Kerosene: Big Black / Magic wand: Sonic Youth / Dutch courage: Rapeman / Bulbs of passion: Ranaldo, Lee / Scratchy heart: Ciccone Youth / Evangelist: Ut / Snake domain: Head Of David / He's a whore: Big Black / Devil's jukebox: Big Stick / 108: Head Of David / Sheikh: A.C. Temple / Just got payed today: Rapeman / Throne of blood: Band Of Susans / Little Hitlers: Arsenal / Jimi: Butthole Surfers
CD _____ BFFP 013CD
Blast First / Mar '89 / Disc.

NOTHING'S GONNA STOP US NOW
CD Set _____ NSCD 015
Newsound / Feb '95 / THE.

NOW DANCE 94
Long train runnin': Doobie Brothers / Got to get it: Culture Beat / Moving on up: M People / Let me show you: K-Klass / Things can only get better: D Ream / Blow your whistle: DJ Duke / Here we go again: Homeboy, A Hippy & A Funki-Dred / Come baby come: K7 / Feelin' alright: EYC / That's how I'm livin': Ice-T / Feels like heaven: Urban Cookie Collective / Lemon: U2 / Welcome to the pleasure dome: Frankie Goes To Hollywood / Alex party: Alex Party / Satisfy my love: Exoterix / Life: Haddaway / Funk dat: Sagat / So in love: Cheeks, Judy / I wish: Gabrielle
CD _____ CDNOD 11
EMI / Jan '94 / EMI.

NOW DANCE 94 - VOL 2
Let the beat control your body: 2 Unlimited / It's alright: East 17 / I like to move it: Reel 2 Real / Sail away: Urban Cookie Collective / Save our love: Eternal / Uptight: Nelson, Shara / Nervous breakdown: Anderson, Carleen / Love and happiness (Yemaya y ochun): River Ocean & India / I want you: Roberts, Juliet / Respect: Sub Sub / Why: D-Mob & Cathy Dennis / Can't wait to be with you: D.J. Jazzy Jeff & The Fresh Prince / I'm in luv: Joe / Spiritual love: Urban Species / Perpetual dawn: Orb / Return to innocence: Enigma / Waterfall: Atlantic Ocean / Music's got me: Bass Bumpers / Beautiful people: Tucker, Barbara / What a life: Negro, Joey
CD _____ CDNOD 12
EMI / Mar '94 / EMI.

NOW DANCE 95
(2CD/MC Set)
Bomb: Bucketheads / Reach out: Perfecto All Stars / Axel F: Clock / Set you free: N-Trance / Runaway: Real McCoy & M.C. Sar / Let love shine: Arnos / U sure do: Strike / Sight for sore eyes: M People / Always something there to remind me: Tin Tin Out & Espiritu / Let me be your fantasy: Baby D / Welcome to tomorrow (are you ready): Snap / Everytime you touch me: Moby / Baby baby: Corona / Cotton eye Joe: Rednex / Here I go: 2 Unlimited / Saturday night: Whigfield / Burning up: De Vit, Tony / Passion: Jon Of The Pleased Wimmin / Boy I gotta have you: Rio & Mars / Eighteen strings: Tinman / Total eclipse of the heart: French, Nicki / Tell me when: Human League / Crazy: Eternal / Respect: Cheeks, Judy / Read my lips: Alex Party / Raise your hands: Mad Stuntman / Bubbling hot: Banton, Pato / You're no good: Aswad / Sweet love: M-Beat / Apparently nothin': Anderson, Carleen / Bump 'n' grind: R. Kelly / Some girls: Ultimate Kaos / Spend some time: Brand New Heavies / Love come rescue: Lovestation / I need somebody: Loveland / Pump up the volume: Greed / Saved: Mr. Roy / No matter what you do: Flavour / Sing it to you: Jones, Lavinia / United: Prince Ital Joe & Marky Mark
CD Set _____ CDNOD 15
EMI / Mar '95 / EMI.

NOW DANCE SUMMER '94
(2CD/MC Set)
You don't love me (no no no): Penn, Dawn / Sweets for my sweet: Lewis, C.J. / Get-away: Maxx / Rock my heart: Haddaway / Renaissance: M People / Real thing: Di Bart, Tony / Crayzy man: Blast / Carry me home: Glowworm / No more tears (Enough is enough): Mazelle, Kym & Jocelyn Brown / Light my fire: Club House / Move on baby: Cappella / Omen III: Magic Affair / UR the best thing: D Ream / Just a step from heaven: Eternal / Because of you: Gabrielle / Dedicated to the one I love: McLean, Bitty / Anything: S.W.V. / High on a happy vibe: Urban Cookie Collective / Doop: Doop / I like to move it: Reel 2 Real / Let the music (lift you up): Loveland / Two can play that game: Brown, Bobby / What you're missing: K-Klass / Shine on: Degrees Of Motion / Waterfall: Atlantic Ocean / Read my lips, Saturday night party: Alex Party / Reach: Cheeks, Judy / Mama said: Robinson, Carleen / How gee: Black Machine / Swamp thing: Grid / Harmonica man: Bravado / Son of a gun: JX / Scream: Disco Anthem / Rockin' for myself: Motiv 8 / When you made the mountain: Opus III / There but for the grace of God: Fire Island / All over you: Level 42 / Hold that sucker down: OT Quartet / Don't go: Awesome 3 / Real thing (2): 2 Unlimited
CD Set _____ CDNOD 13
Virgin / Jun '94 / EMI.

NOW DANCE SUMMER 95
Boom boom boom: Outhere Brothers / In the summertime: Shaggy / Here comes the hotstepper: Kamoze, Ini / Humpin' around: Brown, Bobby / Right in the night: Jam & Spoon / Try me out: Corona / Whoomph (there it is): Clock / Zombie: A.D.A.M. & Amy / Dreamer: Livin' Joy / Heart of glass: Blondie / Your loving arms: Martin, Billie Ray / Not over yet: Grace / Get your hands off my man: Vasquez, Junior / Stay: Isha D / As long as your good to me: Cheeks, Judy / Magic in u: Sugarbabies / Leave home: Chemical Brothers / Misirlou: Spaghetti Surfers / (You're my one and only) Truelove: Smith, Ann-Marie / Love enuff: Soul II Soul
CD _____ CDNOD 16
Virgin / Aug '95 / EMI.

NOW DIG THIS ROULETTE ROCK AND ROLL VOL.3
You're driving me mad: Campbell, Jo Ann / Don't say maybe: Roberts, Don 'Red' / Come dance with me: Ackoff, Bob / Don't stop: Trider, Larry / Ha ha song: Trider, Larry / Sittin' at home with the blues: Elgin, Johnny / High school blues: Vickery, Mack / Hot dog: Curtis, Lee / Sweetness: Lanier, Don / Need your love: Lanier, Don / Hey doll baby: Kelly, Pat / Cloud 13: Kelly, Pat / Patsy: Kelly, Pat / Glow of love: Moonlighters / Broken heart: Moonlighters / School bus: Shades / Baby baby: Shades / Jeri Lee: Shades / Guitar hop: Shades / I looked for you: Gracie, Charlie / Race: Gracie, Charlie / Sorry for you: Gracie, Charlie /

Scenery: Gracie, Charlie / Wassa matter with you baby: Campbell, Jo Ann
CD _____ NEMCD 754
Sequel / Aug '95 / BMG.

NOW THAT'S WHAT I CALL LOVE
For whom the bell tolls: Bee Gees / Come in out of the rain: Moten, Wendy / I don't wanna fight: Turner, Tina / Dreams: Gabrielle / Stay: Eternal / Pray: Take That / Almost unreal: Roxette / Forever in love: Rush, Jennifer / Saving all my love for you: Houston, Whitney / Different corner: Michael, George / Groovy kind of love: Collins, Phil / Now and forever: Marx, Richard / So close: Carroll, Dina / So natural: Stansfield, Lisa / Tracks of my tears: Go West / Delicate: D'Arby, Terence Trent & Des'ree / Heaven help: Kravitz, Lenny / Shed a tear: Wet Wet Wet / Without you: Nilsson, Harry
CD _____ CDEVP 7
EMI / Mar '94 / EMI.

NOW THAT'S WHAT I CALL MUSIC 1994
(2CD/LP/MC Set)
Twist and shout: Demus, Chaka & Pliers / Compliments on your kiss: Red Dragon / Sign: Ace Of Base / Saturday night: Whigfield / Rhythm of the night: Corona / Things can only get better: D Ream / Everything changes: Take That / It's alright: East 17 / Sweets for my sweet: Lewis, C.J. / Shine: Aswad / I like to move it: Reel 2 Real / No good (start the dance): Prodigy / Swamp thing: Grid / Get-a-way: Maxx / What's up: D.J. Miko / Let the beat control your body: 2 Unlimited / Light my fire: Club House / Doop: Doop / Come baby come: K7 / Whatta man: Salt 'N' Pepa & En Vogue / Searching: China Black / You don't love me (no no no): Penn, Dawn / Dedicated to the one I love: McLean, Bitty / Renaissance: M People / Just a step from heaven: Eternal / I miss you: Haddaway / Come in out of the rain: Moten, Wendy / Perfect year: Carroll, Dina / Linger: Cranberries / I'll stand by you: Pretenders / Always: Erasure / Return to innocence: Enigma / Inside: Stiltskin / Rock 'n' roll dreams come through: Meat Loaf / Word up: Gun / Girls and boys: Blur / Trouble: Shampoo / Meet the flintstones: BC-52's / Come on you reds: Manchester United F.C.
CD Set _____ CDNOW 1994
Virgin / Oct '94 / EMI.

NOW THAT'S WHAT I CALL MUSIC 1995
(2CD/MC Set)
Country house: Blur / Alright: Supergrass / Roll with it: Oasis / Girl like you: Collins, Edwyn / Turn on, tune in, cop out: Freakpower / Here comes the hotstepper: Kamoze, Ini / Stayin' alive: N-Trance / Tell me when: Human League / Wake up Boo: Boo Radleys / Hold my body tight: East 17 / Never forget: Take That / Independent love song: Scarlet / Love me for a reason: Boyzone / Search for the hero: M People / You do something to me: Weller, Paul / 74 75: Connells / Sour Don't give me your life: Alex Party / I luv u baby: Original / Push the feeling on: Nightcrawlers / Try me out: Corona / Sunshine after the rain: Berri / Axel F: Clock / Reach up (Papa's got a brand new pigbag): Perfecto All Stars / Your loving arms: Martin, Billie Ray / Cry India: Umboza / Bomb: Bucketheads / Two can play that game: Brown, Bobby / You got a little something for you: RIIII / Boom Boom / Everybody's gotta learn sometime: Baby D / Dreamer: Livin' Joy / Think of you: Whigfield / 3 is family: Dawson, Dana / U sure do: Strike / Call it love: Deuce / Cotton eye Joe: Rednex / I'm only sleeping: Suggs
CD Set _____ CDNOW 1995
Virgin / Oct '95 / EMI.

NOW THAT'S WHAT I CALL MUSIC VOL.27
(2CD/LP/MC Set)
Sign: Ace Of Base / Twist and shout: Demus, Chaka & Pliers / Things can only get better: D Ream / It's alright: East 17 / Moving on up: M People / Save our love: Eternal / Return to innocence: Enigma / For whom the bell tolls: Bee Gees / Come in out of the rain: Moten, Wendy / Perfect year: Carroll, Dina / Everyday: Collins, Phil / Now and forever: Marx, Richard / Linger: Cranberries / Cornflake girl: Amos, Tori / Good as gold (stupid as mud): Beautiful South / Rock 'n' roll dreams come through: Meat Loaf / Rocks: Primal Scream / Hey jealousy: Gin Blossoms / Disarm: Smashing Pumpkins / Doop: Doop / Wonderman: Right Said Fred / Move on baby: Cappella / Anything: Culture Beat / Let the beat control your body: 2 Unlimited / I like to move it: Reel 2 Real / U sure do: Strike / Credit To The Nation / Way you work it: EYC / Here I stand: McLean, Bitty / Sweet lullaby: Deep Forest / Violently happy: Bjork / Uptight: Nelson, Shara / Because of you: Gabrielle / Nervous breakdown: Anderson, Carleen / I want you: Roberts, Juliet / Sail away: Urban Cookie Collective / Shine on: Degrees Of Motion / Lover: Roberts, Joe
CD Set _____ CDNOW 27
EMI / Mar '94 / EMI.

NOW THAT'S WHAT I CALL MUSIC VOL.28
(2CD/LP/MC Set)
Love is all around: Wet Wet Wet / I swear: All 4 One / Don't turn around: Ace Of Base / Shine: Aswad / Meet the flintstones (LP Version): BC 52's / Crazy for you: Let Loose / U R the best thing (Perfecto Radio Mix): D Ream / Everybody's talkin': Beautiful South / I believe: Detroit, Marcella / I'll stand by you: Pretenders / Inside: Stiltskin / Girls and boys: Blur / Renaissance (Radio Mix): M People / Just a step from heaven: Eternal / Another sad love song (Radio Edit): Braxton, Toni / Searching: China Black / You don't love me (no no no): Penn, Dawn / I wanna be your man: Demus, Chaka & Pliers / Always: Erasure / Prayer for the dying: Seal / Swamp thing: Grid / Everybody gonfi gon: Two Cowboys / Get-a-way: Maxx / Go on move: Reel 2 Real & The Mad Stuntman / No good (Start the dance): Prodigy / U and me: Cappella / Rock my heart: Haddaway / Real thing: 2 Unlimited / Don't give it up (Don't You Ever Stop Mix): Sonic Surfers / What's up (Radio Mix): D.J. Miko / Light my fire: Club House / Sweets for my sweet: Lewis, C.J. / Dedicated to the one I love: McLean, Bitty / Whatta man: Salt 'N' Pepa & En Vogue / Your body's calling: R. Kelly / Dream on dreamer: Brand New Heavies / Caught in the middle: Roberts, Juliet / Carry me home: Glowworm / Absolutely fabulous: Absolutely Fabulous
CD Set _____ CDNOW 28
Virgin / Aug '94 / EMI.

NOW THAT'S WHAT I CALL MUSIC VOL.29
(2CD/LP/MC Set)
Baby come back: Banton, Pato / Hey now (Girls just wanna have fun): Lauper, Cyndi / Baby, I love your way: Big Mountain / Sure: Take That / Sweetness: Gayle, Michelle / Saturday night: Whigfield / Another night: M.C. Sar & The Real McCoy / Rhythm of the night: Corona / True faith '94: New Order / Right beside you: Hawkins, Sophie B. / Seven seconds: N'Dour, Youssou & Neneh Cherry / Stay (I missed you): Loeb, Lisa & Nine Stories / Mmm mmm mmm mmm: Crash Test Dummies / We have all the time in the world: Armstrong, Louis / Know by now: Palmer, Robert / What's the frequency, Kenneth: R.E.M. / Cigarettes and alcohol: Oasis / Love is strong: Rolling Stones / Zombie: Cranberries / Around the world: East 17 / Compliments on your kiss: Red Dragon / Gal wine: Demus, Chaka & Pliers / She's got that vibe: R. Kelly / Midnight at the oasis: Brand New Heavies / Stars: China Black / What's going on: Music Relief / Power of love: Dion, Celine / Confide in me: Minogue, Kylie / Sly: Massive Attack / So good: Eternal / Some girls: Ultimate Kaos / Can you feel it: Reel 2 Real & The Mad Stuntman / Incredible: M-Beat & General Levy / Trouble: Shampoo / Parklife: Blur / I love Saturday: Erasure / When do I get to sing 'My Way': Sparks / I want the world: Two Thirds
CD Set _____ CDNOW 29
EMI / Nov '94 / EMI.

NOW THAT'S WHAT I CALL MUSIC VOL.30
(2CD/LP/MC Set)
Turn on, tune in, cop out: Freak Power / Whoops now: Jackson, Janet / Love me for a reason: Boyzone / Love can build a bridge: Cher & Chrissie Hynde/Neneh Cherry / Stay another day: East 17 / Over my shoulder: Mike & The Mechanics / Here I come: Bevell, Vicki / Dum da dum: Melodie MC / Key to my life: Boyzone / Set you free: N-Trance / Tell me where you're going: Banton, Pato / Whoomph (There it is): Clock / Love me for a reason: Boyzone / This cowboy song: Sting / Save it til' the morning after: Shut Up & Dance / Bump 'n' grind: R. Kelly / Oh baby, I: Eternal / Protection: Massive Attack / Glory box: Portishead / Whatever: Oasis / Don't stop (wiggle wiggle): Outhere Brothers / Don't give me your life: Alex Party / U sure do: Strike / Bomb (these sounds fall into my mind): Bucketheads / Push the feeling on: Nightcrawlers / Always something there to remind me: Tin Tin Out & Espiritu / Baby baby: Corona / Axel F: Clock / Set you free: N-Trance / You belong to me: JX / Reach up: Perfecto All Stars / Cotton eye Joe: Rednex / Call it love: Deuce / Here I go: 2 Unlimited / Runaway: Real McCoy & M.C. Sar / Total eclipse of the heart: French, Nicki / Suddenly: Maguire, Sean / Two can play that game: Brown, Bobby / Hoochie booty: Ultimate Kaos / Bubbling hot: Banton, Pato / One: Paris, Mica
CD Set _____ CDNOW 30
EMI / Apr '95 / EMI.

NOW THAT'S WHAT I CALL MUSIC VOL.31
(2CD/MC/LP Set)
I want to forgive me now: Wet Wet Wet / Girl like you: Collins, Edwyn / Common people: Pulp / Alright: Supergrass / In the summertime: Shaggy & Rayvon / Here comes the hotstepper: Kamoze, Ini / Three is family: Dawson, Dana / Right in the night: Jam & Spoon / Hold my body tight: East 17 / Key to my life: Boyzone / Kiss from a rose: Seal / Days: MacColl, Kirsty / One man in my heart: Human League / Sour times: Portishead / I need must say: Oasis / Buddy Holly: Weezer / Roll to me: Del Amitri / I'm

a believer: *EMF/Reeves & Mortimer* / White lines (don't do it): *Duran Duran* / Hurts so good: *Somerville, Jimmy* / Boom boom boom: *Outhere Brothers* / I've got a little something for you: *MN8* / This is how we do it: *Jordan, Montell* / Shoot me with your love: *D Ream* / I need your loving: *Baby D* / Keep warm: *Jinny* / Dreamer: *Livin' Joy* / Think of you: *Whigfield* / Whoomph (there it is): *Clock* / Humpin' around: *Brown, Bobby* / Stuck on you: *PJ & Duncan* / Love city groove: *Love City Groove* / Swing low, sweet chariot: *Ladysmith Black Mambazo & China Black* / Low enuff: *Soul II Soul* / Get your hands off my man: *Vasquez, Junior* / Freedom: *Shiva* / Your loving arms: *Martin, Billie Ray* / I need you: *Deuce* / Only me: *Hyperlogic*

CD Set _____ **CDNOW 31**

Virgin / Aug '95 / EMI.

NOW THAT'S WHAT I CALL MUSIC VOL.32
(2CD/MC/LP Set)

Heaven for everyone: *Queen* / I'd lie for you (and that's the truth): *Meat Loaf* / Fairground: *Simply Red* / Hold me, thrill me, kiss me, kill me: *U2* / Goldeneye: *Turner, Tina* / Walking in Memphis: *Cher* / Friends over the throw: *Beautiful South* / Light of my life: *Louise* / Big river: *Nail, Jimmy* / Wishes of happiness and prosperity (yehanoha): *Sacred Spirit* / Lucky (awicholdj): *Radiohead* / Sorted for Es and wizz: *Pulp* / Country house: *Blur* / Alright: *Cast* / Yes: *McAlmont & Butler* / Broken stones: *Weller, Paul* / I'm only sleeping: *Suggs* / Come together: *Smokin' Mojo Filters* / Gangsta's paradise: *Coolio* / Boombastic: *Shaggy* / Stayin' alive: *N-Trance* / I feel love: *Summer, Donna* / Sunshine after the rain: *Berri* / Try me out: *Corona* / I luv U baby: *Original* / Missing: *Everything But The Girl* / Power of a woman: *Eternal* / I care: *Soul II Soul* / La la la hey hey: *Outhere Brothers* / Big time: *Whigfield* / Wrap me up: *Alex Party* / Higher state of consciousness: *Wink, Josh* / Renegade master: *Wildchild* / Inner city life: *Goldie & The Metalheadz* / Don't you want me: *Human League* / Fe fi fo fum: *Candy Girls* / I believe: *Happy Clappers* / Wild colour: *Dreams* / Runaway: *E'voke* / Roll with it: *Oasis*

CD Set _____ **CDNOW 32**

Virgin / Nov '95 / EMI.

NOW THIS IS REGGAE
CD _____ **MPV 5525**

Movieplay / Oct '92 / Target/BMG.

NU ENERGY

Feeling (Tin Tin Out dub): *Tin Tin Out & Sweet Tee* / Infanta-ci: *Baby Doc & The Dentist* / Cosmonautica (Moontrip mix): *Virtuolisimo* / First rebirth (Hiroshima nu-energy reconstruction): *Jones & Stephenson* / Casablanca (Remix): *Dual Mount* / Energy frenzy: *OCP* / Three minute warning (Scope mix): *Yum Yum* / Catalan rising: *Baby Doc & The Dentist* / For your love: *Elevator* / Mantra to the buddha (Higher state): *Hyperspace* / Dragnet (action hero): *Hiroshima*

CD _____ **CDTOT 19**

Jumpin' & Pumpin' / Oct '94 / 3MV / Sony.

NU GROOVE COMPILATION
CD _____ **NGVCD 1**

Network / Apr '91 / Sony / 3MV.

NU SOUL CLASSICS VOL.1
CD _____ **HOTTCD 2**

Hott / Dec '95 / 3MV / Sony.

NU YORICA - CULTURE CLASH IN NEW YORK CITY
(Experiments In Latin Music 1970-1977 - 2CD/LP Set)

What are you doing for the rest of your life: *Ocho* / Gumbo: *Cortijo & His Time Machine* / La trompeta y la flauta: *Cachao Y Su Descarga* / Babalonia: *Marrero, Ricardo* / Harlem river drive theme: *Harlem River Drive* / Amigos: *Stone Alliance* / Latin strut: *Bataan, Joe* / Anabacoa: *Grupo Folklorico & Experimental Nuevoyorquino* / Tempo 70: *El Gallenton* / Un dia bonita: *Palmieri, Eddie* / Carnaval: *Cortijo & His Time Machine* / Coco may may: *Ocho* / Idle hands: *Harlem River Drive* / Little Rico, little Rico's theme: *Paunetto, Bobby V* / Aftershower funk: *Bataan, Joe* / Macho: *Machito & His Orchestra*

CD Set _____ **SJRCD 029**

Soul Jazz / Jan '96 / New Note / Vital.

NUCLEAR BLAST 100
CD _____ **NB 100**

Nuclear Blast / Feb '94 / Plastic Head.

NUEVO MAMBO
CD _____ **CD 62018**

Saludos Amigos / Apr '94 / Target/BMG.

NUGGETS VOL.1

Dirty water: *Standells* / Pushin' too hard: *Seeds* / Psychotic reaction: *Count Five* / Let's talk about girls: *Chocolate Watch Band* / Friday on my mind: *Easybeats* / I see the light: *Five Americans* / Why pick on me: *Standells* / Little girl: *Syndicate of Sound* / Pleasant Valley Sunday: *Monkees* / Lies: *Knickerbockers* / Laugh laugh: *Beau Brummels* / Wild thing: *Troggs* / Heaven and hell: *Easybeats* / Valleri: *Monkees* / Open my eyes: *Nazz* / Just a little: *Beau Brummels* / Can't seem to make you mine: *Seeds* / Journey to the centre of the mind: *Amboy Dukes*

CD _____ **RNCD 7577**

Rhino / Feb '88 / Warner Music.

NUGGETS VOL.2

(We ain't got) nothin' yet / Mr. Farmer / Sometimes good guys don't wear white / Liar liar / Diddy wah diddy / Are you gonna be there (At the love in) / Talk talk / Live / Western Union / Little black egg / Sunshine girl / You've a very lovely woman / Desire / I wonder what she's doing tonight / Public execution / Try it / Sweet young thing / Gonna have a good time

CD _____ **RNCD 75892**

Rhino / Feb '88 / Warner Music.

NUMBER 1 IN THE UK
CD _____ **CDCD 1276**

Charly / Nov '95 / Charly / THE / Cadillac.

NUMBER 1 IN THE USA
CD _____ **CDCD 1277**

Charly / Nov '95 / Charly / THE / Cadillac.

NUMBER ONE CLASSIC SOUL ALBUM, THE

I heard it through the grapevine: *Gaye, Marvin* / I say a little prayer: *Franklin, Aretha* / (Sittin' on) the dock of the bay: *Redding, Otis* / My cherie amour: *Wonder, Stevie* / Let's stay together: *Green, Al* / Midnight train to Georgia: *Knight, Gladys & The Pips* / Tracks of my tears: *Robinson, Smokey & The Miracles* / Reach out, I'll be there: *Four Tops* / In the midnight hour: *Pickett, Wilson* / Dancing in the streets: *Reeves, Martha* / My guy: *Wells, Mary* / Soul sister brown sugar: *Sam & Dave* / I get the sweetest feeling: *Wilson, Jackie* / Soul city walk: *Bell, Archie & The Drells* / Piece of my heart: *Franklin, Erma* / This old heart of mine (is weak for you): *Isley Brothers* / Just my imagination: *Temptations* / Hey there lonely girl: *Holman, Eddie* / If you don't know me by now: *Melvin, Harold* / Ain't no sunshine: *Jackson, Michael* / Papa was a rollin' stone: *Temptations* / Papa's got a brand new bag: *Brown, James* / Ghetto child: *Detroit Spinners* / Love train: *O'Jays* / Nathan Jones: *Supremes* / Stop her on sight: *Starr, Edwin* / Ms. Grace: *Tymes* / Like sister and brother: *Drifters* / Family affair: *Sly & The Family Stone* / Didn't I (blow your mind this time): *Delfonics* / Homely girl: *Chi-Lites* / Gonna make you an offer you can't refuse: *Helms, Jimmy* / I'm still waiting: *Ross, Diana* / I'll be there: *Jackson Five* / What becomes of the broken hearted: *Ruffin, Jimmy* / Walk on by: *Warwick, Dionne* / Me and Mrs. Jones: *Paul, Billy* / I'm stone in love with you: *Stylistics* / Drift away: *Gray, Dobie* / Easy: *Commodores*

CD _____ **5256562**

PolyGram TV / Jan '96 / PolyGram.

NUMBER ONE HITS VOL 1
CD _____ **DCD 5371**

Disky / Apr '94 / THE / BMG / Discovery / Pinnacle.

NUMBER ONE HITS VOL 2
CD _____ **DCD 5372**

Disky / Apr '94 / THE / BMG / Discovery / Pinnacle.

NUMBER ONE HITS VOL 3
CD _____ **DCD 5373**

Disky / Apr '94 / THE / BMG / Discovery / Pinnacle.

NUMBER ONE HITS VOL 4
CD _____ **DCD 5374**

Disky / Apr '94 / THE / BMG / Discovery / Pinnacle.

NUMBER ONE HITS VOL 5
CD _____ **DCD 5375**

Disky / Apr '94 / THE / BMG / Discovery / Pinnacle.

NUMBER ONE HITS VOL 6
CD _____ **DCD 5376**

Disky / Apr '94 / THE / BMG / Discovery / Pinnacle.

NUMBER ONE HITS VOL 7
CD _____ **DCD 5377**

Disky / Apr '94 / THE / BMG / Discovery / Pinnacle.

NUMBER ONE HITS VOL 8
CD _____ **DCD 5378**

Disky / Apr '94 / THE / BMG / Discovery / Pinnacle.

NUMBER ONE REGGAE ALBUM, THE
(2CD/MC Set)

Bubblin' hot: *Banton, Pato & Ranking Roger* / You're no good: *Aswad* / Love and devotion: *Real McCoy* / Don't turn around: *Ace Of Base* / Baby come back: *Banton, Pato* / You don't love me (no no no): *Penn, Dawn* / Searching: *China Black* / Baby I love your way: *Big Mountain* / Sweets for my sweet: *Lewis, C.J.* / Tease me: *Demus, Chaka & Pliers* / Housecall: *Shabba Ranks & Maxi Priest* / Jamaican in New York: *Shinehead* / Oh Carolina: *Shaggy* / Sweat (A la la la la long): *Inner Circle* / Mr. Loverman: *Shabba Ranks* / Hot hot hot: *Arrow* / Shout: *Louchie Lou & Michie One* / Compliments on your kiss: *Red Dragon* / Dark heart: *Bomb The Bass* / Boom shack-a-lack: *Apache Indian* / Close to you: *Priest, Maxi* / Sweet sensation: *Ladysmith Black Mambazo & China Black* / Keep on moving: *Marley, Bob* / Hurt so good: *Cadogan, Susan* / Now that we've found love: *Third*

World / Silly games: *Kay, Janet* / Dub be good to me: *Beats International & Lindy Layton* / Good thing going: *Minott, Sugar* / I don't wanna dance: *Grant, Eddy* / I want to wake up with you: *Gardiner, Boris* / Israelites: *Dekker, Desmond* / I can see clearly now: *Nash, Johnny* / Double barrel: *Collins, Dave & Ansil* / Young, gifted and black: *Bob & Marcia* / Uptown top ranking: *Althia & Donna* / Don't look back: *Tosh, Peter* / Love of the common people: *Thomas, Nicky* / Help me make it through the night: *Holt, John* / Liquidator: *Johnson, Harry & The All-Stars* / Wonderful world, beautiful people: *Cliff, Jimmy*

CD _____ **5256392**

PolyGram TV / Aug '95 / PolyGram.

NUMBER ONES OF DANCE
CD _____ **TCD 2701**

Telstar / Nov '93 / BMG.

NUMBER ONES OF THE 60'S

Shakin' all over: *Kidd, Johnny & The Pirates* / Poor me: *Faith, Adam* / Walkin' back to happiness: *Shapiro, Helen* / How do you do it: *Gerry & The Pacemakers* / Have I the right: *Honeycombs* / I'm into something good: *Herman's Hermits* / Anyone who had a heart: *Black, Cilla* / Needles and pins: *Searchers* / Always something there to remind me: *Shaw, Sandie* / Go now: *Moody Blues* / House of the rising sun: *Animals* / Yeh yeh: *Fame, Georgie* / It's not unusual: *Jones, Tom* / Make it easy on yourself: *Walker Brothers* / You've lost that lovin' feelin': *Righteous Brothers* / Out of time: *Farlowe, Chris* / All or nothing: *Small Faces* / Sunny afternoon: *Kinks* / Pretty flamingo: *Manfred Mann* / You don't have to say you love me: *Springfield, Dusty* / Release me: *Humperdinck, Engelbert* / With a little help from my friends: *Cocker, Joe* / Fire: *Crazy World Of Arthur Brown* / (If paradise is) half as nice: *Amen Corner* / Something in the air: *Thunderclap Newman*

CD _____ **CDPR 111**

Premier/MFP / Nov '93 / EMI.

NUMBER ONES OF THE 70'S

In the summertime: *Mungo Jerry* / Maggie May: *Stewart, Rod* / Coz I luv you: *Slade* / Get it on: *T. Rex* / See my baby jive: *Wizzard* / Down down: *Status Quo* / Devil gate drive: *Quatro, Suzi* / Rock your baby: *McCrae, George* / Sugar baby love: *Rubettes* / You're the first, the last, my everything: *White, Barry* / Oh boy: *Mud* / Make me smile (Come up and see me): *Harley, Steve & Cockney Rebel* / I'm not in love: *10cc* / Can't give you anything (but my love): *Stylistics* / You to me are everything: *Real Thing* / So you win again: *Hot Chocolate* / When I need you: *Sayer, Leo* / Wuthering Heights: *Bush, Kate* / Rat trap: *Boomtown Rats* / Sunday girl: *Blondie*

CD _____ **CDPR 112**

Premier/MFP / Nov '93 / EMI.

NUMBER ONES OF THE 80'S

Going underground: *Jam* / Use it up and wear it out: *Odyssey* / Tainted love: *Soft Cell* / Prince charming: *Adam Ant* / Ghost town: *Specials* / This ole house: *Stevens, Shakin'* / Come on Eileen: *Dexy's Midnight Runners* / Eye of the tiger: *Survivor* / Down under: *Men At Work* / Too shy: *Kajagoogoo* / Freedom: *Wham* / Nineteen: *Hardcastle, Paul* / Don't leave me this way: *Communards* / Never gonna give you up: *Astley, Rick* / La bamba: *Los Lobos* / Nothing's gonna stop us now: *Starship* / Only way is up: *Yazz* / I owe you nothing: *Bros* / Perfect: *Fairground Attraction* / Eternal flame: *Bangles*

CD _____ **CDPR 113**

Premier/MFP / Nov '93 / EMI.

O

OBLIVAN
CD _____ **OOR 023CD**

Out Of Romford / Nov '95 / Pinnacle / SRD.

OBSESSIVE HOUSE CULTURE
CD _____ **OBRLP 001CD**

Obsessive / Mar '94 / SRD.

OBSESSIVE HOUSE CULTURE VOL.2
CD _____ **OBRCD 2**

Obsessive / Aug '94 / SRD.

OCEAN OF SOUND

Dub fi gwan: *King Tubby* / Rain dance: *Hancock, Herbie* / Analogue bubblebath 1: *Aphex Twin* / Empire III: *Hassell, Jon* / Son of palm badri: *Suryana, Ujang* / Prelude a l'apres midi d'un faune (Debussy): *English Chamber Orchestra* / Vision city: *Baxter, Les* / Loomer: *My Bloody Valentine* / Lizard point: *Eno, Brian* / Shunie Omizutori Buddhist ceremony / Music of horns and whistles: *Vancouver Soundscape* / Howler monkeys / Machine gun: *Brotzmann, Peter Octet* / Yanomami rain song / Bismillah 'rrahmani 'rrahim: *Budd, Harold* / Black satin: *Davis, Miles* / All night flight (extract from Poppy Nogood): *Riley, Terry* / Coyor

Panon: *Kurnia, Detty* / Virgin beauty: *Coleman, Ornette* / Chen pe'i pe'i: *Zorn, John & David Toop* / Rivers of mercury: *Schutze, Paul* / I heard her call my name: *Velvet Underground* / Bearded seals / Boat-woman song: *Czukay, Holger & Rolf Dammers* / Fall breaks and back into winter (Woody Woodpecker symphony): *Beach Boys* / Faraway chant: *African Headcharge* / Cosmo enticement: *Sun Ra* / Untitled 3: *Music Improvisation Company* / Seven-up: *Deep Listening Band* / In a landscape: *Cage, John* / Vexations: *Marks, Alan* / Suikinkutsu water chime

CD _____ **AMBT 10**

Virgin / Jan '96 / EMI.

OFF THE MAP
CD _____ **CHARRMCD 19**

Charrm / Feb '95 / Plastic Head.

OH CHERRY OH BABY
CD _____ **LG 21047**

Lagoon / Feb '93 / Magnum Music Group / THE.

OH HAPPY DAY
CD Set _____ **CDNCBOX 1**

Charly / Sep '91 / Charly / THE / Cadillac.

OH HAPPY DAY
(2CD Set)

Swing low / Old time religion / Long way to go / How great thou art / Alabama / You'll never walk alone / Swing low sweet chariot / Lord's prayer / Glory hallelujah / He's coming soon / Life's railway to heaven / If I could hear my Mother pray again / Will the circle be unbroken / Down by the river side / Keep in touch with Jesus / Rock of ages / So wonderful / I'm a rolling / I'm thankful / Stand by me / Amazing grace / Amen / Hallelujah / There's power in the blood / Just a closer walk with thee / This light is Jesus / Jesus is alright with me / Blood of Jesus / Promised land / Lord I need your love / Land where living waters flow / Camping in Canaan's land / He's got the whole world in his hands / When the saints go marching in / Kneel and pray / Lord will make a way / On Jericho road / Hallelujah special / Oh happy day

CD Set _____ **GP 20092**

Gentle Price / Jan '96 / Target/BMG.

OH NO IT'S THE SEVENTIES

Kung Fu fighting: *Douglas, Carl* / More, more, more: *True, Andrea Connection* / What's your name what's your number: *True, Andrea Connection* / Hold back the night: *Trammps* / Sad sweet dreamer: *Sweet Sensation* / Can you feel the force: *Real Thing* / You to me are everything: *Real Thing* / This is it: *Moore, Melba* / Shame, shame, shame: *Shirley & Company* / Zing went the strings of my heart: *Trammps* / Shaft: *Holmes, Cecil* / We got the funk: *Positive Force* / 7-6-5-4-3-2-1 Blow your whistle: *Rimshots* / Sending out an S.O.S.: *Young, Retta* / It's a better than good time: *Knight, Gladys*

CD _____ **NEMCD 627**

Sequel / Feb '93 / BMG.

OI CHARTBUSTERS VOLS.1 & 2

GLC: *Menace* / Mania: *Strike* / Five minute fashion: *Infa Riot* / Suburban rebels: *Business* / Two pints of lager: *Splodgenessabounds* / Stark raving normal: *Blood* / Police car: *Cockney Rejects* / Blind ambition: *Partizan* / Time bomb: *Blitz* / Rapist: *Combat 84* / Runnin' riot: *Cock Sparrer* / Clockwork skinhead: *4 Skins* / Murder of liddle lovers: *Angelic Upstarts* / Violence in our minds: *Last Resort* / Give a dog a bone (live): *Sham 69* / Riot riot: *Infa Riot* / Borstal breakout: *Accident* / Get outta my 'ouse: *Business* / Two little boys: *Splodgenessabounds* / Such fun: *Blood* / Motorhead: *Cockney Rejects* / Daily news (live): *Exploited* / 4Q: *Blitz* / Poseur: *Combat 84* / Run for cover: *Cock Sparrer* / Plastic gangsters: *4 Skins* / Leave me alone: *Angelic Upstarts* / Held hostage: *Last Resort*

CD _____ **LINKCD 03**

Street Link / Oct '92 / BMG.

OI CHARTBUSTERS VOLS.3 & 4

Joys of oi: *Gonads* / Last year's youth: *Menace* / Blitzkraig bop: *Accident* / Napalm job: *Blood* / Tell us the truth: *Sham 69* / Wiffy woman: *Splodge* / Change: *Partizan* / Outlaw: *Business* / Living next door to Alice: *Chron Gen* / Youth: *Blitz* / Babylon's burning: *Ruts* / F82123: *Combat 84* / Never return to hell: *Angelic Upstarts* / Teenage heart: *Cock Sparrer* / Come clean: *Partizan* / Product: *Business* / Smiling my life away: *Case* / Street rock 'n' roll: *Section 5* / Gonads anthem: *Gonads* / Emergency: *Infa Riot* / Delirious: *Splodge* / When will they learn: *Angelic Upstarts* / Garage land: *Accident* / Escape: *Blitz* / Dead generation: *Cockney Rejects* / Gestapo khazi: *Blood* / Stand strong, stand proud: *Vice Squad*

CD _____ **LINKCD 034**

Street Link / Oct '92 / BMG.

OI CHARTBUSTERS VOLS.5 & 6

On yer bike: *Frankie & The Flames* / You kept me waiting: *Crack* / I won't pay for liberty: *Angelic Upstarts* / Soldier: *Criminal Class* / Cockney kids are innocent: *Sham 69* / School's out: *Infa Riot* / Where have all the boot boys gone: *Slaughter & The Dogs* / Eat the rich: *Gonads* / Time was right: *Partizan* / Chasing rainbows: *Business* / Stab the

judge: *One Way System* / Transvestite: *Peter & The Test Tube Babies* / Computers don't blunder: *Exploited* / Summer holiday: *4 Skins* / Stark raving normal: *Blood* / Twist and turn: *Slaughter & The Dogs* / Brighton bomb: *Angelic Upstarts* / Disco girls: *Business* / Oh: *Case* / Every saturday: *Section 5* / Eight pounds a week: *Last Resort* / I'm on heat: *Lurkers* / Jinx: *Peter & The Test Tube Babies* / Cum on feel the noize: *Crack* / Class war: *Exploited* / It will only ever be: *Cockney Rejects* / Dick Barton: *Frankie & The Flames*
CD _____ LINKCD 081
Street Link / Oct '92 / BMG.

OI OF SEX, THE
CD _____ AHOY 23
Captain Oi / Dec '94 / Plastic Head.

OKEH - A NORTHERN SOUL OBSESSION
CD _____ CDKEND 132
Kent / Feb '96 / Pinnacle.

OKEH RHYTHM'N'BLUES 1949-1957
CD Set _____ CD 48912
Legacy / May '94 / Sony.

OKRA ALL-STARS
CD _____ OKRACD 33021
Normal/Okra / Mar '94 / Direct / ADA.

OLD BELIEVERS
(Songs Of The Nekrasov Cossacks)
CD _____ SFWCD 40462
Smithsonian Folkways / Oct '95 / ADA / Direct / Koch / CM / Cadillac.

OLD BULL AND BUSH, THE
CD _____ GEMMCD 9913
Gemm / Feb '92 / Pinnacle.

OLD SCHOOL RAP - THE ROOTS OF RAP
King Tim III (personality jock): *Fatback Band* / Money (dollar bill y'all): *Spicer, Jimmy* / Rockin': *M.C. Flex & The F.B.I. Crew* / Please stay: *Fatback & Gerry Bledsoe* / Alarm (XX rated): *Hawk* / Rock me down: *Young, Monalisa* / Step by step: *Simon, Joe* / Heobah: *Rae, Fonda* / If I can't have your love: *Brown, Jocelyn* / Workin' out: *Ritz* / We come to jam: *Blaze* / Can you guess what groove this is: *Glory* / Live it up: *Rae, Fonda* / Go with the feeling: *Krystal* / Got to have your lovin': *Feel*
CD _____ CDSEWD 048
Southbound / Jun '92 / Pinnacle.

OLD SCHOOL RAP VOL.2
Adventures of Grand Master Flash on the wheels of steel: *Grandmaster Flash & The Furious Five* / Hey fellas: *Trouble Funk* / Sucker DJ: *Dimples D & Marley Marl* / Got it good: *Tricky Tee* / Success is the word: *12:41* / Fat boys: *Disco 3* / Ya mama: *Wuf Ticket* / Our picture of a man: *Playgirls* / It's good to be the queen: *Sylvia* / Monster jam: *Spoonie Gee & The Treacherous Three*
CD _____ DGPCD 741
Deep Beats / Nov '95 / BMG.

OLD TIME MUSIC ON THE AIR
CD _____ ROUCD 0331
Rounder / Sep '94 / CM / Direct / ADA / Cadillac.

OLD TIME PARTY FAVOURITES VOL. 1
CD _____ SWBCD 203
Sound Waves / Sep '94 / Target/BMG.

OLD TIME PARTY FAVOURITES VOL. 2
CD _____ SWCD 204
Sound Waves / Sep '94 / Target/BMG.

OLD TOWN & BARRY SOUL STIRRERS
Think smart: *Fiestas* / I'm so glad: *Howard, Frank* / Oh oh here comes the heartbreak: *Jones, Thelma* / Try love one more time: *Sparkels* / If I want back your freedom: *Freddie* / You can't trust your best friend: *Height, Donald* / My foolish heart: *Coleman, David* / Gotta find a way: *Jones, Thelma* / We're gonna make it: *Reid, Irene* / Stop, take another look: *Divine Men* / Could this be love: *Rosco & Barbara* / Jerk it: *Gypsies* / Cross my heart: *Yvonne & The Violets* / Baby I need: *Lorraine & The Delights* / Left out: *Johnson, Jesse* / My heart's on fire: *Bland, Billy* / Chills and fever: *Houston, Freddie* / Crown my heart: *Coleman, David* / Barefoon' time in Chinatown: *Young, Lester* / I want a chance for romance: *Rivera, Hector* / It's a woman's world (you better believe it): *Gypsies* / Soul stirrer: *Bobby & Betty Lou* / Gypsy said: *Fiestas* / Things have more meaning now: *Scott, Peggy*
CD _____ CDKEND 111
Kent / Jun '94 / Pinnacle.

OLD TOWN BLUES VOL.1
(Downtown Sides)
Uncle Bud: *Terry, Sonny & Brownie McGhee* / Climbing on top of the hill: *Terry, Sonny & Brownie McGhee* / Sweet sweet woman: *Terry, Sonny & Brownie McGhee* / All hearted woman: *Wayne, James* / Rock and roll: *Wayne, James* / True blues: *Wayne, James* / Slidin': *Terry, Sonny & Brownie McGhee* / Crazy about you baby: *Terry, Sonny & Brownie McGhee* / Chicken hop: *Bland, Billy* / I need a woman: *Terry, Sonny & Brownie McGhee* / Playboy: *Littlefield, Little Willie* / Sweet little girl: *Littlefield, Little Willie* / Hard luck baby: *Littlefield, Little Willie* / Work out: *Littlefield, Little Willie* / Love's a

disease: *Terry, Sonny & Brownie McGhee* / She loves so easy: *Terry, Sonny & Brownie McGhee* / Confusion: *Terry, Sonny & Brownie McGhee* / Reap what you sow: *Terry, Sonny & Brownie McGhee* / Things that I used to do: *Gaddy, Bob* / Could I would I: *Dixon, Willie* / Ugly girls: *Dixon, Willie*
CD _____ CDCHD 469
Ace / Sep '93 / Pinnacle / Cadillac / Complete/Pinnacle.

OLD TOWN BLUES VOL.2
(The Uptown Sides)
CD _____ CDCHD 498
Ace / Jun '94 / Pinnacle / Cadillac / Complete/Pinnacle.

OLD TOWN DOO WOP VOL.1
There's a moon out tonight: *Capris* / Zu zu: *Bonnevilles* / Fool in love: *Keytones* / Walking: *Solitaires* / On Sunday afternoon: *Harptones* / Never let me go: *Royaltones* / Have you ever loved someone: *Vocaleers* / Later later baby: *5 Crowns* / Message of love: *Laurels* / It all depends on you: *Harptones* / Two in love(with one heart): *McFadden, Ruth & The Royaltones* / Last rose of summer: *Symbols* / Remember them: *Earls* / Magic rose: *Solitaires* / Tonight Kathleen: *Valentines* / Seven wonders of the world: *Keytones* / Hey Norman: *Royaltones* / Lorraine: *Bonnevilles* / Why oh why: *Tru-Tones* / I love an angel: *Co-eds* / You're gonna need me: *5 Crowns* / Mambo boogie: *Harptones* / Crying my heart out: *Symbols* / I need your love so bad: *Vocaleers* / I fell in love: *Esquires*
CD _____ CDCHD 433
Ace / Jun '93 / Pinnacle / Cadillac / Complete/Pinnacle.

OLD TOWN DOO WOP VOL.2
So fine: *Fiestas* / My dearest darling: *Cleftones* / What did she say: *Solitaires* / Day we fell in love: *Ovations* / Where I fell in love: *Capris* / Zip boom: *Supremes* / Little girl (I love you madly): *Cleftones* / Life is but a dream: *Harptones* / Ding dong: *Packards* / Lullaby of the bells: *Five Crowns* / My broken heart: *Chimes* / Hong Kong jelly wong: *Royaltones* / School boy: *Harptones* / Love and devotion: *Vocaleers* / Why does the world go round: *Escorts* / Angels sang: *Solitaires* / My babe (she don't want me no more): *Supremes* / (I'm afraid) the masquerade is over: *Cleftones* / Good luck darling: *Five Crowns* / Mexico: *Chimes* / Dream of love: *Packards* / Gee what a girl: *Hummers* / There's something awful nice about you: *Escorts* / I've got a notion: *Harptones* / I give you my word: *Royaltones* / Do you know what I mean: *Hummers* / Our anniversary: *Fiestas* / My lullabye: *Ovations*
CD _____ CDCHD 470
Ace / Aug '93 / Pinnacle / Cadillac / Complete/Pinnacle.

OLD TOWN DOO WOP VOL.3
Crazy love: *Royaltones* / Indian girl: *Capris* / Starlight tonight: *Inspirators* / You know you're doin' me wrong: *Harptones* / I beg your forgiveness: *Co-eds* / Possibility: *Crowns* / My heart (I'm blue without you): *Solitaires* / My faith: *Fi-Tones* / Darling listen to the words of this song: *McFadden, Ruth & The Supremes* / I love you baby: *Farmer, Peggy & The Harptones* / Give me your love: *Four Pharaohs* / Gloria: *Cleftones* / Last round-up: *Supremes* / I'm in love: *Co-eds* / Please give me one more chance: *Mumford, Gene & The Serenaders* / Why must I love you: *Esquires* / Life is but a dream: *Earls* / Tonight: *Supremes* / Think: *Universals* / Oh what a feeling: *Inspirators* / School girl: *Harptones* / Latin lover: *Royaltones* / Guess who: *Cleftones* / China girl: *Four Pharaohs* / Moon shining bright: *Tremaines* / You're gonna need my help someday: *Harptones*
CD _____ CDCHD 471
Ace / Oct '93 / Pinnacle / Cadillac / Complete/Pinnacle.

OLD TOWN DOO WOP VOL.4
Round goes my heart: *Solitaires* / Some people think: *Capris* / I call to you: *Durgass, Vicki* / I won't tell the world: *Blenders* / Night is over: *Gems* / I'll be there: *Vocaleers* / Lonely: *Solitaires* / My heart: *Fi-Tones* / Why do I cry: *Capris* / Night: *Nick & The Nacks* / Walkin' and talkin': *Solitaires* / Lover lover lover: *Symbols* / You for me: *McFadden, Ruth* / It's you: *Earls* / Girl of mine: *Solitaires* / My island in th esun: *Capris* / Summer love: *Valentines* / Crazy love: *Royaltones* / Girl in my dreams: *Capris* / But I know: *Blenders* / Pretty thing: *Solitaires* / Life is but a dream: *Harptones* / Nursery rhymes: *Gems* / Thrill of love: *Solitaires* / When you're smiling: *Mumford, Gene & The Serenaders* / Listen listen baby: *Unknowns*
CD _____ CDCHD 570
Ace / Jan '95 / Pinnacle / Cadillac / Complete/Pinnacle.

OLDIES BUT GOLDIES 1
All or nothing: *Small Faces* / Stairway of love: *Dene, Terry* / Little things: *Berry, Dave* / I wish I could dance: *Poole, Brian & The Tremeloes* / Thunderball: *Jones, Tom* / Put a ring on her finger: *Steele, Tommy* / Why: *Newley, Anthony* / As tears go by: *Faithfull, Marianne* / Here it comes again: *Fortunes* /

In thoughts of you: *Fury, Billy* / I want you to be my baby: *Davis, Billie* / Going nowhere: *Los Bravos* / Memories are made of this: *Doonican, Val* / Dommage dommage: *Humperdinck, Engelbert* / What'cha gonna do about it: *Small Faces* / Mystic eyes: *Them*
CD _____ 15028
Laserlight / Dec '94 / Target/BMG.

OLDIES BUT GOLDIES 2
I can dance: *Poole, Brian & The Tremeloes* / Everything's alright: *Mojos* / Bye bye girl: *Applejacks* / My girl: *Small Faces* / Little love, a little kiss: *Denver, Karl* / Come and stay with me: *Faithfull, Marianne* / Ice cream man: *Tornados* / Besame mucho: *Harris, Jet* / Main title: *Harris, Jet* / Don't bring me your heartaches: *Ryan, Paul & Barry* / Elusive butterfly: *Doonican, Val* / Angel of the morning: *Davis, Billie* / Secret love: *Kirby, Kathy* / Last night was made for love: *Fury, Billy* / Get lost: *Kane, Eden* / Diane: *Bachelors*
CD _____ 15029
Laserlight / Dec '94 / Target/BMG.

OLDIES BUT GOLDIES 3
CD _____ 12388
Laserlight / Feb '95 / Target/BMG.

OLDIES BUT GOLDIES 4
CD _____ 12389
Laserlight / May '95 / Target/BMG.

OLDIES GREATEST HITS
CD _____ SONCD 0059
Sonic Sounds / Mar '94 / Jetstar.

OLDIES KEEP SWINGING
CD _____ SONCD 0057
Sonic Sounds / Jan '94 / Jetstar.

OLDTIME FESTIVAL
CD _____ BLR 84005
L&R / May '91 / New Note.

OLE - BULLFIGHT MUSIC FROM SPAIN
Espana cani / Opera flamenca / Vaya capes / La entrada
CD _____ 15161
Laserlight / '91 / Target/BMG.

OLYMPIC - THE ALBUM
Stay with me forever: *Prolific* / So deep: *Scope* / Question: *7 Grand Housing Authority* / Feel the love: *Perez, Eric* / Shiver: *Powerzone* / Another man: *Shy One* / Your love: *Mr. Peach* / Lies: *Perez, Eric* / You can turn around: *Bottom Dollar* / More to love: *Volcano*
CD _____ ELYACD 001
Olympic / Feb '94 / 3MV / Sony.

ON A DANCE TIP
Cotton eye Joe: *Rednex* / Sight for sore eyes: *M People* / Tell me when: *Human League* / Runaway: *M.C. Sar & The Real McCoy* / Set you free: *N-Trance* / Reach up: *Perfecto All Stars* / Let me be your fantasy: *Baby D* / Them girls: *Zig & Zag* / Saturday night: *Whigfield* / No matter what you do (I'm gonna get with U): *Flavour* / Total eclipse of the heart: *French, Nicki* / Here comes the hotstepper: *I'm A Kamikaze* / Welcome to tomorrow (are you ready): *Snap* / Sweetness: *Gayle, Michelle* / None of your business: *Salt 'N' Pepa* / Saved my life: *Jodeci* / Bump 'n' grind: *R. Kelly*
CD _____ RADCD 07
Global / '95 / BMG.

ON A DANCE TIP '95
CD Set _____ RADCD 27
Global / Nov '95 / BMG.

ON A DANCE TIP 2
CD _____ RADCD 12
Global / May '95 / BMG.

ON A DANCE TIP 3
CD _____ RADCD 20
Global / Jul '95 / BMG.

ON MANA 689 - NEW MUSIC INDONESIA VOL. 2
CD _____ LYRCD 7420
Lyrichord / Aug '93 / Roots / ADA / CM.

ON THE BANKS OF THE DEVERON
Vancouver / Diddler / Hugh MacDonald / Granny Fraser's flitting / Farewell to the creeks / Leaving port Askaig / MacPhersons' lament / Silver darlings / Highland cathedral / Sandy's new chanter / Tak a dram / Dumbarton castle / Craigellachie brig / Left handed fiddler / Trawler song / Rowan tree / Bonnie Gallowa / Old rustic bridge / Carillon / Spirit of Glen Deveron / Here's to Scottish whiskey / Dr Ross's 50th welcome to the Argyllshire gathering / 10th Bn H.L.I. Crossing the Rhine
CD _____ CDGR 151
Ross / Dec '95 / Ross / Duncans.

ON THE BEACH AT WAIKIKI 1914-1952
CD _____ HQCD 57
Harlequin / Aug '95 / Swift / Jazz Music / Wellard / Hot Shot / Cadillac.

ON THE DOWN LOW
CD _____ MAC 4206
Ichiban / May '95 / Koch.

ON THE EDGE OF DEATH
CD _____ 15216
Laserlight / Aug '91 / Target/BMG.

ON THE PHILADELPHIA BEAT VOL.1
Girl across the street: *Smith, Moses* / Got what you need: *Fantastic Johnny C* / Standing in the darkness: *Ethics* / Help wanted: *Volcanos* / This gets to me: *Hudson, Pookie* / If I'm all you got (I'm all you need): *Ambassadors* / Don't set me up for the kill: *Dorothy & The Hesitations* / Ain't it baby: *Gamble, Kenny* / Dynamite exploded: *Honey & The Bees* / Storm warning: *Volcanos* / I want my baby back: *Ashley, Tyrone* / Bobby, is my baby: *Mason, Barbara* / Don't let it happen to you: *Harper, Benny* / Girl I love you: *Temptones* / Joke's on you: *Gamble, Kenny* / Won't find better than me: *Kit Kat's* / Why do you hurt the one who love's you: *Honey & The Bees* / Get me somebody to love you: *Ambassadors* / Don't ever want to lose your love: *Mason, Barbara* / Till then: *Pentagons* / Trying to work out a plan: *Dorothy & The Hesitations* / Let's have a good time: *Nobles, Cliff* / You're number one: *Volcanos* / Love you can depend on: *Brenda & Tabulations* / Let's talk it over: *Kayettes* / Don't care away my love: *Soul Brothers Six* / Better to have loved and lost: *Irwin, Big Dee*
CD _____ BCDAH 15844
Bear Family / Aug '95 / Rollercoaster / Direct / CM / Swift / ADA.

ON THE REAL SIDE
I've got the need: *Jackson, Chuck* / Where did our love go: *Elbert, Donnie* / Sweet baby: *Elbert, Donnie* / Shine shine shine: *Elbert, Donnie* / Hotline: *Jackson, Chuck* / You made me love you: *Wynne, Philippe* / All the way: *Wynne, Philippe* / You ain't going anywhere but home: *Wynne, Philippe* / Let me go, lover: *Wynne, Philippe* / Beautiful woman: *Martin, Derek* / On the real side: *Saunders, Larry* / Love is strange: *Elbert, Donnie*
CD _____ NEMCD 615
Sequel / Jul '91 / BMG.

ON THE REGGAE TIP
CD _____ CIDTV 5
Island / Jun '93 / PolyGram.

ON THE ROAD
CD _____ TUT 771
Wundertute / Oct '94 / CM / Duncans / ADA.

ON THE SUNNY SIDE OF THE STREET 1934
CD _____ PHONTCD 7653
Phontastic / '93 / Wellard / Jazz Music / Cadillac.

ON THE WILD SIDE
CD Set _____ NSCD 003
Newsound / Feb '95 / THE.

ONCE UPON A TIME IN THE WEST
Bonanza / Once upon a time in the West / Good, the bad and the ugly / Magnificent seven / Green leaves of summer / High noon / Fist full of dollars / Hondo / Man with the harmonica / Professional gun / Yankee doodle / Dynamite ringo / Return of the seven / Wandering star / Hang 'em high / Man from Laramie / How the West was won / Alamo / Comancheros / True grit
CD _____ CDGRF 041
Tring / Feb '93 / Tring / Prism.

ONE A.D.
CD _____ WF 841012
Waveform / Jun '94 / Plastic Head / Kudos.

ONE DAY AT A TIME
(20 Songs Of Peace)
One day at a time: *Martell, Lena* / Michael, row the boat ashore: *Donegan, Lonnie* / Where peaceful waters flow: *Knight, Gladys* / Lay down (Candles in the rain): *Melanie & The Edwin Hawkin Singers* / Spirit in the sky: *Morrison, Dorothy* / I don't know how to love him: *Clark, Petula* / Jesu joy of man's desiring: *Black Dyke Mills Band* / Hallelujah chorus: *Black Dyke Mills Band* / Oh happy day: *Hawkins, Edwin Singers* / Amazing grace: *Royal Scots Dragoon Guards* / Ave Maria: *Rose Marie* / Higher and higher: *Wilson, Jackie* / Old rugged cross: *Martell, Lena* / Chorus of the Hebrew slaves: *Sofia National Opera Chorus* / Humming chorus: *Sofia National Opera Chorus* / Peace will come: *Melanie & The Edwin Hawkin Singers* / Border song: *Morrison, Dorothy* / He bought my soul at Calvary: *Alexander Brothers* / Suddenly there's a valley: *Clark, Petula* / Jerusalem: *Walker, Sarah & RPO*
CD _____ TRTCD 120
TrueTrax / Oct '94 / THE.

ONE HELL OF A ROCK ALBUM
She's a lover: *Simple Minds* / Inside: *Stiltskin* / Two princes: *Spin Doctors* / Why can't this be love: *Van Halen* / Living years: *Mike & The Mechanics* / Broken wings: *Mr. Mister* / Bat out of hell: *Meat Loaf* / Driven by you: *May, Brian* / Steamy windows: *Turner, Tina* / Kayleigh: *Marillion* / Viva Las Vegas: *ZZ Top* / Black night: *Deep Purple* / Stay with me: *Faces* / Brass in pockets: *Pretenders* / If I could turn back time: *Cher* / You're the voice: *Farnham, John* / Total eclipse of the heart: *Tyler, Bonnie* / Bad case of lovin' you (Doctor Doctor): *Palmer, Robert* / Can't get enough of your love: *Bad Company* / Waiting for a girl like you: *Foreigner*
CD _____ VISCD 12
Vision / Dec '95 / Pinnacle.

ONE HIT WONDERS
Tell Laura I love her: *Valance, Ricky* / No body's child: *Young, Karen* / Pickin' a chicken: *Boswell, Eve* / Calendar song: *Trinidad Oil Company* / Games people play: *South, Joe* / Tarzan boy: *Baltimore* / With a little help from my friends: *Young Idea* / Softly whispering I love you: *Congregation* / Vaya con dios: *Paul, Les & Mary Ford* / Boogie oogie oogie: *Taste Of Honey* / I'm the urban spaceman: *Bonzo Dog Band* / Let's go all the way: *Sly Fox* / Sukiyaki: *Sakamoto, Kyu* / This ole house: *Stevens, Shakin'* / Up up and away: *Martin, Johnny Singers* / Rock me gently: *Kim, Andy* / Loving you: *Riperton, Minnie* / Unchained melody: *Baxter, Les* / Spanish stroll: *Mink Deville* / I should have known better: *Naturals* / Arrivederci darling: *Savage, Edna* / He's got the whole world in his hands: *London, Laurie*
CD _____ CC 8252
EMI / Nov '94 / EMI.

ONE HUNDRED & TEN BELOW VOL.1
CD _____ BELOW 1CD
New Electronica / Jul '94 / Pinnacle / Plastic Head.

ONE HUNDRED & TEN BELOW VOL.2
CD _____ BELOW 2CD
New Electronica / Mar '95 / Pinnacle / Plastic Head.

ONE HUNDRED & TEN BELOW VOL.3
CD _____ BELOW 3CD
New Electronica / '95 / Pinnacle / Plastic Head.

ONE LITTLE INDIAN TAKES ON THE COWBOYS
CD _____ TPCD 6
One Little Indian / May '88 / Pinnacle.

ONE LOVE - 20 CARIBBEAN CLASSICS
Rivers of babylon: *Boney M* / Brown girl in the ring: *Boney M* / Help me make it through the night: *Holt, John* / Killing me softly: *Holt, John* / Everything I own: *Booth, Ken* / Hurt so good: *Cadogan, Susan* / Nice and easy: *Cadogan, Susan* / Many rivers to cross: *Cliff, Jimmy* / Wonderful world, beautiful people: *Cliff, Jimmy* / Banana boat song (Day O): *Belafonte, Harry* / Side show: *Biggs, Barry* / Dat: *Shevington, Pluto* / Israelites: *Dekker, Desmond* / First time: *Griffiths, Marcia* / Ever I saw your face: *Griffiths, Marcia* / When will I see you again: *Griffiths, Marcia* / I want to wake up with you: *Gardiner, Boris*
CD _____ PLATCD 3913
Platinum Music / Mar '92 / Prism / Ross.

ONE LOVE - THE VERY BEST OF REGGAE
CD _____ ARC 94962
Arcade / Jul '92 / Sony / Grapevine.

ONE LOVE 2 - ANOTHER 20 CARIBBEAN CLASSICS
Amigo: *Black Slate* / Hot hot hot: *Arrow* / Ready for it now: *Lovelady, Bill* / Cupid: *Nash, Johnny* / Let your people be yeah: *Pioneers* / I am what I am: *Greyhound* / Peace to the man: *Hot Chocolate* / Uptown top ranking: *Althia & Donna* / Barbados: *Typically Tropical* / Sing a little song: *Dekker, Desmond* / I'm in the mood for love: *Lord Tanamo* / Hold me tight: *Nash, Johnny* / Double barrel: *Collins, Dave & Ansil* / Liquidator: *Harry J All Stars* / Real fashion, reggae style: *Johnson, Carey* / Money in your pocket: *Brown, Dennis* / You never know what you've got: *Me & You* / Love of the common people: *Thomas, Nicky* / Suzanne beware of the devil: *Livingstone, Dandy* / All in one: *Marley, Bob*
CD _____ PLATCD 3920
Prism / Oct '93 / Prism.

ONE LOVE PRESENTS SENTIMENTAL RAGGA VOL.1
CD _____ KICKCD 16
Kickin' / Oct '94 / SRD.

ONE MAN ONE VOTE
CD _____ GRELCD 160
Greensleeves / Apr '91 / Total/BMG / Jetstar / SRD.

ONE MOMENT IN TIME
(Music Of Whitney Houston - 15 Instrumental Hits)
CD _____ 5708574338158
Carlton Home Entertainment / Sep '94 / Carlton Home Entertainment.

ONE NIGHT STANDS
Geometry / Softly as in a morning sunrise / No going back / Chogui / Little sunflower / Big yellow taxi / My funny valentine / Hello Max / Entertaining Mr. C / Lush life / Cajun / Wind is getting angry
CD _____ BTF 9402
Blow The Fuse / Nov '94 / New Note.

ONE O'CLOCK JUMP
One o'clock jump: *Basie, Count* / Moose the mooch: *Davis, Miles* / Bugle call rag: *Goodman, Benny* / It's only a paper moon: *Cole, Nat King* / Basin Street blues: *Armstrong, Louis* / Rumbo concerto: *Gillespie, Dizzy* / Round midnight: *Parker, Charlie* / Stompin' at the Savoy: *Herman, Woody* / My heart stood still: *Shaw, Artie* / At long last love: *Horne, Lena* / That old black magic: *Fitzgerald, Ella* / Yardbird suite: *Davis, Miles* / Love me or leave me: *Horne,*

Lena / Tiger rag: *Armstrong, Louis* / Feather merchant: *Basie, Count* / Move: *Parker, Charlie* / Get happy: *Goodman, Benny* / Blue prelude: *Horne, Lena* / Three hearts in a triangle: *Gillespie, Dizzy* / Slow boat to China: *Gillespie, Dizzy*
CD _____ CDGRF 125
Tring / '93 / Tring / Prism.

ONE STEP AHEAD TWO TONE DANCE CRAZE
CD _____ BHR 028CD
Burning Heart / Oct '95 / Plastic Head.

ONE VOICE, ONE LOVE
One vision: *Queen* / Let love rule: *Kravitz, Lenny* / Message in the box: *World Party* / Shakin' the tree: *Gabriel, Peter & Youssou N'Dour* / One: *U2* / Future love paradise: *Seal* / Ideal world: *Christians* / Love oh love: *Richie, Lionel* / Sowing the seeds of love: *Tears For Fears* / One love: *Marley, Bob & The Wailers* / Prayer for the world: *Priest, Maxi* / Great heart: *Clegg, Johnny & Savuka* / (Something inside) So strong: *Siffre, Labi* / Where do we go from here: *Birkett, Chris* / Light in the dark: *Brady, Paul* / Brothers in arms: *Dire Straits*
CD _____ 5164172
PolyGram TV / Aug '93 / PolyGram.

ONE WORLD
CD _____ ROUAN 15
Rounder / Oct '94 / CM / Direct / ADA / Cadillac.

ONE WORLD, ONE VOICE
CD _____ CDV 2632
Virgin / Jun '90 / EMI.

ONLY FOR THE HEADSTRONG II
CD _____ 8283162
FFRR / Jun '92 / PolyGram.

ONLY FREEWAYS TO SKINNER KAT
CD _____ RAUCD 12
Raucous / Oct '94 / Nervous / Disc.

ONLY THE POORMAN FEEL IT
Izinziswa / Giya / Siyaya / Mayibuye / Shosholoza / No easy road / Skorokoro / Yivumeni we zinsizw / Uthando lami / Ihlathi / Intsizwa / Thula / Madambadamba
CD _____ CDEMC 3706
EMI / Apr '95 / EMI.

ONLY THE STRONG
CD _____ VR 010CD
Victory / Jun '94 / Plastic Head.

ONLY YOU
(20 Great Hits Of The Sixties)
That's what love will do: *Brown, Joe* / When my little girl is smiling: *Justice, Jimmy* / Only you (And you alone): *Wynter, Mark* / Sailor: *Clark, Petula* / Who put the bomp: *Donegan, Lonnie* / March of the Siamese children: *Ball, Kenny* / Party's over: *Donegan, Lonnie* / Up on the roof: *Grant, Julie* / I wonder who's kissing her now: *Ford, Emile* / Swinging on a star: *Irwin, Big Dee & Little Eva* / It's almost tomorrow: *Wynter, Mark* / Where are you now: *Trent, Jackie* / Counting teardrops: *Ford, Emile* / Alone at last: *Wilson, Jackie* / Ramona: *Bachelors* / Picture of you: *Brown, Joe* / Sukiyaki: *Ball, Kenny* / Michael, row the boat ashore: *Donegan, Lonnie* / Spanish Harlem: *Justice, Jimmy* / Ya ya twist: *Clark, Petula*
CD _____ TRTCD 102
TrueTrax / Dec '94 / THE.

OOH OOH - THE POETS OF RHYTHM: HOTPIE & CANDY RECORDS
(Original Raw Soul Vol.1)
Working on the line: *Soul Saints Orchestra* / Spooky grinder: *Woo Woo's* / South Carolina: *Bus People Express* / Fifty yards of soul: *Whitefield Brothers* / Funky train: *Poets Of Rhythm* / O.R.F. (Pts 1 & 2): *Whitefield Brothers* / Augusta, Georgia (Here I come): *Bus People Express* / Ooh ooh: *Woo Woo's* / Hotpie's popcorn Pt.1: *Poets Of Rhythm* / Bag of soul: *Soul Saints Orchestra* / Sticky sticky sock-a-poo: *Mighty Continentals* / It's your thing
CD _____ ME 000372
Soulciety/Bassism / Sep '95 / EWM.

OPEN T - ON THE ROAD
CD _____ TMPCD 018
Telstar / Dec '95 / BMG.

OPERATIC EUPHONIUM
Celeste aida / Flower duet / Catari, catari / Largo al factotum / Duet from Don Pasquale / Evening prayer / La Donna e mobile / Marriage to Figaro / Pagageno, pagagena / Flower song / On with the motley / Quartet from rigoletto / Softly awakes my heart / Recondita armonia / Panis angelicus / Lohengrin / Oh, beloved father / Le miserere (di travatore) / You are my hearts delight / One fine day / Nun's chorus / Nessum dorma
CD _____ QPRL 072D
Polyphonic / Oct '95 / Conifer.

OPERATION D
CD _____ DBTXCD 2
Sting Ray / Nov '95 / Jetstar.

ORBITS VOL.1
CD _____ CDC 001
Out Of Orbit / Mar '95 / SRD / Plastic Head.

ORCHESTRAL FLEETWOOD MAC
CD _____ EMPRCD 546
Emporio / Nov '94 / THE / Disc / CM.

ORDER ODONATA VOL.1
CD _____ BFLCD 13
Dragonfly / Jul '94 / Pinnacle.

ORDER TO DANCE
Electrowave: *Space Opera* / Get busy time: *Ceejay* / Here we go: *Project* / Theme of St. Baals: *Mental Overdrive* / Brasil (Remix): *Spectrum* / Acid pandemonium: *Mundo Muzique* / Music: *Sonic Solution* / Poison: *Angel*
CD _____ RSCD 1
R & S / Nov '91 / Vital.

ORDER TO DANCE 4
Andromeda: *Mundo Muzique* / Nightbreed: *Bolland, C.J.* / Rise from your grave: *Phuture* / Bounce back: *Angel, Dave* / Neuromancer: *Source* / Mama: *Neuro* / My definition of house music: *D.J. Hell* / Flying dreams: *Afrotrance* / Analogue bubblebath: *Aphex Twin* / Shades: *House Of Usher* / Dream: *Music Of Life Orchestra* / Dreams: *Music Of Life Orchestra*
CD _____ RS 932CD
R & S / Jun '93 / Vital.

ORGANISM 01
CD _____ EFAD 84632
Dossier / Oct '94 / SRD.

ORGANISM 02
CD _____ EFA 084642
Dossier / Mar '95 / SRD.

ORGANISM 03
CD _____ EFA 084682
Dossier / Nov '95 / SRD.

ORGASMIC HOUSE
CD _____ DOWN 1CD
Sun Down / Jun '95 / SRD.

ORIENTAL DREAMS
CD _____ PS 65075
Playasound / Jul '91 / Harmonia Mundi / ADA.

ORIGINAL CHICAGO BLUES HITS
CD _____ CDCD 1265
Charly / Oct '95 / Charly / THE / Cadillac.

ORIGINAL CLUB SKA
CD _____ CDHB 055
Heartbeat / Feb '91 / Greensleeves / Jetstar / Direct / ADA.

ORIGINAL DIXIELAND
CD _____ CDCD 1241
Charly / Jun '95 / Charly / THE / Cadillac.

ORIGINAL HITS
CD Set _____ 4417252
Pilz / Oct '92 / BMG.

ORIGINAL HITS OF GEORGE GERSHWIN
CD _____ DHDL 112
Halcyon / Oct '92 / Jazz Music / Wellard / Swift / Harmonia Mundi / Cadillac.

ORIGINAL HITS OF THE 60'S AND 70'S
CD _____ PKL 514911
K&K / Jul '93 / Jetstar.

ORIGINAL JAZZ CLASSICS
Kid from red bank: *Basie, Count* / Mercy mercy mercy: *Adderley, Cannonball* / Sidewinder: *Henderson, Joe* / Chicago: *Rich, Buddy Band* / I wish I knew (how it would feel to be free): *Taylor, Billy* / Body and soul: *Chaloff, Serge* / Caravan: *Ellington, Duke* / Summertime: *Evans, Gil* / Don't be that way: *Goodman, Benny* / Love me or leave me: *Lewis, John* / Lullaby of birdland: *Shearing, George* / Misty: *Brookmeyer, Bob* / Birdland: *Pastorius, Jaco* / Peanut vendor: *Kenton, Stan* / Midnight blue: *Burrell, Kenny* / Take five: *Brubeck, Dave*
CD _____ CDPR 127
Premier/MFP / Nov '94 / EMI.

ORIGINAL JAZZ MASTERS VOL.1, THE (5CD Set)
CD Set _____ DAMUSIC 76032
DA Music / Dec '95 / Koch.

ORIGINAL JAZZ MASTERS VOL.2, THE (5CD Set)
CD Set _____ DAMUSIC 76042
DA Music / Dec '95 / Koch.

ORIGINAL MAMBO KINGS, THE
CD _____ 5138762
Verve / Jan '93 / PolyGram.

ORIGINAL MEMPHIS FIVE GROUPS
CD _____ VILCD 0162
Village Jazz / Aug '93 / Target/BMG / Jazz Music.

ORIGINAL MEMPHIS FIVE VOLUME 1 1922-1923
My honey's lovin' arms / Cuddle up blues / Hopeless blues / Lonesome mama blues / That's a plenty / Yankee doodle blues / I wish I could shimmy like my sister Kate / Achin' hearted blues / Chicago / Running wild / Ivy / That barking dog / Stop your kidding / Loose feet / Aggravatin' / Great white way blues / Four o'clock blues / Shufflin' Mose / Jelly roll blues / Bunch of blues / Sweet papa Joe / Hootin' de hoot
CD _____ COCD 16
Collector's Classics / Mar '95 / Cadillac / Complete/Pinnacle.

ORIGINAL RAGTIME CLASSICS
(From The Original Piano Rolls)
CD _____ CDCD 1086
Charly / Jun '93 / Charly / THE / Cadillac.

ORIGINAL REGGAE HITS OF THE 60'S & 70'S, THE
CD _____ PKCD 33194
K&K / Sep '94 / Jetstar.

ORIGINAL RHUMBAS
CD _____ 995312
EPM / Aug '93 / Discovery / ADA.

ORIGINAL SOUL CHRISTMAS, THE
CD _____ 8122717882
WEA / Dec '94 / Warner Music.

ORIGINAL STALAG 17-18 AND 19
CD _____ WRCD 1684
Jetstar / Oct '92 / Jetstar.

ORIGINAL VERSIONS OF SONGS BY THE COMMITMENTS
Mustang Sally / Chain of fools / Hard to handle / Mr. Pitiful / I never loved a man (the way I love you) / In the midnight hour / Slip away / Please please please / Shaft / Show me / Try a little tenderness / Dark end of the street / I've got dreams to remember / Do right man / Do right woman, do right man
CD _____ 7567918132
East West / Feb '94 / Warner Music.

ORIGINAL VERSIONS OF THE FAMOUS HITS
CD _____ MPV 5555
Movieplay / Sep '94 / Target/BMG.

ORIGINALS
Wonderful world: *Cooke, Sam* / I heard it through the grapevine: *Gaye, Marvin* / Stand by me: *King, Ben E.* / When a man loves a woman: *Sledge, Percy* / C'mon everybody: *Cochran, Eddie* / Mannish boy: *Waters, Muddy* / Ain't nobody home: *King, B.B.* / Can't get enough: *Bad Company* / Joker: *Miller, Steve Band* / Should I stay or should I go: *Clash* / Twentieth century boy: *T. Rex* / Mad about the boy: *Washington, Dinah* / Piece of my heart: *Franklin, Erma* / Heart attack and vine: *Hawkins, Screamin' Jay*
CD _____ MOODCD 29
Columbia / May '93 / Sony.

ORIGINALS 2
Up on the roof: *Drifters* / It takes two: *Gaye, Marvin & Kim Weston* / (Sittin' on) the dock of the bay: *Redding, Otis* / In crowd: *Gray, Dobie* / La bamba: *Los Lobos* / All right now: *Free* / Move on up: *Mayfield, Curtis* / I get the sweetest feeling: *Wilson, Jackie* / Hey Joe: *Hendrix, Jimi* / Papa's got a brand new bag: *Brown, James* / No particular place to go: *Berry, Chuck* / Heatwave: *Reeves, Martha & The Vandellas* / Bad moon rising: *Creedence Clearwater Revival* / Let's work together: *Canned Heat* / Wander: *Dion* / My baby just cares for me: *Simone, Nina* / Stella Mae: *Hooker, John Lee*
CD _____ MOODCD 31
Columbia / Mar '94 / Sony.

ORIGINALS, THE
I'll be there: *Jackson Five* / It only takes a minute: *Tavares* / Hang on in there baby: *Bristol, Johnny* / Rock your baby: *McCrae, George* / Now that we've found love: *Third World* / Show you the way to go: *Jacksons* / Tired of being alone: *Green, Al* / Summer breeze: *Isley Brothers* / You to me are everything: *Real Thing* / Play that funky music: *Wild Cherry* / It takes two: *Gaye, Marvin & Kim Weston* / Fantasy: *Earth, Wind & Fire* / I believe in miracles: *Jackson Sisters* / Don't leave me this way: *Melvin, Harold & The Bluenotes* / Shame, shame, shame: *Shirley & Company* / Give me just a little more time: *Chairmen Of The Board* / Respect yourself: *Staple Singers* / Tender love: *Force MD's* / Please don't go: *K.C. & The Sunshine Band*
CD _____ DINTVCD 43
Dino / Aug '92 / Pinnacle / 3MV.

ORIGINATION 1974-1984
CD _____ SHCD 6012
Sky High / Oct '95 / Jetstar.

ORIGINS OF A SOUND
(Electro Bass Sound Of Detroit)
Phase 2: *Audiotech* / Countdown has be gun: *Drexciya* / Bass magnetic: *Aux 88* / Twista: *Underground Resistance* / Livin' on the edge: *Drexciya* / Bass camp alpha 808: *Underground Resistance* / Let's dance: *Aux 88* / DJ: *Aux 88* / Wave jumper: *Drexciya* / Deep space 9: *Mad Mike For U.R* / City of fear: *Holland, 808* / Surface Temperature: *Red Planet* / Defying galaxy: *Gigi Galaxy*
CD _____ SVE 004CD
Infonet / Dec '95 / Pinnacle / Vital.

ORKNEY SESSIONS
CD _____ AT 041C
Attic / Oct '95 / CM / ADA.

ORQUESTAS TEJANAS
(Tejano Roots)
CD _____ ARHCD 38
Arhoolie / Apr '95 / ADA / Direct / Cadillac.

ORTHODOX CHANTS
CD _____ AUB 006770
Auvidis/Ethnic / Dec '92 / Harmonia Mundi.

OS IPANEMAS
CD _____ MRBCD 001
Mr. Bongo / May '95 / New Note.

OUD, THE
CD _____ LYRCD 7160
Lyrichord / Dec '94 / Roots / ADA / CM.

OUR HYMNS
O God, our help in ages past: Keaggy, Phil / Holy holy holy: Smith, Michael W. / It is so sweet to trust in Jesus: Grant, Amy / Saviour is waiting: Take 6
CD _____ WSTCD 9107
Nelson Word / Dec '89 / Nelson Word.

OUT CLASSICS
CD _____ 74321312612
RCA / Oct '95 / BMG.

OUT OF MANY, ONE
(Jamaican Music 1962-1975)
Music is my occupation: Drummond, Don / Owe me no pay me: Ethiopians / Jack of my trade: Sir Lord Comic / Run for your life: Bryan, Carl / Sick and tired: Grant, Neville / Don't look back: Brown, Busty / Only yesterday: Parker, Ken / Peace called Africa: Byles, Junior / Hopeful village: Tennors / Better must come: Wilson, Delroy / Stop that man: Crystalites / Space flight: I-Roy / Sun is shining: Marley, Bob & The Wailers / Fever: Byles, Junior / Satan side: Hudson, Keith / Skank in bod: Scotty / Let's start again: Campbell, Cornell & Friends
CD _____ CDTRS 1
Trojan / Jan '89 / Jetstar / Total/BMG.

OUT OF MANY, ONE - VOLUME 2
CD _____ CDTRS 2
Trojan / Nov '90 / Jetstar / Total/BMG.

OUT OF THE BLUE
Theme de yo yo: Art Ensemble Of Chicago / Old gospel: McLean, Jackie / Motystrophe: Taylor, Cecil / Point of many returns: Rivers, Sam / Herzog: Hutcherson, Bobby / Diddy wah: Hill, Andrew / Gazzelloni: Dolphy, Eric / Majestic soul: Young, Larry / We now interrupt for a commercial: Coleman, Ornette
CD _____ CDP 8354142
Blue Note / Oct '95 / EMI.

OUT ON THE FLOOR
Seven days too long: Wood, Chuck / She blew a good thing: Poets / Girls are out to get you: Fascinations / Looking for your: Mimms, Garnet / I can't get a hold of myself: Curry, Clifford / Snake: Wilson, Al / Stay close to me: Stairsteps / I'll do anything: Troy, Doris / Breakout: Ryder, Mitch / What's wrong with me baby: Invitations / Queen of fools: Mills, Barbara / Nobody but me: Human Beinz / I dig your act: O'Jays / Shake a tail feather: Purify, James & Bobby / This thing called love: Wyatt, Johnny / Our love will grow: Showmen / Try a little harder: Fidels / Backfield in motion: Mel & Tim / Don't be sore at me: Parliaments / Reaching for the best: Exciters / Somebody somewhere needs you: Banks, Darrell / Oh my darlin: Dee, Jackie / Groovin' at the go-go: Four Larks / Little piece of leather: Elbert, Donnie / Out on the floor: Gray, Dobie
CD _____ GSCD 058
Goldmine / Mar '95 / Vital.

OUT ON THE LEFT
CD _____ 5198302
Polydor / Aug '93 / PolyGram.

OUT THE LIGHTS VOL.3
CD _____ DTCD 12
Discotex / Jul '92 / Jetstar.

OUT THE LIGHTS VOL.4
CD _____ DTCD 14
Discotex / Nov '92 / Jetstar.

OUT THE LIGHTS VOL.5
CD _____ DTCD 17
Discotex / Jun '93 / Jetstar.

OUT THERE: A THREAD THROUGH TIME
CD Set _____ TBCD 001
T&B / Nov '94 / Plastic Head.

OUTER SPACE COMMUNICATIONS
CD _____ DIS 007CD
Minus Habens / Apr '94 / Plastic Head.

OUTFLUNG NET, THE
CD Set _____ ECMBOX 04
ECM / Nov '92 / New Note.

OUTLAWS
CD _____ PD 81321
RCA / Sep '85 / BMG.

OUTPATIENTS '93
Time and a word: Fish / Mark 13: Dream Disciples / One love: One Eternal / Don't ask me: Joyriders / Seeker: Fish / Swing your bag: Guaranteed Pure / Travellers tales: Avalon / Out of my life: Fish / Best friend: Joyriders / Dream is dead: Dream Disciples
CD _____ FISHYCD 001
Fishy / Nov '93 / Vital.

OUTSIDE THE REACTOR VOL.1
CD _____ BR 1CD
Blue Room Released / Sep '95 / SRD.

OUTSTANDING JAZZ COMPOSITIONS OF THE 20TH CENTURY
(2CD Set)
CD Set _____ 4756392
Sony Jazz / Jan '95 / Sony.

OVCCI VUOMI OVTAA VEAIGGIS
CD _____ DAT 20CD
Dat / Nov '95 / ADA / Direct.

OVER THE EDGE
Got to be emotion: Virginity / I'm coming up: Love Boutique / Love bizarre: Fratelli / Can't stop: Plez / How to win your love: E.C.A. / Throwdown: Bitch / Religion: Awareness / 550 state: Blood Brothers / Just that feelin': T-Boom / Wind theme: Xpulsion / Summer's child: Life Form / Acperience 1: Hardfloor / (You give me) All your love: Progressive
CD _____ CDTOT 9
Debut / May '93 / Pinnacle / 3MV / Sony.

OVER THE RAINBOW
(Gay Classics)
CD _____ BLSTCD 01
Blast / Aug '95 / Total/BMG.

OVER THE TOP
CD _____ TRTCD 180
TrueTrax / Jun '95 / THE.

OVER THERE 1942
CD _____ PHONTCD 7670
Phontastic / Apr '94 / Wellard / Jazz Music / Cadillac.

OVERPOWERED BY FUNK
Theme from Shaft: Hayes, Isaac / One nation under a groove: Funkadelic / Get up off that thing: Brown, James / Fire: Ohio Brothers / Move on up: Mayfield, Curtis / Beginning of the end: Funky Nassau / Funkin' for Jamaica: Brown, Tom / Are you ready (do the bus stop): Fatback Band / Express: B.T. Express / Strawberry letter 23: Brothers Johnson / I need it: Watson, Johnny 'Guitar' / Family affair: Sly & The Family Stone / Papa's got a brand new pig bag: Pig Bag / Word up: Cameo / Ain't gonna bump no more: Tex, Joe / Pick up the pieces: Average White Band / Play that funky music: Wild Cherry / Sunshine day: Osibisa / We got the funk: Positive Funk / Expansion: Smith, Lonnie Liston
CD _____ RENCD 109
Renaissance Collector Series / Oct '95 / BMG.

OW
(All Star Jam Session)
CD _____ MCD 075
Moon / Dec '95 / Harmonia Mundi / Cadillac.

OWLS' HOOT, THE
CD _____ DGF 2
Frog / May '95 / Jazz Music / Cadillac / Wellard.

OXYGENE
(Music Of Jean Michel Jarre - 16 Instrumental Hits)
CD _____ 5708574338028
Carlton Home Entertainment / Sep '94 / Carlton Home Entertainment.

OYE LISTEN
(Compacto Caliente)
Defiendeme Santa Barbara: Leida, Linda / Arroz con manteca: Leida, Linda / Olvidame: Rodriguez, Bobby / La mulata cubana: Valdes, Alfredo / Con carino a Panama: Monguito 'el unico' / Festival in Guarare: Sonora De Baru / Ay se paso la serie: Rolando la serie / Ucana sordi: Los guaracheros de oriente / Como se baila el son: La india del oriente / Ban-con-tin: Super All Star / Prende la vela (on CD and cassette only): Calzado, Rudy / Saludando a los rumberos: Marti, Virgilio
CD _____ CDORB 014
Globestyle / Jan '87 / Pinnacle.

PADDY IN THE SMOKE
Bank of Ireland/Woman of the house/Morning dew: Casey, Bobby / Blue ribbon/Up and away: Clifford, John & Julia / Boys of the lough/Trip to Durrow: Pepper, Noel & Paddy Moran / Paddy man's daughter: Byrne, Packie / Jackie Coleman's/The castle: Power, Jimmy / Kesh jig/Morrison's/Old Joe's: Doonan, John / Bucks of Oranmore/The wind that shakes the barley: O'Halloran Brothers / Rights of man/Honeysuckle hornpipe: Healy, Tommy & Johnny Duffy / Galway shawl: Barry, Margaret / Callaghan's reel: Curtin, Con & Denis McMahon / Ballydesmond/Knocknaboul: Clifford, Julia / Maid behind the bar: Wright Brothers & Paddy Nolan / Coolin': Pepper, Noel / Granuaile: O'Halloran, Des / Follow me down to Limerick/Waltham the fiddler: Power, Jimmy / Shannon breeze/Heathery breeze/Green fields of America: Doonan, John / Cavan lasses/Rose of the heather:

Healy, Tommy & Johnny Duffy / Creel: Byrne, Packie / Moher reel: Farr, Lucy & Bobby Casey / Cherish the ladies: Doonan, John / Dublin porter/Mountain lark: Star Of Munster Trio / Paddy Ryan's dream: Meehan, Danny / Flower of sweet Strabane: Barry, Margaret / Maguire's favourite/Tralee gaol/Maggie in the wood: Barry, Margaret / Coleman's favourite/Promenade: Power, Jimmy / Lucy Campbell/Toss the feathers: McMahon, Tony/Andy Boyce/Mairtin Byrnes / Blackbird: Doonan, John
CD _____ CDORBD 088
Globestyle / Mar '95 / Pinnacle.

PAIN, SORROW & LONLINESS
CD _____ HILOCD 5
Hi / Nov '93 / Pinnacle.

PAISLEY POP
(Pye Psych & Other Colours 1966-1969)
Quiet explosion: Uglys / Good idea: Uglys / Bitter thoughts of little Jane: Timon / Too much on my mind: Gates Of Eden / I wish I was five: Scrugg / Lavender popcorn: Scrugg / All the love in the world: Consortium / You're all things bright and beautiful: Christian, Neil / Blessed: Kytes / Goodbye Thimble Mill Lane: Schadel / Smile a little smile for me: Flying Machine / Timeline: Rainbow People / Cave of clear light: Bystanders / I wonder where my sister's gone: Anan / Black veils of melancholy: Status Quo / Dreams secondhand: Blinkers / That's when happiness begins: Montanas / Tamaris Khan: Onyx / Major to minor: Settlers / Stop, look, listen: Fresh Air / Captain Reale: Gentle Influence / Morning way: Trader Horne
CD _____ NEXCD 188
Sequel / Mar '92 / BMG.

PAKISTAN - THE MUSIC OF THE QAWAL
CD _____ AUD 8082
Unesco / Jun '91 / Harmonia Mundi.

PAKISTAN TREASURES
CD _____ PS 65082
Playasound / Nov '91 / Harmonia Mundi / ADA.

PALACIAO DE LA SALSA
CD _____ 309632
Scratch / Jan '96 / BMG.

PALAIS DE YOGYAKARTA 4
(Concert Music From Java)
CD _____ C 560087
Ocora / Oct '95 / Harmonia Mundi / ADA.

PAN ALL NIGHT
(The Steel Bands Of Trinidad & Tobago)
Birthday party: Phase II Pan Groove / Dus' in dey face: Exodus / All night (reprise): Moods / Mystery band: Amoco Renegades / Pan in yuh pan: Courts Laventille Sound Specialists / Miss supporter: Cordettes / All night: Vat 19 Fonclaire
CD _____ DE 4022
Delos / Feb '94 / Conifer.

PAN GLOSSARY NO.1
CD _____ PAN 2000A
Pan / Oct '94 / ADA / Direct / CM.

PAN IS BEAUTIFUL - THE WORLD'S BEST STEELBANDS
(Calypso & Soca)
Hammer: Trinidad All Stars Steel Band / Set something and wave: Tropical Angel Harps / Jericho: Solo Harmonites / Exodus: Exodus / Musical Volcano: Witco Desperadoes / Nah do that: National Quarries Cordettes / Clmmpor's hall: Trinton loundnn
CD _____ 68962
Tropical / Jul '93.

PAN JAZZ 'N' CALYPSO
California shower / We kinda music / Rhythm in the groove / Take me there / Hy-da / Never can say goodbye / East river drive / Philmore's dream / Sitting through the notes / Iron man / Fire down below
CD _____ DE 4016
Delos / Jan '94 / Conifer.

PAN JAZZ CONVERSATIONS
(Caribbean Carnival Series)
Mauby beach / Dry river blues / What's the name of this song / Reflection / Dadu / De hustler / Karnaval people / Fingers
CD _____ DE 4019
Delos / Apr '94 / Conifer.

PAN PIPE DREAMS
CD _____ PMCD 010
Pure Music / Sep '95 / BMG.

PAN PIPE INSPIRATION
CD _____ PMCD 7011
Pure Music / Apr '95 / BMG.

PAN PIPE MOODS II
CD _____ 5293952
PolyGram TV / Oct '95 / PolyGram.

PAN WOMAN
CD _____ DE 4017
Delos / Sep '95 / Conifer.

PANAUNIE
CD _____ RRTGCD 7705
Rohit / '88 / Jetstar.

PANDEMONIUM NO.1
CD _____ PAN 0100A
Pan / Oct '94 / ADA / Direct / CM.

PANNARAMA
CD _____ BFISHCD 1
Big Fish / Apr '94 / Big Fish.

PANORAMA
(Steel Bands Of Trinidad And Tobago)
Woman is boss / Poom poom / Steel of wheels / Par by storm / Pan in uyh ruck-ungkertungkung / Ramajay / Iron man / Ramjay (reprise)
CD _____ DE 4015
Delos / Jan '94 / Conifer.

P'ANSORI
(Korea's Epic Vocal Art & Instrumental Music)
CD _____ 7559720492
Elektra Nonesuch / Jan '95 / Warner Music.

PARADISE CITY (ONE WORLD - ONE LOVE)
CD Set _____ UKK 4106
UKK / Oct '94 / Total/BMG.

PARADISO
CD _____ CDRAID 503
Rumour / Mar '91 / Pinnacle / 3MV / Sony.

PARAGUAYAN HARP
CD _____ PS 65128
Playasound / May '94 / Harmonia Mundi / ADA.

PARAMOUNT BLUES VOL.3
CD _____ HCD 12013
Black Swan / Oct '93 / Jazz Music.

PARAMOUNTS, THE VOL. 1
CD _____ PYCD 01
Magpie / Apr '90 / Hot Shot.

PARAPHYSICAL CYBERTRONICS
CD _____ PRAXIS 10CD
Praxis / Jul '95 / Plastic Head.

PARASOLS VOLUME 1
CD _____ PLKCD 001
Plink Plonk / Feb '94 / Plink Plonk.

PARIS AFTER DARK
La mer: Trenet, Charles / Hymne a l'amour: Piaf, Edith / J'attendrai: Rossi, Tino / Ma cienne / Vieni vieni: Rossi, Tino / Seul ce soir: Marjane, Leo / J'aime Paris au mois de mai: Aznavour, Charles / Puisque vous parlez d'amour: Delyle, Lucienne / Pigalle: Ulmer, Georges / Le chaland qui passe: Gauty, Lys / Sur ma vie: Les Compagnons De La Chanson / La vie en rose: Piaf, Edith / Parlez-moi d'amour: Boyer, Lucienne / Ces petites choses: Sablon, Jean / Mon homme: Mistinguett / J'ai deux amours: Baker, Josephine / Boum: Trenet, Charles / La java bleue: Frehel / Le fiacre: Sablon, Jean / Les trois cloches: Piaf, Edith et Les Compagnons De La Chansons / C'est a Capri: Rossi, Tino
CD _____ CZ 140
EMI / Sep '88 / EMI.

PARIS BLUES
(French Realist Singers 1926-1958)
Les amants d'un jour (Orchestra: Robert Chauvigny): Piaf, Edith / Ou sont tous mes amants (With orchestra): Frehel / La rue de Notre Amour (Orchestra: Aime Barelli): Delyle, Lucienne / Dans la rue des Blancs Manteaux (Orchestra: P. Arimi.): Greco, Juliette / Tel qu'il est (Maurice Alexander & His Orchestra): Frehel / La serenade due pave (With chorus & orchestra.): Buffet, Eugenie / La chanson de Margaret (Philippe Gerard Ensemble): Montero, Germaine / Mon chapeau (Van Baner): George, Yvonne / Au bal de la chance (Orchestra: Robert Chauvigny.): Piaf, Edith / La complainte de la butte (Orchestra: Francois Rauber.): Vaucaire, Cora / Sombre Dimanche (With Russian chorus.): Damia / Le Noel de la rue (With the Raymond Saint-Paul Chorus.): Piaf, Edith / Lili Marlene (Orchestra: Georges Briez): Solidor, Suzy / Mon amant de St Jean (Orchestra: Aime Barelli): Delyle, Lucienne / Sarah (Orchestra: Franck Pourcel.): Lasso, Gloria / Le chant des partisans (Orchestra: Guy Luypaerts.): Sablon, Germaine / La chanson de Catherine (Orchestra: Robert Chauvigny): Piaf, Edith / La chanson des forfits: Frehel / La fille de Londres (M. Philippe-Gerard & His Ensemble): Montero, Germaine
CD _____ CDEMS 1397
EMI / May '91 / EMI.

PARIS BY NIGHT
Milord: Piaf, Edith / Douce France: Trenet, Charles / Briu d'amour: Alexander, Maurice / Sur les quais du vieux Paris: Delyle, Lucienne / Vieni vieni: Rossi, Tino / Seul ce soir: Marjane, Leo / J'aime Paris au mois de mai: Aznavour, Charles / Puisque vous parlez en voyage: Sablon, Mireille & Jean / Moulin rouge: Les Compagnons De La Chanson / A Paris dans chaque faubourg: Gauty, Lys / Sur le point d'Avignon: Sablon, Jean / Ou est-il donc: Frehel / Ma Louise (Film Chanson De Paris.): Chevalier, Maurice / La cloche de mon coeur: Busch, Eva / Nuages: Reinhardt, Django / Depuis que les bals sont fermes: Damia / Qur reste t'il de nos amours: Trenet, Charles / Ma cabane au Canada: Renaud, Line / Un seul couvert, please, James: Sablon, Jean / Bal dans ma rue: Piaf, Edith
CD _____ CZ 316
EMI / Jun '90 / EMI.

PARIS GROOVE UP
Arabesques / Christ'al / Gardez l'ecoute / Pardonne / Go go motion / K-talk 2 / Elles aimant ca / Bola / Mic mac / Fantaisy / Really groovy / Funky takini / Boom bastic / Just comme ca / Ame saoul-am soul
CD _____ 4509961722
Warner Bros. / Jul '94 / Warner Music.

PARIS, OH QUE J'AIME
CD _____ PASTCD 7069
Flapper / Mar '95 / Pinnacle.

PARIS WASHBOARD VOL.2
CD _____ SOSCD 1261
Stomp Off / Oct '93 / Jazz Music / Wellard.

PARIS...CAFE-CONCERT
C'est un mauvais garcon' / Boum / Gigolette / Maitre Pierre / J'attendrai / Sur le pont d'avignon / C'est un bureaucrate / Un p'tit bock / Chez moi / Vous oubliez votre cheval / Tel qu'il est / Guitare d'amour / Ma douce vallee / Place pigalle / Sombreros et mantillas / As dis ah dis / C'est un chagrin de femme / Je ne donnerais pas ma place / J'ai connu do vous / Oh Suzanna youp youp-la-la / La vie qui va
CD _____ PASTCD 9797
Flapper / Aug '92 / Pinnacle.

PAROXYSN
CD _____ MKTCD 001
Mute / Jul '92 / Disc.

PARTY FEVER
CD _____ SONCD 0062
Sonic Sounds / Mar '94 / Jetstar.

PARTY MEGAMIX
(Over 100 Sensationally Sequenced Songs)
CD _____ PLATCD 3917
Prism / Sep '93 / Prism.

PARTY MIX
CD _____ DINCD 32
Dino / Nov '91 / Pinnacle / 3MV.

PASODOBLES
CD _____ 906662
PMF / Jul '92 / Kingdom / Cadillac.

PASS THE VIBES ON
CD _____ 5352212
PolyGram TV / Jan '96 / PolyGram.

PASSING OF THE REGIMENTS
CD _____ BNA 5065
Bandleader / May '92 / Conifer.

PASSION
(Music For Guitar)
Proven by fire / Love on the beach / Good question / Parasol days / Passion and pride / Gentle touch / Running games / New face / Lover's promise / Explorations / Joy of life
CD _____ ND 61044
Narada / Oct '94 / New Note / ADA.

PASSION TRAX
CD _____ CDPASH 1
Passion / Feb '93 / Pinnacle / 3MV.

PAST PERFECT SAMPLER
(The Great Sound Of The 20's, 30's & 40's)
I never knew: Armstrong, Louis / Doug the Jitterbug: Jordan, Louis / I let a song go out of my heart: Ellington, Duke / King Porter stomp: Crosby, Bob / Home Guard blues: Formby, George / Cuban overture (Gershwin): Whiteman, Paul & Rosa Linda / Carolina shout: Waller, Fats / Just let me look at you: Coward, Sir Noel / La danza: Gigli, Beniamino / Miss Annabelle Lee: Reinhardt, Django & Stephane Grappelli / Muddy water: Lunceford, Jimmie / I guess I'll have to change my plan: Fitzgerald, Ella / Let yourself go: Rogers, Ginger / Taking a chance on love: Fitzgerald, Ella / Shall we dance: Astaire, Fred
CD _____ PPCD 78100
Past Perfect / Feb '95 / THE.

PATH
(An Ambient Journey From Windham Hill)
Tibet (part 2): Isham, Mark / On the forest floor: Holroyd, Bob / Le desert bleu: Descarpentries, Xavier / White spirits: Uman / Ghost dancer: De Roth & The Mirrors / To tree or not to tree: Evenson, Dean / Lydia: Story, Tim / Ancient evenings: Hughes, Gary / Riding windhorse (Buddafields): Heavenly Music Corporation / 12.18: Global Communication
CD _____ 01934111632
Windham Hill / Apr '95 / Pinnacle / BMG / ADA.

PATRONA BAVARIAE
CD _____ 15182
Laserlight / '91 / Target/BMG.

PATTERNS OF JEWISH LIFE
(Highlights Of Series - Traditional & Popular Jewish Music)
CD Set _____ SM 16042
Wergo / Feb '94 / Harmonia Mundi / ADA / Cadillac.

PAUL JONES R&B SHOW VOL 2
CD _____ JSPCD 221
JSP / Oct '88 / ADA / Target/BMG / Direct / Cadillac / Complete/Pinnacle.

PAY IT ALL BACK - US
CD _____ RESTLESS 7269
On-U Sound / Aug '94 / SRD / Jetstar.

PAY IT ALL BACK VOL.2
Train to doomsville: Perry, Lee 'Scratch' & Dub Syndicate / Billy Bonds MBE: Barmy Army / Circular motion: Forehead Bros / What a wonderful day: African Headcharge / No alternative (but to fight): Dub Syndicate & Dr. Pablo / Run them away: Sherman, Bim & Singers & Players / Water the garden: Prince Far-I & Singers & Players / Throw it away: African Headcharge / Digital: Eskimo Fox
CD _____ ONULP 42 CD
On-U Sound / Dec '88 / SRD / Jetstar.

PAY IT ALL BACK VOL.3
Disconnection: Strange Parcels / Heart's desire: Singers & Players / You thought I was dead: Perry, Lee 'Scratch' & Dub Syndicate / Stoned immaculate: Dub Syndicate & Akabu / I think of you: Little Annie / Jack the biscuit: Fairley, Andy / Hey ho: Dub Syndicate / These things happen: Stewart, Mark / Ennio: Frederix, Martin / To be free: Strange Parcels & Bernard Fowler / My God: African Headcharge / Spirit soul: Pillay, Alan / False leader: Clail, Gary / Jacob's pillow: Rae, Jesse / Devo: Barmy Army / Blue moon: Barmy Army / Nightmare: Sherman, Bim
CD _____ ONUCD 53
On-U Sound / May '91 / SRD / Jetstar.

PAY IT ALL BACK VOL.4
CD _____ ONUCD 20
On-U Sound / Feb '93 / SRD / Jetstar.

PAY IT ALL BACK VOL.5
CD _____ ONUCD 75
On-U Sound / Apr '95 / SRD / Jetstar.

PE DE SERRA FORRO BAND, BRAZIL
Wergo / Oct '92 / Harmonia Mundi / ADA / Cadillac.
CD _____ SM 15092

PEACE TOGETHER
Satellite of love: U2 & Lou Reed / Peace in our time: Carter U.S.M. / Religious persuasion: Bragg, Billy & Andy White/Sinead O'Connor / Bad weather: Young Disciples / We have all the time in the world: My Bloody Valentine / Games without frontiers: Pop Will Eat Itself / Oliver's army: Blur / Invisible sun: Therapy / When we were two little boys: Harris, Rolf & Liam O'Maonlai / What a waste: Curve & Ian Dury / John the gun: Fatima Mansions / Be still: Peace Together
CD _____ CID 8018
Island / Jul '93 / PolyGram.

PEACEFUL EASY FEELING
Debut / Sep '95 / Pinnacle / 3MV / Sony.
CD _____ CDTEP 8

PEACEVILLE VOL.4
CD _____ VILE 030 CD
Peaceville / Oct '92 / Pinnacle.

PEBBLES VOL.01
CD _____ AIPCD 5016
AIP / Jul '92 / Disc.

PEBBLES VOL.02
CD _____ AIPCD 5019
AIP / Jul '92 / Disc.

PEBBLES VOL.03
CD _____ AIPCD 5020
AIP / Jul '92 / Disc.

PEBBLES VOL.04
CD _____ AIPCD 5021
AIP / Jul '92 / Disc.

PEBBLES VOL.05
No good woman: Tree / Go away: Plague / You don't know me: Magi / It's a crying shame: Gentlemen / Writing on the wall: 5 Canadians / Why: Dirty Wurds / Universal vagrant: Merry Dragons / I wanna come back (From the world of LSD): Fe Fi Four Plus 2 / I tell no lies: Escapades / You need love: Danny & The Escorts / Yesterday's heroes: Satyrs / Way it used to be: Light & The Night Shadows / Move: State Of Mind / I need love: State Of Mind / Time stoppers: State Of Mind / You'll never be my girl: Thursday's Children / Way I feel: 12 am
CD _____ AIPCD 5022
AIP / Jul '92 / Disc.

PEBBLES VOL.06
CD _____ AIPCD 5023
AIP / Feb '95 / Disc.

PEBBLES VOL.07
CD _____ AIPCD 5024
AIP / Feb '95 / Disc.

PEBBLES VOL.08
CD _____ AIPCD 5025
Backs / Feb '96 / Disc.

PEEL YOUR HEAD
CD _____ SFRCD 129
Strange Fruit / Jan '95 / Pinnacle.

PELHAM'S SOCA PARTY VOL.1
CD _____ CSSCD 001
Cott / Jun '94 / Jetstar.

PENDULUM FLAVA - GOOD LICKIN' VOL.1
Rebirth of slick: Digable Planets / Chief rocka: Lords Of The Underground / Covers:

Lisa Lisa / Desolate one: Papa Chuk / Lords prayer: Lords Of The Underground / Acid rain: Lisa Lisa / Jimmi diggin' cats: Digable Planets / Do me: Walker, Chris
CD _____ CDCHR 6068
Cooltempo / Apr '94 / EMI.

PENETRATE DEEPER
Cassa de x: Elastic Reality / Moment of truth: Transeau, Brian / Lonely winter: Watergate / High frequency: Quench / Feel the fire: Daniel, Naomi / Relativity: Transeau, Brian / After hours: Quench / Feeling (deep feeling): Moods / Dream: Prana / Tmot: Transeau, Brian
CD _____ TRIUK 003CD
Tribal UK / Jan '95 / Vital.

PENSIONERS ON ECSTACY
CD _____ CRECD 082
Creation / Nov '90 / 3MV / Vital.

PENT HOUSE CONCEPT
CD _____ 15205
Laserlight / Aug '91 / Target/BMG.

PENTHOUSE CULTURE CENTRE
CD _____ PHRICD 28
Penthouse / Jan '96 / Jetstar.

PENTHOUSE SAMPLER VOL. 1
CD _____ PHCD 22
Penthouse / Aug '93 / Jetstar.

PEPPERMINT STICK PARADE
CD _____ BUS 10012
Bus Stop / May '95 / Vital.

PERCUSSIONS D'AMERIQUE LATINE
Butucada au carnaval de Rio / Tehuantepec / Cumbia cienaguera / El hombre celoso / Conga au carnival de Santiago de Cuba / Janitzio / Josefa Matia / La llorona / El Ferrocarril de Los Altos / Bateria a Salvador de Bahia / Cancion mixteca / Mapale / El rey Quiche / Descarga barbacoana / Bateria au carnaval de Manaus / Currulao / Chiapas
CD _____ ARN 64023
Arion / '88 / Discovery / ADA.

PERFECT INSTRUMENTAL COLLECTION
CD _____ HRCD 8048
Disky / Dec '93 / THE / BMG / Discovery / Pinnacle.

PERFECT INSTRUMENTAL COLLECTION 2
CD _____ DCD 5253
Disky / Aug '95 / THE / BMG / Discovery / Pinnacle.

PERFECT INSTRUMENTAL LOVE ALBUM
CD _____ CNCD 5993 VT
Disky / Feb '94 / THE / BMG / Discovery / Pinnacle.

PERFECTION - A PERFECTO COMPILATION
CD _____ 0630123482
Perfecto/East West / Oct '95 / Warner Music.

PERFECTO MIXES
Even better than the real thing: U2 / Unfinished sympathy: Massive Attack / U R the best thing: D Ream / Move any mountain: Shamen / World: New Order / Something got me started: Simply Red / Human nature: Clail, Gary / Single: Rise / Doggy dogg world: Snoop Doggy Dogg / Hand in hand: Opus III / Waterfall: Stone Roses / Where love lives: Limerick, Alison / Colour my life: M People / Money love: Cherry, Neneh / Suicide blonde: INXS
CD _____ 4509981312
Perfecto/East West / Oct '94 / Warner Music.

PERSIAN LOVE SONGS
CD _____ LYRCD 7235
Lyrichord / '91 / Roots / ADA / CM.

PERSIAN NIGHTS
CD _____ 340552CD
Koch / Jul '95 / Koch.

PERU
CD _____ G 7501
Sterns / '87 / Sterns / CM.

PERU - HUAYNO, VALSE CREOLE & MARIERA
CD _____ PS 65133CD
Playasound / Jul '94 / Harmonia Mundi / ADA.

PERUVIAN HARPS AND GUITARS
CD _____ PS 65158
Playasound / Dec '95 / Harmonia Mundi / ADA.

PHASE ONE
Void: Exoterix / De niro: Disco Evangelists / Critical: Wall Of Sound / Drop the rock: D-Tek / So in love: Cheeks, Judy / Cosmik byelaw: Disco Evangelists / Give me love: Diddy / Beautiful people: Tucker, Barbara / Raise: Hyper Go Go / I like to move it: Reel 2 Real
CD _____ CDTIVA 1002
Positiva / Mar '94 / EMI.

PHAT JAMS 2
CD _____ EXCDP 4
Debut / Jul '95 / Pinnacle / 3MV / Sony.

PHILADELPHIA CLASSICS
Love is the message: MFSB / Sound of Philadelphia: MFSB & Three Degrees / Dirty ol' man: Three Degrees / I love music: O'Jays / Don't leave me this way: Melvin, Harold & The Bluenotes / Love train: O'Jays / I'll always love my mama: Intruders / Bad luck: Melvin, Harold & The Bluenotes
CD _____ 9833372
Pickwick/Sony Collector's Choice / Oct '93 / Carlton Home Entertainment / Pinnacle / Sony.

PHILADELPHIA SOUL CLASSICS VOL.1
CD _____ STCD 1000
Disky / Jun '93 / THE / BMG / Discovery / Pinnacle.

PHILLY DUST KREW
CD _____ TOODAMNY 52
Too Damn Hype / Feb '95 / SRD.

PHILO SO FAR: 20TH ANNIVERSARY FOLK SAMPLER
CD _____ AN 12
Rounder / Apr '94 / CM / Direct / ADA / Cadillac.

PHOENIX PANORAMA
How about me (pretty baby): Johnson, Jimmy / It's you, you, you: Spellman, Jimmy / Give me some of yours: Spellman, Jimmy / Cat Daddy: Johnson, Jimmy / Lover man: Spellman, Jimmy / Mama Lou: Burnam, Buzz / Time wounds all heels: Clingman, Loy / Don't hate me: Lane, Jack / Wings: Combo, Copa / Queen of hearts: Adair, Ronnie / Mr. Blues (in my shadow): Lane, Jack / Whisper to me: Silvers, Johnny / Five more miles to folsom: Hardin, Doug / King fool: Lane, Jack / Blue and lonesome mood: Silvers, Johnny / Talk to me: Hardin, Doug / All through the night: Lane, Jack / Restless: Lane, Jack / Blue I am: Rollins, Don / That's the way it happened: Rollins, Don / Other woman: Rollins, Don / Other woman (demo): Rollins, Don / If I'm wrong (demo): Rollins, Don / Don't hate me (demo): Rollins, Don / Good bartender (demo): Rollins, Don / Mirror mirror (demo): Rollins, Don / Crazy arms: Lee, Garry / Lady in John's flagpole rock: Roller, Long John / Hay Mama: Roller, Long John / If I'm wrong: Owens, Donnie / Need you: Owens, Donnie / Tomorrow: Owens, Donnie / Shy: Perkins, Dal / Raindance: Self, Alvie / Where, when and how: Self, Alvie / Things I can't forget: Ryan, Ronnie / Devil's den: Turley, Duane / Long gone cat: Turley, Duane / Between midnight and dawn: Owens, Donnie / Ask me anything: Owens, Donnie / On and on: Owens, Donnie / Cry little girlie: Banta, Benny / Gotta get with it: Lemaire, Eddie / Little more wine: Hawks / I ask of you: Johnson, Miriam / Boppin' blue jeans: Leonard Bros / Do da do: Leonard Bros / Still of the night: Langford, Gerry / Tell me: Langford, Gerry / Lonely walk: Self, Alvie / Round and round: Casey, Al / Rockin' down Mexico way: Clinkscale, Jimmy / Doggone lonesome town: Lane, Barry / Rain on the mountain: Q-Zeen / There'll come a day: Wilson, Easy Deal / I don't wantcha: Wilson, Easy Deal / You're still my baby: Banta, Benny / Cruisin' central: Warner, Faron / Stop: Cole, Don / Fussin: Ray, Gerald / Panic: Ray, Gerald / I've got a girl: Smith, Gary / Shummyin': John: Roustabouts / Scotch and soda: Thome, Henry / Scarlett: Thome, Henry / I feel the blues coming on: Clingman, Loy / Li'l O'Bug: Wagoners / Ali Baba: Morgan Condello Combo / Tip: Clingman's Clan / Freshman girl, senior boy: Dansfords / Hard times: McAlisters / Saro Jane: Clingman, Loy / Silly dilly: Terry & Peggy / Cindy's crying: Gray, Jimmie / Forgotten: Versales / Nobody but you: Contessas / Gingerbread: Alan & The Alpines / Was it make believe: Essex, Herb / Bumble bee: Tads / Me, my shadow, and I: Fullylove, Leroy / I want to know: Fullylove, Leroy / Oo, what you do to me: Fullylove, Leroy / One of these days: Fullylove, Leroy / Day after day (master): Fullylove, Leroy / Man like myself: Wild Flowers / More than me: Wild Flowers / Times past: Hobbits / Top of the morning: Hobbits / Sidewalks and avenues: Second Edition / Sad now: Solid Ground / Tell her: Riffs / Don't move girl: Lost & Found / Big wave: Scallywags / Hi-fi baby: Door Knobs / For me: Destiny's Children
CD Set _____ BCDCI 15824
Bear Family / Jun '95 / Rollercoaster / Direct / CM / Swift / ADA.

PHUTURE
CD _____ PCP 194
PCP / Jul '94 / Plastic Head.

PHUTURE BEATS
(2CD Set)
CD Set _____ MM 08941802
Independence / Jan '96 / Plastic Head.

PIANO BLUES
CD _____ DOCD 5192
Blues Document / Oct '93 / Swift / Jazz Music / Hot Shot.

PIANO BLUES SERIES: DALLAS 1927-29
CD Set _____ PYCD 15
Magpie / '92 / Hot Shot.

PIANO BLUES VOL.3: VOCALION 1928-30
(Shake Your Wicked Knees)
Back in the alley / Cow cow blues / Slum gullion stomp / Texas shout / Michigan River blues / You can't come in / I'm so glad / Mexico bound blues band
CD ______ **PYCD 03**
Magpie / Oct '90 / Hot Shot.

PIANO BLUES VOL.5: POSTSCRIPT 1927-33
(Hot Box On My Mind)
CD ______ **PYCD 05**
Magpie / Apr '91 / Hot Shot.

PIANO BLUES, VOL.1: 1923-30
CD ______ **SOBCD 35112**
Story Of The Blues / Mar '92 / Koch / ADA.

PIANO BLUES, VOL.2: 1927-40
CD ______ **DOCD 5220**
Blues Document / Jan '94 / Swift / Jazz Music / Hot Shot.

PIANO BLUES, VOL.2: 1930-39
CD ______ **SOBCD 35122**
Story Of The Blues / Mar '92 / Koch / ADA.

PIANO BLUES, VOL.3: 1924-31
CD ______ **DOCD 5314**
Blues Document / Dec '94 / Swift / Jazz Music / Hot Shot.

PIANO BLUES, VOL.4: 1923-28
CD ______ **DOCD 5336**
Blues Document / May '95 / Swift / Jazz Music / Hot Shot.

PIANO BLUES, VOL.5: 1929-36
CD ______ **DOCD 5337**
Blues Document / May '95 / Swift / Jazz Music / Hot Shot.

PIANO COLLECTION
CD ______ **01934111492**
Windham Hill / Sep '95 / Pinnacle / BMG / ADA.

PIANO DISCOVERIES
(Newly Found Titles & Alt. Takes 1928-43)
CD ______ **BDCD 6045**
Blues Document / Jan '94 / Swift / Jazz Music / Hot Shot.

PIANO IN BLUES
CD ______ **157172**
Blues Collection / Feb '93 / Discovery.

PIANO MOODS
I will always love you / Have you ever really loved a woman / Stay another day / Fragile / Love can build a bridge / Miss you like crazy / Right here waiting / Back for good / No more I love you's / Get here / Think twice / Chains / Key to my life / Endless love / Best in me / Total eclipse of the heart / Whiter shade of pale / Unchained melody / Love is all around
CD ______ **3036000062**
Carlton Home Entertainment / Oct '95 / Carlton Home Entertainment.

PIANO MOODS
Chariots of fire / Way it is / (Everything) I do it for you / Song for guy / Right here waiting / Wonderful tonight / Could it be magic / Power of love / Circle of life / I wish I knew how it would feel to be free / Let it be / Hey Jude / Stars / Another day in paradise / Think twice / Air on a G String / Where do I begin / Swan lake / We've only just begun / As time goes by
CD ______ **DINCD 114**
Dino / Oct '95 / Pinnacle / 3MV.

PIANO TALK
CD ______ **ISCD 105**
Intersound / '88 / Jazz Music.

PIANO VOLUME 1
(The RCA Jazz Collection)
CD Set ______ **74321244622**
RCA / Dec '94 / BMG.

PIANOS WITH BRACES
(The Garlic & Gauloises World Of The French Accordionists)
L'accordeoniste (Singer: Edith Piaf.): *Bonel, Marc* / Balajo: *Privat, Jo* / Quand on s'promene au bord de l'eau (Singer: Jean Gabin. Film: La Belle Equipe): *Deprince, Adolphe* / Polka (Singer: Joli Pinson.): *Deprince, Adolphe* / Tout change dans la vie (Singer: Frehel) / L'ame des poetes/accordion musette: *Huard, Albert Jr.* / C'etait bien (au petit bal perdu) (Singer: Bourvil): *Lorin, Etienne* / Swing valse: *Viseur, Gus* / La Seine (Singer: Denise Ascain): *Alexander, Maurice* / La fete des as: *Azzola, Marcel* / La guinguette a ferme ses volets (With Pierre Chagnon & His Orchestra): *Damia* / Vents d'automne: *Carrara, Emile* / Le plus beau tango du monde (With George Sellers & His 'Marseilles Jazz'.): *Sims, Alibert & Gaby* / Song from Moulin Rouge: *Azzola, Marcel* / Dede de Montmartre: *Prejean, Albert* / Joyeux canari: *Roussel, Gilbert* / Une robe valsait (Includes Marcel Azzola, Andre Astier, Andre & Louis Damergue.): *Paris Accordion Quartet* / Boum: *Vaissade, Jean* / Sous les toits de Paris: *Alexander, Maurice* / Le diable de la Bastille (Singer: Edith Piaf.): *Bonel, Marc*
CD ______ **CDEMS 1400**
EMI / May '91 / EMI.

PICADILLY STORY, THE
Crazy mixed up kid: *Brown, Joe & The Bruvvers* / Half of my heart: *Ford, Emile* / There, I've said it again: *Saxon, Al* / Honest I do: *Storm, Danny* / Z-cars: *Keating, Johnny* / Don't come cryin' to me: *Jones, Davy* / Picture of you: *Brown, Joe & The Bruvvers* / Rivers run dry: *Hill, Vince* / I knew it all the time: *Hill, Vince* / It might as well rain until September: *De Laine Sisters* / All of me: *Lynton, Jackie* / Long gone baby: *Britten, Buddy & The Regents* / Ferryboat ride: *Cudley Dudley* / Walk right in: *Kestrels* / Hey Paula: *Elaine & Derick* / Heavenly: *Eager, Vince* / Let's make a habit: *Guv'nors* / Ain't gonna kiss ya: *Jackson, Simone* / He's so near: *Douglas, Donna* / Tip of my tongue: *Quickly, Tommy* / Don't lie to me: *Jeannie & The Big Guys* / To know her is to love her: *Storme, Robb & Whispers* / He don't want your love anymore: *Doll, Linda & the Sundowners* / Is it true: *D, Tony & the Shakeouts* / Sally go round the roses: *Remo Four* / Where did our love go: *Jay, Peter & The Jaywalkers* / Cast your fate to the wind: *Sounds Orchestral* / Don't cry for me: *Peters, Mark* / You've lost that lovin' feelin': *Ann, Barbara* / Girl who wanted fame: *Wackers* / Baby do it: *McKenna, Val* / Lonely room: *Ryder, Mal & the Spirits* / Poor man's son: *Rockin' Berries* / She's about a mover: *Britten, Buddy & The Regents* / Tossin' and turnin': *Ivy League* / Take a heart: *Sorrows* / Leave my baby alone: *Britt* / Leave it to me: *Band Of Angels* / That's my life (my love and my home): *Lennon, Freddie* / Why don't I run away from you: *Antoinette* / Ask the lonely: *Rio, Bobby* / I know (you don't love me no more): *Felders Orioles* / You don't know like I know: *Powell, Keith & Billie Davis* / Dear Mrs. Applebee: *Garrick, David* / Ain't that peculiar: *Loving Kind* / Whatever will be will be (Que sera sera): *Washington, Geno & The Ram Jam Band* / Ain't love good, ain't love proud: *James, Jimmy & The Vagabonds* / It keeps rainin': *Powell, Keith & The Valets* / Run to the door: *Ford, Clinton* / 98.6: *Bystanders* / I'll always love you: *Time Box* / Almost but not quite there: *Traffic Jam*
CD ______ **NEDCD 240**
Sequel / Oct '93 / BMG.

PICCADILLY NIGHTS
(British Dance Bands Of The 1920's)
That girl over there / Swing on the gait / It's a million to one you're in love / What'll you do / Make my cot where the cot-cot-cotton grows / How long has this been going on / Miss Annabelle Lee / Lila / That's my weakness now / Sunny skies / Matilda Matilda / Saskatchewan / There's a blue ridge round my heart Virginia / 'S wonderful / Crazy rhythm / I'm a one man girl / Spread a little happiness / Out of the dawn / Ida, sweet as apple cider / I don't know why I do it but I do
CD ______ **DHAL 17**
Halcyon / Sep '93 / Jazz Music / Wellard / Swift / Harmonia Mundi / Cadillac.

PICK AND MIX
Higher sun: *Moom* / Time to fly: *Aardvarks* / Ease it: *Suicidal Flowers* / Gil: *Kava Kava* / Corcucopia: *Steppes* / Of the first water: *Sons of Selina* / Tribal elders: *Riff, Nick* / Let the powers: *Nova Express* / Dissolving: *Treatment* / Watching the sky: *Kryptasthesie* / Annihilation: *Omnia Opera* / Inner days: *Nukli* / Solstice song: *Mandagora* / Voyage 34: *Porcupine Tree* / Warmth within: *Dead Flowers* / Psychomuzak: *Extasie* / Root verses of the six bardos: *Liberation Through Hearing* / Goat faced girl: *Zuvuya* / Nindia: *Electric Orange* / Arc of ascent: *Bazaar, Saddar* / Ormithology: *Praise Space Electric* / Can you play: *Praise Space Electric* / Ornithology: *Praise Space Electric* / Purple haze: *Boris & His Bolshie Balalaika* / Gospel according to I.E.M.: *Incredible Expanding Mindfuck*
CD Set ______ **DELECCDD 023**
Delerium / Oct '95 / Vital.

PICTURE YOURSELF BELLY DANCING
CD ______ **MCD 71780**
Monitor / Sep '93 / CM.

PICTURES IN THE SKY
(Rubble Seven)
Pictures in the sky: *Orange Seaweed* / Real life permanent: *Orange Machine* / So sad inside: *Onyx* / My world fell down: *Ivy League* / Better make up your mind: *Koobas* / Within the night: *Velvett Fogg* / You didn't have to be so nice: *Glass Menagerie* / Jump and dance: *Carnaby* / Flying machine: *Flying Machine* / Cloudy: *Factotums* / I'm a hog for you: *Grant Erky/Earwigs*
CD ______ **DOCD 1997**
Drop Out / Mar '91 / Pinnacle.

PIECES OF A DREAM
Flesh: *Tour De Force* / All I'm livin' for: *Drive, She Said* / Heart of mine: *Legs Diamond* / Closer to heaven: *F.M.* / Moonlight: *Lillian Axe* / Attracted: *Romeo's Daughter* / Hard to hold: *Drive, She Said* / Tears: *From The Fire* / Only the strong survive: *F.M.* / True believer: *Lillian Axe* / Be the one: *Legs Diamond* / Inherit the wind: *Tyketto*
CD ______ **CDMFN 165**
Music For Nations / Aug '94 / Pinnacle.

PILGRIM, THE
Himlico's map / Gair na gairbe / Walk in the ocean / Pilgrim / Columcille's farewell to Ireland / Land of the picts / Iona / Briochan and columba / Storm at sea / Whita waves foam over / Ymadawiad Arthur / St Manchans prayer / Samson peccator episcopus / St Mathews point / Danse plin / Bal plin / Danse an dro / Santiago / Vigo / Deer's cry / God be with me / A'ghrian
CD ______ **TARACD 3032**
Tara / Aug '94 / CM / ADA / Direct / Conifer.

PILLOW TALK
Pillow talk: *Sylvia* / Be thankful for what you've got: *DeVaughan, William* / Sad sweet dreamer: *Sweet Sensation* / Girls: *Moments* / Stay with me baby: *Redding, Wilma* / Can't get by without you: *Real Thing* / So sad the song: *Knight, Gladys & The Pips* / There it is: *Shalamar* / Red red wine: *James, Jimmy* / Loving you - losing you: *Hyman, Phyllis* / It's a love thing: *Whispers* / Suspicious minds: *Staton, Candi* / Betcha by golly wow: *Hyman, Phyllis & Michael Henderson* / Come back and finish what you started: *Knight, Gladys & The Pips* / You'll never know: *Hi-Gloss* / Have you seen her: *Chi-Lites* / Valentine love: *Connors, Norman* / You gave me love: *Crown Heights Affair*
CD ______ **TRTCD 117**
TrueTrax / Feb '96 / THE.

PILLOWS AND PRAYERS
(A Cherry Red Compilation 1982-83)
Portrait: *Five Or Six* / Eine symphonie des grauns: *Monochrome Set* / All about you: *Leer, Thomas* / Plain sailing: *Thorn, Tracey* / Some things don't matter: *Watt, Ben* / Love in your heart: *Pillows & Prayers* / Modi 2: *Milesi, Pierro* / Compulsion: *Crow, Joe* / Lazy ways: *Marine Girls* / My face is on fire: *Felt* / No noise: *Eyeless In Gaza* / Xoyo: *Passage* / On my mind: *Everything But The Girl* / Bang and a wimpey: *Attila The Stockbroker* / I unseen: *Misunderstood* / Don't blink: *Nightingales* / Stop the music for a minute: *Crisp, Quentin*
CD ______ **CDMRED 41**
Cherry Red / Jun '88 / Pinnacle.

PINARENO
CD ______ **PIR 372**
Piranha / Oct '92 / SRD.

PIONEER CHRISTMAS
Mistletoe and wine / Frosty the snowman / Step into Christmas / Christmas song / Last Christmas / Stop the cavalry / Lonely this Christmas / Rockin' around the Christmas tree / Blue Christmas / Santa Claus is coming to town / Winter wonderland / Wonderful Christmas time / I saw Mommy kissing Santa Claus / White Christmas
CD ______ **CDMFP 6178**
Music For Pleasure / Nov '95 / EMI.

PIONEERS OF THE BOUNCING BEAT
CD ______ **EFFS 1001CD**
CD ______ **EFFS 1001CDR**
Effective / Oct '94 / Empire / Pinnacle / Amato Disco.

PIPES & DRUMS OF IRELAND
CD ______ **925592**
Buda / Jun '93 / Discovery / ADA.

PIPES & DRUMS OF SCOTLAND
CD ______ **EUCD 1213**
ARC / Sep '93 / ARC Music / ADA.

PIPES & STRINGS OF SCOTLAND
CD ______ **CD ITV 362**
Scotdisc / Dec '86 / Duncans / Ross / Conifer.

PITCH BOGKEMANIA, THE
CD ______ **MONCD 001**
Montana (Jetstar) / Jan '93 / Jetstar.

PITCH, THE
CD ______ **MONCD 001**
Montana / Mar '93 / Jetstar.

PLACE IN THE SUN, A
CD ______ **CRECD 088**
Creation / May '94 / 3MV / Vital.

PLANET DUB
CD Set ______ **BARKCD 015**
Planet Dog / Oct '95 / 3MV / Vital.

PLANET LONDON
High on life: *Sugar Foot* / Let go: *Sound Advice* / Cactus water: *Essen* / J.J.: *Essen* / What you say: *Xangbetos* / Look no further: *Curran, Paul* / First you say you will: *Fumi* / Honeychild: *Shanakies* / Happy people: *Foggis de Taxi Pata Pata* / Call: *Afrobloc*
CD ______ **TNGCD 002**
Tongue 'n' Groove / Oct '93 / Vital.

PLANET SKA
CD ______ **PHZCD 57**
Unicorn / Feb '95 / Plastic Head.

PLANETE BLUES
Della Mae: *Hooker, John Lee* / Hound dog: *Thornton, Willie Mae* / Stormy Monday blues: *Walker, T-Bone* / Diddy wah diddy: *Diddley, Bo* / Key to the highway: *Waters, Muddy* / Wang dang doodle: *Howlin' Wolf* / Crazy for my baby: *Dixon, Willie & Memphis Slim* / Dimples: *Canned Heat* / You can't judge a book by the cover: *Diddley, Bo* / I'm your witch doctor: *Mayall, John* / Boom boom: *Williams, Sonny Boy & The Animals* / Mannish boy: *Waters, Muddy* / Red rooster: *Howlin' Wolf* / Good morning little school girl: *Winter, Johnny* / Steelin': *Beck, Jeff* / Tribute to Elmore: *Beck, Jeff* / I'm a man: *Yardbirds* / Black magic woman: *Fleetwood Mac* / Hoochie coochie man: *Waters, Muddy* / New York City: *Yardbirds* / What kind of man is this: *Taylor, Koko* / Worried life blues: *Berry, Chuck* / Constipation blues: *Hawkins, Screamin' Jay*
CD ______ **GUMBOCD 003**
Cooking Vinyl / Jan '93 / Vital.

PLANETE RAI
Let me cry: *Mami, Cheb* / La Camel: *Khaled, Cheb* / N'sel fik: *Fadela, Chaba* / Sel dem drai: *Kada, Cheb* / Dawili Mali: *Tati, Cheb* / Ana Mazel: *Mami, Cheb* / Rani Meute: *Kada, Cheb* / Zini: *Rai, Raina* / Kutche: *Khaled, Cheb* / Gouloulima: *Zahouania, Chaba* / El awama: *Kada, Cheb* / Rih el gharei: *Moumen, Cheb* / Chabba bent: *Khaled, Cheb* / Douha alia: *Mami, Cheb*
CD ______ **GUMBOCD 004**
Cooking Vinyl / Jan '93 / Vital.

PLANETE ROCK 'N' ROLL
CD Set ______ **302129**
Total / May '94 / Total/BMG.

PLATIPUS RECORDS VOL.2
CD ______ **PLAT 20CD**
Platipus / Nov '95 / SRD.

PLAY ME A POLKA
CD ______ **ROUCD 6029**
Rounder / Dec '94 / CM / Direct / ADA / Cadillac.

PLAY ME THE BLUES
CD ______ **PBCD 101**
Panther / Feb '91 / Sony.

PLAY NEW ROSE FOR ME
CD ______ **ROSE 100CD**
New Rose / Jan '87 / Direct / ADA.

PLAY THAT AMERICAN JUKEBOX
Wake up little Susie: *Everly Brothers* / Hello Mary Lou: *Nelson, Rick* / C'mon everybody: *Cochran, Eddie* / Ain't that a shame: *Domino, Fats* / Dreamin': *Burnette, Johnny Rock 'N' Roll Trio* / Venus: *Avalon, Frankie* / Poetry in motion: *Tillotson, Johnny* / It might as well rain until September: *King, Carole* / Why do fools fall in love: *Lymon, Frankie & The Teenagers* / Unchained melody: *Baxter, Les* / Blue moon: *Marcels* / Will you still love me tomorrow: *Shirelles* / Cry me a river: *London, Julie* / Run to him (CD only.): *Vee, Bobby* / Let the good times roll (CD only.): *Shirley & Lee* / Let's turkey trot (CD only.): *Little Eva* / It's late (CD only.): *Nelson, Rick* / Surf City (CD only.): *Jan & Dean* / Summertime blues: *Cochran, Eddie* / Twenty four hours from Tulsa: *Pitney, Gene* / Don't ever change: *Crickets* / Locomotion: *Little Eva* / Be bop a lula: *Vincent, Gene* / Blueberry Hill: *Domino, Fats* / You got what it takes: *Johnson, Marv* / You're sixteen: *Burnette, Johnny Rock 'N' Roll Trio* / Donna: *Valens, Ritchie* / Party doll: *Knox, Buddy* / Willie and the hand jive: *Otis, Johnny Show* / Bye bye love: *Everly Brothers* / Surfin' USA: *Beach Boys* / Poor little fool: *Nelson, Rick* / Take good care of my baby: *Vee, Bobby* / That old black magic (CD only.): *Prima, Louis & Keely Smith* / Shout (CD only.): *Isley Brothers* / Walk don't run (CD only.): *Ventures* / Tears on my pillow (CD only.): *Imperials* / I'm in love (CD only.): *Domino, Fats*
CD Set ______ **CDDL 1212**
Music For Pleasure / Nov '91 / EMI.

PLAYING FOR LOVE
CD ______ **BLR 84 026**
L&R / May '91 / New Note.

PLAYING HARD TO GET
(West Coast Girls)
You're so fine: *Berry, Dorothy* / Little bit of soap: *Carroll, Yvonne* / Stop shovin' me around: *Delicates* / Dreamworld: *Loren, Donna* / Crying on my pillow: *Berry, Dorothy* / He's a big deal: *Medina, Renee* / Goodbye Jimmie: *Berry, Panda* / You haven't seen nothing: *Young, Dee Dee* / Don't mess around with me: *Sister Rachel* / Nothing to write home about: *Francettes* / Love bells: *Galens* / Date bait: *Maxwell, Diane* / You better watch out boy: *Accents* / Chinese lanterns: *Galens* / Boy I love: *Medina, Renee* / Write me a letter: *Blossoms* / I've been hurt: *Delicates* / How long must this fool pay: *Carroll, Yvonne* / I'll wait: *Blossoms* / I want to get married: *Delicates* / Search is over: *Blossoms* / Hard to get: *Blossoms* / Come on everybody: *Delicates* / I gotta tell it: *Blossoms* / Big talkin' Jim: *Blossoms* / Mr. Loveman: *Carroll, Yvonne* / Comin' down with love: *Delicates* / Muscle bustle: *Loren, Donna*
CD ______ **CDCHD 559**
Ace / May '95 / Pinnacle / Cadillac / Complete/Pinnacle.

PLAYING THE BLUES
Still got the blues (for you): *Moore, Gary* / Boom boom: *Hooker, John Lee* / Down in Mississippi: *Staples, Pops* / Trouble blues: *Hammond, John* / Too many cooks: *Evans, Terry* / I'll be good: *Washington, Walter 'Wolfman'* / Back to my baby: *Sanne* / Iceman: *Collins, Albert* / Green all over: *Jumpin' The Gunn* / Witchin' moon: *McCray, Larry* / Too early to tell: *Kinsey Report* / She

likes to boogie real low: *Winter, Johnny* / Rule the world: *Robillard, Duke*
CD _____ CDVIP 130
Virgin / Oct '94 / EMI.

PLAYING WITH FIRE
Reel *Beatrice/Abbey* reel / Sprig of Shillelagh/Planxty penny / Two reels / Lord Gordon's reel / Foggy dew / Copper plate / Waltz from Orsa / In and out the harbour / Rolling waves/Market town/Scatter the mud / Jenny's welcome to Charlie/Father Francis Cameron / Marquis of Huntly / Con Cassidy's and Nelly O'Boyle's highland reels / Gavotten / Walkin' o' the Fauld / Carraigin ruadh / Curlew/McDermott's reel/Three scones of Boxty
CD _____ GLCD 1101
Green Linnet / Feb '93 / Roots / CM / Direct / ADA.

PLEASURES AND TREASURES
(A Kaleidoscope of Sound)
March by Mr Handel (Boxwood clarinet.): *Hacker, Alan* / Mira O Norma. Polyphon musical box / Jean's reel (Northumbrian small pipes.): *Tickell, Kathryn* / Lezghinka: *Best Of Brass* / Prelude to lute suite in E major (Baroque lute.): *North, Nigel* / Colette (From 78rpm record.): *Whiteman, Paul & His Orchestra* / John come kiss me now (English concertina): *Townsend, Dave* / Music from Compline (Plainsong): *Stanbrook Abbey Nuns & Prinknash Abbey Monks* / Le coucou (Ivory flute): *Preston, Stephen* / Whistling Rufus (Handbells): *Sound In Brass Handbells* / Limerick's lamentation (Celtic harp): *Monger, Eileen* / La quinte estampie real (Treble shawm): *Canter, Robin* / I've got a lovely bunch of coconuts: *Barrel Organ* / Love at the fair (Chinese Er-hu): *Jing Ying Soloists* / Miss Annabelle Lee: *Pianola Roll* / Scherzo (Stradivarius violin): *Holmes, Ralph* / Wibbly wobbly walk (Phonograph cylinder): *Charman, Jack* / Jenny Lind medley (Hammer dulcimer): *Couza, Jim* / Turkish rondo (Viennese fortepiano): *Burnett, Richard* / O Sanctissima (Pan pipes and organ): *Schmitt, Georges* / Reve gourmand (French accordion): *Pauly, Danielle* / Sportive little trifler (English glee with serpents): *Canterbury Clerkes & London Serpent Trio*
CD _____ CDSDLC 362
Saydisc / Sep '86 / Harmonia Mundi / ADA / Direct.

PLEASURES IN LIFE
CD _____ NB 020CD
Nuclear Blast / Dec '90 / Plastic Head.

PLUS FROM US
Obiero: *Ogada, Ayub* / Keep on marching: *Meters* / Oasis: *Hammill, Peter* / Pine tree and on the street: *Pokrovsky, Dmitri* / Best friend paranoia: *Orbit, William* / Lone bear: *Levin, Tony* / Morecambe bay: *Gifford, Alex* / Down by the river: *Rhodes, David* / Triennale: *Eno, Brian* / Rose rhythm: *Serra, Eric* / Silence: *Katche, Manu* / Baladi we hetta: *Ramzy, Hossam* / Dreams: *Shankar 'N' Caroline* / Suheyla: *Erguner, Kudsi* / El Conquistador: *Lanois, Daniel*
CD _____ CDRW 33
Realworld / May '93 / EMI / Sterns.

POETRY PUT TO SONG
CD _____ 7992382
Hispavox / Jan '95 / ADA.

POETRY PUT TO SONG
CD _____ 7996512
Hispavox / Jun '94 / ADA.

POINTS WEST
(New Horizons In Country Music)
CD _____ HCD 8021
Hightone / Oct '94 / ADA / Koch.

POLISH VILLAGE MUSIC 1927-1933
CD _____ ARHCD 7031
Arhoolie / Jun '95 / ADA / Direct / Cadillac.

POLYPHONIC CHANTS OF THE MONGO PEOPLE
CD _____ C 580050
Ocora / Sep '93 / Harmonia Mundi / ADA.

POLYPHONIES OF THE SOLOMON ISLANDS
CD _____ LDX 274663
La Chant Du Monde / Nov '90 / Harmonia Mundi / ADA.

POLYPHONIES VOCALES
(Music From Albania)
CD _____ W 260065
Inedit / Dec '95 / Harmonia Mundi / ADA / Discovery.

POLYPHONY FOR HOLY WEEK
(Religious Vocal Music From Sardinia)
CD _____ LDX 274936
La Chant Du Monde / Jul '92 / Harmonia Mundi / ADA.

POLYPHONY OF SVANETI
CD _____ LDX 274990
La Chant Du Monde / May '94 / Harmonia Mundi / ADA.

POLYPHONY OF THE DORZE
(Ethiopia)
CD _____ 2746461
La Chant Du Monde / Jan '95 / Harmonia Mundi / ADA.

POMELO 01 COMPILATION
CD Set _____ POM 01CD
Pomelo / Jul '94 / Plastic Head.

POP CLASSICS
CD _____ ARC 944422
Arcade / Dec '90 / Sony / Grapevine.

POP CLASSICS
Born to be wild: *Steppenwolf* / Sweet home Alabama: *Lynyrd Skynyrd* / Don't believe a word: *Moore, Gary* / Broken wings: *Mr. Mister* / Saturday night: *Brood, Herman* / Radio girl: *Hiatt, John* / L.B. Boogie: *Livin' Blues* / Lola: *Kinks* / American woman: *Guess Who* / We built this city: *Starship* / Radio Africa: *Latin Quarter* / Rocky mountain way: *Walsh, Joe* / Feelin' alright: *Mason, Dave* / Elvira: *Oak Ridge Boys* / Woodstock: *Matthew's Southern Comfort* / Joy to the world: *Three Dog Night*
CD _____ MCD 30199
Ariola Express / Mar '94 / BMG.

POP CLASSICS
CD _____ DSPCD 105
Disky / Sep '93 / THE / BMG / Discovery / Pinnacle.

POP HIGHLIGHTS
CD Set _____ 4417302
Pilz / Oct '92 / BMG.

POP HITS DELUXE
CD _____ HRCD 8042
Disky / Jul '94 / THE / BMG / Discovery / Pinnacle.

POP HITS GO ON
CD _____ MU 5051
Musketeer / Oct '92 / Koch.

POP HITS OF THE 60'S
CD _____ PWKS 4181
Carlton Home Entertainment / Nov '94 / Carlton Home Entertainment.

POP INSIDE THE 60'S VOL.3
CD _____ SEECD 400
See For Miles/C5 / Jun '94 / Pinnacle.

POP INSIDE THE SIXTIES
Some things just stick in your mind: *Vashti* / Love hit me: *Orchids* / Sleepy city: *Mighty Avengers* / You came along: *Warriors* / Don't make me blue: *Warriors* / Mirror mirror: *Pinkerton's Assorted Colours* / Magic rocking horse: *Pinkerton's Assorted Colours* / I can make it with you: *Douglas, Rob & Dean* / Now it's my turn: *Gunn, Jon* / I just made up my mind: *Gunn, Jon* / Till you say you'll be mine: *Newton-John, Olivia* / For ever: *Newton-John, Olivia* / Give her my love: *Marriott, Steve* / Yes I do: *Wilson, Tony* / Lost without you: *Wilson, Tony* / Lovingly yours: *Mockingbirds* / Lost without Linda: *Essex, David* / Acapulco 1922: *Great, Johnny B* / Girl don't make me wait: *Timebox* / Yellow van: *Timebox*
CD _____ SEECD 386
See For Miles/C5 / Oct '93 / Pinnacle.

POP INSIDE THE SIXTIES VOL. 2
Uncle Willie: *Money, Zoot* / Long tall shorty: *Bond, Graham Organisation* / I'll cry instead: *Cocker, Joe* / Good morning little school girl: *Stewart, Rod* / Money: *Elliott, Bern & The Fenmen* / Buckleshoe stomp: *Snobs* / Just one more chance: *Outer Limits* / London boys: *Bowie, David* / Say you don't mind: *Laine, Denny* / Will you be my lover tonight: *Bean, George* / Surprise surprise: *Lulu* / Now I know: *Beat Chics* / We love the Beatles: *Vernons Girls* / Like dreamers do: *Applejacks* / That's alright mama: *Gonks* / What's new pussycat: *Crying Shames* / Please Mr. Postman: *Elliott, Bern & The Fenmen* / No response: *Hep Stars* / St. James Infirmary: *Gypps 'n' Robbers* / You're on my mind: *Birds* / Lonely weekends: *Bean, George* / Kansas city: *Jay, Peter & The Jaywalkers* / Long legged baby: *Bond, Graham Organisation* / Shang a doo lang: *Posta, Adrienne* / Caroline: *Fortunes* / There got you: *Ryan, Paul & Barry*
CD _____ SEECD 399
See For Miles/C5 / Mar '94 / Pinnacle.

POP MUSIC FROM AFRICA PART 1
CD _____ 15285
Laserlight / '91 / Target/BMG.

POP MUSIC FROM AFRICA PART 2
CD _____ 15286
Laserlight / '91 / Target/BMG.

POP RAI & RACHIO STYLE
CD _____ OVERview 15
Earthworks / Mar '90 / EMI / Sterns.

POP SINGERS ON THE AIR
(Four Complete Broadcasts 1943/58)
CD _____ CDMR 1149
Radiola / Apr '91 / Pinnacle.

POP XMAS
Do they know it's Christmas: *Band Aid* / Have yourself a merry little Christmas: *Williams, Vanessa* / Step into Christmas: *John, Elton* / Silent night: *Bryant, Sharon* / Spaceman came travelling: *De Burgh, Chris* / Funky Christmas: *Sease, Marvin* / Christmas rapping: *Blow, Kurtis* / My Christmas: *Tony Toni Tone* / Christmas song: *Phillips, Shawn* / Merry Christmas everybody: *Metal Gurus* / Winter's tale: *Essex, David* / Christmas day: *Squeeze* / Rent a santa: *Hill, Chris* / It may be winter outside: *Love Unlimited Orchestra*

CD _____ 5504162
Spectrum/Karussell / Nov '94 / PolyGram / THE.

POPCORN'S DETROIT SOUL PARTY
Nothing no sweeter: *Carlton, Carl* / Ooh boy: *Adorables* / Down in the dumps: *Hester, Tony* / Hurting: *Erik & Vikings* / Turn on the heat: *Popcorn & Soul Messengers* / Somebody stop that boy: *Boo, Betty* / Hanky panky: *Wylie, Richard 'Popcorn'* / Tell her: *Clark, Jimmy Soul* / Gotta kind a way: *Lindsay, Therese* / Mighty lover: *Ideals* / Saving all my love for you: *Popcorn Orchestra* / Spaceland: *Hester, Tony* / My baby ain't no play thing: *Harvey, Willy* / Sweet Darling: *Clark, Jimmy Soul* / Arrest me: *Thomas, Jano* / If it's all the same to you babe: *Ingram, Luther* / Nobody love me like you: *Mercer, Barbara* / Going to a happening: *Popcorn Orchestra* / I'll be your champion: *Clark, Jimmy Soul* / Let the sun shine in your window: *Mann, Columbus* / Cool off: *Detroit Executives* / You knew what you was gettin': *Williams, Juanita* / G I Joe we love you: *Fantasions*
CD _____ GSCD 059
Goldmine / Nov '95 / Vital.

POPSICLES AND ICICLES
(Early Girls Vol.1)
Doo wah diddy: *Exciters* / You're no good: *Everett, Betty* / Name game: *Ellis, Shirley* / Chains: *Cookies* / It might as well rain until September: *King, Carole* / I'm into something good: *Earl Jean* / I can't stay mad at you: *Davis, Skeeter* / I wish I were a princess: *March, Little Peggy* / I told every little star: *Scott, Linda* / Triangle: *Grant, Janie* / West of the wall: *Fisher, Toni* / Pink shoelaces: *Stevens, Dodie* / Music music music: *Sensations* / Dear Abby: *Hearts* / Whenever a teenager cries: *Reparata & The Delrons* / I love how you love me: *Paris Sisters* / Dark moon: *Guitar, Bonnie* / You: *Aquatones* / Till: *Angels* / Great pretender: *Young, Kathy* / Angel baby: *Rosie & The Originals* / Eddie my love: *Teen Queens* / He's gone: *Chantels* / Dedicated to the one I love: *Shirelles* / Son in law: *Blossoms* / Easier said than done: *Essex*
CD _____ CDCHD 608
Ace / Sep '95 / Pinnacle / Cadillac / Complete/Pinnacle.

POPTARTZ
Movin to music: *Finito* / My love: *Shades Of Rhythm* / DJ Dubs: *Lock, Eddie* / We got the love: *Erik* / Comes over me: *Stylofoam* / Mooncat: *Shaker* / Changeling: *Tan Ru* / Move and groove: *Basement Of Sound* / Raise the feeling: *Shades Of Rhythm* / Protein: *Tata Box Inhibitors* / Storm: *Space Kittens* / Let the fun begin: *Fluffy Toy IQ* / Think about it: *Stylofoam* / Do me: *Aquarius* / Electroluv: 4th Wave / Hideaway: *De'Lacy* / Deliver me: *Urban Blues Project* / Feeling: *Jasper Street Co* / One love: *Coccoluto, Claudio* / I won't waste your time: *Joi & Jorio* / Reeboot 144: *OLN* / Everlasting picture: *B-Zet* / You can't turn around: *Bottom $* / Do it to me: *Dark, Frankie* / Let no man put a sunder: *First Choice* / Welcome to the factory: *Moraes, Angela* / Work 2 do: *Roach Motel* / Dancing in the year 2000: *From The Soul* / So everybody (get off it): *Sound Design* / Club America: *Club America* / Dreamtime: *Zee* / Same thing in reverse: *Boy George* / El metro: *Disco Volante* / Joanna: *Mrs. Woods* / Fee fi fo fum: *Candy Girls* / Out come the freaks: *Lippy Lou* / Never felt this way: *Hi-Lux* / Indoctrinate: *Castle Trancelot* / Florubunda: *Mothers Pride* / Do you want me: *Mambo Chant* / Love rollercoaster: *Pooley, Ian* / Shake your body: *Ill Disco* / C'mon y'all: *Rhythm Masters* / Come together: *Double FM* / Dive: *Club 69* / Transform: *Mijangos* / Happiness (is just around the bend): *Brooklyn's Soul & Needy* / Let the rythm flow: *Diva Rhythms* / Lost in you: *Matt Bianco* / Geel good: *B-Code* / Forerunner: *Natural Born Groovers* / Who's the badman: *De Patten* / Rock 2 the beat: *RM Project* / In my brain: *Mark NRG* / Unbe: *R.A.W.* / La Casa: *Adrian & Alfared* / Energy tax: *RMS* / If we lose our lovin': *D.M.B.*
CD Set _____ REACTCD 067
React / Nov '95 / Vital.

POPULAR FOLK SONGS FROM NORTH GERMANY
CD _____ EUCD 1180
ARC / '91 / ARC Music / ADA.

POPULAR IRISH BALLADS
CD _____ MATCD 252
Castle / Apr '93 / BMG.

POPULAR MUSIC FROM ANGOLA
CD _____ SOW 90138
Sounds Of The World / Mar '95 / Target/ BMG.

POPULAR MUSIC FROM GUINEA
CD _____ SOW 90140
Sounds Of The World / Mar '95 / Target/ BMG.

POPULAR MUSIC OF CHILE
CD _____ PS 65094
Playasound / Aug '92 / Harmonia Mundi / ADA.

POPULAR PROFESSIONAL MUSICIANS OF RAJASTHAN
CD _____ C 580044
Ocora / May '94 / Harmonia Mundi / ADA.

PORTUGUESE LANDS
CD _____ PS 66003
Playasound / May '94 / Harmonia Mundi / ADA.

PORTUGUESE STRING MUSIC
CD _____ HTCD 05
Heritage / Feb '91 / Swift / Roots / Wellard / Direct / Hot Shot / Jazz Music / ADA.

POSITIVA AMBIENT COLLECTION, THE
O.O.B.E.: *Orb* / Digi out: *Infinite Wheel* / Perfect morning: *Visions Of Shiva* / Hub: *Black Dog* / Halcyon: *Orbital* / Zeroes and ones: *Jesus Jones vs The Aphex Twin* / Sky high: *Irresistable Force* / Mobility: *Moby* / Awakening the soul: *Beaumont & Hannant* / If it really is me: *Polygon Window* / Kaotic harmony: *Rhythm Is Rhythm*
CD _____ CDTIVA 1001
Positiva / Nov '94 / EMI.

POSITIVA PHASE 2
Can you feel it: *Reel 2 Real* / El trago (the drink) (Bottom dollar club mix): *2 In A Room* / Someday (Diesel & ether live & direct mix): *Eddy* / I get lifted (Underground network mix): *Tucker, Barbara* / That's the way you do it (White label mix): *Purple Kings* / Elephant paw (get down to the funk) (Ken mentra remix): *Pan Position* / It's alright (Original mix): *Hyper Go Go* / Only saw today instant karma (Cleveland City vocal mix): *Amos* / Can you feel it (Mix): *Mad Stuntman* / Reach (Brothers In Rhythm club mix): *Cheeks, Judy* / Nothing in the world (Motiv 8 mix): *Mozaic* / Put your handz up (Track orsser edit): *Whooliganz*
CD _____ CDTIVA 1004
Positiva / Nov '94 / EMI.

POSITIVA PHASE 3
As long as you're good to me: *Cheeks, Judy* / Get your hands off my man: *Vasquez, Junior* / (You bring out) The best in me: *Eddy* / Play this house: *BB Club* / Conway: *Reel 2 Real* / Stay together: *Tucker, Barbara* / I'm standing higher: *X-Static* / Let love shine: *Amos* / Raise your hands: *Reel 2 Real* / Respect: *Cheeks, Judy* / Ahora es: *2 In A Room* / Bomb: *Bucketheads* / Church of freedom: *Amos* / Sweetest day of May: *Vannelli, Joe T. Project* / Cry India: *Umboza*
CD _____ CDTIVA 1008
Positiva / Oct '95 / EMI.

POSITIVE ENERGY
CD _____ MM 800282
Moonshine / Jun '95 / Disc.

POSITIVE ROOTS RAGGA
CD _____ CDLINC 005
Lion Inc. / Mar '95 / Jetstar / SRD.

POSITIVELY ELIZABETH STREET
CD _____ CGAS 803CD
Citadel / Apr '89 / ADA.

POSSESSION & POETRY
(Vezo, Mahafaly & Masikoro From Madagascar)
CD _____ C 580046
Ocora / Nov '93 / Harmonia Mundi / ADA.

POUR CEUX QUI S'AIMENT
CD _____ DCD 5294MM
Disky / Apr '94 / THE / BMG / Discovery / Pinnacle.

POW WOW SONGS
(Songs of the Plains Indians)
Slow war dance songs / Contest songs for straight dancers / Contest songs for fancy dancers / Round dance / Sioux flag song / War dance song / Slow war dance, Vietnam song / Grass dance song
CD _____ 803432
New World / Aug '92 / Harmonia Mundi / ADA / Cadillac.

POWER & SOUL
Perfect year: *Carroll, Dina* / Come in out of the rain: *Moten, Wendy* / Get here: *Adams, Oleta* / No more tears (enough is enough): *Mazelle, Kym & Jocelyn Brown* / I will survive: *Gaynor, Gloria* / Ain't no mountain high: *Ross, Diana* / River deep, mountain high: *Turner, Tina* / Respect: *Franklin, Aretha* / Piece of my heart: *Franklin, Erma* / Help me make it through the night: *Knight, Gladys* / And I'm telling you I'm not going: *Holliday, Jennifer* / All woman: *Stansfield, Lisa* / Save the best for last: *Williams, Vanessa* / Sweet love: *Baker, Anita* / It should have been me: *Fair, Yvonne* / Stay with me baby: *Turner, Ruby* / Piano in the dark: *Russell, Brenda* / I will: *Winters, Ruby* / Superwoman: *White, Karyn* / Power of love: *Rush, Jennifer*
CD _____ 5168962
PolyGram TV / Aug '94 / PolyGram.

POWER AND THE GLORY, THE
Suicide blonde: *INXS* / Would I lie to you: *Eurythmics* / Best: *Turner, Tina* / Road to hell: *Rea, Chris* / Listen to your heart: *Roxette* / Black velvet: *Myles, Alannah* / Hard to handle: *Black Crowes* / Hey you: *Quireboys* / Blaze of glory: *Bon Jovi, Jon* / Everybody wants to rule the world: *Tears For Fears* / Good morning Britain: *Aztec Camera & Mick Jones* / Joker: *Miller, Steve* / I can't go for

that (no can do): Hall & Oates / Power of love: Lewis, Huey & The News / Love is a battlefield: Benatar, Pat / Dedication: Thin Lizzy / If right now: Free / Wind of change: Scorpions
CD _____ 5103602
Vertigo / Sep '91 / PolyGram.

POWER OF MEDIA, THE
CD _____ REACTCD 038
React / Apr '94 / Vital.

POWER PLAYS
(19 Classic Tracks)
In my chair: Status Quo / Go now: Moody Blues / No more the fool: Brooks, Elkie / Out of time: Farlowe, Chris / First cut is the deepest: Arnold, P.P. / Tin soldier: Small Faces / America: Nice / Natural born bugie: Humble Pie / Man of the world: Fleetwood Mac / Are you growing tired of my love: Status Quo / You really got me: Kinks / Strange band: Family / Love hurts: Nazareth / Iron man: Black Sabbath / Lay down (Candles in the rain): Melanie & The Edwin Hawkin Singers / In my own time: Family / It's a heartache: Tyler, Bonnie / Operator (That's not the way it feels): Croce, Jim / This flight tonight: Nazareth
CD _____ TRTCD 114
TrueTrax / Oct '94 / THE.

POWERCUTS
Money for nothing: Dire Straits / Addicted to love: Palmer, Robert / Suicide blonde: INXS / One I love: R.E.M. / Sowing the seeds of love: Tears For Fears / I don't want a lover: Texas / Loved walked in: Thunder / First cut is the deepest: Little Angels / Cocaine: Clapton, Eric / Senza una Donna: Zucchero & Paul Young / Broken wings: Mr. Mister / Power of love: Lewis, Huey & The News / All right now: Free / Hard to handle: Black Crowes / Send me an angel: Scorpions / You ain't seen nothin' yet: Bachman-Turner Overdrive / Modern girl: Meat Loaf / All night long: Rainbow
CD _____ 5154152
Polydor / May '92 / PolyGram.

POWERHOUSE
CD _____ PHCD 01
Midtown / Mar '93 / SRD.

POWERPLAY VOL.1
CD _____ FORMCD 02
Formation / Jul '94 / SRD.

PRE-WAR GOSPEL STORY 1902-44, THE
(2CD Set)
CD Set _____ BOG 21
Best Of Gospel / Nov '95 / Discovery.

PRECIOUS COLLECTION, A
Dragging me down: Inspiral Carpets / Weirdo: Charlatans / Fool's guide: Stone Roses / Twisterella: Ride / Drowners: Suede / Loaded: Primal Scream / There's no other way: Blur / Shine on: House Of Love / Sit down: James / Real real real: Jesus Jones / Make it mine: Shamen / Hit: Sugarcubes / For love: Lush / Monsters and angels: Voice Of The Beehive / Size of a cow: Wonder Stuff / Planet of sound: Pixies / Kinky love: Pale Saints / Glad: Spaghetti Head / Soon: My Bloody Valentine / Love your money: Daisy Chainsaw
CD _____ DINCD 38
Dino / Jun '92 / Pinnacle / 3MV.

PRECIOUS METAL
CD _____ TMPCD 014
Telstar / Mar '88 / BMG.

PRECIOUS WATERS, RIVER OF LIFE
Precious waters / Stormlight / Dawn / Mountain shadows / Tears of the Gods / Celebration / First snow / Where the rivers are born / Lonely birds / Shadows of eternity / Snow dreams of becoming water / Warm wind / Return of the sun / Falling water / First sun on the winter ice / Melting waters / In the mountain lake / Raging waters / Desert call / Through the parched land / Flowing toward heaven / Desert flower / River dreams / Cycle continues
CD _____ ND 63917
Narada / May '95 / New Note / ADA.

PRELUDE - DEEP GROOVES
Come on dance, dance: Saturday Night Band / In the bush: Musique / Just let me do my thing: Sine / Check out the groove: Thurston, Bobby / Can you handle it: Redd, Sharon / You'll never know: Hi-Gloss / You're the one for me: D-Train / Body music: Strikers / Never give you up: Redd, Sharon / What I got is what you need: Unique / Love how you feel: Redd, Sharon
Music: D-Train
CD _____ NEDCD 263
Sequel / Oct '93 / BMG.

PREMIER COLLECTION OF INSTRUMENTAL HITS I
CD _____ KNEWCD 733
Disky / Apr '94 / THE / BMG / Discovery / Pinnacle.

PREMIER COLLECTION OF INSTRUMENTAL HITS II
CD _____ KNEWCD 734
Disky / Apr '94 / THE / BMG / Discovery / Pinnacle.

PREMIER COLLECTION OF INSTUMENTAL HITS III
CD _____ KNEWCD 735
Disky / Apr '94 / THE / BMG / Discovery / Pinnacle.

PRENDS DONC COURAGE: SWAMP MUSIC VOL.6
CD _____ US 0202
Trikont / Apr '95 / ADA / Direct.

PRESTIGE FIRST SESSIONS
CD _____ PCD 24115
Prestige / Dec '95 / Complete/Pinnacle / Cadillac.

PRESTIGE FUNKY BEATS
CD _____ PCD 24148
Pablo / Jun '95 / Jazz Music / Cadillac / Complete/Pinnacle.

PRESTIGE JAZZ SAMPLER
CD _____ CDRIVM 002
Riverside / Mar '88 / Jazz Music / Pinnacle / Cadillac.

PRESTIGE SOUL - JAZZ ENCYCLOPAEDIA VOL. 1
CD _____ PCD 24137
Pablo / Jun '95 / Jazz Music / Cadillac / Complete/Pinnacle.

PRESTIGE/FOLKLORE YEARS 1
(All Kinds Of folks)
New York town: Elliot, Jack / Railroad Bill: Elliot, Jack / Rollin' in my sweet baby's arms: Elliot, Jack / Duncan and Brady: Rush, Tom / Rag Mama: Rush, Tom / Barb'ry Allen: Rush, Tom / Wagoner's lad: Seeger, Peggy / Chickens they are crowing: Seeger, Peggy / Green rocky road: Van Ronk, Dave / Whoa Buck: Van Ronk, Dave / Maggie Lauder: Redpath, Jean / Fife overgate: Redpath, Jean / Joshua gone Barbados: Von Schmidt, Eric / She's like a swallow: Dobson, Bonnie / Irish exile song: Dobson, Bonnie / Long chain: Sellers, Maxine / Single girl: Sellers, Maxine / Jesus met the woman at the well: Len & Judy / This life I'm living: Len & Judy
CD _____ CDWIKD 134
Big Beat / Feb '95 / Pinnacle.

PRESTIGE/FOLKLORE YEARS 2
(The New City Blues)
Cocaine blues: Van Ronk, Dave / Death letter: Van Ronk, Dave / Red river blues: Fuller, Jesse / How long blues: Fuller, Jesse / San Francisco Bay blues: Fuller, Jesse / Sleepy man blues: Muldaur, Geoff / Aberdeen Mississippi blues: Muldaur, Geoff / Motherless child blues: Nelson, Tracy / Starting for Chicago: Nelson, Tracy / Ramblin' man: Nelson, Tracy / Crow Jane: Von Schmidt, Eric / Light rain: Von Schmidt, Eric / Kennedy blues: Von Schmidt, Eric / Orphan's blues: Rush, Tom / If you don't want me baby: Larry & Hank / Watchdog blues: Larry & Hank / Four women blues: Larry & Hank / Alberta: New Strangers
CD _____ CDWIKD 135
Big Beat / Feb '95 / Pinnacle.

PRESTIGE/FOLKLORE YEARS 3
(Roots And Branches)
Let us get together right down here: Davis, Rev. Gary / Twelve gates to the city: Davis, Rev. Gary / Maple leaf rag: Davis, Rev. Gary / Bound to lose: Holy Modal Rounders / Euphoria: Holy Modal Rounders / Crowley waltz: Holy Modal Rounders / Blues in the bottle: Holy Modal Rounders / St. Louis tickle: Van Ronk, Dave / Goodbye Maggie: Lilly Brothers / I'm coming back, but I don't know when: West, Harry & Jeanie / I'd like to be your shadow in the moonlight: West, Harry & Jeanie / Beautiful brown eyes: Charles River Valley Boys & Tex Logan / Sally Goodin: Charles River Valley Boys & Tex Logan / Uncle Penn: Charles River Valley Boys & Tex Logan / Salty dog: Keith & Rooney / Teardrops in my eyes: Keith & Rooney / Maggie rag: Greenhill, Mitch / Blues, just blues, that's all: True Endeavor Jug Band / Jug band blues: True Endeavor Jug Band / She's gone: Traum, Artie / High society: Folk Stringers / I don't feel at home in this world anymore: New Strangers
CD _____ CDWIKD 136
Big Beat / Feb '95 / Pinnacle.

PRESTIGE/FOLKLORE YEARS 4
(Singing Out Loud)
Muleskinner blues: Elliot, Jack / Night herding song: Elliot, Jack / Talking fishing blues: Elliot, Jack / Fisherman's luck: Seeger, Mike & Sonny Miller / Sally Ann: Seeger, Mike & Sonny Miller / John Henry: Seeger, Mike & Sonny Miller / Fiddler's bagpipe: Seeger, Mike & Sonny Miller / Peter Emberly: Dobson, Bonnie / First time: Dobson, Bonnie / If I had my way: Davis, Rev. Gary / Sally, where you get your liquor from: Davis, Rev. Gary / You got to move: Davis, Rev. Gary / Devil's dream: Keith & Rooney / Ain't gonna work tomorrow: Keith & Rooney / Gypsy Davey: Aaron, Tossi / I don't want your millions Mister: Seeger, Pete / Here's to Cheshire, here's to cheese: Seeger, Pete
CD _____ CDWIKD 137
Big Beat / Feb '95 / Pinnacle.

PRIDE
(The Very Best Of Scotland)
Dignity: Deacon Blue / Baker Street: Rafferty, Gerry / Vienna: Ultravox / Real gone kid: Deacon Blue / Why: Lennox, Annie /

Caledonia: Miller, Frankie / Sweet dreams (are made of this): Eurythmics / There must be an angel: Eurythmics / Inside: Stiltskin / Perfect: Fairground Attraction / Patience of angels: Reader, Eddi / Party fears two: Associates / If I was: Ure, Midge / Let's go round again: Average White Band / I can feel it: Silencers / Miracle of being: Capercaillie
CD Set _____ 74321284372
RCA / Oct '95 / BMG.

PRIDE '95
CD _____ SR 321CD
Strictly Rhythm / Jul '95 / SRD / Vital.

PRIDE OF INDEPENDENTS
CD _____ TT 6CD
Beechwood / Jun '93 / BMG / Pinnacle.

PRIDE OF THE REGIMENT
(Military Greats)
CD _____ PWK 036
Carlton Home Entertainment / '88 / Carlton Home Entertainment.

PRIMAL BLUE
Bass blues / Uno dos adios / Primal blue / Dear Ruth / Stolen moments / You go to my head
CD _____ HIBD 8006
Hip Bop / Oct '95 / Conifer / Total/BMG / Silva Screen.

PRIME CHOPS VOL. 2
(Blind Pig Sampler)
CD _____ BP 8002CD
Blind Pig / May '94 / Hot Shot / Swift / CM / Roots / Direct / ADA.

PRIME CHOPS VOL. 3
CD _____ BPCD 8003
Blind Pig / Dec '95 / Hot Shot / Swift / CM / Roots / Direct / ADA.

PRIME KUTS VOL 1
Better bring a gun: King Tee / Underwater rimes: Digital Underground / This beat be smooth: Tee, Toddy / N.Y. Rapper: Jimmy, Bobby / My posse: Ice Cube / Six in the mornin': Ice-T / Do you wanna go to the liquor store: Tee, Toddy / Payback's a mutha: King Tee / What I like: 2 Live Crew / All about money: Kool Rock Jay
CD _____ CDINS 5026
Instant / Jul '90 / Charly.

PRIME KUTS VOL 2
Gangster dope: Tee, Toddy / Dog 'n the wax: Ice-T / Coolest: King Tee / I'm about time: Kool Rock Jay / Revelation: 2 Live Crew / Let it go: Mistress & DJ Madame E / It's my turn: Dezo Daz / Ya don't quit: Ice-T / 7 A 3 will rock you: Seven A 3 / Ill legal: Ice Cube
CD _____ CDINS 5027
Instant / Jul '90 / Charly.

PRIME KUTS VOL 3
Off the top of my brain: Real MC Master Rhyme / Rhymes too funky: CMW & Old Man Conway / Vanilla don't play: Vanilla Ice / Get off your butt: Battery Brain & Vicious C / Check is in the mail: Critters & Bobby Jimmy / Mic Jack: Mistress & DJ Madame E / Jamaica funk groove: Invisible Jolly Joe / Quicksand: Quicksand / What's your name: P.G.13 & Shawn / This beat is def: A.T.C.
CD _____ CDINS 5032
Instant / Nov '90 / Charly.

PRIME NUMBERS
Beyond reality: Barnett, Thomas / Body one: Gon Man / Face bass: Sunshower / New age heart core: Trance Induction / Deep: Outerzone / Day in October: Children Of A New Generation / My nude photo: Barnett, Thomas / Robogroove flux remix: Trance Induction / Planet Earth: Zodiac Trax / Kuingia: Mad Doc
CD _____ PRIME 011CD
Prime / Sep '93 / Vital.

PRISON BLUES OF THE SOUTH
CD _____ 17026
Laserlight / Sep '94 / Target/BMG.

PRIVATE COLLECTION OF GERMAN UNDERGROUND...
CD _____ ABB 85CD
Big Cat / Apr '95 / SRD / Pinnacle.

PRIVATE DANCER
(Music Of Tina Turner - 17 Instrumental Hits)
CD _____ 5708574338097
Carlton Home Entertainment / Sep '94 / Carlton Home Entertainment.

PRIVATE SAMPLER
Homeward bound: O'Hearn, Patrick / Piece of time: Summers, Andy / Marrakesh: Tangerine Dream / Wing and a prayer: Tan Tieghem, David / Reunion: O'Hearn, Patrick / Secret agent: Yanni / Keys to imagination: Yanni / Neverland: Ciani, Suzanne / Prarambh: Shankar, Ravi / Tears of joy: Goodman, Jerry / Joy dancing: Colina, Michael / Theme of secrets: Jobson, Eddie / Times twelve: Kottke, Leo
CD _____ 259646
Arista / Aug '89 / BMG.

PRO-CANNABIS
CD _____ EFA 119662
Dope / Jun '94 / SRD.

PRODUCER'S TROPHY
CD _____ HCD 7011
Hightone / Dec '94 / ADA / Koch.

PRODUCTION HOUSE - THE ALBUM
CD _____ PRODHCD 1
Production House / Oct '93 / Jetstar / Total/BMG.

PROFESSOR JORDAN'S MAGIC SOUND SHOW
(Rubble Ten)
Tamaris Iman: Onyx / We don't kiss: Clique / Linda loves Lin: Floribunda Rose / Riding on a wave: Turnstyle / Running wild: Fresh Air / Hungry: 5 AM Event / She's a rainbow: Glass Menagerie / Buffalo: Writing On The Wall / Frederick Johnson: Glass Menagerie / Step in the right direction: Montanas / Lady Caroline: Velvett Fogg / Frosted panes: Kytes / Stay a while: Orange Seaweed / Keep on moving baby: Game / Stay indoors: New Formula / You can all join in: Orange Machine
CD _____ DOCD 1996
Drop Out / Apr '91 / Pinnacle.

PROGRAM ANIHILATOR 2
CD _____ SST 213 CD
SST / Feb '90 / Plastic Head.

PROGRESSION
Fire: Crazy World Of Arthur Brown / Strange kind of woman: Deep Purple / Little bit of love: Free / Devil's answer: Atomic Rooster / Frankenstein: Winter, Edgar / Silver machine: Hawkwind / Race with the devil: Gun / Witch: Rattles / Radar love: Golden Earring / Love like a man: Ten Years After / Standing on the road: Blackfoot Sue / Hold your head up: Argent / Backstreet luv: Curved Air / Living in the past: Jethro Tull / In my own time: Family / Slip and slide: Medicine Head / Sympathy: Rare Bird / Joybringer: Manfred Mann's Earthband / Northern lights: Renaissance / Jig a jig: East Of Eden
CD _____ 5163982
PolyGram TV / Aug '93 / PolyGram.

PROGRESSION
CD _____ PROG 292
Progression / Feb '94 / SRD.

PROGRESSIVE HOUSE CLASSICS
(3 LP Set)
Intoxication: React 2 Rhythm / Difference: Djum Djum / Sack the drummer: Soundclash Republic / LionRock: Lionrock / Speed controller: Acorn Arts / Get out on this dancefloor: D.O.P. / Mighty Ming: Brother Love Dubs / Big mouth: Lemon Interupt / Londress strutt: Smells Like Heaven / Not forgotten: Leftfield / Future te funk: D.O.P. / Who's the badman: Patern, Dee / Pure pleasure: Digital Excitation / Body Medusa: Supereal / Funkatarium: Jump
CD _____ FIRMCD 1
Firm / Feb '96 / Pinnacle.

PROGRESSIVE HOUSE,TRIBAL BEATS AND ADVENTURES IN DUB
CD _____ CDRAID 508
Rumour / Sep '92 / Pinnacle / 3MV / Sony.

PROGRESSIVE POP INSIDE THE 70'S
Who can I trust: Walrus / Yes you do: Pacific Drift / I wrapped her in ribbons: Galliards / I've been moved: Hollywood Freeway / Never gonna let my body touch the ground: Walrus / Goodbye to Baby Jane: Campbell, Junior / Cloudy day: Vehicle / Maybe: Granny's Intentions / Dan the wing: Mellow Candle / Pretty Belinda: Clan / Mr. Horizon: Hemlock / Standing on the corner: Youlden, Chris / Rebels rule: Iron Virgin / Back street luv: Curved Air / Candy baby: Beano / Sweetest tasting candy sugar: Sheriden, Lee / Ultrastar: Rococo / Whizmore kid: Principal Edwards / Sweet illusion: Campbell, Junior / Candy eyes: Fresh Meat / One night affair: Areety, Colin / Jesus come back: Matthews's Revelation / Two sisters: Wolf / Bye and bye: Beano
CD _____ SEECD 424
See For Miles/C5 / May '95 / Pinnacle.

PROLE LIFE
Grand monophonic: Yummy Fur / Fiery Jack: Yummy Fur / Typical of boys: Yummy Fur / All women are robots: Yummy Fur / Vanilla maneli: Yummy Fur / Cosmonauts and cardonauts: Yummy Fur / Eyeball popping madness: Yummy Fur / Human boing: Trout / Owl in the tree: Trout / Divorce at high noon: Blisters / Post-feminist business woman: Blisters / Patrick meets the courgettes: Blisters / Christian chorus: Blisters / Mommy is a punker: Pink Cross / Chopper chix: Pink Cross / Punk outfit: Pink Cross / No time for bimbo: Pink Cross / Toby Mangel: Lugworm / Sweaty says: Lugworm / Disco: Lugworm / Barmitzvah: Lugworm
CD _____ CDKRED 121
Cherry Red / Jul '95 / Pinnacle.

PROPER COMP. 1.0
Grande bassito: Acid Farm / On and on: D.J. Kaay Alexi / Greg Metzger: McBride, Woody / Electric: Stoll, Steve / Infrared: Wild, Damon / Fuken around: Hunt, Gene / Personal carrier: Henze, W.J. / MMMM: Fresh, Freddie / Third eye (CD only): D.J. Capricorn / Dig it (CD only): Carbon Boys

CD _____ **PROPS 008CD**
Proper / Jun '95 / Plastic Head.

PROPHET SPEAKS, THE
(Street Jazz Collection)
CD _____ **SPV 10362**
I.L.C. / Oct '93 / Sony.

PROPRIUS JAZZ SAMPLER 1994
CD _____ **PCD 020**
Proprius / Mar '95 / Jazz Music / May Audio.

PROUD
In the neighbourhood: Sisters Underground / Tuesday's blues: Pacifican Descendants / We're the OMC: Otara Millionaires Club / Based on a lost cause: Radio Backstab & D.J. Payback / Pass it over: Pacifican Descendants / Dawn of the eve: Di-Na-Ve / One too many: Vocal Five / I don't need you: Semi MC's / Ain't it true: Sisters Underground / Save New Zealand: Vocal Five / Pacific beats: Puka Puka / Prove me wrong: MC Slam / Groove me: Rhythm Harmony / Trust me: Semi MC's
CD _____ **VOLTCD 77**
Volition / Oct '95 / Vital / Pinnacle.

PSALMS FOR SOLOMON
CD _____ **BLKMCD 012**
Blakamix / Jun '95 / Jetstar / SRD.

PSEUDOPODIA
CD _____ **BIKE 005CD**
Yellow Books / Nov '92 / Plastic Head.

PSY HARMONICS VOL.1
CD _____ **PSY 009**
PSY Harmonics / Sep '95 / Plastic Head.

PSYCHEDELIA
CD _____ **MUSCD 021**
MCI / Sep '94 / Disc / THE.

PSYCHO MANIA
Loan shark: Guana Batz / Come dancing: Highlanders / I see red: Frenzy / Road to rack 'n' ruin: King Kurt / Holy hack Jack: Demented Are Go / Uncle Sam / Torment / Saints and sinners: Long Tall Texans / Twisted retard: Frantic Flintstones / Mad for it: Deltas / June rhyme: Stingrays / This train: Highlanders / Skitzo mania: Skitzo / For a few burgers more: Coffin Nails / Hellraiser: Radiacs / Rock this town: Guana Batz / Gamblin' man: Fractured / Beast (Live): Rochee & The Sarnos / Call of the wired: Demented Are Go / Rockin' out: Frantic Flintstones / Tuffer than tuff: Deltas / Wazzed 'n' blasted: Batfinks / Dance with the dead: Sugar puff demons / Billy: King Kurt / Rockabilly boogie: Polecats
CD _____ **STR CD 032**
Street Livin / Oct '92 / BMG.

PSYCHOMANIA VOL. 3
CD _____ **DOJOCD 203**
Dojo / Mar '95 / BMG.

PSYCHOTRANCE
CD _____ **MM 800072**
Moonshine / Aug '94 / Disc.

PSYCHOTRANCE 2
CD _____ **MM 800202**
Moonshine / Jan '95 / Disc.

PSYCHOTRANCE 3
CD _____ **MM 800402**
Moonshine / Nov '95 / Disc.

PUCK ROCK VOL.1
CD _____ **WRONG 11**
Wrong / Apr '94 / SRD.

PULP SURFIN'
CD _____ **DOCD 700222**
Del-Fi / Nov '95 / Koch.

PULSATING HITS
CD _____ **PULSE 16CD**
Pulse 8 / Nov '94 / Pinnacle / 3MV.

PULSATING RHYTHMS
CD _____ **PULSECD 1**
Pulse 8 / Aug '91 / Pinnacle / 3MV.

PULSATING RHYTHMS VOL.2
CD _____ **PULSECD 4**
Pulse 8 / Jun '92 / Pinnacle / 3MV.

PULSATING RHYTHMS VOL.3
CD _____ **PULSECD 8**
Pulse 8 / Nov '92 / Pinnacle / 3MV.

PULSATING RHYTHMS VOL.4
CD _____ **PULSECD 10**
Pulse 8 / Jul '93 / Pinnacle / 3MV.

PULSE OF LIFE
CD _____ **ELL 3210C**
Ellipsis Arts / Oct '93 / Direct / ADA.

PUMP UP EUROPE
CD _____ **LDCD 8823**
Play It Again Sam / Aug '89 / Vital.

PUMP YA FIST
(Hip Hop Inspired By The Black Panthers)
Ah yeah: KRS 1 / Pump ya fist: Kam / Black family day: Grand Puba / Shades of black: Rakim / Frustrated nigga: Jeru The Damaja / Throw your hand up 2: 2 Pac / Positive vibe: Speech / Recognition: Fugees / It's the pride: Chuck D / Only if you want it: Ahmad / Crazay: Yo Yo / I gotta get mine: Scott, Dred / Out for just us: Five-O

CD _____ **5276092**
Polydor / Nov '95 / PolyGram.

PUNK
What do I get (Live): Buzzcocks / EMI: Sex Pistols / Personality crisis: New York Dolls / Angels with dirty faces (Live): Sham 69 / Born to lose (Live): Thunders, Johnny / Bored teenagers (Live): Adverts / Looking for a kiss: New York Dolls / Rip off (Live): Sham 69 / One track mind (Live): Thunders, Johnny / Boston babies (Live): Slaughter & The Dogs / Pretty vacant (Live): Sex Pistols / No time to be 21 (Live): Adverts / Hear nothing, see nothing, say nothing: Discharge / Brickfield nights (Live): Boys / Time's me's up (Live): Buzzcocks
CD _____ **MCCD 015**
Music Club / Feb '91 / Disc / THE / CM.

PUNK
(3CD Set)
CD Set _____ **MCBX 017**
Music Club / Dec '94 / Disc / THE / CM.

PUNK AND DISORDERLY
CD _____ **AABT 100CD**
Abstract / Sep '94 / Pinnacle / Total/BMG.

PUNK AND DISORDERLY
I'm in love with a German film star: Passions / It didn't matter: Style Council / Maybe tomorrow: Chords / Beat surrender: Jam / White punks on dope: Tubes / Two pints of lager and a packet of crisps please: Splodgenessabounds / Borstal breakout: Sham 69 / Disguises: Jam / Prime time: Tubes / If the kids are united: Sham 69 / Cowpunk medium: Splodgenessabounds / One more minute: Chords / Swimmer: Passions / Shout to the top: Style Council
CD _____ **5500492**
Spectrum/Karussell / May '83 / PolyGram / THE.

PUNK AND DISORDERLY - FURTHER CHANGES
Sick boy: G.B.H. / Dreaming: Expelled / El salvador: Insane / Stab the judge: One Way System / Gotta get out: Court Martial / London bouncers: Action Pact / Masque: Dark / Gangland: Violators / I've got a gun: Channel 3 / Vicious circle: Abrasive Wheels / Fallen hero: Enemy / Death to humanity: Riot / Hobby for a day: Wall / More than fights: Disorder / Shellshock: Erazerhead / Resurrection: Vice Squad / How much longer: Alternative TV / Corgi crap: Drones / I hate school: Suburban Studs / Run like hell: Peter & The Test Tube Babies
CD _____ **CDPUNK 2**
Anagram / Dec '93 / Pinnacle.

PUNK AND DISORDERLY - THE FINAL SOLUTION
Burn 'em down: Abrasive Wheels / Give us a future: One Way System / Kick out the tories: Newtown Neurotics / Police state: UK Subs / Jailbait: Destructor / Government policy: Expelled / Dead hero: Samples / Woman in disguise: Angelic Upstarts / Viva la revolution: Adicts / Dragnet: Vibrators / Computers don't blunder: Exploited / New barbarians: Urban Dogs / Have you got 10p: Ejected / Outlaw: Chron Gen / Suicide bag: Action Pact / Summer of '81: Violators
CD _____ **CDPUNK 23**
Anagram / Dec '93 / Pinnacle.

PUNK CITY ROCKERS
(4CD Set)
CD Set _____ **MBSCD 440**
Castle / Nov '95 / BMG.

PUNK COMPILATION
CD _____ **EMPRCD 550**
Emporio / Nov '94 / THE / Disc / CM.

PUNK GENERATION
(4 CDST)
CD Set _____ **MBSCD 438**
Castle / Apr '95 / BMG.
CD Set _____ **MBSCD 419**
Castle / Nov '95 / BMG.

PUNK II
Anarchy in the U.K. (live): Sex Pistols / Babylon's burning (Live): Ruts / Nobody's hereo (Live): Stiff Little Fingers / Borstal breakout (Live): Sham 69 / Dead cities: Exploited / Ain't got a clue (Live): Lurkers / Maniac: Peter & The Test Tube Babies / Feeling alright with the crew (Live): 999 / Chinese takeaway (Live): Adicts / Right to work (Live): Chelsea / Holidays in the sun (Live): Sex Pistols / Alternative Ulster: Stiff Little Fingers / Two pints of lager: Splodgenessabounds / Stand strong, stand proud (Live): Vice Squad / Something that I said (Live): Ruts / I hate people (Live): Anti Nowhere League / Teenage warning (Live): Angelic Upstarts / Flares and slippers: Cockney Rejects / Punk's not dead: Exploited / Warriors: Blitz
CD _____ **MCCD 022**
Music Club / May '91 / Disc / THE / CM.

PUNK LIVES
CD _____ **TRTCD 146**
TrueTrax / May '95 / THE.

PUNK ROCK JUKEBOX
I'm against it: No Brain / Bodies: Killing Time / I got your number: Swinging Gutters / Go nowhere: Sweet Diesel / Code blue: Bouncing Souls / In the city: Waterdog / I don't want to hear it: 88 Fingers Louie / Somebody's gonna get their head kicked in

tonight: Murphy's Law / Ready steady go: Trusty / Barbed wire love: Goops / Justification: Brody / Hitman: Jughead's Revenge / Understand: Overcrowd / Police story: Deadguy / I love livin' in the city: Black Velvet Flag / Evil: Awkward thought / Don't need your lovin': New Bomb Turks / Guimo's theme: Plow United / Friends: H2O / Woman: Turbo AC's / Big takeover: Buzzkill / We're only gonna die: Sublime / Civilisation's dying: Leeway
CD _____ **BLK 025ECD**
Blackout / Dec '95 / Vital.

PUNK ROCK RARITIES VOL.1
On me: Bears / Hard time: Mutants / School teacher: Mutants / Lady: Mutants / Office girl: Stoat / Little Jenny: Stoat / Crazy paving: Karloff, Billy / Backstreet Billy: Karloff, Billy / I'm different: Embryo / You know he did: Embryo / Here comes the night: Rivals / Both sides: Rivals / Sound so false: Murder Inc. / Polythene dream: Murder Inc. / Nobody cares: Murder Inc. / Lord of the dance: Jump Squad / Debt: Jump Squad / Kings cross: Charge / Brave new world: Charge / God's kids: Charge
CD _____ **CDPUNK 63**
Anagram / Oct '95 / Pinnacle.

PUNK-O-RAMA
CD _____ **E 864482**
Epitaph / Nov '94 / Plastic Head / Pinnacle.

PUNKS NOT DREAD
CD _____ **PREACH 002CD**
Rhythm Vicar / Mar '94 / Plastic Head.

PURE ATTRACTION
You're my best friend: Queen / Right beside you: Hawkins, Sophie B. / Easy: Faith No More / Just a step from heaven: Eternal / Patience of angels: Reader, Eddi / Return to innocence: Enigma / Don't dream it's over: Crowded House / Now that the magic has gone: Cocker, Joe / Where does my heart beat now: Dion, Celine / Hold me, thrill me, kiss me: Estefan, Gloria / Stay: Shakespears Sister / Someone saved my life tonight: John, Elton / Independent love song: Scarlet / Now and forever: Marx, Richard / Total eclipse of the heart: Tyler, Bonnie / Hold me now: Logan, Johnny / I'll never fall in love again: Deacon Blue / Every breath you take: Police / Careless whisper: Michael, George / Power of love: Rush, Jennifer / Jealous guy: Roxy Music / In dreams: Orbison, Roy / When I fall in love: Dion, Celine / Nothing compares 2 U: O'Connor, Sinead / (Sittin' on) the dock of the bay: Bolton, Michael / In a broken dream: Python Lee Jackson / Eternal flame: Bangles / Always and forever: Vandross, Luther / Time after time: Lauper, Cyndi / Only to be with you: Roachford / Love hurts: Capaldi, Jim / Show me heaven: McKee, Maria / I wonder why: Stigers, Curtis / I'll stand by you: Pretenders / Ordinary world: Duran Duran / Take my breath away: Berlin / Miracle of love: Eurythmics / Whole new world (Aladdin's theme): Bell, Regina
CD _____ **SONYTVCD1**
Columbia / Jun '95 / Sony.

PURE DEVOTION
CD _____ **CDDVN 17**
Music For Nations / Oct '92 / Pinnacle.

PURE ECSTATIC ENERGY
CD _____ **GLOBECD 2**
All Around The World / May '93 / Total/BMG.

PURE IRISH TRADITIONAL ACCORDION
CD _____ **PTICD 1027**
Pure Traditional Irish / Jan '95 / ADA.

PURE JAZZ SAMPLER
CD _____ **CDGATE 1001**
Kingdom Jazz / Oct '90 / Kingdom.

PURE LOVERS VOL.1
CD _____ **CCD 101**
Charm / Oct '92 / Jetstar.

PURE LOVERS VOL.2
CD _____ **CCD 102**
Charm / Sep '90 / Jetstar.

PURE LOVERS VOL.3
CD _____ **CCD 103**
Charm / Apr '91 / Jetstar.

PURE LOVERS VOL.4
I'm so alone: Davis, Richie / Master vibes: Hunningale, Peter / Love u down: Brown, Lloyd / Morning after: Rich, Anthony / I won't stop loving you: Hall, Pam / Daydreaming: Robotiks & Jocelyn Brown / Hypnotic love: Leo, Phillip / Can you feel the love: Pure Silk & Trevor Walters / Hold me: Pinchers / Miss wire waist: Scotty / Emptiness inside: Hammond, Beres / Ecstasy of love: Levi, Sammy / Fire burning: Griffiths, Marcia / I'm only human: Wonder, Wayne / Mrs. Jones: Koffi / Make my dream a reality: Pure Silk & Wendy Walker / Stranger in love: Fluxe, Dave
CD _____ **CCD 104**
Charm / Nov '91 / Jetstar.

PURE LOVERS VOL.5
CD _____ **CCD 105**
Charm / Aug '92 / Jetstar.

PURE LOVERS VOL.6
CD _____ **CCD 106**
Charm / Apr '93 / Jetstar.

PURE LOVERS VOL.7
CD _____ **CCD 107**
Charm / Feb '94 / Jetstar.

PURE LOVERS VOL.8
CD _____ **CCD 108**
Charm / Feb '95 / Jetstar.

PURE MOODS
Return to innocence: Enigma / Sweet lullaby: Deep Forest / Crockett's theme: Hammer, Jan / Oxygene (part IV): Jarre, Jean Michel / Orinoco flow: Enya / Tubular bells: Oldfield, Mike / Chariots of fire: Vangelis / Heart asks pleasure first/The promise: Nyman, Michael / Chi Mai: Morricone, Ennio / Inspector Morse (theme): Pheloung, Barrington / Sadness: Enigma / Little fluffy clouds: Orb / Only you: Praise / Adiemus: Jenkins, Karl / Lily was here: Stewart, David A. & Candy Dulfer / Songbird: Kenny G. / Merry Christmas Mr. Lawrence: Sakamoto, Ryuichi / Twin Peaks theme: Badalmenti, Angelo / Mission: Morricone, Ennio / Another green world: Eno, Brian
CD _____ **VTCD 28**
Virgin / Jun '94 / EMI.

PURE NOSTALGIA
Bei mir bist du schon: Andrews Sisters / Puttin' on the Ritz: Astaire, Fred / When I take my sugar to tea: Boswell Sisters & Dorsey Brothers Orchestra / Very thought of you: Bowlly, Al / Minnie the moocher: Calloway, Cab / Rockin' chair: Carmichael, Hoagy & Louis Armstrong / Louise: Chevalier, Maurice / Temptation: Crosby, Bing / Falling in love again: Dietrich, Marlene / Ten cents a dance: Etting, Ruth / Sally: Fields, Gracie / Leaning on a lamp-post: Formby, George / Over the rainbow: Garland, Judy / All the things you are: Hutch / Java jive: Ink Spots / Sonny boy: Jolson, Al / Medley (What'll I do/All alone/Bye bye blackbird/Always/My blue heaven/It ain't gonna rain no more): Layton & Johnstone / We'll meet again: Lynn, Vera / Dancing on the ceiling: Matthews, Jessie / Moonlight serenade: Miller, Glenn / Tiger rag: Mills Brothers / My curly headed baby: Robeson, Paul / Without a song: Sinatra, Frank & Tommy Dorsey / Marta: Tracy, Arthur / Some of these days: Tucker, Sophie
CD _____ **CDAJA 5118**
Living Era / Mar '94 / Koch.

PURE PUREPECHA
CD _____ **CO 119CD**
Corason / Aug '94 / CM / Direct / ADA.

PURE REGGAE
CD _____ **VSOPCD 198**
Connoisseur / Jun '94 / Pinnacle.

PURE REGGAE VOL.1
You don't love me: Penn, Dawn / Compliments on your kiss: Red Dragon / Program: Morales, David & The Bad Yard Club / Shine: Aswad / Boom shak-a-tack: Born Jamericans / Twist and shout: Demus, Chaka & Pliers / Big things a gwan: Daddy Screw & Donovan Steele / Stress: Brown, Beenie Man / I'm in love (long): Inner Circle / Informer: Snow / Boom shak-a-lak: Apache Indian / Don't turn around: Aswad / Now that we've found love: Third World / 54-46 jeans my property: Toots & The Maytals / Israelites: Dekker, Desmond & The Aces / Johnny B. Badde: Slickers / You can get it if you really want: Cliff, Jimmy / Guns of Navarone: Skatalites / Rivers of Babylon: Melodians / Longshot kick de bucket: Pioneers / Book of rules: Heptones / Breakfast in bed: Bennett, Lorna / Guava jelly: Gray, Owen / Police and thieves: Murvin, Junior / Silly games: Kay, Janet / Somebody's watching you: Black Uhuru / Bed's too big without you: Hylton, Sheila / Sitting and watching: Brown, Dennis / Night nurse: Isaacs, Gregory / Call me: General Grant
CD Set _____ **CIDTV 8**
Island / Jun '94 / PolyGram.

PURE SILK
CD _____ **SGCD 11**
Sir George / Jun '93 / Jetstar / Pinnacle.

PURE SOFT METAL
CD _____ **TMPCD 015**
Telstar / Mar '95 / BMG.

PURE SWING 5
(2CD/MC/LP Set)
Don't be afraid: Hall, Aaron / Where I wanna be boy: Miss Jones / My up and down: Howard, Adina / Something in your eyes: Bell Biv Devoe / Give it 2 you: Da more / Ribbons in the sky: Intro / One more chance: Notorious B.I.G. / I'll be there fo you: Method Man / Just roll: Fabu / Best friend: Brandy / Mary Jane (all night long): Blige, Mary J. / If you love me: Brownstone / Lately: Jodeci / Can't go deep: Silk / I want to: Sweat, Keith / Creep: TLC / Honey dip: Portrait / This is how we do it: Jordan, Montell / Forget I was A G: Whitehead Brothers / I'll make love to you: Boyz II Men / Every little thing I do: Soul For Real / Feel so good: Xscape / Wanna get with you: Guy / Knockin da boots: H-Town / This is for this cool: Babyface / How many way's: Braxton, Toni / I'm so into you: S.W.V. / Party at night: Kreuz / Girlfriend boyfriend: McCrae, Gwen / Sugarhill: A.Z. / Fantasy: Carey, Mariah / Undercover lover: Smooth / Ocean

drive: *Lighthouse Family* / Rock me down: *Benson, Sharon* / Good lover: *Da Influence* / Lay my body down: *Kut Klose* / Rodeo style: *Jamecia* / My cherie amour: *Thompson, Tony* / I've got a little something for you: *MN8* / U will know: *BMU* / Real love: *Driza Bone* / Brand new: *Sista* / You remind me: *R. Kelly* / Finest: *Truce* / Respect: *Troi* / Don't be cruel: *Brown, Bobby* / For the lover in you: *Hewitt, Howard* / Show me: *Nuttin' Nyce*
CD _____ DINCD 116
Dino / Nov '95 / Pinnacle / 3MV.

PURE SWING 1
(20 Bump 'N' Grind Anthems)
CD _____ DINCD 97
Dino / Feb '95 / Pinnacle / 3MV.

PURE SWING 2
Creep: *TLC* / Your love is a 187: *Whitehead Brothers* / U blow my mind: *Blackstreet* / Stroke you up: *Changing Faces* / Freak me: *Silk* / Crazy: *Morrison, Mark* / Make it last forever: *Sweat, Keith* / Get up on it: *Kut Klose* / Taste your love: *Brown, Horace* / Two can play that game: *Brown, Bobby* / Lately: *Jodeci* / Free: *Moore, Chante* / Be happy: *Blige, Mary J.* / Down with the clique: *Aaliyah* / You're body's callin: *R. Kelly* / Hornie lover friend: *R. Kelly* / This is for the cool: *Babyface* / Is it good to you: *Lucas, Tammy & Teddy Riley* / Everyday of the week: *Jade* / Think of you: *Usher* / Slap and tickle: *Kruze* / Here we go again: *Portrait* / Mind blowin: *Smooth* / Freak like me: *Howard, Adina* / Just roll: *Fabu* / Flavour of the old school: *Knight, Beverley*
CD _____ DINCD 98
Dino / May '95 / Pinnacle / 3MV.

PURE SWING 4
Water runs dry: *Boyz II Men* / Freek 'n you: *Jodeci* / How many ways: *Braxton, Toni* / Freak like me: *Howard, Adina* / I've got a little something: *MN8* / Groove of love: *E.V.E.* / Creep: *TLC* / Get up on it: *Kut Klose* / Shy guy: *King, Diana* / Taste your love: *Brown, Horace* / Freak me: *Silk* / It's summertime: *Smooth* / Candy rain: *Soul For Real* / You will know: *BMU* / Best friend: *Brandy* / Forget I was a G: *Whitehead Brothers* / Love me right: *Joy: Blackstreet* / Can we talk: *Campbell, Tevin* / Up and down: *Kreuz* / Don't take it personal: *Monica* / You don't want to mis: *For Real*
CD _____ DINCD 109
Dino / Aug '95 / Pinnacle / 3MV.

PURE SWING 5
Knockin' da boots: *H-Town* / Hanging on a string: *Loose Ends* / Somethin' 4 da honeyz: *Jordan, Montell* / Respect: *Alliance Ethnik* / Treat me right: *Father MC* / This love is forever: *Hewett, Howard* / Can't you see: *Total F Notorious Big* / Love groove: *Smooth* / Slow dance: *R. Kelly* / Get down on it: *Kreuz* / Remedy: *Knight, Beverley* / Funny how time flies: *Intro* / Motown philly: *Boyz II Men* / Smile: *Shanice* / Give it 2 you: *Da Brat* / Hey Mr. D.J.: *Zhane* / I want: *Sweat, Keith* / I wanna be down: *Brandy* / Keep it right there: *Changing Faces* / This is for the cool: *Babyface* / Keep it real: *Jamecia* / Just roll: *Fabu* / Tell me what you want me: *Campbell, Tevin* / Up, Diana* / Make me feel real good: *Porche* / Tell me: *Groove Theory* / Who can I run to: *Xscape* / Hooked on you: *Silk* / Already missing you: *Levert, Gerald*
CD _____ DINCD 117
Dino / Dec '95 / Pinnacle / 3MV.

PURPLE
CD _____ CRELP 032CD
Creation / '88 / 3MV / Vital.

PURPLE PAIN
CD _____ DOL 020CD
Dolores / Jun '95 / Plastic Head.

PURVEYORS OF TASTE
(Creation Compilation)
CD _____ CRECD 010
Creation / May '94 / 3MV / Vital.

PUT ON YOUR BEST DRESS
(Rock Steady 1967-68)
CD _____ CDAT 109
Attack / Nov '94 / Jetstar / Total/BMG.

PUT YA HAND ON DE BUMPER
CD _____ CCD 0021
CRS / Aug '95 / Direct / ADA.

PWEEP
CD Set _____ BFFP 94
Blast First / Apr '95 / Disc.

PYROTECHNICS
CD _____ CDP 799 659 2
Blue Note / Sep '91 / EMI.

Q - COUNTRY
CD _____ AHLCD 16
Hit / May '94 / PolyGram.

Q - RHYTHM & BLUES
Brown eyed girl / I'll go crazy: *Brown, James* / It's all over now: *Cooder, Ry* / I'd rather go blind: *Stewart, Rod* / Fool in love: *Turner, Ike & Tina* / Dr. Brown: *Fleetwood Mac* / Nadine: *Berry, Chuck* / Mockingbird: *Foxx, Inez & Charlie* / Blue Monday: *Domino, Fats* / Everybody needs somebody to love: *Burke, Solomon* / Stepping out: *Mayall, John & Eric Clapton* / Sun ain't gonna bad sign: *King, Albert* / Young blood: *Coasters* / Gimme some lovin': *Davis, Spencer Group* / Hi-heel sneakers: *Tucker, Tommy* / House of the rising sun: *Animals* / Let the good times roll: *Shirley & Lee* / We're gonna make it: *Little Milton* / Roadrunner: *Diddley, Bo* / Long tall shorty: *Kinks* / You'd better move on: *Alexander, Arthur* / Got my mojo working: *Manfred Mann* / My babe: *Little Walter*
CD _____ AHLCD 7
Hit / Mar '93 / PolyGram.

Q - THE ALBUM VOL. 1
CD _____ TCD 2522
Telstar / Sep '91 / BMG.

Q - THE BLUES
CD _____ AHLCD 5
Hit / Jun '92 / PolyGram.

Q.E.D.
Organofonia ramovs: *Laibach* / Ataxia: *Deform* / Untitled excerpt: *2'EV* / Ebony tower in the Orient water: *Radio Rabotnik TV* / Kennen sie koein: *Der Plan* / Delerium 2: *Chris & Cosey* / HLA: *Non Toxique Lost* / Tribal noise 2: *Het Zweet* / Anyway don't do the sport fuck: *Spring As Der Wolken* / Call: *Banablia, Michel* / Restimulation: *Hafler Trio* / Mutation waltz: *Manoton, K. B.* / Menegins: *Einsturzende Neubauten* / Eleven: *De Executie/Klec* / E and E: *Pig D4* / Getuich der miljoenen: *Zegueld, Peter* / L'esprit domine l'etoile: *Etant Donnes* / Oirat / I wanna be injured, the / color or dr: *Club Moral* / Liberal 1:13: *Zero Kama* / C.B.A.: *S.B.O.T.H.I* / Demonomania: *Test Department*
CD _____ NLCD 001
N L Centre / Sep '88 / Vital.

QUADRUPED
CD _____ BARKCD 006
Planet Dog / Oct '94 / 3MV / Vital.

QUARKNOSIS
Dolcevita: *Optica* / Utopia: *Transfinite* / Tapestry: *Quad* / Zoophite: *Optica* / Technozone: *Output & D.J. Oz* / Moonshine: *Zerkel* / Aquaville: *Quad* / Trance dance: *Optic Eye* / Shimmer: *Alien Mutation* / Tokyo: *Centuras* / Something inside: *Deep Joy*
CD _____ KINXCD 1
Kinetix / Apr '94 / Pinnacle.

QUARTER TO TWELVE
CD _____ VPCD 2039
VP / Sep '95 / Jetstar.

QUEENS OF CLUB '95
CD _____ VISCB 9
Vision / Mar '95 / Pinnacle.

QUEENS OF COUNTRY
CD _____ SETCD 102
Stardust / Sep '94 / Carlton Home Entertainment.

QUEENS OF COUNTRY
Rose garden: *Anderson, Lynn* / Misty blue: *Spears, Billie Jo* / Just out of reach: *Cline, Patsy* / Crazy: *Jackson, Wanda* / Both sides now: *Murray, Anne* / Harper Valley PTA: *Riley, Jeannie C.* / End of the world: *Davis, Skeeter* / D.I.V.O.R.C.E.: *West, Dottie* / When I dream: *Anderson, Lynn* / You never can tell: *Spears, Billie Jo* / Poor man's roses: *Cline, Patsy* / It's only make believe: *Jackson, Wanda* / Last thing on my mind: *Murray, Anne* / Box of memories: *Riley, Jeannie C.* / Release me: *Mandrell, Barbara* / No charge: *Montgomery, Melba* / I wish I could fall in love again: *Howard, Jan* / Dallas: *Spears, Billie Jo* / Wishful thinking: *Fargo, Donna* / Blue bayou: *Anderson, Lynn*
CD _____ MUCD 9014
Start / Apr '95 / Koch.

QUEENS OF COUNTRY MUSIC
Just out of reach: *Cline, Patsy* / You belong to me: *Page, Patti* / Am I that easy to forget: *Riley, Jeannie C.* / Walkin' after midnight: *Cline, Patsy* / Stop the world (and let me off): *Cline, Patsy* / I can see an angel: *Cline, Patsy* / Why don't you believe me: *Page, Patti* / Mockin' Bird Hill: *Page, Patti* / Tennessee waltz: *Page, Patti* / Gentle on my mind: *Page, Patti* / Things go better with love: *Riley, Jeannie C.* / Help me make it through the night: *Riley, Jeannie C.* / Before the next teardrop falls: *Riley, Jeannie C.* / Roses and thorns: *Riley, Jeannie C.* / Harper Valley PTA: *Riley, Jeannie C.*
CD _____ PWK 030
Carlton Home Entertainment / '88 / Carlton Home Entertainment.

R & B CONFIDENTIAL NO.1 - THE FLAIR STORY
Romp and stomp blues: *Walton, Mercy Dee* / Baby beat it: *Henderson, Duke* / Cuban getaway: *Turner, Ike Orchestra* / Please find my baby: *James, Elmore* / You better hold me: *Reed, Jimmy* / Night howler: *Gale, Billy* / This is the night for love: *Flairs* / Let's make with some love: *Flairs* / Go Robbie go: *Robinson, Robbie & Binky* / Send him back: *Gunter, Shirley* / Baby, I love you so: *Gunter, Shirley* / Oop shoop: *Gunter, Shirley* / Hey Dr Kinsey: *Henderson, Duke* / Next time: *Berry, Richard* / Hard times: *Fuller, Johnny* / Chop house: *Allen, Blinky* / Have you ever: *Walton, Mercy Dee* / My baby left town (Available on CD only): *Dixie Blues Boys* / People are wonderin' (Available on CD only): *Parham, Baby 'Pee Wee'* / Baby please: *Cockrell, Mat* / Quit hangin' around (Available on CD only): *King, Saunders*
CD _____ CDCHD 258
Ace / Feb '89 / Pinnacle / Cadillac / Complete/Pinnacle.

R & B VOCAL GROUPS VOLUME 1
It's too soon to know: *Orioles* / Lemon squeezin' daddy: *Sultans* / Make me thrill again: *Marylanders* / Hey Bars / Girl that I marry: *Starlings* / I've lost: *Enchanters* / Can't get you off my mind: *Dreamers* / Don't play no mombo: *Charioteers* / You captured my heart: *Sultans* / Prayer: *Teardrops* / Paint a sky for me: *Watkins, Viola & The Crows* / How you move me: *Four Bars* / I'm so all alone: *Marylanders* / Fried chicken: *Marylanders* / Getting tired tired tired: *Orioles* / Music maestro please: *Starlings* / I've got my heart on my sleeve: *Charioteers* / Grief by day, grief by night: *Four Bars* / Blues at dawn: *Sultans* / Fool: *Teardrops* / Today is your birthday: *Enchanters* / These things I miss: *Dreamers* / Teardrops on my pillow: *Orioles* / Don't be angry: *Sultans* / Good old 99: *Marylanders* / If I give my heart to you: *Four Bars*
CD _____ NEMCD 736
Sequel / Jun '95 / BMG.

R & B VOCAL GROUPS VOLUME 2
I'd rather have you under the moon: *Orioles* / Hold me: *Clicks* / Tears of love: *Kari, Sax & Quailtones* / Why do you treat me this way: *Four Bars* / Please love me: *Marylanders* / You are so beautiful: *Five Notes & The Hamil-Tones* / Baby let me bang your box: *Toppers* / My heart: *Teardrops* / You broke my heart: *Clicks* / Fine brown frame: *Starlings* / How I'd feel without you: *Marylanders* / Only you: *Cues* / Feelin' low: *Orioles* / Let me live: *Four Bars* / Ooh baby: *Teardrops* / One fried egg: *Charioteers* / Peace and contentment: *Clicks* / I'm a sentimental fool: *Marylanders* / Stop it suit it: *Four Bars* / I fell for your loving: *Cues* / Broken hearted baby: *Five Notes & The Hamil-Tones* / My plea for love: *Starlings* / Stars are out tonight: *Charioteers* / Come back to me: *Clicks*
CD _____ NEMCD 743
Sequel / Jun '95 / BMG.

R U CONSCIOUS
CD _____ CONCD 011
Conscious / Nov '92 / Jetstar / 3MV.

R.E.R. QUARTERLY VOL.4
CD _____ RER 0401
RER / Jun '93 / Grapevine.

RACE WITH THE DEVIL
Race with the devil: *Girlschool* / War pigs: *Black Sabbath* / Bomber: *Motorhead* / Silver machine: *Hawkwind* / Mean girl: *Status Quo* / Parisienne walkways: *Moore, Gary* / (Don't fear) The Reaper: *Blue Oyster Cult* / Tin soldier: *Small Faces* / Holy roller: *Nazareth* / Invasion: *Magnum* / Look at yourself: *Uriah Heep* / Heartline: *George, Robin* / Born to be wild: *Blue Oyster Cult* / Please don't touch: *Headgirl* / Sudden life: *Man* / Black magic woman: *Fleetwood Mac* / Wrist job: *Humble Pie*
CD _____ TRTCD 115
TrueTrax / Oct '94 / THE.

RADIO 2 - SOUNDS OF THE 60'S
Who put the bomp: *Viscounts* / When we get married: *Dreamlovers* / Have a drink on me: *Donegan, Lonnie* / Venus in blue jeans: *Winter, Mark* / Welcome home baby: *Brook Brothers* / Spanish harlem: *Justice, Jimmy* / Count on me: *Grant, Julie* / He's in town: *Rockin' Berries* / Tossing and turning: *Ivy League* / Thunderbirds theme: *Gray, Barry Orchestra* / Round every corner: *Clark, Petula* / Take a heart: *Sorrows* / Lady Jane: *Garrick, David* / Sittin' on a fence: *Twice As Much* / Baby now that I'v found you: *Foundations* / Green tambourine: *Lemon Pipers* / Handbags and gladrags: *Farlowe, Chris* / David Watts: *Kinks* / Something here in my heart: *Paper Dolls* / Ain't nothing but a house party: *Showstoppers*
CD _____ NEMCD 693
Sequel / Sep '94 / BMG.

RADIO DAYS - BRITISH 30'S RADIO
Radio Times: *Hall, Henry & The BBC Dance Orchestra* / I don't do things like that: *Trinder, Tommy* / Scrimplethorp's talcum (commercial): *Long, Norman* / Coronation girls: *Waters, Elsie & Doris* / Tale of Hector Cramp: *Fletcher, Cyril* / Radio Baloni time signal: *Taunton, Peter* / Schnotzelheimer's suspenders (commercial): *Long, Norman* / All for ten shillings a year: *Stanelli & Norman Long* / There's a small hotel: *Daniels, Bebe & Ben Lyon* / Football commentary: *Keys, Nelson & Ivy St. Helier* / Little Betty Bouncer: *Flotsam & Jetsam* / British mother's big fight: *Desmond, Florence & Max Kester* / Ye B.B.C.: *Flanagan & Allen* / Hi de ho: *Revnell, Ethel & Gracie West* / Gritty granules (commercial): *Taunton, Peter* / In 1992: *Campbell, Big Bill & His Rocky Mountain Rhythm* / I know that sailors do care: *O'Shea, Tessie* / Radio Baloni close-down: *Taunton, Peter* / Ding dong bell: *Askey, Arthur* / Mr. and Mrs. Ramsbottom went off: *Holloway, Stanley* / We can't let you broadcast that: *Long, Norman* / Cricket commentary: *Clapham & Dwyer* / Jubilee baby: *Driver, Betty* / University motors (commercial): *Potter, Gillie* / On the good ship Ballyhoo: *Warner, Jack & Jeff Darnell* / Five-in-one radios: *Pola, Eddie* / Adventures of Lt. Daunton: *Taunton, Peter* / Mirror cleanser: *Fields, Gracie* / Sing as we go: *Dixon, Reginald* / Sandy's own broadcasting station: *Powell, Sandy* / You'll never understand: *Bowlly, Al* / X (commercial): *Taunton, Peter* / We're frightfully BBC: *Western Brothers* / Let me call you sweetheart: *Oliver, Vic & Nellie Wallace* / Next week's film (commercial): *Formby, George* / Dromedary cigarettes (commercial): *Pola, Eddie* / About cruises: *Murgatroyd & Winterbottom* / Here's to the next time: *Hall, Henry & The BBC Dance Orchestra*
CD _____ CDHD 163
Happy Days / '88 / Conifer.

RADIO DREAMSCAPE VOLUME 1
CD _____ DREAMCD 01
Dreamscape / Jun '95 / SRD.

RADIO GOLD
Promised land: *Allan, Johnnie* / La Bamba: *Valens, Ritchie* / When the boy's happy (the girl's happy too): *Four Pennies* / Wake up little Susie: *Everly Brothers* / Wanderer: *Dion* / My true love: *Jive Five* / Dizzy Miss Lizzy: *Williams, Larry* / Mr. Sandman: *Chordettes* / I fought the law: *Fuller, Bobby Four* / Hush-a-bye: *Mystics* / Hello this is Joanie: *Evans, Paul* / Will you still love me tomorrow: *Shirelles* / Where or when: *Dion & The Belmonts* / Venus: *Avalon, Frankie* / Sixteen candles: *Crests* / When will I be loved: *Everly Brothers* / One fine day: *Chiffons* / Rockin' robin: *Day, Bobby* / Twist and shout: *Isley Brothers* / Little bit of soap: *Jarmels* / I'll come running back to you: *Cooke, Sam* / Earth angel: *Penguins* / Runaround Sue: *Dion* / Since I don't have you: *Skyliners* / Good golly Miss Molly: *Little Richard* / Poetry in motion: *Tillotson, Johnny* / Denise: *Randy & The Rainbows* / Tell it like it is: *Neville, Aaron* / Sweet dreams: *McLain, Tommy* / Goodnight my love: *Belvin, Jesse*
CD _____ CDCHD 347
Ace / Feb '92 / Pinnacle / Cadillac / Complete/Pinnacle.

RADIO GOLD VOLUME 2
Long tall Sally: *Little Richard* / Runaway: *Shannon, Del* / Donna: *Valens, Ritchie* / Bye bye love: *Everly Brothers* / Bony Maronie: *Williams, Larry* / Soldier boy: *Shirelles* / Nut rocker: *B. Bumble & The Stingers* / Her Paula: *Paul & Paula* / Let's dance: *Montez, Chris* / Hey baby: *Channel, Bruce* / Nobody needs your love (like I do): *Pitney, Gene* / Lollipop: *Chordettes* / Hippy hippy shake: *Romero, Chan* / Alone: *Shepherd Sisters* / In the mood: *Fields, Ernie Orchestra* / Alley oop: *Hollywood Argyles* / Wayward wind: *Grant, Gogi* / Let the little girl dance: *Bland, Billy* / I'm gonna knock on your door: *Hodges, Eddie* / Ivory tower: *Carr, Cathy* / Gingerbread: *Avalon, Frankie* / Hound dog man: *Fabian* / Send me the pillow that you dream on: *Tillotson, Johnny* / Pretty little angel eyes: *Lee, Curtis* / Birds and the bees: *Akens, Jewel* / Quite a party: *Fireballs* / This diamond ring: *Trondell, Troy* / Shimmy like my sister Kate: *Olympics* / Then you can tell me goodbye: *Casinos* / Louie Louie: *Kingsmen*
CD _____ CDCHD 446
Ace / Sep '93 / Pinnacle / Cadillac / Complete/Pinnacle.

RADIO GOLD VOLUME 3
Love is strange: *Mickey & Sylvia* / Willie and the hand jive: *Otis, Johnny* / Sweet nothin's: *Lee, Brenda* / I'm in love again: *Domino, Fats* / Star dust: *Ward, Billy & The Dominoes* / Chanson d'amour (Song of love): *Todd, Art & Dotty* / I'm gonna sit right down and write myself a letter: *Williams, Billy* / Susie darlin': *Luke, Robin* / Lion sleeps tonight: *Tokens* / Make it easy on yourself: *Butler, Jerry* / It's in his kiss (Shoop shoop song): *Everett, Betty* / Halfway to paradise: *Orlando, Tony* / That'll be the day: *Crickets* / Only the lonely: *Orbison, Roy* / When: *Kalin Twins* / White sports coat and a pink carnation: *Robbins, Marty* / On the rebound: *Cramer, Floyd* / Banana boat song (Day O): *Belafonte, Harry* / Singin' the blues: *Mitchell, Guy* / Twelfth of never: *Mathis, Johnny* / Freight train: *McDevitt, Chas & Nancy*

Whisky / Big man: *Four Preps* / At the hop: *Danny & The Juniors* / Just walking in the rain: *Ray, Johnnie* / Garden of Eden: *Valino, Joe* / Green door: *Lowe, Jim* / I hear you knocking: *Lewis, Smiley* / Seven little girls sitting in the back seat: *Evans, Paul* / Witch doctor: *Seville, David* / I go ape: *Sedaka, Neil*
CD _____ CDCHD 557
Ace / May '95 / Pinnacle / Cadillac / Complete/Pinnacle.

RADIO HELL
Lambs to the slaughter: *Raven* / Hold back the fire: *Raven* / Hard ride: *Raven* / Chainsaw: *Raven* / Black metal: *Venom* / Nightmare: *Venom* / Too loud for the crowd: *Venom* / Bloodlust: *Venom* / Death charge: *Warfare* / Burn down the Kings Road: *Warfare* / Ebony dreams: *Warfare* / Revolution: *Warfare*
CD _____ FRSCD 009
Raw Fruit / Dec '92 / Pinnacle.

RADIO INFERNO
CD _____ RTD 19715982
Our-Choice / Dec '93 / Pinnacle.

RADIO RAP
Boom boom boom: *Outhere Brothers* / Here comes the hotstepper: *Kamoze, Ini* / Whatta man: *Salt 'N' Pepa & En Vogue* / Regulate: *Warren G. & Nate Dogg* / Who am I (what's my name): *Snoop Doggy Dogg* / People everyday: *Arrested Development* / Now that we've found love: *Heavy D & The Boyz* / Boom shake the room: *D.J. Jazzy Jeff & The Fresh Prince* / I like to move it: *Reel 2 Real* / Power: *Snap* / U can't touch this: *M.C. Hammer* / Informer: *Snow* / Boom rock soul: *Benz* / Homie lover friend: *R. Kelly* / Can I kick it: *Tribe Called Quest* / Cantaloop (Flip fantasia): *US 3* / Big poppa: *Notorious B.I.G.* / Throw it out: *Usher* / On a ragga tip: *SL2* / Deep: *East 17*
CD _____ RADCD 22
Global / Oct '95 / BMG.

RAGE TEAM, THE
Back from the grave: *Nekromantix* / We did nothing wrong: *Adolescents UK* / Am I crazy: *Mad Heads* / Jeff's head: *Pikehead* / Rude: *Grind* / Self destruct: *Plastic Bag* / Big wide world: *Strange Behaviour* / And it hurts: *Psycho Bunnies* / Drop dead: *Switchblade* / Everything's so perfect: *Dead Lillies* / Monster metal: *Nekromantix* / Mrs. Thatcher's on the dole: *Adolescents UK* / Now or never: *Mad Heads* / Individuality eagle: *Pikehead* / Paparazzi: *Grind* / Right to remain silent: *Plastic Bag* / It's alright to cry: *Strange Behaviour* / Not with you: *Psycho Bunnies* / I'm your slave: *Switchblade* / Freak show: *Dead Lillies*
CD _____ RAGECD 112
Rage / Sep '93 / Nervous / Magnum Music Group.

RAGGA CLASH
CD _____ FADCD 021
Fashion / Sep '92 / Jetstar / Grapevine.

RAGGA CLASH VOL.2
CD Set _____ FADCD 021
Fashion / Sep '92 / Jetstar / Grapevine.

RAGGA CLASH VOL.3
CD _____ FADCD 29
Fashion / Nov '93 / Jetstar / Grapevine.

RAGGA CLASH VOL.4
CD _____ FADCD 031
Fashion / Dec '95 / Jetstar / Grapevine.

RAGGA DOM
CD _____ 097042
Declic / Apr '95 / Jetstar.

RAGGA HIP HOP VOL. 3
CD _____ CIDM 1096
Mango / Jul '92 / Vital / PolyGram.

RAGGA IN THE JUNGLE
CD _____ STRJCD 1
Street Tuff / Apr '95 / Jetstar.

RAGGA JUNGLE ANTHEMS VOL.1
CD _____ GREZCD 3001
Greensleeves / Dec '95 / Total/BMG / Jetstar / SRD.

RAGGA JUNGLE VOL.1
Talk: *Garnet Silk & Chuckleberry* / Lend me: *F.O.I. & David Thomas* / Limb by limb: *Cutty Ranks* / Hit after hit: *Baby Wayne & Michael Rose* / Connections: *Skeng Gee* / Class: *Bunnie General & Trevor Sax* / Unity remix: *Simpleton & Remarc* / Junglist lover: *Ron Tom & Julie* / Flip flop: *Tenor Senior & Garnet Silk* / Wheel up: *Lion Man* / R.I.P.: *Remarc* / Murder: *Beenie Man & Chuckleberry* / Final chapta (CD/MC): *D.J. Trace* / Soundboy (CD/MC): *Splash* / Selectors roll V.I.P. (CD): *Francis, Errol & Leon Thompson* / Blood, sweat 'n' tears (CD/MC): *Roger Robin & Chuckleberry* / Bad man (CD/MC): *Chuckleberry* / Dead house (CD/MC): *King, Jiggsy & Leroy Smart* / Jungle blanca (MC): *Faze 1 FM*
CD _____ STORM 4 CD
Desert Storm / Jan '96 / Sony.

RAGGA MANIA
CD _____ FABCD 015
Fashion / Sep '95 / Jetstar / Grapevine.

RAGGA MANIA VOL.1
CD _____ CHEMCD 001
Chemist / Aug '95 / Direct / Jetstar.

RAGGA MANIA VOL.2
CD _____ CHEMCD 002
Chemist / Aug '95 / Direct / Jetstar.

RAGGA MEGA MIX
CD _____ SONCD 0054
Sonic Sounds / Aug '93 / Jetstar.

RAGGA PARTY PART 3 - DON'T STOP RAGGA
CD _____ RN 0018 CD
Roof International / Nov '92 / Jetstar.

RAGGA PARTY PART 4 - ROOF ON AIR
CD _____ RN 0019 CD
Roof International / Nov '92 / Jetstar.

RAGGA PITCH
CD _____ MONCD 002
Montana / Nov '93 / Jetstar.

RAGGA RAGGA RAGGA
Don't know: *Jigsy King* / Husband goody-goody: *Capleton* / Movie star: *Galaxy P* / Intimate: *Bounty Killer & Redrose* / Woman fi look good: *Snagapuss* / Living in a dream: *Capleton, Brian & Tony Gold* / Mek noise: *Mad Cobra* / Too young: *Cocoa T & Buju Banton* / Galong so: *Major Mackerel* / Red alert: *Spragga Benz* / Work the body good: *Jigsy King* / Sake a yuh body: *Daddy Screw & Major Christie* / Informer: *Snagapuss, Redrose, Lizard & More* / Return father and son: *Ninja Man & Ninja Ford* / Rude bwoy no powder (Features on cd only.): *Grindsman* / Money (Features on cd only.): *Galaxy P* / Holy moly (Features on cd only.): *Buju Jedd* / Jessica (Features on cd only.): *Red Fox*
CD _____ GRELCD 192
Greensleeves / Nov '93 / Total/BMG / Jetstar / SRD.

RAGGA RAGGA RAGGA 2
Bad boy nuh club scout: *Bounty Killer & Ninjaman* / Dis di program: *Beenie Man* / Sireen: *Papa San* / Run come: *Terror Fabulous* / Wap dem girl: *Sabba Tooth* / Trespass: *Bounty Killer* / Fat piece of goose: *Duck Man* / Hollow point bad boy: *Ninja Man* / Burning up: *Red Dragon* / Not another word: *Bounty Killer* / You must be manical: *Daddy Screw* / Wood stitchie: *Lieutenant Stitchie* / Dem bawling out: *Galaxy P* / Jockey wid di distance: *Tumpa Lion* / Run gal run: *Daddy Lizard* / Hotness: *Mad Cobra* / Spermrod: *Simpleton* / Nuh have no heart: *Bounty Killer*
CD _____ GRELCD 204
Greensleeves / Jun '94 / Total/BMG / Jetstar / SRD.

RAGGA RAGGA RAGGA 3
CD _____ GRELCD 212
Greensleeves / Dec '94 / Total/BMG / Jetstar / SRD.

RAGGA RAGGA RAGGA 4
CD _____ GRELCD 214
Greensleeves / May '95 / Total/BMG / Jetstar / SRD.

RAGGA RAGGA RAGGA 5
CD _____ GRELCD 218
Greensleeves / Aug '95 / Total/BMG / Jetstar / SRD.

RAGGA RAGGA RAGGA 6
CD _____ GRELCD 223
Greensleeves / Nov '95 / Total/BMG / Jetstar / SRD.

RAGGA REVOLUTION
Getting blacker: *Macka B* / Bills: *Thriller Jenna* / Equal rights: *Righteous way: Yabby You* / Kick up a rumpus: *Pepper Seed* / Father of creation: *Harris, Bobby* / Give the poor man a bly: *Pepper Seed* / What's happening to our world: *Shaloma* / Good friend / Tomorrow is another day: *Stewart, Tinga* / Set things straight: *Pepper Seed* / Righteous dub: *Mad Professor*
CD _____ ARICD 086
Ariwa Sounds / Sep '93 / Jetstar / SRD.

RAGGA RIDDIM BHANGRA
CD _____ DMUT 1259
Multitone / Aug '93 / BMG.

RAGGA SUN HIT
CD _____ 0092
Declic / Apr '95 / Jetstar.

RAGGA'S GOT SOUL
CD _____ DTCD 23
Discotex / Aug '95 / 3MV / SRD.

RAGTIME
CD _____ TRTCD 181
TrueTrax / Jun '95 / THE.

RAGTIME BLUES GUITAR (1928-30)
One way gal: *Moore, William* / Ragtime crazy: *Moore, William* / Midnight blues: *Moore, William* / Ragtime millionaire: *Moore, William* / Tillie Lee: *Moore, William* / Barbershop rag: *Moore, William* / Old country rock: *Moore, William* / Raggin' the blues: *Moore, William* / Brownie blues: *Gay, Tarter* / Unknown blues: *Gay, Tarter* / Jamestown exposition: *Baylesse Rose* / Black dog blues: *Baylesse Rose* / Original blues: *Baylesse Rose* / Tricco blues: *Baylesse Rose* / Dupree blues: *Walker, Willie* / Sould Caroline rag: *Walker, Willie*

CD _____ DOCD 5062
Blues Document / Oct '92 / Swift / Jazz Music / Hot Shot.

RAGTIME PIANO HITS
CD _____ MATCD 229
Castle / Dec '92 / BMG.

RAI REBELS
N'sel fik: *Fadela, Chaba & Cheb Sahraoui* / Khadidja: *Hamid, Cheb* / Ya loualid: *Zahouania, Chaba & Cheb Khaled* / Foug-e-ramla: *Benchenet, Houari* / Deblet gualbi: *Sahraoui, Cheb* / Sahr liyali: *Zahouania, Chaba* / Sidi boudmedienne: *Khaled, Cheb* / Mali galbi: *Benchenet, Houari*
CD _____ CDEWV 7
Earthworks / Aug '88 / EMI / Sterns.

**RAIN AND TEARS
(Hit Ballads of the Sixties)**
Yesterday: *Faithfull, Marianne* / You've lost that lovin' feelin': *Righteous Brothers* / I just don't know what to do with myself: *Springfield, Dusty* / Rain and tears: *Aphrodite's Child* / Juliet: *Four Pennies* / I will: *Fury, Billy* / Jesamine: *Casuals* / Joanna: *Walker, Scott* / Someone, someone: *Poole, Brian & The Tremeloes* / Mama: *Berry, Dave* / Sitting in the park: *Fame, Georgie* / Stranger on the shore: *Bilk, Acker*
CD _____ PWK 119
Carlton Home Entertainment / Jul '89 / Carlton Home Entertainment.

RAINDROP GREATEST HITS VOL.1
CD _____ RAINCD 001
Raindrop / Nov '95 / Plastic Head.

RAISE THE ROOF VOL.1
CD Set _____ SCRCD 009
Scratch / Jul '95 / BMG.

RAISE YOUR WINDOW - A CAJUN MUSIC ANTHOLOGY VOL.2
Mama where are you at: *Soileau, Leo & Mayuse Lafleur* / Alone at home: *Guilory, Delin T. & Lewis Lafleur* / Je me suis en alle: *Montet, Bethmost & Joswell Dupois* / You belong to me: *Mistric, Arteleus* / When I meet you at the gate: *Doucet, Oscar & Alius Soileau* / Stop that: *Guilory, Delin T. & Lewis Lafleur* / Waltz of the bayou: *Guidry, Bixy & Percy Babineaux* / La fille que j'aime: *Creduer, Joe & Albert Babindeaux* / Sur le chemin chez moi: *Couzens, Soileau* / Pauvre garcon: *Falcon Trio* / La valse de Ricecville: *Abshire, Nathan & The Rayn-Bo Ramblers* / Raise your window: *Falcon Trio* / Lake Arthur stomp: *Miller's Merrymakers* / La vieux vals an' onc mack: *Thibodeaux Boys* / Si vous moi voudrais aime: *Soileau, Leo & his three aces* / En route chez moi: *Falcon Trio* / Si tu vondroit marriez avec moi: *Joe's Acadians* / Lonesome blues: *Shreve, Floyd & the Three Aces* / Crowley waltz: *Hackberry Ramblers* / Joilie schvr rouge: *Happy Fats & His Rayne-Bo Ramblers*
CD _____ CMF 017D
Country Music Foundation / Aug '93 / Direct / ADA.

RAJASTHAN - MUSICIANS OF THE DESERT
CD _____ C 580058CD
Ocora / Jul '95 / Harmonia Mundi / ADA.

RAJASTHANI FOLK MUSIC
CD _____ CDSDL 401
Saydisc / Mar '94 / Harmonia Mundi / ADA / Direct.

RAK'S - GREATEST HITS
House of the rising sun: *Animals* / I'm into something good: *Herman's Hermits* / Tobacco Road: *Nashville Teens* / Hi ho silver lining: *Beck, Jeff* / To sir with love: *Lulu* / I've been drinking: *Beck, Jeff & Rod Stewart* / Whole lotta love: *CCS* / Oh you pretty thing: *Noone, Peter* / Dance with the devil: *Powell, Cozy* / Journey: *Browne, Duncan* / Tiger feet: *Mud* / So you win again: *Hot Chocolate* / Can the can: *Quatro, Suzi* / Bump: *Kenny* / Motor bikin': *Spedding, Chris* / Lay your love on me: *Racey* / Kids in America: *Wilde, Kim* / Tom, Tom turnaround: *New World* / Classic: *Gurvitz, Adrian* / You sexy thing: *Hot Chocolate*
CD _____ CDSRAK 545
EMI / Aug '91 / EMI.

RAM JAM A GWAAN
CD _____ HBST 161CD
Heartbeat / Aug '94 / Greensleeves / Jetstar / Direct / ADA.

RAMPANT COMPILATION VOL.1
CD _____ SUB 1D
Subversive / Aug '95 / 3MV / SRD.

RANDALL LEE ROSE'S DOO WOP SHOP
I wonder why: *Dion & The Belmonts* / Remember then: *Earls* / Why do kids grow up: *Randy & The Rainbows* / Please love me forever: *Cathy Jean & The Roommates* / You were mine: *Cathy Jean & The Roommates* / Babalu's wedding day: *Eternals* / Church bells may ring: *S.C Cadets* / Pretty little angel eyes: *Lee, Curtis* / I'll follow you: *Jarmels* / Angel baby: *Rosie & The Originals* / Let's start all over again: *Belmonts* / On Sunday afternoon: *Harptones* / Denise: *Randy & The Rainbows* / Eyes: *Earls* / Possibility: *Crowns* / We belong together: *Belmonts* / I'll never know: *Del-Satins* / Once in a while: *Chimes* / Rockin' in the jungle: *Eternals* / Shouldn't

I: *Orients* / I remember: *Five Discs* / Eddie my love: *Teen Queens* / To be loved (forever): *Pentagons* / My true story: *Jive Five* / Who's that knocking: *Genies* / Angels listened in: *Crests* / Hush-a-bye: *Mystics* / There's a moon out tonight: *Capris* / This I swear: *Skyliners* / Till then: *Classics*
CD _____ CDCHD 392
Ace / Oct '92 / Pinnacle / Cadillac / Complete/Pinnacle.

RAP ATTACK
When the ship goes down: *Cypress Hill* / Can I kick it: *Tribe Called Quest* / OPP: *Naughty By Nature* / Boom shake the room: *D.J. Jazzy Jeff & The Fresh Prince* / Wap-babalubop: *Funkdoobiest* / Mr. Wendal: *Arrested Development* / Set adrift on memory bliss: *PM Dawn* / Funky cold medina: *Tone Loc* / Uptown hit: *Kurious* / Jump around: *House Of Pain* / Ghetto jam: *Domino* / Eye know: *De La Soul* / Push it: *Salt 'N' Pepa* / Walk this way: *Run DMC & Aerosmith* / Slam: *Onyx* / Temple: *Fugees* / Lovesick: *Gang Starr* / Around the way girl: *L.L. Cool J* / Shut 'em down: *Public Enemy* / Jump: *Kriss Kross*
CD _____ MOODCD 32
Columbia / Mar '94 / Sony.

RAP AUTHORITY, THE
CD _____ ICH 78032
Ichiban / Apr '94 / Koch.

RAP COMPILATION: ZOMBA
CD _____ EMPRCD 554
Emporio / Nov '94 / THE / Disc / CM.

RAP DECLARES WAR
Rap declares war: *War & Friends* / Funky 4 U: *Nice & Smooth* / New Jack swing: *Wreckx N Effect* / Feels so good: *Brand Nubian* / Potholes in my lawn: *De La Soul* / Short but funky: *Too Short* / Heartbeat: *Ice-T* / Young black male: *2 Pac* / Don't let no-one get you down: *War & Hispanic MC's* / Low rider (on the boulevard): *Latin Alliance* / Ya estuvo (that's it): *Kid Frost* / Slow ride: *Beastie Boys* / Drums of steel: *7A3* / Rhyme fighter: *Mellow Man Ace* / Summatymz ova: *Brotherhood Creed* / Spill the wine: *Lighter Shade Of Brown* / Join me please (homeboys make some noise): *Mantronix*
CD _____ 74321305252
Avenue / Sep '95 / BMG.

RAP HOUSE DANCE PARTY
CD _____ 15376
Laserlight / Aug '91 / Target/BMG.

RAP POWER PLAY
CD _____ 12369
Laserlight / Jun '91 / Target/BMG.

RAP STREET
CD _____ ITM 001459CD
ITM / Jun '93 / Tradelink / Koch.

RAP TO THE MAX
Boom shake the room: *D.J. Jazzy Jeff & The Fresh Prince* / Come baby come: *K7* / Jump around: *House Of Pain* / Boom shak-a-lak: *Apache Indian* / Informer: *Snow* / Whistler: *Honky* / Hip hop hooray: *Naughty By Nature* / That's how I'm livin': *Ice-T* / Can I kick it: *Tribe Called Quest* / Walk this way: *Run DMC & Aerosmith* / Now that we've found love: *Heavy D & The Boyz* / Push it: *Salt 'N' Pepa* / It's a shame (my sister): *Monie Love & True Image* / No matter what U do (I'm gonna get with U): *Flavour* / Here we go: *Stakka Bo* / Feelin' alright: *EYC* / For what it's worth: *Oui 3* / Get a life: *Soul II Soul* / Me, myself and I: *De La Soul* / Can't wait to be with you: *D.J. Jazzy Jeff & The Fresh Prince*
CD _____ VTCD 25
Virgin / Apr '94 / EMI.

RAPSO
CD _____ RAPSOCD 1
Recognition / Oct '94 / Total/BMG.

RARE 1930'S BLUES: 1934-1937
CD _____ DOCD 53331
Blues Document / Apr '95 / Swift / Jazz Music / Hot Shot.

RARE CHICAGO BLUES 1962-1968
CD _____ CDBB 9530
Bullseye Blues / Jun '93 / Direct.

RARE GROOVE
Boogie wonderland: *Earth, Wind & Fire & The Emotions* / Shake your body: *Jacksons* / That's the way I like it: *K.C. & The Sunshine Band* / Use it up and wear it out: *Odyssey* / And the beat goes on: *Whispers* / Contact: *Starr, Edwin* / More than a woman: *Tavares* / If I can't have you: *Gilman, Yvonne* / I will survive: *Gaynor, Gloria* / Ring my bell: *Ward, Anita* / Hang on in there baby: *Bristol, Johnny* / Rock your baby: *McCrae, George* / You bet your love: *Hancock, Herbie* / Now that we've found love: *Third World* / Play that funky music: *Wild Cherry* / It's a disco night (rock don't stop): *Isley Brothers* / Le freak: *Chic* / We are family: *Sister Sledge* / Boogie nights: *Heatwave* / You make me feel (mighty real): *Sylvester* / Don't stop the music: *Yarbrough & Peoples* / Working my way back to you: *Detroit Spinners* / Rock the boat: *Hues Corporation* / Funky town: *Lipps Inc.* / Love come down: *King, Evelyn 'Champagne'* / I can make you feel good: *Shalamar* / Celebration: *Kool & The Gang* / Haven't stopped dancing yet: *Gonzales* / Right back where we started

from: Nightingale, Maxine / Get along with-out you now: Wills, Viola / Jump to the beat: Lattisaw, Stacy / Searching: Change
CD _____ QTVCD 016
Quality / Nov '92 / Pinnacle.

RARE GROOVE CLASSICS VOL.1
CD _____ SGCD 16
Sir George / Jul '93 / Jetstar / Pinnacle.

RARE JAZZ AND BLUES PIANO 1935-37
CD _____ DOCD 5388
Document / Dec '95 / Jazz Music / Hot Shot / ADA.

RARE MANCINI, THE
CD _____ 12430
Laserlight / May '95 / Target/BMG.

RARE MEXICAN CUTS FROM THE SIXTIES
CD _____ 842626
EVA / Jun '94 / Direct / ADA.

RARE ON AIR - LIVE PERFORMANCES VOL.1
Poem: Cohen, Leonard / Silent all these years: Amos, Tori / Cordoba: Cale, John / Always in disguise: Himmelmann, Peter / My drug buddy: Dando, Evan & Juliana Hatfield / Coal: Penn, Michael / Arms for hostages: X / God's hotel: Cave, Nick & The Bad Seeds / Mexico: Beck / Peace: Los Lobos / Never going back again: Buckingham, Lindsey / Moderns: Isham, Mark / Captive heart: Perry, Brendan / How you've grown: Merchant, Natalie / Which will: Williams, Lucinda / Chet Baker's unsung swan song: Wilcox, David
CD _____ MR 0742
Mammoth / May '94 / Vital.

RARE ON AIR - LIVE PERFORMANCES VOL.2
Sugar water: Matto, Cibo / Palomine: Bettie Serveert / Sweet ride: Donnelly, Tanya / Everybody can change: Chesnutt, Vic / Mystery girl: World Party / City sleeps: M.C. 900ft Jesus / Just like this train: Mitchell, Joni / Cajun moon: Cale, J.J. / I've had it: Mann, Aimee / Beautiful friend: Sebadoh / Sunday: Cranberries / Opening: Glass, Philip / Famous blue raincoats: Cole, Lloyd / Late for the sky: Browne, Jackson
CD _____ MR 1072
Mammoth / Sep '95 / Vital.

RARE REGGAE FROM THE VAULTS OF STUDIO ONE
CD _____ HBCD 47
Heartbeat / May '89 / Greensleeves / Jetstar / Direct / ADA.

RARE SOUL: BEACH MUSIC CLASSICS VOL.1
CD _____ R 270277
Rhino / Apr '92 / Warner Music.

RARE SOUL: BEACH MUSIC CLASSICS VOL.2
CD _____ R 270278
Rhino / Apr '92 / Warner Music.

RARE SOUL: BEACH MUSIC CLASSICS VOL.3
CD _____ R 270279
Rhino / Apr '92 / Warner Music.

RARE TERRITORY BANDS
CD _____ IAJRCCD 1002
IAJRC / Oct '93 / Jazz Music.

RAREST ROCKABILLY & HILLBILLY BOOGIE/BEST OF ACE ROCKABILLY
Nothin' but a nuthin': Stewart, Jimmy & His Nighthawks / Darlin': Dale, Jimmie / Baby doll: Dale, Jimmie / Pretending is a game: Jeffers, Sleepy & The Davis Twins / My blackbirds are bluebirds now: Jeffers, Sleepy & The Davis Twins / Don't sweep that dirt on me: Shaw, Buddy / No more: Shaw, Buddy / My baby left me: Rogers, Rock / Little dog blues: Price, Mel / Hen-pecked daddy: Johnson, Ralph & The Hill-billy Show Boys / Umm boy you're my baby: Johnson, Bill & The Dabblers / Stoney mountain boogie: Stoney Mountain Play-boys / Big black cat: Hendon, R.D. / It's a Saturday night: Mack, Billy / Rockin' daddy: Fisher, Sonny / Everybody's movin': Glenn, Glen / One cup of coffee: Glenn, Glen / I can't find the doorknob: Jimmy & Johnny / My big fat baby: Hall, Sonny & The Echoes / How come it: Jones, Thumper / Trucker from Tennessee: Davis, Link / Little bit more: La Beef, Sleepy / I'm through: La Beef, Sleepy / Jitterbop baby: Harris, Hal / Let's get it on: Almond, Hershel / I'm a hobo: Reeves, Danny / Rock it: Jones, George / Sneaky Pete: Fisher, Sonny
CD _____ CDCHD 311
Ace / Jul '91 / Pinnacle / Cadillac / Complete/Pinnacle.

RAS RECORDS PRESENTS A REGGAE CHRISTMAS
We wish you a Merry Christmas / Jingle bells: Carlos, Don & Glenice Spencer / Joy of the world: Lodge, June / O come all ye faithful (Adeste fidelis): McGregor, Freddie / Drummer boy: Michigan & Smiley / Twelve days of Christmas: Broggs, Peter / Silent night: Black, Pablo / Feliz Navidad: McGregor, Freddie / Night before Christmas: Eek-A-Mouse
CD _____ RASCD 3101
Ras / Jan '89 / Jetstar / Greensleeves / SRD / Direct.

RAS, REGGAE AND RYKODISC
CD _____ RCD 20151
Hannibal / Aug '91 / Vital / ADA.

RAST DESTAGAH
CD _____ PANCCD 2017
Pan / May '93 / ADA / Direct / CM.

RASTA REGGAE
CD _____ RB 3018
Reggae Best / Jan '96 / Magnum Music Group / THE.

RASTA SHOWCASE
CD _____ CC 2708
Crocodisc / Jan '94 / THE / Magnum Music Group.

RASTAFARI TEACHINGS
CD _____ ROTCD 004
Reggae On Top / Jun '95 / Jetstar / SRD.

RASTAFARI VOL.1
CD _____ MMCD 3
Melody Muzik / Nov '95 / SRD.

RAUCOUS RECORDS SINGLES COLLECTION
Nightmare: Go Katz / Bedrock: Frantic Flint-stones / Let's go somewhere: Frantic Flint-stones / Last breath: Spellbound / More whiskey: Caravans / Do the hucklebuck: Griswalds / Robbie robot: Griswalds / You can't judge a book by the cover: Deltas / How come you do me: Deltas / Home sweet home: Termites / Old black Joe: Frantic Flintstones / Alchohol buzz: Frantic Flint-stones / Cold cold Sunday: Sergeant Fury / Something gotta give: Nitros / Face the fact: Rattlers / Pink hearse: Radium Cats / Haunted by your love: Radium Cats / Bop pills: Mercurys / Cardillac rest: Deuces Wild / Psycho vision: Sergeant Fury / Kangaroo barndance: Thee Waltons / Fat, drunk and stupid: Thee Waltons / Ready to burn: Thee Rayguns / Caught in a dream: Sergeant Fury / Old man in the woods: Cosmic Voodoo
CD _____ CDMPSYCHO 8
Anagram / Sep '95 / Pinnacle.

RAUNCHY BUSINESS - HOT NUTS AND LOLLIPOPS
Sam the hot dog man: Johnson, Lil / My stove's in good condition: Johnson, Lil / Wipe it off: Johnson, Lonnie / Best jockey in town: Johnson, Lonnie / Shave 'em dry: Bogan, Lucille / He's just my size: Kirkman, Lillie Mae / If it don't fit (don't force it): Barrel House Annie / Furniture man blues: John-son, Lonnie & Victoria Spivey / My pencil don't write no more: Carter, Bo / Banana in your fruit basket: Carter, Bo / Get 'em from the peanut man (hot nuts): Johnson, Lil / Get 'em from the peanut man (the new hot nuts): Johnson, Lil / Drivin' that thing: Mis-sissippi Sheiks / Bed spring poker: Missis-sippi Sheiks / Loophound: Hunter & Jenkins / Meat cuttin' blues: Hunter & Jenkins / You got to give me some of it: Moss, Buddy / Butcher shop blues: Edwards, Bernice
CD _____ 4678892
Columbia / May '91 / Sony.

RAUSCHEN 10
CD _____ FIM 1017
Force Inc / Oct '95 / SRD.

RAUSCHEN 7
CD Set _____ FIM 1013
Force Inc / Jun '94 / SRD.

RAUSCHEN 9
CD _____ FIM 1016
Force Inc / Apr '95 / SRD.

RAVE ANTHEMS
Everybody in the place: Prodigy / Anas-thasia: T99 / Go: Moby / D.J.'s take control: SL2 / (I wanna give you) Devotion: Nomad / Sweet harmony: Liquid / Far out: Sonz Of A Loop Da Loop Era / Charly: Prodigy / Playing with knives: Bizarre Inc / Dub war: Dance Conspiracy / Activ 8: Altern 8 / Take me away: Cappella / Move any mountain: Shamen / Close your eyes: Acen / Insom-niak: DJPC / Get ready for this: 2 Unlimited / Ebeneezer goode: Shamen / We've got to live together: R.A.F. / Bouncer: Kicks Like A Mule / I want you (forever): Cox, Carl / Hard-core heaven: D.J. Seduction / Trip to the moon: Acen / Infinity: Guru Josh / Some-thing good: Utah Saints / Frequency: Altern 8 / Way in my brain: SL2 / Is there anybody out there: SL2 / Night in motion: Cubic 22 / Searching for my rizla: Cubic 22 / Liquid is liquid: Liquid / What time is now: K.L.F. / Feel so real: Dream Frequency / Lock up: Zero B / Hardcore uproar: Together / Let me be your fantasy: Baby D / It's a fine day: Opus III / Nightbird: Convert / 2/231: Anti-cappella / Can you feel the passion: Blue Pearl / Injected with a poison: Khan, Praga
CD _____ DINCD 104
Dino / Jul '95 / Pinnacle / 3MV.

RAVE CLASSICS
CD _____ CCSCD 375
Castle / Jan '96 / BMG.

RAVE COLLISION
CD _____ EWM 41872
Broken Beat / Aug '95 / Plastic Head.

RAVE FLOOR MUSIC FOR RAVE FLOOR PEOPLE VOL.1
CD _____ BB 04209DCD
Broken Beat / Jan '96 / Plastic Head.

RAVE GENER8TOR 2
CD _____ JARCD 4
Cookie Jar / Apr '93 / SRD.

RAVE GENER8TOR, THE
CD _____ JARCD 3
Cookie Jar / May '92 / SRD.

RAVE MASSACRE
CD _____ SPV 08938962
SPV / Oct '94 / Plastic Head.

RAVE MISSION
CD Set _____ SPV 08838952
Subterranean / Aug '94 / Plastic Head.

RAVE MISSION II (Entering Lightspeed)
CD Set _____ SPV 08938232
Subterranean / Dec '94 / Plastic Head.

RAVE MISSION III
CD Set _____ SPV 08938292
Subterranean / May '95 / Plastic Head.

RAVE MISSION IV (2CD Set)
CD Set _____ SPV 08938352
Subterranean / Jul '95 / Plastic Head.

RAVE MISSION V (The Jubilee Box Set)(3CD Set)
CD Set _____ TCD 09238480
Subterranean / Dec '95 / Plastic Head.

RAVE MISSION VOL.5
CD _____ 08938482
CD _____ 09238508
SPV / Jan '96 / Plastic Head.

RAVEALATION
CD _____ STHCCD 1
Strictly Underground / Jun '95 / SRD.

RAVEMEISTER (2CD Set)
CD Set _____ SPV 08938362
SPV / Jun '95 / Plastic Head.

RAVEMEISTER VOL.2 (2CD Set)
CD Set _____ SPV 08938452
Subterranean / Dec '95 / Plastic Head.

RAVING MAD
Trip to Trumpton: Urban Hype / Sesame's treet: Smart E's / Searching for my rizla: Ratpack / Closer to all your dreams: Rhythm Quest / Temple of dreams: Messiah / Sun: Nino / On a rubbish tip: Progression / Papua new guinea: Future Sound Of London / Hot chilli: N.A.M. / No other: Nightbreed / Hu-manoid: Stakker / What's E for dad: Little Jack / Trip to the moon (Part 2): Acen / Re-set: Output & D.J. Oz / Feel the vibe: Tequila Carter
CD _____ CDELV 01
Elevate / Jul '92 / 3MV / Sony.

RAW BLUES VOL.1
CD _____ CDSGP 026
Prestige / Jan '93 / Total/BMG.

RAW BLUES VOL.2
CD Set _____ CDSGP 081
Prestige / Aug '94 / Total/BMG.

RAW COMPILATION VOL.1
CD _____ FNARRCD 009
Damaged Goods / May '92 / SRD.

RAW ELEMENTS VOL.1
Fonky: Goldfinger / Listen carefully: Freak-azoid / Pin pac: Synful Dyme / Clearvoy-ance: Gianelli, Fred / Percussive dub: Closed Circuit / Tri top: Phax & Steve Bug / Fresh: Bug, Steve / Esoteric: Basic Gravity place: Max Da Fly
CD _____ SUPER 2035CD
Superstition / Jun '95 / Vital / BMG.

RAW FLAVAS VOL.1
Up with the boom: S.L. Troopers / Living rhythm and drum: S.L. Troopers / It's the K.O.: Korperayshun / Life: Korperayshun / Can you get with this: Banji / It's like dat: Banji / Fatal attraction: K.I.D. / Big boss: K.I.D. / We ain't tryin' 2 hear it: K.I.D.
CD _____ KSCD 9
Kold Sweat / Mar '94 / 3MV.

RAW JAMS VOL.1
CD _____ HOMEGROWNCD 3
Homegrown / Jun '95 / Jetstar / Mo's Music Machine.

RAW 'N' UNCUT HIP HOP
CD _____ EFA 127772
Ruff 'n' Raw / Nov '95 / SRD.

RAW POWER SAMPLER
Parisienne walkways (live): Moore, Gary / Run to your mama: Moore, Gary / Gypsy: Uriah Heep / Wizard: Uriah Heep / In nomine satanus: Venom / Devil's answer: Atomic Rooster / Walking in the park: Col-osseum / Chase is better than the catch: Motorhead / Bang the drum all day: Rund-gren, Todd / In the beginning: Magnum
CD _____ RAWCD 1000
Raw Power / Mar '88 / BMG.

RAW RAW DUB
CD _____ CEND 2000
Century / Nov '94 / Total/BMG / Jetstar.

RAW RECORDS PUNK COLLECTION, THE
Sick of you: Users / I'm in love with today: Users / Johnny won't go to heaven: Killjoys

/ Naive: Killjoys / Withdrawal: Unwanted / Bleak outlook: Unwanted / 1984: Unwanted / New religion: Some Chicken / Blood on the wall: Some Chicken / Radio call sign: Lockjaw / Young ones: Lockjaw / Arabian daze: Some Chicken / Number seven: Some Chicken / It's my life: Gorillas / My soul's alive: Gorillas / Secret police: Un-wanted / These boots are made for walking: Unwanted / Journalist jive: Lockjaw / I'm not me: Unwanted / End is nigh: Unwanted / Bondage boy: Sick Things / Kids on the street: Sick Things / So young: Psychos / Straight jacket: Psychos / At night: Killjoys / I wish you dead: Acme Sewage Co. / I don't need you: Acme Sewage Co. / Millionaire: G.T.'S / Young British and white: Psychos / I can see you: Acme Sewage Co.
CD _____ CDPUNK 14
Anagram / Sep '93 / Pinnacle.

RAW RUB A DUB VOL.2: EINSTEIN'S THEORY OF DUB
CD _____ GPCD 003
Gussie P / Oct '94 / Jetstar.

RAZOR RECORDS PUNK COLLECTION
CD _____ CDPUNK 45
Anagram / Feb '95 / Pinnacle.

RCA VICTOR JAZZ - THE FIRST HALF-CENTURY (5CD Set)
Black bottom stomp: Morton, Jelly Roll / Heah' me talkin': Dodds, Johnny / Black beauty: Ellington, Duke / Variety stomp: Henderson, Fletcher / Too late: Oliver, King / Peggy: McKinney's Cotton Pickers / Boy in the boat: Johnson, Charlie / Bleeding hearted blues: Johnson, James P. / Handful of keys: Waller, Fats / Glad rag doll: Hines, Earl / Duet stomp: Jones & Collins Astoria Hot Eight / Tiger rag: Original Dixieland Jazz Band / She's cryin for me: New Orleans Rhythm Kings / Lonely melody: Beider-becke, Bix & Paul Whiteman Orchestra / De-lirium: Nichols, Red / Wild cat: Venuti, Joe & Eddie Lang / Waitin' for Katie: Goodman, Benny & Ben Pollack orchestra / Doin' the voom voom: Miley, Bubber & Duke Ellington orchestra / Swing out: Allen, Henry 'Red' / One hour: Hawkins, Coleman & Mound City Blue Blowers / Hello Lola: Russell, Pee Wee, Mound city blue blowers / There's a serious thing: Teagarden, Jack/Eddie Condon's hot shots / South: Moten, Bennie / Basin Street blues: Armstrong, Louis / Daybreak ex-press: Ellington, Duke / Moten swing: Basie, Count & Bennie Moten Orchestra / Hocus pocus: Henderson, Fletcher / King Porter stomp: Goodman, Benny / Swingin' up-town: Lunceford, Jimmie / Song of India: Dorsey, Tommy / XYZ: Hines, Earl / Chero-kee: Barnet, Charlie / Carioca: Shaw, Artie / Any old time: Holiday, Billie & Artie Shaw Orchestra / Body and soul: Wilson, Teddy Trio / Life goes to a party: James, Harry & the Benny Goodman Orchestra / Swing is here: Eldridge, Roy & Gene Krupa's swing band / Shufflin at the Hollywood: Hampton, Lionel / I'm in the mood for swing: Carter, Benny & Lionel Hampton Orchestra / Rockin' chair: Bailey, Mildred / Dinah: Wal-ler, Fats / Really the blues: Bechet, Sidney & Tommy Ladnier / Relaxin' at the Touro: Spanier, Muggsy / Eel: Freeman, Bud / I can't get started (with you): Berigan, Bunny / Jack the bear: Ellington, Duke & Jimmy Blanton / Do nothin' 'til you hear from me: Williams, Cootie & Duke Ellington orchestra / Cotton tail: Webster, Ben & Duke Ellington & his orchestra / Mobile bay: Stewart, Rex / Daydream: Hodges, Johnny / Pennies from heaven: Armstrong, Louis / Little jazz: Eldridge, Roy & Artie Shaw & his orchestra / Manteca: Gillespie, Dizzy / Victory ball: Parker, Charlie & The Metronome All Stars / Epistrophy: Clarke, Kenny / Half step down please: Hawkins, Coleman / Spontaneous combustion: Tristano, Lennie / Stormy Monday blues: Hines, Earl & Billy Eckstine / Bil's mill: Basie, Count / Yes indeed: Dor-sey, Tommy / Summertime: Shaw, Artie / All of me: Carter, Benny / Old man blues: Be-chet, Sidney / Minor swing: Reinhardt, Django / Fifth dimension: Williams, Mary Lou / Erroll's bounce: Garner, Erroll / My blue heaven: Peterson, Oscar / Whisper not: Blakey, Art / Ysabel's table dance: Mingus, Charles / Salt peanuts: Powell, Bud / Black is the colour of my true love's hair: New-born, Phineas Jr. / Concerto for Billy the kid: Russell, George & Bill Evans / Blues for Pablo: Evans, Gil / April in Paris: Evans, Gil / Wailing pot: Ferguson, Maynard / Two de-grees east, three degrees west: Lewis, John / Chiquito loco: Rogers, Shorty & Art Pepper / Roses of picardy: Norvo, Red / East of the sun and west of the moon: Cohn, Al & Zoot Sims / Between the devil and the deep blue sea: Wiley, Lee / Love is just around the corner: Allen, Henry 'Red' / Perdido: Terry, Clark & the Duke Ellington Orchestra / Bridge: Rollins, Sonny / Blood count: Elling-ton, Duke & Billy Strayhorn / So what: John-son, J.J. / Where do go go: The Girl from Ipanema: Getz, Stan / Here's that rainy day: Desmond, Paul / Blight of the fumble bee: Mulligan, Gerry / Old folks: McLean, Jackie / Star eyes: Baker, Chet / Sing me softly of the blues: Burton, Gary / One o'clock jump: Lambert & Hendricks / Come back baby: Williams, Joe / Flying home: Hampton, Lio-nel & Illinois Jacquet
CD _____ 07863660842
Bluebird / Nov '92 / BMG.

REACT - TEST 1
CD _____ REACTCD 31
Southern / Nov '93 / SRD.

REACT TEST THREE
Joanna: *Mrs. Woods* / Shinny: *Elevator* / Magic: *Blu Peter* / Sugar shack: *Seb* / Orange theme: *Cygnus X* / Tip of the iceberg: *G.T.O.* / Spirit: *Kitachi* / Witch doktor: *Van Helden, Armand* / Untitled: *Sharp Tools* / P.A.R.T.Y.: *Movin' Melodies* / Do me: *Aquarius* / Bring it back 2 luv: *Project*
CD _____ REACTCD 070
React / Nov '95 / Vital.

REACTIVATE VOL.10
Osaka acid: *Sushi* / Lost in love: *Legend B* / First rebirth: *Jones & Stephenson* / Access: *X Trax* / Ready to flow: *Urban Trance Plant* / Sizzling love: *PHI* / Ice man on the beach: *Pan & Trex* / Que vous etez: *Friends, Lovers & Family* / Can't stop: *Komakino* / Superstitious: *Luxor* / Point zero: *Li Kwan* / Cybertrance: *Blue Alphabet* / Flagship (On CD2 & MC.): *Blu Peter* / Mighty machine (On CD2 & MC.): *Dream Plant* / Octopus (On CD2 & MC.): *Art Of Trance* / Under siege (On CD2 & MC.): *Project X* / Acid NRG (On CD2 & MC.): *NRG Jams* / Future world (On CD2 £ MC.): *Cenobyte*
CD _____ REACTCD 060
React / May '95 / Vital.

REACTIVATE VOL.10 - REMIX
CD _____ REACTCDX 060
React / May '95 / Vital.

REACTIVATE VOL.5
Age of love: *Age Of Love* / You gotta believe: *Fierce Ruling Diva* / Compnded: *Edge Records 1* / He never lost his hardcore: *NRG* / Eighty eight to piano: *Mainx* / Hablando: *Ramirez & Pizarro* / Cosmotrash: *Trasnman* / Blue oyster: *SIL* / Urban bells: *Passion Flower* / Observing the earth: *Dyewitness* / Mr. Peanut: *West Bam* / Set up 707: *Edge Of Motion*
CD _____ REACTCD 010
React / Jul '92 / Vital.

REACTIVATE VOL.6
CD _____ REACTCD 015
React / Nov '92 / Vital.

REACTIVATE VOL.7
CD _____ REACTCD 019
React / May '93 / Vital.

REACTIVATE VOL.8
CD _____ REACTCD 027
React / Oct '93 / Vital.

REACTIVATE VOL.9
CD _____ REACTCD 044
React / Jul '94 / Vital.

READING FESTIVAL '73
Hands off: *Gallagher, Rory* / Feathered friends: *Greenslade* / Losing you: *Faces* / Earth mother: *Duncan, Lesley* / Hang onto a dream: *Hardin, Tim* / Person to person: *Hardin, Tim* / Roadrunner: *Strider* / Don't waste my time: *Status Quo* / Long legged Linda: *Bown, Andy*
CD _____ SEECD 343
See For Miles/C5 / Mar '92 / Pinnacle.

READY STEADY GO & WIN
Hyde 'n' seek: *Thyrds* / I'll miss you: *Harbour Lights* / Bo Street runner: *Bo Street Runners* / Did you ever hear the sound: *Knight, Tony & The Livewires* / Lonely one: *Deltones & Tony Lane* / She loves to be loved: *Falling Leaves* / You make me go 'oooh': *Dynamos* / Not guilty: *Falling Leaves* / And I do what I want: *Bo Street Runners* / Tell me what you're gonna do: *Bo Street Runners* / I'm leaving you: *Royal, Jimmy & The Hawkes* / So much love: *Planets* / Every time I look at you: *Five Aces* / Anytime: *Scene Five* / Ain't it a shame: *Vibrons* / Mistletoe love: *Fenda, Jaymes & The Vulcans* / Thank of the: *Olympics* / You've come back: *Leasides* / Only girl: *Fenda, Jaymes & The Vulcans* / Get out of my way: *Bo Street Runners* / Baby never say goodbye: *Bo Street Runners*
CD _____ SEECD 202
See For Miles/C5 / Feb '92 / Pinnacle.

REAL BLUES BALLADS, THE
CD _____ MPV 5513
Movieplay / Jun '95 / Target/BMG.

REAL DEAL
CD _____ CDRAID 514
Rumour / Feb '94 / Pinnacle / 3MV / Sony.

REAL DEAL 2
CD _____ CDRAID 517
Rumour / May '94 / Pinnacle / 3MV / Sony.

REAL ESTATE
CD _____ ECD 1015
Recommended / Jul '91 / These / ReR Megacorp.

REAL EXCELLO R&B, THE
Little queen bee (got a brand new king): *Harpo, Slim* / I need money (keep your alibis): *Harpo, Slim* / Still rainin' in my heart: *Harpo, Slim* / I tried so hard: *Smith, Whispering* / Cryin' blues: *Smith, Whispering* / I'm goin' in the valley: *Hogan, Silas* / Dark clouds rollin': *Hogan, Silas* / So glad: *Austin, Leon* / I had a dream last night: *Lonesome Sundown* / She's my crazy little

---

baby: *Lonesome Sundown* / Goin' crazy over T.V.: *Anderson, Jimmy* / You're playin' hookey: *Lonesome Sundown* / It's love baby: *Gaines, Earl* / Nothing in this world (gonna keep you from me): *Anderson, Jimmy* / Let's play house: *Gunter, Arthur* / Winter time blues: *Lightnin' Slim* / Pleasin' for love: *Shelton, Roscoe* / Whoa now: *Lazy Lester* / It's your voodoo working: *Sheffield, Charles 'Mad Dog'* / Rock-a-me all night long: *Nelson, Jay* / Leavin' Tennessee: *Garner, Alan* / Baby, kiss me gain: *Sweet Clifford* / Crazy over you: *Shelton, Roscoe* / Baby I'm stickin' to you: *Friday, Charles*
CD _____ CDCHD 562
Ace / Nov '94 / Pinnacle / Cadillac / Complete/Pinnacle.

REAL JAZZ BALLADS
CD _____ MPV 5519
Movieplay / Oct '92 / Target/BMG.

REAL MUSIC OF PERU, THE
Maria Alejandrina: *Picaflor De Los Andes* / Un pasajero en el camino: *Picaflor De Los Andes* / Fiesta de mayo: *Picaflor De Los Andes* / Aguas del Rio Rimac: *Picaflor De Los Andes* / Cariño de pasatas: *Picaflor De Los Andes* / Verbenita, verbenita: *La Pallasquinta* / Oreganito: *La Pallasquinta* / El guapachoso: *Orquesta Sensacion Del Mantaro* / Llorando a mares: *Flor Pucarina* / Airampito: *Flor Pucarina* / Noche de luna: *Flor Pucarina* / Para que quiero la vida: *Flor Pucarina* / Pichiusita: *Flor Pucarina* / Rompe Macarios: *Orquesta Los Tarumas De Tarma* / Dos Clavelles: *La Princesita De Yungay* / Tus ojos: *Los Borbones Del Peru* / Ya te gane: *Orquesta Los Rebeldes De Huancayo*
CD _____ CDORBD 064
Globestyle / Feb '91 / Pinnacle.

REAL SOUND OF JAZZ, THE
CD _____ LS 2912
Landscape / Nov '92 / THE.

REAL STONES
Come on: *Berry, Chuck* / I just want to be loved: *Waters, Muddy* / Bye bye Johnny: *Berry, Chuck* / You better move on: *Alexander, Arthur* / Money: *Strong, Barrett* / Route 66: *Berry, Chuck* / Caról: *Berry, Chuck* / Mona: *Diddley, Bo* / Fortune teller: *Spellman, Benny* / Confessin' the blues: *Berry, Chuck* / Around and around: *Berry, Chuck* / Don't lie to me: *Berry, Chuck* / Memphis: *Berry, Chuck* / Roadrunner: *Diddley, Bo* / Roll over Beethoven: *Berry, Chuck* / Cops and robbers: *Diddley, Bo* / Down the road apiece: *Diddley, Bo* / I can't be satisfied: *Waters, Muddy* / You can't catch me: *Berry, Chuck* / Suzie Q: *Hawkins, Dale* / Little red rooster: *Howlin' Wolf* / Talkin' about you: *Berry, Chuck* / Look what you've done: *Waters, Muddy* / Little Queenie: *Berry, Chuck* / Let it rock: *Berry, Chuck* / Run Rudolph run: *Berry, Chuck* / Crackin' up: *Diddley, Bo* / I'm a man: *Diddley, Bo* / Rollin' stone: *Waters, Muddy*
CD _____ PRD 70122
Provogue / Dec '89 / Pinnacle.

REAL WORLD SAMPLER 1995
Le voyageur: *Wemba, Papa* / Hazo avo: *Rossy* / Mwanuni: *Eyuphuro* / Al nahla al 'Ali: *Eyuphuro* / Shahbaaz qalandar: *Khan, Nusrat Fateh Ali* / Ya sahib-ul-Jamal: *Sabri Brothers* / Nibiro ghon andare: *Sabri Brothers* / Raga bhairavi: *Sridhar, K. & K Shivakumar* / Enchantment: *Chandra, Sheila* / Sgariunt na Gcompanagh (The parting of friends): *Malloy, Matt*
CD _____ RWSAM 4
Realworld / Oct '95 / EMI / Sterns.

REALWORLD PRESENTS...
CD _____ RWSAM 1
Realworld / Jul '94 / EMI / Sterns.

REBEL MUSIC
(An Anthology of Reggae Music)
You don't know: *Andy, Bob* / Loser: *Harriott, Derrick* / High school dance: *McKay, Freddie* / Russians are coming: *Bennett, Val* / Tonight: *Keith & Tex* / Ain't that lovin' you: *U-Roy* / Them a fe get a beatin': *Tosh, Peter* / God helps the man: *Smart, Leroy* / Hypocrite: *Heptones* / S90 skank: *Big Youth* / Satan side: *Andy, Horace & Earl Flute* / Give praises: *Big Youth* / Rock away: *Isaacs, Gregory* / Saturday night special: *Dyke, Michael* / Cool rasta: *Heptones*
CD Set _____ CDTRD 403
Trojan / Mar '94 / Jetstar / Total/BMG.

REBEL ROUSERS: SOUTHERN ROCK CLASSICS
CD _____ R 270586
Rhino / Mar '92 / Warner Music.

REBIRTH OF COOL
CD _____ BRCD 563
4th & Broadway / Feb '91 / PolyGram.

REBIRTH OF COOL II
i've lost my ignorance (and don't know where to find it): *Dream Warriors* / La raza: *Kid Frost* / Senga abele (lion roar): *Dibango, Manu & MC Mello* / Cool and funky: *Jordan, Ronny* / I should've known better: *Paris, Mica* / All for one: *Brand Nubian* / One to grow on: *UMC's* / Family: *McKoy* / Try my love: *Washburn, Lalomie* / Kickin' jazz: *Outlaw* / Looking at the front door: *Main Source* / Free your feelings: *Slam Slam* / Go with the flow: *Rock, Pete & C.L. Smooth* / Set me free: *Bygraves* / Black whip: *Chapter & Verse* / Slow jam: *Dodge City Productions*
CD _____ BRCD 582
4th & Broadway / Feb '92 / PolyGram.

REBIRTH OF COOL III
CD _____ BRCD 590
4th & Broadway / Apr '93 / PolyGram.

REBIRTH OF COOL IV
Just wanna touch her: *D.J. Krush* / Play my funk: *Simple E* / Rent strike: *Groove Collective* / R U conscious: *Buchanan, Courtney* / My favourite things: *Jordan, Ronny* / Otha fish: *Pharcyde* / Cantamilla: *Tranquility Bass* / Aftermath: *Tricky* / Earthsong: *Batu* / Cool like the blues: *Warfield, Justin* / Straight plays: *F Mob* / Crazy: *Outside* / Spock with a beard: *Palmskin Productions* / World mutations: *Tone Productions* / Tree, air and rain on earth: *Mondo Grosso* / Great men's dub: *Burning Spear* / Soul of the people: *Bread & Butter*
CD _____ BRCD 607
4th & Broadway / Jun '94 / PolyGram.

REBIRTH OF COOL V
(Subterranean Abstract Blues)
Friendly pressure: *Jhelisa* / Eine kleine hedmusik: *Coldcut* / Karmacoma: *Massive Attack* / Boundaries: *Conquest, Leena* / Whipping boy: *Harper, Ben* / Deep shit: *Kruder & Dorfmeister* / Hell is round the corner: *Tricky* / Turn on, tune in, find joy: *Freakpower* / Revenge of the number: *Portishead* / Bug powder dust: *Bomb The Bass* / United Future Airlines: *United Future Organisation* / Iniquity worker: *D-Note* / Release yo'delf: *Method Man* / Kosmos: *Weller, Paul* / Nouveau Western: *M.C. Solaar* / Get it together: *Beastie Boys*
CD _____ BRCD 617
4th & Broadway / Jul '95 / PolyGram.

RECORD
(Ash International Sampler)
CD _____ ASH 2.1
Ash International / Jan '95 / These / Kudos.

RED HEAVEN
(20 Of The Best From The Cherry Red Label)
It's a fine day: *Jane* / An MP speaks: *McCarthy* / Plain sailing: *Thorn, Tracey* / Everybody's problem: *Pulp* / On my mind: *Marine Girls* / Sunbursts in: *Eyeless In Gaza* / Xoyo: *Passage* / All about you: *Leer, Thomas* / Nicky: *Momus* / Black cat: *Bolan, Marc* / Watery song: *Deebank, Maurice* / Trial of Doctor Fancy: *King Of Luxembourg* / Night and day: *Everything But The Girl* / If she doesn't smile: *Fantastic Something* / Walter and John: *Watt, Ben & Robert Wyatt* / Jet set junta: *Monochrome Set* / Parafin brain: *Nightingales* / This brilliant evening: *In Embrace* / You Mary you: *Philippe, Louis* / Reach for your gun: *Bid*
CD _____ NTMCD 520
Nectar / Jan '96 / Pinnacle.

RED HOT AND BLUE
Well did you evah: *Harry, Deborah & Iggy Pop* / Who wants to be a millionaire: *Thompson Twins* / I love Paris: *Les Negresses Vertes* / Love for sale: *Fine Young Cannibals* / After you: *Watley, Jody* / So in love: *Lang, k.d.* / You do something to me: *O'Connor, Sinead* / Down in the depths: *Stansfield, Lisa* / Night and day: *U2* / It's alright for me: *Waits, Tom* / Miss Otis regrets: *MacColl, Kirsty & Pogues* / I get a kick out of you: *Jungle Brothers* / Just one of those things: *MacColl, Kirsty & Pogues* / Begin the beguine: *Keita, Salif* / From this moment on: *Somerville, Jimmy* / Too darn hot: *Erasure* / Every time we say goodbye: *Lennox, Annie* / Do I love you: *Aztec Camera* / Don't fence me in: *Byrne, David* / In the still of the night: *Neville Brothers* / I've got you under my skin: *Cherry, Neneh*
CD Set _____ CCD 1799
Chrysalis / Oct '90 / EMI.

RED HOT AND COUNTRY
CD _____ 5226392
PolyGram / Oct '94 / PolyGram.

RED HOT JAZZ
CD _____ AVM 533
Avid / May '94 / Avid/BMG / Koch.

RED HOT ROCKABILLY
Hip shakin' mama / Bip bop boom / Look out Mabel / Grits / Sunglasses after dark / Okies in the pokie / Hot dog / Made in the shade / Down on the farm / Fool / Snake boogie / Blue swingin' mama
CD _____ CDMF 030
Magnum Force / Jul '90 / Magnum Music Group.

RED HOT ROCKABILLY VOL 7
Rock 'n' roll on a Saturday night / Rock-a-sock a hop / Grandma rock 'n' roll / Servant

---

of love / Knocking on the backside / Walking and a' strolling / Black Cadillac / D.J. blues / Don't cry little darling / Linda Lou / Teenage lover / So help me gal / Snake eyed woman / Depression blues / Quick sand love / Nicotine
CD _____ CDMF 069
Magnum Force / Aug '89 / Magnum Music Group.

RED HOT ROCKABILLY VOL 8
Forty nine women / That'll get it / Lonely heart / Clickety clack / Satellite hop / Dig that crazy driver / My baby's still rockin' / Crawdad hole / Go go heart / You bet I do / It hurts the one who loves you / Puppy love / No doubt about it / Roll over Beethoven / No. 9 train / Rock on Mabel / Long tall Sally / Jitterbuggin' baby / One way ticket / Elvis stole my gal / Fool about you / You don't mean to make me cry / Tore up / Jackson dog / Move over Rover
CD _____ CDMF 082
Magnum Force / Feb '92 / Magnum Music Group.

RED RIVER BLUES - 1934-43
CD _____ TMCD 08
Travellin' Man / '92 / Wellard / CM / Jazz Music.

RED-EYE APPETISER
CD _____ REDCD 32
Normal/Okra / Mar '94 / Direct / ADA.

REDISCOVER THE 50'S & 60'S - HERE COMES SUMMER
(2CD/MC Set)
Summer Place: *Faith, Percy* / Big bad John: *Dean, Jimmy* / Bless you: *Orlando, Tony* / Tower of strength: *Vaughan, Frankie* / Sea of love: *Wilde, Marty* / Halfway to paradise: *Fury, Billy* / Only the lonely: *Orbison, Roy* / Running bear: *Preston, Johnny* / Here comes summer: *Keller, Jerry* / Take five: *Brubeck, Dave Quartet* / Let it be me: *Everly Brothers* / Handyman: *Jones, Jimmy* / Lion sleeps tonight: *Tokens* / Happy birthday sweet sixteen: *Sedaka, Neil* / Language of love: *Loudermilk, John D.* / I will follow him: *March, Little Peggy* / Romeo: *Clark, Petula* / Devil woman: *Robbins, Marty* / Sheila: *Roe, Tommy* / Speedy Gonzalez: *Boone, Pat* / Little town flirt: *Shannon, Del* / Guitar man: *Eddy, Duane* / Peggy Sue got married: *Holly, Buddy* / It's my party: *Gore, Lesley*
CD Set _____ OG 3203
Old Gold / Oct '89 / Carlton Home Entertainment.

REDISCOVER THE 50'S - AT THE HOP
(2CD/MC Set)
High school confidential / At the hop / It's only make believe / Stupid cupid / Baby face / Chantilly lace / See you later alligator / Rave on / Little star / Sorry (I ran all the way) / Twilight theme / Book of love / Teengaer in love / Lollipop / My true love / Pink shoe laces / La Bamba / It's all in the game / Why / Take a message to Mary / Susie darlin' / Mr. Blue / Bad boy / Sweet nothin's
CD Set _____ OG 3214
Old Gold / '92 / Carlton Home Entertainment.

REDISCOVER THE 50'S - MAY YOU ALWAYS
(2CD/MC Set)
Twelfth of never: *Mathis, Johnny* / My happiness: *Francis, Connie* / End: *Grant, Earl* / Maya (always): *McGuire Sisters* / My special angel: *Helms, Bobby* / Love me forever: *Ryan, Marion* / Look homeward angel: *Ray, Johnnie* / Tammy: *Reynolds, Debbie* / Coma prima: *Marini, Marino* / If only I could live my life again: *Morgan, Jane* / For a penny: *Boone, Pat* / My prayer: *Platters* / Answer me: *Whitfield, David* / Sugarbush: *Day, Doris & Frankie Laine* / Mr. Sandman: *Chordettes* / Love me or leave me: *Davis, Sammy Jnr.* / Mr. Wonderful: *Lee, Peggy* / Alone: *Kaye Sisters* / Sixteen tons: *Laine, Frankie* / Tea for two cha cha: *Dorsey, Tommy* / Finger of suspicion: *Valentine, Dickie* / Ivory towers: *Carr, Cathy* / Mangoes: *Clooney, Rosemary* / With all my heart: *Clark, Petula*
CD Set _____ OG 3212
Old Gold / Oct '90 / Carlton Home Entertainment.

REDISCOVER THE 50'S - ROCK WITH THE CAVEMAN
(2CD/MC Set)
Rock-a-bantin' boogie: *Haley, Bill & The Comets* / Rock Island line: *Donegan, Lonnie* / Giddy up a cling dong: *Bell, Freddy & The Bellboys* / Green door: *Vaughan, Frankie* / Start movin' (in my direction): *Mineo, Sal* / Sweet little sixteen: *Berry, Chuck* / Rock with the caveman: *Steele, Tommy* / Great pretender: *Platters* / Banana boat song (Day O): *Belafonte, Harry* / Freight train: *McDevitt, Chas & Nancy Whisky* / Patricia: *Prado, Perez* / We will make love: *Hamilton, Russ* / Little darlin': *Diamonds* / Maybe baby: *Crickets* / Come on-a my house: *Clooney, Rosemary* / Love letters in the sand: *Boone, Pat* / You don't owe me a thing: *Ray, Johnnie* / Love makes the world go round: *Como, Perry* / Oh Carol: *Sedaka, Neil* / Lipstick on your collar: *Francis, Connie* / Broken hearted melody: *Vaughan, Sarah* / Battle of New Orleans: *Horton, Johnny* / Colette: *Fury, Billy* / Peggy Sue: *Holly, Buddy*

868

CD Set _____ OG 3202
Old Gold / Oct '89 / Carlton Home Entertainment.

REDISCOVER THE 50'S - SEALED WITH A KISS
(2CD/MC Set)
Blue bayou: Orbison, Roy / Hey baby: Channel, Bruce / Bobby's girl: Maughan, Susan / Can't get used to losing you: Williams, Andy / Please help me, I'm falling: Locklin, Hank / Island of dreams: Springfields / Cathy's clown: Everly Brothers / Save the last dance for me: Drifters / Tell Laura I love her: Peterson, Ray / Beatnik fly: Johnny & The Hurricanes / Baby sittin' boogie: Clifford, Buzz / El Paso: Robbins, Marty / Telstar: Tornados / Breaking up is hard to do: Sedaka, Neil / Sealed with a kiss: Hyland, Brian / Venus: Avalon, Frankie / Roses are red: Vinton, Bobby / End of the world: Davis, Skeeter / Rawhide: Laine, Frankie / Beyond the sea: Darin, Bobby / Johnny get angry: Summers, Joannie / All alone am I: Lee, Brenda / He'll have to go: Reeves, Jim / Boys cry: Kane, Eden
CD Set _____ OG 3207
Old Gold / Sep '90 / Carlton Home Entertainment.

REDISCOVER THE 50'S - SUGARTIME
(2CD/MC Set)
Music Music: Brewer, Teresa / I see the moon: Stargazers / Hernando's hideaway: Johnston Brothers / Secret love: Day, Doris / Little things mean a lot: Kallen, Kitty / Moonlight gambler: Laine, Frankie / Mambo Italiano: Clooney, Rosemary / Mountain greenery: Torme, Mel / Chances are: Mathis, Johnny / Hey there: Ray, Johnnie / Cara mia: Whitfield, David / Faithful hussar: Heath, Ted / Lay down your arms: Shelton, Anne / (How much is that) doggie in the window: Roza, Lita / Only you: Hilltoppers / Island in the sun: Belafonte, Harry / Cindy oh Cindy: Fisher, Eddie / Love is a many splendoured thing: Four Aces / Unchained melody: Hibbler, Al / Round and round: Como, Perry / Jeepers creepers: Torme, Mel / Naughty lady of Shady Lane: James Brothers / Ricochet: Regan, Joan
CD Set _____ OG 3201
Old Gold / Oct '89 / Carlton Home Entertainment.

REDISCOVER THE 60'S & 70'S - IF I ONLY HAD TIME
(2CD/MC Set)
First of May: Bee Gees / Dedicated to the one I love: Mamas & Papas / Goin' back: Springfield, Dusty / 59th Street bridge song (Feelin' groovy): Harpers Bizarre / Lights of Cincinatti: Walker, Scott / Love in your eyes: Leandros, Vicky / Abraham, Martin and John: Dion / Durham town: Whittaker, Roger / Words: Coolidge, Rita / If I only had time: Rowles, John / Both sides now / You're my soul and inspiration: Righteous Brothers / Never my love: Association / First love never dies: Walker Brothers / It's over: Sandpipers / Anticipation: Simon, Carly / Warm and tender love: Sledge, Percy / Baby don't go: Sonny & Cher / Funny how time slips away: Moore, Dorothy / Going in with my eyes open: Soul, David / Sunny: Hebb, Bobby / Early in the morning: Vanity Fare / What a wonderful world: Armstrong, Louis / Your song: John, Elton
CD Set _____ OG 2214
Old Gold / '92 / Carlton Home Entertainment.

REDISCOVER THE 60'S - FRIDAY ON MY MIND
(2CD/MC Set)
For your love: Yardbirds / Colours: Donovan / Gin house: Amen Corner / Take a heart: Sorrows / All day and all of the night: Kinks / Night of fear: Move / Louie Louie: Kingsmen / Wooly bully: Sam The Sham & The Pharaohs / I put a spell on you: Price, Alan Set / Homburg: Procul Harum / Daydream: Lovin' Spoonful / I fought the law: Fuller, Bobby Four / Lies: Knickerbockers / Delta lady: Cocker, Joe / Friday on my mind: Easybeats / Green tambourine: Lemon Pipers / Liar liar: Castaways / Dirty water: Standells / Out of time: Farlowe, Chris / Pushin' too hard: Seeds / Fire: Crazy World Of Arthur Brown
CD Set _____ OG 3208
Old Gold / Sep '90 / Carlton Home Entertainment.

REDISCOVER THE 60'S - IN THE MIDNIGHT HOUR
(2CD/MC Set)
Harlem shuffle: Bob & Earl / It's all right: Impressions / Twist and shout: Isley Brothers / Hi-heel sneakers: Tucker, Tommy / Green onions: Booker T & The MG's / Under the boardwalk: Drifters / Any day now: Jackson, Chuck / I put a spell on you: Simone, Nina / Papa's got a brand new bag: Brown, James / Knock on wood: Floyd, Eddie / Respect: Franklin, Aretha / Sweet soul music: Conley, Arthur / Rescue me: Bass, Fontella / Working in a coalmine: Dorsey, Lee / Wade in the water: Lewis, Ramsey Trio / Private number: Clay, Judy & William Bell / Treat her right: Head, Roy / Soul man: Sam & Dave / What'cha gonna do about it: Troy, Doris / In the midnight hour: Pickett, Wilson / Mr. Pitiful: Redding, Otis / I'm your puppet: Purify, James & Bobby /

Boogaloo party: Flamingos / Tainted love: Jones, Gloria
CD Set _____ OG 3217
Old Gold / '92 / Carlton Home Entertainment.

REDISCOVER THE 60'S - SOMETHING IN THE AIR
(2CD/MC Set)
Oh pretty woman: Orbison, Roy / Juliet: Four Pennies / When you walk in the room: Searchers / Memphis, Tennessee: Berry, Chuck / She's not there: Zombies / Gloria: Them / What'cha gonna do about it: Small Faces / That's what I want: Marauders / Matthew and son: Stevens, Cat / Heart full of soul: Yardbirds / Wrapping paper: Cream / Dead end street: Kinks / I'd rather go blind: Chicken Shack / Need your love so bad: Fleetwood Mac / My ship is coming in: Walker Brothers / Bringing on back the good times: Love Affair / San Fransiscan nights: Burdon, Eric / This wheel's on fire: Driscoll, Julie & Brian Auger / Hey Joe: Hendrix, Jimi / Race with the devil: Gun / All I really want to do: Byrds / Morning dew: Rose, Tim / Born to be wild: Steppenwolf / Something in the air: Thunderclap Newman
CD Set _____ OG 3204
Old Gold / Oct '89 / Carlton Home Entertainment.

REDISCOVER THE 70'S - WITH A LITTLE HELP FROM MY FRIENDS
(2CD/MC Set)
Unchained melody: Righteous Brothers / California dreamin': Mamas & Papas / Green green: New Christy Minstrels / Hang on to a dream: Hardin, Tim / Woodstock: Matthew's Southern Comfort / Night they drove old dixie down: Baez, Joan / Remember (walkin' in the sand): Shangri-Las / Comin' home baby: Torme, Mel / Black is black: Los Bravos / I got you babe: Sonny & Cher / (Sittin' on) the dock of the bay: Redding, Otis / With a little help from my friends: Cocker, Joe / Sun ain't gonna shine anymore: Walker Brothers / I'm a believer: Monkees / Nano no sloopy: McCoys / Son of Hickory Holler's tramp: Smith, O.C. / Israelites: Dekker, Desmond & The Aces / In the year 2525: Zager & Evans / Mr. Tambourine Man: Byrds / Letter: Box Tops / I had too much to dream last night: Electric Prunes / Somebody to love: Jefferson Airplane / White room: Cream / Eve of destruction: McGuire, Barry
CD Set _____ OG 3215
Old Gold / '92 / Carlton Home Entertainment.

REDISCOVER THE 70'S & 80'S - HOW 'BOUT US
(2CD/MC Set)
CD Set _____ OG 3216
Old Gold / '90 / Carlton Home Entertainment.

REDISCOVER THE 70'S & 80'S - ROCKIN' ALL OVER THE WORLD
(2CD/MC Set)
Walk on the wild side: Reed, Lou / Witch Queen of New Orleans: Redbone / Jeepster: T. Rex / Layla: Derek & The Dominoes / You wear it well: Stewart, Rod / American woman: Guess Who / All the way from Memphis: Mott The Hoople / Wall Street shuffle: 10cc / Radar love: Golden Earring / How long: Ace / Play that funky music: Wild Cherry / Pick up the pieces: Average White Band / Glass of champagne: Sailor / Hanging on the telephone: Blondie / Hold the line: Toto / More than a feeling: Boston / Everyday hurts: Sad Cafe / Run till you're: Lindisfarne / Year of the cat: Stewart, Al / Philadelphia freedom: John, Elton / Rockin' all over the world: Status Quo / Black Betty: Ram Jam / 5-7-0-5: City Boy / Going underground: Jam
CD Set _____ OG 3206
Old Gold / '89 / Carlton Home Entertainment.

REDISCOVER THE 70'S - BOOGIE NIGHTS
(2CD/MC Set)
Best of my love: Emotions / More, more, more: True, Andrea Connection / You can do magic: Limmie & Family Cooking / I love the nightlife: Bridges, Alicia / Gonna get along without you now: Wills, Viola / I will survive: Gaynor, Gloria / Love train: O'Jays / Don't leave me this way: Melvin, Harold / Contact: Starr, Edwin / Shame: King, Evelyn 'Champagne' / Boogie nights: Heatwave / Blame it on the boogie: Jacksons / Celebration: Kool & The Gang / It's a disco night (rock don't stop): Isley Brothers / Best disco in town: Ritchie Family / Ain't gonna bump no more (With no big fat woman): Tex, Joe / Disco lady: Taylor, Johnny / Fantasy: Earth, Wind & Fire / Y.M.C.A.: Village People / This is it: Moore, Melba / What it is: Mimms, Garnet / You can do it: Hudson, Al & The Partners / Turn the music up: Players Association / Use it up and wear it out: Odyssey
CD Set _____ OG 3210
Old Gold / Oct '90 / Carlton Home Entertainment.

REDISCOVER THE 70'S - EMOTIONS
(2CD/MC Set)
It must be love: Siffre, Labi / I'd love you to want me: Lobo / If I had you: Korgis / Moonlight feels right: Starbuck / Cats in the cra-

die: Chapin, Harry / Never let her slip away: Gold, Andrew / Send in the clowns: Collins, Judy / Emotions: Sang, Samantha / Sunshine after the rain: Brooks, Elkie / Torn between two lovers: McGregor, Mary / Don't give up on us: Soul, David / Desiderata: Crane, Les / Seasons in the sun: Jacks, Terry / Everybody's talkin': Nilsson, Harry / Time in a bottle: Croce, Jim / All out of love: Air Supply / Babe: Styx / Help me make it through the night: Holt, John / Best thing that ever happened to me: Knight, Gladys & The Pips / Just when I needed you most: Vanwarmer, Randy / We do it: Stone, R & J / Right thing to do: Simon, Carly / Floating in the wind: Hudson - Ford / Heart on my sleeve: Gallagher & Lyle
CD Set _____ OG 3209
Old Gold / Sep '90 / Carlton Home Entertainment.

REDISCOVER THE 70'S - THE GREATEST LOVE OF ALL
(2CD/MC Set)
Daniel: John, Elton / Arms of Mary: Sutherland Brothers & Quiver / Forever autumn: Hayward, Justin / We do it myself: Carmen, Eric / Amoureuse: Dee, Kiki / Stay with me 'til dawn: Tzuke, Judie / Uptown, uptempo woman: Edelman, Randy / Africa: Toto / Free: Williams, Deniece / Like sister and brother: Drifters / Too much, too little, too late: Mathis, Johnny & Deniece Williams / Greatest love of all: Benson, George / Laughter in the rain: Sedaka, Neil / Woman in love: Three Degrees / Feelings: Albert, Morris / You're a lady: Skellern, Peter / Last farewell: Whittaker, Roger / Always on my mind: Nelson, Willie / For the good times: Como, Perry / I have a dream: Abba / I recall a gypsy woman: Williams, Don / If you go away: Jacks, Terry / I'm not in love: 10cc / Without you: Nilsson, Harry
CD Set _____ OG 3205
Old Gold / Oct '89 / Carlton Home Entertainment.

REDISCOVER THE 70'S - YOU AIN'T SEEN NOTHIN' YET
(2CD/MC Set)
Classical gas: Williams, Mason / Frankenstein: Winter, Edgar / Vicious: Reed, Lou / Rocky mountain way: Walsh, Joe / School's out: Cooper, Alice / Hold your head up: Argent / Pinball wizard: John, Elton / Free electric band: Hammond, Albert / Ballroom blitz: Sweet / Caroline: Status Quo / Sweet home Alabama: Skynyrd, Lynyrd / Jessica: Allman Brothers Band / (Don't fear) the reaper: Blue Oyster Cult / Baby, I love your way: Frampton, Peter / In a broken dream: Python Lee Jackson / Why did you do it: Stretch / My oh my: Sad Cafe / Bat out of hell: Meat Loaf / Life's been good: Walsh, Joe / Jane: Jefferson Starship / Closer to the heart: Rush / You ain't seen nothin' yet: Bachman-Turner Overdrive / Slow down: Miles, John / Hotel California: Eagles
CD Set _____ OG 3211
Old Gold / Oct '90 / Carlton Home Entertainment.

REDISCOVERED BLUES
Ain't nothing like whiskey: Hopkins, Lightin' / Brownie McGee/Sonny Tery/Big Joe Williams / Penitentiary blues: Hopkins, Lightin' / Brownie McGee/Sonny Tery/Big Joe Williams / If you steal my chicken you can't make them say: Hopkins, Lightin'/Brownie McGee/Sonny Tery/Big Joe Williams / First meeting: Hopkins, Lightin'/Brownie McGee/Sonny Tery/Big Joe Williams / How long has it been since you been home: Hopkins, Lightin'/Brownie McGee/Sonny Tery/Big Joe Williams / Wimmin from coast to coast: Hopkins, Lightin'/Brownie McGee/Sonny Tery/Big Joe Williams / Key to the highway: McGhee, Brownie & Sonny Terry / Lose your money: McGhee, Brownie & Sonny Terry / Louise: McGhee, Brownie & Sonny Terry / Sportin' life: McGhee, Brownie & Sonny Terry / New harmonica breakdown: McGhee, Brownie & Sonny Terry / Prison bound: McGhee, Brownie & Sonny Terry / Livin' with the blues: McGhee, Brownie & Sonny Terry / Baby, please don't go: McGhee, Brownie & Sonny Terry / Twelve gates to the city: McGhee, Brownie & Sonny Terry / Pawnship blues: McGhee, Brownie & Sonny Terry / Brownie's guitar blues: McGhee, Brownie & Sonny Terry / Oh baby: Williams, Big Joe / Hand me down my old walking stick: Williams, Big Joe / Shady grover: Williams, Big Joe / Mama don't like me runnin' round: Williams, Big Joe / Sittin' and thinkin': Williams, Big Joe / Scardie Mama: Williams, Big Joe / Blues 'round the world: Williams, Big Joe / Everybody's gonna miss me when I'm gone: Williams, Big Joe / Pearly Mae: Williams, Big Joe / Baby keeps on breaking 'em down: Williams, Big Joe / Church bells ring: Williams, Big Joe / Take it all: Williams, Big Joe / Toledo to Buffalo: Williams, Big Joe / She'll be coming round the mountain: Williams, Big Joe / Old folks tavern: Williams, Big Joe
CD _____ CDEM 1553
Capitol Jazz / Jul '95 / EMI.

REEFER SONGS
(23 Original Jazz and Blues Vocals)
CD _____ JASSCD 7
Jazz / Oct '91 / CM / Jazz Music / ADA / Cadillac / Direct.

REFERENCE JAZZ
CD _____ RRS 2CD
Reference Recordings / '91 / May Audio.

REFLECTIONS -
Brideshead Revisited: Burgon, Geoffrey & Orchestra / Chariots of fire: Hawk & Co / Flame trees of Thika: Video Symphonic / Light of experience: Zamfir, Gheorghe / Cosmos: Vangelis / Deer hunter: Williams, John / Bilitis: Lai, Francis / Midnight express: Moroder, Giorgio / Trois Gymnopedies: Blood, Sweat & Tears / Shepherds song: James, Bob / Albatross: Fleetwood Mac / Don't cry for me Argentina: Shadows / Annie's song: Galway, James / Samba Pati: Santana / Aria: Aske, Oliver & Chi Mai: Morricone, Ennio / Hands and clouds: Vollenweider, Andreas / Arrival: Abba
CD _____ CD 10034
CBS / Nov '90 / Sony.

REGAL RECORDS IN NEW ORLEANS
I'll never be free: Gayten, Paul / Yeah yeah yeah: Gayten, Paul / You ought to know: Gayten, Paul / You shouldn't: Gayten, Paul / Confused: Gayten, Paul / Bear hug: Gayten, Paul / Oooh la la: Gayten, Paul / My last goodbye: Gayten, Paul / I ain't gonna let you in: Gayten, Paul / Kickapoo juice: Gayten, Paul / Each time: Gayten, Paul / Fishtails: Gayten, Paul / Suzette: Gayten, Paul / Happy birthday to you: Gayten, Paul / For you my love: Gayten, Paul / Back trackin' aka Dr. Daddy-o: Gayten, Paul / Gold ain't everything: Gayten, Paul / Baby what's new: Laurie, Annie / My rough and ready man: Laurie, Annie / Low down feeling: Laurie, Annie / Three times seven equals twenty one: Laurie, Annie / I don't marry too soon: Laurie, Annie / Messy Bessy: Bartholomew, Dave / Nickel wine: Bartholomew, Dave / Riding high: Brown, Roy / Brand new baby: Brown, Roy
CD _____ CDCHD 362
Ace / Jan '92 / Pinnacle / Cadillac / Complete/Pinnacle.

REGGAE
Summer in the city: Cocker, Joe / Johnny B. Goode: Tosh, Peter / Wild world: Priest, Maxi / Just another day in paradise: Brown, Dennis / She's a woman: Scritti Politti & Shabba Ranks / Louie Louie: Toots & The Maytals / On and on: Aswad / Now that we've found love: Third World / Tears of a clown: Beat / Some guys have all the luck: Tucker, Junior / Tide is high: Blondie / Knock on wood: Hibbert, Toots / Don't look back: Tosh, Peter & Mick Jagger / Crazy love: Priest, Maxi / (Sittin' on) the dock of the bay: Brown, Dennis / Everything I own: Boy George / Baby I need your loving: Heptones / Minnie the moocher: Reggae Philharmonic Orchestra
CD _____ CDEMD 1068
EMI / Jul '94 / EMI.

REGGAE 93
Boom shak-a-lak: Apache Indian / Tease me: Demus, Chaka & Pliers / It keeps rainin' (tears from my eyes): McLean, Bitty / Sweat (A la la la la long): Inner Circle / All that she wants: Ace Of Base / Work: Levy, Barrington / On and on: Aswad / This carry ja bring come: McGregor, Freddie / Informer: Snow / Love of a lifetime: Tucker, Junior / Twice my age: Krystal & Shabba Ranks / Shout (it out): Louchie Lou & Michie One / Big strong girl: Megaruffian / Rump shaker: Nardo Ranks
CD _____ CIDTV 7
Island / Oct '93 / PolyGram.

REGGAE AFRICA
Lion in a sheep skin: Harley & The Rasta Family / Amagni: Dembele, Koko / Show biz to requin: Tangara Speed Ghoda / Veto de dieu: Alpha Blondy / Nothing but prayer: Senzo / C'est pas da in lio: Kassy, Serges / Wondogbo: Kouame, Lystrone / Unlucky man: Ice T Cool / Sweet reggae: Harley & The Rasta Family / Politic warrior: Pi Ray / Elle: Jah Gunt / Lord say: Tangara Speed Ghoda / N'ka yere: Dembele, Koko / Children of Africa: Ismael Isaac Les Freres Keita
CD _____ CDEMC 3679
FMI / May '94 / FMI.

REGGAE ARCHIVE - US
CD _____ RESTLESS 7268
On-U Sound / Aug '94 / SRD / Jetstar.

REGGAE ARCHIVES VOL.1
CD _____ ONUCD 21
On-U Sound / Mar '93 / SRD / Jetstar.

REGGAE ARCHIVES VOL.2
CD _____ ONUCD 22
On-U Sound / Apr '93 / SRD / Jetstar.

REGGAE BABYLON
CD _____ RB 3031
Reggae Beat / Mar '95 / Magnum Music Group / THE.

REGGAE CHRISTMAS
Silent night / I saw mommy kiss a dreadlocks / Dub it for Christmas / Santa Claus / Flash your dread / Sensimilia
CD _____ PCD 1422
Profile / Nov '91 / Pinnacle.

REGGAE CHRISTMAS
CD _____ CDTRL 364
Trojan / Nov '95 / Jetstar / Total/BMG.

REGGAE CHRISTMAS FROM STUDIO ONE
CD _____ HBCD 118
Heartbeat / Nov '92 / Greensleeves / Jetstar / Direct / ADA.

REGGAE CLASSICS - SERIOUS SELECTIONS VOL. 1
Love the way it should be: Royal Rasses / Back a yard: In Crowd / Bucket bottom: Prince Allah / Here I come: Brown, Dennis / Fade away: Byles, Junior / No man is an island: Motion / Natural collie: McGregor, Freddie / Time is the master: Holt, John / Easy: Lindsay, Jimmy / I'm still waiting: Wilson, Delroy / Man in me: Matumbi / Mr. Ska Beena: Ellis, Alton
CD _____ CDREG 2
Rewind Selecta / Mar '95 / Grapevine.

REGGAE CLASSICS VOL. 4
CD _____ CDTRL 284
Trojan / Mar '94 / Jetstar / Total/BMG.

REGGAE CULTURE
CD _____ HBAN 13CD
Heartbeat / Jul '94 / Greensleeves / Jetstar / Direct / ADA.

REGGAE FAVOURITES
Sweat (A la la la la long) / Iron lion zion / Nightshift / Pass the dutchie / Many rivers to cross / Electric avenue / Reggae night / I got you babe / To love somebody / Everything I own / Could you be loved / Red red wine
CD _____ 399010
Koch / Sep '93 / Koch.

REGGAE FEELING
CD _____ 322936
Koch / Jun '93 / Koch.

REGGAE FEELING III
CD _____ 3411252
Koch / Aug '94 / Koch.

REGGAE FEELINGS
Get up stand up: Tosh, Peter / Reggae night: Cliff, Jimmy / Pass the cup: Aswad / Mr. Loverman: Shabba Ranks / Graveyard rock: Jeffreys, Garland / Legalize jump: Third World / African reggae: Hagen, Nina / Strong me strong: Yellowman / Love is all: Cliff, Jimmy / Legalize it: Tosh, Peter / Try jah love: Third World / Matador: Jeffreys, Garland / Tears on my pillow (I can't take it): Nash, Johnny / One love: Marley, Bob & The Wailers / Crying, waiting, hoping: Mason, Dave
CD _____ 4758312
Columbia / Dec '95 / Sony.

REGGAE FOR KIDS
CD _____ RASCD 3095
Ras / May '92 / Jetstar / Greensleeves / SRD / Direct.

REGGAE FOR LOVERS
CD _____ DCD 5273
Kenwest / Nov '92 / THE.

REGGAE FROM JAMAICA VOL. 1 (Redder Than Red)
CD _____ BB 2801
Blue Beat / Dec '94 / Magnum Music Group / THE.

REGGAE FROM JAMAICA VOL. 2 (Blowin' In The Wind)
CD _____ BB 2802
Blue Beat / Dec '94 / Magnum Music Group / THE.

REGGAE FROM JAMAICA VOL. 3 (Rock Steady)
CD _____ BB 2803
Blue Beat / Dec '94 / Magnum Music Group / THE.

REGGAE FROM JAMAICA VOL. 4 (Mellow Mood)
CD _____ BB 2804
Blue Beat / Dec '94 / Magnum Music Group / THE.

REGGAE FROM JAMAICA VOL. 5 (Girlie Girlie)
CD _____ BB 2805
Blue Beat / Dec '94 / Magnum Music Group / THE.

REGGAE FROM JAMAICA VOL. 6 (Rivers Of Babylon)
CD _____ BB 2806
Blue Beat / Dec '94 / Magnum Music Group / THE.

REGGAE GREATEST HITS
CD Set _____ DCD 5068
Disky / Jul '89 / THE / BMG / Discovery / Pinnacle.

REGGAE GREATS
CD Set _____ TFP 019
Tring / Nov '92 / Tring / Prism.

REGGAE HITS BOX SET 4
CD Set _____ RHBCD 4
Jetstar / Nov '95 / Jetstar.

REGGAE HITS BOX SET 5
CD Set _____ RHBCD 5
Jetstar / Nov '95 / Jetstar.

REGGAE HITS BOX SET 6
CD Set _____ RHBCD 6
Jetstar / Nov '95 / Jetstar.

REGGAE HITS VOL.1
Under me sensi: Levy, Barrington / Herbman hustling: Minott, Sugar / Mix me down: Tuff, Tony / Haul and pull up: Brown, Neville / Lover's magic: Isaacs, Gregory / Someone special: Brown, Dennis / Gimme good loving: Natural Touch / Feel so good: Reid, Sandra / Between me and you: Campbell, Carol / 'Cause you love me baby: Tajah, Paulette / Roots rockin': Aswad / Woman I need your loving: Investigators
CD _____ JECD 1001
Jetstar / Jun '88 / Jetstar.

REGGAE HITS VOL.10
CD _____ JECD 1010
Jetstar / Jul '91 / Jetstar.

REGGAE HITS VOL.12
CD _____ JECD 1012
Jetstar / Apr '92 / Jetstar.

REGGAE HITS VOL.13
Big up: Shaggy & Rayvon / Man kind: Capleton / I spy: General TK / How the world a run: Banton, Buju / Second class: Gonzalez, Carol / Woman a you: Terror Fabulous / Ring the alarm quick: Tenor Saw & Buju Banton / Discovery: Griffiths, Marcia, Tony Rebel, Cutty Ranks & Buju Banton / Missing you now: Sanchez / I was born a winner: McGregor, Freddie / Where is the love: Hammond, Beres, Sugar Minott & Tony Rebel / Who say man nuh cry: Banton, Buju & Beres Hammond / Can this be real: Boom, Barry & Cutty Ranks / I love you too much: Wade, Wayne / You are my lady: Lefty Banton / End of the road: Paul, Frankie / Go round: Jack Reuben & The Riddler / Save the best for last: Singing Sweet
CD _____ JECD 1013
Jetstar / Dec '92 / Jetstar.

REGGAE HITS VOL.14
CD _____ JECD 1014
Jetstar / Aug '93 / Jetstar.

REGGAE HITS VOL.15
CD _____ JECD 1015
Jetstar / Dec '93 / Jetstar.

REGGAE HITS VOL.16
CD _____ JECD 1016
Jetstar / Aug '94 / Jetstar.

REGGAE HITS VOL.17
CD _____ JECD 1017
Jetstar / Dec '94 / Jetstar.

REGGAE HITS VOL.18
CD _____ JECD 1018
Jetstar / Sep '95 / Jetstar.

REGGAE HITS VOL.19
CD _____ JECD 1019
Jetstar / Dec '95 / Jetstar.

REGGAE HITS VOL.2
Wildfire: Holt, John & Dennis Brown / I'll be on my way: Isaacs, Gregory / Inferiority complex: Paul, Frankie / Country living: Mighty Diamonds / Curly locks: Byles, Junior / Senci addick: Fergeson, Horace / Baby be true: Thompson, Carroll / Caught you in a lie: Reid, Sandra / I love you: Sister Audrey & Jazzy: Paula / I'm gonna fall in love: Stewart, Tinga / Horsemove (giddiup): Horseman / House is not a home: Minott, Sugar
CD _____ JECD 1002
Jetstar / '88 / Jetstar.

REGGAE HITS VOL.3
Sweet reggae music: Nitty Gritty / Shub in: Paul, Frankie / Watch how the people dancing: Knots, Kenny / Greetings: Half Pint / Dear Boopsie: Hall, Pam / Boops: Supercats / Girlie girlie: George, Sophia / Members only: Taylor, Tyrone / One dance won't do: Hall, Pam / I've you: Cross, Sandra / Hello darling: Irie, Tippa / Bre yet: Wilson, Jack / Party nite: Undivided Roots / Guilty: Gardiner, Boris
CD _____ JECD 1003
Jetstar / Mar '87 / Jetstar.

REGGAE HITS VOL.4
Wings of love: Sparks, Trevor / Girlfriend: Fraser, Dean / She's mine: Levy, Barrington / She's my lady: Administrators / Holding on: Cross, Sandra / If I give my heart to you: McLean, John / Guilty for loving you: St. Clair, Carl / Dangerous: Smith, Conroy / Chill out: Tenor Saw & Doggie / Debi Debi girl: Metro, Peter & Charmaine / Bad boy: Melody, Courtney / Get ready: Paul, Frankie / Tears: Turner, Chuck / Big in bed: Melody, Lilly
CD _____ JECD 1004
Jetstar / Jun '88 / Jetstar.

REGGAE HITS VOL.5
Woman of moods: Dixon, Trevor / Black pride: Kofi / No way no better than yard: Bailey, Admiral / Am I losing you: Schloss, Cynthia / Ooh la la: LJM / Mi love mi girl bad: Flourgan & Sanchez / Proud to be black: Crucial Robbie / Power of love: Gibbons, Leroy / Cover me: Stewart, Tinga & Ninga Man / Very best: Intense / Life: Frighty & Colonel Mite / I still say: Packings, Juliet / Man in the mirror: Little Kirk
CD _____ JECD 1005
Jetstar / Dec '88 / Jetstar.

REGGAE HITS VOL.6
My commanding wife: Gardiner, Boris / Bun and cheese: Irie, Clement & Robert French / Looking over love: Kofi / Baby can I hold you tonight: Sanchez / New way to say I love you: Wonder, Wayne / Stick by me: Marley, Bob / I want to get next to you: Manifest / Love me ses: Top Cat & Tenor Fly / On my mind: Intense / Lovers affair: Roni / Fatal attraction: Taxman / Mix up: Madoo, U.U. & Captain Barky / Sweet and nice: Douglas, Lambert & Wayne Fire
CD _____ JECD 1006
Jetstar / Jul '89 / Jetstar.

REGGAE HITS VOL.7
CD _____ JECD 1007
Jetstar / Dec '89 / Jetstar.

REGGAE HITS VOL.8
Your love: Prophet, Michael & Ricky Tuff / Know fi move your waist: Major Danger / Ku-klung-klung: Red Dragon / Spirit: Demus, Chaka / Burrp: Nardo Ranks / Money honey: Sweetie Irie / Body tune up: Johnny P. / Buck wild: Paul, Frankie & Papa San / Careless whisper: Thriller U / Mrs. Jones: Levi, Sammy / Sharing the night: Brown, Lloyd / Finders keepers: Mafia, Leroy / One night: Wonder, Wayne/Brian & Tony Gold / 2 a.m.: Calvin / Do you ever think about me: Pure Silk / Ticket to ride: Trisha
CD _____ JECD 1008
Jetstar / Jun '90 / Jetstar.

REGGAE HITS VOL.9
CD _____ JECD 1009
Jetstar / Dec '90 / Jetstar.

REGGAE HITS VOLS.1 & 2
CD Set _____ RHBCD 1
Jetstar / Dec '93 / Jetstar.

REGGAE HITS VOLS.3 & 4
CD Set _____ RHBCD 2
Jetstar / Jan '94 / Jetstar.

REGGAE HITS VOLS.5 & 6
CD Set _____ RHBCD 3
Jetstar / Jan '94 / Jetstar.

REGGAE IN YOUR JEGGAE
CD _____ CDTRL 358
Trojan / Aug '95 / Jetstar / Total/BMG.

REGGAE LEGEND
CD _____ VPCD 1421
VP / Aug '95 / Jetstar.

REGGAE LEGENDS VOL.1
CD _____ RB 3011
Reggae Best / Nov '94 / Magnum Music Group / THE.
CD _____ RNCD 2105
Rhino / Apr '95 / Jetstar / Magnum Music Group / THE.

REGGAE MASSIVE
You don't love me (no no no): Penn, Dawn / Sweat (a la la la long): Inner Circle / Informer: Snow / Don't look back: Tosh, Peter / Baby come back: Banton, Pato / Sweets for my sweet: Lewis, C.J. / Don't turn around: Aswad / Silly games: Kay, Janet / Oh Carolina: Shaggy / Close to you: Priest, Maxi / I shall sing: Griffiths, Marcia / Good thing going: Minott, Sugar / Living on the frontline: Grant, Eddy / Young, gifted and black: Bob & Marcia / Girlie girlie: George, Sophia / I shot the sheriff: Inner Circle / No woman no cry: Boothe, Ken / Hurt so good: Cadogan, Susan / Mr. Loverman: Shabba Ranks / Red red wine: Tribe, Tony / Return to Django: Upsetters / Double barrel: Collins, Dave & Ansil / Liquidator: Harry J All Stars / Help me make it through the night: Holt, John / Lovin' inside: Forrester, Sharon / Twist and shout: Demus, Chaka & Pliers / Police and thieves: Murvin, Junior / Many rivers to cross: Cliff, Jimmy / 54-46 (was my number): Toots & The Maytals / Cherry oh baby: Donaldson, Eric / Sideshow: Biggs, Barry / Night nurse: Isaacs, Gregory / Riddim: US 3 / Stop that train: Eastwood, Clint & General Saint / Bubbling hot: Banton, Pato / Sugar sugar: Basie, Duke / Jungle: Perry, Lee 'Scratch'
CD _____ DINCD 93
Dino / Jan '79 / Pinnacle / 3MV.

REGGAE MEDAL VOL.1
CD _____ CRBCD 001
Carib Jems / Jan '94 / Jetstar.

REGGAE MELODIES
CD _____ RB 3016
Reggae Best / Oct '95 / Magnum Music Group / THE.

REGGAE MUSIC ALL NIGHT LONG (4CD Set)
CD Set _____ CDNCBOX 2
Charly / Sep '91 / Charly / THE / Cadillac.

REGGAE NOW
CD _____ ANCD 9
Heartbeat / Jan '94 / Greensleeves / Jetstar / Direct / ADA.

REGGAE ON THE SEAS
CD _____ SONCD 0075
Sonic Sounds / Mar '95 / Jetstar.

REGGAE REFRESHERS SAMPLER VOL.1
CD _____ RRCDS 101
Reggae Refreshers / Jun '90 / PolyGram / Vital.

REGGAE REFRESHERS SAMPLER VOL.2
Very well: Wailing Souls / Prophecy: Fabian / Gates of Zion: Prophet, Michael / Hypocrite: Wailer, Bunny / Botanical roots: Black Uhuru / Handsworth revolution: Steel Pulse / Jah heavy load: Ijahman Levi / One step forward: Perry, Lee 'Scratch' / Croaking lizard: Upsetters / Invasion: Burning Spear / Fade away: Byles, Junior / Independent in tavernsharn: Johnson, Linton Kwesi / Border: Isaacs, Gregory / Jailbreak: Sly & Robbie / Dub fire: Aswad / Sata: Jah Lion
CD _____ RRCDS 102
Reggae Refreshers / Apr '95 / PolyGram / Vital.

REGGAE REVELATION
CD _____ REO 97CD
Reach Out International / Nov '94 / Jetstar.

REGGAE REVOLUTION
CD _____ LG 21087
Lagoon / Jun '92 / Magnum Music Group / THE.

REGGAE SHOWCASE VOL.1
Stop that train: Eastwood, Clint & General Saint / Tidal wave: Paul, Frankie / I like it: Carlos, Don / Slow down woman: Brown, Dennis / Big ship: McGregor, Freddie / Wado-dem: Eek-A-Mouse / Roots, rock, reggae: Minott, Sugar / Private beach party: Isaacs, Gregory / Zungguzungguguzungguzeng: Yellowman / Boom shaka-a-lak: Red, Junior / Fat she fat: Holt, John
CD _____ MRCD 117
Munich / Oct '86 / CM / ADA / Greensleeves / Direct.

REGGAE SUPERSTARS
CD _____ RRTGCD 7732
Rohit / Mar '89 / Jetstar.

REGGAE SUPERSTARS
CD _____ RNCD 2076
Rhino / Dec '94 / Jetstar / Magnum Music Group / THE.

REGGAE SUPERSTARS BONANZA
CD _____ RNCD 2022
Rhino / Sep '93 / Jetstar / Magnum Music Group / THE.

REGGAE SUPERSTARS OF THE 80'S
CD _____ BSLCD 12003
Rohit / Feb '88 / Jetstar.

REGGAE TIME
CD _____ GLD 63303
Goldies / Jul '94 / THE.

REGGAE TOP 20 VOL. 1
CD _____ SONCD 0029
Sonic Sounds / Jun '92 / Jetstar.

REGGAE TOP 20 VOL. 2
CD _____ SONCD 0030
Sonic Sounds / Jun '92 / Jetstar.

REGGAE'S GREATEST HITS VOL.1
CD _____ CDHB 3601
Heartbeat / Apr '95 / Greensleeves / Jetstar / Direct / ADA.

REGGAE'S GREATEST HITS VOL.2
CD _____ CDHB 3602
Heartbeat / Apr '95 / Greensleeves / Jetstar / Direct / ADA.

REGGAE'S GREATEST HITS VOL.3
CD _____ CDBH 360
Heartbeat / Jun '95 / Greensleeves / Jetstar / Direct / ADA.

REGGAE'S GREATEST HITS VOL.4
CD _____ CDHB 3604
Heartbeat / Jun '95 / Greensleeves / Jetstar / Direct / ADA.

REGGAE'S GREATEST HITS VOL.5
CD _____ CDHB 3605
Heartbeat / Jul '95 / Greensleeves / Jetstar / Direct / ADA.

REGGAE'S GREATEST HITS VOL.6
CD _____ CDHB 3606
Heartbeat / Aug '95 / Greensleeves / Jetstar / Direct / ADA.

REGGAE'S GREATEST HITS VOL.7
CD _____ CDHB 3607
Heartbeat / Aug '95 / Greensleeves / Jetstar / Direct / ADA.

REGGAE'S GREATEST HITS VOL.8
CD _____ CDHB 3608
Heartbeat / Sep '95 / Greensleeves / Jetstar / Direct / ADA.

RELAXING JAZZ
Wave: Desmond, Paul / Softly as in a morning sunrise: Clark, Sonny Trio / Li'l darlin': Basie, Count / Truckin': Brookmeyer, Bob / All of you: Davis, Miles / Satin doll: Three Sounds / Easy living: Quebec, Ike / But beautiful: Pass, Joe / Violets for your furs: Hipp, Jutta / Hundred dreams from now: Bryant, Ray / You got to my heart: Pepper, Art / Easy street: Monkees / Get out of town: Mulligan, Gerry / If I should lose you: Smith, Jimmy
CD _____ CDPR 135
Premier/MFP / May '95 / EMI.

REMEMBER NEW ORLEANS
CD _____ GOJCD 53026
Giants Of Jazz / Aug '88 / Target/BMG / Cadillac.

REMEMBER THE 50'S
CD _____ 12106
Laserlight / Jan '93 / Target/BMG.

REMEMBER THE 60'S - THE GROUPS
Sabre dance: Love Sculpture / Quartermaster's stores: Shadows / It's my life: Animals / Seven daffodils: Cherokees / I'll never get over you: Kidd, Johnny & The Pirates / Greenback dollar: Kingston Trio / Don't let the sun catch you crying: Gerry & The Pacemakers / From a window: Kramer, Billy J. & The Dakotas / William Tell: Sounds Incorporated / You're no good: Swinging Blue Jeans / We're through: Hollies / Livin' above your head: Jay & The Americans / Three rooms with running water: Bennett, Cliff & The Rebel Rousers / One in the middle: Manfred Mann / Heart's symphony: Lewis, Gary & The Playboys / She's lost you: Zephyrs / I think we're alone now: James, Tommy & The Shondells / Going up the country: Canned Heat / For whom the bell tolls: Dupree, Simon & The Big Sound / Break away: Beach Boys
CD _____ CDSL 8249
EMI / Jul '95 / EMI.

REMEMBER THE 70'S
CD _____ CDCD 1240
Charly / Jun '95 / Charly / THE / Cadillac.

REMEMBER THE 70'S
CD Set _____ KBOX 351
Collection / Nov '95 / Target/BMG.

REMEMBER THE 70'S - THE GROUPS
Whole lotta love: CCS / Cotton fields: Beach Boys / Let's work together: Canned Heat / Rag mama rag: Band / Malt and barley blues: McGuinness Flint / Mocking bird: Barclay James Harvest / Strange kind of woman: Deep Purple / Long cool woman in a black dress: Hollies / Do ya: Move / 10538 overture: E.L.O. / Brother Louie: Hot Chocolate / Judy teen: Harley, Steve & Cockney Rebel / Overnight sensation (hit record): Raspberries / Forgotten roads: If / Millionaire: Dr. Hook / Ships in the night: Be-Bop Deluxe / Walk on by: Stranglers / Promises: Buzzcocks / My Sharona: Knack / Dance stance: Dexy's Midnight Runners
CD _____ CDSL 8250
EMI / Jul '95 / EMI.

REMEMBER THEN
(30 Original Doo Wop Classics)
Remember then: Earls / Great pretender: Platters / Why do fools fall in love: Lymon, Frankie & The Teenagers / I love how you love me: Paris Sisters / One fine day: Chiffons / Blue moon: Marcels / You belong to me: Duprees / At the hop: Danny & The Juniors / Born too late: Poni-Tails / My special angel: Helms, Bobby / Duke of Earl: Chandler, Gene / Little darlin': Diamonds / Stay: Williams, Maurice & The Zodiacs / Big man: Four Preps / Tears on my pillow: Imperials / Book of love: Monotones / Earth angel: Crew Cuts / Where or when: Dion & The Belmonts / I only have eyes for you: Flamingoes / It's almost tomorrow: Dream Weavers / Daddy's home: Shep & The Limelites / Sorry (I ran all the way home): Impalas / Sixteen candles: Crests / Little star: Elegants / Come go with me: Del-Vikings / In the still of the nite: Five Satins / Sincerely: Moonglows / Mr. Sandman: Chordettes / Come softly to me: Fleetwoods / Three bells: Browns
CD _____ 5167922
PolyGram / May '94 / PolyGram.

REMEMBER WHEN SINGERS COULD REALLY SING
I left my heart in San Francisco: Bennett, Tony / Been free: Williams, Andy / Crazy: Cline, Patsy / Moon river: Williams, Danny / Portrait of my love: Monro, Matt / Mr. Wonderful: Lee, Peggy / Love letters in the sand: Lester, Ketty / Cry: Ray, Johnnie / On the street where you live: Damone, Vic / Return to me: Martin, Dean / Who's sorry now: Francis, Connie / Around the world: Crosby, Bing / Release me: Humperdinck, Engelbert / Move over darling: Day, Doris / Rose Marie: Whitman, Slim / I'm sorry: Lee, Brenda / It's only make believe: Twitty, Conway / This is my song: Clark, Petula / Distant drums: Reeves, Jim / It's impossible: Como, Perry
CD _____ AHLCD 3
Hit / Nov '92 / PolyGram.

REMEMBERING THE 50'S
(Radio Days)
Finger of suspicion: Valentine, Dickie / Handful of songs: Steele, Tommy / Limelight (theme): Chacksfield, Frank & His Orchestra / Alone: Southlanders / Willie can: Beverley Sisters / Hey there: Rosa, Lita / Ricochet: Regan, Joan / Auf wiedersehen sweetheart: Lynn, Vera / I see the moon: Stargazers / Poor people of Paris: Atwell, Winifred / Hernando's hideaway: Johnston Brothers / Cara mia: Whitfield, David / You need hands: Bygraves, Max / Moulin Rouge theme: Mantovani & His Orchestra / Friends and neighbours: Cotton, Billy / Memories are made of this: King, Dave
CD _____ PWKM 4066P
Carlton Home Entertainment / Jul '91 / Carlton Home Entertainment.

REMIXED REMODELLED
CD _____ CDALMY 1
Almighty / May '95 / Total/BMG.

RENAISSANCE
CD _____ RENMIX 1CD
Network / Sep '94 / Sony / 3MV.

RENEGADE SELECTOR
CD _____ ANIMATE 1CD
Animate / Jun '94 / SRD.

RESPECT - ESSENTIAL ARGO/CADET GROOVES VOL. 5
Charly / Feb '94 / Charly / THE / Cadillac.
CD _____ CDARC 516

RESPECT TO STUDIO ONE
CD Set _____ HBCD 181/182
Heartbeat / Nov '94 / Greensleeves / Jetstar / Direct / ADA.

RESURRECTING THE BLUES
CD _____ NTMCD 505
Nectar / Jun '95 / Pinnacle.

RETRO TECHNO
CD _____ RETROCD 1
Network / Jul '91 / Sony / 3MV.

RETROSPECTIVE 1929-1963, A
(2CD Set)
One hour (if I could be with you one hour tonight): Mound City Blues Blowers / Hello Lola: Mound City Blues Blowers / Miss Hannah: McKinney's Cotton Pickers / Wherever there's a will, baby: McKinney's Cotton Pickers / Sugarfoot stomp: Henderson, Fletcher & His Orchestra / Hocus pocus: Henderson, Fletcher & His Orchestra / When the lights are low: Hampton, Lionel / One sweet letter from you: Hampton, Lionel / Dinah: Hampton, Lionel / Meet Mr Foo: Hawkins, Coleman / Fine dinner: Hawkins, Coleman / She's funny that way: Hawkins, Coleman / Body and soul: Hawkins, Coleman / When day is gone: Hawkins, Coleman / Sheikh of araby: Hawkins, Coleman / My blue heaven: Hawkins, Coleman / Bouncing with bean: Hawkins, Coleman / Bugle call rag: Metronome All Star Band / One o'clock jump: Metronome All Star Band / Say it isn't so: Hawkins, Coleman / Spotlite: Hawkins, Coleman / Indiana winter: Esquire / Indian summer: Esquire / How did she look: Hawkins, Coleman & His Orchestra / April in Paris: Hawkins, Coleman & His Orchestra / How strange: Hawkins, Coleman & His Orchestra / Half step down please: Hawkins, Coleman & His Orchestra / Angel face: Hawkins, Coleman & His Orchestra / There will never be another you: Hawkins, Coleman / Bean stalks again: Hawkins, Coleman & His Orchestra / I love Paris: Hawkins, Coleman / Under Paris skies: Hawkins, Coleman / I've got the world on a string: Allen, Henry 'Red' & His Orchestra / Sweet Lorraine: Allen, Henry 'Red' & His Orchestra / Watermelon man: Lambert, Hendricks/Bavan / All the things you are: Rollins, Sonny
CD Set _____ 786366172
Bluebird / Aug '95 / BMG.

RETROSPECTIVE OF HOUSE VOL.1
CD Set _____ SDIMCD 3
Sound Dimension / Jul '95 / Total/BMG.

RETROSPECTIVE OF HOUSE VOL.2
(2CD/MC/LP Set)
CD Set _____ SDIMCD 4
Sound Dimension / Nov '95 / Total/BMG.

RETURN OF THE DEL-FI & DONNA STORY, THE
Intro / Come on let's go: Valens, Ritchie / Alone and blue: Addrisi Brothers / Wild twist: Roller Coasters / For your love: Romero, Chan / She don't wanna dance (no more): Little Caesar & The Romans / Juliet as it's kept: Nelson, Chip / You're mine: Flamingo, Johnny / Fussy: Hawks / Big top: Nitehawks / Unjamo: Addrisi Brothers / Dancing in the sand: Hollers, Wayne / Watusi bongos: Epps, Preston / Seeing double: Holden, Ron / If I had my way: Romero, Chan / Sugar baby: Romero, Chan / Addrisi Brothers: Romero, Chan / Terror: Grippers / Hockin' Matilda: Swags / Summertime blues: Valens, Ritchie / Hippy hippy shake: Romero, Chan / Rock house party: Romero, Chan / Playboy: Romero, Chan / La Bamba: Romero, Chan / My little Ruby: Romero, Chan / Slauson oax: Romancers / Tell me: Langford, Gerry / Blowin' the blues: Swags / Betty Jean: Little Caesar & The Romans / True love can be: Holden, Ron / Walking alone: Pentagons / I want some more: Romero, Chan
CD _____ CDCHD 489
Ace / Apr '94 / Pinnacle / Cadillac / Complete/Pinnacle.

REVELATION
CD _____ BB 2813
Blue Beat / Oct '95 / Magnum Music Group / THE.

REVENGE OF THE KILLER PUSSIES
Wild women: Alien Sex Fiend / Swamp baby: Sunglasses After Dark / Jazz Butcher meets Count Dracula: Jazz Butcher / Cats terminal: Bone Orchard / Graveyard stomp: Meteors / Seven deadly sins: Outcasts / Running wild: Ricochets / Red headed woman: Panther Burns / Hellbag shuffle: Sunglasses After Dark / Werewolf blues: Guana Batz / She's got fever: Brilliant Corners / Long necked daddy-o: Boneasaurus Wrecks / Hills have eyes: Meteors / Shearing machine: Very Things / Zulu beat: King Kurt / I don't wanna get thin: Blubbery Hellbellies / I wanna be like you: Turnpike Cruisers / Your good girl's gonna go bad: Screaming Sirens / Pointed bra: Orson Family / Stomp it: Raunch Hands
CD _____ CDMGRAM 17
Cherry Red / Oct '93 / Pinnacle.

REVENGE OF THE SURF INSTRUMENTALS
Wipeout: Surfaris / Walk don't run: Ventures / Boss: Rumblers / Move it: Chantays / Victor: Dale, Dick & His Del-Tones / Lonely road to Damascus: Rogers, Milt / Little Linda: Rancheros / Point Panic: Surfaris / Perfidia: Ventures / Angry sea (Weimea): Rumblers / Pipeline: Chantays / Let's go trippin': Dale, Dick & His Del-Tones
CD _____ MCLD 19282
MCA / Sep '95 / BMG.

REVIVAL 1945-49
CD _____ 2512872
Jazztime / Feb '91 / Discovery / BMG.

REVIVAL HITS VOLS.1 & 2
CD _____ MFCD 8
Mafia/Fluxy / May '94 / Jetstar / SRD.

REVIVING A TRADITION
CD _____ PS 65116
Playasound / Nov '93 / Harmonia Mundi / ADA.

REVOLUTIONARY GENERATION
CD _____ ASHADOW 3CD
Moving Shadow / Jan '96 / SRD.

REVOLUTIONS
Wildstyle groove: Paninaro / Make it rock: Cotton Club / Rollercoaster: Chapter 9 / Love the groove: Alpha Motion / Lover number 6: Daydreamer / De dah dah (Spice of life): Mac, Keith / Shock the beat: Electric Choc / In your dance: E-Lustrious / Funkin' crazy: K.G.B. / Rok da house: Tall Paul / It was meant to be: D'Enrico / We are going down: Deadly Sins / Warehouse days of glory: New Deep Society / Club for life: Chris & James / Reach: Cheeks, Judy
CD _____ CDHIGH 1
High On Rhythm / Sep '94 / 3MV / Sony.

REWIND SAMPLER
Lonesome whistle blues: Chicken Shack / Unco-op showband blues: Skid Row / Shake your moneymaker: Fleetwood Mac / Keep on rolling: Argent / Wild witch lady: Donovan / I got a line on you: Spirit / Beat: Only Ones / Lounge lizard: Hunter, Ian / Hello there: Cale, John / He'll break your heart: Walker Brothers / She's a magazine: New Musik / Beasley Street: Cooper Clarke, John
CD _____ 4774532
Columbia / Aug '94 / Sony.

RHYTHM AND BLUES EXPRESS
CD _____ TOLL 002CD
Tollhaus / Jun '92 / Disc.

RHYTHM DIVINE VOL.2
Dance to the music: Stone, Sly / Shake yoru body down to the ground: Jacksons / That lady: Isley Brothers / Best of my love: Emotions / Backstabbers: O'Jays / Rock your baby: McCrae, George / That's the way I like it: K.C. & The Sunshine Band / Boogie oogie oogie: Taste Of Honey / Car wash: Rose Royce / I will survive: Gaynor, Gloria / When will see you again: Three Degrees / Contact: Starr, Edwin / This is it: Moore, Melba / More, more, more: Andrea True Connection / Heaven must be missing an angel: Tavares / Rock the boat: Hues Corporation / Right back where we started from: Nightingale, Maxine / Celebration: Kool & The Gang / Don't stop the music: Yarbrough & Peoples / Use it up wear it out: Odyssey / Shame: King, Evelyn 'Champagne' / Swing your Daddy: Gilstrap, Jim / Don't take away the music: Tavares / Be thankful for what you've got: DeVaughan, William / Respect yourself: Staple Singers / and the beat goes on: Whispers / Love town: Newbury, Booker / Somebody else's guy: Brown, Jocelyn / Change of heart: Change / Burn rubber on me: Gap Band / You gave me love: Crown Heights Affair / Message: Grandmaster Flash / I found love: Fatback Band / Hang on in there baby: Bristol, Johnny
CD _____ DINCD 27
Dino / Oct '91 / Pinnacle / 3MV.

RHYTHM IS A DANCER
CD Set _____ 55524
Laserlight / Nov '94 / Target/BMG.

RHYTHM OF BRAZIL, THE
Mother Brasilier / Bizantina bizancia: Ben, Jorge / Moenda: Machado, Elaine / Tatinvo: De Moraes, Vinicius / Banda da carmen mirandes: Armandinho & Trio Electrico / Joventude moqueta: O Dia Se Zancou / Cinco criancas: Lobo, Edo / Roberto corta essa: Ben, Jorge / Festejando / A Voz doz morro: Melodia, Luiz / Mulato latino: Melodia, Luiz / A bencao bahia: Toquinho & Vincius De Moraes / Salve simpatia: Ben, Jorge / Como diza o poeta: Toquinho & Vinicius De Moraes / Viva meu samba: Casa de samba
CD _____ MCCD 013
Music Club / Feb '91 / Disc / THE / ADA.

RHYTHM OF RESISTANCE
U mama uyajabula: Mlangeni, Babsy / Ke ya le leboha: Mlangeni, Babsy / Perefere: Malomba / Pampa madiba: Malomba / Jesu ot-

soile: Mparanyana & The Cannibals / Umthombowase golgota: Ladysmith Black Mambazo / Yinhleleni: Ladysmith Black Mambazo / Inkunzi ayi hlabi ngokusima: Johnny & Sipho / Igula lamasi: Mahotella Queens / Ubu gowelle: Baseqhudeni, Abafana
CD _____ SHANCD 43018
Shanachie / Apr '88 / Koch / ADA / Greensleeves.

RHYTHM TRACK EXPLOSION VOL.1
CD _____ GSR 70017
Ras / Apr '92 / Jetstar / Greensleeves / SRD / Direct.

RHYTHM WAS OUR BUSINESS
Tiger rag / Mama don't allow it / Hold tight / Apple for the teacher / I can't dance / Bill tell / Anything goes / Out every Friday / Chinatown, my Chinatown / Who's sorry now / Clarinet marmalade / Sea food squabble / Weather man / Give out / It don't mean a thing if it ain't got that swing / Nagasaki / Way down yonder in New Orleans / Potomac jump / I'm forever blowing bubbles / Promenade / Twelfth street rag / Russian salad / Seven day's leave / Someday sweetheart
CD _____ RAJCD 810
Empress / Nov '93 / THE.

RHYTHM ZONE
CD _____ KOOLCD 001
Kool Kat / Jun '89 / Pinnacle.

RHYTHMS OF RAPTURE
(Sacred Music Of Haitian Voodoo)
CD _____ SFWCD 40464
Smithsonian Folkways / Oct '95 / ADA / Direct / Koch / CM / Cadillac.

RIDE DADDY RIDE
Ride daddy ride: Noel, Fats / Sure cure for the blues: Four Jacks / Big ten inch record: Jackson, Bull Moose / One whole day: Drivers / Drill daddy drill: Ellis, Dorothy / Roll roll pretty baby: Swallows / Walkin' blues: Hunter, Fluffy / Rocket 69: Rhodes, Todd / I knew he would: Sharps & Flats / Grandpa can boogie too: Greenwood, Lil / I want a bowlegged woman: Jackson, Bull Moose / I want my Fanny Brown: Harris, Wynonie / My natch'l man: Hunter, Fluffy / Chocolate pork chop man: Lewis, Pete 'Guitar' / It ain't the meat: Swallows / Ride jockey ride: Lamplighters / Mountain oysters: Davis, Eddie 'Lockjaw' / Triflin' woman: Harris, Wynonie / My ding a ling: Bartholomew, Dave / Last of the good rockin' men: Four Jacks / Your daddy's doggin' around: Rhodes, Todd
CD _____ CDCHARLY 272
Charly / Feb '91 / Charly / THE / Cadillac.

RIGHT & EXACT 2
CD _____ KSCD 7
Kold Sweat / Jan '94 / 3MV.

RIGHT TRACKS, THE
CD _____ RNCD 2008
Rhino / May '93 / Jetstar / Magnum Music Group / THE.

RIGHTS OF MAN, THE
CD _____ GLCD 1111
Green Linnet / Feb '92 / Roots / CM / Direct / ADA.

RIGODON SAUVAGE
CD _____ C 560053
Ocora / Nov '95 / Harmonia Mundi / ADA.

RIME OF THE ANCIENT SAMPLER
CD _____ VP 141CD
Voice Print / Jun '93 / Voice Print.

RINE COMPLETE IRISH DANCING SET
CD _____ CHCD 1050
Chyme / Jan '95 / CM / ADA / Direct.

RINGING CLEAR
(The Art of Handbell Ringing)
Entry of the gladiators / Linden Lea / Stephon Foster selection / Grandfather's clock / On wings of song / Lord of the dance / Girl with the flaxen hair / Country gardens / Ashgrove / Ragtime dance / Parade of the tin soldiers / Isle of Capri / Lullaby / Original rags / Silver threads among the gold / Intermezzo from cavalleria rusticana / Bells of St. Mary's / O waly waly / Flow gently sweet Afton / Syncopated clock / O guter mond / Whistling Rufus
CD _____ CDSDL 333
Saydisc / Oct '91 / Harmonia Mundi / ADA / Direct.

RIOT CITY SINGLES COLLECTION
Last rockers: Vice Squad / Young blood: Vice Squad / Politics: Insane / Vicious circle: Abrasive Wheels / Gotta get out: Court Martial / You got me in trouble: Chaotic Dischord / Dreaming: Expelled / Army song: Abrasive Wheels / Fuck the world: Chaotic Dischord / No solution: Court Martial / No security: Chaos UK / Dogsbody: Mayhem / Have you got 10p: Ejected / Dead revolution: Undead / Burn em' down: Abrasive Wheels / Make it alone: Expelled / Nottingham problem: Resistance 77 / Fast 'n' loud: Ejected / Cream of the crop: No Choice / Pints of view: Emergency / Never trust a friend: Chaotic Dischord / Back on the piss again: Sex Aids / Gentle murder: Mayhem / Crime for revenge: Ultra-Violent / East of dachau: Underdogs / Die for your government: Varukers / Russians: Ejected

871

Led to the slaughter: Varukers / Cliff: Chaotic Dischord
CD _______________ CDPUNK 15
Anagram / Sep '93 / Pinnacle.

RIOT CITY SINGLES COLLECTION VOL.2
Living on dreams: Vice Squad / Humane: Vice Squad / Dead and gone: Insane / Voice of youth: Abrasive Wheels / Fight for your life: Court Martial / Kill your baby: Chaos UK / It's corruption: Undead / What justice: Expelled / Juvenile: Abrasive Wheels / You're gonna die: Chaotic Dischord / Too late: Court Martial / What about a future: Chaos UK / Street fight: Mayhem / Class of '82: Ejected / Place is burning: Undead / Urban rebel: Abrasive Wheels / Government policy: Expelled / Join the army: Resistance 77 / I don't care: Ejected / Sadist dream: No Choice / City fun: Emergency / Pop stars: Chaotic Dischord / We are the road crew: Sex Aids / (Your face fits) Lie and die: Mayhem / Dead generation: Ultra Violet / Johnny go home: Underdogs / All systems fail: Varukers / Twenty four years: Ejected / End is nigh: Varukers
CD _______________ CDPUNK 55
Anagram / May '95 / Pinnacle.

RIPE MASTERS
CD _______________ RIPEXD 202
Ripe / Nov '94 / Total/BMG.

RIPE MASTERS #2
Let me love you for tonight: Kariya / Scandalise: Afterlife / Move on: Ray, Cecilia / Need you: Davis, Alvin / Share my love: Waters, Kim / Don't you want it: Edwards, Sandi / Ordinary girl: P-Ski Mac / Naughty but nice: Spice / Money or love: Davis, Alvin / Walking on sunshine: Rockers Revenge / I'll always love my Ma: P-Ski Mac / Round 'n' round: Ray, Cecilia / Lost in the storm: Waters, Kim / I wonder where you are: Edwards, Sandi / Byzantium: Afterlife
CD _______________ RIPECD 216
Ripe / Nov '95 / Total/BMG.

RITMO DE BAHIA
CD _______________ 371001
Justin / Nov '90 / Triple Earth.

RITMO DE LA NOCHE
CD _______________ DCD 5393
Disky / Jul '94 / THE / BMG / Discovery / Pinnacle.

RIVER OF SOUND, A
Ah sweet dancer: Ó Súilleabháin, Mícheál / Johnny Dohertys: Tourish, Ciaran/Dermot Byrne / Two Conneeleys: Moore, Christy/Ó Súilleabháin, Mícheál / Real blues reel: Power, Brendan / Si bheag, si mhor: Ó Súilleabháin, Mícheál/C. Breatnach / Pulsus / Three jigs: Kelly, Laoise / River of sound / Caoineadh na dtri mhuire: O'Lionaird, Iarla / Three reels: Ivers, Eileen / Wind in the woods: O'Connor, M./M. Murray / Turas go tir na nog: Ó Súilleabháin, Mícheál / O'Keefe's slides: Begley, Seamus & Stephen Cooney / Roaring water reels: Vallely, Niall / Barn dances: Gavin, Frankie & Martin O'Connor / Port na bpucai: Browne, Ronan
CD _______________ CDV 2776
Virgin / Dec '95 / EMI.

RIVER TOWN BLUES
CD _______________ HIUKCD 118
Hi / Jul '91 / Pinnacle.

RIVERSIDE HISTORY OF CLASSIC JAZZ (3CD Set)
I'm going to heaven if it takes my life: Gates, Rev. J.M. & Congregation / I've got the blues for Rampart Street: Cox, Ida / Big Bill blues: Broonzy, Big Bill / Cascades: Joplin, Scott / Perfect rag: Morton, Jelly Roll / Pearls: Morton, Jelly Roll / Froggie Moore rag: Oliver, King Jazzband / Memphis maybe man: Cook, Doc & His Dreamland Orchestra / Mama stayed out: Barrelhouse Five / Fives: Yancey, Jimmy / Lone star blues: Johnson, Pete / Royal garden blues: Beiderbecke, Bix & the Wolverines / Friars Point Shuffle: Jungle Kings / Harlem strut: Johnson, James P. / Cake walkin' babies from home: Red Onion Jazz Babies / Stampede: Red & Miffs Stompers / Eccentric: Davison, Wild Bill / Muskrat ramble: Spanier, Muggsy / Hop off: Henderson, Fletcher & His Orchestra / Rainy nights: Ellington, Duke Washingtonians / Make me a pallet on the floor: Johnson, Bunk / Weary blues: Ory, Kid / Antigua blues: Watters, Lu & The Yerba Buena Jazz Band
CD Set _______________ RBCD 005
Riverside / Oct '93 / Jazz Music / Pinnacle / Cadillac.

ROARING 20'S, THE
If you knew Susie like I know Susie: Shilkret, Jack & His Orchestra / Sheikh of Araby: Pianola Roll / I'm tellin' the birds, tellin' the bees: Smith, Jack 'Whispering' / That's my weakness now: Pianola Roll / Canadian capers: Biese, Paul Trio / Rose Marie: Pianola Roll / Colette: Whiteman, Paul & His Orchestra / Where the lazy daisies grow: Pianola Roll / Ain't misbehavin': Hylton, Jack & His Orchestra & Sam Browne / My inspiration is you: Pianola Roll / Wedding of the painted doll: Pianola Roll / Don't bring Lulu: Garber, Jan & His Orchestra / Always: Pianola Roll / Where, oh where do I live: Douglas, Fred & Orchestra / Birth of the blues: Pianola Roll / I miss my Swiss: Golden Gate Orchestra / Ain't she sweet: Pianola Roll / Hello Swanee, hello: Syncopated Four / Ramona: Pianola Roll / Charleston
CD _______________ CDSDL 344
Saydisc / Mar '94 / Harmonia Mundi / ADA / Direct.

ROARING TWENTIES
CD _______________ DCD 5334
Disky / Dec '93 / THE / BMG / Discovery / Pinnacle.

ROBERT BURNS COLLECTION - THE BURNS SUPPER
Selkirk grace / Address to the haggis / Immortal memory of Robert Burns / Toast to the lassies / Reply to the toast to the lassies / Tam o'shanter / Man's a man/Auld lang syne
CD Set _______________ LCOM 6039
Lismor / Nov '95 / Lismor / Direct / Duncans / ADA.

ROBERT BURNS COLLECTION - THE MUSIC
Of a' the airts / Bonnie lass of Ballochmyle / Green grow the rashes / Afton water / Ca' the ewes / Aye waukin' o / Trilogy / John Anderson my jo / Star of Rabbie Burns / Ye banks and braes / O my love is like a red red roae / Ae fond kiss / Man's a man / Bonnie wee thing / Auld lang syne
CD _______________ LCOM 6041
Lismor / Nov '95 / Lismor / Direct / Duncans / ADA.

ROBERT BURNS COLLECTION - THE SONGS
Man's a man / O my love is like a red red rose / Ae fond kiss / Afton water / Bonnie lass of Ballochmyle / Ye banks and braes / Aye waukin' o / De'il's awa wi the exciseman / Rosebud by my early walk / Scots wha hae / I'm ower young to marry yet / There was a lad / Birks o' Aberfeldy / MacPherson's farewell / John Anderson my jo / Auld lang syne
CD _______________ LCOM 6040
Lismor / Nov '95 / Lismor / Direct / Duncans / ADA.

ROBERT PARKER'S JAZZ CLASSICS
Dr. Jazz: Morton, Jelly Roll / Sweet lovin' man: Oliver, King Jazzband / Too tight: Dodds, Johnny Orchestra / Alligator crawl: Armstrong, Louis / Salty dog: Keppard, Freddie / As you like it: Celestin's Original Tuxedo Orchestra / That's a plenty: New Orleans Owls / Franklin Street blues: Dumaine, Louis Jazzola Eight / Mr. Jelly Lord, Panama: New Orleans Rhythm Kings / Pleasin' Paul: Allen, Henry 'Red' & His Orchestra / Astoria strut, damp weather: Jones & Collins Astoria Hot Eight / Sizzling the blues, high society: Hazel, Monk & His Bienville Roof Orchestra / Sweetie dear: New Orleans Feetwarmers / Weatherbird: Armstrong, Louis & Earl Hines / Blue piano stomp: Dodds, Johnny Trio / Clarinet marmalade: Original Dixieland Jazz Band / Sidewalk blues: Morton, Jelly Roll / Someday sweetheart: Oliver, King & His Dixie Syncopators / Savoyager's stomp: Dickerson, Carroll & His Orchestra / African hunch: Jones, Richard M. / Singin' the blues: Trumbauer, Frankie / Nobody's sweetheart: McKenzie & Condon's Chicagoans / Walking the dog: Carmichael Collegians / What do I care what somebody said: Mound City Blues Blowers / Milenberg joys: McKinney's Cotton Pickers / Yellow fire: Reeves, Reuben 'River' / Shake that Jelly Roll: Cobb, J.C. & his Grains of Corn / My oh my: South, Eddie & His International Orchestra / Get 'em again blues: Chicago Foot Warmers / Stomp your stuff: State Street Ramblers / Hear me talkin' to ya: Rainey, Gertrude 'Ma' / Beau Koo Jack: Simeon, Omer / Maple leaf rag: Hines, Earl & His Orchestra / Jump steady blues: Pinetop Slim / Memphis shake: Dixieland Jug Blowers / Burnin' the iceberg: Morton, Jelly Roll / Struggle buggy: Oliver, King Jazzband / Sugarfoot stomp: Henderson, Fletcher / Lock and key: Smith, Bessie / San: Whiteman, Paul / Imagination: Mole, Miff / Makin' friends: Mole, Miff / Minor drag: Waller, Fats / East St. Louis toodle-oo: Ellington, Duke Orchestra / Hot bones and rice: Johnson, Charlie & His Paradise Orchestra / Dr. Blues: Russell, Luis & His Orchestra / Feelin' devilish: Williams, Fess / Happy hour: Scott, Lloyd & his orchestra / Casa Loma stomp: Casa Loma Orchestra / Dog bottom: Jungle Band / Minnie the moocher: Calloway, Cab & His Orchestra / Stratosphere: Lunceford, Jimmie / Cushion foot stomp: Williams, Clarence & His Washboard Band / I can't dance: Jenkins, Freddie & Harlem 7 / Farewell blues: Lang, Eddie & Joe Venuti / Hot town: Williams, Fess & His Royal Flush Orchestra / Everybody loves my baby: Taylor's Dixie Serenaders / Florida rhythm: Ross Deluxe Syncopators / Duck's yas yas yas: Johnson's, Eddie Crackerjacks / Scandinavian stomp: Williamson's Beale Street Frolics Orchestra / In dat mornin': Lunceford, Jimmie & his Chickasaw Syncopators / Stomp: Britt, Mart Orchestra / All muggled up: Blue Steele / To-wa-bac-a-wa: Dumaine, Louis Jazzola Eight / Dreamland blues: Floyd, Troy & His Plaza Hotel Orchestra / Quality shout: Howard, Paul / Skirts: Randall, Slatz & His Orchestra / Corky stomp: Kirk, Andy & His Clouds Of Joy / Butter-fringe blues: Creath, Chas Jazz O Maniacs / Midnight Mama: Moten, Bennie Kansas City Orchestra / Daybreak express: Ellington, Duke Orchestra
CD Set _______________ RP3CD 612
Robert Parker Jazz / Aug '93 / Conifer.

ROCK & POP BALLADS
CD _______________ 12202
Laserlight / May '94 / Target/BMG.

ROCK & ROLL RIOT (GANGWAR)
Rockin' roll riot: Stoltz Brothers / Savage: Barnicoat, Alan / Betty Ann: Cruisers / Tough 'n rough: Saladin / Itch: Cherry, Carl / That cat: Brown, Tommy / Rock 'n' roll saddles: Edwards, Johnny / Baby Sue: Rhythm Tones / Rock 'n' roll rock: Kelly, Roy / Is that wrong: Wynnewoods / Bloodshot: String Kings / Granny went rockin': Scott, Rodney / My baby's casual: Flaharty, Sonny / Rockin' and boppin': Newman, Carl / Rockin' teens: Puckett, Dennis / Little jewel: Taylor, Bill / Keep it swinging: Skelton, Eddie / Rock 'n' roll guitar: Knight, Johnny / Woman can make you blue: Porter, Royce / Wild wild woman: Wright, Steve / Rock rhythm roll: Dash, Frankie / Where's my baby: Giant, Ethan / I know why: Clark, Billy / Scratching on my screen: Cartey, Ric / Rock 'n' roll romance: Big Rocker / Blues in the morning: Foley, Jim / Hard luck: Blank, Billy / Bootleg rock: Bonny, Billy / Robinson Crusoe bop: Cole, Sonny / By by blues: Puckett, Dennis
CD _______________ CDBB 55004
Buffalo Bop / Apr '94 / Rollercoaster.

ROCK AND WATER
CD _______________ ECLCD 9411
Eclectic / Jan '96 / Pinnacle.

ROCK ANTHEMS
CD _______________ STACD 041
Stardust / Aug '93 / Carlton Home Entertainment.

ROCK ANTHEMS
CD _______________ DINCD 101
Dino / Oct '94 / Pinnacle / 3MV.

ROCK BALLADS
CD _______________ STACD 044
Stardust / Sep '94 / Carlton Home Entertainment.

ROCK BALLADS
Once in a lifetime: Kansas / Parisienne walkways: Moore, Gary / Amanda: Boston / Winning man: Krokus / On and on: Bishop, Stephen / Surrender: Trixter / Thrill is gone: King, B.B. / Pusher: Trixter / She's gone: Steelheart / Sara: Starship / Still believe: Starship / Washable ink: Hiatt, John / Gail (live): Cooper, Alice / Just one precious moment: Emergency / Stairway to heaven: Far Corporation
CD _______________ MCD 30202
Ariola Express / Mar '94 / BMG.

ROCK BALLADS
Sowing the seeds of love: Tears For Fears / First time: Beck, Robin / Search is over: Survivor / Cry: Godley & Creme / Stop: Brown, Sam / Should've known better: Diamond, Jim / Sugar box: Then Jerico / Send me an angel: Scorpions / You're the best thing: Style Council / When Smokey sings: ABC / Start talking love: Magnum / Because of you: Dexy's Midnight Runners / Babe: Styx / Street of dreams: Rainbow
CD _______________ 5506482
Spectrum/Karussell / Aug '94 / PolyGram / THE.

ROCK BEFORE ELVIS
CD _______________ STBCD 25162617
Stash / Aug '95 / Jazz Music / CM / Cadillac / Direct / ADA.

ROCK CHARTBUSTERS
I want you to want me: Cheap Trick / Time stood still: Bad English / Africa: Toto / Fight for ourselves: Spandau Ballet / More than a feeling: Boston / Down under: Men At Work / Dead ringer for love: Meat Loaf / Talking in your sleep: Romantics / Take me home tonight (Be my baby): Money, Eddie / Brandy: Looking Glass / Skin deep: Stranglers / Heartbeat: Johnson, Don / Black magic woman: Santana / Who's crying now: Journey / Oh Sherrie: Perry, Steve / Carry on wayward son: Kansas
CD _______________ 4771182
Embassy / Oct '95 / Sony.

ROCK CITY
CD _______________ NTRCD 003
Nectar / May '93 / Pinnacle.

ROCK CITY NIGHTS
One vision: Queen / You give love a bad name: Bon Jovi / Big area: Then Jerico / King of emotion: Big Country / Red sky: Status Quo / Incommunicado: Marillion / Satisfied: Marx, Richard / Some like it hot: Power Station / Rock the night: Europe / Need you tonight: INXS / I don't want a lover: Texas / I won't back down: Petty, Tom / Silent running: Mike & The Mechanics / Africa: Toto / More than a feeling: Boston / Go your own way: Fleetwood Mac / I surrender: Rainbow / Eye of the tiger: Survivor
CD _______________ 8406222
PolyGram TV / Oct '89 / PolyGram.

ROCK CLASSICS
CD _______________ MATCD 236
Castle / Dec '92 / BMG.

ROCK CLASSICS VOLUME 1
CD _______________ 11851
Laserlight / Feb '95 / Target/BMG.

ROCK CLASSICS VOLUME 2
CD _______________ 11852
Laserlight / Feb '95 / Target/BMG.

ROCK CLASSICS VOLUME 3
CD _______________ 11853
Laserlight / Feb '95 / Target/BMG.

ROCK DREAMS
CD _______________ 24064
Laserlight / Mar '95 / Target/BMG.

ROCK DREAMS VOL. 2
CD _______________ 24084
Laserlight / Mar '95 / Target/BMG.

ROCK ERA - MORE OF THE GREATEST HITS
CD _______________ LECD 403
Wisepack / Sep '93 / THE / Conifer.

ROCK EXPERIENCE, THE
CD Set _______________ BOXD 27
Carlton Home Entertainment / Nov '92 / Carlton Home Entertainment.

ROCK FM
CD _______________ STACD 042
Stardust / Aug '93 / Carlton Home Entertainment.

ROCK GIANTS
CD _______________ 12402
Laserlight / Feb '95 / Target/BMG.

ROCK GREATS
CD _______________ STACD 039
Stardust / Sep '94 / Carlton Home Entertainment.

ROCK GUITAR LEGENDS VOL. 2
Mercury blues: Lindley, David / Over and over: Walsh, Joe / Jukebox hero: Foreigner / Lost in the shuffle: Kortchmar, Danny / Long time till I get over you: Little Feat / River of tears: Raitt, Bonnie / Ashphalt jungle: Felder, Don / So wrong: Simmons, Patrick / Stainsby girls: Rea, Chris / Spirit of radio: Rush / I can see for miles: Who / Cocaine: Cale, J.J. / Sky high: Atlanta Rhythm Section / I'm waiting for the man: Velvet Underground / Whiskey in the jar: Thin Lizzy / From little things big things grow: Edmunds, Dave / Confidence man: Healey, Jeff / We can be together: Jefferson Airplane / Built for speed: Stray Cats / Roll with the changes: REO Speedwagon / Don't stop believin': Journey / Honey don't leave L.A.: Taylor, James / Sweet potato pie: Taylor, James / Rock 'n' roll hoochie coo: Winter, Johnny / East of Eden's gate: Thorpe, Billy / Need your love so bad: Fleetwood Mac / Where have you been all my life: Nugent, Ted / Ready for love: Mott The Hoople / Once bitten twice shy: Hunter, Ian / American girl: Petty, Tom / Sweet home Alabama: Lynyrd Skynyrd / Gotta hurry: Yardbirds / No particular place to go: Berry, Chuck / Natural born boogie: Humble Pie / Parisienne walkways (live): Moore, Gary / I'm your witch doctor: Clapton, Eric Allstars / Laundromat: Gallagher, Rory / Bleeding heart: Hendrix, Jimi / You won't see me anymore: Green, Peter / Breakdown: Coverdale, David / I've been born again: Frey, Glenn / Who do you love: Juicy Lucy / Paranoid: Black Sabbath / Rocky mountain way: Walsh, Joe / Drift away: Gray, Dobie / I came to dance: Lofgren, Nils / Show me the way: Frampton, Peter / Dear Mr. Fantasy: Traffic
CD Set _______________ NXTCD 248
Sequel / May '93 / BMG.

ROCK HARD, HARD ROCK
CD _______________ DCD 5369
Disky / Jul '94 / THE / BMG / Discovery / Pinnacle.

ROCK INFERNO
CD _______________ STACD 040
Stardust / Sep '94 / Carlton Home Entertainment.

ROCK IT FOR ME - 1937
One o'clock jump: Basie, Count / Sailboat in the moonlight: Holiday, Billie & Her Orchestra / I can't get started (with you): Berigan, Bunny / Honeysuckle rose: Hawkins, Coleman / Boo hoo: Lombardo, Guy / When we're alone: James, Harry / Alabamy home: Ellington, Duke / Getting some fun out of life: Holiday, Billie & Orchestra/Barney Kessel / Carry me back to old Virginny: Armstrong, Louis / Song of India: Dorsey, Tommy / I can't give you anything but love: Goodman, Benny / Who's sorry now: Crosby, Bob / Loch Lomond: Sullivan, Maxine / Posin': Lunceford, Jimmie / I've got my love to keep me warm: Norvo, Red / Rock it for me: Webb, Chick / Whose babe: Hampton / I must have that man: Wilson, Teddy / Caravan: Ellington, Duke / Topsie
CD _______________ PHONT CD 7663
Phontastic / Apr '90 / Wellard / Jazz Music / Cadillac.

ROCK LEGENDS
CD Set _______________ MBSCD 406
Castle / Nov '93 / BMG.

ROCK LEGENDS
This flight tonight: Nazareth / N.I.B.: Black Sabbath / Sweet Lorraine: Uriah Heep / Sil-

ver machine: *Hawkwind* / Down the dust-pipe: *Status Quo* / Race with the devil: *Girlschool* / Dancin': *Moore, Gary* / Kingdom of madness: *Magnum* / Overkill: *Motorhead* / Who do you love: *Juicy Lucy* / Ace of spades: *Motorhead* / Natural born boogie: *Humble Pie* / Broken down angel: *Nazareth* / Levitation: *Hawkwind* / Ice in the sun: *Status Quo* / Wizard: *Uriah Heep* / All of my life: *Magnum* / Parisienne walkways (lives): *Moore, Gary*
CD _____ MCCD 045
Music Club / Sep '91 / Disc / THE / CM.

ROCK ME SLOWLY
CD _____ MUSCD 020
MCI / Sep '94 / Disc / THE.

ROCK MOODS
CD _____ PMCD 7017
Pure Music / Oct '95 / BMG.

ROCK 'N 'ROLL CLASSICS
CD _____ LECD 054
Wisepack / Jul '94 / THE / Conifer.

ROCK N ROLL HIT PARTY
CD _____ CDCD 1021
Charly / Mar '93 / Charly / THE / Cadillac.

ROCK 'N' ROLL
(2CD Set)
CD Set _____ R2CD 4017
Deja Vu / Jan '96 / THE.

ROCK 'N' ROLL FEVER: THE WILDEST FROM SPECIALITY
Justine: *Don & Dewey* / Moose on the loose: *Jackson, Roddy* / Thunderbird: *Hall, Rene* / My baby's rocking: *Monitors* / Cherokee dance: *Landers, Bob* / Sha sa dat 'Yeah': *Williams, Larry* / Don't stop loving me: *Church, Eugene* / Don't you just know it: *Titans* / Twitchy: *Hall, Rene* / Haunted house: *Fuller, Johnny* / Chicken, baby, chicken: *Harris, Tony* / Sack: *Hughes, Ben* / Arlene: *Titans* / Little bird: *Hollywood Flames* / I've got my sights set on someone new: *Jackson, Roddy* / Lights out: *Byrne, Jerry* / It's spring again: *Pentagons* / Goodbye baby goodbye: *Lowery, Sonny* / Ooh little girl: *Dixon, Floyd* / Rock 'n' roll fever: *Dixon, Floyd* / Swingin' at the creek: *Fuller, Johnny* / Frankenstein's den: *Hollywood Flames* / Carry on: *Byrne, Jerry* / Hiccups: *Jackson, Roddy* / Satisfied: *Casualairs*
CD _____ CDCHD 574
Ace / Jul '94 / Pinnacle / Cadillac / Complete/Pinnacle.

ROCK 'N' ROLL FOREVER
CD _____ DCD 5306
Disky / Dec '93 / THE / BMG / Discovery / Pinnacle.

ROCK 'N' ROLL GOLD
(2CD Set)
CD Set _____ D2CD 4017
Deja Vu / Jun '95 / THE.

ROCK 'N' ROLL GREATS VOL.1
Tutti frutti: *Little Richard* / That'll be the day: *Holly, Buddy & The Crickets* / Blueberry hill: *Domino, Fats* / Take good care of my baby: *Vee, Bobby* / Walk don't run: *Ventures* / Say mama: *Vincent, Gene* / Bird dog: *Everly Brothers* / Sweet little sixteen: *Berry, Chuck* / Something else: *Cochran, Eddie* / We're gonna) Rock around the clock: *Haley, Bill & The Comets* / I'm walkin': *Domino, Fats* / Don't ever change: *Crickets* / Why do fools fall in love: *Lymon, Frankie & The Teenagers* / Be bop a lula: *Vincent, Gene* / Summertime blues: *Cochran, Eddie* / You're sixteen: *Burnette, Johnny* / Peggy Sue: *Holly, Buddy & The Crickets* / Claudette: *Everly Brothers* / Three steps to heaven: *Cochran, Eddie* / Blue Monday: *Domino, Fats* / Blue jean bop: *Vincent, Gene* / Johnny B. Goode: *Berry, Chuck* / Good golly Miss Molly: *Little Richard*
CD _____ CDMFP 5745
Music For Pleasure / Apr '92 / EMI.

ROCK 'N' ROLL GREATS VOL.3
Be my guest: *Domino, Fats* / Night has a thousand eyes: *Vee, Bobby* / Pistol packin' mama: *Vincent, Gene* / Cincinnati fireball: *Burnette, Johnny Rock 'N' Roll Trio* / She's gone: *Knox, Buddy* / Piltdown rides again: *Piltdown Men* / Let's have a party: *Jackson, Wanda* / Get a job: *Silhouettes* / Ha, he's making eyes at me (The Johnny Otis Show with Marie Adams & The Three Tons Of Joy): *Otis, Johnny* / Weekend: *Cochran, Eddie* / Perfidia: *Ventures* / Bony Moronie: *Williams, Larry* / Mother-in-law: *Doe, Ernie K.* / Love potion no.9: *Clovers* / Runaway: *Shannon, Del* / You've got what it takes: *Johnson, Marv* / Stay: *Williams, Maurice & The Zodiacs* / Baby baby (As sung in

film 'Rock, Rock, Rock'.): *Lymon, Frankie & The Teenagers*
CD _____ CDMFP 5941
Music For Pleasure / Apr '92 / EMI.

ROCK 'N' ROLL GREATS VOL.4
Hello Mary Lou: *Nelson, Rick* / Shakin' all over: *Kidd, Johnny & The Pirates* / Run to him: *Vee, Bobby* / Shake, rattle and roll: *Haley, Bill* / Rave on: *Holly, Buddy* / I'm in love again: *Domino, Fats* / Move it: *Richard, Cliff* / No particular place to go: *Berry, Chuck* / Little town flirt: *Shannon, Del* / One sixteen: *Douglas, Craig* / See you later alligator: *Haley, Bill* / It's late: *Nelson, Rick* / Rock 'n' roll music: *Berry, Chuck* / Wild cat: *Vincent, Gene* / Say man: *Diddley, Bo* / Sweetie pie: *Cochran, Eddie* / Hey little girl: *Shannon, Del* / It doesn't matter anymore: *Holly, Buddy*
CD _____ CDMFP 5942
Music For Pleasure / Apr '92 / EMI.

ROCK 'N' ROLL IS HERE TO STAY
CD _____ SETCD 088
Stardust / Sep '94 / Carlton Home Entertainment.

ROCK 'N' ROLL IS HERE TO STAY
C'mon everybody: *Cochran, Eddie* / Hallelujah, I love her so: *Cochran, Eddie* / Something else: *Cochran, Eddie* / I'm a moody guy: *Fenton, Shane & The Fentones* / Five foot two, eyes of blue: *Fenton, Shane & The Fentones* / Stick shift: *Duals* / Party doll: *Knox, Buddy* / Ain't misbehavin': *Bruce, Tommy & The Bruisers* / Let the good times roll: *Shirley & Lee* / Be bop a lula: *Vincent, Gene* / Wild cat: *Vincent, Gene* / Pistol packin' mama: *Vincent, Gene* / Lost and found: *Vernon Girls* / Run to him: *Vee, Bobby* / Take good care of my baby: *Vee, Bobby* / Night has a thousand eyes: *Vee, Bobby* / Saturday night at the duck pond: *Cougars* / Blueberry hill: *Domino, Fats* / Piltdown rides again: *Piltdown Men* / I've got a woman: *McGriff, Jimmy* / Blue moon: *Marcels* / Bap four: Four Preps* / You're sixteen: *Four Preps* / Rubber ball: *Avons* / Love potion no.9: *Clover* / Shakin' all over: *Kidd, Johnny & The Pirates* / Please don't touch: *Kidd, Johnny & The Pirates* / I'll never get over you: *Kidd, Johnny & The Pirates* / You've got what it takes: *Johnson, Marv* / You can't sit down: *Upchurch, Phil Combo* / Ain't that a shame: *Domino, Fats* / I'm a juvenile delinquent: *Lymon, Frankie & The Teenagers* / Why do fools fall in love: *Lymon, Frankie & The Teenagers* / Papa oom mow mow: *Rivingtons* / Western movies: *Olympics* / Baby hully gully: *Olympics* / It's late: *Nelson, Rick* / Hello Mary Lou: *Nelson, Rick* / La Bamba: *Crickets* / Don't ever change: *Crickets* / Tears on my pillow: *Imperials* / Only sixteen: *Douglas, Craig* / Tell Laura I love her: *Valence, Ricky* / Right behind you baby: *Taylor, Vince & Playboys* / Ma, he's making eyes at me: *Otis, Johnny Show/Marie Adams/Three Tons Of Joy* / Gypsy beat: *Packabeats* / Tom Crombie and his Rockets - Teach you to rock: *Packabeats* / Walk don't run: *Ventures*
CD Set _____ CDTRBOX 132
Trio / Oct '94 / EMI.

ROCK 'N' ROLL LEGENDS
CD _____ SETCD 080
Stardust / Sep '94 / Carlton Home Entertainment.

ROCK 'N' ROLL LOVE SONGS
All I have to do is dream: *Everly Brothers* / More than I can say: *Vee, Bobby* / I'm sorry: *Lee, Brenda* / Heartbeat: *Holly, Buddy* / Dear little fool: *Nelson, Rick* / Dreamin': *Burnette, Johnny Rock 'N' Roll Trio* / Three steps to heaven: *Cochran, Eddie* / Poetry in motion: *Tillotson, Johnny* / Teenager in love: *Dion/the belmonts* / Don't ever change: *Crickets* / Why do fools fall in love: *Crickets* / Donna: *Valens, Ritchie* / You don't know what you've got (until you lose it): *Donner, Ral* / Be bop a lula: *Vincent, Gene* / When my little girl is smiling: *Douglas, Craig* / Sealed with a kiss: *Imperials* / All shook up: *Presley, Elvis* / Cumberland gap: *Donegan, Lonnie* / We tonight Josephine: *Ray, Johnnie* / Rockabilly: *Mitchell, Guy* / Hoots mon: *Lord Rockingham's XI* / That'll be the day: *Crickets*
CD _____ OG 3502
Old Gold / May '88 / Carlton Home Entertainment.

ROCK 'N' ROLL ORGY VOL.3
CD _____ FLESHDEN 9603
No Hit / Nov '95 / SRD.

ROCK 'N' ROLL ORIGINALS VOL. 1
Right or wrong: *Cunningham, Buddy* / Why do I cry: *Cunningham, Buddy* / Signifying monkey: *Smokey Joe* / Blue suede shoes: *Perkins, Carl* / Honey don't: *Perkins, Carl* / Ooby dooby: *Orbison, Roy* / Go go go: *Orbison, Roy* / Boppin' the blues: *Perkins, Carl* / All Mama's children: *Perkins, Carl* / Trouble bound: *Riley, Billy Lee* / Rock with me baby: *Riley, Billy Lee* / Welcome to the club: *Chapel, Jean* / I won't be rockin' tonight: *Chapel, Jean* / Rockin' with my baby: *Yelvington, Malcolm* / It's me baby: *Yelvington, Malcolm* / Red headed woman: *Burgess, Sonny* / We wanna boogie: *Burgess, Sonny* / Ubangi stomp: *Smith, Warren* / Black jack David: *Smith, Warren* / You're my baby: *Orbison, Roy* / Rock house: *Orbison, Roy*
CD _____ CDSUN 3
Sun / Feb '88 / Charly.

ROCK 'N' ROLL ORIGINALS VOL. 2
Love crazy baby: *Parchman, Kenny* / I feel like rockin': *Parchman, Kenny* / No matter who's to blame: *Pittman, Barbara* / I need a man: *Pittman, Barbara* / Come on little mama: *Harris, Ray* / Where'd you stay last night: *Harris, Ray* / Take and give: *Rhodes, Slim* / Do what I do: *Rhodes, Slim* / Crazy arms: *Lewis, Jerry Lee* / End of the road: *Lewis, Jerry Lee* / It'll be me: *Lewis, Jerry Lee* / Whole lotta shakin' goin' on: *Lewis, Jerry Lee* / Flyin' saucer rock 'n' roll: *Riley, Billy Lee* / I want you baby: *Riley, Billy Lee* / Restless: *Burgess, Sonny* / Ain't got a thing: *Burgess, Sonny* / I'll be around: *Honeycutt, Glenn* / I'll wait forever: *Honeycutt, Glenn* / Sweet and easy to love: *Orbison, Roy* / Devil doll: *Orbison, Roy* / Matchbox: *Perkins, Carl* / Your true love: *Perkins, Carl*
CD _____ CDSUN 6
Sun / Apr '88 / Charly.

ROCK 'N' ROLL ORIGINALS VOL. 3
Miss Froggie: *Smith, Warren* / So long I'm gone: *Smith, Warren* / Bob bob baby: *Wade & Dick* / Don't need your lovin' baby: *Wade & Dick* / Please don't cry over me: *Williams, Jimmy* / That depends on you: *Williams, Jimmy* / Foolish heart: *Harris, Ray* / Greenback dollar: *Harris, Ray* / That's right: *Perkins, Carl* / Forever yours: *Perkins, Carl* / Rock boppin' baby: *Bruce, Edwin* / More than yesterday: *Bruce, Edwin* / Red hot: *Riley, Billy Lee* / Pearly Lee: *Riley, Billy Lee* / Flatfoot Sam: *Blake, Tommy* / Lordy hoody: *Blake, Tommy* / Love my baby: *Thompson, Hayden* / One broken heart: *Thompson, Hayden* / Two young fools in love: *Pittman, Barbara* / I'm getting better all the time: *Pittman, Barbara* / Midnight man: *Justis, Bill* / Raunchy: *Justis, Bill*
CD _____ CDSUN 9
Sun / Jul '88 / Charly.

ROCK 'N' ROLL ORIGINALS VOL. 4
That's the way I love: *Carroll, Johnny* / I'll wait: *Carroll, Johnny* / Memories never grow old: *Lee, Dickey* / Good lovin': *Lee, Dickey* / You win again: *Lewis, Jerry Lee* / Great balls of fire: *Lewis, Jerry Lee* / Cindy Lou: *Penner, Dick* / Your honey love: *Penner, Dick* / I like love: *Orbison, Roy* / Chicken hearted: *Orbison, Roy* / Sweet misery: *Burgess, Sonny* / My buckets got a hole in it: *Burgess, Sonny* / Got love if you want it: *Smith, Warren* / I fell in love: *Smith, Warren* / Glad all over: *Perkins, Carl* / Lend me your comb: *Perkins, Carl* / Treat me right: *Thomas, Cliff* / I'm on my way home: *Thomas, Cliff* / Cause the time I lost goin' far: *Breathless: Lewis, Jerry Lee* / Wouldn't you know: *Riley, Billy Lee* / Baby wouldn't you know: *Riley, Billy Lee*
CD _____ CDSUN 12
Sun / Nov '89 / Charly.

ROCK 'N' ROLL ORIGINALS VOL. 5
College man: *Justis, Bill* / Stranger: *Justis, Bill* / Wild rice: *Justis, Bill* / Scroungie: *Justis, Bill* / Point of view: *Powers, Wayne* / My love song: *Powers, Wayne* / I think of you: *Grayzell, Rudy* / Judy: *Grayzell, Rudy* / Sweet woman: *Bruce, Edwin* / Part of my life: *Bruce, Edwin* / Love is a stranger: *Sunrays* / Lonely hours: *Sunrays* / Memories of you: *Priesman, Magel* / I feel so blue: *Priesman, Magel* / High school confidential: *Lewis, Jerry Lee* / Fools like me: *Lewis, Jerry Lee* / Dreamy nights: *Lee, Dickey* / Fool, fool, fool: *Lee, Dickey* / So young: *Smith, Ray* / Right behind you baby: *Smith, Ray* / Drinkin' wine: *Simmons, Gene* / I done told you: *Simmons, Gene* / Sweetie pie: *Blake, Tommy* / I dig you baby: *Blake, Tommy*
CD _____ CDSUN 14
Sun / Jan '90 / Charly.

ROCK 'N' ROLL ORIGINALS VOL. 6
CD _____ CDSUN 15
Sun / Apr '90 / Charly.

ROCK 'N' ROLL PARTY
CD Set _____ CDPK 410
Charly / Feb '95 / Charly / THE / Cadillac.

ROCK 'N' ROLL PARTY 1957-1962
Motorbiene (Motorcycle) / Bacara Sera / My happiness / Ein engel ohne fliguel (I can see an angel) / Lippenstift am Jacket / Oh eh oh ah ah (witch doctor) / Plitsch platsch (splish splash) / Speedy Gonzalez / Rock-a-hula

baby / Fur gabi tu ich alles / Fraulein / Norman / Yes tonight Josephine / Kuba rock / Wundrbares madchen (catch a falling star) / Oh, das war schon (oh lonesome me) / Lollipop / Due farbe der liebe (a white sports coat) / Zahn Hag / Japanisches absciedslied
CD _____ BCD 15235
Bear Family / Nov '86 / Rollercoaster / Direct / CM / Swift / ADA.

ROCK 'N' ROLL RADIO
(CBS Radio Broadcasts From The Fifties)
CD _____ CDMR 1087
Derann Trax / Jul '91 / Pinnacle.

ROCK 'N' ROLL ROMANCE
Will you still love me tomorrow: *Shirelles* / Sealed with a kiss: *Hyland, Brian* / Young love: *Hunter, Tab* / Venus: *Avalon, Frankie* / Come go with me: *Del-Vikings* / Born too late: *Poni-Tails* / Since I don't have you: *Skyliners* / Every breath I take: *Pitney, Gene* / Thousand stars: *Young, Karen & The Innocents* / Love letters in the sand: *Boone, Pat* / Heartbeat: *Holly, Buddy* / Donna: *Valens, Ritchie* / Till I kissed you: *Everly Brothers* / Hey baby: *Channel, Bruce* / My true love: *Scott, Jack* / Oh no not my baby: *Brown, Maxine* / Poetry in motion: *Tillotson, Johnny* / Sweet dreams: *McLain, Tommy* / Goodnight sweetheart, goodnight: *Spaniels*
CD _____ PWKS 4197
Carlton Home Entertainment / Feb '96 / Carlton Home Entertainment.

ROCK 'N' ROLL SOUND
Dancing teardrops: *Redd, Barbara* / Why should I dance: *Sheiks* / Night with Daddy: *Church Street Five* / Satan go away: *U.S. Bonds* / Go 'way Christina: *Soul, Jimmy* / Mimi: *Francois & The Anglos* / My last phone call: *Earlington, Lynn* / Sing a song children: *Church Street Five* / Raining teardrops: *Rockmasters* / Up the aisle (just you and I): *Carter, Linda* / I want to know if you love me: *Owens, Garland* / Hey little boy: *Azaleas* / My baby loves to bowl: *Soul, Jimmy* / Hula wobble shake: *Owens, Garland* / In my room: *Payton, George* / Get yo'self married: *Rockmasters* / It's praying time: *Gavin, Maddie* / Hands off: *Azaleas* / I love you so: *Raven Windorof* / Crazy over you: *Day, Margie* / I keep coming back for more: *Soul Cop* / Paper doll: *Russell, Lily* / Give me another chance: *Five Sheiks* / New Orleans: *U.S. Bonds*
CD _____ CDCHD 541
Ace / Jun '94 / Pinnacle / Cadillac / Complete/Pinnacle.

ROCK 'N' ROLL STARS ON STAGE
Great balls of fire: *Lewis, Jerry Lee* / Twist: *Checker, Chubby* / Stagger Lee: *Price, Lloyd* / Little Darlin': *Diamonds* / Tears on my pillow: *Little Anthony* / Tallahassee lassie: *Cannon, Freddy* / Earth angel: *Penguins* / Let the good times roll: *Shirley & Lee* / Short shorts: *Royal Teens* / Kisses sweeter than wine: *Rodgers, Jimmie* / Sea cruise: *Ford, Frankie* / At the harp: *Danny & The Juniors* / Rock around the clock: *Haley, Bill & The Comets*
CD _____ CDZ 2022
Zu Zazz / Nov '95 / Rollercoaster.

ROCK 'N' ROLL SUPER HITS
Peggy Sue: *Holly, Buddy* / I'm sorry: *Lee, Brenda* / Rock 'n' roll music: *Berry, Chuck* / (We're gonna) Rock around the clock: *Haley, Bill* / Rock 'n' roll is here to stay: *Danny & The Juniors* / All by myself: *Burnette, Johnny Rock 'N' Roll Trio* / When: *Kalin Twins* / Mr. Bass man: *Cymbal, Johnny* / 1-2-3: *Barry, Len* / Pipeline: *Chantays* / Wipeout: *Surfaris* / Mona: *Diddley, Bo* / Suzie Q: *Hawkins, Dale* / Come go with me: *Del-Vikings* / Great, gosh and mighty: *Little Richard* / Great balls of fire: *Lewis, Jerry Lee*
CD _____ MCD 30200
Ariola Express / Mar '94 / BMG.

ROCK 'N' ROLL YEARS 1959
Till I kissed you: *Everly Brothers* / Never be anyone else but you: *Nelson, Rick* / What do you want: *Faith, Adam* / Don't touch: *Kidd, Johnny & The Pirates* / C'mon everybody: *Cochran, Eddie* / Teen beat: *Nelson, Sandy* / Sea of love: *Wilde, Marty* / Travellin' light: *Richard, Cliff* / What do you want to make those eyes at me for: *Ford, Emile & The Checkmates* / Lipstick on your collar: *Francis, Connie* / Three bells: *Browns* / It's only make believe: *Twitty, Conway* / Smoke gets in your eyes: *Platters* / Chantilly lace: *Big Bopper* / I go ape: *Sedaka, Neil* / Margie: *Domino, Fats* / Guitar boogie shuffle: *Weedon, Bert* / Teenager in love: *Douglas, Craig* / Petite fleur: *Barber, Chris* / Making love: *Robinson, Floyd* / Venus: *Avalon, Frankie* / It's all in the game: *Edwards, Tommy* / Tomboy: *Como, Perry* / Battle of New Orleans: *Donegan, Lonnie*
CD _____ YRNRCD 59
Connoisseur / Feb '89 / Pinnacle.

ROCK 'N' ROLL YEARS 1960
Only the lonely: *Orbison, Roy* / Shakin' all over: *Kidd, Johnny & The Pirates* / Hit and miss: *Barry, John Seven* / Dreamin': *Burnette, Johnny Rock 'N' Roll Trio* / Let it be me: *Everly Brothers* / Voice in the wilderness: *Richard, Cliff* / You got what it takes: *Johnson, Marv* / Three steps to heaven: *Cochran, Eddie* / Walk don't run: *Ventures* / Colette: *Fury, Billy* / Handyman: *Jones,*

873

Jimmy / Rawhide: Laine, Frankie / Running bear: Preston, Johnny / El paso: Robbins, Marty / Heartaches by the number: Mitchell, Guy / Why: Avalon, Frankie / Someone else's baby: Faith, Adam / Man of mystery: Shadows / Among my souvenirs: Francis, Connie / Harbour lights: Platters / Summer place: Faith, Percy / On a slow boat to China: Ford, Emile & The Checkmates / Bad boy: Wilde, Marty / I'll never fall in love again: Ray, Johnnie
CD _____ **YRNRCD 60**
Connoisseur / Feb '89 / Pinnacle.

ROCK 'N' ROLL YEARS 1961
Poetry in motion: Tillotson, Johnny / You're sixteen: Burnette, Johnny Rock 'N' Roll Trio / Blue moon: Marcels / Are you sure: Allisons / Calendar girl: Sedaka, Neil / Wild wind: Leyton, Johnny / Runaround Sue: Dion / Hats off to Larry: Shannon, Del / On the rebound: Cramer, Floyd / Weekend: Cochran, Eddie / What I'd say: Lewis, Jerry Lee / F.B.I.: Shadows / Hello Mary Lou: Nelson, Rick / Take good care of my baby: Vee, Bobby / Sea of heartbreak: Gibson, Don / War paint: Brook Brothers / Theme for a dream: Richard, Cliff / Sailor: Clark, Petula / Who put the bomp: Viscounts / Perfidia: Ventures / Don't treat me like a child: Shapiro, Helen / Counting teardrops: Ford, Emile & The Checkmates / You're the only good thing: Reeves, Jim / Have a drink on me: Donegan, Lonnie
CD _____ **YRNRCD 61**
Connoisseur / Feb '89 / Pinnacle.

ROCK 'N' ROLL YEARS 1962
Young ones: Richard, Cliff / Speedy Gonzalez: Boone, Pat / Locomotion: Little Eva / Guitar man: Eddy, Duane / Sweet little sixteen: Lewis, Jerry Lee / Breaking up is hard to do: Sedaka, Neil / Let's dance: Montez, Chris / Bobby's girl: Maughan, Susan / Norman: Deene, Carol / Hey little girl: Shannon, Del / It might as well rain until September: King, Carole / Don't ever change: Crickets / Wonderful land: Shadows / Picture of you: Brown, Joe / Sealed with a kiss: Hyland, Brian / Language of love: Loudermilk, John D. / Island of dreams: Springfields / Once upon a dream: Fury, Billy / Twistin' the night away: Cooke, Sam / Forget me not: Kane, Eden / Venus in blue jeans: Wynter, Mark / Love letters: Lester, Ketty / Adios amigo: Reeves, Jim / Moon river: Williams, Danny
CD _____ **YRNRCD 62**
Connoisseur / Oct '88 / Pinnacle.

ROCK 'N' ROLL YEARS 1963
Foot tapper: Shadows / Hippy hippy shake: Swinging Blue Jeans / I only want to be with you: Springfield, Dusty / Night has a thousand eyes: Vee, Bobby / Bad to me: Kramer, Billy J. / You'll never walk alone: Gerry & The Pacemakers / Do you love me: Poole, Brian / Wipeout: Surfaris / It's my party: Gore, Lesley / You were made for me: Freddie & The Dreamers / First time: Faith, Adam / I'll never get over you: Kidd, Johnny & The Pirates / Diamonds: Harris, Jet / Tell him: Davis, Billie / Searchin': Hollies / Rhythm of the rain: Cascades / Hello little girl: Fournotes / Secret love: Kirby, Kathy / Brown eyed handsome man: Holly, Buddy / Good golly Miss Molly: Lewis, Jerry Lee / Mr. Bass man: Cymbal, Johnny / Little town flirt: Shannon, Del / Welcome to my world: Reeves, Jim / End of the world: Davis, Skeeter
CD _____ **YRNRCD 63**
Connoisseur / Oct '88 / Pinnacle.

ROCK 'N' ROLL YEARS 1964
You really got me: Kinks / Shout: Lulu & The Luvvers / Yeh yeh: Fame, Georgie / Needles and pins: Searchers / Have I the right: Honeycombs / I get around: Beach Boys / Do wah diddy diddy: Manfred Mann / Always something there to remind me: Shaw, Sandie / Terry: Twinkle / He's in town: Rockin' Berries / You're no good: Swinging Blue Jeans / Downtown: Clark, Petula / World without love: Peter & Gordon / Little children / Tell me when: Applejacks / I understand: Freddie & The Dreamers / I love you because: Reeves, Jim / Ferry 'cross the Mersey: Gerry & The Pacemakers / You're my world: Black, Cilla / I just don't know what to do with myself: Springfield, Dusty / I'm crying: Animals / Crying game: Berry, Dave / Mockin' Bird Hill: Migil 5 / Juliet: Four Pennies
CD _____ **YRNRCD 64**
Connoisseur / Oct '88 / Pinnacle.

ROCK 'N' ROLL YEARS 1965
Make it easy on yourself: Walker Brothers / You've lost that lovin' feelin': Righteous Brothers / Don't let me be misunderstood: Animals / For your love: Yardbirds / Wooly bully: Sam The Sham & The Pharaohs / 1-2-3: Barry, Len / Tired of waiting for you: Kinks / Eve of destruction: McGuire, Barry / Catch the wind: Donovan / If you gotta go, go now: Manfred Mann / In the middle of nowhere: Springfield, Dusty / It's not unusual: Jones, Tom / To know you is to love you: Peter & Gordon / I'll never find another you: Seekers / You've got your troubles: Fortunes / Game of love: Fontana, Wayne & The Mindbenders / Little things: Berry, Dave / Silhouettes: Herman's Hermits / I'm alive: Hollies / California girls: Beach Boys / Tossing and turning: Ivy League / Poor man's son: Rockin' Berries / Everyone's gone to the moon: King, Jonathan / Clapping song: Ellis, Shirley
CD _____ **YRNRCD 65**
Connoisseur / Oct '88 / Pinnacle.

ROCK 'N' ROLL YEARS 1966
Wild thing: Troggs / Shape of things: Yardbirds / Got to get you into my life: Bennett, Cliff / Working in a coalmine: Dorsey, Lee / Sun ain't gonna shine anymore: Walker Brothers / It's a man's man's man's world: Brown, James / I feel free: Cream / Stop stop stop: Hollies / You don't have to say you love me: Springfield, Dusty / Sorrow: Merseys / All or nothing: Small Faces / Bang bang (my baby shot me down): Cher / Sunny afternoon: Kinks / California dreamin': Mamas & Papas / Pretty flamingo: Manfred Mann / High time: Jones, Paul / No milk today: Herman's Hermits / Elusive butterfly: Lind, Bob / Michelle: Overlanders / God only knows: Beach Boys / Groovy kind of love: Mindbenders / Alfie: Black, Cilla / I couldn't live without your love: Clark, Petula / Bend it: Dee, Dave
CD _____ **YRNRCD 66**
Connoisseur / Oct '88 / Pinnacle.

ROCK 'N' ROLL YEARS 1967
Hey Joe: Hendrix, Jimi Experience / Strange brew: Cream / San Francisco nights: Burdon, Eric & The Animals / Waterloo sunset: Kinks / Excerpt from a teenage opera: West, Keith / Kites: Dupree, Simon / I'm a believer: Monkees / Hi ho silver lining: Beck, Jeff / Ha ha said the clown: Manfred Mann / Massachusetts: Bee Gees / I've been a bad bad boy: Jones, Paul / Baby, now that I've found you: Foundations / Whiter shade of pale: Procul Harum / Let the heartaches begin: Baldry, Long John / Death of a clown: Davies, Dave / Letter: Box Tops / Matthew and son: Stevens, Cat / Nights in white satin: Moody Blues / There's a kind of hush: Herman's Hermits / Let's go to San Francisco: Flowerpot Men / Dedicated to the one I love: Mamas & Papas / Zabadak: Dee, Dave / Carrie Anne: Hollies / Puppet on a string: Shaw, Sandie
CD _____ **YRNRCD 67**
Connoisseur / Jan '90 / Pinnacle.

ROCK 'N' ROLL YEARS 1968
All along the watchtower: Hendrix, Jimi Experience / Fire: Crazy World Of Arthur Brown / Valleri: Monkees / Ice in the sun: Status Quo / Blackberry way: Move / Summertime blues: Cochran, Eddie / With a little help from my friends: Cocker, Joe / Mighty Quinn: Manfred Mann / On the road again: Canned Heat / Weight: Band / Cry like a baby: Box Tops / This wheel's on fire: Driscoll, Julie / Legend of Xanadu: Dave Dee, Dozy, Beaky, Mick & Tich / Build me up buttercup: Foundations / Judy in disguise: Fred, John & His Playboy Band / Bend me, shape me: Amen Corner / Gimme little sign: Wood, Brenton / Urban spaceman: Bonzo Dog Band / I've gotta get a message to you: Bee Gees / Honey: Goldsboro, Bobby / I can't let Maggie go: Honeybus / Jesamine: Casuals / Jennifer Eccles: Hollies / White horses: Jacky
CD _____ **YRNRCD 68**
Connoisseur / Jan '90 / Pinnacle.

ROCK 'N' ROLL YEARS 1969
Suspicious minds: Presley, Elvis / Something in the air: Thunderclap Newman / Badge: Cream / Reflections of my life: Marmalade / Games people play: South, Joe / Dizzy: Roe, Tommy / In the year 2525: Zager & Evans / Aquarius: 5th Dimension / Wonderful world, beautiful people: Cliff, Jimmy / Delta lady: Cocker, Joe / Harlem shuffle: Bob & Earl / Barabajagal: Donovan / Je t'aime: Birkin, Jane / Israelites: Dekker, Desmond & The Aces / Liquidator: Harry J All Stars / Melting pot: Blue Mink / Something's happening: Herman's Hermits / Throw down a line: Richard, Cliff / Where do you go to my lovely: Sarstedt, Peter / I'll never fall in love again: Gentry, Bobbie / He ain't heavy, he's my brother: Hollies / Wichita lineman: Campbell, Glen / Saved by the bell: Gibb, Robin / Move in a little closer: Harmony Grass
CD _____ **YRNRCD 69**
Connoisseur / Jan '90 / Pinnacle.

ROCK 'N' ROLL YEARS 1971
Maggie May: Stewart, Rod / Hot love: T. Rex / Hey girl don't bother me: Tams / I just can't help believin': Presley, Elvis / Didn't I blow your mind this time: Delfonics / Co co: Sweet / I'd like to teach the world to sing: New Seekers / Knock three times: Dawn / Chirpy chirpy cheep cheep: Middle Of The Road / Your song: Elton, John / I believe (in love): Hot Chocolate / Jig a jig: East Of Eden / Resurection shuffle: Ashton Gardener & Dyke / Tap turns on the water: CCS / When I'm dead and gone: McGuinness Flint / Burundi black: Black, Burundi Stephenson / He's gonna step on you again: Kongos, John / Joy to the world: Three Dog Night / Coz I luv you: Slade / Oh you pretty thing: Noone, Peter / Let your yeah be yeah: Pioneers / Freedom come freedom go: Fortunes / Black and white: Greyhound / Double barrel: Collins, Dave & Ansil
CD _____ **YRNRCD 71**
Connoisseur / Oct '88 / Pinnacle.

ROCK 'N' ROLL YEARS 1974
Waterloo: Abba / Never can say goodbye: Gaynor, Gloria / Roll away the stone: Mott

The Hoople / Wall Street shuffle: 10cc / I shot the sheriff: Clapton, Eric / Candle in the wind: John, Elton / Down down: Status Quo / Tiger feet: Mud / Dance with the devil: Powell, Cozy / Sugar baby love: Rubettes / Shang-a-lang: Bay City Rollers / Devil gate drive: Quatro, Suzi / Summer breeze: Isley Brothers / When will I see you again: Three Degrees / Rock the boat: Hues Corporation / Kissin' in the back row of the movies: Drifters / Judy teen: Harley, Steve & Cockney Rebel / Everyday: Slade / Sad sweet dreamer: Sweet Inspiration / Kung fu fighting: Douglas, Carl / Everything I own: Boothe, Ken / You make me feel grand: Stylistics / Seasons in the sun: Jacks, Terry / Gonna make you a star: Essex, David
CD _____ **YRNRCD 74**
Connoisseur / Jan '90 / Pinnacle.

ROCK 'N' ROLL YEARS 1975
Ms. Grace: Tymes / You ain't seen nothin' yet: Bachman-Turner Overdrive / Make me smile (come up and see me): Harley, Steve & Cockney Rebel / There goes my first love: Drifters / Lady Marmalade: Labelle, Patti / Loving you: Riperton, Minnie / You're the first, the last, my everything: White, Barry / Have you seen her: Chi-Lites / Higher and higher: Wilson, Jackie / I can help: Swan, Billy / S.O.S.: Abba / I'm not in love: 10cc / Promised land: Presley, Elvis / Angie baby: Reddy, Helen / I only have the eyes: Essex, David / Hurt so good: Cadogan, Susan / Help me make it through the night: Holt, John / January: Pilot / Give a little love: Bay City Rollers / Bump: Kenny
CD _____ **YRNRCD 75**
Connoisseur / Jan '90 / Pinnacle.

ROCK 'N' ROLL YEARS 1976
Wide eyed and legless: Fairweather-Low, Andy / Let's do the latin hustle: M & O Band / Show me the way: Frampton, Peter / Dr. Kiss Kiss: 5000 Volts / I love to love (but my baby loves to dance): Charles, Tina / Arms of Mary: Sutherland Brothers / Fernando: Abba / Sunshine day: Osibisa / We do it: Stone, R & J / You to me are everything: Real Thing / Uptown uptempo woman: Edelmann, Randy / Midnight train to Georgia: Knight, Gladys & The Pips / Love really hurts without you: Ocean, Billy / Play that funky music: Wild Cherry / Now is the time: James, Jimmy & The Vagabonds / I'm your puppet: Purify, James & Bobby / You see the trouble with me: White, Barry / Blame it on the boogie: Mingo, Moore, Dorothy / Boys are back in town: Thin Lizzy / Glass of champagne: Sailor / You don't have to go: Chi-Lites / You'll never find another love: Rawls, Lou / This is it: Moore, Melba / Music: Miles, John
CD _____ **YRNRCD 76**
Connoisseur / Jan '90 / Pinnacle.

ROCK 'N' ROLL YEARS 1977
red light spells danger: Ocean, Billy / Peaches: Stranglers / All around the world: Jam / Looking after no.1: Boomtown Rats / Year of the cat: Stewart, Al / Torn between two lovers: McGregor, Mary / 2-4-6-8 motorway: Robinson, Tom / Spanish stroll: Mink Deville / Boogie nights: Heatwave / Native New Yorker: Odyssey / Free: Williams, Deniece / Way down: Presley, Elvis / Rockin' all over the world: Status Quo / Don't believe a word: Thin Lizzy / Knowing me, knowing you: Abba / Good morning judge: 10cc / Baby don't change your mind: Knight, Gladys & The Pips / Don't leave me this way: Melvin, Harold / Romeo: Mr. Big / She's not there: Santana / They shoot horses don't they: Racing Cars / Black Betty: Ram Jam / Ain't gonna bump no more (With no big fat woman): Tex, Joe / When I need you: Sayer, Leo
CD _____ **YRNRCD 77**
Connoisseur / Jan '90 / Pinnacle.

ROCK 'N' ROLL YEARS 1978
Denis: Blondie / Don't fear) the reaper: Blue Oyster Cult / Fantasy: Earth, Wind & Fire / More than a woman: Tavares / Love is in the air: Young, John Paul / Take a chance on me: Abba / Forever autumn: Wayward, Justin / In the bush: Musique / Lay your love on me: Racey / I lost my heart: Baccara / Grease: Valli, Frankie / Five minutes: Stranglers / If you can't give me love: Quatro, Suzi / Run for home: Lindisfarne / Rat trap: Boomtown Rats / Every 1's a winner: Hot Chocolate / Baker Street: Rafferty, Gerry / Darlin': Miller, Frankie / Sorry I'm a lady: Darlin' / I lost my heart to a starship trooper: Brightman, Sarah
CD _____ **YRNRCD 78**
Connoisseur / Oct '88 / Pinnacle.

ROCK 'N' ROLL YEARS 1979
Bat out of hell: Meat Loaf / I will survive: Gaynor, Gloria / In a case in a stand: Status Quo / Oliver's army: Costello, Elvis / Ain't no stoppin' us now: McFadden & Whitehead / When you're in love with a beautiful woman / I don't wanna lose you: Kandidate / Can you feel the force: Real Thing / Some girls: Racey / Gangsters: Specials / Milk and alcohol: Dr. Feelgood / I don't like Mondays: Boomtown Rats / Eton rifles: Jam / My Sharona: Knack / On my radio: Selecter / Are friends electric: Tubeway Army / Ring my bell: Ward, Anita / Angel eyes: Abba / Hold the line: Toto / Teen: Regents / Cars: Numan, Gary / You bet your love: Hancock, Herbie

CD _____ **YRNRCD 79**
Connoisseur / Oct '88 / Pinnacle.

ROCK 'N' ROLL YEARS 1980
Tide is high: Blondie / I can't stand up for falling down: Costello, Elvis & The Attractions / Too much too young: Specials / Geno: Dexy's Midnight Runners / Winner takes it all: Abba / Babooshka: Bush, Kate / Let's go round again: Average White Band / Use it up and wear it out: Odyssey / Oops upside your head: Gap Band / Groove: Franklin, Rodney / Funky town: Lipps Inc. / Bourgie bourgie: Knight, Gladys / Going underground: Jam / Modern girl: Easton, Sheena / No doubt about it: Hot Chocolate / Celebration: Kool & The Gang / Never knew love like this before: Mills, Stephanie / Jane: Jefferson Starship / Ant music: Adam & The Ants / Turning Japanese: Vapors / January February: Dickson, Barbara / All out of love: Air Supply / M.A.S.H. (Suicide is painless): M.A.S.H. / Wednesday week: Undertones
CD _____ **YRNRCD 80**
Connoisseur / Nov '88 / Pinnacle.

ROCK 'N' ROLL YEARS 1981
Good year for the roses: Costello, Elvis & The Attractions / Bette Davis eyes: Carnes, Kim / Ghost town: Specials / It's going to happen: Undertones / Favourite shirts (boy meets girl): Haircut 100 / Chant no.1 (I don't need this pressure on): Spandau Ballet / I want to be free: Toyah / Absolute beginners: Jam / Kids in America: Wilde, Kim / Rock this town: Stray Cats / Wedding bells: Godley & Creme / Let's groove: Earth, Wind & Fire / Keep on loving you: REO Speedwagon / One of us: Abba / How 'bout us: Champaign / Japanese boy: Aneka / Hucklebuck: Coast To Coast / Star: Dee, Kiki / Happy birthday: Altered Images / Stand and deliver: Adam & The Ants / For your eyes only: Easton, Sheena / Runaround Sue: Racey / Reward: Teardrop Explodes / Fade to grey: Visage
CD _____ **YRNRCD 81**
Connoisseur / Nov '88 / Pinnacle.

ROCK 'N' ROLL YEARS 1982
Golden brown: Stranglers / Poison arrow: ABC / Sexual healing: Gaye, Marvin / Island of lost souls: Blondie / Message: Grandmaster Flash & The Furious Five / View from a bridge: Wilde, Kim / It started with a kiss: Hot Chocolate / Fame: Cara, Irene / Go wild in the country: Bow Wow Wow / Town called Malice: Jam / Ever so lonely: Monsoon / Harry's Game: Clannad / Dead ringer for love: Meat Loaf / Inside out: Odyssey / Centrefold: Geils, J. Band / T'aint what you do: Fun Boy Three & Bananarama / Lion sleeps tonight: Tight Fit / Seven tears: Goombay Dance Band / Get down on it: Kool & The Gang / Drowning in Berlin: Mobiles / Starmaker: Kids from Fame / Goody two shoes: Adam Ant / Oh Julie: Stevens, Shakin' / Just what I always wanted: Wilson, Mari
CD _____ **YRNRCD 82**
Connoisseur / Dec '88 / Pinnacle.

ROCK 'N' ROLL YEARS 1983
Family man: Hall & Oates / Africa: Toto / True: Spandau Ballet / Down under: Men At Work / Tonight I celebrate my love: Bryson & Flack / Heartbreaker: Warwick, Dionne / Marguerita time: Status Quo / Love town: Newbury, Booker / Give it up: K.C. & The Sunshine Band / We are detectives: Thompson Twins / White lines (don't don't do it): Grandmaster Flash & Melle Mel / Sun goes down (living it up): Level 42 / Total eclipse of the heart: Tyler, Bonnie / In a big country: Big Country / What kinda boy you looking for (girl): Hot Chocolate / Rockit: Hancock, Herbie / Garden party: Marillion / Sign of the times: Belle Stars / Too shy: Kajagoogoo / Dancing tight: Galaxy & Phil Fearon / Boxerbeat: Joboxers / Rip it up: Orange Juice / Only for love: Limahl / Don't talk to me about love: Altered Images
CD _____ **YRNRCD 82**
Connoisseur / Dec '88 / Pinnacle.

ROCK OF AGES
CD _____ **RENCD 104**
Castle / Jul '95 / BMG.

ROCK OF AMERICA
CD _____ **NSCD 018**
Newsound / May '95 / THE.

ROCK ON VOL.1
CD _____ **CDTMR 8014**
Candor / Jul '95 / Else.

ROCK REVOLUTION
CD _____ **STACD 043**
Stardust / Aug '93 / Carlton Home Entertainment.

ROCK STEADY 1966-1967 (Bobby Aitken Presents)
CD _____ **NXBACD 01**
Next Step / Nov '93 / Jetstar / SRD.

ROCK STEADY RAVE
CD _____ **CPCD 8023**
Charly / Feb '94 / Charly / THE / Cadillac.

ROCK STEADY/FUNKY REGGAE
CD _____ **RB 3008**
Reggae Best / May '94 / Magnum Music Group / THE.

ROCK THE FIRST VOL. 1
CD _____ D 2330412
Sandstone / Jul '92 / THE.

ROCK THE FIRST VOL. 2
CD _____ D 2330422
Sandstone / Jul '92 / THE.

ROCK THE FIRST VOL. 3
CD _____ D 2330432
Sandstone / Jul '92 / THE.

ROCK THE FIRST VOL. 4
CD _____ D 2330442
Sandstone / Jul '92 / THE.

ROCK THE FIRST VOL. 5
CD _____ D 2330452
Sandstone / Jul '92 / THE.

ROCK THE FIRST VOL. 6
CD _____ D 2330462
Sandstone / Jul '92 / THE.

ROCK THE NIGHT
(54 Rock And Pop Classics From The 70's And 80's)
Heat is on: Frey, Glenn / Fade to grey: Visage / More than a feeling: Boston / Wishing (If I had a photograph of you): Flock Of Seagulls / Sweetest taboo: Sade / Secrets: Sutherland Brothers / Oh Sherrie: Perry, Steve / Loving you is sweeter than ever: Kamen, Nick / Dark lady: Cher / Heartbeat: Johnson, Don / Rosanna: Toto / You are the girl: Cars / What is love: Jones, Howard / Carrie: Europe / Wide boy: Kershaw, Nik / Bring it on home: Stewart, Rod / Hold on tight: E.L.O. / Can't fight this feeling: REO Speedwagon / Come on Eileen: Dexy's Midnight Runners / Roll on down the highway: Bachman-Turner Overdrive / Gypsies, tramps and thieves: Cher / All day and all of the night: Stranglers / Lucky man: Emerson, Lake & Palmer / Morning dance: Spyro Gyra / Boy from New York City: Darts / I'm not in love: 10cc / Look away: Big Country / Africa: Toto / Cutter: Echo & The Bunnymen / Hold your head up: Argent / Spooky: Atlanta Rhythm Section / Born to be wild: Steppenwolf / Ramblin' man: Allman Brothers Band / St. Elmo's fire: Parr, John / Stop loving you: Toto / 99 red balloons: Nena / Total eclipse of the heart: Tyler, Bonnie / Parisienne walkways: Moore, Gary / Gloria: Branigan, Laura / Cum on feel the noize: Slade / Bat out of hell: Meat Loaf / Silver dagger: Oldfield, Sally / Like to get to know you well: Jones, Howard / Eloise: Damned / Oh no, not my baby: Stewart, Rod / Start: Jam / Hold me close: Essex, David / Take it on the run: REO Speedwagon / God gave rock 'n' roll to you: Argent / Sun goes down (Living it up): Level 42
CD Set _____ BOXD 44
Carlton Home Entertainment / Jan '94 / Carlton Home Entertainment.

ROCK THE NIGHT VOLUME II
Two out of three ain't bad: Meat Loaf / Bad for good: Steinman, Jim / We danced: Hooters / They call me guitar hurricane: Vaughan, Stevie Ray / Flame: Cheap Trick / Grind: Bolin, Tommy / Mr. Skin: Spirit / My back pages: Byrds / No one to depend on: Santana / Mama weer all craxee now: Quiet Riot / Highwire days: Psychedelic Furs / I drove all night: Lauper, Cyndi / Family man: Roachford / Sex: Young, Paul / Just like a baby: Sly & The Family Stone
CD _____ 4803362
Columbia / May '95 / Sony.

ROCK THE WORLD
Man's too strong: Dire Straits / Blue (armed with love) (Live): Wham / Hooked on love: Bananarama / We came here to rock: Saxon / Candles: Rea, Chris / It's not easy: Tyler, Bonnie / Please be good to me: Menudo / Slay the dragon: Johnson, Holly / Never never: Sharkey, Feargal / Something better: Wilde, Kim, Precious Wilson, Daryl Pandy & Bobby Whitlock / Magical: Bucks Fizz / She's gonna love you to death: Iridio Marks & Pete Wylie / Little bit of snow: Jones, Howard / Aqua: Euphermics / You know it makes sense: Starr, Ringo
CD _____ PWKS 4083
Carlton Home Entertainment / Oct '91 / Carlton Home Entertainment.

ROCK THERAPY
We will rock you: Queen / Let's get rocked: Def Leppard / Livin' on a prayer: Bon Jovi / Tragic comic: Extreme / Here I go again: Whitesnake / Wind of change: Scorpions / Wild: Free / Rockin' all over the world: Status Quo / Living after midnight: Jethro Tull / Burning of the Midnight lamp: Hendrix, Jimi / Too old to rock 'n' roll, too young to die: Jethro Tull / Fanfare for the common man: Emerson, Lake & Palmer / Breeze: Lynyrd Skynyrd / Won't get fooled again: Who / Run to the hills: Iron Maiden
CD _____ 5168612
PolyGram TV / Jun '94 / PolyGram.

ROCKABILLY PSYCHOSIS
Surfin' bird: Trashmen / Psycho: Sonics / Crusher: Novas / Paralysed: Legendary Stardust Cowboy / She said: Adkins, Hasil 'Haze' / My daddy is a vampire: Meteors / Radioactive kid: Meteors / Dateless nites: Falco, Tav / Panther Burns / Jack on fire: Gun Club / Folsom prison blues: Geezers / Cut-

man: Stingrays / Just love me: Guana Batz / Love me (Not available on CD): Phantom / Red headed woman: Dickinson, Jimmy & the Cramps / Scream (Available on CD only): Nielsen, Ralph & The Chancellors / Hidden charms (Available on CD only): Wray, Link / Run chicken run (Available on CD only): Milkshakes
CD _____ CDWIK 18
Big Beat / Oct '89 / Pinnacle.

ROCKABILLY RECORD CO. SAMPLER
Rockin' blues: Lewis, Willie / Rock 'n' roll religion: Lewis, Willie / Oh, baby babe: Lewis, Willie / Crazy boogie: Lewis, Willie / Workin' man blues: Lewis, Willie / Mary Lou rock: Billy & The Bob Cats / Train of misery: High Noon / Glory bound: High Noon / Baby let's play house: High Noon / All night long: High Noon / Who was that cat: High Noon / Crazy fever: High Noon / I ain't in love with you/Tonight: Pharaohs / I want my whiskey: Pharaohs / Dollar bill boogie: Pharaohs / A-bop-a-baby: Roadhouse Rockers / Be my baby: Kevin & Todd / Beat up Ford: Leyland, Carl Sonny / I like the boogie woogie: Leyland, Carl Sonny / Whiskey straight up: Frantic Flattops / Rockabilly Willie: King Cat & The Pharaohs / It's Saturday night: King Cat & The Pharaohs / You got no sense: King Cat & The Pharaohs / Ran down Daddy: Three Cats & The Kittens
CD _____ CDGR 6036
Sun Jay / Apr '94 / Magnum Music Group / Rollercoaster.

ROCKABILLY SHAKEOUT - NUMBER 1
Shadow my baby: Barber, Glen / Atom bomb: Barber, Glen / I don't know when: Harris, Hal / My little baby: Jimmy & Johnny / True affection: Johnson, Byron / Slippin' and slidin': Davis, Link / Hey hey little boy blue: Lindsay, Merle / Gee whiz: Dee & Patty / All the time: La Beef, Sleepy / Spin the bottle: Joy, Benny / Chicken bop: Truitt Forse / My big fat baby: Hall, Sonny & The Echoes / Let's just got back in town: Mack, Billy / Tennessee rock: Scoggins, Hoyt / Uranium rock: Gaydts, Ruddy / Prettiest girl at the dance: Wyatt, Gene
CD _____ CDCH 191
Ace / Feb '92 / Pinnacle / Cadillac / Complete/Pinnacle.

ROCKERS AND BALLADEERS 1
CD _____ PLATCD 341
Platinum Music / Oct '90 / Prism / Ross.

ROCKERS AND BALLADEERS 2
CD _____ PLATCD 342
Platinum Music / Oct '90 / Prism / Ross.

ROCKIN' AND BOPPIN'
Preacher man: Smith, Carl & Jive Kings / Johnny machine: Smith, Carl & Jive Kings / Four in the floor: Shutdowns / Little willie: Deram, Richie / Girl and a hot rod: Deram, Richie / I ask her: Country Lads / Salty tears: Country Lads / Teen queen: Avon / Honey honey: Avon / Flying saucer rocket: Duncan, Ferrell / Little Susie: Duncan, Ferrell / So deep rock: Vinyard, Eddie / Big berry: Big Daddy G / Out of the clear blue sky: Frizzell, Billy / Let's rock tonight: Pell Bros / Curfew: Scavengers / R 'n' R rover: King, Jesse Lee / Nervous wreck: King, Jesse Lee / Teen-age partner: Hanson, Ronnie / Cigarettes and coffee blues: Bilhovde, Marv / No doubt about it: Doggett, Ray / What'cha do to me: Clark, Patsy / Stompin': Viscos / Surfin' freeze: Cummings, Pete / Mother, congratulate your son: Baxter, U.L. / Johnnycake mountain: Collins, Lyle / I am my lover: Collins, Lyle / Flamingo rock: Collins, Lyle / Good Jue. Collins, Lyle / Unleash me: Collins, Lyle
CD _____ CDCL 4419
White Label/Bear Family / Apr '94 / Bear Family / Rollercoaster.

ROCKIN' AT THE TAKE 2 VOLS. 1 & 2
CD _____ LOMACD 30
Loma / Aug '94 / BMG.

ROCKIN' AT TOWN HALL
CD _____ RFCD 06
Country Routes / Apr '91 / Jazz Music / Hot Shot.

ROCKIN' THE BLUES
Red house / Blues power / Evil woman blues / Stormy Monday / I got my mojo working / Good morning little school girl / Unlucky boy / Bringing it back / Louisiana blues / Ramblin' on my mind / Bell bottom blues / Statesboro blues / Crossroads / Six days on my mind / Baby, please don't go / Lies / Lonely years / Highway blues / Outside woman blues / Dust my broom
CD _____ MATCD 274
Castle / Apr '93 / BMG.

ROCKIN' THE BLUES
Alley corn: Hooker, Earl / Sweet angel: Hooker, Earl / Jammin': Hooker, Earl / Ride Hooker ride: Hooker, Earl / After hours: Hooker, Earl / Going to New Orleans: Davis, Sam / She's so good to me: Davis, Sam / Goin' home to Mother: Davis, Sam / 1958 Blues: Davis, Sam / Jealous man: Lewis, Johnny / She's taking all my money: Lewis, Johnny / Riding home: Louis, Leslie / Don't do it again: Louis, Leslie / Alley blues: Wilson, Jimmy / Walkin' the streets: Hopkins, Lightnin' / Mussey haired woman: Hopkins, Lightnin' / Goin' back home today: Baker, Willie / Fool no more: Hope, Eddie & The

Mannish Boys / Lost child: Hope, Eddie & The Mannish Boys / Teachin' the blues: Hooker, John Lee / She do the shimmy: Hooker, John Lee / Stoned blues: Hooker, John Lee / You got to reap what you sow: Hooker, John Lee / Meat shakes on her bone: Hooker, John Lee
CD _____ CDCHD 585
Ace / Aug '95 / Pinnacle / Cadillac / Complete/Pinnacle.

ROCKIN' THE CROSSROADS
CD _____ ANT 9904CD
Antones / Jul '94 / Hot Shot / Direct / ADA.

ROCKSTEADY & REGGAE HITS 1969-70
Got to get you off my mind: Rhoden, Pat / Ride your donkey: Rhoden, Pat & Lloyd Campbell / Long shot: Campbell, Lloyd / Hold me tight: Dennis, Denzil / Rough rider: Campbell, Lloyd / Baby why: Rhoden, Pat / Champ: Instrumental Group / Elizabethan reggae: Sterling, Jumbo / Liquidator: King Reggie / Moon hop: King Reggie / Ob La Di Ob La Da: King Reggie / Cool girl: King Reggie / Place in the sun: Rhoden, Pat / Hush: Dennis, Denzil / Red red wine: Smith, Junior / Funny man: King Reggie / Slave driver: Sterling, Jumbo / Put on the pressure: Smith, Junior / Wet dream: Sparkes, Laurel / Swan Lake: Montego Melon / Love of the common people: Smith, Junior
CD _____ PRCD 601
President / Jan '95 / Grapevine / Target/ BMG / Jazz Music / President.

ROCKTASTIC
CD _____ CLACD 999
Castle / Jul '94 / BMG.

RODNY KRAJ
CD _____ CR 0021-2
Czech Radio / Nov '95 / Czech Music Enterprises.

ROGUE TROOPER SAMPLER
CD _____ DBMTR 35
Rogue Trooper / Nov '95 / SRD.

ROLLIN' AND TUMBLIN'
CD _____ IGOCD 2029
Indigo / Apr '95 / Direct / ADA.

ROLLING RIVERS AND SMILING VALLEYS
CD _____ QPRZ 011D
Polyphonic / Jan '93 / Conifer.

ROLLING THUNDER
Eye of the tiger: Survivor / I surrender: Rainbow / Strange kind of woman: Deep Purple / Night games: Bonnet, Graham / Trouble: Gillan / Don't let me be misunderstood: Moore, Gary / Incommunicado: Manillion / Final countdown: Europe / She's a little angel: Little Angels / 747 (Strangers in the night): Saxon / Rhythm of love: Scorpions / Hey you: Quireboys / Living after midnight: Judas Priest / Never say die: Black Sabbath / Ace of spades: Motorhead / Easy livin': Uriah Heep / Race with the devil: Girlschool
CD _____ RENCD 107
Renaissance Collector Series / Oct '95 / BMG.

ROMANCE
(Music For Piano)
Shape of her face / Old family portrait / Sister bay / I always come back to you / Sacred dance / Reasons for moving / Minor truths / Beginning of love / Melusina / In the path of the heart / First light / Over shallow water / State of grace / First kiss / Summer truth / Heart of hearts / Hand in hand
CD _____ ND 61045
Narada / Nov '94 / New Note / ADA.

ROMANIAN GEMS
Incantation / Prelude d'amour / Romance au Claire De Lune / Frenesia / Fiancailles / Pan danse pour la nymphs sprinz / Complaint d'amour / Caprices au bord de l'eau / Taquineries / Consolation / Allegresse en mineur / Porcession nuptiale
CD _____ PV 750004
Disques Pierre Verany / Jul '94 / Kingdom.

ROMANTIC CHRISTMAS
CD _____ DCD 5312
Disky / Dec '93 / THE / BMG / Discovery / Pinnacle.

ROMANTIC CLASSICS
CD _____ DCD 5210
Disky / Jul '92 / THE / BMG / Discovery / Pinnacle.

ROMANTIC CLASSICS
CD _____ DSPCD 104
Disky / Sep '93 / THE / BMG / Discovery / Pinnacle.

ROMANTIC CLASSICS
CD _____ GCC 1002
Disky / Sep '94 / THE / BMG / Discovery / Pinnacle.

ROMANTIC CLASSICS BOX SET
CD Set _____ HRCD 8016
Disky / Feb '93 / THE / BMG / Discovery / Pinnacle.

ROMANTIC CLASSICS VOL.3
CD _____ DCD 5279
Disky / Nov '92 / THE / BMG / Discovery / Pinnacle.

ROMANTIC CLASSICS VOL.4
CD _____ DCD 5280
Disky / Feb '93 / THE / BMG / Discovery / Pinnacle.

ROMANTIC GUITAR
CD _____ GRF 240
Tring / Aug '93 / Tring / Prism.

ROMANTIC INSTRUMENTAL COLLECTION
CD Set _____ HRCD 8015
Disky / Nov '92 / THE / BMG / Discovery / Pinnacle.

ROMANTIC JAZZ
Somewhere: Brubeck, Dave / Easy to love: Garner, Erroll / Goodnight my love: Vaughan, Sarah / My funny valentine: Baker, Chet / Satin doll: Hampton, Lionel / Mood indigo: Ellington, Duke / Moonlight serenade: Miller, Glenn / Body and soul: Goodman, Benny / Round midnight: Davis, Miles / Summertime: Holiday, Billie / I can't stand the rain: Phillips, Esther / Fair weather: Baker, Chet / Theme from "Summer of 42": Benson, George / If I could be with you one hour tonight: Holiday, Billie / I've got a message to you: Laws, Hubert
CD _____ 4811542
Columbia / Dec '95 / Sony.

ROMANTIC LOVE THEMES
CD _____ DCD 5300
Disky / Dec '93 / THE / BMG / Discovery / Pinnacle.

ROMANTIC MUSIC OF SPAIN, THE
CD _____ CD 412
Bescol / May '95 / CM / Target/BMG.

ROMANTIC POP MELODIES
CD _____ DCD 5304
Disky / Dec '93 / THE / BMG / Discovery / Pinnacle.

ROMANTIC RAGGA
CD _____ SIDCD 004
Sinbad / Mar '93 / Jetstar.

ROMANTIC RAGGA VOL II
CD _____ SIDCD 005
Sinbad / Feb '94 / Jetstar.

ROMANTIC REGGAE - 24 GREAT REGGAE LOVE SONGS
I wanna wake up with you: Holt, John / Choose me: Pierre, Marie / Moon river: Greyhound / You are everything: Chosen Few / Stand by me: Junior Soul / Sweet inspiration: Pioneers / Everything I own: Boothe, Ken / Side show: Biggs, Barry / Hurt so good: Cadogan, Susan / Only a smile: Brown, Dennis / Prisoner of love: Barker, Dave / All I have is love: Isaacs, Gregory / Black pearl: Faith, Horace / Spanish harlem: Edwards, Jackie / First time ever I saw your face: Griffiths, Marcia / Runaway with love: Chambers, Lloyd / Crying over you: Boothe, Ken / Everybody plays the fool: Chosen Few / You make me feel brand new: Gardiner, Boris / Still in love: Ellis, Alton / Montego bay: Notes, Freddie & The Rudies / You are everything to me: Holt, John / Let us be: Thomas, Nicky / Save the last dance for me: Heptones
CD _____ VSOPCD 133
Connoisseur / May '89 / Pinnacle.

ROMANTIC ROSES OF IRELAND
CD _____ EMPRCD 549
Emporio / Nov '94 / THE / Disc / CM.

ROMANTIC SOUL
CD _____ STACD 056
Stardust / Sep '94 / Carlton Home Entertainment.

ROMANTIC SOUND SAMPLER II
CD _____ EFA 910092
Zillo / May '95 / SRD.

RONDELET PUNK SINGLES COLLECTION
No government: Anti Pasti / Two years too late: Anti Pasti / Another dead soldier: Anti Pasti / Six guns: Anti Pasti / Burial: Fits / Violent society: Special Duties / Colchester Council: Special Duties / Bomb scare: Dead Mans Shadow / Another Hiroshima: Dead Mans Shadow / East to the West: Anti Pasti / Muscles: Membranes / Police state: Special Duties / Go to hell: Threats / Fuck the Tories: Riot Squad / We are the Riot Squad: Riot Squad / Bullshit Crass: Special Duties / Riot in the city: Riot Squad / Caution in the wind: Anti Pasti / Flower in the gun: Dead Mans Shadow / High Street Yanks: Membranes / Politicians and ministers: Threats / Last laugh: Fits
CD _____ CDPUNK 49
Anagram / Mar '95 / Pinnacle.

ROOF INTERNATIONAL
CD _____ HCD 7008
Hightone / Aug '94 / ADA / Koch.

ROOTS ALL OVER THE GODAMN PLACE
CD _____ EFA 800272
T-Wah / Oct '94 / SRD.

ROOTS AND CULTURE SERIOUS SELECTIONS VOL.1
CD _____ CDREG 3
Rewind Selecta / Jul '95 / Grapevine.

ROOTS DAUGHTERS
Guide and protect: Aisha / Catch the boat: Live Wya / English girl: Sister Audrey / Free South Africa: Cross, Sandra / Fire: Faybienne / Until you come back to me: Just Dale & Robotniks / Place in the sun: Kofi / Mr. Roots man: Rasheda
CD _____ ARICD 039
Ariwa Sounds / Sep '88 / Jetstar / SRD.

ROOTS 'N' CULTURE
(21 Mighty Cuts)
CD _____ MCCD 128
Music Club / Sep '93 / Disc / THE / CM.

ROOTS OF DAVID
CD _____ TWCD 1021
Tamoki Wambesi / Jun '94 / Jetstar / SRD / Roots Collective / Greensleeves.

ROOTS OF DOO WOP
CD _____ RTS 33021
Roots / May '90 / Pinnacle.

ROOTS OF MODERN JAZZ, THE
(The 1948 Sensation Sessions)
Baggy's blues: Jackson, Milt & His All Stars / In a beautiful mood: Jackson, Milt & His All Stars / Baggy eyes: Jackson, Milt & His All Stars / Nobility bop: Thompson, Sir Charles / Yesterdays: Thompson, Sir Charles / It's my turn now: Thompson, Sir Charles / Charles boogie: Thompson, Sir Charles / Don't blame me: Thompson, Sir Charles / Robbin's nest: Thompson, Sir Charles / In a garden: Thompson, Sir Charles / Someone to watch over me: Thompson, Sir Charles / You go to my head: Thompson, Sir Charles / Relaxin': Jacquet, Russell & His All Stars / Lion's roar: Jacquet, Russell & His All Stars / Suede Jacquet: Jacquet, Russell & His All Stars / Scamper roo: Jacquet, Russell & His All Stars / Stardust: Lord Nelson & His Boppers / Red shoes: Lord Nelson & His Boppers / Body and soul (Time to dream): Lord Nelson & His Boppers / Ratio and proportion: Lord Nelson & His Boppers / Royal weddings: Lord Nelson / Be bop blues: the ball: Lord Nelson / Fine and Dandy: Lord Nelson / Third Song: Lord Nelson
CD _____ CDBOPD 017
Bopicity / May '94 / Pinnacle / Cadillac.

ROOTS OF OK JAZZ
CD _____ CRAW 7
Crammed World / Jan '96 / New Note.

ROOTS OF REGGAE
Soul shakedown party: Marley, Bob / Everything I own: Boothe, Ken / You can get it if you really want: Dekker, Desmond / Black and white: Greyhound / Hurt so good: Cadogan, Susan / Man in the street: Drummond, Don / Barber saloon: Dread, Mikey / Let me down easy: Brown, Dennis / I'm a madman: Perry, Lee 'Scratch' / Israelites: Dekker, Desmond / Help me make it through the night: Holt, John / 54-46 (was my number): Toots & The Maytals / Kaya: Marley, Bob / Let your eye be yeah: Pioneers / To the young gifted and black: Bob & Marcia / Rock me in dub: Thompson, Linval / Java: Pablo, Augustus / What you gonna do on judgement day: Prince Far-I
CD _____ MCCD 014
Music Club / Feb '91 / Disc / THE / CM.

ROOTS OF REGGAE VOL. 2
Message to you Rudy: Livingstone, Dandy / Train to Skaville: Ethiopians / 007: Dekker, Desmond / Perfidia: Dillon, Phyllis / Liquidator: Harry J All Stars / Longshot kick de bucket: Pioneers / Phoenix City: Alphonso, Roland / Return of Django: Upsetters / Confucius: Skatalites / Double barrel: Collins, Dave & Ansil / Trenchtown rock: Marley, Bob / Pressure drop: Toots & The Maytals / East of the River Nile: Pablo, Augustus / Skinhead moonstomp: Symarip / All I have is love: Isaacs, Gregory / I shot the sheriff: Inner Circle / Hit the road Jack: Big Youth / Book of rules: Heptones / Shine eye gal: Levy, Barrington / Blood and fire: Niney The Observer
CD _____ MCCD 041
Music Club / Sep '91 / Disc / THE / CM.

ROOTS OF REGGAE VOL. 3
Caution: Marley, Bob & The Wailers / Miss Jamaica: Cliff, Jimmy / Monkey man: Toots & The Maytals / People funny boy: Perry, Lee 'Scratch' / I nah: Dekker, Desmond / Pied Piper: Bob & Marcia / Suzanne beware of the devil: Livingstone, Dandy / Rock steady train: Evan & Jerry/Carib Beats / Stop that train: Tosh, Peter & The Wailers / Skank in bed: Scotty / Keep moving: Marley, Bob & The Wailers / Bartender: Aitken, Laurel / Whip: Ethiopians / Sweet sensation: Melodians / Dreader than dread: Honey Boy Martin / I'm in the mood for ska: Lord Tanamo / Montego bay: Notes, Freddie & The Rudies / Oh ba-a-by (sick and tired): Techniques / African Queen: Pablo, Augustus / Rock steady: Ellis, Alton
CD _____ MCCD 072
Music Club / Jun '92 / Disc / THE / CM.

ROOTS OF RUMBA ROCK
(Zaire Classics Vol.1)
CD _____ CRAW 4
Crammed World / Jan '96 / New Note.

ROOTS OF RUMBA ROCK 2
CD _____ CRAW 10
Crammed Discs / Jul '95 / Grapevine / New Note.

ROOTS OF THE BLUES
Louisiana: Ratcliff, Henry / Field song from Senegal: Bakari Badji / Po' boy blues: Dudley, John / Katy left Memphis: Tangle Eye / Berta berta: Miller, Leyroy & A Group Of Prisoners / Old original blues: McDowell, Fred & Miles Pratcher / Jim and John: Young, Ed & Lonnie Young / Emmaline, take your time: Askew, Alec / Buttermilk: Pratcher, Miles & Bob / Mama Lucy: Gary, Leroy / I'm gonna live, anyhow till I die: Pratcher, Miles & Bob / No more my lord: Tangle Eye & A Group Of Prisoners / Lining hymn and prayer: Rev' Crenshaw & Congregation / Death comes a creepin' in my room: McDowell, Fred / Church house moan: Congregation Of New Brown's Chapel / Beggin the blues: Jones, Bessie / Rolled and tumbled: Hemphill, Rose & Fred McDowell / Goin' down to the races: McDowell, Fred, Miles Pratcher & Fannie Davis / You gotta cut that out: Forest City Joe
CD _____ 802522
New World / Aug '92 / Harmonia Mundi / ADA / Cadillac.

ROOTS PIRAHNA
CD _____ PIR 482
Piranha / Oct '92 / SRD.

ROOTS REALITY
Heartache: Jolly Brothers / Silver and gold: Osbourne, Johnny / Time to unite: Black Uhuru / Ain't gonna turn back: Brown, Barry / Hell and sorrow: Ellis, Hortense / Colly George: Jones, Frankie / Last train to Africa: Prince Allah / Angel of the morning: Lara, Jennifer / Only love can conquer: Fantells / Jah Jah blessing: Fantells / Right track: Minott, Sugar / Great day: Castell, Lacksley
CD _____ MENT 001CD
Mention / Jan '96 / Jetstar.

ROOTS REGGAE
Chalice in the palace: U-Roy / Wear you to the ball: U-Roy / Throw away your gun: Prince Far-I / Message from the king: Prince Far-I / This land is for everyone: Abyssinians / Bluesy baby: Dunbar, Sly / Hearsay: Gladiators / Let Jah be present: Gladiators / Natty dread she want: Big Youth / Never get burn: Twinkle Brothers / Universal tribulation: Isaacs, Gregory / Up town top ranking: Althia & Donna / Too long is slavery: Culture / Song of blood: Johnson, Linton Kwesi / Cry tough: Clark, Johnny
CD _____ CDVIP 125
Virgin / Jul '91 / EMI.

ROOTSMAN SHOWCASE '94
CD _____ RMCD 014
Roots Man / Nov '94 / Jetstar.

ROSE OF TRALEE, THE
CD _____ MU 5065
Musketeer / Oct '92 / Koch.

ROSES ARE RED, VIOLETS ARE BLUE
(Timeless Love Songs)
Roses are red: O'Donnell, Daniel / Donegal shore: O'Donnell, Daniel / Mary from Dungloe: O'Donnell, Daniel / Grace: McCann, Jim / Back in love by Monday: Lynam, Ray / Mona Lisa lost her smile: Lynam, Ray / Before the next teardrop falls: McCann, Susan / Morning glory: Foster & Allen / When I dream: Foster & Allen / Fields of Athenry: Reilly, Paddy / Star of the county down: Reilly, Paddy / Red is the rose: Begley, Philomena / When you were sweet sixteen: Fureys & Davey Arthur / Crazy: Kelly, Sandy / Calypso: Hogan, John / Pretty little girl from Omagh: Duncan, Hugo / Invisible tears: Williamson, Ann / Bunch of violets blue: Big Tom / The tie that binds: Durkin, Kathy / Wild flowers: Flavin, Mick / Pal of my cradle days: Breen, Ann / Spancil hill: Duff, Mary
CD _____ IHCD 56
Irish Music Heritage / Jul '89 / Prism.

ROT RECORDS PUNK SINGLES COLLECTION
Lost cause: Riot Squad / I'm OK fuck you: Riot Squad / There ain't no solution: Riot Squad / Wet dreams: Clockwork Soldiers / Flowers in the gun: Dead Mans Shadow / Enemy: Resistance 77 / Model soldier: Animal Farm / Shattered glass: Paranoia / Last but not least: Enemy / Don't criticise: Patrol / Russia: Resistance 77 / Hate the law: Riot Squad / Massacred millions: Varukers / Will they never learn: Varukers / Incisor: English Dogs / Boot down the door: Oi Polloi / Return to hell: Skeptix / Evil will win: Rattus / Forward into battle: English Dogs / Killed by my mans own hands: Varukers / Bloody road to glory: Rabid / Boys in blue: Rejected / Cider: Expelled / Cities: Cult Maniax
CD _____ CDPUNK 40
Anagram / Oct '94 / Pinnacle.

ROUGH AND FAST
CD _____ EFA 127012
Riot Beats / Jan '95 / SRD.

ROUGH GUIDE TO WEST AFRICAN MUSIC
CD _____ RGNET 1002CD
World Music Network / Oct '95 / New Note.

ROUGH GUIDE TO WORLD MUSIC, THE
Rebellion: Arroyo, Joe / Sama rew: Africando / Dugu kamelenba: Sangare, Oumou / Zaiko wa wa: Zaiko Langa L / Diandioli: De Dabar, Etoile / Rwanamiza: Kayirebwa, Cecile / Jono: Tanka / Tsaliky mboly hely: Georges, Roger / Henna: Kuban, Ali Hassan / Goodbye again: Yue, Guo & Joji Hirota / Tanola nomads: Sainkho / Khosid wedding dances: Muszikas / When I'm up I can't get down: Oyster Band / Hot tamale baby: Buckwheat Zydeco / Theid mi ddhach: MacKenzie, Talitha
CD _____ RGNET 1001CD
World Music Network / Oct '94 / New Note.

ROUGH RIDERS
CD _____ MPV 5538
Movieplay / Sep '93 / Target/BMG.

ROULETTE ROCK 'N' ROLL COLLECTION
Satellite: Tate, Joe / I'm free: Tate, Joe / Rock 'n' roll Mama: Tate, Joe / I guess it's love: Tate, Joe / I got a rocket in my pocket: Lloyd, Jimmy / You're gone baby: Lloyd, Jimmy / Where the Rio de Rosa flows: Lloyd, Jimmy / Rock-a-bop-a-lina: Hart, Billy & Don / Hole in my bucket: Davis, Bob / Rock to the music: Davis, Bob / Never anymore: Davis, Bob / Leapin' guitar: Chaparais / Goin' wild: Isle, Jimmy / Baby take me back: Larue, Roc / You've got what it takes: Strickland, Johnnie / That's baby: Strickland, Johnnie / Sweet talkin' baby: Strickland, Johnnie / Crazy about you: Malloy, Vince / Hubba hubba ding dong: Malloy, Vince / Girls, girls, girls: Hammer, Jack / Private property: Lanier, Don / Ponytail girl: Lanier, Don / Only one: Roberts, Don 'Red' / Goin' back to St. Louis: Vickery, Mack / Romeo Joe: Skee Brothers / Daisy Mae: Dio, Andy
CD _____ NEMCD 619
Sequel / Jul '92 / BMG.

ROULETTE ROCK 'N' ROLL VOL.2
Strange: Hawkins, Screamin' Jay / Whammy: Hawkins, Screamin' Jay / Bloodshot eyes: Harris, Wynonie / Sweet Lucy Brown: Harris, Wynonie / Spread the news: Harris, Wynonie / Saturday night: Harris, Wynonie / Josephine: Harris, Wynonie / Did you get the message: Harris, Wynonie / Everybody's gonna rock 'n' roll: Isley Brothers / I wanna know: Isley Brothers / Drag: Isley Brothers / Rockin' McDonald: Isley Brothers / 7-11: Gone All Stars / Screamin' Ball at Dracula Hall: Duponts / Hippy dippy Daddy: Cookies / Roll over Beethoven: Four Chaps / Hindu baby: Emanons / Ding dong: Echoes / Woo woo train: Valentines / Dance with me: Chaperones / Ain't you gonna: Powell, Jimmy & The Caddies / Alabama rock 'n' roll: King, Mabel
CD _____ NEMCD 670
Sequel / Jun '94 / BMG.

'ROUND MIDNIGHT
Let there be love: Cole, Nat King / Manhattan: Fitzgerald, Ella / My baby just cares for me: Simone, Nina / Your love is king: Sade / Desafinado: Getz, Stan / Air on a G string: Loussier, Jacques / New thought of you: Benoit, Tony / Call me irresponsible: Washington, Dinah / Imagination: Eckstine, Billy / I get a kick out of you: Holiday, Billie / Unsquare dance: Brubeck, Dave / Shiny stockings: Basie, Count / Makin' whoopee: Armstrong, Louis & Oscar Peterson / Lover man: Vaughan, Sarah / When I fall in love: Webster, Ben / Round Midnight: Torme, Mel / Meditation: Gilberto, Astrud / Lullaby of Birdland: Shearing, George / Cat: Smith, Jimmy / What's new: Benson, George
CD _____ 5164712
Verve / Sep '93 / PolyGram.

ROUND TOWER MUSIC VOL.2
CD _____ RTMCD 012
Round Tower / Oct '95 / Pinnacle / ADA / Direct / BMG / CM.

ROUND TOWER MUSIC, VOL. 1
If that's the way you want it / Past the point of rescue / Jesus in a leather jacket / Ordinary town / Fabulous thunderbirds / Putting me in the ground / Only dancing / Drive-in movies / Sister and brother / My love is in America / Lead the knave / Refugee from heaven / Limbo people / Walking on seashells / My love is yours
CD _____ RTMCD 30
Round Tower / Sep '91 / Pinnacle / ADA / Direct / BMG / CM.

ROUNDER BANJO
CD _____ CD 11542
Rounder / '88 / CM / Direct / ADA / Cadillac.

ROUNDER FIDDLE
CD _____ CDROU 11565
Rounder / Dec '90 / CM / Direct / ADA / Cadillac.

ROUNDER FOLK VOLUME 1
CD _____ CD 11511
Rounder / '88 / CM / Direct / ADA / Cadillac.

ROUNDER FOLK VOLUME 2
CD _____ CD 11512
Rounder / '88 / CM / Direct / ADA / Cadillac.

ROUNDER GUITAR
CD _____ CD 11541
Rounder / '88 / CM / Direct / ADA / Cadillac.

ROUNDER OLD TIME MUSIC
CD _____ CD 11510
Rounder / '88 / CM / Direct / ADA / Cadillac.

ROUTES FROM THE JUNGLE
We are E: Lennie Di Ice / Waking up: Nicolette / You held my head: Manix / Open your mind: Foulplay / Last action hero: Doc Scott / Bludclot arttattack: D.J. Ed Rush / Secret summer feeling: Bodysnatch / Dark strangers: Boogie Times Tribe / Nazinja nazaka: Guy Called Gerald / Music box: Roni Size / Deeper love: Dillinja / Apollo 9: Jo / Believe: E-Z Rollers / Scream: Flynn & Flora / Feel it: Randall & Andy C. / Wrinkles in time: 4 Hero / Droppin' science Vol.2: Droppin' Science / Asian love dance: D.J. Krust
CD _____ VTDCD 46
Virgin / Apr '95 / EMI.

ROYAL PALACE OF YOGYAKARTA, JAVA
CD _____ C 560069CD
Ocora / Jul '95 / Harmonia Mundi / ADA.

ROYAL REGIMENTS OF PARADE
Huntsman / Tuba tiger rag / Highland cathedral / Nine O'clock walk / March off / Pipe set / Vivat regina / Desert storm / Amazing grace / Auld lang syne
CD _____ BNA 5111
Bandleader / Jan '95 / Conifer.

ROYAL TOURNAMENT 1989
Firebird suite / I don't want to join the Air Force / Bold aviator was dying / Another thousand revs wouldn't do him any harm / There were three huns sat on his tail / I left the mess room early / Far far away / Glory flying regulations / RAF march past / Bonnie Dundee / Old Towler / Garry Owen / Hunting the hare / Round the Marble Arch / Come lasses and lads / Galloping major / Light cavalry / Post horn gallop / John Peel / Campbells are coming / Royal Artillery slow march / Keel row / In the mood / Little brown jug / String of pearls / Moonlight serenade / St. Louis blues march / Bugle calls from St. Mary's church / Cracow / Sky eagles / March march Polonia / Brothers it is time to fight / Uhlans have come / War, my little war / How nice it is on a little war / March of the 1st brigade / Oka / Victory victory / General Maczek's salute / General salute / Fanfare - Oranges and lemons / Maybe it's because I'm a Londoner / Heart of oak / H.M.S. Pinafore / All the nice girls love a sailor / Alla Marcia (From Karelia March) / Glorious victory / Bond of friendship / Trumpet prelude / Symphony no. 3 in C minor (Saint Saens (excerpt)) / Last post and evening hymn / Hands across the sea / National anthem
CD _____ BNA 5089
Bandleader / Aug '89 / Conifer.

ROYAL TOURNAMENT 1991
CD _____ BNA 5091
Bandleader / Jun '91 / Conifer.

ROYAL TOURNAMENT 1994
CD _____ BNA 5094
Bandleader / Jul '94 / Conifer.

ROYAL TOURNAMENT 1995
(Victory)
CD _____ BNA 5095
Bandleader / Jun '95 / Conifer.

ROYALTIES OVERDUE
In/Flux: D.J. Shadow / Food of my de rhythm: R.P.M. / Slow chase: D.J. Krush / In a silent way: Palm Skin Productions / Harmonium: D.J. Takemura / Like brothers: Palm Skin Productions / Life so free: Federation / If: Step / Sortie des hombres: Step / This is just a dance: Bubba Tunes / Come on: Marden Hill / La doctresse: Le Funk Mob / Hear between the silence: Monday Michiru / Rusty James: Federation / Motor bass get phunked up: Le Funk Mob / Spock with a beard: Palm Skin Productions
CD _____ MWCD 003
Mo Wax / May '94 / Vital.

RUBAB ET DUTAR
(Music From Afghanistan)
CD _____ C 560080
Ocora / Dec '95 / Harmonia Mundi / ADA.

RUBBLE COLLECTION
CD _____ RUBBLE CD1
Bam Caruso / Oct '91 / Vital / Direct.

RUDE AWAKENING
CD _____ WAKE 1CD
Beechwood / Jun '89 / BMG / Pinnacle.

RUDE AWAKENING VOL.2, THE
CD _____ AWAKE 2CD
Beechwood / Jul '94 / BMG / Pinnacle.

RUDER THAN YOU - BEST OF BRITISH SKA
CD _____ RRCD 174
Receiver / Jan '93 / Grapevine.

RUDIES ALL ROUND
Don't be a rude boy: Rulers / Rudie gets plenty: Spanishtonians / Preacher: Ellis, Alton / Blam blam fever: Valentines / Soldiers take over: Rio Grandes / Curfew: Aiken, Bobby / Copasetic: Rulers / Rudie bam

bam: *Clarendonians* / Cool off rudies: *Morgan, Derrick* / Denham town: *Winston & George* / Drop the ratchet: *Stranger Cole* / Blessings of love: *Ellis, Alton* / Rude boy train: *Dekker, Desmond* / Beware: Overtakers / Rudies all round: *White, Joe* / Rudies are the greatest: *Pioneers* / Stop the violence: *Valentines* / What can I say: *Tartans* / Judge Dread in court: *Morgan, Derrick* / Set them free: *Perry, Lee 'Scratch'*
CD _____ CDTRL 322
Trojan / Mar '94 / Jetstar / Total/BMG.

RUDIE'S NIGHT OUT
On my radio: *Selecter* / Are you ready: *International Beat* / Orange Street: *Big 5* / James Bond: *Selecter* / Too nice to talk to: *International Beat* / Live injection: *Big 5* / Too much pressure: *Selecter* / Hard world: *International Beat* / Big 5: *Big 5* / Jackpot: *International Beat* / Can can: *Big 5* / Train to Skaville: *Selecter*
CD _____ CDBM 104
Blue Moon / Jun '95 / Magnum Music Group / Greensleeves / Hot Shot / ADA / Cadillac / Discovery.

RUFF AND READY
CD _____ HLRRCD 1
Higher Limits / Nov '95 / SRD.

RUFF RAGGA
CD _____ RNCD 2052
Rhino / Mar '94 / Jetstar / Magnum Music Group / THE.

RUGBY SONGS
Swing low, sweet chariot / Bye bye blackbird / She's the most immoral lady / If I were the marrying kind / Here's to the good old beer / Good ship Venus / Ivan Skavinski Skavar / Madamoiselle from Armentier / Ring dang doo / Ram from Derbyshire / Dinha Dinha show us your leg / In the shade of the old apple tree / Sing us another one / Horndean school / Doggies meeting / Roll me over / Quartermaster's stores / There was an old segeant / Mayor of Bayswater / In mobile / Poor old Angeline / Bye bye blackbird (version 2) / Bring back seven old ladies / Swing low, sweet Chariot (reprise)
CD _____ CSMCD 571
See For Miles/C5 / Feb '95 / Pinnacle.

RUMBLE IN THE JUNGLE
CD Set _____ MM 800272
Moonshine / Apr '95 / Disc.

RUNNIN' WILD
(The Original Sounds Of The Jazz Age)
Running wild: *Ellington, Duke* / Loveable and sweet: *Hanshaw, Annette* / There's a rainbow 'round my shoulder: *Jolson, Al* / My song: *Vallee, Rudy* / Heebie jeebies: *Boswell Sisters* / Loveless love: *Waller, Fats* / Magnolia: *California Ramblers* / Any old time: *Rodgers, Jimmie* / Egyptian Ella: *Lewis, Ted* / How many times: *Lucas, Nick* / She's got 'It': *Weems, Ted* / Makin' whoopee: *Whiteman, Paul* / Here I come: *Edwards, Cliff* / Me: *Etting, Ruth* / Four or five times: *McKinney's Cotton Pickers* / Without that gal: *Austin, Gene* / Home again blues: *Original Dixieland Jazz Band* / Lindy: *Original Dixieland Jazz Band* / Oh you have no idea: *Tucker, Sophie* / You brought a new kind of love to me: *Chevalier, Maurice* / St. James Infirmary: *Bloom, Rube* / Three little words: *Crumit, Frank* / Painting the clouds with sunshine: *Hylton, Jack*
CD _____ CDAJA 5017
Living Era / Koch.

RUPIE'S GEMS
CD _____ RNCD 2009
Rhino / Jun '93 / Jetstar / Magnum Music Group / THE.

RURAL BLUES
CD _____ 157182
Blues Collection / Feb '93 / Discovery.

RURAL BLUES 1934-56
CD _____ DOCD 5223
Blues Document / Apr '94 / Swift / Jazz Music / Hot Shot.

RUSH HOUR 1, THE
CD _____ REACTCD 021
React / Jun '93 / Vital.

RUSH HOUR 2, THE
Spirits: *Transformer 2* / Do you feel me: *H.O.P.* / Feel so good: *T.H.K.* / Waterfall (Pegasus 4): *Atlantic Ocean* / Feel the magic: *Kiss Of Love* / Esta es la musica: *Cafe Latino* / Dancing through the night: *Sharada House Gang* / Eternity: *Datura* / Apache: *MASI* / Elephant paw (get down to the funk): *Pan Position* / Freedom: *Pan Position* / U People: *Pan Position* / We're going on down: *Deadly Sins*
CD _____ REACTCD 034
React / Jan '94 / Vital.

RUSH HOUR 3, THE
CD _____ REACTCD 048
React / Oct '94 / Vital.

RUSHY MOUNTAIN
Top of Maol/Humours of Ballydesmons: *Kerry Fiddles* / Callaghan's/Right of man: *O'Keeffe, Padraig* / Tom Sullivan's/Johnny Leary's/Jim Keefe's reel: *Daly, Jackie* / Lark in the bog: *Star Of Munster Trio* / Uppercurch polkas: *Clifford, Billy* / Humours of Lisheen: *Clifford, John & Julia* / Doyle's polka: *O'Leary, Johnny* / Chase me Charlie

Kerry Fiddles / Kennedy's favourite/Woman of the house: *Murphy, Dennis* / Banks of Sullane: *Daly, Jackie* / Bill Black's: *Star Of Munster Trio* / Julia Doherty's/Up on the wagon: *Clifford, Billy* / Brosna slide/Scartaglen/Padraig O'Keefe's favourite: *O'Leary, Johnny* / Julia Clifford's/Bill the waiver's: *Clifford, Julia* / Humours of Galtymore/Callaghan's/New mown meadows: *Murphy, Dennis & Julia Clifford* / Trip to the jacks/Where is the cat: *Daly, Jackie* / Palatine's daughter: *Clifford, John & Julia* / Fermoy lasses/Honeymoon: *Clifford, Billy* / Worn torn petticoat/Denis O'Keefe's favourite: *O'Leary, Johnny* / Mountain road/ Paddy Cronin's: *Clifford, Julia & Billy Clifford* / Walsh's hornpipe: *Daly, Jackie* / Mrs. Ryan's/Danny Green's polkas: *Clifford, Billy* / Taimse I'm chodladh: *Clifford, Julia* / Tourmore polkas: *O'Leary, Johnny* / Johnny when you die/Swallow's tail/Miss Mc-Leod's: *Kerry Fiddles* / Danny Ab's: *Clifford, Julia & Dennis Murphy* / Matt Haye's jigs: *Clifford, Billy* / Glenside cottage/Taim gan airgead: *Daly, Jackie* / John Clifford's polka/ Behind the bush in the garden/Going for: *Clifford, John & Julia*
CD _____ CDORBD 85
Globestyle / Aug '94 / Pinnacle.

RUSSIAN COSSACK MUSIC FROM THE URALS
CD _____ 15345
Laserlight / '91 / Target/BMG.

RUSSIAN ORTHODOX MUSIC/GREAT VOICES OF BULGARIA
CD _____ AUB 6786
Auvidis/Ethnic / Feb '94 / Harmonia Mundi.

RUTLES HIGHWAY REVISITED
CD _____ SDE 9028CD
Shimmy Disc / Jan '91 / Vital.

S

SAARBRUCKEN '94
(30 Years Of Mod 1964-1994)
CD _____ DRCD 007
Detour / Oct '95 / Detour.

SABA SABA
Saba saba: *Mil Quilhento 1500 & Conjunto Popombo de Nampula* / Noijukuru: *Conjunto Nimala de lalauah* / Kufera povo: *Mil Quilhento 1500 & Conjunto Popombo de Nampula* / Bainxa: *Conjunto Nimala de lalauah* / Josina: *Mil Quilhento 1500 & Conjunto Popombo de Nampula* / Na muntha-nana: *Conjunto Nimala de lalauah* / Mariana: *Mil Quilhento 1500 & Conjunto Popombo de Nampula* / Nonmualana: *Conjunto Nimala de lalauah* / Arminda: *Mil Quilhento 1500 & Conjunto Popombo de Nampula* / nampula: *Conjunto Nimala de lalauah* / Omahie wa mama kihala e flore: *Mil Quilhento 1500 & Conjunto Popombo de Nampula* / Kamueire Kiwereiaka: *Conjunto Nimala de lalauah*
CD _____ CDORBD 077
Globestyle / Nov '92 / Pinnacle.

SABUROSO
A los rumberos de belen: *Sierra Maestra* / El son de Nicaragua: *Orquesta Chepin* / Chilindron de Chivo: *Conjunto Casino* / Anda ven y muevete: *Los Van Van* / Se que tu sabes que yo se: *Orquesta Reve* / Camina y ven: *Gonzalez, Celina* / Rucu rucu a Santa Clara: *Irakere* / De kabinde a kunene: *Los Karachi* / Vuela la paloma: *Conjunto Rumbavana* / Frutas del caney: *Grupo Monumental*
CD _____ CDEWV 11
Earthworks / Jul '89 / EMI / Sterns.

SACRED MUSIC, SACRED DANCE
CD _____ CD 736
Music & Arts / Oct '92 / Harmonia Mundi / Cadillac.

SACRED SONGS
(Original Performances Classic Years In Digital Stereo)
Sacred hour: *Dawson, Peter* / Bless this house: *McCormack, John* / Nun's chorus: *Frind, Annie* / Lord's prayer: *Thomas, John Charles* / Lost chord: *Butt, Dame Clara* / Star of Bethlehem: *Crooks, Richard* / Rosary: *Novis, Donald* / Ave Maria: *Fields, Gracie* / All through the night: *Crooks, Richard* / In a monastery garden: *Dawson, Peter* / Wings of a dove: *Lough, Master Ernest* / Still night holy night: *Robeson, Paul* / Jesus Christ is risen today: *Crooks, Richard* / Abide with me: *Thomas, John Charles*
CD _____ RPCD 313
Robert Parker Jazz / Nov '94 / Conifer.

SACRED TIBETAN CHANTS FROM THE GREAT PRAYER FESTIVAL
CD _____ CD 735
Music & Arts / Oct '92 / Harmonia Mundi / Cadillac.

SAFE SOUL VOL.1
Just loving you: *Green, Garland* / Once you fall in love: *McLoyd, Eddie* / I'll see you in hell first: *Mitchell, Phillip* / Rising cost of love: *Jackson, Millie* / It takes both of us: *Act One* / If I can't have your love: *Brown, Jocelyn* / Plenty of love: *C-Brand* / Stay with me: *Martin, Daltrey* / Still in love with you: *Bailey, J.R.* / My shining star: *Fatback Band* / Sweet music, soft lights and you: *Jackson, Millie & Isaac Hayes* / I'll see you in hell first (alternative take) (Available on CD only): *Mitchell, Phillip* / Feed me your love (Available on CD only): *Fatback Band*
CD _____ CDSEW 020
Southbound / Jan '90 / Pinnacle.

SAFE SOUL VOL.2
Never like this: *Two Tons* / Hooked on you: *Simmons, David* / I think I love you: *Shock One* / I still love you: *Watson, Johnny 'Guitar'* / Love starved: *Brown, Shirley* / What'cha see is what'cha get: *Dramatics* / Lovin': *Hurtt, Phil* / Shouting out love: *Emotions* / Ghettos of the mind: *Pleasure* / Always there: *Side Effect* / Everybody's singing love songs (Available on CD format only.): *Sweet Thunder* / Ladies night out (Available on CD format only.): *Pleasure*
CD _____ CDSEWD 022
Southbound / Aug '90 / Pinnacle.

SALSA & TRADITION
CD _____ PS 65097
Playasound / Oct '92 / Harmonia Mundi / ADA.

SALSA - THE CALIENTA COMPILATION
Taka taka-ta: *Irakere* / El coco: *Irakere* / Locas por el mambo: *More, Benny* / Mi chiquita: *More, Benny* / Te amo: *More, Benny* / Lo que me paso en la guagua: *Alvarez, Adalberto & Su Son* / Longina: *Burke, Malena & NG La Banda* / Santa Barbara: *Gonzalez, Celina* / Pare Cochero: *Orquesta Aragon* / Yo no quiero que seas celosa: *Reve Y Su Charangon* / Los sitios entero: *NG La Banda* / La protesta de los chivos: *NG La Banda* / Coge el Camaron: *La Origina De Manzanillo* / Se muere la tia: *La Origina De Manzanillo* / Eso que anda: *Los Van Van*
CD _____ PSCCD 1007
Pure Sounds From Cuba / Feb '95 / Henry Hadaway Organisation / THE.

SALSA EXPLOSION
Introduction / Prelude / I just want to hang around you / I want to make it with you / Vivir lo nuestro / Para los rumberos / Disculpeme senora / Mentiras / Son de celia y oscar
CD _____ 66058078
RMM / Oct '95 / New Note.

SALSA FLAMENCA - CON FUERZA Y CON BONDAD
CD _____ EUCD 1262
ARC / Mar '94 / ARC Music / ADA.

SALSA GREATS
Mi negra Mariana: *Rodriguez, Pete* / Che che cole: *Colon, Willie* / Pedro Navaja: *Blades, Ruben* / Arsenio: *Harlow, Larry* / Senor Serano: *Miranda, Ismael* / Aguzate: *Ray, Ricardo* / Oye como va: *Puente, Tito* / Quitate la mascara: *Barretto, Ray* / Juan pena: *Colon, Willie* / El Malecon: *Orchestra Harlow* / Muneca: *Palmieri, Eddie* / Richies jala jala: *Ray, Ricardo* / Tu loco lucoy yo traquillo: *Roena, Roberto* / Huracan: *Valentin, Bobby*
CD _____ CDCHARLY 121
Caliente / Aug '88 / Charly.

SALSA, MERENGUE, MAMBO
La maxima expression: *Ensamble Latino* / La cosecha de Mujeres: *Tribu Band* / Si Sonero: *Raices, Grupo* / Son de Cuba a Puerto Rico: *Delgado, Isaac* / Como se queda: *Ensamble Latino* / Marinata no quiere: *Alvarez, Adalberto* / Adios Carcelero y Carcel: *Rivas, Andrea* / Que ganas: *Delgado, Isaac* / Tres Deseos: *Nazario, Ednita* / Que te pasa mami: *Alvarez, Adalberto* / Tu serenata: *Raices, Grupo* / Mapale: *Rivas, Maria* / No aparentes que no sientes: *Silva, Mauricio* / Fracaso: *Ensamble Latino* / Palanque: *Tribu Band*
CD _____ CDEMC 3701
EMI / Mar '95 / EMI.

SALSA REMIXES
I'll always love you / De mi enamorate / Sonambulo / Almohada / El amor mas bonito / Te amo / Depame vivir / Loco de amor / Necesito una amiga / Voy a conquistar tu amor / Por eso esta conmigo / Eas chica es mia / Darte with me / Gozar / Sueno contigo / La gitana / Disculpeme / Bailemos otra vez / La critica / Lo mio es amor / Ella es / Yo me puedo / Esa mujer / Apartement / El ultimo beso / Si tu no te fueras / Hasta que te conoci / Palabras de alma / Yo soy / Soy la voz / Dale jamon / happy / Los tiempos / Siempre muere con ganas / Un poquito mas / Amame / Llegaste tu / Donde estars / Esa chica es mia / Que le den candela / Fuera de control / No hace falta / Ensename / Escalofrio / Mas / Cuando se necesitan / Bailemos entra vez / Disculpeme senora
CD _____ 66058090
RMM / Feb '96 / New Note.

SALSA SABROSA
Soy antillana: *Cruz, Celia* / Sipriano: *Ray, Ricardo & Bobby Cruz* / Sabo los rumberos: *Canales, Angel* / Sale el sol: *Rivera, Ismael* / Canion: *Sonora Poncena* / Mi debilidad: *Quintana, Ishmael* / Quiero saber: *Fania Allstars* / Arrepientete: *Barretto, Ray* / Anoranzas: *La Serie, Rolando & Johnny Pacheco* / El raton: *Feliciano, Cheo* / No bebo mas: *Sonora Poncena* / De toros maneras rosas: *Rivera, Ismael* / La maleta: *Blades, Ruben* / Periodico de ayer: *Lavoe, Hector*
CD _____ CDHOT 517
Charly / Apr '95 / Charly / THE / Cadillac.

SALSA TROPICAL
CD _____ CD 62039
Saludos Amigos / Nov '93 / Target/BMG.

SALSA/BOLERO/CUBAN
(3CD Set)
CD Set _____ PSCBOX 001
Pure Sounds From Cuba / Feb '95 / Henry Hadaway Organisation / THE.

SALSAMANIA
Ganas / El rey de la puntualidad / Sonaremos el tambo / Nabuco donosor / Dile / Le flor do los lindos campos / Cucala / Yo no soy guapo / Llamame / To loco loco y yo tranquilo / Che che cole / Laye laye
CD _____ CDHOT 515
Charly / Sep '94 / Charly / THE / Cadillac.

SALUDOS AMIGOS
CD _____ CD 62048
Saludos Amigos / Nov '93 / Target/BMG.

SALZBURG VOLKSMUSIK 1910-1949
CD _____ US 0197
Trikont / Jul '95 / ADA / Direct.

SAMBA
Bizantina bizancia: *Ben, Jorge* / La vem o Brasil descendo a ladeira: *Moreira, Moraes* / Prata da noite: *De Sa, Estacio* / O bebado e o equilibrista: *Bosca, Joao* / Meonda: *Machado, Elaine* / Swing de campo grande: *Balonos, Novos* / Flor de lis: *Djavan* / Fruta mulher: *Moreira, Moraes* / Acorda que eu quero ver: *Caymmi, Nana* / O dia que o sol declarou o seu amor pela terra: *Ben, Jorge* / Brasil pandeiro: *Balonos, Novos* / A rita: *Buarque, Chico* / No reino encantado do amor: *Ben, Jorge* / Maria vai com as outras: *Creuza, Maria* / Tem que se tirar da cabeca: *Do Salgueiro, Academicos* / Quilombo do dumba: *De Jesus, Clementina* / Roda viva: *Buarque, Chico* / O dia se zangou: *Negra, Jovelina Perola* / Era umas ves 13 pontos: *Ben, Jorge* / Contraste: *Macale, Jards* / Que maravilha: *Ben, Jorge & Toquinho*
CD _____ NSCD 002
Nascente / Jul '91 / Disc / THE.

SAMBA AND BOSSA NOVA FROM RIO
CD _____ CD 12503
Music Of The World / Nov '92 / Target/ BMG / ADA.

SAMBA COM JAZZ
Milagre: *Quarteto Em Cy* / Agua de beber: *Zimbo Trio* / Tres pontas: *Nascimento, Milton* / Samba do aviao: *Jobim, Antonio Carlos & Mucha* / Reza: *Zimbo Trio* / Mas que nada: *Creuza, Maria* / Samba sem voce: *Passos, Rosa & Emilio Santiago* / Bon tempo: *Buarque, Chico* / Muito obrigado: *Djavan* / Como diza o poeta: *Vinicius & Toquinho* / Noite dos mascarados: *Buarque, Chico* / Consolacao: *Zimbo Trio* / O morro nao engana: *Melodia, Luiz* / Cancao de bussios: *Sa, Sandra* / Samba de verao: *Valle, Marcus* / Bem bem: *Costa, Gal* / Pra fazer o sol nascer: *Gil, Gilberto* / Madalena rui pro mar: *Buarque, Chico* / Requebra que eu dou um doce: *Hime, Olivia & Dory Caymmi* / Um vestido de bolero: *Hime, Olivia & Dory Caymmi* / Onde e que voce esteva: *Buarque, Chico* / Gira giro: *Nascimento, Milton* / Arrastao: *Zimbo Trio* / Espelho christalino: *Valenca, Alceu*
CD _____ NSCD 004
Nascente / Jul '91 / Disc / THE.

SAMBA RUMBA CONGA
CD _____ PASTCD 7071
Flappor / Aug '95 / Pinnacle.

SAMMY'S SALOON
CD _____ 15212
Laserlight / Aug '91 / Target/BMG.

SAMPLE CITY
CD _____ FILECD 442
Profile / Aug '93 / Pinnacle.

SAMPLE CITY II
CD _____ FILECD 450
Profile / Jun '94 / Pinnacle.

SAMPLE SOME OKRA
CD _____ OKSP 001CD
Normal/Okra / Mar '94 / Direct / ADA.

SAN ANTONIO BLUES 1937
CD _____ DOCD 5232
Blues Document / Apr '94 / Swift / Jazz Music / Hot Shot.

SAN ANTONIO'S CONJUNTOS IN THE 1950'S
CD _____ ARHCD 376
Arhoolie / Apr '95 / ADA / Direct / Cadillac.

SAN DIEGO BLUES JAM
CD _____ TCD 5029
Testament / Oct '95 / Complete/Pinnacle / ADA / Koch.

SAN FRANCISCO BLUES FESTIVAL-1980
CD _____ 157732
Blues Collection / Feb '93 / Discovery.

SAN FRANCISCO HOUSE CULTURE
(2CD Set)
CD Set _____ SPV 08638442
Subterranean / Jan '96 / Plastic Head.

SANCTIFIED JUG BANDS 1928-30
CD _____ DOCD 5008
Blues Document / Dec '94 / Swift / Jazz Music / Hot Shot.

SANCTUARY SESSIONS - LIVE AT CRUISE'S HOTEL, ENNIS
CD _____ CCD 001CD
CCD / Oct '94 / ADA.

SANTA CLAUS BLUES
CD _____ JASSCD 3
Jass / Aug '89 / CM / Jazz Music / ADA / Cadillac / Direct.

SANTA'S BAG
O come, o come Emmanuel / O tannenbaum / Silver bells / White Christmas / Have yourself a merry little Christmas / Away in a manger / Christmas song / Christmas blues / It's the time of the year / Jingle bells / Let it snow, let it snow, let it snow / Santa Claus is coming to town / Blue Christmas
CD _____ CD 83352
Telarc / Oct '94 / Conifer / ADA.

SANTIC PRESENTS AN EVEN HARDER SHADE OF BLACK
CD _____ CDPS 001
Pressure Sounds / Mar '95 / SRD / Jetstar.

SARAH 100 THERE AND BACK AGAIN LANE
Sensitive: Field Mice / Atta girl: Heavenly / Ahprahran: Sugargliders / Peaches: Orchids / Joy of living: Blueboy / Six o'clock is rosary: Ministers / Inside out: Brighter / Make a deal with the city: East River Pipe / English rain: Wake / Temporal: Secret Shine / All of a tremble: St. Christopher / Pristine Christine: Sea Urchins / He gets me so hard: Boyracer / Mustard gas: Action Painting / Tell me how it feels: Sweetest Ache / Rio: Another Sunny Day / In Gunnersbury Park: Hit Parade / Drown: Even As We Speak
CD _____ SARAH 100
Sarah / Aug '95 / Vital.

SASHA REMIXES, THE
Nasty rhythm: Creative Thieves / Alright: Urban Soul / Closer: Mr. Fingers / Feel the drop: B.M.EX / Peace and harmony: Brothers In Rhythm / Let you go: Van-Rooy, Marina / Always: Urban Soul / Talk to me: Hysterix / No more: Unique 3 / Everything's gonna change: Rusty / Anambra part 2: Ozo / Sea of tranquility: London Beat
CD _____ KOLDCD 002
Equator / Jun '93 / Pinnacle.

SATIN AND STEEL
If I could turn back time: Cher / Will you be there (in the morning): Heart / Same thing: Carlisle, Belinda / I believe: Detroit, Marcella / Running up that hill: Bush, Kate / Sexcrime (1984): Eurythmics / All fired up: Benatar, Pat / Black velvet: Myles, Alannah / Better be good to me: Turner, Tina / Feel like making love: Henry, Pauline / I want that man: Harry, Deborah / Monsters and angels: Voice Of The Beehive / Going down to Liverpool: Bangles / Stop draggin' my heart around: Nicks, Stevie / Faster than the speed of night: Tyler, Bonnie / I want your love: Transvision Vamp / Pretend we're dead: L7 / Gloria: Branigan, Laura / Bette Davis eyes: Carnes, Kim / Echo beach: Martha & The Muffins
CD _____ 5169712
PolyGram TV / Aug '94 / PolyGram.

SATIN SHEETS
Looking in the eyes of love: Loveless, Patty / I've already loved you in my mind: Twitty, Conway / Feelings: Twitty, Conway / Leave my heart the way you found it: Greenwood, Lee / Hopeless romantics: Earle, Steve & the Dukes / Anyone can be somebody's fool: Griffith, Nanci / Satin sheets: Pruett, Jeanne / Crying: Jennings, Waylon / Don't worry baby: Thomas, B.J. / Break it to me gently: Lee, Brenda / She's got you: Lynn, Loretta / Am I blue (yes I'm blue): Strait, George / Love song: Oak Ridge Boys / Wind beneath my wings: Greenwood, Lee / He called me baby: Cline, Patsy / Turn out the lights) and love me tonight: Williams, Don
CD _____ PWKS 4268
Carlton Home Entertainment / Feb '96 / Carlton Home Entertainment.

SATISFACTION GARANTEED
(Hits Of The Seventies)
CD _____ MU 5047
Musketeer / Oct '92 / Koch.

SATURDAY NIGHT AT HEAVEN, A
CD _____ SATCD 1
Prime Cuts / Mar '94 / Pinnacle.

SATURDAY NIGHT AT THE AMERICAN DINER
(2CD/MC Set)
Reet petite: Wilson, Jackie / Everybody needs somebody: Blues Brothers / Blueberry hill: Domino, Fats / Lucille: Little Richard / No particular place to go: Berry, Chuck / Tequila: Champs / Let's twist again: Checker, Chubby / C'mon everybody: Cochran, Eddie / Leader of the pack: Shangri-Las / In the midnight hour: Pickett, Wilson / Duke of Earl: Chandler, Gene / Goodnight sweetheart: Spaniels / Who put the bomp: Viscounts / (We're gonna) Rock around the clock: Haley, Bill / Grease megamix: Travolta, John & Olivia Newton John / Singin' the blues: Mitchell, Guy / Wanderer: Dion / Green onions: Booker T & The MG's / Great balls of fire: Lewis, Jerry Lee / Wipeout: Surfaris / Wake up little Susie: Everly Brothers / Sweet talking guy: Chiffons / Sherry: Four Seasons / Chantilly lace: Big Bopper / Chapel of love: Dixie Cups / Blue suede shoes: Perkins, Carl / La bamba: Valens, Ritchie / Yakity yak: Coasters / Will you still love me tomorrow: Shirelles / Needle in a haystack: Velvette / I get around: Beach Boys / Rebel rouser: Eddy, Duane / Bony moronie: Williams, Larry / Be bop a lula: Vincent, Gene / My boyfriends back: Angels / Surf city: Jan & Dean / At the hop: Danny & The Juniors / Why do fools fall in love: Lymon, Frankie / Book of love: Monotones / Earth angel: Crew Cuts
CD _____ DINCD 107
Dino / Aug '95 / Pinnacle / 3MV.

SATURDAY NIGHT BLUES
CD _____ SP 1172CD
Stony Plain / Oct '93 / ADA / CM / Direct.

SATURDAY NIGHT'S ALRIGHT
I'm in you: Frampton, Peter / Eighth day: O'Connor, Hazel / Paper plane: Status Quo / Ramblin' man: Allman Brothers / Saturday night's alright for fighting: John, Elton / I'm waiting for the man: Velvet Underground / Stairway to heaven: Far Corporation / Letter: Box Tops / Freebird: Lynyrd Skynyrd / Funk 49: James Gang / Liar: Three Dog Night / Warrior: Wishbone Ash / Parisienne walkways: Moore, Gary / Who do you love: Juicy Lucy / Broken down angel: Nazareth / Lady in the black: Uriah Heep / Ace of spades: Motorhead / America: Nice / You took the words right out of my mouth: Meat Loaf / Rosanna: Toto / God gave rock 'n' roll to you: Argent / All day and all of the night: Stranglers / Holding out for a hero: Tyler, Bonnie / Livin' thing: E.L.O.
CD _____ 3220
Carlton Home Entertainment / Oct '92 / Carlton Home Entertainment.

SAUCY SONGS
(Classic Years In Digital Stereo)
I like a guy what takes his time: West, Mae / Oh you have no idea: Tucker, Sophie / Is there anything wrong: Kane, Helen / When I'm cleaning windows: Formby, George / I found a new way: West, Mae / Say, young lady: Gardener, Dick / Bessie couldn't help it: Randall, Slatz / O'I man mose: Norman, Patricia / It isn't love: Frankau, Ronald / You can't blame me for that: Miller, Max / Come up and see: Edwards, Cliff / You brought a new: Waters, Ethel / I like to do things: Lang, Jeanie / Easy rider: West, Mae / Puleeze Mr. Hemingway: Suter, Anne / I'm wild about that thing: Smith, Bessie / Life begins at forty: Tucker, Sophie / They call me sister: West, Mae
CD _____ RPCD 308
Robert Parker Jazz / Sep '94 / Conifer.

SAUDADE
No dia em que eu vim embora: Regina, Elis / Boca da noite: Toquinho / Cavaleiro: Veloso, Caetano / Bruxa / Joyce / Uma vez um caso: Lobo, Edu & Joyce / Corsario: Regina, Elis / Gongaba: Hime, Olivia & Edu Lobo / Dindi: Creuza, Maria / Vivo sohando: Wanda / Sem fantasia: Buarque, Chico / Ultimo desejo: Bethania, Maria / Umas e outras: Buarque, Chico / Eu sei que vou te amar: Creuza, Maria & Vinicius & Toquinho / Pra nao mais voltar: De Belem, Fafa / Irmao de fe: Nascimento, Milton / How insensitive: Creuza, Maria / Sabia: Buarque, Chico / Da cor do pecado: Creuza, Maria / Acabou chorare: Baianos, Novos / Rosa flor: Vandre, Geraldo / Apelo: Toquinho & Vincius De Moraes
CD _____ NSCD 005
Nascente / Jul '91 / Disc / THE.

SAVE THE LAST DANCE FOR ME
Save the last dance for me: Heptones / Will you still love me tomorrow: Barker, Dave / Shotgun wedding: Campbell, Cornell / Then he kissed me: Marvels / Hang on sloopy: Chosen Few / Da doo ron ron: Heyward, Winston / Darling you send me: Romeo, Max / Oh Carol (vocal): McKay, Freddie / Oh Carol: Brown, Lennox / Sincerely: Edwards, Jackie / (Sittin' on) the dock of the bay: McKay, Freddie / Light my fire: Soul Sam / Come on over to my place: Robinson, Jackie / Wonderful world: Donaldson, Eric / It's in his kiss (Shoop shoop song): Marvels / Blue moon: Platonics / Duke of Earl (Version): McCook, Tommy & The Aggrovators
CD _____ CDTRL 317
Trojan / Mar '94 / Jetstar / Total/BMG.

SAX FOR ROMANTICS
(4CD Set)
CD Set _____ MBSCD 447
Castle / Nov '95 / BMG.

SAXON DANCEHALL SPECIALS VOL.1
CD _____ SAXCD 001
Saxon Studio / Apr '94 / Jetstar.

SAXOPHONE
CD _____ WWCD 2013
West Wind / May '89 / Swift / Charly / CM / McCalmans

SAXOPHONY - HONKERS AND SHOUTERS
Easy rockin': Kohiman, Freddie Orchestra / Flashlight: Wright, Jimmy / Move over: Wright, Jimmy / 2.20 AM: Wright, Jimmy / Blowin' awhile: Hall, Rene / Rene's boogie: Hall, Rene / Blue creek hop: Hall, Rene / Downbeat: Hall, Rene / Jubilee jump: Hall, Rene / Jesse's blues: Hall, Rene / Turnpike: Powell, Jesse / Sopping molasses: Powell, Jesse / Whooping blues: Lucas, Buddy / Pea lily: Lucas, Buddy / Undecided: Lucas, Buddy / Big Bertha: Lucas, Buddy / One taste calls for another: Hall, Rene
CD _____ NEMCD 748
Sequel / Aug '95 / BMG.

SCORPIO RECORDS STORY
Brown eyed girl: Golliwogs / You better be careful: Golliwogs / Fight fire: Golliwogs / Fragile child: Golliwogs / Walking on the water: Golliwogs / You better get it before it gets you: Golliwogs / Call it pretending: Golliwogs / Boots: Spokes / Stop calling me: Group B / She's gone: Group B / I know your name girl: Group B / I never really knew: Group B / Time: Tokays / Hole in the wall: Tokays / It's up to you: Shillings / Made you cry: Shillings / Lusin' you: Newcastle 5 / Yes I'm cryin': Newcastle 5 / Gotta get away: Penn, William / Blow my mind: Penn, William / Far and away: Penn, William / Weatherman: Squires / Anyhow anywhere: Squires / It must be love: Squires / Read all about it: Tears / Rat race: Tears / People through my glasses: Tears
CD _____ CDWIKD 129
Big Beat / Apr '94 / Pinnacle.

SCOTLAND - ACCORDION, HARP & FIDDLE
CD _____ PS 65109
Playasound / Nov '93 / Harmonia Mundi / ADA.

SCOTLAND - THE DANCES AND THE DANCE BANDS
Eightsome reel: Holmes, Ian & Scottish Dance Band / Strip the willow: Johnstone, Jim & His Band / West Highland waltz: MacDonald, Fergie & Highland / Dashing white Sergeant: MacPhail, Ian & His Scottish Dance Band / Canadian barn dance: Johnstone, Jim & His Band / Waltz country dance: Keith, Lex & His Scottish Band / Irish jiggery: MacDonald, Fergie & Highland / Grand march: Wilson, Calum / Jig strathspey and reel: Lothian Scottish Dance Band / St. Bernard's waltz: Johnstone, Jim & His Band / Boston Two Step: Ellis, John & His Highland Country Band / Reel (hoop her and grid her): Glendaruel Scottish Dance Band / Pride o' erin waltz: MacLeod, Bobby & His Music / Gay Gordons: Campbell, Colin & His Highland Band / Two highland schottissches: Ellis, John & His Highland Country Band / Military two step: Johnstone, Jim & His Band / Lothian lads (Only on CD): Lothian Scottish Dance Band / Palais glide (Only on CD): Johnstone, Jim / Hebridean waltz (Only on CD): Carmichael, John / Irish military two step (Only on CD): MacDonald, Fergie
CD _____ LCOM 9003
Lismor / Jul '87 / Lismor / Direct / Duncans / ADA.

SCOTLAND - THE MUSIC OF A NATION
Caddam Woods: Golden Fiddle Orchestra / Strathspeys and reels: Burgess, John D / Bonnie lass o'Bon Accord: Ford, Tommy / Medley: Gonnella, Ron / 4/4 marches: Dysart & Dundonald Pipe Band / Slow air and marches: MacKay, Rhona / Mrs. Hamilton of Pencaitland: Glasgow Caledonian Strathspey & Reel Society / Gay Gordons: Ellis, John & His Highland Country Band / Free and easy: Hunter, Karen / Petronella: Brock, Robin & His Dance Band / March, strathspey and reel: MacFayden, Iain / Hangman's reel: MacLean, Calum / Waltzes: Dysart & Dundonald Pipe Band / Reels: Currie Brothers / Cro cheann 'I Saile: MacKay, Rhona / Marches: Glasgow Caledonian Strathspey & Reel Society / Dumbarton's drums (Only on CD): Gaelforce Orchestra / Mary of Argyll (Only on CD): Gaelforce Orchestra / Trilogy (Only on CD): Gaelforce Orchestra
CD _____ LCOM 9004
Lismor / Aug '87 / Lismor / Direct / Duncans / ADA.

SCOTLAND NOW - THE MUSIC AND THE SONG VOL.2
Fiddle and pipe medley: Hardie, Ian / Forth bridge song: Laing, Robin / Who pays the piper: McCalmans / Wild geese: Redpath, Jean / Slow air and pipe medley: McClain, Alistair / Craig Scottish Dance Band / Chi Mi'n Geamhradh: MacPhee, Catherine-Anne / See the people run: Ceolbeg / Coorie doon: Stramash / Atlantic reels: McNeill, Brian /

MacCrimmon's Lament and slow air: Heywood, Heather / Across the hills of home: Bogle, Eric / Storm in Edinburgh/The streaker: Bogle, Eric / Oor Hamlet: McNaughtan, Adam / Tha Mo Chridhe Sa Ghaidhealtachd: Scott, Eifrida / Fiddle tune medley: Robertson, Arthur Scott / I wish I was in Glasgow: MacKintosh, Iain / Bell: Jackson, William Billy / Rollin' home: McCalmans
CD _____ CDTRAX 060
Greentrax / Dec '92 / Conifer / Duncans / ADA / Direct.

SCOTLAND THE BRAVE
CD _____ MATCD 233
Castle / Dec '92 / BMG.

SCOTLAND THE BRAVE
Scotland the brave: Daly, Glen / Songs of the borders: Alexander Brothers / Scottish trilogy: Martell, Lena / Lass of bon accord: Alexander Brothers / MacNamara's band: Daly, Glen / Marching home: Alexander Brothers / Mary of Skye: Kennedy, Calum / Sky is blue in Scotland: Daly, Glen / Cuckoo waltz: Starr, Will / Auld Scotch sang medley: Alexander Brothers / Grand march: MacLeod, Jim & His Band / Guid Scotch night: Stewart, Andy & Jimmy Blue Band / There's nae toon: Alexander Brothers / Little street where old friends meet: Daly, Glen / Scottish soldier: Stewart, Andy / Duke and Duchess of Edinburgh: MacLeod, Jim & His Band / Dear old Glasgow town: Daly, Glen / Amazing grace: Royal Scots Dragoon Guards / Flower of Scotland: Alexander Brothers
CD _____ TRTCD 136
TrueTrax / Oct '94 / THE.

SCOTLAND THE BRAVE
CD _____ EUCD 1321
ARC / Nov '95 / ARC Music / ADA.

SCOTLAND'S MUSIC
CD _____ CKD 008
Linn / Apr '93 / PolyGram.

SCOTSMAN, THE
(The Bands, Pipes & Drums Of Great Scottish Regiments)
Amazing grace / Medley / Road to the Osles / Athol highlanders/Bugle horn / Green hills of Tyrol / March / Rose of Kelvingrove / Scottish serenade / Tartan tuba / Jacobite sword dance / March off / Highland cathedral / March medley / Scots wha hae / Medley #2 / Wee MacGregor / Bonnie black Isle / Pipe and drum medley / Bays of Harris / March off #2
CD _____ STACD 7006
Valentine / Nov '94 / Conifer.

SCOTTISH BAGPIPES & DRUMS
CD _____ 12249
Laserlight / Sep '94 / Target/BMG.

SCOTTISH COLLECTION
(3CD/MC Set)
CD Set _____ TBXCD 511
TrueTrax / Jan '96 / THE.

SCOTTISH COUNTRY DANCING VOL.1
CD _____ PACD 032
Music Masters / Mar '94 / Target/BMG.

SCOTTISH FOLK FESTIVAL
CD _____ FMS 2036CD
Fenn Music Services / Jul '94 / ADA.

SCOTTISH FOLK FESTIVAL '93
CD _____ FMS 2040CD
Fenn Music Services / Jul '94 / ADA.

SCOTTISH FOLK FESTIVAL '93
CD _____ FMS 2050CD
Fenn Music Services / Jun '94 / ADA.

SCOTTISH GOLD
(In The Celtic Tradition)
CD _____ LCOM 5245
Lismor / May '95 / Lismor / Direct / Duncans / ADA.

SCOTTISH GOLD
(In The Ceilidh & Dance Tradition)
CD _____ LCOM 5246
Lismor / May '95 / Lismor / Direct / Duncans / ADA.

SCOTTISH GOLD
(In The Popular Song)
CD _____ LCOM 5244
Lismor / May '95 / Lismor / Direct / Duncans / ADA.

SCOTTISH GOLD
(In The Piping Tradition)
CD _____ LCOM 5243
Lismor / May '95 / Lismor / Direct / Duncans / ADA.

SCOTTISH PIPES & DRUMS
CD _____ PS 65113
Playasound / Nov '93 / Harmonia Mundi / ADA.

SCOTTISH SONGBOOK, THE
Auld Scotch sangs: McCormack, John / Comin' thro' the rye: Gluck, Alma / My love is like a red red rose: Hislop, Joseph / Annie Laurie: McCormack, John / Turn ye tae me: McCormack, John / Bonnie Mary of Argyle: Hislop, Joseph / Afton water: Hislop, Joseph / Ye banks and braes o bonnie Doon: Melba, Nellie / Road to the isles: Lauder, Harry / Ca' the yowes: Baillie, Isobel / Flowers of the forest: Labette, Dora / March

March Ettrick and Teviotdale: *Dawson, Peter* / Just a song at twilight: *Coleman, Louise* / Robin Adair: *Brola, Jeanne* / An Eriskay love ilt: *Robeson, Paul* / My ain folk: *Butt, Clara* / Ae fond kiss: *Coleman, Esther & Foster Richardson* / Will ye no' come back again: *MacEwan, Sydney* / John Anderson, my jo: *Hill, Carmen* / Bonnie banks of Loch Lomond: *Hislop, Joseph*
CD _____ **MIDCD 001**
Moidart / Jan '95 / Conifer / ADA.

SCOTTISH TRADITION VOL.1
(Bothy Ballads)
Muckin' O' Geordie's byre: *Macbeath, Jimmy* / Stool of repentance: *Bothy Band* / As I came ower the Muir O' Ord: *Bowie, James* / Bold Princess Royal: *Taylor, Jamie* / Shepherd lad o'rhynie: *MacDonald, John* / My last farewell to Stirling: *Murray, Charlie* / Whistle o'er the lave o't: *Macbeath, Jimmy* / Stumpie strathspey: *Macbeath, Jimmy* / Mason's apron: *Macbeath, Jimmy* / Lochiel's welcome to Glasgow march: *Macbeath, Jimmy* / Airlin's fine braes: *Elvin, Bill* / Mrs. Grieg: *Taylor, Jamie* / Hairst o'rettie: *Murray, Charlie* / Smith's a gallant fireman: *Murray, Charlie* / Haill week o' the fair: *Taylor, Jamie* / Old horned sheep: *Taylor, Jamie* / Athol highlanders/March played in jig time: *Taylor, Jamie* / Medley: *Steele, Frank*
CD _____ **CDTRAX 9001**
Greentrax / May '93 / Conifer / Duncans / ADA / Direct.

SCOTTISH TRADITION VOL.2
(Music From The Western Isles)
Ho mandu / Dhoanainn sugradh / Oran do bhean mhie fhraing / Puirt a buel / Cha tillmacrommon
CD _____ **CDTRAX 9002**
Greentrax / Nov '92 / Conifer / Duncans / ADA / Direct.

SCOTTISH TRADITION VOL.3
(Songs From Barra)
We're you in the mountains / My love Alan / One day as I roamed the hills / Woman over there who laughed / Silver whistle / Early today I set out
CD _____ **CDTRAX 9003**
Greentrax / Jan '94 / Conifer / Duncans / ADA / Direct.

SCOTTISH TRADITION VOL.4
(Shetland Fiddle Music)
CD _____ **CDTRAX 9004**
Greentrax / Jan '94 / Conifer / Duncans / ADA / Direct.

SCOTTISH TRADITION VOL.5
(The Muckle Sangs)
Gypsy laddie / False knight upon the road / Bonnie banks o'fordie / Tam lin, the bold pedlar / Two sisters / Young Johnston
CD _____ **CDTRAX 9005**
Greentrax / Nov '92 / Conifer / Duncans / ADA / Direct.

SCOTTISH TRADITION VOL.6
(Gaelic Psalms From Lewis)
Martyrdom / Coleshill / Stroudwater / Dundee / London New / Martyrs
CD _____ **CDTRAX 9006**
Greentrax / Aug '94 / Conifer / Duncans / ADA / Direct.

SCOTTISH TRADITION VOL.9
(The Fiddler & His Art)
Lady Madelina Sinclair/Sandy Cameron: *MacDonnel, Donald* / Mackintosh's lament: *MacDonnel, Donald* / Medley (Atholl Highlander's march to Loch Katrine, The; The Inverness natherinn' Corrimonie's rant, Alexander Duff.): *MacDonnel, Donald* / Gabhaidh sinn an rathad mor: *MacDonnel, Donald* / Renfrewshire Militia/man: *Inkster, Hugh* / Stronsay Waltz/Jock Halcrow: *Shearer, Pat & David Linklater* / Medley #2 (Headlands, The; The Caledonian March; The standing stones of stennes): *Shearer, Pat & David Linklater* / Braes of Tullymet/ Captain Keeler: *Reid, John Snr & John Reid Jnr* / Medley #3 (Jenny Nettles; Cam you here to court and clap; Mither put me to the well; The high road to Linton.): *Poleson, Andrew & William Williamson* / Neil Gow's lament for whiskey: *Stewart, Albert* / Medley #4 (Mill Hills; Pipe Major J. Stewart; The lodge of Glentana; Gavin MacMillan): *MacAndrew, Hector & Sandie Edmondson* / James F. Dickie/J.F. Dickie's delight: *MacAndrew, Hector & Sandie Edmondson* / My heart is broken since thy departure: *MacAndrew, Hector & Sandie Edmondson* / Medley #5 (Mrs Major Stewart of the island Java; Madame Frederick; Earl Grey; Waverley Ball): *MacAndrew, Hector & Sandie Edmondson*
CD _____ **CDTRAX 9009**
Greentrax / May '93 / Conifer / Duncans / ADA / Direct.

SCREWED
CD _____ **ARR 67010CD**
Amphetamine Reptile / Jan '96 / SRD.

SEA SONGS & SHANTIES
Traditional English Songs From The Last Days Of Sail)
Stormy weather boys: *Roberts, A.V. 'Bob'* / Rio Grande: *Fishermen's Group* / Mr. Stormalong: *Copper, Bob & Ron* / Worst old ship: *Roberts, A.V. 'Bob'* / Yarmouth fishermen's song: *Cox, Harry* / Maggie May: *Roberts,*

Gen / Victim: *Strike* / Low life: *4 Skins* / Seems to me: *4 Skins*
CD _____ **CDPUNK 13**
Anagram / Sep '93 / Pinnacle.

SECRET RECORDS PUNK SINGLES COLLECTION VOL.2
Blown to bits: *Exploited* / Fuck the mods: *Exploited* / I belive in anarchy: *Exploited* / Hitler's in the charts again: *Exploited* / Alternative: *Exploited* / Addiction: *Exploited* / Brave new world: *4 Skins* / Justice: *4 Skins* / Employers blacklist: *Business* / Disco girls: *Business* / Subway sadist: *Chron Gen* / Behind closed doors: *Chron Gen* / Disco tech: *Chron Gen* / Punk rock will never die: *Gonads* / Got any Wriggly's John: *Gonads* / She can't whip me: *Gonads* / School's out: *Infa Riot* / Fight for your life: *Angela Rippon's Bum* / I'm thick: *Skin Disease* / Where's dock green: *Venom* / Way it's got to be: *East End Badoes*
CD _____ **CDPUNK 60**
Anagram / Sep '95 / Pinnacle.

SEGADANCE
(Music From Mauritius)
CD _____ **PS 65126**
Playasound / May '94 / Harmonia Mundi / ADA.

SEKUNJALO - NOW IS THE TIME
Hare yeng: *Sankomota* / Hand in hand: *Mkhize, Themba* / Motherland, cry no more / Kopano ke matla: *Tshola, Tsepo* / Bread and roses: *Ferguson, Jennifer* / Phansi ngodlame: *Mlangeni, Babsy* / Sekunjalo: *Ziqubu, Condry* / Come on everybody: *Masekela, Hugh* / Mayihluye: *Louw, Mara* / Set them free: *Morake, Lebo* / Dedication: *Mahene, Blondie* / Time is now: *Powers, P.J.*
CD _____ **CIDM 1110**
Mango / Apr '94 / Vital / PolyGram.

SELECTED CIRCUITS
CD _____ **UPCD 06**
Nitro / Sep '95 / Plastic Head.

SELEKTA SHOWCASE '89
My prerogative: *Sanchez* / Enquirer: *One-two crew* / Lick out: *Ninja Man* / Jah is the way: *Minott, Sugar* / Nice and cute: *Johnny P.* / Special lady: *Gel, Ny* / Vanity crazy: *Demus, Chaka* / Rawborn rub a dub: *Meakes, Carl* / Me no know why: *General Trees* / Step it up: *Antony, Pad*
CD _____ **GRELCD 130**
Greensleeves / Nov '89 / Total/BMG / Jetstar / SRD.

SEMANN AHOI
CD _____ **15261**
Laserlight / Nov '91 / Target/BMG.

SEND ME THE PILLOW YOU DREAM ON
Send me the pillow that you dream on: *Locklin, Hank* / Reuben James: *Rogers, Kenny* / I feel sorry for him: *Nelson, Willie* / Come on in: *Cline, Patsy* / Hey good lookin': *Cash, Johnny* / You'll always have someone: *Nelson, Willie* / Six days on the road: *Dudley, Dave* / Always leaving, always gone: *Rogers, Kenny* / Burning memories: *Jennings, Waylon* / Walkin' after midnight: *Cline, Patsy* / Singin' the blues: *Mitchell, Guy* / Take these chains from my heart: *Drusky, Roy* / Mule train: *Laine, Frankie* / Don't think twice, it's alright: *Jennings, Waylon* / If I don't understand: *Nelson, Willie* / Ramblin' rose: *Cline, Johnny* / Rose garden: *Anderson, Lynn* / Heart you break may be your own: *Cline, Patsy* / Ticket to nowhere: *Rogers, Kenny* / Release me: *Mardell, Barbara* / I can't find the time: *Nelson, Willie* / Waterloo: *Jackson, Stonewall* / Last letter: *Drusky, Roy* / Wild side of life: *Fender, Freddy* / Sunshine: *Rogers, Kenny*
CD _____ **CDGRF 120**
Tring / Feb '93 / Tring / Prism.

SENSATIONAL 70'S
CD _____ **MATCD 203**
Castle / Dec '92 / BMG.

SENSATIONAL 70'S VOL.2
CD _____ **MATCD 241**
Castle / Dec '92 / BMG.

SENSATIONAL HITS OF THE 1960'S
CD _____ **KLMCD 011**
Scratch / Nov '93 / BMG.

SENSATIONAL SOUL
Soul man: *Sam & Dave* / Gimme little sign: *Wood, Brenton* / Backfield in motion: *Mel & Tim* / Rescue me: *Bass, Fontella* / Harlem shuffle: *Bob & Earl* / Letter: *Box Tops* / Under the boardwalk: *Drifters* / Knock on wood: *Floyd, Eddie* / In crowd: *Gray, Dobie* / Dancing in the street: *Reeves, Martha* / Rock your baby: *McCrae, George* / I just can't stop dancing: *Bell, Archie & The Drells* / Sittin' on) the dock of the bay: *Sledge, Percy* / Hey girl don't bother me: *Tams* / Spanish Harlem: *King, Ben E.* / Love I lost: *Melvin, Harold & The Bluenotes* / Indiana wants me: *Taylor, R. Dean* / What becomes of the broken hearted: *Ruffin, Jimmy*
CD _____ **ECD 3056**
K-Tel / Jan '95 / K-Tel.

SENSE OF DIRECTION, A
Sense of direction / Aunt Monk / Theme for a new day / Long as you're living / I'm trying to find a way / Keep the faith / Panther / Cleopatra and the African Knight / To the

establishment / Red clay / Communication / Dorian
CD _____ **CDBGPD 099**
BGP / Oct '95 / Pinnacle.

SENSES
Play dead: *Bjork & D.Arnold* / Robin (The hooded man): *Clannad* / Love theme: *Vangelis* / Between the lines (theme): *Lindes, Hal* / Cockeye's song: *Morricone, Ennio* / Love's theme: *Moroder, Giorgio* / Robinson Crusoe: *Art Of Noise* / Nomads of the wind: *Bennett, Brian* / Oboe concerto in D minor: *Academy Of Ancient Music* / Gymnopedie no.1: *Satie, Erik* / Equinoxe part 4: *Jarre, Jean Michel* / Eve of war: *Wayne, Jeff* / Caschanpaya: *Incantation* / Coisich a ruin (walk my beloved): *Capercaillie* / Rowena's theme: *Edge* / Cavatina: *Williams, John* / Snowman: *Blake, Howard* / Concierto de Aranjuez: *De Angelis, Nicolas* / Oxygene part 1: *Marvin, Hank* / Going home: *Knopfler, Mark*
CD _____ **5166272**
PolyGram TV / Sep '94 / PolyGram.

SENTIMENTAL JOURNEY
It's only a paper moon / Nightingale can sing the blues / Along the Navajo trail / Things ain't what they used to be / Stardust / May you always / As the world turns / Cherokee canyon / I don't mind / Who put the devil in Evelyn's eyes / Far from the madding crowd / Just another blues / Gold cadillac / And the angels sing / In the mood / Mad about him blues / I'll never smile again / On the Atchison, Topeka and the Santa Fe / My very good friend the milkman / That's how love comes / April fool / Don't cry crybaby / You ain't got nothin' / (I'm getting) Corns for my country / It takes a long, long train with a red caboose / Casanova cricket / Finders keepers / I tipped my hat (and slowly rode away)
CD _____ **PWKM 4045**
Carlton Home Entertainment / Feb '96 / Carlton Home Entertainment.

SENTIMENTAL JOURNEY
CD _____ **DCD 5308**
Disky / Dec '93 / THE / BMG / Discovery / Pinnacle.

SENTIMENTAL OVER YOU
Long ago and far away: *Pepper, Art & Carl Perkins* / Farewell: *Kenton, Stan Orchestra* / I'm beginning to see the light: *Hamilton, Chico Quintet* / Once in a blue moon: *Cole, Nat King* / Autumn leaves: *Farmer, Art Tentet* / Autumn in New York: *Stafford, Joe* / I'm getting sentimental over you: *Dickenson, Vic Quartet* / I get the blues when it rains: *Raney, Sue* / Rocker: *Davis, Miles* / Star eyes: *Newborn, Phineas Trio* / September in the rain: *London, Julie* / I've got my love to keep me warm: *Brown, Les & His Orchestra* / Come back to Sorrento: *Napoleon, Phil & His Memphis Five* / Willow weep for me: *Criss, Sonny* / Buji: *Gray, Glen & The Casa Loma Orchestra* / Early Autumn: *Herman, Woody & His Orchestra* / Mercy mercy mercy: *Adderley, Cannonball Quartet* / I concentrate on you: *Torme, Mel*
CD _____ **CDJA 3**
Premier/MFP / Oct '91 / EMI.

SENTIMENTAL SONGS OF WORLD WAR II
CD _____ **VJC 1049**
Vintage Jazz Classics / Apr '94 / Direct / ADA / CM / Cadillac.

SENTIMENTAL SWING - 12 HITS
CD _____ **UP 005**
Hindsight / Sep '92 / Target/BMG / Jazz Music.

SEODA CHONAMARA 1
(Connemara Favourites Vol. 1)
Inis Caltrach/Toss the feathers: *Althneach, Iorras* / Galtee mountain boy: *O Flaharta, John Beag* / Stack of wheat/Stack of barley/ Johnny will you marry me: *O harnain, P.J.* / Green brooms: *Dhonncha, Sean 'ac* / Currachai na Tra Baine: *O Beaglaoch, Sean* / Peigin leitir moir: *O Beaglaoch, Sean* / All the way to Galway fair: *O Lochluinn, Paidraig* / My own dear native land: *MacDonnchadha, Johnny Mhairtin Learai* / Sweet Biddy Daly: *Walsh, John G* / My pretty fair maid: *Walsh, John G* / Cliff, Belfast and Sweeps hornpipes: *O Ceannabhain, Pádraig Tom Photch* / Neansin Bhan: *O Ceannabhain, Pádraig Tom Photch* / Wise maid/Last night's fun: *Connolly, John* / Si do Mhaimeo: *Ni Chathain, Bríd* / High reel: *Learai, Sonai Choilm* / Whistling thief: *Dhonncha, Sean 'ac* / Charlie Mulvihill/ Plains of Boyle: *Na hAncairi* / An Raisin: *Rathcliffe, Peter* / Amhran na gCualain: *Sheainin, Mairtin* / Irish washerwoman: *Ghabha, Michael Mháire* / An Merican mor: *O Flaharta, John Beag* / First house in Connaught: *O harnain, P.J.* / Queen of Connemara: *MacEon, Tomas*
CD _____ **CICD 019**
Clo Iar-Chonnachta / Dec '93 / CM.

SEPTETOS CUBANOS - SONES DE CUBA
CD Set _____ **MT 113/4**
Corason / Jan '94 / CM / Direct / ADA.

SEPTIC CUTS
Sugar Daddy: *Secret Knowledge* / Smokebelch II: *Sabres Of Paradise* / Painkiller: *Slack* / Internal: *Blue* / Untitled: *PT001* / Mu-

A.V. 'Bob' / Caroline and her young sailor bold: *Makem, Sarah* / Whisky Johnny: *Roberts, A.V. 'Bob'* / What shall we do with the drunken sailor: *Fishermen's Group* / Can't you dance the polka: *Roberts, A.V. 'Bob'* / Sailor's alphabet: *Jenkins, Clifford* / Haul away Joe: *Roberts, A.V. 'Bob'* / Cruisin' 'round Yarmouth: *Cox, Harry* / Windy old weather: *Roberts, A.V. 'Bob'* / Farewell and adieu (we'll rant and we'll roar): *Fishermen's Group* / Liverpool packet: *Barber, Bill* / Little boy billee: *Roberts, A.V. 'Bob'* / Johnny Todd: *Roberts, A.V. 'Bob'* / Banks of Claudy: *Copper, Bob & Ron* / Bold Princess Royal: *Roberts, A.V. 'Bob'* / Jack Tarr on the shore: *Cox, Harry* / Smuggler's boy: *Roberts, A.V. 'Bob'* / Smackman: *Brown, Tom* / Hanging Johnny: *Roberts, A.V. 'Bob'*
CD _____ **CDSDL 405**
Saydisc / Feb '94 / Harmonia Mundi / ADA / Direct.

SEALED WITH A KISS
CD _____ **MPV 5549**
Movieplay / Jun '95 / Target/BMG.

SEALED WITH A KISS
Ginny come lately: *West, Albert* / When will I see you again: *Three Degrees* / Kiss and say goodbye: *Manhattans* / White star: *Earth, Wind & Fire* / Longer: *Fogelberg, Dan* / Sylvia's mother: *Dr. Hook* / Ain't no sunshine: *Withers, Bill* / Me and Mrs Jones: *Paul, Billy* / Most beautiful girl: *Rich, Charlie* / How 'bout us: *Champaign* / When I need you: *Hammond, Albert* / Blue velvet: *Vinton, Bobby* / Albatross: *Fleetwood Mac* / Arms of Mary: *Sutherland Brothers & Quiver* / Young girl: *Puckett, Gary & The Union Gap* / Greenfields: *Brothers Four*
CD _____ **4804502**
Embassy / Oct '95 / Sony.

SEASONS IN THE SUN
CD Set _____ **NSCD 014**
Newsound / Feb '95 / THE.

SECRET LIFE OF TRANCE
CD _____ **RSNCD 6**
Rising High / May '93 / Disc.

SECRET LIFE OF TRANCE 3
CD Set _____ **RSNCD 20**
Rising High / Jul '94 / Disc.

SECRET LIFE OF TRANCE 4
CD Set _____ **RSNCD 28**
Rising High / Dec '94 / Disc.

SECRET LIFE OF TRANCE 5
CD _____ **RSNCD 34**
Rising High / May '95 / Disc.

SECRET LIFE OF TRANCE 6
CD Set _____ **RSNCD 6**
Rising High / Aug '95 / Disc.

SECRET LOVERS
Secret lovers: *Atlantic Starr* / Saving all my love for you: *Houston, Whitney* / Have you seen her: *Chi-Lites* / Jealous guy: *Roxy Music* / Who's that girl: *Eurythmics* / Me and Mrs. Jones: *Paul, Billy* / Walking in the rain with the one I love: *White, Barry* / Baby, come to me: *Austin, Patti & James Ingram* / So amazing: *Vandross, Luther* / How can we be lovers: *Bolton, Michael* / Unchained melody: *Righteous Brothers* / Careless whisper: *Michael, George* / Sweet surrender: *Wet Wet Wet* / Nikita: *John, Elton* / I'll never fall in love again: *Deacon Blue* / Cuts both ways: *Estefan, Gloria* / Suspicious minds: *Fine Young Cannibals* / Don't know much: *Ronstadt, Linda & Aaron Neville*
CD _____ **SETVCD 4**
Columbia / Feb '94 / Sony.

SECRET MUSEUM OF MANKIND VOL.1
CD _____ **YAZCD 7004**
Yazoo / Oct '95 / CM / ADA / Roots / Koch.

SECRET MUSEUM OF MANKIND VOL.2
CD _____ **YAZCD 7005**
Yazoo / Oct '95 / CM / ADA / Roots / Koch.

SECRET POLICEMAN'S THIRD BALL
(The music)
Running up that hill: *Bush, Kate & David Gilmour* / Save a prayer: *Duran Duran* / Voices of freedom: *Reed, Lou* / This is the world calling: *Geldof, Bob* / For everyman: *Browne, Jackson* / Victim of love: *Erasure* / Wouldn't it be good: *Kershaw, Nik* / (I love it when you) call me names: *Armatrading, Joan* / Imagine: *Knopfler, Mark & Chet Atkins* / Biko: *Gabriel, Peter* / Ship of fools: *World Party*
CD _____ **CDV 2458**
Virgin / Sep '87 / EMI.

SECRET RECORDS PUNK SINGLES COLLECTION
Dogs of war: *Exploited* / Army life: *Exploited* / Exploited barmy army: *Exploited* / Kids of the 80's: *Infa Riot* / One law for them: *4 Skins* / Dead cities: *Exploited* / Harry May: *Business* / Yesterday's heroes: *4 Skins* / Jet boy jet girl: *Chron Gen* / Attack exploited: *Chron Gen* / I lost my love to a U.K. sub: *Gonads* / Punk city rockers: *Gonads* / Smash the discos: *Business* / H-Bomb: *Business* / T.O.P.: *Exploited* / Computers don't blunder: *Exploited* / Troops of tomorrow: *Exploited* / Feel the rage: *Infa Riot* / Clouded eyes: *Chron Gen* / Outlaw: *Chron*

sical science: *Musical Science* / Vega God: *Jack Of Swords* / Crash bang: *Conemelt*
CD ______________ SOPCD 001
Sabres Of Paradise / Sep '94 / Vital.

SERGEANT SALT & OTHER CONDIMENTS
Venus in furs: *Velvet Underground* / Paper sun: *Traffic* / This wheel's on fire: *Driscoll, Julie & Brian Auger* / Flight from Ashiya: *Kaleidoscope* / Desiree: *Left Banke* / Spin spin spin: *HP Lovecraft* / Gungami: *Quintessence* / San Francisco nights: *Burdon, Eric & The Animals* / Fire: *Crazy World Of Arthur Brown* / Rainbow chaser: *Nirvana* / Beeside: *Tintern Abbey* / Stepping stone: *Flies* / Evil woman: *Spooky Tooth* / (We ain't got) Nothin' yet: *Blues Magoos*
CD ______________ 5501232
Spectrum/Karussell / Oct '93 / PolyGram / THE.

SERIOUS GROOVES
(Detroit's Finest)
I wanna go higher: *Seven Grand Housing Authority* / Woman: *Younger Than Park* / Take it higher: *Disco Revisited* / I can't stop: *Low Key* / Blow your whistle: *Jovan Blade* / Dusk: *Afrodisiac* / Try me baby: *Low Key* / Find sum one new: *Black, Donna* / We got a love: *T.H.D.* / Feeling: *D.J. Tone* / Dialogue: *T.H.D.* / Can't turn back: *Younger Than Park* / Shante: *Jovan Blade* / Witness: *Disco Revisited* / Rainforest: *Low Key* / Pleasure baby: *Alton M* / You took my love: *Plastic Soul Junkies* / Dedication to Joss / Brewster's project: *Younger Than Park*
CD ______________ SGCD 1
Network / Dec '93 / Sony / 3MV.

SERIOUS LISTENING MUSIC VOL.1
CD ______________ DELSDC 1
Delirium / Jan '94 / Plastic Head.

SERIOUS LISTENING MUSIC VOL.2
CD ______________ DELSCD 02
Delirium / Jun '94 / Plastic Head.

SERIOUS REGGAE ALBUM VOLUME 2, THE
CD ______________ CDSGP 0141
Prestige / Aug '95 / Total/BMG.

SERIOUS REGGAE ALBUM VOLUME 3, THE
CD Set ______________ CDSGP 077
Prestige / Jul '94 / Total/BMG.

SERVE CHILLED
Mr. Wendal: *Arrested Development* / Summertime: *D.J. Jazzy Jeff & The Fresh Prince* / Manchild: *Cherry, Neneh* / Ghetto jam: *Domino* / Set adrift on memory bliss: *PM Dawn* / Karmacoma: *Massive Attack* / Rebirth of slick: *Digable Planets* / Spiritual love: *Urban Species* / Eye know: *De La Soul* / Gotta lotta love: *Ice-T* / It was a good day: *Ice Cube* / Can I kick it: *Tribe Called Quest* / Feel me flow: *Naughty By Nature* / I'll be around: *Rappin' 4-Tay* / In the summertime: *Shaggy* / Save it 'til the morning after: *Shut Up & Dance* / My definition of a bombastic jazz style: *Dream Warriors* / That's how I'm livin': *Ice-T* / I need love: *L.L. Cool J* / People everyday: *Arrested Development*
CD ______________ VTCD 56
Virgin / Aug '95 / EMI.

SERVICE BANDS ON THE AIR VOL. 1
Flying home: *Miller, Glenn & The Army Air-force Orchestra* / I couldn't sleep a wink last night: *Skyrockets* / Barrel house boogie: *Skyrockets* / On the sunny side of the street: *Skyrockets* / Swinging on a star: *Skyrockets* / March of the toys: *Canada Dance Band* / It's love love love: *Royal Air Force Dance Orchestra* / Leapfrog: *Royal Air Force Dance Orchestra* / I'll get by: *Royal Air Force Dance Orchestra* / Milkman keep those bottles quiet: *Royal Air Force Dance Orchestra* / Dear old southland: *Royal Air Force Dance Orchestra* / I can't give you anything but love: *U.S. Navy Dance Band* / LST party: *U.S. Navy Dance Band* / With my head in the clouds: *Miller, Glenn & AAF Band* / No compree: *Miller, Glenn & AAF Band* / Lark leaps in: *Royal Marines Commando Forces Band* / Wartime medley: *Canadian Army Radio Orchestra* / Out of this world: *Canadian Army Radio Orchestra* / More than you know: *Royal Army Ordanance Corps Dance Orchestra* / Mr. Ghost goes to town: *Royal Navy Swing Octet* / With a song in my heart: *British Band Of The AEF*
CD ______________ VJB 19442
Vintage Jazz Band / May '94 / Wellard / Cadillac.

SERVICE BANDS ON THE AIR VOL. 2
(V.E. Day Party)
Introduction / Music makers / Let's get lost / Dance with a dolly / My blue heaven / Long ago and far away / Jumpin' Jiminy / Angry / I'm beginning to see the light / Holiday for strings / My heart isn't in it / Introduction (2) / African war dance / All this and heaven too / Down for double / Comedy routine / Jazz me blues / What a difference a day makes / My heart tells me / Woodchopper's ball / Tess's torch song / Way down yonder in New Orleans / I'll be seeing you / When Johnny comes marching home
CD ______________ VJB 19462
Vintage Jazz Band / May '95 / Wellard / Cadillac.

SEVENTIES - A VERY SPECIAL COLLECTION, THE
(3CD Set)
Baby don't change your mind: *Knight, Gladys* / This is it: *Moore, Melba* / Rapper's delight: *Sugarhill Gang* / Now is the time: *James, Jimmy & The Vagabonds* / Where did our love go: *Elbert, Donnie* / Kung fu fighting: *Douglas, Carl* / In the summertime: *Mungo Jerry* / Shooting star: *Dollar* / Light fight: *Pentangle* / Mirrors: *Oldfield, Sally* / Sunshine day: *Osbisa* / Isn't she lovely: *Patron, David* / Lola: *Kinks* / Can't be without you: *Real Thing* / More, more, more: *Andrea True Connection* / Midnight trip to Georgia: *Knight, Gladys & The Pips* / Girls: *Moments* / Who do you love: *Juicy Lucy* / This flight tonight: *Nazareth* / Bomber: *Motorhead* / Boston tea party: *Harvey, Alex Sensational Band* / Roadrunner: *Richman, Jonathan & Modern Lovers* / I saw the light: *Rundgren, Todd* / Overkill: *Motorhead* / In my chair: *Status Quo* / Long legged woman dressed in black: *Mungo Jerry* / Paranoid: *Black Sabbath* / Strange band: *Family* / Bad bad boy: *Nazareth* / Lost in France: *Tyler, Bonnie* / Dellilah: *Harvey, Alex Sensational Band* / Mean girl: *Status Quo* / No class: *Motorhead* / Broken down angel: *Nazareth* / Burlesque: *Family* / I'm the leader of the gang (I am): *Glitter, Gary* / 20th Century boy: *T. Rex* / Angel face: *Glitter Band* / Son of my father: *Chicory Tip* / Do you wanna dance: *Blue, Barry* / Tell him: *Hello* / Sky high: *Jigsaw* / Telegram Sam: *T. Rex* / I love you love me love: *Glitter, Gary* / Rubber bullets: *10cc* / Dancin' (on a saturday night): *Blue, Barry* / New York grove: *Hello* / LL Lucy: *Mud* / Goodbye my love: *Glitter Band* / Metal guru: *T. Rex*
CD Set ______________ BOXD 52T
Old Gold / Oct '95 / Carlton Home Entertainment.

SEVENTIES MIXES
CD ______________ JHD 086
Tring / Mar '93 / Tring / Prism.

SEVENTIES ROCK
CD ______________ CDSR 055
Telstar / Feb '95 / BMG.

SEX OF IT, THE
Sex of it: *Kid Creole & The Coconuts* / Mr. Loverman: *Shabba Ranks* / Move to love: *B.G. The Prince Of Rap* / Things that make you go hmmmm: *C & C Music Factory* / Tonight and forever: *Simon, Carly* / Lady Marmalade: *Labelle, Patti* / Sex drive: *Isley-Jasper-Isley* / Love doctor: *Miracles* / I want to spend the night: *Withers, Bill* / I know you want to: *Vandross, Luther* / I still haven't found what I'm looking for: *Chimes* / Fire: *Mother's Finest* / Love attack: *Hayes, Isaac* / God only knows: *Tzuke, Judie* / Keep on loving you: *REO Speedwagon* / We're all alone: *Scaggs, Boz*
CD ______________ 4758272
Embassy / Oct '95 / Sony.

SEXTETOS CUBANOS VOL.1
CD ______________ FL 7003
Folklyric / Apr '95 / Direct / Cadillac.

SEXTETOS CUBANOS VOL.2
CD ______________ ARHCD 7006
Arhoolie / Sep '95 / ADA / Direct / Cadillac.

SHACK, THE
CD ______________ DOJOCD 145
Dojo / Sep '93 / BMG.

SHAKE 'EM ON DOWN
Shake 'em on down / Sloppy drunk blues / Alabama blues / Need more blues / Judge bushay blues / Pardon denied again / Rabbit blues / Take me out of the bottom / Fred's worried life blues / Poor black Mattie / Come home to me baby / Smokestack lightnin' / Write me a few lines / Mississippi river / Just tippin' in / She left me a mule to ride / Canned heat / Three o'clock in the morning / 'Bout a spoonful / You call yourself a cadillac / Keep your nose out of my business / Oh baby
CD ______________ CDCHD 527
Ace / Oct '94 / Pinnacle / Cadillac / Complete/Pinnacle.

SHAKE, JUMP, SHOUT
Hold me back (remix): *West Bam* / Callas: *Vox Mystica* / Heavy mental: *Heavy Mental* / Saxophone: *West Bam* / Exzess: *Dick* / Alarm clock: *West Bam* / Time: *Beat In Time* / On a mission: *Dick* / Hell or heaven: *L.U.P.O* / Dreams: *Darling, Grace* / Is it raw enough: *Heavy Mental* / Aka aka: *Eastbam*
CD ______________ YOBCD 1
Yobro / Jun '90 / Total/BMG.

SHAKE, RATTLE AND ROLL
CD ______________ 3001172
Scratch / Jul '95 / BMG.

SHAKE THAT THING
(America's Top Bands Of The 20's)
I wanna be loved by you: *Broadway Nitelites* / Shakin' the blues away: *Selvin, Ben & His Orchestra* / Hello Swanee, hello: *Lentz, Al & His Orchestra* / Mighty blue: *Waring's Pennsylvanians* / What a day: *Weems, Ted & His Orchestra* / Melancholy Lou: *Lanin, Howard & His Ben Franklin Dance Orchestra* / Confessin': *Lombardo, Guy & His Royal Canadians* / Shake that thing: *Lyman, Abe & His California Orchestra* / Everything's made for love: *Lopez, Vincent & His Orchestra* / Wabash blues: *Charleston Chasers* / Smile: *Whiteman, Paul & His Orchestra* / Let's misbehave: *Aaronson, Irving & His Commanders* / Just a night for meditation: *Crumit, Frank* / Bugle call rag: *Lewis, Ted & His Band* / S'posin': *Vallee, Rudy & His Connecticut Yankies* / He's the last word: *Bernie, Ben & His Hotel Roosevelt Orchestra*
CD ______________ CDAJA 5002
Living Era / Apr '89 / Koch.

SHAKE YOUR BOOTY
CD ______________ RMB 75033
Remember / Nov '93 / Total/BMG.

SHAMANARCHY IN THE UK
CD ______________ EVO 002CD
Evolution / Jul '92 / Pinnacle.

SHAMROCK AND THISTLE
CD ______________ PLATCD 336
Platinum Music / Jul '92 / Prism / Ross.

SHARKS PATROL THESE WATERS
Super glider: *Drugstore* / Wake up: *Love Spit Love* / Black sheep boy: *Weller, Paul* / Barney (and me): *Boo Radleys* / Pyrotechnician: *Sleeper* / To see the lights: *Gene* / Fake: *Echobelly* / Oily water: *Blur* / Soft: *Elastica* / White belly: *Belly* / Safari: *Breeders* / Vow: *Garbage* / Smile: *Spiritualized* / Stupid car: *Radiohead* / Some velvet morning: *Slowdive* / Only now: *Ride* / Roland navigator: *Madder Rose* / Wheels: *Lanegan, Mark* / Sharks patrol these waters: *Morphine* / Her: *Tindersticks* / Ruby: *Gallon Drunk* / Odio-amor, odio-amor: *Adamson, Barry* / Frosty the snowman: *Cocteau Twins* / Skin diving 1-2-3-4: *James* / Fake '88: *St. Etienne* / Lip tripping: *The The* / Firepile: *Throwing Muses* / My house: *Terrorvision* / Machine drug: *Jesus Jones* / PCP: *Manic Street Preachers* / I believe: *EMF* / Hetero scum: *Sugarcubes* / Innocent X: *Therapy* / Arid Al's dream: *Fall* / She's dead: *Pulp* / My insatiable one: *Suede* / Bailed out: *Auteurs* / Zoo'd out: *Strangelove* / Little girl blue: *Afghan Whigs* / How: *Cranberries* / Super falling star: *Stereolab* / Tinkerbell: *Lush* / Belt: *Teenage Fanclub* / Fuck off: *Mindless Drug Hoover*
CD Set ______________ BOVCD 2
Volume / May '95 / Total/BMG / Vital.

SHAWMS FROM NE CHINA 1
CD ______________ 926132 CD
Buda / Jul '95 / Discovery / ADA.

SHAWMS FROM NE CHINA 2
CD ______________ 926122 CD
Buda / Jul '95 / Discovery / ADA.

SH'BOOM, SH'BOOM
Book of love: *Monotones* / Boy from New York City: *Ad Libs* / Sincerely: *Moonglows* / Oh what a night: *Dells* / Sixteen candles: *Crests* / Goodnight sweetheart, goodnight: *Spaniels* / Duke of Earl: *Chandler, Gene* / Hasppy, happy birthday baby: *Tune Weavers* / Come go with me: *Del-Vikings* / At my front door: *El Dorado* / Since I don't have you: *Skyliners* / Once in a while: *Chimes* / Sea of love: *Phillips, Phil & Twilights* / It's in his kiss (Shoop shoop song): *Everett, Betty* / My true story: *Jive Five* / Long lonely nights: *Andrews, Lee* / Over and over: *Day, Bobby* / For all we know: *Orioles* / Mr. Sandman: *Chordettes* / Alley oop: *Hollywood Argyles*
CD ______________ MCCD 091
Music Club / May '92 / Disc / THE / CM.

SHEEN
CD Set ______________ KK 141CD
KK / Oct '95 / Plastic Head.

SHENANIGANS VOLUME 1
(33 Irish Jigs And Reels)
CD ______________ SOV 023CD
Sovereign / Jun '94 / Target/BMG.

SHERBET-LICK IT
CD ______________ REACTCDX 057
CD ______________ REACTCD 057
React / Feb '95 / Vital.

SHESHWE: SOUNDS OF THE MINES
CD ______________ CD 5031
Rounder / '88 / CM / Direct / ADA / Cadillac.

SHETLAND SESSIONS VOL. 1, THE
CD ______________ LCOM 7021
Lismor / Mar '92 / Lismor / Direct / Duncans / ADA.

SHETLAND SESSIONS VOL. 2, THE
CD ______________ LCOM 7022
Lismor / Mar '92 / Lismor / Direct / Duncans / ADA.

SHINE
Parklife: *Blur* / Cigarettes and alcohol: *Oasis* / Regret: *New Order* / Zombie: *Cranberries* / Animal nitrate: *Suede* / Connection: *Elastica* / Do you remember the first time: *Pulp* / So let me go far: *Dodgy* / Speakeasy: *Shed Seven* / Welcome to paradise: *Green Day* / How soon is now: *Smiths* / Sit down: *James* / Getting away with it: *Electronic* / Size of a cow: *Wonder Stuff* / Altogether now: *Farm* / Dragging me down: *Inspiral Carpets* / Weirdo: *Charlatans* / International bright young thing: *Jesus Jones* / Feel the pain: *Dinosaur Jnr* / Shine on: *House Of Love*
CD ______________ 5255672
PolyGram / May '95 / PolyGram.

SHINE 2
CD ______________ 5258582
PolyGram / Aug '95 / PolyGram.

SHINE 3
CD ______________ 5259652
PolyGram / Oct '95 / PolyGram.

SHINE EYE GAL - BRUKDON FROM BELIZE
CD ______________ CO 118CD
Corason / May '94 / CM / Direct / ADA.

SHOCKS OF MIGHTY (1969-74)
Pound get a blow: *Upsetters* / No bread and butter: *Morris, Milton* / Tackro: *Upsetters* / Set me free: *Barker, Dave* / Shocks of mighty: *Barker, Dave & Upsetters* / Dark moon: *Upsetters* / Civilization: *Classics* / French Connection (chapter 2): *Upsetters* / Black mans time: *Grant, Neville* / Three blind mice: *Graham, Leo* / Three times three: *King Tubby & The Upsetters* / Be thankful: *Clarke, Bunny* / Dubbing in the back seat: *Upsetters* / Woman's gotta have it: *Riley, Jimmy* / Gotta have dub: *Upsetters* / Move out of my way: *Clarke, Bunny* / Move out dub: *Upsetters*
CD ______________ CDAT 104
Attack / May '94 / Jetstar / Total/BMG.

SHOOP SHOOP: SOUTHERN DOO WOP
Shoop shoop: *Gladiolas* / Love you love you love you: *Marigolds* / Won't you let me know: *King Krooners* / Now that she's gone: *King Krooners* / Be bop baby: *Peacheroos* / Little darlin': *Gladiolas* / Love love baby: *Rhythm Casters* / Don't say tomorrow: *Marigolds* / Pretty little girl: *King Krooners* / Memoirs: *King Krooners & Little Rico* / My china doll: *Glad Rags* / Be bop girl: *Gladiolas* / Hey little girl: *Gladiolas* / Rollin' stone: *Marigolds* / There's been a change: *King Krooners* / Sweetheart please don't go: *Gladiolas* / School daze: *King Krooners* / Playboy lover: *King Krooners* / Everyday my love is true: *Peacheroos* / Two strangers: *Marigolds* / Oh my darling: *Rhythm Casters* / Just one love: *Glad Rags* / Don't ever get married: *Meloaires* / Indebted to you: *Meloaires*
CD ______________ CDCHD 529
Ace / Jun '95 / Pinnacle / Cadillac / Complete/Pinnacle.

SHOULD I STAY OR SHOULD I GO
CD ______________ HILOCD 12
Hi / Jan '95 / Pinnacle.

SHOUT AND SCREAM
CD ______________ DRCD 001
Detour / Jul '95 / Detour.

SHOUT BROTHER SHOUT
CD ______________ AL 2800
Alligator / Jul '94 / Direct / ADA.

SHOUT IT OUT 1946-1952
CD ______________ RST 915792
RST / Jun '94 / Jazz Music / Hot Shot.

SHOUT THE FUTURE TRIBE
CD ______________ CDACV 2005
ACV / Jun '95 / Plastic Head / SRD.

SHOUTING THE BLUES
Adam bit the apple: *Turner, Big Joe* / Still in the dark: *Turner, Big Joe* / Feelin' happy: *Turner, Big Joe* / Midnight is here again AKA Dawn is breakin' through: *Turner, Big Joe* / I want my baby (When the rooster crows): *Turner, Big Joe* / Life is a card game: *Turner, Big Joe* / After a while you'll be sorry: *Turner, Big Joe* / Just a travellin' man: *Turner, Big Joe* / Big city blues: *Big Maceo* / Do you remember: *Big Maceo* / Just tell me baby: *Big Maceo* / One Sunday morning: *Big Maceo* / State street boogie: *Johnson, Don Orchestra* / Jackson's blues: *Johnson, Don Orchestra* / Chesterfield baby: *Johnson, Don Orchestra* / Lonesome lover blues: *Smilin' Smokey Lynn* / Run rabbit run: *Smilin' Smokey Lynn* / Feel like ballin' tonight: *Smilin' Smokey Lynn* / Rock-a-bye baby: *Smilin' Smokey Lynn* / Hometown baby (Hip Cat): *Smilin' Smokey Lynn* / She's been gone: *H-Bomb Ferguson* / You made me baby: *H-Bomb Ferguson*
CD ______________ CDCHD 439
Ace / Jan '93 / Pinnacle / Cadillac / Complete/Pinnacle.

SHOVE IT
My man, a sweet man: *Jackson, Millie* / Night fever: *Fatback Band* / Can you get to that: *Funkadelic* / Pain: *Ohio Players* / Baby let me take you (in my arms): *Detroit Emeralds* / Man size job: *Lasalle, Denise* / Keep on stepping: *Fatback Band* / Get down, get down (get on the floor): *Simon, Joe* / Pleasure: *Ohio Players* / It's all over but the shouting: *Jackson, Millie* / Funky dollar bill: *Funkadelic*
CD ______________ CDSEWX 01
Westbound / Oct '89 / Pinnacle.

SHOW GIRLS
CD Set ______________ YDG 251
Movieplay / Oct '92 / Target/BMG.

SHOWCASE VOL. 1
(Scientific Master Mix)
CD ______________ MLCD 00
Mixing Lab / Jul '90 / Jetstar.

SHOWCASE VOL. 2
(Master Mix)
CD _____ MLCD 003
Mixing Lab / Jul '90 / Jetstar.

SHREVEPORT STOMP
Ba Da: Perkins, Roy / Red beans and rice: Scatman Patin / Cheater's can't win: Lewis, Margaret / Flat foot Sam: TV Slim / Mailman mailman: Williamson, Sonny Boy / Come back Betty: Steel, L.C. / I'm leaving: Brannon, Jimmy / Drop top (TK1): Perkins, Roy / Reconsider me: Lewis, Margaret / Hippy Ti Yo: Page, Bobby / Wherever you are: Brannon, Linda / Pow wow: Tennessee, Grace / Let me feel it: Brown, Elgie / Girl in the street: Williams, Vince / Ginning: Scatman Patin / Baby please forgive me: Webb, Troy / What did you do last night: Rocky Robin & the Riff Raffs / Night creature: Run-a-ways / Anyway you do: Brannon, Linda / Eager boy: Lonesome Drifter / Lonesome heart: Hunter, Charlotte / El Rancho Grande Rock: Starmakers / Lover's land: Walker, Ernest / Louisiana twist: Bailey, June Bug
CD _____ CDCHD 495
Ace / Jun '94 / Pinnacle / Cadillac / Complete/Pinnacle.

SHRINE
CD _____ CSR 4 CD
Trident / Jun '93 / Pinnacle.

SHUFFLIN' ON BOND STREET
CD _____ CDTRL 275
Trojan / Aug '94 / Jetstar / Total/BMG.

SHUT UP AND PLAY YER BLUES
CD _____ MCCD 216
Music Club / Oct '95 / Disc / THE / CM.

SI SAFAA
(New Music From The Middle East)
Ghallo Tara: Ahmed, Hamid / Aguluk: Khairy, Saleh / Anta Al Hakam: Sahir, Kazim Al / Matajarahmish: Hanan / Nami: Ayubi, Aida / Sif Safaa: Mounir, Mohamed / Khafet Dhamon: Fouad, Mohamed / Tasadig Wala Ahliflak: Ahmed, Hamdi / Leh Alkhiyana: Hilal, Abu / Ya Leyl A'ah: Hanan / Hawad: Fouad, Mohamed / Alashan Al Malih: Khairy, Saleh
CD _____ CDEMC 3700
EMI / Mar '95 / EMI.

SICK, SICK, SICK
Vibrate: Demented Are Go / Human slug: Demented Are Go / Cast iron arm: Demented Are Go / PVC chair: Demented Are Go / Rubber buccaneer: Demented Are Go / Pervy in the park: Demented Are Go / Rubber love: Demented Are Go / Holy hack Jack: Demented Are Go / Love is for skitzos: Skitzo / I want your lovin': Skitzo / Possessed: Coffin Nails / Werewolf bitch: Coffin Nails / Natural born lover: Coffin Nails / Uncle Willy: Coffin Nails / Wind up dead: Coffin Nails
CD _____ DOJOCD 23
Dojo / Feb '94 / BMG.

SIGNED, SEALED, DELIVERED - 1
Geek U.S.A.: Smashing Pumpkins / Body Count's in the house: Body Count / Real surreal: SMASH / Pinch: Acetone / No honestly: Urban Dance Squad / Shamrock: Daryl-Ann / Wild America: Iggy Pop / Jobs for the boys: These Animal Men / Butterfly: Verve / Street scene: Bark Psychosis / God's green earth: Idaho / Challenger: American Music Club / Sister like you: Auteurs / What are you: Grey, David / Movie star: Cracker / Unworthy (Edit): Thieves
CD _____ VVSAM 21
Virgin / Jun '94 / EMI.

SIGNED, SEALED, DELIVERED - 2
Crashin' the system: Brotherhood / Mr. Businessman green: Anderson, Carleen / Home of the whale: Massive Attack / Boom bastic: Shaggy / Push: Loose Ends / Gotta lotta love (Tubular Bells edit): Ice-T / You the man: Shyheim / No groove sweatin' (A funky space reincarnation): McWilliams, Brigette / Moment of truth: College Boyz / Bring me home: Future Sound Of London / Subliminal aura: Amorphous Androgynous / G.Feel.8.the popsicle: Popsicle / Drippin' wit lust: Knuckles, Frankie / Speaking in tongues III: Chandra, Sheila
CD _____ VVSAM 23
Virgin / Jun '94 / EMI.

SIGNED, SEALED, DELIVERED - 3
Survival in the wind: Belew, Adrian / Same changes: Phillips, Sam / When you smile: Foly, Liane / Come to the water: Sanne / Leave the ground: Duke / Y'a d'la haine: Mitsouko, Rita / Girl I love you: Douglas, Sian / Let it come your way: Six Was Nine / Is this a broken heart: Ruffelle, Frances / Life's funny: Robillard, Duke / More and more: Jumpin' The Gunn / Waiting on an angel: Harper, Ben / Brown dirt: Cale, J.J. / That's the way love turned out for me: Evans, Terry / Here to there: Nyman, Michael / Virgin 21: Wainwright III, Loudon
CD _____ VVSAM 24
Virgin / Jun '94 / EMI.

SILK & STEEL
I found someone: Cher / Night in my veins: Pretenders / Independent love song: Scarlet / Heaven is a place on earth: Carlisle, Belinda / Walking on broken glass: Lennox, Annie / Look: Roxette / Whole world lost its head: Go-Go's / Change of heart: Lauper, Cyndi / We belong: Benatar, Pat / Total eclipse of the heart: Tyler, Bonnie / Rubber band girl: Bush, Kate / Mandinka: O'Connor, Sinead / I touch myself: Divinyls / Crash: Primitives / You're history: Shakespears Sister / Hazy shade of winter: Bangles / Rush hour: Wiedlin, Jane / What I am: Brickell, Edie & New Bohemians / Self control: Branigan, Laura / Baby I don't care: Transvision Vamp
CD _____ 5255692
PolyGram / May '95 / PolyGram.

SILLY SYMPHONIES
CD _____ 70700271363
Essential Dance Music / Nov '95 / Disc.

SILOS AND UTILITY SHEDS
CD _____ GRCD 361
Hypertension / Apr '95 / Total/BMG / Direct / ADA.

SIMON BATES - THE 50'S
Sweet little sixteen: Berry, Chuck / Rave on: Holly, Buddy & The Crickets / Bo Diddley: Diddley, Bo / Rock-a-beatin' boogie: Haley, Bill & The Comets / Born too late: Poni-Tails / Heartbeak: Holly, Buddy & The Crickets / Maybellene: Berry, Chuck / Rock 'n' roll is here to stay: Danny & The Juniors / Oh boy: Holly, Buddy & The Crickets / Hey Bo Diddley: Diddley, Bo / Rockin' through the Rye: Haley, Bill & The Comets / I'm gonna sit right down and write myself a letter: Williams, Billy / Personality: Price, Lloyd / School days: Berry, Chuck
CD _____ PWKS 549
Carlton Home Entertainment / Oct '89 / Carlton Home Entertainment.

SIMON BATES - THE 50'S VOL.2
Great pretender: Platters / Lipstick on your collar: Francis, Connie / Moulin Rouge theme: Mantovani / Giddy up a ding dong: Bell, Freddy & The Bellboys / Broken hearted melody: Vaughan, Sarah / Whole lotta woman: Rainwater, Marvin / Margo: Fury, Billy / Sh-boom: Crew Cuts / Limelight: Chacksfield, Frank / Singin' the blues: Steele, Tommy / It's all in the game: Edwards, Tommy / Passing strangers: Eckstine, Billy & Sarah Vaughan / Rock Island line: Donegan, Lonnie / Memories are made of this: King, Dave / Maybe tomorrow: Fury, Billy / Teenager in love: Wilde, Marty / Earth angel: Crew Cuts / Stupid cupid: Francis, Connie / Chantilly lace: Big Bopper / Smoke gets in your eyes: Platters
CD _____ PWKS 591
Carlton Home Entertainment / Jul '90 / Carlton Home Entertainment.

SIMON BATES - THE 60'S
Delilah: Jones, Tom / Here it comes again: Fortunes / Little things: Berry, Dave / I only want to be with you: Springfield, Dusty / Do you love me: Poole, Brian & The Tremeloes / Tell me when: Applejacks / You've got your troubles: Fortunes / It's not unusual: Jones, Tom / Crying game: Berry, Dave / Yeh yeh: Fame, Georgie & The Australian Blue Flames / It's only make believe: Fury, Billy / Juliet: Four Pennies
CD _____ PWKS 556
Carlton Home Entertainment / Oct '89 / Carlton Home Entertainment.

SIMON BATES - THE 60'S VOL.2
Sha la la lee: Small Faces / I love my dog: Stevens, Cat / Lightning strikes: Christie, Lou / In thoughts of you: Fury, Billy / What's new pussycat: Jones, Tom / Gin house blues: Amen Corner / Candy man: Poole, Brian & The Tremeloes / I feel like a predise: Fury, Billy / Get away: Fame, Georgie & The Blue Flames / Stay awhile: Springfield, Dusty / It's a man's man's world: Brown, James / Girl from Ipanema: Getz, Stan & Astrud Gilberto / Anyway that you want me: Troggs / Summer nights: Faithfull, Marianne / Island of dreams: Springfields / Sunny: Fame, Georgie
CD _____ PWKS 581
Carlton Home Entertainment / May '90 / Carlton Home Entertainment.

SIMON BATES - THE 70'S
Hallelujah freedom: Campbell, Junior / Sugar baby love: Rubettes / One and one is one: Medicine Head / I'm on fire: 5000 Volts / United we stand: Brotherhood Of Man / Walkin' miracle: Limmie & Family Cooking / Don't stay away too long: Peters & Lee / You're a lady: Skellern, Peter / Jukebox jive: Rubettes / You can do magic: Limmie & Family Cooking / Montego Bay: Bloom, Bobby / Dancing with the captain: Nicholas, Paul / High fly: Miles, John / Fisu gun: Medicine Head / My baby loves lovin': White Plains / Welcome home: Peters & Lee
CD _____ PWKS 550
Carlton Home Entertainment / Oct '89 / Carlton Home Entertainment.

SIMON BATES - THE 70'S VOL.2
Rat trap: Boomtown Rats / Angel: Stewart, Rod / Love's theme: Love Unlimited Orchestra / I'm your puppet: Purify, James & Bobby / Reunited: Peaches & Herb / Uptown, uptempo woman: Edelman, Randy / Standing in the road: Blackfoot Sue / What a wonderful world: White, Barry / You wear it well: Stewart, Rod / Crocodile rock: John, Elton / Like clockwork: Boomtown Rats / Radancer: Marmalade / Shuffle: McCoy, Van / Betcha by golly wow: Stylistics / I got the music in me: Dee, Kiki / Giving it all away: Daltrey, Roger
CD _____ PWKS 592
Carlton Home Entertainment / Jul '90 / Carlton Home Entertainment.

SIMON BATES' PARTY ALBUM
(We're gonna) Rock around the clock: Haley, Bill & The Comets / Great balls of fire: Lewis, Jerry Lee / Singin' the blues: Mitchell, Guy / Yes tonight Josephine: Ray, Johnnie / Bye bye love: Everly Brothers / At the hop: Danny & The Juniors / When: Kalin Twins / C'mon everybody: Cochran, Eddie / It's late: Nelson, Rick / Teenager in love: Wilde, Marty / Hound dog: Presley, Elvis / Lollipop: Mudlarks / Hard day's night: Beatles / I only want to be with you: Springfield, Dusty / It's my party: Stewart, Dave & Barbara Gaskin / Locomotion: Little Eva / Needles and pins: Searchers / Just one look: Hollies / Downtown: Clark, Petula / Mr. Tambourine man: Byrds / San Francisco: Mackenzie, Scott / Monday, Monday: Mamas & Papas / Onion song: Gaye, Marvin
CD _____ PWKS 563
Carlton Home Entertainment / Dec '89 / Carlton Home Entertainment.

SIN ALLEY
CD _____ E 11564CD
Crypt / Mar '93 / SRD.

SING DE CHORUS
Country club scandal / Madame Khan / Songs of long ago / Dew and rain / Worker's plea / St. Peter's day / Black market / Leave me alone Dorothy / Ugly woman - trouble and misery / Los crios / Gold in Africa / Treasury scandal / Reign too long / Louise / Graf Zeppelin / Adolf Hitler / Love me or matilda / Money is king / Victory calypso / Coldness of the water / Let the white people fight / Sedition law / Mother's love / Woman called Dorothy / Tribute to executor / Sing de chorus
CD _____ DE 4018
Delos / Feb '94 / Conifer.

SING FOR YOUR SUPPER
CD _____ AVC 529
Avid / Nov '93 / Avid/BMG / Koch.

SING ME A SWING SONG
Troubled waters: Anderson, Ivie / Thanks a million: Armstrong, Louis / More than you know: Bailey, Mildred / What'd ja do to me: Boswell Sisters / I let a song go out of my heart: Boswell, Connie / Zaz zul zaz: Calloway, Cab / Don't try your live on me: Carlisle, Una Mae / Louisiana: Crosby, Bing / When I grow too old to dream: Dandridge, Putney / Ten cents a dance: Etting, Ruth / Sing me a swing song: Fitzgerald, Ella / Loveable and sweet: Hanshaw, Annette / 1-2 Button your shoe: Holiday, Billie / Thursday: Humes, Helen / Isle of Capri: Manone, Wingy / Three little words: Rhythm Boys / I just couldn't take it baby: Teagarden, Jack / I wish I were mine: Valaida / Cream man: Waller, Fats / Restless: Ward, Helen / Am I blue: Waters, Ethel / Drop in next time you're passing: Welch, Elisabeth
CD _____ CD AJA 5077
Living Era / Jan '91 / Koch.

SINGALONG BANJO PARTY
Baby face / Toot toot tootsie / Let's all go down The Strand / You are my sunshine / Pennies from Heaven / Any old iron / Bye bye blackbird / Mammy / Underneath the arches / Shine on harvest moon / On Mother Kelly's doorstep / Birdie song
CD _____ PLATCD 01
Platinum Music / Dec '88 / Prism / Ross.

SINGER & THE SONG, THE
CD _____ STACD 007
Wisepack / Nov '92 / THE / Conifer.

SINGER AND THE SONG, THE
Barcelona: Mercury, Freddie & Montserrat Caballe / Great pretender: Platters / Stand by me: King, Ben E. / Piece of my heart: Franklin, Erma / You've lost that lovin' feelin': Righteous Brothers / Reach out, I'll be there: Four Tops / My cherie amour: Wonder, Stevie / It's over: Orbison, Roy / Sun ain't gonna shine anymore: Walker Brothers / Something's gotten hold of my heart: Almond, Marc & Gene Pitney / It's not unusual: Jones, Tom / I will survive: Gaynor, Gloria / Don't leave me this way: Melvin, Harold & The Bluenotes / Get here: Adams, Oleta / When a man loves a woman: Sledge, Percy / Mad about the boy: Washington, Dinah / When I fall in love: Cole, Nat King / If you go away: Walker, Scott / Crazy: Cline, Patsy / Stand by your man: Wynette, Tammy / Don't let the sun go down on me: Michael, George & Elton John / Nothing compares 2 U: O'Connor, Sinead / Stay: Shakespears Sister / China in your hand: T'Pau / Up where we belong: Cocker, Joe / (Something inside) So strong: Siffre, Labi / Close to you: Carpenters / Lady in red: De Burgh, Chris / Jealous guy: Roxy Music / Air that I breathe: Hollies / Without you: Nilsson, Harry / Send in the clowns: Collins, Judy / I know him so well: Paige, Elaine & Barbara Dickson / I left my heart in San Francisco: Bennett, Tony / You don't have to say you love me: Springfield, Dusty / Goldfinger: Bassey, Shirley / Non, je ne regrette rien: Piaf, Edith / Over the rainbow: Garland, Judy / You'll never walk alone: Gerry & The Pacemakers / Nessun Dorma: Pavarotti, Luciano
CD _____ VTCD 21
Virgin / Oct '93 / EMI.

SINGERS MEET THE DJ'S
CD _____ RNCD 2106
Rhino / Jun '95 / Jetstar / Magnum Music Group / THE.

SINGERS OF IMPERIAL RUSSIA VOL 1
CD Set _____ GEMM CDS 9997-9
Gemm / Sep '92 / Pinnacle.

SINGERS OF IMPERIAL RUSSIA VOL 2
CD Set _____ GEMM CDS 9001-5
Gemm / Oct '92 / Pinnacle.

SINGERS OF IMPERIAL RUSSIA VOL 3
CD Set _____ GEMM CDS 9004-6
Gemm / Nov '92 / Pinnacle.

SINGERS ON TOP
CD _____ 792512
Melodie / Dec '95 / Triple Earth / Discovery / ADA / Jetstar.

SINGIN' THE GOSPEL 1933-36
CD _____ DOCD 5326
Blues Document / Mar '95 / Swift / Jazz Music / Hot Shot.

SINGING IN AN OPEN SPACE
(Zulu Rhythm & Harmony)
CD _____ CDROU 5027
Rounder / Dec '90 / CM / Direct / ADA / Cadillac.

SINGLE MINDED
CD _____ CDWIKD 109
Big Beat / Jun '92 / Pinnacle.

SINNERS & SAINTS
CD _____ DOCD 5106
Blues Document / Nov '92 / Swift / Jazz Music / Hot Shot.

SIREN SONGS OF THE SOUTH SEAS
CD _____ CD 398
Bescol / Aug '94 / CM / Target/BMG.

SISSY MAN BLUES
(Straight/Gay Blues & Jazz Vocals)
CD _____ JASSCD 13
Jass / Oct '91 / CM / Jazz Music / ADA / Cadillac / Direct.

SISTERS 1: FOLKSONG
CD _____ SOW 1001
Sisters Of The World / Oct '95 / Direct.

SISTERS OF SWING
CD _____ 5352252
PolyGram TV / Jan '96 / PolyGram.

SIX FLAGS
CD _____ EYEUKCD 004
Harthouse / Aug '95 / Disc / Warner Music.

SIX STRING BOOGIE
(The Power Of Blues Guitar)
Enter the tornado: Wilson, U.P. & Paul Aorta & The Kingpins / Hold on baby: Wilson, U.P. & Paul Aorta & The Kingpins / Prancing: Turner, Ike / Bessie Mae: Gibson, Lacy & Sunnyland Slim / House rent boogie: Hooker, John Lee / Leave me alone: Benton, Buster / Somebody loan me a dime: Robinson, Fenton / Texas love: Pollock, Mark / Blue light: Mighty Houserockers / Shake 'em on down: McDowell, 'Mississippi' Fred / You're gonna need me: Allison, Luther / All by myself: Murphy, Matt & Memphis Slim / Walked all night long: Smith, Byther / All that's good to me: Cray, Robert / First time I met the blues: Guy, Buddy / Little bit worried: Sharpville, Todd / Dust my broom: Hooker, Earl / Way you dance: Green, Peter & Mick/Enemy Within / Little Stevie's shuffle: Elmores
CD _____ MCCD 151
Music Club / Feb '94 / Disc / THE / CM.

SIXTIES - A VERY SPECIAL COLLECTION, THE
(3CD Set)
(There's) Always something there to remind me: Shaw, Sandie / Don't sleep in the subway: Clark, Petula / Poor man's son: Rockin' Berries / Let the heartbreak begin: Baldry, Long John / Autumn almanac: Kinks / Sugar and spice: Searchers / Pictures of matchstick men: Status Quo / Go away little girl: Wynter, Mark / (I love you) Samantha: Ball, Kenny & His Jazzmen / Waterloo sunset: Kinks / Build me up buttercup: Foundations / Girl don't come: Shaw, Sandie / Midnight in Moscow: Ball, Kenny & His Jazzmen / My love is: Clark, Petula / Where are you now: Clark, Petula / Little bitty tear: Miki & Griff / Goodbye my love: Searchers / Party's over: Donegan, Lonnie / Dedicated follower of fashion: Kinks / Colours: Donovan / What have they done to the rain: Searchers / Other man's grass (is always greener): Clark, Petula / Tossing and turning: Ivy League / I'll stop at nothing: Shaw, Sandie / Baby now that I've found you: Foundations / I couldn't live without your love: Clark, Petula / Universal soldier: Donovan / Dead end street: Kinks / When you walk in the room: Searchers / Downtown: Clark, Petula / Here comes my baby: Tremeloes / All the love in the world: Consortium / Michelle: Overlanders / Turquoise: Donovan / (Underneath the sun in) Mexico:

Baldry, Long John / Till the end of the day: Kinks / Daydream: *Lovin' Spoonful* / Sunny afternoon: *Kinks* / Whiter shade of pale: *Procul Harum* / Itchycoo park: *Small Faces* / Death of a clown: *Davies, Dave* / Blackberry way: *Move* / Lady Jane: *Garrick, David* / Men of the world: *Fleetwood Mac* / Elenore: *Turtles* / Summer in the city: *Lovin' Spoonful* / Green tambourine: *Lemon Pipers* / For your love: *Yardbirds* / Handbags and gladrags: *Farlowe, Chris* / Catch the wind: *Donovan* / Happy together: *Turtles* / Let's go to San Francisco: *Flowerpot Men* / Woodstock: *Matthew's Southern Comfort*
CD Set _____ **BOXD 51T**
Old Gold / Oct '95 / Carlton Home Entertainment.

SIXTIES ARCHIVES VOL.1 - SOUND OF THE SIXTIES
CD _____ 842039
EVA / Jun '94 / Direct / ADA.

SIXTIES ARCHIVES VOL.2 - SCARCE GARAGE RECORDS
CD _____ 842634
EVA / May '94 / Direct / ADA.

SIXTIES ARCHIVES VOL.2 - TEXAS PUNK
CD _____ 842040
EVA / Jun '94 / Direct / ADA.

SIXTIES ARCHIVES VOL.3 - LOUISIANA PUNK
CD _____ 842041
EVA / Jun '94 / Direct / ADA.

SIXTIES ARCHIVES VOL.4 - FLORIDA & NEW MEXICO PUNK
CD _____ 842042
EVA / Jun '94 / Direct / ADA.

SIXTIES ARCHIVES VOL.5 - US PUNK FROM THE 60'S
CD _____ 842043
EVA / Jun '94 / Direct / ADA.

SIXTIES ARCHIVES VOL.6
CD _____ EVA 8420448
EVA / Nov '94 / Direct / ADA.

SIXTIES ARCHIVES VOL.7 - MICHIGAN PUNK
CD _____ 842045
EVA / Jun '94 / Direct / ADA.

SIXTIES ARCHIVES VOL.8 - ACID TRIPS & HEAVY SOUNDS
CD _____ 842046
EVA / May '94 / Direct / ADA.

SIXTIES COLLECTION, THE
King of the road: *Miller, Roger* / Bad boy: *Wilde, Marty* / Running bear: *Preston, Johnny* / Harbour lights: *Platters* / All I see is you: *Springfield, Dusty* / Johnny Rocco: *Wilde, Marty* / I found out the hard way: *Four Pennies* / Bobby's girl: *Maughan, Susan* / Jezebel: *Wilde, Marty* / Bend it: *Dave Dee, Dozy, Beaky, Mick & Tich* / In the middle of nowhere: *Springfield, Dusty* / Tower of strength: *Vaughan, Frankie* / Boys cry: *Kane, Eden* / Little white bull: *Steele, Tommy* / Last night was made for love: *Fury, Billy* / Wimoweh: *Denver, Karl* / I close my eyes and count to ten: *Springfield, Dusty*
CD _____ **PWK 125**
Carlton Home Entertainment / Dec '89 / Carlton Home Entertainment.

SIXTIES DECADE, THE
CD Set _____ **TTP 002**
Tring / Nov '92 / Tring / Prism.

SIXTIES GROUPS
CD _____ **CDSR 053**
Telstar / Feb '95 / BMG.

SIXTIES HEROES
CD _____ **SETCD 089**
Stardust / Sep '94 / Carlton Home Entertainment.

SIXTIES MIXES
CD _____ **JHD 085**
Tring / Mar '93 / Tring / Prism.

SIXTIES SUMMER OF LOVE
Daydream: *Lovin' Spoonful* / Sunny afternoon: *Kinks* / Whiter shade of pale: *Procul Harum* / Itchycoo park: *Small Faces* / Death of a clown: *Davies, Dave* / Blackberry way: *Move* / Lady Jane: *Garrick, David* / Man of the world: *Fleetwood Mac* / Elenore: *Turtles* / Summer in the city: *Lovin' Spoonful* / Green tambourine: *Lemon Pipers* / For your love: *Yardbirds* / Handbags and gladrags: *Farlowe, Chris* / Waterloo sunset: *Kinks* / Happy together: *Turtles* / Let's go to San Francisco: *Flowerpot Men* / Woodstock: *Matthew's Southern Comfort*
CD _____ **PWKS 4182**
Carlton Home Entertainment / Feb '96 / Carlton Home Entertainment.

SIZHU/SILK BAMBOO
CD _____ **PAN 2030CD**
Pan / Feb '95 / ADA / Direct / CM.

SIZZLING THE BLUES (New Orleans 1927-29)
I haven't got a dollar to pay the house rent man: *Davis, Genevieve* / I've got that something: *Davis, Genevieve* / Pretty Audrey: *Dumaine, Louis Jazzola Eight* / To-wa-bac-a-wa: *Dumaine, Louis Jazzola Eight* / Franklin Street blues: *Dumaine, Louis Jazzola Eight*

/ Red onion drag: *Dumaine, Louis Jazzola Eight* / Mama cookie: *Cook, Ann* / He's the sweetest black man in town: *Cook, Ann* / Panama: *Miller, Johnny New Orleans Frollickers* / Dippermouth blues: *Miller, Johnny New Orleans Frollickers* / Sizzling the blues: *Hazel, Monk & His Bienville Roof Orchestra* / Swing society: *Hazel, Monk & His Bienville Roof Orchestra* / Git wit it: *Hazel, Monk & His Bienville Roof Orchestra* / Ideas: *Hazel, Monk & His Bienville Roof Orchestra* / Astoria strut: *Jones & Collins Astoria Hot Eight* / Duet stomp: *Jones & Collins Astoria Hot Eight* / Damp weather: *Jones & Collins Astoria Hot Eight* / Tip easy blues: *Jones & Collins Astoria Hot Eight*
CD _____ **DGF 5**
Frog / May '95 / Jazz Music / Cadillac / Wellard.

SKA BEATS 1
Mental ska (the rap): *Longsy D* / Just keep rockin': *Double Trouble & Rebel MC* / Force ten from Navarone: *Roughneck* / Musical scorcha (Mixes): *Rackit Allstar* / Resolution '99: *Maroon Town* / Rock to dis (house mix): *Jamaica Mean Time* / We play ska: *Children Of The Night* / This is ska (Buster's original ska mix): *Longsy D & Buster Bloodvessel* / Skanking with the toreadors: *Ministry Of Ska* / Rude boy shuffle: *Rude Boys* / Swingin' thing: *Flowers Ltd & BMG*
CD _____ **SKACID 001CD**
Beechwood / Nov '89 / BMG / Pinnacle.

SKA BONANZA
CD Set _____ **CDHB 86**
Heartbeat / Feb '92 / Greensleeves / Jetstar / Direct / ADA.

SKA BOOGIE
You got me rocking: *Aitken, Laurel & Friends* / Millie girl: *Gray, Owen* / Pink Lane shuffle: *Reid, Duke* / Worried over you: *Keith & Enid* / Parapinto boogie: *Clarke, Lloyd* / I wanna love: *Jiving Juniors* / Shake a leg: *Morgan, Derrick* / Humpty Dumpty: *Morris, Eric* / Wasp: *Bubbles* / On the beach: *Gray, Owen* / Open up bartender: *Prince Buster* / Slow boat: *Joe, Al T.* / Never never: *Aitken, Bobby* / South Virginia: *Aitken, Bobby* / Hush baby: *Rudy & Sketto* / Oh Carolina: *Folkes Brothers & Count Ossie* / Midnight train: *Dixon, Errol* / Mash Mr. Lee: *Lee, Byron & The Dragonaires* / I'm on my own: *Joe, Al T.* / Running around: *Joe, Al T.*
CD _____ **NEXCD 254**
Sequel / Oct '93 / BMG.

SKA FANTASTIC
CD _____ **RB 3012**
Reggae Best / Mar '95 / Magnum Music Group / THE.

SKA FOR SKA'S SAKE
Skadansk: *Mark Foggos's Skasters* / It's so easy: *Loafers* / W.L.N.: *Hotknives* / King Hammond shuffle: *King Hammond* / City riot: *Maroon Town* / Off The Shelf tonight: *Off The Shelf* / Blind date: *Riffs* / Another town: *Mr. Review* / Driving me to drink: *Skandal* / One eyed lodger: *Judge Dread* / Ska sax: *Pick it up* / Woman: *Pork Hunts*
CD _____ **DOJOCD 97**
Dojo / Feb '94 / BMG.

SKA IS THE LIMIT/HISTORY OF SKA
CD _____ **RNCD 2073**
Rhino / Oct '94 / Jetstar / Magnum Music Group / THE.

SKA MANIA
CD _____ **DINCD 86**
Dino / May '95 / Pinnacle / 3MV.

SKA SPECTACULAR VOL. 1
CD _____ **CPCD 8021**
Charly / Feb '94 / Charly / THE / Cadillac.

SKA SPECTACULAR VOL. 2
CD _____ **CPCD 8022**
Charly / Feb '94 / Charly / THE / Cadillac.

SKA STARS OF THE 80'S
CD _____ **GAZCD 006**
Gaz's Rockin' Records / May '90 / Pinnacle.

SKA TRAX - THE NEXT GENERATION
CD _____ **EFA 119962**
Heatwave / Dec '94 / SRD.

SKA TRAX - THE NEXT GENERATION PART 2
CD _____ **EFA 127862**
Heatwave / Jan '96 / SRD.

SKA WARS (4CD Set)
CD Set _____ **MBSCD 439**
Castle / Nov '95 / BMG.

SKANK 3 - 15 COMMANDMENTS
CD _____ **DOJOCD 98**
Dojo / May '93 / BMG.

SKANK LICENSED TO SKA
Skinhead love affair: *Busters All Stars* / Fire: *Bluebeat* / Julie Julie: *Braces* / Onion: *Busters* / Laughing loafers: *Loafers* / Ska skank bonch party: *Skaos* / Jump start: *Forest Hill-billies* / Pipeline: *Busters All Stars* / Safety guards: *Bluebeat* / Letter: *Braces* / Keen on games: *Busters* / Melancholy Sally: *Loafers* / Struggle: *Skaos* / Shocker: *Toasters*

CD _____ **DOJOCD 96**
Dojo / Feb '94 / BMG.

SKANKIN' ROUND THE WORLD VOL.1
CD _____ **DOJOCD 175**
Dojo / Nov '93 / BMG.

SKANKIN' ROUND THE WORLD VOL.2
CD _____ **DOJOCD 176**
Dojo / Nov '93 / BMG.

SKANKIN' ROUND THE WORLD VOL.3
CD _____ **DOJOCD 185**
Dojo / Feb '94 / BMG.

SKANKIN' ROUND THE WORLD VOL.4
CD _____ **DOJOCD 186**
Dojo / Feb '94 / BMG.

SKA'S THE LIMIT
CD Set _____ **RNCD 2075**
Rhino / Oct '94 / Jetstar / Magnum Music Group / THE.

SKINHEAD CLASSICS
CD _____ **CDTRL 407**
Trojan / Mar '94 / Jetstar / Total/BMG.

SKINHEAD REVOLT
Skinhead revolt: *Joe The Boss* / What will your mother say: *Jones, Clancy* / If it don't work out: *Kelly, Pat* / Champion: *G.G.All Stars* / Little better: *Parks, Lloyd* / Left with a broken heart: *Paragons* / In the spirit: *Charmers, Lloyd* / Reggae girl: *Tennors* / Death a come: *Charmers, Lloyd* / Skinhead speaks his mind: *Hothead All Stars* / Dark end of the street: *Kelly, Pat* / Shu be du: *Eccles, Clancy* / Come a little closer: *Donaldson, Eric* / Barbabus: *G.G.All Stars* / Loving reggae: *Maytones* / Ease me up officer: *Soul Ofrus* / Got to get away: *Paragons* / To love somebody: *Brown, Buster* / Place called happiness: *Mills, Rudy* / Last call: *Silver Stars*
CD _____ **CDTRL 329**
Trojan / Mar '94 / Jetstar / Total/BMG.

SKIRL OF PIPES VOL. 1, THE
CD _____ **PACD 031**
Music Masters / Mar '94 / Target/BMG.

SKUNK - THIS SOME BAD WEED VOL.1
Dances with fire: *Mojo Risin'* / Return of Rasputin: *Aardvark* / Movement, the message: *Soundcraft* / Sinister footwork: *3rd Alternative* / All of your mind: *Blood Runs Dry* / Out of my paradise: *Aardvark* / Chant 4 freedom: *Vu 2* / Won't cry you: *S.U.L.O.* / Fox on the cut: *Babyfox* / No apologies: *3rd Alternative* / Slider: *Paingang* / One love: *Molara* / 20,000 feet: *Vu 2* / Wibbler: *Soundcraft* / This some bad weed: *Soundcraft*
CD _____ **POOCD 001**
Skunk / Dec '93 / Pinnacle.

SKUNK - THIS SOME BAD WEED VOL.2
CD _____ **POOCD 2**
Skunk / Oct '94 / Pinnacle.

SKY HIGH (20 Smash Hits Of The 70's)
Down the dustpipe: *Status Quo* / Apeman: *Kinks* / Ruby Tuesday: *Melanie* / In the summertime: *Mungo Jerry* / (It's like a) Sad old kinda movie: *Pickettywitch* / You don't mess around with: *Jim* / Croce, *Jim* / Lion sleeps tonight: *Newman, Dave* / Strange band: *Family* / I get the sweetest feeling: *Wilson, Jackie* / Dancing on a Saturday night: *Blue, Barry* / Midnight train to Georgia: *Knight, Gladys & The Pips* / Broken down angel: *Nazareth* / Beach baby: *First Class* / Pillow talk: *Sylvia* / Me and my life: *Tremeloes* / Sky high: *Jigsaw* / Operator (That's not the way it feels): *Croce, Jim* / Mean girl: *Status Quo* / You'll never know what you're missing: *Real Thing* / Natural born bugie: *Humble Pie*
CD _____ **TRTCD 107**
TrueTrax / Oct '94 / THE.

SLAM CHOPS
CD _____ **TX 510202**
Triple X / Jul '95 / Plastic Head.

SLANGED
CD _____ **EFA 04914CD**
City Slang / Nov '92 / Disc.

SLAUGHTERED VOL. 1
CD _____ **SPV 07725162**
SPV / Feb '94 / Plastic Head.

SLAUGHTERED VOL.2
CD _____ **SPV 07725172**
SPV / Jun '94 / Plastic Head.

SLENG TENG EXTRAVAGANZA
CD _____ **GRELCD 209**
Greensleeves / May '95 / Total/BMG / Jetstar.

SLIDE GUITAR - BOTTLES, KNIVES AND STEEL, THE
Bottleneck blues: *Weaver & Beasley* / Untitled: *Barbecue Bob* / God don't never change: *Johnson, Blind Willie* / Dark was the night: *Weaver & Beasley* / Experience blues: *Willis, Ruth & Blind Willie McTell* / Guitar rag: *Weaver, Sylvester* / You can't get that stuff no more: *Tampa Red* / High sheriff blues: *Patton, Charlie* / Homesick and lonesome blues: *Fuller, Blind Boy* / Packin' trunk blues: *Leadbelly* / I believe I'll make a change: *Weldon, Casey Bill* / Don't sell it (don't give it away): *Woods, Buddy* /

Muscat Hill blues: *Woods, Buddy* / Traveling riverside blues: *Johnson, Robert* / Bukka's jitterbug swing: *White, Bukka* / Special stream line: *White, Bukka* / Swing low, sweet chariot: *Terrell, Sister O.M.* / Pearline: *House, Son*
CD _____ 4672512
CBS / Oct '90 / Sony.

SLIDE GUITAR BLUES
CD _____ **IGOCD 2030**
Indigo / Oct '95 / Direct / ADA.

SLIDE GUITAR GOSPEL 1944-64
CD _____ **DOCD 5222**
Blues Document / Apr '94 / Swift / Jazz Music / Hot Shot.

SLIDE GUITAR VOL.2
CD _____ 4721912
Columbia / May '93 / Sony.

SLIDIN'...SOME SLIDE
CD _____ **BB 9533CD**
Bullseye Blues / Jan '94 / Direct.

SLIP 'N' SLIDE VOL.1
You can't touch me: *Pollack, Karen* / Jungle kisses: *Roc & Kato* / Music is so wonderful: *Lee, Vivian* / Time for joy: *Hot house*: *Eq Lateral* / Tank: *Global Logic* / Show 'em how we do it: *Interaction* / Dig deep: *Deep Six* / Open your mind: *Decoy* / All in the same family: *African Dreams* / Digital autopsy: *3 Man Journey* / I don't need you anymore: *H.A.L.F.*
CD _____ **SLIPCD 018**
Slip 'n' Slide / Dec '94 / Vital / Disc.

SLIP 'N' SLIDE VOL.2
Hi loine lo loine: *Basic Soul* / Green: *Firefly* / Love evolution: *Aqua Negra* / Alright: *Roc & Kato* / Let me in: *95 North* / Fire: *BB Boogie Association* / Hideaway: *Delacy* / About you: *Loosse* / Feel it: *TNT* / DC Deepressed: *Deep Dish* / Real good: *Grand Central*
CD _____ **SLIPCD 035**
Slip 'n' Slide / Oct '95 / Vital / Disc.

SLIPMATT TAKES CONTROL
CD _____ **KICKCD 29**
Kickin' / Nov '95 / SRD.

SLIPPING AROUND
CD _____ **HDHCD 010**
HDH / Oct '89 / Pinnacle.

SLOVENIA I.R.P.
CD _____ **CD 13255**
Nika / Mar '93 / SRD.

SLOW MOTION (14 Urban Contemporary Love Ballads)
Your body's calling: *R. Kelly* / Let me do U: *P.O.V.* / All night: *Me 2 U* / Please tell me tonight: *Motiv* / Don't go nowhere: *Riff* / Always: *Mint Condition* / When I need somebody: *Tresvant, Ralph* / I got a thang 4 ya: *Low Key* / La la love: *Avila, Bobby Ross* / Make love 2 me: *Lorenzo* / Baby it's real: *Serenade* / I'll be there for you: *M.L.* / Wait for me: *Chalant* / Gangsta lean: *D.R.S.*
CD _____ **CDELV 16**
Elevate / Jun '94 / 3MV / Sony.

SLOW 'N' MOODY, BLACK 'N' BLUESY
Nothing can change this love: *Hill, Z.Z.* / You messed up my mind: *Hammond, Clay* / I can't stand it: *Holiday, Jimmy* / Directly from my heart: *Little Richard* / I don't need: *Turner, Ike & Tina* / Let's get together: *Arthur & Mary* / Darling I'm standing by you: *Jones, Jeanette* / Baby I'll come right away: *Love, Mary* / If I'd lose you: *Day, Jackie* / I don't wanna lose you: *Young, Tami* / Baby, come to me: *Little Henry & The Shamrocks* / Ain't nobody's business: *King, B.B.* / Every dog has his day: *Copeland, Johnny* / Baby, what you want me to do: *Little Richard* / Baby I'll come: *Love, Mary* / Everybody needs somebody: *Love, Mary* / Weep no more: *Terry & The Tyrants* / It's real: *Robbins, Jimmy* / Can't count the days: *Robbins, Jimmy* / Whenever I can't sleep: *Gauff, Willie & The Love Brothers* / Last one to know: *Haywood, Joe* / Mr. President: *Haywood, Joe* / Woman needs a man: *Baker, Yvonne* / Farewell: *Gauff, Willie & The Love Brothers* / Why should I be the one: *Gauff, Willie & The Love Brothers* / I'll come back to you: *Mighty Hannibal* / Consider yourself: *Johnson, Stacey*
CD _____ **CDKEND 003**
Kent / Nov '94 / Pinnacle.

SLOW PUNANY
CD _____ **GPCD 006**
Gussie P / Dec '93 / Jetstar.

SLY & ROBBIE'S RAGGA PON TOP
Move with the crowd: *Baby Wayne* / Little crook: *Papa San* / Hold me: *Joseph Stepper* / Ole horse: *Red Dragon* / Thief: *Captain Berkley* / Boom boom bye: *Redrose & Round Head* / Rum shaker: *Nardo Ranks* / Love lullaby: *General Degree* / Give her the credit: *Papa San* / Mony fi spend: *Captain Berkley* / Makosa: *Papa San*
CD _____ 111932
Musidisc / Feb '94 / Vital / Harmonia Mundi / ADA / Cadillac / Discovery.

SMALL GROUP SWING
Upstairs: *Smith, Stuff* / I ain't got nobody: *Webb, Chick* / In a little Spanish town: *Webb, Chick* / Chicken and waffles: *Berigan, Bunny* / Swingin' in the coconut trees: *Jordan, Louis* / Doug the Jitterbug: *Jordan,*

Louis / Baby, won't you please come home: Spencer Trio / Lorna Doone shortbread: Spencer Trio / Three little words: Freeman, Bud / Raggin' the scale: Venuti, Joe / Josephine: Rollini, Adrian / Dr. Livingstone, I presume: Shaw, Artie / When the quail come back to San Quentin: Shaw, Artie / Countess blues: Kansas City Six / Home James: James, Harry / Body and soul: Tatum, Art / I'll take the South: Brown, Cleo / Minor Drag: Waller, Fats / Oh Susannah, dust off that old piano: New Orleans Rhythm Kings / 29th and dearborn: Dodds, Johnny / China boy: Goodman, Benny / When the midnight choo-choo leaves for Alabam': Dorsey, Tommy
CD _____ PPCD 78102
Past Perfect / Feb '95 / THE.

SMALL WONDER PUNK SINGLES COLLECTION
Mucky pup: Puncture / Hungry: Zeros / Radio wunderdar: Carpettes / Safety pin stuck in my heart: Fitzgerald, Patrick / G.L.C.: Menace / Buy me sell me: Fitzgerald, Patrick / Nineteen and mad: Leyton Buzzards / Puppet life: Punishment Of Luxury / Small wonder: Carpettes / Little Miss Perfect: Demon Preacher / Never been so stuck: Nicky & The Dots / New way: Wall / Disco love: Molesters / End: Cravats / Last year's youth: Menace / D.N.A.: Murder The Disturbed / End of civilisation: Molesters / Flares and slippers: Cockney Rejects / Violence grows: Fatal Microbes / Exchange: Wall / Time tunnel: English Sub-titles / Soft ground: Prole / Precinct: Cravats / You're driving me: Cravats / Off the beach: Cravats / They've got it all wrong: Anthrax
CD _____ CDPUNK 29
Anagram / Mar '94 / Pinnacle.

SMALL WONDERS PUNK SINGLES VOLUME 2
Can't play rock n roll: Puncture / Radio fun: Zeros / How about me and you: Carpettes / Set we free: Fitzgerald, Patrick / I'm civilised: Menace / Little dippers: Fitzgerald, Patrick / Irrelevant battles: Fitzgerald, Patrick / Youthanasia: Leyton Buzzards / Demon: Punishment Of Luxury / 2 NE 1: Carpettes / Linoleum walk: Nicky & The Dots / Suckers: Wall / Uniforms: Wall / Burning bridges cravats: Cravats / I am the dreg: Cravats / Who's in here with me / Commuter man: Molesters / Carry no banners: Menace / Walking corpses: Murder The Disturbed / Police car: Cockney Rejects / Beautiful picture: Fatal Microbes / Sweat: English Sub-titles / S.M.K.: Prole / What will tomorrow: Anthrax
CD _____ CDPUNK 70
Anagram / Jan '96 / Pinnacle.

SMALLTALK
Colonel Fraser / Mary Ann MacInnes / Famous bridge / Kail and pudding / Cumha coire a 'cheathairch / Jock Hawk / New claret / Low country dance / Advasar Blacksmith / Black haired lad / Shetland fiddler / Over the sea to nova scotia / Rose Anderson / Les vielles bottiness / Heights of casino / 'S truagh nach do dh'fhuirich / Fhorton jig / James Byrne's jig / Duncan McKillop / Bee in the knickers / Fil o ro
CD _____ CDTRAX 079
Greentrax / Sep '94 / Conifer / Duncans / ADA / Direct.

SMASH HITS 94
CD Set _____ TCD 2750
Telstar / Nov '94 / BMG.

SMASH HITS 80 VOL. 1
CD _____ TCD 2764
Telstar / Mar '95 / BMG.

SMASH HITS VOL. 2
CD _____ TCD 2768
Telstar / Jun '94 / BMG.

SMASH HITS VOL. 3
CD _____ TCD 2786
Telstar / Oct '95 / BMG.

SMOKE & FIRE
CD _____ CDTB 022
Magnum Music / Sep '94 / Magnum Music Group.

SMOKE GETS IN YOUR EYES - THOSE ROMANTIC 50'S
Smoke gets in your eyes: Mantovani & His Orchestra / Love letters in the sand: Chacksfield, Frank & His Orchestra / Two different worlds: Mantovani & His Orchestra / Secret lover: Mantovani & His Orchestra / Tender trap: Heath, Ted & His Music / Autumn leaves: Mantovani & His Orchestra / Just in time: Mantovani & His Music / Answer me: Mantovani & His Orchestra / Unforgettable: Ternent, Billy & His Orchestra / Catch a falling star: Mantovani & His Orchestra / Till: Ternent, Billy & His Orchestra / True love: Mantovani & His Orchestra / Unchained melody: Heath, Ted & His Music / When I fall in love: Mantovani & His Orchestra / Smile: Chacksfield, Frank & His Orchestra / Hey there: Mantovani & His Orchestra / I've grown accustomed to her face: Aldrich, Ronnie & His Piano/The Festival Orchestra / Love is a many splendoured thing: Mantovani & His Orchestra
CD _____ 8440642
Eclipse / May '91 / PolyGram.

SMOKE ON THE WATER
CD _____ RR 89672
Roadrunner / Nov '94 / Pinnacle.

SMOKE RINGS
CD _____ PHONTCD 7641
Phontastic / '93 / Wellard / Jazz Music / Cadillac.

SMYRNAIC SONG IN GREECE 1928-35, THE
CD _____ HTCD 27
Heritage / Feb '95 / Swift / Roots / Wellard / Direct / Hot Shot / Jazz Music / ADA.

SNAKEBITE CITY
CD _____ BLU 06
Blue Fire / Apr '95 / SRD.

SNAP - THE ESSENTIAL MIX SHOW
Oasis: Paragliders / Vicious circle: Poltergeist / Love above: Fini Tribe / Where are you: 16 Bit / Original: Leftfield / Flying souls: Sequencer / Luck spray: Redeye / Survive: Brothers Grimm / Raise your hands: Boston Bruins / Drive: Trancesetters / Melt: Leftfield / Aqualite: Wavemaker / Happy nose: Arcus / Tension: Reunification / Dark side of the Moog: Schulze, Klaus / Classix: Arcus / Mushroom shaped: Fini Tribe / Raven: 16 Bit
CD _____ 5286752
Mercury / Oct '95 / PolyGram.

SNAPOLOGY
Cherry man: Wannadies / It's absence: Souls / On your bedroom floor: This Perfect Day / Sheena: Eggstone / Under surface: Baby Lemonade / Miss thing-a-magic: Simpkins / It's not that easy: Poverty Stinks / S.U. song: Singer / Seven years: Scents / Marine love (demo): Easy / Million dollar project: Whipped Cream / Blind: Poodle
CD _____ SNAP 008
Soap / Oct '93 / Vital.

SO BLUE SO FUNKY VOL. 1
(Heroes Of The Hammond)
All about my girl: McGriff, Jimmy / Silver metre: Patton, Big John / I'm movin' on: Smith, Jimmy / Wine, wine, wine (Not on cassette): Roach, Freddie / Brown sugar: Roach, Freddie / Hootin' 'n' tootin': Jackson, Fred / Face to face: Willette, Baby Face / Fat Judy: Patton, Big John / Plaza De Toros: Young, Larry / Boop bop bing bash: Braith, George / Everything I do gonh be funky: Donaldson, Lou / Hot rod (Not on cassette): Wilson, Reuben / Butter for yo' popcorn: McDuff, Brother Jack / Ain't it funky now: Green, Grant
CD _____ BNZ 267
Blue Note / May '91 / EMI.

SO BLUE SO FUNKY VOL. 2
(Heroes Of The Hammond)
Where it's at: McGriff, Jimmy / Meetin' here: Amy, Curtis & Paul Bryant / When Malindy sings: Roach, Freddie / Mary had a little lamb: Braith, George / Can heat: Smith, Jimmy / Morris the minor: Holmes, Richard 'Groove' / Minor soul: Lytell, Jimmy / Somethin' strange: Willette, Baby Face / I want to go home: Patton, Big John / Street scene: Young, Larry / Kid: Donaldson, Lou
CD _____ CDP 8290922
Blue Note / Jun '94 / EMI.

SO WIE ES DAMALS WAR
CD _____ BCD 15712
Bear Family / Mar '93 / Rollercoaster / Direct / CM / Swift / ADA.

SOCA GOLD VOL.1
CD _____ HVCD 015
Hot Vinyl / Apr '92 / Jetstar.

SOCA GOLD VOL.2
CD _____ HVCD 016
Hot Vinyl / Apr '92 / Jetstar.

SOCA GOLD VOL.3
CD _____ HVCD 020
Hot Vinyl / Jan '95 / Jetstar.

SOCA GOLD VOL.4
CD _____ HVCD 021
Hot Vinyl / Jan '95 / Jetstar.

SOCA GOLD VOL.5
CD _____ HVCD 023
Hot Vinyl / Sep '95 / Jetstar.

SOCA GOLD VOL.6
CD _____ HVCD 024
Hot Vinyl / Sep '95 / Jetstar.

SOCCER ROCKERS
(Football Favourites)
Land of hope and glory / We shall not be moved / Battle hymn of the republic / BBC Grandstand theme / I'm forever blowing bubbles / You'll never walk alone / We will rock / When the saints go marching in / Back home / He's got the whole world in his hands / We are the champions / Stars and stripes forever / Match Of The Day theme / Give peace a chance / Red flag
CD _____ 3036000072
Carlton Home Entertainment / Oct '95 / Carlton Home Entertainment.

SOCIAL HARP, THE
CD _____ ROU 0094CD
Rounder / Oct '94 / CM / Direct / ADA / Cadillac.

SOFT METAL
CD _____ TMPCD 013
Telstar / Mar '95 / BMG.

SOFT METAL BALLADS
CD Set _____ ARC 933502
Arcade / Mar '91 / Sony / Grapevine.

SOFT REGGAE
CD _____ RADCD 4
Global / Jan '95 / BMG.

SOFT ROCK
More than a feeling: Boston / She's not there: Santana / European female: Stranglers / Total eclipse of the heart: Tyler, Bonnie / Hold your head up: Argent / Cocaine: Cale, J.J. / Questions: Moody Blues / All the young dudes: Mott The Hoople / Dreadlock holiday: 10cc / You wear it well: Stewart, Rod / Night games: Bonnet, Graham / Jessica: Allman Brothers / Maneater: Hall & Oates / We built this city: Starship / Kyrie: Mr. Mister / All out of love: Air Supply / Eye of the tiger: Survivor
CD _____ STACD 005
Carlton Home Entertainment / Oct '91 / Carlton Home Entertainment.

SOFT ROCK
Suspicious minds: Fine Young Cannibals / Trouble: Buckingham, Lindsey / Little piece of heaven: Godley & Creme / Look away: Big Country / Child in time: Deep Purple / I got you: Split Enz / Cocaine: Cale, J.J. / Don't let the sun go down on me: John, Elton / Reason to believe: Stewart, Rod / Victims of circumstance: Barclay James Harvest / Like flames: Berlin / Mind of a toy: Visage / I'll find my way home: Jon & Vangelis / Reward: Teardrop Explodes
CD _____ 5506472
Spectrum/Karussell / Aug '94 / PolyGram / THE.

SOFT ROCK
CD Set _____ DCDCD 204
Castle / Jun '95 / BMG.

SOFT ROCK
CD _____ 5352482
PolyGram TV / Jan '96 / PolyGram.

SOFT ROCK CLASSICS, VOL.1
You're the voice: Farnham, John / We built this city: Starship / Maneater: Hall & Oates / Kyrie: Mr. Mister / Modern girl: Meat Loaf / Girls talk: Edmunds, Dave / Rock this town: Stray Cats / Mean girl: Status Quo / Get it on: T. Rex / With a little help from my friends: Cocker, Joe / Whiter shade of pale: Procul Harum / House of the rising sun: Animals
CD _____ 74321339202
Camden / Jan '96 / BMG.

SOFT ROCK CLASSICS, VOL.2
Nothing's gonna stop us now: Starship / Rosanna: Toto / Can't fight this feeling: REO Speedwagon / Way it is: Hornsby, Bruce & The Range / Total eclipse of the heart: Tyler, Bonnie / Rock 'n' roll mercenaries: Meat Loaf / More than a feeling: Boston / Final count down: Europe / Manic Monday: Bangles / Living next door to Alice: Smokie / American woman: Guess Who / White rabbit: Jefferson Airplane
CD _____ 74321339212
Camden / Jan '96 / BMG.

SOFT ROCK CLASSICS, VOL.3
Lost in love: Air Supply / It's only make believe: Child / Lily was here: Stewart, David A. & Candy Dulfer / Who's that girl: Eurythmics / Don't answer me: Parsons, Alan Project / Ubangi Stomp: Teen / Up my way / Sad Cafe / Human touch: Springfield, Rick / Burlesque: Family / It's a heartache: Tyler, Bonnie / Love hurts: Nazareth / Mean girl: Status Quo
CD _____ 74321339222
Camden / Jan '96 / BMG.

SOLAR BOX SET
CD Set _____ CDSLBX 1
Street Sounds / Jan '89 / A1.

SOLID GOLD
CD _____ MMGV 014
Magnum Music / Jan '93 / Magnum Music Group.

SOLID GOLD 1960'S
CD _____ CDSR 047
Telstar / May '94 / BMG.

SOLID GOLD 1960'S VOL. 2
CD _____ CDSR 052
Telstar / Feb '95 / BMG.

SOLID GOLD COXSONE STYLE
CD _____ CDHB 80
Heartbeat / May '92 / Greensleeves / Jetstar / Direct / ADA.

SOLID GOLD FROM THE VAULTS
Shocks 71: Barker, Dave / DJ's choice: Williams, Winston / People's choice: Williams, Winston / Ease up: Bleechers / Everything for your fun: Bleechers / Help wanted: Stranger Cole / I'm movin' on: Johnny & The Attractions / Hot sauce: Barker, Dave / New love: Herman / Music keep on playing: Campbell, Cornell / Soup: JJ Allstars / Cloudburst: Hippy Boys / Proud feeling: Rhythm Rulers / Red ash: Carl / Walk with love: Toots & The Maytals / Skanky dog: Scotland, Winston

SON OF STAX FUNK
Title theme (Tough guys): Hayes, Isaac / Type thang: Hayes, Isaac / Steppin' out: Sho Nuff / Mix match man: Sho Nuff / What does it take: Sons Of Slum / Man: Sons Of Slum / Getting funky round here: Black Nasty / Nasty soul: Black Nasty / Watch the

---

CD _____ CDTRL 291
Trojan / Mar '94 / Jetstar / Total/BMG.

SOLID GOLD FROM THE VAULTS VOL.2
CD _____ CDTRLS 293
Trojan / Nov '91 / Jetstar / Total/BMG.

SOLID GOLD FROM THE VAULTS VOL.3
CD _____ CDTRL 295
Trojan / Feb '92 / Jetstar / Total/BMG.

SOLID GOLD FROM THE VAULTS VOL.4
CD _____ CDTRL 302
Trojan / Mar '94 / Jetstar / Total/BMG.

SOLID GOLD HITS
Blue suede shoes: Perkins, Carl / Lucille: Little Richard / Reelin & rockin: Berry, Chuck / Runaway: Shannon, Del / Red river rock: Johnny & The Hurricanes / Poetry inmotion: Tillotson, Johnny / Oh Carol: Sedaka, Neil / Be bop a lula: Vincent, Gene / (Dance with the) Guitar man: Eddy, Duane / Twenty four hours from Tulsa: Pitney, Gene / Duke of Earl: Chandler, Gene / Venus: Avalon, Frankie
CD _____ 74321339322
Camden / Jan '96 / BMG.

SOLID HITBOUND STORY, THE
(A Collection Of Rare Detroit 60's Soul)
I must love you: Davis, Melvin / That's why I love you: Professionals / Hit and run: Owens, Gwen / Watch out: Inst / Friday night: Mancha, Steve / Just can't leave you: Hester, Tony / Baby baby: Tokays / Still in my heart: Davis, Melvin / Just like my baby: Inst / Deeper in love: Mancha, Steve / Headache in my heart: DeBarge, Bunny / I lost you: Holidays / Look what I almost missed: Lewis, Pat / Heartbreaker: Gilford, Jimmy / Never alone: Inst
CD _____ GSCD 053
Goldmine / Oct '94 / Vital.

SOLID SOUNDS - HARDCORE HYPNOTIC DANCE
CD _____ CHAMPCD 1024
Champion / Dec '90 / BMG.

SOLOMON ISLANDS - FATALEKE & BAEGU MUSIC
CD _____ AUD 8027
Unesco / Jun '91 / Harmonia Mundi.

SOLUBLE FISH
CD _____ HMS 1262
Homestead / Apr '93 / SRD.

SOMA COMPILATION
CD _____ SOMACD 1
Soma / Nov '94 / Disc.

SOMA COMPILATION 2
CD _____ SOMACD 003
Soma / Nov '95 / Disc.

SOME LOVE
CD _____ DOG 009CD
Mrs. Ackroyd / Sep '94 / Roots / Direct / ADA.

SOME 'MODERN' SOUL
(The Buddah Collection)
Oh lovin' you: Paragons / Dance and free your mind Pt. 1: Sins of Satan / Sharing: Vitamin E / Midnight lady: Norris, David Jnr. / Deeper and deeper: Wilson, Bobby / Makin' love ain't no fun (without the one you love): Ebonys / I wanna make love to you: Norman, Jimmy / I can't fight your love: Modulations / You and I: Anderson, Joe / Everybody stand and clap your hands (for the entertainer): Black Satin & Fred Parris
CD _____ NEXCD 154
Sequel / Feb '91 / BMG.

SOME OF THESE WERE HOOJ
CD _____ HOOJCD 1
Hooj Choons / Apr '94 / Disc.

SOME OF THESE WERE HOOJ TOO
CD _____ HOOJCD 2
Hooj Choons / Aug '95 / Disc.

SOMEONE'S GONNA GET THEIR HEAD
CD _____ BY 0026CD
Better Youth Organisation / Nov '93 / SRD.

SOMETHING FOR THE WEEKEND
CD _____ FNUN 2
Flying Nun / Oct '94 / Disc.

SOMETHING IN THE AIR
Nights in white satin: Matthew and son / Wild thing / Bend me, shape me / All or nothing / Sun ain't gonna shine anymore / Something in the air / Jackie / Hey Joe / Badge / My mind's eye / Here comes the night
CD _____ PWKS 577
Carlton Home Entertainment / May '90 / Carlton Home Entertainment.

SOMETHING'S GONE WRONG
CD _____ CZ 042 CD
C/Z / Jul '94 / Plastic Head.

SOMETIMES DEATH IS BETTER
CD _____ SHR 007CD
Shiver / Aug '95 / Plastic Head.

883

dog: *Shack* / Patch it up: *Johnson, Roy Lee* / Funky hot grits: *Thomas, Rufus* / Soul town: *Forevers* / Shake your big hips: *Tolbert, Israel* / Bump meat: *Rice, Sir Mack* / Do me: *Knight, Jean* / In the hole: *Bar-Kays* / Watch me do it (CD only): *Sho Nuff* / Right on (CD only): *Sons Of Slum* / Talkin' to the people (CD only): *Black Nasty* / I'd kill a brick for my man (CD only): *Hot Sauce* / Carry on (CD only): *Knight, Jean* / Song and dance (CD only): *Bar-Kays* / Do the funky chicken (CD only): *Thomas, Rufus* / Devil is dope (CD only): *Dramatics*
CD _____ CDSXD 075
Stax / Apr '93 / Pinnacle.

SONA GAIA COLLECTION ONE
CD _____ ND 62761
Lotus / Feb '93 / Jazz Horizons / Impetus.

SONG CREATORS IN EASTERN TURKEY
CD _____ SF 40432CD
Smithsonian Folkways / Jan '94 / ADA / Direct / Koch / CM / Cadillac.

SONGBIRDS
CD _____ MCCD 174
MCI / Sep '94 / Disc / THE.

SONGS & DANCES FROM CUBA
CD _____ EUCD 1235
ARC / Nov '93 / ARC Music / ADA.

SONGS & MUSIC THAT HELPED WIN THE WAR, THE
Colonel Bogey / If a grey-haired lady says How's yer father / Till the lights of London Shine again / Girl who loves a soldier / Lord Haw Haw of Zeesen / Navy's here / Tiggerty boo / Aircraft hand / If I only had wings / Victory roll rag / London I love / I'll get by / There's a land of begin again / Thing-ummy bob (that's going to win the war) / Zoot suite / Pair of silver wings / Swing out to victory / When the lights go on again / We mustn't miss the last bus home / Lit up / Homeward bound / I'll be seeing you / Paper doll / Someday soon / Victory polka / Shine on, victory moon / Sky liner / Cocktails for two / I'm gonna see my baby
CD _____ CDHD 403
Happy Days / Apr '95 / Conifer.

SONGS & RHYTHMS OF MALAWI
CD _____ PS 65140CD
Playasound / Apr '95 / Harmonia Mundi / ADA.

SONGS & RHYTHMS OF MOROCCO
CD _____ LYRCD 7336
Lyrichord / Feb '94 / Roots / ADA / CM.

SONGS FOR A BLACK PLANET (Best Of Goth)
Hex: *Specimen* / Crow baby: *March Violets* / Too many castles in the sky: *Rose Of Avalanche* / Alone she cries: *Skeletal Family* / Boys: *Bauhaus* / Fats terminal: *Bone Orchard* / Creatures of the night: *Screaming Dead* / Propaganda: *Play Dead* / Wake up: *Danse Society* / Under the milky way: *She knows: Balaam & The Angel* / Great expectations: *New Model Army* / Hollow eyes: *Red Lorry Yellow Lorry* / Ignore the machine: *Alien Sex Fiend* / Church of no return: *Christian Death*
CD _____ NTMCD 512
Nectar / Sep '95 / Pinnacle.

SONGS FOR LOVERS
CD _____ DCD 5278
Kenwest / Nov '92 / THE.

SONGS FOR THE 90'S
CD _____ BRAM 199117-2
Brambus / Nov '93 / ADA / Direct.

SONGS FROM BENGAL
CD _____ ARN 64214
Arion / Jun '93 / Discovery / ADA.

SONGS FROM JAHL
CD _____ RB 3005
Reggae Best / May '94 / Magnum Music Group / THE.

SONGS FROM THE EMERALD ISLE
Galway Bay: *Locke, Josef* / Spinning wheel: *Murphy, Delia* / Star of the County Down: *McCormack, John* / Ballyhoe: *McGoldrick, Anna* / Old bog road: *Drennan, Tommy* / Courtin' in the kitchen: *Murphy, Delia* / Mother Machree: *MacEwan, Father Sydney* / Trottin' to the fair: *Murray, Ruby* / Banks of my own lovely Lee: *O Se, Sean* / When Irish eyes are smiling: *Jones, Sandie* / Pretty Irish girl: *O'Dowda, Brendan & Ruby Murray* / Mountains of Mourne: *O'Dowda, Brendan* / Castlebar fair: *Gallagher, Bridie* / Rose of Tralee: *O'Dowda, Brendan* / Eileen O'Grady: *Gallagher, Bridie* / Danny boy: *Ó Sé, Seán* / Connemara: *O'Dowda, Brendan* / Flower of sweet Strabane: *Gallagher, Bridie* / Whiskey in the jar: *Dubliners* / Three drunken maidens: *Planxty* / Galway races: *Dubliners* / Kitty of Coleraine: *Bunratty Singers* / Bantry Bay: *Ó Sé, Seán*
CD Set _____ CDDL 1104
EMI / Nov '92 / EMI.

SONGS FROM THE GREIG DUNCAN COLLECTION
CD _____ CDTRAX 5003
Greentrax / Jul '95 / Conifer / Duncans / ADA / Direct.

SONGS FROM THE SHORES OF THE BLACK SEA
CD _____ LDX 274980
La Chant Du Monde / Jun '94 / Harmonia Mundi / ADA.

SONGS FROM THE SIXTIES
CD Set _____ CDPK 404
Charly / Feb '95 / Charly / THE / Cadillac.

SONGS OF BAKHSHI WOMEN
CD _____ W 260064
Inedit / Sep '95 / Harmonia Mundi / ADA / Discovery.

SONGS OF EARTH, WATER, FIRE & SKY (Music of the American Indian)
CD _____ 802462
New World / Aug '92 / Harmonia Mundi / ADA / Cadillac.

SONGS OF FREEDOM
CD _____ 11815
Music / Jul '95 / Target/BMG.

SONGS OF INDIA
CD _____ MNWCD 156
MNW / Mar '89 / Vital / ADA.

SONGS OF LEIBER & STOLLER, THE
Love potion no.9: *Searchers* / Girls, girls, girls: *Brown, Joe & The Bruvvers* / Yes: *Sandon, Johnny & The Remo Four* / I keep forgettin': *Hi-Fi's* / I who have nothing: *Spectres* / Brother Bill (The Last clean shirt): *Rockin' Berries* / Along came Jones: *Overlanders* / Tricky Dicky: *Searchers* / Trouble: *Ford, Emile & The Checkmates* / Three cool cats: *Ferris Wheel* / If you don't come back: *Takers* / Some other guy: *Searchers* / Dance with me: *Kestrels* / Don't: *Keyes, Ebony* / Hound dog: *Gene & The Gents* / Poison ivy: *Puppets*
CD _____ NEBCD 656
Sequel / Jun '93 / BMG.

SONGS OF LIFE (Music from Mission '89)
CD _____ WSTCD 9710
Nelson Word / Nov '89 / Nelson Word.

SONGS OF LOVE, LUCK, ANIMALS AND MAGIC
Love Song: *Douglas, Frank A.* / Grizzly bear war song: *Douglas, Frank A.* / Rabbit song: *Douglas, Frank A.* / Gambling songs: *Douglas, Frank A.* / Basket song: *Figueirosa, Aileen* / Brush dance: *Figueirosa, Aileen* / Brush dance song: *Figueirosa, Aileen* / Seagull song: *Norris, Ella* / Song to stop the Rain: *Norris, Ella* / Hunting Song: *Shaughnessy, Florence* / Pelican song: *Bommelyn, Loren* / Ceremonial dance / Ending ceremonial dance
CD _____ 8029722
New World / Sep '92 / Harmonia Mundi / ADA / Cadillac.

SONGS OF OLD IRELAND
CD _____ PWK 060
Carlton Home Entertainment / '88 / Carlton Home Entertainment.

SONGS OF OLD RUSSIA
CD _____ MCD 71560
Monitor / Sep '93 / CM.

SONGS OF SCOTLAND, THE
CD _____ EMPRCD 590
Emporio / Oct '95 / THE / Disc / CM.

SONGS OF THE ABORIGINES
CD _____ LYRCD 7331
Lyrichord / '91 / Roots / ADA / CM.

SONGS OF THE BALKANS
CD _____ CNCD 5982
Disky / Apr '94 / THE / BMG / Discovery / Pinnacle.

SONGS OF THE CIVIL WAR
I wish I was in Dixies' land / All quiet along the Potomac tonight / We are coming, Father Abra'am / Mother, is the battle over / Drummer boy of Shiloh / Beauregards's retreat from Shiloh / Jeff in petticoats / Weeping, sad and lonely / It's a gold old rebel
CD _____ NW 202
New World / '88 / Harmonia Mundi / ADA / Cadillac.

SONGS OF THE CIVIL WAR
CD _____ SLCD 9008
Starline / Dec '94 / Jazz Music.

SONGS OF THE DEPRESSION
CD _____ JASSCD 639
Jass / May '94 / CM / Jazz Music / ADA / Cadillac / Direct.

SONGS OF THE LAKOTA SIOUX (North America)
CD _____ 2741000
La Chant Du Monde / Jan '95 / Harmonia Mundi / ADA.

SONGS OF THE RUSSIAN PEOPLE
CD _____ 274978
La Chant Du Monde / Jan '95 / Harmonia Mundi / ADA.

SONGS OF THE TRAVELLING PEOPLE
Won't you buy my sweet blooming lavender: *Penfold, Janet* / Come a' ye tramps an' hawkers: *Stewart, Davie* / Blarney stone: *Barry, Margaret* / Berryfields o'Blair: *Stewart, Belle* / Muckin' o' geordie's byre: *McBeath, Jimmy & Willie Kelby* / Choring song: *Robertson, Jeannie* / Beggar wench: *Stewart, Davie* / Blacksmith courted me: *Smith, Phoebe* / Barnyards o' Delgaty/Gin I were where the Gadie rins: *Kelby, Willie* / On the bonny banks o' the roses: *McPhee, Duncan* / Bard of Armagh: *Barry, Margaret* / Dandling song/Bonny lassie-o/Cuckoo's nest: *Robertson, Jeannie* / I am a romany: *Smith, Phoebe* / Devonshire time and 2 gipsy hornpipes: *Connor, Frank O* / Higher Germanie: *Smith, Phoebe* / Little beggar man: *Doran, Paddy* / Kathleen: *Barry, Margaret* / Lady o' the dainty doon-by: *Robertson, Jeannie* / Tenpenny bit/She moves through the fair: *Stewart, Belle* / Poor smuggler's boy: *Brasil, Angela* / Aul' jockey Bruce o' the Fornet: *Stewart, Davie* / Tuning up: *Hughes, Carolyne & Charlie Lindsay* / Twa heids are better than yin: *Stewart, Kathleen* / Moss O'Burredale: *McBeath, Jimmy* / Gay Gordons: *Kelby, Willie* / Overgate: *Robertson, Jeannie* / Macpherson's rant: *Stewart, Donald & Albert* / Macpherson's lament: *Stewart, Davie*
CD _____ CDSDL 407
Saydisc / Nov '94 / Harmonia Mundi / ADA / Direct.

SONGS OF WARTIME
CD _____ RAJCD 925
Empress / Jun '94 / THE.

SONGS THAT WON THE WAR
CD _____ PLATCD 3928
Prism / May '94 / Prism.

SONGS THAT WON THE WAR
We're gonna hang out the washing on the Siegfried line / This is my army, Mister Jones / There'll always be an England / Roll out the barrel / Lili Marlene / I'll be with you in apple blossom_time / That lovely weekend / I'll never smile again / I've got a lovely bunch of coconuts / Roll me over / Kiss the boys goodbye / Nightingale sang in Berkley Square / Yours / Moonlight serenade / Lords of the air / We'll meet again / I'll get by / Kiss me goodnight, Sergeant Major / Bless 'em all / I'll be seeing you / When the lights go on again / White cliffs of Dover / Run rabbit run / I've got sixpence
CD _____ 4803342
Columbia / Apr '95 / Sony.

SONGWRITERS (3CD Set)
CD _____ CPSC 305
Charly / May '95 / Charly / THE / Cadillac.

SONGWRITERS EXCHANGE
CD _____ STCD 529
Stash / Jan '93 / Jazz Music / CM / Cadillac / Direct / ADA.

SONIC COLLECTION, THE
CD _____ SONCD 0070
Sonic Sounds / Sep '94 / Jetstar.

SONRISAS DE TEXAS
CD _____ MSA 007
Modern Blues / Feb '94 / Direct / ADA.

SONS AND LOVERS
CD _____ RVCD 27
Raven / Feb '93 / Direct / ADA.

SOPHISTICATED GENTLEMEN (2 CD/MCs)
Jump ballerina dance: *Cole, Nat King* / From Russia with love: *Monro, Matt* / That's amore: *Martin, Dean* / You're getting to be a habit with me: *Torme, Mel* / Way you look tonight: *Haymes, Dick* / Fascinating rhythm: *Damone, Vic* / Smile: *Cole, Nat King* / Story of Tina: *Martino, Al* / Stranger in paradise: *MacRae, Gordon* / Return to me: *Martin, Dean* / Portrait of my love: *Monro, Matt* / Spanish eyes: *Martino, Al* / On the street where you live: *Damone, Vic* / Blue moon: *Torme, Mel* / Do you love me: *Haymes, Dick* / Begin the beguine: *MacRae, Gordon* / Pretend: *Cole, Nat King* / Granada (Lara): *Martino, Al* / Impossible dream: *Monro, Matt* / Younger than Springtime: *Damone, Vic* / When I fall in love: *Cole, Nat King* / It might as well be Spring: *MacRae, Gordon* / I've got my love to keep me warm: *Martin, Dean* / How deep is the ocean: *Haymes, Dick* / Again: *Torme, Mel* / Most beautiful girl in the world: *Damone, Vic* / Unchained melody: *Monro, Matt* / Wanted: *Martino, Al* / Volare: *Martin, Dean* / Bewitched: *Torme, Mel* / Memories are made of this: *Martin, Dean* / My funny valentine: *MacRae, Gordon* / Who can I turn to: *Martino, Al* / Til there was you: *Damone, Vic* / Autumn leaves: *MacRae, Gordon* / Blossom fell: *Cole, Nat King* / Kiss: *Martin, Dean* / On days like these: *Monro, Matt* / Isn't it a lovely day (to be caught in the rain): *Haymes, Dick* / Very thought of you: *Cole, Nat King*
CD Set _____ CDDL 1299
Music For Pleasure / Nov '95 / EMI.

SOPHISTICATED LADIES (2CD/MC Set)
Fever: *Lee, Peggy* / Something: *Bassey, Shirley* / Wheel of fortune: *Starr, Kay* / What the world needs now is love: *Horne, Lena* / It must be him: *Carr, Vikki* / I can't give you

anything but love: *Garland, Judy* / I've got you under my skin: *Bassey, Shirley* / Folks who live on the hill: *Lee, Peggy* / Comes along a'love: *Starr, Kay* / Over the rainbow: *Garland, Judy* / Cry me a river: *London, Julie* / By the time I get to Phoenix: *Carr, Vikki* / Unchained melody: *Horne, Lena* / Changing partners: *Starr, Kay* / Long ago (and far away): *Stafford, Jo* / Fools rush in (where angels fear to tread): *Bassey, Shirley* / Occasional man: *London, Julie* / Zing went the strings of my heart: *Garland, Judy* / Mañana: *Lee, Peggy* / I (who have nothing) (Uno dei tanti): *Bassey, Shirley* / Side by side: *Starr, Kay* / It's a good day: *Lee, Peggy* / Old devil moon: *Garland, Judy* / Fly me to the moon: *London, Julie* / Fine romance: *Horne, Lena* / Walk away: *Carr, Vikki* / Cheek to cheek: *Lee, Peggy* / Nearness of you: *Bassey, Shirley* / Diamonds are a girl's best friend: *London, Julie* / In love in vain: *Horne, Lena* / Play me a simple melody: *Stafford, Jo* / Starlighters / My heart belongs to Daddy: *London, Julie* / As long as he needs me: *Bassey, Shirley* / Hello young lovers: *Horne, Lena* / Only love can break a heart: *Carr, Vikki* / I won't dance: *Lee, Peggy* / Always true to you in my fashion: *London, Julie* / That's entertainment: *Garland, Judy* / Yesterdays: *Stafford, Jo* / Puttin' on the Ritz: *Garland, Judy*
CD Set _____ CDDL 1302
Music For Pleasure / Nov '95 / EMI.

SOPHISTICATION (Songs Of The Thirties)
Top hat, white tie and tails: *Gibbons, Carroll* / Things are looking up: *Astaire, Fred* / Way you look tonight: *Astaire, Fred* / Touch of your lips: *Hildegarde* / Darling je vous aime beaucoup: *Hildegarde* / Just let me look at you: *Coward, Sir Noel* / Where are the songs we sung: *Coward, Sir Noel* / Limehouse blues: *Lawrence, Gertrude* / You were meant for me: *Lawrence, Gertrude* / Do do do: *Lawrence, Gertrude* / Someone to watch over me: *Lawrence, Gertrude* / Cup of coffee: *Lawrence, Gertrude* / Wild thyme: *Lawrence, Gertrude* / Experiment: *Lawrence, Gertrude* / Nightfall: *Carter, Benny* / So little time: *Keller, Greta* / I poured my heart into a song: *Hutch* / You do something to me: *Dietrich, Marlene* / Falling in love again: *Dietrich, Marlene* / Dancing honeymoon: *Buchanan, Jack* / And her mother came too: *Buchanan, Jack* / Fancy our meeting: *Buchanan, Jack* / Who: *Buchanan, Jack* / Two little bluebirds: *Buchanan, Jack* / Goodnight Vienna: *Buchanan, Jack* / It's not you: *Buchanan, Jack* / There's always tomorrow: *Buchanan, Jack* / Drop in next time you're passing: *Welch, Elisabeth* / One little kiss from you: *Matthews, Jessie* / Let me give my happiness to you: *Matthews, Jessie* / When you've got a little springtime in your heart: *Matthews, Jessie* / Over my shoulder: *Matthews, Jessie* / I nearly let love go slipping through my fingers: *Matthews, Jessie* / Got to dance my way to heaven: *Matthews, Jessie* / Everything's in rhythm with my heart: *Matthews, Jessie* / I can wiggle my ears: *Matthews, Jessie*
CD _____ PPCD 78108
Past Perfect / Feb '95 / THE.

SORTED, SNORTED AND SPORTED
CD _____ CRECD 117
Creation / Dec '91 / 3MV / Vital.

SOUL BALLADS
Fresh: *Kool & The Gang* / Let the music play: *White, Barry* / Don't walk away: *Four Tops* / Hold on to you: *Ruffin, Jimmy* / Hot pants: *Brown, James* / I really didn't mean it: *Vandross, Luther* / Harvest for the world: *Isley Brothers* / Shake you down: *Abbott, Gregory* / Sexual healing: *Gaye, Marvin* / Hurt: *Manhattans* / Hold me tight: *Nash, Johnny* / Use it up and wear it out: *Odyssey* / Freeway of love: *Franklin, Aretha* / Rock the boat: *Hues Corporation* / System addict: *Five Star* / In the midnight hour: *Reeves, Martha* / If you feel it: *Houston, Thelma* / Close to you: *Guthrie, Gwen* / Girls are more fun: *Parker, Ray Jnr.* / Goin' to the bank: *Commodores*
CD _____ STAMCD 018
Stardust / Oct '92 / Carlton Home Entertainment.

SOUL BALLADS
CD _____ MPV 5550
Movieplay / Apr '94 / Target/BMG.

SOUL BEAT
Going nowhere: *Gabrielle* / How can I love you more: *M People* / Don't walk away: *Jade* / Right here: *S.W.V.* / I love your smile: *Shanice* / Tom's diner: *DNA* / When I'm good and ready: *Sybil* / Please don't go: *KWS* / Now that we've found love: *Heavy D & The Boyz* / I'm doing fine now: *Pasadenas* / Love I lost: *West End & Sybil* / I wanna sex you up: *Color Me Badd* / Gypsy woman: *Waters, Crystal* / Ain't no Cassanova: *Sinclair* / Things that make you go hmmmm: *C & C Music Factory* / I will survive: *Gaynor, Gloria* / Best of my love: *Lovestation* / Everybody dance: *Evolution* / U got 2 let the music: *Cappella* / Motownphilly: *Boyz II Men*
CD _____ JARCD 9
Cookie Jar / Nov '93 / SRD.

SOUL BOX
(3CD/MC Set)
CD Set _____ TBXCD 503
TrueTrax / Jan '96 / THE.

SOUL BROTHERS, SOUL SISTERS
Sweet soul music: Sam & Dave / Operator: Knight, Gladys / Stand by me: King, Ben E. / Under the boardwalk: Drifters / Dancing in the street: Reeves, Martha / Rock your baby: Mcrae, george / Hey girl don't bother me: Tams / Band of gold: Payne, Freda / When a man loves a woman: Sledge, Percy / Something old, something new: Fantastics / Baby: Thomas, Carla / Love really hurts without you: Ocean, Billy / Harlem shuffle: Bob & Earl / It's in his kiss (Shoop shoop song): Everett, Betty / What becomes of the broken hearted: Ruffin, Jimmy / If you don't know me by now: Melvin, Harold & The Bluenotes / Rescue me: Fontella Bass / Knock on wood: Floyd, Eddie / Hey there lonely girl: Holman, Eddie / You'll lose a good thing: Lynn, Barbara
CD _____ MUCD 9026
Start / Apr '95 / Koch.

SOUL CHARTBUSTERS
Lady Marmalade: Labelle, Patti / Lovely one: Jacksons / Fantasy: Earth, Wind & Fire / Shake you down: Abbott, Gregory / Dirty ol' man: Three Degrees / Love train: O'Jays / My love is waiting: Gaye, Marvin / Best of my love: Emotions / Boogie nights: Heatwave / Best of love: Rose Royce / It's raining men: Weather Girls / Disco lady: Taylor, Johnnie / Dance little sister: D'Arby, Terence Trent / Family affair: Sly & The Family Stone / I lead to toe: Lisa Lisa & Cult Jam / Groove: Franklin, Rodney
CD _____ 4771192
Embassy / Oct '95 / Sony.

SOUL CHASERS
Got to get away: Brown, Sheree / Be for real: Miller, Cat / Do it any way you want: Winters, Robert / Trying to get to you: Carter, Valerie / (A case of) Too much love makin': Scott, Gloria / Top of the stairs: Collins & Collins / I want to be your everything: High Fashion / Would you believe in me: Lucien, John / All of my love: Jeter, Genobia / Looking up to you: Wycoff, Michael / And so it begins: Syreeta / Never stopped loving you: Davis, Tyrone / Hold tight: Magic Lady / Call me: Reynolds, L.J.
CD _____ CDEXP 4
Expansion / Nov '92 / Pinnacle / Sony / 3MV.

SOUL CHASERS 2
CD _____ CDEXP 8
Expansion / Nov '94 / Pinnacle / Sony / 3MV.

SOUL CLASSICS
Cry like a baby: Box Tops / Didn't I blow your mind this time: Delfonics / Ms. Grace: Tymes / Kissin' in the back row of the movies: Drifters / Aquarius (let the sunshine in): 5th Dimension / Woman needs love (just like you do): Parker, Ray Jnr. / Givin' up givin' in: Three Degrees / Highwire: Carr, Linda / I am what I am: Gaynor, Gloria / I can't help myself: Real Thing / Caribbean queen (no more love on the run): Ocean, Billy / Hot, wild, unrestricted, crazy love: Jackson, Millie / I'd rather go blind: Turner, Ruby / Hang on in there baby: Bristol, Johnny / Can't give you anything (but my love): Stylistics / I'm your puppet: Purify, James & Bobby / It's in his kiss (Shoop shoop song): Everett, Betty / I can sing a rainbow/Love is blue: Dells / My baby just cared for me: Simone, Nina / Who's the one: Brown, James
CD _____ STAMCD 016
Stardust / Oct '92 / Carlton Home Entertainment.

SOUL CLASSICS
CD _____ 24086
Laserlight / Jan '95 / Target/BMG.

SOUL CLASSICS
This is the album: Moore, Melba / Can't get without you: Real Thing / Hold back the night: Trammps / Come back and finish what you started: Knight, Gladys & The Pips / Dancing in the street: Reeves, Martha / Little piece of leather: Elbert, Donnie / Soul man: Dam & Dave / Harlem shuffle: Bob & Earl / Higher and higher: Wilson, Jackie / Knock on wood: Floyd, Eddie / Your little trustmaker: Tymes / Rock your baby: McCrae, George
CD _____ 74321339282
Camden / Jan '96 / BMG.

SOUL DANCE
CD _____ STACD 058
Wisepack / Sep '94 / THE / Conifer.

SOUL DESIRE
Sexual healing: Gaye, Marvin / Sign your name: D'Arby, Terence Trent / Shake you down: Abbott, Gregory / Rock me tonight: Jackson, Freddie / After the love has gone: Earth, Wind & Fire / Loving you: Riperton, Minnie / Give me the reason: Vandross, Luther / Now 'bout us: Champaign / I still haven't found what I'm looking for: Chimes / Smooth operator: Sade / Ain't no sunshine: Withers, Bill / I need your lovin': Williams, Alyson / Mated: Grant, David & Jaki Graham / Always and forever: Heatwave / Tonight, I celebrate my love to you: Bryson, Peabo &

Roberta Flack / If you don't know me by now: Melvin, Harold & The Bluenotes
CD _____ 4717322
Columbia / Jun '92 / Sony.

SOUL DESIRE VOL.2
On the wings of love: Osborne, Jeffrey / So amazing: Vandross, Luther / Soul provider: Bryson, Peabo / Wind beneath my wings: Knight, Gladys / Cherish: Kool & The Gang / Secret Lovers: Atlantic Starr / Winter in July: Bomb The Bass / Come into my life: Sims, Joyce / Hang on to your love: Sade / See the day: Lee, Dee C. / Show me the way: Belle, Regina / Free: Williams, Deniece / Reunited: Peaches & Herb / Just the way you are: White, Barry / Me and Mrs. Jones: Paul, Billy / Don't leave me this way: Melvin, Harold
CD _____ 4724162
Columbia / Nov '92 / Sony.

SOUL DESIRE VOL.3
Love supreme: Downing, Will / My one temptation: Paris, Mica / Sweetest taboo: Sade / Never too much: Vandross, Luther / I can make you feel good: Shalamar / Finest: S.O.S. Band / Juicy fruit: Mtume / I'm doing fine now: Pasadenas / Piano in the dark: Russell, Brenda / Feel so high: Des'ree / Wishing on a star: Cover Girls / Baby, come to me: Belle, Regina / My love is waiting: Gaye, Marvin / Shining star: Manhattans / Mind blowing decisions: Heatwave / Caravan of love: Isley-Jasper-Isley
CD _____ 4739322
Columbia / Jun '93 / Sony.

SOUL DESIRE VOL.3.1-3
(3CD Set)
Sexual healing: Gaye, Marvin / Sign your name: D'Arby, Terence Trent / Shake you down: Abbott, Gregory / Rock me tonight: Jackson, Freddie / After the love has gone: Earth, Wind & Fire / Lovin' you: Riperton, Minnie / Give me the reason: Vandross, Luther / How 'bout us: Champaign / I still haven't found what I'm looking for: Chimes / Smooth operator: Sade / Ain't no sunshine: Withers, Bill / I need your lovin': Williams, Alyson / Mated: Grant, David & Jaki Graham / Always and forever: Heatwave / Tonight, I celebrate my love to you: Bryson, Peabo & Roberta Flack / If you don't know me by now: Melvin, Harold & The Bluenotes / On the wings of love: Osborne, Jeffrey / So amazing: Vandross, Luther / Soul provider: Bryson, Peabo / Wind beneath my wings: Knight, Gladys / Cherish: Kool & The Gang / Secret lovers: Atlantic Starr / Winter in July: Bomb The Bass / Come into my life: Sims, Joyce / Hang on to your love: Sade / See the day: Lee, Dee C. / Show me the way: Belle, Regina / Free: Williams, Deniece / Reunited: Peaches & Herb / Just the way you are: White, Barry / Me and Mrs. Jones: Paul, Billy / Don't leave me this way: Melvin, Harold / Love supreme: Downing, Will / My one temptation: Paris, Mica / Sweetest taboo: Sade / Never too much: Vandross, Luther / I can make you feel good: Shalamar / Finest: S.O.S. Band / Juicy fruit: Mtume / I'm doing fine now: Pasadenas / Piano in the dark: Russell, Brenda / Feel so high: Des'ree / Wishing on a star: Cover Girls / Baby, come to me: Belle, Regina / My love is waiting: Gaye, Marvin / Shining star: Manhattans / Mind blowing decisions: Heatwave / Caravan of love: Isley-Jasper-Isley
CD Set _____ 4741212
Columbia / Oct '94 / Sony.

SOUL DEVOTION - THE VERY BEST OF HEART & SOUL
Don't be a stranger: Carroll, Dina / My destiny: Richie, Lionel / One moment in time: Houston, Whitney / Change: Stansfield, Lisa / Sign your name: D'Arby, Terence Trent / Save the best for last: Williams, Vanessa / My one temptation: Paris, Mica / Stay with me baby / Three times a lady: Commodores / Being with you: Robinson, Smokey / My cherie amour: Wonder, Stevie / What becomes of the broken hearted: Ruffin, Jimmy / You are everything: Ross, Diana & Marvin Gaye / With you I'm born again: Preston, Billy & Syreeta / Best thing that ever happened to me: Knight, Gladys & The Pips / One day in your life: Jackson, Michael / Touch me in the morning: Ross, Diana / I say a little prayer: Franklin, Aretha / Tired of being alone: Green, Al / (Sittin' on) the dock of the bay: Redding, Otis / When a man loves a woman: Sledge, Percy / Hey there lonely girl: Holman, Eddie / After the love has gone: Earth, Wind & Fire / If you don't know me by now: Melvin, Harold & The Bluenotes / Have you seen her: Chi-Lites / Lovely day: Withers, Bill / Teardrops: Womack & Womack / It's too late: Quartz / If it's too late is good for a way out: Odyssey / Wishing on a star: Rose Royce / One day I'll fly away: Crawford, Randy / Always: Atlantic Starr / Slow hand: Pointer Sisters / Your love is wing: Sade
CD _____ 5166242
PolyGram TV / Mar '94 / PolyGram.

SOUL DREAMING
Like sister and brother: Drifters / Didn't I blow your mind this time: Delfonics / Love come down: King, Evelyn 'Champagne' / Native New Yorker: Odyssey / Woman in love: Three Degrees / You make me feel

brand new: Stylistics / Hold to my love: Ruffin, Jimmy / When she was my girl: Four Tops / Livin' in America: Brown, James / You're the first, my last, my everything: White, Barry / Joanna: Kool & The Gang / Summer breeze: Isley Brothers / I really didn't mean it: Vandross, Luther / Never knew love like this: O'Neal, Alexander / Sexual healing: Gaye, Marvin / Let's hear it for the boy: Williams, Deniece / Come back and finish what you started: Knight, Gladys & The Pips / Kiss and say goodbye: Manhattans
CD _____ STACD 006
Wisepack / Nov '92 / THE / Conifer.

SOUL EMOTION
If you don't know me by now: Simply Red / Mercy mercy me/I want you: Palmer, Robert / Wherever I lay my hat: Young, Paul / Let's stay together: Turner, Tina / Change: Stansfield, Lisa / One moment in time: Houston, Whitney / Walk on by: Warwick, Dionne / Thinking about your love: Thomas, Kenny / Too many walls: Dennis, Cathy / It's too late: Quartz / Never knew love like this before: Mills, Stephanie / There's nothing like this: Omar / Move closer: Nelson, Phyllis / It's a man's man's man's world: Brown, James / In the midnight hour: Pickett, Wilson / Can't get enough of your love: White, Barry / After the love has gone: Earth, Wind & Fire / Solid: Ashford & Simpson
CD _____ 5151882
PolyGram TV / Mar '92 / PolyGram.

SOUL EMOTION
CD Set _____ NSCD 011
Newsound / Feb '95 / THE.

SOUL EXPERIENCE, THE
CD _____ BOXD 28
Carlton Home Entertainment / Nov '92 / Carlton Home Entertainment.

SOUL FOR LOVERS
CD _____ DCD 5274
Kenwest / Nov '92 / THE.

SOUL FROM THE CITY
CD _____ SCD 004
Infonet / Dec '95 / Pinnacle / Vital.

SOUL HITS
CD Set _____ 4417242
Pilz / Oct '92 / BMG.

SOUL HITS
CD _____ LECDD 638
Wisepack / Aug '95 / THE / Conifer.

SOUL HITS DANCE PARTY
Soul man: Sam & Dave / Knock on wood: Floyd, Eddie / Patches: Carter, Clarence / Walking the dog: Thomas, Rufus / Rescue me: Bass, Fontella / In crowd: Gray, Dobie / I know: George, Barbara / Shake: Wilson, Al / Western movies: Olympics / Sweet sixteen: Cooke, Sam / Harlem shuffle: Bob & Earl / You keep me hangin' on: Simon, Joe / That's the way I feel about cha: Womack, Bobby / Hold on to what you've got: Tex, Joe
CD _____ QSCD 6005
Quality (Charly) / Apr '92 / Charly.

SOUL INSPIRATION
My destiny: Richie, Lionel / I love your smile: Shanice / looking through patient eyes: PM Dawn / I never felt like this before: Paris, Mica / Drift away: Gray, Dobie / What's going on: Gaye, Marvin / Got to be there: Jackson, Michael / Sweet love: Baker, Anita / Save the best for last: Williams, Vanessa / Have you seen her: Chi-Lites / What becomes of the broken hearted: Ruffin, Jimmy / Hey there lonely girl: Holman, Eddie / Me and Mrs. Jones: Jackson, Freddie / Piano in the dark: Russell, Brenda / Wake up everybody: Melvin, Harold / Feel so high: Des'ree / Until you come back to me: Franklin, Aretha / Love makes the world go round: Don-E
CD _____ 5162262
PolyGram TV / Jun '93 / PolyGram.

SOUL INSPIRATION
(54 Soul Classics From The 70's And 80's)
Just an illusion: Imagination / I'm so excited: Pointer Sisters / System addict: Five Star / Going back to my roots: Odyssey / Give it up: K.C. & The Sunshine Band / She's strange: Cameo / Rock the boat: Hues Corporation / Jumpin' jack flash: Franklin, Aretha / Let the music play: White, Barry / Boogie wonderland: Earth, Wind & Fire / Can you feel it: Jacksons / Burn rubber on me: Gap Band / Love come down: King, Evelyn 'Champagne' / Mama used to say: Giscombe, Junior / Rockit: Hancock, Herbie / It's a disco night (rock don't stop): King, Evelyn / Livin' in America: Brown, James / Do what you do: Jackson, Jermaine / All the love in the world: Warwick, Dionne / Joanna: Kool & The Gang / Night to remember: Shalamar / Your love is back: Sade / Never knew love like this before: Mills, Stephanie / Secret lovers: Atlantic Starr / Stay with me tonight: Osborne, Jeffrey / There goes my first love: Drifters / Reach out, I'll be there: Gaynor, Gloria / Hundred ways: Jones, Quincy & James Ingram / You make me feel brand new: Stylistics / Never, never gonna give you up: White, Barry / Woman in love: Three Degrees / Summer breeze: Isley Brothers / My

love is waiting: Gaye, Marvin / Lovely day (remix): Withers, Bill / What a fool believes: Franklin, Aretha / Letter: Box Tops / Kissin' in the back row of the movies: Drifters / Hang on in there baby: Bristol, Johnny / Reunited: Peaches & Herb / Best thing that ever happened to me: Knight, Gladys & The Pips / Didn't I: Delfonics / Me and Mrs. Jones: Paul, Billy / Running away: Sly & The Family Stone / Love train: O'Jays / What a difference a day makes: Phillips, Esther / Betcha by golly wow: Stylistics / I'm your puppet: Purify, James & Bobby / That lady: Isley Brothers / I can see clearly now: Nash, Johnny / L.O.D. (on delivery): Ocean, Billy / Can't get enough of your love babe: White, Barry / Where did our love go: Elbert, Donnie / Get up offa that thing: Brown, James
CD Set _____ BOXD 43
Carlton Home Entertainment / Jan '94 / Carlton Home Entertainment.

SOUL INSPIRATION
Newsound / May '95 / THE.
_____ NSCD 020

SOUL JAZZ LOVE STRATA-EAST
Peace go with you, brother: Scott-Heron, Gil / Well you needn't: Ridley, Larry / Prince of peace: Sanders, Pharoah / Changa chikuyo: Ridley, Larry / John Coltrane: Jordan, Clifford / Hopscotch: Rouse, Charlie / Bottle: Scott-Heron, Gil / Travelling man: Cowell, Stanley / First impressions: Farrah, Shamek / Dance of the little children: Parker, Billy / Eddie Harris: Jordan, Clifford / Smiling Billy suite Pt.2: Heath Brothers
CD _____ SJRCD 019
Soul Jazz / Oct '94 / New Note / Vital.

SOUL JAZZ VOL.1
Honky tonk: Butler, Billy / Return of the prodigal son: Green, Byrdie / I've got the blues: Moody, James / Mom and dad: Earland, Charles / 322 wow: Lytle, Johnny / Up to date: Smith, Johnny 'Hammond' / Datdere: Adderley, Cannonball Quartet / Light: Ammons, Gene
CD _____ CDBGP 1028
BGP / Jun '89 / Pinnacle.

SOUL JUKE BOX HITS
CD Set _____ DCD 5064
Disky / Jul '89 / THE / Discovery / Pinnacle.

SOUL LOVE
CD _____ STACD 055
Stardust / Aug '93 / Carlton Home Entertainment.

SOUL MAN
Music / Jul '95 / Target/BMG.
_____ 22513

SOUL MATE
CD _____ DINCD 82
Dino / Feb '94 / Pinnacle / 3MV.

SOUL MESSENGER VOLUME 1
CD _____ RNGCD 002
EC1 / Mar '95 / EC1 / Grapevine.

SOUL MOODS
CD Set _____ NSCD 009
Newsound / Feb '95 / THE.

SOUL NIGHTS
Searching: China Black / Just a step from heaven: Eternal / Don't be a stranger: Carroll, Dina / End of the road: Boyz II Men / Never: Heart / Drift away: Gray, Dobie / Night shift: Commodores / Rainy night in Georgia: Crawford, Randy / Where in the love: Eric Mica & Will Downing / Just another day: Secada, Jon / So close to love: Moten, Wendy / Now I know what made Otis blue: Young, Paul / Stop loving me, stop loving you: Hall, Daryl / Because of you: Gabrielle / Let's stay together: Pasadenas / So amazing: Vandross, Luther / Shake you down: Abbott, Gregory / Everybody's gotta learn sometime: Yazz / Drift away: Gray, Dobie / Tonight, I celebrate my love: Bryson, Peabo & Roberta Flack / Midnight at the Oasis: Muldaur, Maria
CD _____ 5250052
PolyGram TV / Aug '94 / PolyGram.

SOUL OF A WOMAN
CD _____ RENCD 102
Castle / Jul '95 / BMG.

SOUL OF BLACK MUSIC
CD _____ 24010
Laserlight / Mar '95 / Target/BMG.

SOUL OF BLACK PERU, THE
CD _____ 9362458782
Warner Bros. / Jun '95 / Warner Music.

SOUL OF CHRISTMAS
God rest ye merry gentlemen / First Noel / O come all ye faithful (Adeste Fidelis) / Ding dong merrily on high / Once in Royal David's City / Silent night / While shepherds watched their flocks by night / O little town of Bethlehem / We three kings / Away in a manger / Hark the Herald angels sing / Auld lang syne
CD _____ SOV 009CD
Sovereign / '92 / Target/BMG.

SOUL OF DETROIT
CD _____ CDSD 136
Soul Supply / Apr '89 / Pinnacle.

SOUL OF GOSPEL, THE
I'll take you there: Staple Singers / You're all I need to get by: Franklin, Aretha / Have a good time together: Bass, Fontella / Lean on me: Withers, Bill / (Your love keeps lifting me) higher and higher: Wilson, Jackie / People get ready: Impressions / Oh happy day: Hawkins, Edwin Singers / (Take another little) piece of my heart: Franklin, Erma / Let's stay together: Green, Al / I say a little prayer: Franklin, Aretha / Stand by me: King, Ben E. / Yuh mo be there: Ingram, James & Michael McDonald / I'm going all the way: Sounds Of Blackness / Message is love: Baker, Arthur & Backbeat Disciples/ Al Green / Let my people go: Winans / I knew you were waiting (for me): Franklin, Aretha & George Michael / I still haven't found what I'm looking for: Chimes / Anytime you need a friend: New Jersey Gospel Choir / Up where we belong: South Carolina Baptist Choir / If you're ready (come go with me): Staple Singers / Mercy mercy me: Gaye, Marvin
CD _____ RADCD 31
Global / Nov '95 / BMG.

SOUL OF LA, THE
Sweet magic: Servicemen / Wonders of love: Soul Gents / You should have told me: New Yorkers / Under your spell: Paramounts / This is the way I feel: Four Tempos / There's that mountain: Trips / Do this for me: Emotions / It was wrong: Shades Of Jade / Anything for you: Furys / Jealous of you: Mystics / Don't let love get you down: Phonetics / You're good enough for me: Versatiles / (Down in) East LA: Angelenos / You'll never make the grade: Sun Lovers / Sad, sad memories: Tempos / No one else can take your place: Inspirations / (I love her so much) it hurts me: Majestics / Hey hey girls: Vines / Is the feeling still there: Remarkables / Save your love: Soul Patrol / Girl, I love you: Sinceres / Just a little: Prominents / Love is a hurting game: Four Sights / My poor heart: Sun Lovers / Beginning of the end: Young Hearts
CD _____ GSCD 032
Goldmine / Mar '94 / Vital.

SOUL OF LENNON AND MCCARTNEY, THE
Let it be: Franklin, Aretha / Hey Jude: Pickett, Wilson / Long and winding road: Houston, Cissy / Come together: Turner, Ike & Tina / In my life: Havens, Richie / Yesterday: Arnold, P.P. / I want you: Vaughan, Sarah / Can't buy me love: Fitzgerald, Ella / Ticket to ride: Guthrie, Gwen / Day tripper: Redding, Otis / Got to get you into my life: Earth, Wind & Fire / We can work it out: Brown, Maxine / I love him: Detroit Emeralds / Lady Madonna: Booker T Trio / Dear Prudence: Five Stairsteps / Hard days night: Warwick, Dionne / Get back: Green, Al
CD _____ DINCD 112
Dino / Nov '95 / Pinnacle / 3MV.

SOUL OF RHYTHM 'N' BLUES REVUE
(Live At The Lone Star Roadhouse)
CD _____ SHAN 9005CD
Shanachie / Oct '93 / Koch / ADA / Greensleeves.

SOUL OF THE 80'S VOL. 2
CD _____ JHD 043
Tring / Jun '92 / Tring / Prism.

SOUL ON THE STREETS VOL. 1
Take care of yourself: Dan-Elle / Love and devotion: Marshall, Wayne / 24-7 Love: Irini / Save your love: S.L.O. / Hooked on you: Everis / Don't let them know: Irini / You turn me on: Everis / Sexual thing: Marshall, Wayne / Sweet lovin': 3rd Zone / Fire and desire (Remixes): Dan-Elle / Everybody's gotta rave: Marshall, Wayne / Don't let them know (remix): Irini / She want's a 24/7: Hyper Man
CD _____ SCGCD 201
SCG / May '94 / Jetstar.

SOUL ON THE STREETS VOL. 2
CD _____ SCGCD 3
Stone Cold Gentleman / Dec '94 / Jetstar.

SOUL POWER
Sign your name: D'Arby, Terence Trent / Paradise: Sade / Never too much: Vandross, Luther / Can you feel it: Jacksons / Let's hear it for the boy: Williams, Deniece / That lady: Isley Brothers / Ain't no sunshine: Withers, Bill / Crazy: Manhattans / Sweet understanding love: Four Tops / Something old, something new: Fantastics / Wedding bell blues: 5th Dimension / Slightest touch: Five Star / Ain't nothin' goin' on but the rent: Guthrie, Gwen / Livin' in America: Brown, James / Come into my life: Sims, Joyce / Down on the street: Shakatak / Secret lovers: Atlantic Starr / What a difference a day makes: Phillips, Esther / Gonna get along without you now: Wills, Viola
CD _____ STACD 015
Telstar / Oct '92 / BMG.

SOUL PRESSURE
CD _____ CDMISH 2
Debut / Jun '95 / Pinnacle / 3MV / Sony.

SOUL PRESSURE 2
(14 Urban Soul Flavours)
Never make love: Troi / Total satisfaction: Heron, Dee / Could you be mine: Ballin, Chris / Get down on it: Kreuz / Something

good tonight: Trichelle / Do me that way: Damage / Come go away: Truce / First time: Haynes, Victor / Giving my all: Phillips, Jennifer / In love: Campbell, Roger / Lover come back: Sha Sha / Heaven: SCG & Inni / Closer than close: McNeish, Carol / Do you really: Ruude
CD _____ CDMISH 4
Mission / Dec '95 / 3MV / Sony.

SOUL QUEENS, THE
CD _____ 15168
Laserlight / Aug '91 / Target/BMG.

SOUL REFLECTION
Three times a lady: Commodores / I don't wanna lose you: Turner, Tina / Have you seen her: M.C. Hammer / Stop to love: Vandross, Luther / Criticize: O'Neal, Alexander / Yah mo be there: Ingram, James & Michael McDonald / There'll be sad songs (to make you cry): Ocean, Billy / Almaz: Crawford, Randy / If you don't know me by now: Melvin, Harold & The Bluenotes / Just my imagination: Temptations / I second that emotion: Robinson, Smokey & The Miracles / Too busy thinking about my baby: Gaye, Marvin / Hold back the night: Trammps / Just the way you are: White, Barry / You sexy thing: Hot Chocolate / Always: Atlantic Starr / Baby, come to me: Austin, Patti & James Ingram
CD _____ 8453342
PolyGram TV / Feb '91 / PolyGram.

SOUL SEARCHING
Could it be I'm falling in love: Detroit Spinners / Used to be my girl: O'Jays / I can see clearly now: Cliff, Jimmy / Don't let love get you down: Bell, Archie & The Drells / Let's get it on: Gaye, Marvin / Reunited: Peaches & Herb / Me and Mrs. Jones: Paul, Billy / Right here (Human Nature radio mix): S.W.V. / I still haven't found what I'm looking for: Chimes / Special kind of love (Radio edit): Carroll, Dina / Stay: Eternal / I miss you: Haddaway / Walk on by: Warwick, Dionne / Almaz: Crawford, Randy / Feel so high: Des'ree / Lovely day: Withers, Bill / Night to remember: Shalamar / Don't let it go to your head: Carne, Jean / I've made me feel like) a natural woman: Franklin, Aretha / Delicate: D'Arby, Terence Trent / I love your smile: Hughes, Jimmy / These arms of mine: Redding, Otis / On the wings of love: Osborne, Jeffrey / Your body's calling: R. Kelly / Hearts run free: Staton, Candi / Whole town's laughing at me: Pendergrass, Teddy / Show me the way: Bell, Regina / Private number: Clay, Judy & William Bell / I want your love: Chic / Sweet love: Baker, Anita / Woman to woman: Brown, Shirley / I'm doing fine now: New York City / Winter in July: Bomb The Bass / Misty blue: Moore, Dorothy
CD Set _____ MOODCD 34
Columbia / Jul '94 / Sony.

SOUL SEARCHING
CD _____ HILOCD 11
Hi / Jan '95 / Pinnacle.

SOUL SENSATION
CD _____ MATCD 204
Castle / Dec '92 / BMG.

SOUL SENSATION
CD Set _____ NSCD 012
Newsound / Feb '95 / THE.

SOUL SENSITIVITY
CD Set _____ NSCD 010
Newsound / Feb '95 / THE.

SOUL SISTERS
CD _____ NTRCD 028
Nectar / Sep '94 / Pinnacle.

SOUL SOLDIERS
I'm the one who loves you: Banks, Darrell / No one blinder (than a man who won't see): Banks, Darrell / Just because your love has gone: Banks, Darrell / Only the strong survive: Banks, Darrell / Got to get rid of you: Barnes, J.J. / Snowflakes: Barnes, J.J. / I like everything about you: Hughes, Jimmy / I'm so glad: Hughes, Jimmy / Did you forget: Hughes, Jimmy / Chains of love: Hughes, Jimmy / I just ain't strong as I used to be: Hughes, Jimmy / Since I lost my baby's love: Lance, Major / I I wanna make up (before we break up): Lance, Major / That's the story of my life: Lance, Major / Girl come on home: Lance, Major / Ain't no sweat: Lance, Major / Beautiful feeling (CD only): Banks, Darrell / When a man loves a woman (CD only): Banks, Darrell / Let 'em down baby (CD only): Hughes, Jimmy / I'm not ashamed to beg or plead (CD only): Hughes, Jimmy / Sweet Sherry (CD only): Barnes, J.J. / Baby, please come back home (CD only): Barnes, J.J.
CD _____ CDSX 012
Stax / Aug '88 / Pinnacle.

SOUL SOUNDS OF THE 90'S
CD _____ SOUNDSCD 7
Street Sounds / Oct '95 / BMG.

SOUL STIRRINGS - THE NU INSPIRATIONAL
CD _____ BRCD 599
4th & Broadway / Oct '93 / PolyGram.

SOUL TO SOUL
CD _____ CDTRL 356
Trojan / Jul '95 / Jetstar / Total/BMG.

SOUL TRACKS
CD _____ CDSR 046
Telstar / May '94 / BMG.

SOUL TRAIN VOL.1
CD _____ CDSGP 0149
Prestige / Jan '95 / Total/BMG.

SOUL UNDERGROUND
Two sides to every story: Love, Jimmy / Baby I'm serious: Tillman, Charlotta / Don't accuse me: Squires / I feel good (all over): Lavette, Bettye / Come back baby: Stoppers / (I know) Your love has gone away: Drapers / Only your love can save me: Lavette, Bettye / He's got the nerve: True Tones / Another time another place: Starr, Harry / If you ask me (because I love you): Williams, Jerry / Fell in love with you baby: Elliot, Linda / Dance dance dance: Casualeers / What shall I do: Frankie & Classicals / Don't refuse my love: Intrigues / Stand up like a man: Lavette, Bettye / Nothing can help you now: Curtis, Lenny / I'll do anything: Troy, Doris / Too long without some loving: Clovers / What did I do: Humes, Anita & The Essex / Walkin': Jones, Jimmy / I'm just a fool for you: Lavette, Bettye / Mama's got a bag of her own: King, Anna / Can't help lovin' dat man: Vann, Ila / Step into my world: Vann, Ila
CD _____ NEMCD 759
Sequel / Oct '95 / BMG.

SOUL'D TOGETHER VOL.2
(The Soul Of Black America)
CD _____ ATCD 016
About Time / Nov '92 / Target/BMG.

SOUL'D TOGETHER VOL.3
(The Soul Of Black America)
Close to you: Bush, Charles / I want you: Smith, Antoine / Second go around: Cornelious, Eve / House my love: Blount, Carlton / Never go back: Ledford, Kenne / G.o.o.d. times: DeBarge / I knew I could always count on you: Brown, Shirley / Thank you lady: Brittan, James / Nine to five (who said it): Floyd, Jeff / Reaching for the sky: Riley, Walter / Drug free society: Mozie B / Never give up: Mathis, Diane / One more night: Gaines, Rosie / Let me kiss you where it hurts: Burris, Warren / Girl I miss you: Group Life / If you need it: Bush, Charles
CD _____ ATCD 017
About Time / Aug '93 / Target/BMG.

SOUL'D TOGETHER VOL.4
(The Soul Of Black America)
Walking in rhythm: Foxx Empire / I'll give my love: Thin Line / Take U to the top: Bush, Charles / Taking it as it comes: Desi / Tell me to stay: Kiass / Reach out your hand: Mason, Laverna / Baby I know: McNeir, Ronnie / Nothing like this: Greene, Mark / Call me: Nash, Kevin / Straight from the heart: Brittan, James / Throw her love: Floyd, Jeff / Peaceful: Eddie M
CD _____ ATCD 023
About Time / Aug '95 / Target/BMG.

SOULED ON REGGAE
CD _____ EMPRCD 577
Emporio / Jul '95 / THE / Disc / CM.

SOULED OUT - THE BEST OF CHELSEA
CD _____ CHELD 1007
Start / May '89 / Koch.

SOULFUL KINDA 70'S
(2CD Set)
Shy guy: Baker, Johnny / Man of value: Berklay, Tyrone / Your smallest wish: 21st Century Ltd / Dancing on a daydream: Souivation Army / You live only once: Imperial Wonders / Happy: Velvet Hammer / It's not where you start: Davis, Luckey / Like taking candy from a baby: Brown, J.T. / Ain't nothing wrong: Jones, Jimmy / This economy: Michel, Lee / Shady lady: Newton, Bobby / Baby hard times: Love, Dave / In a world so cold: St. Germain, Tyrone / Over the top: Dawson, Roy / Secret place: Brothers / If it wasn't for you: Four Sonics / Loneliness: Will, David / Let's spend some time together: Houston, Larry / Dance all night: Masterplan / You're my main squeeze: Crystal Motion / Game players: Silverspoon, Dooley / Wrong crowd: Prince George / Bet you if you ask around: Velvet / You better keep her: Holmes, Marvin / You can win: Bileo / Heartache and pain: Pages / He's always around: Gerrard, Donny / I can't make it: Simmons, Vessie / I want to be loved: Stevens & Foster / Love's built on a strong foundation: Big Jim's Border Crossing / Ho happy day: Flame 'n' King / Turning point: Simmons, Mack / Honey baby: Innervision / Have love will travel: Jones, Rosey / When the fuel runs out: Ambros / Spellbound: Everett, Frank / I won't desert: Family Circle / Come back: Fantastic Puzzles / What goes up: Cody, Black / Don't you leave: Hughes, Freddie / Operator operator: Baker, Johnny / Some kinda man: Pride & Passion / All I want: Neal, C.C. / Come and ask me: 5 Wagers / From the bottom of your heart: Steelers / Give in to the power of love: Committee / Let's get nasty: Stephens, Chuck / What: Weathers, Oscar / Love will turn around: Entertains / I'm a winner: Just Bobby
CD Set _____ GSCD 050
Goldmine / Nov '95 / Vital.

SOULFUL LOVE DUETS #1
CD _____ SCL 2512
Ichiban Soul Classics / Nov '95 / Koch.

SOULFUL LOVE DUETS #2
CD _____ SCL 2513
Ichiban Soul Classics / Nov '95 / Koch.

SOULINN'
Wake up in the city: Pure Instinct / All by myself: Backbone / Light: G.E.M. / Who's got the muthafunk: Muthafunk / Race: Fumi / You blow my mind away: Sugarfalls / Thankful: Egidio / Skyline: Pure Instinct
CD _____ SDS 41722
Three / Sep '95 / EWM.

SOUND BOY KILLING
CD _____ SH 45018
Shanachie / Dec '94 / Koch / ADA / Greensleeves.

SOUND GALLERY, THE
Oh Calcutta: Pell, Dave / Black rite: Mandingo / Headhunter: Mandingo / Snake pit: Mandingo / Punch bowl: Parker, Allan / Night rider: Hawkshaw, Alan / Girl in a sportscar: Hawkshaw, Alan / It's all at the co-op now: Hawkshaw, Alan / Blarney's stoned: Hawkshaw, Alan / Riviera affair: Richardson, Neil / Jetstream: Gregory, John / Jaguar: Gregory, John / Half forgotten daydreams: Gregory, John / Life of leisure: Mansfield, Keith / Young scene: Mansfield, Keith / Music to drive by: Loss, Joe / Detectives: Tew, Alan / Boogie juice: Bennett, Brian / Penthouse suite: Dale, Syd / I feel the earth move: Keating, Johnny / Jesus Christ superstar: Keating, Johnny / Earthmen: Kingsland, Paddy / Shout about pepsi: Wright, Denny / Funky fever: Morehouse, Alan
CD _____ CDTWO 2001
EMI / Apr '95 / EMI.

SOUND INFORMATION
CD _____ WWCD 9
Wibbly Wobbly / Feb '95 / SRD.

SOUND NAVIGATOR
(Setting Sail For A Outernational Reggae Style)
CD _____ BTT 0332
Buback / Oct '95 / SRD.

SOUND OF CHRISTMAS PANPIPES, THE
When a child is born / Have yourself a very merry Christmas / Sleigh ride / O little town of Bethlehem / Way in a manger / In Dulci jubilo / Once in Royal David's city / Hark the herald angels sing / Silent night / God rest ye merry gentlemen / White Christmas / Christmas dreams / First Noel / Little Drummer Boy / Walking in the air (The snowman) / In the bleak mid winter / Happy Christmas (war is over) / I'll be home for Christmas / Mistletoe and wine / Christmas song / Go rest ye merry gentlemen
CD _____ 3036000052
Carlton Home Entertainment / Oct '95 / Carlton Home Entertainment.

SOUND OF CLEVELAND CITY
CD _____ CLECD 333
Cleveland City / Aug '94 / Grapevine / Sony / 3MV.

SOUND OF CLUB, THE
CD Set _____ VKCD 1
Total / Jun '95 / Total/BMG.

SOUND OF COLUMBIA
CD _____ CPCD 8165
Charly / Jan '96 / Charly / THE / Cadillac.

SOUND OF COOLTEMPO, VOL. 2
Ring my bell: Love, Monie Vs Adeva / Outstanding: Thomas, Kenny / Lovesick: Gang Starr / Keep the dream alive: Light Of The World / Matter of fact: Innocence / Alright: Four: G.T.O. / My heart: Beat / D-shake: Mainline
CD _____ CCD 1867
Cooltempo / Jun '91 / EMI.

SOUND OF DETROIT/RARE STAMPS/HERE TO STAY
(Don Davis Presents)
Baby, please come back home: Barnes, J.J. / Chains of love: Barnes, J.J. / Now that I got you back: Barnes, J.J. / Easy living: Barnes, J.J. / Sweet Sherry: Barnes, J.J. / Don't make me a storyteller: Mancha, Steve / Love like yours: Mancha, Steve / Keep the faith: Mancha, Steve / I don't wanna lose you: Mancha, Steve / I hate yourself in the morning: Mancha, Steve / Just keep on loving: Mancha, Steve / Just because your love has gone: Banks, Darrell / Forgive me: Banks, Darrell / Only the strong survive: Banks, Darrell / Don't know what to do: Banks, Darrell / When a man loves a woman: Banks, Darrell / We'll get over: Banks, Darrell / Beautiful feeling: Banks, Darrell / I could never hate her: Banks, Darrell / Never alone: Banks, Darrell / No one blinder than a man who won't see): Banks, Darrell / My love is strictly reserved: Banks, Darrell
CD _____ CDSXD 061
Stax / Jul '92 / Pinnacle.

SOUND OF FUNK VOL 1
Damph T'aint: Johnson, Herb Settlement / Sad chicken: Leroy & The Drivers / How long shall I wait: Fields, James Lewis / Hec-

tor: *Village Callers* / *Let the groove move you: Lewis, Gus 'The Groove'* / *Groovy world: Fabulous Caprices* / Jan jan: *Various Narrators* / *Iron leg: Mickey & The Soul Generation* / *You got to be a man: Williams, Frank* / *Searching for soul: Various Narrators* / *Push and pull: Sons Of Slum* / *Take this woman off the corner: Spencer, James* / *Everything gonna be alright: Various Narrators* / *Tramp Part 1: Showmen Inc.* / *I'm the man: Showmen Inc.* / *Whip: Brown, Al* / *You: Wilson, Spanky* / *Brother Brown: Bob, Camille* / *Happy soul: Cortez, Dave & The Moon People* / *Let my people go: Darondo* / *Nefertiti: Wysdom*

CD _____ GSCD 007

Goldmine / Nov '92 / Vital.

SOUND OF FUNK VOL.2

Gat or bat / *Humpty dumpty: Vibrettes* / *I've got reasons: Hooper, Mary Jane* / *Got to get me a job: Alford, Ann* / *Love got a piece of your mind: 5 Ounces Of Earth* / *African strut: Westbrook, Lynn* / *Spin-II jug: Brooks, Smokey* / *Girl chooses the boy: Collins, Lashdown* / *Funk I-Tus: Warm excursion* / *Chocolate sugar: Six Feet Under* / *Screwdriver: Austin, Lee* / *Skin II black: Bush, Tommy* / *Communication is where it's at: Billy the baron* / *World: 1619 Bab* / *Fun and funk: Fantastic epics* / *Marvin's groove: B.W. Souls* / *Hot butter 'n' all: Darondo*

CD _____ GSCD 012

Goldmine / Apr '93 / Vital.

SOUND OF FUNK VOL.3

Got a thing for you baby: Mr. Percolator / *Funky funky hot pants: Mason, Wee Willie* / *J.B.'s latin: Spittin' Image* / *New bump and twist: Kats* / *Hit drop: Explosions* / *African Propositions* / *Got a gig on my back: Kelly & The Soul Explosion* / *Soul drippin's: Interns* / *Let's get together: George, Cassietta* / *Baby I've got it: King George & The Fabulous Souls* / *Fon-kin love: Love international* / *Candlelit kick: Campbell, Don* / *Funky soul shake: White, E.T. & The Potential Band* / *Hot pants (pt 1): 20th Century* / *Closed minds: Different Bags* / *Give a damn: Gordon, Benny* / *Stop (what'cha doing to me): Roberts, Roy* / *Gimme some tonight: Holmes Justice, Marvin* / *How you get higher: Hunter & His Games*

CD _____ GSCD 023

Goldmine / Sep '93 / Vital.

SOUND OF FUNK VOL.4

Funky buzzard: Little Oscar / *Fun in your thang: Phelps, Bootsey & The Soul Invaders* / *Funky fat man: Bynum, Burnett & The Soul Invaders* / *Keep on brother keep on: Fatback Band* / *Crumbs for the table: Young Disciples & Co.* / *Moon walk: King Solomon* / *Bumping: Chestnut, Tyrone* / *Open up your heart: Raw Soul & Frankie Beverly* / *Get some: Wee Willie & The Winners* / *(Ride on) iron horse: Marlboro Men* / *Funky funk: Big Al & The Star Treks* / *Funky moon meditation: Moonlighters* / *Wait a minute: Xplosions* / *Do the funky donkey: Turner, Otis & The Mighty Kingpins* / *Funky line part 1: Fabulous Shalimars* / *Hold tight: McNutt, Bobby* / *Funky book, Little Joe* / *Be black baby: Tate, Grady* / *Can you dig it: Chico & Buddy*

CD _____ GSCD 028

Goldmine / Jan '94 / Vital.

SOUND OF FUNK VOL.5

Dynamite: Colt, Steve / *Crazy legs: Soul Tornadoes* / *Breakdown: Memphians* / *Revolution rap (Part 1): Green, Cal* / *Wait a minute: Xplosions* / *Funkie moon: Johnson, Unlikely & Company* / *Our combination: Soul Combination* / *Afro bush: Gaunichaux, E. & the Skeptics* / *Football: Mickey & The Soul Generation* / *Whip (Part 1): Simpkins, Darnell & the Family Tree* / *Give a man a break: Mintz, Charles* / *I laugh and talk (but I don't play): Strong, Zeke & the Ladyetts* / *Kurt kun: Diety* / *Hot pants: Bee, Jimmy* / *Bear funk: Revolution Funk* / *Do the yum yum man: Contributors Of Soul* / *Whip (Part 2): Simpkins, Darnell & the Family Tree* / *I laugh and talk (instrumental): Strong, Zeke & the Ladyetts* / *Revolution rap (Part 2): Green, Cal*

CD _____ GSCD 036

Goldmine / Apr '94 / Vital.

SOUND OF FUNK VOL.6

Gigolo: Anderson, Gene / *You did it: Robinson, Ann* / *Foxy little Mama: Stone, Bob & His Band* / *Oof (Do anything I want): Colbert, Chuck* / *Funky soul: Campbell, Milton & The R-D-M Band* / *Rerun: King Hannibal* / *Atlanta boogaloo: Inclines* / *Rough nut: Zodiacs* / *Fussin and cussin (part 1): Four Wheel Drive* / *(Get ready for) Changes: Marva & Melvin* / *Funky John: Cameron, Johnny & The Camerons* / *Soul chills: Soul, Dede & The Spidels* / *Loneliest one: Anderson, Gene* / *Life is like a puzzle: Village Soul Choir* / *Sunshine: Scacy & The Sound Service* / *Take it where you found it: Jackson, Lorraine* / *Fussin and cussin (Part 2): Four Wheel Drive* / *Soul chills (Part 2): Soul, Dede & The Spidels* / *Boogie man: Jones, Rufus R*

CD _____ GSCD 045

Goldmine / Aug '94 / Vital.

SOUND OF GARAGE CITY, THE

CD _____ CTC 0404

Coast 2 Coast / May '95 / Jetstar.

SOUND OF KISS 100FM, THE

Blow your whistle: D.J. Duke / *Big time sensuality: Bjork* / *Just to know (ain't no use): Sub Sub & Melanie Williams* / *U got 2 let the music: Cappella* / *What is love: Haddaway* / *Love I lost: West End & Sybil* / *When I'm good and ready: Sybil* / *Show me love: Robin S* / *Funk DAT: Sagat* / *Dreams: Gabrielle* / *There's nothing like this: Omar* / *Apparently nothin': Young Disciples* / *I love your smile: Shance* / *Right here: S.W.V.* / *Don't walk away: Jade* / *I shall sing: Griffiths, Marcia* / *People everyday: Arrested Development* / *Chime: Orbital* / *On a ragga tip: SL2* / *Key, the secret: Urban Cookie Collective* / *Don't you want me: Felix* / *It's a fine day: Opus III* / *I'm gonna get you: Bizarre Inc.* / *Everybody's free: Rozalla* / *L.S.I: Love sex intelligence: Shamen* / *Seize the day: FKW* / *I'll be there for you: House Of Virginham* / *Give it up: Goodmen* / *Shout: Louchie Lou & Michie One* / *Jump around: House Of Pain* / *Oh Carolina: Shaggy* / *Boom shak-a-lak: Apache Indian* / *Come baby come: K7* / *Boom shake the room: D.J. Jazzy Jeff & The Fresh Prince*

CD _____ 5164862

PolyGram TV / Jan '94 / PolyGram.

SOUND OF LIGHT, THE

CD _____ ND 63914

Narada / Oct '94 / New Note / ADA.

SOUND OF MUSIC, THE

CD _____ CZ 33CD

Bring On Bull / Nov '93 / Vital / SRD.

SOUND OF PHILADELPHIA

Me and Mrs. Jones: Paul, Billy / *I love music: O'Jays* / *Don't leave me this way: Melvin, Harold & The Bluenotes* / *Nights over Egypt: Jones Girls* / *Year of decision: Three Degrees* / *Love train: O'Jays* / *Love TKO: Pendergrass, Teddy* / *When will I see you again: Three Degrees* / *Show me the way to go: Jacksons* / *If you don't know me by now: Melvin, Harold & The Bluenotes* / *Backstabbers: O'Jays* / *You'll never find another love like mine: Rawls, Lou* / *Wake up everybody: Melvin, Harold & The Bluenotes* / *TSOP: MFSB* / *Soul City walk: Bell, Archie & The Drells* / *Love I lost: Melvin, Harold & The Bluenotes*

CD _____ PWKS 588

Carlton Home Entertainment / Jul '90 / Carlton Home Entertainment.

SOUND OF PHILADELPHIA VOL.1

CD _____ 312161

Arcade / Aug '89 / Sony / Grapevine.

SOUND OF PHILADELPHIA VOL.2

CD _____ 312261

Arcade / Aug '89 / Sony / Grapevine.

SOUND OF PHILADELPHIA, THE

CD _____ 3057

Scratch / Mar '95 / BMG.

SOUND OF ROME

CD _____ ACV 204 CD

ACV / Oct '95 / Plastic Head / SRD.

SOUND OF SKA

CD _____ QTVCD 001

Quality / May '92 / Pinnacle.

SOUND OF SOUND VOL. 2

CD _____ 111902

Musidisc / Feb '94 / Vital / Harmonia Mundi / ADA / Cadillac / Discovery.

**SOUND OF SUMMER, THE
(The Ultimate Beach Party)**

Surf city: Jan & Dean / *Surfin' safari: Beach Boys* / *Hey little cobra: Regents* / *Little Honda: Hondells* / *Tequila: Cannon, Ace* / *Indian lake: Cowsills* / *Ride the wild surf: Jan & Dean* / *Wipeout: Surfaris* / *Surfer girl: Beach Boys* / *Baby talk: Jan & Dean* / *G.T.O.: Regents* / *Remember (walkin' in the sand): Shangri-Las* / *Summer song: Chad & Jeremy* / *Beach baby: Regents* / *Surfin': Beach Boys* / *Pipeline: Chantays*

CD _____ ECD 3047

K-Tel / Jan '95 / K-Tel.

SOUND OF SUPERSTITION VOL.1, THE

Beginning: Mind Abuse / *Schoneberg: Marmion* / *Your ears are mine: Bassxpansion* / *Brainkiller: Azid Force* / *Loops and tings: Jens* / *Far from K: Azid Force* / *Flight 101: Phax* / *Acid bird: Bassxpansion* / *First contact (On CD only): Marmion* / *Fragile: Open House*

CD _____ SUPER 2008CD

Superstition / Dec '93 / Vital / SRD.

SOUND OF SUPERSTITION VOL.2, THE

Loops and tings (Fruit loops remix): Jens / *Schoneberg: Marmion* / *Paraglide: Paragliders* / *Odyssey (Single version): L.S.G.* / *Lust: Velocity* / *Bagdad: Paragliders* / *Fragile: L.S.G.* / *Spacetribe: Humate* / *Nothern lights: Basic Gravity* / *Spring the wildlife: Mijks Magic Marble Box* / *Firechild: Marmion*

CD _____ SUPER 2017CD

Superstition / Jul '94 / Vital / SRD.

SOUND OF SUPERSTITION VOL.3, THE

3.1: Humate / *Phi: Paragliders* / *Voyager: Arte Bionico* / *Fox hunt: Gianelli, Fred* / *Uplift: Velocity* / *East: Humate & Rabbit In The Moon* / *Tumble dry: Goldfinger* / *For men: Bug, Steve* / *First contact (Telepathic remix.): Marmion* / *3.3: Humate*

CD _____ SUPER 2033CD

Superstition / Feb '95 / Vital / SRD.

SOUND OF THE ABSOLUTE

CD _____ OMCD 1

OM / Mar '94 / SRD.

SOUND OF THE SUBURBS, THE

Eton rifles: Jam / *Ant music: Adam & The Ants* / *Ever fallen in love: Buzzcocks* / *Another girl another planet: Only Ones* / *Teenage kicks: Undertones* / *Echo beach: Martha & The Muffins* / *Happy birthday: Altered Images* / *Oliver's army: Costello, Elvis* / *2-4-6-8 Motorway: Robinson, Tom Band* / *Hit me with your rhythm stick: Dury, Ian & The Blockheads* / *Call me: Blondie* / *Reward: Teardrop Explodes* / *I don't like Mondays: Boomtown Rats* / *Pretty in pink: Psychedelic Furs* / *No more heroes: Stranglers* / *Turning Japanese: Vapors* / *Do anything you wanna do: Eddie & The Hot Rods* / *Sound of the suburbs: Members*

CD _____ MOODCD 18

Columbia / Aug '91 / Sony.

SOUND OF THE SYNTHS VOL.2

CD _____ 15426

Laserlight / Jun '93 / Target/BMG.

**SOUND OF THE UNDERGROUND VOL.1
(Sour Cream)**

CD _____ SOURCD 1

SOUR / Feb '95 / SRD.

SOUND SPECTRUM, THE

Get carter: Budd, Roy / *Love is a four letter word: Budd, Roy* / *Getting nowhere in a hurry: Budd, Roy* / *Plaything: Budd, Roy* / *Hurry to me: Budd, Roy* / *Grow your own: Schroeder, John Orchestra* / *Headband: Schroeder, John Orchestra* / *Touch of velletto: Rey, Chico & The Jett Band* / *Heavy Mach 1: Davies, Ray & His Funky Trumpet* / *Speakin' of spoken: Lovin' Spoonful* / *Supershine No.9: Sister Goose And The Ducklings* / *Loner: Hunter, Milton* / *Fancy: Birds* / *Dicks, Ted* / *Birds: Hatch, Tony Orchestra* / *2001: Holmes, Cecil Soulful Sound* / *Pegasus: Vickers, Mike* / *Hot wheels: Badder Than Evil*

CD _____ WENCD 005

When / Nov '95 / BMG / Pinnacle.

SOUNDS AND PRESSURE VOL.1

Barbican dub: Hudson, Keith / *Problems: Andy, Horace* / *Ras menilik Congo: Pablo, Augustus* / *Red blood: Black Skin The Prophet* / *Mansion of invention: Prince Far-I & The Arabs* / *Black belt Jones: Hudson, Keith* / *Tribal war: Little Roy* / *Sinners: Hudson, Keith* / *Bass ace: Prince Far-I & The Arabs* / *Same song: Israel Vibration* / *King Tubby's dub song: Pablo, Augustus*

CD _____ PSCD 005

Pressure Sounds / Sep '95 / SRD / Jetstar.

SOUNDS OF AFRICA

CD _____ SOW 90120

Sounds Of The World / Jan '94 / Target/BMG.

SOUNDS OF ONE, THE

CD _____ ORCD 017

One / Apr '95 / Vital.

SOUNDS OF SUDAN

CD _____ WCD 018

World Circuit / Jan '91 / New Note / Direct / Cadillac / ADA.

**SOUNDS OF THE 70'S
(4CD Set)**

CD Set _____ MBSCD 402

Castle / Nov '95 / BMG.

SOUNDS OF THE 70'S, THE

CD _____ RADCD 1

Global / Nov '94 / BMG.

SOUNDS OF THE CITY

CD Set _____ SCCD 1

Sounds Of The City / Jan '94 / Total/BMG.

SOUNDS OF THE FIFTIES

Secret love: Day, Doris / *Jezebel: Laine, Frankie* / *Oh mein Papa: Calvert, Eddie* / *Unchained melody: Hibbler, Al* / *Singin' the blues: Mitchell, Guy* / *True love: Crosby, Bing & Grace Kelly* / *When I fall in love: Cole, Nat King* / *Here in my heart: Martino, Al* / *Rock 'n' roll waltz: Starr, Kay* / *Softly, softly: Murray, Ruby* / *No other love: Hilton, Ronnie* / *Blue Tango: Martin, Ray* / *Blueberry Hill: Domino, Fats* / *(We're gonna) rock around the clock: Haley, Bill* / *Cumberland gap: Donegan, Lonnie* / *Cry me a river: London, Julie* / *Tammy: Reynolds, Debbie* / *Little things mean a lot: Kallen, Kitty* / *Fever: Lee, Peggy* / *Petite fleur: Barber, Chris Jazz Band & Monty Sunshine*

CD _____ CDPR 122

Premier/MFP / Oct '94 / Vital.

SOUNDS OF THE SEVENTIES-REGGAE STYLE

I can't get next to you: Charmers / *You're a big girl now: Chosen Few* / *Rainy night in Georgia: Thomas, Nicky* / *Groove me: Beckford, Keeling* / *Just my imagination: Barber, Dave* / *Sister big stuff: Holt, John* / *Shaft: Charmers, Lloyd* / *Help me make it through the night: Parker, Ken* / *Been: Elaine, Margaret* / *Lean on me: Seaton, B.B.* / *Have you seen her: Harriott, Derrick* / *First time ever I*

---

saw your face: Griffiths, Marcia / *Let me down easy: Brown, Dennis* / *Break up to make up: Sibbles, Leroy* / *Hurt so good: Cadogan, Susan* / *Too late to turn back: Ellis, Alton* / *Living a little, laughing a little: Spence, Barrington* / *If you're ready: Richards, Cynthia* / *You make me feel brand new: Gardiner, Boris* / *When will I see you again: Inner Circle*

CD _____ CDTRL 321

Trojan / Mar '94 / Jetstar / Total/BMG.

SOUNDS OF THE SIXTIES

Up on the roof: Drifters / *Same old feeling: Fortunes* / *End of the world: Davis, Skeeter* / *Ferry 'cross the Mersey: Gerry & The Pacemakers* / *Those were the days: Hopkin, Mary* / *98.6: Keith* / *Do you want to know a secret: Kramer, Billy J.* / *If I had a hammer: Lopez, Trini* / *Billy, don't be a hero: Paper Lace* / *Great pretender: Platters* / *Lady Willpower: Puckett, Gary* / *Poetry in motion: Tillotson, Johnny* / *Forty Miles of bad road: Eddy, Duane* / *That's where the music takes me: Sedaka, Neil* / *Mr. Bass Man: Cymbal, Johnny* / *Raunchy: Justis, Bill* / *Speedy Gonzalez: Boone, Pat* / *Turn me loose: Faubian* / *Dreaming dreams: Benton, Brook* / *Put your hand: Platters* / *Raindrops keep falling on my head: Warwick, Dionne* / *Remember (walkin' in the sand): Shangri-Las* / *Room in your heart: Knight, Gladys* / *King of the road: Miller, Roger* / *Red roses for a blue lady: Dana, Vic*

CD _____ LECD 408

Stardust / Aug '93 / Carlton Home Entertainment.

SOUNDS OF THE WORLD, VOL.1: LATIN AMERICA

CD _____ PS 65991

Playasound / Mar '93 / Harmonia Mundi / ADA.

SOUNDSITE

Angular art: Parker & Morley / *Sons of the subway: Da Tunnelz* / *Noskin (funky hornsey): Golden Palaminos* / *Crisis a gwan: Bandulu* / *Clesestial funk: Space DJ's* / *Munk: Koh Tao* / *Year 2000: Bandulu* / *You make me do night: Shyman & D.J. LJK* / *Bouyancy: Bissmire & Long* / *Yard style: Bandulu*

CD _____ INF 007CD

Infonet / Oct '95 / Pinnacle / Vital.

SOUTH AMERICA - HISPANIC

CD _____ AUB 006782

Auvidis/Ethnic / Sep '93 / Harmonia Mundi.

SOUTH AMERICA - INDIAN

CD _____ AUB 006783

Auvidis/Ethnic / Sep '93 / Harmonia Mundi.

SOUTH INDIA - RITUAL MUSIC & THEATRE OF KERALA

CD _____ LDX 274910

La Chant Du Monde / Nov '90 / Harmonia Mundi / ADA.

SOUTH SIDE BLUES - CHICAGO: LIVING LEGENDS

Wonderful thing: Mississippi Sheiks / *I knew you were kiddin' all the time: Mississippi Sheiks* / *Things 'bout comin' my way: Mississippi Sheiks* / *Four o'clock blues: Mama Yancey* / *How long blues: Mama Yancey* / *Mama yancey's blues: Mama Yancey* / *Make me a pallet on the floor: Mama Yancey* / *Jelly Jelly: Benson, Henry* / *Jelly Roll Baker: Benson, Henry* / *New satellite blues: Montgomery, Little Brother*

CD _____ CD500 500

Original Blues Classics / Apr '94 / Complete/Pinnacle / Wellard / Cadillac.

SOUTH SIDE CHICAGO JAZZ

CD _____ VILCD 0192

Village Jazz / Sep '92 / Target/BMG / Jazz Music.

SOUTHERN FRIED SOUL

You're so good to me baby: Spencer, Eddie / *It takes a whole lotta woman: Gauff, Willie & The Love Brothers* / *When she touches me: Martin, Rodge* / *Good man is hard to find: Martin, Rodge* / *Can you handle it: Allison, Levert* / *You can get it now: Middleton, Gene* / *Man who will do anything: Middleton, Gene* / *So many times: Lewis, Levina* / *Look a little higher: Up Tights* / *Just a dream: Up Tights* / *Sad, sad song: Crawford, Charles* / *Fa fa fa fa fa (sad song): McDade, Joe* / *My girl's a soul girl: Rogers, Lon* / *Too good to be true: Rogers, Lon* / *You're being unfair to me: Sample, Hank* / *So in love with you: Sample, Hank* / *I'll always love you: Moutrie, Sam* / *I found what I wanted: Lacour, Bobby* / *Cry like a baby: Lacour, Bobby* / *Love waits for no man: Curlee, Bobby & The Preachers* / *Why is it taking so long: Baxter, Tony* / *I'm surprised: Vann, Paul*

CD _____ GSCD 025

Goldmine / Nov '93 / Vital.

SOUTHERN GROOVES

CD _____ CPCD 8067

Charly / Nov '94 / Charly / THE / Cadillac.

SOUTHERN NIGHTS

Keep on lovin' you: REO Speedwagon / *I love you more than you'll ever know: Blood, Sweat & Tears* / *(Don't fear) The reaper: Blue Oyster Cult* / *Don't stop believin': Jour-*

ney / Foolish heart: Perry, Steve / Arms of Mary: Sutherland Brothers & Quiver / I'll have to say I love you in a song: Croce, Jim / I saw the light: Rundgren, Todd / Perfect lovers: Kansas / Why do lovers break each others hearts: Hall & Oates / Jessie's girl: Springfield, Rick / Jane: Jefferson Starship / Broken wings: Mr. Mister / Even the nights are better: Air Supply / Ramblin' man: All-man Brothers / Spooky: Atlanta Rhythm Section / Fooled around and fell in love: Bishop, Elvin / Witch Queen of New Orleans: Redbone

CD _____ **STACD 010**
Stardust / Nov '92 / Carlton Home Entertainment.

SOUTHERN STATES SOUND
CD _____ **MCCD 135**
Music Club / Jan '92 / Disc / THE / CM.

SOUVENIR DE PARIS
(The Great French Stars)
C'est un p'tit rien: Mistinguett & Jean Gabin / Tango de Marilou: Rossi, Tino / Si j'etais Blanche: Baker, Josephine / Oui, papa: Chevalier, Maurice / Parlez-moi d'amour: Boyer, Lucienne / St. Louis blues: Ventura, Ray & Ses Collegiens / Plaisir d'amour: Printemps, Yvonne / Pauvre grand: Frehel / Vous avez: Sablon, Jean / Le fiacre: Guilbert, Yvette / Plus rien, je n'ai plus rien qu'un chien: Sablon, Jean / Ca c'est Paris: Mistinguett / Ca c'est fou: Alibert / Le chaland qui passe: Gauty, Lys / Valentine: Chevalier, Maurice / C'est mon gigolo: Damina / La petite Tonkinoise: Baker, Josephine / Couche dans le toin: Pills & Tabet / Papa n'a pas voulou: mirielle / La Marseillaise: Thill, Georges

CD _____ **CD AJA 5028**
Living Era / Koch.

SOUVENIR OF WALES IN SONG
CD _____ **SCD 9006**
Sain / Feb '95 / Direct / ADA.

SOVEREIGN SOLOISTS
CD _____ **DOYCD 003**
Doyen / Jun '93 / Conifer.

SOWETO NEVER SLEEPS
CD _____ **SHANCD 43041**
Shanachie / Apr '88 / Koch / ADA / Greensleeves.

SPACE DAZE
(The History And Mystery Of Electronic Ambient Space Rock)
CD Set _____ **CLEO 76162**
Cleopatra / Jan '95 / Disc.

SPACE INVADERS
CD _____ **RE 201CD**
Panorama / Aug '95 / Plastic Head.

SPACE LOG 1.1
CD _____ **GAMMA 01**
Gamma / Mar '95 / Plastic Head.

SPACE MOUNTAIN
CD _____ **JAC 002CD**
Oasis / Oct '95 / Plastic Head.

SPACEFROGS VOL.2, THE
CD _____ **EFA 290102**
Superstition / Dec '95 / Vital / SRD.

SPANISH RAGGA
CD _____ **SM 3110**
Declic / Apr '95 / Jetstar.

SPECIAL COLE PORTER
CD _____ **JASSCD 632**
Jass / Feb '92 / CM / Jazz Music / ADA / Cadillac / Direct.

SPECIAL GUITARS VOL. 2 1943-56
CD _____ **7899522**
Jazztime / Jan '95 / Discovery / BMG.

SPECIALTY LEGENDS OF BOOGIE WOOGIE
X-temporaneous boogie: Howard, Camille / Rock that voot: Alexander, Nelson Trio / Rockin' boogie: Lutcher, Joe & His Society Cats / Doin' the boogie-woogie: Alexander, Nelson Trio / Society boogie: Lutcher, Joe & His Society Cats / Barcarolle boogie: Howard, Camille / Instantaneous boogie: Howard, Camille / State street boogie: Johnson, Don Orchestra / Miraculous boogie: Howard, Camille / Milton's boogie: Milton, Roy / Ferocious boogie: Howard, Camille / Unidentified instrumental no. 1: McDaniel, Willard / Boogie woogie Lou: Liggins, Joe / Fire-ball boogie: Howard, Camille / Boogie woogie barber shop: Milton, Roy / 3 a.m. boogie: McDaniel, Willard / Bangin' the boogie: Howard, Camille / Ciribiribin boogie: McDaniel, Willard / Unidentified boogie no. 1: Howard, Willard / Million dollar boogie: Howard, Camille / Boogie in the groove: Jackson, Jo Jo

CD _____ **CDCHD 422**
Ace / Sep '92 / Pinnacle / Cadillac / Complete/Pinnacle.

SPECIALTY LEGENDS OF JUMP BLUES VOL.1
Honeydripper: Liggins, Joe / Oh babe: Milton, Roy / Blues for sale: Lutcher, Joe / Duck's yas yas yas: King, Perry & His Pied Pipers / I can't stop it: Liggins, Jimmy / That song is gone: Liggins, Jimmy / Well, well baby: Alexander, Nelson Trio / Rag mop: Liggins, Joe / One sweet letter: Liggins, Joe / Pink champagne: Liggins, Joe / Happy

---

home blues: Banks, Buddy / Muffle shoe shuffle: Wynn, Big Jim / I ain't got a dime: Perry, King / Saturday night boogie woogie man: Liggins, Jimmy / Jack of diamonds: Thomas, Jesse / I dare you baby: Mayfield, Percy / I'm your rockin' man: Manzy, Herman / Natural born lover: King, Perry & His Pied Pipers / I wonder who's boogin' my woogie: King, Perry & His Pied Pipers / I can't lose with the stuff I use: Williams, Lester / Country girl: Henderson, Duke / Hucklebuck: Milton, Roy / Heavy weight baby: Motley, Frank / Traffic gong: Lutcher, Joe

CD _____ **CDCHD 573**
Ace / Jul '94 / Pinnacle / Cadillac / Complete/Pinnacle.

SPECIALTY ROCK'N'ROLL
Lights out: Bryne, Jerry / Moose on the loose: Jackson, Roddy / Bim bam: Don & Dewey / Don't you just know it: Titans / (We're gonna) Rock around the clock: Millet, Lil / My baby's rockin': Monitors / Hickory dickory dock: Myles, Big Boy / Tip: Marvin & Johnny / Good golly Miss Molly: Little Richard / Rockin' pneumonia and the boogie woogie flu: Neville, Art / Goodbye baby goodbye: Lowery, Sonny / Short fat Fannie: Williams, Larry / Rock 'n' roll dance: Price, Lloyd / Girl can't help it: Little Richard / Haunted house: Fuller, Jerry / Slow down: Williams, Larry / Cherokee dance: Landers, Bob / Hiccups: Jackson, Roddy / Zing zing: Neville, Art / Carry on: Byrne, Jerry

CD _____ **CDCH 291**
Ace / May '90 / Pinnacle / Cadillac / Complete/Pinnacle.

SPECIALTY STORY, THE
Boogie number one: Sepia-Tones / Voo-it voo-it: Blues Woman / Milton's boogie: Milton, Roy / R.M. Blues: Milton, Roy / Rainy day blues: Jackson, Jump Band / Ice Cream Freezer: Blues Man / True blues: Milton, Roy / Rockin' boogie: Lutcher, Joe & His Society Cats / Thrill me: Milton, Roy / Tear drop blues: Liggins, Jimmy / Cadillac boogie: Liggins, Jimmy / Keep a dollar in your pocket: Milton, Roy & His Solid Senders / X-temporaneous boogie: Howard, Camille / You don't love me: Howard, Camille / Fat meat: Wynn, Big Jim / Everything I do is wrong: Milton, Roy / Hop, skip and jump: Milton, Roy / Careful love: Liggins, Jimmy / Big city blues: Maceo, Big / I want a roller: Hogg, Smokey / Hucklebuck: Milton, Roy & His Solid Senders / Fiesta on old Mexico: Howard, Camille / Honeydripper: Liggins, Joe / Don't put me down: Liggins, Joe / Information blues: Milton, Roy / Rag mop: Liggins, Joe / Pink champagne: Liggins, Joe / Junior jives: Milton, Roy / Where there is no love: Milton, Roy / Everything gonna be alright: King, Perry & His Pied Pipers / Please send me someone to love: Mayfield, Percy / Strange things happening: Mayfield, Percy / Little Joe's boogie: Liggins, Joe / Oh Babe: Milton, Roy / Lost love: Mayfield, Percy / Frankie Lee: Liggins, Joe / What a fool I was: Mayfield, Percy / Money blues: Howard, Camille / It's later than you think: Milton, Roy / T-twist twist: Milton, Roy / I have news for you: Milton, Roy / Prayin' for your return: Mayfield, Percy / Strange angel: Easton, Amos / Best wishes: Milton, Roy / Cry baby: Mayfield, Percy / Love will make you a slave: Greenwood, Lil / I can't lose with the stuff I use: Williams, Lester / Wheel of fortune: Four Flames / Big question: Mayfield, Percy / Lawdy Miss Clawdy: Price, Lloyd / So tired: Milton, Roy / Night and day (I miss you so): Milton, Roy / Oooh oooh oooh: Price, Lloyd / Restless heart: Price, Lloyd / Tell me: Milton, Roy / Ain't it a shame: Price, Lloyd / Frantic: Crawford, Jimmy & Frank Motley / Too close to heaven: Bradford, Alex / I'm coming home: Swan Silvertones / I've got a new home: Pilgrim Travelers / One room country shack: Walton, Mercy Dee / Lucy Mae blues: Sims, Frankie Lee / Early in the morning: Milton, Roy / She's been gone: H-Bomb Ferguson / Hard living alone: Dixon, Floyd / Drunk: Liggins, Jimmy / I ate the wrong part: Temple Little & His 88 / Blood stains on the wall: Honey Boy / Baby doll: Marvin & Johnny / Things that I used to do: Guitar Slim / I'm your best bet baby: King, Earl / No room in the hotel: Chosen Gospel Singers / I'm mad: Hooker, John Lee / Something's going on in my room: Cleanhead, Daddy / Zindy Lou: Chimes / One more river: Soul Stirrers / Where's my girl: Belvin, Jesse / Nite owl: Allen, Tony & The Champs / Tutti frutti: Little Richard / Eternity: Kador, Ernest / Rich woman: Millet, Lil / Squeeze box boogie: Chenier, Clifton / Touch the hem of his garment: Soul Stirrers / Long tall Sally: Little Richard / Slippin' and slidin': Little Richard / Oh-Rooba-Lee: Maye, Arthur Lee & The Crowns / Gloria: Maye, Arthur Lee & The Crowns / Cherokee dance: Landers, Bob & Willie Joe & His Unitar / Rip it up: Little Richard / Ready teddy: Little Richard / Sweet breeze: Green, Vernon & The Phantoms / Everytime I hear that mellow saxophone: Montrell, Roy / She's got it: Little Richard / Heebie jeebies: Little Richard / Should i ever love again: Carr, Wynona & The Bumps Blackwell Band / Just hold my hand: Myles, Big Boy & Sha-Weez / Girl can't help it: Little Richard / All around the world: Little Richard / Oooh-whee baby: Neville, Art / Just because: Williams, Larry / Lucille: Little Ri-

---

chard / Send me some livin': Little Richard / Open up your heart: Church, Eugene / Our romance: King, Clydie / Jenny Jenny: Little Richard / Miss Ann: Little Richard / Short fat fannie: Williams, Larry / Leavin' it all up to you: Don & Dewey / Keep a knockin': Little Richard / Bony moronie: Williams, Larry / Twitchy: Hall, Rene Orchestra & Willie Joe / I'll come running back to you: Cooke, Sam / Good golly Miss Molly: Little Richard / Slow down: Williams, Larry / Dizzy Miss Lizzy: Williams, Larry / Justine: Don & Dewey / True fine mama: Little Richard / Ooh my soul: Little Richard / Lights out: Byrne, Jerry / Love of god: Soul Stirrers / Koko Joe: Don & Dewey / Baby face: Little Richard / There's a moose on the loose: Jackson, Roddy / Haunted house: Fuller, Johnny / She said yeah: Williams, Larry / Bad boy: Williams, Larry / Farmer John: Don & Dewey / Big boy Pete: Don & Dewey / Bama lama bama loo: Little Richard

CD Set _____ **5 SPCD 4412**
Fantasy / Mar '94 / Pinnacle / Jazz Music / Wellard / Cadillac.

SPECTRUM
Kindred: John / Smokin' a blunt: Chuck E / Warning: Firefox & 4 Tree / Drum, a bass and a piano: Nookie / Joker jump up: Dynamic Duo / Timestretch: Roni Size / Love inside: Forrester, Sharon / Dred bass: Dead Dred / Presha III: Keith, Ray / Sound murderer: Remarc / Fire: Prisoner / Chill pill: Reece, Alex / Burial: Leviticus / Sweet vibrations: D.M.S. & Boneman X / You don't know: Dillinja / Inner city life: Goldie & The Metalheadz / Worries in the dance: New Blood / Girls: London's Most Wanted / Way: D.J. Taktix / Special dedication: D.J. Nut Nut & Top Cat/Frankie Paul

CD _____ **8286092**
FFRR / Mar '95 / PolyGram.

SPEED KILLS VOL.4
(Speed Kills But Who's Dying?)
CD _____ **CDFLAG 33**
Under One Flag / Jun '89 / Pinnacle.

SPEED KILLS VOL.5
(Head Crushing Metal)
CD _____ **CDFLAG 46**
Under One Flag / Oct '90 / Pinnacle.

SPEED KILLS VOL.6
CD _____ **CDFLAG 69**
Music For Nations / Jul '92 / Pinnacle.

SPEED LIMIT
CD _____ **MM 890502**
Moonshine / Jan '96 / Disc.

SPEED OF THE SOUND
CD _____ **GRCD 314**
Glitterhouse / Apr '94 / Direct / ADA.

SPERM BANK, THE
CD _____ **SPERM 2001**
Sperm / Nov '95 / Grapevine / Mo's Music Machine.

SPICE OF LIFE REMIXES VOL.1
Hott / Feb '95 / 3MV / Sony.
_____ **HOTTCD 1**

SPIRIT CRIES, THE
Abelagudahani / Grating song / Abaimahani / Paranda / Combination / Punta / Duga song / Healing song / Shipibo song / Ashaninka song / Aleke / Songe / Lonsei / Mato (Solo) / Mato (Leader and chorus) / Awasa / Kumanti / Agwado song / Susa / Dance song / Love song / Papa / Tambu

CD _____ **RCD 10250**
Rykodisc / Mar '93 / Vital / ADA.

SPIRIT OF '73
(Rock For Choice)
CB radio / If I can't have you: Eve's Plum / AM DJ: Babes In Toyland / More more more (pt 1): Babes In Toyland / We are family: Ebony Vibe Everlasting / Hairdryer: Letters To Cleo / Dreams: Letters To Cleo / Dancing barefoot: Napolitano, Johnette / Disco: L7 & Joan Jett / Cherry bomb: L7 & Joan Jett / Midnight at the Oasis: That Dog / Van: Cash, Rosanne / Have you ever been making love: Cash, Rosanne / Waterbed: Cash, Rosanne / River: Cash, Rosanne / Feel like makin' love: Ferrick, Melissa / PM DJ: Wilson, Cassandra / Killing me softly with his song: Wilson, Cassandra / Blue: McLachlan, Sarah / It won't take long: Hawkins, Sophie B. / Lip gloss: Hawkins, Sophie B. / Night they drove Old Dixie down: Hawkins, Sophie B. / Anti disco / CB radio (2)

CD _____ **4809812**
Epic / Sep '95 / Sony.

SPIRIT OF AFRICAN SANCTUS
(Compiled By David Fanshawe)
Acholi bwala dance / Call to prayer / Egyptian wedding / Islamic prayer school / Reed pipe and grass cutting song / Courtship dances / Four men on the prayer mat / Zebaidir song with Rebabah / Hadandua cattle boys song / Hadandua love songs and bells / Zande song of flight and frogs / Tamboura song / Edongo dance / Busoga fishermen / Bowed harp / Teso fishermen / Acholi enanga / Dingy dingy dance / Rainsong of latigo oteng / Bunyoro madinda / Bwala dance / Rowing chant of the Samia / Song of Lamentation / Masai milking song / Love song of the river, Karamoja / Karamajong children's song / Turkana cattle song / Luo ritual burial dance / War drums / Aluar horns

CD _____ **CDSDL 389**

Saydisc / Mar '94 / Harmonia Mundi / ADA / Direct.

SPIRIT OF CALIFORNIA
CD _____ **NTRCD 005**
Nectar / May '93 / Pinnacle.

SPIRIT OF INDIA, THE
(The Best Of Indian Classical Music)
Raga mishra piloo / Raga pahadi / Bhajan / Tal ektal / Dhun bhairavi / Raga bhairavi

CD _____ **PLATCD 3931**
Prism / Mar '95 / Prism.

SPIRIT OF MICRONESIA
CD _____ **CDSDL 414**
Saydisc / Oct '95 / Harmonia Mundi / ADA / Direct.

SPIRIT OF POLYNESIA
Aitutaki drum dance / Himene tarava / Popoi - taro pounding / Song of Papa Teora / Himene Ruau / Bird dance hula / Haka Maori welcome / Song of Papa Kiko / Kai kai of Mama Amelia / Hoko war dance / Meke wesi spear dance / Tau 'a' alo / Fangufangu nose flute / Fakawa love song / Chiefs and orators sasa / Tagi lullaby / Tawhoe - oar dance / Copra bugle call / Mokaone's harmonica / Song of Anili / Frigate bird dance, Nauru / Funafuti chorus, Tuvalu / Imenetuki - Gospel chant / Mere of Eamaki / Ute - cutting nuts / tapa cloth beating / Palmerston shanties / Imenetuki / Mako of Mama Lulutangi / Canoe racing and wrestling / Children's games / Akatikatika drum dance / Mako chant / Haka tapatapa / Pig dance/Kuu chant / Himene tarava (Tahiti) / Himene Nota / Otea drum dance

CD _____ **CDSDL 403**
Saydisc / Mar '94 / Harmonia Mundi / ADA / Direct.

SPIRIT OF ROCK
CD _____ **STACD 038**
Wisepack / Sep '94 / THE / Conifer.

SPIRIT OF SCOTLAND, THE
CD _____ **RECD 473**
REL / Nov '94 / THE / Gold / Duncans.

SPIRIT OF VICTORY, THE
(Hits from the 40's)
Happy and glorious: Somers, Debroy & His Band / In the land of beginning again: Lewis, Archie & Geraldo / Waiting in Sweetheart Valley (Vocalist: Paul Rich): Preager, Lou & His Orchestra / Little things that mean so much (Vocalist: Jane Lee): Payne, Jack & His Orchestra / Memories of you: Squires, Dorothy / It's been a long, long time (Vocalist: Rita Williams): Gibbons, Carroll & Savoy Hotel Orpheans / Dream: Foster, Teddy & The Band / What a difference a day makes: Green, Paula & Her Orchestra / There, I've said it again (Vocalist: Howard Jones): Loss, Joe & His Orchestra / Candy: Roy, Harry & His Band / Seems like old times (Vocalist: Rita Williams): Geraldo & His Orchestra / Goodnight darling (Vocalist: Dorothy Carless): Roy, Harry & His Band / June comes around every year (Vocalist: Archie Lewis. CD only): Geraldo & His Orchestra / One-zy-two-zy, I love you-zy (Vocalist: Maureen Moreton. CD only): Simpson, Jack & His Sextet / Remember me (Vocalist: Rita Williams. CD only): Preager, Lou & His Orchestra / Let's wait until tomorrow (Vocalist: Edna Kaye. CD only): Roy, Harry & His Band / I'm gonna love that guy (like he's never been loved before) (Vocalists: Carole Carr, 3 Boys & A Girl. CD only): Green, Paula & Her Orchestra / I'm beginning to see the light (Vocalist: Benny Lee. CD only): Geraldo & His Orchestra / I should care (Vocalist: Betty Kent): Roy, Harry & His Band / Sentimental journey (Vocalist: Betty Kent): Foster, Teddy & The Band / Squires, Dorothy / You came along (from out of nowhere) (Vocalist: Eunice Metcalf): Foster, Teddy & The Band / Did you ever get that feeling in the moonlight (Vocalist: Rita Williams): Preager, Lou & His Orchestra / I dream of you: Lewis, Archie & Geraldo / Bell bottom trousers: Roy, Harry & His Band / Dreams of yesterday: Squires, Dorothy / Anywhere (Vocalist: Julie Dawn): Winstone, Eric & His Band / Just a blue serge suit: Preager, Lou & His Orchestra / Till all our prayers are answered: Green, Paula & Her Orchestra / I walked right in (Vocalist: Benny Lee. CD only): Winstone, Eric & His Band / I'd rather be me (Vocalist: Dorothy Carless. CD only): Roy, Harry & His Band / Takin' the trains out (chasin' after you) (Vocalist: Betty Kent. CD only): Foster, Teddy & The Band / It's a grand night for singing (Vocalist: Rita Williams. CD only): Gibbons, Carroll & Savoy Hotel Orpheans / We'll gather lilacs (Vocalist: Sally Douglas. CD only): Geraldo & His Orchestra / Cavalry patrol (With The Geraldo Ensemble. CD only): Geraldo & His Orchestra / Celebration medley: Somers, Debroy & His Band

CD Set _____ **CDDL 1218**
Music For Pleasure / Nov '91 / EMI.

SPIRIT SAMPLER VOL.2
CD _____ **DW 092CD**
Deathwish / Jan '96 / Plastic Head.

SPIRITUAL
(The Best Of Outland)
Emotions: Jaimy & Con-Am / Organs in rhythm: Basic Bastard / Concerto in E: Dimitri / Movin' up: Digital Cartel / Equipment chasing: Rachmad Project Vol.2 / Fluid har-

mony: *Dimitri & Jaimy* / Moods a feeling: *Paardekooper, Maurits* / Yellow brass mix: *Colours* / Spend the night: *Digital Cartel* / Do you feel what I'm feeling: *Luvspunge* / Burning: *Daniel, Naomi* / Taste like funk: *Men With Rhythm* / Voices of K.A.: *Van Leeuwen, Sjef* / Devaradja: *Nouhan, Eric*
CD _____ BESTOFCD 001
Outland / Jul '94 / Vital / Plastic Head.

SPIRITUALLY IBIZA
Barefoot in the head: *Man Called Adam* / Moments in love: *Art Of Noise* / 60 Seconds: *Audio Deluxe* / Real life: *Corporation Of One* / Drop the deal: *Code 61* / Autumn love: *Electra* / Zobi la mouche: *Les Negresses Vertes* / Cafe del mar: *Mental Generation* / Love's got a feeling: *Neutron 9000* / Free spirit: *Orchestra J.B.* / Why can't we live together: *Illusion* / Solid gold easy amex: *Enjoy* / Jesus on the payroll: *Thrashing Doves* / Hoomba hoomba: *Voices Of Africa* / Whole of the moon: *Waterboys* / Only love can break your heart: *St. Etienne* / La passionara: *Blow Monkeys* / Come together: *Primal Scream*
CD _____ DINCD 111
Dino / Oct '95 / Pinnacle / 3MV.

SPLENDOUR OF THE KOTO
CD _____ PS 65131
Playasound / May '94 / Harmonia Mundi / ADA.

SPLENDOUR OF THE SHAKUHACHI
CD _____ PS 65130
Playasound / May '94 / Harmonia Mundi / ADA.

SPLENDOUR OF THE SHAMISEN
CD _____ PS 65129
Playasound / May '94 / Harmonia Mundi / ADA.

SPOONFUL OF BLUES
CD _____ 422490
New Rose / May '94 / Direct / ADA.

SPOTLIGHT ON BLUES
Boom boom boom: *Hooker, John Lee* / Honest I do: *Reed, Jimmy* / Dust my broom: *James, Elmore* / Baby, let me hold your hand: *Charles, Ray* / Need him: *Little Richard* / Rooster blues: *Lightnin' Slim* / I put a spell on you: *Hawkins, Screamin' Jay* / Caldonia: *Jordan, Louis* / Blueberry Hill: *Domino, Fats* / Dimples: *Hooker, John Lee* / She's a winner: *Taylor, Ted* / When the sun goes down: *Turner, Big Joe* / Moppers blues: *Stewart, Rod* / Shame, shame, shame: *Reed, Jimmy* / Rollin' and tumblin': *Canned Heat* / Polk salad Annie: *White, Tony Joe*
CD _____ HADCD 146
Javelin / Feb '94 / THE / Henry Hadaway Organisation.

SPOTLIGHT ON COUNTRY
Ruby, don't take your love to town: *Rogers, Kenny* / Rawhide: *Laine, Frankie* / Walkin' after midnight: *Cline, Patsy* / Wasted days and wasted nights: *Fender, Freddy* / Rose garden: *Anderson, Lynn* / Medley: *Boxcar Willie* / Here comes my baby: *West, Dottie* / Let it be me: *Tillotson, Johnny* / Let your love flow: *Bellamy Brothers* / Ball and chain: *Mattea, Kathy* / He stopped loving her today: *Jones, George* / Mr. Bojangles: *Nitty Gritty Dirt Band* / Total woman: *Riley, Jeannie C.* / Key largo: *Higgins, Bertie* / Okie from Muskogee: *Haggard, Merle* / Wine me up: *Young, Faron*
CD _____ HADCD 150
Javelin / Feb '94 / THE / Henry Hadaway Organisation.

SPOTLIGHT ON HITS OF THE SIXTIES
Sweets for my sweet: *Searchers* / You've got your troubles: *Fortunes* / Love is all around: *Troggs* / Wild thing: *Troggs* / I am the world: *Bee Gees* / Ferry 'cross the Mersey: *Gerry & The Pacemakers* / When you walk in the room: *Searchers* / Storm in a teacup: *Fortunes* / I can't control myself: *Troggs* / Needles and pins: *Searchers* / How do you do it: *Gerry & The Pacemakers* / Caroline: *Fortunes* / Monday's rain: *Bee Gees* / Sugar and spice: *Searchers*
CD _____ HADCD 143
Javelin / Feb '94 / THE / Henry Hadaway Organisation.

SPOTLIGHT ON JAZZ
n the mood: *Miller, Glenn* / One o'clock ump: *Basie, Count* / Tuxedo junction: *Hirt, Al* / Misty: *Vaughan, Sarah* / Ring dem bells: *Hampton, Lionel* / C Jam blues: *Ellington, Duke* / How high the moon: *Fitzgerald, Ella*

/ Scrape from the apple: *Parker, Charlie* / Sawnuff: *Davis, Miles* / Sweet Georgia Brown: *Cole, Nat King* / Tip toe topic: *Ellington, Duke* / Mr. Paganini: *Fitzgerald, Ella* / Curros: *Byrd, Donald* / Court: *Hubbard, Freddie* / If you could see me now: *Vaughan, Sarah* / All the things you are: *Benson, George*
CD _____ HADCD 144
Javelin / Feb '94 / THE / Henry Hadaway Organisation.

SPOTLIGHT ON PAUL SIMON PLUS
Play me a sad song: *Simon, Paul* / It means a lot: *Simon, Paul* / Flame: *Simon, Paul* / While I dream: *Sedaka, Neil* / Ring-a-rock: *Sedaka, Neil* / Ding dong: *Orlando, Tony* / You're the one: *Rivers, Johnny* / Hole in the ground: *Rivers, Johnny* / This is real: *Valli, Frankie* / Comme si bella: *Valli, Frankie* / Please me forever: *Edwards, Tommy* / It's all in the game: *Edwards, Tommy*
CD _____ HADCD 141
Javelin / Feb '94 / THE / Henry Hadaway Organisation.

SPOTLIGHT ON REGGAE
CD _____ RGCD 0011
Rocky One / Nov '94 / Jetstar.

SPOTLIGHT ON ROCK 'N' ROLL
(We're gonna) Rock around the clock: *Haley, Bill & The Comets* / Tutti frutti: *Little Richard* / Rockin' robin: *Day, Bobby* / Blue suede shoes: *Perkins, Carl* / Venus: *Avalon, Frankie* / Red river rock: *Johnny & The Hurricanes* / Let's dance: *Montez, Chris* / Surfin' bird: *Trashmen* / Louie Louie: *Kingsmen* / Walk don't run: *Ventures* / I fought the law: *Fuller, Bobby* / Hey little girl: *Clark, Dee* / Tiger: *Fabian* / Ooby dooby: *Orbison, Roy* / Ring-a-rock: *Sedaka, Neil* / Great balls of fire: *Lewis, Jerry Lee*
CD _____ HADCD 147
Javelin / Feb '94 / THE / Henry Hadaway Organisation.

SPOTLIGHT ON ROCK 'N' ROLL - LIVE
Rubber ball: *Vee, Bobby* / I'm gonna make you mine: *Christie, Lou* / Twilight time: *Platters* / Ginny come lately: *Hyland, Brian* / Charlie Brown: *Coasters* / Runaway: *Shannon, Del* / Motor running: *Lewis, Jerry Lee* / Dizzy: *Roe, Tommy* / Way down yonder in New Orleans: *Cannon, Freddy* / Why do fools fall in love: *Diamonds* / Roberta: *Ford, Frankie* / La bamba: *Tokens* / Peggy Sue: *Crickets* / Keep on running: *Davis, Spencer* / My guy: *Wells, Mary* / Rock 'n' roll is here to stay: *Original Juniors*
CD _____ HADCD 148
Javelin / Feb '94 / THE / Henry Hadaway Organisation.

SPOTLIGHT ON SOUL
Soul man: *Sam & Dave* / Knock on wood: *Floyd, Eddie* / Harlem shuffle: *Bob & Earl* / My guy: *Wells, Mary* / Stay: *Williams, Maurice & The Zodiacs* / Stagger Lee: *Price, Lloyd* / Tell it like it is: *Neville, Aaron* / Every beat of my heart: *Knight, Gladys & The Pips* / So fine: *Turner, Ike & Tina* / Mockingbird: *Foxx, Inez* / Oh no, not my baby: *Brown, Maxine* / Precious and few: *Climax Blues Band* / Show and tell: *Wilson, Al* / Seems like I gotta do wrong: *Whispers* / Stand by me: *King, Ben E.* / When a man loves a woman: *Sledge, Percy*
CD _____ HADCD 145
Javelin / Feb '94 / THE / Henry Hadaway Organisation.

SPRING STORY, THE
(Essential '70s Soul)
Tom the peeper: *Act 1* / My way, a smooth man: *Jackson, Millie* / Step by step: *Simon, Joe* / I can see him making love to you: *Mayberry Movement* / Too through: *Brown, Jocelyn* / I found lovin': *Fatback Band* / I gotta get away (from my own self): *Godfrey, Ray* / He didn't know (he kept on talkin'): *Green, Garland* / You've come a long way baby: *Flower Shoppe* / Baby you got it all: *Street People* / Just a little misunderstanding: *Jones, Busta* / S.O.S. (stop her on sight): *Barker, Winfield* / Get ready: *Harris, Eva* / Uptight: *Harris, Eva* / (Are you ready) Do the bus stop: *Fatback Band* / It's my life: *Mainstreeters* / Jody, come back and get your shoes: *Newsome, Bobby* / If we get caught I don't know you: *Mitchell, Phillip* / Drowning in the sea of love: *Simon, Joe* / (If loving you is wrong) I don't wanna be right: *Jackson, Millie* / Friends or lovers: *Act 1* / Magic's in the air: *Walker, Ronnie* / Loves contest: *Joneses* / How about a little hand (for the boys in the band): *Boys In The Band* / Bumpin' and stompin': *Green, Garland* / Come and get these memories: *Godfrey, Ray*
CD _____ CWSEWD 103
Southbound / Oct '95 / Pinnacle.

SQUASBOX
CD _____ Y 225107CD
Silex / Jul '95 / ADA.

SST ACOUSTIC
CD _____ SST 276 CD
SST / May '93 / Plastic Head.

ST. LOUIS 1927-1933
CD _____ DOCD 5181
Blues Document / Oct '93 / Swift / Jazz Music / Hot Shot.

ST. LOUIS BLUES 1925-41
CD _____ 158392
Blues Collection / Sep '95 / Discovery.

ST. LOUIS GIRLS 1927-1934
CD _____ DOCD 5182
Blues Document / Oct '93 / Swift / Jazz Music / Hot Shot.

ST. LOUIS GIRLS 1929-1937
CD _____ SOB 035362
Story Of The Blues / Oct '92 / Koch / ADA.

ST. LOUIS TOWN 1929-1933
CD _____ YAZCD 1003
Yazoo / Apr '91 / CM / ADA / Roots / Koch.

STAND BY ME
CD _____ YDG 74609
Yesterday's Gold / Feb '93 / Target/BMG.

STANDING STONES
CD _____ NAGE 5CD
Art Of Landscape / Feb '86 / SNY.

STAR O'RABBIE BURNS, THE
Star O'Rabbie Burns: *Dawson, Peter* / Auld lang syne: *Dawson, Peter* / Man's a man for a' that: *Watson, Robert* / My love is like a red red rose: *Hislop, Joseph* / Of a' the airts the wind can blaw: *Hislop, Joseph* / My love she's but a lassie yet: *Hislop, Joseph* / Corn rigs: *Hislop, Joseph* / Afton water: *Hislop, Joseph* / Ye banks and braes o' bonnie Doon: *MacEwan, Sydney* / Comin' thro' the rye: *Teyte, Maggie* / Blue eyed lassie: *Burnett, Robert* / Ca' the yowes: *Brunskill, Muriel* / Green grow the rashes: *MacKinley, Jean Sterling* / I'll meet thee on the Lea rig: *Murray, Laidlaw* / Mary Morison: *Harrison, John* / Tam Glen: *Day, Jean* / De'il's awa' wi' the exciseman: *Henderson, Roy* / Oh Willie brewed a peck o'malt: *Henderson, Roy* / I'm owre young tae marry yet: *Baillie, Isobel* / John Anderson, my Jo: *Baillie, Isobel* / Bonnie wee thing: *McCormack, John* / Ae fond kiss: *Coleman, Esther & Foster Richardson* / Scots wha hae: *Glasgow Orpheus Choir* / Charming Chloe: *Suddaby, Elsie* / O'whistle an' I'll come tae ye, my lad: *Scotney, Evelyn* / Mary Morison (2): *MacGregor, Alexander*
CD _____ MIDCD 004
Moidart / Jan '95 / Conifer / ADA.

STAR POWER
CD _____ EFA 201172
Pravda / May '95 / SRD.

STARDUST MEMORIES
With a shot in my heart: *Sinatra, Frank* / If I give my heart to you: *Day, Doris* / Georgia on my mind: *Laine, Frankie* / Welcome to my world: *Reeves, Jim* / In the mood: *Miller, Glenn* / Changing partners: *Crosby, Bing* / Hey there: *Clooney, Rosemary* / As time goes by: *Holiday, Billie* / Catch a falling star: *Como, Perry* / Three coins in a fountain: *Four Aces* / It's almost tomorrow: *Dreamweavers* / What a wonderful world: *Armstrong, Louis* / Little white cloud that cried: *Ray, Johnnie* / Autumn leaves: *Bennett, Tony* / Tear fell: *Brewer, Teresa* / Moon river: *Mancini, Henry* / Stormy weather: *Vaughan, Sarah* / May each day: *Williams, Andy* / Mr Wonderful: *Lee, Peggy* / Because you're mine: *Lanza, Mario* / Under the bridges of Paris: *Kitt, Eartha* / Smoke gets in your eyes: *Platters*
CD _____ NTRCD 045
Nectar / Oct '95 / Pinnacle.

STARS AT CHRISTMAS
White Christmas: *Crosby, Bing* / It's Christmas all over the world: *Davis, Sammy Jnr.* / Jolly old St. Nicholas: *Conniff, Ray* / We wish you a Merry Christmas: *Conniff, Ray* / Santa Claus is coming to town: *Bennett, Tony* / Christmas time is here again: *Whittaker, Roger* / Let it snow, let it snow, let it snow: *Williams, Andy* / Rockin' around the Christmas tree: *Lee, Brenda* / Christmas wonderland: *Kaempfert, Bert* / Rudolph the red nosed reindeer: *Crosby, Bing* / Baby's first Christmas: *Francis, Connie* / I'll be home for Christmas: *Day, Doris* / Home for the holidays: *Como, Perry* / Joy to the world: *Wynette, Tammy* / Hark the herald angels sing: *Andrews, Julie* / O come all ye faithful (Adeste Fidelis): *Reeves, Jim* / Ave Maria: *Lanza, Mario* / Christmas song: *Bennett, Tony* / What child is this: *Charles, Ray* / Special time of year: *Knight, Gladys* / Snowflake: *Clooney, Rosemary* / When a child is born: *Mathis, Johnny* / Count your blessings: *Conniff, Ray* / May each day: *Williams, Andy* / Have yourself a merry little Christmas: *Como, Perry* / Jingle bell rock: *Lee, Brenda* / Holiday for bells: *Kaempfert, Bert* / Snowfall: *Bennett, Tony* / Silver bells: *Day, Doris* / O little town of Bethlehem: *Francis, Connie* / Twelve days of Christmas: *Whittaker, Roger* / I saw mommy kissing Santa Claus: *Beverly Sisters* / Little drummer boy: *Whittaker, Roger* / I believe in Christmas: *Boone, Pat* / Carol of the bells: *Mathis, Johnny* / Jingle bells: *Mancini, Henry* / Frosty the snowman: *Lee, Brenda* / Do you hear what I hear: *Williams, Andy* / Christmas time: *Charles, Ray* / All I want for Christmas: *Ben-*

ton, Brook* / I walk with God: *Lanza, Mario* / Let there be peace: *Knight, Gladys* / Silent night: *Crosby, Bing* / White Christmas (2): *Mantovani*
CD _____ STADD 1000
Wisepack / Oct '94 / THE / Conifer.

STARS OF COUNTRY MUSIC, THE
Oh lonesome me: *Gibson, Don* / Peace in the valley: *Jordanaires* / Mexican Joe: *Reeves, Jim* / Crazy arms: *Lewis, Jerry Lee* / Next in line: *Cash, Johnny* / These boots are made for walking: *Hazlewood, Lee* / World's worst loser: *Jones, George* / Sally was a good old girl: *Jennings, Waylon* / Rose Marie: *Whitman, Slim* / Settin' the woods on fire: *Williams, Hank* / Honky tonk angels: *Parton, Dolly* / Race is on: *Jones, George* / Yonder comes a sucker: *Reeves, Jim* / Broken heart: *Twitty, Conway* / El Paso: *Robbins, Marty* / Train of love: *Cash, Johnny* / Please release me: *Parton, Dolly*
CD _____ 22518
Music / Dec '95 / Target/BMG.

STARS OF LAS VEGAS
Take the 'A' train: *Ellington, Duke* / I left my heart in San Francisco: *Bennett, Tony* / God bless the children: *Minnelli, Liza* / I'm coming home: *Jones, Tom* / What now my love: *Bassey, Shirley* / Man without love: *Humperdinck, Engelbert* / Lady: *Rogers, Kenny* / All the love in the world: *Warwick, Dionne* / My way: *Anka, Paul* / Passing strangers: *Eckstine, Billy & Sarah Vaughan* / April in Paris: *Basie, Count* / Every time we say goodbye: *Fitzgerald, Ella* / Very thought of you: *Damone, Vic* / Moon river: *Williams, Andy* / September in the rain: *Washington, Dinah* / For the good times: *Como, Perry* / Volare: *Martin, Dean* / Blue spanish eyes: *Martino, Al* / Move over darling: *Day, Doris* / Unforgettable: *Cole, Nat King*
CD _____ VSOP CD 181
Connoisseur / Mar '93 / Pinnacle.

STARS OF REGGAE SUNSPLASH
Charly / Feb '94 / Charly / THE / Cadillac.
CD _____ CPCD 8025

STARS OF ROCK 'N' ROLL
Tutti frutti: *Little Richard* / Rock around the clock: *Haley, Bill* / Mr Bassman: *Cymbal, Johnny* / Wooly bully: *Sam The Sham & The Pharaohs* / Da doo ron ron: *Crystals* / Tallahassie lassie: *Cannon, Freddy* / Rubber ball: *Vee, Bobby* / Good golly Miss Molly: *Swinging Blue Jeans* / Shake, rattle and roll: *Haley, Bill* / Maybelline: *Berry, Chuck* / Keep a knockin': *Little Richard* / Lucille: *Little Richard* / Long Tall Sally: *Little Richard* / Wild thing: *Troggs* / Sheila: *Roe, Tommy* / At the hop: *Danny & The Juniors* / Speddy Gonzalez: *Boone, Pat* / It's my party: *Gore, Lesley*
CD _____ 22524
Music / Dec '95 / Target/BMG.

STARS OF THE 50'S
Softly, softly: *Murray, Ruby* / Heartbeat: *Murray, Ruby* / My special angel: *Vaughan, Malcolm* / Every day of my life: *Vaughan, Malcolm* / Stairway of love: *Holliday, Michael* / Starry eyed: *Holliday, Michael* / Dreamboat: *Cogan, Alma* / Never do a tango with an window: *Cogan, Alma* / Around the world: *Hilton, Ronnie* / Wake up little Susie: *King Brothers* / White sports coat and a pink carnation: *King Brothers* / My thanks to you: *Conway, Steve* / Zambesi: *Calvert, Eddie* / Mandy: *Calvert, Eddie* / Pickin' a chicken: *Boswell, Eve* / Blue star: *Boswell, Eve* / Lollicop: *Mudlarks* / Tammy: *Lotis, Dennis* / Be my girl: *Dale, Jim* / China tea: *Conway, Russ* / Cindy Oh Cindy: *Brent, Tony* / Very sixteen: *Douglas, Craig* / Don't laugh at me: *Wisdom, Norman*
CD _____ CC 205
Music For Pleasure / May '88 / EMI.

STARS SALUTE SINATRA
Night and day: *Astaire, Fred* / How about you: *Garland, Judy* / Sunday, Monday or always: *Crosby, Bing* / Fools rush in: *Miller, Glenn* / One for my baby: *Horne, Lena* / They can't take that away from me: *Dorsey, Jimmy* / I get a kick out of you: *Merman, Ethel* / Sweet Lorraine: *Tatum, Art* / Yesterdays: *Holiday, Billie* / Jeepers creepers: *Armstrong, Louis* / Imagination: *Fitzgerald, Ella* / I'll follow my secret heart: *Coward, Sir Noel* / Lady is a tramp: *Dorsey, Tommy* / All or nothing: *Haymes, Dick* / Glad to be unhappy: *Wiley, Lee* / I'll never smile again: *Shelton, Anne* / I didn't know what time was: *Shaw, Artie* / Where are you: *Bailey, Mildred* / Embraceable you: *Hackett, Bobby* / Blues in the night: *Shore, Dinah* / River, stay 'way from my door: *Waters, Ethel* / When your love has gone: *Austin, Gene* / Always: *Durbin, Deanna* / Mood indigo: *Ellington, Duke*
CD _____ CECD 2
Collector's Edition / Nov '95 / Magnum Music Group.

STARTREFF VOLKSMUSIK
CD _____ 15257
Laserlight / Nov '91 / Target/BMG.

STASH SAMPLER
(Salvador, Turre, Pizzarelli, Thielmans etc.)
CD _____ STCD 526
Stash / Mar '90 / Jazz Music / CM / Cadillac / Direct / ADA.

889

STASH SAMPLER 2, THE
CD _____ STCD 599
Stash / Jan '93 / Jazz Music / CM / Cadillac / Direct / ADA.

STATE OF THE UNION
CD _____ DIS 23CD
Dischord / Mar '95 / SRD.

STATESIDE SMASHES
CD _____ PLATCD 345
Platinum Music / Oct '90 / Prism / Ross.

STATESIDE SWEET MUSIC
Love and learn: Fields, Shep / If the moon turns green: Kassel, Art / Little rendezvous in Honolulu: Lopez, Vincent / I have eyes: Shaw, Artie & His Orchestra / One cigarette for two: Martin, Freddy & His Orchestra / Pessimistic character: Ayres, Mitchell & His Orchestra / Can't get Indiana off my mind: Gordon, Gay & The Mince Pies / I don't want to cry any more: Barnet, Charlie / Apple blossom and chapel bells: Martin, Freddy & His Orchestra / I threw a bean bag at the moon: Kassel, Art / That sentimental sandwich: Nelson, Ozzie & His Orchestra / On a little bamboo bridge: Fields, Shep / Whispering grass: Dorsey, Jimmy Orchestra / Strange enchantment: Nelson, Ozzie & His Orchestra / Meet the sun halfway: Ayres, Mitchell & His Orchestra / Whitemen, Paul & His Orchestra / Never took a lesson in my life: Gordon, Gay & His Orchestra / Why don't we do this more often: Martin, Freddy & His Orchestra / That's for me: Barnet, Charlie & His Orchestra / Moonlight and shadows: Shaw, Artie & His Orchestra / Who's afraid of love: Bengar, Bunny & His Orchestra / Flamingo: Martin, Freddy & His Orchestra
CD _____ PASTCD 9787
Flapper / Apr '92 / Pinnacle.

STAX BLUES MASTERS, VOL 1: BLUE MONDAY
They want money: Little Sonny / Drivin' wheel: King, Albert / Creeper: Robinson, Freddie / Eight men, four women: Little Milton / Things that I used to do: Little Sonny / Bad luck: King, Albert / More bad luck: King, Albert / Born under a bad sign: King, Albert / Blues with a feeling: Little Sonny / Married woman: Little Milton / Ronettes: Robinson, Freddie / Blue Monday: Little Milton / After hours: Robinson, Freddie / Open the door to your heart: Little Milton / Blues after hours: Robinson, Freddie / River's invitation: Robinson, Freddie / It's hard going up (but twice as hard coming down): Little Sonny
CD _____ CDSXE 080
Stax / Nov '92 / Pinnacle.

STAX FUNK - GET UP AND GET DOWN
Shaft: Hayes, Isaac / Castle of joy: Tar Larry's Band / What goes around (must come around): Sons Of Slum / Dark skin woman (On CD/MC only): Rice, Sir Mack / What'cha see is what'cha get: Dramatics / Son of Shaft: Bar-Kays / Dryer part 1: Johnson, Roy Lee & The Villagers / Cool strut part one (On CD/MC only): Hayes, Bernie / Mr. Big Stuff: Knight, Jean / Funkaaize you: Sho Nuff / Holy ghost: Bar-Kays / Men (On CD/MC only): Hayes, Isaac / Circuits overloaded: Foxx, Inez & Charlie / FLB: Tar Larry's Band / Black: Mar-Keys / Get up and get down: Dramatics / Moving on: Dynamic Soul Machine / You chose me (On CD/MC only): Sho Nuff / Dryer part 2 (On CD/MC only): Johnson, Roy Lee & The Villagers / Cool strut part 1 (On CD/MC only): Hayes, Bernie
CD _____ CDSX 020
Stax / May '89 / Pinnacle.

STAX GOLD
(Hits 1968-1971)
Soul limbo: Booker T & The MG's / Time is tight: Booker T & The MG's / Private number: Clay, Judy & William Bell / Who's making love: Taylor, Johnnie / Bring it on home to me: Floyd, Eddie / I forgot to be your lover: Bell, William / I like what you're doing (to me): Thomas, Carla / Do the push and pull (part 1): Thomas, Rufus / Mr. Big Stuff: Knight, Jean / What'cha see is what'cha get: Dramatics / Respect yourself: Staple Singers / I'll take you there: Staple Singers / Shaft: Hayes, Isaac / Son of Shaft: Bar-Kays / I've been lonely for so long: Knight, Frederick / Starting all over again: Mel & Tim / Woman to woman: Brown, Shirley / I'll be the other woman: Soul Children / So I can love you (Not on LP): Emotions / I have learned to do without you (Not on LP): Staples, Mavis / In the rain (Not on LP): Dramatics / Dedicated to the one I love (Not on LP): Temprees / Short stoppin' (Not on LP): Brown, Veda / Cheaper to keep her (Not on LP): Taylor, Johnnie
CD _____ CDSXD 043
Stax / Sep '91 / Pinnacle.

STAX GREATEST HITS
In the rain: Dramatics / I'll take you there: Staple Singers / Who's making love: Taylor, Johnnie / Do the funky chicken: Thomas, Rufus / Hearsay: Soul Children / Dedicated to the one I love: Temprees / I could never be president: Taylor, Johnnie / Woman to woman: Brown, Shirley / Good woman turning bad / Respect yourself: Staple Singers / I've been lonely for so long: Knight, Frederick / Shaft: Hayes, Isaac / Mr. Big Stuff: Knight, Jean / Private number: Clay, Judy & William

William Bell / So I can love you: Emotions / Starting all over again: Mel & Tim / That's what love will make us do: Little Milton / What'cha see is what'cha get: Dramatics
CD _____ JCD 7021110
Stax / Mar '87 / Pinnacle.

STAX O' SOUL: SAMPLER OF STAX TRAX
Will you still love me tomorrow: Bell, William / Stolen angel: Tonettes / Zip a dee doo dah: Booker T & The MG's / Little boy: Thomas, Carla / Last clean shirt: Thomas, Rufus / Cupid: Redding, Otis / Sweet devil: John, Mable / Need your love so bad: Johnson, Ruby / I've never found a girl: Floyd, Eddie / I could never be president: Taylor, Johnnie / What side of the door: Hughes, Jimmy / Open the door to your heart: Little Milton / I can't break away (from your love): Lewis, Barbara / When something is wrong with my baby: Weston, Kim / I finally got you: McCracklin, Jimmy / Takin' all the love I can: Joseph, Margie / Wade in the water: Little Sonny / I've been lonely for so long: Knight, Frederick / Respect yourself: Staple Singers / Getting funky round here: Black Nasty / Flat tire: King, Albert / We need each other, girl: Hayes, Isaac / Move me move me: Brown, Shirley
CD _____ CDSXX 100
Stax / Oct '93 / Pinnacle.

STAX REVUE LIVE AT THE 54 BALLROOM
Green onions: Booker T & The MG's / You can't sit down: Booker T & The MG's / Summertime: Booker T & The MG's / Soul twist: Booker T & The MG's / Boot-leg: Booker T & The MG's / Don't have to shop around: Mad Lads / Candy: Astors / Last night: Mar-Keys / Any other way: Bell, William / You don't miss your water: Bell, William / Every ounce of strength: Thomas, Carla / I've done the dog: Thomas, Rufus / Walking the dog: Thomas, Rufus
CD _____ CDSXD 040
Stax / Sep '91 / Pinnacle.

STAX SIRENS AND VOLT VAMPS
Try a little tenderness: Sweet Inspirations / I've got to go on without you: Brown, Shirley / Take it off her (and put it on me): Brown, Veda / Love slave: Alexander, Margie / Shouldn't I love him: John, Mable / Got to be the man: Emotions / Save the last kiss for me: Knight, Jean / Nobody: Joseph, Margie / Who could be loving you: Ross, Jackie / Standing in the need of your love: Jeanne & The Darlings / I'll never grow old: Charmells / Give love to save love: Clay, Judy / You hurt me for the last time: Foxx, Inez & Charlie / I like what you're doing (to me): Thomas, Carla / If I had it my way: Weston, Kim / How can you mistreat the one you love (Available on CD only): Love, Katie / Love changes (Available on CD only): Charlene & The Soul Serenaders / What happened to our good thing (Available on CD only): Haywood, Kitty / Where would you be today (Available on CD only): Ilana
CD _____ CDSX 013
Stax / Jun '88 / Pinnacle.

STAX/VOLT REVUE, VOL 1: LIVE IN LONDON
Green onions: Booker T & The MG's / Philly dog: Mar-Keys / If I had a hammer: Floyd, Eddie / Knock on wood: Floyd, Eddie / Shake: Redding, Otis / Yesterday: Thomas, Carla / B-A-B-Y: Thomas, Carla / I take what I want: Sam & Dave / When something is wrong with my baby: Sam & Dave / Hold on I'm comin': Sam & Dave
CD _____ 756823412
Carlton Home Entertainment / Nov '94 / Carlton Home Entertainment.

STAX/VOLT REVUE, VOL 3: LIVE IN EUROPE
Introduction (London): Emperor Rosko / Red beans and rice: Booker T & The MG's / Booker-loo: Booker T & The MG's / Green onions: Booker T & The MG's / Hip hug-her: Booker T & The MG's / Introduction (Paris): Hubert / Let me be good to you: Thomas, Carla / Yesterday: Thomas, Carla / Something good: Thomas, Carla / B-A-B-Y: Thomas, Carla / Introduction (London) 2: Emperor Rosko / I don't want to cry: Floyd, Eddie / Raise your hand: Floyd, Eddie / Knock on wood: Floyd, Eddie / Introduction (London): Emperor Rosko / Respect: Redding, Otis / My girl: Redding, Otis / Day tripper: Redding, Otis / Introduction: Redding, Otis / Fa fa fa fa (Sad song): Redding, Otis / Introduction (2): Redding, Otis / Try a little tenderness: Redding, Otis
CD _____ CDSXD 044
Stax / May '92 / Pinnacle.

STEAL THIS DISC
CD _____ RCD 00210
Rykodisc / Jun '92 / Vital / ADA.

STEAMIN'
(Hardcore '92)
It's grim up north: JAMMS / Get ready for 2 Unlimited / D.J.'s take control: SL2 / Faith (in the power of love): Rozalla / A 8 (come with me): Altern 8 / 2/231: Anticappella / Ring my bell: D.J. Jazzy Jeff & The Fresh Prince / Best of you: Thomas, Kenny / Apparently nothin': Young Disciples / Something got me started: Simply Red / Killer: Seal / Dance with me: Control /

Change: Stansfield, Lisa / Love will bring us together: Cookie Crew & Roy Ayers / Alright: Urban Soul / Give it to me baby (sample free zone): Love Revolution / Peter and the wolf: Zero G / I want you (forever): Cox, Carl / O. P. P.: Naughty By Nature / Keepin' the faith: De La Soul
CD _____ JARCD 1
Cookie Jar / Dec '91 / SRD.

STEEL BAND MUSIC OF THE CARIBBEAN
CD _____ 12176
Laserlight / Aug '95 / Target/BMG.

STEEL BANDS OF TRINIDAD AND TOBAGO
Sunset / Pan in the minor / Love's theme / To be continued / Unknown band / I just called to say I love you / Sparrow medley / Calypso music / Brisad del zolla / Somewhere out there / Hammer
CD _____ DE 4011
Delos / Jan '94 / Conifer.

STEPPIN' OUT - THE ALBUM 1
CD _____ STEP 001CD
Steppin' Out / Oct '94 / Pinnacle / Steppin' Out / Vital.

STEPPING IT OUT
CD _____ VT 1CD
Veteran Tapes / Oct '93 / Direct / ADA.

STEWED MOONBEAMS IN WAVY GRAVY
(Okeh Black Rock'n'Roll)
CD _____ EDCD 283
Edsel / Mar '92 / Pinnacle / ADA.

STILL GOT THE BLUES
CD _____ EMPRBX 004
Empress / Sep '94 / THE.

STILL GOT THE BLUES VOL.1
CD _____ EMPRCD 502
Emporio / Apr '94 / THE / Disc / CM.

STILL GOT THE BLUES VOL.2
CD _____ EMPRCD 508
Emporio / Apr '94 / THE / Disc / CM.

STILL SPICY GUMBO STEW
I don't want to be hurted: George, Barbara / Losing battle: Adams, Johnny / Check Mr. Popeye: Bo, Eddie / Now let's Popeye: Bo, Eddie / Shrimp boat: Dr. John / Somebody's got to go: Tick tocks / Why lie: Tee, Willie / I found a little girl: Bo, Eddie / Love as true as mine: Johnson, Wallace / I got a feelin': Nooky Boy / Money (that's what I want): Afo executives / Who knows: Tee, Willie / Heart for sale: Lee, Robbie / Point: Dr. John / Roamin-itis: Bo, Eddie / Baby: Lynn, Tammi / Love love love: Wood Brothers / Nancy: Afo executives / Serpent and the flame: Robinson, Alvin / Soulful woman: Robinson, Alvin / 'bout drive me wild: Robinson, Alvin / End of a dream (Booker's ballad): Booker, James / Cry cry cry: Robinson, Alvin
CD _____ CDCHD 520
Ace / Jun '94 / Pinnacle / Cadillac / Complete/Pinnacle.

STINGRAY THE COLLCTION VOL.1
CD _____ STINGCD 1
Sting Ray / Feb '95 / Jetstar.

STOLEN MOMENTS - RED, HOT & COOL
Time is moving on: Byrd, Donald & Guru / Un angel en danger: M.C. Solaar & Ron Carter / Positive: Franti, Michael / Nocturnal sunshine: Ndegeocello, Me'shell / Flyin' high in the Brooklyn sky: Digable Planets / Lester Bowie/Wah Wah Watson / Stolen moments: UFO / Righteous: Parcyde / I shall proceed: Roots & Roy Ayers / Trouble don't last always: Incognito/Carleen Anderson/Ramsey Lewis / Rent strike: Groove Collective & Bernie Worrell / Scream: Us3 / Joshua Redman/Tony Remy / This is madness: Last Poets & Pharoah Sanders / Apprehension: Cherry, Don & The Watts Prophets / Love supreme: Marsalis, Branford / Love supreme (1) (CD only): Coltrane, Alice / Creator has a master plan (CD only): Sanders, Pharoah
CD Set _____ GRP 97942
GRP / Oct '94 / BMG / New Note.

STOMPIN' AT THE KLUB FOOT VOLS 1 & 2
Ghost town: Restless / Baby, please don't go: Restless / Bottle on the beach: Restless / Long black shiny car: Restless / Red monkey: Milkshakes / Did I hear you: Milkshakes / It's you: Milkshakes / Sweet little sixteen: Milkshakes / Joe 90: Guana Batz / Train kept a rollin': Guana Batz / Dizzy miss lizzy one something: Guana Batz / Devil's guitar: Guana Batz / I can satisfy you: Stingrays / Escalator: Stingrays / Time is after you: Stingrays / Blue girl: Stingrays / St. Jack: Primevals / Low down: Primevals / Transvestite blues: Demented Are Go / Fucked and preserved: Demented Are Go / Misdemeanour: Demented Are Go / Where's my baby: Pharaohs / Listen pretty baby: Pharaohs / Real cool chick: Styngrites / Reptile (Man): Styngrites / Legend of the lost: Rapids / Raid: Rapids / Ride this torpedo: Tall Boys / Action woman: Tall Boys
CD _____ SLOG CD 6
Slogan / Oct '92 / BMG.

STOMPIN' AT THE KLUB FOOT VOLS 3 & 4
Pass it on: Torment / Last time: Torment / Rip it up: Rochee & The Sarnos / High class power: Wigsville Spliffs / Psycho disease: Coffin Nails / Bamboo land: Batmobile / Baby that's where you're wrong: Caravans / Edge on you: Restless / No particular place to go: Guana Batz / Ghost train: Frenzy / Be bop a lula: Demented Are Go / Shake it up: Styngrites / Dizzy Miss Lizzy: Milkshakes / Uncle Sam: Torment / Beast: Rochee & The Sarnos / Al Capone: Wigsville Spliffs / Let's wreck: Coffin Nails / Cold sweat: Batmobile / Ballroom blitz: Batmobile / Gonna love ya: Caravans / You're so fine: Guana Batz / Hall of mirrors: Frenzy / Killed love: Pharaohs / Spiritual: Primevals / Fun time: Tall Boys
CD _____ SLOG CD 7
Slogan / Oct '92 / BMG.

STOMPIN' AT THE SAVOY
Stompin' at the Savoy: Armstrong, Louis / In the mood: Miller, Glenn / It started all over again: Dorsey, Tommy / Nutcracker suite: Brown, Les / Northwest passage: Herman, Woody / Tea for two: Armstrong, Louis / April in Paris: Miller, Glenn / Nearness of you: Dorsey, Jimmy / Nightmare: Shaw, Artie / How about you: Brown, Les / C'est si bon: Armstrong, Louis / Frankie and Johnny: Goodman, Benny / Chattanooga choo choo: Miller, Glenn / Fools rush in: Dorsey, Jimmy / Pretty woman: Ellington, Duke / Good for nothin' Joe: Barnet, Charlie / Tiger rag: Armstrong, Louis / After glow: Herman, Woody / I've got rhythm: Dorsey, Jimmy / That old black magic: Miller, Glenn
CD _____ CDGRF 129
Tring / '93 / Tring / Prism.

STOMPING PARTY
Rockin' all over the world: Status Quo / Venus: Bananarama / Come on Eileen: Dexy's Midnight Runners / Crocodile rock: John, Elton / Come on feel the noise: Slade / Wild thing: Troggs / Twist and shout: Beatles / Brian & The Tremeloes / Shout: Lulu / La Bamba: Los Lobos / Monster mash: Pickett, Bobby / All right now: Free / Tainted love: Soft Cell / Only way is up: Yazz / Kiss: Art Of Noise / Spirit in the sky: Greenbaum, Norman / Tequila: Champs / Addicted to love: Palmer, Robert / Shakin' all over: Kidd, Johnny / Respectable: Mel & Kim / See my baby jive: Wizzard / 5-4-3-2-1: Manfred Mann / Let's work together: Canned Heat / Mony mony: James, Tommy / Hippy hippy shake: Swinging Blue Jeans / Hi ho silver lining: Beck, Jeff / Locomotion: Little Eva / Hit me with your rhythm stick: Dury, Ian / (We're gonna) Rock around the clock: Haley, Bill / Roll over beethoven: Berry, Chuck / Time warp: Damian / Dizzy: Remy, Tommy / Let's twist again: Checker, Chubby / My baby just cares for me: Simone, Nina / Israelites: Dekker, Desmond / Double barrel: Collins, Dave & Ansil / Reet petite: Wilson, Jackie / Can can: Buster / I'm the leader of the gang (I am): Glitter, Gary / Lond tall Sally: Little Richard / Let's dance: Montez, Chris
CD _____ DINCD 52
Dino / Nov '92 / Pinnacle / 3MV.

STONE LOVE ON THE ROAD VOL.1
CD _____ SGCD 13
Sir George / Mar '93 / Jetstar / Pinnacle.

STONE LOVE ON THE ROAD VOL.2
CD _____ SGCD 18
Sir George / Nov '94 / Jetstar / Pinnacle.

STONE LOVE VOL.3
CD _____ VPCD 1448
VP / Nov '95 / Jetstar.

STONE LOVE VOL.6 - CHAMPION SOUND
CD _____ SGCD 17
Sir George / Nov '94 / Jetstar / Pinnacle.

STONE ROCK BLUES
CD _____ CHLD 19264
Chess/MCA / Oct '94 / BMG / New Note.

STONED ALCHEMY
(27 Blues And R&B Hits That Inspired The Rolling Stones)
Come on: Berry, Chuck / Red rooster: Howlin' Wolf / Fortune teller: Spellman, Benny / I just want to make love to you: Waters, Muddy / Roadrunner: Diddley, Bo / Down home girl: Robinson, Alvin / Bright lights big city: Reed, Jimmy / Down the road apiece: Berry, Chuck / Around and around: Berry, Chuck / Ruler of my heart: Thomas, Irma / I can't be satisfied: Waters, Muddy / Fannie Mae: Brown, Buster / Cops and robbers: Diddley, Bo / Down in the bottom: Howlin' Wolf / You can't catch me: Berry, Chuck / Diddley daddy: Diddley, Bo / Hoochie coochie man: Waters, Muddy / Honest I do: Reed, Jimmy / How many more years: Howlin' Wolf / You can make it if you try: Allison, Gene / Feel so good: Berry, Chuck / Carol: Berry, Chuck / I need you baby: Diddley, Bo / Suzie Q: Hawkins, Dale / Pretty thing: Diddley, Bo / Got my mojo working: Waters, Muddy / It's all over now: Womack, Bobby
CD Set _____ CDINS 5016
Instant / Sep '89 / Charly.

STOP SAMPLER
CD _____ 74321308452
Arista / Sep '95 / BMG.

STORMY MONDAY
CD _____ NTRCD 023
Nectar / Sep '94 / Pinnacle.

STORMY WEATHER
CD _____ PHONTCD 7647
Phontastic / '94 / Weillard / Jazz Music / Cadillac.

STORY OF GOLDBAND RECORDS, THE
Stormy weather: Phillips, Phil / Let's boogie: Bonner, Juke Boy / Sugar Bee: Cleveland Crochet / Let's go boppin' tonight: Ferrier, Al / Crawl: Guitar Junior / So what: Duhan, Johnny / Cindy Lou: Terry, Gene / You're lonesome now: Perrywell, Charles / Boogie in the mud: James, Danny / Going crazy baby: Guitar Junior / Rooster strut: Savoy, Ashton / No future: Rockin' Sidney / You're so fine: Kershaw, Pee Wee / Frosty: James, Danny / San Antonio: Big Walter / Please accept my love: Wilson, Jimmy / Blue bayou shuffle: Cookie & The Cupcakes / Teenage baby: Herman, Sticks / Crisis / Straight of tune: Anderson, Elton / Chicken stuff: Wilson, Hop / Teardrops in my eyes: Terry, Gene / Puppy love: Parton, Dolly / Don't leave me: Phillips, Phil
CD _____ CDCHD 424
Ace / Nov '92 / Pinnacle / Cadillac / Complete/Pinnacle.

STORY OF THE CIVIL RIGHTS MOVEMENT THROUGH ITS SONG, THE
CD _____ SFWCD 40032
Smithsonian Folkways / Dec '94 / ADA / Direct / Koch / CM / Cadillac.

STORY SO FAR, THE
(Essential Argo/Cadet Grooves)
Slick Eddie: Stitt, Sonny / I am the blackgold of the sun: New Rotary Connection / Straussmania: Salinas, Daniel / Ordinary Joe: Callier, Terry / City bump: McDuff, Jack / California soul: Shaw, Marlena / Moondance: Tate, Grady / Golden ring: American Gypsy / Samba blues: Foster, Frank / Mo' blues: Willette, Baby Face
CD _____ ARCD 517
Charly / Feb '94 / Charly / THE / Cadillac.

STORYTELLERS
Fisherman's blues: Waterboys / Sunshine on leith: Proclaimers / This beautiful pain: Runrig / Candle in the wind: John, Elton / Anchorage: Shocked, Michelle / Don't go: Hothouse Flowers / My old friend the blues: Reader, Eddi / Copperhead road: Earle, Steve / Walk on the wild side: Reed, Lou / Shipbuilding: Wyatt, Robert / War baby: Robinson, Tom / Cry cry: Oyster Band / Find my love: Fairground Attraction / Riverboat song: Cale, J.J. / All the way from America: Armatrading, Joan / Hawaiian island world: World Party
CD _____ NTRCD 012
Nectar / Mar '94 / Pinnacle.

STRAIGHT NO CHASER
Pee Wee Marquette's intro / Cantaloupe island / Ronnie's bonnie / Comment on ritual / straight no chaser / Sookie sookie / Goin' down south / Song for my father / Blind man / Filthy McNasty / Jeannine / Steppin' into tomorrow
CD _____ CDS 8282632
Blue Note / Apr '94 / EMI.

STRAIGHT TO I ROY'S HEAD
CD _____ OO 2718
Crocodisc / Apr '95 / THE / Magnum Music Group.

STRAIGHT TO PRINCE JAZZBO'S HEAD
CD _____ CC 2718
Crocodisc / Apr '95 / THE / Magnum Music Group.

STREET CAROLS DECEMBER VOICES
CD _____ STG 4217
Street Gold / Nov '95 / Koch.

STREET JAZZ - WHERE HIP HOP MEETS JAZZ
Breakfast at Denny's: Buckshot Lefonque / Behaviour the sickness: B'Zar Behaviour / Montuno funk: Solsonics / Street jazz: Tribeca Sound / No pain, no gain: Buckshot Lefonque / Proceed 3: Roots / Pride (she loves me she loves me not): Tribeca Sound / Old school rule: Da Phenoms / Drum major instinct: Joey, Pal / Words I misinterpret: Gang Starr / Bless ya life: K.G.B. / Murder 1: Powerful
CD _____ DLCD 001
Downlow Entertainment / Sep '95 / Vital.

STREET JAZZ 1
Natasha: Like Young / Klute: F.R.I.S.K. / Theme from the underground bowling alley: T.U.B.A. / West by South Wash: As One / Be bop breakdance: Little Eye / Candyfloss: Forest Mighty Black / A.W.O.L.: British Underground Productions / Get up, get down: Fishbelly Black / London kills me: Groove Nation / Don't rub another man's rhubarb: Innuendo / You know what it's like: Doverney, Ondrea / Free your mind: Action People / Seasons of my mind: Batu / Apple strudle: Up Bustle & Out
CD _____ CDTEP 4
Step 2 / Jun '94 / 3MV / Sony.

STREET JAZZ VOL.2
CD _____ CDTEP 6
Step 2 / Dec '94 / 3MV / Sony.

STREET JAZZ VOL.3
CD _____ CDTEP 7
Step 2 / Aug '95 / 3MV / Sony.

STREET MUSIC OF PANAMA
CD _____ OMCD 008
Original Music / Nov '90 / SRD / Jetstar.

STREET PARADE '95
Sound: Humate / C5: D.J. Edge / Level X: Bad Boy: Advent / Eclos: Random Fluctuations / Pure energy: Freakazoid / Mechatech: Mijks Magic Marble Box / I like that: A.W.E.X. / I feel so detuned: No Soul / Clap your hands: Koenig / Audio strike: Synectics
CD _____ SUPER 2043CD
Superstition / Aug '95 / Vital / SRD.

STREET PARTY SING-A-LONG - 45 ENGLISH FAVOURITES
CD _____ PLATCD 3937
Prism / Mar '95 / Prism.

STREET SOUL
Two can play that game: Brown, Bobby / She's got that vibe: R. Kelly / Motownphilly: Boyz II Men / Right here: S.W.V. / Flavour of the old school: Knight, Beverley / Just a step from heaven: Eternal / Don't walk away: Jade / Back and forth: Aaliyah / I love your smile: Shanice / That's the way love goes: Jackson, Janet / I swear: All 4 One / Down that road: Nelson, Shara / Don't look any further: M People / Don't be a fool: Loose Ends / Back to life: Soul II Soul / One: Paris, Mica / Searching: China Black / Some girls: Ultimate Kaos / Sweetness: Gayle, Michelle / Unfinished sympathy: Massive Attack / Bump 'n' grind: R. Kelly / Sensitivity: Tresvant, Ralph / Cry for you: Jodeci / 69: Father MC / Poison: Bell Biv Devoe / Can't stop: After 7 / Ghetto heaven: Family Stand / My lovin': En Vogue / Express: Carroll, Dina / Finally: Peniston, Ce Ce / Midnight at the oasis: Brand New Heavies / Mama said: Anderson, Carleen / Real love: Driza Bone / Carry me home: Gloworm / Down 4 whatever: Nuttin' Nyce / Hey D.J.: Lighter Shade Of Brown / Buddy X: Cherry, Neneh / Whatta man: Salt 'N' Pepa & En Vogue / People everyday: Arrested Development / Summertime: D.J. Jazzy Jeff & The Fresh Prince
CD Set _____ VTDCD 41
Virgin / May '95 / EMI.

STREET SOUNDS ANTHEMS 1
(The Official Week-Enders Album)
I found lovin': Fatback Band / Funkin' for Jamaica: Browne, Tom / Bring the family back: Paul, Billy / Ain't no stoppin' us now: McFadden & Whitehead / Dominoes: Byrd, Donald / Movin': Brass Construction / Encore: Lynn, Cheryl / Hard work: Handy, John / Groove: Franklin, Rodney / Prance on: Henderson, Eddie
CD _____ SOUNDSCD 3
Street Sounds / Mar '95 / BMG.

STREET WALKIN' BLUES
CD _____ JASSCD 626
Jass / Oct '92 / CM / Jazz Music / ADA / Cadillac / Direct.

STREETS OF FEAR
Streets of fear: Caldonia / Goin' to Albert Lea: Higham, Daniel / Hot rhythm blue love: Kyme, Peter / Rollin' Danny: Phillips, Dave / Do you have to go: Hayward, Ronnie / You better watch out: Blue Jeans / Sleepless night: Vortex, Eddie / Rattlin' man: Twenty Flight Rock / Blue moon: Lightnin' Jay / Money: Muskrats / Say what you mean: Flapjacks / 1000 miles: Outer Miles / Too fast to live, too young to die: Sabrejets / Rock 'n' roll planet: Chalky The Yorkie / C'mon little girl: Cobras / Rattlesnake: Haywire / Cosmic star of rock 'n' roll: Power, Will / That's you: Rimshots / Down in the jungle: Clive's Jive Five / Losers never win: Caldonia
CD _____ FCD 3037
Fury / Mar '95 / Magnum Music Group / Nervous.

STREETS OF SKA
CD _____ CDHB 198
Heartbeat / Nov '95 / Greensleeves / Jetstar / ADA.

STREETWALKING BLUES
CD _____ JCD 626
Jass / Feb '91 / CM / Jazz Music / ADA / Cadillac / Direct.

STRICTLY HARDCORE
CD _____ STHCCD 1
Strictly Underground / '92 / SRD.

STRICTLY RHYTHM
CD _____ REACTCD 016
React / Feb '93 / Vital.

STRICTLY RHYTHM - THE EARLY YEARS
CD _____ SR 307CD
React/Strictly Rhythm / Mar '94 / Vital.

STRICTLY RHYTHM 2
Deep inside: Hardrive / Pressure: Quick, Butch / Watching you: Washington, Joey / Nothin': Levi, Ira / Beat that makes you move: Bass Hitt / Go on move: Reel 2 Real / Inside out: Phuture / Feel my love: Odyssey / Live and die: Audio Clash / House of love: Smooth Touch / Work it out: Mood Live / Who keeps changing your mind: South Street Players
CD _____ REACTCD 026
React / Sep '93 / Vital.

STRICTLY RHYTHM 3
CD _____ REACTCD 043
React / Jul '94 / Vital.

STRICTLY RHYTHM 4
Theme (Legend mix): Loop 7 / Unnecessary changes (Club mix): Morel's Grooves / Let's talk about me (Fierce mix): Androgeny / Tearin' me apart (Main klub mix): Inner Soul / Goin' clear: Caucasion Boy / Witch doktor: Van Helden, Armand / Sumba luma (S-Man's got you in a trance mix): Tribal Infusion / Paul's pain (Demoral mix): Phantom Inc. / Chosen path (Trance mix): Sole Fusion / Get up and get moving: Morel's Grooves / Flavor of love (Mixes): Logic
CD _____ REACTCD 058
React / Mar '95 / Vital.

STRICTLY RHYTHM 5
CD _____ SR 322CD
Strictly Rhythm / Oct '95 / SRD / Vital.

STRICTLY THE BEST
CD _____ VPCD 1227
VP / Apr '92 / Jetstar.

STRICTLY THE BEST VOL.15
CD _____ VPCD 1459
VP / Nov '95 / Jetstar.

STRICTLY THE BEST VOL.18
CD _____ VPCD 1460
VP / Nov '95 / Jetstar.

STRICTLY THE BEST VOL.4
CD _____ VPCD 1186
VP / Jul '92 / Jetstar.

STRICTLY THE BEST VOL.7
CD _____ VPCD 1251
VP / Nov '92 / Jetstar.

STRICTLY THE BEST VOL.8
CD _____ VPCD 1252
VP / Nov '92 / Jetstar.

STRICTLY UNDERGROUND
Protein: Sonic Experience / Moonstompin': Undercover Movement / Mind, body and soul: Fantasy UFO / Burial: Soundclash / Let's go: Noise Engineer / Answer: Equation / Thru the night: Noise Engineer / Music's gonna rule the world: Sonic Experience / Untitled revolution: Tigers In Space / Best: Full Dread / Check it out: Masters Of The Universe / Do you want me: Skeletor
CD _____ STURCD 1
Strictly Underground / Nov '91 / SRD.

STRICTLY UNDERGROUND 2
CD _____ STURCD 3
Strictly Underground / Feb '94 / SRD.

STRICTLY UNDERGROUND 3
CD _____ STURCD 5
Strictly Underground / Feb '94 / SRD.

STRICTLY WORLDWIDE VOL.3
CD _____ PIR 36
Piranha / Jun '94 / Direct.

STRIKE A DEEP CHORD
CD _____ JR 000032
Justice / Dec '92 / Koch.

STRING BANDS 1926-1929
CD _____ DOCD 5167
Blues Document / May '93 / Swift / Jazz Music / Hot Shot.

STRING OF SWINGING PEARLS, A
Annie Laurie: Manone, Wingy Orchestra / Eel: Freeman, Bud Summa Cum Laude / Troubled: Trumbauer, Frank & His Orchestra / That's a serious thing: Condon, Eddie / I've found a new baby: Freeman, Bud Summa Cum Laude / Nothin' but the blues: Gifford, Gene & His Orchestra / Blue Lou: All Star Band / Blues: All Star Band / Limehouse blues: Manone, Wingy Orchestra / Easy to get: Freeman, Bud Summa Cum Laude / It's only a paper moon: Stacy, Jess / China boy: Freeman, Bud Summa Cum Laude / I'm gonna stomp Mr. Henry Lee: Condon, Eddie / New Orleans twist: Gifford, Gene & His Orchestra
CD _____ 74321130352
RCA / Sep '93 / BMG.

STRUMMIN' MENTAL PART 2
CD _____ EFA 115792
Crypt / Jun '95 / SRD.

STRUT YOUR FUNKY STUFF
CD _____ DCD 5394
Scratch / Oct '94 / BMG.

SUB POP 200
CD _____ TUPCD 4
Tupelo / Jul '89 / Disc.

SUBCONSCIOUS VOL.1
CD _____ EEG 1CD
Subconscious / Oct '95 / 3MV.

SUBLIME HARMONIE
(Victorian Musical Boxes & Polyphons)
March of the Toreadors / Hallelujah Chorus / Ave Maria / War march of the priests / Lost chord / Waltz from Faust (Gounod) / Largo (Handel) / Wedding song (Wagner) / Wedding march (Mendelssohn) / I have a song to sing (Sullivan) / Behold the Lord High Executioner (Sullivan) / Valse des fees
CD _____ CDSDL 303
Saydisc / Feb '93 / Harmonia Mundi / ADA / Direct.

SUBSONIC BLEEPS
CD _____ BLEEPSCD 1
Upfront / Nov '90 / Serious Records.

SUBURBS FROM HELL
CD _____ SOHO 13CD
Suburbs Of Hell / Jan '94 / Pinnacle / Plastic Head / Kudos.

SUDDEN IMPACT VOL. 1
CD _____ VPCD 1241
Shocking Vibes / Jul '92 / Jetstar.

SUE BOX, THE
Vengeance: Matadors / Itchy twichy feeling: Hendricks, Bobby / Thousand dreams: Hendricks, Bobby / Psycho: Hendricks, Bobby / Written in the stars: Four Jokers / Believe it or not: Covay, Don / Betty Jean: Covay, Don / I feel like a million: Bradley, Mamie / Chicken scratch: Commandos / Hand in hand: Darrow, Johnny / Don't start me talkin': Darrow, Johnny / Don't leave: Adams, Bobby / Fool in love: Turner, Ike & Tina / I idolize you: Turner, Ike & Tina / I'm jealous: Turner, Ike & Tina / Can't work even out fine: Turner, Ike & Tina / Poor fool: Turner, Ike & Tina / Tra la la la la: Turner, Ike & Tina / You shoulda treated me right: Turner, Ike & Tina / Worried and hurtin' inside: Turner, Ike & Tina / Two is a couple: Turner, Ike & Tina / Stagger Lee and Billy: Turner, Ike & Tina / That's all I need: Turner, Ike & The Kings Of Rhythm / Trouble up the road: Brenston, Jackie / You ain't the one: Brenston, Jackie / I wanna marry you: Jimmy & Jean / I can't believe it: Jimmy & Jean / My man Rockhead: Carter, Eloise / My love: Turner, Ike & The Kings Of Rhythm / My love: Turner, Ike & Tina / Night riders / Night riders to yourself: Woods, Pearl / Stick shift: Duals / She put the hurt on me: Prince La La / Gettin' married soon: Prince La La / Come back to me: Prince La La / I know you don't love me no more): George, Barbara / You talk about love: George, Barbara / Send for me: George, Barbara / She's got everything: George, Barbara / May I have this dance: Senors / Graveyard: Blenders / I've got a woman: McGriff, Jimmy / All about my girl: McGriff, Jimmy / Last minute (Part 1): McGriff, Jimmy / Handful of memories: Washington, Baby / That's how heartaches are made: Washington, Baby / Leave me alone: Washington, Baby / I can't wait until I see my baby: Washington, Baby / Only those in love: Washington, Baby / Come on let me try: Linda & The Del Rios / Prancing: Ike & Tina's Kings Of Rhythm / It seemed like heaven to me: Morris, Elmore / Let's shimmy: Coleman, King / Hitch hike (pt 1): Byrd, Russell / Any other way: Shane, Jackie / In my tenement: Shane, Jackie / Hold on baby: Hockadays / Summer's love: Barrett, Richie / Mockingbird: Foxx, Inez / Ask me: Foxx, Inez / I see you my love: Foxx, Inez / Hurt by love: Foxx, Inez / La de da I love you: Foxx, Inez / Daddy rollin' stone: Martin, Derek / Don't put me down like this: Martin, Derek / Count to ten: Martin, Derek / If you go: Martin, Derek / I can't stand it: Soul Sisters / Good time tonight: Soul Sisters / Loop de loop: Soul Sisters / Think about the good times: Soul Sisters / So far away: Jacobs, Hank / Monkey hips and rice: Jacobs, Hank / Everybody but me: Smith, O.C. / You're mine you: Helms, Jimmy / I can't tell you: Robbins, Sylvia / Dreams: Watkins, Lovelace / Limbo Lucy: Everglades / Yesterday: Glenn, Tyree Jr. / Ain't that bad: Villa, Pancho & The Bandits / You succeeded: Phillips, Sandra / World without sunshine: Phillips, Sandra / Time waits for no one: Eddie & Ernie / Outcast: Eddie & Ernie / I'm going for myself: Eddie & Ernie / I can't do it: Eddie & Ernie / Fast back: Doggett, Bill / Real thing: Britt, True / Annie don't love me no more: Hollywood Flames / I'm gonna stand by you: Hollywood Flames / One more hurt: Black Marjorie / Love in my heart: Entertainers / What can I do: Prophet, Billy / New breed: Turner, Ike / She blew a good thing: Poets / So young: Poets / I was born a loser: Lee, Bobby / If you've ever loved someone: Wells, Jean / She's called a woman: Magnificent Seven / Soul at sunrise: Juggy
CD Set _____ SUEBOX 1
EMI / Jun '94 / EMI.

SUFFERERS CHOICE
CD _____ CDAT 101
Attack / May '94 / Jetstar / Total/BMG.

SUGARHILL - THE 12" REMIXES
Message: Grandmaster Flash & The Furious Five / Freedom: Grandmaster Flash & The Furious Five / Apache: Sugarhill Gang / Rapper's delight: Sugarhill Gang / Eighth wonder: Sugarhill Gang / White lines (don't don't do it): Grandmaster Flash & Melle Mel
CD _____ CLACD 345
Castle / Jun '94 / BMG.

SUITCASE FULL OF BLUES, A
CD _____ HCD 23
Black Swan / Dec '95 / Jazz Music.

SUMMER DANCE ENERGY
CD _____ JHD 106
Tring / Aug '93 / Tring / Prism.

SUMMER DANCE PARTY
CD _____ RADCD 18
Global / Jul '95 / BMG.

SUMMER FUN
CD _____ MUSCD 027
Music Club / Jul '95 / Disc / THE / CM.

SUMMER IN THE CITY
CD _____ MATCD 251
Castle / Apr '93 / BMG.

SUMMER OF LOVE
CD _____ MUSCD 022
MCI / Sep '94 / Disc / THE.

SUMMER OF LOVE
California dreamin': Mamas & Papas / Happy together: Turtles / Albatross: Fleetwood Mac / Let's go to San Francisco: Flowerpot Men / Eve of destruction: McGuire, Barry / Summer in the city: Lovin' Spoonful / She'd rather be with me: Turtles / Oh happy day: Hawkins, Edwin Singers / Sunshine of your love: Cream / Delta lady: Cocker, Joe / Mr. Tambourine man: Byrds / Daydream: Lovin' Spoonful / San Franciso (be sure to wear some flowers): McKenzie, Scott / Green tambourine: Lemon Pipers / Ruby Tuesday: Melanie / Monday, Monday: Mamas & Papas / Venus: Shocking Blue / Eight miles high: Byrds / Something in the air: Thunderclap Newman / Woodstock: Matthew's Southern Comfort
CD _____ DINCD 10
Dino / Jul '90 / Pinnacle / 3MV.

SUMMER OF LOVE, THE - 20 CLASSIC HITS OF 1967
Dedicated to the one I love: Mamas & Papas / Creeque Alley: Mamas & Papas / Heroes and villains: Beach Boys / San Franciso nights: Burdon, Eric / Itchycoo Park: Small Faces / Waterloo sunset: Kinks / Gin house blues: Amen Corner / Night of the long grass: Troggs / From the underworld: Herd / Kites: Dupree, Simon & The Big Sound / Hi ho silver lining: Beck, Jeff / I'm gonna get me a gun: Stevens, Cat / Autumn almanac: Kinks / Walking in the rain: Walker Brothers / Baby, now that I've found you: Foundations / Puppet on a string: Shaw, Sandie / Carrie Anne: Hollies / Ha ha said the clown: Manfred Mann / Mellow yellow: Donovan / Let's go to San Francisco: Flowerpot Men
CD _____ CDPR 109
Premier/MFP / May '93 / EMI.

SUMMER SIZZLERS
Walking on sunshine: Katrina & The Waves / Fantastic day: Haircut 100 / Beach baby: First Class / Hot hot hot: Arrow / In the summertime: Mungo Jerry / Happy together: Turtles / Sunny afternoon: Kinks / Lazy Sunday: Small Faces / Summer in the city: Lovin' Spoonful / I Remember (walking in the sand): Shangri-Las / Seasons in the sun: Jacks, Terry / Hang on sloopy: McCoys
CD _____ 74321339292
Camden / Jan '96 / BMG.

SUMMER SWING
Humpin' around: Brown, Bobby / Freak like me: Howard, Adina / Party all night: Kreuz / Candy rain: Soul For Real / Oh baby, I: Eternal': R. Kelly / Down with the clique: Aaliyah / I wanna be down: Brandy / Your love is a 187: Whitehead Brothers / Here comes the hotstepper: Kamoze, Ini / Rump shaker: Wreckx N Effect / Hoochie booty: Ultimate Kaos / Real love: Blige, Mary J. / Everyday: Incognito / Apparently nothin': Anderson, Carleen / Too many fish: Knuckles, Frankie & Adeva / Lifted: Lighthouse Family / Joy: Blackstreet / There's nothing like this: Omar
CD _____ VTCD 33
Virgin / Jul '95 / EMI.

SUMMER WIND
CD _____ BLR 84 017
L&R / May '91 / New Note.

SUMMERTIME HITS FROM THE WORLD
CD _____ DCD 5305
Disky / Nov '93 / THE / BMG / Discovery / Pinnacle.

SUMMERTIME SOUL
CD _____ 5258002
PolyGram TV / Aug '95 / PolyGram.

SUN OF JAMAICA
CD Set _____ 4417202
Pilz / Oct '92 / BMG.

SUN RECORDS STORY, THE (4CD Set)
Cool down Mama: Hunter, Long John / Boogie in the park: Louis, Joe Hill / Howlin' tom cat: Floyd, Frankie / Rocket 88: Branston, Jackie / Registration daily blues: Estes, Sleepy John / Highway man: Howlin' Wolf / How long will it last: Turner, Ike / Juiced: Love, Billy / T model boogie: Gordon, Roscoe / Driving slow: Thomas, Rufus / Tiger man: Thomas, Rufus / Love my baby: Parker, Junior / Come back baby: Dr. Ross / I feel so worried: Lewis, Sammy & Willie Johnson / Easy: Jimmy & Walter / Time has made a change: Deberry, Jimmy / Seems like a million years: Nix, Willie / Cotton crop blues: Cotton, James / I'm gonna murder my baby: Hare, Pat / Red hot: Emerson, Billy / If you love me: Little Milton / Look to Jesus: Jones Brothers / I betcha gonna like it: Stuart, Jeb / Dark muddy bottom: Riley, Billy Lee / Hello, hello baby: Lewis, Jerry Lee / Listen to me baby: Baugh, Smokey Joe / Charlie's boogie: Rich, Charlie / Woodchuck: Emerson, Billy / Boogie blues: Peterson, Earl / Blues waltz: Ripley Cotton Choppers / Rockin' chair Daddy: Floyd, Frankie / Walkin' shoes: Wheeler, Onie / Troublesome waters: Sergt. Howard / Gonna dance all night: Gunter, Hardrock / Don't believe: Rhodes, Slim / Sure to fall: Perkins, Carl / Defrost your heart: Feathers, Charlie / Don't make me go: Cash, Johnny / Back street glidin': Bond, Eddie / You pass me by: Blake, Buddy / Fool proof: Vickery, Mack / Big river: Cash, Johnny / Turn around: Perkins, Carl / I'd rather be safe than sorry: Smith, Warren / Jump right out of this: Wheeler, Onie / You're the only star in my blue heaven: Lewis, Jerry Lee / Fool for lovin' you: Earl, Jack / New Mexico: Cash, Johnny / Finders keepers: Miller Sisters / It's me baby: Yelvington, Malcolm / Rockin' Daddy: Bond, Eddie / Mean little Mama: Orbison, Roy / Red headed woman: Burgess, Sonny / God love it you want it: Smith, Warren / Crawdad song: Lewis, Jerry Lee / Her love rubbed off: Perkins, Carl / Flyin' saucer rock'n'roll: Riley, Billy Lee & The Little Green Men / Mad man: Wages, Jimmy / Miss Froggie: Smith, Warren / Pearly Lee: Riley, Billy Lee / Deep elem blues: Lewis, Jerry Lee / That don't move me: Perkins, Carl / All night rock: Honeycutt, Glenn / Come on little Mama: Harris, Ray / Rock with me baby: Riley, Billy Lee / Fine little baby: Penner, Dick / Rockin' with my baby: Yelvington, Malcolm / Baby that's good: Bruce, Edwin / That's right: Perkins, Carl / My baby don't rock: McDaniel, Luke / Miss Pearl: Wages, Jimmy / So glad you're mine: Burgess, Sonny / Willing & ready: Smith, Ray / Shake around: Blake, Tommy / Crazy woman: Simmons, Gene / Judy: Grayzell, Rudy / Good rockin' tonight: Lewis, Jerry / Bear cat: Thomas, Rufus / Just walkin' in the rain: Prisonaires / Feelin' good: Parker, Junior / Blue suede shoes: Perkins, Carl / When it rains it pours: Emerson, Billy / Mystery train: Parker, Junior / Boppin' the blues: Perkins, Carl / Whole lotta shakin' goin' on: Lewis, Jerry Lee / I walk the line: Cash, Johnny / Ubangi stomp: Orbison, Roy / We wanna boogie: Burgess, Sonny / Dixie fried: Perkins, Carl / Great balls of fire: Lewis, Jerry Lee / Rock'n'roll Ruby: Smith, Warren / Red hot (2): Riley, Billy Lee / Breathless: Lewis, Jerry Lee / Honey don't: Perkins, Carl / Ballad of a teenage Queen: Cash, Johnny / High School confidential: Lewis, Jerry Lee / Matchbox: Perkins, Carl / Lonely weekends: Rich, Charlie / I'm coming home: Mann, Carl / Who will the next fool be: Rich, Charlie / What'd I say: Lewis, Jerry Lee / Guess things happen that way: Cash, Johnny / Raunchy: Justis, Bill / Mona Lisa: Mann, Carl / Whirlwind: Rich, Charlie
CD Set _____ CDSUNBOX 6
Sun / Oct '95 / Charly.

SUN SINGLES VOL.1
Flat tire: London, Johnny / Drivin' slow: London, Johnny / Got my application baby: Garth, Gay / Trouble (will bring you down): Jackson, Handy / We all gotta go sometime: Louis, Joe Hill / Some may be like yours: Louis, Joe Hill / Baker shop boogie: Nix, Willie / Seems like a million years: Nix, Willie / Easy: Jimmy & Walter / Before long: Jimmy & Walter / Bear cat: Thomas, Rufus / Walkin' in the rain: Thomas, Rufus / Heaven or fire: Brooks, Dusty / Tears and wine: Brooks, Dusty / Lonesome old jail: Hunt, D.A. / Greyhound blues: Hunt, D.A. / Call ma anything, but call me: Big Memphis Marainey / Baby no no: Big Memphis Marainey / Take a little chance: De Berry, Jimmy / Time has made a change: De Berry, Jimmy / Baby please: Prisonaires / Just walking in the rain: Prisonaires / Feelin' good: Prisonaires / The Blue Flames / Fussing and fighting: Parker, Junior & The Blue Flames / Tiger man: Thomas, Rufus / Save that money: Thomas, Rufus / My God is real: Prisonaires / Softly and tenderly: Prisonaires / Blues waltz: Ripley Cotton Choppers / Silver bells: Ripley Cotton Choppers / Prisoner's prayer: Prisonaires / I know: Prisonaires / Mystery train: Parker, Junior & The Blue Flames / Love my baby: Parker, Junior & The Blue Flames / Come back baby: Ross, Dr. Isiah / Chicago breakdown: Ross, Dr. Isiah / Beggin' my baby: Little Milton / No teasing around: Emerson, Billy 'The Kid' / If love is believing: Emerson, Billy 'The Kid' / Wolf call boogie: Hot Shot Love / Harmonica jam: Hot Shot Love / Boogie blues: Peterson, Earl / In the dark: Emerson, Billy 'The Kid' / Troublesome waters: Seratt, Howard / I must be saved: Seratt, Howard / My baby: Cotton, James / Straighten up baby: Cotton, James / If you love me: Little Milton / Alone and blue: Little Milton / Gonna dance all night: Gunter, Hardrock / Fallen angel: Gunter, Hardrock / Now she cares no more for me: Poindexter, Doug / My kind of woman: Poindexter, Doug / I'm not going home: Emerson, Billy 'The Kid' / Woodchuck: Emerson, Billy 'The Kid' / Bourbon street jump: Hill, Raymond / Snuggle: Hill, Raymond / Great medical menagerist: Harmonica Frank / Rockin' chair Daddy: Harmonica Frank / Cotton crop blues: Cotton, James / Hold me in your arms: Cotton, James / There is love in you: Prisonaires / What'll you do next: Prisonaires / Right or wrong: Cunningham, Buddy / Who do I cry: Prisonaires / That's all right: Presley, Elvis / Blue moon of Kentucky: Presley, Elvis / Good rockin' tonight: Presley, Elvis / I don't care if the sun don't shine: Presley, Elvis / Drinkin' wine spo-dee-o-dee: Yelvington, Malcolm / Just rolling along: Yelvington, Malcolm / Boogie disease: Ross, Dr. Isiah / Jukebox boogie: Ross, Dr. Isiah / Look to Jesus: Jones Brothers / Every night: Jones Brothers / Move baby move: Emerson, Billy 'The Kid' / When it rains it pours: Emerson, Billy 'The Kid' / Milkcow blues boogie: Presley, Elvis / You're a heartbreaker: Presley, Elvis / Don't believe: Rhodes, Slim / Uncertain love: Rhodes, Slim / I'm left, you're right, she's gone: Presley, Elvis / Baby let's play house: Presley, Elvis / I feel so worried: Lewis, Sammy & Willie Johnson / So long baby, goodbye: Lewis, Sammy & Willie Johnson / Red hot: Emerson, Billy 'The Kid' / No greater love: Emerson, Billy 'The Kid' / Homesick for my baby: Little Milton / Lookin' for my baby: Little Milton / Cry cry: Cash, Johnny / Hey porter: Cash, Johnny / Don't do that: Five Tinos / Sitting by my window: Five Tinos / I forgot to remember to forget: Presley, Elvis / Let the jukebox keep on playing: Perkins, Carl / Gone gone gone: Perkins, Carl / House of sin: Rhodes, Slim / Are you ashamed of me: Rhodes, Slim / Ain't that right: Snow, Eddie / Bring your love back home to me: Snow, Eddie / Just love me baby: Gordon, Roscoe / Weeping blues: Gordon, Roscoe / Signifying monkey: Smokey Joe / Listen to my baby: Smokey Joe / Movie magg: Perkins, Carl / Turn around: Perkins, Carl / Lonely sweetheart: Taylor, Bill / Split personality: Taylor, Bill / I've been deceived: Feathers, Charlie / Peepin' eyes: Feathers, Charlie / Someday you will pay: Miller Sisters / You didn't think I would: Miller Sisters
CD _____ BCDDI 15801
Bear Family / Nov '94 / Rollercoaster / Direct / CM / Swift / ADA.

SUN SINGLES VOL.2
Daydreams come true: Wimberly, Maggie Sue / How long: Wimberly, Maggie Sue / There's no right way to do me wrong: Miller Sisters / You can tell me: Miller Sisters / Defrost your heart: Feathers, Charlie / Wedding gown of white: Feathers, Charlie / Folsom prison blues: Cash, Johnny / So doggone lonesome: Cash, Johnny / Little fine healthy thing: Emerson, Billy 'The Kid' / Something for nothing: Emerson, Billy 'The Kid' / Blue suede shoes: Perkins, Carl / Honey don't: Perkins, Carl / Sure to fall: Perkins, Carl / Tennessee: Perkins, Carl / No more, no more: Haggett, Jimmy / They call our love a sin: Haggett, Jimmy / Chicken: Gordon, Roscoe / Love for you baby: Gordon, Roscoe / Gonna romp and stomp: Rhodes, Slim / Shake that girl: Rhodes, Slim / Rock 'n' roll Ruby: Smith, Warren / I'd rather be safe than sorry: Smith, Warren / Slow down: Earls, Jack / Fool for loving you: Earls, Jack / Get rhythm: Cash, Johnny / I walk the line: Cash, Johnny / Ooby dooby: Orbison, Roy / Go go go: Orbison, Roy / Boppin' the blues: Perkins, Carl / All Mama's children: Perkins, Carl / Welcome to the club: Chapel, Jean / I won't be rockin' tonight: Chapel, Jean / Trouble bound: Riley, Billy Lee / Rock with me baby: Riley, Billy Lee / Rockin' with my baby: Yelvington, Malcolm / It's me baby: Yelvington, Malcolm / Red headed woman: Burgess, Sonny / We wanna boogie: Burgess, Sonny / Fishdle bop: Rhythm Rockers / Jukebox help me find my baby: Rhythm Rockers / I'm sorry: Perkins, Carl / I'm not going home: Carl / Dixie fried: Perkins, Carl / Black Jack David: Smith, Warren / Unbangi stomp: Smith, Warren / You're my baby: Orbison, Roy / Rock house: Orbison, Roy / Love crazy baby: Parchman, Kenny / I feel like rockin': Parchman, Kenny / I need a man: Pitman, Barbara / No matter who's to blame: Pitman, Barbara / Come on little Mama: Harris, Ray / Where'd you stay last night: Harris, Ray / Ten cats down: Miller Sisters / Finders keepers: Miller Sisters / Take and give: Rhodes, Slim / Do what I do: Rhodes, Slim / Snoobee doobee: Gordon, Roscoe / Cheese and crackers: Gordon, Roscoe / There you go: Cash, Johnny / Train of love: Cash, Johnny / Crazy arms: Lewis, Jerry Lee / End of the road: Lewis, Jerry Lee / Flyin' saucer rock 'n' roll: Riley, Billy Lee / I want you baby: Riley, Billy Lee / Matchbox: Perkins, Carl / Your true love: Perkins, Carl / Feelin' low: Chaffin, Ernie / Lonesome for my baby: Chaffin, Ernie / Restless: Burgess, Sonny / Ain't got a thing: Burgess, Sonny / I'll be around: Honeycutt, Glenn / I'll wait forever: Honeycutt, Glenn / Sweet and easy: Orbison, Roy / Devil doll: Orbison, Roy / Don't make me go: Cash, Johnny / Nest in line: Cash, Johnny / It'll be me: Lewis, Jerry Lee / Whole lotta shakin' goin' on: Lewis, Jerry Lee / So long I've been gone: Smith, Warren / Miss Froggie: Smith, Warren / Bop bop baby: Wake & Dick / Don't need your lovin' baby: Wake & Dick / Please don't cry over me: Williams, Jimmy / That depends on you: Williams, Jimmy / Fools hall of fame: Richardson, Rudi / Why should I cry: Richardson, Rudi / Greenback dollar: Harris, Ray / Foolish heart: Harris, Ray / Easy to love: Self, Mack / Every day: Self, Mack / Forever yours: Perkins, Carl / That's right: Perkins, Carl / I'm lonesome: Chaffin, Ernie / Laughin' and jokin': Chaffin, Ernie / More than yesterday: Bruce, Edwin / Rock boppin' baby: Bruce, Edwin / Red hot: Riley, Billy Lee / Pearly Lee: Riley, Billy Lee / Flat foot Sam: Blake, Tommy / Lordy hoody: Blake, Tommy
CD Set _____ BCDDI 15802
Bear Family / Jun '95 / Rollercoaster / Direct / CM / Swift / ADA.

SUN STUDIO STORY, THE (2CD/MC Set)
Matchbox: Perkins, Carl / Breathless: Lewis, Jerry Lee / Mystery train: Parker, Junior / Guess things happen that way: Cash, Johnny / Just walkin' in the rain: Prisonaires / Tootsie: McVoy, Carl / Red hot: Emerson, Billy / Baby, please don't go: Riley, Billy Lee / I won't be rockin' tonight: Chapel, Jean / Ooby dooby: Orbison, Roy / Ubangi stomp: Smith, Warren / You made a hit: Smith, Ray / Rebound: Rich, Charlie / Cheese and crackers: Gordon, Roscoe / Ain't got a thing: Burgess, Sonny / Lovestruck: McGill, Jerry / Raunchy: Justis, Bill / Uncle Jonah's place: Dorman, Harold / Cadillac man: Jerry / Mona Lisa: Mann, Carl / Rocket 88: Thomas, Rufus / Walkin' in the rain: Thomas, Rufus / Baby I love you: Randy & The Radiants / Everything's gonna be alright: Randy & The Radiants / Really some good: Thomas, Rufus & Carla / Early in the morning: Laury, Booker T. / Booker's boogie: Laury, Booker T. / Prayin' at the crossroads: McMinn, Don / 12 Bar blues: McMinn, Don / Lonely weekends: Swan, Billy / Rockabilly B: Swan, Billy / Man would be crazy: Duren, Van / Buy your love on time: Duren, Van / Disappointed: Yelvington, Malcolm / Yaknety yak: Yelvington, Malcolm / Dream girl: Bilys / Boppin' the blues: Billys / Rockhouse: Hardy, Guy & The Sun Studio Trio / C.C. Rider: Moorman, Sonny & The Dogs / Wet my lips: Roe, Joe & The Hellhounds
CD Set _____ 3036400012
Elite/Old Gold / Oct '95 / Carlton Home Entertainment.

SUNDAY MATINEE (The Best Of NY Hardcore)
Sailin' on: Bad Brains / We gotta know: Cro-Mags / Anthem: Agnostic Front / Anytown: Reagan Youth / Quest for herb: Murphy's Law / Injustice system: Sick Of It All / As one: Warzone / Expectations: Youth Of Today / Clear: Bold / Step forward: Mob / Enforcer: Leeway / Over the edge: Underdog / Away: American Standard Band / Here to stay: Sheer Terror / Where it went: Judge / Brightside: Raw Deal / Public opinion: Urban Waste
CD _____ ANPCD 6001
Another Planet / Sep '94 / Vital.

SUNDAY MORNING SESSIONS
CD _____ MRCD 176
Munich / Sep '95 / CM / ADA / Greensleeves / Direct.

SUNDAZED SAMPLER, THE
Water baby boogie: Maphis, Joe / Nancy: Barker Bros. / Ain't that too much: Vincent, Gene / Rockabilly yodel: Larue, Roc & The Three Pals / Loophole: Royal Coachmen / Four in the floor: Shutdowns / Bustin' floor boards: Tornadoes / Twist and shout: Isley Brothers / Mama here comes the bride: Shirelles / Western Union: Five Americans / One track mind: Knickerbockers / Cadillac: Colony Six / Dirty water: Standells / Little latin lupe lu: Ryder, Mitch & The Detroit Wheels / Louie Louie: Kingsmen / Surfin' bird: Trashmen / Dimples: Animals / I got my mojo working: Shadows Of Knight / I've been wrong before: H.P. Lovecraft / Rollercoaster: 13th Floor Elevators / I not no miracle worker: Brogues / Spend your life: First Crow To The Moon / Last time around: Delvetts / Anyway I can: Choir / Sweetgina: Things To Come
CD _____ CDSC 01
Sundazed / Apr '94 / Rollercoaster.

SUNNY AFTERNOON (Hits Of Summer)
In the summertime: Mungo Jerry / Beach baby: First Class / Hello Susie: Amen Corner / Do you wanna dance: Blue, Barry / Let's go to San Francisco: Flowerpot Men / El bimbo: Bimbo Jet / Baby, now that I've found you: Foundations / Sunny afternoon: Kinks / Green tambourine: Lemon Pipers / Simon says: 1910 Fruitgum Company / Sunshine day: Osibisa / Egyptian reggae: Richman, Jonathan & Modern Lovers / Sky high: Jigsaw / Brand new key: Melanie / Summer in the city: Lovin' Spoonful / Itchycoo Park: Small Faces / I wanna hold your hand: Dollar / That same old feeling: Pickettywitch / Swing your daddy: Gilstrap, Jim / Elenore: Turtles
CD _____ TRTCD 145
TrueTrax / Oct '94 / THE.

SUNNY AFTERNOONS
Sunny afternoon: Kinks / Daydream: Lovin' Spoonful / 59th Street Bridge song: Simon & Garfunkel / Happy together: Turtles / Wouldn't it be nice: Beach Boys / Lazy Sunday: Small Faces / Daydream believer: Monkees / Sunshine superman: Donovan /

Sitting in the park: *Fame, Georgie* / Sunny: *Hebb, Bobby* / Dedicated to the one I love: *Mamas & Papas* / Mr. Tambourine Man: *Byrds* / San Francisco: *McKenzie, Scott* / Woodstock: *Matthew's Southern Comfort* / Paper sun: *Traffic* / Badge: *Cream* / Green tambourine: *Lemon Pipers* / Let's go to San Francisco: *Flowerpot Men* / For what it's worth: *Buffalo Springfield* / I can't let Maggie go: *Honeybus* / In Keith: *Kites: Dupree, Simon & The Big Sound* / Good vibrations: *Beach Boys* / Itchycoo Park: *Small Faces* / Mellow yellow: *Donovan* / Waterloo sunset: *Kinks* / She'd rather be with me: *Turtles* / Friday on my mind: *Cure* / Jesamine: *Casuals* / Love grows (Where my Rosemary grows): *Edison Lighthouse* / My name is Jack: *Manfred Mann* / Early in the morning: *Vanity Fare* / Jennifer Eccles: *Hollies* / Flowers in the rain: *Move* / I'm a believer: *Monkees* / Summer in the city: *Lovin' Spoonful* / We gotta get out of this place: *Animals* / With a girl like you: *Troggs* / Monday Monday: *Mamas & Papas* / Morning has broken: *Stevens, Cat* / Good day sunshine: *Tremeloes* / Judy in disguise: *Fred, John & His Playboy Band* / Sorrow: *Merseys* / Elusive butterfly: *Lind, Bob* / Windy: *Association* / Groovy kind of love: *Mindbenders* / Goo goo Barabajagal (Love is hot): *Donovan & Jeff Beck Group* / Hole in my shoe: *Traffic*
CD _____ 5256002
PolyGram TV / Jul '95 / PolyGram.

SUNNY SUNDAY SMILE
CD _____ SUNDAY 640CD
Sunday / May '94 / SRD.

SUNSET SWING
CD _____ BLC 760171
Black Lion / Oct '92 / Jazz Music / Cadillac / Wellard / Koch.

SUNSHINE DAY
(20 Smash Hits Of The Seventies)
It's a heartache: *Tyler, Bonnie* / Sunshine day: *Osibisa* / Egyptian reggae: *Richman, Jonathan & Modern Lovers* / Best thing that ever happened to me: *Knight, Gladys & The Pips* / Shooting star: *Dollar* / Making up again: *Goldie* / You to me are everything: *Real Thing* / Girls: Moments / I'll have to say I love you in a song: *Croce, Jim* / Isn't she lovely: *Parton, David* / Lady rose: *Mungo Jerry* / So sad the song: *Knight, Gladys & The Pips* / Purely by coincidence: *Sweet Sensation* / Matchstalk men and matchstalk cats and dogs: *Brian & Michael* / In Zaire: *Wakelin, Johnny* / Summer of my life: *May, Simon* / Now is the time: *James, Jimmy & The Vagabonds* / Show me you're a woman: *Mud* / Car 67: *Driver 67* / Can't get by without you: *Real Thing*
CD _____ TRTCD 109
TrueTrax / Oct '94 / THE.

SUNSHINE GIRLS
(TK Deep Soul 2)
Make me feel like a woman: *Moore, Jackie* / Jazz freak: *Reades, Philette* / Puttin' it down to you: *Moore, Jackie* / One woman's trash: *Brandye* / Your real good thing's about to come to an end: *Reades, Philette* / It's harder to leave: *Moore, Jackie* / Loving you, loving me: *Serton, Ann* / Secret lover: *Reades, Philette* / Tired of hiding: *Moore, Jackie* / I'll be right here (when you return): *Wilson, Ruby & The Blue Chips* / Bridge that lies between us: *Moore, Jackie* / God bless this man of mine: *Reades, Philette* / Hurtin' inside out: *Moore, Jackie* / Man and a baby boy: *Wilson, Ruby* / Somebody loves you: *Moore, Jackie*
██ ▪ _____ ПЕМОЯ Т 11
Sequel / Jun '95 / BMG.

SUNSHINE REGGAE
CD _____ SBCD 009
Soul Beat / Jun '95 / Jetstar.

SUNSPLASH SHOWCASE
CD _____ TWCD 1055
Tamoki Wambesi / Nov '95 / Jetstar / SRD / Roots Collective / Greensleeves.

SUPER ALL STAR
Francisco guayabal / El platanal de bartolo / Tres linda cubanas / Ban-con-tim / Alto songo / Malanga / El sopon / La cascara
CD _____ CDORB 017
Globestyle / Jul '90 / Pinnacle.

SUPER GROUPS
CD _____ STACD 046
Wisepack / Sep '93 / THE / Conifer.

SUPER HIT TROPICAL
CD _____ VGCD 670017
Vogue / Jan '93 / THE.

SUPER MERENGAZO
Que no me adivino / Amandote / Caliente / Que la pasa a mi mujer / Cuando me enamoro / Toitico tuyo / Rondando / Ala talala / Suegra / Merengue internacional / Mambo mix
CD _____ 66058070
RMM / Sep '95 / New Note.

SUPER ROCK SESSION VOL.1
Bat out of hell: *Meat Loaf* / Are you ready: *Pacific Gas & Electric* / Time of the season: *Argent* / With Queen of New Orleans: *Redbone* / Gamma ray: *Birth Control* / Mental health: *Quiet Riot* / You took the words right out of my mouth (hot summer night): *Meat Loaf* / Betty Black: *Ram Jam* / On the run:

Lake / (Don't fear) the reaper: *Blue Oyster Cult* / I want you to want me: *Cheap Trick* / Roll away the stone: *Mott The Hoople* / Any way you want it: *Journey* / Take it on the run: *REO Speedwagon* / Carry me, Carrie: *Dr. Hook & The Medicine Show* / Hi-de-ho (that old sweet roll): *Blood, Sweat & Tears*
CD _____ 4804452
Columbia / Dec '95 / Sony.

SUPER SALSA HITS
Abueleta: *Colon, Willie* / Indestructible: *Barretto, Ray* / Abandonada fue: *Orchestra Harlow* / Nina Y semora: *Puente, Tito* / Mi disengana: *Roena, Roberto* / Cafe: *Palmieri, Eddie* / Acuzar mami: *Pacheco, Johnny* / Senora: *Ray, Ricardo* / Soy Boricua: *Valentin, Bobby* / Acere Ko: *Sonora Poncena*
CD _____ CDHOT 500
Charly / Oct '93 / Charly / THE / Cadillac.

SUPER SKA
CD _____ PHZCD 011
Unicorn / Dec '93 / Plastic Head.

SUPER SUPER BLUES BAND, THE
(Charly Blues Masterworks Vol.26)
Long distance call / Goin' down slow / You don't love me / I'm a man / Who do you love / Red rooster / Diddley daddy / I just want to make love to you
CD _____ CDBM 26
Charly / Apr '92 / Charly / THE / Cadillac.

SUPERBAD BLUES
(18 Chicago Blues Classics)
CD _____ CDCD 1098
Charly / Jun '93 / Charly / THE / Cadillac.

SUPERFUNK
CD _____ VTCD 20
Virgin / Jun '94 / EMI.

SUPERMARKET
CD _____ EFA 122682
Disko B / Apr '95 / SRD.

SUPERSTAR LINE UP 2
CD _____ CDNNM 005
New Name / Jun '92 / Jetstar.

SUPERSTARS AT THE DANCE HALL
CD _____ RNCD 2093
Rhino / Mar '95 / Jetstar / Magnum Music Group / THE.

SURF PARTY
CD _____ 295720
Ariola / Jul '93 / BMG.

SURF SET, THE
Surfbeat: *Dale, Dick & His Del-Tones* / Surfin' USA: *Beach Boys* / Wipeout: *Surfaris* / Surf city: *Jan & Dean* / Pipeline: *Chantays* / Summer means fun: *Fantastic Baggys* / Penetration: *Pyramids* / This little woodie surfin' craze: *Rip Chords* / Baja: *Astronauts* / Beach boy: *Ronny & The Daytonas* / Surfin' safari: *Beach Boys* / Surfer's stomp: *Marketts* / Three surfer bops: *Usher, Gary* / Shoot the curl: *Honeys* / Let's go trippin': *Hot Doggers* / Surfer Joe: *Surfaris* / Tell 'em I'm surfin': *Fantastic Baggys* / Move it: *Chantays* / Draggin' wagon: *Surfer Girls* / Surf route 101: *Super Stocks* / Black denim: *Surfaris* / Bucket T: *Jan & Dean* / 409: *Rip Chords* / My stingray: *Four Speeds* / Don't worry baby: *Beach Boys* / Burnin' rubber: *Moles, Gene & The Softwinds* / Readin', ridin' and racin': *Super Stocks* / Hot rod high: *Knights* / New girl in school: *Jan & Dean* / Chug-a-lug: *Sunsets* / Be true to your school: *Beach Boys* / Drive-in: *Beach Boys* / Gidget: *Darren, James* / Theme from the endless summer: *Sandals* / Muscle beach party: *Super Stocks* / Surfin': *Jan & Dean* / Surfer girl: *Beach Boys* / Surfin' round the world: *Johnson, Bruce* / I wanna take a trip to the islands: *Surfaris* / Big breaker: *Ambassadors* / (Dance with the) surfin' band: *Blaine, Hal* / Don't back down: *Beach Boys* / Misericuz: *Dale, Dick & His Del-Tones* / Drag city: *Jan & Dean* / Little deuce coupe: *Beach Boys* / G.T.O.: *Ronny & The Daytonas* / Hey little cobra: *Rip Chords* / R.P.M.'s: *Four Speeds* / Little street machine: *Hot Rod Rog* / Competition coupe: *Astronauts* / Dead man's curve: *Jan & Dean* / Move out little Mustang: *Rally packs* / Hot rod USA: *Rip Chords* / Cycle set: *Loren, Donna* / Boss barracuda: *Surfaris* / Surf party: *Astronauts* / Girls on the beach: *Beach Boys* / Ride the wild surf: *Jan & Dean* / Gone: *Rip Chords* / Little scrambler: *Ronny & The Daytonas* / She rides with me: *Petersen, Pete* / Honda bike: *Devonnes* / My buddy seat: *Surfaris* / Little Honda: *Beach Boys* / She's my summer girl: *Jan & Dean* / Beach girl: *Boone, Pat* / Your baby's gone surfin': *Eddy, Duane* / Surfin' John Brown: *Ambassadors* / Sidewalk surfin': *Jan & Dean* / I'll think of summer: *Ronny & The Daytonas* / New York's a lonely town: *Tradewinds* / Do it again: *Beach Boys*
CD _____ NXTCD 249
Sequel / Jul '93 / BMG.

SURREALITY
Drive: *Boddy, Ian* / Journeyman: *Tranceport* / Winter's passage: *River Of Dreams* / Into Battle: *Shipway, Michael* / Xiological sky: *Lloyd-Jones, Glyn* / Alchemist: *Ward, Paul* / In search of new horizons: *Wasatch* / No more questions: *Cooper, Simon* / I'm here to set fire to the world: *Whitlan, Stephan* / Assassin: *Shreeve, Mark* / Child's eye: *Hi-Q* / Timenode: *Dyson, J & Friends*
CD _____ REAL 101

Surreal / Aug '91 / Surreal To Real / C & D Compact Disc Services.

SURRENDER TO THE VIBE
CD _____ PTM 132
Phantasm / Sep '95 / Vital/SAM / Plastic Head.

SURVIVAL 2000
CD _____ TRIBECD 1
Survival / Oct '94 / Total/BMG.

SURVIVAL INTERNATIONAL BENEFIT ALBUM
CD _____ TRIBECD 2
Survival / Feb '96 / Total/BMG.

SURVIVAL-THE DANCE COMPILATION
One nation: *Supereal* / Little bullet part 1: Spooky / Boss drum: *Shamen* / Choice: Orbital / Djapana: *Yothu Yindi* / King of the funky zulus: *Moody Blues* / Release the dub: *Leftfield* / Aquarium: *Grid* / Flowing nile: *Zion Train* / Freeality (CD only): *Freeality* / Predator (CD only): *Spiral Tribe*
CD _____ GRCD 008
Guerilla / May '93 / Pinnacle.

SWALLOW RECORDS LOUISIANA CAJUN SPECIAL VOL.2
Choupique two step: *Abshire, Nathan* / Cypress in special: *Cormier, Lionel* / Chinaball blues: *Pitre, Austin* / Cameron two step: *Barro* / Calcasieu rambler's special: *Broussard, August* / Hold at trouble: *Cormier, Lionel* / Little cajun boy: *Leger, Bobby* / Zydeco cha cha: *Mouzas & Lignos* / Mamou hot step: *Mamou Playboys* / Every night when it's dark: *Hebert, Adam* / La valse de grand bois: *Balfa Brothers* / Cankton two step: *Prejean, Leeman* / She didn't know I was married: *Menard, D L* / Family waltz: *Menard, Phil & Don Guillory* / Two steps de vieux temps: *Rambling Aces* / One step de duson: *Cormier, Louis*
CD _____ CDCH 368
Ace / Mar '92 / Pinnacle / Cadillac / Complete/Pinnacle.

SWAN'S SOUL SIDES
Run run: *Persianettes* / You're everything: *Showmen* / Misery: *Carlton, Eddie* / Never too young to fall in love): *Modern Redcaps* / In love: *Galla, Tony* / Trying to find my baby: *Dodds, Troy* / I'm just your clown: *Teddy & The Twilights* / Two steps ahead: *Johnson, Herb* / No sign of you: *Modern Redcaps* / Put yourself in my place: *Mortimor, Azie* / In return: *Ferguson, Sheila* / Have faith in me: *Sugar & Spice* / Handsome boy: *Ladybirds* / Gotta find a way: *Wilson, Naomi* / Hey sah-lo-ney: *Lane, Mickey Lee* / No good: *Anthony, Richard* / Our love will grow: *Showmen* / Hot hot: *Buena Vistas* / You got to tell me: *Rivieras* / Who do you love: *Sapphires* / Gotta draw the line: *Three Degrees* / Heartbroken memories: *Ferguson, Sheila* / I do love you: *Styles* / Put that woman down: *Leach, John* / It will be done: *Carlton, Eddie* / Everybody crossfire: *Stevens, Sammy*
CD _____ CDKEND 120
Kent / Jan '96 / Pinnacle.

SWEDEN'S ALTERNATIVE
CD _____ RA 91332
Roadrunner / Aug '92 / Pinnacle.

SWEDISH JAZZ FROM THE 70'S
CD _____ 2002
Caprice / Nov '89 / CM / Complete/ Pinnacle / Cadillac / ADA.

SWEET DREAMS
CD Set _____ 4417392
Pilz / Oct '92 / BMG.

SWEET HOME CHICAGO
Delmark / Mar '95 / Hot Shot / ADA / CM / Direct / Cadillac.

SWEET LORD
(Charly Gospel Greats)
Uncloudy day: *Staple Singers* / Jesus is the answer: *Argo Singers* / No coward soldier: *Caravans* / Have I told you about my religion: *Bells Of Joy* / I'm thinkin': *Five Blind Boys Of Mississippi* / My one good book: *Soul Stirrers* / His eye is on the sparrow: *Harmonizing Four* / Somewhere to lay my head: *Highway QC's* / What he's done for me: *Five Blind Boys Of Alabama* / He saved my soul: *Swan Silvertones* / He has a way: *Greater Harvest Choir* / Too close to heaven: *Bradford, Alex* / Will the circle be unbroken: *Pilgrim Travelers* / God is moving: *Sallie Martin Singers* / Step by step: *Original Gospel Harmonettes* / Precious Lord (part 1): *Franklin, Aretha* / Precious Lord (part 2): *Franklin, Aretha* / We shall overcome: *Jackson, Mahalia*
CD _____ CPCD 8090
Charly / Apr '95 / Charly / THE / Cadillac.

SWEET MEMORIES FROM BIG BAND
CD _____ UP 004
Hindsight / Sep '92 / Target/BMG / Jazz Music.

SWEET SOUL CLASSICS
CD Set _____ DCDCD 217
Castle / Nov '95 / BMG.

SWEET SOUL DREAMS
CD _____ 290426
Ariola / Dec '92 / BMG.

SWEET SOUL HARMONIES
My lovin': *En Vogue* / Stay: *Eternal* / I wanna sex you up: *Color Me Badd* / Right here (Human Nature Radio Mix): *S.W.V.* / Motownphilly: *Boyz II Men* / I'm doing fine now: *Pasadenas* / Love train: *O'Jays* / My girl: *Temptations* / If you don't know me by now: *Melvin, Harold & The Bluenotes* / Best thing that ever happened to me: *Knight, Gladys & The Pips* / Back to life (Accapella): *Soul II Soul & Caron Wheeler* / Apparently nothin' (Edit): *Young Disciples* / Ghetto heaven (Remix Edit): *Family Stand* / Sexual healing: *Gaye, Marvin* / After the love has gone: *Earth, Wind & Fire* / There's nothing like this: *Omar* / Ghetto child: *Detroit Spinners* / Casanova: *Levert* / Don't walk away: *Jade* / Thinking of you (Rampo Radio Remix): *Sister Sledge*
CD _____ VTCD 20
Virgin / Jan '94 / EMI.

SWEET SOUL HARMONIES 2
Could it be I'm falling in love: *Detroit Spinners* / Summer breeze: *Isley Brothers* / I love music: *O'Jays* / Save our love: *Eternal* / Crazy: *Seal* / Zoom: *Fat Larry's Band* / Downtown: *S.W.V.* / Would I lie to you: *Charles & Eddie* / What's going on: *Gaye, Marvin* / Don't look any further: *M People* / Hold on: *En Vogue* / Slowhand: *Pointer Sisters* / Tribute (Right on): *Pasadenas* / Ain't no sunshine: *Withers, Bill* / Everything must change: *Young, Paul* / Too young to die: *Jamiroquai* / Let's stay together: *Green, Al*
CD _____ VTCD 31
Virgin / Aug '94 / EMI.

SWEET SOUL MUSIC
CD _____ SETCD 083
Stardust / Sep '94 / Carlton Home Entertainment.

SWEET SOUND OF SUCCESS
You've got the power: *Esquires* / If I had you: *O'Dell, Brooks* / There's still tomorrow: *Diplomats* / Same old story: *Big Maybelle* / Don't say goodnight and mean goodbye: *Shirelles* / Invisible: *Miles, Lenny* / That's enough: *Robinson, Roscoe* / Baby take me: *Jackson, Chuck* / Keep on searchin': *Candy & The Kisses* / Finders keepers, losers weepers: *Dodds, Nella* / If I catch you: *Shaw, Timmy* / Hand it over: *Jackson, Chuck* / He's no good: *Hughes, Freddie* / Love of my man: *Kilgore, Theola* / Look over your shoulder: *Jackson, Chuck* / One step at a time: *Brown, Maxine* / Door is open: *Hunt, Tommy* / It's mine: *Montgomery, Tammy* / Lonely people do foolish things: *Clay, Judy* / How much pressure: *Robinson, Roscoe* / Come see about me: *Dodds, Nella* / Half a man: *Cooke, L.C.* / This world's in a hell of a shape: *Ross, Jackie* / Do it now: *Basses / Ask me: Brown, Maxine* / Can't let you out of my sight: *Jackson, Chuck & Maxine Brown* / Gonna send you back to Georgia: *Shaw, Timmy* / Don't believe him Donna: *Miles, Lenny*
CD _____ CDKEND 112
Kent / Jun '94 / Pinnacle.

SWEET, SOFT AND LAZY
CD _____ 12203
Laserlight / Dec '94 / Target/BMG.

SWEET STUFF
I'll erase away: *Whatnauts* / I dig your act: *Whatnauts* / Friends by day (lovers by night): *Whatnauts* / Blues flyaway: *Whatnauts* / I too forgot too easy: *Whatnauts* / I just can't lose your love: *Whatnauts* / Please make love go away: *Whatnauts* / Tweedly dum-dum: *Whatnauts* / To the bottle: *Brother To Brother* / Hurry sundown: *Staton, Candi* / Count on me: *Staton, Candi* / Suspicious minds: *Staton, Candi* / Me and my gemini this is it: *First Class* / Sweet stuff: *Sylvia* / Love is God almighty: *Optimystic* / Where were you: *Mills, Eleonore* / Those ol' O'Jays / Soul je t'aime: *Sylvia & Ralfi Pagan*
CD _____ NEMCD 616
Sequel / Jun '91 / BMG.

SWEETER THAN THE DAY BEFORE
(28 Classic Cuts From The Chess Stable)
Strange change: *Ward, Herb* / Baby you've got it: *McAllister, Maurice & The Radiants* / Such a pretty thing: *Chandler, Gene* / Chained to your heart: *Moore, Bobby & The Rhythm Aces* / Love reputation: *Lasalle, Denise* / Let's wade in the water: *Shaw, Marlena* / Make sure (you have someone who loves you): *Dells* / What can I do: *Kirby, George* / Lucky boy: *Hutton, Harold* / Later than you think: *Mack, Andy* / Sweeter than the day before: *Valentinos* / If I would marry you: *Montgomery, Tammy* / Is it a sin: *Timoi* / Whole new plan: *Garrett, Joan* / Look at me now: *Callier, Terry* / Strange feeling: *Nash, Johnny* / Mighty good lover: *Vashonettes* / My baby's good: *Williams, Johnny* / Sometimes: *Little Milton* / Can't you hear the beat: *Carltons* / I can't stand it: *Seminoles* / I just kept on dancing: *Banks, Doug* / Pay back: *James, Etta* / Pain: *Collier, Mitty* / Landslide: *Clarke, Tony* / Thinkin' about you: *Dells* / Ain't got no problems: *Sunday* / Count me out: *Stewart, Billy*
CD _____ CDARC 515
Charly / Jun '91 / Charly / THE / Cadillac.

SWEETEST FEELING - THE GOLDEN AGE OF SOUL
(4CD Set)
CD Set _____ CDDIG 7
Charly / Feb '95 / Charly / THE / Cadillac.

SWEETS FOR MY SWEET
CD _____ TMPCD 008
Telstar / Jan '95 / BMG.

SWING CLASSICS OF THE GOLDEN ERA
CD _____ CDSVL 211
Saville / '92 / Conifer.

SWING ERA, THE
CD Set _____ CDDIG 2
Charly / Feb '95 / Charly / THE / Cadillac.

SWING FOR A CRIME
CD _____ 842623
EVA / May '94 / Direct / ADA.

SWING HITS
CD _____ DINCD 46
Dino / Sep '92 / Pinnacle / 3MV.

SWING INTO BOP
CD _____ TPZ 1028
Topaz Jazz / Oct '95 / Pinnacle / Cadillac.

SWING INTO CHRISTMAS
Cradle in Bethleham: *Washington, Grover Jr.* / Blue Christmas: *Washington, Grover Jr. & Terence Blanchard* / O come all ye faithful: *Roberts, Marcus* / Winter wonderland: *Roberts, Marcus* / Christmas time is here: *Blanchard, Terence* / Amazing grace: *Hawkins, Tramaine* / Carols of the bells: *Marsalis, Wynton Septet* / Let it snow: *Marsalis, Wynton Septet*
CD _____ 4814112
Sony Jazz / Nov '95 / Sony.

SWING INTO SPRING
CD _____ CDSH 2057
Derann Trax / Nov '91 / Pinnacle.

SWING NOT AGAIN
Swing's the thing / Begin the beguine / Serenade in blue / I've got you under my skin / Compulsory / Blue room / Zec / Alone together / Rubberneck / Mean to me / Sweet and lovely / Take me out to the ball game
CD _____ SV 0188
Savoy Jazz / Jan '94 / Conifer / ADA.

SWING OUT AGAIN
Solo hop: *Miller, Glenn Orchestra* / Strictly jive: *Webb, Chick & His Orchestra* / Flea on a spree: *Powell, Teddy & His Orchestra* / Flat foot floogie: *Manone, Wingy Orchestra* / At the Darktown strutter's ball: *Dorsey, Jimmy Orchestra* / Keep a knockin': *Jordan, Louis & His Tympany Five* / And the angels sing: *Elman, Ziggy & His Orchestra* / Don't miss your baby: *Basie, Count Orchestra* / Swinging 'em down: *Jenkins, Freddie & Harlem 7* / Miss Otis regrets: *Lunceford, Jimmie & Orchestra* / Dusk in upper Sandusky: *Dorsey, Jimmy Orchestra* / In a little Spanish town: *Miller, Glenn Orchestra*
CD _____ SMS 50
Pickwick/Sony Collector's Choice / Apr '92 / Carlton Home Entertainment / Pinnacle / Sony.

SWING PARTY
CD _____ ENTCD 209
Entertainers / '89 / Target/BMG.

SWING, SWING, SWING
Moonlight serenade: *Miller, Glenn* / Sunrise serenade: *Miller, Glenn* / My prayer: *Miller, Glenn* / Little brown jug: *Miller, Glenn* / Blueberry hill: *Miller, Glenn* / Fresh as a daisy: *Miller, Glenn* / Boogie woogie piggly: *Miller, Glenn* / Kiss polka: *Miller, Glenn* / It happened in Sun Valley: *Miller, Glenn* / Chattanooga choo choo: *Miller, Glenn* / Don't sit under the apple tree: *Miller, Glenn* / Adios: *Miller, Glenn* / South Rampart street parade: *Crosby, Bob* / Slow mood: *Crosby, Bob* / Big noise from winnetka: *Crosby, Bob* / It was a lover and his lass: *Crosby, Bob* / My inspiration: *Crosby, Bob* / Ja da: *Crosby, Bob* / What's new: *Crosby, Bob* / Rose of Washington Square: *Crosby, Bob* / Fidgety feet: *Crosby, Bob* / Begin the beguine: *Crosby, Bob* / Hindustan: *Crosby, Bob* / Riffin' at the Ritz: *Goodman, Benny* / Fat and greasy: *Waller, Fats* / Minnie the moocher: *Calloway, Cab* / Dinah: *Noble, Ray* / Night ride: *Henderson, Fletcher* / After you've gone: *Hawkins, Coleman* / Music goes round and round: *Dorsey, Tommy* / Fine romance: *Holiday, Billie* / Hot and anxious: *Henderson, Fletcher*
CD Set _____ HDBOX 003
Happy Days / Sep '94 / Conifer.

SWING THAT MUSIC
(20 Original Swing Hits)
CD _____ CDCD 1181
Charly / Apr '94 / Charly / THE / Cadillac.

SWING TIME
CD _____ CWNCD 2007
Javelin / Jun '95 / THE / Henry Hadaway Organisation.

SWING VOLUME 1
CD Set _____ 74321248182
RCA / Oct '94 / BMG.

SWING WAS OUR BUSINESS
St. Louis blues / Don't let your jive on me / Ridin' high / Spring fever / Frankie and Johnny / How'm I doin' / China boy / Sing

sing sing / Calling all keys / Chopsticks / Dedication / Get hot / Mozelton / Fate let's go / Ol' man river / Sheik of araby / Archer street drag / Patty cake patty cake / There's a plenty / Yankee doodle blues fugue / Hot lips
CD _____ RAJCD 859
Empress / Oct '95 / THE.

SWINGIN' 'ROUND THE CLOCK: NEW YEAR'S EVE 1944
CD _____ VJCD 1050
Vintage Jazz Classics / Feb '94 / Direct / ADA / CM / Cadillac.

SWINGIN' UPTOWN
CD _____ CDHD 185
Happy Days / Oct '92 / Conifer.

SWINGING 60'S
CD _____ MATCD 210
Castle / Dec '92 / BMG.

SWINGING GROOVES FROM 20 PHONTASTIC YEARS
CD _____ PHONTCD 9315
Phontastic / Nov '95 / Wellard / Jazz Music / Cadillac.

SWINGING SIXTIES
Blue moon / Midnight in Moscow / Always something there to remind me / Have I the right / Downtown / Something here in my heart / Michelle / Sunny afternoon / Baby, now that I've found you / Let the heartaches begin / Pictures of matchstick men / Make me an island / Autumn almanac / Red red wine / Warpaint / Goodbye my love
CD _____ PWKS 4068
Carlton Home Entertainment / Jul '91 / Carlton Home Entertainment.

SWINGING THE BLUES
Swingin' the blues: *Basie, Count* / Jelly roll blues: *Berigan, Bunny* / Just blues: *Connie's Inn Orchestra* / Dogtown blues: *Crosby, Bob* / Savoy blues: *Crosby, Bob* / Dippermouth blues: *Dorsey, Jimmy & Louis Armstrong* / Tin roof blues: *Dorsey, Tommy* / St. Louis blues: *Dorsey Brothers* / Bundle of blues: *Ellington, Duke* / Roll 'em: *Goodman, Benny* / Memphis blues: *Henderson, Fletcher* / At the woodchoppers' ball: *Herman, Woody* / Sweet sorrow blues: *Hughes, Spike* / That too, do: *Moten, Bennie* / Hot and anxious: *Redman, Don* / New call of the freaks: *Russell, Luis* / Blues: *Shaw, Artie* / Ridin' but walkin': *Waller, Fats*
CD _____ CD AJA 5088
Living Era / Oct '91 / Koch.

SWINGING THE BLUES
(1931-39)
CD _____ DOCD 5354
Blues Document / Jun '95 / Swift / Jazz Music / Hot Shot.

SWISS BLUES AUTHORITY
CD _____ LAKE 2028
Lakeside / Aug '95 / Magnum Music Group.

SWITCHED ON COUNTRY: THE RANCH HANDS
CD _____ GRF 214
Tring / Mar '93 / Tring / Prism.

SWITCHED ON SWING
CD _____ EMPRCD 519
Emporio / Jul '94 / THE / Disc / CM.

SWITZERLAND - YODELS OF APPENZELL
CD _____ AUD 8026
Unesco / Jun '91 / Harmonia Mundi.

SYMPHONIC BOSSA NOVA
CD _____ 4509908772
WEA / Feb '95 / Warner Music.

SYNEWAVE NEW YORK VOL.1
CD _____ KICKCD 27
Kickin' / Sep '95 / SRD.

SYNOPTICS
CD _____ EFA 003162
Reflective / May '95 / SRD.

SYNTHESISER ALBUM, THE
Chariots of fire / Oxygene / Love theme from Midnight Express / Miami vice / Autobahn / Axel F / Magic fly / Popcorn / Metropolis / Mammagamma / Aurora / I hear you now / Equinoxe / Forbidden colours / Lucifer / Das madchen auf der treppe / Chi mai / Song for Guy
CD _____ MCCD 061
Music Club / Mar '92 / Disc / THE / CM.

SYNTHESIZER GOLD
CD _____ HRCD 8052
Disky / Apr '94 / THE / BMG / Discovery / Pinnacle.

SYNTHESIZER HITS
CD _____ 22521
Music / Aug '95 / Target/BMG.

SYNTHESIZER HITS
CD _____ 55137
Laserlight / Oct '95 / Target/BMG.

SYNTHESIZER HITS
(4CD Set)
CD Set _____ MBSCD 446
Castle / Nov '95 / BMG.

SYNTHESIZER HITS VOL.2
CD _____ MU 5005
Musketeer / Oct '92 / Koch.

SYRIA: MUEZZINS D'ALEP
CD _____ C 580038
Ocora / Nov '92 / Harmonia Mundi / ADA.

T-BIRD PARTY
CD _____ EFA 115962
Crypt / Dec '95 / SRD.

TAARAB MUSIC OF ZANZIBAR VOL.3
Mapenzi kiapo / Wembe / Mwana mtifu / Mbaya kufanya jema / Sitakila wama / Juwa toka / Sema / Wambea / Machozi yananimwaika / Mpeni pole / Pakacha
CD _____ CDORBD 040
Globestyle / Jul '90 / Pinnacle.

TABASKO - THE SALSOUL REMIX PROJECT
CD _____ SALSARCD 1
Beechwood / Nov '93 / BMG / Pinnacle.

TABLE IN MONTMARTRE, A
La goualante du pauvre Jean: *Piaf, Edith* / La ballade Irlandaise: *Bourvil* / Mademoiselle Hortensia: *Giraud, Yvette* / Sous le lit de Lili: *Trenet, Charles & Johnny Hess* / Le marchand de poesie: *Micheyl, Mick* / Ferme jusqu'a Lundi: *Mireille/Jean Sablon* / Le coeur de Paris: *Trenet, Charles* / C'est a Robinson: *Boyer, Lucienne* / Tickled pink: *Les Freres Dommergue* / Tristesse: *Rossi, Tino* / Paris - chansons: *Danno, Jaqueline* / Louise: *Sipers, Pierre* / Rendezvous sous la pluie: *Sablon, Jean* / Erlin le printemps: *Piaf, Edith* / Clopin - clopant: *Dudan, Pierre* / Ca c'est Paris: *Mistinguett* / Coeur en chomage: *Fragson* / Fleur de Paris (With French cine Aubret and Zappy Max): *Helian, Jacques Orchestra*
CD _____ CDEMS 1445
EMI / Apr '92 / EMI.

TAHITI: BELLE EPOQUE 3
CD _____ S 65811
Manuiti / Nov '92 / Harmonia Mundi.

TAHITI: SONGS OF THE ATOLLS & ISLANDS
CD _____ S 65816CD
Manuiti / Aug '94 / Harmonia Mundi.

TAJIK MUSIC OF BADAKHSHAN
CD _____ AUD 0082212
Auvidis/Ethnic / Dec '93 / Harmonia Mundi.

TAKE THE ROUGH WITH THE SMOOTH
CD _____ EFA 116802
Mzee / May '95 / SRD.

TAKIN' A DETOUR VOLUME 1
Catastrophe theory: *Dilemmas* / Jenny Diablo: *Protectors* / Piece of the action: *Most* / Doin' me in: *Mourning After* / Emily against the world: *Curtains* / You know I need you: *Route 66* / Rackin' my mind: *Logue / Down the tubestation a midnight: *Persuaders* / Threw her a line: *Aardvarks* / Secondry modern Miss: *Now* / Harder I try: *Nuthins* / Airwaves: *Strike* / Mr. Cooper: *Sharp Kiddie* / Wish you were here: *Buzz* / Water: *Knave*
CD _____ DRCD 006
Detour / Jan '96 / Detour.

TAKIN' LIBERTIES
CD _____ TTPCD 005
Totem / Nov '94 / Grapevine / THE.

TALE OF ALE, THE
CD _____ FRCD 23
Free Reed / Nov '93 / Direct / ADA.

TALES FROM YESTERDAY
Roundabout: *Berry, Robert* / Siberian khatru: *Stanley Snail* / Mood for a day: *Morse, Steve* / Don't kill the whale: *Magellan* / Turn of the century: *Howe, Steve* / Release release: *Shadow Gallery* / Wondrous stories: *World Trade* / South of the sky: *Cairo* / Soon: *Moraz, Patrick* / Changes: *Enchant* / Astral traveller: *Banks, Peter* / Clap: *Morse, Steve* / Starship trooper: *Jeronimo Road*
CD _____ RR 89142
Roadrunner / Oct '95 / Pinnacle.

TALES OF THE UNEXPECTED
CD _____ RFCD 001
Rainforest / Jun '95 / SRD.

TALK ME DADDY
(Anthology Of Women Singers From Gothic)
CD _____ FLYCD 37
Flyright / Oct '91 / Hot Shot / Wellard / Jazz Music / CM.

TALKIN' JAZZ
Hip walk: *Herbolzheimer, Peter* / See you later: *Grauer, Joanne* / New morning: *Winter, Kitty* / Join us: *Reith, Dieter* / Someday: *Duke, George* / Upa neguinho: *Lobo, Edo* /

My soul: *Duke, George* / Sconsolato: *Murphy, Mark* / Carmell's black forest waltz: *Davis, Nathan* / Secret site: *Novi Singers* / All blues (CD only): *Ross, Annie & Pony Pointdexter* / Colours of excitement: *Francis, Rimona* / Frog child: *Grauer, Joanne*
CD _____ 5188612
Talkin' Loud / Nov '93 / PolyGram.

TALKIN' JAZZ II
Mathar: *Pike, Dave Set* / Take off your shoes to feel the setting sun: *Dauner, Wolgang* / Love me: *Teupen, Johnny* / Get out of my life woman: *Barry, Dee Dee & The Movements* / Big schlepp: *Pike, Dave Set* / Roll on the left side: *Kiesewetter, Knut Train* / Onkel Joe: *Catch Up* / Wives and lovers: *Reith, Dieter Trio* / Nude: *Velebny, Karel* / Espresso loco: *Boland, Francy* / Cantaloupe Island: *Krog, Karin* / Feet: *Duke, George*
CD _____ 5235292
Talkin' Loud / Sep '94 / PolyGram.

TALKIN' LOUD SAMPLER 1
Young Disciples Theme: *Young Disciples & MC Mello* / Get it: *Steps Ahead* / Mean machine 90: *Jalal* / Step right on: *Young Disciples & Outlaw Posse* / Glide: *Incognito* / Tribal knight: *Ace Of Clubs* / Wild and peaceful: *Bassic* / Little ghetto boy: *Galliano*
CD _____ 8467922
Talkin' Loud / Sep '90 / PolyGram.

TALKIN' LOUD SAMPLER 2
Hide and seek: *Urban Species* / Hungry like a baby: *Galliano* / Colibri: *Incognito* / You've got to move: *Omar* / Back to the real world: *K-Creative* / All I have in me: *Young Disciples* / Theme from Marxman: *Marxman* / Qui semme le vente recolte le tempo: *M.C. Solaar* / Serious love: *Perception* / I commit: *Powell, Bryan* / Take me now: *Payne, Tammy* / Apparently nothin': *Young Disciples* / There's nothing like this: *Omar* / Prince of peace: *Galliano* / Always there: *Incognito*
CD _____ 5159362
Talkin' Loud / Jan '93 / PolyGram.

TALKING BLUES
CD _____ LG 21067
Lagoon / May '93 / Magnum Music Group / THE.

TALKING SPIRITS
(Native American Peublo Music)
CD _____ CDT 126
Topic / Apr '93 / Direct / ADA.

TANGO
Jealousy: *Geraldo's Gaucho Tango Orchestra* / There's heaven in your eyes: *La Plata Tango Band* / Marushka: *Sesta, Don Gaucho Tango Band* / From a kiss springs happiness: *La Plata Tango Band* / Madame, you're lovely: *Mantovani & His Tipica Orchestra* / Tangled tangos No. 1 (part 1): *Rinaldo, Don & His Tango Orchestra* / Dolores: *Geraldo & His Gaucho Tango Orchestra* / Spider of the night: *Mantovani & His Tipica Orchestra* / Summer evening in Santa Cruz: *Silvester, Victor & His Ballroom Orchestra* / I could be happy with you: *Geraldo's Gaucho Tango Orchestra* / Dear madam: *Silvester, Victor & His Ballroom Orchestra* / Te quiero dijiste: *Geraldo & His Gaucho Tango Orchestra* / Tangled tangos No. 1 (part 2): *Rinaldo, Don & His Tango Orchestra* / At the balalaika: *Geraldo & His Orchestra* / Blue sky: *Mantovani & His Tipica Orchestra* / If the world were mine: *Geraldo & His Orchestra* / South of the border: *Harris, Jack & His Orchestra* / El pescador: *Loss, Joe & His band* / Isle of Capri: *Geraldo & His Gaucho Tango Orchestra* / Serenade in the night: *Mantovani & His Tipica Orchestra* / Flowers I may not offer: *La Plata Tango Band* / Lamento gitano: *Loss, Joe & His band*
CD _____ PASTCD 9752
Flapper / Jan '92 / Pinnacle.

TANGO AND MAMBO CALIENTE
(2CD Set)
CD Set _____ R2CD 4021
Deja Vu / Jan '96 / THE.

TANGO ARGENTINA
Vuelo al sur / Ventanita florida / Voy cantando tangos por el mundo / Sur / Volver / Tango-tango / Yuyo verde / Los argentinos / Comos dos extranos / Loca bohemia / Buenos aires conoce / Los suenos / Maipo / La vida es Linda, pibe / Milonga del tarnamundo / Corrientes arriba / Tango del eco / Ausencias / Adios arrabal / Oblivion / Tal vez no tenga fin / Como abrazado a un rencor / Typical one
CD _____ MCCD 098
Music Club / Mar '93 / Disc / THE / CM.

TANGO LADIES
CD _____ HQCD 34
Harlequin / Feb '94 / Swift / Jazz Music / Wellard / Hot Shot / Cadillac.

TANGO LADIES 1923-1954
CD _____ HQCD 52
Harlequin / Jun '95 / Swift / Jazz Music / Wellard / Hot Shot / Cadillac.

TANGOS PARA AFICIONADOS VOL. 2
(The '50's)
CD _____ PHONTCD 7582
Phontastic / Jun '94 / Wellard / Jazz Music / Cadillac.

TANTRANCE
(2CD Set)
CD Set _____ SPV 08938582
Subterranean / Jan '96 / Plastic Head.

TANZANIA SOUND
CD _____ OMCD 018
Original Music / May '93 / Direct.

TAPESTRY REVISITED
CD _____ 7567926042
Atlantic / Nov '95 / Warner Music.

TARTAN DISC, THE
(Scotland The Brave)
CD _____ CDITV 480
Scotdisc / Jul '89 / Duncans / Ross / Conifer.

TASTE OF 3RD STONE RECORDS VOL.1, A
Sooner or later: State Of Grace / Smile: State Of Grace / Deep blue breath: A.R. Kane / I know: Bark Psychosis / So cold: Popguns / Someone to dream of: Popguns / Basking: Mali Rain / Callow hill 508am: Mali Rain / Alaska pt.1: Transambient Communications / River: Transambient Communications / California nocturne: E.A.R. / Ecstasy in slow motion: Spacemen 3 / Revolution (live): Spacemen 3 / Paddington Bear: Goober Patrol / Grabbers: Goober Patrol
CD _____ STONE 021CD
3rd Stone / Sep '95 / Vital / Plastic Head.

TASTE OF OLD IRELAND, A
CD _____ HCD 115
GTD / Apr '95 / Direct.

TASTE OF THE INDESTRUCTIBLE BEAT OF SOWETO, A
Kwa volondiya / Mazuzu / Heyi wena / Kulukhuni / Thuto kelefa / Madyisa mbitsi / Ngayivuye / Jabula mfana / Asambeni sonke / Mubi umakhelwane / Nomacala / Emandulu
CD _____ CDEWV 32
Virgin / Nov '93 / EMI.

TASTE TEST NO.1
CD _____ NAR 045 CD
New Alliance / Sep '90 / Pinnacle.

TEACHING YOU NO FEAR
CD _____ BHR 015
Burning Heart / Feb '95 / Plastic Head.

TEARDROPS, LOVE, HEARTBREAK
CD _____ DCD 5302
Disky / Nov '93 / THE / BMG / Discovery / Pinnacle.

TECHNO CLASSICS VOL.1
CD _____ FRCD 003
Flex / '95 / Jetstar.

TECHNO CLASSICS VOL.2
CD _____ RSNCD 3
Rising High / Oct '92 / Disc.

TECHNO DANCE HIGHFLYER
CD _____ 12371
Laserlight / Jun '94 / Target/BMG.

TECHNO EUROPA
CD _____ 5350002
Polydor / Nov '95 / PolyGram.

TECHNO HYPER DANCE
CD _____ 12611
Laserlight / Oct '95 / Target/BMG.

TECHNO I & II - ELECTRONIC DANCE
It is what it is: Rythim Is Rythim / Forever and a day: Baxter, Blake / Time to express: Fowlkes, Eddie 'Flashin' / Electronic dance: H.B. Experience / Bhaa a'bla house: Members Of The House / Feel surreal: A Tongue & D Groove / Spark: Hesterley, Mia / Techno music: Juan / Big fun: Inner City / Ride 'em boy: Baxter, Blake / Sequence 10: Shakir / Un, deux, trois: Idol Making / Love takes me over: Area 10 / Aftermath: Reel By Real / Stark: K.G.B. / Mirror mirror: MK / I believe: Octave One & Lisa Newberry / Techno pour favor: Infinity / Elements: Psyche / Ritual: Vice
CD _____ DIXCD 123
10 / Mar '92 / EMI.

TECHNO NATIONS 2
CD _____ KICKCD 9
Kickin' / Apr '94 / SRD.

TECHNO NATIONS 3
CD _____ KICKCD 14
Kickin' / Jan '95 / SRD.

TECHNO NATIONS 4
CD _____ KICKCD 25
Kickin' / Jun '95 / SRD.

TECHNO NIGHTS, AMBIENT DAWN
(2CD/MC Set)
Destination Eschaton: Shamen / Minus 61 in Detroit: Holmes, David / Leave home: Chemical Brothers / Winter: Clarke, Dave / Hot flush: Red Snapper / Smokebelch II: Sabres Of Paradise / Sprung aus den wolken: D.J. Hell / FUK: Plastikman / Go: Moby / Pacific 707: 808 State / Papillon: N-Joi / Spice: Eon / Playing with knives: Bizarre Inc. / Big fun: Inner City / Texas cowboys: Grid / NRG: Adamski / Weather experience: Prodigy / S.A.X.: Yello / Lush: Orbital / Age of loneliness (Carly's song): Enigma / Water from a vine leaf: Orbit, William / L'Esperanca: Vath, Sven / Labyrinth: Glass, Philip / Hispanos in space: Jam & Spoon / Age of love: Age Of Love / Raxos: Black Dog / Landcruising: Craig, Carl / Donkey rhubarb: Aphex Twin / Mass observation: Scanner / Film me and finish me off: Apollo 440 / One day: Bjork / Oxbrow lakes: Orb / Barefoot in the head: Man Called Adam / Sun rising: Beloved / Autumn leaves: Coldcut / Love theme from Blade Runner: Vangelis / Ending (Ascent): Eno, Brian
CD Set _____ CDEMTV 97
EMI / Sep '95 / EMI.

TECHNO SOUND OF DISTANCE
CD _____ DI 182
Distance / Dec '95 / 3MV.

TECHNOHEAD
(Mix Hard Or Die)
CD _____ REACTCD 022
React / Aug '93 / Vital.

TECHNOHEAD 2
(Harder & Faster)
CD _____ REACTCD 035
React / Mar '94 / Vital.

TECHNOHEAD 3
(Out Of Control)
CD _____ REACTCD 051
React / Oct '94 / Vital.

TECHNOPHUNK
CD _____ BAZZCD 2
Rumour / Mar '95 / Pinnacle / 3MV / Sony.

TECHNOSTATE
Everybody in the place: Prodigy / Bouncer: Kicks Like A Mule / Running out of time: Digital Orgasm / Different strokes: Isotonik / Take me away: Cappella / Can you feel the passion: Blue Pearl / Playing with knives: Bizarre Inc. / Frequency: Altern 8 / Get down: M D Emm / What can you do for me: Utah Saints / Are you ready to fly: Rozalla / Pure pleasure: Digital Excitation / Rave generator: Tribeka / Rescue me: Malone, Debbie / Uptempo: Tronikhouse / Stand up (earthquake): Rave Nation & Juliette / U.H.F.: UHF / Wicked love: Oceanic / Put the hammer down: Set The Tone / Out: Sonz Of A Loop Da Loop Era
CD _____ JARCD 2
Cookie Jar / Mar '92 / SRD.

TECHNOVISIONS
CD _____ CDRAID 510
Rumour / Mar '93 / Pinnacle / 3MV / Sony.

TECHNOVISIONS 2
CD _____ CDRAID 510
Rumour / Mar '93 / Pinnacle / 3MV / Sony.

TECHNOZONE
CD _____ OZONCD 2
Ozone / Mar '92 / SRD.

TEDDY BOY ROCK'N'ROLL
CD _____ PEPCD 104
Pollytone / Jun '95 / Pollytone.

TEEN BEAT
Teen beat: Nelson, Sandy / Swanee river hop: Domino, Fats / Raunchy: Freeman, Ernie / Rumble: Wray, Link / Green mosquito: Tune Rockers / Poor boy: Royaltones / Topsy II: Cole, Cozy / So rare: Dorsey, Jimmy / Orchestra / Tequila: Champs / Happy organ: Cortez, Dave 'Baby' / Clouds: Spacemen / Twitchy: Hall, Rene / Organ boogie shuffle: Virtues / Wild bird: Jive-A-Tones / Midnighter: Champs / Fast freight: Aliens, Arvee / In the mood: Fields, Ernie / Orchestra / So wild: Yellow Jackets / Wild weekend: Rockin' Rebels / Torquay: Fireballs / Bongo rock: Epps, Preston / Walk don't run: Ventures / Nut rocker: B. Bumble & The Stingers / Wheels: String-A-Longs / Bulldog: Fireballs / Rockin' crickets: Hot-Toddys / Wham: Mack, Lonnie / Slumber party: Van-Dells / Spunky: Jenkins, Johnny / Memphis: Mack, Lonnie
CD _____ CDCHD 406
Ace / Sep '93 / Pinnacle / Cadillac / Complete/Pinnacle.

TEEN BEAT
Wipeout: Safaris / Batman: Marketts / Let there be drums: Nelson, Sandy / Walk don't run: Ventures / Predator: Billy Joe & The Checkmates / Red river rock: Johnny & The Hurricanes / Let's go: Routers / Sleep walk: Santo & Johnny / Teen rocker: Eddy, Duane / Teen beat: Nelson, Sandy / Pipeline: Chantays / Hawaii Five-O: Ventures / Reveille rock: Johnny & The Hurricanes / Happy organ: Cortez, Dave 'Baby' / Forty miles of bad road: Eddy, Duane / Raunchy: Justis, Bill / Tequila: Cannon, Ace / Nut rocker: B. Bumble & The Stingers
CD _____ ECD 3058
K-Tel / Jan '95 / K-Tel.

TEEN BEAT TEQUILA
CD _____ 12546
Laserlight / Jun '95 / Target/BMG.

TEEN BEAT VOL.2
Calif boogie: Teenbeats / El rancho rock: Champs / Mathilda: String-A-Longs / Flip, flop and bop: Cramer, Floyd / Mule train stomp: Buchanan, Roy / Manhattan spiritual: Owen, Reg / Wiggle wobble: Cooper, Les / Ramrod: Eddy, Duane / Boo boo stick beat: Atkins, Chet / Fickle chicken: Atmospheres / Cerveza: Brown, Boots / Wild twist: Roller Coasters / Blue eagle: Rivers, Jimmy / Big jump: Nelson, Sandy / Patricia: Prado, Perez / Teensville: Atkins, Chet / Mardi gras: Cortez, Dave 'Baby' / Carioca: Fireballs / Rebel rouser: Eddy, Duane / Cast your fate to the wind: Guaraldi, Vince / Machine gun: Rip Tides / Power shift: Usher, Gary / Havana: Atmospheres / Hucklebuck: Fields, Ernie / Guitar rhumba: Guitar Gable / Pretty please: Buchanan, Roy / Apple knocker: B. Rumble & The Stingers / Doin' the horse: Brooks, Skippy / Soul twist: King Curtis & The Noble Knights / Dish rag: Kendrick, Nat
CD _____ CDCHD 522
Ace / Aug '94 / Pinnacle / Cadillac / Complete/Pinnacle.

TEEN BEAT VOL.3
CD _____ CDCHD 602
Ace / Feb '96 / Pinnacle / Cadillac / Complete/Pinnacle.

TEENAGE HEART THROBS
CD _____ CDCD 1242
Charly / Jun '95 / Charly / THE / Cadillac.

TEENAGE KICKS
Pretty vacant: Sex Pistols / Going underground: Jam / My perfect cousin: Undertones / Do anything you wanna do: Eddie & The Hot Rods / If the kids are united: Sham 69 / Pump it up: Costello, Elvis & The Attractions / No more heroes: Stranglers / She's so modern: Boomtown Rats / Hit me with your rhythm stick: Dury, Ian & The Blockheads / Ever fallen in love: Buzzcocks / Working for the Yankee dollar: Skids / Turning Japanese: Vapors / King rocker: Generation X / Germ free adolescents: X-Ray Spex / What a waste: Dury, Ian & The Blockheads / Is Vic there: Department S / Go wild in the country: Bow Wow Wow / Eighth day: O'Connor, Hazel / Automatic lover: Vibrators / Lucky number: Lovich, Lena / Rich kids: Rich Kids / Start: Jam / Teenage kicks: Undertones / Hanging on the telephone: Blondie / Brass in pocket: Pretenders / Airport: Motors / Take me, I'm yours: Squeeze / Can't stand losing you: Police / I got you: Split Enz / Pretty in pink: Psychedelic Furs / 2-4-6-8 Motorway: Robinson, Tom / I want you to want me: Cheap Trick / Shake some action: Flamin' Groovies / Swords of a thousand men: Tenpole Tudor / Back of my hand: Jags / My best friend's girl: Cars / My Sharona: Knack / Time for action: Secret Affair / Generals and Majors: XTC / Reward: Teardrop Explodes / Clean clean: Buggles / Roxette: Dr. Feelgood / Hey Lord don't ask me questions: Parker, Graham / Spanish stroll: Mink Deville / Roadrunner: Richman, Jonathan / Real wild child: Iggy Pop
CD _____ 5253382
PolyGram TV / Jul '95 / PolyGram.

TEENAGE REPRESSION VOL. 1
CD _____ 642041
EVA / May '94 / Direct / ADA.

TEENAGE ROCK 'N' ROLL PARTY
All night long / Old folk's boogie / Slow down / Blue jeans and a boy's shirt / That's alright baby / Sweetheart please don't go / Crying my heart out / Roll hot rock roll / Jump Jack jump / Yama yama pretty mama / You know you're doin' me wrong / These golden rings / My desire / Night of the werewolf / Dance to it / Have mercy Miss Percy / Hands off / Can't believe you wanna leave me / (I'm afraid) the masquerade is over / Those lonely, lonely nights / Wet back hop / Hey girl, hey boy / Let a go boppin' tonight / I hit, git and split / Right now / Shake your hips / Look out Miss James / Who's been jivin' you / Sweet dreams
CD _____ CDCHD 555
Ace / Sep '94 / Pinnacle / Cadillac / Complete/Pinnacle.

TEENBEAT 50
Earle Hotel: Scaley Andrew / Sketch for Sleepy: Bastro / Marbles: Circus Lupus / Block of wood: Vomit Launch / Strange pair: Vomit Launch / Capitalist joyride: Unrest / Dr. Seuss: Autoclave / Time loop: Cohen, Johnny / On tape: Teenage Gang Debs / California: Sexual Milkshake / I'm going to blow your fucking head off: Superconductor / Not at all: Velocity Girl / It's hard to be an egg: Eggs / Shaniko: Love, Courtney / Teenbeat theme: Love, Courtney / Teenbeat epilepue: Love, Courtney / Sweet Georgia Brown: Krokodiloes / Look out: Helter Skelter / Teenage suicide: Naomi Wolff / Love affair is over: Clarence / Merry go round: Coral / Equator of her navel: Jungle George / Holiday New England: Superstar, Mark E / You fucking English bastard: S.C.U.D. / 23rd rocker: Wills, Butch / Peace: Wall Drug
CD _____ OLE 025-2
Matador / Mar '94 / Vital.

TEENBEAT SAMPLER
CD _____ TEENBEAT 141CD
Teenbeat / Sep '94 / SRD.

TEJANO ROOTS
(24 Hits From Discos Ideal 1946-1966)
CD _____ ARHCD 341
Arhoolie / Apr '95 / ADA / Direct / Cadillac.

TEJANO ROOTS - THE WOMEN
CD _____ ARHCD 343
Arhoolie / Apr '95 / ADA / Direct / Cadillac.

TEKNO ACID BEATS
CD _____ TOPY 39 CD
Temple / Feb '89 / Pinnacle / Plastic Head.

TELARC SAMPLER 4
CD _____ CD 80004
Telarc / '89 / Conifer / ADA.

TELARCHIVE
Seven come eleven / Line for Lyons / Cherokee / So long Eric / I know that you know / Stardust / Sweet Sue, just you / Slop / Gerry meets Hamp
CD _____ 83318
Telarc / Jun '92 / Conifer / ADA.

TELEPATHY
CD _____ BDRCD 8
Breakdown / Jun '95 / SRD.

TEMPLE OF ELECTRONICA
CD _____ TEMPNYC 2CD
Temple / Oct '95 / Pinnacle / Plastic Head.

TEMPLE RECORDS VOL.1
CD _____ TEMPNYC 1CD
Temple / Oct '95 / Pinnacle / Plastic Head.

TEMPLE SAMPLER, THE
CD _____ COMD 2049
Temple / Feb '94 / CM / Duncans / ADA / Direct.

TEMPO DE BAHIA
CD _____ BMCD 123
Blue Moon / Mar '89 / Magnum Music Group / Greensleeves / Hot Shot / ADA / Cadillac / Discovery.

TEMPTED
If I ever lose my faith in you: Sting / More than words: Extreme / Love song for a vampire: Lennox, Annie / Too much love will kill you: May, Brian / One: U2 / Easy: Faith No More / Womankind: Little Angels / Twenty nine pains: Plant, Robert / Tempted: Squeeze / Beautiful girl: INXS / Just another day: Secada, Jon / Emotional time: Hothouse Flowers / Deep: East 17 / All woman: Stansfield, Lisa / This time: Carroll, Dina / Love makes no sense: O'Neal, Alexander / Hello (Turn your radio on): Shakespears Sister / Young at heart: Bluebells
CD _____ 5163052
PolyGram TV / Jul '93 / PolyGram.

TENDER LOVE
(17 Romantic Love Songs)
Tender love: Thomas, Kenny / When you tell me that you love me: Stansfield, Lisa / All woman: Stansfield, Lisa / Way of the world: Turner, Tina / Every time you go away: Young, Paul / Don't dream it's over: Crowded House / Careless whisper: Michael, George / Your song: John, Elton / Saving all my love for you: Houston, Whitney / Try a little tenderness: Redding, Otis / She makes my day: Palmer, Robert / Right here waiting: Marx, Richard / Best of me: Richard, Cliff / Promise me: Craven, Beverley / True: Spandau Ballet / It's my own way with me now: Minogue, Kylie & Keith Washington / If you don't know me by now: Simply Red
CD _____ CDEMTV 64
EMI / Feb '92 / EMI.

TENOR SAX & TROMBONE SPECTACULAR
CD _____ PCD 7019
Progressive / Jun '93 / Jazz Music.

TERMINAL CITY RICOCHET
CD _____ VIRUS 75CD
Alternative Tentacles / Nov '89 / Pinnacle.

TERRORDROME 1
(Hardcore Nightmare)
CD Set _____ DB 47982
Deep Blue / Mar '95 / Pinnacle.

TERRORDROME 1
(Darkside From Hell)
CD _____ 0041512COM
Edel / Oct '95 / Pinnacle.

TERRORDROME 2
(Hardcore Cyberpunk)
Introdrome: Chosen Few / Tyrannofuck: D.J. Fistfuck / String X: Cyanide / I'll show you my gun (mixes): Annihilator / Base U (Smash TV): Shadowrun / Accelerator 4: Technohead / One day: Wedlock / Maniac: Chosen Few / Cocksuckers: Tellurian / F.T.S.: Vinyl Killer / Doomsday mixes: Maniac Of Noise / Victim of trance: Analyzer / Cause a riot: Blunted Vision, A / Power dominion: Dee, Lenny & Ralphie Dee / 20,000 / High Energy / Suck it: Oral Maniac / Terrordrome: High Energy / Fuck this: Reanimator / Accelerator 3: Technohead / Fucking Speedloader: Speedloader / Relatic: Cyanide / Mokurmania: Maniac Of Noise / Goddamn mind: Noisegate / Invasion of the intruders: Sons of Aliens / In 16 beats time second (mixes): Vitamin / C.T.X. (Mirror mix): Original Gabber / Eat za pizza: Salami Brothers / Insane: Strontium 9000 / Psychic 909: Milan / Move it faster: Triplet / Quetsch: Haardcore / Outrodrome: Origi-

nal Gabber / I control your body: Dee, Lenny & Ralphie Dee / Maniac (mix): Chosen Few / Suck it (mix): Oral Maniac / Accelerator: Technohead / Mokummania (mix): Maniac Of Noise / Relatic (mix): Cyanide / My house is your house: Vitamin / Victim of trance (mix): Analyzer / Eat zat pizza (mix): Salami Brothers / Cocksuckers (mix): Tellurian / 20,000 volt (mix): High Energy

CD Set _____ DB 47972
Deep Blue / Mar '95 / Pinnacle.

TERRORDROME 3
(Party Animal)
CD Set _____ DB 47992
Deep Blue / Nov '94 / Pinnacle.

TERRORDROME 4
(Supersonic Guerilla)
CD _____ DB 47962
PolyGram TV / Apr '95 / PolyGram.

TERRORIST GENERATION
CD _____ CCSCD 355
Castle / Nov '92 / BMG.

TERYAKI ASTHMA VOL 1-5
CD _____ CZ 037CD
C/Z / Nov '92 / Plastic Head.

TEST 1
CD _____ REACTCD 031
React / '94 / Vital.

TEST 2
CD _____ REACTCD 052
React / Nov '94 / Vital.

TESTAMENT RECORDS SAMPLER
CD _____ TCD 4001
Testament / May '95 / Complete/Pinnacle / ADA / Koch.

TEX-MEX FIESTA
Ay te dejo en San Antonio / La ratita / Amor bonito / Corine Corina / La tracionera / El desperado / Caballo viejo / Que cobarde / Viva seguin / La duena de la llave / Por esos montes / Cuatro o cinco farolazos / Quiereme vidita / Las gaviotas / Tomando y fumando / Puentes quemados / Saludamos a texas / Mi unico camino real / Medio vuelo / Tarde pa' appepentirnos / Magia de amor / Juarez
CD _____ CDCHD 528
Ace / Oct '94 / Pinnacle / Cadillac / Complete/Pinnacle.

TEXAS BLACK COUNTRY DANCE 1927-35
CD _____ DOCD 5162
Blues Document / May '93 / Swift / Jazz Music / Hot Shot.

TEXAS BLUES
CD _____ ARHCD 352
Arhoolie / Apr '95 / ADA / Direct / Cadillac.

TEXAS BLUES 1927-37
CD _____ DOCD 5161
Blues Document / May '93 / Swift / Jazz Music / Hot Shot.

TEXAS BLUES GUITAR 1929-35
Story Of The Blues / Apr '95 / Koch / ADA.
CD _____ SOB 35332CD

TEXAS BOHEMIA
CD _____ TRIKONTUS 201
Trikont / Jan '95 / ADA / Direct.

TEXAS COUNTRY BLUES 1948-1951
CD _____ FLYCD 941
Flyright / Aug '94 / Hot Shot / Wellard / Jazz Music / CM.

TEXAS CZECH & BOHEMIAN BANDS, THE
(1928-1958)
CD _____ ARHC 9031
Arhoolie / Apr '95 / ADA / Direct / Cadillac.

TEXAS CZECH, BOHEMIAN & MORAVIAN BANDS, THE
(1929-1959)
CD _____ FL 7026
Folklyric / Apr '95 / Direct / Cadillac.

TEXAS FIELD RECORDINGS 1934-39
CD _____ DOCD 5231
Blues Document / Apr '94 / Swift / Jazz Music / Hot Shot.

TEXAS FOLK AND OUTLAW MUSIC
CD _____ EDCD 352
Edsel / Jun '92 / Pinnacle / ADA.

TEXAS GIRLS
CD _____ DOCD 5163
Blues Document / May '93 / Swift / Jazz Music / Hot Shot.

TEXAS PIANO 1923-35
CD _____ DOCD 5224
Blues Document / Apr '94 / Swift / Jazz Music / Hot Shot.

TEXAS PIANO 1927-38
CD _____ DOCD 5225
Blues Document / Apr '94 / Swift / Jazz Music / Hot Shot.

TEXAS PIANO BLUES, 1929-48
CD _____ SOB 35092CD
Story Of The Blues / Apr '95 / Koch / ADA.

TFSM 03
CD _____ EFA 127662
Gaia / Jul '95 / SRD.

THANKS FOR THE MEMORY
CD _____ MCCD 164
MCI / Jul '94 / Disc / THE.

THAT HIGH LONESOME SOUND
(The Best Of Bluegrass Through The Years)
If I should wander back tonight: Hot Rize / Looking for the stone: O'Brien, Tim & Mollie / Blue yodel # 3: Johnson Mountain Boys / My hands are tied: Lonesome Standard Time / I'm going back to the old home: Watson, Doc / Blue moon of Kentucky: Osborne Brothers / Trains make me lonesome: Auldridge, Mike / Rock salt and nails: Crowe, J.D. & The New South / I ain't brok but I'm badly bent: Grisman, David / I was left on the street: McCoury Brothers / Where the soul man never dies: Skaggs, Ricky & Tony Rice / When God dips his pen of love in my heart: Krauss, Alison / Running hard on a broken heart: Lonesome River Band / Kentucky King: Lonesome Standard Time / That high lonesome sound: Rowan, Peter & The Nashville Bluegrass Band / Molly & teenbrooks: Crowe, J.D. / Blue ridge express: Munde, Alan / One way track: Boone Creek / Darlin' Corey: Clifton, Bill / Roll jordan roll: Nashville Bluegrass Band / Foggy mountain chimes: Here Today / Tramp on the street: Blue Sky Boys / Come on home: Clements, Vassar
CD _____ NTMCD 514
Nectar / Jan '96 / Pinnacle.

THAT LOVING FEELING
Unchained melody: Righteous Brothers / One and one is one: Medicine Head / Things we do for love: 10cc / Night you murdered love: ABC / Reunited: Peaches & Herb / My friend the wind: Roussos, Demis / Little piece of heaven: Godley & Creme / First time: Beck, Robin / Say hello, wave goodbye: Soft Cell / Down on the street: Shakatak / Come what may: Leandros, Vicky / Pearl's a singer: Brooks, Elkie / Fooled around and fell in love: Bishop, Elvin / Only love: Mouskouri, Nana
CD _____ 5501482
Spectrum/Karussell / Jan '94 / PolyGram / THE.

THAT LOVING FEELING VOL.7
Power of love: Rush, Jennifer / Don't let the sun go down on me: John, Elton / Show me heaven: McKee, Maria / Ain't no sunshine: Jackson, Michael / Everywhere: Fleetwood Mac / Best: Turner, Tina / Everytime you go away: Young, Paul / Who's that girl: Eurythmics / Would I lie to you: Charles & Eddie / Wishing on a star: Rose Royce / It's a man's man's man's world: Brown, James / Baby, I love your way: Frampton, Peter / I was made to love her: Wonder, Stevie / Another day: McCartney, Paul / Miss you like crazy: Cole, Natalie / When I fall in love: Cole, Nat King / Real thing: Di Bart, Tony / Dedicated to the one I love: McLean, Bitty / Right here: S.W.V. / I miss you: Haddaway / Stay: Eternal / How can I love you more: M People / U R the best thing: D Ream / So natural: Stansfield, Lisa / Just another day: Secada, Jon / Don't wanna lose you: Estefan, Gloria / If only for one night: Vandross, Luther / Come on in out of the rain: Moten, Wendy / I can see clearly now: Cliff, Jimmy / Everything but the girl: Cliff, Jimmy / I don't want to talk about it: Everything But The Girl / Every little thing she does is magic: Police / Kissing a fool: Michael, George
CD Set _____ DINCD 83
Dino / Aug '94 / Pinnacle / 3MV.

THAT WAS THE SWINGING 60'S VOL.1
What do you want to make those eyes at me for: Ford, Emile & The Checkmates / Be mine: Fortune, Lance / Michael, row the boat ashore: Donegan, Lonnie / War paint: Brook Brothers / Venus in blue jeans: Wynter, Mark / Little bitty tear: Miki & Griff / Sugar and spice: Searchers / Suckiyaki Hill: Kenny & His Jazzmen / Mockingbird Hill: Migil 5 / Downtown: Clark, Petula / Poor man's son: Rockin' Berries / Funny how love can be: Ivy League / Daydream: Lovin' Spoonful / Dedicated follower of fashion: Kinks / Flowers in the rain: Move / Puppet on a string: Shaw, Sandie / Build me up buttercup: Foundations / Mexico: Baldry, Long John / Oh happy day: Hawkins, Edwin Singers / Make me an island: Dolan, Joe
CD _____ CDMFP 5897
Music For Pleasure / Oct '90 / EMI.

THAT'LL FLAT GIT IT VOL. 1
(RCA Rockabillies)
Sixteen chicks: Clay, Joe / Born to love one woman: Cartey, Ric / Sugar sweet: Houston, David / New shoes: Denson, Lee / Little boy blue: Johnson, Hoyt / Drug store rock 'n' roll: Martin, Janis / Rosie let's get cozy: Rich, Dave / Catty Town: Glasser, Dick / Star light, star bright: Castle, Nan / TV hop: Morgan Twins / Honky tonk mind: Blake, Tommy / Teen billy baby: Sprouts / Don't bug me baby: Allen, Milt / Now stop: Carson, Martha / Milkcow blues: Rodgers, Jimmie / Duck tail: Clay, Joe / Heart throb:

Cartey, Ric / One and only: Houston, David / I've got a dollar: Dell, Jimmy / Lovin' honey (2): Morris, Gene / Barefoot baby: Martin, Janis / Rock-a-bye baby: Bonn, Skeeter / That ain't nothing but right: Castle, Joey / Mary Nell: Inman, Autrey / Hey jibbo: Wood, Art / All night long: Blake, Tommy / Full grown cat: McCoys / Just thought I'd set you straight: Harris, Ted / Oooh-wee baby: Cartey, Ric / Shake it up baby: Dee, Frankie / Lovin' honey (1): Morris, Gene
CD Set _____ BCD 15622
Bear Family / May '93 / Rollercoaster / Direct / CM / Swift / ADA.

THAT'LL FLAT GIT IT VOL. 2
(Decca Rockabillies)
Hot rock wild: Carroll, Johnny / Wild women - crazy: Carroll, Johnny / Crazy lovin': Carroll, Johnny / Tryin' to get you: Carroll, Johnny / Corine Corina: Carroll, Johnny / Rock 'n' Roll Ruby: Carroll, Johnny / Flip, flop and fry: Carroll, Johnny / Baby don't leave me: Five Chavis Brothers / Way out there: Chuck & Bill / Ruby Pearl: Cochran, Jackie Lee / Mamy don't you think I know: Cochran, Jackie Lee / Lorraine: Covelle, Buddy / Cool it baby: Fontaine, Eddie / Whole lotta shakin' goin' on: Hall, Roy / Off beat boogie: Hall, Roy / See you later alligator: Hall, Roy / Three alley cats: Hall, Roy / Diggin' the boogie: Hall, Roy / I wanna bop: Harlan, Billy / I would be a doggone lie: Harlan, Billy / Be bop baby: Harlan, Billy / Sweet love on my mind: Jimmy & Johnny / Teenage love is misery: Kennedy, Jerry / Crazy baby: Maltais, Gene / Ten little women: Noland, Terry / Teenage boogie: Pierce, Webb / Cast iron arm: Wilson, Peanuts / You're barking up the wrong tree: Woody, Don / Make like a rock and roll: Woody, Don
CD _____ BCD 15623
Bear Family / Jun '92 / Rollercoaster / Direct / CM / Swift / ADA.

THAT'LL FLAT GIT IT VOL. 3
(Capitol Rockabillies)
You oughta see Grandma rock: McDonald, Skeets / Heartbreakin' Mama: McDonald, Skeets / My little baby: Maddox, Rose / Sebbin' come elebbin: Heap, Jimmy / Go ahead on: Heap, Jimmy / Try me: Luman, Bob / Cash on the barrelhead: Louvin Brothers / Red hen hop: Louvin Brothers / Worryin' kind: Sands, Tommy / My gal Gertie: Dickerson, Dub / When I found you: Reed, Jerry / I've bad enough: Reed, Jerry / Mr. Big feet: Charlie Bop Trio / Cool down Mame: Farmer Boys / My baby done left me: Farmer Boys / Party kiss: Fallin, Johnny / Party line: Fallin, Johnny / There's gonna be a ball: Grayzell, Rudy / Bop cat bop: Crum, Simon / Jeopardy: Shepard, Jean / He's my baby: Shepard, Jean / Alone with you: Young, Faron / I can't dance: Young, Faron / Black cat: Collins, Tommy / I chickened out: Loran, Kenny / Slow down brother: Huskey, Ferlin / I went rockin': Norris, Bobby / You mostest girl: Trammell, Bobby Lee
CD _____ BCD 15624
Bear Family / Jun '92 / Rollercoaster / Direct / CM / Swift / ADA.

THAT'LL FLAT GIT IT VOL. 4
They call me Willie: Barry, Billy / Wild one: Barry, Billy / My love is true: Barry, Billy / Baby I'm a king: Barry, Billy / Weepin' and wailin': Barry, Billy / On too much: Barry, Billy / Do the oop-poo-pah-doo: Dio, Ronnie / Love pains: Dio, Ronnie / Motorcycle: Balls, Billy / Till time stands still: Starr, Charlie / Sick and tired: Starr, Charlie / Black jack Joey: Starr, Charlie / Christmas twist: Starr, Charlie / One broken heart for sale: Blackwell, Otis
CD _____ BCD 15630
Bear Family / Apr '94 / Rollercoaster / Direct / CM / Swift / ADA.

THAT'LL FLAT GIT IT VOL. 6
All by myself: Hall, Roy / Rock it down to my house: Tubb, Justin / Alligator come across: Duff, Arlie / Wee Willie Brown: Graham, Lou / Hey babe let's go downtown: Therien, Joe Jnr. / Everybody's tryin' to be my baby: York Brothers / Morse code: Woody, Don / Juke joint Johnny: Sovine, Red / Don't stop now: Hall, Roy / Come back to me darling: Therien, Joe Jnr. / You gotta move: Smith, Chester / Knock knock: Allen, Rex / Crazy little guitar man: Foley, Red / Sputnik (satellite girl): Engler, Jerry / You're long gone: Therien, Joe Jnr. / Baby's gone: Claud, Vernon / Sweet Willie: Allen, Barbara / Move on: Hall, Roy / She wanna rock: Derksen, Arnie / Wheels: Therien, Joe Jnr. / Crazy chicken: Gallagher, James / Don't go baby (don't go): Coker, Al / School house rock: Harlan, Billy / Bring my cadillac back: Knightmares / Rockabilly boogie: Therien, Joe Jnr. / Poo-a-chicka: Mack, Warner / Cheat on me baby: Rockin' Saints / Tennessee Tody: Billy & Western Okies / One and only: Fontaine, Eddie / Shake baby shake: Raney, Wayne
CD _____ BCDAH 15733
Bear Family / Nov '94 / Rollercoaster / Direct / CM / Swift / ADA.

THAT'S CHRISTMAS
(2CD/MC Set)
I wish it could be Christmas every day: Wizzard / Happy Christmas (war is over): Len-

non, John & Yoko Ono / Step into Christmas: John, Elton / Pipes of peace: McCartney, Paul / Winter's tale: Essex, David / Gaudette: Steeleye Span / Do they know it's Christmas: Band Aid / Another rock'n'roll Christmas: Glitter, Gary / Little saint Nick: Beach Boys / December will be magic again: Bush, Kate / Mary's boy child: Boney M / In dulci jubilo: Oldfield, Mike / Fairy tale of New York: Pogues & Kirsty MacColl / Merry Christmas everyone: Stevens, Shakin' / I'll be coming home for Christmas: Beach Boys / Last Christmas: Wham / Wonderful Christmas time: McCartney, Paul / Lonely this Christmas: Mud / Stop the cavalry: Lewie, Jona / Driving home for Christmas: Rea, Chris / Ring out, solstice bells: Jethro Tull / Silent night: O'Connor, Sinead / White Christmas: Crosby, Bing / Little town: Richard, Cliff / When a child is born: Mathis, Johnny / Winter wonderland: Martin, Dean / Merry Christmas darling: Carpenters / Rockin' around the Christmas tree: Lee, Brenda / Christmas song: Cole, Nat King / Santa Claus is coming to town: Lee, Peggy / Do you hear what I hear: Crosby, Bing / Have yourself a merry little Christmas: Campbell, Glen / God rest ye merry gentlemen: Richard, Cliff / Little boy that Santa Claus forgot: Cole, Nat King / Walking in the air: Jones, Aled / O come all ye faithful (Adeste fidelis): Locke, Josef / We have all the time in the world: Armstrong, Louis / We wish you a Merry Christmas: Halle Orchestra / First nowell: King's College Cambridge Choir / Troika: London Philharmonic Orchestra / Sleigh ride: Halle Orchestra / Away in a manger: King's College Cambridge Choir / Puernatus est nobis (modo VII): Coro De Montes Del Monasterio Benedicto De Santo
CD Set _____ CDEMTV 88
EMI / Nov '94 / EMI.
CD Set _____ CDEMTVD 105
EMI / Nov '95 / EMI.

THAT'S COUNTRY
(2CD/MC Set)
Your cheating heart: Williams, Hank / I love you because: Reeves, Jim / El Paso: Robbins, Marty / Crying: Orbison, Roy / Weight: Band / Galveston: Campbell, Glen / Southern nights: Campbell, Glen / Everybody's talkin': Nilsson / Boy named Sue: Cash, Johnny / Help me make it through the night: Kristofferson, Kris / Take me home country roads: Newton-John, Olivia / More like the movies: Dr. Hook / I will always love you: Parton, Dolly / Always on my mind: Nelson, Willie / Crazy: Cline, Patsy / Stand by your man: Spears, Billie Jo / Take it to the limit: Bogguss, Suzy / Night they drove old Dixie down: Baez, Joan / Talking in your sleep: Gayle, Crystal / Angel of the morning: Newton, Juice / You're my best friend: Williams, Don / Horse with no name: America / Carolina on my mind: Taylor, James / Ruby, don't take your love to town: Rogers, Kenny / Most beautiful girl: Rich, Charlie / D.I.V.O.R.C.E.: Wynette, Tammy / From a distance: Griffith, Nanci / I'll never fall in love again: Gentry, Bobbie / Wind beneath my wings: Greenwood, Lee / Rose garden: Anderson, Lynn / Blue bayou: Ronstadt, Linda / Delta dawn: Tucker, Tanya / It not you: Dr. Hook / Achy breaky heart: Cyrus, Billy Ray / Here, there and everywhere: Harris, Emmylou / Brass buttons: Parsons, Gram / Feels so right: Alabama / What I've got in mind: Spears, Billie Jo
CD Set _____ CDEMTVD 103
EMI / Oct '95 / EMI.

THAT'S JAZZ
(2CD/MC Set)
Birdland: Weather Report / Morning dance: Spyro Gyra / Cantaloupe island: Hancock, Herbie / Have you ever had it blue: Style Council / Girl from Ipanema: Gilberto, Astrud / My baby just cares for me: Simone, Nina / Fever: Lee, Peggy / Thinking about your body: McFerrin, Bobby / At last: Rawls, Lou & Diana Reeves / Songbird: Kenny G. / Midnight at the Oasis: Muldaur, Maria / Lily was here: Stewart, David A. & Candy Dulfer / Walk on the wild side: Smith, Jimmy / Moanin': Blakey, Art / I wish I knew (how it would be to feel free): Taylor, Billy / Take five: Brubeck, Dave / Song for my father: Silver, Horace / Always there: Laws, Ronnie / Walkin' in rhythm: Blackbyrds / Change (makes you want to hustle): Byrd, Donald / Let's face the music: Cole, Nat King / Every time we say goodbye: Fitzgerald, Ella / We have all the time in the world: Armstrong, Louis / Mack the knife: Darin, Bobby / Body and soul: Manhattan Transfer / I've got the world on a string: O'Day, Anita / Love for sale: Franklin, Aretha / Passing strangers: Vaughan, Sarah & Billy Eckstine / Cry me a river: London, Julie / My funny valentine: Baker, Chet / Yesterday's: Davis, Miles / Tea in tain: Ellington, Duke / Ain't misbehavin': Waller, Fats / Call me irresponsible: Washington, Dinah / Stormy Monday blues: Basie, Count & Billy Eckstine / Summertime: Vaughan, Sarah / Misty: Garner, Erroll / Round midnight: Torme, Mel / Let there be love: Cole, Nat King / Chicago: Bennett, Tony
CD Set _____ CDEMTVD 104
EMI / Nov '95 / EMI.

THAT'S LOVE
(2CD/MC Set)
Goodnight girl: *Wet Wet Wet* / Three times a lady: *Commodores* / Tracks of my tears: *Robinson, Smokey & The Miracles* / Up were we belong: *Cocker, Joe & Jennifer Warnes* / Little time: *Beautiful South* / Don't be a stranger: *Carroll, Dina* / I'll make love to you: *Boyz II Men* / Endless love: *Richie, Lionel & Diana Ross* / One day in your life: *Jackson, Michael* / Reason to believe: *Stewart, Rod* / Without you: *Nilsson* / There must be an angel: *Eurythmics* / Million love songs: *Take That* / Why: *Lennox, Annie* / Stand by me: *King, Ben E.* / Waiting for a girl like you: *Foreigner* / When a man loves a woman: *Sledge, Percy* / I'll stand by you: *Pretenders* / Make it with you: *Bread* / Power of love: *Rush, Jennifer* / Slave to love: *Ferry, Bryan* / Alison: *Costello, Elvis* / Nothing compares 2 U: *O'Connor, Sinead* / Tender love: *Thomas, Kenny* / Suddenly: *Ocean, Billy* / Little bit more: *Dr. Hook* / It started with a kiss: *Hot Chocolate* / When you tell me that you love me: *Ross, Diana* / It must have been love: *Roxette* / Move closer: *Nelson, Phyllis* / Miss you nights: *Richard, Cliff* / My love: *McCartney, Paul & Wings* / Now and forever: *Marx, Richard* / She makes my day: *Palmer, Robert* / We have all the time in the world: *Armstrong, Louis* / This woman's world: *Bush, Kate* / God only knows: *Beach Boys* / Jessie: *Kadison, Joshua* / Unchained melody: *Righteous Brothers* / Let's stay together: *Turner, Tina*
CD Set _____ CDEMTVD 102
EMI / Nov '95 / EMI.

THAT'S ROCK 'N' ROLL
(2CD/MC Set)
C'mon everybody: *Cochran, Eddie* / Tutti frutti: *Little Richard* / Johnny B. Goode: *Berry, Chuck* / Rave on: *Crickets* / It's late: *Nelson, Rick* / Stagger Lee: *Price, Lloyd* / Be bop a lula: *Vincent, Gene* / Reveille rock: *Johnny & The Hurricanes* / I'm walkin': *Domino, Fats* / Tallahassie lassie: *Cannon, Freddy* / Willie and the hand jive: *Otis, Johnny Show* / I go ape: *Sedaka, Neil* / See you later alligator: *Haley, Bill & The Comets* / Fleet petite: *Wilson, Jackie* / Bony moronie: *Williams, Larry* / Chantilly lace: *Big Bopper* / Nutrocker: *B. Bumble & The Stingers* / Whole lotta woman: *Rainwater, Marvin* / Let's have a party: *Jackson, Wanda* / Runaround Sue: *Dion* / Tell Laura I love her: *Valence, Ricky* / Claudette: *Everly Brothers* / Donna: *Wilde, Marty* / Move it: *Richard, Cliff* / Whole lotta shakin' goin' on: *Lewis, Jerry Lee* / Rock around the clock: *Haley, Bill & The Comets* / Lucille: *Little Richard* / Weekend: *Cochran, Eddie* / Cannonball: *Eddy, Duane* / Sweet little sixteen: *Berry, Chuck* / Ain't that a shame: *Domino, Fats* / At the hop: *Danny & The Juniors* / High class baby: *Richard, Cliff* / Lonesome town: *Nelson, Rick* / Why do fools fall in love: *Lymon, Frankie & The Teenagers* / Dreamin': *Burnette, Johnny* / Hoots mon: *Lord Rockingham's XI* / Rock with the caveman: *Steele, Tommy* / Big man: *Four Preps* / Shakin' all over: *Kidd, Johnny & The Pirates* / Little bitty pretty one: *Harris, Thurston & The Sharps* / Walk don't run: *Ventures* / Blue moon: *Marcels* / La bamba: *Valens, Ritchie* / Pistol packin' mama: *Vincent, Gene* / Party doll: *Knox, Buddy* / Let there be drums: *Nelson, Sandy* / McDonald's cave: *Piltdown Men* / Halfway to paradise: *Fury, Billy* / Oh boy: *Holly, Buddy & The Crickets*
CD Set _____ CDEMTVD 100
EMI / Oct '95 / EMI.

THAT'S THE 70'S
(2CD/MC Set)
Hello hello I'm back again: *Glitter, Gary* / You to me are everything: *Real Thing* / Make me smile (come up and see me): *Harley, Steve & Cockney Rebel* / Blockbuster: *Sweet* / Down down: *Status Quo* / I will survive: *Gaynor, Gloria* / All right now: *Free* / Live and let die: *Wings* / Baker Street: *Rafferty, Gerry* / Gudbye't Jane: *Slade* / 20th Century boy: *T. Rex* / Sunday girl: *Blondie* / I'm not in love: *10cc* / Let's stick together: *Ferry, Bryan* / That's the way (I like it): *K.C. & The Sunshine Band* / Theme from Shaft: *Hayes, Isaac* / Go west: *Village People* / Maggie May: *Stewart, Rod* / Venus: *Shocking Blue* / I'm still waiting: *Ross, Diana* / Harvest for the world: *Isley Brothers* / Wuthering heights: *Bush, Kate* / Sylvia's mother: *Dr. Hook* / Lola Kinks / More than a woman: *Tavares* / Walk on the wild side: *Reed, Lou* / Angel fingers: *Wizzard* / Nutbush city limits: *Turner, Ike & Tina* / Rock your baby: *McCrae, George* / Saturday night's alright for fighting: *John, Elton* / Tiger feet: *Mud* / American pie: *McLean, Don* / All the young dudes: *Mott The People* / I want you back: *Jackson Five* / You can get it if you really want it: *Dekker, Desmond & The Aces* / Dancing in the city: *Marshall Hain* / So you win again: *Hot Chocolate* / School's out: *Cooper, Alice* / Wishing on a star: *Rose Royce* / Stay with me: *Faces & Rod Stewart*
CD Set _____ CDEMTVD 110
EMI / Nov '95 / EMI.

THELMA RECORD CO STORY, THE
(Legendary Detroit Soul)
Love is the only solution: *Star, Martha* / I'm a peace loving man: *Laskey, Emanuel* / Lucky to be loved by you: *Hargreaves, Silky* / I just cant leave you: *Inst* / You got the

---

best of me: *Hill, Eddie* / I just cant leave you: *Batiste, Rose* / Sorry ain't good enough: *Matthews, Joe* / I love you: *Inst* / Gonna cry a river: *Ward, Robert* / I've got to run for my life: *Laskey, Emanuel* / Someday: *Batiste, Rose* / Whirlpool: *Inst* / You better mend your ways: *Matthews, Joe* / No part time love for me: *Star, Martha* / Nobody loves me like my baby: *Gilford, Jimmy*
CD _____ GSCD 055
Goldmine / Nov '94 / Vital.

THEM DIRTY BLUES
(2CD Set)
Jass / Oct '91 / CM / Jazz Music / ADA / Cadillac / Direct.
CD Set _____ JASSCD 11/12

THEMES AND DREAMS
CD _____ RADCD 11
Global / Jun '95 / BMG.

THEMES FOR DREAMS
(The Magic Sound Of The Panpipes)
Light of experience / Bright eyes / Feelings / Miss you nights / White shade of pale / Don't cry for me Argentina / Love story / Ave Maria / Stranger on the shore / Annie's song / Concierto de aranjuez / You don't bring me flowers / Aria / Forever autumn / Sailing / Nights in white satin / Amazing grace / I can't stop loving you
CD _____ MCCD 156
Music Club / May '94 / Disc / THE / CM.

THEMES FROM VAPOURSPACE
CD _____ TRUCD 4
Internal / Jun '94 / PolyGram / Pinnacle.

THEN THAT'S WHAT THEY CALL DISCO
We got the funk: *Positive Force* / Lookin' for love tonight: *Fat Larry's Band* / Hi tension: *Hi-Tension* / Can you feel the force: *Real Thing* / You can do it: *One Way & Al Hudson* / Shake your groove thing: *Peaches & Herb* / Sir Dancealot: *Olympic Runners* / You make me feel (mighty real): *Sylvester* / Space bass: *Slick* / Get down: *Chandler, Gene* / Everything is great: *Inner Circle* / White lines (don't don't do it): *Grandmaster Flash & Melle Mel*
CD _____ CDELV 05
Debut / May '93 / Pinnacle / 3MV / Sony.

THERE ARE TOO MANY FOOLS FOLLOWING TOO MANY RULES
CD Set _____ 501 RDOOM2CD
Irdial / Jun '95 / Disc.

THERE IS SOME FUN GOING FORWARD
(Dandelion - Rarities)
Only do what is true: *Medicine Head* / Anticipation: *Ward, Clifford T.* / Pretty little girl: *Coxhill-Bedford Duo* / Neil's song: *Hart, Mike* / All ends up: *Tractor* / Fly high: *St. John, Bridget* / Sky dance: *Trevor, John* / Mama keep your big mouth shut: *Stackwaddy* / Colour is blue: *Country Sun* / Sand all yellow: *Coyne, Kevin* / Vorblifa exit: *Coxhill, Lol* / Fetch me my woman: *Siren* / War is over: *Siren* / Autumn lady dancing: *Principle Edward's Magic Theatre* / Early morning song: *St. John, Bridget* / Sleeping town: *Beau* / Girl form Ipanema: *Stackwaddy*
CD _____ SEECD 427
See For Miles/C5 / Jul '95 / Pinnacle.

THERE WHERE THE AVALANCHE STOPS
(Albanian Folk Festival)
CD _____ T 33.11
Touch / '90 / These / Kudos.

THERE'LL ALWAYS BE AN ENGLAND
(24 War-Time Songs From 1939)
There'll always be an England: *Loss, Joe* / Wishing: *Lynn, Vera* / We must all stick together: *Geraldo* / Sying the Tommies sang (Fall in and follow me/Hello, who's your lady friend/Mlle from Armentieres): *Stone, Lew* / Adolf: *Ambrose* / F.D.R. Jones: *Flanagan & Allen* / We're gonna hang out the washing on the Siegfried Line: *Waters, Elsie & Doris* / Handsome Territorial: *Gonella, Nat* / Till the lights of London shine again: *Henderson, Chick & Joe Loss* / They can't black out the moon: *Roy, Harry* / Kiss me goodnight, Sergeant Major: *Cotton, Billy* / We'll meet again: *Henderson, Chick & Joe Loss* / If a grey-haired lady says I love's yer fether: *Flanagan & Allen* / Wish me luck as you wave me goodbye: *Hylton, Jack* / Goodnight children everywhere: *Henderson, Chick & Joe Loss* / Wings over the navy: *Cotton, Billy* / Run rabbit run: *Flanagan & Allen* / I'm sending a letter to Santa Claus: *Fields, Gracie* / Nasty Uncle Adolf: *Ambrose* / Somewhere in France with you: *Henderson, Chick & Joe Loss* / Mother's prayer at twilight: *Lynn, Vera* / Rhymes of the times: *Ambrose*
CD _____ CD AJA 5069
Living Era / Feb '90 / Koch.

THERE'S A GRIOT GOING ON
CD _____ FMS 5029
Rogue / Jan '94 / Sterns.

THESE ARMS OF MINE
CD _____ YDG 74633
Yesterday's Gold / Feb '93 / Target/BMG.

THEY CALLED IT CROONING
(Recordings From 1928-1932)
Where the blue of the night meets the gold of the day: *Crosby, Bing* / Cheerful little earful: *Ellis, Segar* / My song: *Bullock, Chick* /

She's a new kind of old-fashioned girl: *Smith, Jack* / Got a date with an angel: *O'Malley, Pat* / Living in dreams: *Columbo, Russ* / Orange blossom time: *Edwards, Cliff* / She's wonderful: *Shalson, Harry* / Am I blue: *Bellew, Smith* / Here lies love: *Brownie, Sam* / Thrill is gone: *Vallee, Rudy* / Ain't misbehavin': *Austin, Gene* / My sweet Virginia: *Bowlly, Al* / Please: *Rosing, Val* / Little by little: *Marvin, Johnny* / You're a real sweetheart: *Coslow, Sam* / Sweet Sue, just you: *Metaxa, George* / Thank your father: *Richman, Harry*
CD _____ CD AJA 5026
Living Era / Koch.

THEY PLAYED THE HACKNEY EMPIRE
Summer sweetheart: *Cortez, Leon & His Coster Band/Dorren Harris* / Beer barrel polka: *Cortez, Leon & His Coster Band/Guv'nor & The Boys* / He said Kiss Me: *O'Shea, Tessie & Her Banjulele & Orchestra* / Hymie and Amy sing sing: *O'Shea, Tessie & Her Banjulele & Orchestra* / Serenade in the night: *Loss, Joe & His band* / When the poppies bloom: *Loss, Joe & His band* / Again: *Loss, Joe & His band* / Did I remember: *Loss, Joe & His band* / Forty four thousand and five: *Sarony, Leslie & Leslie Holmes* / Cut yourself a little piece of cake: *Sarony, Leslie & Leslie Holmes* / He's an angel: *Masters, Kitty & Orchestra* / Ready for the river: *Gonella, Nat & His Georgians* / Deep river: *Gonella, Nat & His Georgians* / Two rivers flow through: *Gonella, Nat & His Georgians* / Harlem: *Gonella, Nat & His Georgians* / Sandy furnishes the home: *Powell, Sandy & Company* / Arp experience: *Miller, Max* / Grand old man: *Miller, Max* / Swimming instructor: *Miller, Max* / Georgia's got a moon: *Roy, Harry* / I'm looking for the Sheik Of Araby: *Millward, Sid & His Nitwits* / Good morning: *Murgatroyd & Winterbottom* / Lonesome trail ain't lonesome anymore: *Campbell, Big Bill* / London pride: *Waters, Elsie & Doris* / Button up your shoes and dance: *Wall, Max* / My All: *Tarri, Suzette* / Stormy weather: *Carless, Dorothy* / Lady of Spain: *Geraldo & His Gaucho Tango Orchestra*
CD _____ RAJCD 848
Empress / May '95 / THE.

THEY SHALL NOT PASS
Lean on me: *Redskins* / Unionize: *Redskins* / Adrenochrome: *Sisters Of Mercy* / Body electric: *Sisters Of Mercy* / Mindless violence: *Newtown Neurotics* / Kick out the tories: *Newtown Neurotics* / Pink headed bug: *Three Johns* / Men like monkeys: *Three Johns*
CD _____ AABT 400CD
Abstract / Jul '91 / Pinnacle / Total/BMG.

THIN ICE 2
(The Second Shiver)
Telstar / Aug '91 / BMG.
CD _____ STCD 2535

THING CALLED LOVE
Dreaming with my eyes open: *Walker, Clay* / You'd be home by now: *Norwood, Daron* / I can't understand: *Yearwood, Trisha* / I don't remember your name (But I remember you): *Oslin, K.T.* / Diamonds and tears: *Berg, Matraca* / Ready and waiting: *Allen, Deborah* / Until now: *Crowell, Rodney* / Looking for a thing called love: *Robbins, Dennis* / Streets of love: *Welch, Kevin* / Partners in wine: *Travis, Randy* / Blame it on your heart: *Allen, Deborah* / Standing on a rock: *Crowell, Rodney*
CD _____ 74321157932
Giant / Apr '94 / BMG.

THINGS WE SAY FOR LOVE
Everybody's talkin': *Nilsson, Harry* / Light my fire: *Feliciano, Jose* / Cherish: *Kool & The Gang* / Never knew love like this before: *Mills, Stephanie* / Right time of the night: *Warnes, Jennifer* / Whistle down the wind: *Heyward, Nick* / Everyday hurts: *Sad Cafe* / Things we do for love: *10cc* / All the love in the world: *Warwick, Dionne* / Answer me: *Dickson, Barbara* / Give me the reason: *Vandross, Luther* / Look of love: *ABC* / Midnight lady: *Gaye, Marvin* / Weak in the presence of beauty: *Moyet, Alison* / Love really hurts without you: *Ocean, Billy* / Sign your name: *D'Arby, Terence Trent* / Best of my love: *Emotions* / Sweetest taboo: *Sade*
CD _____ STACD 008
Stardust / Nov '91 / Carlton Home Entertainment.

THINKING OF YOU
Here we are: *Estefan, Gloria* / Fool (if you think it's over): *Brooks, Elkie* / I'll never fall in love again: *Deacon Blue* / Promise me: *Craven, Beverley* / Two out of three ain't bad: *Meat Loaf* / All cried out: *Moyet, Alison* / Everytime you go away: *Young, Paul* / Neither one of us: *Knight, Gladys & The Pips* / If you were here tonight: *O'Neal, Alexander* / Sorry seems to be the hardest word: *John, Elton* / Ain't no sunshine: *Withers, Bill* / Blue velvet: *Vinton, Bobby* / Stay with me 'til dawn: *Tzuke, Judie* / How am I supposed to live without you: *Bolton, Michael* / Eternal flame: *Bangles* / Let's stay together: *Green, Al* / Still: *Commodores*
CD _____ MOODCD 15
CBS / Feb '91 / Sony.

THIS AIN'T TRIP HOP
CD _____ MM 800212
Moonshine / Feb '95 / Disc.

THIS AIN'T TRIP HOP 2
CD _____ MM 800392
Moonshine / Oct '95 / Disc.

THIS BRUTAL HOUSE
Tighten up: *Wally 'Jump' Jnr* / House that Jack built: *Jack 'n' Chill* / Who's gonna ease the pressure: *Thornhill, Mac* / Love won't turn around: *Farley Jackmaster Funk* / Turn up the bass: *Tyree* / Tired of getting pushed around: *Two Men, A Drum Machine & A Trumpet* / Pump up the volume: *M/A/R/R/S* / Jack the groove: *Raze* / Beat dis: *Bomb The Bass* / Theme from S'Express: *S'Express* / Rok da house: *Beatmasters* / I'll house you: *Richie Rich & Jungle Bros*
CD _____ OG 3304 CD
Carlton Home Entertainment / Oct '92 / Carlton Home Entertainment.

THIS HOUSE IS NOT A MOTEL
CD _____ EFA 4481 CD
Glitterhouse / Jul '89 / Direct / ADA.

THIS IS 2 KOOL
CD _____ TKCD 1
2 Kool / Mar '95 / SRD.

THIS IS BLACK TOP
I can't stop loving you: *Fundeburgh, Anson & Sam Myers* / Iron cupid: *King, Earl* / That certain door: *Eaglin, Snooks* / Woman's gotta have it: *Neville Brothers* / Stick around: *Radcliff, Bobby* / Can't call you no: *Sumlin, Hubert & Mighty Sam* / Lemonade: *Fundeburgh, Anson & Sam Myers* / Young girl: *Eaglin, Snooks* / If I don't get involved: *Welch, Michael* / Joe & Grady Gaines* / Hello sundown: *Davis, James 'Thunderbird'* / Party in Nogales: *Levy, Ron*
CD _____ BTSCD 1
Black Top / Dec '89 / CM / Direct / ADA.

THIS IS DANCEHALL
Sugar Wogga man: *Griffiths, Marcia* / How else can I ease the pain: *Haughton, Anthony* / Best friends: *Singing Melody* / My love: *Paul, Frankie* / Every kinda people: *Kevin B* / Sax-a-rock: *Johnson, Jerry* / Send down some: *Reverend Badoo* / Work it out: *J.R. Demus* / Struggle: *Ravon* / Science: *Shaggy* / New talk: *Dollar Man* / Pretty girls: *Judas* / Love's gone: *White Mice* / Dub dis': *Livin' Crew*
CD _____ CDCTUM 1
Continuum / Jun '93 / Pinnacle.

THIS IS DANCEHALL VOL. 4
CD _____ CDCTUM 6
Continuum / Dec '93 / Pinnacle.

THIS IS DISCO
(2CD Set)
Hotshot: *Young, Karen* / Is it all over my face: *Loose Joints* / Don't make me wait: *Peech Boys* / Heartbeat times: *McCall Allie* / Rescue me: *Thomas, Sybil* / Another man: *Mason, Barbara* / Heartbeat: *Gardner, Taana*
CD _____ CDSTROB 1
Street Sounds / Oct '88 / BMG.

THIS IS HIP HOP
Ultrasound / Feb '95 / Grapevine.
CD _____ USCD 002

THIS IS IT
Music Club / Mar '95 / Disc / THE / CM.
CD _____ MCCD 196

THIS IS JUNGLE
Ultrasound / Sep '94 / Grapevine.
CD _____ USCD 001

THIS IS MERSEYBEAT
Edsel / Feb '91 / Pinnacle / ADA.
CD _____ EDCD 070

THIS IS MOD VOL.1 - RARITIES 1979-1981
Opening up: *Circles* / Billy: *Circles* / We can go dancing: *Amber Squad* / You should see what I do to you in my dreams: *Amber Squad* / Can't sleep at night: *Cigarettes* / It's the only way to live: *Cigarettes* / All I want is your money: *Cigarettes* / I've forgotten my number: *Cigarettes* / They're back again: *Cigarettes* / Choose you: *Deadbeats* / Julies new boyfriend: *Deadbeats* / Oh no: *Deadbeats* / Nobody loves me: *Letters* / Don't want you back: *Letters* / Happy song: *Nips* / Nobody to love: *Nips* / Saturday night: *Odds* / Not another love song: *Odds* / Circles: *Circles* / Summer nights: *Circles*
CD _____ CDMGRAM 98
Anagram / Oct '95 / Pinnacle.

THIS IS NORTHERN SOUL
Silent treatment: *Demain, Arin* / My sugar baby: *Clark, Connie* / Double cookin': *Checkerboard Squares* / I've got to get myself together: *Turner, Spyder* / Love makes me lonely: *Chandlers* / Walk with me heart: *Smith, Bobby* / Emperor of my baby's heart: *Harris, Kurt* / Nobody knows: *Wonder, Dianna* / You're on top girl: *Empires* / Are you angry: *Servicemen* / No right to cry: *Galore, Mamie* / So sweet so satisfying: *Treetop, Bobby* / Not me baby: *Silhouettes* / Love's just begun: *Grayson, Calvin* / Falling in love with you baby: *Cook, Little Joe* / Those lonely nights: *Soul Communicators* / Bar track: *Burdock, Doni* / He broke your game wide open: *Deil, Frank* / I've had it: *Andrews, Lee* / I'll always love you: *Moultrie, Sam* / Sister Lee: *Ward, Sam* / Prove your-

THIS IS NORTHERN SOUL
self a lady: Bounty, James / Psychedelic soul: Russell, Saxie
CD _____ GSCD 014
Goldmine / Jun '93 / Vital.

THIS IS NOT A LOVE COLLECTION
This is not a love song: Public Image Ltd / Ever fallen in love: Buzzcocks / Walk on by: Stranglers / Forget about you: Motors / Jilted John: Jilted John / (I'm always touched by your) presence dear: Blondie / Mary of the fourth form: Boomtown Rats / Is she really going out with him: Jackson, Joe / Another girl another planet: Only Ones / Little girl: Banned / Julie Ocean: Undertones / Whole wide world: Wreckless Eric / Love song: Damned / Wake up and make love with me: Dury, Ian / Morning of our lives: Modern Lovers / Have I the right: Dead End Kids / Irene: Photos / Automatic lover: Vibrators / Young Parisians: Adam & The Ants
CD _____ VSOPCD 193
Connoisseur / Feb '94 / Pinnacle.

THIS IS OI
(A Street Punk Compilation)
CD _____ AHOYCD 6
Captain Oi / Sep '93 / Plastic Head.

THIS IS SCOTLAND
Hundred thousand welcomes / Amazing grace / Come to the Ceilidah-John Worth's jig / Dancing in Kyle / Abide with me / Massacre of Glencoe / Jaqueline waltz / Always Argyil / Punch bowl reel / Archaracle midgie / Bonnie Mary of Argyle / Skyline of Skye / Reels / 4/4 marches
CD _____ CDITV 354
Scotdisc / Aug '88 / Duncans / Ross / Conifer.

THIS IS SKA
Al Capone: Prince Buster / Liquidator: Harry J All Stars / Gangsters: Special AKA / 007: Dekker, Desmond / Double barrel: Collins, Dave & Ansil / Irie feelings: Edwards, Rupie / Sweet sensation: Melodians / Wet dream: Romeo, Max / Train to skaville: Ethiopians / Guns of Navarone: Skatalites / Return of Django: Upsetters / Dat: Pluto / Longshot kick de bucket: Pioneers / Tears of a clown: Beat / Red red wine: Tribe, Tony / Montego Bay: Note, Freddie & Rudies / Big 7: Judge Dread / Suzanne beware of the devil: Livingstone, Dandy / Monkey man: Toots & The Maytals / Elizabethan reggae: Gardiner, Boris
CD _____ TCD 2366
Telstar / Jun '89 / BMG.

THIS IS SOUL
CD _____ AVC 501
Avid / Dec '92 / Avid/BMG / Koch.

THIS IS SOUL
(A Collection Of Soul Smashes)
Soul man: Sam & Dave / Knock on wood: Floyd, Eddie / That's the way I feel about cha: Womack, Bobby / Ruler of my heart: Thomas, Irma / Rainy night in Georgia: Benton, Brook / What you see is what you get: Joe / Hello stranger: Lewis, Barbara / If you need me: Burke, Solomon / Patches: Carter, Clarence / Rescue me: Fontella Bass / Gimme little sign: Wood, Brenton / Walking the dog: Thomas, Rufus / Turn back the hand of time: Davis, Tyrone / B-A-B-Y: Thomas, Carla / Troilodyte: Castor, Jimmy Bunch / Snake: Wilson, Al
CD _____ CDCD 1026
Charly / Mar '93 / Charly / THE / Cadillac.

THIS IS SOUL
Dance to the music: Sly & The Family Stone / Love the one you're with: Isley Brothers / Grazing in the grass: Friends Of Distinction / Rescue me: Fontella Bass / You little trustmaker: Tymes / Back stabbers: O'Jays / Native New Yorker: Odyssey / K-jee: Nite Liters / I can understand it: New Birth / To each his own: Faith, Hope & Charity / Whispering: Dr. Buzzard's Original Savannah Band / Everybody plays the fool: Main Ingredient / Lean on me: Withers, Bill / La la means I love you: Delfonics / I wanna get next to you: Rose Royce / Don't walk away: General Johnson / I'm your puppet: Purify, James & Bobby / Hey there lonely girl: Holman, Eddie
CD _____ 74321275262
Arista / May '95 / BMG.

THIS IS SOUL II
CD _____ AVC 516
Avid / Dec '92 / Avid/BMG / Koch.

THIS IS SOUL VOL.2
Higher and higher: Wilson, Jackie / One monkey don't stop no show: Tex, Joe / Lipstick traces: Spellman, Benny / I cried my last tear: K-Doe, Ernie / You're no good: Everett, Betty / Hey girl don't bother me: Tams / I'd rather go blind: James, Etta / Any day now: Jackson, Chuck / He will break your heart: Butler, Jerry / Summertime: Stewart, Billy / Soulful dress: Desanto, Sugar Pie / Reconsider me: Adams, Johnny / Every little bit hurts: Scott, Peggy / Hurt: Yuro, Timi / Boo hoo hoo: Burke, Solomon / When a man loves a woman: Sledge, Percy / Barefootin': Parker, Robert / Dresses too short: Johnson, Syl / Ruler of my heart: Thomas, Irma / Looking for a love: Womack, Bobby
CD _____ CDCD 1176
Charly / Apr '94 / Charly / THE / Cadillac.

THIS IS THE BLUES
(24 Electric Blues Hits)
Mona: Diddley, Bo / You can't judge a book by the cover: Diddley, Bo / I'm a man: Diddley, Bo / Who do you love: Diddley, Bo / Spoonful: Howlin' Wolf / Smokestack lightnin': Howlin' Wolf / Help me: Williamson, Sonny Boy / I'd rather go blind: James, Etta / Rock me baby: James, Etta / Almost grown: Berry, Chuck / Memphis: Berry, Chuck / I just want to make love to you: Waters, Muddy / Hoochie coochie man: Waters, Muddy / Baby, please don't go: Waters, Muddy / I've got my mojo working: Waters, Muddy / Let's work together: Harrison, Wilbert / Nadine: James, Elmore / Dust my broom: James, Elmore / Bright lights big city: Reed, Jimmy / Dimples: Hooker, John Lee / Boom boom: Hooker, John Lee / Born under a bad sign: King, Albert / Hi-heel sneakers: Tucker, Tommy
CD _____ PLATCD 3909
Platinum Music / Oct '90 / Prism / Ross.

THIS IS THE SOUND OF TRIBAL UNITED KINGDOM
Get your hands off my man (Fire Island Remix): Vasquez, Junior / Y (Original Fuzzy Fruit Mix): Kiwi Dreams & Darrell Martin / What am I gonna do with you (Rushmore Attack That Track): Wood, Matt / Nervaas (Original Mix): Vasquez, Junior & The Spastic Babies / Bottom heavy (Original Mix): Tenaglia, Danny / K-scope theme (Album Mix): Kupper, Eric / Beams of light (Voice In The Jungle Mix): Banton, Pato / Feeling free (Masters And Servants Mix): Liquid City / Are you satisfied (Tao Of def Mix And Bad Yard Dub (CD & MC)): Daou / Sound Factory Mix (CD & MC)): Vasquez, Junior / Beams of light (Depth of an ocean's love) (CD & MC): Banton, Pato / U dig (U Dig Mix & Pacific Dub (CD & MC)): Eastmen / Little hot body (Erotic Vocal Mix (CD & MC)): Misbehavin' & Joi Cardwell / Montobi's raindance (CD & MC): Sextravaganza / Love and contradiction (CD & MC): Lost Children / Horn ride: E-N
CD _____ TRIUK 001CD
Tribal UK / Jul '94 / Vital.

THIS IS THE SOUND OF TRIBAL UNITED KINGDOM 2
Get your hands off my man: Vasquez, Junior / Sugar pie guy: Club 69 / That's what I got: Liberty City / Horn ride: E-N / There will a day: Absolute Us / Love to heart: Atom / Love breakdown: Streetlife / Only you: Balo / Storm: Salt City Orchestra / Wear the hat: Deep Dish / Story of my life: Hidden Agenda / I believe: Absolute Us / Love songs: Chocolate City / It all begins here: Ofunwa / Look ahead: Tenaglia, Danny / What do you want: Fallout / Cassade X: Elastic Reality / Organism: K-Scope / In the presence of angels: Spiritual Experience / After hours: Quench DC / Love yourself to you: Daou / Love is the message: Club 69 / World of plenty: Tenaglia, Danny
CD _____ TRIUK 010CDX
CD _____ TRIUK 010CD
Tribal UK / Oct '95 / Vital.

THIS YEARS LOVE
Think twice: Dion, Celine / Back for good: Take That / Stay another day: East 17 / Oh baby I: Eternal / Missing: Everything But The Girl / No more I love you's: Lennox, Annie / Love me for a reason: Boyzone / If you love me: Brownstone / I'll find you: Gayle, Michelle / I'll make love to you: Boyz II Men / Your body's callin': Boyz II Men / Always and forever: Vandross, Luther / Hold me thrill me kiss me: Estefan, Gloria / Chains: Arena, Tina / Jesse: Kadison, Joshua / You gotta be: Des'ree / Search for the hero: M People / Independent love song: Scarlet / Unchained melody: Robson & Jerome / Careless whisper: Michael, George
CD _____ MOODCD 42
Sony Music / Nov '95 / Sony.

THOSE FABULOUS FORTIES
Boogie woogie bugle boy: Andrews Sisters / It's a sin to tell a lie: Ink Spots / Golden wedding: Herman, Woody / For me and my gal: Garland, Judy / There, I've said it again: Monroe, Vaughan / Frenesi: Shaw, Artie / Chica chica boom chic: Miranda, Carmen / Paper doll: Mills Brothers / Honey hush: Waller, Fats & his Rhythm Orchestra / Skylark: James, Harry / Daybreak: Dorsey, Tommy / My adobe hacienda: Baker, Kenny / Harlem nocturne: Anthony, Ray / Fools rush in: Martin, Tony / In the mood: Miller, Glenn / Tangerine: Dorsey, Jimmy
CD _____ HADCD 159
Javelin / May '94 / THE / Henry Hadaway Organisation.

THOSE WERE THE DAYS
CD _____ KWCD 809
Disky / Jul '94 / THE / BMG / Discovery / Pinnacle.

THOUGHTS OF COUNTRY
Stand beside me: O'Donnell, Daniel / Almost persuaded: Kirwan, Dominic / Jennifer Johnson and me: Flavin, Mick / Dear God: Duff, Mary / Four in the morning: Pride, Charley / You old friends do: Begley, Philomena / Back in love by Monday: Lynam, Ray / Still got a crush on you: Hogan, John

/ Daisy chain: Begley, Philomena & Mick Flavin / Apologising roses: Spears, Billie Jo / Queen of the Silver Dollar: Begley, Philomena / Travellin' light: Flavin, Mick / Amy's eyes: Pride, Charley / Forever and ever Amen: Duff, Mary / Just between you and me: Begley, Philomena & Mick Flavin / I'm no stranger to the rain: Curtis, Sonny / Take good care of her: O'Donnell, Daniel / Don't fight the feeling: Hogan, John / Sweethearts in heaven: Margo / Sea of heartbreak: Kirwan, Dominic
CD _____ RITZRCD 518
Ritz / May '92 / Pinnacle.

THOUGHTS OF IRELAND
Summertime in Ireland: O'Donnell, Daniel / Isle of Innisfree: Foster & Allen / Beautiful meath: Duff, Mary / Golden dreams: Kirwan, Dominic / Shanagolden: Margo / Home to Donegal: Flavin, Mick / Red is the rose: Begley, Philomena / Spancil Hill: Duff, Mary / If we only had old Ireland over here: McCaffrey, Frank / Carrickfergus: Quinn, Brendan / Girl from Wexford town: Flavin, Mick / Bunch of thyme: Foster & Allen / Galway Bay: Begley, Philomena / Give an Irish girl to me: Nerney, Declan / Noreen Bawn: Kirwan, Dominic / Moonlight in Mayo: McCaffrey, Frank / Lady from Glenfarne: Quinn, Brendan / Rose of Allendale: Morrisey, Louise / Forty miles to Donegal: Margo / Sing me an old Irish song: O'Donnell, Daniel
CD _____ RITZRCD 519
Ritz / May '92 / Pinnacle.

THOUGHTS OF YESTERDAY
I need you: O'Donnell, Daniel / Do what you do do well: Pride, Charley / Crazy: Duff, Mary / More than I can say: Curtis, Sonny / Maggie: Foster & Allen / Before the next teardrop falls: Kirwan, Dominic / Pal of my cradle days: Gloria / Seven lonely days: Spears, Billie Jo / Sentimental old you: Begley, Philomena / More than yesterday: McCaffrey, Frank / Roses are red: O'Donnell, Daniel / China doll: Hogan, John / Say you'll stay until tomorrow: Kirwan, Dominic / After all these years: Foster & Allen / Ramblin' rose: Pride, Charley / Little things mean a lot: Dana / It's over: McCaffrey, Frank / Yellow roses: Duff, Mary / He stopped loving her today: Lynam, Ray / Old flames: Begley, Philomena
CD _____ RITZRCD 520
Ritz / Apr '92 / Pinnacle.

THRACE ANTHOLOGY VOL.3
(Bulgaria)
CD _____ 274977
La Chant Du Monde / Jan '95 / Harmonia Mundi / ADA.

THRASH THE WALL
CD _____ RR 93932
Roadrunner / Mar '90 / Pinnacle.

THREADGILL'S SUPPER SESSION
CD _____ WM 1013CD
Watermelon / May '94 / ADA / Direct.

THREE FROM THE FRONTLINE SERIES
CD Set _____ TPAK 14
Virgin / Oct '90 / EMI.

THREE MINUTE HEROES
CD _____ VTCD 9
Virgin Television / Feb '92 / EMI.

THREE SHADES OF THE BLUES
CD _____ BCD 107
Biograph / '92 / Wellard / ADA / Hot Shot / Jazz Music / Cadillac / Direct.

THREE STEPS TO HEAVEN
CD _____ QTVCD 011
Quality / Aug '92 / Pinnacle.

THREE WAY MIRROR
Treme terra / Misturada / Return / Threeway mirror / San Francisco River / Starting over again / Lilia / Plane to the trane
CD _____ RR 24CD
Reference Recordings / Sep '91 / May Audio.

THREE WORLDS OF TRIKOLA, THE
(The Collection)
CD _____ 3201932
Trikola / Jul '92 / New Note.

THUNDERBOLT
(Searing RNB Sax Instrumentals)
Paradise rock / Thunderbolt / Paradise roll / Fish bait / Melancholy horn / Jay bird / Strollin' out / Flying with the king / King is blue / Big wind / Royal crown blues / Sweet Georgia Brown / Easy ridin' / Joyride
CD _____ FLYCD 29
Flyright / Apr '91 / Hot Shot / Wellard / Jazz Music / CM.

THUNDERDOME - THE MEGAMIX
CD _____ AR 9902205
Arcade / May '94 / Sony / Grapevine.

THUNDERDOME VI - FROM HELL TO EARTH
CD Set _____ AR 9902212
Arcade / Nov '94 / Sony / Grapevine.

THUNDERING DRAGON
CD _____ SM 1519CD
Wergo / Oct '94 / Harmonia Mundi / ADA / Cadillac.

TIBETAN BUDDHISM - RITUAL ORCHESTRA/CHANTS
CD _____ 7559720712
Elektra Nonesuch / Jan '95 / Warner Music.

TIBETAN RITUAL MUSIC
CD _____ LYRCD 7181
Lyrichord / '91 / Roots / ADA / CM.

TIGER RAG
CD _____ PHONTCD 7619
Phontastic / '93 / Wellard / Jazz Music / Cadillac.

TIGHTEN UP VOL. 1 & 2
Tighten up: Perry, Lee 'Scratch' / Kansas City: Landis, Joya / Spanish Harlem: Bennett, Val / Place in the sun: Isaacs, David / Win your love: Penny, George A. / Donkey returns: Brother Dan Allstars / Ob la di ob la da: Bond, Joyce / Angel of the morning: Landis, Joya / Fat man: Morgan, Derrick / Soul limbo: Lee, Byron / Mix it up: Kingstonians / Watch this squad: Uniques / Longshot kick de bucket: Pioneers / John Hones: Mills, Rudy / Fire corner: Eccles, Clancy / Wreck a buddy: Soul Sisters / Reggae in your jeggae: Livingstone, Dandy / Fattie fattie: Eccles, Clancy / Return of Django: Upsetters / Sufferer: Kingstonians / Moonlight lover: Landis, Joya / Come into my parlour: Bleechers / Them a laugh and a ki ki: Soulmates / Live injection: Upsetters
CD _____ CDTRL 306
Trojan / Mar '94 / Jetstar / Total/BMG.

TIGHTEN UP VOL. 3 & 4
Monkey man / Shocks of mighty / Freedom Street / Raining in my heart / Man from Carolina / Leaving Rome / Singer man / Suffering / Herbsman / Barbwire / Stay a little bit longer / Queen of the world / Blood and fire / Johnny too bad / Selah / One eye enos / Hard life / I shall sing / Grooving out on life / Starvation / Bush doctor / Good ambition / I got it / Stand by your man
CD _____ CDTRL 307
Trojan / Mar '94 / Jetstar / Total/BMG.

TIGHTEN UP VOL. 5 & 6
Better must come: Wilson, Delroy / In paradise: Edwards, Jackie & Julie Anne / Hello mother: Dynamites / Rod of correction: Eccles, Clancy / Ripe cherry: Alcapone, Dennis / Three in one: Dunkley, Errol / Joy to the world: Julien & The Chosen Few / Know Far I: Herman, Bongo & Bunny / It's you: Toots & The Maytals / Bridge over troubled water: London, Jimmy / Shaft: Chosen Few / Duppy conqueror: Marley, Bob & The Wailers / Pitta patta: Smith, Ernie / Do your thing: Chosen Few / Breezing: Chung, Mikie / As long as you love me: Maytones / Down side up: Harry J All Stars / Suzanne beware of the devil: Livingstone, Dandy / Struggling man: Cimarons / Redemption song: Toots & The Maytals / Hot bomb: I-Roy & The Jumpers / President mash up the resident: Shortie / Who told you so: Edwards, Jackie / Unite tonight: Eccles, Clancy
CD _____ CDTRL 320
Trojan / Mar '94 / Jetstar / Total/BMG.

'TIL THE NIGHT IS GONE
(A Doc Pomus Tribute)
CD _____ 8122718782
Warner Bros. / Apr '95 / Warner Music.

TIME CAPSULE VOLUME 1
CD Set _____ CHIMIKCD 1
Hos Wasp / Nov '95 / Total/BMG.

TIME FOR LOVE
(More Songs For Lovers)
It's time for love: Chi-Lites / Zoom: Fat Larry's Band / Time in a bottle: Croce, Jim / Now is the time: James, Jimmy / I can see clearly now: Knight, Gladys / Hot love: Marie, Kelly / Girls: Moments / Can't get by without you: Real Thing / Night to remember: Shalamar / Purely by coincidence: Sweet Sensation / Band of gold: Sylvester / Pillow talk: Sylvia / Hold back the night: Trammps / And the beat goes on: Whispers / I get the sweetest feeling: Wilson, Jackie / It's in his kiss (Shoop shoop song): Everett, Betty / She'd rather be with me: Turtles / Gimme little sign: Wood, Brenton / Caroline goodbye: Blunstone, Colin
CD _____ TRTCD 159
TrueTrax / Jan '96 / THE.

TIME FOR LOVING, A
CD Set _____ NSCD 005
Newsound / Feb '95 / THE.

TIME WARP DUB CLASH
Indiana James (man next door): Paragons / Whip that tarantula (moulding): Ijahman Levi / Monkey is a spy: Black Uhuru / Pit of snakes (social living): Burning Spear / Well of souls (feel the spirit): Wailing Souls / Dub of gold (heart made of stone): Viceroys / Who's in the tomb (guess who's coming to dinner): Black Uhuru / Convoy hijack (sponji reggae): Black Uhuru / Bazooka blast (Fort Augustus): Delgado, Junior / Fire and brimstone (journey): Black Uhuru / Dub so hard: Mad Professor / Absentee: Manasseh / Smiling dub: Jah Shaka / One prayer: Alpha & Omega / Mixman: Zulu Warriors / Kumbia dub: Jah Shaka / Warrior dance: Mixman / Rastafari: Alpha & Omega / What happened: Dub Syndicate
CD _____ CIDM 1105
Mango / Jan '94 / Vital / PolyGram.

TIMELESS COMPILATION
CD _____ PWMCD 1
Total / Oct '89 / Total/BMG.

TIMELESS TRADITIONAL JAZZ FESTIVAL
Schlafe mein prinzchen: Bue, Papa Viking Jazz Band / Muskrat ramble: Collie, Max & his Rhythm Aces / Mood indigo: Ball, Kenny & His Jazzmen / Bourbon Street Parade: Dutch Swing College Band / Flyin' house: Dr. Dixie / That's a plenty: Prowizorka Dzez Bed / Stranger on the shore: Bilk, Acker & His Paramount Jazz Band / Struttin' with some barbecue: Down Town Jazzband / Ice cream: Sunshine, Monty Jazz Band / Basin Street blues: Sunshine, Monty Jazz Band / Jumpin' at the Woodside: Jansens, Huub / World is waiting for the sunrise: Jansens, Huub / Bye and bye: Boutte, Lillian / Petite fleur: Lightfoot, Terry / West End blues: Barber, Chris & Rod Mason's Hot Five / At the Jazz Band Ball: World's Greatest Jazz Band / Jambalaya: Barber, Chris & his Jazz Band / As I go to the Quick River: Uralski All Stars
CD Set _____ CDTTD 522-23
Timeless Traditional / Jul '94 / New Note.

TIP OF THE ICEBERG
CD _____ REACTCD 028
React / Nov '93 / Vital.

TIROLER-ABEND
CD _____ 499422
Koch / Jul '91 / Koch.

TO THE BEAT Y'ALL - OLD SCHOOL RAP
Rapper's delight: Sugarhill Gang / Radio commercial: Sugarhill Gang / That's the joint: Funky 4 Plus 1 / Adventures of grandmaster flash on the wheels of steel: Grandmaster Flash / Good times: Grandmaster Flash / Another one bites the dust: Grandmaster Flash / Rapture: Grandmaster Flash / Flash to the beat: Grandmaster Flash / White lines (don't don't do it): Grandmaster Flash & Melle Mel / Drop the bomb: Trouble Funk / Pump me up: Trouble Funk / Hey fellas: Trouble Funk / Freedom: Grandmaster Flash & The Furious Five / Message: Grandmaster Flash & The Furious Five / It's nasty (genius of love): Grandmaster Flash & The Furious Five / Scorpio: Grandmaster Flash & The Furious Five / Spoonin' rap: Gee, Spoonie / And you know that: Sequence / Funk you up: Sequence / To the beat y'all: Lady B / Super wolf can do it: Super-Wolf / Eighth Wonder: Sugarhill Gang / Monster jam: Spoonie Gee & The Sequence / Yes we can-can: Treacherous Three / Break dancin': West Street Mob / Electric boogie: West Street Mob / Busy bee's groove: Busy Bee / Making cash money: Busy Bee / Jesse: Grandmaster Flash & Melle Mel / Message II (Survival): Melle Mel & Duke Bootee / We are known as emcees (we turn the party out): Crash Crew / Breaking bells (take me to the mardi gras): Crash Crew / Scratching: Crash Crew / Check it out: Wayne & Charlie / All night long (Waterbed): Kevie Kev / Mirda rock: Griffin, Reggie / King heroin: Funky Four / Mayor: Melle Mel
CD _____ NXTCD 217
Sequel / Oct '92 / BMG.

TODO TANGO
CD _____ 188232
Milan / Nov '94 / BMG / Silva Screen.

TODOS ESTOS ANOS
CD _____ 21067CD
Sonifolk / Nov '95 / ADA / CM.

TOGETHER
Too much, too little, too late: Mathis, Johnny & Deniece Williams / There's nothing better than love: Vandross, Luther & Gregory Hines / Rockin' good way: Stevens, Shakin' & Bonnie Tyler / Wake me up before you go go: Wham / Reunited: Peaches & Herb / Saturday love: O'Neal, Alexander & Cherreile / Do that to me one more time: Captain & Tennille / Don't go breaking my heart: John, Elton & Kiki Dee / Je t'aime: Birkin, Jane & Serge Gainsbourgh / Day by day: Shakatak & Al Jarreau / Hot together: Pointer Sisters / Love is strange: Mickey & Sylvia / Just we two (Mona Lisa): Momen Talking / Waiting for a star to fall: Boy Meets Girl / In the year 2525: Zager & Evans / I can't go for that (no can do): Hall & Oates / Every step of the way: Francis, Joe & Mary Carew / Reservations for two: Warwick, Dionne & Kashif
CD _____ STACD 001
Stardust / Nov '91 / Carlton Home Entertainment.

TOGETHER
CD _____ STACD 001
Wisepack / Nov '92 / THE / Conifer.

TOGETHER
I knew you were waiting (for me): Franklin, Aretha & George Michael / Sometimes love just ain't enough: Smyth, Patty & Don Henley / Where is the love: Paris, Mica & Will Downing / Baby, come to me: Austin, Patti & James Ingram / Don't know much: Ronstadt, Linda & Aaron Neville / We've got tonight: Rogers, Kenny & Sheena Easton / If you were with me now: Minogue, Kylie & Keith Washington / You are everything: Ross, Diana & Marvin Gaye / Ain't nothing like the real thing: Gaye, Marvin & Tammi

Terrell / Up where we belong: Cocker, Joe & Jennifer Warnes / Endless love: Ross, Diana & Lionel Richie / With you from born again: Preston, Billy & Syreeta / Tonight I celebrate my love: Bryson, Peabo & Roberta Flack / You're all I need to get by: Gaye, Marvin & Tammi Terrell / Stop, look, listen (to your heart): Gaye, Marvin & Diana Ross / It takes two: Gaye, Marvin & Kim Weston / Too much, too little, too late: Mathis, Johnny & Deniece Williams / Reunited: Peaches & Herb / Solid: Ashford & Simpson / Teardrops: Womack & Womack
CD _____ 5254612
PolyGram / Mar '95 / PolyGram.

TOGETHER - THE EASTBOUND JAZZ YEARS
Baby let me take you (in my arms): Chandler, Gary / Crazy legs: Person, Houston / For the love of you: Person, Houston / Gettin' off: Mason, Bill / Lester leaps in: Person, Houston / Blow top blues: Jones, Etta / Flamingo: Chandler, Gary / Gathering together: Sparks, Melvin / When I'm kissing my love: Wilson, Spanky / Jet set: Chandler, Gary / Mr. Jay: Mason, Bill
CD _____ CDBGPD 071
BGP / Aug '93 / Pinnacle.

TOKYO FLASHBACK #4
CD _____ PSFD 69
PSF / Dec '95 / Harmonia Mundi.

TOLEKI BANGO
CD _____ CRAW 1
Crammed World / Jan '96 / New Note.

TOM WILSON'S BOUNCIN' BEATS 2
CD _____ BNCCD 2
Rumour / Jul '95 / Pinnacle / 3MV / Sony.

TOM WILSON'S TARTAN TECHNO
CD _____ TOONCD 101
Tempo Toons / Oct '95 / 3MV / Sony.

TOMATO DELTA BLUES PACKAGE
No shoes: Hooker, John Lee / Lightnin's discourse on the cadillac: Hopkins, Lightnin' / Big car blues: Hopkins, Lightnin' / Talkin' Casey: Hurt, Mississippi John / Walters blues: Little Walter & Otis Rush / Nahavo trail: Peg Leg Sam / That's all right mama: Crudup, Arthur / Some day: McDowell, Mississippi Fred / Trouble's all I see: Shines, Johnny / Walk on: Terry, Sonny & Brownie McGhee / Walk all over Georgia: Louisiana Red / Christina: McGhee, Brownie / Ride in my new car blues: Williams, Big Joe / Commit a crime: Howlin' Wolf / That's alright: Lightnin' Slim / John Hardy: Leadbelly
CD _____ 598109520
Tomato / Nov '93 / Vital.

TOMBSTONE AFTER DARK
Honky tonk masquerade (#): Shepard, Jean & Ray Pillow / Gypsy rider: Clark, Gene & Carla Olsen / Hey good lookin': Sledge, Percy / Shady was a lady from Louisville: Alexander, Larry 'Jinx' / Fools fall in love: Hancock, Butch / Further: Halley, David / My baby don't dance to nothing but Ernest Tubb: Brown, Junior / Where I grew up: Durham, Bobby / West Texas waltz: Hancock, Butch / Dallas (#): Hancock, Butch / Me and Billy the Kid: Ely, Joe / Border radio: Alvin, Dave / Big beaver: Asleep At The Wheel
CD _____ FIENDCD 713
Demon / Apr '92 / Pinnacle / ADA.

TONE TALES FROM TOMORROW VOL.2 (Ntone Compilation)
CD _____ NTONECD 008
Ntone / Oct '95 / Vital.

TONGUE SANDWICH
Whole affair: Izit / Sharing our lives: Izit / Caterpillar: Mustard Spoon / Crack the crackers: Sidewinder / Stimela (coaltrain): Masekela, Hugh / Charge of the large brigade: Powdered Rhino Horns / Spring in your step: Nodding Dog Productions / Awake: K-Creative / Maybe tomorrow: Yerbouti / From the city to the sea: Mighty Truth / Better way: Fumi
CD _____ TNGCD 005
Tonguo 'n' Groovo / Oct '94 / Vital.

TOO GOOD TO BE FORGOTTEN
CD _____ CDTRL 362
Trojan / Oct '95 / Jetstar / Total/BMG.

TOO LATE, TOO LATE VOL. 2 - 1897-1935
Blues Document / Jan '94 / Swift / Jazz Music / Hot Shot.

TOO LATE, TOO LATE VOL. 4 - 1892-1937
CD _____ DOCD 5321
Blues Document / Mar '95 / Swift / Jazz Music / Hot Shot.

TOO PURE - PEEL SESSIONS
Coffee commercial couples: Faith Healers / Bobby kopper: Faith Healers / Jesus freak: Faith Healers / Super electric: Stereolab / Changer: Stereolab / Doubt: Stereolab / Difficult fourth title: Stereolab / Oh my space: PJ Harvey / Victory: PJ Harvey / Sheela na gig: PJ Harvey / Water: PJ Harvey
CD _____ SFRCD 119
Strange Fruit / Feb '94 / Pinnacle.

TOO PURE SAMPLER
CD _____ PURECD 034
Too Pure / Apr '94 / Vital.

TOO YOUNG (20 Hits Of The Fifties)
Reet petite: Wilson, Jackie / Tomorrow: Brandon, Johnny & The Phantoms / Little shoemaker: Clark, Petula / Cumberland gap: Donegan, Lonnie / I'm walking behind you: Squires, Dorothy / Young and foolish: Hockridge, Edmund / Hold back tomorrow: Miki & Griff / Too young: Young, Jimmy / Suddenly there's a valley: Clark, Petula / Happy anniversary: Regan, Joan / Love me forever: Ryan, Marion / Wayward wind: Grant, Gogi / Gamblin' man: Donegan, Lonnie / Venus: Valentine, Dickie / Why: Avalon, Frankie / Petite fleur: Barber, Chris / Be anything (but be mine): Young, Jimmy / Side saddle: Conway, Russ / Alone: Clark, Petula / Dead or alive: Donegan, Lonnie
CD _____ TRTCD 111
TrueTrax / Oct '94 / THE.

TOP 12 DISCO SINGLES
CD _____ PKCD 03893
K&K / Jul '93 / Jetstar.

TOP COUNTRY STARS
CD _____ 15214
Laserlight / Aug '91 / Target/BMG.

TOP GEAR
Jessica: Allman Brothers Band / Killer queen: Queen / Sharp dressed man: ZZ Top / You took the words right out of my mouth: Meat Loaf / Two princes: Spin Doctors / We don't need another hero: Turner, Tina / More than a feeling: Boston / Big log: Plant, Robert / Inside: Stiltskin / Wishing well: Free / Roll away the stone: Mott The Hoople / Maggie May: Stewart, Rod / Tuff enuff: Fabulous Thunderbirds / Because the night: Smith, Patti / Call me: Blondie / Rhiannon (Will you ever win): Fleetwood Mac / You: Frampton, Peter / When tomorrow comes: Eurythmics / Power of love: Lewis, Huey & The News / Do anything you wanna do: Eddie & The Hot Rods / 2-4-6-8 Motorway: Robinson, Tom / Bad case of lovin' you (Doctor Doctor): Palmer, Robert / Boys are back in town: Thin Lizzy / Brown eyed girl: Morrison, Van / Rocky mountain way: Walsh, Joe / Talking back to the night: Cocker, Joe / Show me the way: Frampton, Peter / I want you to want me (live): Cheap Trick / Long train runnin': Doobie Brothers / American pie: McLean, Don / Black magic woman: Santana / Everybody wants to rule the world: Tears For Fears / Walk on the wild side: Reed, Lou / Wicked game: Isaak, Chris / Venus in furs: Velvet Underground
CD _____ MOODCD 33
Columbia / May / Sony.

TOP GEAR 2
I want to breake free: Queen / I drove all night: Lauper, Cyndi / My brother Jake: Free / Drive: Cars / Change: Lightning Seeds / Can't get enough: Bad Company / Final countdown: Europe / Peace pipe: Cry Of Love / Africa: Toto / Damn, I wish I was your love: Hawkins, Sophie B. / Owner of a lonely heart: Yes / Heart of stone: Stewart, Dave / Atomic: Blondie / Since you've been gone: Rainbow / Satellite: Hooters / Once bitten twice shy: Hunter, Ian / Addicted to love: Palmer, Robert / Free bird: Lynyrd Skynyrd / Dead ringer for love: Meat Loaf / Little Miss can't be wrong: Spin Doctors / Seven wonders: Fleetwood Mac / Driver's seat: Sniff 'N' The Tears / Good feeling: Reef / Gimme all your lovin': ZZ Top / Flame: Cheap Trick / If I could see him: Cher / Twenty nine palms: Plant, Robert / Hold your head up: Argent / Life's been good: Walsh, Joe / Missing you: Waite, John / Night games: Bonnet, Graham / Motorcycle emptiness: Manic Street Preachers / (Don't fear) The reaper: Blue Oyster Cult
CD _____ MOODCD 44
Columbia / May '95 / Sony.

TOP HITS DER VOLKSMUSIK
CD _____ 15258
Laserlight / Nov '91 / Target/BMG.

TOP OF THE HILL
CD _____ SHCD 9201
Sugarhill / Dec '95 / Roots / CM / ADA / Direct.

TOP OF THE POPS
CD _____ 24034
Laserlight / Mar '95 / Target/BMG.

TOP OF THE POPS
Think twice: Dion, Celine / Chains: Arena, Tina / If you love me: Brownstone / Open up your heart: M People / Guaglione: Prado, Perez / Wake up: Boo Radleys / Change: Lightning Seeds / Some might say: Oasis / I wanna go where the people go: Wildhearts / Crush with eyeliner: R.E.M. / Vegas: Sleeper / Waking up: Elastica / Over my shoulder: Mike & The Mechanics / Over the river: McLean, Bitty / Everlasting love: Estefan, Gloria / Cowboy dreams: Nail, Jimmy / Independent love song: Scarlet / As I lay me down: Hawkins, Sophie B. / Space cowboy: Jamiroquai / You gotta be: Des'ree / I've got a little something for you: MN8 / My girl Josephine: Super Cat / Here comes the hotstepper: Kamoze, Ini / Scatman John:

Scatman John / Love and devotion: Real McCoy / Dreamer '95: Livin' Joy / Love city groove: Love City Groove / Your body's calling: R. Kelly / Feel so good: Xscape / Right in the night: Jam & Spoon / Not over yet: Grace / U sure do: Strike / Lifting me higher: Gems For Jem / Move: H Block X / Don't stop (wiggle wiggle): Outhere Brothers / One man in my heart: Human League / Two can play that game: Brown, Bobby / Give it to you: Da Brat / Crazy: Morrison, Mark / Baby baby: Corona / First, the last eternity: Snap
CD _____ MOODCD 40
Columbia / May '95 / Sony.

TOP OF THE POPS 2
Fairground: Simply Red / Gangstas paradise: Coolio / Shy guy: King, Diana / Baby it's you: Dion, Celine / Four que tu m'ames encore: Dion, Celine / Power of love: Vandross, Luther / Walking in Memphis: Cher / Never forget: Take That / Heaven help my heart: Arena, Tina / If you leave me now: Riverseries / U krazy katz: PJ & Duncan / We've got it goin' on: Backstreet Boys / Stay with me: Erasure / He's on the phone: St. Etienne / I'm only sleeping: Suggs / Girl like you: Collins, Edwyn / Raoul and the Kings of Spain: Tears For Fears / You do: McAlmont & Butler / 74-75: Connells / Where the wild roses grow: Cave, Nick & Kylie Minogue / Wonderwall: Oasis / Lucky you: Lightning Seeds / Common people: Pulp / What do I do now: Sleeper / Kings of the kerb: Echobelly / From the bench at Belvidere: Boo Radleys / Love rendezvous: M People / Missing: Everything But The Girl / I lideaway: Delacy / Happy just to be with you: Gayle, Michelle / I can't tell you why: Brownstone / You remind me of something: R. Kelly / Stayin' alive: N-Trance / Found love: Double Dee & Dany / My prerogative: Brown, Bobby / 1st of tha month: Bone Thugs 'N' Harmony / Exodus: Sunscreem / Transamazonia: Shamen / La la la hey hey: Outhere Brothers / Angel: Jam & Spoon
CD _____ SONYTV 9CD
Sony Music / Nov '95 / Sony.

TOP RANK EXPLOSION
CD _____ LG 21096
Lagoon / May '94 / Magnum Music Group / THE.

TOP ROCK STEADY
CD _____ LG 21070
Lagoon / Feb '93 / Magnum Music Group / THE.

TOP TEN
CD _____ NWSCD 6
New Sound / Apr '93 / Jetstar.

TOP TEN HITS OF THE 60'S
House of the rising sun: Animals / Do it again: Beach Boys / Got to get you into my life: Bennett, Cliff & The Rebel Rousers / Someone else's baby: Faith, Adam / little lovin': Fourmost / Ferry 'cross the Mersey: Gerry & The Pacemakers / Something is happening: Herman's Hermits / In the country: Richard, Cliff / Look through my window: Hollies / Little town: Jones, Paul / I'm a tiger: Lulu / F.B.I.: Shadows / Hippy hippy shake: Swinging Blue Jeans / Pasadena: Temperance Seven / Twelfth of never: Richard, Cliff / Let's go to San Francisco: Flowerpot Men / Seven little girls sitting in the back seat: Avons / You were made for me: Freddie & The Dreamers
CD _____ CDMFP 6040
Music For Pleasure / Sep '88 / EMI.

TOP TEN HITS OF THE 60'S, 70'S, 80'S
CD Set _____ CDMFPBOX 1
Music For Pleasure / Oct '90 / EMI.

TOP TEN HITS OF THE 70'S
Wuthering Heights: Bush, Kate / American pie: McLean, Don / Baker Street: Rafferty, Gerry / Roll over Beethoven: E.L.O. / Tap turns on the water: CCS / 2-4-6-8 motorway: Robinson, Tom / You sexy thing: Hot Chocolate / Angie baby: Reddy, Helen / Air that I breathe: Hollies / Make me smile (come up and see me): Harley, Steve & Cockney Rebel / Let's work together: Canned Heat / Some girls: Racey / Heaven must be missing an angel: Tavares / 48 crash: Quatro, Suzi / Cotton fields (CD only.): Beach Boys / Cat crept in (CD only.): Mud / Little bit more (CD only.): Dr. Hook / Years may come years may go (CD only.): Herman's Hermits
CD _____ CDMFP 6078
Music For Pleasure / Oct '89 / EMI.

TOP TEN HITS OF THE 80'S
Girls on film: Duran Duran / Running up that hill: Bush, Kate / Geno: Dexy's Midnight Runners / Golden brown: Stranglers / Kids in America: Wilde, Kim / Tainted love: Brother Beyond / Bette Davis eyes: Carnes, Kim / Tonight I celebrate my love: Bryson, Peabo & Roberta Flack / Kayleigh: Marillion / Set me free: Graham, Jaki / Model: Kraftwerk / Too shy: Kajagoogoo / Turning Japanese: Vapors / Searchin': Dean, Hazell / Walking on sunshine: Katrina & The Waves / Tarzan boy: Baltimora / Election day (CD only.): Arcadia / Sexy eyes (CD only.): Dr. Hook / No doubt about it (CD only.): Hot Chocolate / Let's go all the way (CD only.): Sly Fox
CD _____ CDMFP 5893
Music For Pleasure / Sep '90 / EMI.

TOP TEN HITS OF THE 80'S - VOL.2

Reflex: Duran Duran / Perfect: Fairground Attraction / Babooshka: Bush, Kate / Lifeline: Spandau Ballet / Lavender: Marillion / System addict: Five Star / Fantastic day: Haircut 100 / Living in a box: Living In A Box / We close our eyes: Go West / Better love next time: Dr. Hook / Atomic: Blondie / Use it up and wear it out: Odyssey / Tunnel of love: Fun Boy Three / Broken wings: Mr. Mister / Girl you know it's true: Milli Vanilli / Rat race: Specials / You'll never stop me loving you: Sonia / Rise to the occasion: Climie Fisher / Who's leaving who: Dean, Hazell / There there my dear: Dexy's Midnight Runners
CD _____ CDMFP 5975
Music For Pleasure / Dec '92 / EMI.

TOPAZ BOX, THE
(5CD Set)
CD Set _____ TPZS 1030
Topaz Jazz / Nov '95 / Pinnacle / Cadillac.

TORONTO TATTOO
CD _____ LCOM 8015
Lismor / Oct '93 / Lismor / Direct / Duncans / ADA.

TOTAL DEVOTION
Rage: Scritt Acht / Codeine, glue and you: Chemlab / Chikasaw: Pigface / Do ya think I'm sexy: Revolting Cocks / Boomerang: Sugarsmack / Picasso trigger: Skrew / Never trust a whin: Evil Mothers / Cut and divide: Deep Throat / Fuck it up: Pigface / Open up your mind: Lab Report
CD _____ CDDVN 32
Devotion / Aug '94 / Pinnacle.

TOTAL KAOS
(Underground House From Kaos Portugal)
CD _____ TRIUK 006CD
Tribal UK / Feb '95 / Vital.

TOTAL RECALL 8
CD _____ VPCD 1334
VP / Aug '94 / Jetstar.

TOTAL SCIENCE
Firin' line: Droppin' Science / Sovereign melody: Dillinger / Never as good: Wax Doctor / Feenin: Jodeci / It's a jazz thing: Roni Size / Sky: Just Jungle / Peace sign: Shades Of Rhythm / Kan ya feel it: Skool Of Hard Knocks / Dance hall style: J.J. Rock
CD _____ MCD 11332
MCA / Aug '95 / BMG.

TOTAL TOGETHERNESS
CD _____ CRCD 27
Charm / Mar '94 / Jetstar.

TOTAL TOGETHERNESS 2
CD _____ CRCD 37
Charm / Nov '94 / Jetstar.

TOTAL TOGETHERNESS 3
CD _____ FAMCD 001
Famous / Jul '95 / Jetstar.

TOTAL TOGETHERNESS 4
Nah fi watch nuh mate: Cobra / Oh yes no guess: Beenie Man / Babylon drop: Bounty Killer / Noise of the ghetto: Tony Rebel / Darness thing: Lady Saw / Oh Mama: Jigsy King / Sis: Galaxy P / House mouse: Shabba Ranks / Turn around: Beenie Man / No interview: Bounty Killer / Search: Culture, Louie / Top rankin: Althia & Donna / Tek yuh man: Buccaneer / Want you back: Lady G
CD _____ FAMCD 002
Famous / Jan '96 / Jetstar.

TOTALLY SOLID HITBOUND
Good things: Hatcher, Willie / Our love is in this pocket): Barnes, J.J. / My darling: Griffin, Herman / Never alone: Holidays / Hit and run: Revilot Orchestra / I need my baby: Beavers, Jackie / Somebody somewhere (needs you): Lebaron Orchestra / I lost you: Holidays / You better wake up: Debonaires / I love that never grows cold: Beavers, Jackie / Did my baby call: Mancha, Steve / Girl crazy: Gigi & The Charmaines / I need you like a baby: Henry, Andrea / I must love you: Davis, Melvin / When you lose the one you love: Smith, Buddy / Poor unfortunate me: Gigi & The Charmaines / I won't hurt anymore: Anderson, Eddie / Happiness is here: Trapper Ensemble / Open the door to your heart: Banks, Daryl
CD _____ GSCD 070
Goldmine / Jan '96 / Vital.

TOTALLY TRADITIONAL TIN WHISTLES
CD _____ OSS 53CD
Ossian / Jan '94 / ADA / Direct / CM.

TOTALLY TRANCED
Your touch: R 2001 / Purity: Aloof / Feel: Chameleon Project / Hello San Francisco: Dance 2 Trance / Slide: Contact / Music is movin' DHK: Fargetta / World evolution: Trance / La yerba del diablo: Datura / Spirit in me: Vibe Alive / Land of oz: Spooky / Peace and happiness: Hullabaloo / Orcana: Void / Hit music: Marmalade / Passing thru' the surface: Flux / Time to rock: Industrial / Forever people: Biologix
CD _____ CDELV 03
Debut / Dec '92 / Pinnacle / 3MV / Sony.

TOTALLY WIRED 1
Love me to death: Man Called Adam / Dance wicked: New Jersey Kings / Odd one (part 1): What's What / Bolivia: Sandberg,

Ulf Quartet / Olumo rock: Leo, Bukky Quintet / Frederic lies still: Galliano / Latin jam: Haryon / Lock out: Hip Joints / Playing for real: Jazz Renegades / Batu casu: Bangs A Bongo / Freedom principle: Leo, Bukky & Galliano / Sweet cakes (Added to the reissued CD): New Jersey Kings
CD _____ JAZIDCD 013
Acid Jazz / Nov '93 / Pinnacle.

TOTALLY WIRED 10
Time and space time: Time & Space / Would you believe in me: Lucien, John / Corduroy orgasm club: Corduroy / Ladder: One Creed / Real gone turn it on: Cloud 9 / It's all in: Whole Thing / Sweet feeling: Esperanto / Cucaraca macarra: Averne, Harvey / Never change: Quiet Boys / Bone: Wizards of Ooze / Nature never repeats itself: Emperor's New Clothes
CD _____ JAZIDCD 072
Acid Jazz / Jul '93 / Pinnacle.

TOTALLY WIRED 11
Three mile island: Taylor, James Quartet / Fresh in my mind: Forest Mighty Black / Never will I stop loving you: Clark, Alice / Freakin': Freak Power / Joyous: Pleasure / Theme from Millenium Falcon: Janson Window / To the bone: Children Of Judah / Who me: Ghosof / Monsieur Taylor's new brand: Monsieur Kamayatsu / Do you like it: Skunkhour / Anger: Mondo Grosso / Clear air: Purdey, Samuel / Astral space: Quiet Boys
CD _____ JAZIDCD 101
Acid Jazz / Jun '94 / Pinnacle.

TOTALLY WIRED 12
Life eternal: Mother Earth / Akimbo: Bartholomew, Simon / Funky jam: Primal Scream / Mental: Dub War / Swinging foot: Swinging Foot / Gimme one of those: Brand New Heavies / Couldn't take missing you: Square Window / Summertime: O.O.K.E. / Art is the message: Stickman / Don't you let me down: Planet / Work on a dream: Birtha / In deep: Red Snapper / Indian rope man: Phaze
CD _____ JAZIDCD 120
Acid Jazz / Mar '95 / Pinnacle.

TOTALLY WIRED 2
Beads, things and flowers: Humble Souls / Monkey drop (Added to the re-issued CD): New Jersey Kings / Trinkets and trash: Cool Beats / A.P.B.: Man Called Adam / Break for jazz: Break for Jazri / Nzuri beat: White, Steve & Gary Wallace / Homegrown: Jones, Ed / Tilldens: Sandberg, Ulf Quartet / Gimme one of those: Brand New Heavies / Killer: Night Trains
CD _____ JAZIDCD 016
Acid Jazz / Nov '93 / Pinnacle.

TOTALLY WIRED 3
CD _____ JAZIDCD 022
Acid Jazz / Nov '93 / Pinnacle.

TOTALLY WIRED 4
CD _____ JAZIDCD 028
Acid Jazz / Break for jazz / Pinnacle.

TOTALLY WIRED 5
CD _____ JAZIDCD 031
Acid Jazz / Dec '91 / Pinnacle.

TOTALLY WIRED 6
CD _____ JAZID 36CD
Acid Jazz / May '91 / Pinnacle.

TOTALLY WIRED 7
Theme from riot on 103rd street: Mother Earth / Taurus woman: Subterraneans / That's how it is: Grand Oral Disceminator / Machine shop (pt.1): Untouchable Machine Shop / Don't you care: Clark, Alice / Sunship: Sunship / Sim ting: Quiet Boys / Believe in me: Vibraphonic / Change had better come: Dimmond, Mark
CD _____ JAZIDCD 043
Acid Jazz / Nov '91 / Pinnacle.

TOTALLY WIRED 8
CD _____ JAZIDCD 050
Acid Jazz / Apr '92 / Pinnacle.

TOTALLY WIRED 9
Mr. Jeckle: Beesley's, Max High Vibes / Warlock of pendragon: Mother Earth / Dat's slammin': Gordon, Robbie / Peter and the wolf in sheep's clothing: Sons Of Judah / Got a groove: Wiggs, Supa & Jonzi / I can't stand it: George, Brenda / Electric soup: Corduroy / That's it: Grass Snakes / Dreams: Raw
CD _____ JAZIDCD 057
Acid Jazz / Oct '92 / Pinnacle.

TOTALLY WIRED ITALIA
CD _____ JAZIDCD 079
Acid Jazz / Sep '93 / Pinnacle.

TOTALLY WIRED SWEDEN
CD _____ JAZIDCD 103
Acid Jazz / Aug '94 / Pinnacle.

TOUCH ME IN THE MORNING
CD _____ CDTRL 337
Trojan / Apr '94 / Jetstar / Total/BMG.

TOUCH OF DEATH
Perpetual dawn: Fleshcrawl / Primeval transubstantiation: Agressor / Where the rivers of madness stream: Cemetary / Who will not be dead: Seance / Within the silence: Rosicrucian / Excursion demise: Invocator / Solace: Necrosanct / Born Bizarre: Tribulation / Enigma: Edge Of Sanity / Blood And Iron: Bathory

CD _____ BMCD 026
Black Mark / Sep '92 / Plastic Head.

TOUCH OF ROMANCE 1, A
CD _____ KNEWCD 725
Disky / Apr '94 / THE / BMG / Discovery / Pinnacle.

TOUCH OF ROMANCE 2, A
CD _____ KNEWCD 726
Disky / Apr '94 / THE / BMG / Discovery / Pinnacle.

TOUCH OF ROMANCE 3, A
CD _____ KNEWCD 727
Disky / Apr '94 / THE / BMG / Discovery / Pinnacle.

TOUCH OF ROMANCE 4, A
CD _____ KNEWCD 728
Disky / Apr '94 / THE / BMG / Discovery / Pinnacle.

TOUCH SAMPLER
Mind loss: H3OH / PS one: Jeck, Philip / Valley of the Kings and Queens: Gamil, Soliman / Orgasmatron: Sandoz / Sudurgate: Hilmarsson, Hilmar Orn / I remain...: Hafler Trio / Mara river at night: Watson, Chris / Supermind's light becommes part of the Earth: Seymour, Daren & Mark Van Hoen / Mule river of Grebene: Fara, Eli & Liza Mica / Ghettoes of the mind: Sweet Exorcist / Mesmerised: Drome / In the compound: Rax Werx / Radio KPFK: Z'Ev / Knowledge: S.E.T.I. / Supplication: Gamil, Soliman / Calcutta: Marutani, Koji
CD _____ T 01
Touch / Oct '95 / These / Kudos.

TOUCHE COMPILATION
CD _____ TOU 96015
Vermoth / Jan '96 / Disc.

TOUCHED BY THE HAND OF GOTH
CD Set _____ SPV 08638302
SPV / Aug '95 / Plastic Head.

TOUGHER THAN TOUGH
CD _____ CDTRL 304
Trojan / Mar '94 / Jetstar / Total/BMG.

TOUGHER THAN TOUGH
(The Story Of Jamaican Music)
Oh Carolina: Folkes Brothers / Boogie in my bones: Aitken, Laurel / Midnight track: Gray, Owen / Easy snappin': Beckford, Theophilus / Housewives' choice: Derrick & Patsy / Forward march: Morgan, Derrick / Miss Jamaica: Cliff, Jimmy / My boy lollipop: Millie / Six and seven books of Moses: Toots & The Maytals / Simmer down: Wailers / Man in the street: Drummond, Don / Carry go bring home: Hinds, Justin / Guns of navarone: Skatalites / Al Capone: Prince Buster / Hard man fe dead: Prince Buster / Tougher than tough: Morgan, Derrick / Girl I've got a date: Ellis, Alton / Happy go lucky girl: Paragons / Dancing mood: Wilson, Delroy / Train is coming: Boothe, Ken / Take it easy: Lewis, Hopeton / Ba ba boom: Jamaicans / 007: Dekker, Desmond / I've got to go back home: Andy, Bob / Queen majesty: Techniques / Loving pauper: Dobson, Dobby / Don't stay away: Dillon, Phyllis / Israelites: Dekker, Desmond / 54-46 (was my number): Toots & The Maytals / Reggae hit the town: Ethiopians / Wet dream: Romeo, Max / My conversation: Uniques / Bangarang: Stranger Cole / Return of Django: Upsetters / Liquidator: Harry J All Stars / Rivers of Babylon: Melodians / Harder they come: Cliff, Jimmy / Young, gifted and black: Bob & Marcia / Wake the town: U-Roy / How long: Kelly, Pat / Double barrel: Collins, Dave & Ansil / Blood and fire: Niney The Observer / Cherry oh baby: Donaldson, Eric / Better must come: Wilson, Delroy / Money in my pocket: Brown, Dennis / Stick by me: Holt, John / Teach the children: Alcapone, Dennis / S.90 skank: Big Youth / Everything I own: Boothe, Ken / Westbound train: Brown, Dennis / Move out a Babylon: Clarke, Johnny / Curly locks: Byles, Junior / Country boy: Heptones / Welding: I-Roy / Marcus Garvey: Burning Spear / Right time: Mighty Diamonds / Natty sing hit songs: Stewart, Roman / Ballistic affair: Smart, Leroy / Tenement yard: Miller, Jacob / War in a Babylon: Romeo, Max / Police and thieves: Murvin, Junior / Two sevens clash: Culture / I'm still waiting: Wilson, Delroy / No woman, no cry: Marley, Bob & The Wailers / Uptown top ranking: Althia & Donna / My number one: Isaacs, Gregory / Bredda gravalicious: Wailing Souls / River Jordan: Minott, Sugar / Armagideon time: Williams, Willie / Guess who's coming to dinner: Black Uhuru / Fort Augustus: Delgado, Junior / Jogging: McGregor, Freddie / Sitting and watching: Brown, Dennis / Night nurse: Isaacs, Gregory / Mad over me: Yellowman / Diseases: Michigan & Smiley / Water pumping: Osbourne, Johnny / Pass the tu-sheng-peng: Smith, Wayne / Tempo: Redrose / Boops: Super Cat / Greetings: Half Pint / Punanny: Bailey, Admiral / Hol' a fresh: Red Dragon / Rumours: Isaacs, Gregory / Cover me: Stewart, Tinga & Ninjaman / Legal rights: Papa San & Lady G / Wicked in bed: Shabba Ranks / Bandelero: Pliers / Hot this year: Tiger / Bogle dance: Banton, Buju / Murder she wrote: Demus, Chaka & Pliers / O Carolina: Shaggy
CD Set _____ IBXCD 1
Mango / Oct '93 / Vital / PolyGram.

TOUR DE CHANT
CD _____ DCD 5325
Disky / Nov '93 / THE / BMG / Discovery / Pinnacle.

TOURNEE 95
CD _____ GWP 010CD
Gwerz Productions / Nov '95 / ADA.

TOUVAN CHANTS FROM CENTRAL ASIA
CD _____ Y 225222CD
Silex / Jul '95 / ADA.

TOWER ROCKS
CD _____ 9548326482
WEA / Mar '94 / Warner Music.

TOWN HALL PARTY 1958-61
CD _____ RFCD 15
Country Routes / Dec '95 / Jazz Music / Hot Shot.

TOWNSHIP SWING JAZZ VOL.1
(1954-58)
CD _____ HQCD 08
Harlequin / Oct '91 / Swift / Jazz Music / Wellard / Hot Shot / Cadillac.

TOX UTHAT
CD _____ PS 9329
Pulse Sonic / Jul '93 / Plastic Head.

TOX UTHAT II
CD _____ SR 9465
Silent / Jul '94 / Plastic Head.

TRAD AT HEART
CD _____ DARTECD 171
Dara / Oct '93 / Roots / CM / Direct / ADA / Koch.

TRAD FIDDLE IN FRANCE
CD _____ Y 225110CD
Silex / Feb '95 / ADA.

TRAD JAZZ FAVOURITES
CD _____ 5501242
Spectrum/Karussell / Oct '93 / PolyGram / THE.

TRAD JAZZ FESTIVAL
CD _____ MATCD 224
Castle / Dec '92 / BMG.

TRADE VOL.1
(2CD/MC Set)
Back from the dead EP: Sound Design / Up and down: Raw Junkies / Horny toad: Cajmere / Fusion journey: Aqua Boogie / Don't you want me: PV Project / Everybody reach: Millennium / Kick it in: Hit Junkie / Movin' K Hand / Fanakio: Underground Vibes Sessions III / Can you feel what I feel: Bell, Louise / Itty bitty boozy woozy: Tempo fiesta / Indoctrinate: Castle Trancelot / It's alright: S.A.I.N. / Cut the midrange: Watchman 3 / If we lose our lovin': Movin' Melodies / If we lose our lovin': D.M.B. / Ultimate: Antic / Ga ga: Yo Yo / Let's rock: E-Trax / Forces of nature: D.J. Eric Sneo / Feel the generation: Mind X / Underrave: Disciples / Chemical hostage: Sigma 2 / Eine kleine nacht music: Kleinboiz / Controller: Sigma 2
CD Set _____ FVRCD 1001
Feverpitch / Sep '95 / EMI.

TRADITIONAL AND MODERN JAZZ MASTERWORKS
Back o' town blues: Armstrong, Louis & His Allstars / Panama: Armstrong, Louis & His Allstars / Jack-Armstrong blues: Armstrong, Louis & His Allstars / Beale Street blues: Nichols, Red & His Five Pennies / Pennies from heaven: Nichols, Red & His Five Pennies / Music goes round and round: Dorsey, Tommy & His Clambake Seven / Maple leaf rag: Condon, Eddie / Polka dot stomp rag: Condon, Eddie / Carolina shout: Condon, Eddie / Margie: Condon, Eddie / Riverboat shuffle: Condon, Eddie / Walkin' my baby back home: Condon, Eddie / Runnin' wild: Condon, Eddie / Add Hagar's blues: Condon, Eddie / Swing dat music: Condon, Eddie / Heebie jeebies: Condon, Eddie / Oh babe: Prima, Louis & Swing Band / How high the moon: Prima, Louis & Swing Band
CD _____ 17052
Laserlight / Nov '95 / Target/BMG.

TRADITIONAL ARABIC MUSIC
CD _____ D 8002
Auvidis/Ethnic / Jun '89 / Harmonia Mundi.

TRADITIONAL CHILEAN MUSIC
CD _____ D 8001
Auvidis/Ethnic / Jun '89 / Harmonia Mundi.

TRADITIONAL IRISH FAVOURITES (Trad Irish Favourites/Back To The Glen/Pipe On The Hob)
CD SET _____ HBOXCD 78
Carlton Home Entertainment/Jul '94 / Carlton Home Entertainment.

TRADITIONAL JAZZ MASTERWORKS
Trouble in mind: Armstrong, Louis & Chippie Hill / New York blues: Graves, Roosevelt / I ain't no iceman: Davenport, Cow Cow / You do me any old way: Broonzy, Big Bill / I'm tired of fattnin' frogs for snakes: Crawford, Rosetta & James P. Johnson's Hep Cats / Freight train blues: Smith, Trixie / Cherry red: Turner, Big Joe & Pete Johnson's Boogie Woogie Boys / Billie's blues:

Holiday, Billie & Her Orchestra / Boogie woogie: Rushing, Jimmy & The Jones-Smith Inc. / Lockwood boogie: Lockwood, Robert Jr. & The Aces / Jumpin' in the moonlight: Williams, Big Joe & J.D. Short / Sykes gumboogie: Sykes, Roosevelt & King Kolax Band / Good morning schoolgirl: Wells, Junior/Buddy Guy/Jack Myers/Billy Warren / Take five: Johnson, Jimmy/Carl Snyder/Ike Anderson/Dino Alvarez / Young Hawk's crawl: Hutto, J.B. & His Hawks / Everyday I have the blues: Rush, Otis Blues Band / Blues and trouble: Lockwood, Robert Jr. & The Aces / Things I used to do: Young, Mighty Joe & His Chicago Blues Band
CD _____ 17050
Laserlight / Nov '95 / Target/BMG.

TRADITIONAL MUSIC
CD _____ D 8004
Auvidis/Ethnic / Jun '89 / Harmonia Mundi.

**TRADITIONAL MUSIC FROM CONNEMARA
(The Gaelic Heritage)**
CD _____ C 580029
Ocora / Mar '93 / Harmonia Mundi / ADA.

TRADITIONAL MUSIC FROM THE AZORES
CD _____ PS 65125
Playasound / Apr '94 / Harmonia Mundi / ADA.

TRADITIONAL MUSIC FROM THE CARPATHIANS
CD _____ QUI 903029
Quintana / Jul '91 / Harmonia Mundi.

TRADITIONAL MUSIC FROM THE UKRAINE
CD _____ Y 225216CD
Silex / Apr '95 / ADA.

TRADITIONAL MUSIC OF CAPE BRETON
CD _____ NIM 5383CD
Nimbus / Nov '93 / Nimbus.

TRADITIONAL MUSIC OF CHINA
CD _____ 824912
Buda / Nov '90 / Discovery / ADA.

TRADITIONAL MUSIC OF ETHIOPIA
CD _____ PS 65074
Playasound / Jun '91 / Harmonia Mundi / ADA.

TRADITIONAL MUSIC OF GREECE
CD _____ QUI 903060
Quintana / Nov '91 / Harmonia Mundi.

**TRADITIONAL MUSIC OF PERU 1
(Festivals Of Cusco)**
CD _____ SFWCD 40466
Smithsonian Folkways / Dec '95 / ADA / Direct / Koch / CM / Cadillac.

**TRADITIONAL MUSIC OF PERU 2
(The Mantaro Valley)**
CD _____ SFWCD 40467
Smithsonian Folkways / Dec '95 / ADA / Direct / Koch / CM / Cadillac.

TRADITIONAL MUSIC OF THE BRAZILIAN RAIN FOREST
CD _____ CD 410
Bescol / May '95 / CM / Target/BMG.

TRADITIONAL MUSIC OF VIETNAM
CD _____ ARN 64303
Arion / Jul '95 / Discovery / ADA.

TRADITIONAL PORTUGUESE MUSIC
CD _____ D 8008
Auvidis/Ethnic / Jun '89 / Harmonia Mundi.

TRADITIONAL SONGS OF IRELAND
Warrior's chant: McPeake Family Trio / Moorlough shore: O'Neill, Jim / Wild colonial boy: Barry, Margaret / My singing bird: McPeake Family Trio / Whistling thief: Ennis, Seamus / Factory girl: Barry, Margaret / When you go to the fair: Devaney, Hudie / Jug of punch: McPeake Family Trio / Moses ritoolarilay: Barry, Margaret / Keening song: Gallagher, Kitty / Verdant braes of skreen: McPeake Family Trio / Her mantle so green: O'Neill, Jim / As I roved out: Ennis, Seamus / Factory girl (2): Makem, Sarah / Brian O'Linn: Moran, Thomas / Hawk and the crow: O Connor, Liam / She moves through the fair: Barry, Margaret / Bridget O Mally: Devaney, Hudie / Wild mountain thyme: McPeake Family Trio / Blackbird: McKearn, Francis / Turfman from Ardee: Barry, Margaret / Nursemaid: Gallagher, Kitty / Monaghan fair: McPeake, Frank / Magpie's nest: Kelly, Annie Jane / Dance to your daddy: Cronin, Elizabeth / Siubhan ni dhuibhir: McPeake Family Trio
CD _____ CDSDL 411
Saydisc / May '95 / Harmonia Mundi / ADA / Direct.

TRADITIONAL THAI MUSIC
CD _____ D 8007
Auvidis/Ethnic / Jun '89 / Harmonia Mundi.

TRADITIONS OF BALI
CD Set _____ 926002 CD
Buda / Oct '94 / Discovery / ADA.

TRADITIONS OF BRITTANY - BAGPIPES
CD _____ SCM 026CD
Diffusion Breizh / Apr '94 / ADA.

TRADITIONS OF BRITTANY - CLARINET
CD _____ SCM 025CD
Diffusion Breizh / Apr '94 / ADA.

TRADITIONS OF BRITTANY - HURDY GURDY
CD _____ SCM 024CD
Diffusion Breizh / Apr '94 / ADA.

TRADITIONS OF BRITTANY - VIOLIN
CD _____ SCM 031CD
Diffusion Breizh / Apr '94 / ADA.

TRANCE 2
CD _____ CDRAID 509
Rumour / Dec '92 / Pinnacle / 3MV / Sony.

TRANCE 3
CD _____ CDRAID 511
Rumour / May '93 / Pinnacle / 3MV / Sony.

TRANCE 4
CD _____ CDRAID 513
Rumour / Oct '93 / Pinnacle / 3MV / Sony.

TRANCE 5
Dreams: Quench / Kruspolska: Hedningarna / Fluid: Marine Boy / Rich girl: Crimes, Tori / Agent o: Aloof / Move in motion: Hanson & Nelson / Torwart: Deep Piece / Kiss the baby: United State Of Sound / X-tribe: X-Tribe / Space man: Miro / Solar VS1: Remould
CD _____ CDRAID 515
Rumour / Mar '94 / Pinnacle / 3MV / Sony.

TRANCE 6
CD _____ CDRAID 521
Rumour / Feb '95 / Pinnacle / 3MV / Sony.

TRANCE ATLANTIC
CD _____ TACD 1
Volume / Jan '95 / Total/BMG / Vital.

**TRANCE ATLANTIC 2
(2CD Set)**
CD Set _____ TACD 2
Volume / Sep '95 / Total/BMG / Vital.

TRANCE ATLANTIC HIGHWAYS VOLUME 4
CD _____ SUN 49942
Mokum / Mar '95 / Pinnacle.

TRANCE CENTRAL
CD _____ KICKCD 18
Kickin' / Mar '95 / SRD.

TRANCE CENTRAL 3
CD _____ KICKCD 030
Kickin' / Nov '95 / SRD.

TRANCE CENTRAL VOLUME 2
CD _____ KICKCD 22
Kickin' / May '95 / SRD.

TRANCE EUROPE
CD _____ CLEO 9243-2
Cleopatra / Mar '94 / Disc.

**TRANCE EUROPE EXPRESS
(2CD/MC 4LP Set)**
Semi detatched: Orbital / Gravity pull: Bandulu / Face the day: Readymade / Desir: System 7 / Persuasion: Spooky & Billy Ray Martin / Praying mantra: Material / Xeper: Black Dog / Celestial symphony: Scubad-evils / Midnight in vegas: Drum 030 / Space Eclipse / Random: Boiland, C.J. / Colour of the sun: MI O / It's a kind of magic: Source / Analogue bubblebath: Aphex Twin / Majestic: Orb / Glitch: Moody Boyz / Move: Moby / Washed over by mastemah: DIY / Follow the sun: Drum Club / Dust: Psychik Warriors Ov Gaia / Mission: Barbarella / Inter/lergen/ten/ko: Sabres Of Paradise / N: Trance Induction
CD Set _____ TEEXCD 1
Volume / May '94 / Total/BMG / Vital.

**TRANCE EUROPE EXPRESS 2
(2CD/MC 4LP Set)**
Trust: Microglobe / Fun equations: Speedy J / Today: Van Dyke, Paul / Camillo: Analogical / Lotus position: Irresistable Force / Pleidean communication: Positive Life / Dreams: Saint Tack / Life's little pleasures: Angel, Dave / Element 115: Eat Static / Symbols: Megalon / Aphelion: Pressure Of Speech / Afterworld: Secret Knowledge / Lucky sadle: FFWD / Safety: Scanner / Frendman: New London School Of Electronics / Oneski: Kirk, Richard H. / Real: Pentatonik / Rockerfella: Pluto / Orbit: Human Beings / Escape to earth: Escape / Justice loop: Auto Creation / Reverberate opinion: Hardfloor / Sun: Ambush
CD Set _____ TEEXCD 2
Volume / May '94 / Total/BMG / Vital.

**TRANCE EUROPE EXPRESS 3
(2CD/MC 4LP Set)**
Chromoplastic: Air Liquide / Mondonet: 808 State / Kincajou: Banco De Gaia / Pearl: Luke Slaters 7th Pain / Carino (silencio): Pulse / Judgement: Beltram, Joey / Whoshe: Sun Electric / Energy: Holy Language & Dr. Motte / Unknown: Resistance D / Lava trader: Kinesthesia / Roy Castle: u-Ziq / Cunt: Caustic Window / Maus mobil: Mouse On Mars / Before: Ultramarine / San Fran: Coco Steel & Love-

bomb / Barbarik: Orbit, William / Araqua: Inner Space / Avatar: Link / Ancient memory: Nuw Idol / Big foot: Grid / Sex and gender: Alter Ego / Third planet: Biosphere / i-94: Infinity / Track 4: Fowlkes, Eddie 'Flashin' / 3:78: Emergency Broadcast Network
CD Set _____ TEEXCD 3
Volume / Oct '94 / Total/BMG / Vital.

**TRANCE EUROPE EXPRESS 4
(The Final Chapter) (2CD/MC 4LP Set)**
CD Set _____ TEEXCD 4
Volume / Jun '95 / Total/BMG / Vital.

TRANCE MUSIC
CD _____ LDX 2741008
La Chant Du Monde / Sep '95 / Harmonia Mundi / ADA.

TRANCE PLANET VOL.2
Kothbiro / Walk like a pygmy / Sacred stones / Angelica in delirium / Boto / Matinal / Monsoon / Through the hill / Touba fame ke / Third chamber part 4 / True to the times / Improvisation / N'cosi sikelel' afica
CD _____ 3202102
Triloka / May '95 / New Note.

TRANCE TRIPPIN'
Sanction: Emtorino / Kollo: Pan Pacific / Bandos: Villivaru / Shadow: Nyali / Argentine dawn: Mullos / Insatiable: Emtorino / Mission to love: Coyaba Tribe / Three walls two ceilings: Delirious Pink Dog / Topkapi: Canabisis / 5 a.m. in Barringo: Mashed / Satyagrahi: Meallo
CD _____ CDTOT 11
Jumpin' & Pumpin' / Jun '94 / 3MV / Sony.

TRANCEFLOOR
CD _____ XPS 2CDU
CD _____ XPS 2CDM
X:Press / Oct '95 / SRD.

TRANCEMITTER
CD _____ WIGWAM 1
Wigwam / Oct '93 / Plastic Head.

TRANCEPORTER
CD _____ 70001271363
Essential Dance Music / Jan '95 / Disc.

TRANQUIL IRISH MELODIES
CD _____ HCD 006
GTD / Apr '95 / Else / ADA.

TRANS EUROPA 2
CD _____ 150 BPMCD
Contempo / Aug '93 / Plastic Head.

TRANS SLOVENIA EXPRESS
CD _____ CDSTUMM 131
Mute / Aug '94 / Disc.

TRANSATLANTIC SAMPLER
CD _____ TRACD 002
Transatlantic / Oct '94 / BMG / Pinnacle / ADA.

TRANSFORMATIONS & MODULATIONS
CD _____ EFA 6512
Mille Plateau / Apr '94 / SRD.

TRANSIENT - NEW ENERGY & TRANCE
CD _____ TRANRCD 1
Transient / Apr '95 / Total/BMG.

TRANSIENT VOLUME 2
CD _____ TCD 602
Transient / Oct '94 / Total/BMG.

TRANSISTOR REVENGE
CD _____ IRB 59992
Deep Blue / Jan '96 / Pinnacle.

TRANZMISSION
CD _____ TRANZ 001CD
Bunce Net / Sep '95 / Plastic Head.

TRAS-OS-MONTES (BEYOND THE MOUNTAINS)
CD _____ C 580035
Ocora / Mar '93 / Harmonia Mundi / ADA.

TRAVELLIN' LIGHT
C jam blues: Parlan, Horace/Sam Jones/Al Harwood / Begin the beguine: Shaw, Artie & His Orchestra / I won't dance: Lee, Peggy / Soul serenade: King Curtis / What is there to say: Hawkins, Coleman / One I love (belongs to somebody else): London, Julie & Howard Roberts / Violets for your furs: Nipp, Jutta & Zoot Sims/Jerry Lloyd / 9.20 special: Basie, Count Orchestra / Come on let's play with Pearlie Mae: Bailey, Pearl / Travellin' light: Holiday, Billie & Paul Whiteman Orchestra / M.G. Blues: McGriff, Jimmy / All of you: Ross, Annie & Gerry Mulligan/Art Farmer / Thinkin' about your body: McFerrin, Bobby / Makin' whoopee: Cole, Bobby / Just in time: Vaughan, Sarah / But not for me: Baker, Chet / Sister Sadie: Silver, Horace / Easy street: London, Julie & Barney Kessel / Bye bye blackbird: Martin, Dean / Baby, won't you please come home: Hackett, Bobby & Jack Teagarden
CD _____ CDJA 1
Premier/MFP / Oct '91 / EMI.

**TRAVELLING THROUGH THE JUNGLE
(Fife & Drum Bands From The Deep South)**
CD _____ TCD 5017
Testament / Mar '95 / Complete/Pinnacle / ADA / Koch.

TREASURE CHEST OF NORTHERN SOUL, A
I must love you: Wilson, Timothy / Remember: Whispers / I'll be there: Gems / Day my

heart stood still: Jackson, Ollie / I found true love: Hambric, Billy / Watch yourself: Hester, Tony / Hole in the wall: J.J. Barnes / You will never get away: Maye, Cholli / Shin-a-ling: Cooperettes / Mixed up: Furys / What is this: Womack, Bobby / You don't mean it: Barnes, Towanda / What good am I without you: Fletcher, Darrow / I'll never let you go: O'Jays / Going going gone: Black, Cody / Lovingly yours: Wilson, Timothy / My kind of woman: Starr, Edwin / Now you've got the upper hand: Staton, Candi / Daddy-o: Lindsay, Therese / What is this (vox): Womack, Bobby / This won't change: Tipton, Lester / Lies: Owens, Gwen / Feel good all over: Huey, Claude 'Baby' / I still want for you: Batiste, Rose / Love bandit: Chi-Lites / Very next time: Marlynns / Gee baby: Wilson, Micky / I got the power: Masqueraders / My baby ain't no plaything: Harvey, Willy
CD _____ GSCD 075
Goldmine / Oct '95 / Vital.

TREASURE ISLE DUB VOLS 1 & 2
CD _____ LG 21090
Lagoon / Aug '93 / Magnum Music Group / THE.

TREASURE ISLE GREATEST HITS
CD _____ SONCD 0041
Sonic Sounds / Sep '95 / Jetstar.

TREASURE ISLE MEETS TIPTOP
CD _____ SONCD 0047
Sonic Sounds / Jul '93 / Jetstar.

TREASURE ISLE MOOD
CD _____ CBHB 195
Heartbeat / Oct '95 / Greensleeves / Jetstar / Direct / ADA.

TREASURE ISLE TIME
CD _____ RNCD 2092
Rhino / Feb '95 / Jetstar / Magnum Music Group / THE.

TREASURE ISLE TIME
CD _____ CDHB 196
Heartbeat / Oct '95 / Greensleeves / Jetstar / Direct / ADA.

TREASURE OF MY HEART
Munster Buttermilk: Andrews, William / Johnny will you marry me: Sullivan, Dan & Shamrock Band / Farewell to Ireland: Morrison, James / Paddy in London: Flanagan Brothers / Me husband's flannel shirt: Gillespie, Hugh / Tippin' it up to Nancy: Reilly, John / Bruachna carriage baine: Clancy, Willie / Bunch of keys/Buckley's dream: Rowsome, Leo / My father's a hedger and ditcher: Carolan, Mary-Ann / Muckross Abbey/Mulvihill's: Murphy, Dennis / Turfman from Ardee: Barry, Margaret / Choice white: Barry, Margaret / Heaney, Joe / Wild mountain thyme: McPeake Clan / Roaring Mary: Doherty, John / Off to California: Russell, Micho / Wind that shakes the barley: Makem, Sarah / Rakish Paddy: Doran, Felix / Rollicking boys around Tandaragee: Tunney, Paddy / New demesne: Ennis, Seamus / Micko Russell's reel/trip to Birmingham: Harte, Frank / Silver spear/Flax in bloom: Glackin, Paddy / Murphy's/Going to the well for water: Daly, Jackie / Eclipse/Tailor's twist: Boys Of The Lough / Willie Clarke's/ Green grow the rushes-o: Holmes, Joe / Micho Russels/Sporting nell: Four Men & A Dog
CD _____ ORB 081CD
Globestyle / Oct '93 / Pinnacle.

TREASURY OF IRISH MUSIC 1, A
CD _____ CDTCD 004
Gael Linn / Aug '95 / Roots / CM / Direct / ADA.

TREASURY OF IRISH MUSIC 2, A
CD _____ CDTCD 005
Gael Linn / Aug '95 / Roots / CM / Direct / ADA.

TREASURY OF IRISH MUSIC 3, A
CD _____ CDTCD 006
Gael Linn / Aug '95 / Roots / CM / Direct / ADA.

TREASURY OF IRISH SONGS, A
CD _____ SHCD 79094
Shanachie / Oct '95 / Koch / ADA / Greensleeves.

TRENCH TOWN DUB
CD _____ OMCD 27
Original Music / Oct '93 / SRD / Jetstar.

TRESOR 2
CD _____ CDNOMU 14
Nova Mute / May '93 / Disc.

TRESOR 3
Solid sleep: Mills, Jeff / Ten four: Beltram, Joey / Rhythm of vision: Hood, Robert / Science fiction: Bell, Daniel / Allerseelen: D.J. Hell / Motor music-maerz: 3 Phase / Energizer: Baxter, Blake / Protection: Vision / Monolith: Sun Electric / Schizophrenia: Schizophrenia
CD _____ NOMU 43CD
Nova Mute / Apr '95 / Disc.

TRIBAL HEART
CD _____ AIM 1042
Aim / May '95 / Direct / ADA / Jazz Music.

TRIBES OF DA UNDERGROUND VOL.II
(2CD/LP Set)
CD Set _____ IC 012CD
Inftacom / Jan '96 / Plastic Head.

TRIBUTE BY THE GIANTS OF JAZZ
CD _____ GOJCD 53015
Giants Of Jazz / Mar '90 / Target/BMG /
Cadillac.

TRIBUTE TO BERRY GORDY, A
CD _____ 5304362
Motown / Jul '95 / PolyGram.

TRIBUTE TO BOB MARLEY VOLUME II
CD _____ CDTRL 341
Trojan / May '94 / Jetstar / Total/BMG.

**TRIBUTE TO DUKE ELLINGTON - LIVE
AT THE MONTREUX JAZZ FESTI**
CD _____ BLCD 760208
Black Lion / Nov '95 / Jazz Music /
Cadillac / Wellard / Koch.

TRIBUTE TO HARRY CHAPIN
CD _____ 4677262
Epic / May '91 / Sony.

TRIBUTE TO JEROME KERN, A
Folks who live on the hill: Lee, Peggy / Fine
romance: Tilton, Martha / Last time I saw
Paris: Four Freshmen / Way you look to-
night: Haymes, Dick / I'm old fashioned:
Garland, Judy / Look for the silver lining:
Brent, Tony / Ol' man river: Wiata, Iniate /
Yesterdays: Stafford, Jo / They don't be-
lieve me: Alberghetti, Anna Maria / Long
ago and far away: Cardinal, Roberto & the
Rita Williams singers / I still suits me: Wiata,
Iniate / How do you like to spoon with me:
Hunt, Jan / Why was I born: Washington,
Dinah / Sure thing: Simpson, Carole / Bo-
jangles of Harlem: Gonella, Nat / All through
the day: Geraldo / Who: Shore, Dinah / Bill:
Laine, Cleo / Lovely to look at: MacRae,
Gordon / I won't dance: Lee, Peggy /
Smoke gets in your eyes: Hilton, Ronnie /
Song is you: Smith, Keely / Make believe:
Lee, Peggy / Nobody else but me: Laine,
Cleo / Who do I love you: Dallas, Lorna /
Pick yourself up: Cordell, Frank / Can't help
lovin' dat man: Bassey, Shirley / You were
never lovelier: Lewis, Archie / Can I forget
you: Lewis, Archie / You are love: Dallas,
Lorna / Life upon the wicked stage: Bryan,
Dora / I might fall back on you: Bryan, Dora
/ Moon love: Silvester, Victor / I've told
every little star: Vernon Girls / You wouldn't
be cute: Geraldo / Waltz in swingtime: Mar-
tin, Skip / Dearly beloved: Wilson, Nancy /
Daydreaming: Osbourne, Tony / All the
things you are: May, Billy / In love in vain:
Horne, Lena
CD Set _____ CDDL 1290
EMI / Jun '95 / EMI.

**TRIBUTE TO NEW ORLEANS - MARDE
GRAS PARADE**
CD _____ GOJCD 53084
Giants Of Jazz / Mar '90 / Target/BMG /
Cadillac.

TRIBUTE TO NEWCASTLE F.C, A
Black 'n' white / We will follow united /
Home Newcastle / Never been defeated /
Harry Geordie medley / Blaydon races / Ho-
way the lads 93 / Toon toon army / Andy
Cole song / United, Newcastle united /
Thank you mention from the team / Head
over heals in love / Move on down / Fog on
the Tyne / Geordie boys / Santa is a
Geordie
CD _____ CDGAFFER 3
Cherry Red / Nov '95 / Pinnacle.

TRIBUTE TO OTIS REDDING
I can't turn you loose / (Sittin' on) the dock
of the bay / These arms of mine / Respect
/ I've been loving you too long / Good to
me / Let me come on home / Tribute to a
king
CD _____ JD 3320
JVC / Jun '90 / New Note.

TRIBUTE TO TI FRERE, A
CD _____ C560019
Ocora / Jun '91 / Harmonia Mundi / ADA.

TRIGGER
CD _____ HAIR 5
Hair / May '94 / SRD.

**TRINIDAD LOVES TO PLAY CARNIVAL
1914-39**
CD _____ MBCD 302-2
Matchbox / Nov '93 / Roots / CM / Jazz
Music / Cadillac.

**TRIP 'N' GROOVE - LE SON DE RADIO
NOVA**
CD _____ 325022
Melodie / Nov '95 / Triple Earth /
Discovery / ADA / Jetstar.

TRIP TO MARS
CD Set _____ SPV 899605
Scratch / Feb '94 / BMG.

TRIP TO MARS II
CD Set _____ SPV 0899626
Scratch / Jul '94 / BMG.

TRIPHOPRISY
CD _____ SQUCD 1
Rumour / Jun '95 / Pinnacle / 3MV / Sony.

TRIPHOPRISY II
CD _____ SQUCD 2
Rumour / Nov '95 / Pinnacle / 3MV /
Sony.

TRISKEDEKAPHILIA
CD _____ ANKST 61CD
Ankst / Oct '95 / SRD.

TRIUMPH OF DEATH
CD _____ TURBO 011CD
Turbo Music / Nov '92 / Plastic Head.

TROJAN EXPLOSION
(20 Reggae Hits)
You can get it if you want: Desmond
Dekker & The Aces / Reggae in your jeggae:
Livingstone, Dandy / Johnny too bad: Slick-
ers / Liquidator: Harry J All Stars / Wonder-
ful world, beautiful people: Cliff, Jimmy /
Them a laugh and a kiki: Soulmates / 54-46
(was my number): Toots & The Maytals /
Cherry oh baby: Donaldson, Eric / Let your
yeah be yeah: Pioneers / Dollar of soul:
Ethiopians / Young, gifted and black: Bob
& Marcia / Sweet sensation: Melodians /
Elizabethan reggae: Gardiner, Boris / Mama
look deh: Pioneers / Double barrel: Collins,
Dave & Ansil / Small axe: Marley, Bob /
Pomp and pride: Toots & The Maytals / Re-
turn of Django: Upsetters / 007: Dekker,
Desmond & The Aces / Phoenix city: Al-
phonso, Roland
CD _____ CDTRL 246
Trojan / Mar '94 / Jetstar / Total/BMG.

TROJAN STORY VOL.1
Bartender: Aitken, Laurel / Humpty dumpty:
Morris, Eric / Housewives' choice: Derrick &
Patsy / Don't stay out late: Patrick, Kentrick
/ Rough and tough: Cole, Stranger / Man to
man: Patrick, Kentrick / Confucius: Drum-
mond, Don / Soon you'll be gone: Blues
Busters / Yeah yeah: Riots / Dreader than
dread: Martin, Honeyboy / Syncopate: As-
tronauts / Keep the pressure on: Winston,
George / Oh babe: Techniques / Train to
Skaville: Ethiopians / Pretty Africa: Cliff,
Jimmy / Rock steady: Ellis, Alton / Perfidia:
Dillon, Phyllis / Way of life: Tait, Lynn / Sec-
ond fiddle: Tennors / Nana: Slickers / Black
and white
CD _____ CDTAL 100
Trojan / Mar '94 / Jetstar / Total/BMG.

TROJAN STORY, THE
Guns of Navarone: Skatalites / Phoenix City:
Alphonso, Roland / Oh ba-a-by: Tech-
niques / Rock steady: Ellis, Alton / Do the
reggae: Toots & The Maytals / Stand by
your man: Webber, Marlene / Red red wine:
Tribe, Tony / Miss Jamaica: Cliff, Jimmy /
Version galore: U-Roy / Screaming target:
Big Youth / Cassius Clay: Alcapone, Dennis
/ Black man time: Roy, I. / Silhouette:
Brown, Dennis / Jimmie Brown: Parker, Ken
/ Just can't figure it out: Diamonds / Enter
into his gates: Clark, Johnnie / Pretty Afri-
can: Dekker, Desmond / Save the last
dance tonight: Heptones / Nice nice time:
Zap Pow / Take me home country roads:
Toots & The Maytals / Time is the master:
Simon, Tito / Mama look deh: Pioneers / Big
8: Judge Dread / Them a fe get a beatin':
Tosh, Peter / Wonder Boy: Notes, Freddie
& The Rudies / Elizabethan reggae: Lee, By-
ron & The Dragonaires / 007: Dekker, Des-
mond / Crying over you: Boothe, Ken / Re-
turn of Django: Upsetters / Mr. Bojangles:
Holt, John / Reggae in your jeggae: Living-
stone, Dandy / Longshot kick de bucket:
Pioneers
CD Set _____ CDTRD 402
Trojan / Mar '94 / Jetstar / Total/BMG.

TROPICAL EXTRAVAGANZA
CD _____ TUMICD 028
Tumi / Oct '92 / Sterns / Discovery.

TROPICAL FESTIVAL
Kwassa kwassa: Kanda Bongo Man / Cach-
ita: La Charanga Almendra / Forward Jah
Jah children: Inner Circle / La revancha: Los
Diablitos / Bomba camara: Grupo Melao /
Cuban medley (Son De La Loma/Danzon/
Cha Cha Cha/Que Rico Mambo/Guantan-
amera/Cochero/Buenos Dias America/Re-
cogan Los Guantes/Traigo La Ultima): La
Origina De Manzanillo / Workey workey:
Burning Flames / Cascara Bellagua: Castro,
Poldo / Suma sume: Godzom / Maria La
Hoz: Grupo Caneo
CD _____ CPCD 8131
Charly / Oct '95 / Charly / THE / Cadillac.

**TROUBADOURS OF THE FOLK ERA
VOL.1**
CD _____ R 270262
Rhino / Apr '92 / Warner Music.

**TROUBADOURS OF THE FOLK ERA
VOL.2**
CD _____ R 270263
Rhino / Apr '92 / Warner Music.

**TROUBADOURS OF THE FOLK ERA
VOL.3**
CD _____ R 270264
Rhino / Apr '92 / Warner Music.

TROUBLE, HEARTACHES & SADNESS
Trouble, heartaches and sadness: Peebles,
Ann / What more do you want from me:
Starks, Veniece / Lonely soldier: Bryant,
Don / That's just my luck: Johnson, Syl /
Ain't no love in my life: Mitchell, Phillip / I
must be losin' you: Clayton, Willie / I can't
let you go: Peebles, Ann / I've been hurt:

Big Lucky Carter / Can't hide the hurt: Bryant, Don / I can't take it: Clay, Otis / Heartaches, heartaches: Peebles, Ann / Love you
left behind: Johnson, Syl / Trying to live my
life without you: Clay, Otis / About to make
me leave home: Johnson, Syl / You're
gonna make me cry: Peebles, Ann / I die a
little each day: Clay, Otis / I'm leavin' you:
Peebles, Ann / Please don't give up on me:
Johnson, Syl / Everytime I think about you
I get the blues: One Plus One / Won't you
try me: Peebles, Ann / Please don't leave:
One Plus One
CD _____ HILOCD 10
Hi / Mar '94 / Pinnacle.

TRUCKIN' MY BLUES AWAY
(Collection Of Contemporary Blues
Songs From Texas)
CD _____ TX 1009CD
Taxim / Jan '94 / ADA.

TRUE BRITS II
CD _____ ASBCD 003
Scratch / Nov '94 / BMG.

TRUE FAITH 1ST PHASE
CD _____ NTWCD 1
Network / Nov '91 / Sony / 3MV.

TRUE LOVE
(16 Songs From The Heart)
True love: Cline, Patsy / Blue velvet: Mc-
Cann, Susan / May I have the next dream
with you: Roberts, Malcolm / As usual: Lee,
Brenda / Marianne: O'Donnell, Daniel / Por-
trait of my love / I need to give me roses:
Ray, Stacey / Let it be me: Everly Brothers
/ Take good care of my baby: Vee, Bobby
/ Country hits medley: McCann, Susan / It's
our anniversary: McCaffrey, Frank / Tennes-
see waltz / If those lips could only speak:
Foster & Allen / I'll never find another you:
Seekers / When I dream: Gayle, Crystal / All
I have to do is dream: Everly Brothers
CD _____ PLATCD 3912
Prism / '91 / Prism.

TRUE LOVE
CD _____ STACD 054
Wisepack / Sep '93 / THE / Conifer.

TRUE LOVE WAYS
CD _____ MCCD 119
Music Club / Aug '93 / Disc / THE / CM.

TRUE LOVE WAYS
True love ways: Peter & Gordon / Will you
still love me tomorrow: Shirelles / Groovy
kind of love: Mindbenders / Make it easy on
yourself: Walker Brothers / When a man
loves a woman: Sledge, Percy / Don't let
the sun catch you crying: Gerry & The Pacemakers / I think of you: Merseybeats / God
only knows: Beach Boys / I can't stop loving
you: Charles, Ray / Everlasting love: Love
Affair / Save the last dance for me: Drifters
/ Stand by me: King, Ben E. / You don't
have to say you love me: Springfield, Dusty
/ Halfway to paradise: Fury, Billy / In
dreams: Orbison, Roy / Take good care of
my baby: Vee, Bobby / All I have to do is
dream: Everly Brothers
CD _____ MOODCD 28
Columbia / Dec '93 / Sony.

**TRUE PEOPLE: THE DETROIT TECHNO
ALBUM**
(2CD/5LP/1MC Set)
Davy Jones Locker: Dresciya / Aura: K.T.
19941 / Life of a planet rider: Shakir, An-
thony / Fusion part 2: Atkins, Juan / Wiggin:
May, Derrick / R.M.F. 60: Fowlkes, Eddie /
8th Wonder: Pullne, Stacey / Emperor: Kech
& B. Bonds / Carma: Young, Claude /
Morph: Larkin, Kenny / Where is the love:
Baxter, Blake / Sources: Echols, Santonio /
T.M.F. 61: Fowlkes, Eddie / Operation 10:
Barnett, Thomas / E-Dancer: Saunderson,
Kevin / D May 87: Oldham, Alan / Don't
blame it on me: 365 Black / Art of stalking:
Suburban Knight / Gama: Brown, Tom /
C.R.X.: Little Joe
CD Set _____ REACTCD 071
React / Jan '96 / Vital.

TRUE STORY OF COUNTRY, THE
Rose garden: Anderson, Lynn / It's only
make believe: Jackson, Wanda / Big bad
John: Dean, Jimmy / Harper valley P.T.A.:
Riley, Jeannie C. / Mad: Dudley, Dave / Girl
on the billboard: Reeves, Del / Heartbreak
U.S.A.: Wells, Kitty / Hallo walls: Young, Faron / Tennessee: Jack & Misty / He took me
for a ride: La Costa Tucker / I'm a truck:
Simpson, Red / Rednecks, white socks,
blue ribbon beer: Russell, Johnny / No
charge: Montgomery, Melba / Nashville:
Houston, David / It only hurts for a little
while: Smith, Margo / Help me make it
through the night: Smith, Sammi
CD _____ 11813
Music / Dec '95 / Target/BMG.

TRUE VOICES
Changes / Devil eyes / Lady came from Baltimore / Thank you for being there / Simple
song of freedom / Which will / To love
someone / At the end of the day / Loving
arms / Across the great divide / Dreamer
CD _____ FIENDCD 115
Demon / Jun '90 / Pinnacle / ADA.

TRULY UNFORGETTABLE
(32 Truly Unforgettable Songs)
When I fall in love: Cole, Nat King / Be my
love: Lanza, Mario / Who you: Platters / It's
all in the game: Edwards, Tommy / Spanish

eyes: Martino, Al / On the street where you
live: Damone, Vic / He'll have to go: Reeves,
Jim / Misty: Mathis, Johnny / Can't get used
to losing you: Williams, Andy / Dream lover:
Darin, Bobby / Move over darling: Day,
Doris / Never be anyone else but you: Nelson, Rick / It's only make believe: Twitty,
Conway / End of the world: Davis, Skeeter
/ More than I can say: Vee, Bobby / It's
over: Orbison, Roy / Cry me a river: London,
Julie / Love letters: Lester, Ketty / I left my
heart in San Francisco: Bennett, Tony /
Make it easy on yourself: Walker Brothers /
Joanna: Walker, Scott / You don't have to
say you love me: Springfield, Dusty / Look
homeward angel: Ray, Johnnie / Every time
we say goodbye: Fitzgerald, Ella / God
bless the child: Holiday, Billie / Passing
strangers: Eckstine, Billy & Sarah Vaughan /
What a wonderful world: Armstrong, Louis /
Folks who live on the hill: Lee, Peggy /
Stand by me: King, Ben E. / Save the last
dance for me: Drifters / Unforgettable: Cole,
Nat King
CD Set _____ CDEMTVD 55
EMI / Nov '90 / EMI.

TRUMPET SPECTACULAR
CD _____ PCD 7015
Progressive / Jun '93 / Jazz Music.

TRUMPETS IN JAZZ
CD _____ CDCH 556
Milan / Feb '91 / BMG / Silva Screen.

TRUMPETS IN MODERN JAZZ
Will you still be mine: Farmer, Art / For now:
Baker, Chet / Swingin' the blues: Clark,
Terry / Bubba and the whale: Conexion La-
tina / Adriatica: Goykovich, Dusko / One
bright glance: D'Earth, John / Jeffuso:
Brooks, Roy / Little song: Blue Box / Kush:
Gillespie, Dizzy / Body and soul: Jones, El-
vin / Fairy boat to Rio: Ambrosetti, Franco /
Siempre junto a ti: Gonzalez, Jerry
CD _____ ENJ 80002
Enja / Mar '94 / New Note / Vital/SAM.

TRUTH AND RIGHTS
CD _____ HBCD 78
Heartbeat / Jun '94 / Greensleeves /
Jetstar / Direct / ADA.

TULIKULKKU
CD _____ KICD 30
KICD / Dec '93 / ADA.

TUMI CUBA CLASSICS 1 - SON
CD _____ TUMICD 049
Tumi / Aug '95 / Sterns / Discovery.

TUMI CUBA CLASSICS 3 - RUMBA
CD _____ TUMICD 052
Tumi / Aug '95 / Sterns / Discovery.

**TUMI CUBA CLASSICS 4 - THE BIG
SOUND**
CD _____ TUMICD 053
Tumi / Aug '95 / Sterns / Discovery.

**TUMI CUBA CLASSICS 5 - SON, THE
FUTURE**
CD _____ TUMICD 055
Tumi / Sep '95 / Sterns / Discovery.

**TUMI CUBA CLASSICS 6 - MUSICA
CAMPESINO**
CD _____ TUMICD 057
Tumi / Dec '95 / Sterns / Discovery.

TUN IT OVER
CD _____ CIDM 110
Mango / Nov '91 / Vital / PolyGram.

TUN IT OVER 2
(Bogle Meets Armstrong)
CD _____ CIDM 1099
Mango / Jan '93 / Vital / PolyGram.

TURKEY - THE MUSIC OF THE YAYLA
CD _____ C 560050
Ocora / Aug '94 / Harmonia Mundi / ADA.

TURQUERIE
CD _____ SPNO 11
Spin / Oct '94 / Direct.

TUVALU
CD _____ PAN 2055CD
Pan / Dec '94 / ADA / Direct / CM.

TWANGS FOR THE MEMORY
(20 Rockin' Instrumental Hits)
Charly / Jul '93 / Charly / THE / Cadillac.

TWELVE DAYS OF CHRISTMAS, THE
Introducing the twelve days of christmas /
Jingle bells / Sleigh ride through the snow /
Christmas together / O Christmas tree /
Dear Santa / Gift of love / Here we come a-
carolling / We wish you a merry Christmas
/ Snow ho ho ho / Santa Claus is coming
to town / Downtown holiday hullabaloo / I'd
like to have a elephant for Christmas / Deck
the halls / He delivers / Around the world
Christmas / Twelve days of Christmas
CD _____ DSBCD 476
Disney / Oct '95 / Carlton Home
Entertainment.

**TWENTY BEST OF TODAY'S FOLK
MUSIC**
CD _____ EUCD 1071
ARC / '89 / ARC Music / ADA.

TWENTY GOSPEL GREATS
CD _____ CDCD 1074
Charly / Mar '93 / Charly / THE / Cadillac.

TWIST
CD ______________ **TBCD 003**
T&B / Sep '95 / Plastic Head.

TWISTED
CD Set ______________ **TVCD 1**
Tearin' Vinyl / Dec '95 / Total/BMG.

TWISTED WHEEL STORY, THE
Good time tonight: *Soul Sisters* / Shotgun and the duck: *Lee, Jackie* / Fife piper: *Dynatones* / You get your kicks: *Ryder, Mitch* / Everybody's going to a love in: *Brady, Bob* / Karate boogaloo: *Jerry O* / Gonna fix you good: *Little Anthony* / Lil lovin' sometimes: *Patton, Alexander* / Ain't no soul: *Milsap, Ronnie* / Humphrey stomp: *Harrison, Earl* / That driving beat: *Mitchell, Willie* / There's nothing else to say: *Incredibles* / Any day now: *Jackson, Chuck* / Dr Love: *Sheen, Bobby* / Love is after me: *Rich, Charlie* / Little Queenie: *Blacks, Bill* / Secret agent: *Olympics* / Tightrope: *Inez & Charlie Foxx* / I got what it takes: *Inez & Charlie Foxx* / That's enough: *Robinson, Roscoe* / Open the door to your heart: *Banks, Darrell* / My elusive dreams: *Dillard, Moses & Joshua* / Next in line: *Lands, Hoagy* / It keeps rainin: *Domino, Fats* / Get out of my heart: *Dillard, Moses & Joshua* / Never love a robin: *Barbara & Brenda*
CD ______________ **GSCD 066**
Goldmine / Nov '95 / Vital.

TWO FRIENDS TING AND TING
Sound ting: *Gold, Brian & Tony* / Idle talk ting: *Cutty Ranks* / Keeping a fat ting: *Pedrose* / Gun ting: *Lindo, Hopeton* / Pretend ting: *Papa San* / Love ting: *Home-T* / Oil ting: *Cocoa T* / Bow ting: *Flourgan* / Procrastinate ting: *Mann, Peter* / Bun ting / Cheat ting: *Chevelle* / Gyow ting: *Sister Charmaine*
CD ______________ **GRELCD 155**
Greensleeves / Feb '91 / Total/BMG / Jetstar / SRD.

TWO RIDDIMS CLASH
CD ______________ **GPCD 002**
Gussie P / Jun '92 / Jetstar.

TWO RYDIM CLASH
CD ______________ **NWSCD 9**
New Sound / May '94 / Jetstar.

TWO TONE JUMP
CD ______________ **RKCD 9306**
Rockhouse / May '93 / Charly / CM / Nervous.

TWO WAY FAMILY FAVOURITES
With a song in my heart: *Kostelanetz, Andre* / When I fall in love: *Cole, Nat King* / Boum: *Trenet, Charles* / Up, up and away: *Mann, Johnny Singers* / 633 Squadron: *Goodwin, Ron & His Orchestra* / With pen in hand: *Carr, Vikki* / Here in my heart: *Martino, Al* / All in the April evening: *Glasgow Orpheus Choir* / Memories are made of this: *Martin, Dean* / Side by side: *Starr, Kay* / Portrait of my love: *Monro, Matt* / Genevieve: *Adler, Larry* / Home cooking: *Hope, Bob* / Waltzing Matilda: *Ifield, Frank* / Count your blessings: *Luton Girls Choir* / Where do you go to my lovely: *Sarstedt, Peter* / Serenade (fair maid of Perth): *Nash, Heddle* / Anyone who had a heart: *Black, Cilla* / Hey neighbour: *Flanagan & Allen* / Too young: *Cole, Nat King* / Creed: *Russian Metropolitan Church Choir* / Big spender: *Bassey, Shirley* / Bad penny blues: *Lyttelton, Humphrey* / Let there be love: *Cole, Nat King* / I know that my redeemer liveth: *Baillie, Isobel* / Softly whispering I love you: *Congregation* / Roses of Picardy: *Hill, Vince* / Spinning wheel: *Murphy, Delia* / Side saddle: *Conway, Russ* / Nymphs and shepherds: *Manchester Childrens Choir* / Willie can: *Cogan, Alma* / Just a wearyin' for you: *Robeson, Paul* / Snowbird: *Murray, Anne* / Ramblin' rose: *Cole, Nat King* / O my beloved father: *Hammond, Joan* / Born free: *Monro, Matt* / How wonderful to know: *Carr, Pearl & Teddy Johnson* / Nun's chorus: *Frind, Annie* / Milord: *Piaf, Edith* / Starry eyed: *Holiday, Michael* / Good luck, good health, God bless you: *Conway, Steve* / Crimond: *Glasgow Orpheus Choir*
CD ______________ **CDEM 1465**
EMI / Sep '93 / EMI.

TYPES - A KUDOS SAMPLER
About this: *Pentatonik* / Rotation: *Angel, Dave* / Zycoon: *Synectics* / Point of no return: *Stasis* / Contrapoint: *Fugue* / Isatai: *As One* / Penguins: *Eco Tourist* / Tknoh: *Germ* / Intelligence: *Sandoz* / Vein: *Scanner* / All over hair piece: *Conemelt* / Crystalline existences: *White Funks On Dope*
CD ______________ **KUDCD 005**
Kudos / Jul '94 / Kudos / Pinnacle.

TYRANNY OF THE BEAT
CD ______________ **SPV 05622172**
SPV / May '95 / Plastic Head.

TYROLEAN EVENING, A
CD ______________ **399422**
Koch / Sep '92 / Koch.

U

U.F.O.'S ARE REAL
CD ______________ **BBLP 001**
Bionic Beats / Nov '93 / Plastic Head.

UGANDA: AUX SOURCES DU NIL
CD ______________ **C 560032**
Ocora / Nov '92 / Harmonia Mundi / ADA.

UK REGGAE ALL STARS
CD ______________ **CONQ 999CD**
Conqueror / Nov '94 / Jetstar / SRD.

UK UNDERGROUND
CD ______________ **AZNY 1001**
Azuli / Oct '92 / Azuli / Empire.

UK/DK
U.S.A.: *Exploited* / Joker in the pack / No security: *Chaos UK* / Life: *Disorder* / Blind justice: *Business* / Things that need / Fighter pilot: *Vibrators* / Ignite: *Damned* / You talk, we talk: *Pressure* / Viva la revolution / Jerusalem: *One Way System* / Soldier boy: *Varukers* / 42nd Street: *Angelic Upstarts* / Stand strong, stand proud: *Vice Squad* / U.S.A. #2
CD ______________ **CDPUNK 47**
Anagram / Feb '95 / Pinnacle.

UKRAINIAN VILLAGE MUSIC (Historic Recordings 1928-1933)
CD ______________ **FL 7030**
Folklyric / Apr '95 / Direct / Cadillac.

UKRAINIAN VOICES
CD ______________ **PS 65114**
Playasound / Nov '93 / Harmonia Mundi / ADA.

ULTIMATE 80'S
U2
Under pressure: *Queen & David Bowie* / New year's day / It's a sin: *Pet Shop Boys* / Sexcrime (1984): *Eurythmics* / Relax: *Frankie Goes To Hollywood* / Is there something I should know: *Duran Duran* / Need you tonight: *INXS* / I'm still standing: *John, Elton* / Everywhere: *Fleetwood Mac* / Every breath you take: *Police* / Road to hell: *Rea, Chris* / I want to know what love is: *Foreigner* / Big log: *Plant, Robert* / Wonderful life: *Black* / Love of the common people: *Young, Paul* / Road to nowhere: *Talking Heads* / Reward: *Teardrop Explodes* / Something about you: *Level 42* / Do you really want to hurt me: *Culture Club* / She drives me crazy: *Fine Young Cannibals* / Money for nothing: *Dire Straits* / Wonderland: *Big Country* / White wedding: *Idol, Billy* / Start: *Jam* / Big area: *Then Jerico* / Dead ringer for love: *Meat Loaf* / Atomic: *Blondie* / I'm your man: *Wham* / Look of love: *ABC* / Young at heart: *Bluebells* / Come on Eileen: *Dexy's Midnight Runners* / Blue Monday: *New Order* / Only you: *Yazoo* / (Keep feeling) Fascination: *Human League* / Enola Gay: *O.M.D.* / Shout: *Tears For Fears* / To cut a long story short: *Spandau Ballet* / Tainted love: *Soft Cell* / We close our eyes: *Go West* / Vienna: *Ultravox*
CD ______________ **5168312**
PolyGram / Jun '94 / PolyGram.

ULTIMATE 80'S
CD ______________ **74321271042**
RCA / Aug '95 / BMG.

ULTIMATE 80'S BALLADS
Save me: *Queen* / Different corner: *Michael, George* / All I want is you: *U2* / Absolute beginners: *Bowie, David* / Every little thing she does is magic: *Police* / Sweet surrender: *Wet Wet Wet* / Save a prayer: *Duran Duran* / True: *Spandau Ballet* / Power of love: *Frankie Goes To Hollywood* / Eternal flame: *Bangles* / Here comes the rain again: *Eurythmics* / I go to sleep: *Pretenders* / Don't dream it's over: *Crowded House* / Avalon: *Roxy Music* / Waiting for a girl like you: *Foreigner* / Hard habit to break: *Chicago* / She makes my day: *Palmer, Robert* / Little lies: *Fleetwood Mac* / Total eclipse of the heart: *Tyler, Bonnie* / Romeo and Juliet: *Dire Straits* / Right here waiting: *Marx, Richard* / Wherever I lay my hat: *Young, Paul* / One day in your life: *Jackson, Michael* / Leaving me now: *Level 42* / Long hot summer: *Style Council* / Hands to heaven: *Breathe* / Love don't live here anymore: *Nail, Jimmy* / It's different for girls: *Jackson, Joe* / Golden brown: *Stranglers* / Chance: *Big Country* / Kayleigh: *Marillion* / All of my heart: *ABC* / No regrets: *Ure, Midge* / Human: *Human League* / Souvenir: *O.M.D.* / One of us: *Abba* / China in your hands: *T'Pau* / I second that emotion: *Japan* / Hold me now: *Thompson Twins* / Victims: *Culture Club*
CD ______________ **5251132**
PolyGram TV / Nov '94 / PolyGram.

ULTIMATE CAJUN COLLECTION
J'aime grand gueydan: *Allan, Johnnie* / Colinda: *Raven, Eddy* / Jolie blon: *Thibodeaux, Rufus* / Grand Texas: *Roger, Aldus* / Gabriel: *Broussard, Alex* / Cajun two-step: *Forester, Blackie* / Le sud de la Louisianne: *Bruce, Vin* / Allons a Lafayette: *Thibodeaux, Rufus* / Pine grove blues: *Abshire, Nathan* / Creole stomp: *Roger, Aldus* / Tout son amour: *Foret, L.J.* / Pauvre hobo: *Thibodeaux, Rufus* / Married life: *Cormier, Louis* / La Lou special: *Broussard, Pee-Wee* / Tous les deux pour la meme: *Forester, Blackie* / Crawfish festival time: *Raven, Eddy* / Mon tit baille: *Newman, Jimmy C.* / Chere Alice: *Richard, Zachary* / One scotch, one bourbon, one beer: *Roger, Aldus* / Tee Maurice: *Guidry, Doc* / Mamou two-step: *Walker, Lawrence* / la valse de amite: *Thibodeaux, Rufus* / Comment ca se fait: *Newman, Jimmy C.* / I'm Cajun cool: *Storm, Warren* / Evangeline: *Dusenberry Family* / La maison a deux portes: *Storm, Warren* / La valse de KLFY: *Doucet, Michael* / Fais do do: *Thibodeaux, Rufus* / La valse d'anniversaire: *Forester, Blackie* / Le two-step de l'acadien: *Abshire, Nathan* / Grand mamou: *Thibodeaux, Rufus* / Chemin des coeurs casser: *Foret, L.J.* / Le nouveau two-step: *Richard, Zachary* / One more chance: *Roger, Aldus* / Dans la Louisianne: *Bruce, Vin* / Alligator Bayou: *Raven, Eddy* / Lake Arthur stomp: *Thibodeaux, Rufus* / Ma belle Evangeline: *Allan, Johnnie* / Le two-step de choupique: *Abshire, Nathan* / Bayou Sam: *Forester, Blackie* / Elle n'est pas la plus belle: *Foret, L.J.* / Tu es la mienne pour toujours: *West, Clint* / La valse de Quebec: *Thibodeaux, Rufus* / Lafayette two-step: *Roger, Aldus* / Le blues Francais: *Abshire, Nathan* / Cotton fields: *Forester, Blackie*
CD ______________ **DCD 5254**
Disky / Aug '92 / THE / BMG / Discovery / Pinnacle.

ULTIMATE COLLECTION, THE
CD ______________ **8453002**
Philips / May '91 / PolyGram.

ULTIMATE COUNTRY COLLECTION
Most beautiful girl in the world: *Rich, Charlie* / I recall a gypsy woman: *Williams, Don* / I fall to pieces: *Cline, Patsy* / Crystal chandeliers: *Pride, Charley* / Stand by your man: *Wynette, Tammy* / Walk on by: *Van Dyke, Leroy* / Before the next teardrop falls: *Fender, Freddy* / Poor boy blues: *Atkins, Chet & Mark Knopfler* / Blanket on the ground: *Spears, Billie Jo* / Make the world go away: *Arnold, Eddy* / He'll have to go: *Reeves, Jim* / He stopped loving her today: *Jones, George* / Ring of fire: *Cash, Johnny* / Rose garden: *Anderson, Lynn* / I couldn't leave you if I tried: *Crowell, Rodney* / Lucille: *Rogers, Kenny* / Legend in my time: *Milsap, Ronnie* / Rhinestone cowboy: *Campbell, Glen* / I'm movin' on: *Snow, Hank* / Feel so right: *Alabama* / Always on my mind: *Nelson, Willie* / Please help me, I'm falling: *Locklin, Hank* / For the good times: *Price, Ray* / Coal miner's daughter: *Lynn, Loretta* / Oh lonesome me: *Gibson, Don* / Hillbilly girl with the blues: *Dalton, Lacy J* / Abilene: *Hamilton, George IV* / Four in the morning: *Young, Faron* / Loving her was easier (than anything I'll ever do again): *Kristofferson, Kris* / Baby don't get hooked on me: *Davis, Mac* / Lone star state of mind: *Griffith, Nanci* / If I said you had a beautiful body: *Bellamy Brothers* / Here you come again: *Parton, Dolly* / Dukes of Hazzard: *Jennings, Waylon* / Down at the twist and shout: *Carpenter, Mary-Chapin* / El Paso: *Robbins, Marty* / Don't close your eyes: *Whitley, Keith* / Wind beneath my wings: *Greenwood, Lee* / Talking in your sleep: *Gayle, Crystal* / Don't rock the jukebox: *Jackson, Alan*
CD ______________ **MOODCD 26**
Columbia / Oct '92 / Sony.

ULTIMATE DANCE
CD ______________ **12580**
Laserlight / Oct '95 / Target/BMG.

ULTIMATE DISCO COLLECTION
CD ______________ **QTVCD 021**
Quality / Mar '93 / Pinnacle.

ULTIMATE DOO-WOP COLLECTION
CD ______________ **NEMCD 618**
Sequel / Feb '92 / BMG.

ULTIMATE DRUM AND BASS (2CD/MC Set)
CD Set ______________ **QPMCD 2**
Total / Dec '95 / Total/BMG.

ULTIMATE HOTWIRE SAMPLER
CD ______________ **EFA 128172**
Hotwire / May '95 / SRD.

ULTIMATE HOUSE
CD ______________ **CHAMPCD 1016**
Champion / Oct '88 / BMG.

ULTIMATE HOUSE, THE
CD ______________ **GRF 210**
Tring / Mar '93 / Tring / Prism.

ULTIMATE JUNGLE COLLECTION
CD Set ______________ **DINCD 105**
Dino / Dec '94 / Pinnacle / 3MV.

ULTIMATE LOVERS VOL.1
CD ______________ **ARKCD 101**
Arawak / Nov '92 / Jetstar.

ULTIMATE LOVERS VOL.2
CD ______________ **ARKCD 104**
Arawak / Dec '93 / Jetstar.

ULTIMATE MEMPHIS COUNTRY COLLECTION VOL. 1 (2CD Set)
Hey porter: *Cash, Johnny* / Cold cold heart: *Lewis, Jerry Lee* / (Tell me) Who: *Smith, Warren* / Turn around: *Perkins, Carl* / Uncertain love: *Rhodes, Slim* / Daisy bread boogie: *Steele, Gene* / Feelin' low: *Chaffin, Ernie* / Chains of love: *Miller Sisters* / My kind of carryin' on: *Poindexter, Doug* / Show me: *Bond, Eddie* / Blues in the bottom of my shoes (Way down blues): *Yelvington, Malcolm* / When you stop loving me: *King, Cast* / Easy to love: *Self, Mack* / Home of the blues: *Cash, Johnny* / Let the jukebox keep on playing: *Perkins, Carl* / Tonight will be the last night: *Smith, Warren* / Will the circle be unbroken: *Lewis, Jerry Lee* / Standing in your window: *Bond, Eddie* / Down on the border: *Simmons, Gene* / How long: *Wimberly, Maggie Sue* / Heartbreakin' love: *Wages, Jimmy* / I'm bluer than anyone can be: *Mann, Carl* / Muddy ole river: *Stinit, Dane* / Tragedy: *Wayne, Thomas* / Your the nearest thing to heaven: *Cash, Johnny* / This old heart of mine: *Bond, Eddie* / That black haired man: *Clement, Jack* / Who will the next fool be: *Rich, Charlie* / Wayward wind: *Mann, Carl* / Bummin' around: *Feathers, Charlie* / In the dark: *Peterson, Earl* / Just rolling along: *Yelvington, Malcolm* / Fool for loving you: *Earls, Jack* / Jump right out of this jukebox: *Wheeler, Onie* / I'd rather be safe than sorry: *Smith, Warren* / Someday you will pay: *Miller Sisters* / That's what I tell my heart: *McDaniel, Luke* / Country boy: *Cash, Johnny* / Sure to fall: *Perkins, Carl* / Jambalaya: *Lewis, Jerry Lee* / Take and give: *Rhodes, Slim* / We're getting closer to being apart: *Feathers, Charlie* / Tell 'em off: *Wheeler, Onie* / Everyday: *Self, Mack* / I'm lonesome: *Chaffin, Ernie* / When I dream: *Earls, Jack* / Nothing to lose but my heart: *Peterson, Earl* / I've been deceived: *Feathers, Charlie* / Day I found you: *Bond, Eddie* / Ten years: *Clement, Jack* / Sittin' and thinkin': *Rich, Charlie* / Goodbye Mr. Love: *Smith, Warren* / If I could change you: *Mann, Carl* / Who's gonna shoe your pretty little feet: *Anthony, Rayburn* / I know what it means: *Lewis, Jerry Lee* / Tennessee: *Perkins, Carl*
CD Set ______________ **MEMPHIS 01**
Disky / Jan '93 / THE / BMG / Discovery / Pinnacle.

ULTIMATE PARTY MIX ALBUM, THE
Buddy Holly medley: *Berry, Mike* / Beatles medley: *Starsound* / That's what I like: *Jive Bunny* / Beach boys gold: *Gidea Park* / Tribut to Motown: *Motor City Allstars* / Hi NRG megamix: *Thomas, Evelyn* / Chuck Berry megamix: *Berry, Chuck* / Kylie megamix: *Minogue, Kylie* / Back to the 60's: *Tight Fit* / Abba medley: *Starsound*
CD ______________ **NTRCD 044**
Nectar / Nov '95 / Pinnacle.

ULTIMATE RECORDING COMPANY, THE
CD ______________ **TOPPCD 004**
Ultimate / Jul '94 / 3MV / Vital.

ULTIMATE REGGAE PARTY
CD ______________ **TCD 2731**
Telstar / Oct '94 / BMG.

ULTIMATE ROCK
Wishing well: *Free* / Sixty eight guns: *Alarm* / Down at the doctors: *Dr. Feelgood* / Do anything you wanna do: *Eddie & The Hot Rods* / Gimme some lovin': *Davis, Spencer Group* / Stray cat strut: *Stray Cats* / Real wild child: *Iggy Pop* / Some like it hot: *Power Station* / I want a new drug: *Lewis, Huey & The News* / I don't want a lover: *Texas* / Whiskey in the jar: *Thin Lizzy* / Fields of fire: *Big Country* / Comin' on strong: *Broken English* / American woman: *Guess Who* / Who's crying now: *Journey* / Can't fight this feeling: *REO Speedwagon* / God gave rock 'n' roll to you: *Argent* / All the young dudes: *Mott The Hoople* / Walk on the wild side: *Reed, Lou* / Radar love: *Golden Earring*
CD ______________ **CDPR 129**
Premier/MFP / Nov '94 / EMI.

ULTIMATE ROCK 'N' ROLL COLLECTION
(We're gonna) Rock around the clock: *Haley, Bill & The Comets* / Chantilly lace: *Big Bopper* / Johnny B. Goode: *Berry, Chuck* / Say mama: *Vincent, Gene* / Little bitty pretty one: *Lymon, Frankie* / Sea cruise: *Ford, Frankie* / Girl can't help it: *Little Richard* / Something else: *Cochran, Eddie* / Reet petite: *Wilson, Jackie* / Tequila: *Champs* / Good golly miss molly (Live): *Lewis, Jerry Lee* / That's alright: *Perkins, Carl* / I'm walkin': *Domino, Fats* / Hats off to Larry: *Shannon, Del* / Stagger Lee: *Price, Lloyd* / Red river rock: *Johnny & The Hurricanes* / Baby let's play house: *Feathers, Charlie* / Claudette: *Everly Brothers* / Barbara Ann: *Regents* / That'll be the day: *Holly, Buddy* / Stay: *Maurice & The Zodiacs* / Walk don't run: *Ventures* / Tutti frutti: *Little Richard* / Rockin' robin: *Day, Bobby* / Wake up little Susie: *Everly Brothers* / Ah poor little baby: *Craddock, Billy Crash* / It's late: *Nelson, Rick* / Book of love: *Monotones* / Runaround Sue: *Dion* / All Mama's children: *Perkins, Carl* / Bony moronie: *Williams, Larry* / Nut rocker: *B Bumble & The Stingers* / Blue suede shoes: *Cochran, Eddie* / At the

hop: *Danny & The Juniors* / Oh boy: *Holly, Buddy* / Little darlin': *Diamonds* / Rebel rouser: *Eddy, Duane* / I'm number one rock 'n' roll C&W boogie blues man: *Gilley, Mickey* / Whole lotta shakin' goin' on: *Lewis, Jerry Lee* / Rip it up: *Haley, Bill & The Comets* / Shame, shame, shame: *La Beef, Sleepy* / Oh carol: *Berry, Chuck*
CD _____ **MOODCD 36**
Columbia / Oct '94 / Sony.

ULTIMATE SKA COLLECTION
CD _____ **DCD 5295**
Disky / Nov '93 / THE / BMG / Discovery / Pinnacle.

ULTIMATE SOUL COLLECTION
CD _____ **9548333402**
Warner Bros. / Feb '95 / Warner Music.

ULTIMATE SOUL COLLECTION 2
CD _____ **9548338402**
Warner Bros. / Oct '95 / Warner Music.

ULTIMATE SUN COUNTRY COLLECTION
(56 Legendary Original Sun Recordings)
Hey porter: *Cash, Johnny* / Cold cold heart: *Lewis, Jerry Lee* / (Tell me) who: *Smith, Warren* / Turn around: *Perkins, Carl* / Uncertain love: *Rhodes, Slim* / Daisy bread boogie: *Steele, Gene* / Feelin' low: *Chaffin, Ernie* / Cranes of love: *Miller Sisters* / My kind of carryin' on: *Poindexter, Doug* / Show me: *Bond, Eddie* / Blues in the bottom of my shoes (way down blues): *Yelvington, Malcolm* / When you stop loving me: *King, Carl* / Easy to love: *Self, Mack* / Home of the blues: *Cash, Johnny* / Let the jukebox keep on playing: *Perkins, Carl* / Tonight will be the last night: *Smith, Warren* / Will the circle be unbroken: *Lewis, Jerry Lee* / Standing in your window: *Bond, Eddie* / Down on the border: *Simmons, Gene* / How long: *Wimberly, Maggie Sue* / Heartbreakin' love: *Wages, Jimmy* / I'm bluer than anyone can be: *Mann, Carl* / Muddy ole river: *Stinit, Dane* / Tragedy: *Wayne, Thomas* / You're the nearest thing to heaven: *Cash, Johnny* / This old heart of mine: *Bond, Eddie* / That black haired man: *Clement, Jack* / Who will the next fool be: *Rich, Charlie* / Wayward wind: *Mann, Carl* / Bummin' around: *Feathers, Carl* / In the dark: *Peterson, Earl* / Just rolling along: *Yelvington, Malcolm* / Fool for loving you: *Earls, Jack* / Jump right out of this jukebox: *Wheeler, Onie* / I'd rather be safe than sorry: *Smith, Warren* / Someday you will pay: *Miller Sisters* / That's what I tell my heart: *McDaniel, Luke* / Country boy: *Cash, Johnny* / Sure to fail: *Perkins, Carl* / Jambalaya: *Lewis, Jerry Lee* / Take and give: *Rhodes, Slim* / We're getting closer to being apart: *Feathers, Charlie* / Tell 'em off: *Wheeler, Onie* / Everyday: *Self, Mack* / I'm lonesome: *Chaffin, Ernie* / When I dream: *Earls, Jack* / Nothing to lose but my heart: *Peterson, Earl* / I've been deceived: *Feathers, Charlie* / Day I found you: *Bond, Eddie* / Ten years: *Clement, Jack* / Sittin' and thinkin': *Rich, Charlie* / Goodbye Mr. Love: *Smith, Warren* / If I could change you: *Mann, Carl* / Who's gonna shoe your pretty little feet: *Anthony, Rayburn* / I know what it means: *Lewis, Jerry Lee* / Tennessee: *Perkins, Carl*
CD _____ **DCD 5201**
Disky / Aug '91 / THE / BMG / Discovery / Pinnacle.

ULTRAMETAL
CD _____ **MONITOR 1**
Monitor / Jan '92 / CM.

UNCHAINED MELODIES 1
CD _____ **TMPCD 001**
Telstar / Nov '94 / BMG.

UNCHAINED MELODIES 2
CD _____ **TMPCD 002**
Telstar / Nov '94 / BMG.

UNCHAINED MELODIES 3
CD _____ **TMPCD 003**
Telstar / Nov '94 / BMG.

UNCOLLECTED BIG BANDS VOL 1, THE
Dipsy doodle: *Clinton, Larry* / Imagination: *Dorsey, Jimmy* / My baby just cares for me: *James, Harry* / Serenade in blue: *Spivak, Charlie* / Meet me tonight in dreamland: *Gray, Glen* / I've got my love to keep me warm: *Brown, Les* / Somebody else is taking my place: *Nelson, Ozzie* / I'm making believe: *Brown, Les* / Exactly like you: *Herman, Woody* / Contrasts: *Dorsey, Jimmy* / Heart and soul: *Barron, Blue* / I didn't know what time it was: *Cavallaro, Carmen*
CD _____ **HCD 301**
Hindsight / Sep '92 / Target/BMG / Jazz Music.

UNCOVERED
Walk on by: *Franklin, Aretha* / Let's stay together: *Pasadenas* / Every night: *Snow, Phoebe* / They won't go when I go: *Michael, George* / Until you come back to me: *Williams, Deniece & Johnny Mathis* / (Sittin' on) the dock of the bay: *Bolton, Michael* / Don't dream it's over: *Young, Paul* / Stop lovin' me, stop lovin' you: *Hall, Daryl* / What's going on: *Lauper, Cyndi* / Summertime: *Benson, George* / Stand by me: *White, Maurice* / Why can't we live together: *Sade* / Still haven't found what I'm looking for: *Chimes* / Superstar (Don't you remember): *Vandross, Luther* / I'll never fall in love again:

Deacon Blue / Georgia on my mind: *Nelson, Willie*
CD _____ **MOODCD 38**
Sony Music / Feb '95 / Sony.

UNDER DOCTORS ORDERS
CD _____ **VPCD 02038**
VP / Sep '95 / Jetstar.

UNDER THE COVERS
(18 Classic Cover Versions)
Don't let the sun go down on me: *Michael, George & Elton John* / Jealous guy: *Roxy Music* / Let's stay together: *Turner, Tina* / Angel: *Stewart, Rod* / No regrets: *Ure, Midge* / Nothing compares 2 U: *O'Connor, Sinead* / Crying game: *Boy George* / When I fall in love: *Astley, Rick* / You've lost that lovin' feelin': *Hall & Oates* / Where is the love: *Paris, Mica & Will Downing* / Have you seen her: *M.C. Hammer* / It's too late: *Quartz & Dina Carroll* / Don't you worry about a thing: *Incognito* / Why can't we live together: *Sade* / Just the way you are: *White, Barry* / Loving you: *Shanice* / Crying in the rain: *A-Ha* / Baby I love your way/ Freebird: *Will To Power*
CD _____ **5160742**
PolyGram TV / Apr '93 / PolyGram.

UNDERCOVER VOL.3
CD _____ **SPV 08438202**
SPV / Jul '95 / Plastic Head.

UNDERGROUND DANCE
CD _____ **LOWCDX 26**
Low Price Music / Aug '95 / Total/BMG.

UNDERGROUND HOUSE PARTY, THE
(Roger S Presents)
CD _____ **2101535**
Scratch / Jul '95 / BMG.

UNDERGROUND LONDON
CD _____ **KICKCD 31**
Kickin' / Dec '95 / SRD.

UNDERGROUND VOL.1
CD _____ **JARCD 6**
Cookie Jar / Mar '93 / SRD.

UNEARTHED GOLD OF ROCK STEADY VOL.1
Ossie / Nov '95 / Jetstar. _____ **OHCD 004**

UNFORGETTABLE BIG BANDS
CD _____ **UP 006**
Hindsight / Sep '92 / Target/BMG / Jazz Music.

UNFORGETTABLE MELODIES
Bridge over troubled water: *Goodwin, Ron & His Orchestra* / Never on a Sunday: *Love, Geoff & His Orchestra* / Honeymoon song: *Manuel & The Music Of The Mountains* / Snowbird: *Pourcel, Franck & His Orchestra* / What the world needs now is love: *Goodwin, Ron & His Orchestra* / Moon river: *Manuel & The Music Of The Mountains* / True love: *Love, Geoff & His Orchestra* / Godfather love theme: *Pourcel, Franck & His Orchestra* / Misty: *Love, Geoff & His Orchestra* / Fool on the hill: *Goodwin, Ron & His Orchestra* / Spanish Harlem: *Manuel & The Music Of The Mountains* / Forever and ever: *Pourcel, Franck & His Orchestra* / Spartacus love theme: *Love, Geoff & His Orchestra* / Autumn leaves: *Manuel & The Music Of The Mountains* / Summertime: *Pourcel, Franck & His Orchestra* / When I fall in love: *Love, Geoff & His Orchestra* / Elizabethan serenade: *Goodwin, Ron & His Orchestra* / Shadow of your smile: *Manuel & The Music Of The Mountains* / On a clear day: *Pourcel, Franck & His Orchestra* / Misty: *Love, Geoff & His Orchestra* / Walk in the Black Forest: *Love, Geoff & His Orchestra* / Rhapsody on a theme by Paganini: *Goodwin, Ron & His Orchestra* / Night from serenade for strings: *Manuel & The Music Of The Mountains* / Summertime: *Pourcel, Franck & His Orchestra* / When I fall in love: *Love, Geoff & His Orchestra* / Ballade pour Adeline: *Love, Geoff & His Orchestra* / Walk on by: *Goodwin, Ron & His Orchestra* / White rose of Athens: *Manuel & The Music Of The Mountains* / Blue moon: *Pourcel, Franck & His Orchestra* / Walk in the Black Forest: *Love, Geoff & His Orchestra* / Rhapsody on a theme by Paganini: *Goodwin, Ron & His Orchestra*
CD Set _____ **CDDL 1120**
Music For Pleasure / Aug '91 / EMI.

UNFORGETTABLE SESSION, AN
CD _____ **CD 53097**
Giants Of Jazz / Jan '95 / Target/BMG / Cadillac.

UNIDENTIFIED FLOATING AMBIENCE
CD _____ **SR 9454**
Silent / May '94 / Plastic Head.

UNISSUED SUN MASTERS
CD _____ **CPCD 8137**
Charly / Nov '95 / Charly / THE / Cadillac.

UNITED ARTISTS OF MESSIDOR SAMPLER
CD _____ **MES 158232**
Messidor / Apr '93 / Koch / ADA.

UNITED DANCE ALBUM 3
(2CD/MC/LP Set)
CD _____ **FBRCD 334**
4 Beat / Jan '96 / Pinnacle.

UNITED FLAVA OF BRITISH RAP
Listen again nation species: *Urban Species* / Here we go: *NSO Force* / Nang 'em high: *Kaliphz* / Bring it on: *Cash Crew* / Who you loving: *Krispy Three* / Making moves: *M.C. Ni* / Big

---

trouble in little Asia: *Hustlers HC* / Yabba dabba doo: *Darkman* / Free man: *11 - 59* / Colourcode: *Gunshot* / Coming eqipped: *3 P.M.* / Hell hath no fury: *Evey* / Wha cha' all paid: *Scientists Of Sound* / How's life in London: *London Posse* / What's going on: *Black Twang* / All about Eve: *Marxman*
CD _____ **WOLCD 1063**
Ticking Time/China / Jul '95 / Pinnacle.

UNITED FREQUENCIES OF TRANCE VOL. 6
CD _____ **E 11943/2**
United Frequencies Of Trance / Dec '93 / SRD.

UNITED NATIONS OF HOUSE
Shine on: *Degrees Of Motion* / Saturday night, Sunday morning: *T-Empo* / Why: *D-Mob* / Do you want it right now: *Degrees Of Motion* / Back in my life: *Roberts, Joe* / What can you do for me: *Utah Saints* / I'll be there for you: *House Of Virginism* / We are going down: *Deadly Sins* / You and me: *Lisa B* / Back to love: *Brand New Heavies* / New York express: *Hardheads* / Blow your whistle: *D.J. Duke*
CD _____ **828549-2**
FFRR / Aug '94 / PolyGram.

UNITED RAVERS COMPILATION VOL.1
CD _____ **URRC 1**
United Ravers / Nov '95 / Plastic Head.

UNITED SPEAKEASY COLLECTIVE NU JAZZ PRINCIPLES
CD _____ **MM 890002**
Moonshine / Jun '95 / Disc.

UNITY
CD _____ **TTPCD 1**
Totem / Sep '94 / New Note / Jazz Music.

UNIVERSAL SOUNDS OF AMERICA
Space 2: *Durrah, David* / Theme de yoyo: *Art Ensemble Of Chicago* / Lions of judah: *Reid, Steve* / Astral travelling: *Sanders, Pharoah* / Space odyssey: *Belgrave, Marcus* / Empty street: *Reid, Steve* / Kitty bey: *Morris, Byron* / Space 1: *Durrah, David* / Space is the place: *Sun Ra*
CD _____ **SJRCD 027**
Soul Jazz / Jul '95 / New Note / Vital.

UNIVERSE - WORLD TECHNO TRIBE (The Most Progressive Dance Party Organisation In The World)
Pioneers of the universe: *Hypnotist* / List 1: *Bolland, C.J.* / .215061: *AFX* / List 2: *Suburban Hell* / Tremora del terra: *Illuminatae* / Virtual reality: *Two Thumbs* / Joba: *Dr. Fernando* / Flying deeper: *Skyflyer* / Cosmic love (approach and identify): *Resistance D* / Virtual breakdown (mind your head): *Garnier, Laurent* / Sequential (the dune mix): *Sequential* / First symphony: *Angel, Dave* / Barbarella: *Vath, Sven*
CD _____ **VERSECD 1**
Universe/Rising High / Apr '93 / SRD.

UNIVERSE PRESENTS THE TRIBAL GATHERING
Are we here (who are they): *Orbital* / Voodoo people: *Prodigy* / Song for life: *Leftfield* / Spastik: *Plastikman* / Infinite mass: *Faith Department* / Every time you touch me: *Moby* / Starship universe: *Bolland, C.J.* / Crisis a gwan: *Bandulu* / Lagoon: *Angel, Dave* / Her jazz: *Chemical Brothers* / Mother Earth: *Biosphere* / Def 29-62: *Cox, Carl* / Heart: *Loop 8.2* / Hypnotic Eastern rhythm: *Soundclash Republic* / Violator: *Transmakus* / Bug: *Drum Club* / Dark and long: *Underworld*
CD Set _____ **8284522**
Internal / Jul '95 / PolyGram / Pinnacle.

UNNECESSARY NICENESS
CD _____ **TRAIL 2 CD**
Beechwood / Jun '93 / BMG / Pinnacle.

UNPLUGGED COLLECTION VOL.1
Before you accuse me: *Clapton, Eric* / Deep dark truthful mirror: *Costello, Elvis & The Rude 5* / Come rain or come shine: *Henley, Don* / Don't let the sun go down on me: *John, Elton* / Are you gonna go my way: *Kravitz, Lenny* / Barefoot: *Lang, k.d.* / Why: *Lennox, Annie* / We can work it out: *McCartney, Paul* / Pink houses: *Mellencamp, John* / Half a world away: *R.E.M.* / Graceland: *Simon, Paul* / Somebody to shove: *Soul Asylum* / Gasoline alley: *Stewart, Rod* / Don't talk: *10,000 Maniacs* / Pride and joy: *Vaughan, Stevie Ray* / Like a hurricane: *Young, Neil*
CD _____ **9362457742**
WEA / Dec '94 / Warner Music.

UNRELEASED III
CD _____ **PRESAGE 04CD**
Semantic / Feb '94 / Plastic Head.

UNSUNG HEROES - THE PHASE II MOD COLLECTION
CD _____ **PHZCD 17**
Unicorn / Nov '94 / Plastic Head.

UP & DOWN CLUB SESSIONS VOL.1
Soft target: *Jones, Josh Ensemble* / Mr. Puffy: *Dry Look* / Funky niblets: *Hunter, Charlie Trio* / Music in my head: *Alphabet Soup* / Knucklebean: *Brooks, Kenny Trio* / Up and around: *Bernad, Will Trio* / New flavor: *Marshall, Eddie Hip Hop Jazz Band* / 20 30 40 50 60: *Dead: Hunter, Charlie Trio* / Jonesintime: *Jones, Josh Ensemble* / Up and down: *Alphabet Soup*

CD _____ **MR 1032**
Mammoth / Jul '95 / Vital.

UP & DOWN CLUB SESSIONS VOL.2
Round midnight: *Hueman Flavour* / As I reach: *Hueman Flavour* / Up: *Up & Down Allstars* / Here on earth: *Jones, Josh Ensemble* / Cherry suite: *Hueman Flavour* / Acafona yare: *Jones, Josh Ensemble* / Blues in Havana: *Jones, Josh Ensemble* / Vision sets you free: *Hueman Flavour* / Destiny: *Hueman Flavour* / Down: *Up & Down Allstars* / Ache: *Jones, Josh*
CD _____ **MR1042**
Mammoth / Aug '95 / Vital.

UP ALL NIGHT
(30 Northern Soul Classics)
Nothing can stop me: *Chandler, Gene* / Getting mighty crowded: *Everett, Betty* / Nothing worse than being alone: *Ad Libs* / That other place: *Flemons, Wade* / I keep tryin': *Hughes, Freddie* / You're the dream: *Shelton, Roscoe* / I hurt on the other side: *Barnes, Sidney* / Lonely for you baby: *Dee, Sonny* / Come on train: *Thomas, Don* / Breakaway: *Valentines* / You're gonna need me: *Ford, Ted* / Being without you: *Williams, Maurice* / Why don't you write: *Bates, Lee* / But I couldn't: *Harper, Willie* / Just another heartbreak: *Little Richie* / Touch me, hold me, kiss me: *Inspirations* / Tear stained face: *Varner, Don* / Hung up on your love: *Montclairs* / Running for my life: *Shelton, Roscoe* / My man don't think I know: *Davies, Gwen* / Hold on: *Beavers, Jackie* / You've been gone too long: *Sexton, Ann* / That's enough: *Robinson, Roscoe* / I'd think it over twice (if I were you): *Fletcher, Sam* / You'll always be in style: *Barnes, Sidney* / Don't let me down: *Hughes, Freddie* / Humphrey, Amanda* / Now I'm in love with you: *Sims, Marvin L.* / I'm a fool, I must love you: *Falcons*
CD _____ **CDINS 5028**
Charly / Apr '90 / Charly / THE / Cadillac.

UP ALL NIGHT VOL 2
(30 Hits From The Original Soul Underground)
CD _____ **CDGRM 500**
Charly / Jan '93 / Charly / THE / Cadillac.

UP COUNTRY
CD _____ **SOV 014CD**
Sovereign / Jan '93 / Target/BMG.

UP FRONT 1 (NEW SERIES)
CD _____ **UPCD 901**
Upfront / Jun '90 / Serious Records.

UP TO ZION
I hear a sound / Day of the Lord / He is good / Bless the Lord / Let us rejoice and be glad / Praise the Lord / Ascribe unto the Lord / He shall reign / We give you thanks / By your blood / Who is like me / Worthy is the lamb / Great and marvellous / Sond of Moses / Come let us get up to Zion / Come let us get up
CD _____ **HMD 41**
Hosanna / Mar '92 / Nelson Word.

UP WITH THE CURTAIN
(Stars of the Variety Theatre)
That's what you think: *Bermon, Len* / Stormy weather: *Carless, Dorothy* / I'll take romance: *Driver, Betty* / Can't we meet again: *Flanagan & Allen* / Million tears: *Flanagan & Allen* / Underneath the arches: *Flanagan & Allen* / Caught in the act: *Forsythe, Seamon & Farrell* / I have an ear for music: *Geraldo & Arthur Tracy* / Love in bloom: *Geraldo* / Pretty girl is like a melody: *Geraldo & Arthur Tracy* / Up with the curtain: *Geraldo* / I'm a different me they say: *Hutch* / Melody maker: *Hutch* / Oh they're tough, mighty tough in the West: *Hylton, Jack* / Was it rain: *Hylton, Jack* / Me and my girl: *Lane, Lupino & Teddie St. Denis* / Every Sunday afternoon: *Miller, Max* / You can't go away like that: *Miller, Max* / Georgia's got a moon: *Nesbitt, Max & Harry* / Hit medley: *Reid, Billy Accordion Band* / My honey's loving arms: *Rosing, Val* / On behalf of the working classes: *Russell, Billy* / I don't do things like that: *Trinder, Tommy* / Lads tell a few: *Western Brothers*
CD _____ **CD AJA 5076**
Living Era / '91 / Koch.

UP YER RONSON - ORIGINAL SOUNDTRACK VOL.1
You can't touch me / You won't be mix): *Pollack, Karen & Fire Island* / U (K Klass radio mix): *Clark, Loni* / I know a place (E-Smoove remix): *English, Kim* / Back to love (Graeme Park club mix): *Brand New Heavies* / I believe (Classic gospel mix): *Sounds Of Blackness* / Another sleepness night: *Christopher, Shawn* / Lost in love (Graeme Park club mix): *Hutch* / Show me loves (Classic mix): *Limerick, Alison* / Lover (K Klass klub mix): *Roberts, Joe* / Keep the jam goin' (live): *Ill Disco* / Nite life (English, Kim / Colour of my skin (Swing remix): *Swing 52* / Gimmie luv: *Bad Yard Club* / Real: *Allen, Donna* / Take me back to love: *Sledge, Kathy* / Mings incredible disco machine: *Brothers Love Dubs* / All over me (Association squeeze mix): *Carr, Suzi* / Blow your whistle (Demo mix): *D.J. Duke* / Dreamer (Original club mix): *Livin' Joy* / Theme from Outrage (That piano mix): *Outrage* / On the dance floor (Roach motel dub): *D.J. Disciple* / U girls (Radio edit): *Nush* / Will you love

---

me in the morning (Mollison remix): Mollison, Sam / Get yourself together (Extended disco groovathon): Hustlers Convention / Someday (Sasha's full tension mix): M People / 100% pure (Radio mix): Waters, Crystal / Renegade master (Original mix): Wildchild / On ya way (Original mix): Helicopter / Everybody dance (Chic inspirational mix): Evolution
CD _____ 5350762
Hi Life / Nov '95 / PolyGram.

UPPERS ON THE SOUTH DOWNS
CD _____ DOJOCD 196
Dojo / Nov '94 / BMG.

UPTOWN, DOWN SOUTH
I've got to hold back / Sweetest girl in the world / Judy / That's loving you / I'm not your regular woman / Since I met you baby / Don't let our love fade away / Even if the signs are wrong / Childhood days / Just another guy / Bigger and better / Cryin' days are over / Save a foolish man / That's my man / No more tears / Set your soul on fire / Our love is getting better / Crystal blue persuasion / What price for love / Thanks a lot / I would if I could / Keep on running away / Running away from love / Just the other day
CD _____ CDKEND 121
Kent / Feb '95 / Pinnacle.

URAL: TRADITIONAL MUSIC FROM BASHKORTOSTAN
CD _____ PAN 2018CD
Pan / Mar '95 / ADA / Direct / CM.

URBAN BLACK VOL. 1
CD _____ SOUNDSCD 1
Street Sounds / Oct '94 / BMG.

UZLYAU
(Music Of The Tuva, Sayan, Altai & Urais)
CD _____ PAN 2019CD
Pan / Jan '94 / ADA / Direct / CM.

V AS IN VICTIM
CD _____ AVANT 027CD
Avant / Oct '94 / Harmonia Mundi / Cadillac.

V DISC COLLECTION
CD Set _____ 269032
Milan / Dec '95 / BMG / Silva Screen.

V DISC COLLECTION VOL.1
(The Big Bands)
CD _____ 269042
Milan / Jun '95 / BMG / Silva Screen.

V DISC COLLECTION VOL.2
(Combos & Soloists)
CD _____ 269052
Milan / Jun '95 / BMG / Silva Screen.

V DISC COLLECTION VOL.3
(The Singers)
CD _____ 269062
Milan / Jun '95 / BMG / Silva Screen.

V.E. DAY - THE DANCE BANDS
Germany surrenders: Churchill, Sir Winston / I've got a heart filled with love: Preager, Lou & His Band / Together: Winick, Fred & His Astor Club Seven / Marlene: Loss, Joe & His Orchestra / If I had only known: Geraldo & His Orchestra / Opus one: Heath, Ted & His Music / Sitting on a cloud: Simpson, Jack & His Sextet / Swinging on a star: Geraldo & His Orchestra / Barrelhouse boogie: Roy, Harry & His Band / So dumb but so beautiful: Geraldo & His Orchestra / Shine on harvest moon: Geraldo & His Orchestra / You're in love: Preager, Lou & His Band / Don't sweetheart me: Geraldo & His Orchestra / It had to be you: Loss, Joe & His Orchestra / Dance with a Dolly: Ambrose & His Orchestra / Time on my hands: Gonella, Nat & His Georgians / Someday I'll meet you again: Geraldo & His Orchestra / What do you think those ruby lips were made for: Thorburn, Billy & Robinson Cleaver / That's sabotage: Geraldo & His Orchestra / Don't ask me why: Gibbons, Carroll & The Savoy Hotel Orpheans / Undecided: Silvester, Victor & His Jive Orchestra / Amor amor: Ambrose & His Orchestra / I'll get by: Barriteau, Carl & His Orchestra / You'll be a happy little sweetheart in the spring: Cotton, Billy & His Band / I'm going to build a future world around you: Geraldo & His Orchestra
CD _____ RAJCD 844
Empress / Feb '95 / THE.

V.E. DAY - THE OFFICIAL BRITISH LEGION COLLECTION
Run rabbit run: Flanagan & Allen / We'll meet again: Lynn, Vera / We're gonna hang out the washing on the Siegfried Line: Cotton, Billy & His Band / Over the rainbow: Garland, Judy / In the mood: Loss, Joe & His Band / Puss in the backroom: Dietrich, Marlene / If I had my way: Crosby, Bing / Nightingale sang in Berkley Square: Hutch-

inson, Leslie / Beer barrel polka: Andrews Sisters / I'll never smile again: Dorsey, Tommy / I've got sixpence: Organ Dance Band & Me / Room 504: Hale, Binnie / Last time I saw paris: Coward, Sir Noel / Frensi: Shaw, Artie & His Orchestra / Beneath the lights of home: Geraldo / I yi yi yi yi (I like you very much): Miranda, Carmen / London pride: Coward, Sir Noel / Yours: Lynn, Vera / American patrol: Loss, Joe & His band / Anniversary waltz: Crosby, Bing / You made me love you: Foster, Teddy / White cliffs of Dover: Lynn, Vera / I don't want to walk without you: Gibbons, Carroll / You are my sunshine: Crosby, Bing / Don't sit under the apple tree: Andrews Sisters / Chattanooga choo choo: Miller, Glenn / Deep in the heart of Texas: Crosby, Bing / Silver wings in the moonlight: Shelton, Anne / Whispering grass: Ink Spots / Moonlight becomes you: Crosby, Bing / Praise the Lord and pass the ammunition: Macs, Merry / As time goes by: Layton, Turner / Begin the beguine: Haywood, Eddie / I had the craziest dream: Gibbons, Carroll / I'm gonna get lit up (when the lights go on in London): Crosby, Bing / A nightingale sang and a prayer: Ambrose / Tico tico: Smith, Ethel / You'll never know: Haymes, Dick / This is the army Mr. Jones: Berlin, Irving / Besame mucho: Dorsey, Jimmy / Roll me over: Cotton, Billy & His Band / Paper doll: Mills Brothers / Lovely way to spend an evening: Gibbons, Carroll / I'll be seeing you: Crosby, Bing / Lili Marlene: Shelton, Anne / Swinging on a star: Crosby, Bing / No love, no nothin': Carless, Dorothy / Dance with a dolly: Geraldo & His Dance Orchestra / Jukebox Saturday night: Miller, Glenn / My guy's come home: Loss, Joe
CD Set _____ CDEM 1549
EMI / Apr '95 / EMI.

V.E. DAY - THE VOCALISTS
Victory: Churchill, Sir Winston / There's a new world: Lynn, Vera / Shine on Victory moon: Bonn, Issy / It's been a long, long time: Hall, Adelaide / Let me love you tonight: Melachrino, George / I got it bad: Davis, Beryl / (All of a sudden) My heart sings: Hall, Adelaide / Goodnight wherever you are: Green, Johnny / It could happen to you: Lynn, Vera / Tonight I kissed you: Shelton, Anne / Come out come out where ever you are: Green, Johnny / Don't believe everything you dream: Bonn, Issy / Then you kissed me: Green, Johnny / Long ago and far away: Lynn, Vera / You're in love: Peers, Donald / Pistol packin' Mama: Dennis, Johnny / Shine on harvest moon: Flanagan & Allen / In a friendly little harbour: Layton, Turner / It's love love love: Morrow, Dorothy / Dreaming: Flanagan & Allen / Lili Marlene: Shelton, Anne / MacNamara's band: Morrow, Dorothy / Dare I love you: Hutch / Things that mean so much to me: Bonn, Issy / Fool with a dream: O'Connor, Cavan
CD _____ RAJCD 845
Empress / Feb '95 / THE.

V.E. DAY MUSIC COLLECTION VOL.1, THE
We'll meet again / Run rabbit run / Bless 'em all / Wish me luck as you wave me goodbye / London pride / Beneath the lights of home / Kiss the boys of home / Johnny zero / When that man is dead and gone / Somewhere in France / It's that man again / I couldn't sleep a wink last night / This is the army / My heart and I / Chattanooga choo choo / All over the place / Warsaw concerto / Blues in the night / Calling all workers / Lambeth walk / Bandwagon
CD Set _____ HDBOX 004
Happy Days / Apr '95 / Conifer.

V.E. DAY MUSIC COLLECTION VOL.2, THE
Kiss me goodnight, Sergeant Major / Beer barrel polka / My brother int he life guards / Corporal McDougall / I fell in love with an airman / Biggest aspidistra in the world / Der fuhrer's face / Sam goes to it / Munition worker / New kind of old fashioned girl / Viv Oliver joins the army / Darling daughter / Amapola / I'm going to see you today / Pistol packin' mama / You'd be so nice to come home to / Paper doll
CD Set _____ HDBOX 005
Happy Days / Apr '95 / Conifer.

V.E. DAY MUSICAL TRIBUTE - NOW IS THE HOUR
CD _____ VEDAY 1945
Start / Apr '95 / Koch.

V.E. DAY PARTY
CD _____ PASTCD 7063
Flapper / May '95 / Pinnacle.

VALLEY AND PAMPAS
CD _____ PS 65152
Playasound / Sep '95 / Harmonia Mundi / ADA.

VALLEY OF DEATH
CD _____ VPCD 1443
VP / Nov '95 / Jetstar.

VALLEYS SING, THE
Old rugged cross / Love divine / Day thou gavest Lord is ended / All in the April evening / Guide me o thou great / Jehovah / Where you there / What a friend we have in Jehovah / Lord's prayer / Give thanks / There is a redeemer / Majesty / Steal away / Kymbayah / Abide with me / Onward

Christian soldiers / When I survey the wondrous cross / You'll never walk alone / Praise my soul the king of heaven
CD _____ WSTCD 9725
Nelson Word / Apr '92 / Nelson Word.

VAMPIROS LESBOS: SEXADELIC DANCE PARTY
CD _____ EFA 119502
Crippled Dick Hot Wax / Nov '95 / SRD.

VARIATIONS ON A CHILL
CD Set _____ SSR 147
SSR / Aug '95 / Grapevine.

VARIOUS AMBIENT COLLABORATIONS
CD _____ RSNCD 11
Rising High / Oct '93 / Disc.

VARIOUS ANTHEMS
(Tunes Vol.1)
CD _____ DANCECD 002
D-Zone / May '92 / Pinnacle.

VASSAR
CD _____ KFWCD 120
Knitting Factory / Nov '94 / Grapevine.

VAULT CLASSICS VOL.1
CD _____ DGVCD 2023
Grapevine & Dynamite / Jun '93 / Jetstar.

VERABRA RETROSPECTIVE '80/'90
Bob the bob: Lounge Lizards / Minha rua: Xiame / Sundown: Cerletti, Marco / Pipeland: Schaffer, Janne / Bagus: Toshiyuki Honda / Act natural: Grolnick, Don / D.U.V.: De Winkel & Hattler / Yellow fellow: Mynta / No name: Von Senger, Dominik / Algodoal: Herting, Mike / Flamencos en Nueva York: Nunez, Gerardo / Lilo and Max: De Winkel, Torsten / Azure treasure: Shlomo Bat-Ain / Cousin butterfly: Never Been There / Joyride: Thompson, Barbara Paraphernalia / At the top of the hill: Marsh, Hug / De sabado pra domingunhes: Pascoal, Hermeto
CD _____ VBR 20402
Vera Bra / Nov '90 / Pinnacle / New Note.

VERSION 1.1
CD _____ NOMU 17CD
Mute / Oct '93 / Disc.

VERSION LIKE RAIN
I want a wine: Graham, Leo / Double wine: Upsetters / Hot and cold (version 1): Pablo & Upsetters / Fever: Cadogan, Susan / Beat down Babylon: Byles, Junior / Outformer version: Upsetters / Beat version: Upsetters / Iron wolf: Upsetters / Stick together: U-Roy / This world: Milton, Henry / Influenza version: Upsetters / Informer man: Byles, Junior / Babylon burning: Maxie / Freedom fighter: Bunny & Ricky / Bet you don't know: Duffus, Shenley
CD _____ CDTRL 278
Trojan / Mar '92 / Jetstar / Total/BMG.

VERVE JAZZ MASTERS SAMPLER
CD _____ 5198532
Verve / Apr '93 / PolyGram.

VERVE'S GRAMMY WINNERS
CD _____ 5214852
Verve / May '94 / PolyGram.

VERY BEST IRISH CEILI MUSIC
CD _____ CHCD 1039
Chyme / Aug '94 / CM / ADA / Direct.

VERY BEST OF BLUES GUITAR
CD _____ VBCD 306
Charly / Jan '96 / Charly / THE / Cadillac.

VERY BEST OF CHARLY BLUES MASTERWORKS, THE
(4CD Box Set)
Breachin' blues: Johnson, Robert / If I had possession over judgement day: Johnson, Robert / Midnight steppers: Broonzy, Big Bill / Rockin' chair blues: Broonzy, Big Bill / I love the life I live, I live the life I love: Waters, Muddy / Rock me: Waters, Muddy / I don't know: Mabon, Willie / Sloppy drunk: Rogers, Jimmy / Mama talk to your daughter: Lenoir, J.B. / How many more years: Howlin' Wolf / Sky is crying: James, Elmore / Dust my broom: James, Elmore / Honest I do: Reed, Jimmy / Shame, shame, shame: Reed, Jimmy / I'll play the blues for you: King, Albert / Big town playboy: Taylor, Eddie / Don't start me talkin': Williamson, Sonny Boy / Help me: Williamson, Sonny Boy / First time I met the blues: Guy, Buddy / Stone crazy: Guy, Buddy / Good morning little school girl: Williamson, Sonny Boy / Juke: Little Walter / Rattin' and runnin' around: Boyd, Eddie / I ain't got you: Reed, Jimmy / My babe: Little Walter / I wish you would: Arnold, Billy Boy / Smokestack lightnin': Howlin' Wolf / Natchez burning: Howlin' Wolf / All your love: Magic Sam / Twenty one days in jail: Magic Sam / Rockin' the house: Memphis Slim / So many roads, so many trains: Rush, Otis / Searching for a woman: King, Albert / Got my mojo working: Waters, Muddy / Bring it on home: Williamson, Sonny Boy / I'm a man: Spoon / Super blues Band / Killing floor: Howlin' Wolf / Highway 49: Howlin' Wolf / Can't get no grindin' What's the matter with the mill): Waters, Muddy / After hours: Waters, Muddy / Crawl: Guitar Junior / Inspiration blues: Walker, T-Bone / T-Bone shuffle: Walker, T-Bone / Reconsider baby: Fulson, Lowell / Coffee house blues: Hopkins, Lightnin' / Letter to my (back door friend): Hopkins, Lightnin' / Fishing colins: Hopkins, Lightnin' / Person to person: James,

Elmore / Downhearted blues: Smith, Bessie / Careless love blues: Smith, Bessie / I see you when you're weak: Hooker, John Lee / Walkin' the boogie: Hooker, John Lee / Hard feeling: Dupree, Champion Jack / That's all right: Crudup, Arthur 'Big Boy' / Shake your moneymaker: James, Elmore / Dimples: Hooker, John Lee / Ain't nobody's business: Witherspoon, Jimmy / Jelly roll king: Frost, Frank / Boom boom: Hooker, John Lee / Family rules (Angel child): Guitar Junior / Score: Cray, Robert / Shake it baby: Hooker, John Lee / Last time: Mayall, John & The Bluesbreakers / I'm bad: Diddley, Bo / Long way home: Brown, Clarence 'Gatemouth' / It's raining in my life: Washington, Walter 'Wolfman' / Five long years: Clapton, Eric & The Yardbirds / Three times a fool: Rush, Otis / I can't quit you baby: Rush, Otis / Honky tonk: Washington, Walter 'Wolfman' / Mellow fellow: Robinson, Fenton / Getaway: Robinson, Fenton / Waterfront: Hooker, John Lee / My love is real: Guy, Buddy / It's a bloody life: Page, Jimmy & Sonny Boy Williamson / I'm gonna forget about you: Cray, Robert / For now so long: Brown, Clarence 'Gatemouth' / I cry and sing the blues: Guy, Buddy / Who do you love: Diddley, Bo / Sweet home Chicago: Allison, Luther
CD Set _____ CDBM 103-4
Charly / Feb '94 / Charly / THE / Cadillac.

VERY BEST OF CHARLY BLUES MASTERWORKS, THE
(2CD Set)
CD Set _____ CDBMD 01
Charly / Feb '94 / Charly / THE / Cadillac.

VERY BEST OF COUNTRY, THE
CD _____ AHLCD 23
Hit / Sep '94 / PolyGram.

VERY BEST OF IRISH FOLK
CD _____ DCDCD 203
Castle / Jun '95 / BMG.

VERY BEST OF SUN ROCK 'N' ROLL
Whole lotta shakin' goin' on: Lewis, Jerry Lee / Ain't got a thing: Burgess, Sonny / Boppin' the blues: Perkins, Carl / Devil doll: Orbison, Roy / Red hot: Riley, Billy Lee / Got love if you want it: Smith, Warren / All night rock: Honeycutt, Glenn / Love my baby: Thompson, Hayden / Flatfoot Sam: Blake, Tommy / Love crazy baby: Parchman, Kenny / Put your cat clothes on: Perkins, Carl / Baby, please don't go: Riley, Billy Lee / Wild one: Lewis, Jerry Lee / Domino: Orbison, Roy / My bucket's got a hole in it: Burgess, Sonny / Blue suede shoes: Perkins, Carl / Come on little mama: Harris, Ray / Ubangi stomp: Smith, Warren / Break up: Smith, Ray / Madman: Wages, Jimmy / We wanna boogie: Burgess, Sonny / That don't move me: Perkins, Carl
CD _____ MCCD 024
Music Club / May '91 / Disc / THE / CM.

VERY BEST OF THAT LOVING FEELING, THE
CD _____ DINCD 78
Dino / Nov '93 / Pinnacle / 3MV.

VERY BEST OF THE FESTIVALS OF ONE THOUSAND WELSH MALE VOICES
Llanfair / Ar hyd y nos / Rhyfelgyrch gwyr Harlech (Men of Harlech) / Cyfri'r geifr / Laudamus / Deus salutis / Silver birch / tyd a roddiaist / Crimond / Dies irae / Go down Moses / Chorus of the Hebrew slaves / Pilgrims chorus / Nile chorus / O Isis and Osiris / Sailor's chorus / Soldier's chorus / Roman war song / Battle hymn of the Republic / Myfanwy / Cwm Rhondda / Hen wlad fy rhadau (Land of my fathers)
CD _____ CDEMS 1448
EMI / May '92 / EMI.

VERY NOSTALGIC CHRISTMAS, A
White Christmas: Crosby, Bing / Winter wonderland: Walsh & Parker / I'm sending a letter to Santa Claus: Robins, Phyllis / God bless you every gentlemen: Crosby, Bing / Fairy on the Christmas tree: Hall, Henry Orchestra / Little boy that Santa Claus forgot: Tracy, Arthur / Silent night: Langford, Frances / O come all ye faithful (Adeste Fidelis): Langford, Frances / Christmas bells at Eventide: Fields, Gracie / Jingle bells: Miller, Glenn / I'm spending Christmas with the old folks: Rabin, Oscar / Christmas bells are ringing: Winn, Mae / Santa Claus express: Wilbur, Jay / I'm going home for Christmas: Hall, Henry Orchestra / I took my harp to a party: Fields, Gracie / Jolly old Christmas: Cotton, Billy / Cradle song: Miller, Glenn / Ave Maria: Lynn, Vera / Good morning blues: Lynn, Vera / Aladdin - A potty pantomime: Payne, Jack
CD _____ RAJCD 839
Empress / Oct '95 / THE.

VERY SPECIAL CHRISTMAS 2, A
Christmas all over again: Petty, Tom & The Heartbreakers / Jingle bell rock: Travis, Randy / Christmas song: Vandross, Luther / Santa Claus is coming to town: Sinatra, Frank & Cyndi Lauper / Birth of Christ: Boyz II Men / Please come home for Christmas: Bon Jovi, Jon / What Christmas means to me: Young, Paul / O Christmas tree: Franklin, Aretha / Rockin' around the Christmas tree: Spector, Ronnie & Darlene Love / White Christmas: Bolton, Michael / Christmas is: Run DMC / Christmas time again: Extreme / Merry Christmas baby: Raitt,

Bonnie & Charles Brown / O holy night: Campbell, Tevin / Sleigh ride: Gibson, Debbie / What child is this: Williams, Vanessa / Blue Christmas: Wilson, A.N. / Silent night: Wilson Phillips / I believe in you: O'Connor, Sinead
CD _____ 5400032
A&M / Nov '95 / PolyGram.

VERY SPECIAL CHRISTMAS, A
Santa Claus is coming to town: Pointer Sisters / Winter Wonderland: Eurythmics / Do you hear what I say: Houston, Whitney / Merry Christmas baby: Springsteen, Bruce & The E Street Band / Have yourself a merry little Christmas: Pretenders / I saw Mommy kissing Santa Claus: Mellencamp, John Cougar / Gabriel's message: Sting / Christmas in Hollis: Run DMC / Christmas (baby please come home): U2 / Santa baby: Madonna / Little drummer boy: Seger, Bob & The Silver Bullet Band / Run Rudolph run: Adams, Bryan / Back door Santa: Bon Jovi / Coventry carol: Moyet, Alison / Silent night: Nicks, Stevie
CD _____ CDA 3911
A&M / Nov '94 / PolyGram.

VETERAN COMPILATION
CD _____ VTC 1
Veteran Tapes / Jun '93 / Direct / ADA.

VIBE (THE SOUND OF SWING)
Love nu minit: Blige, Mary J. / Realize: Wilson, Charlie / That's the way love is: Brown, Bobby / If you feel the need: Shomari / I like your style: Bubba / Don't keep me waiting: Rhythm Within / Real love: Lorenzo / One night stand: Father MC / Do you wanna chill with me: Solid State Sound / Yo - that's a lot of body: Ready For The World / Baby, baby: TLC / Right here: S.W.V. / Helluva: Brotherhood Creed / I dream, I dream: Jackson, Jermaine
CD _____ CDELV 07
Debut / Jul '93 / Pinnacle / 3MV / Sony.

VIBE 2
CD _____ CDELV 17
Elevate / Jun '94 / 3MV / Sony.

VIBE MUSIC - THE SOULFUL SOUND OF CHICAGO
CD _____ PLUGCD 2
CD _____ PLUGMD 2
Produce / Jul '95 / 3MV / Sony.

VICTORIAN MUSICAL BOXES
CD _____ CDSDL 408
Saydisc / Sep '94 / Harmonia Mundi / ADA / Direct.

VICTORIAN SUNDAY, A
Abide with me / Judas Maccabaeus / Lost chord / When I survey the wondrous cross / How sweet the name of Jesus sounds / Lead kindly light / Nearer my god to thee / Shall we meet beyond the river / Only an armour bearer / I will sing of my redeemer / Scatter seeds of kindness / Shall we gather at the river / Beaulah land / Hold City / Morning hymn / Evening hymn / Onward Christian Soldiers / Rescue the perishing / What shall the harvest be / We'll work 'til Jesus comes / Washed in the blood of the lamb / What a friend we have in Jesus / Sicilian mariners / Helmsley / Luther's hymn / London new / Mountain Ephraim / God save the Queen
CD _____ CDSDL 331
Saydisc / Oct '91 / Harmonia Mundi / ADA / Direct.

VIETNAM - THE DAN TRANH
CD _____ C 560055CD
Ocora / Aug '94 / Harmonia Mundi / ADA.

VIETNAM - TRADITION DU SUD
CD _____ C 580043
Ocora / Nov '92 / Harmonia Mundi / ADA.

VILE VIBES
CD _____ VILE 15CD
Peaceville / Feb '90 / Pinnacle.

VILLAGE MUSIC
(Songs & Dances From Bosnia/Croatia/Macedonia)
CD _____ 7559722422
Elektra Nonesuch / Jan '95 / Warner Music.

VINE YARD REVIVAL SAMPLER
CD _____ VYDCD 1
Vine Yard / Sep '95 / Grapevine.

VINTAGE BANDS, THE
Music, Maestro, please: Hylton, Jack & His Orchestra / Alexander's ragtime band: Roy, Harry & His Orchestra / Nagasaki: Gonella, Nat & His Georgians / Nobody loves a fairy when she's forty: Cotton, Billy & His Band / My brother makes the noises for the talkies: Payne, Jack & The BBC Dance Orchestra / Stay as sweet as you are: Stone, Lew & His Orchestra / In the mood: Loss, Joe & His Orchestra / Let's face the music and dance: Fox, Roy & His Orchestra / Nightingale sang in Berkeley Square: Gibbons, Carroll & The Savoy Hotel Orpheans / Dancing in the dark: Ambrose / Here's to the next time: Hall, Henry & The BBC Dance Orchestra / Say it with music: Payne, Jack & The BBC Dance Orchestra / I'm gonna get lit up (when the lights go on in London): Gibbons, Carroll & The Savoy Hotel Orpheans / Change partners: Loss, Joe & His Orchestra / Did you ever see a dream walking: Hall,

Henry & The BBC Dance Orchestra / Shine: Cotton, Billy & His Band / She had to go and lose it at the Astor: Roy, Harry & His Orchestra / Easy to remember: Stone, Lew & His Orchestra / Have you met Miss Jones: Hylton, Jack & His Orchestra / I can't dance: Gonella, Nat & His Georgians / Night is young and you're so beautiful: Fox, Roy & His Orchestra / Let's put out the lights: Ambrose
CD _____ CC 206
Music For Pleasure / May '88 / EMI.

VINTAGE CHRISTMAS, A
Little boy that Santa Claus forgot / Winter wonderland / Gracie Fields' christmas party / I'm sending a letter to Santa Claus / Gert and Daisy make a christmas pudding / Silent night / I'm going home for christmas / Christmas in the rockies / Santa with the Air Force at christmas / Santa Claus express / Lambeth walk christmas party / O come all ye faithful (Adeste Fidelis) / Christmas bells at eventide / Robinson cleaver's christmas medley / White Christmas
CD _____ PASTCD 9768
Flapper / Nov '91 / Pinnacle.

VINTAGE COUNTRY
My little lady: Rodgers, Jimmie / Daddy and me: Rodgers, Jimmie / Waiting for a train: Rodgers, Jimmie / Any old time: Rodgers, Jimmie / Back in the saddle again: Autry, Gene / It makes no difference now: Autry, Gene / You are my sunshine: Autry, Gene / Time changes everything: Wills, Bob & His Texas Playboys / New San Antonio Rose: Wills, Bob & His Texas Playboys / Take me back to Tulsa: Wills, Bob & His Texas Playboys / Great speckled bird: Acuff, Roy & His Smokey Mountain Boys / Night train to Memphis: Acuff, Roy & His Smokey Mountain Boys / Wreck on the highway: Acuff, Roy & His Smokey Mountain Boys / Wabash cannonball: Monroe, Bill & His Blue Grass Boys / No letter in the mail: Monroe, Bill & His Blue Grass Boys / Orange blossom special: Monroe, Bill & His Blue Grass Boys
CD _____ HADCD 161
Javelin / May '94 / THE / Henry Hadaway Organisation.

VINTAGE MELLOW JAZZ
(3CD Set)
When the saints go marching in: Armstrong, Louis / I'm confessin': Armstrong, Louis / Our Monday date: Armstrong, Louis / You are my lucky star: Armstrong, Louis / As long as you live you'll be dead if you die: Armstrong, Louis / On the sunny side of the street: Armstrong, Louis / Lyin' to myself: Armstrong, Louis / Solitude: Armstrong, Louis / Shoe shine boy: Armstrong, Louis / So little time: Armstrong, Louis / I double dare you: Armstrong, Louis / Love walked in: Armstrong, Louis / Public melody number one: Armstrong, Louis / True confession: Armstrong, Louis / Thankful: Armstrong, Louis / Red sails in the sunset: Armstrong, Louis / Falling in love with you: Armstrong, Louis / Yours and mine: Armstrong, Louis / Hear me talkin' to ya: Armstrong, Louis / Save it pretty Mama: Armstrong, Louis / You rascal you: Armstrong, Louis / When it's sleepy time down south: Armstrong, Louis / Hot mallets: Hampton, Lionel / Shufflin' at the Hollywood: Hampton, Lionel / Central Avenue breakdown: Hampton, Lionel / Dinah: Hampton, Lionel / Four or five times: Hampton, Lionel / Twelfth street rag: Hampton, Lionel / Chasin' with chase: Hampton, Lionel / Rythm: Hampton, Lionel / China stomp: Hampton, Lionel / Blue: Hampton, Lionel / Pig boot boogie: Hampton, Lionel / Three quarter beacon: Hampton, Lionel / Ain't cha comin' home: Hampton, Lionel / Munson street breakdown: Hampton, Lionel / When the lights are low: Hampton, Lionel / Shoe shiners drag: Hampton, Lionel / Ring dem bells: Hampton, Lionel / I've found a new baby: Hampton, Lionel / Singin' the blues: Hampton, Lionel / Take the 'A' train: Ellington, Duke / Perdido: Ellington, Duke / Five O'clock whistle: Ellington, Duke / Sidewalks of New York: Ellington, Duke / Sophisticated lady: Ellington, Duke / Harlem air shaft: Ellington, Duke / Me and you: Ellington, Duke / Concerto for cootie: Ellington, Duke / My greatest mistake: Ellington, Duke / Johnny come lately: Ellington, Duke / Cotton tail: Ellington, Duke / Don't get around much anymore: Ellington, Duke / Blue goose: Ellington, Duke / In a mellotone: Ellington, Duke / Warm valley: Ellington, Duke / Printer panther patter: Ellington, Duke / Raincheck: Ellington, Duke / Hayfoot, strawfoot: Ellington, Duke / Moon mist: Ellington, Duke / Morning glory: Ellington, Duke / Saratoga swing: Ellington, Duke
CD Set _____ EMPRESS 1003
Empress / Oct '95 / THE.

VINTAGE MELODIES
(Songs of the Victorian era)
Come into the garden Maud / Won't you buy my pretty flowers / Mistletoe bough / End of a perfect day / My pretty Jane / Drinking / I'll be your sweetheart / Silent worship / In the gloaming / Road to Mandalay / Mother take the wheel away / Excelsior
CD _____ LCDM 9040

Lismor / Oct '90 / Lismor / Direct / Duncans / ADA.

VINTAGE MUSIC FROM INDIA
CD _____ ROU 1083CD
Rounder / May '93 / CM / Direct / ADA / Cadillac.

VINYL JUNKIE: COUNTRY
CD _____ VJCD 1
Vinyl Junkie / Jul '95 / Direct / ADA.

VIP VOLUME ONE
CD Set _____ BASHD 1
VIP Champagne Bash / Jun '95 / Grapevine.

VIPER MAD BLUES
(16 songs of dope and depravity)
CD _____ JASSCD 630
Jass / Oct '92 / CM / Jazz Music / ADA / Cadillac / Direct.

VIRGINIA TRADITIONS - BALLADS & SONGS
CD _____ GVM 1004CD
Global Village / Jul '95 / ADA / Direct.

VIRGINIA TRADITIONS - SECULAR BLACK MUSIC
CD _____ GVM 1001CD
Global Village / Jul '95 / ADA / Direct.

VIRTUAL SEX
CD _____ 2100008
Indisc / May '93 / Pinnacle.

VISIONS
CD _____ TCD 2687
Telstar / Mar '94 / BMG.

VIVA SALSA
(4CD Set)
CD Set _____ CDHOTBOX 1
Caliente / Sep '91 / Charly.

VIVATIONAL COMPILATION
Intro: Musical Director / Supervisor error: Diceman / Purpuss: Bob & Ian / Tempest: Diceman / Silcock express: L.M.N.O / In wildebeest: Bob & Ian / Hold me now: Diceman / Le noir: Diceman / Y: L.M.N.O / Bad data from disc: Zamurknaya petstotin aisle: Diceman / Purpuss (Secret knowledge mix): Bob & Ian / L.M.N.O / Quad (Spooky's magi remix): Diceman / Silcock express (remix): L.M.N.O / Sonic system: Diceman / Hold me now (John Digweeds mix): Solace
CD _____ VTTCD 01
Vivational / Feb '94 / Grapevine.

VOCAL AND INSTRUMENTAL MUSIC OF MONGOLIA
CD _____ TSCD 909
Topic / Sep '94 / Direct / ADA.

VOCAL COLLECTION, THE
Kalerka / Erienda / Africando / Bluer than blue / Horse I used to ride / Little red rooster / I cover the waterfront / Wave / Zoot walked in / Remind me / Tell me what you're gonna do
CD _____ VC 94
Chesky / Nov '94 / Complete/Pinnacle.

VOCAL GROUPS, THE
CD _____ PLATCD 343
Platinum Music / Oct '90 / Prism / Ross.

VOCAL REFRAIN
CD Set _____ MAK 103
Avid / Nov '94 / Avid/BMG / Koch.

VOCAL TRADITIONS OF BULGARIA
Mari Maro / Snoshti vecher u vas byah / Polegnala bela pshenitza / Momne le mari hubava / Vido dva vetra veyat / Ziadi mi rayo / Dosto, mome dosto / Shto yubavo sofiskoto pole / Zamurknaya petstotin aisle / Senkya pada / Bre Nikola Nikola / Devolko Mari Hubava / Rechenski kamuk reka zaglavya / Rasti bore / Zazhena se niva / Pominalo e devoiche / Rodilo se muzhko dete / Zluntzeto trepti zauda / Pusni ma maicho / Doide mi obed pladnina / Done ide ot manastir
CD _____ CDSDL 396
Saydisc / Mar '94 / Harmonia Mundi / ADA / Direct.

VOCALS & INSTRUMENTALS POLYPHONIES OF ETHIOPIA
CD Set _____ C 580055/56
Ocora / May '94 / Harmonia Mundi / ADA.

VOCIFEROUS MACHIAVUVIAN HATE
CD _____ E 0001
Osmose / Apr '94 / Plastic Head.

VOICE
Tribe: Gruntruck / Business: Biohazard / Let the world on fire: Exhorder / Isolation: Waltari / Cinderella's daydream: Zu Zu's Petals / Skin: Optimum Wound Profile / Never too late: Phantom Blue / Monarch of the sleeping marches: Disincarnate / Boy can sing the blues: Hughes, Glenn / Monotony: Willard / Face: Innerstate / Sky turned red: Atrocity / Ghost rider: Bloodstar / Fugitive soul: Treponem Pal / Scapegoat: Fear Factory / Throb: Skin Chamber / It's like that: Dog Eat Dog / Black no. 1 (Little Miss Scare-all): Type O Negative
CD _____ CDRR 90742
Roadrunner / Apr '93 / Pinnacle.

VOICE OF MUSIC
CD _____ 710083
Magnum Music / Jun '89 / Magnum Music Group.

VOICES
(Hannibal Sampler)
CD _____ HNCD 8301
Hannibal / Feb '90 / Vital / ADA.

VOICES
CD _____ FECD 87
Fellside / Nov '95 / Target/BMG / Direct / ADA.

VOICES FROM THE GHETTO - YIDDISH
CD _____ 242066
FNAC / Aug '93 / Discovery.

VOICES OF THE RAIN FOREST
From morning night to real morning / Making sago / Cutting trees / Clearing the brush / Bamboo Jew's harp / From afternoon to afternoon darkening / Evening rainstorm / Drumming / Song ceremony / From night to inside night / Relaxing by the creek
CD _____ RCD 10173
Rykodisc / Jul '91 / Vital / ADA.

VOICES OF THE SPIRITS - SONGS AND CHANTS
CD _____ ELL 3210A
Ellipsis Arts / Oct '93 / Direct / ADA.

VOICES OF THE UKRAINE
CD _____ PS 65145CD
Playasound / Jul '95 / Harmonia Mundi / ADA.

VOICES OF WONDER
CD _____ VOW 36CD
Voices Of Wonder / May '94 / Plastic Head.

VOILA
Kebou: Khaled, Hadj Brahim / D'abord, D'abord: Taha, Rachid / N'ssi N'ssi: Khaled, Hadj Brahim / Chebba: Khaled, Cheb & Safy Boutella / Time fax: Sakan / Voila voila: Taha, Rachid / Bakala: Maden, Alex / Yeke yeke: Kante, Mory / Mogo djolo: Kante, Mory / Indie (The game is about): Taha, Rachid / Mongo djolo: Kante, Mory
CD _____ 5273922
Barclay / May '95 / PolyGram.

VOLCANO
(20 Super Hits)
CD _____ SONCD 0005
Sonic Sounds / Oct '90 / Jetstar.

VOLCANO ERUPTION, THE
CD _____ SONCD 0050
Sonic Sounds / Jul '93 / Jetstar.

VOLCANO SPECIAL COMPILATION VOL.1
Nyam Up / Apr '95 / Conifer.
CD _____ CY 78934

VOLKSTUMLICHE FAVORITEN
CD _____ 15396
Laserlight / Nov '91 / Target/BMG.

VOLUME ELEVEN
Super glider: Drugstore / Jailbird: Primal Scream / Pyrotechnician: Sleeper / Eject: Senser / Dairy thief: Shed Seven / Terrorvision / Lick a shot: Cypress Hill / Dis MX: Collapsed Lung / Stepping out: Jale / Violins and happy endings: Deus / Spangle: Wedding Present / Good under pressure: Scrawl / Lord of this world: Helmet / Curious George Blues: Dig / PCP (live): Manic Street Preachers / Remember me: Kitchens Of Distinction / Man with a box: Salad / Machine gun: Shed Seven / Verbal diary: Rollins, Henry / Divine: Noce / Good times (Pure phase): Spiritualized / Foetus: Goya Dress / Vow: Garbage / Visa for violet and van: Prolapse / Girl meets girl: Shriek / Son of John Doe: Pet Lamb / What love: Moby / Tomorrow night: G-Love & Special Sauce / Karmacoma (Bumper ball dub): Massive Attack / Space theme (Tribute to John Cage in C, A, G and E): E.A.R. / Lower than stars: Laika / Only now (US remix): Ride / Dream on: Catatonia / Wake up (acoustic): Love Spit Love / Pond life: Novocaine / Days: Flinch / In decline: Nitzer Ebb
CD _____ 11VCD11
Volume / Oct '95 / Total/BMG / Vital.

VOLUME FIFTEEN
(Technology Alert/2CD Set)
Springs and magnets part 2: Rhythmicon / Quiet storm: Life's Addiction / Outside: Solid / Circling girl: Cocteau Twins / Alan Ladd: Baby Bird / Vanishing: Lhooq / MK 2A: Shamen / Hypo full of love: Alabama 3 / Altered ego: Ultramarine / Everybody's gone green: New Order / Everybody say yeah: Joi / Thierry Lacroix: Nectarine No.9 / Don't know why: Scheer / Bring me the rest of Alfredo Garcia: Flaming Stars / Who's in, who's out: Harvey, Mick / Perfect and wild: State Of Grace / Let go oh oh: Wannadies / Better get ready: Law One / Sam the ant tamer: Alien / Ambient jazz suit no.2: Bonjour Monsieur Basie
CD Set _____ 15 VCD 015
Volume / Jan '96 / Total/BMG / Vital.

VOLUME FOURTEEN
(Reading 1995 Special)
Volume / Aug '95 / Total/BMG / Vital.
CD _____ 14VCD14

VOLUME NINE
Wheels: *Lanegan, Mark* / Sharks patrol these waters: *Morphine* / One summer night: *That Dog* / Soda jerk: *Buffalo Tom* / Black sheep boy: *Weller, Paul* / Roland navigator: *Madder Rose* / Doctor's orders: *Sonic Youth* / Gas fish: *Wagon Christ* / Emile: *Pressure Of Speech* / Aqualung: *Spooky* / Life's what you make it: *Divine Comedy* / How: *Cranberries* / Her: *Tindersticks* / Close your eyes: *Hersh, Kristin* / Whisky priests: *Jah Wobble* / New world order: *Fun-Da-Mental* / Suspend: *Rub Ultra* / Daisy: *Blessed Ethel* / Top of the world: *Compulsion*
CD _____ 9 VCD 9
Volume / Mar '94 / Total/BMG / Vital.

VOLUME TEN
Deep blue breath: *A.R. Kane* / First language: *Disco Inferno* / Naked freak shadow: *Scarce* / To see the lights: *Gene* / Might as well be dumbo: *High Llamas* / Joy-riders (Acoustic version): *Pulp* / Cream bun (Acoustic version): *Tiny Monroe* / Fake: *Echobelly* / They don't know: *Gigolo Aunts* / Tinkaballi. Lush / You don't: *Tricky* / Come dancing: *Credit To The Nation* / La boheme: *Loop Guru* / Khan: *Transglobal Underground* / Re-volvaluation: *Transcendental Love Machine* / Tikky: *Insides* / Sweetest place: *Oracle* / Daughter: *Perrett, Peter*
CD _____ 10VCD10
Volume / Oct '95 / Total/BMG / Vital.

VOLUME THIRTEEN
Listen up: *Krispy Three* / Polyester blues: *Whiteout* / Reaching out from here: *Boo Radleys* / East street O'Neill: *Animals That Swim* / Waves: *Hatfield, Juliana* / Games we play: *Elcka* / Just because: *Interact* / Hillbilly: *Throwing Muses* / Sex, horror, violence: *Kaliphz* / Daddy: *Luscious Jackson* / Look at yourself: *Tribute To Nothing* / Vanity fair: *Flying Medallions* / No promise have I made: *Nova Mob* / Bolus: *Done Lying Down* / Frost bitten: *Rosa Mota* / In a nutshell: *Collins, Edwyn* / Tiny tears: *Tindersticks* / Nice dream: *Radiohead* / Jesus let me in: *Velo Deluxe* / It's all over now: *Reverberation* / Maybe an angel: *Nova, Heather*
CD _____ 13 VCD 13
Volume / Feb '95 / Total/BMG / Vital.

VOLUME TWELVE
Olivine: *Node* / Good times: *Spiritualized* / Foetus: *Goya Dress* / Vow: *Garbage* / Visa for violet and van: *Prolapse* / Girl meets girl: *Shriek* / Son of John Doe: *Pet Lamb* / What love: *Moby* / Tomorrow night: *G Love & Special Sauce* / Karma coma: *Massive Attack* / Space theme (Tribute to John Cage in C, A, G & E): *E.A.R.* / Lower than stars: *Laika* / Only now: *Ride* / Dream on: *Catatonia* / Wake up: *Love Spit Love* / Pond life: *Novocaine* / Days: *Flinch* / In decline: *Nitzer Ebb*
CD _____ 12 VCD 12
Volume / Dec '94 / Total/BMG / Vital.

VORSPRUNG DURCH LOGIC, VOLUME 1
Do you see the light: *Snap* / Brain ticket (Remix): *Ramin Vol.II* / P.ower of A.merican N.atives: *Dance 2 Trance* / Do u feel 4 me: *Eden* / Fly high: *Whirlpool* / Sing hallelujah: *Dr. Alban* / 2 the rhythm: *Sound Factory* / One more time: *Baxter, Blake* / Here's my A: *Rapination & Carol Kenyon* / Turn me out: *Fowlkes, Eddie* / Feel the rhythm: *Jinny* / What is love: *Haddaway* / Rhythm is a dancer: *Snap*
CD _____ 74321158692
Arista / Aug '93 / BMG.

VOYAGE INTO TRANSE, A
CD _____ BFLCD 11
Big Life / May '93 / Pinnacle.

VOZES
Para-raio: *Djavan* / Ole ola: *Buarque, Chico* / Cavalgada: *De Belem, Fafa* / Mariano: *Camargo, Cesar* / Bodas de prata: *Regina, Elis* / Outubro: *Nascimento, Milton* / Denise rei: *Ben, Jorge* / Viramundo: *Bethania, Maria* / Maravilha: *Hime, Francis & Chico Buarque* / Abre alas: *Lins, Ivan* / I ve brussel: *Ben, Jorge & Caetano Veloso* / Toada: *Lobo, Edo* / Doce magica: *De Belem, Fafa* / Ate segunda feira: *Buarque, Chico* / Curumin chama cunhata que eu vou contar: *Ben, Jorge* / Travessia: *Nascimento, Milton* / Preta pretinha: *Buarque, Chico* / Casas cristalinas: *Wando* / Ventos do norte: *Djavan* / Faz parte do meu show: *Creuza, Maria*
CD _____ NSCD 001
Nascente / Jul '91 / Disc / THE.

WA-CHI-KA-NOCKA
Wigwam Willie: *Phillips, Carl* / Indian Joe: *Adams, Art* / Warrior Sam: *Willis, Don* / Warpath: *Lenny & The Star Chiefs* / Cherokee stomp: *Tidwell, Bobby* / Cherokee rock: *Wheeler, Chuck* / Cherokee rock and roll: *Jerome, Ralph* / War paint: *Warriors* / Kawliga: *Porter, Bruce* / Rock my warriors rock:

Jackson, Joe / Wa-chic-ka-noka: *Holmes, Tommy* / Witchapoo: *Cathey, Frank* / Geronimo: *Renegade* / Indian squaw: *Kellwoods* / Geronimo stomp: *Darvell, Barry* / Big indian: *Downs, Tommy* / Chief whoopin' koff: *Royal Knights* / Little brave: *Smalling, Eddie* / Little bull and buttercup: *Homer, Chris* / Massacre: *Ronny & Johnny* / Wahoo: *Bennett, Arnold* / Bobby sox squaw: *Impacts* / Tomahawk: *Brown, Tom* / Rockin' redwing: *Masters, Sammy* / Red wing: *Wayne, Gordon* / Indian moon: *Chieftones* / Medicine man: *Warren, Bobby Five* / Rattlesnake: *Bayou, Billy* / Cowboys and indians: *Brent, Ronnie* / Indian rock: *Musical Lynn Twins*
CD _____ CDBB 55011
Buffalo Bop / Apr '94 / Rollercoaster.

WADE IN THE WATERS VOL. 1 - SPIRITUALS
CD _____ SFWCD 40072
Smithsonian Folkways / Jun '94 / ADA / Direct / Koch / CM / Cadillac.

WADE IN THE WATERS VOL. 2 - CONGREGATION SINGING
CD _____ SFWCD 40073
Smithsonian Folkways / Jun '94 / ADA / Direct / Koch / CM / Cadillac.

WADE IN THE WATERS VOL. 3 - GOSPEL PIONEERS
CD _____ SFWCD 40074
Smithsonian Folkways / Jun '94 / ADA / Direct / Koch / CM / Cadillac.

WADE IN THE WATERS VOL. 4 - COMMUNITY GOSPEL
CD _____ SFWCD 40075
Smithsonian Folkways / Jun '94 / ADA / Direct / Koch / CM / Cadillac.

WAKE UP DEAD MAN
CD _____ ROUCD 2013
Rounder / Aug '94 / CM / Direct / ADA / Cadillac.

WAKE UP JAMAICA
CD _____ CDTRL 331
Trojan / Mar '94 / Jetstar / Total/BMG.

WALES - LAND OF SONG
CD _____ PWK 061
Carlton Home Entertainment / '88 / Carlton Home Entertainment.

WALKING ON SUNSHINE
CD Set _____ NSCD 016
Newsound / Feb '95 / THE.

WALKING ON THE MOON
CD _____ CRESTCD 001
Mooncrest / Dec '95 / Direct / ADA.

WALL OF SOUND VS PUSSYFOOTS
CD _____ WALLPUSSCD 1
Wall Of Sound / Mar '96 / Disc / Soul Trader.

WAREHOUSE RAVES
Numero uno: *Starlight* / Guitarra: *Raul* / Love is life: *Candy Flip* / Te amo: *Navarro, Raimunda* / Love sensation: *Holloway, Loleatta* / 8: *Brooklyn Express* / Paradhouse: *Koxo Club Band* / Why can't we live together: *Illusion* / It's a dream: *Amnesia* / Let me love you for tonight: *Kariya* / Just a little bit: *Total Science* / Strings of life: *Rhythm Is Rhythm*
CD _____ CDRUMD 101
Rumour / Sep '89 / Pinnacle / 3MV / Sony.

WAREHOUSE RAVES VOL. 2
CD _____ CDRUMD 102
Rumour / May '92 / Pinnacle / 3MV / Sony.

WAREHOUSE RAVES VOL. 3
CD _____ CDRUMD 103
Rumour / Mar '90 / Pinnacle / 3MV / Sony.

WARM AND TENDER LOVE
CD _____ YDG 74622
Yesterday's Gold / Feb '93 / Target/BMG.

WARNING FOR PUNK (3CD Set)
CD Set _____ DISTCD 0
Dolores / Jan '95 / Plastic Head.

WARTIME FAVOURITES VOL.1 - THE EARLY YEARS
They can't black out the moon: *Roy, Harry & His Orchestra* / God bless you Mr. Chamberlain: *Roy, Harry & His Orchestra* / Oh ain't it grand to be in the navy: *Roy, Harry & His Orchestra* / Nasty Adolf Hitler: *Ambrose & His Orchestra* / Rhymes of the times: *Ambrose & His Orchestra* / Spitfire song: *Loss, Joe & His Orchestra* / Adolf: *Ambrose & His Orchestra* / Run rabbit: *Geraldo & His Dance Orchestra* / Run rabbit run: *Roy, Harry & His Orchestra* / Wings over the navy: *Cotton, Billy & His Band* / Kiss me goodnight, Sergeant Major: *Cotton, Billy & His Band* / F.D.R insine: *Roy, Harry & His Orchestra* / Lords of the air: *Loss, Joe & His band* / Tipperary: *Roy, Harry & His Band* / It's a paor of wings for me: *Gonella, Nat & His Band* / Nice kind Sergeant Major: *Long, Norman* / There'll always be an England: *Loss, Joe & His band*

CD _____ RAJCD 825
Empress / Aug '94 / THE.

WARTIME FAVOURITES VOL.2 - SONGS OF D-DAY
Homeward bound: *Hall, Henry Orchestra* / Don't ask me why/Whistling in the dark/Hey good looking: *Preager, Lou & His Orchestra* / I never mention your name: *Roy, Harry & His Band* / Milkman keep those bottles quiet: *Squadronaires* / I heard you cried last night: *Preager, Lou & His Orchestra* / My heart tells me: *Roy, Harry & His Band* / San fernando valley: *Skyrockets Dance Orchestra* / Shoo shoo baby: *Preager, Lou & His Orchestra* / How sweet you are: *Roy, Harry & His Band* / Do you believe in dreams: *Skyrockets Dance Orchestra* / I left my heart at the stage door canteen: *Ambrose & His Orchestra* / Is you is or is you an't my baby: *Skyrockets Dance Orchestra* / Spring will be a little late this year: *Skyrockets Dance Orchestra* / Dreamer: *Hall, Henry Orchestra* / Close to you: *Ambrose & His Orchestra* / Is my baby blue tonight: *Crowe, George & The Blue Mariners* / Chocolate soldier from the USA: *Parry, Harry & His Radio Rhythm Club Sextet* / Mairzy doats and dozy doats: *Preager, Lou & His Orchestra* / October mood: *Skyrockets Dance Orchestra*
CD _____ RAJCD 826
Empress / Aug '94 / THE.

WARTIME FAVOURITES VOL.3 - VICTORY
Keep an eye on your heart: *Geraldo & His Orchestra* / What more can I say: *Thorburn, Billy* / Don't sit under the apple tree: *Crosby, Bob & His Orchestra* / In my arms: *Geraldo & His Orchestra* / It costs so little: *Thorburn, Billy* / Smiths and the Jones: *Geraldo & His Orchestra* / All over the place: *New Mayfair Dance Orchestra* / You are my sunshine: *Roy, Harry & His Band* / You can't say no to a soldier: *Geraldo & His Orchestra* / It's foolish but it's fun: *Thorburn, Billy* / Five o'clock whistle: *Loss, Joe & His Orchestra* / We three: *Gonella, Nat & His Georgians* / Hey Mabel: *Winstone, Eric* / Aurora: *Dorsey, Jimmy Orchestra* / Jingle jangle jingle: *Winstone, Eric & His Band* / Sailor with the navy blue eyes: *Roy, Harry & His Band* / Six lessons from Madame La Zonga: *Dorsey, Jimmy Orchestra* / I've got a girl in Kalamazoo: *Geraldo & His Orchestra* / I'm nobody's baby: *Gonella, Nat & His Georgians* / Yours: *Winstone, Eric & His Band* / Why don't you fall in love with me: *Roy, Harry & His Band* / Zoot suit: *Crosby, Bob & His Orchestra* / White cliffs of Dover: *Thorburn, Billy* / Pennsylvania polka: *Roy, Harry & His Band*
CD _____ RAJCD 827
Empress / Aug '94 / THE.

WARTIME KITCHEN & GARDEN
CD _____ DSHCD 7012
D-Sharp / Nov '93 / Pinnacle.

WASSOULOU SOUND
CD _____ STCD 1035
Sterns / Oct '91 / Sterns / CM.

WASSOULOU SOUND VOL.2
Kani kassi / Gnoumna ke la / Kankeletigui / Nale nale / Ni la kani / Mougakan / Ita dia / Simbo / Barika bognala / Djina Mousso
CD _____ STCD 1048
Sterns / Mar '94 / Sterns / CM

WASTED
Reefer spin in the galaxy: *Orb* / Low cool: *Cabaret Voltaire* / Fallen: *One Dove* / One day: *Bjork* / Hyperreal: *Shamen* / Bullet proof: *Pop Will Eat Itself* / Cybernetic: *Grid* / Miracle: *System 7* / Why why why: *Underworld* / Anything you want: *Delta Lady* / One tribe: *Drum Club* / Lick wid nit wit: *Sabres Of Paradise* / Aqualung: *Spooky* / Belfast: *Orbital* / Wasted: *Orbital* / Karmacoma: *Massive Attack* / You don't: *Tricky* / Lick a shot: *Cypress Hill* / Come dancing: *Credit To The Nation* / 15 to 4: *Little Axe* / Venice groove: *Sandals* / Elevate my mind: *Stereo MC's* / Whisky priests: *Jah Wobble* / Olivine: *Node* / Confusion: *New Order* / Go: *Moby* / Slow down Speedy: *LFO* / Lanx 3: *Autechre* / En trange to exit: *Aphex Twin* / Reefer song: *Mindless Drug Hoover*
CD Set _____ BOVCD 1
Volume / May '95 / Total/BMG / Vital.

WATCH HOW YOU FLEX (Reggae Dancehall vol.2)
CD _____ SHCD 45002
Shanachie / Jun '93 / Koch / ADA.

WATERHOUSE REVISITED
CD _____ HCD 7012
Hightone / Dec '94 / ADA / Koch.

WATERHOUSE REVISITED - CHAPTER 2
CD _____ HCD 7013
Hightone / Mar '95 / ADA / Koch.

WATERLOO SUNSET (20 Hits Of The Sixties)
Waterloo sunset: *Kinks* / Tomorrow: *Shaw, Sandie* / Call me number one: *Tremeloes* /

Universal: *Small Faces* / Suzannah's still alive: *Davies, Dave* / Other man's grass: *Clark, Petula* / Something's gotten hold of my heart: *Pitney, Gene* / I'm gonna make you mine: *Christie, Lou* / Make me an island: *Dolan, Joe* / It's too late now: *Baldry, Long John* / Are you growing tired of my love: *Status Quo* / Simon says: *1910 Fruitgum Company* / Oh happy day: *Hawkins, Edwin Singers* / Just one smile: *Pitney, Gene* / Puppet on a string: *Shaw, Sandie* / In the bad bad old days: *Foundations* / Green tambourine: *Lemon Pipers* / Man of the world: *Fleetwood Mac* / Let's go to San Francisco: *Flowerpot Men* / America: *Nice*
CD _____ TRTCD 106
TrueTrax / Oct '94 / THE.

WATERMELON FILES OF TEXAS MUSIC, THE
CD _____ MSACD 9
Munich / Dec '94 / CM / ADA / Greensleeves / Direct.

WATT WORKS FAMILY ALBUM
Fleur carnivore: *Bley, Carla* / Best of friends: *Mantler, Karen* / Walking batteriewoman: *Bley, Carla* / A l'abattoir: *Mantler, Michael* / Crab alley: *Swallow, Steve* / When I run: *Mantler, Michael* / I can't stand...: *Weisberg, Steve* / Alien (part 2): *Mantler, Michael* / Talking hearts: *Bley, Carla* / Twenty: *Mantler, Michael* / I hate to sing: *Bley, Carla* / Movie six: *Mantler, Michael* / A.D. infinitum: *Bley, Carla* / Doubtful guest: *Mantler, Michael* / Funny bird: *Bley, Carla*
CD _____ 8414782
Watt / Jan '90 / New Note

WAVE PARTY
Goody two shoes: *Adam Ant* / Feels like heaven: *Fiction Factory* / This is the day: *The The* / Skin deep: *Stranglers* / Pretty in pink: *Psychedelic Furs* / Dog good: *Fruer* / Who can it be now: *Men At Work* / You spin me round (like a record): *Dead Or Alive* / Talking in your sleep: *Romantics* / Real gone kid: *Deacon Blue* / Wheel: *Spear Of Destiny* / Birth, school, work, death: *Godfathers* / Heaven: *Psychedelic Furs* / Be free with your love: *Spandau Ballet* / Dutch mountains: *Nits*
CD _____ 4758322
Columbia / Dec '95 / Sony.

WAVE ROMANTICS VOL. 2
Do you love me: *Cave, Nick* / Green and grey: *New Model Army* / Golden brown: *Stranglers* / Beside you: *Iggy Pop* / Vienna: *Ultravox*
CD _____ SPV 08438992
SPV / Feb '95 / Plastic Head.

WAVY GRAVY (For Adult Enthusiasts)
CD _____ BEWARECD 01
No Hit / Aug '95 / SRD.

WAY FOR BRITTANY, A
CD _____ CD 819
Escalibur / Aug '93 / Roots / ADA / Discovery.

WAY FOR IRELAND, A
CD _____ CD 314
Arfolk / Aug '93 / Roots / ADA.

WAY FOR SCOTLAND, A
CD _____ CD 313
Arfolk / Aug '93 / Roots / ADA.

WAY IT USED TO BE, THE (Great Love Songs)
Way it used to be: *Humperdinck, Engelbert* / You're a lady: *Skellern, Peter* / Without love: *Jones, Tom* / Laughter in the rain: *Sedaka, Neil* / Little green apples: *Miller, Roger* / Lights of Cincinnati: *Walker, Scott* / Last farewell: *Whittaker, Roger* / Music: *Miles, John* / I'll never fall in love again: *Jones, Tom* / I don't believe in it anymore: *Whittaker, Roger* / Winter world of love: *Humperdinck, Engelbert* / Way you look tonight: *Woodward, Edward* / Our last song together: *Sedaka, Neil*
CD _____ PWKS 554
Carlton Home Entertainment / Oct '89 / Carlton Home Entertainment.

WAY WE WERE, THE
CD _____ CDSR 045
Telstar / May '94 / BMG.

WAY WE WERE, THE
Best thing that ever happened to me: *Knight, Gladys & The Pips* / Sad sweet dreamer: *Sweet Sensation* / Dolly my love: *Moments* / You to me are everything: *Real Thing* / Love hurts: *Nazareth* / More than a lover: *Tyler, Bonnie* / I'll go where your music takes me: *James, Jimmy & The Vagabonds* / Making up again: *Goldie* / Love's got a hold on me: *Dollar* / Pillow talk: *Sylvia* / Hold back the night: *Trammps* / So sad the song: *Knight, Gladys & The Pips* / Where did our love go: *Elbert, Donnie* / Time in a bottle: *Croce, Jim* / Ruby Tuesday: *Melanie* / You'll never know what you're missing: *Real Thing* / Aria: *Bilk, Acker* / Try to remember (the way we were): *Knight, Gladys & The Pips* / Arms of Mary: *Sutherland Brothers* / If you don't know me by now: *Melvin, Harold & The Bluenotes* / Take good care of yourself: *Three Degrees* / Behind closed doors: *Rich, Charlie* / Every night: *Snow, Phoebe* / You'll never find another love like mine: *Rawls, Lou* / Shining

star: *Manhattans* / *Angel of the morning*: *Mason, Mary* / *Anyway that you want me*: *Mason, Mary* / *I can help*: *Swan, Billy* / *Tears on my pillow*: *Nash, Johnny* / *Say you don't mind*: *Blunstone, Colin* / *Summer breeze*: *Isley Brothers* / *Kiss and say goodbye*: *Manhattans* / *Stand by your man*: *Wynette, Tammy* / *When will I see you again*: *Three Degrees* / *Lean on me*: *Withers, Bill* / *Midnight train to Georgia*: *Knight, Gladys & The Pips* / *It's a heartache*: *Tyler, Bonnie* / *Free*: *Williams, Deniece* / *I can see clearly now*: *Nash, Johnny* / *Zing went the strings of my heart*: *Trampps* / *I'll have to say I love you in a song*: *Croce, Jim* / *Rose garden*: *Anderson, Lynn* / *January February*: *Dickson, Barbara* / *That same old feeling*: *Pickettywitch* / *Isn't she lovely*: *Parton, David* / *Summer of my life*: *May, Simon* / *After the goldrush*: *Prelude* / *Most beautiful girl in the world*: *Rich, Charlie* / *Hurt*: *Manhattans* / *Who were you with in the moonlight*: *Dollar* / *Can't get by without you*: *Real Thing*
CD Set _____ BOXD 47T
Carlton Home Entertainment / Oct '94 / Carlton Home Entertainment.

WAY WITH THE GIRLS
(30 Female Soul Rarities From The 1960's)
You will never get away: *Maye, Cholli* / *Here come the heartaches*: *Lovells* / *I'm a sad girl*: *Johnson, Deena* / *If you can stand me*: *Lewis, Tamala* / *Thrills and chills*: *Smith, Helene* / *I feel strange*: *Wonderettes* / *Lost without your love*: *Carlettes* / *Now that I found you baby*: *Mirettes* / *It's over*: *Lindsay, Terry* / *It's all over*: *Gee's* / *Why weren't you there*: *Lindsay, Thelma* / *Step aside baby*: *Lollipops* / *It happens every day*: *Persianettes* / *Source of love*: *Marie, Gina* / *Sweet sweet love*: *Durettes* / *Pretty boy*: *Hall, Dora* / *Big man*: *Starr, Karen* / *Ain't gonna hurt my pride*: *Judi & The Affections* / *You're the guy*: *Angie & The Arketts* / *There's something the matter (with your heart)*: *Cynthia & The Imaginations* / *Wonderful one*: *Lindsey, Theresa* / *My, my sweet love*: *Lee, Barbara* / *If you love me (show me)*: *Monique* / *Sugar boy*: *Charmettes* / *Don't cha tell nobody*: *Vont Claires* / *Don't cry*: *Irma & The Larks* / *My fault*: *Passionettes* / *Try my love*: *Sequins* / *How can I get to you*: *Soul, Sharon* / *His way with the girls*: *Lornettes*
CD _____ GSCD 029
Goldmine / Mar '94 / Vital.

WAYS OF LOVE, THE
Careless whisper: *Michael, George* / *Your love is king*: *Sade* / *So amazing*: *Vandross, Luther* / *Softly whispering i love you*: *Young, Paul* / *I'll never fall in love again*: *Deacon Blue* / *Eternal flame*: *Bangles* / *Time and tide*: *Basia* / *Wishing you were here*: *Moyet, Alison* / *Through the barricades*: *Spandau Ballet* / *Castle in the clouds*: *Craven, Beverley* / *Stay with me 'til dawn*: *Tzuke, Judie* / *Unconditional love*: *Hoffs, Susanna* / *Toy soldiers*: *Martika* / *Baby I love your way/Freebird*: *Will To Power*
CD _____ 4720732
Columbia / Aug '92 / Sony.

WE ARE ICERINK
Birth of Sharon: *Brutus, Earl* / *When I get to heaven*: *Sensuround* / *Don't destroy me*: *Golden* / *V neck*: *Elizabeth City State* / *Supermarket*: *Supermarket* / *Why don't you)* *Ring me*: *Hard Muscle* / *Love hour*: *Oval* / *Bob cool*: *Spring* / *Don't worry baby*: *Melody Dog* / *Bouffant headbutt*: *Shampoo* / *Dub to the stars (instrumental)*: *Parallel Universe* / *New electric pop and soul*: *World Of Twist*
CD _____ DAVO 001CD
Icerink / May '94 / Pinnacle.

WE ARE ONE
(Griot Songs From Mali)
CD _____ PAN 2015CD
Pan / Aug '94 / ADA / Direct / CM.

WE ARE THE BLUES
CD _____ 5238382
PolyGram Jazz / Feb '95 / PolyGram.

WE BITE 100
CD _____ WB 10002
We Bite / Jan '96 / Plastic Head.

WE BITE LIVE '91
CD _____ WBCD 076
Wildebeest / Jan '92.

WE BITE TOO
CD _____ WB 100012
We Bite / Jan '96 / Plastic Head.

WE CAME TO DANCE
CD _____ SPV 08438822
SPV / Jul '95 / Plastic Head.

WE DIED IN HELL - THEY CALLED IT PASSCHENDAELE
CD _____ MAPCD 93004CD
Map / Jan '94 / ADA / Direct.

WE GOT A PARTY
(Best Of Ron Records Vol.1)
CD _____ CD 2076
Rounder / CM / Direct / ADA / Cadillac.

WE WILL ROCK YOU
CD _____ DINCD 2
Dino / Sep '91 / Pinnacle / 3MV.

WE WISH YOU A MERRY CHRISTMAS
CD _____ PWKS 598
Carlton Home Entertainment / Oct '95 / Carlton Home Entertainment.

WEDDING ALBUM, THE
(To Have And To Hold)
CD _____ QTVCD 006
Quality / Jun '92 / Pinnacle.

WEDDING MUSIC OF MARAMURES
CD _____ C 580052
Ocora / Jan '94 / Harmonia Mundi / ADA.

WEEK IN THE REAL WORLD, A - PART I
CD _____ CDRW 25
Realworld / Jul '92 / EMI / Sterns.

WEEK OR TWO IN THE REAL WORLD
CD _____ CDRW 30
Realworld / Jul '94 / EMI / Sterns.

WEEKENDER
(12 Extended Dance Classics)
CD _____ MUSCD 010
MCI / Sep '93 / Disc / THE.

WEIRD & WONDERFUL
Hello or goodbye: *Magnolias* / *Grid of absence*: *Brick Supply* / *Endless fall*: *Lunch, Lydia & Roland S.Howard* / *Ghost of Lonnie Mack*: *Beat Poets* / *He's dead*: *Suede* / *Light of life*: *Celibate Rifles* / *God cries*: *Zu Zu's Petals* / *Everytime*: *Sofa Head* / *Slack*: *Bivouac* / *Loretta's scars*: *Pavement* / *Worship*: *Wyatt, Robert* / *While you were out*: *Carter U.S.M.* / *Rennen*: *Ride* / *Jigsaw blues*: *Sudden, Nikki* / *Here's Johnny*: *Blaggers ITA* / *Springtime*: *Leatherface* / *Buffalo bill*: *Boo Radleys* / *Burning hole*: *Crane* / *My right..*: *Unsane*
CD _____ JAC 001CD
Oasis / Jul '93 / Plastic Head.

WELCOME TO NORTHERN IRELAND
CD _____ CDN 100
Outlet / Oct '95 / ADA / Duncans / CM / Ross / Direct / Koch.

WELCOME TO SCOTLAND
Teviot brig: *Shand, Jimmy Jnr.* / *Quaker's wife*: *Shand, Jimmy Jnr.* / *Ishbel's jig*: *Shand, Jimmy Jnr.* / *Comin' thro' the rye*: *MacLeod, Jim* / *My love is like a red red rose*: *MacLeod, Jim* / *Bonnie Galloway*: *MacLeod, Jim* / *Soft lowland tongue*: *MacLeod, Jim* / *Uist tramping song*: *Anderson, Moira* / *Roamin' in the gloamin'*: *Shand, Jimmy Jnr.* / *I love a lassie*: *Shand, Jimmy Jnr.* / *Stop your ticklin' jock*: *Shand, Jimmy Jnr.* / *Wee Deoch an' Doris*: *Shand, Jimmy Jnr.* / *Northern lights of old Aberdeen*: *Logan, Jimmy* / *Battle o'er*: *Shand, Jimmy Jnr.* / *I see mull*: *Anderson, Moira* / *Mairi's wedding*: *MacLeod, Jim & His Band* / *Bill Thomson's farewell to Dublane*: *MacLeod, Jim & His Band* / *Rabbie's visit*: *MacLeod, Jim & His Band* / *Carronades*: *MacLeod, Jim & His Band* / *Pheonix*: *MacLeod, Jim & His Band* / *Lassie come and dance with me*: *MacLeod, Jim & His Band* / *I lo'e nae a laddie*: *MacLeod, Jim & His Band* / *Muckin' O' Geordie's byre*: *MacLeod, Jim & His Band* / *Wi' a hundred pipers*: *MacLeod, Jim & His Band* / *Dancing in Kyle*: *Anderson, Moira* / *Jock McKay*: *Shand, Jimmy Jnr.* / *Gordon for me*: *Shand, Jimmy Jnr.* / *Lass of lowrie*: *Shand, Jimmy Jnr.* / *The glen*: *Logan, Jimmy* / *Memories of Orkney*: *Shand, Jimmy Jnr.* / *Macfarlane O' the sproats*: *MacLeod, Jim & His Band* / *Bonnie lass o'Fyvie*: *MacLeod, Jim & His Band* / *Barnyards o'Delgaty*: *MacLeod, Jim & His Band* / *Mormond braes*: *MacLeod, Jim & His Band* / *Polka danska*: *Shand, Jimmy Jnr.* / *My ain' folk*: *Logan, Jimmy*
CD _____ CDMFP 5926
Music For Pleasure / Nov '91 / EMI.

WELCOME TO THE BLUES VOL.1
CD _____ 157572
Blues Collection / Feb '93 / Discovery.

WELCOME TO THE BLUES VOL.2
CD _____ 157592
Blues Collection / Feb '93 / Discovery.

WELCOME TO THE FUTURE
CD _____ TPLP 50CD
One Little Indian / Mar '93 / Pinnacle.

WELCOME TO THE FUTURE 2
Human behaviour: *Bjork* / *Beautiful morning*: *Soul Family Sensation* / *Sugar daddy*: *Secret Knowledge* / *Comin' on*: *Shamen* / *Devo*: *Crunch* / *God*: *Hypnotist* / *U.K. :* *U.S.A.: Eskimos & Egypt* / *F.U.2.: F.U.S.E.* / *Obsession*: *Wishdokta & Vibes*
CD _____ TPLP 60CD
One Little Indian / Jan '94 / Pinnacle.

WELCOME TO THE FUTURE 3
CD _____ TPLP 80CD
One Little Indian / Oct '95 / Pinnacle.

WELCOME TO THE LAND OF HONEYDIPPED
CD _____ DIPAL 001CD
Honeydipped / Sep '95 / Jumpstart / Kudos.

WELCOME TO THE SUMMER OF LOVE '93
CD _____ HFCD 29
PWL / Jul '93 / Warner Music / 3MV.

WELCOME TO THE WORLD OF DEMI-MONDE
CD _____ DMCD 1030
Demi-Monde / Oct '95 / Disc / Magnum Music Group.

WE'LL KEEP A WELCOME
We'll keep a welcome / *Bryan Myrddin* / *How great thou art* / *Memory* / *Aberystwyth* / *Sound of silence* / *Hymn (from Finlandia)* / *Christus redemptor (hyfrydol)* / *Softly as I leave you* / *Comrades in arms* / *Let it be me* / *Creation's hymn* / *You'll never walk alone* / *Martyrs of the arena*
CD _____ PWK 087
Carlton Home Entertainment / May '89 / Carlton Home Entertainment.

WE'LL MEET AGAIN
CD Set _____ DBG 53038
Double Gold / Jan '95 / Target/BMG.

WELL TRODDEN PATH, THE
CD _____ CR 0009-2
Czech Radio / Nov '95 / Czech Music Enterprises.

WELSH CHORAL FAVOURITES
My little Welsh home: *Dunvant Male Choir* / *Soldier's farewell*: *Dunvant Male Choir* / *Close thing eyes*: *Dunvant Male Choir* / *Stodole pumpa*: *Gwalia Male Choir* / *Hiraeth*: *Gwalia Male Choir* / *Marching song*: *Gwalia Male Choir* / *Steal away*: *Gwalia Male Choir* / *Hiraeth*: *Morriston Orpheus Choir* / *Hyder*: *Morriston Orpheus Choir* / *American trilogy*: *Morriston Orpheus Choir* / *My dearest dear*: *Morriston Orpheus Choir* / *Martyrs of the arena*: *Morriston Orpheus Choir* / *My hero*: *Morriston Orpheus Choir* / *Ride the chariot*: *Pontarddulais Male Choir* / *Windmills of your mind*: *Pontarddulais Male Choir* / *Mill harddach wyt na'r rhosyn Gwyn*: *Pontarddulais Male Choir* / *Memory*: *Canoldir Male Voice Choir* / *Eli Jenkin's prayer*: *Canoldir Male Voice Choir* / *My love is like a red red rose*: *Canoldir Male Voice Choir*
CD _____ CC 265
Music For Pleasure / May '91 / EMI.

WEMBLEY MILITARY TATTOO
CD _____ MATCD 238
Castle / Dec '92 / BMG.

WE'RE HERE BECAUSE WE'RE HERE - PASCHENDALE
CD _____ NMCD 9CD
No Master's Voice / Jul '95 / ADA.

WE'RE HERE BECUASE WE'RE HERE
CD _____ NMCD 8
NMC / Jan '96 / Direct.

WEST 25TH
CD _____ CHIP 151
Jive / Aug '94 / BMG.

WEST 25TH CLASSICS
CD _____ CHIP 152
Jive / Oct '94 / BMG.

WEST 25TH VOL.2
CD _____ CHIP 157
Jive / Jul '95 / BMG.

WEST COAST RAP VOL. 1
CD _____ CDSEWM 050
Southbound / Jul '92 / Pinnacle.

WEST COAST RAP VOL. 2
CD _____ CDSEWM 051
Southbound / Jul '92 / Pinnacle.

WEST COAST RAP VOL. 3
CD _____ CDSEWM 052
Southbound / Jul '92 / Pinnacle.

WEST END GIRLS
CD _____ 12215
Laserlight / Aug '94 / Target/BMG.

WEST END STORY VOL.1
Heartbeat: *Gardner, Taana* / *Let's go dancin'*: *Sparque* / *Heat you up (melt you down)*: *Lites, Shirley* / *Do it to the music*: *Raw Silk* / *Can't you feel it*: *Michelle* / *Rescue me*: *Thomas, Sybil* / *Time*: *Stone* / *You can't have your cake*: *Taylor, Brenda*
CD _____ 110652
Musidisc / Jun '93 / Vital / Harmonia Mundi / ADA / Cadillac / Discovery.

WEST END STORY VOL.2
Work that body: *Gardner, Taana* / *It's all over my face*: *Loose Joints* / *Another man*: *Mason, Barbara* / *Give your body up to music*: *Nichols, Billy* / *Ride on the rhythm*: *Mahogany* / *Girl I like the way you move*: *Stone* / *Doin' the best that I can*: *Lavette, Bettye* / *Just in time*: *Rawsilk*
CD _____ 110692
Musidisc / Aug '93 / Vital / Harmonia Mundi / ADA / Cadillac / Discovery.

WEST END STORY VOL.3
When you touch me: *Gardner, Taana* / *Let me feel your heartbeat*: *Glass* / *Music turns me on*: *Sparque* / *When the shit hits the fan*: *Master Boogie's song & dance* / *Disco dance*: *Michele* / *Chillin' out*: *Brooks, Inez* / *Speak well*: *Philly U.S.A.* / *Keep on dancin'*: *Phrase II*
CD _____ 110942
Musidisc / Nov '93 / Vital / Harmonia Mundi / ADA / Cadillac / Discovery.

WEST END STORY VOL.4
No frills: *Gardner, Taana* / *Take some time*: *Sparque* / *Searchin' for some lovin'*: *Trusty,*

Debbie / *I get lifted*: *Sweet Life* / *Hot summer nights*: *Love Club* / *Don't I ever cross your mind*: *Mason, Barbara* / *Hold me, squeeze me*: *Michele* / *People come dance*: *Holt, Ednah & Starluv*
CD _____ 111872
Musidisc / Jan '94 / Vital / Harmonia Mundi / ADA / Cadillac / Discovery.

WEST INDIES - AN ISLAND CARNIVAL
CD _____ 7559720912
Elektra Nonesuch / Jan '95 / Warner Music.

WESTBOUND SOUND OF DETROIT
Gonna spread the news: *Unique Blend* / *Does he treat you better*: *Unique Blend* / *Monny and Daddy*: *Unique Blend* / *Old fashioned woman*: *Unique Blend* / *Lonely in a crowd*: *Superlatives* / *I don't know how (to say I love you)*: *Superlatives* / *Things are looking up*: *Detroit Emeralds* / *Rosetta Stone*: *Detroit Emeralds* / *That's all I got*: *Detroit Emeralds* / *If you need me, call me (and I'm come running)*: *Fantastic Four* / *I'm falling in love (I feel good all over)*: *Fantastic Four* / *What's it all about*: *Counts* / *Happy days*: *Magictones* / *Everything's gonna be alright*: *Magictones* / *I've changed*: *Magictones* / *I'll make it up to you*: *Magictones* / *Trying real hard (to make the grade)*: *Magictones* / *I don't what it is but it sho is funky*: *Mighty Elegant* / *I find myself falling in love with you*: *Mighty Elegant* / *What am I gonna do*: *Houston outlaws* / *I'm loving you, you're leaving me*: *Motivations* / *I love you*: *Motivations* / *My baby ain't no plaything*: *New Holidays* / *When I'm back on my feet*: *Various Narrators*
CD _____ CDSEWD 065
Westbound / Aug '94 / Pinnacle.

WESTERN COUNTRY HITS
CD _____ 55135
Laserlight / Oct '95 / Target/BMG.

WESTERN SWING ON THE AIR 1948-61
CD _____ RFCD 07
Country Routes / Oct '91 / Jazz Music / Hot Shot.

WE'VE GOT ONE WICKED BOGLE
CD _____ SGCD 12
Sir George / Dec '92 / Jetstar / Pinnacle.

WHAAM BAM THANK YOU DAN
In the afternoon: *Revolving Paint Dream* / *I know where*: *Syd Barrett* / *TV Personalities* / *Never find time*: *Mixers* / *You're my kind of girl*: *Page Boys* / *Only the sky children know*: *Page Boys* / *Too shy*: *Direct Hits* / *Dream inspires*: *TV Personalities* / *Still dreaming*: *Marbie Staircase* / *Art of love*: *1000 Mexicans* / *Dancing with the dead*: *E* / *I'm sad*: *Dmochowski, Jedrez* / *Wouldn't you*: *Laughing Apples* / *Bike*: *TV Personalities* / *I'm in love with you*: *Page Boys* / *Naughty little boys*: *Direct Hits* / *My favourite films*: *Gifted Children* / *Dark ages*: *Marble Staircase* / *Love hurts*: *Mixers* / *Painting by numbers*: *Gifted Children* / *News of you*: *1000 Mexicans* / *No use in little girl*: *TV Personalities* / *What killed Alesiter Crowley*: *Direct Hits*
CD _____ ASKCD 043
Vinyl Japan / May '95 / Vital.

WHAT A DIFFERENCE A DAY MADE
CD _____ AVC 526
Avid / Nov '93 / Avid/BMG / Koch.

WHAT A WONDERFUL WORLD
CD _____ MATCD 240
Castle / Nov '93 / BMG.

WHAT DO YOU WANT A JAPANESE TO DO
Just ask why: *Revs* / *Big yellow taxi*: *Elmerhassel* / *She's gone*: *Saturn V* / *House of god*: *Monochrome Set* / *Pistols of colour*: *Tokyo Skunx* / *Dead head baby*: *Fat Tulips* / *Back again*: *Grape* / *I never loved you*: *Strawberry Story* / *Orange county*: *Bluebells* / *Cathedral high*: *St. Christopher* / *Come clean*: *BMX Bandits* / *I won't be there*: *Milkshakes* / *My boyfriend's learning karate*: *Thee Headcoatees* / *My favourite girl*: *Hit Parade* / *Locks and bolts*: *Carousel* / *Special to me*: *Speedway Stars* / *Aware of all*: *McCluskey Brothers* / *Mirror man*: *Looking Glass* / *Rosanna*: *Haywains* / *Nobody better*: *S.K.A.W.* / *Nine or seven*: *Beatnik Filmstars* / *Christmas tears*: *Fletcher, Amelia & Hit Parade*
CD _____ ASKCD 015
Vinyl Japan / Feb '93 / Vital.

WHAT ELSE DO YOU DO
CD _____ SDE 9021CD
Shimmy Disc / Nov '90 / Vital.

WHAT IS FUNK
(12 Funk Classics)
Do it ('til you're satisfied): *B T Express* / *What is funk*: *Rare Gems Odyssey* / *Get the funk out my face*: *Brothers Johnson* / *Take your time (do it right)*: *S.O.S. Band* / *Spirit of the boogie*: *Kool & The Gang* / *Don't stop the music*: *Yarbrough & Peoples* / *Funky nassau*: *Beginning Of The End* / *Love injection*: *Trussel* / *U + Me = Love*: *Undisputed Truth* / *Yum yum (gimme some)*: *Fatback Band* / *Finders keepers*: *Chairmen Of The Board* / *Express*: *B T Express*

CD _____ RNBCD 108
Connoisseur / Apr '94 / Pinnacle.

WHAT IS JAZZ
CD _____ KFWCD 109
Knitting Factory / Nov '94 / Grapevine.

WHAT IS THIS THING CALLED LOVE
(Cool Love Songs Of The 30s & 40s)
Taking a chance on love: Fitzgerald, Ella / Sweet Lorraine: Cole, Nat King / What is this thing called love: Dorsey, Tommy & Connie Haines / Sunshine of your smile: Dorsey, Tommy & Frank Sinatra / All of me: Dorsey, Jimmy & Helen O'Connell / Sposin': Crosby, Bing / Say it with a kiss: Shaw, Artie & Helen Forrest / May I never love again: Weems, Ted & Perry Como / He's funny that way: Hawkins, Coleman & Thelma Carpenter / These foolish things: Goodman, Benny / More than you know: Wilson, Teddy & Billie Holiday / When somebody thinks you're wonderful: Waller, Fats / Body and soul: Shore, Dinah / Why do I love you: Langford, Frances & Tony Martin / I can't give you anything but love: Armstrong, Louis / Think it over: Wynn, Nan / Old fashioned love: Mills Brothers / Here's love in your eyes: Wilson, Teddy & Helen Ward / Two in love: Krupa, Gene, Anita O'Day & Johnny Desmond / Journey to a star: Garland, Judy / Nearness of you: Miller, Glenn & Ray Eberle / Man I love: Lamour, Dorothy
CD _____ PPCD 78114
Past Perfect / Feb '95 / THE.

WHAT SWEET MUSIC THEY MAKE VOL.1
CD _____ VAMPCD 001
3PV / Feb '95 / Plastic Head.

WHAT SWEET MUSIC THEY MAKE VOL.2
CD _____ VAMPCD 002
Vampire Guild / Aug '95 / Plastic Head.

WHATCHA GONNA SWING TONIGHT
CD _____ RHRCD 50
Red House / Oct '95 / Koch / ADA.

WHAT'S THE QUESTION
CD _____ HILOCD 4
Hi / Nov '93 / Pinnacle.

WHAT'S THE QUESTION VOL.2
Is that asking too much: Bryant, Don / What have you done to my heart: Imported Moods / What is this feeling: Green, Al / What made you change: McGee, Eddie / Will you be my man (in the morning): Quiet Elegance / How can you mend a broken heart: Green, Al / How can I believe in you: Known Facts / How's your love life: Quiet Elegance / Hello, how have you been: Clayton, Willie / Baby, what's wrong with you: Green, Al / How strong is a woman: Peebles, Ann / Did you ever have the blues: Bryant, Don / Who's gonna love you: Johnson, Syl / Baby please: West, Norm
CD _____ HILOCD 9
Hi / Mar '94 / Pinnacle.

WHAT'S THIS MUSIC ALL ABOUT
CD _____ 15204
Laserlight / Aug '91 / Target/BMG.

WHEN A MAN LOVES A WOMAN
CD _____ HRCD 8053
Disky / May '94 / THE / BMG / Discovery / Pinnacle.

WHEN A MAN LOVES A WOMAN
CD _____ DINCD 88
Dino / Aug '94 / Pinnacle / 3MV.

WHEN A MAN LOVES A WOMAN (16 Love Songs With Soul)
When a man loves a woman: Sledge, Percy / Higher and higher: Wilson, Jackie / Have you seen her: Chi-Lites / So in love: Mayfield, Curtis / I'd rather go blind: James, Etta / That's the way I feel about cha: Womack, Bobby / Shoop shoop song (It's in his kiss): Everett, Betty / Gimme little sign: Wood, Brenton / Rescue me: Bass, Fontella / Ruler of my heart: Thomas, Irma / Tell it like it is: Neville, Aaron / I had a talk with my man: Collier, Mitty / (If loving you is wrong) I don't want to be right: Ingram, Luther / Every beat of my heart: Knight, Gladys & The Pips / You send me: Cooke, Sam / Hold what you've got: Tex, Joe
CD _____ CPCD 8057
Charly / Feb '95 / Charly / THE / Cadillac.

WHEN A MAN LOVES A WOMAN
When a man loves a woman: Sledge, Percy / Sitting on the dock of the bay: Sledge, Percy / Blue moon: Marcels / My special angel: Vogues / Hey Paula: Paul & Paula / Softly whispering I love you: New English Congregation / Solitaire: Yarborough, Glenn / Deep purple: Tempo, Nino / I'd love you to want me: Lobo / Silence is golden: Tremeloes / Whispering: Tempo, Nino / Come softly to me: Fleetwoods / Rainy night in Georgia: Benton, Brook / Little darlin': Diamonds / Where have all the flowers gone: Kingston Trio
CD _____ 22503
Music / Dec '95 / Target/BMG.

WHEN HEMP WAS HIP
CD _____ VN 167
Viper's Nest / Aug '95 / Direct / Cadillac / ADA.

WHEN I FALL IN LOVE
CD _____ YDG 74621
Yesterday's Gold / Feb '93 / Target/BMG.

WHEN THE MAY IS ALL IN BLOOM (Traditional Singing From SE England)
CD _____ VT 131CD
Veteran Tapes / Jul '95 / Direct / ADA.

WHEN THE SAINTS GO MARCHING IN
When the saints go marching in: Armstrong, Louis / Something new: Basie, Count / Bird of paradise: Davis, Miles / Street heat: Parker, Charlie / Basin Street blues: Fitzgerald, Ella / More than you know: Horne, Lena / Sweet Georgia Brown: Cole, Nat King / Northwest passage: Herman, Woody / Don't blame me: Davis, Miles / (Back home again in) Indiana: Armstrong, Louis / Study in Soulphony: Gillespie, Dizzy / Somebody stole my gal: Goodman, Benny / All of me: Basie, Count / Scuttlebut: Shaw, Artie / Flying home: Fitzgerald, Ella / Little girl blue: Horne, Lena / Bijou: Herman, Woody / Yes sir that's my baby: Cole, Nat King / On the sunny side of the street: Armstrong, Louis / Blue juice: Barnet, Charlie
CD _____ CDGRF 124
Tring / '93 / Tring / Prism.

WHEN THE SUN SETTLES DOWN
CD _____ EFA 064712
Foundation 2000 / Jan '94 / Plastic Head.

WHEN THE SUN SETTLES DOWN VOLUME 2
CD _____ EFA 064722
Foundation 2000 / May '95 / Plastic Head.

WHEN YOUR LOVER HAS GONE
When your lover has gone: Holiday, Billie / Dimples: Hooker, John Lee / Baby, please don't go: Waters, Muddy / Who's been talkin': Howlin' Wolf / Catfish blues: King, B.B. / Ain't nobody's business: Holiday, Billie / Hand in hand: James, Elmore / Born blind: Williamson, Sonny Boy / Boogie chillun: Hooker, John Lee / Trainfare blues: Waters, Muddy / Wang dang doodle: Howlin' Wolf / Easy to remember: Holiday, Billie / B.B. boogie: King, B.B. / Coming home: James, Elmore / Poor Howard green corn: Leadbelly / Settin' here drinkin': Waters, Muddy / Tupelo: Hooker, John Lee / Down in the bottom: Howlin' Wolf / My babe: Little Walter / Don't explain: Holiday, Billie / Don't lose your eye: Williamson, Sonny Boy / Everyday I have the blues: King, B.B. / You gonna miss me: Waters, Muddy / Look on yonder wall: James, Elmore / Drug store woman: Hooker, John Lee
CD _____ CDGRF 126
Tring / '93 / Tring / Prism.

WHERE BLUES MEETS ROCK
CD _____ PRD 70712
Provogue / Oct '94 / Pinnacle.

WHERE JAZZ WAS BORN
CD _____ CD 56021
Jazz Roots / Aug '94 / Target/BMG.

WHIP 1983-1993 (Various Goths)
CD _____ FREUDCD 43
Jungle / Sep '93 / Disc.

WHIP, THE
CD _____ SATE 06
Talitha / Aug '93 / Plastic Head.

WHIPLASH
CD _____ RNCD 2051
Rhino / Mar '94 / Jetstar / Magnum Music Group / THE.

WHITE BOY BLUES
CD _____ TRTCD 01
TrueTrax / Dec '94 / THE.

WHITE BOY BLUES VOL.1
Snake drive: Clapton, Eric / West coast idea: Clapton, Eric / Choker: Clapton, Eric & Jimmy Page / I'm your witch doctor: Mayall, John & The Bluesbreakers / Tribute to Elmore: Clapton, Eric / Freight loader: Clapton, Eric & Jimmy Page / Miles road: Clapton, Eric & Jimmy Page / Telephone blues: Mayall, John & The Bluesbreakers / Draggin' my tail: Clapton, Eric & Jimmy Page / I'm down in the boots: All Stars & Jimmy Page / Stealin': All Stars & Jeff Beck / Chuckles: All Stars & Jeff Beck / L.A. breakdown: All Stars & Jimmy Page / Piano shuffle: All Stars & Nicky Hopkins / Some day baby: Davies, Cyril & The All Stars / Porcupine juice: Santa Barbara Machine Head / Rubber monkey: Santa Barbara Machine Head / Albert: Santa Barbara Machine Head / Who's knocking: Spencer, Jeremy / Look down at my woman: Spencer, Jeremy
CD _____ CCSCD 103
Castle / May '86 / BMG.

WHITE BOY BLUES VOL.2
Tried: Savoy Brown Blues Band / Cold blooded woman: Savoy Brown Blues Band / Can't quit you baby: Savoy Brown Blues Band / True blue: Savoy Brown Blues Band / I feel so good: Kelly, Jo Ann / Ain't gonna worry no more: McPhee, Tony / You don't love me: McPhee, Tony / When you got a good friend: McPhee, Tony / Someone to love me: McPhee, Tony / Dealing with the devil: Dharma Blues Band / Roll 'em Pete: Dharma Blues Band / Water on my fire: Lee, Albert / Crosstown link: Lee, Albert / Flapjacks: Masonry, Stones / Not fade away: Davis,

Cyril & The All Stars / So much to say: Stewart, Rod / On top of the world (featuring Eric Clapton.): Mayall, John & The Bluesbreakers / Hideaway (featuring Eric Clapton.): Mayall, John & The Bluesbreakers / Supernatural: Mayall, John & The Bluesbreakers / Standing at the crossroads: Ten Years After / I want to know: Ten Years After / Next milestone: Lee, Albert
CD _____ CCSCD 142
Castle / '86 / BMG.

WHITE CHRISTMAS (28 Famous Christmas Melodies)
CD _____ CNCD 3132
Hermanex / Nov '92 / THE.

WHITE CHRISTMAS
CD _____ CDCD 1135
Charly / Mar '93 / Charly / THE / Cadillac.

WHITE CHRISTMAS
CD _____ 290609
RCA / Nov '93 / BMG.

WHITE CHRISTMAS VOL.1
CD _____ LECD 030
Wisepack / Nov '92 / THE / Conifer.

WHITE CHRISTMAS VOL.1 & 2
CD Set _____ LECDD 602
Wisepack / Oct '94 / THE / Conifer.

WHITE CHRISTMAS VOL.2
CD _____ LECD 031
Wisepack / Nov '92 / THE / Conifer.

WHITE COUNTRY BLUES 1926-1938 (A Lighter Shade Of Blue)
CD _____ 4728862
Columbia / May '93 / Sony.

WHITE HEATHER CLUB, THE
CD _____ CC 263
Music For Pleasure / May '91 / EMI.

WHITE LABEL VOLUME 2
CD _____ WLCD 3002
White Label/SRD / Jan '95 / SRD.

WHITE LIGHTNING (30 Original Hits That Lit Up The Sixties)
Roll over Beethoven: Berry, Chuck / Boom boom: Hooker, John Lee / Roadrunner: Diddley, Bo / Spoonful: Howlin' Wolf / Walkin' thru the park: Waters, Muddy / My babe: Little Walter / I wish you would: Arnold, Billy Boy / Kansas City: Harrison, Wilbert / Dust my broom: James, Elmore / I'm talking about you: Berry, Chuck / Reconsider baby: Fulson, Lowell / Certain girl: Doe, Ernie K. / Dimples: Hooker, John Lee / Smokestack lightnin': Howlin' Wolf / You can't judge a book by the cover: Diddley, Bo / I ain't got you: Arnold, Billy Boy / No more doggin': Gordon, Roscoe / First time I met the blues: Guy, Buddy / Too much monkey business: Berry, Chuck / I like it like that: Kenner, Chris / Go now: Banks, Bessie / Baby, what you want me to do: Reed, Jimmy / Rollin' and tumblin': James, Elmore / Help me: Williamson, Sonny Boy / Night time is the right time: Turner, Big Joe / I'd rather go blind: James, Etta / Pretty thing: Diddley, Bo / Going down slow: Howlin' Wolf / Standing at the crossroads: James, Elmore / I can't quit you baby: Rush, Otis
CD _____ CDINS 5017
Instant / Jan '90 / Charly.

WHITE MAN BLUES
Dock of the bay: Spatz / Hungry man blues: Sumlin, Willie / It's too late: Head, Roy / Black cat bone: Blanchard, Terence / Hard symmetry: Long, Joe / Mercury blues: Owens, Steve / Milk cow blues: Terrapin Jackson / Red neck blues: Holzhaus, Chris / Please come home for Christmas: Winter, Johnny & Edgar / Rough girl: Maly, Ed / Gonna get my baby: Brooks, Bruce / Lay down gal of mine: Winter, Johnny / Nobody but me tells me when my eagle to fly: Head, Roy / Something to ease my pain: Long, Joey
CD _____ CDTB 168
Thunderbolt / Oct '95 / Magnum Music Group.

WHITE MANSIONS (A Tale From The American Civil War 1861-65)
Story to tell / Dixie, hold on / Join around the flag / White trash / Last chance and the Kentucky racehorse / Southern boys / Union mare and confederate grey / No one would believe a summer could be so cold / Southland's bleeding / Bring up the twelve pounders / They laid waste to our land / Praise the lord / King has called me home / Bad man / Dixie now your done
CD _____ CDMID 182
A&M / '93 / PolyGram.

WHITE ROSE, THE (A Festival Of Yorkshire Music)
Soldier's chorus / Monte christe / Prelude to Act III / Lohengrin / Portrait of my love / Westminster waltz / Fishermen of England / Tribute to Ivor Novello / White rose / Battle hymn of the Republic / Gladiator's farewell / Love could I only tell thee / Lost chord / Colonel Bogey / Roman war song / Clog day closes / Fantasia on British sea songs / On Ilkley moor baht'at
CD _____ QPRZ 016D
Polyphonic / Apr '95 / Conifer.

WHITE SPIRITUALS FROM THE SACRED HARP
CD _____ 802052
New World / Aug '92 / Harmonia Mundi / ADA / Cadillac.

WHITER SHADE OF DOO-WOP, A
Little star: Elegants / Little boy blue: Elegants / I'll close my eyes: Skyliners / Door is still open: Skyliners / Little Eva: Locomotions / Adios my love: Locomotions / Read between the lines: Dell Satins / I'll pray for you: Dell Satins / Bermuda: Four Seasons / Spanish lace: Four Seasons / Barbara Ann: Regents / Over the rainbow: Regents / Runaround: Regents / Cruise to the moon: Chaperones / Shining star: Chaperones / Picture in my wallet: Darrell & Oxfords / Roses are red: Darrell & Oxfords / Can't you tell: Darrell & Oxfords / Reasons for love: Darrell & Oxfords / Rip Van Winkle: Devotions / (I love you) for sentimental reasons: Devotions / Snow White: Devotions / Zindy Lou: Devotions / Tears from a broken heart: Devotions / Sunday kind of love: Devotions
CD _____ NEMCD 715
Sequel / Nov '94 / BMG.

WHO COVERS WHO
CD _____ CM 006CD
Trident / Aug '93 / Pinnacle.

WHO GAVE THE PERMISSION
CD _____ RIZ 00032
Riz / Nov '95 / Jetstar.

WHO WILL CALM THE STORM
CD _____ SCR 26
Strictly Country / Jul '95 / ADA / Direct.

WHOLE LOTTA ROCK 'N' ROLL
CD Set _____ MCBX 011
Music Club / Apr '94 / Disc / THE / CM.

WHY DO FOOLS FALL IN LOVE
Why do fools fall in love: Lymon, Frankie & The Teenagers / Party doll: Knox, Buddy / Kisses sweeter than wine: Rodgers, Jimmie / Goody goody: Lymon, Frankie & The Teenagers / Do ya wanna dance: Freeman, Bobby / Tears on my pillow: Imperials / Book of love: Monotones / Beep beep: Playmates / Oh-oh I'm falling in love again: Rodgers, Jimmie / Poor boy: Royaltones / Happy organ: Cortez, Dave 'Baby' / I only have eyes for you: Flamingos / Mary Lou: Hawkins, Ronnie / Woo hoo: Rock A Teens / You talk too much: Jones, Joe / Fannie Mae: Brown, Buster / Girl of my best friend: Donner, Ral / Daddy's home: Shep & The Limelites / Blue moon: Marcels / Goodbye cruel world: Darren, Jimmy
CD _____ CDROU 1044
Roulette / Aug '91 / EMI.

WIBBLY WOBBLY WALK, THE (From Original Phonograph Cylinders)
Wibbly wobbly walk: Charman, Jack / Oh by jingo: Billy boy / Little Ford rambled right along: He: Merson, Billy / Tickle me Timothy: Williams, Billy / Little Ford rambled right along: Williams, Billy / Wallaperoo: Osmond, Arthur / I love me: Broadway Dance Orchestra / All by yourself in the moonlight: Sarony, Leslie / Little wooden whistle wouldn't whistle: Columbia Novelty Orchestra / Why did I kiss that girl: Savoy Havana Band / Felix keeps on walking: Savoy Havana Band / I parted my hair in the middle: Formby, George / There's a rickety rackety shack: Tin Pan Band / Down south: Inter-national Novelty Quartet / Parade of the wooden soldiers: International Novelty Orchestra
CD _____ CDSDL 350
Saydisc / Mar '94 / Harmonia Mundi / ADA / Direct.

WIBBLY, WOBBLY WORLD
CD _____ WWCD 4
Wibbly Wobbly / Mar '94 / SRD.

WIEN - VOLKSMUSIK 1906-1937
CD _____ US 0198
Trikont / Jun '95 / Direct.

Baby mine: Houston, Thelma / Love slipped through my fingers: Williams, Sam / Superlove: David & The Giants / Hey little way out girl: Construction / Double cookin': Checkerboard Squares / Take me home: King, Donna / Panic: Reparata & The Delrons / My sugar baby: Clarke, Connie / Psychedelic soul: Russell, Saxie / Ten miles high: David & The Giants / What shall I do: Frankie & Classicals / Hey little girl: Phillips, D.D. / Rosemary: Wylie, Richard / If that's what you wanted: Beverly, Frankie / Champion: Mitchell, Willie / Ever again: Williams, Bernie / So is the sun: World Column / Breakaway: Carmen, Steve / I'm where it's at: Jades / I'm comin' home in the morning: Pride, Lou / I'm gettin' on life: Wombats / You got me where you want me: Santos, Larry / I travel alone: Ragland, Lou / End of our love: Wilson, Nancy / Meet me halfway: Little Bryany / Manifesto: Case Of Tyme / I walked away: Paris, Bobby
CD _____ GSCD 072
Goldmine / Sep '95 / Vital.

WIGAN CASINO STORY, THE
Flasher: Mistura / Long after tonight is all over: Radcliffe, Jimmy / We go together: August & Duneen / Tears: Roye, Lee / You've been away: Roye, Lee / Take away the pain stain: Austin, Patti / Live Adam and Eve: Reflections / Dance, dance, dance: Casualeers / If you ask me: Williams, Jerry / Better use your head: Imperials / Joker: Mysiestones / Ski-ing in the snow: Invitations / Time will pass you by: Legend, Tobi / I can't help lovin' you: Anka, Paul / I'll always need you: Courtney, Dean / Stick by me baby: Salvadors / You don't love me: Epitome Of Sound / I never knew: Foster, Eddie / Put your arms around me: Sherry's / I really love you: Tomangoes / I'm on my way: Parrish, Dean
CD _____ GSCD 051
Goldmine / Sep '94 / Vital.

WILD BUNCH
(27 Instrumental Reggae Classics)
CD _____ CDTRL 346
Trojan / Mar '95 / Jetstar / Total/BMG.

WILD CONSERVES - THE FLAVOURS OF SCOTLAND
(In Aid Of Scottish Wildlife Trust)
CD _____ LCOM 5226CD
Lismor / Jan '94 / Lismor / Direct / Duncans / ADA.

WILD PARTY SOUNDS
Woodpecker sound: Jah Woosh Machine Gun / Bedbound saga: Hogg & Co / Quante jubila: Prince Far-I & Creation Rebel / Quit the body: Chicken Rebel / Parasitic machine: Pellay, Alan / Dreams are better: London Underground / Asian rebel: Suns Of Arqa / Demonic forces: Pellay, Alan / Afghani dub: Mothmen / Things that made U.S.: Loy, Jeb & The Oilwell / Yippee-I-ay: New Age Steppers / Dice: Nylon, Judy
CD _____ CDBRED 24
Cherry Red / Feb '94 / Pinnacle.

WILD ROCK & ROLL INSTRUMENTALS
Rampage: Thunderrocks / Shadow: Thunderrocks / Travelers rock: Dave's Travelers / Roy's romp: Kountry Kings / Line drive: Terry & The Renegades / Pig bone: Abootay's / Skip's boogie: Haston, Skip & The Phantoms / Royal B: Roy & The Royals / Wildcat: Nitecaps / Brand: Devrons / Trance: Scott, Dean & The Dominoes / Clip clop: Royaltones / Jamboree rock: Wilson, Robert & Gene / Mad surfer: Stingrays / Shaften: Duzan, Bill & The Corvettes / Fasnach-kuechel: Fendermen / Ramrod: Rogers, Johnny / Blue Saturday: Checkers / Big gass: Gassaway, El & C. Stacey Trio / Scalping party: Tornados / Jorris boogie: Hennessee, J. & Roundup Boys / Go Daddy rock: Hendrix, Al & Jolly Jody / Space needle: Starfires / Anchor park: P.J. & His Headliners / Moovin 'n' groovin: Rockets / Mad gass: Royal Teens / Dennis boogie: Volk, Dennis / Ghost train: Swanks / Spitfire: Logsdon, Bill / Lariat: Legends
CD _____ CDCL 4418
White Label/Bear Family / Apr '94 / Bear Family / Rollercoaster.

WILD ROVER
(A Feast Of Irish Folk)
Rocky road to Dublin: Dubliners / Lonesome boatman: Furey, Finbar & Eddie / Medley: Renbourn, John / Barleycorn: Johnstons / Leaving of Liverpool: Johnstons / Medley #3: Maloney, Michael / Foggy dew: Imlach, Hamish / Flowers in the valley: Furey, Finbar & Eddie / Newry highwayman: Johnstons / Wild rover: Dubliners / Bill Hart's favourite: Furey, Finbar & Eddie / Killarney boys of pleasure: Swarbrick, Dave / Medley #2: Renbourn, John / Spanish cloak: Furey, Finbar & Eddie / I'll tell me ma: Dubliners / Reels: Kilfenora Ceili Band / Norwegian song: Maloney, Michael / Golden jubilee: Glenside Ceilidh Band / Lentram fancy: Maloney, Michael / Home boys home: Dubliners
CD _____ TRTCD 125
TrueTrax / Dec '94 / THE.

WILD SUMMER WOW
(A Creation Sampler)
CD _____ CRECD 002
Creation / May '94 / 3MV / Vital.

WILDFLOWERS
(The New York Loft Jazz Sessions)
Jays: Kalaprusha / New times: McIntyre, Ken / Over the rainbow: Murray, Sunny / Rainbows: Rivers, Sam / U.S.O. Dance: Air / Need to smile: Flight To Sanity / Naomi: McIntyre, Ken / 730 S Kelvin: Braxton, Anthony / Then they dance: Brown, Marion
CD _____ 3000332
Gravity / May '95 / New Note.

WILDFLOWERS 2
(The New York Loft Jazz Sessions)
Push pull: Lyons, Jimmy / Zaki: Lake, Oliver / Shout song: Murray, David / Something's cookin': Murray, Sunny / Chant: Mitchell, Roscoe
CD _____ 3000342
Gravity / Jun '95 / New Note.

WIND AND REED
Sunderlal: Renbourn, Nancy / Rose water: Siebert, Budi / Meisoroku (edit): Lee, Riley / Thunder's windmill: Brewer, Spencer / To the willow: Wynberg, Simon / Night tribe: Rumbel, Nancy / Guinevere's tears: Arken-

stone, David / Sad memories: Illenberger, Ralf / Awakening: Stein, Ira / Surrender: Gettel, Michael / Northeast wind: Lauria, Nando
CD _____ ND 61037
Narada / Nov '93 / New Note / ADA.

WIND DOWN ZONE VOL.3
Sexy girl: Thomas, Lillo / Every little bit: Scott, Millie / Genie: B B & Q Band / There isn't nothin' (like your lovin'): Laurence, Paul / I'm the one for you: Whispers / Get in touch with me: Collage / Your smile: Rene & Angela / I need your lovin': Williams, Alyson / My sensitivity: Vandross, Luther / Addictive love: Winans, Bebe & Cece / Never say goodbye to love: Moore, Rene / Can't wait: Payne, Freda / When we're making love: Lasalle, Denise / Are you ready: Robbins, Rockie
CD _____ CDELV 11
Elevate / Dec '93 / 3MV / Sony.

WIND DOWN ZONE VOL.4
Make it last forever: Sweat, Keith / Games: Booker, Chuckii / Please be mine: Belle, Regina / Let's start love over: Jaye, Miles / Nite and day: Sure, Al B. / You can't turn me away: Striplin, Sylvia / I believe in love: Harris, Major / Rockin' you eternally: Ware, Leon / Don't stop doin' what cha' do: Mills, Stephanie / In the mood: Davis, Tyrone / Warm weather: Pieces Of A Dream / Feels like I'm falling in love: Bar-Kays / Strung out for your love: Four Tops / Lovers everywhere: L.T.D.
CD _____ CDELV 14
Elevate / Apr '94 / 3MV / Sony.

WIND DOWN ZONE VOL.5
CD _____ CDELV 18
Elevate / Dec '94 / 3MV / Sony.

WIND DOWN ZONE VOL.6
CD _____ CDELV 20
Elevate / Jun '95 / 3MV / Sony.

WINDHAM HILL - THE FIRST TEN YEARS
(2CD Set)
Bricklayer's beautiful daughter: Ackerman, Will / White rain: De Grassi, Alex / Colors/dance: Winston, George / Angel's flight: Shadowfax / Bradley's dream: Storey, Liz / Afternoon postlude soliloquy: Hecht, Daniel / Second gymnopedie (1888): Quist, Bill / Homefield suite: Qualey, David / Rickover's dream: Hedges, Michael / Variations on clair de lune: Basho, Robbie / Oristano sojourn: Cossu, Scott / Clockwork: De Grassi, Alex / Peace: Winston, George / Aerial boundaries: Hedges, Michael / Egrets: Montreux Band / On the threshold of liberty: Isham, Mark / Welcoming: Manring, Michael / 19a: Nightnoise / Montana ball: Aaberg, Philip / Shadowdance: Shadowfax / Pittsburgh 1901: Isham, Mark / Calling: Stein & Walder / Gwenlaise: Cossu, Scott & Friesen, Eugene / Dolphins: Marshall, Mike & Darol Anger / Wishing well: Schonherz & Scott / Theme for Naomi Uemura: Aaberg, Philip / Toys not ties: Nightnoise / Close cover: Mertens, Wim / To the well: Mathieu, W.A. / Hot beach: Interior / New waltz: Dalglish, Malcolm / Processional: Ackerman, Will / Woman at the well: Story, Tim
CD Set _____ WD 1095
Windham Hill / May '91 / Pinnacle / BMG / ADA.

WINDHAM HILL SAMPLER '92
CD _____ 111092
Windham Hill / Sep '91 / Pinnacle / BMG / ADA.

WINDHAM HILL SAMPLER '94
Bright sky: De Grassi, Alex / Love on three levels: Psychograss / Sentimental walk from diva: Aaberg, Philip / Pavanne: Erquiaga, Steve / Night in that land: Nightnoise / Patu: Aquarela Carioca / Firewater: Gaia / How insensitive: Storey, Liz / Happy home in Kathmandu: Ackerman, Will / Redonda: Modern Mandolin Quartet / Pas de deux: Cossu, Scott / My heart: Sevag, Oystein / Ivory: Lynch, Ray
CD _____ 01934111382
Windham Hill / Feb '94 / Pinnacle / BMG / ADA.

WINDOWS - C.T.I. COLLECTION VOL.1
CD _____ ESJCD 233
Essential Jazz / Oct '94 / BMG.

WINDOWS - C.T.I. COLLECTION VOL.2
CD _____ ESJCD 234
Essential Jazz / Oct '94 / BMG.

WINDY CITY BLUES
CD _____ 77002
Laserlight / Jan '93 / Target/BMG.

WINGS OF LOVE
Get here: Adams, Oleta / Sacrifice: John, Elton / Senza una Donna: Zucchero & Paul Young / Because I love you (The postman song): Stevie B / Let's wait awhile: Jackson, Janet / Different corner: Michael, George / Every breath you take: Police / Wonderful tonight: Clapton, Eric / On the wings of love: Osborne, Jeffrey / Anything for you: Estefan, Gloria / Love and affection: Armatrading, Joan / Unchained melody: Righteous Brothers / I'm not in love: 10cc / Angel eyes: Wet Wet Wet / Fool (if you think it's over): Brooks, Elkie / Goodbye to love: Carpenters

CD _____ 8455062
A&M / Jun '91 / PolyGram.

WINNERS
CD _____ RITZRCD 551
Ritz / Nov '95 / Pinnacle.

WINNERS CIRCLE 2
Romantically inspired: Tashan / Light of love: Angie & Debbie / Wanna make love 2U: Mansfield, Rodney / You can't go wrong: Vertical Hold / Come a little closer: Rice, Gene / Quiet time: Belle, Regina / Love tonight: Walker, Chris / Where do we go from here: Steele, Jevetta / I wanna love: Moore, Chante / If you ever loved someone and lost: Beasley, Walter / Never too late: Goodman, Gabrielle / Wait a minute: Mahogany Blue / More today than yesterday: Company / Wonderin': Moten, Wendy
CD _____ CDEXP 7
Expansion / Dec '93 / Pinnacle / Sony / 3MV.

WINNERS, THE
(The Great British Country Music Awards)
Follow your dream: O'Donnell, Daniel / Light years away: West Virginia / Before I call it love: Jory, Sarah / Charlie: Froggatt, Raymond / Your love is like a flower: Down County Boys / Fireside dreaming: Landsborough, Charlie / If tomorrow never comes: Pride, Charley / Born to run: Young Country / You're the first thing I think of: O'Donnell, Daniel / Never had it so good: Jory, Sarah / Just between you and me: Pride, Charley / Going nowhere fast: Young Country / Don't make me cry again: Froggatt, Raymond / Come and sit by the river with me: Down County Boys / Blue rendezvous: West Virginia / What colour is the wind: Landsborough, Charlie
CD _____ RCD 551
Ritz / Nov '95 / Pinnacle.

WINTER WONDERLAND
Winter wonderland: Day, Doris / Jingle bells: Streisand, Barbra / Santa Claus is coming to town: Bennett, Tony / Christmas spirit: Charles, Ray / Christmas song: Mathis, Johnny / It came upon a midnight clear: Andrews, Julie / O holy night: Vinton, Bobby / When a child is born: Mathis, Johnny & Gladys Knight / Blue Christmas: Nelson, Willie / Little drummer boy: Cash, Johnny / First Noel: Williams, Andy / Silent night: Wynette, Tammy / Christmas time is here again: Robbins, Marty / Mary's boy child: Humperdinck, Engelbert / White Christmas: Sinatra, Frank
CD _____ 4677042
Columbia / Nov '95 / Sony.

WINTER'S SOLSTICE II, A
CD _____ WD 1077
Windham Hill / Oct '91 / Pinnacle / BMG / ADA.

WINTER'S SOLSTICE III, A
CD _____ WD 1098
Windham Hill / Oct '91 / Pinnacle / BMG / ADA.

WINTER'S SOLSTICE, A
CD _____ 01934111742
Windham Hill / Nov '95 / Pinnacle / BMG / ADA.

WINTERS OF DISCONTENT
CD _____ SFRCD 204
Strange Fruit / Sep '91 / Pinnacle.

WIPEOUT
Afro ride: Leftfield / Chemical beats: Chemical Brothers / Blue Monday (Hardfloor mix): New Order / Age of love: Jam & Spoon / Wipeout (P.E.T.R.O.L.): Orbital / Love (Narcotic suite): Prodigy / In a tristesse durera (Scream to a sigh) (Dust Brothers mix): Manic Street Preachers / When (K-Klass/Pharmacy mix): Sunscreem / Good enough (Gemini's psychosis mix): B.B. & Angie Brown / Circus bells (Hardfloor remix): Armani, Robert / Captain dread: Dreadzone / Transamazonia (Deepdish rockit express dub mix): Shamen
CD _____ SONYTV 6CD
Sony Music / Nov '95 / Sony.

WISH ME LUCK AS YOU WAVE ME GOODBYE
(Popular Songs Of The War Years)
We must all stick together / Absent friends / We'll meet again / Run rabbit run / There'll always be an England / (We're gonna hang out the) washing on the Siegfried Line / They can't black out the moon / Wish me luck as you wave me goodbye / Somewhere in France / Berlin or bust / Old lady of Armentieres / Bless 'em all / Beneath the lights of home / When that man is dead and gone / Oh what a surprise for the duce / London pride / Grand old man / I'll walk beside you / Kiss the boys goodbye / White cliffs of Dover / Bombardier song / This is something worth fighting for / Johnny zero / Don't let's be beastly to the Germans / Coming in on a wing and a prayer
CD _____ CDHD 301
Happy Days / Aug '94 / Conifer.

WITH A SONG IN OUR HEARTS AGAIN
They say it's wonderful: Crosby, Bing / Sentimental me: Anthony, Ray & His Orchestra / Undecided: Anthony, Ray & His Orchestra / It's magic: Anthony, Ray & His Orchestra

/ Steppin' out with my baby: Anthony, Ray & His Orchestra / How lucky are you: Andrews Sisters / Do you love me: Haymes, Dick / You're getting to be a habit with me: Torme, Mel / Again: Torme, Mel / I'll string along with you: Stafford, Jo & Gordon MacRae / To each his own: Ink Spots / No orchids for my lady: Ink Spots / Where or when: Dinning Sisters / I can't begin to tell you: Crosby, Bing & Carmen Cavallaro / Hurry on down: Lutcher, Nellie / My mother's eyes: Lutcher, Nellie / Song is ended (but the melody lingers on): Lutcher, Nellie / Put 'em in a box: Cole, Nat King / My one and only highland fling: Haymes, Dick & Dorothy Carless / Hop scotch polka: Garber, Jan & His Orchestra / That lucky old sun: Martin, Dean / Powder your face with sunshine: Martin, Dean / Day by day: Crosby, Bing / Riders in the sky: Crosby, Bing / Teresa: Haymes, Dick & The Andrews Sisters / I get sentimental over nothing: Cole, Nat King / Tenderly: Dennis, Clark / Bluebird of happiness: Stafford, Jo & Gordon MacRae / With a song in my heart: Day, Dennis / This is the moment: Stafford, Jo / There's a train out for dreamland: Cole, Nat King / Kiss in the dark: MacRae, Gordon / Far away places: Whiting, Margaret / Mañana: Lee, Peggy / How high the moon: Cole, Nat King / Jealous heart: Garber, Jan / On a slow boat to China: Goodman, Benny / Buttons and bows: Dinning Sisters / You was: Lee, Peggy & Dean Martin / When my dreamboat comes home: Crosby, Bing
CD Set _____ CDDL 1266
Music For Pleasure / May '94 / EMI.

WITNESS VOL.1
(Spirituals And Gospels)
Witness / Hush somebody's calling my name / Death is gonna lay his cold icy hands on me / Walk together chillin' / Were you there / Elijah rock / This train / Jesu lover of my soul / My Lord, what a morning / Go down Moses / In dat great gittin' up mornin' / Crucifixion / Go where I send thee / Swing low, sweet chariot / Go, tell it on the mountain / What a mighty God
CD _____ 14492
Collins Classics / Apr '95 / Conifer.

WIZARD OF OZ
CD _____ JASSCD 629
Jass / Feb '92 / CM / Jazz Music / ADA / Cadillac / Direct.

WOHLSTAND - GERMAN/JAPANESE NOISE COMPILATION
Human Wreckords / Oct '95 / SRD.

WOKE UP THIS MORNING
CD _____ MCLD 19238
Chess/MCA / Nov '90 / BMG / New Note.

WOMAN IN LOVE, A
CD _____ MATCD 263
Castle / May '93 / BMG.

WOMAN IN ME, THE
(18 Superb Vocal Performances)
I say a little prayer: Franklin, Aretha / Right thing to do: Simon, Carly / Love me: Elliman, Yvonne / Don't it make my brown eyes blue: Gayle, Crystal / I just don't know what to do with myself: Springfield, Dusty / Something: Bassey, Shirley / One day I'll fly away: Crawford, Randy / Every time we say goodbye: Fitzgerald, Ella / Anyone who had a heart: Warwick, Dionne / Cry me a river: London, Julie / Loving you: Riperton, Minnie / Memory: Paige, Elaine / Torn between two lovers: MacGregor, Mary / Best thing that ever happened to me: Knight, Gladys & The Pips / Ain't got no...I got life: Simone, Nina / This is my song: Clark, Petula / Wishing you were somehow here again: Brightman, Sarah / We're all alone: Coolidge, Rita
CD _____ MUSCD 019
MCI / May '94 / Disc / THE.

WOMAN TO WOMAN
Woman to woman: Brown, Shirley / I never loved a man (the way I love you): Franklin, Aretha / Rescue me: Bass, Fontella / I can't stand the rain: Peebles, Ann / Oh no not my baby: Brown, Maxine / I'd rather go blind: James, Etta / Dirty man: Lee, Laura / Mockingbird: Foxx, Inez & Charlie / When something is wrong with my baby: Weston, Kim / B-A-B-Y: Thomas, Carla / Misty blue: Moore, Dorothy / Time is on my side: Thomas, Irma / What cha gonna do about it: Troy, Doris / Fire: Taylor, Koko / Greatest love: Clay, Judy / Mr. Bigstuff: Knight, Jean / Let me down easy: Lavette, Bettye / Clean up woman: Wright, Betty / (If loving you is wrong) I don't want to be right: Jackson, Millie / Stay with me baby: Ellison, Lorraine
CD _____ VSOPCD 188
Connoisseur / Apr '93 / Pinnacle.

WOMAN TO WOMAN 2
Silent all these years: Amos, Tori / Constant craving: Lang, k.d. / Venus as a boy: Bjork / Rubber band girl: Bush, Kate / Marlene on the wall: Vega, Suzanne / Cold: Lennox, Annie / Show me heaven: McKee, Maria / Don't wanna lose you: Estefan, Gloria / In your care: Archer, Tasmin / Will you: O'Connor, Hazel / Power of love: Rush, Jennifer / Stop: Brown, Sam / Late night Grand Hotel: Griffith, Nanci / Willow: Armatrading, Joan / Loves scenes: Craven, Beverley / Good tradition: Tikaram, Tanita / Climb on (that's strong): Colvin, Shawn / Ho-

neychild: *Reader, Eddi* / I am woman:
Reddy, Helen / Stay: *Shakespears Sister*
CD _____ 5163302
PolyGram TV / Apr '94 / PolyGram.

WOMAN'S HEART 2, A
CD _____ DARA 3063
Dara / Jan '95 / Roots / CM / Direct / ADA
/ Koch.

WOMAN'S HEART, A
Only a woman's heart: *McEvoy, Eleanor &
Mary Black* / Caledonia: *Keane, Dolores* /
Vanities: *Keane, Dolores* / Blackbird: *Shan-
non, Sharon* / Wall of tears: *Black, Frances*
/ Summerfly: *O'Connell, Maura* / Island:
Keane, Dolores / I hear you breathing:
McEvoy, Eleanor / Sonny: *Black, Mary* /
Coridinio: *Shannon, Sharon* / Living in these
troubled times: *O'Connell, Maura* / After the
ball: *Black, Frances*
CD _____ DARA 3158
Dara / Jan '95 / Roots / CM / Direct / ADA
/ Koch.

WOMAN'S LOVE, A
Fare thee well, my own true love: *Black,
Mary* / Amhran Peter Baille: *Black, Mary* /
Casting my shadow on the road: *Murray,
Sinead* / New love story: *Murray, Sinead* /
Chomaraigh Aoibhinn O: *O'Sullivan, Maire* /
Carraig: *O'Sullivan, Maire* / Johnny lovely
Johnny: *Keane, Dolores* / Low low lands of
Holland: *Keane, Dolores* / Pluirin na mBan
Don Og: *Na Chathain, Bríd* / Aililiu na
Gamha: *Na Chathain, Bríd* / Memories of
Father Angus MacDonald: *Roach, Nancy* /
Golden keyboard: *Roach, Nancy* / An Seán-
duine: *Ní Bheaglaoich, Eilin* / Jimmy Mo
Mhíle Stór: *Ní Bheaglaoich, Eilin* / Workin'
man: *Taggart, Mairead* / Scolar: *Taggart,
Mairead* / Cre na Cille: *Dhonncha, Ann Ma-
rie Nic* / Slan leis an Oige: *Dhonncha, Ann
Marie Nic*
CD _____ CICD 091
Clo Iar-Chonnachta / Dec '93 / CM.

WOMAN'S WORLD
CD _____ EFA 064612
Metalimbo / Oct '94 / SRD.

WOMEN IN (E)MOTION FESTIVAL
CD _____ T&M 109
Tradition & Moderne / Jan '95 / Direct /
ADA.

WOMEN IN LOVE
CD _____ STACD 050
Stardust / Sep '94 / Carlton Home
Entertainment.

WOMEN IN LOVE
Talking in your sleep: *Gayle, Crystal* / Don't
it make my brown eyes blue: *Gayle, Crystal*
/ Way we were: *Knight, Gladys* / Best thing
that ever happened to me: *Knight, Gladys* /
It's a heartache: *Tyler, Bonnie* / I don't know
how to love him: *Reddy, Helen* / First cut is
the deepest: *Arnold, P.P.* / I honestly love
you: *Newton-John, Olivia* / What I've got in
mind: *Spears, Billie Jo* / Bette Davis eyes:
Carnes, Kim / All I have is the love we started
from: *Nightingale, Maxine* / Answer me:
Dickson, Barbara / This will be: *Cole, Natalie*
/ He was beautiful (Cavatina): *Williams, Iris*
/ Ruby Tuesday: *Melanie* / I'll never fall in
love again: *Gorney, Bobbie* / One man
woman: *Easton, Sheena* / Loving you: *Riperton, Minnie*
CD _____ CDMFP 5998
Music For Pleasure / Nov '93 / EMI.

WOMEN IN LOVE
CD _____ NTRCD 017
Nectar / Jan '94 / Pinnacle.

**WOMEN OF GOSPEL'S GOLDEN AGE
VOL 1**
More like Jesus: *Griffin, Bessie* / Blessed
mother: *Griffin, Bessie* / Whosoever will:
Griffin, Bessie / Heaven: *Griffin, Bessie* /
Nobody but you: *Griffin, Bessie* / All of my
burdens (ain't that good news): *Griffin, Bes-
sie* / Sit dowm children: *Robinson, Helen
Youth Choir* / I'm not gonna let nobody stop
you: *Princess Stewart* / Tired, Lord: *Prin-
cess Stewart* / Blind Barbara Dues: *Argo
Singers* / Lookin' this way: *Argo Singers* /
Get away Jordan: *Love Coates, Dorothy* /
Every day will be Sunday (by and by): *Love
Coates, Dorothy* / I'm going to die with the
staff in my hand: *Love Coates, Dorothy* /
Take your burden to the Lord and leave it
there: *Love Coates, Dorothy* / I must see
Jesus (for myself): *Greenwood, Lil* / Tell Jesus all: *Simmons-Akers Trio* / Going to Canaan's shore: *Simmons-Akers Trio* / Glory
to his name: *Simmons-Akers Trio* / God is
a battle axe: *Carr, Sister Wynona* / I'm a
pilgrim traveller: *Carr, Sister Wynona* / See
his blessed face: *Carr, Sister Wynona* / How
good God is: *Carr, Sister Wynona* / Till we
meet again: *Martin, Sallie Singers & Cora
Martin* / Jesus: *Martin, Sallie Singers & Cora
Martin* / Thank you Jesus: *Martin, Sallie
Singers & Cora Martin* / How far am I from
Canaan (pts 1 & 2): *Famous Ward Singers
of Philadelphia*
CD _____ CDCHD 567
Ace / Mar '94 / Pinnacle / Cadillac / Com-
plete/Pinnacle.

WONDERFUL CHRISTMAS
CD _____ DCD 5346
Disky / Dec '93 / THE / BMG / Discovery /
Pinnacle.

WONDERFUL WORLD
CD _____ DINCD 89
Dino / May '94 / Pinnacle / 3MV.

**WONDERFUL WURLITZER, THE
(Featuring Robert Wolfe & Nicholas
Martin)**
RAF march past / Medley 1 (Take these
chains from my heart/Nobody's child/Your
cheatin' heart/Crystal chandeliers) / Medley
2 (Mairzy doats and dozy doats/We're
gonna hang out the washing on the Siegfried Line/Don't fence me in) / Parade of the
tin soldiers / Medley 3 (I'm beginning to see
the light/I've got a girl in Kalamazoo/It don't
mean a thing if it ain't got that swing) / Medley 4 - Me and my girl (The sun has got his
hat on/Leaning on a lamp post/Love makes
the world go round/Me and my girl) / Gymnopedie no.1 / Our director / Tiger rag / Kitten on the keys / Medley 5 (You're never
fully dressed without a smile/Smile/Smiling
through/Smile darn ya, smile) / Medley 6
(Happy days are here again/I wonder where
my baby is tonight/Saturday rag) / Rondo
all turca / Medley 7 (The touch of your lips /
The very thought of you Cherokee) / Elean-
ora / Buffoon / Light of foot march
CD _____ 12722
Laserlight / Nov '95 / Target/BMG.

WOODSTOCK '94
Selling the drama: *Live* / Just like a man:
Del Amitri / I'm the only one: *Etheridge,
Melissa* / Feelin' alright: *Cocker, Joe* /
Dreams: *Cranberries* / Soup: *Blind Melon* /
When I come around: *Green Day* / Shoop:
Salt 'N' Pepa / Blood sugar sex magik: *Red
Hot Chili Peppers* / Sometimes: *James* /
Porno for pyros: *Porno For Pyros* / These
damned blue collar tweeders: *Primus* /
Draw the line/F.I.N.E.: *Aerosmith* / Happi-
ness in slavery: *Nine Inch Nails* / For whom
the bell tolls: *Metallica* / Come together: *Ne-
ville Brothers* / Generations: *N'Dour, Yous-
sou* / Mama: *Zucchero* / Run baby run:
Crow, Sheryl / Dance, motherfucker, dance:
Violent Femmes / Kiss off: *Violent Femmes*
/ Shine: *Collective Soul* / Arrow: *Candlebox*
/ How I could just kill a man: *Cypress Hill* /
Right here too much: *Rollins, Henry* / High-
way 61 revisited: *Dylan, Bob* / Pearly
Queen: *Traffic* / Biko: *Gabriel, Peter*
CD _____ 5403222
A&M / Dec '94 / PolyGram.

**WOODSTOCK - 3 DAYS OF PEACE AND
MUSIC**
CD Set _____ 7567826362
Warner Bros. / Sep '94 / Warner Music.

WOODSTOCK GENERATION
CD _____ NTRCD 020
Nectar / Jul '94 / Pinnacle.

WOODSTOCK GENERATION
CD _____ EDL 28612
Edel / Oct '94 / Pinnacle.

WOODSTOCK GENERATION 2
CD _____ NTRCD 032
Nectar / Mar '95 / Pinnacle.

WOODSTOCK MOUNTAINS
CD _____ CD 11520
Rounder / '88 / CM / Direct / ADA /
Cadillac.

WORD SOUN' 'AVE POWER
CD _____ HBCD 15
Heartbeat / Jun '94 / Greensleeves /
Jetstar / Direct / ADA.

WORLD ACCORDING TO CRAMMED
Shimmering warm and bright: *Canto, Bel* /
Granite and sand: *Lone, Kent* / Look of love:
Dalcan, Dominique / Habitual dream in duba
/ If I sleep will the plane crash: *Lune, John* /
L'oeuil de la nuit: *Matta, Ramuntcho* / I
don't care: *Gruesome Twosome* / Tanola
nomads: *Sainkho* / Brrrlak: *Zap Mama* / No
tears: *Tuxedo Moon* / Ay triste: *Boban /
Amdyaz: Zazou, Hector* / Soul magic:
Y.B.U. & Jonell / Monna: *Black Maria* / Dra-
goste de la clejani: *Taraf De Haidouks* / Et
tout est parti je sais: *Lew, Benjamin* / Ban-
zanza: *Roots Of OK Jazz*
CD _____ CRAM 087
Crammed Discs / Jan '94 / Grapevine / New
Note.

WORLD DOMINATION
CD _____ OPCD 032
Osmose / May '95 / Plastic Head.

WORLD DOMINATION OF DEATH
CD _____ PLAYCD 012
Workers Playtime / Apr '90 / Pinnacle.

WORLD IN UNION ANTHEMS
World in union '95: *Ladysmith Black Mam-
bazo* / Swing low, sweet chariot: *Ladysmith
Black Mambazo & China Black* / Bread of
heaven: *Ball, Michael & Ladysmith Black
Mambazo* / Haka 95/Pokarekare Ana: *Union
& Ngati Ranana* / Burning in your heart: *Un-
ion* / Ye olde alegria a mi Corazon: *Union &
Marie Claire D'Ubaldo* / Shoshaloza: *Lad-
ysmith Black Mambazo* / Samoa Tula'i: *Un-
ion & The Samoan Choir* / Sakura: *Union* /
Flower of Scotland: *Dickson, Barbara* / Otua
Mafimafi: *Union & The Tongan Choir* / Ire-
land's call: *Strong, Andrew & The Irish
Rugby Squad* / Ya Penisese: *Union* / O Can-
ada: *Union* / Vis-a-vis: *Union & Monique
Seka* / Romualo Cu Trifoi: *Union & Nick
Magnus* / Run wallaby run: *Parkinson, Doug*
/ Le monde uni: *Union*

CD _____ 5278072
PolyGram TV / Jul '95 / PolyGram.

WORLD IS A WONDERFUL PLACE, THE
CD _____ HPR 2003CD
Hokey Pokey / May '93 / ADA / Direct.

WORLD MUSIC
CD _____ NI 7008
Nimbus / Sep '94 / Nimbus.

WORLD MUSIC ALBUM
Finale: *Piazzolla, Astor* / Neend koyi: *Najma*
/ Bolingo: *Doudongo, M Poto* / Puente de
Los Alunados: *Nunez, Gerardo* / Milagre
dos peixes: *Nascimento, Milton* / Humpty
dumpty: *Palmieri, Eddie* / Alvorada: *Mariano
/ Souareba: Keita, Salif* / Flash of the spirit
(laughter): *Hassell, Jon & Farafina* / Chebba:
Khaled, Cheb / Galapagos: *Nuemann &
Zapf*
CD _____ INT 30102
Intuition / May '91 / New Note.

**WORLD MUSIC COLLECTION :
IRELAND**
Are you my girl: *Something Happens* /
Sweet time: *Aslan* / Capercaille: *Revenants*
/ Captured: *Kennedy, Brian* / This is the mo-
ment: *Wilkinson, Colm* / Against the wind:
Brennan, Maire / When you and I were
young Maggie: *Galway, James* / Clannad* / In
a lifetime: *Clannad* / In your eyes:
Kavanagh, Niamh / Fear is the enemy of
love: *Sweetmouth* / Misty eyes adventure:
Brennan, Maire / Almost seems (too late to
turn): *Clannad* / Waiting for the wheel to
turn: *Capercaillie* / Rose of Tralee: *Nightnoise* / Rose: *Fury, Finbar* / Give me your
hand: *Galway, James & The Chieftains*
CD _____ 74321258802
Arista / Mar '95 / BMG.

WORLD MUSIC OF AMERICA, THE
CD _____ WLD 002
Tring / Aug '93 / Tring / Prism.

WORLD MUSIC SAMPLER 2
CD _____ NI 7014
Nimbus / Sep '94 / Nimbus.

**WORLD MUSIC VOL. 1
(N. Europe/S. America)**
Buda / Jul '91 / Discovery / ADA.
CD _____ 825052

WORLD OF BRASS, THE
Stars and stripes forever / Ash grove / Scottish rhapsody / Flowert duet / Blue danube
waltz / Last spring / Australian fantasy / Excerpts from Capriccio Espagnol / Largo /
Blaydon races / Rose of tralee / Three tenors fantasy / Russian fantasy
CD _____ CHAN 4511
Chandos / Aug '92 / Chandos.

WORLD OF DELIRIUM
CD _____ DELCD 01
Delirium / '95 / Plastic Head.

WORLD OF DELIRIUM VOL.2
CD _____ DELWCD 002
Delirium / Jul '94 / Plastic Head.

WORLD OF DELIRIUM VOL.3
CD _____ DELWCD 003
Delirium / May '95 / Plastic Head.

WORLD OF SOCA, THE
CD Set _____ GC 900003/4
ITM / Dec '93 / Tradelink / Koch.

WORLD OF THE ZOMBIES, THE
CD _____ PLCD 85
Blue Rose / Feb '95 / 3MV.

WORLD OF TRADITIONAL MUSIC, THE
CD _____ C 56006166
Ocora / May '94 / Harmonia Mundi / ADA.

**WORLD PIPE BAND CHAMPIONSHIPS
1987**
Selection / March, strathspey and reel / Se-
lection (2) / Selection (3) / March, strathspey
and reel #2 / Selection (4) / Selection (5) /
March, strathspey and reel #3 / Selection
(6) / March, strathspey and reel #4 / Selec-
tion (7) / March, strathspey and reel #5 /
March, strathspey and reel #6
CD _____ LCOM 9005
Lismor / '87 / Lismor / Direct / Duncans /
ADA.

**WORLD PIPE BAND CHAMPIONSHIPS
1989**
March, strathspey and reel: *Strathclyde Po-
lice Pipe Band* / Selection: *Strathclyde Po-
lice Pipe Band*
CD _____ LCDM 9019
Lismor / '89 / Lismor / Direct / Duncans /
ADA.

**WORLD PIPE BAND CHAMPIONSHIPS
1990**
CD _____ CDMON 816
Monarch / Sep '90 / CM / ADA / Duncans
/ Direct.

**WORLD PIPE BAND CHAMPIONSHIPS
1991**
CD _____ CDMON 816
Klub / Jul '94 / CM / Ross / Duncans /
ADA / Direct.

**WORLD PIPE BAND CHAMPIONSHIPS
1992**
CD _____ CDMON 818
Klub / Jul '94 / CM / Ross / Duncans /
ADA / Direct.

**WORLD PIPE BAND CHAMPIONSHIPS
1993**
CD _____ MON 820CD
Monarch / Nov '93 / CM / ADA / Duncans
/ Direct.

**WORLD PIPE BAND CHAMPIONSHIPS
1994**
CD _____ MON 825CD
Klub / Oct '94 / CM / Ross / Duncans /
ADA / Direct.

**WORLD PIPE BAND CHAMPIONSHIPS
1995**
CD _____ ZCM 2825C
Monarch / Oct '94 / CM / ADA / Duncans
/ Direct.
CD _____ CDMON 827
Monarch / Sep '95 / CM / ADA / Duncans
/ Direct.

WORLD RECORDS SAMPLER
CD _____ WWCD 03
World / Dec '88 / Grapevine.

WORLD RECORDS SAMPLER VOL.1
CD _____ WRCD 012
World / Dec '90 / Jetstar / Total/BMG.

WORLD RECORDS SAMPLER VOL.2
CD _____ WRCD 014
World / Oct '95 / Jetstar / Total/BMG.

WORLD ROOTS LIVE 1992-93
CD _____ MW 3007CD
Music & Words / Jun '94 / ADA / Direct.

WORLD SONIC DOMINATION
CD _____ KICKCD 11
Kickin' / Jul '94 / SRD.

WORLD STARS FOR FREEDOM
Don't give up: *Gabriel, Peter & Kate Bush* /
Man's too strong: *Dire Straits* / It's my life:
Talk Talk / We don't need another hero:
Turner, Tina / Hostage: *Oldfield, Mike* /
Happy ending: *Dorsey, Gail Ann* / Almost
seems (too late to turn): *Clannad* / Candle:
Rea, Chris / Everybody's gotta learn some-
time: *Korgis* / Perfect strangers: *Deep Pur-
ple* / Belfast child: *Simple Minds* / War
baby: *Robinson, Tom* / Driftwood: *Moody
Blues* / Morning side: *Winwood, Steve* /
Give blood: *Townshend, Pete*
CD _____ MPG 74014
Movieplay Gold / Jan '93 / Target/BMG.

WORLD WIDEST YOUR GUIDEST
CD _____ CDORBD 073
Globestyle / May '92 / Pinnacle.

**WORLD'S GREATEST JAZZ CONCERT
VOL.1**
CD _____ JCD 301
Jazzology / Oct '93 / Swift / Jazz Music.

**WORLD'S GREATEST JAZZ CONCERT
VOL.2**
CD _____ JCD 302
Jazzology / Oct '93 / Swift / Jazz Music.

WORLDWIDE: TEN YEARS OF WOMAD
Live at real world (extract): *Voices Of
Burundi* / Amina: *Kanda Bongo Man* / Allah
hoo allah hoo: *Khan, Nusrat Fateh Ali* / In-
vaders of the heart: *Jah Wobble* / Lion -
Gainde: *N'Dour, Youssou* / Pacifica and
pacifica medley inc aloha: *Sandii* / If things
were perfect: *James* / Runidera: *Orquesta
Reve* / Gum: *Scott-Heron, Gil* / Wake of the
Medusa: *Pogues* / Sina: *Keita, Salif* / Diaka:
Toumani Diarate / Legend of the old moun-
tain man: *Terem Quartet* / Entrada: *Cabral,
Pedro Caldiera* / Muchadura: *Mapfumo,
Thomas* / Will the circle be unbroken:
Holmes Brothers
CD _____ RWDR 1
Realworld / Jul '92 / EMI / Sterns.

WOW - LET THE MUSIC LIFT YOU UP
CD _____ ARC 3100112
Arcade / May '94 / Sony / Grapevine.

WRESTLING ALBUM, THE
Land of 1000 dances: *Wrestlers* / Grab
them cakes: *Junk Yard Dog* / Real Ameri-
can: *Derringer, Rick* / Eat your heart out
Rick Springfield: *Hart, Jimmy* / Captain
Lou's history of music/Captain Lou: *Captain
Lou Albano* / Hulk Hogan's theme: *WWF* /
For everybody: *Piper, Rowdy Roddy* / Tutti
frutti: *Okerlund, Gene* / Don't go messin'
with a country boy: *Hillbilly Jim* / Cara Mia:
Volkow, Niklai
CD _____ 4757192
Epic / Apr '94 / Sony.

WURLITZER CHRISTMAS
CD _____ AVC 545
Avid / Nov '94 / Avid/BMG / Koch.

WURLITZER WONDERLAND
California here I come / Five foot two, eyes
of blue / When you're smiling / I should be
so lucky / Rockin' all over the world / Knock
three times / Oh la de oh la da / Beautiful
Sunday / Rhinestone cowboy / Can't take
my eyes off you / Sugar sugar / American
patrol / Little brown jug / Don't sit under the
apple tree / Chattanooga choo choo / Locomotion / That's livin' alright / Atmosphere
/ Amarillo / I only want to be with you / Will
you still love me tomorrow / Fame / Happy
heart / Young ones / It's a sin to tell a lie /
Who's taking you home tonight / Always /
Now is the hour / Can't help falling in love
/ Wonder of you

CD _____ SOV 003CD
Sovereign / '92 / Target/BMG.

WURLITZER WONDERLAND - SUMMERTIME SPECIAL
CD _____ SOV 018CD
Sovereign / Jul '93 / Target/BMG.

WURLITZER WONDERLAND - WARTIME HITS
CD _____ SOV 019CD
Sovereign / Jul '93 / Target/BMG.

WURLITZER WONDERLAND VOL.1
Hello hello, who's your lady friend / Ship ahoy / Jolly good company / Take me back to dear old blighty / Ivory rag / Lucky day / Everything's in rhythm with my heart / Don't dilly dally on the way / Sally / I wonder what's become of Sally / Answer me / Love everlasting / Says my heart / Count your blessings and smile / Back home in Tennessee / I'm sitting on top of the world / Roses of Picardy / When I fall in love / I don't want to walk without you / I'm looking over a four leaf clover / On the crest of a wave / Oh johnny oh / Chicago / La cumparsita / Play to me gypsy / I just called to say I love you / It's de-lovely / Crazy carioca / Lambeth walk / For me and my gal / Rock-a-bye baby / With a Dixie melody / Anything goes / Second hand rose / Beyond the blue horizon / Music music music / I was never kissed before / I wonder who's kissing her now / Boomps a daisy / Too-ra-loo-ra-loo-ra / Comin' thro' the rye / Charlie is my darling / Keel row / Scottish washerwoman
CD _____ SOV 011CD
Sovereign / Jun '92 / Target/BMG.

WURLITZER WONDERLAND VOL.2
Around the world / Pal of my cradle days / Edelweiss / Are you lonesome tonight / When I grow too old to dream / Don't dilly dally on the way / Happy wanderer / Pack up your troubles / Who were you with last night / It's a long way to Tipperary / Raining in my heart / Downtown / Do wah diddy diddy / Teenager in love / Y.M.C.A. / Jesus / (We're gonna) Rock around the clock / Teddy bear (let me be your teddy bear) / When the saints go marching in / Let's twist again / Let's dance / Oh boy / Bless 'em all / After the ball / I'm forever blowing bubbles / My bonnie lies over the ocean / Down at the old bull and bush / In the news / I just called to say I love you / Secret love / Singin' in the rain / Paloma blanca / Save the last dance for me / Birdie song / Sweet Caroline / Hi ho silver lining / My boy lollipop / What'll I do / At the end of the day / Till we meet again / Walkin' my baby back home / Maybe it's because I'm a Londoner / You made me love you / For me and my girl / Show me the way to go home / Over the rainbow / Unchained melody / You'll never walk alone
CD _____ SOV 010CD
Sovereign / '92 / Target/BMG.

WURLITZER WONDERLAND VOL.3
Whistling Rufus / Twelfth street rag / Black and white rag / Root beer / All by yourself in the moonlight / Remember me / Happy together / Have you ever been lonely / Sonny boy / Agadoo / Lambada / Conga / Simon Sez / March of the Mods / When you tell me that you love me / After the ball / Cruising down the river / Ash grove / Skye boat song / Mountains of mourne / Joshua / I'm getting sentimental over you / Poor butterfly / September song / Unforgettable / In the mood / You light up my life / Try to remember / At the end of the day / Hello Dolly / Alexander's ragtime band / Best things in life are free / Pasadena / Spanish gypsy dance / Scotland the brave / Comin' thro' the rye / Scotch on the rocks / Johnny B. Goode / You drive me crazy / (We're gonna) Rock around the clock
CD _____ SOV 012CD
Sovereign / Jun '92 / Target/BMG.

X-MAS PROJECT
CD _____ SHARK 005 CD
Shark / Jan '90 / Plastic Head.

X-MIX 2: DESTINATION PLANET DREAM
CD _____ K 7027CD
Studio K7 / Apr '94 / Disc.

X-MIX 3
CD _____ K 7032CD
Studio K7 / Nov '94 / Disc.

X:TREME POWER D.J. DUKE VS POWER
CD _____ XTR 19CDM
CD _____ XTR 19CDU
X:Treme / Jan '96 / Pinnacle / SRD.

XL RECORDINGS - THE FIFTH CHAPTER
CD _____ XLCD 116
XL / Jul '95 / Warner Music.

XL RECORDINGS - THE FIRST CHAPTER
CD _____ XLCD 105
XL / Oct '90 / Warner Music.

XL RECORDINGS - THE FOURTH CHAPTER
(Further Adventures In Hard Dance)
CD _____ XLCD 112
XL / Dec '93 / Warner Music.

XL RECORDINGS - THE SECOND CHAPTER
CD _____ XLCD 108
XL / Sep '91 / Warner Music.

XL RECORDINGS - THE THIRD CHAPTER
CD _____ XLCD 109
XL / Apr '92 / Warner Music.

XMIX 5 - WILDSTYLE
(DJ Hell)
Studio K7 / Nov '95 / Disc.
_____ K 7039CD

XOURCISE YOUR MIND
CD _____ XOUCD 9501
Xource / Apr '95 / ADA / Cadillac.

XRATED GANG VOL.1, THE
CD _____ RN 0037
Runn / Nov '94 / Jetstar / SRD.

Y

Y VIVA ESPANA
CD _____ 16124
Laserlight / Aug '94 / Target/BMG.

YABBA DABBA DANCE
(21 Rockin' Hits Of The Year)
CD _____ ARC 3100182
Arcade / Aug '94 / Sony / Grapevine.

YARD VIBES
CD _____ ICD 951
Imaj / Apr '95 / Jetstar.

YEAR ZERO SURROUND SOUNDBITES VOL.1
CD _____ SUSCD 1
Aura Surround Sounds / Jan '95 / Grapevine / PolyGram.

YEH YEH
CD _____ TMPCD 007
Telstar / Jan '95 / BMG.

YELE BRAZIL
Yele congo / Coche viejo (carro velho) / Venha me amar / Kizomba festa da raca / Embala-eu / Volte para o seu lar / Felicidade / Epilogo / Jogo de angola / Swqura este samba (ogunhe) / De onde eu vim / Nego laranja / Alagados / Canto de nana / Toque e seducao / Canto da cor
CD _____ CDEMC 3694
EMI / Nov '94 / EMI.

YELLOW UNLIMITED
CD _____ EFA 2222CD
Yellow / May '89 / SRD.

YESTERDAY - THOSE ROMANTIC 60'S
Yesterday: Mantovani & His Orchestra / Sunny: Aldrich, Ronnie & His Piano/The Festival Orchestra / Almost there: Mantovani & His Orchestra / Somethin' stupid: Aldrich, Ronnie & His Orchestra / Love is blue: Howard, Johnny Orchestra & Singers / Softly as I leave you: Aldrich, Ronnie & His Orchestra / Leaving on a jet plane: Mantovani & His Orchestra / Moon river: Chacksfield, Frank & His Orchestra / Release me: Aldrich, Ronnie & His Piano/The Festival Orchestra / Strangers in the night: Mantovani & His Orchestra / I can't stop loving you: Stapleton, Cyril & His Show Band / Didn't we: Aldrich, Ronnie & His Piano/The Festival Orchestra / I left my heart in San Francisco: Howard, Johnny Orchestra & Singers / My cherie amour: Aldrich, Ronnie & His Piano/The Festival Orchestra / What now my love: Mantovani & His Orchestra / Goin' out of my head: Aldrich, Ronnie & His Piano/The Festival Orchestra / What kind of fool am I: Mantovani & His Orchestra / I'll never fall in love again: Chacksfield, Frank & His Orchestra / Joanna: Howard, Johnny Orchestra & Singers / Cherish: Aldrich, Ronnie & His Piano/The Festival Orchestra
CD _____ 8440652
Eclipse / May '91 / PolyGram.

YESTERDAY ONCE MORE
CD _____ CDTRL 294
Trojan / Mar '94 / Jetstar / Total/BMG.

YESTERDAY PART II
(The Black Album)
CD _____ CDTRL 338
Trojan / Apr '94 / Jetstar / Total/BMG.

YESTERDAY'S
Pick yourself up: Astaire, Fred / Look for the silver lining: Matthews, Jessie / Song is you: BBC Dance Orchestra / Smoke gets in your eyes: Robins, Phyllis / Last time I saw paris: Shelton, Anne / I've told every little star: Ellis, Mary / She didn't say Yes: Wood, Peggy / Make believe: Goodman, Benny Orchestra / Yesterday's: Holiday, Billie / Whose baby are you: Gershwin, George / Why was I born: Holiday, Billie / Why do I love you: Beiderbecke, Bix / Can't help lovin' dat man: Morgan, Helen / I might grow fonder of you: Hulbert, Jack / I'll be hard to handle: Rivera Orchestra / They didn't believe me: Ambrose & His Orchestra / You couldn't be cuter: Stone, Lew & His Orchestra / Never gonna dance: Astaire, Fred / Something had to happen: Whiteman, Paul & His Orchestra / Ol' man river: Robeson, Paul / Folks who live on the hill: Crosby, Bing
CD _____ AVC 519
Avid / Apr '93 / Avid/BMG / Koch.

YESTERDAYS VOL 1
CD _____ 12101
Laserlight / Dec '94 / Target/BMG.

YESTERDAYS VOL 2
CD _____ 12102
Laserlight / Dec '94 / Target/BMG.

YESTERDAYS VOL 3
CD _____ 12103
Laserlight / Dec '94 / Target/BMG.

YESTERDAYS VOL 4
CD _____ 12104
Laserlight / Dec '94 / Target/BMG.

YESTERYEARS VOL.1
Memories are made of this: King, Dave / Swedish rhapsody: Mantovani & His Orchestra / Finger of suspicion: Valentine, Dickie / (How much is that) doggie in the window: Roza, Lita / Cara mia: Whitfield, David / Poor people of Paris: Atwell, Winifred / Crying in the chapel: Lawrence, Lee / Someone else's roses: Regan, Joan / Hernando's hideaway: Johnston Brothers / Swingin' shepherd blues: Heath, Ted Orchestra / Tulips from Amsterdam: Bygraves, Max / Little drummer boy: Beverley Sisters / Friends and neighbours: Cotton, Billy & His Band / Limelight (theme): Chacksfield, Frank & His Orchestra / Man from Laramie: Young, Jimmy / I see the moon: Stargazers / Personality: Newley, Anthony / Auf wiedersehen sweetheart: Lynn, Vera
CD _____ 5501002
Spectrum/Karussell / Oct '93 / PolyGram / THE.

YESTERYEARS VOL.2
Unchained melody: Young, Jimmy / Ricochet: Regan, Joan / Happy whistler: Stapleton, Cyril & Orchestra / Handful of songs: Steele, Tommy / My son, my son: Lynn, Vera / Mono: Southlanders / Daddy's little girl: Vaughan, Frankie / Ebb tide: Chacksfield, Frank Orchestra / Willie can: Beverley Sisters / You need hands: Bygraves, Max / Story of my life: King, Dave / Isle of Innisfree: Shelton, Anne / Piano medley no 114 (Part 1): Kunz, Charlie / In the middle of the road: Johnston Brothers / Happy wanderer: Stargazers / Don't let the stars get in your eyes: Lotis, Dennis / Dragnet: Heath, Ted Orchestra / Bimbo: Miller, Suzi
CD _____ 5501012
Spectrum/Karussell / Oct '93 / PolyGram / THE.

YESTERYEARS VOL.3
Mr. Sandman: Valentine, Dickie / Hey there: Roza, Lita / Broken wings: Stargazers / Moulin rouge theme: Mantovani & His Orchestra / Cinnamon sinner: Lotis, Dennis / Rock 'n' roll waltz: Klooger, Annette / Answer me: Whitfield, David / Tom Hark: Heath, Ted Orchestra / Garden of Eden: Monro, Matt / I dreamed: Beverley Sisters / Flirtation waltz: Atwell, Winifred / Hole in the hole: Southlanders / Shiralee: Steele, Tommy / Prize of gold: Regan, Joan / Love is a golden ring: King, Dave / I talk to the trees: Shelton, Anne / Blue star (the medic theme): Stapleton, Cyril & Orchestra
CD _____ 5501022
Spectrum/Karussell / Oct '93 / PolyGram / THE.

YODELLING AND SCHULPLATTER FOLK DANCE
CD _____ 399200
Koch / Sep '92 / Koch.

YONDER COMES THE BLUES
(Jazz Classics)
CD _____ SOSCD 1061
Stomp Off / Nov '92 / Jazz Music / Wellard.

YOU ARE THERE - A LEGENDARY LABEL
CD _____ 4425412
Mercury / Feb '95 / PolyGram.

YOU BE
CD _____ MMCD 8007
Minor Music / Apr '90 / Vital/SAM.

YOU CAN'T GET THAT STUFF NO MORE
(The Slide Guitar)
CD _____ IMP 938
IMP / Nov '93 / Discovery / ADA.

YOU DESERVE EVEN WORSE
CD _____ LF 063CD
Lost & Found / Jun '94 / Plastic Head.

YOU DIRTY MISTREATER
Deep water blues: Thomas, Hociel / Jealous woman like me: Wallace, Sippie / Mail train blues: Wallace, Sippie / Dead drunk blues: Wallace, Sippie / Lazy man blues: Wallace, Sippie / Lovesick blues: Hill, Bertha / Trouble in mind: Hill, Bertha / You dirty mistreater: Wilson, Grant / Come on coot do that thing: Wilson, Grant / Down hearted blues: Smith, Bessie / My sweetie went away: Smith, Bessie / Sobbin' hearted blues: Smith, Bessie / I used to be: Taylor, Eva / Coal cart blues: Taylor, Eva / Mandy, make up your mind: Taylor, Eva / Was it a dream: Christian, Lillie Delk / How do you do it that way: Spivey, Victoria / Ain't misbehavin': Ellis, Segar / Nobody know's the way I feel 'dis morning: Hunter, Alberta / Broken busted blues: Smith, Clara / You've got to beat me to keep me: Smith, Trixie
CD _____ RAJCD 870
Empress / Oct '95 / THE.

YOU KNOW THE SCORE
CD _____ DCSR 003
Clubscene / Oct '94 / Clubscene / Mo's Music Machine / Grapevine.

YOU MUST HAVE BEEN A BEAUTIFUL BABY
CD _____ AVC 525
Avid / Nov '93 / Avid/BMG / Koch.

YOU MUST REMEMBER THIS
You'll never know: Lynn, Vera / Night and day: Astaire, Fred / As time goes by: Hale, Binnie / Folks who live on the hill: Sullivan, Maxine / I'd climb the highest mountain: Ink Spots / Love walked in: Baker, Kenny / It's always you: Crosby, Bing / Stairway to the stars: Keller, Greta / Please believe me: Froman, Jane / Falling in love again: Dietrich, Marlene / How deep is the ocean: Goodman, Benny & Peggy Lee / I wish I knew a bigger word than love: Gideon, Melville / All the things you are: Martin, Tony / Starlight serenade: Rey, Monte / There, I've said it again: Carter, Benny & Roy Felton / Nearness of you: Welch, Elisabeth / Two sleepy people: Geraldo & Al Bowlly / I only have eyes for you: Hutch / Dream lover: MacDonald, Jeanette / When a man loves a woman: Robins, Phyllis / You were meant for me: Boswell, Connie / Man I love: Langford, Frances / Nightingale sang in Berkeley Square: Layton, Turner / I know why: Miller, Glenn & Paula Kelly / Night is young and you're so beautiful: Sinatra, Frank & Dinah Shore / As time goes by (extract): Wilson, Dooley & Ingrid Bergman
CD _____ UCD 252
Happy Days / Feb '94 / Conifer.

YOU MUST REMEMBER THIS
Signature tune: Payne, Cy / Who is that man who looks like Charlie Chaplin: Handley, Tommy / Wish me luck as you wave me goodbye: Fields, Gracie / I didn't really oughter 'ave went: Hare, Doris / I did what I could with my gas mask: Formby, George / Washing of the Siegfried Line: 2 Leslies / Kiss me Goodnight, Sergeant Major: Askey, Arthur / It was a lover and his lass: Bowlly, Al / We'll meet again: Lynn, Vera / As time goes by: Wilson, Dooley / Coming in on a wing and a prayer: Shelton, Anne / Calling all workers: Coates, Eric / Yes my darling daughter: Shore, Dinah / Thingummy Bob: Fields, Gracie / All over the place: Trinder, Tommy / London pride: Coward, Sir Noel / Deepest shelter: Desmond, Florence / Grand old man: Miller, Max / Run rabbit run: Flanagan & Allen / When can I have a banana again: Roy, Harry / Thanks for dropping in Mr. Hess: Askey, Arthur / Moonlight serenade: Miller, Glenn / This is the army: Berlin, Irving / Why don't you right: Lee, Peggy / In the mood: Miller, Glenn / That lovely weekend: Geraldo / My British buddy: Berlin, Irving / Jersey bounce: Squadronaires / Tico tico: Smith, Ethel / I's Marlene: Andersen, Lale / Cocktails for two: Jones, Spike / Oh what a surprise for the duce: Carlisle, Elsie / Swing out to victory: Waller, Fats / I'd climb the highest mountain: Ink Spots / Victory roll rag: Roy, Harry / Wings over the navy: Stones, Lew & His Band / You'd be so nice to come home to: Shelton, Anne / Last time i saw paris: Coward, Sir Noel / White cliffs of Dover: Lynn, Vera / Body and soul: Miller, Glenn / Saturday night is the loneliest night of the week: Sinatra, Frank / Don't fence me in: Crosby, Bing
CD Set _____ CDHD 265
Happy Days / May '95 / Conifer.

YOU THRILL MY SOUL
(Female & Girl Groups From The Early Stax Sessions)
Same thing: Thomas, Carla / Here it comes again: Thomas, Carla / I can't stay: Thomas, Carla / Heavenly angel: Tonettes / Stolen angel: Tonettes / Unhand that man: Tonettes / Gone for good: Rene, Wendy / Same guy: Rene, Wendy / Love at first sight: Rene, Wendy / If she should ever break your heart: Stephens, Barbara / Heartbreaker: Parker, Deanie / Ask him: Parker, Deanie / Love is like a seesaw: Stephens, Barbara / Just one touch: Parker, Deanie / Ain't enough hours in the day: Thomas,

Carla / Gosh I'm lucky: Thomas, Carla / He hasn't failed me yet: Rene, Wendy / Crying all by myself: Rene, Wendy / Last love: Rene, Wendy / Crowded park: Rene, Wendy / Can't stay away: Rene, Wendy / Tell me: Tonettes / Come to me: Tonettes / Do boys keep diaries: Thomas, Carla
CD _____ CDSXD 088
Stax / Sep '93 / Pinnacle.

YOU WIN AGAIN
(20 Classic Country Tracks)
Jambalaya: Jones, George / Crystal chandeliers: Spears, Billie Jo / You win again: Cash, Johnny / Deep in the heart of Texas: Jones, Ed / Walk right in: Lewis, Jerry Lee / Oh, lonesome me: Gibson, Don / Sticks and stones: Fargo, Donna / Daddy sang bass: Perkins, Carl / Love hurts: Parsons, Gram & Emmylou Harris / Indian reservation: Fardon, Don / Send me the pillow that you dream on: Locklin, Hank / Harper valley PTA: Riley, Jeannie C. / El paso: Robbins, Marty / Blizzard: Reeves, Jim / Today, tomorrow and forever: Cline, Patsy / Who needs your love: Paycheck, Johnny / Making believe: Wells, Kitty / From a jack to a king: Miller, Ned / Take these chains from my heart: Drusky, Roy / Rose garden: Anderson, Lynn
CD _____ TRTCD 116
TrueTrax / Oct '94 / THE.

YOU'D BE SO NICE TO COME HOME TO
In the mood / Nightingale sang in Berkeley Square / It was a lover and his lass / Oh, Johnny, oh / Whispering grass / I'm nobody's baby / Yes my darling daughter / Our love affair / Amapola / Boa noite / That lovely weekend / Jingle jangle jingle / Don't sit under the apple tree / Elmer's tune / Paper doll / Pennsylvania polka / Moonlight cocktail / Sergeant / Jersey bounce / I'm going to see you today / You'd be so nice to come home to / Pistol packin' Mama / I left my heart at the stage door canteen / It can't be wrong / Lovely way to spend an evening
CD _____ CDHD 304
Happy Days / Sep '94 / Conifer.

YOU'LL NEVER WALK ALONE
CD _____ WH 12001
Whitehouse / May '95 / Mo's Music Machine / Jetstar / Grapevine / Target/ BMG.

YOUNG FLAMENCOS, THE
CD _____ HNCD 1370
Hannibal / Dec '91 / Vital / ADA.

YOUNG FOGIES
CD _____ ROU 0319CD
Rounder / Jul '94 / CM / Direct / ADA / Cadillac.

YOUNG FOGIES VOL.2
CD _____ ROUCD 0369
Rounder / Oct '95 / CM / Direct / ADA / Cadillac.

YOUNG LIONS AND OLD TIGERS - A 75TH BIRTHDAY CELEBRATION
Roy Hargrove / How high the moon / Michael Brecker waltz / Here comes McBride / Joe Lovano tango / In your own sweet way / Joshua Redman / Together / Moody / Gerry-go-round / Ronnie Buttacavoli / Deep in a dream
CD _____ CD 83349
Telarc / Nov '95 / Conifer / ADA.

YOUNG SOUL REBEL
CD _____ RADCD 19
Transatlantic / Jan '96 / BMG / Pinnacle / ADA.

YOUNG, WILD AND FREE
CD _____ DCD 5360
Disky / May '94 / THE / BMG / Discovery / Pinnacle.

YOUNG ZYDECO DESPERADOS: SWAMP MUSIC VOL.8
CD _____ US 0204
Trikont / Apr '95 / ADA / Direct.

YOUNGBLOOD STORY, VOL.1
Do wah diddy diddy: Dave Dee, Dozy, Beaky, Mick & Tich / Brandy: English, Scott / Get ready for love: Easybeats / Planetary cruiser: McGlynn, Pat Band / Sea trip: Shelley, Peter / On the run: Ocean, Billy / Rhythm on the radio: ABC / True love for-

gives: Kissoon, Mac & Katie / Crazy feeling: Douglas, Carl / Ain't nothing but a house party: Show Stoppers / Personality crisis: New York Dolls / Take a heart: Fardon, Don / Mr. Station Master: Harper, Roy / Morning bird: Damned / C'mon round to my place: Wayne, Carl / When I was 16: Page, Jimmy / Captain man: Powell, Jimmy / Let the live live: Fardon, Don / You keep me hangin' on (Available on CD only): Kissoon, Mac / Don't ever change (Available on CD only): Berry, Mike / Spread myself around (Available on CD only): King, Ben E. / Can you feel it (Available on CD only): Ocean, Billy / Sleepwalk (Available on CD only): Los Indianos
CD _____ C5CD-549
See For Miles/C5 / '89 / Pinnacle.

YOUR CHEATIN' HEART
CD _____ YDG 74630
Yesterday's Gold / Feb '93 / Target/BMG.

YOUR GENERATION
(18 Punk & New Wave Classics)
CD _____ MUSCD 009
MCI / Sep '93 / Disc / THE.

YOUR INVITATION TO SUICIDE
CD _____ MRCD 040
Munster / May '94 / Plastic Head.

YOUR OWN, YOUR VERY OWN
(Stars Of The Music Hall 1901-1929)
Don't do it again, Matilda: Champion, Harry / Every little movement has a meaning of its own: Lloyd, Marie / Two lovely black eyes: Coburn, Charles / Mrs. Kelly: Leno, Dan / One of the boys: Formby, George / Jocular joker: Cherqwin, G.H. / Let's all go where all the crowd goes: Williams, Billy / Photo of the girl I left behind me: Merson, Billy / I'm twenty-one today: Pleasante, Jack / Flower of the heather: Lauder, Sir Harry / If the managers only thought the same as mother: Scott, Maidie / She sells seashells: Bard, Wilkie / By the sea: Sheridan, Mark / Don't have any more, Mrs. Moore: Morris, Lily / Dinah: Elliott, G.H. / Hello, sunshine, hello: Whelan, Albert
CD _____ CDAJA 5004
Living Era / Apr '92 / Koch.

YOU'RE DRIVING ME CRAZY
Ring dem bells / Confessin' / Rockin' chair / Happy feet / Somebody loves me / You're driving me crazy / New Orleans hop scop blues / Sheikh of Araby / Mood indigo / I got rhythm / Here comes Emily Brown / If I could be with you one hour tonight / When I'm alone / Heebie jeebies / I can't believe that you're in love with me / Okay baby
CD _____ PHONTCD 7618
Phontastic / '93 / Wellard / Jazz Music / Cadillac.

YOU'RE THE TOPS - THE SONGS OF COLE PORTER
Begin the beguine: Shaw, Artie & His Orchestra / My heart belongs to Daddy (With Count Basie & his orchestra.): Humes, Helen / Let's' do it: Crosby, Bing & The Dorsey Brothers Orchestra / In the still of the night: Reinhardt, Django & Quintette Du Hot Club De France / Love for sale: Holman, Libby / What is this thing called love: Johnson, James P. / Experiment: Bowlly, Al & Lew Stone Band / Easy to love: Holiday, Billie / I get a kick out of you: BBC Dance Orchestra / Miss Otis regrets: Mills Brothers / Night and day: Dorsey, Tommy Orchestra / Anything goes: Stone, Lew & His Band / Moi (I've got you under my skin): Baker, Josephine / Soloman: Welch, Elisabeth / Physician: Lawrence, Gertrude / Just one of those things: Himber, Richard & His Orchestra / I'm a gigolo: Porter, Cole / All through the night: Ambrose & His Orchestra / It's de-lovely: Day, Frances / You're the top: Aubert, Jeanne & Jack Whiting
CD _____ AVC 518
Avid / Apr '93 / Avid/BMG / Koch.

YU BODY GOOD
CD _____ WRCD 008
Techniques / Dec '93 / Jetstar.

YUGOSLAVIA: LES BOUGIES DU PARADIS
CD _____ C 580041
Ocora / Nov '92 / Harmonia Mundi / ADA.

YULE COOL
I wish it could be Christmas forever: Como, Perry / Happy holiday: Crosby, Bing / Little boy that Santa Claus forgot: Cole, Nat King

/ Senor Santa Claus: Reeves, Jim / Holly and the ivy: Steeleye Span / White Christmas: Boone, Pat / Let it snow, let it snow, let it snow: Martin, Dean / I want Elvis for Christmas: Cochran, Eddie / Jingle bells: Fitzgerald, Ella / Wonderful land: Shadows / Mary's boy child: Monro, Matt / Frosty the snowman: Ventures / What Christmas means to me: Green, Al / Baby's first Christmas: Francis, Connie / Song angels sing: Lanza, Mario / Snow coach: Conway, Russ / Never do a tango with an eskimo: Cogan, Alma / Lonely pup in a Christmas shop: Faith, Adam / Christmas waltz: Lee, Peggy / Warm December: London, Julie / Silent night: Locke, Josef / Bells of St. Mary's: Neville, Aaron / Holly jolly Christmas: Ives, Burl / Rockin' around the Christmas tree: Lee, Brenda / Christmas on the range: Wills, Bob / Christmas is paintin' the town: Oak Ridge Boys / Rockin' around the Christmas tree #2: Cannon, Ace / Deck the halls with boughs of holly: Crickets / Sleigh ride: Ferrante & Teicher / O'Holy night: Rodgers, Jimmie / Parade of the wooden soldiers: Garber, Jan / I saw Mommy kissing Santa Claus: Gleason, Jackie / Jingle bell rock: Hollyridge Strings / Silver bells: Dunstedter, Eddie / Christmas trumpets: Anthony, Ray / Auld lang syne: Alexander, Van / Christmas song: Mancini, Henry / O Holy night: Danny & The Juniors / Must be Santa: Steele, Tommy / Baby, it's cold outside: Montgomery, Wes & Jimmy Smith
CD Set _____ VTDCD 36
Virgin / Oct '95 / EMI.

Z

ZAIRE: SUPER GUITAR SOUKOUS
Sana: Kanda Bongo Man / Africa: Depeu, Dave / Sango ya mawa: Dabany, Patience / Mukaji wani: Yogo, Dindo / Guelo: Gueatan System / Pa moi: Delly, Joyce / N'nanele: Zoukunion / Guede guina: Guede, Olives / Mosolo na ngai: General Defao / Soso ya tongo: Empire Bakuba Et Pepe Kalle / Makoule: Seliko
CD _____ CDEMC 3678
EMI / May '94 / EMI.

ZAMBIANCE
Kambowa: Shalawambe / Mao: Amayenge / Nyina kataila: Kalambo hit parade / By air / Tai atuya: Julizya / Icupo cha kuala pa mpapa: Shalawambe / Itumba: Kalusha, Alfred Chisala Jnr. / Ni Maggie: Kalusha, Alfred Chisala Jnr.
CD _____ CDORB 037
Globestyle / Jun '89 / Pinnacle.

ZANCE
(A Decade Of Dance From ZTT)
Welcome to the pleasure dome: Frankie Goes To Hollywood / Liverpool: Frankie Goes To Hollywood / Who's afraid (of the Art of Noise): Art Of Noise / Daft: Art Of Noise / Wishful thinking: Propaganda / Secret wish: Propaganda / Alphabed: Poppy, Andrew / Beating of wings: Poppy, Andrew / Everything could be so perfect: Pigalle, Anne
CD _____ 4509960552
ZTT / May '94 / Warner Music.

ZIMBABWE - THE SOUL MUSIC OF MBIRA
Elektra Nonesuch / Jan '95 / Warner Music.

ZOMBA SOUL COMPILATION
CD _____ EMPRCD 548
Emporio / Nov '94 / THE / Disc / CM.

ZOO, THE
CD _____ DCD 001
Blues Document / Oct '90 / Swift / Jazz Music / Hot Shot.

ZOOM CLASSICS
CD _____ ZOOMCD 2
Zoom / Sep '95 / Disc.

ZOOM, ZOOM, ZOOM
Get a job / Stranded in the jungle / Remember then / Come go with me / Zoom, zoom, zoom / Stay / I understand / Sixteen candles / Lover's island / One summer night / Church bells may ring / Earth angel / Since I don't have you / For all we know / When you dance / Deserie / At last up on a mountain / Why don't you write me / Crazy over you / Clock / Music music music / Tears on my pillow / You painted pictures
CD _____ CPCD 8000
Charly / Oct '93 / Charly / THE / Cadillac.

ZOOP, ZOOP, ZOOP
(Traditional Music Of The Virgin Islands)
CD _____ 804272
New World / Nov '93 / Harmonia Mundi / ADA / Cadillac.

ZORBA'S DANCE - MEMORIES FROM GREECE
CD _____ 15180
Laserlight / '91 / Target/BMG.

ZORBA'S DANCE/BOUZOUKI MAGIC
CD _____ MATCD 242
Castle / Nov '93 / BMG.

ZULU BEATS
CD _____ FILECD 466
Profile / Oct '95 / Pinnacle.

ZULU JIVE
CD _____ HNCD 4410
Hannibal / Aug '93 / Vital / ADA.

ZYDECO - THE EARLY YEARS (1961-63)
CD _____ ARHCD 307
Arhoolie / Apr '95 / ADA / Direct / Cadillac.

ZYDECO CHAMPS
CD _____ ARHCD 328
Arhoolie / Apr '95 / ADA / Direct / Cadillac.

ZYDECO DANCE PARTY
Gator man / Chere duloone / Hello Rosa Lee / Zydeco round the world / Capitaine Gumbo / Boogie in New Orleans / Just a little girl / They all ask for you / Tyrone / Mazuka / Ay tet fee / Zydeco / I'm gonna take you home tonight / Creole de Lake Charles / My baby she's gone / Fais deaux deaux / Bayou polka / La bas two step
CD _____ GNPD 2220
GNP Crescendo / Sep '95 / Silva Screen.

ZYDECO HOTSTEPPERS
Zydeco sont pas sale: Chenier, Clifton / Baby, please don't go: Beausoleil / Hack a step: Daigrepont, Bruce / Cajun life: Sonnier, Jo El / Walkin' to New Orleans: Buckwheat Zydeco / La pointe aux pins: Riley, Steve & Mamou Playboys / Cajun two step: Newman, Joe / Zarico est pas sale: Riley, Steve & Mamou Playboys / Flame will never die: Beausoleil / Les flammes d'enfer: Pitre, Austin / I'm gone and I won't be back: Delafose, John / Hot tamale baby: Buckwheat Zydeco / Lacassine special: Sonnier, Jo El / La valse du bambocheur: Balfa Freres / Let's talk it over: Chenier, Clifton / Frisco zydeco: Daigrepont, Bruce
CD _____ NTMCD 515
Nectar / Jan '96 / Pinnacle.

ZYDECO PARTY
Zydeco groove: August, Lynn / I'm on my way: Zydeco Force / I'm coming home: Brothers, Bon Ton / Johnny can't dance: Chenier, Clifton / Zydeco hee haw: Chavis, Boozoo / Jalapena lena: Rockin' Sidney / Whatever boils your crawfish: August, Lynn / Leon's Zydeco: Brothers, Sam Five / Dopsie's Cajun Stomp: Rockin' Dopsie / Down east: Zydeco Brothers / Loan me your handkerchief: Delafose, John / Do it all night long: Chavis, Boozoo / Fun in acadiana: Francis, Morris / Eh mon allons dancer le zydeco: Chavis, Wilfred / You used to call me: Chenier, Clifton / Shake, rattle and roll: Rockin' Sidney / Keep on dreaming: Chavis, Wilfred / Deacon Jones: Chavis, Boozoo / Reach out: Zydeco Brothers
CD _____ CDCHD 430
Ace / Oct '92 / Pinnacle / Cadillac / Complete/Pinnacle.

Soundtracks

13 DAYS IN FRANCE
Lai, Francis C
CD _____ MANTRA 052
Silva Screen / Jan '93 / Conifer / Silva Screen.

32 SHORT FILMS ABOUT GLENN GOULD
Gould, Glenn C on
CD _____ SK 46686
Sony Classical / Jan '94 / Sony.

42ND STREET
1980 Broadway Cast
Warren, Harry C
Dubin, Al L
Overture / Audition / Shadow waltz / Young and healthy / Go into your dance / You're getting to be a habit with me / Getting out of town / We're in the money / Dames / Sunny side to every situation / Lullaby of Broadway / About a quarter to nine / Shuffle off to Buffalo / 42nd Street / Finale / 42nd Street (reprise)
CD _____ BD 83891
RCA Victor / '85 / BMG.

55 DAYS AT PEKING
Tiomkin, Dimitri C
CD _____ VSD 5233
Varese Sarabande/Colosseum / Feb '90 / Pinnacle / Silva Screen.

70 GIRLS 70
1991 London Cast
Kander, John C
Ebb, Fred L
CD _____ CDTER 1186
TER / Sep '91 / Koch.

70 GIRLS 70
1971 Broadway Cast
Kander, John C
Ebb, Fred L
Kosarin, O. C on
Sony Broadway / Nov '92 / Sony. SK 30589

1776
Broadway Cast
Edwards, Sherman C
CD _____ SK 48215
Sony Broadway / Nov '92 / Sony.

1984
(For The Love Of Big Brother)
Eurythmics
Stewart, David A./Annie Lennox C
I did it just the same / Sexcrime (1984) / For the love of big brother / Winston's diary / Greetings from a dead man / Julia / Doubleplusgood / Ministry of love / Room 101
CD _____ CDVIP 135
Virgin / Sep '95 / EMI.

2001: A SPACE ODYSSEY
Also sprach Zarathustra (Main title) / Requiem for soprano, mezzo-soprano, two mixed choirs and orc (Monolith) / Lux aeterna (Lunar landscape) / Blue Danube (Space station) / Gayaneh ballet suite: Adagio (Discovery) / Atmospheres (Beyond the infinite) / Blue Danube (reprise) (End titles) / Also sprach Zarathustra (reprise) (Star child)
CD _____ CDMGM 6
MGM/EMI / Jan '90 / EMI.

2001: A SPACE ODYSSEY
(Alex North Score)
National Philharmonic Orchestra
North, Alex C
Goldsmith, Jerry C on
CD _____ VSD 5400
Varese Sarabande/Colosseum / Oct '93 / Pinnacle / Silva Screen.

100,000 DOLLARS FOR RINGO
Nicolai, Bruno C
CD _____ PAN 2501
Silva Screen / May '95 / Conifer / Silva Screen.

A BOUT DE SOUFFLE
CD _____ 873008
Milan / May '92 / BMG / Silva Screen.

A LA FOLIE
Nyman, Michael Band
Nyman, Michael C
CD _____ 399492
Delabel / Nov '94 / EMI.

A-TEAM, THE
Caine, Daniel Orchestra
Post, Mike & Pete Carpenter C
Caine, Daniel C on
Theme / Young Hannibal / B.A.'s ride / A-Team in New York city / Bandits / Taxi chase / A-Team escape / A-Team prepare for war / Showtime / Move, sucker / Let's get busted / Murdock's "face" / Helicopters / More bandits / Theme (reprise)
CD _____ FILMCD 701
Silva Screen / Nov '90 / Conifer / Silva Screen.

A.D. - ANNO DOMINI
Paris Philharmonic Orchestra
Schifrin, Lalo C
Golgatha / Valerius and Sarah / King Herod's march / Eternal land / Fisherman / Peter and Thomas trek / Roman celebration / Road to Damascus / New love / Gladiator school / Majesty of Rome / Corina and Caleb / Roman legion / Wedding procession / Nero the lover / Martyrdom / Exalted love
CD _____ PCD 112
Prometheus / Apr '92 / Silva Screen.

A.W.O.L.
Scott, John C
CD _____ MAF 7011D
Intrada / Jan '93 / Silva Screen / Koch.

ABOUT LAST NIGHT
So far, so good: Easton, Sheena / Shape of things to come: Hall & Oates / Natural love: Easton, Sheena / Words into action: Jackson, Jermaine / Step by step: Souther, J.D. / Living inside my heart: Seger, Bob / Trials of the heart: Shanks, Nancy / Till you love somebody: Henderson, Michael / If we can get through the night: Davis, Paul / True love: Del Lords / If anybody had a heart: Waite, John
CD _____ 465602
EMI/Silva Screen / Feb '90 / Conifer / Silva Screen.

ABOVE THE RIM
Anything: S.W.V. / Old time's sake: Sweet Sable / Part time lover: H-Town / Big pimpin': Dogg Pound Gangstas / Didn't mean to turn you on: 2nd II None / Doggie style: D.J. Rogers / Regulate: Warren G. & Nate Dogg / Pour out a little liquor: Thug Life / Gonna give it to ya: Jewell & Aaron Hall / Afro puffs: Lady Of Rage / Jus' so ya no: CPO - Boss Hog / Hoochies need love too: Paradise / I'm still in love with you: Sure, Al B. / Crack 'em: O.F.T.B. / U bring da dog out: Rhythm & Knowledge / Blowed away: Rezell, B. / It's not deep enough: Jewell / Dogg pound 4 life: Dogg Pound Gangstas
CD _____ 6544923592
Death Row / Apr '94 / Warner Music.

ABSOLUTE BEGINNERS
(Soundtrack Highlights)
Absolute beginners: Bowie, David / Killer blow: Sade / Have you ever had it blue: Style Council / Quiet life: Davies, Ray / Va va voom: Evans, Gil / That's motivation: Roderigo Bay: Working Week / Selling out: Gaillard, Slim / Riot City: Dammers, Jerry / Boogie stop shuffle: Evans, Gil / Ted ain't dead: Tenpole Tudor / Volare: Bowie, David / Napoli: Jonas / Little cat you've never had it so good: Jonas / Better git it in your soul: Evans, Gil / So what: Smiley Culture / Absolute beginners (refrain): Bowie, David
CD _____ CDV 2386
Virgin / Jul '87 / EMI.
CD _____ VVIPD 112
Virgin VIP / May '91 / Carlton Home Entertainment / THE / EMI.

ABYSS, THE
Silvestri, Alan C
Main title / Search the Montana / Crane / Manta ship / Pseudopod / Fight / Sub battle / Lindsey drowns / Resurrection / Bud's big dive / Bud on the ledge / Back on the air / Finale
CD _____ VSD 5235
Varese Sarabande/Colosseum / Oct '89 / Pinnacle / Silva Screen.

ACE VENTURA - PET DETECTIVE
Power of suggestion: Stevens, Steve / All Ace's: Stevens, Steve / Lion sleeps tonight: John, Robert / Psychoville/Ace Race: John, Robert / Mission Impossible / Ace of hearts / Hammer smashed face: Cannibal Corpse / Warehouse / Ficklo and Einhorn / Ace in the hole / Ace is in the house: Tone Loc
CD _____ 5230002
Polydor / May '94 / PolyGram.

ACE VENTURA II
CD _____ MCD 11374
MCA / Jan '96 / BMG.

ACT OF PIRACY/THE GREAT WHITE
Stevens, Morton C
CD _____ PCD 111
Prometheus / '92 / Silva Screen.

ACT, THE
Broadway Cast
Kander, John C

ACT, THE
Minnelli, Liza/Broadway Cast
Kander, John C
Ebb, Fred L
CD _____ MSCD 8
Music De-Luxe / Nov '94 / Magnum Music Group.

ADDAMS FAMILY VALUES
(Score)
Shaiman, Marc C
CD _____ VSD 5465
Varese Sarabande/Colosseum / Dec '93 / Pinnacle / Silva Screen.

ADDAMS FAMILY, THE
(Music From TV Series)
Mizzy, Vic C
CD _____ 610572
RCA/Silva Screen / '86 / Silva Screen.

ADVENTURES OF PRISCILLA, QUEEN OF THE DESERT
I've never been to me: Charlene / Go west: Village People / Billy, don't be a hero: Paper Lace / My baby loves lovin': White Plains / I love the nightlife: Bridges, Alicia / Can't help lovin' dat man: Richards, Trudy & Billy May / I will survive: Gaynor, Gloria / Fine romance: Horne, Lena / Shake your groove thing: Peaches & Herb / I don't care if the sun don't shine: Page, Patti / Finally: Peniston, Ce Ce / Take a letter Maria: Peniston, Ce Ce / Mamma mia: Abba / Save the best for last: Williams, Vanessa
CD _____ MUMCD 9416
Mother / Oct '94 / PolyGram.

ADVENTURES OF ROBIN HOOD, THE
Utah Symphony Orchestra
Korngold, Erich C
CD _____ EK 57568
Silva Screen / Jan '93 / Conifer / Silva Screen.

ADVENTURES OF ROBIN HOOD, THE
Korngold, Erich C
CD _____ CDTER 1066
TER / May '89 / Koch.

ADVENTURES OF ROBIN HOOD, THE/ REQUIEM FOR A CAVALIER
Korngold, Erich C
Korngold, Erich C on
CD _____ VSD 47202
Varese Sarabande/Colosseum / Aug '91 / Pinnacle / Silva Screen.

ADVENTURES OF ROBINSON CRUSOE, THE
Mellin, Robert & Gian-Piero Reverberi C
Reverberi, Gian-Piero C on
Opening titles / Main theme / Friday / Crusoe's youth remembered / Away from home / Adrift / Solitude / Shelter / Scanning the horizon/Flashback - escapades in York / Cannibals / Wild goats / Palm trees / In search of rescue / Civilised man / Distant shores / Alone / Catching dinner / Poor Robinson / Danger / Closing titles
CD _____ FILMCD 705
Silva Screen / Dec '90 / Conifer / Silva Screen.

AFTER DARK MY SWEET
Jarre, Maurice C
After dark my sweet (Suite I) / Collie and Fay (suite II) / Uncle Bud (suite III) / Kidnapping (suite IV)
CD _____ VSD 5274
Varese Sarabande/Colosseum / Jul '90 / Pinnacle / Silva Screen.

AFTER MIDNIGHT
Gordon, Dexter C
CD _____ SCCD 31226
Southern Cross / Jul '88 / Silva Screen.

AGAINST ALL ODDS
Against all odds: Collins, Phil / Violet and blue: Nicks, Stevie / Walk through the fire: Gabriel, Peter / Balcony: Big Country / Making a big mistake: Rutherford, Mike / My male curiosity: Kid Creole & The Coconuts / Search: Carlton, Larry & Michel Colombier / El solitario: Carlton, Larry & Michel Colombier / Rock 'n' roll jaguar: Carlton, Larry & Michel Colombier / For love alone: Carlton, Larry / Race: Carlton, Larry / Murder: Carlton, Larry
CD _____ CDVIP 112
Virgin VIP / Nov '93 / Carlton Home Entertainment / THE / EMI.

AIN'T MISBEHAVIN'
1979 Broadway Cast
Waller, Fats L

Ebb, Fred L
Shine it on / It's the strangest thing / Bobo's / Turning / Little do they know / Arthur in the afternoon / Money tree / City lights / There when I need him / Hot enough for you / Little do they know (reprise) / My own space / Walking papers
CD _____ DRGCD 6101
DRG / '87 / New Note.

ACT, THE
Minnelli, Liza/Broadway Cast
Kander, John C
Ebb, Fred L
CD _____ MSCD 8
Music De-Luxe / Nov '94 / Magnum Music Group.

ADDAMS FAMILY VALUES
(Score)
Shaiman, Marc C

Ain't misbehavin' (medley with Lookin' good but feelin' bad/T'ain't nobody's business if I do) / Honeysuckle Rose / Squeeze me / Handful of keys / I've got a feeling I'm falling / How ya baby / Jitterbug waltz / Ladies who sing with the band / Yacht Club swing / When the nylons bloom again / Cash for your trash / Off-time / Joint is jumpin' / Entr'acte / Spreadin' rhythm around / Lounging at the Waldorf / Viper's drag/The reefer song / Mean to me / Your feet's too big / That ain't right / Keepin' out of mischief now / Find out what they like / Fat and greasy / Black and blue / I'm gonna sit right down and write myself a letter / Two sleepy people/I've got my fingers crossed (Finale medley inc. I can't give you anything but love/It's a sin to tell a lie/Honeysuckle Rose)
2CD _____ BD 82965
RCA Victor / Aug '90 / BMG.

AIRHEADS
Born to raise hell: Motorhead / I'm the one: 4 Non Blondes / Feed the gods: White Zombie / No way out: D-Generation / Bastardizing jellikit: Primus / London: Anthrax / Can't give in: Candlebox / Curious George blues: Dig / Inheritance: Prong / Degenerated: Lone Rangers / I'll talk my way out of: Stuttering John / Fuel: Stick / We want the airwaves: Ramones
CD _____ 07822110142
Arista / Oct '94 / BMG.

AIRPORT
Newman, Alfred C
CD _____ VSD 5436
Varese Sarabande/Colosseum / Aug '93 / Pinnacle / Silva Screen.

AKIRA
(Japanese Score)
Shoji, Yamashiro C
CD _____ DSCD 6
Demon / Nov '93 / Pinnacle / ADA.

AKIRA
Shoji, Yamashiro C
Kaneda / Battle against clown / Tetsuo (pts I & II) / Akira / Winds over Neo-Tokyo / Exodus from the underground fortress / Illusion / Requiem
CD _____ DSCD 7
Demon / Jun '94 / Pinnacle / ADA.

ALADDIN
1958 Television Cast
Porter, Cole C
Perelman, S.J. L
CD _____ SK 48205
Sony Broadway / May '95 / Sony.

ALICE'S RESTAURANT
Guthrie, Arlo C
Alice's restaurant massacre / Chilling of the evening / Ring around a rosy rag / Now and then I'm going home / Motorcycle song / Highway in the wind
CD _____ 244045
WEA / Feb '94 / Warner Music.

ALIEN
National Philharmonic Orchestra
Goldsmith, Jerry C
Newman, Lionel C on
Main title / Face hugger / Breakaway / Acid test / Landing / Droid / Recovery / Alien planet / Shaft / End titles
CD _____ FILMCD 003
Silva Screen / Jun '87 / Conifer / Silva Screen.

ALIEN EMPIRE
(The Ocellus Suite)
Munich Symphony Orchestra
Kiszko, Martin C
Journey to the Alien Empire / Ocellus voyage / Battle zone / Angels and warriors / Slipstreams / Earthstalkers / Insectarium / Solus odyssey / Ancient enemies / Three visions / Firstborn / Distant swarm / Colony and metropolis / Earthrise / Return voyage
CD _____ CDEMC 3730
Soundtrack Music / Jan '96 / EMI.

ALIEN NATION - THE SERIES
Dorff, Steve/Larry Herbstritt/David Kurtz C
Dorff, Steve/Larry Herbstritt/David Kurtz C on
CD _____ GNPD 8024
GNP Crescendo / '94 / Silva Screen.

ALIVE
Howard, James Newton C
CD _____ EA 614542
Silva Screen / Jan '93 / Conifer / Silva Screen.

ALL AMERICAN
1962 Broadway Cast
Strouse, Charles C
Adams, Lee L
CD _____ SK 48216
Sony Broadway / Nov '92 / Sony.

ALL THAT JAZZ
On Broadway: Benson, George / Michelle: Burns, Ralph / Take off with us: Bergman,

914

Sandahl & Chorus Vavaldi / Ponte vecchio:
Burns, Ralph / Everything old is new again:
Allen, Peter / South Mt Sinai parade: Burns,
Ralph / After you've gone: Palmer, Leland /
There'll be some changes made: Reinking,
Ann / Who's sorry now: Burns, Ralph /
Some of these days: Foldi, Erzsebet / Going
home now: Burns, Ralph / Bye bye love:
Vereen, Ben & Roy Scheider / Vivaldi con-
certi in G: Burns, Ralph / Main Title: Burns,
Ralph
CD _____ 5512692
Spectrum/Karussell / Sep '95 / PolyGram /
THE.

ALLONSANFAN/METELLO
Morricone, Ennio C
2CD _____ OST 103
Milano Dischi / Jan '95 / Silva Screen.

ALMOST AN ANGEL
Jarre, Maurice C
Jarre, Maurice Con
CD _____ VSD 5307
Varese Sarabande/Colosseum / Jan '91 /
Pinnacle / Silva Screen.

ALWAYS
Williams, John C
Smoke gets in your eyes / Cowboy man /
Fool in love / Follow me / Saying goodbye
/ Return / Seeing Dorinda / Promise to Hap
/ Dorinda solo flight / Boomerang love /
Give me your heart / Among the clouds /
Pete in heaven / Pete and Dorinda / Rescue
operation / Intimate conversation / Old ti-
mer's shack
CD _____ MCAD 8036
MCA/Silva Screen / Jan '93 / Silva Screen.

AMADEUS
Academy Of St. Martin In The Fields
Mozart, W.A. C
Marriner, Neville Con
2CD _____ 8251262
London / Feb '85 / PolyGram.

AMADEUS: MORE AMADEUS
Academy Of St. Martin In The Fields
Mozart, W.A. C
Marriner, Neville Con
CD _____ 8272672
London / Aug '85 / PolyGram.

**AMAHL AND THE NIGHT VISITORS,
THE**
Royal Opera House
Menotti, Gian Carlo C
CD _____ CDTER 1124
TER / Jan '93 / Koch.

AMATEUR
Taylor, Jeff/Ned Rifle C
CD _____ 7567925002
Warner Bros. / Jan '95 / Warner Music.

AMAZING GRACE AND CHUCK
Bernstein, Elmer C
CD _____ VCD 47285
Varese Sarabande/Colosseum / Jan '89 /
Pinnacle / Silva Screen.

AMAZING GRACE AND CHUCK, AN
CD _____ VSD 5441
Varese Sarabande/Colosseum / Dec '93 /
Pinnacle / Silva Screen.

AMERICAN GIGOLO
Moroder, Giorgio
Moroder, Giorgio C
Call me: Blondie / Love and passion:
Barnes, Cheryl / Night drive / Hello Mr.
W.A.M. / Apartment / Palm Springs Drive /
Night drive (reprise) / Seduction (Love
Theme)
CD _____ 5511032
Spectrum/Karussell / Sep '95 / PolyGram /
THE.

AMOK
Piovani, Nicola C
CD _____ 887898
Milan / Jan '95 / BMG / Silva Screen.

**ANASTASIA
(The Mystery Of Anna)**
Munich Philharmonic Orchestra
Rosenthal, Laurence C
Main title (part 1) / Ballroom / Sled
/ Family only / The cellar / Berlin bridge /
Confronting Sophie / After the intrusion /
Railroad car / Main title (part 2) / Denial /
Shopping spree / Romanoffs / At the Astor
/ Russian antiques / Darya says no / Lunch-
eonette / Anna and Erich / Ekaterinburg /
Back to Europe
CD _____ SCCD 1015
Southern Cross / Jan '89 / Silva Screen.

AND DO THEY DO
Nyman, Michael Band
Nyman, Michael C
CD _____ CDTER 1123
TER / Aug '93 / Koch.

AND THE BAND PLAYED ON
Burwell, Carter C
Burwell, Carter Con
CD _____ VSD 5449
Varese Sarabande/Colosseum / Apr '94 /
Pinnacle / Silva Screen.

ANDRE
Rowland, Bruce C
CD _____ 8122718022
Warner Bros. / Jan '95 / Warner Music.

**ANDY WARHOL'S DRACULA/ANDY
WARHOL'S FRANKENSTEIN**
Gizzi, Claudio C
CD _____ OST 119
Milano Dischi / Jan '94 / Silva Screen.

ANGEL AT MY TABLE, AN
McGlashan, Don C
CD _____ A 8925
Alhambra / Jan '92 / Silva Screen.

ANGEL AT MY TABLE, AN
McGlashan, Don C
CD _____ DRGCD 12603
DRG / Jan '95 / New Note.

ANGEL HEART
Jones, Trevor C
Harry Angel: Jones, Trevor & Courtney Pine
/ Honeymoon blues: Smith, Bessie / Night-
mare: Jones, Trevor & Courtney Pine / Girl
of ...: Gray, Glen & The Casa Loma Orches-
tra / I got this thing about chickens: Jones,
Trevor & Courtney Pine / Right key but the
wrong keyhole / Rainy rainy day: McGhee,
Brownie / Looking for Johnny: Jones, Tre-
vor & Courtney Pine / Soul on fire: Baker,
LaVern / Bloodmare: Jones, Trevor & Court-
ney Pine / Johnny Favourite: Jones, Trevor
& Courtney Pine
CD _____ IMCD 76
Island / '89 / PolyGram.

ANGIE
Goldsmith, Jerry C
Goldsmith, Jerry Con
CD _____ VSD 5469
Varese Sarabande/Colosseum / Jun '94 /
Pinnacle / Silva Screen.

ANGST
Schulze, Klaus
Schulze, Klaus C
Freeze / Pain / Memory / Surrender /
Beyond
CD _____ CDTB 027
Thunderbolt / Feb '86 / Magnum Music
Group.

ANGUS
CD _____ 9362459602
Warner Bros. / Aug '95 / Warner Music.

ANIMAL HOUSE
Faber College theme / Louie Louie: Belushi,
John / Twistin' the night away: Cooke, Sam
/ Tossin' and turnin': Lewis, Bobby / Shama
lama ding dong / Hey Paula: Paul & Paula /
Animal house: Bishop, Stephen / Money
(that's what I want): Belushi, John / Let's
dance: Montez, Chris / Dream girl: Bishop,
Stephen / What a wonderful world: Cooke,
Sam / Shout / Intro
CD _____ MCLD 19086
MCA / Jun '92 / BMG.

ANIMANIACS
CD _____ 8122715702
Atlantic / Apr '94 / Warner Music.

ANNIE
1982 Film Cast
Strouse, Charles C
Charnin, Martin L
Tomorrow / It's the hard-knock life / Maybe
/ Dumb dog / Sandy / I think I'm gonna like
it here / Little girls / We got Annie / Let's go
to the movies / Sign / You're never fully
dressed without a smile / Easy Street / To-
morrow reprise / Finale
CD _____ 4676082
CBS / Dec '90 / Sony.

ANNIE GET YOUR GUN
Criswell, Kim & Thomas Hampson/Studio
Cast/Ambrosian Chorus/London Sinfonietta
Berlin, Irving C
Fields, Dorothy L
McGlinn, John Con
CD _____ CDANNIE 1
EMI Classics / Aug '91 / EMI.

**ANNIE GET YOUR GUN
(Featuring Ethel Merman)**
Berlin, Irving C
Fields, Dorothy L
Overture / Colonel Buffalo Bill / I'm a bad,
bad man / Doin' what comes natur'lly / Girl
that I marry / You can't get a man with a
gun / There's no business like show business / They say it's wonderful / Moonshine
lullaby / There's no business like show business (reprise) / My defenses are down / I'm
an Indian too / I got lost in his arms / I got
the sun in the morning / Old fashioned wedding / Anything you can do / Finale (There's
no business like show business/They say
it's wonderful)
CD _____ RD 81124
RCA Victor / Jan '89 / BMG.

ANNIE GET YOUR GUN
1986 London Cast
Berlin, Irving C
Fields, Dorothy L
Overture / Colonel Buffalo Bill / I'm a bad
bad man / Doin' what comes natur'lly / Girl
that I marry / You can't get a man with a
gun / There's no business like show business / They say it's wonderful / Wild horse
ceremonial dance / I'm an Indian too / I got
lost in his arms / I got the sun in the morning
/ Old fashioned wedding / Anything you can
do / Finale
CD _____ OCRCD 6024
First Night / Oct '95 / Pinnacle.

ANNIE GET YOUR GUN
Broadway Cast
Berlin, Irving C
Fields, Dorothy L
CD _____ ZDM 7647652
EMI Classics / Apr '93 / EMI.

ANNIE GET YOUR GUN
Cast Recording
Berlin, Irving C
Fields, Dorothy L
CD _____ CDTER 1229
TER / Aug '95 / Koch.

ANNIE WARBUCKS
Broadway Cast
CD _____ CDQ 5550402
EMI / Mar '94 / EMI.

ANTARTIDA
Cale, John
Cale, John C
CD _____ TWI 1008
Les Disques Du Crepuscule / Nov '95 / Dis-
covery / ADA.

ANTONY AND CLEOPATRA
Royal Philharmonic Orchestra
Scott, John C
Main title / Give me to drink Mandragora
(Cleopatra's theme) / Confrontation with
Pompey / Antony and Octavia (Caesar's
sister) / Barge she sat in / One will tear the
other / Battle of Actium / Prelude to part 2
(love theme) / Whither hast thou led me
Egypt / Death of Enobarbus / He goes forth
gallantly / Sometimes we see a cloud that's
dragonish / Death of Antony (love theme) /
Pretty worm of Nilus / She shall be buried
by her Antony (end titles)
CD _____ JSCD 114
Silva Screen / Jan '93 / Conifer / Silva
Screen.

ANYONE CAN WHISTLE
1964 Broadway Cast
Sondheim, Stephen C
CD _____ CK 02480
CBS/Silva Screen / Jan '89 / Conifer / Silva
Screen.

ANYTHING GOES
1989 London Cast
Porter, Cole C
Prelude / There's no cure like travel / You're
the top / I want to row on the crew / Friendship / Anything goes / Public enemy No.1 /
Goodbye little dream goodbye / All through
the night / Buddie beware / I get a kick out
of you / Bon voyage / Easy to love / Sailor's
chantey / It's de-lovely / Entr'acte / Blow
Gabriel blow / Be like the bluebird / Gypsy
in me
CD _____ OCRCD 6038
First Night / Oct '95 / Pinnacle.

ANYTHING GOES
Cast Recording
Porter, Cole C
CD _____ EK 15100
Silva Screen / Jan '89 / Conifer / Silva
Screen.

ANYTHING GOES
1969 London Cast
Porter, Cole C
CD _____ CDTER 1219
TER / Jan '94 / Koch.

ANYTHING GOES
Criswell, Kim & Chris Groenendaal/Jack Gil-
ford/Frederica Von Stade/Ambrosian Cho-
rus/London Symphony Orchestra
Porter, Cole C
Overture / I get a kick out of you / Bon voyage / All through the night / There'll always
be a lady fair / Where are the men / You're
the top / You're the top (encore) / There'll
always be a lady fair (reprise) / Anything
goes (finale) / Entr'acte / Public enemy No.1
/ What a joy to be young / Blow Gabriel
blow / Be like the bluebird / Buddie beware
/ Gypsy in me / Finale ultimo / Kate the
great / Waltz down the aisle
CD _____ CDC 7498482
EMI Classics / Oct '89 / EMI.

ANYWHERE I WANDER
Cast Recording
Loesser, Frank C
CD _____ VSD 5434
Varese Sarabande/Colosseum / Oct '93 /
Pinnacle / Silva Screen.

APOCALYPSE NOW
Coppola, Carmine C
2CD _____ 900012
Elektra/Silva Screen / Jan '89 / Silva
Screen.

APOLLO 13
Horner, James C
Horner, James Con
Night train: Brown, James / Groovin': Young
Rascals / Somebody to love: Jefferson Air-
plane / I can see for miles: Who / Purple
haze: Hendrix, Jimi / Spirit in the sky: Gree-
baum, Norman / Honky tonkin': Williams,
Hank / Blue moon: Mavericks
CD _____ MCD 11241
MCA / Jul '95 / BMG.

**APRES LA GUERRE
(After The War)**
Knieper, Jurgen C
CD _____ CDCH 386
Milan / Feb '90 / BMG / Silva Screen.

ARCADIANS, THE
London Cast
Monckton, Lionel & Howard Talbot C
Wimperis, Arthur L
Overture / Opening chorus: Arcadians are
we / Joy of life / Pipes of Pan are calling /
To all and each (Finale Act 1) / Back your
fancy / Girl with the brogue / Arcady is ever
young / Somewhere / Charming weather / I
like London / Half past two / All down Piccadilly / Truth is beautiful / My motter / All
down Piccadilly (Reprise) / Pipes of Pan /
Girl with a brogue / Arcady is ever young
(2) / My motter (2) / Bring me a rose / Come
back to Arcady / Light is my heart
CD _____ CDANGEL 1
Angel / Apr '93 / EMI.

ARE YOU LONESOME TONIGHT
1985 London Cast
Peace in the valley / Heartbreak hotel /
That's alright mama / I don't care if the sun
don't shine / Loving you / Blue suede shoes
/ Moody blue / If I can dream / All my trials
/ NBC-TV special 1968 / You gave me a
mountain / I was the one / If we never meet
again / Are you lonesome tonight
CD _____ OCRCD 6027
First Night / Dec '95 / Pinnacle.

ARISTOCATS, THE
Sherman, Richard & Robert C
Aristocats / Scales and Arpeggios / Thomas
O'Malley cat / Everybody wants to be a cat
/ Pretty melody (My Paree) / Cats love
theme / Butler sneak / Nine lives / Goose
steps high / Windmill/The butler speak /
Blues / After her/Cat fight / My Paree /
Chords in blue / Nice melody / Two dogs
and a cycle / Everybody wants to be a cat
(reprise)
CD _____ DSMCD 473
Carlton Home Entertainment / Jul '94 / Carl-
ton Home Entertainment.

AROUND THE WORLD IN 80 DAYS
Young, Victor C
Young, Victor Con
CD _____ MCAD 31164
MCA/Silva Screen / Jan '93 / Silva Screen.

ARRIVAL, THE
Band, Richard C
CD _____ MAF 7032D
Intrada / Nov '92 / Silva Screen / Koch.

ASPECTS OF LOVE
London Cast
Lloyd Webber, Andrew C
Love changes everything / Seeing is believ-
ing / Chason d'enfante / She's far better off
without you / Leading lady / There's more
to love / First man you remember / Falling /
Anything but lonely / Cafe / Memory of a
happy moment / Everybody loves a hero /
Stop wait please / Other pleasures / Mer-
maid song / Journey of a lifetime / Hand me
the wine and the dice
CD _____ 8411262
Really Useful / Aug '89 / PolyGram.

ASPECTS OF LOVE/CATS
Cast Recording
Lloyd Webber, Andrew C
CD _____ 340832
Koch / Oct '95 / Koch.

ASSASSINS
1991 Broadway Cast
Sondheim, Stephen C
Everybody's got the right / Ballad of Booth
/ How I saved Roosevelt / Gun song / Ballad
of Czolgosz / Unworthy of your love / Ballad
of Guiteau / Another national anthem / No-
vember 22, 1963 / Final sequence - You
can close the New York Stock Exchange /
Everybody's got the right (reprise)
CD _____ RD 60737
RCA Victor / '91 / BMG.

ASTRONOMERS, THE
Redford, J.A.C. C
CD _____ MAF 7018D
Intrada / Jan '93 / Silva Screen / Koch.

AT PLAY IN THE FIELDS OF THE LORD
Polish Radio Grand Symphony Orchestra
Preisner, Zbigniew C
Wit, Antoni Con
CD _____ FCD 210072
Fantasy / Jan '93 / Pinnacle / Jazz Music /
Wellard / Cadillac.

**IT HAPPENED AT THE WORLD'S FAIR/
FUN IN ACAPULCO**
Presley, Elvis
Beyond the bend / Relax / Take me to the
fair / They remind me too much of you / One
broken heart for sale (Film version) / I'm falling in love tonight / Cotton candy land /
World of our own / How would you like to
be / Happy ending / One broken heart for
sale / Fun in Acapulco / Vino, dinero y amor
/ Mexico / El toro / Marguerita / Bullfighter
was a lady / No room to rhumba in a sports
car / I think I'm gonna like it here / Bossa
nova baby / You can't say no in Acapulco
/ Guadalajara
CD _____ 74321134312
RCA / Mar '93 / BMG.

ATLANTIC CITY
Legrand, Michel C
Casta diva / Slot machine baby / Bellini rock
variation city / My old friend / Balcon / Piano blackjack / Steel pier / Song of India /
Roadmap for a free jazz group / No
gambling allowed / AC/DC / Trio jazz

CD _____ CDRG 6104
DRG / Jan '89 / New Note.

ATLANTIS
Serra, Eric C
CD _____ 30867
Silva Screen / Jan '93 / Conifer / Silva Screen.

ATTACK AND RETREAT/THE CAMP FOLLOWERS
(Italiani Brava Gente/Le Soldatesse)
Trovajoli, Armando/Mario Nascimbene C
CD _____ OST 112
Milano Dischi / Apr '92 / Silva Screen.

ATTENTION BANDITS
Lai, Francis C
CD _____ MANTRA 055
Silva Screen / Jan '93 / Conifer / Silva Screen.

AUF OFFENER STRASSE/L 627
Sarde, Philippe C
CD _____ 873131
Milan / Jan '95 / BMG / Silva Screen.

AUX YEAUX DU MONDE
Wonder, Stevie
Torikian, G. C
CD _____ CH 403
Milan / Jan '95 / BMG / Silva Screen.

AVALON
Newman, Randy
Newman, Randy C
CD _____ 9264372
Silva Screen / Jan '93 / Conifer / Silva Screen.

AVENGERS, THE/THE NEW AVENGERS/ THE PROFESSIONALS
London Studio Orchestra
Johnson, Laurie C
CD _____ VCD 47270
Varese Sarabande/Colosseum / Jan '89 / Pinnacle / Silva Screen.

AWAKENINGS
Newman, Randy
Newman, Randy C
Leonard / Dr. Sayer / Lucy / Catch / Rilke's panther / L dopa / Awakenings / Time of the season / Outside / Escape attempt / Ward five / Dexter's tune / Reality of miracles / End titles
CD _____ 7599264662
Reprise / Mar '91 / Warner Music.

AWFULLY BIG ADVENTURE, AN
Hartley, Richard C
CD _____ TRXCD 2001
Silva Screen / Apr '95 / Conifer / Silva Screen.

AY, CARMELA
Masso, Alejandro C
CD _____ CH 557
Milan / Jan '95 / BMG / Silva Screen.

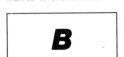

BABE
Bernstein, Elmer C
CD _____ VSD 5661
Varese Sarabande/Colosseum / Oct '95 / Pinnacle / Silva Screen.

BABES IN ARMS
Film Cast
Rodgers, Richard C
Hart, Lorenz L
CD _____ NW 3862
New World / Aug '92 / New World.

BABY
Broadway Cast
Shire, David C
Maltby, Richard Jr. L
Opening / We start today / What could be better / Plaza song / Baby, baby, baby / I want it all / At night she comes home to me / Fatherhood blues / Romance / I chose right / Story goes on / Ladies singing their song / Romance / Romance 2 / Easier to love / Romance 3 / Two people in love / With you / And what if we had loved like that / Birth / Finale
CD _____ CDTER 1089
TER / Mar '84 / Koch.

BABY OF MACON, THE
CD _____ 340142
Koch / Sep '93 / Koch.

BABYLON 5
Franke, Christopher C
Chrysalis / Mindwar / Parliament of dreams / Geometry of shadows
CD _____ S 185022
CDS / Mar '95 / Pinnacle.

BACK TO THE FUTURE
Johnny B. Goode: McFly, Marty & the Starlighters / Power of love: Lewis, Huey & The News / Time bomb town: Buckingham, Lindsey / Back to the future: Silvestri, Alan / Heaven is one step away: Clapton, Eric / Back in time: Lewis, Huey & The News /

Back to the future overture: Silvestri, Alan / Wallflower (dance with me, Henry): James, Etta / Night train: Berry, Marvin & the Starlighters / Earth angel: Berry, Marvin & the Starlighters
CD _____ MCLD 19151
MCA / Apr '93 / BMG.

BACK TO THE FUTURE III
Silvestri, Alan C
Main title / It's Clara / Train / Hill Valley / Hanging / At first sight / Indians / Goodbye Clara / Doc returns / Point of no return / Future isn't written / Showdown / Doc to the rescue / Kiss / We're out of gas / Wake up juice / Science experiment / Doubleback: ZZ Top / End credits
CD _____ VSD 5272
Varese Sarabande/Colosseum / Sep '90 / Pinnacle / Silva Screen.

BACKBEAT
Backbeat Band
Money / Long tall Sally / Bad boy / Twist and shout / Please Mr. Postman / C'mon everybody / Rock 'n' roll music / Slow down / Roadrunner / Carol / Good golly Miss Molly / Twenty flight rock
CD _____ CDV 2729
Virgin / Apr '94 / EMI.

BACKBEAT
(Score)
Was, Don C
You asked I came / Darkroom / What do they call this drink / He's wearing my bathrobe / Just read the poems / You asked I came (2) / He's wearing my bathrobe (2)
CD _____ CDV 2740
Virgin / Apr '94 / EMI.

BACKDRAFT
Zimmer, Hans C
CD _____ 262023
Milan / '95 / BMG / Silva Screen.

BAD BOYS
Shy guy: King, Diana / So many ways: Warren G. / Five o'here they come): 69 / Boom boom boom: Juster / Me against the world: 2 Pac / Someone to love: Jon B / I've got a little something for you: MN8 / Never find someone like you: Martin, Keith / Theme from Bad Boys: Mancina, Mark / Bad boys reply: Inner Circle / Juke joint jezebel: K.M.F.D.M. / Cloud of smoke: Cali O'da Wild / Work me slow: Xscape / Da B side: Da Brat / Call the police: Kamoze, Ini
CD _____ 4804532
Columbia / Jun '95 / Sony.

BAD GIRLS
Goldsmith, Jerry C
CD _____ 220542
Milan / Jan '95 / BMG / Silva Screen.

BAD INFLUENCE
Spiritual healing: Toots / Bird boy: Vasconcelos, Nana & Bushdances / Downtown: Cole, Lloyd / Out of the rain: James, Etta / N'sel Fik: Fadela, Chaba / Corruption: Mapfumo, Thomas / Who's laughing now: Skinny Puppy / Orane: Les Negresses Vertes / I've got what he wanted: Friday, Gavin / Shades for the night: Jones, Trevor / Main theme: Jones, Trevor / Wilshire corridor: Jones, Trevor
CD _____ 5511022
Spectrum/Karussell / Sep '95 / PolyGram / THE.

BAD SEED, THE
North, Alex C
CD _____ TSU 0124
Tsunami / Jan '95 / Silva Screen.

BAD TASTE
CD _____ QDK CD 002
Normal/Okra / Sep '94 / Direct / ADA.

BAGDAD CAFE
Calling you: Steele, Jevetta / Zwifach: Blasmusik, Deihinger / C major prelude: Flagg, Darron / Blues harp: Galison, William / Brenda, Brenda: Steele, Jevetta / Calliope: Telson, Bob
CD _____ IMCD 102
Island / Feb '90 / PolyGram.

BAKER'S WIFE, THE
London Cast
Schwartz, Stephen C
2CD _____ CDTER 1175
TER / Jul '90 / Koch.

BALANCING ACT
Original New York Cast
Goggin, Dan C
Life is a balancing act / Next stop: New York City / Home sweet home / Play away the blues / Tough town / I left you there / Twist of fate / Fifth from the right / You heard it here first / Long long way / Women of the century / Welcome bienvenue / Where is the rainbow / I am yours / That kid's gonna make it / Chew chew chow / Hollywood 'n' vinyl / California suite / I knew the music
CD _____ DRGCD 19004
DRG / Jan '95 / New Note.

BALLAD OF LITTLE JOE
Mansfield, David & Kate/Anne McGarrigle
Mansfield, David C
CD _____ MAF 7053D
Intrada / Jan '93 / Silva Screen / Koch.

BALLAD OF THE IRISH HORSE, THE
Chieftains
Moloney, Paddy C
Ballad of the Irish horse / Green pastures / Birth of the foals / Lady Hemphill / Horses of Ireland - part 1 / Chasing the fox / Going to the fair / Galway races / Story of the horse / Boyne hunt/Mullingar races/Fivemile chase / Horses of Ireland - part 2
CD _____ CCF 15CD
Claddagh / May '93 / ADA / Direct.

BANANAS IN PYJAMAS
(16 New Songs)
Bananas in Pyjamas
Bananas in pyjamas / Hello song / Banana holiday / Un deux trois (1,2,3,) / Roly poly rat / Happy birthday for two / Walking in the park / Amy's magic act / Twins / Hey there everybody / Shopping with Lulu / At the beach / Banana's fixing song / I love the ballet / Amy shake / We like wearing pyjamas
CD _____ PWMCD 2500
Carlton Home Entertainment / Aug '94 / Carlton Home Entertainment.

BANDOLERO
Goldsmith, Jerry C
Trap / El jefe / Bait / Ambushed / Sabinas / Dee's proposal / Across the river / Bad day for a hanging / Better way
CD _____ TCS 10012
Edel / Jan '90 / Pinnacle.

BARAKA
Stearns, Michael
Stearns, Michael C
CD _____ 153062
Milan / Feb '94 / BMG / Silva Screen.

BARBARIANS, THE
Donaggio, Pino C
CD _____ MAF 7008D
Intrada / Jan '93 / Silva Screen / Koch.

BARCELONA
Suozzo, Mark C
CD _____ 237942
Milan / Jan '95 / BMG / Silva Screen.

BARMITZVAH BOY
1978 London Cast
Styne, Jule C
CD _____ 4804532
Overture / Why / If only a little bit sticks / Bar mitzvah of Elliot Green / This time tomorrow / Thou shalt not / Harolds of this world / We've done alright / Simchas / You wouldn't be you / Rita's request / Sun shines out of your eyes / Where is the music coming from / I've just begun
CD _____ SMK 53498
Sony West End / Nov '92 / Sony.

BARNUM
1980 Broadway Cast
Coleman, Cy C
Stewart, Michael L
CD _____ CK 36576
CBS/Silva Screen / Jan '89 / Conifer / Silva Screen.

BARRY LYNDON
Moloney, Paddy C
Sarabande (main title) / Women of Ireland / Piper's maggot jig / Seamaiden / Tin whistle / British Grenadiers / Hohenfriedberger march / Lilliburlero / March: Idomeneo / Sarabande-duel / German dance no.1 in C major / Il barbiere di siviglia / Cello concerto / Concerto for two harpsichords and orchestra in / Piano trio in E flat / Sarabande (end title)
CD _____ 7559259842
Warner Bros. / Jan '95 / Warner Music.

BASHVILLE
1983 London Cast
King, Denis C
Green, Benny L
Prelude / Fancy Free / Lydia / 8-9-10 / One pair of hands / Gentleman's true to his code / Because I love her / Take the road to the ring / Entr'acte / Hymn to law and order / Blackman's burden / He is my son / Bashville / Boats are burned / Finale
CD _____ CDTER 1072
TER / Aug '95 / Koch.

BASIC INSTINCT
Goldsmith, Jerry C
Goldsmith, Jerry Con
CD _____ VSD 5360
Varese Sarabande/Colosseum / Mar '92 / Pinnacle / Silva Screen.

BASIL THE GREAT MOUSE DETECTIVE
Mancini, Henry C
CD _____ VSD 5359
Varese Sarabande/Colosseum / Feb '92 / Pinnacle / Silva Screen.

BASKET CASE II/FRANKENHOOKER
Renzetti, Joe
Renzetti, Joe C
I'm pregnant, I'm dead / Granny at break tent / Barbecue / Original main titles / Out of hospital / Out of window / Big escape / Room of memories / In the attic / Granny meeting / In love / Frankenhooker (main titles) / Lookin' for hookers / Jeffrey and parts / Creation / Eyeball / Happy day / Jeffrey fixes Elizabeth / Zoro killing
CD _____ FILMCD 073
Silva Screen / '89 / Conifer / Silva Screen.

BASKETBALL DIARIES
CD _____ 5240934
Island / Jul '95 / PolyGram.

BAT 21
CD _____ VSD 5202
Varese Sarabande/Colosseum / Dec '88 / Pinnacle / Silva Screen.

BATMAN
(Score)
Sinfonia Of London
Elfman, Danny C
Walker, S. Con
Batman theme / First confrontation / Clown attack / Roasted dude / Descent into mystery / Joker's poem / Charge of the Batmobile / Up the cathedral / Final confrontation / Roof fight / Flowers / Batman to the rescue / Photos / Beautiful dreamer / Bat cave / Love theme / Attack of the batwing / Waltz to the death / Finale
CD _____ K 9259772
WEA / Aug '89 / Warner Music.

BATMAN
Prince
Prince C
Future / Electric chair / Arms of Orion / Partyman / Vicki waiting / Trust / Lemon crush / Scandalous / Batdance
CD _____ 9259362
WEA / Feb '95 / Warner Music.

BATMAN FOREVER
CD _____ 7567827592
Warner Bros. / Jun '95 / Warner Music.

BATMAN RETURNS
Elfman, Danny C
Birth of Penguin / Lair / Selina transforms / Cemetary / Cat suite / Batman Vs The Circus / Rise and fall from grace / Sore spots / Rooftops / Wild ride / Children's hour / Final confrontation / Finale / End credits / Face to face: Siouxsie & the Banshees
CD _____ 7599269722
WEA / Jun '92 / Warner Music.

BATMAN: MASK OF THE PHANTOM
Walker, Shirley C
CD _____ WA 454842
Silva Screen / Jan '93 / Conifer / Silva Screen.

BATTLE OF ALGIERS/MASSACRE IN ROME
Pontecorvo, Gillo C
CD _____ OST 105
Milano Dischi / Jan '93 / Silva Screen.

BATTLE OF BRITAIN
Goodwin, Ron C
Battle of Britain / Aces high / Lull before the storm / Work and play / Death and destruction / Briefing and the Lutwaffe / Prelude to battle / Victory assured / Defeat / Hitler's headquarters / Return to base / Threat / Civilian tragedy / Offensive build-up / Absent friends / Battle of Britain (End title) / Operation Crossbow (theme) / Monte Carlo or bust (theme) / Trap (theme) / Those magnificent men in their flying machines
CD _____ CDMGM 21
MGM/EMI / Aug '90 / EMI.

BATTLE OF NERETVA, THE
London Philharmonic Orchestra
Herrmann, Bernard C
Prelude / Retreat / Separation / From Italy / Chetnik's march / Farewell / Partisan march / Pastorale / Turning point / Death of Danica / Victory
CD _____ SCCD 5005
Southern Cross / Jan '89 / Silva Screen.

BATTLERS, THE
Tall Poppies Orchestra
Vine, Carl C
Stanhope, D. Con
CD _____ TP 024
Tall Poppies / '94 / Complete/Pinnacle.

BATTLESHIP POTEMKIN/THE HOLY MOUNTAIN
Orchestra Della Svizzera Italiana
2CD _____ EDL 29062
Edel / Oct '95 / Pinnacle.

BATTLESTAR GALACTICA
Los Angeles Philharmonic Orchestra
Phillips, Stu & Glen Larson C
CD _____ TCS 1042
Silva Screen / Jan '93 / Conifer / Silva Screen.

BEACHES
Midler, Bette
Under the boardwalk / I've still got my health / Otto Titsling / Glory of love / Oh industry / Wind beneath my wings / I think it's going to rain today / I know you by heart / Baby mine / Friendship theme
CD _____ 7819332
WEA / Feb '95 / Warner Music.

BEASTMASTER II
CD _____ MAF 7019D
Intrada / Mar '92 / Silva Screen / Koch.

BEAT GIRL/STRINGBEAT
Barry, John Seven & Orchestra
Barry, John C
CD _____ PLAY 001
Play It Again / Jan '95 / Total/BMG.

BEAUTY AND THE BEAST
Menken, Alan *C*
Ashman, Howard *L*
Prologue / Belle: *Dion, Celine & Peabo Bryson* / Belle (reprise) / Gaston / Gaston (reprise) / Be our guest: *Dion, Celine & Peabo Bryson* / Something there / Mob song / Beauty and the beast / To the fair / West wing / Beast lets Belle go / Battle on the tower / Transformation / Beauty and the beast (duet): *Dion, Celine & Peabo Bryson*
CD _____ DSTCD 458
Disney / Jun '92 / Carlton Home Entertainment.

BEAUTY AND THE BEAST
2CD _____ MBOCD 1
MBO / Dec '95 / Total/BMG.

BEETHOVEN
Edelman, Randy *C*
Edelman, Randy *Con*
CD _____ MCAD 10600
MCA/Silva Screen / Jan '94 / Silva Screen.

BEETLEJUICE
Elfman, Danny
Elfman, Danny *C*
Banana boat song (Day O): *Belafonte, Harry* / Jump in the line: *Belafonte, Harry* / Main title / Travel music / Book / Enter... the family/Sand worm planet / Fly / Lydia discovers / In the model / Juno's theme / Beetlesnake / Sold / Flyer (inc. Lydia's pep talk) / Incantation / Lydia strikes a bargain / Showtime / Laughs / Wedding / Aftermath / End credits
CD _____ GFLD 19296
Geffen / Oct '95 / BMG.

BEIDERBECKE CONNECTION, THE
Ricotti, Frank All Stars
Connection / Viva le van / Morgans mystery / Tulips for Chris / Barney's walk / Boys in blue / Hobson's chase / Tiger jive / Scouting ahead / Jennie's tune / Live at the Limping Whippet / Russian over / Dormouse delights / Crying all day
CD _____ DMCD 20
Dormouse / Dec '88 / Jazz Music / Target/BMG.

BEING HUMAN
Gibbs, Michael *C*
Snell, D. *Con*
CD _____ VSD 5479
Varese Sarabande/Colosseum / May '94 / Pinnacle / Silva Screen.

BELLE OF NEW YORK/GOOD NEWS/RICH YOUNG & PRETTY
When I'm out with the belle of New York / Oops: *Astaire, Fred* / Naughty but nice: *Ellis, Anita* / Bachelor's dinner song: *Astaire, Fred* / Baby doll: *Astaire, Fred* / Bride's wedding day: *Ellis, Anita* / Seeing's believing: *Astaire, Fred* / I wanna be a dancin' man: *Astaire, Fred* / Good news: *McCracken, Joan* / He's a ladies man: *Lawford, Peter* / Lucky in love: *Marshall, Pat/Peter Lawford/June Allyson* / French lesson: *Allyson, June & Peter Lawford* / Best things in life are free: *Allyson, June & Peter Lawford* / Pass that peace pipe: *McCracken, Joan* / Just imagine: *Allyson, June* / Varsity drag: *Allyson, June & Peter Lawford* / Wonder why: *Powell, Jane* / Dark is the night: *Powell, Jane* / Paris: *Lamas, Fernando* / We never talk much: *Darrieux, Danielle* / There's danger in your eyes, cherie: *Darrieux, Danielle*
CD _____ CDMGM 23
MGM/EMI / Aug '94 / EMI.

BELLS ARE RINGING
1956 Broadway Cast
Styne, Jule *C*
Comden, Betty & Adolph Green *L*
Overture / Bells are ringing / It's a perfect relationship / On my own / It's a simple little system / It is a crime / Hello, hello there / I met a girl / Long before I knew you / Mucha-cha / Just in time / Drop that name / Party's over / Saltzburg / Midas touch / I'm goin' back
CD _____ CK 02006
CBS/Silva Screen / Jan '89 / Conifer / Silva Screen.

BEN FRANKLIN IN PARIS
1964 Broadway Cast
Sandrich, Mark *C*
Michaels, Sidney *L*
CD _____ ZDM 5651342
EMI Classics / Apr '94 / EMI.

BEN HUR
(New Score For 1925 Silent Movie)
Royal Liverpool Philharmonic Orchestra
Davis, Carl *C*
Davis, Carl *Con*
Opening titles / Nativity (The cave of David/Star of Bethlehem/The adoration of the Magi) / Esther and the young prince / Roman march and disaster (Gratus' entry into Jerusalem/Storming the palace and arrest) / Galley slave / Pirate battle / Iras the Egyptian / Chariot race (The gathering of the chariots/The race) / Ben Hur's return (The palace of Hur/Lepers) / Via Dolorosa (The way of the cross/Miracle) / Earthquake and new dawn (Collapse of the Senate/The resurrection)
CD _____ FILMCD 043
Silva Screen / Nov '89 / Conifer / Silva Screen.

BEN HUR
Rome Symphony Orchestra
Rozsa, Miklos *C*
Savina, Carlos *Con*
Prelude / Adoration of the Magi / Roman march / Friendship / Love theme / Rowing desert / Rowing of the galley slaves / Naval battle / Return to Judaea / Victory parade / Mother's love / Leper's search for the Christ / Procession to Calvary / Miracle and finale
CD _____ CDMGM 8
MGM/EMI / Jan '90 / EMI.

BEN HUR
National Philharmonic Orchestra
Rozsa, Miklos *C*
Rozsa, Miklos *Con*
Fanfare to prelude / Star of Bethlehem and adoration of the Magi / Friendship / Rowing desert / Arrius / Rowing of the galley slaves / Parade of the charioteers / Mother's love / Return to Judaea / Ring for freedom / Leper's search for the Christ / Procession to Calvary / Miracle and finale
CD _____ 4178492
Decca / '86 / PolyGram.

BEN HUR
Rozsa, Miklos *C*
2CD _____ A2K 47020
Silva Screen / Jan '93 / Conifer / Silva Screen.

BENNY AND JOON
Portman, Rachel *C*
Redford, J.A.C. *Con*
CD _____ 151682
Milan / Feb '94 / BMG / Silva Screen.

BERLIN BLUES
Schifrin, Lalo *C*
CD _____ CDCH 357
Milan / Jan '89 / BMG / Silva Screen.

BEST FOOT FORWARD
Revival Cast
Martin, Hugh & Ralph Blane *C*
Wish I may / Three men on a date / Hollywood story / Three B's / Ev'ry time / Alive and kicking/The guy who bought me / Shady lady bird / Buckle down Winsocki / You're lucky / What do you think I am / Raving beauty / Just a little joint with a juke box / You are for loving / Finale: Buckle down Winsocki
CD _____ DRGCD 15003
DRG / Sep '93 / New Note.

BEST LITTLE WHOREHOUSE GOES PUBLIC, THE
Broadway Cast
Hall, Carol *C*
CD _____ VSD 5542
Varese Sarabande/Colosseum / Jan '95 / Pinnacle / Silva Screen.

BEST OF THE BEST II
Frank, David Michael *C*
CD _____ CIN 22012
Silva Screen / Jan '93 / Conifer / Silva Screen.

BEST SHOT
(aka Hoosiers)
Goldsmith, Jerry *C*
Goldsmith, Jerry *Con*
Best shot / You did good / Coach stays / Pivot / Get the ball / Town meeting / Finals
CD _____ CDTER 1141
TER / Aug '87 / Koch.

BEST YEARS OF OUR LIVES, THE
London Philharmonic Orchestra
Friedhofer, Hugo *C*
Best years of our lives / Homecoming / Elevator / Boone City / Peggy / Fred and Peggy / Nightmare / Fred asleep / Neighbours / Homer goes upstairs / Citation / Exit music
CD _____ PRCD 1779
Preamble / Jan '89 / Silva Screen.

BETRAYED
Conti, Bill *C*
Main title / Way / Shoot the horse / Bank robbery / Kill me Kathy / To the bank / Riding to work / Guns / Passing time / End titles
CD _____ CDTER 1163
TER / Jul '89 / Koch.

BETTY BLUE
Yared, Gabriel
Yared, Gabriel *C*
Betty et Zorg / Des orages pour la nuit / Cargo voyage / La poubelle cuisine / Humecter la monture / Le petit Nicolas / Gyneco zebre / Comme les deux doigts de la main / Zorg et Betty / Chili con carne / C'est le vent, Betty / Un coucher de soleil accroche dans les arbres / Lisa rock / Le coeur en skai mauve / Bungalow zen / 37-2 le matin / Maudits maneges
CD _____ CDV 2396
Virgin / Sep '86 / EMI.

BEVERLY HILLBILLIES, THE
CD _____ 663132
Silva Screen / Jan '93 / Conifer / Silva Screen.

BEVERLY HILLS 90210
Bend time back around: *Abdul, Paula* / Got 2 have U: *Color Me Badd* / Right kind of love: *Jordan, Jeremy* / Love is: *Williams, Vanessa & Brian McKnight* / Just wanna be your friend: *Puck & Natty* / Let me be your baby: *Williams, Geoffrey* / Saving forever for you: *Shanice* / All the way to heaven: *Watley, Jody* / Why: *Dennis, Cathy & D-Mob* / Time to be lovers: *McDonald, Michael & Chaka Khan* / Action speaks louder than words: *Kemp, Tara* / Beverly Hills 90210 (theme): *Davis, John*
CD _____ 74321147982
Giant / Nov '94 / BMG.

BEVERLY HILLS 90210 - THE COLLEGE YEARS
Make it right: *Stansfield, Lisa* / Not one more time: *Piersa, Stacey* / Every day of the week: *Jade* / Not enough hours in the...: *After 7* / S.O.S.: *Dennis, Cathy* / No intermission: *5th Power* / Cantaloop (Flip fantasia): *US 3* / Moving on up: *M People* / Saturday: *Omar* / Touch my light: *Big Mountain* / I'll love you anyway: *Neville, Aaron* / What your love means to me: *Hi-Five* / Forever yours: *Moten, Wendy*
CD _____ 74321203032
Giant / Nov '94 / BMG.

BEVERLY HILLS COP
New attitude: *Labelle, Patti* / Don't get stopped in Beverly Hills: *Shalamar* / Do you really want my love: *Giscombe, Junior* / Emergency: *Robbins, Rockie* / Neutron dance: *Pointer Sisters* / Heat is on: *Frey, Glenn* / Gratitude: *Elfman, Danny* / Stir it up: *Labelle, Patti* / Rock 'n' roll me again: *System* / Axel F: *Faltermeyer, Harold*
CD _____ MCLD 19087
MCA / Sep '94 / BMG.

BEYOND RANGOON
CD _____ 286652
Milan / Jul '95 / BMG / Silva Screen

BEYOND THE CLOUDS/PURSUING THE CLOUDS
Fenton, George
Fenton, George *C*
CD _____ CDWM 109
Westmoor / Sep '94 / Target/BMG.

BEYOND THE LAW/DAY OF ANGER
Ortolani, Riz *C*
CD _____ OST 110
Milano Dischi / Jan '93 / Silva Screen.

BHAJI ON THE BEACH
Altman, John & Craig Pruess *C*
Summer holiday / Uchiya lumbia / Queen / Ha la la la / Mera laung glawacha / Na bada / Nachna / Greenhouse fantasy / Main theme / Ginder and Amrik theme, brothers fight in tower / Oliver and Hashida theme, at the museum / Ladies getting ready / Under the pier / Brothers theme, Ranjit hits Ginder and runs / Ambrose and Asha in theatre / Oliver's theme / Ginder's theme / End titles / Summer holiday (2)
CD _____ KEDCD 23
Keda / Feb '94 / Grapevine.

BIBLE, THE
Mayuzumi, Toshiro *C*
CD _____ OST 115
Milano Dischi / '94 / Silva Screen.

BIG BATTALIONS, THE
Gunning, Christopher *C*
CD _____ AHLCD 6
Hit / Nov '92 / PolyGram.

BIG BLUE, THE
Serra, Eric *C*
Big Blue overture / Rescue in a wreck / Huacracocha / Remembering a heart beat / Homo delphinus / Virgin Island / For Enzo / My lady blue / Deep blue dream / In raya (instr.) / Synchronised instant / Monastery of Amorgos / Leaving this world behind
CD _____ CDV 2541
Virgin / Nov '88 / EMI.

BIG BLUE, THE II
Serra, Eric *C*
CD _____ 30667
Silva Screen / Jan '93 / Conifer / Silva Screen.

BIG BLUE, THE II/THE MISSION/BETTY BLUE
3CD _____ TPAK 33
Virgin / Jan '95 / EMI.

BIG BLUE, THE: COMPLETE
Serra, Eric *C*
2CD _____ 30193
Silva Screen / Jan '93 / Conifer / Silva Screen.

BIG CHILL, THE
I heard it through the grapevine: *Gaye, Marvin* / My girl: *Temptations* / Good lovin': *Rascals* / Tracks of my tears: *Robinson, Smokey* / Joy to the world: *Three Dog Night* / Ain't too proud to beg: *Temptations* / (You make me feel like) a natural woman: *Franklin, Aretha* / I second that emotion: *Robinson, Smokey* / Whiter shade of pale: *Procul Harum*
CD _____ 530017-2
Motown / Jan '93 / PolyGram.

BIG COUNTRY, THE
Philharmonia Orchestra
Moross, Jerome *C*
Bremner, Tony *Con*
Main title / Julie's house / Welcoming / Courtin' time / Old thunder / Raid/Capture / Major Terrill's party: Dance/Waltz/Polka / McKay's ride/McKay is missing/Old house / Waiting / Big muddy / McKay alone/Night at Ladder Ranch/The fight / Cattle at the river / War party gathers/McKay in Blanco Canyon/Major alone / Duel/Death of Buck Hannassey / End title
CD _____ FILMCD 030
Silva Screen / Nov '95 / Conifer / Silva Screen.

BIG EASY, THE
Iko iko: *Dixie Cups* / Tipitina: *Professor Longhair* / Ma 'tit fille: *Buckwheat Zydeco* / Colinda: *Newman, Jimmy C.* / Tell it like it is: *Neville, Aaron & The Neville Brothers* / Zydeco gris gris: *Beausoleil* / Oh yeah: *Simien, T. & The Mallet Playboys* / Hey hey: *Wild Tchoupitoulas* / Closer to you: *Quaid, Dennis* / Savour, pass...: *Swan Silvertones*
CD _____ 5511592
Spectrum/Karussell / Sep '95 / PolyGram / THE.

BIG JAKE/THE SHOOTIST/CAHILL US MARSHALL
(Music From John Wayne Westerns Vol. 2)
Bernstein, Elmer *C*
Shootist / Ride / In the fire / Necktie party / Nocturne / Riders / Reunion / All Jake / Buzzards / Going home (finale)
CD _____ VCD 47264
Varese Sarabande/Colosseum / Jan '89 / Pinnacle / Silva Screen.

BIG RIVER
(The Adventures Of Huckleberry Finn)
1985 Broadway Cast
Miller, Roger *C*
Big River - Overture / Do you wanna go to heaven / Boys / Waitin' for the light to shine / Guv'ment / Hand for the hog / I, Huckleberry, me / Muddy water / Crossing / River in the rain / When the sun goes down in the south / Arte'cate / Royal nonesuch / Worlds apart / Arkansas / How blest we are / You oughta be here with me / Leavin's not the only way to go / Waitin' for the light to shine (reprise) / Free at last / Muddy water (reprise)
CD _____ MCAD 6147
MCA/Silva Screen / Jan '89 / Silva Screen.

BIG TROUBLE IN LITTLE CHINA
Carpenter, John *C*
Big trouble in little China: *Coup De Villes* / Pork chop express / Alley / Here come the storms / Lo Pan's domain / Escape from Wing Kong / Into the spirit path / Great arcade / Final escape
CD _____ DSCD 2
Demon / Aug '91 / Pinnacle / ADA.

BILITIS
Lai, Francis *C*
Bilitis / Promenade / Les deux nudites / Spring time ballet / L'abre / I need a man / Melissa / La campagne / Scene d'amour / Rainbow
CD _____ 800342
Silva Screen / Jan '93 / Conifer / Silva Screen.

BILL AND TED'S BOGUS JOURNEY
Shout it out: *Slaughter* / Battle stations: *Winger* / God gave rock 'n' roll to you II: *Kiss* / Drinking again: *Neverland* / Dream of a new day: *Kotzen, Richie* / Reaper: *Vai, Steve* / Perfect crime: *Faith No More* / Go to hell: *Megadeth* / Tommy the cat: *Primus* / Junior's gone wild: *Kings X* / Showdown: *Love on Ice* / Reaper rap: *Vai, Steve*
CD _____ 7567917252
Interscope / Jan '92 / Warner Music.

BILL AND TED'S EXCELLENT ADVENTURE
Play with me: *Extreme* / Boys and girls are living in: *Vital* / Not so far away: *Burtnick, Glenn* / Dancing with a gypsy: *Tora Tora* / Father time: *Shark Island* / I can't breakaway: *Big Pig* / Dangerous: *Shark Island* / Walk away: *Bricklin* / In time: *Robb, Robbie* / Two heads are better than one: *Power Tools*
CD _____ 3939152
A&M / Feb '92 / PolyGram.

BILLY
1974 London Cast
Barry, John *C*
Black, Don *L*
Overture / Ambrosia / Some of us belong to the stars / Happy to be themselves / Witch / Lies / It were all green hills / Aren't you Billy Fisher / Is there when I wake up / Billy / Remembering / Any minute now / Lady from L.A. / I missed the last rainbow / Finale / Some of us belong to the stars (reprise) / Ambrosia (reprise)
CD _____ 4728182
Columbia / Dec '92 / Sony.

BILLY BATHGATE
Isham, Mark *C*
CD _____ 262495
Milan / Jan '95 / BMG / Silva Screen.

BILLY CONNOLLY'S MUSICAL TOUR OF SCOTLAND
CD _____ 5298162
PolyGram TV / Dec '95 / PolyGram.

BING BOYS ARE HERE
Cast Recording
Grey, Clifford *L*
Orchestral selection: *Orchestra* / In other words: *Robey, George* / If you were the only

917

girl in the world: Robey, George & Violet Loraine / Whistler: Intermezzo / Another little drink: Robey, George & Violet Loraine / Shoeblack's dance: Orchestra / Right side of Bond Street: Morrison, Jack / Kipling walk: Orchestra / Lady of a thousand charms: Lester, Alfred & Violet Loraine / Kiss trot dance: Orchestra / Dear old Shepherd's Bush: Lester, Alfred / I start my day over again: Morrison, Jack / Languid melody: Orchestra / I stopped, I looked and I listened: Robey, George / Ragging the dog: Orchestra / Vocal gems: Columbia Revue Company / Orchestral finale: Orchestra
CD _____ PAST CD 9716
Flapper / '90 / Pinnacle.

BIOGRAPH GIRL, THE
1980 London Cast
Heneker, David C
Heneker, David & Warner Brown L
Reed, Michael Con
CD _____ CDTER 1003
TER / May '92 / Koch.

BIRD WITH THE CRYSTAL PLUMAGE, THE/FOUR FLIES ON GREY VELVET
Morricone, Ennio C
CD _____ CDCIA 5087
Cinevox / Jan '93 / Conifer / Silva Screen.

BIRD WITH THE CRYSTAL PLUMAGE, THE/FOUR FLIES ON GREY VELVET/CAT O'NINE TAILS
Morricone, Ennio C
CD _____ DRGCD 32911
DRG / Sep '95 / New Note.

BIRDMAN OF ALCATRAZ, THE
Bernstein, Elmer C
CD _____ TSU 0126
Tsunami / Jan '95 / Silva Screen.

BIRDS OF PARADISE
Off-Broadway Cast
Evans, David C
Holzman, Winnie L
CD _____ CDTER 1196
TER / Apr '93 / Koch.

BIRDY
Gabriel, Peter
Gabriel, Peter C
At night / Floating dogs / Quiet and alone / Close up (from Family Snapshot) / Slow water / Dressing the wound / Birdy's flight (from Not One Of Us) / Slow marimbas / Heat (from Rhythm Of The Heat) / Sketchpad with trumpet and voice / Under lock and key (from Wallflower) / Powerhouse at the foot of the mountain (from San Jacinto)
CD _____ CASCD 1167
Charisma / Mar '85 / EMI.

BIRTH OF A NATION, THE
Breil, Joseph C
Bringing the African to America / Abolitionists / Austin Stoneman / Elsie Stoneman / Old Southland / Boys at play / Cotton fields / Love strain / Stoneman library / Lydia Brown
CD _____ LSCD 701
Silva Screen / Jan '90 / Conifer / Silva Screen.

BITTER SWEET
1988 London Cast
Coward, Sir Noel C
Reed, Michael Con
Opening / That wonderful melody / Call of life / If you could only come with me / I'll see you again / Polka / What is love / Last dance / Finale / Opening chorus (Life in the morning) / Ladies of the town / If love were all / Dear little cafe / Bittersweet waltz / Officer's chorus (we wish to order wine) / Tokay / Bonne nuit, merci / Kiss me / Ta-ra-ra-boom-de-ay / Alas the time is past / We all wear a green carnation / Zigeuner
2CD _____ CDTER2 1160
TER / Mar '94 / Koch.

BITTER SWEET
(Highlights)
1988 London Cast
Coward, Sir Noel C
Reed, Michael Con
CD _____ CDTEO 1001
TER / Nov '89 / Koch.

BIX
Beiderbecke, Bix
Idolizing / Dardanella / Singing the blues (till my dad) / My pretty girl / Maple leaf rag / Riverboat shuffle (2) / Since my best gal turned me down / Jazz me blues (2) / Somebody stole my gal / Stardust / I'll be a friend with pleasure / In a mist / Tin roof blues / Riverboat shuffle / I'm coming Virginia / Davenport blues / Singing the blues (till my dad) (2) / Bix
CD _____ PD 74766
RCA / Aug '91 / BMG.

BLACK AND BLUE
Broadway Cast
CD _____ DRG 19001
DRG / Jan '95 / New Note.

BLACK AND WHITE MINSTREL SHOW, THE
(Stars From...)
Black & White Minstrels
CD _____ URCD 105
Upbeat / Apr '91 / Target/BMG / Cadillac.

BLACK CAULDRON, THE
Bernstein, Elmer C
CD _____ VCD 47241
Varese Sarabande/Colosseum / Jan '89 / Pinnacle / Silva Screen.

BLACK EAGLE
Plumeri, Terry C
Plumeri, Terry Con
CD _____ CIN 22202
Silva Screen / Oct '94 / Conifer / Silva Screen.

BLACK ORPHEUS
CD _____ 8307832
Silva Screen / Jan '93 / Conifer / Silva Screen.

BLACK RAIN
Zimmer, Hans
Zimmer, Hans C
Livin' on the edge of the night: Iggy Pop / Way you do the things you do: UB40 / Back to life: Soul II Soul / Laser man: Sakamoto, Ryuichi / Singing in the shower: Les Rita Mitsouko & The Sparks / I'll be holding on: Allman, Gregg / Sato (Black Rain Suite) / Charlie loses his head / Sugai / Nick and Masa
CD _____ CDV 2607
Virgin / Feb '90 / EMI.

BLADERUNNER
Vangelis
Vangelis C
Main title / Blush response / Wait for me / Rachel's song / Love theme / One more kiss, Dear / Bladerunner blues / Memories of green / Tales of the future / Damask rose / End titles / Tears in rain
CD _____ 4509965742
Warner Bros. / May '94 / Warner Music.

BLANKMAN
Super hero: New Power Generation / Do you wanna get down: Portrait / Dig deep: Tag Team / Cry on: Silk / Do you like it baby: Domino / Here he comes: G Wiz & Big House / Could it be I'm falling in love: II D Extreme / Anyone can be a hero: Hathaway, Lalah / Live into the future: Ball, Keith K.B. / Never say never: Funky Poets / Talk of the town: K-Dee
CD _____ 4768212
Epic / Oct '94 / Sony.

YOUNG GUNS II
(Blaze Of Glory)
Bon Jovi, Jon
Billy get your guns / Blaze of glory / Santa Fe / Never say die / Bang a drum / Guano City / Miracle / Blood money / Justice in the barrel / You really got me now / Dyin' ain't much of a livin'
CD _____ 846 473 2
Vertigo / Aug '90 / PolyGram.

BLIND DATE
Myers, Stanley C
Simply meant to be: Morris, Gary & Jennifer Warnes / Let you get away: Vera, Billy / Oh what a nite: Vera, Billy / Anybody seen her: Vera, Billy / Talked about lover: L'Neire, Keith / Crash band boom: Tubbs, Hubert / Something for Nash / Treasures: Jordan, Stanley
CD _____ FILMCD 016
Silva Screen / Aug '87 / Conifer / Silva Screen.

BLINK
Fiedel, Brad C
CD _____ 191902
Milan / May '94 / BMG / Silva Screen.

BLOOD BROTHERS
1983 London Cast
Russell, Willy C
Narration / Marilyn Monroe / My child / Devil's got your number / Easy terms / Just a game / Sunday afternoon / My friend / Bright new day / One summer narration / Saying a word / Miss Jones (sign of the times) / Prison song / Light romance / There's a madman / Tell me it's not true
CD _____ CLACD 270
Castle / May '93 / BMG.

BLOOD BROTHERS
1988 London Cast
Russell, Willy C
CD _____ 09026616892
RCA Victor / Jul '91 / BMG.
CD _____ CASTCD 49
First Night / Jul '95 / Pinnacle.

BLOOD BROTHERS
International Cast
Russell, Willy C
CD _____ CASTCD 50
First Night / Nov '95 / Pinnacle.

BLOOD IN BLOOD OUT
Conti, Bill C
CD _____ VSD 5396
Varese Sarabande/Colosseum / Mar '93 / Pinnacle / Silva Screen.

BLOOD OF HEROES, THE
Boekelheide, Todd C
Adler, M. Con
CD _____ MAF 7060D
Intrada / May '95 / Silva Screen / Koch.

BLOODMOON
May, Brian C
CD _____ IMICD 1006
Silva Screen / Jan '93 / Conifer / Silva Screen.

BLOODSPORT
Hertzog, Paul C
CD _____ FILMCD 055
Silva Screen / Sep '90 / Conifer / Silva Screen.

BLOWN AWAY
In the morning: Big Head Todd & The Monsters / Return to me: October Project / With or without you: U2 / All night long: Franklin, Aretha / Tuesday morning: Pogues / Here's where the story ends: Sundays / Darling today: Jayhawks / You'll lose a good thing: Franklin, Aretha / Take me home: Cocker, Joe & Bekka Bramlett
CD _____ 476823 2
Epic / Sep '94 / Sony.

BLUE CITY
Cooder, Ry
Cooder, Ry C
Blue city down / Elevation 13 foot / True believers/Marianne / Nice bike / Greenhouse / Billy and Annie / Pops and timer / Tell me something slick / Blue city / Don't take your guns to town / Leader of men / Not even key west
CD _____ 7599253862
WEA / Jan '96 / Warner Music.

BLUE COLLAR
Nitzsche, Jack
Nitzsche, Jack C
Hard workin' man: Captain Beefheart / Zeke, Jerry & Smokie / Satin sheets: Pruett, Jeanne / Party / Wang dang doodle / Coke machine / Quittin' time / Easy listening / F.B.I. / Goodbye so long: Turner, Ike & Tina / Saturday night: Lynyrd Skynyrd
CD _____ EDCD 435
Edsel / Aug '95 / Pinnacle / ADA.

BLUE HAWAII
Presley, Elvis
Blue Hawaii / Almost always true / Aloha oe / No more / Can't help falling in love / Rock-a-hula baby / Moonlight swim / Ku-u-i-po / Ito eats / Slicin' sand / Hawaiian sunset / Beach boy blues / Island of love / Hawaiian wedding song
CD _____ ND 83683
RCA / Oct '87 / BMG.

BLUE LAGOON, THE
Poledouris, Basil C
Poledouris, Basil Con
Blue lagoon (love theme) / Fire / Island / Sands of time / Paddy's death / Children grow / Lord of the lagoon / Underwater courtship / Kiss
CD _____ SCCD 1018
Southern Cross / Jun '88 / Silva Screen.

BLUE MAX, THE
Goldsmith, Jerry C
CD _____ CB 57890
CBS/Silva Screen / Apr '95 / Conifer / Silva Screen.

BLUE MAX, THE
Goldsmith, Jerry C
Dream machine / Sing song blues / Bad bad amigo / Hangman / Need your love / Flying to Moscow / Paid assassin / Camera camera / Photographing gold / Murder at the movies / I know you're there / Wait for the new one
CD _____ VCD 47238
Varese Sarabande/Colosseum / Jan '89 / Pinnacle / Silva Screen.

BLUE PLANET/THE DREAM IS ALIVE
Erbe, Micky C
Erbe, Micky Con
CD _____ CDC 1010
Silva Screen / Mar '92 / Conifer / Silva Screen.

BLUE VELVET
Badalamenti, Angelo C
Badalamenti, Angelo Con
Night streets/Sandy and Jeffrey / Frank Jeffrey's dark side / Mysteries of love (2 versions) / Frank returns / Blue velvet: Vinton, Bobby / Lumberton USA/Going down to Lincoln / Akron meets the blues / In dreams: Orbison, Roy / Honky tonk: Doggett, Bill / Love letters: Lester, Ketty / Mysteries of love / Blue star
CD _____ CDTER 1127
TER / May '87 / Koch.

BLUES BROTHERS, THE
Blues Brothers
Shake a tailfeather: Charles, Ray / Think: Franklin, Aretha / Minnie the moocher: Calloway, Cab / Rawhide / Jailhouse rock / She caught the Katy / Gimme some lovin' / Old landmark / Sweet home Chicago / Peter Gunn / Everybody needs somebody to love
CD _____ 7567827872
Atlantic / Nov '95 / Warner Music.

BLUES BROTHERS, THE
(A Tribute To The Blues Brothers)
1991 Cast
CD _____ CASTCD 25
First Night / '94 / Pinnacle.

BLUES IN THE FACE
CD _____ 9362460132
WEA / Jan '96 / Warner Music.

BLUES IN THE NIGHT
1987 London Cast
Epps, Sheldon C
CD _____ OCRCD 6029
First Night / Oct '95 / Pinnacle.

BOCCACCIO '70
Rota, Nino/Armando Trovaiolo/Piero Umiliani C
CD _____ OST 116
Milano Dischi / Jan '93 / Silva Screen.

BODIES, REST AND MOTION
Convertino, Michael C
CD _____ 9245062
Silva Screen / Jan '93 / Conifer / Silva Screen.

BODY BAGS
Carpenter, John & Jim Lang C
CD _____ VSD 5448
Varese Sarabande/Colosseum / Feb '94 / Pinnacle / Silva Screen.

BODY LOVE
Schulze, Klaus
Schulze, Klaus C
Stardancer / Blanche / P.T.O.
CD _____ CDTB 123
Thunderbolt / Jan '92 / Magnum Music Group.

BODY OF EVIDENCE
Revell, Graeme C
CD _____ 127202
Milan / Feb '94 / BMG / Silva Screen.

BODY PARTS
Dikker, Loek C
CD _____ VSD 5337
Varese Sarabande/Colosseum / Aug '91 / Pinnacle / Silva Screen.

BODY, THE
Waters, Roger & Ron Geesin
Our song / Seashell and soft stone / Red stuff writhe / Gentle breeze through life / Lick your partners / Bridge passage for three plastic teeth / Chain of life / Womb bit / Embryo thought / March past of the embryos / More than seven dwarfs in Penisland / Dance of the red corpuscles / Body transport / Hand dance - full evening dress / Breathe / Old folks ascension / Bedtime climb / Piddle in perspex / Embryonic womb walk / Mrs. Throat goes walking / Give birth to a smile
CD _____ CDFA 3299
Fame / '95 / EMI.

BODYGUARD, THE
I will always love you: Houston, Whitney / I have nothing: Houston, Whitney / I'm every woman: Houston, Whitney / Run to you: Houston, Whitney / Queen of the night: Houston, Whitney / Jesus loves me: Houston, Whitney / Even if my heart would break: Kenny G. & Aaron Neville / Someday (I'm coming back): Stansfield, Lisa / It's gonna be a lovely day: S.O.U.L. System & Michelle Visage / Peace, love and understanding: Stigers, Curtis / Waiting for you: Kenny G. / Trust in me: Cocker, Joe
CD _____ 07822186992
Arista / Jan '93 / BMG.

BODYWORK
Stilgoe, Richard C
CD _____ CASTCD 15
First Night / Oct '88 / Pinnacle.

BOLERO
Bernstein, Peter C
CD _____ PCD 124
Prometheus / Mar '93 / Pinnacle.

BONANZA
Bonanza Cast
Bonanza / Sourwood mountain / Sky ball paint / Early one morning / Ponderosa / Careless love / Skip to my Lou / In the pines / Happy birthday / My sons, my sons / Hangin' blues / Shenandoah / Miss Cindy / Hark the herald angels sing / Deck the halls with boughs of holly / New born King / First Christmas trees (story) / Oh fir tree dear / Christmas is a comin' / O come all ye faithful (Adeste Fidelis) / Jingle bells / Santa got lost in Texas / Stuck in the chimney / Why we light candles on the Christmas tree (story) / Merry Christmas neighbour / Merry Christmas and goodnight / Intro / Alamo: Greene, Lorne / Pony Express: Greene, Lorne / An ol' tin cup: Greene, Lorne / Endless prairie: Greene, Lorne / Ghost riders in the sky: Greene, Lorne / Ringo: Greene, Lorne / Blue guitar: Greene, Lorne / Sand: Greene, Lorne / Saga of the Ponderosa: Greene, Lorne / Five card stud: Greene, Lorne / Cool water: Greene, Lorne / Devil's grin: Greene, Lorne / Devil cat: Greene, Lorne / Ol' Chisholm trail: Greene, Lorne / Wagon wheels: Greene, Lorne / Frightened town: Greene, Lorne / Shadow of the cactus: Greene, Lorne / Tumbling tumbleweeds: Greene, Lorne / Gold: Greene, Lorne / Whoopee ti yi yo: Greene, Lorne / Search: Greene, Lorne / Dig, dig, dig, dig (there's no more water...): Greene, Lorne / Ol' cyclone: Greene, Lorne / Twilight on the trail: Greene, Lorne / Geronimo: Greene, Lorne / Mule train: Greene, Lorne / I'm a gun: Greene, Lorne / Gunslinger's prayer: Greene, Lorne / Nellie Cole: Greene, Lorne / Home on the range: Greene, Lorne / Virginia town: Greene, Lorne / Place where I

worship: *Greene, Lorne* / Pop goes the
hammer: *Greene, Lorne* / End of the track:
Greene, Lorne / Nine pound hammer:
Greene, Lorne / Bring on the dancin' girls:
Greene, Lorne / Oh what a town: *Greene,
Lorne* / Fourteen men: *Greene, Lorne* / Destiny: *Greene, Lorne* / Sixteen tons: *Greene,
Lorne* / Trouble now: *Greene, Lorne* / Chickasaw mountain: *Greene, Lorne* / Darling my
darling: *Greene, Lorne* / Man: *Greene,
Lorne* / Ringo (French): *Greene, Lorne* / Du
sable: *Greene, Lorne* / Bold soldier: *Roberts, Pernell* / Mary Ann: *Roberts, Pernell* /
They call the mind Maria: *Roberts, Pernell* /
Sylvie: *Roberts, Pernell* / Lily of the west:
Roberts, Pernell / Water is wide: *Roberts,
Pernell* / Rake and the rambling boy: *Roberts, Pernell* / Quiet girl: *Roberts, Pernell* /
Shady grove: *Roberts, Pernell* / Alberta:
Roberts, Pernell / Empty pocket blues:
Roberts, Pernell / Come all ye fair and
tender ladies: *Roberts, Pernell* / Springfield
mountain: *Blocker, Dan & John Mitchum* /
Roll out heave that cotton: *Blocker, Dan &
John Mitchum* / Battle hymn of the Republic: *Blocker, Dan & John Mitchum* / Erie canal: *Blocker, Dan & John Mitchum* / Paiute
sunrise chant: *Blocker, Dan & John Mitchum* / Charles, steal away: *Blocker, Dan &
John Mitchum* / He never said a mumblin':
Blocker, Dan & John Mitchum
4CD _____ BCD 15684
Bear Family / May '93 / Rollercoaster /
Direct / CM / Swift / ADA.

BONFIRE OF THE VANITIES, THE
Grusin, Dave *C*
CD _____ 821772
Silva Screen / Jan '92 / Conifer / Silva
Screen.

BOPHA
Horner, James *C*
CD _____ 9245352
Silva Screen / Jan '93 / Conifer / Silva
Screen.

BORGIAS
Delerue, Georges *C*
CD _____ PCD 109
Prometheus / Jan '93 / Silva Screen.

BOUND BY HONOUR
Rosenthal, Laurence *C*
Silva Screen / Jan '93 / Conifer / Silva
Screen.   HR 614782

BOURNE IDENTITY, THE
Rosenthal, Laurence *C*
Bourne identity (Main title) / French children
/ Fishing village / Arrival in Zurich / Attack
at the bank / Jason and Marie / Red door /
Discovery / Chernak dead / Valois bank /
Wild goose chase / Carlos as confessor /
Trocadero
CD _____ RVF 6005D
Intrada / Jan '90 / Silva Screen / Koch.

BOY WHO GREW TOO FAST, THE
1986 Royal Opera House Cast
Menotti, Gian Carlo *C*
CD _____ CDTER 1125
TER / Jan '93 / Koch.

BOYFRIEND, THE
1954 Broadway Cast
Wilson, Sandy *C*
Overture / Perfect young ladies / Boyfriend
/ Won't you Charleston with me / Fancy forgetting / I could be happy with you / Sur la
plage / Room in Bloomsbury / You-don't-want-to-play-with-me blues / Safety in
numbers / Riviera / It's never too late to fall
in love / Carnival tango / Poor little Pierrette
/ Finale
CD _____ GD 60056
RCA Victor / Oct '89 / BMG.

BOYFRIEND, THE
1984 London Cast
Wilson, Sandy *C*
Overture / Perfect young ladies / Boyfriend
/ Won't you Charleston with me / Fancy forgetting / I could be happy with you / Sur la
plage / Room in Bloomsbury / It's nicer in
Nice / You-don't-want-to-play-with-me
blues / Safety in numbers / Riviera / It's
never too late too fall in love / Poor little
Pierrette / Finale
CD _____ CDTER 1095
TER / Dec '84 / Koch.

**BOYFRIEND, THE/GOODBYE MR.
CHIPS**
Cast Recording
Wilson, Sandy *C*
Overture (The Boyfriend) / Perfect young ladies / I could be happy with you / Fancy
forgetting / Sur la plage / You are my lucky
star / It's never too late to fall in love / Won't
you Charleston with me / You-don't-want-to-play-with-me blues / Room in Blooms-
bury / It's nicer in Nice / All I do is dream
of you / Safety in numbers / Poor little Pier-
rette / Riviera/Finale / Overture (2) (Goodbye
Mr. Chips) / London is London: *Clark, Pe-
tula* / And the sky smiled: *Clark, Petula* /
When I am older / Walk through the world:
Clark, Petula / Schooldays: *Clark, Petula &
Boys* / When I was younger: *O'Toole, Peter
You and I: *Clark, Petula* Fill the world with
love: *O'Toole, Peter & Boys*
CD _____ CDMGM 20
MGM/EMI / Apr '90 / EMI.

BOYFRIEND, THE/ME AND MY GIRL
Cast Recording
Wilson, Sandy *C*
CD _____ 340802
Koch / Oct '95 / Koch.

BOYS FROM SYRACUSE, THE
1953 Studio Cast
Rodgers, Richard *C*
Engel, L. *Con*
CD _____ SK 53329
Sony Broadway / Nov '94 / Sony.

BOYS FROM SYRACUSE, THE
Off-Broadway Cast
Rodgers, Richard *C*
Hart, Lorenz *L*
CD _____ ZDM 7646952
EMI Classics / Apr '93 / EMI.

BOYS ON THE SIDE
You got it: *Raitt, Bonnie* / I take you with
me: *Etheridge, Melissa* / Keep on growing:
Crow, Sheryl / Power of two: *Indigo Girls* /
Somebody stand by me: *Nicks, Stevie* /
Everyday is like Sunday: *Pretenders* /
Dreams: *Cranberries* / Why: *Lennox, Anna-
trading, Joan* / Crossroads: *Mosser, Jonell*
CD _____ 07822187482
Arista / May '95 / BMG.

BOYZ N THE HOOD
How to survive in South Central: *Ice Cube*
/ Just ask me to: *Campbell, Tevin* / Mama
don't take no mess: *Yo Yo* / Growin' up in
the hood: *Compton's Most Wanted* / Just a
friendly game of baseball: *Main Source* / Me
and you: *Tony Toni Tone* / Work it out:
Love, Monie / Every single weekend: *Karn* /
Too young: *Hi-Five* / Hangin' out: *2 Live
Crew* / It's your life: *Too Short* / Spirit: *Force
One Network* / Setembro: *Jones, Quincy* /
Black on black crime
CD _____ 7599266432
WEA / Aug '91 / Warner Music.

BRADY BUNCH, THE
CD _____ 279322
Milan / Jun '95 / BMG / Silva Screen.

BRAINDEAD
CD _____ QDKCD 006
Normal/Okra / Sep '94 / Direct / ADA.

BRAZIL
Kamen, Michael *C*
CD _____ 111242
Milan / Feb '94 / BMG / Silva Screen.

BREAKFAST AT TIFFANY'S
Mancini, Henry *C*
Moon river / Something for cat / Sally's to-
mato / Mr. Yunioshi / Big blow-out / Hub
caps and tail lights / Breakfast at Tiffany's
/ Latin Golightly / Holly / Loose caboose /
Big heist / Moon river cha cha
CD _____ 23622
Silva Screen / Feb '90 / Conifer / Silva
Screen.

BREAKFAST CLUB, THE
Don't you forget about me: *Simple Minds* /
Fire in the twilight: *Wang Chung* / We are
not alone: *De Vito, Karla* / Heart too hot to
hold: *Johnson, Jesse* / Waiting: *Daly, Elizabeth* / Didn't I tell you: *Kennedy, Joyce* / I'm
the dude: *Forsey, Keith* / Dream montage:
Forsey, Keith / Reggae: *Forsey, Keith* / Love
theme: *Forsey, Keith*
CD _____ CDMID 179
A&M / Jan '94 / PolyGram.

BREAKING GLASS
O'Connor, Hazel
Writing on the wall / Monsters in disguise /
Come into the air / Big brother / Who needs
it / Will you / Eighth day / Top of the wheel
/ Calls the tune / Blackman / Give me an
inch / If only
CD _____ 5513562
Spectrum/Karussell / Sep '95 / PolyGram /
THE.

BREAKING THE RULES
CD _____ VSD 5386
Varese Sarabande/Colosseum / Sep '92 /
Pinnacle / Silva Screen.

BRIDE OF FRANKENSTEIN, THE
Westminster Philharmonic Orchestra
Waxman, Franz *C*
Alwyn, Kenneth *Con*
Main title / Prologue - Menuetto and storm
/ Monster entrance / Processional march /
Strange aggregation/Pretorius' entrance/You
will need a coat / Bottle sequence / Female
monster music/Pastorale/Village/Chase /
Crucifixion/Monster breaks out / Fire in the
hut/Graveyard / Dance macabre / Creation
/ Tower explodes/Finale / Invisible ray suite
CD _____ FILMCD 135
Silva Screen / Mar '94 / Conifer / Silva
Screen.

BRIDES OF CHRIST, THE
Millo, Mario *C*
CD _____ A 8936
Alhambra / Feb '92 / Silva Screen.

BRIDESHEAD REVISITED
Burgon, Geoffrey *C*
Brideshead revisited / Going to Brideshead
/ First visit / Venice nocturne / Sebastian's
summer / Hunt / Sebastian against the
world / Julia in love / Julia / Rain in Venice
/ General strike / Fading light / Julia's theme

/ Sebastian alone / Orphans of the storm /
Finale
CD _____ CDMFP 6172
Music For Pleasure / Sep '95 / EMI.

BRIDGE, THE
Mitchell, Richard G. *C*
Opening titles (Painting) / Quay house / Arriving in Suffolk / Storm / Reginald and Isobel return to London / Sitting / Walberswick
fete / Fireworks / France / Kiss / Love theme
(I only have one subject now) / Reginald's
proposition / Mrs. Todd's release / What did
you see Emma / Garden / Leaving without
saying goodbye / We've come to an
arrangement / End titles (Steer's theme)
CD _____ DSCD 5
Demon / Feb '92 / Pinnacle / ADA.

BRIGADOON
1988 London Cast
Loewe, Frederick *C*
Lerner, Alan Jay *L*
CD _____ OCRCD 6018
First Night / Oct '95 / Pinnacle.

BRIGADOON
Studio Cast & Ambrosian Chorus/London
Sinfonietta
Loewe, Frederick *C*
Lerner, Alan Jay *L*
McGlinn, John *Con*
CD _____ CDC 7544812
EMI Classics / Apr '93 / EMI.

BRIGADOON
Cast Recording
Loewe, Frederick *C*
Lerner, Alan Jay *L*
2CD _____ CDTER2 1218
TER / Aug '95 / Koch.

BRIGHT ANGEL
Utah Symphony Orchestra
Intrada / Mar '92 / Silva Screen / Koch.
MAF 7014D

BRONX TALE, A
Streets of the bronx: *Cool Change* / I won-
der why: *Dion & The Belmonts* / Little girl of
mine: *Cleftones* / Don't you know: *Reese,
Della* / For your precious love: *Butler, Jerry*
/ Ain't that a kick in the head: *Cool Change*
/ Father and son: *Cool Change* / Beautiful
morning: *Rascals* / Tell it like it is: *Neville,
Aaron* / Bus talk: *Watson, Bobby* / I only
have eyes for you: *Niewood, Gerry Quartet*
/ Ninety nine and a half (won't do): *Pickett,
Wilson* / Nights in white satin: *Moody Blues*
/ Baby I need your loving: *Four Tops* / Re-
grets: *Barbella, Butch* / All along the watch-
tower: *Hendrix, Jimi Experience* / I'm so
proud: *Impressions* / It's a man's man's
man's world: *Brown, James* / Christo redemptor: *Byrd, Donald*
CD _____ 474806 2
Epic / Mar '94 / Sony.

BROTHERS MCMULLEN, THE
CD _____ 7822188032
RCA / Dec '95 / BMG.

BROWNING VERSION, THE
Isham, Mark *C*
CD _____ 213012
Milan / Oct '94 / BMG / Silva Screen.

BUBBLING BROWN SUGAR
1977 London Cast
Harlem '70 / Bubbling Brown Sugar / That's
what Harlem is to me: *Delmar, Elaine* / Bill
Robinson speciality: *Augins, Charles* / Harlem sweet Harlem / Nobody: *Daniels, Billy* /
Goin' back in time: *Augins, Charles* / Some
of these days: *Lawrence, Stephanie* / Moving Uptown: *Augins, Charles* / Strolling:
Cameron, David & others / I'm gonna tell
God all my troubles: *Taylor, Mel* / His eye is
on the sparrow/Swing low sweet chariot
(medley): *Brown, Miquel & Company* /
Sweet Georgia Brown: *Gelzer, Helen/New-
ton Winters/David Cameron* / Honeysuckle
Rose: *Delmar, Elaine/Billy Daniels* / Stormy
Monday blues: *Brown, Miquel* / Sophisticated lady: *Peters, Clarke* / In honeysuckle
time, when Emaline said she'd be mine:
Satton, Lon/Billy Daniels / Rosetta: *Collins,
Ray/David Cameron/Newton Winters* / Solitude: *Gelzer, Helen/Newton Winters/Ray
Collins/David Cameron* / C'mon up to Jive
Time: *Augins, Charles* / Stompin' at the Sa-
voy/Take the 'A' train / Harlem-time: *Au-
gins, Charles* / Bubbling Brown Sugar II: *Pe-
ters, Clarke/Amii Stewart* / Ain't
misbehavin': *Daniels, Billy* / Pray for the
lights to go out: *Satton, Lon* / I got it bad:
Stewart, Amii / Harlem makes me feel:
Sharpe, Bernard / Jim, jam, jumpin' jive: *Au-
gins, Charles/Newton Winters/Ray Collins* /
There'll be some changes made: *Delmar,
Elaine* / Memories of you: *Daniels, Billy* /
God bless the child: *Peters, Helen* / It don't
mean a thing: *Peters, Clarke & Company* /
Bubbling Brown Sugar (reprise)
2CD _____ CDSBL 13106
DRG / Oct '92 / New Note.

BUBBLING BROWN SUGAR
Broadway Cast
CD _____ AMH 93310
Silva Screen / Jan '89 / Conifer / Silva
Screen.

BUCCANEER, THE
Bernstein, Elmer *C*
CD _____ VSD 5214
Varese Sarabande/Colosseum / Feb '90 /
Pinnacle / Silva Screen.

BUCCANEERS, THE
London Filmworks Orchestra
Towns, Colin *C*
Towns, Colin *Con*
Allfriars / Lov'd I not / Buccaneers / Nun
and Julius / Trevenick ruins / Newport New
Jersey / Birth of an heir / Waltz of a lost
room / Capture (Christmas) / This is Miss
Annabelle / Love theme / Turn out like you
/ Runnymede / Nothing to love for / Willows
whiten / Card games and summer lawns /
Correggio room / Visitors / Lov'd I not #2
CD _____ 5268662
Mercury / Mar '95 / PolyGram.

BUDDHA OF SUBURBIA, THE
Bowie, David
Bowie, David *C*
Buddha of Suburbia / Sex and the church /
South horizon / Mysteries / Bleed like a
craze, Dad / Strangers when we meet /
Dead against it / Untitled No.1 / Ian Fish,
UK heir
CD _____ 74321170042
Arista / Nov '93 / BMG.

BUDDY
London Cast
Holly, Buddy *C*
CD _____ QUEUE CD1
First Night / Jan '90 / Pinnacle.

BULL DURHAM
CD _____ 905864
Silva Screen / Jan '93 / Conifer / Silva
Screen.

**BURNING SECRET/FRUIT MACHINE/
DIAMOND SKULLS**
Zimmer, Hans *C*
CD _____ CDCH 530
Silva Screen / Feb '90 / BMG / Silva Screen.

BUSTER
Two hearts: *Collins, Phil* / Just one look:
Hollies / Big noise: *Collins, Phil* / Robbery:
Dudley, Anne / I got you babe: *Sonny &
Cher* / Keep on running (Not on CD): *Davis,
Spencer Group* / Loco in Acapulco: *Four
Tops* / How do you do it: *Gerry & The Pace-
makers* / I just don't know what to do with
myself: *Springfield, Dusty* / Sweets for my
sweet: *Searchers* / Will you still be waiting:
Dudley, Anne / Groovy kind of love: *Collins,
Phil*
CD _____ CDV 2544
Virgin / Apr '92 / EMI.

**BUTCH CASSIDY AND THE SUNDANCE
KID**
Bacharach, Burt *C*
Sundance kid: *Bacharach, Burt* / Raindrops
keep fallin' on my head: *Bacharach, Burt* /
Not goin' home anymore: *Bacharach, Burt*
/ South American getaway: *Bacharach, Burt*
/ Old fun city: *Bacharach, Burt* / Come
touch the sun: *Bacharach, Burt* / On a bi-
cycle built for joy: *Bacharach, Burt*
CD _____ 5514332
Spectrum/Karussell / Aug '95 / PolyGram /
THE.

BUTTERFLY
Morricone, Ennio *C*
CD _____ PCD 108
Prometheus / Jan '93 / Silva Screen.

BY THE BEAUTIFUL SEA
Broadway Cast
CD _____ ZDM 7648892
EMI Classics / Apr '93 / EMI.

BYE BYE BIRDIE
1960 Broadway Cast
Strouse, Charles *C*
Adams, Lee *L*
CD _____ CK 02025
CBS/Silva Screen / Feb '90 / Conifer / Silva
Screen.

BYE BYE BIRDIE
Film Cast
Strouse, Charles *C*
Adams, Lee *L*
CD _____ 10812
Silva Screen / Jan '89 / Conifer / Silva
Screen.

CABARET
Film Cast
Kander, John *C*
Ebb, Fred *L*
Wilkommen / Mein herr / Two ladies /
Maybe this time / Sitting pretty / Tiller girls
/ Money, money / Heiraten / If you could
see her / Tomorrow belongs to me / Cab-
aret / Finale
CD _____ MCLD 19088
MCA / Jun '92 / BMG.

CABARET
1986 London Cast
Kander, John *C*
Ebb, Fred *L*
Wilkommen / So what / Don't tell mama /
Perfectly marvellous / Two ladies / It

CABARET
couldn't please me more / Why should I wake up / Money, money, money / Married / Meeskite / Tomorrow belongs to me / If you could see her / Maybe this time / What would you do / Cabaret / Auf wiedersehen (Finale)
CD _____ OCRCD 6010
First Night / Mar '93 / Pinnacle.

CABARET (Highlights)
Cast Recording
Kander, John C
Ebb, Fred L
Wilkommen / Don't tell Mama / Telephone song / Perfectly marvellous / Two ladies / Tomorrow belongs to me / Why should I wake up / Maybe this time / Sitting pretty / Money, money / If you could see her / Cabaret
CD _____ SHOWCD 021
Showtime / Feb '95 / Disc / THE.

CABARET
Cast Recording
Kander, John C
Ebb, Fred L
2CD _____ CDTER2 1210
TER / Aug '95 / Koch.

CABIN IN THE SKY
Duke, Vernon C
Latouche, John L
CD _____ 873108
Milan / Jun '92 / BMG / Silva Screen.

CABIN IN THE SKY
Broadway Cast
Duke, Vernon C
Latouche, John L
CD _____ ZDM 7648932
EMI Classics / Aug '93 / EMI.

CADDYSHACK II
CD _____ CK 44317
CBS/Silva Screen / Jan '89 / Conifer / Silva Screen.

CALAMITY JANE
Cast Recording
Fain, Sammy C
Webster, Paul Francis L
CD _____ CDTER 1215
TER / Aug '95 / Koch.

CALAMITY JANE/PYJAMA GAME
Deadwood stage / I can do without you / Black hills of Dakota / Just blew in from the Windy City / Woman's touch / Higher than a hawk (deeper than a well) / 'Tis Harry I'm planning to marry / Secret love / Pajama game / And racing with the clock / I'm not at all in love / I'll never be jealous again / Once a year day / Small talk / There once was a man / Hernando's hideaway / Finale
CD _____ 4676102
CBS / Dec '90 / Sony.

CALIFORNIA DREAMS
This time / Castles on quicksand / Everybody's got someone / It's gonna be rain / Let me be the one / If only you knew / One world / If you lean on me / If it wasn't for you / Love is not like this / Heart don't lie / California dreams theme
CD _____ MCLD 19301
MCA / Oct '95 / BMG.

CALL ME MADAM
Revival Cast
Berlin, Irving C
CD _____ DRGCD 94761
DRG / Jun '95 / New Note.

CAMELOT
Film Cast
Loewe, Frederick C
Lerner, Alan Jay L
Overture / I wonder what the king is doing tonight / Simple joys of maidenhood / Camelot and the wedding ceremony / C'est moi / Lusty month of May / Follow me / How to handle a woman / Take me to the fair / If ever I would leave you / What do the simple folk do / I loved you once in silence / Guenevere / Finale
CD _____ 7599273252
Warner Bros. / Mar '94 / Warner Music.

CAMELOT
1982 London Cast
Loewe, Frederick C
Lerner, Alan Jay L
Overture / I wonder what the king is doing tonight / Simple joys of maidenhood / I wonder what the king is doing tonight / C'est moi / Follow me / Joust / Lusty month of May / Resolution / Then you may take me to the fair / How to handle a woman / Entracle madrigal / Before I gaze at you again / If ever I would leave you
CD _____ CDTER 1030
TER / Mar '89 / Koch.

CAMELOT (Highlights)
1982 London Cast
Loewe, Frederick C
Lerner, Alan Jay L
Overture / I wonder what the king is doing tonight / Simple joys of maidenhood / Camelot / Follow me / C'est moi / Lusty month of May / How to handle a woman / Before I gaze at you again / If ever I would leave you / I loved you once in silence
CD _____ SHOWCD 013
Showtime / Feb '95 / Disc / THE.

CAMELOT/MY FAIR LADY
Cast Recording
Loewe, Frederick C
Lerner, Alan Jay L
CD _____ 340792
Koch / Oct '95 / Koch.

CAMILLE CLAUDEL
Yared, Gabriel C
CD _____ 30673
Silva Screen / Jan '93 / Conifer / Silva Screen.

CAN-CAN
1953 Broadway Cast
Porter, Cole C
CD _____ ZDM 7646642
EMI Classics / Apr '93 / EMI.

CANDIDE
1988 Scottish Opera
Bernstein, Leonard C
Wilbur, Richard L
CD _____ CDTER 1156
TER / Jul '88 / Koch.

CANDIDE
1956 Broadway Cast
Bernstein, Leonard C
Wilbur, Richard L
Overture / Best of all possible worlds / What's the use / It must be so / Glitter and be gay / Oh happy me / Mazurka / You were dead you know / My love / I am easily assimilated / Eldorado / Quiet / Bon Voyage / Gavotte / Make our garden grow
CD _____ SK 48017
Sony Broadway / Dec '91 / Sony.

CANDIDE
1982 New York Opera Cast
Bernstein, Leonard C
Wilbur, Richard L
Fanfare/Life is happiness indeed / Best of all possible worlds / Happy instrumental/Oh happy we / Candide begins his travels / It must be so (Candide's meditation) / Westphalian fanfare/Chorale/Battle music / Entrance of the Jew / Glitter and be gay / Earthquake music/Dear boy / Auto da fe / Candide's lament / You were dead you know / Travel/(to the stables)/I am easily assimilated / Quartet finale / Entr'acte / Ballad of the new world / My love / Barcarolle / Alleluia / Eldorado / Sheep song / Governor's waltz / Bon voyage / Quiet / Constantinople/What's the use / Finale: Make our garden grow
CD _____ NWCD 3401
New World / Oct '86 / New World.

CANDIDE
Hadley, Jerry & June Anderson/London Symphony Orchestra/Chorus
Bernstein, Leonard C
Wilbur, Richard L
Bernstein, Leonard Con
2CD _____ 4297342
Deutsche Grammophon / Aug '91 / PolyGram.

CANDIDE (Highlights)
1988 Scottish Opera
Bernstein, Leonard C
Wilbur, Richard L
CD _____ CDTEO 1006
TER / Jul '88 / Koch.

CANICULE (DOG DAY)
Lai, Francis C
CD _____ MANTRA 056
Silva Screen / Jan '94 / Conifer / Silva Screen.

CANNONBALL FEVER
Wheatley, David C
CD _____ CST 348042
Varese Sarabande/Colosseum / Feb '90 / Pinnacle / Silva Screen.

CAPITAL CITY
Towns, Colin C
CD _____ SCENECD 8
First Night / '94 / Pinnacle.

CAPTAIN FROM CASTILE
Newman, Alfred C
CD _____ FCD 8103
Fantasy / Mar '84 / Pinnacle / Jazz Music / Wellard / Cadillac.

CAPTIVE
Edge
Edge C
Rowena's theme / Heroine (featuring Sinead O'Connor) / One foot in heaven / Strange party / Hiro's theme / Drift / Dream theme / Djinn / Island / Hiro's theme 2
CD _____ CDV 2401
Virgin / Sep '86 / EMI.

CARAVAGGIO 1610
Fisher-Turner, Simon
Fisher-Turner, Simon C
Hills of Abruzzi / Dog star / All paths lead to Rome / Fantasia, childhood memories / How blue sky was / Light and dark / From Missa Lux Et Orrigo / Umber wastes / Cafe of the moors / Timeout and mind / In the still of the night / Michele of the shadows / Waters of forgetfulness / Running running / Frescobaldi, the greatest organist of our time / Hourglass / I love you more than my eyes
CD _____ DSCD 10
Demon / Jul '95 / Pinnacle / ADA.

CARD, THE
1994 London Cast
Hatch, Tony C
Trent, Jackie L
CD _____ CASTCD 45
First Night / Sep '94 / Pinnacle.

CARDINAL, THE
Moross, Jerome C
Stonebury / Dixieland / Tango / Cardinal's faith / They haven't got the girls in the USA / Cardinal in Vienna / Anne-Marie / Cardinal's decision / Way down South / Cardinal themes
CD _____ PRCD 1778
Preamble / Jan '94 / Silva Screen.

CARLITO'S WAY
I love music: Rozalla / Rock the boat: Hues Corporation / Rock your baby: Terry, Ed / Perece mentira: Anthony, Mark / Backstabbers: O'Jays / Sound of Philadelphia: MFSB / Got to be real: Lynn, Cheryl / Lady Marmalade: Labelle / Pillow talk: Sinoa / El watusi: Barretto, Ray / Oye como va: Santana / You are so beautiful: Preston, Billy
CD _____ 474994 2
Columbia / Jan '94 / Sony.

CARLITO'S WAY (Score)
Doyle, Patrick C
CD _____ VSD 5463
Varese Sarabande/Colosseum / Jan '94 / Pinnacle / Silva Screen.

CARMEN JONES
1954 Film Cast
Bizet, Georges C
Hammerstein II, Oscar L
Overture / Opening medley / Dat's love (Habanera) / You talk jus' like my maw / Dere's a cafe on de corner / Dis flower / Beat out that rhythm on a drum / Stan' up an' fight / Whizzin' away along de track / Card song / My Joe / Duet and finale
CD _____ GD 81881
RCA Victor / Nov '92 / BMG.

CARMEN JONES
London Cast
Bizet, Georges C
Hammerstein II, Oscar L
Lewis, Henry Con
CD _____ CDC 7543512
EMI Classics / Apr '93 / EMI.

CARNIVAL
1961 Broadway Cast
Kaper, Bronislaw C
CD _____ 8371952
Silva Screen / Feb '90 / Conifer / Silva Screen.

CAROUSEL
Film Cast
Rodgers, Richard C
Hammerstein II, Oscar L
Carousel waltz / You're a queer one Julie Jordan / Mr. Snow / If I loved you / When the children are asleep / June is bustin' out all over / Soliloquy / Blow high, blow low / Real nice clambake / Stonecutters cut it on stone / What's the use of wonderin' / You'll never walk alone
CD _____ ZDM 7646922
EMI Classics / Apr '93 / EMI.

CAROUSEL
1993 London Cast
Rodgers, Richard C
Hammerstein II, Oscar L
CD _____ CASTCD 40
First Night / Oct '93 / Pinnacle.

CAROUSEL
1945 Broadway Cast
Rodgers, Richard C
Hammerstein II, Oscar L
Carousel waltz / You're a queer one Julie Jordan / Mr. Snow / If I loved you / Soliloquy / June is bustin' out all over / When the children are asleep / Blow high, blow low / Real nice clambake / There's nothin' so bad for a woman / What's the use of wonderin' / Highest judge of all / You'll never walk alone
CD _____ MCLD 19152
MCA / Jul '92 / BMG.

CAROUSEL (Highlights - The Shows Collection)
Cast Recording
Rodgers, Richard C
Hammerstein II, Oscar L
If I loved you / You're a queer one Julie Jordan / Mr. Snow / June is bustin' out all over / Soliloquy / Blow high, blow low / Real nice clambake / Stonecutters cut it on stone / What's the use of wonderin' / Highest judge of all / You'll never walk alone
CD _____ PWKS 4144
Carlton Home Entertainment / Oct '93 / Carlton Home Entertainment.

CARRIE/DRESSED TO KILL/BODY DOUBLE
Donaggio, Pino C
CD _____ CDCH 384
Milan / Mar '90 / BMG / Silva Screen.

CARTOUCHE
Delerue, Georges C
CD _____ PCD 104
Prometheus / Feb '90 / Silva Screen.

CASINO ROYALE
Bacharach, Burt C
Casino Royale theme: Alpert, Herb / Money penny goes for broke / Home James and don't spare the horses / Look of love / Little French boy / Venerable Sir James Bond / Big cowboys and indians / Le chiffre's torture of ... / Sir James' trip to find ... / Hi there Miss Good Thighs / Flying saucer / Dream on James
CD _____ VSD 5265
Varese Sarabande/Colosseum / Nov '90 / Pinnacle / Silva Screen.

CASABLANCO
Goldsmith, Jerry C
CD _____ PCD 127
Prometheus / Jan '94 / Silva Screen.

CASPER (Score)
Horner, James C
Horner, James Con
CD _____ MCD 11240
MCA / Jul '95 / BMG.

CASPER
Casper / Daddy never understood / Nothing gonna stop / Jenny's theme / Simean groove / Casper the friendly ghost / Natural one / Spoiled / Crash / Wet stuff / Mad fright night / Raise the bell / Good morning Casper
CD _____ 8286402
London / Sep '95 / PolyGram.

CASSANDRA CROSSING
Goldsmith, Jerry C
CD _____ OST 102
Milano Dischi / Jan '93 / Silva Screen.

CAT PEOPLE
Moroder, Giorgio C
Cat people (putting out fires): Bowie, David & Giorgio Moroder / Autopsy / Irena's theme / Night rabbit / Leopard tree dream / Paul's theme / Myth / To the bridge / Transformation seduction / Bring the prod
CD _____ MCLD 19302
MCA / Oct '95 / BMG.

CATCH ME IF YOU CAN
Tangerine Dream
Tangerine Dream C
CD _____ CIN 22132
Silva Screen / May '94 / Conifer / Silva Screen.

CATS
1981 London Cast
Lloyd Webber, Andrew C
Eliot, T.S./Trevor Nunn/Richard Stilgoe L
Jellicle songs for jellicle cats / Old gumbie cat / Naming of cats / Rum tum tugger / Grizabella / Bustopher Jones / Memory / Mungojerrie and Rumpleteazer / Old Deuteronomy / Moments of happiness / Gus the theatre cat / Overture/Prologue / Invitation to the Jellicle ball / Jellicle ball / Journey to the heavy side / Ad - dressing of cats / Growltiger's last stand / Ballad of Billy McCaw's Skimbleshanks / Macavity / Mr. Mistofelees
2CD _____ 8178102
Really Useful / Jun '84 / PolyGram.

CATS (Highlights)
1981 London Cast
Lloyd Webber, Andrew C
Eliot, T.S./Trevor Nunn/Richard Stilgoe L
Prologue: Jellicle songs for jellicle cats / Solo dance / Old gumbie cat / Rum tum tugger / Mungojerrie and rumpelteazer / Old deuteronomy / Jellicle ball / Grizabella the glamour cat / Gus the theatre cat / Shimbleshanks: The railway cat / Macavity / Mr. Mistoffelees / Memory / Journey to the heaviside layer / Ad - dressing of cats
CD _____ 8394152
Really Useful / Aug '88 / PolyGram.

CB4
Thirteenth message: Public Enemy / Livin' in a zoo: Public Enemy / Black cop: Boogie Down Productions / May Day on the front line: M.C. Ren / Stick em up: Hurricane & Beastie Boys / Lifeline: Parental Advisory / Nocturnal is in the house: P.M. Dawn / Baby be mine: Blackstreet & Teddy Riley / It's allright: Spencer, Tracie / Straight out of Locash: CB4 / Rapper's delight: CB4 / Sweat of my balls: CB4 / Creepin' up on ya: Fu-Schnickens
CD _____ MCD 10758
MCA / Apr '93 / BMG.

CEMETERY CLUB, THE
Bernstein, Elmer C
CD _____ VSD 5412
Varese Sarabande/Colosseum / Mar '93 / Pinnacle / Silva Screen.

CHALLENGE, THE
London Cast
2CD _____ CDTER 1201
TER / Aug '93 / Koch.

CHAPLIN
Barry, John C
Barry, John Con
Main theme / Early days in London/Honeysuckle and the Bee / Charlie proposes / To California/The cutting room / Discovering the tramp/The wedding chase / Chaplin's studio opening / Salt Lake City episode / Roll dance / News of Hetty's death / Smile / From London to L.A / John Barry trouble/

Oona arrives / Remembering Hetty / Roll dance (reprise)
CD _____ 472602 2
Epic / Dec '92 / Sony.

CHAPLIN PUZZLE, THE
Czech Symphony Orchestra
Hyldgaard, Soren C
Bremner, Tony Con
Main title / Clergyman and the drunk / Flophouse / Kitchen waltz (Edna's theme) / Since my father died (Mabel's theme)/Pillow fight / Putting the drunk to sleep / Burglar / Robbed - by an old friend / Dinner is served / He's my husband / Cops/Music hall / Finale - The tramp / Finale
CD _____ FILMCD 128
Silva Screen / Jan '93 / Conifer / Silva Screen.

CHARADE
Mancini, Henry C
CD _____ 27552
Silva Screen / Jan '89 / Conifer / Silva Screen.

CHARLIE CHALK
CD _____ CDHARL 1
Redrock / Aug '89 / THE / Target/BMG.

CHARLIE GIRL
1986 London Cast
Heneker, David & John Taylor C
McMillan, I. Con
Overture / Most ancestral home of all / Bells will ring / I love him, I love him / What would I get from being married / Let's do a deal / My favourite occupation / What's the magic / When I hear music I dance / I 'ates money / Charlie Girl waltz / Party of a lifetime / Like love / That's it / Washington / Fish and chips / Society twist / You never know what you can do / Finale
CD _____ OCRCD 6009
First Night / Jan '96 / Pinnacle.

CHARLIE GIRL
1965 London Cast
Heneker, David & John Taylor C
Alwyn, Kenneth Con
CD _____ SMK 66174
Sony West End / Nov '92 / Sony.

CHARLOTTE SWEET
Cast Recording
At the music hall / Forever / Liverpool sunset / Layers of underwear / Quartet agonistes / Circus of voices / Keep it low / Bubbles in me bonnet / Vegetable Reggie / My baby and me / A-weaving / Your high note / Kantika / Darkness / You see me in a bobby / Christmas buche / Letter / Volley of indecision/Good things come / It could only happen in the theatre / Lonely canary / Queenly comments / Farewell to auld lang syne/Finale
CD _____ DRGCD 6300
DRG / Jan '95 / New Note.

CHASE, THE
Barry, John C
CD _____ VSD 5229
Varese Sarabande/Colosseum / Feb '90 / Pinnacle / Silva Screen.

CHESS
1984 London Cast
Ulvaeus, Bjorn & Benny Andersson C
Rice, Tim L
Merano / Russian and Molokov / Where I want to be / Opening ceremony / Quartet (A model of decorum and tranquility) / American and Florence / Nobody's side / Chess / Mountain duet / Florence quits / Embassy lament / Anthem / Bangkok / One night in Bangkok / Heaven help my heart / Argument / I know him so well / Deal (no deal) / Pity the child / Endgame / Epilogue - You and I / Story of Chess
2CD _____ PD 70500
RCA / Nov '84 / BMG.

CHEYENNE AUTUMN
North, Alex C
Indians arrive / Friend Deborah / School house / Archer / Rejection / truth / Entr'acte / River crossing / Sick girl / Battle / Dodge city / Old chief / Lead our people home / Death
CD _____ LXCD 2
Silva Screen / Jun '88 / Conifer / Silva Screen.

CHILDREN OF A LESSER GOD
Convertino, Michael C
Silence and sound / Sarah sleeping / Rain pool / Underwater love / On the ferry / James and Sarah / Goodnight / Boomerang
CD _____ GNPD 8007
GNP Crescendo / Jan '89 / Silva Screen.

CHILDREN OF EDEN
Cast Recording
Schwartz, Stephen C
Let there be: Page, Ken & Company / Naming: Smith, Martin & Shezwae Powell / Spark of creation: Powell, Shezwae / In pursuit of excellence: Lloyd King, Richard & snake / World without you: Smith, Martin / Wasteland / Lost in the wilderness / Close to home / Children of Eden: Powell, Shezwae & Company / Generations: Shell, Ray Company / Civilised society: Colson, Kevin & Company / Shipshape / Return of the animals / Stranger in the house: Ruffelle, Frances / In whatever time we have: Barclay, Anthony & Frances Ruffelle / Degen-

erations: Page, Ken / Dove song: Ruffelle, Frances / Hardest part of love: Colson, Kevin / Ain't it good: Dubois, Jacqui & Company / In the beginning
CD _____ 8282342
London / Apr '91 / PolyGram.

CHILDREN OF NATURE
Hilmarsson, Hilmar Orn
Hilmarsson, Hilmar Orn C
Touch / Oct '95 / These / Kudos.

CHILDREN'S THIEF, THE/ON MY OWN
Piersanti, Franco C
CD _____ OST 117
Milano Dischi / Jul '93 / Silva Screen.

CHILD'S PLAY
Renzetti, Joe C
CD _____ CDCH 382
Milan / Feb '90 / BMG / Silva Screen.

CHILLER
Cincinnati Pops Orchestra
Kunzel, Erich C
CD _____ CD 80189
Telarc / Aug '90 / Conifer / ADA.

CHINA 9 LIBERTY 37
Donaggio, Pino C
CD _____ PCD 117
Prometheus / Jan '93 / Silva Screen.

CHINATOWN
Goldsmith, Jerry C
CD _____ VSD 5677
Varese Sarabande/Colosseum / Feb '96 / Pinnacle / Silva Screen.

CHORUS LINE, A
1975 Broadway Cast
Hamlisch, Marvin C
Kleban, Edward L
I hope I get it / I can do that / At the ballet / Sing / Hello twelve, hello thirteen, hello love / Nothing / Music and the mirror / Dance:Ten looks three / One / What I did for love / One (Reprise) / Chorus line (finale)
CD _____ CK 33581
CBS/Silva Screen / Jan '89 / Conifer / Silva Screen.

CHRISTINE
(Score)
Carpenter, John C
CD _____ VSD 5240
Varese Sarabande/Colosseum / Jan '90 / Pinnacle / Silva Screen.

CHRISTOPHER COLUMBUS
(The Discovery)
Eidelman, Cliff C
CD _____ VSD 5389
Varese Sarabande/Colosseum / Sep '92 / Pinnacle / Silva Screen.

CHU CHIN CHOW
1959 London Cast
Norton, Frederic C
Asche, Oscar L
Prelude: Orchestra / Here be oysters stewed in honey: Te Wiata, Inia / I am Chu Chin Chow: Te Wiata, Inia / Cleopatra's Nile: Bryan, Julie / When a pullet is plump: Te Wiata, Inia / Serenade: Mahbubah: Chorus / I'll sing and dance / I long for the sun: Leigh, Barbara / Robber's chorus: Te Wiata, Inia / I love thee so: Bryan, Julie / Behold: Te Wiata, Inia / Anytime's kissing time: Bryan, Julie & Inia Te Wiata / Cobbler's song: Te Wiata, Inia / I built a fairy palace in the sky: Connors, Ursula / We bring ye fruits: Williams Singers / Finale: Chorus
CD _____ CDANGEL 5
Angel / Apr '94 / EMI.

CHULAS FRONTERAS/DEL MERO CORAZON
CD _____ ARHCD 425
Arhoolie / Sep '95 / ADA / Direct / Cadillac.

CINDERELLA
1957 TV Musical Cast
Rodgers, Richard C
Hammerstein II, Oscar L
CD _____ CK 02005
CBS/Silva Screen / Jan '89 / Conifer / Silva Screen.

CINEMA PARADISO
Morricone, Ennio C
CD _____ DRGCD 12598
DRG / Jul '93 / New Note.

CIRCLE OF FRIENDS
CD _____ 0630109572
East West / Jun '95 / Warner Music.

CITIZEN KANE
Australian Philharmonic Orchestra
Herrmann, Bernard C
Bremner, Tony Con
CD _____ PRCD 1788
Preamble / Jul '93 / Silva Screen.

CITIZEN X
Edelman, Randy C
CD _____ VSD 5601
Varese Sarabande/Colosseum / Mar '95 / Pinnacle / Silva Screen.

CITY LIGHTS
City Lights Orchestra
Chaplin, Charlie C
Davis, Carl Con
Overture/Unveiling the statue / Flower girl (Violetera) / Evening/Meeting the millionaire

/ At the millionaire's home / Nightclub (Dance suite)/ Limousine / Sober dawn / Party and the morning after / Eviction/The road sweeper/At the girl's home / Boxing match / Burglars / Reunited
CD _____ FILMCD 078
Silva Screen / Jan '93 / Conifer / Silva Screen.

CITY OF ANGELS
1993 London Cast
Coleman, Cy C
Zippel, David L
Blakemore, M. Con
Prelude (theme from City Of Angels) / Double talk / What you don't know about women / Ya gotta look after yourself / Buddy system / With every breath I take / Tennis song / Everybody's gotta be somewhere / Lost and found / All ya have to do is wait / You're nothing without me / Stay with me / You can always count on me / It needs work / With every breath I take (Reprise) / Funny
CD _____ CAST CD34
First Night / Jul '93 / Pinnacle.

CITY OF JOY
Morricone, Ennio C
CD _____ ACCD 1025
Audiorec / Nov '92 / Audiorec.

CITY OF LOST CHILDREN, THE
CD _____ 0630102512
East West / Nov '95 / Warner Music.

CITY OF VIOLENCE (CITTA VIOLENTA) (& Svegliati E Uccidi)
Morricone, Ennio C
CD _____ OST 127
Milano Dischi / May '95 / Silva Screen.

CITY SLICKERS
Shaiman, Marc C
CD _____ VSD 5321
Varese Sarabande/Colosseum / Sep '91 / Pinnacle / Silva Screen.

CITY SLICKERS II (The Legend Of Curly's Gold)
Shaiman, Marc C
Kane, A. Con
Mitch's dream / Main title / Found / One smile / Discovering the map / On brother / Gold diggers of 1994 / Map is real...and on fire / On the trail / Real men / Let's get that gold / Duke saves the day / Come and get me / Stampede / Look who's bonding too / Over the buffalo's back / Under the frozen people / To the bat cave / There's gold in them thar hills / Box full of lead / Jackpot
CD _____ 4768152
Sony Music / Sep '94 / Sony.

CIVIL WAR, THE
Burns, Ken C
CD _____ 7559792562
Elektra Nonesuch / Mar '91 / Warner Music.

CLEAR AND PRESENT DANGER
Horner, James C
Horner, James Con
CD _____ 224012
Milan / Sep '94 / BMG / Silva Screen.

CLERKS
Clerks: Love Among Freaks / Kill the sexplayer: Girls Against Boys / Got me wrong: Alice In Chains / Making me sick: Bash & Pop / Chewbacca: Super Nova / Family in Cicero: Jesus Lizard / Shooting star: Golden Smog / Leaders and followers: Bad Religion / Violent moodswings: Stabbing Westward / Berserker: Love Among Freaks / Big problems: Corrosion Of Conformity / Go your own way: Seaweed / Can't even tell: Bad Asylum
CD _____ 4778022
Columbia / May '95 / Sony.

CLIFFHANGER
London Philharmonic Orchestra
Jones, Trevor C
Snell, D. Con
CD _____ 5144552
Polydor / Jun '94 / PolyGram.

CLOCKWORK ORANGE, A
Carlos, Walter/Rossini/Beethoven/Elgar/Rimsky-Korsakov C
Clockwork orange / Thieving magpie (La gazza ladra) (overture) / Symphony no. 9 (second movement - abridged) / March: Clockwork Orange / William Tell (overture) / Timesteps (excerpt) / Overture to the sun / I want to marry a lighthouse keeper / Suicide Scherzo / Singin' In The Rain: Astaire, Fred
CD _____ K2 46127
WEA / Oct '93 / Warner Music.

CLOSE ENCOUNTERS OF THE THIRD KIND
National Philharmonic Orchestra
Williams, John C
Close Encounters of the Third Kind / Nocturnal pursuit / Abduction of Barry / I can't believe it's real / Climbing devil's tower / Arrival of sky harbour
CD _____ A 8915
Alhambra / Jan '92 / Silva Screen.

CLUELESS
Kids in America: Muffs / Shake some action: Cracker / Ghost in you: Counting Crows / Here: Luscious Jackson / All the young dudes: World Party / Fake plastic

trees: Radiohead / Change: Lightning Seeds / Need you around: Smoking Popes / Mullet head: Beastie Boys / Where'd you go: Mighty Mighty Bosstones / Rollin' with my homies: Coolio / Alright: Supergrass / My Forgotten favourite: Velocity Girl / Supermodel: Sobule, Jill
CD _____ CDEST 2267
Capitol / Sep '95 / EMI.

COBRA
Levay, Sylvester C
Voice of America's son: Cafferty, John & The Beaver Brown Band / Feel the heat: Beauvoir, Jean / Loving on borrowed time: Knight, Gladys & Bill Medley / Skyline: Levay, Sylvester / Hold on to your vision: Wright, Gary / Suave: Miami Sound Machine / Cobra: Levay, Sylvester / Angel of the city: Tepper, Robert / Chase: Levay, Sylvester / Two into one: Medley, Bill & Carmen Twillie
CD _____ 752392
Scotti Bros/Silva Screen / Apr '92 / Silva Screen.

COBRA VERDE
Popul Vuh
Popul Vuh C
Der tod des Cobra Verde / Nachts, schnee / Der marktplatz / Eine andere welt / Grab der mutter / Die singenden madchen von ho, ziavi / Sieh nicht uberm meer ist's / Ha-'mut bis dass die nacht mit ruh
CD _____ CH 353
Milan / Feb '88 / BMG / Silva Screen.

COCKTAIL
Wild again: Starship / Powerful stuff: Fabulous Thunderbirds / Since when: Nevil, Robbie / Don't worry be happy: McFerrin, Bobby / Hippy hippy shake: Georgia Satellites / Kokomo: Beach Boys / Rave on: Mellencamp, John / All shook up: Cooder, Ry / Oh, I love you so: Smith, Preston / Tutti frutti: Little Richard
CD _____ 9608062
Elektra / Oct '88 / Warner Music.

COCOON: THE RETURN
Horner, James C
CD _____ VSD 5211
Varese Sarabande/Colosseum / Feb '90 / Pinnacle / Silva Screen.

COLD FEET
Bahler, Tom C
Afternoon roundup / Shoot the doc / Just remember / Watch my lips / Cowboy reggae / Monty shows off infidel / Maureen and Kenny on the road / Survival camp / Infidel's and inspiration / Isometrics / Monty stole the horse / It's a sham/ Workin' man / Sheriff's a preacher / Lizard boots, size 100 / Good morning / Maureen's monologue / Sceered fitless / Monty hides infidel / Have a Turkish fig / Chasin' Monty / Kenny's in the vat / Happy now and forever
CD _____ VSD 5231
Varese Sarabande/Colosseum / Feb '90 / Pinnacle / Silva Screen.

COLD ROOM, THE
Nyman, Michael C
CD _____ FILMCD 157
Silva Screen / Jan '95 / Conifer / Silva Screen.

COLLETTE COLLAGE
1993 Studio Cast
CD _____ VSD 5473
Varese Sarabande/Colosseum / Jun '94 / Pinnacle / Silva Screen.

COLOR OF MONEY, THE
Who owns this place: Henley, Don / It's in the way that you use it: Clapton, Eric / Let yourself in for it: Palmer, Robert / Don't tell me nothin': Dixon, Willie / Two brothers and a stranger: Knopfler, Mark / Standing on the edge of love: King, B.B. / Modern blues: Robertson, Robbie / Werewolves of London: Zevon, Warren / My baby's in love with another guy: Palmer, Robert / Color of money: Robertson, Robbie
CD _____ MCAD 6189
MCA/Silva Screen / Jan '91 / Silva Screen.

COLOR PURPLE, THE
Jones, Quincy C
Overture / Main title / Celie leaves with Mr. / Corrine and Olivia / Nettie teaches Celie / Separation / Celie and Harpo grow up / Mr. dresses to see Shug / Sophia leaves Harpo / Celie cooks Shug breakfast / Three on the road / Bus pulls out / First letter / Letter search / Nellie's letters / High life / Heaven belongs to you / Katutoka Corrine / Celie shaves Mr. / Scarification ceremony / I'm here / Champagne train / Reunion / Finale / Careless love: Vega, Tata / Dirty dozens: Vega, Tata / Miss Celie's blues: Vega, Tata / Junk bucket blues: Get Happy Band / Don't make me, no never mind: Hooker, John Lee / My heart will always lead me back to you / Body and soul: Hawkins, Coleman / Maybe God is tryin' to tell you something: Vega, Tata & Jacquelyn Farris
2CD _____ 9253892
Qwest/Silva Screen / Jan '89 / Silva Screen.

COLORS
Colors: Ice-T / Six gun: Decadent Dub Team / Let the rhythm run: Salt 'N' Pepa / Butcher shop: Kool G Rap / Paid in full: Eric B & Rakim / Raw: Big Daddy Kane / Mad mad world: Seven A 3 / Go on girl: Shante,

Roxanne / Mind is a terrible thing to waste:
M.C. Shan / Everywhere I go: James, Rick
CD _____ K 925/132
WEA / Apr '88 / Warner Music.

COLOURS OF BRAZIL
CD _____ 233872
Milan / Mar '95 / Silva Screen.

COLUMBUS & THE AGE OF DISCOVERY
Mirowitz, Sheldon *C*
Overture / Idea takes shape / Crossing / Worlds found / Worlds lost / In search of Columbus
CD _____ CD 6002
Narada / Jun '92 / New Note / ADA.

COMA
Goldsmith, Jerry *C*
CD _____ BCD 3027
Bay Cities / Mar '92 / Silva Screen.

COME AND SEE THE PARADISE
Edelman, Randy *C*
CD _____ CH 614
Milan / Jan '95 / BMG / Silva Screen.

COMMANCHEROS/TRUE GRIT
Bernstein, Elmer *C*
CD _____ VCD 47236
Varese Sarabande/Colosseum / Jan '89 / Pinnacle / Silva Screen.

COMMITMENTS, THE
CD _____ MCAD 10286
MCA / Aug '91 / BMG.

COMMITMENTS, THE - VOL.2
Hard to handle / Grits ain't groceries / I thank you / That's the way love is / Show me / Saved / Too many fish in the sea / Fa fa fa fa fa (sad song) / Land of the 1000 dances / Nowhere to run / Bring it on home to me
CD _____ MCLD 19312
MCA / Oct '95 / BMG.

COMPANY
1970 Broadway Cast
Sondheim, Stephen *C*
CD _____ CK 03550
CBS/Silva Screen / '89 / Conifer / Silva Screen.

COMPANY
1972 London Cast
Sondheim, Stephen *C*
CD _____ SMK 53496
Sony West End / Nov '93 / Sony.

COMPANY
(In Jazz)
Trotter Trio
Sondheim, Stephen *C*
CD _____ VSD 5673
Varese Sarabande/Colosseum / Nov '95 / Pinnacle / Silva Screen.

COMPANY BUSINESS
Kamen, Michael *C*
CD _____ A 8931
Alhambra / Mar '92 / Silva Screen.

COMPANY OF WOLVES, THE
Fenton, George
Fenton, George *C*
Message and main theme / Rosaleen's first dream / Story of the bride and groom / The village wedding/The return of the groom) / Forest and the huntsman's theme / Wedding party (based on Beethoven's String Trio Op. 9 No. 1) / Boy and the devil / One Sunday afternoon / All the better to eat you with / (Arriving at Granny's cottage/The promise and transformation) / Wolfgirl / Liberation
CD _____ CDTER 1094
TER / '90 / Koch.

CONAN THE BARBARIAN
Poledouris, Basil *C*
Anvil of crom / Riddle of steel - riders of doom / Gift of fury / Wheel of pain / Atlantean sword / Theology civilization wifeing / Search / Orgy / Funeral pyre / Battle of the mounds / Orphans of doom / Awakening
CD _____ 111262
Milan / Feb '94 / BMG / Silva Screen.

CONAN THE BARBARIAN
(American Score)
Poledouris, Basil *C*
CD _____ VSD 5390
Varese Sarabande/Colosseum / Jan '93 / Pinnacle / Silva Screen.

CONEHEADS
Magic carpet ride: *Slash* / Tainted love: *Soft Cell* / No more tears (enough is enough): *Lang, k.d. & Andy Bell* / Kodachrome: *Simon, Paul* / Can't take my eyes off you: *Harket, Morten* / It's a free world baby: *R.E.M.* / Soul to squeeze: *Red Hot Chili Peppers* / Fight the power: *Barenaked Ladies* / Little Renee: *Digable Planets* / Chat jao: *Babble* / Conehead love: *Beldar*
CD _____ 9362453452
Warner Bros. / Jul '93 / Warner Music.

CONFESSIONS OF A POLICE CAPTAIN/ IN THE GRIP OF THE SPIDER
Ortolani, Riz *C*
CD _____ OST 114
Milano Dischi / Jul '93 / Silva Screen.

CONGO
Goldsmith, Jerry *C*
Spirit of Africa / Bail out / No customs / Deep jungle / Hippo attack / Crash site / Gates of zinj / Amy's nightmare / Kahega / Amy's farewell
CD _____ 4809382
Epic / Jul '95 / Sony.

CONNECTION, THE
Redd, Freddie/Howard McGhee/Tina Brooks/Milt Hinton
Redd, Freddie *C*
Who killed cock robin / Music forever / Wigglin' / O.D. / Jim Dunn's dilemma / Time to smile / Sister salvation
CD _____ CDBOP 019
Boplicity / Jul '95 / Pinnacle / Cadillac.

CONSENTING ADULTS
Small, Michael *C*
CD _____ 124792
Milan / Jan '95 / BMG / Silva Screen.

COOK, THE THIEF, HIS WIFE AND HER LOVER, THE
Nyman, Michael Band
Nyman, Michael *C*
Nyman, Michael *C*
Memorial / Misere paraphase: *Nyman, Michael & Alexander Balanescu* / Miserere: *London Voices* / Coupling / Book depository
CD _____ CDVE 53
Virgin / May '90 / EMI.

COOL RUNNINGS
Wild wild life: *Wailing Souls* / I can see clearly now: *Cliff, Jimmy* / Stir it up: *King, Diana* / Cool me down: *Tiger* / Picky picky head: *Wailing Souls* / Jamaican bobsledding chant: *Worl-A-Girl* / Sweet Jamaica: *Tony Rebel* / Dolly my baby: *Super Cat* / Love you want: *Wailing Souls* / Countrylypso: *Zimmer, Hans* / Walk home: *Zimmer, Hans*
CD _____ 474840 2
Columbia / Feb '94 / Sony.

COOLEY HIGH
CD _____ 5515472
Spectrum/Karussell / Aug '93 / PolyGram / THE.

COPACABANA
1994 London Cast
Manilow, Barry *C*
CD _____ CASTCD 42
First Night / Jun '94 / Pinnacle.

CORNBREAD, EARL AND ME
Blackbyrds
Cornbread / One eye two step / Mother Son theme / Heavy town / One gun salute / Gym fight / Riot / Soulful source / Mother Son talk / At the carnival / Candy store dilemna / Wilford's gone / Mother Son bedroom talk / Courtroom emotions / Cornbread (2)
CD _____ CDBGPM 094
BGP / May '95 / Pinnacle.

COSI COME SEI
(Stay The Way You Are)
Morricone, Ennio *C*
CD _____ PCD 115
Prometheus / Mar '92 / Silva Screen.

COTTON CLUB, THE
Mooche / Cotton Club stomp no.2 / Drop me off in Harlem / Creole love call / Ring dem bells / East St. Louis toodle-oo / Truckin' / Ill wind / Cotton Club stomp / Mood indigo / Minnie the moocher / Copper coloured gal / Dixie kidnaps Vera / Depression shits / Best beats sandman / Daybreak Express medley
CD _____ GEF 24062
MCA/Silva Screen / Feb '90 / Silva Screen.

COUNT DRACULA
(Il Conte Dracula)
Nicolai, Bruno *C*
CD _____ PAN 2502
Silva Screen / May '95 / Conifer / Silva Screen.

COUNT OF LUXEMBOURG, THE
New Sadler's Wells Opera Chorus/ Orchestra
Lehar, Franz *C*
Maschwitz, Eric *L*
CD _____ CDTER 1050
TER / May '89 / Koch.

COUNT OF LUXEMBOURG, THE
(Highlights)
New Sadler's Wells Opera Chorus/ Orchestra
Lehar, Franz *C*
Maschwitz, Eric *L*
CD _____ CDTEO 1004
TER / May '89 / Koch.

COUNT OF MONTE CRISTO, THE/THE MAN IN THE IRON MASK
London Studio Symphony Orchestra
Ferguson, Allyn *C*
Ferguson, Allyn Con
CD _____ PCD 130
Prometheus / Oct '94 / Silva Screen.

COUNTESS MARITZA
New Sadler's Wells Opera Chorus/ Orchestra
Kalman, Emmerich *C*
Douglas, Nigel *L*
CD _____ CDTER 1051
TER / May '89 / Koch.

COUNTESS MARITZA
(Highlights)
New Sadler's Wells Opera Chorus/ Orchestra
Kalman, Emmerich *C*
Douglas, Nigel *L*
CD _____ CDTEO 1007
TER / May '89 / Koch.

COUNTRYMAN
Natural mystic: *Marley, Bob* / Rastaman chant: *Marley, Bob* / Theme from Countryman: *Bacárou, Wally* / Rat race: *Marley, Bob* / Jah live: *Marley, Bob* / Three o'clock roadblock: *Marley, Bob* / Ramble: *Rico* / Sound system: *Steel Pulse* / Mosman skank: *Aswad* / Small axe: *Marley, Bob* / Sitting and watching: *Brown, Dennis*
CD _____ RRCD 44
Reggae Refreshers / May '94 / PolyGram / Vital.

COUSTEAU'S PAPUA NEW GUINEA JOURNEY
Scott, John *C*
CD _____ JSCD 112
Silva Screen / Jan '93 / Conifer / Silva Screen.

COWBOY WAY, THE
Good guys don't always wear white: *Bon Jovi* / Cowboy way: *Tritt, Travis* / Mama's don't let your babies grow up to be cowboys / Blue Danube blues: *Cracker* / No one to run with: *Allman Brothers* / On Broadway: *Beck, Jeff* / Days gone by: *House, James* / Candy says: *Blind Melon* / Too far gone: *Harris, Emmylou* / Sonny rides again: *Hargood, George* / Free your mind: *En Vogue*
CD _____ 4768222
Columbia / Apr '95 / Sony.

COWBOYS, THE
Williams, John *C*
Williams, John (1) *Con*
CD _____ VSD 5540
Varese Sarabande/Colosseum / Jul '95 / Pinnacle / Silva Screen.

CRADLE WILL ROCK, THE
1985 London Cast
Blitzstein, Marc *C*
Moll's song / I'll show you guys / Solicitin' / Hard times/The sermon / Croon spoon / Freedom of the press / Let's do something / Honolulu / Summer weather / Love duet (Gus and Sadie) / Don't let me keep you / Ask us again / Art for art's sake / Nickel under your foot / Cradle will rock / Joe worker / Cradle will rock (Final scene)
CD _____ CDTER 1105
TER / Oct '85 / Koch.

CRASH AND BURN
Band, Richard
Band, Richard *C*
CD _____ MAF 7033D
Intrada / Nov '92 / Silva Screen / Koch.

CRAZY FOR YOU
1993 London Cast
Gershwin, George *C*
Gershwin, Ira *L*
CD _____ CASTCD 37
First Night / Oct '93 / Pinnacle.

CRAZY FOR YOU
Broadway Cast
Gershwin, George *C*
Gershwin, Ira *L*
CD _____ CDC 7546182
EMI Classics / Apr '93 / EMI.

CRIMES OF PASSION
Wakeman, Rick
Wakeman, Rick *C*
CD _____ RWCDP 3
President / Nov '93 / Grapevine / Target/ BMG / Jazz Music / President.

CRIMINAL LAW
Goldsmith, Jerry *C*
CD _____ VSD 5210
Varese Sarabande/Colosseum / Dec '88 / Pinnacle / Silva Screen.

CRISS CROSS
Jones, Trevor *C*
CD _____ MAF 7021D
Intrada / Sep '92 / Silva Screen / Koch.

CRITTERS II
(The Main Course)
Pike, Nicholas *C*
CD _____ MAF 7045D
Intrada / Jul '93 / Silva Screen / Koch.

CROCODILE DUNDEE
Best, Peter
Best, Peter *C*
Mick and his mate / Cyril / Walkabout bounce / Goodnight Walter / In the truck / Buffalo / In the boat / Never never land / Death roll / Sunset / Nice one Skippy / Walk in the bush / Would you mind / Nick meets New York / G'day / Sydney / Mad, bad and dangerous / Pimp / Stone the crows / That's not a knife / Oh Richard / Pimp returns / Crocodile Dundee (theme)
CD _____ FILMCD 009
Silva Screen / Dec '86 / Conifer / Silva Screen.

CROSS OVER USA
Bolling, Claude *C*
New York, New York / Way down yonder / Do you know what it means to miss New Orleans / Chicago / Georgia on my mind / Mississippi (old man river) / On the atchsion, topeka and the santa fe / Stars fell on Alabama / Moonlight in vermont / (Back home again) in Indiana
CD _____ 14080-2
Milan / Jun '93 / BMG / Silva Screen.

CROSSING DELANCEY
Chihara, Paul *C*
CD _____ VSD 5205
Varese Sarabande/Colosseum / Dec '88 / Pinnacle / Silva Screen.

CROSSROADS
Cooder, Ry *C*
See you in hell, blind boy / Nitty gritty Mississippi / He made a woman out of me / Feeling bad blues / Somebody's calling my name / Willie Brown blues / Walkin' away blues / Crossroads / Down in Mississippi / Cotton needs pickin' / Viola lee blues
CD _____ 9253992
WEA / Oct '91 / Warner Music.

CROW, THE
Burn: *Cure* / Golgotha tenement blues: *Machines Of Loving Grace* / Big empty: *Stone Temple Pilots* / Dead souls: *Nine Inch Nails* / Darkness: *Rage Against The Machine* / Color me once: *Violent Femmes* / Ghost rider: *Rollins, Henry* / Milktoast: *Helmet* / Badge: *Pantera* / Sip slide melting: *For Love Not Lisa* / After the flesh: *My Life With The Thrill Kill Kult* / Snakedriver: *Jesus & Mary Chain* / Time baby II: *Medicine* / It can't rain all the time: *Siberry, Jane*
CD _____ 7567825192
WEA / Mar '94 / Warner Music.

CROW, THE
(score)
Revell, Graeme *C*
CD _____ VSD 5499
Varese Sarabande/Colosseum / Jun '94 / Pinnacle / Silva Screen.

CRUMB
Boeddinghaus, David & Craig Ventresco *C*
Ragtime nightingale / Sensation rag / Harlem strut / Abraham Jefferson / Washington Lee / Belle of the Philippines / Last kind word blues / Radiator cap blues / Gabby glide medley / Frog-I-more Reg / Cocaine / Won't you fondle me medley / Pass the jug / Skinny leg blues / Buffalo rag / 35th Street blues / Mabel's dream / Wall Street rag / Hateful blues / Real slow drag / Comic montage stomp / Someday sweetheart / Rag pickings / Black diamond rag
CD _____ RCD 10322
Rykodisc / Jul '95 / Vital / ADA.

CRY BABY
King cry baby: *Intveld, James* / Doin' time: *Intveld, James* / Please, Mr. Jailer: *Sweet, Rachel* / Teardrops are falling: *Intveld, James* / Mr. Sandman: *Baldwin & The Whiffles* / Bad boy: *Jive Bombers* / I'm so young: *Students* / I'm a bad bad girl: *Phillips, Esther* / Cherry: *Jive Bombers* / Sh-boom: *Baldwin & The Whiffles* / Teenage prayer: *Sweet, Rachel* / Cry baby: *Honey Sisters* / Nosey Joe: *Jackson, Bull Moose* / High school hellcats: *Intveld, James* / Flirt: *Shirley & Lee* / My heart goes: *Brown, Nappy* / Jungle drums: *Bostic, Earl* / Rubber biscuit: *Chips*
CD _____ MCLD 19260
MCA / Jun '94 / BMG.

CRY IN THE DARK, A
Smeaton, Bruce *C*
CD _____ SIL 15272
Silva Screen / Mar '93 / Conifer / Silva Screen.

CRYING GAME, THE
CD _____ 5170242
Polydor / Jan '93 / PolyGram.

CURE, THE
Grusin, Dave
Grusin, Dave *C*
First visit / Battleship / Shopping cart ride / Soon as they find a cure / Candy montage / Gathering leaves / Bedtime/Big changes / Mississippi montage / Make mine a T-bone / Million light years / Found money / Chase and confrontation / Going home / We call it a miracle / Rain/Realization / Requiem / Last visit / Down the river/End credits
CD _____ GRP 98282
GRP / Jun '95 / BMG / New Note.

CYBERCITY 808
CD _____ DSCD 8
Demon / Jan '95 / Pinnacle / ADA.

CYBORG
Bassinson, Kevin *C*
CD _____ FILMCD 050
Silva Screen / Dec '89 / Conifer / Silva Screen.

CYRANO DE BERGERAC
Petit, Jean Claude *C*
CD _____ ETKY 310CD
Enteleky / Apr '91 / Pinnacle.

CYRANO DE BERGERAC
Petit, Jean Claude *C*
Cyrano / Chandeliers / Magic lantern / Due / Gate of Nesle / Roxane / No thank you

Letters / Count's visit / Marriage / Lute / Affected young ladies / Cyrano's declaration / Mad man / File / Arrival of Roxane / Spaniard's mass / Death of Christian / Song of the nuns / Revelation / Death of Cyrano
CD _____ DRGCD 12602
DRG / Jan '95 / New Note.

CYRANO DE BERGERAC
Paris Opera Orchestra
Petit, Jean Claude *C*
Petit, Jean Claude *Con*
CD _____ CST 348046
Pinnacle / Silva Screen / Jul '90 / Pinnacle / Silva Screen.

D.O.A.
Jankel, Chas *C*
CD _____ VCD 70461
Varese Sarabande/Colosseum / Aug '91 / Pinnacle / Silva Screen.

D.R.O.P. SQUAD, THE
Drop Squad theme / Keep that same old feeling / Never forget where you come from / Lenora / Gently in the night / Forever yours / Come back / Rocky's theme / When I needed you / Never say never
CD _____ GRM 40282
GRP / Feb '95 / BMG / New Note.

DADDY NOSTALGIE
CD _____ 4671342
Silva Screen / Jan '93 / Conifer / Silva Screen.

DAMAGE
Preisner, Zbigniew *C*
CD _____ VSD 5406
Varese Sarabande/Colosseum / Feb '93 / Pinnacle / Silva Screen.

DAMES AT SEA
1989 Touring Cast
Wise, Jim *C*
Wall Street / It's you / Broadway baby / That mister man of mine / Choo choo honeymoon / Sailor of my dreams / Singapore Sue / Broadway baby (reprise) / Good times are here to stay / Entr'acte / Dames at sea / Beguine / Raining in my heart / There's something about you / Echo waltz / Star tar / Let's have a simple wedding / Dames at sea (overture)
CD _____ CDTER 1169
TER / Jul '89 / Koch.

DAMES AT SEA
1968 Broadway Cast
Wise, Jim *C*
Haimsohn, George & Robin Miller *L*
CD _____ SK 48214
Sony Broadway / Nov '92 / Sony.

DAMNED, THE/A SEASON IN HELL/FOR THOSE I LOVED
Jarre, Maurice *C*
CD _____ DRGCD 32906
DRG / Jul '95 / New Note.

D'AMORE SI MUORE/LE DUE STAGIONI BELLA VITA
(For Love One Could Die/The Two Seasons Of Life)
Morricone, Ennio *C*
Preamble / Jan '95 / Silva Screen.
CD _____ PRCD 106

DANCE A LITTLE CLOSER
1983 Broadway Cast
Strouse, Charles *C*
Lerner, Alan Jay *L*
CD _____ CDTER 1174
TER / Jul '90 / Koch.

DANCERS
CD _____ CD 42565
CBS / '89 / Sony.

DANCES WITH WOLVES
Barry, John *C*
Barry, John *Con*
Main title / Looks like a suicide / John Dunbar / Journey to Fort Sedgewick / Ride to Fort Hays / Death of Timmons / Two Socks - the wolf theme / Pawnee Attack / Kicking Bird's gift / Journey to the buffalo killing ground / Buffalo hunt / Stands with a fist / Remembers / I love theme / John Dunbar theme / Two Socks at play / Death of Cisco / Rescue of Dances With Wolves / Loss of the journal and the return to winter camp / Farewell and the end
CD _____ 4675912
Epic / Feb '91 / Sony.
CD _____ ZK 66817
Columbia / Nov '95 / Sony.

DANCING THRU THE DARK
Paradise / Power and the glory / Jam it jam / Dancin' thru the dark / Shoe shine / I'm livin' a life of love / Caribbean queen (no more love on the run) / Get busy / People all around the world / So many people / Once in a lifetime

CD _____ CHIP 92
Jive / Mar '90 / BMG.

DANGEROUS LIAISONS
Fenton, George
Fenton, George *C*
Dangerous liasons / O Malheureuse iphigenie / Beneath the surface / Her eyes are closing / Tourvel's flight / Concerto in A minor for 4 harpsichords / Success / Madame de Tourvel / Valmont's first move / Staircase / Key / Ombra mau fu / Ombra mau fu reprise / the mirror / Beyond my control
CD _____ CDV 2583
Virgin / Mar '89 / EMI.

DANGEROUS MINDS
Gangsta's paradise: *Coolio* / Curiosity: *Hall, Aaron* / Havin' thangs: *Big Mike* / Problems: *Rappin' 4-Tay* / True O.G.: *Mr. Dalvin & Static* / Put ya back into it: *Tre Black* / Don't go there: *Rappin' 4-Tay* / Feel the funk: *Immature* / It's alright: *Sista* / Message for your mind: *Rappin' 4-Tay* / Gin & juice: *Devante* / This is the life: *Wendy & Lisa*
CD _____ MCD 11228
MCA / Oct '95 / BMG.

DANZON
Black tears / Traveller / To love and to live / Blue / Schubert's serenade / Magic flute / Long distance telephone / Perjured woman / Moorish woman
CD _____ DRGCD 12605
DRG / Jan '95 / New Note.

DARK HALF, THE
Munich Symphony Orchestra
Young, Christopher *C*
Young, Christopher *Con*
CD _____ VSD 5340
Varese Sarabande/Colosseum / Apr '93 / Pinnacle / Silva Screen.

DARK STAR
Carpenter, John *C*
CD _____ VSD 5327
Varese Sarabande/Colosseum / Nov '92 / Pinnacle / Silva Screen.

DARLING BUDS OF MAY, THE
English Light Concert Orchestra
Guard, Barry *C*
Perfick / Pop's rolls royce / Home farm / Strawberry time / Devil's gallop / Calling all workers / Breath of French air / Gore Court march / One the river / Dinner in the shade / Hop picker's hop / Puffin' Billy / In a party mood / Girl in yellow / Gymkhana / Darling buds of May
CD _____ CDMFP 6128
EMI / Jul '94 / EMI.

D'ARTAGNAN'S DAUGHTER
(La Fille De D'Artagnan)
CD _____ SK 66364
CBS/Silva Screen / Jan '95 / Conifer / Silva Screen.

DAS BARBECU
1995 US Cast
CD _____ VSD 5593
Varese Sarabande/Colosseum / Aug '95 / Pinnacle / Silva Screen.

DAS BOOT
Doldinger, Klaus
Doldinger, Klaus *C*
Anfang / Das boot (The boat) / Appell (inspection) / U96 / Auslaufen (pulling out) / Erinnerung (rememberance) / Konvoi / Angriff (attack) / Heimkehr (returning home) / Das boot / Bodrohung (threat) / Erinnerung / Gibralter / Warlen (waiting) / Eingeschlossen (locked in) / Rettung (rescue) / Ruckzug (retreat) / Ende
CD _____ 2292405812
WEA / Feb '92 / Warner Music.

DAVE
Howard, James Newton *C*
CD _____ 9255102
Silva Screen / Jan '93 / Conifer / Silva Screen.

DAWN OF THE DEAD/TENEBRAE
Goblin
Simonetti, Claudio *C*
CD _____ CDCIA 5035
Cinevox / Feb '90 / Conifer / Silva Screen.

DAY IN HOLLYWOOD, A NIGHT IN THE UKRAINE, A
1980 Broadway Cast
Lazarus, Frank *C*
Vosburgh, Dick *L*
Just go to the movies / Famous feet / I love a film cliche / Nelson / It all comes out of the piano / Best in the world / Doin' the production code / Night in the Ukraine / Samovar the lawyer
CD _____ DRGCD 12580
DRG / Mar '92 / New Note.

DAY THE EARTH STOOD STILL, THE
Herrmann, Bernard *C*
CD _____ 07822110102
Fox Film Scores / Apr '94 / BMG.

DAY THE FISH CAME, THE
Theodorakis, Mikis
Theodorakis, Mikis *C*
CD _____ SR 50088
Varese Sarabande/Colosseum / May '94 / Pinnacle / Silva Screen.

DAYS OF HOPE
1991 London Cast
Goodall, Howard *C*
CD _____ CDTER 1183
TER / Sep '91 / Koch.

DAYS OF THUNDER
Last note of freedom: *Coverdale, David* / Deal for life: *Waite, John* / Break through the barrier: *Turner, Tina* / Hearts in trouble: *Chicago* / Trail of broken hearts: *Cher* / Knockin' on Heaven's door: *Guns N' Roses* / You gotta love someone: *John, Elton* / Show me heaven: *McKee, Maria* / Tinder box: *Appollo Smile* / Long live the night: *Jett, Joan & The Blackhearts* / Gimme some lovin': *Reid, Terry*
CD _____ 4571592
Epic / Aug '90 / Sony.

DAZED AND CONFUSED
CD _____ 74321166752
Medicine / Sep '94 / BMG / Vital.

DE ESO NON SE HABLA
Piovani, Nicola *C*
CD _____ 88765
Milan / Jan '95 / BMG / Silva Screen.

DEAD AGAIN
Doyle, Patrick *C*
CD _____ D5339
Varese Sarabande/Colosseum / Aug '91 / Pinnacle / Silva Screen.

DEAD MAN
WEA / Feb '96 / Warner Music.
CD _____ 9362461712

DEAD MEN DON'T WEAR PLAID
Rozsa, Miklos *C*
CD _____ PCD 126
Prometheus / Jan '93 / Silva Screen.

DEAD POETS SOCIETY
(& The Year Of Living Dangerously)
Jarre, Maurice *C*
CD _____ CDCH 558
Milan / Feb '94 / BMG / Silva Screen.

DEAD SOLID PERFECT
Tangerine Dream
Tangerine Dream *C*
Theme / In the pond / Beverly leaves / Of cads and caddies / Tournament montage / Whore in one / Sand trap / In the rough / Nine iron / U.S. Open / My name is bad hair / In the hospital room / Welcome to Bushwood/Golfus interruptus / Deja vu (I've heard this before) / Birdie / Divot / Kenny and Donny montage / Off to see Beverly / Phone to Beverly / Nice shots / Sinking putts / Kenny's winning shot
CD _____ FILMCD 079
Silva Screen / Mar '91 / Conifer / Silva Screen.

DEAD, THE
North, Alex *C*
CD _____ VCD 47341
Varese Sarabande/Colosseum / Jan '89 / Pinnacle / Silva Screen.

DEAD ZONE, THE
Kamen, Michael *C*
CD _____ 239762
Milan / Jan '95 / BMG / Silva Screen.

DEADLY CARE
Tangerine Dream
Tangerine Dream *C*
CD _____ FILMCD 121
Silva Screen / Nov '92 / Conifer / Silva Screen.

DEAD RIADY
Piovani, Nicola *C*
CD _____ 210542
Milan / Nov '94 / BMG / Silva Screen.

DEAR WORLD
1969 Broadway Cast
Herman, Jerry *C*
CD _____ SK 48220
Sony Broadway / Nov '92 / Sony.

DEATH BECOMES HER
Silvestri, Alan *C*
CD _____ VSD 5375
Varese Sarabande/Colosseum / Aug '92 / Pinnacle / Silva Screen.

DEATH BEFORE DISHONOUR
May, Brian *C*
CD _____ PCD 118
Prometheus / Mar '93 / Silva Screen.

DEATH IN BRUNSWICK
Judd, Philip *C*
CD _____ A 8933
Alhambra / Jan '92 / Silva Screen.

DEATH RIDES A HORSE/A PISTOL FOR RINGO
Morricone, Ennio *C*
CD _____ OST 107
Milano Dischi / Jan '93 / Silva Screen.

DEATH WISH IV
Bisharat, John & Val McCallum *C*
CD _____ SIL 15292
Silva Screen / Mar '93 / Conifer / Silva Screen.

DEATH WISH V
Plumeri, Terry *C*
CD _____ CIN 22142
Silva Screen / May '94 / Conifer / Silva Screen.

DEEP COVER
Deep cover: *Snoop Doggy Dogg* / Love or lust: *Jewell* / Down with my nigga: *Paradise* / Sex is on: *Po', Broke & Lonely* / Way (is in love: *3RD Avenue* / John and Betty's theme: *Colombier, Michel* / Mr. Loverman: *Nickei slick nigga: Ko-Kane* / Typical relationship: *Times 3* / Digits: *Deele* / Sound of one hand clapping: *Calloway* / Why you frontin' on me: *Emmage*
CD _____ 471669 2
Epic / Feb '93 / Sony.

DEEP STAR SIX
Manfredini, Harry *C*
Shock wave / On the edge / Our baby's heartbeat / Seatrack attack / That morning / Rescue / Alone / Plan / Shark darts / Snyder snaps / Swim to the mini-sub
CD _____ MAF 7004D
Intrada / Jan '90 / Silva Screen / Koch.

DEERHUNTER, THE
Myers, Stanley *C*
CD _____ 920582
Silva Screen / Jan '93 / Conifer / Silva Screen.

DEF CON 4
Young, Christopher *C*
CD _____ MAF 7010D
Intrada / Jan '94 / Silva Screen / Koch.

DEFENDING YOUR LIFE
Gore, Michael *C*
CD _____ CK 47836
CBS/Silva Screen / Jan '94 / Conifer / Silva Screen.

DEJA VU/GOING BANANAS/ORDEAL OF INNOCENCE
Donaggio, Pino *C*
CD _____ FILMCD 093
Silva Screen / Jan '93 / Conifer / Silva Screen.

DELICATESSEN
CD _____ 8493452
Polydor / Jan '93 / PolyGram.

DELINQUENTS, THE
CD _____ HFCD 11
PWL / Mar '90 / Warner Music / 3MV.

DELIVERANCE
Weissberg, Eric & Steve Mandell
Weissberg, Eric *C*
Duellin' banjos / Little Maggie / Shuckin' the corn / Pony Express / Old Joe Clark / Eight more miles to Louisville / Farewell blues / Earl's breakdown / End of a dream / Buffalo gals / Reuben's train / Riding the waves / Fire on the mountain / Eighth of January / Bugle call rag / Hard, ain't it hard / Mountain dew / Rawhide
CD _____ K 246214
WEA / Sep '88 / Warner Music.

DELLAMORTE DELLAMORTE
De Sica, Manuel *C*
De Sica, Manuel *C*
CD _____ GDM 2004
Silva Screen / Jan '95 / Conifer / Silva Screen.

DELORES CLAIBORNE
Elfman, Danny
Elfman, Danny *C*
CD _____ VSD 5602
Varese Sarabande/Colosseum / Mar '95 / Pinnacle / Silva Screen.

DELTA FORCE II
European Symphony Orchestra
Talgorn, Frederic *C*
CD _____ A 8921
Alhambra / Feb '92 / Silva Screen.

DELTA FORCE/KING SOLOMON'S MINES
Goldsmith, Jerry *C*
CD _____ CH 290
Milan / Jan '89 / BMG / Silva Screen.

DEMOLITION MAN
Goldenthal, Elliot *C*
Sheffer, Jonathan/A.Kane *Con*
CD _____ VSD 5447
Varese Sarabande/Colosseum / Nov '93 / Pinnacle / Silva Screen.

DEMONS/RAGE/LOVE THREAT/ NIGHTMARE BEACH
Simonetti, Claudio
Simonetti, Claudio *C*
CD _____ OST 104
Milano Dischi / Apr '93 / Silva Screen.

DENNIS
Goldsmith, Jerry *C*
CD _____ 9255142
Silva Screen / Jan '94 / Conifer / Silva Screen.

DESERT SONG/THE NEW MOON/THE BLUE TRAIN
Cast Recording
CD _____ GEMMCD 9100
Pearl / May '94 / Harmonia Mundi.

DESPERADO
Cancion del Mariachi: *Los Lobos & Antonio Banderas* / Six blade knife: *Dire Straits* / Jack the ripper: *Link & His Ray Men* / Manifold de amor: *Latin Playboys* / Forever night shade Mary: *Latin Playboys* / Pass the hatchet: *Roger & The Gypsies* / Bar fight:

Los Lobos / Strange face of love: *Tito & Ta-rantula* / Bucho's gragias/Navajas attacks: *Los Lobos* / Bulletproof: *Los Lobos* / Bella: *Santana* / Quedate aqui: *Hayek, Salma* / Rooftop action: *Los Lobos* / Phone call: *Los Lobos* / White train: *Tito & Tarantula* / Back to the house that love built: *Tito & Tarantula* / Let love reign: *Los Lobos* / Mariachi suite: *Los Lobos*
CD _____ 4809442
Epic / Jan '96 / Sony.

DESPERATE HOURS
Mansfield, David *C*
Chase / Nancy slashes the jaguar / Jail-break / Tim leaves with Zeck / Too many bad memories / Into the lake / Tim meets Bosworth / Nancy's apartment / May meets Bosworth / Tim stabbed / Tim and Nora's theme / Albert leaves / Dumping the body / I'll be back / Albert persued / Give me the Gun / Tim and Nora / Bosworth and the FBI / Stadium / Aftermath / End credits
CD _____ VSD 5284
Varese Sarabande/Colosseum / Oct '90 / Pinnacle / Silva Screen.

DESPERATE REMEDIES
Scholes, Peter *C*
CD _____ 887938
Milan / May '94 / BMG / Silva Screen.

DESPERATELY SEEKING SUSAN
Newman, Thomas *C*
CD _____ VSD 47291
Varese Sarabande/Colosseum / Feb '90 / Pinnacle / Silva Screen.

DESPERATELY SEEKING SUSAN/ MAKING MR RIGHT
Newman, Thomas *C*
CD _____ VCD 47291
Varese Sarabande/Colosseum / Aug '91 / Pinnacle / Silva Screen.

DESTRY RIDES AGAIN
1979 London Cast
Rome, Harold *C*
Bottle neck / Ladies / Hoop-de-dingle / To-morrow morning / Ballad of gun / I know your kind / I hate him / Anyone would love you / Every once in a while / Destry rides again: Finale act I / Are you ready Gyp Wat-son / Not guilty / Only time will tell / That ring on the finger / I say hello / Destry rides again: Finale act II / Curtain call
CD _____ CDTER 1034
TER / Dec '94 / Koch.

DEVIL IN A BLUE DRESS
West side baby: *Walker, T-Bone* / Ain't no-body's business: *Witherspoon, Jimmy* / El-lignton, duke / Hy-ah Su: *Ellington, Duke* / Hop skip and jump: *Milton, Roy* / Good rockin' tonight: *Harris, Wyonie* / Blues after hours: *Crayton, Pee Wee* / I can't go on without you: *Jackson, Bull Moose* / Round midnight: *Monk, Thelonius* / Chicken shack boogie: *Milburn, Amos* / Messin' around: *Memphis Slim* / Chica boo: *Glenn, Lloyd* / Theme from Devil In A Blue Dress: *Bern-stein, Elmer* / Malibu chase: *Bernstein, Elmer*
CD _____ 4813792
Columbia / Dec '95 / Sony.

DI QUESTO NON SI PARLA
Piovani, Nicola *C*
CD _____ 887865
Milan / Jan '95 / BMG / Silva Screen.

DIAMONDS ARE FOREVER
Barry, John *C*
Diamonds are forever: *Bassey, Shirley* / Moon buggy ride / Bond meets Bambi and Thumper / Circus, circus / Death at the Whyte house / Bond smells a rat / Tiffany case / 007 and counting / Q's trick / To hell with blofeld
CD _____ CZ 554
Premier / Dec '95 / EMI.

DIARY OF ANNE FRANK, THE
Newman, Alfred *C*
Newman, Alfred *Con*
CD _____ TSU 0122
Tsunami / May '95 / Silva Screen.

DICK TRACY
Elfman, Danny *C*
Dick Tracy (theme) / After the kid / Crime spree / Breathless theme / Big boy, bad boy / Tess' theme / Slimy D.A. / Breathless comes on / Meet the blank / Story unfolds / Tess' theme (reprise) / Chase / Showdown / Dick Tracy (finale)
CD _____ 7599262362
WEA / Jun '90 / Warner Music.

DIE HARD II
Kamen, Michael
Kamen, Michael *C*
Colonel Stuart / General Esperanza / Church / Runaway / Icicle / Terminal / Bag-gage handling / Annexe skywalk / Doll / In the plane / Snowmobiles / Finlandia
CD _____ VSD 5273
Varese Sarabande/Colosseum / Jul '90 / Pinnacle / Silva Screen.

DIE HARD WITH A VENGEANCE
Kamen, Michael
Kamen, Michael *C*
Summer in the city: *Lovin' Spoonful* / Good-bye Bosworth / John & Zeus / Papaya King / Take another train / Waltz of the bankers / Gold vault / Surfing in the aquaduct / Got it

covered: *Fu-Schnickens* / In front of the kids: *Extra Prolific* / Iron foundry: *Mosolov*
CD _____ 09026683062
RCA / Aug '95 / BMG.

DIE TIGERIN
Dikker, Loek *C*
CD _____ 118462
Milan / Jan '95 / BMG / Silva Screen.

DIE ZWEITE HEIMAT
Mamangakis, Nikos *C*
CD _____ 887881
Milan / Jan '95 / BMG / Silva Screen.

DIEN BIEN PHU
Delerue, Georges *C*
CD _____ 5132892
Silva Screen / Jan '93 / Conifer / Silva Screen.

DINER
Brody, Bruce *C*
2CD _____ 601072
Silva Screen / Jan '89 / Conifer / Silva Screen.

DINGO
Davis, Miles & Michel Legrand
Legrand, Michel *C*
Kimberly / Arrival / Concert on the runway / Departure / Dingo howl / Letter as hero / Trumpet cleaning / Dream / Paris walking / Kimberly trumpet in Paris / Music room / Club entrance / Jam session / Going home / Surprise
CD _____ 7599264382
WEA / Feb '92 / Warner Music.

DIRTY DANCING
I've had the time of my life: *Medley, Bill & Jennifer Warnes* / Be my baby: *Ronettes* / She's like the wind: *Swayze, Patrick & Wendy Fraser* / Hungry eyes: *Carmen, Eric* / Stay: *Williams, Maurice & The Zodiacs* / Yes: *Clayton, Merry* / You don't own me: *Blow Monkeys* / Hey baby: *Channel, Bruce* / Overload: *Zappacosta* / Love is strange: *Mickey & Sylvia* / Where are you tonight: *Johnston, Tom* / In the still of the nite: *Five Satins*
CD _____ BD 86408
RCA / Oct '87 / BMG.

DIRTY DANCING - LIVE IN CONCERT
Cast Recording
Yes: *Clayton, Merry* / Overload: *Clayton, Merry* / Steamroller blues: *Clayton, Merry* / Make me lose control: *Carmen, Eric* / Al-most paradise: *Carmen, Eric & Merry Clay-ton* / Hungry eyes: *Carmen, Eric* / Get ready: *Contours* / Higher and higher: *Con-tours* / Cry to me: *Contours* / Do you love me: *Contours* / Let the good times roll: *Medley, Bill* / Sea cruise: *Medley, Bill* / You've lost that lovin' feelin': *Medley, Bill* / Old time rock 'n' roll: *Medley, Bill* / I've had the time of my life: *Medley, Bill* / Encore
CD _____ ND 90672
RCA / Aug '92 / BMG.

DIRTY DANCING: MORE DIRTY DANCING
I've had the time of my life: *Morris, John* / Orchestra / Big girls don't cry: *Four Seasons* / Merengue: *Lloyd, Michael & Le Disc* / Some kind of wonderful: *Drifters* / Johnny's mambo: *Lloyd, Michael & Le Disc* / Do you love me: *Contours* / Love man: *Redding, Otis* / Wipeout: *Surfaris* / These arms of mine: *Redding, Otis* / De todo un poco: *Lloyd, Michael & Le Disc* / Cry to me: *Burke, Solomon* / Trot the fox: *Lloyd, Michael & Le Disc* / Will you still love me tomorrow: *Shi-relles* / Kellerman's anthem: *Emile Bergstein Chorale*
CD _____ BD 86965
RCA / Apr '88 / BMG.

DIRTY WEEKEND
(Score)
National Philharmonic Orchestra
Fanshawe, David *C*
Coleman, John *Con*
Titles / Bella / Brighton Neapolitana / Peep-ing Tim / Brunswick Square / Dirty phone calls / Fate found Bella / Nimrod - Iranian clairvoyant / Bella's revenge - Tim's death / Bella - beautiful dreamer / Thinking guns / Target practice / Bella burning for a man / Bella's fantasy / Bella's waltz / Bondage game - Bella and Norman / Bella's tooth-ache - Reggie's end / Minuet / Bella res-cues Mary / Dawn in Brighton / Serial killer / Finale / Mountain earth harp (solo)
CD _____ FILMCD 140
Silva Screen / Sep '93 / Conifer / Silva Screen.

DISCLOSURE
Morricone, Ennio *C*
Serene family / Unusual approach / With energy and decision / Virtual reality / Pre-paration and victory / Disclosure / Sad fam-ily / Unemployed / Sex and computers / Computers and work / Sex and power / First passacaglia / Second passacaglia / Third passacaglia / Sex, power and computers
CD _____ CDVMM 16
Virgin / Feb '95 / EMI.

DISORDERLIES
Don't treat me like this: *Anita* / Edge of a broken heart: *Bon Jovi* / Trying to dance: *Kimmel, Tom* / Roller one: *Art Of Noise* / Fat off my back: *Guthrie, Gwen* / Work me down: *Hunter, Laura* / Baby, you're a rich

man: *Fat Boys* / I heard a rumour: *Banan-arama* / Disorderly conduct: *Latin Rascals* / Big money: *Cashflow*
CD _____ 5511372
Spectrum/Karussell / Aug '95 / PolyGram / THE.

DIVA
Cosma, Vladimir *C*
CD _____ CDCH 061
Milan / Feb '94 / BMG / Silva Screen.

DIVINE MADNESS
Midler, Bette
CD _____ 7567814762
Atlantic / Feb '92 / Warner Music.

DJANGO REINHARDT
Reinhardt, Django
CD _____ 873138
Milan / Mar '93 / BMG / Silva Screen.

DO I HEAR A WALTZ
Broadway Cast
Rodgers, Richard *C*
Sondheim, Stephen *L*
CD _____ SK 48206
Sony Broadway / Jan '93 / Sony.

DOCTOR WHO: EARTHSHOCK
(Classic Music From The BBC Radiophonic Workshop I)
BBC Radiophonic Workshop
Tardis / Sea devils / Meglos / Keeper of Traken / Four to doomsday / Leisure hive / Arc of infinity / Warrior's gate / Earthshock
CD _____ FILMCD 709
Silva Screen / Nov '92 / Conifer / Silva Screen.

DOCTOR WHO: GHOSTLIGHT
Ayres, Mark
Ayres, Mark *C*
Madhouse / Redvers, I presume / Un-charted territory / Heart of the interior / En-ter Josiah Indoor lightning / Nimrod ob-served / Time to emerge / Burnt toast / Ace's adventures underground / Where's is Mamma / Way to the zoo / Memory teller / Lighting the touchpaper / Homo victorianus ineptus / Light enlightened / Tropic of fan-ivale / Tricks of the light / Judgement in stone / Requiem / Passing thoughts
CD _____ FILMCD 133
Silva Screen / Jun '93 / Conifer / Silva Screen.

DOCTOR WHO: MYTHS AND OTHER LEGENDS
Ayres, Mark *C*
CD _____ FILMCD 088
Silva Screen / '94 / Conifer / Silva Screen.

DOCTOR WHO: PYRAMIDS OF MARS
Blair, Heathcliff
Simpson, Dudley *C*
Ark in space / Planet of evil / Brain of Mor-bius / Genesis of the Daleks / Pyramids of Mars
CD _____ FILMCD 134
Silva Screen / '94 / Conifer / Silva Screen.

DOCTOR WHO: THE CURSE OF FENRIC
Ayres, Mark
Ayres, Mark *C*
Introduction: Doctor Who / Boats / Beach-head and rat-trap / Sealed orders / Eyes watching / Commander Milington / Viking graves / Maidens' point / Translations / Au-drey and Millington's office / Curse of Fenric / High stakes / Crypt / Ambush / Well of Vergelmir / Ultima machine / Dangerous un-dercurrents / Seduction of Prozorov / Half-time score / Exit Miss Hardaker/The vicar and the vampires / Stop the machine / Hae-movores / Battle for St. Jude's / Mineshaft / Sealing the hatch / House guests / Tele-gram / Evil from the dawn of time / Storm breaks / Ancient enemies / Shadow dimen-sions / Chemical grenade / Great serpent / Pawns in the game / Kathleen's escape / Wolves of Fenric / Black wins, Time Lord / Final battle / Epilogue: Doctor Who
CD _____ FILMCD 087
Silva Screen / Apr '94 / Conifer / Silva Screen.

DOCTOR WHO: THE FIVE DOCTORS
(Classic Music From The BBC Radiophonic Workshop II)
BBC Radiophonic Workshop
Five doctors / King's demons / Enlighten-ment / Warriors of the deep / Awakening / Resurrection of the Daleks / Planet of fire / Caves of Androzani
CD _____ FILMCD 710
Silva Screen / Nov '92 / Conifer / Silva Screen.

DOCTOR WHO: THE GREATEST SHOW IN THE GALAXY
Ayres, Mark
Ayres, Mark *C*
Introduction: Doctor Who / Psychic rap / In-vitation to segorax / Bellboy and Deadbeat child / Warning / Fellow explorers / Robot attacks / Something sinister / Welcome one and all / Circus ring / Deadbeat / Eaves-dropping / Let me entertain you/Stone arch-way / Well / Powers on the move / Sifting dreams / Survival of the fittest / Bellboy's sacrifice / Plans / Werewolf/Request stop / Gods of Ragnarok / Playing for time / Entry of the psychic clowns / Liberty who / Psy-chic carnival / Coda: Kingpin's new circus / Epilogue: Doctor Who
CD _____ FILMCD 114

Silva Screen / Feb '92 / Conifer / Silva Screen.

DOCTOR WHO: THE WORLDS OF DOCTOR WHO
(Music Sampler)
CD _____ FILMCD 715
Silva Screen / Apr '94 / Conifer / Silva Screen.

DOCTOR WHO: VARIATIONS ON A THEME
Doctor Who - Mood version: *Ayres, Mark* / Doctor Who - Terror version: *Glynn, Domi-nic* / Doctor Who - Latin version: *Mc-Culloch, Keff* / Panopticon eight (Regener-ation mix): *Ayres, Mark*
CD _____ FILMCD 706
Silva Screen / '94 / Conifer / Silva Screen.

DOCTOR ZHIVAGO/RYAN'S DAUGHTER
Jarre, Maurice *C*
Dr. Zhivago overture / Dr. Zhivago / Lara leaves Yuri / At the student cafe / Koma-rovsky and Lara's rendezvous / Revolution / Lara's theme / Funeral / Sventytski's waltz / Yuri escapes / Tonya arrives at Varykino / Yuri writes a poem for Lara / Ryan's Daugh-ter (main title) / Major / You don't want me then / Michael's theme / Ride through the woods / Obsession / Shakes / Rosy on the beach / Song of the Irish rebels / Rosy and the schoolmaster / Michael shows Ran-dolph his strange treasure / Rosy's theme
CD _____ CDMGM 3
MGM/EMI / Jan '90 / EMI.

DOMINICK AND EUGENE
Jones, Trevor *C*
CD _____ VCD 70454
Varese Sarabande/Colosseum / Jan '89 / Pinnacle / Silva Screen.

DON'T BE A MENACE
CD _____ 5241462
Island / Feb '96 / PolyGram.

DON'T LOOK NOW
Donaggio, Pino *C*
John's theme / Candles for Christine / John's vision / Through the street / Dead end / Christine is dead / Strange happen-ings / Searching for Laura / Laura comes back / Laura's theme
CD _____ CDTER 1007
TER / Oct '89 / Koch.

DOORS, THE
Doors
Movie / Riders on the storm / Love street / Break on through / End / Light my fire / Ghost song / Roadhouse blues / Heroin / Carmina buruna / Stoned immaculate / When the music's over / Severed garden / L.A. Woman
CD _____ 7559610472
WEA / Mar '91 / Warner Music.

DOUBLE IMPACT
Kempel, Arthur *C*
CD _____ FILMCD 110
Silva Screen / '91 / Conifer / Silva Screen.

DOUBLE LIFE OF VERONIKA, THE
Preisner, Zbigniew *C*
CD _____ SID 001
Sidonie / Feb '92 / Conifer.

DOWN BY LAW
Lurie, John *C*
CD _____ MTM 14CD
Made To Measure / May '87 / Grapevine.

DOWNTIME
Levine, Ian *C*
CD _____ FILMCD 717
Silva Screen / Nov '95 / Conifer / Silva Screen.

DR. GIGGLES
May, Brian *C*
May, Brian (2) *Con*
CD _____ MAF 7043D
Intrada / Feb '93 / Silva Screen / Koch.

DR. NO
Norman, Monty *C*
Norman, Monty *Con*
James Bond / Kingston calypso / Island speaks / Under the mango tree / Jump up / Dr. No's fantasy / Boy chase / Love at last / Jamaican rock / Audio bongo / Twisting with James / Jamaica jazz
CD _____ CZ 558
Premier / Dec '95 / EMI.

DRACULA
(1992 version)
Kilar, Wojciech *C*
Dracula / Beginning / Vampire hunters / Mi-na's photo / Lucy's party / Brides / Storm / Love remembered / Hunt builds / Hunter's prelude / Green mist / Mina/Dracula / Ring of fire / Love eternal / Ascension / End cred-its / Love song for a vampire: *Lennox, Annie*
CD _____ 472746 2
Columbia / Jan '93 / Sony.

DRACULA
(Hammer Presents)
Lee, Christopher & Hammer City Orchestra
Bernard, James *C*
Dracula / Four faces of evil (Fear in the night/She/Vampire lovers/Dr Jeckyll & Siste Hyde)
CD _____ BGOCD 246
Beat Goes On / Mar '95 / Pinnacle.

DRAGON
(The Bruce Lee Story)
Edelman, Randy *C*
Dragon theme (A father's nightmare) / Yip man's kwoon / Lee Hoi Chuen's love / Bruce and Linda / Challenge fight warm-up / Sailing on the South China Sea / Fists of fury / Tao of Jeet Kune Do / Victory at Ed Parker's / Chopsaki / Brandon / Mountain of gold / Premiere of The Big Boss / Fighting demons / Dragon's heartbeat / First date / Hong Kong Cha-Cha
CD _____ MCAD 10827
MCA / Oct '94 / BMG.

DRAUGHTSMAN'S CONTRACT, THE
Nyman, Michael *C*
Queen of the night / Disposition of the linen / Watery death / Garden is becoming a robe room / Chasing sheep is best left to shepherds / Eye for optical theory / Bravura in the face of grief
CD _____ CASCD 1158
Charisma / Aug '95 / EMI.

DRAW/RED RIVER
National Philharmonic Orchestra/Little Mountain Studio Symphony Orchestra
Wannberg, Ken *C*
Wannberg, Ken *Con*
CD _____ PCD 129
Prometheus / Oct '94 / Silva Screen.

DREAM LOVER
Young, Christopher *C*
Anthony, P. *Con*
CD _____ 387002
Koch / Dec '94 / Koch.

DRESSED TO KILL
Donaggio, Pino *C*
CD _____ VCD 47148
Varese Sarabande/Colosseum / Jan '89 / Pinnacle / Silva Screen.

DRIVING MISS DAISY
Zimmer, Hans *C*
CD _____ VSD 5246
Varese Sarabande/Colosseum / Feb '90 / Pinnacle / Silva Screen.

DROP ZONE
Zimmer, Hans *C*
CD _____ VSD 5581
Varese Sarabande/Colosseum / Dec '94 / Pinnacle / Silva Screen.

DROWNING BY NUMBERS
Nyman, Michael Band
Nyman, Michael *C*
Trysting fields / Sheep and tides / Great death game / Drowning by number 3 / Wheelbarrow walk / Dead man's catch / Drowning by number 2 / Bees in trees / Fish beach / Wedding tango / Crematorium conspiracy / Knowing the ropes / End game
CD _____ CDVE 23
Venture / Aug '88 / EMI.

DUBARRY, THE/MADAME POMPADOUR
London Cast
Millocker, Carl/Leo Fall *C*
Leigh, Rowland/Harry Graham *L*
CD _____ GEMMCD 9068
Pearl / Nov '93 / Harmonia Mundi.

DUCK YOU SUCKER
Morricone, Ennio *C*
Morricone, Ennio *Con*
Main title / Love / Green table / March of the beggars / Sean song / Addio / Jokes on the side / Mexico and Ireland / Inventions for John / Counter revolution / After the explosion
CD _____ A 8917
Alhambra / Feb '92 / Silva Screen.

DUCK YOU SUCKER
(A Fistful Of Dynamite)
Morricone, Ennio *C*
CD _____ CDCIA 5003
Cinevox / Jan '89 / Conifer / Silva Screen.

DUMB AND DUMBER
Ballad of Peter Pumpkinhead: Crash Test Dummies / New age girl: Deadeye Dick / Insomniac: Echobelly / If you don't love me (I'll kill myself): Droge, Pete / Crash: Primitives / Whiney, whiney (what really drives me crazy): Willie One Blood / Too much of a good thing: Sons / You sexy thing: Deee-Lite / Where I find my heaven: Gigolo Aunts / Hurdy gurdy man: Butthole Surfers / Take: Lupins / Bear song: Green Jelly / Get ready: Proclaimers
CD _____ 07863665232
RCA / Apr '95 / BMG.

DUNE
Eno, Brian/Toto *C*
Dune / Dune prologue / Dune main title / Robot fight / Leto's theme / Box / Floating fat man / Trip to Arrakis / First attack / Prophecy theme / Dune (desert home) / Paul meets Chani / Prelude (take my hand) / Paul takes the water of life / Big battle / Paul kills Feyd / Final dream / Take my hand
CD _____ TCS 1032
Silva Screen / Jan '94 / Conifer / Silva Screen.

DUTCH
CD _____ D5336
Varese Sarabande/Colosseum / Aug '91 / Pinnacle / Silva Screen.

DYING YOUNG
Howard, James Newton *C*
Dying Young (Theme from): Kenny G. / Driving North/Moving in / Clock / Love montage / Maze / All the way: Osborne, Jeffrey / Hillary's theme / Victor teaches art / Bluff / San Francisco / Victor / All the way (2): King Curtis / I'll never leave you (Love theme)
CD _____ 261952
Arista / Aug '91 / BMG.

E.T.
Williams, John *C*
Three million light years from home / Abandoned and pursued / E.T.'s halloween / Flying / E.T. phone home / Over the moon / Adventure on Earth
CD _____ MCLD 19021
MCA / Apr '92 / BMG.

EARTHQUAKE
Williams, John *C*
CD _____ VSD 5262
Varese Sarabande/Colosseum / Apr '91 / Pinnacle / Silva Screen.

EASY COME, EASY GO/SPEEDWAY
Presley, Elvis
Easy come, easy go / Love machine / Yoga is as yoga does / You gotta stop / Sing you children / I'll take love / She's a machine / Love machine (alternate take) / Sing you children (alternate take) / She's a machine (alternate take 13) / Speedway (alternate master) / Your time hasn't come yet, baby / Who are you, who am I / He's your uncle, not your dad / Let yourself go / Five sleepy heads / Suppose / Your groovy self
CD _____ 07863665582
RCA / Mar '95 / BMG.

EASY RIDER
Pusher: Steppenwolf / Born to be wild: Steppenwolf / Weight: Band / I wasn't born to follow: Byrds / If you want to be a bird: Holy Modal Rounders / Don't Bogart me: Fraternity of Man / If six was nine: Hendrix, Jimi Experience / Kyrie Eleison Mardi Gras: McGuinn, Roger / It's alright Ma (I'm only bleeding): McGuinn, Roger / Ballad of Easy Rider: McGuinn, Roger
CD _____ MCLD 19153
MCA / Nov '92 / BMG.

EASY RIDER
(Songs From & Inspired By The Film)
CD _____ NTRCD 027
Quality / Sep '94 / Pinnacle.

EDDIE AND THE CRUISERS II
(Eddie Lives)
Runnin' thru the fire / Open road / Emotional storm / Garden of Eden / Some like it hot / Just a matter of time / Maryia / Pride and passion / NYC song / (Keep my love) alive
CD _____ 842 046-2
Polydor / Jul '90 / PolyGram.

EDUCATING RITA
Hentschel, David
Hentschel, David *C*
Educating Rita / Franks theme Pt. 1 (A dead good poet) / Franks theme Pt. 2 / Variations on Frank and Rita (Innocence and experience) / Educating Rita (reprise) / Thought for Rita Pt. 1 / University challenge / Burning books / Franks theme pt. 3 (Virginia, Charlotte, Jane or Emily) / Thought for Rita Pt. 2 / Educated woman / Macbeth
CD _____ C5CD 587
See For Miles/C5 / Jun '92 / Pinnacle.

EDWARD SCISSORHANDS
Elfman, Danny
Elfman, Danny *C*
Main title / Story time / Castle on the hill / Cookie factory / Edwardo the barber / Etiquette lesson / Ballet de suburbia (suite) / Death / Final confrontation / Finale / Farewell / Ice dance / Home sweet home / Esmerelda / Helst / Rampage / Plot unfolds / End credits / Beautiful new world / With these sands
CD _____ MCLD 19003
MCA / Oct '95 / BMG.

EIGER SANCTION, THE
Williams, John (1)
Williams, John (1) *Con*
CD _____ VSD 5277
Varese Sarabande/Colosseum / Mar '91 / Pinnacle / Silva Screen.

EL DORADO
Masso, Alejandro *C*
CD _____ CD 342
Milan / Jan '89 / BMG / Silva Screen.

EL GRECO/GIORDANO BRUNO
Morricone, Ennio *C*
CD _____ OST 111
Milano Dischi / Mar '92 / Silva Screen.

EL LADO OSCURO DEL CORAZON
Montes, Oswaldo *C*
CD _____ 887880
Milan / Jan '95 / BMG / Silva Screen.

EL VIAJE
CD _____ 262579
Milan / Jan '95 / BMG / Silva Screen.

ELECTRA
Theodorakis, Mikis *C*
CD _____ SR 50090
Varese Sarabande/Colosseum / May '94 / Pinnacle / Silva Screen.

ELECTRIC DREAMS
Moroder, Giorgio *C*
Electric dreams: Arnold, P.P. / Video: Lynne, Jeff / Dream: Culture Club / Duel: Moroder, Giorgio / Now you are mine: Terry, Helen / Love is love: Culture Club / Chase runner: Heaven 17 / Let it run: Lynne, Jeff / Madeline's theme: Moroder, Giorgio / Together in electric dreams: Moroder, Giorgio & Philip Oakey
CD _____ CDVIP 127
Virgin / Oct '94 / EMI.

ELECTRIC HORSEMAN, THE
Grusin, Dave *C*
Midnight rider: Nelson, Willie / My heroes have always been cowboys: Nelson, Willie / Mamas don't let your babies grow up to be cowboys: Nelson, Willie / Hands on the wheel: Nelson, Willie / Electro-phantasma / Rising star / Electric horseman / Tumbleweed morning / Disco magic / Freedom / Epilogue
CD _____ CK 36327
CBS/Silva Screen / Jan '89 / Silva Screen.

ELEGIES
1993 London Cast
Hood, Janet *C*
Russell, Bill *L*
CD _____ CASTCD 35
First Night / Sep '93 / Pinnacle.

ELEPHANT MAN, THE
Morris, John *C*
Morris, John *Con*
CD _____ 199862
Milan / May '94 / BMG / Silva Screen.

ELIZABETH AND ESSEX
Munich Symphony Orchestra
Korngold, Erich *C*
Davis, Carl *Con*
CD _____ 873122
Silva Screen / Jul '93 / Conifer / Silva Screen.

ELIZABETH TAYLOR IN LONDON/FOUR IN THE MORNING
(The Ember Years Vol.1)
Barry, John *C*
Barry, John *Con*
Elizabeth in London / Elizabeth walk / English garden / London theme / London waltz / Lovers / Fire of London / Elizabeth theme / Four in the morning / River walk / Lover's clasp / Norman's return / River ride / Lover's tension / First reconciliation / Norman leaves / Moment of decision / Judi comes back
CD _____ PLAY 002
Play It Again / Mar '92 / Total/BMG.

EMERALD FOREST, THE
Homrich, Junior & Brian Gascoigne *C*
CD _____ VCD 47251
Varese Sarabande/Colosseum / Jan '89 / Pinnacle / Silva Screen.

EMPIRE OF THE SUN
Williams, John *C*
Williams, John (1) *Con*
Suo Gan / Cadillac of the skies / Jim's new life / Lost in the crowd / Imaginary air battle / Liberation: exsultate justi / Return of the city / British Grenadiers / Toy planes, home and hearth / Streets of Shangai / Pheasant hunt / No road home/seeing the bomb / Exsultate justi
CD _____ 9256682
WEA / Feb '91 / Warner Music.

ENCHANTED APRIL
Bennett, Richard Rodney *C*
CD _____ BCD 3035
Bay Cities / Mar '93 / Silva Screen.

ENCIRCLED SEA, THE
Boyle, Robert *C*
Boyle, Robert *Con*
Waters edge / Earth, fire and water / Heart of the Mediterranean / Fishermen / Shipbuilders / Navigators / Great exchange / Gateways and haven / Theatre of war / Sea of belief
CD _____ FILMCD 076
Silva Screen / Sep '90 / Conifer / Silva Screen.

ENEMIES
(A Love Story)
Jarre, Maurice *C*
Herman / Tamara / In the wood / Masha / Third wife / Kertchmar Country Club / Rumba / Baby Masha
CD _____ VSD 5253
Varese Sarabande/Colosseum / May '90 / Pinnacle / Silva Screen.

ENGLISHMAN WHO WENT UP A HILL BUT CAME DOWN A MOUNTAIN, THE
Edelman, Stephen *C*
Opening credits / English drive / Johnny's triumph / Hustle and bustle / Johnny's barrow / Never ending rain / Brothers tup / Lovers on the mountain / Reverend Jones' death / It's a hill / Villagers begin building / Sermon / Rain / Anson and Betty / Tommy two strokes / Men of Harlech / Ffignnon garn / Magnificent peak
CD _____ 4809452
Epic / Jul '95 / Sony.

EQUINOX
Mystery man: Rypdal, Terje / Milonga del angel: Piazzolla, Astor / Al Bine: Toure, Ali Farke / Left alone: Shepp, Archie / Mirage: Rypdal, Terje / Istoria ne Edna Lyubov: Paposov, Ivo / Symphonic dances: Paposov, Ivo / Once upon a time: Rypdal, Terje
CD _____ VSD 5424
Varese Sarabande/Colosseum / May '93 / Pinnacle / Silva Screen.

ETOILE/THE VISITOR
Knieper, Jurgen/Franco Micalizzi *C*
CD _____ OST 108
Milano Dischi / Jul '93 / Silva Screen.

EUROPEANS
CD _____ CDQ 5551022
EMI / Apr '94 / EMI.

EVEN COWGIRLS GET THE BLUES
Lang, k.d.
Lang, k.d./Ben Mink *C*
Just keep me moving / Much finer place / Or was I / Hush sweet lover / Myth / Apogee / Virtual vortex / Lifted by love / Overture / Kundalini yoga waltz / In perfect dreams / Curious soul astray / Ride of Bonanza Jellybean / Don't be a lemming polka / Sweet Cherokee / Cowgirl pride
CD _____ 9362454332
WEA / Oct '93 / Warner Music.

EVERLASTING SECRET FAMILY
(& A Halo For Athuan/Kindred Spirits)
Bremner, Tony *C*
Everlasting secret family / Halo for Athuan / Kindred spirit
CD _____ SCCD 1020
Southern Cross / Jul '88 / Silva Screen.

EVERYBODY'S ALL AMERICAN
CD _____ C 21Z91184
Silva Screen / Jan '89 / Conifer / Silva Screen.

EVIL DEAD
Loduca, Joseph
Loduca, Joseph *C*
CD _____ VSD 5362
Varese Sarabande/Colosseum / Jun '93 / Pinnacle / Silva Screen.

EVIL DEAD II
Loduca, Joseph *C*
Behemoth / Book of evil / Fresh panic / Other side of your dream) / Purified forest under her skin
CD _____ CDTER 1142
TER / Jul '87 / Koch.

EVIL DEAD III
(Army Of Darkness)
Loduca, Joseph *C*
CD _____ VSD 5411
Varese Sarabande/Colosseum / Mar '93 / Pinnacle / Silva Screen.

EVITA
1976 Studio Cast
Lloyd Webber, Andrew *C*
Rice, Tim *L*
Cinema in Buenos Aires 26 July 1952 / Requiem for Evita/Oh what a circus / On this night of a thousand stars / Buenos Aires / Goodnight and thank you / Lady's got potential / Charity concert/I'd be surprisingly good for you / Another suitcase in another hall / Dangerous Jade / New Argentina / On the balcony of the Casa Rosada / High flying adored / Rainbow high / Rainbow tour / Actress hasn't learned the lines (you'd like to hear) / And the money kept rolling in (and out) / Santa Evita / Waltz for Eva and Che / She is a diamond / Dice are rolling/Eva's sonnet / Eva's final broadcast / Montage / Lament
2CD _____ DMCX 503
MCA / Nov '90 / BMG.

EVITA
1978 London Cast
Lloyd Webber, Andrew *C*
Rice, Tim *L*
Requiem for Evita / Oh what a circus / On this night of a thousand stars / Eva and Magaldi / Eva beware of the city / Buenos Aires / Goodnight and thank you / Lady's got potential / Charity concert / I'd be surprisingly good for you / Another suitcase in another hall / On the balcony of the Casa Rosada / Don't cry for me Argentina / High flying adored / Rainbow high / Rainbow tour / Actress hasn't learned the lines (you'd like to hear) / And the money kept rolling in (and out) / Santa Evita / Waltz for Eva and Che / She is a diamond / Dice are rolling / Eva's sonnet / Eva's final broadcast / Montage / Lament / Cinema in Buenos Aires 26 July 1952 / Art of the possible / Peron's latest flame
CD _____ DMCG 3527
MCA / Jul '85 / BMG.

925

EVITA
Webb, Marti
Lloyd Webber, Andrew *C*
Rice, Tim *L*
CD _____ **PWKS 4233**
Carlton Home Entertainment / Feb '95 /
Carlton Home Entertainment.

EVITA
(Sung In Korean)
Korean Cast
Lloyd Webber, Andrew *C*
Rice, Tim *L*
2CD _____ **DRGCD 13104**
DRG / Jan '95 / New Note.

EXIT
Tangerine Dream
Tangerine Dream *C*
Kiew mission / Pilots of purple twilight /
Choronzon / Exit / Network 23 / Remote
viewing
CD _____ **TAND 13**
Virgin / Jul '95 / EMI.

EXIT TO EDEN
Doyle, Patrick *C*
CD _____ **VSD 5553**
Varese Sarabande/Colosseum / Jun '95 /
Pinnacle / Silva Screen.

EXODUS
Gold, Ernest *C*
Exodus / Summer in Cyprus/Escape / Ari /
Karen / Valley of Jezreel / Fight for survival
/ In Jerusalem / Brothers / Conspiracy /
Prison break / Dawn / Fight for peace /
Hatikvah
CD _____ **10582**
Silva Screen / Jan '89 / Conifer / Silva
Screen.

EXODUS/CAST A GIANT SHADOW
Gold, Ernest *C*
Cast a giant shadow (prologue) (Cast A Giant Shadow.) / Land of hope / War in the
desert / Magda / Cast a giant shadow /
Love me true / Road to Jerusalem / Gathering of the forces / Victory on the beach /
Garden of Abu Gosh / Cast a giant shadow
(finale) / Exodus (Exodus) / Summer in Cyprus / Escape / Ari / Karen / Valley of Jezreel / Fight for survival / Brothers / Conspiracy / Prison break / Dawn / Fight for
peace / Hatikvah
CD _____ **CDMGM 11**
MGM/EMI / Apr '90 / EMI.

EXODUS/JUDITH
Gold, Ernest/Sol Kaplan *C*
CD _____ **TSU 0115**
Tsunami / Jan '95 / Silva Screen.

EXOTICA
Danha, Mychael *C*
CD _____ **VSD 5543**
Varese Sarabande/Colosseum / Mar '95 /
Pinnacle / Silva Screen.

EXTREME JUSTICE
Frank, David Michael *C*
CD _____ **887879**
Milan / Jan '95 / BMG / Silva Screen.

FABULOUS BAKER BOYS, THE
Main title (Jack's theme): *Grusin, Dave* /
Welcome to the road: *Grusin, Dave* / Makin'
whoopee: *Pfeiffer, Michelle* / Suzie and
Jack: *Grusin, Dave* / Shop till you bop: *Gru-
sin, Dave* / Soft on me: *Grusin, Dave* / Do
nothin' 'til you hear from me: *Ellington, Duke
Orchestra* / Moment of truth: *Grusin, Dave* /
Moonglow: *Goodman, Benny* / Lullaby of
birdland: *Palmer, Earl Trio* / My funny val-
entine: *Pfeiffer, Michelle*
CD _____ **GRP 20022**
GRP / Jun '93 / BMG / New Note.

FACE TO FACE/THE BIG GUNDOWN
(Faccia A Faccia/La Resa Dei Conti)
Morricone, Ennio *C*
CD _____ **MASK MK701**
Silva Screen / May '95 / Conifer / Silva
Screen.

FALL OF A NATION/GLORIA'S
ROMANCE
CD _____ **OMP 103**
Silva Screen / Jan '89 / Conifer / Silva
Screen.

FALL OF THE ROMAN EMPIRE
Tiomkin, Dimitri *C*
Tiomkin, Dimitri *Con*
CD _____ **VSD 5228**
Varese Sarabande/Colosseum / Feb '90 /
Pinnacle / Silva Screen.

FALL OF THE ROMAN EMPIRE
(More Music From The Film)
Tiomkin, Dimitri *C*
Tiomkin, Dimitri *Con*
CD _____ **ACN 7016**
Cloud Nine / Sep '91 / Conifer / Silva
Screen.

FALSETTOLAND
Cast Recording
Finn, William *C*
Finn, William & James Lapine *L*
Falsettoland / About time / Year of the child
/ Miracle of Judaism / Baseball game / Day
in falsettoland / Round tables, square tables
/ Everyone hates his parents / What more
can I say / Something bad is happening /
More racquetball / Holding to the ground /
Days like this / Cancelling the Barmitzvah /
Unlikely lovers
CD _____ **DRGCD 12601**
DRG / Mar '92 / New Note.

FAME
1995 London Cast
Margoshes, Steve *C*
Levy, Jacques *L*
Hard work / I want to make magic / Can't
keep it down / Tyrone's rap / There she
goes/Fame / Let's play a love scene /
Teacher's argument / Hard work (reprise) /
I want to make magic (reprise) / Mabel's
prayer / Think of Meryl Streep / Dancin' on
the sidewalk / These are my children / In
L.A. / Let's play a love scene (reprise) /
Bring on tomorrow / Fame
CD _____ **5291092**
Really Useful / Aug '95 / PolyGram.

FAME - THE KIDS FROM FAME
Kids From Fame
Starmaker / I can do anything better than
you can / I still believe in me / Life is a cel-
ebration / Step up to the mike / Hi fidelity /
We got the power / It's gonna be a long
night / Desdemona / Be my music
CD _____ **ND 90427**
RCA / Jun '95 / BMG.

FANTASIA
Toccata and fugue in D minor / Sorcerer's
apprentice / Nutcracker suite (Part 1) / Nutcracker suite (Part 2) / Night on a bare
mountain / Ave Maria
CD _____ **4178512**
Decca / '85 / PolyGram.

FANTASTICKS
1960 Broadway Cast
Schmidt, Harvey *C*
Jones, Tom *L*
Try to remember / Much much more / Met-
aphor / Never say no / It depends on what
you pay / You wonder how these things be-
gin / Soon it's gonna rain / Rape ballet / I
can see it / Plant a radish / Round and round /
There is a curious paradox / They were you
/ Try to remember (reprise)
CD _____ **CDTER 1099**
TER / Aug '90 / Koch.

FANTASTICKS
Japan Tour Cast
Schmidt, Harvey *C*
Jones, Tom *L*
Overture / Try to remember / Much more /
Metaphor / Never say no / It depends on
what you pay / Soon it's gonna rain / Ab-
duction ballet / Happy ending / This plum is
too ripe / I can see it / Plant a radish /
Round and round / They were you
CD _____ **DRGCD 19005**
DRG / Jun '93 / New Note.

FANTOZZI/IL SECONDO TRAGICO
FANTOZZI
Bixio, Franco & Fabio Frozzi/Vince
Tempera *C*
CD _____ **CDCIA 5096**
Cinevox / Jul '92 / Conifer / Silva Screen.

FAR FROM THE MADDING CROWD
Bennett, Richard Rodney *C*
CD _____ **AK 47023**
Cinevox / Jul '93 / Conifer / Silva Screen.

FAR NORTH
Far north / Blue duluth / Amy's theme
(Kitchen)/Gourd part 1 / Amy's theme (Field)
/ Roll on Buddy/Montage / Gangar / Big
ships / Karlie's ride / Train through the big
woods / Night harps / Run sister run /
Camptown races/Amy's theme / Amy's
theme (Over the hill) / Gourd, part 2
CD _____ **SHCD 8502**
Sugarhill / '89 / Roots / CM / ADA / Direct.

FARAWAY, SO CLOSE
Faraway, so close: *Cave, Nick* / Stay (fara-
way, so close): *U2* / Why can't I be good:
Reed, Lou / Chaos: *Gronemeyer, Herbert* /
Travellin' on: *Bonney, Simon* / Wanderer:
U2 / Cassiel's song: *Cave, Nick* / Slow
tango: *Siberry, Jane* / Call me: *House Of
Love* / All God's children: *Bonney, Simon* /
Tightrope: *Anderson, Laurie* / Speak my
language: *Anderson, Laurie*
CD _____ **CDEMC 3660**
EMI / Sep '93 / EMI.

FARENHEIT 451
Seattle Symphony Orchestra
Herrmann, Bernard *C*
CD _____ **VSD 5551**
Varese Sarabande/Colosseum / Jul '95 /
Pinnacle / Silva Screen.

FAREWELL TO ARMS, A/THE
BAREFOOT CONTESSA
Nascimbene, Mario *C*
CD _____ **LEGENDCD 11**
Legend / Sep '93 / Conifer / Silva Screen /
Discovery.

FAREWELL TO THE KING
Poledouris, Basil *C*
CD _____ **CDCH 375**
Milan / Feb '90 / BMG / Silva Screen.

FATHER CHRISTMAS
Phoenix Chamber Orchestra
Hewer, Mike *C*
Bigg, Julian *Con*
CD _____ **4694752**
Columbia / Nov '95 / Sony.

FATHER OF THE BRIDE II
CD _____ **1620202**
Hollywood / Feb '96 / PolyGram.

FATTI DI GENTE PERBENE/DIVINE
CREATURE
Morricone, Ennio *C*
CD _____ **CDCIA 5087**
Cinevox / Jan '93 / Conifer / Silva Screen.

FEARLESS
Jarre, Maurice/Gorecki *C*
CD _____ **793342**
Silva Screen / Jan '93 / Conifer / Silva
Screen.

FEDS
Edelman, Randy
Edelman, Randy *C*
CD _____ **GNPD 8014**
GNP Crescendo / Jan '95 / Silva Screen.

FIDDLER ON THE ROOF
1971 Film Cast
Bock, Jerry *C*
Harnick, Sheldon *L*
Williams, John (1) *Con*
Prologue/Tradition/Main title / If I were a
rich man / Sabbath prayer / To life / Miracle
of miracles / Tevye's dream / Sunrise sun-
set / Wedding celebration and the bottle
dance / Do you love me / Far from the home
I love / Chava ballet sequence / Anatevka /
Finale / Matchmaker, matchmaker / Bottle
dance / Now I have everything
CD _____ **CDP 7460912**
EMI / Jul '94 / EMI.

FIDDLER ON THE ROOF
1964 Broadway Cast
Bock, Jerry *C*
Harnick, Sheldon *L*
Greene, M. *Con*
Prologue - Tradition / Matchmaker, match-
maker / If I were a rich man / Sabbath
prayer / To life. / Miracle of miracles. /
Dream / Sunrise, sunset / Wedding dance /
Now I have everything / Do you love me /
Rumour / Far from the home I love /
Anatevka
CD _____ **RD 87060**
RCA Victor / Aug '90 / BMG.

FIDDLER ON THE ROOF
1967 London Cast
Bock, Jerry *C*
Harnick, Sheldon *L*
Davies, G. *Con*
CD _____ **SMK 53499**
Sony Classical / Jul '94 / Sony.

FIELD OF DREAMS
Horner, James *C*
Horner, James *Con*
Cornfield / Deciding to build the field /
Shoeless Joe / Timeless street / Old ball
players / Drive home / Field of dreams / Li-
brary / Moonlight Graham / Night mists /
Doc's memories / Place where dreams
come true / End credits
CD _____ **30602**
Silva Screen / Feb '90 / Conifer / Silva
Screen.

FIELD OF HONOUR/SECRET OF THE
ICE CAVE
Unione Musiciti Di Roma Orchestra
Budd, Roy/Robert Esty *C*
CD _____ **SIL 15022**
Silva Screen / Jan '93 / Conifer / Silva
Screen.

FINAL JUDGEMENT
(& Scores From Stepmother & The
Terror Within II)
Plumeri, Terry *C*
CD _____ **CIN 2224**
Silva Screen / Jan '95 / Conifer / Silva
Screen.

FINE ROMANCE, A
Kern, Jerome *C*
Fields, Dorothy *L*
CD _____ **C 537**
Milan / Aug '92 / BMG / Silva Screen.

FIORELLO
Broadway Cast
Bock, Jerry *C*
Harnick, Sheldon *L*
CD _____ **ZDM 5650232**
EMI Classics / Dec '93 / EMI.

FIORILE
Piovani, Nicola *C*
CD _____ **873148**
Milan / May '95 / BMG / Silva Screen.

FIRE IN THE SKY
Isham, Mark *C*
CD _____ **VSD 5417**
Varese Sarabande/Colosseum / Apr '93 /
Pinnacle / Silva Screen.

FIRESTARTER
Tangerine Dream
Tangerine Dream *C*

Crystal voice / Testlab / Escaping point /
Burning force / Shop territory / Out of the
heat / Run / Charly the kid / Rainbirds move
/ Between realities / Flash final
CD _____ **VSD 5251**
Varese Sarabande/Colosseum / '90 / Pin-
nacle / Silva Screen.

FIRM, THE
Grusin, Dave
Grusin, Dave *C*
Firm / Stars on the water / Mitch and Abby
/ Money / Memphis stomp / Never mind /
Ray's blues / Dance class / Plan / Blues:
The death of love and trust / Start it up /
Mud island chase / How could you lose me
CD _____ **GRM 20072**
GRP / Jul '93 / BMG / New Note.

FIRST KNIGHT
Goldsmith, Jerry *C*
Arthur's fanfare / Promise me / Camelot /
Raid on Leonesse / New life / To Leonesse
/ Night battle / Village ruins / Arthur's fare-
well / Camelot lives
CD _____ **4809372**
Epic / Jul '95 / Sony.

FIRST MEN IN THE MOON, THE
Johnson, Laurie *C*
Johnson, Laurie *Con*
Prelude / Modern moon landing / News-
casters/Union Jack/Journey to Dymchurch
/ Cherry cottage/Kate and Bedford / Argu-
ments / Cavor's experiments / The sphere
/ Love theme / To the moon / Lunar landing/
Moonscpae/Weightlessness/Planting the
Union Ja / Lens pit/Shadows / Battle with
the Selenites / Search for the sphere/Kate
in peril / Moon beast / Lens complex/Dis-
mantling the sphere/Cocooning Selenites/
The / End of the eclipse/The grand lunar /
Bedford shoots at the grand lunar / Pursuit
and escape from the moon/End title
CD _____ **ACN 7015**
Cloud Nine / Jul '91 / Conifer / Silva Screen.

FIRST NUDIE MUSICAL, THE
(& Stages/Spaceship/The Good One)
Kimmel, Bruce *C*
CD _____ **XCD 1002**
Silva Screen / Feb '90 / Conifer / Silva
Screen.

FISH CALLED WANDA, A
Du Prez, John *C*
Du Prez, John *Con*
CD _____ **887878**
Milan / '95 / BMG / Silva Screen.

FITZWILLY
Williams, John *C*
CD _____ **TSU 0121**
Tsunami / Jan '95 / Silva Screen.

FIVE CORNERS
Howard, James Newton *C*
CD _____ **VCD 47354**
Varese Sarabande/Colosseum / Jan '89 /
Pinnacle / Silva Screen.

FIVE GUYS NAMED MOE
1991 London Cast
Jordan, Louis *C*
CD _____ **CASTCD 23**
First Night / Jun '91 / Pinnacle.

FIVE HEARTBEATS, THE
Heart Is A House For Love: *Dells* / We hav-
en't finished yet: *Labelle, Patti & Thomas,
Tressa* / Nights Like This: *After 7* / Bring
Back The Days: *U.S. Male* / Baby stop run-
ning around: *Bird & The Midnight Falcons* /
In The Middle: *Flash & The Five Heartbeats*
/ Nothing but Love: *Five Heartbeats* / Are
you ready for love: *Flash & The Ebony Sparks*
/ Stay in my corner: *Dells* / I feel like going
on: *Eddie, Baby Doll & The LA Mass Choir/
Billy Valentine*
CD _____ **CDVMM 4**
Virgin / Sep '92 / EMI.

FIVE SUMMER STORIES
Honk
Honk *C*
Creation / Blue of your backdrop / Brad and
David's theme / High in the middle / Hum
drums / Bear's country / Made my state-
ment (Love you baby) / Don't let your good-
bye stand / Lopez / Blue of your backdrop
(instrumental) / Tunnel of love
CD _____ **GNPD 8027**
GNP Crescendo / Jan '91 / Silva Screen.

FLAHOOLEY
Broadway Cast
Lane, Burton *C*
Harburg, E.Y. 'Yip' *L*
CD _____ **ZDM 7647642**
EMI Classics / Apr '93 / EMI.

FLAMING STAR/WILD IN THE
COUNTRY/FOLLOW THAT DREAM
Presley, Elvis
Flaming star / Summer kisses, winter tears
/ Britches a cane and a high starched collar
/ Black star / Flaming star (end title version)
/ Wild in the country / I slipped, I stumbled,
I fell / Lonely man / In my way / Forget me
never / Lonely man (solo) / I slipped, I stum-
bled, I fell (Alternate master) / Follow that
dream / Angel / What a wonderful life / I'm
not the marrying kind / Whistling tune /
Sound advice
CD _____ **07863665572**
RCA / Mar '95 / BMG.

FLAMINGO KID
Breakaway / Heatwave / He's so fine / One fine day / Stranger on the shore / Runaround Sue / Good golly Miss Molly / Money (Thats what I want) / It's alright / Finger poppin' time / Get a job / Boys will be boys
CD _____ 5515392
Spectrum/Karussell / Aug '95 / PolyGram THE.

FLASH FEARLESS
I'm Flash: Cooper, Alice / Space pirates: Cooper, Alice / Trapped: Brooks, Elkie / Sacrifice: Brooks, Elkie / Country cookin: Dandy, Jim / Blast off: Dandy, Jim / What's happening: Trower, Robin / Let's go to the chop: Entwistle, John / All around my hat: Prior, Maddy / Georgia syncopator: Prior, Maddy
CD _____ RPM 148
RPM / Mar '95 / Pinnacle.

FLASH GORDON
Queen
Flash's theme / in the space capsule (The love theme) / Ming's theme (in the court of Ming the merciless) / Ring / Football fight / In the death cell (Love theme reprise) / Execution of Flash / Kiss / Arboria (planet of the tree men) / Escape from the swamp / Flash to the rescue / Vultan's theme (attack of the hawk men) / Battle theme / Wedding march / Marriage of Dale and Ming, and Flash approaching) / Crash dive on Mingo city / Flash's theme reprise (victory celebrations) / Hero
CD _____ CDPCSD 137
Parlophone / Apr '94 / EMI.

FLASHDANCE
Moroder, Giorgio C
Flashdance (what a feeling): Cara, Irene / He's a dream: Shandi / Flashdance love theme: St. John, Helen / Manhunt: Kamon, Karen / Lady lady lady: Esposito, Joe / Imagination: Branigan, Laura / Romeo: Summer, Donna / Seduce me tonight: Cycle V / I'll be here where the heart is: Carnes, Kim / Maniac: Sembello, Michael
CD _____ 8114922
Casablanca / Dec '83 / PolyGram.

FLASHPOINT
Tangerine Dream
Tangerine Dream C
Going west / Afternoon in the desert / Plane ride / Mystery tracks / Lost in the dunes / Highway patrol / Love phantasy / Madcap story / Dirty cross roads / Flashpoint
CD _____ HMIXD 29
Heavy Metal / Apr '87 / Sony.

FLINTSTONES, THE
Stone Age Project
Meet the Flintstones / Human Being (Bedrock Steady) / Hit and run holiday / Prehistoric daze / Rock with the caveman / I showed a caveman how to rock / Bedrock twitch / I wanna be a flintstone / In the days of the caveman / Anarchy in the U.K. / Walk the dinosaur / Bedrock anthem / Mesozic music
CD _____ AAOHP 93552
Start / Oct '94 / Koch.

FLINTSTONES, THE
CD _____ 32532
Scratch / Mar '95 / BMG.

FLORA, THE RED MENACE
1987 Off-Broadway Cast
Kander, John C
Ebb, Fred L
Prologue/Unafraid / Street song I / Kall herself / All I need is one good break / Not every day of the week / Street song II / Sign here / Street song III / Quiet thing / Flame / Not every day of the week (reprise) / Street song IV / Dear love / Keepin' it hot / Street song V / Express yourself / Where did everybody go / Street song VI / You are you / Quiet thing (reprise) / Sing happy / Closing scene
CD _____ CDTER 1159
TER / May '89 / Koch.

FLORA, THE RED MENACE
1965 Broadway Cast
Kander, John C
Ebb, Fred L
Hastings, Harold Con
Overture / Prologue/Unafraid / All I need (is one good break) / Not every day of the week / Sign here / Flame / Palomino pal / Quiet thing / Hello, waves / Dera love / Express yourself / Knock knock / Sing happy / You are you
CD _____ GD 60821
RCA Victor / Dec '92 / BMG.

FLOWER DRUM SONG
1960 London Cast
Rodgers, Richard C
Hammerstein II, Oscar L
Lowe, R. Con
Overture / You are beautiful / Hundred million miracles / I enjoy being a girl / I am going to like it here / Like a god / Chop suey / Don't marry me / Grant Avenue / Love look away / Fan Tan Fannie / Gliding through my memoree / Other generation / Sunday / Finale
CD _____ CDANGEL 7
Angel / Apr '94 / EMI.

FLOWER DRUM SONG
1958 Broadway Cast
Rodgers, Richard C
Hammerstein II, Oscar L
Dell'Isola, S. Con
CD _____ SK 53536
Sony Broadway / Nov '93 / Sony.

FLOWERING PASSIONS
Shaw, Francis C
CD _____ FILMCD 116
Silva Screen / Feb '02 / Conifer / Silva Screen.

FLOWERS IN THE ATTIC
Young, Christopher C
CD _____ MAF 7009D
Intrada / Jul '92 / Silva Screen / Koch.

FLY, THE
London Philharmonic Orchestra
Shore, Howard C
Main title / Last visit / Phone call / Ronnie calls back / Particle magazine / Ronnie's visit / Fingernails / Creature / Maggot, The/ Fly graphic / Ultimate family / Plasma pool / Stathis enters / Seth goes through / Jump / Armwrestle / Stairs / Baboon teleportation / Steak montage / Success with baboon / Finale
CD _____ VCD 47272
Varese Sarabande/Colosseum / Jan '89 / Pinnacle / Silva Screen.

FLY, THE II
Young, Christopher C
Fly II / Fly variations / Spider and the fly / Fly march / Bay 17 mysteries / What's the magic word / Come fly with me / Musica domestica metastasis / More is coming / Accelerated Brundle disease / Bartok barbaro / Dad
CD _____ VSD 5220
Varese Sarabande/Colosseum / May '89 / Pinnacle / Silva Screen.

FLY, THE/OMEN III (THE FINAL CONFLICT)
CD _____ VSD 47272
Varese Sarabande/Colosseum / Feb '90 / Pinnacle / Silva Screen.

FOG, THE
Carpenter, John C
Carpenter, John Con
CD _____ VCD 47267
Varese Sarabande/Colosseum / Jan '89 / Pinnacle / Silva Screen.

FOLLIES
1985 Lincoln Center Revival Cast
Sondheim, Stephen C
Overture / Beautiful girls / Don't look at me / Waiting for the girls upstairs / Rain on the roof / Ah Paree / Broadway baby / Road you didn't take / In Buddy's eyes / Who's that woman / I'm still here / Too many mornings / Right girl / One more kiss / Could I leave you / Loveland / You're gonna love tomorrow/Love will see us through / Buddy's blues / Losing my mind / Story of Lucy and Jessie / Live, laugh, love / Finale (Waiting for the girls upstair/Beautiful girls - reprises)
2CD _____ RD 87128
RCA Victor / Aug '90 / BMG.

FOLLIES
1987 London Cast
Sondheim, Stephen C
CD _____ OCRCD 6019
First Night / Oct '95 / Pinnacle.

FOLLIES
1971 Broadway Cast
Sondheim, Stephen C
CD _____ ZDM 7646662
EMI Classics / Apr '93 / EMI.

FOOLS OF FORTUNE
Zimmer, Hans C
CD _____ CH 334
Milan / Jan '95 / BMG / Silva Screen.

FOOTLOOSE
Footloose: Loggins, Kenny / Let's hear it for the boy: Williams, Deniece / Almost paradise: Wilson, Ann & Mike Reno / Holding out for a hero: Tyler, Bonnie / Dancing in the street: Shalamar / I'm free (heaven helps the man): Loggins, Kenny / Somebody's eyes: Bonoff, Karla / Girl gets around: Hagar, Sammy / Never: Moving Pictures
CD _____ 4630002
CBS / Nov '86 / Sony.

FOR LOVE OR MONEY (THE CONCIERGE)
Broughton, Bruce C
CD _____ 9245152
Silva Screen / Jul '93 / Conifer / Silva Screen.

FOR THE BOYS
Midler, Bette
Billy-a-dick / Stuff like that there / P.S. I love you / Girlfriend of the whirling dervish / I remember you / Dixie's dream / Baby, it's cold outside / Dreamland / Vickie and Mr. Valves / For all we know / Come rain or come shine / In my life / Every road leads back to you
CD _____ 7567823292
Atlantic / Feb '92 / Warner Music.

FOR THE TERM OF HIS NATURAL LIFE
Walker, Simon
Walker, Simon C

CD _____ IMICD 1001
Silva Screen / Feb '90 / Conifer / Silva Screen.

FOR WHOM THE BELL TOLLS
Warner Brothers Studio Orchestra
Young, Victor C
Heindorf, Ray Con
CD _____ STZ 112
Stanyan / Jul '93 / Silva Screen.

FORBIDDEN BROADWAY
Unoriginal Cast
Alessandrini, Gerard L
CD _____ DRGCD 12585
DRG / Mar '92 / New Note.

FORBIDDEN BROADWAY II
Unoriginal Cast
Alessandrini, Gerard L
CD _____ CDSBL 12599
DRG / Mar '92 / New Note.

FORBIDDEN BROADWAY III
Unoriginal Cast
Alessandrini, Gerard L
Carol Channing sequence / Forbidden Broadway III / Ya got troubles / Guys And Dolls sequence / Topol / Anna Karenina: the musical / Julie Andrews / Grim hotel / Barbara: The Broadway album / Dustin Hoffman / Return to Merman and Martin / Ms. Saigon / Michael Crawford sequence / Robert Goulet sequence / Mess of the spider woman / Back to Barbara / Mug brothers / Who's Tommy / Finale
CD _____ DRGCD 12609
DRG / Apr '94 / New Note.

FORBIDDEN HOLLYWOOD
Cast Recording
CD _____ VSD 5669
Varese Sarabande/Colosseum / Nov '95 / Pinnacle / Silva Screen.

FORBIDDEN PLANET
Barron, Louis & Bebe C
Barron, Louis & Bebe Con
CD _____ PRD 001
GNP Crescendo / Sep '95 / Silva Screen.

FOREST FLOWER
Lloyd, Charles C
CD _____ 812271746-2
Warner Bros. / Aug '94 / Warner Music.

FOREVER PLAID
1993 London Cast
Three coins in the fountain / Gotta be this or that undecided / Moments to remember / Crazy about ya baby / Not too much / Perfidia / Cry / Sixteen tons/Chain gang / Tribute to Mr. C (Sing to me Mr.C, Dream along with me, Catch a falling star) / Caribbean dreamin' (Kingston market, Jamaica farewell, Matilada, Matilada) / Heart and soul / Lady of Spain / Scotland the brave / Shangri-la/ Rags to riches / Love is a many splendoured thing
CD _____ CASTCD 33
First Night / Jul '93 / Pinnacle.

FOREVER YOUNG
Goldsmith, Jerry C
CD _____ WA 244822
Silva Screen / Jul '93 / Conifer / Silva Screen.

FORREST GUMP
Hound dog: Presley, Elvis / Rebel rouser: Eddy, Duane / But I do: Henry, Clarence 'Frogman' / Walk right in: Rooftop Singers / Land of 1000 dances: Pickett, Wilson / Blowin' in the wind: Baez, Joan / Fortunate son: Creedence Clearwater Revival / I can't help myself: Four Tops / Respect: Franklin, Aretha / Rainy day women 12/35: Dylan, Bob / Sloop John B: Beach Boys / California dreamin': Mamas & Papas / For what it's worth: Buffalo Springfield / What the world needs now is love: De Shannon, Jackie / Break on through (to the other side): Doors / Mrs. Robinson: Simon & Garfunkel / Volunteers: Jefferson Airplane / Let's get together: Youngbloods / San Francisco: McKenzie, Scott / Turn turn turn: Byrds / Aquarius (let the sunshine in): 5th Dimension / Everybody's talkin': Nilsson, Harry / Joy to the world: Three Dog Night / Stoned love: Supremes / Raindrops keep falling on my head: Thomas, B.J. / Mr. President (Have pity on the working man): Newman, Randy / Sweet home Alabama: Lynyrd Skynyrd / It keeps you runnin': Doobie Brothers / I've got to use my imagination: Knight, Gladys & The Pips / Against the wind: Nelson, Willie / Suite from Forrest Gump: Silvestri, Alan
2CD _____ 4769412
Epic / Oct '94 / Sony.

FORREST GUMP
(Score)
Silvestri, Alan
Silvestri, Alan C
I'm Forrest... Forrest Gump / You're no different / You can't sit here / Run Forrest run / Pray with me / Crimson Gump / They're sendingme to Vietnam / I ran and ran / I had a destiny / Washington reunion / Jesus on the mainline / That's my boat / I never thanked you / Jenny returns / Crusade / Forrest meets Forrest / Wedding guest / Where heaven ends / Jenny's grave / I'll be right here / Suite from Forrest Gump
CD _____ 4773692
Epic / Oct '94 / Sony.

FOUR MUSKETEERS, THE
(& The Eagle Has Landed/Voyage Of The Damned)
Schifrin, Lalo C
Four Musketeers / Eagle Has Landed / Voyage of the Damned
CD _____ LXCD 5
Silva Screen / '88 / Conifer / Silva Screen.

FOUR WEDDINGS AND A FUNERAL
Love is all around: Wet Wet Wet / But not for me: Wet Wet Wet / You're the first, my last, my everything: White, Barry / Smoke gets in your eyes: Nu Colours / I will survive: Gaynor, Gloria / La la (means I love you): Swing Out Sister / Crocodile rock: John, Elton / Right time: I to I / It should have been me: Knight, Gladys / Loving you tonight: Squeeze / Can't smile without you: Flagbe, Lena / Four weddings and a funeral/Funeral blues / Secret marriage: Sting / Chapel of love: John, Elton
CD _____ 516751-2
Vertigo / Jun '94 / PolyGram.

FRANKENSTEIN
Doyle, Patrick C
Snell, D. Con
To think of a story / What's out there / There's an answer / I won't if you won't / Perilous direction / Risk worth taking / Victor begins / Even if you die / Creation / Evil stitched to evil / Escape / Reunion / Journal / Friendless / William / Death of Justine/Sea of ice / Yes I speak / God forgive me / Please wait / Honeymoon / Wedding night / Elizabeth / She's beautiful / He was my father
CD _____ 4779872
Epic / Nov '94 / Sony.

FRANKIE AND JOHNNY/PARADISE, HAWAIIAN STYLE
Presley, Elvis
Frankie and Johnny / Come along / Petunia, the gardener's daughter / Chesay / What every woman lives for / Look out, Broadway / Beginner's luck / Down by the riverside/ When the saints go marching in / Shout it out / Hard luck / Please don't stop loving me / Everybody come aboard / Paradise, Hawaiian style / Queenie Wahine's papaya / Scratch my back / Drums of the islands / Datin' / Dog's life / House of sand / Stop where you are / This is my heaven / Sand castles
CD _____ 07863663602
RCA / Jun '94 / BMG.

FRANKIE STARLIGHT
Bernstein, Elmer C
CD _____ VSD 5679
Varese Sarabande/Colosseum / Nov '95 / Pinnacle / Silva Screen.

FRANKIE'S HOUSE
Beck, Jeff & Jed Stoller
Jungle / Requiem of the Bao-Chi / Hi-heel sneakers / Thailand / Love and death / Cathouse / In the dark / Sniper patrol / Peace Island / White mice / Tunnel rat / Vihn's funeral / Apocalypse / Innocent victim
CD _____ 472494 2
Epic / Nov '92 / Sony.

FRANTIC
Morricone, Ennio C
I'm gonna lose you: Simply Red / Frantic / On the roofs of Paris / One flugel horn / Six short interludes / Nocturne for Michel / In the garage / Paris project / Sadly nostalgic
CD _____ 7559607822
WEA / Oct '93 / Warner Music.

FREE WILLY II
(The Adventure Home)
Childhood: Jackson, Michael / Forever young: Jackson, Rebbie / Sometimes dancing: Brownstone / What it will take: 3 T / I'll say goodbye for the two of us: Expose / Lou's blues: Cavalieri, Nathan / White room: Poledouris, Basil / Reunion: Poledouris, Basil / Childhood (instrumental): Jackson, Michael
CD _____ 4807392
Epic / Jul '95 / Sony.

FREEJACK
CD _____ 5131052
Polydor / May '91 / PolyGram.

FRENCH KISS
Someone like you: Morrison, Van / La vie en rose: Armstrong, Louis / Dream a little dream: Beautiful South / Via con me: Conte, Paolo / I love Paris: Thielemans, Toots / La mer: Kline, Kevin / I love Paris (2): Fitzgerald, Ella / Verlaine: Trenet, Charles / C'est trop beau: Rossi, Tino / Les yeux ouverts: Beautiful South / I want you (theme from French Kiss): Howard, James Newton / Les yeux de ton pere: Les Negresses Vertes
CD _____ 5263212
Mercury / Jun '95 / PolyGram.

FRENCH LIEUTENANT'S WOMAN, THE
Davis, Carl C
Sarah's walk / Proposal / Period research / Her story / Decision taken / Towards love / Location lunch / Together / Domestic scene / Resurrection / House in Windermere / End of shoot party / Happy ending
CD _____ DRGCD 6106
DRG / '88 / New Note.

FRIDAY
Friday: Ice Cube / Keep their heads ringin': Dr. Dre / Friday night: Scarface / Lettin' nig-

gas know: *Threat* / Roll it up, light it up, smoke it up: *Cypress Hill* / Take a hit: *Mack 10* / Tryin' to see another day: *Isley Brothers* / You got me wide open: *Collins, Bootsy & Bernie Worrell* / Mary Jane: *James, Rick* / I wanna get next to you: *Rose Royce* / Superhoes: *Funkdoobiest* / Coast II coast: *Alkaholiks* / Blast if I have to: *E-A-Ski* / Hoochie mama: *2 Live Crew* / I heard it through the grapevine: *Roger*
CD _____ CDPTY 117
Priority/Virgin / Apr '95 / EMI.

FRIDAY THE 13TH
(Parts 1 - 3)
CD _____ CDFMC 10
Silva Screen / Feb '90 / Conifer / Silva Screen.

FRIDAY THE 13TH - THE SERIES
Molin, Fred
Molin, Fred *C*
CD _____ GNPD 8018
GNP Crescendo / Jan '90 / Silva Screen.

FRITZ THE CAT
CD _____ FCD 4532
Fantasy / Jan '94 / Pinnacle / Jazz Music / Wellard / Cadillac.

FROG DREAMING/WILD DUCK, THE
May, Brian & Simon Walker *C*
CD _____ SCCD 1019
Southern Cross / Jan '89 / Silva Screen.

FROM RUSSIA WITH LOVE
Barry, John *C*
Opening titles / James Bond is back/From Russia with love/James Bond theme / Tania meets Klebb / Meeting in St. Sophia / Golden horn / Girl trouble / Bond meets Tania / 007 / Gypsy camp / Death of Grant / Spectre island / Guitar lament / Man overboard - SMERSH in action / James Bond with bongos / Stalking / Leila dances / Death of Kerim / 007 takes the lektor
CD _____ CZ 550
Premier / Dec '95 / EMI.

FRUIT MACHINE, THE
Zimmer, Hans *C*
CD _____ CDCH 520
Milan / '88 / BMG / Silva Screen.

FUGITIVE, THE
Howard, James Newton *C*
Howard, James Newton *Con*
Main title / Storm drain / Kimble dyes his hair / Helicopter chase / Fugitive theme / Subway fight / Kimble returns / No press / Stairway chase / Sykes' apt / It's over
CD _____ 7559615922
Elektra / Sep '93 / Warner Music.

FULL CIRCLE
(The Haunting Of Julia)
Towns, Colin *C*
Towns, Colin *Con*
CD _____ 387032
Koch / Apr '95 / Koch.

FULL METAL JACKET
Mead, Abigail *C*
Full metal jacket / Hello Vietnam / Chapel of love / Wooly bully / I like it like that / These boots are made for walking / Surfin' bird / Marines' hymn / Transition / Parris Island / Ruins / Leonard / Attack / Time suspended / Sniper
CD _____ 925613 2
WEA / Sep '87 / Warner Music.

FUNNY GIRL
Styne, Jule *C*
Merrill, Bob *L*
Funny girl overture / I'm the greatest star / If a girl isn't pretty / Roller skate rag / I'd rather be blue over you (than happy with somebody else) / His love makes me beautiful / People / You are woman / Don't rain on my parade / Sadie Sadie / Swan / Funny girl / My man (mon homme) / Finale
CD _____ 462545 2
Columbia / Apr '94 / Sony.

FUNNY GIRL
1964 Broadway Cast
Styne, Jule *C*
Merrill, Bob *L*
Rosenstock, Milton *Con*
Overture / If a girl isn't pretty / I'm the greatest star / Cornet man / Who taught her everything / His love makes me beautiful / I want to be seen with you tonight / Henry Street / People / You are woman / Don't rain on my parade / Sadie Sadie / Find yourself a man / Rat-tat-tat-tat / Who are you now / Music that makes me dance / Finale
CD _____ ZDM 7646612
EMI Classics / Apr '93 / EMI.

FUNNY THING HAPPENED ON THE WAY TO THE FORUM
1962 Broadway Cast
Sondheim, Stephen *C*
CD _____ ZDM 7647702
EMI Classics / Apr '93 / EMI.

FUNNY THING HAPPENED ON THE WAY TO THE FORUM
1963 London Cast
Sondheim, Stephen *C*
CD _____ CDANGEL 3
Angel / Apr '93 / EMI.

FURY, THE
London Symphony Orchestra
Williams, John *C*

Williams, John (1) *Con*
Main title / Vision on the stairs / Gillian's escape / Death on the carousel / For Gillian / Hester's theme and the house, / Search for Robin / Gillian's vision / End titles / Epilogue
CD _____ A 8914
Alhambra / Feb '92 / Silva Screen.

G.B.H.
Costello, Elvis & Richard Harvey
Costello, Elvis & Richard Harvey *C*
Life and times of Michael Murray / It wasn't me / Men of alloy / Lambs to the slaughter / Bubbles / Goldilocks theme / Perfume the odour of money / Assassin: *Douglas, Barbara* / Pursuit suite / Roaring boy: *Prufrock Quartet* / So I used five / Love from a cold land / In a cemetery garden / Smack 'im / Woodlands - Oh joy / It's cold up there / Going home service / Grave music / Puppet masters' work / He's so easy / Another time, another place / Closing titles
CD _____ DSCD 4
Demon / Jul '91 / Pinnacle / ADA.

G.I. BLUES
Presley, Elvis
Tonight is so right for love / What's she really like / Frankfurt special / Wooden heart / G.I. blues / Pocket full of rainbows / Shopping around / Big boots / Didja ever / Blue suede shoes / Doin' the best I can
CD _____ ND 83735
RCA / Oct '87 / BMG.

GADFLY, THE
USSR Cinema Symphony Orchestra
Shostakovich, Dmitry *C*
Overture / Contradance / National holiday / Prelude and waltz / Galop / Introduction into the dance / Romance / Intermezzo / Nocturne / Scene / Finale
CD _____ CDCFP 4463
Classics For Pleasure / Nov '88 / EMI.

GAMBLE, THE
Donaggio, Pino *C*
CD _____ OST 106
Milano Dischi / Jul '93 / Silva Screen.

GAME OF DEATH/NIGHT GAMES
Barry, John *C*
CD _____ FILMCD 123
Silva Screen / Jan '93 / Conifer / Silva Screen.

GARDEN OF THE FINZI-CONTINIS, THE
De Sica, Manuel *C*
Micol's theme / Tennis match / Giorgio and Micol (love theme) / Persecution / Garden of the Finzi-Continis / Meeting at Easter / Declaration of war / Leaving for Genocide / Giorgio's delusion / Villa / Childhood memories / Finale / Micol's theme (reprise)
CD _____ OST 125
Milano Dischi / Aug '94 / Silva Screen.

GAY LIFE, THE
Broadway Cast
Schwartz, Arthur *C*
Dietz, Howard *L*
CD _____ ZDM 7647632
EMI Classics / Apr '93 / EMI.

GENESIS
Shankar, Ravi
Shankar, Ravi *C*
Genesis theme / Woman reminiscing / Fair / Return from the film / Passion / Jealousy and fighting / Variation on Genesis theme / Bounty full of crops / Song in the rain / Swing / Camel / Genesis: Title
CD _____ CDCH 287
Milan / Nov '86 / BMG / Silva Screen.

GENOCIDE
Bernstein, Elmer *C*
CD _____ FMT 8007D
Intrada / Jan '93 / Silva Screen / Koch.

GENTLEMEN PREFER BLONDES
(inc. Unreleased Songs/Never Before And Never Again)
Monroe, Marilyn
Robin, Leo *L*
Gentlemen prefer blondes / Diamonds are a girl's best friend / Little girl from Little Rock / Ain't there anyone here for love / When love goes wrong / Bye bye baby / Do it again / Kiss / You'd be surprised / Fine romance / She acts like a woman should / Heatwave / Happy birthday Mr. President
CD _____ DRGCD 15005
DRG / Jan '95 / New Note.

GENTLEMEN PREFER BLONDES
1949 Broadway Cast
Styne, Jule *C*
Robin, Leo *L*
CD _____ SK 48013
Sony Broadway / Dec '91 / Sony.

GENTLEMEN PREFER BLONDES
Monroe, Marilyn
Styne, Jule *C*

Robin, Leo *L*
CD _____ DRGCD 94762
DRG / Jun '95 / New Note.

GERMINAL
Roques, Jean-Louis *C*
Germinal (Generique debut) / Les machines / La descente a la mine / Catherine et etienne / Une piece de cent sous... / La remonte / Montsou l'ete / Bal du bon joyeux / Le voreux occupe / Catherine n'est pas rentree / En bas... / La greve / Catherine et chaval / Saccage a jean bart / Le viol / La revolte / Mort de maheu / Apres l'ecroulement de voreux / Germinal (Generique fin)
CD _____ CDVIR 28
Virgin / Jun '94 / EMI.

GERONIMO: AN AMERICAN LEGEND
Cooder, Ry
Cooder, Ry *C*
Geronimo: Main title / Restoration / Goyakla is coming / Bound for Canaan (The 6th Cavalry) / Cibecue / Governer's ball / Get off the track/Danza/Battle cry of freedom / Wayfaring stranger / Judgement day / Bound for Canaan (Siber and Davis) / Embudos / Sand fight / Army brass band / Young recruit/The girl I left behind me/ Come come away / Yaqui village / Have I seen my power / La vista / Davis / Train to Florida
CD _____ 745645 2
Columbia / Apr '94 / Sony.

GETTYSBURG
Edelman, Randy *C*
Edelman, Randy *Con*
CD _____ 170082
Milan / Oct '94 / BMG / Silva Screen.

GHOST
Jarre, Maurice *C*
Jarre, Maurice *Con*
CD _____ 883617
Milan / Sep '94 / BMG / Silva Screen.

GHOST AND MRS. MUIR, THE
Herrmann, Bernard *C*
Bernstein, Elmer *Con*
CD _____ VCD 47254
Varese Sarabande/Colosseum / Jan '89 / Pinnacle / Silva Screen.

GHOST STORY
Sarde, Philippe *C*
CD _____ VSD 5259
Varese Sarabande/Colosseum / Apr '91 / Pinnacle / Silva Screen.

GHOST TOWN/SLAUGHTER ON TENTH AVENUE/LA PRINCESSE ZENOBIA
Rodgers, Richard *C*
CD _____ CDTER 1114
TER / '88 / Koch.

GHOSTS OF THE CIVIL DEAD
Cave, Nick & The Bad Seeds
Cave, Nick *C*
CD _____ CDIONIC 3
Mute / Apr '89 / Disc.

GIANT
Tiomkin, Dimitri *C*
CD _____ TSU 0106
Tsunami / Jan '94 / Silva Screen.

GIANT/EAST OF EDEN/REBEL WITHOUT A CAUSE
Tiomkin, Dimitri *C*
CD _____ TSU 0201
Tsunami / Jan '95 / Silva Screen.

GIGI
1985 London Cast
Loewe, Frederick *C*
Lerner, Alan Jay *L*
Paris is Paris again / It's a bore / Earth and other minor things / Thank heaven for little girls / She's not thinking of me / Night they invented champagne / I remember it well / Gigi / Entr'acte / Contract / I'm not young anymore / Wide wide world / Finale
CD _____ OCRCD 6007
First Night / Jan '96 / Pinnacle.

GIGI/AN AMERICAN IN PARIS
Cast Recording
Loewe, Frederick/George Gershwin *C*
Lerner, Alan Jay/Ira Gershwin *L*
Gigi (overture) / Thank heavens for little girls / It's a bore / Parisians / Waltz at Maxim's / Night they invented champagne: *Caron, Leslie/Louis Jordan/Hermione Gingold* / I remember it well / Say a prayer for me tonight / I'm glad I'm not young anymore / Gigi (finale) / 'S wonderful / Love is here to stay / I'll build a stairway to paradise / I got rhythm / American in Paris (ballet)
CD _____ CDMGM 1
MGM/EMI / Jan '90 / EMI.

GIN'GER ALE AFTERNOON
Dixon, Willie
Dixon, Willie *C*
CD _____ VSD 5234
Varese Sarabande/Colosseum / Oct '89 / Pinnacle / Silva Screen.

GIOVANNI FALCONE
Donaggio, Pino *C*
CD _____ LEGENDCD 12
Legend / Jan '93 / Conifer / Silva Screen / Discovery.

GIRL CRAZY
Cast Recording
Gershwin, George *C*
Gershwin, Ira *L*

Mauceri, John *Con*
CD _____ 7559792502
Elektra Nonesuch / Feb '91 / Warner Music.

GIRL WHO CAME TO SUPPER, THE
(Noel Coward Sings His Score)
Coward, Sir Noel
Coward, Sir Noel *C*
CD _____ DRGCD 5178
DRG / Oct '95 / New Note.

GIRL WHO CAME TO SUPPER, THE
1963 Broadway Cast
Coward, Sir Noel *C*
Blackton, Jay *Con*
CD _____ SK 48210
Sony Broadway / Nov '93 / Sony.

GIRLFRIEND, THE
1987 Colchester Cast
Rodgers, Richard *C*
Hart, Lorenz *L*
CD _____ CDTER 1148
TER / Aug '95 / Koch.

GIVE MY REGARDS TO BROAD STREET
McCartney, Paul
McCartney, Paul *C*
No more lonely nights / Good day sunshine / Corridor music / Yesterday / Here, there and everywhere / Wanderlust / Ballroom dancing / Silly love songs / Silly love songs (reprise) / Not such a bad boy / So bad / No values / No more lonely nights (reprise) / For no one / Eleanor Rigby / Eleanor's dream / Long and winding road / No more lonely nights (version) / Goodnight princess
CD _____ CDPMCOL 14
EMI / Jun '93 / EMI.

GLADIATORS - RETURN OF THE GLADIATORS
Unbelievable: *EMF* / Three little pigs: *Green Jelly* / Everything's ruined: *Faith No More* / Pretend we're dead: *L7* / Cats in the cradle: *Ugly Kid Joe* / Under the bridge: *Red Hot Chili Peppers* / Too much too young: *Little Angels* / Boys are back in town: *Thin Lizzy* / Calling all the heroes: *It Bites* / One and only: *Hawks, Chesney* / When the going gets tough (the tough get going): *Ocean, Billy* / We are family: *Sister Sledge* / We've got the power: *Gladiators* / War: *Starr, Edwin* / Gladiator's rap: *Gus* / Wild thing: *Troggs* / Main theme: *Storm* / Return of the Gladiators: *Storm* / Chase: *Storm* / Joust: *Storm* / Skytrack: *Storm* / Power ball: *Storm* / Tilt: *Storm* / Suspension bridge: *Storm* / Gladiator power: *Storm*
CD _____ 5165172
PolyGram TV / Nov '93 / PolyGram.

GLADIATORS - THE ALBUM
Main theme: *Gladiators* / Everything about you: *Ugly Kid Joe* / Holding out for a hero: *Tyler, Bonnie* / Final Countdown: *Europe* / Bat out of hell: *Meat Loaf* / Since you've been gone: *Rainbow* / Burning heart: *Survivor* / Hold the line: *Toto* / More than a feeling: *Boston* / All right now: *Free* / Power: *Snap* / War: *Starr, Edwin* / Wild thing: *Troggs* / You seem nothin' yet: *Bachman-Turner Overdrive* / Gladiator's endzone: *Warren's world* / Duel: *Storm* / Eliminator: *Storm* / Wall: *Storm* / Atlaspheres: *Storm* / You're a winner: *Storm* / Danger zone: *Storm* / Hang tough: *Storm* / Swingshot: *Storm* / There are no losers: *Storm*
CD _____ 515 877-2
PolyGram TV / Nov '92 / PolyGram.

GLAM METAL DETECTIVES
CD _____ 650103392
Warner Bros. / Apr '95 / Warner Music.

GLENGARRY GLEN ROSS
CD _____ 7559613842
WEA / Nov '92 / Warner Music.

GLENN MILLER STORY, THE
Gershenson, Joseph *Con*
Moonlight serenade / Tuxedo Junction / Little brown jug / St. Louis blues / In the mood / String of pearls / Pennsylvania 6-5000 / American patrol / Basin Street blues / Chchi-tchor-hi-ya
CD _____ MCLD 19025
MCA / May '93 / BMG.

GLINT OF SILVER, A
Silly Wizard
CD _____ GLCD 1070
Green Linnet / Mar '87 / Roots / CM / Direct / ADA.

GLORY
Harlem Boys Choir
Horner, James *C*
Horner, James *Con*
Call to arms / After antietam / Lonely Christmas / Forming the regiment / Whipping / Burning the town of darien / Brave words / Braver deeds / Year of jubilee / Preparations for battle / Charging for Wagner / Epitaph / Closing credits
CD _____ CDV 2614
Virgin / '90 / EMI.

GO WEST
(New Jazz Score For Buster Keaton Film)
Frisell, Bill *C*
CD _____ 755979350?
Elektra / Jan '95 / Warner Music.

GOBLIN MARKET
1985 Off-Broadway Cast
Pen, Polly C
Rosetti, Christine L
CD _____ CDTER 1144
TER / Mar '90 / Koch.

GODFATHER SUITE, THE
(Music Featured In The Godfather Trilogy)
Milan Philharmonia Orchestra
Rota, Nino/Carmine Coppola/Francesco Pennino C
Coppola, Carmine Con
Love theme / Godfather's tarantella / Godfather's mazurka / Every time I look in your eyes / Godfather's waltz / Michael's theme / Godfather's fox-trot / Senza mamma (Without a mother) / Naple ve salute (Goodbye to Naples) / Marcia religiosa / Festa march / Kay's theme / New carpet / Immigrant (Main theme)
CD _____ FILMCD 077
Silva Screen / Mar '91 / Conifer / Silva Screen.

GODFATHER, THE
Rota, Nino C
Godfather waltz / I have but one heart / Pick-up / Connie's wedding / Halls of fear / Sicilian pastorale / Godfather (love theme) / Appollonia / New godfather / Baptism / Godfather finale
CD _____ MCLD 19022
MCA / Apr '92 / BMG.

GODFATHER, THE II
Rota, Nino/Carmine Coppola C
CD _____ MCAD 10232
MCA/Silva Screen / Apr '93 / Silva Screen.

GODFATHER, THE III
Rota, Nino/Carmine Coppola C
Godfather part III main title / Godfather waltz / Marcia Religioso / Michael's letter / Immigrant / Godfather part III love theme / Godfather waltz (2) / To each his own / Vincent's theme / Altobella / Godfather intermezzo / Sicilian medley / Promise me you'll remember (love theme) / Preludio and Siciliano / A case amiche / Preghiera / Godfather finale / Coda: The Godfather finale
CD _____ 4678132
Epic / Mar '91 / Sony.

GODSPELL
Cast Recording
Schwartz, Stephen C
Prepare ye the way of the Lord / Save the people / Day by day / Learn your lessons well/Bless the Lord / All for the best / All good gifts / Turn back old man / Alas for you / By my side / We beseech thee / On the willow / Finale
CD _____ SHOWCD 012
Showtime / Feb '95 / Disc / THE.

GODSPELL
Cast Recording
Schwartz, Stephen C
CD _____ CDTER 1204
TER / Jan '94 / Koch.

GODSPELL/JESUS CHRIST SUPERSTAR
(Highlights - The Songs Collection)
Cast Recording
Schwartz, Stephen/Andrew Lloyd Webber C
Schwartz, Stephen/Tim Rice L
CD _____ PWKS 4220
Carlton Home Entertainment / Nov '94 / Carlton Home Entertainment.

GOLD DIGGERS
Cooper, Lindsay
McNeely, Joel C
CD _____ VSD 5633
Varese Sarabande/Colosseum / Nov '95 / Pinnacle / Silva Screen.

GOLDEN BOY
1959 Broadway Cast
Strouse, Charles C
Adams, Lee L
CD _____ ZDM 5650242
EMI Classics / Nov '93 / EMI.

GOLDEN GATE
Goldenthal, Elliot C
CD _____ VSD 5470
Varese Sarabande/Colosseum / Aug '94 / Pinnacle / Silva Screen.

GOLDENEYE
Serra, Eric C
Goldeneye: Turner, Tina / Goldeneye overture / Ladies first / We share the same passions / Little surprise for you / Severnaya suite / Our lady of Smolensk / Whispering statues / Run, shoot and jump / Pleasant drive in St. Petersburg / Fatal weakness / That's what keeps you alone / Dish out of water / Scale to hell / For ever, James / Experience of love
CD _____ CDVUSX 100
Virgin / Nov '95 / EMI.

GOLDFINGER
Barry, John C
Teasing the Korean / Main title / Alpine drive / Auric's factory / Oddjob's pressing engagement / Bond back in action again / Gassing the gangsters / Goldfinger (instrumental version) / Dawn raid on Fort Knox / Arrival of the bomb and countdown / Death of Goldfinger / End titles

GOLDILOCKS
1958 Broadway Cast
Anderson, Leroy C
Ford, Joan/Jean & Walter Kerr L
Engel, L. Con
CD _____ SK 48222
Sony Broadway / Nov '92 / Sony.

GONDOLIERS, THE
D'Oyly Carte Opera Chorus/New Symphony Orchestra
Sullivan, Sir Arthur C
Gilbert, W.S. L
Godfrey, I. Con
2CD _____ 4251772
Decca / Jan '90 / PolyGram.

GONDOLIERS, THE
Evans, Geraint & Alexander Young/Glyndebourne Festival Choir/Pro Arte Orchestra
Sullivan, Sir Arthur C
Gilbert, W.S. L
Sargent, Sir Malcolm Con
2CD _____ CMS 7643942
EMI Classics / Apr '94 / EMI.

GONDOLIERS, THE
D'Oyly Carte Opera Chorus/Orchestra
Sullivan, Sir Arthur C
Gilbert, W.S. L
Pryce Jones, J. Con
2CD _____ CDTER2 1187
TER / May '92 / Koch.

GONDOLIERS, THE/PATIENCE
D'Oyly Carte Opera Chorus/New Symphony Orchestra
Sullivan, Sir Arthur C
Gilbert, W.S. L
Sargent, Sir Malcolm Con
CD _____ Z 80952
Arabesque / Jul '89 / Seaford Music.

GONDOLIERS, THE/TRIAL BY JURY
D'Oyly Carte Opera Chorus/Orchestra
Sullivan, Sir Arthur C
Gilbert, W.S. L
Sargent, Malcolm/H. Norris Con
2CD _____ GEMMCDS 9961
Pearl / Sep '93 / Harmonia Mundi.

GONE WITH THE WIND
Steiner, Max C
Main title / Scarlett and Rhett's first meeting / Ashley and Scarlett / Mammy / Christmas during the war in Atlanta / Atlanta in flames / Reconstruction / Ashley returns to Tara from the war prison / Scarlett makes her demands of Rhett / Scarlett's fall down the staircase / Bonnie's fatal pony ride / Finale
CD _____ AK 45438
Cinevox / Jul '93 / Conifer / Silva Screen.

GONE WITH THE WIND
National Philharmonic Orchestra
Steiner, Max C
Gerhardt, Charles Con
Selznick international trademark/Main title / Opening sequence / Driving home / Dance montage - Charleston heel and toe polka / Grazioso/Love theme / Civil war/Fall of the South/Scarlett walks among the wounded / True love/Ashley returns to Tara from the war/Tara in ruins / Belle Watling / Reconstruction/Nightmare/Tara rebuilt/Bonnie/ The accident / Mammy and Melanie on the staircase/Rhett's sorrow / Apotheosis - Melanie's death/Scarlett and Rhett/Tara
CD _____ GD 80452
RCA Victor / Mar '90 / BMG.

GONE WITH THE WIND
London Sinfonietta
Steiner, Max C
CD _____ 12436
Laserlight / Jun '95 / Target/BMG.

GONE WITH THE WIND
(Film score/Unissued material)
Steiner, Max C
CD _____ 96762
Silva Screen / Feb '90 / Conifer / Silva Screen.

GOOD COMPANIONS, THE
1974 London Cast
Previn, Andre C
Mercer, Johnny L
Camaraderie / Pools / Footloose / Pleasure of your company / Stage struck / Dance of life / Slippin' around the corner / Good companions / Little travelling music / And points beyond / Darkest before the dawn / Susie for everybody / Ta luv / I'll tell the world / Stage door John
CD _____ DRGCD 15020
DRG / Jan '95 / New Note.

GOOD MORNING VIETNAM
Nowhere to run: Reeves, Martha / I get around: Beach Boys / Game of love: Fontana, Wayne & The Mindbenders / Sugar and spice: Searchers / Liar liar: Castaways / Warmth of the sun: Beach Boys / I got you (I feel good): Brown, James / Baby, please don't go: Them / Danger, heartbreak dead ahead: Marvelettes / Five o'clock world: Vogues / California sun: Rivieras / What a wonderful world: Armstrong, Louis
CD _____ CDMID 163
A&M / Oct '92 / PolyGram.

GOOD NEWS
1994 American Cast
Henderson, Ray C

De Sylva, B.G. & Lew Brown L
CD _____ CDTER 1230
TER / Aug '95 / Koch.

GOOD ROCKIN' TONITE
1992 London Cast
CD _____ CASTCD 26
First Night / Mar '92 / Pinnacle.

GOOD SON, THE
Bernstein, Elmer C
CD _____ FOX 110132
Fox Film Scores/Silva Screen / Jan '93 / Silva Screen.

GOOD, THE BAD AND THE UGLY, THE
Morricone, Ennio C
Good, the bad and the ugly / Sundown / Strong / Desert / Carriage of the spirits / Marcia / Story of a soldier / Marcia without hope / Death of a soldier / Ecstasy of gold / Trio (Main title theme)
CD _____ CDP 7484082
EMI Manhattan / Sep '88 / EMI.

GOOD, THE BAD AND THE UGLY, THE
Morricone, Ennio C
CD _____ 464082
Silva Screen / Jul '93 / Conifer / Silva Screen.

GOOD, THE BAD AND THE UGLY, THE/A FISTFUL OF DOLLARS
(& For A Few Dollars More - The Dollars Trilogy)
Morricone, Ennio C
CD _____ ND 74021
RCA/Silva Screen / Jan '92 / Silva Screen.

GOODBYE MR. CHIPS
1982 Chichester Festival Cast
Bricusse, Leslie C
Roll call / Fill the world with love / Would I had lived my life then / Schooldays / That's a boy / Where did my childhood go / Boring / Take a chance / Walk through the world / When I am older / Miracle / Day has a hundred packets / You and I / What a lot of flowers / When I was younger / Goodbye, Mr Chips
CD _____ CDTER 1025
TER / Apr '91 / Koch.

GOODFELLAS
Rags to riches: Bennett, Tony / Sincerely: Moonglows / Speedo: Cadillacs / Stardust: Ward, Billy / Look in my eyes: Chantels / Life is but a dream: Harptones / Remember (walkin' in the sand): Shangri-Las / Baby I love you: Franklin, Aretha / Beyond the sea: Darin, Bobby / Sunshine of your love: Cream / Mannish boy: Waters, Muddy / Layla (piano edit): Derek & The Dominoes
CD _____ 7567821522
Atlantic / Nov '90 / Warner Music.

GORKY PARK
Horner, James C
Horner, James C
Main title / Following Kirwill / Irina's theme / Following KGB / Chase through the park / Arkady and Irina / Faceless bodies / Irina's chase / Sable shed / Airport farewell / Releasing the sables / End title
CD _____ VCD 47260
Varese Sarabande/Colosseum / Jan '89 / Pinnacle / Silva Screen.

GOSPEL AT COLONUS, THE
Broadway Cast
Live where you can / Stop do not go on / How shall I see you through my tears / Voice foretold prayer / Never drive you away / Numberless are the world's wonders / Lift me up (like a dove) / Sunlight of no light / Eternal sleep / Lift him up / Now let the weeping cease
CD _____ 7559791912
Elektra Nonesuch / Jan '95 / Warner Music.

GOTHIC
Dolby, Thomas C
Dolby, Thomas C
Fantasmagoria / Byronic love / Shelleymania / Mary's theme / Party games / Gypsy girl / Crucifix / Fundamental source / Sin and buggery / Impalement / Leech juice / Restless sleep 1,2 and 3 / It's his / Coitus per stigmata / Once we vowed eternal love / Riddled with guilt / Metamorphosis / Hangman / Beast in the crypt / Final seance / Funeral by the lake / No ghosts in daylight / To the grave / Devil is an Englishman (Featuring Screamin' Lord Byron) / Skull pulse / Trickle of blood
CD _____ CDV 2417
Virgin / Feb '87 / EMI.

GRADUATE, THE
Simon & Garfunkel
Simon, Paul C
Sound of silence / Jungleman party foxtrot / Mrs. Robinson / Sunporch cha-cha-cha / Scarborough Fair / On the strip / April come she will / Great effect / Big bright green pleasure machine
CD _____ CD 32359
CBS / Feb '94 / Sony.

GRADUATE, THE/WEST SIDE STORY/MY FAIR LADY
Sound of silence / Singleman party foxtrot / Mrs. Robinson / Sunporch cha-cha-cha / Scarborough Fair/Canticle / On the strip / April come she will / Folks / Great affect / Big bright green pleasure machine / Maria! / Prologue / Jet song / Something's coming / dance at the gym / Maria / America / To-

night / Gee officer Krupke / I feel pretty / One hand / Rumble / Cool / Boy like that / I had a love / Somewhere / Overture / Why can't the English / Would'nt it be loverly / I'm just an ordinary man / With a little bit of luck / Just you wait / Rain in Spain / I could have danced all night / Ascot gavotte / On the street where you live / You did it / Show me / Get me to the church on time / Hymn to him / Without you / I've grown accustomed to her face
2CD _____ 4775212
Columbia / Oct '94 / Sony.

GRAFFITI BRIDGE
Prince
Prince C
Can't stop this feeling I got / Question of U / Round and round: Campbell, Tevin / Joy in repetition / Tick tick bang / Thieves in the temple / Elephants and flowers / We can funk / Love machine / Shake: Time / Latest fashion / Still would stand all time / New power generation (pts I and II)
CD _____ 7599274932
WEA / Aug '90 / Warner Music.

GRAND CANYON
Howard, James Newton C
CD _____ 262493
Milan / Feb '94 / BMG / Silva Screen.

GRAND DUKE, THE
D'Oyly Carte Opera Chorus/Royal Philharmonic Orchestra
Sullivan, Sir Arthur C
Gilbert, W.S. L
Nash, R. Con
London / Jun '92 / PolyGram. _____ 4368132

GRAND HOTEL
1992 Broadway Cast
Forrest, George C
Forrest, George & Robert Wright L
Lee, J. Con
Grand parade/Some have, some have not/ As it should be / Look at him (dialogue) / At the Grand Hotel/Table with a view / Maybe my baby loves me / Fire and ice/Twenty-two years/Villa on a hill / I want to go to Hollywood / Sorry to report (dialogue) / Crooked path/Some have, some have not/ As it should be / Who couldn't dance with you / So tell me Baron (dialogue) / Love can't happen / What you need / Bonjour amour / Happy/We'll take a glass together / I waltz alone / No creature on this planet (dialogue) / Bolero / How can I tell her / Final scene (As it should be/At the Grand Hotel/ Some have, some have not/The grand parade) / Grand waltz
CD _____ 09026613272
RCA Victor / Jul '92 / BMG.

GRAND NIGHT FOR SINGING, A
Cast Recording
CD _____ VSD 5516
Varese Sarabande/Colosseum / Dec '94 / Pinnacle / Silva Screen.

GRAND TOUR/LONDON MORNING
(The Ballet Music Of Noel Coward)
City Of Prague Philharmonic Orchestra
Coward, Sir Noel C
CD _____ SILKD 6007
Silva Classics / Sep '95 / Conifer / Silva Screen.

GREASE
Film Cast
Grease: Valli, Frankie / Summer nights: Travolta, John & Olivia Newton John / Hopelessly devoted to you: Newton-John, Olivia / Sandy: Travolta, John / Look at me I'm Sandra Dee: Channing, Stockard / Greased lightnin': Travolta, John / It's raining on prom night: Bullens, Cindy / You're the one that I want: Travolta, John & Olivia Newton John / Beauty school dropout: Avalon, Frankie / Alone at the drive-in movie: Watts, Ernie / Blue moon: Sha Na Na / Rock 'n' roll is here to stay: Sha Na Na / Those magic changes: Sha Na Na / Hound dog: Sha Na Na / Born to hand jive: Sha Na Na / Tears on my pillow: Sha Na Na / Mooning: Bullens, Cindy / Freddy my love: Bullens, Cindy / Rock 'n' roll party queen: St. Louis, Louis / There are worse things I could do: Channing, Stockard / Look at me I'm Sandra Dee (reprise): Newton-John, Olivia / We go together: Travolta, John & Olivia Newton John / Love is a many splendoured thing: Studio Orchestra / Grease (reprise): Valli, Frankie
2CD _____ 8179982
Polydor / Feb '91 / PolyGram.

GREASE
1972 Broadway Cast
CD _____ 8275482
Polydor / Feb '90 / PolyGram.

GREASE
1993 London Cast
Radio WAXX jingle / Vince Fontaine / Sandy (opening) / Grease / Summer nights / Those magic changes / Freddie my love / Look at me I'm Sandra Dee / Greased lightnin' / Rydell fight song / Mooning / We go together / Sing, Stockard / Look at me I'm Sandra Dee (reprise) / Beauty school dropout / Hopelessly devoted to you / Beauty school dropout / Sandy / Rock 'n' roll party queen / There are worse things I could do / Look at me I'm Sandra Dee (reprise) / You're the one that I want / Finale (medley)

929

GREASE
CD _____ 4746322
Epic / Sep '93 / Sony.

GREASE
(Highlights - The Shows Collection)
1993 Studio Cast
Grease / Summer nights / You're the one that I want / Sandy / Beauty school dropout / Greased lightnin' / Blue moon / Rock 'n' roll is here to stay / Hound dog / Tears on my pillow / Hopelessly devoted to you / Look at me I'm Sandra Dee / Freddy my love / It's raining on prom night
CD _____ PWKS 4176
Carlton Home Entertainment / Oct '93 / Carlton Home Entertainment.

GREASE
New Broadway Cast
Alma Mater / We go together / Summer nights / Those magic changes / Freddy, my love / Greased lightnin' / Greased lightnin' (Reprise) / Rydell fight song / Mooning / Look at me I'm Sandra Dee / Since I don't have you / We go together (Reprise) / Shakin' at the High School Hop / It's raining on Prom night / Born to hand jive / Beauty school dropout / Alone at a drive-in movie / Rock 'n' roll party Queen / There are worse things I could do / Look at me I'm Sandra Dee (reprise) / Finale
CD _____ 09026627032
RCA / Sep '94 / BMG.

GREASE
1994 Studio Cast
Jacobs, Jim & Warren Casey C
Yates, M. Con
CD _____ CDTER 1220
TER / Dec '94 / Koch.

GREASE
Cast Recording
Grease / Summer nights / Freddy my love / Greased lightnin' / Look at me I'm Sandra Dee / Hopelessly devoted to you / We go together / Shakin' at the high school hop / Beauty school dropout / There are worse things I could do / Sandy / You're the one that I want
CD _____ SHOWCD 007
Showtime / Feb '95 / Disc / THE.

GREASE II
Back to school again: Four Tops / Cool rider: Pfeiffer, Michelle / Score tonight: T-Birds & Pink Ladies / Girl for all seasons: Teefy, Maureen/Lorna Luft/Alison Price/ Michelle Pfeiffer / Do it for our country: Frechette, Peter / Who's that guy: Cast / Prowlin': T-Birds / Reproduction: Hunter, Tab / Charades: Caulfield, Maxwell / Turn back the hands of time: Caulfield, Maxwell & Michelle Pfeiffer / Rock-a-hula: Cast / We'll be together: Caulfield, Maxwell
CD _____ 825096-2
Polydor / Apr '94 / PolyGram.

GREAT ESCAPE, THE
Bernstein, Elmer C
Bernstein, Elmer Con
Main title / Premature plans / Cooler and Mole / Blythe / Discovery / Various troubles / On the road / Betrayal / Hendley's risk / Road's end / More action / Chase / Finale
CD _____ MAF 7025D
Intrada / Jul '92 / Silva Screen / Koch.

GREAT EXPECTATIONS
1993 Clwyd Cast
CD _____ CDTER 1209
TER / Mar '94 / Koch.

GREAT MOGHULS, THE
Souster, Tim & Shanti Sharma C
CD _____ FILMCD 064
Silva Screen / Feb '90 / Conifer / Silva Screen.

GREAT MUPPET CAPER, THE
Muppets
Main title / Hey, a movie / Big red bus / Happiness hotel / Lady Holiday / Steppin' out with a star / Apartment / Night life / First time it happens / Couldn't we ride / Piggy's fantasy / Great muppet caper / Homeward bound / Finale
CD _____ 74321 18246-2
BMG Kidz / Jan '94 / BMG.

GREAT ROCK 'N' ROLL SWINDLE, THE
Sex Pistols
God save the Queen (Symphony) / Johnny B. Goode / Roadrunner / Anarchy in the U.K. / Don't give me no lip child / Stepping stone / L'anarchie pour le UK / Silly thing / My way / I wanna be me / Something else / (We're gonna) Rock around the clock: Tenpole Tudor / Lonely boy / EMI (orchestral) / Great rock 'n' roll swindle / Friggin' in the riggin' / You need hands: McLaren, Malcolm / Who killed Bambi: Tenpole Tudor / Belsen was a gas (live) / Black arabs: Black Arabs / Substitute / No one is innocent: Biggs, Ronnie / C'mon everybody / Belsen was a gas: Biggs, Ronnie
CD _____ CDVDX 2510
Virgin / Jan '95 / EMI.

GREED IN THE SUN/PAUL GAUGIN
Delerue, Georges C
CD _____ PCD 101
Prometheus / Jan '89 / Silva Screen.

GREEN CARD
Zimmer, Hans C
CD _____ VSD 5309

Varese Sarabande/Colosseum / Apr '91 / Pinnacle / Silva Screen.

GREENWILLOW
1960 Broadway Cast
Loesser, Frank C
CD _____ DRGCD 19006
DRG / Jun '95 / New Note.

GREMLINS
Goldsmith, Jerry C
Gremlins mega madness / Make it shine / Out out: Gabriel, Peter / Gift / Gizmo / Mrs. Deagle / Gremlin rag
CD _____ GED 24044
Geffen / Oct '89 / BMG.

GREMLINS II
(The New Batch)
Goldsmith, Jerry C
Just you wait / Gizmo escapes / Leaky faucet / Cute / Pot luck / Visitors / Teenage mutant gremlins / Keep it quiet / No rats / Gremlin pudding / New trends / Gremlin credits
CD _____ VSD 5269
Varese Sarabande/Colosseum / Aug '90 / Pinnacle / Silva Screen.

GREY FOX, THE
Chieftains
Moloney, Paddy C
Main title / Oyster bed sequence / Country store sequence / Ride to Kamloops / Meeting tram at Ducks Siding / Chase / End titles / Sweet Betsy from Pike: Farnsworth, Richard
CD _____ DRGCD 9515
DRG / Jan '95 / New Note.

GRIFTERS, THE
Bernstein, Elmer C
CD _____ VSD 5290
Varese Sarabande/Colosseum / Dec '90 / Pinnacle / Silva Screen.

GRIND
1985 Broadway Cast
Grossman, Larry C
Fitzhugh, Ellen L
This must be the place / Cadava / Sweet thing like me / I get myself out / My daddy always taught me to share / All things to one man / Line / Katie, my love / Grind / Never put it in writing / I talk, you talk / Timing / These eyes of mine / New man / Down / Century of progress / Finale
CD _____ CDTER 1103
TER / Sep '95 / Koch.

GROUNDHOG DAY
Fenton, George C
Weatherman: McClinton, Delbert / Clouds / I got you babe: Sonny & Cher / Quartet No. 1 in D: Dukov, Bruce / Ground hog: Dukov, Bruce / Take me around again: Stevens, Susie / Drunks / You like boats but not the ocean / Phil getz the girl / Phil steals the money / Pennsylvania polka: Yankovic, Frank / You don't know me: Liebert, Ottmar & Luna Negra / Kidnap and the quarry / Sometimes people just die / Eighteenth variation from a rhapsody on a theme of Paganini: Buccheri, Elizabeth / Medley (Phil's piano solo, Eighteenth variation from rhapsodie on a theme of Paganini): Fryer, Terry / Ice sculpture / New day / Almost like being in love: Cole, Nat King
CD _____ 4736742
Epic / May '93 / Sony.

GUILTY BY SUSPICION
Howard, James Newton C
CD _____ VSD 5310
Varese Sarabande/Colosseum / Apr '91 / Pinnacle / Silva Screen.

GUITARRA
Bream, Julian
CD _____ BCM 314 CD
BCM / Oct '89 / Pinnacle.

GUNS FOR SAN SEBASTIAN/HANG 'EM HIGH
Morricone, Ennio C
CD _____ AK 47705
Cinevox / Jan '93 / Conifer / Silva Screen.

GUNS OF NAVARONE, THE
Tiomkin, Dimitri C
CD _____ VSD 5236
Varese Sarabande/Colosseum / Feb '90 / Pinnacle / Silva Screen.

GUYS AND DOLLS
1982 London Cast
Loesser, Frank C
Runyonland music / Fugue for tinhorns / Follow the fold / Oldest established craps game in New York / I'll know / Bushel and a peck / Adelaide's lament / Guys and dolls / If I were a bell / My time of day / I've never been in love before / Take back your mink / Adelaide's lament (reprise) / More I cannot wish you / Craps shooter's ballet / Luck be a lady / Sue me / Sit down you're the rockin' the boat / Marry the man today / Guys and dolls (reprise)
CD _____ CDMFP 5978
Music For Pleasure / Dec '92 / EMI.

GUYS AND DOLLS
1991 Broadway Cast
Loesser, Frank C
CD _____ 09026613172
RCA Victor / Oct '92 / BMG.

GUYS AND DOLLS
Original Broadway Cast
Loesser, Frank C
CD _____ MCLD 19155
MCA / Jan '93 / BMG.

GUYS AND DOLLS
Cast Recording
Loesser, Frank C
CD _____ CDTER2 1228
TER / Aug '95 / Koch.

GYPSIES
Milan / Apr '90 / BMG / Silva Screen.
CD _____ CDCH 305

GYPSY
1993 Film Cast
Styne, Jule C
Sondheim, Stephen L
Overture / May we entertain you / Some people / Small world / Baby June and her newsboys / Mr. Goldstone / Little lamb / You'll never get away from me / Dainty June and her farmboys / If Momma was married / All I need is the girl / Everthing's coming up roses / Together, wherever we go / You gotta get a gimmick / Let me entertain you / Rose's tune / End credits
CD _____ 7567825512
WEA / Mar '94 / Warner Music.

GYPSY
Ross, Annie & Buddy Bregman Band
CD _____ CDP 8335742
Pacific Jazz / Jan '96 / EMI.

HAIR
1968 Broadway Cast
MacDermot, Galt C
Ragni, Jerome & James Rado L
Aquarius / Donna / Hashish / Sodomy / Coloured spade / Manchester, England / I'm black / Ain't got no air / Initials / I got life / Hair / My conviction / Don't put it down / Frank Mills / Be in / Where do I go / Black boys / Where do I go / Easy to be hard / Walking in space / Abie baby / Three five zero zero / What a piece of work is man / Good morning starshine / Let the sunshine in
CD _____ 74321289852
RCA Victor / Aug '95 / BMG.

HAIR
1968 London Cast
MacDermot, Galt C
Ragni, Jerome & James Rado L
Aquarius: Edward, Vince & The Company / Donna: Dolas, Oliver & The Company / Sodomy: Feast, Michael & The Company / Coloured spade: Straker, Peter & The Company / Ain't got no: Feast, Michael/Peter Straker/Joanne White/The Company / Air: Kendrick, Linda & The Company / I got life: Nicholas, Paul & The Company / Hair: Nicholas, Paul/Oliver Tobias/The Company / My conviction: Forray, Andy / Easy to be hard: Leventon, Annabel / Frank Mills: Kristina, Sonja / Where do I go: Nicholas, Paul & The Company / Electric blues: Gulliver, John/ Rohan McCullough/Andy Forray/Jimmy Winston / Black boys: Kelly, Colette/Rohan McCullough/Lucy Fenwick / White boys: Hunt, Marsha/Ethel Coley/Joanne White / Walking in space / Able baby: Straker, Peter/Limbert Spencer/Leighton Robinson / Three five zero zero / What a piece of work is man: Edward, Vince & Leighton Robinson / Good morning starshine / Bed / Let the sunshine in
CD _____ 5199732
Polydor / Sep '93 / PolyGram.

HAIR
1993 London Cast
MacDermot, Galt C
Ragni, Jerome & James Rado L
Aquarius / Donna/Hashish / Holy orgy / Coloured spade / Manchester, England / I'm black / Ain't got no / Dead end / I believe in love / Ain't got / I got life / Initials / Going down / Hair / My conviction / Easy to be hard / Frank Mills / Hare Krishna / Where do I go / Electric blues / White boys / Walking in space / Yes, it's finished / Abie baby / All you have to do / Three five zero / Good morning starshine / Let the sunshine in
CD _____ CDEMC 3663
EMI / Nov '93 / EMI.

HAIR
1968 Broadway Cast
MacDermot, Galt C
Ragni, Jerome & James Rado L
CD _____ 11502
Silva Screen / Jan '89 / Conifer / Silva Screen.

HALF A SIXPENCE
1963 London Cast
Heneker, David C
Overture / All in the cause of economy / Half a sixpence / Money to burn / Oak and the ash / She's too far above me / I'm not talk-

ing to you / If the rain's got to fall / Old military canal / One that's run away / Long ago / Flash bang wallop / I know what i am / I'll build a palace / I only want a little house / Finale
CD _____ 8205892
Deram / Nov '90 / PolyGram.

HALF COCKED
Dragnalus: Unwound / Time expired: Slant 6 / Iron: Rodan / CB: Sleepyhead / Dusty: Ruby Falls / Drunk friend: Freakwater / Be-9: Versus / Can I hold: Polvo / (We got) Flowers in our hair: Big Heifer / Invertebrate: Boondoggie / Hey man went out: Dungbeetle / Truckstop theme: Dungbeetle / Want: Grifters / Thirty seven push-ups (LP only): Smog / Sex 60 (LP only): 2 Dollar Guitar / Satellite (LP only): Kicking Giant / Crazy man (LP only): Freakwater
CD _____ OLE 1522
Matador / Aug '95 / Vital.

HALLELUJAH TRAIL, THE
Bernstein, Elmer C
CD _____ TSU 0103
Tsunami / Jan '93 / Silva Screen.

HALLELUJAH, BABY
1967 Broadway Cast
Styne, Jule C
Comden, Betty & Adolph Green L
CD _____ SK 48218
Sony Broadway / Nov '92 / Sony.

HALLOWEEN
Carpenter, John C
CD _____ VCD 47230
Varese Sarabande/Colosseum / Jan '89 / Pinnacle / Silva Screen.

HALLOWEEN II
Carpenter, John & Alan Howarth C
CD _____ VCD 47152
Varese Sarabande/Colosseum / Jan '89 / Pinnacle / Silva Screen.

HALLOWEEN III
(Season Of The Witch)
Carpenter, John & Alan Howarth C
CD _____ VSD 5243
Varese Sarabande/Colosseum / Feb '90 / Pinnacle / Silva Screen.

HALLOWEEN IV
(The Return Of Michael Myers)
Howarth, Alan C
CD _____ VSD 5205
Varese Sarabande/Colosseum / Dec '88 / Pinnacle / Silva Screen.

HALLOWEEN V
(The Revenge Of Michael Myers)
Howarth, Alan C
Romeo Romeo: Becca / Dancin' on Churchill: Churchill / Sporting woman: Diggy/ Chosak/Clark / Shape also rises / First victim / Tower farm / Trapped / Jailbreak / Anything for money: DVB / Second time around: Rhythm Tribe / Halloween 5 - the revenge / Evil child must die / Stranger in the house / Stop the rage / Attic / Halloween finale
CD _____ VSD 5239
Varese Sarabande/Colosseum / Dec '89 / Pinnacle / Silva Screen.

HALLOWEEN VI
Howarth, Alan C
CD _____ VSD 5678
Varese Sarabande/Colosseum / Nov '95 / Pinnacle / Silva Screen.

HAMLET
Morricone, Ennio C
Hamlet (version 1) / King is dead / Ophelia (version) / What a piece of work is man / Prayer / Ghost / Play / Banquet / Dance for the queen / Ophelia (version 2) / Hamlet's madness / Hamlet (version 2) / Simulated madness / Closet / Second madness / To be or not to be / Solid flesh / Vaults
CD _____ 916002
Silva Screen / Jan '94 / Conifer / Silva Screen.

HAND THAT ROCKS THE CRADLE, THE
Revell, Graeme C
CD _____ HR 613042
Reprise / Mar '92 / Warner Music.

HANDMAID'S TALE, THE
Sakamoto, Ryuichi
Sakamoto, Ryuichi C
CD _____ GNPD 8020
GNP Crescendo / Dec '90 / Silva Screen.

HANNAH... 1939
Off-Broadway Cast
Merrill, Bob C
CD _____ CDTER 1192
TER / Jan '93 / Koch.

HANNA'S WAR/THE ASSIS UNDERGROUND
Seltzer, Dov C
CD _____ FILMCD 094
Silva Screen / Jun '92 / Conifer / Silva Screen.

HANS CHRISTIAN ANDERSON/THE COURT JESTER
Kaye, Danny
CD _____ VSD 5498
Varese Sarabande/Colosseum / Jun '94 / Pinnacle / Silva Screen.

HAPPY END
Cologne Pro Musica/Konig Ensemble
Weill, Kurt C
Brecht, Bertolt L
Latham Konig, J. Con
CD _____ 600151
Capriccio / Jun '90 / Target/BMG.

HAPPY END/THE SEVEN DEADLY SINS
Lenya, Lotte & Chorus/Orchestra
Weill, Kurt C
Brecht, Bertolt L
Bruckner Ruggenberg, W. Con
CD _____ CD 45886
CBS / Apr '91 / Sony.

HARD DAY'S NIGHT, A
Beatles
Beatles C
I should have known better / If I fell / I'm
happy just to dance with you / And I love
her / Tell me why / Can't buy me love / Hard
day's night / Anytime at all / I'll cry instead
/ Things we said today / When I get home
/ You can't do that / I'll be back
CD _____ CDP 7464372
Parlophone / Feb '87 / EMI.

HARD TARGET
Kodo Japanese Drum Ensemble
Revell, Graeme C
Simonec, T. Con
CD _____ VSD 5445
Pinnacle / Silva Screen.

HARD TO KILL/ABOVE THE LAW/OUT FOR JUSTICE
(Music From The Films Of Steven Seagal)
Frank, David Michael C
CD _____ GNPD 8028
GNP Crescendo / May '92 / Silva Screen.

HARD WAY, THE
Rubinstein, Arthur C
CD _____ VSD 5315
Varese Sarabande/Colosseum / Apr '91 / Pinnacle / Silva Screen.

HARDER THEY COME, THE
You can get it if you really want: Cliff, Jimmy / Many rivers to cross: Cliff, Jimmy / Harder they come: Cliff, Jimmy / Sitting in limbo: Cliff, Jimmy / Draw your brakes: Scotty / Rivers of Babylon: Melodians / Sweet and Dandy: Toots & The Maytals / Pressure drop: Toots & The Maytals / Johnny too bad: Slickers / Shanty town: Dekker, Desmond
CD _____ RRCD 11
Reggae Refreshers / Sep '90 / PolyGram / Vital.

HARDWARE
Boswell, Simon
Boswell, Simon C
CD _____ CDCH 627
Milan / Feb '94 / BMG / Silva Screen.

HARLEQUIN/THE DAY AFTER HALLOWEEN
May, Brian C
CD _____ IMICD 1010
Silva Screen / Jan '94 / Conifer / Silva Screen.

HARUM SCARUM/GIRL HAPPY
Presley, Elvis
Harem holiday / My desert serenade / Go eat young man / Mirage / Kismet / Shake that tambourine / Hey little girl / Golden coins / So close, yet so far / Animal instinct / Wisdom of the ages / Girl happy / Spring fever / Fort Lauderdale chamber of commerce / Startin' tonight / Wolf call / Do not disturb / Cross my heart and hope to die / Meanest girl in town / Do the clam / Puppet on a string / I've got to find my baby
CD _____ 74321 13433-2
RCA / Mar '93 / BMG.

HATARI
CD _____ 25592
Silva Screen / Jan '89 / Conifer / Silva Screen.

HAUNTED
Wiseman, Debbie C
CD _____ TRXCD 2002
Silva Screen / Nov '95 / Conifer / Silva Screen.

HAUNTED SUMMER
Young, Christopher
Young, Christopher C
Haunted summer / Menage / Villa diodati / Night was made for loving / Polidori's potions / Ariel / Confreres / Geneva / Alby / Unquiet dream / Hauntings
CD _____ FILMCD 037
Silva Screen / Jan '89 / Conifer / Silva Screen.

HAWAII
Bernstein, Elmer C
CD _____ TSU 0105
Tsunami / Jul '93 / Silva Screen.

HEAD
Monkees
CD _____ 4509976592
Warner Bros. / Dec '94 / Warner Music.

HEAR MY SONG
Altman, John C
Hear my song (main title) / Heartley's boogie / Nancy with the laughing face / Whis-

tling dance / Jenny picking cockies / I'll take you home again Kathleen / Foxhunter's reel/Mason's apron / Peter Byrne's fancy / Movin' / Getting Joe / Truth and beauty / Come back to Sorrento / Goodbye / Hear my song
CD _____ 7599244562
WEA / Apr '92 / Warner Music.

HEART OF MIDNIGHT
Yanni
Yanni C
Overture / Carol's theme / Welcome to "Midnight" / Carol through the rooms / Oh Daddy / Carol sees Fletcher/Rathead on ice / Carol's theme - soft interlude / Rape (parts I and II) / Aftermath / Carol talks to Maria / Sharpe no.2 dies/Carol's nightmare / Carol's theme - sadness of the heart / Library of porn / Cabinet falls / Carol out in the street / Dinner and downstairs in the club / S and M room / End sequence / Final confrontation / Carol's theme - sisters in pain / Sonny's death / Finale - Carol's theme
CD _____ FILMCD 119
Silva Screen / Apr '92 / Conifer / Silva Screen.

HEART OF THE STAG
CD _____ SCCD 1017
Southern Cross / Jan '89 / Silva Screen.

HEARTBEAT
Heartbeat: Berry, Nick / Hippy hippy shake: Swinging Blue Jeans / Always something there to remind me: Shaw, Sandie / Little Children: Kramer, Billy J. & The Dakotas / All day and all of the night: Kinks / World without love: Peter & Gordon / House of the rising sun: Animals / Shout: Lulu & The Luvvers / Don't let the sun catch you crying: Gerry & The Pacemakers / I'm into something good: Herman's Hermits / Needles and pins: Searchers / I believe: Bachelors / I like it: Gerry & The Pacemakers / Picture of you: Brown, Joe & The Bruvvers / Stranger on the shore: Bilk, Acker
CD _____ 4719002
Columbia / Jun '92 / Sony.

HEARTBEAT - THE BEST OF HEARTBEAT
CD _____ MOODCD 37
Columbia / Jan '95 / Sony.

HEARTBEAT II
Look through my window: Hollies / Go now: Moody Blues / Tired of waiting for you: Kinks / Bend me, shape me: Amen Corner / Sunny: Fame, Georgie / FBI: Shadows / Itchycoo Park: Small Faces / Crying game: Berry, Dave / They were made for me: Freddie & The Dreamers / Heartbeat: Berry, Nick / Hi ho silver lining: Beck, Jeff / Do you love me: Poole, Brian & The Tremeloes / Bad to me: Kramer, Billy J. & The Dakotas / You've got your troubles: Fortunes / When you walk in the room: Searchers / Gimme some lovin': Davis, Spencer Group / Mighty Quinn: Manfred Mann / Catch the wind: Donovan / Let it be: Cocker, Joe / Daydream believer: Berry, Nick
CD _____ 475529 2
Columbia / Nov '93 / Sony.

HEARTBREAK HIGH
CD _____ 4509999382
Warner Bros. / May '95 / Warner Music.

HEARTBREAKERS
Tangerine Dream
Tangerine Dream C
CD _____ FILMCD 163
Silva Screen / Jun '95 / Conifer / Silva Screen.

HEARTS AND SOULS
Shaiman, Marc C
CD _____ MCAD 10919
MCA/Silva Screen / Jul '94 / Silva Screen.

HEAT
CD _____ 9362461442
Warner Bros. / Jan '96 / Warner Music.

HEAT AND DUST
Robbins, Richard C
CD _____ CDQ 5551012
EMI / Apr '94 / EMI.

HEATHCLIFF
(Songs from)
Richard, Cliff
Misunderstood man / Sleep of the good / Gypsy bundle / Had to be: Richard, Cliff & Olivia Newton-John / When you thought of me / Dream tomorrow: Richard, Cliff & Olivia Newton-John / I do not love you Isabella (Heathcliff's wedding song): Richard, Cliff / Olivia Newton-John/Kristina Nichols / Choosing (when it's too late): Richard, Cliff & Olivia Newton-John / Marked with death: Richard, Cliff & Olivia Newton-John / Be with me always
CD _____ CDEMD 1091
EMI / Oct '95 / EMI.

HEAVEN AND EARTH
Kitaro
Kitaro C
Heaven and earth (land theme) / Sau dau tree / Ahn and Le Ly love theme / Saigon reunion / Arvn / Sau nightmare / V.C. Bonfire / Trong com / Ahn's house / Destiny / Last phone call / Child without a father / Village attack/The arrest / Walk to the village / Steve's ghosts / Return to Vietnam / End titles

CD _____ GED 24614
Geffen / Jan '94 / BMG.

HEIDI
Williams, John C
CD _____ LXE 707
CBS/Silva Screen / May '95 / Conifer / Silva Screen.

HELEN MORGAN STORY, THE
CD _____ 10302
Silva Screen / Jan '89 / Conifer / Silva Screen.

HELL CAN BE HEAVEN
1983 London Cast
Kaye, Hereward C
CD _____ CDTER 1068
TER / Aug '95 / Koch.

HELLO DOLLY
1967 Broadway Cast
Herman, Jerry C
CD _____ GD 81147
RCA Victor / Aug '91 / BMG.

HELLO DOLLY
1994 Studio Cast
Herman, Jerry C
CD _____ VSD 5557
Varese Sarabande/Colosseum / Jan '95 / Pinnacle / Silva Screen.

HELLO DOLLY
1964 Broadway Cast
Herman, Jerry C
Lang, P.J. Con
Prologue (Overture) / I put my hand in / It takes a woman / Put on your Sunday clothes / Ribbons down my back / Motherhood / Dancing / Before the parade passes by / Elegance / Hello Dolly / It only takes a moment / So long dearie / Finale
CD _____ GD 83814
RCA Victor / Oct '89 / BMG.

HELLO DOLLY
Film Cast
Herman, Jerry C
CD _____ 8103682
Silva Screen / May '84 / Conifer / Silva Screen.

HELLRAISER
Young, Christopher
Young, Christopher C
Resurrection / Hellbound heart / Lament configuration / Reunion / Quick death / Seduction and pursuit / In love's name / Cenobites / Rat slice quartet / Re-resurrection / Uncle Frank / Brought on by night / Another puzzle
CD _____ FILMCD 021
Silva Screen / Nov '87 / Conifer / Silva Screen.

HELLRAISER II
(Hellbound)
Graunke Symphony Orchestra
Young, Christopher C
Young, Christopher Con
Hellbound / Second sight seance / Looking through a woman / Something to think about / Skin her alive / Stringing the puppet / Hall of mirrors / Dead or living / Leviathan / Sketch with fire
CD _____ GNPD 8015
GNP Crescendo / Jan '89 / Silva Screen.

HELLRAISER III
Hellraiser / Go with me / What girls want / I feel like Steve / Troublemaker / Ooh-la-la / Baby universal / Divine thing / Down down down / Hell on earth / Waltzing with a jugular / Elected
CD _____ 8283602
London / Jan '93 / PolyGram.

HELLRAISER III
(Score)
Mosfilm State Orchestra & Choir
Miller, Randy C
CD _____ GNPD 8033
GNP Crescendo / Nov '92 / Silva Screen.

HELP
Beatles
Beatles C
Help / Night before / You've got to hide your love away / I need you / Another girl / You're going to lose that girl / Ticket to ride / Act naturally / It's only love / You like me too much / Tell me what you see / I've just seen a face / Yesterday / Dizzy Miss Lizzy
CD _____ CDP 7464392
Parlophone / Apr '87 / EMI.

HEMINGWAY'S ADVENTURES OF A YOUNG MAN
Waxman, Franz C
CD _____ LXCD 1
Silva Screen / Jan '89 / Conifer / Silva Screen.

HENRY
(Portrait Of A Serial Killer)
Normal/Okra / Sep '94 / Direct / ADA.
CD _____ QDKCD 004

HENRY AND JUNE
Splet, Alan
Splet, Alan C
CD _____ VSD 5294
Varese Sarabande/Colosseum / Apr '91 / Pinnacle / Silva Screen.

HENRY V
City Of Birmingham Symphony Orchestra
Doyle, Patrick C
Rattle, Simon Con
Oh for a muse of fire / Henry V (The boar's head) / Three traitors / Now, lords, for France / Death of Falstaff / Once more unto the breach / Threat to the governor of Harfleur / Katherine of France / March to Calais / Death of Bardolph / Upon the king / St. Crispin's day (The battle of Agincourt) / Day is come / Non nobis domine / Wooing of Katherine / Let this acceptance take / End titles
CD _____ CDC 7499192
EMI / Sep '89 / EMI.

HERE'S LOVE
1963 Broadway Cast
Willson, Meredith C
Lawrence, E. Con
CD _____ SK 48204
Sony Classical / '90 / Sony.

HERITAGE: CIVILISATION AND THE JEWS
(Symphonic Dances)
Royal Philharmonic Orchestra
Bernstein, Leonard/John Duffy C
Williams, Richard Con
On the Town (dance episodes) / Heritage symphonic dances / Heritage fanfare and chorale / Heritage suite for orchestra
CD _____ CDDCA 630
ASV / Oct '88 / Koch.

HERO AND THE TERROR
Frank, David Michael C
Obsession / Workout / Terror / Hero's seduction / San Pedro bust / Ladies room / Breakout / Birthday wishes / Discovery / Showtime / Angela / Subterranean terror / Simon's lair / Search / Living nightmare / Love and obsession
CD _____ EDL 25082
Edel / Jan '90 / Pinnacle.

HEROES, THE/HEROES II: THE RETURN
Best, Peter
Best, Peter C
CD _____ FILMCD 112
Silva Screen / Jul '92 / Conifer / Silva Screen.

HIDDEN, THE
Convertino, Michael C
CD _____ VCD 47349
Varese Sarabande/Colosseum / Jan '89 / Pinnacle / Silva Screen.

HIDEAWAY
Fine Line / Jun '95 / Disc.
CD _____ IONIC 12CD

HIDER IN THE HOUSE
Young, Christopher C
CD _____ MAF 7007D
Intrada / Jan '94 / Silva Screen / Koch.

HIGH HEELS
Sakamoto, Ryuichi C
CD _____ 5108552
Silva Screen / Jul '94 / Conifer / Silva Screen.

HIGH NOON
Foster Radio Symphony Orchestra
Tiomkin, Dimitri C
CD _____ 09026626582
RCA / Nov '95 / BMG.

HIGH NOON
(Also Includes The Alamo, Cyrano De Bergerac, 55 Days At Peking, The High And The Mighty)
Berlin Radio Symphony Orchestra
Tiomkin, Dimitri C
Foster, Lawrence Con
CD _____ 9026656582
RCA Victor / Nov '95 / BMG.

HIGH SIGN, THE
(New Jazz Score For Buster Keaton Film)
Frisell, Bill
Frisell, Bill C
CD _____ 7559793512
Elektra / Jan '95 / Warner Music.

HIGH SOCIETY
Film Cast
Porter, Cole C
Overture / Calypso / Little one / You're sensational / I love you Samantha / Now you has jazz / Well did you evah / Mind if I make love to you
CD _____ CDP 7937872
Capitol / Apr '95 / EMI.

HIGH SOCIETY
(Highlights - The Shows Collection)
1994 Studio Cast
Porter, Cole C
CD _____ PWKS 4193
Carlton Home Entertainment / Mar '94 / Carlton Home Entertainment.

HIGH SPIRITS
Fenton, George
Fenton, George C
Overture / Castle Plunkett / Plunkett's lament / Ghost bus tours / Ghostly reflections / She is from the far land / Bumps in the knight / Mary appears
CD _____ GNPD 8016
GNP Crescendo / '88 / Silva Screen.

HIGH SPIRITS
(inc. Four Bonus Songs Performed By
Noel Coward)
1964 London Cast
Martin, Hugh & Timothy Gray *C*
Overture / Was she prettier than I / Bicycle
song / You'd better love me / Where is the
man I married / Go into your trance / Forever and a day / Something tells me / I
know your heart / Faster than sound / If I
gave you / Talking to you / Home sweet
heaven / Something is coming to tea / What
in the world did you want / Faster than
sound (reprise) / High spirits / Something to
tell me
CD _____ CDSBL 13107
DRG / Oct '92 / New Note.

HIGH VELOCITY
National Philharmonic Orchestra
Goldsmith, Jerry *C*
CD _____ PCD 134
Prometheus / Sep '94 / Silva Screen.

HIGHER LEARNING
Higher: *Ice Cube* / Something to think
about: *Ice Cube* / Soul searchin' (I wanna
know if it's mine): *Ndegeocello, Me'shell* /
Situatuion grimm: *Mista Grimm* / Ask of you:
Saadiq, Raphael / Losing my religion: *Amos,
Tori* / Butterfly: *Amos, Tori* / Time for a
change: *Brand New Heavies* / Learning
curve: *Clarke, Stanley* / Eye: *Eve's Plum* /
By your side: *Zhane* / Don't have time:
Phair, Liz / Phobia: *Outkast* / Higher learn-
ing: *Brand New Heavies* / My new friend:
Hauser, Les & Michael Paraport / Year of
the boomerang: *Rage Against The Machine*
CD _____ 4783512
Epic / Feb '95 / Sony.

HIGHLANDER - THE FINAL DIMENSION
(Highlander I/II/III)
Kamen, Michael/Stewart Copeland/J.Peter
Robinson *C*
CD _____ EDL 28892
Edel / Oct '95 / Pinnacle.

HIGHLANDER II
(The Quickening)
Copeland, Stewart *C*
Trust / One dream / Who's that man part 1
/ Haunted / Here we go / As time goes by
/ It's a perfect, perfect world / Bird flight /
Destroy shield / Sun shield/Dam escape
CD _____ 9031736572
Bronze / Apr '91 / Warner Music.

HIGHLANDER III
Honest Joe: *James* / Immortality: *Fall* / Yalili
ya aini: *Jah Wobble's Invaders Of The Heart*
/ High in your face: *House Of Love* / Cry
mercy judge: *Verlaine, Tom* / Jam 3: *James*
/ Sept Marins/Hanter Dro: *Whirling Pope
Joan* / Bonny Portmore: *McKennitt, Loreena*
/ Quiet mind - for Joe: *Ruby Blue* / Ce he
mise le ulaingt: *McKennitt, Loreena* / Two
trees: *McKennitt, Loreena* / Little muscle:
Catherine Wheel / Dummy crusher: *Kerb-
dog* / Becoming more like God: *Jah Wob-
ble's Invaders Of The Heart* / Bluebeard:
Cocteau Twins
CD _____ 5267472
Mercury / Mar '95 / PolyGram.

HILL STREET BLUES
Caine, Daniel Orchestra
Post, Mike *C*
Caine, Daniel *Con*
Theme / Cruising on the hill / Field of honour
/ Blues in the day / Wasted / City / No jive
/ Freedom's end / Night on the hill / Forever
/ Conviction / Captain / Friend on the hill /
Officer down / Suite from the Hill Street
Blues
CD _____ FILMCD 702
Silva Screen / '91 / Conifer / Silva Screen.

HIRED MAN, THE
1992 London Cast
Goodall, Howard *C*
Song of the hired men / Scene: the Tallen-
tire boys / Fill it to the top / Now for the first
time / Narration 3 / Work song: It's all right for
you / Narration II / Who will you marry then
/ Scene: Jackson and Emily / Get up and
go lad / I wouldn't be the first / Scene: Emily
did you get the message / Fade away / Hear
your voice / What a fool I've been / If I could
/ Narration III / You never see the sun /
Scene: Jackson meets May / Scene: Harry,
you're not going down the pit / What would
you say to your son / Union song: Men of
stone / Narration IV / Farewell song / War
song: So tell your children / Narration V /
No choir of angels / Scene: the mining disaster / Scene: John and Seth / Re-hiring
2CD _____ CDTER2 1189
TER / May '92 / Koch.

HITCHER, THE
Isham, Mark *C*
CD _____ FILMCD 118
Silva Screen / Mar '92 / Conifer / Silva
Screen.

HMS PINAFORE
New Sadler's Wells Opera Chorus/
Orchestra
Sullivan, Sir Arthur *C*
Gilbert, W.S. *L*
Phipps, S. *Con*
2CD _____ CDTER2 1150
TER / May '88 / Koch.

HMS PINAFORE
D'Oyly Carte Opera Chorus/New Sym-
phony Orchestra
Sullivan, Sir Arthur *C*
Gilbert, W.S. *L*
Godfrey, I. *Con*
2CD _____ 4142832
Decca / Jan '90 / PolyGram.

HMS PINAFORE
Welsh National Opera/Orchestra
Sullivan, Sir Arthur *C*
Gilbert, W.S.L
Mackerras, C. *Con*
CD _____ CD 80374
Telarc / Jan '95 / Conifer / ADA.

HMS PINAFORE/THE MIKADO
D'Oyly Carte Opera Chorus/New Sym-
phony Orchestra
Sullivan, Sir Arthur *C*
Gilbert, W.S.L
Sargent, Sir Malcolm *Con*
2CD _____ CDHD 253/4
Happy Days / Jan '94 / Conifer.

HMS PINAFORE/TRIAL BY JURY
Baker, George & John Cameron/Glynde-
bourne Festival Choir/Pro Arte Orchestra
Sullivan, Sir Arthur *C*
Gilbert, W.S.L
Sargent, Sir Malcolm *Con*
2CD _____ CMS 7643972
EMI Classics / Apr '94 / EMI.

HOFFA
Newman, David *C*
CD _____ 07822110012
Fox Film Scores / Jan '94 / BMG.

HOME ALONE II
(Score)
Williams, John *C*
CD _____ 07822110002
Fox Film Scores / Dec '92 / BMG.

HOME ALONE II
All alone on Christmas: *Love, Darlene* /
Holly jolly Christmas: *Jackson, Alan* / Some-
where in my memory: *Midler, Bette* / My
Christmas tree: *Home Alone Children's
Choir* / Sombras de otros tiempos (Some-
where in my memory): *Belen, Ana* / Merry
Christmas, Merry Christmas: *Williams, John*
/ Cool jerk (Christmas mix): *Capitols* / It's
beginning to look a lot like Christmas:
Mathis, Johnny / Christmas star: *Williams,
John* / O come all ye faithful: *Fischer, Lisa*
CD _____ 74321165162
Arista / Oct '93 / BMG.

HOMEBOY
Clapton, Eric
Kamen, Michael & Eric Clapton *C*
I want to love you baby: *Benson, Jo* / Hom-
eboy / Call me if you need me: *Magic Sam*
/ Final fight / Travelling East / Bridge
CD _____ CDV 2574
Virgin / Dec '88 / EMI.

HOMEWARD BOUND
Broughton, Bruce *C*
CD _____ MAF 7041D
Intrada / Jan '94 / Silva Screen / Koch.

HOMO FABER (THE VOYAGE)
CD _____ CDCH 804
Milan / Mar '92 / BMG / Silva Screen.

HONEY, I BLEW UP THE KIDS
Broughton, Bruce *C*
Broughton, Bruce *Con*
CD _____ MAF 7030D
Intrada / Sep '92 / Silva Screen / Koch.

HONEYMOON IN VEGAS
Newman, David *C*
All shook up: *Joel, Billy* / Wear my ring
around your neck: *Van Shelton, Ricky* /
Love me tender: *Grant, Amy* / Burning love:
Tritt, Travis / Heartbreak hotel: *Joel, Billy* /
Are you lonesome tonight: *Ferry, Bryan* /
Suspicious minds: *Yoakam, Dwight* / Devil
in disguise: *Yearwood, Trisha* / Hound dog:
Beck, Jeff & Jed Leiber / That's all right: *Gill,
Vince* / Jailhouse rock: *Mellencamp, John* /
Blue Hawaii: *Nelson, Willie* / Can't help fall-
ing in love: *Bono*
CD _____ 471925 2
Epic / Aug '94 / Sony.

HOOP DREAMS
Hoop dreams / Traveling music / Original
lesson / Float / Tide (keeps lifting me) /
Above the rim / Low post / Fast break / Un-
der the knife / Junior moved / Walking the
walk / Face / Sweet dreams
CD _____ GFLD 19305
Geffen / Oct '95 / BMG.

HOPE AND GLORY
Martin, Peter *C*
CD _____ VCD 47290
Varese Sarabande/Colosseum / Jan '89 /
Pinnacle / Silva Screen.

HORROR OF DRACULA, THE
Bernard, James *C*
Main theme / Inside castle Dracula / Lure of
the vampire woman / Dracula's rage / Intro-
duction / Hammer house of horror / Lord of
the vampiric hordes / Horror of Dracula /
Legend / Castle Dracula / Kiss of living
death / Blood-splashed bride / Death of
Dracula / Final horror / Epilogue / Funeral in
Carpathia / Romance: At dusk / Pursuit/
Death of Lucy / Victory of love

HMS PINAFORE
CD _____ FILMCD 708
Silva Screen / '92 / Conifer / Silva Screen.

HOT MIKADO
London Cast
CD _____ CASTCD 48
First Night / Jul '95 / Pinnacle.

HOT SHOE SHUFFLE
1993 Australian Cast
CD _____ CASTCD 41
First Night / Mar '94 / Pinnacle.

HOT SHOE SHUFFLE
Cast Recording
CD _____ FLHSSCD 1
JVO / Dec '95 / Pinnacle.

HOT SHOTS
Levay, Sylvester *C*
CD _____ VSD 5338
Varese Sarabande/Colosseum / Sep '91 /
Pinnacle / Silva Screen.

HOUR OF THE GUN
Goldsmith, Jerry *C*
CD _____ MAF 7020D
Intrada / Jan '93 / Silva Screen / Koch.

HOUSE OF ELIOT
Parker, Jim *C*
House of Eliot / Tango De La Luna / Shopping spree / Evie's tune / Eliott rag / Manhattan blues / Brooklands / Highgate memories / Jack's blues / Fashion parade / Tiger
moth / Paris morning / Wedding / Paris by
night / Hermitage (A new ballet) / Beatrice
and Jack / New apartment / Paraquay /
Funny man blues / Charity waltz / Reunion
blues / Leaving for America
CD _____ CDSTM 5
Soundtrack Music / Jul '93 / EMI.

**HOUSE OF FRANKENSTEIN/GHOST OF
FRANKENSTEIN**
RTE Concert Orchestra
Salter, Hans *C*
Penny, A. *Con*
CD _____ 8223477
Marco Polo / Aug '94 / Select.

**HOUSE ON SORORITY ROW, THE/THE
ALCHEMIST**
London Philharmonic Orchestra
Band, Richard *C*
Band, Richard *Con*
CD _____ MAF 7046D
Intrada / '93 / Silva Screen / Koch.

HOUSE PARTY II
Announcement of pajama jammi jam /
House party (Don't know what you come to
do) / Christopher Robinson scholarship
fund / Ready or not / Kid 'n' play wreck
shop / Ain't gonna hurt nobody / I like your
style (House Party II swing theme) / Kid and
Sydney break up candelight and you / I just
4 U (House Party II passion theme) / Bilal
gets off / Let me know something (House
Party II mental theme) / Yo baby yo / F.F.F.
Rap what's on your mind (House Party II
rap theme) / Big ol' jazz (House Party II memorial) / You gotta pay what you owe / It's
so hard to say goodbye to yesterday / Confidence / It's so hard to say goodbye to yesterday (Acapella) / Kid's goodbye thanks to
Pope
CD _____ MCLD 19246
MCA / Apr '94 / BMG.

HOUSE/HOUSE II
Manfredini, Harry *C*
CD _____ VCD 47295
Varese Sarabande/Colosseum / Jan '89 /
Pinnacle / Silva Screen.

HOUSEKEEPING
Gibbs, Michael
Gibbs, Michael *C*
CD _____ VCD 47308
Varese Sarabande/Colosseum / Jan '89 /
Pinnacle / Silva Screen.

HOW GREEN WAS MY VALLEY
Newman, Alfred *C*
CD _____ 07822110082
Fox Film Scores / Apr '94 / BMG.

HOW THE WEST WAS WON
Newman, Alfred *C*
CD _____ AK 47024
Cinevox / Jan '93 / Conifer / Silva Screen.

HOW TO MAKE LOVE TO A NEGRO
Dibango, Manu
Dibango, Manu *C*
CD _____ CDCH 513
Milan / Feb '90 / BMG / Silva Screen.

HOW TO STEAL A MILLION
Williams, John *C*
CD _____ TSU 0109
Tsunami / Jan '93 / Silva Screen.

HOWARD'S END
Robbins, Richard *C*
CD _____ NI 5339
Nimbus / Apr '92 / Nimbus.

**HOWARD'S END/MAURICE/A ROOM
WITH A VIEW**
Robbins, Richard *C*
Rabinowitz, H. *Con*
3CD _____ CMS 5652202
EMI / Jan '91 / EMI.

HUDSON HAWK
Kamen, Michael *C*
CD _____ VSD 5323

Varese Sarabande/Colosseum / Jul '91 /
Pinnacle / Silva Screen.

HUMANOID, THE/NIGHTMARE CASTLE
Morricone, Ennio *C*
CD _____ OST 118
Milano Dischi / Jan '93 / Silva Screen.

HUNDRA, THE
Morricone, Ennio *C*
CD _____ PCD 107
Prometheus / Jan '93 / Silva Screen.

HUNGER, THE
Rubini, Michael & Denny Jaeger *C*
CD _____ VSD 47261
Varese Sarabande/Colosseum / Oct '94 /
Pinnacle / Silva Screen.

**HUNGER, THE/THE YEAR OF LIVING
DANGEROUSLY**
CD _____ CDCH 004
Milan / Feb '94 / BMG / Silva Screen.

HUNT FOR RED OCTOBER, THE
Poledouris, Basil *C*
CD _____ MCLD 19306
MCA / Oct '95 / BMG.

HUNTERS, THE
Residents
CD _____ 311692
Milan / Dec '95 / BMG / Silva Screen.

HUNTING OF THE SNARK
1991 London Cast
Batt, Mike *C*
CD _____ CASTCD 24
First Night / Nov '91 / Pinnacle.

HYPERSPACE
(Inc. Symphonic Suite From Beauty &
The Beast)
Davis, Don *C*
CD _____ PCD 120
Prometheus / Jan '93 / Silva Screen.

I AND ALBERT
1972 London Cast
Strouse, Charles *C*
Adams, Lee *L*
Draw the blinds / I and Albert / Leave it
alone / I've 'eard the bloody 'indoos
CD _____ CDTER 1004
TER / Aug '95 / Koch.

I LIKE IT LIKE THAT
Try a little tenderness: *Barrio Boyzz* / I like
it: *Blackout Allstars* / Latin lingo (Blackout
mix): *Cypress Hill* / Like Father, like son:
Main One - Ghetto Child / I'm tryin' to tell
'em: *Fat Joe* / Come baby come: *K7* / Forever: *C & C Music Factory* / You better
change: *Cover Girls* / Si tu no te fuera: *Anthony, Mark* / Eres tu: *Rivera, Jerry* / Brin-
quen salten: *Shabbakan*
CD _____ 4773342
Columbia / Jan '95 / Sony.

I LOVE MY WIFE
Broadway Cast
Coleman, Cy *C*
Stewart, Michael *L*
We're still friends / Monica / By threes /
Love revolution / Mover's life / Someone
wonderful I missed / Sexually free / Hey
there / Good times / By the way if you are
free tonight / Lovers on Christmas Eve /
Scream / Ev'rybody today is turning on /
Married couple seeks married couple / I
love my wife / In conclusion
CD _____ DRGCD 6109
DRG / Jan '89 / New Note.

I LOVE YOU PERFECT
Yanni
Yanni *C*
Theme / Lovers quarrel / Allan fired / Chair
shower and court room montage / Setting
the horse free / Lovers make up / Cabaret
quintet K.581 - allegretto: *Camerata Aca-
demica Salzburg* / Marry me / I'll be by your
side / Temper tantrum / But I have some
good days / Hospital montage / Christina
dies / I love you perfect (reprise)
CD _____ FILMCD 122
Silva Screen / Jun '93 / Conifer / Silva
Screen.

I NEVER TOLD YOU
Hersch, Fred *C*
CD _____ VSD 5547
Varese Sarabande/Colosseum / Jul '95 /
Pinnacle / Silva Screen.

I REMEMBER MAMA
1985 Studio Cast
Rodgers, Richard *C*
Charnin, Martin *L*
I remember Mama / Little bit more / Writer
writes at night / Ev'ry day (comes something beautiful) / You could not please me
more / Most disagreeable man/Uncle Chris
/ Lullaby / Easy come, easy go / It's not the
end of the world / Entr'acte / Mama always
makes it better / When / Fair trade / I write,

you read (fair trade) / It's going to be good to be gone / Time / Finale
CD _____ **CDTER 1102**
TER / Oct '85 / Koch.

ICE CASTLES
Hamlisch, Marvin C
CD _____ **ARCD 8317**
Silva Screen / Jan '89 / Conifer / Silva Screen.

ICEMAN
Smeaton, Bruce C
CD _____ **SCCD 1006**
Southern Cross / Jan '89 / Silva Screen.

IGNACIO
Vangelis
Vangelis C
CD _____ **813 042 2**
Phonogram / Jul '85 / PolyGram.

IL SOLE ANCHE DI NOTTE
Piovani, Nicola C
CD _____ **CH 605**
Milan / Jan '95 / BMG / Silva Screen.

I'LL DO ANYTHING
Zimmer, Hans C
Glennie-Smith, Nick Con
CD _____ **VSD 5474**
Varese Sarabande/Colosseum / '94 / Pinnacle / Silva Screen.

I'M GETTING MY ACT TOGETHER AND TAKING IT ON THE ROAD
1981 London Cast
Ford, Nancy C
Cryer, Grotchen L
Natural high / Smile / In a simple way / Miss Africa / Strong woman number / Dear Tom / Old friend / Put in a package and sold / If only things were different / Feel the love / Lonely lady / Happy birthday
CD _____ **CDTER 1006**
TER / May '89 / Koch.

IMMORTAL BELOVED
Beethoven, Ludvig Van C
Solti, George Con
CD _____ **SK 66301**
Sony Classical / Mar '95 / Sony.

IN CUSTODY
CD _____ **CDQ 5550972**
EMI / Apr '94 / EMI.

IN SEARCH OF ANGELS
In search of angels: Story, Tim / Angel of the elegies: Story, Tim / Voices in the liquid air: Story, Tim / Angelos: Story, Tim / Woman at the well: Story, Tim / Theme reprise: Story, Tim / Calling all angels: Story, Jane & K D Lang / Requiem in paradisium: Trinity Boys Choir / Close cover: Mertens, Wim / Assumpta est Maria in coelum: Schroeder-Sheker, Terese / Star in the east: St. Olaf Choir / Good thing (angels running): Larkin, Patty / Love's ash dissolves: Isham, Mark / Oh of pleasure: Sevag, Oystein / Jesus Christ the apple tree: American Boys' Choir
CD _____ **01934111532**
Windham Hill / Nov '94 / Pinnacle / BMG / ADA.

IN THE ARMY NOW
Sinfonia Of London
Folk, Robert C
CD _____ **MAF 7058D**
Intrada / Sep '94 / Silva Screen I.

IN THE BLOOD
CD _____ **RCD 20174**
Rykodisc / Aug '91 / Vital / ADA.

IN THE GOOD OLD SUMMERTIME/ GOOD NEWS/TWO WEEKS
Cast Recording
Henderson, Ray C
De Sylva, B.G. & Lew Brown L
CD _____ **MCAD 5951**
MCA/Silva Screen / Jan '89 / Silva Screen.

IN THE LINE OF DUTY
Snow, Mark C
CD _____ **MAF 7034D**
Intrada / Dec '92 / Silva Screen I.

IN THE MOUTH OF MADNESS
Carpenter, John & Jim Lang
Carpenter, John & Jim Lang C
In the mouth of madness / Robby's office / Axe man / Bookstore creep / Alley nightmare / Trent makes the map / Boy and his bike / Don't look down / Hobb's end / Pickman Hotel / Picture changes / Black church / You're wrong, Trent / Mommy's day / Do you like my ending / I'm losing me / Main street / Hobb's end escape / Portal opens / Old ones return / Book comes back / Madness outside / Just a bedtime story
CD _____ **DRGCD 12611**
DRG / Mar '95 / New Note.

IN THE NAME OF THE FATHER
Jones, Trevor C
In the name of the Father: Bono & Gavin Friday / Voodoo chile: Hendrix, Jimi / Billy Boola: Bono & Gavin Friday / Dedicated follower of fashion: Kinks / Interrogation: Jones, Trevor / Is this love: Marley, Bob / Walking the circle: Jones, Trevor / Whiskey in the jar: Thin Lizzy / Passage of time: Jones, Trevor / You made me the thief of your heart: O'Connor, Sinead
CD _____ **IMCD 208**
Island / Apr '95 / PolyGram.

IN WITH THE OLD
1986 BBC Radio 2 Cast
Prelude / Music goes round and around / I want to be happy / Did you ever see a dream walking / Stompin' at the Savoy / I'm putting all my eggs in one basket / Only a glass of champagne / Ten cents a dance / Goody goody / Zing went the strings of my heart / Lulu's back in town / Pretty baby / Where are the songs we sung / Storm / And her mother came too / With plenty of money and you / Playout
CD _____ **CDTER 1122**
TER / Aug '95 / Koch.

INCHON
Goldsmith, Jerry C
Goldsmith, Jerry Con
CD _____ **FMT 8002D**
Intrada / Feb '90 / Silva Screen / Koch.

INDIAN RUNNER, THE
Feelin' alright: Traffic / Comin' back to me: Jefferson Airplane / Fresh air: Quicksilver Messenger Service / Green river: Creedence Clearwater Revival / Brothers for good: Haller, Eric & Bert / Summertime: Joplin, Janis & Big Brother & The Holding Company / I shall be released: Band / Cold day in Omaha / Flop house / Goin' to Columbus / Brothers / Bye Mommy / Indian runner / Bad news / Criminal blood / My brother Frank
CD _____ **CDEST 2163**
Capitol / Nov '91 / EMI.

INDIANA JONES AND THE LAST CRUSADE
Williams, John C
Williams, John (1) Con
Indy's very first adventure / X marks the spot / Scherzo for motorcycle and orchestra / Ah rats / Escape from Venice / No ticket / Keeper of the grail / Keeping up with the Joneses / Brother of the cruciform sword / Belly of the steel beast / Canyon of the crescent moon / Penitent man will pass / End credits (raiders march)
CD _____ **K 9258832**
WEA / Jun '89 / Warner Music.

INDOCHINA
Doyle, Patrick C
CD _____ **VSD 5397**
Varese Sarabande/Colosseum / Jan '93 / Pinnacle / Silva Screen.

INFERNO
Emerson, Keith
Emerson, Keith C
Inferno / Rose's descent into the cellar / Taxi ride / Library / Sarah in the library vaults / Bookbinder's delight / Rose leaves the apartment / Rose gets / Elisa's story / Cat attic attack / Kazanians tarantella / Mark's discovery / Mater tenebrarum / Inferno (finals) / Cigarettes, ices, etc.
CD _____ **CDCIA 5022**
Cinevox / Jan '93 / Conifer / Silva Screen.

INKWELL, THE
Dancing machine: Jade / Let's get it on: Jade / On and on: Knight, Gladys & The Pips / Lets get it on: Gaye, Marvin / Fire: Ohio Players / Do you like it: B.T. Express / This house is smokin': B.T. Express / Do it (till you're satisfied): B.T. Express / Everything good to you: B.T. Express / Jam: Graham Central Station / I don't know what it is but it sure is funky: Graham Central Station
CD _____ **74321 21568-2**
Giant / Jul '94 / BMG.

INNER CIRCLE, THE
Artemyev, Eduard C
CD _____ **262494**
Milan / Jan '95 / BMG / Silva Screen.

INNOCENT, THE
Gouriet, Gerald C
CD _____ **164622**
Milan / Jan '95 / BMG / Silva Screen.

INSPECTOR MORSE (The Essential Collection)
PhellOung, Barrington
PhellOung, Barrington C
Inspector Morse (theme) / Evolving mystery / Andantino (from Debussy's String Quartet op10) / Lewis and Morse / Mi tradi quell alma ingrata (from Mozart's Don Giovanni k527) / Student's death / Eirl theme / Dark suspicion / Adieu notre petite table (from Massenet's Manon) / Worrying dilemma / La fille aux cheveux de lin (from Debussy's Preludes For Piano book 1) / Sad suspicion / Senza mamma (from Puccini's Suor Angelica) / Sad echoes / Terzettino - soave sia il vento (from Mozart's Cosi Fan Tutte k588) / Morse's remorse / String quartet in C minor d.703 - Quartettsatz (Schubert) / Inspector Morse theme (piano version)
CD _____ **VTCD 62**
Virgin / Nov '95 / EMI.

INSPECTOR MORSE I
PhellOung, Barrington
PhellOung, Barrington C
Main theme / Oxfordshire country home / Overture from Die Zauberflöte / K 620 / Student's death / Morse's optimism / O Isis and Osiris / Potential murder / Morse on the case / Macabre pursuit / Sad discovery / Senza mama / Hunt / Oxford college / Lewis / Gothic ritual / Closing credits

CD _____ **VTCDX 2**
Virgin Television / Jan '95 / EMI.

INSPECTOR MORSE II
PhellOung, Barrington
PhellOung, Barrington C
Main theme / Warmer side of Morse / Che faro senza Eurydice (From 'Orfed et Eurydice') / Gently sinister revelation / Concerto for 2 mandolini in G (Vivaldi arr: Barrington PhellOung) / Sad echoes / Mitradi quell alma ingrata (From 'Don Giovanni') / Gentle loving / Andante (Wolfgan Amadeus Mozart) / Lewis and Morse / Chorale 'er kenne mich mein huter' (From St Matthew Passion) / Morse's sympathetic ear / Adagio quintet in C / Tenderness / Tersettino 'soave sia il vento' (From 'Cosi Fan Tutte') / Morse's second chance / Signore Ascolta (From 'Turandot')
CD _____ **VTCD 14**
Virgin Television / Feb '92 / EMI.

INSPECTOR MORSE III
PhellOung, Barrington
PhellOung, Barrington C
Eirl theme / Oxford / Duet: Bei Mannern - Welche Liebe Fühlen / Cryptic contemplation / Adante from string sextet No 1 in Bb OP 18 / Reflections / Traume from wesendonk-lieder / Generic Morse theme / Dark suspicion / Adagio from piano concert K488 in A / Apprension - confession - resolution / Promised land / Hab'mir's gelbot from der rosenkavalier / Painful admissions / Adieu notre petite from manon / Quiet awakening / Brunnhilde's immolation from gotterdammerung / Main theme
CD _____ **VTCD 16**
Virgin Television / Jan '95 / EMI.

INSPECTOR MORSE VOLS I-III
PhellOung, Barrington
PhellOung, Barrington C
3CD _____ **TPAK 27**
Virgin / Jan '95 / EMI.

INTERSECTION
Howard, James Newton C
CD _____ **191912**
Milan / May '94 / BMG / Silva Screen.

INTERVIEW WITH THE VAMPIRE
Goldenthal, Elliot C
Sheffer, Jonathan Con
Libera me / Born to darkness / Lestat's tarantella / Madeleine's lament / Claudia's allegro agitato / Escape to Paris / Marche funebre / Lestat's recitative / Santiago's waltz / Theatre des vampires / Armand's seduction / Plantation pyre / Forgotten lore / Scent of death / Abduction and absolution / Armand rescues Louis / Louis revenge / Born to darkness part II / Sympathy for the devil: Guns N' Roses
CD _____ **GED 24719**
Geffen / Jan '95 / BMG.

INTO THE WEST
Doyle, Patrick C
CD _____ **SBK 890492**
SBK/Silva Screen / Jan '93 / Conifer / Silva Screen.

INTO THE WOODS
Broadway Cast
Sondheim, Stephen C
Prologue - Into the woods / Cinderella at the grave / Hello little girl / I guess this is goodbye / Maybe they're magic / I know what / Ending / Very nice prince / First midnight / Giants in the sky / Agony / It takes two / Stay with me / On the steps of the palace / Ever after / Act 2 Prologue - So happy / Agony (2) / Lament / Any moment / Moments in the woods / Your fault / Last midnight / No more / No one is alone / Finale - Children will listen
CD _____ **07863567962**
RCA Victor / Jun '94 / BMG.

INTO THE WOODS
1990 London Cast
Sondheim, Stephen C
Prologue - Once upon a time (Into the woods/Fly bird.../Witch's entrance/Jack Jack Jack.../You wish to have the curse reversed?/Ladies, our carriage waits/The curse is on my house) / Cinderella at the grave / Hello little girl / I guess this is goodbye / Maybe they're magic / Our little world / I know things now / Very nice Prince / First midnight / Giants in the sky / Agony / It takes two / Stay with me / On the steps of the palace / Finale - Ever after / Act 2 Prologue - So happy / Agony (2) / Lament / Any moment / Moments in the woods / Your fault / Last midnight / No more / No one is alone / Finale - Children will listen
CD _____ **RD 60752**
RCA Victor / Jun '93 / BMG.

INTOLERANCE
Davis, Carl C
CD _____ **PCD 105**
Prometheus / Jan '93 / Silva Screen.

INVADE MY PRIVACY
1993 London Cast
Landesman, Frans L
Brown, D. Con
CD _____ **CDTER 1202**
TER / Sep '93 / Koch.

INVESTIGATION OF A CITIZEN ABOVE SUSPICION
Morricone, Ennio C
CD _____ **CDCIA 5086**
Cinevox / Jan '93 / Conifer / Silva Screen.

IOLANTHE
Baker, George & Ian Wallace/Glyndebourne Festival Choir/Pro Arte Orchestra
Sullivan, Sir Arthur C
Gilbert, W.S. L
Sargent, Sir Malcolm Con
2CD _____ **CMS 7644002**
EMI Classics / Apr '94 / EMI.

IOLANTHE
D'Oyly Carte Opera Chorus/New Symphony Orchestra/Grenadier Guards Band
Sullivan, Sir Arthur C
Gilbert, W.S. L
Godfrey, I. Con
2CD _____ **4141452**
Decca / Jan '90 / PolyGram.

IOLANTHE
D'Oyly Carte Opera Chorus/Orchestra
Sullivan, Sir Arthur C
Gilbert, W.S. L
Pryce Jones, J. Con
2CD _____ **CDTER2 1188**
TER / May '92 / Koch.

IPHIGENIA
Theodorakis, Mikis C
CD _____ **SR 50089**
Varese Sarabande/Colosseum / May '94 / Pinnacle / Silva Screen.

IRMA LA DOUCE
1960 Broadway Cast
Monnot, Marguerite C
Breffort, Alexandre L
CD _____ **SK 48018**
Sony Broadway / Dec '91 / Sony.

IRMA LA DOUCE
Broadway Cast
Monnot, Marguerite C
Breffort, Alexandre L
CD _____ **MCAD 6178**
MCA / Jan '89 / BMG.

IRON EAGLE III (Aces)
Utah Symphony Orchestra
Manfredini, Harry C
CD _____ **MAF 7022D**
Intrada / Mar '92 / Silva Screen / Koch.

IRON WILL
McNeely, Joel C
McNeely, Joel Con
CD _____ **VSD 5467**
Varese Sarabande/Colosseum / Aug '94 / Pinnacle / Silva Screen.

IS PARIS BURNING
Jarre, Maurice C
CD _____ **VSD 5222**
Varese Sarabande/Colosseum / Feb '90 / Pinnacle / Silva Screen.

IS PARIS BURNING
Jarre, Maurice C
CD _____ **4768422**
Silva Screen / Aug '94 / Conifer / Silva Screen.

ISLANDS IN THE STREAM
Hungarian State Symphony Orchestra
Goldsmith, Jerry C
Goldsmith, Jerry Con
Island / Boys arrive / Pillow fight / Is ten too old / Night attack / Marlin / Boys leave / Letter / How long can you stay / I can't have him / Refugees / Eddie's death / Is it all true
CD _____ **RVF 6003D**
Intrada / Jan '89 / Silva Screen / Koch.

IT COULD HAPPEN TO YOU
Burwell, Carter C
Young at heart: Bennett, Tony & Shaun Colvin / They can't take that away from me: Holiday, Billie / Now it can be told: Bennett, Tony / Swingtown, sweetown: Marsalis, Wynton / She's no lady: Lovett, Lyle / Always: Bennett, Tony / Overture: Burwell, Carter / I feel lucky: Carpenter, Mary-Chapin / Round of blues: Colvin, Shawn / Search: Burwell, Carter / Young at heart (2): Sinatra, Frank
CD _____ **476817 2**
Columbia / Nov '94 / Sony.

IT'S A BIRD, IT'S A PLANE, IT'S SUPERMAN
1966 Broadway Cast
Strouse, Charles C
Adams, Lee L
CD _____ **SK 48207**
Sony Broadway / Nov '92 / Sony.

IT'S ALIVE II
Herrmann, Bernard C
Johnson, Laurie Con
Main title / Birth traumas / Evil evolving / Savage trilogy / Nightmares / Beautiful and bizarre / Revulsion / Basement nursery / Lamentation / Living with fear / Stalking the infants / Climax
CD _____ **FILMCD 074**
Silva Screen / Jan '91 / Conifer / Silva Screen.

IVAN THE TERRIBLE
Kitaenko, Dmitri
Prokofiev, Sergei C
CD _____ **9026619542**
RCA Victor / Nov '95 / BMG.

IVANHOE
Sinfonia Of London
Rozsa, Miklos C
Broughton, Bruce Con

CD _____ **MAF 7055D**
Intrada / Jan '95 / Silva Screen / Koch.

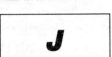

JACOB'S LADDER
Jarre, Maurice C
CD _____ **VSD 5291**
Varese Sarabande/Colosseum / Dec '90 /
Pinnacle / Silva Screen.

**JACQUES BREL IS ALIVE AND WELL
AND LIVING IN PARIS**
Brel, Jacques C
Blau, Eric & Mort Shuman L
CD _____ **CGK 40817**
Silva Screen / Jan '89 / Conifer / Silva
Screen.

**JACQUES BREL IS ALIVE AND WELL
AND LIVING IN PARIS**
London Cast
Brel, Jacques C
2CD _____ **CDTER2 1231**
TER / Jan '94 / Koch.

JAKE'S PROGRESS
Costello, Elvis & Richard Harvey C
Costello, Elvis & Richard Harvey C
CD _____ **DSCD 14**
Demon / Nov '95 / Pinnacle / ADA.

JAMAICA GO GO
Mango / Oct '90 / Vital / PolyGram.
CD _____ **CIDM 1064**

JAMON JAMON
Piovani, Nicola C
CD _____ **873139**
Milan / Jun '93 / BMG / Silva Screen.

JANE EYRE
Williams, John C
Jane Eyre / Overture (main title) / Lowood /
To Thornfield / String quartet - Festivity at
Thornfield / Grace Poole and Mason's arri-
val / Trrio - The meeting / Thwarted wed-
ding / Across the Moors / Restoration /
Reunion
CD _____ **FILMCD 031**
Silva Screen / Sep '88 / Conifer / Silva
Screen.

JANE EYRE
Bratislava Symphony Orchestra
Herrmann, Bernard C
CD _____ **8223535**
Marco Polo / Nov '93 / Select.

JANE EYRE/LAURA
Herrmann, Bernard/David Raskin C
CD _____ **07822110062**
Fox Film Scores / Jul '92 / BMG.

JASON'S LYRIC
CD _____ **5229152**
Mercury / Mar '95 / PolyGram.

JAWS
Williams, John C
Main title / Chrissie's death / Promenade /
Out to sea / Indianapolis story / Sea attack
no. 1 / One barrel chase / Preparing the
cage / Night search / Underwater siege /
Hand to hand combat / End titles
CD _____ **MCLD 19281**
MCA / Jun '95 / BMG.

JAZZ SINGER, THE
Diamond, Neil
Diamond, Neil C
America / Adorn o lume / You baby / Love
on the rocks / Amazed and confused / Rob-
ert E. Lee / Summer love / Hello again / Ac-
apulco / Hey Louise / Songs of life / Jeru-
salem / Kol nidre / My name is Yussel /
America (reprise)
CD _____ **CDEAST 12120**
Capitol / Jul '84 / EMI.

**JEAN DE FLORETTE/MANON DE
SOURCES**
Petit, Jean Claude C
CD _____ **CDCH 378**
Milan / Jan '89 / BMG / Silva Screen.

JEFFREY
Endelman, Stephen C
CD _____ **VSD 5649**
Varese Sarabande/Colosseum / Aug '95 /
Pinnacle / Silva Screen.

JENATSCH
Donaggio, Pino C
CD _____ **CDCH 036**
Milan / Jan '89 / BMG / Silva Screen.

JENNIFER 8
Skywalker Symphony Orchestra
Young, Christopher C
CD _____ **661202**
Silva Screen / Jan '93 / Conifer / Silva
Screen.

JERKY BOYS
Jerky Boys
CD _____ **7567827082**
WEA / Jan '95 / Warner Music.

JEROME KERN GOES TO HOLLYWOOD
1985 London Cast
Kern, Jerome C
Song is you/I've told every little star / I'll be
hard to handle / Smoke gets in your eyes /
Yesterdays / I won't dance / I'm old fashioned / Dearly beloved / Pick yourself up /
She didn't say yes / Folks who live on the
hill / Long ago and far away / Lovely to look
at/Just let me look at you / Remind me /
Last time I saw Paris / Ol' man river / Why
was I born / Can't help lovin' dat man / All
the things you are/They didn't believe me
CD _____ **OCRCD 6014**
First Night / Oct '93 / Pinnacle.

**JEROME ROBBINS' BROADWAY
(Musical Revue Of Shows Staged By
Robbins)**
1989 Broadway Cast
Gemignani, Paul Con
2CD _____ **601502**
RCA/Silva Screen / Jan '95 / Silva Screen.

JERRY'S GIRLS
1984 Broadway Cast
Herman, Jerry C
Jerry's girls / Put on your Sunday clothes /
It only takes a moment / Wherever he ain't
/ We need a little Christmas / I won't send
roses / Tap your troubles away / Two a day
/ Bosom buddies / Man in the moon / So
long dearie / Take it all off / Shalom / Milk
and honey / Showturn / If he walked into
my life / Hello Dolly / Nelson / Just go to
the movies / Movies were movies / Look
what happened to Mabel / Time heals
everything / It's today / Mame / Kiss her
now / That's how young I feel / Gooch's
song / Before the parade passes by / I don't
want to know / La cage aux folles / Song
on the sand / I am what I am / Best of times
/ Jerry's turn
2CD _____ **CDTER2 1093**
TER / Mar '85 / Koch.

**JESUS CHRIST SUPERSTAR
(The 20th Anniversary Recording)**
1992 London Cast
Lloyd Webber, Andrew C
Rice, Tim L
2CD _____ **09026614342**
RCA Victor / Jan '93 / BMG.
CD _____ **ENCORECD 7**
First Night / '94 / Pinnacle.

**JESUS CHRIST SUPERSTAR
(Highlights From The 20th Anniversary
Recording)**
1992 London Cast
Lloyd Webber, Andrew C
Rice, Tim L
CD _____ **OCRCD 6031**
First Night / Dec '95 / Pinnacle.

JESUS CHRIST SUPERSTAR
Cast Recording
Lloyd Webber, Andrew C
Rice, Tim L
2CD _____ **CDTER2 1216**
TER / Aug '95 / Koch.

JFK
Williams, John C
Prologue / Motorcade / Drummer's salute /
J.F.K. (theme) / Eternal father / Strong to
save / Garrison's obsession / On the sunny
side of the street / Conspirators / Death of
David Ferrie / Maybe September / Garrison
family theme / Ode to Buckwheat / El wa-
tusi / Witnesses / Concerto no. 2/Horn and
orchestra (K 417) / Arlington / Finale
CD _____ **7559612932**
WEA / Feb '93 / Warner Music.

JOHNNY AND THE DEAD
Girandet, Stefan C
CD _____ **CDWEEK 106**
Weekend / Jul '95 / Total/BMG.

JOHNNY GUITAR
Young, Victor C
Young, Victor Con
CD _____ **VSD 5377**
Varese Sarabande/Colosseum / May '93 /
Pinnacle / Silva Screen.

JOHNNY HANDSOME
Cooder, Ry
Cooder, Ry C
Main theme / I can't walk this time - the
prestige / Angola / Clip joint rhumba / Sad
story / Fountain walk / Cajun metal / First
week at work / Greasy oysters / Smells like
money / Sunny's tune / I like your eyes /
Adios Donna / Cruising with Rafe / How's
my face / End theme
CD _____ **925996 2**
WEA / Sep '89 / Warner Music.

JOHNNY JOHNSON
1955 Cast
Weill, Kurt C
CD _____ **8313842**
Silva Screen / Jan '89 / Conifer / Silva
Screen.

JONATHAN LIVINGSTONE SEAGULL
Diamond, Neil
Diamond, Neil C
Jonathan Livingstone Seagull (prologue) /
Flight of the gull / Dear father (Parts 1 - 3)
/ Skybird (part 1) / Lonely looking sky / Od-
yssey / Anthem / Be (part 1) / Skybird (part
2) / Be (part 3)
CD _____ **4676072**
CBS / Dec '90 / Sony.

**JOSEPH AND THE AMAZING
TECHNICOLOUR DREAMCOAT**
1973 London Cast
Lloyd Webber, Andrew C
Rice, Tim L
Jacob and sons / Joseph's coat / Joseph's
dreams / Poor, poor Joseph / One more an-
gel in heaven / Potiphar / Close every door
/ Go go go Joseph / Pharaoh story / Poor,
poor Pharaoh / Song of the king / Pharaoh's
dreams explained / Stone the crows /
Those Canaan days / Brothers come to
Egypt / Grovel, grovel / Who's the thief /
Benjamin calypso / Joseph all the time / Ja-
cob in Egypt / Any dream will do
CD _____ **MCLD 19023**
MCA / Apr '92 / BMG.

**JOSEPH AND THE AMAZING
TECHNICOLOUR DREAMCOAT
(Highlights - The Shows Collection)**
Cast Recording
Lloyd Webber, Andrew C
Rice, Tim L
Jacob and sons / Joseph's coat / Any
dream will do / Joseph's dreams / One
more angel in heaven / Potiphar / Close
every door / Go go go Joseph / Poor, poor
Pharaoh / Song of the king / Those Canaan
days / Benjamin calypso
CD _____ **PWKS 4163**
Carlton Home Entertainment / Sep '93 /
Carlton Home Entertainment.

**JOSEPH AND THE AMAZING
TECHNICOLOUR DREAMCOAT**
1991 London Cast
Lloyd Webber, Andrew C
Rice, Tim L
CD _____ **5111302**
Really Useful / Sep '91 / PolyGram.

**JOSEPH AND THE AMAZING
TECHNICOLOUR DREAMCOAT
(Featuring Paul Jones, Tim Rice and
The Mike Sammes Singers)**
Studio Cast
Lloyd Webber, Andrew C
Rice, Tim L
Love, Geoff Con
Jacob and sons/Joseph's coat / Joseph's
dreams / Poor, poor Joseph / One more an-
gel in Heaven / Potiphar / Close every door
/ Go, go, go Joseph / Pharaoh story / Poor,
poor Pharaoh / Song of the king / Pharaoh's
dreams explained / Stone the crows /
Those Canaan days / Brothers come to
Egypt/Grovel, grovel / Who's the thief /
Benjamin Calypso / Joseph all the time /
Jacob in Egypt / Any dream will do
CD _____ **CC 242**
Classics For Pleasure / May '89 / EMI.

JOURNEY THROUGH THE PAST
Young, Neil
Young, Neil C
For what it's worth / Mr. Soul / Rock 'n' roll
woman / Find the cost of freedom / Ohio /
Southern man / Alabama / Are you ready
for the country / Words / Soldier
CD _____ **7599261232**
Reprise / Jun '94 / Warner Music.

JOY LUCK CLUB, THE
Portman, Rachel C
CD _____ **74321184562**
Milan / Mar '94 / BMG / Silva Screen.

JUDGE DREDD
Dredd song: Cure / Darkness falls: The The
/ Super charger: White Zombie / Heaven:
White Zombie / Need fire: Cocteau Twins /
Release the pressure: Leftfield / Time: Aska
/ You come closer: Worldbeaters & Youssou
N'Dour
CD _____ **4808552**
Epic / Jul '95 / Sony.

JUDGEMENT NIGHT
I love you Mary Jane: Cypress Hill & Sonic
Youth / Judgement night: Onyx & Biohazard
/ Just another victim: House of Pain & Hel-
met / Me, myself and my microphone: Run
DMC & Living Colour / Disorder: Ice-T &
Slayer / Missing link: Del The Funky Hom-
osapien & Dinosaur Jr / Fallin': De La Soul
& Teenage Fanclub / Freak momma: Sir
Mix-A-Lot & Mudhoney / Another body
murdered: Boo-Yaa T.R.I.B.E. & Faith No
More / Come and die: Fatal & Therapy / Real
thing: Cypress Hill & Pearl Jam
CD _____ **474183-2**
Epic / Oct '93 / Sony.

JUICE
CD _____ **MCLD 19308**
MCA / Oct '95 / BMG.

JULES ET JIM/LA CLOCHE TIBETAINE
Delerue, Georges C
CD _____ **PCD 103**
Prometheus / Feb '90 / Silva Screen.

JULIA AND JULIA
Jarre, Maurice C
CD _____ **VCD 47327**
Varese Sarabande/Colosseum / Jan '89 /
Pinnacle / Silva Screen.

JUMPIN' JACK FLASH
Newman, Thomas C
Set me free: Rene & Angela / Trick of the
night: Bananarama / Misled: Kool & The
Gang / Rescue me: Jumpin' Jack Flash:
Rolling Stones / You can't hurry love: Su-
premes / Hold on: Branigan, Laura / Win-
dow to the world: Voice To Face / Breaking

the code: Newman, Thomas / Love music:
Newman, Thomas
CD _____ **5511382**
Spectrum/Karussell / Aug '95 / PolyGram /
THE.

**JUNGLE BOOK, THE/THE THIEF OF
BAGHDAD**
Rozsa, Miklos C
CD _____ **CST 348044**
Varese Sarabande/Colosseum / Sep '90 /
Pinnacle / Silva Screen.

JUST CAUSE
Howard, James Newton C
CD _____ **VSD 5596**
Varese Sarabande/Colosseum / Feb '95 /
Pinnacle / Silva Screen.

JUST IN TIME
Kuhn, Judy C
CD _____ **VSD 5472**
Varese Sarabande/Colosseum / Feb '95 /
Pinnacle / Silva Screen.

JUST LIKE A WOMAN
Return to sender: Presley, Elvis / Wife's re-
turn / (You're the) devil in disguise: Presley,
Elvis / Transformation / Big girls don't cry:
Pasdar, Adrian / La senorita: Latin Touch /
Sisters are doin' it for themselves: Euryth-
mics & Aretha Franklin / Geraldine / Love
letters: Presley, Elvis / Waltz / End titles /
Politics of love: Blunstone, Colin
CD _____ **74321110702**
RCA / Sep '92 / BMG.

JUSTINE
Goldsmith, Jerry C
CD _____ **TSU 0119**
Tsunami / May '95 / Silva Screen.

JUSTIZ
Loef, Frank C
CD _____ **CIN 22102**
Silva Screen / Jan '95 / Conifer / Silva
Screen.

JUTE CITY
Stewart, David A.
Stewart, David A. C
Jute City / Dead planets / Last love / In
Duncan's arms / Black wedding / Jute City
revisited / Contaminated / See no evil / Ji-
gula / Lords theme / Hats off to Hector /
Deep waters / Dark wells
CD _____ **ZD 75187**
RCA / Nov '91 / BMG.

K2
Zimmer, Hans C
CD _____ **VSD 5354**
Varese Sarabande/Colosseum / Sep '91 /
Pinnacle / Silva Screen.

KAOS
Piovani, Nicola C
CD _____ **FMC 11**
Milan / Jan '95 / BMG / Silva Screen.

KAPO/ROSOLINO PATERNO SOLDATO
Rustichelli, Carlo C
CD _____ **CDCIA 5091**
Cinevox / Jan '93 / Conifer / Silva Screen.

KARA BEN NEMSI EFFENDI
Bottcher, Martin C
CD _____ **SP 10002**
Silva Screen / Jan '93 / Conifer / Silva
Screen.

KARATE KID
Moment of truth: Survivor / On the beach:
Flirts & Jan & Dean Bop Bop / No shelter:
Broken Edge / It takes two to tango: Davis,
Paul / Tough love: Shandi / Rhythm man:
St. Regis / Feel the night: Robertson, Baxter
/ Desire: Gang Of Four / You're the best:
Esposito, Joe
CD _____ **5511362**
Spectrum/Karussell / Sep '95 / PolyGram /
THE.

KEEPER OF THE CITY
Utah Symphony Orchestra
Rosenman, Leonard C
CD _____ **MAF 7024D**
Intrada / Apr '92 / Silva Screen / Koch.

**KENTUCKIAN, THE
(& Music By Steiner/Friedhofer/
Newman)**
Herrmann, Bernard C
CD _____ **PRCD 1777**
Preamble / Sep '87 / Silva Screen.

KEY TO REBECCA, THE
Redford, J.A.C. C
CD _____ **PCD 123**
Prometheus / Mar '93 / Silva Screen.

KID GALAHAB/GIRLS GIRLS GIRLS
Presley, Elvis
King of the whole wide world / This is living
/ Riding the rainbow / Home is where the
heart is / I got lucky / Whistling tune / Girls,
girls, girls - girls, girls, girls / I don't wanna

be tied / Where do you come from / I don't
want to / We'll be together / Boy like me, a
girl like you / Return to sender / Because of
love / Thanks to the rolling sea / Song of
the shrimp / Walls have ears / We're coming
in loaded / Mama / Plantation rock / Dainty
little moonbeams / Girls, girls, girls
CD _____ 74321 13430-2
RCA / Mar '93 / BMG.

KILLING FIELDS, THE
Oldfield, Mike
Oldfield, Mike C
Pran's theme / Requiem for a city / Evac-
uation / Capture / Execution / Bad news /
Pran's departure / Work site / Year zero /
Blood sucking / Pran's escape / Trek /
Boy's burial, The/Pran sees the red cross /
Good news / Etude / Pran's theme - 2 /
Year zero (2)
CD _____ CDV 2328
Virgin / Nov '84 / EMI.

KINDERGARTEN COP
Edelman, Randy C
CD _____ VSD 5305
Varese Sarabande/Colosseum / Jan '91 /
Pinnacle / Silva Screen.

KING AND I, THE
Film Cast
Rodgers, Richard C
Hammerstein II, Oscar L
Newman, Alfred Con
I whistle a happy tune / My lord and master
/ Hello, young lovers / March of the Sia-
mese children / Puzzlement / Getting to
know you / We kiss in a shadow / I have
dreamed / Shall I tell you what I think of you
/ Something wonderful / Song of the King /
Shall we dance
CD _____ ZDM 7646932
EMI Classics / Apr '93 / EMI.

KING AND I, THE
1951 Broadway Cast
Rodgers, Richard C
Hammerstein II, Oscar L
Overture / I whistle a happy tune / My lord
and master / Hello, young lovers / March of
the Siamese children / Puzzlement / Getting
to know you / We kiss in a shadow / Shall
I tell you what I think of you / Something
wonderful / I have dreamed / Shall we
dance
CD _____ MCLD 19156
MCA / Dec '92 / BMG.

KING AND I, THE
1977 Broadway Cast
Rodgers, Richard C
Hammerstein II, Oscar L
Overture / Arrival at Bangkok/I whistle a
happy tune / My lord and master / Hello
young lovers / March of the Siamese children / Children sing, priests chant / Puzzlement / Royal Bangkok Academy / Getting
to know you / So big a world / We kiss in a
shadow / Puzzlement (reprise) / Shall I tell
you what I think of you / Something wonderful / Finale (Act 1) / Western people
funny / Dance of Anna and Sir Edward / I
have dreamed / Song of the king / Shall we
dance / Finale
CD _____ RD 82610
RCA Victor / Aug '90 / BMG.

KING AND I, THE
1964 Broadway Cast
Rodgers, Richard C
Hammerstein II, Oscar L
Engel, L. Con
CD _____ SK 53328
Sony Broadway / Nov '93 / Sony.

KING AND I, THE
Cast Recording
Rodgers, Richard C
Hammerstein II, Oscar L
2CD _____ CDTER2 1214
TER / Aug '95 / Koch.

KING AND I, THE/OKLAHOMA
Cast Recording
Rodgers, Richard C
Hammerstein II, Oscar L
CD _____ 340772
Koch / Oct '95 / Koch.

KING CREOLE
Presley, Elvis
King Creole / As long as I have you / Hard
headed woman / Trouble / Dixieland rock /
Don't ask me why / Lover doll / Crawfish /
Young dreams / Steadfast, loyal and true /
New Orleans
CD _____ ND 83733
RCA / Oct '87 / BMG.

KING KONG
Steiner, Max C
CD _____ LXCD 10
Silva Screen / Jan '93 / Conifer / Silva
Screen.

KING OF KINGS
(& Unreleased Material)
Rozsa, Miklos C
Cinevox / Jan '94 / Conifer / Silva Screen.
CD _____ AK 52424

KING SOLOMON'S MINES
Hungarian State Opera Orchestra
Goldsmith, Jerry C
Goldsmith, Jerry Con
CD _____ FMT 8005D
Intrada / Mar '92 / Silva Screen / Koch.

**KINGS GO FORTH/SOME CAME
RUNNING**
Bernstein, Elmer C
Bernstein, Elmer Con
Kings go forth / Riviera / Bunker / Sam's
theme / Monique's theme / Le chat noir /
Quiet drive / Britt's kiss / Monique's despair
/ Displaced / Finale / Prelude / To love and
be loved / Dave's double life / Dave and
Gwen / Fight / Gwen's theme / Ginny /
Short noise / Live it up / Tryst / Seduction
/ Smitty's place / Rejection / Pursuit
CD _____ CNS 5004
Cloud Nine / Sep '92 / Conifer / Silva
Screen.

KINGS ROW
National Philharmonic Orchestra
Korngold, Erich C
Gerhardt, Charles Con
Main title / Children (Parris and Cassie) /
Parris and grandmother / Cassie's party /
Icehouse / Operation / Cassie's farewell /
Parris goes to Dr. Tower / Winter / Grand-
mother's last will / Seduction / All is quiet /
Grandmother dies / Sunset / Parris leaves
Kings Row / Flirtation / Vienna and Happy
New Year 1900 / Randy and Drake / Finan-
cial ruin / Accident and amputation / Drake
awakens / Vienna/Cable/Randy and Drake /
Letters across the ocean / Parris comes
back / Kings Row / Elise / Parris' decision
/ Finale
CD _____ VCD 47203
Varese Sarabande/Colosseum / Jan '89 /
Pinnacle / Silva Screen.

KISMET
Cast Recording
Forrest, George & Robert Wright C
Overture/Sands of time / Rhymes have I /
Fate / Not since nineveh / Baubles, bangles
and beads / Stranger in paradise / Gesticu-
late / Night of my nights / Was I wazir / Ra-
hadakum / This is my beloved / Olive tree
CD _____ SHOWCD 014
Showtime / Feb '95 / Disc / THE.

KISMET
1953 Broadway Cast
Forrest, George & Robert Wright C
CBS/Silva Screen / Jan '93 / Conifer / Silva
Screen.
CD _____ CK 32605

**KISMET
(Highlights)**
1990 Studio Cast/Ambrosian Chorus/Phil-
harmonia Orchestra
Forrest, George & Robert Wright C
Edwards, John Owen Con
CD _____ CDTEO 1002
TER / Jan '93 / Koch.

KISMET
Ambrosian Singers/New York Concert Cho-
rale/London Symphony Orchestra
Benjamin, Paul Con
CD _____ SK 46438
Sony Broadway / Mar '92 / Sony.

KISMET/TIMBUKTU
1990 Studio Cast/Ambrosian Chorus/Phil-
harmonia Orchestra
Forrest, George & Robert Wright C
Edwards, John Owen Con
2CD _____ CDTER2 1170
TER / Jan '93 / Koch.

KISS ME KATE
1987 Royal Shakespeare Cast
Porter, Cole C
CD _____ OCRCD 6020
First Night / Oct '95 / Pinnacle.

KISS ME KATE
Broadway Cast
Porter, Cole C
CD _____ ZDM 7647602
EMI Classics / Apr '93 / EMI.

KISS ME KATE
Barstow, Josephine & Thomas Hampson/
Kim Criswell/Ambrosian Chorus/London
Sinfonietta
Porter, Cole C
McGlinn, John Con
2CD _____ CDS 7540332
EMI Classics / Apr '93 / EMI.

KISS ME KATE
Cast Recording
Porter, Cole C
2CD _____ CDTER2 1212
TER / Aug '95 / Koch.

KISS OF DEATH
CD _____ 280282
Milan / Jun '95 / BMG / Silva Screen.

KISS OF THE SPIDER WOMAN
1992 London Cast
Kander, John C
Ebb, Fred L
CD _____ 09026615792
RCA Victor / Jan '90 / BMG.
CD _____ OCRCD 6030
First Night / Oct '95 / Pinnacle.

**KISSIN' COUSINS/CLAMBAKE/STAY
AWAY, JOE**
Presley, Elvis
Kissin' cousins (2) / Smoky mountain bay /
There's gold in the mountains / One boy
two little girls / Catchin' on fast / Tender
feeling / Anyone (could fall in love with you)
/ Barefoot ballad / Once is enough / Kissin'

cousins / Clambake / Who needs money /
House that has everything / Confidence /
Hey hey hey / You don't know me / Girl I
never loved / How can you lose what you
never had / Clambake (Reprise) / Stay
away, Joe / Dominic / All I needed was the
rain / Goin' home / Stay away
CD _____ 07863663622
RCA / Jun '94 / BMG.

KNIGHT MOVES
Dudley, Anne C
Dudley, Anne Con
CD _____ 262753
Milan / Sep '92 / BMG / Silva Screen.

KNIGHTS OF THE ROUND TABLE
Rozsa, Miklos C
CD _____ VCD 47269
Varese Sarabande/Colosseum / Jan '89 /
Pinnacle / Silva Screen.

KRAMER VS KRAMER
Mandolin and harpsichord concerto / Scott
Kuney / Frederick Hand / New York / Trum-
pet sonata / Gordion knot untied
CD _____ MK 35873
Silva Screen / Feb '90 / Conifer / Silva
Screen.

KRULL
London Symphony Orchestra
Horner, James C
Horner, James Con
Riding the fire mares / Slayer's attack / Wi-
dow's web / Widow's lullaby / Destruction
of the black fortress / Epilogue
CD _____ SCCD 1004
Southern Cross / Nov '06 / Silva Screen.

KUFFS
Faltermeyer, Harold
Faltermeyer, Harold C
CD _____ 101512
Milan / Jan '94 / BMG / Silva Screen.

KUNG FU - THE LEGEND CONTINUES
Danna, Jeff
Danna, Jeff C
From out of the past / Theme from Kung Fu
/ Place of light and song / Promise / Long-
est night / Omeishan / Reunion / Yellow
flower in her hair / Tomb/Searching for Tan
/ Dragon's eye / Posse / Father and son /
Emperor
CD _____ ND 66008
Narada / May '94 / New Note / ADA.

KWAMINA
Broadway Cast
CD _____ ZDM 7648912
EMI Classics / Aug '93 / EMI.

![L]

LA CALIFFA
Morricone, Ennio C
CD _____ A 8928
Alhambra / Feb '92 / Silva Screen.

**LA CLASSE OPERAIA VA IN PARADISO/
LA PROPRIETA NON E PIU UN F**
Morricone, Ennio C
CD _____ OST 122
Milano Dischi / Jul '92 / Silva Screen.

**LA DONNA DELLA DOMENICA/LA
MOGLIE PIU BELLA**
Morricone, Ennio C
CD _____ PCD 119
Prometheus / Apr '92 / Silva Screen.

LA HAINE
(Score)
CD _____ 319662
Milan / Nov '95 / BMG / Silva Screen.

LA HAINE
Intro / Sacrifice de poulets: Ministere Amer
/ Le vent tourne: Sons Unik / La 25eme im-
age: Nuttea, Iam & Daddy / Dealer pour sur-
vivre: Expression Direkt / C'est la meme his-
toire: Ste Strausz / Requiem: La Cliqua /
Comme dance un film: M.C. Solaar / La
vague a l'arme: FF / Sors avec ton gun:
Raggasonic / Bons baisers du poste: Les
Sages Poetes De La Rue / L'etat assassine:
Assassin
CD _____ CDVIR 45
Virgin / Nov '95 / EMI.

LA PASSION BEATRICE
Boulanger, Lili C
Markevitch, Igor Con
CD _____ BD 314
Milan / Jan '89 / BMG / Silva Screen.

**LA PETITE VOLEUSE
(The Little Thief)**
Jomy, Alain C
CD _____ CH 399
Milan / Jan '93 / BMG / Silva Screen.

LA REINA DE LA NOCHE
Pecanins, Betsy
CD _____ 887960
Milan / Jan '95 / BMG / Silva Screen.

LA REINE MARGOT
Begovic, Goran C
CD _____ 5226552
Silva Screen / Jan '95 / Conifer / Silva
Screen.

LA REVOLUTION FRANCAISE
Schonberg, Claude-Michel C
Boublil, Alain L
CD _____ OCRCD 6006
First Night / Dec '95 / Pinnacle.

LA STRADA/NIGHTS OF CABIRIA
Rota, Nino C
CD _____ LEGENDCD 7
Legend / Apr '92 / Conifer / Silva Screen /
Discovery.

LA TRAVERSE A PARIS
Nyman, Michael C
CD _____ 899002
Silva Screen / Jan '93 / Conifer / Silva
Screen.

LABYRINTH
Bowie, David
Bowie, David C
Underground / Into the labyrinth / Magic
dance / Sarah / Chilly down / Hallucination
/ As the world falls down / Goblin battle /
Within you / Thirteen o'clock / Home at last
/ Underground (reprise)
CD _____ CDFA 3322
Fame / Jul '95 / EMI.

LADY BE GOOD
Cast Recording
Gershwin, George C
Gershwin, Ira L
Stern, Eric Con
CD _____ 7559793082
Elektra Nonesuch / Jul '93 / Warner Music.

LADY IN WHITE
Laloggia, Frank C
CD _____ VCD 47530
Varese Sarabande/Colosseum / Jan '89 /
Pinnacle / Silva Screen.

**LADY OF THE CAMELIAS (LA DAME
AUX CAMELIAS)**
Morricone, Ennio C
CD _____ PCD 116
Prometheus / Mar '92 / Silva Screen.

LADY SINGS THE BLUES
Ross, Diana
Lady sings the blues / Baltimore brothel /
Billie sneaks into Dean and Dean's / Swinging uptown / T'ain't nobody's business if I
do / Big Ben / C.C. rider / All of me / Man
I love / Them there eyes / Gardenias from
Louis / Cafe Manhattan / Had you been
around / Love theme / Country tune / I cried
for you / Billy and Harry / Mean to me / Fine
and mellow / What a little moonlight can do
/ Louis visits Billie on tour / Persuasion /
Agent's office / Love is here to stay / Lover
man / You've changed / Gimme a pigfoot
and a bottle of beer / Good morning heartache / My man (mon homme) / Don't explain / Strange fruit / God bless the child /
Closing theme
CD _____ 5301352
Motown / Jan '93 / PolyGram.

LADY SINGS THE BLUES
1989 Musical Cast
CD _____ BEARCD 33
Big Bear / Oct '90 / BMG.

L'AMANT
Yared, Gabriel
Yared, Gabriel C
CD _____ CDVMM 9
Virgin / Jan '95 / EMI.

LAMERICA
Piersanti, Franco C
CD _____ GDM 2006
Silva Screen / Jan '95 / Conifer / Silva
Screen.

LAND OF THE PHAROAHS
Tiomkin, Dimitri C
CD _____ TCI 0608
Silva Screen / May '95 / Conifer / Silva
Screen.

LANDRAIDERS, THE
Nicolai, Bruno C
CD _____ PCD 128
Prometheus / Jul '93 / Silva Screen.

LAST ACTION HERO, THE
Big gun: AC/DC / What the hell have I: Alice
In Chains / Angry again: Megadeth / Real
world: Queensryche / Two steps behind:
Def Leppard / Poison my eyes: Anthrax /
Dream on: Aerosmith / Cock the hammer:
Cypress Hill / Swim: Fishbone / Last action
hero: Tesla / Jack and the Ripper: Kamen,
Michael & The Los Angeles Rock 'n' Roll
Ensemble / Little bitter: Alice In Chains
CD _____ 473990 2
Columbia / Jul '93 / Sony.

LAST DAYS OF CHEZ NOUS, THE
Grabowsky, Paul
Grabowsky, Paul C
Last days of chez nous / Last days / Inver-
sions / Warm hands / Conversations / New
life / New lives / Big car people / Small car
people / Two hands / Lover man / Donna
Lee / Day's end
CD _____ DRGCD 12607
DRG / Jun '93 / New Note.

935

LAST EMPEROR, THE
Sakamoto, Ryuichi & David Byrne *C*
First coronation / Open the door / Where is
Armo / Picking up brides / Last Emperor,
The (theme) (variation 1) / Rain / Picking up
Bed / Wind, rain and water / Paper emperor
/ Rain (I want a divorce) / Baby was born
dead / Last Emperor, The (theme) (variation
2) / Last Emperor, The (theme) / Main title /
Lunch / Red guard / Emperor's waltz / Red
guard dance
CD _____ CDV 2485
Virgin / Nov '87 / EMI.

LAST EXIT TO BROOKLYN
Knopfler, Mark
Knopfler, Mark *C*
Last exit to Brooklyn / Victims / Think fast /
Love idea / Tralala / Riot / Reckoning / As
low as it gets / Finale
CD _____ 8387252
Vertigo / Nov '89 / PolyGram.

LAST KLEZMER, THE
Kozlowski, Leopold
CD _____ GVCD 168
Global Village / Nov '94 / ADA / Direct.

**LAST METRO, THE (LE DERNIER
METRO)/LA FEMME D'A COTE**
Delerue, Georges *C*
CD _____ PCD 113
Prometheus / Apr '92 / Silva Screen.

LAST OF ENGLAND
Fisher-Turner, Simon *C*
CD _____ CDIONIC 1
Mute / Oct '87 / Disc.

LAST OF THE MOHICANS, THE
Edelman, Randy *C*
CD _____ 5174922
Polydor / Dec '92 / PolyGram.

LAST PICTURE SHOW, THE
Cold cold heart / Give me more, more, more
(of your kisses) / Wish you were here / Slow
poke / Blue velvet / Rose rose I love you /
Belong to me / Fool such as I / Please Mr.
Sun / Solitaire
CD _____ CK 31143
CBS/Silva Screen / Jan '92 / Conifer / Silva
Screen.

LAST STARFIGHTER, THE
Safan, Craig *C*
Outer space chase / Into the starscape /
Planet of Rylos / Death blossom / Incom-
municado / Never crossed my mind / Re-
turn to Earth / Hero's march / Centauri dies
CD _____ LXE 705
Silva Screen / Jan '93 / Conifer / Silva
Screen.

**LAST TEMPTATION OF CHRIST, THE
(Passion)**
Gabriel, Peter
Gabriel, Peter *C*
Feeling begins / Gethsemane / Of these,
hope / Lazarus raised / Of these hope (re-
prise) / In doubt / Different drum / Zaar /
Troubled / Open / Before night falls / With
this love / Sandstorm / Stigmata / Passion
/ Disturbed / It is accomplished / Wall of
breath / Promise of shadows / Bread and
wine
CD _____ RWCD 1
Realworld / Jun '89 / EMI / Sterns.

LAST WALTZ, THE
Band
Last waltz / Up on Cripple Creek / Who do
you love / Helpless / Stage fright / Coyote
/ Dry your eyes / It makes no difference /
Such a night / Night they drove old Dixie
down / Mystery train / Mannish boy / Fur-
ther on up the road / Shape I'm in / Down
South in New Orleans / Ophelia / Tura lura
larai (That's an Irish lullaby) / Caravan / Life
is a carnival / Baby let me follow you down
/ I don't believe you (she acts like we never
have met) / Forever young / I shall be re-
leased / Last waltz suite / Well / Evangeline
/ Out of the blue / Weight
CD _____ K 266076
WEA / Mar '88 / Warner Music.

LAURA/JANE EYRE
Herrmann, Bernard *C*
CD _____ 07822110062
RCA / Apr '94 / BMG.

L'AVVENTURIERO/OCEANO
Morricone, Ennio *C*
CD _____ OST 120
Milano Dischi / Jan '93 / Silva Screen.

LAWRENCE OF ARABIA
London Philharmonic Orchestra
Jarre, Maurice *C*
Overture / Main title / Miracle / Nefud mi-
rage / Rescue of Gasim / Bringing Gasim
into camp / Arrival at Auda's camp / Voice
of the guns / Continuation of the miracle /
Sun's anvil / Lawrence and his bodyguard
/ That is the desert / End titles
CD _____ VSD 5263
Varese Sarabande/Colosseum / Apr '91 /
Pinnacle / Silva Screen.
CD _____ CLACD 271
Castle / '92 / BMG.

LAWRENCE OF ARABIA
Philharmonia Orchestra
Jarre, Maurice *C*
Bremner, Tony *Con*
Overture/Main titles / First entrance to the
desert - night and stars / Lawrence and Ta-

fas / Miracle / That is the desert / Nefud
mirage/Sun's anvil / Rescue of Gasim/
Bringing Gasim into camp / Arrival at Au-
da's camp / On to Akaba/The beach at
night / Sinai desert / Voice at the guns /
Horse stampede - All rescues Lawrence /
Lawrence and his bodyguard / End/Playoff
music
CD _____ FILMCD 036
Silva Screen / Jan '89 / Conifer / Silva
Screen.

LE BON ET LES MECHANTS
Lai, Francis *C*
CD _____ MANTRA 054
Silva Screen / Jan '93 / Conifer / Silva
Screen.

LE NOUVELLE VAGUE
CD _____ 887825
Milan / Jun '95 / BMG / Silva Screen.

LEAVE IT TO JANE/OH KAY
Broadway Cast
Kern, Jerome/George Gershwin *C*
Wodehouse, P.G./Ira Gershwin *L*
Just you watch my step (Leave It To Jane)
/ Leave it to Jane / Siren's song / Cleopat-
terer / Crickets are calling / Sun shines
brighter / Sir Galahad / Wait 'til tomorrow /
I'm going to find a girl / Good old amateur /
There it is again / Poor prune / Finale / Over-
ture (Oh Kay) / Woman's touch / Twenties
are here to stay / Home / Stiff upper lip /
Maybe / Pophams / Do do do / Clap yo'
hands
CD _____ DRGCD 15017
DRG / Apr '91 / New Note.

**LEGEND
(American Score)**
Tangerine Dream
Tangerine Dream *C*
CD _____ VSD 5645
Varese Sarabande/Colosseum / Sep '95 /
Pinnacle / Silva Screen.

LEGEND
National Philharmonic Orchestra
Goldsmith, Jerry *C*
Goldsmith, Jerry *Con*
Main title/Goblins / My true love's eyes/Cot-
tage / Unicorns / Living river/Bumps and
hollows/Freeze / Faeries/Riddle / Sing the
wee / Forgive me / Faerie dance / Armour /
Oona/Jewels / Dress waltz / Darkness fails
/ Ring / Re-united
CD _____ FILMCD 045
Silva Screen / Jan '90 / Conifer / Silva
Screen.

LEGENDS OF THE FALL
Horner, James *C*
Legends of the fall / Ludlows / Off to war /
To the boys / Samuel's death / Alfred
moves to Helena / Farewell/Descent into
madness / Changing seasons / Wild horses
/ Tristan's return / Wedding / Isabel's mur-
der / Recollections of Samuel / Revenge /
Goodbyes / Alfred / Tristan / Colonel /
Legend
CD _____ 4785112
Epic / May '95 / Sony.

LEGS DIAMOND
Broadway Cast
Allen, Peter *C*
CD _____ 79832
Silva Screen / Feb '90 / Conifer / Silva
Screen.

LENIN: THE TRAIN
Piovani, Nicola
CD _____ CDCH 381
Milan / Feb '90 / BMG / Silva Screen.

LEON
Serra, Eric
Serra, Eric *C*
Noon / Cute name / Ballad for Mathilde /
What's happening out there / Bird in New
York / She is dead / Fatman / Leon the
cleaner / Can I have a word with you /
Game is over / Feel the breath / Room 4602
/ Very special delivery / When Leon does
his beast / Back on the crime scene / Bird
of storm / Thony the IBM / How do you
know this it's love / Fight (The SWAT
squad/Bring me everyone/Big weapon/One
is alive) / Two ways / Out, hey little angel
CD _____ 4783232
Columbia / Feb '95 / Sony.

LEON THE PIG FARMER
Murphy, John & David Hughes *C*
I fell in love with the moon / Feels so right
/ Mon dieu / Jump out of your skin (Instru-
mental) / Siman Tov / Asher Bara / Feelings
/ Gallery / Every valley shall be exalted /
Nothing ever goes to plan / Yorkshire theme
/ Jewish transformation / Leon's theme (In-
strumental) / Jump out of your skin / Leon
chase / Hava nagila / If I'd never known you
/ Mess around
CD _____ CDSTY 1
Soundtrack Music / May '94 / EMI.

LEPRECHAUN
Kiner, Kevin *C*
CD _____ MAF 7050D
Intrada / Mar '93 / Silva Screen / Koch.

LES CLES DU PARADIS
Lai, Francis *C*
CD _____ MANTRA 066
Silva Screen / Jul '92 / Conifer / Silva
Screen.

LES MISERABLES
Broadway Cast
Schonberg, Claude-Michel *C*
Kretzmar, Herbert *L*
2CD _____ 9241512
Silva Screen / Jan '89 / Conifer / Silva
Screen.

**LES MISERABLES
(Highlights)**
International Cast
Schonberg, Claude-Michel *C*
Kretzmer, Herbert *L*
CD _____ CASTCD 20
First Night / Oct '91 / Pinnacle.

LES MISERABLES
1985 London Cast
Schonberg, Claude-Michel *C*
Kretzmer, Herbert *L*
Koch, Martin *Con*
At the end of the day / I dreamed a dream
/ Lovely ladies / Who am I / Come to me /
Confrontation / Castle on a cloud / Master
of the house / Stars / Look down / Little
people / Red and black / Do you hear the
people sing / I saw him once / In my life /
Heart full of love / One day more / On my
own / Attack / Little fall of rain / Drink with
me to days gone by / Bring him home / Dog
eats dog / Soliloquy / Empty chairs at
empty tables / Wedding chorale / Beggars
at the feast / Finale
2CD _____ ENCORECD 1
First Night / Dec '85 / Pinnacle.

LES MISERABLES
Cast Recording
Schonberg, Claude-Michel *C*
Kretzmer, Herbert *L*
CD _____ WMCD 5672
Woodford Music / Feb '93 / THE.

LES MISERABLES
Cast Recording
Schonberg, Claude-Michel *C*
Kretzmer, Herbert *L*
CD _____ GRF 197
Tring / Jan '93 / Tring / Prism.

**LES MISERABLES
(Highlights - The Shows Collection)**
1993 Studio Cast
Schonberg, Claude-Michel *C*
Kretzmer, Herbert *L*
At the end of the day / I dreamed a dream
/ Master of the house / Stars / Heart full of
the people sing / In my life / Heart full of
love / On my own / Little fall of rain / Drink
with me / Bring him home / Empty chairs at
empty tables
CD _____ PWKS 4175
Carlton Home Entertainment / Oct '93 /
Carlton Home Entertainment.

**LES MISERABLES
(Complete Symphonic Score)**
International Cast
Schonberg, Claude-Michel *C*
Kretzmer, Herbert *L*
2CD _____ MIZCD 1
First Night / Dec '88 / Pinnacle.

**LES MISERABLES
(Five Outstanding Performances From
The Symphonic Score)**
International Cast
Schonberg, Claude-Michel *C*
Kretzmer, Herbert *L*
Empty chairs at empty tables / Stars / One
day more / I dreamed a dream / On my own
CD _____ SCORECD 17
First Night / Apr '89 / Pinnacle.

**LES MISERABLES
(The Original French Concept Album)**
Cast Recording
Schonberg, Claude-Michel *C*
Boublil, Alain *L*
CD _____ DOCRCD 1
First Night / '94 / Pinnacle.

**LES MISERABLES/MISS SAIGON
(Orchestral suites from...)**
Royal Philharmonic Orchestra
Schonberg, Claude-Michel *C*
At the end of the day / I dreamed a dream
/ Lovely ladies / Fantines death / Master of
the house / Stars / Do you hear the people
sing / Heart full of love / On my own / Drink
with me / Bring him home / Final battle /
Valjean's death / Heat is on in Saigon /
Move in my mind / Why God why / Sun and
moon / Ceremony / Last night of the world
/ Fall of Saigon / I still believe / If you want
to die in bed / Truth inside your head / Little
god of my heart
CD _____ PWKS 4079
Carlton Home Entertainment / Aug '91 /
Carlton Home Entertainment.

LES PASSIONS AMOREUSES
Lai, Francis *C*
CD _____ 887974
Milan / Jun '95 / BMG / Silva Screen.

LES SILENCES DU PALAIS
Amal hayeti / Lecon de oud / Lessa faker /
Bachraf mazmoum / Elegie (chant patrio-
tique version radio) / Danse 1 / Fogue acha-
jera / Notes / Taalila / Vocalises, cris de
douleurs / Danse II / Ghanili cheoui cheoui
/ Bachraf / Elegie (chant patriotique) /
Theme alia
CD _____ CDVIR 35
Virgin / Apr '95 / EMI.

LES UNS ET LES AUTRES
Legrand, Michel/Francis Lai *C*
CD _____ 800432
Silva Screen / Jan '93 / Conifer / Silva
Screen.

LET IT BE
Beatles
Beatles *C*
Two of us / Dig a pony / Across the universe
/ I me mine / Dig it / Let it be / Maggie Mae
/ I've got a feeling / One after 909 / Long
and winding road / Get back
CD _____ CDPCS 7096
Parlophone / Oct '87 / EMI.

LETHAL WEAPON III
Kamen, Michael
Kamen, Michael *C*
It's probably me: *Sting* / Runaway train:
John, Elton & Eric Clapton / Grab the cat /
Leo Getz goes to the hockey game / Darryl
dies / Riggs and Roger / Roger's boat / Ar-
mour piercing bullets / God judges us by
our scars / Lorna - a quiet evening by the
fire
CD _____ 7599269892
WEA / Jun '92 / Warner Music.

**LET'S DO IT
(A Celebration Of Noel Coward & Cole
Porter)**
1994 Chichester Festival Cast
Coward, Sir Noel/Cole Porter *C*
My heart belongs to Daddy / Blow Gabriel
blow / Mrs. Worthington / It's de-lovely /
London pride / Throwing a ball tonight /
You're the top / I wonder what happened
to him / Mad dogs and Englishmen
CD _____ SONGCD 910
Silva Classics / Aug '94 / Conifer / Silva
Screen.

LET'S MAKE LOVE
Cahn, Sammy *C*
CD _____ 8369642
Silva Screen / Feb '90 / Conifer / Silva
Screen.

LEVIATHAN
Goldsmith, Jerry *C*
CD _____ VSD 5226
Varese Sarabande/Colosseum / Feb '90 /
Pinnacle / Silva Screen.

**LIFE AND ADVENTURES OF NICHOLAS
NICKLEBY, THE**
1982 London Cast
Oliver, Stephen *C*
London / Home in Devonshire / Dotheboys'
Hall / Journey to Portsmouth / Farewell
waltz / Mantini chase / Wedding anthem /
Patriotic song / Milliners' sewing room / Sir
Mulberry Hawk / Mrs. Grudden's goodbye
/ Wititterly gavotte / At the opera / Cheer-
ybyle brothers / Christmas carol
CD _____ CDTER 1029
TER / Aug '95 / Koch.

**LIFE IS FOR LIVING/A MAN AND A
WOMAN**
Lelouch, Claude & Francis Lai *C*
CD _____ 101292
Musidisc / Aug '90 / Vital / Harmonia Mundi
/ ADA / Cadillac / Discovery.

LIFEFORCE
London Symphony Orchestra
Mancini, Henry *C*
Lifeforce / Spacewalk / Into the alien craft /
Exploration / Sleeping vampires / Evil visi-
tations / Carson's story / Girl in the raincoat
/ Web of destiny (parts 1-3)
CD _____ CDFM 256
Milan / Feb '90 / BMG / Silva Screen.

**LIFETIMES
(To Live)**
Jiping, Zhao *C*
CD _____ 210532
Milan / Oct '94 / BMG / Silva Screen.

**LIGHT AT THE EDGE OF THE WORLD,
THE**
CD _____ A 8934
Alhambra / May '92 / Silva Screen.

LIGHTHORSEMAN, THE
Millo, Mario *C*
CD _____ IMICD 1009
Silva Screen / Jan '93 / Conifer / Silva
Screen.

LIGHTNING JACK
Rowland, Bruce *C*
CD _____ TVD 93405
Primetime / Aug '94 / Silva Screen.

L'ILE (THE ISLAND)
Petit, Jean Claude *C*
CD _____ CD 340
Milan / Jan '89 / BMG / Silva Screen.

LILI MARLENE/LOLA
Schygulla, H.
Raben, Peer *C*
CD _____ CH 123
Milan / Jan '95 / BMG / Silva Screen.

LILLIES OF THE FIELD
Goldsmith, Jerry *C*
CD _____ TSU 0101
Tsunami / Sep '93 / Silva Screen.

**LINCOLN
(inc. Traditional Civil War Music/
Lincoln's Speeches)**
Menken, Alan *C*

CD _____ 547522
Silva Screen / Jan '93 / Conifer / Silva Screen.

LINGUINI INCIDENT, THE
Newman, Thomas C
CD _____ VSD 5372
Varese Sarabande/Colosseum / Jun '93 / Pinnacle / Silva Screen.

LINK
Goldsmith, Jerry C
CD _____ VCD 47276
Varese Sarabande/Colosseum / Jan '89 / Pinnacle / Silva Screen.

L'INTEGRALE COMPLETE
CD _____ 887988
Milan / Jun '95 / BMG / Silva Screen.

LION IN WINTER, THE
Barry, John C
CD _____ VSD 5217
Varese Sarabande/Colosseum / Feb '90 / Pinnacle / Silva Screen.

LION KING, THE
John, Elton
John, Elton C
Rice, Tim L
Circle of life: Twillie, Carmen / I just can't wait to be King: Weaver, Jason / Be prepared: Irons, Jeremy / Hakuna matata: Lane, Nathan & Ernie Sabella / Can you feel the love tonight: Williams, Joseph & Sally Dworsky / This land: Zimmer, Hans / To die for / Under the stars / King of Pride Rock / Circle of life (2) / I just can't wait to be King (2) / Can you feel the love tonight (2)
CD _____ 5226902
Rocket / Jun '94 / PolyGram.

LION KING, THE
(Sing-along)
John, Elton C
Rice, Tim L
CD _____ DSMCD 477
Carlton Home Entertainment / Oct '94 / Carlton Home Entertainment.

LION KING, THE
John, Elton C
Rice, Tim L
CD _____ 32542
Scratch / Mar '95 / BMG.

LION KING, THE
Overtures
John, Elton C
Rice, Tim L
Circle of life / I just can't wait to be king / Be prepared / Hakuna Matara / Can you feel the love tonight / This land / To die for / Under the stars / King of Pride Rock / I just can't wait to be king (2) / Can you feel the love tonight (2) / Lion king of the jungle
CD _____ MSCD 13
Music De-Luxe / Dec '94 / Magnum Music Group.

LIONHEART
Goldsmith, Jerry C
CD _____ VSD 5484
Varese Sarabande/Colosseum / Apr '94 / Pinnacle / Silva Screen.

LIONHEART VOL 2
Goldsmith, Jerry C
CD _____ VCD 47288
Varese Sarabande/Colosseum / Jan '89 / Pinnacle / Silva Screen.

LIPSTICK
Polnareff, Michel C
CD _____ 4669942
Silva Screen / Jan '93 / Conifer / Silva Screen.

LIPSTICK ON YOUR COLLAR
Lipstick on your collar: Francis, Connie / Don't be cruel: Presley, Elvis / Great pretender: Platters / Earth angel: Crew Cuts / Little bitty pretty one: Thurston / Green door: Vaughan, Frankie / Only you: Platters / Story of my life: Holliday, Michael / Blueberry Hill: Domino, Fats / It's almost tomorrow: Dream Weavers / Your cheatin' heart: Williams, Hank / Garden of Eden: Vaughan, Frankie / My prayer: Platters / Blue suede shoes: Perkins, Carl / Raining in my heart: Holly, Buddy & The Crickets / Unchained melody: Baxter, Les / I see the moon: Stargazers / Be bop a lula: Vincent, Gene / I'm in love again: Domino, Fats / Young love: James, Sonny / Fool: Clark, Sanford / It'll be me: Lewis, Jerry Lee / Love is strange: Mickey & Sylvia / Sh-boom: Crew Cuts / Lotta lovin': Vincent, Gene / Lay down your arms: Shelton, Anne / Making love: Robinson, Floyd / Man with the golden arm: May, Billy & His Orchestra
CD _____ 5160862
PolyGram TV / Mar '93 / PolyGram.

LIQUID SKY
CD _____ VCD 47181
Varese Sarabande/Colosseum / Jan '89 / Pinnacle / Silva Screen.

LITTLE BUDDHA
Sakamoto, Ryuichi C
Sakamoto, Ryuichi Con
CD _____ 180312
Milan / Apr '94 / BMG / Silva Screen.

LITTLE BUDDHA
(The Secret Score)
Sakamoto, Ryuichi C

CD _____ 227452
Milan / Jun '95 / BMG / Silva Screen.

LITTLE MARY SUNSHINE
1962 London Cast
Besoyan, Rick C
Overture / Forest rangers / Little Mary Sunshine / Look for a sky of blue / You're the fairest flower / Swingin' - how do you do / Colorado love call / What has happened (finale Act 1) / Tell a handsome stranger / Once in a blue moon / Every little nothing / Such a merry party / Say Uncle / Heap big Injun / Mata Hari / Do you ever dream of Vienna / Coo coo / Finale
CD _____ CDSBL 13108
DRG / Nov '92 / New Note.

LITTLE MARY SUNSHINE
Broadway Cast
Besoyan, Rick C
CD _____ ZDM 7647742
EMI Classics / Apr '93 / EMI.

LITTLE ME
London Cast
Coleman, Cy C
Leigh, Carolyn L
Overture / Truth / On the other side of the tracks / Rich kids rag / I love you / Deep down inside / To be a performer / Le grand boom-boom / I've got your number / Real live girl / Poor little Hollywood star / Little me / Goodbye / Here's to us
CD _____ CDSBL 13111
DRG / Aug '93 / New Note.

LITTLE ME
1962 Broadway Cast
Coleman, Cy C
Leigh, Carolyn L
CD _____ 09026614822
RCA Victor / Jul '93 / BMG.

LITTLE MERMAID, THE
Menken, Alan C
Ashman, Howard L
Fathoms below / Fanfare / Daughters of Triton / Part of your world / Poor unfortunate souls / Les poissons / Kiss the girl / Firework / Jig / Storm / Destruction of the grotto / Flotsam and Jetsam / Tour of the kingdom / Bedtime / Wedding announcement / Eric to the rescue / Happy ending
CD _____ DSTCD 451
Disney / Sep '90 / Carlton Home Entertainment.

LITTLE NIGHT MUSIC, A
1975 London Cast
Sondheim, Stephen C
Wheller, H. L
Overture and night waltz / Now, later, soon / Glamorous life / Remember / You must meet my wife / Liaisons / In praise of women / Every day a little death / Weekend in the country / Sun won't set / It would have been wonderful / Perpetual anticipation / Send in the clowns / Miller's son / Finale (Reprise - Send in the clowns/Night waltz)
CD _____ GD 85090
RCA Victor / Apr '90 / BMG.

LITTLE NIGHT MUSIC, A
Cast Recording
Sondheim, Stephen C
Wheller, H. L
Edwards, John Owen Con
CD _____ CDTER 1179
TER / Jan '93 / Koch.

LITTLE PRINCESS
Doyle, Patrick C
CD _____ VSD 5628
Varese Sarabande/Colosseum / Feb '95 / Pinnacle / Silva Screen.

LITTLE RED RIDING HOOD
London Philharmonic Orchestra
Patterson, Paul C
Dahl, Roald L
Weiser-Most, Franz Con
CD _____ CDC 5555532
EMI Classics / Nov '95 / EMI.

LITTLE ROMANCE, A
Delerue, Georges C
Delerue, Georges Con
CD _____ VSD 5367
Varese Sarabande/Colosseum / Nov '92 / Pinnacle / Silva Screen.

LITTLE SHOP OF HORRORS
1987 Film Cast
Menken, Alan C
Ashman, Howard L
Prologue / Da doo / Grow for me / Somewhere that's green / Dentist / Feed me / Suddenly, Seymour / Suppertime / Meek shall inherit / Mean green mother from outer space / Finale / Skid Row (downtown)
CD _____ GFLD 19289
Geffen / Oct '95 / BMG.

LITTLE SHOP OF HORRORS
Cast Recording
Menken, Alan C
Ashman, Howard L
Prologue / Skid row / Da doo / Grow for me / Somewhere that's green / Be a dentist / Mushnik and son / Git it (feed me) / Suddenly, Seymour / Suppertime / Finale / Megamix
CD _____ LS 94CD01
Dreamtime / Apr '94 / Kudos / Pinnacle.

LITTLE TRAMP
1992 Studio Cast
Pomeranz, David C
In America again / Something no one could ever take away / When the world stops turning / Number one / 'Less it ends with a chase / Tramp/He's got to be someone / Chaplin films / Thank you / Heaven / He's got to be someone (reprise) / Too many words / I got me a red/There's got to be a law / This is what I dreamed / Finale
CD _____ 4509913872
WEA / Nov '92 / Warner Music.

LITTLE VERA
CD _____ CDCH 368
Milan / Apr '90 / BMG / Silva Screen.

LITTLE WOMEN
Newman, Thomas C
CD _____ SK 66922
Sony Classical / Mar '95 / Sony.

LIVE A LITTLE.../TROUBLE WITH GIRLS/CHANGE OF HEART/CHARRO
Presley, Elvis.
Almost in love / Little less conversation / Wonderful world / Edge of reality / Little less conversation (album version) / Charro / Let's forget about the stars / Clean up your own backyard / Swing low, sweet chariot (2) / Swing low, sweet chariot / Signs of the zodiac / Almost / Whiffenpoof song / Violet / Clean up your own backyard (undubbed version) / Almost (undubbed version) / Have a happy / Let's be friends / Change of habit / Let us pray / Rubberneckin'
CD _____ 07863665592
RCA / Mar '95 / BMG.

LIVE AND LET DIE
Martin, George C
Live and let die: McCartney, Paul & Wings / Just a closer walk with thee / New second line: Dejan, Harold A. 'Duke' & The Olympia Brass Band / Bond meets Solitaire / Whisper who dares / Snakes alive / Baron Samedi's dance of death / San Monique / Fillet of soul / Bond drops in / If he finds it, kill him / Trespassers will be eaten / Solitaire gets her cards / Sacrifice / James Bond
CD _____ CZ 553
Premier / Dec '95 / EMI.

LOCAL HERO
Knopfler, Mark
Knopfler, Mark C
Rocks and the water / Wild theme / Freeway flyer / Boomtown / Way it always starts / Rocks and the thunder / Ceilidh and the Northern lights / Mist covered mountain / Ceilidh / Louis favourite Billy tune / Whistle / Smooching / Stargazer / Going home (theme from Local Hero)
CD _____ 8110382
Phonogram / Jan '94 / PolyGram.

LOGAN'S RUN
Goldsmith, Jerry C
CD _____ BCD 3024
Bay Cities / Mar '92 / Silva Screen.

LOMA/VIXEN/FASTER PUSSYCAT KILL KILL
(Russ Meyer Original Soundtracks Vol. 1)
CD _____ QDKCD 008
Normal/Okra / Jul '94 / Direct / ADA.

LONDON'S BURNING
Brint, Simon & Roddy Matthews C
Blue watch / Dixie's rescue / Bus / Sicknote plays golf / Naked fear / Dormitory / Bogus fireman / Donald's theme / Boats / Water kids / Basketball / Blackwall bomb / Billy falls in / Skate race / Sandra suspects / Chip fire / Nick's decision time / Kevin is homeless / Junkies / Helicopter / Kevin's brother / Convertible / Blue watch (long version)
CD _____ CDEMC 3729
Premier / Nov '95 / EMI.

LONE WOLF MCQUADE
De Masi, Francesco C
CD _____ VSD 5573
Varese Sarabande/Colosseum / Nov '95 / Pinnacle / Silva Screen.

LONESOME DOVE
Poledouris, Basil C
CD _____ CFM 9722
Silva Screen / Jan '93 / Conifer / Silva Screen.

LONG GOOD FRIDAY, THE
Monkman, Francis
Monkman, Francis C
Long good Friday / Overture / Scene is set / At the pool / Discovery / Icehouse / Talking to the police / Guitar interludes / Realization / Fury / Taken
CD _____ FILMCD 020
Silva Screen / Jan '89 / Conifer / Silva Screen.

LONG RIDERS, THE
Cooder, Ry
Cooder, Ry C
Long riders / I'm a good old rebel / Seneca square dance / Archie's funeral (hold to God's unchanging hand) / I always knew that you were the one / Rally round the flag / Better things to think about / My grandfather / Cole Younger / Escape from Northfield / Leaving Missouri / Jesse James

CD _____ 7599234482
WEA / Jan '96 / Warner Music.

LONG WALK HOME, THE
Fenton, George
Fenton, George C
CD _____ VSD 5304
Varese Sarabande/Colosseum / Apr '91 / Pinnacle / Silva Screen.

LORD OF ILLUSION
CD _____ IONIC 13CD
Fine Line / Jul '95 / Disc.

LORD OF THE FLIES
London Symphony Orchestra
Sarde, Philippe C
Lord of the flies / Island / Demons / Fire on the mountain / Cry of the hunters / Last hope / Savages / After the storm / Bacchanalia / Lord Of The Flies (finale)
CD _____ FILMCD 067
Silva Screen / Jun '90 / Conifer / Silva Screen.

LORD OF THE RINGS
Rosenman, Leonard C
CD _____ FMT 8003D
Intrada / Apr '92 / Silva Screen / Koch.

LOST BOYS, THE
To the shock of Miss Louise: Newman, Thomas / Good times: INXS & Jimmy Barnes / Lost in the shadows: Gramm, Lou / Don't let the sun go down on me: Daltrey, Roger / Laying down the law: INXS & Jimmy Barnes / People are strange: Echo & The Bunnymen / Cry little sister: McMann, Gerard / Power play: Eddie & The Tide / I still believe: Cappello, Tim / Beauty has her way: Mummy Calls
CD _____ 7817672
Atlantic / Aug '87 / Warner Music.

LOST EMPIRE, THE/RETRIBUTION
Howarth, Alan C
Howarth, Alan Con
CD _____ FILMCD 068
Silva Screen / Jan '91 / Conifer / Silva Screen.

LOST EMPIRES
Hilton, Derek C
Lost empires theme / Army of today's alright / Your king and country / Pure white rose / Somewhere / Oh Flo / They didn't believe me / Wedding glide / Cigar girl / Honeysuckle and the bee / Mother Machree / Alexander's ragtime band / Land of hope and glory / Rule Britannia / I don't want to play in your yard / Yankee doodle boy / Shine on harvest moon / Love's old sweet song / Trombone song / Take me on the flip flap / Nobody knows, nobody cares / Mr. Knick Knock / Poor little Dolly / Waiting for the Robert E. Lee / Catari, catari / Nightingale and the star / Julia's theme
CD _____ CDTER 1119
TER / Nov '86 / Koch.

LOUISIANA STORY
New London Orchestra
Thomson, Virgil C
Corp, R. Con
Power among men / Louisiana story / Acadian songs and dances / Plow that broke the plains
CD _____ CDA 66576
Hyperion / Feb '92 / Select.

LOVE HURTS
Hawkshaw, Alan C
Love hurts (Tessa's theme) / Chance encounter / St. Petersburg / Frank's theme / Marisha / Jade's theme / Nikolai / Everyone needs someone to love / New beginnings / Lynne's theme / Crisis for Diane / Jade confides in Mum / Frank and Tessa / Simon and Diane / Jade joins Seed / Frank owns up / Love hurts (closing title song): Polycarpou, Peter
CD _____ CDSTM 4
Soundtrack Music / Feb '93 / EMI.

LOVE ME TENDER
Presley, Elvis
CD _____ 295 052
RCA / May '95 / BMG.

LOVE STORY
Lai, Francis C
Love story / Snow frolic / Sonata No.12 in F major / I love you Phil / Christmas tree / Search for Jenny / Bozo Barrett / Skating in Central Park / Long walk home / Concerto No.3 in D Major / Love story (finale)
CD _____ MCLD 19157
MCA / Jun '93 / BMG.

LOVED UP
Smoke belch II: Sabres Of Paradise / Crystal clear: Grid / Prologue: 10th Chapter / Two full moons and a trout: Union Jack / Little bullet: Spooky / Gut drum mix: Funtopia / Plastic dream: Jaydee / Break and enter: Prodigy / Acperience: Hardfloor / Surjestive: Advances / Melt: Leftfield
CD _____ PRIMACD 002
Prima Vera / Oct '95 / Vital.

LOVING YOU
Presley, Elvis
Mean woman blues / Teddy bear / Got a lot of livin' to do / Lonesome cowboy / Hot dog / Party / Blueberry Hill / True love / Don't leave me now / Have I told you lately that I love you / I need you so / Loving you

LOVING YOU
CD _____ ND 81515
RCA / Oct '87 / BMG.

LOVING YOU
Herman, Jerry C
CD _____ VSD 5586
Varese Sarabande/Colosseum / Aug '95 /
Pinnacle / Silva Screen.

LOW DOWN DIRTY SHAME, A
CD _____ CHIP 156
Jive / Apr '95 / BMG.

LUBITSCH TOUCH
Film Orchestra Babelsberg
Sasse, Karl-Ernst C
Rosenberg, Manfred Con
CD _____ 09026626562
RCA Victor / Nov '95 / BMG.

LUCIFER RISING
Beausoleil, Bobby C
CD _____ DIGUST 2
Masters Of Disgust / Feb '94 / Pinnacle.

LUCKY STIFF
Flaherty, Stephen C
Something funny's going on / Mr. Wither-
spoon's friday night / Uncle's last request /
Good to be alive / Rita's confession / Lucky
/ Dogs versus you / Phone call / Monte
Carlo / Speaking French / Times like this /
Fancy meeting you here / Him, them, it, her
/ Nice / Welcome back Mr. Witherspoon /
Confession no.2 / Finale: Good to be alive
CD _____ VSD 5461
Varese Sarabande/Colosseum / Apr '94 /
Pinnacle / Silva Screen.

LULU
Segarra, Carlos C
CD _____ CH 703
Milan / Jan '95 / BMG / Silva Screen.

LUNCH
(The Studio Recording)
Dorff, Steve C
Bettis, John L
Lunch / He'll never know / I never danced
with you / Requiem for a sandwich / Man
like me / Skyline / Time stands still / I'm no
angel / Why fall at all / Perfectly alone /
Lunch concerto
CD _____ DRGCD 12610
DRG / Mar '95 / New Note.

M. BUTTERFLY
Shore, Howard C
Shore, Howard Con
CD _____ VSD 5435
Varese Sarabande/Colosseum / Oct '93 /
Pinnacle / Silva Screen.

M.A.S.H.
M.A.S.H. (Suicide is painless) / Duke and
Hawkeye arrive at MASH / Jeep ride to
camp / Tokyo shoe shine boy / Onward
christian soldiers / My blue Heaven / Operating theatre / Happy days are here again
/ Major Houlihan and Major Burns / Hi ho hi
lo / Hail to the chief / Sayonara, painless
suicide, funeral and resurrection / Jig is up
/ Tent scene, Hot Lip's shows her true colours / Chattanooga choo choo / Moments
to remember / Football game / March
post march
CD _____ CK 66804
CBS/Silva Screen / Apr '95 / Conifer / Silva
Screen.

MACARTHUR
(The Rebel General)
Goldsmith, Jerry C
CD _____ VSD 5260
Varese Sarabande/Colosseum / Oct '90 /
Pinnacle / Silva Screen.

MACHINE GUN MCCAIN
Morricone, Ennio C
Morricone, Ennio Con
CD _____ A 8922
Alhambra / Feb '92 / Silva Screen.

MACK AND MABEL
1974 Broadway Cast
Herman, Jerry C
Overture: Orchestra / Movies were movies:
Preston, Robert / Look what happened to
Mabel: Mack & Mabel / Big time: Kirk, Lisa
/ I won't send roses: Preston, Robert / I
wanna make the world laugh: Preston, Rob-
ert / Wherever he ain't: Peters, Bernadette
/ Hundreds of girls: Preston, Robert & The
Bathing Beauties / When Mabel comes in
the room: Simmonds, Stanley / My heart
leaps up: Preston, Robert / Time heals
everything: Peters, Bernadette / Tap your
troubles away: Kirk, Lisa / I promise you a
happy ending: Preston, Robert
CD _____ MCLD 19089
MCA / Oct '92 / BMG.

MACK AND MABEL
(In Concert)
1988 London Cast
Herman, Jerry C

Overture / Introduction / When movies were
movies / Look what happened to Mabel /
Big time / I won't send roses (with first re-
prise) / I wanna make the world laugh /
Wherever he ain't / Hundreds of girls / En-
tr'acte / When Mabel comes in the room /
Hit 'em on the head / Time heals everything
/ Tap your troubles away / I promise you a
happy ending / I won't send roses (reprise)
CD _____ CDEMC 3734
Premier / Dec '95 / EMI.
CD _____ OCRCD 6015
First Night / Oct '95 / Pinnacle.

MACK THE KNIFE
CD _____ CD 45630
CBS / '89 / Sony.

MACROSS PLUS
National anthem of Macross / Fly up in the
air - tension / After, in the dark - torch song
/ Myung theme / Bees and honey / In cap-
tivity / More than 3cm / Voices / Break out
- cantabile / Very little wishes / Santi-U
CD _____ DSCD 12
Demon / May '95 / Pinnacle / ADA.

MCVICAR
Bitter and twisted / Escape / Free me: Dal-
trey, Roger / Just a dream away / McVicar
/ My time is gonna come / Waiting for a
friend / White City lights / Without your love:
Daltrey, Roger
CD _____ 5273412
Polydor / Jan '94 / PolyGram.

MAD DOG AND GLORY
Bernstein, Elmer C
Bernstein, Elmer Con
CD _____ VSD 5415
Varese Sarabande/Colosseum / Mar '93 /
Pinnacle / Silva Screen.

MAD MAX
May, Brian C
CD _____ VCD 47144
Varese Sarabande/Colosseum / Jan '89 /
Pinnacle / Silva Screen.

MAD MAX II
(The Road Warrior)
May, Brian C
Opening titles / Montage / Confrontation /
Marauder's massacre / Max enters com-
pound / Feral boy strikes / Gyro tank: Max
/ Gyro flight / Breakout / Chase continues /
Journey over the mountain / Finale and
largo / End title
CD _____ VCD 47262
Varese Sarabande/Colosseum / Jan '89 /
Pinnacle / Silva Screen.

MAD MAX III
(Beyond The Thunderdome)
Royal Philharmonic Orchestra
Jarre, Maurice C
We don't need another hero: Turner, Tina /
One of the living: Turner, Tina / We don't
need another hero (instrumental) / Barter-
town / Children / Coming home
CD _____ GNPD 8037
GNP Crescendo / Sep '92 / Silva Screen.

MAD MONKEY
Duhamel, Antoine C
CD _____ CH 397
Milan / Jan '95 / BMG / Silva Screen.

MADAME SOUSATZKA
Gouriet, Gerald C
CD _____ VSD 5204
Varese Sarabande/Colosseum / Dec '88 /
Pinnacle / Silva Screen.

MADE IN AMERICA
Go Away: Estefan, Gloria / Does he do it
good: Sweat, Keith / Made in America: Del
Tha Funky Homosapien / Colours of love:
Fischer, Lisa / What is this: Mendes, Sergio
/ Made in Love: Isham, Mark / I know I don't
walk on water: Satterfield, Laura & Ephraim
Lewis / Dance or die: D.J. Jazzy Jeff & The
Fresh Prince / Smoke on the water: Deep
Purple / If you need a miracle: King, Ben E.
/ Stand: Y.T Staple
CD _____ 7559614982
WEA / Jun '93 / Warner Music.

MADE IN HEAVEN
Isham, Mark C
CD _____ 9607292
Silva Screen / Jan '89 / Conifer / Silva
Screen.

MADNESS OF KING GEORGE, THE
Fenton, George C
Opening the Houses of Parliament / Prel-
ude/Front titles / Smile, it's what you're paid
for / King goes riding / Family matter /
Cricket match / King wakes up early / Do it
England / Concert / We have no time / He
will be restrained / London is flooding / Go-
ing to Kew / Starting to recover / Chancellor
drives to London / Prince Regent / Mr. and
Mrs. King / End credits
CD _____ 4784772
Epic / Apr '95 / Sony.

**MADWOMAN OF CENTRAL PARK
WEST, THE**
Broadway Cast
CD _____ DRGCD 5212
DRG / Jan '95 / New Note.

MAGDALENE
Munich Symphony Orchestra
Eidelman, Cliff C
Eidelman, Cliff Con

CD _____ MAF 7029D
Intrada / Sep '92 / Silva Screen / Koch.

MAGIC RIDDLE, THE
Ordinary miracles / When I was just a little
girl / I will find the will / Mean mean mean /
My darling daughters / Sisters sisters /
Cindy do it now / Try not to cry so / Pig
song / Oh silver bright reflection / Grandma
dear grandma / Now how did it get / Girl in
the snow white dress / I'm alive / Cinderella's wedding day / Instrumental score
excerpts
CD _____ A 8937
Alhambra / May '92 / Silva Screen.

MAGNIFICENT AMBERSONS
Australian Philharmonic Orchestra
Herrmann, Bernard C
Bremner, Tony Con
CD _____ PRCD 1783
Preamble / Jan '93 / Silva Screen.

**MAGNIFICENT SEVEN, THE/RETURN
OF THE SEVEN**
Bernstein, Elmer C
Magnificent Seven / Bandidos / Return of
the seven / Defeat / Mariachis de Mexico /
El toro / Journey / Council / Petra's decla-
ration / In the trap / Battle / Finale
CD _____ TSU 0102
Tsunami / Jan '95 / Silva Screen.

MAHABHARATA
Tchuchitori, Toshi
Tchuchitori, Toshi C
Nibiro ghono anobua / Draupadi / Ontoro
momo / Satvati / Virata / Bushi ok sudure /
Cities / Bhima / Markandeya (part 1) / Dur-
yodhana / Dhire / Markandeya (part 2) /
Svetasvatara upanisad
CD _____ RWCD 9
Realworld / Jan '90 / EMI / Sterns.

MAIN EVENT
Melvoin, Michael C
Main event / Fight / Body shop / Copeland
meets the Coasters / Get a job / Big girls
don't cry / It's your foot again / Angry eyes
/ I'd clean a fish for you
CD _____ 4749062
Columbia / '95 / Sony.

MAJOR DUNDEE
Amfitheatrof, Daniele C
CD _____ TSU 0111
Tsunami / Jan '95 / Silva Screen.

MAJOR LEAGUE II
Boom bapa boom: Vaughan, Jimmy /
(Everything I do) Got to be funky: Vaughan,
Jimmy / Wild thing '94: X / Shake me up:
Little Feat / Rude mood: Vaughan, Stevie
Ray / All my love is gone: Lovett, Lyle / Born
under a bad sign: King, Albert / House is
rockin': Vaughan, Stevie Ray & Double
Trouble / Wild thing: X
CD _____ 523245-2
Morgan Creek / Jun '94 / PolyGram.

MALCOLM X
Revolution: Arrested Development / Roll
'em Pete / Flying home: Hampton, Lionel /
My prayer: Ink Spots / Big stuff / Don't cry
baby / Beans and cornbread / Azure: Fitz-
gerald, Ella / Alabama: Coltrane, John /
Lucky old sun just rolls around heaven /
Arabesque cooke / Shotgun / Someday
we'll all be free: Franklin, Aretha
CD _____ 9362451302
WEA / Nov '92 / Warner Music.

MALCOLM X
(Score)
Blanchard, Terence C
Opening credits / Young Malcolm / Cops
and robbers / Earl's death / Flashback /
Numbers / Fire / Back to Boston / Malcolm
meets Baines / Black and white / Little lamb
vision / Malcolm's letter / Malcolm meets
Elijah / Old days / Betty's theme / Fruit of
Islam / First minister / Betty's conflict / Mal-
colm speaks to secretaries / Malcolm con-
fronts Baines / Chickens come home / Go-
ing to Mecca / Firebomb / Assassins /
Assassination / Eulogy
CD _____ 472806 2
Columbia / Mar '93 / Sony.

MALICE
Goldsmith, Jerry C
Goldsmith, Jerry Con
CD _____ VSD 5442
Varese Sarabande/Colosseum / Jan '94 /
Pinnacle / Silva Screen.

MALLRATS
MCA / Nov '95 / BMG.
CD _____ MCD 11294

MAMA, I WANT TO SING
London Cast
Treasure of love / On Christ / Solid rock /
You are my child / Faith can move a moun-
tain / I know who hold tomorrow / He'll be
your strength / Gifted is / This bitter earth /
Stormy weather / In my solitude / God bless
the child / Mama I want to sing / I'll do an-
ything / What do you win when you win /
Take my hand (precious Lord) / His eye is
on the sparrow / Take my hand (precious
Lord) (1) / Know when to leave the party /
Just one look / One who will love me
CD _____ CDEMC 3709
EMI / May '95 / EMI.

MAMBO KINGS, THE
La dicha mia / Ran kan kan / Cuban Pete /
Mambo caliente / Quiereme mucho / Sunny
ray / Melao da cana (moo la lah) / Para los
rumberos / Perfidia / Guantanamera / Tea
for two / Accidental mambo / Come fue /
Tanga / Rumba afro cubana / Beautiful Ma-
ria of my soul
CD _____ 7559612402
Elektra / May '92 / Warner Music.

MAME
1966 Broadway Cast
Herman, Jerry C
CD _____ CK 03000
CBS/Silva Screen / Jan '89 / Conifer / Silva
Screen.

MAN BITES DOG
CD _____ 873142
Milan / Jan '93 / BMG / Silva Screen.

MAN CALLED MOON, A
Bacalov, Luis Enriquez C
CD _____ A 8935
Silva Screen / Jan '93 / Conifer / Silva
Screen.

MAN FROM SNOWY RIVER, THE
Rowland, Bruce C
CD _____ VCD 47217
Varese Sarabande/Colosseum / Jan '89 /
Pinnacle / Silva Screen.

MAN FROM U.N.C.L.E., THE
Montenegro, Hugo C
Montenegro, Hugo Con
Man from U.N.C.L.E. / Meet Mr. Solo / Mar-
tini built for two / Wild bike / Solo on a raft
/ Fiddlesticks / Man from THRUSH / Illya /
Invaders / Solo's samba / Bye bye Jill /
Watch out / Sandals only / Solo busanova
/ Off and running / Boo-bam-boo baby /
Slink / Run spy run / Jungle beat / Wiggely
pig walk / Lament for a trapped spy / There
they go / Jo Jo's torch thing / Dance of the
flaming swords
CD _____ 74321241792
RCA / Jan '95 / BMG.

MAN ON FIRE
Graunke Symphony Orchestra
Scott, John C
CD _____ VCD 47314
Varese Sarabande/Colosseum / Jan '89 /
Pinnacle / Silva Screen.

MAN WHO WOULD BE KING, THE
Jarre, Maurice C
CD _____ 873127
Milan / Jan '95 / BMG / Silva Screen.

MAN WITH THE GOLDEN GUN, THE
Barry, John C
Man with the golden gun: Lulu / Scraman-
ga's fun house / Chew mee in Grisly land /
Man with the golden gun (jazz instrumental)
/ Getting the bullet / Goodnight, goodnight
/ Let's go get em / Hip's trip / Kung fu fight
/ In search of Scaramanga's island / Return
to Scaramanga's fun house / Man with the
golden gun (reprise): Lulu
CD _____ CZ 102
Premier / Dec '95 / EMI.

MAN WITHOUT A FACE
Horner, James C
CD _____ 5182442
Silva Screen / Jul '93 / Conifer / Silva
Screen.

MANHATTAN
Gershwin, George C
Rhapsody in blue / Someone to watch over
me / I've got a crush on you / Embraceable
you / Land of the gay caballero / Do do do
/ 'S Wonderful / Mine / He loves and she
loves / Bronco buster's ball / Lady be good
/ Love is here to stay / Sweet and low down
/ Blue blue blue / But not for me / Strike up
the band / Love is sweeping the country
CD _____ MK 36020
CBS / Jun '87 / Sony.

MANNAJA/TE DEUM
De Angelis, G. & M. C
CD _____ OST 121
Milano Dischi / Jul '94 / Silva Screen.

**MANON DE SOURCES/JEAN DE
FLORETE**
Petit, Jean Claude
Petit, Jean Claude C
CD _____ CDCH 241
Milan / Feb '94 / BMG / Silva Screen.

MARCH OF THE FALSETTOS
1981 Off-Broadway Cast
Finn, William C
Finn, William L
Four Jews in a room bitching / Tight-knit
family / Love is blind / Thrill of first love /
Marvin at the psychiatrist / My Father's a
homo / Everyone tells Jason to see a psy-
chiatrist / This had better come to a stop /
Please come to my house / Jason's therapy
/ Marriage proposal / Trina's song / March
of the falsettos / Chess game / Making a
home
CD _____ DRGCD 12581
DRG / Mar '92 / New Note.

**MARCH OF THE FALSETTOS/
FALSETTOLAND**
Cast Recording
Finn, William C
Finn, William & James Lapine L

2CD _____ DRGCD 22600
DRG / Jan '95 / New Note.

MARIA'S LOVERS
CD _____ CDEMC 362
Milan / Apr '90 / BMG / Silva Screen.

MARKED FOR DEATH
CD _____ BRCD 561
4th & Broadway / Jan '94 / PolyGram.

MARNIE
Herrmann, Bernard C
CD _____ TCI 0601
Silva Screen / Jan '95 / Conifer / Silva Screen.

MARRY ME A LITTLE
1981 Broadway Cast
Sondheim, Stephen C
Saturday night / Two fairy tales / Can that boy foxtrot / All things bright and beautiful / Bang (All things bright and beautiful pt. 2) / Girls of Summer / Uptown, downtown / So many people / Your eyes are blue / Moment with you / Marry me a little / Happily ever after / Pour le sport / Silly people / There won't be trumpets / It wasn't meant to happen / Who could be blue/Little white house
CD _____ 71422
RCA/Silva Screen / '88 / Silva Screen.

MARTIN CHUZZLEWIT
Burgon, Geoffrey C
CD _____ DMUSCD 107
Destiny / Dec '94 / Total/BMG.

MARY POPPINS
Sherman, Richard & Robert C
Overture / Sister Suffragette / Life I lead / Perfect nanny / Spoonful of sugar / Pavement artist (chim chim cher-ee) / Jolly holiday / Supercalifragilisticexpialidocious / Stay awake / I love to laugh / British bank (the life I lead) / Feed the birds (tuppence a bag) / Fidelity diduciary bank / Chim chim cheree / Step in time / Man has dreams / Let's go and fly a kite
CD _____ DSM CD 459
Disney / Jul '92 / Carlton Home Entertainment.

MASK, THE
Cuban Pete (Edit: _Carrey, Jim_ / Cuban Pete: _Carrey, Jim_ / Who's that man: _Xscape_ / This business of love: _Domino_ / Bounce around: _Tony Toni Tone_ / (I could only) Whisper your name: _Connick, Harry Jr._ / You would be my baby: _Williams, Vanessa_ / Hi de ho: _K7_ / Let the good times roll: _Fishbone_ / Straight up: _Setzer, Brian Orchestra_ / Hey pachuco: _Royal Crown Revue_ / Gee baby ain't I good to you: _Boyd, Susan_
CD _____ 477316-2
Columbia / Aug '94 / Sony.

MASTERS OF THE UNIVERSE
Graunke Symphony Orchestra
Conti, Bill C
Main title / Gwildor's quadrille / Quiet escape / Earthly encounter / Battle at the gym / Procession of the mercenaries / Evilyn's decption / Centurion attack / Skeletor the destroyer / He-Man enslaved / Transformation of Skeletor / Kevin's plight/After them / Julie's muzal / Power of Greyskull / Good journey / He-Man victorious
CD _____ FILMCD 095
Silva Screen / May '92 / Conifer / Silva Screen.

MATADOR
Overture / There's no way out of here / To be a Matador / I was born to me / Only other people / Manolete, Belmonte, Joselito / Boy from nowhere / Wake up Madrid / I'll take you out to dinner / This incredible journey / Don't be deceived / I'll dress you in mourning / Dance with death / Panama hat
CD _____ VIVA CD 1
Epic / Apr '91 / Sony.

MATEWAN
CD _____ DARING 1011CD
Daring / Feb '95 / Direct / CM / ADA.

MAVERICK
Newman, Randy C
Renegades, rebels and rogues / Good run of bad luck / Maverick / Ophelia / Something already gone / Dream on Texas ladies / Ladies love outlaws / Solitary travelers / Rainbow down the road / You don't mess around with me / Ride gambler ride / Amazing grace
CD _____ 756782595-2
Warner Bros. / Mar '94 / Warner Music.

MAXIMUM OVERDRIVE
(Who Made Who)
AC/DC
Who made who / You shook me all night long / D.T. / Sink the pink / Ride on / Hell's bells / Shake your foundations / Chase the ace / For those about to rock (we salute you)
CD _____ 7816402
Atlantic / May '86 / Warner Music.

MAYRIG
Petit, Jean Claude C
CD _____ 752001
Silva Screen / Jul '93 / Conifer / Silva Screen.

ME AND MY GIRL
1985 London Cast
Gay, Noel C

Furber, Douglas & L. Arthur Rose L
Overture / Weekend at Hareford / Thinking of no one but me / Family solicitor / Me and my girl / English gentleman / You would if you could / Lambeth walk / Sun has got his hat on / Once you lose your heart / Take it on the chin / Song of Hareford / Love makes the world go round / Leaning on a lamp-post / If only you cared for me / Finale
CD _____ CDP 7463932
EMI / Jun '92 / EMI.

ME AND MY GIRL
(Highlights - The Shows Collection)
Cast Recording
Gay, Noel C
Furber, Douglas & L. Arthur Rose L
CD _____ PWKS 4143
Carlton Home Entertainment / Jan '95 / Carlton Home Entertainment.

ME AND MY GIRL
1987 Broadway Cast
Gay, Noel C
Furber, Douglas & L. Arthur Rose L
CD _____ CDTER 1145
TER / May '89 / Koch.

MEDAL OF HONOUR
Stone, Richard C
CD _____ PCD 106
Prometheus / Jul '94 / Silva Screen.

MEDICINE MAN
Goldsmith, Jerry C
Goldsmith, Jerry Con
CD _____ VSD 5350
Varese Sarabande/Colosseum / Mar '92 / Pinnaole / Silva Screen.

MEET ME IN ST. LOUIS
1989 Broadway Cast
Martin, Hugh & Ralph Blane C
CD _____ DRGCD 19002
DRG / Jan '95 / New Note.

MEET THE FEEBLES
CD _____ QDKCD 003
Normal/Okra / Sep '94 / Direct / ADA.

MEGAZONE 23
Eden the last city / Sleepless beauty in the woods / Eiji / Netjacker / Ryo / G form / Artifact / Wall of Eden / Another story of megazone / Tragedy of an idol / Wang dai / Netpolice / Bahamoud / Cyberspace force / Project heaven / Pandora's boat / Mother Earth
CD _____ DSCD 9
Demon / May '95 / Pinnacle / ADA.

MELANCHOLIA
Fisher-Turner, Simon
Fisher-Turner, Simon C
Holiday snaps and raincoat / Wrench and pull and blue / Flirt / Drinking at a stream / Butcher and Musak / Sergio electro / Bom bom bom / Sarah / Runner
CD _____ FILMCD 061
Silva Screen / Dec '89 / Conifer / Silva Screen.

MELROSE PLACE
That's just what you are: _Mann, Aimee_ / Back on me: _Urge Overkill_ / Baby I can't please you: _Phillips, Sam_ / Blah: _Dinosaur Jnr_ / Ordinary angels: _Frente_ / Precious: _Lennox, Annie_ / I'm jealous: _Divinyls_ / Kids, this is fabulous: _Seed_ / Here and now: _Letters To Cleo_ / How was it for you: _James_ / Star is bored: _Westerberg, Paul_
CD _____ 74321226082
Giant / Nov '94 / BMG.

MEMPHIS BELLE
Fenton, George C
Fenton, George Con
Londonderry air/Front titles / Green eyes / Flying home / Steel lady / Prepare for take-off / Final mission / With deep regret... / I know why and so do you / Bomb run / Limping home / Crippled Belle: The landing / Resolution / End title suite / Danny Boy
CD _____ VSD 5293
Varese Sarabande/Colosseum / Nov '90 / Pinnacle / Silva Screen.

MENACE 2 SOCIETY
CD _____ CHIP 137
Jive / Jun '93 / BMG.

MER DE CHINE
Coe, Tony
Coe, Tony C
Binh a la sortie de l'ecole / Le secretaire / Conversation sous la pluie / Troop long temps / La famille de binh / Sans cesse / La criee / Le departe de la famille / Le bus / L'arrestation de l'oncle / La mission / Vers le refuge / La fuite / La mort de la mere / Le delta / Boat people / La rencontre des boats / Pirates / Mer a boire / Enfin / Les eaux internationales / Marine de la nuit / I never held one before / Marine de jour / Nuit de boat / Les visages / Le bateau de binh / Sur le point / La seperation / L'arrivee / Binh et joy / La bicyclette / Mer de chine
CD _____ 626506
Nato / Aug '91 / Discovery.

MERLIN OF THE CRYSTAL CAVE
Munich Symphony Orchestra
Shaw, Francis C
Shaw, Francis Con
Main titles / Young Merlin - a strange boy / King Gorlan / Young Merlin / Galapas the teacher / Red dragon medallion / Young lovers - Ninianne and Ambrose / Merlin

journeys to the palace / Merlin's adventures / Ambrosius kills the sacred bull / Vision explained / Merlin returns to England / Death of Galapas / Merlin captured by King Vortigern / Attack on the rafts / Vision of Stonehenge / Killary battle / Sacred stone / Rebuilding Stonehenge / Funeral of Ninianne and Ambrosius / Sunrise / Arthur - who shall be King / Merlin's theme
CD _____ FILMCD 089
Silva Screen / May '92 / Conifer / Silva Screen.

MERRILY WE ROLL ALONG
1981 Broadway Cast
Sondheim, Stephen C
CD _____ RCD 15840
RCA/Silva Screen / Jan '89 / Silva Screen.

MERRILY WE ROLL ALONG
1994 Cast
Sondheim, Stephen C
CD _____ VSD 5548
Varese Sarabande/Colosseum / Jan '95 / Pinnacle / Silva Screen.

MERRILY WE ROLL ALONG
1993 Haymarket Theatre Cast
Sondheim, Stephen C
CD _____ CDTER 1225
TER / Dec '94 / Koch.

MERRILY WE ROLL ALONG
Cast Recording
Sondheim, Stephen C
CD _____ CDTEM 21203
TER / Jan '93 / Koch.

MERRY CHRISTMAS MR. LAWRENCE
Sakamoto, Hyuichi
Sakamoto, Ryuichi C
Batavia / Germination / Hearty breakfast / Before the war / Seed and the sower / Brief encounter / Ride ride ride / Flight / Father Christmas / Dismissed / Assembly / Beyond reason / Sowing the seed / 23rd Psalm / Forbidden colours: _Sakamoto, Ryuichi_ & _David Sylvian_ / Merry Christmas Mr. Lawrence
CD _____ 220482
Milan / Aug '94 / BMG / Silva Screen.

MERRY WIDOW, THE
1986 London Cast/New Sadler's Wells Opera Choir/Orchestra
Lehar, Franz C
Wordsworth, Barry Con
CD _____ CDTER 1111
TER / Sep '86 / Koch.

MERRY WIDOW, THE
(Highlights)
1986 London Cast/New Sadler's Wells Opera Choir/Orchestra
Lehar, Franz C
Wordsworth, Barry Con
CD _____ CDTEO 1003
TER / Sep '86 / Koch.

MERRY WIDOW, THE
Schwarzkopf, Elisabeth & Nicolai Gedda/Erich Kunz/Philharmonia Chorus & Orchestra
Lehar, Franz C
Ackermann, Otto Con
CD _____ CDH 7695202
EMI Classics / Apr '93 / EMI.

MERRY WIDOW, THE
Schwarzkopf, Elisabeth & Nicolai Gedda/Hanny Steffek/Philharmonia Chorus/Orchestra
Lehar, Franz C
Von Matacic, Lovro Con
2CD _____ CDC 7471788
EMI Classics / Apr '93 / EMI

MERRY WIDOW, THE
Studer, Cheryl & Monteverdi Choir/Wiener Philharmoniker
Lehar, Franz C
Gardiner, John Eliot Con
CD _____ 4399112
Deutsche Grammophon / Jan '95 / PolyGram.

MERRY WIDOW, THE
Harwood, Elizabeth & Teresa Stratas/Berliner Philharmoniker
Lehar, Franz C
Von Karajan, Horbort Con
2CD _____ 4357122
Deutsche Grammophon / Jan '95 / PolyGram.

MESSAGE, THE/LION OF THE DESERT
(The Epic Film Music Of Maurice Jarre)
Royal Philharmonic Orchestra/London Symphony Orchestra
Jarre, Maurice C
Jarre, Maurice Con
Message (inc. Hegira/Building the first mosque/Sura/Presence of Mohammed/Entry to Mecca/Declaration/First martyrs/Fight/Spread of Islam/Broken idols/Faith of Islam): _Royal Philharmonic Orchestra_ / Lion of the desert (Omar the teacher/Italian invasion/Resistance/Lion of the desert/Displacement/ Concentration camp/Death/ March of freedom): _London Symphony Orchestra_
CD _____ FILMCD 060
Silva Screen / Feb '90 / Conifer / Silva Screen.

METISSE
CD _____ 887821
Milan / Jan '95 / BMG / Silva Screen.

METROPOLIS
CD _____ CK 39526
CBS/Silva Screen / Feb '90 / Conifer / Silva Screen.

METROPOLIS
1988 London Cast
Brooks, Joe C
Brooks, Joe & Dusty Hughes L
101.11 / Hold back the night / Machines are beautiful / He's distant from me now / Elitists' dance / Oh my, what a beautiful city / This is the vision we're forbidden / Children of Metropolis / 50,000 pounds of power / One more morning / It's only love / Bring on the night / Pressure chant / Day after day / When Maria comes / You are the light / Curl is a witch / It's only love (reprise) / Sun / Almost done / I don't need help from you / There's a girl down below / Futura / We're the cream / I've seen a nightmare / This is life / Look at this girl who stands before you / Futura's dance / Where do you think she's gone, your precious Maria / If that was love / Listen to me / Learning song / Old friends / When Maria wakes / Futura's promise / Maria's insane / Perfect face / Haven't you finished with me / Let's watch the world go to the devil / One of those nights / Requiem / Metropolis / Finale
2CD _____ CDTER2 1168
TER / Jul '89 / Koch.

METROPOLIS
(1984 Restored Version)
Moroder, Giorgio C
Love kills: _Mercury, Freddie_ / Here's my heart: _Benatar, Pat_ / Cage of freedom: _Anderson, Jon_ / Blood from a stone: _Cycle V_ / Legend of Babel: _Moroder, Giorgio_ / Here she comes: _Tyler, Bonnie_ / Destruction: _Loverboy_ / On your own: _Squier, Billy_ / What's going on: _Adam Ant_ / Machines: _Moroder, Giorgio_
CD _____ 4602042
Columbia / Apr '94 / Sony.

MIAMI VICE
Hammer, Jan
Hammer, Jan C
Miami Vice (instrumental theme) / Smuggler's blues: _Frey, Glenn_ / Own the night: _Khan, Chaka_ / You belong to the city: _Frey, Glenn_ / In the air tonight: _Collins, Phil_ / Vice / Better be good to me: _Turner, Tina_ / Flashback / Chase / Evan
CD _____ MCLD 19024
MCA / Apr '92 / BMG.

MIAMI VICE II
Mercy: _Jones, Steve_ / Last unbroken heart: _Labelle, Patti_ / Crockett's theme: _Hammer, Jan_ / Lives in the balance: _Browne, Jackson_ / Miami Vice (original theme): _Hammer, Jan_ / Send it to me: _Knight, Gladys & The Pips_ / When the rain comes down: _Taylor, Andy_ / Lover: _Roxy Music_ / In dulce decorum: _Damned_
CD _____ MCLD 19090
MCA / Apr '93 / BMG.

MIDNIGHT EXPRESS
Moroder, Giorgio C
Chase / Love's theme / Midnight express, Theme from / Istanbul blues / Wheel / Istanbul opening / Cacaphoney / Billy's theme
CD _____ 8242062
Phonogram / Apr '85 / PolyGram.

MIDNIGHT STING
(Diggstown)
Howard, James Newton C
CD _____ VSD 5379
Varese Sarabande/Colosseum / Sep '92 / Pinnacle / Silva Screen.

MIGHTY MORPHIN' POWER RANGERS
CD _____ 7567827772
Warner Bros. / Jul '95 / Warner Music.

MIGHTY MORPHIN' POWER RANGERS
(Score)
Revell, Graeme C
CD _____ VSD 5672
Varese Sarabande/Colosseum / Nov '95 / Pinnacle / Silva Screen.

MIKADO, THE
(Highlights)
English National Opera
Sullivan, Arthur C
Gilbert, W.S. L
If you want to know who we are / Wandering minstrel, I / Our great Mikado / Young man/Despair / Behold the Lord/High executioner / I've got a little list / Three little maids / Braid with raven hair / Sun, whose rays / Flowers that bloom in the spring / On a tree by a river (tit' willow) / There is a beauty in the bellow of the blast
CD _____ SHOWCD 005
Showtime / Feb '95 / Disc / THE.

MIKADO, THE
Brannigan, Owen & Richard Lewis/Glyndebourne Festival Choir/Pro Arte Orchestra
Sullivan, Sir Arthur C
Gilbert, W.S. L
Sargent, Sir Malcolm Con
2CD _____ CMS 7644802
EMI Classics / Apr '94 / EMI.

MIKADO, THE
D'Oyly Carte Opera Chorus/Royal Philharmonic
Sullivan, Sir Arthur C
Gilbert, W.S. L

MIKADO, THE
Nash, R. Con
2CD _____ 4251902
London / Jan '00 / PolyGram.

MIKADO, THE
D'Oyly Carte Opera Chorus/Orchestra
Sullivan, Sir Arthur C
Gilbert, W.S. L
Pryce Jones, J. Con
2CD _____ CDTER2 1178
TER / Sep '90 / Koch.

MIKADO, THE
Welsh National Opera/Orchestra
Sullivan, Sir Arthur C
Gilbert, W.S. L
Mackerras, C. Con
CD _____ CD 80284
Telarc / May '92 / Conifer / ADA.

MIKADO, THE
Sadler's Wells Opera Chorus/Orchestra
Sullivan, Sir Arthur C
Gilbert, W.S. L
Faris, A. Con
2CD _____ CDCFPD 4730
Classics For Pleasure / Apr '94 / EMI.

MIKADO, THE
(Highlights)
English National Opera
Sullivan, Sir Arthur C
Gilbert, W.S. L
CD _____ CDTER 1121
TER / Jan '93 / Koch.

MILLENIUM
(Tribal Wisdom & The Modern World)
Mancina, Mark
Zimmer, Hans C
Shaman's song / Stories for a thousand years / Journey begins / Stone drag / Courting song/Love in the Himalayas / Inventing reality / Fiddlers/Pilgrimage to Wirikuta / Shock of the other / Race of the initiates / Art of living / Geerewol celebrations / Song for the dead / Pilgrims' chant/In the land of the ancestors / Ecology of mind / Well song/A desert home / Initiation chant/Rites of passage / Journey continues / Millenium theme
CD _____ C 6001
Narada / May '92 / New Note / ADA.

MIRACLE ON 34TH STREET
Jingle bells: Cole, Natalie / It's beginning to look like Christmas: Warwick, Dionne / Have yourself a merry little Christmas: Kenny G. / Santa Claus is coming to town: Charles, Ray / You're all I want for Christmas: Franklin, Aretha / Santa Claus is back in town: Presley, Elvis / Singing: McLachlan, Sarah / Bellevue carol: McLachlan, Sarah / Song for a winter's night: McLachlan, Sarah
CD _____ 07822110222
Arista / Nov '94 / BMG.

MISERY
Shaiman, Marc C
CD _____ BCD 3011
Bay Cities / Jun '93 / Silva Screen.

MISFITS, THE
North, Alex C
CD _____ TCI 0609
Silva Screen / May '95 / Conifer / Silva Screen.

MISHIMA
Glass, Philip C
Opening / Morning 1934 / Grandmother and Kimitake / Temple of the golden pavillion / Osamu's theme / Kyoko's house / 1937 / St. Sebastian / November 25th / Ichigaya / 1957 / Award montage / Runaway horses / 1962 / Bodybuilding / Last day / F 104 / Epilogue from sun and steel / Closing
CD _____ 7559791132
Elektra Nonesuch / Nov '85 / Warner Music.

MISS LIBERTY
1949 Broadway Cast
Berlin, Irving C
Overture / What do I have to do to get my picture took / Most expensive statue in the world / Little fish in a big pond / Let's take an old fashioned walk / Homework / Paris wakes and smiles / Only for Americans / Just one way to say I love you / You can have him / Policemen's ball / Falling out of love can be fun / Give me your tired, your poor
CD _____ SK 48015
Sony Broadway / Dec '91 / Sony.

MISS SAIGON
(Highlights)
1989 London Cast
Schonberg, Claude-Michel C
Maltby, Richard Jnr. & Alain Boublil L
CD _____ CASTCD 38
First Night / Oct '93 / Pinnacle.

MISS SAIGON
(Music From The Show)
Criswell & Wayne
Schonberg, Claude-Michel C
CD _____ PWKS 4229
Carlton Home Entertainment / Nov '94 / Carlton Home Entertainment.

MISS SAIGON
(Complete Symphonic Suite)
1989 London Cast
Schonberg, Claude-Michel C
CD _____ ENCORECD 5
First Night / '94 / Pinnacle.

2CD _____ KIMCD 1
First Night / Jul '95 / Pinnacle.

MISS SAIGON/LES MISERABLES
(Symphonic Suites)
Bournemouth Symphony Orchestra
Schonberg, Claude-Michel C
CD _____ CASTCD 39
First Night / Oct '93 / Pinnacle.

MISSING IN ACTION
Chattaway, Jay & Brian May C
CD _____ FILMCD 056
Silva Screen / '90 / Conifer / Silva Screen.

MISSION IMPOSSIBLE
Schifrin, Lalo C
CD _____ GNPD 8029
GNP Crescendo / Nov '92 / Silva Screen.

MISSION, THE
London Philharmonic Orchestra
Morricone, Ennio C
On earth as it is in Heaven / Mission / Falls / River / Gabriel's oboe / Ave Maria Guarani / Te Deum Guarani / Brothers / Refusal / Carlotta / Asuncion / Vita nostra / Alone / Climb / Guarani / Remorse / Sword / Penance / Miserere
CD _____ CDV 2402
Virgin / Oct '86 / EMI.

MISSION, THE/THE LAST EMPEROR/ DANGEROUS LIAISONS
2CD _____ TPAK 24
Virgin / Nov '92 / EMI.

MISSISSIPPI BLUES
CD _____ FMC 246
Milan / Jan '95 / BMG / Silva Screen.

MISSISSIPPI BURNING
Jones, Trevor C
Take my hand, precious Lord: Jackson, Mahalia / Murder in Mississippi (Part 1) / Some things are worth dying for / Murder in Mississippi (Part 2) / Anderson and Mrs Pell / When we all get to Heaven: Choral / Try Jesus: Williams, Vesta / Abduction / You live it, you breathe it, you marry it / Murder in Mississippi (Part 3) / Requiem for three young men / Burning cross / Justice in Mississippi / Walk by faith: McBride, Lannie / Walk on by faith: McBride, Lannie
CD _____ 5511002
Spectrum/Karussell / Sep '95 / PolyGram THE.

MISSISSIPPI MASALA
Subramaniam, L. C
CD _____ CASTCD 27
First Night / '94 / Pinnacle.

MO' MONEY
Mo' money groove: Mo' Money Allstars / Best things in life are free: Vandross, Luther & Janet Jackson / Ice cream dream: M.C. Lyte / Let's just run away: M.C. Lyte / I adore you: Wheeler, Caron / Get off my back: Public Enemy & Flavor Flav / Forever love: Color Me Badd / Money can't buy you love: Tresvant, Ralph / Let's get together (so groovy now): Krush / Joy: Sounds Of Blackness / New style: Jam & Lewis / Job ain't nuthin' but work: Big Daddy Kane & Lo-Key / My dear: Mint Condition / Brother Will: Harlem Yacht Club
CD _____ 3610042
A&M / Apr '95 / PolyGram.

MOBY DICK
1992 London Cast
Kaye, Hereward C
Longden, Robert L
2CD _____ DICKCD 2
First Night / Nov '92 / Pinnacle.

MOBY DICK
(Highlights)
1992 London Cast
Kaye, Hereward C
Longden, Robert L
CD _____ SCORECD 35
First Night / '92 / Pinnacle.

MODERNS, THE
Isham, Mark
Isham, Mark C
Les modernes / Cafe Selavy / Paris la nuit / Really the blues / Madame Valentin / Dada je suis / Parlez-moi d'amour / La valse moderne / Les peintres / Death of Irving Fagelman / Je ne veux pas de tes chocolats / Selavy
CD _____ CDV 2530
Virgin / May '88 / EMI.

MOLL FLANDERS
1993 London Cast
Stiles, George & Paul Leigh C
CD _____ OCRCD 6036
First Night / Dec '95 / Pinnacle.

MOLLY MAGUIRES, THE
Mancini, Henry C
Molly Maguires / Molly's strike / Main title / Fiddle and fife / Work montage / Jamie and Mary (the hills of yesterday) / Room and board (theme from the Molly Maguires) / Hills of yesterday / Penny whistle jig / Sandwiches and tea / Trip to town / Molly's strike again / Brew with the boys / Suit for Grandpa / End
CD _____ BCD 3029
Bay Cities / Mar '93 / Silva Screen.

MON DERNEIR REVE SERA
Duhamel, Antoine C
CD _____ CH 517
Milan / Jan '95 / BMG / Silva Screen.

MONEY TRAIN
Train is coming: Shaggy & Ken Boothe / Top of the stairs: Skee Lo / Do you know: Total / Show you the way to go: Men Of Vision / Hiding place: Assorted Phlavors & Patra / Making love: 112 / Thrill I'm in: Vandross, Luther / Still not over you: Lorenz, Trey / It's alright: Terri & Monica / Oh baby: 4.0 / Merry go round: UBU / Hold on I'm coming: Neville Brothers / Money train suite: Mancina, Mark
CD _____ 4815622
Epic / Jan '96 / Sony.

MONSIGNOR QUIXOTE SUITE
English Chamber Orchestra
Monsignor Quixote / Rocinante / Streets of Toboso / Twilight in La Mancha / Companeros / Windmills or giants / Let me feel temptation / Dulcinea / Adventures in the mind / In a certain village / Thoughts of a distant friend
CD _____ CDRBLP 1010
Red Bus / Dec '85 / Total/BMG.

MONTY PYTHON AND THE HOLY GRAIL
Monty Python
Jeunesse / Honours list / Big country / Homeward bound / God choir / Fanfare / Camelot song / Sunrise music / Magic finger / Sir Robin's song / In the shadows / Desperate moment / Knights of Ni / Circle of danger / Love theme / Magenta / Starlet in the starlight / Monk's chat / Promised land
CD _____ CASCD 1103
Charisma / Nov '89 / EMI.

MOON 44
Graunke Symphony Orchestra
Goldsmith, Joel C
Goldsmith, Joel Con
CD _____ FILMCD 075
Silva Screen / '90 / Conifer / Silva Screen.

MOONLIGHTING
Moonlighting: Jarreau, Al / Limbo rock: Checker, Chubby / This old heart of mine: Isley Brothers / I told ya I love ya, now get out: Shepherd, Cybill / Good lovin': Willis, Bruce / Since I fell for you: James, Bob & David Sanborn / When a man loves a woman: Sledge, Percy / Someone to watch over me: Ronstadt, Linda / Stormy weather: Holiday, Billie
CD _____ MCLD 19091
MCA / Oct '92 / BMG.

MOONRAKER
Barry, John C
Main title / Space laser battle / Miss Goodhead meets Bond / Cable car and snake fight / Bond lured to pyramid / Flight into space / Bond arrives in Rio/Boat chase / Centrifuge and Corrine put down / Bond smells a rat / End title
CD _____ CZ 551
Premier / Dec '95 / EMI.

MORE
Pink Floyd
Pink Floyd C
Cirrus minor / Nile song / Crying song / Up the Khyber / Green is the colour / Cymbaline / Party sequence / Main theme / Ibiza bar / More blues / Quicksilver / Spanish piece / Dramatic theme
CD _____ CDP 7463862
EMI / Mar '87 / EMI.

MORITURI - THE SABOTEUR
(& Music From In Harm's Way)
Goldsmith, Jerry C
CD _____ TCI 0604
Silva Screen / Jan '95 / Conifer / Silva Screen.

MORTAL KOMBAT
Taste of things to come: Clinton, George / Goodbye: Gravity Kills / Juke joint Jezebel: KMFDM / Unlearn: Psykosonik / Control: Lords, Traci / Halcyon + on + on: Orbital / Utah Saints take on the theme from Mortal Kombat: Utah Saints / Invisible: G/Z/R / Zero signal: Fear Factory / Burn: Sister Machine Gun / Blood and fire: Type O Negative / I reject: Bile / Twist the knife (slowly): Napalm Death / What u see/We all bleed red: Mutha's Day Out / Techno syndrome: Immortals / Goro Vs. art: Clinton, George
CD _____ 8288972
London / Oct '95 / PolyGram.

MORTAL KOMBAT
(Score)
Clinton, George C
CD _____ 8287152
London / Jan '96 / PolyGram.

MOSES THE LAWGIVER
Morricone, Ennio C
2CD _____ OST 113
Milano Dischi / Jan '93 / Silva Screen.

MOSQUITO COAST, THE
Jarre, Maurice C
Jarre, Maurice Con
Mosquito Coast / Goodbye America / Gimme soca: Lee, Byron & The Dragonaires / Up the river / Geronimo / Fat boy / Destruction / Storm / Allie's theme
CD _____ FCD 210052

Fantasy / Jan '89 / Pinnacle / Jazz Music / Wellard / Cadillac.

MOST HAPPY FELLA, THE
1956 Broadway Cast
Loesser, Frank C
2CD _____ SK 48010
Sony Broadway / Dec '91 / Sony.

MR. AND MRS. BRIDGE
Robbins, Richard C
Opening title / Boogie woogie: Dorsey, Tommy Orchestra / Painting class / String of pearls: Miller, Glenn Orchestra / Little brown jug: Miller, Glenn Orchestra / Rhumba jumps: Miller, Glenn Orchestra / Ruth's journey / Jeepers creepers: Waters, Ethel & Edward Mallory / Blues in the night: Shore, Dinah / Stormy weather: Horne, Lena, Lou Bring & His Orchestra / She was my best friend / Take me, I'm yours / Choo choo conga / Down on the farm / Locking up / Closing credits
CD _____ PD 83100
Novus / Mar '91 / BMG.

MR. CINDERS
1983 London Cast
Ellis, Vivian & Richard Myers C
Grey, Clifford & Greatrex Newman L
Tennis / Blue blood / True to two / I want the world to know / One man girl / On with the dance / At the ball / Spread a little happiness / Ent'racte / Eighteenth century dance / She's my lovely / Please Mr. Cinders / On the Amazon / Every little moment / I've got you, you've got me / Honeymoon for four / Finale
CD _____ CDTER 1069
TER / Sep '83 / Koch.

MR. DESTINY
Newman, David
Newman, David C
CD _____ VSD 5299
Varese Sarabande/Colosseum / '90 / Pinnacle / Silva Screen.

MR. LUCKY
Mancini, Henry C
CD _____ 21982
Silva Screen / Feb '90 / Conifer / Silva Screen.

MR. PRESIDENT
1962 Broadway Cast
Berlin, Irving C
CD _____ SK 48212
Sony Broadway / Nov '92 / Sony.

MR. SATURDAY NIGHT
Shaiman, Marc C
CD _____ 124682
Milan / Feb '94 / BMG / Silva Screen.

MRS. DOUBTFIRE
Horner, James C
Mrs. Doubtfire / Divorce / My name is Euphegenia / Meeting Mrs. Doubtfire / Tea time with Mrs Seliner / Dinner is served / Daniel and the kids / Cable cars / Bridges restaurant / Show's over / Kids need you / Figaro/Papa's got a brand new bag
CD _____ 07822110112
Arista / Jan '94 / BMG.

MRS. PARKER AND THE VICIOUS CIRCLE
Isham, Mark C
CD _____ VSD 5471
Varese Sarabande/Colosseum / Jan '95 / Pinnacle / Silva Screen.

MUCH ADO ABOUT NOTHING
Doyle, Patrick C
Snell, D. Con
Picnic / Overture / Sweetest lady / Conspirators / Masked ball / Prince woos hero / Star danced / Rich she shall be / Sigh no more ladies / Gulling of Benedick / It must be requited / Gulling of Beatrice / Contempt farewell / Lady is disloyal / Hero's wedding / Take her back again / Die to live / You have killed a sweet lady / Choose your revenge / Pardon Goddess of the night / Did I not tell you / Hero revealed / Benedick the married man / Strike up pipers
CD _____ MOODCD 30
Epic / Sep '93 / Sony.

MUPPET CHRISTMAS CAROL, THE
Muppets
Overture / Scrooge / Room in your heart / Good king Wenceslas / One more sleep till Christmas / Marley and Marley / Christmas past / Chairman of the board / Fozziwigs party / When love is gone / It feels like Christmas / Christmas scat / Bless us all / Christmas future / Christmas morning / Thankful heart / Finale
CD _____ 7432112194-2
Arista / Nov '93 / BMG.

MUPPET MOVIE, THE
Muppets
Rainbow connection / Movin' right along / Never before never again / I hope that something better comes along / Can you picture that / I'm going to go back there someday / God bless America / Come back animal / Magic stone
CD _____ 74321182472
BMG Kidz / Jan '94 / BMG.

MURDER ON THE ORIENT EXPRESS/ DEATH ON THE NILE
Bennett, Richard Rodney/Nino Rota C
CD _____ CNS 5007

Cloud Nine / Aug '93 / Conifer / Silva
Screen.

MURDER WAS THE CASE
Murder was the case (remix): Snoop Doggy
Dogg / Natural born killaz: Dr. Dre & Ice
Cube / What would you do: Dogg Pound /
21 Jumpstreet: Snoop Doggy Dogg & Tray
Deee / One more day: Dogg, Nate / Harvest
for the world: Jewell / Who got some
gangsta shit: Snoop Doggy Dogg & Tha
Dogg Pound / Come when I call: Boy,
Danny / U better recognise: Sneed, Sam &
Dr. Dre / Come up to my room: Jodeci &
Tha Dogg Pound / Woman to woman: Jew-
ell / Dollars and sense: D.J. Quik / Eulogy:
Capone, Slip & CPO / Horny: Rezell, B /
East side, west side: Young Soldierz
CD _____ 6544924842
Death Row / Oct '94 / Warner Music.

MURDERERS AMONG US
Conti, Bill C
CD _____ BCD 3004
Bay Cities / Jan '93 / Silva Screen.

MURIEL'S WEDDING
CD _____ 5274932
Polydor / May '95 / PolyGram.

MUSIC BRUT-INSECT
Revell, Graeme C
CD _____ BRUT 1CD
Grey Area / Jul '94 / Pinnacle.

MUSIC MAN, THE
1957 Broadway Cast
Willson, Meredith C
Overture/Rock island / Iowa stubborn / Ya
got trouble / Piano lesson / Goodnight my
someone / Seventy six trombones / Sincere
/ Sadder but wiser girl for me / Pick-a-little,
take-a-little/Goodnight ladies / Marian the
librarian / My white knight / Wells Fargo
wagon / It's you / Shipoopi / Lida Rose/Will
I ever tell you / Gary, Indiana / Till there was
you / Finale
CD _____ ZDM 7646632
EMI Classics / Nov '93 / EMI.

**MUSIC TEACHER (LE MAITRE DE
MUSIQUE)**
Cortigiani, vil razza dannata / Alcandro, lo
confessa...non so d'onde viene / Waltz /
Das lied von der erde / Symphony no. 4 in
g major / Deh vieni alla finestra / Wohl denk
ich oft / Du meine seele, du mein herz /
Stille tranen / Sorgio, o padre / An die mu-
sik, d547 / Caro nome / Tanton duol / Ich
bin der welt abhanden
CD _____ PCOM 1109
President / Nov '90 / Grapevine / Target/
BMG / Jazz Music / President.

MUTANT
National Philharmonic Orchestra
Band, Richard C
CD _____ MAF 7052D
Intrada / Jan '93 / Silva Screen / Koch.

**MUTINY ON THE BOUNTY/TARAS
BULBA**
Mutiny on the bounty theme / Portsmouth
harbour / Storm at sea / Girls and sailors /
Mutiny / Follow me (Tahitian) / Leaving har-
bour / Arrival in Tahiti / Pitcairn island / Fol-
low me (English) / Outrigger chase / Chris-
tian's death / Taras bulba (overture) / Birth
of Andrei / Sleighride / Chase at night / No
retreat / Ride to Dubno / Wishing star /
Black plague / Taras' pledge / Battle of
Dubno and finale
CD _____ CDMGM 26
MGM/EMI / Aug '90 / EMI.

MY COUSIN VINNY
Edelman, Randy
Edelman, Randy C
CD _____ VSD 5364
Varese Sarabande/Colosseum / Apr '92 /
Pinnacle / Silva Screen.

MY FAIR LADY
Film Cast
Loewe, Frederick C
Lerner, Alan Jay L
Previn, Andre Con
Overture / Why can't the English / Wouldn't
it be lovely / I'm just an ordinary man / With
a little bit of luck / Just you wait / Rain in
Spain / I could have danced all night / Ascot
gavotte / On the street where you live / You
did it / Show me / Get me to the church on
time / Hymn to him / Without you / I've
grown accustomed to her face
CD _____ SK 66711
Sony Broadway / May '95 / Sony.

MY FAIR LADY
1956 Broadway Cast
Loewe, Frederick C
Lerner, Alan Jay L
CD _____ CK 05090
CBS/Silva Screen / Jan '89 / Conifer / Silva
Screen.

MY FAIR LADY
1959 London Cast
Loewe, Frederick C
Lerner, Alan Jay L
Overture / Why can't the English / Wouldn't
it be lovely / With a little bit of luck / I'm
just an ordinary man / Just you wait / Rain
in Spain / I could have danced all night /
Ascot gavotte / On the street where you live
/ You did it / Show me / Get me to the
church on time / Hymn to him / Without you
/ I've grown accustomed to her face

CD _____ CK 02105
CBS/Silva Screen / Jan '89 / Conifer / Silva
Screen.

MY FAIR LADY
(Highlights - The Shows Collection)
Cast Recording
Loewe, Frederick C
Lerner, Alan Jay L
Why can't the English / Wouldn't it be lov-
erly / With a little bit of luck / I'm just an
ordinary man / Just you wait / Rain in Spain
/ I could have danced all night / On the
street where you live / Show me / Get me
to the church on time / Hymn to him / With-
out you / I've grown accustomed to her
face
CD _____ PWKS 4174
Carlton Home Entertainment / Oct '93 /
Carlton Home Entertainment.

MY FAIR LADY
Cast Recording
Loewe, Frederick C
Lerner, Alan Jay L
2CD _____ CDTER2 1211
TER / Aug '95 / Koch.

**MY FATHER'S GLORY/MY MOTHER'S
CASTLE**
Cosma, Vladimir C
Cosma, Vladimir Con
CD _____ DRGCD 12604
DRG / Jan '95 / New Note.

**MY FATHER'S GLORY/MY MOTHER'S
CASTLE**
Cosma, Vladimir C
CD _____ 50050
Silva Screen / Jan '93 / Conifer / Silva
Screen.

MY GIRL
My girl: Temptations / More today than yesterday: Spiral Starecase / Hot fun in the
summertime: Sly & The Family Stone / Wedding bell blues: 5th Dimension / Do wah
diddy diddy: Manfred Mann & Todd Rundgren / Good lovin': Rascals / Bad moon rising: Creedence Clearwater Revival / If you
don't know me by now: Melvin, Harold &
The Bluenotes / I only have eyes for you:
Flamingos / Saturday in the park: Chicago /
My girl (Theme from): Howard, James
Newton
CD _____ 4692132
Epic / Sep '94 / Sony.

MY GIRL II
My girl: Temptations / Don't worry baby:
Beach Boys / Reason to believe: Stewart,
Rod / Walk away Renee: Price, Rick / Tiny
dancer: John, Elton / Swingtown: Miller, Steve /
John, Elton / Swingtown: Miller, Steve /
Doctor my eyes: Browne, Jackson / Baby
love: Supremes / Our house: Crosby, Stills,
Nash & Young / Rockin' pneumonia and the
boogie woogie fly: Rivers, Johnny
CD _____ 475734 2
Columbia / Apr '95 / Sony.

**MY HEROES HAVE ALWAYS BEEN
COWBOYS**
Horner, James C
CD _____ 23382
Silva Screen / Jan '93 / Conifer / Silva
Screen.

MY LIFE
Barry, John C
Barry, John Con
Main title / Childhood wish / Pictures from
the past / I'm still in the game / My life -
love theme / Old neighbourhood / I used to
hide in there / You're a believer / My last
trip home / Moments D-day / Child's play /
Circus / Nice to meet you Brian / Roller-
coaster / End titles
CD _____ EK 57683
Silva Screen / Jan '93 / Conifer / Silva
Screen.

MY NAME IS NOBODY
Morricone, Ennio C
Morricone, Ennio Con
CD _____ A 8918
Alhambra / Feb '92 / Silva Screen.

MY RIFLE, MY PONY & ME
My rifle, my pony and me: Martin, Dean &
Ricky Nelson / Legend of Shenandoah:
Stewart, James / Montana/The searchers/
Wagons west/Song of the wagonmaster:
Sons Of The Pioneers / Nevada Smith: Kil-
gore, Merle / Ballad of the Alamo/ The
hanging tree: Robbins, Marty / Ballad of
Paladin: Western, Johnny / Sons of Katie
Elder/Rebel Johnny Yuma: Cash, Johnny /
Rawhide/Gunfight at the O.K. Corral: Laine,
Frankie / Ballad of Davy Crockett: Parker,
Fess / Rio Bravo: Martin, Dean / I'm a run-
away: Hunter, Tab / Bonanza: Greene,
Lorne / North to Alaska: Horton, Johnny /
High noon: Ritter, Tex / And the river will
flow: Adamson, Barry / Day the niggaz took
over: Dr. Dre / Born bad: Lewis, Juliette /
Fall of the rebel angels: Cervetti, Sergio /
Peace: Nine Inch Nails / Allah, Mohammed,
Char, Yarr (inc. Judgement Day by Dia-
manda Galas): Khan, Nusrat Fateh Ali &
Party / Future: Cohen, Leonard / What
would you do: Dogg Pound
CD _____ 6544924602
Interscope / Sep '94 / Warner Music.

MY SO CALLED LIFE
CD _____ 7567827212
Warner Bros. / Jan '95 / Warner Music.

MY STEPMOTHER IS AN ALIEN
Pump up the volume: M/A/R/R/S / Room to
move: Animotion / Be the one: Jackson,
Jackie / One good lover: Siren / Klystron /
Not just another girl: Neville, Ivan / I like the
world: Cameo / Hot wives: Aykroyd, Dan /
Enjoy / Celeste
CD _____ 5511352
Spectrum/Karussell / Sep '95 / PolyGram /
THE.

MYSTERIOUS ISLAND
London Symphony Orchestra
Herrmann, Bernard C
CD _____ ACN 7017
Cloud Nine / Mar '93 / Conifer / Silva
Screen.

MYSTERY OF EDWIN DROOD
Broadway Cast
Holmes, Rupert C
There you are / Man could go quite mad /
Two kinsmen / Moonfall / Wages of sin /
Ceylon / Both sides of the coin / Perfect
strangers / No good can come from bad /
Never the luck / Name of love / Setting up
the score / Off to the races / Don't quit while
you're ahead / Garden path to hell / Out on
a limerick / Jasper's confession / Puffer's
confession / Writing on the wall
CD _____ VSD 5597
Varese Sarabande/Colosseum / Oct '95 /
Pinnacle / Silva Screen.

MYSTERY TRAIN
Lurie, John C
CD _____ CH 509
Milan / Jul '95 / BMG / Silva Screen.

NAILS
Conti, Bill C
CD _____ VSD 5384
Varese Sarabande/Colosseum / Sep '92 /
Pinnacle / Silva Screen.

**NAKED GUN 2 1/2, THE
(The Smell Of Fear)**
Newborn, Ira C
CD _____ VSD 5331
Varese Sarabande/Colosseum / Aug '91 /
Pinnacle / Silva Screen.

NAKED LUNCH, THE
London Philharmonic Orchestra
Shore, Howard/Ornette Coleman C
CD _____ 262732
Milan / Feb '94 / BMG / Silva Screen.

NAME OF THE ROSE, THE
Horner, James C
Horner, James Con
Beta viscera / First recognition / Lesson /
Kyrie / Scriptorium / Veri sancti spiritus /
Confession / Flashbacks / Discovery / Be-
trayed / Epilogue / Name Of The Rose end
title
CD _____ 30046
Silva Screen / Jan '89 / Conifer / Silva
Screen.

NAPOLEON
(New Score For 1927 Silent Film)
Wren Orchestra
Davis, Carl C
Davis, Carl Con
Eagle of destiny / Teaching the Marseillaise
/ Reunion in Corsica / Pursued / Double
storm / Drums of the 6th Regiment / Victor
of Toulon / Gigue / Fan / Tambourin / Acting
lesson / Ghosts / Peroration / Strange con-
ductor in the sky
CD _____ FILMCD 149
Silva Screen / Mar '94 / Conifer / Silva
Screen.

NATURAL BORN KILLERS
Waiting for the miracle: Cohen, Leonard /
Shitlist: L7 / Moon over Greene County: Za-
nes, Dan / Rock 'n' roll nigger: Smith, Patti
/ Sweet Jane: Cowboy Junkies / You belong
to me: Dylan, Bob / Trembler: Eddy, Duane
/ Burn: Nine Inch Nails / Route 666: Downey
Jr, Robert & 'BB Tone' Brian Berdan / Totally hot: Ongala, Remmy & Orchestra /
Back in baby's arms: Cline, Patsy / Taboo:
Gabriel, Peter & Nusrat Fateh Ali Khan / Sex
is violent (inc. Ted, just admit it/I put a spell
on you): Jane's Addiction & Diamanda Galas / History (repeats itself): A.O.S. / Something I can never have: Nine Inch Nails / I
will take you home: Means, Russel / Drums
a go go: Hollywood Persuaders / Hungry
ants: Adamson, Barry / Day the niggaz took
over: Dr. Dre / Born bad: Lewis, Juliette /
Fall of the rebel angels: Cervetti, Sergio /
Peace: Nine Inch Nails / Allah, Mohammed,
Char, Yarr (inc. Judgement Day by Diamanda Galas): Khan, Nusrat Fateh Ali &
Party / Future: Cohen, Leonard / What
would you do: Dogg Pound
CD _____ 6544924602
Interscope / Sep '94 / Warner Music.

NATURAL, THE
Newman, Randy
Newman, Randy C
CD _____ 9251162
Silva Screen / Feb '90 / Conifer / Silva
Screen.

NATURE: GREAT AFRICAN MOMENTS
Whalen, Michael
Whalen, Michael C
Elephants / Night on the Serengeti / Fire
and ice / Killer instinct / Rain the rain / Lost
on the plains / After the rain / Cheetah hunt
/ Jacana and the fish eagle / Hyena and the
melons / Chimps / Journey of the
thousands / Mountain gorillas / Wild pups /
Meerkats / Flamingoes / African sunset /
Vultures / Slowpake club / Cycles of life
CD _____ ND 66066
Narada / Apr '94 / New Note / ADA.

NATURE: PHANTOM OF THE FOREST
Whalen, Michael
Whalen, Michael C
Spirits / Sea of trees / Hawk appears / Kill-
ing to survive / Wood cock / Open spaces
/ New forests / Building a nest / Feather /
Life in the nest / Cathedral of the woods /
Sunrise dance / Night creatures / Forest
edge / Brink of extinction / Quite beauty /
Winter rain / Predators of the predators /
Woodland lullaby / Soliloquy
CD _____ ND 66007
Narada / Apr '94 / New Note / ADA.

NAVIGATOR, THE
Tabrizi, Davood A. C
Forging the cross / Vision / Ascent / Plain-
song / Queenfish / Macedonian pipes /
Paean (The dance) / Refugees / Connor's
return / Storm / Work song / Escape / Fall
/ Celtic refrain / Requiem / Knell / Panpipes
and drums (Loading the horse) / Seeing the
celestial city / Pilgrimage / Brotherhood /
Cantus / Chase / Falcon call/Thunder
dream / Azan - the caller from the East /
Death / Quest / Asunder/Trumpet call /
Celtic refrain (2)
CD _____ FILMCD 039
Silva Screen / Jun '89 / Conifer / Silva
Screen.

NEAR DARK
Tangerine Dream
Caleb's blues / Pick up at high noon / Rain
in the threo house / Bus station / Good times
/ She's my sister / Mae comes back / Father
and son / Severin dies / Flight at dawn /
Mae's transformation
CD _____ FILMCD 026
Silva Screen / Jun '90 / Conifer / Silva
Screen.

NEEDFUL THINGS
Doyle, Patrick C
Snell, D. Con
CD _____ VSD 5438
Varese Sarabande/Colosseum / Jul '93 /
Pinnacle / Silva Screen.

NELL
Isham, Mark C
CD _____ 4448162
PolyGram / Mar '95 / PolyGram.

NET, THE
Isham, Mark
Isham, Mark C
CD _____ VSD 5662
Varese Sarabande/Colosseum / Oct '95 /
Pinnacle / Silva Screen.

NEVADA SMITH
Newman, Alfred C
CD _____ TSU 0113
Tsunami / Jan '95 / Silva Screen.

NEVER SAY NEVER AGAIN
Legrand, Michel C
Legrand, Michel Con
Bond back in action / Never say never
again: Hall, Lani / Prologue - enter 007 /
Fatima Blush/A very bad lady / Dinner with
007 / Bahama island / Bond smells a rat/
Nurse Blush / Plunder of a nuclear missile /
Big band death of Jack Petachi / Bond and
Domino / Fight to death with the Tiger
sharks / Una Chanson d'amour / Video
duel/Victory / Nuclear nightmare / Tango to
the death / Bond returns home / Death of
Nicole / Chase her / Felix and James exit /
Jealousy / Largo's waltz / Bond to the rescue / Big escape / Tears of Allah / Under-
water cave / Fight to the death / Bond in
retirement / End title - Never say never
again: Hall, Lani
CD _____ FILMCD 145
Silva Screen / Apr '95 / Conifer / Silva
Screen.

NEVER-ENDING STORY III
CD _____ 4509983092
WEA / Dec '94 / Warner Music.

NEW JACK CITY
New jack hustler: Ice-T / I'm dreaming: Wil-
liams, Christopher / I wanna sex you up:
Color Me Badd / I'm still waiting: Gill,
Johnny / (There you go) tellin' me no again:
Sweat, Keith / Facts of life: Madden, Danny
/ For the love of money/Living for the city
(medley): Troop/Levert / Lyrics 2 the
rhythm: Essence / Get it together (black is
back): Black Is A Force / In the dust: 2
Live Crew / New jack city (CD only): Guy

NEW JACK CITY
CD _____ 7599244092
Giant / Apr '91 / BMG.

NEW JERSEY DRIVE VOL.1
CD _____ TBCD 1114
Tommy Boy / Mar '95 / Disc.

NEW JERSEY DRIVE VOL.2
CD _____ TBCD 1130
Tommy Boy / Apr '95 / Disc.

NEW ORLEANS
Holiday, Billie & Louis Armstrong
Free as a bird / When the saints go marching in / Westend blues / Do you know what it means to miss New Orleans / Brahms lullaby / Tiger rag / Buddy Bolden's blues / Basin Street blues / Raymond Street blues / Melenberg joys / Where the blues was born in New Orleans / Farewell to Storyville / Beale Street stomp / Dippermouth blues (Slow & fast versions) / Shimme sha wobble / Ballin' the Jack / King Porter stomp / Mahogany Hall stomp / Endie / Blues are brewin'
CD _____ GOJCD 1025
Giants Of Jazz / Jan '95 / Target/BMG / Cadillac.

NEW YORK ROCK
Cast Recording
Ono, Yoko C
It happened / I'll always be with you / Speck of dust / Midsummer New York / What a bastard the world is / Loneliness / Give me something / Light on the other side / Tomorrow may never come / Don't be scared / Growing pains / Warzone / Never say goodbye / O'sanity / I want my love to rest tonight / I felt like smashing my face in a clear glass window / Now or never / We're all water / Yes, I'm your angel / Where do we go from here / Sleepless night / No, no, no / Even when you're far away / Hell in paradise / Toyboat / Story of an oak tree / Goodbye sadness
CD _____ CDP 8298432
Capitol / Aug '95 / EMI.

NEW YORK STORIES
Coppola, Carmine C
CD _____ 9608572
Elektra / Nov '89 / Warner Music.

NEW YORK, NEW YORK
You brought a new kind of love to me / Flip the dip / V.J. Stomp / Opus No. 1 / Once in a while / You are my lucky star / Game over / It's a wonderful world / Man I love / Hazoy / Just you, just me / There goes the ball game / Blue moon / Don't be that way / Happy endings / But the world goes 'round / New York, New York / Honeysuckle rose / Once again right away / Bobby's dream / Finale
CD _____ ACD 373
Milan / Jan '89 / BMG / Silva Screen.

NEW YORK, NEW YORK
(A Broadway Extravaganza)
New York City Gay Men's Chorus
CD _____ CDD 594
Silva Screen / Jul '92 / Conifer / Silva Screen.

NEWSIES
Menken, Alan C
CD _____ DIS 60832
Silva Screen / Jan '93 / Conifer / Silva Screen.

NEXT OF KIN
Brother to brother / Hillbilly heart / Paralysed / My sweet baby's gone / Brothers / On a Spanish Highway (revised) / Hey backwoods / Straight and narrow / Yard sale / Pyramids of cans / Wailing sax
CD _____ 4662402
Epic / May '90 / Sony.

NICK AND NORA
1991 Broadway Cast
Strouse, Charles C
Maltby, Richard Jr. L
CD _____ CDTER 1191
TER / Sep '92 / Koch.

NIE WIEDER SCHLAFEN
Dikker, Loek C
CD _____ 873143
Milan / Jan '95 / BMG / Silva Screen.

NIGHT AND THE CITY
Great pretender: Mercury, Freddie / Cool jerk: Capitols / Money (That's what i want): Walker, Junior & The All Stars / You really got a hold on me: Robinson, Smokey & The Miracles / Wooly bully: Sam The Sham & The Pharaohs / Love doesn't matter: Saulsberry, Rodney / Deep water: Champlin, Bill / Forgiveness: Davis, Lynn / Never gonna stop: Cole, Gardner / Boxing gym: Howard, James Newton
CD _____ CDPCSD 126
EMI / Nov '92 / EMI.

NIGHT CROSSING
National Philharmonic Orchestra
Goldsmith, Jerry C
Goldsmith, Jerry Con
Main title / All in vain / Picnic / Plans / Success / First flight / Patches / Tomorrow we go / No time to vain / Final flight / In the West
CD _____ RVF 6004D
Intrada / Jan '89 / Silva Screen / Koch.

NIGHT OF THE GENERALS
Jarre, Maurice C
Jarre, Maurice Con
CD _____ FMT 8004D
Intrada / Mar '92 / Silva Screen / Koch.

NIGHT ON EARTH
Waits, Tom
Waits, Tom C
CD _____ 5109292
Island / Mar '92 / PolyGram.

NIGHTINGALE
1982 London Cast
Strouse, Charles C
Prologue / Perfect harmony / Why am I so happy / Take us to the forest / Who are these people / Never speak directly to an Emperor / Nightingale / Emperor is a man / I was lost / Entr'acte / Charming / Singer must be free / Mechanical bird / Rivers cannot flow upwards / Death duet / We are China / Finale
2CD _____ CDTER2 1031
TER / Aug '95 / Koch.

NIGHTMARE BEFORE CHRISTMAS
Elfman, Danny C
CD _____ DIS 608557
Silva Screen / Jan '95 / Conifer / Silva Screen.

NIGHTMARE CAFE
Robinson, J. Peter C
CD _____ VSD 5363
Varese Sarabande/Colosseum / Jul '92 / Pinnacle / Silva Screen.

NIGHTMARE ON ELM STREET - THE BEST OF NIGHTMARE ON ELM STREET (Freddy's Favourites)
Young, Christopher C
CD _____ VSD 5427
Varese Sarabande/Colosseum / Nov '93 / Pinnacle / Silva Screen.

NIGHTMARE ON ELM STREET I & II
CD _____ VCD 47255
Varese Sarabande/Colosseum / Jan '89 / Pinnacle / Silva Screen.

NIGHTMARE ON ELM STREET III (Dream Warriors)
Badalamenti, Angelo
Badalamenti, Angelo C
CD _____ VCD 47293
Varese Sarabande/Colosseum / Jan '89 / Pinnacle / Silva Screen.

NIGHTMARE ON ELM STREET IV (The Dream Master/Score)
Safan, Craig
Safan, Craig C
CD _____ VCD 5203
Varese Sarabande/Colosseum / Jan '89 / Pinnacle / Silva Screen.

NIGHTMARE ON ELM STREET V (Dream Child/Score)
Ferguson, Jay
Ferguson, Jay C
CD _____ VSD 5238
Varese Sarabande/Colosseum / Oct '89 / Pinnacle / Silva Screen.

NIGHTMARE ON ELM STREET VI (Freddy's Dead: The Final Nightmare/ Score)
May, Brian C
CD _____ VSD 5333
Varese Sarabande/Colosseum / Sep '91 / Pinnacle / Silva Screen.

NIKITA
Serra, Eric
Serra, Eric C
Rico's gang suicide / Playing on saucepans / As cold as ice / Sentence / Paradise / Failed escape / Leaning time / Smile / Fancy face / First night out / Tpokmop / Last time I kiss you / Free side / I am on duty / Josephine and the big duster / Mission in Venice / Fall / Let's welcome Victor / Last mission / We will miss you / Dark side of time
CD _____ CDVMM 2
Virgin / Nov '90 / EMI.

NINE
1992 London Cast
Yeston, Maury C
Higgs, Timothy Con
2CD _____ CDTER 1193
TER / Oct '92 / Koch.

NINE
Australian Cast
Yeston, Maury C
CD _____ CDTER 1190
TER / May '93 / Koch.

NINE AND A HALF WEEKS
I do what I do: Taylor, John / Best is yet to come: Luba / Slave to love: Ferry, Bryan / Black on black: Dalbello / Eurasian eyes: Hart, Corey / You can leave your hat on: Cocker, Joe / Bread and butter: Devo / This city never sleeps: Eurythmics / Cannes: Copeland, Stewart / Let it go: Luba
CD _____ CDEST 2003
EMI / Sep '94 / EMI.

NO MAN'S LAND
Poledouris, Basil C
Jewel movement / Med.sa's refrain (pts 1 & 2) / Spark from the infinite (pts 1 & 2) / Return of the dream collector / Jaipur local / Blue anthem

NO NO NANETTE
CD _____ VCD 47352
Varese Sarabande/Colosseum / Jan '89 / Pinnacle / Silva Screen.

NO NO NANETTE
1971 Revival Cast
Youmans, Vincent C
Harbach, Otto & Irving Caesar L
CD _____ CK 30563
CBS/Silva Screen / Jan '89 / Conifer / Silva Screen.

NO NO NANETTE
London Cast
Youmans, Vincent C
Harbach, Otto & Irving Caesar L
CD _____ SMK 66173
Sony West End / Jul '94 / Sony.

NO RETREAT, NO SURRENDER
Gilreath, Paul C
Gilreath, Paul Con
CD _____ FILMCD 150
Silva Screen / Mar '94 / Conifer / Silva Screen.

NO STRINGS
Broadway Cast
Rodgers, Richard C
CD _____ ZDM 7646942
EMI Classics / Apr '93 / EMI.

NO WAY OUT/THE YEAR OF LIVING DANGEROUSLY
Jarre, Maurice C
No way out / National security / Cover up / In the Pentagon / We can interface / Susan
CD _____ CDTER 1149
TER / Feb '88 / Koch.

NOBLE HOUSE
Chihara, Paul C
CD _____ VCD 47360
Varese Sarabande/Colosseum / Jan '89 / Pinnacle / Silva Screen.

NOBODY'S FOOL
CD _____ 249032
Milan / Aug '95 / BMG / Silva Screen.

NOEL AND GERTIE
1986 London Cast
Coward, Sir Noel C
Overture / Some day I'll find you / Mrs. Worthington / Touring days / Parisian pierrot / Dance little lady / Play orchestra play / We were dancing / Man about town / I travel alone / Sail away / Why must the show go on / Come the wild, wild weather / I'll remember her / I'll see you again / Curtain music
CD _____ CDTER 1117
TER / Aug '95 / Koch.

NORTH
Hawaiian war chant / Tiny bubbles / My little grass shack / Blue Hawaii / Aloha oe / North heads north / Alaska / Winter wonderland / Winchell's master plan / World traveller / Amazing grace / Can-can / Bedford / Homesick / Winchell / Lies and videotape / New York City / North figures it out / Race to the finish / Reunion
CD _____ 4772802
Columbia / Apr '95 / Sony.

NORTH AND SOUTH/THE RIGHT STUFF
London Symphony Orchestra
Conti, Bill C
Conti, Bill Con
CD _____ VCD 47250
Varese Sarabande/Colosseum / Jan '89 / Pinnacle / Silva Screen.

NORTH BY NORTHWEST
London Studio Symphony Orchestra
Herrmann, Bernard C
CD _____ VCD 47205
Varese Sarabande/Colosseum / '90 / Pinnacle / Silva Screen.

NORTHERN EXPOSURE
Northern Exposure (theme): Schwartz, David / Jolie Louise: Lanois, Daniel / Hip hugher: Booker T & The MG's / At last: James, Etta / Everybody be yourself: Chic Street Man / Alaskan nights: Schwartz, David / Don Quichotte: Magazine 60 / When I grow too old to dream: Cole, Nat King / Emabhaceni: Makeba, Miriam / Gimme three steps: Lynyrd Skynyrd / Bailero (From Chant's D'Auvergne): Von Stade, Frederica & The Royal Philharmonic Orchestra / Medley: Funeral in my brain (Woody the indian, The Tellakutans): Schwartz, David
CD _____ MCD 10685
MCA / Mar '93 / BMG.

NOSFERATU
Brandenburg Philharmonic Orchestra
Erdmann, Hans C
Anderson, Gillian Con
CD _____ 9026681432
RCA Victor / Nov '95 / BMG.

NOSTRADAMUS
Pheloung, Barrington C
CD _____ 4439462
Decca / Jan '95 / PolyGram.

NOT WITHOUT MY DAUGHTER
Goldsmith, Jerry C
CD _____ FILMCD 091
Silva Screen / May '91 / Conifer / Silva Screen.

NOTHING BUT TROUBLE
Kamen, Michael C
CD _____ 9264912
Silva Screen / Jan '93 / Conifer / Silva Screen.

NOW AND THEN
Eidelman, Cliff C
CD _____ VSD 5675
Varese Sarabande/Colosseum / Nov '95 / Pinnacle / Silva Screen.

NUNS ON THE RUN
Race: Yello / Comin' to you: Hidden Faces / Roll with it: Winwood, Steve / Moon on ice: Yello / Sacred heart: Shakespears Sister / On the run: Yello / Hawaiian chance: Yello / Blow away: Harrison, George / Tied up: Yello / Dr. Van Steiner: Yello / Gold rush: Yello / Nun's medley: Hidden Faces
CD _____ 8460432
Mercury / Jun '90 / PolyGram.

NUN'S STORY, THE
Waxman, Franz C
CD _____ STZ 114
Stanyan / Jan '94 / Silva Screen.

NUNSENSE
1986 Off-Broadway Cast
Goggin, Dan C
Nunsense is habit forming / Difficult transition / Benedicte/Biggest ain't best: Hubert & Leo / Playing second fiddle: Anne, Robert / So you want to be a Nun: Amnesia, Mary / Turn up the spotlight: Cardelia, Mary / Lilacs bring back memories / Tackle that temptation with a time-step: Hubert & Cast / Growing up Catholic: Anne, Robert & Cast / Drive-in: St. Andrew's Sister / I could go to Nashville: Amnesia, Mary / Holier than thou: Hubert & Cast / Finale
CD _____ CDSBL 12589
DRG / Apr '87 / New Note.

NUNSENSE II (The Second Coming)
Cast Recording
Goggin, Dan C
Jubilate deo/Nunsense - The magic word / Winning is just the beginning / Prima ballerina / Biggest still ain't the best / I've got pizazz / Country nun / Look Ma, I made it / Padre polka / Classic Queens / Hat and cane song / Angeline / We're the nuns to come to / What would Elvis do / Yes we can / I am here to stay / No one cared like you / There's only one way to end your prayers / Nunsense - The magic word (Reprise)
CD _____ DRGCD 12608
DRG / Jun '93 / New Note.

O PIONEERS
Broughton, Bruce C
Broughton, Bruce Con
CD _____ MAF 7023D
Intrada / Apr '92 / Silva Screen / Koch.

OBSCURED BY CLOUDS (La Vallee)
Pink Floyd
Pink Floyd C
Obscured by clouds / When you're in / Burning bridges / Gold it's in the... / Wot's... uh, the deal / Mudmen / Childhood's end / Free four / Stay / Absolutely curtains
CD _____ CDP 7463852
EMI / Mar '87 / EMI.

OBSESSION (Includes Welles Raises Kane/The Devil and Daniel Webster)
National Philharmonic Orchestra
Herrmann, Bernard C
Herrmann, Bernard Con
CD _____ UKCD 2065
Unicorn-Kanchana / Nov '94 / Harmonia Mundi.

OCCHIO ALLA PENNA
Morricone, Ennio C
CD _____ A 8916
Alhambra / Jan '92 / Silva Screen.

OCTOPUS/ALL ABOUT THE MAFIA
Morricone, Ennio C
CD _____ EDL 25492
Edel / Jan '93 / Pinnacle.

OF THEE I SING
Kaufman, George S. & Morrie Ryskind C
CD _____ ZDM 5650252
EMI Classics / Feb '94 / EMI.

OFF LIMITS (aka Saigon)
Howard, James Newton C
CD _____ VCD 70445
Varese Sarabande/Colosseum / Jan '89 / Pinnacle / Silva Screen.

OFFICER AND A GENTLEMAN, AN
Officer and a gentleman: Ritenour, Lee / Up where we belong: Cocker, Joe & Jennifer Warnes / Hungry for your love: Morrison, Van / Tush: ZZ Top / Treat me right: Ben-

atar, Pat / Be real: *Sir Douglas Quintet* / Tunnel of love: *Dire Straits*
CD _____ IMCD 77
Island / Jan '93 / PolyGram.

OH, KAY
Upshaw, Dawn & Orchestra Of St. Luke's
Gershwin, George *C*
Gershwin, Ira *L*
Stern, Eric *Con*
CD _____ 7559793612
Elektra Nonesuch / May '95 / Warner Music.

OIL CITY SYMPHONY
Broadway Cast
Ohio afternoon / Beaver ball / Dear Miss Reaves / Old Kentucky rock 'n' roll home / Bus ride / Beehive polka / In a gaddada vida / Baby it's cold outside / Exodus song / Getting acquainted / End of the world / Dizzy fingers
CD _____ CDSBL 12594
DRG / Jan '89 / New Note.

OKLAHOMA
Film Cast
Rodgers, Richard *C*
Hammerstein II, Oscar *L*
Blackton, Jay *Con*
Overture / Oh what a beautiful morning / Surrey with the fringe on top / Kansas City / I cain't say no / Many a new day / People will say we're in love / Poor Jud is dead / Out of my dreams / Farmer and the cow-man / All er nothin' / Oklahoma
CD _____ ZDM 7646912
EMI Classics / Apr '93 / EMI.

OKLAHOMA
1943 Broadway Cast
Rodgers, Richard *C*
Hammerstein II, Oscar *L*
Oh what a beautiful morning / Surrey with the fringe on top / Out of my dreams / Kansas City / I cain't say no / People will say we're in love / Farmer dance / Poor Jud is dead / It's a scandal, it's an outrage / Many a new day / All er nothin' / Oklahoma
CD _____ MCLD 19026
MCA / Apr '92 / BMG.

OKLAHOMA
1980 London Cast
Rodgers, Richard *C*
Hammerstein II, Oscar *L*
CD _____ CDTER 1208
TER / Mar '94 / Koch.

OKLAHOMA
1980 London Cast
Rodgers, Richard *C*
Hammerstein II, Oscar *L*
Overture / OH what a beautiful morning / Surrey with the fringe on top / Kansas City / I cain't say no / Many a new day / People will say we're in love / Pore Jud is dead / Out of my dreams / Farmer and the cow-man / All er nothin' / Oaklahoma
CD _____ SHOWCD 001
Showtime / Feb '95 / Disc / THE.

OKLAHOMA
1952 Broadway Cast
Rodgers, Richard *C*
Hammerstein II, Oscar *L*
Engel, L. *Con*
CD _____ SK 53326
Sony Broadway / Nov '93 / Sony.

OLD GRINGO
Holdridge, Lee *C*
Ride to the hacienda / Battle / Harriet's theme / Bitter's last ride / Mirrors / Nightime / Bell tower / Sigh / Battle (resolution) / Bitter's destiny / Finale
CD _____ GNPD 8017
GNP Crescendo / Nov '89 / Silva Screen.

OLD MAN AND THE SEA, THE
Tiomkin, Dimitri *C*
CD _____ VSD 5232
Varese Sarabande/Colosseum / Feb '90 / Pinnacle / Silva Screen.

OLD MAN AND THE SEA, THE
(TV Version)
Broughton, Bruce *C*
CD _____ RVF 6008D
Intrada / Jul '93 / Silva Screen / Koch.

OLIVER
1963 Broadway Cast
Bart, Lionel *C*
Food, glorious food / Oliver / I shall scream / Boy for sale / Where is love / Consider yourself / You've got to pick a pocket or two / It's a fine life / I'd do anything / Be back soon / Oom-pah-pah / My name / As long as he needs me / Who will buy / Reviewing the situation / As long as he needs me (reprise) / Reviewing the situation (reprise) / Finale
CD _____ GD 84113
RCA Victor / Oct '89 / BMG.

OLIVER
1960 London Cast
Bart, Lionel *C*
CD _____ 8205902
London / Jan '95 / PolyGram.

OLIVER
Film Cast
Bart, Lionel *C*
Overture / Food glorious food / Boy for sale / Where is love / You've got to pick a pocket or two / Consider yourself / I'd do anything / Be back soon / As long as he needs me /

Who will buy / It's a fine life / Reviewing the situation / Oom pah pah / Finale (Where is love/Consider yourself)
CD _____ ND 90311
RCA / Mar '89 / BMG.

OLIVER
(Highlights - The Shows Collection)
1994 Studio Cast
Bart, Lionel *C*
CD _____ PWKS 4194
Carlton Home Entertainment / Mar '94 / Carlton Home Entertainment.

OLIVER
1966 Studio Cast
Bart, Lionel *C*
Food, glorious food / Oliver / I shall scream / Where is love / Consider yourself / Pick a pocket or two / It's a fine life / Be back soon / I'd do anything / Oom pah pah / My name / As long as he needs me / Who will buy this wonderful morning / Reviewing the situation
CD _____ CC 8253
Music For Pleasure / Oct '94 / EMI.

OLIVER
1994 London Cast
Bart, Lionel *C*
CD _____ CASTCD 47
First Night / Mar '95 / Pinnacle.

OLIVER
Cast Recording
Bart, Lionel *C*
Overture/Food glorious food / Oliver / Where is love / Consider yourself / You've got to pick a pocket or two / It's a fine life / I'd do anything / Be back soon / Oom-pah-pah / As long as he needs me / Who will buy / Reviewing the situation
CD _____ SHOWCD 004
Showtime / Feb '95 / Disc / THE.

OLIVER
Holloway, Stanley & Alma Cogan/Tony Osborne Orchestra
Bart, Lionel *C*
CD _____ ZDM 7648902
EMI Classics / Aug '93 / EMI.

OLIVER
1991 Cast
Bart, Lionel *C*
CD _____ CDTER 1184
TER / Jan '92 / Koch.

OLIVER AND COMPANY
Redford, J.A.C. *C*
CD _____ PWK 450
Carlton Home Entertainment / Jul '90 / Carlton Home Entertainment.

OLIVER TWIST/MALTA G.C.
Royal Philharmonic Orchestra
Bax, Sir Arnold *C*
Prelude / Storm / Fight / Oliver's sleepless night / Oliver and the Artful Dodger / Fagin's romp / Chase / Oliver and Brownlow / Nancy and Browlow / Finale / Convoy / Old valletta / Air raid / Ruins / Quick march / Intermezzo / Work and play
CD _____ ACN 7012
Cloud Nine / Jan '89 / Conifer / Silva Screen.

OLIVIER OLIVIER/EUROPA EUROPA
Preisner, Zbigniew *C*
Main title / Affection et amour / Arrivee au cafe / Elizabeth S'evancuit / Olivier / Exode / Attaque aerienne / Bataille / Troubles / Hitler Staline
CD _____ DRGCD 12606
DRG / Jun '93 / New Note.

OLYMPUS ON MY MIND
1986 US Cast
Sturiale, Grant *C*
Harman, Barry *L*
Welcome to Greece: *Chorus* / Heaven on earth: *Jupiter, Alchmene* / Gods on top: *Delores, Jupiter* / Surprise: *Sosia & Mercury* / Love - what...: *Jupiter, Mercury & Delores* / Enter the husband: *Chorus* / I know my wife: *Amphitryon* / Back so soon: *Amphitryon, Sosia & Orchestra* / Wonderful: *Alchmene* / At liberty...: *Charis & The Chorus* / Jupiter slept here: *Jupiter & All* / Something of yourself: *Mercury* / Star is born: *Delores & all* / Final sequence: *Amphitryon, alchmene*
CD _____ CDTER 1131
TER / Aug '95 / Koch.

OMEN, THE
Goldsmith, Jerry *C*
Goldsmith, Jerry *Con*
CD _____ VSD 5281
Varese Sarabande/Colosseum / '91 / Pinnacle / Silva Screen.

OMEN, THE II
(Damien)
National Philharmonic Orchestra
Goldsmith, Jerry *C*
Newman, Lionel *Con*
Main title / Runaway train / Claws / Thoughtful night / Broken ice / Fallen temple / I love you, Mark / Shafted / Knife / All the power (End title)
CD _____ FILMCD 002
Silva Screen / Nov '89 / Conifer / Silva Screen.

OMEN, THE III
(The Final Conflict)
Goldsmith, Jerry *C*

Goldsmith, Jerry *Con*
CD _____ VCD 47242
Varese Sarabande/Colosseum / Sep '86 / Pinnacle / Silva Screen.

OMEN, THE IV
Sheffer, Jonathan *C*
CD _____ VSD 5318
Varese Sarabande/Colosseum / Jul '91 / Pinnacle / Silva Screen.

ON A CLEAR DAY YOU CAN SEE FOREVER
1970 Film Cast
Lane, Burton *C*
Lerner, Alan Jay *L*
Hurry it's lovely up here / On a clear day (you can see forever) / Love with all the trimmings / Melinda / Go to sleep / He isn't you / What did I have that I don't have / Come back to me
CD _____ 4749072
Columbia / '95 / Sony.

ON A CLEAR DAY YOU CAN SEE FOREVER
1965 Broadway Cast
Lane, Burton *C*
Lerner, Alan Jay *L*
CD _____ 09026608202
RCA Victor / Jan '90 / BMG.

ON DEADLY GROUND
Poledouris, Basil *C*
Poledouris, Basil *Con*
CD _____ VSD 5468
Varese Sarabande/Colosseum / Mar '94 / Pinnacle / Silva Screen.

ON HER MAJESTY'S SECRET SERVICE
Barry, John *C*
We have all the time in the world (feat. Louis Armstrong) / This never happened to the other fella / Try / Ski chase / Do you know how Christmas trees are grown / Main theme / Journey to Blofeld's hideaway / Over and out / Battle at Piz Gloria / We have all the time in the world/James Bond theme (medley)
CD _____ CZ 549
Premier / Dec '95 / EMI.

ON THE BIG HILL
Croker, Brendan & Guy Fletcher
Opening shot / Best laid plans / Mountain madness / Thru the window / Try not to fall / Higher ground / There are times / Things look different / Take a short walk / Some people get hurt / Long walk / Across the bridge / Dougie's march / Each night you die a little / In the back of your mind / Home Dougie, home
CD _____ ORECD 501
Silvertone / Mar '94 / Pinnacle.

ON THE TOWN
1963 London Cast
Bernstein, Leonard *C*
Comden, Betty & Adolph Green *L*
CD _____ SMK 53497
Sony West End / Nov '93 / Sony.

ON THE TOWN
Von Stade, Frederica & Thomas Hampson/London Voices/London Symphony Orchestra
Bernstein, Leonard *C*
Comden, Betty & Adolph Green *L*
Tilson Thomas, Michael *Con*
CD _____ 4375162
Deutsche Grammophon / Oct '93 / PolyGram.

ON THE TOWN
Cast Recording
Bernstein, Leonard *C*
Comden, Betty & Adolph Green *L*
CD _____ CDTER 1217
TER / Aug '95 / Koch.

ON THE WATERFRONT
1995 Broadway Cast
Amran, David *C*
Schulberg, Bud *L*
CD _____ VSD 5638
Varese Sarabande/Colosseum / Aug '95 / Pinnacle / Silva Screen.

ON YOUR TOES
1983 Broadway Cast
Rodgers, Richard *C*
Hart, Lorenz *L*
Overture / Two a day for Keith / It's got to be love / Too good for the average man / There's a small hotel / Heart is quicker than the eye / Quite night / Questions and answers / Glad to be unhappy / On your toes / Princess Zenobia ballet (edit) / Slaughter on 10th Avenue (edit)
CD _____ CDTER 1063
TER / Jul '83 / Koch.

ON YOUR TOES/PAL JOEY
Cast Recording
Rodgers, Richard *C*
Hart, Lorenz *L*
CD _____ 340822
Koch / Oct '95 / Koch.

ONCE AROUND
Horner, James *C*
Horner, James *Con*
CD _____ VSD 5308
Varese Sarabande/Colosseum / Apr '91 / Pinnacle / Silva Screen.

ONCE ON THIS ISLAND
Broadway Cast
Ahrens, Lynn *C*
CD _____ CDTER 1224
TER / Nov '94 / Koch.

ONCE UPON A FOREST
Horner, James *C*
CD _____ 662862
Silva Screen / Jul '92 / Conifer / Silva Screen.

ONCE UPON A TIME IN AMERICA
Morricone, Ennio *C*
Once upon a time in America / Poverty / Deborah's theme / Childhood memories / Amapola / Friends / Prohibition dirge / Cockeye's song / Childhood poverty / Photographic memories / Friendship and love / Speakeasy
CD _____ 8223342
Phonogram / Dec '84 / PolyGram.

ONCE UPON A TIME IN THE WEST
Morricone, Ennio *C*
Once upon a time in the West / As a judgement / Farewell to Cheyenne / Transgression / First tavern / Second tavern / Man with a harmonica / Dimly lit room / Bad orchestra / Man / Jill's America / Death rattle / Finale
CD _____ 47362
Silva Screen / Feb '90 / Conifer / Silva Screen.

ONCE WERE WARRIORS
CD _____ 249022
Milan / Mar '95 / BMG / Silva Screen.

ONE AGAINST THE WIND
Holdridge, Lee *C*
CD _____ MAF 7039D
Intrada / Jul '93 / Silva Screen / Koch.

ONE EYED JACKS
Friedhofer, Hugo *C*
CD _____ TSU 0114
Tsunami / Jan '95 / Silva Screen.

ONE FLEW OVER THE CUCKOO'S NEST
Nitzsche, Jack *C*
CD _____ FCD 4531
Fantasy / Jan '96 / Pinnacle / Jazz Music / Wellard / Cadillac.

ONE FROM THE HEART
Waits, Tom & Crystal Gayle
Waits, Tom *C*
Opening montage / Tom's piano / Once upon a town / Wages of love / Is there any way out of this dream / Presents / Picking up after you / Old boy friends / Broken bicycles / I beg your pardon / Little boy blue / Instrumental montage / Tango / Circus girl / You can't unring a bell / This one's from the heart / Take me home
CD _____ 4676092
CBS / Dec '90 / Sony.

ONE MILLION YEARS B.C.
(& When Dinosaurs Ruled The Earth/The Creatures The World Forgot)
Nascimbene, Mario *C*
CD _____ LEGENDCD 13
Legend / Jun '94 / Conifer / Silva Screen / Discovery.

ONE TRICK PONY
Simon, Paul
Simon, Paul *C*
Late in the evening / That's why God made the movies / One-trick pony / How the heart approaches what it yearns / Oh Marion / Ace in the hole / Nobody / Jonah / God bless the absentee / Long long day
CD _____ 256846
WEA / Feb '94 / Warner Music.

ONE WEEK
(New Jazz Score For Buster Keaton Film)
Frisell, Bill *C*
CD _____ 7559793522
Elektra / Jan '95 / Warner Music.

ONLY THE LONELY
Jarre, Maurice *C*
CD _____ VSD 5324
Varese Sarabande/Colosseum / Jul '91 / Pinnacle / Silva Screen.

ONLY THE LONELY
(The Roy Orbison Story)
London Cast
CD _____ CASTCD 51
First Night / Aug '95 / Pinnacle.

ONLY YOU
Portman, Rachel *C*
Once in a lifetime: *Bolton, Michael* / Only you (theme) / Do you love him / Venice / Arriving at Damon's resturant / Running after Damon / Positano / Quartet in B flat major / Only you (you alone): *Armstrong, Louis* / Some enchanted evening: *Pinza, Enzio* / O sole mio: *Quartetto Gelato* / La traviata: *Balsta, Agnes & Jose Carreras* / Lost in Tuscanny
CD _____ 4768182
Columbia / Jan '95 / Sony.

OPERA
CD _____ CDCIA 5074
Cinevox / Jan '93 / Conifer / Silva Screen.

OPERATION DUMBO DROP
CD _____ 1620322
Hollywood / Feb '96 / PolyGram.

ORCA - KILLER WHALE
Morricone, Ennio *C*
CD _____ LEGENDCD 10
Legend / Jul '93 / Conifer / Silva Screen /
Discovery.

ORLANDO
Motton, David & Sally Potter *C*
CD _____ VSD 5413
Varese Sarabande/Colosseum / Mar '93 /
Pinnacle / Silva Screen.

ORPHEUS IN THE UNDERWORLD
English National Opera
Offenbach, Jacques *C*
Wilson, Snoo & David Pontney *L*
CD _____ CDTER 1134
TER / May '89 / Koch.

ORPHEUS IN THE UNDERWORLD
(Highlights)
English National Opera
Offenbach, Jacques *C*
Wilson, Snoo & David Pontney *L*
CD _____ CDTEO 1008
TER / May '89 / Koch.

ORSON WELLES' OTHELLO
Lavagnino, Angelo Francesco *C*
CD _____ VSD 5420
Varese Sarabande/Colosseum / Feb '94 /
Pinnacle / Silva Screen.

OSCAR
Bernstein, Elmer *C*
CD _____ VSD 5313
Varese Sarabande/Colosseum / Apr '91 /
Pinnacle / Silva Screen.

OTHELLO
Mayes, Sally *C*
CD _____ VSD 5689
Varese Sarabande/Colosseum / Dec '95 /
Pinnacle / Silva Screen.

OUR PRIVATE WORLD
Mayes, Sally *C*
CD _____ VSD 5529
Varese Sarabande/Colosseum / Mar '95 /
Pinnacle / Silva Screen.

OUT FOR JUSTICE
(Score/Songs)
Frank, David Michael *C*
Don't stand in my way: *Allman, Gregg* /
Shake the firm: *Cool J.T.* / Temptation: *Bel-
mont James, Teresa* / When the night
comes down: *Smallwood, Todd* / One good
man: *Armstrong, Kymberli* / Puerto Ri-
queno: *Jimenez, Michael* / Bad side of
town: *Ball, Sherwood* / Bigger they are:
Cool J.T.
CD _____ VSD 5317
Varese Sarabande/Colosseum / Aug '91 /
Pinnacle / Silva Screen.

OUT OF AFRICA
Barry, John *C*
Barry, John *Con*
I had a farm in Africa / I'm better at hello
(Karen's theme I) / Have you got a story for
me / Concerto for clarinet in A / Safari / Kar-
en's journey / Siyawe / Flying over Africa /
I had a compass from Denys (Karen's
theme II) / Alone on the farm / Let the rest
of the world go by / If I know a song from
Africa (Karen's theme III) / You are Karen
(end theme) / Music of goodbye (feat. Mel-
issa Manchester & Al Jarreau)
CD _____ MCLD 19092
MCA / Oct '92 / BMG.

OUT OF THE RUINS
Nyman, Michael *C*
Meykhanejian, K. *Con*
CD _____ FILMCD 063
Silva Screen / Dec '89 / Conifer / Silva
Screen.

OUT OF THIS WORLD
1950 Broadway Cast
Porter, Cole *C*
CD _____ SK 48223
Sony Broadway / Nov '92 / Sony.

OUTBREAK
Howard, James Newton *C*
CD _____ VSD 5599
Varese Sarabande/Colosseum / Mar '95 /
Pinnacle / Silva Screen.

OUTER LIMITS
Frontiere, Dominic *C*
CD _____ GNPD 8032
GNP Crescendo / Apr '93 / Silva Screen.

OUTLAND/CAPRICORN ONE
Goldsmith, Jerry *C*
Goldsmith, Jerry *Con*
CD _____ GNPD 8035
GNP Crescendo / Nov '93 / Silva Screen.

OUTSIDE EDGE
CD _____ LBWCD 1
Echo / Feb '95.

OUTSIDERS, THE
Coppola, Carmine *C*
CD _____ FILMCD 051
Silva Screen / Jan '90 / Conifer / Silva
Screen.

OVER HERE
Cast Recording
Sherman, Richard & Robert *C*

CD _____ SK 32961
Sony Broadway / Nov '92 / Sony.

PACIFIC HEIGHTS
Zimmer, Hans *C*
Zimmer, Hans *Con*
CD _____ VSD 5286
Varese Sarabande/Colosseum / Feb '91 /
Pinnacle / Silva Screen.

PACIFIC OVERTURES
(Highlights)
London Cast/English National Opera
Sondheim, Stephen *C*
Weidman, J. *L*
2CD _____ CD2TER 1151
TER / Mar '90 / Koch.

PACIFIC OVERTURES
(Complete)
London Cast/English National Opera
Sondheim, Stephen *C*
Weidman, J. *L*
2CD _____ CDTER2 1152
TER / May '89 / Koch.

PAGEMASTER, THE
Horner, James *C*
Dream away: *Stansfield, Lisa & Babyface* /
Whatever you imagine: *Moten, Wendy* /
Main title / Stormy ride to the library / Pa-
gemaster / Dr. Jekyll and Mr. Hyde / Narrow
escape / Towards the open sea / Pirates /
Loneliness / Flying dragon / Swallowed
alive / Wonder in books / New courage /
Magic of imagination
CD _____ 07822110192
RCA / Nov '94 / BMG.

PAINT YOUR WAGON
Film Cast
Loewe, Frederick *C*
Lerner, Alan Jay *L*
I'm on my way / I still see Elisa / First thing
you know / Hand me down that can o'
beans / They call the wind Maria / Million
miles away behind the door / There's a
coach comin' in / Whoop-ti-ay (shivaree) / I
talk to the trees / Gospel of no name city /
Best things / Wandering star / Gold fever /
Finale
CD _____ MCLD 19310
MCA / Oct '95 / BMG.

PAINT YOUR WAGON
1951 Broadway Cast
Loewe, Frederick *C*
Lerner, Alan Jay *L*
Allers, Franz *Con*
I'm on my way / Rumson / What's goin' on
here / I talk to the trees / They call the wind
Maria / I still see Elsa / How can I wait / In
between / Whoop-ti-ay / Carino mio / The-
re's a coach comin' in / Hand me down that
can o' beans / Another autumn / All for him
/ Wandrin' star
CD _____ GD 60243
RCA Victor / Jan '90 / BMG.

PAL JOEY
1980 London Cast
Rodgers, Richard *C*
Hart, Lorenz *L*
CD _____ CDTER 1005
TER / Sep '91 / Koch.

PAL JOEY
(Highlights)
London Cast
Rodgers, Richard *C*
Hart, Lorenz *L*
You mustn't kick it around / I could write a
book / That terrific rainbow / What is a man
/ Happy hunting horn / Bewitched, bothered
and bewildered / Flower garden of my heart
/ Zip / Plant you now, dig you later / In our
little den / Do it the hard way / Take him
CD _____ SHOWCD 008
Showtime / Feb '95 / Disc / THE.

PAL JOEY
Broadway Cast
Rodgers, Richard *C*
Hart, Lorenz *L*
CD _____ ZDM 7646962
EMI Classics / Apr '93 / EMI.

PAL JOEY
Rodgers, Richard *C*
Hart, Lorenz *L*
CD _____ DRGCD 94763
DRG / Oct '95 / New Note.

PAPER, THE
Newman, Randy *C*
Newman, Randy *Con*
Opening / Clocks / Henry goes to work /
Sun / Bernie calls deanne / Busting the
guys / Marty and Henry / Newsroom 7.00
P.M / More clocks / Henry leaves with
McDougal / Bernie finds Deanne / Bernie /
Stop the presses / Henry's fired / Marty /
Marty's in trouble / To the hospital / Little
polenta is born / New day / 7.00 A.M. /
Make up your mind

CD _____ 9362456162
WEA / Feb '94 / Warner Music.

PAPERHOUSE
Zimmer, Hans & Stanley Myers *C*
CD _____ ACD 374
Milan / Jan '89 / BMG / Silva Screen.

PAPILLON
Goldsmith, Jerry *C*
Goldsmith, Jerry *Con*
Papillon / Camp / Reunion / New friend /
Freedom / Gift from the sea / Antonio's
death / Cruel sea / Hospital / Survival
CD _____ FILMCD 029
Silva Screen / Sep '88 / Conifer / Silva
Screen.

PARADISE ALLEY
Conti, Bill *C*
CD _____ TCS 1052
Silva Screen / Jul '93 / Conifer / Silva
Screen.

PARADISE BEACH
Elated / Holiday / Laughing (on the outside)
/ Train of thought / Freedom / Satisfy me /
Under the sun / R U sexin' me / It's the love
/ This isn't love / 747 / Break in the weather
/ We got it goin' on / Juliette / Weekend /
Faith in love / Choir girl / Boy
CD _____ 450993447-2
East West / Apr '93 / Warner Music.

PARDON MY ENGLISH
Cast Recording
Gershwin, George *C*
Gershwin, Ira *L*
Stern, Eric *Con*
CD _____ 7559793382
Elektra Nonesuch / Nov '94 / Warner Music.

PARIS, TEXAS
Cooder, Ry
Cooder, Ry *C*
Paris, Texas / Brothers / Nothing out there
/ Cancion mixteca / No safety zone / Hous-
ton in two seconds / She's leaving the bank
/ On the couch / I knew these two people /
Dark was the night
CD _____ 9252702
WEA / Feb '92 / Warner Music.

PARK IS MINE, THE
Tangerine Dream
Tangerine Dream *C*
CD _____ FILMCD 080
Silva Screen / Oct '91 / Conifer / Silva
Screen.

PART OF YOUR WORLD
Shapiro, Debbie *C*
CD _____ VSD 5452
Varese Sarabande/Colosseum / Jun '94 /
Pinnacle / Silva Screen.

PARTY PARTY
Party party: *Costello, Elvis* / Run Rudolph
run: *Edmunds, Dave* / No woman, no cry:
Black, Pauline / Yakety yak: *Bad Manners* /
Elizabethan reggae: *Bad Manners* / Tutti
frutti: *Sting* / Need your love so bad: *Sting*
/ No feelings: *Bananarama* / Band of gold:
Modern Romance / Little town flirt: *Altered
Images* / Man who sold the world: *Cox,
Midge* / Auld lang syne: *Chas & Dave*
CD _____ 5514402
Spectrum/Karussell / Aug '95 / PolyGram /
THE.

PASSION
Broadway Cast
Sondheim, Stephen *C*
CD _____ CDQ 5552512
EMI Classics / Apr '93 / EMI.

PASSION FISH
Daring / Apr '93 / Direct / CM / ADA.
CD _____ DR 3008

PASSION FLOWER HOTEL
1965 German Cast
Barry, John *C*
Peacock, Trevor *L*
Holmes, Richard *Con*
CD _____ SMK 66175
Sony West End / Jul '94 / Sony.

PASSION IN JAZZ
Sondheim, Stephen *C*
CD _____ VSD 5556
Varese Sarabande/Colosseum / Nov '94 /
Pinnacle / Silva Screen.

PAT GARRET AND BILLY THE KID
Dylan, Bob
Dylan, Bob *C*
Pat Garret and Billy the Kid (Main title) /
Workin' for the law (Cantina theme) / Billy 1
/ Bunkhouse theme / River theme / Turkey
chase / Knockin' on Heaven's door / Pat
Garret and Billy the Kid (Final theme) / Billy
4 / Billy 7
CD _____ CD 32098
Columbia / Feb '91 / Sony.

PATIENCE
D'Oyly Carte Opera Chorus/New Sym-
phony Orchestra
Sullivan, Sir Arthur *C*
Gilbert, W.S. *L*
Godfrey, I. *Con*
2CD _____ 4251932
London / Jan '90 / PolyGram.

PATIENCE
Shaw, John & Trevor Anthony/Glynde-
bourne Festival Choir/Pro Arte Orchestra

Sullivan, Sir Arthur *C*
Gilbert, W.S. *L*
Sargent, Sir Malcolm *Con*
2CD _____ CMS 7644062
EMI Classics / Apr '93 / EMI.

PATIENCE
D'Oyly Carte Opera Chorus
Sullivan, Sir Arthur *C*
Gilbert, W.S. *L*
2CD _____ CDTER2 1213
TER / Jan '94 / Koch.

PATRIOT GAMES
Horner, James *C*
Horner, James *Con*
CD _____ 101502
Milan / Feb '94 / BMG / Silva Screen.

PEAK PRACTICE
Altman, John *C*
Title music / Still life / Drive / From the heart
/ Don't throw stones / Leaving Africa /
Beth's theme / Will and Sarah / Got to run
/ Breathing space / Elegy / BB's groove /
Last dance
CD _____ CDSTM 7
Soundtrack Music / Mar '94 / EMI.

**PEE WEE'S BIG ADVENTURE/BACK TO
SCHOOL**
Elfman, Danny *C*
CD _____ VCD 47281
Varese Sarabande/Colosseum / Jan '89 /
Pinnacle / Silva Screen.

PEG
1984 London Cast
Heneker, David *C*
CD _____ CDTER 1024
TER / Dec '94 / Koch.

PELICAN BRIEF, THE
Horner, James *C*
CD _____ WA 245442
Silva Screen / Feb '95 / Conifer / Silva
Screen.

PELLE THE CONQUERER
CD _____ CHCH364
Milan / Feb '90 / BMG / Silva Screen.

PENITENT
CD _____ VCD 47299
Varese Sarabande/Colosseum / '87 /
Pinnacle / Silva Screen.

PENNIES FROM HEAVEN
CD _____ POTTCD 300
Connoisseur / May '93 / Pinnacle.

PEOPLE UNDER THE STAIRS
Revell, Graeme & Don Peake *C*
CD _____ 873105
Milan / Jan '95 / BMG / Silva Screen.

PERCY
Kinks
Davies, Ray *C*
God's children / Lola / Way love used to be
/ Completely / Running round town / Mo-
ments / Animals in the zoo / Just friends /
Whip lady / Dreams / Helga / Willesden
Green / End titles
CD _____ CLACD 164
Castle / Dec '89 / BMG.

PERFECT WORLD, A
Niehaus, Lennie *C*
Ida red (likes the boogie): *Wills, Bob & His
Texas Playboys* / Blue blue day: *Gibson,
Don* / Guess things happen that way: *Cash,
Johnny* / Sea of heartbreak: *Gibson, Don* /
Don't worry: *Robbins, Marty* / Abilene:
Hamilton, George IV / Please help me, I'm
falling: *Locklin, Hank* / Dark moon: *Isaak,
Chris* / Catch a falling star: *Como, Perry* /
Little white cloud that cried: *Isaak, Chris* /
Night life: *Draper, Rusty* / Big Fran's baby:
Niehaus, Lennie / End credits medley: *Nie-
haus, Lennie*
CD _____ 936245516-2
WEA / Jan '94 / Warner Music.

PERFORMANCE
Nitzsche, Jack *C*
Gone dead train: *Jagger, Mick* / Perform-
ance / Get away / Powis Square / Rolls
Royce / Dyed, dead, red / Harry Flowers /
Memo from Turner: *Jagger, Mick* / Hash-
ishin / Wake up niggers / Poor white hound
dog / Natural magic / Turner's murder
CD _____ 7599264002
WEA / Oct '93 / Warner Music.

PET SEMATARY
Goldenthal, Elliot
Goldenthal, Elliot *C*
CD _____ VSD 5227
Varese Sarabande/Colosseum / Jul '89 /
Pinnacle / Silva Screen.

PETALIA
Gavarentz, George *C*
CD _____ 873155
Milan / May '94 / BMG / Silva Screen.

PETER PAN
USA Television Cast
Styne, Jule/Betty Comden/Adolph Green/
Mark Charlap/Carolyn Leigh *C*
Tender shepherd / I've gotta crow / Never
never land / I'm flying / Pirate song / Hook's
tango / Indians / Wendy / Tarantella / I
won't grow up / Oh, my mysterious lady /
Ygg-a-wugg / Distant melody / Captain
Hook's waltz
CD _____ 37622
RCA/Silva Screen / Jan '89 / Silva Screen.

PETER PAN
1950 Broadway Cast
Bernstein, Leonard C
CD _____ CK 04312
CBS/Silva Screen / Jan '89 / Conifer / Silva Screen.

PETER PAN
1994 London Cast
CD _____ CASTCD 46
First Night / Dec '94 / Pinnacle.

PETER PAN
(The British Musical)
London Cast
Overture / Darlings / Peter / What happens when you're grown up / Come away / Rich damp cake / Wendy's song / Braves to war / Why / Goodbye Peter Pan / You gotta believe / We're going home / Darlings (Reprise) / Don't say goodbye
CD _____ CDEMC 3696
EMI / Dec '94 / EMI.

PETER THE GREAT
Rosenthal, Laurence C
Main title / Cathedral / Alexander / Tartars / Two living tears / His first sail / Foreign colony / Eudoxia / Peter's wedding / Tsar and Tsaritsa / New Tsarevich / Death of Natalyda - The slap / Great embassy / Gopak / Alexis and Danilo / Battle of Poltova / Sophia and Alexis - Ordeal - Martyrdom / Requiem / Peter's theme
CD _____ SCCD 1011
Southern Cross / Jan '95 / Silva Screen.

PETER'S FRIENDS
Everybody wants to rule the world: Tears For Fears / My baby just cares for me: Simone, Nina / You're my best friend: Queen / Girls just wanna have fun: Lauper, Cyndi / If you let me stay: D'Arby, Terence Trent / Hungry heart: Springsteen, Bruce / Don't get me wrong: Pretenders / King of rock 'n' roll: Prefab Sprout / What's love got to do with it: Turner, Tina / Give me strength: Clapton, Eric / Love and regret: Deacon Blue / Let's stay together: Pasadenas / Rio: Nesmith, Michael / Wherever I lay my hat: Young, Paul / I guess that's why they call it the blues: John, Elton / As the days go by: Braithwaite, Daryl
CD _____ MOODCD 27
Epic / Nov '92 / Sony.

PHAEDRA
Theodorakis, Mikis C
Love theme from Phaedra / Rendezvous / Ship to shore / London's fog / One more time / Agapimou / Only you / Fling / Candlelight / Rodostimo / Love theme: Mercouri, Melina / Goodbye John Sebastian
CD _____ SR 50060
Sakkaris / Oct '93 / Pinnacle.

PHANTASM/PHANTASM II
Myrow, Fred & Malcolm Seagrave C
CD _____ FILMCD 071
Silva Screen / Apr '91 / Conifer / Silva Screen.

PHANTOM
1993 Broadway Cast
Yeston, Maury C
CD _____ 09026616602
RCA Victor / May '93 / BMG.

PHANTOM OF THE OPERA
Budapest Studio Symphony Orchestra
Segal, Misha C
Segal, Misha Con
Phantom of the opera - main title / Don Juan triumphant/Travel through time / Phantom's lair/Hellbound (Freddy at the opera)/Maddie / Young Phantom's piano etude (Davis' unpleasant surprise/Carlotta's head) / You are him/Into the lair / Phantom on fire/The Phantom's face / Salon talk / Jewel song (from Faust) / Music of the knife/Killing Joseph / Graveyard violin/Pact with the devil/Richard gets killed / Ride to the cemetery/The cursed manuscript/ What's in the clo / Wedding/The intruder from Springwood/Christine's decision / Mott stalks the Phantom/Davis' death/ Phantom's fiery death / Finale/End title
CD _____ FILMCD 069
Silva Screen / Jun '90 / Conifer / Silva Screen.

PHANTOM OF THE OPERA
1986 London Cast
Lloyd Webber, Andrew C
Hart, Charles L
Overture / Think of me / Angel of music / Little Lotte / Mirror / Phantom of the opera / Music of the night / I remember / Stranger than you dreamt it / Magical lasso / Prima donna / Poor fool, he makes me laugh / All I ask of you / Entr'acte / Masquerade / Why so silent / Twisted every way / Wishing you were somewhere here again / Wandering child / Point of no return / Down once more / Phantom of the opera (finale)
CD _____ 8312732
Polydor / Feb '87 / PolyGram.

PHANTOM OF THE OPERA
(Highlights)
Cast Recording
Lloyd Webber, Andrew C
Hart, Charles L
CD _____ CDTER 1207
TER / Dec '93 / Koch.

PHANTOM OF THE OPERA
(Highlights)
1986 London Cast
Lloyd Webber, Andrew C
Hart, Charles L
Overture / Angel of music / Mirror / Phantom of the opera / Music of the night / Prima donna / All I ask of you / Masquerade / Wishing you were somewhere here again / Point of no return / Down once more
CD _____ 8315632
Polydor / Nov '87 / PolyGram.

PHANTOM OF THE OPERA/ASPECTS OF LOVE
(Highlights - The Shows Collection)
Cast Recording
Lloyd Webber, Andrew C
Hart, Charles & Don Black L
Phantom of the Opera / All I ask of you / Wishing you were somewhere here again / Think of me / Music of the night / Love changes everything / There is more to love / First man you remember / Chanson d'enfance / Anything but lonely / Seeing is believing / Journey of a lifetime
CD _____ PWKS 4164
Carlton Home Entertainment / Oct '93 / Carlton Home Entertainment.

PHANTOM OF THE OPERA/CATS
Cast Recording
Lloyd Webber, Andrew C
Hart, Charles L
CD _____ 340782
Koch / Oct '95 / Koch.

PHENOMENA
Goblin
Simonetti, Claudio C
CD _____ CDCIA 5062
Cinevox / Feb '93 / Conifer / Silva Screen.

PHILADELPHIA
(Songs)
Streets of Philadelphia: Springsteen, Bruce / Love town: Gabriel, Peter / It's in your eyes: Washington, Pauletta / Ibo Lele (dreams come true): Ram / Please send me someone to love: Sade / Have you ever seen the rain: Spin Doctors / I don't want to talk about it: Indigo Girls / La mama morta: Callas, Maria / Philadelphia: Young, Neil / Precedent: Shore, Howard
CD _____ 474998 2
Epic / Mar '94 / Sony.

PHILADELPHIA
(Score)
Shore, Howard C
Senior associate Beckett / Minor catastrophe / Birth / Non temer amayo bene: Popp, Lucia / I have a case / Essence of discrimination / Going home / Trial / Ebben, ne andro Iotana: Callas, Maria / Trying to survive / La mama morta: Callas, Maria / Excellent lawyer / Calculated risks / Verdict / I'm ready / Non temer amato bene: Popp, Lucia / Ebben, ne andro Iotana: Callas, Maria
CD _____ 4758002
Epic / Mar '94 / Sony.

PHILADELPHIA EXPERIMENT/MOTHER LODE
Wannberg, Ken C
CD _____ PCD 121
Prometheus / Mar '93 / Silva Screen.

PIAF
Paige, Elaine
La vie en rose / La goualante du pauvre jean / Hymne a l'amour / C'est a hambourg / Les trois cloches / Mon dieu / Les amants d'un jour / La belle histoire d'amour / Je sais comment / Non, je ne regrette rien / L'accordeoniste
CD _____ 450994641-2
WEA / Nov '94 / Warner Music.

PIANO, THE
Munich Philharmonic Orchestra
Nyman, Michael C
Nyman, Michael Con
To the edge of the earth / Big my secret / Wild and distant shore / Heart asks pleasure first / Here to there / Promise / Bed of ferns / Fling / Scent of love / Deep in the forest / Mood that passes through you / Lost and found / Embrace / Little impulse / Sacrifice / I clipped your wing / Wounded / All imperfect things / Dreams of a journey / Heart asks pleasure first/The promise
CD _____ CDVEX 919
Venture / May '94 / EMI.

PIAZZA DI SPAGNA
Morricone, Ennio C
CD _____ PRCD 107
Preamble / Jan '95 / Silva Screen.

PICKWICK
1993 Chichester Festival Cast
Ornadel, Cyril C
Bricusse, Leslie L
CD _____ CDTER 1205
TER / Dec '93 / Koch.

PICKWICK/SCROOGE
Cast Recording
Bricusse, Leslie L
CD _____ 340812
Koch / Oct '95 / Koch.

PICTURE BRIDE
Eidelman, Cliff C
CD _____ VSD 5651

Varese Sarabande/Colosseum / Jul '95 / Pinnacle / Silva Screen.

PINK PANTHER, THE
Mancini, Henry & His Orchestra
Mancini, Henry C
Mancini, Henry Con
Pink Panther / It had better be tonight / Royal blue / Champagne and quail / Village Inn / Titoer twist / Cortina / Lonely princess / Something for Sellers / Piano and strings / Shades of Sennett
CD _____ 27952
Silva Screen / Feb '90 / Conifer / Silva Screen.

PIPPIN
Broadway Cast
Schwartz, Stephen C
CD _____ MOTD 9088
Silva Screen / Jan '89 / Conifer / Silva Screen.

PIRATE, THE/PAGAN LOVE SONG
Porter, Cole C
CD _____ MCAD 5950
MCA/Silva Screen / Jan '89 / Silva Screen.

PIRATES
Paris Orchestra
Sarde, Philippe C
Pirates / Sauves mais captifs / Linares se meurt / Mutinerie a bord / C'ptain red maitre du galion / Red, la grenouille et le requin / Dolores / C'ptain Red's empare du tresor / Red et la grenouille voguent vers de nouvelles
CD _____ CDCH 233
Milan / '86 / BMG / Silva Screen.

PIRATES OF PENZANCE, THE
(Highlights)
D'Oyly Carte Opera Chorus
Sullivan, Sir Arthur C
Gilbert, W.S. L
Overture / When Fred'ric was a little lad / Oh better far to live and die / Oh is there not one maiden breast / Poor wandering one / I am the very model / Oh dry the glistening tear / When the foreman bares his steel / When you had left our pirates fold / When a felon's not engaged in his employment / With cat-like tread / Finale
CD _____ SHOWCD 010
Showtime / Feb '95 / Disc / THE.

PIRATES OF PENZANCE, THE
D'Oyly Carte Opera Chorus/Royal Philharmonic Orchestra
Sullivan, Sir Arthur C
Gilbert, W.S. L
Godfrey, I. Con
2CD _____ 4251962
Decca / Jan '90 / PolyGram.

PIRATES OF PENZANCE, THE
Glyndebourne Festival Choir/Pro Arte Orchestra
Sullivan, Sir Arthur C
Gilbert, W.S. L
Sargent, Sir Malcolm Con
2CD _____ CMS 7644092
EMI Classics / Apr '94 / EMI.

PIRATES OF PENZANCE, THE
D'Oyly Carte Opera Chorus/Orchestra
Sullivan, Sir Arthur C
Gilbert, W.S. L
Pryce Jones, J. Con
2CD _____ CDTER2 1177
TER / Sep '90 / Koch.

PIRATES OF PENZANCE, THE
Welsh National Opera/Orchestra
Sullivan, Sir Arthur C
Gilbert, W.S. L
Mackerras, C. Con
CD _____ CD 80353
Telarc / Nov '93 / Conifer / ADA.

PIRATES OF PENZANCE, THE/THE SORCERER
D'Oyly Carte Opera Chorus/New Symphony Orchestra
Sullivan, Sir Arthur C
Gilbert, W.S. L
Sargent, Sir Malcolm Con
2CD _____ Z 80682
Arabesque / Nov '87 / Seaford Music.

PLAIN AND FANCY
Broadway Cast
Hague, Albert C
Horwitt, Arnold L
CD _____ ZDM 7647622
EMI Classics / Apr '93 / EMI.

PLANET OF THE APES
(Remastered With Extra Music)
Goldsmith, Jerry C
Goldsmith, Jerry Con
CD _____ FMT 8006D
Intrada / Dec '92 / Silva Screen / Koch.

PLATOON
Village: Vancouver Symphony Orchestra / Tracks of my tears: Robinson, Smokey / Okie from Muskogee: Haggard, Merle / Hello I love you: Doors / White rabbit: Jefferson Airplane / Barnes shoots Elias: Vancouver Symphony Orchestra / Respect: Franklin, Aretha / (Sittin' on) the dock of the bay: Redding, Otis / When a man loves a woman: Sledge, Percy / Groovin': Rascals / Adagio for strings: Vancouver Symphony Orchestra

CD _____ 7817422
Atlantic / Jun '87 / Warner Music.

PLATOON LEADER
Clinton, George C
CD _____ GNPD 8013
GNP Crescendo / Jan '89 / Silva Screen.

PLAYER, THE
Newman, Thomas C
CD _____ VSD 5366
Varese Sarabande/Colosseum / May '92 / Pinnacle / Silva Screen.

POINT BREAK
Isham, Mark C
CD _____ MCAD 10202
MCA / Nov '91 / BMG.

POINT OF NO RETURN/THE ASSASSIN
Zimmer, Hans C
CD _____ 143022
Milan / Feb '94 / BMG / Silva Screen.

POLTERGEIST II
Goldsmith, Jerry C
Power / Late call / Smoke / Worm / Reaching out
CD _____ VCD 47266
Varese Sarabande/Colosseum / Jan '89 / Pinnacle / Silva Screen.
CD _____ CDTER 1116
TER / Jan '92 / Koch.
Intrada / Jan '93 / Silva Screen / Koch.
CD _____ RVF 6002D

POLTERGEIST II
(& Unreleased Music)
Goldsmith, Jerry C
CD _____ VJD 5002D
Silva Screen / Jan '95 / Conifer / Silva Screen.

POLTERGEIST III
Renzetti, Joe C
CD _____ VCD 70462
Varese Sarabande/Colosseum / Jan '89 / Pinnacle / Silva Screen.

POPPIE NONGENA
1983 Cast
Mgcina, Sophie C
Kotze, Sandra & Elsa Joubert L
Amen / Taru bawo / Wenzeni na / U Jehovah / Uzubale / Makoti / Lalasana / Jerusalem / Nkosi Sikela l'Afrika / Zisana abantwane / Bantwana besikolo / Liza Lisi Dinga / Mampondo mse
CD _____ HNCD 1351
Hannibal / Jan '87 / Vital / ADA.

PORGY AND BESS
1942 Broadway Cast
Gershwin, George C
Gershwin, Ira & DuBose Heyward L
Overture/Summertime / Woman is a sometime thing / My man's gone now / It takes a long pull to get there / I got plenty o' nuttin' / Buzzard song / Bess, you is my woman now / It ain't necessarily so / What you want wid Bess / Strawberry woman's call - crab man's call / I loves you Porgy / Requiem / There's a boat dat's leavin' now for New York / Porgy's lament/Finale
CD _____ MCLD 19158
MCA / Jan '94 / BMG.

PORGY AND BESS
(Scenes)
Price, Leontyne
Gershwin, George C
Gershwin, Ira & DuBose Heyward L
CD _____ GD 85234
RCA / Mar '95 / BMG.

PORGY AND BESS
(Highlights)
Houston Grand Opera
Gershwin, George C
Gershwin, Ira & DuBose Heyward L
DeMain, J. Con
CD _____ RD 84680
RCA Victor / '88 / BMG.

PORGY AND BESS
White, Willard & Cynthia Haymon/Glyndebourne Festival Opera Cast/London Philharmonic Orchestra
Gershwin, George C
Gershwin, Ira & DuBose Heyward L
Rattle, Simon Con
3CD _____ CDS 7495682
EMI Classics / Apr '93 / EMI.

PORGY AND BESS
(Highlights)
White, Willard & Cynthia Haymon/Glyndebourne Festival Opera Cast/London Philharmonic Orchestra
Gershwin, George C
Gershwin, Ira & DuBose Heyward L
Rattle, Simon Con
CD _____ CDC 7543252
EMI Classics / Apr '93 / EMI.

PORGY AND BESS
Cleveland Orchestra/Choir/Children's Choir
Gershwin, George C
Gershwin, Ira & DuBose Heyward L
Maazel, L. Con
3CD _____ 4145592
Decca / Feb '86 / PolyGram.

PORGY AND BESS
London Cast
Gershwin, George C
Gershwin, Ira & DuBose Heyward L

POSSE
Posse (Shoot 'em up): *Intelligent Hoodlum* / Posse love: *Tone Loc* / One night of love: *Bad Boys Of The Industry* / Cruel Jim Crow (Please don't play that): *Van Peebles, Melvin* / I think to myself: *Top Choice Clique* / Jesse: *Colombier, Michel* / Tell me: *Vesta* / Free at last: *David & David* / If I knew at all: *Richardson, Salli* / Freemansville (Homecoming): *Sounds Of Blackness* / Ride of your life: *Vesta* / Let the hammer fall: *Neville Brothers*
CD _____ 5400812
A&M / Apr '95 / PolyGram.

POWAQQATSI
Glass, Philip C
Riesman, Michael Con
CD _____ 755991922
Elektra Nonesuch / Aug '88 / Warner Music.

POWER OF ONE, THE
Zimmer, Hans C
Rainmaker / Mother Africa / Of death and dying / Limpopo river song / Power of one / Woza Mfana / Southland concerto / Senzenina / Penny whistle song / Funeral song / Wangal unozipho / Mother Africa (reprise)
CD _____ 7559613352
Elektra / Oct '92 / Warner Music.

POWER, THE
(with Choral Pieces From King Of Kings & Ben Hur)
Rozsa, Miklos C
CD _____ PCD 122
Prometheus / Jan '93 / Silva Screen.

PREDATOR II
Silvestri, Alan C
CD _____ VSD 5302
Varese Sarabande/Colosseum / Jan '91 / Pinnacle / Silva Screen.

PRELUDE TO A KISS
Shore, Howard C
CD _____ 111252
Milan / May '94 / BMG / Silva Screen.

PRESUMED INNOCENT
Williams, John C
CD _____ VSD 5280
Varese Sarabande/Colosseum / Oct '90 / Pinnacle / Silva Screen.

PRET-A-PORTER
Here comes the hotstepper: *Kamoze, Ini* / My girl Josephine: *Super Cat* / Here we come: *Salt 'N' Pepa* / Natural thing: *M People* / 70's love groove: *Jackson, Janet* / Jump on top of me: *Rolling Stones* / These boots were made for walkin': *Phillips, Sam* / Pretty: *Cranberries* / Martha: *Deep Forest* / Close to you: *Brand New Heavies* / Keep givin' me your love: *Peniston, Ce Ce* / Get wild: *New Power Generation* / Supermodel sandwich: *D'Arby, Terence Trent* / Lemon (Perfecto mix): *U2*
CD _____ 4782262
Columbia / Feb '95 / Sony.

PRETTY IN PINK
Left of centre: *Vega, Suzanne* / Get to know ya: *Johnson, Jesse* / Do wot you do: *INXS* / Pretty in pink: *Psychedelic Furs* / Shellshock: *New Order* / Round round: *Belouis Some* / Wouldn't it be good: *Hutton, June* / Bring on the dancing horses: *Echo & The Bunnymen* / Please, please, please let me get what I want: *Smiths* / If you leave: *O.M.D.*
CD _____ CDMID 157
A&M / Oct '92 / PolyGram.

PRETTY WOMAN
Wild women do: *Cole, Natalie* / Fame '90: *Bowie, David* / King of wishful thinking: *Go West* / Tangled: *Wiedlin, Jane* / It must have been love: *Roxette* / Life in detail: *Palmer, Robert* / No explanation: *Cetera, Peter* / Real wild child: *Otcasek, Christopher* / Fallen: *Wood, Lauren* / Oh pretty woman: *Orbison, Roy* / Show me your soul: *Red Hot Chili Peppers*
CD _____ CDMTL 1052
EMI Manhattan / Apr '90 / EMI.

PRETTYBELLE
Broadway Cast
CD _____ VSD 5439
Varese Sarabande/Colosseum / Sep '93 / Pinnacle / Silva Screen.

PRIDE AND PREJUDICE
Pride and prejudice / Netherfield ball montage / Elizabeth observed / Piano summary (Episodes 1 - 5) / Canon Collins / Gardeners / Winter into Spring / Parting / Rosings / Telling the truth / Farewell to the regiment / Darcy returns / Thinking about Lizzie / Lydia's elopement / Return of Bingley / Double wedding
CD _____ CDEMC 3726
EMI / Sep '95 / EMI.

PRIEST OF LOVE
Lawrence / English hotel trio / Variations / Mabel's tango / Frieda's theme (part 1) / Frieda's theme (part 2) / Italy / Cornwall / Fugue / Lawrence's death / Priest of love (finale) / Way we get it together
CD _____ DSCD 1003
D-Sharp / Nov '85 / Pinnacle.

PRINCE OF DARKNESS
Carpenter, John C
CD _____ VCD 47310
Varese Sarabande/Colosseum / Jan '89 / Pinnacle / Silva Screen.

PRINCESS BRIDE, THE
Knopfler, Mark
Knopfler, Mark C
Once upon a time...storybook love / I will never love again / Florin dance / Morning ride / Friends' song / Cliffs of insanity / Sword fight / Guide my sword / Fire swamp and the rodents of unusual size / Revenge / Happy ending / Storybook love
CD _____ 832 864-2
Vertigo / Nov '87 / PolyGram.

PRINCESS CARABOO
Hartley, Richard C
CD _____ VSD 5544
Varese Sarabande/Colosseum / Dec '94 / Pinnacle / Silva Screen.

PRINCESS IDA/PINEAPPLE POLL
D'Oyly Carte Opera Chorus/Royal Philharmonic Orchestra/Philharmonia Orchestra
Sullivan, Sir Arthur C
Gilbert, W.S. L
Sargent, Malcolm/C. Mackerras Con
2CD _____ 4368102
London / Jan '90 / PolyGram.

PRISONER VOL.2, THE
Grainer, Ron/Wilfred Josephs/Albert Elms C
Arrival / Chimes of Big Ben / A B And C / Many happy returns / Checkmate / Dance of the dead / Do not forsake me oh my darling / Girl who was death / Fall out
CD _____ FILMCD 084
Silva Screen / Jun '92 / Conifer / Silva Screen.

PRISONER VOL.3, THE
Grainer, Ron/Wilfred Josephs/Albert Elms C
Arrival / Chimes of Big Ben / A B and C / Free for all / General / Dance of the dead / Hammer into anvil / Change of mind / Do not forsake me oh my darling / Girl who was death / Fall out
CD _____ FILMCD 126
Silva Screen / Nov '92 / Conifer / Silva Screen.

PRISONER, THE
Grainer, Ron/Wilfred Josephs/Albert Elms C
Arrival (Theme/No.6 attempts helicopter escape/Band marches into main village square/Chimes) / A, B & C (Engadine's dreamy party) / Free For All (Mini Moke and speedboat escape/Cat and mouse nightclub mechanical band/No.6 wins village election/Violent capture of No.6 in rover cave) / General / Fall Out (Theme) / Many Happy Returns (No.6 aboard gunrunners' boat) / Dance Of The Dead (Village square carnival procession/No.6 steals a lifebelt) / Checkmate (Escapers attack searchlight tower) / Hammer Into Anvil (No.2 has No.6 followed to the stone boat/Farandelle played by village band/Fight between No.6 and No.14) / Girl Who Was Death (Village green cricket match) / Once Upon A Time (No.6's regression to childhood/No.6's schooldays revisited/Main title theme reprise)
CD _____ FILMCD 042
Silva Screen / Nov '89 / Conifer / Silva Screen.

PRIVATE PARTS/RICHTHOFEN AND BROWN
Graunke Symphony Orchestra
Friedhofer, Hugo C
Graunke, K. Con
CD _____ FE 8105
Facet / Mar '94 / Conifer.

PROFESSIONALS, THE
Jarre, Maurice C
Jarre, Maurice Con
CD _____ 2504302
Silva Screen / Jan '93 / Conifer / Silva Screen.

PROFUNDO ROSSO/SUSPIRIA
Goblin
Simonetti, Claudio C
CD _____ CDCIA 5005
Cinevox / Jan '89 / Conifer / Silva Screen.

PROMISED LAND
CD _____ 20352
Silva Screen / Feb '90 / Conifer / Silva Screen.

PROOF
Not Drowning, Waving
Not Drowning, Waving C
CD _____ A 8927
Alhambra / Jan '92 / Silva Screen.

PROSPERO'S BOOKS
Nyman, Michael C
Nyman, Michael Con
CD _____ 4252242
Decca / Nov '91 / PolyGram.

PSYCHO
Herrmann, Bernard C
CD _____ CDCH 022
Milan / Feb '90 / BMG / Silva Screen.

PSYCHO
National Philharmonic Orchestra
Herrmann, Bernard C
Herrmann, Bernard Con
CD _____ UKCD 2021

PUBLIC EYE, THE
Isham, Mark C
CD _____ VSD 5374
Varese Sarabande/Colosseum / Nov '92 / Pinnacle / Silva Screen.

PULP FICTION
Misirlou: *Dale, Dick & His Del-Tones* / Jungle boogie: *Kool & The Gang* / Let's stay together: *Green, Al* / Bustin' surfboards: *Tornadoes* / Lonesome town: *Nelson, Ricky* / Son of a preacher man: *Springfield, Dusty* / Bullwinkle (part 2): *Centurions* / You never can tell: *Berry, Chuck* / Girl, you'll be a woman soon: *Urge Overkill* / If love is a red dress (hang me in rags): *McKee, Maria* / Comanche: *Revels* / Flowers on the wall: *Statler Brothers* / Surf rider: *Lively Ones*
CD _____ MCD 11103
MCA / Sep '94 / BMG.

PUMP UP THE VOLUME
Everybody knows: *Concrete Blonde* / Why can't I fall in love: *Neville, Ivan* / Stand: *Liquid Jesus* / Wave of mutilation: *Pixies* / I've got a secret minature camera: *Murphy, Peter* / Kick out the jams: *Bad Brains & Henry Rollins* / Freedom of speech: *Above The Law* / Heretic: *Soundgarden* / Titanium express: *Sonic Youth* / Me and the Devil blues: *Cowboy Junkies*
CD _____ DMCG 6121
MCA / Nov '90 / BMG.

PUPPET MASTERS, THE
London Filmworks Orchestra
Towns, Colin C
Wilson, Allan Con
CD _____ STC 77104
Klavier / Jan '95 / Quantum Audio / UK Distribution.

PURE LUCK
Sheffer, Jonathan C
CD _____ VSD 5330
Varese Sarabande/Colosseum / Aug '91 / Pinnacle / Silva Screen.

PURPLE RAIN
Prince & The Revolution
Prince C
Let's go crazy / Take me with U / Beautiful ones / Computer blue / Darling Nikki / When doves cry / I would die 4 U / Baby I'm a star / Purple rain
CD _____ 9251102
WEA / Feb '95 / Warner Music.

PUTTING IT TOGETHER
1993 US Cast
Sondheim, Stephen C
Invocation and instructions to the audience / Putting it together / Rich and happy / Merrily we roll along / Everybody ought to have a maid / Sooner or later / Ah but underneath / Hello little girl / My husband the pig / Every day a little death / Have I got a girl for you / Pretty women / Now / Bang / Country house / Could I leave you / Back in business / Night waltzes / Love takes time / Remember / In praise of women / Perpetual anticipation / Sun won't set / Game sequence / What would we do without you / Gun song / Little priest / Miller's son / Live alone and like it / Sorry / Grateful / Sweet Polly Plunket / I could drive a person crazy / Marry me a little / Getting married today / Being alive / Like it was / Old friends
CD _____ 09026617292
RCA Victor / Jan '94 / BMG.

PYROMANIACS LOVE STORY
Portman, Rachel C
CD _____ VSD 5620
Varese Sarabande/Colosseum / Jun '95 / Pinnacle / Silva Screen.

Q

QUADROPHENIA
I am the sea: *Who* / Real me: *Who* / I'm one: *Who* / 5.15: *Who* / I've had enough: *Who* / Love reign o'er me: *Who* / Dr. Jimmy: *Who* / Helpless dancer: *Who* / Dr. Jimmy: *Who* / Four faces: *Who* / Get out and stay out: *Who* / Joker James: *Who* / Punk and the Godfather: *Who* / Louie Louie: *Kingsmen* / Zoot suit: *High Numbers* / Hi-heel sneakers: *Cross Section* / Night train: *Brown, James* / Green onions: *Booker T & The MG's* / He's so fine: *Chiffons* / Rhythm of the rain: *Cascades* / Be my baby: *Ronettes* / Da doo ron ron: *Crystals*
CD _____ 519 999 2
Polydor / Sep '93 / PolyGram.

QUANTUM LEAP
Post, Mike C
CD _____ GNPD 8036
GNP Crescendo / Nov '93 / Silva Screen.

QUARTET
CD _____ CDQ 5551002
EMI / Apr '94 / EMI.

QUEST FOR FIRE
Sarde, Philippe C
CD _____ CDFMC 1
Silva Screen / Jan '89 / Conifer / Silva Screen.

QUI C'EST CE GARCON
Sarde, Philippe C
CD _____ CD 312
Milan / Jan '89 / BMG / Silva Screen.

QUICK AND THE DEAD, THE
Silvestri, Alan C
Redemption / Gunfight montage / Couldn't tell us apart / John Herod / Ellen's first round / Lady's the winner / Dinner tonight / Cort's story / Ellen vs. Dred / Kid vs. Herod / I don't wanna die / Big day / Ellen returns / Law's come back to town / Quick and the dead (End credits)
CD _____ VSD 5595
Varese Sarabande/Colosseum / Oct '95 / Pinnacle / Silva Screen.

QUIEN SABE
Bacalov, Luis Enriquez C
CD _____ A 8932
Alhambra / Jan '93 / Silva Screen.

QUIET MAN, THE
Dublin Screen Orchestra
Young, Victor C
Alwyn, Kenneth Con
CD _____ SFC 1501
Silva Screen / Sep '95 / Conifer / Silva Screen.

QUIET MAN, THE/SAMSON AND DELILAH
Young, Victor C
Young, Victor Con
CD _____ VSD 5497
Varese Sarabande/Colosseum / Jun '94 / Pinnacle / Silva Screen.

QUIGLEY DOWN UNDER
Poledouris, Basil C
CD _____ MAF 7006D
Intrada / Jan '93 / Silva Screen / Koch.

QUILLER MEMORANDUM, THE
Barry, John C
CD _____ VSD 5218
Varese Sarabande/Colosseum / Feb '90 / Pinnacle / Silva Screen.

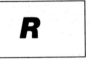

R

RACE FOR THE YANKEE ZEPHYR/SURVIVOR
May, Brian C
CD _____ IMICD 1008
Silva Screen / Jan '93 / Conifer / Silva Screen.

RADIO FLYER
Zimmer, Hans C
CD _____ 244542
Silva Screen / Jan '93 / Conifer / Silva Screen.

RADIO GALS
Cast Recording
CD _____ VSD 5604
Varese Sarabande/Colosseum / Jul '95 / Pinnacle / Silva Screen.

RAGE OF THE HEART
Garzilli, Enrico C
CD _____ ROLECD 1
First Night / Apr '89 / Pinnacle.

RAGGEDY RAWNEY, THE
Kamen, Michael
Kamen, Michael C
Tribe / You should see Nellie pass water: *Hoskins, Bob & Cast* / Caravans / Horse race / Farmyard / Rolling home: *Tams, John* / Jessie and Tom / Daisy chain / Wedding dress / Bullroarer/Band of lace / Peacock polka (Darky's polka) / Simon drowned / Funeral lament: *Bell, Maggie* / Prayer / Officer / Children / Raggedy rawney
CD _____ FILMCD 033
Silva Screen / Sep '88 / Conifer / Silva Screen.

RAIDERS OF THE LOST ARK
(Digitally Remastered)
London Symphony Orchestra
Williams, John C
Williams, John (1) Con
CD _____ RAIDERS 001
Silva Screen / Nov '95 / Conifer / Silva Screen.

RAIN
Takemitsu, Toru C
CD _____ FMC 5
Milan / Jan '95 / BMG / Silva Screen.

RAINBOW, THE
Graunke Symphony Orchestra
Davis, Carl C
Davis, Carl Con
Prelude and opening titles / Walking home / Swingboats / Ursula and Winifred / Seduction / Exam results / School assembly / Mr. Harby / Wedding / Moonlight lovers /

Military two step / Waterfull / Cottage Idyll / Pursuit through the forest / Ursula's dream / Rainbow
CD _____ FILMCD 040
Silva Screen / Nov '89 / Conifer / Silva Screen.

RAINMAKER, THE
North, Alex C
CD _____ TSU 0120
Tsunami / Jan '95 / Silva Screen.

RAINTREE COUNTY
Green, John C
2CD _____ 2PRCD 1781
Silva Screen / Jan '90 / Conifer / Silva Screen.

RAISE THE RED LANTERN
Jiping, Zhao C
CD _____ 887952
Milan / Jan '95 / BMG / Silva Screen.

RAISING CAIN
Donaggio, Pino C
CD _____ 101302
Milan / Nov '92 / BMG / Silva Screen.

RAMBO
Goldsmith, Jerry C
CD _____ VCD 47234
TER / Jan '89 / Koch.

RAMBO I
Goldsmith, Jerry C
CD _____ FMT 8001D
Intrada / Jan '89 / Silva Screen / Koch.

RAMBO II
Goldsmith, Jerry C
Main title / Preparation / Jump / Snake / Stories / Cage / Betrayed / Peace in our life / Escape from torture / Ambush / Revenge / Bowed down / Pilot over / Home flight / Day by day
CD _____ VSD 47234
Varese Sarabande/Colosseum / Feb '90 / Pinnacle / Silva Screen.

RAMBO III
(Score)
Hungarian State Opera Orchestra
Goldsmith, Jerry C
Goldsmith, Jerry Con
CD _____ RVF 6006D
Intrada / Jan '90 / Silva Screen / Koch.

RANSOM
(AKA The Terrorist & The Chairman)
Goldsmith, Jerry C
Goldsmith, Jerry Con
CD _____ FILMCD 081
Silva Screen / Jul '91 / Conifer / Silva Screen.

RAPA NUI
Copeland, Stewart C
CD _____ 214402
Milan / Nov '94 / BMG / Silva Screen.

RAPID FIRE
Young, Christopher C
CD _____ VSD 5388
Varese Sarabande/Colosseum / Sep '92 / Pinnacle / Silva Screen.

RAW DEAL
Bahler, Tom C
CD _____ VSD 47286
Varese Sarabande/Colosseum / Feb '93 / Pinnacle / Silva Screen.

RAZOR'S EDGE
London Studio Symphony Orchestra
Nitzsche, Jack C
Bla.., Stanley Con
CD _____ PRCD 1794
Preamble / Jan '93 / Silva Screen.

RE-ANIMATOR/BRIDE OF THE RE-ANIMATOR
Band, Richard C
CD _____ FILMCD 082
Silva Screen / '92 / Conifer / Silva Screen.

RE-JOYCE
Lipman, Maureen
Addinsell, Richard C
CD _____ SCENECD 21
First Night / '94 / Pinnacle.

REAL MCCOY, THE
Fiedel, Brad C
Walker, S. Con
Varese Sarabande/Colosseum / Oct '93 /
CD _____ VSD 5450
Pinnacle / Silva Screen.

REALITY BITES
My Sharona: Knack / Spin the bottle: Hatfield, Juliana / Bed of roses: Indians / When you come back to me: World Party / Going going gone: Posies / Stay: Loeb, Lisa & Nine Stories / All I want is you: U2 / Locked out: Crowded House / Spinning around after the music / Turnip farm: Dinosaur Jnr / Revival: Me Phi Me / Tempted (94): Squeeze / Baby, I love your way: Big Mountain
CD _____ 07863663642
MCA / Apr '94 / BMG.

REBECCA
ft. Alf Newman's Selznick International (Pictures Fanfare)
Bratislava Symphony Orchestra
Waxman, Franz C
CD _____ 8223399
Marco Polo / Oct '92 / Select.

REBEL WITHOUT A CAUSE/EAST OF EDEN/GIANT
(James Dean - Rebel)
Czech Symphony Orchestra
Rosenman, Leonard/Dimitri Tiomkin C
2CD _____ CIN 22062
Silva Screen / Nov '93 / Conifer / Silva Screen.

RECIDIVE
Musy, Jean C
CD _____ 873146
Milan / Jan '95 / BMG / Silva Screen.

RED DAWN
Poledouris, Basil C
Invasion / Drive-in / Let it turn / Woverines / Flowers / Eulogy / Robert's end / Death and freedom / End titles
CD _____ RVF 6001D
Intrada / Jan '89 / Silva Screen / Koch.

RED KNIGHT, WHITE KNIGHT
Scott, John C
CD _____ MAF 7016D
Intrada / Jan '89 / Silva Screen / Koch.

RED SCORPION
Chattaway, Jay C
Chattaway, Jay C
CD _____ VSD 5230
Varese Sarabande/Colosseum / Sep '89 / Pinnacle / Silva Screen.

RED TENT, THE
Morricone, Ennio C
Love theme / Do dreams go on / Death at the Pole / Love like the snow / Message from Rome / They're alive / Farewell / Others, who will follow us
CD _____ LEGENDCD 15
Legend / Aug '94 / Conifer / Silva Screen / Discovery.

REIVERS, THE
Williams, John C
Williams, John (1) Con
CD _____ CK 66130
Columbia / Apr '95 / Sony.

REMAINS OF THE DAY, THE
Robbins, Richard C
Rabinowitz, H. Con
Angel / Aug '94 / EMI.
CD _____ CDQ 5550292

RENAISSANCE MAN
Zimmer, Hans C
CD _____ VSD 5502
Varese Sarabande/Colosseum / Aug '94 / Pinnacle / Silva Screen.

RENT-A-COP
Rent a cop / Bust / Lonely cop / Russian roulette / Station / Worth a lot / Lights out / This is the Guy / They need me / Room / Lake forest / Jump
CD _____ FILMCD 025
Silva Screen / Apr '88 / Conifer / Silva Screen.

REPO MAN
CD _____ MCLD 19311
MCA / Oct '95 / BMG.

RESERVOIR DOGS
Little green bag: Baker, George Selection / Hooked on a feeling: Blue Swede / I gotcha: Tex, Joe / Magic carpet ride: Bedlam / Fool for love: Rogers, Sandy / Stuck in the middle with you: Stealer's Wheel / Harvest moon: Bedlam / Coconut: Nilsson, Harry
CD _____ MCD 10793
MCA / Jan '93 / BMG.

RETURN OF THE JEDI
Williams, John C
Main title / Into the trap / Luke and Leia / Bot got Jarraz / Han Solo returns / Parade of the Ewoks / Forest / Rebel briefing / Emperor / Return of the Jedi / Ewok celebration and finale
CD _____ 8117672
RSO / May '83 / PolyGram.

RETURN OF THE JEDI
National Philharmonic Orchestra
Williams, John C
Gerhardt, Charles Con
Approaching the Death Star / Parade of the Ewoks / Luke and Leia / Jabba the Hutt / Return of the Jedi / Ewok battle / Han Solo returns / Into the trap (Fight in the dungeon) / Heroic Ewok / Battle in the forest / Finale
CD _____ GD 80767
RCA Victor / Jun '91 / BMG.

RETURN OF THE LIVING DEAD
Surfin' dead: Cramps / Party time (Zombie version): 45 Grave / Nothing for you: T.S.O.L. / Eyes without a face: Flesh Eaters / Burn the flames: Erickson, Roky / Dead beat dance: Damned / Take a walk: Tall Boys / Love under will: Jet Black Berries / Tonight (we'll make love until we die): SSQ / Trash's theme: SSQ
CD _____ CDWIK 38
Big Beat / Jun '88 / Pinnacle.

RETURN OF THE MUSKETEERS
Petit, Jean Claude C
CD _____ CDCH 383
Milan / Feb '90 / BMG / Silva Screen.

RETURN TO OZ
London Symphony Orchestra
Shire, David C

CD _____ BCD 3001
Bay Cities / Jan '93 / Silva Screen.

RETURN TO SNOWY RIVER
Rowland, Bruce C
CD _____ VCD 70451
Varese Sarabande/Colosseum / Jan '89 / Pinnacle / Silva Screen.

REVENGE
Nitzsche, Jack C
Love theme / Friendship / Miryea / Betrayal / Jeep ride / On the beach / Illicit love / Tibey's revenge / Whorehouse and healing / Dead Texan / Confrontation / Miryea's death
CD _____ FILMCD 065
Silva Screen / Aug '90 / Conifer / Silva Screen.

REVENGE IN EL PASO
Rustichelli, Carlo C
Cinevox / Jan '93 / Conifer / Silva Screen.
CD _____ CDCIA 5094

REVENGE OF THE PINK PANTHER
Mancini, Henry C
Pink Panther / Simone / Give me some mo'l / Thar she blows / Balls caprice / Move 'em out / Touch of red / After the shower / Hong Kong fireworks / Almond eyes
CD _____ 911132
Silva Screen / Jan '93 / Conifer / Silva Screen.

REVOLVER
Morricone, Ennio C
Alhambra / Feb '92 / Silva Screen.
CD _____ A 8919

RICHIE RICH
Silver Screen Orchestra
Silvestri, Alan C
CD _____ VSD 5582
Varese Sarabande/Colosseum / Mar '95 / Pinnacle / Silva Screen.

RIDER ON THE RAIN
Lai, Francis C
CD _____ A 8926
Alhambra / Mar '92 / Silva Screen.

RIGHT AS THE RAIN
Cast Recording
Previn, Andre C
Price, Leontyne L
Right as rain / Sunrise sunset / It's good to have you near again / It never entered my mind / Nobody's heart / My melancholy baby / Sleepin' bee / They didn't believe me / Hello, young lovers / Love walked in / Where, I wonder
CD _____ GD 82983
RCA / Apr '90 / BMG.

RINK, THE
1983 Broadway Cast
Kander, John C
Ebb, Fred L
Colored lights / Chief cook and bottle washer / Don't ah ma me / Blue crystal / Under the roller coaster / Not enough magic / Here's to the rink / We can make it / After all these years / Angel's rink... / What... / Marry me / Mrs. A / Rink / Wallflower / All the children / Coda
CD _____ CDTER 1091
TER / Sep '84 / Koch.

RINK, THE
1988 London Cast
Kander, John C
Ebb, Fred L
TER / Jan '90 / Koch.
CD _____ CDTERS 1155

RIO CONCHOS
(& The Artist Who Did Not Want To Paint/Prelude From Agony & The Ecstasy)
London Symphony Orchestra
Goldsmith, Jerry C
Goldsmith, Jerry Con
CD _____ RVF 6007D
Intrada / Feb '90 / Silva Screen / Koch.

RIO GRANDE
Sons Of The Pioneers
Young, Victor C
I'll take you home again Kathleen / Cattle call / Erie canal / Yellow stripes / My gal is purple / Down by the glenside / Footstore cavalry
CD _____ VSD 5378
Varese Sarabande/Colosseum / Aug '93 / Pinnacle / Silva Screen.

RIOT ON SUNSET STRIP
(& Standells Rarities)
Riot on Sunset Strip: Standells / Sunset Sally: Mugwumps / Sunset theme: Sidewalk Sounds / Old country: Travis, Debra / Don't need your lovin': Chocolate Watch Band / Children of the night: Mom's Boys / Make the music pretty: Sidewalk Sounds / Get away from here: Standells / Like my baby: Drew / Sitting there standing: Chocolate Watch Band / Love me: Standells / Batman: Standells / Our candidate: Standells / Boy who is lost: Standells / It's all in your mind: Standells / School girl: Standells / I hate to leave you: Standells / Looking at tomorrow: Standells / Don't say nothing at all: Standells / Try it (alternate vocal): Standells / Rari (extended): Standells
CD _____ CDWIKD 113
Big Beat / Jun '93 / Pinnacle.

RIPOUX CONTRE RIPOUX
Lai, Francis C
CD _____ MANTRA 051
Silva Screen / Jan '93 / Conifer / Silva Screen.

RISING SUN
Takemitsu, Toru C
CD _____ 07822110032
Arista / Feb '94 / BMG.

RISKY BUSINESS
Old time rock 'n' roll: Seger, Bob / Dream is always the same: Tangerine Dream / No future: Tangerine Dream / Mannish boy: Waters, Muddy / Pump: Beck, Jeff / D.M.S.R.: Prince / After the fall: Journey / In the air tonight: Collins, Phil / Love on a real train: Tangerine Dream / Guido the killer pimp: Tangerine Dream / Lana: Tangerine Dream
CD _____ CDV 2302
Virgin / May '87 / EMI.

RIVER OF DEATH
Matson, Sasha C
CD _____ FILMCD 053
Silva Screen / '90 / Conifer / Silva Screen.

RIVER RUNS THROUGH IT, A
Isham, Mark C
CD _____ 124692
Milan / Feb '93 / BMG / Silva Screen.

RIVER, THE
Williams, John C
CD _____ VSD 5298
Varese Sarabande/Colosseum / May '91 / Pinnacle / Silva Screen.

ROAD TO WELLVILLE
Portman, Rachel C
CD _____ VSD 5512
Varese Sarabande/Colosseum / Jan '95 / Pinnacle / Silva Screen.

ROADGAMES/PATRICK
May, Brian C
CD _____ IMICD 1014
Silva Screen / Jan '93 / Conifer / Silva Screen.

ROB ROY
CD _____ CDVMM 18
Virgin / May '95 / EMI.

ROBBERY UNDER ARMS
CD _____ IMICD 1013
Silva Screen / Jan '93 / Conifer / Silva Screen.

ROBE, THE
Newman, Alfred C
Newman, Alfred Con
Farewell to Diana / Palm Sunday / Carriage of the cross / Marcellus returns to Capri / Village of Cana / Redemption of Marcellus / Miriam / Catacombs / Rescue of Demetrius / Better kingdom
CD _____ 07822110112
Fox Film Scores / Apr '94 / BMG.

ROBERT AND ELIZABETH
1987 Chichester Festival Cast
Grainer, Ron C
Millar, Ronald L
Here on the corner of Wimpole Street / Family Moulton-Barrett / World outside / Moon in my pocket / I said love / You only to love me / Real thing / In a simple way / I know now / Escape me never / Soliloquy / Pass the eau de cologne / I'm the master here / Hate me please / Girls that boys dream about / Long ago I loved you / What the world calls love / Woman and man / Frustration
CD _____ UCHCD 6032
First Night / Oct '95 / Pinnacle.

ROBERT ET ROBERT
Lai, Francis C
CD _____ MANTRA 053
Silva Screen / Jan '93 / Conifer / Silva Screen.

ROBIN HOOD
Burgon, Geoffrey C
Burgon, Geoffrey Con
CD _____ FILMCD 063
Silva Screen / May '91 / Conifer / Silva Screen.

ROBIN HOOD - MEN IN TIGHTS
Mann, Hummie C
Brooks, Mel L
Mann, Hummie Con
CD _____ 176392
Milan / Feb '94 / BMG / Silva Screen.

ROBIN HOOD - PRINCE OF THIEVES
Kamen, Michael C
CD _____ 5110502
Polydor / Jul '91 / PolyGram.

ROBOCOP
Poledouris, Basil C
Poledouris, Basil Con
Main title / Van chase / Murphy's death / Rock shop / Home / Robo vs. ED-209 / Dream / Across the board / Betrayal / Clarence frags Bob / Drive to Jones' office / We killed you / Directive IV / Robo tips his hat / Showdown
CD _____ CDTER 1146
TER / Nov '87 / Koch.
CD _____ VSD 47298
Varese Sarabande/Colosseum / Apr '91 / Pinnacle / Silva Screen.

ROBOCOP
(A Future To This Life)
Walsh, Joe
CD _____ ESSCD 285
Essential / Feb '95 / Total/BMG.

ROBOCOP II
Rosenman, Leonard C
Rosenman, Leonard Con
Overture / City mayhem / Happier days / Robo cruiser / Robo memories / Robo and Nuke / Robo fanfare / Robo and Cain chase / Creating the monster / Robo I vs Robo II
CD _____ VSD 5271
Varese Sarabande/Colosseum / Aug '90 / Pinnacle / Silva Screen.

ROBOCOP III
Poledouris, Basil C
Poledouris, Basil/M. Boddicker Con
CD _____ VSD 5416
Varese Sarabande/Colosseum / Nov '93 / Pinnacle / Silva Screen.

ROBOTJOX
Talgorn, Frederic C
CD _____ PCD 125
Prometheus / Jan '93 / Silva Screen.

ROCKERS
We 'a' rockers: Inner Circle / Money worries: Maytones / Police and thieves: Murvin, Junior / Book of rules: Heptones / Stepping razor: Tosh, Peter / Tenement yard: Miller, Jacob / Fade away: Byles, Junior / Rockers: Wailer, Bunny / Slave master: Isaacs, Gregory / Dread lion: Perry, Lee 'Scratch' & The Upsetters / Graduation in Zion: Kiddus 1 / Jah no dead: Burning Spear / Satta a massagana: Third World / Natty takes over: Hinds, Justin & The Dominoes / Driving me backwards: Eno, Brian / Baby's on fire: Eno, Brian / Heartbreak hotel: Cale, J.J. / Standing in a buketful of blues: Ayers, Roy / Stranger in blue suede shoes: Ayers, Roy / Everybody's sometime and some people's all the time blues: Ayers, Roy / Two goes into four: Ayers, Roy
CD _____ RRCD 45
Reggae Refreshers / May '94 / PolyGram / Vital.

ROCKETEER, THE
Horner, James C
CD _____ 611172
Silva Screen / Jan '93 / Conifer / Silva Screen.

ROCKY HORROR PICTURE SHOW, THE
1990 London Cast
O'Brien, Richard C
Science fiction / Dammit Janet / Over at the Frankenstein place / Time warp / Sweet transvestite / Rocky's birth/Sword of Damocles / I can make you a man / Hot patootie - Bless my soul / I can make you a man (reprise) / Touch-a-touch-a-touch-a-touch me / Once in a while / Eddie's teddy / Planet Schmanet / Floor show - Rose tint my world / Fanfare - Don't dream it / Wild and untamed thing / I'm going home / Super heroes / Science fiction (reprise)
CD _____ CDMFP 5977
Music For Pleasure / Dec '92 / EMI.

ROCKY HORROR PICTURE SHOW, THE
Cast Recording
O'Brien, Richard C
CD _____ ESSCD 286
Essential / Apr '95 / Total/BMG.

ROCKY HORROR PICTURE SHOW, THE
Cast Recording
O'Brien, Richard C
CD _____ GRF 231
Tring / Aug '93 / Tring / Prism.

ROCKY HORROR SHOW, THE
Original Cast
O'Brien, Richard C
First Night / '94 / Pinnacle.
CD _____ SCENECD 17

ROCKY HORROR SHOW, THE
Cast Recording
O'Brien, Richard C
CD _____ CDTER 1221
TER / Jul '94 / Koch.

ROCKY I
Conti, Bill C
Gonna fly now (Rocky theme) / Philadelphia morning / Going the distance / Reflections / Marine's hymn/Yankee doodle / Take you back / First date / You take my heart away / Fanfare for Rocky / Butkus / Alone in the ring / Final bell / Rocky's reward
CD _____ 460812
Silva Screen / Jan '93 / Conifer / Silva Screen.

ROCKY II
Conti, Bill C
Redemption / Gonna fly now (Rocky theme) / Conquest / Vigil / All of my life / Overture / Two kinds of love
CD _____ 460822
Silva Screen / Jan '93 / Conifer / Silva Screen.

ROCKY III
Conti, Bill C
Eye of the tiger: Survivor / Take you back (Tough Gym) / Pushin' / Reflections / Mickey / Take you back / Decision / Gonna fly now (Rocky theme) / Adrian / Conquest
CD _____ 465612

Silva Screen / Jan '93 / Conifer / Silva Screen.

ROCKY IV
Burning heart: Survivor / Heart's on fire: Gafferty, John / Double or nothing: Loggins, Kenny & Gladys Knight / Eye of the tiger: Survivor / War fanfare from Rocky: Dicola, Vince / Livin' in America: Brown, James / No easy way out: Tepper, Robert / One way street: Go West / Sweetest victory: Touch / Training montage: Dicola, Vince
CD _____ 752402
Scotti Bros/Silva Screen / Apr '92 / Silva Screen.

ROMANCE ROMANCE
1988 Broadway Cast
Herrmann, Keith & Barry Harman C
Little comedy / Goodbye Emily / I'll always remember the song / Night it had to end / Think of the odds / Let's not talk about it / Through a window / Small craft warnings / So glad I married her / Letters / It's not too late / Oh what a performance / Women of Vienna / Summer share / Plans A and B / Words he doesn't say / Romantic notions / Romance romance
CD _____ CDTER 1161
TER / Feb '89 / Koch.

ROMEO AND JULIET
Rota, Nino C
Rota, Nino Con
Prologue and fanfare for the prince / Romeo / Juliet / Feast at the house of capulet / Their first meeting / What is a youth / What light through yonder window breaks / Parting is such sweet sorrow / But this I pray consent to marry us today / Romeo and Juliet are wed / Death of Mercutio and Tybalt / Night's candles are burnt out / Adieu / Likeness of death / Ride from Mantua / Death hath sucked the honey of thy breath / Love theme from "Romeo and Juliet" / O' happy dagger / Epilogue
CD _____ CNS 5000
Cloud Nine / Feb '90 / Conifer / Silva Screen.

ROSE AND THE GUN, THE
Johnson, Laurie C
CD _____ FLYCD 103
Fly / Aug '95 / Bucks Music.

ROSE, THE
Midler, Bette
Midnight in Memphis / Concert monologue / When a man loves a woman / Sold my soul to rock'n'roll / Keep on rockin' / Love me with a feeling / Camellia / Homecoming monologue / Stay with me / Let me call you sweetheart / Rose / Whose side are you on
CD _____ 7567827782
East West / Nov '95 / Warner Music.

ROSEMARY'S BABY
Komeda, Christopher C
CD _____ TSU 0116
Tsunami / Jan '95 / Silva Screen.

ROSENEMIL
Kalman, Charles/Stefan Zorzor C
CD _____ CIN 22072
Silva Screen / Jan '95 / Conifer / Silva Screen.

ROTHSCHILDS, THE
Cast Recording
Bock, Jerry C
Harnick, Sheldon L
CD _____ SK 30337
Sony Broadway / Nov '92 / Sony.

ROXANNE
Smeaton, Bruce C
Roxanne / Starry sky / Just honest - we did it / Roxanne's theme / Game, set and match / Panache / Roxanne's eyes / Blue Danube / Written in the wind / Roxanne (End title)
CD _____ CDC 1000
Silva Screen / Jul '88 / Conifer / Silva Screen.

RUBY
Scott, John C
CD _____ MAF 7026D
Intrada / Jan '93 / Silva Screen / Koch.

RUDDIGORE
Light Opera Company
Sullivan, Sir Arthur C
Gilbert, W.S. L
CD _____ CDHD 255
Happy Days / May '95 / Conifer.

RUDDIGORE
New Sadler's Wells Opera Chorus/ Orchestra
Sullivan, Sir Arthur C
Gilbert, W.S. L
Phipps, S. Con
2CD _____ CDTER2 1128
TER / Aug '87 / Koch.

RUDDIGORE
Baker, George & Richard Lewis/Glyndebourne Festival Choir/Pro Arte Orchestra
Sullivan, Sir Arthur C
Gilbert, W.S. L
Godfrey, I. Con
CD _____ CMS 7644122
EMI Classics / Apr '94 / EMI.

RUDDIGORE/COX AND BOX
D'Oyly Carte Opera Chorus/Orchestra Of The Royal Opera House

Sullivan, Sir Arthur C
Gilbert, W.S. L
Godfrey, I. Con
2CD _____ 4173552
London / Jan '90 / PolyGram.

RUNAWAY
Goldsmith, Jerry C
CD _____ VCD 47221
Varese Sarabande/Colosseum / Jan '89 / Pinnacle / Silva Screen.

RUNAWAY TRAIN
Jones, Trevor C
Jailbreak / Moving on / Destination unknown / Clear the track / Reflections / Runaway train / Prison memories / Yellow rose of Texas / Collision course / Past, present and future / Red for danger / Gloria / End of the line
CD _____ CDCH 267
Milan / '86 / BMG / Silva Screen.

RUNNING MAN, THE
Faltermeyer, Harold
Faltermeyer, Harold C
CD _____ VCD 47356
Varese Sarabande/Colosseum / Jan '89 / Pinnacle / Silva Screen.

RUSH
Clapton, Eric
Clapton, Eric C
New recruit / Tracks and lines / Realization / Kristen and Jim / Preludin fugue / Cold turkey / Will gaines / Help me up / Don't know which way to go / Tears in heaven
CD _____ 7599267942
WEA / Oct '94 / Warner Music.

RUTH RENDELL MYSTERIES
Bennett, Brian
Bennett, Brian C
Sleeping life / No crying he makes / Guilty thing surprised / Shake hands for ever / Ruth Rendell
CD _____ PWKS 546
Carlton Home Entertainment / Oct '89 / Carlton Home Entertainment.

RUTH RENDELL MYSTERIES, THE
Bennett, Brian
Bennett, Brian C
Ruth Rendell Mysteries / Wexford in L.A. / Put on by cunning / Search for Mina / Love from Doon / Castle / Kissing the gunner's daughter / New lease of death / Let me believe / Letters from the past / Cry from the tomb / Strange confessions / Corsica / Day in Provence / Achilles heel / Mouse in the corner / Mother and daughter / Means of evil / Premonition / Speaker of Mandarin
CD _____ CDSTM 2
Soundtrack Music / May '94 / EMI.

RUTHLESS - THE MUSICAL
Los Angeles Cast
CD _____ VSD 5476
Varese Sarabande/Colosseum / Oct '94 / Pinnacle / Silva Screen.

RYAN'S DAUGHTER
(& Selections From The Train & Grand Prix)
Jarre, Maurice C
Cinevox / Jan '93 / Conifer / Silva Screen.
CD _____ AK 47989

S.F.W.
Jesus Christ Pose: Soundgarden / Get your gunn: Manson, Marilyn / Can I stay: Pretty Mary Sunshine / Teenage whore: Hole / Negasonic teenage warhead: Monster Magnet / Like suicide: Cornell, Chris / No fuckin' problem: Suicidal Tendencies / Surrender: Paw / Creep: Radiohead / Two at a time: Cop Shoot Cop / Say what you want: Babes In Toyland / S.F.W.: GWAR / Spab'n'Janet evening/Green Room: Revell, Graeme
CD _____ 540246-2
A&M / Sep '94 / PolyGram.

SABRINA
CD _____ 5404562
A&M / Dec '95 / PolyGram.

SAFE
Tomney, Ed C
CD _____ IONIC 14CD
Fine Line / Aug '95 / Disc.

SAHARA
Morricone, Ennio C
Morricone, Ennio Con
CD _____ MAF 7047D
Intrada / Mar '93 / Silva Screen / Koch.

SAIL AWAY
Broadway Cast
Coward, Sir Noel C
CD _____ ZDM 7647592
EMI Classics / Apr '94 / EMI.

SALAAM BOMBAY
Subramaniam, L.
Subramaniam, L. C
Subramaniam, L. Con

CD _____ DRGCD 12595
DRG / Jan '95 / New Note.

SALAD DAYS
1982 London Cast
Slade, Julian C
Slade, Julian & Dorothy Reynolds L
Things that are done by a Don / We said we wouldn't look back / Find yourself something to do / I sit in the sun / Oh, look at me / Hush-hush / Out of breath / Cleopatra / Sand in my eyes / It's easy to sing / We're looking for a piano / I've had the time of my life / Saucer song / We don't understand our children
CD _____ CDTER 1018
TER / Apr '94 / Koch.

SALAD DAYS
(Highlights)
London Cast
Slade, Julian C
Slade, Julian & Dorothy Reynolds L
Things that are done by a Don / We said we wouldn't look back / Find yourself something to do / I sit in the sun / Oh, look at me / Hush-hush / Cleopatra / Sand in my eyes / It's easy to sing / We're looking for a piano / I've had the time of my life / We don't understand our children
CD _____ SHOWCD 009
Showtime / Feb '95 / Disc / THE.

SALAD DAYS
London Cast
Slade, Julian C
Slade, Julian & Dorothy Reynolds L
CD _____ SMK 66176
Sony West End / Jul '94 / Sony.

SAMANTHA
McNeely, Joel C
CD _____ MAF 7040D
Intrada / Feb '93 / Silva Screen / Koch.

SAND PEBBLES, THE
Goldsmith, Jerry C
CD _____ TSU 0107
Tsunami / Jan '93 / Silva Screen.

SANTA CLAUSE, THE
Convertino, Michael C
CD _____ 323642
RCA Victor / Nov '95 / BMG.

SANTA SANGRE
Boswell, Simon C
Fin del mundo / Alma / Alejandra: Circus Orgo / Triste / Besame mucho: Silver Hombre / Acid revenge / Herbage / Truck / Dejame llorar: Concha Y Fenix / Holy guitar / Grave business / Heart / Kid's theme / Wingbeat / Church tattoo / Sweet dreams / Karnival
CD _____ PCOM 1104
President / Apr '90 / Grapevine / Target/ BMG / Jazz Music / President.

SARAFINA
Broadway Cast
Ngema, Mbongeni C
Zibuyilile emasisweni / Sarafina / Lord's prayer / Yes, mistress it's a pity / Give us power / Afunani amaphoyisa e Soweto (What is the army doing in Soweto) / Nkois sikeleli Afrika / Freedom is coming tomorrow / Entr'acte (Excuse me baby, please if you don't mind baby, thank you) / Meeting tonight / Stand and fight / Uyamemeza umgoma / Sewe lami / Wawungalahla / Mama Sechaba / Isizwe (the nation is dying) / Goodbye / Kilimanjaro / Africa is coming in the sun / Olyaithi (It's all right) / Bring back Nelson Mandela / Freedom is coming (reprise)
2CD _____ RD 89307
RCA Victor / Jul '89 / BMG.

SARAFINA
(The Sound Of Freedom)
Myers, Stanley C
Sarafina / Lord's prayer / Nkonyane kandaba / Freedom is coming tomorrow / Sabela / Sechaba / Safa saphel' isizwe / Thank you mama / Vuma dlozi lami / Lizobuya / One more time
CD _____ 9362450602
Warner Bros. / Jan '91 / Warner Music.

SATURDAY NIGHT FEVER
Stayin' alive: Bee Gees / How deep is your love: Bee Gees / Night fever: Bee Gees / More than a woman: Bee Gees / Jive talkin': Bee Gees / You should be dancing: Bee Gees / Calypso breakdown: Donaldson, Ralph / If I can't have you: Elliman, Yvonne / Fifth of Beethoven: Murphy, Walter / Open sesame: Kool & The Gang / Boogie shoes: K.C. & The Sunshine Band / M.F.S.B.: K.C. & The Sunshine Band / K. Jee: K.C. & The Sunshine Band / Disco inferno: Tramps / Manhattan skyline: Tramps / Night on disco mountain: Tramps / Salsation: Tramps
2CD _____ 8253892
Polydor / Oct '95 / PolyGram.

SAVAGE NIGHTS
Collard, Cyril C
CD _____ 5158622
Silva Screen / Jan '93 / Conifer / Silva Screen.

SAY AMEN, SOMEBODY
Dorsey, Thomas A. C
Highway to heaven / Singing in my soul / What manner of man is this / When I've done my best / Take my hand, precious Lord / I'm his child / He chose me / No ways

tired / Jesus dropped the charges / I'll never turn back / Storm is passing over / It's gonna rain / He brought us / Canaan
CD _____ DRGCD 12584
DRG / Jan '95 / New Note.

SAYONARA
Berlin Radio Symphony Orchestra
Waxman, Franz C
Bernstein, Elmer Con
CD _____ 09026626572
RCA Victor / Nov '95 / BMG.

SCARLET LETTER
Barry, John C
Theme / Arrival / Search for home / Hester rides to town / Bird / Swimmer / Very exhilarating read / I'm not the man I seem / Agnus dei / I can see what others cannot / Love scene / Are you with child / Small act of contrition / Birth / I baptise this child / Pearl / She will not speak / Dr. Roger Prynne / Hester walks through town / Poor fatherless child / Attempt at rape / Savages have killed him / Round up / I am the father of her child / Indians attack / Letter has served a purpose / End title
CD _____ 4835772
Epic / Jan '96 / Sony.

SCARLETT
(Sung In Japanese)
Japanese Cast
Rome, Harold C
He loves me / We belong to you / Two of a kind / Blissful Christmas / My soldier / Goodbye my honey / Lonely stranger / Time for love / What is love / Gambling man / Which way is home / Bonnie blue flag / O'Hara / Newlywed's song / Strange and wonderful / Blueberry eyes / Little wonder / Bonnie gone
2CD _____ DRGCD 13105
DRG / Jan '95 / New Note.

SCENT OF GREEN PAPAYA
Tiet, Ton That C
CD _____ 887794
Milan / May '94 / BMG / Silva Screen.

SCHINDLER'S LIST
Boston Symphony Orchestra with Itzhak Perlman
Williams, John C
Williams, John (1) Con
Theme / Jewish town / Immolation / Remembrances / Schindler's workforce / Oyf'n pripetshok / And nacht aktion / I could have done more / Auschwitz-Birkenau / Stolen memories / Making the list / Give me your names / Yeroushalaim chel zahav / Theme (reprise)
CD _____ MCD 10969
MCA / Feb '94 / BMG.

SCHOOL TIES
Jarre, Maurice C
CD _____ 244762
Silva Screen / Jan '93 / Conifer / Silva Screen.

SCOOP
Donaggio, Pino C
CD _____ 4711842
Silva Screen / Jan '93 / Conifer / Silva Screen.

SCRAMBLED FEET
Broadway Cast
Driver, John & Jeffrey Haddow C
CD _____ DRGCD 6105
DRG / Jan '95 / New Note.

SCROOGE
1992 Cast
Bricusse, Leslie C
CD _____ CDTER 1194
TER / Jan '93 / Koch.

SCROOGED
Put a little love in your heart: Green, Al & Annie Lennox / Wonderful life: Lennon, Julian / Sweetest thing: New Voices Of Freedom / Love you take: Hartman, Dan & Denise Lopez / Get up 'n' dance: Kool Moe Dee / We three kings of Orient are: Davis, Miles & Larry Carlton / Christmas must be tonight: Robertson, Robbie / Brown eyed girl: Poindexter, Buster / Christmas song: Cole, Natalie
CD _____ 5513202
Spectrum/Karussell / Sep '95 / PolyGram / THE.

SEA HAWK, THE
Utah Symphony Orchestra
Korngold, Erich C
CD _____ VCD 47304
Varese Sarabande/Colosseum / Jan '89 / Pinnacle / Silva Screen.

SEA HAWK, THE
Korngold, Erich C
CD _____ CDTER 1164
TER / Jan '91 / Koch.

SEA OF LOVE
Jones, Trevor C
Sea of love: Phillips, Phil & Twilights / Poetic Killing / Cocktails and fingerprints / Fear and passion / Helen's 45 / Is she or isn't she / Sea of love Reprise
CD _____ 5501302
Spectrum/Karussell / Oct '93 / PolyGram / THE.

SEA POWER
Whalen, Michael
Whalen, Michael C
CD _____ ND 66005
Narada / Nov '93 / New Note / ADA.

SEAFORTH
Petit, Jean Claude C
Seaforth / Light / Bri / In a public house / First kiss / Love / I can do anything / Tension / Obsession / Bob's family / Petite fugue / Waiting / Diana / Don't call here / Diana drama / Paula and Bob / Suspense / Melancholly / In private / Paula / End
CD _____ DSHCD 7016
D-Sharp / Oct '94 / Pinnacle.

SEAQUEST DSV
Debney, John C
Debney, John Con
CD _____ VSD 5565
Varese Sarabande/Colosseum / Jul '95 / Pinnacle / Silva Screen.

SEARCHING FOR BOBBY FISHER
Horner, James C
CD _____ 9245322
Silva Screen / Jan '93 / Conifer / Silva Screen.

SEASON IN HELL, A
Jarre, Maurice C
CD _____ A 8923
Alhambra / Feb '92 / Silva Screen.

SECOND BEST
Boswell, Simon C
CD _____ 246312
Milan / Aug '95 / BMG / Silva Screen.

SECOND TIME LUCKY
Stone, Laurie & Garry MacDonald C
CD _____ IMCD 1016
Silva Screen / Jan '93 / Conifer / Silva Screen.

SECRET GARDEN, THE
Cracow Boys Choir/Sinfonia Varsovia
Preisner, Zbigniew C
Michniewski, W. Con
CD _____ VSD 5443
Varese Sarabande/Colosseum / Sep '93 / Pinnacle / Silva Screen.

SECRET GARDEN, THE
Cast Recording
CD _____ VSD 5451
Varese Sarabande/Colosseum / Oct '94 / Pinnacle / Silva Screen.

SECRET OF NIMH, THE
Goldsmith, Jerry C
Goldsmith, Jerry Con
CD _____ VSD 5541
Varese Sarabande/Colosseum / Mar '95 / Pinnacle / Silva Screen.

SECRET OF ROAN INISH, THE
CD _____ DARING 3015CD
Daring / Sep '95 / Direct / CM / ADA.

SECRET POLICEMAN'S CONCERT, THE
Cast Recording
CD _____ CCSCD 351
Castle / Nov '92 / BMG.

SEESAW
1973 Broadway Cast
Coleman, Cy C
Fields, Dorothy L
Seesaw / My city / Nobody does it like me / In tune / Spanglish / Welcome to Holiday Inn / You're a loveable lunatic / He's good for me / Ride out the storm / Certainly / We've got it / Poor everybody else / Chapter 54, Number 1909 / Seesaw ballet / It's not where you start / I'm way ahead and seesaw (finale) / It's not where you start (bows)
CD _____ DRGCD 6108
DRG / Jun '92 / New Note.

SELFISH GIANT, THE
1993 Cast
Jenkins, Michael C
Williams, Nigel L
CD _____ CDTER 1206
TER / Nov '93 / Koch.

SENZA PELLE
(No Skin)
Ovadia, Moni/Alfredo Lacosegliaz C
CD _____ GDM 2005
Silva Screen / Jan '95 / Conifer / Silva Screen.

SEPOLTA VIVA/THE ANTICHRIST
Morricone, Ennio C
CD _____ CDCR 17
Silva Screen / Jul '94 / Conifer / Silva Screen.

SERPENT AND THE RAINBOW, THE
Fiedel, Brad C
CD _____ VCD 47362
Varese Sarabande/Colosseum / Jan '89 / Pinnacle / Silva Screen.

SERPICO
Theodorakis, Mikis C
CD _____ SR 50061
Sakkaris / Oct '93 / Pinnacle.

SEVEN
CD _____ 0022432CIN
Edel / Jan '96 / Pinnacle.

SEVEN BRIDES FOR SEVEN BROTHERS
1986 London Cast
De Paul, Gene C
Mercer, Johnny L
Yates, M. Con
Overture / Bless your beautiful hide / Wonderful wonderful day / One man / Goin' courtin' / I love never goes away / Sobbin' women / Townsfolk's lament / Woman ought to know her place / We gotta make it through the winter / We gotta make it through the winter (Reprise) / Spring spring spring / Woman ought to know her place (Reprise) / Glad that you were born / Wedding dance / Goin' courtin/Wonderful wonderful day (finale)
CD _____ OCRCD 6008
First Night / Oct '95 / Pinnacle.

SEVEN BRIDES FOR SEVEN BROTHERS
De Paul, Gene C
Mercer, Johnny L
Bless your beautiful hide / Spring, spring, spring / Wonderful, wonderful day / When you're in love / Goin' cotin / Hoedown / Lonesome polecat / Sobbin' women / June bride
CD _____ PWKS 4209
Carlton Home Entertainment / Jul '94 / Carlton Home Entertainment.

SEVEN DEADLY SINS
Reaux, Angelina & New York Philharmonic Orchestra
Weill, Kurt C
Brecht, Bertolt L
Masur, Kurt Con
CD _____ 4509950292
Teldec Classics / Jan '95 / Warner Music.

SEVEN DEADLY SINS
Van Otter, A./North German Symphony Orchestra
Weill, Kurt C
Brecht, Bertolt L
Gardiner, John Eliot Con
CD _____ 4398942
Deutsche Grammophon / Dec '94 / PolyGram.

SEVEN DEADLY SINS
Lemper, Ute/Cast & Berlin RIAS Sinfonietta
Weill, Kurt C
Brecht, Bertolt L
Mauceri, John Con
CD _____ 4301682
Decca / Apr '91 / PolyGram.

SEVENTH SIGN
Nitzsche, Jack C
Opening, fish, desert, wrath, 1st seal / Nightmare / David's apartment / Abby follows David to the synagogue / World in trouble / Parchment 2.29 / Stabbing / Attempted suicide / Lazzri revealed / Last martyr / Walk to the gas chamber / Birth / Abby's death / End credits
CD _____ EDL 25062
Edel / Jan '89 / Pinnacle.

SEVENTH VOYAGE OF SINBAD, THE
Herrmann, Bernard C
CD _____ VCD 47256
Varese Sarabande/Colosseum / Jan '89 / Pinnacle / Silva Screen.

SHADOW OF THE WOLF
Jarre, Maurice C
CD _____ 121462
Milan / Jan '95 / BMG / Silva Screen.

SHADOW, THE
(Score/Songs)
Goldsmith, Jerry C
Goldsmith, Jerry Con
CD _____ 07822187632
Arista / Sep '94 / BMG.

SHADOWLANDS
London Symphony Orchestra
Fenton, George C
CD _____ CDQ 5550932
Angel / Mar '94 / EMI.

SHAFT
Hayes, Isaac C
Hayes, Isaac C
Shaft / Bumpy's lament / Walk from Regio's / Ellie's love theme / Shaft's cab ride / Cafe Regio's / Early Sunday morning / Be yourself / Friend's place / Soulsville / No name bar / Bumpy's blues / Shaft strikes again / Do your thing / End theme
CD _____ CDSXD 021
Stax / Oct '89 / Pinnacle.

SHAKA ZULU
Pollecutt, Dave C
CD _____ CDC 1002
Silva Screen / Mar '92 / Conifer / Silva Screen.

SHALLOW GRAVE
Boswell, Simon C
Shallow grave: Leftfield / Shallow grave theme / My baby just cares for me: Simone, Nina / Laugh not riot / Release the dubs: Leftfield / Strips the willo: Carmichael, John & His Band / Loft conversion / Spade we need a spade / Shallow grave, deep depression / Hugo's last trip / Happy heart: Williams, Andy
CD _____ CDEMC 3699
EMI / Feb '95 / EMI.

SHANGHAI TRIAD
Guangtian, Zhang C
Beddy-bye, beddy-bye over Grandma's bridge / Main theme / Go away / Bright moon / Bijou cries / Lilac menuet / Murder on a rainy night / Express train / Garden / Tree under the bright moon / Shui Sheng climbs the stairs / False pretenses / Umbrella / Game (Mah Jong) / Russian hills / Shusheng and bijou / Escape from Shanghai / Eyes of Shui Sheng / Bright moon (instrumental) / Conversation at night / Main theme (reprise) / Beddy-bye, beddy-bye over Grandma's bridge (reprise)
CD _____ CDVIR 44
Virgin / Nov '95 / EMI.

SHATTERED
Silvestri, Alan C
CD _____ 262208
Milan / Jan '95 / BMG / Silva Screen.

SHAWSHANK REDEMPTION, THE
Newman, Thomas C
May / Shawshank prison (stoic theme) / New fish / Rock hammer / Inch by inch / If I didn't care: Ink Spots / Brooks was here / His judgement cometh / Suds on the roof / Workfield / Shawshank redemption / Love-sick blues: Williams, Hank / Elmo blatch / Sisters Zihuatanejo / Marriage of Figaro: Deutsch Opera Berlin/Karl Bohm / Lovely Raquel / And that night soon / Compass and guns / So was red / End titles
CD _____ 4783322
Epic / Feb '95 / Sony.

SHE DEVIL
I will survive: Sa-Fire / You can have him: Carmel / C'mon and get my love: D-Mob / Always: Kimmel, Tom / You're the devil in disguise: Presley, Elvis / Party up: Checker, Chubby / Tren d'amour: Stewart, Jermaine / That's what I call love: Ceberano, Kate / Tied up: Yello / It's getting hot: Fat Boys
CD _____ 5511342
Spectrum/Karussell / Aug '95 / PolyGram / THE.

SHE LOVES ME
1963 Broadway Cast
Bock, Jerry C
Harnick, Sheldon L
Loud, D. Con
CD _____ VSD 5464
Varese Sarabande/Colosseum / Jun '94 / Pinnacle / Silva Screen.

SHE LOVES ME
1994 London Cast
Bock, Jerry C
Harnick, Sheldon L
Scott, R. Con
CD _____ CASTCD 44
First Night / Sep '94 / Pinnacle.

SHE LOVES ME
1964 London Cast
Bock, Jerry C
Harnick, Sheldon L
Ainsworth, A. Con
Overture/Good morning, good day / Sounds while selling / No more chocolates / Letters / Tonight at eight / Perspective / Ilona / Heads I win / Romantic atmosphere / Dear friend / Try me / Ice cream / She loves me / Trip to the library / Grand knowing you / Twelve days of Christmas / Ice cream (reprise)
CD _____ CDANGEL 6
Angel / Apr '94 / EMI.

SHELTERING SKY, THE
Sakamoto, Ryuichi C
Sacred koran / Sheltering sky / Belly / Port's composition / On the bed (dream) / Lunch ness / On the hill / Kyoto / Cemetry / Dying / Market / Grand Hotel / Louange au prophet houria aaichi flute / Je chante / Midnight sun / Fever ride / Chantavec ristre / Marnia's tent / Goula lima / Happy bus ride / Night train / Guedra
CD _____ CDV 2652
Virgin / Nov '90 / EMI.

SHERLOCK HOLMES
(The Sign of Four/The Adventures of.../ The Return of...)
Gowers, Patrick C
Gowers, Patrick Con
CD _____ CDTER 1136
TER / Mar '90 / Koch.

SHERLOCK HOLMES
London Cast
Bricusse, Leslie C
Sherlock Holmes / Without him, there can be no me / London is London / Vendetta / Anything you want to know / Her face / Men like you / Lousy life / I shall find her / No reason / Halcyon days / Without him, there can be no me (reprise) / Down the apples 'n' pairs / He's back / Million years ago or was it yesterday / Best of you, the best of me / Sherlock Holmes (reprise)
CD _____ BD 74145
RCA / Jan '89 / BMG.

SHERLOCK HOLMES
1993 Cast
Bricusse, Leslie C
CD _____ CDTER 1198
TER / Jan '94 / Koch.

SHINING THROUGH
Kamen, Michael C
CD _____ 262742
Milan / Jan '95 / BMG / Silva Screen.

SHIPHUNTERS
Morricone, Ennio C
CD _____ OST 109
Milano Dischi / Jan '93 / Silva Screen.

SHIRLEY VALENTINE
Russell, Willy & George Hatzinassios
Russell, Willy & George Hatzinassios C
Girl who used to be me: Austin, Patti / Shirley Valentine (theme) / Affection / Crumbling resolve / Dreams / Costas / Coming to Greece / Nocturne / Arrival in Mykonos
CD _____ FILMCD 062
Silva Screen / Nov '89 / Conifer / Silva Screen.

SHOES OF THE FISHERMAN, THE
North, Alex C
CD _____ GAD 94009
Silva Screen / Jan '95 / Conifer / Silva Screen.

SHOGUN MAYEDA
Utah Symphony Orchestra
Scott, John C
CD _____ MAF 7017D
Intrada / Mar '92 / Silva Screen / Koch.

SHOOTING PARTY, THE
Royal Philharmonic Orchestra
Scott, John C
CD _____ JSCD 113
Silva Screen / Jan '93 / Conifer / Silva Screen.

SHOW BOAT
(Highlights - The Shows Collection)
Cast Recording
Kern, Jerome C
Hammerstein II, Oscar L
Ol' man river / Where's the mate for me / Make believe / Can't help lovin' dat man / I might fall back on you / Life upon the wicked stage / You are love / Why do I love you / Bill / Goodbye my lady love / After the ball / Ol' man river (reprise)
CD _____ PWKS 4161
Carlton Home Entertainment / Sep '93 / Carlton Home Entertainment.

SHOW BOAT
(1946 Broadway Revival Version)
1993 Studio Cast
Kern, Jerome C
Hammerstein II, Oscar L
Edwards, John Owen Con
CD _____ CDTER 1199
TER / Nov '93 / Koch.

SHOW BOAT
1987 Studio Cast & Ambrosian Chorus/London Sinfonietta
Kern, Jerome C
Hammerstein II, Oscar L
McGlinn, John Con
3CD _____ CDRIVER 1
EMI Classics / Sep '88 / EMI.

SHOW BOAT
1962 Studio Cast
Kern, Jerome C
Hammerstein II, Oscar L
CD _____ CK 02220
CBS/Silva Screen / Jan '89 / Conifer / Silva Screen.

SHOW BOAT
Cast Recording
Kern, Jerome C
Hammerstein II, Oscar L
Overture / Where's the mate for me / Make believe / Ol' man river / Can't help lovin' dat man / Life on the wicked stage / Queenie's ballyhoo / You are love / Why do I love you / Bill / Goodbye my lady love / After the ball
CD _____ SHOWCD 011
Showtime / Feb '95 / Disc / THE.

SHOW BOAT
(Highlights)
1987 Studio Cast & Ambrosian Chorus/London Sinfonietta
Kern, Jerome C
Hammerstein II, Oscar L
McGlinn, John Con
Overture / Cotton blossom / Where's the mate for me / Make believe / Ol' man river / Can't help lovin' dat man / Life on the wicked stage / Till good luck comes my way / I might fall back on you / Queenie's ballyhoo / You are love / Showboat / At the fair / Why do I love you / Bill / Goodbye my Lady love / After the ball / Hey feller / Finale ultimo
CD _____ CDC 7498472
EMI Classics / Oct '89 / EMI.

SHOW BOAT
Previn, Andre & Mundell Lowe/Ray Brown/Grady Tate
Kern, Jerome C
Hammerstein II, Oscar L
Make believe / Can't help lovin' dat man / Ol' man river / Bill / Life on the wicked stage / Why do I love you / I might fall back on you / Nobody else but me
CD _____ 4476392
Deutsche Grammophon / Jan '95 / PolyGram.

SHOW BOAT/BAND WAGON
Cast Recording
Ol' man river (Showboat): Warfield, William / Make believe: Keel, Howard & Kathryn Grayson / I might fall back on you: Champion, Gower & Marge / Can't help lovin' dat man: Gardner, Ava / Why do I love you:

Keel, Howard & Kathryn Grayson / Bill: Gardner, Ava / Life upon the wicked stage: Champion, Gower & Marge / You are love: Keel, Howard & Kathryn Grayson / Ol' man river (reprise): Warfield, William / Shine on your shoes (Band Wagon): Astaire, Fred / By myself: Astaire, Fred / Dancing in the dark / Triplets: Astaire, Fred/Nanette Fabray/Jack Buchanan / New sun in the sky / I guess I'll have to change my plan: Adams, India / Louisiana hayride: Fabray, Nanette / I love Louisa: Astaire, Fred / That's entertainment: Astaire, Fred/Nanette Fabray/Jack Buchanan
CD _____ CDMGM 10
MGM/EMI / Jan '90 / EMI.

SHOW OF FORCE, A
Delerue, Georges C
Delerue, Georges Con
CD _____ XCD 1005
Varese Sarabande/Colosseum / Apr '91 / Pinnacle / Silva Screen.

SHOW, THE
CD _____ 5290212
Def Jam / Aug '95 / PolyGram.

SHOWGIRLS
CD _____ 6544926612
Warner Bros. / Jan '96 / Warner Music.

SHVITZ, THE
CD _____ KFWCD 144
Knitting Factory / Feb '95 / Grapevine.

SHY PEOPLE
Tangerine Dream
Tangerine Dream C
Shy people / Joe's place / Harbour / Nightfall / Dancing on a white moon / Civilized illusions / Swamp voices / Transparent days / Shy people (reprise)
CD _____ FILMCD 027
Silva Screen / Jun '90 / Conifer / Silva Screen.

SICILIAN, THE
Hungarian State Symphony Orchestra
Mansfield, David C
Sicilian / Camilla returns from riding / Stealing grain / Camilla's horses / On the stairs / Monastery ride / I'm not leaving... yet / Off to Palermo / Giuliano recovered / Monastery / Fire from heaven / Terranova / They join him / Little Guiliano / Don Massino in Rome / Jewel robbery / With this ring / Silvio's blessing / To Frisella's / Confession / That's life, gentlemen / Meeting ends / Ginestra massacre / Giuliano's funeral / End titles
CD _____ 906822
Silva Screen / Jan '89 / Conifer / Silva Screen.

SIDE BY SIDE BY SONDHEIM
1976 London Cast
Sondheim, Stephen C
Comedy tonight / Love is in the air / Little things you do together / You must meet my wife / Getting married today / I remember / Can that boy foxtrot / Too many mornings / Company / Another hundred people / Barcelona / Being alive / I never do anything twice (Madam's song) / Bring on the girls / Ah Paree / Buddy's blues / Broadway baby / You could drive a person crazy / Everybody says don't / There won't be trumpets / Anyone can whistle / Send in the clowns / Pretty lady / We're gonna be alright / Boy like that / Boy from... / If momma was married / Losing my mind / Could I leave you / I'm still here / Side by side by side
2CD _____ GD 81851
RCA Victor / Apr '90 / BMG.

SILK STOCKINGS
1955 Broadway Cast
Porter, Cole C
CD _____ 11022
Silva Screen / Jan '92 / Conifer / Silva Screen.

SILKWOOD
Delerue, Georges C
Drew's theme / Ride to Texas / Ride from Texas / Largo / Karen is contaminated / Legato / Karen and Drew on the porch / Down the highway / Love theme / Down the highway (reprise) / Drew leaves Karen / Karen looks through files / Pretty little horses lullaby / Karen has a car accident / After stripping Karen's house of her possessions / Drew walks through the empty house / Largo desolato / Amazing grace / Epilogue and end titles
CD _____ DRGCD 6107
DRG / Jun '95 / New Note.

SILVERADO
Broughton, Bruce C
CD _____ MAF 7035D
Intrada / Feb '93 / Silva Screen / Koch.

SIMPLE MAN, A
English Chamber Orchestra
Davis, Carl C
White on white / Characters appear / Organ grinder / Sitting / Death of mother / Going to work / Coming from the hill / Waiting / Golden room / Three Anns / Seascape / Man with red eyes / Clogs / Homage
CD _____ OCRCD 6039
First Night / Jan '96 / Pinnacle.

SIMPLE TWIST OF FATE, A
Eidelman, Cliff C
CD _____ VSD 5538

Varese Sarabande/Colosseum / Jul '95 / Pinnacle / Silva Screen.

SING FOR SONG DRIVES AWAY THE WOLVES
Popul Vuh
Popul Vuh C
CD _____ 139142
Milan / May '93 / BMG / Silva Screen.

SINGIN' IN THE RAIN
1983 London Cast
Freed, Arthur C
Brown, Nacio Herb L
Reed, Michael Con
Overture / Fit as a fiddle / Temptation / I can't give you anything but love / Be a clown / Too marvellous for words / You are my lucky star / Moses / Good morning / Singin' in the rain / Would you / Fascinating rhythm / Finale
CD _____ OCRCD 6013
First Night / Oct '93 / Pinnacle.

SINGIN' IN THE RAIN/EASTER PARADE
Singin' in the rain (Singin' In The Rain): Kelly, Gene / Fit as a fiddle: Kelly, Gene & Donald O'Connor / All I do is dream of you: Reynolds, Debbie & Girly Chorus / Make 'em laugh: O'Connor, Donald / You were meant for me: Kelly, Gene / Good morning: Reynolds, Debbie & Gene Kelly/Donald O'Connor / Moses: Kelly, Gene & Debbie O'Connor / Broadway ballet: Kelly, Gene / You are my lucky star: Kelly, Gene & Debbie Reynolds / Steppin' out with my baby (Easter Parade): Astaire, Fred / Fella with an umbrella: Garland, Judy & Peter Lawford / Shaking the blues away: Miller, Ann / I love a piano / Snooky Ookums / When the midnight choo choo leaves for Alabam' / Couple of swells: Garland, Judy & Fred Astaire / It only happens when I dance with you: Astaire, Fred / Better luck next time: Garland, Judy / Easter parade: Garland, Judy & Fred Astaire
CD _____ CDMGM 4
MGM/EMI / Jan '90 / EMI.

SINGING DETECTIVE, THE/OTHER SIDE OF THE SINGING DETECTIVE
Umbrella man: Kaye, Sammy Orchestra / Copenhagen: Ambrose & His Orchestra / I'll just close my eyes: Shelton, Anne / Old Moses put Pharoah in his place: Waring, Fred & His Pennsylvanians / Stop crying: Oliver, King Orchestra / Three caballeros: Crosby, Bing & Andrews Sisters / That's for me: Haynes, Dick / I'll be around: Mills Brothers / Sing nightingale sing: Anderson, Lale / There's something wrong with the weather: Stone, Lew & His Band / Java jive: Ink Spots / There's a fellow waiting in Poughkeepsie: Crosby, Bing & Andrews Sisters / Till then: Mills Brothers / Chinatown, my Chinatown: Jolson, Al / Let the people sing: Payne, Jack & His Orchestra / I'm making believe: Ink Spots & Ella Fitzgerald / Little Dutch mill: Noble, Ray & His Orchestra & Al Bowlly / Hush hush hush, here comes the bogeyman: Hall, Henry Orchestra / Later on: Lynn, Vera / Birdsong at Eventide: Ronalde, Ronnie & Robert Farnon Orchestra
2CD _____ POTTCD 200
Connoisseur / May '93 / Pinnacle.

SINGLES
Would: Alice In Chains / Breath: Pearl Jam / Seasons: Cornell, Chris / Dyslexic heart: Westerberg, Paul / Battle of Evermore: Lovemongers / Chloe dancer/Crown of thorns: Mother Love Bone / Birth ritual: Soundgarden / State of love and trust: Pearl Jam / Overblown: Mudhoney / Waiting for somebody: Westerberg, Paul / May this be love: Hendrix, Jimi / Nearly lost you: Screaming Trees / Drown: Smashing Pumpkins
CD _____ 4714382
Epic / Jul '92 / Sony.

SIRENS
Portman, Rachel C
CD _____ 213022
Milan / Jul '94 / BMG / Silva Screen.

SISTERS
Herrmann, Bernard C
Herrmann, Bernard Con
Dressing room / Ferry / Scar / Cake / Phillip's murder / Clean up / Plastic bag / Apartment house / Couch / Siamese twins
CD _____ SCCD 903
Southern Cross / Jan '89 / Silva Screen.

SIX DEGREES OF SEPARATION
Goldsmith, Jerry C
CD _____ 616232
Silva Screen / Jan '93 / Conifer / Silva Screen.

SKIN, THE
Schifrin, Lalo C
CD _____ CDCIA 5095
Cinevox / Jan '93 / Conifer / Silva Screen.

SKY PIRATES
May, Brian C
CD _____ IMICD 1002
Silva Screen / Jan '96 / Conifer / Silva Screen.

SKYSCRAPER
Cast Recording
Van Heusen, James C
Cahn, Sammy L

CD _____ ZDM 5651322
EMI Classics / Apr '94 / EMI.

SLEEPLESS IN SEATTLE
As time goes by: Durante, Jimmy / Kiss to build a dream on: Armstrong, Louis / Stardust: Cole, Nat King / Makin' whoopee: Dr. John & Rickie Lee Jones / In the wee small hours of the morning: Simon, Carly / Back in the saddle again: Autry, Gene / Bye bye blackbird: Cocker, Joe / Wink and a smile: Connick, Harry Jr. / Stand by your man: Wynette, Tammy / Affair to remember: Durante, Jimmy / Make someone happy: Durante, Jimmy / When I fall in love: Dion, Celine & Clive Griffin
CD _____ 473594 2
Epic / Sep '93 / Sony.

SLEEPWALKERS
Pike, Nicholas C
CD _____ 101322
Milan / Feb '94 / BMG / Silva Screen.

SLICE OF SATURDAY NIGHT, A
1989 London Cast
Heather Brothers C
CD _____ OCRCD 6041
First Night / Oct '95 / Pinnacle.

SLIVER
Can't help falling in love: UB40 / Carly's song: Enigma / Slid: Fluke / Unfinished sympathy: Massive Attack / Most wonderful girl: Lords Of Acid / Oh Carolina: Shaggy / Move with me: Cherry, Neneh / Principles of lust: Enigma / Slave to the vibe: Aftershock / Penthouse and pavement: Heaven 17 / Skinflowers: Young Gods / Star sail: Verve / Wild at heart: Bigod 20 / Carly's loneliness: Enigma
CD _____ CDVMM 11
Virgin / Jul '93 / EMI.

SNOOPY
1981 New York Cast
Grossman, Larry C
Hackady, Hal L
CD _____ DRGCD 6103
DRG / Jan '95 / New Note.

SNOOPY
1982 London Cast
Grossman, Larry C
Hackady, Hal L
Overture: The world according to Snoopy / Edgar Allen Poe / Woodstock's theme / I know now / Vigil / Clouds / Where did that little dog go / Friend / Great winter (It was a dark and stormy night) / Poor sweet baby / Don't be anything less / Big wow-wow / Just one person
CD _____ CDTER 1073
TER / Sep '93 / Koch.

SNOW WHITE AND THE SEVEN DWARFS
Churchill, Frank E. C
Overture / Magic mirror / I'm wishing / Queen theme / Far into the forest / Animal friends/With a smile and a song / Just like a doll's house / Whistle while you work / Heigh ho / Let's see what's upstairs / There's trouble a-brewin' / It's a girl / Hooray she stays / Bluddle-uddle-um-dum (The washing song) / I've been tricked / Silly song / Someday my Prince will come / Pleasant dreams / Special sort of death / Why grumpy, you do care / Makin' pies / Have a bite / Chorale for Snow White / Love's first kiss / Music in your soup / You're never too old to be young
CD _____ DSTCD 472
Carlton Home Entertainment / Jun '94 / Carlton Home Entertainment.

SNOWMAN, THE
Blake, Howard
CD _____ 4071136
Columbia / Nov '95 / Sony.

SO I MARRIED AN AXE MURDERER
Brother: Toad The Wet Sprocket / Break: Soul Asylum / Starve to death: Whitley, Chris / Rush: Big Audio Dynamite II / This poem sucks: Myers, Mike / Saturday night: Ned's Atomic Dustbin / Long day in the universe: Darling Buds / Two princes: Spin Doctors / My insatiable one: Suede / Maybe baby: Sun 60 / There she goes: La's
CD _____ 474273 2
Columbia / Nov '93 / Sony.

SOAPDISH
Silvestri, Alan C
CD _____ VSD 5322
Varese Sarabande/Colosseum / Aug '91 / Pinnacle / Silva Screen.

SOLDIER SOLDIER
Parker, Jim
Parker, Jim C
Soldier soldier / Kate's tune / Night patrol / Absent without leave / La Ci Darem (from Mozart: Don Giovanni) / Girls hitch a ride / Lament from Vinny / Tony's Kiwi blues / Von Fremden Landern Und Menschen (Schumann) / Cyprus laments / Peacos / Beach assault / Dave and Donna / Aria (from Mozart: Die Zauberflote) / Hong Kong / Chinese affair / Showing the flag / An Die Music (Schumann) / Paddy's German romance / Cycling in the rain / King's chorale / Munster Square / Albumblat (Schumann) / Amsterdam adventure / Variations on a theme of Mozart / Leaving for Bosnia
CD _____ CDSTM 8
Soundtrack Music / Sep '94 / EMI.

SOLO
CD _____ CHAN 8769
Chandos / Jul '89 / Chandos.

SOME KIND OF WONDERFUL
Do anything: Shelley, Peter / Brilliant mind: Furniture / Cry like this: Blue Room / I go crazy: Flesh For Lulu / She loves me: Duffy, Stephen 'Tin Tin' / Hardest walk: Jesus & Mary Chain / Shyest time: Apartments / Miss Amanda Jones: March Violets / Can't help falling in love: Lick The Tins / Turn to the sky: March Violets / Dr. Mabuse: Propaganda
CD _____ BGOCD 178
Beat Goes On / Feb '95 / Pinnacle.

SOME LIKE IT HOT
1992 London Cast
Styne, Jule C
Merrill, Bob L
CD _____ CASTCD 28
First Night / '94 / Pinnacle.

SOMETHING TO TALK ABOUT
Zimmer, Hans & Graham Preskett C
CD _____ VSD 5664
Varese Sarabande/Colosseum / Nov '95 / Pinnacle / Silva Screen.

SOMETHING WILD
Loco de amor: David Y Celia / Ever fallen in love: Fine Young Cannibals / Zero zero seven Charlie: UB40 / Not my slave: Oingo Boingo / You don't have to cry: Cliff, Jimmy / With or without you: Jones, Steve / High life: Okossun, Sonny / Man with a gun: Harrison, Jerry / Temptation: New Order / Wild thing: Sister Carol
CD _____ MCAD 6194
MCA / Jan '89 / BMG.

SOMEWHERE IN TIME
Barry, John C
Somewhere in time / Old woman / Journey back in time / Day together / Rhapsody on a theme of Paganini / Is he the one / Man of my dreams / Return to the present
CD _____ BGOCD 222
Beat Goes On / Feb '95 / Pinnacle.

SOMMERSBY
Elfman, Danny C
Sheffer, Jonathan/T. Pasatieri Con
Main title / Homecoming / Welcoming / First love / At work / Alone / Return montage / Mortal sin / Horner / Going to nashville / Baby / Tea cups / Townsend's tale / Death / Finale / End credits
CD _____ 7559614912
WEA / Apr '93 / Warner Music.

SON OF DARKNESS
(To Die For II)
McKenzie, Mark C
CD _____ PCD 110
Prometheus / Jan '93 / Silva Screen.

SON OF THE MORNING STAR
Safan, Craig C
CD _____ MAF 7037D
Intrada / Feb '93 / Silva Screen / Koch.

SON OF THE PINK PANTHER
Mancini, Henry C
CD _____ 164612
Milan / Dec '94 / BMG / Silva Screen.

SONATINE
CD _____ 293452
Milan / Sep '95 / BMG / Silva Screen.

SONG AND DANCE
Broadway Cast
Lloyd Webber, Andrew C
Black, Don L
CD _____ RCD 1 7162
RCA/Silva Screen / Jan '89 / Silva Screen.

SONG OF NORWAY, THE
Broadway Cast/Ambrosian Chorus/Philharmonia Orchestra
Forrest, George & Robert Wright C
Edwards, John Owen Con
2CD _____ CDTER2 1173
TER / Jan '91 / Koch.

SONG OF SINGAPORE
Cast Recording
Song of Singapore / Inexpensive tango / I miss my home in Harlem / You gotta do what you gotta do / Rose of Rangoon / Necrology / Sunrise / Never pay musicians what they're worth / Harbour of love / I can't remember / I want to get offa this island/ Harbour of love / Foolish geese / Serve it up / Fly away Rose / I remember / Shake shake shake / We're rich / Sunrise/Song of Singapore
CD _____ DRGCD 19003
DRG / Jan '95 / New Note.

SONS OF KATIE ELDER, THE
Bernstein, Elmer C
CD _____ TSU 0104
Tsunami / Jan '93 / Silva Screen.

SOPHIE'S CHOICE
Hamlisch, Marvin C
Sophie's choice / Train ride to Brooklyn / Returning the tray / Coney Island fun / Songs without words / Op 30, no 1 / Emily Dickenson / Aren't all women like you / Rite on the Brooklyn Bridge / Stingo; Polish lullaby / Nathan returns / Southern plantation / I'll never leave you / Stingo and Sophie together / Ample make this bed / Sophie's choice end credits

CD _____ SCCD 902
Southern Cross / Jan '89 / Silva Screen.

SORCERER, THE
Tangerine Dream
Tangerine Dream C
Search / Call / Creation / Vengeance / Journey / Grind / Rainforest / Abyss / Mountain road / Impressions of sorcerer / Betrayal
CD _____ MCLD 19159
MCA / May '93 / BMG.

SORCERER, THE/THE ZOO
D'Oyly Carte Opera Chorus/Royal Philharmonic Orchestra
Sullivan, Sir Arthur C
Gilbert, W.S. L
Godfrey, I./R. Nash Con
2CD _____ 4368072
London / Jan '90 / PolyGram.

SOUL MAN
Soul man: Moore, Sam & Lou Reed / Outside: Nu Shooz / Bang, bang, bang (who's on the phone): Ricky / Totally academic: Russell, Brenda / Suddenly it's magic: Williams, Vesta / Sweet Sarah: Scott, Tom / Black girls: Chong, Rae Dawn / Misadventures of: Evolution / Love and affection: Davis, Martha & Sly Stone / Eek-ah-boo-static automatic: Stone, Sly
CD _____ 5514312
Spectrum/Karussell / Sep '95 / PolyGram / THE.

SOUND BARRIER, THE
Royal Philharmonic Orchestra
Arnold, Sir Malcolm C
Alwyn, Kenneth Con
CD _____ CNS 5446
Cloud Nine / Jan '89 / Conifer / Silva Screen.

SOUND OF MUSIC, THE
Royal Liverpool Philharmonic Orchestra
Rodgers, Richard C
Hammerstein II, Oscar L
CD _____ CDCFP 4573
Classics For Pleasure / Sep '90 / EMI.

SOUND OF MUSIC, THE
1959 Broadway Cast
Rodgers, Richard C
Hammerstein II, Oscar L
CD _____ CK 32601
CBS/Silva Screen / Jan '89 / Conifer / Silva Screen.
CD _____ SK 53537
Sony Broadway / Nov '93 / Sony.

SOUND OF MUSIC, THE
Film Cast
Rodgers, Richard C
Hammerstein II, Oscar L
Climb every mountain / So long, farewell / Edelweiss / Maria / Processional / Something good / Do re mi / Sound of music / Lonely goatherd / My favourite things / Sixteen going on seventeen / Mornign hymn / Alleluia / I have confidence in me
CD _____ 07863665872
RCA / Apr '95 / BMG.

SOUND OF MUSIC, THE
(Highlights - The Shows Collection)
Cast Recording
Rodgers, Richard C
Hammerstein II, Oscar L
CD _____ PWKS 4145
Carlton Home Entertainment / Jan '95 / Carlton Home Entertainment.

SOUND OF MUSIC, THE
Studio Cast/May Fest Choir/Cincinnati Pops Orchestra
Rodgers, Richard C
Hammerstein II, Oscar L
Kunzel, Erich Con
CD _____ CD 80162
Telarc / Dec '88 / Conifer / ADA.

SOUND OF MUSIC, THE/SOUTH PACIFIC/THE KING AND I
Denon / Nov '92 / Conifer.
CD _____ CO 75077

SOUTH PACIFIC
1958 Film Cast
Rodgers, Richard C
Hammerstein II, Oscar L
Newman, Alfred Con
South Pacific overture / Dites moi / Cock-eyed optimist / Twin soliloquies / Some enchanted evening / Bloody Mary / My girl back home / There is nothin' like a dame / Bali Ha'i / I'm gonna wash that man right outa my hair / I'm in love with a wonderful guy / Younger than Springtime / Happy talk / Honey bun / Carefully taught / This nearly was mine / Finale
CD _____ ND 83681
RCA / Feb '89 / BMG.

SOUTH PACIFIC
1986 Studio Cast
Rodgers, Richard C
Hammerstein II, Oscar L
Overture / Dites moi / Cock-eyed optimist / Twin soliloquies / Some enchanted evening / Bloody Mary / There is nothin' like a dame / Bali Ha'i / I'm gonna wash that man right outa my hair / I'm in love with a wonderful guy / Younger than Springtime / This is how it feels / Entr'acte / Happy talk / Honey bun / Carefully taught / This nearly was mine / March / Take off / Communications established / Finale ultimo

CD _____ CD 42205
CBS / '86 / Sony.

SOUTH PACIFIC
1988 London Cast
Rodgers, Richard C
Hammerstein II, Oscar L
CD _____ OCRCD 6023
First Night / Jan '96 / Pinnacle.

SOUTH PACIFIC
1949 Broadway Cast
Rodgers, Richard C
Hammerstein II, Oscar L
CD _____ CK 32604
CBS/Silva Screen / Jan '89 / Conifer / Silva Screen.
CD _____ SK 53327
Sony Broadway / Nov '93 / Sony.

SOUTH PACIFIC
(Highlights - The Shows Collection)
Cast Recording
Rodgers, Richard C
Hammerstein II, Oscar L
South Pacific overture / Dites moi / Twin soliloquys / Some enchanted evening / Bloody Mary / Cock-eyed optimist / There is nothin' like a dame / I'm gonna wash that man right outa my hair / Younger than springtime / Happy talk / Honey bun / Carefully taught / This nearly was mine / Ditas moi / I'm in love with a wonderful guy
CD _____ PWKS 4162
Carlton Home Entertainment / Sep '93 / Carlton Home Entertainment.

SOUTHERN MAID
1920 London Cast
Fraser Simson, Harold C
Clayton Calthorp, Dion & Harry Graham L
CD _____ GEMMCD 9115
Pearl / Jan '93 / Harmonia Mundi.

SPECIALIST, THE
Turn the beat around: Estefan, Gloria / Jambala: Miami Sound Machine / Shower me with love: Lagaylia / El baile de la vela: Cheito / Slip away: Lagaylia / El duro so yo: Tatis, Tony / Mental picture: Secada, Jon / Que manera de quererte: Albita / Love is the thing: Allen, Donna / El amor: Moreno, Azucar / Did you call me: Barry, John Orchestra / Specialist: Barry, John Orchestra
CD _____ 4776662
Epic / Jan '95 / Sony.

SPECIALIST, THE
(Score)
Barry, John C
Barry, John C
Main title / Bogota 1984 / Specialist in Miami / Ray and May at the cemetry / Nay dances with Thomas / Did you call me / Ray covers May / After Thomas / First bomb / Ray's place / Explosive trent / Parking lot bomb / Don't touch me Ned / Bomb for Thomas / Death of Thomas
CD _____ 4778102
Epic / Jan '95 / Sony.

SPECIALIST, THE
(Remixes)
Turn the beat around (Def classic mix): Estefan, Gloria / Love is the thing (Spike boys club remix): Allen, Donna / El amor (Multiple orgasm mix): Moreno, Azucar / El baile de la vela (Ralph's tribalground mix): Cheito / Jambala (Alternative mix): Miami Sound Machine / Real (X-tended R&B mix): Allen, Donna / Shower me with love (Smoove soul 12"): Lagaylia / Turn the beat around (Damien's fountainbleu mix): Allen, Donna / Real (def house mix): Allen, Donna
CD _____ 4778092
Epic / Jan '95 / Sony.

SPEED
Speed: Idol, Billy / Million miles away: Plimsouls / Soul deep: Gin Blossoms / Let's go for a ride: Cracker / Go outside and drive: Blues Traveller / Crash: Ocasek, Ric / Rescue me: Benatar, Pat / Hard road: Stewart, Rod / Cot: Carnival Strippers / Cars ('93 sprint): Numan, Gary / Like a motorway: St. Etienne / Mr. Speed: Kiss
CD _____ 07822110182
Arista / Aug '94 / BMG.

SPEED
(Score)
Mancina, Mark C
CD _____ 234652
Milan / Jun '95 / BMG / Silva Screen.

SPIES LIKE US
Bernstein, Elmer C
Williams, John C
Ace tomato company / Off to spy / Russians in the desert / Pass in the tent / Escape / To the bus / Road to Russia / Rally 'round / W.A.M.P. / Martian act / Arrest / Recall / Winners
CD _____ VCD 47246
Varese Sarabande/Colosseum / Jan '89 / Pinnacle / Silva Screen.

SPINOUT/DOUBLE TROUBLE
Presley, Elvis
Stop, look and listen / Adam and evil / All that I am / Never say yes / Am I ready / Beach shack / Spinout / Smorgasbord / I'll be back / Double trouble / Baby, if you'll give me all your love / Could I fall in love / Long legged girl with the short dress on / City by night / Old MacDonald / I love only one girl / There's so much world to see / It won't be long

CD _____ 07863663612
RCA / Jun '94 / BMG.

SPITTING IMAGE: SPIT IN YOUR EAR
Spitting Image (theme) / Ronnie and Maggie goodbye / Royal singalong / Weather forecast / Coleman peaks / We've got beards (ZZ Top) / Second coming / Someone famous has died / Tea at Johnnies / Trendy Kinnock / Da doo ron Ron / Ronnie's birthday / One man and his bitch / Special relationship / Clean rugby songs / O'Toole's night out / Spock the actor / Line of celebrities / Price is right / Botha tells the truth / I've never met a nice South African / End announcement / Andy and Fergie / Pete Townsend appeals / Our generation (The who) / Three Davids / Party system / Hello you must be going / Naming the Royal baby / Ronnie and Ruthless / South Bank show on Ronnie Hazelhurst / Bernard Manning newsflash / Juan Carlos meets the Queen / Chicken song (Celebrity megamix) / Lawson goes bonkers / Talk bollocks / Snooker games / Good old British bloke / Black moustache (Prince.) / Uranus / Denis Thatcher's pacemaker / John And Tatum - the young marrieds / We're scared of Bob / Trooping the colour / Night thoughts
CD _____ VVIP0 110
Virgin VIP / Nov '90 / Carlton Home Entertainment / THE / EMI.

SPLIT SECOND
Parsons, S./F. Haines C
CD _____ 873117
Milan / Jun '92 / BMG / Silva Screen.

SPY WHO LOVED ME, THE
Hamlisch, Marvin C
Nobody does it better: Simon, Carly / Bond 77 / Ride to Atlantis / Mojave club / Anya / Tanker / Pyramids / Eastern lights / Conclusion / Spy who loved me, The (end titles) / Bond 77
CD _____ CZ 555
Premier / Dec '95 / EMI.

ST. ELMO'S FIRE
St. Elmo's fire: Parr, John / Shake down: Squier, Billy / Young and innocent: Elefante / This time it was really right: Anderson, Jon / Saved my life: Waybill, Fee / Love theme: Foster, David / Georgetown: Foster, David / If I turn you away: Moss, Vikki / Stressed out (Close to the edge): Airplay / St. Elmo's fire (man in motion) / ehake down
CD _____ 7567812612
Atlantic / Feb '95 / Warner Music.

ST. LOUIS WOMAN
Broadway Cast
Arlen, Harold C
Mercer, Johnny L
CD _____ ZDM 7646622
EMI Classics / Apr '93 / EMI.

STAIRWAY TO THE STARS
1989 London Cast
That's dancing / Who's sorry now / You stepped out of a dream / Fine romance / Three little words / Bye bye baby / Chattanooga choo choo / Rose's turn / Finale, hooray for Hollywood / Ma belle Marguerite / 'S Wonderful / Not even nominated / Life upon the wicked stage / Buttons and bows / I got a gal in Kalamazoo / Lucky numbers / Bosom buddies
CD _____ OCRCD 6021
First Night / Dec '95 / Pinnacle.

STAND AND DELIVER
Safan, Craig C
CD _____ VCD 70459
Varese Sarabande/Colosseum / Jan '89 / Pinnacle / Silva Screen.

STAND BY ME
Everyday: Holly, Buddy / Let the good times roll: Shirley & Lee / Come go with me: Del-Vikings / Whispering bells: Del-Vikings / Get a job: Silhouettes / Lollipop: Chordettes / Yakety yak: Coasters / Great balls of fire: Lewis, Jerry Lee / Mr. Lee: Bobbettes / Stand by me: King, Ben E.
CD _____ 7567816772
Atlantic / Feb '94 / Warner Music.

STAND, THE
Walden, W.G. 'Snuffy'
Walden, W.G. 'Snuffy' C
CD _____ VSD 5496
Varese Sarabande/Colosseum / Aug '94 / Pinnacle / Silva Screen.

STANLEY AND IRIS
Williams, John C
Williams, John (1) Con
Stanley and Iris / Bicycle / Back to school / Finding a family / Putting it all together / Letters / Reading lessons / Factory work / Stanley at work / Stanley and Iris end credits / Stanley's invention
CD _____ VSD 5255
Varese Sarabande/Colosseum / May '90 / Pinnacle / Silva Screen.

STAR
(& Alfred Newman's 20th Century Fox Fanfare)
Andrews, Julie & Film Cast
CD _____ 07822110092
Fox Film Scores / May '94 / BMG.

STAR IS BORN, A
Garland, Judy
Arlen, Harold C
Gershwin, Ira L

951

Gotta have me go with you / Man that got away / Born in a trunk / I'll get by / You took advantage of me / Black bottom / Peanut vendor / My melancholy baby / Swanee / Here's what I'm here for / It's a new world / Someone at last / Lose that long face / Overture
CD _____ CK 44389
CBS/Silva Screen / Jan '89 / Conifer / Silva Screen.

STAR IS BORN, A
(with Barbra Streisand)
1976 Film Cast
Williams, Paul & Others C
Watch closely now / Queen Bee / Everything / Lost inside of you / Hellacious acres / Love theme (Evergreen) / Woman in the moon / I believe in love / Crippled crow / With one more look at you / Watch closely now (2) / Reprise
CD _____ 4749052
Columbia / Apr '95 / Sony.

STAR TREK - VOL.1
(The Cage/Where No Man Has Gone Before)
Royal Philharmonic Orchestra
Courage, Alexander C
Courage, Alexander Con
CD _____ GNPD 8006
GNP Crescendo / '88 / Silva Screen.

STAR TREK - VOL.2
(The Doomsday Machine/Amok Time)
Kaplan, Sol & Gerald Fried C
Kaplan, Sol & Gerald Fried C
CD _____ GNPD 8025
GNP Crescendo / Sep '90 / Silva Screen.

STAR TREK - VOL.3
(Shore Leave/The Naked Time)
Fried, Gerald & Alexander Courage C
CD _____ GNPD 8030
GNP Crescendo / Nov '92 / Silva Screen.

STAR TREK CLASSIC BOX SET
3CD _____ GNPBX 3006
GNP Crescendo / Sep '93 / Silva Screen.

STAR TREK I: THE MOTION PICTURE
Goldsmith, Jerry C
Goldsmith, Jerry Con
Main title / Klingon battle / Leaving drydock / Cloud / Enterprise / Ilia's theme / Vejur flyover / Meld / Spock walk / End titles
CD _____ 9833812
Pickwick/Sony Collector's Choice / Feb '94 / Carlton Home Entertainment / Pinnacle / Sony.

STAR TREK II: THE WRATH OF KHAN
Horner, James C
Main title / Surprise attack / Spock / Kirk's explosive reply / Khan's pets / Enterprise clears moorings / Battle in the Mutara Nebula / Genesis countdown / Epilogue (End title)
CD _____ GNPD 8022
GNP Crescendo / Jul '91 / Silva Screen.

STAR TREK III: THE SEARCH FOR SPOCK
Horner, James C
Horner, James Con
Prologue and main title / Klingons / Stealing the Enterprise / Mind meld / Bird Of Prey decloaks / Returning to Vulcan / Katra ritual / End titles
CD _____ FILMCD 070
Silva Screen / Aug '90 / Conifer / Silva Screen.

STAR TREK VI: THE UNDISCOVERED COUNTRY
Eidelman, Cliff C
Eidelman, Cliff Con
CD _____ MCAD 10512
MCA / Feb '92 / BMG.

STAR TREK VII: GENERATIONS
McCarthy, Dennis C
CD _____ GNPD 8040
GNP Crescendo / Feb '95 / Silva Screen.

STAR TREK: DEEP SPACE NINE
McCarthy, Dennis C
McCarthy, Dennis Con
CD _____ GNPD 8034
GNP Crescendo / May '93 / Silva Screen.

STAR TREK: THE ASTRAL SYMPHONY
(Music From films I-V)
CD _____ 262832
Milan / Feb '94 / BMG / Silva Screen.

STAR TREK: THE NEXT GENERATION
McCarthy, Dennis C
CD _____ GNPD 8012
GNP Crescendo / Jan '89 / Silva Screen.

STAR TREK: THE NEXT GENERATION VOL.2
Jones, Ron C
CD _____ GNPD 8026
GNP Crescendo / Sep '90 / Silva Screen.

STAR TREK: THE NEXT GENERATION VOL.3
McCarthy, Dennis C
CD _____ GNPD 8031
GNP Crescendo / Nov '92 / Silva Screen.

STAR TREK: THE NEXT GENERATION VOLS. 1-3
3CD _____ GNPBX 3007
GNP Crescendo / Sep '93 / Silva Screen.

STAR TREK: TV SCORES VOL.1
Royal Philharmonic Orchestra
Duning, George/Gerald Freid C
Bremner, Tony Con
Is there in truth no beauty / Paradise syndrome
CD _____ LXE 703
CBS/Silva Screen / Jan '94 / Conifer / Silva Screen.

STAR TREK: TV SCORES VOL.2
Royal Philharmonic Orchestra
Conscience of the king / Spectre of the gun / Enemy within / I, Mudd
CD _____ LXE 704
CBS/Silva Screen / Jan '94 / Conifer / Silva Screen.

STAR TREK: TV SERIES VOL.1
Royal Philharmonic Orchestra
CD _____ VCD 47235
Varese Sarabande/Colosseum / Jan '89 / Pinnacle / Silva Screen.

STAR TREK: TV SERIES VOL.2
Royal Philharmonic Orchestra
Empath / Trouble with the Tribbles / Mirror mirror / By any other name
CD _____ VSD 47240
Varese Sarabande/Colosseum / Jan '90 / Pinnacle / Silva Screen.

STAR TREK: VOYAGER
Chattaway, Jay C
CD _____ GNPD 8041
GNP Crescendo / Jun '95 / Silva Screen.

STAR WARS TRILOGY
(Music From The Films)
Utah Symphony Orchestra
Williams, John C
Star Wars main title / Princess Leia's theme / Here they come / Asteroid field / Yoda's theme / Imperial march / Parade of the Ewoks / Luke and Leia / Funeral with the tigers / Jabba the Hutt / Darth Vader's death / Forest battle / Star Wars (finale)
CD _____ CDTER 1067
TER / Dec '83 / Koch.

CD _____ VCD 47201
Varese Sarabande/Colosseum / Jan '89 / Pinnacle / Silva Screen.

STAR WARS TRILOGY
London Symphony Orchestra
Williams, John C
Williams, John (1) Con
4CD _____ FOX 110122
Fox Film Scores/Silva Screen / Jan '94 / Silva Screen.

STARGATE
Sinfonia Of London
Arnold, David C
Dodd, N. Con
Stargate overture / Giza, 1928 / Unstable / Coverstones / Orion / Stargate opens / You're on the team / Entering the Stargate / Other side / Mastadge drag / Mining pit / King of the slaves / Caravan to Nagado / Daniel and Shauri / Symbol discovery / Sarcophagus opens / Daniel's mastadge / Leaving Nagada / Ra - The Sun God / Destruction of Nagada / Myth, faith, belief / Procession / Slave rebellion / Seventh symbol / Quartz shipment / Battle at the pyramid / We don't want to die / Surrender / Kasuf returns / Going home
CD _____ 74321249012
Milan / May '95 / BMG / Silva Screen.

STARLIGHT EXPRESS
1984 London Cast
Lloyd Webber, Andrew C
Stilgoe, Richard L
Overture / Rolling stock / Call me Rusty / Lotta locomotion / Pumping iron / Freight / AC/DC / Hitching and switching / He whistled at me / Race - heat one / There's me / Blues / Belle / Race - heat two / Race - heat three / Starlight Express / Rap / Uncoupled / Rolling stock (reprise) / C.B. / Race - uphill final / Right place, right time / Race - downhill final / No comeback / One rock 'n' roll too many / Only He / Only you / Light at the end of the tunnel
2CD _____ 8215972
Polydor / Jun '84 / PolyGram.

STARLIGHT EXPRESS
1993 London Cast
Lloyd Webber, Andrew C
Stilgoe, Richard L
CD _____ 5190412
Really Useful / Apr '93 / PolyGram.

STARLIGHT EXPRESS/CATS
(Highlights - The Shows Collection)
Cast Recording
Lloyd Webber, Andrew C
Stilgoe, Richard L
Starlight express / Rolling stock / U.N.C.O.U.P.L.E.D. / Crazy / Pumping iron / One rock'n' roll too many / Next time we fall in love / Light at the end of the tunnel / Memory / Grizabella / Gus / Mr. Mistoffelees / Old deuteronomy / Macavity / Memory (Reprise)
CD _____ PWKS 4192
Carlton Home Entertainment / Jul '94 / Carlton Home Entertainment.

STARMAN
Nitzsche, Jack C
CD _____ VCD 47220
Epic / Jan '96 / Sony.

Varese Sarabande/Colosseum / Jan '89 / Pinnacle / Silva Screen.
CD _____ CDTER 1097
TER / Aug '90 / Koch.

STARTING HERE, STARTING NOW
London Cast
Shire, David C
Maltby, Richard Jr. L
CD _____ CDTER 1200
TER / Jan '93 / Koch.

STATE OF SIEGE
Theodorakis, Mikis C
CD _____ SR 50063
Sakkaris / Oct '93 / Pinnacle.

STAY TUNED
Polydor / Dec '92 / PolyGram.
CD _____ 517 472-2

STEALING HEAVEN
Bicat, Nick C
CD _____ CDTER 1166
TER / Jui '89 / Koch.

STEEL MAGNOLIAS
Delerue, Georges C
CD _____ 8415822
Silva Screen / Jan '93 / Conifer / Silva Screen.

STEPPING OUT
Minnelli, Liza
Kander, John C
Ebb, Fred L
Matz, Peter Con
CD _____ 262062
Milan / Feb '94 / BMG / Silva Screen.

STING, THE
Hamlisch, Marvin & Scott Joplin C
Solace / Entertainer / Easy winners / Pineapple rag / Gladiolus rag / Merry go round music / Listen to the mockingbird / Darling Nellie Gray / Turkey in the straw / Ragtime dance / Hooker's hooker / Luther / Glove / Little girl
CD _____ MCLD 19027
MCA / Apr '92 / BMG.

STONE KILLER, THE
Budd, Roy C
CD _____ LEGENDCD 6
Legend / Jan '94 / Conifer / Silva Screen / Discovery.

STOP IN THE NAME OF LOVE
(With The Fabulous Singlettes)
1988 London Cast
Do wah diddy diddy / Da doo ron ron / My guy / Be my baby / It's in his kiss (Shoop shoop song) / Needle in a haystack / Walk in the room / Time is on my side / Dum dum ditty / Leader of the pack / It's my party / Maybe / Born too late / I only want to be with you / You don't own me / Will you still love me tomorrow / Dancing in the streets / Supremes medley / Thank you and good night
CD _____ OCRCD 6017
First Night / Jan '96 / Pinnacle.

STOP THE WORLD I WANT TO GET OFF
1961 London Cast
Newley, Anthony & Leslie Bricusse C
ABC / I wanna be rich / Typically English / Lumbered / Gonna build a mountain / Glorious Russia / Mellinki Meilchick / Typiache Deutsche / Nag nag nag / All American / Once in a lifetime / Mumbo jumbo / Someone nice like you / What kind of fool am I
CD _____ CDTER 1226
TER / Aug '95 / Koch.

STORMY WEATHER
(inc. Alfred Newman's 20th Century Fox Fanfare)
Calloway, Cab & Film Cast
CD _____ 07822110072
Fox Film Scores / Apr '94 / BMG.

STORYVILLE
Burwell, Carter C
CD _____ VSD 5347
Varese Sarabande/Colosseum / Sep '92 / Pinnacle / Silva Screen.

STRAIGHT TO HELL
Good, the bad and the ugly: Pogues / Rake at the gates of hell: Pogues / If I should fall from grace with God: Pogues / Rabinga: Pogues / Danny boy: Pogues / Evil darling: Strummer, Joe / Ambush or mystery rock: Strummer, Joe / Money guns and coffee: Pray For Rain / Killers: Pray For Rain / Salsa y ketchup: Zander Schloss / Big nothing: MacManus Gang
CD _____ REP 4224-WY
Repertoire / Aug '91 / Pinnacle / Cadillac.

STRANGE DAYS
Selling Jesus: Skunk Anansie / Real thing: Lords Of Acid / Overcome: Tricky / Coral lounge: Deep Forest / No white clouds: Strange Fruit / Hardly wait: Lewis, Juliette / Here we come: Me Phi Me & Jungle Funk / Feed: Skunk Anansie / Strange days: Prong & Ray Manzarek / Walk in freedom: Satchel / Dance me to the end of love: Hate Gibson / Fall in the night: Carson, Lori & Graeme Revell / While the earth sleeps: Deep Forest
CD _____ 4809842

STRANGER THAN PARADISE
Lurie, John C
CD _____ MTM 7CD
Made To Measure / Mar '86 / Grapevine.

STRATAGEM
Big Head Todd & The Monsters
Kensington line / Stratagem / Wearing only flowers / Neckbreaker / Magdalena / Angel leads me on / In the morning / Candle / Ninety nine / Greyhound / Poor miss / Shadowlands
CD _____ 74321229042
Giant / Oct '94 / BMG.

STREET FIGHTER
Revell, Graeme
Revell, Graeme C
CD _____ VSD 5560
Varese Sarabande/Colosseum / May '95 / Pinnacle / Silva Screen.

STREET FIGHTER
Street fighter: Ice Cube / Come widdit: Ahmad & Ras Kass/Saafir / One on one: Nas / Pandemonium: Pharcyde / Street soldier: Paris / Something kinda funky: Rally Ral / It's a street fight: B.U.M.S. / Life as...: L.L. Cool J / Do you have what it takes: Mack, Craig / Straight to my feet: Hammer & Deion Sanders / Rumbo in da jungo: Public Enemy & Wreck League / Rap commando: Anotha Level / Worth fighting for: Kidjo, Angelique / Something there: Chage & Aska
CD _____ CDPTY 114
Priority/Virgin / Dec '94 / EMI.

STREET SCENE
1991 London Cast
Weill, Kurt C
Hughes, Langston L
2CD _____ CDTER2 1185
TER / Jan '94 / Koch.

STREETCAR NAMED DESIRE, A
(& Since You Went Away/Now Voyager/ The Informer)
North, Alex/Max Steiner C
Heindorf, Ray/Max Steiner Con
Streetcar / Four deuces / Belle Reve / Blanche / Della Robia blue / Flores para Los Muertos / Mania / Lust / Soliloquy and redemption / Since you went away / Now Voyager / Informer
CD _____ CNS 5003
Cloud Nine / Jun '92 / Conifer / Silva Screen.

STREETCAR NAMED DESIRE, A
North, Alex C
CD _____ VSD 5500
Varese Sarabande/Colosseum / Oct '95 / Pinnacle / Silva Screen.

STREETS OF FIRE
Steinman, Jim C
Nowhere fast: Fire Inc. / Sorcerer: Martin, Marilyn / Deeper and deeper: Fixx / Countdown to love: Phillinganes, Greg / One bad stud: Blasters / Tonight is what it means to be young: Fire Inc. / Never be you: McKee, Maria / I can dream about you: Hartman, Dan / Hold that snake: Cooder, Ry / Blue shadows: Blasters
CD _____ BGOCD 220
Beat Goes On / Feb '95 / Pinnacle.

STRICTLY BALLROOM
Love is in the air: Young, John Paul / Perhaps, perhaps, perhaps: Day, Doris / La cumparsita: Hirschfelder, David & The Bogo Pogo Orchestra / Tango please: Hirschfelder, David & The Bogo Pogo Orchestra / Tequila: Hirschfelder, David & The Bogo Pogo Orchestra / Sinful samba: Hirschfelder, David & The Bogo Pogo Orchestra / Rumba de burros: Jones, Ignatius / Doug's tearful waltz/First kiss: Hirschfelder, David & The Bogo Pogo Orchestra / Time after time: Williams, Mark & Monroe, Tara / Standing in the rain: Young, John Paul / Scott's sinful solo: Hirschfelder, David & The Bogo Pogo Orchestra / Blue Danube: Hirschfelder, David & The Bogo Pogo Orchestra / Scott and Fran's paso doble: Hirschfelder, David & The Bogo Pogo Orchestra / Yesterday's hero: Jones, Ignatius
CD _____ 472300-2
Columbia / Nov '92 / Sony.

STRIKE UP THE BAND
Cast Recording
Gershwin, George C
Gershwin, Ira L
Mauceri, John Con
2CD _____ 7559792732
Elektra Nonesuch / Jan '92 / Warner Music.

STUDENT PRINCE, THE
Lanza, Mario
Brodszky, Nicholas C
Callinicos, C. Con
Overture / Serenade / Golden days / Drink, drink, drink / Summertime in Heidelberg / I'll walk with God / Thoughts will come back / Student life / Just we two / Beloved / Gaudeamus igitur / Deep in my heart
CD _____ GD 60048
RCA / Sep '89 / BMG.

STUDENT PRINCE, THE
1990 Studio Cast/Ambrosian Chorus/Philharmonia Orchestra
Romberg, Sigmund C
Donnelly, Dorothy L
Edwards, John Owen Con

2CD _____ CDTER2 1172
TER / Mar '91 / Koch.

STUDENT PRINCE, THE
(Highlights)
1990 Studio Cast/Ambrosian Chorus/Philharmonia Orchestra
Romberg, Sigmund C
Donnelly, Dorothy L
Edwards, John Owen Con
CD _____ CDTEO 1005
TER / Mar '91 / Koch.

SUBWAY
Serra, Eric C
Subway / Guns and people / Burglary / Masquerade / Childhood drama / Man Y / Congabass / Song to Xavier / Speedway / It's only mystery / Drumskate / Dolphin dance / Racked animal / Pretext / Dark passage II
CD _____ GMD 9702
Silva Screen / Jan '89 / Conifer / Silva Screen.

SUDDEN DEATH
Debney, John C
CD _____ VSD 5663
Varese Sarabande/Colosseum / Nov '95 / Pinnacle / Silva Screen.

SUGAR BABIES
(The Burlesque Musical)
Broadway Cast
McHugh, Jimmy C
Sugar babies overture / Good old burlesque show / Welcome to the Gaiety - Intro / Let me be your sugar baby / In Louisiana / I feel a song coming on / Going back to New Orleans / Broken Arms Hotel / Sally / Don't blame me / Immigration rose / Little red house / Sugar baby bounce / Introduction Mme Rentz / Down at the Gaiety Burlesque / Mr. Banjo man / When my sugar walks down the street / Candy butcher / Entr'Acte / I'm keeping myself available for you / Exactly like you / I'm in the mood for love / I just can't give you anything but love / I'm shooting high / When you and I were young Maggie / On the sunny side of the street / You can't blame your Uncle Sammy
CD _____ VSD 5453
Varese Sarabande/Colosseum / Dec '93 / Pinnacle / Silva Screen.

SUGAR HILL
CD _____ 07822110162
Arista / Jun '94 / BMG.

SULEYMAN THE MAGNIFICENT
CD _____ CDCEL 023
Celestial Harmonies / Feb '88 / ADA / Select.

SUMMER HOLIDAY
Richard, Cliff & The Shadows
Seven days to a holiday / Summer holiday / Let us take you for a ride / Les girls / Foot tapper / Round and round / Stranger in town / Orlando's mine / Bachelor boy / Swingin' affair / Really waltzing / All at once / Dancing shoes / Yugoslav wedding / Next time / Big news
CD _____ CDMFP 6021
Music For Pleasure / Apr '88 / EMI.

SUNDAY IN THE PARK WITH GEORGE
1984 Broadway Cast
Sondheim, Stephen C
Sunday in the park with George / No life / Color and light / Goodby / Day off / Everybody loves Louis / Finishing the hat / We do not belong together / Children and art / Lesson 8 / Move on / Sunday
CD _____ RD 85042
RCA Victor / '91 / BMG.

SUNDOWN
(The Vampire In Retreat)
Graunke Symphony Orchestra
Stone, Richard A
Wilson, Allan Con
CD _____ FILMCD 044
Silva Screen / Jan '90 / Conifer / Silva Screen.

SUNNY/SHOW BOAT/LIDO LADY
Cast Recording
Kern, Jerome/Richard Rodgers C
Harbach, Otto & Oscar Hammerstein II L
CD _____ GEMMCD 9105
Pearl / May '94 / Harmonia Mundi.

SUNSET
Off-Broadway Cast
Friedman, Gary William C
Holt, Will L
CD _____ CDTER 1180
TER / May '91 / Koch.

SUNSET BOULEVARD
1993 London Cast
Lloyd Webber, Andrew C
Black, Don & Christopher Hampton L
White, D. Con
Prologue / Let's have lunch / Sheldrake's office / On the road / Surrender / With one look / Salome / Greatest star of all / Let's have lunch (reprise)/Girl meets boy / House on Sunset / New ways to dream / Lady's paying / Perfect year (plus dialogue) / Artie Green's apartment / This time next year / Sunset Boulevard / Perfect year (reprise) / Journey to Paramount / As if we never said

goodbye / Girl meets boy (reprise) / Eternal youth / Too much in love to care / Sunset Boulevard (reprise) / Greatest star of all (reprise)
2CD _____ 5197672
Really Useful / Aug '93 / PolyGram.

SUNSET BOULEVARD
1994 US Cast
Lloyd Webber, Andrew C
Black, Don & Christopher Hampton L
Bogaev, P. Con
Overture/ I guess it was 5am / Let's have lunch / Every movie's a circus / Car chase / At the house on Sunset / Surrender / With one look / Salome / Greatest star of all / Every movie's a circus (reprise) / Girl meets boy / Back at the house on Sunset / New ways to dream / Completion of the script / Lady's paying / New Year's Eve / Perfect year / This time next year / New Year's Eve (Back at the house on Sunset) / Entr'acte / Sunset Boulevard / There's been a call/ Journey to Paramount / As if we never said goodbye / Paramount conversations/Surrender / Girl meets boy (reprise) / Eternal youth is worth a little suffering / Who's Betty Schaefer / Betty's office at Paramount / Too much love to care / New ways to dream (reprise) / Phone call / Final Scene
2CD _____ 5235072
Really Useful / Oct '94 / PolyGram.

SUPERFLY
Mayfield, Curtis
Little child runnin' wild / Freddie's dead / Give me your love (Love song) / No thing on mo (cocaine song) / Superfly / Pusherman / Junkie chase (Instrumental) / Eddie you should know better / Think (Instrumental)
CD _____ MPG 74028
Movieplay Gold / Nov '93 / Target/BMG.
CD _____ CPCD 8039
Charly / Jun '94 / Charly / THE / Cadillac.

SUPERGIRL
National Philharmonic Orchestra
Goldsmith, Jerry C
Goldsmith, Jerry Con
Overture / Main title & Argo city / Argo city / Butterfly / Journey begins / Arrival on earth / Flying ballet / Chicago light / Street attack / Superman / New school / Spellbound / Monster tractor / Map / Bracelet / First kiss / Monster storm / Where is she / Monster bumper cars / Flying bumper car / Where's Linda / Black magic / Phantom zone / Vortex / End of Zaltar / Final showdown & victory / End title
CD _____ FILMCD 132
Silva Screen / May '93 / Conifer / Silva Screen.

SUPERMAN
Williams, John C
Main title / Planet Krypton / Destruction of Krypton / Trip to Earth / Growing up / Superman love theme / Leaving home / Fortress of solitude / Flying sequence/Can you read my mind / Super rescues / Lex Luther's lair / Superfeats / March of the villains / Chasing rockets / Turning back the world / End titles
CD _____ 32572
Silva Screen / Feb '90 / Conifer / Silva Screen.

SURRENDER
Colombier, Michel C
CD _____ VCD 47312
Varese Sarabande/Colosseum / Jan '89 / Pinnacle / Silva Screen.

SUSPECT
Kamen, Michael C
CD _____ VCD 47315
Varese Sarabande/Colosseum / Jan '89 / Pinnacle / Silva Screen.

SWAN DOWN GLOVES, THE
1982 London Cast
Hess, Nigel C
Hess, Nigel & Bille Brown L
Overture / With the sun arise / Everything's going to be fine / Catastrophe / Let's be friends / Make your own world / How's the way / Going into town / Stuck in a muddle / Best foot forward / Demwer but dangerous / Muck / Any old rose / Firedown / Finale
CD _____ CDTER 1017
TER / Aug '95 / Koch.

SWEENEY TODD
(Jazz Version)
Cast Recording
Sondheim, Stephen C
CD _____ VSD 5603
Varese Sarabande/Colosseum / Jul '95 / Pinnacle / Silva Screen.

SWEENEY TODD
(Highlights)
Broadway Cast
Sondheim, Stephen C
CD _____ RCD 1 5033
RCA/Silva Screen / Jan '89 / Silva Screen.

SWEET CHARITY
Cast Recording
Coleman, Cy C
Fields, Dorothy L
2CD _____ CDTER2 1222
TER / Aug '95 / Koch.

SWEET CHARITY
1967 London Cast
Coleman, Cy C
Fields, Dorothy L
CD _____ SMK 66172
Sony West End / Jul '94 / Sony.

SWELL PARTY, A
(A Celebration Of Cole Porter)
1991 London Cast
Porter, Cole C
I'm throwing a ball tonight / I get a kick out of you / Anything goes / From this moment on / You've got that thing / I'm unlucky at gambling / I've got you under my skin / Red, hot and blue / Love for sale / Find me a primitive man / Blow, Gabriel, blow / Begin the beguine / Miss Otis regrets / Down in the depths / Rap tap on wood / Night and day / In the still of the night / I concentrate on you / Who said gay paree / Always true to you in my fashion / I happen to like New York / You're sensational / Can-can / I gaze in your eyes / Let's do it lets fall in love / You're the top / Well, did you evah / Ev'ry time we say goodbye
CD _____ SONGCD 905
Silva Classics / Jul '92 / Conifer / Silva Screen.

SWING KIDS
Horner, James C
Horner, James Con
CD _____ 142102
Milan / Feb '94 / BMG / Silva Screen.

TAFFETAS, THE
1988 Off-Broadway Cast
Lewis, Rick C
Sh-boom / Mr. Sandman / Three bells / I'm sorry / Ricochet / I cried / Cry / Smile / Achoo cha-cha / Mockin' Bird Hill / Tonight you belong to me / Happy wanderer / Constantinople / My little grass shack / C'est si bon / Sweet song of India / Arrivederci Roma / See the USA in your Chevrolet / Allegheny moon / Tennessee waltz / Old Cape Cod / Fly me to the moon / Nel blue de pinto di blue / Around the world / Music music music / You're just in love / Love letters in the sand / L.O.V.E. / I-M-4-U / Rag mop / You, you, you / Puppy love / (How much is that) doggie in the window / Hot canary / Tweedlee dee / Lollipop / Sincerely / Johnny Angel / Mr. Lee / Dedicated to the one I love / Where the boys are / I'll think of you / Little darlin' / Spotlight on the music
CD _____ CDTER 1167
TER / Jun '90 / Koch.

TAGGART
CD _____ CDSTM 1
EMI / Oct '92 / EMI.

TAI PAN
Jarre, Maurice C
CD _____ VCD 47274
Varese Sarabande/Colosseum / Jan '89 / Pinnacle / Silva Screen.

TALES FROM THE CRYPT
CD _____ 7567827252
Warner Bros. / Jan '95 / Warner Music.

TALES FROM THE CRYPT
(TV Soundtrack)
CD _____ 9244622
Silva Screen / Jan '95 / Conifer / Silva Screen.

TALES FROM THE DARKSIDE
CD _____ GNPD 8021
GNP Crescendo / Jan '95 / Silva Screen.

TALES FROM THE HOOD
Let me at them: Wu Tang Clan / Face mob: Face Mob / Tales from the hood: Domino / Born II die: Spice 1 / Ol' Dirty's back: Ol' Dirty Bastard / I'm talkin' to myself: NME & Grench The Mean 1 / Hood got me feelin' the pain: Havoc & Prodeje / One less nigga: M.C. Eiht / From the dark side: Gravediggaz / Death represents my hood: Bokie Loc / Hot ones echo thru the ghetto: Click / Grave: Click
CD _____ Click
MCA / Jun '95 / BMG.

TALES OF BEATRIX POTTER
Lanchberry, John C
CD _____ CDC 7545372
EMI / Nov '94 / EMI.

TALES OF THE CITY
Love to love you baby: Summer, Donna / Never can say goodbye: Gaynor, Gloria / Jive talkin': Bee Gees / Philadelphia freedom: John, Elton / That's the way I like it: K.C. & The Sunshine Band / Lady marmalade: Labelle / You sexy thing: Hot Chocolate / H.A.P.P.Y. radio: Starr, Edwin / You're the first, the last, my everything: White, Barry / It's a man's man's man world: White, Barry / Cry me a river: London, Julie / I'm not in love: 10cc / Cocaine: Cale, J.J. / Hang on in there: Bristol, Johnny / Don't

take away the music: Tavares / Disco inferno: Soul Station
CD _____ 5165152
PolyGram TV / Oct '93 / PolyGram.

TALK RADIO/WALL STREET
Copeland, Stewart C
Unpredictable: Kent / We know where you live: Tick / He has a heart: Trend / Bud's scam: Copeland, Stewart / Trading begins: Copeland, Stewart / End titles: Copeland, Stewart / Break up: Copeland, Stewart / Just come right in here please: Dietz / We feel too much: Tick / Are you mine: Copeland, Stewart / Tall weeds: Copeland, Stewart / Anacott steel: Copeland, Stewart
CD _____ VSD 5215
Varese Sarabande/Colosseum / Feb '90 / Pinnacle / Silva Screen.

TANGO ARGENTINA
1991 London Cast
Quejas de bandoneon / El choclo / La cumparsita / Uno / Nostalgias / La punalada / Cuesta abajo / Jealousy / Balada pars mi muerte / Milonguita/Divina/Melenita de oro/ Ra-fa-si / Milongueando en el 40 / Nunca tuvo novio / Orgullo criollo / De mi barrio / Verano porteno / La ultima curda / Canaro en Paris / Mi noche triste / Tanguera / Desencuentro / Adios nonino / Danzarin
CD _____ 7567816362
East West / Apr '91 / Warner Music.

TANK GIRL
CD _____ 7559617602
Warner Bros. / Apr '95 / Warner Music.

TANTIE DANIELLE
Yared, Gabriel C
CD _____ 30761
Silva Screen / Jul '93 / Conifer / Silva Screen.

TAP DANCE KID, THE
1984 Broadway Cast
Krieger, Henry C
Lorick, Robert L
Overture / Another day / Four strikes against me / Class act / They never hear what I say / Dancing is everything / Fabulous feet / I could get used to him / Man in the moon / Like him / My luck is changing / Someday / I remember how it was / Tap tap / Dance if it makes you happy / William's song / Finale
CD _____ CDTER 1096
TER / Mar '95 / Koch.

TARAS BULBA
Waxman, Franz C
Bernstein, Elmer Con
CD _____ 09026626572
RCA / Nov '95 / BMG.

TAXI DRIVER
Herrmann, Bernard C
Theme / I work the whole city / Betsy in a white dress / Days do not end / All the animals come out at night / 44 Magnum is a monster / Sport and Iris
CD _____ A 8912
Alhambra / Jan '92 / Silva Screen.

TEEN WOLF
Goodman, Miles C
Flesh on fire: House, James / Big bad wolf: Wolf Sisters / Win in the end: Safan, Mark / Shootin' for the moon: Holland, Amy / Silhouette: Palmer, David / Way to go: Viena, Mark / Good news: Morgan, David / Transformation: Teen Wolf / Boof: Teen Wolf
CD _____ 8290922
Silva Screen / Jan '89 / Conifer / Silva Screen.

TELL ME ON A SUNDAY
Webb, Marti
Lloyd Webber, Andrew C
Black, Don L
Capped teeth and Caesar salad / I'm very you, you're very me / It's not the end of the world / If he's married, if he's younger, if I lose him / Let me finish / Let's talk about you / Letter home to England / Nothing like you've ever known / Second letter home / Sheldon bloom / Take that look off your face / Tell me on a Sunday / You made me think you were in love
CD _____ 8334472
Polydor / Jan '90 / PolyGram.

TEN COMMANDMENTS, THE
Bernstein, Elmer C
Prelude / In the bulrushes / Bitter life / Love and ambition / Hard bondage / Egyptian dance / Crucible of God / And Moses watered Jethro's flock / Bedouin dance / I am that I am / Overture / Thus says the lord / Plagues / Exodus / Pillar of fire / Red sea / Ten commandments / Go, proclaim liberty
CD _____ MCAD 42320
MCA/Silva Screen / Jan '92 / Silva Screen.

TENDERLOIN
Broadway Cast
Bock, Jerry C
Harnick, Sheldon L
CD _____ ZDM 5650222
EMI Classics / Dec '93 / EMI.

TERMINATOR, THE
(Complete Score)
Fiedel, Brad C
CD _____ CIN 22082
Silva Screen / Aug '94 / Conifer / Silva Screen.

TERMINATOR, THE
Fiedel, Brad C
CD _____ FILMCD 101
Silva Screen / Jul '92 / Conifer / Silva Screen.

TERMINATOR, THE II
(Judgement Day)
Fiedel, Brad C
CD _____ VSD 5335
Varese Sarabande/Colosseum / Aug '91 / Pinnacle / Silva Screen.

TEX AVERY
Bradley, Scott C
CD _____ 124702
Milan / Jan '95 / BMG / Silva Screen.

THAT'S THE WAY IT IS
Presley, Elvis
I just can't help believin' / Twenty days and twenty nights / How the web was woven / Patch it up / Mary in the morning / You don't have to say you love me / You've lost that lovin' feelin' / I've lost you / Just pretend / Stranger in the crowd / Next step is love / Bridge over troubled water
CD _____ 7432114690-2
RCA / Jul '93 / BMG.

THELMA AND LOUISE
Zimmer, Hans C
CD _____ MCLD 19313
MCA / Oct '95 / BMG.

THEY LIVE
Carpenter, John
Carpenter, John & Alan Howarth C
Coming to L.A. / Message / Siege of Justiceville / Return to church / All out of bubblegum / Back to the street / Kidnapped / Transient hotel / Underground / Wake up
CD _____ DSCD 1
Demon / Oct '90 / Pinnacle / ADA.

THEY'RE PLAYING OUR SONG
1980 London Cast
Hamlisch, Marvin C
Bayer Sager, Carole L
Hossack, Grant Con
Overture / Fallin' / If he really knew me / Workin' it out / They're playing my song / If she really knew me / Right / Entr'acte / Just for tonight / When you're in my arms / Fill in the words / They're playing our song (finale)
CD _____ CDTER 1035
TER / May '89 / Koch.

THIBEAUD THE CRUSADER
Delerue, Georges C
CD _____ PCD 114
Prometheus / Jan '93 / Silva Screen.

THIEF
Tangerine Dream
Tangerine Dream C
Beach theme / Dr. Destructo / Diamond diary / Burning bar / Beach scene / Scrap yard / Trap feeling / Igneous
CD _____ TAND 12
Virgin / Jul '95 / EMI.

THIN BLUE LINE, THE
Glass, Philip Ensemble
Glass, Philip C
Riesman, Michael Con
Opening credits / Interrogation / Turko (part one) / Vidor / Adam's story / Defense attorney's / Judge / Trial (part two) / Mystery eyewitness (part two) / Thin blue line / Defense attorney's II / Hell on earth / Confession / Prologue / Interrogation (part two) / Turko (part two) / Harris' story / Comets and Vegas / Harris' crimes (pts 1 & 2) / Trial (part one) / Mystery eyewitness (part one) / Mystery eyewitness (part three) / Electric chair / Harris' testimony / Mystery eyewitness (part five) / Harris' childhood / End credits
CD _____ 7559792092
Elektra Nonesuch / Apr '89 / Warner Music.

THIN LINE BETWEEN LOVE AND HATE, THE
CD _____ 9362461342
WEA / Feb '96 / Warner Music.

THING, THE
Morricone, Ennio C
Morricone, Ennio C
CD _____ VSD 5278
Varese Sarabande/Colosseum / Aug '91 / Pinnacle / Silva Screen.

THIRST
May, Brian C
CD _____ IMICD 1003
Silva Screen / Jan '93 / Conifer / Silva Screen.

THIS FILM'S CRAP LET'S SLASH THE SEATS
Holmes, David
Holmes, David C
Holmes, David L
No man's land / Slash the seats / Shake ya brain / Got fucked up along the way / Gone / Atom in you / Minus 61 in Detroit / Inspired by Leyburn / Coming home to the sun
2CD _____ 8286312
Go Discs / Jun '95 / PolyGram.

THIS IS MY LIFE
Simon, Carly
Simon, Carly L
Love of my life / Back the way (Dottie's point of view) / Moving day / Easy on the eyes / Walking and kissing / Show must go on / Back the way (girls' point of view) / Little troupers / Night before christmas / This is my life suite / Love of my life (drive to the city)
CD _____ 7599269012
Qwest / May '92 / Warner Music.

THIS IS SPINAL TAP
Spinal Tap
CD _____ 8178462
Polydor / Aug '90 / PolyGram.

THOMAS AND THE KING
1975 London Cast
Williams, John C
Harbert, James L
CD _____ CDTER 1009
TER / Aug '95 / Koch.

THREE GUYS NAKED FROM THE WAIST DOWN
1985 Off-Broadway Cast
Rupert, Michael & Jerry Colker C
Overture / Promise of greatness / Angry guy/Lovely day / Don't wanna be no super-star / Screaming clocks (The dummies song) / History of stand-up comedy / Dreams of heaven / Kamikaze kaberaet / American dream / What a ride / Hello fellas TV special world tour / Father now / Three guys naked from the waist down (theme) / I don't believe in heroes anymore / Finale
CD _____ CDTER 1100
TER / May '93 / Koch.

THREE MUSKETEERS
Kamen, Michael C
All for love: Adams, Bryan & Rod Stewart/Sting / Cavern of Cardinal Richelieu / D'Artagnan / Athos, Porthos and Aramis / Sword fight / King Louis XIII, Queen Anne and Constance / Cardinal's coach / Cannonballs / M'lady de winter / Fourth musketeer
CD _____ 5401902
A&M / Apr '94 / PolyGram.

THREE O'CLOCK HIGH
Tangerine Dream
Tangerine Dream C
CD _____ VCD 47307
Varese Sarabande/Colosseum / Jan '89 / Pinnacle / Silva Screen.

THREE STEPS TO HEAVEN
2CD _____ DBG 53034
Double Gold / Sep '94 / Target/BMG.

THREE WISHES
Magic begins / Tom remembers / Magic comes closer / Highway / Betty Jane appears / Hide and seek / Jack / Left out / Journal / Jack's life / Phil / Explorers / In the yard / Monster / Catch / Gunny / Tom gets his wish / Homecoming / Gunny flies / Jack and Jeanne / Jack's wish / Gunny's wish / Coach / Jack's cast comes off / Light creature / Love / Home run / Bad news / Bather's day / End credits
CD _____ CDEMD 1093
Premier / Dec '95 / EMI.

THREE WISHES FOR JAMIE
Broadway Cast
Moloney, Paddy C
CD _____ ZDM 7648882
EMI Classics / Apr '93 / EMI.

THREE WORLDS OF GULLIVER, THE
Herrmann, Bernard C
CD _____ ACN 7018
Cloud Nine / Apr '95 / Conifer / Silva Screen.

THREEPENNY OPERA, THE
1954 Broadway Cast
Weill, Kurt C
Brecht, Bertolt L
Overture / Ballad of Mack the Knife / Morning anthem / Instead-of-song / Wedding song / Pirate Jenny / Army song / Love song / Ballad of dependency / Melodrama / Polly's song / Ballad of the easy life / World is mean / Barbara song / Tango ballad / Jealousy duet / How to survive / Useless song / Solomon song / Call from the grave / Death message / Finale / Mounted messenger
CD _____ CDTER 1101
TER / Jul '89 / Koch.

THREEPENNY OPERA, THE
1995 London Cast
Weill, Kurt C
Brecht, Bertolt L
CD _____ CDTER 1227
TER / Aug '95 / Koch.

THREEPENNY OPERA, THE
Lenya, Lotte/Marlene Dietrich
Weill, Kurt C
Brecht, Bertolt L
CD _____ 9031720252
Teldec Classics / Jan '95 / Warner Music.

THREEPENNY OPERA, THE
Berlin RIAS Chamber Choir/Sinfonietta
Weill, Kurt C
Brecht, Bertolt L
Mauceri, John Con
CD _____ 4300752
Decca / Mar '90 / PolyGram.

THREEPENNY OPERA, THE
Bulgarian TV/Radio Mixed Choir/Symphony Orchestra
Weill, Kurt C

BRECHT, Bertolt L
CD _____ 370062
Koch / Feb '91 / Koch.

THREESOME
New star: Tears For Fears / I'll take you there: General Public / Dancing barefoot: U2 / Like a virgin: Teenage Fanclub / Boom shak-a-lak: Apache Indian / Is your love strong enough: Ferry, Bryan / Bizarre love triangle: New Order / Make me smile (come up and see me): Duran Duran / He's my best friend: Jellyfish / Buttercup: Brad / What does sex mean to me: Human Sexual Response / That was the day: The The
CD _____ 4765782
Epic / Oct '94 / Sony.

THUNDERBALL
Barry, John C
Thunderball, Theme from: Jones, Tom / Chateau flight / Electrocution - searching Lippe's room / Switching the body / Vulcan crash landing - loading bombs into disc / Cape Martinique - Mr. Kiss Kiss Bang Bang / Thunderball / Death of Fiona / Bond below / Disco Volante / Search for vulcan / 007 / Mr. Kiss Kiss Bang Bang
CD _____ CZ 556
Premier / Dec '95 / EMI.

THUNDERHEART
Horner, James C
Intrada / Jan '93 / Silva Screen / Koch.

TILL WE MEET AGAIN
CD _____ XCD 1003
Varese Sarabande/Colosseum / Apr '91 / Pinnacle / Silva Screen.

TIME MACHINE, THE
Garcia, Russell C
London 1900 / Time machine model / Time machine / Quick trip into the future / All the time in the world / Beautiful forest / Great hall / Fear / Weena / Rescue
CD _____ GNPD 8008
GNP Crescendo / Jan '89 / Silva Screen.

TIME OF DESTINY, A
Morricone, Ennio C
CD _____ 7909382
Silva Screen / Jan '89 / Conifer / Silva Screen.

TIME OF THE GYPSIES
Bregovic, Goran C
CD _____ 8427622
Silva Screen / Jul '92 / Conifer / Silva Screen.

TIMECOP
Isham, Mark
Isham, Mark C
CD _____ VSD 5532
Varese Sarabande/Colosseum / Nov '94 / Pinnacle / Silva Screen.

TINTYPES
Broadway Cast
CD _____ CDXP 5196
DRG / Jan '89 / New Note.

TITO
Theodorakis, Mikis C
CD _____ SR 50087
Varese Sarabande/Colosseum / May '94 / Pinnacle / Silva Screen.

TO DIE FOR
Elfman, Danny C
CD _____ VSD 5646
Varese Sarabande/Colosseum / Nov '95 / Pinnacle / Silva Screen.

TO THE ENDS OF THE EARTH
Scott, John C
CD _____ PCD 102
Prometheus / Jan '89 / Silva Screen.

TOGETHER WITH MUSIC
(Archive Recording Of The Television Event)
Martin, Mary & Noel Coward
Together with music / Uncle Harry / Nina / Mad dogs and Englishmen / Dites moi / Cockeyed optimist / Some enchanted evening / Wash that man right out of my hair / Wonderful guy / My heart belongs to Daddy
CD _____ DRGCD 1103
DRG / Jan '94 / New Note.

TOM AND VIV
Palm Court Theatre Orchestra
Wiseman, Debbie C
Wiseman, Debbie Con
CD _____ SK 64381
Sony Classical / Nov '94 / Sony.

TOMBSTONE
Broughton, Bruce C
CD _____ MAF 7038D
Intrada / Jan '93 / Silva Screen / Koch.

TOMMY
Who
Townshend, Pete C
Overture / It's a boy / 1921 / Amazing journey / Sparks / Eyesight to the blind / Miracle cure / Sally Simpson / I'm free / Welcome / Tommy's holiday camp / We're not gonna take it / Christmas / Cousin Kevin / Acid queen / Underture / Do you think it's alright / Fiddle about / Pinball wizard / There's a doctor / Go to the mirror / Tommy can you hear me / Smash the mirror / Sensation
2CD _____ 8000772

TOMMY
Polydor / Apr '89 / PolyGram.
CD _____ 73145310432
Polydor / Mar '96 / PolyGram.

TOMMY
Cast Recording
Townshend, Pete C
CD _____ CCSCD 406
Castle / Nov '94 / BMG.

TOMMY
1993 Broadway Cast
Townshend, Pete C
2CD _____ 09026618742
RCA Victor / '93 / BMG.

TOMMY
Townshend, Pete C
Overture from Tommy / Prologue / Captain Walker/It's a boy / Bernie's holiday camp 1951/What about the boy / Amazing journey / Christmas / Eyesight to the blind / Acid Queen / Do you think it's alright / Cousin Kevin / Do you think it's alright #2 / Fiddle about / Do you think it's alright #3 / Sparks / Extra extra extra / Pinball wizard / Champagne / There's a doctor / Go to the mirror / Tommy can you hear me / Smash the mirror / I'm free / Mother and son / Sensation / Miracle cure / Sally Simpson / Welcome TV studio / Tommy's holiday camp / We're not gonna take it / Listening to you/See you, feel me
2CD _____ 8411212
Polydor / Jan '94 / PolyGram.

TOMMY BOY
CD _____ 9362459042
Warner Bros. / Aug '95 / Warner Music.

TONITE LET'S ALL MAKE LOVE IN LONDON
1967 Film Cast
CD _____ SEECD 258
See For Miles/C5 / '90 / Pinnacle.

TOP BANANA
Broadway Cast
Mercer, Johnny C
CD _____ ZDM 7647722
EMI Classics / Apr '93 / EMI.

TOP GUN
Danger zone: Loggins, Kenny / Mighty wings: Cheap Trick / Playing with the boys: Loggins, Kenny / Lead me on: Marie, Teena / Take my breath away (Love theme from Top Gun): Berlin / Hot summer nights: Miami Sound Machine / Heaven in your eyes: Loverboy / Through the fire: Greene, Larry / Destination unknown: Marietta / Top Gun anthem: Faltermeyer, Harold & Steve Stevens
CD _____ CD 70296
CBS / Sep '86 / Sony.

TORN CURTAIN
Addison, John C
Addison, John Con
CD _____ VSD 5296
Varese Sarabande/Colosseum / Apr '91 / Pinnacle / Silva Screen.

TOTAL RECALL
Goldsmith, Jerry C
Goldsmith, Jerry Con
Dream / Hologram / Big jump / Mutant / Cleaver girl / First meeting / Treatment / Where am I / End of a dream / New life
CD _____ VSD 5267
Varese Sarabande/Colosseum / Aug '90 / Pinnacle / Silva Screen.

TOTO LE HEROS
Van Dormael, Pierre C
CD _____ BM 001
Milan / Jan '95 / BMG / Silva Screen.

TOUCH OF EVIL, A
Mancini, Henry C
Mancini, Henry Con
CD _____ VSD 5414
Varese Sarabande/Colosseum / Jul '93 / Pinnacle / Silva Screen.

TOUGH GUYS/TRUCK TURNER
Hayes, Isaac
Title theme / Randolph and Dearborn / Red rooster / Joe Bell / Hung up on my baby / Kidnapped / Run Fay run / Buns o'plenty / End theme / Main title: Truck Turner / House of beauty / Blue's crib / Driving in the sun / Breakthrough / Now we're one / Duke / Dorinda's party / Persuit of the pimpmobile / We need each other, girl / House full of girls / Hospital shootout / You're in my arms again / Give it to me / Drinking / Insurance company
CD _____ CDSXE 2095
Stax / Jul '93 / Pinnacle.

TOUS LES MATINS DU MONDE
CD _____ AUE 004640
Auvidis/Ethnic / Feb '93 / Harmonia Mundi.

TOVARICH
Broadway Cast
CD _____ ZDM 7648932
EMI Classics / Apr '93 / EMI.

TOWN FOX, THE
(And Other Musical Tales)
Royal Liverpool Philharmonic Orchestra
Davis, Carl Con
CD _____ SCENECD 19
First Night / '94 / Pinnacle.

TOWN LIKE ALICE, A
Smeaton, Bruce C
CD _____ SCCD 1013
Southern Cross / Jan '89 / Silva Screen

TOY SOLDIERS
Folk, Robert C
CD _____ MAF 7015D
Intrada / Jan '93 / Silva Screen / Koch.

TOYS
Tchaikovsky's Symphony No.1 (excerpt) /
Closing of the year: Wendy & Lisa/Cast /
Etudae: Enya / Happy worker: Amos, Tori /
Alsatia's lullaby: Migenes, Julia & Hans Zim-
mer / Workers: Cast of Toys / Let joy and
innocence prevail: Metheny, Pat / General:
Gambon, Michael & Hans Zimmer / Mirror
song: Dolby, Thomas & Robin Williams/
John Cusack / Battle introduction: Williams,
Robin / Welcome to the pleasure dome:
Frankie Goes To Hollywood / Let joy and
innocence prevail (2): Jones, Grace / Clos-
ing of the year/Happy Workers (Reprise):
Siberry, Jane
CD _____ 450991603-2
ZTT / Mar '93 / Warner Music.

TRAIL OF THE PINK PANTHER
Mancini, Henry & His Orchestra
Mancini, Henry C
Trail of the pink panther / Greatest gift /
Hong Kong fireworks / Shot in the dark /
Simone / I had better be tonight / Easy life
in Paris / Come to me / Bierfest polka / After
the shower / Inspector Clouseau theme /
Return of the Pink Panther
CD _____ 906272
Silva Screen / Jan '89 / Conifer / Silva
Screen.

TRANSFORMERS
Touch: Bush, Stan / Instruments of destruc-
tion: NRG / Death of Optimus prime: Dicola,
Vince / Dare: Bush, Stan / Nothin's gonna
stand in our way: Spectre General / Trans-
formers (theme): Lion / Escape: Dicola,
Vince / Hunger: Spectre General / Autobot:
Dicola, Vince / Decepticon battle: Dicola,
Vince / Dare to be stupid: Yankovic, Weird
Al
CD _____ 752422
Silva Screen / Mar '92 / Conifer / Silva
Screen.

TRAVELLING MAN
Browne, Duncan & Sebastian Graham
Jones
CD _____ CDSGP 0114
Prestige / Sep '95 / Total/BMG.

TREE GROWS IN BROOKLYN, A
1951 Broadway Cast
Schwartz, Arthur C
Fields, Dorothy L
Goberman, M. Con
CD _____ SK 48014
Sony Broadway / Dec '91 / Sony.

TRESPASS
Trespass: Ice-T & Ice Cube / Gotta do what
I gotta do: Public Enemy / Depths of hell:
Ice-T / I check my bank: Sir Mix-a-Lot / I'm
a playa (bitch): Penthouse Players Clique /
On the wall: Black Sheep / Don't be a 304:
AMG / Gotta get over (taking loot): Gang
Starr / You know what I'm about: Lord Fi-
nesse / I'm gonna smoke him: Donald D /
Quick way out: W.C. & the Maad Circle /
King of the street: Cooder, Ry
CD _____ 7599269782
Sire / Feb '93 / Warner Music.

TRESPASS
(Score)
Cooder, Ry C
Cooder, Ry C
CD _____ 9362452202
Warner Bros. / Jan '94 / Warner Music.

TRIAL, THE
Davis, Carl C
CD _____ 873150
Milan / Feb '94 / BMG / Silva Screen.

TRIPODS, THE
Freeman, Ken C
Freeman, Ken C
CD _____ GERCD 1
Pinnacle / Nov '95 / Pinnacle.

TRIUMPH OF THE SPIRIT
Eidelman, Cliff C
Main title / Dark tunnel to Aushwitz / Answer
us / Avram refuses to work / Hard felt rest /
Elena's false dreams / Begging for bread
/ Slaughter / Hunger / Salamo desperately
finds Allegra / New assignment / Epilogue /
Love in wedlock / There was a time / Mi dyo
mi / Longing for home / Hell realization /
There was a memory / Mourning / It was a
month before we left / Mercy on to us / Al-
legra's punishment / Death march
CD _____ VSD 5254
Varese Sarabande/Colosseum / Apr '90 /
Pinnacle / Silva Screen.

TROIS COULEURS - BLEU
Preisner, Zbigniew
Preisner, Zbigniew C
Chant pour l'unification d'Europe / Van den
budenmayer - musique funebre / Les images d'enterrement / Memento - premiere
apparition / Lutte de carnaval contre la careme / Memento / Julie avec Olivier / Ellipse
1 / Premiere flute / Julie - dans son nouvel
appartement / Memento - Julie dans l'es-
calier / Deuxieme flute / Ellipse 2 / Lutte de

carnaval contre le careme II / Memento -
flute / Ellipse 3 / Theme d'Olivier - piano /
Olivier et Julie - essai de composition /
Theme d'Olivier - version finale / Bolero -
annonce du film "Rouge" / Chant pour
l'unification d'Europe - version de Julie /
Generique de fin / Memento - orgue / Bo-
lero - film "Rouge"
CD _____ CDVMM 12
Virgin / Oct '93 / EMI.

**TROIS COULEURS - BLEU, BLANC,
ROUGE**
Preisner, Zbigniew
Preisner, Zbigniew C
3CD _____ CDVMMX 15
Virgin / Nov '94 / EMI.

TROIS COULEURS - ROUGE
Preisner, Zbigniew
Preisner, Zbigniew C
Fashion show (1) / Meeting the judge /
Tapped conversation / Leaving the judge /
Psychoanalysis / Today is my birthday / Do
not take another man's wife / Treason /
Fashion show (2) / Conversation at the
theatre / Rest of the conversation at the
theatre / Do not take another man's wife (2)
/ Catastrophe / Finale
CD _____ CDVMM 14
Virgin / Nov '94 / EMI.

TROUBLE IN MIND
Isham, Mark C
CD _____ 905012
Silva Screen / Jan '89 / Conifer / Silva
Screen.

TROUBLE IN PARADISE
Newman, Randy
Newman, Randy C
I love L.A. / Christmas in Capetown / Blues
/ Same girl / Mikey's / My life is good / Mi-
ami / Real emotional girl / Take me back /
There's a party at my house / I'm different
/ Song for the dead
CD _____ 923755 2
WEA / Jan '83 / Warner Music.

TROUBLE MAN
Gaye, Marvin
Gaye, Marvin C
Trouble man main theme (2) / T plays it cool
/ Poor Abbey Walsh / Break in (police shoot
big) / Cleo's apartment / Trouble man /
Trouble man, Theme from / T stands for
trouble / Trouble man main theme (1) / Life
is a gamble / Deep in it / Don't mess with
Mr. T / There goes mister 'T'
CD _____ 530097-2
Motown / Jan '92 / PolyGram.

TRUE GRIT/COMANCHEROS
**(Music From John Wayne Westerns Vol.
1)**
Bernstein, Elmer C
CD _____ VSD 47236
Varese Sarabande/Colosseum / Jan '89 /
Pinnacle / Silva Screen.

TRUE LIES
Fiedel, Brad C
Sunshine of your love (2 mixes): Living Col-
our / Darkness darkness: Screaming Trees
/ Alone in the dark: Hiatt, John / Entity:
Mother Tongue / Main title: Harry makes his
entrance / Escape from the chateau / Har-
ry's sweet home / Harry rides again / Spy-
ing on Helen / Juno's place / Caught in the
act / Shadow lover / Island suite / Cause-
way/Helicopter rescue / Nuclear Kiss /
Harry saves the day
CD _____ 4769392
Columbia / Aug '94 / Sony.

TRUE ROMANCE
Zimmer, Hans C
CD _____ 5199542
Polydor / Nov '93 / PolyGram.

TRUSTING BEATRICE/COLD HEAVEN
Myers, Stanley C
CD _____ MAF 7048D
Intrada / Mar '93 / Silva Screen / Koch.

TRYOUT
**(Songs From Where Do We Go From
Here/One Touch Of Venus)**
Weill, Kurt & Ira Gershwin
CD _____ DRGCD 904
DRG / Jan '95 / New Note.

TUCKER
Jackson, Joe
Captain of industry (overture) / Car of to-
morrow - today / No chance blues / (He's
a shape) In a drape / Factory / Vera / It pays
to advertise / Tiger rag / Showtime in Chi-
cago / Lone bank loan blues / Speedway /
Marilee / Hangin' in Howard Hughes' han-
gar / Toast of the town / Abe's blues / Trial
/ Freedom swing / Rhythm delivery
CD _____ 5512672
Spectrum/Karussell / Sep '95 / PolyGram /
THE.

TURTLE BEACH
Neal, Chris C
Main theme / Minou's theme / Judith / Let
the fates decide / Riot / Children without
tears / Batu caves / Whispering knives /
Love theme / Sacrifice / For the refugees /
Homecoming
CD _____ FILMCD 120
Silva Screen / Jun '92 / Conifer / Silva
Screen.

TUSITALA, TELLER OF TALES
(Music From BBC's Stevenson's Tales)
Stevenson, Savourna
CD _____ ECLCD 9412
Eclectic / Jan '95 / Pinnacle.

TWILIGHT ZONE, THE - VOL. 1
(Music From The TV Series)
Invaders / Where is everybody / I sing the
body electric / Jazz themes / Nervous man
in a four dollar room / Walking distance /
Main title / End titles
CD _____ VCD 47233
Varese Sarabande/Colosseum / Jan '89 /
Pinnacle / Silva Screen.

TWILIGHT ZONE, THE - VOL. 2
(Music From The TV Series)
Main theme / Back there / And when the
sky was opened / Passerby / Lonely / Two
/ End theme
CD _____ VCD 47247
Varese Sarabande/Colosseum / Jan '89 /
Pinnacle / Silva Screen.

TWILIGHT'S LAST GLEAMING
Graunke Symphony Orchestra
Goldsmith, Jerry C
Goldsmith, Jerry Con
Silo 3 / Takeover begins / General Macken-
zie arrives / He has launch control / Special
forces arrive / Bubble / Nuclear nightmare /
Reflective interlude / After you Mr President
/ Heading for home / President falls / Taking
of silo 3 / Operation going begins / Watching
and waiting / Tanks / Down the elevator
shaft / Gold bomb / Gold team enters silo
3 / Final betrayal
CD _____ FILMCD 111
Silva Screen / Apr '92 / Conifer / Silva
Screen.

TWIN PEAKS
Badalamenti, Angelo
Badalamenti, Angelo C
Twin Peaks (theme) / Laura Palmer's theme
/ Audrey's dance / Nightingale / Freshly
squeezed / Bookhouse boys / Into the night
/ Night life in Twin Peaks / Dance of the
dream man / Love theme from Twin Peaks
/ Falling: Cruise, Julee
CD _____ 7599263162
Warner Bros. / Nov '90 / Warner Music.

TWIN PEAKS - FIRE WALK WITH ME
Badalamenti, Angelo
Badalamenti, Angelo C
Twin Peaks - fire walk with me (theme) /
Pine float / Sycamore trees / Don't do any-
thing (I wouldn't do) / Real indication /
Questions in a world of blue / Pink room /
Black dog runs at night / Best friends /
Moving through time / Montage from Twin
Peaks
CD _____ 9362450192
WEA / Feb '95 / Warner Music.

TWINS
Twins: Little Richard & Phil Bailey / Brother
to brother: Spinners / It's too late: Nayobe
/ I only have eyes for you: Scott, Marilyn /
Yakety yak: 2 Live Crew / No way of
knowin': Summer, Henry Lee / Train kept a
rollin': Beck, Jeff / I'd die for this: Laser-
son, Nicolette / Going to Santa Fe: Mc-
Ferrin, Bobby & Herbie Hancock / Main title
CD _____ SPK 45036
CBS/Silva Screen / Jan '89 / Conifer / Silva
Screen.

TWO MOON JUNCTION
Elias, Jonathan C
CD _____ VSD 5518
Varese Sarabande/Colosseum / Oct '94 /
Pinnacle / Silva Screen.

U

U BOATS: THE WOLF PACK
Young, Christopher C
CD _____ CEUR 0214
Silva Screen / Jan '93 / Conifer / Silva
Screen.

ULYSSES
Cicognini, Alessandro C
CD _____ LEGENDCD 8
Legend / Apr '96 / Conifer / Silva Screen /
Discovery.

ULYSSES' GAZE
Karaindrou, Eleni
CD _____ 4491532
ECM / Oct '95 / New Note.

UMBRELLAS OF CHERBOURG, THE
Legrand, Michel C
CD _____ 8341392
Silva Screen / Jan '89 / Conifer / Silva
Screen.

UN COEUR EN HIVER
Sarde, Philippe C
CD _____ 4509924082
WEA / Jan '95 / Warner Music.

UN EROE BORGHESE
Donaggio, Pino C
CD _____ LEGENDCD 19
Legend / May '96 / Conifer / Silva Screen /
Discovery.

**UNBEARABLE LIGHTNESS OF BEING,
THE**
Janacek, Leos C
Fairytale III / Holy Virgin of Frydek / In the
mists / Hey Jude / Joy joy joy / String quartet no. 2 / Sonata for violin and piano / Bird
of ill omen lingers on / On the overgrown
path, set 2 / String quartet no. 3 / Blow
away leaf / Goodnight / Idyll for string orchestra, II
CD _____ FCD 21006
Fantasy / Jan '89 / Pinnacle / Jazz Music /
Wellard / Cadillac.

UNDER SIEGE
Chang, Gary
Chang, Gary C
CD _____ VSD 5409
Varese Sarabande/Colosseum / Feb '93 /
Pinnacle / Silva Screen.

UNDER SIEGE II
Poledouris, Basil C
CD _____ VSD 5648
Varese Sarabande/Colosseum / Oct '95 /
Pinnacle / Silva Screen.

UNDER THE CHERRY MOON
(Parade)
Prince & The Revolution
Prince C
Christopher Tracy's parade / New position
/ I wonder U / Under the cherry moon / Girls
and boys / Life can be so nice / Venus de
Milo / Mountains / Do U lie / Kiss / Anoth-
erloverholenyohead / Sometimes it snows
in April
CD _____ 925395 2
WEA / Apr '86 / Warner Music.

UNDERNEATH
Soderbergh, Steven C
CD _____ VSD 5587
Varese Sarabande/Colosseum / Mar '95 /
Pinnacle / Silva Screen.

UNDERNEATH THE ARCHES
1982 London Cast
Old bull and bush / Just for laughs / Un-
derneath the arches / Maybe it's because
I'm a Londoner / Home town / Umbrella
man / Strollin' / Siegfried line
CD _____ CDTER 1015
TER / Aug '95 / Koch.

UNFORGIVEN
Niehaus, Lennie C
CD _____ VSD 5380
Varese Sarabande/Colosseum / Sep '92 /
Pinnacle / Silva Screen.

UNFORGIVEN, THE
Tiomkin, Dimitri C
CD _____ TSU 0108
Tsunami / Jan '95 / Silva Screen.

UNIVERSAL SOLDIER
Franke, Christopher C
CD _____ VSD 5373
Varese Sarabande/Colosseum / Nov '92 /
Pinnacle / Silva Screen.

UNKNOWN TIME, THE
Dikker, Loek C
CD _____ 887902
Milan / Jan '95 / BMG / Silva Screen.

UNLAWFUL ENTRY
Horner, James C
CD _____ MAF 7031D
Intrada / Dec '92 / Silva Screen / Koch.

UNSINKABLE MOLLY BROWN, THE
Willson, Meredith C
CD _____ CDP 92054
Silva Screen / Feb '90 / Conifer / Silva
Screen.

UNSINKABLE MOLLY BROWN, THE
Broadway Cast
Willson, Meredith C
CD _____ ZDM 7647612
EMI Classics / Apr '93 / EMI.

UNTAMED HEART
Eidelman, Cliff C
CD _____ VSD 5404
Varese Sarabande/Colosseum / Mar '93 /
Pinnacle / Silva Screen.

UNTIL SEPTEMBER/STAR CRASH
Barry, John C
Barry, John Con
CD _____ FILMCD 085
Silva Screen / Sep '91 / Conifer / Silva
Screen.

UNTIL THE END OF THE WORLD
Opening titles / Sax and violins: Talking
Heads / Summer kisses, winter tears / Move
with me / Adversary / What's good: Reed,
Lou / Last night sleep / Fretless: R.E.M. /
Days / Claire's theme / Till the end of the
world / It takes time / Death's door / Love
theme / Calling all angels: Siberry, Jane /
Humans from earth / Sleeping in the devil's
bed / Until the end of the world: U2
CD _____ 7599267072
WEA / Dec '91 / Warner Music.

UP/MEGA VIXENS/BENEATH THE VALLEY OF THE ULTRA VIXENS
(Russ Meyer Original Soundtracks Vol. 2)
CD _____ QDKCD 009
Normal/Okra / Jul '94 / Direct / ADA.

UPTIGHT
Booker T & The MG's
Johnny I love you / Cleveland now / Children don't get weary / Tank's lament / Blues in the gutter / We've got Johnny Wells / Down at Ralph's joint / Deadwood Dick / Run tank run / Time is tight
CD _____ CDSXE 024
Stax / Jan '90 / Pinnacle.

URSUS - SCORES FROM 4 ITALIAN FANTASY FILMS
(Ursus/Ursus In The Valley Of Lions/Ursus In The Land Of Fire/The Three Invincibles)
CD _____ CDCIA 5090
Cinevox / Jan '92 / Conifer / Silva Screen.

USED PEOPLE
Portman, Rachel C
CD _____ WA 244812
Silva Screen / Jul '93 / Conifer / Silva Screen.

UTOPIA LIMITED
D'Oyly Carte Opera Chorus/Royal Philharmonic Orchestra
Sullivan, Sir Arthur C
Gilbert, W.S. L
Nash, R. Con
2CD _____ 4368162
London / Jan '90 / PolyGram.

UTU
Charles, John C
CD _____ LXCD 6
Silva Screen / Jan '92 / Conifer / Silva Screen.

V

VAGRANT, THE
Young, Christopher C
Young, Christopher Con
CD _____ MAF 7028D
Intrada / Sep '92 / Silva Screen / Koch.

VALMOUTH
1982 Chichester Festival Cast
Wilson, Sandy C
Valmouth / Magic fingers / Mustapha / I loved a man / All the girls were pretty / What do I want with love / Just once more / Lady of de manor / Big best shoes / Niri Esther / Cry of the peacock
CD _____ CDTER 1019
TER / May '89 / Koch.

VALMOUTH
1958 London Cast
Wilson, Sandy C
Valmouth / Magic fingers / Mustapha / I love a man / All the girls were pretty / What do I want with love / Just one more / Lady of de manor / Big best shoes / Niri Esther / Cry of the peacock / Little girl baby / Cathedral of Clemenza / Only a passing phase / Where the trees are green with parrots / My talking day / I will miss you / Finale
CD _____ CDSBL 13109
DRG / Nov '92 / New Note.

VERY GOOD EDDIE
1975 Broadway Cast
Kern, Jerome C
Greene, Schuyler L
Overture / We're on our way / Some sort of somebody / Thirteen collar / Bungalow in Quogue / Isn't it great to be married / Good night boat / Left all alone again / Hot dot / If you're a friend of mine / Wedding bells are calling me / Honeymoon Inn / I've got to dance / Moon of love / Old boy neutral / Babes in the wood / Katy D / Nodding roses / Finale
CD _____ DRGCD 6100
DRG / '88 / New Note.

VICTOR VICTORIA
Mancini, Henry C
You and me / Shady dame from Seville / Alone in Paris / King's can can / Le jazz hot / Crazy world / Chicago Illinois / Cat and mouse / Gay Paree / Finale
CD _____ GNPD 8038
GNP Crescendo / Sep '94 / Silva Screen.

VICTORY AT SEA
Cincinnati Pops Orchestra
Rodgers, Richard C
Kunzel, Erich Con
CD _____ CD 80175
Telarc / Aug '90 / Conifer / ADA.

VICTORY AT SEA
RCA Victor Symphony Orchestra
Rodgers, Richard C
Bennett, Robert Russell Con
Song of the high seas / Pacific boils over / Guadalcanal march / D-Day / Hard work and horseplay / Theme of the fast carriers / Beneath the Southern Cross / Mare nos-

trum / Victory at sea / Fire on the waters / Danger down deep / Mediterranean mosaic / Magnetic North
CD _____ 09026609632
RCA Victor / '90 / BMG.

VICTORY AT SEA
(More Victory At Sea)
RCA Victor Symphony Orchestra
Rodgers, Richard C
Bennett, Robert Russell Con
Allies on the march / Voyage into fate / Peleliu / Sound of victory / Rings around Rabaul / Full fathom five / Turkey shoot / Ships that pass / Two if by sea / Turning point / Symphonic scenario
CD _____ 09026609642
RCA Victor / '90 / BMG.

VIKINGS, THE/SOLOMON & SHEBA
Nascimbene, Mario C
CD _____ LEGENDCD 9
Legend / Jan '93 / Conifer / Silva Screen / Discovery.

VILLAGE OF THE DAMNED
Carpenter, John C
CD _____ VSD 5629
Varese Sarabande/Colosseum / Jun '95 / Pinnacle / Silva Screen.

VISION QUEST
CD _____ GED 24063
MCA/Silva Screen / Jan '93 / Silva Screen.

VIVA LAS VEGAS/ROUSTABOUT
Presley, Elvis
Viva Las Vegas / If you think I don't need you / If you need somebody to lean on / You're the boss / What I'd say / Do the Vega / C'mon everybody / Lady love me (With Ann Margaret) / Night life / Today, tomorrow and forever / Yellow rose of Texas / The eyes of Texas / Santa Lucia / Roustabout / Little Egypt / Poison ivy league / Hard knocks / It's a wonderful world / Big love, big heartache / One track heart / It's carnival time / Carmy town / There's a brand new day on the horizon / Wheels on my heels
CD _____ 74321 13432-2
RCA / Mar '93 / BMG.

VOICES
I will always wait for you / Rose Marie's theme / Disco if you want to / Children's song / Family theme / Anything that's rock 'n' roll / I will always wait for you (instrumental) / On a stage / Across the river / Bubbles in my beer / Rose Marie and drew / Drunk as a punk / Children's song (instrumental) / Rose Marie's dance
CD _____ DINTVCD 44
Dino / Sep '92 / Pinnacle / 3MV.

VON RYAN'S EXPRESS/OUR MAN FLINT/IN LIKE FLINT
Goldsmith, Jerry C
CD _____ TCI 0602
Silva Screen / Jan '95 / Conifer / Silva Screen.

VOYAGE OF TERROR
(The Achille Lauro Affair)
Morricone, Ennio C
CD _____ OST 101
Milano Dischi / Jan '93 / Silva Screen.

VOYAGES
Silvestri, Alan
Silvestri, Alan C
CD _____ VSD 5641
Varese Sarabande/Colosseum / Oct '95 / Pinnacle / Silva Screen.

W

WAITING TO EXHALE
Babyface C
Exhale: Houston, Whitney / Count on me: Houston, Whitney / Let it flow: Braxton, Toni / This is how it works: TLC / Sittin' in my room: Brandy / Not gonna try: Blige, Mary J. / All night long: S.W.V. / Kissing you: Evans, Faith / My funny valentine: Khan, Chaka / My love, sweet love: Labelle, Patti / Hurts like hell: Franklin, Aretha / Wey it: Moore, Chante / How could you call her baby: Shanna / Love will be waiting at home: For Real / And I give you love: Marie, Sonja
CD _____ 07822187962
Arista / Nov '95 / BMG.

WALK IN THE CLOUDS, A
Jarre, Maurice C
CD _____ 286662
RCA Victor / Nov '95 / BMG.

WALKING HAPPY
1966 Broadway Cast
Van Heusen, James C
Cahn, Sammy L
CD _____ ZDM 5651332
EMI Classics / Apr '94 / EMI.

WALL STREET/SALVADOR
Copeland, Stewart/Georges Delerue C
Bud's scam: Copeland, Stewart / Are you with me: Copeland, Stewart / Trading begins: Copeland, Stewart / Tall weeds: Copeland, Stewart / Break up: Copeland, Stewart / Anacott steel: Copeland, Stewart / El playon: Vancouver Symphony Orchestra / Siege at Santa Fe: Vancouver Symphony Orchestra / Goodby Maria: Vancouver Symphony Orchestra / At the border: Vancouver Symphony Orchestra / Roadblock: Vancouver Symphony Orchestra / Love theme: Finale: Vancouver Symphony Orchestra
CD _____ CDTER 1154
TER / May '88 / Koch.

WANDERERS, THE
You really got a hold on me: Miracles / Shout: Isley Brothers / Big girls don't cry: Four Seasons / Ya ya: Dorsey, Lee / My boyfriend's back: Angels / Soldier boy: Shirelles / Pipeline: Chantays / Do you love me: Contours / Wipeout: Surfans / Wanderer: Dion / Stand by me: King, Ben E. / Tequila: Champs
CD _____ NEMCD 765
Sequel / Oct '95 / BMG.

WAR AND PEACE
Ovchinnikov, Vyacheslav
Ovchinnikov, Vyacheslav C
CD _____ VSD 5225
Varese Sarabande/Colosseum / Feb '90 / Pinnacle / Silva Screen.

WAR LORD, THE
Moross, Jerome C
CD _____ VSD 5536
Varese Sarabande/Colosseum / Apr '95 / Pinnacle / Silva Screen.

WAR LORD, THE/THE CARDINAL
Moross, Jerome C
CD _____ TSU 0117
Tsunami / Jan '95 / Silva Screen.

WAR OF THE BUTTONS
Portman, Rachel C
CD _____ VSD 5554
Varese Sarabande/Colosseum / Oct '94 / Pinnacle / Silva Screen.

WAR REQUIEM
City Of Birmingham Symphony Orchestra
Britten, Benjamin C
Rattle, Simon Con
2CD _____ CDS 7470348
EMI / '88 / EMI.

WARLOCK
Melbourne Symphony Orchestra
Goldsmith, Jerry C
Goldsmith, Jerry Con
Sentence / Ill wind / Ring / Trance / Old age / Growing pains / Weather vane / Nails / Uninvited / Salt water attack / Salt flats
CD _____ FILMCD 038
Silva Screen / Jun '89 / Conifer / Silva Screen.

WARLOCK II - THE ARMAGEDDON
McKenzie, Mark C
CD _____ MAF 7049D
Intrada / Jan '93 / Silva Screen / Koch.

WARNING SIGN
Safan, Craig C
CD _____ SCCD 1012
Southern Cross / Jan '89 / Silva Screen.

WARRIORS
In the city: Walsh, Joe / Warriors theme: De Vorzon, Barry / Nowhere to run: Mandrill / Nowhere to run: McCuller, Arnold / In Havana: Vance, Kenny & Ismael Miranda / Love is a fire: Ravan, Genya / You're movin' too slow: Vastano, Johnny / Last of an ancient breed: Child, Desmond
CD _____ 235152
Spectrum/Karussell / Sep '95 / PolyGram THE.

WATERWORLD
Howard, James Newton C
Main titles / Escaping the smokers / Atoll / Prodigal child / Smokers sighted / Swimming / Sky boat / National geographic / Speargun / Bubble / Helen Frees the mariner / Helen sews / Slide for life / Half an hour / We're gonna die / Arriving at the deez / Deacons' speech / Haircuts / Gills / Why aren't you rowing / Balloon flight / Dry land / Mariner's goodbye / Main credits
CD _____ MCD 11282
MCA / Aug '95 / BMG.

WATTSTAX
Oh la de da: Staple Singers / I like the things about you: Staple Singers / Respect yourself: Staple Singers / I'll take you there: Staple Singers / Knock on wood: Floyd, Eddie / Lay your loving on me: Floyd, Eddie / I like what you're doing (to me): Thomas, Carla / Gee Whiz: Thomas, Carla / I have a God who loves: Thomas, Carla / Do the breakdown: Thomas, Rufus / Do the funky chicken: Thomas, Rufus / Do the funky penguin: Thomas, Rufus / Son of Shaft: Bar-Kays / Feel it: Bar-Kays / I can't turn you loose: Bar-Kays / Killing floor: King, Albert / I'll play the blues for you: King, Albert / Angel of mercy: King, Albert / I don't know what this world is coming to: Soul Children / Hearsay: Soul Children / Ain't no sunshine: Hayes, Isaac

2CD _____ CDSXE2 079
Stax / Nov '92 / Pinnacle.

WAVELENGTH
Tangerine Dream
Tangerine Dream C
CD _____ VCD 47223
Varese Sarabande/Colosseum / Jan '89 / Pinnacle / Silva Screen.

WAY WE WERE, THE
Streisand, Barbra
Hamlisch, Marvin C
Bergman, Marilyn L
Being at war with each other / Something so right / Best thing you've ever done / Way we were / All in love is fair / What are you doing the rest of your life / Summer me, Winter me / Pieces of dreams / I've never been a woman before / My buddy / How about me
CD _____ 474911 2
Columbia / Jan '94 / Sony

WAYNE'S WORLD
Bohemian rhapsody: Queen / Hot and bothered: Cinderella / Rock candy: Bulletboys / Dream weaver: Wright, Gary / Silkamikanico: Red Hot Chili Peppers / Time machine: Black Sabbath / Wayne's world theme: Myers, Mike / Ballroom blitz: Carrere, Tia / Foxy lady: Hendrix, Jimi / Feed my Frankenstein: Cooper, Alice / Why you wanna break my heart: Carrere, Tia
CD _____ 7599268052
Reprise / Feb '95 / Warner Music.

WAYNE'S WORLD II
Dude (looks like a lady) (live): Aerosmith / Shut up and dance: Aerosmith / Louie Louie: Plant, Robert / Superstar: Superfan / Frankenstein: Winter, Edgar / Radar love: Golden Earring / Spirit in the sky: Greenbaum, Norman / Can't get enough: Bad Company / Out there: Dinosaur Jnr / Idiot summer: Gin Blossoms / Mary's house: 4 Non Blondes / Y.M.C.A.: Village People
CD _____ 9362454852
Warner Bros. / Feb '94 / Warner Music.

WE BEGIN
Isham, Mark & Art Lande
Isham, Mark C
Melancholy of departure / Ceremony in starlight / We begin / Lord Ananea / Surface and symbol / Sweet circle / Fanfare
CD _____ 8316212
ECM / Jul '87 / New Note.

WE OF THE NEVER NEVER/DEVIL IN THE FLESH
Best, Peter/Philippe Sarde C
CD _____ IMICD 1012
Silva Screen / Jan '93 / Conifer / Silva Screen.

WEDLOCK
(Deadlock)
Gibbs, Richard C
Gibbs, Richard C
CD _____ FILMCD 086
Silva Screen / Sep '91 / Conifer / Silva Screen.

WEEDS
Badalamenti, Angelo C
CD _____ VCD 47313
Varese Sarabande/Colosseum / Jan '89 / Pinnacle / Silva Screen.

WENDY CRACKED A WALNUT
Smeaton, Bruce C
CD _____ IMICD 1007
Silva Screen / Jan '93 / Conifer / Silva Screen.

WES CRAVEN'S NEW NIGHTMARE
Robinson, J. Peter C
CD _____ 235152
Milan / Jan '95 / BMG / Silva Screen.

WEST SIDE STORY
1961 Film Cast
Bernstein, Leonard C
Sondheim, Stephen L
Green, John Con
Jet song / Something's coming / dance at the gym / America / Maria / Tonight / Gee officer Krupke / I feel pretty / One hand, one heart / Quintet / Rumble / Cool / Boy like that / I have a love / Somewhere
CD _____ 4676062
CBS / Dec '90 / Sony.
CD _____ SK 48211
Sony Music / Aug '93 / Sony.

WEST SIDE STORY
(Highlights)
Te Kanawa, Dame Kiri & Jose Carreras/ 1984 Studio Cast
Bernstein, Leonard C
Sondheim, Stephen L
Bernstein, Leonard Con
Jet song / Something's coming / Maria / Tonight / America / Cool / One hand, one heart / I feel pretty / Somewhere / Gee Officer Krupke / Boy like that / I have a love / Taunting scene / Finale
CD _____ 4159632
Deutsche Grammophon / May '85 / PolyGram.

WEST SIDE STORY
1957 Broadway Cast
Bernstein, Leonard C
Sondheim, Stephen L
CD _____ CK 32603

CBS/Silva Screen / Jan '95 / Conifer / Silva Screen.

WEST SIDE STORY
Te Kanawa, Dame Kiri & Jose Carreras/ 1984 Studio Cast
Bernstein, Leonard C
Sondheim, Stephen L
Bernstein, Leonard Con
Prologue/Jet song / Something's coming / Dance at the gym (Blues/Promenade/Jump) / Maria / Tonight / Rumble / I feel pretty / Somewhere / Gee Officer Krupke / Boy like that / I have a love / Finale
2CD _____ 4152532
Deutsche Grammophon / May '85 / PolyGram.

WEST SIDE STORY
1993 Studio Cast
Bernstein, Leonard C
Sondheim, Stephen L
Wordsworth, Barry Con
Prologue / Jet Song / Something's coming / Blues / Promenade / Mambo / Cha cha / Meeting scene / Jump / Maria / Balcony scene (Tonight) / America / Cool / One hand, one heart / Tonight / Rumble / I feel pretty / Scherzo / Somewhere / Procession/ Adagio / Gee Officer Krupke / Boy like that / I have a love / Taunting scene / Finale
CD _____ IMGCD 1801
IMG / Mar '93 / Carlton Home Entertainment / Complete/Pinnacle.

WEST SIDE STORY
London Cast
Bernstein, Leonard C
Sondheim, Stephen L
Jet song / Something's coming / Maria / America / Cool / One hand, one heart / Quintet (tonight) / I feel pretty / Somewhere / Gee officer Krupke / Boy like that / I have a love
CD _____ SHOWCD 006
Showtime / Feb '95 / Disc / THE.

WEST SIDE STORY
Broadway Cast
Bernstein, Leonard C
Sondheim, Stephen L
Prologue / Jet song / Something's coming / Dance at the gym / Maria / Tonight / America / Cool / One hand, one heart / Rumble / I feel pretty / Somewhere / Gee Officer Krupke / Boy like that / I have a love / Finale
CD _____ CK 64419
Sony Music / Feb '95 / Sony.

WEST SIDE STORY
Chorus & National Symphony Orchestra
Bernstein, Leonard C
Sondheim, Stephen L
Edwards, John Owen Con
2CD _____ CDTER2 1197
TER / Feb '94 / Koch.

WEST SIDE STORY/MY FAIR LADY
Previn, Andre/Shelly Manne/Leroy Vinnegar
Bernstein, Leonard/Frederick Loewe C
Sondheim, Stephen/Alan Jay Lerner L
CD _____ CDCOPD 942
Contemporary / Aug '94 / Jazz Music / Cadillac / Pinnacle / Wellard.

WHALES OF AUGUST, THE
Price, Alan C
CD _____ VCD 47311
Varese Sarabande/Colosseum / Jan '89 / Pinnacle / Silva Screen.

WHAT ABOUT LUV
Marren, Howard C
1000 Cent
Birkenhead, Susan L
CD _____ CDTER 1171
TER / Jul '90 / Koch.

WHAT'S LOVE GOT TO DO WITH IT
Turner, Tina
I don't wanna fight / Rock me baby / Disco inferno / Why must we wait until tonight / Stay awhile / Nutbush City Limits / You know I love you / Proud Mary / Fool in love / It's gonna work out fine / Shake a tailfeather / I might have been Queen / What's love got to do with it (live) / Tina's wish
CD _____ CDP3CD 120
EMI / Jun '93 / EMI.

WHEN HARRY MET SALLY
Connick, Harry Jr.
It had to be you / Love is here to stay / Stompin' at the Savoy / But not for me / Winter wonderland / Don't get around much anymore / Autumn in New York / I could write a book / Let's call the whole thing off / Where or when / It had to be you (instrumental)
CD _____ 4657532
CBS / Nov '89 / Sony.

WHEN THE WHALES CAME
Gunning, Christopher C
Gunning, Christopher Con
Bryher and the curse of Samson / Gracie plays truant / Birdman's gift / Islanders / Tempest - and first visit to the birdman / Crown investigators / Daniel's gift for the Birdman / War and Jack's dilemma / Birdman's warning / Lured to Samson / Clemmie's lament / Whale beached / Saving the whale / Torches in the sea / Daniel / Well full/The sailor returns/Re-united / Redeemed
CD _____ FILMCD 049

CBS/Silva Screen / Nov '89 / Conifer / Silva Screen.

WHEN THE WIND BLOWS
Waters, Roger
When the wind blows: Bowie, David / Facts and figures: Cornwell, Hugh / Brazilian: Genesis / What have they done: Squeeze / Shuffle: Hardcastle, Paul / Towers of faith / Russian missile / Hilda's dream / American bomber / Anderson shelter / British submarine / Attack / Fallout / Hilda's hair / Folded flags
CD _____ CDVIP 132
Virgin VIP / Apr '95 / Carlton Home Entertainment / THE / EMI.

WHERE THE RIVER RUNS BLACK
Horner, James C
CD _____ VCD 47273
Varese Sarabande/Colosseum / Jan '89 / Pinnacle / Silva Screen.

WHILE YOU WERE SLEEPING
Edelman, Randy C
CD _____ VSD 5627
Varese Sarabande/Colosseum / Jun '95 / Pinnacle / Silva Screen.

WHISPERS IN THE DARK
Newman, Thomas C
CD _____ VSD 5387
Varese Sarabande/Colosseum / Sep '92 / Pinnacle / Silva Screen.

WHITE MISCHIEF
Fenton, George C
CD _____ CDTER 1153
TER / Feb '90 / Koch.

WHITE PALACE
Fenton, George C
CD _____ VSD 5289
Varese Sarabande/Colosseum / Nov '90 / Pinnacle / Silva Screen.

WHOOP-UP
1958 Broadway Cast
Charlap, Mark C
CD _____ 8371962
Silva Screen / Feb '90 / Conifer / Silva Screen.

WHO'S AFRAID OF VIRGINIA WOOLF
North, Alex C
CD _____ TSU 0112
Tsunami / Jan '95 / Silva Screen.

WHO'S THAT GIRL
Who's that girl: Madonna / Causing a commotion: Madonna / Look of love: Madonna / Twenty four hours / Turn it up / Best thing ever / Can't stop: Madonna / El loco loco
CD _____ 9256112
Sire / Feb '95 / Warner Music.

WILD AT HEART
Im abendrot / Slaughterhouse / Cool cat walk / Love me / Baby, please don't go / Up in flames / Wicked game / Be bop a lula / Smoke rings / Perdita / Blue Spanish sky / Dark Spanish symphony / Dark Lolita / Love me tender
CD _____ 8451282
London / Sep '90 / PolyGram.

WILD BOYS
CD _____ REP 4120-WZ
Repertoire / Aug '91 / Pinnacle / Cadillac.

WILD IS THE WIND
Tiomkin, Dimitri C
CD _____ TSU 0110
Tsunami / Jan '95 / Silva Screen.

WILD ORCHID
Wild orchid: Paradise / Elejibo: Menezes, Margereth / Dark secret: Rudder, David & Margareth Menezes / Shake the Sheikh: Dissidenten / I want to fly: Haza, Ofra / Slave dream: Haza, Ofra / Bird boy: Vasconcelos, Nana & Bushdances / Twistin' with Annie: Ballard, Hank / Magic jewelled limousine: Nasa / Oxossi: Geronimo / Children of fire: Rudder, David / Promised land: Underworld / Flor cubana: Moreno, Simone / Wheeler's howl: Rhythm Methodists / Just a carnival: Rudder, David
Sire / Aug '90 / Warner Music.

WILD WEST
Nowhere road: Earle, Steve / I ain't ever satisfied: Honky Tonk Cowboys & Steve Earle / River: Honky Tonk Cowboys / Fearless heart: Earle, Steve / No. 29: Honky Tonk Cowboys & Steve Earle / Love wore a halo: Honky Tonk Cowboys & Nanci Griffiths / Anyone can be somebody's fool: Honky Tonk Cowboys & Nanci Griffiths / Akhan naz akhan: Anaara / Wild west: Honky Tonk Cowboys / Guitars and cadillacs: Yoakam, Dwight
CD _____ COOKCD 056
Cooking Vinyl / May '93 / Vital.

WILLOW
London Symphony Orchestra/King's College Choir
Horner, James C
Horner, James Con
Elora Danan / Escape from the tavern / Canyon of mazes / Tir asleen / Willow's theme / Willow's journey begins / Bavmorda's spell is cast / Willow the sorcerer
CD _____ CDV 2538
Virgin / Nov '88 / EMI.

WIND AND THE LION, THE
Goldsmith, Jerry C
Goldsmith, Jerry Con
CD _____ RVF 7005D
Intrada / Feb '90 / Silva Screen / Koch.

WINDY CITY
1982 London Cast
Macaulay, Tony C
Vosburgh, Dick L
Bowles, A. Con
Overture: Orchestra / Hey hallelujah: Waterman, Dennis & Company / Wait till I get you on your own: Redman, Amanda & Dennis Waterman / Waltz for Mollie: Langton, Diane & Reporters / Saturday: Allen, Arhlene/Terese Stevens/Tracey Booth & Reporters / Long night again tonight / No one walks out on me: Rodgers, Anton / Saturday (reprise): Waterman, Dennis/Anton Rodgers/Leonard Lowe / Windy city: Waterman, Dennis & Reporters / Round in circles / I can just imagine it: Waterman, Dennis & Anton Rodgers / I can talk to you: Langton, Diane / Perfect casting: Redman, Amanda / Besinger's poem: Spinetti, Victor / Water under the bridge: Waterman, Dennis / Windy city (reprise) / Shake the city: Waterman, Dennis
CD _____ CDANGEL 7
Angel / Apr '94 / EMI.

WINGS OF COURAGE
Yared, Gabriel C
CD _____ SK 68350
CBS/Silva Screen / May '95 / Conifer / Silva Screen.

WINGS OF DESIRE, THE
(aka Der Himmel Uber Berlin)
Knieper, Jurgen C
CD _____ CD 316
Milan / Jan '89 / BMG / Silva Screen.

WINGS OF DESIRE, THE
CD _____ CDIONIC 2
Mute / Aug '88 / Disc.

WINNETOU: THUNDER ON THE BORDERLINE
Thomas, Peter C
CD _____ SP 10001
Silva Screen / Jan '94 / Conifer / Silva Screen.

WINTER IN LISBON
Gillespie, Dizzy C
CD _____ CDCH 704
Milan / Feb '93 / BMG / Silva Screen.

WIRED
(Score/Songs)
Poledouris, Basil C
I'm a king bee / Soul man / Raven's theme / Two thousand pounds / Still looking for a way / You are so beautiful / I can't turn you loose / You don't know like I know / Choice / Bee / Angel of death
CD _____ VSD 5237
Varese Sarabande/Colosseum / Oct '89 / Pinnacle / Silva Screen.

WISDOM
Elfman, Danny C
CD _____ VSD 5209
Varese Sarabande/Colosseum / Jan '89 / Pinnacle / Silva Screen.

WITH HONORS
Thank you: Duran Duran / I'll remember: Madonna / She sells sanctuary: Cult / It's not unusual: Belly / Cover me: Candlebox / Your ghost: Hersh, Kristin / Forever young: Pretenders / Fuzzy: Grant Lee Buffalo / Run shithead run: Mudhoney / Tribe: Babble / Rlna skies: I nyett / yle / On the wrong side: Buckingham, Lindsey
CD _____ 9362455492
Warner Bros. / Mar '94 / Warner Music.

WITHNAIL AND I/HOW TO GET AHEAD IN ADVERTISING
Dundas, David & Rick Wentworth C
Boilbusters / While my guitar gently weeps: Beatles / Barbara Simmons / Voodoo chile: Hendrix, Jimi Experience / Marwood returns / It looks just like me / Julia / Whiter shade of pale: King Curtis / Sit down / Mother black cap / Crow crag / After the dinner party / Boil in a bag / All along the watchtower: Hendrix, Jimi / Bandages come off / Chevel blanc / La fite / Get out of the bloody bath / Range rover / Wolf / Going for the briefcase / Margeaux / To the crow / Monty remembers / Marwood leaves / Withnail's theme
CD _____ FILMCD 041
Silva Screen / Sep '89 / Conifer / Silva Screen.

WITHOUT APPARENT MOTIVE
Morricone, Ennio C
Morricone, Ennio Con
CD _____ A 8924
Alhambra / Feb '92 / Silva Screen.

WITNESS
Jarre, Maurice C
CD _____ CDTER 1098
TER / '88 / Koch.

WIZARD OF OZ, THE
1939 Film Cast
Arlen, Harold C
Harburg, E.Y. 'Yip' L
Wizard of Oz / Dialogues / Over the rainbow / Munchkin land / Ding dong the witch is dead / Follow the yellow brick road / If I only had a brain / We're off to see the wizard /

If I only had a heart / If I only had the nerve / If I were king of the forest / Courage / Home sweet home
CD _____ CDMGM 7
MGM/EMI / Jan '90 / EMI.

WIZARD OF OZ, THE
1988 Royal Shakespeare Cast
Arlen, Harold C
Harburg, E.Y. 'Yip' L
CD _____ CDTER 1165
TER / Mar '89 / Koch.

WIZARD OF OZ, THE
(Highlights)
London Cast
Arlen, Harold C
Harburg, E.Y. 'Yip' L
Overture / Over the rainbow / Munchkinland / If only I had a brain / We're off to see the Wizard / If I only had a brain / See the Wizard (reprise) / If I only had the nerve / Merry old land of Oz / If I were the King of the forest/Courage / Jitterbug / Finale
CD _____ SHOWCD 003
Showtime / Feb '95 / Disc / THE.

WOLF
Morricone, Ennio C
Wolf and love / Barn / Dream and the deer / Moon / Laura goes to join wolf / Laura and wolf united / First transition / Howl and the city / Animals and encounters / Laura transformed / Wolf / Second transition / Will's fina / Goodbye / Chase / Confirmed doubts / Talisman / Third transition / Shock for Laura / Laura and Will / Laura
CD _____ 4766012
Columbia / Aug '94 / Sony.

WOLVES OF WILLOUGHBY CHASE, THE
Graunke Symphony Orchestra
Towns, Colin C
Jones, A. Con
CD _____ CDTER 1162
TER / Dec '89 / Koch.

WOMAN IN RED, THE
Wonder, Stevie
Wonder, Stevie C
Woman in red / It's you: Wonder, Stevie & Dionne Warwick / It's more than you / I just called to say I love you / Love light in flight / Moments aren't moments / Weakness: Wonder, Stevie & Dionne Warwick / Don't drive drunk
CD _____ 5300302
Motown / Jan '93 / PolyGram.

WONDERFUL COUNTRY
North, Alex C
CD _____ TSU 0118
Tsunami / Jan '95 / Silva Screen.

WONDERFUL TOWN
1953 Broadway Cast
Bernstein, Leonard C
Comden, Betty & Adolph Green L
Christopher Street / Ohio / Hundred ways to lose a man / What a waste / Little bit in love / Pass the football / Conversation piece / Quiet girl / Conga / My darlin' Eileen / Swing / Ohio (reprise) / It's love / Vortex ballet / Wrong note rag / It's love (reprise)
CD _____ SK 48021
Sony Broadway / Dec '91 / Sony.
CD _____ MCAD 10050
MCA/Silva Screen / Jan '95 / Silva Screen.

WONDERFUL TOWN
1986 London Cast
Bernstein, Leonard C
Comden, Betty & Adolph Green L
Overture / Christopher Street / Ohio / Hundred ways to lose a man / What a waste / Little bit in love / Pass the football / Conversation piece / Quiet girl / Conga / My darlin' Eileen / Swing / It's love / Vortex ballet / Wrong note rag / Finale
CD _____ OCRCD 11
First Night / Mar '93 / Pinnacle.

WONDERFUL TOWN
Cast Recording
Bernstein, Leonard C
Comden, Betty & Adolph Green L
2CD _____ CDTER2 1223
TFR / Aug '95 / Koch.

WONDERWALL MUSIC
Harrison, George
Harrison, George C
Microbes / Red lady too / Table and Pakavai / in the park / Drilling a home / Guru vandana / Greasy legs / Ski-ing / Gat kirwani / Dream scene / Party seacombe / Love scene / Crying / Cowboy music / Fantasy sequins / On the bed / Glass box / Wonderwall to be here / Singing om
CD _____ CDSAPCOR 1
Apple / Jun '92 / EMI.

WOODSTOCK
I had a dream: Sebastian, John B. / Going up the country: Canned Heat / Freedom: Havens, Richie / Rock and soul music: Country Joe & The Fish / Coming into Los Angeles: Guthrie, Arlo / At the hop: Sha Na Na / Fish cheer: McDonald, Country Joe / I feel like I'm fixin' to die rag / Drug store truck drivin' man: Baez, Joan / Sea of madness: Crosby, Stills & Nash / Wooden ships: Crosby, Stills & Nash / We can gonna take it: Who / With a little help from my friends: Cocker, Joe / Crowd rain chant: Cocker, Joe / Soul sacrifice: Santana / I'm going

home: *Ten Years After* / Volunteers: *Jefferson Airplane* / Rainbows all over your blues: *Sebastian, John* / Love march: *Butterfield Blues Band* / Star spangled banner: *Hendrix, Jimi*
2CD _____ 7567805932
Warner Bros. / Aug '94 / Warner Music.

WOODSTOCK DIARIES
CD _____ 7567826342
Warner Bros. / Sep '94 / Warner Music.

WOODSTOCK II
Jam back at the house: *Hendrix, Jimi* / Izabella: *Hendrix, Jimi* / Get my heart back together: *Hendrix, Jimi* / Saturday afternoon: *Jefferson Airplane* / Eskimo blue day: *Jefferson Airplane* / Everything's gonna be alright: *Butterfield Blues Band* / Sweet Sir Galahad: *Baez, Joan* / Guinevere: *Crosby, Stills, Nash & Young* / Four plus twenty: *Crosby, Stills, Nash & Young* / Marrakesh express: *Crosby, Stills, Nash & Young* / My beautiful people: *Melanie* / Birthday of the sun: *Melanie* / Blood of the sun: *Mountain* / Theme for an imaginary western: *Mountain* / Woodstock boogie: *Canned Heat* / Let the sunshine in: *Audience*
2CD _____ 7567805942
Warner Bros. / Aug '94 / Warner Music.

WORKING GIRL
Let the river run: *Simon, Carly* / In love (instrumental): *Simon, Carly* / Man that got away: *Mounsey, Rob/George Young/Chip Jackson/Grady Tate* / Scar (instrumental): *Simon, Carly* / Carlotta's heart: *Simon, Carly* / Looking through Katherine's house: *Simon, Carly* / Poor butterfly: *Rollins, Sonny* / I'm so excited: *Pointer Sisters* / Let the river run (2): *Thomas Choir of Men & Boys*
CD _____ 259767
Arista / '89 / BMG.

WORLD APART, A
Zimmer, Hans *C*
CD _____ CD 302
Silva Screen / Jan '89 / Conifer / Silva Screen.

WORLD OF JEEVES AND WOOSTER, THE
Jeeves and Wooster / Jeeves and Wooster say what ho / Blue room / Meanwhile in Berkeley Square / Barmy's choice / Nagazaki / Amateur dictator (suite for Spode) / Because my baby don't mean maybe now / Midnight in Mayfair / Minnie the moocher is alive and well (and living in Berkeley Square) / Minnie the moocher / Weekend in the country / Changes / Fire / If I had a talking picture of you / Jeeves and Wooster say tinkerty tonk / Daily grind
CD _____ CDEMC 3623
EMI / Mar '92 / EMI.

WRESTLING ERNEST HEMINGWAY
Convertino, Michael *C*
CD _____ 5188972
Silva Screen / Jan '93 / Conifer / Silva Screen.

WUTHERING HEIGHTS
(The Musical)
Cast/Philharmonic Orchestra & Chorus
Taylor, Bernard J. *C*
Raine, Nic *Con*
Prelude / Wuthering Heights / Cathy / They say he's a gypsy / You were my first love / I see a change in you / One rules my heart / I have no time for them / He's gone / Let her live/I will have my vengeance / Gypsy waltz / I belong to the earth / Coming home to you / Pleasure of your company / If only / Heathcliff's lament / Up here with you
CD _____ SONGCD 904
Silva Classics / Jul '92 / Conifer / Silva Screen.

WYATT EARP
Hollywood Recording Musicians' Orchestra
Howard, James Newton *C*
Paich, M. *Con*
CD _____ 9362456602
Warner Bros. / Sep '94 / Warner Music.

YAKSA
Winter green and Summer blue / Prologue / Joy / Love and solitude / Uminari / Gentle snow / Man once lived in Miami / Dear memories / Black overcoat / Tatto yaksa / Dark wind
CD _____ C38 7556
Denon / '85 / Conifer.

YEAR IN PROVENCE, A
Davis, Carl *C*
Davis, Carl *Con*
Bonnie Annee Mr Mayle / Learning the language / Black gold / Tony awards / Daylight robbery / Bread winner / Room service / Frogbusters / Chateau Mayle / War of the worlds / Old boys / Year in Provence
CD _____ FILMCD 131
Silva Screen / Mar '93 / Conifer / Silva Screen.

YEAR OF LIVING DANGEROUSLY, THE
Jarre, Maurice *C*
CD _____ VCD 47222
Varese Sarabande/Colosseum / '85 / Pinnacle / Silva Screen.

YEAR OF THE COMET
Mann, Hummie *C*
CD _____ VSD 5365
Varese Sarabande/Colosseum / Nov '92 / Pinnacle / Silva Screen.

YELLOW SUBMARINE
Beatles
Beatles *C*
Yellow submarine / Only a northern song / All you need is love / Hey bulldog / It's all too much / All together now / Pepperland / Sea of time / Sea of holes / Sea of monsters / March of the meanies / Pepperland laid to waste / Yellow submarine in Pepperland
CD _____ CDPCS 7070
Parlophone / Aug '87 / EMI.

YEOMAN OF THE GUARD
Dowling, Denis & Richard Lewis/Glyndebourne Festival Choir/Pro Arte Orchestra
Sullivan, Sir Arthur *C*
Gilbert, W.S. *L*
Sargent, Sir Malcolm *Con*
2CD _____ CMS 7644152
EMI Classics / Jan '95 / EMI.

YEOMAN OF THE GUARD
D'Oyly Carte Opera Chorus/Orchestra
Sullivan, Sir Arthur *C*
Gilbert, W.S. *L*
Edwards, John Owen *Con*
2CD _____ CDTER2 1195
TER / Mar '93 / Koch.

YEOMAN OF THE GUARD
Academy & Chorus Of St. Martin In The Fields
Sullivan, Sir Arthur *C*
Gilbert, W.S. *L*
Marriner, Neville *Con*
2CD _____ 4381382
Philips / Nov '93 / PolyGram.

YEOMAN OF THE GUARD
(Highlights)
Academy & Chorus Of St. Martin In The Fields
Sullivan, Sir Arthur *C*
Gilbert, W.S. *L*
Marriner, Neville *Con*
CD _____ 4424362
Philips / Jan '90 / PolyGram.

YEOMAN OF THE GUARD/TRIAL BY JURY
D'Oyly Carte Opera Chorus/Royal Philharmonic Orchestra/Orchestra Of The Royal Opera House
Sullivan, Sir Arthur *C*

Gilbert, W.S. *L*
Sargent, Malcolm/I. Godfrey *Con*
2CD _____ 4173582
Decca / Jan '90 / PolyGram.

YOR - HUNTER FROM THE FUTURE
Scott, John *C*
CD _____ LXCD 7
Silva Screen / Jan '95 / Conifer / Silva Screen.

YOU ONLY LIVE TWICE
Barry, John *C*
You only live twice: *Sinatra, Nancy* / Capsule in space / Fight at Kobe Dock / Halga / Tanaka's world / Drop in the ocean / Death of Aki / Mountains and sunsets / Wedding / James Bond astronaut / Countdown for Blofeld / Bond averts World War III / Twice is the only way to live
CD _____ CZ 559
Premier / Dec '95 / EMI.

YOUNG AMERICANS
CD _____ CID 8019
Island / Oct '93 / PolyGram.

YOUNG GIRLS OF ROCHEFORT
Legrand, Michel *C*
CD _____ 8341402
Silva Screen / Jan '95 / Conifer / Silva Screen.

YOUNG INDIANA JONES CHRONICLES I, THE
(Paris, 1916/Verdun, 1916)
Munich Symphony Orchestra
McNeely, Joel *C*
McNeely, Joel *Con*
CD _____ VSD 5381
Varese Sarabande/Colosseum / May '93 / Pinnacle / Silva Screen.

YOUNG INDIANA JONES CHRONICLES II, THE
(German East Africa, 1916/London, 1916/The Congo, 1917)
Munich Symphony Orchestra
McNeely, Joel *C*
McNeely, Joel *Con*
CD _____ VSD 5391
Varese Sarabande/Colosseum / Sep '93 / Pinnacle / Silva Screen.

YOUNG INDIANA JONES CHRONICLES III, THE
(The Mystery Of The Blues/The Scandal Of 1920)
McNeely, Joel *C*
McNeely, Joel *Con*
Rhapsody in blue / Swanee / Somebody loves me / Sounds like perfection / Scandal walk / Sweetie Dear / My handyman / 12th Street rag / Blue horizon / Tiger rag / I can't believe that you're in love with me / Twinkle Dixie
CD _____ VSD 5401
Varese Sarabande/Colosseum / Jun '93 / Pinnacle / Silva Screen.

YOUNG INDIANA JONES CHRONICLES IV, THE
(Ireland 1916/Northern Italy 1918)
Munich Philharmonic Film Orchestra/West Australian Philharmonic Orchestra
Rosenthal, Laurence/Joel McNeely *C*
Rosenthal, Laurence/Joel McNeely *Con*
CD _____ VSD 5421
Varese Sarabande/Colosseum / Jan '95 / Pinnacle / Silva Screen.

YOUNG LIONS, THE/THE EARTH IS MINE
Friedhofer, Hugo *C*
Friedhofer, Hugo *Con*
2CD _____ VSD 25403
Varese Sarabande/Colosseum / Jun '93 / Pinnacle / Silva Screen.

YOUNG ONES, THE
Richard, Cliff & The Shadows
Friday night / Got a funny feeling / Peace pipe / Nothing's impossible / Young ones / All for one / Lessons in love / No one for me but Nicky / What d'you know, we've got

a show / Vaudeville routine / Mambo / Savage / We say yeah
CD _____ CDMFP 6020
Music For Pleasure / Apr '88 / EMI.

YOUNG POISONERS'S HANDBOOK, THE
CD _____ 8444292
Deram / Jan '96 / PolyGram.

YOUNG SOUL REBELS
CD _____ BLRCD 10
Big Life / Sep '91 / Pinnacle.

Z
Theodorakis, Mikis *C*
CD _____ SR 50062
Sakkaris / Oct '93 / Pinnacle.

ZED AND TWO NOUGHTS, A
Zoo Orchestra
Nyman, Michael *C*
Nyman, Michael *Con*
Angelfish decay / Car crash / Time lapse / Prawn watching / Bisocosis populi / Swan rot / Delft waltz / Up for crabs / Vermeer's wife / Venus de Milo / Lady in the red hat / L'escargot
CD _____ CDVE 54
Virgin / Feb '90 / EMI.

ZELLY AND ME
Donaggio, Pino *C*
CD _____ VCD 70422
Varese Sarabande/Colosseum / Jan '89 / Pinnacle / Silva Screen.

ZERO PATIENCE
Schellenberg, Glenn *C*
CD _____ 887971
Milan / Jan '95 / BMG / Silva Screen.

ZOO/NOTTACACCIA/UOVA DI GARAFONA
CD _____ CDCIA 5092
Cinevox / Jul '93 / Conifer / Silva Screen.

ZORBA
Broadway Cast
Kander, John *C*
Ebb, Fred *L*
CD _____ ZDM 7646652
EMI Classics / Apr '93 / EMI.

ZORBA
1968 Broadway Cast
Kander, John *C*
Ebb, Fred *L*
CD _____ 920532
Silva Screen / Jan '95 / Conifer / Silva Screen.

ZULU
(& Other Themes)
Barry, John *C*
Barry, John *Con*
Istanchiwania / News of the massacre / First Zulu / Wagons over / Durnford's horses arrive and depart / Zulu's final appearance and salute / V.C. roll/Men of Harlech / Elizabeth theme / From Russia with love / Four in the morning
CD _____ FILMCD 022
Silva Screen / Nov '89 / Conifer / Silva Screen.

ZULU DAWN
Royal Philharmonic Orchestra
Bernstein, Elmer *C*
CD _____ CD 0201
Silva Screen / Jan '89 / Conifer / Silva Screen.

Collections

4 AMERICA
Caine, Daniel Orchestra
Caine, Daniel Con
Roseanne / Thirtysomething / My Two Dads
/ Cheers / Cosby Show / Hill Street Blues /
St. Elsewhere / Newhart / Bronx Zoo / Rem-
ington Steele / North And South / L.A. Law
/ White Shadow / Lou Grant
CD _____ TVPMCD 801
Primetime / Feb '92 / Silva Screen.

4 AMERICA TWO
Caine, Daniel Con
Waltons / I'll Fly Away / Northern Exposure
/ Land of the Giants / Dream On / Mork and
Mindy / Blossom / Munsters / Evening
Shade / Different World / Hogan's Heroes /
Barney Miller / Little House on the Prairie /
Street / Johnny Staccato / Eerie, Indiana /
Family Ties / Waltons (reprise)
CD _____ TVPMCD 803
Primetime / Aug '93 / Silva Screen.

007 CLASSICS
London Symphony Orchestra
James Bond / Thunderball / Goldfinger /
From Russia With Love / Diamonds Are For-
ever / You Only Live Twice / Look of love /
On Her Majesty's Secret Service / Man With
The Golden Gun
CD _____ EDL 25132
Edel / Dec '89 / Pinnacle.

18 WONDERFUL FILM THEMES
CD _____ EMPRCD
Emporio / Jul '94 / THE / Disc / CM.

20 GREAT WESTERN THEMES
CD _____ EMPRCD 514
Emporio / Jul '94 / THE / Disc / CM.

28 FAMOUS WESTERN FILM THEMES
Entertainers / Mar '92 / Target/BMG.
CD _____ ENT CD 258

32 MOVIE & TV HITS
CD _____ 24005
Music / Mar '95 / Target/BMG.

**50 YEARS OF CLASSIC HORROR FILM
MUSIC**
Omen (suite) / She (suite) / Rosemary's
Baby (suite) / Dr. Jekyll And Mr. Hyde / King
Kong (suite) / Vampire Lovers (suite) / Fear
In The Night (suite) / Exorcist 2 / Hellraiser
(suite) / Dr. Jekyll And Sister Hyde
CD _____ FILMCD 017
Silva Screen / Nov '89 / Conifer / Silva
Screen.

100 YEARS OF CINEMA GOLD
2CD _____ D2CD 4025
Deja Vu / Jun '95 / THE.

A-Z OF BRITISH TV THEMES
(1960's/70's)
Avengers: Johnson, Laurie / Captain Scar-
let: Gray, Barry / Catweazle: Dicks, Ted /
Champions: Hatch, Tony / Crossroads:
Hatch, Tony / Dad's Army (Who do you
think you are kidding Mr. Hitler): Taverner,
Perry / Danger Man (High Wire) / Depart-
ment S / Doctor In The House / Dr. Who:
Grainer, Ron / Emmerdale Farm: Hatch,
Tony / Fireball XL5 / Forsyth Saga / Had-
leigh: Hatch, Tony / Hancock: Scott, Derek
/ Maigret: Grainer, Ron / Man In A Suitcase:
Grainer, Ron / No Hiding Place: Johnson,
Laurie / Please Sir: Fonteyn, Sam / Power
Game / Return Of The Saint: Dee, Martin /
Saint / Sportsnight: Hatch, Tony / Steptoe
And Son: Grainer, Ron / Stingray: Gray,
Barry / Thank Your Lucky Stars: Knight, Pe-
ter / Thunderbirds: Gray, Barry / Top Secret
/ Z Cars
CD _____ PLAY 004
Play It Again / Oct '92 / Total/BMG.

A-Z OF BRITISH TV THEMES VOL.2
All Creatures Great And Small / Angels /
Bergerac / Animal Magic / Bread / BBC
Cricket / Auf Wiedersehen Pet / Doctor Who
/ Grandstand / Four Feather Falls / Juke
Box Jury / Liver Birds / Man About The
House / New Avengers / Persuaders / Su-
percar / Tales Of The Unexpected / Van Der
Valk / Upstairs Downstairs / Whatever Hap-
pened To The Likely Lads
CD _____ PLAY 006
Play It Again / Jul '94 / Total/BMG.

**ABSOLUTE COLLECTION - CLASSIC
FILM & TELEVISION**
CD _____ LECD 427
Wisepack / Jul '93 / THE / Conifer.

ABSOLUTELY DISNEY
Bare necessities / Hakuna matata / Super-
califragilisticexpialidocius / Winnie the Pooh
/ Work song / I've got no strings / Be our
guest / Who's afraid of the big bad wolf /
Yo-ho (a pirate's life for me) / Under the sea
/ When I see an elephant fly / Mickey mouse
club march / Everybody wants to be a cat
/ Let's go fly a kite / Ballad of Davy Crockett
/ Zip a dee doo dah / Beautiful briny / I
wanna be like you / Whistle while you work
/ Little April showers / Wonderful thing
about tiggers / Monkey's uncle / One jump
ahead / Bibbidi bobbidi boo / Once upon a
dream / Ten feet off the ground / Aristocats
/ Heigh ho / Jolly holiday / Swamp fox / Hi
diddle dee dee / Higgitus figitus / Whale of
a tale / Following the leader / Circle of life /
Colours of the wind / Can you feel the love
tonight / Animal friends/With a smile and a
song
CD _____ DISACD 7001
Disney / Oct '95 / Carlton Home
Entertainment.

ACADEMY AWARD THEMES
London Philharmonic Orchestra
CD _____ PWK 037
Carlton Home Entertainment / '88 / Carlton
Home Entertainment.

ACADEMY AWARD WINNERS VOL. 2
Baker, Tony & His Orchestra
In the cool, cool, cool of the evening / High
noon / Screen love / Three coins in the
fountain / Love is a many splendoured thing
/ Whatever will be will be (Que sera sera) /
All the way / Gigi / High hopes / Never on
a Sunday / Moon river / Days of wine and
roses / Call me irresponsible / Chim chim
cheree / Shadows of your smile / Born free
/ Talk to the animals
CD _____ PWKM 661
Carlton Home Entertainment / Nov '90 /
Carlton Home Entertainment.

ACTION HERO
True Lies / Last Action Hero / Terminator /
Total Recall / Conan The Barbarian / Red
Heat / Predator / Red Sonja
CD _____ CIN 22232
Silva Screen / Oct '94 / Conifer / Silva
Screen.

ACTION MOVIE THEMES
We don't need another hero / I can dream
about you / Delta force theme / Take my
breath away / Ride of the Valkyries / Brains
and trains / It's a long road / Eye of the tiger
/ Love theme / Glory of love / When the
going get tough, the tough get going / One
vision / Voice of America's son's
CD _____ 22527
Music / Aug '95 / Target/BMG.

ACTION THEMES
Power Pack Orchestra
Cagney and Lacey / Rocky 3 (Gonna fly
now - Rocky theme) / Magnum P.I. / Great
escape / Superman / Crazy like a fox / 633
Squadron / Hill Street Blues / Reamington
Steele / Hunter / Operation crossbow /
Sweeney / Mike Hammer / Miami Vice /
Longest day / Bond theme / Hawaii Five-O
/ New avengers / Bergerac / Bill / Starsky
and Hutch / A-Team / T.J. Hooker / Shoe-
string / Dempsey and Makepeace / Knots
landing / Scarecrow and Mrs. King / Hart to
Hart / Where eagles dare / Indiana Jones
CD _____ CC 8247
EMI / Nov '94 / EMI.

ALWAYS CHASING RAINBOWS
(The Young Judy Garland)
Garland, Judy
All God's chillun got rhythm / Buds won't
bud / Cry baby cry / Embraceable you / End
of the rainbow / Everybody sing / F.D.R.
Jones / I'm always chasing rainbows / I'm
just wild about Harry / I'm nobody's baby /
In between / It never rains but it pours /
Oceans apart / Our love affair / Over the
rainbow / Sleep my baby sleep / Stompin'
at the Savoy / Sweet sixteen / Swing Mister
Charlie / Ten pins in the sky / You can't
have everything / Zing went the strings of
my heart
CD _____ CD AJA 5093
Living Era / Jul '92 / Koch.

**AMERICAN AND ITALIAN WESTERN
SCREEN THEMES**
CD _____ 873038
Milan / Oct '92 / BMG / Silva Screen.

**AMERICAN TELEVISION THEMES VOL.
1**
(Twin Peaks)
Caine, Daniel Con
Midnight caller / L.A. Law / Twin Peaks /
Star Trek: the next generation / North and
South / Hooperman / Murder she wrote /
Spenser for hire / 21 Jump Street / Newhart
/ Hunter / Bronx Zoo / Sonny Spoon
CD _____ TVPMCD 400
Primetime / Mar '91 / Silva Screen.

**AMERICAN TELEVISION THEMES VOL.
2**
(Thirtysomething)
Caine, Daniel Con
Thirtysomething / Falcon Crest / Doogie
Howser M.D. / Highway to Heaven / Quan-
tum Leap / McGyver / Slap Maxwell Story /
Head of the class / Alf / Wiseguy / Nutt
House / Remington Steele / Men / Bring 'em
back alive
CD _____ TVPMCD 401
Primetime / Mar '91 / Silva Screen.

**AMERICAN TELEVISION THEMES VOL.
3**
Caine, Daniel Con
Law and order / Capital News / Sledgeham-
mer / China Beach / B.L. Stryker / Days and
Nights of Molly Dodd / Parker Lewis Can't
Lose / Young Riders / Night Court / Stingray
/ Houston Knights / Over My Dead Body /
Buck James / Top of the Hill
CD _____ TVPMCD 404
Primetime / Oct '91 / Silva Screen.

**AMERICAN TELEVISION'S GREATEST
HITS**
A-Team / Airwolf / Barnaby Jones / Battles-
tar Galactica / Baywatch / Cheers / Beverly
Hills 90210 / Cagney and Lacey / Cosby
Show / Falcon Crest / Knight Rider / Quan-
tum leap / Roseanne / Twin Peaks / Incred-
ible Hulk / Waltons / Equalizer / Hunter /
Little house on the prairie / Melrose Place /
North and South / Taxi / V
2CD _____ TVPMCD 804
Primetime / Aug '94 / Silva Screen.

**ANOTHER OPENIN', ANOTHER SHOW -
BROADWAY'S OVERTURES**
Engel, L. Con
CD _____ SK 53540
Sony Classical / Jul '94 / Sony.

APOCALYPSE NAM
(The 10,000 Day War)
Apocalypse Now / Vietnam Texas / Deer
Hunter / Airwolf / Platoon Leader / First
Blood / Purple Hearts / Missing in Action /
Missing in Action III / Platoon
CD _____ CIN 22042
Silva Screen / Jan '95 / Conifer / Silva
Screen.

ARGENTO VIVO
CD _____ MAF 170D
Intrada / Jan '93 / Silva Screen / Koch.

ARGENTO VIVO II
CD _____ MAF 185D
Intrada / Jan '92 / Silva Screen / Koch.

ARNOLD
(Great Music From The films Of Arnold
Schwarzenegger)
CD _____ VSD 5398
Varese Sarabande/Colosseum / Jul '93 /
Pinnacle / Silva Screen.

AS TIME GOES BY
(Classic Movie Love Songs)
Mancini, Henry & Mancini Pops Orchestra
CD _____ RD 60974
RCA / Jul '92 / BMG.

AT THE MOVIES
CD _____ 11816
Music / Jul '95 / Target/BMG.

AT THE THEATRE
Mantovani
CD _____ CDSIV 6108
Horatio Nelson / Jul '95 / THE / BMG / Avid/
BMG / Koch.

**AUDREY HEPBURN - FAIR LADY OF
THE SCREEN**
Dobson, Rudi
Audrey Hepburn - Fair lady of the screen /
Belgian rock / Fight for time / Dark city /
Broadway melody / Little dog called "Mr Fa-
mouse" / Sister Audrey / Moon river /
Breakfast at Tiffany's / Charade / My fair
lady (Medley) / Desert anthem / Lac Geni-
eve (Lake Geneva) / Moon river (Reprise)
CD _____ PCOM 1136
President / Aug '94 / Grapevine / Target/
BMG / Jazz Music / President.

AUSTRALIAN TV'S GREATEST HITS
Neighbours / Prisoner Cell Block H / Sulli-
vans / Sons and daughters / Anzacs / The
Skippy / Paul Hogan show / Young Doctors
/ Chopper Squad / Country Practice / Car-
son's Law
CD _____ FILMCD 028
Silva Screen / Nov '88 / Conifer / Silva
Screen.

B

BACK TO BROADWAY
Streisand, Barbra
Some enchanted evening / Everybody says
don't / Music of the night / Speak low / As
if we never said goodbye / Children will lis-
ten / I have a love / I've never been in love
before / Luck be a lady / With one look /
Man I love / Move on
CD _____ 473880 2
Columbia / Jun '93 / Sony.

BBC SPORTING THEMES
Grandstand / Wimbledon / Match of the day
/ Ski Sunday (pop goes Bach) / Test cricket
/ Snooker / Rugby special / Sportsnight /
Question of sport / Darts / Commonwealth
games / World Cup / Rugby / Sport on Two
/ Athletics / Bowls
CD _____ PWKS 648
Carlton Home Entertainment / '88 / Carlton
Home Entertainment.

**BEATRIX POTTER MUSIC
COLLECTION, THE**
London Film Orchestra
Perfect day / Peter Rabbit theme / Mrs.
Tiggy Winkle / Foxy gentleman / Tailor of
Gloucester / Songs from Gloucester / Silent
falls of snow / Cuckoo / Beatrix and the
lakes / Tom, Tom, the piper's son / Tom
Lost / Tom Kitten / Chase / Room full of
tales / Themes reprise / Perfect day (2)
CD _____ PWKS 4200
Carlton Home Entertainment / Jun '94 /
Carlton Home Entertainment.

**BERLIN FILMHARMONIC CONCERTS,
THE**
Berlin RIAS Youth Orchestra
CD _____ CDCH 037
Milan / Jan '89 / BMG / Silva Screen.

**BEST OF ARNOLD
SCHWARZENEGGER, THE**
City Of Prague Philharmonic Orchestra
Conan the Barbarian / Conan the Destroyer
/ Predator / Terminator / Terminator II / Kin-
dergarten Cop / Twins / Junior / Running
Man / Commando / Red Heat / Raw Deal /
Total Recall
CD _____ FILMCD 164
Silva Screen / Oct '95 / Conifer / Silva
Screen.

**BEST OF ARNOLD
SCHWARZENEGGER, THE - VOL. 2**
City Of Prague Philharmonic Orchestra
Conan the Barbarian / Conan the Destroyer
/ Commando / Raw Deal / Running
Cop / Red Sonja / Running Man / Termi-
nator / Red Heat / Twins / Christmas in
Connecticut / Predator / Total Recall / Ter-
minator 2
CD _____ CIN 22052
Silva Screen / Sep '93 / Conifer / Silva
Screen.

BEST OF BBC TV THEMES
Singing detective / Tender is the night / Dr.
Who / Dallas / Howard's Way / Bergerac /
My family and other animals / Ski Sunday /
Eastenders / Miss Marple / Maigret /
Neighbours / Tomorrow's world / Star cops
/ Shoestring / Knots Landing / Whicker's
world / Life and loves of a she devil / Flight
of the Condor / Fawlty Towers / Who pays
the ferryman / Life and times of David Lloyd
George / Fortunes of war
CD _____ PWKS 645
Carlton Home Entertainment / Jan '88 /
Carlton Home Entertainment.

BEST OF BRITISH TV MUSIC
London's burning / Forever green / Profes-
sionals / Agatha Christie's Poirot / To have
and to hold / Upstairs, downstairs / Thomas
and Sarah / Gentle touch / Bouquet of
barbed wire / Partners in crime / Budgie /
Wish me luck as you wave me goodbye /
Love for Lydia / Lillie / Black beauty /
Dempsey and Makepeace
CD _____ CDSTM 3
Soundtrack Music / May '94 / EMI.

BEST OF CHINESE FILM MUSIC, THE
CD _____ VSD 5455
Varese Sarabande/Colosseum / Jan '95 /
Pinnacle / Silva Screen.

**BEST OF JACK NICHOLSON FILMS,
THE**
Wolf / Shining / Few Good Men / Batman /
Terms of Endearment / Prizzi's Honor / Chi-
natown / Postman Always Rings Twice /
Heartburn / Red / Missouri Breaks / Witches
of Eastwick / One Flew Over the Cuckoo's
Nest

959

CD _____ **CIN 22312**
Edel / Oct '95 / Pinnacle.

BEST OF JAMES BOND, THE
(30th Anniversary Collection)
James Bond: Norman, Monty & Studio Orchestra / Goldfinger: Bassey, Shirley / Nobody does it better: Simon, Carly / View to a kill: Duran Duran / Mr. Kiss Kiss Bang Bang: Warwick, Dionne / For your eyes only: Easton, Sheena / We have all the time in the world: Armstrong, Louis / Live and let die: McCartney, Paul / All time high: Coolidge, Rita / Living daylights: A-Ha / Licence to kill: Knight, Gladys / From Russia with love: Monro, Matt / Thunderball: Jones, Tom / You only live twice: Sinatra, Nancy / Moonraker: Bassey, Shirley / On her Majesty's Secret Service: Barry, John & Studio Orchestra / Man with the golden gun / Diamonds are forever / 007: Barry, John & Studio Orchestra
CD _____ **CDBOND 007**
EMI / Dec '95 / EMI.

BEST OF JEAN-CLAUDE VAN DAMME
(Death Warrant/Double Impact/
Kickboxer/Bloodsport/Cyborg)
CD _____ **FILMCD 103**
Silva Screen / Jun '92 / Conifer / Silva Screen.

BEST OF SCANDANAVIAN FILM MUSIC
Milan / Dec '93 / BMG / Silva Screen.
CD _____ **CDCH 760**

BEST OF STEPHEN KING FILMS, THE
CD _____ **CIN 22002**
Silva Screen / Aug '93 / Conifer / Silva Screen.

BEST OF THE HOLLYWOOD MUSICALS
CD _____ **PWKS 4213**
Carlton Home Entertainment / Nov '94 /
Carlton Home Entertainment.

BEST OF THE TV DETECTIVES VOL.1
Overkill (The Bill) / Inspector Morse / Taggart / Between the lines / Prime suspect 3 / Gentle touch / Juliet bravo / Chandler and co / Miss Marples / Van Der Valk / Agatha Christie's Poirot / Maigret / Bergerac / Cade's theme (The Chief) / Ruth Rendell mysteries / Insector Wexford / Shoestring / Professionals / Dempsey and makepeace
CD _____ **CDDEC 9**
Soundtrack Music / Feb '95 / EMI.

BEST OF WEST END MUSICALS, THE
Consider yourself / All I ask of you / I don't know how to love him / Spread a little happiness / I could be happy with you / Thank you very much / Leaning on a lamp-post / Reviewing the situation / If I ruled the world / Ta-ra-ra-boom-de-ay / Wishing you were somehow here again / Oh look at me
CD _____ **SHOWCD 019**
Showtime / Feb '95 / Disc / THE.

BETWEEN THE LINES
(Music From UK Primetime Television)
Bill / Chief / Brideshead revisited / Casualty / Medics / London's burning / Chronicles of Narnia / Captain Scarlet / Star Trek: Deep space 9 / Seaquest DSV / Tinker tailor soldier spy / Thunderbirds / Twin Peaks / Baywatch / Trial
CD _____ **TVPMCD 805**
Primetime / Oct '94 / Silva Screen.

BIG SCREEN ADVENTURE
Budd, Roy & London Symphony Orchestra
CD _____ **DSHCD 7004**
D-Sharp / Dec '92 / Pinnacle.

BIG SCREEN CLASSICS
CD _____ **BIGSCD 1**
Dino / Nov '93 / Pinnacle / 3MV.

BIT OF A SHOWMAN, A
Hobbs, Jeremy
Applause / Mascara / I promise you a happy ending / Time heals eveything / I won't send roses / Movies were movies / Maybe this time / And yet and yet / Hurt / My way / Ballad of the sad young men / I am what I am / Look over there
CD _____ **CDGRS 1285**
Grosvenor / Jan '96 / Target/BMG.

BLADE RUNNER
(Synthesizer Soundtracks)
Hitcher / Big trouble in Little China / Haunted summer / Revenge / Lock up / Halloween / Blade runner
CD _____ **SILVAD 3008**
Silva Treasury / Aug '91 / Conifer / Silva Screen.

BLOOD AND THUNDER
Ben Hur / Captain from Castile / Cleopatra / Wind and the lion / North by northwest / Ten commandments / Taras bulba / Mutiny on the bounty
CD _____ **VSD 5561**
Varese Sarabande/Colosseum / May '95 / Pinnacle / Silva Screen.

BOND AND BEYOND
Cincinnati Pops Orchestra
Kunzel, Erich Con
CD _____ **CD 80251**
Telarc / May '92 / Conifer / ADA.

BOND COLLECTION, THE
(The 30th Anniversary)
Bassey, Shirley

View to a kill / Nobody does it better / From Russia with love / We have all the time in the world / You only live twice / Diamonds are forever / Live and let die / Moonraker / For your eyes only / All time high / Thunderball / Goldfinger
CD _____ **ICOCD 007**
Icon / Mar '93 / Pinnacle.

BORN ON THE FOURTH OF JULY
(Music From The Films Of Tom Cruise)
Born On The Fourth Of July (End credits) / Risky Business (Love on a real train) / Days Of Thunder (Main title/Car building) / Color of Money (Main title) / Outsiders (Stay gold) / Legend (Unicorns/Opening/Unicorn theme) / Top Gun (Anthem/Take my breath away) / Rain Man (Las Vegas/End credits) / Cocktail (Jordan) / Firm (Main title) / Few Good Men (Code red/Facts and figures/Honor) / Far And Away (Book of days/End credits)
CD _____ **FILMCD 152**
Silva Screen / Sep '94 / Conifer / Silva Screen.

BOX OFFICE BLASTS
Movin' Dream Orchestra
Color purple / Round Midnight / Take my breath away / Livin' in America / Surprise surprise / Left of centre / So far, so good / Earth angel / Absolute beginners / Say you, say me / Separate lives / Ghostbusters / Goonies 'r' good enough / Young Sherlock Holmes / Tonight is what it means to be young
CD _____ **DC 8501**
Denon / '88 / Conifer.

BRITISH FILM MUSIC
(From The 1940s & 1950s)
Way to the stars / Blithe spirit (Prelude and waltz) / Night has eyes (Theme) / Western approaches (Seascape) / Passionate friends (Film theme) / Man between / Sound barrier (Rhapsody Op.38) / Matter of life and death (Prelude) / Kid for two farthings / Hungry hill (waltz into jig) / Rake's progress (Calypso music) / Wanted for murder (A voice in the night) / Ha'penny breeze (Film theme) / Carnival (Intermezzo) / Scott of the Antartic / Pony march, penguins, climbing the glacier, final music
CD _____ **CDGO 2059**
EMI / May '94 / EMI.

BROADWAY
Andrew Lloyd Webber suite / Harold Arlen suite / Hart and Hammerstein by Rodgers suite / Cole Porter suite / Royal Philharmonic Orchestra suite / Paul Gemingnani suite
CD _____ **PWK 075**
Carlton Home Entertainment / Jan '89 /
Carlton Home Entertainment.

BROADWAY CHRISTMAS
Be a Santa / Chtistmas eve / Pine cones and holly berries / Turkey lurkey time / Christmas gifts / That man over there / Hard candy Christmas / Christmas child / I thank you for your love / I don't remember Christmas / We need a little Christmas / Greenwillow Christmas / Lovers on Christmas eve / Happy New Year blues / Have yourself a merry little Christmas
CD _____ **VSD 5517**
Varese Sarabande/Colosseum / Jan '95 / Pinnacle / Silva Screen.

BROADWAY CLASSICS
CD _____ **MCAD 10051**
MCA/Silva Screen / Jan '95 / Silva Screen.

BROADWAY HITS
CD _____ **CDCD 1231**
Charly / Jun '95 / Charly / THE / Cadillac.

BROADWAY MAGIC I
(1950s)
CD _____ **CK 40660**
CBS/Silva Screen / Feb '90 / Conifer /
Silva Screen.

BROADWAY MAGIC II
(1960s)
CD _____ **CK 40698**
CBS/Silva Screen / Feb '90 / Conifer /
Silva Screen.

BROADWAY MAGIC III
(1970s)
CD _____ **CK 40699**
CBS/Silva Screen / Feb '90 / Conifer /
Silva Screen.

BROADWAY SHOWSTOPPERS
Casts & Ambrosian Chorus/London Sinfonietta
CD _____ **CDC 7545862**
EMI Classics / Apr '93 / EMI.

BROADWAY SHOWSTOPPERS
CD _____ **CDTEZ 7002**
TER / Jan '95 / Koch.

BUGS BUNNY ON BROADWAY
(New Recordings Of Music From Bugs
Bunny Cartoons)
CD _____ **9264942**
Silva Screen / Sep '93 / Conifer / Silva Screen.

BUSBY BERKELY ALBUM, THE
Barrett, Brent & Judy Blazer/Ann Morrison/London Sinfonietta & Chorus
CD _____ **CDC 5551892**
EMI Classics / Apr '93 / EMI.

C

CAGNEY AND LACEY
(And Other American Television
Themes)
Caine, Daniel Orchestra
Caine, Daniel Con
Cagney and Lacey / Mike Hammer / Lou Grant / St. Elsewhere / Magnum P.I. / Taxi / Simon and Simon / Hill Street Blues / Blues in the day / Night on the hill / Officer down / Captain / Suite from Hill Street blues
CD _____ **FILMCD 704**
Silva Screen / Jun '92 / Conifer / Silva Screen.

CAROUSEL WALTZ
Philharmonia/National Symphony/D'Oyly Carte Opera/New Sadler's Wells/Scottish Opera Orchestras
Edwards, John Owen/J. Pryce Jones/M. Reed/G. Hossack Con
CD _____ **CDVIR 8315**
TER / Oct '91 / Koch.

CASABLANCA
(Classic Film Scores For Humphrey
Bogart)
National Philharmonic Orchestra
Gerhardt, Charles Con
Casablanca / Passage to Marseille (Rescue at sea) / Treasure of the Sierra Madre / Big Sleep (Love themes) / Two Mrs Carrolls / Caine Mutiny (March) / To Have and Have Not (Main title - Martinique) / Sabrina (Main title (The Larrabee estate) / Virginia City (Stagecoach/Love scene) / Key Largo / Left Hand of God (Love theme) / Sahara (Main theme)
CD _____ **GD 80422**
RCA Victor / '90 / BMG.

CELEBRATE BROADWAY
Sing happy: Minnelli, Liza / Blow Gabriel blow: Lupone, Patti / Freedom: Theodore, Donna & Chip Ford / Crossword square!: Goodman, Michael / I've gotta crow: Martin, Mary & Kathy Nolan / Good morning starshine: Kellogg, Lyn / Born again: Martin, Mary / Our time: Walton, Jim / Hey look me over: Ball, Lucille / Before the parade passes by: Channing, Carol / I got love: Moore, Melba / To life: Mostel, Zero / Certain girl: Wayne, David / Little me: Andrews, Nancy / H-A-P-P-Y/We'll take a glass together: Jackson, David / Best of times: Hearn, George
CD _____ **09026619872**
RCA / Apr '94 / BMG.

CELEBRATE BROADWAY VOL. 2
I've got your number: Swenson, Swen / Step to the rear: Roberts, Anthony & Charlotte Jones / I can't say no: Ebersole, Christine / Mama will provide: Lewis, Kecia / Caribbean plaid (medley): Kingston market/ Matilda Matilda: Chandler, Stan / Dream: Mostel, Zero / Lizzie Borden: Lautner, Joe / Arthur in the afternoon: Ziemba, Karn / Your feet's too big: Page, Ken / Crossword puzzle: Ackerman, Loni / Well known fact: Preston, Robert / Shuffle off to Buffalo: Prunczik, Karen / Siberia: Lascoe, Henry / Another wedding song: Barrett, Brent / So long dearie: Bailey, Pearl / Little more mascara: Shapiro, Debbie
CD _____ **09026619882**
RCA / Apr '94 / BMG.

CENTRE STAGE
Warlow, Anthony
Music of the night / Easy to love / Luck be a lady / Somewhere / This nearly was mine / I am what I am / Anthem / Bring him home / You're nothing without me / Impossible dream / Johanna / Colours of my life / Soliloquy
CD _____ **5112232**
London / Nov '91 / PolyGram.

CHANSONS POUR FELLINI
CD _____ **CDCH 330**
Milan / Feb '94 / BMG / Silva Screen.

CHARLES BRONSON
(Original Motion Picture Soundtracks)
Kinjite / Forbidden subjects / Assassination / Messenger of death
CD _____ **FILMCD 052**
Silva Screen / Dec '89 / Conifer / Silva Screen.

CHARLIE
(Music From The Films Of Charlie
Chaplin)
Munich Symphony Orchestra
Shaw, Francis Con
Limelight / Modern times / King in New York / City lights / Great dictator / Countess from Hong Kong
CD _____ **FILMCD 711**
Silva Screen / Jan '93 / Conifer / Silva Screen.

CHUMMA DO
(Hit Hindi Film Songs In Bengali)
Jooma chumma de / Khullam khulla pyaar / Chura liya tune / Pyaar bina chain ka-

han re / Yeh ladka hai allah / Oh romeo / Ole ole / Tama tama loge / Dil afri dam
CD _____ **ARCD 2035**
Audiorec / '91 / Audiorec.

CINEMA DU MONDE
(18 Film Soundtrack Masterpieces)
CD _____ **MCCD 127**
Music Club / Sep '93 / Disc / THE / CM.

CINEMA MOODS
Heart asks pleasure first/The promise: Nyman, Michael / Sheltering sky theme: Sakamoto, Ryuichi / Dangerous liasons (Vivaldi) / On earth as it is in heaven: Morricone, Ennio / Veni sancte spiritus: Fenton, George / Jean De Florette: Petit, Jean Claude / Darlington Hall: Robbins, Richard / Germinal: Roques, Jean-Louis / Betty et Zorg: Yared, Gabriel / Last emperor: Byrne, David / Etude: Tarrega, Francisco / Chasing sheep is best left to shepherds: Nyman, Michael / Age of innocence: Bernstein, Leonard / Hamlet: Morricone, Ennio / Pensione Bertollini: Robbins, Richard / Cinema paradiso: Morricone, Ennio / Adagio for strings (Samuel Barber) / Big Blue overture: Serra, Eric
CD _____ **CDV 2774**
Virgin / Mar '95 / EMI.

CINEMA OF THE '80S
CD _____ **CDCH 394**
Milan / Feb '91 / BMG / Silva Screen.

CINEMATIC PIANO - SOLO PIANO
MUSIC FROM THE MOVIES
Chertock, M.
CD _____ **CD 80357**
Telarc / Jul '94 / Conifer / ADA.

CLASSIC FILM SCORES FOR BETTE
DAVIS
National Philharmonic Orchestra
Gerhardt, Charles Con
Now Voyager / Dark Victory / Stolen Life / Private Lives of Elizabeth and Essex / Mr. Skeffington / In This Our Life / All About Eve / Jezebel / Beyond the Forest / Juarez / Letter / All This and Heaven Too
CD _____ **GD 80183**
RCA Victor / '89 / BMG.

CLASSIC FILM THEMES
Carter, Gaylord
King's row / Bad and the beautiful / How green was my valley / High noon / Uninvited / Exodus / Gone with the wind / Best years of our lives / Spellbound / Place in the sun / Raintree county
CD _____ **FA 8102**
Facet / May '94 / Conifer.

CLASSIC FILM THEMES
CD _____ **TRTCD 202**
TrueTrax / Jun '95 / THE.

CLASSIC GREEK FILM MUSIC
City Of Prague Philharmonic Orchestra
Zorba the Greek / 300 Spartans / Topkapi / Never on a Sunday / Chariots of Fire / 1492 (Conquest of Paradise) / Z / Phaedra / Honeymoon / State of Siege / Blue / Serpico / Shirley Valentine / Missing
CD _____ **FILMCD 165**
Silva Screen / Oct '95 / Conifer / Silva Screen.

CLASSIC HOLLYWOOD
New World Philharmonic
CD _____ **FMICD 1**
FMI / Feb '95 / Total/BMG.

CLASSIC ITALIAN SOUNDTRACKS
(The Horror Film Collection)
Deep red / Night of the devils / Nightmare / City / Planet of the vampires / Monk / Throne of fire / Seven notes in black / Mysterious island of Dr Nemo / Deadly steps lost in the dark
CD _____ **DRGCD 32903**
DRG / Jun '95 / New Note.

CLASSIC ITALIAN SPAGHETTI
WESTERN THEMES
CD _____ **DRGCD 32909**
DRG / Oct '95 / New Note.

CLASSIC MOVIE SONGS OF THE 40'S
Haran, Mary Cleere
CD _____ **VSD 5482**
Varese Sarabande/Colosseum / Oct '94 / Pinnacle / Silva Screen.

CLASSICAL FILM MUSIC
CD _____ **889706**
Milan / May '93 / BMG / Silva Screen.

CLASSICAL FILM THEMES
2CD _____ **MBSCD 421**
Castle / Nov '93 / BMG.

CLASSICAL HOLLYWOOD VOL.1
CD _____ **873126**
Milan / Sep '92 / BMG / Silva Screen.

CLASSICAL HOLLYWOOD VOL.2
CD _____ **873128**
Milan / Sep '92 / BMG / Silva Screen.

CLASSICS FROM HOLLYWOOD TO
BROADWAY
Holliday, Melanie & Frankfurt Radio Orchestra
CD _____ **310642**
Koch Schwann / Dec '95 / Koch.

CLASSICS OF THE SILVER SCREEN
Kunzel, Erich & Cincinnati Pops Orchestra
CD _____ CD 80221
Telarc / Aug '90 / Conifer / ADA.

CLASSICS TO BROADWAY
Paratore, A. & J.
CD _____ 310115
Koch / Oct '92 / Koch.

CLIFFHANGERS
(Action & Adventure In The Movies)
City Of Prague Philharmonic Orchestra
Motzing, William Con
Bear Island / Flight of the Intruder / Duellists
/ Shoot to Kill / Riddle of the Sands / Remo
/ Savage Islands / Jaws IV / Last of the Mo-
hicans / Arachnophobia / First Blood / King
Solomon's Mines / Farewell to the King /
Young Indiana Jones / 1492 (Conquest of
Paradise) / Cliffhanger
CD _____ FILMCD 155
Silva Screen / Sep '94 / Conifer / Silva
Screen.

COLLECTION
Monroe, Marilyn
CD _____ COL 042
Collection / Mar '95 / Target/BMG.

COLLECTION: DORIS DAY
(20 Golden Greats)
Day, Doris
Secret love / Whatever will be will be (Que
sera sera) / My blue Heaven / Pillow talk /
Sentimental journey / Blue skies / Move
over darling / Somebody loves me / At sundown / Fine and dandy / Please don't talk
about me when I'm gone / You made me
love you / Lullaby of Broadway / Just one
of those things / It's magic / Mean to mo /
Please don't eat the daisies / Do not disturb
/ Everybody loves my baby / Love me or
leave me
CD _____ DVCD 2088
Deja Vu / Jan '87 / THE.

COLLECTION: MARILYN MONROE
(20 Golden Greats)
Monroe, Marilyn
Diamonds are a girl's best friend / River of
no return / Heatwave / Do it again / Kiss /
My heart belongs to daddy / I'm gonna file
my claim / This is a fine romance / Little girl
from Little Rock / Happy birthday Mr. President / After you get what you want, you
don't want it / You'd be surprised / She acts
like a woman should / Lazy / When love
goes wrong nothing goes right / One silver
dollar / When I fall in love / Things / Bye bye
duet (With Jane Russell.) / Bye bye baby
CD _____ DVCD 2001
Deja Vu / Jul '87 / THE.

COMMERCIAL BREAKS VOL 3
Only you: Praise / Lovely day: Withers, Bill
/ Summer breeze: Isley Brothers / Love
train: O'Jays / How 'bout us: Champaign /
Turn turn turn: Byrds / It's over: Orbison,
Roy / Move over darling: Day, Doris / I can
see clearly now (remix): Nash, Johnny /
Stand by your man: Wynette, Tammy / Al-
ways on my mind: Nelson, Willie / Blue vel-
vet: Vinton, Bobby / I can help: Swan, Billy
/ Take five: Brubeck, Dave / Summertime:
Vaughan, Sarah / Mannish boy: Waters,
Muddy / Should I stay or should I go: Clash
CD _____ 4690482
Columbia / Nov '91 / Sony.

COMPLETE CINEMA CLASSICS COLLECTION, THE
Piano (The heart asks pleasure first/The
promise) / Shadowlands / Schindler's List
(theme) / Remains of the Day (A portrait re-
turns/Darlington Hall) / Philadelphia (La
mamma morta) / Diva (Fhhen? No porta
Juliatta) / Apocalypse Now (The ride of the
Valkyries) / Platoon (Adagio for strings) / My
Left Foot (Un'aura amorosa) / Fatal Attraction (Un bel di vedremo) / Room With A
View (O mio babbino caro) / Immortal Beloved (Piano sonata - Moonlight) / Jefferson
in Paris (Violin sonata - La Follia) / Sleeping
With The Enemy (Symphonic fantastique -
Dream of a Witches' Sabbath) / Madness of
King George (Zadok the priest) / Out of Africa (Adagio from clarinet concerto) / Driving
Miss Daisy (Song to the moon) / Raging Bull
(Intermezzo - Cavalleria rusticana) / Untouchables (Verdi la giubba) / Gallipoli (Adagio) / Amadeus (Introitus: requiem aeter-
nam) / Pretty Woman (Dammi tu forza -
Violetta's farewell) / Brief Encounter (Piano
concerto no.2) / Moonstruck (Che gelida
manina) / True Romance (Flower duet) /
Children of a Lesser God (Double violin
concerto) / Dead Poets Society (Symphony
no.9 choral - Ode to joy)
2CD _____ CDEMTVD 106
EMI / Oct '95 / EMI.

COPS AND PRIVATE EYES
Caine, Daniel Con
L.A. Law / Sledgehammer / Hill Street Blues
/ Spenser For Hire / Remington Steele / Law
and Order / Mike Hammer / Riptide / Mid-
night Caller / Hooperman / Over My Dead
Body / Houston Knights / Twin Peaks /
Magnum P.I.
CD _____ TVPMCD 405
Primetime / Jul '92 / Silva Screen.

CORONATION STREET ALBUM, THE
Devoted to you: Richard, Cliff & Denise
Black / Blue eyes: Tarmey, Bill / He ain't
heavy, he's my brother: Hollies & Corona-

tion Street Cast / I remember it well: Barlow,
Thelma & Peter Baldwin / Life on the street:
Deuce featuring Sherrie Hewson / Tra la la
la: Waddington, Bill / Something stupid:
Barrie, Amanda & Johnny Briggs / Baby's in
black: Kennedy, Kevin / Didn't we: Ball, Michael & Barbara Knox / Teardrops: Griffin,
Angela & Chloe Newsome / I'll string along
with you: Nicholls, Sue / Always look on the
bright side of life: Coronation Street Cast
featuring Bill Waddington
CD _____ CDCOROTV 1
Premier / Nov '95 / EMI.

DAY AT THE MOVIES, A
Day, Doris
CD _____ CK 44371
CBS/Silva Screen / Jan '89 / Conifer / Silva
Screen.

DIAL M FOR MURDER
(A History Of Hitchcock)
City Of Prague Philharmonic Orchestra
Bateman, Paul Con
Psycho / North by Northwest / Rebecca /
Spellbound / Under Capricorn / Vertigo /
Topaz / Marnie / Frenzy / Suspicion / Dial
M for murder
CD _____ FILMCD 137
Silva Screen / Sep '93 / Conifer / Silva
Screen.

DIAMOND COLLECTION, THE
Monroe, Marilyn
CD _____ WWRCD 6002
Wienerworld / Jun '95 / Disc.

DIAMONDS ARE A GIRL'S BEST FRIEND
Monroe, Marilyn
CD _____ CDGFR 135
IMD / Jun '92 / BMG.

DIGITAL SPACE
London Symphony Orchestra
Star Wars / Tribute to a bad man / Lady
Hamilton / Airport / Things to come / Wind-
jammer / Big Country / Red pony / 49th Par-
allel / Spitfire prelude and fugue
CD _____ VCD 47229
Varese Sarabande/Colosseum / Jan '89 /
Pinnacle / Silva Screen.

DIGITAL THEMES SPECTACULAR
Dallas / My name is Bond / Rocky medley
/ Chariots of Fire / Knots landing / Raiders
of the Lost Ark / Falcon Crest / Only love /
Where no man has gone before / Chi Mai /
Dynasty / Those Magificent Men in their Fly-
ing Machine / Rockford files / Eastenders /
Warship / Barwick Green / Dambusters
march / Longest Day / Concert march-
Cockleshell Heroes
CD _____ BNA 5011
Bandleader / Feb '88 / Conifer.

DIGITAL THEMES SPECTACULAR VOL. 2
2001 / Superman / Hill Street Blues / Kojak
/ Cagney and Lacey / Dempsey and mak-
epeace / Dad's Army / TV Sports themes /
Cavatina / 633 Squadron / Swing march /
Trap / Howard's Way / Last starfighter /
Masterpiece / Nobilmente / Things to come
(Bridge Too Far / Squadron) / In party mood
/ Liberty bell / Black Hole / Lawrence of Ara-
bia / Elizabeth Tudor / Battle of Britain
CD _____ BNA 5031
Bandleader / Aug '89 / Conifer.

DIRTY HARRY
(Heroes And Tough Guys At The Movies)
Dirty Harry (Suite): San Diego Symphony
Pops / Hunt For Red October (Hymn of the
Red Army): San Diego Symphony Pops /
Godfather Part Two (The immigrant/Theme):
Milan Philharmonia Orchestra / Big Trouble
In Little China (Pork chop express/Theme):
Caine, Daniel Orchestra / Cool Hand Luke
(Symphonic sketches): Rochester Pops Or-
chestra / Running Man (Theme): Hollywood
Sound Orchestra / Robin Hood (Attack on
the castle/The wedding): Bullitt (Theme):
San Diego Symphony Pops / Heroes
(Theme) / Revenge (Love theme): San
Diego Symphony Pops / Hitcher (Head-
lights/Theme): High Road To China (Waziri
village attack/Escape): Crocodile Dundee
(Overture) / Missing In Action II (End titles)
/ Long Good Friday (Taken) / Double Impact
(The brother's revenge) / Raiders Of The
Lost Ark (Raiders march): San Diego Sym-
phony Pops
CD _____ SILVAD 3001
Silva Treasury / '92 / Conifer / Silva Screen.

DISNEY BABIES - WAKE UP
Morning / Good morning starshine / Get
outta bed / French toast / Zip a dee doo
dah / Mom is the sweetest alarm clock /
Here comes the sun / Rising early in the
morning / Cock-a-doodle-doo / Beautiful
morning / Morning glory / New morning /

Early in the morning / Wake up symphony /
Morning song
CD _____ DSMCD 474
Carlton Home Entertainment / Aug '94 /
Carlton Home Entertainment.

DISNEY COLLECTION VOLUME 1, THE
Under the sea / I wanna be like you / Mickey
Mouse alma mater / It's a small world / Fol-
lowing the leader / Spoonful of sugar / Hi
diddle dee dee / Zip a dee doo dah / Whis-
tle while you work / Who's afraid of the big
bad wolf / Give a little whistle / Work song
/ Yo ho (a pirates life for me) / Bibbidi-bob-
bidi-boo / Supercalifragilisticexpialidocious
CD _____ DSTCD 453
Carlton Home Entertainment / Aug '94 /
Carlton Home Entertainment.

DISNEY COLLECTION VOLUME 2, THE
Kiss the girl / Chim chim cheree / Bare ne-
cessities / He's a tramp / Cruella de vil /
Everybody wants to be a cat / Siamese cat
song / Feed the birds (tuppence a bag) /
Let's go fly a kite / When I see an elephant
fly / You can fly, you can fly, you can fly /
I've got no strings / Ballad of Davy Crockett
/ Zorro / Saludos amigos / Little April show-
ers / Lavender blue / With a smile and a
song
CD _____ DSTCD 454
Carlton Home Entertainment / Aug '94 /
Carlton Home Entertainment.

DISNEY COLLECTION VOLUME 3, THE
Part of your world / Candle on the water /
Bella notte / So this is love / Someone's
waiting for you / When you wish upon a star
/ Winnie the Pooh / Best of friends / Casey
junior / Jolly holiday / Once upon a dream
/ One song / Ronettes / Someday my Prince
will come / Second star to the right / Baby
mine / Love is a song / Dream is a wish your
heart makes
CD _____ DSTCD 455
Carlton Home Entertainment / Aug '94 /
Carlton Home Entertainment.

DISNEY HITS
When you wish upon a star: Sammes, Mike
Singers / Thomas O'Malley cat: Hilton, Ronnie / When I see an elephant fly: Sammes,
Mike Singers / When I see an elephant fly: Peterson, Clive / Who's afraid of the big bad
wolf: Sammes, Mike Singers / Ugly bug ball:
Hilton, Ronnie / Whistle while you work /
Winnie the Pooh / Heigh ho / Siamese cat
song: Sammes, Mike Singers / Bare necessities: Sammes, Mike Singers / Supercalifragilisticexpialidocious / Colonel Hathi's
march: Sammes, Mike Singers / Trust in me:
Curtis, Nick / That's what friends are for:
Sammes, Mike Singers / I wanna be like
you: Sammes, Mike Singers / Never smile
at a crocodile: Peterson, Clive / Feed the
birds: Dawn, Julie / Aristocats: Hilton, Ronnie / Hi diddle dee dee: Sammes, Mike
Singers / Everybody wants to be a cat: Hilton, Ronnie / My own home: Heard, Enid /
I've got no strings: Sammes, Mike Singers
CD _____ CC 262
Music For Pleasure / Oct '90 / EMI.

DISNEY SPECTACULAR
Cincinnati Pops Orchestra
When you wish upon a star / It's a small
world / Alice in Wonderland / March of the
cards / Mary Poppins / Cinderella / Jungle
book / Who's afraid of the big bad wolf /
Snow White and the seven dwarfs / Disney
fantasy medley
CD _____ CD 80196
Telarc / '89 / Conifer / ADA.

DIVA - SOPRANO AT THE MOVIES
Garrett, Lesley
CD _____ SONGCD 903
Silva Classics / Jan '94 / Conifer / Silva
Screen.

DIVA BY DIVA
Kaye, Judy
CD _____ VSD 5589
Varese Sarabande/Colosseum / Nov '95 /
Pinnacle / Silva Screen.

DIVAS OF THE SILVER SCREEN
(Essential Recordings/Songs From The Stage & Screen/Marlene)
Monroe, Marilyn/Judy Garland/Marlene
Dietrich
3CD _____ MCBX 016
Music Club / Dec '94 / Disc / THE / CM.

DRACULA
(Classic Scores From Hammer Horror)
Philharmonia Orchestra
Richardson, Neil Con
Dracula / Dracula has risen from the grave
/ Taste the blood of Dracula / Vampire cir-
cus / Hands of the ripper / Dracula, prince
of darkness
CD _____ FILMCD 714
Silva Screen / May '93 / Conifer / Silva
Screen.

E

EARFUL OF MERMAN, AN
Merman, Ethel
I got rhythm / Sam and Delilah / Shake well
/ Eadie was a lady / Animal in me / Spanish
custom / He reminds me of you / Earful of
music / Shake it off with rhythm / You're the
top / Shanghai-de-ho / Riding high / It's de-
lovely / Hot and happy / You are the music
to the words in my heart / Heatwave /
Marching along with time / This is it / I'll pay
the check / Friendship / Make it another
old-fashioned please / Let's be buddies
CD _____ CMSCD 015
Movie Stars / May '94 / Conifer.

EMBRACEABLE YOU - BROADWAY IN LOVE
Broadway Casts
CD _____ SK 53542
Sony Classical / Jul '94 / Sony.

EMPIRE MOVIE MUSIC COLLECTION
On Earth as it is in heaven: London Phil-
harmonic Orchestra / Last Emperor (main ti-
tle): Byrne, David / Merry Christmas Mr.
Lawrence: Sakamoto, Ryuichi / Black rain
suite: Zimmer, Hans / Looks like a stain-
cloth: Martinez, Cliff / Homeboy: Clapton,
Eric / C'est le vent, Betty: Yared, Gabriel /
Key: Fenton, George / Etude: Oldfield, Mike
/ Call to arms: Horner, James / Les mod-
ernes: Krause, Steven
CD _____ CDVMM 1
Virgin / Nov '90 / EMI.

ENCORE, ENCORE
(Hits From The West End Stage Show)
London Theatre Orchestra & Singers
Only He / Memory / Maria / Another suit-
case in another hall / I know him so well /
Aquarius / Edelweiss / One night in Bang-
kok / She's so beautiful / Tomorrow /
Grease / Hey there / Prepare the way of the
Lord / People / Don't cry for me Argentina
/ I don't know how to love him / Impossible
dream / Day by day / Sound of music / Till
there was you
CD _____ OP 0002
MCI / Apr '87 / Disc / THE.

EPIC FILM SCORES
King of Kings / Nativity / Miracles of Christ
/ Salome's dance / Way of the cross / Res-
urrection and finale / Ben Hur / Victory pa-
rade / Miracle and finale / El Cid overture /
Palace music / Legend and epilogue
CD _____ VCD 47268
Varese Sarabande/Colosseum / '88 / Pin-
nacle / Silva Screen.

EROTIC CINEMA
CD _____ 12167
Laserlight / Sep '93 / Target/BMG.

ESSENTIAL COLLECTION
Monroe, Marilyn
2CD _____ LECD 621
Wisepack / Apr '95 / THE / Conifer.

ESSENTIAL JAMES BOND, THE
City Of Prague Philharmonic Orchestra
Raine, Nic Con
Dr. No / From Russia With Love / 007 /
Goldfinger / Thunderball / You Only Live
Twice / On Her Majesty's Secret Service /
Diamonds Are Forever / Man With the
Golden Gun / Spy Who Loved Me / Moon-
raker / For Your Eyes Only / Octopussy /
Living Daylights / View to a Kill / Licence to
Kill
CD _____ FILMCD 007
Silva Screen / '93 / Conifer / Silva Screen.

ETHEL MERMAN'S BROADWAY
Merman, Ethel
CD _____ VSD 5665
Varese Sarabande/Colosseum / Nov '95 /
Pinnacle / Silva Screen.

EUROPE GOES TO HOLLYWOOD
CD _____ CO 75470
Denon / Sep '93 / Conifer.

EVERYBODY SING
(Great Songs From The Hollywood Musicals)
Everybody sing: Garland, Judy / If it's you:
Martin, Tony / When I love you: Miranda,
Carmen / Boljanglers of Harlem: Astaire, Fred
/ Ain't it a shame about Mame: Martin, Mary
/ When my ship comes in: Cantor, Eddie /
I'm no angel: West, Mae / Treat me rough:
Rooney, Mickey / Let yourself go: Rogers,
Ginger / With plenty of money and you:
Powell, Dick / Easy to love: Langford, Fr-
ances / Two sleepy people: Hope, Bob &
Shirley Ross / Sand in my shoes: Boswell,
Connie / Ol' man river: Robeson, Paul /
Never in a million years: Faye, Alice / Sweet
little headache: Crosby, Bing / Moon of
Manakoora: Lamour, Dorothy / You are too
beautiful: Jolson, Al / It's raining sunbeams:
Durbin, Deanna / Lovely way to spend an
evening: Sinatra, Frank
CD _____ PPCD 78113
Past Perfect / Feb '95 / THE.

FAMOUS STAGE AND SCREEN PERSONALITIES
CD _____ CDSVL 209
Saville / Oct '91 / Conifer.

FAMOUS THEMES
(Radio/TV/Newsreel Themes From 1940's/50's)
Queens Hall Light Orchestra
Portrait of a flirt/Willo the wisp/Jumping bean (In Town Tonight) / Journey into melody / Sapphires and sables / Invitation waltz (Ring Round the Moon) / By the sleepy lagoon (Desert Island Discs) / Puffin' Billy (Children's Favourites) / Coronation Scot (Paul Temple) / Rhythm on rails (Morning Music) / Music everywhere (Rediffusion's call sign) / Horse guards, Whitehall (Down Your Way) / Devil's gallop (Dick Barton Special Agent) / Destruction by fire (Pathe News) / On a spring note (Pathe Gazette) / All sports march (Pathe News) / Cavalcade of youth (Barlows of Beddington) / Drum majorette (Match of the Day) / Girls in grey (BBC TV news) / Elizabethan serenade (Music in Miniature) / Melody on the move / Alpine pastures (My Word) / Young ballerina (Potters wheel interlude) / Horse feathers (Meet the Huggetts) / Sportsmaster (Peter Stuyvesvant)
CD _____ GRCD 10
Grasmere / May '86 / Target/BMG / Savoy.

FAMOUS THEMES
New World Philharmonic
CD _____ CDRBL 7782
Red Bus / '88 / Total/BMG.

FANTASTIC JOURNEY
Kunzel, Erich & Cincinnati Pops Orchestra
CD _____ CD 8023
Telarc / Aug '90 / Conifer / ADA.

FANTASTIC TELEVISION THEMES
Caine, Daniel Con
Quantum Leap / V the series / Freddy's Nightmares / Star Trek - The Next Generation / Knight Rider / Highway to Heaven / Streethawk / Battlestar Galactica / Airwolf / Buck Rogers in the 25th Century / North Star (The TV movie) / Bring 'Em Back Alive / Return of the Man From U.N.C.L.E. / Tales of the Gold Monkey
CD _____ TVPMCD 402
Primetime / May '91 / Silva Screen.

FANTASTIC VOYAGE
(A Journey Through Classic Fantasy Film Music)
City Of Prague Philharmonic Orchestra
Motzing, William Con
Alien (End title) / Terminator (Theme) / My Stepmother Is An Alien (The Klystron) / Dead Zone (Main title) / Gremlins 2: The New Batch (End title) / Countdown (Main theme) / 2010 (Finale) / Seconds (Suite) / Ghostbusters (Main theme) / Flash Gordon (Suite) / V For Victory (Main title) / Mad Max 2 (Journey over the mountain) / Fantastic Voyage (Ocean of life) / Explorers (The construction) / Fortress (Main title) / Philadelphia Experiment (Main theme) / Illustrated Man (Main title
Frightened Willie) / Battle For The Planet Of The Apes (Main title) / Total Recall (Main title) / Batman (March)
CD _____ FILMCD 146
Silva Screen / Jan '94 / Conifer / Silva Screen.

FANTASY FESTIVAL
(Themes From Italian Fantasy/Horror Films)
CD _____ CDCIA 5093
Cinevox / Apr '94 / Conifer / Silva Screen.

FANTASY MOVIE THEMES
London Symphony Orchestra
CD _____ HRM 7002
Hermes / Jan '86 / Nimbus.

FASCINATING RHYTHM
Astaire, Fred
Shall we dance / Fascinating rhythm / Night and day / Crazy feet / Puttin' on the ritz / My one and only / Babbitt and the bromide / I've got you on my mind / Foggy day / Let's call the whole thing off / New sun in the sky / High hat / Hang on to me / Funny face / They can't take that away from me / Nice work if you can get it
CD _____ HADCD 163
Javelin / May '94 / THE / Henry Hadaway Organisation.

FAVOURITE MOVIE CLASSICS
CD _____ CDCFP 4606
Classics For Pleasure / Jan '95 / EMI.

FAVOURITE TV CLASSICS
CD _____ CDCFP 4613
Classics For Pleasure / Jan '95 / EMI.

FAVOURITE TV CLASSICS II
CD _____ CDCFP 4626
Classics For Pleasure / Jan '95 / EMI.

FAVOURITE TV THEMES
Inspector Morse / Ruth Rendell mysteries / Upstairs and downstairs / She (Seven faces of woman) / Agatha Christie's Poirot / Woman of substance / The match (Goal crazy) / Avengers / Forever green / New adventures of Black Beauty / Chimera (Rosheen du) / London's burning / Dr. Who / Saylon Dola (One game) / World Cup '90 (Tutti al mondo) / Hundred acres / On the line / Wish me luck as you wave me goodbye / Summer's lease (Carmina Valles) / ITV Athletics (Hot foot) / Good guys / Classic adventures
CD _____ MCCD 069
Music Club / Jun '92 / Disc / THE / CM.

FELLINI FILM THEMES
Amarcord / Juliet of the spirits / 8-1/2 / La dolce vita / Satyricon Roma / White sheik / I vitteloni / Il bidone / Nights of Cabiria / La strada
CD _____ HNCD 9301
Hannibal / Jan '87 / Vital / ADA.

FILM AND MUSICAL FAVOURITES
Keel, Howard
CD _____ 15093
Laserlight / May '94 / Target/BMG.

FILM COLLECTION, THE
CD _____ 11818
Music / Aug '95 / Target/BMG.

FILM FANTASY
National Philharmonic Orchestra
Journey to the Centre of the Earth / Seventh voyage of Sinbad / Day the earth stood still / Fahrenheit
CD _____ 4212662
Decca / '88 / PolyGram.

FILM FAVOURITES
Mancini, Henry
Love story / Pink panther / Windmills of your mind / Moon river / Raindrops keep falling on my head
CD _____ 295469
Ariola Express / Aug '95 / BMG.

FILM FAVOURITES
Mantovani & His Orchestra
Love story / Big country / Secret love / Wand'rin' star / Tammy / Never on a Sunday / When you wish upon a star / Born free / Que sera sera / Alfie / High Noon / Trolley song / Moon river / Windmills of your mind / Moulin Rouge theme / Chim chim cher-ee / As time goes by / My foolish heart
CD _____ 5516012
Spectrum/Karussell / Nov '95 / PolyGram / THE.

FILM STAR PARADE
I wanna be loved by you: Kane, Helen / Please: Crosby, Bing / Ich bin von kopf bis fuss auf liebe eingestellt (Falling in love again): Dietrich, Marlene / My wife is on a diet: Cantor, Eddie / You're always in my arms (but only in my dreams): Daniels, Bebe / Living in clover: Buchanan, Jack / Let me sing and I'm happy: Jolson, Al / What'll I do: Pidgeon, Walter / Dance of the cuckoos: Laurel & Hardy / Eadie was a lady: Merman, Ethel / All I need is just one girl: MacMurray, Fred / Love your magic spell is everywhere: Swanson, Gloria / I could make a good living at that: Formby, George / Don't tell him what's happened to me: Bankhead, Tallulah / My rock-a-bye baby: Moore, Grace / (I'd like to be) A bee in your boudoir: Rogers, Charles 'Buddy' / Love me tonight: MacDonald, Jeanette & Maurice Chevalier / Goodnight Vienna: Buchanan, Jack
CD _____ CDAJA 5020
Living Era / Jul '89 / Koch.

FILM THEMES
Mantovani
CD _____ CDSIV 6105
Horatio Nelson / Jul '95 / THE / BMG / Avid/BMG / Koch.

FILM WORKS 1986-1990
Zorn, John
CD _____ 7559792702
Elektra Nonesuch / Jan '95 / Warner Music.

FILMS CONCERT
Diva / Kramer vs Kramer / Apocalypse Now / Clockwork orange / Runaway Train / 2001 / Death in Venice / E la Nave Va
CD _____ CDCH 249
Milan / May '87 / BMG / Silva Screen.

FILMS OF JEAN CLAUDE VAN DAMME
CD _____ FILMCD 092
Silva Screen / Sep '91 / Conifer / Silva Screen.

FLIGHT INTO FANTASY
Movin' Dream Orchestra
Danger zone / Harold the duck / Power of love / E.T. (theme) / Star Wars / Close encounters of the third kind / Superman / Convoy / We may never love like this again / Jaws II / View to a kill / From Russia with love / Speak softly love / Stranger in the night / Exodus / Laurence of Arabia
CD _____ DC 8502
Denon / '88 / Conifer.

FOUR ALFRED HITCHCOCK FILMS
Ketcham, Charles & Utah Symphony Orchestra

Family Plot (end credits) / Strangers on a Train (suite) / Suspicion (suite) / Notorious (suite)
CD _____ VCD 47225
TER / Sep '86 / Koch.

FROG PRINCE, THE
Train to Paris / First day / Mack the knife / Let it be me / With Jean-Phillipe / Jenny / Reflections / Frog Prince / Dreams / Kiss / Sweet Georgia Brown / Georgia on my mind / Kiss by the fountain / Jenny and Roz / Les flon-flons du bal / Epilogue
CD _____ 5510992
Spectrum/Karussell / Jun '95 / PolyGram / THE.

FROM THE BIG SCREEN
Band Of The Life Guards
Jurassic Park / Medley from The Lion King / E.T. (theme) / Robin Hood, Prince of Thieves / Medley from Indiana Jones and the Temple of Doom / Medley: an Aladdin fantasy / Star Trek (Through the Generations medley) / Medley from The Bodyguard / Evening at tops
CD _____ BNA 5116
Bandleader / Jul '95 / Conifer.

G

GALA NIGHT
(Classic Songs From The Shows)
CD _____ SILVAD 3005
Silva Treasury / Apr '94 / Conifer / Silva Screen.

GARY WILMOT - THE ALBUM
Wilmot, Gary & The London Symphony Orchestra
Luck be a lady / I've never been in love before / We're off to see the wizard / Somewhere over the rainbow / If I only had a brain / Younger than springtime / Bali ha'i / Night they invented champagne / Gigi / Where is love / Consider yourself / Who will buy / Stan' up and fight / Beat out dat rhythm on a drum / Perfect year / Sunset Boulevard
CD _____ 3036000092
Carlton Home Entertainment / Oct '95 / Carlton Home Entertainment.

GHOST
(Classic Fantasy Film Music Vol.2)
City Of Prague Philharmonic Orchestra
Motzing, William Con
Conan The Barbarian (Main title) / Highlander (The castle - Anno Domini 1518/Ramirez Arrives/Training montage/Heather death - Who wants to live forever/Forge battle - There can be only one) / Addams Family (End credits) / Demolition Man (Main title) / Excalibur (End credits) / Ladyhawke (She was sad at first) / Witches Of Eastwick (Ballroom scene) / Rocketeer (End credits) / Island Of Dr. Moreau (Main title) / Super Mario Brothers (Main title/Prison chase) / Short Circuit (Getaway/Night camp/Finale) / Monkey Shines (Main title) / Wolfen (Epilogue/End credits) / Ghost (End credits)
CD _____ FILMCD 156
Silva Screen / Sep '94 / Conifer / Silva Screen.

GODFATHER, THE
(& Other Movie Themes)
London Symphony Orchestra/Philadelphia Orchestra Pops
Mancini, Henry Con
CD _____ 09026614782
RCA Victor / Jan '90 / BMG.

GOLD
(18 Epic Sporting Themes)
CD _____ CDSR 042
Telstar / Feb '94 / BMG.

GOLDEN VOICES FROM THE SILVER SCREEN VOL.1
Jaadugar kaatil: Bhosle, Asha / Dil cheez kya hai: Bhosle, Asha / Aplam chaplam: Mangeshkar, Lata & Usha / Toote hue khwabon ne: Rafi, Mohammed / Chahe koi mujhe: Rafi, Mohammed / Bechain dil khoi si nazar: Mangeshkar, Lata & Geeta Dutt / Sari sari raat: Mangeshkar, Lata / Inhi logon ne: Mangeshkar, Lata / Na to karavankitalash hai / Yeh hai ishq ishq / Aaj phir jeene ki (Available on CD format only.): Mangeshkar, Lata / Yashomati maiya se bole nandlala (Available on CD format only.): Mangeshkar, Lata & Manna Dey
CD _____ CDORBD 054
Globestyle / Mar '90 / Pinnacle.

GOLDEN VOICES FROM THE SILVER SCREEN VOL.2
Daiya re daiya: Bhosle, Asha / O megha re bole: Rafi, Mohammed / Babuji dheere chalna: Dutt, Geeta / Na jao saiyan: Dutt, Geeta / Chhalia mera naam: Mukesh / O hasina zulfonwau: Bhosle, Asha & Mohammed Rafi / Sar pe topi laal: Bhosle, Asha & Mohammed Rafi / Chalte chalte: Mangeshkar, Lata / Tere bina aag yeh chandini (Available on CD format only.): Mangeshkar, Lata & Manna Dey / Ghar aaya mera pardesi

(Available on CD format only.): Mangeshkar, Lata
CD _____ CDORBD 056
Globestyle / Apr '90 / Pinnacle.

GOLDEN VOICES FROM THE SILVER SCREEN VOL.3
Dhoondo dhoondo re: Mangeshkar, Lata / Saqiya aaj mujhe: Bhosle & Chorus, Asha / Satyam shivam (part 1): Mangeshkar, Lata / Ab reat guzarne vali: Mangeshkar, Lata / Leke pahla ahla pyar: Bhosle/Begum/Rafi / Hondton pe aisi: Mangeshkar/Bupinder / Salam e ishq: Mangeshkar, Lata / Aaj ki raat: Bhosle & Chorus, Asha / Satyam shivam (part 2): Mangeshkar, Lata / Jean Pehchaan no: Rafi, Mohammed / Toote na dil toote na: Mukesh
CD _____ CDORBD 059
Globestyle / May '90 / Pinnacle.

GREAT AMERICAN SONGWRITERS
Te Kanawa, Dame Kiri & Thomas Hampson/Frederica Von Stade/Bruce Hubbard
EMI Classics / Apr '93 / EMI.
CD _____ CDM 7646702

GREAT CLASSICAL THEMES
Mantovani
CD _____ MU 5011
Musketeer / Oct '92 / Koch.

GREAT FILM MUSICALS, THE
Lullaby of Broadway / Lulu's back in town / Jeepers creepers / Moonlight becomes you / Over the rainbow / Singin' in the rain / Love walked in / Boogie woogie bugle boy / Chatamooga choo-choo / Thanks for the memory / Isn't this a lovely day / I yi yi yi yi like you very much / Smoke gets in your eyes / Let yourself go / Keep young and beautiful / Road to Morocco / Puttin' on the Ritz / Wake up and live / Lover come back to me / I'm in the mood for love / Dearly beloved / I've got you under my skin / Yankee doodle boy / Hooray for Hollywood
CD _____ CDMOIR 514
Memoir / Jan '96 / Target/BMG.

GREAT FILM THEMES
CD _____ 8200402
London / Feb '88 / PolyGram.

GREAT FILM THEMES
2CD _____ TFP 024
Tring / Nov '92 / Tring / Prism.

GREAT FILMS AND SHOWS
Sinatra, Frank
Night and day / I wish I were in love again / I got plenty o' nuttin' / I guess I'll have to change my plan / Nice work if you can get it / I won't dance / You'd be so nice to come home to / I got it bad and that ain't good (CD only.) / From this moment on / Blue moon / September in the rain / It's only a paper moon / You do something to me / Taking a chance on love / Get happy / Just one of those things / I love Paris / Chicago / High hopes / I believe / Lady is a tramp / Let's do it (With Shirley MacLaine.) / C'est magnifique / Tender trap / Three coins in the fountain / Young at heart / Girl next door / They can't take that away from me / Someone to watch over me / Little girl blue / Like someone in love / Foggy day / I get a kick out of you / My funny valentine / Embraceable you / That old feeling / I've got a crush on you / Dream / September song / I'll see you again / As time goes by / There will never be another you / I'll remember April / Stormy weather / I can't get started (with you) / Around the world / Something's gotta give / Just in time / Dancing in the dark / Too close for comfort / I could have danced all night / Cheek to cheek / Song is you / Baubles, bangles and beads / Almost like being in love / Lover / On the sunny side of the street / That old black magic / I've heard that song before / You make me feel so young / Too marvellous for words / It happened in Monterey / I've got you under my skin / How about you / Pennies from Heaven / You're getting to be a habit with me / You brought a new kind of love to me / Love is here to stay / Old devil moon / Makin' whoopee / Anything goes / What is this thing called love / Glad to be unhappy / I get along without you very well / Dancing on the ceiling / Can't we be friends / All the way / To love and be loved / All my tomorrows / I couldn't sleep a wink last night / Spring is here / One for my baby / Time after time / It's all right with me / It's the same old dream / Johnny Concho theme (wait for me) / Wait till you see her / Where are you / Lonely town / Where or when / I concentrate on you / Love and marriage
4CD _____ CDFS 1
Capitol / Apr '89 / EMI.

GREAT MGM HOLLYWOOD MUSICALS
CD _____ CD 023
Silva Screen / Jan '89 / Conifer / Silva Screen.

GREAT MGM STARS: FRED ASTAIRE
Astaire, Fred
Steppin' out with my baby / It only happens when I dance with you / Oops / Bachelor's dinner song / Baby doll / Seeing's believing / I wanna be a dancin' man / Every night at seven / I left my hat in Haiti / You're all the world to me / How could you believe me when I said I love you (when you know I've been a liar all my life) / Fated to be mated: Astaire, Fred/Cyd Charisse/Carol Richards /

Paris loves lovers: *Astaire, Fred/Cyd Charisse/Carol Richards* / Ritz roll and rock / Nevertheless: *Astaire, Fred/Red Skelton/ Anita Ellis* / Where did you get that girl: *Astaire, Fred & Anita Ellis* / Three little words / Shine on your shoes / By myself / Triplets: *Astaire, Fred/Nanette Fabray/Jack Buchanan* / I love Louisa / That's entertainment: *Astaire, Fred/Nanette Fabray/Jack Buchanan* / All of you
CD _____ CDMGM 28
MGM/EMI / Feb '91 / EMI.

GREAT MOVIE SOUNDTRACKS
Aliens / Star Wars / Rambo / Escape from New York
CD _____ PWK 055
Carlton Home Entertainment / Jan '89 / Carlton Home Entertainment.

GREAT MOVIE SOUNDTRACKS VOL.2
Empire strikes back / White mischief / Running man / Robocop / Master of the Universe / Final conflict / Fly / Hope and Glory / Wall Street / Brainstorm / Prince of Darkness / Seventh voyage of Sinbad / No Way Out / Boy Who Could Fly / Xtro / Zed and two noughts / Secret of N.Y.M.H.
CD _____ PWK 110
Carlton Home Entertainment / May '89 / Carlton Home Entertainment.

GREAT MOVIE THEMES
London Symphony Orchestra
Black, Stanley *Con*
Raiders of the Lost Ark / Star Wars / Superman / 2001 / Magnificent seven / Big country / Lawrence of Arabia / Deer hunter / 633 Squadron / Medley: Themes from James Bond films (James Bond theme/ Thunderball/From Russia with love/ Goldfinger.)
CD _____ PWKS 4203
Carlton Home Entertainment / May '94 / Carlton Home Entertainment.

GREAT MUSICAL STANDARDS
CD _____ HCD 327
Hindsight / Jun '95 / Target/BMG / Jazz Music.

GREAT OVERTURES FROM THE MUSICALS
CD _____ CDVIR 8324
TER / Aug '95 / Koch.

GREAT SCREEN LOVERS COLLECTION
Who is there among...: *Nicholson, Jack* / Chattanooga choo choo: *Power, Tyrone* / Louise: *Chevalier, Maurice* / Manhattan: *Rooney, Mickey* / Let's do it: *Coward, Sir Noel* / Foolish pride: *Mitchum, Robert* / Puttin' on the Ritz: *Gable, Clarke* / Two of us: *Curtis, Tony & Gloria De Haven* / Let's make love: *Montand, Yves* / Day after day: *Stewart, James* / Did I remember: *Grant, Cary* / Kashmiri love song: *Valentino, Rudolph* / Pillow talk: *Hudson, Rock* / Mary's a grand old name: *Cagney, James* / Woman in love: *Brando, Marlon & Jean Simmons* / As long as there is music: *Sinatra, Frank* / Chico's choo choo: *Wagner, Robert & Debbie Reynolds* / Lover come back to me / I do is dream of you: *Kelly, Gene* / Gotta bran' new suit: *Astaire, Fred & Nanette Fabray*
CD _____ DVCD 2117
Deja Vu / Dec '87 / THE.

GREAT SHAKESPEARE FILMS
National Philharmonic Orchestra & London Festival Orchestra
CD _____ 4212682
Decca / '88 / PolyGram.

GREAT SONGS FROM GREAT SHOWS
CD _____ MATCD 297
Castle / Sep '00 / DMB.

GREAT SONGS FROM THE MUSICALS
CD _____ MCCD 162
MCI / Jul '94 / Disc / THE.

GREAT STAGE MUSICALS 1924–41, THE
CD _____ CDMOIR 531
Memoir / Jul '93 / Target/BMG.

GREAT STAGE MUSICALS VOL.2
Strike up the band / Lady be good / 'S Wonderful / High hat / Embraceable you / Body and soul / On the sunny side of the street / Love me or leave me / Makin' whoopee / It's de lovely / All through the night / Friendship / Everything I love / Hey good lookin' / My heart belongs to Daddy / Solomon / September song / Tchaikovsky / Saga of Jenny / My ship / Easter parade / Heatwave / Oh how I hate to get up in the morning / Hand in hand / Make believe / Who / They didn't believe me
CD _____ CDMOIR 509
Memoir / Jun '94 / Target/BMG.

GREAT TV THEMES
2CD _____ TFP 029
Tring / Nov '92 / Tring / Prism.

GREAT WAR THEMES
Dam Busters / Longest Day / Bridge Too Far / Colditz march / High On A Hill / Colonel Bogey / Top Gun / Aces High / Great Escape / Lawrence Of Arabia / Cockleshell Heroes / M.A.S.H. (Suicide is painless) / Road To Vitez / Raiders march and Imperial march / Cavalry of the clouds / Cavatina / Berliner luft / Normandy veterans / Battle Of Britain march
CD _____ PWKS 4208

Carlton Home Entertainment / Aug '94 / Carlton Home Entertainment.

GREAT WESTERN FILM THEMES
Rio bravo / Man with the harmonica / Fistful of dollars / Magnificent seven / Once upon a time in the west / My name is nobody / High noon / Ballad of the Alamo / Johnny guitar / Comancheros / Shane / Vera cruz / Virginian / Bonanza / Riders in the sky
CD _____ 22526
Music / Dec '95 / Target/BMG.

GREATEST LOVE SONGS FROM THE MUSICALS, THE
Love changes everything / Hello, young lovers / On the street where you live / As long as he needs me / All I ask of you / Human heart / Hopelessly devoted to you / I don't know how to love him / If ever I would leave you / You are love / Stranger in paradise / So in love
CD _____ SHOWCD 020
Showtime / Feb '95 / Disc / THE.

GREATEST SCIENCE FICTION HITS, VOL 1
Norman, Neil & his Orchestra
Alien / Moonraker / Star Wars / Superman / 2001 / Battlestar Galactica / Space 1999 / Star trek / Black hole
CD _____ GNPD 2128
GNP Crescendo / Jan '89 / Silva Screen.

GREATEST SCIENCE FICTION HITS, VOL 2
Norman, Neil & his Orchestra
Empire strikes back / Twilight zone / Buck Rogers / Time tunnel / Dr. Who / Voyage to the bottom of the sea / Dark star / Sinbad and the eye of the tiger
CD _____ GNPD 2133
GNP Crescendo / Jan '89 / Silva Screen.

GREATEST SCIENCE FICTION HITS, VOL 3
Norman, Neil & his Orchestra
E.T. (theme) / War of the worlds / Lost in space / Bladerunner / Flash Gordon / Thing / Prisoner / Land of giants / Space 1999 / Angry red planet / Capricorn one / Raiders of the Lost Ark / Invaders / U.F.O. / Vena's dance / Return of the jedi
CD _____ GNPD 2163
GNP Crescendo / Jan '89 / Silva Screen.

HITS & MOVIES
CD _____ 11817
Music / Aug '95 / Target/BMG.

HITS FROM THE MOVIES
Crying game / Heat is on / Axel F / Power of love / Nothing has been proved / More than a woman / Call me / Born to be wild / Sisters are doin' it for themselves / Everybody's talkin' / Midnight cowboy / Joy to the world / Warmth of the sun / Woodstock / Gonna fly now (Rocky theme)
CD _____ CDMFP 6138
Music For Pleasure / Jun '95 / EMI.

HITS FROM THE MOVIES
Charly / Jun '95 / Charly / THE / Cadillac.
CD _____ CCD 1230

HOLLYWOOD
London Festival Orchestra
Man and a woman / Il silenzio / Love story / Affair to remember / Hello, young lovers / Sound of music / Moon river / La ronde / Tara's theme / Three coins in the fountain / Shane / Anything goes / Dancing in the dark / Days of wine and roses / Love is a many splendoured thing / Tammy / Pennies from Heaven / It's magic / Magnificent seven / High noon
CD _____ OP 0004
MCI / Apr '87 / Disc / THE.

HOLLYWOOD '94
McNeely, Joel & Seattle Symphony Orchestra
CD _____ VSD 5531
Varese Sarabande/Colosseum / Jan '95 / Pinnacle / Silva Screen.

HOLLYWOOD '95
McNeely, Joel & Seattle Symphony Orchestra
CD _____ VSD 5671
Varese Sarabande/Colosseum / Nov '95 / Pinnacle / Silva Screen.

HOLLYWOOD BACKLOT 3
CD _____ VSD 5361
Varese Sarabande/Colosseum / Dec '92 / Pinnacle / Silva Screen.

HOLLYWOOD CHRONICLE - GREAT MOVIE CLASSICS VOL. 1
CD _____ VSD 5351
Varese Sarabande/Colosseum / Nov '92 / Pinnacle / Silva Screen.

HOLLYWOOD COLLECTION
Singin' in the rain: *Kelly, Gene* / Over the rainbow: *Garland, Judy* / Entertainer: *Joplin,*

Scott / Cheek to cheek: *Astaire, Fred* / Mammy: *Jolson, Al* / Let's face the music and dance: *Rogers, Ginger* / Couple of swells: *Astaire, Fred* / Diamonds are a girl's best friend: *Monroe, Marilyn* / Night and day: *Sinatra, Frank* / In the mood: *Miller, Glenn* / Trail of the lonesome pine: *Laurel & Hardy* / Ol' man river: *Robeson, Paul* / I'm in the mood for love: *Hutton, Betty* / Hello Dolly: *Armstrong, Louis* / Zip: *Haworth, Rita* / I've got my love to keep me warm: *Bogart, Humphrey* / Gentlemen prefer blondes: *Russell, Jane & Marilyn Monroe* / Hi lili hi lo: *Caron, Leslie & Mel Ferrer* / Who's sorry now: *De Haven, Gloria* / It had to be you: *Lamour, Dorothy*
CD _____ DVCD 2054
Deja Vu / May '86 / THE.

HOLLYWOOD DREAMS
Hollywood Bowl Symphony Orchestra
Mauceri, John *Con*
CD _____ 4321092
Philips / Sep '91 / PolyGram.

HOLLYWOOD GOLDEN CLASSICS
Carreras, Jose
CD _____ 9031737932
WEA / Jul '93 / Warner Music.

HOLLYWOOD LADIES SING (I'm Ready For My Close Up)
CD _____ 85972
Silva Screen / Feb '90 / Conifer / Silva Screen.

HOLLYWOOD LEGENDS
CD _____ LECD 120
Wisepack / Apr '95 / THE / Conifer.

HOLLYWOOD MAGIC 1 (1950s)
CD _____ CK 44374
CBS/Silva Screen / Jan '89 / Conifer / Silva Screen.

HOLLYWOOD MAGIC 2 (1960s)
CD _____ CK 44373
CBS/Silva Screen / Jan '89 / Conifer / Silva Screen.

HOLLYWOOD MUSICALS
Mammy: *Jolson, Al* / Cheek to cheek: *Astaire, Fred* / Over the rainbow: *Garland, Judy* / Yankee doodle boy: *Cagney, James* / Road to Morocco: *Hope, Bob/Bing Crosby/Judy Garland* / Put the blame on mame: *Hayworth, Rita* / White Christmas: *Crosby, Bing* / Best things in life are free: *Allyson, June & Peter Lawford* / Johnny one note: *Garland, Judy* / Couple of swells: *Garland, Judy & Fred Astaire* / Who's sorry now: *De Haven, Gloria* / 'S Wonderful: *Kelly, Gene* / diamonds are a girl's best friend: *Monroe, Marilyn* / Bye bye baby: *Monroe, Marilyn & Jane Russell* / Too darn hot: *Miller, Arthur* / Hi lili hi lo: *Caron, Leslie & Mel Ferrer* / Indian love call: *Blyth, Ann & Fernando Lamas* / Rose Marie: *Keel, Howard* / Stranger in paradise: *Blyth, Ann & Vic Damone* / Thank heavens for little girls: *Chevalier, Maurice* / Hello Dolly: *Armstrong, Louis* / There's no business like show business: *Merman, Ethel* / Move over darling: *Day, Doris* / Oh what a beautiful morning: *McRae, Gordon*
2CD _____ DVRECD 26
Deja Vu / '89 / THE.

HOLLYWOOD SINGS (Stars Of The Silver Screen)
Happy feet: *Whiteman, Paul & Rhythm Boys* / Toot toot Tootsi: *goodbye: Jolson, Al* / Johnny: *Dietrich, Marlene* / Day after day: *Clayton, Jackson & Durante* / If you haven't got love: *Swanson, Gloria* / Down the new low down: *Robinson, Bill 'Bojangles'* / Keep your sunny side up: *Gaynor, Janet* / Kashmiri love song: *Valentino, Rudolph* / Broadway melody: *King, Charles* / Puttin' on the ritz: *Richman, Harry* / How long will it last: *Crawford, Joan* / Hooray for Captain Spaulding: *Marx, Groucho & Zeppo* / Just like a butterfly: *Morgan, Helen* / I love Louisa: *Astaire, Fred* / Can't get along: *Rogers, Ginger* / You've got that thing: *Chevalier, Maurice* / Beyond the blue horizon: *MacDonald, Jeanette* / White dove: *Tibbett, Lawrence* / Yes yes (my baby says yes): *Cantor, Eddie*
CD _____ CD AJA 5011
Living Era / Feb '87 / Koch.

HOLLYWOOD SOUNDSTAGE, VOL. 1
CD _____ VSD 5301
Varese Sarabande/Colosseum / Jul '91 / Pinnacle / Silva Screen.

HOLLYWOOD STARS GO TO WAR
Vintage Jazz Classics / Jul '93 / Direct / ADA / CM / Cadillac.
CD _____ VJC 1048

HOLLYWOOD'S GREATEST HITS
Tring / Jan '93 / Tring / Prism.
CD _____ GRF 192

HOLLYWOOD'S GREATEST HITS
Tritt, W./Cincinnati Pops Orchestra
Kunzel, Erich *Con*
CD _____ CD 80168
Telarc / Sep '88 / Conifer / ADA.

HOLLYWOOD'S GREATEST HITS, VOL 2
Cincinnati Pops Orchestra
CD _____ CD 80319
Telarc / Aug '93 / Conifer / ADA.

HOMAGE A MARCEL CARNE (Musique De Films)
Orchestre Du Capitole De Toulouse
Plasson, Michel *Con*
CD _____ CDC 75477642
EMI Classics / Apr '94 / EMI.

HOORAY FOR HOLLYWOOD
CD _____ TQ 157
Compact Selection / Jun '88 / Conifer.

HORROR AND SCIENCE FICTION
CD _____ 889707
Milan / '92 / BMG / Silva Screen.

HORROR AND SCIENCE FICTION VOL. 2
Escape from New York / Mad Max / Phantasm / Day after Halloween / Tourist trip / Daytime ended / Maniac / Videodrome / Evil dead / Hunger / Friday 13th / Forbidden zone / Liquid sky / Red Sonja / Lifeforce / Elephant man
CD _____ CDCH 157
Milan / Feb '90 / BMG / Silva Screen.

HORROR AND SCIENCE FICTION VOL. 3
CD _____ CH 363
Milan / Jan '95 / BMG / Silva Screen.

HORRORVISIONS
CD _____ EDL 25772
Edel / Jan '92 / Pinnacle.

HOT MOVIE THEMES
CD _____ 24030
Music / Mar '95 / Target/BMG.

I WANTS TO BE A ACTOR LADY
Cincinnati Uni Singers/Orchestra
Rivers, E. *Con*
CD _____ 802212
New World / Apr '94 / New World.

I WISH IT SO (Songs By Sondheim/Bernstein/Weill/ Blitzstein)
Upshaw, Dawn
Stern, Eric *Con*
CD _____ 7559793452
Elektra Nonesuch / Dec '94 / Warner Music.

IF I LOVED YOU - LOVE DUETS FROM THE MUSICALS
Allen, Thomas & Valerie Masterson/Philharmonia Orchestra
Edwards, John Owen *Con*
CD _____ CDVIR 8317
TER / May '94 / Koch.

IF I RULED THE WORLD
Secombe, Harry
Be my love / Bless this house / Falling in love with love / I believe in love / If I ruled the world / Mama / O Sole Mio / Speak to me of love / This is my song / Younger than Springtime
CD _____ PWK 095
Carlton Home Entertainment / '89 / Carlton Home Entertainment.

IL CINEMA ITALIANO (Music From The Films Of Marcello Mastroianni)
Nakamura, Yoshiro et al
La dolce vita / Intervista / Splendor / Generique des jeux noirs / Sunflower / Galanterie / Macaroni / La dolce vita (guitar solo) / Valzer / Ginger e Fred / A Marcello / 8% / La dolce vita (bossa nova)
CD _____ CY 79543
Denon / Apr '92 / Conifer.

IN LOVE IN HOLLYWOOD
Jones, Salena
CD _____ CDVIR 8328
TER / Jan '95 / Koch.

IN LOVE ON BROADWAY
Jones, Salena
CD _____ CDVIR 8327
TER / May '94 / Koch.

IN THE REAL WORLD
Hadley, Jerry & American Theatre Orchestra
Gemignani, Paul *Con*
CD _____ 09026619372
RCA Victor / Apr '94 / BMG.

INDIANA JONES (Music From The Films Of Harrison Ford)
City Of Prague Philharmonic Orchestra
Bateman, Paul *Con*
Witness / Regarding Henry / Mosquito coast / Patriot games / Fugitive / Blade runner / Presumed innocent / Star Wars / Empire strikes back / Return of the Jedi / Raiders of the Lost Ark / Indiana Jones and the temple of doom / Indiana Jones and the last crusade / Hanover Street
CD _____ FILMCD 154

Silva Screen / Oct '94 / Conifer / Silva Screen.

IS IT REALLY ME
Philharmonia/Symphony/Scottish Opera/ New Sadler's Wells Opera Orchestras
CD _____ CDVIR 8314
TER / Oct '91 / Koch.

ITV CHILDREN'S THEMES
Silver Screen Orchestra
Super gran / Knight rider / Joe 90 / Captain Scarlet / Fall guy / Sooty show theme / Dangermouse / Fraggle rock / Stingray / Ghostbusters / A-Team / Batman theme / Black Beauty / Thunderbird / Dogtanian / Handful of songs / Blockbusters (Theme) / Follyfoot farm
CD _____ PWK 108
Carlton Home Entertainment / May '89 / Carlton Home Entertainment.

JAMES BOND THEMES
London Theatre Orchestra
CD _____ EMPRCD 576
Emporio / Jul '95 / THE / Disc / CM.

JAZZ GOES TO HOLLYWOOD
Karlin, Fred
CD _____ VSD 5639
Pinnacle / Silva Screen.

JOHN TRAVOLTA
Travolta, John
CD _____ EMPRCD 524
Empress / Sep '94 / THE.

JOSE CARRERAS SINGS MUSICALS
Carreras, Jose
CD _____ 4169732
Philips / Jan '88 / PolyGram.

KIDS
CD _____ 8286402
London / Jan '96 / PolyGram.

KIRI ON BROADWAY
Te Kanawa, Dame Kiri
My fair lady / One touch of Venus / Too many girls / Carousel / Kiss me Kate / West Side Story / Sound of music
CD _____ 4402802
Decca / Jan '94 / PolyGram.

KISS
Monroe, Marilyn
You'd be surprised / River of no return / I wanna be loved by you / When I fall in love / Bye bye baby / Diamonds are a girl's best friend / One silver dollar / I'm gonna file my claim / When love goes wrong, nothing goes right / After you get what you want, you don't want it / Runnin' wild / Specialisation / My heart belongs to Daddy / Two little girls from Little Rock / Heat wave / Kiss
CD _____ CD 3555
Cameo / Nov '95 / Target/BMG.

LADIES OF THE 20TH CENTURY, THE
Monroe, Marilyn
Kiss / Do it again / She acts like a woman should / Little girl from Little Rock / Bye bye bye / Diamonds are a girl's best friend / When love goes wrong / Fine romance / River of no return / Down in the meadow / After you get what you want, you don't want it / Heatwave
CD _____ JD 1238
Jazz Door / Aug '93 / Koch.

**LAUREL AND HARDY'S MUSIC BOX
(New Recordings Of Laurel & Hardy Scores)**
Ku-ku / On to the show / Bells / Dash and dot / We're out for fun / Drunk / Rockin' chairs / Give us a hand / Riding along / Gangway Charlie / Here we go / Moon and you / You are the one I love / Beautiful lady / Look at him now / Funny faces / On a sunny afternoon / Sons of the Desert
CD _____ LH 10012

Silva Screen / Oct '94 / Conifer / Silva Screen.

LAUREL AND HARDY'S MUSIC BOX II
CD _____ LH 10022
Silva Screen / Nov '89 / Conifer / Silva Screen.

LEGENDS IN MUSIC - DORIS DAY
Day, Doris
CD _____ LECD 091
Wisepack / Sep '94 / THE / Conifer.

LEGENDS IN MUSIC - JUDY GARLAND
Garland, Judy
CD _____ LECD 094
Wisepack / Sep '94 / THE / Conifer.

LEGENDS IN MUSIC - MARILYN MONROE
Monroe, Marilyn
CD _____ LECD 067
Wisepack / Jul '94 / THE / Conifer.

LES FILMS NOIR
CD _____ 887976
Milan / Jun '95 / BMG / Silva Screen.

LET'S FACE THE MUSIC
Astaire, Fred
Let's face the music and dance / Fine romance / Foggy day / Change partners / I'm old fashioned / They can't take that away from me / Flying down to Rio / Let yourself go / Fascinating rhythm / They all laughed / Pick yourself up / Nice work if you can get it / Isn't this a lovely day / Dearly beloved / Way you look tonight / Let's call the whole thing off / Cheek to cheek / Funny face / Bojangles of Harlem / Shall we dance / Love of my life / Top hat, white tie & tails / I'm putting all my eggs in one basket / I used to be colour blind / Dream dancing
CD _____ AVC 537
Avid / Oct '95 / Avid/BMG / Koch.

LET'S FACE THE MUSIC AND DANCE
Astaire, Fred
Change partners / Cheek to cheek / I used to be colour blind / I'm putting all my eggs in one basket / Let's face the music and dance / No strings / Top hat, white tie and tails / Yam / Foggy day / I can't be bothered now / I've got beginner's luck / Let's call the whole thing off / Nice work if you can get it / Shall we dance / Slap that bass / They all laughed / They can't take that away from me / Things are looking up / Poor Mr. Chisholm / Dearly Beloved / Fine romance / I'm old fashioned / Never gonna dance / Pick yourself up / Way you look tonight / You were never lovelier / Since I kissed my baby goodbye
CD _____ CDAJA 5123
Living Era / Mar '94 / Koch.

**LET'S GO ON WITH THE SHOW
(Hits From The West End & Broadway)**
America / If my friends could see me now / Send in the clowns / Wilkommen / I am what I am / Wunderbar / OH what a beautiful morning / Shall we dance / You'll never walk alone / Camelot / Get me to the church on time / Stranger in Paradise
CD _____ SHOWCD 016
Showtime / Feb '95 / Disc / THE.

LET'S GO TO THE MOVIES VOL.1
CD _____ C32 7074
Denon / '88 / Conifer.

LET'S GO TO THE MOVIES VOL.2
Tara's theme / Over the rainbow / Love is a many splendoured thing / Summertime in Venice / East of Eden / Plein soliel / Raindrops keep falling on my head / Speak softly love / Man and a woman / Live for life / Romeo and Juliet / Love story / Sunflower / Way we were
CD _____ C32 7099
Denon / '88 / Conifer.

LINO VENTURA FILM MUSIC
CD _____ CH 302
Milan / Jan '95 / BMG / Silva Screen.

**LONGEST DAY, THE
(Music From The Classic War Films)**
City Of Prague Philharmonic Orchestra
Bateman, Paul Con
Longest Day (March) / 633 Squadron / Guns Of Navarone (The Legend of Navarone) / Dambusters / Battle Of Britian / Mac-Arthur/Patton (The generals suite) / Night Of The Generals / Bridge On The River Kwai (Colonel Bogey) / Where Eagles Dare / Das Boot (The Boat) / Great Escape / Battle Of Midway (March) / Battle Of The Bulge (Prelude) / Force 10 From Navarone / In Harm's Way (The rock/First victory) / Sink The Bismark / Bridge At Remagen / Bridge Too Far (Overture) / 1941 (March) / Is Paris Burning
CD _____ FILMCD 151
Silva Screen / Mar '94 / Conifer / Silva Screen.

**LORELEI, THE
(Songs By Gershwin, Porter & Berlin)**
Criswell, Kim & Ambrosian Chorus/London Sinfonietta
McGlinn, John Con
CD _____ CDC 7548022
EMI Classics / Apr '94 / EMI.

LOST IN BOSTON
CD _____ VSD 5475
Varese Sarabande/Colosseum / Aug '94 / Pinnacle / Silva Screen.

LOST IN BOSTON II
CD _____ VSD 5485
Varese Sarabande/Colosseum / Mar '95 / Pinnacle / Silva Screen.

**LOST IN BOSTON III
(Lost Gems From The Greatest Shows & Composers)**
CD _____ VSD 5563
Varese Sarabande/Colosseum / Aug '95 / Pinnacle / Silva Screen.

LOUIS DE FUNES FILM MUSIC
CD _____ 887901
Milan / Jan '95 / BMG / Silva Screen.

LOVE AT THE MOVIES
CD _____ 889708
Milan / Jan '93 / BMG / Silva Screen.

LOVE AT THE THEATRE
CD _____ PMCD 7006
Pure Music / Nov '94 / BMG.

**LOVE IN THE CINEMA
(A Collection Of Romantic Movie Music)**
CD _____ 191892
Milan / Jun '95 / BMG / Silva Screen.

LOVE IS HERE TO STAY
Henshall, Ruthie
Love is here to stay / Somebody loves me / Someone to watch over me / Nice work if you can get it / Lady be good / 'S wonderful / But not for me / Summertime / Man I love / Embraceable you / Boy what love has done to me / They all laughed / Swanee / Love walked in
CD _____ BRCD 6000
Bravo / Mar '94 / Carlton Home Entertainment.

LOVE MOVIE THEMES
CD _____ 15070
Laserlight / Dec '94 / Target/BMG.

LOVE MOVIE THEMES
Exodus / Alfie / Lara's theme / Your eyes / I just called to say I love you / Gilr from Ipanema / Maria / Sound of music / Charmaine / Against all odds / Mrs. Robinson / Raindrops keep falling on my head / Man and a woman / Chim-chim cheree / This is my song / Bilitis
CD _____ 22510
Music / Jul '95 / Target/BMG.

LOVE THEMES FROM THE MOVIES
I will always love you / Rose / Do you know where you're going to / Greatest love of all / It must have been love / Nobody loves it better / Hard to say I'm sorry / Hopelessly devoted to you / Wind beneath my wings / Beauty and the beast / Take my breath away / First time ever I saw your face / Up where we belong / Endless love / Way we were / Love touch / Evergreen / My own true love
CD _____ ECD 3132
K-Tel / Jan '95 / K-Tel.

MAGIC FROM THE MUSICALS
Only you: Blessed, Brian / Good morning starshine: Clark, Petula / If I were a rich man: Topol / Luck be a lady: Jones, Paul / Memory: Clark, Petula / Send in the clowns: Webb, Marti / Impossible dream: Blessed, Brian / Bless your beautiful hide: Keel, Howard / Thank heavens for little girls: Topol / Lullaby of Broadway: Jones, Paul / If he walked into my life: Webb, Marti / Annie get your gun medley: Keel, Howard / I don't know how to love him: Webb, Marti / I've grown accustomed to her face: Jones, Paul
CD _____ MCCD 012
Music Club / Feb '91 / Disc / THE / CM.

MAGIC OF THE BRITISH MUSICALS, THE
CD _____ CDTEZ 7003
TER / Jan '95 / Koch.

**MAGIC OF THE MUSICALS, THE
(40 Hits From 40 Great Musicals Of Stage & Screen)**
There's no business like show business: Silver Screen Orchestra / Couple of swells: Silver Screen Orchestra / It's a lovely day today: Silver Screen Orchestra / Let's face the music and dance: Silver Screen Orchestra / Cheek to cheek (CD only): Silver Screen Orchestra / Cooking my mind / melody (CD only): Silver Screen Orchestra / Play a simple melody: Silver Screen Orchestra / Heatwave: Silver Screen Orchestra / I love a piano: Silver Screen Orchestra / Stepping out with my baby: Silver Screen Orchestra / Change partners and dance (CD only): Silver Screen Orchestra / Everything's coming up roses: Bassey, Shirley / People: Bassey, Shirley / Tonight: Bassey, Shirley / Lady is a tramp: Bassey, Shirley / Big spender: a kick out of you: Bassey, Shirley / It might as well be spring: Bassey, Shirley / As long as he needs me: Bassey, Shirley / I've never been in love before (CD only): Bassey, Shirley / Any dream will do: Jones, Paul / Take

it on the chin: O'Hara, Mary / Unusual way: O'Hara, Mary / How to handle a woman: Young, Robert / Love changes everything: Keel, Howard / Music of the night (CD only): Keel, Howard / O what a beautiful morning: Keel, Howard / Hello, young lovers: Monro, Matt / Who can I turn to: Monro, Matt / I can give you the starlight: Hill, Vince / Someday my heart will awake (CD only): Hill, Vince / Edelweiss: Hill, Vince / Shine through my dreams (CD only): Hill, Vince / Sunrise sunset: Cogan, Alma / This is my lovely day: Wallace, Ian / Mr. Mistoffelees (Don't cry for me Argentina (CD only): Morriston Orpheus Choir / Starlight Express: Morriston Orpheus Choir / Don't cry for me Argentina (CD only): Morriston Orpheus Choir & Margaret Williams / Day by day: Laine, Cleo / Prepare ye the way of the Lord: Laine, Cleo / All I do is dream of you: Cogan, Alma / I've got my love to keep me warm (CD only): Berlin, Irving
2CD _____ CDDL 1227
Music For Pleasure / Apr '92 / EMI.

MAGIC OF THE MUSICALS, THE
Webb, Marti & Mark Rattray
Lullaby of broadway / I got rhythm / I get a kick out of you / It ain't necessarily so / Got plenty of nothing / There's a boat dat's leavin' soon for New York / Porgy, I's your woman now / Summertime / Blow Gabriel blow / Losing my mind / Not while I'm around / Send in the clowns / Do you hear the people sing / Empty chairs at empty tables / I dreamed a dream / Last night of the world / Bui-doi / Don't cry for me Argentina / Jesus Christ superstar / Mama a rainbow / Take that look off your face / In one of my weaker moments / Anthem / You and I / Tell me it's not true / Only he / Love changes everything / Music of the night / Memory
CD _____ MCCD 149
Music Club / Feb '94 / Disc / THE / CM.

MAGIC OF THE MUSICALS, THE
3CD _____ MCBX 014
Music Club / Dec '94 / Disc / THE / CM.

MAGICAL MUSIC OF DISNEY, THE
Cincinnati Pops Orchestra
Circle of life / I just can't wait to be king / Hakuna matata / Be prepared / Can you feel the love tonight / Arabian nights / One jump ahead / Whole new world / Prince Ali / Part of your world / Under the sea / Poor unfortunate souls / Le poissons / Kiss the girl / Happy ending / She's a funny girl / That Belle / Be our guest / Gaston / Beauty and the beast
CD _____ CD 80381
Telarc / Jun '95 / Conifer / ADA.

**MAGNUM, P.I.
(The American TV Hits Album)**
Caine, Daniel Orchestra
Caine, Daniel Con
Magnum, P.I. / Airwolf / Cosby Show / Mike Hammer (Harlem nocturne) / Lou Grant / Cheers (Where everybody knows your name) / Hill Street Blues / Hollywood Wives / Cagney And Lacey / St. Elsewhere / Touch Of Scandal / Taxi / Simon And Simon / Rockford Files
CD _____ FILMCD 703
Silva Screen / Nov '90 / Conifer / Silva Screen.

**MAN FROM U.N.C.L.E., THE
(Cult TV Classics)**
Man From U.N.C.L.E.: Fahey, Brian Orchestra / Mission: Impossible (The plot/Theme): San Diego Symphony Pops / Captain Scarlet (Mysterons Theme): Gray, Barry Orchestra / Stingray (Marina theme): Fahey, Brian Orchestra / Matnix: San Diego Symphony Pops / Batman: Fahey, Brian Orchestra / Adventures Of Robinson Crusoe: Mellin, Robert Orchestra / Tommorow People: Simpson, Dudley / Stingray: Gray, Barry Orchestra / March Of The Oysters: Gray, Barry Orchestra / Aqua Marina: Gray, Barry Orchestra / Saint: Fahey, Brian Orchestra / Joe 90 (Hi-jacked/Theme/Theme remix): Gray, Barry Orchestra / Avengers: Fahey, Brian Orchestra / Thunderbirds (Parker, well done/Theme): Gray, Barry Orchestra
CD _____ FILMCD 712
Silva Screen / Nov '92 / Conifer / Silva Screen.

MANTOVANI AT THE MOVIES
Mantovani
CD _____ CDMOIR 506
Memoir / Oct '93 / Target/BMG.

MARCOVICCI SINGS MOVIES
Marcovicci, Andrea
As time goes by / It might be you / On such a night as this / Folks who live on the hill / Two for the road / Happy endings / Don't ever leave me / Here lies love / Let's not talk about love / Girl medley / Someone to love / Mad about the boy / World War II medley / Too late now / Love is here to stay
CD _____ DRGCD 91405
DRG / Mar '92 / New Note.

MARILYN SINGS
Monroe, Marilyn
CD _____ CDCD 1195
Charly / Sep '94 / Charly / THE / Cadillac.

**MARLENE DIETRICH COLLECTION
(20 Golden Greats)**
Dietrich, Marlene

Lili Marlene / Boys in the backroom / Lola / Illusions / Johnny / I've been in love before / Black market / Lazy afternoon / Another spring another love / Symphonie / You do something to me / Falling in love again / You go to my head / You've got that look / If he swings by the string / This world of ours / Near you / Candles glowing / Kisses sweeter than wine / Such trying times
CD _____ **DVCD 2098**
Deja Vu / Jun '88 / THE.

MISS SHOWBUSINESS
Garland, Judy
Zing went the strings of my heart / Stompin' at the savoy / All God's chillun got rhythm / Everybody sing / You made me love you / Over the rainbow / Sweet sixteen / Embraceable you / (Can this be) The end of the rainbow / I'm nobody's baby / Pretty girl milking her cow / It's a great day for the Irish / Sunny side of the street / For me and my gal / That old black magic / When you wore a tulip
CD _____ **HADCD 156**
Javelin / May '94 / THE / Henry Hadaway Organisation.

MOVIE CLASSICS
CD _____ **CDZ 76772542**
EMI Classics / Apr '93 / EMI.

MOVIE HITS
CD _____ **TCD 2615**
Telstar / Oct '92 / BMG.

MOVIE HITS
CD _____ **12196**
Laserlight / Apr '95 / Target/BMG.

MOVIE HITS, THE
Crosby, Bing
Apple for the teacher / Man and his dream / If I had my way / Too romantic / I haven't time to be a millionaire / Meet the sun halfway / My heart is taking lessons / Funny old hills / I have eyes / Still the bluebird sings / Moonburn / Love thy neighbour / Waiter and the porter and the upstairs maid / Small fry / Moon got in my eyes / Smarty / Without a word of warning / My heart and I / Let's call a heart a heart / Go fly a kite / Empty saddles / Birth of the blues
CD _____ **PASTCD 9784**
Flapper / Mar '92 / Pinnacle.

MOVIE LOVE SONGS
Philadelphia Orchestra
Ormandy, Eugene _Con_
Love Story (theme) / Elvira Madigan (Piano concert no.21, Andante): _Wild, Earl_ / Yesterday / Thomas Crown Affair (The windmills of your mind) / Romeo and Juliet (Love theme) / Heart is a Lonely Hunter (theme) / West Side Story (Somewhere) / Tristan and Isolde (Liebestod) / Now, Voyager (Romeo and Juliet, overture fantasy)
CD _____ **09026609652**
RCA Victor / Jan '92 / BMG.

MOVIE LOVE THEMES
Tritt, W./A. Romero/Cincinnati Pops Orchestra
Kunzel, Erich _Con_
CD _____ **CD 80243**
Telarc / Feb '91 / Conifer / ADA.

MOVIE MEMORIES
Nuremberg Symphony Orchestra
CD _____ **CST 348052**
Colosseum / Nov '95 / Pinnacle.

MOVIE MUSIC
CD _____ **PCD 887**
Prometheus / '88 / Silva Screen.

MOVIE MUSICALS
Fine romance / My Mammy / My man / Three little words / Beyond the blue horizon / What would you do / I love to croon / What I hate you / It's only a paper moon / I'm no angel / 42nd Street / Learn to croon / On the good ship Lollipop / Okay Toots / Lulu's back in town / Ol' man river / Bojangles of Harlem / Broadway melody / Lullaby of Broadway / Everybody sing / Swing me an old fashioned song / Let's sing again / Someday my Prince will come / Song of the dawn / Yours and mine / Rose Marie / Indian love call / Dear Mr. Gable / I'm putting all my eggs in one basket / Get thee behind me, Satan / Let's face the music and dance / About a quarter to nine / Lullaby of Broadway (2) / Little Miss Broadway / Some of these days / Broadway melody (2)
2CD _____ **RPCD 310**
Robert Parker Jazz / Mar '95 / Conifer.

MOVIE'S GREATEST LOVE SONGS
Play dead: _Arnold, David & Bjork_ / Love song for a vampire: _Lennox, Annie_ / No ordinary love: _Sade_ / Unchained melody: _Righteous Brothers_ / Licence to kill: _Knight, Gladys_ / Show me heaven: _McKee, Maria_ / Falling: _Cruise, Julee_ / Forbidden colours: _Sakamoto, Ryuichi & David Sylvian_ / Going home: _Knopfler, Mark_ / Book of days: _Enya_ / Take my breath away: _Berlin_ / Glory of love: _Cetera, Peter_ / Up where we belong: _Cocker, Joe & Jennifer Warnes_ / Nothing has been proved: _Springfield, Dusty_ / I guess that's why they call it the blues: _John, Elton_ / Arthur's theme: _Cross, Christopher_ / Love is in the air: _Young, John Paul_ / My girl: _Temptations_ / Try a little tenderness: _Commitments_ / Brown eyed girl: _Morrison, Van_

CD _____ **516651-2**
PolyGram TV / Feb '94 / PolyGram.

MURDER SHE WROTE
(ITV America)
Caine, Daniel _Con_
Murder she wrote / Beverly Hills 90210 / Magnum P.I. / Baywatch / Highway to Heaven / Sledgehammer / Bring 'Em Back Alive / Streethawk / A-Team / Men / Airwolf / B.L. Stryker / Simon and Simon / Hooperman / Young Riders / Hardcastle and McCormick
CD _____ **TVPMCD 802**
Primetime / '92 / Silva Screen.

MUSIC FOR FILMS
CD _____ **ASCD 04**
All Saints / Jun '92 / Vital / Discovery.

MUSIC FROM DEANNA DURBIN FILMS,
THE
My heart is singing / It's raining sunbeams / Heart that's free / Libiamo / Chapel bells / I love to whistle / Serenade to the stars / You're as pretty as a picture / My own / Je veux vivre / Last rose of summer / Love is all / Loch Lomond / Ave Maria / When April sings / When I sing / Goin' home / Mighty lak' a rose / Begin the beguine / Say a prayer for the boys over there / Kashmiri song / In the spirit of the moment / When you're away / Russian melody / None shall sleep
CD _____ **CMSCD 013**
Movie Stars / Aug '94 / Conifer.

MUSIC FROM GREAT AUSTRALIAN
FILMS
Australian Broadcasting Commission Philharmonic Orchestra
Motzing, William _Con_
Newsfront / Gallipoli / My brilant career / Tall timbers / Cathy's child / Eliza Frazer / Breaker morant / Chant of Jimmy Blacksmith / Picture show man / Picnic at hanging Rock / Mango tree / Dimboola / Caddie
CD _____ **DRGCD 12582**
DRG / Jan '95 / New Note.

MUSIC FROM HOLLYWOOD
CD _____ **CK 66691**
CBS/Silva Screen / Apr '95 / Conifer / Silva Screen.

MUSIC FROM JACQUES TATI FILMS
CD _____ **8369832**
Silva Screen / Feb '90 / Conifer / Silva Screen.

MUSIC FROM SYLVESTER STALLONE
FILMS, THE
CD _____ **CDCIA 5064**
Cinevox / Jan '93 / Conifer / Silva Screen.

MUSIC FROM THE FILMS OF ANDRE
TECHINE
CD _____ **CD 343**
Milan / Jan '89 / BMG / Silva Screen.

MUSIC FROM THE FILMS OF AUDREY
HEPBURN
CD _____ **9245032**
Silva Screen / Jan '93 / Conifer / Silva Screen.

MUSIC FROM THE FILMS OF CLINT
EASTWOOD
City Of Prague Philharmonic Orchestra
Wadsworth, Derek _Con_
Where Eagles Dare (Main title) / Outlaw Josey Wales (The war is over) / Good, the Bad and the Ugly (Theme/The ecstasy of gold) / Fistful Of Dollars / For A Few Dollars More / Play Misty For Me (Misty) / Hang 'Em High / In The Line Of Fire / Rawhide / Dirty Harry (' Sudden impact / Magnum Force / Two Mules For Sister Sara / Unforgiven
CD _____ **FILMCD 138**
Silva Screen / '93 / Conifer / Silva Screen.

MUSIC FROM THE FILMS OF JEAN-
PIERRE MOCKY
CD _____ **MANTRA 033**
Silva Screen / Jan '93 / Conifer / Silva Screen.

MUSIC FROM THE FILMS OF KEVIN
COSTNER
Dances With Wolves (The John Dunbar Theme): _City Of Prague Philharmonic Orchestra_ / Revenge (Love theme on the beach) / No Way Out (Suite) / JFK (Theme): _City Of Prague Philharmonic Orchestra_ / Field Of Dreams (Suite) / Untouchables (The Ness Family theme): _City Of Prague Philharmonic Orchestra_ / Fandango (Theme) / Silverado (Suite): _City Of Prague Philharmonic Orchestra_ / Robin Hood Prince Of Thieves (Marian Everything I do (I do for you))
CD _____ **FILMCD 143**
Silva Screen / Nov '93 / Conifer / Silva Screen.

MUSIC FROM THE FILMS OF SEAN
CONNERY
City Of Prague Philharmonic Orchestra
Dr. No (James Bond theme) / Medicine Man (Medley) / From Russia With Love / Untouchables (The Ness Family theme) / Highlander (A kind of magic) / Goldfinger / Name Of The Rose / Thunderball / Presidio / You Only Live Twice / Russia House / Diamonds Are Forever / Marnie / Never Say Never Again: _Hall, Lani_ / Robin And Marian
CD _____ **FILMCD 142**

Silva Screen / Nov '93 / Conifer / Silva Screen.

MUSIC FROM THE HAMMER FILMS
Philharmonia Orchestra
Dracula suite / Dracula, Prince of Darkness suite / Hands of the Ripper suite / Taste the blood of Dracula suite / Vampire Circus suite
CD _____ **FILMCD 066**
Silva Screen / Jan '90 / Conifer / Silva Screen.

MUSIC FROM THE MOVIES
CD _____ **CD MFP 5915**
Music For Pleasure / '91 / EMI.

MUSIC FROM THE NEW YORK STAGE
(1890-1908)
3CD _____ **GEMMCDS 90502**
Pearl / Aug '93 / Harmonia Mundi.

MUSIC FROM THE NEW YORK STAGE
II
(1908-1913)
3CD _____ **GEMMCDS 90535**
Pearl / Nov '93 / Harmonia Mundi.

MUSIC FROM THE NEW YORK STAGE
III
(1913-1917)
3CD _____ **GEMMCDS 90568**
Pearl / Nov '93 / Harmonia Mundi.

MUSIC FROM THE NEW YORK STAGE
IV
(1917-1920)
3CD _____ **GEMMCDS 905961**
Pearl / Nov '93 / Harmonia Mundi.

MUSIC OF THE MOVIES
CD _____ **GRF 241**
Tring / Aug '93 / Tring / Prism.

MUSICAL
CD _____ **15 400**
Laserlight / Jan '93 / Target/BMG.

MUSICAL HIGHLIGHTS
CD _____ **22536**
Music / Jul '95 / Target/BMG.

MUSICAL SELECTIONS FROM THE
RIDICULOUS THEATRICAL COMPANY
(The 25th Anniversary)
Original Casts
Reverse psychology / Heterosexual Heidi / Conquerer / Sophisticated love / Humanity / Thank God he made me a drag queen / Artificial jungle overture / Eddie's swing / Illusory thing is love / You've changed / Valkyrie dance and song / Yah yah yah - The music has me so confused
CD _____ **DRGCD 6301**
DRG / Jan '95 / New Note.

MUSICAL WORLD HITS
CD _____ **15086**
Laserlight / Dec '94 / Target/BMG.

MUSICALS
Ambrosian Chorus & London Sinfonietta
McGlinn, John _C_
Cafe song / Empty chairs at empty tables / Maria / It must be so / Gigi / How to handle a woman / There but for you go / I / Never will I marry / Way you look tonight / Fine romance / Love song / Johanna / Finishing the hat / Silly people / Alone together / You do something to me / Gay divorcee / Night and day
CD _____ **CDC 7497922**
EMI Classics / Aug '93 / EMI.

MUSICALS
(15 Hit Songs From Classic Musical
Shows)
EMI Classics / Apr '93 / EMI.

MUSICALS II
(Highlights From Porgy & Bess/
Oklahoma/King And I/West Side Story)
Royal Liverpool Philharmonic Orchestra
Davis, Carl _Con_
CD _____ **CDCFP 4601**
Classics For Pleasure / Jan '95 / EMI.

MUSICALS, THE
Royal Philharmonic Pops Orchestra
CD _____ **DCDCD 215**
Castle / Nov '95 / BMG.

OVER THE RAINBOW
Garland, Judy
CD _____ **PWK 022**
Carlton Home Entertainment / '88 / Carlton Home Entertainment.

CD _____ **77015**
Discovery / Feb '95 / Warner Music.

PARTY'S OVER
(Broadway Sings The Blues)
Broadway Casts
CD _____ **SK 53543**
Sony Classical / Jul '94 / Sony.

PERFORMANCE
Webb, Marti & The Philharmonia Orchestra
CD _____ **OCRCD 6033**
First Night / Dec '95 / Pinnacle.

PORTRAIT OF BROADWAY, A
Pierce, Joshua & Dorothy Jonas
CD _____ **CDPC 5003**
Prestige / Aug '90 / Complete/Pinnacle / Cadillac.

POWER THEMES '90
Thunderbirds are go / Joe 90 / U.F.O / Captain Scarlet / Space 1999 / Stingray / Prisoner / Saint / Avengers / Danger Man / Department S / Persuaders
CD _____ **CDSR 022**
Telstar / Sep '93 / BMG.

PRINCE AND THE PAUPER, THE
(& Other Film Music)
National Philharmonic Orchestra
Gerhardt, Charles _Con_
Revivers / Jane Eyre / Lost weekend / Between two worlds / Constant nymph / Prince and the pauper / Escape me never / Spectre of the rose / Madwoman of Chaillot / Cleopatra / Julie / Who's afraid of Virginia Woolf / Anne of the 1000 days / Henry V / Henry V suite
CD _____ **VSD 5207**
Varese Sarabande/Colosseum / '90 / Pinnacle / Silva Screen.

PSYCHO
(Horror & Fantasy At The Movies)
Krull (Main title/Colwyn's arrival) / It's Alive II (Main title) / Bride Of The Re-animator (Prologue/Main title) / Moon 44 (First training flight) / Near Dark (Mae's theme) / Empire Strikes Back (The Imperial march): _San Diego Symphony Pops_ / Halloween (Theme) / Phantom Of The Opera (Finale/End title) / Sundown (Redemption of the damned) / Psycho (Prelude/The murder/Finale: _San Diego Symphony Pops_ / Dark Star (Suite) / Masters Of The Universe (He-Man victorious/End title) / Hellraiser (Resurrection) / They Live (End title) / Dragonslayer (The white horse/Into the sunset) / Dracula Has Risen From The Grave (Finale) / Superman (March): _San Diego Symphony Pops_
CD _____ **SILVAD 3003**
Silva Treasury / '92 / Conifer / Silva Screen.

PUBLIC TV'S GREATEST HITS
CD _____ **604702**
Silva Screen / Jul '92 / Conifer / Silva Screen.

PUTTIN' ON THE RITZ
Cincinnati Pops Orchestra
CD _____ **CD 80356**
Telarc / Nov '95 / Conifer / ADA.

RED SHOES - CLASSIC BRITISH FILM
MUSIC
(Coastal Command/Conquest Of The
Air/Attack & Celebration/Red Shoes
Ballet)
Philharmonia Orchestra
Alwyn, Kenneth _Con_
Red shoes ballet (The Red Shoes) / Prelude (Coastal Command) / Hebrides / U-Boat alert / Taking off at night / Hudsons take off from Iceland / Dawn patrol / Battle of the Beauforts / Finale / Attack and celebration (Attack On The Iron Coast/Two-Headed Spy) / Wind (Conquest Of The Air) / Vision of Leonardo Da Vinci / Stunting / Over the Arctic / Gliding / March - Conquest of the air
CD _____ **FILMCD 713**
Silva Screen / May '93 / Conifer / Silva Screen.

RICHARD III
CD _____ **8287192**
London / Jan '96 / PolyGram.

ROMANCING THE FILM
Rochester Pops Orchestra
Gone with the wind / Wizard of Oz / Casablanca / Breakfast at Tiffany's / Lawrence of Arabia / Dr. Zhivago / Cool hand Luke / Godfather / 2001 / Star Wars / Dirty dancing / Little mermaid
CD _____ CDS 577
Prometheus / May '92 / Silva Screen.

SAX AND VIOLENCE
CD _____ VSD 5562
Varese Sarabande/Colosseum / Apr '95 / Pinnacle / Silva Screen.

SCIENCE FICTION THEMES
Star Trek / X files / Close encounters of the third kind / E.T. / Star wars / Twilight zone / Robocop 2 / Superman / Timecop / Battleship galactica / Dune / Batdance / Stark Trek 3 / Flash / Blade runner / Terminator 2 / Empire strikes back / Star trek: The next generation
CD _____ ECD 3225
K-Tel / Jan '95 / K-Tel.

SCREEN ACTION
Power Pack Orchestra
Superman / Miami Vice / Magnum P.I. / Hunter / Professionals / Starsky and Hutch / Shoestring / Hawaii Five-O / Dempsey and Makepeace / Indiana Jones and the Temple of Doom / T.J. Hooker / James Bond / New Avengers theme / Rockford files / Street hawk / Good, the bad and the ugly / A-Team / Knight rider / Crazy like a fox / Mike Hammer theme / Fall guy / Sweeney / Chinese detective / Highway patrol / Airwolf
CD _____ CDMFP 6017
Music For Pleasure / Apr '88 / EMI.

SCREEN SINATRA
Sinatra, Frank
From here to eternity / Three coins in the fountain / Young at heart / Just one of those things / Someone to watch over me / Not as a stranger / Tender trap / Wait for me / Johnny Concho theme / All the way / Chicago / Monique-Song from Kings Go Forth / They came to Cordura / To love and be loved / High hopes / All my tomorrows / It's all right with me / C'est magnifique / Dream
CD _____ CDMFP 6052
Music For Pleasure / Mar '89 / EMI.

SCREEN THEMES
Royal Philharmonic Orchestra
Scott, John Con
Die Hard / Big / Who Framed Roger Rabbit / Milagro Beanfield War / Beetlejuice / Crossing Delancey / Cocoon – the Return / Madame Sousatzka / Criminal Law / Nightmare on Elm Street IV / Betrayed / Coming to America / Masquerade / Da
CD _____ VSD 5208
Varese Sarabande/Colosseum / Dec '88 / Pinnacle / Silva Screen.

SCREEN THEMES '93
Garson, Michael
Jurassic park (Theme) / Schindler's list (Theme) / Indecent proposal (Instrumental Suite) / Fugitive (Main Title) / Age of innocence / Shadowlands / Pelican brief (Main Title) / Piano (Heart asks for pleasure) / Beau (Closing Credits) / Heaven and earth (End Title) / Firm (Main Title) / Mrd.Doubtfire (Snow's over) / Philadelphia (Streets of Philadelphia) / Sleepless in Seattle
CD _____ 77009
Discovery / Jun '94 / Warner Music.

SECRET AGENT FILE
Norman, Neil & his Orchestra
Reilly, ace of spies / Octopussy / I spy / Rockford files / Man from U.N.C.L.E. / Casino Royale / Ipcress file / Get smart / Thunderball / Spy who came in from the cold
CD _____ GNPD 2166
GNP Crescendo / '88 / Silva Screen.

SHOW STOPPERS
CD _____ 95902
Silva Screen / Feb '90 / Conifer / Silva Screen.

SHOW STOPPERS
(18 Unforgettable Songs...18 Unforgettable Shows)
Starsound Singers & Orchestra
Music of the night / Memory / If ever I would leave you / Send in the clowns / America / If I were a rich man / I enjoy being a girl / Some enchanted evening / If my friends could see me now / Cabaret / Good morning starshine / I don't know how to love him / Stranger in paradise / I could have danced all night / Sound of music / Hello young lovers / I can't give you anything but love / There's no business like show business
CD _____ ECD 3133
K-Tel / Jan '95 / K-Tel.

SHOW STOPPERS - TIMELESS HITS FROM THE MUSICALS
Big spender / Consider yourself / Cabaret / Somewhere / You're the one that I want / Send in the clowns / Ol' man river / Oklahoma / Windy city / I won't send roses / I could write a book / Memory
CD _____ SHOWCD 018
Showtime / Feb '95 / Disc / THE.

SHOWS COLLECTION, THE
CD _____ PWKS 4142
Carlton Home Entertainment / Jan '95 / Carlton Home Entertainment.

SHOWS ORCHESTRAL
Royal Philharmonic Orchestra
Phantom of the opera / Think of me / Angel of music / Point of no return / Music of the night / Masquerade / All I ask of you / Wishing you were somehow here again / Overture / Heaven on their minds / What's the buzz / Everything's alright / I don't know how to love him / Damned for all time / Blood money / Last supper / Gethsemane / Pilate and Herod / Trial before Pilate / Jesus Christ superstar / Prologue / At the end of the day / I dreamed a dream / Lovely ladies / Fantine's death / Master of the house / Stars / Do you hear the people sing / Heart full of love / On my own / Drink with me / Bring him home / Final battle / Epilogue / Valjean's death / Heat is on Saigon / Movie in my mind / Why God why / Sun and moon / Ceremony / Last night of the world / Fall of Saigon / I still believe / If you want to die in bed / Truth inside your head / Little God of my heart / Love changes everything / Seeing is believing / Memeory of a happy moment / Chanson D'Enfance / Everybody loves a hero / She'd be far better off without you / Stop, wait please / There is more to love / First man you remember / Hand me the wine and the dice / Anything but lonely / Jacob and sons / Joseph's dreams / Poor, poor Joseph / One more angel in heaven / Potiphar / Close every door / Pharaoh story / Those canaan days / Jacob in Egypt / Any dream will do / Give me my coloured coat / Old Gumbie cat / Rum tum tugger / Grizabella / Glamour cat / Bustopher Jones / Old deuteronomy / Jellicle ball / Gus / Skimbleshanks / Macavity / Memeory / Journey to the heaviside layer
3CD _____ BOXD 38T
Carlton Home Entertainment / Oct '94 / Carlton Home Entertainment.

SHOWSTOPPERS
(The Greatest Show Songs)
CD _____ DINCD 118
Dino / Nov '95 / Pinnacle / 3MV.

SHOWTIME
4CD _____ CDPK 417
Charly / Oct '93 / Charly / THE / Cadillac.

SMASH HITS OF BROADWAY
CD _____ CDTEZ 7005
TER / Jan '95 / Koch.

SO IN LOVE - SAMUEL RAMEY ON BROADWAY
Ramey, Samuel & London Studio Symphony Orchestra
Stratta, Ettore Con
CD _____ 4509908652
Teldec Classics / Jan '95 / Warner Music.

SOME LIKE IT HOT
Monroe, Marilyn
Diamonds are a girl's best friend / Man chases a girl / Every baby needs a da da daddy / Happy birthday Mr. President / Incurably romantic / Down in the meadow / Some like it hot / I found a dream / Anyone can see I love you / Specialization / Heatwave / Ladies of the chorus / When I fall in love / Let's make love / Bye bye baby / Fine romance / One silver dollar / That old black magic / There's no business like show business / I wanna be loved by you
CD _____ HADCD 153
Javelin / May '94 / THE / Henry Hadaway Organisation.

SONGS FROM THE MOVIES
Astaire, Fred
No strings / Isn't this a lovely day (to be caught in the rain) / Top hat, white tie and tails / Cheek to cheek / Piccolino / We saw the sea / Let yourself go / I'd rather lead a band / I'm putting all my eggs in one basket / Let's face the music and dance / Pick yourself up / Way you look tonight / Fine romance / Bojangles of Harlem / Never gonna dance / Beginner's luck / Slap that bass / They all laughed / Let's call the whole thing off / They can't take that away from me / Shall we dance / I can't be bothered now / Things are looking up / Foggy day / Nice work if you can get it
CD _____ PPCD 78115
Past Perfect / Feb '95 / THE.

SONGS FROM THE STAGE & SCREEN
Garland, Judy
CD _____ MCCD 101
MCI / May '93 / Disc / THE.

SOUND STAGE & STORY, THE
Easy going fellow: Shelton, Roscoe / Hymn no. 5: Gaines, Earl / I'm his wife, you're just a friend: Shelton, Ann / I love you: Baker, Sam / Only time you say you love me: Smith, Charles / You keep me hangin' on:

Simon, Joe / Whole lot of man: Davis, Geator / All the time: Washington, Ella / Sometimes you have to cry: Baker, Sam / Chokin' kind: Simon, Joe / He called me baby: Washington, Ella / Your heart is so cold: Davis, Geator / Strain on my heart: Shelton, Roscoe / You're gonna miss me: Sexton, Ann / I'll take care of you: Gaines, Earl / I'm not through loving you: Brown, Latimore / I don't care who knows: Church, Jimmy / Soon as darkness falls: Shelton, Roscoe / What made you change your mind: King, Bobby / Human / Judge of hearts: Hobbs, Willie / Someone bigger than you or me: Baker, Sam / We've got to save it: Scott, Moody / Let me come on home: King, Bobby / I'm ready to love you now: Shelton, Roscoe / Just a glance away: Baker, Sam / Try something new: Billups, Eddie / Ooh I love you: Cashmeres / I got love: Byrd, Leon / Woman's touch: Scott, Moody / My faith in you: Church, Jimmy / I know your heart has been broken: Shelton, Roscoe
CD _____ CDCHARLY 191
Charly / Aug '89 / Charly / THE / Cadillac.

SPACE MOVIE THEMES
(Star Wars/Empire Strikes Back/Return Of The Jedi/etc)
London Symphony Orchestra
CD _____ HRM 7001
Hermes / Jan '86 / Nimbus.

SPAGHETTI WESTERNS VOL.1
2CD _____ DRGCD 32905
DRG / Jun '95 / New Note.

SPECTACULAR WORLD OF CLASSIC FILM SCORES
National Philharmonic Orchestra
Gerhardt, Charles Con
Studio fanfares / Star Wars / Captain Blood / Now, Voyager / Gone With the Wind / Elizabeth and Essex / Peyton Place / Citizen Kane / Caine Mutiny / Knights of the Round Table / Objective Burma / Guns of Navarone / Julius Caesar / Thing from Another World / King of the Khyber Rifles / Salome
CD _____ GD 82792
RCA Victor / '92 / BMG.

STAGE AND SCREEN FAVOURITES
Royal Philharmonic Orchestra
Lewis, Vic Con
Don't cry for me Argentina / M.A.S.H. (Suicide is painless) (theme) / Serenade for strings / Coco / Always Madamoiselle / Hannie Caulder / 49th Parallel / So much you loved me / Louise / Escape me never / My ship / Little Prince
CD _____ PWK 126
Carlton Home Entertainment / Jun '90 / Carlton Home Entertainment.

STALLONE
(Music From The Films Of Sylvester Stallone)
Rocky (Fanfare/Gonna fly now/Going the distance/The final bell): London Screen Orchestra / F.I.S.T. (Theme): City Of Prague Philharmonic Orchestra / Paradise Alley (Victor's big match): London Screen Orchestra / Rocky II (Redemption): London Screen Orchestra / Nighthawks (Theme): London Screen Orchestra / Rocky III (Eye of the tiger) / First Blood (It's a long road): City Of Prague Philharmonic Orchestra / Rambo: First Blood Part 2 (Theme/Day by day/Pilot over): City Of Prague Philharmonic Orchestra / Cobra (Theme/Chase): Ayres, Mark / Over The Top (In this country/The fight/Meet me halfway): Ayres, Mark / Rambo III (Questions): City Of Prague Philharmonic Orchestra / Lock Up (Theme/Breaking point/Release): Ayres, Mark / Cliffhanger (Theme/Rabbit hole/End title): City Of Prague Philharmonic Orchestra
CD _____ FILMCD 139
Silva Screen / Nov '93 / Conifer / Silva Screen.

STAND BY ME
(Love Songs From TV Commercials)
Stand by me: King, Ben E. / Only you: Platters / Drift away: Gray, Dobie / Will you still love me tomorrow: Shirelles / When a man loves a woman: Sledge, Percy / Rescue me: Fontella Bass / Games people play: South, Joe / I'm into something good: Herman's Hermits / My baby heaven: Domino, Fats / Walkin' the dog: Thomas, Rufus / I got you (I feel good): Brown, James / Be bop a lula: Vincent, Gene / Up on the roof: Drifters / Leader of the pack: Shangri-Las / I put a spell on you: Hawkins, Screamin' Jay / Man with tender love: Sledge, Percy / But I do: Henry, Clarence / Venus: Avalon, Frankie / Runaway: Shannon, Del / Goodnight sweetheart, well it's time to go: Spaniels
CD _____ MU 3013 CD
Musketeer / Oct '95 / Koch.

STANDING ROOM ONLY
(Broadway Favourites)
Hadley, Jerry
CD _____ 09026613702
RCA Victor / Jul '93 / BMG.

STAR TRACKS II
Nimoy, L.D. Dorsey/Cincinnati Pops Orchestra
Kunzel, Erich Con
CD _____ CD 80146
Telarc / Nov '87 / Conifer / ADA.

STAR WARS/2001: A SPACE ODYSSEY
(Classic Symphonic Film Music)
Lawrence Of Arabia (Suite): Philharmonia Orchestra / Gone With The Wind (Tara's theme): Rochester Pops Orchestra / Star Wars/2001: A Space Odyssey (Space medley): Rochester Pops Orchestra / Best Years Of Our Lives (The homecoming): London Philharmonic Orchestra / Vertigo (Suite): San Diego Symphony Pops / Big Country (Suite): Philharmonia Orchestra / Time After Time (End title): Royal Philharmonic Orchestra / British film scores suite
CD _____ SILVAD 3002
Silva Treasury / '92 / Conifer / Silva Screen.

STORY GOES ON, THE
Callaway, Liz
CD _____ VSD 5585
Varese Sarabande/Colosseum / Oct '95 / Pinnacle / Silva Screen.

SUPPLY AND DEMAND
(Songs by Brecht, Weill & Eisler)
Krause, Dagmar
CD _____ HNCD 1317
Hannibal / Mar '86 / Vital / ADA.

SYMPHONIC SUITE OF THE ANIMATED CLASSICS
Kingston Symphony
CD _____ MACD 2501
Hindsight / Mar '95 / Target/BMG / Jazz Music.

SYNTHESIZER HITS
(TV Themes)
CD _____ MU 5006
Musketeer / Oct '92 / Koch.

SYNTHESIZER HITS
(Film Themes)
CD _____ MU 5003
Musketeer / Oct '92 / Koch.

SYNTHESIZER HITS
(James Bond Themes)
CD _____ MU 5004
Musketeer / Oct '92 / Koch.

SYNTHESIZER HITS OF CINEMA AND TV
CD _____ 22528
Music / Jul '95 / Target/BMG.

TELEVISION'S GREATEST HITS
CD _____ GRF 198
Tring / Jan '93 / Tring / Prism.

THAT'S ENTERTAINMENT
London Symphony Orchestra
That's entertainment / Crazy girl (overture) / My Fair Lady (symphonic picture) / Don't rain on my parade / Evita (Intro) / Fiddler on the roof (overture) / Me and my girl (concert overture) / Showboat / Mack and Mabel (overture) / Everything's coming up roses
CD _____ PWKS 4204
Carlton Home Entertainment / May '94 / Carlton Home Entertainment.

THAT'S MUSICAL
CD _____ 12554
Laserlight / Jun '95 / Target/BMG.

THEATRE ROYAL DRURY LANE
Rose Marie / Door of my dreams / Desert song / One alone / Can't help lovin' dat man / Ol' man river / Why do I love you / Lover come back to me / Wanting you / March of the musketeers / You are my heart's delight / Keep smiling / Hand in hand / Fold your wings / Shine through my dreams / Music in May / Why is there ever goodbye / Rose of England / River God / Waltz of my heart / I can give you the starlight
CD _____ CDHD 233
Happy Days / Sep '95 / Conifer.

THEMES FROM ACADEMY AWARD WINNERS
Gerhardt, Charles/Arthur Fiedler/Henry Mancini/David Raksin Con
Star Wars / Tom Jones / Casablanca / Ben Hur / Breakfast at Tiffany's (Moon river) / Exodus / West Side Story / Airport / High Noon / Laura / Lawrence of Arabia / Doctor Zhivago / Gone With the Wind
CD _____ 09026609662
RCA Victor / Jan '92 / BMG.

THEMES FROM CHILDREN'S BBC
Postman Pat / Fireman Sam / Dr. Who / Muppet babies / Jim'll fix it / Grange Hill / Mop 'n' Smiff / Trumpton / Heads and tails / Family Ness / Paddington Bear / Willy Fog / Camberwick Green / Hokey cokey / Magic roundabout / Bertha / Henry's cat / Will o' the wisp / Playschool / Dogtanian and the three muskehounds
CD _____ PWKS 650
Carlton Home Entertainment / Jul '88 / Carlton Home Entertainment.

THEMES FROM SUSPENSE MOVIES
CD _____ 873040
Milan / Jan '95 / BMG / Silva Screen.

THEMES FROM THE SIXTIES
Avengers: *Grave* / To Sir with love: *Studio 68* / On her Majesty's secret sevice: *Editors* / Prisoner: *Kitch* / Man in a suitcase: *Ministry of Defiance* / Up the junction: *Eleanor Rigby* / You only live twice: *Eleanor Rigby* / Man from U.N.C.L.E.: *Grave* / Mission impossible: *Ministry of Defiance* / Captain Zeppo: *Beatboy* / Stingray: *C.B.U.* / Addams family: *Perestroika* / Batman: *Waterloo Sunset Allstars*
CD _____ FLEG 1CD
Future Legend / Mar '93 / Future Legend.

THEMES FROM THE SIXTIES VOL. 3
CD _____ FLEG 5CD
Future Legend / Sep '95 / Future Legend.

THEMES FROM THE SIXTIES VOL.2
CD _____ FLEGCD 2
Future Legend / Mar '94 / Future Legend.

THEMES OF STAGE & SCREEN
CD _____ MATCD 254
Castle / Apr '93 / BMG.

THERE'S NO BUSINESS LIKE SHOW BUSINESS
(Broadway's Showstoppers)
Original Broadway/London/Film Casts
CD _____ SK 53541
Sony Classical / Jul '94 / Sony.

THERE'S NOTHIN' LIKE A DAME - BROADWAY'S BROADS
Broadway Casts
CD _____ SK 53539
Sony Classical / Jul '94 / Sony.

THIS IS CULT FICTION
Little green bag: *Baker, George Selection* / Misirlou: *Dale, Dick & His Del-Tones* / Mission impossible: *Schifrin, Lalo* / Shaft: *Hayes, Isaac* / Jungle boogie: *Kool & The Gang* / Man from U.N.C.L.E.: *Montenegro, Hugo* / Everybody's talkin': *Nilsson, Harry* / Stuck in the middle with you: *Stealer's Wheel* / Blue velvet: *Vinton, Bobby* / Touch of evil: *Mancini, Henry* / We have all the time in the world: *Armstrong, Louis* / James Bond: *Barry, John Seven* / Joe 90: *Gray, Barry Orchestra* / Harder they come: *Cliff, Jimmy* / Here comes the hotstepper: *Kamoze, Ini* / Guaglione: *Prado, Perez 'Prez'* / Play dead: *Arnold, David & Bjork* / Avengers: *Johnson, Laurie Orchestra* / You never can tell: *Berry, Chuck* / Rumble: *Wray, Link* / Saint: *Reed, Les* / Hawaii five o: *Ventures* / Streets of San Francisco: *Gregory, John* / Long good Friday: *Monkman, Francis* / Sweeney: *Power Pack Orchestra* / Dangerman: *Leaper, Bob Orchestra* / Twin peaks: *Baladamenti, Angelo* / All the animals come out at night: *Herrmann, Bernard*
CD _____ VTCD 59
Virgin / Aug '95 / EMI.

THOSE FABULOUS BUSBY BERKELEY MUSICALS
(Radio Versions From The Thirties)
CD _____ CDMR 1161
Radiola / Jan '91 / Pinnacle.

THOSE MAGNIFICENT MGM MUSICALS (Vol. 1 1939-1952)
Over the rainbow (Wizard of Oz.): *Garland, Judy* / Ol' man river (Till the clouds roll by.): *Peterson, Caleb* / Look for the silver lining (Till the clouds roll by.): *Garland, Judy* / Leave it to Jane and Cleopatterer (Till the clouds roll by.): *Allyson, June* / Can't help lovin' dat man (Till the clouds roll by.): *Horne, Lena* / Who (Till the clouds roll by.): *Garland, Judy* / Best things in life are free (Good news.): *Allyson, June* / A Fellow Law ford* / Pass that peace pipe (Good news.): *McCracken, Joan* / Lucky in love (Good news.): *Marshall, Pat/Peter Lawford/June Allyson* / Varsity drag (Good news.): *Allyson, June & Peter Lawford* / Steppin' out with my baby (Easter parade): *Astaire, Fred* / Fella with an umbrella (Easter Parade.): *Garland, Judy & Peter Lawford* / Shaking the blues (Easter Parade.): *Miller, Ann* / Couple of swells (Easter Parade.): *Garland, Judy & Fred Astaire* / Easter parade (Easter Parade.): *Garland, Judy & Fred Astaire* / Manhattan (Words and music.): *Rooney, Mickey* / Johnny one note (Words and music.): *Garland, Judy* / Lady is a tramp (Words and music.): *Horne, Lena* / I wish I were in love again (Words and music.): *Rooney, Mickey & Judy Garland* / Where or when (Words and music.): *Horne, Lena* / Thou swell (Words and music.): *Allyson, June* / Be a clown (The Pirate.): *Garland, Judy & Gene Kelly* / Love of my life (The Pirate.): *Garland, Judy* / I don't care (In the good old summertime.): *Garland, Judy* / Meet me tonight in dreamland (In the good old summertime.): *Garland, Judy* / Play that barber shop chord (In the good old summertime.): *Garland, Judy & The King's Men* / Last night when we were young (In the good old summertime.): *Garland, Judy* / Put your arms around me honey (In the good old summertime.): *Garland, Judy* / Merry Christmas (In the good old summertime.) / Pagan love song (Pagan love song.): *Keel, Howard* / House of singing bamboo (Pagan love song.): *Keel, Howard* / Who's sorry now (Three little words.): *De Haven, Gloria* / I wanna be loved by you (Three little words.): *Kane, Helen* / Nevertheless I'm in love with you (Three little words.): *Astaire, Fred/Red Skelton/Anita Ellis* / I love you so much (Three little words.): *Dahl, Arlene* / Where

did you get that girl (Three little words.): *Astaire, Fred & Anita Ellis* / Get happy (Summer Stock (UK: If you feel like singing)): *Garland, Judy* / (Howdy neighbour) happy harvest: *Garland, Judy* / You wonderful you (Summer Stock (UK: If you feel like singing)): *Kelly, Gene* / Friendly star (Summer Stock (UK: If you feel like singing)): *Garland, Judy* / Heavenly music (Summer Stock (UK: If you feel like singing)): *Kelly, Gene & Phil Silvers* / If you feel like singing, sing (Summer Stock (UK: If you feel like singing)): *Garland, Judy* / Dig dig dig dig for your dinner (Summer Stock (UK: If you feel like singing)): *Kelly, Gene & Phil Silvers* / Aba daba honeymoon (Two weeks with love.): *Carpenter, Carleton & Debbie Reynolds* / By the light of the silvery moon (Two weeks with love.): *Powell, Jane* / Row row row (Two weeks with love.): *Carpenter, Carleton & Debbie Reynolds* / My hero (Two weeks with love.): *Powell, Jane* / Make believe (Showboat.): *Keel, Howard & Kathryn Grayson* / I might fall back on you (Showboat.): *Champion, Marge & Gower* / Why do I love you (Showboat.): *Keel, Howard & Kathryn Grayson* / Bill (Showboat.): *Gardner, Ava* / Life upon the wicked stage (Showboat.): *Champion, Marge & Gower* / You are love (Showboat.): *Keel, Howard & Kathryn Grayson* / Wonder why (Rich, young and pretty.): *Powell, Jane* / Paris (Rich, young and pretty.): *Lamas, Fernando* / I can see you (Rich, young and pretty.): *Powell, Jane* / There's danger in your eyes, cherie (Rich, young and pretty.): *Darrieux, Danielle* / Too late now (Royal wedding (UK: Wedding bells).): *Powell, Jane* / Every night at seven (Royal wedding (UK: Wedding bells).): *Powell, Jane* / Happiest day of my life (Royal wedding (UK: Wedding bells).): *Powell, Jane* / I left my hat in Haiti (Royal wedding (UK: Wedding bells).): *Astaire, Fred* / You're all the world to me (Royal wedding (UK: Wedding bells).): *Astaire, Fred* / How could you believe me when I said I love you (when you know I've been a liar all my life): *Astaire, Fred & Jane Powell* / 'S wonderful (An American in Paris.): *Kelly, Gene & George Guetary* / Love is here to stay (An American in Paris.): *Kelly, Gene* / I'll build a stairway to paradise (An American in Paris.): *Guetary, Georges* / I got rhythm (An American in Paris.): *Kelly, Gene* / Singin' in the rain (Singin' in the rain.): *Kelly, Gene* / Fit as a fiddle (Singin' in the rain.): *Kelly, Gene & Donald O'Connor* / You were meant for me (Singin' in the rain.): *Kelly, Gene* / Make 'em laugh (Singin' in the rain.): *O'Connor, Donald* / Good morning (Singin' in the rain.): *Kelly, Gene & Donald O'Connor* / All I do is dream of you (Singin' in the rain.): *Kelly, Gene* / Moses (Singin' in the rain.): *Kelly, Gene & Donald O'Connor* / You are my lucky star (Singin' in the rain.): *Kelly, Gene & Debbie Reynolds* / Oops (Belle of New York.): *Astaire, Fred* / Naughty but nice (Belle of New York.): *Ellis, Anita* / Seeing's believing (Belle of New York.): *Astaire, Fred* / I wanna be a dancin' man (Belle of New York.): *Astaire, Fred* / Everything I have is yours/Seventeen thousand telephones (Everything I have is yours.): *Astaire, Fred* / Maxim's (Merry widow.): *Lamas, Fernando* / Girls, girls, girls (Merry widow.): *Night (Merry widow.): *Lamas, Fernando* / Merry widow waltz (Merry widow.): *Lamas, Fernando & Trudy Erwin*
4CD _____ CDMGB 1
MGM/EMI / May '90 / EMI.

THOSE MAGNIFICENT MGM MUSICALS VOL.2
(1952-1971)
Shine of your shoes / Be myself / Triplets / New sun in the sky / I guess I'll have to change my plan / I love Louisa / That's entertainment / Smoke gets in your eyes / I'll be hard to handle / Yesterdays / Touch of my hand / Lovely to look at / Hi lili hi lo / Too darn hot / So in love / Tom, Dick or Harry / Were thine that special face / Why can't you behave / Wunderbar / Always true to you in my fashion / I hate men / From this moment on / Brush up your Shakespeare / Spring, spring, spring / Bless your heart / Wonderful, wonderful day / Goin' cotin / Sobin' women / Sometimes I'm happy / Chiribiribee (Ciribiribin) / More than you know / I know that you know / Rose Marie / I'm a mountie who never got his man / Indian love call / Softly as in a morning sunrise / Serenade / Lover come back to me / Road to paradise / Will you remember / Once in the highlands / Brigadoon / Heather on the hill / Waitin' for my dearie / I'd go home with Bonnie Jean / Come to me, bend to me / Fate / Not since Nineveh / Baubles, bangles and beads / Stranger in paradise / Gesticulate / Night of my nights / Bored / Olive tree / Rahadakum / And this is my beloved / March march / Thanks a lot, but no thanks / Blue Danube / Music is better than words / I like myself / Les Girls / You're just too too / Ca, c'est l'amour / Ladies in waiting / Why am I so gone / Thank heavens for little girls / Say a prayer for me tonight / I remember it well / Gaston's soliloquy / I'm glad I'm not young anymore / Night they invented champagne / Paris loves lovers / All of you / Fated to be mated / Siberia / Ritz roll and rock / I ain't down yet / I'll never say no / Belly up to the bar, boys / London is London / You

and I / I could be happy with you / It's never too late to fall in love / Room in Bloomsbury / Riviera / Boy friend finale
2CD _____ CDMGB 2
MGM/EMI / May '90 / EMI.

THOSE SENSATIONAL SWINGING SIRENS OF THE SILVER SCREEN
CD _____ VJC 1002-2
Victorious Discs / Aug '90 / Jazz Music.

TIMELESS TV THEMES
Thunderbirds: *Gray, Barry Orchestra* / Avengers theme: *Johnson, Laurie Orchestra* / Man in a suitcase: *Grainer, Ron Orchestra* / Z-cars: *Keating, Johnny & The Z Men* / Captain Scarlet: *Gray, Barry Orchestra* / Champions: *Hatch, Tony Orchestra* / Fugitive: *Schroeder, John Orchestra* / Emmerdale Farm: *Hatch, Tony Orchestra* / Danger man: *Leaper, Bob Orchestra* / Stranger on the shore: *Bilk, Acker* / Maigret: *Eagles* / Stingray: *Gray, Barry Orchestra & The Gary Miller Orchestra* / Crossroads: *Hatch, Tony Orchestra* / Forsyte saga (Elizabeth Tudor): *Stapleton, Cyril & Orchestra* / Mysterons theme: *Gray, Barry Orchestra* / Return of the Saint (theme): *Gray, Barry Orchestra* / Dr. Who: *Winstone, Eric & His Orchestra* / Fireball: *Flee-Rekkers* / Steptoe And Son (Old Ned): *Grainer, Ron Orchestra*
CD _____ TRTCD 122
TrueTrax / Oct '94 / THE.

TIMEWARP
Dorsey, D./Cincinnati Pops Orchestra
Kunzel, Erich Con
CD _____ CD 80106
Telarc / May '85 / Conifer / ADA.

TO CATCH A THIEF
(A History Of Hitchcock Vol. 2)
City Of Prague Philharmonic Orchestra
Bateman, Paul Con
Thirty Nine Steps / Lady Vanishes / Stagefright / Rope / Lifeboat / To Catch a Thief / Vertigo / Torn Curtain / Family Plot / North by Northwest / Strangers on a Train / Trouble with Harry / Rear Window
CD _____ FILMCD 159
Silva Screen / Apr '95 / Conifer / Silva Screen.

TOP HAT
(Music From The Films Of Astaire & Rogers)
Mancini Pops Orchestra
Mancini, Henry Con
Roberta / Flying Down to Rio / Gay Divorcee / Follow the Fleet / Shall We Dance / Swing Time
CD _____ 09026607952
RCA Victor / Nov '92 / BMG.

TOP OF THE BILL
(Over 60 Of Their Greatest Successes)
CD _____ PASTCD 9753
Flapper / Apr '92 / Pinnacle.

TOP TV & MOVIE THEMES
Star trek / High noon / 2001 / Shaft / Howard's Way / Eastenders
2CD _____ 2802
Sound / Jan '89 / Direct / ADA.

TOP TV THEMES
CD _____ 887978
Milan / Jan '95 / BMG / Silva Screen.

TRUE GRIT
(Music From The Classic Films Of John Wayne)
City Of Prague Philharmonic Orchestra
Bateman, Paul Con
Stagecoach / She Wore a Yellow Ribbon / Quiet Man / Searchers / Alamo / True Grit / Cowboys / How the West Was Won / High and the Mighty / In Harm's Way
CD _____ FILMCD 153
Silva Screen / Jul '94 / Conifer / Silva Screen.

TRUFFAUT FILM MUSIC
CD _____ 887790
Milan / Jan '95 / BMG / Silva Screen.

TV AND FILM THEMES II
CD _____ 3024 DDD
CRC / Oct '89.

TV CLASSICS
4CD _____ MBSCD 412
Castle / Feb '93 / BMG.

TV THEMES AMERICA
Dallas / Perfect Strangers / Knots Landing / Midnight Caller / Head of the Class / Mission Impossible / McGyver / Cagney and Lacey / Dynasty / Odd Couple / High Chapparal / M.A.S.H. (Suicide is painless) / Bonanza / Taxi / Rockford Files / Dr. Kildare
CD _____ EMPRCD 556
Emporio / Mar '95 / THE / Disc / CM.

TV THEMES II
(Best Of UK Gold)
Casualty / Overkill (theme from The Bill) / Dallas / Dynasty / Eastenders / Home (theme from Bread) / Juliet Bravo / Miss Marple / Bergerac / Dr. Who / Duchess of Duke Street / Pallisers / To serve them all our days / Poldark / Shoestring / Brothers / Onedin Line
CD _____ CDSTM 6
Soundtrack Music / Jan '94 / EMI.

U

UNFORGETTABLE
Boston Pops Orchestra
Williams, John (1) Con
CD _____ SK 53380
Sony Classical / Jan '94 / Sony.

UNIVERSAL SOLDIERS
CD _____ SIL 51072
Silva Screen / Jan '93 / Conifer / Silva Screen.

UNSUNG MUSICALS
Fay, T. Con
Smile / Postcards / Will we ever know each other / Ragtime Romeo / Starfish / Silverware / Her laughter in my life / In the name of love / There are days and there are days / In our hands / Sherry / She's a star / At my side / Disneyland / New words
CD _____ VSD 5462
Varese Sarabande/Colosseum / Apr '94 / Pinnacle / Silva Screen.

UNSUNG MUSICALS II
CD _____ VSD 5564
Varese Sarabande/Colosseum / Jun '95 / Pinnacle / Silva Screen.

V

VAMPIRE CIRCUS
(The Essential Vampire Theme Collection)
Return of Dracula / Vampire circus / Fright night / Transylvania twist / Vamp / Children of the night / Thirst / Transylvania / Forever knight / To die for / Son of darkness: To die for II / Sundown: The vampire in retreat / Hunger
CD _____ FILMCD 127
Silva Screen / Mar '93 / Conifer / Silva Screen.

VERY BEST OF DISNEY, THE
I wanna be like you / Give a little whistle / Little April showers / Everybody wants to be a cat / Heigh ho / Cruella De Vil / Whole new world / Spoonful of sugar / Part of your world / He's a tramp / Once upon a dream / Zip a dee doo dah / Beauty and the beast / Following the leader / Bare necessities / I've got no strings / Whistle while you work / Supercalifragilisticexpialidocious / Second star to the right / Love is a song / Under the sea / Friend like me / When I see an elephant fly / You can fly, you can fly, you can fly / Bibbidi-bobbidi-boo / Bella Notte / Be our quest / When you wish upon a star
CD _____ DISGD 471
Disney / Oct '93 / Carlton Home Entertainment.

VERY BEST OF ERICH KUNZEL
Laine, F./R. Leech/Central St. Uni. Choir/Cincinnati Pops Orchestra
Kunzel, Erich Con
Round up / Star Trek (theme) / Sing, sing, sing / Tara's theme (Gone with the wind) / Unchained melody / Nessun dorma / Little fugue in G minor / Star Wars / Batman / Grand Canyon suite / From Russia with love / Olympic fanfare / Opening sequence from Chiller / Overture to the Phantom Of The Opera / Godfather (theme) / Pink Panther (theme) / O mio babbino caro / Non-stop fast polka / Op 112 / Honor, honor, do lord / Cybergenesis / Terminator / Jurassic lunch
CD _____ CD 80401
Telarc / Sep '94 / Conifer / ADA.

VERY BEST OF THE BOSTON POPS, THE
Boston Pops Orchestra
Williams, John (1) Con
CD _____ 4328022
Philips / Dec '92 / PolyGram.

VISIONS
Flying (theme from ET) / Harry's Game / M.A.S.H. (Suicide is painless) / Hill Street Blues / Chariots of fire / Brideshead revisited / Arthur's theme / I don't know how to love him / Don't cry for me Argentina / Eve of the war / Star Wars / Fame / For your eyes only / Dallas / Shoestring / Chain / Angela / Take that look off your face
CD _____ MCCD 190
Music Club / Nov '94 / Disc / THE / CM.

WESTERN MOVIE THEMES
CD _____ 15 492
Laserlight / Jan '93 / Target/BMG.

WHEN I GROW TOO OLD TO DREAM
(Her Greatest Musical Comedy
Successes)
Laye, Evelyn
Lover come back to me / Girl on the prowl / One kiss / You've done something to my heart / Let the people sing / Night is young / When I grow too old to dream / Glass of golden baubles / Butterfly song / Brave hearts / Near and yet so far / Princess is awakening / Love is a song / Ensa / Zigeuner / I'll see you again / All thro' a glass of champagne / If you look into her eyes
CD _____ PAST CD 9717
Flapper / Mar '91 / Pinnacle.

WHITE HEAT - FILM NOIR
Jazz At The Movies Band
This gun for hire / Bad and the beautiful / White heat / Double indemnity / Touch of evil / Key largo / Laura / Lost weekend / Postman always rings twice / Asphalt jungle / Big sleep / Strange love of Martha Ivers / Naked city

CD _____ 77008
Discovery / Jun '94 / Warner Music.

WHY EVER DID THEY
(Hollywood Stars At The Microphone)
Kashmiri love song: *Valentino, Rudolph* / El relicario: *Valentino, Rudolph* / Long ago in Alcala: *Novarro, Ramon* / Two white arms: *Menjou, Adolphe* / Not for all the rice in China: *Webb, Clifton* / One little drink: *Beery, Noah* / Whip: *Beery, Noah* / Where the lighthouse shines: *Veidt, Conrad* / Tout la-bas: *Boyer, Charles* / Salue la lune: *Boyer, Charles* / Matrosenlied: *Albers, Hans* / Where is the song of songs for me: *Velez, Lupe* / Mi amado: *Velez, Lupe* / Ramona: *Del Rio, Dolores* / Ya va cayendo: *Del Rio, Dolores* / Come to me: *Swanson, Gloria* / What do I care: *Bankhead, Tallulah* / Don't tell him: *Bankhead, Tallulah* / It's all so new to me: *Crawford, Joan* / I'm in love with the Honourable Mr. So and So: *Crawford, Joan* / Little bit bad: *Brody, Estelle* / Lorna's song: *Hopper, Victoria*
CD _____ PAST CD 9735
Flapper / Mar '91 / Pinnacle.

WILD BUNCH, THE
(Best Of The West)
Czech Symphony Orchestra
Motzing, William Con
Sons of Katie Elder / Dances with wolves / Silverado / High noon / Once upon a time in the west / Magnificient seven / Alamo / Lonesome dove / Blue and the grey / Fistful of dynamite / TV Western themes / Ballad of Cable Hogue / Young guns II / Return of

a man called horse / Gunfight at the O.K. Corral / Wild bunch / Big country
CD _____ FILMCD 136
Silva Screen / Jun '93 / Conifer / Silva Screen.

WILD, WILD WEST, THE
(16 Great Western Tracks)
Good, the bad and the ugly / Ghost riders in the sky / Fistful of dollars / Man who shot Liberty Valance / Hanging tree / Streets of Loredo / Hang 'em high / High noon (Do not forsake me) / High chaparal / Bonanza / For a few dollars more / Big country / Magnificent seven / Shenandoah / Red river valley / Once upon a time in the West
CD _____ ECD 3043
K-Tel / Jan '95 / K-Tel.

WIM WENDERS' FILMMUSIC
CD _____ 873089
Milan / Nov '91 / BMG / Silva Screen.

WOODY ALLEN CLASSICS
CD _____ SK 53549
Sony Classical / Jul '94 / Sony.

WORKING IN A COALMINE
(Songs From TV Commercials)
CD _____ SMP 850007
Movieplay / Jan '94 / Target/BMG.

WORLD WAR II FILM THEMES
Royal Military School Of Music
Dambusters march / Where eagles dare / Bridge too far / 633 Squadron / Battle of the river plate / Great escape march / Reach for the sky / Aces high / Operation

crossbow / Longest day / Cockleshell heroes / River Kwai march / Battle of Britain
CD _____ CDPR 131
Premier/MFP / Apr '95 / EMI.

WORLD'S GREATEST MUSICALS, THE
CD _____ MU 5064
Musketeer / Oct '92 / Koch.

Y

YESTERDAY'S DREAM
(Movie Theme Classics)
Movin' Dream Orchestra
Moon river / Way we were / Shadow of your smile / Time for us / Over the rainbow / Melody fair / East of Eden / To love again / Windmills of your mind / Third man, Theme from / Sunflower / Where do I begin / Both sides now / Sound of silence / Let it be / Raindrops keep falling on my head / Born free / Tara's theme
CD _____ DC 8503
Denon / '88 / Conifer.

Composer Collections

Alwyn, William

ALWYN: FILM MUSIC
London Symphony Orchestra
Hickox, Richard Con
Rake's progress / Odd man out / Fallen idol
/ History of Mr. Polly
CD _____ CHAN 9243
Chandos / Mar '94 / Chandos.

Arlen, Harold

SINGS THE HAROLD ARLEN SONGBOOK
Wilson, Julie
Blues in the night / Man that got away / Fun
to be fooled / This time / Dream's on me /
Buds won't bud / Last night when we were
young / One for my baby / Lydia the tat-
tooed the lady / Out of this world
CD _____ DRG 5211
DRG / Jan '95 / New Note.

Arnold, Sir Malcolm

ARNOLD: FILM MUSIC
London Symphony Orchestra
Hickox, Richard Con
Bridge on the River Kwai / Inn of the sixth
happiness / Hobson's choice / Whistle
down the wind / Sound barrier
CD _____ CHAN 9100
Chandos / Feb '93 / Chandos.

Baird, Tadeusz

TADEUSZ BAIRD: FILM MUSIC
Polish Symphony Orchestra
Baird, Tadeusz Con
Room for one / Warsaw in Canaletto paint-
ings / Visit at the kings / Year one / Pas-
senger / Manhunter / Panic on a train / April
/ Rugged creativeness / When love was a
crime
CD _____ OCD 604
Olympia / Aug '94 / Priory.

TADEUSZ BAIRD: FILM MUSIC II
Polish Symphony Orchestra
Baird, Tadeusz Con
Between the shores / Burning mountains /
Every day / Sky of stone / Those who are
late / Samson
CD _____ OCD 607
Olympia / Aug '94 / Priory.

Barry, John

007 AND OTHER GREAT SOUNDTRACK THEMES
CD _____ CDCD 1225
Charly / Jun '95 / Charly / THE / Cadillac.

16 JOHN BARRY THEMES, THE
(The Ember Years Vol.2)
Barry, John
CD _____ PLAY 003
Play It Again / Mar '92 / Total/BMG.

CLASSIC JOHN BARRY, THE
City Of Prague Philharmonic Orchestra
Raine, Nic Con
Zulu / Out Of Africa / Midnight Cowboy /
Last Valley (Main title/Death of the captain/
End title) / Eleanor And Franklin / Hanover
Street / Born Free / Chaplin / Dances with
Wolves / Raise The Titanic / Indecent Pro-
posal / Persuaders / Robin And Marian /
Body Heat / Somewhere In Time / Lion In
Winter (Lion in winter/Eleanor's arrival/We-
're jungle creatures)
CD _____ FILMCD 141
Silva Screen / Oct '93 / Conifer / Silva
Screen.

EMI YEARS VOL.1, THE
(1957-1960)
Barry, John
CD _____ CDEMS 1497
EMI / Jul '93 / EMI

EMI YEARS VOL.2, THE
(1960-1962)
Barry, John
Magnificent seven / Skid row / Twist it /
Watch your step / Dark rider / Matter of who
/ Iron horse / It doesn't matter anymore /
Sweet talk / Moon river / There's life in the
old boy yet / Handful of songs / Like waltz
/ Rodeo / Donna's theme / Starfire / Bau-
bles, bangles and beads / Zapata / Rum-
de-dum-de-da / Spanish Harlem / Man
from Madrid / Challenge / Menace / Satin
smooth / Agressor / Rocco's theme /
Spinnerree
CD _____ CDEMS 1501
EMI / Jul '93 / EMI.

EMI YEARS VOL.3, THE
(1962-1964)
Barry, John Seven & Orchestra
James Bond theme / Blacksmith blues /
Curly Sark (Dateline TV theme) / Lost patrol
/ Roman Spring of Mrs Stone (theme from):
Loewe, Frederick / Tears: Loewe, Frederick
/ Blueberry Hill: Barry, John Seven &
Cherry pink and apple blossom white:

Barry, John Orchestra / Smokey Joe: Barry,
John / Unchained melody: Barry, John Or-
chestra / Party's over / Lolly theme / March
of the Mandarins / Human jungle (alt. ver-
sion) / Big safari: 1989 Broadway Cast /
Mouse on the moon: 1989 Broadway Cast
/ Twangin' cheek / I'll be with you in apple
blossom time: Barry, John Orchestra / Vo-
lare: Barry, John Orchestra / Human jungle
/ Onward Christian spacemen / Seven faces
/ Twenty four hours ago: Stone, Richard /
Jolly Bad Fellow (theme from): Belen, Ana /
Oublie ca: Barry, John Orchestra / Seance
on a Wet Afternoon: Barry, John / That fatal
kiss: Barry, John
CD _____ CDEMS 1555
EMI / Sep '95 / EMI.

MOVIOLA
Out of Africa / Midnight cowboy / Body heat
/ Somewhere in time / Mary Queen of Scots
/ Born free / Dances With Wolves / Chaplin
/ Cotton club / Walkabout / Frances / We
have all the time in the world / Moviola
CD _____ 4724902
Epic / Nov '92 / Sony.

Bart, Lionel

SONGS OF LIONEL BART
CD _____ MCCD 176
MCI / Sep '94 / Disc / THE.

Berlin, Irving

BERLIN ALWAYS
(The Songs Of Irving Berlin)
Cheek to cheek: Astaire, Fred / Let yourself
go: Astaire, Fred / This year's kisses: Faye,
Alice / Alexander's ragtime band: Goodman, Benny Orchestra / Always: Goodman,
Benny Orchestra / Slummin' on Park Avenue: Lunceford, Jimmy / I'm putting all my
eggs in one basket: Armstrong, Louis /
Waiting at the end of the road: Waters, Ethel
/ Harlem on my mind: Waters, Ethel / Isn't
this a lovely day: Ambrose & His Orchestra
/ Shakin' the blues away: Etting, Ruth /
When I lost you: Crosby, Bing / How deep
is the ocean: Crosby, Bing / He ain't got
rhythm: Holiday, Billie / I've got my love to
keep me warm: Tatum, Art / Blue skies:
Dorsey, Tommy Orchestra / When the midnight choo-choo leaves for Alabam': Dorsey, Tommy Orchestra / I want to be in
Dixie: American Ragtime Octette / How's
chances: Hall, Henry Orchestra / Russian
lullaby: Berigan, Bunny / Now it can be told:
Bowly, Al
CD _____ AVC 517
Avid / Apr '95 / Avid/BMG / Koch.

ELIZABETH WELCH SINGS IRVING BERLIN
Welch, Elizabeth
CD _____ CDVIR 8305
TER / Jan '89 / Koch.

IRVING BERLIN SHOWCASE, THE
Follow the fleet: Anton & The Paramount
Theatre Orchestra / I can't remember:
Wood, Scott & His Orchestra / Puttin' on the
Ritz: Alfredo & His Band / Reaching for the
moon: Da Costa, Raie / Piccolino: Manto-
vani & His Tipica Orchestra / With you: Man-
vin, Johnny / Berlin waltz medley: Coventry
Hippodrome Orchestra / Say it isn't so: Vallee, Rudy & His Connecticut Yankees / I
miss you in the evening: Davidson, Harry /
Song of paradise: Hilo Hawaiian Orches-
tra / Cocoanuts: Light Opera Company /
Russian lullaby: Savoy Orpheans / Mammy:
Bidgood, Harry & His Broadcasters / Be-
cause I love you: Fillis, Len / I never had a
chance: Leader, Harry & His Band / Top hat:
Arnold, Doris & Harry S. Pepper / I'm play-
ing with fire: Rabin, Oscar & His Band / How
many times: Brox Sisters / Just a little
longer: Spitalny, Philip & His Orchestra /
Song is ended (but the melody lingers on):
Richardson, Foster / On the Avenue: Levy,
Louis & His Gaumont British Symphony
Orchestra
CD _____ PASTCD 9733
Flapper / Feb '91 / Pinnacle.

SONG IS...IRVING BERLIN, THE
I'm putting all my eggs in one basket: Bos-
well Sisters / Let yourself go: Bowly, Al &
the Ray Noble Orchestra / Marie: Bowly, Al
& the Ray Noble Orchestra / Cheek to
cheek: Browne, Sam & Lew Stone / Pretty
girl is like a melody: Dennis, Denny & Ray
Noble Orchestra / Say it isn't so: Dorsey
Brothers / Heat wave: Farnon, Robert /
Slumming on Park Avenue: Farnon, Robert
/ Alexander's ragtime band: Geraldo & His
Orchestra / White christmas: Geraldo & His
Orchestra / He ain't got rhythm: Goodman,
Nat / Blue skies: Goodman, Benny / This
year's kisses: Gibbons, Carroll / You keep
coming back like a song: James, Dick / Let
me sing and I'm happy: Joyson, Al / I never
had a chance: Joyce, Teddy & Jimmy Mes-
ene / I've got my love to keep me warm:
Melachrino, George & Carroll Gibbons /

Let's face the music and dance: Roy, Harry
& His Orchestra / Piccolino: Roy, Harry & His
Orchestra / We saw the sea: Roy, Harry &
His Orchestra / All alone: Shaw, Artie & His
Orchestra / Because I love you: Shaw, Artie
& His Orchestra
CD _____ CDAJA 5068
Living Era / Oct '95 / Koch.

SONGS OF IRVING BERLIN
CD _____ MCCD 188
Music Club / Nov '94 / Disc / CM.

SPOTLIGHT ON IRVING BERLIN
Cheek to cheek / Anything you can do / Top
hat, white tie and tails / Let's face the music
and dance / Easter parade / There's no
business like show business / You're just in
love / Girl that I marry / Always / White
Christmas / They say it's wonderful
CD _____ HADCD 137
Javelin / Feb '94 / THE / Henry Hadaway
Organisation.

STARS SALUTE IRVING BERLIN, THE
Various Artists C
CD _____ CDCD 1247
Charly / Jun '95 / Charly / THE / Cadillac.

TRIBUTE TO IRVING BERLIN, A
CD _____ CDDL 1248
Music For Pleasure / Jan '94 / EMI.

UNSUNG IRVING BERLIN
(31 Hidden Treasures)
2CD _____ VSD 25632
Varese Sarabande/Colosseum / Nov '95 /
Pinnacle / Silva Screen.

Bernstein, Elmer

ELMER BERNSTEIN WITH THE RPO POPS
Royal Philharmonic Pops Orchestra
CD _____ CO 75288
Denon / Apr '93 / Conifer.

Bernstein, Leonard

BERNSTEIN CONDUCTS BERNSTEIN
New York Philharmonic Orchestra
Bernstein, Leonard Con
West Side Story / Candide (Overture) /
Rhapsody in blue / American in Paris
CD _____ SMK 47529
Sony Classical / Nov '92 / Sony.

BERNSTEIN CONDUCTS BERNSTEIN
New York Philharmonic Orchestra
Bernstein, Leonard Con
On the Waterfront (suite) / On the Town /
Fancy Free (complete)
CD _____ SMK 47530
Sony Classical / Nov '92 / Sony.

BERNSTEIN ON BROADWAY
(Highlights - West Side Story/Candide/
On The Town)
Casts/London Symphony Chorus &
Orchestra
Bernstein, Leonard/Michael Tilson
Thomas Con
CD _____ 4478982
Deutsche Grammophon / Jan '95 /
PolyGram.

**THEATRE WORKS (ON THE TOWN/
FANCY FREE/TROUBLE IN TAHITI)**
(& Candide/West Side Story/On The
Waterfront excerpts)
Bernstein, Leonard Con
3CD _____ SM3K 47154
Sony Classical / May '92 / Sony.

Black, Don

DON BLACK SONGBOOK, THE
Black, Don L
Born free: Monro, Matt / To sir with love:
Lulu / Girl with the sun in her hair: Clinton,
Davy / True grit: Street, Danny / On days
like these: Monro, Matt / This was then: Monro,
Matt / Curiouser and curiouser: Monro, Matt
/ Me I never knew: Monro, Matt / Billy: Mar-
tell, Lena / Lady from L.A.: Crawford, Mi-
chael / I missed the last rainbow: Crawford,
Michael / Play it again: Reading, Wilma / I'll
put you together again: Hot Chocolate / Tell
me on a Sunday: Webb, Marti / Last man
in my life: Webb, Marti / Anyone can fall in
love: Webb, Marti / Always there: Webb,
Marti / There is love and there is love: Faith,
Adam / In one of my weaker moments:
Dobson, Anita / Anything but lonely: Webb,
Marti / Love changes everything: Webb,
Marti
CD _____ PLAY 005
Play It Again / Sep '93 / Total/BMG.

Bliss, Arthur

BLISS - FILM MUSIC
Slovak Philharmonic Choir/Bratislava Sym-
phony Orchestra
Capova, S. Con

CD _____ 8223315
Marco Polo / Dec '91 / Select.

Bolling, Claude

BOLLING FILMS
Bolling, Claude
CD _____ 111982
Musidisc / Nov '94 / Vital / Harmonia Mundi
/ ADA / Cadillac / Discovery.

Burgon, Geoffrey

BRIDESHEAD REVISITED
(The Television Scores Of Geoffrey
Burgon)
Philharmonia Orchestra
Burgon, Geoffrey Con
Brideshead Revisited / Julia / Julia's theme
/ Hunt / Fading light / Farewell to Brides-
head / Testament of youth (Testament of
youth) / Intimations of war / Elegy / Finale /
Bleak house (Bleak House) / Streets of Lon-
don / Dedlock versus Boython / Lady Ded-
lock's quest / Finale (2) / Opening music
(Tinker, Tailor, Soldier, Spy) / Nunc Dimittis
/ Aslan's theme (Chronicles of Narnia) /
Great battle / Mr. Tumnus' tune / Storm at
sea / Aslan sacrificed / Journey to Harlang
/ Farewell to Narnia
CD _____ FILMCD 117
Silva Screen / Feb '95 / Conifer / Silva
Screen.

Caesar, Irving

THE GREAT ONES
CD _____ PASTCD 7075
Flapper / Nov '95 / Pinnacle.

Cahn, Sammy

EVENING WITH SAMMY CAHN, AN
Cahn, Sammy & Bobbi Baird/Shirley Lem-
mon/Jon Peck
Cahn, Sammy L
CD _____ DRG 5172
DRG / Jan '95 / New Note.

Carmichael, Hoagy

SONG IS...HOAGY CARMICHAEL, THE
Ev'ntide: Armstrong, Louis / Lazy river:
Armstrong, Louis / Lyin' to myself: Arms-
trong, Louis / Rockin' chair: Armstrong,
Louis / Judy in the morning: Bowly, Al / One
morning in May: Bowly, Al / Two sleepy
people: Bowly, Al / Heart and soul: Carless,
Dorothy & Billy Mayerl / Doctor, lawyer, In-
dian chief: Carr, Carole / Nearness of you:
Carr, Carole / Blue orchids: Dennis, Denny
Denny & Jack Hylton / Little old lady: Dennis,
Denny & Jack Hylton / Sing me a swing
song: Fitzgerald, Ella / Down 't Uncle Bill's:
Gonella, Nat / Jubilee: Gonella, Nat / Moon
country: Gonella, Nat / Small fry: Gonella,
Nat / I get along without you very well: Lay-
ton, Turner / Georgia on my mind: Mills
Brothers / Stardust: Mills Brothers / Sing it
way down low: Prima, Louis / Snowball:
Roy, Harry & His Orchestra / Lazybones:
Stone, Lew & His Band
CD _____ CDAJA 5074
Living Era / Oct '95 / Koch.

SONGS OF HOAGY CARMICHAEL, THE
CD _____ CDGRF 094
Tring / '93 / Tring / Prism.

TRIBUTE TO HOAGY CARMICHAEL, A
CD _____ CDDL 1280
EMI / Nov '92 / EMI.

Carpenter, John

HALLOWEEN
(The Best Of John Carpenter)
Halloween (Main title) / Fog (End title) /
Christine (Bad to the bone/Main title) / Thing
(End title) / They live (End title) / Prince of
Darkness (End title) / Starman (End title) /
Escape from New York (End title) / Dark
Star (Suite) / Big trouble in Little China (Main
title) / Assault on Precinct 13 (Julie's dead/
Main title & remixes)
CD _____ FILMCD 113
Silva Screen / Sep '93 / Conifer / Silva
Screen.

JOHN CARPENTER'S GREATEST HITS
CD _____ VSD 5266
Varese Sarabande/Colosseum / Nov '92 /
Pinnacle / Silva Screen.

JOHN CARPENTER'S GREATEST HITS II
CD _____ VSCD 345336
Varese Sarabande/Colosseum / Jul '93 /
Pinnacle / Silva Screen.

Cirque Du Soleil

CIRQUE DE SOLEIL
Cirque Du Soleil

CD _____ 9026625232
RCA Victor / Jan '96 / BMG.

MYSTERE
Cirque Du Soleil
CD _____ 9026626862
RCA Victor / Jan '96 / BMG.

NOUVELLE EXPERIENCE
Cirque Du Soleil
CD _____ 9026615312
RCA Victor / Jan '96 / BMG.

Comden & Green

COMDEN AND GREEN SONGBOOK, THE
Broadway Casts
Comden, Betty & Adolph Green L
CD _____ SK 48202
Sony Classical / Feb '93 / Sony.

PARTY WITH BETTY COMDEN AND ADOLPH GREEN
Comden, Betty & Adolph Green L
CD _____ ZDM 7647732
EMI Classics / Apr '93 / EMI.

Cosma, Vladimir

VERY BEST OF VLADIMIR COSMA, THE
2CD _____ DRGCD 32900
DRG / Jan '95 / New Note.

Coward, Sir Noel

GREAT BRITISH DANCE BANDS PLAY NOEL COWARD
CD _____ PASTCD 9758
Flapper / Aug '91 / Pinnacle.

TALENT TO AMUSE, A
(The Songs Of Noel Coward)
Greenwell, Peter
CD _____ SILVAD 3009
Silva Treasury / Sep '95 / Conifer / Silva Screen.

De Angelis, G. & M.

BEST OF BUD SPENCER & TERENCE HILL FILMS
CD _____ FILMCD 106
Silva Screen / Sep '93 / Conifer / Silva Screen.

BEST OF BUD SPENCER & TERENCE HILL FILMS II
CD _____ SIL 15302
Silva Screen / Sep '93 / Conifer / Silva Screen.

De Masi, Francesco

FILM MUSIC OF FRANCESCO DE MASI, THE
CD _____ VCDS 7007
Varese Sarabande/Colosseum / May '95 / Pinnacle / Silva Screen.

Delerue, Georges

BEST FILM MUSIC OF GEORGES DELERUE VOL 1
(Le Mepris/La Peau Douce/Mona/Les Deux Anglaises Et La Continent)
CD _____ CD 319
Milan / Jan '89 / BMG / Silva Screen.

BEST FILM MUSIC OF GEORGES DELERUE VOL 2
CD _____ CD 320
Milan / Jan '89 / BMG / Silva Screen.

LONDON SESSIONS VOL 1, THE
Rich and famous / Platoon / Beaches
CD _____ VSD 5241
Varese Sarabande/Colosseum / Apr '90 / Pinnacle / Silva Screen.

LONDON SESSIONS VOL 2, THE
Hommage a Francois Truffaut
CD _____ VSD 5245
Varese Sarabande/Colosseum / Sep '90 / Pinnacle / Silva Screen.

LONDON SESSIONS VOL 3, THE
CD _____ VSD 5256
Varese Sarabande/Colosseum / Jul '91 / Pinnacle / Silva Screen.

MUSIC FROM THE FILMS OF FRANCOIS TRUFFAUT
CD _____ CH 220
Milan / Jan '89 / BMG / Silva Screen.

TRUFFAUT AND DELERUE ON THE SCREEN
(Confidentially Yours/A Beautiful Girl Like Me/Day For Night/The Last Metro/The Woman Next Door)
Confidentially yours / Beautiful girl like me / Day for night / Last metro / Woman next door
CD _____ DRGCD 32902
DRG / Sep '93 / New Note.

Devreese, Frederic

DEVREESE - FILM MUSIC
Belgian Radio & TV Orchestra
Devreese, Frederic Con
CD _____ 8223681
Marco Polo / Nov '94 / Select.

Donaggio, Pino

BRIAN DE PALMA FILM MUSIC
CD _____ 191922
Milan / Jan '95 / BMG / Silva Screen.

Ellis, Vivian

SPREAD A LITTLE HAPPINESS
CD _____ PASTCD 7076
Flapper / Nov '95 / Pinnacle.

SPREAD A LITTLE HAPPINESS
2CD _____ CDHD 2578
Happy Days / Oct '95 / Conifer.

Erskine, Peter

BIG THEATRE
(Scores Based On 12th Night/Richard III/Midsummer Night's Dream)
Cast Recording
CD _____ AHUM 004
Ah-Um / Jul '90 / New Note / Cadillac.

Fielding, Jerry

JERRY FIELDING FILM MUSIC
2CD _____ BCDLE 4001/2
Silva Screen / Jan '94 / Conifer / Silva Screen.

JERRY FIELDING FILM MUSIC II
CD _____ BCDLE 4003
Silva Screen / Jan '94 / Conifer / Silva Screen.

Fisher-Turner, Simon

MANY MOODS OF SIMON TURNER, THE
Fisher-Turner, Simon
Isles of spice / Exotic hats / Esperanza / Caravaggio 1986 / Sloane Square / Gourmet's love song / Colours of my life / Violet crumble
CD _____ MONDE 14CD
Cherry Red / Apr '93 / Pinnacle.

Friml, Rudolf

ROMANTIC WORLD OF RUDOLF FRIML, THE
Song of the vagabonds / Only a rose / Blue kitten / Indian love call / One kiss / Rose Marie / Love me tonight / Three musketeers / Huguette waltz / Ma belle / Totem Tom / Twelve o'clock girl in a nine o'clock town / Sympathy waltz / Love everlasting / Vagabond King
CD _____ PASTCD 9764
Flapper / Jul '92 / Pinnacle.

Gay, Noel

SONG IS...NOEL GAY, THE
Sun has got his hat on: Ambrose & His Orchestra / Hold my hand: Bowlly, Al / Girl who loves a soldier: Cotton, Billy & His Band / I took my harp to a party: Cotton, Billy & His Band / That started it: Cotton, Billy & His Band / There's something about a soldier: Courtneidge, Cicely / Run rabbit run: Flanagan & Allen / Leaning on a lamp post: Formby, George / All over the place: Gieraldo & His Orchestra / Who's been polishing the sun: Hulbert, Jack / Love makes the world go round: Hutch / Melody maker: Hylton, Jack / Lambeth walk: Lane, Lupino / Let the people sing: Laye, Evelyn / You've done something to my heart: Laye, Evelyn / Oh what a wonderful night: Laye, Evelyn / Who's little what's-it are you: London Piano Accordion Band / Me and my girl: Munro, Ronnie / Fleet's in port again: Payne, Jack & His Orchestra / Moonlight Avenue: Silvester, Victor
CD _____ CDAJA 5081
Living Era / Oct '95 / Koch.

Gershwin, George

BARBARA HENDRICKS SINGS GERSHWIN
Hendricks, Barbara
CD _____ 4164602
Philips / Jan '87 / PolyGram.

CRAZY FOR GERSHWIN
Carlton Home Entertainment / Jan '94 / Carlton Home Entertainment.

CRAZY FOR GERSHWIN
Someone to watch over me: Fitzgerald, Ella / Love is here to stay: Jones, Jack / But not for me: Crosby, Bing / Embraceable you: Garland, Judy / Nice work if you can get it: Fitzgerald, Ella / I got plenty o' nuttin': Crosby, Bing / Swanee: Jolson, Al / How long has this been going on: Fitzgerald, Ella / They can't take that away from me: Lee, Peggy / Mine: Garland, Judy & Bing Crosby / Oh lady be good: Fitzgerald, Ella / I got rhythm: Garland, Judy / I loves you Porgy: Holiday, Billie / Love walked in: Crosby, Bing / Liza (all the clouds'll roll away): Jolson, Al / I've got a crush on you: Fitzgerald, Ella
CD Set _____ CDMOIR 502
Memoir / Jul '93 / Target/BMG.

GEORGE GERSHWIN COLLECTION, THE
Parkin, Eric
CD _____ SILVAD 3007
Silva Treasury / Apr '94 / Conifer / Silva Screen.

GERSHWIN IN THE MOVIES VOLS 1 & 2
St. Louis Symphony Orchestra
Slatkin, Leonard Con
2CD _____ CDCH 249/250
Milan / May '87 / BMG / Silva Screen.

GLORY OF GERSHWIN, THE
Summertime: Gabriel, Peter / Do what you do: De Burgh, Chris / Nice work if you can get it: Sting / They can't take that away from me: Stansfield, Lisa / Someone to watch over me: John, Elton / Our love is here to stay: John, Elton / I've got a crush on you: Simon, Carly / But not for me: Costello, Elvis / It ain't necessarily so: Cher / Man I love: Bush, Kate / How long has this been going on: Bon Jovi, Jon / Bidin' my time: White, Willard / My man's gone now: O'Connor, Sinead / I got rhythm: Palmer, Robert / Somebody loves me: Meat Loaf / Stairway to paradise: Van Randwyck, Issy / Rhapsody in blue: Adler, Larry
CD _____ 5227272
Mercury / Jul '94 / PolyGram.

KIRI SINGS GERSHWIN
Te Kanawa, Dame Kiri & The New Princess Theater Orchestra
McGlinn, John Con
CD _____ CDC 7474542
EMI Classics / Apr '93 / EMI.

MARNI NIXON SINGS GERSHWIN
Nixon, Marni
CD _____ RR 19
Reference Recordings / Sep '91 / May Audio.

S'MARVELLOUS
Gershwin, Ira L
CD _____ 5216582
Verve / Feb '94 / PolyGram.

SONG IS...GEORGE GERSHWIN, THE
Half of it, dearie blues: Astaire, Fred / I found a four leaf clover: Audrey, Irene & Charles Hart / Fascinating rhythm: Edwards, Cliff / When do we dance: Gershwin, George / My one and only: Gershwin, George / Little jazz bird: Hylton, Jack / Oh lady be good: Hylton, Jack / Liza: Jolson, Al / Someone to watch over me: Lawrence, Gertrude / Do what you do: O'Neal, Zelma / Sweet and low down: Selvin, Ben / That certain feeling: Selvin, Ben / Funny face: Smith, Jack / I got plenty o' nuttin': Tibbett, Lawrence / I got rhythm: Waller, Fats / Nashville nightingale: Waring, Fred & His Pennsylvanians / Man I love: Welch, Elizabeth / I'll build a stairway to paradise: Whiteman, Paul & Rhythm Boys / S'wonderful: Winter, Marius B. & His Dance Band
CD _____ CDAJA 5048
Living Era / Oct '95 / Koch.

SONGS & DUETS
Kaye, J./W. Sharp/S. Blier
CD _____ 370282
Koch / Jul '91 / Koch.

SPOTLIGHT ON GEORGE GERSHWIN
Fascinating rhythm / 'S wonderful / Summertime / Embraceable you / Foggy day / It ain't necessarily so / Nice work / Man I love / Somebody loves me / They can't take that away from me / I got rhythm
CD _____ HADCD 139
Javelin / Feb '94 / THE / Henry Hadaway Organisation.

S'WONDERFUL
(The Songs Of George & Ira Gershwin)
Gershwin, Ira L
Swanee: Jolson, Al / I got plenty o' nuttin': Tibbett, Lawrence / Love walked in: Armstrong, Louis / Embraceable you: Garland, Judy / Liza: Webb, Chick / How long has this been going on: Lee, Peggy / Nice work if you can get it: Dorsey, Tommy Orchestra / Funny face: Smith, Jack / Oh lady be good: Hawkins, Coleman / Somebody loves me: Carter, Benny / Someone to watch over me: Gershwin, George / I've got a crush on you: Wiley, Lee / S'Wonderful: Goodman, Benny / I'll build a stairway to paradise: Whiteman, Paul & Rhythm Boys / I got rhythm: Waller, Fats / Man I love: Forrest, Helen / They all laughed: Astaire, Fred / Summertime: Robeson, Paul / I was doing alright: Fitzgerald, Ella / Fascinating rhythm: Lee, Buddy / They can't take that away from me: Holiday, Billie
CD _____ AVC 520
Avid / Apr '95 / Avid/BMG / Koch.

S'WONDERFUL - THE MUSIC OF GEORGE GERSHWIN
Nice work if you can get it / Someone to watch over me / Looking for a boy / Liza / Foggy day / S'wonderful / Lady be good / Do do do / Somebody loves me / I got rhythm / I'll build a stairway to paradise / They can't take that away from me / Funny face / Fascinating rhythm / They all laughed / That certain feeling / Maybe / My one and only / Summertime / Swanee / Let's call the whole thing off / I got plenty o' nuttin'
CD _____ PASTCD 9777
Flapper / Dec '92 / Pinnacle.

TRIBUTE TO GEORGE GERSHWIN, A
CD _____ CDDL 1278
EMI / Nov '94 / EMI.

Gilbert & Sullivan

ARIAS AND DUETS
(The Best Of Gilbert & Sullivan)
Sullivan, Sir Arthur C
Gilbert, W.S. L
Three little maids / When a felon's not engaged in his employment / Poor wandering one / Loudly let the trumpet bray / Take a pair of sparkling eyes / I have a song to sing / I know a youth / I'm called little buttercup / On a tree by a river / If somebody there chanced to be / Wandering minstrel / When the foreman bares his steel
CD _____ SHOWCD 017
Showtime / Feb '95 / Disc / THE.

ARIAS AND DUETS OF GILBERT & SULLIVAN
Sullivan, Sir Arthur C
Gilbert, W.S. L
CD _____ CDVIR 8325
TER / Aug '95 / Koch.

BEST OF GILBERT & SULLIVAN, THE
Sullivan, Sir Arthur C
Gilbert, W.S. L
CD _____ CDTEZ 7004
TER / Jan '95 / Koch.

BEST OF GILBERT & SULLIVAN, THE
Sullivan, Sir Arthur C
Sargent, Sir Malcolm Con
CD _____ CDZ 7625312
EMI Classics / Apr '93 / EMI.

GILBERT & SULLIVAN - EXCERPTS
Soloists & Glyndebourne Festival Choir/Pro Arte Orchestra
Sullivan, Sir Arthur C
Gilbert, W.S. L
Sargent, Sir Malcolm Con
CD _____ CDCFP 4238
Classics For Pleasure / Jan '95 / EMI.

GILBERT & SULLIVAN CLASSICS
(Selections From The Mikado/Pirates Of Penzance/The Gondoliers/HMS Pinafore)
Sullivan, Sir Arthur C
Gilbert, W.S. L
Alwyn, Kenneth/Richard Hickox Con
CD _____ HMV 58
HMV / Jan '95 / EMI.

GILBERT & SULLIVAN CLASSICS II
Sullivan, Sir Arthur C
Gilbert, W.S. L
Sargent, Sir Malcolm Con
CD _____ HMV 102
HMV / Jan '95 / EMI.

GILBERT & SULLIVAN OVERTURES
Pro Arte Orchestra
Sullivan, Sir Arthur C
Gilbert, W.S. L
Sargent, Sir Malcolm Con
CD _____ CDCFP 4529
Classics For Pleasure / Jan '95 / EMI.

GILBERT & SULLIVAN SPECTACULAR
English Corale/London Concert Orchestra
Sullivan, Sir Arthur C
Dods, M. Con
CD _____ PWK 1157
Carlton Home Entertainment / Jun '90 / Carlton Home Entertainment.

OVERTURES
New Sadler's Wells/D'Oyly Carte Opera Orchestra
Sullivan, Sir Arthur C
Gilbert, W.S. L
Pryce Jones, J./S. Phipps/John Owen Edwards Con
CD _____ CDVIR 8316
TER / May '93 / Koch.

OVERTURES
Academy Of St. Martin In The Fields
Sullivan, Sir Arthur C
Gilbert, W.S. L
Marriner, Neville Con
CD _____ 4349162
Philips / Jun '93 / PolyGram.

VERY BEST OF GILBERT & SULLIVAN, THE
Sullivan, Sir Arthur C
Gilbert, W.S. L
CD _____ CDMOIR 413
Memoir / Aug '93 / Target/BMG.

WORLD OF GILBERT & SULLIVAN II, THE
Sullivan, Sir Arthur C
Gilbert, W.S. L
HMS Pinafore / Mikado / Patience / Iolanthe / Gondoliers / Ruddigore / Sorcerer / Yeoman of the guard / Princess Ida / Pirates of Penzance
CD _____ 4338682
Decca / Feb '93 / PolyGram.

WORLD OF GILBERT & SULLIVAN, THE
Sullivan, Sir Arthur C
Gilbert, W.S. L
HMS Pinafore / Mikado / Yeoman of the guard / Pirates of Penzance / Iolanthe / Gondoliers
CD _____ 4300952
Decca / Jun '91 / PolyGram.

Glass, Philip

FILM WORKS
(Anima Mundi/Mishima/Powaqattsi/The Thin Blue Line)
Glass, Philip Ensemble/Kronos Quartet
4CD _____ 7559793772
Elektra Nonesuch / Jan '95 / Warner Music.

Goodwin, Ron

MISS MARPLE FILMS, THE
(& Other Film Suites)
Murder she said / Murder at the gallop / Murder most foul / Murder ahoy / Force 10 from Navarone / Lancelot and Guinevere
CD _____ LXE 706
Silva Screen / Mar '93 / Conifer / Silva Screen.

Grainer, Ron

DOCTOR WHO
(And Other Classic Ron Grainer TV Themes)
Maigret / Steptoe and son / Some people / Man in s suitcase / Prisoner / Assassination bureau / Only when I larf / Paul Temple / Tales of the unexpected / Edward and Mrs. Simpson / Dr. Who
CD _____ PLAY 008
Play It Again / Sep '94 / Total/BMG.

Gray, Barry

FAB
(Music From The Gerry Anderson TV Shows)
Royal Philharmonic Orchsotra
Pavlov, Konstantin Con
Thunderbirds (Prelude
Overture
Tracy Island
Alan's reverie
Dirty work
Heading for disaster
Thunderbird's are go
Finale) / Space 1999 / Joe 90 / Stingray (Medley) / U.F.O. / Captain Scarlet
CD _____ FILMCD 124
Silva Screen / Nov '92 / Conifer / Silva Screen.

NO STRINGS ATTACHED
Gray, Barry Orchestra
Thunderbirds / Captain Scarlet / Hijacked / Aqua Marina / Stingray / Mysterons / Joe 90 / Parker - well done
CD _____ CLACD 204
Castle / Oct '90 / BMG.

THUNDERBIRDS ARE GO
Gray, Barry Con
Thunderbirds theme / Alan's dream / Joie de vivre / Martian mystery / Thunderbirds theme (reprise) / Astronauts in trouble / Zero X theme / That dangerous game / Swinging star / San Marino / Jeremiah / Tracy Island
CD _____ FILMCD 018
Silva Screen / Aug '90 / Conifer / Silva Screen.

Harnell, Joe

FILM & TV MUSIC OF JOE HARNELL
2CD _____ FJCD 001/2
Silva Screen / Jan '92 / Conifer / Silva Screen.

Harnick, Sheldon

EVENING WITH SHELDON HARNICK, AN
Harnick, Sheldon & Margery GrayMary Louise
Harnick, Sheldon L
Suave young man / How could I / Merry little minuet / Boston beguine / At the Basilica of St. Anne / Garbage / Worlds apart / Little tin box / Till tomorrow / Picture of happiness / She loves me / Dear friend / Sunrise sunset / Do you love me / When Messiah comes / How much richer could one man be / If I were a rich man / In my own lifetime
CD _____ DRG 5174
DRG / Jan '95 / New Note.

Henderson, Ray

GOOD NEWS
(Music & Songs Of B.G. De Sylva, Lew Brown & Ray Henderson)
De Sylva, B.G. & Lew Brown L
Black bottom / Good news / Varsity drag / You're the cream in my coffee / I'm on the crest of a wave / Sonny boy / It all depends on you / Button up your overcoat / I want to be bad / You wouldn't fool me, would you / I'm a dreamer (aren't we all) / Little gal / Never swat a fly / Don't tell her what happened to me / If I had a talking picture of you / Turn on the heat / If you haven't got love / You try somebody else / One more time
CD _____ CDHD 182
Happy Days / Mar '92 / Conifer.

Herbert, Victor

VICTOR HERBERT SHOWCASE, A
CD _____ PASTCD 9796
Flapper / Oct '92 / Pinnacle.

Herman, Jerry

EVENING WITH JERRY HERMAN, AN
Herman, Jerry & Lisa Kirk/Joe Masiell/Carol Dorian
Salome salome / Just leave everything to me / Put on your Sunday clothes / Ribbons down my back / Before the parade passes by / It only takes a moment / It's today / Open a new window / Man in the moon / Hooch's song / We need a little Christmas / Bosom buddies / If he walked into my life / I don't want to know / And I was beautiful
CD _____ CDSL 5173
DRG / Jan '93 / New Note.

JERRY HERMAN SONGBOOK, THE
Feinstein, Micahel & Jerry Herman
CD _____ 7559793152
Elektra Nonesuch / Jan '95 / Warner Music.

Herrmann, Bernard

BERNARD HERRMANN FILM SCORES
Royal Philharmonic Orchestra
Bernstein, Elmer Con
Citizen Kane / Psycho / Vertigo / Taxi driver / Farenheit 451
CD _____ 140812
Milan / Feb '94 / BMG / Silva Screen.

CITIZEN KANE
London Philharmonic Orchestra
Citizen Kane:Overture / Jane Eyre / Devil and Daniel Webster / Snows of Kilimanjaro / Jason and the argonauts / Citizen Kane:Variations / Citizen Kane:Ragtime / Citizen Kane:Finale / Swing your partners / Memory waltz
CD _____ 4178522
Decca / Aug '88 / PolyGram.

CITIZEN KANE
(Classic Film Scores Of Bernard Herrmann)
National Philharmonic Orchestra
Gerhardt, Charles Con
Citizen Kane (Prelude - Xanadu/Snow picture/Theme and variations - Breakfast montage/Aria from Salammbo/Rosebud and Finale) / On Dangerous Ground (The sea/Death hunt) / Beneath the 12-Mile Reef (The sea/ The lagoon/Descending/The octopus/Homecoming) / Hangover Square (Concerto macabre for piano and orchestra) / White Witch Doctor (Talking drums/Prelude/Riverboat/Petticoat dance/Safari/Tarantula/ Lion/Nocturne/Abduction of the Bakuba boy/Skulls/Lonni bound by ropes/ Departure)
CD _____ GD 80707
RCA Victor / Jun '91 / BMG.

CLASSIC FANTASY FILM SCORES
Three Worlds Of Gulliver / Mysterious Island / Seventh Voyage Of Sinbad / Jason And The Argonauts
CD _____ ACN 7014
Cloud Nine / Jun '88 / Conifer / Silva Screen.

INQUIRER, THE
(The Film Music Of Bernard Herrmann)
CD _____ PRCD 1789
Preamble / Sep '92 / Silva Screen.

MARVELLOUS FILM WORLD OF BERNARD HERRMANN, THE
Cape Fear / Garden of Evil / Beneath the 12-Mile Reef / King of the Khyber Rifles
CD _____ TCI 0605
Silva Screen / May '95 / Conifer / Silva Screen.

TORN CURTAIN
(Classic Film Music Of Bernard Herrmann)
City Of Prague Philharmonic Orchestra
Bateman, Paul Con
Torn Curtain / Cape Fear / Psycho / Ghost and Mrs. Muir / Obsession / Snows of Kilimanjaro / Taxi driver / On dangerous ground / Man who knew too much / Ray Harryhausen fantasy film suite
CD _____ FILMCD 162
Silva Screen / Sep '95 / Conifer / Silva Screen.

Holdridge, Lee

FILM MUSIC OF LEE HOLDRIDGE, THE
London Symphony Orchestra
Gerhardt, Charles Con
Wizards and warriors / Splash / Great Whales (theme) / Hemingway play - Parisian sketch / Going home / Journey / Beastmaster suite / Music for strings / East of Eden (suite)
CD _____ VCD 47244
Varese Sarabande/Colosseum / Jan '89 / Pinnacle / Silva Screen.

Honegger, Arthur

HONEGGER: FILM MUSIC
Bratislava Symphony Orchestra
Crime et chatiment suite / Deserteur fragment / Farinet suite / Grand barrage image / Idee
CD _____ 8223466
Marco Polo / Jun '94 / Select.

HONEGGER: FILM SCORES
Slovak Philharmonic Choir/Bratislava Symphony Orchestra
Mayering / Regain / Demons d'Himalaya

CD _____ 8223467
Marco Polo / Jun '94 / Select.

Ibert, Jacques

IBERT - FILM MUSIC
Bratislava Symphony Orchestra
Macbeth suite / Golgotha suite / Don Quichotte / Chansons de Don Quichotte
CD _____ 8223287
Marco Polo / Mar '91 / Select.

Jacobs, Dick

THEMES FROM CLASSIC SCIENCE FICTION, FANTASY & HORROR FILMS
CD _____ VSD 5407
Varese Sarabande/Colosseum / Feb '93 / Pinnacle / Silva Screen.

Jarre, Maurice

DOCTOR ZHIVAGO
(The Classic Film Music Of Maurice Jarre)
City Of Prague Philharmonic Orchestra
Bateman, Paul Con
Dr. Zhivago / Passage to India / Ryan's daughter / Lawrence of Arabia / Ghost / Witness / Is Paris Burning / Night of the Generals / Man Who Would Be King / Villa Rides / Fatal Attraction / El Condor / Fixer / Jesus of Nazareth
CD _____ FILMCD 158
Silva Screen / May '95 / Conifer / Silva Screen.

LEAN BY JARRE
(Maurice Jarre's Musical Tribute To David Lean)
Royal Philharmonic Orchestra
Jarre, Maurice Con
Ryan's Daughter / Passage to India / Lawrence of Arabia / Dr. Zhivago
CD _____ 101312
Milan / Feb '94 / BMG / Silva Screen.

MAURICE JARRE AT ABBEY ROAD
Royal Philharmonic Orchestra
Jarre, Maurice Con
CD _____ 262321
Milan / Sep '93 / BMG / Silva Screen.

Jaubert, Maurice

MUSIC FROM THE FILMS OF FRANCOIS TRUFFAUT VOL 2
CD _____ CH 293
Milan / Jan '89 / BMG / Silva Screen.

Kander & Ebb

EVENING WITH KANDER & EBB, AN
Kander, John & Fred Ebb
Kander, John C
Ebb, Fred L
Sara Lee / Liza with a 'z' / My colouring book / Ring them bells / Life is / Cabaret / Quiet thing / Money money money / Maybe this time / Tomorrow morning / Please sing / All that jazz / Roxie / Yes
CD _____ DRG 5171
DRG / Jan '95 / New Note.

Kaper, Bronislaw

BRONISLAW KAPER PLAYS HIS FAMOUS FILM THEMES
Kaper, Bronislaw
Mutiny on the bounty / Lili / Glass slipper / Butterfield 8 / Auntie Mame / Chocolate soldier / Invitation / Brothers Karamazov / Green Dolphin Street / Swan / Lord Jim / San Francisco
CD _____ FE 8101
Facet / Feb '91 / Conifer.

FILM MUSIC OF BRONISLAW KAPER
Mutiny on the bounty / Lilli / Glass slipper / Butterfield 8 / Auntie Mame / Chocolate soldier / Invitation / Brother Karamazov / Green Dolphin Street / Swan / Lord Jim / San Francisco
CD _____ FA 8101
Facet / May '94 / Conifer.

Kazanecki, Waldemar

WALDEMAR KAZANECKI: FILM MUSIC
Polish Symphony Orchestra
Kazanecki, Waldemar Con
Night and days / House / Love will forgive you everything / By journey / Eva's madness / Boat to Sweden / Dark haired man / Gypsy Autumn / Harbours / Pacific 88
CD _____ OCD 603
Olympia / Aug '94 / Priory.

Kern, Jerome

ELIZABETH WELCH SINGS JEROME KERN
Welch, Elizabeth
CD _____ CDVIR 8310
TER / Jan '90 / Koch.

JEROME KERN COLLECTION, THE
Parkin, Eric
CD _____ SILVAD 3006
Silva Treasury / Apr '94 / Conifer / Silva Screen.

JEROME KERN SHOWCASE, A
Back to the heather / D'ye love me / Showboat / Who / Try to forget / Song is you / I

might grow fond of you / Cabaret girl / Look for the silver lining / Do I do wrong / Fine romance / Cat and the fiddle / I've loved every little star / Sunny / Reckless / Sweet Adeline / High, wide and handsome / Waltz / New love is old / Sally
CD _____ PAST CD 9767
Flapper / Nov '91 / Pinnacle.

JEROME KERN TREASURY
London Sinfonietta
McGlinn, John Con
CD _____ CDC 7548832
EMI Classics / Apr '94 / EMI.

KIRI SINGS KERN
Te Kanawa, Dame Kiri & London Sinfonietta
Tunick, Jonathan Con
CD _____ CDC 7545272
EMI Classics / Apr '93 / EMI.

MARNI NIXON SINGS CLASSIC KERN
Nixon, Marni
CD _____ RR 28
Reference Recordings / '90 / May Audio.

SILVER LININGS
(Songs Of Jerome Kern)
Morris, Joan & William Bolcom
CD _____ Z 6515
Arabesque / Nov '85 / New Note.

SONG IS...JEROME KERN, THE
She didn't say yes: Ambrose & His Orchestra / They didn't believe me: Ambrose & His Orchestra / Song is you: BBC Dance Orchestra / I'll be hard to handle: Coleman, Emil / Let's begin: Coleman, Emil / Make believe: Crosby, Bing & Paul Whiteman / I've told ev'ry little star: Ellis, Mary / Who. Hopkins, Claude / Look for the silver lining: Hopkins, Claude / Bill: Morgan, Helen / Can't help lovin' dat man: Morgan, Helen / Ol' man river: Robeson, Paul / Hand in hand: Stone, Lew & Al Bowlly / Sunny: Ipana Troubadours / Smoke gets in your eyes: Whiteman, Paul & Rhythm Boys / Something had to happen: Whiteman, Paul & Rhythm Boys
CD _____ CDAJA 5036
Living Era / Oct '95 / Koch.

SONGS OF JEROME KERN
CD _____ MCCD 187
Music Club / Nov '94 / Disc / THE / CM.

SURE THING
(The Jerome Kern Songbook)
Philips / Dec '94 / PolyGram.
CD _____ 4421292

TRIBUTE TO JEROME KERN, A
2CD _____ CDDL 1290
EMI / Jun '95 / EMI.

YESTERDAYS
(The Unforgettable Music Of Jerome Kern)
Pick yourself up: Astaire, Fred / Never gonna dance: Astaire, Fred / Look for the silver lining: Matthews, Jessie / Song is you: BBC Dance Orchestra / Smoke gets in your eyes: Robins, Phyllis / Last time I saw Paris: Shelton, Anne / I've told ev'ry little star: Ellis, Mary / She didn't say yes: Wood, Peggy / Make believe: Goodman, Benny / Yesterdays: Holiday, Billie / Why was I born: Holiday, Billie / Whose baby are you: Gershwin, George / Why do I love you: Beiderbecke, Bix / Can't help lovin' dat man: Morgan, Helen / I might grow fond of you: Randolph, Elsie / It'll be hard to handle: Coleman, Emil / They didn't believe me: Stone, Lew & Al Bowlly / Something had to happen: Whiteman, Paul & Rhythm Boys / Ol' man river: Robeson, Paul / Folks who live on the hill: Crosby, Bing
CD _____ AVC 519
Avid / Apr '95 / Avid/BMG / Koch.

Kilar, Wojciech

FILM MUSIC
Polish Symphony Orchestra
Kilar, Wojciech Con
Land of promise / Balance / Hypothesis / Polaniecki family / Silence / Taste of black earth / Pearl in the crown / Salto / Jealousy and medicine / Leper
CD _____ OCD 602
Olympia / Aug '94 / Priory.

King, Denis

LOVEJOY AND OTHER TV THEMES
King, Denis Con
Lovejoy / We'll meet again / Dick Turpin / All at No. 20 / Wish me luck as you wave me goodbye / Within these walls / Hannay / Moon and Son / Day to remember / Running wild / Between the wars / Galloping home / About face
CD _____ CDWM 104
Westmoor / '91 / Target/BMG.

Knopfler, Mark

SCREENPLAYING
Knopfler, Mark
Irish boy / Irish love / Father and son / Potato picking / Long road / Love idea / Victims / Finale (Last Exit to Brooklyn) / Once upon a time ..... storybook love / Morning ride / Friends song / Guide my sword / Happy ending / Wild theme / Boomtown / Mist covered mountains / Smooching / Going home (theme from Local Hero)

CD _____ 518327-2
Vertigo / Nov '93 / PolyGram.

Korngold, Erich

ELIZABETH AND ESSEX
(The Classic Film Scores Of Erich Wolfgang Korngold)
National Philharmonic Orchestra
Gerhardt, Charles *Con*
Private Lives of Elizabeth and Essex / Prince and the Pauper / Sea Wolf / Deception / Of Human Bondage / Anthony Adverse / Another Dawn
CD _____ GD 80185
RCA Victor / Jun '91 / BMG.

Korzynski, Andrzej

FILM MUSIC
Korzynski, Andrzej *Con*
Man of iron / Man of marble / Birchwood / Hunting flies
CD _____ OCD 601
Olympia / Aug '94 / Priory.

Kurylewicz, Andrzej

ANDRZEJ KURYLEWICZ: FILM MUSIC
Warsaw National Philharmonic/Lodz Philharmonic Orchestras
Kurylewicz, Andrzej *Con*
Polish roads / On the Niemen river / Doll / Pan Tudeusz
CD _____ OCD 605
Olympia / Aug '94 / Priory.

Lai, Francis

FILM MUSIC OF FRANCIS LAI
CD _____ CDCIA 5034
Cinevox / Sep '92 / Conifer / Silva Screen.

INEDITS
(Rare Film Themes)
CD _____ MANTRA 057
Silva Screen / Sep '93 / Conifer / Silva Screen.

Lane, Burton

BURTON LANE SONGBOOK, THE
Feinstein, Michael
CD _____ 7559792832
Elektra Nonesuch / Aug '94 / Warner Music.

Leiber & Stoller

SONGS OF LEIBER & STOLLER
CD _____ NEBCD 656
Sequel / Jun '93 / BMG.

Lerner & Lowe

LERNER & LOEWE SONGBOOK
Cincinnati Pops Orchestra
Loewe, Frederick *C*
CD _____ CD 80375
Telarc / Jan '94 / Conifer / ADA.

SPOTLIGHT ON LERNER & LOEWE
I've grown accustomed to her face / Gigi / Wouldn't it be lovely / Almost like being in love / I talk to the trees / They call the wind Maria / On the street where you live / Waltz at Maxim's / Get me to the church on time / If ever I would leave you / Rain in Spain / Thank heaven for little girls
CD _____ HADCD 138
Javelin / Feb '94 / THE / Henry Hadaway Organisation.

Lerner, Alan Jay

EVENING WITH ALAN JAY LERNER, AN
Lerner, Alan Jay *L*
CD _____ OCRCD 12
First Night / Jun '93 / Pinnacle.

EVENING WITH ALAN JAY LERNER, AN
Lerner, Alan Jay & Bobbi Baird/J.T. Cromwell/Barbara Williams
Lerner, Alan Jay *L*
How to handle a woman / Why can't a woman / I talk to the trees / Wouldn't it be lovely / Oh come to the ball / On the street where you live / Come back to me / What did I have that I don't have / I'm glad I'm not young anymore / I loved you in silence / Gigi / Camelot / On a clear day / I've grown accustomed to her face
CD _____ DRG 5175
DRG / Jan '95 / New Note.

Lloyd Webber, Andrew

ANDREW LLOYD WEBBER ALBUM, THE
Beechman, Laurie
CD _____ VSD 5583
Varese Sarabande/Colosseum / Aug '95 / Pinnacle / Silva Screen.

ANDREW LLOYD WEBBER COLLECTION, THE
Starlight express: *Wayne, Carl* / Unexpected song: *Jones, Paul* / Macavity: *Lawrence, Stephanie* / Memory: *Lawrence, Stephanie* / Gus the theatre cat: *Jones, Paul* / Pumping iron: *Conrad, Jess* / Tell me on a Sunday: *Wayne, Carl* / I don't know how to love him: *Hendley, Fiona* / Any dream will do: *Conrad, Jess* / Love changes everything: *Lawrence, Stephanie* / All I ask of you: *Lawrence, Stephanie* / Oh what a cir-

cus: *Conrad, Jess* / Wishing you were somehow here again: *Lawrence, Stephanie*
CD _____ PWKS 4065
Carlton Home Entertainment / Aug '91 / Carlton Home Entertainment.

ANDREW LLOYD WEBBER SONGBOOK, THE
CD _____ PWKS 4046
Carlton Home Entertainment / Jan '95 / Carlton Home Entertainment.

ANDREW LLOYD WEBBER'S CLASSIC MUSICALS
(Phantom Of The Opera/Jesus Christ Superstar)
Royal Philharmonic Pops Orchestra
Gemignani, Paul *Con*
Think of me (prelude)/ Phantom of the opera / Think of me / Angel of music / Phantom (reprise) / Music of the night / Masquerade / Think of me (reprise) / All I ask of you / Wishing you were somehow here again / Overture / Heaven on their minds / What's the buzz / Everything's alright / I don't know how to love him / Damned for all time/Blood money / Last supper / Pilate and Herod / Trial before Pilate
CD _____ PWKS 506
Carlton Home Entertainment / Aug '88 / Carlton Home Entertainment.

ANDREW LLOYD WEBBER'S GREATEST HITS
CD _____ CDTEZ 7001
TER / Jan '95 / Koch.

BEST OF ANDREW LLOYD WEBBER
Journey of a lifetime / Last man in my life / Rolling stock / Another suitcase in another hall / Close every door / Everything's alright / Gethsemane / There is more to love / Old deuteronomy / High flying adored / Don't cry for me Argentina / First man you remember / Pie jesu / Starlight express / Unexpected song / Memory / Macavity / Gus the theatre cat / Pumping iron / Tell me on a Sunday / I don't how to love him / Any dream will do / Love changes everything / All I ask of you / Oh what a circus / Wishing you were here again / Superstar / Chanson d'enfance / Mr. Mistoffelees / One more angel in heaven / Anything but lonely / Half a moment / Take that look off your face / On this night of a thousand stars / Seeing is believing / Think of me / Music of the night / Phantom of the opera
2CD _____ BOXCD 39T
Carlton Home Entertainment / Oct '94 / Carlton Home Entertainment.

CLASSIC ANDREW LLOYD WEBBER
West End Theatre Orchestra & Chorus
Superstar / Memory / Starlight Express / Don't cry for me Argentina / Take that look off your face / Journey of a lifetime / Any dream will do / Close every door / I don't know how to love him / Tell me on a Sunday / Love changes everything / Music of the night / All I ask of you
CD _____ CDMFP 6106
Music For Pleasure / Nov '93 / EMI.

CLASSIC SONGS
(Featuring Lesley Garrett)
Royal Philharmonic Concert Orchestra
Bateman, Paul *Con*
CD _____ SONGCD 909
Silva Classics / Sep '93 / Conifer / Silva Screen.

ESSENTIALS
Memory: *Friedman, Maria* / Any dream will do: *Barrowman, John* / Think of me: *Moore, Claire & John Barrowman* / Don't cry for me Argentina: *Friedman, Maria* / There's me: *Carter, Clive* / All I ask of you: *Moore, Claire & John Barrowman* / Another suitcase in another hall: *Renihan, Grania* / Mr. Mistoffelees: *Carter, Clive* / Tell me on a Sunday: *Robertson, Liz* / High flying adored: *Barrowman, John & Maria Friedman* / I don't know how to love him: *Friedman, Maria* / Only you: *Renihan, Grania* / Music of the night: *Dietrich, John* / Seeing is believing: *Barrowman, John & Janis Kelly* / Close every door: *Carter, Clive* / Wishing you were somehow here again: *Moore, Claire* / Love changes everything: *Barrowman, John*
CD _____ 322634
Koch / Mar '92 / Koch.

GREATEST HITS
Lloyd Webber, Andrew
Perfect year / Music of the night / Memory / Friends for life / Starlight express / Jesus Christ Superstar / Don't cry for me Argentina / Love changes everything / Any dream will do / Take that look off your face / I don't know how to love him / Only he (has the power to move me) / As if we never said goodbye / Another suitcase in another hall / All I ask of you / Pie jesu / Magical Mr. Mistoffelees
CD _____ 11956
Music / Dec '95 / Target/BMG.

GREATEST SONGS, THE
Bateman, Paul *Con*
Superstar / I don't know how to love him / Everything's alright / Close every door / High flying adored / Another suitcase in another hall / Oh what a circus / Don't cry for me Argentina / Tell me on a Sunday / Take that look off your face / Unexpected song / Macavity / Mystery cat / Memory / Starlight express / Next time you fall in love / Only

you / Pie Jesu / Phantom of the opera / Wishing you were here / Music of me / Angel of music / Point of no return / All I ask of you / Seeing is believing / Love changes everything / Sunset boulevard / Perfect year / With one look / Too much in love to care / As if we never say goodbye
2CD _____ SONGCD 911
Silva Classics / Apr '95 / Conifer / Silva Screen.

HIT SONGS OF ANDREW LLOYD WEBBER, THE
Music of the night / I don't know how to love him / Any dream will do / Don't cry for me Argentina / Wishing you were somehow here again / Mr. Mistoffelees / Another suitcase in another hall / Memory / Only you / Take that look off your face / Love changes everything / Superstar
CD _____ SHOWCD 015
Showtime / Feb '95 / Disc / THE.

LOVE SONGS
(& Lesley Garrett & Dave Willetts)
Royal Philharmonic Pops Orchestra
Bateman, Paul *Con*
CD _____ SONGCD 908
Silva Classics / Jan '93 / Conifer / Silva Screen.

MAGIC OF ANDREW LLOYD WEBBER, THE
CD _____ PWKS 4110
Carlton Home Entertainment / Jan '95 / Carlton Home Entertainment.

MUSIC OF ANDREW LLOYD WEBBER
Power Pack Orchestra
Jesus Christ superstar / Phantom of the opera / Tell me on a Sunday / Starlight express / Mr. Mistoffelees / Music of the night / Take that look off your face / Another suitcase in another hall / I don't know how to love him / Any dream will do / Don't cry for me Argentina / Old Deuteronomy / All I ask of you / Pumping iron (CD only) / King Herod's song (CD only) / One more angel in heaven (CD only) / Love changes everything (CD only)
CD _____ CDMFP 6065
Music For Pleasure / Aug '89 / EMI.

MUSIC OF ANDREW LLOYD WEBBER
Royal Philharmonic Orchestra
Reed, Michael *Con*
Music of the night / Memory / Jesus Christ superstar / Take that look off your face / Don't cry for me Argentina / All I ask of you
CD _____ LLOYDCD 1
First Night / Sep '88 / Pinnacle.

MUSIC OF ANDREW LLOYD WEBBER
2CD _____ TFP 030
Tring / Nov '92 / Tring / Prism.

MUSICAL THEATRE GREATS
CD _____ CDVIR 8320
TER / Aug '95 / Koch.

OVATION
(The Best Of Andrew Lloyd Webber)
Don't cry for me Argentina: *Dickson, Barbara* / Another suitcase in another hall: *Dickson, Barbara* / I don't know how to love him: *Savage: Storm, Rebecca* / King Herod's song / One more angel in heaven / Pumping iron / Starlight express / Pie Jesu: *New Scottish Concert Choir* / Old deuteronomy: *Quilley, Denis* / Introduction: variations
CD _____ CLACD 298
Castle / '92 / BMG.

OVATION
(A Musical Tribute To Andrew Lloyd Webber)
Take that look off your face / Phantom of the opera / Don't cry for me Argentina / Close every door / Only he has the power to move me / Jesus Christ superstar / Sunset boulevard / Mr. Mistoffelees / Music of the night / Memory / All I ask of you / I don't know how to love him / Pie Jesu / Love changes everything / Another suitcase in another hall / Tell me on a Sunday / Joseph's coat / Starlight express
CD _____ ECD 3062
K-Tel / Jan '95 / K-Tel.

PERFORMS ANDREW LLOYD WEBBER
Crawford, Michael
CD _____ TCD 2544
Telstar / Nov '91 / BMG.

PERFORMS RICE AND LLOYD WEBBER
London Symphony Orchestra
CD _____ VISCD 4
Vision / Oct '94 / Pinnacle.

PREMIERE COLLECTION
(Best Of Andrew Lloyd Webber)
Phantom of the opera: *Harley, Steve & Sarah Brightman* / Take that look off your face / Mr. Mistoffelees / All I ask of you: *Richard, Cliff & Sarah Brightman* / Don't cry for me Argentina: *Covington, Julie* / Mr. Mistoffelees: *Nicholas, Paul* / Variations 1-4: *LLoyd Webber, Julian* / Superstar: *Head, Murray* / Memory: *Paige, Elaine* / Starlight express: *Shell, Ray* / Tell me on a Sunday: *Webb, Marti* / Music of the night: *Crawford, Michael* / Another suitcase in another hall: *Dickson, Barbara* / I don't know how to love him: *Elliman, Yvonne* / Pie Jesu: *Brightman, Sarah & Paul Miles Kingston*

CD _____ 8372822
Really Useful / Oct '88 / PolyGram.

PREMIERE COLLECTION ENCORE
Lloyd Webber, Andrew
CD _____ 5173662
Really Useful / Nov '92 / PolyGram.

SONGS OF ANDREW LLOYD WEBBER
Lloyd Webber, Andrew
CD _____ SHOWCD 915
Showtime / Mar '95 / Disc / THE.

SONGS OF ANDREW LLOYD WEBBER, THE
CD _____ MCCD 210
MCI / Jul '95 / Disc / THE.

SYMPHONIC LLOYD WEBBER, THE
(Phantom Of The Opera/Cats/Evita/Aspects Of Love)
Royal Philharmonic Orchestra
Stratta, Ettore *Con*
CD _____ 9031737422
Teldec Classics / Jan '95 / Warner Music.

VARIATIONS
Lloyd Webber, Andrew
CD _____ MCLD 19126
MCA / Apr '92 / BMG.

VERY BEST OF ANDREW LLOYD WEBBER, THE
Lloyd Webber, Andrew
Memory: *Paige, Elaine* / Music of the night: *Crawford, Michael* / Take that look off your face: *Webb, Marti* / Any dream will do: *Donovan, Jason* / Don't cry for me Argentina: *Brightman, Sarah* / Love changes everything: *Ball, Michael* / Perfect year: *Carroll, Dina* / Phantom of the opera: *Harley, Steve* / Oh what a circus: *Essex, David* / Tell me on a Sunday: *Webb, Marti* / Close every door: *Schofield, Philip* / With one look: *Streisand, Barbra* / All I ask of you: *Richard, Cliff & Sarah Brightman* / Sunset Boulevard: *Ball, Michael* / As if we never said goodbye: *Close, Glenn* / Next time you fall in love: *Rice, Reva & Greg Ellis* / Amigos Para Siempra: *Carreras, Jose & Sarah Brightman*
CD _____ 523860-2
Really Useful / Oct '94 / PolyGram.

Loesser, Frank

EVENING WITH FRANK LOESSER, AN
(Performing Songs From His Great Shows)
Loesser, Frank
Fugue from tinhorns / I'll know / Luck be a lady / I've never been in love before / Sit down you're rockin' the boat / Sue me / Traveling light / Adelaide / Happy to keep his dinner warm / Organization man / Secretary is not a toy / Been a long day / Grand old Ivy / Paris original / Rosemary / Love from a heart of gold / I believe in you / Ooh my feet / Love letter / Wanting to be wanted / House and garden
CD _____ DRGCD 5169
DRG / Jan '95 / New Note.

LOESSER BY LOESSER
(A Salute To Frank Loesser)
Loesser, Jo Sullivan & Emily/Don Stephenson
Romoff, Colin *Con*
CD _____ DRGCD 5170
DRG / Jan '95 / New Note.

MacKeben, Theo

ORIGINAL FILM SCORES
CD _____ 10705
Total / Oct '95 / Total/BMG.

Mancini, Henry

IN THE PINK
Mancini, Henry & His Orchestra
Mancini, Henry & Others *C*
Pink Panther theme / Moon river / Days of wine and roses / Baby elephant walk / Hatari (theme) / Charade / Thorn Birds (theme) / Blue satin / Two for the road / Mr. Lucky / Molly Maguires (theme) / Moment to moment / As time goes by / Shot in the dark / Misty / Love Story (theme) / Pennywhistle jig / Everything I do (I do it for you) / Moonlight sonata / Tender is the night / Mommie Dearest (theme) / Raindrops keep falling on my head / Crazy world / Mona Lisa / Peter Gunn / Unchained melody / Summer knows / Experiment in terror / Windmills of your mind / Till there was you / Speedy Gonzales (theme) / Dream a little dream of me / Lonesome / Pie in the face polka / Love is a many splendored thing / By the time I get to Phoenix / Dear heart / Charade (opening titles) / Shadow of your smile / One for my baby / Breakfast at Tiffany's / That old black magic / Evergreen / Midnight cowboy
2CD _____ 74321242832
RCA Victor / Nov '95 / BMG.

PINK PANTHER, MOON RIVER, BABY ELEPHANT WALK AND OTHER HITS
Mancini, Henry & His Orchestra
Pink Panther / Royal blue / Champagne and quail / Lonely princess / It had'' better be tonight / Charade (with chorus) / Megeve / Latin snowfall / Bateau mouche / Bistro / Hatari (theme) / Baby elephant walk / Night side / Your father's feathers / Sounds of Hatari / Breakfast at Tiffany's / Something for

the cat / Sally's tomato / Holly / Latin go-
lightly / Moon river
CD _____ RD 85938
RCA Victor / Feb '92 / BMG.

Martin & Blane

SING MARTIN & BLANE
Martin, Hugh & Ralph Blane
Martin, Hugh & Ralph Blane *C*
Wish I may, wish I might / Every time /
That's how I love the blues / Buckle down
winsocki / Have yourself a merry little christ-
mas / Love / Trolley song / Boy next door /
Pass that peace pipe / Connecticut / Oc-
casional man / Venezia
CD _____ DRGCD 5168
DRG / Apr '94 / New Note.

Martin, Hugh

HUGH MARTIN SONGBOOK, THE
Feinstein, Michael
CD _____ 7559793142
Elektra Nonesuch / Jan '95 / Warner Music.

Mercer, Johnny

EVENING WITH JOHNNY MERCER, AN
Mercer, Johnny & Margaret Whiting/Robert
Sands
I'm old fashioned / And the angels sing /
Out of this world / Glow worm / Hit the road
to dreamland / Lazy bones / Jeepers creep-
ers / Satin doll / That old black magic /
Fools rush in / Come rain or come shine /
Hooray for Hollywood / Laura / Skylark / Au-
tumn leaves / Moon river / Days of wine and
roses
CD _____ DRG 5176
DRG / Jan '95 / New Note.

PORTRAIT OF JOHNNY MERCER, A
Syms, Sylvia
CD _____ DRG 91433
DRG / Feb '95 / New Note.

**STARS SALUTE JOHNNY MERCER,
THE**
95CD _____ CDCD 1238
Charly / Jun '95 / Charly / THE / Cadillac.

Moross, Jerome

VALLEY OF GWANGI, THE
(Film Scores Of Jerome Moross)
City Of Prague Philharmonic Orchestra
Adventures of Huckleberry Finn / Sharkfigh-
ters / Mountain Road / Rachel Rachel / War
lord / Valley of the Gwangi / Five finger ex-
ercise / Wagon train
CD _____ FILMCD 161
Silva Screen / Sep '95 / Conifer / Silva
Screen.

Morricone, Ennio

BEST OF ENNIO MORRICONE
For a few dollars more / Fistful of dollars /
Sacco and Vanzetti / Moses the lawgiver /
Metello / God with us / Once upon a time
in the west / 1900 / Death rides a horse /
Life's tough, isn't it / Cirbinibin / Scetate
CD _____ 74321289842
RCA / Aug '95 / BMG.

**BIG GUNDOWN, THE
(The Music Of Ennio Morricone)**
Zorn, John
CD _____ 7559791392
Elektra Nonesuch / Jan '95 / Warner Music.

CINEMA ITALIANO
(Music Of Ennio Morricone/Nino Rota)
Mancini Pops Orchestra
Morricone, Ennio/Nino Rota *C*
Mancini, Henry *Con*
Cinema Paradiso / Boccaccio 70 / Once
Upon a Time in the West / Once Upon a
Time in America / Godfather
CD _____ RD 60706
RCA Victor / Apr '91 / BMG.

CINEMA PARADISO
(The Classic Ennio Morricone)
City Of Prague Philharmonic Orchestra
Motzing, William/Derek Wadsworth *Con*
Cinema Paradiso / Mission (Gabriel's oboe/
Theme/On earth as it is in heaven) / Good,
The Bad And The Ugly (Theme/Ecstasy of
gold) / Once Upon A Time In America (De-
borah's theme) / Two Mules For Sister Sara
/ Marco Polo / Once Upon A Time In The
West (Suite) / 1900 (Romanze) / In The Line
Of Fire: Ayres, Mark / Untouchables (Death
theme) / Red Sonja / Casualties Of War (El-
egy for Brown) / Fistful Of Dollars / For A
Few Dollars More / Hamlet / Fistful Of Dy-
namite (Duck You Sucker) / Thing: Caine,
Daniel
CD _____ FILMCD 148
Silva Screen / Jan '94 / Conifer / Silva
Screen.

ENNIO MORRICONE ANTHOLOGY, AN
La cage aux folles III / Professional / This
kind of love / Serpent / Without apparent
motive / What am I doing in the middle of
this revolution
CD _____ DRGCD 32908
DRG / Sep '95 / New Note.

ENNIO MORRICONE LIVE IN CONCERT
Morricone, Ennio/Nino Rota *C*
CD _____ T 8710

Silva Screen / Jan '89 / Conifer / Silva
Screen.

**ENNIO MORRICONE WESTERN
QUINTET, AN**
Fistful of dynamite / My name is nobody /
Fist goes west / Blood and guns /
Companeros
CD _____ DRGCD 32907
DRG / Aug '95 / New Note.

FILM FAVOURITES
CD _____ 295714
Ariola / Oct '94 / BMG.

FILM HITS
Once upon a time in the West / For a few
dollars more / Moses theme / Bye bye Colonel / Fistful of dollars / Gun for Ringo / Ballad of Sacco and Vanzetti / Here's to you /
Vice of killing / Paying off scores: Morricone, Ennio / Adventurer / What have you
done to Solange / Violent city / Mertelli
CD _____ ND 70091
RCA / May '90 / BMG.

**FILM MUSIC OF ENNIO MORRICONE,
THE**
Good, the bad and the ugly / Sicilian clan
/ Chi mai / Man with the harmonica / La
califfa / Gabriel's oboe / Fistful of dynamite
/ Once upon a time in the west / Once upon
a time in America / Mission / Come Mad-
diena / Moses theme / Falls / My name is
nobody / Le vent, le cri: Morricone, Ennio
/ Virgin VIP / Sep '93 / Carlton Home Enter-
tainment / THE / EMI.
CD _____ CDVIP 123

GREATEST FILM THEMES
CD _____ 402222
Musidisc / Aug '90 / Vital / Harmonia
Mundi / ADA / Cadillac / Discovery.

GREATEST MOVIE THEMES
CD _____ 139220
Accord / '86 / Discovery / Harmonia
Mundi / Cadillac.

MUSIC OF ENNIO MORRICONE, THE
London Studio Orchestra
North, Nicky *Con*
For A Few Dollars More / Man with the har-
monica / Cockeye's song / Good, The Bad
and The Ugly / Once Upon A Time in the
West / Once Upon A Time in America (main
theme) / Fl mercenario / My Name is No-
body / It etait une fois la revolution / Chi mai
/ Here's to you / Exorcist II / La libertad /
Fistful of Dollars (1st/2nd themes) / Square
dance / Fistful of Dynamite / Apres
l'explosion
CD _____ CD 3509
Cameo / Nov '95 / Target/BMG.

SPAGHETTI WESTERN
Gun for Ringo / Grotesque suspense / Heroic Mexico / Wait / Slaughter / Angel face
/ At times life is very hard, isn't that fate /
McGregor's march / Santa Fe express /
Gringo like me / Lonesome Billy / Indians /
Young girl and the sheriff / Bullets don't ar-
gue / Woman for the McGregors / Death
rides a horse / Mystic and severe / Guitar
and nocturne / Anger and sorrow / We'll be
back, isn't that fate / Mouth to mouth / Gal-
lop / Return of Ringo / Disguise / Fuentes /
Funeral / Wedding and the revenge / Peace
comes in Mimbres
CD _____ 74321264952
RCA / May '95 / BMG.

**VERY BEST OF ENNIO MORRICONE,
THE**
8B _____ 323122
Koch / Feb '94 / Koch.

Newman, Alfred

**CAPTAIN FROM CASTILE
(Classic Film Scores Of Alfred Newman)**
National Philharmonic Orchestra
Gerhardt, Charles *Con*
Captain from Castile (Pedro and Catana/
Conquest) / How to Marry a Millionaire (Ex-
tension and Street scene) / Wuthering
Heights (Cathy's theme) / Down to the Sea
in Ships (Hornpipe) / Bravados (Main title) /
Anastasia (Main title) / Best of Everything
(London calling) / Airport (Main title) / Song
of Bernadette (Prelude/The vision) / Robe
(Main title/Elegy/Caligula's march) / Map of
Jerusalem
CD _____ GD 80184
RCA Victor / Oct '90 / BMG.

Nicastro, Michelle

REEL IMAGINATION
CD _____ VSD 5537
Varese Sarabande/Colosseum / Jun '95 /
Pinnacle / Silva Screen.

North, Alex

CINERAMA SOUTH SEAS ADVENTURE
CD _____ LXCD 4
Silva Screen / Jan '92 / Conifer / Silva
Screen.

FILM MUSIC OF ALEX NORTH
CD _____ 14452
Silva Screen / Feb '90 / Conifer / Silva
Screen.

**UNCHAINED MELODIES
(The Film Music Of Alex North)**
CD _____ BCD 3010
Bay Cities / Sep '92 / Silva Screen.

Novello, Ivor

**IVOR NOVELLO - CENTENARY
CELEBRATION**
CD _____ GEMMCD 9062
Pearl / Nov '93 / Harmonia Mundi.

Porter, Cole

**CENTENARY TRIBUTE TO COLE
PORTER, A**
Let's do it / What is this thing called love /
You do something to me / You've got that
thing / Miss Otis regrets / My heart belongs
to Daddy
CD _____ DOLD 15
Old Bean / Apr '91 / Jazz Music / Wellard.

**CENTENARY TRIBUTE TO COLE
PORTER, THE**
You're the top / Anything goes / Solomon /
Jubilee selections / What is this thing called
love / My heart belongs to Daddy / Swingin'
the jinx away / Goodbye, little dream, goodbye / Gypsy in me / I've got you under my
skin / Let's do it (Let's fall in love) / Something for the boys selections / There'll always be a lady fair / Nymph errant / Thank
you so much / Mrs. Lowsborough-Goodby
/ All through the night / Night and day / Rap
tap on wood / How could we be so wrong
/ Begin the beguine
CD _____ PASTCD 9751
Flapper / Feb '91 / Pinnacle.

CENTENNIAL GALA CONCERT
CD _____ 9031752712
Teldec Classics / Jan '95 / Warner Music.

COLE PORTER COLLECTION, A
CD _____ JCD 632
Jass / Jan '92 / CM / Jazz Music / ADA /
Cadillac / Direct.

GEORGE FEYER PLAYS COLE PORTER
Feyer, George
Feyer, George *Con*
Anything goes / Leave it to me / Miss Otis
regrets / Jubilee / Red hot and blue / Fifty
million Frenchman / Gay divorce / Rosalie /
Born to dance / New Yorkers / Can can /
Let's face it / Don't fence me in / Broadway
medley / Mexican hayride / Kiss me Kate /
Where oh where / Seven lively arts / Silk
stockings / High society / From this mo-
ment on
CD _____ 08601471
Vanguard Classics / Jun '91 / Complete/
Pinnacle.

KIRI SINGS PORTER
Te Kanawa, Dame Kiri & New World Phil-
harmonic Orchestra
Matz, Peter *Con*
CD _____ CDC 5550502
EMI Classics / Apr '93 / EMI.

LOVE FOR SALE
Moonlight Serenaders
CD _____ PWKM 4060
Carlton Home Entertainment / Feb '96 /
Carlton Home Entertainment.

**NIGHT AND DAY
(Sings Cole Porter)**
Hampson, Thomas & Ambrosian Chorus/
London Symphony Orchestra
McGlinn, John *Con*
CD _____ CDC 7542032
EMI Classics / Apr '93 / EMI.

OVERTURES
London Sinfonietta
McGlinn, John *Con*
CD _____ CDC 7543002
EMI Classics / Apr '93 / EMI.

**RED HOT AND BLUE
(The Songs Of Cole Porter)**
2CD _____ CCD 1799
Chrysalis / Oct '90 / EMI.

SINGS THE COLE PORTER SONGBOOK
Wilson, Julie
Most gentlemen don't like love / My heart
belongs to Daddy / Easy to love / All of you
/ You'd be so nice to come home to / I
Experiment / Dream dancing / Queen of
Terre Haute / You've got that thing
CD _____ DRG 5208
DRG / Jan '95 / New Note.

SONG IS...COLE PORTER, THE
All through the night: Ambrose & His Orchestra / Lady Fair: Anything Goes Foursome / Night and day: Astaire, Fred / I'm in
love again: Bernie, Ben / How could we be
wrong: Bowlly, Al / Miss Otis regrets: Byng,
Douglas / Let's do it: Crosby, Bing / Just
one of those things: Himber, Richard / Love
for sale: Holman, Libby / They all fall in love:
Hylton, Jack / Experiment: Lawrence, Gertrude / I get a kick out of you: Merman,
Ethel / Anything goes: Porter, Cole / Be like
the bluebird: Porter, Cole / I'm a gigolo:
Porter, Cole / Thank you so much, Mrs.
Lowsborough-Goodby: Porter, Cole /
You're the top: Porter, Cole / What is this
thing called love: Reisman, Leo
CD _____ CDAJA 5044
Living Era / Oct '95 / Koch.

SONGS OF COLE PORTER
CD _____ MCCD 175
MCI / Sep '94 / Disc / THE.

SPOTLIGHT ON COLE PORTER
I love Paris / What is this thing called love /
Begin the beguine / Can can / My heart be-
longs to daddy / Night and day / So in love
/ C'est magnifique / From this moment on /
It's alright with me / Wunderbar / True love
CD _____ HADCD 136
Javelin / Feb '94 / THE / Henry Hadaway
Organisation.

TRIBUTE TO COLE PORTER, A
2CD _____ CDDL 1203
Music For Pleasure / Jun '91 / EMI.

**YOU'RE THE TOPS
(The Songs Of Cole Porter)**
Begin the beguine: Shaw, Artie & His Or-
chestra / My heart belongs to Daddy: Hu-
mes, Helen / Let's do it: Crosby, Bing / In
the still of the night: Reinhardt, Django /
Love for sale: Holman, Libby / What is this
thing called love: Johnson, James P. /
Experiment: Bowlly, Al / Easy to love: Holi-
day, Billie / I get a kick out of you: BBC
Dance Orchestra / Miss Otis regrets: Mills
Brothers / Night and day: Dorsey, Tommy
Orchestra / Anything goes: Stone, Lew &
His Band / Vous faites partie de moi: Baker,
Josephine / Soloman: Welch, Elizabeth /
Physician: Lawrence, Gertrude / Just one of
those things: Himber, Richard / I'm a gigolo:
Porter, Cole / All through the night: Am-
brose & His Orchestra / It's D'Lovely: Day,
Frances / You're the top: Aubert, Jeanne &
Jack Whiting / Night and day (2): Adams,
Fred
CD _____ AVC 518
Avid / Apr '95 / Avid/BMG / Koch.

**YOU'RE THE TOPS
(Music & Songs Of Cole Porter)**
Happy Days / Mar '92 / Conifer.
CD _____ CDHD 181

Post, Mike

INVENTIONS FROM THE BLUE LINE
Post, Mike
NYPD Blue (theme) / One five open for busi-
ness / Blue line / Rough wolf / Song for
Rudy / Has the heart of a lion / Law and
order / Silk stockings / Theme from Rene-
gade / Cop files
CD _____ AGCD 450
American Gramophone / May '94 / New
Note.

**TELEVISION MUSIC OF MIKE POST &
PETE CARPENTER, THE**
Post, Mike & Pete Carpenter *C*
Caine, Daniel *Con*
Doogie Howser M.D. / L.A. Law / A-Team /
Quantum Leap / Hunter / Magnum P.I. / Hill
Street Blues / Riptide / Hooperman / Wise-
eguy / Rockford Files / Tales of the Gold
Monkey / Studio 5B / Hardcastle and Mc-
Cormick / Sonny Spoon / White Shadow
CD _____ TVPMCD 403
Primetime / '92 / Silva Screen.

Rice, Tim

**I KNOW THEM SO WELL
(The Best Of Tim Rice)**
Rice, Tim *L*
Golden boy: Mercury, Freddie & Montserrat
Caballe / Oh what a circus: Essex, David / I
know him so well: Elaine & Barbara
Dickson / Don't cry for me Argentina: Covington, Julie / Gethsemane's alright: Dillman,
Yvonne & Ian Gillan / I don't know how to
love him: Elliman, Yvonne / Ziggy: Dion, Celine / All time high: Coolidge, Rita / World is
stone: Lauper, Cyndi / One night in Bang-
kok: Head, Murray / Another suitcase in an-
other hall: Dickson, Barbara / Any dream will
do: Donovan, Jason / Second time: Paige,
Elaine / Least of my troubles: Nicholas, Paul
/ Close every door: Schofield, Philip / Song
the play: Daltrey, Dave / Winter's tale: Essex, David / Legal boys: John, Elton / Only
the very best: Kingsberry, Peter / Superstar:
Head, Murray / Whole new world: Bryson,
Peabo
CD _____ 516650-2
PolyGram TV / Mar '94 / PolyGram.

Rodgers & Hammerstein

COMPLETE OVERTURES
Hollywood Bowl Symphony Orchestra
Rodgers, Richard *C*
Hammerstein II, Oscar *L*
Mauceri, John *Con*
CD _____ 4341272
Philips / Sep '92 / PolyGram.

**GREATEST HITS: RODGERS &
HAMMERSTEIN**
Rodgers, Richard *C*
Hammerstein II, Oscar *L*
CD _____ U 4039
Spectrum/Karussell / Jun '88 / PolyGram /
THE.

**RODGERS & HAMMERSTEIN
SONGBOOK, THE**
Rodgers, Richard *C*
Hammerstein II, Oscar *L*
CD _____ SK 53331
Sony Classical / Dec '93 / Sony.

SPOTLIGHT ON RODGERS AND HAMMERSTEIN
Rodgers, Richard C
Hammerstein II, Oscar L
Hello, young lovers / Oh what a beautiful morning / Carousel waltz / Climb every mountain / It might as well be spring / Oklahoma / If I loved you / Bali Ha'i / Shall we dance / You'll never walk alone / Sound of music
CD _____ HADCD 135
Javelin / Feb '94 / THE / Henry Hadaway Organisation.

Rodgers & Hart

HITS OF RODGERS & HART, THE
Rodgers, Richard C
Hart, Lorenz L
There's a small hotel / Little girl blue / My romance / On your toes / You took advantage of me / My heart stood still / This can't be love / My man is on the make / Atlantic blues / Where's that rainbow / Isn't it romantic / It never entered my mind / Where or when / Sing for your supper / Blue moon a tree in the park / With a song in my heart / Girl friend / Ten cents a dance / Lover / You are too beautiful / Lady is a tramp / Slaughter on 10th Avenue
CD _____ PASTCD 9794
Flapper / Dec '92 / Pinnacle.

MUSIC AND SONGS OF RODGERS & HART
Rodgers, Richard C
Hart, Lorenz L
Manhattan / Here in my arms / Girlfriend / Mountain greenery / Blue room / Where's the rainbow / My heart stood still / Thou swell / You took advantage of me / With a song in my heart / Ten cents a dance / I've a song in my heart / Isn't it romantic / Dancing on the ceiling / You are too beautiful / That's the rhythm of the day / Fly away to Iowa / That's love / Bad in every man / Blue moon / Soon / There's a small hotel / On your toes / Lady is a tramp / This can't be love / Sing for your supper / I didn't know what time it was / Bewitched, bothered and bewildered
CD _____ CDHD 223
Happy Days / Jul '94 / Conifer.

MY FUNNY VALENTINE
(Sings Rodgers & Hart)
Von Stade, Frederica & Ambrosian Chorus/ London Symphony Orchestra
Rodgers, Richard C
Hart, Lorenz L
McGlinn, John Con
CD _____ CDC 7540712
EMI Classics / Apr '93 / EMI.

RODGERS & HART - WITH A SONG IN THEIR HEARTS
Rodgers, Richard C
Hart, Lorenz L
With a song in my heart: Hutch / Ten cents a dance: Etting, Ruth / Manhattan: Todd, Dick / There's a small hotel: Thornhill, Claude / Ship without a sail: Wiley, Lee / Glad to be unhappy: Wiley, Lee / Maybe it's me: Hutch, Jack / Where or when: Horne, Lena / Give her a kiss: Coslow, Sam / Dancing on the ceiling: Matthews, Jessie / It's easy to remember: Crosby, Bing / On your toes: Whiting, Jack / Spring is here: Sullivan, Maxine / Blue moon: Trumbauer, Frankie / Lady is a tramp: Dickson, Dorothy / Where's that rainbow: Dickson, Dorothy / Thou swell: Waller, Fats / My heart stood still: Baker, Edith / I didn't know what time it was: Shaw, Artie & His Orchestra / Sing for your supper: Basie, Count / You took advantage of me: Mole, Miff / Blue room: Dorsey Brothers / C'est un nid Charmant: Baker, Josephine / This can't be love: Langford, Frances
CD _____ AVC 538
Avid / May '94 / Avid/BMG / Koch.

SONG IS...RODGERS & HART, THE
Rodgers, Richard C
Hart, Lorenz L
We'll be the same: Arden, Victor / Thou swell: Beiderbecke, Bix / Give her a kiss: Coslow, Sam / It's easy to remember: Crosby, Bing / Little things you do: Hutch / With a song in my heart: Hutch / Maybe it's me: Whiting, Jack / Little birdie told me so: Kahn, Roger Wolfe / Girlfriend: Light Opera Company / Mountain in the useful: Light Opera Company / Step on the blues: Light Opera Company / What's the use of talking: Light Opera Company / Hello: Light Opera Company / Where's that rainbow: Light Opera Company / Tree in the park: Light Opera Company / Dancing on the ceiling: Matthews, Jessie / My heart stood still: Matthews, Leo / Who do you suppose: Ross & Sargent / Blue room: Savoy Orpheans
CD _____ CDAJA 5041
Living Era / Oct '95 / Koch.

STARS SALUTE RODGERS AND HART, THE
CD _____ CDCD 1180
Charity / Apr '94 / M.I.S.Records.

WORDS AND MUSIC
Rodgers, Richard C
Hart, Lorenz L
CD _____ AK 47711
Cinevox / Jan '95 / Conifer / Silva Screen.

Rodgers, Richard

MUSICAL THEATRE GREATS
CD _____ CDVIR 8321
TER / Aug '95 / Koch.

TRIBUTE TO RICHARD RODGERS, A
2CD _____ CDDL 1287
EMI / Jun '94 / EMI.

Romberg, Sigmund

GOLDEN DAYS
(The Songs Of Romberg, Friml & Herbert)
Hadley, Jerry
Romberg, Sigmund & Rudolf Friml/Victor Herbert C
Song of the vagabonds / Stout hearted men / I'm falling in love with someone / Streets of New York / Neapolitan love song / Desert song / One alone / Every day is ladies day with me / Donkey serenade / Softly as in a morning sunrise / Drining song / When you're away / I love to go swimmin' with wimmin / I might be your once in a while / Marianne / Serenade / Indian summer / Gypsy love song / Golden days
CD _____ 09026626812
RCA Victor / Nov '94 / BMG.

GREAT HITS FROM SIGMUND ROMBERG
It / Who are we to say / Gaucho march / Waltz / Song of love / In old Granada / Farewell to dreams / Your smiles / Marienne / Softly as in a morning sunrise / My first love, my last love / I bring a love song / When I grow to old to dream
CD _____ PASTCD 9761
Flapper / Feb '92 / Pinnacle.

Rota, Nino

SYMPHONIC FELLINI/ROTA, THE
(Nino Rota's Music From The Films Of Frederico Fellini)
Czech Symphony Orchestra
Wadsworth, Derek Con
White Sheikh / I vitelloni / La strada / Swindle (Il bidone) / La notti di cabiria / La dolce vita / 8/1/2 / Juliet of the spirits / Toby Dammit - The clowns / Satyricon Roma / Amarcord / Il casanova (o venezia, venaga) / Il casanova (pin penin) / Orchestra rehearsal
CD _____ FILMCD 129
Silva Screen / Apr '93 / Conifer / Silva Screen.

Rozsa, Miklos

CLASSIC MIKLOS ROZSA FILM THEMES, THE
CD _____ CDTER 1135
TER / May '89 / Koch.

HOLLYWOOD SPECTACULAR
CD _____ BCD 3028
Bay Cities / Mar '93 / Silva Screen.

KNIGHT WITHOUT ARMOUR: FILM MUSIC FOR PIANO
Robbins, D. Con
Knight without armour / Lydia / Man in half moon street / Because of him / Strange love of Martha Ivers / Killers / Macomber affair / Time out of mind / Other love / Woman's vengeance / Kiss the blood off my hands / Fedora
CD _____ MAF 7057D
Intrada / Jan '94 / Silva Screen / Koch.

Salter, Hans

SALTER: A SYMPHONY OF FILM MUSIC
Creature from the black lagoon / Incredible shrinking man / Black shield of Falworth / Hitler
CD _____ MAF 7054D
Intrada / Jan '94 / Silva Screen / Koch.

Schneider, Romy

ROMY SCHNEIDER FILM MUSIC
CD _____ CH 306
Milan / Jan '95 / BMG / Silva Screen.

Schnittke, Alfred

ALFRED SCHNITTKE: FILM MUSIC
USSR Cinema Symphony Orchestra
Khachaturian, E. Con
Story of an unknown actor / Sport sport sport / Agony / Music for an imaginary play
CD _____ OCD 606
Olympia / Aug '94 / Priory.

Schurmann, Gerard

HORRORS OF THE BLACK MUSEUM
(The Film Music Of Gerard Schurmann)
Horrors Of The Black Museum (Prelude/ Streets of London/Spiked binoculars/Investigations/Headline news/Tunnel of death/ Bancroft's demise/End credits) / Cone Of Silence (Overture) / Bedford Incident (Atlantic encounters) / Smugglers' Rhapsody (Fantasy for orchestra) / Konga (Konga unchained/End titles) / Lost Continent (Sargasso sea/Romanza/Action stations) / Ceremony (Main theme/Memories of Tangier/ Freedom) / Long Arm (Prelude/Safe-cracking/Dawn/Investigations/Tailing the suspect/Finale) / Attack On The Iron Coast

(Prelude/Celebration/The mission) / Claretta (The drama of Claretta/Waltz/Claretta's theme/Finale)
CD _____ CNS 5005
Cloud Nine / Jan '93 / Conifer / Silva Screen.

Schwartz, Arthur

DANCING IN THE DARK
(Music & Songs of Arthur Schwartz)
I guess I'll have to change my plan / She's such a comfort to me / Something to remember you by / I'll always remember / I'm like a sailor / Hot / Dancing in the dark / I love Louisa / High and low / Hoops / Louisiana hayride / Shine on your shoes / To-night / After all, you're all I'm after / You and the night and the music / Then I'll be tired of you / Got a bran' new suit / Love is a dancing thing / This is it
CD _____ CDHD 180
Happy Days / Mar '92 / Conifer.

Shore, Howard

DEAD RINGERS
(Symphonic Suites From The Films Of David Cronenberg)
Shore, Howard
Shore, Howard Con
Scanners (Main title/Vale captured/Ephemerol/The ripe program/The injection/Dirge for the assassins/Vale's lonely walk/The dart/Scanner duel) / Brood (The shape of rage - a suite for 21 strings) / Dead ringers (Main title/Bondage/Twins/Growing awareness/Dependence/Helpless/The operating room/In delirium/Birthday party/Suicide/Finale): London Philharmonic Orchestra
CD _____ FILMCD 115
Silva Screen / Jul '92 / Conifer / Silva Screen.

Simonetti, Claudio

MYSTERY, MAGIC & MADNESS
Simonetti Project
Profondo rosso / Tenebre / Phenomena / Suspiria / Opera / Crows / I'll take the night / Searching / Albinoni in rock / Carmina burana / Days of confusion / Demon
CD _____ PCOM 1137
President / Aug '94 / Grapevine / Target/ BMG / Jazz Music / President.

RARE TRACKS AND OUTTAKES COLLECTION 1975-1989
Goblin
CD _____ DRGCD 32904
DRG / Jun '95 / New Note.

Sondheim, Stephen

COLLECTOR'S SONDHEIM, A
3CD _____ RCD3 5359
RCA/Silva Screen / Jan '89 / Silva Screen.

COLOUR AND LIGHT
(Jazz Sketches on Sondheim)
CD _____ SK 66566
Sony Classical / Sep '95 / Sony.

MUSICAL THEATRE GREATS
CD _____ CDVIR 8322
TER / Aug '95 / Koch.

SINGS THE STEPHEN SONDHEIM SONGBOOK
Wilson, Julie
Can that boy foxtrot / Good thing going / Not a day goes by / Love I hear / I do like you / Not while I'm around / I never do anything twice / With so little to be sure of / Too many mornings / Beautiful girls
CD _____ DRG 5206
DRG / Jan '95 / New Note.

SONDHEIM
(A Celebration At Carnegie Hall)
2CD _____ 09026614842
RCA Victor / '93 / BMG.

SONDHEIM
(A Celebration At Carnegie Hall - Highlights)
CD _____ 09026615162
RCA Victor / '93 / BMG.

SONDHEIM EVENING: A MUSICAL TRIBUTE
2CD _____ 605152
Silva Screen / Jan '95 / Conifer / Silva Screen.

SONDHEIM SONGBOOK, THE
Broadway Casts
CD _____ SK 48201
Sony Classical / Feb '93 / Sony.

STEPHEN SONDHEIM SONGBOOK, THE
Turner, Geraldine
Like it was / Old friends / Losing my mind / Not while I'm around / Could I leave you / With so much to be sure of / Miller's son / Buddy's blues / I remember / Parade in town / There won't be trumpets / Being alive / Anyone can whistle / Another hundred people / Goodbye for now
CD _____ SILVAD 3009
Silva Treasury / '95 / Conifer / Silva Screen.

UNSUNG SONDHEIM
Saturday Night / Love's a bond: Willison, Walter / All for you: Gaines, Davis / In the movies: Cooper, Marilyn / What can you lose: Kuhn, Judy / Invitation to a march /

That old piano roll: Groener, Harry & Lynette Perry / They asked me why I believed in you: Luker, Rebecca / No, Mary Ann: Grace, Jason / Truly content: Kaye, Judy / Water under the bridge: Gravitte, Debbie Shapiro / Enclave / There's always a woman: Ballard, Kaye & Sally Mayes / Two of you: Moore, Christa / Multitudes of Amys: Rupert, Michael / Goodbye for now: Callaway, Liz
CD _____ VSD 5433
Varese Sarabande/Colosseum / Sep '93 / Pinnacle / Silva Screen.

Stalling, Carl

CARL STALLING PROJECT, THE
(Original Music From Warner Brothers Cartoons 1936-1958)
CD _____ 9260272
Silva Screen / Jan '93 / Conifer / Silva Screen.

CARL STALLING PROJECT, THE II
CD _____ 9454302
Silva Screen / May '95 / Conifer / Silva Screen.

Stein, Ronald

NOT OF THIS EARTH
Stein, Ronald
Attack of the 50 foot woman / Attack of the crab monsters / Spider baby / Not of this earth
CD _____ VSD 5634
Varese Sarabande/Colosseum / Oct '95 / Pinnacle / Silva Screen.

Steiner, Max

GONE WITH THE WIND
(The Classic Max Steiner)
Westminster Philharmonic Orchestra
Alwyn, Kenneth Con
Adventures of Mark Twain (Overture) / Distant Trumpet (Prelude) / Casablanca (Prelude/Rick's Bar/Paris/The airport/The beginning of a beautiful friendship) / Summer Place (Main title/Young love) / Treasure of the Sierra Madre (Overture) / Helen of Troy (Prelude/The voyage/The gates of Troy/The siege and aftermath/Finale) / Caine Mutiny (March) / Gone With the Wind (Prelude/Invitation to Twelve Oaks/Tara/Mammy/The fall of the South/Scarlett walks among the wounded/Rhett's leaving/Melanie's death/ Finale)
CD _____ FILMCD 144
Silva Screen / Mar '94 / Conifer / Silva Screen.

NOW VOYAGER
(Classic Film Scores Of Max Steiner)
National Philharmonic Orchestra
Gerhardt, Charles Con
Now Voyager (Main title/Love scene/Finale) / King Kong / Saratoga Trunk (As long as I live) / Charge of the Light Brigade (Forward the Light Brigade) / Four Wives (Symphonie moderne) / Big Sleep / Johnny Belinda (suite) / Since You Went Away (Main title) / Informer (Main title/Love scene/Sancta Maria) / Fountainhead
CD _____ GD 80136
RCA Victor / Oct '90 / BMG.

Styne, Jule

CELEBRATES THE MUSIC OF JULE STYNE
Tompkins, Ross
CD _____ PCD 7103
Progressive / Nov '95 / Jazz Music.

EVERYTHING'S COMING UP ROSES: OVERTURES VOL. 1
National Symphony Orchestra
Everly, Jack Con
CD _____ CDVIR 8318
TER / May '94 / Koch.

OVERTURES VOL. 2
National Symphony Orchestra
Everly, Jack Con
CD _____ CDVIR 8319
TER / May '94 / Koch.

Tangerine Dream

DREAM MUSIC
(The Movie Music Of Tangerine Dream)
Tangerine Dream
Park Is Mine (Victory
Letter
Taking Central Park
Helicopter attack) / Deadly Care (Hospital Clean and sober) / Dead Solid Perfect (Theme
Suite)
CD _____ FILMCD 165
Silva Screen / Feb '93 / Conifer / Silva Screen.

DREAM MUSIC II
Tangerine Dream
CD _____ FILMCD 166
Silva Screen / Nov '95 / Conifer / Silva Screen.

Theodorakis, Mikis

MIKIS THEODORAKIS ON THE SCREEN
(4 Complete Soundtracks - Z/Serpico/ Phaedra/State of Siege)

Z / Serpico / Phaedra / State of siege
2CD _____ **DRGCD 32901**
DRG / Sep '93 / New Note.

Tiomkin, Dimitri

FILM MUSIC OF DIMITRI TIOMKIN
Royal College Of Music Orchestra
Roman Empire overture / Pax Romana /
Guns of Navarone / Wild is the wind / Rhap-
sody of steel / President's country
CD _____ **DKPCD 9047**
Unicorn-Kanchana / Dec '88 / Harmonia
Mundi.

GREAT EPIC FILM SCORES
(Music From The Samuel Bronston
Productions)
Tiomkin, Dimitri/Miklos Rozsa C
Webster, Paul Francis L
Tiomkin, Dimitri/Miklos Rozsa Con
Overture (El Cid) / Main title / Thirteen
knights / Pride and sorrow / Scene d'amour
/ El Cid march / Falcon and the dove / Over-
ture (2) (55 Days At Peking) / Prelude / Mur-
der of the German ambassador / Orphan
and the Major / Attack on the French lega-
tion / Intermezzo: So little time / Fanfares
and flourishes (Fall Of The Roman Empire)
/ Prelude (2) / Livius' arrival / Old acquaint-
ances / Decoy patrol / Battle in the forest /
Reinforcements / Intermezzo: Livius and
Lucilla / New God / John Wayne march
(Magnificent Showman) / Main title 'Circus
World' / Buffalo gal / Toni and Giovanna /
In old Vienna / Exit music 'Circus World'
CD _____ **UKCD 2011**
Cloud Nine / Nov '92 / Conifer / Silva
Screen.

WESTERN FILM WORLD OF DIMITRI
TIOMKIN, THE
London Studio Symphony Orchestra
Johnson, L. Con
Giant (prelude) / Red River (Prelude/Wagon
train/Red River crossing/Challenge and Fi-
nale) / Duel in the Sun (Prelude and Legend/
Buggy ride/Trek to the sun/Love - death
and Finale) / High Noon (Clock and The
showdown) / Night Passage (Follow the
river) / Rio Bravo (DeGuella/Love theme/
Main titles)
CD _____ **UKCD 2011**
Unicorn-Kanchana / Jan '89 / Harmonia
Mundi.

Trovajoli, Armando

FILM MUSIC OF ARMANDO
TROVAJOLI, THE
CD _____ **VCDS 7005**
Varese Sarabande/Colosseum / May '95 /
Pinnacle / Silva Screen.

Vangelis

THEMES
Vangelis
Bladerunner (end titles) / Missing (main
theme) / L'Enfant / Chung kuo (the long
march) / Hymn / Tao of love / Antarctica /
Bladerunner love theme / Mutiny on the
Bounty (opening titles/closing titles) / Mem-
ories of green / La petite fille de la mer /
Chariots of Fire / Five circles
CD _____ **8395182**
Polydor / Jul '89 / PolyGram.

Walton, Sir William

FILM MUSIC OF SIR WILLIAM WALTON
London Philharmonic Orchestra
Davis, Carl Con
Henry V (suite) / Battle of Britain / Troilus
and Cressida / As You Like It / History of
English Speaking Peoples
CD _____ **CDM 5655852**
EMI Classics / Oct '90 / EMI.

WALTON: FILM MUSIC VOL. 1
Academy Of St. Martin In The Fields
Marriner, Neville Con
Hamlet / As you like it
CD _____ **CHAN 8842**
Chandos / Jun '90 / Chandos.

WALTON: FILM MUSIC VOL. 2
Academy Of St. Martin In The Fields
Marriner, Neville Con
Battle of Britain / Spitfire prelude and fugue
/ Escape me never / Three sisters / Wartime
sketchbook
CD _____ **CHAN 8870**
Chandos / Dec '90 / Chandos.

WALTON: FILM MUSIC VOL. 3
Westminster Cathedral Choir/Academy Of
St. Martin In The Fields
Marriner, Neville Con
Henry V / Rosa solis / Watkin's ale / Chants
d'Auvergne
CD _____ **CHAN 8892**
Chandos / Apr '91 / Chandos.

WALTON: FILM MUSIC VOL. 4
Academy Of St. Martin In The Fields
Marriner, Neville Con
Richard III / Macbeth / Major Barbara
CD _____ **CHAN 8841**
Chandos / May '91 / Chandos.

Warren, Harry

LULLABY OF BROADWAY
(The Music Of Harry Warren)
Pasadena / I found a million dollar baby /
Lullaby of Broadway / Love is where you
find it / You're my everything / I yi yi yi /
You're gotting to be a habit with me / Sep
tember in the rain / Shadow waltz / Keep
young and beautiful / Nagasaki / You must
have been a beautiful baby / With plenty of
money and you / Jeepers creepers / I only
have eyes for you / I've got to sing a torch
song / About a quarter to nine / Lulu's back
in time / Man with the lollipop / Boulevard
of broken dreams / I'll string along with you
/ She's a latin from Manhattan / By a waterfall / 42nd Street / Medley
CD _____ **PASTCD 9795**
Flapper / Jul '93 / Pinnacle.

SONG IS...HARRY WARREN, THE
Love is where you find it: Andrews Sisters /
42nd Street: Boswell Sisters & Dorsey
Brothers / Shuffle off to Buffalo: Boswell
Sisters & Dorsey Brothers / I'll string along
with you: Bowlly, Al & the Ray Noble Or-
chestra / Shadow waltz: Browne, Sam /
You're my everything: Carlisle, Elsie / You
must have been a beautiful baby: Crosby,
Bing / Young and beautiful: Crosby, Bing /
Ooh that kiss: Day, Frances / Keep young
and beautiful: Dennis, Denny & Roy Fox / I
only have eyes for you: Duchin, Eddie /
You're getting to be a habit with me: Four
Musketeers / You'll never know: Haymes,
Dick / Nagasaki: Henderson, Fletcher / I've
got to sing a torch song: Hutch / September
in the rain: Hutch / Serenade in blue: Lang-
ford, Frances / I found a million dollar baby:
Langford, Frances / At last: Miller, Glenn /
Chattanooga choo choo: Miller, Glenn /
Jeepers creepers: Mills Brothers / I yi yi yi
yi (I like you very much): Miranda, Carmen /
Lullaby of Broadway: Roy, Harry & His Or-
chestra / Lulu's back in town: Roy, Harry &
His Orchestra / Would you like to take a
walk: Sanderson, Julia & Frank Crumit
CD _____ **CDAJA 5139**
Living Era / Apr '95 / Koch.

Waxman, Franz

LEGENDS OF HOLLYWOOD VOL.1
CD _____ **VSD 5242**
Varese Sarabande/Colosseum / Apr '90 /
Pinnacle / Silva Screen.

LEGENDS OF HOLLYWOOD VOL.3
CD _____ **VSD 5480**
Varese Sarabande/Colosseum / Jun '94 /
Pinnacle / Silva Screen.

Webb, Roy

CURSE OF THE CAT PEOPLE, THE
(The Film Music Of Roy Webb)
Out of the past / Crossfire / Bedlam / Sin-
bad the sailor / Dick Tracy / Ghost ship /
Mighty Joe Young / Notorious / Locket /
Cornered / Curse of the cat people
CD _____ **CNS 5008**
Cloud Nine / May '95 / Conifer / Silva
Screen.

Weill, Kurt

BARBARA SONG
(Arranged For Saxophone & String
Quartet)
Thompson, Barbara & The Medici String
Quartet
Je te n'aime pas / Barbara song / Mack the
Knife / Zuhalterballade / It never was you /
Speak low / Surabaya / Johnny / Septem-
ber song / Bilbao song / Nanas lied / My
ship
CD _____ **VC 5451672**
Virgin Classics / Nov '95 / EMI.

KURT WEILL - A MUSICAL PORTRAIT
Wust, Stefanie
CD _____ **AS 20102**
Al Segno / Mar '95 / Koch.

SINGS THE KURT WEILL SONGBOOK
Wilson, Julie
One touch of venus / That's him / Septem-
ber song / There's nowhere to go but up /
Surabaya Johnny / Sing me not a ballad /
Foolish heart / This is new / Speak low /
Trouble man / Stay well / Jenny
CD _____ **DRG 5207**
DRG / Jan '95 / New Note.

STRATAS SINGS WEILL
Stratas, Teresa & Chamber Symphony
Schwarz, Gerard Con
CD _____ **7559791312**
Elektra Nonesuch / Jan '95 / Warner Music.

UNKNOWN KURT WEILL
Stratas, Teresa
Woitach, Richard Con
CD _____ **7559790192**
Elektra Nonesuch / Jan '95 / Warner Music.

UTE LEMPER SINGS KURT WEILL
Lemper, Ute
CD _____ **CH 341**
Milan / Jan '95 / BMG / Silva Screen.

UTE LEMPER SINGS KURT WEILL
Lemper, Ute & Berlin Radio Ensemble
Mauceri, John/W. Meyer/K.
Rautenberg Con
CD _____ **4252042**
Decca / Mar '89 / PolyGram.

UTE LEMPER SINGS KURT WEILL VOL.
2
Lemper, Ute/J. Cohen/London Voices/Ber-
lin RIAS Sinfonietta
Mauceri, John Con
Happy end / Marie Galante / Lady in the
dark / Youkali
CD _____ **4364172**
Decca / Jul '93 / PolyGram.

Williams, John

FILM WORKS
Jurassic park - end credits / Jurassic park
- My friend the brachiosaurus / Always - fol
low me / Always - Dorinda solo flight /
Earthquake (Theme) / Jaws - out to sea /
Jaws II - end title/cast / Eiger sanction
(theme) / Midway - midway march / Dracula

- Main title/Storm sequence / Schindler's
list / E.T. The extra terrestrial - Over the
moon / E.T. The extra terrestrial - Flying /
River / Far and away - County Galway June
1982 / Far and away - End credits
CD _____ **MCD 32877**
MCA / Jun '95 / BMG.

GREAT MUSIC OF JOHN WILLIAMS
CD _____ **873044**
Milan / Jan '95 / BMG / Silva Screen.

JURASSIC PARK
(The Classic John Williams)
Motzing, William Con
Jurassic Park (Main title) / Jaws (Main title
Chrissie's death
Out of the sea
End titles) / Raiders Of The Lost Ark (Raiders
march) / E.T. - The Extra-Terrestrial (The de-
parture) / Presumed Innocent (End credits)
/ Close Encounters Of The Third Kind (Jim
activities) / Accidental Tourist (Main title) /
Return Of The Jedi (Parade of the Ewoks) /
JFK (Main title) / Superman (Main theme) /
Black Sunday (Preparation
Blimp and the bomb
Air chase
The explosion
End cast) / Star Wars (Main theme)
CD _____ **FILMCD 147**
Silva Screen / Jan '94 / Conifer / Silva
Screen.

SCHINDLER'S LIST
(The Classic Film Music Of John
Williams)
City Of Prague Philharmonic Orchestra
Bateman, Paul Con
CD _____ **FILMCD 160**
Silva Screen / Apr '95 / Conifer / Silva
Screen.

SPACE AND TIME
Williams, John & The Boston Pops
Orchestra
2001: A space odyssey / Superman (March)
/ Star Trek (Motion picture main title) / Twi-
light Zone (Theme and variations) / Alien
(Closing title) / Star wars (Main theme) /
Empire Strikes Back (Imperial march) / Re-
turn Of The Jedi (Luke and Leia) / Close En-
counters Of The Third Kind (Suite) / E.T.
(Flying theme)
CD _____ **5501062**
Spectrum/Karussell / Jul '95 / PolyGram /
THE.

SPIELBERG/WILLIAMS
COLLABORATION, THE
Boston Pops Orchestra
Williams, John (1) Con
CD _____ **CD 45997**
Sony Classical / Nov '91 / Sony.

STAR TRACKS
Cincinnati Pops Orchestra
Kunzel, Erich Con
CD _____ **CD 80094**
Telarc / May '85 / Conifer / ADA.

STAR WARS/CLOSE ENCOUNTERS
(Classic Film Scores Of John Williams)
National Philharmonic Orchestra
Gerhardt, Charles Con
Star Wars (Main title/The little people work/
Here they come/Princess Leia/The final bat-
tle/The throne room/End title) / Close En-
counters of the Third Kind (Horizon/
Barnstorming/Arrival of the mother ship/The
pilot's return/The visitors/Final scene)
CD _____ **GD 82698**
RCA Victor / Sep '91 / BMG.

Zimmer, Hans

HANS ZIMMER FILM MUSIC
CD _____ **CH 530**
Milan / Jan '95 / BMG / Silva Screen.